DIANA GABALDON

DRAGONFLY IN AMBER

A NOVEL

A DELL BOOK

For my husband,
Doug Watkins—
In thanks for the Raw Material

Dragonfly in Amber is a work of fiction. Names, characters, places,
and incidents either are the product of the author's imagination or
are used fictitiously. Any resemblance to actual persons, living or
dead, events, or locales is entirely coincidental.

2016 Dell Mass Market Edition

Copyright © 1992 by Diana Gabaldon
Excerpt from *Voyager* by Diana Gabaldon copyright © 1994
by Diana Gabaldon

Published in the United States by Dell, an imprint of Random
House, a division of Penguin Random House LLC, New York.

DELL and the HOUSE colophon are registered trademarks of
Penguin Random House LLC.

Originally published in hardcover in the United States by
Delacorte Press, an imprint of Random House, a division of
Penguin Random House LLC, in 1992.

ISBN 978-0-440-21562-2
eBook ISBN 978-0-440-33518-4

Cover design: Marietta Anastassatos

Printed in the United States of America

randomhousebooks.com

60 62 64 66 67 65 63 61 59

Dell mass market edition: March 2016

By Diana Gabaldon

(in chronological order)
Outlander
Dragonfly in Amber
Voyager
Drums of Autumn
The Fiery Cross
A Breath of Snow and Ashes
An Echo in the Bone
Written in My Own Heart's Blood

The Outlandish Companion
(nonfiction)

The Exile
(graphic novel)

The Outlandish Companion, Volume Two
(nonfiction)

(in chronological order)
Lord John and the Hellfire Club (novella)
Lord John and the Private Matter
Lord John and the Succubus (novella)
Lord John and the Brotherhood of the Blade
Lord John and the Haunted Soldier (novella)
The Custom of the Army (novella)
Lord John and the Hand of Devils (collected novellas)
The Scottish Prisoner
A Plague of Zombies (novella)

Other Outlander-related novellas
A Leaf on the Wind of All Hallows
The Space Between

Prologue

I woke three times in the dark predawn. First in sorrow, then in joy, and at the last, in solitude. The tears of a bone-deep loss woke me slowly, bathing my face like the comforting touch of a damp cloth in soothing hands. I turned my face to the wet pillow and sailed a salty river into the caverns of grief remembered, into the subterranean depths of sleep.

I came awake then in fierce joy, body arched bowlike in the throes of physical joining, the touch of him fresh on my skin, dying along the paths of my nerves as the ripples of consummation spread from my center. I repelled consciousness, turning again, seeking the sharp, warm smell of a man's satisfied desire, in the reassuring arms of my lover, sleep.

The third time I woke alone, beyond the touch of love or grief. The sight of the stones was fresh in my mind. A small circle, standing stones on the crest of a steep green hill. The name of the hill is Craigh na Dun; the fairies' hill. Some say the hill is enchanted, others say it is cursed. Both are right. But no one knows the function or the purpose of the stones.

Except me.

PART ONE

Through a
Looking Glass, Darkly

INVERNESS, 1968

PART ONE

Mustering the Roll

R oger Wakefield stood in the center of the room, feeling surrounded. He thought the feeling largely justified, insofar as he *was* surrounded: by tables covered
with bric-a-brac and mementos, by heavy Victorian-style furniture, replete with antimacassars, plush and afghans, by tiny
braided rugs that lay on the polished wood, craftily awaiting
an opportunity to skid beneath an unsuspecting foot. Surrounded by twelve rooms of furniture and clothing and papers. And the books—my God, the books!

The study where he stood was lined on three sides by
bookshelves, every one crammed past bursting point. Paper-
back mystery novels lay in bright, tatty piles in front of calf-
bound tomes, jammed cheek by jowl with book-club selec-
tions, ancient volumes pilfered from extinct libraries, and
thousands upon thousands of pamphlets, leaflets, and hand-
sewn manuscripts.

A similar situation prevailed in the rest of the house.
Books and papers cluttered every horizontal surface, and every closet groaned and squeaked at the seams. His late adoptive father had lived a long, full life, a good ten years past his
biblically allotted threescore and ten. And in eighty-odd
years, the Reverend Mr. Reginald Wakefield had never
thrown anything away.

Roger repressed the urge to run out of the front door,
leap into his Morris Minor, and head back to Oxford, abandoning the manse and its contents to the mercy of weather
and vandals. Be calm, he told himself, inhaling deeply. You
can deal with this. The books are the easy part; nothing more
than a matter of sorting through them and then calling someone to come and haul them away. Granted, they'll need a
lorry the size of a railcar, but it can be done. Clothes—no
problem. Oxfam gets the lot.

He didn't know what Oxfam was going to do with a lot of
vested black serge suits, circa 1948, but perhaps the deserving
poor weren't all that picky. He began to breathe a little eas-

ier. He had taken a month's leave from the History department at Oxford in order to clear up the Reverend's affairs. Perhaps that would be enough, after all. In his more depressed moments, it had seemed as though the task might take years.

He moved toward one of the tables and picked up a small china dish. It was filled with small metal rectangles; lead "gaberlunzies," badges issued to eighteenth-century beggars by parishes as a sort of license. A collection of stoneware bottles stood by the lamp, a ramshorn snuff mull, banded in silver, next to them. Give them to a museum? he thought dubiously. The house was filled with Jacobite artifacts; the Reverend had been an amateur historian, the eighteenth century his favorite hunting ground.

His fingers reached involuntarily to caress the surface of the snuff mull, tracing the black lines of the inscriptions—the names and dates of the Deacons and Treasurers of the Incorporation of Tailors of the Canongate, from Edinburgh, 1726. Perhaps he should keep a few of the Reverend's choicer acquisitions . . . but then he drew back, shaking his head decidedly. "Nothing doing, cock," he said aloud, "that way madness lies." Or at least the incipient life of a pack rat. Get started saving things, and he'd end up keeping the lot, living in this monstrosity of a house, surrounded by generations of rubbish. "Talking to yourself, too," he muttered.

The thought of generations of rubbish reminded him of the garage, and he sagged a bit at the knees. The Reverend, who was in fact Roger's great-uncle, had adopted him at the age of five when his parents had been killed in World War II; his mother in the Blitz, his father out over the dark waters of the Channel. With his usual preservative instincts, the Reverend had kept all of Roger's parents' effects, sealed in crates and cartons in the back of the garage. Roger knew for a fact that no one had opened one of those crates in the past twenty years.

Roger uttered an Old Testament groan at the thought of pawing through his parents' memorabilia. "Oh, God," he said aloud. "Anything but that!"

The remark had not been intended precisely as prayer, but the doorbell pealed as though in answer, making Roger bite his tongue in startlement.

The door of the manse had a tendency to stick in damp weather, which meant that it was stuck most of the time. Roger freed it with a rending screech, to find a woman on the doorstep.

"Can I help you?"

She was middle height and very pretty. He had an overall impression of fine bones and white linen, topped with a wealth of curly brown hair in a sort of half-tamed chignon. And in the middle of it all, the most extraordinary pair of light eyes, just the color of well-aged sherry.

The eyes swept up from his size-eleven plimsolls to the face a foot above her. The sidelong smile grew wider. "I hate to start right off with a cliché," she said, "but my, how you have grown, young Roger!"

Roger felt himself flushing. The woman laughed and extended a hand. "You *are* Roger, aren't you? My name's Claire Randall; I was an old friend of the Reverend's. But I haven't seen you since you were five years old."

"Er, you said you *were* a friend of my father's? Then, you know already. . . ."

The smile vanished, replaced by a look of regret.

"Yes, I was awfully sorry to hear about it. Heart, was it?"

"Um, yes. Very sudden. I've only just come up from Oxford to start dealing with . . . everything." He waved vaguely, encompassing the Reverend's death, the house behind him, and all its contents.

"From what I recall of your father's library, that little chore ought to last you 'til next Christmas," Claire observed.

"In that case, maybe we shouldn't be disturbing you," said a soft American voice.

"Oh, I forgot," said Claire, half-turning to the girl who had stood out of sight in the corner of the porch. "Roger Wakefield—my daughter, Brianna."

Brianna Randall stepped forward, a shy smile on her face. Roger stared for a moment, then remembered his manners. He stepped back and swung the door open wide, momentarily wondering just when he had last changed his shirt.

"Not at all, not at all!" he said heartily. "I was just wanting a break. Won't you come in?"

He waved the two women down the hall toward the Reverend's study, noting that as well as being moderately attractive, the daughter was one of the tallest girls he'd ever seen close-to. She had to be easily six feet, he thought, seeing her head even with the top of the hall stand as she passed. He unconsciously straightened himself as he followed, drawing up to his full six feet three. At the last moment, he ducked, to avoid banging his head on the study lintel as he followed the women into the room.

"I'd meant to come before," said Claire, settling herself deeper in the huge wing chair. The fourth wall of the Reverend's study was equipped with floor-to-ceiling windows, and the sunlight winked off the pearl clip in her light-brown hair. The curls were beginning to escape from their confinement, and she tucked one absently behind an ear as she talked.

"I'd arranged to come last year, in fact, and then there was an emergency at the hospital in Boston—I'm a doctor," she explained, mouth curling a little at the look of surprise Roger hadn't quite managed to conceal. "But I'm sorry that we didn't; I would have liked so much to see your father again."

Roger rather wondered why they had come now, knowing the Reverend was dead, but it seemed impolite to ask. Instead, he asked, "Enjoying a bit of sightseeing, are you?"

"Yes, we drove up from London," Claire answered. She smiled at her daughter. "I wanted Bree to see the country; you wouldn't think it to hear her talk, but she's as English as I am, though she's never lived here."

"Really?" Roger glanced at Brianna. She didn't really look English, he thought; aside from the height, she had thick red hair, worn loose over her shoulders, and strong, sharp-angled bones in her face, with the nose long and straight—maybe a touch too long.

"I was born in America," Brianna explained, "but both Mother and Daddy are—were—English."

"Were?"

"My husband died two years ago," Claire explained. "You knew him, I think—Frank Randall."

"*Frank* Randall! Of course!" Roger smacked himself on the forehead, and felt his cheeks grow hot at Brianna's giggle.

"You're going to think me a complete fool, but I've only just realized who you are."

The name explained a lot; Frank Randall had been an eminent historian, and a good friend of the Reverend's; they had exchanged bits of Jacobite arcana for years, though it was at least ten years since Frank Randall had last visited the manse.

"So—you'll be visiting the historical sites near Inverness?" Roger hazarded. "Have you been to Culloden yet?"

"Not yet," Brianna answered. "We thought we'd go later this week." Her answering smile was polite, but nothing more.

"We're booked for a trip down Loch Ness this afternoon," Claire explained. "And perhaps we'll drive down to Fort William tomorrow, or just poke about in Inverness; the place has grown a lot since I was last here."

"When was that?" Roger wondered whether he ought to volunteer his services as tour guide. He really shouldn't take the time, but the Randalls had been good friends of the Reverend's. Besides, a car trip to Fort William in company with two attractive women seemed a much more appealing prospect than cleaning out the garage, which was next on his list.

"Oh, more than twenty years ago. It's been a long time." There was an odd note in Claire's voice that made Roger glance at her, but she met his eyes with a smile.

"Well," he ventured, "if there's anything I can do for you, while you're in the Highlands . . ."

Claire was still smiling, but something in her face changed. He could almost think she had been waiting for an opening. She glanced at Brianna, then back to Roger.

"Since you mention it," she said, her smile broadening.

"Oh, Mother!" Brianna said, sitting up in her chair. "You don't want to bother Mr. Wakefield! Look at all he's got to do!" She waved a hand at the crowded study, with its overflowing cartons and endless stacks of books.

"Oh, no bother at all!" Roger protested. "Er . . . what is it?"

Claire shot her daughter a quelling look. "I wasn't planning to knock him on the head and drag him off," she said tartly. "But he might well know someone who could help. It's a small historical project," she explained to Roger. "I need someone who's fairly well versed in the eighteenth-century Jacobites—Bonnie Prince Charlie and all that lot."

Roger leaned forward, interested. "Jacobites?" he said. "That period's not one of my specialties, but I do know a bit —hard not to, living so close to Culloden. That's where the final battle was, you know," he explained to Brianna. "Where the Bonnie Prince's lot ran up against the Duke of Cumberland and got slaughtered for their pains."

"Right," said Claire. "And that, in fact, has to do with what I want to find out." She reached into her handbag and drew out a folded paper.

Roger opened it and scanned the contents quickly. It was a list of names—maybe thirty, all men. At the top of the sheet was a heading: "JACOBITE RISING, 1745—CULLODEN"

"Oh, the '45?" Roger said. "These men fought at Culloden, did they?"

"They did," Claire replied. "What I want to find out is— how many of the men on this list survived that battle?"

Roger rubbed his chin as he perused the list. "That's a simple question," he said, "but the answer might be hard to find. So many of the Highland clansmen who followed Prince Charles were killed on Culloden Field that they weren't buried individually. They were put into mass graves, with no more than a single stone bearing the clan name as a marker."

"I know," Claire said. "Brianna hasn't been there, but I have—a long time ago." He thought he saw a fleeting shadow in her eyes, though it was quickly hidden as she reached into her handbag. No wonder if there was, he thought. Culloden Field was an affecting place; it brought tears to his own eyes, to look out over that expanse of moorland and remember the gallantry and courage of the Scottish Highlanders who lay slaughtered beneath the grass.

She unfolded several more typed sheets and handed them to him. A long white finger ran down the margin of one sheet. Beautiful hands, Roger noted; delicately molded, carefully kept, with a single ring on each hand. The silver one on her right hand was especially striking; a wide Jacobean band in the Highland interlace pattern, embellished with thistle blossoms.

"These are the names of the wives, so far as I know them. I thought that might help, since if the husbands were killed at Culloden, you'd likely find these women remarrying or emigrating afterward. Those records would surely be in the parish register? They're all from the same parish; the church was in Broch Mordha—it's a good bit south of here."

"That's a very helpful idea," Roger said, mildly surprised. "It's the sort of thing an historian would think of."

"I'm hardly an historian," Claire Randall said dryly. "On the other hand, when you live with one, you do pick up the occasional odd thought."

"Of course." A thought struck Roger, and he rose from his chair. "I'm being a terrible host; please, let me get you a drink, and then you can tell me a bit more about this. Perhaps I could help you with it myself."

Despite the disorder, he knew where the decanters were kept, and quickly had his guests supplied with whisky. He'd put quite a lot of soda in Brianna's, but noticed that she sipped at it as though her glass contained ant spray, rather than the best Glenfiddich single malt. Claire, who took her whisky neat by request, seemed to enjoy it much more.

"Well." Roger resumed his seat and picked up the paper again. "It's an interesting problem, in terms of historical research. You said these men came from the same parish? I suppose they came from a single clan or sept—I see a number of them were named Fraser."

Claire nodded, hands folded in her lap. "They came from the same estate; a small Highland farm called Broch Tuarach—it was known locally as Lallybroch. They were part of clan Fraser, though they never gave a formal allegiance to Lord Lovat as chief. These men joined the Rising early; they fought in the Battle of Prestonpans—while Lovat's men didn't come until just before Culloden."

"Really? That's interesting." Under normal eighteenth-century conditions, such small tenant-farmers would have died where they lived, and be filed tidily away in the village churchyard, neatly docketed in the parish register. However, Bonnie Prince Charlie's attempt to regain the throne of Scotland in 1745 had disrupted the normal course of things in no uncertain terms.

In the famine after the disaster of Culloden, many Highlanders had emigrated to the New World; others had drifted from the glens and moors toward the cities, in search of food and employment. A few stayed on, stubbornly clinging to their land and traditions.

"It would make a fascinating article," Roger said, thinking aloud. "Follow the fate of a number of individuals, see what happened to them all. Less interesting if they all *were* killed at Culloden, but chances were that a few made it out." He would be inclined to take on the project as a welcome break even were it not Claire Randall who asked.

"Yes, I think I can help you with this," he said, and was gratified at the warm smile she bestowed on him.

"Would you really? That's wonderful!" she said.

"My pleasure," Roger said. He folded the paper and laid it on the table. "I'll start in on it directly. But tell me, how did you enjoy your drive up from London?"

The conversation became general as the Randalls regaled him with tales of their transatlantic journey, and the drive from London. Roger's attention drifted slightly, as he began to plan the research for this project. He felt mildly guilty about taking it on; he really shouldn't take the time. On the other hand, it was an interesting question. And it was possible that he could combine the project with some of the necessary clearing-up of the Reverend's material; he knew for a fact that there were forty-eight cartons in the garage, all labeled JACOBITES, MISCELLANEOUS. The thought of it was enough to make him feel faint.

With a wrench, he tore his mind away from the garage, to find that the conversation had made an abrupt change of subject.

"Druids?" Roger felt dazed. He peered suspiciously into his glass, checking to see that he really had added soda.

"You hadn't heard about them?" Claire looked slightly disappointed. "Your father—the Reverend—he knew about them, though only unofficially. Perhaps he didn't think it worth telling you; he thought it something of a joke."

Roger scratched his head, ruffling the thick black hair. "No, I really don't recall. But you're right, he may not have thought it anything serious."

"Well, I don't know that it is." She crossed her legs at the knee. A streak of sunlight gleamed down the shin of her stockings, emphasizing the delicacy of the long bone beneath.

"When I was here last with Frank—God, that was

twenty-three years ago!—the Reverend told him that there was a local group of—well, modern Druids, I suppose you'd call them. I've no idea how authentic they might be; most likely not very." Brianna was leaning forward now, interested, the glass of whisky forgotten between her hands.

"The Reverend couldn't take official notice of them—paganism and all that, you know—but his housekeeper, Mrs. Graham, was involved with the group, so he got wind of their doings from time to time, and he tipped Frank that there would be a ceremony of some kind on the dawn of Beltane—May Day, that is."

Roger nodded, trying to adjust to the idea of elderly Mrs. Graham, that extremely proper person, engaging in pagan rites and dancing round stone circles in the dawn. All he could remember of Druid ceremonies himself was that some of them involved burning sacrificial victims in wicker cages, which seemed still more unlikely behavior for a Scottish Presbyterian lady of advanced years.

"There's a circle of standing stones on top of a hill, fairly nearby. So we went up there before dawn to, well, to spy on them," she continued, shrugging apologetically. "You know what scholars are like; no conscience at all when it comes to their own field, let alone a sense of social delicacy." Roger winced slightly at this, but nodded in wry agreement.

"And there they were," she said. "Mrs. Graham included, all wearing bedsheets, chanting things and dancing in the midst of the stone circle. Frank was fascinated," she added, with a smile. "And it *was* impressive, even to me."

She paused for a moment, eyeing Roger rather speculatively.

"I'd heard that Mrs. Graham had passed away a few years ago. But I wonder . . . do you know if she had any family? I believe membership in such groups is often hereditary; maybe there's a daughter or granddaughter who could tell me a bit."

"Well," Roger said slowly. "There is a granddaughter—Fiona's her name, Fiona Graham. In fact, she came to help out here at the manse after her grandmother died; the Reverend was really too elderly to be left all on his own."

If anything could displace his vision of Mrs. Graham dancing in a bedsheet, it was the thought of nineteen-year-old

Fiona as a guardian of ancient mystic knowledge, but Roger rallied gamely and went on.

"She isn't here just now, I'm afraid. I could ask her for you, though."

Claire waved a slender hand in dismissal. "Don't trouble yourself. Another time will do. We've taken up too much of your time already."

To Roger's dismay, she set down her empty glass on the small table between the chairs and Brianna added her own full one with what looked like alacrity. He noticed that Brianna Randall bit her nails. This small evidence of imperfection gave him the nerve to take the next step. She intrigued him, and he didn't want her to go, with no assurance that he would see her again.

"Speaking of stone circles," he said quickly. "I believe I know the one you mentioned. It's quite scenic, and not too far from town." He smiled directly at Brianna Randall, registering automatically the fact that she had three small freckles high on one cheekbone. "I thought perhaps I'd start on this project with a trip down to Broch Tuarach. It's in the same direction as the stone circle, so maybe . . . aaagh!"

With a sudden jerk of her bulky handbag, Claire Randall had bumped both whisky glasses off the table, showering Roger's lap and thighs with single malt whisky and quite a lot of soda.

"I'm terribly sorry," she apologized, obviously flustered. She bent and began picking up pieces of shattered crystal, despite Roger's half-coherent attempts to stop her.

Brianna, coming to assist with a handful of linen napkins seized from the sideboard, was saying "Really, Mother, how they ever let you do surgery, I don't know. You're just not safe with anything smaller than a bread-box. Look, you've got his shoes soaked with whisky!" She knelt on the floor, and began busily mopping up spilled Scotch and fragments of crystal. "And his pants, too."

Whipping a fresh napkin from the stack over her arm, she industriously polished Roger's toes, her red mane floating deliriously around his knees. Her head was rising, as she peered at his thighs, dabbing energetically at damp spots on the corduroy. Roger closed his eyes and thought frantically of terrible car crashes on the motorway and tax forms for the

Inland Revenue and the Blob from Outer Space—anything
that might stop him disgracing himself utterly as Brianna
Randall's warm breath misted softly through the wet fabric of
his trousers.

"Er, maybe you'd like to do the rest yourself?" The voice
came from somewhere around the level of his nose, and he
opened his eyes to find a pair of deep blue eyes facing him
above a wide grin. He rather weakly took the napkin she was
offering him, breathing as though he had just been chased by
a train.

Lowering his head to scrub at his trousers, he caught
sight of Claire Randall watching him with an expression of
mingled sympathy and amusement. There was nothing else
visible in her expression; nothing of that flash he thought he'd
seen in her eyes just before the catastrophe. Flustered as he
was, it was probably his imagination, he thought. For why on
earth should she have done it on purpose?

————————————

*"Since when are you interested in Druids, Mama?"
Brianna seemed disposed to find something hilarious in
the idea; I had noticed her biting the insides of her cheeks
while I was chatting with Roger Wakefield, and the grin
she had been hiding then was now plastered across her
face. "You going to get your own bedsheet and join up?"*

*"Bound to be more entertaining than hospital staff
meetings every Thursday," I said. "Bit drafty, though."
She hooted with laughter, startling two coal tits off the
walk in front of us.*

*"No," I said, switching to seriousness. "It isn't the
Druid ladies I'm after, so much. There's someone I used
to know in Scotland that I wanted to find, if I can. I
haven't an address for her—I haven't been in touch with
her for more than twenty years—but she had an interest in
odd things like that: witchcraft, old beliefs, folklore. All
that sort of thing. She once lived near here; I thought if
she was still here, she might be involved with a group like
that."*

"What's her name?"

I shook my head, grabbing at the loosened clip as it

slid from my curls. It slipped through my fingers and bounced into the deep grass along the walk.

"Damn!" *I said, stooping for it. My fingers were unsteady as I groped through the dense stalks, and I had trouble picking up the clip, slippery with moisture from the wet grass. The thought of Geillis Duncan tended to unnerve me, even now.*

"I don't know," *I said, brushing the curls back off my flushed face.* "I mean—it's been such a long time, I'm sure she'd have a different name by now. She was widowed; she might have married again, or be using her maiden name."

"Oh." *Brianna lost interest in the topic, and walked along in silence for a little. Suddenly she said,* "What did you think of Roger Wakefield, Mama?"

I glanced at her; her cheeks were pink, but it might be from the spring wind.

"He seems a very nice young man," *I said carefully.* "He's certainly intelligent; he's one of the youngest professors at Oxford." *The intelligence I had known about; I wondered whether he had any imagination. So often scholarly types didn't. But imagination would be helpful.*

"He's got the grooviest eyes," *Brianna said, dreamily ignoring the question of his brain.* "Aren't they the greenest you've ever seen?"

"Yes, they're very striking," *I agreed.* "They've always been like that; I remember noticing them when I first met him as a child."

Brianna looked down at me, frowning.

"Yes, Mother, really! Did you* have *to say 'My, how you've grown?' when he answered the door? How embarrassing!"

I laughed.

"Well, when you've last seen someone hovering round your navel, and suddenly you find yourself looking up his nose," *I defended myself,* "you can't help remarking the difference."

"Mother!" *But she fizzed with laughter.*

"He has a very nice bottom, too," *I remarked, just to keep her going.* "I noticed when he bent over to get the whisky."

"Mo-THERRR! They'll hear *you!"*

We were nearly at the bus stop. There were two or three women and an elderly gentleman in tweeds standing by the sign; they turned to stare at us as we came up.

"Is this the place for the Loch-side Tours bus?" I asked, scanning the bewildering array of notices and advertisements posted on the signboard.

"Och, aye," one of the ladies said kindly. "The bus will be comin' along in ten minutes or so." She scanned Brianna, so clearly American in blue jeans and white windbreaker. The final patriotic note was added by the flushed face, red with suppressed laughter. "You'll be going to see Loch Ness? Your first time, is it?"

I smiled at her. "I sailed down the loch with my husband twenty-odd years ago, but this is my daughter's first trip to Scotland."

"Oh, is it?" This attracted the attention of the other ladies and they crowded around, suddenly friendly, offering advice and asking questions until the big yellow bus came chugging round the corner.

Brianna paused before climbing the steps, admiring the picturesque drawing of green serpentine loops, undulating through a blue-paint lake, edged with black pines.

"This will be fun," she said, laughing. "Think we'll see the monster?"

"You never know," I said.

Roger spent the rest of the day in a state of abstraction, wandering absently from one task to another. The books to be packed for donation to the Society for the Preservation of Antiquities lay spilling out of their carton, the Reverend's ancient flatbed lorry sat in the drive with its bonnet up, halfway through a motor check, and a cup of tea sat half-drunk and milk-scummed at his elbow as he gazed blankly out at the falling rain of early evening.

What he should do, he knew, was get at the job of dismantling the heart of the Reverend's study. Not the books; massive as that job was, it was only a matter of deciding which to keep himself, and which should be dispatched to the SPA or the Reverend's old college library. No, sooner or later he would have to tackle the enormous desk, which had papers filling each huge drawer to the brim and protruding from its dozens of pigeonholes. And he'd have to take down and dispose of all of the miscellany decorating the cork wall that filled one side of the room; a task to daunt the stoutest heart.

Aside from a general disinclination to start the tedious job, Roger was hampered by something else. He didn't *want* to be doing these things, necessary as they were; he wanted to be working on Claire Randall's project, tracking down the clansmen of Culloden.

It was an interesting enough project in its way, though probably a minor research job. But that wasn't it. No, he thought, if he were being honest with himself, he wanted to tackle Claire Randall's project because he wanted to go round to Mrs. Thomas's guesthouse and lay his results at the feet of Brianna Randall, as knights were supposed to have done with the heads of dragons. Even if he didn't get results on that scale, he urgently wanted some excuse to see her and talk with her again.

It was a Bronzino painting she reminded him of, he decided. She and her mother both gave that odd impression of having been outlined somehow, drawn with such vivid strokes and delicate detail that they stood out from their background as though they'd been engraved on it. But Brianna had that brilliant coloring, and that air of absolute physical presence that made Bronzino's sitters seem to follow you with their eyes, to be about to speak from their frames. He'd never seen a Bronzino painting making faces at a glass of whisky, but if there had been one, he was sure it would have looked precisely like Brianna Randall.

"Well, bloody hell," he said aloud. "It won't take a lot of time just to look over the records at Culloden House tomorrow, will it? You," he said, addressing the desk and its multiple burdens, "can wait for a day. So can you," he said to the wall, and defiantly plucked a mystery novel from the shelf. He glanced around belligerently, as though daring any of the furnishings to object, but there was no sound but the whirring of the electric fire. He switched it off and, book under his arm, left the study, flicking off the light.

A minute later, he came back, crossing the room in the dark, and retrieved the list of names from the table.

"Well, bloody hell anyway!" he said, and tucked it into the pocket of his shirt. "Don't want to forget the damn thing in the morning." He patted the pocket, feeling the soft crackle of the paper just over his heart, and went up to bed.

———————————

We had come back from Loch Ness blown with wind and chilled with rain, to the warm comfort of a hot supper and an open fire in the parlor. Brianna had begun to yawn over the scrambled eggs, and soon excused herself to go and take a hot bath. I stayed downstairs for a bit, chatting with Mrs. Thomas, the landlady, and it was nearly ten o'clock before I made my way up to my own bath and nightgown.

Brianna was an early riser and an early sleeper; her soft breathing greeted me as I pushed open the bedroom door. An early sleeper, she was also a sound one; I moved carefully around the room, hanging up my clothes and tidying things away, but there was little danger of waking her. The house grew quiet as I went about my work, so that the rustle of my own movements seemed loud in my ears.

I had brought several of Frank's books with me, intending to donate them to the Inverness Library. They were laid neatly in the bottom of my suitcase, forming a foundation for the more squashable items above. I took them out one by one, laying them on the bed. Five hardbound volumes, glossy in bright dust covers. Nice, substantial things; five or six hundred pages each, not counting index and illustrations.

My late husband's Collected Works, in the Fully Annotated editions. Inches of admiring reviews covered the jacket flaps, comments from every recognized expert in the historical field. Not bad for a Life's Work, I thought. An accomplishment to be proud of. Compact, weighty, authoritative.

I stacked the books neatly on the table next to my bag, so as not to forget them in the morning. The titles on the spines were different, of course, but I stacked them so that the uniform "Frank W. Randall"'s at the ends lined up, one above the other. They glowed jewel-bright in the small pool of light from the bedside lamp.

The bed-and-breakfast was quiet; it was early in the year for guests, and those there were had long since gone to sleep. In the other twin bed, Brianna made a small whuffling noise and rolled over in her sleep, leaving long strands of red hair draped across her dreaming face. One long, bare foot protruded from the bedclothes, and I pulled the blanket gently over it.

The impulse to touch a sleeping child never fades, no matter that the child is a good deal larger than her mother, and a woman—if a young one—in her own right. I smoothed the hair back from her face and stroked the crown of her head. She smiled in her sleep, a brief reflex of contentment, gone as soon as it appeared. My own smile lingered as I watched her, and whispered to her sleep-deaf ears, as I had so many times before, "God, you are so like him."

I swallowed the faint thickening in my throat—it was nearly habit, by now—and took my dressing gown from the chairback. It was bloody cold at night in the Scottish Highlands in April, but I wasn't yet ready to seek the warm sanctuary of my own twin bed.

I had asked the landlady to leave the fire burning in the sitting room, assuring her that I would bank it before retiring. I closed the door softly, still seeing the sprawl of long limbs, the splash and tumble of red silk across the quilted blue spread.

"Not bad for a Life's Work, either," I whispered to the dark hallway. "Maybe not so compact, but damned authoritative."

The small parlor was dark and cozy, the fire burnt down to a steady glow of flame along the backbone of the main log. I pulled a small armchair up before the fire and propped my feet on the fender. I could hear all the small usual sounds of modern life around me; the faint whirr of the refrigerator in the basement below, the hum and whoosh of the central heating that made the fire a comfort rather than a necessity; the passing rush of an occasional car outside.

But under everything was the deep silence of a Highland night. I sat very still, reaching for it. It had been twenty years since I last felt it, but the soothing power of the dark was still there, cradled between the mountains.

I reached into the pocket of my dressing gown and pulled out the folded paper—a copy of the list I had given Roger Wakefield. It was too dark to read by firelight, but I didn't need to see the names. I unfolded the paper on my silk-clad knee and sat blindly staring at the lines of illegible type. I ran my finger slowly across each line, murmuring each man's name to myself like a prayer. They belonged to the cold spring night, more than I did. But I kept looking into the flames, letting the dark outside come to fill the empty places inside me.

And speaking their names as though to summon them, I began the first steps back, crossing the empty dark to where they waited.

The Plot Thickens

R oger left Culloden House next morning with twelve pages of notes and a growing feeling of bafflement. What had at first seemed a fairly straightforward job of historical research was turning up some odd twists, and no mistake.

He had found only three of the names from Claire Randall's list among the rolls of the dead of Culloden. This in itself was nothing remarkable. Charles Stuart's army had rarely had a coherent roll of enlistment, as some clan chieftains had joined the Bonnie Prince apparently on whim, and many had left for even less reason, before the names of their men could be inscribed on any official document. The Highland army's record-keeping, haphazard at best, had disintegrated almost completely toward the end; there was little point in keeping a payroll, after all, if you had nothing with which to pay the men on it.

He carefully folded his lanky frame and inserted himself into his ancient Morris, automatically ducking to avoid bumping his head. Taking the folder from under his arm, he opened it and frowned at the pages he had copied. What was odd about it was that nearly all of the men on Claire's list *had* been shown on another army list.

Within the ranks of a given clan regiment, men might have deserted as the dimensions of the coming disaster became clearer; that would have been nothing unusual. No, what made the whole thing so incomprehensible was that the names on Claire's list had shown up—entire and complete—as part of the Master of Lovat's regiment, sent late in the campaign to fulfill a promise of support made to the Stuarts by Simon Fraser, Lord Lovat.

Yet Claire had definitely said—and a glance at her original sheets confirmed it—that these men had all come from a small estate called Broch Tuarach, well to the south and west of the Fraser lands—on the border of the MacKenzie clan lands, in fact. More than that, she had said these men had been with the Highland army since the Battle of Prestonpans, which had occurred near the beginning of the campaign.

Roger shook his head. This made no kind of sense. Granted, Claire might have mistaken the timing—she had said herself that she was no historian. But not the location, surely? And how could men from the estate of Broch Tuarach, who had given no oath of allegiance to the chief of clan Fraser, have been at the disposal of Simon Fraser? True, Lord Lovat had been known as "the Old Fox," and for good reason, but Roger doubted that even that redoubtable old Earl had had sufficient wiliness to pull off something like this.

Frowning to himself, Roger started the car and pulled out of the parking lot. The archives at Culloden House were depressingly incomplete; mostly a lot of picturesque letters from Lord George Murray, beefing about supply problems, and things that looked good in the museum displays for the tourists. He needed a lot more than that.

"Hold on, cock," he reminded himself, squinting in the rearview mirror at the turn. "You're meant to be finding out what happened to the ones that *didn't* cark it at Culloden. What does it matter how they got there, so long as they left the battle in one piece?"

But he couldn't leave it alone. It was such an odd circumstance. Names got muddled with enormous frequency, especially in the Highlands, where half the population at any given moment seemed to be named "Alexander." Consequently, men had customarily been known by their place-names, as well as their clan or surnames. Sometimes *instead* of the surnames. "Lochiel," one of the most prominent Jacobite chieftains, was in fact Donald Cameron, *of* Lochiel, which distinguished him nicely from the hundreds of other Camerons named Donald.

And all the Highland men who hadn't been named Donald or Alec had been named John. Of the three names that he'd found on the death rolls that matched Claire's list, one was Donald Murray, one was Alexander MacKenzie Fraser, and one was John Graham Fraser. All without place-names attached; just the plain name, and the regiment to which they'd belonged. The Master of Lovat's regiment, the Fraser regiment.

But without the place-name, he couldn't be sure that

they *were* the same men as the names on Claire's list. There were at least six John Frasers on the death roll, and even that was incomplete; the English had given little attention to completeness or accuracy—most of the records had been compiled after the fact, by clan chieftains counting noses and determining who hadn't come home. Frequently the chieftains themselves hadn't come home, which complicated matters.

He rubbed his hand hard through his hair with frustration, as though scalp massage might stimulate his brain. And if the three names *weren't* the same men, the mystery only deepened. A good half of Charles Stuart's army had been slaughtered at Culloden. And Lovat's men had been in the thick of it, right in the center of the battle. It was inconceivable that a group of thirty men had survived in that position without one fatality. The Master of Lovat's men had come late to the Rising; while desertion had been rife in other regiments, who had served long enough to have some idea what they were in for, the Frasers had been remarkably loyal —and suffered in consequence.

A loud horn-blast from behind startled him out of his concentration, and he pulled to the side to let a large, annoyed lorry rumble past. Thinking and driving were not compatible activities, he decided. End up smashed against a stone wall, if he kept this up.

He sat still for a moment, pondering. His natural impulse was to go to Mrs. Thomas's bed-and-breakfast, and tell Claire what he had found to date. The fact that this might involve basking for a few moments in the presence of Brianna Randall enhanced the appeal of this idea.

On the other hand, all his historian's instincts cried out for more data. And he wasn't at all sure that Claire was the person to provide it. He couldn't imagine why she should commission him to do this project, and at the same time, interfere with its completion by giving him inaccurate information. It wasn't sensible, and Claire Randall struck him as an eminently sensible person.

Still, there was that business with the whisky. His cheeks grew hot in memory. He was positive she'd done it on purpose—and as she didn't really seem the sort for practical jokes, he was compelled to assume she'd done it to stop him inviting Brianna to Broch Tuarach. Did she want to keep him away from the place, or only to stop him taking Brianna there? The more he thought about the incident, the more convinced he became that Claire Randall was keeping something from her daughter, but what it was, he couldn't imagine. Still less could he think what connection it had with him, or the project he had undertaken.

He'd give it up, were it not for two things. Brianna, and simple curiosity. He wanted to know what was going on, and he bloody well intended to find out.

He rapped his fist softly against the wheel, thinking, ignoring the rush of passing traffic. At last, decision made, he started the engine again and pulled into the road. At the next roundabout, he went three-quarters round the circle and headed for the town center of Inverness, and the railroad station.

The Flying Scotsman could have him in Edinburgh in five hours. The curator in charge of the Stuart Papers had been a close friend of the Reverend. And he had one clue to start with, puzzling as it was. The roll that had listed the names in the Master of Lovat's regiment had shown those thirty men as being under the command of a Captain James Fraser—of Broch Tuarach. This man was the only apparent link between Broch Tuarach and the Frasers of Lovat. He wondered why James Fraser had not appeared on Claire's list.

The sun was out; a rare event for mid-April, and Roger made the most of it by cranking down the tiny window on the driver's side, to let the bright wind blow past his ear.

He had had to stay overnight in Edinburgh, and coming back late the next day, had been so tired from the long train ride that he had done little more than eat the hot supper Fiona insisted on fixing him before he fell into bed. But today he had risen full of renewed energy and determination, and motored down to the small village of Broch Mordha, near the site of the estate called Broch Tuarach. If her mother didn't want Brianna Randall going to Broch Tuarach, there was nothing stopping *him* from having a look at the place.

He had actually found Broch Tuarach itself, or at least he

assumed so; there was an enormous pile of fallen stone, surrounding the collapsed remnant of one of the ancient circular brochs, or towers, used in the distant past both for living and for defense. He had sufficient Gaelic to know that the name meant "north-facing tower," and had wondered briefly just how a circular tower could have come by such a name.

There was a manor house and its outbuildings nearby, also in ruins, though a good deal more of it was left. An estate agent's sign, weathered almost to illegibility, stood tacked to a stake in the dooryard. Roger stood on the slope above the house, looking around. At a glance, he could see nothing that would explain Claire's wanting to keep her daughter from coming here.

He parked the Morris in the dooryard, and climbed out. It was a beautiful site, but very remote; it had taken him nearly forty-five minutes of careful maneuvering to get his Morris down the rutted country lane from the main highway without fracturing his oil pan.

He didn't go into the house; it was plainly abandoned, and possibly dangerous—there would be nothing there. The name FRASER was carved into the lintel, though, and the same name adorned most of the small tombstones in what must have been the family graveyard—those that were legible. Not a great help, that, he reflected. None of these stones bore the names of men on his list. He'd have to go on along the road; according to the AA map, the village of Broch Mordha was three miles farther on.

As he'd feared, the small village church had fallen into disuse and been knocked down years ago. Persistent knockings on doors elicited blank stares, dour looks, and finally a doubtful speculation from an aged farmer that the old parish records might have gone to the museum in Fort William, or maybe up to Inverness; there was a minister up that way who collected such rubbish.

Tired and dusty, but not yet discouraged, Roger trudged back to his car, sheltering in the lane by the village pub. This was the sort of setback that so often attended historical field research, and he was used to it. A quick pint—well, two, maybe, it was an unusually warm day—and then on to Fort William.

Serve him right, he reflected wryly, if the records he was

looking for turned out to be in the Reverend's archives all along. That's what he got for neglecting his work to go on wild-goose chases to impress a girl. His trip to Edínburgh had done little more than serve to eliminate the three names he'd found at Culloden House; all three men proved to have come from different regiments, not the Broch Tuarach group.

The Stuart Papers took up three entire rooms, as well as untold packing cases in the basement of the museum, so he could hardly claim to have made an exhaustive study. Still, he had found a duplicate of the payroll he'd seen at Culloden House, listing the joining of the men as part of a regiment under the overall command of the Master of Lovat—the Old Fox's son, that would have been, Young Simon. Cagy old bastard split his vote, Roger thought; sent the heir to fight for the Stuarts, and stayed home himself, claiming to have been a loyal subject of King Geordie all along. Much good it did him.

That document had listed Simon Fraser the Younger as commander, and made no mention of James Fraser. A James Fraser was mentioned in a number of army dispatches, memoranda, and other documents, though. If it was the same man, he'd been fairly active in the campaign. Still, with only the name "James Fraser," it was impossible to tell if it was the Broch Tuarach one; James was as common a Highland name as Duncan or Robert. In only one spot was a James Fraser listed with additional middle names that might help in identification, but that document made no mention of his men.

He shrugged, irritably waving off a sudden cloud of voracious midges. To go through those records in coherent fashion would take several years. Unable to shake the attentions of the midges, he ducked into the dark, brewery atmosphere of the pub, leaving them to mill outside in a frenzied cloud of inquiry.

Sipping the cool, bitter ale, he mentally reviewed the steps taken so far, and the options open to him. He had time to go to Fort William today, though it would mean getting back to Inverness late. And if the Fort William museum turned up nothing, then a good rummage through the Reverend's archives was the logical, if ironic, next step.

And after that? He drained the last drops of bitter, and signaled the landlord for another glass. Well, if it came down to it, a tramp round every kirkyard and burying ground in the general vicinity of Broch Tuarach was likely the best he could do in the short term. He doubted that the Randalls would stay in Inverness for the next two or three years, patiently awaiting results.

He felt in his pocket for the notebook that is the historian's constant companion. Before he left Broch Mordha, he should at least have a look at what was left of the old kirkyard. You never knew what might turn up, and it would at least save him coming back.

The next afternoon, the Randalls came to take tea at Roger's invitation, and to hear his progress report.

"I've found several of the names on your list," he told Claire, leading the way into the study. "It's very odd; I haven't yet found any who died for sure at Culloden. I thought I had three, but they turned out to be different men with the same names." He glanced at Dr. Randall; she was standing quite still, one hand clasping the back of a wing chair, as though she'd forgotten where she was.

"Er, won't you sit down?" Roger invited, and with a small, startled jerk, she nodded and sat abruptly on the edge of the seat. Roger eyed her curiously, but went on, pulling out his folder of research notes and handing it to her.

"As I say, it's odd. I haven't tracked down all the names; I think I'll need to go nose about among the parish registers and graveyards near Broch Tuarach. I found most of these records among my father's papers. But you'd think I'd have turned up one or two battle-deaths at least, given that they were all at Culloden. Especially if, as you say, they were with one of the Fraser regiments; those were nearly all in the center of the battle, where the fighting was thickest."

"I know." There was something in her voice that made him look at her, puzzled, but her face was invisible as she bent over the desk. Most of the records were copies, made in Roger's own hand, as the exotic technology of photocopying had not yet penetrated to the government archive that guarded the Stuart Papers, but there were a few original sheets, unearthed from the late Reverend Wakefield's hoard of eighteenth-century documents. She turned over the records with a gentle finger, careful not to touch the fragile paper more than necessary.

"You're right; that *is* odd." Now he recognized the emotion in her voice—it was excitement, but mingled with satisfaction and relief. She had been in some way expecting this—or hoping for it.

"Tell me . . ." She hesitated. "The names you've found. What happened to them, if they didn't die at Culloden?"

He was faintly surprised that it should seem to matter so much to her, but obligingly pulled out the folder that held his research notes and opened it. "Two of them were on a ship's roll; they emigrated to America soon after Culloden. Four died of natural causes about a year later—not surprising, there was a terrible famine after Culloden, and a lot of people died in the Highlands. And this one I found in a parish register—but not the parish he came from. I'm fairly sure it's one of your men, though."

It was only as the tension went out of her shoulders that he noticed it had been there.

"Do you want me to look for the rest, still?" he asked, hoping that the answer would be "yes." He was watching Brianna over her mother's shoulder. She was standing by the cork wall, half-turned as though uninterested in her mother's project, but he could see a small vertical crease between her brows.

Perhaps she sensed the same thing he did, the odd air of suppressed excitement that surrounded Claire like an electric field. He had been aware of it from the moment she walked into the room, and his revelations had only increased it. He imagined that if he touched her, a great spark of static electricity would leap between them.

A knock on the study door interrupted his thoughts. The door opened and Fiona Graham came in, pushing a tea cart, fully equipped with teapot, cups, doilies, three kinds of sandwiches, cream-cakes, sponge cake, jam tarts, and scones with clotted cream.

"Yum!" said Brianna at the sight. "Is that all for us, or are you expecting ten other people?"

Claire Randall looked over the tea preparations, smiling. The electric field was still there, but damped down by major effort. Roger could see one of her hands, clenched so hard in the folds of her skirt that the edge of her ring cut into the flesh.

"That tea is so high, we won't need to eat for weeks," she said. "It looks wonderful!"

Fiona beamed. She was short, plump and pretty as a small brown hen. Roger sighed internally. While he was pleased to be able to offer his guests hospitality, he was well aware that the lavish nature of the refreshments was intended for his appreciation, not theirs. Fiona, aged nineteen, had one burning ambition in life. To be a wife. Preferably of a professional man. She had taken one look at Roger when he arrived a week earlier to tidy up the Reverend's affairs, and decided that an assistant professor of history was the best prospect Inverness offered.

Since then, he had been stuffed like a Christmas goose, had his shoes polished, his slippers and toothbrush laid out, his bed turned down, his coat brushed, the evening paper bought for him and laid alongside his plate, his neck rubbed when he had been working over his desk for long hours, and constant inquiries made concerning his bodily comfort, state of mind, and general health. He had never before been exposed to such a barrage of domesticity.

In short, Fiona was driving him mad. His current state of unshaven dishabille was more a reaction to her relentless pursuit than it was a descent into that natural squalor enjoyed by men temporarily freed from the demands of job and society.

The thought of being united in bonds of holy wedlock with Fiona Graham was one that froze him to the marrow. She would drive him insane within a year, with her constant pestering. Aside from that, though, there was Brianna Randall, now gazing contemplatively at the tea cart, as though wondering where to start.

He had been keeping his attention firmly fixed on Claire Randall and her project this afternoon, avoiding looking at her daughter. Claire Randall was lovely, with the sort of fine bones and translucent skin that would make her look much the same at sixty as she had at twenty. But looking at Brianna Randall made him feel slightly breathless.

She carried herself like a queen, not slumping as tall girls so often do. Noting her mother's straight back and graceful posture, he could see where that particular attribute had come from. But not the remarkable height, the cascade of waist-length red hair, sparked with gold and copper, streaked with amber and cinnamon, curling casually around face and shoulders like a mantle. The eyes, so dark a blue as almost to be black in some lights. Nor that wide, generous mouth, with a full lower lip that invited nibbling kisses and biting passion. Those things must have come from her father.

Roger was on the whole rather glad that her father was not present, since he would certainly have taken paternal umbrage at the sorts of thoughts Roger was thinking; thoughts he was desperately afraid showed on his face.

"Tea, eh?" he said heartily. "Splendid. Wonderful. Looks delicious, Fiona. Er, thanks, Fiona. I, um, don't think we need anything else."

Ignoring the broad hint to depart, Fiona nodded graciously at the compliments from the guests, laid out the doilies and cups with deft economy of motion, poured the tea, passed round the first plate of cake, and seemed prepared to stay indefinitely, presiding as lady of the house.

"Have some cream on your scones, Rog—I mean, Mr. Wakefield," she suggested, ladling it on without waiting for his reply. "You're much too thin; you want feeding up." She glanced conspiratorially at Brianna Randall, saying, "You know what men are; never eat properly without a woman to look after them."

"How lucky that he's got you to take care of him," Brianna answered politely.

Roger took a deep breath, and flexed his fingers several times, until the urge to strangle Fiona had passed.

"Fiona," he said. "Would you, um, could you possibly do me a small favor?"

She lit up like a small jack-o'-lantern, mouth stretched in an eager grin at the thought of doing something for him. "Of course, Rog—Mr. Wakefield! Anything at all!"

Roger felt vaguely ashamed of himself, but after all, he argued, it was for her good as much as his. If she didn't leave, he was shortly going to cease being responsible and commit some act they would both regret.

"Oh, thanks, Fiona. It's nothing much; only that I'd ordered some . . . some"—he thought frantically, trying to remember the name of one of the village merchants—"some tobacco, from Mr. Buchan in the High Street. I wonder if you'd be willing to go and fetch it for me; I could just do with a good pipe after such a wonderful tea."

Fiona was already untying her apron—the frilly, lace-trimmed one, Roger noted grimly. He closed his eyes briefly in relief as the study door shut behind her, dismissing for the moment the fact that he didn't smoke. With a sigh of relief, he turned to conversation with his guests.

"You were asking whether I wanted you to look for the rest of the names on my list," Claire said, almost at once. Roger had the odd impression that she shared his relief at Fiona's departure. "Yes, I do—if it wouldn't be too much trouble?"

"No, no! Not at all," Roger said, with only slight mendacity. "Glad to do it."

Roger's hand hovered uncertainly amid the largesse of the tea cart, then snaked down to grasp the crystal decanter of twelve-year-old Muir Breame whisky. After the skirmish with Fiona, he felt he owed it to himself.

"Will you have a bit of this?" he asked his guests politely. Catching the look of distaste on Brianna's face, he quickly added, "Or maybe some tea?"

"Tea," Brianna said with relief.

"You don't know what you're missing," Claire told her daughter, inhaling the whisky fumes with rapture.

"Oh yes I do," Brianna replied. "That's why I'm missing it." She shrugged and quirked an eyebrow at Roger.

"You have to be twenty-one before you can drink legally in Massachusetts," Claire explained to Roger. "Bree has another twenty months to go, so she really isn't used to whisky."

"You act as though not liking whisky was a crime," Brianna protested, smiling at Roger above her teacup.

He raised his own brows in response. "My dear woman," he said severely. "This is *Scotland*. Of course not liking whisky is a crime!"

"Oh, aye?" said Brianna sweetly, in a perfect imitation of his own slight Scots burr. "Well, we'll hope it's no a capital offense like murrderrr, shall we?"

Taken by surprise, he swallowed a laugh with his whisky and choked. Coughing and pounding himself on the chest, he glanced at Claire to share the joke. A forced smile hung on her lips, but her face had gone quite pale. Then she blinked, the smile came back more naturally, and the moment passed.

Roger was surprised at how easily conversation flowed among them—both about trivialities, and about Claire's project. Brianna clearly had been interested in her father's work, and knew a great deal more about the Jacobites than did her mother.

"It's amazing they ever made it as far as Culloden," she said. "Did you know the Highlanders won the battle of Prestonpans with barely two thousand men? Against an English army of eight thousand? Incredible!"

"Well, and the Battle of Falkirk was nearly that way as well," Roger chimed in. "Outnumbered, outarmed, marching on foot . . . they should never have been able to do what they did . . . but they did!"

"Um-hm," said Claire, taking a deep gulp of her whisky. "They did."

"I was thinking," Roger said to Brianna, with an assumed air of casualness. "Perhaps you'd like to come with me to some of the places—the battle sites and other places? They're interesting, and I'm sure you'd be a tremendous help with the research."

Brianna laughed and smoothed back her hair, which had a tendency to drop into her tea. "I don't know about the help, but I'd love to come."

"Terrific!" Surprised and elated with her agreement, he fumbled for the decanter and nearly dropped it. Claire fielded it neatly, and filled his glass with precision.

"The least I can do, after spilling it the last time," she said, smiling in answer to his thanks.

Seeing her now, poised and relaxed, Roger was inclined to doubt his earlier suspicions. Maybe it had been an accident after all? That lovely cool face told him nothing.

A half-hour later, the tea table lay in shambles, the decanter stood empty, and the three of them sat in a shared stupor of content. Brianna shifted once or twice, glanced at Roger, and finally asked if she might use his "rest room."

"Oh, the W.C.? Of course." He heaved himself to his feet, ponderous with Dundee cake and almond sponge. If he didn't get away from Fiona soon, he'd weigh three hundred pounds before he got back to Oxford.

"It's one of the old-fashioned kind," he explained, pointing down the hall in the direction of the bathroom. "With a tank on the ceiling and a pull-chain."

"I saw some of those in the British Museum," Brianna said, nodding. "Only they weren't in with the exhibits, they were in the ladies' room." She hesitated, then asked, "You haven't got the same sort of toilet paper they have in the British Museum, do you? Because if you do, I've got some Kleenex in my purse."

Roger closed one eye and looked at her with the other. "Either that's a very odd non sequitur," he said, "or I've drunk a good deal more than I thought." In fact, he and Claire had accounted very satisfactorily for the Muir Breame, though Brianna had confined herself to tea.

Claire laughed, overhearing the exchange, and got up to hand Brianna several folded facial tissues from her own bag. "It won't be waxed paper stamped with 'Property of H. M. Government,' like the Museum's, but it likely won't be much better," she told her daughter. "British toilet paper is commonly rather a stiff article."

"Thanks." Brianna took the tissues and turned to the door, but then turned back. "Why on earth would people deliberately make toilet paper that feels like tinfoil?" she demanded.

"Hearts of oak are our men," Roger intoned, "stainless steel are their bums. It builds the national character."

"In the case of Scots, I expect it's hereditary nerve-deadening," Claire added. "The sort of men who could ride horseback wearing a kilt have bottoms like saddle leather."

Brianna fizzed with laughter. "I'd hate to see what they used for toilet paper *then*," she said.

"Actually, it wasn't bad," Claire said, surprisingly. "Mullein leaves are really very nice; quite as good as two-ply bathroom tissue. And in the winter or indoors, it was usually a bit of damp rag; not very sanitary, but comfortable enough."

Roger and Brianna both gawked at her for a moment.

"Er . . . read it in a book," she said, and blushed amazingly.

As Brianna, still giggling, made her way off in search of the facilities, Claire remained standing by the door.

"It was awfully nice of you to entertain us so grandly,"

she said, smiling at Roger. The momentary discomposure had vanished, replaced by her usual poise. "And remarkably kind of you to have found out about those names for me."

"My pleasure entirely," Roger assured her. "It's made a nice change from cobwebs and mothballs. I'll let you know as soon as I've found out anything else about your Jacobites."

"Thank you." Claire hesitated, glanced over her shoulder, and lowered her voice. "Actually, since Bree's gone for the moment . . . there's something I wanted to ask you, in private."

Roger cleared his throat and straightened the tie he had donned in honor of the occasion.

"Ask away," he said, feeling cheerfully expansive with the success of the tea party. "I'm completely at your service."

"You were asking Bree if she'd go with you to do field research. I wanted to ask you . . . there's a place I'd rather you didn't take her, if you don't mind."

Alarm bells went off at once in Roger's head. Was he going to find out what the secret was about Broch Tuarach?

"The circle of standing stones—they call it Craigh na Dun." Claire's face was earnest as she leaned slightly closer. "There's an important reason, or I wouldn't ask. I want to take Brianna to the circle myself, but I'm afraid I can't tell you why, just now. I will, in time, but not quite yet. Will you promise me?"

Thoughts were chasing themselves through Roger's mind. So it hadn't been Broch Tuarach she wanted to keep the girl away from, after all! One mystery was explained, only to deepen another.

"If you like," he said at last. "Of course."

"Thank you." She touched his arm once, lightly, and turned to go. Seeing her silhouetted against the light, he was suddenly reminded of something. Perhaps it wasn't the moment to ask, but it couldn't do any harm.

"Oh, Dr. Randall—Claire?"

Claire turned back to face him. With the distractions of Brianna removed, he could see that Claire Randall was a very beautiful woman in her own right. Her face was flushed from the whisky, and her eyes were the most unusual light golden-brown color, he thought—like amber in crystal.

"In all the records that I found dealing with these men,"

Roger said, choosing his words carefully, "there was a mention of a Captain James Fraser, who seems to have been their
leader. But he wasn't on your list. I only wondered; did you
know about him?"

She stood stock-still for a moment, reminding him of the
way she had behaved upon her arrival that afternoon. But
after a moment, she shook herself slightly, and answered with
apparent equanimity.

"Yes, I knew about him." She spoke calmly, but all the
color had left her face, and Roger could see a small pulse
beating rapidly at the base of her throat.

"I didn't put him on the list because I already knew what
happened to him. Jamie Fraser died at Culloden."

"Are you sure?"

As though anxious to leave, Claire scooped up her handbag, and glanced down the hall toward the bathroom, where
the rattling of the ancient knob indicated Brianna's attempts
to get out.

"Yes," she said, not looking back. "I'm quite sure. Oh,
Mr. Wakefield . . . Roger, I mean." She swung back now,
fixing those oddly colored eyes on him. In this light, they
looked almost yellow, he thought; the eyes of a big cat, a
leopard's eyes.

"Please," she said, "don't mention Jamie Fraser to my
daughter."

It was late, and he should have been abed long since, but
Roger found himself unable to sleep. Whether from the ag-
gravations of Fiona, the puzzling contradictions of Claire
Randall, or from exaltation over the prospect of doing field
research with Brianna Randall, he was wide-awake, and likely
to remain so. Rather than toss, turn, or count sheep, he resolved to put his wakefulness to good use. A rummage
through the Reverend's papers would probably put him to
sleep in no time.

Fiona's light down the hall was still on, but he tiptoed
down the stair, not to disturb her. Then, snapping on the
study light, he stood for a moment, contemplating the magnitude of the task before him.

The wall exemplified the Reverend Wakefield's mind.

Completely covering one side of the study, it was an expanse of corkboard measuring nearly twenty feet by twelve. Virtually none of the original cork was visible under the layers upon layers of papers, notes, photographs, mimeographed sheets, bills, receipts, bird feathers, torn-off corners of envelopes containing interesting postage stamps, address labels, key rings, postcards, rubber bands, and other impedimenta, all tacked up or attached by bits of string.

The trivia lay twelve layers deep in spots, yet the Reverend had always been able to set his hand unerringly on the bit he wanted. Roger thought that the wall must have been organized according to some underlying principle so subtle that not even American NASA scientists could discern it.

Roger viewed the wall dubiously. There was no logical point at which to start. He reached tentatively for a mimeographed list of General Assembly meeting dates sent out by the moderator's office, but was distracted by the sight underneath of a crayoned dragon, complete with artistic puffs of smoke from the flaring nostrils, and green flames shooting from the gaping mouth.

ROGER was written in large, straggling capitals at the bottom of the sheet. He vaguely remembered explaining that the dragon breathed green fire because it ate nothing but spinach. He let the General Assembly list fall back into place, and turned away from the wall. He could tackle that lot later.

The desk, an enormous oak rolltop with at least forty stuffed-to-bursting pigeonholes, seemed like pie by comparison. With a sigh, Roger pulled up the battered office chair and sat down to make sense of all the documents the Reverend thought worth keeping.

One stack of bills yet to be paid. Another of official-looking documents: automobile titles, surveyor's reports, building-inspection certificates. Another for historical notes and records. Another for family keepsakes. Another—by far the largest—for rubbish.

Deep in his task, he didn't hear the door open behind him, or the approaching footsteps. Suddenly a large teapot appeared on the desk next to him.

"Eh?" He straightened up, blinking.

"Thought you might do with some tea, Mr. Wake—I

mean, Roger." Fiona set down a small tray containing a cup and saucer and a plate of biscuits.

"Oh, thanks." He was in fact hungry, and gave Fiona a friendly smile that sent the blood rushing into her round, fair cheeks. Seemingly encouraged by this, she didn't go away, but perched on the corner of the desk, watching him raptly as he went about his job between bites of chocolate biscuit.

Feeling obscurely that he ought to acknowledge her presence in some way, Roger held up a half-eaten biscuit and mumbled, "Good."

"Are they? I made them, ye know." Fiona's flush grew deeper. An attractive little girl, Fiona. Small, rounded, with dark curly hair and wide brown eyes. He found himself wondering suddenly whether Brianna Randall could cook, and shook his head to clear the image.

Apparently taking this as a gesture of disbelief, Fiona leaned closer. "No, really," she insisted. "A recipe of my gran's, it is. She always said they were a favorite of the Reverend's." The wide brown eyes grew a trifle misty. "She left me all her cookbooks and things. Me being the only granddaughter, ye see."

"I was sorry about your grandmother," Roger said sincerely. "Quick, was it?"

Fiona nodded mournfully. "Oh, aye. Right as rain all day, then she said after supper as she felt a bit tired, and went up to her bed." The girl lifted her shoulders and let them fall. "She went to sleep, and never woke up."

"A good way to go," Roger said. "I'm glad of it." Mrs. Graham had been a fixture in the manse since before Roger himself had come, a frightened, newly orphaned five-year-old. Middle-aged even then, and widowed with grown children, still she had provided an abundant supply of firm, no-nonsense maternal affection during school holidays when Roger came home to the manse. She and the Reverend made an odd pair, and yet between them they had made the old house definitely a home.

Moved by his memories, Roger reached out and squeezed Fiona's hand. She squeezed back, brown eyes suddenly melting. The small rosebud mouth parted slightly, and she leaned toward Roger, her breath warm on his ear.

"Uh, thank you," Roger blurted. He pulled his hand out

of her grasp as though scorched. "Thanks very much. For the
. . . the . . . er, tea and things. Good. It was good. Very
good. Thanks." He turned and reached hastily for another
stack of papers to cover his confusion, snatching a rolled bundle of newspaper clippings from a pigeonhole chosen at random.

He unrolled the yellowed clippings and spread them on
the desk, holding them down between his palms. Frowning in
apparent deep concentration, he bent his head lower over the
smudged text. After a moment Fiona rose with a deep sigh,
and her footsteps receded toward the door. Roger didn't look
up.

Letting out a deep sigh of his own, he closed his eyes
briefly and offered a quick prayer of thanks for the narrow
escape. Yes, Fiona was attractive. Yes, she was undoubtedly a
fine cook. She was also nosy, interfering, irritating, and firmly
bent on marriage. Lay one hand on that rosy flesh again, and
they'd be calling the banns by next month. But if there was
any bann-calling to be done, the name linked with Roger
Wakefield in the parish register was going to be Brianna Randall's, if Roger had anything to say about it.

Wondering just how much he *would* have to say about it,
Roger opened his eyes and then blinked. For there in front of
him was the name he had been envisioning on a wedding
license—Randall.

Not, of course, Brianna Randall. Claire Randall. The
headline read RETURNED FROM THE DEAD. Beneath was a picture
of Claire Randall, twenty years younger, but looking little
different than she did now, bar the expression on her face.
She had been photographed sitting bolt upright in a hospital
bed, hair tousled and flying like banners, delicate mouth set
like a steel trap, and those extraordinary eyes glaring straight
into the camera.

With a sense of shock, Roger thumbed rapidly through
the bundle of clippings, then returned to read them more
carefully. Though the papers had made as much sensation as
possible of the story, the facts were sparse.

Claire Randall, wife of the noted historian Dr. Franklin
W. Randall, had disappeared during a Scottish holiday in Inverness, late in the spring of 1945. A car she had been driving
had been found, but the woman herself was gone without

trace. All searches having proved futile, the police and bereaved husband had at length concluded that Claire Randall
must have been murdered, perhaps by a roving tramp, and
her body concealed somewhere in the rocky crags of the area.

And in 1948, nearly three years later, Claire Randall had
returned. She had been found, disheveled and dressed in
rags, wandering near the spot at which she had disappeared.
While appearing to be in good physical health, though slightly
malnourished, Mrs. Randall was disoriented and incoherent.

Raising his eyebrows slightly at the thought of Claire
Randall ever being incoherent, Roger thumbed through the
rest of the clippings. They contained little more than the information that Mrs. Randall was being treated for exposure
and shock at a local hospital. There were photographs of the
presumably overjoyed husband, Frank Randall. He looked
stunned rather than overjoyed, Roger thought critically, not
that one could blame him.

He examined the pictures curiously. Frank Randall had
been a slender, handsome, aristocratic-looking man. Dark,
with a rakish grace that showed in the angle of his body as he
stood poised in the door of the hospital, surprised by the
photographer on his way to visit his newly restored wife.

He traced the line of the long, narrow jaw, and the curve
of the head, and realized that he was searching for traces of
Brianna in her father. Intrigued by the thought, he rose and
fetched one of Frank Randall's books from the shelves. Turning to the back jacket, he found a better picture. The jacket
photograph showed Frank Randall in color, in full-face view.
No, the hair was definitely dark brown, not red. That blazing
glory must have come from a grandparent, along with the
deep blue eyes, slanted as a cat's. Beautiful they were, but
nothing like her mother's. And not like her father's either.
Try as he might, he could see nothing of the flaming goddess
in the face of the famous historian.

With a sigh, he closed the book and gathered up the
clippings. He really must stop this mooning about and get on
with the job, or he'd be sitting here for the next twelvemonth.

He was about to put the clippings into the keepsake pile,
when one, headlined KIDNAPPED BY THE FAIRIES?, caught his
eye. Or rather, not the clipping, but the date that appeared
just above the headline. May 6, 1948.

He set the clipping down gently, as though it were a bomb that might go off in his hand. He closed his eyes and tried to summon up that conversation with the Randalls. "You have to be twenty-one to drink in Massachusetts," Claire had said. "Brianna still has eight months to go." Twenty, then. Brianna Randall was twenty.

Unable to count backward fast enough, he rose and scrabbled through the perpetual calendar that the vicar had kept, in a clear space to itself on his cluttered wall. He found the date and stood with his finger pressed to the paper, blood draining from his face.

Claire Randall had returned from her mysterious disappearance disheveled, malnourished, incoherent—and pregnant.

In the fullness of time, Roger slept at last, but in consequence of his wakefulness, woke late and heavy-eyed, with an incipient headache, which neither a cold shower nor Fiona's chirpiness over breakfast did much to dispel.

The feeling was so oppressive that he abandoned his work and left the house for a walk. Striding through a light rain, he found the fresh air improved his headache, but unfortunately cleared his mind enough to start thinking again about the implications of last night's discovery.

Brianna didn't know. That was clear enough, from the way she spoke about her late father—or about the man she *thought* was her father, Frank Randall. And presumably Claire didn't mean her to know, or she would have told the girl herself. Unless this Scottish trip were meant to be a prelude to such a confession? The real father must have been a Scot; after all, Claire had disappeared—and reappeared—in Scotland. Was he still here?

That was a staggering thought. Had Claire brought her daughter to Scotland in order to introduce her to her real father? Roger shook his head doubtfully. Bloody risky, a thing like that. Bound to be confusing to Brianna, and painful as hell to Claire herself. Scare the shoes and socks off the father, too. And the girl plainly was devoted to Frank Randall. What was she going to feel like, realizing that the man she'd loved and idolized all her life in fact had no blood ties to her at all?

Roger felt bad for all concerned, including himself. He hadn't asked to have any part of this, and wished himself in the same state of blissful ignorance as yesterday. He liked Claire Randall, liked her very much, and he found the thought of her committing adultery distasteful. At the same time, he jeered at himself for his old-fashioned sentimentality. Who knew what her life with Frank Randall had been like? Perhaps she'd had good reason for going off with another man. But then why had she come back?

Sweating and moody, Roger wandered back to the house. He shed his jacket in the hallway and went up to have a bath. Sometimes bathing helped to soothe him, and he felt much in need of soothing.

He ran a hand along the row of hangers in his closet, groping for the fuzzy shoulder of his worn white toweling robe. Then, pausing for a moment, he reached instead far to the back of the closet, sweeping the hangers along the rod until he could grasp the one he wanted.

He viewed the shabby old dressing gown with affection. The yellow silk of the background had faded to ochre, but the multicolored peacocks were bold as ever, spreading their tails with lordly insouciance, regarding the viewer with eyes like black beads. He brought the soft fabric to his nose and inhaled deeply, closing his eyes. The faint whiff of Borkum Riff and spilled whisky brought back the Reverend Wakefield as not even his father's wall of trivia could do.

Many were the times he had smelled just that comforting aroma, with its upper note of Old Spice cologne, his face pressed against the smooth slickness of this silk, the Reverend's chubby arms wrapped protectively around him, promising him refuge. He had given the old man's other clothes to Oxfam, but somehow he couldn't bear to part with this.

On impulse, he slipped the robe over his bare shoulders, mildly surprised at the light warmth of it, like the caress of fingers across his skin. He shifted his shoulders pleasurably under the silk, then wrapped it closely about his body, tying the belt in a careless knot.

Keeping a wary eye out in case of raids by Fiona, he made his way along the upper hall to the bathroom. The hot-water geyser stood against the head of the bath like the guardian of a sacred spring, squat and eternal. Another of his youthful memories was the weekly terror of trying to light the geyser with a flint striker in order to heat the water for his bath, the gas escaping past his head with a menacing hiss as his hands, sweaty with the fear of explosion and imminent death, slipped ineffectively on the metal of the striker.

Long since rendered automatic by an operation on its mysterious innards, the geyser now gurgled quietly to itself, the gas ring at its base rumbling and whooshing with unseen flame beneath the metal shield. Roger twisted the cracked "Hot" tap as far as it would go, added a half-turn of the "Cold," then stood to study himself in the mirror while waiting for his bath to fill.

Nothing much wrong with him, he reflected, sucking in his stomach and pulling himself upright before the full-length reflection on the back of the door. Firm. Trim. Long-legged, but not spindle-shanked. Possibly a bit scrawny through the shoulders? He frowned critically, twisting his lean body back and forth.

He ran a hand through his thick black hair, until it stood on end like a shaving brush, trying to envision himself with a beard and long hair, like some of his students. Would he look dashing, or merely moth-eaten? Possibly an earring, while he was about it. He might look piratical then, like Edward Teach or Henry Morgan. He drew his brows together and bared his teeth.

"Grrrrr," he said to his reflection.

"Mr. Wakefield?" said the reflection.

Roger leaped back, startled, and stubbed his toe painfully against the protruding claw-foot of the ancient bath.

"Ow!"

"Are you all right, Mr. Wakefield?" the mirror said. The porcelain doorknob rattled.

"Of course I am!" he snapped testily, glaring at the door. "Go away, Fiona, I'm bathing!"

There was a giggle from the other side of the door.

"Ooh, twice in one day. *Aren't* we the dandy, though? Do you want some of the bay-rum soap? It's in the cupboard there, if you do."

"No, I don't," he snarled. The water level had risen midway in the tub, and he cut off the taps. The sudden silence was soothing, and he drew a deep breath of steam into his lungs. Wincing slightly at the heat, he stepped into the water and lowered himself gingerly, feeling a light sweat break out on his face as the heat rushed up his body.

"Mr. Wakefield?" The voice was back, chirping on the other side of the door like a hectoring robin.

"Go *away*, Fiona," he gritted, easing himself back in the tub. The steaming water rose around him, comforting as a lover's arms. "I have everything I want."

"No, you haven't," said the voice.

"Yes, I have." His eye swept the impressive lineup of bottles, jars, and implements arrayed on the shelf above the tub. "Shampoo, three kinds. Hair conditioner. Shaving cream. Razor. Body soap. Facial soap. After-shave. Cologne. Deodorant stick. I don't lack a thing, Fiona."

"What about towels?" said the voice, sweetly.

After a wild glance about the completely towel-less confines of the bathroom, Roger closed his eyes, clenched his teeth and counted slowly to ten. This proving insufficient, he made it twenty. Then, feeling himself able to answer without foaming at the mouth, he said calmly.

"All right, Fiona. Set them outside the door, please. And then, please . . . please, Fiona . . . *go.*"

A rustle outside was succeeded by the sound of reluctantly receding footsteps, and Roger, with a sigh of relief, gave himself up to the joys of privacy. Peace. Quiet. No Fiona.

Now, able to think more objectively about his upsetting discovery, he found himself more than curious about Brianna's mysterious real father. Judging from the daughter, the man must have had a rare degree of physical attractiveness; would that alone have been sufficient to lure a woman like Claire Randall?

He had wondered already whether Brianna's father might have been a Scot. Did he live—or *had* he lived—in Inverness? He supposed such proximity might account for Claire's nervousness, and the air she had of keeping secrets. But did it account for the puzzling requests she had made of him? She didn't want him to take Brianna to Craigh na Dun, nor to mention the captain of the Broch Tuarach men to her daughter. Why on earth not?

A sudden thought made him sit upright in the tub, water sloshing heedlessly against the cast-iron sides. What if it were not the eighteenth-century Jacobite soldier she was concerned about, but *only his name*? What if the man who had fathered her daughter in 1947 was also named James Fraser? It was a common enough name in the Highlands.

Yes, he thought, that might very well explain it. As for Claire's desire to show her daughter the stone circle herself, perhaps that was also connected with the mystery of her father; maybe that's where she'd met the man, or perhaps that's where Brianna had been conceived. Roger was well aware that the stone circle was commonly used as a trysting spot; he'd taken girls there himself in high school, relying on the circle's air of pagan mystery to loosen their reserve. It always worked.

He had a sudden startling vision of Claire Randall's fine white limbs, locked in wild abandon with the naked, straining body of a red-haired man, the two bodies slick with rain and stained with crushed grass, twisting in ecstasy among the standing stones. The vision was so shocking in its specificity that it left him trembling, sweat running down his chest to vanish into the steaming water of the bath.

Christ! How was he going to meet Claire Randall's eyes, next time they met? What was he going to say to Brianna, for that matter? "Read any good books lately?" "Seen any good flicks?" "D'you know you're illegitimate?"

He shook his head, trying to clear it. The truth was that he didn't know what to do next. It was a messy situation. He wanted no part in it, and yet he did. He liked Claire Randall; he liked Brianna Randall, too—much more than liked her, truth be told. He wanted to protect her, and save her whatever pain he could. And yet there seemed no way to do that. All he could do was keep his mouth shut until Claire Randall did whatever it was she planned to do. And then be there to pick up the pieces.

3

Mothers and Daughters

I wondered just how many tiny tea shops there were in Inverness. The High Street is lined on both sides with small cafes and tourist shops, as far as the eye can see. Once Queen Victoria had made the Highlands safe for travelers by giving her Royal approval of the place, tourists had flocked north in ever-increasing numbers. The Scots, unaccustomed to receiving anything from the South but armed invasions and political interference, had risen to the challenge magnificently.

You couldn't walk more than a few feet on the main street of any Highland town without encountering a shop selling shortbread, Edinburgh rock, handkerchiefs embroidered with thistles, toy bagpipes, clan badges of cast aluminum, letter-openers shaped like claymores, coin purses shaped like sporrans (some with an anatomically correct "Scotchman" attached underneath), and an eye-jangling assortment of spurious clan tartans, adorning every conceivable object made of fabric, from caps, neckties, and serviettes down to a particularly horrid yellow "Buchanan" sett used to make men's nylon Y-front underpants.

Looking over an assortment of tea towels stenciled with a wildly inaccurate depiction of the Loch Ness monster singing "Auld Lang Syne," I thought Victoria had a lot to answer for.

Brianna was wandering slowly down the narrow aisle of the shop, head tilted back as she stared in amazement at the assortment of merchandise hanging from the rafters.

"Do you think those are *real*?" she said, pointing upward at a set of mounted stag's antlers, poking their tines inquisitively through an absolute forest of bagpipe drones.

"The antlers? Oh, yes. I don't imagine plastics technology's got quite *that* good, yet," I replied. "Besides, look at the price. Anything over one hundred pounds is very likely real."

Brianna's eyes widened, and she lowered her head.

"Jeez. I think I'll get Jane a skirt-length of tartan instead."

"Good-quality wool tartan won't cost a lot less," I said dryly, "but it will be a lot easier to get home on the plane. Let's go across to the Kiltmaker store, then; they'll have the best quality."

It had begun to rain—of course—and we tucked our paper-wrapped parcels underneath the raincoats I had prudently insisted we wear. Brianna snorted with sudden amusement.

"You get so used to calling these things 'macs,' you forget what they're really called. I'm not surprised it was a Scot that invented them," she added, looking up at the water sheeting down from the edge of the canopy overhead. "Does it rain *all* the time here?"

"Pretty much," I said, peering up and down through the downpour for oncoming traffic. "Though I've always supposed Mr. Macintosh was rather a lily-livered sort; most Scots I've known were relatively impervious to rain." I bit my lip suddenly, but Brianna hadn't noticed the slip, minor as it was; she was eyeing the ankle-deep freshet running down the gutter.

"Tell you what, Mama, maybe we'd better go up to the crossing. We aren't going to make it jaywalking here."

Nodding assent, I followed her up the street, heart pounding with adrenaline under the clammy cover of my mac. *When are you going to get it over with?* my mind demanded. *You can't keep watching your words and swallowing half the things you start to say. Why not just tell her?*

Not yet, I thought to myself. I'm not a coward—or if I am, it doesn't matter. But it isn't quite time yet. I wanted her to see Scotland first. Not this lot—as we passed a shop offering a display of tartan baby booties—but the countryside. And Culloden. Most of all, I want to be able to tell her the end of the story. And for that, I need Roger Wakefield.

As though my thought had summoned it into being, the bright orange top of a battered Morris caught my eye in the parking lot to the left, glowing like a traffic beacon in the foggy wet.

Brianna had seen it too—there couldn't be many cars in Inverness of that specific color and disreputability—and

pointed at it, saying, "Look, Mama, isn't that Roger Wakefield's car?"

"Yes, I think so," I said. There was a cafe on the right,
from which the scent of fresh scones, stale toast, and coffee
drifted to mingle with the fresh, rainy air. I grabbed Brianna's
arm and pulled her into the cafe.

"I think I'm hungry after all," I explained. "Let's have
some cocoa and biscuits."

Still child enough to be tempted by chocolate, and young
enough to be willing to eat at any time, Bree offered no argument, but sat down at once and picked up the tea-stained
sheet of green paper that served as the daily menu.

I didn't particularly want cocoa, but I did want a moment
or two to think. There was a large sign on the concrete wall of
the parking lot across the street, reading PARKING FOR SCOTRAIL
ONLY, followed by various lowercase threats as to what would
happen to the vehicles of people who parked there without
being train riders. Unless Roger knew something about the
forces of law and order in Inverness that I didn't know,
chances were that he had taken a train. Granted that he could
have gone anywhere, either Edinburgh or London seemed
most likely. He was taking this research project seriously,
dear lad.

We had come up on the train from Edinburgh ourselves.
I tried to remember what the schedule was like, with no particular success.

"I wonder if Roger will be back on the evening train?"
Bree said, echoing my thoughts with an uncanniness that
made me choke on my cocoa. The fact that she wondered
about Roger's reappearance made *me* wonder just how much
notice she had taken of young Mr. Wakefield.

A fair amount, apparently.

"I was thinking," she said casually, "maybe we should get
something for Roger Wakefield while we're out—like a
thank-you for that project he's doing for you?"

"Good idea," I said, amused. "What do you think he'd
like?"

She frowned into her cocoa as though looking for inspiration. "I don't know. Something nice; it looks like that project could be a lot of work." She glanced up at me suddenly,
brows raised.

"Why did you ask him?" she said. "If you wanted to trace people from the eighteenth century, there're companies that do that. Genealogies and like that, I mean. Daddy always used Scot-Search, if he had to figure out a genealogy and didn't have time to do it himself."

"Yes, I know," I said, and took a deep breath. We were on shaky ground here. "This project—it was something special to . . . to your father. He would have wanted Roger Wakefield to do it."

"Oh." She was silent for a while, watching the rain spatter and pearl on the cafe window.

"Do you miss Daddy?" she asked suddenly, nose buried in her cup, lashes lowered to avoid looking at me.

"Yes," I said. I ran a forefinger up the edge of my own untouched cup, wiping off a drip of spilled cocoa. "We didn't always get on, you know that, but . . . yes. We respected each other; that counts for a lot. And we liked each other, in spite of everything. Yes, I do miss him."

She nodded, wordless, and put her hand over mine with a little squeeze. I curled my fingers around hers, long and warm, and we sat linked for a little while, sipping cocoa in silence.

"You know," I said at last, pushing back my chair with a squeak of metal on linoleum, "I'd forgotten something. I need to post a letter to the hospital. I'd meant to do it on the way into town, but I forgot. If I hurry, I think I can just catch the outgoing post. Why don't you go to the Kiltmaker's—it's just down the street, on the other side—and I'll join you there after I've been to the post office?"

Bree looked surprised, but nodded readily enough.

"Oh. Okay. Isn't the post office a long way, though? You'll get soaked."

"That's all right. I'll take a cab." I left a pound note on the table to pay for the meal, and shrugged back into my raincoat.

In most cities, the usual response of taxicabs to rain is to disappear, as though they were soluble. In Inverness, though, such behavior would render the species rapidly extinct. I'd walked less than a block before finding two squatty black cabs lurking outside a hotel, and I slid into the warm, tobacco-scented interior with a cozy feeling of familiarity. Besides the greater leg room and comfort, British cabs smelled different than American ones; one of those tiny things I had never realized I'd missed during the last twenty years.

"Number sixty-four? Tha's the auld manse, aye?" In spite of the efficiency of the cab's heater, the driver was muffled to the ears in a scarf and thick jacket, with a flat cap guarding the top of his head from errant drafts. Modern Scots had gone a bit soft, I reflected; a long way from the days when sturdy Highlanders had slept in the heather in nothing but shirt and plaid. On the other hand, I wasn't all that eager to go sleep in the heather in a wet plaid, either. I nodded to the driver, and we set off in a splash.

I felt a bit subversive, sneaking round to interview Roger's housekeeper while he was out, and fooling Bree into the bargain. On the other hand, it would be difficult to explain to either of them just what I was doing. I hadn't yet determined exactly how or when I would tell them what I had to say, but I knew it wasn't time yet.

My fingers probed the inner pocket of my mac, reassured by the scrunch of the envelope from Scot-Search. While I hadn't paid a great deal of attention to Frank's work, I did know about the firm, which maintained a staff of half a dozen professional researchers specializing in Scottish genealogy; not the sort of place that gave you a family tree showing your relationship to Robert the Bruce and had done with it.

They'd done their usual thorough, discreet job on Roger Wakefield. I knew who his parents and grandparents had been, back some seven or eight generations. What I didn't know was what he might be made of. Time would tell me that.

I paid off the cab and splashed up the flooded path to the steps of the old minister's house. It was dry on the porch, and I had a chance to shake off the worst of the wet before the door was opened to my ring.

Fiona beamed in welcome; she had the sort of round, cheerful face whose natural expression was a smile. She was attired in jeans and a frilly apron, and the scent of lemon polish and fresh baking wafted from its folds like incense.

"Why, Mrs. Randall!" she exclaimed. "Can I be helpin' ye at all, then?"

"I think perhaps you might, Fiona," I said. "I wanted to talk to you about your grandmother."

⊷

"Are you sure you're all right, Mama? I could call Roger and ask him to go tomorrow, if you'd like me to stay with you." Brianna hovered in the doorway of the guesthouse bedroom, an anxious frown creasing her brow. She was dressed for walking, in boots, jeans, and sweater, but she'd added the brilliant orange and blue silk scarf Frank had brought her from Paris, just before his death two years before.

"Just the color of your eyes, little beauty," he'd said, smiling as he draped the scarf around her shoulders, "—orange." It was a joke between them now, the "little beauty," as Bree had topped Frank's modest five feet ten since she was fifteen. It was what he'd called her since babyhood, though, and the tenderness of the old name lingered as he reached up to touch the tip of her nose.

The scarf—the blue part—was in fact the color of her eyes; of Scottish lochs and summer skies, and the misty blue of distant mountains. I knew she treasured it, and revised my assessment of her interest in Roger Wakefield upward by several notches.

"No, I'll be fine," I assured her. I gestured toward the bedside table, adorned with a small teapot, carefully keeping warm under a knitted cozy, and a silver-plated toast rack, just as carefully keeping the toast nice and cold. "Mrs. Thomas brought me tea and toast; perhaps I'll be able to nibble a little later on." I hoped she couldn't hear the rumbling of my empty stomach under the bedclothes, registering appalled disbelief at this prospect.

"Well, all right." She turned reluctantly to the door. "We'll come right back after Culloden, though."

"Don't hurry on my account," I called after her.

I waited until I heard the sound of the door closing below, and was sure she was on her way. Only then did I reach into the drawer of the bedtable for the large Hershey bar with almonds that I had hidden there the night before.

Cordial relations with my stomach reestablished, I lay back against the pillow, idly watching the gray haze thicken in the sky outside. The tip of a budding lime branch flicked intermittently against the window; the wind was rising. It was warm enough in the bedroom, with the central-heating vent roaring away at the foot of the bed, but I shivered nonetheless. It would be cold on Culloden Field.

Not, perhaps, as cold as it had been in the April of 1746, when Bonnie Prince Charlie led his men onto that field, to stand in the face of freezing sleet and the roar of English cannon fire. Accounts of the day reported that it was bitterly cold, and the Highland wounded had lain heaped with the dead, soaked in blood and rain, awaiting the mercies of their English victors. The Duke of Cumberland, in command of the English army, had given no quarter to the fallen.

The dead were heaped up like cordwood and burned to prevent the spread of disease, and history said that many of the wounded had gone to a similar fate, without the grace of a final bullet. All of them lay now beyond the reach of war or weather, under the greensward of Culloden Field.

I had seen the place once, nearly thirty years before, when Frank had taken me there on our honeymoon. Now Frank was dead, too, and I had brought my daughter back to Scotland. I wanted Brianna to see Culloden, but no power on earth would make me set foot again on that deadly moor.

I supposed I had better stay in bed, to maintain credence in the sudden indisposition that had prevented me accompanying Brianna and Roger on their expedition; Mrs. Thomas might blab if I got up and put in an order for lunch. I peeked into the drawer; three more candy bars and a mystery novel. With luck, those would get me through the day.

The novel was good enough, but the rush of the rising wind outside was hypnotic, and the embrace of the warm bed welcoming. I dropped peacefully into sleep, to dream of kilted Highland men, and the sound of soft-spoken Scots, burring round a fire like the sound of bees in the heather.

4

Culloden

"What a mean little piggy face!" Brianna stooped to peer fascinated at the red-coated mannequin that stood menacingly to one side of the foyer in the Culloden Visitors Centre. He stood a few inches over five feet, powdered wig thrust belligerently forward over a low brow and pendulous, pink-tinged cheeks.

"Well, he was a fat little fellow," Roger agreed, amused. "Hell of a general, though, at least as compared to his elegant cousin over there." He waved a hand at the taller figure of Charles Edward Stuart on the other side of the foyer, gazing nobly off into the distance under his blue velvet bonnet with its white cockade, loftily ignoring the Duke of Cumberland.

"They called him 'Butcher Billy.'" Roger gestured at the Duke, stolid in white knee breeches and gold-braided coat. "For excellent reason. Aside from what they did here"—he waved toward the expanse of the spring-green moor outside, dulled by the lowering sky—"Cumberland's men were responsible for the worst reign of English terror ever seen in the Highlands. They chased the survivors of the battle back into the hills, burning and looting as they went. Women and children were turned out to starve, and the men shot down where they stood—with no effort to find out whether they'd ever fought for Charlie. One of the Duke's contemporaries said of him, 'He created a desert and called it peace'—and I'm afraid the Duke of Cumberland is still rather noticeably unpopular hereabouts."

This was true; the curator of the visitors' museum, a friend of Roger's, had told him that while the figure of the Bonnie Prince was treated with reverent respect, the buttons of the Duke's jacket were subject to constant disappearance, while the figure itself had been the butt of more than one rude joke.

"He said one morning he came in early and turned on the light, to find a genuine Highland dirk sticking in His

Grace's belly," Roger said, nodding at the podgy little figure. "Said it gave him a right turn."

"I'd think so," Brianna murmured, looking at the Duke with raised brows. "People still take it that seriously?"

"Oh, aye. Scots have long memories, and they're not the most forgiving of people."

"Really?" She looked at him curiously. "Are you Scottish, Roger? Wakefield doesn't sound like a Scottish name, but there's something about the way you talk about the Duke of Cumberland . . ." There was the hint of a smile around her mouth, and he wasn't sure whether he was being teased, but he answered her seriously enough.

"Oh, aye." He smiled as he said it. "I'm Scots. Wakefield's not my own name, see; the Reverend gave it to me when he adopted me. He was my mother's uncle—when my parents were killed in the War, he took me to live with him. But my own name is MacKenzie. As for the Duke of Cumberland"—he nodded at the plate-glass window, through which the monuments of Culloden Field were plainly visible. "There's a clan stone out there, with the name of MacKenzie carved on it, and a good many of my relatives under it."

He reached out and flicked a gold epaulet, leaving it swinging. "I don't feel quite so personal about it as some, but I haven't forgotten, either." He held out a hand to her. "Shall we go outside?"

It was cold outside, with a gusty wind that lashed two pennons, flying atop the poles set at either side of the moor. One yellow, one red, they marked the positions where the two commanders had stood behind their troops, awaiting the outcome of the battle.

"Well back out of the way, I see," Brianna observed dryly. "No chance of getting in the way of a stray bullet."

Roger noticed her shivering, and drew her hand further through his arm, bringing her close. He thought he might burst from the sudden swell of happiness touching her gave him, but tried to disguise it with a retreat into historical monologue. "Well, that was how generals led, back then— from the rear. Especially Charlie; he ran off so fast at the end of the battle that he left behind his sterling silver picnic set."

"A *picnic* set? He brought a picnic to the battle?"

"Oh, aye." Roger found that he quite liked being Scottish for Brianna. He usually took pains to keep his accent modulated under the all-purpose Oxbridge speech that served him at the university, but now he was letting it have free rein for the sake of the smile that crossed her face when she heard it.

"D'ye know why they called him 'Prince Charlie'?" Roger asked. "English people always think it was a nickname, showing how much his men loved him."

"It wasn't?"

Roger shook his head. "No, indeed. His men called him Prince *Tcharlach*"—he spelled it carefully—"which is the Gaelic for Charles. *Tcharlach mac Seamus,* 'Charles, son of James.' Very formal and respectful indeed. It's only that *Tcharlach* in Gaelic sounds the hell of a lot like 'Charlie' in English."

Brianna grinned. "So he never was 'Bonnie Prince Charlie'?"

"Not then." Roger shrugged. "Now he is, of course. One of those little historical mistakes that get passed on for fact. There are a lot of them."

"And you an historian!" Brianna said, teasing,

Roger smiled wryly. "That's how I know."

They wandered slowly down the graveled paths that led through the battlefield, Roger pointing out the positions of the different regiments that had fought there, explaining the order of battle, recounting small anecdotes of the commanders.

As they walked, the wind died down, and the silence of the field began to assert itself. Gradually their conversation died away as well, until they were talking only now and then, in low voices, almost whispers. The sky was gray with cloud from horizon to horizon, and everything beneath its bowl seemed muted, with only the whisper of the moor plants speaking in the voices of the men who fed them.

"This is the place they call the Well of Death." Roger stooped by the small spring. Barely a foot square, it was a tiny pool of dark water, welling under a ridge of stone. "One of the Highland chieftains died here; his followers washed the blood from his face with the water from this spring. And over there are the graves of the clans."

The clan stones were large boulders of gray granite,

rounded by weather and blotched with lichens. They sat on
patches of smooth grass, widely scattered near the edge of the
moor. Each one bore a single name, the carving so faded by
weather as to be nearly illegible in some cases. MacGillivray.
MacDonald. Fraser. Grant. Chisholm. MacKenzie.

"Look," Brianna said, almost in a whisper. She pointed
at one of the stones. A small heap of greenish-gray twigs lay
there; a few early spring flowers mingled, wilted, with the
twigs.

"Heather," Roger said. "It's more common in the summer, when the heather is blooming—then you'll see heaps
like that in front of every clan stone. Purple, and here and
there a branch of the white heather—the white is for luck,
and for kingship; it was Charlie's emblem, that and the white
rose."

"Who leaves them?" Brianna squatted on her heels next
to the path, touching the twigs with a gentle finger.

"Visitors." Roger squatted next to her. He traced the
faded letters on the stone—FRASER. "People descended from
the families of the men who were killed here. Or just those
who like to remember them."

She looked sidelong at him, hair drifting around her
face. "Have you ever done it?"

He looked down, smiling at his hands as they hung between his knees.

"Yes. I suppose it's very sentimental, but I do."

Brianna turned to the thicket of moor plants that edged
the path on the other side.

"Show me which is heather," she said.

On the way home, the melancholy of Culloden lifted, but
the feeling of shared sentiment lingered, and they talked and
laughed together like old friends.

"It's too bad Mother couldn't come with us," Brianna
remarked as they turned into the road where the Randalls'
bed-and-breakfast was.

Much as he liked Claire Randall, Roger didn't agree at
all that it was too bad she hadn't come. Three, he thought,
would have been a crowd, and no mistake. But he grunted
noncommitally, and a moment later asked, "How *is* your
mother? I hope she's not terribly ill."

"Oh, no, it's just an upset stomach—at least that's what

she says." Brianna frowned to herself for a moment, then turned to Roger, laying a hand lightly on his leg. He felt the muscles quiver from knee to groin, and had a hard time keeping his mind on what she was saying. She was still talking about her mother.

". . . think she's all right?" she finished. She shook her head, and copper glinted from the waves of her hair, even in the dull light of the car. "I don't know; she seems awfully preoccupied. Not ill, exactly—more as though she's kind of worried about something."

Roger felt a sudden heaviness in the pit of his stomach.

"Mphm," he said. "Maybe just being away from her work. I'm sure it will be all right." Brianna smiled gratefully at him as they pulled up in front of Mrs. Thomas's small stone house.

"It was great, Roger," she said, touching him lightly on the shoulder. "But there wasn't much here to help with Mama's project. Can't I help you with some of the grubby stuff?"

Roger's spirits lightened considerably, and he smiled up at her. "I think that might be arranged. Want to come tomorrow and have a go at the garage with me? If it's filth you want, you can't get much grubbier than that."

"Great." She smiled, leaning on the car to look back in at him. "Maybe Mother will want to come along and help."

He could feel his face stiffen, but kept gallantly smiling.

"Right," he said. "Great. I hope so."

In the event, it was Brianna alone who came to the manse the next day.

"Mama's at the public library," she explained. "Looking up old phone directories. She's trying to find someone she used to know."

Roger's heart skipped a beat at that. He had checked the Reverend's phonebook the night before. There were three local listings under the name "James Fraser," and two more with different first names, but the middle initial "J."

"Well, I hope she finds him," he said, still trying for casualness. "You're really sure you want to help? It's boring, filthy work." Roger looked at Brianna dubiously, but she nodded, not at all discomposed at the prospect.

"I know. I used to help my father sometimes, dredging through old records and finding footnotes. Besides, it's Mama's project; the least I can do is help you with it."

"All right." Roger glanced down at his white shirt. "Let me change, and we'll go have a look."

The garage door creaked, groaned, then surrendered to the inevitable and surged suddenly upward, amid the twanging of springs and clouds of dust.

Brianna waved her hands back and forth in front of her face, coughing. "Gack!" she said. "How long since anyone's been in this place?"

"Eons, I expect." Roger replied absently. He shone his torch around the inside of the garage, briefly lighting stacks of cardboard cartons and wooden crates, old steamer trunks smeared with peeling labels, and amorphous tarpaulin-draped shapes. Here and there, the upturned legs of furniture poked through the gloom like the skeletons of small dinosaurs, protruding from their native rock formations.

There was a sort of fissure in the junk; Roger edged into this and promptly disappeared into a tunnel bounded by dust and shadows, his progress marked by the pale spot of his torch as it shone intermittently on the ceiling. At last, with a cry of triumph, he seized the dangling tail of a string hanging from above, and the garage was suddenly illuminated in the glare of an oversized bulb.

"This way," Roger said, reappearing abruptly and taking Brianna by the hand. "There's sort of a clear space in back."

An ancient table stood against the back wall. Perhaps originally the centerpiece of the Reverend Wakefield's dining room, it had evidently gone through several successive incarnations as kitchen block, toolbench, sawhorse, and painting table, before coming to rest in this dusty sanctuary. A heavily cobwebbed window overlooked it, through which a dim light shone on the nicked, paint-splattered surface.

"We can work here," Roger said, yanking a stool out of the mess and dusting it perfunctorily with a large handkerchief. "Have a seat, and I'll see if I can pry the window open; otherwise, we'll suffocate."

Brianna nodded, but instead of sitting down, began to

poke curiously through the nearer piles of junk, as Roger
heaved at the warped window frame. He could hear her behind him, reading the labels on some of the boxes. "Here's
1930–33," she said, "And here's 1942–46. What are these?"

"Journals," said Roger, grunting as he braced his elbows
on the grimy sill. "My father—the Reverend, I mean—he always kept a journal. Wrote it up every night after supper."

"Looks like he found plenty to write about." Brianna
hoisted down several of the boxes, and stacked them to the
side, in order to inspect the next layer. "Here's a bunch of
boxes with names on them—'Kerse,' 'Livingston,' 'Balnain.'
Parishioners?"

"No. Villages." Roger paused in his labors for a moment,
panting. He wiped his brow, leaving a streak of dirt down the
sleeve of his shirt. "Luckily both of them were dressed in old
clothes, suitable for rootling in filth. "Those will be notes on
the history of various Highland villages. Some of those boxes
ended up as books, in fact; you'll see them in some of the
local tourist shops through the Highlands."

He turned to a pegboard from which hung a selection of
dilapidated tools, and selected a large screwdriver to aid his
assault on the window.

"Look for the ones that say 'Parish Registers,'" he advised. "Or for village names in the area of Broch Tuarach."

"I don't know any of the villages in the area," Brianna
pointed out.

"Oh, aye, I was forgetting." Roger inserted the point of
the screwdriver between the edges of the window frame,
grimly chiseling through layers of ancient paint. "Look for
the names Broch Mordha . . . um, Mariannan, and . . .
oh, St. Kilda. There's others, but those are ones I know had
fair-sized churches that have been closed or knocked down."

"Okay." Pushing aside a hanging flap of tarpaulin, Brianna suddenly leaped backward with a sharp cry.

"What? What is it?" Roger whirled from the window,
screwdriver at the ready.

"I don't know. Something skittered away when I touched
that tarp." Brianna pointed, and Roger lowered his weapon,
relieved.

"Oh, that all? Mouse, most like. Maybe a rat."

"A *rat!* You have *rats* in here?" Brianna's agitation was noticeable.

"Well, I hope not, because if so, they'll have been chewing up the records we're looking for," Roger replied. He handed her the torch. "Here, shine this in any dark places; at least you won't be taken by surprise."

"Thanks a lot." Brianna accepted the torch, but still eyed the stacks of cartons with some reluctance.

"Well, go on then," Roger said. "Or did you want me to do you a rat satire on the spot?"

Brianna's face split in a wide grin. "A rat satire? What's that?"

Roger delayed his answer, long enough for another try at the window. He pushed until he could feel his biceps straining against the fabric of his shirt, but at last, with a rending screech, the window gave way, and a reviving draft of cool air whooshed in through the six-inch gap he'd created.

"God, that's better." He fanned himself exaggeratedly, grinning at Brianna. "Now, shall we get on with it?"

She handed him the torch, and stepped back. "How about *you* find the boxes, and *I'll* sort through them? And what's a rat satire?"

"Coward," he said, bending to rummage beneath the tarpaulin. "A rat satire is an old Scottish custom; if you had rats or mice in your house or your barn, you could make them go away by composing a poem—or you could sing it—telling the rats how poor the eating was where they were, and how good it was elsewhere. You told them where to go, and how to get there, and presumably, if the satire was good enough—they'd go."

He pulled out a carton labeled JACOBITES, MISCELLANEOUS, and carried it to the table, singing,

> *"Ye rats, ye are too many,*
> *If ye would dine in plenty,*
> *Ye mun go, ye mun go."*

Lowering the box with a thump, he bowed in response to Brianna's giggling and turned back to the stacks, continuing in stentorian voice.

> *"Go to Campbell's garden,*
> *Where nae cat stands warden,*
> *And the kale, it grows green.*
>
> *Go and fill your bellies,*
> *Dinna stay and gnaw my wellies—*
> *Go, ye rats, go!"*

Brianna snorted appreciatively. "Did you just make that up?"

"Of course." Roger deposited another box on the table with a flourish. "A good rat satire must always be original." He cast a glance at the serried ranks of cartons. "After that performance, there shouldn't be a rat within miles of this place."

"Good." Brianna pulled a jackknife from her pocket and slit the tape that sealed the topmost carton. "You should come do one at the bed-and-breakfast place; Mama says she's sure there's mice in the bathroom. Something chewed on her soap case."

"God knows what it would take to dislodge a mouse capable of eating bars of soap; far beyond my feeble powers, I expect." He rolled a tattered round hassock out from behind a teetering stack of obsolete encyclopedias, and plumped down next to Brianna. "Here, you take the parish registers, they're a bit easier to read."

They worked through the morning in amiable companionship, turning up occasional interesting passages, the odd silverfish, and recurrent clouds of dust, but little of value to the project at hand.

"We'd better stop for lunch soon," Roger said at last. He felt a strong reluctance to go back into the house, where he would once more be at Fiona's mercy, but Brianna's stomach had begun to growl almost as loudly as his own.

"Okay. We can do some more after we eat, if you're not worn out." Brianna stood and stretched herself, her curled fists almost reaching the rafters of the old garage. She wiped her hands on the legs of her jeans, and ducked between the stacks of boxes.

"Hey!" She stopped short, near the door. Roger, following her, was brought up sharp, his nose almost touching the back of her head.

"What is it?" he asked. "Not another rat?" He noted with approval that the sun lit her thick single braid with glints of copper and gold. With a small golden nimbus of dust surrounding her, and the light of noon silhouetting her long-nosed profile, he thought she looked quite medieval; Our Lady of the Archives.

"No. Look at this, Roger!" She pointed at a cardboard carton near the middle of a stack. On the side, in the Reverend's strong black hand, was a label with the single word "Randall."

Roger felt a stab of mingled excitement and apprehension. Brianna's excitement was unalloyed.

"Maybe that's got the stuff we're looking for!" she exclaimed. "Mama said it was something my father was interested in; maybe he'd already asked the Reverend about it."

"Could be." Roger forced down the sudden feeling of dread that had struck him at sight of the name. He knelt to extract the box from its resting place. "Let's take it in the house; we can look in it after lunch."

The box, once opened in the Reverend's study, held an odd assortment of things. There were old photostats of pages from several parish registers, two or three army muster lists, a number of letters and scattered papers, a small, thin notebook, bound in gray cardboard covers, a packet of elderly photographs, curling at the edges, and a stiff folder, with the name "Randall" printed on the cover.

Brianna picked up the folder and opened it. "Why, it's Daddy's family tree!" she exclaimed. "Look." She passed the folder to Roger. Inside were two sheets of thick parchment, with lines of descent neatly ruled across and down. The beginning date was 1633; the final entry, at the foot of the second page, showed

**Frank Wolverton Randall m. Claire Elizabeth
Beauchamp, 1937**

"Done before you were born," Roger murmured.

Brianna peered over his shoulder as his finger passed slowly down the lines of the genealogical table. "I've seen it before; Daddy had a copy in his study. He used to show it to me all the time. His had me at the bottom, though; this must be an early copy."

"Maybe the Reverend did some of the research for him." Roger handed Brianna back the folder, and picked up one of the papers from the stack on the desk.

"Now here's an heirloom for you," he said. He traced the coat of arms embossed at the head of the sheet. "A letter of commission in the army, signed by His Royal Majesty, King George II."

"George the *Second?* Jeez, that's even before the American Revolution."

"Considerably before. It's dated 1735. In the name of Jonathan Wolverton Randall. Know that name?"

"Yeah." Brianna nodded, stray wisps of hair falling in her face. She wiped them back carelessly and took the letter. "Daddy used to talk about him every now and then; one of the few ancestors he knew much about. He was a captain in the army that fought Bonnie Prince Charlie at Culloden." She looked up at Roger, blinking. "I think maybe he was killed in that battle, in fact. He wouldn't have been buried there, would he?"

Roger shook his head. "I shouldn't think so. It was the English who cleared up after the battle. They shipped most of their own dead back home for burial—the officers, anyway."

He was prevented from further observation by the sudden appearance in the doorway of Fiona, bearing a feather duster like a battle standard.

"Mr. Wakefield," she called. "There's the man come to take awa' the Reverend's truck, but he canna get it started. He says will ye be givin' him a hand, like?"

Roger started guiltily. He had taken the battery to a garage for testing, and it was still sitting in the backseat of his own Morris. No wonder the Reverend's truck wasn't starting.

"I'll have to go sort this out," he told Brianna. "I'm afraid it might take a while."

"That's okay." She smiled at him, blue eyes narrowing to triangles. "I should go too. Mama will be back by now; we thought we might go out to the Clava Cairns, if there was time. Thanks for the lunch."

"My pleasure—and Fiona's." Roger felt a stab of regret at being unable to offer to go with her, but duty called. He glanced at the papers spread out on the desk, then scooped them up and deposited them back in the box.

"Here," he said. "This is all your family records. You take it. Maybe your mother would be interested."

"Really? Well, thanks, Roger. Are you sure?"

"Absolutely," he said, carefully laying the folder with the genealogical chart on top. "Oh, wait. Maybe not all of it." The corner of the gray notebook stuck out from under the letter of commission; he pulled it free, and tidied the disturbed papers back into the box. "This looks like one of the Reverend's journals. Can't think what it's doing in there, but I suppose I'd better put it with the others; the historical society says they want the whole lot."

"Oh, sure." Brianna had risen to go, clutching the box to her chest, but hesitated, looking at him. "Do you—would you like me to come back?"

Roger smiled at her. There were cobwebs in her hair, and a long streak of dirt down the bridge of her nose.

"Nothing I'd like better," he said. "See you tomorrow, eh?"

The thought of the Reverend's journal stayed with Roger, all during the tedious business of getting the ancient truck started, and the subsequent visit of the furniture appraiser who came to sort the valuable antiques from the rubbish, and set a value on the Reverend's furnishings for auction.

This disposition of the Reverend's effects gave Roger a sense of restless melancholy. It was, after all, a dismantling of his own youth, as much as the clearing away of useless bric-a-brac. By the time he sat down in the study after dinner, he could not have said whether it was curiosity about the Randalls that compelled him to pick up the journal, or simply the urge somehow to regain a tenuous connection with the man who had been his father for so many years.

The journals were kept meticulously, the even lines of

ink recording all major events of the parish and the community of which the Reverend Mr. Wakefield had been a part for so many years. The feel of the plain gray notebook and the sight of its pages conjured up for Roger an immediate vision of the Reverend, bald head gleaming in the glow of his desk lamp as he industriously inscribed the day's happenings.

"It's a discipline," he had explained once to Roger. "There's a great benefit to doing regularly something that orders the mind, you know. Catholic monks have services at set times every day, priests have their breviaries. I'm afraid I haven't the knack of such immediate devotion, but writing out the happenings of the day helps to clear my mind; then I can say my evening prayers with a calm heart."

A calm heart. Roger wished he could manage that himself, but calmness hadn't visited him since he'd found those clippings in the Reverend's desk.

He opened the book at random, and slowly turned the pages, looking for a mention of the name "Randall." The dates on the notebook's cover were January–June, 1948. While what he had told Brianna about the historical society was true, that had not been his chief motive in keeping the book. In May of 1948, Claire Randall had returned from her mysterious disappearance. The Reverend had known the Randalls well; such an event was sure to have found mention in his journal.

Sure enough, the entry for May 7:

"Visit w. Frank Randall this evening; this business about his wife. So distressing! Saw her yesterday—so frail, but those eyes staring—made me uneasy to sit w. her, poor woman, though she talked sensibly.

Enough to unhinge anyone, what she's been through—whatever it was. Terrible gossip about it all—so careless of Dr. Bartholomew to let on that she's pregnant. So hard for Frank—and for her, of course! My heart goes out to them both.

Mrs. Graham ill this week—she could have chosen a better time; jumble sale next week, and the porch full of old clothes . . ."

Roger flipped rapidly through the pages, looking for the next mention of the Randalls, and found it, later the same week.

"May 10—Frank Randall to dinner. Doing my best to associate publicly both w. him and his wife; I sit with her for an hour most days, in hopes of quelling some of the gossip. It's almost pitying now; word's gone round that she's demented. Knowing Claire Randall, I'm not sure that she would not be more offended at being thought insane than at being considered immoral—must be one or the other though?

Tried repeatedly to talk to her about her experiences, but she says nothing of that. Talks all right about anything else, but always a sense that she's thinking of something else.

Must make a note to preach this Sunday on the evils of gossip—though I'm afraid calling attention to the case with a sermon will only make it worse."

"May 12—. . . Can't get free of the notion that Claire Randall is not deranged. Have heard the gossip, of course, but see nothing in her behaviour that seems unstable in the slightest.

Do think she carries some terrible secret; one she's determined to keep. Spoke—cautiously—to Frank of this; he's reticent, but I'm convinced she has said something to him. Have tried to make it clear I wish to help, in any way I can."

"May 14—A visit from Frank Randall. Very puzzling. He has asked my help, but I can't see why he asked what he has. Seems very important to him, though; he keeps himself under close rein, but wound tight as a watch. I fear the release—if it comes.

Claire well enough to travel—he means to take her back to London this week. Assured him I would communicate any results to him by letter at his University address; no hint to his wife.

Have several items of interest on Jonathan Randall, though I can't imagine the significance of Frank's ancestor to this sorry business. Of James Fraser, as I told Frank—no inkling; a complete mystery."

A complete mystery. In more ways than one, Roger thought. What had Frank Randall asked the Reverend to do? To find out what he could about Jonathan Randall and about James Fraser, apparently. So Claire had told her husband about James Fraser—told him something, at least, if not everything.

But what conceivable connection could there be between an English army captain who had died at Culloden in 1746, and the man whose name seemed inextricably bound up with the mystery of Claire's disappearance in 1946—and the further mystery of Brianna's parentage?

The rest of the journal was filled with the usual miscellany of parish happenings; the chronic drunkenness of Derick Gowan, culminating in that parishioner's removal from the River Ness as a water-logged corpse in late May; the hasty wedding of Maggie Brown and William Dundee, a month before the christening of their daughter, June; Mrs. Graham's appendectomy, and the Reverend's attempts to cope with the resultant influx of covered dishes from the generous ladies of the parish—Herbert, the Reverend's current dog, seemed to have been the beneficiary of most of them.

Reading through the pages, Roger found himself smiling, hearing the Reverend's lively interest in his flock come to life once more in the old minister's words. Browsing and skimming, he nearly missed it—the last entry concerning Frank Randall's request.

"June 18—Had a brief note from Frank Randall, advising me that his wife's health is somewhat precarious; the pregnancy is dangerous and he asks my prayers.

Replied with assurances of prayers and good wishes for both him and his wife. Enclosed also the information I had so far found for him; can't say what use it will be to him, but that must be his own judgement. Told him of the surprising discovery of Jonathan Randall's grave at St. Kilda; asked if he wishes me to photograph the stone."

And that was all. There was no further mention of the Randalls, or of James Fraser. Roger laid the book down and massaged his temples; reading the slanting lines of handwriting had given him a mild headache.

Aside from confirming his suspicions that a man named James Fraser was mixed up in all this, the matter remained as impenetrable as ever. What in the name of God did Jonathan Randall have to do with it, and why on earth was the man buried at St. Kilda? The letter of commission had given Jonathan Randall's place of birth as an estate in Sussex; how did he end up in a remote Scottish kirkyard? True, it wasn't all that far from Culloden—but why hadn't he been shipped back to Sussex?

"Will ye be needin' anything else tonight, Mr. Wakefield?" Fiona's voice roused him from his fruitless meditations. He sat up, blinking, to see her holding a broom and a polishing cloth.

"What? Er, no. No, thanks, Fiona. But what are you doing with all that clobber? Not still cleaning at this time of night?"

"Well, it's the church ladies," Fiona explained. "You remember, ye told them they could hold their regular monthly meeting here tomorrow? I thought I'd best tidy up a bit."

The church ladies? Roger quailed at the thought of forty housewives, oozing sympathy, descending on the manse in an avalanche of tweeds, twin-sets, and cultured pearls.

"Will ye be takin' tea with the ladies?" Fiona was asking. "The Reverend always did."

The thought of entertaining Brianna Randall and the church ladies simultaneously was more than Roger could contemplate with equanimity.

"Er, no," he said abruptly. "I've . . . I've an engagement tomorrow." His hand fell on the telephone, half-buried in the debris of the Reverend's desk. "If you'll excuse me, Fiona, I've got to make a call."

Brianna wandered back into the bedroom, smiling to herself. I looked up from my book and arched a brow in inquiry.

"Phone call from Roger?" I said.

"How'd you know?" She looked startled for a moment, then grinned, shucking off her robe. "Oh, because he's the only guy I know in Inverness?"

"I didn't think any of your boyfriends would be calling long-distance from Boston," I said. I peered at the clock on the table. "Not at this hour, anyway; they'll all be at football practice."

Brianna ignored this, and shoved her feet under the covers. "Roger's invited us to go up to a place called St. Kilda tomorrow. He says it's an interesting old church."

"I've heard of it," I said, yawning. "All right, why not? I'll take my plant press; maybe I can find some crown vetch—I promised some to Dr. Abernathy for his research. But if we're going to spend the day tramping round reading old gravestones, I'm turning in now. Digging up the past is strenuous work."

There was a brief flicker in Brianna's face, and I thought she was about to say something. But she merely nodded, and reached to turn out the light, the secretive smile still lurking in the corners of her mouth.

I lay looking up into the darkness, hearing her small tossings and turnings fade into the regular cadences of her sleeping breath. St. Kilda, eh? I had never been there, but I knew of the place; it was an old church, as Brianna had said, long deserted and out of the way for tourists—only the occasional researcher ever went there. Perhaps this was the opportunity I had been waiting for, then?

I would have Roger and Brianna together there, and alone, with little fear of interruption. And perhaps it was a suitable place to tell them—there among the long-dead parishioners of St. Kilda. Roger had not yet verified the whereabouts of the rest of the Lallybroch men, but it seemed fairly sure that they had at least left Culloden Field alive, and that was really all I needed to know, now. I could tell Bree the end of it, then.

My mouth grew dry at the thought of the coming interview. Where was I to find the words for this? I tried to visualize how it might go; what I might say, and how they might react, but imagination failed me. More than ever, I regretted my promise to Frank that had kept me from writing to the Reverend Wakefield. If I had, Roger at least might already know. Or perhaps not; the Reverend might not have believed me.

I turned restlessly, seeking inspiration, but weariness crept over me. And at last I gave up and turned onto my back, closing my eyes on the dark above me. As though my thinking of him had summoned the Reverend's spirit, a biblical quotation drifted into my fading consciousness: *Sufficient unto the day,* the Reverend's voice seemed to murmur to me, *sufficient unto the day is the evil thereof.* And then I slept.

$\blacktriangleright$

I woke up in the shadowed dark, hands clenched in the bedclothes, heart beating with a force that shook me like the skin of a kettledrum. "Jesus!" I said.

The silk of my nightgown was hot and clinging; looking down, I could dimly see my nipples thrusting through it, hard as marbles. The quivering spasms were still rippling through wrists and thighs, like the aftershocks of an earthquake. I hoped I hadn't cried out. Probably not; I could hear Brianna's breathing, untroubled and regular across the room.

I fell back on the pillow, shaking with weakness, the sudden flush washing my temples with damp.

"Jesus H. Roosevelt Christ," I muttered, breathing deeply as my heart slowly returned to normal.

One of the effects of a disturbed sleep cycle is that one stops dreaming coherently. Through the long years of early motherhood, and then of internship, residency, and nights on-call, I had got used to falling at once into oblivion when I lay down, with such dreams as occurred nothing more than fragments and flashes, restless flickers in the dark as synapses fired at random, recharging themselves for the work of the day that would come too soon.

In more recent years, with the resumption of something resembling a normal schedule, I had begun to dream again. The usual kinds of dreams, whether nightmare or good dream—long sequences of images, wanderings in the wood of the mind. And I was familiar with this kind of dream, too; it was common to what might politely be called periods of deprivation.

Usually, though, such dreams came floating, soft as the touch of satin sheets, and if they woke me, I fell at once back into sleep, glowing dimly with a memory that would not last 'til morning.

This was different. Not that I remembered much about it, but I had a vague impression of hands that gripped me, rough and urgent, not wooing but compelling. And a voice, nearly shouting, that echoed in the chambers of my inner ear, along with the sound of my fading heartbeat.

I put my hand on my chest over the leaping pulse, feeling the soft fullness of my breast beneath the silk. Brianna's breath caught in a soft snore, then resumed its even cadence. I remembered listening for that sound when she was small; the slow, stertorous rhythm of reassurance, sounding through the darkened nursery, even as a heartbeat.

My own heartbeat was slowing under my hand, under the deep rose silk, the color of a baby's sleep-flushed cheek. When you hold a child to your breast to nurse, the curve of the little head echoes exactly the curve of the breast it suckles, as though this new person truly mirrors the flesh from which it sprang.

Babies are soft. Anyone looking at them can see the tender, fragile skin and know it for the rose-leaf softness that invites a finger's touch. But when you live with them and love them, you feel the softness going inward, the round-cheeked flesh wobbly as custard, the boneless splay of the tiny hands. Their joints are melted rubber, and even when you kiss them hard, in the passion of loving their existence, your lips sink down and seem never to find bone. Holding them against you, they melt and mold, as though they might at any moment flow back into your body.

But from the very start, there is that small streak of steel within each child. That thing that says "I am," and forms the core of personality.

In the second year, the bone hardens and the child stands upright, skull wide and solid, a helmet protecting the softness within. And "I am" grows, too. Looking at them, you can almost see it, sturdy as heartwood, glowing through the translucent flesh.

The bones of the face emerge at six, and the soul within is fixed at seven. The process of encapsulation goes on, to reach its peak in the glossy shell of adolescence, when all softness then is hidden under the nacreous layers of the mul-

tiple new personalities that teenagers try on to guard themselves.

In the next years, the hardening spreads from the center,
as one finds and fixes the facets of the soul, until "I am" is set,
delicate and detailed as an insect in amber.

I had thought I was well beyond that stage, had lost all
trace of softness and was well set on my way to a middle age
of stainless steel. But now I thought that Frank's death had
cracked me in some way. And the cracks were widening, so
that I could no longer patch them with denial. I had brought
my daughter back to Scotland, she with those bones strong as
the ribs of Highland mountains, in the hope that her shell was
strong enough to hold her together, while the center of her "I
am" might still be reachable.

But my own core held no longer in the isolation of "I
am," and I had no protection to shield me from the softness
from within. I no longer knew what I was or what she would
be; only what I must do.

For I had come back, and I dreamed once more, in the
cool air of the Highlands. And the voice of my dream still
echoed through ears and heart, repeated with the sound of
Brianna's sleeping breath.

"You are mine," it had said. "Mine! And I will not let
you go."

5

Beloved Wife

The kirkyard of St. Kilda lay quiet in the sun. Not entirely flat, it occupied a plateau carved from the side of the hill by some geological freak. The land sloped and curved, so that the gravestones lay hidden in small hollows or jutted suddenly from the crest of a rise. The shifting of the earth had moved many, tilting them drunkenly or toppling them altogether, to lie flattened and broken in the long grass.

"It's a bit untidy," Roger said, apologetically. They paused in the kirkyard gate, looking over the small collection of ancient stones, overgrown and shadowed by the row of giant yews, planted long ago as a windbreak against the storms that rolled in from the northern sea. Clouds massed there now, far out over the distant firth, but the sun shone on the hilltop, and the air was still and warm.

"My father used to get together a gang of men from the church once or twice a year, and bring them up to keep the place in order, but I'm afraid it's rather gone to seed lately." He swung the lych-gate experimentally, noting the cracked hinge and the latch-fitting, dangling by one nail.

"It's a lovely, quiet place." Brianna edged carefully past the splintery gate. "Really old, isn't it?"

"Aye, it is. Dad thought the kirk itself was built on the site of an early church or an even older temple of some kind; that's why it's up here in such an inconvenient spot. One of his friends from Oxford was always threatening to come up and excavate the place to see what was under it, but of course he couldn't get clearance from the Church authorities, even though the place has been deconsecrated for years."

"It's kind of a climb." The flush of exertion was beginning to fade from Brianna's face as she fanned her cheeks with a guidebook. "Beautiful, though." She eyed the facade of the kirk with appreciation. Built into a natural opening in the crag, the stones and timbers of the kirk had been fitted by hand, the chinks caulked with peat and mud, so that it seemed to have grown there, a natural part of the cliff face.

Ancient carvings decorated door sill and window frame, some showing the symbols of Christianity, some obviously much older.

"Is Jonathan Randall's stone over there?" She waved toward the kirkyard, visible beyond the gate. "Mother will be so surprised!"

"Aye, I expect so. Haven't seen it myself." He hoped the surprise would be a pleasant one; when he had mentioned the stone cautiously to Brianna over the phone the night before, she had been enthusiastic.

"I know about Jonathan Randall," she was telling Roger. "Daddy always admired him; said he was one of the few interesting people in the family tree. I guess he was a good soldier; Daddy had lots of commendations and things he'd gotten."

"Really?" Roger looked back, in search of Claire. "Does your mother need help with that plant press?"

Brianna shook her head. "Nah. She just found a plant by the path she couldn't resist. She'll be up in a minute."

It was a silent place. Even the birds were quiet as midday approached, and the dark evergreens that edged the plateau were still, with no breeze to stir their branches. Without the raw scars of recent graves or the flags of plastic flowers as testimony to still-fresh grief, the kirkyard breathed only the peace of the long-dead. Removed from strife and trouble, only the fact of their life remained to give the comfort of a human presence on the lonely heights of an empty land.

The progress of the three visitors was slow; they wandered their way casually through the old kirkyard, Roger and Brianna pausing to read aloud quaint inscriptions from the weathered stones, Claire, on her own, stooping now and then to clip a vine or uproot a small flowering plant.

Roger bent over one stone, and grinning, beckoned Brianna to read the inscription.

" 'Approach and read, not with your hats on,' " she read. " 'For here lies Bailie William Watson / Who was famous for his thinking / And moderation in his drinking.' " Brianna rose from examining the stone, her face flushed with laughter. "No dates—I wonder when William Watson lived."

"Eighteenth century, most likely," Roger said. "The seventeenth-century stones are mostly too weathered to read, and no one's been buried here in two hundred years; the church was deconsecrated in 1800."

A moment later, Brianna let out a muffled whoop. "Here it is!" She stood up and waved to Claire, who was standing on the far side of the kirkyard, peering inquisitively at a length of greenery she held in one hand. "Mama! Come look at this!"

Claire waved back, and made her way to where they stood beside the flat, square stone, stepping carefully across the crowded graves.

"What is it?" she asked. "Find an interesting grave?"

"I think so. Recognize this name?" Roger stepped back, so she could have a clear view.

"Jesus H. Roosevelt Christ!" Mildly startled, Roger glanced at Claire, and was alarmed to see how pale she was. She stared down at the weathered stone, and the muscles of her throat moved in a convulsive swallow. The plant she had pulled was crushed in her hand, unregarded.

"Dr. Randall—Claire—are you all right?"

The amber eyes were blank, and she appeared not to hear him for a moment. Then she blinked, and looked up. She was still pale, but seemed better now; back in control.

"I'm fine," she said, voice flat. She stooped, and ran her fingers over the letters of the stone as though reading them in Braille.

"Jonathan Wolverton Randall," she said softly, "1705–1746. I told you, didn't I? You bastard, I *told* you!" Her voice, so flat an instant before, was suddenly vibrant, filled with a restrained fury.

"Mama! Are you all right?" Brianna, obviously upset, pulled at her mother's arm.

Roger thought it was as though a shade had dropped behind Claire's eyes; the feeling that had shone there was suddenly hidden, as she snapped back to a realization of the two people staring at her, aghast. She smiled, a brief, mechanical grimace, and nodded.

"Yes. Yes, of course. I'm fine." Her hand opened, and the stalk of limp greenery dropped to the ground.

"I thought you'd be surprised." Brianna was looking worriedly at her mother. "Isn't this Daddy's ancestor? The soldier who died at Culloden?"

Claire glanced down at the gravestone near her feet.

"Yes, it is," she said. "And he *is* dead, isn't he?"

Roger and Brianna exchanged looks. Feeling responsible, Roger touched Claire on the shoulder.

"It's rather a hot day," he said, trying for a note of casual matter-of-factness. "Perhaps we should go into the church for a little shade. There are some very interesting carvings on the font; well worth seeing."

Claire smiled at him. A real smile this time, a little tired, but eminently sane.

"You go," she said, including Brianna with a tilt of her head. "I need a little air. I'll stay out here for a bit."

"I'll stay with you." Brianna was hovering, clearly unwilling to leave her mother on her own, but Claire had recovered both her equanimity and her air of command.

"Nonsense," she said briskly. "I'm perfectly all right. I'll go sit in the shade of the trees over there. You go along. I'd rather be by myself for a bit," she added firmly, seeing Roger opening his mouth to protest.

With no further ado, she turned and walked off, toward the line of dark yew trees that edged the kirkyard to the west. Brianna hesitated, looking after her, but Roger took the girl by the elbow, and drew her toward the church.

"Best leave her alone," he murmured. "After all, your mother's a doctor, isn't she? She'll know if it's all right."

"Yeah . . . I suppose so." With a final troubled glance after Claire's retreating figure, Brianna allowed him to lead her away.

The kirk was no more than an empty wood-floored room, with the abandoned font left in place only because it could not be removed. The shallow basin had been scooped out of the stone ledge that ran along one side of the room. Above the basin, the carved visage of St. Kilda gazed emptily toward the ceiling, eyes piously upturned.

"It was probably one of the pagan gods to start with," Roger said, tracing the line of the carving with a finger. "You can see where they added the veil and wimple to the original figure—not to mention the eyes."

"Like poached eggs," Brianna agreed, rolling her own up

in imitation. "What's this carving over here? It looks a lot like the patterns on those Pictish stones outside Clava."

They strolled casually around the walls of the kirk, breathing the dusty air, examining the ancient carvings in the stone walls, and reading the small wooden plaques affixed by long-vanished parishioners in memory of ancestors gone still longer. They spoke quietly, both keeping an ear out for any sounds from the kirkyard, but all was quiet, and slowly they began to relax again.

Roger followed Brianna toward the front of the room, watching the curling tendrils that escaped from her braid to coil damply on her neck.

All that remained now at the front of the kirk was a plain wooden ledge above the hole where the altarstone had been removed. Still, Roger felt something of a quiver up his spine as he stood beside Brianna, facing the vanished altar.

The sheer intensity of his feelings seemed to echo in the empty place. He hoped she couldn't hear them. They had known each other barely a week, after all, and had had scarcely any private conversation. She would be taken aback, surely, or frightened, if she knew what he felt. Or worse yet, she would laugh.

Yet, when he stole a glance at her, her face was calm and serious. It was also looking back at him, with an expression in the dark blue of her eyes that turned him toward her and made him reach for her without conscious thought.

The kiss was brief and gentle, scarcely more than the formality that concludes a wedding, yet as striking in its impact as though they had this minute plighted a troth.

Roger's hands fell away, but the warmth of her lingered, in hands and lips and body, so that he felt as though he held her still. They stood a moment, bodies grazing, breathing each other's air, and then she stepped back. He could still feel the touch of her on the palms of his hands. He curled his fingers into fists, seeking to hold the feeling.

The still air of the church shivered suddenly into bits, the echoes of a scream scattering the dust motes. Without conscious thought, Roger was outside, running, stumbling and scrambling over the tumbled stones, heading for the dark line of the yews. He pushed his way between the overgrown branches, not bothering to hold back the scaly twigs for Brianna, hot on his heels.

Pale in the shadows, he saw Claire Randall's face. Completely drained of color, she looked like a wraith against the dark branches of the yew. She stood for a moment, swaying, then sank to her knees in the grass, as though her legs would no longer support her.

"Mother!" Brianna dropped to her knees beside the crouching figure, chafing one of the limp hands. "Mama, what is it? Are you faint? You should put your head between your knees. Here, why don't you lie down?"

Claire resisted the helpful proddings of her offspring, and the drooping head came upright on its slender neck once more.

"I don't want to lie down," she gasped. "I want. . . . oh, God. Oh, dear holy God." Kneeling among the unmowed grass she stretched out a trembling hand to the surface of the stone. It was carved of granite, a simple slab.

"Dr. Randall! Er, Claire?" Roger dropped to one knee on her other side, putting a hand under her other arm to support her. He was truly alarmed at her appearance. A fine sweat had broken out on her temples and she looked as though she might keel over at any moment. "Claire," he said again, urgently, trying to rouse her from the staring trance she had fallen into. "What is it? Is it a name you know?" Even as he spoke, his own words were ringing in his ears. *No one's been buried here since the eighteenth century,* he'd told Brianna. *No one's been buried here in two hundred years.*

Claire's fingers brushed his own away, and touched the stone, caressing, as though touching flesh, gently tracing the letters, the grooves worn shallow, but still clear.

"'JAMES ALEXANDER MALCOLM MACKENZIE FRASER,'" she read aloud. "Yes, I know him." Her hand dropped lower, brushing back the grass that grew thickly about the stone, obscuring the line of smaller letters at its base.

"'Beloved husband of Claire,'" she read.

"Yes, I knew him," she said again, so softly Roger could scarcely hear her. "I'm Claire. He was my husband." She looked up then, into the face of her daughter, white and shocked above her. "And your father," she said.

Roger and Brianna stared down at her, and the kirkyard was silent, save for the rustle of the yews above.

"No!" I said, quite crossly. "For the fifth time—no! I don't want a drink of water. I have not got a touch of the sun. I am not faint. I am not ill. And I haven't lost my mind, either, though I imagine that's what you're thinking."

Roger and Brianna exchanged glances that made it clear that that was precisely what they were thinking. They had, between them, got me out of the kirkyard and into the car. I had refused to be taken to hospital, so we had gone back to the manse. Roger had administered medicinal whisky for shock, but his eyes darted toward the telephone now as though wondering whether to dial for additional help—like a straitjacket, I supposed.

"Mama." Brianna spoke soothingly, reaching out to try to smooth the hair back from my face. "You're upset."

"Of course I'm upset!" I snapped. I took a long, quivering breath and clamped my lips tight together, until I could trust myself to speak calmly.

"I am certainly upset," I began, "but I'm not mad." I stopped, struggling for control. This wasn't the way I'd intended to do it. I didn't know quite what I *had* intended, but not this, blurting out the truth without preparation or time to organize my own thoughts. Seeing that bloody grave had disrupted any plan I might have formed.

"Damn you, Jamie Fraser!" I said, furious. "What are you doing there anyway; it's *miles* from Culloden!"

Brianna's eyes were halfway out on stalks, and Roger's hand was hovering near the telephone. I stopped abruptly and tried to get a grip on myself.

Be calm, Beauchamp, I instructed myself. Breathe deeply. Once . . . twice . . . once more. Better. Now. It's very simple; all you have to do is tell them the truth. That's what you came to Scotland for, isn't it?

I opened my mouth, but no sound came out. I closed my mouth, and my eyes as well, hoping that my nerve would return, if I couldn't see the two ashen faces in front of me. Just . . . let . . . me . . . tell . . . the . . . truth, I prayed, with no idea who I was talking to. Jamie, I thought.

I'd told the truth once before. It hadn't gone well.

I pressed my eyelids shut more tightly. Once more I could smell the carbolic surroundings of a hospital, and feel the unfamiliar starched pillowcase beneath my cheek. From the corridor outside came Frank's voice, choked with baffled rage.

"What do you mean, don't press her? Don't *press* her? My wife's been gone for nearly three years, and come back filthy, abused, and *pregnant,* for God's sake, and I'm not to ask *questions*?"

And the doctor's voice, murmuring soothingly. I caught the words "delusion," and "traumatic state," and "leave it for later, old man—just for a bit" as Frank's voice, still arguing and interrupting, was gently but firmly eased down the hall. That so-familiar voice, which raised anew the storm of grief and rage and terror inside me.

I had curled my body into a defensive ball, pillow clutched to my chest, and bitten it, as hard as I could, until I felt the cotton casing give way and the silky grit of feathers grinding between my teeth.

I was grinding them now, to the detriment of a new filling. I stopped, and opened my eyes.

"Look," I said, as reasonably as I could. "I'm sorry, I know how it sounds. But it's true, and nothing I can do about it."

This speech did nothing to reassure Brianna, who edged closer to Roger. Roger himself had lost that green-about-the-gills look, though, and was exhibiting signs of cautious interest. Could it be possible that he really did have enough imagination to be able to grasp the truth?

I took hope from his expression, and unclenched my fists.

"It's the bloody stones," I said. "You know, the standing stone circle, on the fairies' hill, to the west?"

"Craigh na Dun," Roger murmured. "That one?"

"Right." I exhaled consciously. "You may know the legends about fairy hills—do you? About people who get trapped in rocky hills and wake up two hundred years later?"

Brianna was looking more alarmed by the moment.

"Mother, I really think you ought to go up and lie

down," she said. She half-rose from her seat. "I could go get Fiona . . ."

Roger put a hand on her arm to stop her.

"No, wait," he said. He looked at me, with the sort of suppressed curiosity a scientist shows when putting a new slide under the microscope. "Go ahead," he said to me.

"Thanks," I said dryly. "Don't worry, I'm not going to start driveling about fairies; I just thought you'd like to know there's some basis to the legends. I haven't any idea what it actually is up there, or how it works, but the fact is . . ." I took a deep breath, "Well, the fact is, that I walked through a bloody cleft stone in that circle in 1946, and I ended up on the hillside below in 1743."

I'd said exactly that to Frank. He'd glared at me for a moment, picked up a vase of flowers from my bedside table, and smashed it on the floor.

Roger looked like a scientist whose new microbe has come through a winner. I wondered why, but was too engrossed in the struggle to find words that sounded halfway sane.

"The first person I ran into was an English dragoon in full fig," I said. "Which rather gave me a hint that something was wrong."

A sudden smile lighted Roger's face, though Brianna went on looking horrified. "I should think it might," he said.

"The difficulty was that I couldn't get back, you see." I thought I'd better address my remarks to Roger, who at least seemed disposed to listen, whether he believed me or not.

"The thing is, ladies then didn't go about the place unescorted, and if they did, they didn't do it wearing print dresses and oxford loafers," I explained. "Everyone I met, starting with that dragoon captain, knew there was something wrong about me—but they didn't know what. How could they? I couldn't explain then any better than I can now—and lunatic asylums back then were much less pleasant places than they are now. No basket weaving," I added, with an effort at a joke. It wasn't noticeably successful; Brianna grimaced and looked more worried than ever.

"That dragoon," I said, and a brief shudder went over

me at the memory of Jonathan Wolverton Randall, Captain of His Majesty's Eighth Dragoons. "I thought I was hallucinating at first, because the man looked so very like Frank; at first glance, I thought it was he." I glanced at the table where a copy of one of Frank's books lay, with its back-cover photograph of a dark and handsome lean-faced man.

"That's quite a coincidence," Roger said. His eyes were alert, fixed on mine.

"Well, it was and it wasn't," I told him, wrenching my eyes with an effort from the stack of books. "You know he was Frank's ancestor. All the men in that family have a strong family resemblance—physically, at least," I added, thinking of the rather striking nonphysical differences.

"What—what was he like?" Brianna seemed to be coming out of her stupor, at least slightly.

"He was a bloody filthy pervert," I said. Two pairs of eyes snapped open wide and turned to each other with an identical look of consternation.

"You needn't look like that," I said. "They had perversion in the eighteenth century; it isn't anything new, you know. Only it was worse then, maybe, since no one really cared, so long as things were kept quiet and decent on the surface. And Black Jack Randall was a soldier; he captained a garrison in the Highlands, charged with keeping the clans under control—he had considerable scope for his activities, all officially sanctioned." I took a restorative gulp from the whisky glass I still held.

"He liked to hurt people," I said. "He liked it a lot."

"Did he . . . hurt you?" Roger put the question with some delicacy, after a rather noticeable pause. Bree seemed to be drawing into herself, the skin tightening across her cheekbones.

"Not directly. Or not much, at least." I shook my head. I could feel a cold spot in the pit of my stomach, which the whisky was doing little to thaw. Jack Randall had hit me there, once. I felt it in memory, like the ache of a long-healed wound.

"He had fairly eclectic tastes. But it was Jamie that he . . . wanted." Under no circumstances would I have used the word "loved." My throat felt thick, and I swallowed the last drops of whisky. Roger held up the decanter, one brow raised questioningly, and I nodded and held out my glass.

"Jamie. That's Jamie Fraser? And he was . . ."

"He was my husband," I said.

Brianna shook her head like a horse driving off flies.

"But you *had* a husband," she said. "You couldn't . . . even if . . . I mean . . . you *couldn't.*"

"I had to," I said flatly. "I didn't do it on purpose, after all."

"Mother, you can't get married accidentally!" Brianna was losing her kindly-nurse-with-mental-patient attitude. I thought this was probably a good thing, even if the alternative was anger.

"Well, it wasn't precisely an accident," I said. "It was the best alternative to being handed over to Jack Randall, though. Jamie married me to protect me—and bloody generous of him, too," I finished, glaring at Bree over my glass. "He didn't have to do it, but he did."

I fought back the memory of our wedding night. He was a virgin; his hands had trembled when he touched me. I had been afraid too—with better reason. And then in the dawn he had held me, naked back against bare chest, his thighs warm and strong behind my own, murmuring into the clouds of my hair, "Dinna be afraid. There's the two of us now."

"See," I turned to Roger again, "I couldn't get back. I was running away from Captain Randall when the Scots found me. A party of cattle-raiders. Jamie was with them, they were his mother's people, the MacKenzies of Leoch. They didn't know what to make of me, but they took me with them as a captive. And I couldn't get away again."

I remembered my abortive efforts to escape from Castle Leoch. And then the day when I had told Jamie the truth, and he—not believing, any more than Frank had, but at least willing to act as though he did—had taken me back to the hill and the stones.

"He thought I was a witch, perhaps," I said, eyes closed, smiling just a bit at the thought. "Now they think you're mad; then they thought you were a witch. Cultural mores," I explained, opening my eyes. "Psychology is just what they call it these days instead of magic. Not the hell of a lot of difference." Roger nodded, seeming a little stunned.

"They tried me for witchcraft," I said. "In the village of Cranesmuir, just below the castle. Jamie saved me, though, and then I told him. And he took me to the hill, and told me to go back. Back to Frank." I paused and drew a deep breath, remembering that October afternoon, where control of my destiny, taken from me for so long, had been suddenly thrust back into my hands, and the choice not given, but demanded of me.

"Go back!" he had said. "There's nothing here for ye! Nothing save danger."

"Is there really nothing here for me?" I had asked. Too honorable to speak, he had answered nonetheless, and I had made my choice.

"It was too late," I said, staring down at my hands, lying open on my knees. The day was darkening to rain, but my two wedding rings still gleamed in the fading light, gold and silver. I hadn't taken Frank's gold band from my left hand when I married Jamie, but had worn Jamie's silver ring on the fourth finger of my right hand, for every day of the twenty-odd years since he put it there.

"I loved Frank," I said quietly, not looking at Bree. "I loved him a lot. But by that time, Jamie was my heart and the breath of my body. I couldn't leave him. I *couldn't*," I said, raising my head suddenly to Bree in appeal. She stared back at me, stone-faced.

I looked down at my hands again, and went on.

"He took me to his own home—Lallybroch, it was called. A beautiful place." I shut my eyes again, to get away from the look on Brianna's face, and deliberately summoned the image of the estate of Broch Tuarach—Lallybroch, to the people who lived there. A beautiful Highland farm, with woods and streams; even a bit of fertile ground—rare for the Highlands. A lovely, peaceful place, sealed within high hills above a mountain pass that kept it remote from the recurrent strife that troubled the Highlands. But even Lallybroch had proved only a temporary sanctuary.

"Jamie was an outlaw," I said, seeing behind my closed eyelids the scars of flogging that the English had left on his back. A network of thin white lines that webbed the broad shoulders like a branded grid. "There was a price on his head. One of his own tenants betrayed him to the English. They captured him, and took him to Wentworth Prison—to hang him."

Roger gave a long, low whistle.

"Hell of a place," he remarked. "Have you seen it? The walls must be ten feet thick!"

I opened my eyes. "They are," I said wryly. "I've been inside them. But even the thickest walls have doors." I felt a small flicker of the blaze of desperate courage that had taken me inside Wentworth Prison, in pursuit of my heart. If I could do that for you, I told Jamie silently, I can do this as well. But help me, you bloody big Scot—help me!

"I got him out," I said, taking a deep breath. "What was left of him. Jack Randall commanded the garrison at Wentworth." Now I didn't want to remember the images that my words brought back, but they wouldn't stop. Jamie, naked and bloody, on the floor of Eldridge Manor, where we had found sanctuary.

"I wilna let them take me back again, Sassenach," he'd said to me, teeth clenched against the pain as I'd set the crushed bones of his hand and cleansed his wounds. "Sassenach." He had called me that from the first; the Gaelic word for an outlander, a stranger. An Englishman. First in jest, and then in affection.

And I hadn't let them find him; with the help of his kinsman, a little Fraser clansman called Murtagh, I'd gotten him across the Channel to France, and to refuge in the Abbey of Ste. Anne de Beaupré, where one of his Fraser uncles was abbot. But once there in safety, I had found that saving his life was not the end of the task set me.

What Jack Randall had done to him had sunk into his soul as surely as the flails of the lash had sunk in his back, and had left scars every bit as permanent. I was not sure, even now, what I had done, when I had summoned his demons and fought them single-handed, in the dark of his mind; there is very little difference between medicine and magic, when it comes to some kinds of healing.

I could still feel the cold, hard stone that bruised me, and the strength of the fury that I had drawn from him, the hands that closed round my neck and the burning creature who had hunted me through the dark.

"But I did heal him," I said softly. "He came back to me."

Brianna was shaking her head slowly back and forth, bewildered, but with a stubborn set to her head that I knew very well indeed. "Grahams are stupid, Campbells are deceitful, MacKenzies are charming but sly, and Frasers are stubborn," Jamie had told me once, giving me his view of the general characteristics of the clans. He hadn't been far wrong, either; Frasers *were* extremely stubborn, not least him. Nor Bree.

"I don't believe it," she said flatly. She sat up straighter, eyeing me closely. "I think maybe you've been thinking too much about those men at Culloden," she said. "After all, you've been under a strain lately, and maybe Daddy's death . . ."

"Frank wasn't your father," I said bluntly.

"He was!" She flashed back with it immediately, so fast that it startled both of us.

Frank had, in time, bowed to the doctors' insistence that any attempt to "force me to accept reality," as one of them put it, might be harmful to my pregnancy. There had been a lot of murmuring in corridors—and shouting, now and then—but he had given up asking me for the truth. And I, in frail health and sick at heart, had given up telling it to him.

I wasn't going to give up, this time.

"I promised Frank," I said. "Twenty years ago, when you were born. I tried to leave him, and he wouldn't let me go. He loved you." I felt my voice soften as I looked at Brianna. "He couldn't believe the truth, but he knew—of course—that he wasn't your father. He asked me not to tell you—to let him be your only father—as long as he lived. After that, he said, it was up to me." I swallowed, licking dry lips.

"I owed him that," I said. "Because he loved you. But now Frank's dead—and you have a right to know who you are."

"If you doubt it," I said, "go to the National Portrait Gallery. They've a picture there of Ellen MacKenzie; Jamie's mother. She's wearing these." I touched the pearl necklace at my throat. A string of baroque freshwater pearls from Scottish rivers, strung with roundels of pierced gold. "Jamie gave them to me on our wedding day."

I looked at Brianna, sitting tall and stiff, the bones of her face stark in protest. "Take along a hand mirror," I said. "Take a good look at the portrait and then in the mirror. It's not an exact likeness, but you're very like your grandmother."

Roger stared at Brianna as though he'd never seen her before. He glanced back and forth between us, then, as though making up his mind, suddenly squared his shoulders and rose from the sofa where he had been sitting beside her.

"I've something I think you should see," he said firmly. He crossed quickly to the Reverend's old rolltop desk and pulled a rubber-banded bundle of yellowed newspaper clippings from one of the pigeonholes.

"When you've read them, look at the dates," he told Brianna, handing them to her. Then, still standing, he turned to me and looked me over, with the long, dispassionate gaze that I recognized as that of a scholar, schooled in objectivity. He didn't yet believe, but he had the imagination to doubt.

"Seventeen forty-three," he said, as though to himself. He shook his head, marveling. "And I thought it was a man you'd met here, in 1946. God, I would *never* have thought—well, Christ, who would?"

I was surprised. "You knew? About Brianna's father?"

He nodded at the clippings in Brianna's hands. She hadn't yet looked at them, but was staring at Roger, half-bewildered, half-angry. I could see the storm gathering in her eyes, and so, I thought, could Roger. He looked hastily away from her, turning back to me in question.

"Then those men whose names you gave me, the ones who fought at Culloden—you *knew* them?"

I relaxed, ever so slightly. "Yes, I knew them." There was a grumble of thunder to the east, and the rain broke in a spatter against the long windows that lined the study from floor to ceiling on one side. Brianna's head was bent over the clippings, the wings of her hair hiding everything but the tip of her nose, which was bright red. Jamie always went red when he was furious or upset. I was all too familiar with the sight of a Fraser on the verge of explosion.

"And you were in France," Roger murmured as though to himself, still studying me closely. The shock in his face was fading into surmise, and a kind of excitement. "I don't suppose you knew . . ."

"Yes, I did," I told him. "That's why we went to Paris. I'd told Jamie about Culloden—the '45, and what would happen. We went to Paris to try to stop Charles Stuart."

PART TWO

The Pretenders

LE HAVRE, FRANCE: FEBRUARY 1744

6

Making Waves

"**B**read," I muttered feebly, keeping my eyes tightly closed. There was no response from the large, warm object next to me, other than the faint sigh of his breathing.

"Bread!" I said, a little louder. There was a sudden startled heave of the bedclothes, and I grasped the edge of the mattress and tightened all my muscles, hoping to stabilize the pitch and yaw of my internal organs.

Fumbling noises came from the far side of the bed, followed by the sliding of a drawer, a muffled exclamation in Gaelic, the soft thud of a bare foot stamping planks, and then the sinking of the mattress under the weight of a heavy body.

"Here, Sassenach," said an anxious voice, and I felt the touch of a dry bread crust against my lower lip. Groping blindly without opening my eyes, I grasped it and began to chew gingerly, forcing each choking bite down a parched throat. I knew better than to ask for water.

The desiccated wads of bread crumbs gradually made their way down my throat and took up residence in my stomach, where they lay like small heaps of ballast. The nauseating roll of my inner waves slowly calmed, and at last my innards lay at anchor. I opened my eyes, to see the anxious face of Jamie Fraser hovering a few inches above me.

"Ak!" I said, startled.

"All right, then?" he asked. When I nodded and feebly began to sit up, he put an arm around my back to help me. Sitting down beside me on the rough inn bed, he pulled me gently against him and stroked my sleep-tousled hair.

"Poor love," he said. "Would a bit of wine help? There's a flask of hock in my saddlebag."

"No. No, thank you." I shuddered briefly at the thought of drinking hock—I seemed to smell the dark, fruity fumes, just at the mention of it—and pushed myself upright.

"I'll be fine in a moment," I said, with forced cheerfulness. "Don't worry, it's quite normal for pregnant women to feel sick in the morning."

With a dubious look at me, Jamie rose and went to retrieve his clothes from the stool near the window. France in February is cold as hell frozen over, and the bubbled-glass panes of the window were coated thick with frost.

He was naked, and a ripple of gooseflesh brushed his shoulders and raised the red-gold hairs on his arms and legs. Accustomed to cold, though, he neither shivered nor hurried as he pulled on stockings and shirt. Pausing in his dressing, he came back to the bed and hugged me briefly.

"Go back to bed," he suggested. "I'll send up the chambermaid to light the fire. Perhaps ye can rest a bit, now you've eaten. You won't be sick now?" I wasn't entirely sure, but nodded reassuringly.

"I don't think so." I cast an eye back at the bed; the quilts, like most coverings supplied by public inns, were none too clean. Still, the silver in Jamie's purse had procured us the best room in the inn, and the narrow bed was stuffed with goose feathers rather than with chaff or wool.

"Um, perhaps I *will* just lie down a moment," I murmured, pulling my feet off the freezing floor and thrusting them under the quilts, in search of the last remnants of warmth. My stomach seemed to have settled sufficiently to risk a sip of water, and I poured a cupful from the cracked bedroom ewer.

"What were you stamping on?" I asked, sipping carefully. "There aren't spiders up here, are there?"

Fastening his kilt about his waist, Jamie shook his head.

"Och, no," he said. Hands busy, he tilted his head toward the table. "Just a rat. After the bread, I expect."   ·

Glancing down, I saw the limp gray form on the floor, a small pearl of blood glistening on the snout. I made it out of bed just in time.

"It's all right," I said faintly, a bit later. "There isn't anything left to throw up."

"Rinse your mouth, Sassenach, but don't swallow, for God's sake." Jamie held the cup for me, wiped my mouth with a cloth as though I were a small and messy child, then lifted me and laid me carefully back in the bed. He frowned worriedly down at me.

"Perhaps I'd better stay here," he said. "I could send word."

"No, no, I'm all right," I said. And I was. Fight as I would to keep from vomiting in the mornings, I could hold nothing down for long. Yet once the bout was over, I felt entirely restored. Aside from a sour taste in my mouth, and a slight soreness in the abdominal muscles, I felt quite my normal self. I threw back the covers and stood up, to demonstrate.

"See? I'll be fine. And you have to go; it wouldn't do to keep your cousin waiting, after all."

I was beginning to feel cheerful again, despite the chilly air rushing under the door and beneath the folds of my nightgown. Jamie was still hesitating, reluctant to leave me, and I went to him and hugged him tightly, both in reassurance and because he was delightfully warm.

"Brrr," I said. "How on earth can you be warm as toast, dressed in nothing but a kilt?"

"I've a shirt on as well," he protested, smiling down at me.

We clung together for a bit, enjoying each other's warmth in the quiet cold of the early French morning. In the corridor, the clash and shuffle of the chambermaid with her scuttle of kindling grew nearer.

Jamie shifted a bit, pressing against me. Because of the difficulties of traveling in the winter, we had been nearly a week on the road from Ste. Anne to Le Havre. And between the late arrivals at dismal inns, wet, filthy, and shivering with fatigue and cold, and the increasingly unsettled wakenings as my morning sickness got worse, we had scarcely touched each other since our last night at the Abbey.

"Come to bed with me?" I invited, softly.

He hesitated. The strength of his desire was obvious through the fabric of his kilt, and his hands were warm on the cool flesh of my own, but he didn't move to take me in his arms.

"Well . . ." he said doubtfully.

"You want to, don't you?" I said, sliding a chilly hand under his kilt to make sure.

"Oh! er . . . aye. Aye, I do." The evidence at hand bore out this statement. He groaned faintly as I cupped my hand between his legs. "Oh, Lord. Don't do that, Sassenach; I canna keep my hands from ye."

He did hug me then, wrapping long arms about me and pulling my face into the snowy tucks of his shirt, smelling faintly of the laundry starch Brother Alfonse used at the Abbey.

"Why should you?" I said, muffled in his linen. "You've a bit of time to spare, surely? It's only a short ride to the docks."

"It isna that," he said, smoothing my riotous hair.

"Oh, I'm too fat?" In fact, my stomach was still nearly flat, and I was thinner than usual because of the sickness. "Or is it . . . ?"

"No," he said, smiling. "Ye talk too much." He bent and kissed me, then scooped me up and sat down on the bed, holding me on his lap. I lay down and pulled him determinedly down on top of me.

"Claire, no!" he protested as I started unbuckling his kilt.

I stared at him. "Whyever not?"

"Well," he said awkwardly, blushing a bit. "The child . . . I mean, I dinna want to hurt it."

I laughed.

"Jamie, you can't hurt it. It's no bigger than the tip of my finger yet." I held up a finger in illustration, then used it to trace the full, curving line of his lower lip. He seized my hand and bent to kiss me abruptly, as though to erase the tickle of my touch.

"You're sure?" he asked. "I mean . . . I keep thinking he wouldna like being jounced about . . ."

"He'll never notice," I assured him, hands once more busy with the buckle of his kilt.

"Well . . . if you're sure of it."

There was a peremptory rap at the door, and with impeccable Gallic timing, the chambermaid pushed her way in backward, carelessly gouging the door with a billet of wood as she turned. From the scarred surfaces of door and jamb, it appeared that this was her usual method of operations.

"*Bonjour,* Monsieur, Madame," she muttered, with a curt nod toward the bed as she shuffled toward the hearth. All right for *some* people, said her attitude, louder than

words. Used by this time to the matter-of-factness with which
servants treated the sight of inn patrons in any form of dishabille, I merely murmured *"Bonjour,* Mademoiselle," in return
and let it go at that. I also let go of Jamie's kilt, and slid under
the covers, pulling the quilt up to hide my scarlet cheeks.

Possessed of somewhat greater sang-froid, Jamie placed
one of the bolsters strategically across his lap, parked his
elbows on it, rested his chin on upturned palms, and made
pleasant conversation with the maid, praising the cuisine of
the house.

"And from where do you procure the wine, Mademoiselle?" he asked politely.

"From here, from there." She shrugged, stuffing kindling
rapidly under the sticks with a practiced hand. "Wherever it's
cheapest." The woman's plump face creased slightly as she
gave Jamie a sidelong look from the hearth.

"I gathered as much," he said, grinning at her, and she
gave a brief snort of amusement.

"I'll wager I can match the price you're getting, and
double the quality," he offered. "Tell your mistress."

One eyebrow rose skeptically. "And what's your own
price, Monsieur?"

He made an altogether Gallic gesture of self-abnegation.
"Nothing, Mademoiselle. I go to call upon a kinsman who
sells wine. Perhaps I can bring him some new business to
ensure my welcome, no?"

She nodded, seeing the wisdom of this, and grunted as
she rose from her knees.

"Well enough, Monsieur. I'll speak to the *patronne.*"

The door thumped to behind the maid, aided by a skillful
swing of her hip in passing. Putting the bolster aside, Jamie
stood up and began to rebuckle his kilt.

"Where do you think you're going?" I protested.

He glanced down at me, and a reluctant smile curved the
wide mouth.

"Oh. Well . . . you're sure you're up to it, Sassenach?"

"I am if you are," I said, unable to resist.

He eyed me austerely.

"Just for that, I should go at once," he said. "Still, I've
heard that ye ought to humor expectant mothers." He let the

kilt fall to the floor and sat down beside me in his shirt, the bed creaking beneath his weight.

His breath rose in a faint cloud as he turned back the quilt and spread the front of the nightdress to expose my breasts. Bending his head, he kissed each one, touching the nipple delicately with his tongue, so it rose as though by magic, a swelling dark pink against the white skin of my breast.

"God, they're so lovely," he murmured, repeating the process on the other side. He cupped both breasts, admiring them.

"They're heavier," he said, "just a bit. And the nipples are darker, too." One forefinger traced the springing curve of a single fine hair that rose near the dark areola, silver in the frosted light of the morning.

Lifting the quilt, he rolled next to me and I turned into his arms, clasping the solid curves of his back, letting my hands cup the firm rounds of his buttocks. His bare flesh was chilled by the morning air, but the goose bumps smoothed away under the warmth of my touch.

I tried to bring him to me at once, but he resisted me gently, forcing me down onto the pillow as he nibbled the edges of neck and ear. One hand slid up my thigh, the thin material of the nightgown gliding in waves before it.

His head dipped lower, and his hands gently spread my thighs apart. I shivered momentarily as the cold air hit the bare skin of my legs, then relaxed completely into the warm demand of his mouth.

His hair was loose, not yet laced back for the day, and the soft red tickle of it brushed my thighs. The solid weight of his body rested comfortably between my legs, broad hands cupped on the roundness of my hips.

"Mmmm?" came an interrogative sound from below.

I arched my hips slightly in response, and a brief chuckle grazed my skin with warmth.

The hands slid beneath my hips and raised me, and I relaxed into deliquescence as the tiny shudder grew and spread, rising in seconds to a fulfillment that left me limp and gasping, Jamie's head resting on my thigh. He waited a moment for me to recover, caressing the slope of my leg, before returning to his self-appointed task.

I smoothed the tumbled hair back, caressing those ears, so incongruously small and neat for such a large, blunt man. The upper curve glowed with a faint, translucent pink, and I ran my thumb along the edge of the curve.

"They're pointed at the tips," I said. "Just a bit. Like a faun's."

"Oh, aye?" he said, interrupting his labors for a moment. "Like a small deer, ye mean, or the things ye see in classical paintings wi' goat's legs, chasing naked women?"

I lifted my head and peered down across the roil of bedclothes, nightgown, and naked flesh, to the deep blue cat-eyes, gleaming above damp curls of brown hair.

"If the shoe fits," I said, "wear it." And let my head fall back on the pillow as the resultant muffled laugh vibrated against my all too sensitive flesh.

"Oh," I said, straining upward. "Oh, my. Jamie, come here."

"Not yet," he said, doing something with the tip of his tongue that made me squirm uncontrollably.

"Now," I said.

He didn't bother to reply, and I had no more breath to speak with.

"Oh," I said, a bit later. "That's . . ."

"Mmmm?"

"Good," I murmured. "Come here."

"No, I'll do," he said, face invisible behind the tangle of roan and cinnamon. "Would ye like it if I . . ."

"Jamie," I said. "I want you. Come *here.*"

Sighing in resignation, he rose to his knees and let me pull him upward, settling at last with his weight balanced on his elbows, but comfortingly solid on top of me, belly to belly and lips to lips. He opened his mouth to protest further, but I promptly kissed him, and he slid between my thighs before he could stop himself. He moaned slightly in involuntary pleasure as he entered me, muscles tensing as he gripped my shoulders.

He was gentle and slow, pausing now and then to kiss me deeply, moving again only at my silent urging. I ran my hands softly down the slope of his back, careful not to press on the healing ridges of the fresh scars. The long muscles of his thigh trembled briefly against my own, but he held back, unwilling to move as quickly as he needed to.

I moved my hips against him, to bring him deeper.

He closed his eyes, and his brow furrowed slightly in concentration. His mouth was open, and his breath came hard.

"I can't . . ." he said. "Oh, God, I canna help it." His buttocks clenched suddenly, taut beneath my hands.

I sighed with deep satisfaction, and pulled him hard against me.

"You're all right?" he asked, a few moments later.

"I won't break, you know," I said, smiling into his eyes.

He laughed huskily. "Maybe not, Sassenach, but *I* may." He gathered me close against him, his cheek pressed against my hair. I flipped the quilt up and tucked it around his shoulders, sealing us in a pocket of warmth. The heat of the fire had not yet reached the bed, but the ice on the window was thawing, the crusted edge of the rime melted into glowing diamonds.

We lay quiet for a time, listening to the occasional crack of the burning applewood in the hearth and the faint sounds of the inn as the guests stirred to life. There were callings to and fro from the balconies across the courtyard, the swish and clop of hooves on the slushy stones outside, and the odd squeal now and then from below, from the piglets the land-lady was raising in the kitchen behind the stove.

"Très français, n'est-ce pas?" I said, smiling at the sounds of an altercation drifting up through the floorboards, an ami-able settling of accounts between the innkeeper's wife and the local vintner.

"Diseased son of a pox-ridden whore," the female voice remarked. "The brandy from last week tasted like horse-piss."

I didn't need to see the reply to imagine the one-shoul-dered shrug that went with it.

"How would you know, Madame? After the sixth glass, it all tastes the same, is it not so?"

The bed shook slightly as Jamie laughed with me. He lifted his head from the pillow and sniffed appreciatively at the scent of frying ham that filtered through the drafty chinks of the floorboards.

"Aye, it's France," he agreed. "Food, and drink—and love." He patted my bare hip before tugging the wrinkled gown down over it.

"Jamie," I said softly, "are you happy about it? About the baby?" Outlawed in Scotland, barred from his own home, and with only vague prospects in France, he could pardonably have been less than enthused about acquiring an additional obligation.

He was silent for a moment, only hugging me harder, then sighed briefly before answering.

"Aye, Sassenach." His hand strayed downward, gently rubbing my belly. "I'm happy. And proud as a stallion. But I am most awfully afraid, too."

"About the birth? I'll be all right." I could hardly blame him for apprehension; his own mother had died in childbirth, and birth and its complications were the leading cause of death for women in these times. Still, I knew a thing or two myself, and I had no intention whatever of exposing myself to what passed for medical care here.

"Aye, that—and everything," he said softly. "I want to protect ye, Sassenach—spread myself over ye like a cloak and shield you and the child wi' my body." His voice was soft and husky, with a slight catch in it. "I would do anything for ye . . . and yet . . . there's nothing I *can* do. It doesna matter how strong I am, or how willing; I canna go with you where ye must go . . . nor even help ye at all. And to think of the things that might happen, and me helpless to stop them . . . aye, I'm afraid, Sassenach."

"And yet"—he turned me toward him, hand closing gently over one breast—"yet when I think of you wi' my child at your breast . . . then I feel as though I've gone hollow as a soap bubble, and perhaps I shall burst with joy."

He pressed me tight against his chest, and I hugged him with all my might.

"Oh, Claire, ye do break my heart wi' loving you."

I slept for some time, and woke slowly, hearing the clang of a church bell ringing in the nearby square. Fresh from the Abbey of Ste. Anne, where all the day's activities took place to the rhythm of bells, I automatically glanced at the window, to gauge the intensity of the light and guess the time of day. Bright, clear light, and a window free of ice. The bells rang for the Angelus then, and it was noon.

I stretched, enjoying the blissful knowledge that I needn't get up at once. Early pregnancy made me tired, and the strain of travel had added to my fatigue, making the long rest doubly welcome.

It had rained and snowed unceasingly on the journey as the winter storms battered the French coast. Still, it could have been worse. We had originally intended to go to Rome, not Le Havre. That would have been three or four weeks' travel, in this weather.

Faced with the prospect of earning a living abroad, Jamie had obtained a recommendation as a translator to James Francis Edward Stuart, exiled King of Scotland—or merely the Chevalier St. George, Pretender to the Throne, depending on your loyalties—and we had determined to join the Pretender's court near Rome.

It had been a near thing, at that; we had been on the point of leaving for Italy, when Jamie's uncle Alexander, Abbot of Ste. Anne's, had summoned us to his study.

"I have heard from His Majesty," he announced without preamble.

"Which one?" Jamie asked. The slight family resemblance between the two men was exaggerated by their posture —both sat bolt upright in their chairs, shoulders squared. On the abbot's part, the posture was due to natural asceticism; on Jamie's, to reluctance to let the newly healed scars on his back contact the wood of the chair.

"His Majesty King James," his uncle replied, frowning slightly at me. I was careful to keep my face blank; my presence in Abbot Alexander's study was a mark of trust, and I didn't want to do anything to jeopardize it. He had known me a bare six weeks, since the day after Christmas, when I had appeared at his gate with Jamie, who was near death from torture and imprisonment. Subsequent acquaintance had presumably given the abbot some confidence in me. On the other hand, I was still English. And the English King's name was George, not James.

"Aye? Is he not in need of a translator, then?" Jamie was still thin, but he had been working outdoors with the Brothers who minded the stables and fields of the Abbey, and his face was regaining tinges of its normal healthy color.

"He is in need of a loyal servant—and a friend." Abbot Alexander tapped his fingers on a folded letter that lay on his desk, the crested seal broken. He pursed his lips, glancing from me to his nephew and back.

"What I tell you now must not be repeated," he said sternly. "It will be common knowledge soon, but for now—" I had tried to look trustworthy and close-mouthed; Jamie merely nodded, with a touch of impatience.

"His Highness, Prince Charles Edward, has left Rome, and will arrive in France within the week," the Abbot said, leaning slightly forward as though to emphasize the importance of what he was saying.

And it was important. James Stuart had mounted an abortive attempt to regain his throne in 1715—an ill-considered military operation that had failed almost immediately for lack of support. Since then—according to Alexander—the exiled James of Scotland had worked tirelessly, writing ceaselessly to his fellow monarchs, and particularly to his cousin, Louis of France, reiterating the legitimacy of his claim to the throne of Scotland and England, and the position of his son, Prince Charles, as heir to that throne.

"His royal cousin Louis has been distressingly deaf to these entirely proper claims," the Abbot had said, frowning at the letter as though it were Louis. "If he's now come to a realization of his responsibilities in the matter, it's cause for great rejoicing among those who hold dear the sacred right of kingship."

Among the Jacobites, that was, James's supporters. Of whom Abbot Alexander of the Abbey of Ste. Anne—born Alexander Fraser of Scotland—was one. Jamie had told me that Alexander was one of the exiled King's most frequent correspondents, in touch with all that touched the Stuart cause.

"He's well placed for it," Jamie had explained to me, discussing the endeavor on which we were about to embark. "The papal messenger system crosses Italy, France, and Spain faster than almost any other. And the papal messengers canna be interfered with by government customs officers, so the letters they carry are less likely to be intercepted."

James of Scotland, exiled in Rome, was supported in large part by the Pope, in whose interest it very much was to have a Catholic monarchy restored to England and Scotland. Therefore, the largest part of James's private mail was carried by papal messenger—and passed through the hands of loyal supporters within the Church hierarchy, like Abbot Alexander of Ste. Anne de Beaupré, who could be depended on to communicate with the King's supporters in Scotland, with less risk than sending letters openly from Rome to Edinburgh and the Highlands.

I watched Alexander with interest, as he expounded the importance of Prince Charles's visit to France. A stocky man of about my own height, he was dark, and considerably shorter than his nephew, but shared with him the faintly slanted eyes, the sharp intelligence, and the talent for discerning hidden motive that seemed to characterize the Frasers I had met.

"So," he finished, stroking his full, dark-brown beard, "I cannot say whether His Highness is in France at Louis's invitation, or has come uninvited, on behalf of his father."

"It makes a wee bit of difference," Jamie remarked, raising one eyebrow skeptically.

His uncle nodded, and a wry smile showed briefly in the thicket of his beard.

"True, lad," he said, letting a faint hint of his native Scots emerge from his usual formal English. "Very true. And that's where you and your wife may be of service, if ye will."

The proposal was simple; His Majesty King James would provide travel expenses and a small stipend, if the nephew of his most loyal and most esteemed friend Alexander would agree to travel to Paris, there to assist his son, His Highness Prince Charles Edward, in whatever ways the latter might require.

I was stunned. We had meant originally to go to Rome because that seemed the best place to embark on our quest: the prevention of the second Jacobite Rising—the '45. From my own knowledge of history, I knew that the Rising, financed from France and carried out by Charles Edward Stuart, would go much farther than had his father's attempt in 1715—but not nearly far enough. If matters progressed as I thought they would, then the troops under Bonnie Prince

Charlie would meet with disastrous defeat at Culloden in 1746, and the people of the Highlands would suffer the repercussions of defeat for two centuries thereafter.

Now, in 1744, apparently Charles himself was just beginning his search for support in France. Where better to try to stop a rebellion, than at the side of its leader?

I glanced at Jamie, who was looking over his uncle's shoulder at a small shrine set into the wall. His eyes rested on the gilded figure of Ste. Anne herself and the small sheaf of hothouse flowers laid at her feet, while his thoughts worked behind an expressionless face. At last he blinked once, and smiled at his uncle.

"Whatever assistance His Highness might require? Aye," he said quietly, "I think I can do that. We'll go."

And we had. Instead of proceeding directly to Paris, though, we had come down the coast from Ste. Anne to Le Havre, to meet first with Jamie's cousin, Jared Fraser.

A prosperous Scottish émigré, Jared was an importer of wines and spirits, with a small warehouse and large town house in Paris, and a very large warehouse indeed here in Le Havre, where he had asked Jamie to meet him, when Jamie had written to say we were en route to Paris.

Sufficiently rested by now, I was beginning to feel hungry. There was food on the table; Jamie must have told the chambermaid to bring it while I slept.

I had no dressing gown, but my heavy velvet traveling cloak was handy; I sat up and pulled the warm weight of it over my shoulders before rising to relieve myself, add another stick of wood to the fire, and sit down to my late breakfast.

I chewed hard rolls and baked ham contentedly, washing them down with the jug of milk provided. I hoped Jamie was being adequately fed as well; he insisted that Jared was a good friend, but I had my doubts about the hospitality of some of Jamie's relatives, having met a few of them by now. True, Abbot Alexander had welcomed us—insofar as a man in the abbot's position could be said to welcome having an outlaw nephew with a suspect wife descend upon him unexpectedly. But our sojourn with Jamie's mother's people, the MacKenzies of Leoch, had come within inches of killing me the autumn before, when I had been arrested and tried as a witch.

"Granted," I'd said, "this Jared's a Fraser, and they seem a trifle safer than your MacKenzie relatives. But have you actually met him before?"

"I lived with him for a time when I was eighteen," he told me, dribbling candle-wax onto his reply and pressing his father's wedding ring on the resultant greenish-gray puddle. A small cabochon ruby, its mount was engraved with the Fraser clan motto, *je suis prest:* "I am ready."

"He had me to stay with him when I came to Paris to finish my schooling, and learn a bit of the world. He was verra kind to me; a good friend of my father's. And there's no one knows more about Parisian society than the man who sells it drink," he added, cracking the ring loose from the hardened wax. "I want to talk to Jared before I walk into Louis's court by the side of Charles Stuart; I should like to feel that I have some chance of getting out again," he finished wryly.

"Why? Do you think there'll be trouble?" I asked. "Whatever assistance His Highness might require" seemed to offer quite a bit of latitude.

He smiled at my worried look.

"No, I dinna expect any difficulty. But what is it the Bible says, Sassenach? 'Put not your trust in princes'?" He rose and kissed me quickly on the brow, tucking the ring back in his sporran. "Who am I to ignore the word of God, eh?"

❧

I spent the afternoon in reading one of the herbals that my friend Brother Ambrose had pressed upon me as a parting gift, then in necessary repairs with needle and thread. Neither of us owned many clothes, and while there were advantages in traveling light, it meant that holey socks and undone hems demanded immediate attention. My needlecase was nearly as precious to me as the small chest in which I carried herbs and medicines.

The needle dipped in and out of the fabric, winking in the light from the window. I wondered how Jamie's visit with Jared was going. I wondered still more what Prince Charles would be like. He would be the first historically famous person I had met, and while I knew better than to believe all the legends that had (not had, *would,* I reminded myself) sprung up around him, the reality of the man was a mystery. The

Rising of the '45 would depend almost entirely on the personality of this one young man—its failure or success. Whether it took place at all might depend upon the efforts of another young man—Jamie Fraser. And me.

I was still absorbed in my mending and my thoughts, when heavy footsteps in the corridor aroused me to the realization that it was late in the day; the drip of water from the eaves had slowed as the temperature dropped, and the flames of the sinking sun glowed in the ice spears hanging from the roof. The door opened, and Jamie came in.

He smiled vaguely in my direction, then stopped dead by the table, face absorbed as though he were trying to remember something. He took his cloak off, folded it, and hung it neatly over the foot of the bed, straightened, marched over to the other stool, sat down on it with great precision, and closed his eyes.

I sat still, my mending forgotten in my lap, watching this performance with considerable interest. After a moment, he opened his eyes and smiled at me, but didn't say anything. He leaned forward, studying my face with great attention, as though he hadn't seen me in weeks. At last, an expression of profound revelation passed over his face, and he relaxed, shoulders slumping as he rested his elbows on his knees.

"Whisky," he said, with immense satisfaction.

"I see," I said cautiously. "A lot of it?"

He shook his head slowly from side to side, as though it were very heavy. I could almost hear the contents sloshing.

"Not me," he said, very distinctly. "You."

"Me?" I said indignantly.

"Your eyes," he said. He smiled beatifically. His own eyes were soft and dreamy, cloudy as a trout pool in the rain.

"My eyes? What have my eyes got to do with . . ."

"They're the color of verra fine whisky, wi' the sun shining through them from behind. I thought this morning they looked like sherry, but I was wrong. Not sherry. Not brandy. It's whisky. That's what it is." He looked so gratified as he said this that I couldn't help laughing.

"Jamie, you're terribly drunk. What have you been doing?"

His expression altered to a slight frown.

"I'm not drunk."

"Oh, no?" I laid the mending aside and came over to lay a hand on his forehead. It was cool and damp, though his face was flushed. He at once put his arms about my waist and pulled me close, nuzzling affectionately at my bosom. The smell of mingled spirits rose from him like a fog, so thick as almost to be visible.

"Come here to me, Sassenach," he murmured. "My whisky-eyed lass, my love. Let me take ye to bed."

I thought it a debatable point as to who was likely to be taking whom to bed, but didn't argue. It didn't matter why he thought he was going to bed, after all, provided he got there. I bent and got a shoulder under his armpit to help him up, but he leaned away, rising slowly and majestically under his own power.

"I dinna need help," he said, reaching for the cord at the neck of his shirt. "I told ye, I'm not drunk."

"You're right," I said. " 'Drunk' isn't anywhere near sufficient to describe your current state. Jamie, you're completely pissed."

His eyes traveled down the front of his kilt, across the floor, and up the front of my gown.

"No, I'm not," he said, with great dignity. "I did that outside." He took a step toward me, glowing with ardor. "Come here to me, Sassenach; I'm ready."

I thought "ready" was a bit of an overstatement in one regard; he'd gotten his buttons half undone, and his shirt hung askew on his shoulders, but that was as far as he was likely to make it unaided.

In other respects, though . . . the broad expanse of his chest was exposed, showing the small hollow in the center where I was accustomed to rest my chin, and the small curly hairs sprang up joyous around his nipples. He saw me looking at him, and reached for one of my hands, clasping it to his breast. He was startlingly warm, and I moved instinctively toward him. The other arm swept round me and he bent to kiss me. He made such a thorough job of it that I felt mildly intoxicated, merely from sharing his breath.

"All right," I said, laughing. "If you're ready, so am I. Let me undress you first, though—I've had enough mending today."

He stood still as I stripped him, scarcely moving. He

didn't move, either, as I attended to my own clothes and turned down the bed.

I climbed in and turned to look at him, ruddy and magnificent in the sunset glow. He was finely made as a Greek statue, long-nosed and high-cheeked as a profile on a Roman coin. The wide, soft mouth was set in a dreamy smile, and the slanted eyes looked far away. He was perfectly immobile.

I viewed him with some concern.

"Jamie," I said, "how, exactly, do you decide whether you're drunk?"

Aroused by my voice, he swayed alarmingly to one side, but caught himself on the edge of the mantelpiece. His eyes drifted around the room, then fixed on my face. For an instant, they blazed clear and pellucid with intelligence.

"Och, easy, Sassenach. If ye can stand up, you're not drunk." He let go of the mantelpiece, took a step toward me, and crumpled slowly onto the hearth, eyes blank, and a wide, sweet smile on his dreaming face.

"Oh," I said.

The yodeling of roosters outside and the clashing of pots below woke me just after dawn the next morning. The figure next to me jerked, waking abruptly, then froze as the sudden movement jarred his head.

I raised up on one elbow to examine the remains. Not too bad, I thought critically. His eyes were screwed tightly shut against stray beams of sunlight, and his hair stuck out in all directions like a hedgehog's spines, but his skin was pale and clear, and the hands clutching the coverlet were steady.

I pried up one eyelid, peered within, and said playfully, "Anybody home?"

The twin to the eye I was looking at opened slowly, to add its baleful glare to the first. I dropped my hand and smiled charmingly at him.

"Good morning."

"That, Sassenach, is entirely a matter of opinion," he said, and closed both eyes again.

"Have you got any idea how much you weigh?" I asked conversationally.

"No."

The abruptness of the reply suggested that he not only didn't know, he didn't care, but I persisted in my efforts.

"Something around fifteen stone, I make it. About as much as a good-sized boar. Unfortunately, I didn't have any beaters to hang you upside down from a spear and carry you home to the smoking shed."

One eye opened again, and looked consideringly at me, then at the hearthstone on the far side of the room. One corner of his mouth lifted in a reluctant smile.

"How did you get me in bed?"

"I didn't. I couldn't budge you, so I just laid a quilt over you and left you on the hearth. You came to life and crawled in under your own power, somewhere in the middle of the night."

He seemed surprised, and opened the other eye again.

"I did?"

I nodded and tried to smooth down the hair that spiked out over his left ear.

"Oh, yes. Very single-minded, you were."

"Single-minded?" He frowned, thinking, and stretched, thrusting his arms up over his head. Then he looked startled.

"No. I couldn't have."

"Yes, you could. Twice."

He squinted down his chest, as though looking for confirmation of this improbable statement, then looked back at me.

"Really? Well, that's hardly fair; I dinna remember a thing about it." He hesitated for a moment, looking shy. "Was it all right, then? I didna do anything foolish?"

I flopped down next to him and snuggled my head into the curve of his shoulder.

"No, I wouldn't call it foolish. You weren't very conversational, though."

"Thank the Lord for small blessings," he said, and a small chuckle rumbled through his chest.

"Mm. You'd forgotten how to say anything except 'I love you,' but you said that a lot."

The chuckle came back, louder this time. "Oh, aye? Well, could have been worse, I suppose."

He drew in his breath, then paused. He turned his head and sniffed suspiciously at the soft tuft of cinnamon under his raised arm.

"Christ!" he said. He tried to push me away. "Ye dinna want to put your head near my oxter, Sassenach. I smell like a boar that's been dead a week."

"And pickled in brandy after," I agreed, snuggling closer. "How on earth did you get so—ahem—stinking drunk, anyway?"

"Jared's hospitality." He settled himself in the pillows with a deep sigh, arm round my shoulder.

"He took me down to show me his warehouse at the docks. And the storeroom there where he keeps the rare vintages and the Portuguese brandy and the Jamaican rum." He grimaced slightly, recalling. "The wine wasna so bad, for that you just taste, and spit it on the floor when you've done wi' a mouthful. But neither of us could see wasting the brandy that way. Besides, Jared said ye need to let it trickle down the back of your throat, to appreciate it fully."

"How much of it did you appreciate?" I asked curiously.

"I lost count in the middle of the second bottle." Just then, a church bell started to ring nearby; the summons to early Mass. Jamie sat bolt upright, staring at the windowpane, bright with sun.

"Christ, Sassenach! What time is it?"

"About six, I suppose," I said, puzzled. "Why?"

He relaxed slightly, though he stayed sitting up.

"Oh, that's all right, then. I was afraid it was the Angelus bell. I'd lost all track of time."

"I'd say so. Does it matter?"

In a burst of energy, he threw back the quilts and stood up. He staggered a moment, but kept his balance, though both hands went to his head, to make sure it was still attached.

"Aye," he said, gasping a bit. "We've an appointment this morning down at the docks, at Jared's warehouse. The two of us."

"Really?" I clambered out of bed myself, and groped for the chamber pot under the bed. "If he's planning to finish the job, I shouldn't think he'd want witnesses."

Jamie's head popped through the neck of his shirt, eyebrows raised.

"Finish the job?"

"Well, most of your other relatives seem to want to kill

you or me; why not Jared? He's made a good start at poisoning you, seems to me."

"Verra funny, Sassenach," he said dryly. "Have ye something decent to wear?"

I had been wearing a serviceable gray serge gown on our travels, acquired through the good offices of the almoner at the Abbey of Ste. Anne, but I did also have the gown in which I had escaped from Scotland, a gift from Lady Annabelle MacRannoch. A pretty leaf-green velvet, it made me look rather pale, but was stylish enough.

"I think so, if there aren't too many saltwater stains on it."

I knelt by the small traveling chest, unfolding the green velvet. Kneeling next to me, Jamie flipped back the lid of my medicine box, studying the layers of bottles and boxes and bits of gauze-wrapped herbs.

"Have ye got anything in here for a verra vicious headache, Sassenach?"

I peered over his shoulder, then reached in and touched one bottle.

"Horehound might help, though it's not the best. And willow-bark tea with sow fennel works fairly well, but it takes some time to brew. Tell you what—why don't I make you up a recipe for hobnailed liver? Wonderful hangover cure."

He bent a suspicious blue eye on me.

"That sounds nasty."

"It is," I said cheerfully. "But you'll feel lots better after you throw up."

"Mphm." He stood up and nudged the chamber pot toward me with one toe.

"Vomiting in the morning is *your* job, Sassenach," he said. "Get it over with and get dressed. I'll stand the headache."

Jared Munro Fraser was a small, spare, black-eyed man, who bore more than a passing resemblance to his distant cousin Murtagh, the Fraser clansman who had accompanied us to Le Havre. When I first saw Jared, standing majestically in the gaping doors of his warehouse, so that streams of longshoremen carrying casks were forced to go around him, the resemblance was strong enough that I blinked and rubbed my eyes. Murtagh, so far as I knew, was still at the inn, attending a lame horse.

Jared had the same lank, dark hair and piercing eyes; the same sinewy, monkey-like frame. But there all resemblance stopped, and as we drew closer, Jamie gallantly clearing a path for me through the mob with elbows and shoulders, I could see the differences as well. Jared's face was oblong, rather than hatchet-shaped, with a cheerful snub nose that effectively ruined the dignified air conferred at a distance by his excellent tailoring and upright carriage.

A successful merchant rather than a cattle-raider, he also knew how to smile—unlike Murtagh, whose natural expression was one of unrelieved dourness—and a broad grin of welcome broke out on his face as we were jostled and shoved up the ramp into his presence.

"My dear!" he exclaimed, clutching me by the arm and yanking me deftly out of the way of two burly stevedores rolling a gigantic cask through the huge door. "So pleased to see you at last!" The cask bumped noisily on the boards of the ramp, and I could hear the rolling slosh of its contents as it passed me.

"You can treat rum like that," Jared observed, watching the ungainly progress of the enormous barrel through the obstructions of the warehouse, "but not port. I always fetch that up myself, along with the bottled wines. In fact, I was just setting off to see to a new shipment of Belle Rouge port. Would you perhaps be interested in accompanying me?"

I glanced at Jamie, who nodded, and we set off at once in Jared's wake, sidestepping the rumbling traffic of casks and hogsheads, carts and barrows, and men and boys of all descriptions carrying bolts of fabric, boxes of grain and foodstuffs, rolls of hammered copper, sacks of flour, and anything else that could be transported by ship.

Le Havre was an important center of shipping traffic, and the docks were the heart of the city. A long, solid wharf ran nearly a quarter-mile round the edge of the harbor, with smaller docks protruding from it, along which were anchored three-masted barks and brigantines, dories and small galleys; a full range of the ships that provisioned France.

Jamie kept a firm hold on my elbow, the better to yank

me out of the way of oncoming handcarts, rolling casks, and careless merchants and seamen, who were inclined not to look where they were going but rather to depend on sheer momentum to see them through the scrum of the docks.

As we made our way down the quay, Jared shouted genteelly into my ear on the other side, pointing out objects of interest as we passed, and explaining the history and ownership of the various ships in a staccato, disjointed manner. The *Arianna,* which we were on our way to see, was in fact one of Jared's own ships. Ships, I gathered, might belong to a single owner, more often to a company of merchants who owned them collectively, or, occasionally, to a captain who contracted his vessel, crew, and services for a voyage. Seeing the number of company-owned vessels, compared to the relatively few owned by individuals, I began to form a very respectful idea of Jared's worth.

The *Arianna* was in the middle of the anchored row, near a large warehouse with the name FRASER painted on it in sloping, whitewashed letters. Seeing the name gave me an odd little thrill, a sudden feeling of alliance and belonging, with the realization that I shared that name, and with it, an acknowledged kinship with those who bore it.

The *Arianna* was a three-masted ship, perhaps sixty feet long, with a wide bow. There were two cannon on the side of the ship that faced the dock; in case of robbery on the high seas, I supposed. Men were swarming all over the deck with what I assumed was some purpose, though it looked like nothing so much as an ant's nest under attack.

All sails were reefed and tied, but the rising tide shifted the vessel slightly, swinging the bowsprit toward us. It was decorated with a rather grim-visaged figurehead; with her formidable bare bosom and tangled curls all spangled with salt, the lady looked as though she didn't enjoy sea air all that much.

"Sweet little beauty, is she not?" Jared asked, waving a hand expansively. I assumed he meant the ship, not the figurehead.

"Verra nice," said Jamie politely. I caught his uneasy glance at the boat's waterline, where the small waves lapped dark gray against the hull. I could see that he was hoping we would not be obliged to go on board. A gallant warrior, brilliant, bold, and courageous in battle, Jamie Fraser was also a landlubber.

Definitely not one of the hardy, seafaring Scots who hunted whales from Tarwathie or voyaged the world in search of wealth, he suffered from a seasickness so acute that our journey across the Channel in December had nearly killed him, weakened as he then was by the effects of torture and imprisonment. And while yesterday's drinking orgy with Jared wasn't in the same league, it wasn't likely to have made him any more seaworthy.

I could see dark memories crossing his face as he listened to his cousin extolling the sturdiness and speed of the *Arianna,* and drew near enough to whisper to him.

"Surely not while it's at anchor?"

"I don't know, Sassenach," he replied, with a look at the ship in which loathing and resignation were nicely mingled. "But I suppose we'll find out." Jared was already halfway up the gangplank, greeting the captain with loud cries of welcome. "If I turn green, can ye pretend to faint or something? It will make a poor impression if I vomit on Jared's shoes."

I patted his arm reassuringly. "Don't worry. I have faith in you."

"It isna *me,*" he said, with a last, lingering glance at terra firma, "it's my stomach."

The ship stayed comfortably level under our shoes, however, and both Jamie and his stomach acquitted themselves nobly—assisted, perhaps, by the brandy poured out for us by the captain.

"A nice make," Jamie said, passing the glass briefly under his nose and closing his eyes in approval of the rich, aromatic fumes. "Portuguese, isn't it?"

Jared laughed delightedly and nudged the captain.

"You see, Portis? I told you he had a natural palate! He's only tasted it once before!"

I bit the inside of my cheek and avoided Jamie's eye. The captain, a large, scruffy-looking specimen, looked bored, but grimaced politely in Jamie's direction, exhibiting three gold teeth. A man who liked to keep his wealth portable.

"Ung," he said. "This the lad's going to keep your bilges dry, is it?"

Jared looked suddenly embarrassed, a slight flush rising

under the leathery skin of his face. I noticed with fascination that one ear was pierced for an earring, and wondered just what sort of background had led to his present success.

"Aye, well," he said, betraying for the first time a hint of Scots accent, "that's to be seen yet. But I think—" He glanced through the port at the activity taking place on the dock, then back at the captain's glass, drained in three gulps while the rest of us were sipping. "Um, I say, Portis, would you allow me to use your cabin for a moment? I should like to confer with my nephew and his wife—and I see that the aft hold seems to be having a bit of trouble with the cargo nets, from the sound of it." This craftily added observation was enough to send Captain Portis out of the cabin like a charging boar, hoarse voice uplifted in a Spanish-French patois that I luckily didn't understand.

Jared stepped delicately to the door and closed it firmly after the captain's bulky form, cutting down the noise level substantially. He returned to the tiny captain's table and cere-moniously refilled all our glasses before speaking. Then he looked from Jamie to me and smiled once more, in charming deprecation.

"It's a bit more precipitous than I'd meant to make such a request," he said. "But I see the good captain has rather given away my hand. The truth of the matter is"—he raised his glass so the watery reflections from the port shivered through the brandy, striking patches of wavering light from the brass fittings of the cabin—"I need a man." He tipped the cup in Jamie's direction, then brought it to his lips and drank.

"A good man," he amplified, lowering the glass. "You see, my dear," bowing to me, "I have the opportunity of mak-ing an exceptional investment in a new winery in the Moselle region. But the evaluation of it is not one I should feel com-fortable in entrusting to a subordinate; I should need to see the facilities myself, and advise in their development. The undertaking would require several months."

He gazed thoughtfully into his glass, gently swirling the fragrant brown liquid so its perfume filled the tiny cabin. I had drunk no more than a few sips from my own glass, but began to feel slightly giddy, more from a rising excitement than from drink.

"It's too good a chance to be missed," Jared said. "And

there's the chance of making several good contracts with the wineries along the Rhône; the products there are excellent, but relatively rare in Paris. God, they'd sell among the nobility like snow in summer!" His shrewd black eyes gleamed momentarily with visions of avarice, then sparkled with humor as he looked at me.

"But—" he said.

"But," I finished for him, "you can't leave your business here without a guiding hand."

"Intelligence as well as beauty and charm. I congratulate you, Cousin." He tilted a well-groomed head toward Jamie, one eyebrow cocked in humorous approval.

"I confess that I was at something of a loss to see how I was to proceed," he said, setting the glass down on the small table with the air of a man putting aside social frivolity for the sake of serious business. "But when you wrote from Ste. Anne, saying you intended to visit Paris . . ." He hesitated a moment, then smiled at Jamie, with an odd little flutter of the hands.

"Knowing that you, my lad"—he nodded to Jamie—"have a head for figures, I was strongly inclined to consider your arrival an answer to prayer. Still, I thought that perhaps we should meet and become reacquainted before I took the step of making you a definite proposal."

You mean you thought you'd better see how presentable *I* was, I thought cynically, but smiled at him nonetheless. I caught Jamie's eye, and one of his brows twitched upward. This was our week for proposals, evidently. For a dispossessed outlaw and a suspected English spy, our services seemed to be rather in demand.

Jared's proposal was more than generous; in return for Jamie's running the French end of the business during the next six months, Jared would not only pay him a salary but would leave his Paris town house, complete with staff, at our disposal.

"Not at all, not at all," he said, when Jamie tried to protest this provision. He pressed a finger on the end of his nose, grinning charmingly at me. "A pretty woman to host dinner parties is a great asset in the wine business, Cousin. You have no idea how much wine you can sell, if you let the customers taste it first." He shook his head decidedly. "No, it will be a great service to me, if your wife would allow herself to be troubled by entertaining."

The thought of hosting supper parties for Parisian society was in fact a trifle daunting. Jamie looked at me, eyebrows raised in question, but I swallowed hard and smiled, nodding. It was a good offer; if he felt competent to take over the running of an importing business, the least I could do was order dinner and brush up my sprightly conversational French.

"Not at all," I murmured, but Jared had taken my agreement for granted, and was going on, intent black eyes fixed on Jamie.

"And then, I thought perhaps you'd be needing an establishment of sorts—for the benefit of the other interests which bring you to Paris."

Jamie smiled noncommittally, at which Jared uttered a short laugh and picked up his brandy glass. We had each been provided a glass of water as well, for cleansing the palate between sips, and he pulled one of these close with the other hand.

"Well, a toast!" he exclaimed. "To our association, Cousin—and to His Majesty!" He lifted the brandy glass in salute, then passed it ostentatiously over the glass of water and brought it to his lips.

I watched this odd behavior in surprise, but it apparently meant something to Jamie, for he smiled at Jared, picked up his own glass and passed it over the water.

"To His Majesty," he repeated. Then, seeing me staring at him in bewilderment, he smiled and explained, "To His Majesty—over the water, Sassenach."

"Oh?" I said, then, realization dawning, "oh!" The king over the water—King James. Which did a bit to explain this sudden urge on the part of everyone to see Jamie and myself established in Paris, which would otherwise have seemed an improbable coincidence.

If Jared were also a Jacobite, then his correspondence with Abbot Alexander was very likely more than coincidental; chances were that Jamie's letter announcing our arrival had come together with one from Alexander, explaining the commission from King James. And if our presence in Paris fitted in with Jared's own plans—then so much the better. With a sudden appreciation for the complexities of the Jacobite network, I raised my own glass, and drank to His Majesty across the water—and our new partnership with Jared.

Jared and Jamie then settled down to a discussion of the business, and were soon head to head, bent over inky sheets of paper, evidently manifests and bills of lading. The tiny cabin reeked of tobacco, brandy fumes, and unwashed sailor, and I began to feel a trifle queasy again. Seeing that I wouldn't be needed for a while, I stood up quietly and found my way out on deck.

I was careful to avoid the altercation still going on around the rear cargo hatch, and picked my way through coils of rope, objects which I assumed to be belaying pins, and tumbled piles of sail fabric, to a quiet spot in the bow. From here, I had an unobstructed view over the harbor.

I sat on a chest against the taffrail, enjoying the salty breeze and the tarry, fishy smells of ships and harbor. It was still cold, but with my cloak pulled tight around me, I was warm enough. The ship rocked slowly, rising on the incoming tide; I could see the beards of algae on nearby dock pilings lifting and swirling, obscuring the shiny black patches of mussels between them.

The thought of mussels reminded me of the steamed mussels with butter I had had for dinner the night before, and I was suddenly starving. The absurd contrasts of pregnancy seemed to keep me always conscious of my digestion; if I wasn't vomiting, I was ravenously hungry. The thought of food led me to the thought of menus, which led back to a contemplation of the entertaining Jared had mentioned. Dinner parties, hm? It seemed an odd way to begin the job of saving Scotland, but then, I couldn't really think of anything better.

At least if I had Charles Stuart across a dinner table from me, I could keep an eye on him, I thought, smiling to myself at the joke. If he showed signs of hopping a ship for Scotland, maybe I could slip something into his soup.

Perhaps that wasn't so funny, after all. The thought reminded me of Geillis Duncan, and my smile faded. Wife of the procurator fiscal in Cranesmuir, she had murdered her husband by dropping powdered cyanide into his food at a banquet. Accused as a witch soon afterward, she had been arrested while I was with her, and I had been taken to trial myself; a trial from which Jamie had rescued me. The memories of several days spent in the cold dark of the thieves' hole at Cranesmuir were all too fresh, and the wind seemed suddenly very cold.

I shivered, but not altogether from chill. I could not think of Geillis Duncan without that cold finger down my spine. Not so much because of what she had done, but because of who she had been. A Jacobite, too; one whose support of the Stuart cause had been more than slightly tinged with madness. Worse than that, she was what I was—a traveler through the standing stones.

I didn't know whether she had come to the past as I had, by accident, or whether her journey had been deliberate. Neither did I know precisely *where* she had come from. But my last vision of her, screaming defiance at the judges who would condemn her to burn, was of a tall, fair woman, arms stretched high, showing on one arm the telltale round of a vaccination scar. I felt automatically for the small patch of roughened skin on my own upper arm, beneath the comforting folds of my cloak, and shuddered when I found it.

I was distracted from these unhappy memories by a growing commotion on the next quay. A large knot of men had gathered by a ship's gangway, and there was considerable shouting and pushing going on. Not a fight; I peered over at the altercation, shading my eyes with my hand, but could see no blows exchanged. Instead, an effort seemed to be under way to clear a pathway through the milling crowd to the doors of a large warehouse on the upper end of the quay. The crowd was stubbornly resisting all such efforts, surging back like the tide after each push.

Jamie suddenly appeared behind me, closely followed by Jared, who squinted at the mob scene below. Absorbed by the shouting, I hadn't heard them come up.

"What is it?" I stood and leaned back into Jamie, bracing myself against the increasing sway of the ship underfoot. I was aware at close quarters of his scent; he had bathed at the inn and he smelled clean and warm, with a faint hint of sun and dust. A sharpening of the sense of smell was another effect of pregnancy, apparently; I could smell him even among the myriad stenches and scents of the seaport, much as you can hear a low-pitched voice close by in a noisy crowd.

"I don't know. Some trouble with the other ship, looks like." He reached down and put a hand on my elbow, to steady me. Jared turned and barked an order in gutteral French to one of the sailors nearby. The man promptly hopped over the rail and slid down one of the ropes to the quay, tarred pigtail dangling toward the water. We watched from the deck as he joined the crowd, prodded another seaman in the ribs, and received an answer, complete with expressive gesticulations.

Jared was frowning, as the pigtailed man scrambled back up the crowded gangplank. The sailor said something to him in that same thick-sounding French, too fast for me to follow it. After a few more words' conversation, Jared swung abruptly around and came to stand next to me, lean hands gripping the rail.

"He says there's sickness aboard the *Patagonia*."

"What sort of sickness?" I hadn't thought of bringing my medicine box with me, so there was little I could do in any case, but I was curious. Jared looked worried and unhappy.

"They're afraid it might be smallpox, but they don't know. The port's inspector and the harbor master have been called."

"Would you like me to have a look?" I offered. "I might at least be able to tell you whether it's a contagious disease or not."

Jared's sketchy eyebrows disappeared under the lank black fringe of his hair. Jamie looked mildly embarrassed.

"My wife's well known as a healer, Cousin," he explained, but then turned and shook his head at me.

"No, Sassenach. It wouldna be safe."

I could see the *Patagonia*'s gangway easily; now the gathered crowd moved suddenly back, jostling and stepping on each other's toes. Two seamen stepped down from the deck, a length of canvas slung between them as a stretcher. The white sail-fabric sagged heavily under the weight of the man they carried, and a bare, sun-darkened arm lolled from the makeshift hammock.

The seamen wore strips of cloth tied round their noses and mouths, and kept their faces turned away from the stretcher, jerking their heads as they growled at each other, maneuvering their burden over the splintered planks. The pair passed under the fascinated noses of the crowd and disappeared into a nearby warehouse.

Making a quick decision, I turned and headed for the rear gangplank of the *Arianna*.

"Don't worry," I called to Jamie over one shoulder, "if it is smallpox, I can't get that." One of the seamen, hearing me, paused and gaped, but I just smiled at him and brushed past.

The crowd was still now, no longer surging to and fro, and it was not so difficult to make my way between the muttering clusters of seamen, many of whom frowned or looked startled as I ducked past them. The warehouse was disused; no bales or casks filled the echoing shadows of the huge room, but the scents of sawn lumber, smoked meat, and fish lingered, easily distinguishable from the host of other smells.

The sick man had been hastily dumped near the door, on a pile of discarded straw packing. His attendants pushed past me as I entered, eager to get away.

I approached him cautiously, stopping a few feet away. He was flushed with fever, his skin a queer dark red, scabbed thick with white pustules. He moaned and tossed his head restlessly from side to side, cracked mouth working as though in search of water.

"Get me some water," I said to one of the sailors standing nearby. The man, a short, muscular fellow with his beard tarred into ornamental spikes, merely stared as though he had found himself suddenly addressed by a fish.

Turning my back on him impatiently, I sank to my knees by the sick man and opened his filthy shirt. He stank abominably; probably none too clean to start with, he had been left to lie in his own filth, his fellows afraid to touch him. His arms were relatively clear, but the pustules clustered thickly down his chest and stomach, and his skin was burning to the touch.

Jamie had come in while I made my examination, accompanied by Jared. With them was a small, pear-shaped man in a gold-swagged official's coat and two other men, one a nobleman or a rich bourgeois by his dress; the other a tall, lean individual, clearly a seafarer from his complexion. Probably the captain of the plague ship, if that's what it was.

And that's what it appeared to be. I had seen smallpox

many times before, in the uncivilized parts of the world to which my uncle Lamb, an eminent archaeologist, had taken me during my early years. This fellow wasn't pissing blood, as sometimes happened when the disease attacked the kidneys, but otherwise he had every classic symptom.

"I'm afraid it is smallpox," I said.

The *Patagonia*'s captain gave a sudden howl of anguish, and stepped toward me, face contorted, raising his hand as though to strike me.

"No!" he shouted. "Fool of a woman! *Salope! Femme sans cervelle!* Do you want to ruin me?"

The last word was cut off in a gurgle as Jamie's hand closed on his throat. The other hand twisted hard in the man's shirtfront, lifting him onto his toes.

"I should prefer you to address my wife with respect, Monsieur," Jamie said, rather mildly. The captain, face turning purple, managed a short, jerky nod, and Jamie dropped him. He took a step back, wheezing, and sidled behind his companion as though for refuge, rubbing his throat.

The tubby little official was bending cautiously over the sick man, holding a large silver pomander on a chain close to his nose as he did so. Outside, the level of noise dropped suddenly as the crowd pulled back from the warehouse doors to admit another canvas stretcher.

The man before us sat up suddenly, startling the little official so that he nearly fell over. The man stared wildly around the warehouse, then his eyes rolled back in his head, and he fell back onto the straw as though he'd been poleaxed. He hadn't, but the end result was much the same.

"He's dead," I said, unnecessarily.

The official, recovering his dignity along with his pomander, stepped in once more, looked closely at the body, straightened up and announced, "Smallpox. The lady is correct. I'm sorry, Monsieur le Comte, but you know the law as well as anyone."

The man he addressed sighed impatiently. He glanced at me, frowning, then jerked his head at the official.

"I'm sure this can be arranged, Monsieur Pamplemousse. Please, a moment's private conversation . . ." He motioned toward the deserted foreman's hut that stood some distance away, a small derelict structure inside the larger building. A nobleman by dress as well as by title, Monsieur le Comte was a slender, elegant sort, with heavy brows and thin lips. His entire attitude proclaimed that he was used to getting his way.

But the little official was backing away, hands held out before him as though in self-defense.

"*Non,* Monsieur le Comte," he said, "*Je le regrette, mais c'est impossible.* . . . It cannot be done. Too many people know about it already. The news will be all over the docks by now." He glanced helplessly at Jamie and Jared, then waved vaguely at the warehouse door, where the featureless heads of spectators showed in silhouette, the late afternoon sun rimming them with gold halos.

"No," he said again, his pudgy features hardening with resolve. "You will excuse me, Monsieur—and Madame," he added belatedly, as though noticing me for the first time. "I must go and institute proceedings for the destruction of the ship."

The captain uttered another choked howl at this, and clutched at his sleeve, but he pulled away, and hurried out of the building.

The atmosphere following his departure was a trifle strained, what with Monsieur le Comte and his captain both glaring at me, Jamie glowering menacingly at them, and the dead man staring sightlessly up at the ceiling forty feet above.

The Comte took a step toward me, eyes glittering. "Have you any notion what you have done?" he snarled. "Be warned, Madame; you will pay for this day's work!"

Jamie moved suddenly in the Comte's direction, but Jared was even faster, tugging at Jamie's sleeve, pushing me gently in the direction of the door, and murmuring something unintelligible to the stricken captain, who merely shook his head dumbly in response.

"Poor bugger," Jared said outside, shaking his head. "Phew!" It was chilly on the quay, with a cold gray wind that rocked the ships at anchor, but Jared mopped his face and neck with a large, incongruous red sailcloth handkerchief pulled from the pocket of his coat. "Come on, laddie, let's find a tavern. I'm needing a drink."

Safely ensconced in the upper room of one of the quayside taverns, with a pitcher of wine on the table, Jared collapsed into a chair, fanning himself, and exhaled noisily.

"God, what luck!" He poured a large dollop of wine into his cup, tossed it off, and poured another. Seeing me staring at him, he grinned and pushed the pitcher in my direction.

"Well, there's wine, lassie," he explained, "and then there's stuff you drink to wash the dust away. Toss it back quick, before you have time to taste it, and it does the job handily." Taking his own advice, he drained the cup and reached for the pitcher again. I began to see exactly what had happened to Jamie the day before.

"Good luck or bad?" I asked Jared curiously. I would have assumed the answer to be "bad," but the little merchant's air of jovial exhilaration seemed much too pronounced to be due to the red wine, which strongly resembled battery acid. I set down my own cup, hoping the enamel on my molars was intact.

"Bad for St. Germain, good for me," he said succinctly. He rose from his chair and peered out the window.

"Good," he said, sitting down again with a satisfied air. "They'll have the wine off and into the warehouse by sunset. Safe and sound."

Jamie leaned back in his chair, surveying his cousin with one eyebrow raised, a smile on his lips.

"Do we take it that Monsieur le Comte St. Germain's ship also carried spirits, Cousin?"

An ear-to-ear grin in reply displayed two gold teeth in the lower jaw, which made Jared look still more piratical.

"The best aged port from Pinhão," he said happily. "Cost him a fortune. Half the vintage from the Noval vineyards, and no more available for a year."

"And I suppose the other half of the Noval port is what's being unloaded into your warehouse?" I began to understand his delight.

"Right, my lassie, right as rain!" Jared chortled, almost hugging himself at the thought. "D'ye know what that will sell for in Paris?" he demanded, rocking forward and banging his cup down on the table. "A limited supply, and me with the monopoly? God, my profit's made for the year!"

I rose and looked out the window myself. The *Arianna* rode at anchor, already noticeably higher in the water, as the huge cargo nets swung down from the boom mounted on the rear deck, to be carefully unloaded, bottle by bottle, into handcarts for the trip to the warehouse.

"Not to impair the general rejoicing," I said, a little diffidently, "but did you say that your port came from the same place as St. Germain's shipment?"

"Aye, I did." Jared came to stand next to me, squinting down at the procession of loaders below. "Noval makes the best port in the whole of Spain and Portugal; I'd have liked to take the whole bottling, but hadn't the capital. What of it?"

"Only that if the ships are coming from the same port, there's a chance that some of your seamen might have smallpox too," I said.

The thought blanched the wine flush from Jared's lean cheeks, and he reached for a restorative gulp.

"God, what a thought!" he said, gasping as he set the cup down. "But I think it's all right," he said, reassuring himself. "The port's half unloaded already. But I'd best speak to the captain, anyway," he added, frowning. "I'll have him pay the men off as soon as the loading's finished—and if anyone looks ill, they can have their wages and leave at once." He turned decisively and shot out of the room, pausing at the door just long enough to call over his shoulder, "Order some supper!" before disappearing down the stair with a clatter like a small herd of elephants.

I turned to Jamie, who was staring bemusedly into his undrunk cup of wine.

"He shouldn't do that!" I exclaimed. "If he has got smallpox on board, he could spread it all over the city by sending men off with it."

Jamie nodded slowly.

"Then I suppose we'll hope he hasna got it," he observed mildly.

I turned uncertainly toward the door. "But . . . shouldn't we do something? I could at least go have a look at his men. And tell them what to do with the bodies of the men from the other ship . . ."

"Sassenach." The deep voice was still mild, but held an unmistakable note of warning.

"What?" I turned back to find him leaning forward, regarding me levelly over the rim of his cup. He looked at me thoughtfully for a minute before speaking.

"D'ye think what we've set ourselves to do is important, Sassenach?"

My hand dropped from the door handle.

"Stopping the Stuarts from starting a rising in Scotland? Yes, of course I do. Why do you ask?"

He nodded, patient as an instructor with a slow pupil.

"Aye, well. If ye do, then you'll come here, sit yourself down, and drink wine wi' me until Jared comes back. And if ye don't . . ." He paused and blew out a long breath that stirred the ruddy wave of hair above his forehead.

"If ye don't, then you'll go down to a quay full of seamen and merchants who think women near ships are the height of ill luck, who are already spreading gossip that you've put a curse on St. Germain's ship, and you'll tell them what they must do. With luck, they'll be too afraid of ye to rape you before they cut your throat and toss you in the harbor, and me after you. If St. Germain himself doesna strangle you first. Did ye no see the look on his face?"

I came back to the table and sat down, a little abruptly. My knees were a trifle wobbly.

"I saw it," I said. "But could he . . . he wouldn't . . ."

Jamie raised his brows and pushed a cup of wine across the table to me.

"He could, and he would if he thought it could be managed inconspicuously. For the Lord's sake, Sassenach, you've cost the man close on a year's income! And he doesna look the sort to take such a loss philosophically. Had ye not told the harbor master it was smallpox, out loud in front of witnesses, a few discreet bribes would have taken care of the matter. As it is, why do ye think Jared brought us up here so fast? For the quality of the drink?"

My lips felt stiff, as though I'd actually drunk a good bit of the vitriol from the pitcher.

"You mean . . . we're in danger?"

He sat back, nodding.

"Now you've got it," he said kindly. "I dinna suppose Jared wanted to alarm you. I expect he's gone to arrange a guard of some kind for us, as well as to see to his crew. He'll likely be safe enough—everyone knows him, and his crew and loaders are right outside."

I rubbed my hands over the gooseflesh that rippled up my forearms. There was a cheerful fire in the hearth, and the room was warm and smoky, but I felt cold.

"How do you know so much about what the Comte St. Germain might do?" I didn't doubt Jamie at all—I remembered all too well the malevolent black glare the Comte had shot at me in the warehouse—but I did wonder how he knew the man.

Jamie took a small sip of the wine, made a face and put it down.

"For the one thing, he's some reputation for ruthlessness —and other things. I heard a bit about him when I lived in Paris before, though I had the luck never to run afoul of the man then. For another, Jared spent some time yesterday warning me about him; he's Jared's chief business rival in Paris."

I rested my elbows on the battered table, and parked my chin on my folded hands.

"I've made rather a mess of things, haven't I?" I said ruefully. "Got you off on a fine footing in business."

He smiled, then got up and came behind me, bending to put his arms around me. I was still rather unnerved from his sudden revelations, but felt much better to feel the strength and the bulk of him behind me. He kissed me lightly on top of the head.

"Dinna worry, Sassenach," he said. "I can take care of myself. And I can take care of you, too—and you'll let me." There was a smile in his voice, but a question as well, and I nodded, letting my head fall back against his chest.

"I'll let you," I said. "The citizens of Le Havre will just have to take their chances with the pox."

It was nearly an hour before Jared came back, ears reddened with cold, but throat unslit, and apparently none the worse for wear. I was happy to see him.

"It's all right," he announced, beaming. "Nothing but scurvy and the usual fluxes and chills aboard. No pox." He looked around the room, rubbing his hands together. "Where's supper?"

His cheeks were wind-reddened and he looked cheerful and capable. Apparently dealing with business rivals who settled contentions by assassination was all in a day's work to this merchant. And why not? I thought cynically. He was a bloody Scot, after all.

As if to confirm this view, Jared ordered the meal, acquired an excellent wine to go with it by the simple expedient of sending to his own warehouse for it, and sat down to a genial postprandial discussion with Jamie on ways and means of dealing with French merchants.

"Bandits," he said. "Every man jack o' them would stab ye in the back as soon as look at ye. Filthy thieves. Don't trust them an inch. Half on deposit, half on delivery, and never let a nobleman pay on credit."

Despite Jared's assurances that he had left two men below on watch, I was still a bit nervous, and after supper, I placed myself near the window, where I could see the comings and goings along the pier. Not that my watching out was likely to do a lot of good, I thought; every second man on the dock looked like an assassin to me.

The clouds were closing in over the harbor; it was going to snow again tonight. The reefed sails fluttered wildly in the rising wind, rattling against the spars with a noise that nearly overwhelmed the shouts of the loaders. The harbor glowed with a moment of dull green light as the setting sun was driven into the water by the pressing clouds.

As it grew darker, the bustle to and fro died down, the loaders with their handcarts disappearing up the streets into the town, and the sailors disappearing into the lighted doors of establishments like the one in which I sat. Still, the place was far from deserted; in particular, there was a small crowd still gathered near the ill-fated *Patagonia*. Men in some sort of uniform formed a cordon at the foot of the gangplank; no doubt to prevent anyone going aboard or bringing the cargo off. Jared had explained that the healthy members of the crew would be allowed to come ashore, but not permitted to bring anything off the ship save the clothes that they wore.

"Better than they'd do under the Dutch," he said, scratching the rough black stubble that was beginning to emerge along his jaw. "If a ship's coming in from a port known to have plague of some kind, the damned Hollanders make the sailors swim ashore naked."

"What do they do for clothes once they get ashore?" I asked curiously.

"I don't know," said Jared absently, "but since they'll find a brothel within moments of stepping on land, I don't suppose they'd need any—begging your pardon, m'dear," he added hastily, suddenly remembering that he was talking to a lady.

Covering his momentary confusion with heartiness, he rose and came to peer out of the window beside me.

"Ah," he said. "They're getting ready to fire the ship. Given what she's carrying, they'd best tow it a good way out into the harbor first."

Towropes had been attached to the doomed *Patagonia,* and a number of small boats manned by oarsmen were standing ready, waiting for a signal. This was given by the harbor master, whose gold braid was barely visible as a gleam in the dying light of the day. He shouted, waving both hands slowly back and forth above his head like a semaphore.

His shout was echoed by the captains of the rowboats and galleys, and the towropes slowly lifted from the water as they tautened, water sluicing down the heavy hemp spirals with a splash audible in the sudden silence that struck the docks. The shouts from the towboats were the only sound as the dark hulk of the condemned ship creaked, quivered, and turned into the wind, shrouds groaning as she set out on her last brief voyage.

They left her in the middle of the harbor, a safe distance away from the other ships. Her decks had been soaked with oil, and as the towropes were cast off and the galleys pulled away, the small round figure of the harbor master rose from the seat of the dinghy that had rowed him out. He bent down, head close to one of the seated figures, then rose with the bright sudden flame of a torch in one hand.

The rower behind him leaned away as he drew back his arm and threw the torch. A heavy club wrapped with oil-soaked rags, it turned end over end, the fire shrinking to a blue glow, and landed out of sight behind the railing. The harbor master didn't wait to see the effects of his action; he sat down at once, gesturing madly to the rower, who heaved on the oars, and the small boat shot away across the dark water.

For long moments, nothing happened, but the crowd on the dock stood still, murmuring quietly. I could see the pale reflection of Jamie's face, floating above my own in the dark glass of the window. The glass was cold, and misted over quickly with our breath; I rubbed it clear with the edge of my cloak.

"There," Jamie said softly. The flame ran suddenly behind the railing, a small blue glowing line. Then a flicker, and the forward shrouds sprang out, orange-red lines against the sky. A silent leap, and the tongues of fire danced along the oil-drenched rails, and one furled sail sparked and burst into flame.

In less than a minute, the shrouds of the mizzen had caught, and the mainsail unfurled, its moorings burnt through, a falling sheet of flame. The fire spread too rapidly then to watch its progress; everything seemed alight at once.

"Now," Jared said suddenly. "Come downstairs. The hold will catch in a minute, and that will be the best time to make away. No one will notice us."

He was right; as we crept cautiously out of the tavern door, two men materialized beside Jared—his own seamen, armed with pistols and marlinspikes—but no one else noticed our appearance. Everyone was turned toward the harbor, where the superstructure of the *Patagonia* was visible now as a black skeleton inside a body of rippling flame. There was a series of pops, so close together they sounded like machine-gun fire, and then an almighty explosion that rose from the center of the ship in a fountain of sparks and burning timbers.

"Let's go." Jamie's hand was firm on my arm, and I made no protest. Following Jared, guarded by the sailors, we stole away from the quay, surreptitious as though we had started the fire.

7

Royal Audience

Jared's house in Paris stood in the Rue Trémoulins. It was a wealthy district, with stone-faced houses of three, four, and five stories crowded cheek by jowl together. Here and there a very large house stood alone in its own park, but for the most part, a reasonably athletic burglar could have leaped from rooftop to rooftop with no difficulty.

"Mmphm" was Murtagh's solitary observation, upon beholding Jared's house. "I'll find my own lodging."

"And if it makes ye nervous to have a decent roof above your head, man, ye can sleep in the stables," Jamie suggested. He grinned down at his small, dour godfather. "We'll ha' the footman bring ye out your parritch on a silver tray."

Inside, the house was furnished with comfortable elegance, though as I was later to realize, it was Spartan by comparison with most of the houses of the nobility and the wealthy bourgeois. I supposed that this was at least in part because the house had no lady; Jared had never married, though he showed no signs of feeling the lack of a wife.

"Well, he has a mistress, of course," Jamie had explained when I speculated about his cousin's private life.

"Oh, of course," I murmured.

"But she's married. Jared told me once that a man of business should never form entanglements with unmarried ladies—he said they demand too much in terms of expense and time. And if ye marry them, they'll run through your money and you'll end up a pauper."

"Fine opinion he's got of wives," I said. "What does he think of your marrying, in spite of all this helpful advice?"

Jamie laughed. "Well, I havena got any money to start with, so I can hardly be worse off. He thinks you're verra decorative; he says I must buy ye a new gown, though."

I spread the skirt of the apple-green velvet, more than a little the worse for wear.

"I suppose so," I agreed. "Or I'll go round wrapped in a bedsheet after a while; this is already tight in the waist."

"Elsewhere, too," he said, grinning as he looked me over. "Got your appetite back, have ye, Sassenach?"

"Oaf," I said coldly. "You know perfectly well that Annabelle MacRannoch is the general size and shape of a shovel handle, whereas I am not."

"You are not," he agreed, eyeing me with appreciation. "Thank God." He patted me familiarly on the bottom.

"I'm to join Jared at the warehouse this morning to go over the ledgers, then we're going to call on some of his clients, to introduce me. Will ye be all right by yourself?"

"Yes, of course," I said. "I'll explore the house a bit, and get acquainted with the servants." I had met the servants en masse when we had arrived late in the previous afternoon, but since we had dined simply in our room, I had seen no one since but the footman who brought the food, and the maid who had come in early in the morning to put back the curtains, lay and light the fire, and carry away the chamber pot. I quailed a bit at the thought of suddenly being in charge of a "staff," but reassured myself by thinking that it couldn't be much different from directing orderlies and junior nurses, and I'd done that before, as a senior nurse at a French field station in 1943.

After Jamie's departure, I took my time in making what toilette could be made with a comb and water, which were the only grooming implements available. If Jared was serious about my holding dinner parties, I could see that a new gown was going to be merely the start of it.

I did have, in the side pocket of my medicine chest, the frayed willow twigs with which I cleaned my teeth, and I got one of these and set to work, thinking over the amazing fortune which had brought us here.

Essentially barred from Scotland, we would have had to find a place to make our future, either in Europe or by emigrating to America. And given what I now knew about Jamie's attitude toward ships, I wasn't at all surprised that he should have looked to France from the start.

The Frasers had strong ties with France; many of them, like Abbot Alexander and Jared Fraser, had made lives here, seldom if ever returning to their native Scotland. And there were many Jacobites as well, Jamie had told me, those who had followed their king into exile, and now lived as best they could in France or Italy while awaiting his restoration.

"There's always talk of it," he had said. "In the houses, mostly, not the taverns. And that's why nothing's come of it. When it gets to the taverns, you'll know it's serious."

"Tell me," I said, watching him brush the dust from his coat, "are all Scots born knowing about politics, or is it just you?"

He laughed, but quickly sobered as he opened the huge armoire and hung up the coat. It looked worn and rather pathetic, hanging by itself in the enormous, cedar-scented space.

"Well, I'll tell ye, Sassenach, I'd as soon not know. But born as I was, between the MacKenzies and the Frasers, I'd little choice in the matter. And ye don't spend a year in French society and two years in an army without learning how to listen to what's being said, and what's being meant, and how to tell the difference between the two. Given these times, though, it isna just me; there's neither laird nor cottar in the Highlands who can stand aside from what's to come."

"What's to come." What *was* to come? I wondered. What *would* come, if we were not successful in our efforts here, was an armed rebellion, an attempt at restoration of the Stuart monarchy, led by Prince Charles Edward Casimir Maria Sylvester Stuart, the son of the exiled king.

"Bonnie Prince Charlie," I said softly to myself, looking over my reflection in the large pier glass. He was here, now, in the same city, perhaps not too far away. What would he be like? I could think of him only in terms of his usual historical portrait, which showed a handsome, slightly effeminate youth of sixteen or so, with soft pink lips and powdered hair, in the fashion of the times. Or the imagined paintings, showing a more robust version of the same thing, brandishing a broadsword as he stepped out of a boat onto the shore of Scotland.

A Scotland he would ruin and lay waste in the effort to reclaim it for his father and himself. Doomed to failure, he would attract enough support to cleave the country, and lead his followers through civil war to a bloody end on the field of Culloden. Then he would flee back to safety in France, but the retribution of his enemies would be exacted upon those he left behind.

It was to prevent such a disaster that we had come. It seemed incredible, thinking about it in the peace and luxury of Jared's house. How did one stop a rebellion? Well, if risings were fomented in taverns, perhaps they could be stopped over dinner tables. I shrugged at myself in the mirror, blew an errant curl out of one eye, and went down to cozen the cook.

The staff, at first inclined to view me with frightened suspicion, soon realized that I had no intention of interfering with their work, and relaxed into a mood of wary obligingness. I had thought at first, in my blur of fatigue, that there were at least a dozen servants lined up in the hallway for my inspection. In fact, there were sixteen of them, counting the groom, the stable-lad and the knife-boy, whom I hadn't noticed in the general scrum. I was still more impressed at Jared's success in business, until I realized just how little the servants were paid: a new pair of shoes and two livres per year for the footmen, a trifle less for the housemaids and kitchenmaids, a little more for such exalted personages as Madame Vionnet, the cook, and the butler, Magnus.

While I explored the mechanics of the household and stored up what information I could glean at home from the gossip of the parlormaids, Jamie was out with Jared every day, calling upon customers, meeting people, preparing himself to "assist His Highness" by making those social connections that might prove of value to an exiled prince. It was among the dinner guests that we might find allies—or enemies.

"St. Germain?" I said, suddenly catching a familiar name in the midst of Marguerite's chatter as she polished the parquet floor. "The Comte St. Germain?"

"*Oui*, Madame." She was a small, fat girl, with an oddly flattened face and popeyes that made her look like a turbot, but she was friendly and eager to please. Now she pursed her mouth up into a tiny circle, portending the imparting of some really scandalous tidbit. I looked as encouraging as possible.

"The Comte, Madame, has a very bad reputation," she said portentously.

Since this was true—according to Marguerite—of virtually everyone who came to dinner, I arched my brows and waited for further details.

"He has sold his soul to the Devil, you know," she confided, lowering her voice and glancing around as though that gentleman might be lurking behind the chimney breast. "He celebrates the Black Mass, at which the blood and flesh of innocent children are shared amongst the wicked!"

A fine specimen you picked to make an enemy of, I thought to myself.

"Oh, everyone knows, Madame," Marguerite assured me. "But it does not matter; the women are mad for him, anyway; wherever he goes, they throw themselves at his head. But then, he is rich." Plainly this last qualification was at least sufficient to balance, if not to outweigh, the blood-drinking and flesh-eating.

"How interesting," I said. "But I thought that Monsieur le Comte was a competitor of Monsieur Jared; doesn't he also import wines? Why does Monsieur Jared invite him here, then?"

Marguerite looked up from her floor-polishing and laughed.

"Why, Madame! It is so that Monsieur Jared can serve the best Beaune at dinner, tell Monsieur le Comte that he has just acquired ten cases, and at the conclusion of the meal, generously offer him a bottle to take home!"

"I see," I said, grinning. "And is Monsieur Jared similarly invited to dine with Monsieur le Comte?"

She nodded, white kerchief bobbing over her oil-bottle and rag. "Oh, yes, Madame. But not as often!"

The Comte St. Germain was fortunately not invited for this evening. We dined simply en famille, so that Jared could rehearse Jamie in the few details left to be arranged before his departure. Of these, the most important was the King's *lever* at Versailles.

Being invited to attend the King's *lever* was a considerable mark of favor, Jared explained over dinner.

"Not to you, lad," he said kindly, waving a fork at Jamie. "To me. The King wants to make sure I'm coming back from Prussia—or Duverney, the Minister of Finance, does, at least. The latest wave of taxes hit the merchants hard, and a good many of the foreigners left—with the ill effects on the

Royal Treasury you can imagine." He grimaced at the thought of taxes, scowling at the baby eel on his fork.

"I mean to be gone by Monday-week. I'm waiting only for word that the *Wilhelmina*'s come in safe to Calais; then I'm off." Jared took another bite of eel and nodded at Jamie, talking around the mouthful of food. "I'm leaving the business in good hands, lad; I've no worry on that score. We might talk a bit before I go about other matters, though. I've arranged with the Earl Marischal that we'll go with him to Montmartre two days hence, for you to pay your respects to His Highness, Prince Charles Edward."

I felt a sudden thump of excitement in the pit of my stomach, and exchanged a quick glance with Jamie. He nodded at Jared, as though this were nothing startling, but his eyes sparkled with anticipation as he looked at me. So this was the start of it.

"His Highness lives a very retired life in Paris," Jared was saying as he chased the last eels, slick with butter, around the edge of the plate. "It wouldn't be appropriate for him to appear in society, until and unless the King receives him officially. So His Highness seldom leaves his house, and sees few people, save those supporters of his father who come to pay their respects."

"That isn't what I've heard," I interjected.

"What?" Two pairs of startled eyes turned in my direction, and Jared laid down his fork, abandoning the final eel to its fate.

Jamie arched an eyebrow at me. "What have ye heard, Sassenach, and from whom?"

"From the servants," I said, concentrating on my own eels. Seeing Jared's frown, it occurred to me for the first time that it might not be considered quite the thing for the lady of the house to be gossiping with parlormaids. Well, the hell with it, I thought rebelliously. There wasn't much else for me to do.

"The parlormaid says that His Highness Prince Charles has been paying calls on the Princesse Louise de La Tour de Rohan," I said, plucking a single eel off the fork and chewing slowly. They were delicious, but felt rather disconcerting if swallowed whole, as though the creature were still alive. I swallowed carefully. So far, so good.

"In the absence of the lady's husband," I added delicately.

Jamie looked amused, Jared horrified.

"The Princesse de Rohan?" Jared said. "Marie-Louise-Henriette-Jeanne de La Tour d'Auvergne? Her husband's family are very close to the King." He rubbed his fingers across his lips, leaving a buttery shine around his mouth. "That could be very dangerous," he muttered, as though to himself. "I wonder if the wee fool . . . but no. Surely he's more sense than that. It must be only inexperience; he's not been so much in society, and things are different in Rome. Still . . ." He left off muttering and turned to Jamie with decision.

"That will be your first task, lad, in the service of His Majesty. You're much of an age with His Highness, but you have the experience and the judgment of your time in Paris— and my training, I flatter myself." He smiled briefly at Jamie. "You can befriend his Highness; smooth his path as much as may be with those men that will be of use to him; you've met most of them by now. And explain to His Highness—as tactfully as ye can—that gallantry in the wrong direction may do considerable damage to the aims of his father."

Jamie nodded absently, plainly thinking of something else.

"How does our parlormaid come to know about His Highness's visits, Sassenach?" he asked. "She doesna leave the house more than once a week, to go to Mass, does she?"

I shook my head, and swallowed the next mouthful in order to reply.

"So far as I've worked it out, our kitchenmaid heard it from the knife-boy, who heard it from the stable-lad, who got it from the groom next door. I don't know how many people there are in between, but the Rohan house is three doors down the street. I'd imagine the Princesse knows all about us, too," I added cheerfully. "At least she does, if she talks to her kitchenmaid."

"Ladies do *not* gossip with their kitchenmaids," Jared said coldly. He narrowed his eyes at Jamie in a silent adjuration to keep his wife in better order.

I could see the corner of Jamie's mouth twitching, but he merely sipped his Montrachet and changed the subject to a discussion of Jared's latest venture; a shipment of rum, on its way from Jamaica.

When Jared rang the bell for the dishes to be cleared and the brandy brought out, I excused myself. One of Jared's idiosyncrasies was the enjoyment of long black cheroots with his brandy, and I had the distinct feeling that, carefully chewed or not, the eels I had eaten wouldn't benefit from being smoked.

I lay on my bed and tried, with limited success, not to think about eels. I closed my eyes and tried to think of Jamaica—pleasant white beaches under tropical sun. But thoughts of Jamaica led to thoughts of the *Wilhelmina* and thoughts of ships made me think of the sea, which led directly back to images of giant eels, coiling and writhing through the heaving green waves. I greeted the distraction of Jamie's appearance with relief, sitting up as he came in.

"Phew!" He leaned against the closed door, fanning himself with the loose end of his jabot. "I feel like a smoked sausage. I'm fond of Jared, but I shall be verra pleased when he's taken his damned cheroots to Prussia."

"Well, don't come near me, if you smell like a cheroot," I said. "The eels don't like smoke."

"I dinna blame them a bit." He took off his coat and unbuttoned his shirt. "I think it's a plan, ye ken," he confided, tossing his head toward the door as he took his shirt off. "Like the bees."

"Bees?"

"How ye move a hive of bees," he explained, opening the window and hanging his shirt outside from the crank of the casement. "You get a pipe full of the strongest tobacco ye can find, stick it into the hive and blow smoke up into the combs. The bees all fall down stunned, and you can take them where ye like. I think that's what Jared does to his customers; he smokes them into insensibility, and they've signed orders for three times more wine than they meant to before they recover their senses."

I giggled and he grinned, putting a finger to his lips as the sound of Jared's light footsteps came down the corridor, passing our door on his way to his own room.

Danger of discovery past, he came and stretched out beside me, wearing only his kilt and stockings.

"Not too bad?" he asked. "I can sleep in the dressing room, if it is. Or put my head out of the window for airing."

I sniffed his hair, where the scent of tobacco lingered among the ruddy waves. The candlelight shot the red with strands of gold, and I ruffled my fingers through it, enjoying the thick softness of it, and the hard, solid feel of the bone beneath.

"No, it's not too bad. You're not worried about Jared leaving so soon, then?"

He kissed my forehead and lay down, head on the bolster. He smiled up at me, shaking his head.

"No. I've met all the chief customers and the captains, I know all the warehousemen and the officials, I've the price lists and the inventories committed to memory. What's left to learn about the business I must just learn by trying; Jared canna teach me more."

"And Prince Charles?"

He half-closed his eyes and gave a small grunt of resignation. "Aye, well. For that, I must trust to the mercy of God, not Jared. And I daresay it will be easier if Jared isn't here to see what I'm doing."

I lay down beside him, and he turned toward me, sliding an arm around my waist so that we lay close together.

"What *shall* we do?" I asked. "Have you any idea, Jamie?"

His breath was warm on my face, scented with brandy, and I tilted my head up to kiss him. His soft, wide mouth opened on mine, and he lingered in the kiss for a moment before answering.

"Oh, I've ideas," he said, drawing back with a sigh. "God knows what they'll amount to, but I've ideas."

"Tell me."

"Mmphm." He settled himself more comfortably, turning on his back and cradling me in one arm, head on his shoulder.

"Well," he began, "as I see it, it's a matter of money, Sassenach."

"Money? I should have thought it was a matter of politics. Don't the French want James restored because it will cause the English trouble? From the little I recall, Louis wanted—*will* want"—I corrected myself—"Charles Stuart to distract King George from what Louis is up to in Brussels."

"I daresay he does," he said, "but restoring kings takes money. And Louis hasna got so much himself that he can be using it on the one hand to fight wars in Brussels, and on the other to finance invasions of England. You heard what Jared said about the Royal Treasury and the taxes?"

"Yes, but . . ."

"No, it isna Louis that will make it happen," he said, instructing me. "Though he's something to say about it, of course. No, there are other sources of money that James and Charles will be trying as well, and those are the French banking families, the Vatican, and the Spanish Court."

"James covering the Vatican and the Spanish, and Charles the French bankers, you think?" I asked, interested.

He nodded, staring up at the carved panels of the ceiling. The walnut panels were a soft, light brown in the flickering candle-glow, darker rosettes and ribbons twining from each corner.

"Aye, I do. Uncle Alex showed me correspondence from His Majesty King James, and I should say the Spanish are his best opportunity, judging from that. The Pope's compelled to support him, ye ken, as a Catholic monarch; Pope Clement supported James for a good many years, and now Clement's dead, Benedict continues it, but not at such a high level. But both Philip of Spain and Louis are James's cousins; it's the obligation of Bourbon blood he calls on there." He smiled wryly at me, sidelong. "And from the things I've seen, I can tell ye that Royal blood runs damn thin when it comes to money, Sassenach."

Lifting one foot at a time, he stripped off his stockings one handed and tossed them onto the bedroom stool.

"James got some money from Spain thirty years ago," he observed. "A small fleet of ships, and some men as well. That was the Rising in 1715. But he had ill luck, and James's forces were defeated at Sheriffmuir—before James himself even arrived. So I'd say the Spanish are maybe none too eager to finance a second try at the Stuart restoration—not without a verra good idea that it might succeed."

"So Charles has come to France to work on Louis and

the bankers," I mused. "And according to what I know of history, he'll succeed. Which leaves us where?"

Jamie's arm left my shoulders as he stretched, the shift of his weight tilting the mattress under me.

"It leaves me selling wine to bankers, Sassenach," he said, yawning. "And you talking to parlormaids. And if we blow enough smoke, perhaps we'll stun the bees."

Just before Jared's departure, he took Jamie to the small house in Montmartre where His Highness, Prince Charles Edward Casimir, etc. Stuart was residing, biding his time while waiting to see what Louis would or would not do for an impecunious cousin with aspirations to a throne.

I had seen them off, both dressed in their best, and spent the time while they were gone picturing the encounter in my mind, wondering how it had gone.

"How did it go?" I asked Jamie, the moment I got him alone upon his return. "What was he like?"

He scratched his head, thinking.

"Well," he said at last, "he had a toothache."

"What?"

"He said so. And it looked verra painful; he kept his face screwed up to one side with his jaw puffed a bit. I canna say whether he's stiff in his manner usually, or if it was only that it hurt him to talk, but he didna say much."

After the formal introductions, in fact, the older men, Jared, the Earl Marischal, and a rather seedy-looking specimen referred to casually as "Balhaldy," had gravitated together and begun talking Scottish politics, leaving Jamie and His Highness more or less to themselves.

"We had a cup of brandywine each," Jamie obediently reported, under my goading. "And I asked him how he found Paris, and he said he was finding it rather tiresomely confining, as he couldna get any hunting. And so then we talked of hunting. He prefers hunting wi' dogs to hunting with beaters, and I said I did, too. Then he told me how many pheasants he'd shot on one hunting trip in Italy. He talked about Italy until he said the cold air coming in through the window was hurting his tooth—it's no a verra well-built house; just a small villa. Then he drank some more brandywine for his tooth, and

I told him about stag-hunting in the Highlands, and he said he'd like to try that sometime, and was I a good shot with a bow? And I said I was, and he said he hoped he would have the opportunity to invite me to hunt with him in Scotland. And then Jared said he needed to stop at the warehouse on the way back, so His Highness gave me his hand and I kissed it and we left."

"Hmm," I said. While reason asserted that naturally the famous—or about-to-be-famous, or possibly-famous, at any rate—were bound to be much like everyone else in their daily behavior, I had to admit that I found this report of the Bonnie Prince a bit of a letdown. Still, Jamie had been invited back. The important thing, as he pointed out, was to become acquainted with His Highness, in order to keep an eye on his plans as any developed. I wondered whether the King of France would be a trifle more impressive in person.

We were not long in finding out. A week later, Jamie rose in the cold, black dark and dressed himself for the long ride to Versailles, to attend the King's *lever*. Louis awoke punctually at six o'clock every morning. At this hour, the favored few chosen to attend the King's toilette should be assembled in the antechamber, ready to join the procession of nobles and attendants who were necessary to assist the monarch in greeting the new day.

Wakened in the small hours by Magnus the butler, Jamie stumbled sleepily out of bed and made ready, yawning and muttering. At this hour, my insides were tranquil, and I luxuriated in that delightful feeling that comes when we observe someone having to do something unpleasant that we are not required to do ourselves.

"Watch carefully," I said, my voice husky with sleep. "So you can tell me everything."

With a sleepy grunt of assent, he leaned over to kiss me, then shuffled off, candle in hand, to see to the saddling of his horse. The last I heard before sinking back under the surface of sleep was Jamie's voice downstairs, suddenly clear and alert in the crisp night air, exchanging farewells with the groom in the street outside.

Given the distance to Versailles, and the chance—of

which Jared had warned—of being invited to lunch, I wasn't surprised when he didn't return before noon, but I couldn't help being curious, and waited in increasing impatience until his arrival—finally—near teatime.

"And how was the King's *lever*?" I asked, coming to help Jamie remove his coat. Wearing the tight pigskin gloves de rigueur at Court, he couldn't manage the crested silver buttons on the slippery velvet.

"Oh, that feels better," he said, flexing his broad shoulders in relief as the buttons sprang free. The coat was much too tight in the shoulders; peeling him out of it was like shelling an egg.

"Interesting, Sassenach," he said, in answer to my question, "at least for the first hour or so."

As the procession of nobles came into the Royal Bed-chamber, each bearing his ceremonial implement—towel, razor, alecup, royal seal, etc.—the gentlemen of the bedchamber drew back the heavy curtains that kept out the dawn, unveiled the draperies of the great bed of state, and exposed the face of *le roi Louis* to the interested eye of the rising sun.

Assisted to a sitting position on the edge of his bed, the King had sat yawning and scratching his stubbled chin while his attendants pulled a silk robe, heavy with embroidery of silver and gold, over the royal shoulders, and knelt to strip off the heavy felt stockings in which the King slept, to be re-placed with hose of lighter silk, and soft slippers lined with rabbit fur.

One by one, the nobles of the court came to kneel at the feet of their sovereign, to greet him respectfully and ask how His Majesty had passed the night?

"Not verra well, I should say," Jamie broke off to observe here. "He looked like he'd slept little more than an hour or two, and bad dreams with it."

Despite bloodshot eyes and drooping jowls, His Majesty had nodded graciously to his courtiers, then risen slowly to his feet and bowed to those favored guests hovering in the back of the chamber. A dispirited wave of the hand summoned a gentleman of the bedchamber, who led His Majesty to the waiting chair, where he sat with closed eyes, enjoying the ministrations of his attendants, while the visitors were led forward one at a time by the Duc d'Orléans, to kneel before the King and offer a few words of greeting. Formal petitions would be offered a little later, when there was a chance of Louis being awake enough to hear them.

"I wasna there for petitioning, but only as a mark of favor," Jamie explained, "so I just knelt and said, 'Good morning, Your Majesty,' while the Duc told the King who I was."

"Did the King say anything to you?" I asked.

Jamie grinned, hands linked behind his head as he stretched. "Oh, aye. He opened one eye and looked at me as though he didna believe it."

One eye still open, Louis had surveyed his visitor with a sort of dim interest, then remarked, "Big, aren't you?"

"I said, 'Yes, Your Majesty,' " Jamie said. "Then he said, 'Can you dance?' and I said I could. Then he shut his eye again, and the Duc motioned me back."

Introductions complete, the gentlemen of the bedchamber, ceremoniously assisted by the chief nobles, had then proceeded to make the King's toilette. As they did so, the various petitioners came forward at the beckoning of the Duc d'Orléans, to murmur into the King's ear as he twisted his head to accommodate the razor, or bent his neck to have his wig adjusted.

"Oh? And were you honored by being allowed to blow His Majesty's nose for him?" I asked.

Jamie grinned, stretching his linked hands until the knuckles cracked.

"No, thank God. I skulked about against the wardrobe, trying to look like part of the furniture, wi' the bitty wee comtes and ducs all glancing at me out of the sides of their eyes as though Scottishness were catching."

"Well, at least you were tall enough to see everything?"

"Oh, aye. That I did, even when he eased himself on his *chaise percée.*"

"He really did that? In front of everyone?" I was fascinated. I'd read about it, of course, but found it difficult to believe.

"Oh, aye, and everyone behaving just as they did when he washed his face and blew his nose. The Duc de Neve had the unspeakable honor," he added ironically, "of wiping His

Majesty's arse for him. I didna notice what they did wi' the towel; took it out and had it gilded, no doubt.

"A verra wearisome business it was, too," he added, bending over and setting his hands on the floor to stretch the muscles of his legs. "Took forever; the man's tight as an owl."

"Tight as an owl?" I asked, amused at the simile. "Constipated, do you mean?"

"Aye, costive. And no wonder, the things they eat at Court," he added censoriously, stretching backward. "Terrible diet, all cream and butter. He should eat parritch every morning for breakfast—that'd take care of it. Verra good for the bowels, ye ken."

If Scotsmen were stubborn about anything—and, in fact, they tended to be stubborn about quite a number of things, truth be known—it was the virtues of oatmeal parritch for breakfast. Through eons of living in a land so poor there was little to eat but oats, they had as usual converted necessity into a virtue, and insisted that they liked the stuff.

Jamie had by now thrown himself on the floor and was doing the Royal Air Force exercises I had recommended to strengthen the muscles of his back.

Returning to his earlier remark, I said, "Why did you say 'tight as an owl'? I've heard that before, to mean drunk, but not costive. Are owls constipated, then?"

Completing his course, he flipped over and lay on the rug, panting.

"Oh, aye." He blew out a long sigh, and caught his breath. He sat up and pushed the hair out of his eyes. "Or not really, but that's the story ye hear. Folk will tell ye that owls havena got an arsehole, so they canna pass the things they eat —like mice, aye? So the bones and the hairs and such are all made up into a ball, and the owl vomits them out, not bein' able to get rid of them out the other end."

"Really?"

"Oh, aye, that's true enough, they do. That's how ye find an owl-tree; look underneath for the pellets on the ground. Make a terrible mess, owls do," he added, pulling his collar away from his neck to let air in.

"But they have got arseholes," he informed me. "I knocked one out of a tree once wi' a slingshot and looked."

"A lad with an inquiring mind, eh?" I said, laughing.

"To be sure, Sassenach." He grinned. "And they do pass things that way, too. I spent a whole day sitting under an owl-tree with Ian, once, just to make sure."

"Christ, you *must* have been curious," I remarked.

"Well, I wanted to know. Ian didna want to sit still so long, and I had to pound on him a bit to make him stop fidgeting." Jamie laughed, remembering. "So he sat still wi' me until it happened, and then he snatched up a handful of owl pellets, jammed them down the neck of my shirt, and was off like a shot. God, he could run like the wind." A tinge of sadness crossed his face, his memory of the fleet-footed friend of his youth clashing with more recent memories of his brother-in-law, hobbling stiffly, if good-naturedly, on the wooden leg a round of grapeshot taken in a foreign battle had left him with.

"That sounds an awful way to live," I remarked, wanting to distract him. "Not watching owls, I don't mean—the King. No privacy, ever, not even in the loo."

"I wouldna care for it myself," Jamie agreed. "But then he's the King."

"Mmm. And I suppose all the power and luxury and so forth makes up for a lot."

He shrugged. "Well, if it does or no, it's the bargain God's made for him, and he's little choice but to make the best of it." He picked up his plaid and drew the tail of it through his belt and up to his shoulder.

"Here, let me." I took the silver ring-brooch from him and fastened the flaming fabric at the crest of his shoulder. He arranged the drape, smoothing the vivid wool between his fingers.

"I've a bargain like that myself, Sassenach," he said quietly, looking down at me. He smiled briefly. "Though thank God it doesna mean inviting Ian to wipe my arse for me. But I was born laird. I'm the steward of that land and the people on it, and I must make the best of my own bargain wi' them."

He reached out and touched my hair lightly.

"That's why I was glad when ye said we'd come, to try and see what we might do. For there's a part of me would like no better than to take you and the bairn and go far away, to spend the rest of my life working the fields and the beasts, to come in in the evenings and lie beside ye, quiet through the night."

The deep blue eyes were hooded in thought, as his hand returned to the folds of his plaid, stroking the bright checks of the Fraser tartan, with the faint white stripe that distinguished Lallybroch from the other septs and families.

"But if I did," he went on, as though speaking more to himself than to me, "there's a part of my soul would feel forsworn, and I think—I think I would always hear the voices of the people that are mine, calling out behind me."

I laid a hand on his shoulder, and he looked up, a faint lopsided smile on the wide mouth.

"I think you would, too," I said. "Jamie . . . whatever happens, whatever we're able to do . . ." I stopped, looking for words. As so often before, the sheer enormity of the task we had taken on staggered me and left me speechless. Who were we, to alter the course of history, to change the course of events not for ourselves, but for princes and peasants, for the entire country of Scotland?

Jamie laid his hand over mine and squeezed it reassuringly.

"No one can ask more of us than our best, Sassenach. Nay, if there's blood shed, it wilna lie on our hands at least, and pray God it may not come to that."

I thought of the lonely gray clanstones on Culloden Moor, and the Highland men who might lie under them, if we were unsuccessful.

"Pray God," I echoed.

8

Unlaid Ghosts
and Crocodiles

Between Royal audiences and the daily demands of
Jared's business, Jamie seemed to be finding life full.
He disappeared with Murtagh soon after breakfast
each morning, to check new deliveries to the warehouse,
make inventories, visit the docks on the Seine, and conduct
tours of what sounded from his description to be extremely
unsavory taverns.

"Well, at least you've got Murtagh with you," I remarked, taking comfort from the fact, "and the two of you
can't get in too much trouble in broad daylight." The wiry
little clansman was unimpressive to look at, his attire varying
from that of the ne'er-do-wells on the docks only by the fact
that the lower half was tartan plaid, but I had ridden through
half of Scotland with Murtagh to rescue Jamie from Wentworth Prison, and there was no one in the world whom I
would sooner have trusted with his welfare.

After luncheon, Jamie would make his rounds of calls—
social and business, and an increasing number of both—and
then retire into his study for an hour or two with the ledgers
and account books before dinner. He was busy.

I was not. A few days of polite skirmishing with Madame
Vionnet, the head-cook, had left it clear who was in charge of
the household, and it wasn't me. Madame came to my sitting
room each morning, to consult me on the menu for the day,
and to present me with the list of expenditures deemed necessary for the provisioning of the kitchen—fruit, vegetables,
butter, and milk from a farm just outside the city, delivered
fresh each morning, fish caught from the Seine and sold from
a barrow in the street, along with fresh mussels that poked
their sealed black curves from heaps of wilting waterweed. I
looked over the lists for form's sake, approved everything,
praised the dinner of the night before, and that was that.
Aside from the occasional call to open the linen cupboard,

the wine cellar, the root cellar, or the pantry with a key from my bunch, my time was then my own, until the hour came to dress for dinner.

The social life of Jared's establishment continued much as it had when he was in residence. I was still cautious about entertaining on a large scale, but we held small dinners every night, to which came nobles, chevaliers, and ladies, poor Jacobites in exile, wealthy merchants and their wives.

However, I found that eating and drinking and preparing to eat and drink was not really sufficient occupation. I fidgeted to the point that Jamie at last suggested I come and copy ledger entries for him.

"Better do that than be gnawin' yourself," he said, looking critically at my bitten nails. "Beside, ye write a fairer hand than the warehouse clerks."

So it was that I was in the study, crouched industriously over the enormous ledger books, when Mr. Silas Hawkins came late one afternoon, with an order for two tuns of Flemish brandy. Mr. Hawkins was stout and prosperous; an émigré like Jared, he was an Englishman who specialized in the export of French brandies to his homeland.

I supposed that a merchant who looked like a teetotaler would find it rather difficult to sell people wines and spirits in quantity. Mr. Hawkins was fortunate in this regard, in that he had the permanently flushed cheeks and jolly smile of a reveler, though Jamie had told me that the man never tasted his own wares, and in fact seldom drank anything beyond rough ale, though his appetite for food was a legend in the taverns he visited. An expression of alert calculation lurked at the back of his bright brown eyes, behind the smooth bonhomie that oiled his transactions.

"My best suppliers, I do declare," he declared, signing a large order with a flourish. "Always dependable, always of the first quality. I shall miss your cousin sorely in his absence," he said, bowing to Jamie, "but he's done well in his choice of a substitute. Trust a Scotsman to keep the business in the family."

The small, bright eyes lingered on Jamie's kilt, the Fraser red of it bright against the dark wood paneling of the drawing room.

"Just over from Scotland recently?" Mr. Hawkins asked casually, feeling inside his coat.

"Nay, I've been in France for a time." Jamie smiled, turning the question away. He took the quill pen from Mr. Hawkins, but finding it too blunted for his taste, tossed it aside, pulling a fresh one from the bouquet of goose feathers that sprouted from a small glass jug on the sideboard.

"Ah. I see from your dress that you are a Highland Scot; I had thought perhaps you would be able to advise me as to the current sentiments prevailing in that part of the country. One hears such rumors, you know." Mr. Hawkins subsided into a chair at the wave of Jamie's hand, his round, rosy face apparently intent on the fat leather purse he had drawn from his pocket.

"As for rumors—well, that's the normal state of affairs in Scotland, no?" Jamie said, studiously sharpening the fresh quill. "But sentiments? Nay, if ye mean politics, I'm afraid I've little attention for such things myself." The small penknife made a sharp snicking sound as the horny slivers shaved off the thick stem of the quill.

Mr. Hawkins brought out several silver pieces from his purse, stacking them neatly in a tidy column between the two men.

" 'Strewth?" he said, almost absently. "If so, you're the first Highlander I've met who hadn't."

Jamie finished his sharpening and held the point of the quill up, squinting to judge its angle.

"Mm?" he said vaguely. "Aye, well, I've other matters that concern me; the running of a business such as this is time-consuming, as you'll know yourself, I imagine."

"So it is." Mr. Hawkins counted over the coins in his column once more and removed one, replacing it with two smaller ones. "I've heard that Charles Stuart has recently arrived in Paris," he said. His round tippler's face showed no more than mild interest, but the eyes were alert in their pockets of fat.

"Oh, aye," Jamie muttered, his tone of voice leaving it open whether this was acknowledgment of fact, or merely an expression of polite indifference. He had the order before him, and was signing each page with excessive care, crafting the letters rather than scribbling them, as was his usual habit.

A left-handed man forced as a boy to write right-handed, he always found letters difficult, but he seldom made such a fuss of it.

"You do not share your cousin's sympathies in that direction, then?" Hawkins sat back a little, watching the crown of Jamie's bent head, which was naturally rather noncommittal.

"Is that any concern of yours, sir?" Jamie raised his head, and fixed Mr. Hawkins with a mild blue stare. The plump merchant returned the look for a moment, then waved a podgy hand in airy dismissal.

"Not at all," he said smoothly. "Still, I am familiar with your cousin's Jacobite leanings—he makes no secret of them. I wondered only whether all Scots were of one mind on this matter of the Stuart pretensions to the throne."

"If you've had much to do wi' Highland Scots," Jamie said dryly, handing across a copy of the order, "then ye'll know that it's rare to find two of them in agreement on anything much beyond the color of the sky—and even that is open to question from time to time."

Mr. Hawkins laughed, his comfortable paunch shaking under his waistcoat, and tucked the folded paper away in his coat. Seeing that Jamie was not eager to have this line of inquiry pursued, I stepped in at this point with a hospitable offer of Madeira and biscuits.

Mr. Hawkins looked tempted for a moment, but then shook his head regretfully, pushing back his chair to rise.

"No, no, I thank you, milady, but no. The *Arabella* docks this Thursday, and I must be at Calais to meet her. And the devil of a lot there is to do before I set foot in the carriage to leave." He grimaced at a large sheaf of orders and receipts he had pulled from his pocket, added Jamie's receipt to the heap, and stuffed them back into a large leather traveling wallet.

"Still," he said, brightening, "I can do a bit of business on the way; I shall call in at the inns and public houses between here and Calais."

"If ye call in at *all* the taverns 'twixt here and the coast, you'll no reach Calais 'til next month," observed Jamie. He fished his own purse from his sporran and scooped the small column of silver into it.

"Too true, milord," Mr. Hawkins said, frowning ruefully.

"I suppose I must give one or two the miss, and catch them up on my way back."

"Surely you could send someone to Calais in your place, if your time is so valuable?" I suggested.

He rolled his eyes expressively, pursing his jolly little mouth into something as close to mournfulness as could be managed within the limitations of its shape.

"Would that I could, milady. But the shipment the *Arabella* carries is, alas, nothing I can consign to the good offices of a functionary. My niece Mary is aboard," he confided, "bound even as we speak for the French coast. She is but fifteen, and has never been away from her home before. I am afraid I could scarce leave her to find her way to Paris alone."

"I shouldn't think so," I agreed politely. The name seemed familiar, but I couldn't think why. Mary Hawkins. Undistinguished enough; I couldn't connect it with anything in particular. I was still musing over it when Jamie rose to see Mr. Hawkins to the door.

"I trust your niece's journey will be pleasant," he said politely. "Does she come for schooling, then? Or to visit relatives?"

"For marriage," said her uncle with satisfaction. "My brother has been fortunate in securing a most advantageous match for her, with a member of the French nobility." He seemed to expand with pride at this, the plain gold buttons straining the fabric of his waistcoat. "My elder brother is a baronet, you know."

"She's fifteen?" I said, uneasily. I knew that early marriages were not uncommon, but fifteen? Still, I had been married at nineteen—and again at twenty-seven. I knew the hell of a lot more at twenty-seven.

"Er, has your niece been acquainted with her fiancé for very long?" I asked cautiously.

"Never met him. In fact"—Mr. Hawkins leaned close, laying a finger next to his lips and lowering his voice—"she doesn't yet know about the marriage. The negotiations are not quite complete, you see."

I was appalled at this, and opened my mouth to say something, but Jamie clutched my elbow tightly in warning.

"Well, if the gentleman is of the nobility, perhaps we shall see your niece at Court, then," he suggested, shoving me firmly toward the door like the blade of a bulldozer. Mr. Hawkins, moving perforce to avoid my stepping on him, backed away, still talking.

"Indeed you may, milord Broch Tuarach. Indeed, I should deem it a great honor for yourself and your lady to meet my niece. I am sure she would derive great comfort from the society of a countrywoman," he added with a smarmy smile at me. "Not that I would presume upon what is merely a business acquaintance, to be sure."

The hell you wouldn't presume, I thought indignantly. You'd do anything you could to squeeze your family into the French nobility, including marrying your niece to . . . to . . .

"Er, who *is* your niece's fiancé?" I asked bluntly.

Mr. Hawkins's face grew cunning, and he leaned close enough to whisper hoarsely into my ear.

"I really should not say until the contracts have been signed, but seeing as it is your ladyship. . . . I can tell you that it is a member of the House of Gascogne. And a very high-ranking member indeed!"

"Indeed," I said.

Mr. Hawkins went off rubbing his hands together in a perfect frenzy of anticipation, and I turned at once to Jamie.

"Gascogne! He must mean . . . but he can't, can he? That revolting old beast with the snuff stains on his chin who came to dinner last week?"

"The Vicomte Marigny?" Jamie said, smiling at my description. "I suppose so; he's a widower, and the only single male of that house, so far as I know. I dinna think it's snuff, though; it's only the way his beard grows. A bit moth-eaten," he admitted, "but it's bound to be a hellish shave, wi' all those warts."

"He can't marry a fifteen-year-old girl to . . . to . . . *that*! And without even asking her!"

"Oh, I expect he can," Jamie said, with infuriating calmness. "In any case, Sassenach, it isna your affair." He took me firmly by both arms and gave me a little shake.

"D'ye hear me? I know it's strange to ye, but that's how matters are. After all"—the long mouth curled up at one corner—"you were made to wed against your will. Reconciled yourself to it yet, have ye?"

"Sometimes I wonder!" I yanked, trying to pull my arms free, but he merely gathered me in, laughing, and kissed me. After a moment, I gave up fighting. I relaxed into his embrace, admitting surrender, if only temporarily. I *would* meet with Mary Hawkins, I thought, and we'd see just what she thought about this proposed marriage. If she didn't want to see her name on a marriage contract, linked with the Vicomte Marigny, then . . . Suddenly I stiffened, pushing away from Jamie's embrace.

"What is it?" he looked alarmed. "Are ye ill, lass? You've gone all white!"

And little wonder if I had. For I had suddenly remembered where I had seen the name of Mary Hawkins. Jamie was wrong. This *was* my affair. For I had seen the name, written in a copperplate hand at the top of a genealogy chart, the ink old and faded by time to a sepia brown. Mary Hawkins was not meant to be the wife of the decrepit Vicomte Marigny. She was to marry Jonathan Randall, in the year of our Lord 1746.

"Well, she can't, can she?" Jamie said. "Jack Randall is dead." He finished pouring the glass of brandy, and held it out to me. His hand was steady on the crystal stem, but the line of his mouth was set and his voice clipped the word "dead," giving it a vicious finality.

"Put your feet up, Sassenach," he said. "You're still pale." At his motion, I obediently pulled up my feet and stretched out on the sofa. Jamie sat down near my head, and absently rested a hand on my shoulder. His fingers felt warm and strong, gently massaging the small hollow of the joint.

"Marcus MacRannoch told me he'd seen Randall trampled to death by cattle in the dungeons of Wentworth Prison," he said again, as though seeking to reassure himself by repetition. "A 'rag doll, rolled in blood.' That's what Sir Marcus said. He was verra sure about it."

"Yes." I sipped my brandy, feeling the warmth come back into my cheeks. "He told me that, too. No, you're right, Captain Randall is dead. It just gave me a turn, suddenly remembering about Mary Hawkins. Because of Frank." I glanced down at my left hand, resting on my stomach. There was a small fire burning on the hearth, and the light of it caught the smooth gold band of my first wedding ring. Jamie's ring, of Scottish silver, circled the fourth finger of my other hand.

"Ah." Jamie's touch on my shoulder stilled. His head was bent, but he glanced up to meet my gaze. We had not spoken of Frank since I had rescued Jamie from Wentworth, nor had Jonathan Randall's death been mentioned between us. At the time it had seemed of little importance, except insofar as it meant that no more danger menaced us from that direction. And since then, I had been reluctant to bring back any memory of Wentworth to Jamie.

"You know he is dead, do ye not, *mo nighean donn*?" Jamie spoke softly, his fingers resting on my wrist, and I knew he spoke of Frank, not Jonathan.

"Maybe not," I said, my eyes still fixed on the ring. I raised my hand, so the metal gleamed in the fading afternoon light. "If he's dead, Jamie—if he won't exist, because Jonathan is dead—then why do I still have the ring he gave me?"

He stared at the ring, and I saw a small muscle twitch near his mouth. His face was pale, too, I saw. I didn't know whether it would do him harm to think of Jonathan Randall now, but there seemed little choice.

"You're sure that Randall had no children before he died?" he asked. "That would be an answer."

"It would," I said, "but no, I'm sure not. Frank"—my voice trembled a bit on the name, and Jamie's grip on my wrist tightened—"Frank made quite a bit of the tragic circumstances of Jonathan Randall's death. He said that he—Jack Randall—had died at Culloden Field, in the last battle of the Rising, and his son—that would be Frank's six-times great-grandfather—was born a few months after his father's death. His widow married again, a few years later. Even if there were an illegitimate child, it wouldn't be in Frank's line of descent."

Jamie's forehead was creased, and a thin vertical line ran between his brows. "Could it be a mistake, then—that the child was not Randall's at all? Frank may come only of Mary Hawkins's line—for we know she still lives."

I shook my head helplessly.

"I don't see how. If you'd known Frank—but no, I suppose I've never told you. When I first met Jonathan Randall, I thought for the first moment that he *was* Frank—they weren't the same, of course, but the resemblance was . . . startling. No, Jack Randall was Frank's ancestor, all right."

"I see." Jamie's fingers had grown damp; he took them away and wiped them absently on his kilt.

"Then . . . perhaps the ring means nothing, *mo nighean donn*," he suggested gently.

"Perhaps not." I touched the metal, warm as my own flesh, then dropped my hand helplessly. "Oh, Jamie, I don't know! I don't know anything!"

He rubbed his knuckles tiredly on the crease between his eyes. "Neither do I, Sassenach." He dropped his hand and tried to smile at me.

"There's the one thing," he said. "You said that Frank told you Jonathan Randall would die at Culloden?"

"Yes. In fact, I told Jack Randall that myself, to scare him—at Wentworth, when he put me out in the snow, before . . . before going back to you." His eyes and mouth clamped shut in sudden spasm, and I swung my feet down, alarmed.

"Jamie! Are you all right?" I tried to put a hand on his head, but he pulled away from my touch, rising and going to the window.

"No. Yes. It's all right, Sassenach. I've been writing letters all the morning, and my head's fit to burst. Dinna worry yourself." He waved me away, pressing his forehead against the cold pane of the window, eyes tight closed. He went on speaking, as though to distract himself from the pain.

"Then, if you—and Frank—knew that Jack Randall would die at Culloden, but we know that he shall not . . . then it can be done, Claire."

"What can be done?" I hovered anxiously, wanting to help, but not knowing what to do. Clearly he didn't want to be touched.

"What you know will happen can be changed." He raised his head from the window and smiled tiredly at me. His face was still white, but the traces of that momentary spasm were gone. "Jack Randall died before he ought, and Mary Hawkins will wed another man. Even if that means that your Frank wilna be born—or perhaps will be born some other way," he added, to be comforting, "then it also means that we have a chance of succeeding in what we've set ourselves to do. Perhaps Jack Randall didna die at Culloden Field, because the battle there will never happen."

I could see him make the effort to stir himself, to come to me and put his arms around me. I held him about the waist, lightly, not moving. He bent his head, resting his forehead on my hair.

"I know it must grieve ye, *mo nighean donn.* But may it not ease ye, to know that good may come of it?"

"Yes," I whispered at last, into the folds of his shirt. I disengaged myself gently from his arms and laid my hand along his cheek. The line between his eyes was deeper, and his eyes slightly unfocused, but he smiled at me.

"Jamie," I said, "go and lie down. I'll send a note to the d'Arbanvilles, to say we can't come tonight."

"Och, no," he protested. "I'll be fine. I know this kind of headache, Sassenach; it's only from the writing, and an hour's sleep will cure it. I'll go up now." He turned toward the door, then hesitated and turned back, half-smiling.

"And if I should call out in my sleep, Sassenach, just lay your hand upon me, and say to me, 'Jack Randall's dead.' And it will aye be well wi' me."

Both food and company at the d'Arbanvilles were good. We came home late, and I fell into a sound sleep the instant my head hit the pillow. I slept dreamlessly, but waked suddenly in the middle of the night, knowing something was wrong.

The night was cold, and the down quilt had slithered off onto the floor, as was its sneaky habit, leaving only the thin woolen blanket over me. I rolled over, half-asleep, reaching for Jamie's warmth. He was gone.

I sat up in bed, looking for him, and saw him almost at once, sitting on the window seat, head in his hands.

"Jamie! What is it? Have you got a headache again?" I groped for the candle, meaning to find my medicine box, but something in the way he sat made me abandon the search and go to him at once.

He was breathing hard, as though he had been running, and cold as it was, his body was drenched with sweat. I touched his shoulder and found it hard and cold as a metal statue.

He jerked back at my touch and sprang to his feet, eyes seeming wide and black in the night-filled room.

"I didn't mean to startle you," I said. "Are you all right?"

I wondered briefly if he were sleepwalking, for his expression didn't change; he looked straight through me, and whatever he saw, he didn't like it.

"Jamie!" I said sharply. "Jamie, wake up!"

He blinked then, and saw me, though his expression stayed fixed in the desperate lines of a hunted beast.

"I'm all right," he said. "I'm awake." He spoke as though wanting to convince himself of the fact.

"What is it? Did you have a nightmare?"

"A dream. Aye. It was a dream."

I stepped forward and put a hand on his arm.

"Tell me. It will go away if you tell me about it."

He grasped me hard by the forearms, as much to keep me from touching him as for support. The moon was full, and I could see that every muscle of his body was tensed, hard and motionless as stone, but pulsing with furious energy, ready to explode into action.

"No," he said, still sounding dazed.

"Yes," I said. "Jamie, talk to me. Tell me. Tell me what you see."

"I canna . . . see anything. Nothing. I can't see."

I pulled, turning him from the shadows of the room to face the bright moonlight from the window. The light seemed to help, for his breathing slowed, and in halting, painful bits, the words came out.

It was the stones of Wentworth Prison that he dreamed of. And as he spoke, the shape of Jonathan Randall walked the room. And lay naked in my bed, atop the woolen blanket.

There had been the sound of hoarse breathing close behind him, and the feel of sweat-drenched skin, sliding against his own. He gritted his teeth in an agony of frustration. The man behind him sensed the small movement and laughed.

"Oh, we've some time yet before they hang you, my boy," he whispered. "Plenty of time to enjoy it." Randall moved suddenly, hard and abrupt, and he made a small involuntary sound.

Randall's hand stroked back the hair from his brow and smoothed it around his ear. The hot breath was close to his ear and he turned his head to escape, but it followed him, breathing words.

"Have you ever seen a man hanged, Fraser?" The words went on, not waiting for him to reply, and a long, slim hand came around his waist, gently stroking the slope of his belly, teasing its way lower with each word.

"Yes, of course you have; you were in France, you'll have seen deserters hanged now and then. A hanged man looses his bowels, doesn't he? As the rope tightens fast round his neck." The hand was gripping him, lightly, firmly, rubbing and stroking. He clenched his good hand tight around the edge of the bed and turned his face hard into the scratchy blanket, but the words pursued him.

"That will happen to you, Fraser. Just a few more hours, and you'll feel the noose." The voice laughed, pleased with itself. "You'll go to your death with your arse burning from my pleasure, and when you lose your bowels, it will be my spunk running down your legs and dripping on the ground below the gallows."

He made no sound. He could smell himself, crusted with filth from his imprisonment, acrid with the sweat of fear and anger. And the man behind him, the rank stench of the animal breaking through the delicate scent of the lavender toilet water.

"The blanket," he said. His eyes were closed, face strained in the moonlight. "It was rough under my face, and all I could see were the stones of the wall before me. There was nothing there to fix my mind to . . . nothing I could see. So I kept my eyes closed and thought of the blanket under my cheek. It was all I could feel besides the pain . . . and him. I . . . held to it."

"Jamie. Let me hold you." I spoke quietly, trying to calm the frenzy I could feel running through his blood. His grip on my arms was tight enough to numb them. But he wouldn't let me move closer; he held me away as surely as he clung to me.

Suddenly he freed me, jerking away and turning toward

the moon-filled window. He stood tense and quivering as a bowstring just fired, but his voice was calm.

"No. I willna use ye that way, lassie. Ye shallna be part of it."

I took a step toward him, but he stopped me with a quick motion. He turned his face back to the window, calm now, and blank as the glass he looked through.

"Get ye to bed, lassie. Leave me to myself a bit; I'll be well enough presently. There's naught to worry ye now."

He stretched his arms out, grasping the window frame, blotting out the light with his body. His shoulders swelled with effort, and I could tell that he was pushing against the wood with all his might.

"It was only a dream. Jack Randall is dead."

I had at length fallen asleep, with Jamie still poised at the window, staring out into the face of the moon. When I woke at dawn, though, he was asleep, curled in the window seat, wrapped in his plaid, with my cloak dragged over his legs for warmth.

He woke to my stirring, and seemed his normal, irritatingly cheerful morning self. But I was not likely to forget the happenings of the night, and went to my medicine box after breakfast.

To my annoyance, I lacked several of the herbs I needed for the sleeping tonic I had in mind. But then I remembered the man Marguerite had told me about. Raymond the herb-seller, in the Rue de Varenne. A wizard, she had said. A place worth seeing. Well, then. Jamie would be at the warehouse all the morning. I had a coach and a footman at my disposal; I would go and see it.

A clean wooden counter ran the length of the shop on both sides, with shelves twice the height of a man extending from floor to ceiling behind it. Some of the shelves were enclosed with folding glass doors, protecting the rarer and more expensive substances, I supposed. Fat gilded cupids sprawled abandonedly above the cupboards, tooting horns, waving their draperies, and generally looking as though they had been imbibing some of the more alcoholic wares of the shop.

"Monsieur Raymond?" I inquired politely of the young woman behind the counter.

"*Maître* Raymond," she corrected. She wiped a red nose inelegantly on her sleeve and gestured toward the end of the shop, where sinister clouds of a brownish smoke floated out over the transom of a half-door.

Wizard or not, Raymond had the right setting for it. Smoke drifted up from a black slate hearth to coil beneath the low black beams of the roof. Above the fire, a stone table pierced with holes held glass alembics, copper "pelicans"—metal cans with long noses from which sinister substances dripped into cups—and what appeared to be a small but serviceable still. I sniffed cautiously. Among the other strong odors in the shop, a heady alcoholic note was clearly distinguishable from the direction of the fire. A neat lineup of clean bottles along the sideboard reinforced my original suspicions. Whatever his trade in charms and potions, Master Raymond plainly did a roaring business in high-quality cherry brandy.

The distiller himself was crouched over the fire, poking errant bits of charcoal back into the grate. Hearing me come in, he straightened up and turned to greet me with a pleasant smile.

"How do you do?" I said politely to the top of his head. So strong was the impression that I had stepped into an enchanter's den that I would not have been surprised to hear a croak in reply.

For Master Raymond resembled nothing so much as a large, genial frog. A touch over four feet tall, barrel-chested and bandy-legged, he had the thick, clammy skin of a swamp dweller, and slightly bulbous, friendly black eyes. Aside from the minor fact that he wasn't green, all he lacked was warts.

"Madonna!" he said, beaming expansively. "What may I have the pleasure of doing for you?" He lacked teeth altogether, enhancing the froggy impression still more, and I stared at him in fascination.

"Madonna?" he said, peering up at me questioningly.

Snapped abruptly to a realization of how rudely I had been staring, I blushed and said without thinking, "I was just wondering whether you'd ever been kissed by a beautiful young girl."

I went still redder as he shouted with laughter. With a broad grin, he said "Many times, madonna. But alas, it does not help. As you see. *Ribbit.*"

We dissolved in helpless laughter, attracting the notice of the shopgirl, who peered over the half-door in alarm. Master Raymond waved her away, then hobbled to the window, coughing and clutching his sides, to open the leaded panes and allow some of the smoke to escape.

"Oh, that's better!" he said, inhaling deeply as the cold spring air rushed in. He turned to me, smoothing back the long silver hair that brushed his shoulders. "Now, madonna. Since we are friends, perhaps you will wait a moment while I attend to something?"

Still blushing, I agreed at once, and he turned to his firing shelf, still hiccupping with laughter as he refilled the canister of the still. Taking the opportunity to restore my poise, I strolled about the workroom, looking at the amazing array of clutter.

A fairly good-sized crocodile, presumably stuffed, hung from the ceiling. I gazed up at the yellow belly-scutes, hard and shiny as pressed wax.

"Real, is it?" I asked, taking a seat at the scarred oak table.

Master Raymond glanced upward, smiling.

"My *crocodile*? Oh, to be sure, madonna. Gives the customers confidence." He jerked his head toward the shelf that ran along the wall just above eye height. It was lined with white fired-porcelain jars, each ornamented with gilded curlicues, painted flowers and beasts, and a label, written in elaborate black script. Three of the jars closest to me were labeled in Latin, which I translated with some difficulty—crocodile's blood, and the liver and bile of the same beast, presumably the one swinging sinisterly overhead in the draft from the main shop.

I picked up one of the jars, removed the stopper and sniffed delicately.

"Mustard," I said, wrinkling my nose, "and thyme. In walnut oil, I think, but what did you use to make it nasty?" I tilted the jar, critically examining the sludgy black liquid within.

"Ah, so your nose is not purely decorative, madonna!" A wide grin split the toadlike face, revealing hard blue gums.

"The black stuff is the rotted pulp of a gourd," he confided, leaning closer and lowering his voice. "As for the smell . . . well, that actually *is* blood."

"Not from a crocodile," I said, glancing upward.

"Such cynicism in one so young," Raymond mourned. "The ladies and gentlemen of the Court are fortunately more trusting in nature, not that trust is the emotion that springs immediately to mind when one thinks of an aristocrat. No, in fact it is pig's blood, madonna. Pigs being so much more available than crocodiles."

"Mm, yes," I agreed. "That one must have cost you a pretty penny."

"Fortunately, I inherited it, along with much of my present stock, from the previous owner." I thought I saw a faint flicker of unease in the depths of the soft black eyes, but I had become oversensitive to nuances of expression of late, from watching the faces at parties for tiny clues that might be useful to Jamie in his manipulations.

The stocky little proprietor leaned still closer, laying a hand confidentially on mine.

"A professional, are you?" he said. "I must say, you don't look it."

My first impulse was to jerk my hand away, but his touch was oddly comfortable; quite impersonal, but unexpectedly warm and soothing. I glanced at the frost riming the edge of the leaded-glass panes, and thought that that was it; his ungloved hands were warm, a highly unusual condition for anyone's hands at this time of year.

"That depends entirely upon what you mean by the term 'professional,' " I said primly. "I'm a healer."

"Ah, a healer?" He tilted back in his chair, looking me over with interest. "Yes, I thought so. Anything else, though? No fortune-telling, no love philtres?"

I felt a twinge of conscience, recalling my days on the road with Murtagh, when we had sought Jamie through the Highlands of Scotland, telling fortunes and singing for our suppers like a couple of Gypsies.

"Nothing like that," I said, blushing only slightly.

"Not a professional liar, at any rate," he said, eyeing me

in amusement. "Rather a pity. Still, how may I have the pleasure of serving you, madonna?"

I explained my needs, and he nodded sagely as he listened, the thick gray hair swinging forward over his shoulders. He wore no wig within the sanctum of his shop, nor did
he powder his hair. It was brushed back from a high, wide
forehead, and fell straight as a stick to his shoulders, where it
ended abruptly, as though cut with a blunt pair of scissors.

He was easy to talk to, and very knowledgeable indeed
about the uses of herbs and botanicals. He took down small
jars of this and that, shaking bits out and crushing the leaves
in his palm for me to smell or taste.

Our conversation was interrupted by the sound of raised
voices in the shop. A nattily-dressed footman was leaning
across the counter, saying something to the shopgirl. Or
rather, trying to say something. His feeble attempts were being thrown back in his teeth by a gale of withering Provençale
from the other side of the counter. It was too idiomatic for
me to follow entirely, but I caught the general drift of her
remarks. Something involving cabbages and sausages, none of
it complimentary.

I was musing on the odd tendency of the French to bring
food into virtually any kind of discussion, when the shop door
banged suddenly open. Reinforcements swept in behind the
footman, in the guise of a rouged and flounced Personage of
some sort.

"Ah," murmured Raymond, peering interestedly beneath my arm at the drama unfolding in his shop. "La Vicomtesse de Rambeau."

"You know her?" The shopgirl evidently did, for she
abandoned her attack on the footman and shrank back
against the cabinet of purges.

"Yes, madonna," said Raymond, nodding. "She's rather
expensive."

I saw what he meant, as the lady in question picked up
the evident source of altercation, a small jar containing a
pickled plant of some kind, took aim, and flung it with considerable force and accuracy into the glass front of the cabinet.

The crash silenced the commotion at once. The Vicomtesse pointed one long, bony finger at the girl.

"You," she said, in a voice like metal shavings, "fetch me the black potion. At once."

The girl opened her mouth as though to protest, then, seeing the Vicomtesse reaching for another missile, shut it and fled for the back room.

Anticipating her entrance, Raymond reached resignedly above his head and thrust a bottle into her hand as she came through the door.

"Give it to her," he said, shrugging. "Before she breaks something else."

As the shopgirl timidly returned to deliver the bottle, he turned to me, pulling a wry face.

"Poison for a rival," he said. "Or at least she thinks so."

"Oh?" I said. "And what is it really? Bitter cascara?"

He looked at me in pleased surprise.

"You're very good at this," he said. "A natural talent, or were you taught? Well, no matter." He waved a broad palm, dismissing the matter. "Yes, that's right, cascara. The rival will fall sick tomorrow, suffer visibly in order to satisfy the Vicomtesse's desire for revenge and convince her that her purchase was a good one, and then she will recover, with no permanent harm done, and the Vicomtesse will attribute the recovery to the intervention of the priest or a counterspell done by a sorcerer employed by the victim."

"Mm," I said. "And the damage to your shop?" The late-afternoon sun glinted on the shards of glass on the counter, and on the single silver écu that the Vicomtesse had flung down in payment.

Raymond tilted a palm from side to side, in the immemorial custom of a man indicating equivocation.

"It evens out," he said calmly. "When she comes in next month for an abortifacient, I shall charge her enough not only to repair the damage but to build three new cases. And she'll pay without argument." He smiled briefly, but without the humor he had previously shown. "It's all in the timing, you know."

I was conscious of the black eyes flickering knowledgeably over my figure. I didn't show at all yet, but I was quite sure he knew.

"And does the medicine you'll give the Vicomtesse next month work?" I asked.

"It's all in the timing," he replied again, tilting his head quizzically to one side. "Early enough, and all is well. But it is dangerous to wait too long."

The note of warning in his voice was clear, and I smiled at him.

"Not for me," I said. "For reference only."

He relaxed again.

"Ah. I didn't think so."

A rumble from the street below proclaimed the passing of the Vicomtesse's blue-and-silver carriage. The footman waved and shouted from behind as pedestrians were forced to scramble for the shelter of doors and alleyways to avoid being crushed.

"A la lanterne," I murmured under my breath. It was rare that my unusual perspective on current affairs afforded me much satisfaction, but this was certainly one occasion when it did.

"Ask not for whom the tumbril calls," I remarked, turning to Raymond. "It calls for thee."

He looked mildly bewildered.

"Oh? Well, in any case, you were saying that black betony is what you use for purging? I would use the white, myself."

"Really? Why is that?"

And with no further reference to the recent Vicomtesse, we sat down to complete our business.

9

The Splendors of Versailles

I closed the door of the drawing room quietly behind me and stood still a moment, gathering courage. I essayed a restorative deep breath, but the tightness of the whalebone corseting made it come out as a strangled gasp.

Jamie, immersed in a handful of shipping orders, glanced up at the sound and froze, eyes wide. His mouth opened, but he made no sound.

"How do you like it?" Handling the train a bit gingerly, I stepped down into the room, swaying gently as the seamstress had instructed, to show off the filmy gussets of silk plissé let into the overskirt.

Jamie shut his mouth and blinked several times.

"It's . . . ah . . . red, isn't it?" he observed.

"Rather." *Sang-du-Christ,* to be exact. Christ's blood, the most fashionable color of the season, or so I had been given to understand.

"Not every woman could wear it, Madame," the seamstress had declared, speech unhampered by a mouthful of pins. "But you, with that skin! Mother of God, you'll have men crawling under your skirt all night!"

"If one tries, I'll stamp on his fingers," I said. That, after all, was not at all the intended effect. But I did mean to be visible. Jamie had urged me to have something made that would make me stand out in the crowd. Early-morning fog notwithstanding, the King had evidently remembered him from his appearance at the *lever,* and we had been invited to a ball at Versailles.

"I'll need to get the ears of the men with the money," Jamie had said, making plans with me earlier. "And as I've neither great position nor power myself, it will have to be managed by making them seek my company." He heaved a sigh, looking at me, decidedly unglamorous in my woolen bedgown.

"And I'm afraid in Paris that means we'll have to go out a bit in society; appear at Court, if it can be managed. They'll know I'm a Scot; it will be natural for folk to ask me about Prince Charles, and whether Scotland is eagerly awaiting the return of the Stuarts. Then I can assure them discreetly that most Scots would pay a good price *not* to have the Stuarts back again—though it goes against the grain a bit to say so."

"Yes, you'd better be discreet," I agreed. "Or the Bonnie Prince may set the dogs on you next time you go to visit." In accordance with his plan to keep abreast of Charles's activities, Jamie had been paying weekly duty calls on the small house at Montmartre.

Jamie smiled briefly. "Aye. Well, so far as His Highness, and the Jacobite supporters are concerned, I'm a loyal upholder of the Stuart cause. And so long as Charles Stuart is not received at Court and I am, the chances of his finding out what I'm saying there are not great. The Jacobites in Paris keep to themselves, as a rule. For the one thing, they haven't the money to appear in fashionable circles. But we have, thanks to Jared."

Jared had concurred—for entirely different reasons—in Jamie's proposal that we widen the scope of Jared's usual business entertaining, so that the French nobility and the heads of the wealthy banking families might beat a path to our door, there to be seduced and cozened with Rhenish wine, good talk, fine entertainment, and large quantities of the good Scotch whisky that Murtagh had spent the last two weeks shepherding across the Channel and overland to our cellars.

"It's entertainment of one kind or another that draws them, ye ken," Jamie had said, sketching out plans on the back of a broadsheet poem describing the scurrilous affair between the Comte de Sévigny and the wife of the Minister of Agriculture. "All the nobility care about is appearances. So to start with, we must offer them something interesting to look at."

Judging from the stunned look on his face now, I had made a good beginning. I sashayed a bit, making the huge overskirt swing like a bell.

"Not bad, is it?" I asked. "Very visible, at any rate."

He found his voice at last.

"Visible?" he croaked. "*Visible?* God, I can see every inch of ye, down to the third rib!"

I peered downward.

"No, you can't. That isn't me under the lace, it's a lining of white charmeuse."

"Aye well, it *looks* like you!" He came closer, bending to inspect the bodice of the dress. He peered into my cleavage.

"Christ, I can see down to your navel! Surely ye dinna mean to go out in public like that!"

I bristled a bit at this. I had been feeling a trifle nervous myself over the general revealingness of the dress, the fashionable sketches the seamstress had shown me notwithstanding. But Jamie's reaction was making me feel defensive, and thus rebellious.

"*You* told me to be visible," I reminded him. "And this is absolutely nothing, compared to the latest Court fashions. Believe me, I shall be modesty personified, in comparison with Madame de Pérignon and the Duchesse de Rouen." I put my hands on my hips and surveyed him coldly. "Or do you want me to appear at Court in my green velvet?"

Jamie averted his eyes from my décolletage and tightened his lips.

"Mphm," he said, looking as Scotch as possible.

Trying to be conciliatory, I came closer and laid a hand on his arm.

"Come now," I said. "You've been at Court before; surely you know what ladies dress like. You know this isn't terribly extreme by those standards."

He glanced down at me and smiled, a trifle shamefaced.

"Aye," he said. "Aye, that's true. It's only . . . well, you're my wife, Sassenach. I dinna want other men to look at you the way I've looked at those ladies."

I laughed and put my hands behind his neck, pulling him down to kiss me. He held me around the waist, his thumbs unconsciously stroking the softness of the red silk where it sheathed my torso. His touch traveled upward, sliding across the slipperiness of the fabric to the nape of my neck. His other hand grasped the soft roundness of my breast, swelling up above the tethering grip of the corsets, voluptuously free under a single layer of sheer silk. He let go at last and straightened up, shaking his head doubtfully.

"I suppose ye'll have to wear it, Sassenach, but for Christ's sake be careful."

"Careful? Of what?"

His mouth twisted in a rueful smile.

"Lord, woman, have ye no notion what ye look like in that gown? It makes me want to commit rape on the spot. And these damned frog-eaters havena got my restraint." He frowned slightly. "You couldna . . . cover it up at bit at the top?" He waved a large hand vaguely in the direction of his own lace jabot, secured with a ruby stickpin. "A . . . ruffle or something? A handkerchief?"

"Men," I told him, "have no notion of fashion. But not to worry. The seamstress says that's what the fan is for." I flipped the matching lace-trimmed fan open with a gesture that had taken fifteen minutes' practice to perfect, and fluttered it enticingly over my bosom.

Jamie blinked meditatively at this performance, then turned to take my cloak from the wardrobe.

"Do me the one favor, Sassenach," he said, draping the heavy velvet over my shoulders. "Take a larger fan."

In terms of attracting notice, the dress was an unqualified success. In terms of the effects on Jamie's blood pressure, it was somewhat more equivocal.

He hovered protectively at my elbow, glaring ferociously at any male who glanced in my direction, until Annalise de Marillac, spotting us from across the room, came floating in our direction, her delicate features wreathed in a welcoming smile. I felt the smile freezing on my own face. Annalise de Marillac was an "acquaintance"—he said—of Jamie's, from his former residence in Paris. She was also beautiful, charming, and exquisitely tiny.

"Mon petit sauvage!" she greeted Jamie. "I have someone you must meet. Several someones, in fact." She tilted a head like a china doll in the direction of a group of men, gathered around a chess table in the corner, arguing heatedly about something. I recognized the Duc d'Orléans, and Gérard Gobelin, a prominent banker. An influential group, then.

"Come and play chess with them," Annalise urged, placing a mothlike hand on Jamie's arm. "It will be a good place for His Majesty to meet you, later."

The King was expected to appear after the supper he was

attending, sometime in the next hour or two. In the meantime, the guests wandered to and fro, conversing, admiring
the paintings on the walls, flirting behind fans, consuming
confits, tartlets, and wine, and disappearing at more or less
discreet intervals into the odd little curtained alcoves. These
were cleverly fitted into the paneling of the rooms, so that
you scarcely noticed them, unless you got close enough to
hear the sounds inside.

Jamie hesitated, and Annalise pulled a bit harder.

"Come along," she urged. "Have no fear for your lady"
—she cast an appreciative glance at my gown—"she won't be
alone long."

"That's what I'm afraid of," Jamie muttered under his
breath. "All right, then, in a moment." He disengaged himself
momentarily from Annalise's grasp and bent to whisper in my
ear.

"If I find ye in one of those alcoves, Sassenach, the man
you're with is dead. And as for you . . ." His hands twitched
unconsciously in the direction of his swordbelt.

"Oh, no, you don't!" I said. "You swore on your dirk you'd
never beat me again. What price the Holy Iron, eh?"

A reluctant grin tugged at his mouth.

"No, I wilna beat ye, much as I'd like to."

"Good. What do you mean to do, then?" I asked, teasing.

"I'll think of something," he replied, with a certain grimness. "I dinna ken what, but ye wilna like it."

And with a final glare round and a proprietary squeeze
of my shoulder, he allowed Annalise to lead him away, like a
small but enthusiastic tug towing a reluctant barge.

Annalise was right. No longer deterred by Jamie's glowering presence, the gentlemen of the Court descended upon
me like a flock of parrots on a ripe passion fruit.

My hand was kissed repeatedly and held lingeringly, dozens of flowery compliments were paid me, and cups of spiced
wine were brought me in endless procession. After half an
hour of this, my feet began to hurt. So did my face, from
smiling. And my hand, from fan-wielding.

I had to admit some gratitude to Jamie for his intransigence in the matter of the fan. Bowing to his sensibilities, I
had brought the largest I possessed, a foot-long whopper

painted with what purported to be Scottish stags leaping through the heather. Jamie had been critical of the artistry, but approving of the size. Graciously fanning away the attentions of an ardent young man in purple, I then spread the thing inconspicuously beneath my chin to deflect crumbs while I nibbled at a piece of toast with salmon on it.

And not only toast crumbs. While Jamie, from his vantage point a foot above me, had claimed to be able to see my navel, my umbilicus was by and large safe from scrutiny by the French courtiers, most of whom were shorter than I was. On the other hand . . .

I had often enjoyed snuggling into Jamie's chest, my nose fitting comfortably into the small hollow in the center. A few of the shorter and bolder souls among my admirers seemed bent on enjoying a similar experience, and I was kept busy, flapping my fan hard enough to blow their curls back from their faces, or if that didn't suffice to discourage them, snapping the fan shut and rapping them smartly on the head with it.

It came as a considerable relief ᵼᴐ hear the footman at the door suddenly draw himself up and intone, *"Sa Majesté, Le Roi Louis!"*

While the King might rise at dawn, apparently he blossomed at night. Not much taller than my own five feet six, Louis entered with the carriage of a much taller man, glancing left and right, nodding in gracious acknowledgment of his bowing subjects.

Now this, I thought, looking him over, was a good deal more in line with my ideas of what a king *ought* to look like. Not particularly handsome, he acted as though he were; an impression enhanced not only by the richness of his clothes, but by the attitude of those around him. He wore the latest backswept wig, and his coat was cut velvet, embroidered all over with hundreds of frivolous silk butterflies. It was cut away at the middle to display a waistcoat of voluptuous cream-colored silk with diamond buttons, matching the wide, butterfly-shaped buckles on his shoes.

The dark, hooded eyes swept restlessly over the crowd, and the haughty Bourbon nose lifted as though smelling out any item of interest.

Dressed in kilt and plaid, but with a coat and waistcoat

of stiffened yellow silk, and with his flaming hair loose to his
shoulders, a single small braid down one side in ancient Scots
fashion, Jamie definitely qualified. At least I thought it was
Jamie who had attracted the King's attention, as *Le Roi Louis*
purposefully changed direction and swerved toward us, parting the crowd before him like the waves of the Red Sea.
Madame Nesle de La Tourelle, whom I recognized from a
previous party, followed close behind him like a dinghy in his
wake.

I had forgotten the red dress; His Majesty halted directly
in front of me and bowed extravagantly, hand over his waist.
"Chère Madame!" he said. "We are enchanted!"

I heard a deep intake of breath from Jamie, and then he
stepped forward and bowed to the King.

"May I present my wife, Your Majesty—my lady Broch
Tuarach." He rose and stepped back. Attracted by a quick
flutter of Jamie's fingers, I stared at him for a moment of
incomprehension, before suddenly realizing that he was signaling me to curtsy.

I dipped automatically, struggling to keep my eyes on the
floor and wondering where I would look when I bobbed up
again. Madame Nesle de la Tourelle was standing just behind
Louis, watching the introduction with a slightly bored look on
her face. Gossip said that "Nesle" was Louis's current favorite. She was, in current vogue, wearing a gown cut *below* both
breasts, with a bit of supercedent gauze which was clearly
meant for the sake of fashion, as it couldn't possibly function
for either warmth or concealment.

It was neither the gown nor the prospect it revealed that
had rattled me, though. The breasts of "Nesle," while reasonably adequate in size, pleasant in proportion, and tipped with
large brownish areolae, were further adorned with a pair of
nipple jewels that caused their settings to recede into insignificance. A pair of diamond-encrusted swans with ruby eyes
stretched their necks toward each other, swinging precariously in their gold-hooped perches. The workmanship was
superb and the materials stunning, but it was the fact that
each gold hoop passed *through* her nipple that made me feel
rather faint. The nipples themselves were rather seriously in-
verted, but this fact was disguised by the large pearl that cov-

ered each one, dangling on a thin gold chain that looped from side to side of the main hoop.

I rose, red-faced and coughing, and managed to excuse myself, hacking politely into a handkerchief as I backed away. I felt a presence in my rear and stopped just in time to avoid backing into Jamie, who was watching the King's mistress with no pretense whatever of tactful obliviousness.

"She told Marie d'Arbanville that Master Raymond did the piercing for her," I remarked under my breath. His fascinated gaze didn't waver.

"Shall I make an appointment?" I asked. "I imagine he'd do it for me if I gave him the recipe for caraway tonic."

Jamie glanced down at me at last. Taking my elbow, he steered me toward a refreshment alcove.

"If you so much as *speak* to Master Raymond again," he said, out of the corner of his mouth, "I'll pierce them for ye myself—wi' my teeth."

The King had by now wandered off toward the Salon of Apollo, the space left by his passage quickly filled by others coming from the supper room. Seeing Jamie distracted into conversation with a Monsieur Genet, head of a wealthy shipping family, I looked surreptitiously about for a place in which to remove my shoes for a moment.

One of the alcoves was at hand and, from the sounds of it, unoccupied. I sent a lingering admirer off to fetch some more wine, then, with a quick glance round, slid into the alcove.

It was furnished rather suggestively with a couch, a small table, and a pair of chairs—more suitable for laying aside garments than for sitting upon, I thought critically. I sat down nonetheless, pried my shoes off, and with a sigh of relief, propped my feet up on the other chair.

A faint jingling of curtain rings behind me announced the fact that my departure had not been unnoticed after all.

"Madame! At last we are alone!"

"Yes, more's the pity," I said, sighing. It was one of the countless Comtes, I thought. Or no, this one was a Vicomte; someone had introduced him to me earlier as the Vicomte de Rambeau. One of the short ones. I seemed to recall his beady little eyes gleaming up at me in appreciation from below the edge of my fan.

Wasting no time, he slid adroitly onto the other chair, lifting my feet into his lap. He clasped my silk-stockinged toes fervently against his crotch.

"Ah, *ma petite*! Such delicacy! Your beauty distracts me!"

I thought it must, if he was under the delusion that my feet were particularly delicate. Raising one to his lips, he nibbled at my toes.

"*C'est un cochon qui vit dans la ville, c'est un cochon qui vit . . .*"

I jerked my foot from his grasp and stood up hastily, rather impeded by my voluminous petticoats.

"Speaking of *cochons* who live in the city," I said, rather nervously, "I don't think my husband would be at all pleased to find you here."

"Your husband? Pah!" He dismissed Jamie with an airy wave of the hand. "He will be occupied for some time, I am sure. And while the cat's away . . . come to me, *ma petite souris*; let me hear you squeak a bit."

Presumably intending to fortify himself for the fray, the Vicomte produced an enameled snuffbox from his pocket, deftly sprinkled a line of dark grains along the back of his hand, and wiped it delicately against his nostrils.

He took a deep breath, eyes glistening in anticipation, then jerked his head as the curtain was suddenly thrust aside with a jangling of brass rings. His aim distracted by the intrusion, the Vicomte sneezed directly into my bosom with considerable vigor.

I shrieked.

"You *disgusting* man!" I said, and walloped him across the face with my closed fan.

The Vicomte staggered back, eyes watering. He tripped over my size-nine shoes, which lay on the floor, and fell headfirst into the arms of Jamie, who was standing in the doorway.

~

"Well, you *did* attract a certain amount of notice," I said at last.

"Bah," he said. "The *salaud*'s lucky I didna tear off his head and make him swallow it."

"Well, that would have provided an interesting spectacle," I agreed dryly. "Sousing him in the fountain was nearly as good, though."

He looked up, his frown replaced with a reluctant grin. "Aye, well. I didna drown the man, after all."

"I trust the Vicomte appreciates your restraint."

He snorted again. He was standing in the center of a sitting room, part of a small *appartement* in the palace, to which the King, once he had stopped laughing, had assigned us, insisting that we should not undertake the return journey to Paris tonight.

"After all, *mon chevalier,*" he had said, eyeing Jamie's large, dripping form on the terrace, "we should dislike exceedingly for you to take a chill. I feel sure that the Court would be deprived of a great deal of entertainment in such a case, and Madame would never forgive me. Would you, sweetheart?" He reached out and pinched Madame de La Tourelle playfully on one nipple.

His mistress looked mildly annoyed, but smiled obediently. I noticed, though, that once the King's attention had been distracted, it was Jamie on whom her gaze lingered. Well, he was impressive, I had to admit, standing dripping in the torchlight with his clothes plastered to his body. That didn't mean I liked her doing it.

He peeled his wet shirt off and dropped it in a sodden heap. He looked even better without it.

"As for you," he said, eyeing me in a sinister manner, "did I not tell ye to stay away from those alcoves?"

"Yes. But aside from that, Mrs. Lincoln, how did you enjoy the play?" I asked politely.

"What?" He stared at me as though I had lost my mind on the spot.

"Never mind; it's a bit out of your frame of reference. I only meant, did you meet anyone useful before you came to defend your marital rights?"

He rubbed his hair vigorously with a towel plucked from the washstand. "Oh, aye. I played a game of chess with Monsieur Duverney. Beat him, too, and made him angry."

"Oh, that sounds promising. And who's Monsieur Duverney?"

He tossed me the towel, grinning. "The French Minister of Finance, Sassenach."

"Oh. And you're pleased because you made him angry?"

"He was angry at himself for losing, Sassenach," Jamie explained. "Now he won't rest until he's beaten me. He's coming round to the house on Sunday to play again."

"Oh, well done!" I said. "And in the process, you can assure him that the Stuarts' prospects are exceedingly dim, and convince him that Louis doesn't want to assist them financially, blood kin or not."

He nodded, combing back his wet hair with both hands. The fire had not yet been lit, and he shivered slightly.

"Where did you learn to play chess?" I asked curiously. "I didn't know you knew how."

"Colum MacKenzie taught me," he said. "When I was sixteen, and spent a year at Castle Leoch. I had tutors for French and German and mathematics and such, but I'd go up to Colum's room for an hour every evening to play chess. Not that it usually took him an hour to beat me," he added ruefully.

"No wonder you're good," I said. Jamie's uncle Colum, the victim of a deforming disease that had deprived him of most of his mobility, made up for it with a mind that would have put Machiavelli to shame.

Jamie stood up and unbuckled his swordbelt, narrowing his eyes at me. "Dinna think I don't know what you're up to, Sassenach. Changing the subject and flattering me like a courtesan. Did I not tell ye about those alcoves?"

"You said you didn't mean to beat me," I reminded him, sitting a bit farther back in my chair, just to be on the safe side.

He snorted again, tossing the swordbelt onto the chest of drawers and dropping his kilt next to the sodden shirt.

"Do I look the sort of man would beat a woman who's with child?" he demanded.

I eyed him doubtfully. Stark naked, with his hair in damp red snarls and the white scars still visible on his body, he looked as though he had just leaped off a Viking ship, rape and pillage on his mind.

"Actually, you look capable of just about anything," I told him. "As for the alcoves, yes, you told me. I suppose I should have gone outside to take my shoes off, but how was I to know that idiot would follow me in and begin nibbling on my toes? And if you don't mean to beat me, just what did you have in mind?" I took a firm grip on the arms of my chair.

He lay down on the bed and grinned at me.

"Take off that whore's dress, Sassenach, and come to bed."

"Why?"

"Well, I canna wallop you, or drench ye in the fountain." He shrugged. "I meant to give ye a terrible scolding, but I dinna think I can keep my eyes open long enough." He gave a terrific yawn, then blinked and grinned at me again. "Remind me to do it in the morning, eh?"

"Better, is it?" Jamie's dark-blue eyes were clouded with worry. "Is it right for ye to be sick so much, Sassenach?"

I pushed the hair back from my sweaty temples and dabbed a damp towel over my face.

"I don't know whether it's *right*," I said weakly, "but at least I believe it's normal. Some women are sick all through." Not a pleasant thought at the moment.

Jamie glanced, not at the gaily painted clock on the table, but as usual, out the window at the sun.

"Do ye feel well enough to go down to breakfast, Sassenach, or ought I to tell the chambermaid to bring up something on a tray?"

"No. I'm quite all right now." And I was. In the odd way of morning sickness, once the inexorable nausea had had its way with me, I felt perfectly fine within a moment or two. "Let me just rinse my mouth."

As I bent over the basin, sluicing cool water over my face, there was a rap at the door of the *appartement*. Likely the servant who had been dispatched to the house in Paris to bring us fresh clothes, I thought.

To my surprise, though, it was a courtier, with a written invitation to lunch.

"His Majesty is dining today with an English nobleman," the courtier explained, "newly arrived in Paris. His Majesty has summoned several of the prominent English merchants from the Cité to lunch, for the purpose of providing His Grace the Duke with the company of some of his countrymen. And someone pointed out to His Majesty that Madame your wife is an English lady, too, and thus should be invited to attend."

"All right," Jamie said, after a quick glance at me. "You may tell His Majesty that we will be honored to remain."

Soon thereafter, Murtagh had arrived, dour as ever, bearing a large bundle of fresh clothes, and my medicine box, which I had asked for. Jamie took him into the sitting room to give him instructions for the day, while I hastily struggled into my fresh gown, for the first time rather regretting my refusal to employ a lady's maid. Always unruly, the state of my hair had not been improved by sleeping in close embrace with a large, damp Scot; wild tangles shot off in several directions, resisting all attempts to tame them with brush and comb.

At length I emerged, pink and cross with effort, but with my hair in some semblance of order. Jamie looked at me and murmured something about hedgehogs under his breath, but caught a searing glance in return and had the good sense to shut up.

A stroll among the parterres and fountains of the palace gardens did a good bit to restore my equanimity. Most of the trees were still leafless, but the day was unexpectedly warm for late March, and the smell of the swelling buds on the twigs was green and pungent. You could almost feel the sap rising in the towering chestnuts and poplars that edged the paths and sheltered the hundreds of white marble statues.

I paused beside a statue of a half-draped man with grapes in his hair and a flute at his lips. A large, silky goat nibbled hungrily at more grapes that were cascading from the marble folds of the draperies.

"Who's this?" I asked, "Pan?"

Jamie shook his head, smiling. He was dressed in his old kilt and a worn, if comfortable coat, but he looked much better to me than did the luxuriously clad courtiers who passed us in chattering groups.

"No, I think there is a statue of Pan about, but it isna that one. That's one of the Four Humors of Man."

"Well, he looks fairly humorous," I said, glancing up at the goat's smiling friend.

Jamie laughed.

"And you a physician, Sassenach! Not that sort of humor. Do ye not know the four humors that make up the human body? That one's Blood"—he motioned at the flute-player, then pointed down the path—"and there's Melancholy." This was a tall man in a sort of toga, holding an open book.

Jamie pointed across the path. "And over there is Choler"—a nude and muscular young man, who certainly was scowling ferociously, without regard to the marble lion that was about to bite him smartly in the leg—"and that's Phlegm."

"Is it, by Jove?" Phlegm, a bearded gent with a folded hat, had both arms crossed on his chest, and a tortoise at his feet.

"Hum," I remarked.

"Do physicians not learn about humors in your time?" Jamie asked curiously.

"No," I said. "We have germs, instead."

"Really? Germs," he said to himself, trying the word over, rolling it on his tongue with a Scottish burr, which made it sound sinister in the extreme. "Gerrrms. And what do germs look like?"

I glanced up at a representation of "America," a nubile young maiden in a feathered skirt and headdress, with a croc-odile at her feet.

"Well, they wouldn't make nearly such picturesque statues," I said.

The crocodile at America's feet reminded me of Master Raymond's shop.

"Did you mean it about not wanting me to go to Master Raymond's?" I asked. "Or do you just not want me to pierce my nipples?"

"I most definitely dinna want ye to pierce your nipples," he said firmly, taking me by the elbow and hurrying me onward, lest I derive any untoward inspiration from America's bare breasts. "But no, I dinna want ye to go to Master Raymond's, either. There are rumors about the man."

"There are rumors about everyone in Paris," I observed, "and I'd be willing to bet that Master Raymond knows all of them."

Jamie nodded, hair glinting in the pale spring sunshine. "Oh, aye, I expect so. But I think I can learn what's needful in the taverns and drawing rooms. Master Raymond's said to be at the center of a particular circle, but it isna Jacobite sympathizers."

"Really? Who, then?"

"Cabalists and occultists. Witches, maybe."

"Jamie, you aren't seriously worried about witches and demons, are you?"

We had arrived at the part of the gardens known as the "Green Carpet." This early in the spring, the green of the huge lawn was only a faint tinge, but people were lounging on it, taking advantage of the rare balmy day.

"Not witches, no," he said at last, finding a place near a hedge of forsythia and sitting down on the grass. "The Comte St. Germain, possibly."

I remembered the look in the Comte St. Germain's dark eyes at Le Havre, and shivered, in spite of the sunshine and the woolen shawl I wore.

"You think he's associated with Master Raymond?"

Jamie shrugged. "I don't know. But it was you told me the rumors about St. Germain, no? And if Master Raymond is part of that circle—then I think you should keep the hell away from him, Sassenach." He gave me a wry half-smile. "After all, I'd as soon not have to save ye from burning again."

The shadows under the trees reminded me of the cold gloom of the thieves' hole in Cranesmuir, and I shivered and moved closer to Jamie, farther into the sunlight.

"I'd as soon you didn't, either."

The pigeons were courting on the grass below a flowering forsythia bush. The ladies and gentlemen of the Court were performing similar activities on the paths that led through the sculpture gardens. The major difference was that the pigeons were quieter about it.

A vision in watered aqua silk hove abaft our resting place, in loud raptures over the divinity of the play the night before. The three ladies with him, while not so spectacular, echoed his opinions faithfully.

"Superb! Quite superb, the voice of La Couelle!"

"Oh, superb! Yes, wonderful!"

"Delightful, delightful! Superb is the only word for it!"

"Oh, yes, superb!"

The voices—all four of them—were shrill as nails being pulled from wood. By contrast, the gentleman pigeon doing his turn a few feet from my nose had a low and mellifluous coo, rising from a deep, amatory rumble to a breathy whistle as he puffed his breast and bowed repeatedly, laying his heart at the feet of his ladylove, who looked rather unimpressed so far.

I looked beyond the pigeon toward the aqua-satined courtier, who had hastened back to snatch up a lace-trimmed handkerchief, coyly dropped as bait by one of his erstwhile companions.

"The ladies call that one 'L'Andouille,' " I remarked. "I wonder why?"

Jamie grunted sleepily, and opened one eye to look after the departing courtier.

"Mm? Oh, 'The Sausage.' It means he canna keep his roger in his breeches. You know the sort . . . ladies, footmen, courtesans, pageboys. Lapdogs, too, if rumor is right," he added, squinting in the direction of the vanished aqua silk, where a lady of the Court was now approaching, a fluffy white bundle clasped protectively to her ample bosom. "Reckless, that. I wouldna risk mine anywhere near one o' those wee yapping hairballs."

"Your roger?" I said, amused. "I used to hear it called peter, now and again. And the Yanks, for some peculiar reason, used to call theirs a dick. I once called a patient who was teasing me a 'Clever Dick,' and he nearly burst his stitches laughing."

Jamie laughed himself, stretching luxuriously in the warming spring sun. He blinked once or twice and rolled over, grinning at me upside down.

"You have much the same effect on me, Sassenach," he said. I stroked back the hair from his forehead, kissing him between the eyes.

"Why do men call it names?" I asked. "John Thomas, I mean. Or Roger, for that matter. Women don't do that."

"They don't?" Jamie asked, interested.

"No, of course not. I'd as soon call my nose Jane."

His chest moved up and down as he laughed. I rolled on top of him, enjoying the solid feel of him beneath me. I pressed my hips downward, but the layers of intervening petticoats rendered it more of a gesture than anything else.

"Well," Jamie said logically, "yours doesna go up and down by itself, after all, nor go carryin' on regardless of your own wishes in the matter. So far as I know, anyway," he added, cocking one eyebrow questioningly.

"No, it doesn't, thank God. I wonder if Frenchmen call theirs 'Pierre,' " I said, glancing at a passing dandy in green velvet-faced moiré.

Jamie burst into a laugh that startled the pigeons out of the forsythia bush. They flapped off in a ruffle of indignation, scattering wisps of gray down in their wake. The fluffy white lapdog, hitherto content to loll in its mistress's arms like a bundle of rags, awoke at once to an awareness of its responsibilities. It popped out of its warm nest like a Ping-Pong ball and galloped off in enthusiastic pursuit of the pigeons, barking dementedly, its mistress in similar cry behind it.

"I dinna ken, Sassenach," he said, recovering enough to wipe the tears from his eyes. "The only Frenchman I ever heard call it a name called his 'Georges.' "

"Georges!" I said, loudly enough to attract the attention of a small knot of passing courtiers. One, a short but vivacious specimen in dramatic black slashed with white satin, stopped alongside and bowed deeply, sweeping the ground at my feet with his hat. One eye was still swelled shut, and a livid welt showed across the bridge of his nose, but his style was unimpaired.

"À votre service, Madame," he said.

I might have managed if it weren't for the bloody nightingales. The dining salon was hot and crowded with courtiers and onlookers, one of the stays in my dress frame had come loose and was stabbing me viciously beneath the left kidney each time I drew breath, and I was suffering from that most ubiquitous plague of pregnancy, the urge to urinate every few minutes. Still, I might have managed. It was, after all, a serious breach of manners to leave the table before the King, even though luncheon was a casual affair, in comparison with the formal dinners customary at Versailles—or so I was given to understand. "Casual," however, is a relative term.

True, there were only three varieties of spiced pickle, not eight. And one soup, clear, not thick. The venison was merely roasted, not presented *en brochette,* and the fish, while tastily poached in wine, was served fileted, not whole and riding on a sea of aspic filled with shrimp.

As though frustrated by so much rustic simplicity, though, one of the chefs had provided a charming hors d'oeuvre—a nest, cunningly built from strips of pastry, ornamented with real sprigs of flowering apple, on the edge of which perched two nightingales, skinned and roasted, stuffed with apple and cinnamon, then redressed in their feathers. And in the nest was the entire family of baby birds, tiny stubs of outstretched wings brown and crispy, tender bare skins glazed with honey, blackened mouths agape to show the merest hint of the almond-paste stuffing within.

After a triumphal tour of the table to show it off—to the accompaniment of murmurs of admiration all round—the dainty dish was set before the King, who turned from his conversation with Madame de La Tourelle long enough to pluck one of the nestlings from its place and pop it into his mouth.

Crunch, crunch, crunch went Louis's teeth. Mesmerized, I watched the muscles of his throat ripple, and felt the rubble of small bones slide down my own gullet. Brown fingers reached casually for another baby.

At this point, I concluded that there were probably worse things than insulting His Majesty by leaving the table, and bolted.

Rising from my knees amid the shrubbery a few minutes later, I heard a sound behind me. Expecting to meet the eye of a justifiably irate gardener, I turned guiltily to meet the eye of an irate husband.

"Damn it, Claire, d'ye have to do this all the time?" he demanded.

"In a word—yes," I said, sinking exhaustedly onto the rim of an ornamental fountain. My hands were damp, and I smoothed them over my skirt. "Did you think I did it for fun?" I felt light-headed, and closed my eyes, trying to regain my internal balance before I fell into the fountain.

Suddenly there was a hand at the small of my back, and I

half-leaned, half-fell into his arms as he sat beside me and gathered me in.

"Oh, God. I'm sorry, *mo nighean donn.* Are ye all right, Claire?"

I pushed away enough to look up at him and smile.

"I'm all right. Just a bit light-headed, is all." I reached up and tried to smooth away the deep line of concern on his forehead. He smiled back, but the line stayed, a thin vertical crease between the thick sandy curves of his eyebrows. He swished a hand in the fountain and smoothed it over my cheeks. I must have looked rather pale.

"I'm sorry," I added. "Really, Jamie, I couldn't help it."

His damp hand squeezed the back of my neck reassuringly, strong and steady. A fine spray of droplets from the mouth of a bug-eyed dolphin misted my hair.

"Och, dinna mind me, Sassenach. I didna mean to snap at ye. It's only . . ." He made a helpless gesture with one hand. ". . . only that I feel such a thick-heided clot. I see ye in a misery, and I know I've done it to ye, and there isna the slightest thing I can do to aid you. So I blame ye for it instead, and act cross and growl at your . . . why do ye no just tell me to go to the devil, Sassenach?" he burst out.

I laughed until my sides hurt under the tight corseting, holding on to his arm.

"Go to hell, Jamie," I said at last, wiping my eyes. "Go directly to hell. Do not pass Go. Do not collect two hundred dollars. There. Do you feel better now?"

"Aye, I do," he said, his expression lightening. "When ye start to talk daft, I know you're all right. Do *you* feel better, Sassenach?"

"Yes," I said, sitting up and beginning to take notice of my surroundings. The grounds of Versailles were open to the public, and small groups of merchants and laborers mingled oddly with the brightly colored nobles, all enjoying the good weather.

Suddenly the nearby door onto the terrace burst open, spilling the King's guests out into the garden in a tide of chatter. The exodus from luncheon had been augmented by a new deputation, apparently just decanted from the two large coaches I could see driving past the edge of the garden toward distant stables.

It was a large group of people, men and women, soberly clad by comparison with the bright colors of the courtiers around them. It was the sound of them, though, rather than the appearance, that had caught my attention. French, spoken by a number of people at a distance, strongly resembles the quacking conversation of ducks and geese, with its nasal elements. English, on the other hand, has a slower pace, and much less rise and fall in its intonations. Spoken at a distance where individual voices are impossible to distinguish, it has the gruff, friendly monotony of a sheepdog's barking. And the general effect of the mass exodus presently coming in our direction was of a gaggle of geese being driven to market by a pack of dogs.

The English party had arrived, somewhat belatedly. No doubt they were being tactfully shooed into the garden while the kitchen staff hastily prepared another dinner and reset the massive table for them.

I scanned the group curiously. The Duke of Sandringham I knew, of course, having met him once before in Scotland at Castle Leoch. His barrel-chested figure was easy to pick out, walking side by side with Louis, modish wig tilted in polite attention.

Most of the other people were strangers, though I thought the stylish lady of middle age just coming through the doors must be the Duchess of Claymore, whom I had heard was expected. The Queen, normally left behind at some country house to amuse herself as best she could, had been trotted out for the occasion. She was talking to the visitor, her sweet, anxious face flushed with the unaccustomed excitement of the occasion.

The young girl just behind the Duchess caught my eye. Quite plainly dressed, she had the sort of beauty that would make her stand out in any crowd. She was small, fine-boned but nicely rounded in figure, with dark, shiny, unpowdered hair and the most extraordinary white skin, flushed across the cheeks with a clear deep pink that made her look exactly like a flower petal.

Her coloring reminded me of a dress I'd once had in my own time, a light cotton frock decorated with red poppies. The thought for some reason struck me with a sudden unexpected wave of homesickness, and I gripped the edge of the marble bench, eyelids prickling with longing. It must be hearing plain bluff English spoken, I thought, after so many months among the lilt of Scotland and the quacking of France. The visitors sounded like home.

Then I saw him. I could feel all of the blood draining from my head as my eye traced disbelievingly over the elegant curve of the skull, dark-haired and bold amid the powdered wigs around it. Alarms rang in my head like air-raid sirens, as I fought to accept and repel the impressions that assaulted me. My subconscious saw the line of the nose, thought "Frank," and turned my body to fly toward him in welcome. "Not-Frank," came the slightly higher, rational center of my brain, freezing me in my tracks as I saw the familiar curve of a half-smiling mouth, repeating, "You *know* it's not Frank," as the muscles of my calves knotted. And then the lurch into panic and the clenching of hands and stomach, as the slower processes of logical thought came doggedly on the trail of instinct and knowledge, seeing the high brow and the arrogant tilt of the head, assuring me of the unthinkable. It could not be Frank. And if it were not, then it could only be . . .

"Jack Randall." It wasn't my voice that spoke, but Jamie's, sounding oddly calm and detached. Attention attracted by my peculiar behavior, he had looked where I was looking, and had seen what I had seen.

He didn't move. So far as I could tell through the increasing haze of panic, he didn't breathe. I was dimly aware of a nearby servant peering curiously upward at the towering form of the frozen Scottish warrior next to me, silent as a statue of Mars. But all my concern was for Jamie.

He was entirely still. Still as a lion is still, part of the grass of the plain, its stare hot and unblinking as the sun that burns the veldt. And I saw something move in the depths of his eyes. The telltale twitch of the stalking cat, the tiny jerk of the tuft at the end of the tail, precursor to carnage.

To draw arms in the presence of the King was death. Murtagh was on the far side of the garden, much too far away to help. Two more paces would bring Randall within hearing distance. Within sword's reach. I laid a hand on his arm. It was rigid as the steel of the swordhilt under his hand. The blood roared in my ears.

"Jamie," I said. "Jamie!" And fainted.

10

A Lady, with Brown Hair Curling Luxuriantly

I swam up out of a flickering yellow haze composed of sunlight, dust, and fragmented memories, feeling completely disoriented.

Frank was leaning over me, face creased in concern. He was holding my hand, except that he wasn't. The hand I held was much larger than Frank's, and my fingers brushed the wiriness of coarse hairs on the wrist. Frank's hands were smooth as a girl's.

"Are you all right?" The voice was Frank's, low and cultured.

"Claire!" That voice, deeper and rougher, wasn't Frank's at all. Neither was it cultured. It was full of fright and anguish.

"Jamie." I found the name at last to match the mental image for which I had been seeking. "Jamie! Don't . . ." I sat bolt upright, staring wildly from one face to the other. I was surrounded by a circle of curious faces, courtiers two and three deep around me, with a small clear space left for His Majesty, who was leaning over, peering down at me with an expression of sympathetic interest.

Two men knelt in the dust beside me. Jamie on the right, eyes wide and face pale as the hawthorn blossoms above him. And on my left . . .

"Are you all right, Madame?" The light hazel eyes held only respectful concern, the fine dark brows arched over them in inquiry. It wasn't Frank, of course. Neither was it Jonathan Randall. This man was younger than the Captain by a good ten years, perhaps close to my own age, his face pale and unlined by exposure to weather. His lips had the same chiseled lines, but lacked the marks of ruthlessness that bracketed the Captain's mouth.

"You. . . ." I croaked, leaning away from him. "You're . . ."

"Alexander Randall, Esquire, Madame," he answered quickly, making an abortive gesture toward his head, as though to doff a hat he wasn't wearing. "I don't believe we have met?" he said, with a hint of doubt.

"I, er, that is, no, we haven't," I said, sagging back against Jamie's arm. The arm was steady as an iron railing, but the hand holding mine was trembling, and I pulled our clasped hands into the fold of my skirt to hide it.

"Rather an informal introduction, Mrs., er, no . . . it's Lady Broch Tuarach, is it not?" The high, piping voice pulled my attention back above me, to the flushed, cherubic countenance of the Duke of Sandringham peering interestedly over the shoulders of the Comte de Sévigny and the Duc d'Orléans. He pushed his ungainly body through the narrow opening afforded, and extended a hand to help me to my feet. Still holding my sweaty palm in his own, he bowed in the direction of Alexander Randall, Esquire, who was frowning in a puzzled sort of way.

"Mr. Randall is in my employ as secretary, Lady Broch Tuarach. Holy Orders is a noble calling, but unfortunately nobility of purpose does not pay the cobbler's bill, does it, Alex?" The young man flushed slightly at this barb, but he inclined his head civilly toward me, acknowledging his employer's introduction. Only then did I notice the sober dark suit and high white stock that marked him as a junior cleric of some sort.

"His Grace is correct, my lady. And that being so, I must hold his offer of employment in the deepest gratitude." A faint tightening of the lips at this speech seemed to indicate that the gratitude felt might not perhaps go so deep as all that, pleasant words notwithstanding. I glanced at the Duke, to find his small blue eyes creased against the sun, his expression blandly impenetrable.

This little tableau was broken by a clap of the King's hands summoning two footmen, who, at Louis's direction, grasped me by both arms and lifted me forcibly into a sedan chair, despite my protests.

"Certainly not, Madame," he said, graciously dismissing both protests and thanks. "Go home and rest; we do not wish you to be indisposed for the ball tomorrow, *non*?" His large brown eyes twinkled at me as he raised my hand to his lips.

Not taking his eyes from my face, he bowed formally toward Jamie, who had gathered his wits sufficiently to be making a gracious speech of thanks, and said, "I shall perhaps accept your thanks, my lord, in the form of your permission to request a dance from your lovely wife."

Jamie's lips tightened at this, but he bowed in return and said, "My wife shares my honor at your attention, Your Majesty." He glanced in my direction. "If she is well enough to attend the ball tomorrow evening, I am sure she will look forward to dancing with Your Majesty." He turned without waiting for formal dismissal, and jerked his head toward the chair-bearers.

"Home," he said.

Home at last after a hot, jolting ride through streets that smelled of flowers and open sewers, I shed my heavy dress and its uncomfortable frame in favor of a silk dressing gown.

I found Jamie sitting by the empty hearth, eyes closed, hands on his knees as though thinking. He was pale as his linen shirt, glimmering in the shadow of the mantelpiece like a ghost.

"Holy Mother," he muttered, shaking his head. "Dear God and saints, so close. I came within a hairsbreadth of murdering that man. Do ye realize, Claire, if ye hadna fainted . . . Jesus, *I meant to kill him,* with every last morsel of will I had." He broke off, shuddering again with reaction.

"Here, you'd better put your feet up," I urged, tugging at a heavy carved footstool.

"No, I'm all right now," he said, waving it away. "He's . . . Jack Randall's brother, then?"

"I should think it likely in the extreme," I said dryly. "He could scarcely be anyone else, after all."

"Mm. Did ye know he worked for Sandringham?"

I shook my head. "I didn't—don't—know anything about him other than his name and the fact that he's a curate. F-Frank wasn't particularly interested in him, as he wasn't a direct ancestor of his." The slight quaver of my voice as I spoke Frank's name gave me away.

Jamie put down the flask and came toward me. Stooping purposefully, he picked me up and cradled me against his

chest. The smell of the gardens of Versailles rose sharp and
fresh from the folds of his shirt. He kissed the top of my head
and turned toward the bed.

"Come lay your head, Claire," he said quietly. "It's been
a long day for us both."

I had been afraid that the encounter with Alexander
Randall would set Jamie dreaming again. It did not happen
often, but now and again, I would feel him wake beside me,
body tensed in sudden battle. He would lurch out of bed then,
and spend the night by the window as though it offered escape, refusing any form of solace or interference. And by the
morning, Jack Randall and the other demons of the dark
hours had been forced back into their box, battened down
and held fast by the steel bands of Jamie's will, and all was
well again.

But Jamie fell asleep quickly, and the stresses of the day
had already fled from his face, leaving it peaceful and smooth
by the time I put out the candle.

It was bliss to lie unmoving, with the warmth growing
about my cold limbs, the myriad small aches of back and neck
and knees fading into the softness of oncoming sleep. But my
mind, released from watchfulness, replayed a thousand times
that scene outside the palace—a quick glimpse of a dark head
and a high brow, close-set ears and a fine-edged jaw—that
first harsh flash of mistaken recognition, which struck my
heart with a blow of joy and anguish. Frank, I had thought.
Frank. And it was Frank's face I saw as I sank into sleep.

The lecture room was one of those at London University; ancient timbered ceiling and modern floors, lino scuffed
by restless feet. The seats were the old smooth benches; new
desks were saved for the science lectures. History could make
do with sixty-year-old scarred wood; after all, the subject was
fixed and would not change—why should its accommodation?

"Objects of *vertu*," Frank's voice said, "and objects of
use." His long fingers touched the rim of a silver candlestick,
and the sun from the window sparked from the metal, as
though his touch were electric.

The objects, all borrowed from the collections of the
British Museum, were lined up along the edge of the table,

close enough for the students in the front row to see the tiny cracks in the yellowed ivory of the French counter-box, and the stains of tobacco smoked long ago that browned the edges of the white clay pipe. An English gold-mounted scent bottle, a gilt-bronze inkstand with gadrooned lid, a cracked horn spoon, and a small marble clock topped with two swans drinking.

And behind the row of objects, a row of painted miniatures, laid flat on the table, features obscured by the light reflecting off their surfaces.

Frank's dark head bent over the objects, absorbed. The afternoon sun picked up a stray reddish gleam in his hair. He lifted the clay pipe, cupped one-handed like an eggshell.

"For some periods of history," he said, "we have history itself; the written testimony of the people who lived then. For others, we have only the objects of the period, to show us how men lived."

He put the pipe to his mouth and pursed his lips around the stem, puffing out his cheeks, brows raised comically. There was a muffled giggle from the audience, and he smiled and laid the pipe down.

"The art, and the objects of *vertu*"—he waved a hand over the glittering array—"these are what we most often see, the decorations of a society. And why not?" He picked an intelligent-looking brown-haired boy to address. An accomplished lecturer's trick; pick one member of the audience to talk to as though you were alone with him. A moment later, shift to another. And everyone in the room will feel the focus of your remarks.

"These are pretty things, after all." A finger's touch set the swans on the clock revolving, curved necks stately in two-fold procession. "Worth preserving. But who'd bother keeping an old, patched tea cozy, or a worn-out automobile-tire?" A pretty blonde in glasses this time, who smiled and tittered briefly in response.

"But it's the useful objects, the things that aren't noted in documents, which are used and broken and discarded without a second thought, that tell you how the common man lived. The numbers of these pipes, for example, tell us something about the frequency and types of tobacco use among the classes of society, from high"—a finger tap on the lid of the enameled snuffbox—"to low." The finger moved to stroke the long, straight pipestem with affectionate familiarity.

Now a middle-aged woman, scribbling frantically to catch every word, hardly aware of the singular regard upon her. The lines creased beside smiling hazel eyes.

"You needn't take down *everything*, Miss Smith," he chided. "It's an hour's lecture, after all—your pencil will never last."

The woman blushed and dropped her pencil, but smiled shyly in answer to the friendly grin on Frank's lean, dark face. He had them now, everyone warmed by the glow of good humor, attention attracted by the small flashes of gilt and glitter. Now they would follow him without flagging or complaint, along the path of logic and into the thickets of discussion. A certain tenseness left his neck as he felt the students' attention settle and fix on him.

"The best witness to history is the man—or woman"—a nod to the pretty blonde—"who's lived it, right?" He smiled and picked up the cracked horn spoon. "Well, perhaps. After all, it's human nature to put the best face on things when you know someone will read what you've written. People tend to concentrate on the things they think important, and often enough, they tidy it up a bit for public consumption. It's rare to find a Pepys who records with equal interest the details of a Royal procession, and the number of times each night that he's obliged to use his chamber pot."

The laugh this time was general, and he relaxed, leaning casually back against the table, gesturing with the spoon.

"Similarly, the lovely objects, the artful artifacts, are the ones most often preserved. But the chamber pots and the spoons and the cheap clay pipes can tell us as much or more about the people who used them.

"And what about those people? We think of historical persons as something different than ourselves, sometimes halfway mythological. But someone played games with this" —the slender index finger stroked the counter-box—"a lady used this"—nudged the scent bottle—"dabbing scent behind her ears, on her wrists . . . where else do you ladies dab scent?" Lifting his head suddenly, he smiled at the plump blond girl in the front row, who blushed, giggled, and touched herself demurely just above the V of her blouse.

"Ah, yes. Just there. Well, so did the lady who owned this."

Still smiling at the girl, he unstoppered the scent bottle and passed it gently under his nose.

"What is it, Professor? Arpège?" Not so shy, this student; dark-haired, like Frank, with gray eyes that held more than a hint of flirtation.

He closed his eyes and inhaled deeply, nostrils flaring over the mouth of the bottle.

"No. It's L'Heure Bleue. My favorite."

He turned back to the table, hair falling over his brow in concentration as his hand hovered over the row of miniatures.

"And then there's a special class of objects—portraits. A bit of art, and at the same time, as much as we can see of the people themselves. But how real are they to us?"

He lifted a tiny oval and turned it to face the class, reading from the small gummed label affixed to its back.

"A Lady, by Nathaniel Plimer, signed with initials and dated 1786, with curled brown hair piled high, wearing a pink dress and a ruffle-collared chemise, cloud and sky background." He held up a square beside it.

"A Gentleman, by Horace Hone, signed with monogram and dated 1780, with powdered hair *en queue,* wearing a brown coat, blue waistcoat, lawn jabot, and an Order, possibly the Most Honorable Order of the Bath."

The miniature showed a round-faced man, mouth rosily pursed in the formal pose of eighteenth-century portraits.

"The artists we know," he said, laying the portrait down. "They signed their work, or they left clues to their identity in the techniques and the subjects they used. But the people they painted? We see them, and yet we know nothing of them. The strange hairstyles, the odd clothes—they don't seem people that you'd know, do they? And the way so many artists painted them, the faces are all alike; pudding-faced and pale, most of them, and not a lot more you can say about them. Here and there, one stands out. . . ." Hand hovering over the row, he selected another oval.

"A Gentleman . . ."

He held up the miniature, and Jamie's blue eyes blazed out under the fiery thatch of his hair, combed for once, braided and ribboned into an unaccustomed formal order. The knife-edged nose was bold above the lace of his stock, and the long mouth seemed about to speak, half-curled at one corner.

"But they *were* real people," Frank's voice insisted. "They did much the same things you do—give or take a few small details like going to the pictures or driving down the motorway"—there were appreciative titters among the class —"but they cared about their children, they loved their husbands or wives . . . well, sometimes they did . . ." More laughter.

"A Lady," he said softly, cradling the last of the portraits in his palm, shielding it for the moment. "With brown hair curling luxuriantly to her shoulders, and a necklace of pearls. Undated. The artist unknown."

It was a mirror, not a miniature. My cheeks were flushed, and my lips trembled as Frank's finger gently traced the edge of my jaw, the graceful line of my neck. The tears welled in my eyes and spilled down my cheeks as I heard his voice, still lecturing, as he laid down the miniature, and I stared upward at the timbered ceiling.

"Undated. Unknown. But once . . . once, she was real."

I was having trouble breathing, and thought at first that I was being smothered by the glass over the miniature. But the material pressing on my nose was soft and damp, and I twisted my head away and came awake, feeling the linen pillow wet with tears beneath my cheek. Jamie's hand was large and warm on my shoulder, gently shaking me.

"Hush, lassie. Hush! You're but dreaming—I'm here."

I turned my face into the warmth of his naked shoulder, feeling the tears slick between cheek and skin. I clung tightly to his solidness, and the small night sounds of the Paris house came slowly to my ears, bringing me back to the life that was mine.

"I'm sorry," I whispered. "I was dreaming about . . . about . . ."

He patted my back, and reached under the pillow for a handkerchief.

"I know. Ye were calling his name." He sounded resigned.

I laid my head back on his shoulder. He smelled warm and rumpled, his own sleepy scent blending with the smell of the down-filled quilt and the clean linen sheets.

"I'm sorry," I said again.

He snorted briefly, not quite a laugh.

"Well, I'll no say I'm not wicked jealous of the man," he said ruefully, "because I am. But I can hardly grudge him your dreams. Or your tears." His finger gently traced the wet track down one cheek, then blotted it with the handkerchief.

"You don't?"

His smile in the dimness was lopsided.

"No. Ye loved him. I canna hold it against either of you that ye mourn him. And it gives me some comfort to know . . ." He hesitated, and I reached up to smooth the rumpled hair off his face.

"To know what?"

"That should the need come, you might mourn for me that way," he said softly.

I pressed my face fiercely into his chest, so my words were muffled.

"I *won't* mourn you, because I won't have to. I won't lose you, I won't!" A thought struck me, and I looked up at him, the faint roughness of his beard stubble a shadow on his face.

"You aren't afraid I would go back, are you? You don't think that because I . . . think of Frank. . . ."

"No." His voice was quick and soft, a response fast as the possessive tightening of his arms around me.

"No," he said again, more softly. "We are bound, you and I, and nothing on this earth shall part me from you." One large hand rose to stroke my hair. "D'ye mind the blood vow that I swore ye when we wed?"

"Yes, I think so. 'Blood of my blood, bone of my bone . . .'"

"I give ye my body, that we may be one," he finished. "Aye, and I have kept that vow, Sassenach, and so have you." He turned me slightly, and one hand cupped itself gently over the tiny swell of my stomach.

"Blood of my blood," he whispered, "and bone of my bone. You carry me within ye, Claire, and ye canna leave me now, no matter what happens. You are mine, always, if ye will it or no, if ye want me or nay. Mine, and I wilna let ye go."

I put a hand over his, pressing it against me.

"No," I said softly, "nor can you leave me."

"No," he said, half-smiling. "For I have kept the last of the vow as well." He clasped both hands about me, and bowed his head on my shoulder, so I could feel the warm breath of the words upon my ear, whispered to the dark.

"For I give ye my spirit, 'til our life shall be done."

Useful Occupations

"Who is that peculiar little man?" I asked Jamie curiously. The man in question was making his way slowly through the groups of guests gathered in the main salon of the de Rohans' house. He would pause a moment, scanning the group with a critical eye, then either shrug a bony shoulder and pass on, or suddenly step in close to a man or woman, hold something to their face and issue some sort of command. Whatever he was doing, his actions appeared to be the occasion of considerable hilarity.

Before Jamie could answer, the man, a small, wizened specimen in gray serge, spotted us, and his face lit up. He swooped down on Jamie like a tiny bird of prey suddenly descending upon a large and startled rabbit.

"Sing," he commanded.

"Eh?" Jamie blinked down at the little figure in astonishment.

"I said 'Sing,' " answered the man, patiently. He prodded Jamie admiringly in the chest. "With a resonating cavity like that, you should have a wonderful volume."

"Oh, he has volume," I said, amused. "You can hear him across three squares of the city when he's roused."

Jamie shot me a dirty look. The little man was circling him, measuring the breadth of his back and tapping on him like a woodpecker sampling a prime tree.

"I can't sing," he protested.

"Nonsense, nonsense. Of course you can. A nice, deep baritone, too," the little man murmured approvingly. "Excellent. Just what we need. Here, a bit of help for you. Try to match this tone."

Deftly whipping a small tuning fork from his pocket, he struck it smartly against a pillar and held it next to Jamie's left ear.

Jamie rolled his eyes heavenward, but shrugged and obligingly sang a note. The little man jerked back as though he'd been shot.

"No," he said disbelievingly.

"I'm afraid so," I said sympathetically. "He's right, you know. He really *can't* sing."

The little man squinted accusingly at Jamie, then struck his fork once more and held it out invitingly.

"Once more," he coaxed. "Just listen to it, and let the same sound come out."

Patient as ever, Jamie listened carefully to the "A" of the fork, and sang again, producing a sound wedged somewhere in the crack between E-flat and D-sharp.

"Not possible," said the little man, looking thoroughly disillusioned. "No one could be that dissonant, even on purpose."

"*I* can," said Jamie cheerfully, and bowed politely to the little man. We had by now begun to collect a small crowd of interested onlookers. Louise de Rohan was a great hostess, and her salons attracted the cream of Parisian society.

"Yes, he can," I assured our visitor. "He's tone-deaf, you see."

"Yes, I do see," the little man said, looking thoroughly depressed. Then he began to eye me speculatively.

"Not me!" I said, laughing.

"You surely aren't tone-deaf as well, Madame?" Eyes glittering like a snake slithering toward a paralyzed bird, the little man began to move toward me, tuning fork twitching like the flicking tongue of a viper.

"Wait a minute," I said, holding out a repressive hand. "Just who *are* you?"

"This is Herr Johannes Gerstmann, Sassenach." Looking amused, Jamie bowed again to the little man. "The King's singing-master. May I present you to my wife, Lady Broch Tuarach, Herr Gerstmann?" Trust Jamie to know every last member of the Court, no matter how insignificant.

Johannes Gerstmann. Well, that accounted for the faint accent I had detected under the formality of Court French. German, I wondered, or Austrian?

"I am assembling a small impromptu chorus," the little singing-master explained. "The voices need not be trained, but they must be strong and true." He cast a glance of disillusionment at Jamie, who merely grinned in response. He took the tuning fork from Herr Gerstmann and held it inquiringly in my direction.

"Oh, all right," I said, and sang.

Whatever he heard appeared to encourage Herr Gerstmann, for he put away the tuning fork and peered at me interestedly. His wig was a trifle too big, and tended to slide forward when he nodded. He did so now, then pushed the wig carelessly back, and said "Excellent tone, Madame! Really very nice, very nice indeed. Are you acquainted perhaps with 'Le Papillon'?" He hummed a few bars.

"Well, I've heard it at least," I replied cautiously. "Um, the melody, I mean; I don't know the words."

"Ah! No difficulty, Madame. The chorus is simplicity; like this . . ."

My arm trapped in the singing-master's grip, I found myself being ineluctably drawn away toward the sound of harpsichord music in a distant room, Herr Gerstmann humming in my ear like a demented bumblebee.

I cast a helpless glance back at Jamie, who merely grinned and raised his cup of sorbet in a farewell salute before turning to take up a conversation with Monsieur Duverney the younger, the son of the Minister of Finance.

The Rohans' house—if you could use a mere word like "house" in description of such a place—was alight with lanterns strung through the back garden and edging the terrace. As Herr Gerstmann towed me through the corridors, I could see servants hurrying in and out of the supper rooms, laying linen and silver for the dining that would take place later. Most "salons" were small, intimate affairs, but the Princesse Louise de La Tour de Rohan was an expansive personality.

I had met the Princesse a week before, at another evening party, and had found her something of a surprise. Plump and rather plain, she had a round face with a small round chin, pale lashless blue eyes, and a star-shaped false beauty mark that did very little to fulfill its function in life. So this was the lady who enticed Prince Charles into ignoring the dictates of propriety? I thought, curtsying in the receiving line.

Still, she had an air of lively animation about her that was quite attractive, and a lovely soft pink mouth. Her mouth was the most animated part of her, in fact.

"But I am charmed!" she had exclaimed, grabbing my hand as I was presented to her. "How wonderful to meet you at last! My husband and my father have both sung the praises of milord Broch Tuarach unendingly, but of his delightful wife they have said nothing. I am enchanted beyond measure by your coming, my dear, sweet lady—must I really say Broch Tuarach, or won't it do if I only say Lady Tuarach? I'm not sure I could remember all of it, but one word, surely, even if such a strange-sounding word—is it Scottish? How enchanting!"

In fact, Broch Tuarach meant "the north-facing tower," but if she wanted to call me "Lady North-facing," it was all right with me. In the event, she quickly gave up trying to remember "Tuarach," and had since called me only *"ma chère Claire."*

Louise herself was with the group of singers in the music room, fluttering plumply from one to another, talking and laughing. When she saw me, she dashed across the room as fast as her draperies would allow, her plain face alight with animation.

"Ma chère Claire!" she exclaimed, ruthlessly commandeering me from Herr Gerstmann. "You are just in time! Come, you must talk to this silly English child for me."

The "silly English child" was in fact very young; a girl of not more than fifteen, with dark, shiny ringlets, and cheeks flushed so hotly with embarrassment that she reminded me of a brilliant poppy. In fact, it was the cheeks that recalled her to me; the girl I had glimpsed in the garden at Versailles, just before the unsettling appearance of Alexander Randall.

"Madame Fraser is English, too," Louise was explaining to the girl. "She will soon make you feel at home. She's shy," Louise explained, turning to me without pausing to draw breath. "Talk to her; persuade her to sing with us. She has a delightful voice, I am assured. There, *mes enfants,* enjoy yourselves!" And with a pat of benediction, she was off to the other side of the room, exclaiming, cajoling, marveling at a new arrival's gown, pausing to fondle the overweight youth who sat at the harpsichord, twisting ringlets of his hair around her finger as she chattered to the Duc di Castellotti.

"Makes you rather tired just to watch her, doesn't it?" I said in English, smiling at the girl. A tiny smile appeared on her own lips and she bobbed her head briefly, but didn't speak. I thought this must all be rather overwhelming; Louise's parties tended to make my own head spin, and the little poppy girl could scarcely be out of the schoolroom.

"I'm Claire Fraser," I said, "but Louise didn't remember to tell me your name." I paused invitingly, but she didn't reply. Her face got redder and redder, lips pressed tight together, and her fists clenched at her sides. I was a trifle alarmed at her appearance, but she finally summoned the will to speak. She took a deep breath, and raised her chin like one about to mount the scaffold.

"M-m-my name is . . . M-M-M," she began, and at once I understood her silence and her painful shyness. She closed her eyes, biting her lip savagely, then opened her eyes and gamely had another try. "M-M-Mary Hawkins," she managed at last. "I d-d-don't sing," she added defiantly.

If I had found her interesting before, I was fascinated now. So this was Silas Hawkins's niece, the baronet's daughter, the intended fiancée of the Vicomte Marigny! It seemed a considerable weight of male expectation for such a young girl to bear. I glanced around to see whether the Vicomte was in evidence, and was relieved to find that he wasn't.

"Don't worry about it," I said, stepping in front of her, to shield her from the waves of people now filling the music room. "You needn't talk if you don't want to. Though perhaps you should try to sing," I said, struck by a thought. "I knew a physician once who specialized in the treatment of stammering; he said that people who stammer don't do it when they sing."

Mary Hawkins's eyes grew wide with astonishment at this. I looked around and saw a nearby alcove, curtained to hide a cozy bench.

"Here," I said, taking her by the hand. "You can sit in here, so you don't have to talk to people. If you want to sing, you can come out when we start; if not, just stay in here 'til the party's over." She stared at me for a minute, then gave me a sudden blinding smile of gratitude, and ducked into the alcove.

I loitered outside, to prevent any nosy servants from disturbing her hiding place, chatting with passersby.

"How lovely you look tonight, *ma chère!*" It was Ma-

dame de Ramage, one of the Queen's ladies. An older, dignified woman, she had come to supper in the Rue Trémoulins
once or twice. She embraced me warmly, then looked around
to be sure that we were unobserved.

"I had hoped to see you here, my dear," she said, leaning
a bit closer and lowering her voice. "I wished to advise you to
take care concerning the Comte St. Germain."

Half-turning in the direction of her gaze, I saw the lean-
faced man from the docks of Le Havre, entering the music
room with a younger, elegantly dressed woman on his arm.
He hadn't seen me, apparently, and I hastily turned back to
Madame de Ramage.

"What . . . has he . . . I mean . . ." I could feel myself flushing still more deeply, rattled by the appearance of
the saturnine Comte.

"Well, yes, he has been heard to speak of you," Madame
de Ramage said, kindly helping me out of my confusion. "I
gather that there was some small difficulty in Le Havre?"

"Something of the kind," I said. "All I did was to recognize a case of smallpox, but it resulted in the destruction of
his ship, and . . . he wasn't pleased about it," I concluded
weakly.

"Ah, so that was it." Madame de Ramage looked
pleased. I imagined having the inside story, so to speak,
would give her an advantage in the trade of gossip and information that was the commerce of Parisian social life.

"He has been going about telling people that he believes
you to be a witch," she said, smiling and waving at a friend
across the room. "A fine story! Oh, no one believes it," she
assured me. "Everyone knows that if anyone is mixed up in
such matters, it is Monsieur le Comte himself."

"Really?" I wanted to ask just what she meant by this,
but just then Herr Gerstmann bustled up, clapping his hands
as though shooing a flock of hens.

"Come, come, mesdames!" he said. "We are all complete; the singing commences!"

As the chorale hastily assembled near the harpsichord, I
looked back toward the alcove where I had left Mary Hawkins. I thought I saw the curtain twitch, but wasn't sure. And
as the music began, and the joined voices rose, I thought I

heard a clear, high soprano from the direction of the alcove—
but again, I wasn't sure.

"Verra nice, Sassenach," Jamie said when I rejoined him,
flushed and breathless, after the singing. He grinned down at
me and patted my shoulder.

"How would you know?" I said, accepting a glass of
wine-punch from a passing servant. "You can't tell one song
from another."

"Well, ye were loud, anyway," he said, unperturbed. "I
could hear every word." I felt him stiffen slightly beside me,
and turned to see what—or whom—he was looking at.

The woman who had just entered was tiny, scarcely as
high as Jamie's lowest rib, with hands and feet like a doll's,
and brows delicate as Chinese tracery, over eyes the deep
black of sloes. She advanced with a step that mocked its own
lightness, so she looked as though she were dancing just
above the ground.

"There's Annalise de Marillac," I said, admiring her.
"Doesn't she look lovely?"

"Oh, aye." Something in his voice made me glance
sharply upward. A faint pink tinged the tips of his ears.

"And here I thought you spent your years in France
fighting, not making romantic conquests," I said tartly.

To my surprise, he laughed at this. Catching the sound,
the woman turned toward us. A brilliant smile lit her face as
she saw Jamie looming among the crowd. She turned as
though to come in our direction, but was distracted by a gentleman, wigged and resplendent in lavender satin, who laid an
importuning hand on her fragile arm. She flicked her fan
charmingly at Jamie in a gesture of regretful coquetry before
devoting her attention to her new companion.

"What's so funny?" I asked, seeing him still grinning
broadly after the lady's gently oscillating lace skirts.

He snapped suddenly back to an awareness of my presence, and smiled down at me.

"Oh, nothing, Sassenach. Only what ye said about fighting. I fought my first duel—well, the only one, in fact—over
Annalise de Marillac. When I was eighteen."

His tone was mildly dreamy, watching the sleek, dark

head bob away through the crowd, surrounded wherever it
went by white clusters of wigs and powdered hair, with here
and there a fashionably pink-tinged peruke for variety.

"A duel? With whom?" I asked, glancing around warily
for any male attachments to the China doll who might feel
inclined to follow up an old quarrel.

"Och, he isna here," Jamie said, catching and correctly
interpreting my glance. "He's dead."

"You *killed* him?" Agitated, I spoke rather louder than
intended. As a few nearby heads turned curiously in our direction, Jamie took me by the elbow and steered me hastily
toward the nearest French doors.

"Mind your voice, Sassenach," he said, mildly enough.
"No, I didna kill him. Wanted to," he added ruefully, "but
didn't. He died two years ago, of the morbid sore throat.
Jared told me."

He guided me down one of the garden paths, lit by lan-
tern-bearing servants, who stood like bollards at five-yard intervals from the terrace to the fountain at the bottom of the
path. In the midst of a big reflecting pool, four dolphins
sprayed sheets of water over an annoyed-looking Triton in the
center, who brandished a trident rather ineffectually at them.

"Well, don't keep me in suspense," I urged as we passed
out of hearing of the groups on the terrace. "What happened?"

"All right, then," he said, resigned. "Well, ye will have
observed that Annalise is rather pretty?"

"Oh, really? Well, perhaps, now that you mention it, I
can see something of the kind," I answered sweetly, provoking a sudden sharp look, followed by a lopsided smile.

"Aye. Well, I wasna the only young gallant in Paris to be
of the same opinion, nor the only one to lose his head over
her, either. Went about in a daze, tripping over my feet.
Waited in the street, in hopes of seeing her come out of her
house to the carriage. Forgot to eat, even; Jared said my coat
hung on me like a scarecrow's, and the state of my hair didna
much help the resemblance." His hand went absently to his
head, patting the immaculate queue that lay clubbed tight
against his neck, bound with blue ribbon.

"Forgot to eat? Christ, you *did* have it bad," I remarked.
He chuckled. "Oh, aye. And still worse when she began

to flirt wi' Charles Gauloise. Mind ye," he added fairly, "she flirted with everyone—that was all right—but she chose him for her supper partner ower-often for my taste, and danced with him too much at the parties, and . . . well, the long and the short of it, Sassenach, is that I caught him kissing her in the moonlight on her father's terrace one night, and challenged him."

By this time, we had reached the fountain in our promenade. Jamie drew to a stop and we sat on the rim of the fountain, upwind of the spray from the puff-lipped dolphins. Jamie drew a hand through the dark water and lifted it dripping, abstractedly watching the silver drops run down his fingers.

"Dueling was illegal in Paris then—as it is now. But there were places; there always are. It was his to choose, and he picked a spot in the Bois de Boulogne. Close by the road of the Seven Saints, but hidden by a screen of oaks. The choice of weapon was his, too. I expected pistols, but he chose swords."

"Why would he do that? You must have had a six-inch reach on him—or more." I was no expert, but was perforce learning a small bit about the strategy and tactics of swordfighting; Jamie and Murtagh took each other on every two or three days to keep in practice, clashing and parrying and lunging up and down the garden, to the untrammeled delight of the servants, male and female alike, who all surged out onto the balconies to watch.

"Why did he choose smallswords? Because he was bloody good with one. Also, I suspected he thought I might kill him accidentally with a pistol, while he knew I'd be satisfied only to draw blood with a blade. I didna mean to kill him, ye ken," he explained. "Only to humiliate him. And he knew it. No fool, was our Charles," he said, ruefully shaking his head.

The mist from the fountain was making ringlets escape from my coiffure, to curl around my face. I brushed back a wisp of hair, asking, "And did you humiliate him?"

"Well, I wounded him, at least." I was surprised to hear a small note of satisfaction in his voice, and raised an eyebrow at him. "He'd learnt his craft from LeJeune, one of the best swordmasters in France," Jamie explained. "Like fighting a damn flea, it was, and I fought him right-handed, too." He pushed a hand through his hair once more, as though checking the binding.

"My hair came loose, midway through," he said. "The thong holding it broke, and the wind was blowing it into my eyes, so all I could see was the wee white shape of Charles in his shirt, darting to and fro like a minnow. And that's how I got him, finally—the way ye spear a fish with a dirk." He snorted through his nose.

"He let out a skelloch as though I'd run him through, though I knew I'd but pinked him in one arm. I got the hair out of my face at last and looked beyond him to see Annalise standing there at the edge of the clearing, wi' her eyes wide and dark as yon pool." He gestured out over the silver-black surface beside us.

"So I sheathed my blade and smoothed back my hair, and stood there—half-expectin' her to come and throw herself into my arms, I suppose."

"Um," I said, delicately. "I gather she didn't?"

"Well, I didna ken anything about women then, did I?" he demanded. "No, she came and threw herself on *him*, of course." He made a Scottish noise deep in his throat, one of self-derision and humorous disgust. "Married him a month later, I heard."

"Aye, well." He shrugged suddenly, with a rueful smile. "So my heart was broken. Went home to Scotland and moped about for weeks, until my father lost patience wi' me." He laughed. "I even thought of turning monk over it. Said to my father over supper one night as I thought perhaps in the spring I'd go across to the Abbey and become a novice."

I laughed at the thought. "Well, you'd have no difficulty with the vow of poverty; chastity and obedience might come a bit harder. What did your father say?"

He grinned, teeth white in a dark face. "He was eating brose. He laid down the spoon and looked at me for a moment. Then he sighed and shook his head, and said, 'It's been a long day, Jamie.' Then he picked up the spoon again and went back to his supper, and I never said another word about it."

He looked up the slope to the terrace, where those not

dancing strolled to and fro, cooling off between dances, sipping wine and flirting behind fans. He sighed nostalgically.

"Aye, a verra pretty lass, Annalise de Marillac. Graceful as the wind, and so small that ye wanted to tuck her inside your shirt and carry her like a kitten."

I was silent, listening to the faint music from the open doors above, as I contemplated the gleaming satin slipper that encased my size-nine foot.

After a moment, Jamie became aware of my silence.

"What is it, Sassenach?" he asked, laying a hand on my arm.

"Oh, nothing," I said with a sigh. "Only thinking that I rather doubt anyone will ever describe me as 'graceful as the wind.' "

"Ah." His head was half-turned, the long, straight nose and firm chin lighted from behind by the glow of the nearest lantern. I could see the half-smile on his lips as he turned back toward me.

"Well, I'll tell ye, Sassenach, 'graceful' is possibly not the first word that springs to mind at thought of you." He slipped an arm behind me, one hand large and warm around my silk-clad shoulder.

"But I talk to you as I talk to my own soul," he said, turning me to face him. He reached up and cupped my cheek, fingers light on my temple.

"And, Sassenach," he whispered, "your face is my heart."

It was the shifting of the wind, several minutes later, that parted us at last with a fine spray from the fountain. We broke apart and rose hastily, laughing at the sudden chill of the water. Jamie inclined his head inquiringly toward the terrace, and I took his arm, nodding.

"So," I observed, as we made our way slowly up the wide steps to the ballroom, "you've learnt a bit more about women now, I see."

He laughed, low and deep, tightening his grasp on my waist.

"The most important thing I've learned about women, Sassenach, is which one to choose." He stepped away, bowing to me, and gesturing through the open doors to the brilliant scene inside. "May I have this dance, milady?"

I spent the next afternoon at the d'Arbanvilles', where I met the King's singing-master once again. This time, we found time for a conversation, which I recounted to Jamie after supper.

"You what?" Jamie squinted at me, as though he suspected me of pulling some practical joke.

"I said, Herr Gerstmann suggested that I might be interested in meeting a friend of his. Mother Hildegarde is in charge of L'Hôpital des Anges—you know, the charity hospital down near the cathedral."

"I know where it is." His voice was marked by a general lack of enthusiasm.

"He had a sore throat, and that led to me telling him what to take for it, and a bit about medicines in general, and how I was interested in diseases and, well, you know how one thing leads to another."

"With you, it customarily does," he agreed, sounding distinctly cynical. I ignored his tone and went on.

"So, I'm going to go to the hospital tomorrow." I stretched on tiptoe to reach down my medicine box from its shelf. "Maybe I won't take it along with me the first time," I said, scanning the contents meditatively. "It might seem too pushing. Do you think?"

"Pushing?" He sounded stunned. "Are ye meaning to visit the place, or move into it?"

"Er, well," I said. I took a deep breath. "I, er, thought perhaps I could work there regularly. Herr Gerstmann says that all the physicians and healers who go there donate their time. Most of them don't turn up every day, but I have plenty of time, and I could—"

"Plenty of time?"

"Stop repeating everything I say," I said. "Yes, plenty of time. I know it's important to go to salons and supper parties and all that, but it doesn't take all day—at least it needn't. I could—"

"Sassenach, you're with child! Ye dinna mean to go out to nurse beggars and criminals?" He sounded rather helpless now, as though wondering how to deal with someone who had suddenly gone mad in front of him.

"I hadn't forgotten," I assured him. I pressed my hands against my belly, squinting down.

"It isn't really noticeable yet; with a loose gown I can get away with it for a time. And there's nothing wrong with me except the morning sickness; no reason why I shouldn't work for some months yet."

"No reason, except I wilna have ye doing it!" Expecting no company this evening, he had taken off his stock and opened his collar when he came home. I could see the tide of dusky red advancing up his throat.

"Jamie," I said, striving for reasonableness. "You know what I am."

"You're my wife!"

"Well, that, too." I flicked the idea aside with my fingers. "I'm a doctor, Jamie. A healer. You have reason to know it."

He flushed hotly. "Aye, I do. And because ye've mended me when I'm wounded, I should think it right for ye to tend beggars and prostitutes? Sassenach, do ye no ken the sort of people that L'Hôpital des Anges takes in?" He looked pleadingly at me, as though expecting me to return to my senses any minute.

"What difference does that make?"

He looked wildly around the room, imploring witness from the portrait over the mantelpiece as to my unreasonableness.

"You could catch a filthy disease, for God's sake! D'ye have no regard for your child, even if ye have none for me?"

Reasonableness was seeming a less desirable goal by the moment.

"Of course I have! What kind of careless, irresponsible person do you think I am?"

"The kind who would abandon her husband to go and play with scum in the gutter!" he snapped. "Since you ask." He ran a big hand through his hair, making it stick up at the crown.

"Abandon you? Since when is it abandoning you to suggest really doing something, instead of rotting away in the d'Arbanvilles' salon, watching Louise de Rohan stuff herself with pastry, and listening to bad poetry and worse music? I want to be useful!"

"Taking care of your own household isna useful? Being

married to me isna useful?" The lacing round his hair broke under the stress, and the thick locks fluffed out like a flaming halo. He glared down his nose at me like an avenging angel.

"Sauce for the gander," I retorted coldly. "Is being married to *me* sufficient occupation for *you*? I don't notice you hanging round the house all day, adoring me. And as for the household, bosh."

"Bosh? What's bosh?" he demanded.

"Stuff and nonsense. Rot. Horsefeathers. In other words, don't be ridiculous. Madame Vionnet does everything, and does it several dozen times better than I could."

This was so patently true that it stopped him for a moment. He glared down at me, jaw working.

"Oh, aye? And if I forbid ye to go?"

This stopped me for a moment. I drew myself up and looked him up and down. His eyes were the color of rain-dark slate, the wide, generous mouth clamped in a straight line. Shoulders broad and back erect, arms folded across his chest like a cast-iron statue, "forbidding" was precisely the word that best described him.

"*Do* you forbid me?" The tension crackled between us. I wanted to blink, but wouldn't give him the satisfaction of breaking off my own steely gaze. What *would* I do if he forbade me to go? Alternatives raced through my mind, everything from planting the ivory letter-opener between his ribs to burning down the house with him in it. The only idea I rejected absolutely was that of giving in.

He paused, and drew a deep breath before speaking. His hands were curled into fists at his sides, and he uncurled them with conscious effort.

"No," he said. "No, I dinna forbid ye." His voice shook slightly with the effort to control it. "But if I asked you?"

I looked down then, and stared at his reflection in the polished tabletop. At first, the idea of visiting L'Hôpital des Anges had seemed merely an interesting idea, an attractive alternative to the endless gossip and petty intrigues of Parisian society. But now . . . I could feel the muscles of my arms swell as I clenched my own fists. I didn't just *want* to work again; I *needed* to.

"I don't know," I said at last.

He took a deep breath, and let it out slowly.

"Will ye think about it, Claire?" I could feel his eyes on me. After what seemed a long time, I nodded.

"I'll think about it."

"Good." His tension broken, he turned restlessly away. He wandered round the drawing room, picking up small objects and putting them down at random, finally coming to roost by the bookshelf, where he leaned, staring unseeingly at the leather-bound titles. I came tentatively up beside him, and laid a hand on his arm.

"Jamie, I didn't mean to upset you."

He glanced down at me and gave me a sidelong smile.

"Aye, well. I didna mean to fight wi' you, either, Sassenach. I'm short-tempered and ower-touchy, I expect." He patted my hand in apology, then moved aside, to stand looking down at his desk.

"You've been working hard," I said soothingly, following him.

"It's not that." He shook his head, and reached out to flip open the pages of the huge ledger that lay in the center of the desk.

"The wine business; that's all right. It's a great deal of work, aye, but I dinna mind it. It's the other." He gestured at a small stack of letters, held down by an alabaster paperweight. One of Jared's, it was carved in the shape of a white rose—the Stuarts' emblem. The letters it secured were from Abbot Alexander, from the Earl of Mar, from other prominent Jacobites. All filled with veiled inquiry, misty promises, contradictory expectations.

"I feel as though I'm fighting feathers!" Jamie said, violently. "A real fight, something I could get my hands on, that I could do. But this . . ." He snatched up the handful of letters from the desk, and tossed them into the air. The room was drafty, and the papers zigzagged wildly, sliding under furniture and fluttering on the carpet.

"There's nothing to get hold of," he said helplessly. "I can talk to a thousand people, write a hundred letters, drink wi' Charles 'til I'm blind, and never know if I'm getting on or not."

I let the scattered letters lie; one of the maids could retrieve them later.

"Jamie," I said softly. "We can't do anything but try."

He smiled faintly, hands braced on the desk. "Aye. I'm glad you said 'we,' Sassenach. I do feel verra much alone with it all sometimes."

I put my arms around his waist and laid my face against his back.

"You know I wouldn't leave you alone with it," I said. "I got you into it in the first place, after all."

I could feel the small vibration of a laugh under my cheek.

"Aye, you did. I wilna hold it against ye, Sassenach." He turned, leaned down, and kissed me lightly on the forehead. "You look tired, *mo nighean donn.* Go up to bed, now. I've a bit more work to do, but I'll join ye soon."

"All right." I *was* tired tonight, though the chronic sleepiness of early pregnancy was giving way to new energy; I was beginning to feel alert in the daytime, brimming with the urge to be active.

I paused at the door on my way out. He was still standing by the desk, staring down into the pages of the open ledger.

"Jamie?" I said.

"Aye?"

"The hospital—I said I'd think about it. You think, too, hm?"

He turned his head, one brow sharply arched. Then he smiled, and nodded briefly.

"I'll come to ye soon, Sassenach," he said.

It was still sleeting, and tiny particles of frozen rain rattled against the windows and hissed into the fire when the night wind turned to drive them down the flue. The wind was high, and it moaned and grumbled among the chimneys, making the bedroom seem all the cozier by contrast. The bed itself was an oasis of warmth and comfort, equipped with goose-down quilts, huge fluffy pillows, and Jamie, faithfully putting out British Thermal Units like an electric storage heater.

His large hand stroked lightly across my stomach, warm through the thin silk of my nightdress.

"No, there. You have to press a little harder." I took his hand and pressed the fingers downward, just above my pubic bone, where the uterus had begun to make itself obvious, a round, hard swelling a little larger than a grapefruit.

"Aye, I feel it," he murmured. "He's really there." A tiny smile of awed delight tugged at the corner of his mouth, and he looked up at me, eyes sparkling. "Can ye feel him move, yet?"

I shook my head. "Not yet. Another month or so, I think, from what your sister Jenny said."

"Mmm," he said, kissing the tiny bulge. "What d'ye think of 'Dalhousie,' Sassenach?"

"What do I think of 'Dalhousie' as *what*?" I inquired.

"Well, as a name," he said. He patted my stomach. "He'll need a name."

"True," I said. "Though what makes you think it's a boy? It might just as easily be a girl."

"Oh? Oh, aye, that's true," he admitted, as though the possibility had just occurred to him. "Still, why not start with the boys' names? We could name him for your uncle who raised you."

"Umm." I frowned at my midsection. Dearly as I had loved my uncle Lamb, I didn't know that I wanted to inflict either "Lambert" or "Quentin" on a helpless infant. "No, I don't think so. On the other hand, I don't think I'd want to name him for one of *your* uncles, either."

Jamie stroked my stomach absently, thinking.

"What was your father's name, Sassenach?" he asked.

I had to think for a moment to remember.

"Henry," I said. "Henry Montmorency Beauchamp. Jamie, I am *not* having a child named 'Montmorency Fraser,' no matter what. I'm not so keen on 'Henry,' either, though it's better than Lambert. How about 'William'?" I suggested. "For your brother?" His older brother, William, had died in late childhood, but had lived long enough for Jamie to remember him with great affection.

His brow was furrowed in thought. "Hmm," he said. "Aye, maybe. Or we could call him . . ."

"James," said a hollow, sepulchral voice from the flue.

"*What?*" I said, sitting straight up in bed.

"James," said the fireplace, impatiently. "James, James!"

"Sweet bleeding Jesus," said Jamie, staring at the leaping flames on the hearth. I could feel the hair standing up on his forearm, stiff as wire. He sat frozen for a moment; then, a thought occurring to him, he jumped to his feet and went to the dormer window, not bothering to put anything on over his shirt.

He flung up the sash, admitting a blast of frigid air, and thrust his head out into the night. I heard a muffled shout, and then a scrabbling sound across the slates of the roof. Jamie leaned far out, rising on his toes to reach, then backed slowly into the room, rain-dampened and grunting with effort. He dragged with him, arms clasped about his neck, the form of a handsome boy in dark clothing, thoroughly soaked, with a bloodstained cloth wrapped around one hand.

The visitor caught his foot on the sill and landed clumsily, sprawling on the floor. He scrambled up at once, though, and bowed to me, snatching off his slouch hat.

"Madame," he said, in thickly accented French. "I must beg your pardon, I arrive so without ceremony. I intrude, but it is of necessity that I call upon my friend James at such an unsocial hour."

He was a sturdy, good-looking lad, with thick, light-brown hair curling loose upon his shoulders, and a fair face, cheeks flushed red with cold and exertion. His nose was running slightly, and he wiped it with the back of his wrapped hand, wincing slightly as he did so.

Jamie, both eyebrows raised, bowed politely to the visitor.

"My house is at your service, Your Highness," he said, with a glance that took in the general disorder of the visitor's attire. His stock was undone and hung loosely around his neck, half his buttons were done up awry, and the flies of his breeches flopped partially open. I saw Jamie frown slightly at this, and he moved unobtrusively in front of the boy, to screen me from the indelicate sight.

"If I may present my wife, Your Highness?" he said. "Claire, my lady Broch Tuarach. Claire, this is His Highness, Prince Charles, son of King James of Scotland."

"Um, yes," I said. "I'd rather gathered that. Er, good evening, Your Highness." I nodded graciously, pulling the bedclothes up around me. I supposed that under the circumstances, I could dispense with the usual curtsy.

The Prince had taken advantage of Jamie's long-winded

introduction to fumble his trousers into better order, and now
nodded back at me, full of Royal dignity.

"It is my pleasure, Madame," he said, and bowed once
more, making a much more elegant production of it. He
straightened and stood turning his hat in his hands, obviously
trying to think what to say next. Jamie, standing bare-legged
in his shirt alongside, glanced from me to Charles, seemingly
at an equal loss for words.

"Er . . ." I said, to break the silence. "Have you had an
accident, Your Highness?" I nodded at the handkerchief
wrapped around his hand, and he glanced down as though
noticing it for the first time.

"Yes," he said, "ah . . . no. I mean . . . it is nothing,
my lady." He flushed redder, staring at his hand. His manner
was odd; something between embarrassment and anger. I
could see the stain on the cloth spreading, though, and put
my feet out of bed, groping for my dressing gown.

"You'd better let me have a look at it," I said.

The injury, exposed with some reluctance by the Prince,
was not serious, but it was unusual.

"That looks like an animal bite," I said incredulously,
dabbing at the small semicircle of puncture wounds in the
webbing between thumb and forefinger. Prince Charles
winced as I squeezed the flesh around it, meaning to cleanse
the wound by bleeding before binding it.

"Yes," he said. "A monkey bite. Disgusting, flea-ridden
beast!" he burst out. "I told her she must dispose of it. Undoubtedly the animal is diseased!"

I had found my medicine box, and now applied a thin
layer of gentian ointment. "I don't think you need worry," I
said, intent on my work. "So long as it isn't rabid, that is."

"Rabid?" The Prince went quite pale. "Do you think it
could be?" Plainly he had no idea what "rabid" might mean,
but wanted no part of it.

"Anything's possible," I said cheerfully. Surprised by his
sudden appearance, it was just beginning to dawn on me that
it would save everyone a great deal of trouble in the long run,
if this young man would succumb gracefully to some quick
and deadly disease. Still, I couldn't quite find it in my heart to
wish him gangrene or rabies, and I tied up his hand neatly in
a fresh linen bandage.

He smiled, bowed again, and thanked me very prettily in a mixture of French and Italian. Still apologizing effusively for his untimely visit, he was towed away by Jamie, now respectably kilted, for a drink downstairs.

Feeling the chill of the room seep through gown and robe, I crawled back into bed and drew the quilts up under my chin. So this was Prince Charles! Bonnie enough, to be sure; at least to look at. He seemed very young—much younger than Jamie, though I knew Jamie was only a year or so younger. His Highness did have considerable charm of manner, though, and quite a bit of self-important dignity, despite his disordered dress. Was that really enough to take him to Scotland, at the head of an army of restoration? As I drifted off, I wondered exactly what the heir to the throne of Scotland had been doing, wandering over the Paris rooftops in the middle of the night, with a monkey bite on one hand.

The question was still on my mind when Jamie woke me sometime later by sliding into bed and planting his large, ice-cold feet directly behind my knees.

"Don't scream like that," he said, "you'll wake the servants."

"What in hell was Charles Stuart doing running about the rooftops with monkeys?" I demanded, taking evasive action. "Take those bloody ice cubes off me."

"Visiting his mistress," said Jamie succinctly. "All right, then; stop kicking me." He removed the feet and embraced me, shivering, as I turned to him.

"He has a mistress? Who?" Stimulated by whiffs of cold and scandal, I was quickly waking up.

"It's Louise de La Tour," Jamie explained reluctantly, in response to my prodding. His nose looked longer and sharper than usual, with the thick brows drawn together above it. Having a mistress was bad enough, in his Scottish Catholic view, but it was well known that royalty had certain privileges in this regard. The Princesse Louise de La Tour was married, however. And royalty or not, taking a married woman as one's mistress was positively immoral, his cousin Jared's example notwithstanding.

"Ha," I said with satisfaction. "I knew it!"

"He says he's in love with her," he reported tersely, yanking the quilts up over his shoulders. "He insists she loves him too; says she's been faithful only to him for the last three months. Tcha!"

"Well, it's been known to happen," I said, amused. "So he was visiting her? How did he get out on the roof, though? Did he tell you that?"

"Oh, aye. He told me."

Charles, fortified against the night with several glasses of Jared's best aged port, had been quite forthcoming. The strength of true love had been tried severely this evening, according to Charles, by his inamorata's devotion to her pet, a rather ill-tempered monkey that reciprocated His Highness's dislike and had more concrete means of demonstrating its opinions. Snapping his fingers under the monkey's nose in derision, His Highness had suffered first a sharp bite in the hand, and then the sharper bite of his mistress's tongue, exercised in bitter reproach. The couple had quarreled hotly, to the point that Louise, Princesse de Rohan, had ordered Charles from her presence. He had expressed himself only too willing to go—never, he emphasized dramatically, to return.

The Prince's departure, however, had been considerably hampered by the discovery that the Princesse's husband had returned early from his evening of gaming, and was comfortably ensconced in the anteroom with a bottle of brandy.

"So," said Jamie, smiling despite himself at the thought, "he wouldna stay with the lassie, but he couldna go out of the door—so he threw up the sash and jumped out on the roof. He got down almost to the street, he said, along the drainage pipes; but then the City guard came along, and he had to scramble back up to stay out of their sight. He had a rare time of it, he said, dodging about the chimneys and slipping on the wet slates, until it occurred to him that our house was only three houses down the row, and the rooftops close enough to hop them like lily pads."

"Mm," I said, feeling warmth reestablish itself around my toes. "Did you send him home in the coach?"

"No, he took one of the horses from the stable."

"If he's been drinking Jared's port, I hope they both make it to Montmartre," I remarked. "It's a good long way."

"Well, it will be a cold, wet journey, no doubt," said Jamie, with the smugness of a man virtuously tucked up in a

warm bed with his lawfully wedded wife. He blew out the
candle and pulled me close against his chest, spoon-fashion.

"Serve him right," he murmured. "A man ought to be
married."

The servants were up before dawn, polishing and cleaning in preparation for entertaining Monsieur Duverney at a
small, private supper in the evening.

"I don't know why they bother," I told Jamie, lying in
bed with my eyes closed, listening to the bustle downstairs.
"All they need do is dust off the chess set and put out a bottle
of brandy; he won't notice anything else."

He laughed and bent to kiss me goodbye. "That's all
right; I'll need a good supper if I'm to go on beating him." He
patted my shoulder in farewell. "I'm going to the warehouse,
Sassenach; I'll be home in time to dress, though."

In search of something to do that would take me out of
the servants' way, I finally decided to have a footman escort
me down to the Rohans'. Perhaps Louise could use a bit of
solace, I thought, after her quarrel of the night before. Vulgar
curiosity, I told myself primly, had nothing whatsoever to do
with it.

When I returned in the late afternoon, I found Jamie
slouched in a chair near the bedroom window with his feet
propped on the table, collar undone and hair rumpled as he
pored over a sheaf of scribbled papers. He looked up at the
sound of the door closing, and the absorbed expression
melted into a broad grin.

"Sassenach! There you are!" He swung his long legs
down and came across to embrace me. He buried his face in
my hair, nuzzling, then drew back and sneezed. He sneezed
again, and let go of me to grope in his sleeve for the handkerchief he carried there, military style.

"What do ye smell like, Sassenach?" he demanded,
pressing the linen square to his nose just in time to muffle the
results of another explosive sneeze.

I reached into the bosom of my dress and plucked the
small sachet from between my breasts.

"Jasmine, roses, hyacinth, and lily of the valley. . . . ragweed, too, apparently," I added as he snorted and wheezed into the capacious depths of the handkerchief. "Are you all right?" I looked around for some means of disposal, and settled for dropping the sachet into a stationery box on my desk at the far side of the room.

"Aye, I'll do. It's the hya . . . hya . . . hyaCHOO!"

"Goodness!" I hastily flung the window open, and motioned to him. He obligingly stuck his head and shoulders out into the wet drizzle of the morning, breathing in gusts of fresh, hyacinth-free air.

"Och, that's better," he said with relief, pulling in his head a few minutes later. His eyes widened. "What are ye doing now, Sassenach?"

"Washing," I explained, struggling with the back laces of my gown. "Or getting ready to, at least. I'm covered with oil of hyacinth," I explained, as he blinked. "If I don't wash it off, you're liable to explode."

He dabbed meditatively at his nose and nodded.

"You've a point there, Sassenach. Shall I have the footman fetch up some hot water?"

"No, don't bother. A quick rinse should take most of it off," I assured him, unbuttoning and unlacing as quickly as possible. I raised my arms, reaching behind my head to gather my hair into a bun. Suddenly Jamie leaned forward and grasped my wrist, pulling my arm into the air.

"What are you doing?" I said, startled.

"What have *you* done, Sassenach?" he demanded. He was staring under my arm.

"Shaved," I said proudly. "Or rather, waxed. Louise had her *servante aux petits soins*—you know, her personal groomer?—there this morning, and she did me, too."

"Waxed?" Jamie looked rather wildly at the candlestick by the ewer, then back at me. "You put wax in your oxters?"

"Not that kind of wax," I assured him. "Scented beeswax. The grooming lady heated it, then spread the warm wax on. Once it's cooled, you just jerk it off," I winced momentarily in recollection, "and Bob's your uncle."

"My uncle Bob wouldna countenance any such goings-on," said Jamie severely. "What in hell would ye do that for?" He peered closely at the site, still holding my wrist up.

"Didn't it hur . . . hurt . . . choof!" He dropped my hand and backed up rapidly.

"Didn't it hurt?" he asked, handkerchief to nose once more.

"Well, a bit," I admitted. "Worth it, though, don't you think?" I asked, raising both arms like a ballerina and turning slightly to and fro. "First time I've felt entirely clean in months."

"Worth it?" he said, sounding a little dazed. "What's it to do wi' clean, that you've pulled all of the hairs out from under your arms?"

A little belatedly, I realized that none of the Scottish women I had encountered employed any form of depilation. Furthermore, Jamie had almost certainly never been in sufficiently close contact with an upper-class Parisienne to know that many of them *did.* "Well," I said, suddenly realizing the difficulty an anthropologist faces in trying to interpret the more singular customs of a primitive tribe. "It smells much less," I offered.

"And what's wrong wi' the way ye smell?" he said heatedly. "At least ye smelt like a woman, not a damn flower garden. What d'ye think I am, a man or a bumblebee? Would ye wash yourself, Sassenach, so I can get within less than ten feet of ye?"

I picked up a cloth and began sponging my torso. Madame Laserre, Louise's groomer, had applied scented oil all over my body; I rather hoped it would come off easily. It was disconcerting to have him hovering just outside sniffing range, glaring at me like a wolf circling its prey.

I turned my back to dip the cloth into the bowl, and said offhandedly over my shoulder, "Er, I did my legs, too."

I stole a quick glance over my shoulder. The original shock was fading into a look of total bewilderment.

"Your legs dinna smell like anything," he said. "Unless you've been walkin' knee-deep in the cow-byre."

I turned around and pulled my skirt up to my knees, pointing one toe forward to display the delicate curves of calf and shin.

"But they look so much nicer," I pointed out. "All nice and smooth; not like Harry the hairy ape."

He glanced down at his own fuzzy knees, offended.

"An ape, am I?"

"Not you, me!" I said, getting exasperated.

"My legs are any amount hairier than yours ever were!"

"Well, they're *supposed* to be; you're a man!"

He drew in breath as though about to reply, then let it out again, shaking his head and muttering something to himself in Gaelic. He flung himself back into the chair and sat back, watching me through narrowed eyes, every now and then muttering to himself again. I decided not to ask for a translation.

After most of my bath had been accomplished in what might best be described as a charged atmosphere, I decided to attempt conciliation.

"It might have been worse, you know," I said, sponging the inside of one thigh. "Louise had *all* her body hair removed."

That startled him back into English, at least temporarily.

"What, she's taken the hairs off her honeypot?" he said, horrified into uncharacteristic vulgarity.

"Mm-hm," I replied, pleased that this vision had at least distracted him from my own distressingly hairless condition. "Every hair. Madame Laserre plucked out the stray ones."

"Mary, Michael, and Bride!" He closed his eyes tightly, either in avoidance, or the better to contemplate the prospect I had described.

Evidently the latter, for he opened his eyes again and glared at me, demanding, "She's goin' about now bare as a wee lassie?"

"She says," I replied delicately, "that men find it erotic."

His eyebrows nearly met his hairline, a neat trick for someone with such a classically high brow.

"I do wish you would stop that muttering," I remarked, hanging the cloth over a chairback to dry. "I can't understand a word you say."

"On the whole, Sassenach," he replied, "that's as well."

12

L'Hôpital des Anges

"All right," Jamie said resignedly over breakfast. He pointed a spoon at me in warning. "Go ahead, then. But you'll take Murtagh as escort, besides the footman; it's a poor neighborhood near the cathedral."

"Escort?" I sat up straight, pushing back the bowl of parritch which I had been eyeing with something less than enthusiasm. "Jamie! Do you mean you don't mind if I visit L'Hôpital des Anges?"

"I don't know if I mean that, exactly," he said, spooning in his own parritch in a businesslike way. "But I expect I'll mind a lot more if ye don't. And if ye work at the Hôpital, at least it will keep ye from spending all your time with Louise de Rohan. I suppose there are worse things than associating wi' beggars and criminals," he said darkly. "At least I don't expect you'll come home from a hospital wi' your privates plucked bare."

"I'll try not," I assured him.

I had seen a number of good hospital matrons in my time, and a few of the really excellent ones, who had exalted a job into a vocation. With Mother Hildegarde, the process had been reversed, with impressive results.

Hildegarde de Gascogne was the most suitable person I could imagine to be in charge of a place like L'Hôpital des Anges. Nearly six feet tall, her gaunt, rawboned frame swathed in yards of black wool, she loomed over her nursing sisters like a broomstick scarecrow guarding a field of pumpkins. Porters, patients, sisters, orderlies, novices, visitors, apothecaries, all were swept up by the force of her presence, to be tidied away into neat heaps, wherever Mother Hildegarde might decree.

With that height, plus a face of an ugliness so transcendent as to be grotesquely beautiful, it was obvious why she had embraced a religious life—Christ was the only man from whom she might expect embrace in return.

Her voice was deep and resonant; with its nasal Gascony accent, it bonged through the corridors of the hospital like the echo of the church bells next door. I could hear her sometime before I saw her, the powerful voice increasing in volume as she came down the hall toward the office where six ladies of the Court and I huddled behind Herr Gerstmann, like island dwellers awaiting the arrival of a hurricane behind a flimsy barricade.

She filled the narrow doorway with a swoosh of batwings, and descended upon Herr Gerstmann with a cry of rapture, kissing him soundly on both cheeks.

"*Mon cher ami!* How unexpected a pleasure—and so much the more sweet for its unexpectedness. What brings you to me?"

Straightening, she turned a wide smile on the rest of us. The smile remained wide as Herr Gerstmann explained our mission, though a less experienced fortune-teller than I could have seen the tightening cheek muscles that turned it from a social grace to a rictus of necessity.

"We are most appreciative of your thoughts and your generosity, mesdames." The deep, bell-like voice went on with a gracious speech of gratitude. Meanwhile, I could see the small, intelligent eyes, set deep beneath bony brow ridges, darting back and forth, deciding how best to dispose of this nuisance in short order, while still extracting such money as these pious ladies might be induced to part with for the good of their souls.

Having come to a decision, she clapped her hands sharply. A short nun, on the general order of Cock-Robin, popped up in the doorway like a jack-in-the-box.

"Sister Angelique, be so kind as to take these ladies to the dispensary," she ordered. "Give them some suitable garments and then show them the wards. They may assist with the distribution of food to the patients—if they are so inclined." A slight twitch of the wide, thin mouth made it evident that Mother Hildegarde did not expect the ladies' pious inclination to survive the tour of the wards.

Mother Hildegarde was a shrewd judge of human nature. Three of the ladies made it through the first ward, with its cases of scrofula, scabies, eczema, defluxions, and stinking pyemia, before deciding that their charitable inclinations could be entirely satisfied by a donation to L'Hôpital, and fleeing back to the dispensary to shed the rough hopsacking gowns with which we had been furnished.

In the center of the next ward, a tall, gangly man in a dark frock coat was carrying out what appeared to be the skillful amputation of a leg; particularly skillful in that the patient was not sedated in any visible way, and was being restrained at the moment by the efforts of two husky order-lies and a solidly built nun who was sitting upon the patient's chest, her flowing draperies fortunately obscuring the man's face.

One of the ladies behind me made a small gagging sound; when I looked round, all I saw was the rather wide rear aspect of two of the would-be Samaritans, jammed hip to hip in the narrow doorway leading toward the dispensary and freedom. With a last desperate tug and the rending of silk, they burst through and fled precipitately down the dark hall-way, nearly knocking over an orderly coming on the trot with a tray piled high with linens and surgical instruments.

I glanced to the side, and was amused to find Mary Haw-kins still there. Somewhat whiter than the surgical linens—which were quite a disgraceful shade of gray, truth be told—and a bit green about the gills, but still there.

"Vite! Dépêchez-vous!" the surgeon uttered a peremptory shout, aimed presumably at the shaken orderly, who hastily reassembled his tray and came on the gallop to the spot where the tall, dark man was poised, bone saw in hand, ready to sever an exposed thigh bone. The orderly bent to tie a second tourniquet above the site of operation, the saw de-scended with an indescribable grating sound, and I took pity on Mary Hawkins, turning her in the other direction. Her arm trembled under my hand, and the peony lips were blanched and pinched as a frostbitten flower.

"Would you like to leave?" I asked politely. "I'm sure Mother Hildegarde could summon a carriage for you." I glanced over one shoulder to the vacant darkness of the hall-way. "I'm afraid the Comtesse and Madame Lambert have left already."

Mary gulped audibly, but tightened an already firm jaw in determination.

"N-no," she said. "If you stay, I'll stay."

I definitely intended staying; curiosity and the urge to worm my way into the operations of L'Hôpital des Anges were much too strong to weigh against any pity I might feel for Mary's sensibilities.

Sister Angelique had gone some distance before noticing that we had stopped. Returning, she stood patiently waiting, a small smile on her plump face, as though expecting that we, too, would turn and run. I bent over a pallet at the edge of the floor. A very thin woman lay listlessly under a single blanket, her eyes drifting dully over us without interest. It wasn't the woman who had attracted my attention, so much as the oddly shaped glass vessel standing on the floor alongside her pallet.

The vessel was brimming with a yellow fluid—urine, undoubtedly. I was mildly surprised; without chemical tests, or even litmus paper, what conceivable use could a urine sample be? Thinking over the various things one tested urine for, though, I had an idea.

I picked up the vessel carefully, ignoring Sister Angelique's exclamation of alarmed protest. I sniffed carefully. Sure enough; half-obscured by sour ammoniac fumes, the fluid smelled sickly sweet—rather like soured honey. I hesitated, but there was only one way to make sure. With a moue of distaste, I gingerly dipped the tip of one finger into the liquid and touched it delicately to my tongue.

Mary, watching bug-eyed at my side, choked slightly, but Sister Angelique was watching with sudden interest. I placed a hand on the woman's forehead; it was cool—no fever to account for the wasting.

"Are you thirsty, Madame?" I asked the patient. I knew the answer before she spoke, seeing the empty carafe near her head.

"Always, Madame," she replied. "And always hungry, as well. Yet no flesh gathers on my bones, no matter how much I eat." She raised a stick-thin arm, displaying a bony wrist, then let it fall as though the effort had exhausted her.

I patted the skinny hand gently, and murmured something in farewell, my exhilaration at having made a correct diagnosis substantially quenched by the knowledge that there was no possible cure for diabetes mellitus in this day; the woman before me was doomed.

In subdued spirits, I rose to follow Sister Angelique, who slowed her bustling steps to walk next to me.

"Could you tell from what she suffers, Madame?" the nun asked curiously. "Only from the urine?"

"Not only from that," I answered. "But yes, I know. She has—" Drat. What would they have called it now? "She has . . . um, sugar sickness. She gets no nourishment from the food she eats, and has a tremendous thirst. Consequently, she produces large quantities of urine."

Sister Angelique was nodding, a look of intense curiosity stamped on her pudgy features.

"And can you tell whether she will recover, Madame?"

"No, she won't," I said bluntly. "She's far gone already; she may not last out the month."

"Ah." The fair brows lifted, and the look of curiosity was replaced by one of respect. "That's what Monsieur Parnelle said."

"And who's he, when he's at home?" I asked flippantly.

The plump nun frowned in bewilderment. "Well, at his own establishment, I believe he is a maker of trusses, and a jeweler. When he comes here, though, he acts usually as a urinoscopist."

I felt my own brows rising. "A urinoscopist?" I said unbelievingly. "There actually are such things?"

"*Oui*, Madame. And he said just what you said, about the poor thin lady. I have never seen a woman who knew about the science of urinoscopy," Sister Angelique said, staring at me in frank fascination.

"Well, there are more things in heaven and on earth than are dreamt of in your philosophy, Sister," I said graciously. She nodded seriously, making me feel rather ashamed of my facetiousness.

"That is true, Madame. Will you have a look at the gentleman in the end bed? He has a complaint of the liver, we believe."

We continued, from one bed to another, making the complete circuit of the enormous hall. We saw examples of diseases I had seen only in textbooks, and every kind of traumatic injury, from head wounds inflicted in drunken brawls to a carter whose chest had been crushed by a rolling wine barrel.

I paused by some beds, asking questions of those patients who seemed able to answer. I could hear Mary breathing through her mouth behind my shoulder, but didn't check to see whether she was in fact holding her nose.

At the conclusion of the tour, Sister Angelique turned to me with an ironic smile.

"Well, Madame? Do you still desire to serve the Lord by helping his unfortunates?"

I was already rolling up the sleeves of my gown.

"Bring me a basin of hot water, Sister," I said, "and some soap."

"How was it, Sassenach?" Jamie asked.

"Horrible!" I answered, beaming broadly.

He raised one eyebrow, smiling down at me as I lay sprawled on the chaise.

"Oh, enjoyed yourself, did ye?"

"Oh, Jamie, it was so nice to be useful again! I mopped floors and I fed people gruel, and when Sister Angelique wasn't looking, I managed to change a couple of filthy dressings and lance an abscess."

"Oh, good," he said. "Did ye remember to eat, in the midst of all this frivolity?"

"Er, no, as a matter of fact, I didn't," I said guiltily. "On the other hand, I forgot to be sick, too." As though reminded of delinquency, the walls of my stomach took a sudden lurch inward. I pressed a fist under my breastbone. "Perhaps I should have a bite."

"Perhaps ye should," he agreed, a little grimly, reaching for the bell.

He watched as I obediently downed meat pie and cheese, describing L'Hôpital des Anges and its inmates in enthusiastic detail between bites as I ate.

"It's very crowded in some of the wards—two or three to a bed, which is awful, but—don't you want some of this?" I broke off to ask. "It's very good."

He eyed the piece of pastry I was holding out to him.

. "If ye think ye can keep from telling me about gangrenous toenails long enough for a bite to make it from my gullet
to my stomach, then yes."

Belatedly, I noticed the slight pallor on his cheeks, and
the faint pinching of his nostrils. I poured a cup of wine and
handed it to him before picking up my own plate again.

"And how was *your* day, my dear?" I asked demurely.

L'Hôpital des Anges became a refuge for me. The blunt
and unsophisticated directness of nuns and patients was a
wonderful refreshment from the continual chattering intrigues of the Court ladies and gentlemen. I was also positive
that without the relief of allowing my facial muscles to relax
into their normal expressions at the Hôpital, my face would
quickly have frozen into an expression of permanent simpering vapidity.

Seeing that I appeared to know what I was doing, and
required nothing of them beyond a few bandages and linens,
the nuns quickly accepted my presence. And after an initial
shock at my accent and title, so did the patients. Social prejudice is a strong force, but no match for simple competence
when skill is in urgent demand and short supply.

Mother Hildegarde, busy as she was, took somewhat
more time to make her own assessment of me. She never
spoke to me at first, beyond a simple "*Bonjour,* Madame," in
passing, but I often felt the weight of those small, shrewd eyes
boring into my back as I stooped over the bed of an elderly
man with shingles, or smeared aloe ointment on the blisters
of a child burned in one of the frequent house fires that beset
the poorer quarters of the city.

She never gave the appearance of hurrying, but covered
an immense amount of ground during the day, pacing the flat
gray stones of the Hôpital wards with a stride that covered a
yard at a time, her small white dog Bouton hurrying at her
heels to keep up.

A far cry from the fluffy lapdogs so popular with the
ladies of the Court, he looked vaguely like a cross between a
poodle and a dachshund, with a rough, kinky coat whose
fringes fluttered along the edges of a wide belly and stumpy,
bowed legs. His feet, splay-toed and black-nailed, clicked

frantically over the stones of the floor as he trotted after Mother Hildegarde, pointed muzzle almost touching the sweeping black folds of her habit.

"Is that a *dog*?" I had asked one of the orderlies in amazement, when I first beheld Bouton, passing through the Hôpital at the heels of his mistress.

He paused in his floor-sweeping to look after the curly, plumed tail, disappearing into the next ward.

"Well," he said doubtfully, "Mother Hildegarde says he's a dog. I wouldn't like to be the one to say he isn't."

As I became more friendly with the nuns, orderlies, and visiting physicians of the Hôpital, I heard various other opinions of Bouton, ranging from the tolerant to the superstitious. No one knew quite where Mother Hildegarde had got him, nor why. He had been a member of the Hôpital staff for several years, with a rank—in Mother Hildegarde's opinion, which was the only one that counted—well above that of the nursing sisters, and equal to that of most of the visiting physicians and apothecaries.

Some of the latter regarded him with suspicious aversion, others with jocular affability. One chirurgeon referred to him routinely—out of Mother's hearing—as "that revolting rat," another as "the smelly rabbit," and one small, tubby truss-maker greeted him quite openly as "Monsieur le Dishcloth." The nuns considered him something between a mascot and a totem, while the junior priest from the cathedral next door, who had been bitten in the leg when he came to administer the sacraments to the patients, confided to me his own opinion that Bouton was one of the lesser demons, disguised as a dog for his own fell purposes.

In spite of the unflattering tone of the priest's remarks, I thought that he had perhaps come the closest to the truth. For after several weeks of observing the pair, I had come to the conclusion that Bouton was in fact Mother Hildegarde's familiar.

She spoke to him often, not in the tone one generally uses for dogs, but as one discussing important matters with an equal. As she paused beside this bed or that, often Bouton would spring onto the mattress, nuzzling and sniffing at the startled patient. He would sit down, often on the patient's legs, bark once, and glance up inquiringly at Mother, wagging his silky plumed tail as though asking her opinion of his diagnosis—which she always gave.

Though I was rather curious about this behavior, I had had no opportunity of closely observing the odd pair at work until one dark, rainy morning in March. I was standing by the bed of a middle-aged carter, making casual conversation with him while I tried to figure out what in bloody hell was wrong with the man.

It was a case that had come in the week before. He had had his lower leg caught in the wheel of a cart when he carelessly dismounted before the vehicle had stopped moving. It was a compound fracture, but a fairly uncomplicated one. I had reset the bone, and the wound seemed to be healing nicely. The tissue was a healthy pink, with good granulation, no bad smell, no telltale red streaks, no extreme tenderness, nothing at all to explain why the man still smoldered with fever and produced the dark, odorous urine of a lingering infection.

"*Bonjour,* Madame." The deep, rich voice spoke above me, and I glanced up at the towering form of Mother Hildegarde. There was a *whish* past my elbow, and Bouton landed on the mattress with a thump that made the patient groan slightly.

"What do you think?" said Mother Hildegarde. I wasn't at all sure whether she was addressing me or Bouton, but took the benefit of the doubt and explained my observations.

"So, there must be a secondary source of infection," I concluded, "but I can't find it. I'm wondering now whether perhaps he has an internal infection that's not related to the leg wound. A mild appendicitis, or a bladder infection, perhaps, though I don't find any abdominal tenderness, either."

Mother Hildegarde nodded. "A possibility, certainly. Bouton!" The dog cocked his head toward his mistress, who jerked an oblong chin in the direction of the patient. "*A la bouche,* Bouton," she ordered. With a mincing step, the dog pushed the round black nose that presumably gave him his name into the carter's face. The man's eyes, heavy-lidded with fever, sprang open at this intrusion, but a glance at the imposing presence of Mother Hildegarde stopped whatever complaint he might have been forming.

"Open your mouth," Mother Hildegarde instructed, and

such was her force of character that he did so, even though his lips twitched at the nearness of Bouton's. Dog-kissing plainly wasn't on his agenda of desirable activities.

"No," said Mother Hildegarde thoughtfully, watching Bouton. "That isn't it. Have a look elsewhere, Bouton, but carefully. The man has a broken leg, remember."

As though he had in fact understood every word, the dog began to sniff curiously at the patient, nosing into his armpits, putting stubby feet on his chest in order to investigate, nudging gently along the crease of the groin. When it came to the injured leg, he stepped carefully over the limb before putting his nose to the surface of the bandages round it.

He returned to the groin area—well, what else, I thought impatiently, he's a dog, after all—nudged at the top of the thigh, then sat down and barked once, wagging triumphantly.

"There it is," said Mother Hildegarde, pointing to a small brown scab just below the inguinal crease.

"But that's almost healed," I protested. "It isn't infected."

"No?" The tall nun placed a hand on the man's thigh and pressed hard. Her muscular fingers dented the pale, clammy flesh, and the carter screamed like a banshee.

"Ah," she said in satisfaction, observing the deep prints left by her touch. "A pocket of putrefaction."

It was; the scab had loosened at one edge, and a thick ooze of yellow pus showed under it. A little probing, with Mother Hildegarde holding the man by leg and shoulder, revealed the problem. A long sliver of wood, flying free of the splintered cartwheel, had driven upward, deep into the thigh. Disregarded because of the apparently insignificant entrance wound, it had gone unnoticed by the patient himself, to whom the whole leg was one giant pain. While the tiny entrance wound had healed cleanly, the deeper wound had festered and formed a pocket of pus around the intrusion, buried in the muscle tissue where no surface symptoms were visible—to human senses, at least.

A little scalpel work to enlarge the entrance wound, a quick grip with a pair of long-nosed forceps, a smooth, forceful pull—and I held up a three-inch sliver of wood, coated with blood and slime.

"Not bad, Bouton," I said, with a nod of acknowledgment. A long pink tongue lolled happily, and the black nostrils sniffed in my direction.

"Yes, she's a good one," said Mother Hildegarde, and this time there was no doubt which of us she was speaking to, Bouton being male. Bouton leaned forward and sniffed politely at my hand, then licked my knuckles once in reciprocal acknowledgment of a fellow professional. I repressed the urge to wipe my hand on my gown.

"Amazing," I said, meaning it.

"Yes," said Mother Hildegarde, casually, but with an unmistakable note of pride. "He's very good at locating tumors beneath the skin, as well. And while I cannot always tell what he finds in the odors of breath and urine, he has a certain tone of bark that indicates unmistakably the presence of a derangement of the stomach."

Under the circumstances, I saw no reason to doubt it. I bowed to Bouton, and picked up a vial of powdered St.-John's-wort to dress the infection.

"Pleased to have your assistance, Bouton. You can work with me anytime."

"Very sensible of you," said Mother Hildegarde, with a flash of strong teeth. "Many of the physicians and *chirurgiens* who work here are less inclined to take advantage of his skills."

"Er, well. . . ." I didn't want to disparage anyone's reputation, but my glance across the hall at Monsieur Voleru must have been transparent.

Mother Hildegarde laughed. "Well, we take what God sends us, though occasionally I wonder whether He sends them to us only in order to keep them out of greater trouble elsewhere. Still, the bulk of our physicians are better than nothing—even if only marginally so. You"—and the teeth flashed once more, reminding me of a genial draft horse—"are a great deal better than nothing, Madame."

"Thanks."

"I have wondered, though," Mother Hildegarde went on, watching as I applied the medicated dressing, "why you see only the patients with wounds and broken bones? You avoid those with spots and coughs and fevers, yet it is more common for *les maîtresses* to deal with such things. I don't think I have ever seen a female *chirurgien* before." *Les maîtresses* were the unlicensed healers, mostly from the provinces, who dealt in herbals, poultices, and charms. *Les maîtresses sage-femme* were the midwives, the top of the heap so far as popular healers were concerned. Many were accorded more respect than the licensed practitioners, and were much preferred by the lower-class patients, as they were likely to be both more capable and much less expensive.

I wasn't surprised that she had observed my proclivities; I had gathered long since that very little about her Hôpital escaped Mother Hildegarde's notice.

"It isn't lack of interest," I assured her. "It's only that I'm with child, so I can't expose myself to anything contagious, for the child's sake. Broken bones aren't catching."

"Sometimes I wonder," said Mother Hildegarde, with a glance at an incoming stretcher. "We're having a plague of them this week. No, don't go." She motioned me back. "Sister Cecile will see to it. She'll call you if there's need."

The nun's small gray eyes regarded me with curiosity, mingled with appraisal.

"So, you are not only a milady, but you are with child, but your husband does not object to your coming here? He must be a most unusual man."

"Well, he's Scottish," I said, by way of explanation, not wishing to go into the subject of my husband's objections.

"Oh, Scottish." Mother Hildegarde nodded understandingly. "Just so."

The bed trembled against my thigh as Bouton leaped off and trotted toward the door.

"He smells a stranger," Mother Hildegarde remarked. "Bouton assists the doorkeeper as well as the physicians— with no more gratitude for his efforts, I fear."

The sounds of peremptory barks and a high voice raised in terror came through the double doors of the entryway.

"Oh, it's Father Balmain again! Curse the man, can't he learn to stand still and let Bouton smell him?" Mother Hildegarde turned in haste to the succor of her companion, turning back at the last moment to smile engagingly at me. "Perhaps I will send him to assist you with your tasks, Madame, while I soothe Father Balmain. While no doubt a most holy man, he lacks true appreciation for the work of an artist."

She strode toward the doors with her long, unhurried

stride, and with a last word for the carter, I turned to Sister Cecile and the latest stretcher case.

Jamie was lying on the carpet in the sitting room when I came back to the house, with a small boy sitting cross-legged on the floor beside him. Jamie was holding a bilboquet in one hand, and had the other poised over one eye.

"Of course I can," he was saying. "Anyday and twice on Sundays. Watch."

Placing the hand over his eye, he fixed the other piercingly on the bilboquet and gave the ivory cup a toss. The tethered ball leaped from its socket into an arc, and dropped as though guided by radar, landing back in its cup with a snug little plop.

"See?" he said, removing the hand from his eye. He sat up and handed the cup to the boy. "Here, you try it." He grinned at me, and slid a hand under the hem of my skirt, clasping my green silk ankle in greeting.

"Having fun?" I inquired.

"Not yet," he replied, giving the ankle a squeeze. "I was waiting for you, Sassenach." The long, warm fingers curled around my ankle slid higher, playfully stroking the curve of my calf, as a pair of limpid blue eyes gazed up at me, all innocence. His face had a streak of dried mud down one side, and there were dirty blotches on his shirt and kilt.

"Is that so?" I said, trying to pull my leg free of his grasp inconspicuously. "I should have thought your little playmate would have been all the company you needed."

The boy, understanding none of the English in which these exchanges were conducted, ignored them, intent on trying to work the bilboquet with one eye closed. The first two attempts having failed, he opened the second eye and glared at the toy, as though daring it not to work. The second eye closed again, but not all the way; a small slit remained, gleaming alertly below the thick fringe of dark lashes.

Jamie clicked his tongue disapprovingly, and the eye hastily snapped tight shut.

"Nah, then, Fergus, we'll have nay cheatin', if ye please," he said. "Fair's fair." The boy obviously caught the meaning, if not the words; he grinned sheepishly, displaying a pair of large, white, gleamingly perfect front teeth, square as a squir-rel's.

Jamie's hand exerted an invisible pull, obliging me to move closer to him to avoid being toppled off my moroccan heels.

"Ah," he said. "Well, Fergus here is a man of many tal-ents, and a boon companion for the idle hours when a man's wife has deserted him and left him to seek his own pursuits amidst the wickedness of the city"—the long fingers curled delicately into the hollow behind my knee, tickling sugges-tively—"but he isna qualified as a partner for the pastime I had in mind."

"Fergus?" I said, eyeing the boy, and trying to ignore the goings-on below. The lad was possibly nine or ten, but small for his age, and fine-boned as a ferret. Clad in clean, worn clothes several sizes too big for him, he was also as French as they come, with the pale, sallow skin and big, dark eyes of a Parisian street child.

"Well, his name is really Claudel, but we decided that didna sound verra manly, so he's to be called Fergus instead. A suitable warrior's name, that." Catching the sound of his name—or names—the boy glanced up and grinned shyly at me.

"This is Madame," Jamie explained to the boy, gesturing to me with his free hand. "You may call her milady. I dinna think he could manage 'Broch Tuarach,' " he added to me, "or even Fraser, for that matter."

" 'Milady' will be fine," I said, smiling. I wriggled my leg harder, trying to shake off the leechlike grip. "Er, *why*, if I may ask?"

"Why what? Oh, why Fergus, ye mean?"

"That's what I mean, all right." I wasn't sure just how far his arm would reach, but the hand was creeping slowly up the back of my thigh. "Jamie, take your hand away this minute!"

The fingers darted to one side, and deftly pulled loose the ribbon garter that held up my stocking. The stocking slith-ered down my leg to puddle round my ankle.

"You beast!" I kicked at him, but he dodged aside, laughing.

"Oh, beast, is it? What kind?"

"A cur!" I snapped, trying to bend over to pull up my

stocking without falling off my heels. The child Fergus, after a brief, incurious glance at us, had resumed his trials with the bilboquet.

"As for the lad," he continued blithely, "Fergus is now in my employ."

"To do what?" I asked. "We already have a boy who cleans the knives and boots, and a stable-lad."

Jamie nodded. "Aye, that's true. We havena got a pickpocket, though. Or rather, we hadn't; we have, now."

I drew in my breath and blew it out again slowly.

"I see. I suppose it would be dense of me to ask exactly why we need to add a pickpocket to the household?"

"To steal letters, Sassenach," Jamie said calmly.

"Oh," I said, light beginning to dawn.

"I canna get anything sensible out of His Highness; when he's with me, he wilna do anything but moan about Louise de La Tour, or grind his teeth and curse because they've been quarreling again. In either case, all he wants to do is to get drunk as quickly as possible. Mar is losing all patience with him, for he's haughty and sullen by turns. And I canna get anything out of Sheridan."

The Earl of Mar was the most respected of the exiled Scottish Jacobites in Paris. A man whose long and illustrious prime was only now beginning to edge into elderliness, he had been the primary supporter of King James at the abortive Rising in 1715, and had followed his king into exile after the defeat at Sheriffmuir. I had met the Earl and liked him; an elderly, courtly man with a personality as straight as his backbone. He was now doing his best—with little reward, it seemed—for his lord's son. I had met Thomas Sheridan, too; the Prince's tutor—an elderly man who handled His Highness's correspondence, translating impatience and illiteracy into courtly French and English.

I sat down and pulled my stocking back up. Fergus, apparently hardened to the sight of female limbs, ignored me altogether, concentrating grimly on the bilboquet.

"Letters, Sassenach," he said. "I need the letters. Letters from Rome, sealed with the Stuart crest. Letters from France, letters from England, letters from Spain. We can get them either from the Prince's house—Fergus can go with me, as a page—or possibly from the papal messenger who brings them; that would be a bit better, as we'd have the information in advance."

"So, we've made the bargain," Jamie said, nodding at his new servant. "Fergus will do his best to get what I need, and I will provide him with clothes and lodging and thirty écus a year. If he's caught while doing my service, I'll do my best to buy him off. If it canna be done, and he loses a hand or an ear, then I maintain him for the rest of his life, as he wilna be able to pursue his profession. And if he's hanged, then I guarantee to have Masses said for his soul for the space of a year. I think that's fair, no?"

I felt a cold hand pass down my spine.

"Jesus Christ, Jamie" was all I could find to say.

He shook his head, and reached out a hand for the bilboquet. "Not our Lord, Sassenach. Pray to St. Dismas. The patron saint of thieves and traitors."

Jamie reached over and took the bilboquet from the boy. He flicked his wrist sharply and the ivory ball rose in a perfect parabola, to descend into its cup with an inevitable plop.

"I see," I said. I eyed the new employee with interest as he took the toy Jamie offered him and started in on it once more, dark eyes gleaming with concentration. "Where did you get him?" I asked curiously.

"I found him in a brothel."

"Oh, of course," I said. "To be sure." I eyed the dirt and smears on his clothes. "Which you were visiting for some really excellent reason, I expect?"

"Oh, aye," he said. He sat back, arms wrapped about his knees, grinning as he watched me make repairs to my garter. "I thought you'd prefer me to be found in such an establishment, to the alternative of bein' found in a dark alleyway, wi' my head bashed in."

I saw the boy Fergus's eyes focus at a spot somewhat past the bilboquet, where a tray of iced cakes stood on a table near the wall. A small, pointed pink tongue darted out across his lower lip.

"I think your protégé is hungry," I said. "Why don't you feed him, and then you can tell me just what in bloody hell happened this afternoon."

"Well, I was on my way to the docks," he began, obediently rising to his feet, "and just past the Rue Eglantine, I began to have a queer feeling up the back of my neck."

Jamie Fraser had spent two years in the army of France, fought and stolen with a gang of Scottish "broken men," and been hunted as an outlaw through the moors and mountains of his native land. All of which had left him with an extreme sensitivity to the sensation of being followed.

He couldn't have said whether it was the sound of a footfall, too close behind, or the sight of a shadow that shouldn't be there, or something less tangible—the scent of evil on the air, perhaps—but he had learned that the prickle of warning among the short hairs of his neck was something to be ignored at his peril.

Promptly obeying the dictates of his cervical vertebrae, he turned left instead of right at the next corner, ducked around a whelk-seller's stall, cut between a barrow filled with steamed puddings and another of fresh vegetable marrows, and into a small charcuterie.

Pressed against the wall near the doorway, he peered out through a screen of hanging duck carcasses. Two men entered the street no more than a second later, walking close together, glancing quickly from side to side.

Every workingman in Paris carried the marks of his trade upon his person, and it didn't take much of a nose to detect the whiff of sea-salt on these two. If the small gold hoop in the shorter man's ear had not been a dead giveaway, the deep reddish-brown of their faces would have made it clear they were deep-water sailors.

Accustomed to the cramped quarters of shipboard and quay taverns, seamen seldom walked in a straight line. These two slid through the crowded alley like eels through rocks, eyes flicking past beggars, servingmaids, housewives, merchants; sea wolves assessing potential prey.

"I let them get well past the shop," Jamie explained, "and I was just about to step out and go back the other way, when I saw another of them at the mouth of the alley."

This man wore the same uniform as the other two; sidelocks heavily coated with grease, a fish knife at his side and a marlinspike the length of a man's forearm thrust through his belt. Short and thickset, the man stood still at the end of the alley, holding his ground against the buffeting waves of commerce that ebbed and flowed through the narrow passage. Clearly he had been left on guard, while his fellows quested ahead.

"So I was left wondering what best to do," Jamie said, rubbing his nose. "I was safe enough where I was, but there was no back way from the shop, and the moment I stepped from the doorway, I'd be seen." He glanced down reflectively, smoothing the crimson fabric of his kilt across his thigh. An enormous red barbarian was going to be conspicuous, no matter how thick the crowd.

"So what did you do?" I asked. Fergus, ignoring the conversation, was stuffing his pockets methodically with cakes, pausing for a hasty bite every so often in the process. Jamie caught my glance at the boy and shrugged.

"He'll not have been in the habit of eating regularly," he said. "Let him be."

"All right," I said. "But go on—what did you do?"

"Bought a sausage," he said promptly.

A Dunedin, to be exact. Made of spiced duck, ham and venison, boiled, stuffed and sun-dried, a Dunedin sausage measured eighteen inches from end to end and was as hard as seasoned oakwood.

"I couldna step out wi' my sword drawn," Jamie explained, "but I didna like the idea of stepping past the fellow in the alleyway wi' no one at my back, and empty hands."

Bearing the Dunedin at port arms, and keeping a weather eye on the passing crowd, Jamie had stepped boldly down the alley, toward the watcher at its mouth.

The man had met his gaze quite calmly, showing no sign of any malign intent. Jamie might have thought his original premonition mistaken, had he not seen the watcher's eyes flick briefly to something over Jamie's shoulder. Obeying the instincts that had kept him alive thus far, he had dived forward, knocking the watcher down and sliding on his face across the filthy cobbles of the street.

The crowd scattered before him with shrieks of alarm, and he rolled to his feet to see the flung knife that had missed him, quivering in the boards of a ribbon stall.

"If I'd had a bit of doubt it was me they wanted, I didna fret about it longer," he said dryly.

He had kept hold of the sausage, and now found use for it, swinging it smartly across the face of one attacker.

"I broke his nose, I think," he said meditatively. "Anyway, he reeled back, and I shoved past and took off running, down the Rue Peletier."

The inhabitants of the street scattered before him like geese, startled by the sight of a hurtling Scotsman, kilt flying around his churning knees. He didn't stop to look behind; by the shouts of indignant passersby, he could tell that the assailants were still in pursuit.

This part of the city was seldom patrolled by the King's Guard, and the crowd itself offered little protection other than a simple obstruction that might slow his pursuers. No one was likely to interfere in a matter of violence on a foreigner's behalf.

"There are no alleys off the Rue Peletier. I needed at least to get to a place where I could draw my sword and have a wall at my back," Jamie explained. "So I pushed at the doors as I passed, 'til I hit one that opened."

Dashing into a gloomy hallway, past a startled porter, and through a hanging drape, he had shot into the center of a large, well-lighted room, and come to a screeching halt in the middle of one of Madame Elise's salon, the scent of perfume heavy in his nostrils.

"I see," I said, biting my lip. "I, um, trust you didn't draw your sword in there?"

Jamie narrowed his eyes at me, but didn't deign to reply directly.

"I'll leave it to you, Sassenach," he said dryly, "to imagine what it feels like to arrive unexpectedly in the midst of a brothel, in possession of a verra large sausage."

My imagination proved fully equal to this task, and I burst out laughing.

"God, I wish I could have seen you!" I said.

"Thank God ye didn't!" he said fervently. A furious blush glowed on his cheekbones.

Ignoring remarks from the fascinated inmates, Jamie had made his way awkwardly through what he described, shuddering, as "tangles o' bare limbs," until he had spotted Fergus against one wall, regarding the intruder with a round-eyed astonishment.

Seizing upon this unexpected manifestation of maleness, Jamie had gripped the lad by the shoulder, and fervently implored him to show the way to the nearest exit, without loss of a moment.

"I could hear a hurly-burly breakin' out in the hallway," he explained, "and I kent they were in after me. I didna want to be having to fight for my life wi' a lot of naked women getting in the way."

"I can see that the prospect might be daunting," I agreed, rubbing my upper lip. "But obviously he got you out."

"Aye. He didna hesitate a moment, the dear lad. 'This way, Monsieur!' he says, and it was up the stair, and through a room, and out a window onto the roof, and awa' wi' us both." Jamie cast a fond glance at his new employee.

"You know," I observed, "there are *some* wives who wouldn't believe one word of a story like that."

Jamie's eyes opened wide in astonishment.

"They wouldna? Whyever not?"

"Possibly," I said dryly, "because they aren't married to *you*. I'm pleased that you escaped with your virtue intact, but for the moment, I'm rather more interested in the chaps who chased you in there."

"I didna have a great deal of leisure to think about it at the time," Jamie replied. "And now that I have, I still couldna say who they were, or why they were hunting me."

"Robbery, do you think?" The cash receipts of the wine business were conveyed between the Fraser warehouse, the Rue Trémoulins, and Jared's bank by strongbox, under heavy guard. Still, Jamie was very visible among the crowds near the river docks, and was undoubtedly known to be a wealthy foreign merchant—wealthy by contrast with most of the denizens of that neighborhood, at any rate.

He shook his head, flicking crumbs of dried mud off his shirtfront.

"It might be, I suppose. But they didna try to accost me; it was straight-out murder they meant."

His tone was quite matter-of-fact, but it gave me rather a

wobbly feeling in the knees, and I sank down onto a settee. I licked my lips, gone suddenly dry.

"Who—who do you think . . . ?"

He shrugged, frowning as he scooped up a dab of icing from the plate and licked it off his finger.

"The only man I could think of who's threatened me is the Comte St. Germain. But I canna think what he'd gain from having me killed."

"He's Jared's business rival, you said."

"Oh, aye. But the Comte's no interest in German wines, and I canna see him going to the trouble of killing me, only to ruin Jared's new enterprise by bringing him back to Paris. That seems a trifle extreme," he said dryly, "even for a man wi' the Comte's temper."

"Well, do you think . . ." The idea made me mildly ill, and I swallowed twice before going on. "Do you think it might have been . . . revenge? For the *Patagonia* being burned?"

Jamie shook his head, baffled.

"I suppose it could be, but it seems a long time to wait. And why me, come to that?" he added. "It's you annoyed him, Sassenach. Why not kill you, if that's what he meant?"

The sick feeling got slightly worse.

"Do you have to be so bloody logical?" I said.

He saw the look on my face, and smiled suddenly, putting an arm around me for comfort.

"Nay, *mo nighean donn.* The Comte's a quick temper, but I canna see him going to the trouble and expense of killing either of us, only for revenge. If it might get him his ship back, then yes," he added, "but as it is, I expect he'd only think the price of three hired assassins throwing good money after bad."

He patted my shoulder and stood up.

"Nay, I expect it was only a try at robbery, after all. Dinna trouble yourself about it. I'll take Murtagh with me to the docks from now on, to be safe."

He stretched himself, and brushed the last of the crumbling dirt from his kilt. "Am I decent to go in to supper?" he asked, looking critically down his chest. "It must be nearly ready by now."

"What's ready?"

He opened the door, and a rich, spicy scent wafted up at once from the dining room below.

"Why, the sausage, of course," he said, with a grin over one shoulder. "Ye dinna think I'd let it go to waste?"

13

Deceptions

"barberry leaves, three handfuls in a decoction, steeped overnight, poured over half a handful of black hellebore." I laid the list of ingredients down on the inlaid table as though it were slightly slimy to the touch. "I got it from Madame Rouleaux. She's the best of the angel-makers, but even she says it's dangerous. Louise, are you sure you want to do this?"

Her round pink face was blotched, and the plump lower lip had a tendency to quiver.

"What choice do I have?" She picked up the recipe for the abortifacient and gazed at it in repulsed fascination.

"Black hellebore," she said, and shuddered. "The very name of it sounds evil!"

"Well, it's bloody nasty stuff," I said bluntly. "It will make you feel as though your insides are coming out. But the baby may come, too. It doesn't always work." I remembered Master Raymond's warning—*It is dangerous to wait too long*—and wondered how far gone she might be. Surely no more than six weeks or so; she had told me the instant she suspected.

She glanced at me, startled, with red-rimmed eyes.

"You have used it yourself?"

"God, no!" I startled myself with the vehemence of my exclamation, and took a deep breath.

"No. I've seen women who have, though—at L'Hôpital des Anges." The abortionists—the angel-makers—practiced largely in the privacy of homes, their own or their clients'. Their successes were not the ones that came to the hospital. I laid a hand unobtrusively over my own abdomen, as though for protection of its helpless occupant. Louise caught the gesture and hurled herself into the sofa, burying her head in her hands.

"Oh, I wish I were dead!" she moaned. "Why, why couldn't I be as fortunate as you—to be bearing the child of a husband I loved?" She clutched her own plump stomach with both hands, staring down at it as though expecting the child to peek out between her fingers.

There were any number of answers to that particular question, but I didn't think she really wanted to hear any of them. I took a deep breath and sat down beside her, patting a heaving damask shoulder.

"Louise," I said. "Do you want the child?"

She lifted her head and stared at me in astonishment.

"But of course I want it!" she exclaimed. "It's his—it's Charles's! It's . . ." Her face crumpled, and she bowed her head once more over her hands, clasped so tightly over her belly. "It's mine," she whispered. After a long moment, she raised her streaming face, and with a pathetic attempt to pull herself together, wiped her nose on a trailing sleeve.

"But it's no good," she said. "If I don't . . ." She glanced at the recipe on the table and swallowed heavily. "Then Jules will divorce me—he'll cast me out. There would be the most terrible scandal. I might be excommunicated! Not even Father could protect me."

"Yes," I said. "But . . ." I hesitated, then cast caution to the winds. "Is there any chance Jules might be convinced the child is his?" I asked bluntly.

She looked blank for a moment, and I wanted to shake her.

"I don't see how, unless—oh!" Light dawned, and she looked at me, horrified.

"Sleep with Jules, you mean? But Charles would be furious!"

"Charles," I said through my teeth, "is not pregnant!"

"Well, but he's . . . that is . . . I couldn't!" The look of horror was fading, though, being slowly replaced with the growing realization of possibility.

I didn't want to push her; still, I saw no good reason for her to risk her life for the sake of Charles Stuart's pride, either.

"Do you suppose Charles would want you to endanger yourself?" I said. "For that matter—does he know about the child?"

She nodded, mouth slightly open as she thought about it, hands still clenched together over her stomach.

"Yes. That's what we quarreled about last time." She

sniffed. "He was angry; he said it was all my fault, that I should have waited until he had reclaimed his father's throne. Then he would be king someday, and he could come and take me away from Jules, and have the Pope annul my marriage, and his sons could be heirs to England and Scotland . . ." She gave way once more, sniveling and wailing incoherently into a fold of her skirt.

I rolled my eyes in exasperation.

"Oh, do be quiet, Louise!" I snapped. It shocked her enough to make her stop weeping, at least momentarily, and I took advantage of the hiatus to press my point.

"Look," I said, as persuasively as possible, "you don't suppose Charles would want you to sacrifice his son, do you? Legitimate or not?" Actually, I rather thought Charles would be in favor of any step that removed inconvenience from his own path, regardless of the effects on Louise or his putative offspring. On the other hand, the Prince did have a marked streak of romanticism; perhaps he could be induced to view this as the sort of temporary adversity common to exiled monarchs. Obviously, I was going to need Jamie's help. I grimaced at the thought of what he was likely to say about it.

"Well. . . ." Louise was wavering, wanting desperately to be convinced. I had a momentary pang of pity for Jules, Prince de Rohan, but the vision of a young servant-girl, dying in protracted, blood-smeared agony on a pallet spread in the stone hallway of L'Hôpital des Anges was brutally clear in my mind.

It was nearly sunset when I left the de Rohans', footsteps dragging. Louise, palpitating with nervousness, was upstairs in her boudoir, her maid putting up her hair and arraying her in her most daring gown before she went down to a private supper with her husband. I felt completely drained, and hoped that Jamie hadn't brought anyone home for supper; I could use a spot of privacy, too.

He hadn't; when I entered the study, he was seated at the desk, poring over three or four sheets of close-written paper.

"Do you think 'the fur merchant' is more likely to be Louis of France, or his minister Duverney?" he asked, without looking up.

"Fine, thank you, darling, and how are *you*?" I said.

"All right," he said absently. The cowlicks on the top of his head were sticking up straight; he massaged his scalp vigorously as I watched, scowling down his long nose at the paper.

"I'm sure 'the tailor from Vendôme' must be Monsieur Geyer," he said, running a finger along the lines of the letter, "and 'our mutual friend'—that could be either the Earl of Mar, or possibly the papal envoy. I think the Earl, from the rest of it, but the—"

"What on earth is that?" I peered over his shoulder, and gasped when I saw the signature at the foot of the letter. James Stuart, by the grace of God King of England and Scotland.

"Bloody Christ! It worked, then!" Swinging around, I spotted Fergus, crouched on a stool in front of the fire, industriously stuffing pastries into his face. "Good lad," I said, smiling at him. He grinned back at me, cheeks puffed like a chipmunk's with chestnut tart.

"We got it from the papal messenger," Jamie explained, coming to the surface long enough to realize I was there. "Fergus took it from the bag while he was eating supper in a tavern. He'll spend the night there, so we'll have to put this back before morning. No difficulties there, Fergus?"

The boy swallowed and shook his head. "No, milord. He sleeps alone—not trusting his bedmates not to steal the contents of his bag." He grinned derisively at this. "The second window on the left, above the stables." He waved an airy hand, the deft, grubby fingers reaching for another pie. "It is nothing, milord."

I had a sudden vision of that fine-boned hand held squirming on a block, with an executioner's blade raised above the broomstick wrist. I gulped, forcing down the sudden lurch of my stomach. Fergus wore a small greenish copper medal on a string about his neck; the image of St. Dismas, I hoped.

"Well," I said, taking a deep breath to steady myself, "what's all this about fur merchants?"

There was no time then for leisurely inspection. In the end, I made a quick fair copy of the letter, and the original was carefully refolded and its original seal replaced with the aid of a knife blade heated in a candle flame.

Watching this operation critically, Fergus shook his head at Jamie. "You have the touch, milord. It is a pity that the one hand is crippled."

Jamie glanced dispassionately at his right hand. It really wasn't too bad; a couple of fingers set slightly askew, a thick scar down the length of the middle finger. The only major damage had been to the fourth finger, which stuck out stiffly, its second joint so badly crushed that the healing had fused two finger-bones together. The hand had been broken in Wentworth Prison, less than four months ago, by Jack Randall.

"Never mind," he said, smiling. He flexed the hand and flicked the fingers playfully at Fergus. "My great paws are too big to make a living picking pockets, anyway." He had regained an astounding degree of movement, I thought. He still carried the soft ball of rags I had made for him, squeezing it unobtrusively hundreds of times a day as he went about his business. And if the knitting bones hurt him, he never complained.

"Off with ye, then," he told Fergus. "Come and find me when you're safe back, so I'll know ye havena been taken up by the police or the landlord of the tavern."

Fergus wrinkled his nose scornfully at such an idea, but nodded, tucking the letter carefully inside his smock before disappearing down the back stair toward the night that was both natural element and protection for him.

Jamie looked after him for a long minute, then turned to me. He truly looked at me for the first time, and his brows flew up.

"Christ, Sassenach!" he said. "You're pale as my sark! Are ye all right?"

"Just hungry," I said.

He rang at once for supper, and we ate it before the fire, while I told him about Louise. Rather to my surprise, while he knit his brows over the situation and muttered uncomplimentary things under his breath in Gaelic about both Louise and Charles Stuart, he agreed with my solution to the problem.

"I thought you'd be upset," I said, scooping up a mouthful of succulent cassoulet with a bit of bread. The warm, bacon-spiced beans soothed me, filling me with a sense of peaceful well-being. It was cold and dark outside, and loud with the rushing of the wind, but it was warm and quiet here by the fire together.

"Oh, about Louise de La Tour foisting a bastard on her husband?" Jamie frowned at his own dish, running a finger around the edge to pick up the last of the juice.

"Well, I'm no verra much in favor of it, I'll tell ye, Sassenach. It's a filthy trick to play on a man, but what's the poor bloody woman to do otherwise?" He shook his head, then glanced at the desk across the room and smiled wryly.

"Besides, it doesna become me to be takin' a high moral stand about other people's behavior. Stealing letters and spying and trying generally to subvert a man my family holds as King? I shouldna like to have someone judging me on the grounds of the things I'm doing, Sassenach."

"You have a damn good reason for what you're doing!" I objected.

He shrugged. The firelight flickering on his face hollowed his cheeks and threw shadows into the orbits of his eyes. It made him look older than he was; I tended to forget that he was not quite twenty-four.

"Aye, well. And Louise de La Tour has a reason, too," he said. "She wants to save one life, I want ten thousand. Does that excuse my risking wee Fergus—and Jared's business—and you?" He turned his head and smiled at me, the light gleaming from the long, straight bridge of his nose, glowing like sapphire in the one eye turned toward the fire.

"Nay, I think I wilna lose my sleep over the need for opening another man's letters," he said. "It may come to much worse than that before we've done, Claire, and I canna say ahead of time what my conscience will stand; it's best not to test it too soon."

There was nothing to be said to that; it was all true. I reached out and laid my hand against his cheek. He laid his own hand over mine, cradling it for a moment, then turned his head and gently kissed my palm.

"Well," he said, drawing a deep breath and returning to business. "Now that we've eaten, shall we have a look at this letter?"

The letter was coded; that much was obvious. To foil possible interceptors, Jamie explained.

"Who would want to intercept His Highness's mail?" I asked. "Besides us, I mean."

Jamie snorted with amusement at my naiveté.

"Almost anyone, Sassenach. Louis's spies, Duverney's spies, Philip of Spain's spies. The Jacobite lords and the ones who think they might turn Jacobite if the wind sets right. Dealers in information, who dinna care a fart in a breeze who lives or dies by it. The Pope himself; the Holy See's been supporting the Stuarts in exile for fifty years—I imagine he keeps an eye on what they're doing." He tapped a finger on the copy I'd made of James's letter to his son.

"The seal on this letter had been removed maybe three times before I took it off myself," he said.

"I see," I said. "No wonder James codes his letters. Do you think you can make out what he says?"

Jamie picked up the sheets, frowning.

"I don't know; some, yes. Some other things, I've no idea. I think perhaps I can work it out, though, if I can see some other letters King James has sent. I'll see what Fergus can do for me there." He folded the copy and put it carefully away in a drawer, which he locked.

"Ye canna trust anyone, Sassenach," he explained, seeing my eyes widen. "We might easily have spies among the servants." He dropped the small key in the pocket of his coat, and held out his arm to me.

I took the candle in one hand and his arm in the other, and we turned toward the stairs. The rest of the house was dark, the servants—all but Fergus—virtuously asleep. I felt a trifle creepy, with the realization that one or more of the silent sleepers below or above might not be what they seemed.

"Doesn't it make you feel a bit nervous?" I asked as we went up the stairs. "Never being able to trust anyone?"

He laughed softly. "Well, I wouldna say *anyone,* Sassenach. There's you—and Murtagh, and my sister Jenny and her husband Ian. I'd trust the four of you wi' my life—I have, for that matter, more than once."

I shivered as he pulled back the drapes of the big bed.

The fire had been banked for the night, and the room was growing cold.

"Four people you can trust doesn't seem like all that many," I said, unlacing my gown.

He pulled his shirt over his head and tossed it on the chair. The scars on his back shone silver in the faint light from the night sky outside.

"Aye, well," he said matter-of-factly. "It's four more than Charles Stuart has."

There was a bird singing outside, though it was long before first light. A mockingbird, practicing his trills and runs over and over, perched on a rain gutter somewhere in the dark nearby.

Moving sleepily, Jamie rubbed his cheek against the smooth skin of my freshly waxed underarm, then turned his head and planted a soft kiss in the warm hollow that sent a small, delicious shudder down my side.

"Mm," he murmured, running a light hand over my ribs. "I like it when ye come out all gooseflesh like that, Sassenach."

"Like this?" I answered, running the nails of my right hand gently over the skin of his back, which obligingly rippled into goose bumps under the teasing of the touch.

"Ah."

"Ah, yourself, then," I answered softly, doing it some more.

"Mmmm." With a luxurious groan, he rolled to the side, wrapping his arms around me as I followed, enjoying the sudden contact of every inch of our naked skins, all down the front from head to toe. He was warm as a smothered fire, the heat of him safely banked for the night, to kindle again to a blaze in the black cold of dawn.

His lips fastened gently on one nipple, and I groaned myself, arching slightly to encourage him to take it deeper into the warmth of his mouth. My breasts were growing fuller, and more sensitive by the day; my nipples ached and tingled sometimes under the tight binding of my gowns, wanting to be suckled.

"Will ye let me do this later?" he murmured, with a soft

bite. "When the child's come, and your breasts fill wi' milk? Will ye feed me, too, then, next to your heart?"

I clasped his head and cradled it, fingers deep in the baby-soft hair that grew thick at the base of his skull.

"Always," I whispered.

14

Meditations on the Flesh

Fergus was more than adept at his profession, and nearly every day brought in a new selection of His Highness's correspondence; sometimes I was hard pressed to copy everything before Fergus's next expedition, when he would replace the items abstracted, before stealing the new letters.

Some of these were further coded communications from King James in Rome; Jamie put aside the copies of these, to puzzle over at leisure. The bulk of His Highness's correspondence was innocuous—notes from friends in Italy, an increasing number of bills from local merchants—Charles had a taste for gaudy clothing and fine boots, as well as for brandy-wine—and the occasional note from Louise de La Tour de Rohan. These were fairly easy to pick out; aside from the tiny, mannered handwriting she employed, that made her letters look as though a small bird had been making tracks on them, she invariably saturated the paper with her trademark hyacinth scent. Jamie resolutely refused to read these.

"I willna be reading the man's love letters," he said firmly. "Even a plotter must scruple at *something*." He sneezed, and dropped the latest missive back into Fergus's pocket. "Besides," he added more practically, "Louise tells ye everything, anyway."

This was true; Louise had become a close friend, and spent nearly as much time in my drawing room as she did in her own, wringing her hands over Charles, then forgetting him in the fascination of discussing the marvels of pregnancy—*she* never had morning sickness, curse her! Scatterbrained as she was, I liked her very much; still, it was a great relief to escape from her company to L'Hôpital des Anges every afternoon.

While Louise was unlikely ever to set foot within L'Hôpital des Anges, I was not without company when I went there. Undaunted by her first exposure to the Hôpital, Mary Hawkins summoned up the courage to accompany me again.

And yet again. While she couldn't quite bring herself to look directly at a wound yet, she was useful at spooning gruel into people and sweeping floors. Apparently she considered these activities a welcome change from either the gatherings of the Court or the life at her uncle's house.

While she was frequently shocked at some of the behavior she saw at Court—not that she saw much, but she was easily shocked—she didn't betray any particular distaste or horror at the sight of the Vicomte Marigny, which led me to conclude that her wretched family had not yet completed the negotiations for her marriage—and therefore hadn't told her about it.

This conclusion was borne out one day in late April, when, en route to L'Hôpital des Anges, she blushingly confided to me that she was in love.

"Oh, he's so handsome!" she enthused, her stammer entirely forgotten. "And so . . . well, so *spiritual*, as well."

"Spiritual?" I said. "Mm, yes, very nice." Privately I thought that that particular quality was not one which would have topped my own list of desirable attributes in a lover, but then tastes differed.

"And who is the favored gentleman, then?" I teased gently. "Anyone I know?"

The rosy blush deepened. "No, I shouldn't think so." She looked up then, eyes sparkling. "But—oh, I shouldn't tell you this, but I can't help myself. He wrote to my father. He's coming back to Paris next week!"

"Really?" This was interesting news. "I'd heard that the Comte de Palles is expected at Court next week," I said. "Is your, um, intended, one of his party?"

Mary looked aghast at the suggestion.

"A Frenchman! Oh, no, Claire; really, how could I marry a Frenchman?"

"Is there something wrong with Frenchmen?" I asked, rather surprised at her vehemence. "You do speak French, after all." Perhaps that was the trouble, though; while Mary did speak French very nicely, her shyness made her stammer even worse in that language than in English. I had come across a couple of kitchen-boys only the day before, entertaining each other with cruel imitations of *"la petite Anglaise maladroite."*

"You don't know about Frenchmen?" she whispered, eyes wide and horrified. "Oh, but of course, you wouldn't. Your husband is so gentle and so kind . . . he wouldn't, I m-mean I know he d-doesn't trouble you that way . . ." Her face was suffused with a rich peony that reached from chin to hairline, and the stammer was about to strangle her.

"Do you mean . . ." I began, trying to think of some tactful way of extricating her without entangling myself in speculations about the habits of Frenchmen. However, considering what Mr. Hawkins had told me about Mary's father and his plans for her marriage, I rather thought perhaps I should try to disabuse her of the notions that she had clearly picked up from the gossip of salon and dressing room. I didn't want her to die of fright if she *did* end up married to a Frenchman.

"What they d-do . . . in . . . in *bed*!" she whispered hoarsely.

"Well," I said matter-of-factly, "there are only so many things you *can* do in bed with a man, after all. And since I see quite a large number of children about the city, I'd assume that even Frenchmen are fairly well versed in the orthodox methods."

"Oh! Children . . . well, yes, of course," she said vaguely, as though not seeing much connection. "B-b-but they said"—she cast her eyes down, embarrassed, and her voice sank even lower—"th-that he . . . a Frenchm-man's *thing*, you know. . . ."

"Yes, I know," I said, striving for patience. "So far as I know, they're much like any other man's. Englishmen and Scotsmen are quite similarly endowed."

"Yes, but they, they . . . p-p-put it between a lady's l-l-legs! I mean, right up *inside* her!" This bit of stop-press news finally out, she took a deep breath, which seemed to steady her, for the violent crimson of her face receded slightly. "An Englishman, or even a Scot . . . oh, I didn't m-mean it *that* way . . ." Her hand flew to her mouth in embarrassment. "But a decent man like your husband, surely he would n-never dream of forcing a wife to endure s-something like that!"

I placed a hand on my slightly bloated stomach and re-

garded her thoughtfully. I began to see why spirituality
ranked so highly in Mary Hawkins's catalog of manly virtues.

"Mary," I said, "I think we must have a small talk."

I was still smiling privately to myself when I walked out
into the Great Hall of the Hôpital, my own dress covered
with the drab, sturdy fabric of a novice's habit.

A good many of the *chirurgiens,* urinoscopists, boneset-
ters, physicians, and other healers were donating their time
and services as a charity; others came to learn or refine their
skills. The hapless patients of L'Hôpital des Anges were in no
position to protest being the subjects of assorted medical experiments.

Aside from the nuns themselves, the medical staff
changed almost daily, depending upon who found themselves
without paying patients that day, or who had a new technique
that needed trial. Still, most of the free-lance medicos came
often enough that I learned to recognize the regulars in short
order.

One of the most interesting was the tall, gaunt man
whom I had seen amputating a leg on my first visit to the
Hôpital. Upon inquiry, I determined that his name was Monsieur Forez. Primarily a bonesetter, occasionally he would attempt the trickier types of amputation, particularly when a
whole limb, rather than a joint, was involved. The nuns and
orderlies seemed a bit in awe of Monsieur Forez; they never
chaffed him or exchanged rude jokes, as they did with most of
the other volunteer medical help.

Monsieur Forez was at work today. I approached quietly,
to see what he was doing. The patient, a young workman, lay
white-faced and gasping on a pallet. He had fallen from the
scaffolding on the cathedral—always under construction—
and broken both an arm and a leg. I could see that the arm
was no particular challenge to a professional bonesetter—
only a simple fracture of the radius. The leg, though, was
something else; an impressive double compound fracture, involving both the mid-femur and the tibia. Sharp bone fragments protruded through the skin of both thigh and shin, and
the lacerated flesh was blue with traumatic bruising over most
of the upper aspect of the leg.

I didn't wish to distract the bonesetter's attention to his case, but Monsieur Forez appeared sunk in thought, slowly circling the patient, sidling back and forth like a large carrion crow, cautious lest the victim not be really dead yet. He did look rather like a crow, I thought, with that prominent beak of a nose, and the smooth black hair that he wore unpowdered, slicked back to a wispy knot at the nape of his neck. His clothes, too, were black and somber, though of good quality—evidently he had a profitable practice outside the Hôpital.

At last deciding on his course of action, Monsieur Forez lifted his chin from his hand and glanced around for assistance. His eye lighted on me, and he beckoned me forward. I was dressed in a coarse linen novice's gown, and lost in his concentration, he did not notice that I didn't wear the wimple and veil of a nursing sister.

"Here, *ma soeur*," he directed, taking hold of the patient's ankle. "Grasp it tightly just behind the heel. Do not apply pressure until I tell you, but when I give the word, draw the foot directly toward you. Pull very slowly, but with force— it will take considerable strength, you understand."

"I understand." I grasped the foot as directed, while Monsieur Forez made his slow and gangling way toward the other end of the pallet, glancing contemplatively at the fractured leg.

"I have a stimulant here to assist," he said, drawing a small vial out of his coat pocket and setting it beside the patient's head. "It constricts the blood vessels of the surface skin, and drives the blood inward, where it may be of more use to our young friend." So speaking, he grasped the patient by the hair and thrust the vial into the young man's mouth, skillfully decanting the medicine down his throat without spilling a drop.

"Ah," he said approvingly as the man gulped and breathed deeply. "That will help. Now, as to the pain—yes, it is better if we can numb the leg, so he will be less inclined to resist our efforts as we straighten it."

He reached into his capacious pocket once more, this time coming out with a small brass pin, some three inches in length, with a wide, flat head. One bony, thick-jointed hand tenderly explored the inside of the patient's thigh near the groin, following the thin blue line of a large vein beneath the skin. The groping fingers hesitated, paused, palpated in a small circle, then settled on a point. Digging a sharp forefinger into the skin as though to mark his place, Monsieur Forez brought the point of the brass pin to bear in the same place. Another quick reach into the pocket of marvels produced a small brass hammer, with which he drove the pin straight into the leg with one blow.

The leg twitched violently, then seemed to relax into limpness. The vasoconstrictor administered earlier did in fact seem to be working; the ooze of blood from the severed tissues was markedly less.

"That's amazing!" I exclaimed. "What did you do?"

Monsieur Forez smiled shyly, a faint rosiness staining his blue-shadowed cheeks with pleasure at my admiration.

"Well, it does not always work quite so well," he admitted modestly. "Luck was with me this time." He pointed at the brass pin, explaining, "There is a large bundle of nerve endings there, Sister, what I have heard the anatomists call a *plexus*. If you are fortunate enough to pierce it directly, it numbs a great deal of the sensations in the lower extremity." He straightened abruptly, realizing that he was wasting time in talk that might better be spent in action.

"Come, *ma soeur*," he ordered. "Back to your post! The action of the stimulant is not long-lasting; we must work now, while the bleeding is suppressed."

Almost limp, the leg straightened easily, the splintered ends of bone drawing back through the skin. Following Monsieur Forez's orders, I now grasped the young man about the torso, while he maneuvered the foot and lower leg, so that we applied a constant traction while the final small adjustments were made.

"That will do, Sister. Now, if you will but hold the foot steady for a moment." A shout summoned an orderly with a couple of stout sticks and some rags for binding, and in no time we had the limb neatly splinted and the open wounds firmly dressed with pressure bandages.

Monsieur Forez and I exchanged a broad smile of congratulation over the body of our patient.

"Lovely work, that," I praised, shoving back a lock of hair that had come unbound during our exertions. I saw Mon-

sieur Forez's face change suddenly, as he realized that I wore
no veil, and just then the loud bonging of the Vespers bell
rang from the adjacent church. I glanced openmouthed at the
tall window at the end of the ward, left unglassed to allow
unwholesome vapors to pass out. Sure enough, the oblong of
sky was the deep half-indigo of early evening.

"Excuse me," I said, starting to wriggle out of the covering gown. "I must go at once; my husband will be worried
about me coming home so late. I'm so glad to have had the
chance of assisting you, Monsieur Forez." The tall bonesetter
watched this disrobing act in patent astonishment.

"But you . . . well, no, of course you are not a nun, I
should have realized that before . . . but you . . . who are
you?" he asked curiously.

"My name's Fraser," I told him briefly. "Look, I *must* go,
or my husband . . ."

He drew himself up to his full gawky height, and bowed
with deep seriousness.

"I should esteem it a privilege if you would allow me to
see you home, Madame Fraser."

"Oh . . . why, thank you," I said, touched at his
thoughtfulness. "I have an escort, though," I said, looking
vaguely around the hall for Fergus, who had taken over escort
duty from Murtagh, when he was not needed to steal something. He was there, leaning against the doorjamb, twitching
with impatience. I wondered how long he had been there—
the sisters wouldn't allow him into the main hall or the wards,
always insisting that he wait for me by the door.

Monsieur Forez eyed my escort dubiously, then took me
firmly by the elbow.

"I will see you to your door, Madame," he declared.
"This section of the city is much too dangerous in the evening
hours for you to be abroad with no more than a child for
protection."

I could see Fergus swelling with indignation at being
called a child, and hastened to protest that he was an excellent escort, always taking care to guide me by the safest
streets. Monsieur Forez paid no attention to either of us,
merely nodding in a stately manner to Sister Angelique as he
steered me through the huge double doors of the Hôpital.

Fergus trotted at my heels, plucking at my sleeve. "Madame!" he said in an urgent whisper. "Madame! I promised the master that I would see you safely home each day, that I would not allow you to associate with undesirable—"

"Ah, here we are. Madame, you sit here; your boy may have the other seat." Ignoring Fergus's yapping, Monsieur Forez picked him up and tossed him casually into the waiting carriage.

The carriage was a small open one, but elegantly equipped, with deep blue velvet seats and a small canopy to protect the passengers from sudden inclemencies of weather or slops flung from above. There was no coat of arms or other decoration on the equipage's door; Monsieur Forez was not of the nobility—must be a rich bourgeois, I thought.

We made polite conversation on the way home, discussing medical matters, while Fergus sulked in the corner, glowering under the ragged thatch of his hair. When we pulled up in the Rue Trémoulins, he leaped over the side without waiting for the coachman to open the door, and sprinted inside. I stared after him, wondering what ailed him, then turned to take my farewell of Monsieur Forez.

"Really, it is nothing," he assured me graciously, in response to my profuse thanks. "Your residence lies along the path I take to my own house, in any case. And I could not have trusted the person of such a gracious lady to the Paris streets at this hour." He handed me down from the carriage, and was opening his mouth to say more, when the gate slammed open behind us.

I turned in time to see Jamie's expression change from mild annoyance to startled surprise.

"Oh!" he said. "Good evening, Monsieur." He bowed to Monsieur Forez, who returned the salute with great solemnity.

"Your wife has allowed me the great pleasure of delivering her safely to your door, milord. As for her late arrival, I beg you will lay the blame for that on my own shoulders; she was most nobly assisting me in a small endeavor at L'Hôpital des Anges."

"I expect she was," said Jamie in a resigned tone. "After all," he added in English, raising an eyebrow at me, "ye couldna expect a mere husband to hold the same sort of appeal as an inflamed bowel or a case of bilious spots, could ye?" The corner of his mouth twitched, though, and I knew he wasn't really annoyed, only concerned that I hadn't come home; I felt a twinge of regret at having worried him.

Bowing once more to Monsieur Forez, he grasped me by the upper arm and hustled me through the gate.

"Where's Fergus?" I asked, as soon as the gate was closed behind us. Jamie snorted.

"In the kitchen, awaiting retribution, I expect."

"Retribution? What do you mean by that?" I demanded. Unexpectedly, he laughed.

"Well," he said, "I was sittin' in the study, wondering where in bloody hell you'd got to, and on the verge of going down to the Hôpital myself, when the door flew open, and young Fergus shot in and threw himself on the floor at my feet, begging me to kill him on the spot."

"Kill him? Whatever for?"

"Well, that's what I asked him myself, Sassenach. I thought perhaps you and he had been waylaid by footpads along the way—there are dangerous gangs of ruffians about the streets, ye ken, and I thought losin' you that way would be the only thing would make him behave so. But he said you were at the gate, so I came tearing along to see were ye all right, with Fergus at my heels, babbling about betraying my trust and being unworthy to call me master, and begging me to beat him to death. I found it a bit difficult to think, what wi' all that going on, so I told him I'd attend to him later, and sent him to the kitchen."

"Oh, bloody hell!" I said. "Does he really think he's betrayed your trust, just because I've come home a bit late?"

Jamie glanced aside at me.

"Aye, he does. And so he did, for that matter, letting ye ride in company with a stranger. He swears that he would ha' thrown himself in front of the horses before he would let ye enter the carriage, save that *you,*" he added pointedly, "seemed on good terms wi' the man."

"Well, of course I was on good terms with him," I said indignantly. "I'd just been helping him set a leg."

"Mphm." This line of argument appeared to strike him as unconvincing.

"Oh, all right," I agreed reluctantly. "Perhaps it was a bit unwise. But he really did seem entirely respectable, and I *was*

in a hurry to get home—I knew you'd be worried." Still, I was
now wishing I had paid a little more attention to Fergus's
frantic mumblings and pluckings at my sleeve. At the time, I
had been concerned only to reach home as soon as possible.

"You aren't really going to beat him, are you?" I asked in
some alarm. "It wasn't his fault in the slightest—I insisted on
going with Monsieur Forez. I mean, if anyone deserves beating, it's me."

Turning in the direction of the kitchen, Jamie cocked a
sardonic eyebrow at me.

"Aye, it is," he agreed. "Having sworn to refrain from
any such actions, though, I may have to settle for Fergus."

"Jamie! You wouldn't!" I stopped dead, yanking on his
arm. "Jamie! Please!" Then I saw the smile hidden in the
corner of his mouth, and sighed in relief.

"No," he said, letting the smile become visible. "I dinna
mean to kill him—or even beat him, for that matter. I may
have to go clout him over the ear a time or two, though, if
only to save his honor," he added. "He thinks he's committed
a major crime by not following my orders to guard ye—I can
hardly let it pass without some sign of official displeasure."

He paused outside the baize door to the kitchens to
fasten his cuffs and rewind the stock about his throat.

"Am I decent?" he inquired, smoothing back his thick,
unruly hair. "Perhaps I should go and fetch my coat—I'm not
sure what's proper for administering rebukes."

"You look fine," I said, suppressing a smile. "Very severe."

"Oh, that's good," he said, straightening his shoulders
and compressing his lips. "I hope I don't laugh, that wouldna
do at all," he muttered, pushing open the door to the kitchen
stair.

The atmosphere in the kitchen was far from hilarious,
though. At our entrance, the customary gabble ceased at
once, and there was a hasty drawing up of the staff at one side
of the room. Everyone stood stock-still for a moment, then
there was a small stir between two kitchenmaids, and Fergus
stepped out into the open space before us.

The boy's face was white and tracked with tears, but he
was not weeping now. With considerable dignity, he bowed,
first to me and then Jamie, in turn.

"Madame, Monsieur, I am ashamed," he said, low-voiced but distinct. "I am unworthy to be in your employment, but still I beg that you will not dismiss me." His high-pitched voice quavered a little at the thought, and I bit my lip. Fergus glanced aside at the ranks of the servants, as though for moral support, and received a nod of encouragement from Fernand the coachman. Drawing a deep breath for courage, he straightened up and addressed Jamie directly.

"I am ready to suffer my punishment now, milord," he said. As though this had been the signal, one of the footmen stepped out of the rigid crowd, led the boy to the scrubbed plank table, and passing on the other side, took hold of the lad's hands, pulling him half across the surface of the table and holding him so extended.

"But . . ." Jamie began, taken aback by the speed of events. He got no further before Magnus, the elderly butler, stepped gravely up and presented him with the leather strop used for sharpening the kitchen knives, laid ceremonially atop the meat platter.

"Er," Jamie said, looking helplessly at me.

"Um," I said, and took one step back. Eyes narrowed, he grabbed my hand, squeezing it tightly.

"No, ye don't, Sassenach," he muttered in English. "If I have to do it, you have to watch it!"

Glancing desperately back and forth between his would-be victim and the proffered instrument of execution, he hesitated for a moment longer, then gave up.

"Oh, bloody fucking hell," he muttered under his breath in English, grabbing the strop from Magnus. He flexed the broad strap dubiously between his hands; three inches wide and a quarter-inch thick, it was a formidable weapon. Clearly wishing himself anywhere else, he advanced upon the prone body of Fergus.

"All right, then," he said, glaring ferociously round the room. "Ten strokes, and I don't wish to hear a fuss about it." Several of the female servants blanched visibly at this, and clung to each other for support, but there was dead silence in the big room as he raised the strop.

The resultant crack at impact made me jump, and there were small squeaks of alarm from the kitchenmaids, but no sound from Fergus. The small body quivered, and Jamie closed his eyes briefly, then set his lips and proceeded to inflict the remainder of the sentence, strokes evenly spaced. I felt sick, and surreptitiously wiped my damp palms on my skirt. At the same time, I felt an unhinged urge to laugh at the terrible farce of the situation.

Fergus endured everything in total silence, and when Jamie had finished and stepped back, pale and sweating, the small body lay so still that I was afraid for a moment that he had died—of shock, if not from the actual effects of the beating. But then a deep shudder seemed to run over the small frame, and the boy slid backward and raised himself stiffly off the table.

Jamie leaped forward to grasp him by an arm, anxiously smoothing back the sweat-drenched hair from his forehead.

"Are ye all right, man?" he asked. "God, Fergus, tell me you're all right!"

The boy was white to the lips, and his eyes were the size of saucers, but he smiled at this evidence of goodwill on the part of his employer, buck teeth gleaming in the lamplight.

"Oh yes, milord," he gasped. "Am I forgiven?"

"Jesus Christ," Jamie muttered, and clasped the boy tightly against his chest. "Yes, of course ye are, fool." He held the boy at arm's length and shook him slightly. "I dinna want to do that ever again, d'ye hear me?"

Fergus nodded, eyes glowing, then broke away and fell to his knees before me.

"Do you forgive me also, Madame?" he asked, folding his hands formally in front of him, and looking trustfully up, like a chipmunk begging for nuts.

I thought I would expire on the spot of mortification, but mustered sufficient self-possession to reach down and raise the boy to his feet.

"There is nothing to forgive," I told him firmly, my cheeks burning. "You're a very courageous lad, Fergus. Why . . . er, why don't you go and have some supper now?"

At this, the atmosphere of the kitchen relaxed, as though everyone had drawn a massive sigh of relief at once. The other servants pushed forward, babbling concern and congratulations, and Fergus was swept off to a hero's reception, while Jamie and I beat a precipitous retreat back to our quarters abovestairs.

"Oh, God," Jamie said, collapsing into his chair as though completely drained. "Sweet bleeding Jesus. Mary, Michael, and Bride. Lord, I need a drink. Don't ring!" he exclaimed in alarm, though I hadn't made a move toward the bell rope. "I couldna bear to face one of the servants just now."

He got up and rummaged in the cupboard. "I think I've a bottle in here, though."

He had indeed, a nice aged Scotch. Removing the cork unceremoniously with his teeth, he lowered the level of the spirit by an inch or so, then handed the bottle to me. I followed his example without hesitation.

"Jesus Christ," I said, when I had recovered breath enough to speak.

"Yes," he said, taking the bottle back and taking another gulp. Setting the bottle down, he clutched his head, running his fingers through his hair until it stood on end in wild disarray. He laughed weakly.

"I've never felt so foolish in my entire life. God, I felt a clot-heid!"

"So did I," I said, taking my turn at the bottle. "Even more than you, I imagine. After all, it was all my fault. Jamie, I can't tell you how sorry I am; I never imagined . . ."

"Ah, dinna worry yourself." The tension of the last half-hour released, he squeezed my shoulder affectionately. "You couldna have any idea. Neither did I, for that matter," he added reflectively. "I suppose he thought I'd dismiss him, and he'd be back in the streets . . . poor little bugger. No wonder he thought himself lucky to take a beating instead."

I shuddered briefly, remembering the streets through which Monsieur Forez's carriage had traveled. Beggars dressed in rags and sores clung stubbornly to their territories, sleeping on the ground even on the coldest nights, lest some rival steal a profitable corner from them. Children much smaller than Fergus darted through the market crowds like hungry mice, eyes always watching for the dropped crumb, the unguarded pocket. And for those too unhealthy to work, too unattractive to sell to the brothels, or simply too unlucky —it would be a short life indeed, and far from merry. Little wonder if the prospect of being thrust from the luxury of three meals a day and clean clothes back into that sordid stew had been sufficient to send Fergus into paroxysms of needless guilt.

"I suppose so," I said. My manner of intake had declined from gulps to a more genteel sipping by this time. I sipped genteelly, then handed the bottle back, noting in a rather detached manner that it was more than half empty. "Still, I hope you didn't hurt him."

"Weel, nay doubt he'll be a bit sore." His Scots accent, usually faint, always grew more pronounced when he drank a lot. He shook his head, squinting through the bottle to judge the level of spirit remaining. "D'ye know, Sassenach, I never 'til tonight realized just how difficult it must ha' been for my father to beat me? I always thought it was me had the hardest part of that particular transaction." He tilted his head back and drank again, then set down the bottle and stared owl-eyed into the fire. "Being a father might be a bit more complicated than I'd thought. I'll have to think about it."

"Well, don't think too hard," I said. "You've had a lot to drink."

"Och, don't worry," he said cheerfully. "There's another bottle in the cupboard."

15

In Which Music Plays a Part

We stayed up late with the second bottle, going over and over the latest of the abstracted letters from the Chevalier St. George—otherwise known as His Majesty, James III—and the letters to Prince Charles from Jacobite supporters.

"Fergus got a large packet, bound for His Highness," Jamie explained. "There was a lot of stuff in it, and we couldna copy it all quickly enough, so I kept some to go back the next time."

"See," he said, extracting one sheet from the pile and laying it on my knee, "the majority of the letters are in code, like this one—'I hear that the prospects for grouse seem most favorable this year in the hills above Salerno; hunters in that region should find themselves successful.' That's easy; it's a reference to Manzetti, the Italian banker; he's from Salerno. I found that Charles had been dining with him, and managed to borrow fifteen thousand livres—apparently James's advice was good. But here—" He shuffled through the stack, pulling out another sheet.

"Look at this," Jamie said, handing me a sheet covered with his lopsided scrawls.

I squinted obediently at the paper, from which I could pick out single letters, connected with a network of arrows and question marks.

"What language is that?" I asked, peering at it. "Polish?" Charles Stuart's mother, the late Clementina Sobieski, had been Polish, after all.

"No, it's in English," Jamie said, grinning. "You canna read it?"

"You can?"

"Oh, aye," he said smugly. "It's a cipher, Sassenach, and no a verra complicated one. See, all ye must do is break the letters up into groups of five, to start—only ye don't count the letters *Q* or *X*. The *X's* are meant as breaks between sentences, and the *Q's* are only stuck in here and there to make it more confusing."

"If you say so," I said, looking from the extremely confusing-looking letter, which began "Mrti ocruti dlopro qahstmin . . ." to the sheet in Jamie's hand, with a series of five-letter groups written on one line, single letters printed in carefully above them, one at a time.

"So, one letter is only substituted for another, but in the same order," Jamie was explaining, "so if you have a fair amount of text to work from, and you can guess a word here or there, then all ye need do is to translate from one alphabet to the other—see?" He waved a long strip of paper under my nose, with two alphabets printed one above the other, slightly offset.

"Well, more or less," I said. "I gather you do, though, which is what's important. What does it say?"

The expression of lively interest with which Jamie greeted all manner of puzzles faded a bit, and he let the sheet of paper fall to his knee. He looked at me, lower lip caught between his teeth in introspection.

"Well," he said, "that's what's odd. And yet I dinna see how I can be mistaken. The tone of James's letters overall tend one way, and this ciphered one spells it out clearly."

Blue eyes met mine under thick, ruddy brows.

"James wants Charles to find favor with Louis," he said slowly, "but he isna looking for support for an invasion of Scotland. James has no interest in seeking restoration to the throne."

"What?" I snatched the sheaf of letters from his hand, my eyes feverishly scanning the scribbled text.

Jamie was right; while the letters from supporters spoke hopefully of the impending restoration, James's letters to his son mentioned no such thing, but were all concerned with Charles's making a good impression upon Louis. Even the loan from Manzetti of Salerno had been sought to enable Charles to live with the appearance of a gentleman in Paris; not to support any military end.

"Well, I'm thinking James is a canny wee man," Jamie had said, tapping one of the letters. "For see, Sassenach, he's verra little money of his own; his wife had a great deal, but Uncle Alex told me that she left it all to the Church when she died. The Pope has been maintaining James's establishment —after all, he's a Catholic monarch, and the Pope is bound to uphold his interests against those of the Elector of Hanover."

He clasped his hands around one knee, gazing meditatively at the pile of papers now laid between us on the sofa.

"Philip of Spain and Louis—the Old King, I mean—gave him a small number of troops and a few ships, thirty years ago, with which to try to regain his throne. But it all went wrong; bad weather sank some of the ships, and the rest had no pilots and landed in the wrong place—everything went awry, and in the end, the French simply sailed off again, with James not even setting foot upon the soil of Scotland. So perhaps in the years since, he gave up any thought of getting back his throne. But still, he had two sons coming to manhood, and no way to see them properly settled in life.

"So I ask myself, Sassenach"—he rocked backward a bit —"what would I do, in such a situation? The answer being, that I might try and see if my good cousin Louis—who's King of France, after all—might maybe see one son established in a good position; given a military appointment, maybe, and men to lead. A General of France is no bad position in life."

"Mm." I nodded, thinking. "Yes, but if I were a very smart man, I might not just come to Louis and beg, as a poor relation. I might send my son to Paris, and try to shame Louis into accepting him at Court. And meanwhile keep alive the illusion that I was actively seeking restoration."

"For once James admits openly that the Stuarts will never rule Scotland again," Jamie added softly, "then he has no more value to Louis."

And without the possibility of an armed Jacobite invasion to occupy the English, Louis would have little reason to give his young cousin Charles anything beyond the pittance that decency and public opinion would force him to provide.

It wasn't certain; the letters Jamie had been able to get, a few at a time, went back only as far as last January, when Charles had arrived in France. And, couched in code, cipher, and guarded language generally, the situation was far from clear. But taken all in all, the evidence did point in that direction.

And if Jamie's guess as to the Chevalier's motives was

correct—then our task was accomplished already; had never in fact existed at all.

Thinking over the events of the night before, I was abstracted all the next day, through a visit to Marie d'Arbanville's morning salon to hear a Hungarian poet, through a visit to a neighborhood herbalist's to pick up some valerian and orris root, and through my rounds at L'Hôpital des Anges in the afternoon.

Finally, I abandoned my work, afraid that I might accidentally damage someone while wool-gathering. Neither Murtagh nor Fergus had yet arrived to escort me home, so I changed out of my covering gown and sat down in Mother Hildegarde's vacant office to wait, just inside the vestibule of the Hôpital.

I had been there for perhaps half an hour, idly pleating the stuff of my gown between my fingers, when I heard the dog outside.

The porter was absent, as he often was. Gone to buy food, no doubt, or run an errand for one of the nuns. As usual in his absence, the guardianship of the Hôpital's portals was given into the capable paws—and teeth—of Bouton.

The first warning yip was followed by a low, burring growl that warned the intruder to stay where he was, on pain of instant dismemberment. I rose and stuck my head out of the office door, to see whether Father Balmain might be braving the peril of the demon once more, in pursuit of his sacramental duties. But the figure outlined against the huge stained-glass window of the entry hall was not the spare form of the junior priest. It was a tall figure, whose silhouetted kilt swayed gracefully around his legs as he drew back from the small, toothed animal at his feet.

Jamie blinked, brought up short by the assault. Shading his eyes against the dazzle from the window, he peered down into the shadows.

"Oh, hallo there, wee dog," he said politely, and took a step forward, knuckles stretched out. Bouton raised the growl a few decibels, and he took a step back.

"Oh, like that, is it?" Jamie said. He eyed the dog narrowly.

"Think it over, laddie," he advised, squinting down his long, straight nose. "I'm a damn sight bigger than you. I wouldna undertake any rash ventures, if I were you."

Bouton shifted his ground slightly, still making a noise like a distant Fokker.

"Faster, too," said Jamie, making a feint to one side. Bouton's teeth snapped together a few inches from Jamie's calf, and he stepped back hastily. Leaning back against the wall, he folded his arms and nodded down at the dog.

"Well, you've a point there, I'll admit. When it comes to teeth, ye've the edge on me, and no mistake." Bouton cocked an ear suspiciously at this gracious speech, but went back to the low-pitched growl.

Jamie hooked one foot over the other, like one prepared to pass the time of day indefinitely. The multicolored light from the window washed his face with blue, making him look like one of the chilly marble statues in the cathedral next door.

"Surely you've better things to do than harry innocent visitors?" he asked, conversationally. "I've heard of you— you're the famous fellow that sniffs out sickness, no? Weel, then, why are they wastin' ye on silly things like door-guarding, when ye might be makin' yourself useful smelling gouty toes and pustulant arseholes? Answer me that, if ye will!"

A sharp bark in response to his uncrossing his feet was the only answer.

There was a stir of robes behind me as Mother Hildegarde entered from the inner office.

"What is it?" she asked, seeing me peering round the corner. "Have we visitors?"

"Bouton seems to be having a difference of opinion with my husband," I said.

"I don't have to put up wi' this, ye ken," Jamie was threatening. One hand was stealing toward the brooch that held his plaid at the shoulder. "One quick spring wi' my plaid, and I'll have ye trussed like a—oh, *bonjour,* Madame!" he said, changing swiftly to French at sight of Mother Hildegarde.

"*Bonjour,* Monsieur Fraser." She inclined her veil gracefully, more to hide the broad smile on her face than in greeting, I thought. "I see you have made the acquaintance of Bouton. Are you perhaps in search of your wife?"

This seeming to be my cue, I sidled out of the office behind her. My devoted spouse glanced from Bouton to the office door, plainly drawing conclusions.

"And just how long have ye been standin' there, Sassenach?" he asked dryly.

"Long enough," I said, with the smug self-assurance of one in Bouton's good books. "What would you have done with him, once you'd got him wrapped up in your plaid?"

"Thrown him out the window and run like hell," he answered, with a brief glance of awe at Mother Hildegarde's imposing form. "Does she by chance speak English?"

"No, luckily for you," I answered. I switched to French for the introductions. *"Ma mère, je vous présente mon mari, le seigneur de Broch Tuarach."*

"Milord." Mother Hildegarde had by now mastered her sense of humor, and greeted him with her usual expression of formidable geniality. "We shall miss your wife, but if you require her, of course—"

"I didn't come for my wife," Jamie interrupted. "I came to see you, *ma mère.*"

Seated in Mother Hildegarde's office, Jamie laid the bundle of papers he carried on the shining wood of her desk. Bouton, keeping a wary eye on the intruder, lay down at his mistress's feet. He laid his nose upon his feet, but kept his ears cocked, lip raised over one eyetooth in case he should be called upon to rend the visitor limb from limb.

Jamie narrowed his eyes at Bouton, pointedly pulling his feet away from the twitching black nose. "Herr Gerstmann recommended that I consult you, Mother, about these documents," he said, unrolling the thick sheaf and flattening it beneath his palms.

Mother Hildegarde regarded Jamie for a moment, one heavy brow raised quizzically. Then she turned her attention to the sheaf of papers, with that administrator's trick of seeming to focus entirely on the matter at hand, while still keeping her sensitive antennae tuned to catch the faintest vibration of emergency from the far-off reaches of the Hôpital.

"Yes?" she said. One blunt finger ran lightly over the lines of scribbled music, one by one, as though she heard the notes by touching them. A flick of the finger, and the sheet slid aside, half-exposing the next.

"What is it that you wish to know, Monsieur Fraser?" she asked.

"I don't know, Mother." Jamie was leaning forward, intent. He touched the black lines himself, dabbing gently at the smear where the writer's hand had carelessly brushed the staves before the ink had dried.

"There is something odd about this music, Mother."

The nun's wide mouth moved slightly in what might have been a smile.

"Really, Monsieur Fraser? And yet I understand—you will not be offended, I trust—that to you, music is . . . a lock to which you have no key?"

Jamie laughed, and a sister passing in the hallways turned, startled by such a sound in the confines of the Hôpital. It was a noisy place, but laughter was unusual.

"That is a very tactful description of my disability, Mother. And altogether true. Were you to sing one of these pieces"—his finger, longer and more slender, but nearly the same size as Mother Hildegarde's, tapped the parchment with a soft rustling noise—"I could not tell it from the Kyrie Eleison or from 'La Dame fait bien'—except by the words," he added, with a grin.

Now it was Mother Hildegarde's turn to laugh.

"Indeed, Monsieur Fraser," she said. "Well, at least you listen to the words!" She took the sheaf of papers into her hands, riffling the tops. I could see the faint swelling of her throat above the tight band of her wimple as she read, as though she was singing silently to herself, and one large foot twitched slightly, keeping time.

Jamie sat very still upon his stool, good hand folded over the crooked one on his knee, watching her. The slanted blue eyes were intent, and he paid no attention to the ongoing noise from the depths of the Hôpital behind him. Patients cried out, orderlies and nuns shouted back and forth, family members shrieked in sorrow or dismay, and the muted clang of metal instruments echoed off the ancient stones of the building, but neither Jamie nor Mother Hildegarde moved.

At last she lowered the pages, peering at him over the tops. Her eyes were sparkling, and she looked suddenly like a young girl.

"I think you are right!" she said. "I cannot take time to think it over carefully just now"—she glanced toward the doorway, momentarily darkened by the form of an orderly dashing past with a large sack of lint—"but there is something odd here." She tapped the pages on the desk, straightening them into an orderly stack.

"How extraordinary," she said.

"Be that as it may, Mother—can you, with your gift, discern what this particular pattern is? It would be difficult; I have reason to suppose that it is a cipher, and that the language of the message is English, though the text of the songs is in German."

Mother Hildegarde uttered a small grunt of surprise.

"English? You are sure?"

Jamie shook his head. "Not sure, no, but I think so. For one reason, there is the country of origin; the songs were sent from England."

"Well, Monsieur," she said, arching one eyebrow. "Your wife speaks English, does she not? And I imagine that you would be willing to sacrifice her company to assist me in performing this endeavor for you?"

Jamie eyed her, the half-smile on his face the mirror image of hers. He glanced down at his feet, where Bouton's whiskers quivered with the ghost of a growl.

"I'll make ye a bargain, Mother," he said. "If your wee dog doesna bite me in the arse on the way out, you can have my wife."

◆━━▶

And so, that evening, instead of returning home to Jared's house in the Rue Trémoulins, I took supper with the sisters of the Couvent des Anges at their long refectory table, and then retired for the evening's work to Mother Hildegarde's private rooms.

There were three rooms in the Superior's suite. The outer one was furnished as a sitting room, with a fair degree of richness. This, after all, was where she must often receive official visitors. The second room was something of a shock, simply because I wasn't expecting it. At first, I had the impression that there was nothing in the small room but a large harpsichord, made of gleaming, polished walnut, and decorated with small, hand-painted flowers sprouting from a twisting vine that ran along the sounding board above glowing ebony keys.

On second look, I saw a few other bits of furniture in the room, including a set of bookshelves that ran the length of one wall, stuffed with works on musicology and hand-stitched manuscripts much like the one Mother Hildegarde now laid on the harpsichord's rack.

She motioned me to a chair placed before a small secretary against one wall.

"You will find blank paper and ink there, milady. Now, let us see what this little piece of music may tell us."

The music was written on heavy parchment, the lines of the staves cleanly ruled across the page. The notes themselves, the clef signs, rests, and accidentals, were all drawn with considerable care; this was plainly a final clean copy, not a draft or a hastily scribbled tune. Across the top of the page was the title "Lied des Landes." A Song of the Country.

"The title, you see, suggests something simple, like a *volkslied*," Mother Hildegarde said, pointing one long, bony forefinger at the page. "And yet the form of the composition is something quite different. Can you read music at sight?" The big right hand, large-knuckled and short-nailed, descended on the keys with an impossibly delicate touch.

Leaning over Mother Hildegarde's black-clad shoulder, I sang the first three lines of the piece, making the best I could of the German pronunciation. Then she stopped playing, and twisted to look up at me.

"That is the basic melody. It then repeats itself in variations—but *such* variations! You know, I have seen some things reminiscent of this. By a little old German named Bach; he sends me things now and again—" She waved carelessly at the shelf of manuscripts. "He calls them 'Inventions,' and they're really quite clever; playing off the variations in two or three melodic lines simultaneously. *This*"—she pursed her lips at the 'Lied' before us—"is like a clumsy imitation of one of his things. In fact, I would swear that. . . ." Muttering to herself, she pushed back the walnut bench and went to the shelf, running a finger rapidly down the rows of manuscripts.

She found what she was looking for, and returned to the bench with three bound pieces of music.

"Here are the Bach pieces. They're fairly old, I haven't looked at them in several years. Still, I'm almost sure . . ." She lapsed into silence, flipping quickly through the pages of the Bach scripts on her knee, one at a time, glancing back now and then at the "Lied" on the rack.

"Ha!" she let out a cry of triumph, and held out one of the Bach pieces to me. "See there?"

The paper was titled "Goldberg Variations," in a crabbed, smeared hand. I touched the paper with some awe, swallowed hard, and looked back at the "Lied." It took only a moment's comparison to see what she meant.

"You're right, it's the same!" I said. "A note different here and there, but basically it's exactly the same as the original theme of the Bach piece. How very peculiar!"

"Isn't it?" she said, in tones of deep satisfaction. "Now, why is this anonymous composer stealing melodies and treating them in such an odd fashion?"

This was clearly a rhetorical question, and I didn't bother with an answer, but asked one of my own.

"Is Bach's music much in vogue these days, Mother?" I certainly hadn't heard any at the musical salons I attended.

"No," she said, shaking her head as she peered at the music. "Herr Bach is not well known in France; I believe he had some small popularity in Prussia and in Austria fifteen or twenty years ago, but even there his music is not performed much publicly. I am afraid his music is not the sort to endure; clever, but no heart. Hmph. Now, see here?" The blunt forefinger tapped here, and here, and here, turning pages rapidly.

"He has repeated the same melody—almost—but changed the key each time. I think this is perhaps what attracted your husband's notice; it is obvious even to someone who doesn't read music, because of the changing signatures— the *note tonique*."

It was; each key change was marked by a double vertical line followed by a new treble clef sign and the signature of sharps or flats.

"Five key changes in such a short piece," she said, tapping the last one again for emphasis. "And changes that make no sense at all, in terms of music. Look, the basic line is precisely the same, yet we move from the key of two flats, which is B-flat major, to A-major, with three sharps. Stranger yet, now he goes to a signature of two sharps, and yet he uses the G-sharp accidental!"

"How very peculiar," I said. Adding a G-sharp accidental to the section in D-major had the effect of making the musical line identical with the A-major section. In other words, there was no reason whatsoever to have changed the key signature.

"I don't know German," I said. "Can you read the words, Mother?"

She nodded, the folds of her black veil rustling with the movement, small eyes intent on the manuscript.

"What truly execrable lyrics!" she murmured to herself. "Not that one expects great poetry from Germans in general, but really . . . still—" She broke off with a shake of her veil. "We must assume that if your husband is correct in assuming this to be a cipher of some sort, that the message lies embedded in these words. They may therefore not be of great import in themselves."

"What does it say?" I asked.

" 'My shepherdess frolics with her lambs among the verdant hills,' " she read. "Horrible grammar, though of course liberties are often taken in writing songs, if the lyricist insists upon the lines rhyming, which they nearly always do if it is a love song."

"You know a lot about love songs?" I asked curiously. Full of surprises tonight, was Mother Hildegarde.

"Any piece of good music is in essence a love song," she replied matter-of-factly. "But as for what you mean—yes, I have seen a great many. When I was a young girl"—she flashed her large white teeth in a smile, acknowledging the difficulty of imagining her as a child—"I was something of a prodigy, you understand. I could play from memory anything I heard, and I wrote my first composition at the age of seven." She gestured at the harpsichord, the rich veneer shining with polish.

"My family has wealth; had I been a man, no doubt I

would have been a musician." She spoke simply, with no trace of regret.

"Surely you could still have composed music, if you'd married?" I asked curiously.

Mother Hildegarde spread her hands, grotesque in the lamplight. I had seen those hands wrench loose a dagger embedded in bone, guide a displaced joint back into alignment, cup the blood-smeared head of a child emerging from between its mother's thighs. And I had seen those fingers linger on the ebony keys with the delicacy of moths' feet.

"Well," she said, after a moment's contemplation, "it is the fault of St. Anselm."

"It is?"

She grinned at my expression, her ugly face quite transformed from its stern public facade.

"Oh, yes. My godfather—the Old Sun King," she added casually, "gave to me a book, *Lives of the Saints*, for my own Saint's Day when I was eight. It was a beautiful book," she said reminiscently, "with gilded pages and a jeweled cover; intended more as a work of art than a work of literature. Still, I read it. And while I enjoyed all of the stories—particularly those of the martyrs—still there was one phrase in the story of St. Anselm that seemed to strike a response in my soul."

She closed her eyes and tilted back her head, recalling.

"St. Anselm was a man of great wisdom and great learning, a Doctor of the Church. But also a bishop, a man who cared for the people of his flock, and looked after their temporal needs as well as those of the spirit. The story detailed all of his works, and then concluded in these words—'And so he died, at the conclusion of an eminently useful life, and thus obtained his crown in Paradise.'" She paused, flexing her hands lightly on her knees.

"There was something about that that appealed most strongly to me. 'An eminently useful life.'" She smiled at me. "I could think of many worse epitaphs than that, milady." She spread her hands suddenly and shrugged, an oddly graceful gesture.

"I wished to be useful," she said. Then, dismissing idle conversation, she turned abruptly back to the music on the rack.

"So," she said. "Plainly the change in the key signatures

—the *note tonique*—that is the oddity. Where can we go with that?"

My mouth dropped open with a small exclamation. Speaking in French as we had been, I hadn't noticed before. But observing Mother Hildegarde as she told her story, I had been thinking in English, and when I glanced back at the music it hit me.

"What is it?" the nun asked. "You have thought of something?"

"The key!" I said, half-laughing. "In French, a musical key is the *note tonique,* but the word for an object that unlocks . . ." I pointed to the large bunch of keys—normally carried on her girdle—that Mother Hildegarde had laid aside on the bookshelf when we came in. "That is a *passe-partout,* isn't it?"

"Yes," she said, watching me in puzzlement. She touched the skeleton key in turn. "*Une passe-partout.* That one," she said, pointing to a key with barrel and wards, "is more likely called a *clef.*"

"A clef!" I exclaimed joyously. "Perfect!" I stabbed a finger at the sheet of music before us. "See, *ma mère,* in English, the words are the same. A 'key' gives the basis of a piece of music, and a 'key' unlocks. In French, the *clef* is a key, and in English, the 'clef' is also part of the musical signature. And the key of the music is also the key to the cipher. Jamie *said* he thought it was an English cipher! Made by an Englishman with a really diabolical sense of humor, too," I added.

With that small insight, the cipher proved not too difficult to unravel. If the maker was English, the ciphered message likely was in English, too, which meant that the German words were provided only as a source of letters. And having seen Jamie's earlier efforts with alphabets and shifting letters, it took only a few tries to determine the pattern of the cipher.

"Two flats means you must take every second letter, starting from the beginning of the section," I said, frantically scribbling down the results. "And three sharps means to take every third letter, beginning at the end of the section. I suppose he used German both for concealment and because it's so bloody wordy; it takes nearly twice as many words to say the same thing as it would in English."

"You have got ink on your nose," Mother Hildegarde observed. She peered over my shoulder. "Does it make sense?"

"Yes," I said, my mouth gone suddenly dry. "Yes, it makes sense."

Deciphered, the message was brief and simple. Also deeply disturbing.

"His Majesty's loyal subjects of England await his lawful restoration. The sum of fifty thousand pounds is at your disposal. As an earnest of good faith, this will be paid only in person, upon His Highness's arrival on the soil of England," I read. "And there's a letter left over, an *S*. I don't know if that's a signature of sorts, or only something the maker needed to make the German word come out right."

"Hmph." Mother Hildegarde glanced curiously at the scribbled message, then at me. "You will know already, of course," she said, with a nod, "but you may assure your husband that I will keep this in confidence."

"He wouldn't have asked your help if he didn't trust you," I protested.

The sketchy brows rose to the edge of her wimple, and she tapped the scribbled paper firmly.

"If this is the sort of endeavor in which your husband engages, he takes considerable risk in trusting anyone. Assure him that I am sensible of the honor," she added dryly.

"I'll do that," I said, smiling.

"Why, *chère Madame*," she said, catching sight of me, "you are looking quite pale! I myself often stay awake far into the night when I am working on a new piece, so I tend to pay little attention to the hour, but it must be late for you." She glanced at the hour-candle burning on the little table near the door.

"Gracious! It *is* growing late. Shall I summon Sister Madeleine to take you to your chamber?" Jamie had agreed, reluctantly, with Mother Hildegarde's suggestion that I spend the night at the Couvent des Anges, so that I need not return home through the dark streets late at night.

I shook my head. I was tired, and my back ached from sitting on the stool, but I didn't want to go to bed. The implications of the musical message were too disturbing to permit me to sleep right away, in any case.

"Well, then, let us take a little refreshment, in celebration of your accomplishment." Mother Hildegarde rose and went to the outer room, where I heard the ringing of a bell. Shortly one of the serving sisters came, bearing a tray of hot milk and small, iced cakes, and followed by Bouton. The serving sister placed a cake on a small china plate and set it on the floor before him as a matter of course, laying beside it a bowl of milk.

While I sipped my own hot milk, Mother Hildegarde set aside the source of our labors, laying it on the secretary, and instead placed a loose sheaf of music manuscript on the rack of the harpsichord.

"I shall play for you," she announced. "It will help to compose your mind for sleep."

The music was light and soothing, with a singing melody that wove back and forth from treble voice to bass in a pattern of pleasing complexity, but without the driving force of Bach.

"Is that yours?" I asked, choosing a pause as she lifted her hands at the conclusion of the piece.

She shook her head without turning around.

"No. A friend of mine, Jean Philippe Rameau. A good theorist, but he does not write with great passion."

I must have dozed, the music lulling my senses, for I woke suddenly to the murmur of Sister Madeleine's voice in my ear, and her warm, firm grip under my arm, lifting me to my feet and leading me away.

Looking back, I could see the broad span of Mother Hildegarde's black-swathed back, and the flex of powerful shoulders beneath the drape of her veil as she played, oblivious now to the world beyond the sanctum of her chamber. On the boards near her feet lay Bouton, nose on his paws, small body laid straight as the needle of a compass.

"So," Jamie said, "it's gone a little further than talk—maybe."

"Maybe?" I echoed. "An offer of fifty thousand pounds sounds fairly definite." Fifty thousand pounds, by current standards, was the yearly income of a good-sized duchy.

He raised one eyebrow cynically at the musical manuscript I had brought back with me from the convent.

"Aye, well. An offer like that is fairly safe, if it's contingent on either Charles or James setting foot in England. If Charles is in England, it means he's gotten sufficient backing from other places to get him to Scotland, first. No," he said, rubbing his chin thoughtfully, "what's interesting about this offer is that it's the first definite sign we've seen that the Stuarts—or one of them, at least—are actually making an effort at mounting a restoration attempt."

"One of them?" I caught the emphasis. "You mean you think James isn't in on this?" I looked at the coded message with even more interest.

"The message came to Charles," Jamie reminded me, "and it came from England—not through Rome. Fergus got it from a regular messenger, in a packet marked with English seals; not from a papal messenger. And everything I've seen in James's letters—" He shook his head, frowning. He hadn't yet shaved, and the morning light caught random sparks of copper among the auburn stubble of his beard.

"The packet had been opened; Charles has seen this manuscript. There was no date on it, so I dinna ken how long ago it came to him. And of course, we don't have the letters Charles has sent to his father. But there's no reference in any of James's letters to anyone who could possibly be the composer, let alone to any definite promises of support from England."

I could see the direction in which he was heading.

"And Louise de La Tour was babbling about how Charles meant to have her marriage annulled and claim her as his wife, once he was king. So you think perhaps Charles wasn't just talking through his hat to impress her?"

"Maybe not," he said. He poured water from the bedroom ewer into the basin and laved his face with water, preparatory to shaving.

"So it's possible that Charles is acting on his own?" I said, horrified and intrigued by the possibility. "That James has set him up for a masquerade of pretending to start a restoration attempt, in order to keep Louis impressed with the Stuarts' potential value, but—"

"But Charles isn't pretending?" Jamie interrupted. "Aye,

that's how it seems. Is there a towel there, Sassenach?" Eyes screwed shut and face dripping, he was patting about on the surface of the table. I moved the manuscript to safety and found the towel, draped over the foot of the bed.

He examined his razor critically, decided it would do, and leaned over my dressing table to look in the mirror as he applied shaving soap to his cheeks.

"Why is it barbaric of me to take the hair off my legs and armpits, and it isn't barbaric for you to take it off your face?" I asked, watching him draw his upper lip down over his teeth as he scraped under his nose with tiny, delicate strokes.

"It is," he replied, squinting at himself in the mirror. "But it itches like a fiend if I don't."

"Have you ever grown a beard?" I asked curiously.

"Not on purpose," he replied, half-smiling as he scraped one cheek, "but I've had one now and then when I couldna help it—when I lived as an outlaw in Scotland. When it came to a choice between shaving in a cold burn with a dull razor every morning or itching, I chose to itch."

I laughed, watching him draw the razor along the edge of his jawbone with one long sweep.

"I can't imagine what you'd look like with a full beard. I've only seen you in the stubbly stage."

He smiled on one side of his mouth, drawing the other up as he scraped under the high, broad cheekbone on that side.

"Next time we're invited to Versailles, Sassenach, I'll ask if we may visit the Royal zoo. Louis has a creature there that one of his sea-captains brought him from Borneo, called an orangutan. Ever seen one?"

"Yes," I said, "the zoo in London had a pair before the war."

"Then you'll know what I look like in a beard," he said, smiling at me as he finished his shave with a careful negotiation of the curve of his chin. "Scraggly and moth-eaten. Rather like the Vicomte Marigny," he added, "only red."

As though the name had reminded him, he returned to the main topic of discussion, wiping the remains of soap off his face with the linen towel.

"So I suppose what we must do now, Sassenach," he said, "is to keep a sharp eye out for Englishmen in Paris." He picked up the manuscript off the bed and riffled the pages thoughtfully. "If anyone is actually willing to contemplate support on this scale, I think they might be sending an envoy to Charles. If I were risking fifty thousand pounds, I might like to see what I was getting for my money, wouldn't you?"

"Yes, I would," I answered. "And speaking of Englishmen—does His Highness patriotically buy his brandywine from you and Jared, or does he by chance patronize the services of Mr. Silas Hawkins?"

"Mr. Silas Hawkins, who is so eager to know what the political climate is like in the Scottish Highlands?" Jamie shook his head at me admiringly. "And here I thought I married you because ye had a fair face and a fine fat arse. To think you've a brain as well!" He neatly dodged the blow I aimed at his ear, and grinned at me.

"I don't know, Sassenach, but I will before the day is out."

16

The Nature of Sulfur

Prince Charles *did* purchase his brandywine from Mr. Hawkins. Beyond that discovery, though, we made little progress over the course of the next four weeks. Things continued much as before. Louis of France continued to ignore Charles Stuart. Jamie continued to run the wine business and to visit Prince Charles. Fergus continued to steal letters. Louise, Princesse de Rohan, appeared in public on the arm of her husband, looking doleful, but blooming. I continued to throw up in the mornings, work at the Hôpital in the afternoons, and smile graciously over the supper table in the evenings.

Two things happened, though, that seemed to signify progress toward our goal. Charles, bored at confinement, began to invite Jamie to go to taverns with him in the evenings —often without the restraining and discretionary presence of his tutor, Mr. Sheridan, who professed himself much too old for such revels.

"God, the man drinks like a fish!" Jamie had exclaimed, returning from one of these jaunts reeking of cheap wine. He examined a large stain on the front of his shirt critically.

"I'll have to order a new shirt," he said.

"Worth it," I said, "if he tells you anything while he's drinking. What does he talk about?"

"Hunting and women," Jamie said succinctly, and declined firmly to elaborate further. Either politics did not weigh as heavily on Charles's mind as did Louise de La Tour, or else he was capable of discretion, even in the absence of his tutor Mr. Sheridan.

The second thing that happened was that Monsieur Duverney, the Minister of Finance, lost at chess to Jamie. Not once, but repeatedly. As Jamie had foreseen, the effect of losing was merely to make Monsieur Duverney more determined to win, and we were invited frequently to Versailles, where I circulated, collecting gossip and avoiding alcoves, and Jamie played chess, generally collecting an admiring crowd to watch, though I didn't myself consider it much of a spectator sport.

Jamie and the Minister of Finance, a small, round man with stooped shoulders, were bent over the chessboard, both apparently so intent on the game as to be oblivious to their surroundings, despite the murmur of voices and the clink of glasses just beyond their shoulders.

"I have seldom seen anything so wearisome as chess," murmured one of the ladies to another. "Amusement, they call it! I should be more amused watching my maid pick fleas off the black pageboys. At least they squeal and giggle a bit."

"I shouldn't mind making the red-haired lad squeal and giggle a bit," said her companion, smiling charmingly at Jamie, who had lifted his head and was gazing absently past Monsieur Duverney. Her companion caught sight of me, and dug the lady, a luscious blonde, in the ribs.

I smiled pleasantly at her, rather nastily enjoying the deep flush that rose from her low neckline, leaving her complexion in rosy blotches. As for Jamie, she could have twined her plump fingers in his hair for all the notice he would have paid, so abstracted did he seem.

I wondered just what was occupying his concentration. Surely it wasn't the game; Monsieur Duverney played a dogged game of cautious positioning, but used the same gambits repeatedly. The middle two fingers of Jamie's right hand moved slightly against his thigh, a brief flutter of quickly masked impatience, and I knew that whatever he was thinking of, it wasn't the game. It might take another half-hour, but he held Monsieur Duverney's king in the palm of his hand.

The Duc de Neve was standing next to me. I saw his dark little eyes fix on Jamie's fingers, then flick away. He paused meditatively for a moment, surveying the board, then glided away to increase his wager.

A footman paused by my shoulder and dipped obsequiously, offering me yet another glass of wine. I waved him away; I had had enough during the evening that my head was feeling light and my feet dangerously far away.

Turning to look for a place to sit down, I caught sight of the Comte St. Germain across the room. Perhaps he was what Jamie had been looking at. The Comte in turn was looking at me; staring at me, in fact, with a smile on his face. It wasn't his normal expression, and it didn't suit him. I didn't care for it at all, in fact, but bowed as graciously as I could in his direction, and then pushed off into the throng of ladies, chatting of this and that, but trying wherever possible to lead the conversation in the direction of Scotland and its exiled king.

By and large, the prospects for a Stuart restoration did not seem to be preoccupying the aristocracy of France. When I mentioned Charles Stuart now and then, the usual response was a rolling of the eyes or a shrug of dismissal. Despite the good offices of the Earl of Mar and the other Paris Jacobites, Louis was stubbornly refusing to receive Charles at Court. And a penniless exile who was not in the King's favor was not going to find himself invited out in society to make the acquaintance of wealthy bankers.

"The King is not particularly pleased that his cousin should have arrived in France without seeking his permission," the Comtesse de Brabant told me when I had introduced the topic. "He has been heard to say that England can stay Protestant, so far as he himself is concerned," she confided. "And if the English burn in hell with George of Hanover, so much the better." She pursed her lips in sympathy; she was a kindly sort. "I am sorry," she said. "I know that must be disappointing to you and your husband, but really . . ." She shrugged.

I thought we might be able to accommodate this sort of disappointment, and scouted eagerly for further bits of gossip along these lines, but met with little success this evening. Jacobites, I was given to understand, were a bore.

"Rook to queen's pawn five," Jamie mumbled later that evening as we prepared for bed. We were staying as guests in the palace once more. As the chess game had lasted well past midnight, and the Minister would not hear of our undertaking the journey back to Paris at such an hour, we had been accommodated in a small *appartement*—this one a notch or two above the first, I noted. It had a featherbed, and a window overlooking the south parterre.

"Rooks, eh?" I said, sliding into the bed and stretching out with a groan. "Are you going to dream about chess tonight?"

Jamie nodded, with a jaw-cracking yawn that made his eyes water.

"Aye, I'm sure I will. I hope it wilna disturb ye, Sassenach, if I castle in my sleep."

My feet curled in the sheer joy of being unfettered and relieved of my increasing weight, and my lower spine sent out sharp jolts of a mildly pleasant pain as it readjusted to lying down.

"You can stand on your head in your sleep if you want," I said, yawning myself. "Nothing will bother me tonight."

I have seldom been more wrong.

I was dreaming of the baby. Grown almost to the birthing, it kicked and heaved in my swollen belly. My hands went to the mound, massaging the stretched skin, trying to quiet the turmoil within. But the squirming went on, and in the unexcited fashion of dreams, I realized that it was not a baby, but a snake that writhed in my belly. I doubled, drawing up my knees as I wrestled the serpent, my hands groping and pummeling, searching for the head of the beast that darted and thrust under my skin. My skin was hot to the touch, and my intestines coiled, turning into snakes themselves, biting and thrashing as they twined together.

"Claire! Wake up, lass! What's amiss?" The shaking and calling roused me at last to a fuzzy apprehension of my surroundings. I was in bed, and it was Jamie's hand on my shoulder, and the linen sheets over me. But the snakes continued to writhe in my belly, and I moaned loudly, the sound alarming me almost as much as it did Jamie.

He flung back the sheets and rolled me onto my back, trying to push my knees down. I stayed stubbornly rolled into a ball, clutching my stomach, trying to contain the pangs of sharp agony that stabbed through me.

He yanked the quilt back over me and rushed out of the room, barely pausing to snatch his kilt from the stool.

I had little attention to spare for anything other than my inner turmoil. My ears were ringing, and a cold sweat soaked my face.

"Madame? Madame!"

I opened my eyes enough to see the maid assigned to our *appartement,* eyes frantic and hair awry, bending over the bed. Jamie, half-naked and still more frantic, was behind her. I shut my eyes, groaning, but not before I saw him grab the maid by the shoulder, hard enough to shake her curls loose from her nightcap.

"Is she losing the child? Is she?"

It seemed extremely likely. I twisted on the bed, grunting, and doubled tighter, as though to protect the burden of pain I contained.

There was an increasing babble of voices in the room, mostly female, and a number of hands poked and prodded at me. I heard a male voice speaking amid the babble; not Jamie, someone French. At the voice's direction, a number of hands fastened themselves to my ankles and shoulders and stretched me flat upon the bed.

A hand reached under my nightdress and probed my belly. I opened my eyes, panting, and saw Monsieur Flèche, the Royal Physician, kneeling by the bed as he frowned in concentration. I should have felt flattered at this evidence of the King's favor, but had little attention to spare for it. The character of the pain seemed to be changing; while it grew stronger in spasms, it was more or less constant, and yet it seemed to be almost *moving,* traveling from somewhere high up in my abdomen to a lower spot.

"Not a miscarriage," Monsieur Flèche was assuring Jamie, who hovered anxiously over his shoulder. "There is no bleeding." I saw one of the attending ladies staring in rapt horror at the scars on his back. She grasped a companion by the sleeve, calling her attention to them.

"Perhaps an inflammation of the gallbladder," Monsieur Flèche was saying. "Or a sudden chill of the liver."

"Idiot," I said through clenched teeth.

Monsieur Flèche stared haughtily down his rather large nose at me, belatedly adding his gold-rimmed pince-nez to increase the effect. He laid a hand upon my clammy brow, incidentally covering my eyes so that I could no longer glare at him.

"Most likely the liver," he was saying to Jamie. "Impaction of the gallbladder causes this accumulation of bilious humors in the blood, which cause pain—and temporary derangement," he added authoritatively, pressing down harder as I thrashed to and fro. "She should be bled at once. Plato, the basin!"

I yanked one hand free and batted the restraining hand off my head.

"Get away from me, you bloody quack! Jamie! Don't let them touch me with that!" Plato, Monsieur Flèche's assistant, was advancing upon me with lancet and basin, while the ladies in the background gasped and fanned each other, lest they be overcome with excitement at this drama.

Jamie, white-faced, glanced helplessly between me and Monsieur Flèche. Coming to a sudden decision, he grabbed the hapless Plato and pulled him back from the bed, turned him and propelled him toward the door, lancet stabbing the air. The maids and ladies fell back shrieking before him.

"Monsieur! Monsieur *le chevalier*!" The physician was expostulating. He had clapped his wig professionally upon his head when called, but had not taken time to dress, and the sleeves of his bedgown flapped like wings as he followed Jamie across the room, waving his arms like a demented scarecrow.

The pain increased once more, a vise squeezing my insides, and I gasped and doubled up once more. As it eased a bit, I opened my eyes and saw one of the ladies, her eyes fixed alertly on my face. A look of dawning realization passed over her features, and still looking at me, she leaned over to whisper to one of her companions. There was too much noise in the room to hear, but I read her lips clearly.

"Poison," she said.

The pain shifted abruptly lower with an ominous interior gurgle, and I realized finally what it was. Not a miscarriage. Not appendicitis, still less a chilled liver. Nor was it poison, precisely. It was bitter cascara.

❦

"You," I said, advancing menacingly on Master Raymond, crouched defensively behind his worktable, beneath the protective aegis of his stuffed crocodile. "You! You bloody frog-faced little worm!"

"Me, madonna? I have done you no harm, have I?"

"Aside from causing me to have violent diarrhea in the presence of thirty-odd people, making me think I was having a miscarriage, and scaring my husband out of his skin, no harm at all!"

"Oh, your husband was present?" Master Raymond looked uneasy.

"He was," I assured him. It was in fact with considerable difficulty that I had succeeded in preventing Jamie from coming up to the apothecary's shop and extracting, by force, such information as Master Raymond possessed. I had finally persuaded him to wait with the coach outside, while I talked to the amphibious proprietor.

"But you aren't dead, madonna," the little herbalist pointed out. He had no brows to speak of, but one side of his wide, heavy forehead crinkled upward. "You could have been, you know."

In the stress of the evening and the physical shakiness that followed, I had rather overlooked this fact.

"So it wasn't just a practical joke?" I said, a little weakly. "Someone really meant to poison me, and I'm not dead only because you have scruples?"

"Perhaps my scruples are not entirely responsible for your survival, madonna; it is possible that it was a joke—I imagine there are other purveyors from whom one might obtain bitter cascara. But I have sold that substance to two persons within the last month—and neither of them asked for it."

"I see." I drew a long breath, and wiped the perspiration from my brow with my glove. So we had *two* potential poisoners loose; just what I needed.

"Will you tell me who?" I asked bluntly. "They might buy from someone else, next time. Someone without your scruples."

He nodded, his wide, froggy mouth twitching in thought.

"It is a possibility, madonna. As for the actual purchasers, I doubt that information would help you. They were servants; plainly acting on the orders of a master. One was maid to the Vicomtesse de Rambeau; the other a man I did not recognize."

I drummed my fingers on the counter. The only person who had made threats against me was the Comte St. Germain. Could he have hired an anonymous servant to procure what he thought was poison, and then slipped it into my glass himself? Casting my mind back to the gathering at Versailles, I thought it certainly possible. The goblets of wine had been passed around on trays by servants; while the Comte had not come within arm's length of me himself, it would have been no great problem to bribe a servant to give me a particular glass.

Raymond was eyeing me curiously. "I would ask you, madonna, have you done something to antagonize la Vicomtesse? She is a very jealous woman; this would not be the first time she has sought my aid in disposing of a rival, though fortunately her jealousies are short-lived. The Vicomte has a roving eye, you understand—there is always a new rival to displace her thoughts of the last one."

I sat down, uninvited.

"Rambeau?" I said, trying to attach the name to a face. Then the mists of memory cleared, revealing a stylishly dressed body and a homely round face, both liberally splashed with snuff.

"Rambeau!" I exclaimed. "Well, yes, I've met the man, but all I did was to smack him across the face with my fan when he bit my toes."

"In some moods, that would be sufficient provocation for la Vicomtesse," Master Raymond observed. "And if so, then I believe you are likely safe from further attacks."

"Thanks," I said dryly. "And if it wasn't the Vicomtesse?"

The little apothecary hesitated for a moment, his eyes narrowed against the glare of the morning sun that shone through the lozenged panes behind me. Then he made up his mind, and turned toward the stone table where his alembics simmered, jerking his head at me to follow.

"Come with me, madonna. I have something for you."

To my surprise, he ducked beneath the table and disappeared. As he didn't come back, I bent down and peered under the table myself. A bed of charcoal was glowing on the hearth, but there was space to either side of it. And in the wall beneath the table, concealed by the shadows, was the darker space of an opening.

With only a little hesitation, I kilted up my skirts and waddled under the table after him.

On the other side of the wall, there was room to stand up, though the room was quite small. The building's outer structure gave no hint of it.

Two walls of the hidden room were taken up by a honey-comb of shelves, each cell dustless and immaculate, each displaying the skull of a beast. The impact of the wall was enough to make me take a step backward; all the empty eyes seemed trained on me, teeth bared in gleaming welcome.

I blinked several times before I was able to locate Raymond, crouched cautiously at the foot of this ossuary like the resident acolyte. He held his arms raised nervously before him, eying me rather as though he expected me either to scream or to throw myself upon him. But I had seen sights a good deal more grisly than a mere rank of polished bone, and walked forward calmly to examine them more closely.

He had everything, it seemed. Tiny skulls, of bat, mouse and shrew, the bones transparent, little teeth spiked in pinpoints of carnivorous ferocity. Horses, from the huge Percherons, with massive scimitar-shaped jaws looking eminently suitable for flattening platoons of Philistines, down to the skulls of donkeys, as stubbornly enduring in their miniature curves as those of the enormous draft horses.

They had a certain appeal, so still and so beautiful, as though each object held still the essence of its owner, as if the lines of bone held the ghost of the flesh and fur that once they had borne.

I reached out and touched one of the skulls, the bone not cold as I would have expected, but strangely inert, as though the vanished warmth, long gone, hovered not far off.

I had seen human remains treated with far less reverence; the skulls of early Christian martyrs jammed cheek by bony jowl together in heaps in the catacombs, thigh bones tossed in a pile like jackstraws underneath.

"A bear?" I said, speaking softly. A big skull, this one, the canine teeth curved for ripping, but the molars oddly flattened.

"Yes, madonna." Seeing that I was not afraid, Raymond relaxed. His hand floated out, barely skimming the curves of the blunt, solid skull. "You see the teeth? An eater of fish, of meat"—a small finger traced the long, wicked curve of the canine, the flat serrations of molar—"but a grinder of berries, of grubs. They seldom starve, because they will eat anything."

I turned slowly from side to side, admiring, touching one here and there.

"They're lovely," I said. We spoke in quiet tones, as though to speak loudly might rouse the silent sleepers.

"Yes." Raymond's fingers touched them as mine did, stroking the long frontal bones, tracing the delicate squamosal arch of the cheek. "They hold the character of the animal, you see. You can tell much about what was, only from what is left."

He turned over one of the smaller skulls, pointing out the swelling bulges on the underside, like small, thin-walled balloons.

"Here—the canal of the ear enters into these, so that the sounds echo within the skull. Hence the sharp ears of the rat, madonna."

"Tympanic bullae," I said, nodding.

"Ah? I have but little Latin. My names for such things are . . . my own."

"Those . . ." I gestured upward. "Those are special, aren't they?"

"Ah. Yes, madonna. They are wolves. Very old wolves." He lifted down one of the skulls, handling it with reverent care. The snout was long and canid, with heavy canines and broad carnassial teeth. The sagittal crest rose stark and commanding from the back of the skull, testimony to the heavy muscles of the brawny neck that had once supported it.

Not a soft dull white like the other skulls, these were stained and streaked with brown, and shone glossy with much polishing.

"Such beasts are no more, madonna."

"No more? Extinct, you mean?" I touched it once more, fascinated. "Where on earth did you get them?"

"Not *on* the earth, madonna. Under it. They came from a peat bog, buried many feet down."

Looking closely, I could see the differences between these skulls and the newer, whiter ones on the opposite wall. These animals had been larger than ordinary wolves, with jaws that might have cracked the leg bones of a running elk or torn the throat from a fallen deer.

I shuddered slightly at the touch, reminded of the wolf I had killed outside Wentworth Prison, and its pack-mates who had stalked me in the icy twilight, barely six months ago.

"You do not care for wolves, madonna?" Raymond

asked. "Yet the bears and the foxes do not trouble you? They also are hunters, eaters of flesh."

"Yes, but not mine," I said wryly, handing him back the age-dark skull. "I feel a good deal more sympathy with our friend the elk." I patted the high jutting nose with some affection.

"Sympathy?" The soft black eyes regarded me curiously. "It is an unusual emotion to feel for a bone, madonna."

"Well . . . yes," I said, slightly embarrassed, "but they don't really seem like just bones, you know. I mean, you can tell something about them, and get a feeling for what the animal was like, looking at these. They aren't just inanimate objects."

Raymond's toothless mouth stretched wide, as though I had inadvertently said something that pleased him, but he said nothing in reply.

"Why do you have all these?" I asked abruptly, suddenly realizing that racks of animal skulls were hardly the usual appurtenances of an apothecary's shop. Stuffed crocodiles, possibly, but not all this lot.

He shrugged good-naturedly.

"Well, they are company, of a sort, while I pursue my work." He gestured toward a cluttered workbench in one corner. "And while they may talk to me of many things, they are not so noisy as to attract the attention of the neighbors. Come here," he said, changing subjects abruptly. "I have something for you."

I followed him toward a tall cabinet at the end of the room, wondering.

He was not a naturalist, certainly not a scientist, as I understood the term. He kept no notes, made no drawings, no records that others might consult and learn from. And yet I had the odd conviction that he wanted very much to teach me the things that he knew—a sympathy for bones, perhaps?

The cabinet was painted with a number of odd signs, tailed and whorled, among what appeared to be pentagons and circles; Cabbalistic symbols. I recognized one or two, from some of Uncle Lamb's historical references.

"Interested in the Cabbala, are you?" I asked, eyeing the symbols with some amusement. That would account for the hidden workroom. While there was a strong interest in occult matters among some of the French literati and the aristocracy, it was an interest kept highly clandestine, for fear of the Church's cleansing wrath.

To my surprise, Raymond laughed. His blunt, short-nailed fingers pressed here and there on the front of the cabinet, touching the center of one symbol, the tail of another.

"Well, no, madonna. Most Cabbalists tend to be rather poor, so I do not seek their company often. But the symbols *do* keep curious people out of my cabinet. Which, if you think of it, is no small power for a bit of paint to exercise. So perhaps the Cabbalists are right, after all, when they say these signs hold power?"

He smiled mischievously at me, as the cabinet door swung open. I could see that it was in fact a double cabinet; if a nosy person ignored the warning of the symbols and merely opened the door, he or she would no doubt see only the harmless contents of an apothecary's closet. But if the proper sequence of hidden catches was pressed, then the inner shelves swung out as well, revealing a deep cavity behind them.

He pulled out one of the small drawers that lined the cavity, and upended it into his hand. Stirring the contents, he plucked out a single large white crystalline stone and handed it to me.

"For you," he said. "For protection."

"What? Magic?" I asked cynically, tilting the crystal from side to side in my palm.

Raymond laughed. He held his hand over the desk and let a handful of small colored stones trickle through his fingers, to bounce on the stained felt blotting-pad.

"I suppose you can call it so, madonna. Certainly I can charge more for it when I do." One fingertip nudged a pale greenish crystal free from the pile of colored stones.

"They have no more—and surely no less—magic than the skulls. Call them the bones of the earth. They hold the essence of the matrix in which they grew, and whatever powers that held, you may find here as well." He flicked a small yellowish nodule in my direction.

"Sulfur. Grind it with a few other small things, touch it with a match, and it will explode. Gunpowder. Is that magic? Or is it only the nature of sulfur?"

"I suppose it depends who you're talking to," I observed, and his face split in a delighted grin.

"If you ever seek to leave your husband, madonna," he said, chuckling, "be assured that you won't starve. I *said* you were a professional, did I not?"

"My husband!" I exclaimed, paling. My mind suddenly made sense of the muffled noises coming from the distant shop. There was a loud thump, as of a large fist brought down with considerable force on a countertop, and the deep rumble of a voice inclined to brook no interference made itself heard amid the babble of other sounds.

"Bloody Christ! I forgot Jamie!"

"Your husband is here?" Raymond's eyes went wider even than usual, and had he not already been so pale, I imagine he would have gone white, too.

"I left him outside," I explained, stooping to cross back through the secret opening. "He must have got tired of waiting."

"Wait, madonna!" Raymond's hand gripped my elbow, stopping me. He put his other hand over mine, the one that held the white crystal.

"That crystal, madonna. I said it is for your protection."

"Yes, yes," I said impatiently, hearing my name being shouted outside with increasing volume. "What does it do, then?"

"It is sensitive to poison, madonna. It will change color, in the presence of several harmful compounds."

That stopped me. I straightened up and stared at him.

"Poison?" I said, slowly. "Then . . ."

"Yes, madonna. You may be still in some danger." Raymond's froglike face was grim. "I cannot say for sure, or from which direction, for I do not know. If I find out, be assured I will tell you." His eyes flicked uneasily toward the entrance through the hearth. A thunder of blows sounded on the outer wall. "Assure your husband as well, please, madonna."

"Don't worry," I told him, ducking under the low lintel. "Jamie doesn't bite—I don't think."

"I was not worried about his *teeth,* madonna" came from behind me as I walked duckfooted over the ashes of the hearth.

Jamie, in the act of raising his dagger-hilt to hammer

again on the paneling, caught sight of me emerging from the fireplace and lowered it.

"Och, there ye are," he observed mildly. He tilted his head to one side, watching me brush soot and ashes from the hem of my gown, then scowled at the sight of Raymond peeping cautiously out from under the drying table.

"Ah, and there's our wee toadling, as well. Has he some explanation, Sassenach, or had I best pin him up wi' the rest?" Not taking his eyes off Raymond, he nodded toward the wall of the outer workshop, where a number of dried toads and frogs were pinned to a long strip of hanging felt.

"No, no," I said hastily as Raymond made to duck back into his sanctuary. "He's told me everything. In fact, he's been *most* helpful."

With some reluctance, Jamie put up his dirk, and I reached down a hand to draw Raymond out of hiding. He flinched slightly at the sight of Jamie.

"This man is your husband, madonna?" he asked, in the tones of someone hoping the answer would be "no."

"Yes, of course," I answered. "My husband, James Fraser, my lord Broch Tuarach," I said, waving at Jamie, though I could scarcely have been referring to anyone else. I waved in the other direction. "Master Raymond."

"So I gathered," said Jamie dryly. He bowed and extended a hand toward Raymond, whose head reached a few inches past Jamie's waist. Raymond touched the outstretched hand briefly and yanked his own back, unable to repress a mild shiver. I stared at him in amazement.

Jamie merely raised one eyebrow, then leaned back and settled himself against the edge of the table. He crossed his arms across his chest.

"All right, then," he said. "What about it?"

I made most of the explanations, Raymond contributing only monosyllables of confirmation from time to time. The little apothecary seemed deprived of all his normal sly wit, and huddled on a stool near the fire, shoulders hunched in wariness. Only when I had finished with an explanation of the white crystal—and the presumed need for it—did he stir and seem to take on a little life once more.

"It is true, milord," he assured Jamie. "I do not know, in fact, whether it is your wife or yourself that may be in danger, or perhaps the two of you together. I have heard nothing specific; only the name 'Fraser,' spoken in a place where names are seldom named in blessing."

Jamie glanced sharply at him. "Aye? And you frequent such places, do you, Master Raymond? Are the people you speak of associates of yours?"

Raymond smiled, a little wanly. "I should be inclined to describe them more as business rivals, milord."

Jamie grunted. "Mmmphm. Aye, well, and anyone who tries something may get a bit more of a blessing than he's bargained for." He touched the dirk at his belt, and straightened up.

"Still, I thank ye for the warning, Master Raymond." He bowed to the apothecary, but didn't offer his hand again. "As for the other"—he cocked an eyebrow at me—"if my wife is disposed to forgive your actions, then it isna my place to say more about it. Not," he added, "that I wouldna advise ye to pop back in your wee hole, the next time the Vicomtesse comes into your shop. Come along then, Sassenach."

As we rattled toward the Rue Trémoulins, Jamie was silent, staring out the window of the coach as the stiff fingers of his right hand tapped against his thigh.

"A place where names are seldom named in blessing," he murmured as the coach turned into the Rue Cambodge. "What might that be, I wonder?"

I remembered the Cabbalistic signs on Raymond's cabinet, and a small shiver raised the hairs on my forearms. I remembered Marguerite's gossip about the Comte St. Germain, and Madame de Ramage's warning. I told Jamie about them, and what Raymond had said.

"*He* may regard it as paint and window dressing," I finished, "but plainly he knows people who don't, or who is he looking to keep out of his cabinet?"

Jamie nodded. "Aye. I've heard a bit—only a bit—about such goings-on around the Court. I paid no attention at the time, thinking it only silliness, but now I'll find out a bit more." He laughed, suddenly, and drew me close to his side. "I'll set Murtagh to follow the Comte St. Germain. That'll give the Comte a *real* demon to play with."

17

Possession

$\mathcal{M}$urtagh was duly set to watch the comings and goings of the Comte St. Germain, but beyond reporting that the Comte entertained a remarkable number of persons in his home—of both sexes and all classes—detected nothing particularly mysterious. The Comte did have one visitor of note, though—Charles Stuart, who came one afternoon, stayed for an hour, and left.

Charles had begun to require Jamie's company more frequently on his expeditions through the taverns and low places of the city. I personally thought this had more to do with Jules de La Tour de Rohan's party, held to celebrate the announcement of his wife's pregnancy, than it did with any sinister influence of the Comte's.

These expeditions sometimes lasted well into the night, and I became accustomed to going to bed without Jamie, waking when he crawled in beside me, his body chilled with walking through the evening fog, and the smell of tobacco smoke and liquor clinging to his hair and skin.

"He's so distraught about that woman that I dinna think he even remembers he's the heir to the thrones of Scotland and England," Jamie said, returning from one of these expeditions.

"Goodness, he *must* be upset," I said, sarcastically. "Let's hope he stays that way."

A week later, though, I woke to the cold gray light of dawn to find the bed beside me still vacant, the coverlet flat and undisturbed.

"Is milord Broch Tuarach in his study?" I leaned over the banister in my nightgown, startling Magnus, who was passing through the lower hall. Perhaps Jamie had chosen to sleep on the sofa in the study, so as not to disturb me.

"No, milady," he answered, staring up at me. "I came to unbolt the front door, and found that it had never been bolted. Milord did not come home last night."

I sat down heavily on the top step. I must have looked

rather alarming, because the elderly butler nearly sprinted up the stairs to me.

"Madame," he said, anxiously chafing one of my hands. "Madame, are you all right?"

"I've been better, but it isn't important. Magnus, send one of the footmen to Prince Charles's house in Montmartre at once. Have him see if my husband is there."

"At once, milady. And I will send Marguerite up to attend you, as well." He turned and hurried down the stairs, the soft felt slippers he wore for his morning duties making a soft, shushing noise on the polished wood.

"And Murtagh!" I called after Magnus's departing back. "My husband's kinsman. Bring him to me, please!" The first thought that had sprung into my mind was that Jamie had perhaps stayed the night at Charles's villa; the second, that something had happened to him, whether by accident or by someone's deliberate intent.

"Where is he?" Murtagh's cracked voice spoke at the foot of the stair. He had obviously just awakened; his face was creased from whatever he had been lying on, and there were bits of straw in the folds of his ratty shirt.

"How should I know?" I snapped. Murtagh always looked as though he suspected everyone of something, and being rudely wakened had not improved his habitual scowl. The sight of him was nonetheless reassuring; if anything rough was in the offing, Murtagh looked the person to be dealing with it.

"He went out with Prince Charles last night, and didn't come back. That's all I know." I pulled myself up by the banister railing and smoothed down the silk folds of my nightgown. The fires had been lit, but hadn't had time to warm the house, and I was shivering.

Murtagh rubbed a hand over his face to assist thought. "Mphm. Has someone gone to Montmartre?"

"Yes."

"Then I'll wait 'til they come back with word. If Jamie's there, well and good. If he isn't, mayhap they'll know when he parted company with His Highness, and where."

"And what if they're both gone? What if the Prince didn't come home either?" I asked. If there were Jacobites in Paris, there were also those who opposed the restoration of the Stuart line. And while assassinating Charles Stuart might not assure the failure of a potential Scottish Rising—he did, after all, have a younger brother, Henry—it might go some way toward damping James's enthusiasm for such a venture— if he had any to start with, I thought distractedly.

I remembered vividly the story Jamie had told me, of the attempt on his life during which he had met Fergus. Street assassinations were far from uncommon, and there were gangs of ruffians who hunted the Paris streets after dark.

"You'd best go dress yourself, lassie," Murtagh remarked. "I can see the gooseflesh from here."

"Oh! Yes, I suppose so." I glanced down at my arms; I had been hugging myself as suppositions raced through my mind, but to little effect; my teeth were beginning to chatter.

"Madame! You will give yourself a chill, surely!" Marguerite came stumping rapidly up the stairs, and I allowed her to shoo me into the bedroom, glancing back to see Murtagh below, carefully examining the point of his dirk before ramming it home in its sheath.

"You should be in bed, Madame!" Marguerite scolded. "It isn't good for the child, for you to let yourself be chilled like that. I will fetch a warming pan at once; where is your nightrobe? Get into it at once, yes, that's right . . ." I shrugged the heavy woolen nightrobe over the thin silk of my nightgown, but ignored Marguerite's clucking to go to the window and open the shutters.

The street outside was beginning to glow as the rising sun struck the upper facades of the stone houses along the Rue Trémoulins. There was a good deal of activity on the street, early as it was; maids and footmen engaged in scrubbing steps or polishing brass gate-fittings, barrowmen selling fruit, vegetables, and fresh seafood, crying their wares along the street, and the cooks of the great houses popping up from their basement doors like so many jinni, summoned by the cries of the barrowmen. A delivery cart loaded with coal clopped slowly along the street, pulled by an elderly horse who looked as though he would much rather be in his stable. But no sign of Jamie.

I at last allowed an anxious Marguerite to persuade me into bed, for the sake of warmth, but couldn't go back to sleep. Every sound from below brought me to the alert, hoping that each footstep on the pavement outside would be followed by Jamie's voice in the hall below. The face of the Comte St. Germain kept coming between me and sleep. Alone among the French nobility, he had some connection with Charles Stuart. He had, in all likelihood, been behind the earlier attempt on Jamie's life . . . and on mine. He was known to have unsavory associations. Was it possible that he had arranged to have both Charles and Jamie removed? Whether his purposes were political or personal made little difference, at this point.

When at last the sound of steps below did come, I was so occupied with visions of Jamie lying in a gutter with his throat cut, that I didn't realize he was home until the bedroom door opened.

"Jamie!" I sat up in bed with a cry of joy.

He smiled at me, then yawned immensely, making no effort to cover his mouth. I could see a goodly distance down his throat, and observed with relief that it wasn't cut. On the other hand, he looked distinctly the worse for wear. He lay down on the bed next to me and stretched, long and rackingly, then settled with a half-contented groan.

"What," I demanded, "happened to *you*?"

He opened one red-rimmed eye.

"I need a bath," he said, and closed it again.

I leaned toward him and sniffed delicately. The nose detected the usual smoky smell of closed rooms and damp wool, underlying a truly remarkable combination of alcoholic stenches—ale, wine, whisky, and brandy—which matched the variety of stains on his shirt. And forming a high note to the mixture, a horrible cheap cologne, of a particularly penetrating and noxious pungency.

"You do," I agreed. I scrambled out of bed and leaning out into the corridor, shouted for Marguerite, sending her on arrival for a hip bath and sufficient water to fill it. As a parting gift from Brother Ambrose, I had several cakes of a fine-milled hard soap, made with attar of roses, and told her to fetch those, as well.

As the maid set about the tedious business of bringing up the huge copper bath-cans, I turned my attention to the hulk on the bed.

I stripped off his shoes and stockings, then loosening the

buckle of his kilt, I flipped it open. His hands went reflexively to his crotch, but my eyes were focused elsewhere.

"*What*," I said again, "happened to you?"

Several long scratches marked his thighs, angry red welts against the pale skin. And high on the inside of one leg was what could be nothing other than a bite; the toothmarks were plainly visible.

The maid, pouring hot water, cast an interested eye at the evidence and thought fit to put in her tuppence at this delicate moment.

"*Un petit chien?*" she asked. A little dog? Or something else. While I was far from fluent in the idiom of the times, I *had* learned that *les petits chiens* often walked the street on two legs with painted faces.

"Out," I said briefly in French, with a Head Matron intonation. The maid picked up the cans and left the room, pouting slightly. I turned back to Jamie, who opened one eye, and after a glance at my face, closed it again.

"Well?" I asked.

Instead of answering, he shuddered. After a moment, he sat up and rubbed his hands over his face, the stubble making a rasping noise. He cocked one ruddy eyebrow interrogatively. "I wouldna suppose a gently reared young lady such as yourself would be familiar wi' an alternate meaning for the term *soixante-neuf* ?"

"I've heard the term," I said, folding my arms across my chest and regarding him with a certain amount of suspicion. "And may I ask just where *you* encountered that particular interesting number?"

"It was suggested to me—with some force—as a desirable activity by a lady I happened to meet last night."

"Was that by any chance the lady who bit you in the thigh?"

He glanced down and rubbed the mark meditatively.

"Mm, no. As a matter of fact, it wasn't. That lady seemed preoccupied wi' rather lower numbers. I think she meant to settle for the six, and the nine could go hang."

"Jamie," I said, tapping my foot in a marked manner, "*where* have you been all night?"

He scooped up a handful of water from the basin and

splashed it over his face, letting the rivulets run down among the dark red hairs on his chest.

"Mm," he said, blinking drops from his thick lashes, "well, let me see. First there was supper at a tavern. We met Glengarry and Millefleurs there." Monsieur Millefleurs was a Parisian banker, while Glengarry was one of the younger Jacobites, chief of one sept of the MacDonell clan. A visitor in Paris, rather than a resident, he had been much in Charles's company lately, by Jamie's report. "And after supper, we went to the Duc di Castellotti's, for cards."

"And then?" I asked.

A tavern, apparently. And then another tavern. And then an establishment which appeared to share some of the characteristics of a tavern, but was embellished by the addition of several ladies of interesting appearance and even more interesting talents.

"Talents, eh?" I said, with a glance at the marks on his leg.

"God, they did it in public," he said, with a reminiscent shudder. "Two of them, on the table. Right between the saddle of mutton and the boiled potatoes. With the quince jelly."

"Mon dieu," said the newly returned maid, setting down the fresh bath-can long enough to cross herself.

"You be quiet," I said, scowling at her. I turned my attention back to my husband. "And then what?"

Then, apparently, the action had become somewhat more general, though still accomplished in fairly public fashion. With due regard to Marguerite's sensibilities, Jamie waited until she had left for another round of water before elaborating further.

". . . and then Castellotti took the fat one with red hair and the small blond one off to a corner, and—"

"And what were *you* doing all this time?" I broke in on the fascinating recitative.

"Watching," he said, as though surprised. "It didna seem decent, but there wasna much choice about it, under the circumstances."

I had been groping in his sporran as he talked, and now fished out not only a small purse, but a wide metal ring, embellished with a coat of arms. I tried it curiously on a finger; it was much larger than any normal ring, and hung like a quoit on a stick.

"Whoever does this belong to?" I asked, holding it out. "It looks like the Duc di Castellotti's coat of arms, but whoever it belongs to must have fingers like sausages." Castellotti was an etiolated Italian stringbean, with the pinched face of a man with chronic dyspepsia—no wonder, judging from Jamie's story. Quince jelly, forsooth!

I glanced up to find Jamie blushing from navel to hairline.

"Er," he said, taking an exaggerated interest in a mud stain on one knee, "it . . . doesna go on a man's finger."

"Then what . . . oh." I looked at the circular object with renewed interest. "Goodness. I've heard of them before . . ."

"You have?" said Jamie, thoroughly scandalized.

"But I've never seen one. Does it fit you?" I reached out to try it. He clasped his hands reflexively over his private parts.

Marguerite, arriving with more water, assured him, "*Ne vous en faites pas,* Monsieur. *J'en ai déjà vu un.*" Don't worry yourself, monsieur; I've already seen one.

Dividing a glare between me and the maid, he pulled a quilt across his lap.

"Bad enough to spend all night defending my virtue," he remarked with some asperity, "without havin' it subjected to comment in the morning."

"Defending your virtue, hm?" I tossed the ring idly from hand to hand, catching it on opposing index fingers. "A gift, was it?" I asked, "or a loan?"

"A gift. Don't do that, Sassenach," he said, wincing. "It brings back memories."

"Ah yes," I said, eying him. "Now *about* those memories . . ."

"Not *me!*" he protested. "Surely ye dinna think I'd do such things? I'm a married man!"

"Monsieur Millefleurs isn't married?"

"He's not only married, he has two mistresses," Jamie said. "But he's French—that's different."

"The Duc di Castellotti isn't French—he's Italian."

"But he's a duke. That's different, too."

"Oh, it is, is it? I wonder if the Duchess thinks so."

"Considering a few things the Duc claimed he learnt from the Duchess, I would imagine so. Isn't that bath ready yet?"

Clutching the quilt about him, he lumbered from the bed to the steaming tub and stepped in. He dropped the quilt and lowered himself quickly, but not quite quickly enough.

"Énorme!" said the maid, crossing herself.

"C'est tout," I said repressively. *"Merci bien."* She dropped her eyes, blushed, and scuttled out.

As the door closed behind the maid, Jamie relaxed into the tub, high at the back to allow for lounging; the feeling of the times seemed to be that once having gone to the trouble of filling a bath, one might as well enjoy it. His stubbled face assumed an expression of bliss as he sank gradually lower into the steaming water, a flush of heat reddening his fair skin. His eyes were closed, and a faint mist of moisture gleamed across the high, broad cheekbones and shone in the hollows beneath his eyesockets.

"Soap?" he asked hopefully, opening his eyes.

"Yes, indeed." I fetched a cake and handed it to him, then sat down on a stool alongside the bath. I watched for some time as he scrubbed industriously, fetching him a cloth and a pumice stone, with which he painstakingly rasped the soles of his feet and his elbows.

"Jamie," I said at last.

"Aye?"

"I don't mean to quarrel with your methods," I said, "and we agreed that you might have to go to some lengths, but . . . did you *really* have to . . ."

"To what, Sassenach?" He had stopped washing and was watching me intently, head on one side.

"To . . . to . . ." To my annoyance, I was flushing as deeply as he was, but without the excuse of hot water.

A large hand rose dripping out of the water and rested on my arm. The wet heat burned through the thin fabric of my sleeve.

"Sassenach," he said, "what do ye think I've been doing?"

"Er, well," I said, trying and failing to keep my eyes away

from the marks on his thigh. He laughed, though he didn't sound truly amused.

"O ye of little faith!" he said sardonically.

I withdrew beyond his reach.

"Well," I said, "when one's husband comes home covered with bites and scratches and reeking with perfume, admits he's spent the night in a bawdy house, and . . ."

"And tells ye flat-out he's spent the night watching, not doing?"

"You didn't get those marks on your leg from watching!" I snapped suddenly, then clamped my lips together. I felt like a jealous biddy, and I didn't care for it. I had vowed to take it all calmly, like a woman of the world, telling myself that I had complete faith in Jamie and—just in case—that you can't make omelets without breaking eggs. Even if something *had* happened . . .

I smoothed the wet spot on my sleeve, feeling the air chill through the cooling silk. I struggled to regain my former light tone.

"Or are those the scars of honorable combat, gained in defending your virtue?" Somehow the light tone didn't quite come off. Listening to myself, I had to admit that the overall tone was really quite nasty. I was rapidly ceasing to care.

No slouch at reading tones of voice, Jamie narrowed his eyes at me and seemed about to reply. He drew in his breath, then apparently thought better of whatever he had been going to say and let it out again.

"Yes," he said calmly. He fished about in the tub between his legs, coming up at length with the cake of soap, a roughly shaped ball of white slickness. He held it out on his palm.

"Will ye help me to wash my hair? His Highness vomited on me in the coach coming home, and I reek a bit, all things considered."

I hesitated a moment, but accepted the olive branch, temporarily at least.

I could feel the solid curve of his skull under the thick, soapy hair, and the welt of the healed scar across the back of his head. I dug my thumbs firmly into his neck muscles, and he relaxed slightly under my hands.

The soap bubbles ran down across the wet, gleaming

curves of his shoulders, and my hands followed them, spreading the slickness so that my fingers seemed to float on the surface of his skin.

He *was* big, I thought. Near him so much, I tended to forget his size, until I saw him suddenly from a distance, towering among smaller men, and I would be struck anew by his grace and the beauty of his body. But he sat now with his knees nearly underneath his chin, and his shoulders filled the tub from one side to the other. He leaned forward slightly to assist my ministrations, exposing the hideous scars on his back. The thick red welts of Jack Randall's Christmas gift lay heavily over the thin white lines of the earlier floggings.

I touched the scars gently, my heart squeezed by the sight. I had seen those wounds when they were fresh, seen him driven to the edge of madness by torture and abuse. But I had healed him, and he had fought with all the power of a gallant heart to be whole once more, to come back to me. Moved by tenderness, I brushed the trailing ends of his hair aside, and bent to kiss the back of his neck.

I straightened abruptly. He felt my movement and turned his head slightly.

"What is it, Sassenach?" he asked, voice slow with drowsy contentment.

"Not a thing," I said, staring at the dark-red blotches on the side of his neck. The nurses in the quarters at Pembroke used to conceal them with jaunty scarves tied about their necks the morning after their dates with soldiers from the nearby base. I always thought the scarves were really meant as a means of advertisement, rather than concealment.

"No, not a thing," I said again, reaching for the ewer on the stand. Placed near the window, it was ice-cold to the touch. I stepped behind Jamie and upended it on his head.

I lifted the silk skirts of my nightdress to avoid the sudden wave that spilled over the side of the bath. He was sputtering from the cold, but too shocked yet to form any of the words I could see gathering force on his lips. I beat him to it.

"Just watched, did you?" I asked coldly. "I wouldn't suppose you enjoyed it a bit, did you, poor thing?"

He thrust himself back in the tub with a violence that made the water slosh over the sides, splattering on the stone floor, and twisted around to look up at me.

"What d'ye want me to say?" he demanded. "Did I want to rut with them? Aye, I did! Enough to make my balls ache with not doing it. And enough to make me feel sick wi' the thought of touching one of the sluts."

He shoved the sopping mass of his hair out of his eyes, glaring at me.

"Is that what ye wanted to know? Are ye satisfied now?"

"Not really," I said. My face was hot, and I pressed my cheek against the icy pane of the window, hands clenched on the sill.

"Who looks on a woman with lust in his heart hath committed adultery with her already. Is that how ye see it?"

"Is it how *you* see it?"

"No," he said shortly. "I don't. And what would ye do if I *had* lain wi' a whore, Sassenach? Slap my face? Order me out of your chamber? Keep yourself from my bed?"

I turned and looked at him.

"I'd kill you," I said through my teeth.

Both eyebrows shot up, and his mouth dropped slightly with incredulity.

"Kill *me*? God, if I found you wi' another man, I'd kill *him*." He paused, and one corner of his mouth quirked wryly.

"Mind ye," he said, "I'd no be verra pleased wi' *you*, either, but still, it's him I'd kill."

"Typical man," I said. "Always missing the point."

He snorted with a bitter humor.

"Am I, then? So you dinna believe me. Want me to prove it to ye, Sassenach, that I've lain wi' no one in the last few hours?" He stood up, water cascading down the stretches of his long legs. The light from the window highlighted the reddish-gold hairs of his body and the steam rose off his flesh in wisps. He looked like a figure of freshly molten gold. I glanced briefly down.

"Ha," I said, with the maximum of scorn it was possible to infuse into one syllable.

"Hot water," he said briefly, stepping out of the tub. "Dinna worry yourself, it won't take long."

"That," I said, with delicate precision, "is what *you* think."

His face flushed still more deeply, and his hands curled involuntarily into fists.

"No reasoning wi' you, is there?" he demanded. "God, I spend the night torn between disgust and agony, bein' tormented by my companions for being unmanly, then come home to be tormented for being unchaste! *Mallaichte bàs!*"

Looking wildly about, he spotted his discarded clothing on the floor near the bed and lunged for it.

"Here, then!" he said, scrabbling for his belt. "Here! If lusting is adultery and you'll kill me for adultery, then ye'd best do it, hadn't ye!" He came up with his dirk, a ten-inch piece of dark steel, and thrust it at me, haft first. He squared his shoulders, presenting the broad expanse of his chest to me, and glared belligerently.

"Go ahead," he insisted. "Ye dinna mean to be forsworn, I hope? Being so sensitive to your honor as a wife and all?"

It was a real temptation. My clenched hands quivered at my sides with the longing to take the dagger and plant it firmly between his ribs. Only the knowledge that, all his dramatizing aside, he certainly wouldn't allow me to stab him, stopped me from trying. I felt sufficiently ridiculous, without humiliating myself further. I whirled away from him in a flurry of silk.

After a moment, I heard the clank of the dirk on the floorboards. I stood without moving, staring out of the window at the back courtyard below. I heard faint rustling sounds behind me, and glanced into the faint reflections of the window. My face showed in the windowpane as a smudged oval in a nimbus of sleep-snarled brown hair. Jamie's naked figure moved dimly in the glass like someone seen underwater, searching for a towel.

"The towel is on the bottom shelf of the ewer-stand," I said, turning around.

"Thank you." He dropped the dirty shirt with which he had begun gingerly dabbing himself and reached for the towel, not looking at me.

He wiped his face, then seemed to make some decision. He lowered the towel and looked directly at me. I could see the emotions struggling for mastery on his face, and felt as though I were still looking into the mirror of the window. Sense triumphed in both of us at once.

"I'm sorry," we said, in unison. And laughed.

The damp of his skin soaked through the thin silk, but I
didn't care.

Minutes later, he mumbled something into my hair.

"What?"

"Too close," he repeated, moving back a bit. "It was too
damn close, Sassenach, and it scared me."

I glanced down at the dirk, lying forgotten on the floor.

"Scared? I've never seen anyone less scared in my life.
You knew damned well I wouldn't do it."

"Oh, that." He grinned. "No, I didna think you'd kill me,
much as ye might like to." He sobered quickly. "No, it was
. . . well, those women. What I felt like with them. I didna
want them, truly not . . ."

"Yes, I know," I said, reaching for him, but he wasn't
stopping there. He held back from me, looking troubled.

"But the . . . the lusting, I suppose ye'd call it . . .
that was . . . too close to what I feel sometimes for you, and
it . . . well, it doesna seem right to me."

He turned away, rubbing at his hair with the linen towel,
so his voice came half-muffled.

"I always thought it would be a simple matter to lie wi' a
woman," he said softly. "And yet . . . I want to fall on my
face at your feet and worship you"—he dropped the towel
and reached out, taking me by the shoulders—"and still I
want to force ye to your knees before me, and hold ye there
wi' my hands tangled in your hair, and your mouth at my
service . . . and I want both things *at the same time,* Sassenach." He ran his hands up under my hair and gripped my
face between them, hard.

"I dinna understand myself at all, Sassenach! Or maybe I
do." He released me and turned away. His face had long
since dried, but he picked up the fallen towel and wiped the
skin of his jaw with it, over and over. The stubble made a
faint rasping sound against the fine linen. His voice was still
quiet, barely audible from a few feet away.

"Such things—the knowledge of them, I mean—it came
to me soon after . . . after Wentworth." Wentworth. Where
he had given his soul to save my life, and suffered the tortures
of the damned in retrieving it.

"I thought at the first that Jack Randall had stolen a bit
of my soul, and then I knew it was worse than that. All of it

was my own, and had been all along; it was only he'd shown it to me, and made me know it for myself. That's what he did that I canna forgive, and may his own soul rot for it!"

He lowered the towel and looked at me, face worn with the strains of the night, but eyes bright with urgency.

"Claire. To feel the small bones of your neck beneath my hands, and that fine, thin skin on your breasts and your arms . . . Lord, you are my wife, whom I cherish and I love wi' all my life, and still I want to kiss ye hard enough to bruise your tender lips, and see the marks of my fingers on your skin."

He dropped the towel. He raised his hands and held them trembling in the air before his face, then very slowly brought them down to rest on my head as though in benediction.

"I want to hold you like a kitten in my shirt, *mo nighean donn,* and still I want to spread your thighs and plow ye like a rutting bull." His fingers tightened in my hair. "I dinna understand myself!"

I pulled my head back, freeing myself, and took a half-step backward. The blood seemed all to be on the surface of my skin, and a chill ran down my body at the brief separation.

"Do you think it's different for me? Do you think I don't feel the same?" I demanded. "That I don't sometimes want to bite you hard enough to taste blood, or claw you 'til you cry out?"

I reached out slowly to touch him. The skin of his breast was damp and warm. Only the nail of my forefinger touched him, just below the nipple. Lightly, barely touching, I drew the nail upward, downward, circling round, watching the tiny nub rise hard amid the curling ruddy hairs.

The nail pressed slightly harder, sliding down, leaving a faint red streak on the fair skin of his chest. I was trembling all over by this time, but did not turn away.

"Sometimes I want to ride you like a wild horse, and bring you to the taming—did you know that? I can do it, you know I can. Drag you over the edge and drain you to a gasping husk. I can drive you to the edge of collapse and sometimes I delight in it, Jamie, I do! And yet so often I want"— my voice broke suddenly and I had to swallow hard before continuing—"I want . . . to hold your head against my breast and cradle you like a child and comfort you to sleep."

My eyes were so full of tears that I couldn't see his face clearly; couldn't see if he wept as well. His arms went tight around me and the damp heat of him engulfed me like the breath of a monsoon.

"Claire, ye do kill me, knife or no," he whispered, face buried in my hair. He bent and picked me up, carrying me to the bed. He sank to his knees, laying me amid the rumpled quilts.

"You'll lie wi' me now," he said quietly. "And I shall use ye as I must. And if you'll have your revenge for it, then take it and welcome, for my soul is yours, in all the black corners of it."

The skin of his shoulders was warm with the heat of the bath, but he shivered as with cold as my hands traveled up to his neck, and I pulled him down to me.

And when I had at length taken my last revenge of him, I did cradle him, stroking back the roughened, half-dry locks.

"And sometimes," I whispered to him, "I wish it could be you inside me. That I could take you into me and keep you safe always."

His hand, large and warm, lifted slowly from the bed and cupped the small round swell of my belly, sheltering and caressing.

"You do, my own," he said. "You do."

I felt it for the first time while lying in bed the next morning, watching Jamie dress for the day. A tiny fluttering sensation, at once entirely familiar and completely new. Jamie had his back turned to me, as he wriggled into his knee-length shirt and stretched his arms, settling the folds of white linen across the breadth of his shoulders.

I lay quite still, waiting, hoping for it to come again. It did, this time as a series of infinitesimal quick movements, like the bursting of bubbles rising to the surface of a carbonated liquid.

I had a sudden memory of Coca-Cola; that odd, dark, fizzy American drink. I had tasted it once, while having supper with an American colonel, who served it as a delicacy— which it was, in wartime. It came in thick greenish bottles, smooth-ribbed and tapered, with a high-waisted nip to the glass, so that the bottle was roughly woman-shaped, with a rounded bulge just below the neck, swelling to a broader one farther down.

I remembered how the millions of tiny bubbles had rushed into the narrow neck when the bottle was opened, smaller and finer than the bubbles of champagne, bursting joyous in the air. I laid one hand very gently on my abdomen, just above the womb.

There it was. There was no sense of him, or her, as I had thought there might be—but there was certainly a sense of Someone. I wondered whether perhaps babies had no gender —physical characteristics aside—until birth, when the act of exposure to the outside world set them forever as one or the other.

"Jamie," I said. He was tying back his hair, gathering it into a thick handful at the base of his neck and winding a leather lace about it. Head bent in the task, he looked up at me from under his brows and smiled.

"Awake, are ye? It's early yet, *mo nighean donn.* Go back to sleep for a bit."

I had been going to tell him, but something stopped me. He couldn't feel it, of course, not yet. It wasn't that I thought he wouldn't care, but there was something about that first awareness that seemed suddenly private; the second shared secret between me and the child—the first being our knowledge of its existence, mine a conscious knowing, the embryo's a simple being. The sharing of that knowledge linked us close as did the blood that passed through both of us.

"Do you want me to braid your hair for you?" I asked. When he went to the docks, sometimes he would ask me to plait his ruddy mane in a tight queue, proof against the tugging winds on deck and quay. He always teased that he would have it dipped in tar, as the sailors did, to solve the problem permanently.

He shook his head, and reached for his kilt.

"No, I'm going to call on His Highness Prince Charles today. And drafty as his house is, I think it wilna be blowing my hair in my eyes." He smiled at me, coming to stand by the bed. He saw my hand lying on my stomach, and put his own lightly over it.

"Feeling all right, are ye, Sassenach? The sickness is better?"

"Much." The morning sickness had in fact abated, though waves of nausea still assailed me at odd moments. I found I could not bear the smell of frying tripe with onions, and had had to ban this popular dish from the servants' menu, since the smell crept from the basement kitchen like a ghost up the back stairs, to pop out at me unexpectedly when I opened the door of my sitting room.

"Good." He raised my hand, and bent over to kiss my knuckles in farewell. "Go back to sleep, *mo nighean donn*," he repeated.

He closed the door gently behind him, as though I were already sleeping, leaving me to the early morning silence of the chamber, with the small busy noises of the household safely barred by paneled wood.

Squares of pale sunlight from the casement window lay bright on the opposite wall. It would be a beautiful day, I could tell, the spring air ripening with warmth, and the plum blossoms bursting pink and white and bee-rich in the gardens of Versailles. The courtiers would be outside in the gardens today, rejoicing in the weather as much as the barrowmen who wheeled their wares through the streets.

So did I rejoice, alone and not alone, in my peaceful cocoon of warmth and quiet.

"Hello," I said softly, one hand over the butterfly wings that beat inside me.

PART THREE

Malchance

18

Rape in Paris

There was an explosion at the Royal Armory, near the beginning of May. I heard later that a careless porter had put down a torch in the wrong place, and a minute later, the largest assortment of gunpowder and firearms in Paris had gone up with a noise that startled the pigeons off Notre Dame.

At work in L'Hôpital des Anges, I didn't hear the explosion itself, but I certainly noticed the echoes. Though the Hôpital was on the opposite side of the city from the Armory, there were sufficient victims of the explosion that a good many of them overflowed the other hospitals and were brought to us, mangled, burned, and moaning in the backs of wagons, or supported on pallets by friends who carried them through the streets.

It was full dark before the last of the victims had been attended to, and the last bandage-swathed body laid gently down among the grubby, anonymous ranks of the Hôpital's patients.

I had dispatched Fergus home with word that I would be late, when I saw the magnitude of the task awaiting the sisters of des Anges. He had come back with Murtagh, and the two of them were lounging on the steps outside, waiting to escort us home.

Mary and I emerged wearily from the double doors, to find Murtagh demonstrating the art of knife-throwing to Fergus.

"Go on then," he was saying, back turned to us. "Straight as ye can, on the count of three. One . . . two . . . three!" At "three," Fergus bowled the large white onion he was holding, letting it bounce and hop over the uneven ground.

Murtagh stood relaxed, arm drawn back at a negligent cock, dirk held by the tip between his fingers. As the onion spun past, his wrist flicked once, quick and sharp. Nothing else moved, not so much as a stir of his kilts, but the onion leaped sideways, transfixed by the dirk, and fell mortally wounded, rolling feebly in the dirt at his feet.

"B-bravo, Mr. Murtagh!" Mary called, smiling. Startled, Murtagh turned, and I could see the flush rising on his lean cheeks in the light from the double doors behind us.

"Mmmphm," he said.

"Sorry to take so long," I said apologetically. "It took rather a time to get everyone squared away."

"Och, aye," the little clansman answered laconically. He turned to Fergus. "We'll do our best to find a coach, lad; it's late for the ladies to be walking."

"There aren't any here," Fergus said, shrugging. "I've been up and down the street for the last hour; every spare coach in the Cité has gone to the Armory. We might get something in the Rue du Faubourg St.-Honoré, though." He pointed down the street, at a dark, narrow gap between buildings that betrayed the presence of a passageway through to the next street. "It's quick through there."

After a short, frowning pause for thought, Murtagh nodded agreement. "All right, lad. Let's go, then."

It was cold in the alleyway, and I could see my breath in small white puffs, despite the moonless night. No matter how dark it got in Paris, there was always light somewhere; the glow of lamps and candles seeped through shutters and chinks in the walls of wooden buildings, and light pooled around the stalls of the street vendors and scattered from the small horn and metal lanterns that swung from cart tails and coach trees.

The next street was one of merchants, and here and there the proprietors of the various businesses had hung lanterns of pierced metal above their doors and shopyard entrances. Not content to rely upon the police to protect their property, often several businessmen would join together and hire a watchman to guard their premises at night. When I saw one such figure in front of the sailmaker's shop, sitting hunched in the shadows atop a pile of folded canvas, I nodded in response to his gruff *"Bonsoir,* Monsieur, mesdames."

As we passed the sailmaker's shop, though, I heard a sudden cry of alarm from the watchman.

"Monsieur! Madame!"

Murtagh swung round at once to meet the challenge,

sword already hissing from its scabbard. Slower in my reflexes, I was only halfway turned as he stepped forward, and
my eye caught the flicker of movement from the doorway
behind him. The blow took Murtagh from behind before I
could shout a warning, and he went sprawling facedown in
the street, arms and legs gone loose and nerveless, sword and
dirk flying from his hands to clatter on the stones.

I stooped quickly for the dirk as it slid past my foot, but a
pair of hands seized my arms from behind.

"Take care of the man," ordered a voice behind me.
"Quickly!"

I wrenched at my captor's grip; the hands dropped to my
wrists and twisted them sharply, making me cry out. There
was a billow of white, ghostlike in the dim street, and the
"watchman" bent over Murtagh's prone body, a length of
white fabric trailing from his hands.

"Help!" I shrieked. "Leave him alone! Help! Brigands!
Assassins! HELP!"

"Be still!" A quick clout over the ear made my head spin
for a moment. When my eyes stopped watering, I could make
out a long, white sausage-shape in the gutter; Murtagh,
shrouded and neatly secured in a canvas sail-bag. The false
watchman was crouched over him; he rose, grinning, and I
could see that he was masked, a dark strip of fabric extending
from forehead to upper lip.

A thin strip of light from the nearby chandler's fell
across his body as he rose. In spite of the cold evening, he was
wearing no more than a shirt that glowed momentarily emerald green in the passing light. A pair of breeches, buckled at
the knee, and what amazingly appeared to be silk hose and
leather shoes, not the bare feet or sabots I had expected. Not
ordinary bandits, then.

I caught a quick glimpse of Mary, at one side. One of the
masked figures had her in a tight grip from behind, one arm
clasped across her midriff, the other rummaging its way under
her skirts like a burrowing animal.

The one in front of me put a hand ingratiatingly behind
my head and pulled me close. The mask covered him from
forehead to upper lip, leaving his mouth free for obvious reasons. His tongue thrust into my mouth, tasting strongly of

drink and onions. I gagged, bit it, and spat as it was removed. He cuffed me heavily, knocking me to my knees in the gutter.

Mary's silver-buckled shoes were kicking dangerously near my nose as the ruffian holding her unceremoniously yanked her skirt above her waist. There was a tearing of satin, and a loud screech from above as his fingers plunged between her struggling thighs.

"A virgin! I've got a virgin!" he crowed. One of the men bowed mockingly to Mary.

"Mademoiselle, my congratulations! Your husband will have cause to thank us on his wedding night, as he will encounter no awkward obstructions to hinder his pleasure. But we are selfless—we ask for no thanks for the performance of our duties. The doing of service is pleasure in itself."

If I had needed anything beyond the silk hose to tell me that our assailants were not street ruffians, this speech— greeted with howls of laughter—would have done it. Fitting names to the masked faces was something else again.

The hands that grasped my arm to haul me to my feet were manicured, with a small beauty mark just above the fork of the thumb. I must remember that, I thought grimly. If they let us live afterward, it might be useful.

Someone else grabbed my arms from behind, yanking them back so strongly that I cried out. The posture thus induced made my breasts stand out in the low-cut bodice as though they were being offered on a platter.

The man who seemed in charge of operations wore a loose shirt of some pale color, decorated with darker spots— embroidery perhaps. It gave him an imprecise outline in the shadows, making it difficult to look at him closely. As he leaned forward and ran a finger appraisingly over the tops of my breasts, though, I could see the dark hair greased flat to his head and smell the heavy pomade. He had large ears, the better to hold up the strings of his mask.

"Do not worry yourselves, mesdames," Spotted-shirt said. "We mean you no harm; we intend only to give you a little gentle exercise—your husbands or fiancés need never know—and then we shall release you."

"Firstly, you may honor us with your sweet lips, mesdames," he announced, stepping back and tugging at the lacings of his breeches.

"Not that one," protested Green-shirt, pointing at me. "She bites."

"Not if she wants to keep her teeth," replied his companion. "On your knees, Madame, if you please." He shoved down strongly on my shoulders, and I jerked back, stumbling. He grabbed me to keep me from getting away, and the full hood of my cloak fell back, freeing my hair. Pins loosened in the struggle, it fell over my shoulders, strands flying like banners in the night wind, blinding me as they whipped across my face.

I staggered backward, pulling away from my assailant, shaking my head to clear my eyes. The street was dark, but I could see a few things in the faint gleam of lanterns through the shuttered shop windows, or in the glow of starlight that struck through the shadows to the street.

Mary's silver shoe buckles caught the light, kicking. She was on her back, struggling, with one of the men on top of her, swearing as he fought to get his breeches down and to control her at the same time. There was the sound of tearing cloth, and his buttocks gleamed white in a shaft of light from a courtyard gate.

Someone's arms seized me round the waist and dragged me backward, raising my feet off the ground. I scraped my heel down the length of his shin, and he squealed in outrage.

"Hold her!" ordered Spotted-shirt, coming out of the shadows.

"You hold her!" My captor thrust me unceremoniously into the arms of his friend, and the light from the courtyard shone into my eyes, temporarily blinding me.

"Mother of God!" The hands clutching my arms slackened their grip, and I yanked loose, to see Spotted-shirt, mouth hanging open in horrified amazement below the mask. He backed away from me, crossing himself as he went.

"In nomine Patris, et Filii, et Spiritus Sancti," he babbled, crossing and recrossing. "La Dame Blanche!"

"La Dame Blanche!" The man behind me echoed the cry, in tones of terror.

Spotted-shirt was still backing away, now making signs in the air which were considerably less Christian than the sign of the Cross, but which presumably had the same intent. Pointing index and little fingers at me in the ancient horned sign against evil, he was working his way steadily down a list of spiritual authorities, from the Trinity to powers on a considerably lower level, muttering the Latin names so fast that the syllables blurred together.

I stood in the street, shaken and dazed, until a terrible shriek from the ground near my feet recalled me to my senses. Too occupied with his own business to pay any attention to matters above him, the man on top of Mary made a gutteral sound of satisfaction and began to move his hips rhythmically, to the accompaniment of throat-tearing screams from Mary.

Acting purely from instinct, I took a step toward them, drew back my leg, and kicked him as hard as I could in the ribs. The breath exploded from his lungs in a startled "Oof!" and he rocked to one side.

One of his friends darted forward and seized him by the arm, shouting urgently, "Up! Up! It's La Dame Blanche! Run!"

Still sunk in the frenzy of rape, the man stared stupidly and tried to turn back to Mary, who was frantically writhing and twisting, trying to free the folds of her skirts from the weight that held her trapped. Both Green-shirt and Spotted-shirt were now pulling on her assailant's arms, and succeeded in getting him to his feet. His torn breeches drooped about his thighs, the blood-smeared rod of his erection trembling with mindless eagerness between the dangling shirttails.

The clatter of running feet approaching seemed finally to rouse him. His two helpers, hearing the sound, dropped his arms and fled precipitately, leaving him to his fate. With a muffled curse, he made his way down the nearest alley, hopping and hobbling as he tried to yank his breeches up around his waist.

"Au secours! Au secours! Gendarmes!" A breathless voice was shouting down the alleyway for help, as its owner fumbled his way in our direction, stumbling over rubbish in the dark. I hardly thought a footpad or other miscreant would be staggering down an alleyway shouting for the gendarmerie, though in my present state of shock, almost nothing would have surprised me.

I *was* surprised, though, when the black shape that flapped out of the alley proved to be Alexander Randall, swathed in black cape and slouch hat. He glanced wildly around the small cul-de-sac, from Murtagh, masquerading as a bag of rubbish, to me, standing frozen and gasping against a wall, to the huddled shape of Mary, nearly invisible among the other shadows. He stood helpless for a moment, then whirled and clambered up the iron gate from which our assailants had emerged. From the top of this, he could just reach the lantern suspended from the rafter above.

The light was a comfort; pitiful as was the sight it revealed, at least it banished the lurking shadows that threatened at any moment to turn into new dangers.

Mary was on her knees, curled into herself. Head buried in her arms, she was shaking, in total silence. One shoe lay on its side on the cobbles, silver buckle winking in the swaying light of the lantern.

Like a bird of ill omen, Alex swooped down beside her. "Miss Hawkins! Mary! Miss Hawkins! Are you all right?"

"Of all the damn-fool questions," I said with some asperity as she moaned and shrank away from him. "Naturally she isn't all right. She's just been raped." With a considerable effort, I pried myself from the comforting wall at my back, and started toward them, noting with clinical detachment that my knees were wobbling.

They gave way altogether in the next moment as a huge, batlike shape swooped down a foot in front of me, landing on the cobbles with a substantial thud.

"Well, well, look who's dropped in!" I said, and started to laugh in an unhinged sort of way. A large pair of hands grabbed me by the shoulders and administered a good shake.

"Be quiet, Sassenach," said Jamie, blue eyes gleaming black and dangerous in the lanternlight. He straightened up, the folds of his blue velvet cloak falling back over his shoulders as he stretched his arms toward the roof from which he had jumped. He could just grasp the edge of it, standing on his toes.

"Well, come down, then!" he said impatiently, looking up. "Put your feet over the edge onto my shoulders, and ye can slide down my back." With a grating of loose roof slates, a small black figure wriggled its way cautiously backward, then swarmed down the tall figure like a monkey on a stick.

"Good man, Fergus." Jamie clapped the boy casually on the shoulder, and even in the dim light I could see the glow of pleasure that rose in his cheeks. Jamie surveyed the landscape with a tactician's eye, and with a muttered word, sent the lad down the alley to keep watch for approaching gendarmes. The essentials taken care of, he squatted down before me once more.

"Are ye all right, Sassenach?" he inquired.

"Nice of you to ask," I said politely. "Yes, thanks. She's not so well, though." I waved vaguely in Mary's direction. She was still rolled into a ball, shuddering and quaking like a jelly, oozing away from Alex's fumbling efforts to pat her.

Jamie spared no more than a glance at her. "So I see. Where in hell is Murtagh?"

"Over there," I answered. "Help me up."

I staggered over to the gutter, where the sack that held Murtagh was heaving to and fro like an agitated caterpillar, emitting a startling mixture of muffled profanities in three languages.

Jamie drew his dirk, and with what seemed to be a rather callous disregard for the contents, slit the sack from end to end. Murtagh popped out of the opening like a Jack out of its box. Half his spiky black hair was pasted to his head by whatever noisome liquid the bag had rested in. The rest stood on end, lending a fiercer cast to a face rendered already sufficiently warlike by a large purple knot on the forehead and a rapidly darkening eye.

"Who hit me?" he barked.

"Well, it wasn't me," answered Jamie, raising one eyebrow. "Come along, man, we havena got all night."

⟡

"This is never going to work," I muttered, stabbing pins decorated with brilliants at random through my hair. "She ought to have medical care, for one thing. She needs a doctor!"

"She has one," Jamie pointed out, lifting his chin and peering down his nose into the mirror as he tied his stock. "You." Stock tied, he grabbed a comb and pulled it hurriedly through the thick, ruddy waves of his hair.

"No time to braid it," he muttered, holding a thick tail

behind his head as he rummaged in a drawer. "Have ye a bit of ribbon, Sassenach?"

"Let me." I moved swiftly behind him, folding under the ends of the hair and wrapping the club in a length of green ribbon. "Of all the bloody nights to have a dinner party on!"

And not just any dinner party, either. The Duke of Sandringham was to be guest of honor, with a small but select party to greet him. Monsieur Duverney was coming, with his eldest son, a prominent banker. Louise and Jules de La Tour were coming, and the d'Arbanvilles. Just to make things interesting, the Comte St. Germain had also been invited.

"St. Germain!" I had said in astonishment, when Jamie had told me the week before. "Whatever for?"

"I do business with the man," Jamie had pointed out. "He's been to dinner here before, with Jared. But what I want is to have the opportunity of watching him talk to you over dinner. From what I've seen of him in business, he's not the man to hide his thoughts." He picked up the white crystal that Master Raymond had given me and weighed it thoughtfully in his palm.

"It's pretty enough," he had said. "I'll have it set in a gold mounting, so you can wear it about your neck. Toy with it at dinner until someone asks ye about it, Sassenach. Then tell them what it's for, and make sure to watch St. Germain's face when ye do. If it was him gave ye the poison at Versailles, I think we'll see some sign of it."

What I wanted at the moment was peace, quiet, and total privacy in which to shake like a rabbit. What I had was a dinner party with a duke who might be a Jacobite or an English agent, a Comte who might be a poisoner, and a rape victim hidden upstairs. My hands shook so that I couldn't fasten the chain that held the mounted crystal; Jamie stepped behind me and snicked the catch with one flick of his thumb.

"Haven't you got any nerves?" I demanded of him. He grimaced at me in the mirror and put his hands over his stomach.

"Aye, I have. But it takes me in the belly, not the hands. Have ye some of that stuff for cramp?"

"Over there." I waved at the medicine box on the table, left open from my dosing of Mary. "The little green bottle. One spoonful."

Ignoring the spoon, he tilted the bottle and took several healthy gulps. He lowered it and squinted at the liquid within.

"God, that's foul stuff! Are ye nearly ready, Sassenach? The guests will be here any minute."

Mary was concealed for the moment in a spare room on the second floor. I had checked her carefully for injuries, which seemed limited to bruises and shock, then dosed her quickly with as large a slug of poppy syrup as seemed feasible.

Alex Randall had resisted all Jamie's attempts to send him home, and instead had been left to stand guard over Mary, with strict instructions to fetch me if she woke.

"How on earth did that idiot happen to be there?" I asked, scrabbling in the drawer for a box of powder.

"I asked him that," Jamie replied. "Seems the poor fool's in love with Mary Hawkins. He's been following her to and fro about the town, drooping like a wilted flower because he knows she's to wed Marigny."

I dropped the box of powder.

"*H-h-he's* in love with *her*?" I wheezed, waving away the cloud of floating particles.

"So he says, and I see nay reason to doubt it," Jamie said, brushing powder briskly off the bosom of my dress. "He was a bit distraught when he told me."

"I should imagine so." To the conflicting welter of emotions that filled me, I now added pity for Alex Randall. Of course he wouldn't have spoken to Mary, thinking the devotion of an impoverished secretary nothing compared to the wealth and position of a match with the House of Gascogne. And now what must he feel, seeing her subjected to brutal attack, virtually under his nose?

"Why in hell didn't he speak up? She would have run off with him in a moment." For the pale English curate, of course, must be the "spiritual" object of Mary's speechless devotion.

"Randall's a gentleman," Jamie replied, handing me a feather and the pot of rouge.

"You mean he's a silly ass," I said uncharitably.

Jamie's lip twitched. "Well, perhaps," he agreed. "He's also a poor one; he hasna the income to support a wife, should her family cast her off—which they certainly would, if she eloped with him. And his health is feeble; he'd find it hard to find another position, for the Duke would likely dismiss him without a character."

"One of the servants is bound to find her," I said, returning to an earlier worry in order to avoid thinking about this latest manifestation of tragedy.

"No, they won't. They'll all be busy serving. And by the morning, she may be recovered enough to go back to her uncle's house. I sent round a note," he added, "to tell them she was staying the night with a friend, as it was late. Didna want them searching for her."

"Yes, but—"

"Sassenach." His hands on my shoulders stopped me, and he peered over my shoulder to meet my eyes in the mirror. "We canna let her be seen by anyone, until she's able to speak and to act as usual. Let it be known what's happened to her, and her reputation will be ruined entirely."

"Her reputation! It's hardly her fault she was raped!" My voice shook slightly, and his grip on my shoulders tightened.

"It isna right, Sassenach, but it's how it is. Let it be known that she's a maid no more, and no man will take her— she'll be disgraced, and live a spinster to the end of her days." His hand squeezed my shoulder, left it, and returned to help guide a pin into the precariously anchored hair.

"It's all we can do for her, Claire," he said. "Keep her from harm, heal her as best we can—and find the filthy bastards who did it." He turned away and groped in my casket for his stick pin. "Christ," he added softly, speaking into the green velvet lining, "d'ye think I don't know what it is to her? Or to him?"

I laid my hand on his groping fingers and squeezed. He squeezed back, then lifted my hand and kissed it briefly.

"Lord, Sassenach! Your fingers are cold as snow." He turned me around to look earnestly into my face. "Are *you* all right, lass?"

Whatever he saw in my face made him mutter "Christ" again, sink to his knees, and pull me against his ruffled shirtfront. I gave up the pretense of courage, and clung to him, burying my face in the starchy warmth.

"Oh, God, Jamie. I was so scared. I *am* so scared. Oh, God, I wish you could make love to me now."

His chest vibrated under my cheek with his laugh, but he hugged me closer.

"You think that would help?"

"Yes."

In fact, I thought that I would not feel safe again, until I lay in the security of our bed, with the sheltering silence of the house all about us, feeling the strength and the heat of him around and within me, buttressing my courage with the joy of our joining, wiping out the horror of helplessness and near-rape with the sureness of mutual possession.

He held my face between his hands and kissed me, and for a moment, the fear of the future and the terror of the night fell away. Then he drew back and smiled. I could see his own worry etched in the lines of his face, but there was nothing in his eyes but the small reflection of my face.

"On account, then," he said softly.

➤

We had reached the second course without incident, and I was beginning to relax slightly, though my hand still had a tendency to tremble over the consommé.

"How perfectly fascinating!" I said, in response to a story of the younger Monsieur Duverney's, to which I wasn't listening, my ears being tuned for any suspicious noises abovestairs. "Do tell me more."

I caught Magnus's eye as he served the Comte St. Germain, seated across from me, and beamed congratulations at him as well as I could with a mouthful of fish. Too well trained to smile in public, he inclined his head a respectful quarter-inch and went on with the service. My hand went to the crystal at my neck, and I stroked it ostentatiously as the Comte, with no sign of perturbation on his saturnine features, dug into the trout with almonds.

Jamie and the elder Duverney were close in conversation at the other end of the table, food ignored as Jamie scribbled left-handed figures on a scrap of paper with a stub of chalk. Chess, or business? I wondered.

As guest of honor, the Duke sat at the center of the table. He had enjoyed the first courses with the gusto of a natural-born trencherman, and was now engaged in animated conversation with Madame d'Arbanville, on his right. As the

Duke was the most obviously prominent Englishman in Paris at the time, Jamie had thought it worthwhile cultivating his acquaintance, in hopes of uncovering any rumors that might lead to the sender of the musical message to Charles Stuart. My attention, though, kept straying from the Duke to the gentleman seated across from him—Silas Hawkins.

I had thought I might just die on the spot and save trouble all round when the Duke had walked through the door, gesturing casually over his shoulder, and saying, "I say, Mrs. Fraser, you do know Hawkins here, don't you?"

The Duke's small, merry blue eyes had met mine with a look of guileless confidence that his whims would be accommodated, and I had had no choice but to smile and nod, and tell Magnus to be sure another place was set. Jamie, seeing Mr. Hawkins as he came through the door of the drawing room, had looked as though he were in need of another dose of stomach medicine, but had pulled himself together enough to extend a hand to Mr. Hawkins and start a conversation about the quality of the inns on the road to Calais.

I glanced at the carriage clock over the mantelpiece. How long before they would all be gone? I mentally tallied the courses already served, and those to come. Nearly to the sweet course. Then the salad and cheese. Brandy and coffee, port for the men, liqueurs for the ladies. An hour or two for stimulating conversation. Not too stimulating, please God, or they would linger 'til dawn.

Now they were talking of the menace of street gangs. I abandoned the fish and picked up a roll.

"And I have heard that some of these roving bands are composed not of rabble, as you would expect, but of some of the younger members of the nobility!" General d'Arbanville puffed out his lips at the monstrousness of the idea. "They do it for sport—sport! As though the robbery of decent men and the outraging of ladies were nothing more than a cockfight!"

"How extraordinary," said the Duke, with the indifference of a man who never went anywhere without a substantial escort. The platter of savouries hovered near his chin, and he scooped half a dozen onto his plate.

Jamie glanced at me, and rose from the table.

"If you'll excuse me, mesdames, messieurs," he said with a bow, "I have something rather special in the way of port that I would like to have His Grace taste. I'll fetch it from the cellar."

"It must be the Belle Rouge," said Jules de La Tour, licking his lips in anticipation. "You have a rare treat in store, Your Grace. I have never tasted such a wine anywhere else."

"Ah? Well, you soon will, Monsieur le Prince," the Comte St. Germain broke in. "Something even better."

"Surely there is nothing better than Belle Rouge!" General d'Arbanville exclaimed.

"Yes, there is," the Comte declared, looking smug. "I have found a new port, made and bottled on the island of Gostos, off the coast of Portugal. A color rich as rubies, and a flavor that makes Belle Rouge taste like colored water. I have a contract for delivery of the entire vintage in August."

"Indeed, Monsieur le Comte?" Silas Hawkins raised thick, graying brows toward our end of the table. "Have you found a new partner for investment, then? I understood that your own resources were . . . depleted, shall we say? following the sad destruction of the *Patagonia*." He took a cheese savoury from the plate and popped it delicately into his mouth.

The Comte's jaw muscles bulged, and a sudden chill descended on our end of the table. From Mr. Hawkins's sidelong glance at me, and the tiny smile that lurked about his busily chewing mouth, it was clear that he knew all about my role in the destruction of the unfortunate *Patagonia*.

My hand went again to the crystal at my neck, but the Comte didn't look at me. A hot flush had risen from his lacy stock, and he glared at Mr. Hawkins with open dislike. Jamie was right; not a man to hide his emotions.

"Fortunately, Monsieur," he said, mastering his choler with an apparent effort, "I *have* found a partner who wishes to invest in this venture. A fellow countryman, in fact, of our gracious host." He nodded sardonically toward the doorway, where Jamie had just appeared, followed by Magnus, who bore an enormous decanter of the Belle Rouge port.

Hawkins stopped chewing for a moment, his mouth unattractively open with interest. "A Scotsman? Who? I didn't think there were any Scots in the wine business in Paris besides the house of Fraser."

A definite gleam of amusement lit the Comte's eyes as

he glanced from Mr. Hawkins to Jamie. "I suppose it is debatable whether the investor in question could be considered Scottish at the moment; nonetheless, he is milord Broch Tuarach's fellow countryman. Charles Stuart is his name."

This bit of news had all the impact the Comte might have hoped for. Silas Hawkins sat bolt upright with an exclamation that made him choke on the remnants of his mouthful. Jamie, who had been about to speak, closed his mouth and sat down, regarding the Comte thoughtfully. Jules de La Tour began to spray exclamations and globules of spit, and both d'Arbanvilles made ejaculations of amazement. Even the Duke took his eyes off his plate and blinked at the Comte in interest.

"Really?" he said. "I understood the Stuarts were poor as church mice. You're sure he's not gulling you?"

"I have no wish to cast aspersions, or arouse suspicions," chipped in Jules de La Tour, "but it is well known at Court that the Stuarts have no money. It is true that several of the Jacobite supporters have been seeking funds lately, but without luck, so far as I have heard."

"That's true," interjected the younger Duverney, leaning forward with interest. "Charles Stuart himself has spoken privately with two bankers of my acquaintance, but no one is willing to advance him any substantial sum in his present circumstances."

I shot a quick glance at Jamie, who answered with an almost imperceptible nod. This came under the heading of good news. But then what about the Comte's story of an investment?

"It is true," he said belligerently. "His Highness has secured a loan of fifteen thousand livres from an Italian bank, and has placed the entire sum at my disposal, to be used in commissioning a ship and purchasing the bottling of the Gostos vineyard. I have the signed letter right here." He tapped the breast of his coat with satisfaction, then sat back and looked triumphantly around the table, stopping at Jamie.

"Well, milord," he said, with a wave at the decanter that sat on the white cloth in front of Jamie, "are you going to allow us to taste this famous wine?"

"Yes, of course," Jamie murmured. He reached mechanically for the first glass.

Louise, who had sat quietly eating through most of the dinner, noted Jamie's discomfort. A kind friend, she turned to me in an obvious effort to change the course of the conversation to a neutral topic.

"That is a beautiful stone you wear about your neck, *ma chère*," she said, gesturing at my crystal. "Where did you get it?"

"Oh, this?" I said. "Well, in fact—"

I was interrupted by a piercing scream. It stopped all conversation, and the brittle echoes of it chimed in the crystals of the chandelier overhead.

"Mon Dieu," said the Comte St. Germain, into the silence. "What—"

The scream was repeated, and then repeated again. The noise spilled down the wide stairway and into the foyer.

The guests, rising from the dinner table like a covey of flushed quail, also spilled into the foyer, in time to see Mary Hawkins, clad in the shredded remnants of her shift, lurch into view at the top of the stair. There she stood, as though for maximum effect, mouth stretched wide, hands splayed across her bosom, where the ripped fabric all too clearly displayed the bruises left by grappling hands on her breasts and arms.

Her pupils shrunk to pinpoints in the light of the candelabra, her eyes seemed blank pools in which horror was reflected. She looked down, but plainly saw neither stairway nor crowd of gaping onlookers.

"No!" she shrieked. "No! Let me go! Please, I beg you! DON'T TOUCH ME!" Blinded by the drug as she was, apparently she sensed some movement behind her, for she turned and flailed wildly, hands clawing at the figure of Alex Randall, who was trying vainly to get hold of her, to calm her.

Unfortunately, from below, his attempts looked rather like those of a rejected seducer bent on further attack.

"Nom de Dieu," burst out General d'Arbanville. *"Racaille!* Let her go at once!" The old soldier leaped for the stair with an agility belying his years, hand reaching instinctively for his sword—which, luckily, he had laid aside at the door.

I hastily thrust myself and my voluminous skirts in front of the Comte and the younger Duverney, who showed symptoms of following the General to the rescue, but I could do nothing about Mary's uncle, Silas Hawkins. Eyes popping from his head, the wine merchant stood stunned for a moment, then lowered his head and charged like a bull, forcing his way through the onlookers.

I looked wildly about for Jamie, and found him on the edge of the crowd. I caught his eye and raised my brows in silent question; in any case, nothing I said could have been heard above the hubbub in the foyer, punctuated by Mary's steam-whistle shrieks from above.

Jamie shrugged at me, then glanced around him. I saw his eyes light for a moment on a three-legged table near the wall, holding a tall vase of chrysanthemums. He glanced up, measuring the distance, closed his eyes briefly as though commending his soul to God, then moved with decision.

He sprang from the floor to the table, grasped the banister railing and vaulted over it, onto the stairway, a few feet in advance of the General. It was such an acrobatic feat that one or two ladies gasped, little cries of admiration intermingled with their exclamations of horror.

The exclamations grew louder as Jamie bounded up the remaining stairs, elbowed his way between Mary and Alex, and seizing the latter by the shoulder, took careful aim and hit him solidly on the point of the jaw.

Alex, who had been staring at his employer below in openmouthed amazement, folded gently at the knees and crumpled into a heap, eyes still wide, but gone suddenly blank and empty as Mary's.

19

An Oath Is Sworn

The clock on the mantelpiece had an annoyingly loud tick. It was the only sound in the house, other than the creakings of the boards, and the far-off thumps of servants working late in the kitchens below. I had had enough noise to last me some time, though, and wanted only silence to mend my frazzled nerves. I opened the clock's case and removed the counterweight, and the tick ceased at once.

It had undeniably been the dinner party of the season. People not fortunate enough to have been present would be claiming for months that they had been, bolstering their case with bits of repeated gossip and distorted description.

I had finally got my hands on Mary long enough to force another strong dose of poppy juice down her throat. She collapsed in a pitiful heap of bloodstained clothes, leaving me free to turn my attention to the three-sided argument going on among Jamie, the General, and Mr. Hawkins. Alex had the good sense to stay unconscious, and I arranged his limp form neatly alongside Mary's on the landing, like a couple of dead mackerel. They looked like Romeo and Juliet laid out in the public square as a reproach to their relatives, but the resemblance was lost on Mr. Hawkins.

"Ruined!" he kept shrieking. "You've ruined my niece! The Vicomte will never have her now! Filthy Scottish prick! You and your strumpet"—he swung on me—"whore! Procuress! Seducing innocent young girls into your vile clutches for the pleasure of bastardly scum! You—" Jamie, with a certain long-suffering grimness, put a hand on Mr. Hawkins's shoulders, turned him about, and hit him, just under the fleshy jaw. Then he stood abstractedly rubbing his abused knuckles, watching as the stout wine merchant's eyes rolled upward. Mr. Hawkins fell back against the paneling and slid gently down the wall into a sitting position.

Jamie turned a cold blue gaze on General d'Arbanville, who, observing the fate of the fallen, wisely put down the wine bottle he had been waving, and took a step back.

"Oh, go ahead," urged a voice behind my shoulder. "Why stop now, Tuarach? Hit all three of them! Make a clean sweep of it!" The General and Jamie focused a glance of united dislike on the dapper form behind me.

"Go away, St. Germain," Jamie said. "This is none of your affair." He sounded weary, but raised his voice in order to be heard above the uproar below. The shoulder seams of his coat had been split, and folds of his linen shirt showed white through the rents.

St. Germain's thin lips curved upward in a charming smile. Plainly the Comte was having the time of his life.

"Not my affair? How can such happenings not be the affair of every public-spirited man?" His amused gaze swept the landing, littered with bodies. "After all, if a guest of His Majesty has so perverted the meaning of hospitality as to maintain a brothel in his house, is that not the—no, you don't!" he said, as Jamie took a step toward him. A blade gleamed suddenly in his hand, appearing as though by magic from the ruffled lace cascading over his wrist. I saw Jamie's lip curl slightly, and he shifted his shoulders inside the ruins of his coat, settling himself for battle.

"Stop it at once!" said an imperious voice, and the two Duverneys, older and younger, pushed their way onto the already overcrowded landing. Duverney the younger turned and waved his arms commandingly at the herd of people on the stairs, who were sufficiently cowed by his scowl to move back a step.

"You," said the elder Duverney, pointing at St. Germain. "If you have any feeling of public spirit, as you suggest, you will employ yourself usefully in removing some of those below."

St. Germain locked eyes with the banker, but after a moment, the noble shrugged, and the dagger disappeared. St. Germain turned without comment and made his way downstairs, pushing those before him and loudly urging them to leave.

Despite his exhortations, and those of Gérard, the younger Duverney, behind him, the bulk of the dinner guests departed, brimming with scandal, only upon the arrival of the King's Guard.

Mr. Hawkins, recovered by this time, at once lodged a

charge of kidnapping and pandering against Jamie. For a moment, I really thought Jamie was going to hit him again; his muscles bunched under the azure velvet, but then relaxed as he thought better of it.

After a considerable amount of confused argument and explanation, Jamie agreed to go to the Guard's headquarters in the Bastille, there—perhaps—to explain himself.

Alex Randall, white-faced, sweating, and clearly having no idea what was going on, was taken, too—the Duke had not waited to see the fate of his secretary, but had discreetly summoned his coach and left before the arrival of the Guard. Whatever his diplomatic mission, being involved in a scandal wouldn't help it. Mary Hawkins, still insensible, was removed to her uncle's house, wrapped in a blanket.

I had narrowly avoided being included in the roundup when Jamie flatly refused to allow it, insisting that I was in a delicate condition and could on no account be removed to a prison. At last, seeing that Jamie was more than willing to start hitting people again in order to prove his point, the Guard Captain relented, on condition that I agreed not to leave the city. While the thought of fleeing Paris had its attractions, I could hardly leave without Jamie, and gave my *parole d'honneur* with no reservations.

As the group milled confusedly about the foyer, lighting lanterns and gathering hats and cloaks, I saw Murtagh, bruised face set grimly, hovering on the outskirts of the mob. Plainly he intended to accompany Jamie, wherever he was going, and I felt a quick stab of relief. At least my husband wouldn't be alone.

"Dinna worry yourself, Sassenach." He hugged me briefly, whispering in my ear. "I'll be back in no time. If anything goes wrong . . ." He hesitated, then said firmly, "It wilna be necessary, but if ye need a friend, go to Louise de La Tour."

"I will." I had no time for more than a glancing kiss, before the Guardsmen closed in about him.

The doors of the house swung open, and I saw Jamie glance behind him, catch sight of Murtagh, and open his mouth as though to say something. Murtagh, setting hands to his swordbelt, glared fiercely and pushed his way toward Jamie, nearly shoving the younger Duverney into the street. A short, silent battle of wills ensued, conducted entirely by means of ferocious glares, and then Jamie shrugged and tossed up his hands in resignation.

He stepped out into the street, ignoring the Guardsmen who pressed close on all sides, but stopped at sight of a small figure standing near the gate. He stooped and said something, then straightened, turned toward the house and gave me a smile, clearly visible in the lanternlight. Then, with a nod to the elder Monsieur Duverney, he stepped into the waiting coach and was borne away, Murtagh clinging to the rear of the carriage.

Fergus stood in the street, looking after the coach as long as it was in sight. Then, mounting the steps with a firm tread, he took me by the hand and led me inside.

"Come, milady," he said. "Milord has said I am to care for you, 'til his return."

Now Fergus slipped into the salon, the door closing silently behind him.

"I have made the rounds of the house, milady," he whispered. "All buttoned up." Despite the worry, I smiled at his tone, so obviously an imitation of Jamie's. His idol had entrusted him with a responsibility, and he plainly took his duties seriously.

Having escorted me to the sitting room, he had gone to make the rounds of the house as Jamie did each night, checking the fastenings of the shutters, the bars on the outer doors —which I knew he could barely lift—and the banking of the fires. He had a smudge of soot from forehead to cheekbone on one side, but had rubbed his eye with a fist at one point, so his eye blinked out of a clear white ring, like a small raccoon.

"You should rest, milady," he said. "Don't worry, I'll be here."

I didn't laugh, but smiled at him. "I couldn't sleep, Fergus. I'll just sit here for a bit. Perhaps you should go to bed, though; you've had an awfully long night of it." I was reluctant to order him to bed, not wanting to impair his new dignity as temporary man of the house, but he was clearly exhausted. The small, bony shoulders drooped, and dark smudges showed beneath his eyes, darker even than the coating of soot.

He yawned unashamedly, but shook his head.

"No, milady. I will stay with you . . . if you do not mind?" he added hastily.

"I don't mind." In fact, he was too tired either to talk or to fidget in his usual manner, and his sleepy presence on the hassock was comforting, like that of a cat or a dog.

I sat gazing into the low-burning flames, trying to conjure up some semblance of serenity. I tried summoning images of still pools, forest glades, even the dark peace of the Abbey chapel, but nothing seemed to be working; over all the images of peace lay those of the evening: hard hands and gleaming teeth, coming out of a darkness filled with fear; Mary's white and stricken face, a twin to Alex Randall's; the flare of hatred in Mr. Hawkins's piggy eyes; the sudden mistrust on the faces of the General and the Duverneys; St. Germain's ill-concealed delight in scandal, shimmering with malice like the crystal drops of the chandeliers. And last of all, Jamie's smile, reassurance and uncertainty mingled in the shifting light of jostling lanterns.

What if he didn't come back? That was the thought I had been trying to suppress, ever since they took him away. If he was unable to clear himself of the charge? If the magistrate was one of those suspicious of foreigners—well, more suspicious than usual, I amended—he could easily be imprisoned indefinitely. And above and beyond the fear that this unlooked-for crisis could undo all the careful work of the last weeks, was the image of Jamie in a cell like the one where I had found him at Wentworth. In light of the present crisis, the news that Charles Stuart was investing in wine seemed trivial.

Left alone, I now had plenty of time to think, but my thoughts didn't seem to be getting me anywhere. Who or what was "La Dame Blanche"? What sort of "white lady," and why had the mention of that name made the attackers run off?

Thinking back over the subsequent events of the dinner party, I remembered the General's remarks about the criminal gangs that roamed the streets of Paris, and how some of them included members of the nobility. That was consistent with the speech and the dress of the leader of the men who had attacked me and Mary, though his companions seemed a good deal rougher in aspect. I tried to think whether the man reminded me of anyone I knew, but the memory of him was indistinct, clouded by darkness and the receding haze of shock.

In general form, he had been not unlike the Comte St. Germain, though surely the voice was different. But then, if the Comte was involved, surely he would take pains to disguise his voice as well as his face? At the same time, I found it almost impossible to believe that the Comte could have taken part in such an attack, and then sat calmly across the table from me two hours later, sipping soup.

I ran my fingers through my hair in frustration. There was nothing that could be done before morning. If morning came, and Jamie didn't, then I could begin to make the rounds of acquaintances and presumed friends, one of whom might have news or help to offer. But for the hours of the night, I was helpless; powerless to move as a dragonfly in amber.

My fingers jammed against one of the decorated hairpins, and I yanked at it impatiently. Tangled in my hair, it stuck.

"Ouch!"

"Here, milady. I'll get it."

I hadn't heard him pass behind me, but I felt Fergus's small, clever fingers in my hair, disentangling the tiny ornament. He laid it aside, then, hesitating, said, "The others, milady?"

"Oh, thank you, Fergus," I said, grateful. "If you wouldn't mind."

His pickpocket's touch was light and sure, and the thick locks began to fall around my face, released from their moorings. Little by little, my breathing slowed as my hair came down.

"You are worried, milady?" said the small, soft voice behind me.

"Yes," I said, too tired to keep up a false bravado.

"Me, too," he said simply.

The last of the hairpins clinked on the table, and I slumped in the chair, eyes closed. Then I felt a touch again, and realized that he was brushing my hair, gently combing out the tangles.

"You permit, milady?" he said, feeling it as I tensed in surprise. "The ladies used to say it helped them, if they were feeling worried or upset."

I relaxed again under the soothing touch.

"I permit," I said. "Thank you." After a moment, I said, "What ladies, Fergus?"

There was a momentary hesitation, as of a spider disturbed in the building of a web, and then the delicate ordering of strands resumed.

"At the place where I used to sleep, milady. I couldn't come out because of the customers, but Madame Elise would let me sleep in a closet under the stairs, if I was quiet. And after all the men had gone, near morning, then I would come out and sometimes the ladies would share their breakfast with me. I would help them with the fastening of their underthings —they said I had the best touch of anyone," he added, with some pride, "and I would comb their hair, if they liked."

"Mm." The soft whisper of the brush through my hair was hypnotic. Without the clock on the mantel, there was no telling time, but the silence of the street outside meant it was very late indeed.

"How did you come to sleep at Madame Elise's, Fergus?" I asked, barely suppressing a yawn.

"I was born there, milady," he answered. The strokes of the brush grew slower, and his voice was growing drowsy. "I used to wonder which of the ladies was my mother, but I never found out."

The opening of the sitting-room door woke me. Jamie stood there, red-eyed and white-faced with fatigue, but smiling in the first gray light of the day.

"I was afraid you weren't coming back," I said, a moment later, into the top of his head. His hair had the faint acrid scent of stale smoke and tallow, and his coat had completed its descent into total disreputability, but he was warm and solid, and I wasn't disposed to be critical about the smell of the head I was cradling next my bosom.

"So was I," he said, somewhat muffled, and I could feel

his smile. The arms around my waist tightened and released, and he sat back, smoothing my hair out of my eyes.

"God, you are so beautiful," he said softly. "Unkempt and unslept, wi' the waves of your hair all about your face. Bonny love. Have ye sat here all night long, then?"

"I wasn't the only one." I motioned toward the floor, where Fergus lay curled up on the carpet, head on a cushion by my feet. He shifted slightly in his sleep, mouth open a bit, soft pink and full-lipped as the baby he so nearly was.

Jamie laid a big hand gently on his shoulder.

"Come on, then, laddie. Ye've done well to guard your mistress." He scooped the boy up and laid him against his shoulder, mumbling and sleepy-eyed. "You're a good man, Fergus, and ye've earned your rest. Come on to your bed." I saw Fergus's eyes flare wide in surprise, then half-close as he relaxed, nodding in Jamie's arms.

I had opened the shutters and rekindled the fire by the time Jamie returned to the sitting room. He had shed his ruined coat, but still wore the rest of last night's finery.

"Here." I handed him a glass of wine, and he drank it standing, in three gulps, shuddered, then collapsed onto the small sofa, and held out the cup for more.

"Not a drop," I said, "until you tell me what's going on. You aren't in prison, so I assume everything's all right, but—"

"Not all right, Sassenach," he interrupted, "but it could be worse."

After a great deal of argument to and fro—a good deal of it Mr. Hawkins's reiterations of his original impressions—the judge-magistrate who had been hustled out of his cozy bed to preside over this impromptu investigation had ruled grumpily that since Alex Randall was one of the accused, he could hardly be considered an impartial witness. Nor could I, as the wife and possible accomplice of the other accused. Murtagh had been, by his own testimony, insensible during the alleged attack, and the child Claudel was not legally capable of bearing witness.

Clearly, Monsieur le Juge had said, aiming a vicious glare at the Guard Captain, the only person capable of providing the truth of the matter was Mary Hawkins, who was by all accounts incapable of doing so at the present time. Therefore, all the accused should be locked up in the Bastille until such time as Mademoiselle Hawkins could be interviewed, and surely Monsieur le Capitaine should have been able to think that out for himself?

"Then why aren't you locked up in the Bastille?" I asked.

"Monsieur Duverney the elder offered security for me," Jamie replied, pulling me down onto the sofa beside him. "He sat rolled up in the corner like a hedgehog, all through the clishmaclaver. Then when the judge made his decision, he stood up and said that, having had the opportunity to play chess with me on several occasions, he didna feel that I was of a moral character so dissolute as to permit of my having conspired in the commission of an act so depraved—" He broke off and shrugged.

"Well, ye ken what he talks like, once he's got going. The general idea was that a man who could take him at chess six times in seven wouldna lure innocent young lasses to his house to be defiled."

"Very logical," I said dryly. "I imagine what he really meant was, if they locked you up, you wouldn't be able to play with him anymore."

"I expect so," he agreed. He stretched, yawned, and blinked at me, smiling.

"But I'm home, and right now, I don't greatly care why. Come here to me, Sassenach." Grasping my waist with both hands, he boosted me onto his lap, wrapped his arms around me, and sighed with pleasure.

"All I want to do," he murmured in my ear, "is to shed these filthy clouts, and lie wi' you on the hearthrug, go to sleep straight after, with my head on your shoulder, and stay that way 'til tomorrow."

"Rather an inconvenience to the servants," I remarked. "They'll have to sweep round us."

"Damn the servants," he said comfortably. "What are doors for?"

"To be knocked on, evidently," I said as a soft rap sounded outside.

Jamie paused a moment, nose buried in my hair, then sighed, and raised his head, sliding me off his lap onto the sofa.

"Thirty seconds," he promised me in an undertone, then said, *"Entrez!"* in a louder voice.

The door swung open and Murtagh stepped into the room. I had rather overlooked Murtagh in the bustles and confusion of the night before, and now thought to myself that his appearance had not been improved by neglect.

He lacked as much sleep as Jamie; the one eye that was open was red-rimmed and bloodshot. The other had darkened to the color of a rotten banana, a slit of glittering black visible in the puffed flesh. The knot on his forehead had now achieved full prominence: a purple goose-egg just over one brow, with a nasty split through it.

The little clansman had said barely a word since his release from the bag the night before. Beyond a brief inquiry as to the whereabouts of his knives—retrieved by Fergus, who, questing in his usual rat-terrier fashion, had found both dirk and *sgian dubh* behind a pile of rubbish—he had preserved a grim silence through the exigencies of our getaway, guarding the rear as we hurried on foot through the dim Paris alleys. And once arrived at the house, a piercing glance from his operating eye had been sufficient to quell any injudicious questions from the kitchen servants.

I supposed he must have said something at the *commissariat de police* if only to bear witness to the good character of his employer—though I did wonder just how much credibility I would be inclined to place in Murtagh, were I a French judge. But now he was silent as the gargoyles on Notre Dame, one of which he strongly resembled.

However disreputable his appearance, though, Murtagh never seemed to lack for dignity, nor did he now. Back straight as a ramrod, he advanced across the carpet, and knelt formally before Jamie, who looked nonplussed at this behavior.

The wiry little man drew the dirk from his belt, without flourishes, but with a good deal of deliberateness, and held it out, haft first. The bony, seamed face was expressionless, but the one black eye rested unwaveringly on Jamie's face.

"I've failed ye," the little man said quietly. "And I'll ask ye, as my chief, to take my life now, so I needna live longer wi' the shame of it."

Jamie drew himself slowly upright, and I felt him push away his own tiredness as he brought his gaze to bear on his retainer. He was quite still for a moment, hands resting on his knees. Then he reached out and placed one hand gently over the purple knot on Murtagh's head.

"There's nay shame to ha' fallen in battle, *mo caraidh*," he said softly. "The greatest of warriors may be overcome."

But the little man shook his head stubbornly, black eye unwinking.

"Nay," he said. "I didna fall in battle. Ye gave me your trust; your own lady and your child unborn to guard, and the wee English lassie as well. And I gave the task sae little heed that I had nay chance to strike a blow when the danger came. Truth to tell, I didna even see the hand that struck me down." He did blink then, once.

"Treachery—" Jamie began.

"And now see what's come of it," Murtagh interrupted. I had never heard him speak so many words in a row in all the time I had known him. "Your good name smirched, your wife attacked, and the wee lass . . ." The thin line of his mouth clamped tight for a moment, and his stringy throat bobbed once as he swallowed. "For that alone, the bitter sorrow chokes me."

"Aye." Jamie spoke softly, nodding. "Aye, I do see, man. I feel it, too." He touched his chest briefly, over his heart. The two men might have been alone together, their heads inches apart as Jamie bent toward the older man. Hands folded in my lap, I neither moved nor spoke; it was not my affair.

"But I'm no your chief, man," Jamie went on, in a firmer tone. "Ye've sworn me no vow, and I hold nay power ower ye."

"Aye, that ye do." Murtagh's voice was firm as well, and the haft of the dirk never trembled.

"But—"

"I swore ye my oath, Jamie Fraser, when ye were no more than a week old, and a bonny lad at your mother's breast."

I could feel the tiny start of astonishment as Jamie's eyes opened wide.

"I knelt at Ellen's feet, as I kneel now by yours," the little clansman went on, narrow chin held high. "And I swore to her by the name o' the threefold God, that I would follow ye always, to do your bidding, and guard your back, when ye became a man grown, and needing such service." The harsh voice softened then, and the eyelid drooped over the one tired eye.

"Aye, lad. I do cherish ye as the son of my own loins. But I have betrayed your service."

"That ye havena and never could." Jamie's hands rested on Murtagh's shoulders, squeezing firmly. "Nay, I wilna have your life from ye, for I've need of ye still. But I will lay an oath on ye, and you'll take it."

There was a long moment's hesitation, then the spiky black head nodded imperceptibly.

Jamie's voice dropped still further, but it was not a whisper. Holding the middle three fingers of his right hand stiff, he laid them together over the hilt of the dirk, at the juncture of haft and tang.

"I charge ye, then, by your oath to me and your word to my mother—find the men. Hunt them, and when they be found, I do charge ye wi' the vengeance due my wife's honor —and the blood of Mary Hawkins's innocence."

He paused a moment, then took his hand from the knife. The clansman raised it, holding it upright by the blade. Acknowledging my presence for the first time, he bowed his head toward me and said, "As the laird has spoken, lady, so I will do. I will lay vengeance at your feet."

I licked dry lips, not knowing what to say. No response seemed necessary, though; he brought the dirk to his lips and kissed it, then straightened with decision and thrust it home in its sheath.

20

La Dame Blanche

The dawn had broadened into day by the time we had changed our clothes, and breakfast was on its way up the stairs from the kitchen.

"What I want to know," I said, pouring out the chocolate, "is who in bloody hell is La Dame Blanche?"

"La Dame Blanche?" Magnus, leaning over my shoulder with a basket of hot bread, started so abruptly that one of the rolls fell out of the basket. I fielded it neatly and turned round to look up at the butler, who was looking rather shaken.

"Yes, that's right," I said. "You've heard the name, Magnus?"

"Why, yes, milady," the old man answered. "La Dame Blanche is *une sorcière.*"

"A sorceress?" I said incredulously.

Magnus shrugged, tucking in the napkin around the rolls with excessive care, not looking at me.

"The White Lady," he murmured. "She is called a wise-woman, a healer. And yet . . . she sees to the center of a man, and can turn his soul to ashes, if evil be found there." He bobbed his head, turned, and shuffled off hastily in the direction of the kitchen. I saw his elbow bob, and realized that he was crossing himself as he went.

"Jesus H. Christ," I said, turning back to Jamie. "Did you ever hear of La Dame Blanche?"

"Um? Oh? Oh, aye, I've . . . heard the stories." Jamie's eyes were hidden by long auburn lashes as he buried his nose in his cup of chocolate, but the blush on his cheeks was too deep to be put down to the heat of the rising steam.

I leaned back in my chair, crossed my arms, and regarded him narrowly.

"Oh, you have?" I said. "Would it surprise you to hear that the men who attacked Mary and me last night referred to me as La Dame Blanche?"

"They did?" He looked up quickly at that, startled.

I nodded. "They took one look at me in the light, shouted 'La Dame Blanche,' and then ran off as though they'd just noticed I had plague."

Jamie took a deep breath and let it out slowly. The red color was fading from his face, leaving it pale as the white china plate before him.

"God in heaven," he said, half to himself. "God . . . in . . . heaven!"

I leaned across the table and took the cup from his hand.

"Would you like to tell me just what you know about La Dame Blanche?" I suggested gently.

"Well . . ." He hesitated, but then looked at me sheepishly. "It's only . . . I told Glengarry that you were La Dame Blanche."

"You told Glengarry *what*?" I choked on the bite of roll I had taken. Jamie pounded me helpfully on the back.

"Well, it was Glengarry and Castellotti, was what it was," he said defensively. "I mean, playing at cards and dice is one thing, but they wouldna leave it at that. And they thought it verra funny that I'd wish to be faithful to my wife. They said . . . well, they said a number of things, and I . . . I got rather tired of it." He looked away, the tips of his ears burning.

"Mm," I said, sipping chocolate. Having heard Castellotti's tongue in action, I could imagine the sort of merciless teasing Jamie had taken.

He drained his own cup at one swallow, then occupied himself with carefully refilling it, keeping his eyes fixed on the pot to avoid meeting mine. "But I couldna just walk out and leave them, either, could I?" he demanded. "I had to stay with His Highness through the evening, and it would do no good to have him thinkin' me unmanly."

"So you told them I was La Dame Blanche," I said, trying hard to keep any hint of laughter out of my voice. "And if you tried any funny business with ladies of the evening, I'd shrivel your private parts."

"Er, well . . ."

"My God, they *believed* it?" I could feel my own face flushing as hotly as Jamie's, with the effort to control myself.

"I was verra convincing about it," he said, one corner of

his mouth beginning to twitch. "Swore them all to secrecy on their mothers' lives."

"And how much did you all have to drink before this?"

"Oh, a fair bit. I waited 'til the fourth bottle."

I gave up the struggle and burst out laughing.

"Oh, Jamie!" I said. "You darling!" I leaned over and kissed his furiously blushing cheek.

"Well," he said awkwardly, slathering butter over a chunk of bread. "It was the best I could think of. And they did stop pushing trollops into my arms."

"Good," I said. I took the bread from him, added honey, and gave it back.

"I can hardly complain about it," I observed. "Since in addition to guarding your virtue, it seems to have kept me from being raped."

"Aye, thank God." He set down the roll and grasped my hand. "Christ, if anything had happened to you, Sassenach, I'd—"

"Yes," I interrupted, "but if the men who attacked us knew I was supposed to be La Dame Blanche . . ."

"Aye, Sassenach." He nodded down at me. "It canna have been either Glengarry nor Castellotti, for they were with me at the house where Fergus came to fetch me when you were attacked. But it must have been someone they told of it."

I couldn't repress a slight shiver at the memory of the mask and the mocking voice behind it.

With a sigh, he let go of my hand. "Which means, I suppose, that I'd best go and see Glengarry, and find out just how many people he's been regaling wi' tales of my married life." He rubbed a hand through his hair in exasperation. "And then I must go call on His Highness, and find out what in hell he means by this arrangement with the Comte St. Germain."

"I suppose so," I said thoughtfully, "though knowing Glengarry, he's probably told half of Paris by now. I have some calls to make this afternoon, myself."

"Oh, aye? And who are you going to call upon, Sassenach?" he asked, eyeing me narrowly. I took a deep breath, bracing myself at the thought of the ordeal that lay ahead.

"First, on Master Raymond," I said. "And then, on Mary Hawkins."

"Lavender, perhaps?" Raymond stood on tiptoe to take a jar from the shelf. "Not for application, but the aroma is soothing; it calms the nerves."

"Well, that depends on whose nerves are involved," I said, recalling Jamie's reaction to the scent of lavender. It was the scent Jack Randall had favored, and Jamie found exposure to the herb's perfume anything but soothing. "In this case, though, it might help. Do no harm, at any rate."

"Do no harm," he quoted thoughtfully. "A very sound principle."

"That's the first bit of the Hippocratic Oath, you know," I said, watching him as he bent to rummage in his drawers and bins. "The oath a physician swears. 'First, do no harm.' "

"Ah? And have you sworn this oath yourself, madonna?" The bright, amphibious eyes blinked at me over the edge of the high counter.

I felt myself flushing before that unblinking gaze.

"Er, well, no. Not actually. I'm not a real physician. Not yet." I couldn't have said what made me add that last sentence.

"No? Yet you are seeking to mend that which a 'real' physician would never try, knowing that a lost maidenhead is not restorable." His irony was evident.

"Oh, isn't it?" I answered dryly. Fergus had, with encouragement, told me quite a bit about the "ladies" at Madame Elise's house. "What's that bit with the shoat's bladder full of chicken blood, hm? Or do you claim that things like that fall into an apothecary's realm of competence, but not a physician's?"

He had no eyebrows to speak of, but the heavy shelf of his forehead lifted slightly when he was amused.

"And who is harmed by that, madonna? Surely not the seller. Not the buyer, either—he is likely to get more enjoyment for his money than the purchaser of the genuine article. Not even the maidenhead itself is harmed! Surely a very moral and Hippocratic endeavor, which any physician might be pleased to assist?"

I laughed. "And I expect you know more than a few who do?" I said. "I'll take the matter up with the next Medical Review Board I see. In the meantime, short of manufactured miracles, what can we do in the present case?"

"Mm." He laid out a gauze square on the counter and poured a handful of finely shredded dried leaves into the center of it. A sharp, pleasant tang rose from the small heap of grayish-green vegetation.

"This is Saracen's consound," he said, skillfully folding the gauze into a tidy square with the ends tucked in. "Good for soothing irritated skin, minor lacerations, and sores of the privy parts. Useful, I think?"

"Yes, indeed," I said, a little grimly. "As an infusion or a decoction?"

"Infusion. Warm, probably, under the circumstances." He turned to another shelf and abstracted one of the large white jars of painted porcelain. This one said CHELIDONIUM on the side.

"For the inducement of sleep," he explained. His lipless mouth stretched back at the corners. "I think perhaps you had better avoid the use of the opium-poppy derivatives; this particular patient appears to have an unpredictable response to them."

"Heard all about it already, have you?" I said resignedly. I could hardly have hoped he hadn't. I was well aware that information was one of the more important commodities he sold; consequently the little shop was a nexus for gossip from dozens of sources, from street vendors to gentlemen of the Royal Bedchamber.

"From three separate sources," Raymond replied. He glanced out the window, craning his neck to see the huge *horloge* that hung from the wall of the building near the corner. "And it's barely two o'clock. I expect I will hear several more versions of the events at your dinner before nightfall." The wide, gummy mouth opened, and a soft chuckle emerged. "I particularly liked the version in which your husband challenged General d'Arbanville to a duel in the street, while you more pragmatically offered Monsieur le Comte the enjoyment of the unconscious girl's body, if he would refrain from calling the King's Guard."

"Mmphm," I said, sounding self-consciously Scottish.

"Have you any particular interest in knowing what actually *did* happen?"

The horned-poppy tonic, a pale amber in the afternoon sunlight, sparkled as he poured it into a small vial.

"The truth is always of use, madonna," he answered, eyes fixed on the slender stream. "It has the value of rarity, you know." He set the porcelain jar on the counter with a soft thump. "And thus is worth a fair price in exchange," he added. The money for the medicines I had bought was lying on the counter, the coins gleaming in the sun. I narrowed my eyes at him, but he merely smiled blandly, as though he had never heard of frog legs in garlic butter.

The *horloge* outside struck two. I calculated the distance to the Hawkins's house in Rue Malory. Barely half an hour, if I could get a carriage. Plenty of time.

"In that case," I said, "shall we step into your private room for a bit?"

———◆———

"And that's it," I said, taking a long sip of cherry brandy. The fumes in the workroom were nearly as strong as those rising from my glass, and I could feel my head expanding under their influence, rather like a large, cheerful red balloon. "They let Jamie go, but we're still under suspicion. I can't imagine that will last long, though, do you?"

Raymond shook his head. A draft stirred the crocodile overhead, and he rose to shut the window.

"No. A nuisance, nothing more. Monsieur Hawkins has money and friends, and of course he is distraught, but still. Plainly you and your husband were guilty of nothing more than excessive kindness, in trying to keep the girl's misfortune a secret." He took a deep swallow from his own glass.

"And that is your concern at present, of course. The girl?"

I nodded. "One of them. There's nothing I can do about her reputation at this point. All I can do is try to help her to heal."

A sardonic black eye peered over the rim of the metal goblet he was holding.

"Most physicians of my acquaintance would say, 'All I can do is try to heal her.' You will help her to heal? It's interesting that you perceive the difference, madonna. I thought you would."

I set down the cup, feeling that I had had enough. Heat was radiating from my cheeks, and I had the distinct feeling that the tip of my nose was pink.

"I told you I'm not a real physician." I closed my eyes briefly, determined that I could still tell which way was up, and opened them again. "Besides, I've . . . er, dealt with a case of rape once before. There isn't a great deal you can do, externally. Maybe there isn't a great deal you can do, period," I added. I changed my mind and picked up the cup again.

"Perhaps not," Raymond agreed. "But if anyone is capable of reaching the patient's center, surely it would be La Dame Blanche?"

I set the cup down, staring at him. My mouth was unbecomingly open, and I closed it. Thoughts, suspicions, and realizations were rioting through my head, colliding with each other in tangles of conjecture. Temporarily sidestepping the traffic jam, I seized on the other half of his remark, to give me time to think.

"The patient's center?"

He reached into an open jar on the table, withdrew a pinch of white powder, and dropped it into his goblet. The deep amber of the brandy immediately turned the color of blood, and began to boil.

"Dragon's blood," he remarked, casually waving at the bubbling liquid. "It only works in a vessel lined with silver. It ruins the cup, of course, but it's most effective, done under the proper circumstances."

I made a small, gurgling noise.

"Oh, the patient's center," he said, as though recalling something we had talked about many days ago. "Yes, of course. All healing is done essentially by reaching the . . . what shall we call it? the soul? the essence? say, the center. By reaching the patient's center, from which they can heal themselves. Surely you have seen it, madonna. The cases so ill or so wounded that plainly they will die—but they don't. Or those who suffer from something so slight that surely they must recover, with the proper care. But they slip away, despite all you can do for them."

"Everyone who minds the sick has seen things like that," I replied cautiously.

"Yes," he agreed. "And the pride of the physician being what it is, most often he blames himself for those that die, and congratulates himself upon the triumph of his skill for those that live. But La Dame Blanche sees the essence of a man, and turns it to healing—or to death. So an evildoer may well fear to look upon her face." He picked up the cup, raised it in a toast to me, and drained the bubbling liquid. It left a faint pink stain on his lips.

"Thanks," I said dryly. "I think. So it wasn't just Glengarry's gullibility?"

Raymond shrugged, looking pleased with himself. "The inspiration was your husband's," he said modestly. "And a really excellent idea, too. But of course, while your husband has the respect of men for his own natural gifts, he would not be considered an authority on supernatural manifestations."

"You, of course, *would.*"

The massive shoulders lifted slightly under the gray velvet robe. There were several small holes in one sleeve, charred around the edges, as though a number of tiny coals had burned their way through. Carelessness while conjuring, I supposed.

"You have been seen in my shop," he pointed out. "Your background is a mystery. And as your husband noted, my own reputation is somewhat suspect. I do move in . . . circles, shall we say?"—the lipless mouth broadened in a grin—"where a speculation as to your true identity may be taken with undue seriousness. And you know how people talk," he added with an air of prim disapproval that made me burst out laughing.

He set down the cup and leaned forward.

"You said that Mademoiselle Hawkins's health was *one* concern, madonna. Have you others?"

"I have." I took a small sip of brandy. "I'd guess that you hear a great deal about what goes on in Paris, don't you?"

He smiled, black eyes sharp and genial. "Oh, yes, madonna. What is it that you want to know?"

"Have you heard anything about Charles Stuart? Do you know who he is, for that matter?"

That surprised him; the shelf of his forehead lifted

briefly. Then he picked up a small glass bottle from the table
in front of him, rolling it meditatively between his palms.

"Yes, madonna," he said. "His father is—or should be—
King of Scotland, is he not?"

"Well, that depends on your perspective," I said, stifling
a small belch. "He's either the King of Scotland in exile, or
the Pretender to the throne, but that's of no great concern to
me. What I want to know is . . . is Charles Stuart doing
anything that would make one think he might be planning an
armed invasion of Scotland or England?"

He laughed out loud.

"Goodness, madonna! You are a most uncommon
woman. Have you any idea how rare such directness is?"

"Yes," I admitted, "but there isn't really any help for it.
I'm not good at beating round bushes." I reached out and
took the bottle from him. "*Have* you heard anything?"

He glanced instinctively toward the half-door, but the
shopgirl was occupied in mixing perfume for a voluble customer.

"Something small, madonna, only a casual mention in a
letter from a friend—but the answer is most definitely yes."

I could see him hesitating in how much to tell me. I kept
my eyes on the bottle in my hand, to give him time to make
up his mind. The contents rolled with a pleasant sensation as
the little vial twisted in my palm. It was oddly heavy for its
size, and had a strange, dense, fluid feel to it, as though it was
filled with liquid metal.

"It's quicksilver," Master Raymond said, answering my
unspoken question. Apparently whatever mind-reading he
had been doing had decided him in my favor, for he took
back the bottle, poured it out in a shimmering silver puddle
on the table before us, and sat back to tell me what he knew.

"One of His Highness's agents has made inquiries in
Holland," he said. "A man named O'Brien—and a man more
inept at his job I hope never to employ," he added. "A secret
agent who drinks to excess?"

"Everyone around Charles Stuart drinks to excess," I
said. "What was O'Brien doing?"

"He wished to open negotiations for a shipment of
broadswords. Two thousand broadswords, to be purchased in

Spain, and sent through Holland, so as to conceal their place of origin."

"Why would he do that?" I asked. I wasn't sure whether I was naturally stupid, or merely fuddled with cherry brandy, but it seemed a pointless undertaking, even for Charles Stuart.

Raymond shrugged, prodding the puddle of quicksilver with a blunt forefinger.

"One can guess, madonna. The Spanish king is a cousin of the Scottish king, is he not? As well as of our good King Louis?"

"Yes, but . . ."

"Might it not be that he is willing to help the cause of the Stuarts, but not openly?"

The brandy haze was receding from my brain.

"It might."

Raymond tapped his finger sharply downward, making the puddle of quicksilver shiver into several small round globules, that shimmied wildly over the tabletop.

"One hears," he said mildly, eyes still on the droplets of mercury, "that King Louis entertains an English duke at Versailles. One hears also that the Duke is there to seek some arrangements of trade. But then it is rare to hear *everything*, madonna."

I stared at the rippling drops of mercury, fitting all this together. Jamie, too, had heard the rumor that Sandringham's embassage concerned more than trade rights. What if the Duke's visit really concerned the possibilities of an agreement between France and England—perhaps with regard to the future of Brussels? And if Louis was negotiating secretly with England for support for his invasion of Brussels —then what might Philip of Spain be inclined to do, if approached by an impecunious cousin with the power to distract the English most thoroughly from any attention to foreign ventures?

"Three Bourbon cousins," Raymond murmured to himself. He shepherded one of the drops toward another; as the droplets touched, they merged at once, a single shining drop springing into rounded life as though by magic. The prodding finger urged another droplet inward, and the single drop grew larger. "One blood. But one interest?"

The finger struck down again, and glittering fragments ran over the tabletop in every direction.

"I think not, madonna," Raymond said calmly.

"I see," I said, with a deep breath. "And what do you think about Charles Stuart's new partnership with the Comte St. Germain?"

The wide amphibian smile grew broader.

"I have heard that His Highness goes often to the docks these days—to talk with his new partner, of course. And he looks at the ships at anchor—so fine and quick, so . . . expensive. The land of Scotland *does* lie across the water, does it not?"

"It does indeed," I said. A ray of light hit the quicksilver with a flash, attracting my attention to the lowering sun. I would have to go.

"Thank you," I said. "Will you send word? If you hear anything more?"

He inclined his massive head graciously, the swinging hair the color of mercury in the sun, then jerked it up abruptly.

"Ah! Do not touch the quicksilver, madonna!" he warned as I reached toward a droplet that had rolled toward my edge of the table. "It bonds at once with any metal it touches." He reached across and tenderly scooped the tiny pellet toward him. "You do not wish to spoil your lovely rings."

"Right," I said. "Well, I'll admit you've been helpful so far. No one's tried to poison me lately. I don't suppose you and Jamie between you are likely to get me burnt for witchcraft in the Place de la Bastille, do you?" I spoke lightly, but my memories of the thieves' hole and the trial at Cranesmuir were still fresh.

"Certainly not," he said, with dignity. "No one's been burnt for witchcraft in Paris in . . . oh, twenty years, at least. You're perfectly safe. As long as you don't kill anyone," he added.

"I'll do my best," I said, and rose to go.

Fergus found me a carriage with no difficulty, and I spent the short trip to the Hawkins house musing over recent developments. I supposed that Raymond had in fact done me a service by expanding on Jamie's original wild story to his more superstitious clients, though the thought of having my name bandied about in séances or Black Masses left me with some misgivings.

It also occurred to me that, rushed for time, and beset with speculations of kings and swords and ships, I had not had time to ask Master Raymond where—if anywhere—the Comte St. Germain entered into his own realm of influence.

Public opinion seemed to place the Comte firmly in the center of the mysterious "circles" to which Raymond referred. But as a participant—or a rival? And did the ripples of these circles spread as far as the King's chamber? Louis was rumored to take interest in astrology; could there be some connection, through the dark channels of Cabbalism and sorcery, among Louis, the Comte, and Charles Stuart?

I shook my head impatiently, to clear it of brandy fumes and pointless questions. The only thing that could be said for certain was that he had entered into a dangerous partnership with Charles Stuart, and that was concern enough for the present.

The Hawkins residence on the Rue Malory was a solid, respectable-looking house of three stories, but its internal disruption was apparent even to the casual observer. The day was warm, but all the shutters were still sealed tight against any intrusion of prying eyes. The steps had not been scrubbed this morning, and the marks of dirty feet smeared the white stone. No sign of cook or housemaid out front to bargain for fresh meat and gossip with the barrowmen. It was a house battened down against the coming of disaster.

Feeling not a little like a harbinger of doom myself, despite my relatively cheerful yellow gown, I sent Fergus up the steps to knock for me. There was some give-and-take between Fergus and whoever opened the door, but one of Fergus's better character traits was an inability to take "no" for an answer, and shortly I found myself face-to-face with a woman who appeared to be the lady of the house, and therefore Mrs. Hawkins, Mary's aunt.

I was forced to draw my own conclusions, as the woman seemed much too distraught to assist me by offering any sort of tangible information, such as her name.

"But we can't see anybody!" she kept exclaiming, glancing furtively over her shoulder, as though expecting the bulky form of Mr. Hawkins suddenly to materialize accusingly behind her. "We're . . . we have . . . that is . . ."

"I don't want to see you," I said firmly. "I want to see your niece, Mary."

The name seemed to throw her into fresh paroxysms of alarm.

"She . . . but . . . Mary? No! She's . . . she's not well!"

"I don't suppose she is," I said patiently. I lifted my basket into view. "I've brought some medicines for her."

"Oh! But . . . but . . . she . . . you . . . aren't you . . . ?"

"Havers, woman," said Fergus in his best Scots accent. He viewed this spectacle of derangement disapprovingly. "The maid says the young mistress is upstairs in her room."

"Just so," I said. "Lead on, Fergus." Waiting for no further encouragement, he ducked under the outstretched forearm that barred our way, and made off into the gloomy depths of the house. Mrs. Hawkins turned after him with an incoherent cry, allowing me to slip past her.

There was a maid on duty outside Mary's door, a stout party in a striped apron, but she offered no resistance to my statement that I intended to go in. She shook her head mournfully. "I can do nothing with her, Madame. Perhaps you will have better luck."

This didn't sound at all promising, but there was little choice. At least I wasn't likely to do further harm. I straightened my gown and pushed open the door.

It was like walking into a cave. The windows were covered with heavy brown velvet draperies, drawn tight against the daylight, and what chinks of light seeped through were immediately quenched in the hovering layer of smoke from the hearth.

I took a deep breath and let it out again at once, coughing. There was no stir from the figure on the bed; a pathetically small, hunched shape under a goose-feather duvet. Surely the drug had worn off by now, and she couldn't be asleep, after all the racket there had been in the hallway. Probably playing possum, in case it was her aunt come back for further blithering harangues. I would have done the same, in her place.

I turned and shut the door firmly in Mrs. Hawkins's wretched face, then walked over to the bed.

"It's me," I said. "Why don't you come out, before you suffocate in there?"

There was a sudden upheaval of bedclothes, and Mary shot out of the quilts like a dolphin rising from the sea waves, and clutched me round the neck.

"Claire! Oh, Claire! Thank God! I thought I'd n-never see you again! Uncle said you were in prison! He s-said you—"

"Let go!" I managed to detach her grip, and force her back enough to get a look at her. She was red-faced, sweaty, and disheveled from hiding beneath the covers, but otherwise looked fine. Her brown eyes were wide and bright, with no sign of opium intoxication, and while she looked excited and alarmed, apparently a night's rest, coupled with the resilience of youth, had taken care of most of her physical injuries. The others were what worried me.

"No, I'm not in prison," I said, trying to stem her eager questions. "Obviously not, though it isn't for any lack of trying on your uncle's part."

"B-but I *told* him—" she began, then stammered and let her eyes fall. "—at least I *t-t-tried* to tell him, but he—but I . . ."

"Don't worry about it," I assured her. "He's so upset he wouldn't listen to anything you said, no matter how you said it. It doesn't matter, anyway. The important thing is you. How do you feel?" I pushed the heavy dark hair back from her forehead and looked her over searchingly.

"All right," she answered, and gulped. "I . . . bled a little bit, but it stopped." The blood rose still higher in her fair cheeks, but she didn't drop her eyes. "I . . . it's . . . sore. D-does that go away?"

"Yes, it does," I said gently. "I brought some herbs for you. They're to be brewed in hot water, and as the infusion cools, you can apply it with a cloth, or sit in it in a tub, if one's handy. It will help." I got the bundles of herbs from my reticule and laid them on her side table.

She nodded, biting her lip. Plainly there was something

more she wanted to say, her native shyness battling her need for confidence.

"What is it?" I asked, as matter-of-factly as I could.

"Am I going to have a baby?" she blurted out, looking up fearfully. "You said . . ."

"No," I said, as firmly as I could. "You aren't. He wasn't able to . . . finish." In the folds of my skirt, I crossed both pairs of fingers, hoping fervently that I was right. The chances were very small indeed, but such freaks had been known to happen. Still, there was no point in alarming her further over the faint possibility. The thought made me faintly ill. Could such an accident be the possible answer to the riddle of Frank's existence? I put the notion aside; a month's wait would prove or dispel it.

"It's hot as a bloody oven in here," I said, loosening the ties at my throat in order to breathe. "And smoky as hell's vestibule, as my old uncle used to say." Unsure what on earth to say to her next, I rose and went round the room throwing back drapes and opening windows.

"Aunt Helen said I mustn't let anyone see me," Mary said, kneeling up in bed as she watched me. "She says I'm d-disgraced, and people will point at me in the street if I go out."

"They might, the ghouls." I finished my airing and came back to her. "That doesn't mean you need bury yourself alive and suffocate in the process." I sat down beside her, and leaned back in my chair, feeling the cool fresh air blow through my hair as it swept the smoke from the room.

She was silent for a long time, toying with the bundles of herbs on the table. Finally she looked up at me, smiling bravely, though her lower lip trembled slightly.

"At least I won't have to m-marry the Vicomte. Uncle says he'll n-never have me now."

"No, I don't suppose so."

She nodded, looking down at the gauze wrapped square on her knee. Her fingers fiddled restlessly with the string, so that one end came loose and a few crumbs of goldenrod fell out onto the coverlet.

"I . . . used to th-think about it; what you told me, about how a m-man . . ." She stopped and swallowed, and I saw a single tear fall onto the gauze. "I didn't think I could

stand to let the Vicomte do that to me. N-now it's been done
. . . and n-nobody can undo it and I'll never have to d-do it
again . . . and . . . and . . . oh, Claire, Alex will never
speak to me again! I'll never see him again, never!"

She collapsed into my arms, weeping hysterically and
scattering herbs. I clutched her against my shoulder and patted her, making small shushing noises, though I shed a few
tears myself that fell unnoticed into the dark shininess of her
hair.

"You'll see him again," I whispered. "Of course you will.
It won't make a difference to him. He's a good man."

But I knew it would. I had seen the anguish on Alex
Randall's face the night before, and at the time thought it
only the same helpless pity for suffering that I saw in Jamie
and Murtagh. But since I had learned of Alex Randall's professed love for Mary, I had realized how much deeper his own
pain must go—and his fear.

He seemed a good man. But he was also a poor, younger
son, in ill health and with little chance of advancement; what
position he did have was entirely dependent on the Duke of
Sandringham's goodwill. And I had little hope that the Duke
would look kindly on the idea of his secretary's union with a
disgraced and ruined girl, who had now neither social connections nor dowry to bless herself with.

And if Alex found somewhere the courage to wed her in
spite of everything—what chance would they have, penniless,
cast out of polite society, and with the hideous fact of the
rape overshadowing their knowledge of each other?

There was nothing I could do but hold her, and weep
with her for what was lost.

It was twilight by the time I left, with the first stars coming out in faint speckles over the chimneypots. In my pocket
was a letter written by Mary, properly witnessed, containing
her statement of the events of the night before. Once this was
delivered to the proper authorities, we should at least have no
further trouble from the law. Just as well; there was plenty of
trouble pending from other quarters.

Mindful, this time, of danger, I made no objection to

Mrs. Hawkins's unwilling offer to have me and Fergus transported home in the family carriage.

I tossed my hat on the card table in the vestibule, observing the large number of notes and small nosegays that overflowed the salver there. Apparently we weren't yet pariahs, though the news of the scandal must long since have spread through the social strata of Paris.

I waved away the anxious inquiries of the servants, and drifted upward toward the bedchamber, shedding my outer garments carelessly along the way. I felt too drained to care about anything.

But when I pushed open the bedchamber door and saw Jamie, lying back in a chair by the fire, my apathy was at once supplanted by a surge of tenderness. His eyes were closed and his hair sticking up in all directions, sure sign of mental turmoil at some point. But he opened his eyes at the slight noise of my entrance and smiled at me, eyes clear and blue in the warm light of the candelabrum.

"It's all right" was all he whispered to me as he gathered me into his arms. "You're home." Then we were silent, as we undressed each other and went finally to earth, each finding delayed and wordless sanctuary in the other's embrace.

21

Untimely Resurrection

y mind was still on bankers when our coach pulled up to the Duke's rented residence on the Rue St. Anne. It was a large, handsome house, with a long, curving drive lined with poplar trees, and extensive grounds. A wealthy man, the Duke.

"Do you suppose it was the loan Charles got from Manzetti that he's investing with St. Germain?" I asked.

"It must be," Jamie replied. He pulled on the pigskin gloves suitable for a formal call, grimacing slightly as he smoothed the tight leather over the stiff fourth finger of his right hand. "The money his father thinks he's spending to maintain himself in Paris."

"So Charles really is trying to raise money for an army," I said, feeling a reluctant admiration for Charles Stuart. The coach came to a halt, and the footman hopped down to open the door.

"Well, he's trying to raise money, at least," Jamie corrected, handing me out of the coach. "For all I ken, he wants it to elope with Louise de La Tour and his bastard."

I shook my head. "I don't think so. Not from what Master Raymond told me yesterday. Besides, Louise says she hasn't seen him since she and Jules . . . well . . ."

Jamie snorted briefly. "At least she's got some sense of honor, then."

"I don't know whether that's it," I observed, taking his arm as we climbed the steps to the door. "She said Charles was so furious at her for sleeping with her husband that he stormed off, and she hasn't seen him since. He writes her passionate letters from time to time, swearing to come and take her and the child away with him as soon as he comes into his rightful place in the world, but she won't let him come to see her; she's too afraid of Jules finding out the truth."

Jamie made a disapproving Scottish noise.

"God, is there any man safe from cuckoldry?"

I touched his arm lightly. "Likely some more than others."

"Ye think so?" he said, but smiled down at me.

The door swung open to reveal a short, tubby butler, with a bald head, a spotless uniform, and immense dignity.

"Milord," he said, bowing to Jamie, "and milady. You are expected. Please come in."

The Duke was charm itself as he received us in the main drawing room.

"Nonsense, nonsense," he said, dismissing Jamie's apologies for the contretemps of the dinner party. "Damned excitable fellows, the French. Make an ungodly fuss over everything. Now, do let us look over all these fascinating propositions, shall we? And perhaps your good lady would like to . . . um, amuse herself with a perusal of . . . eh?" He waved an arm vaguely in the direction of the wall, leaving it open to question whether I might amuse myself by looking at the several large paintings, the well-furnished bookshelf, or the several glass cases in which the Duke's collection of snuffboxes resided.

"Thank you," I murmured, with a charming smile, and wandered over to the wall, pretending to be absorbed in a large Boucher, featuring the backview of an amply endowed nude woman seated on a rock in the wilderness. If this was a reflection of current tastes in female anatomy, it was no wonder that Jamie appeared to think so highly of my bottom.

"Ha," I said. "What price foundation garments, eh?"

"Eh?" Jamie and the Duke, startled, looked up from the portfolio of investment papers that formed the ostensible reason for our visit.

"Never mind me," I said, waving a gracious hand. "Just enjoying the art."

"I'm deeply gratified, ma'am," said the Duke politely, and at once reimmersed himself in the papers, as Jamie began the tedious and painstaking real business of the visit—the inconspicuous extraction of such information as the Duke might be willing to part with regarding his own sympathies—or otherwise—toward the Stuart cause.

I had my own agenda for this visit, as well. As the men

became more immersed in their discussions, I edged my way toward the door, pretending to look through the well-furnished shelves. As soon as the coast looked clear, I meant to slip out into the hallway and try to find Alex Randall. I had done what I could to repair the damage done to Mary Hawkins; anything further would have to come from him. Under the rules of social etiquette, he couldn't call upon her at her uncle's house, nor could she contact him. But I could easily make an opportunity for them to meet at the Rue Trémoulins.

The conversation behind me had dropped to a confidential murmur. I stuck my head into the hall, but didn't see a footman immediately. Still, one couldn't be far away; a house of this size must have a staff numbering in the dozens. As large as it was, I would need directions in order to locate Alexander Randall. I chose a direction at random and walked along the hallway, looking for a servant of whom to inquire.

I saw a flicker of motion at the end of the hall, and called out. Whoever it was made no answer, but I heard a surreptitious scuttle of feet on polished boards.

That seemed curious behavior for a servant. I stopped at the end of the hall and looked around. Another hall extended at right angles to the one I stood in, lined on one side with doors, on the other with long windows that opened on the drive and the garden. Most of the doors were closed, but the one closest to me was slightly ajar.

Moving quietly, I stepped up to it and put my ear next to the paneling. Hearing nothing, I took hold of the handle and boldly pushed the door open.

"What in the name of God are *you* doing here?" I exclaimed in astonishment.

"Oh, you scared me! Gracious, I thought I was g-going to die." Mary Hawkins pressed both hands against her bodice. Her face was blanched white, and her eyes dark and wide with terror.

"You're not," I said. "Unless your uncle finds out you're here; then he'll probably kill you. Or does he know?"

She shook her head. "No. I didn't t-tell anyone. I took a public fiacre."

"*Why*, for God's sake?"

She glanced around like a frightened rabbit looking for a

bolthole, but failing to find one, instead drew herself up and tightened her jaw.

"I had to find Alex. I had to t-talk to him. To see if he—if he . . ." Her hands were wringing together, and I could see the effort it cost her to get the words out.

"Never mind," I said, resigned. "I understand. Your uncle won't, though, and neither will the Duke. His Grace doesn't know you're here, either?"

She shook her head, mute.

"All right," I said, thinking. "Well, the first thing we must do is—"

"Madame? May I assist you?"

Mary started like a hare, and I felt my own heart leap uncomfortably into the back of my throat. Bloody footmen; never in the right place at the right time.

There was nothing to do now but brazen it out. I turned to the footman, who was standing stiff as a ramrod in the doorway, looking dignified and suspicious.

"Yes," I said, with as much hauteur as I could summon on short notice. "Will you please tell Mr. Alexander Randall that he has visitors."

"I regret that I cannot do so, Madame," said the footman, with remote formality.

"And why not?" I demanded.

"Because, Madame," he answered, "Mr. Alexander Randall is no longer in His Grace's employ. He was dismissed." The footman glanced at Mary, then lowered his nose an inch and unbent sufficiently to say, "I understand that Monsieur Randall has taken ship back to England."

"No! He can't be gone, he can't!"

Mary darted toward the door, and nearly cannoned into Jamie as he entered. She drew up short with a startled gasp, and he stared at her in astonishment.

"What—" he began, then saw me behind her. "Oh, there ye are, Sassenach. I made an excuse to come and find ye—His Grace just told me that Alex Randall—"

"I know," I interrupted. "He's gone."

"No!" Mary moaned. "No!" She darted toward the door, and was through it before either of us could stop her, her heels clattering on the polished parquet.

"Bloody fool!" I kicked off my own shoes, picked up my

skirts, and whizzed after her. Stocking-footed, I was much faster than she in her high-heeled slippers. Maybe I could catch her before she ran into someone else and was caught, with the concomitant scandal *that* would involve.

I followed the whisk of her disappearing skirts round the bend of the hall. The floor here was carpeted; if I didn't hurry, I might lose her at an intersection, unable to hear from the footsteps which way she had gone. I put my head down, charged round the last corner, and crashed head-on into a man coming the other way.

He let out a startled "Whoof!" as I struck him amidships, and clutched me by the arms to keep upright as we swayed and staggered together.

"I'm sorry," I began, breathlessly. "I thought you were— oh, Jesus H. fucking Christ!"

My initial impression—that I had encountered Alexander Randall—had lasted no more than the split second necessary to see the eyes above that finely chiseled mouth. The mouth was much like Alex's, bar the deep lines around it. But those cold eyes could belong to only one man.

The shock was so great that for a moment everything seemed paradoxically normal; I had an impulse to apologize, dust him off, and continue my pursuit, leaving him forgotten in the corridor, as just a chance encounter. My adrenal glands hastened to remedy this impression, dumping such a dose of adrenaline into my bloodstream that my heart contracted like a squeezed fist.

He was recovering his own breath by now, along with his momentarily shattered self-possession.

"I am inclined to concur with your sentiments, Madam, if not precisely with their manner of expression." Still clutching me by the elbows, he held me slightly away from him, squinting to see my face in the shadowed hall. I saw the shock of recognition blanch his features as my face came into the light. "Bloody hell, it's you!" he exclaimed.

"I thought you were dead!" I wrenched at my arms, trying to free them from the iron-tight grip of Jonathan Randall.

He let go of one arm, in order to rub his middle, surveying me coldly. The thin, fine-cut features were bronzed and healthy; he gave no outward sign of having been trampled five months before by thirty quarter-ton beasts. Not so much as a hoofprint on his forehead.

"Once more, Madam, I find myself sharing your sentiments. I was under a very similar misapprehension concerning *your* state of health. Possibly you are a witch, after all—what did you do, turn yourself into a wolf?" The wary dislike stamped on his face was mingled with a touch of superstitious awe. After all, when you turn someone out into the midst of a pack of wolves on a cold winter evening, you rather expect them to cooperate by being eaten forthwith. The sweatiness of my own palms and the drumlike beating of my heart were testimony to the unsettling effect of having someone you thought safely dead suddenly rise up in front of you. I supposed he must be feeling a trifle queasy as well.

"Wouldn't *you* like to know?" The urge to annoy him—to disturb that icy calm—was the first emotion to surface from the seething mass of feelings that had erupted within me at sight of his face. His fingers tightened on my arm, and his lips thinned. I could see his mind working, starting to tick off possibilities.

"If it wasn't yours, whose body did Sir Fletcher's men take out of the dungeon?" I demanded, trying to take advantage of any break in his composure. An eyewitness had described to me the removal of "a rag doll, rolled in blood"—presumably Randall—from the scene of the cattle stampede that had masked Jamie's escape from that same dungeon.

Randall smiled, without much humor. If he was as rattled as I, he didn't show it. His breathing was a trifle faster than usual, and the lines that edged mouth and eyes cut deeper than I remembered, but he wasn't gasping like a landed fish. I was. I took in as much oxygen as my lungs would allow and tried to breathe through my nose.

"It was my orderly, Marley. Though if you aren't answering my questions, why should I answer yours?" He looked me up and down, carefully evaluating my appearance: silk gown, hair ornaments, jewelry, and stockinged feet.

"Married a Frenchman, did you?" he asked. "I always did think you were a French spy. I trust your new husband keeps you in better order than . . ."

The words died in his throat as he looked up to see the source of the footsteps that had just turned into the hall behind me. If I had wanted to discompose him, that urge was now fully gratified. No Hamlet on the stage had ever reacted to the appearance of a ghost with more convincing terror than I saw stamped on that aristocratic face. The hand still holding my arm clawed deep into my flesh, and I felt the jolt of shock that surged through him like an electric charge.

I knew what he saw behind me, and was afraid to turn. There was a deep silence in the hall; even the wash of the cypress branches against the windows seemed part of the quiet, like the ear-roaring silence that waves make, at the bottom of the sea. Very slowly, I disengaged my arm from his grasp, and his hand fell nerveless to his side. There was no sound behind me, though I could hear voices start up from the room at the end of the hall. I prayed that the door would stay closed, and tried desperately to remember how Jamie was armed.

My mind went blank, then blazed with the reassuring vision of his smallsword, hung by its belt from a hook on the wardrobe, sun glowing on the enameled hilt. But he still had his dirk, of course, and the small knife he habitually carried in his stocking. Come to that, I was entirely sure that in a pinch, he would consider his bare hands perfectly adequate. And if you cared to describe my present situation, standing between the two of them, as a pinch . . . I swallowed once and slowly turned around.

He was standing quite still, no more than a yard behind me. One of the tall, paned casements was open near him, and the dark shadows of the cypress needles rippled over him like water over a sunken rock. He showed no more expression than a rock, either. Whatever lived behind those eyes was hidden; they were wide and blank as windowpanes, as though the soul they mirrored were long since flown.

He didn't speak, but after a moment, reached out one hand to me. It floated open in the air, and I finally summoned the presence of mind to take it. It was cool and hard, and I clung to it like the wood of a raft.

He drew me in, close to his side, took my arm and turned me, all without speaking or changing expression. As we reached the turning of the hall, Randall spoke behind us.

"Jamie," he said. The voice was hoarse with shock, and held a note halfway between disbelief and pleading.

Jamie stopped then, and turned to look at him. Randall's face was a ghastly white, with a small red patch livid on each cheekbone. He had taken off his wig, clenched in his hands, and sweat pasted the fine dark hair to his temples.

"No." The voice that spoke above me was soft, almost expressionless. Looking up, I could see that the face still matched it, but a quick, hot pulse beat in his neck, and the small, triangular scar above his collar flushed red with heat.

"I am called Lord Broch Tuarach for formality's sake," the soft Scottish voice above me said. "And beyond the re-quirements of formality, you will never speak to me again—until you beg for your life at the point of my sword. Then, you may use my name, for it will be the last word you ever speak."

With sudden violence, he swept around, and his flaring plaid swung wide, blocking my view of Randall as we turned the corner of the hall.

The carriage was still waiting by the gate. Afraid to look at Jamie, I climbed in and absorbed myself in tucking the folds of yellow silk around my legs. The click of the carriage door shutting made me look up abruptly, but before I could reach the handle, the carriage started with a jerk that threw me back in my seat.

Struggling and swearing, I fought my way to my knees and peered out of the back window. He was gone. Nothing moved on the drive but the swaying shadows of cypress and poplar.

I hammered frenziedly on the roof of the carriage, but the coachman merely shouted to the horses and urged them on faster. There was little traffic at this hour, and we hurtled through the narrow streets as though the devil were after us.

When we drew up in the Rue Trémoulins, I sprang out of the coach, at once panicked and furious.

"Why didn't you stop?" I demanded of the coachman. He shrugged, safely impervious atop his perch.

"The master ordered me to drive you home without de-lay, Madame." He picked up the whip and touched it lightly to the off-horse's rump.

"Wait!" I shouted. "I want to go back!" But he only

hunched himself turtle-like into his shoulders, pretending not to hear me, as the coach rattled off.

Fuming with impotence, I turned toward the door, where the small figure of Fergus appeared, thin brows raised questioningly at my appearance.

"Where's Murtagh?" I snapped. The little clansman was the only person I could think of who might be able first, to find Jamie, and secondly, to stop him.

"I don't know, Madame. Maybe down there." The boy nodded in the direction of the Rue Cambodge, where there were several taverns, ranging in respectability from those where a traveling lady might dine with her husband, to the dens near the river, which even an armed man might hesitate to enter alone.

I laid a hand on Fergus's shoulder, as much for support as in exhortation.

"Run and find him, Fergus. Quickly as you can!"

Alarmed by my tone, he leaped off the step and was gone, before I could add "Be careful!" Still, he knew the lower levels of Paris life much better than I did; no one was better adapted to eeling through a tavern crowd than an ex-pickpocket. At least I hoped he was an ex-pickpocket.

But I could worry effectively about only one thing at a time, and visions of Fergus being captured and hanged for his activities receded before the vision Jamie's final words to Randall had evoked.

Surely, *surely* he would not have gone back into the Duke's house? No, I reassured myself. He had no sword. Whatever he might be feeling—and my soul sank within me to think of what he felt—he wouldn't act precipitously. I had seen him in battle before, mind working in an icy calm, severed from the emotions that could cloud his judgment. And for this, above all things, surely he would adhere to the formalities. He would seek the rigid prescriptions, the formulae for the satisfaction of honor, as a refuge—something to cling to against the tides that shook him, the bone-deep surge of bloodlust and revenge.

I stopped in the hallway, mechanically shedding my cloak and pausing by the mirror to straighten my hair. *Think, Beauchamp,* I silently urged my pale reflection. If he's going to fight a duel, what's the first thing he'll need?

A sword? No, couldn't be. His own was upstairs, hanging on the armoire. While he might easily borrow one, I couldn't imagine his setting out to fight the most important duel of his life armed with any but his own. His uncle, Dougal MacKenzie, had given it to him at seventeen, seen him schooled in its use, taught him the tricks and the strengths of a left-handed swordsman, using that sword. Dougal had made him practice, left hand against left hand, for hours on end, until, he told me, he felt the length of Spanish metal come alive, an extension of his arm, hilt welded to his palm. Jamie had said he felt naked without it. And this was not a fight to which he would go naked.

No, if he had needed the sword at once, he would have come home to fetch it. I ran my hand impatiently through my hair, trying to think. Damn it, what was the protocol of dueling? Before it came to swords, what happened? A challenge, of course. Had Jamie's words in the hallway constituted that? I had vague ideas of people being slapped across the face with gloves, but had no idea whether that was really the custom, or merely an artifact of memory, born of a film-maker's imagination.

Then it came to me. First the challenge, then a place must be arranged—a suitably circumspect place, unlikely to come to the notice of the police or the King's Guard. And to deliver the challenge, to arrange the place, a second was required. Ah. That was where he had gone, then; to find his second. Murtagh.

Even if Jamie found Murtagh before Fergus did, still there would be the formalities to arrange. I began to breathe a little easier, though my heart was still pounding, and my laces still seemed too tight. None of the servants was visible; I yanked the laces loose and drew a deep, expanding breath.

"I didna know ye were in the habit of undressing in the hallways, or I would ha' stayed in the drawing room," said an ironic Scots voice behind me.

I whirled, my heart leaping high enough to choke me. The man standing stretched in the drawing room doorway, arms outspread to brace him casually against the frame, was big, nearly as large as Jamie, with the same taut grace of movement, the same air of cool self-possession. The hair was dark, though, and the deep-set eyes a cloudy green. Dougal

MacKenzie, appearing suddenly in my home as though called by my thought. Speak of the devil.

"What in God's name are you doing here?" The shock of seeing him was subsiding, though my heart still pounded. I hadn't eaten since breakfast, and a sudden wave of queasiness washed over me. He stepped forward and grasped me by the arm, pulling me toward a chair.

"Sit ye down, lass," he said. "Ye'll no be feeling just the thing, it looks like."

"Very observant of you," I said. Black spots floated at the edge of my vision, and small bright flashes danced before my eyes. "Excuse me," I said politely, and put my head between my knees.

Jamie. Frank. Randall. Dougal. The faces flickered in my mind, the names seemed to ring in my ears. My palms were sweating, and I pressed them under my arms, hugging myself to try to stop the tremblings of shock. Jamie wouldn't be facing Randall immediately; that was the important thing. There was a little time, in which to think, to take preventive action. But what action? Leaving my subconscious to wrestle with this question, I forced my breathing to slow and turned my attention to matters closer to hand.

"I repeat," I said, sitting up and smoothing back my hair, "what are you doing here?"

The dark brows flickered upward.

"Do I need a reason to visit a kinsman?"

I could still taste the bile at the back of my throat, but my hands had stopped trembling, at least.

"Under the circumstances, yes," I said. I drew myself up, grandly ignoring my untied laces, and reached for the brandy decanter. Anticipating me, Dougal took a glass from the tray and poured out a teaspoonful. Then, after a considering glance at me, he doubled the dose.

"Thanks," I said dryly, accepting the glass.

"Circumstances, eh? And which circumstances would those be?" Not waiting for answer or permission, he calmly poured out another glass for himself and lifted it in a casual toast. "To His Majesty."

I felt my mouth twist sideways. "King James, I suppose?" I took a small sip of my own drink, and felt the hot aromatic fumes sear the membranes behind my eyes. "And does the fact that you're in Paris mean that you've converted Colum to your way of thinking?" For while Dougal MacKenzie might be a Jacobite, it was his brother Colum who led the MacKenzies of Leoch as chieftain. Legs crippled and twisted by a deforming disease, Colum no longer led his clan into battle; Dougal was the war chieftain. But while Dougal might lead men into battle, it was Colum who held the power to say whether the battle would take place.

Dougal ignored my question, and having drained his glass, immediately poured out another drink. He savored the first sip of this one, rolling it visibly around his mouth and licking a final drop from his lips as he swallowed.

"Not bad," he said. "I must take some back for Colum. He needs something a bit stronger than the wine, to help him sleep nights."

This was indeed an oblique answer to my question. Colum's condition was degenerating, then. Always in some pain from the disease that eroded his body, Colum had taken fortified wine in the evenings, to help him to sleep. Now he needed straight brandy. I wondered how long it would be before he might be forced to resort to opium for relief.

For when he did, that would be the end of his reign as chieftain of his clan. Deprived of physical resources, still he commanded by sheer force of character. But if the strength of Colum's mind were lost to pain and drugs, the clan would have a new leader—Dougal.

I gazed at him over the rim of my glass. He returned my stare with no sign of abashment, a slight smile on that wide MacKenzie mouth. His face was much like his brother's—and his nephew's—strong and boldly modeled, with broad, high cheekbones and a long, straight nose like the blade of a knife.

Sworn as a boy of eighteen to support his brother's chieftainship, he had kept that vow for nearly thirty years. And would keep it, I knew, until the day that Colum died or could lead no longer. But on that day, the mantle of chief would descend on his shoulders, and the men of clan MacKenzie would follow where he led—after the saltire of Scotland, and the banner of King James, in the vanguard of Bonnie Prince Charlie.

"Circumstances?" I said, turning to his earlier question. "Well, I don't suppose one would consider it in the best of taste to come calling on a man whom you'd left for dead and whose wife you'd tried to seduce."

Being Dougal MacKenzie, he laughed. I didn't know quite what it would take to disconcert the man, but I certainly hoped I was there to see it when it finally happened.

"Seduction?" he said, lips quirked in amusement. "I offered ye marriage."

"You offered to rape me, as I recall," I snapped. He had, in fact, offered to marry me—by force—after declining to help me in rescuing Jamie from Wentworth Prison the winter before. While his principal motive had been the possession of Jamie's estate of Lallybroch—which would belong to me upon Jamie's death—he hadn't been at all averse to the thought of the minor emoluments of marriage, such as the regular enjoyment of my body.

"As for leaving Jamie in the prison," he went on, ignoring me as usual, "there seemed no way to get him out, and no sense in risking good men in a vain attempt. He'd be the first to understand that. And it was my duty as his kinsman to offer his wife my protection, if he died. I was the lad's foster father, no?" He tilted back his head and drained his glass.

I took a good gulp of my own, and swallowed quickly so as not to choke. The spirit burned down my throat and gullet, matching the heat that was rising in my cheeks. He was right; Jamie hadn't blamed him for his reluctance to break into Wentworth Prison—he hadn't expected *me* to do it, either, and it was only by a miracle that I had succeeded. But while I had told Jamie, briefly, of Dougal's intention of marrying me, I hadn't tried to convey the carnal aspects of that intention. I had, after all, never expected to see Dougal MacKenzie again.

I knew from past experience that he was a seizer of opportunities; with Jamie about to be hanged, he had not even waited for execution of the sentence before trying to secure me and my about-to-be-inherited property. If—no, I corrected myself, *when*—Colum died or became incompetent, Dougal would be in full command of clan MacKenzie within a week. And if Charles Stuart found the backing he was seeking, Dougal would be there. He had some experience in being a power behind the throne, after all.

I tipped up the glass, considering. Colum had business

interests in France; wine and timber, mostly. These undoubtedly were the pretext for Dougal's visit to Paris, might even be his major ostensible reason. But he had other reasons, I was sure. And the presence in the city of Prince Charles Edward Stuart was almost certainly one of them.

One thing to be said for Dougal MacKenzie was that an encounter with him stimulated the mental processes, out of the sheer necessity of trying to figure out what he was actually up to at any given moment. Under the inspiration of his presence and a good slug of Portuguese brandy, my subconscious was stirring with the birth of an idea.

"Well, be that as it may, I'm glad you're here now," I said, replacing my empty glass on the tray.

"You are?" The thick dark brows rose incredulously.

"Yes." I rose and gestured toward the hall. "Fetch my cloak while I do up my laces. I need you to come to the *commissariat de police* with me."

Seeing his jaw drop, I felt the first tiny upsurge of hope. If I had managed to take Dougal MacKenzie by surprise, surely I could stop a duel?

"D'ye want to tell me what you think you're doing?" Dougal inquired, as the coach bumped around the Cirque du Mireille, narrowly avoiding an oncoming barouche and a cart full of vegetable marrows.

"No," I said briefly, "but I suppose I'll have to. Did you know that Jack Randall is still alive?"

"I'd not heard he was dead," Dougal said reasonably.

That took me up short for a moment. But of course he was right; we had thought Randall dead only because Sir Marcus MacRannoch had mistaken the trampled body of Randall's orderly for the officer himself, during Jamie's rescue from Wentworth Prison. Naturally no news of Randall's death would have gone round the Highlands, since it hadn't occurred. I tried to gather my scattered thoughts.

"He *isn't* dead," I said. "But he is in Paris."

"In Paris?" That got his attention; his brows went up, and then his eyes widened with the next thought.

"Where's Jamie?" he asked sharply.

I was glad to see he appreciated the main point. While

he didn't know what had passed between Jamie and Randall in Wentworth Prison—no one was ever going to know that, save Jamie, Randall, and, to some extent, me—he knew more than enough about Randall's previous actions to realize exactly what Jamie's first impulse would be on meeting the man here, away from the sanctuary of England.

"I don't know," I said, looking out the window. We were passing Les Halles, and the smell of fish was ripe in my nostrils. I pulled out a scented handkerchief and covered my nose and mouth. The strong, sharp tang of the wintergreen with which I scented it was no match for the reek of a dozen eel-sellers' stalls, but it helped a bit. I spoke through the spicy linen folds.

"We met Randall unexpectedly at the Duke of Sandringham's today. Jamie sent me home in the coach, and I haven't seen him since."

Dougal ignored both the stench and the raucous cries of fishwives calling their wares. He frowned at me.

"He'll mean to kill the man, surely?"

I shook my head, and explained my reasoning about the sword.

"I can't let a duel happen," I said, dropping the handkerchief in order to speak more clearly. "I won't!"

Dougal nodded abstractedly.

"Aye, that would be dangerous. Not that the lad couldna take Randall with ease—I taught him, ye ken," he added with some boastfulness, "but the sentence for dueling . . ."

"Got it in one," I said.

"All right," he said slowly. "But why the police? You dinna mean to have the lad locked up beforehand, do ye? Your own husband?"

"Not Jamie," I said. "Randall."

A broad grin broke out on his face, not unmixed with skepticism.

"Oh, aye? And how d'ye mean to work that one?"

"A friend and I were . . . attacked on the street a few nights ago," I said, swallowing at the memory. "The men were masked; I couldn't tell who they were. But one of them was about the same height and build as Jonathan Randall. I mean to say that I met Randall at a house today and recognized him as one of the men who attacked us."

Dougal's brows shot up and then drew together. His cool gaze flickered over me. Suddenly there was a new speculation in his appraisal.

"Christ, you've the devil's own nerve. Robbery, was it?" he asked softly. Against my will, I could feel the rage rising in my cheeks.

"No," I said, clipping the word between my teeth.

"Ah." He sat back against the coach's squabs, still looking at me. "Ye'll have taken no harm, though?" I glanced aside, at the passing street, but could feel his eyes, prying at the neck of my gown, sliding over the curve of my hips.

"Not me," I said. "But my friend . . ."

"I see." He was quiet for a moment, then said meditatively, "Ever heard of 'Les Disciples du Mal,' have you?"

I jerked my head back around to him. He lounged in the corner like a crouching cat, watching me through eyes narrowed against the sun.

"No. What are they?" I demanded.

He shrugged and sat upright, peering past me at the approaching bulk of the Quai des Orfèvres, hovering gray and dreary above the glitter of the Seine.

"A society—of a sort. Young men of family, with an interest in things . . . unwholesome, shall we say?"

"Let's," I said. "And just what do you know about Les Disciples?"

"Only what I heard in a tavern in the Cité," he said. "That the society demands a good deal from its members, and the price of initiation is high . . . by some standards."

"That being?" I dared him with my eyes. He smiled rather grimly before replying.

"A maidenhead, for one thing. The nipples of a married woman, for another." He shot a quick glance at my bosom. "Your friend's a virgin, is she? Or was?"

I felt hot and cold by turns. I wiped my face with the handkerchief and tucked it into the pocket of my cloak. I had to try twice, for my hand trembled.

"She was. What else have you heard? Do you know who's involved with Les Disciples?"

Dougal shook his head. There were threads of silver in the russet hair over his temples, that caught the light of the afternoon.

"Only rumors. The Vicomte de Busca, the youngest of the Charmisse sons—perhaps. The Comte St. Germain. Eh! Are ye all right, lass?"

He leaned forward in some consternation, peering at me.

"Fine," I said, breathing deeply through my nose. "Bloody fine." I pulled out the handkerchief and wiped the cold sweat off my brow.

"We mean you no harm, mesdames." The ironic voice echoed in the dark of my memory. The green-shirted man was medium-height and dark, slim and narrow-shouldered. If that description fit Jonathan Randall, it also fit the Comte St. Germain. Would I have recognized his voice, though? Could any normal man conceivably have sat across from me at dinner, eating salmon mousse and making genteel conversation, barely two hours after the incident in the Rue du Faubourg St.-Honoré?

Considered logically, though, why not? *I* had, after all. And I had no particular reason for supposing the Comte to be a normal man—by my standards—if rumor were true.

The coach was drawing to a halt, and there was little time for contemplation. Was I about to ensure that the man responsible for Mary's violation went free, while I also ensured the safety of Jamie's most loathed enemy? I took a deep, quivering breath. Damn little choice about it, I thought. Life was paramount; justice would just have to wait its turn.

The coachman had alighted and was reaching for the door handle. I bit my lip and glanced at Dougal MacKenzie. He met my gaze with a slight shrug. What did I want of him?

"Will you back my story?" I asked abruptly.

He looked up at the towering bulk of the Quai des Orfèvres. Brilliant afternoon light blazed through the open door.

"You're sure?" he asked.

"Yes." My mouth was dry.

He slid across the seat and extended a hand to me.

"Pray God we dinna both end in a cell, then," he said.

An hour later, we stepped into the empty street outside the *commissariat de police*. I had sent the coach home, lest anyone who knew us should see it standing outside the Quai

des Orfèvres. Dougal offered me an arm, and I took it perforce. The ground here was muddy underfoot, and the cobbles in the street made uncertain going in high-heeled slippers.

"Les Disciples," I said as we made our way slowly along
the banks of the Seine toward the towers of Notre Dame.
"Do you really think the Comte St. Germain might have been
one of the men who . . . who stopped us in the Rue du
Faubourg St.-Honoré?" I was beginning to tremble with reaction and fatigue—and with hunger; I had had nothing since
breakfast, and the lack was making itself felt. Sheer nerve had
kept me going through the interview with the police. Now the
need to think was passing, and with it, the ability to do so.

Dougal's arm was hard under my hand, but I couldn't
look up at him; I needed all my attention to keep my footing.
We had turned into the Rue Elise and the cobbles were shiny
with damp and smeared with various kinds of filth. A porter
lugging a crate paused in our path to clear his throat and
hawk noisily into the street at my feet. The greenish glob
clung to the curve of a stone, finally slipping off to float sluggishly onto the surface of a small mud puddle that lay in the
hollow of a missing cobble.

"Mphm." Dougal was looking up and down the street for
a carriage, brow creased in thought. "I canna say; I've heard
worse than that of the man, but I havena had the honor of
meeting him." He glanced down at me.

"You've managed brawly so far," he said. "They'll have
Jack Randall in the Bastille within the hour. But they'll have
to let the man go sooner or later, and I wouldna wager much
on the chances of Jamie's temper cooling in the meantime.
D'ye want me to speak to him—convince him to do nothing
foolish?"

"No! For God's sake, stay out of it!" The thunder of
carriage wheels was loud on the cobbles, but my voice rose
high enough to make Dougal's brows lift in surprise.

"All right, then," he said, mildly. "I'll leave it to you to
manage him. He's stubborn as a stone . . . but I suppose
you have your ways, no?" This was said with a sidelong glance
and knowing smirk.

"I'll manage." I would. I would have to. For everything I
had told Dougal was true. All true. And yet so far from the

truth. For I would send Charles Stuart and his father's cause to the devil gladly, sacrifice any hope of stopping his headlong dash to folly, even risk the chance of Jamie's imprisonment, for the sake of healing the breach Randall's resurrection had opened in Jamie's mind. I would help him to kill Randall, and feel only joy in the doing of it, except for the one thing. The one consideration strong enough to outweigh Jamie's pride, loom larger than his sense of manhood, than his threatened soul's peace. Frank.

That was the single idea that had driven me through this day, sustained me well past the point where I would have welcomed collapse. For months I had thought Randall dead and childless, and feared for Frank's life. But for those same months I had been comforted by the presence of the plain gold ring on the fourth finger of my left hand.

The complement to Jamie's silver ring upon my right, it was a talisman in the dark hours of the night, when doubts came on the heels of dreams. If I wore his ring still, then the man who had given it to me would live. I had told myself that a thousand times. No matter that I didn't know how a man dead without issue could sire a line of descent that led to Frank; the ring was there, and Frank would live.

Now I knew why the ring still shone on my hand, metal chilly as my own cold finger. Randall was alive, could still marry, could still father the child who would pass life on to Frank. Unless Jamie killed him first.

I had taken what steps I could for the moment, but the fact I had faced in the Duke's corridor remained. The price of Frank's life was Jamie's soul, and how was I to choose between them?

The oncoming fiacre, ignoring Dougal's hail, barreled past without stopping, wheels passing close enough to splash muddy water on Dougal's silk hose and the hem of my gown.

Desisting from a volley of heartfelt Gaelic, Dougal shook a fist after the retreating coach.

"Well, and now what?" he demanded rhetorically.

The blob of mucus-streaked spittle floated on the puddle at my feet, reflecting gray light. I could feel its cold slime viscid on my tongue. I put out a hand and grasped Dougal's arm, hard as a smooth-skinned sycamore branch. Hard, but it seemed to be swaying dizzily, swinging me far out over the cold and glittering, fish-smelling, slimy water nearby. Black spots floated before my eyes.

"Now," I said, "I'm going to be sick."

It was nearly sunset when I returned to the Rue Trémoulins. My knees trembled, and it was an effort to put one foot in front of the other on the stairs. I went directly to the bedroom to shed my cloak, wondering whether Jamie had returned yet.

He had. I stopped dead in the doorway, surveying the room. My medicine box lay open on the table. The scissors I used for cutting bandages lay half-open on my dressing table. They were fanciful things, given to me by a knifemaker who worked now and then at L'Hôpital des Anges; the handles were gilt, worked in the shape of storks' heads, with the long bills forming the silver blades of the scissors. They gleamed in the rays of the setting sun, lying amid a cloud of reddish gold silk threads.

I took several steps toward the dressing table, and the silky, shimmering strands lifted in the disturbed air of my movement, drifting across the tabletop.

"Jesus bloody Christ," I breathed. He had been here, all right, and now he was gone. So was his sword.

The hair lay in thick, gleaming strands where it had fallen, littering dressing table, stool and floor. I plucked a shorn lock from the table and held it, feeling the fine, soft hairs separate between my fingers like the threads of embroidery silk. I felt a cold panic that started somewhere between my shoulder blades and prickled down my spine. I remembered Jamie, sitting on the fountain behind the Rohans' house, telling me how he had fought his first duel in Paris.

"The lace that held my hair back broke, and the wind whipped it into my face so I could scarcely see what I was doing."

He was taking no chance of that happening again. Seeing the evidence left behind, feeling the lock of hair in my hand, soft and alive-feeling still, I could imagine the cold deliberation with which he had done it; the snick of metal blades against his skull as he cut away all softness that might obscure his vision. Nothing would stand between him and the killing of Jonathan Randall.

Nothing but me. Still holding the lock of his hair, I went to the window and stared out, as though hoping to see him in the street. But the Rue Trémoulins was quiet, nothing moving but the flickering shadows of the poplar trees by the gates and the small movement of a servant, standing at the gate of the house to the left, talking to a watchman who brandished his pipe to emphasize a point.

The house hummed quietly around me, with dinner preparations taking place belowstairs. No company was expected tonight, so the usual bustle was subdued; we ate simply when alone.

I sat down on the bed and closed my eyes, folding my hands across my swelling stomach, the lock of hair gripped tight, as though I could keep him safe, so long as I didn't let go.

Had I been in time? Had the police found Jack Randall before Jamie did? What if they had arrived concurrently, or just in time to find Jamie challenging Randall to a formal duel? I rubbed the lock of hair between thumb and forefinger, splaying the cut ends in a small spray of roan and amber. Well, if so, at least they would both be safe. In prison, perhaps, but that was a minor consideration by contrast to other dangers.

And if Jamie had found Randall first? I glanced outside; the light was fading fast. Duels were traditionally fought at dawn, but I didn't know whether Jamie would have waited for morning. They might at this moment be facing each other, somewhere in seclusion, where the clash of steel and the cry of mortal wounding would attract no attention.

For a mortal fight it would be. What lay between those two men would be settled only by death. And whose death would it be? Jamie's? Or Randall's—and with him, Frank's? Jamie was likely the better swordsman, but as the challenged, Randall would have the choice of weapons. And success with pistols lay less with the skill of the user than with his fortune; only the best-made pistols aimed true, and even those were prone to misfire or other accidents. I had a sudden vision of Jamie, limp and quiet on the grass, blood welling from an empty eye socket, and the smell of black powder strong among the scents of spring in the Bois de Boulogne.

"What in hell are you doing, Claire?"

My head snapped up, so hard I bit my tongue. Both his eyes were present and in their correct positions, staring at me from either side of the knife-edged nose. I had never seen him with his hair so close-clipped before. It made him look like a stranger, the strong bones of his face stark beneath the skin and the dome of his skull visible under the short, thick turf of his hair.

"What am I doing?" I echoed. I swallowed, working some moisture back into my dry mouth. "What am I doing? I'm sitting here with a lock of your hair in my hand, wondering whether you were dead or not! That's what I'm doing!"

"I'm not dead." He crossed to the armoire and opened it. He wore his sword, but had changed clothes since our visit to Sandringham's house; now he was dressed in his old coat—the one that allowed him free movement of his arms.

"Yes, I noticed," I said. "Thoughtful of you to come tell me."

"I came to fetch my clothes." He pulled out two shirts and his full-length cloak and laid them across a stool while he went to rummage in the chest of drawers for clean linen.

"Your clothes? Where on earth are you going?" I hadn't known what to expect when I saw him again, but I certainly hadn't expected this.

"To an inn." He glanced at me, then apparently decided I deserved more than a three-word explanation. He turned and looked at me, his eyes blue and opaque as azurite.

"When I sent ye home in the coach, I walked for a bit, until I had a grip on myself once more. Then I came home to fetch my sword, and returned to the Duke's house to give Randall a formal challenge. The butler told me Randall had been arrested."

His gaze rested on me, remote as the ocean depths. I swallowed once more.

"I went to the Bastille. They told me you'd sworn to an accusation against Randall, saying he'd attacked you and Mary Hawkins the other night. Why, Claire?"

My hands were shaking, and I dropped the lock of hair I

had been holding. Its cohesion disturbed by handling, it disintegrated, and the fine red hairs spilled loose across my lap.

"Jamie," I said, and my voice was shaking, too, "Jamie, you can't kill Jack Randall."

One corner of his mouth twitched, very slightly.

"I dinna ken whether to be touched at your concern for my safety, or to be offended at your lack of confidence. But in either case, you needna worry. I can kill him. Easily." The last word was spoken quietly, with an underlying tone that mingled venom with satisfaction.

"That isn't what I mean! Jamie—"

"Fortunately," he went on, as though not hearing me, "Randall has proof that he was at the Duke's residence all during the evening of the rape. As soon as the police finish interviewing the guests who were present, and satisfy themselves that Randall is innocent—of *that* charge, at least—then he'll be let go. I shall stay at the inn until he's free. And then I shall find him." His eyes were fixed on the wardrobe, but plainly he was seeing something else. "He'll be waiting for me," he said softly.

He stuffed the shirts and linen into a traveling-bag and slung his cloak over his arm. He was turning to go through the door when I sprang up from the bed and caught him by the sleeve.

"Jamie! For God's sake, Jamie, listen to me! You can't kill Jack Randall because I won't let you!"

He stared down at me in utter astonishment.

"Because of Frank," I said. I let go of his sleeve and stepped back.

"Frank," he repeated, shaking his head slightly as though to clear a buzzing in his ears. "Frank."

"Yes," I said. "If you kill Jack Randall now, then Frank . . . he won't exist. He won't be born. Jamie, you can't kill an innocent man!"

His face, normally a pale, ruddy bronze, had faded to a blotchy white as I spoke. Now the red began to rise again, burning the tips of his ears and flaming in his cheeks.

"An innocent man?"

"Frank is an innocent man! I don't care about Jack Randall—"

"Well, I do!" He snatched up the bag and strode toward

the door, cloak streaming over one arm. "Jesus God, Claire! You'd try to stop me taking my vengeance on the man who made me play whore to him? Who forced me to my knees and made me suck his cock, smeared with my own blood? *Christ*, Claire!" He flung the door open with a crash and was in the hallway by the time I could reach him.

It had grown dark by now, but the servants had lit the candles, and the hallway was aglow with soft light. I grasped him by the arm and yanked at him.

"Jamie! Please!"

He jerked his arm impatiently out of my grasp. I was almost crying, but held back the tears. I caught the bag and pulled it out of his hand.

"Please, Jamie! Wait, just for a year! The child—Randall's—it will be conceived next December. After that, it won't matter. But please—for my sake, Jamie—wait that long!"

The candelabra on the gilt-edged table threw his shadow huge and wavering against the far wall. He stared up at it, hands clenched, as though facing a giant, blank-faced and menacing, that towered above him.

"Aye," he whispered, as though to himself, "I'm a big chap. Big and strong. I can stand a lot. Yes, I can stand it." He whirled on me, shouting.

"I can stand a lot! But just because I can, does that mean I must? Do I have to bear everyone's weakness? Can I not have my own?"

He began to pace up and down the hall, the shadow following in silent frenzy.

"You canna ask it of me! You, you of all people! You, who know what . . . what . . ." He choked, speechless with rage.

He hit the stone wall of the passage repeatedly as he walked, smashing the side of his fist viciously into the limestone wall. The stone swallowed each blow in soundless violence.

He turned back and came to a halt facing me, breathing heavily. I stood stock-still, afraid to move or speak. He nodded once or twice, rapidly, as though making up his mind about something, then drew the dirk from his belt with a hiss and held it in front of my nose. With a visible effort, he spoke calmly.

"You may have your choice, Claire. Him, or me." The candle flames danced in the polished metal as he turned the knife slowly. "I canna live while he lives. If ye wilna have me kill him, then kill me now, yourself!" He grabbed my hand and forced my fingers around the handle of the dirk. Ripping the lacy jabot open, he bared his throat and yanked my hand upward, fingers hard around my own.

I pulled back with all my strength, but he forced the tip of the blade against the soft hollow above the collarbone, just below the livid cicatrix that Randall's own knife had left there years before.

"Jamie! Stop it! Stop it right now!" I brought my other hand down on his wrist as hard as I could, jarring his grip enough to jerk my fingers free. The knife clattered to the floor, bouncing from the stones to a quiet landing on a corner of the leafy Aubusson carpet. With that clarity of vision for small details that afflicts life's most awful moments, I saw that the blade lay stark across the curling stem of a bunch of fat green grapes, as though about to sever it and cut them free of the weft to roll at our feet.

He stood frozen before me, face white as bone, eyes burning. I gripped his arm, hard as wood beneath my fingers.

"Please believe me, please. I wouldn't do this if there were any other way." I took a deep, quivering breath to quell the leaping pulse beneath my ribs.

"You owe me your life, Jamie. Not once, twice over. I saved you from hanging at Wentworth, and when you had fever at the Abbey. You owe me a life, Jamie!"

He stared down at me for a long moment before answering. When he did, his voice was quiet again, with an edge of bitterness.

"I see. And ye'll claim your debt now?" His eyes burned with the clear, deep blue that burns in the heart of a flame.

"I have to! I can't make you see reason any other way!"

"Reason. Ah, reason. No, I canna say that reason is anything I see just now." He folded his arms behind his back, gripping the stiff fingers of his right hand with the curled ones of his left. He walked slowly away from me, down the endless hall, head bowed.

The passage was lined with paintings, some lighted from below by torchère or candelabra, some from above by the gilded sconces; a few less favored, skulked in the darkness between. Jamie walked slowly between them, glancing up now and again as though in converse with the wigged and painted gallery.

The hall ran the length of the second floor, carpeted and tapestried, with enormous stained-glass windows set into the walls at either end of the corridor. He walked all the way to the far end, then, wheeling with the precision of a soldier on parade, all the way back, still at a slow and formal pace. Down and back, down and back, again and again.

My legs trembling, I subsided into a *fauteuil* near the end of the passage. Once one of the omnipresent servants approached obsequiously to ask if Madame required wine, or perhaps a biscuit? I waved him away with what politeness I could muster, and waited.

At last he came to a halt before me, feet planted wide apart in silver-buckled shoes, hands still clasped behind his back. He waited for me to look up at him before he spoke. His face was set, with no twitch of agitation to betray him, though the lines near his eyes were deep with strain.

"A year, then" was all he said. He turned at once and was several feet away by the time I struggled out of the deep green-velvet chair. I had barely gained my feet when he suddenly whirled back past me, reached the huge stained-glass window in three strides, and smashed his right hand through it.

The window was made up of thousands of tiny colored panes, held in place by strips of melted lead. Though the entire window, a mythological scene of the Judgment of Paris, shuddered in its frame, the leading held most of the panes intact; in spite of the crash and tinkle, only a jagged hole at the feet of Aphrodite let in the soft spring air.

Jamie stood a moment, pressing both hands tight into his midriff. A dark red stain grew on the frilled cuff, lacy as a bridal shirt. He brushed past me once again as I moved toward him, and stalked away unspeaking.

I collapsed once more into the armchair, hard enough to make a small puff of dust rise from the plush. I lay there limp, eyes closed, feeling the cool night breeze wash over me. The hair was damp at my temples, and I could feel my pulse, quick as a bird's, racing at the base of my throat.

Would he ever forgive me? My heart clenched like a fist at the memory of the knowledge of betrayal in his eyes. *"How could you ask it?"* he had said. *"You, you who know . . ."* Yes, I knew, and I thought the knowing might tear me from Jamie as I had been torn from Frank.

But whether Jamie could forgive me or not, I could never forgive myself, if I condemned an innocent man—and one I had once loved.

"The sins of the fathers," I murmured to myself. "The sins of the fathers shall not be visited upon the children."

"Madame?"

I jumped, opening my eyes to find an equally startled chambermaid backing away. I put a hand to my pounding heart, gasping for air.

"Madame, you are unwell? Shall I fetch—"

"No," I said, as firmly as I could. "I am quite well. I wish to sit here for a time. Please go away."

The girl seemed only too anxious to oblige. *"Oui,* Madame!" she said, and vanished down the corridor, leaving me gazing blankly at a scene of amorous love in a garden, hanging on the opposite wall. Suddenly cold, I drew up the folds of the cloak I had had no time to shed, and closed my eyes again.

<hr />

It was past midnight when I went at last to our bedroom. Jamie was there, seated before a small table, apparently watching a pair of lacewings fluttering dangerously around the single candlestick which was all the light there was in the room. I dropped my cape on the floor and went toward him.

"Don't touch me," he said. "Go to bed." He spoke almost abstractedly, but I halted in my tracks.

"But your hand—" I started.

"It doesn't matter. Go to bed," he repeated.

The knuckles of his right hand were laced with blood, and the cuff of his shirt was stiff with it, but I would not have dared touch him then had he had a knife stuck in his belly. I left him staring at the death-dance of the lacewings and went to bed.

I woke sometime near dawn, with the first light of the coming day fuzzing the outlines of the furniture in the room. Through the double doors to the anteroom, I could see Jamie as I had left him, still seated at the table. Now the candle was burnt out, the lacewings gone, and he sat with his head in his hands, fingers furrowed in the brutally cropped hair. The light stole all color from the room; even the hair spiking up like flames between his fingers was quenched to the color of ashes.

I slid out of bed, cold in the thin embroidered nightdress. He didn't turn as I came up behind him, but he knew I was there. When I touched his hand he let it drop to the table, and allowed his head to fall back until it rested just below my breasts. He sighed deeply as I rubbed it, and I felt the tension begin to go out of him. My hands worked their way down over neck and shoulders, feeling the chill of his flesh through the thin linen. Finally I came around in front of him. He reached up and grasped me around the waist, pulling me to him and burying his head in my nightdress, just above the round swell of the unborn child.

"I'm cold," I said at last, very softly. "Will you come and warm me?"

After a moment, he nodded, and stumbled blindly to his feet. I led him to bed, stripped him as he sat unresisting, and tucked him under the quilts. I lay in the curve of his arm, pressed tight against him, until the chill of his skin had faded and we lay ensconced in a pocket of soft warmth.

Tentatively, I laid a hand on his chest, stroking lightly back and forth until the nipple stood up, a tiny nub of desire. He laid his hand over mine, stilling it. I was afraid he would push me away, and he did, but only so that he could roll toward me.

The light was growing stronger, and he spent a long time just looking down at my face, stroking it from temple to chin, drawing his thumb down the line of my throat and out along the wing of my collarbone.

"God, I do love you," he whispered, as though to himself. He kissed me, preventing response, and circling one breast with his maimed right hand, prepared to take me.

"But your hand—" I said, for the second time that night.

"It doesn't matter," he said, for the second time that night.

PART FOUR

Scandale

22

The Royal Stud

The coach bumped slowly over a particularly bad stretch
of road, one left pitted and holed by the winter freeze
and the beating of spring rains. It had been a wet year;
even now, in early summer, there were moist, boggy patches
under the lush growth of gooseberry bushes by the sides of
the road.

Jamie sat beside me on the narrow, padded bench that
formed one seat of the coach. Fergus sprawled in the corner
of the other bench, asleep, and the motion of the coach made
his head rock and sway like the head of a mechanical doll
with a spring for its neck. The air in the coach was warm, and
dust came through the windows in small golden spurts whenever we hit a patch of dry earth.

We had talked desultorily at first of the surrounding
countryside, of the Royal stables at Argentan for which we
were headed, of the small bits of gossip that composed the
daily fare of conversation in Court and business circles. I
might have slept, too, lulled by the coach's rhythm and the
warmth of the day, but the changing contours of my body
made sitting in one position uncomfortable, and my back
ached from the jolting. The baby was becoming increasingly
active, too, and the small flutters of the first movements had
developed into definite small pokes and proddings; pleasant
in their own fashion, but distracting.

"Perhaps ye should have stayed at home, Sassenach,"
Jamie said, frowning slightly as I twisted, adjusting my position yet again.

"I'm all right," I said with a smile. "Just twitchy. And it
would have been a shame to miss all this." I waved at the
coach window, where the broad sweep of fields shone green
as emeralds between the windbreak rows of dark, straight
poplars. Dusty or not, the fresh air of the countryside was rich
and intoxicating after the close, fetid smells of the city and
the medicinal stenches of L'Hôpital des Anges.

Louis had agreed, as a gesture of cautious amity toward

the English diplomatic overtures, to allow the Duke of Sandringham to purchase four Percheron broodmares from the
Royal stud at Argentan, with which to improve the bloodlines
of the small herd of draft horses which His Grace maintained
in England. His Grace was therefore visiting Argentan today,
and had invited Jamie along to give advice on which mares
should be chosen. The invitation was given at an evening
party, and one thing leading to another, the visit had ended
up as a full-scale picnic expedition, involving four coaches
and several of the ladies and gentlemen of the Court.

   "It's a good sign, don't you think?" I asked, with a cautious glance to be sure our companions were indeed fast
asleep. "Louis giving the Duke permission to buy horses, I
mean. If he's making gestures toward the English, then he's
presumably not inclined to be sympathetic to James Stuart—
at least not openly."

   Jamie shook his head. He declined absolutely to wear a
wig, and the bold, clean shape of his polled head had occasioned no little excitement at Court. It had its advantages at
the present moment; while a faint sheen of perspiration
glowed on the bridge of his long, straight nose, he wasn't
nearly as wilted as I.

   "No, I'm fairly sure now that Louis means to have nothing to do with the Stuarts—at least so far as any move toward
restoration goes. Monsieur Duverney assures me that the
Council is entirely opposed to any such thing; while Louis
may eventually yield to the Pope's urgings so far as to make
Charles a small allowance, he isna disposed to bring the
Stuarts into any kind of prominence in France, wi' Geordie of
England looking over his shoulder." He wore his plaid today
pinned with a brooch at the shoulder—a beautiful thing his
sister had sent him from Scotland, made in the shape of two
running stags, bodies bent so that they joined in a circle,
heads and tails touching. He pulled up a fold of the plaid and
wiped his face with it.

   "I think I've spoken with every banker in Paris of any
substance over the last months, and they're united in basic
disinterest." He smiled wryly. "Money's none so plentiful that
anyone wants to back a dicey proposition like the Stuart restoration."

"And that," I said, stretching my back with a groan, "leaves Spain."

Jamie nodded. "It does. And Dougal MacKenzie." He looked smug, and I sat up, intrigued.

"Have you heard from him?" Despite an initial wariness, Dougal had accepted Jamie as a devoted fellow Jacobite, and the usual crop of coded letters had been augmented by a series of discreet communications sent by Dougal from Spain, meant to be read by Jamie and passed on to Charles Stuart.

"I have indeed." I could tell from his expression that it was good news, and it was—though not for the Stuarts.

"Philip has declined to lend any assistance to the Stuarts," Jamie said. "He's had word from the papal office, ye ken; he's to keep awa' from the whole question of the Scottish throne."

"Do we know why?" The latest interception from a papal messenger had contained several letters, but as these were all addressed to James or Charles Stuart, they might well contain no reference to His Holiness's conversations with Spain.

"Dougal thinks he knows." Jamie laughed. "He's fair disgusted, is Dougal. Said he'd been kept cooling his heels in Toledo for nearly a month, and sent awa' at last with no more than a vague promise of aid 'in the fullness of time, *Deo volente.*'" His deep voice captured a pious intonation perfectly, and I laughed myself.

"Benedict wants to avoid friction between Spain and France; he doesna want Philip and Louis wasting money that he might have a use for, ye ken," he added cynically. "It's hardly fitting for a pope to say so, but Benedict has his doubts as to whether a Catholic king could hold England anymore. Scotland's got its Catholic chiefs among the Highland clans, but it's some time since England owned a Catholic king— likely to be the hell of a lot longer before they do again—*Deo volente*," he added, grinning.

He scratched his head, ruffling the short red-gold hair above his temple. "It looks verra dim for the Stuarts, Sassenach, and that's good news. No, there'll be no aid from the Bourbon monarchs. The only thing that concerns me now is this investment Charles Stuart's made with the Comte St. Germain."

"You don't think it's just a business arrangement, then?"

"Well, it is," he said, frowning, "and yet there's more behind it. I've heard talk, aye?"

While the banking families of Paris were not inclined to take the Young Pretender to the throne of Scotland with any seriousness, that situation might easily change, were Charles Stuart suddenly to have money to invest.

"His Highness tells me he's been talking to the Gobelins," Jamie said. "St. Germain introduced him; otherwise they'd not give him the time o' day. And old Gobelin thinks him a wastrel and a fool, and so does one of the Gobelin sons. The other, though—he says that he'll wait and see; if Charles succeeds with this venture, then perhaps he can put other opportunities in his way."

"Not at all good," I observed.

Jamie shook his head. "No. Money breeds money, ye ken. Let him succeed at one or two large ventures, and the bankers will begin to listen to him. The man's no great thinker," he said, with a wry twist of his mouth, "but he's verra charming in person; he can persuade people into things against their better judgment. Even so, he'll make no headway without a small bit of capital to his name—but he'll have that, if this investment succeeds."

"Mm." I shifted my position once more, wriggling my toes in their hot leather prison. The shoes had fit when made for me, but my feet were beginning to swell a bit, and my silk stockings were damp with sweat. "Is there anything we can do about it?"

Jamie shrugged, with a lopsided smile. "Pray for bad weather off Portugal, I suppose. Beyond the ship sinking, I dinna see much way for the venture to fail, truth be told. St. Germain has contracts already for the sale of the entire cargo. Both he and Charles Stuart stand to triple their money."

I shivered briefly at the mention of the Comte. I couldn't help recalling Dougal's speculations. I had not told Jamie about Dougal's visit, nor about his speculations as to the Comte's nocturnal activities. I didn't like keeping secrets from him, but Dougal had demanded my silence as his price for helping me in the matter of Jonathan Randall, and I had had little choice but to agree.

Jamie smiled suddenly at me, and stretched out a hand.

"I'll think of something, Sassenach. For now, give me your feet. Jenny said it helped to have me rub her feet when she was wi' child."

I didn't argue, but slipped my feet out of the hot shoes and swung them up onto his lap with a sigh of relief as the air from the window cooled the damp silk over my toes.

His hands were big, and his fingers at once strong and gentle. He rubbed his knuckles down the arch of my foot and I leaned back with a soft moan. We rode silently for several minutes, while I relaxed into a state of mindless bliss.

Head bent over my green silk toes, Jamie remarked casually, "It wasna really a debt, ye ken."

"What wasn't?" Fogged as I was by warm sun and foot massage, I hadn't any idea what he meant.

Not stopping his rubbing, he looked up at me. His expression was serious, though the hint of a smile lit his eyes.

"You said that I owed ye a life, Sassenach, because you'd saved mine for me." He took hold of one big toe and wiggled it. "But I've been reckoning, and I'm none so sure that's true. Seems to me that it's nearly even, taken all in all."

"What you do mean, even?" I tried to pull my foot loose, but he held tight.

"If you've saved my life—and ye have—well, I've saved yours as well, and at least as often. I saved ye from Jack Randall at Fort William, you'll recall—and I took ye from the mob at Cranesmuir, no?"

"Yes," I said cautiously. I had no idea where he was going, but he wasn't just making idle conversation. "I'm grateful for it, of course."

He made a small Scottish noise of dismissal, deep in his throat. "It isna a matter for gratitude, Sassenach, on your part *or* mine—my point is only that it's no a matter of obligation, either." The smile had vanished from his eyes, and he was entirely serious.

"I didna give ye Randall's life as an exchange for my own —it wouldna be a fair trade, for one thing. Close your mouth, Sassenach," he added practically, "flies will get in." There were in fact a number of the insects present; three were resting on Fergus's shirtfront, undisturbed by its constant rise and fall.

"Why did you agree, then?" I stopped struggling, and he

wrapped both hands around my feet, running his thumbs slowly over the curves of my heels.

"Well, it wasna for any of the reasons you tried to make me see. As for Frank," he said, "well, it's true enough that I've taken his wife, and I do pity him for it—more sometimes than others," he added, with an impudent quirk of one eyebrow. "Still, is it any different than if he were my rival here? You had free choice between us, and you chose me—even with such luxuries as hot baths thrown in on his side. Oof!" I jerked one foot loose and drove it into his ribs. He straightened up and grabbed it, in time to prevent me repeating the blow.

"Regretting your choice, are you?"

"Not yet," I said, struggling to repossess my foot, "but I may any minute. Keep talking."

"Well then. I couldna see that the fact that you picked me entitled Frank Randall to particular consideration. Besides," he said frankly, "I'll admit to bein' just a wee bit jealous of the man."

I kicked with my other foot, aiming lower. He caught that one before it landed, twisting my ankle skillfully.

"As for owing him his life, on general principles," he continued, ignoring my attempts to escape, "that's an argument Brother Anselm at the Abbey could answer better than I. Certainly I wouldna kill an innocent man in cold blood. But there again, I've killed men in battle, and is this different?"

I remembered the soldier, and the boy in the snow that I had killed in our escape from Wentworth. I no longer tormented myself with memories of them, but I knew they would never leave me.

He shook his head. "No, there are a good many arguments ye might make about that, but in the end, such choices come down to one: You kill when ye must, and ye live with it after. I remember the face of every man I've killed, and always will. But the fact remains, I am alive and they are not, and that is my only justification, whether it be right or no."

"But that's not true in this case," I pointed out. "It isn't a case of kill or be killed."

He shook his head, dislodging a fly that had settled on his hair. "Now there you're wrong, Sassenach. What it is that lies between Jack Randall and me will be settled only when one of us is dead—and maybe not then. There are ways of killing other than with a knife or a gun, and there are things worse than physical death." His tone softened. "In Ste. Anne, you pulled me back from more than one kind of death, *mo nighean donn,* and never think I don't know it." He shook his head. "Perhaps I do owe you more than you owe me, after all."

He let go my feet and rearranged his long legs. "And that leads me to consider your conscience as well as mine. After all, you had no idea what would happen when ye made your choice, and it's one thing to abandon a man, and another to condemn him to death."

I did not at all like this manner of describing my actions, but I couldn't shirk the facts. I had in fact abandoned Frank, and while I could not regret the choice I had made, still I did and always would regret its necessity. Jamie's next words echoed my thoughts eerily.

He continued, "If ye had known it might mean Frank's— well, his death, shall we say—perhaps you would have chosen differently. Given that ye did choose me, have I the right to make your actions of more consequence than you intended?"

Absorbed in his argument, he had been oblivious of its effect on me. Catching sight of my face now, he stopped suddenly, watching me in silence as we jostled our way through the greens of the countryside.

"I dinna see how it can have been a sin for you to do as ye did, Claire," he said at last, reaching out to lay a hand on my stockinged foot. "I am your lawful husband, as much as he ever was—or will be. You do not even know that ye could have returned to him; *mo nighean donn,* ye might have gone still further back, or gone forward to a different time altogether. You acted as ye thought ye must, and no one can do better than that." He looked up, and the look in his eyes pierced my soul.

"I'm honest enough to say that I dinna care what the right and wrong of it may be, so long as you are here wi' me, Claire," he said softly. "If it was a sin for you to choose me . . . then I would go to the Devil himself and bless him for tempting ye to it." He lifted my foot and gently kissed the tip of my big toe.

I laid my hand on his head; the short hair felt bristly but soft, like a very young hedgehog.

"I don't think it was wrong," I said softly. "But if it was . . . then I'll go to the Devil with you, Jamie Fraser."

He closed his eyes and bowed his head over my foot. He held it so tightly that I could feel the long, slender metatarsals pressed together; still, I didn't pull back. I dug my fingers into his scalp and tugged his hair gently.

"Why then, Jamie? Why did you decide to let Jack Randall live?"

He still gripped my foot, but opened his eyes and smiled at me.

"Well, I thought a number of things, Sassenach, as I walked up and down that evening. For one thing, I thought that you would suffer, if I did kill the filthy scut. I would do, or not do, quite a few things to spare you distress, Sassenach, but—how heavily does your conscience weigh, against my honor?

"No." He shook his head again, disposing of another point. "Each one of us can be responsible only for his own actions and his own conscience. What I do canna be laid to your account, no matter what the effects." He blinked, eyes watering from the dusty wind, and passed a hand across his hair in a vain attempt to smooth the disheveled ends. Clipped short, the spikes of a cowlick stood up on the crest of his skull in a defiant spray.

"Why, then?" I demanded, leaning forward. "You've told me all the reasons why not; what's left?"

He hesitated for a moment, but then met my eyes squarely.

"Because of Charles Stuart, Sassenach. So far we have stopped all the earths, but with this investment of his—well, he might yet succeed in leading an army in Scotland. And if so . . . well, ye ken better than I do what may come, Sassenach."

I did, and the thought turned me cold. I could not help remembering one historian's description of the Highlanders' fate at Culloden—"the dead lay four deep, soaking in rain and their own blood."

The Highlanders, mismanaged and starving, but ferocious to the end, would be wasted in one decisive half-hour. They would be left to lie in heaps, bleeding in a cold April rain, the cause they had cherished for a hundred years dead along with them.

Jamie reached forward suddenly and took my hands.

"I think it will not happen, Claire; I think we will stop him. And if not, then still I dinna expect anything to happen to me. But if it should . . ." He was in deadly earnest now, speaking soft and urgently. "If it does, then I want there to be a place for you; I want someone for you to go to if I am . . . not there to care for you. If it canna be me, then I would have it be a man who loves you." His grasp on my fingers grew tighter; I could feel both rings digging into my flesh, and felt the urgency in his hands.

"Claire, ye know what it cost me to do this for you—to spare Randall's life. Promise me that if the time should come, you'll go back to Frank." His eyes searched my face, deep blue as the sky in the window behind him. "I tried to send ye back twice before. And I thank God ye wouldna go. But if it comes to a third time—then promise me you will go back to him—back to Frank. For that is why I spare Jack Randall for a year—for your sake. Promise me, Claire?"

"Allez! Allez! Montez!" the coachman shouted from above, encouraging the team up a slope. We were nearly there.

"All right," I said at last. "I promise."

The stables at Argentan were clean and airy, redolent of summer and the smell of horses. In an open box stall, Jamie circled a Percheron mare, enamored as a horsefly.

"Ooh, what a bonnie wee lass ye are! Come here, sweetheart, let me see that beautiful fat rump. Mm, aye, that's grand!"

"I wish my husband would talk that way to *me*," remarked the Duchesse de Neve, provoking giggles from the other ladies of the party, who stood in the straw of the central aisle, watching.

"Perhaps he would, Madame, if your own back view provided such stimulation. But then, perhaps your husband does not share my lord Broch Tuarach's appreciation for a finely shaped rump." The Comte St. Germain allowed his eyes to drift over me with a hint of contemptuous amusement. I tried to imagine those black eyes gleaming through the slits of a mask, and succeeded only too well. Unfortunately, the lace of his wrist frills fell well past his knuckles; I couldn't see the fork of his thumb.

Catching the byplay, Jamie leaned comfortably on the mare's broad back, only his head, shoulders and forearms showing above the bulk of the Percheron.

"My lord Broch Tuarach appreciates beauty wherever it may be encountered, Monsieur le Comte; in animal or woman. Unlike some I might name, though, I am capable of telling the difference between the two." He grinned maliciously at St. Germain, then patted the mare's neck in farewell as the party broke out laughing.

Jamie took my arm to lead me toward the next stable, followed more slowly by the rest of the party.

"Ah," he said, inhaling the mixture of horse, harness, manure, and hay as though it were incense. "I do miss the smell of a stable. And the country makes me sick for Scotland."

"Doesn't look a lot like Scotland," I said, squinting in the bright sun as we emerged from the dimness of the stable.

"No, but it's country," he said, "it's clean, and it's green, and there's nay smoke in the air, or sewage underfoot—unless ye count horse dung, which I don't."

The sun of early summer shone on the roofs of Argentan, nestled among gently rolling green hills. The Royal stud was just outside the town, much more solidly constructed than the houses of the King's subjects nearby. The barns and stables were of quarried stone, stone-floored, slate-roofed, and maintained in a condition of cleanliness that surpassed that of L'Hôpital des Anges by a fair degree.

A loud whooping came from behind the corner of the stable, and Jamie stopped short, just in time to avoid Fergus, who shot out in front of us as though fired from a slingshot, hotly pursued by two stable-lads, both a good deal bigger. A dirty green streak of fresh manure down the side of the first boy's face gave some clue as to the cause of the altercation.

With considerable presence of mind, Fergus doubled on his tracks, shot past his pursuers, and whizzed into the middle of the party, whence he took refuge behind the bulwark of Jamie's kilted hips. Seeing their prey thus safely gone to earth, his pursuers glanced fearfully at the oncoming phalanx of courtiers and gowns, exchanged a look of decision, and, as one, turned and loped off.

Seeing them go, Fergus stuck his head out from behind my skirt and yelled something in gutter French that earned him a sharp cuff on the ear from Jamie.

"Off wi' ye," he said brusquely. "And for God's sake, dinna be throwin' horse apples at people bigger than you are. Now, go and keep out of trouble." He followed up this advice with a healthy smack on the seat of the breeches that sent Fergus staggering off in the opposite direction to that taken by his erstwhile assailants.

I had been of two minds as to the wisdom of taking Fergus with us on this expedition, but most of the ladies were bringing pageboys with them, to run errands and carry the baskets of food and other paraphernalia deemed essential to a day's outing. And Jamie had wanted to show the lad a bit of country, feeling that he'd earned a holiday. All well and good, except that Fergus, who had never been outside Paris in his life, had got the exhilaration of air, light, and beautiful huge animals right up his nose, and, demented with excitement, had been in constant trouble since our arrival.

"God knows what he'll do next," I said darkly, looking after Fergus's retreating form. "Set one of the hayricks on fire, I expect."

Jamie was unperturbed at the suggestion.

"He'll be all right. All lads get into manure fights."

"They do?" I turned around, scrutinizing St. Germain, immaculate in white linen, white serge, and white silk, bending courteously to listen to the Duchesse, as she minced slowly across the straw-strewn yard.

"Maybe *you* did," I said. "Not him. Not the Bishop, either, I don't think." I was wondering whether this excursion had been a good idea, at least on my part. Jamie was in his element with the giant Percherons, and the Duke was clearly impressed with him, which was all to the good. On the other hand, my back ached miserably from the carriage ride, and my feet felt hot and swollen, pressing painfully against the tight leather of my shoes.

Jamie looked down at me and smiled, pressing my hand where it lay on his arm.

"None so long now, Sassenach. The guide wants to show us the breeding sheds, and then you and the other ladies can go and sit down wi' the food, while the men stand about makin' crude jests about the size of each other's cock."

"Is that the general effect of watching horses bred?" I asked, fascinated.

"Well, on men it is; I dinna ken what it does to ladies. Keep an ear out, and ye can tell me later."

There was in fact an air of suppressed excitement among the members of the party as we all pressed into the rather cramped quarters of a breeding shed. Stone, like the other buildings, this one was equipped not with partitioned stalls down both sides, but with a small fenced pen, with holding stalls at either side, and a sort of chute or runway along the back, with several gates that could be opened or closed to control a horse's movement.

The building itself was light and airy, owing to huge, unglazed windows that opened at either end, giving a view of a grassy paddock outside. I could see several of the enormous Percheron mares grazing near the edge of this; one or two seemed restless, breaking into a rocking gallop for a few paces, then dropping back to a trot or a walk, shaking heads and manes with a high, whinnying noise. Once, when this happened, there was a loud, nasal scream from one of the holding stalls at the end of the shed, and the paneling shook with the thud of a mighty kick from its inhabitant.

"*He's* ready," a voice murmured appreciatively behind me. "I wonder which is the lucky mademoiselle?"

"The one nearest the gate," the Duchesse suggested, always ready to wager. "Five livres on that one."

"Ah, no! You're wrong, Madame, she's too calm. It will be the little one, under the apple tree, rolling her eyes like a coquette. See how she tosses her head? That one's my choice."

The mares had all stopped at the sound of the stallion's cry, lifting inquiring noses and flicking their ears nervously. The restless ones tossed their heads and whickered; one stretched her neck and let out a long, high call.

"That one," Jamie said quietly, nodding at her. "Hear her call him?"

"And what is she saying, my lord?" the Bishop asked, a glint in his eye.

Jamie shook his head solemnly.

"It is a song, my lord, but one that a man of the cloth is deaf to—or should be," he added, to gales of laughter.

Sure enough, it was the mare who had called who was chosen. Once inside, she stopped dead, head up, and stood testing the air with flaring nostrils. The stallion could smell her; his cries echoed eerily off the timbered roof, so loud that conversation was impossible.

No one wanted to talk now, anyway. Uncomfortable as I was, I could feel the quick tingle of arousal through my breasts, and a tightening of my swollen belly as the mare once more answered the stallion's call.

Percherons are very large horses. A big one stands over five feet at the shoulder, and the rump of a well-fed mare is almost a yard across, a pale, dappled gray or shining black, adorned with a waterfall of black hair, thick as my arm at the root of it.

The stallion burst from his stall toward the tethered mare with a suddenness that made everyone fall back from the fence. Puffs of dust flew up in clouds as the huge hooves struck the packed dirt of the pen, and drops of saliva flew from his open mouth. The groom who had opened his stall door jumped aside, tiny and insignificant next to the magnificent fury let loose in the pen.

The mare curvetted and squealed in alarm, but then he was on her, and his teeth closed on the sturdy arch of her neck, forcing her head down into submission. The great swathe of her tail swept high, leaving her naked, exposed to his lust.

"Jésus," whispered Monsieur Prudhomme.

It took very little time, but it seemed a lot longer, watching the heaving of sweat-darkened flanks, and the play of light on swirling hair and the sheen of great muscles, tense and straining in the flexible agony of mating.

Everyone was very quiet as we left the shed. Finally the Duke laughed, nudged Jamie, and said, "You are accustomed to such sights, my lord Broch Tuarach?"

"Aye," Jamie answered. "I've seen it a good many times."

"Ah?" the Duke said. "And tell me, my lord, how does the sight make you feel, after so many times?"

One corner of Jamie's mouth twitched as he replied, but he remained otherwise straight-faced.

"Verra modest, Your Grace," he said.

➤

"What a sight!" the Duchesse de Neve said. She broke a biscuit, dreamy-eyed, and munched it slowly. "So arousing, was it not?"

"What a prick, you mean," said Madame Prudhomme, rather coarsely. "I wish Philibert had one like that. As it is . . ." She cocked an eyebrow toward a plate of tiny sausages, each perhaps two inches long, and the ladies seated on the picnic cloth broke into giggles.

"A bit of chicken, please, Paul," said the Comtesse St. Germain to her pageboy. She was young, and the bawdy conversation of the older ladies was making her blush. I wondered just what sort of marriage she had with St. Germain; he never took her out in public, save on occasions like this, where the presence of the Bishop prevented his appearing with one of his mistresses.

"Bah," said Madame Montresor, one of the ladies-in-waiting, whose husband was a friend of the Bishop's. "Size isn't everything. What difference if it's the size of a stallion's, if he lasts no longer than one? Less than two minutes? I ask you, what good is that?" She held up a cornichon between two fingers and delicately licked the tiny pale-green pickle, the pink tip of her tongue pointed and dainty. "It isn't what they have in their breeches, I say; it's what they do with it."

Madame Prudhomme snorted. "Well, if you find one who knows how to do anything with it but poke it into the nearest hole, tell me. I would be interested to see what else can be done with a thing like that."

"At least you have one who's interested," broke in the Duchesse de Neve. She cast a glance of disgust at her husband, huddled with the other men near one of the paddocks, watching a harnessed mare being put through her paces.

"Not tonight, my dearest," she imitated the sonorous, nasal tones of her husband to perfection. "I am *fatigued.*" She put a hand to her brow and rolled her eyes up. "The press of business is so wearing." Encouraged by the giggles, she went on with her imitation, now widening her eyes in horror and crossing her hands protectively over her lap. "What, *again*? Do you not know that to expend the male essence gratuitously is to court ill-health? Is it not enough that your demands have worn me to a nubbin, Mathilde? Do you wish me to have an *attack*?"

The ladies cackled and screeched with laughter, loud enough to attract the attention of the Bishop, who waved at us and smiled indulgently, provoking further gales of hilarity.

"Well, at least he is not expending all his male essence in brothels—or elsewhere," said Madame Prudhomme, with an eloquently pitying glance at the Comtesse St. Germain.

"No," said Mathilde gloomily. "He hoards it as though it were gold. You'd think there was no more to be had, the way he . . . oh, Your Grace! Will you not have a cup of wine?" She smiled charmingly up at the Duke, who had approached quietly from behind. He stood smiling at the ladies, one fair brow slightly arched. If he had heard the subject of our conversation, he gave no sign of it.

Seating himself beside me on the cloth, His Grace made casual, witty conversation with the ladies, his oddly high-pitched voice forming no contrast to theirs. While he seemed to pay close attention to the conversation, I noticed that his eyes strayed periodically to the small cluster of men who stood by the paddock fence. Jamie's kilt was bright even amid the gorgeous cut velvets and stiffened silk.

I had had some hesitation in meeting the Duke again. After all, our last visit had ended in the arrest of Jonathan Randall, upon my accusation of attempted rape. But the Duke had been all charming urbanity on this outing, with no mention of either of the Randall brothers. Neither had there been any public mention of the arrest; whatever the Duke's diplomatic activities, they seemed to rank highly enough to merit a Royal seal of silence.

On the whole, I welcomed the Duke's appearance at the picnic cloth. For one thing, his presence kept the ladies from asking me—as some bold souls did every so often, at parties —whether it was true about what Scotsmen wore beneath their kilts. Given the mood of the present party, I didn't think my customary reply of "Oh, the usual" would suffice.

"Your husband has a fine eye for horses," the Duke observed to me, freed for a moment when the Duchesse de Neve, on his other side, leaned across the cloth to talk to Madame Prudhomme. "He tells me that both his father and his uncle kept small but quite fine stables in the Highlands."

"Yes, that's true." I sipped my wine. "But you've visited Colum MacKenzie at Castle Leoch; surely you've seen his stable for yourself." I had in fact first met the Duke at Leoch the year before, though the meeting had been brief; he had left on a hunting expedition shortly before I was arrested for witchcraft. I thought surely he must have known about that, but if so, he gave no sign of it.

"Of course." The Duke's small, shrewd blue eyes darted left, then right, to see whether he was observed, then shifted into English. "At the time, your husband informed me that he did not reside upon his own estates, owing to an unfortunate —and mistaken—charge of murder laid against him by the English Crown. I wondered, my lady, whether that charge of outlawry still holds?"

"There's still a price on his head," I said bluntly.

The Duke's expression of polite interest didn't change. He reached absently for one of the small sausages on the platter.

"That is not an irremediable matter," he said quietly. "After my encounter with your husband at Leoch, I made some inquiries—oh, suitably discreet, I assure you, my dear lady. And I think that the matter might be arranged without undue difficulty, given a word in the right ear—from the right sources."

This was interesting. Jamie had first told the Duke of Sandringham about his outlawry at Colum MacKenzie's suggestion, in the hopes that the Duke might be persuaded to intervene in the case. As Jamie had not in fact committed the crime in question, there could be little evidence against him; it was quite possible that the Duke, a powerful voice among the nobles of England, could indeed arrange to have the charges dismissed.

"Why?" I said. "What do you want in return?"

The sketchy blond brows shot upward, and he smiled, showing small white even teeth.

"My word, you *are* direct, are you not? Might it not be

only that I appreciate your husband's expertise and assistance in the selection of horses, and would like to see him restored to a place where that skill might once again be profitably exercised?"

"It might be, but it isn't," I said. I caught Madame Prudhomme's sharp eyes on us, and smiled pleasantly at the Duke. "Why?"

He popped the sausage whole in to his mouth and chewed it slowly, his bland round face reflecting nothing more than enjoyment of the day and the meal. At last he swallowed and patted his mouth delicately with one of the linen napkins.

"Well," he said, "as a matter of supposition only, you understand—"

I nodded, and he went on. "*As* a matter of supposition, then, perhaps we may suppose that your husband's recent friendship with—a certain personage recently arrived from Rome? Ah, I see you understand me. Yes. Let us suppose that that friendship has become a matter of some concern to certain parties who would prefer this personage to return peaceably to Rome—or alternatively, to settle in France, though Rome would be better—safer, you know?"

"I see." I took a sausage myself. They were richly spiced, and little bursts of garlic wafted up my nose at each bite. "And these parties take a sufficiently serious view of this friendship to offer a dismissal of the charges against my husband in return for its severance? Again, why? My husband is no one of great importance."

"Not now," the Duke agreed. "But he may be in future. He has linkages to several powerful interests among the French banking families, and more among the merchants. He is also received at Court, and has some access to Louis's ear. In short, if he does not at present hold the power to command substantial sums of money and influence, he is likely to do so soon. He is also a member of not one but *two* of the more powerful Highland clans. And the parties who wish the personage in question to return to Rome harbor a not unreasonable fear that this influence might be exerted in undesirable directions. So much better if your husband were to return—his good name restored—to his lands in Scotland, do you not think?"

"It's a thought," I said. It was also a bribe, and an attractive one. Sever all connection with Charles Stuart, and be free to return to Scotland and Lallybroch, without the risk of being hanged. The removal of a possibly troublesome supporter of the Stuarts, at no expense to the Crown, was an attractive proposition from the English side, too.

I eyed the Duke, trying to figure out just where he fitted in to the scheme of things. Ostensibly an envoy from George II, Elector of Hanover and King—so long as James Stuart remained in Rome—of England, he could well have a dual purpose in his visit to France. To engage with Louis in the delicate exchange of civility and threat that constituted diplomacy, and simultaneously to quash the specter of a fresh Jacobite rising? Several of Charles's usual coterie had disappeared of late, pleading the press of urgent business abroad. Bought off or scared away? I wondered.

The bland countenance gave no clue to his thoughts. He pushed back the wig from a balding brow and scratched his head unselfconsciously.

"Do think about it, my dear," he urged. "And when you have thought—speak to your husband."

"Why don't you speak to him yourself?"

He shrugged and took more sausages, three this time. "I find that so often men are more amenable to a word spoken from the home quarter, from one they trust, rather than to what they may perceive as pressure from an outside source." He smiled. "There is the matter of pride to be considered; that must be handled delicately. And for delicate handling—well, they do talk of 'the woman's touch,' do they not?"

I hadn't time to respond to this, when a shout from the main stable jerked all heads in that direction.

A horse was coming toward us, up the narrow alley between the main stable and the long, open shed that held the forge. A Percheron colt, and a young one, no more than two or three, judging from the dappling of his hide. Even young Percherons are big, and the colt seemed huge, as he blundered to and fro at a slow trot, tail lashing from side to side. Plainly the colt was not yet broken to a saddle; the massive shoulders twitched in an effort to dislodge the small form that straddled his neck, both hands buried deep in the thick black mane.

"Bloody hell, it's Fergus!" The ladies, disturbed by the shouting, had all gotten to their feet by now, and were peering interestedly at the sight.

I didn't realize that the men had joined us until one woman said, "But how dangerous it seems! Surely the boy will be injured if he falls!"

"Well, if he doesna hurt himself falling off, I'll attend to it directly, once I've got my hands on the wee bugger," said a grim voice behind me. I turned to see Jamie peering over my head at the rapidly approaching horse.

"Should you get him off?" I asked.

He shook his head. "No, let the horse take care of it."

In fact, the horse seemed more bewildered than frightened by the strange weight on his back. The dappled gray skin twitched and shivered as though beset by hordes of flies, and the colt shook its head confusedly, as though wondering what was going on.

As for Fergus, his legs were stretched nearly at right angles across the Percheron's broad back; clearly the only hold he had on the horse was his death-grip on the mane. At that, he might have managed to slide down or at least tumble off unscathed, had the victims of the manure fight not completed their plan to exact a measure of revenge.

Two or three grooms were following the horse at a cautious distance, blocking the alleyway behind it. Another had succeeded in running ahead, and opening the gate to an empty paddock that stood near us. The gate was between the group of visiting picnickers and the end of the alleyway between the buildings; clearly the intention was to nudge the horse quietly into the paddock, where it could trample Fergus or not as it chose, but at least would itself be safe from escape or injury.

Before this could be accomplished, though, a lithe form popped its head through a small loft window, high above the alleyway. The spectators intent on the horse, no one noticed but me. The boy in the loft observed, withdrew, and reappeared almost at once, holding a large flake of hay in both hands. Judging the moment to a nicety, he dropped it as Fergus and his mount passed directly beneath.

The effect was much like a bomb going off. There was an explosion of hay where Fergus had been, and the colt gave a

panicked whinny, got its hindquarters under it, and took off
like a Derby winner, heading straight for the little knot of
courtiers, who scattered to the four winds, screeching like
geese.

Jamie had flung himself on me, pushing me out of the
way and knocking me to the ground in the process. Now he
rose off my supine form, cursing fluently in Gaelic. Without
pausing to inquire after my welfare, he raced off in the direction taken by Fergus.

The horse was rearing and twisting, altogether spooked,
churning forelegs keeping at bay a small gang of grooms and
stable-lads, all of whom were rapidly losing their professional
calm at the thought of one of the King's valuable horses damaging itself before their eyes.

By some miracle of stubbornness or fear, Fergus was still
in place, skinny legs flailing as he slithered and bounced on
the heaving back. The grooms were all shouting at him to let
go, but he ignored this advice, eyes squeezed tight shut as he
clung to the two handfuls of horsehair like a lifeline. One of
the grooms was carrying a pitchfork; he waved this menacingly in the air, causing a shriek of dismay from Madame
Montresor, who plainly thought he meant to skewer the child.

The shriek didn't ease the colt's nerves to any marked
extent. It danced and skittered, backing away from the people
who were beginning to surround it. While I didn't think the
groom actually intended to stab Fergus off the horse's back,
there was a real danger that the child would be trampled if he
fell off—and I didn't see how he was going to avoid that fate
for much longer. The horse made a sudden dash for a small
clump of trees that grew near the paddock, either seeking
shelter from the mob, or possibly having concluded that the
incubus on its back might be scraped off on a branch.

As it passed beneath the first branches, I caught a
glimpse of red tartan among the greenery, and then there was
a flash of red as Jamie launched himself from the shelter of a
tree. His body struck the colt a glancing blow and he tumbled
to the ground in a flurry of plaid and bare legs that would
have revealed to a discerning observer that this particular
Scotsman wasn't wearing anything under his kilt at the moment.

The party of courtiers rushed up as one, concentrating

on the fallen Lord Broch Tuarach, as the grooms pursued the disappearing horse on the other side of the trees.

Jamie lay flat on his back under the beech trees, his face a dead greenish-white, both eyes and mouth wide open. Both arms were locked tight around Fergus, who clung to his chest like a leech. Jamie blinked at me as I dashed up to him, and made a faint effort at a smile. The faint wheezings from his open mouth deepened into a shallow panting, and I relaxed in relief; he'd only had his wind knocked out.

Finally realizing that he was no longer moving, Fergus raised a cautious head. Then he sat bolt upright on his employer's stomach and said enthusiastically, "That was fun, milord! Can we do it again?"

Jamie had pulled a muscle in his thigh during the rescue at Argentan, and was limping badly by the time we returned to Paris. He sent Fergus—none the worse either for the escapade or the scolding that followed it—down to the kitchen to seek his supper, and sank into a chair by the hearth, rubbing the swollen leg.

"Hurt much?" I asked sympathetically.

"A bit. All it needs is rest, though." He stood up and stretched luxuriously, long arms nearly reaching the blackened oak beams above the mantel. "Cramped in that coach; I'd've sooner ridden."

"Mmm. So would I." I rubbed the small of my back, aching with the strain of the trip. The ache seemed to press downward through my pelvis to my legs—joints loosening from pregnancy, I supposed.

I ran an exploratory hand over Jamie's leg, then gestured to the chaise.

"Come and lie on your side. I've some nice ointment I can rub your leg with; it might ease the ache a bit."

"Well, if ye dinna mind." He rose stiffly and lay down on his left side, kilt pulled above his knee.

I opened my medicine box and rummaged through the boxes and jars. Agrimony, slippery elm, pellitory-of-the-wall . . . ah, there it was. I pulled out the small blue glass jar Monsieur Forez had given me and unscrewed the lid. I sniffed cautiously; salves went rancid easily, but this one appeared to have a good proportion of salt mixed in for preservation. It had a nice mellow scent, and was a beautiful color—the rich yellow-white of fresh cream.

I scooped out a good bit of the salve and spread it down the long muscle of the thigh, pushing Jamie's kilt above his hip to keep out of the way. The flesh of his leg was warm; not the heat of infection, only the normal heat of a young male body, flushed with exercise and the glowing pulse of health. I massaged the cream gently into the skin, feeling the swell of the hard muscle, probing the divisions of quadriceps and hamstring. Jamie made a small grunting sound as I rubbed harder.

"Hurt?" I asked.

"Aye, a bit, but don't stop," he answered. "Feels as though it's doing me good." He chuckled. "I wouldna admit it to any but you, Sassenach, but it *was* fun. I havena moved like that in months."

"Glad you enjoyed yourself," I said dryly, taking another dab of cream. "I had an interesting time myself." Not pausing in the massage, I told him of Sandringham's offer.

He grunted in response, wincing slightly as I hit a tender spot. "So Colum was right, when he thought the man might be able to help with the charges against me."

"So it would seem. I suppose the question is—do you want to take him up on it?" I tried not to hold my breath, as I waited for his answer. For one thing, I knew what it would be; the Frasers as a family were renowned for stubbornness, and despite his mother's having been a MacKenzie, Jamie was a Fraser through and through. Having made up his mind to stopping Charles Stuart, he was hardly likely to abandon the effort. Still, it was tempting bait—to me, as well as to him. To be able to go back to Scotland, to his home; to live in peace.

But there was another rub, of course. If we did go back, leaving Charles's plans to run their course into the future I knew, then any peace in Scotland would be short-lived indeed.

Jamie gave a small snort, apparently having followed my own thought processes. "Well, I'll tell ye, Sassenach. If I thought that Charles Stuart might succeed—might free Scotland from English rule—then I would give my lands, my liberty, and life itself to help him. Fool he might be, but a royal fool, and not an ungallant one, I think." He sighed.

"But I know the man, and I've talked with him—and with all the Jacobites that fought with his father. And given what you tell me will happen if it comes to a Rising again . . . I dinna see that I've any choice but to stay, Sassenach. Once he is stopped, then there may be a chance to go back— or there may not. But for now, I must decline His Grace's offer wi' thanks."

I patted his thigh gently. "That's what I thought you'd say."

He smiled at me, then glanced down at the yellowish cream that coated my fingers. "What's that stuff?"

"Something Monsieur Forez gave me. He didn't say what it's called. I don't think it's got any active ingredients, but it's a nice, greasy sort of cream."

The body under my hands stiffened and Jamie glanced over his shoulder at the blue jar.

"Monsieur Forez gave it ye?" he said uneasily.

"Yes," I answered, surprised. "What's the matter?" For he had put aside my cream-smeared hands and, swinging his legs over the side of the chaise longue, was reaching for a towel.

"Has that jar a fleur-de-lys on the lid, Sassenach?" he asked, wiping the ointment from his leg.

"Yes, it has," I said. "Jamie, what's wrong with that salve?" The look on his face was peculiar in the extreme; it kept vacillating between dismay and amusement.

"Oh, I wouldna say there's anything *wrong* about it, Sassenach," he answered finally. Having rubbed his leg hard enough to leave the curly red-gold hair bristling above reddened skin, he tossed the towel aside and looked thoughtfully at the jar.

"Monsieur Forez must think rather highly of ye, Sassenach," he said. "It's expensive stuff, that."

"But—"

"It's not that I dinna appreciate it," he assured me hastily. "It's only that havin' come within a day's length of being one of the ingredients myself, it makes me feel a bit queer."

"Jamie!" I felt my voice rising. "*What* is that stuff?" I grabbed the towel, hastily swabbing my salve-coated hands.

"Hanged-men's grease," he answered reluctantly.

"H-h-h . . ." I couldn't even get the word out, and started over. "You mean . . ." Goose bumps rippled up my arms, raising the fine hairs like pins in a cushion.

"Er, aye. Rendered fat from hanged criminals." He spoke cheerfully, regaining his composure as quickly as I was losing mine. "Verra good for the rheumatism and joint-ill, they say."

I recalled the tidy way in which Monsieur Forez had gathered up the results of his operations in L'Hôpital des Anges, and the odd look on Jamie's face when he had seen the tall *chirurgien* escort me home. My knees were watery, and I felt my stomach flip like a pancake.

"Jamie! Who in bloody fucking hell is Monsieur Forez?" I nearly screamed.

Amusement was definitely getting the upper hand in his expression.

"He's the public hangman for the Fifth Arrondissement, Sassenach. I thought ye knew."

Jamie returned damp and chilled from the stableyard, where he had gone to scrub himself, the required ablutions being on a scale greater than the bedroom basin could provide.

"Don't worry, it's all off," he assured me, skinning out of his shirt and sliding naked beneath the covers. His flesh was rough and chilly with gooseflesh, and he shivered briefly as he took me in his arms.

"What is it, Sassenach? I don't still smell of it, do I?" he asked, as I huddled stiff under the bedclothes, hugging myself with my arms.

"No," I said. "I'm scared. Jamie, I'm bleeding."

"Jesus," he said softly. I could feel the sudden thrill of fear that ran through him at my words, identical to the one that ran through me. He held me close to him, smoothing my hair and stroking my back, but both of us felt the awful helplessness in the face of physical disaster that made his actions futile. Strong as he was, he couldn't protect me; willing he might be, but he couldn't help. For the first time, I wasn't safe in his arms, and the knowledge terrified both of us.

"D'ye think—" he began, then broke off and swallowed. I could feel the tremor run down his throat and hear the gulp as he swallowed his fear. "Is it bad, Sassenach? Can ye tell?"

"No," I said. I held him tighter, trying to find an anchorage. "I don't know. It isn't heavy bleeding; not yet, anyway."

The candle was still alight. He looked down at me, eyes dark with worry.

"Had I better fetch someone to ye, Claire? A healer, one of the women from the Hôpital?"

I shook my head and licked dry lips.

"No. I don't . . . I don't think there's anything they could do." It was the last thing I wanted to say; more than anything, I wanted there to be someone we could find who knew how to make it all right. But I remembered my early nurse's training, the few days I had spent on the obstetrical ward, and the words of one of the doctors, shrugging as he left the bed of a patient who'd had a miscarriage. "There's really nothing you can do," he'd said. "If they're going to lose a child, they generally do, no matter what you try. Bed rest is really the only thing, and even that often won't do it."

"It may be nothing," I said, trying to hearten both of us. "It isn't unusual for women to have slight bleeding sometimes during pregnancy." It wasn't unusual—during the first three months. I was more than five months along, and this was by no means usual. Still, there were many things that could cause bleeding, and not all of them were serious.

"It may be all right," I said. I laid a hand on my stomach, pressing gently. I felt an immediate response from the occupant, a lazy, stretching push that at once made me feel better. I felt a rush of passionate gratitude that made tears come to my eyes.

"Sassenach, what can I do?" Jamie whispered. His hand came around me and lay over mine, cupping my threatened abdomen.

I put my other hand on top of his, and held on.

"Just pray," I said. "Pray for us, Jamie."

23

The Best-laid Plans of Mice and Men . . .

The bleeding had stopped by the morning. I rose very cautiously, but all remained well. Still, it was obvious that the time had come for me to stop working at L'Hôpital des Anges, and I sent Fergus with a note of explanation and apology to Mother Hildegarde. He returned with her prayers and good wishes, and a bottle of a brownish elixir much esteemed—according to the accompanying note—by *les maîtresses sage-femme* for the prevention of miscarriage. After Monsieur Forez's salve, I was more than a little dubious about using any medication I hadn't prepared myself, but a careful sniff reassured me that at least the ingredients were purely botanical.

After considerable hesitation, I drank a spoonful. The liquid was bitter and left a nasty taste in my mouth, but the simple act of doing something—even something I thought likely to be useless—made me feel better. I spent the greater part of each day now lying on the chaise longue in my room, reading, dozing, sewing, or simply staring into space with my hands over my belly.

When I was alone, that is. When he was home, Jamie spent most of his time with me, talking over the day's business, or discussing the most recent Jacobite letters. King James had apparently been told of his son's proposed investment in port wine, and approved it wholeheartedly as ". . . a very sounde scheme, which I cannot but feel will go a great way in providing for you as I should wish to see you established in France."

"So James thinks the money's intended merely to establish Charles as a gentleman, and give him some position here," I said. "Do you think that could be all he has in mind? Louise was here this afternoon; she says Charles came to see her last week—insisted on seeing her, though she refused to receive him at first. She says he was very excited and puffed up about something, but he wouldn't tell her what; just kept hinting mysteriously about something great he was about to do. 'A great adventure' is what she says he said. That doesn't sound like a simple investment in port, does it?"

"It doesn't." Jamie looked grim at the thought.

"Hm," I said. "Well, all things taken together, it seems a good bet that Charles isn't meaning just to settle down upon the profits of his venture and become an upstanding Paris merchant."

"If I were a wagering man, I'd lay my last garter on it," Jamie said. "The question now is, how do we stop him?"

The answer came several days later, after any amount of discussion and useless suggestions. Murtagh was with us in my bedroom, having brought up several bolts of cloth from the docks for me.

"They say there's been an outbreak of pox in Portugal," he observed, dumping the expensive watered silk on the bed as though it were a load of used burlap. "There was a ship carrying iron from Lisbon came in this morning, and the harbor master was over it with a toothcomb, him and three assistants. Found naught, though." Spotting the brandy bottle on my table, he poured a tumbler half-full and drank it like water, in large, healthy swallows. I watched this performance openmouthed, pulled from the spectacle only by Jamie's exclamation.

"Pox?"

"Aye," said Murtagh, pausing between swallows. "Smallpox." He lifted the glass again and resumed his systematic refreshment.

"Pox," Jamie muttered to himself. "Pox."

Slowly, the frown left his face and the vertical crease between his eyebrows disappeared. A deeply contemplative look came over him, and he lay back in his chair, hands linked behind his neck, staring fixedly at Murtagh. The hint of a smile twitched his wide mouth sideways.

Murtagh observed this process with considerable skeptical resignation. He drained his cup and sat stolidly hunched on his stool as Jamie sprang to his feet and began circling the little clansman, whistling tunelessly through his teeth.

"I take it you have an idea?" I said.

"Oh, aye," he said, and began to laugh softly to himself. "Oh, aye, that I have."

He turned to me, eyes alight with mischief and inspiration.

"Have ye anything in your box of medicines that would make a man feverish? Or give him flux? Or spots?"

"Well, yes," I said slowly, thinking. "There's rosemary. Or cayenne. And cascara, of course, for diarrhea. Why?"

He looked at Murtagh, grinning widely, then, overcome with his idea, cackled and ruffled his kinsman's hair, so it stuck up in black spikes. Murtagh glared at him, exhibiting a strong resemblance to Louise's pet monkey.

"Listen," Jamie said, bending toward us conspiratorially. "What if the Comte St. Germain's ship comes back from Portugal wi' pox aboard?"

I stared at him. "Have you lost your mind?" I inquired politely. "What if it did?"

"If it did," Murtagh interrupted, "they'd lose the cargo. It would be burnt or dumped in the harbor, by law." A gleam of interest showed in the small black eyes. "And how d'ye mean to manage that, lad?"

Jamie's exhilaration dropped slightly, though the light in his eyes remained.

"Well," he admitted, "I havena got it thought out all the way as yet, but for a start . . ."

The plan took several days of discussion and research to refine, but was at last settled. Cascara to cause flux had been rejected as being too debilitating in action. However, I'd found some good substitutes in one of the herbals Master Raymond had lent me.

Murtagh, armed with a pouch full of rosemary essence, nettle juice, and madder root, would set out at the end of the week for Lisbon, where he would gossip among the sailors' taverns, find out the ship chartered by the Comte St. Germain, and arrange to take passage on it, meanwhile sending back word of the ship's name and sailing date to Paris.

"No, that's common," said Jamie, in answer to my question as to whether the captain might not find this behavior fishy. "Almost all cargo ships carry a few passengers; however many they can squeeze between decks. And Murtagh will have enough money to make him a welcome addition, even if they have to give him the captain's cabin." He wagged an admonitory finger at Murtagh.

"And get a cabin, d'ye hear? I don't care what it costs; ye'll need privacy for taking the herbs, and we dinna want the chance of someone seeing ye, if you've naught but a hammock slung in the bilges." He surveyed his godfather with a critical eye. "Have ye a decent coat? If you go aboard looking like a beggar, they're like to hurl ye off into the harbor before they find out what ye've got in your sporran."

"Mmphm," said Murtagh. The little clansman usually contributed little to the discussion, but what he did say was cogent and to the point. "And when do I take the stuff?" he asked.

I pulled out the sheet of paper on which I had written the instructions and dosages.

"Two spoonfuls of the rose madder—that's this one"—I tapped the small clear-glass bottle, filled with a dark pinkish fluid—"to be taken four hours before you plan to demonstrate your symptoms. Take another spoonful every two hours after the first dose—we don't know how long you'll have to keep it up."

I handed him the second bottle, this one of green glass filled with a purplish-black liquor. "This is concentrated essence of rosemary leaves. This one acts faster. Drink about one-quarter of the bottle half an hour before you mean to show yourself; you should start flushing within half an hour. It wears off quickly, so you'll need to take more when you can manage inconspicuously." I took another, smaller vial from my medicine box. "And once you're well advanced with the 'fever,' then you can rub the nettle juice on your arms and face, to raise blisters. Do you want to keep these instructions?"

He shook his head decidedly. "Nay, I'll remember. There's more risk to being found wi' the paper than there is to forgetting how much to take." He turned to Jamie.

"And you'll meet the ship at Oviedo, lad?"

Jamie nodded. "Aye. She's bound to make port there; all the wine haulers do, to take on fresh water. If by chance she doesna do so, then—" He shrugged. "I shall hire a boat and try to catch her up. So long as I board her before we reach Le Havre, it should be all right, but best if we can do it while we're still close off the coast of Spain. I dinna mean to spend longer at sea than I must." He pointed with his chin at the bottle in Murtagh's hand.

"Ye'd best wait to take the stuff 'til ye see me come on board. With no witnesses, the captain might take the easy way out and just put ye astern in the night."

Murtagh grunted. "Aye, he might try." He touched the hilt of his dirk, and there was the faintest ironic emphasis on the word "try."

Jamie frowned at him. "Dinna forget yourself. You're meant to be suffering from the pox. With luck, they'll be afraid to touch ye, but just in case . . . wait 'til I'm within call and we're well offshore."

"Mmphm."

I looked from one to the other of the two men. Farfetched as it was, it might conceivably work. If the captain of the ship could be convinced that one of his passengers was infected with smallpox, he would under no circumstances take his ship into the harbor at Le Havre, where the French health restrictions would require its destruction. And, faced with the necessity of sailing back with his cargo to Lisbon and losing all profit on the voyage, or losing two weeks at Oviedo while word was sent to Paris, he might very well instead consent to sell the cargo to the wealthy Scottish merchant who had just come aboard.

The impersonation of a smallpox victim was the crucial role in this masquerade. Jamie had volunteered to be the guinea pig for testing the herbs, and they had worked magnificently on him. His fair skin had flushed dark red within minutes, and the nettle juice raised immediate blisters that could easily be mistaken for those of pox by a ship's doctor or a panicked captain. And should any doubt remain, the madder-stained urine gave an absolutely perfect illusion of a man pissing blood as the smallpox attacked his kidneys.

"Christ!" Jamie had exclaimed, startled despite himself at the first demonstration of the herb's efficacy.

"Oh, jolly good!" I said, peering over his shoulder at the white porcelain chamber pot and its crimson contents. "That's better than I expected."

"Oh, aye? How long does it take to wear off, then?" Jamie had asked, looking down rather nervously.

"A few hours, I think," I told him. "Why? Does it feel odd?"

"Not odd, exactly," he said, rubbing. "It itches a bit."

"That's no the herb," Murtagh interjected dourly. "It's just the natural condition for a lad of your age."

Jamie grinned at his godfather. "Remember back that far, do ye?"

"Farther back than you were born or thought of, laddie," Murtagh had said, shaking his head.

The little clansman now stowed the vials in his sporran, methodically wrapping each one in a bit of soft leather to prevent breakage.

"I'll send word of the ship and her sailing so soon as I may. And I'll see ye within the month off Spain. You'll have the money before then?"

Jamie nodded. "Oh, aye. By next week, I imagine." Jared's business had prospered under Jamie's stewardship, but the cash reserves were not sufficient to purchase entire shiploads of port, while still fulfilling the other commitments of the House of Fraser. The chess games had borne fruit in more than one regard, though, and Monsieur Duverney the younger, a prominent banker, had willingly guaranteed a sizable loan for his father's friend.

"It's a pity we can't bring the stuff into Paris," Jamie had remarked during the planning, "but St. Germain would be sure to find out. I expect we'll do best to sell it through a broker in Spain—I know a good man in Bilbao. The profit will be much smaller than it would be in France, and the taxes are higher, but ye canna have everything, can ye?"

"I'll settle for paying back Duverney's loan," I said. "And speaking of loans, what's Signore Manzetti going to do about the money he's loaned Charles Stuart?"

"Whistle for it, I expect," said Jamie cheerfully. "And ruin the Stuarts' reputation with every banker on the Continent while he's about it."

"Seems a bit hard on poor old Manzetti," I observed.

"Aye well. Ye canna make an omelet wi'out breakin' eggs, as my auld grannie says."

"You haven't got an auld grannie," I pointed out.

"No," he admitted, "but if I had, that's what she'd say." He had dropped the playfulness then, momentarily. "It's no verra fair to the Stuarts, forbye. In fact, should any of the Jacobite lords come to know what I've been doing, I expect they'd call it treason, and they'd be right." He rubbed a hand over his brow, and shook his head, and I saw the deadly seriousness that his playfulness covered.

"It canna be helped, Sassenach. If you're right—and I've staked my life so far on it—then it's a choice between the aspirations of Charles Stuart and the lives of a hell of a lot of Scotsmen. I've no love for King Geordie—me, wi' a price on my head?—but I dinna see that I can do otherwise."

He frowned, running a hand through his hair, as he always did when thinking or upset. "If there were a chance of Charles succeeding . . . aye, well, that might be different. To take a risk in an honorable cause—but your history says he wilna succeed, and I must say, all I know of the man makes it seem likely that you're right. They're my folk and my family at stake, and if the cost of their lives is a banker's gold . . . well, it doesna seem more a sacrifice than that of my own honor."

He shrugged in half-humorous despair. "So now I've gone from stealing His Highness's mail to bank robbery and piracy on the high seas, and it seems there's nay help for it."

He was silent for a moment, looking down at his hands, clenched together on the desk. Then he turned his head to me and smiled.

"I always wanted to be a pirate, when I was a bairn," he said. "Pity I canna wear a cutlass."

I lay in bed, head and shoulders propped on pillows, hands clasped lightly over my stomach, thinking. Since the first alarm, there had been very little bleeding, and I felt well. Still, any sort of bleeding at this stage was cause for alarm. I wondered privately what would happen if any emergency arose while Jamie was gone to Spain, but there was little to be gained by worrying. He had to go; there was too much riding on that particular shipload of wine for any private concerns to intrude. And if everything went all right, he should be back well before the baby was due.

As it was, all personal concerns would have to be put aside, danger or no. Charles, unable to contain his own excitement, had confided to Jamie that he would shortly require two ships—possibly more—and had asked his advice on hull design and the mounting of deck cannon. His father's most recent letters from Rome had betrayed a slight tone of questioning—with his acute Bourbon nose for politics, James Stuart smelled a rat, but plainly hadn't yet been informed of what his son was up to. Jamie, hip-deep in decoded letters, thought it likely that Philip of Spain had not yet mentioned Charles's overtures or the Pope's interest, but James Stuart had his spies, as well.

After a little while, I became aware of some slight change in Jamie's attitude. Glancing toward him, I saw that while he was still holding a book open on his knee, he had ceased to turn the pages—or to look at them, for that matter. His eyes were fixed on me instead; or, to be specific, on the spot where my nightrobe parted, several inches lower than strict modesty might dictate, strict modesty hardly seeming necessary in bed with one's husband.

His gaze was abstracted, dark blue with longing, and I realized that if not socially required, modesty in bed with one's husband might be at least considerate, under the circumstances. There were alternatives, of course.

Catching me looking at him, Jamie blushed slightly and hastily returned to an exaggerated interest in his book. I rolled onto my side and rested a hand on his thigh.

"Interesting book?" I asked, idly caressing him.

"Mphm. Oh, aye." The blush deepened, but he didn't take his eyes from the page.

Grinning to myself, I slipped my hand under the bedclothes. He dropped the book.

"Sassenach!" he said. "Ye know you canna . . ."

"No," I said, "but you can. Or rather, I can for you."

He firmly detached my hand and gave it back to me.

"No, Sassenach. It wouldna be right."

"It wouldn't?" I said, surprised. "Whyever not?"

He squirmed uncomfortably, avoiding my eyes.

"Well, I . . . I wouldna feel right, Sassenach. To take my pleasure from ye, and not be able to give ye . . . well, I wouldna feel right about it, is all."

I burst into laughter, laying my head on his thigh.

"Jamie, you are too sweet for words!"

"I am not sweet," he said indignantly. "But I'm no such a selfish—Claire, stop that!"

"You were planning to wait several more months?" I asked, not stopping.

"I could," he said, with what dignity was possible under the circumstances. "I waited tw-twenty-two years, and I can . . ."

"No, you can't," I said, pulling back the bedclothes and admiring the shape so clearly visible beneath his nightshirt. I touched it, and it moved slightly, eager against my hand. "Whatever God meant you to be, Jamie Fraser, it wasn't a monk."

With a sure hand, I pulled up his nightshirt.

"But . . ." he began.

"Two against one," I said, leaning down. "You lose."

Jamie worked hard for the next few days, readying the wine business to look after itself during his absence. Still, he found time to come up and sit with me for a short time after lunch most days, and so it was that he was with me when a visitor was announced. Visitors were not uncommon; Louise came every other day or so, to chatter about pregnancy or to moan over her lost love—though I privately thought she enjoyed Charles a great deal more as the object of noble renunciation than she did as a present lover. She had promised to bring me some Turkish sweetmeats, and I rather expected her plump pink face to peek through the door.

To my surprise, though, the visitor was Monsieur Forez. Magnus himself showed him into my sitting room, taking his hat and cloak with an almost superstitious reverence.

Jamie looked surprised at this visitation, but rose to his feet to greet the hangman politely and offer him refreshment.

"As a general rule, I take no spirits," Monsieur Forez said with a smile. "But I would not insult the hospitality of my esteemed colleague." He bowed ceremoniously in the direction of the chaise where I reclined. "You are well, I trust, Madame Fraser?"

"Yes," I said cautiously. "Thank you." I wondered to what we owed the honor of the visit. For while Monsieur Forez enjoyed considerable prestige and a fair amount of wealth in return for his official duties, I didn't think his job got him many dinner invitations. I wondered suddenly whether hangmen had any social life to speak of.

He crossed the room and laid a small package on the chaise beside me, rather like a fatherly vulture bringing home dinner for his chicks. Keeping in mind the hanged-men's grease, I picked the package up gingerly and weighed it in my hand; light for its size, and smelling faintly astringent.

"A small remembrance from Mother Hildegarde," he explained. "I understand it is a favorite remedy of *les maîtresses sage-femme.* She has written directions for its use, as well." He withdrew a folded, sealed note from his inner pocket and handed it over.

I sniffed the package. Raspberry leaves and saxifrage; something else I didn't recognize. I hoped Mother Hildegarde had included a list of the ingredients as well.

"Please thank Mother Hildegarde for me," I said. "And how is everyone at the Hôpital?" I greatly missed my work there, as well as the nuns and the odd assortment of medical practitioners. We gossiped for some time about the Hôpital and its personnel, with Jamie contributing the occasional comment, but usually just listening with a polite smile, or—when the subject turned to the clinical—burying his nose in his glass of wine.

"What a pity," I said regretfully, as Monsieur Forez finished his description of the repair of a crushed shoulder blade. "I've never seen that done. I do miss the surgical work."

"Yes, I will miss it as well," Monsieur Forez nodded, taking a small sip from his wineglass. It was still more than half-full; apparently he hadn't been joking about his abstention from spirits.

"You're leaving Paris?" Jamie said in some surprise.

Monsieur Forez shrugged, the folds of his long coat rustling like feathers.

"Only for a time," he said. "Still, I will be gone for at least two months. In fact, Madame," he bowed his head toward me again, "that is the main reason for my visit today."

"It is?"

"Yes. I am going to England, you understand, and it occurred to me that if you wished it, Madame, it would be a matter of the greatest simplicity for me to carry any message that you desired. Should there be anyone with whom you wished to communicate, that is," he added, with his usual precision.

I glanced at Jamie, whose face had suddenly altered, from an open expression of polite interest to that pleasantly smiling mask that hid all thoughts. A stranger wouldn't have noticed the difference, but I did.

"No," I said hesitantly. "I have no friends or relatives in England; I'm afraid I have no connections there at all, since I was—widowed." I felt the usual small stab at this reference to Frank, but suppressed it.

If this seemed odd to Monsieur Forez, he didn't show it. He merely nodded, and set down his half-drunk glass of wine.

"I see. It is fortunate indeed that you have friends here, then." His voice seemed to hold a warning of some kind, but he didn't look at me as he bent to straighten his stocking before rising. "I shall call upon you on my return, then, and hope to find you again in good health."

"What is the business that takes you to England, Monsieur?" Jamie said bluntly.

Monsieur Forez turned to him with a faint smile. He cocked his head, eyes bright, and I was struck once more by his resemblance to a large bird. Not a carrion crow at the moment, though, but a raptor, a bird of prey.

"And what business should a man of my profession travel on, Monsieur Fraser?" he asked. "I have been hired to perform my usual duties, at Smithfield."

"An important occasion, I take it," said Jamie. "To justify the summoning of a man of your skill, I mean." His eyes were watchful, though his expression showed nothing beyond polite inquiry.

Monsieur Forez's eyes grew brighter. He rose slowly to his feet, looking down at Jamie where he sat near the window.

"That is true, Monsieur Fraser," he said softly. "For it is a matter of skill, make no mistake. To choke a man to death at the end of a rope—pah! Anyone can do that. To break a neck cleanly, with one quick fall, that requires some calculation in terms of weight and drop, and a certain amount of practice in the placing of the rope, as well. But to walk the line between these methods, to properly execute the sentence of a traitor's death; that requires great skill indeed."

My mouth felt suddenly dry, and I reached for my own glass. "A traitor's death?" I said, feeling as though I really didn't want to hear the answer.

"Hanging, drawing, and quartering," Jamie said briefly. "That's what you mean, of course, Monsieur Forez?"

The hangman nodded. Jamie rose to his feet, as though against his will, facing the gaunt, black-clad visitor. They were much of a height, and could look each other in the face without difficulty. Monsieur Forez took a step toward Jamie, expression suddenly abstracted, as though he were about to make a demonstration of some medical point.

"Oh, yes," he said. "Yes, that is the traitor's death. First, the man must be hanged, as you say, but with a nice judgment, so that the neck is not broken, nor the windpipe crushed—suffocation is not the desired result, you understand."

"Oh, I understand." Jamie's voice was soft, with an almost mocking edge, and I glanced at him in bewilderment.

"Do you, Monsieur?" Monsieur Forez smiled faintly, but went on without waiting for an answer. "It is a matter of timing then; you judge by the eyes. The face will darken with blood almost immediately—more quickly if the subject is of fair complexion—and as choking proceeds, the tongue is forced from the mouth. That is what delights the crowds, of course, as well as the popping eyes. But you watch for the signs of redness at the corners of the eyes, as the small blood vessels burst. When that happens, you must give at once the signal for the subject to be cut down—a dependable assistant is indispensable, you understand," he half-turned, to include me in this macabre conversation, and I nodded, despite myself.

"Then," he continued, turning back to Jamie, "you must administer at once a stimulant, to revive the subject while the shirt is being removed—you must insist that a shirt opening down the front is provided; often it is difficult to get them off over the head." One long, slender finger reached out, pointing at the middle button of Jamie's shirt, but not quite touching the fresh-starched linen.

"I would suppose so," Jamie said.

Monsieur Forez retracted the finger, nodding in approval at this evidence of comprehension.

"Just so. The assistant will have kindled the fire beforehand; this is beneath the dignity of the executioner. And then the time of the knife is at hand."

There was a dead silence in the room. Jamie's face was still set in inscrutability, but a slight moisture gleamed on the side of his neck.

"It is here that the utmost of skill is required," Monsieur Forez explained, raising a finger in admonition. "You must work quickly, lest the subject expire before you have finished. Mixing a dose with the stimulant which constricts the blood vessels will give you a few moments' grace, but not much."

Spotting a silver letter-opener on the table, he crossed to it and picked it up. He held it with his hand wrapped about the hilt, forefinger braced on top of the blade, pointed down at the shining walnut of the tabletop.

"Just there," he said, almost dreamily. "At the base of the breastbone. And quickly, to the crest of the groin. You can see the bone easily in most cases. Again"—and the letter-opener flashed to one side and then the other, quick and delicate as the zigzag flight of a hummingbird—"following the arch of the ribs. You must not cut deeply, for you do not wish to puncture the sac which encloses the entrails. Still, you must get through skin, fat, and muscle, and do it with one stroke. This," he said with satisfaction, gazing down at his own reflection in the tabletop, "is artistry."

He laid the knife gently on the table, and turned back to Jamie. He shrugged pleasantly.

"After that, it is a matter of speed and some dexterity, but if you have been exact in your methods, it will present little difficulty. The entrails are sealed within a membrane, you see, resembling a bag. If you have not severed this by accident, it is a simple matter, needing only a little strength, to force your hands beneath the muscular layer and pull free the entire mass. A quick cut at stomach and anus"—he glanced disparagingly at the letter-opener—"and then the entrails may be thrown upon the fire."

"Now"—he raised an admonitory finger—"if you have been swift and delicate in your work, there is now a moment's leisure, for mark you, as yet no large vessels will have been severed."

I felt quite faint, although I was sitting down, and I was sure that my face was as white as Jamie's. Pale as he was, Jamie smiled, as though humoring a guest in conversation.

"So the . . . subject . . . can live a bit longer?"

"*Mais oui,* Monsieur." The hangman's bright black eyes swept over Jamie's powerful frame, taking in the width of shoulder and the muscular legs. "The effects of such shock are unpredictable, but I have seen a strong man live for more than a quarter of an hour in this state."

"I imagine it seems a lot longer to the subject," Jamie said dryly.

Monsieur Forez appeared not to hear this, picking up the letter-opener again and flourishing it as he spoke.

"As death approaches, then, you must reach up into the cavity of the body to grasp the heart. Here skill is called upon again. The heart retracts, you see, without the downward anchorage of the viscera, and often it is surprisingly far up. In addition, it is most slippery." He wiped one hand on the skirt of his coat in pantomime. "But the major difficulty lies in severing the large vessels above very quickly, so that the organ may be pulled forth while still beating. You wish to please the crowd," he explained. "It makes a great difference to the remuneration. As to the rest—" He shrugged a lean, disdainful shoulder. "Mere butchery. Once life is extinct, there is no further need of skill."

"No, I suppose not," I said faintly.

"But you are pale, Madame! I have detained you far too long in tedious conversation!" he exclaimed. He reached for my hand, and I resisted the very strong urge to yank it back. His own hand was cool, but the warmth of his lips as he brushed his mouth lightly across my hand was so unexpected that I tightened my own grasp in surprise. He gave my hand a slight, invisible squeeze, and turned to bow formally to Jamie.

"I must take my leave, Monsieur Fraser. I shall hope to meet you and your charming wife again . . . under such pleasant circumstances as we have enjoyed today." The eyes of the two men met for a second. Then Monsieur Forez appeared to recall the letter-opener he was still holding in one hand. With an exclamation of surprise, he held it out on his

open palm. Jamie arched one brow, and picked the knife up
delicately by the point.

"*Bon voyage,* Monsieur Forez," he said. "And I thank
you"—his mouth twisted wryly—"for your most instructive
visit."

He insisted upon seeing our visitor to the door himself.
Left alone, I got up and went to the window, where I stood
practicing deep-breathing exercises until the dark-blue carriage disappeared around the corner of the Rue Cambodge.

The door opened behind me, and Jamie stepped in. He
still held the letter-opener. He crossed deliberately to the
large famille rose jar that stood by the hearth and dropped
the paper knife into it with a clang, then turned to me, doing
his best to smile.

"Well, as warnings go," he said, "that one was verra effective."

I shuddered briefly.

"Wasn't it, though?"

"Who do you think sent him?" Jamie asked. "Mother
Hildegarde?"

"I expect so. She warned me, when we decoded the music. She said what you were doing was dangerous." The fact of
just *how* dangerous had been lost upon me, until the hangman's visit. I hadn't suffered from morning nausea for some
time, but I felt my gorge rising now. *If the Jacobite lords knew
what I was doing, they'd call it treason.* And what steps might
they take, if they did find out?

To all outward intents, Jamie was an avowed Jacobite
supporter; in that guise, he visited Charles, entertained the
Earl Marischal to dinner, and attended court. And so far, he
had been skillful enough, in his chess games, his tavern visits,
and his drinking parties, to undercut the Stuart cause while
seeming outwardly to support it. Besides the two of us, only
Murtagh knew that we sought to thwart a Stuart rising—and
even he didn't know why, merely accepting his chief's word
that it was right. That pretense was necessary, while operating
in France. But the same pretense would brand Jamie a traitor, should he ever set foot on English soil.

I had known that, of course, but in my ignorance, had
thought that there was little difference between being hanged

as an outlaw, and executed as a traitor. Monsieur Forez's visit had taken care of *that* bit of naiveté.

"You're bloody calm about it," I said. My own heart was still thumping erratically, and my palms were cold, but sweaty. I wiped them on my gown, and tucked them between my knees to warm them.

Jamie shrugged slightly and gave me a lopsided smile.

"Well, there's the hell of a lot of unpleasant ways to die, Sassenach. And if one of them should fall to my lot, I wouldna like it much. But the question is: Am I scairt enough of the possibility that I would stop what I'm doing to avoid it?" He sat down on the chaise beside me, and took one of my hands between his own. His palms were warm, and the solid bulk of him next to me was reassuring.

"I thought that over for some time, Sassenach, in those weeks at the Abbey while I healed. And again, when we came to Paris. And again, when I met Charles Stuart." He shook his head, bent over our linked hands.

"Aye, I can see myself standing on a scaffold. I saw the gallows at Wentworth—did I tell ye that?"

"No. No, you didn't."

He nodded, eyes gone blank in remembrance.

"They marched us down to the courtyard; those of us in the condemned cell. And made us stand in rows on the stones, to watch an execution. They hanged six men that day, men I knew. I watched each man mount the steps—twelve steps, there were—and stand, hands bound behind his back, looking down at the yard as they put the rope around his neck. And I wondered then, how I would manage come my turn to mount those steps. Would I weep and pray, like John Sutter, or could I stand straight like Willie MacLeod, and smile at a friend in the yard below?"

He shook his head suddenly, like a dog flinging off drops of water, and smiled at me a little grimly. "Anyway, Monsieur Forez didna tell me anything I hadna thought of before. But it's too late, *mo nighean donn.*" He laid a hand over mine. "Aye, I'm afraid. But if I would not turn back for the chance of home and freedom, I shallna do it for fear. No, *mo nighean donn.* It's too late."

$\mathcal{M}$onsieur Forez's visit proved merely to be the first of a series of unusual disruptions.

"There is an Italian person downstairs, Madame," Magnus informed me. "He would not give me his name." There was a pinched look about the butler's mouth; I gathered that if the visitor would not give his name, he had been more than willing to give the butler a number of other words.

That, coupled with the "Italian person" designation, was enough to give me a clue as to the visitor's identity, and it was with relatively little surprise that I entered the drawing room to find Charles Stuart standing by the window.

He swung about at my entrance, hat in his hands. He was plainly surprised to see *me;* his mouth dropped open for a second, then he caught himself and gave me a quick, brief bow of acknowledgment.

"Milord Broch Tuarach is not at home?" he inquired. His brows drew together in displeasure.

"No, he isn't," I said. "Will you take a little refreshment, Your Highness?"

He looked around the richly appointed drawing-room with interest, but shook his head. So far as I knew, he had been in the house only once before, when he had come over the rooftops from his rendezvous with Louise. Neither he nor Jamie had thought it appropriate for him to be invited to the dinners here; without official recognition by Louis, the French nobility scorned him.

"No. I thank you, Madame Fraser. I shall not stay; my servant waits outside, and it is a long ride to return to my lodgings. I wished only to make a request of my friend James."

"Er . . . well, I'm sure that my husband would be happy to oblige Your Highness—if he can," I answered cautiously, wondering just what the request was. A loan, probably; Fergus's gleanings of late had included quite a number of impatient letters from tailors, bootmakers, and other creditors.

Charles smiled, his expression altering to one of surprising sweetness.

"I know; I cannot tell you, Madame, how greatly I esteem the devotion and service of your husband; the sight of his loyal face warms my heart amid the loneliness of my present surroundings."

"Oh?" I said.

"It is not a difficult thing I ask," he assured me. "It is only that I have made a small investment; a cargo of bottled port."

"Really?" I said. "How interesting." Murtagh had left for Lisbon that morning, vials of nettle juice and madder root in his pouch.

"It is a small thing," Charles flipped a lordly hand, disdaining the investment of every cent he had been able to borrow. "But I wish that my friend James shall accomplish the task of disposing of the cargo, once it shall arrive. It is not appropriate, you know"—and here he straightened his shoulders and elevated his nose just a trifle, quite unconsciously—"for a—a person such as myself, to be seen to engage in trade."

"Yes, I quite see, Your Highness," I said, biting my lip. I wondered whether he had expressed this point of view to his business partner, St. Germain—who undoubtedly regarded the young pretender to the Scottish throne as a person of less consequence than any of the French nobles—who engaged in "trade" with both hands, whenever the chance of profit offered.

"Is Your Highness quite alone in this enterprise?" I inquired innocently.

He frowned slightly. "No, I have a partner; but he is a Frenchman. I should much prefer to entrust the proceeds of my venture to the hands of a countryman. Besides," he added thoughtfully, "I have heard that my dear James is a most astute and capable merchant; it is possible that he might be able to increase the value of my investment by means of judicious sale."

I supposed whoever had told him of Jamie's capability hadn't bothered to add the information that there was probably no wine merchant in Paris whom St. Germain more disliked. Still, if everything worked out as planned, that shouldn't matter. And if it didn't, it was possible that St. Germain would solve all of our problems by strangling Charles Stuart, once he found out that the latter had contracted delivery of half his exclusive Gostos port to his most hated rival.

"I'm sure that my husband will do his utmost to dispose of Your Highness's merchandise to the maximum benefit of all concerned," I said, with complete truth.

His Highness thanked me graciously, as befitting a prince accepting the service of a loyal subject. He bowed, kissed my hand with great formality, and departed with continuing protestations of gratitude to Jamie. Magnus, looking dourly unimpressed by the Royal visit, closed the door upon him.

In the event, Jamie didn't come home until after I had fallen asleep, but I told him over breakfast of Charles's visit, and his request.

"God, I wonder if His Highness will tell the Comte?" he said. Having ensured the health of his bowels by disposing of his parritch in short order, he proceeded to add a French breakfast of buttered rolls and steaming chocolate on top of it. A broad grin spread across his face in contemplation of the Comte's reaction, as he sipped his cocoa.

"I wonder is it *lèse-majesté* to hammer an exiled prince? For if it's not, I hope His Highness has Sheridan or Balhaldy close by when St. Germain hears about it."

Further speculation along these lines was curtailed by the sudden sound of voices in the hallway. A moment later, Magnus appeared in the door, a note borne on his silver tray.

"Your pardon, milord," he said, bowing. "The messenger who brought this desired most urgently that it be brought to your attention at once."

Brows raised, Jamie took the note from the tray, opened and read it.

"Oh, bloody hell!" he said in disgust.

"What is it?" I asked. "Not word from Murtagh already?"

He shook his head. "No. It's from the foreman of the warehouse."

"Trouble at the docks?"

An odd mixture of emotions was visible on Jamie's face; impatience struggling with amusement.

"Well, not precisely. The man's got himself into a coil at a brothel, it seems. He humbly begs my pardon"—he waved ironically at the note—"but hopes I'll see fit to come round and assist him. In other words," he translated, crumpling his napkin as he rose, "will I pay his bill?"

"Will you?" I said, amused.

He snorted briefly and dusted crumbs from his lap.

"I suppose I'll have to, unless I want to supervise the warehouse myself—and I havena time for that." His brow creased as he mentally reviewed the duties of the day. This was a task that might take some little time, and there were orders waiting on his desk, ship's captains waiting on the docks, and casks waiting in the warehouse.

"I'd best take Fergus wi' me to carry messages," he said, resigned. "He can maybe go to Montmartre wi' a letter, if I'm too short of time."

"Kind hearts are more than coronets," I told Jamie as he stood by his desk, ruefully flipping through the impressive pile of waiting paperwork.

"Oh, aye?" he said. "And whose opinion is that?"

"Alfred, Lord Tennyson, I think," I said. "I don't believe he's come along yet, but he's a poet. Uncle Lamb had a book of famous British poets. There was a bit from Burns in there, too, I recall—he's a Scot," I explained. "He said, 'Freedom and Whisky gang teqither.' "

Jamie snorted. "I canna say if he's a poet, but he's a Scot, at least." He smiled then, and bent to kiss me on the forehead. "I'll be home to my supper, *mo nighean donn.* Keep ye well."

I finished my own breakfast, and thriftily polished off Jamie's toast as well, then waddled upstairs for my morning nap. I had had small episodes of bleeding since the first alarm, though no more than a spot or two, and nothing at all for several weeks. Still, I kept to my bed or the chaise as much as possible, only venturing down to the salon to receive visitors, or to the dining room for meals with Jamie. When I descended for lunch, though, I found the table laid for one.

"Milord has not come back yet?" I asked in some surprise. The elderly butler shook his head.

"No, milady."

"Well, I imagine he'll be back soon; make sure there's food waiting for him when he arrives." I was too hungry to wait for Jamie; the nausea tended to return if I went too long without eating.

After lunch, I lay down to rest again. Conjugal relations being temporarily in abeyance, there wasn't that much one could do in bed, other than read or sleep, which meant I did quite a lot of both. Sleeping on my stomach was impossible, sleeping on my back uncomfortable, as it tended to make the baby squirm. Consequently, I lay on my side, curling around my growing abdomen like a cocktail shrimp round a caper. I seldom slept deeply, but tended rather to doze, letting my mind drift to the gentle random movements of the child.

Somewhere in my dreams, I thought I felt Jamie near me, but when I opened my eyes the room was empty, and I closed them again, lulled as though I, too, floated weightless in a blood-warm sea.

I was wakened at length, somewhere in the late afternoon, by a soft tap on the bedroom door.

"Entrez," I said, blinking as I came awake. It was the butler, Magnus, apologetically announcing more visitors.

"It is the Princesse de Rohan, Madame," he said. "The Princesse wished to wait until you awakened, but when Madame d'Arbanville also arrived, I thought perhaps . . ."

"That's all right, Magnus," I said, struggling upright and swinging my feet over the side of the bed. "I'll come down."

I looked forward to the visitors. We had stopped entertaining during the last month, and I rather missed the bustle and conversation, silly as much of it was. Louise came frequently to sit with me and regale me with the latest doings of the Court, but I hadn't seen Marie d'Arbanville in some time. I wondered what brought her here today.

I was ungainly enough to take the stairs slowly, my increased weight jarring upward from the soles of my feet on each step. The paneled door of the drawing room was closed, but I heard the voice inside clearly.

"Do you think she *knows*?"

The question, asked in the lowered tones that portended

the juiciest of gossip, reached me just as I was about to enter the drawing room. Instead, I paused at the threshold, just out of sight.

It was Marie d'Arbanville who had spoken. Welcome everywhere because of her elderly husband's position, and gregarious even by French standards, Marie heard everything worth hearing within the environs of Paris.

"Does she know what?" The reply was Louise's; her high, carrying voice had the perfect self-confidence of the born aristocrat, who doesn't care who hears what.

"Oh, you haven't heard!" Marie pounced on the opening like a kitten, delighted to find a new mouse to play with. "Goodness! Of course, I only heard myself an hour ago."

And raced directly over here to tell me about it, I thought. Whatever "it" was. I thought I stood a better chance of hearing the unexpurgated version from my position in the hallway.

"It is my lord Broch Tuarach," Marie said, and I didn't need to see her, to imagine her leaning forward, green eyes darting back and forth, snapping with enjoyment of her news. "Only this morning, he challenged an Englishman to a duel—over a whore!"

"What!" Louise's cry of astonishment drowned out my own gasp. I grabbed hold of a small table and held on, black spots whirling before my eyes as the world came apart at the seams.

"Oh, yes!" Marie was saying. "Jacques Vincennes was there; he told my husband all about it! It was in that brothel down near the fish market—imagine going to a brothel at that hour of the morning! Men are so odd. Anyway, Jacques was having a drink with Madame Elise, who runs the place, when all of a sudden there was the most frightful outcry upstairs, and all kinds of thumping and shouting."

She paused for breath—and dramatic effect—and I heard the sound of liquid being poured.

"So, Jacques of course raced to the stairs—well, that's what he *says,* anyway; I expect he actually hid behind the sofa, he's such a coward—and after more shouting and thumping, there was a terrible crash, and an English officer came hurtling down the stairs, half-undressed, with his wig off, staggering and smashing into the walls. And who should appear at

the top of the stairs, looking like the vengeance of God, but
our own *petit* James!"

"No! And I would have sworn he was the last . . . but
go on! What happened then?"

A teacup chimed softly against its saucer, followed by
Marie's voice, released by excitement from the modulations
of secrecy.

"Well—the man reached the foot of the stairs still on his
feet, by some miracle, and he turned at once, and looked up
at Lord Tuarach. Jacques says the man was very self-possessed, for someone who'd just been kicked downstairs with
his breeches undone. He smiled—not a real smile, you know,
the nasty sort—and said, 'There's no need for violence, Fraser; you could have waited for your turn, surely? I should
have thought you get enough at home. But then, some men
derive pleasure from paying for it.' "

Louise made shocked noises. "How awful! The *canaille*!
But of course, it is no reproach to milord Tuarach—" I could
hear the strain in her voice as friendship warred with the urge
to gossip. Not surprisingly, gossip won.

"Milord Tuarach cannot enjoy his wife's favors at the
moment; she carries a child, and the pregnancy is dangerous.
So of course he would relieve his needs at a brothel; what
gentleman would do otherwise? But go on, Marie! What happened then?"

"Well." Marie drew breath as she approached the high
point of the story. "Milord Tuarach rushed down the stairs,
seized the Englishman by the throat, and shook him like a
rat!"

"Non! Ce n'est pas vrai!"

"Oh, yes! It took three of Madame's servants to restrain
him—such a wonderful big man, isn't he? So fierce-looking!"

"Yes, but then what?"

"Oh—well, Jacques said the Englishman gasped for a
bit, then straightened up and said to milord Tuarach, 'That's
twice you've come near killing me, Fraser. Someday you may
succeed.' And then milord Tuarach cursed in that terrible
Scottish tongue—I don't understand a word, do you?—and
then he wrenched himself free from the men holding him,
struck the Englishman across the face with his bare hand"—
Louise gasped at the insult—"and said, 'Tomorrow's dawn

will see you dead!' Then he turned about and ran up the stairs, and the Englishman left. John said he looked quite white—and no wonder! Just imagine!"

I imagined, all right.

"Are you well, Madame?" Magnus's anxious voice drowned out Louise's further exclamations. I put out a hand, groping, and he took it at once, putting his other hand under my elbow in support.

"No. I'm not well. Please . . . tell the ladies?" I waved weakly toward the drawing room.

"Of course, Madame. In a moment; but now let me see you to your chamber. This way, *chère Madame* . . ." He led me up the stairs, murmuring consolingly as he supported me. He escorted me to the bedroom chaise, where he left me, promising to send up a maid at once to attend me.

I didn't wait for assistance; the first shock passing, I could navigate well enough, and I stood and made my way across the room to where my small medicine box sat on the dressing table. I didn't think I was going to faint now, but there was a bottle of spirits of ammonia in there that I wanted handy, just in case.

I turned back the lid and stood still, staring into the box. For a moment, my mind refused to register what my eyes saw; the folded white square of paper, carefully wedged upright between the multicolored bottles. I noted rather abstractedly that my fingers shook as I took the paper out; it took several tries to unfold it.

I am sorry. The words were bold and black, the letters carefully formed in the center of the sheet, the single letter "J" written with equal care below. And below that, two more words, these scrawled hastily, done as a postscript of desperation: *I must!*

"You must," I murmured to myself, and then my knees buckled. Lying on the floor, with the carved panels of the ceiling flickering dimly above, I found myself thinking that I had always heretofore assumed that the tendency of eighteenth-century ladies to swoon was due to tight stays; now I rather thought it might be due to the idiocy of eighteenth-century men.

There was a cry of dismay from somewhere nearby, and then helpful hands were lifting me, and I felt the yielding softness of the wool-stuffed mattress under me, and cool cloths on my brow and wrists, smelling of vinegar.

I was soon restored to what senses I had, but strongly disinclined to talk. I reassured the maids that I was in fact all right, shooed them out of the room, and lay back on the pillows, trying to think.

It was Jack Randall, of course, and Jamie had gone to kill him. That was the only clear thought in the morass of whirling horror and speculation that filled my mind. Why, though? What could have made him break the promise he had made me?

Trying to consider carefully the events Marie had related —third-hand as they were—I thought there had to have been something more than just the shock of an unexpected encounter. I knew the Captain, knew him a great deal better than I wanted to. And if there was one thing of which I was reasonably sure, it was that he would not have been purchasing the usual services of a brothel—the simple enjoyment of a woman was not in his nature. What he enjoyed—needed— was pain, fear, humiliation.

These commodities, of course, could also be purchased, if at a somewhat higher price. I had seen enough, in my work at L'Hôpital des Anges, to know that there were *les putains* whose chief stock in trade lay not between their legs, but in strong bones overlaid with expensive fragile skin that bruised at once, and showed the marks of whips and blows.

And if Jamie, his own fair skin scarred with the marks of Randall's favor, had come upon the Captain, enjoying himself in similar fashion with one of the ladies of the establishment— That, I thought, could have carried him past any thought of promises or restraint. There was a small mark on his left breast, just below the nipple; a tiny whitish pucker, where he had cut from his skin the branded mark of Jonathan Randall's heated signet ring. The rage that had led him to suffer mutilation rather than bear that shameful mark could easily break forth again, to destroy its inflictor—and his hapless progeny.

"Frank," I said, and my left hand curled involuntarily over the shimmer of my gold wedding ring. "Oh, dear God. Frank." For Jamie, Frank was no more than a ghost, the dim possibility of a refuge for me, in the unlikely event of necessity. For me, Frank was the man I had lived with, had shared my bed and body with—had abandoned, at the last, to stay with Jamie Fraser.

"I can't," I whispered, to the empty air, to the small companion who stretched and twisted lazily within me, undisturbed by my own distress. "I can't let him do it!"

The afternoon light had faded into the gray shades of dusk, and the room seemed filled with all the despair of the world's ending. *Tomorrow's dawn will see you dead.* There was no hope of finding Jamie tonight. I knew he would not return to the Rue Trémoulins; he wouldn't have left that note if he were coming back. He could never lie beside me through the night, knowing what he intended doing in the morning. No, he had undoubtedly sought refuge in some inn or tavern, there to ready himself in solitude for the execution of justice that he had sworn.

I thought I knew where the place of execution would be. With the memory of his first duel strong in his mind, Jamie had shorn his hair in preparation. The memory would have come to him again, I was sure, when choosing a spot to meet his enemy. The Bois de Boulogne, near the path of the Seven Saints. The Bois was a popular place for illicit duels, its dense growth sheltering the participants from detection. Tomorrow, one of its shady clearings would see the meeting of Jamie Fraser and Jack Randall. And me.

I lay on the bed, not bothering to undress or cover myself, hands clasped across my belly. I watched the twilight fade to black, and knew I would not sleep tonight. I took what comfort I could in the small movements of my unseen inhabitant, with the echo of Jamie's words ringing in my ears: *Tomorrow's dawn will see you dead.*

The Bois de Boulogne was a small patch of almost-virgin forest, perched incongruously on the edge of Paris. It was said that wolves as well as foxes and badgers were still to be found lurking in its depths, but this story did nothing to discourage the amorous couples that dallied under the branches on the grassy earth of the forest. It was an escape from the noise and dirt of the city, and only its location kept it from becoming a playground for the nobility. As it was, it was patronized largely by those who lived nearby, who found a moment's respite in the shade of the large oaks and pale birches of the Bois, and by those from farther away who sought privacy.

It was a small wood, but still too large to quarter on foot, looking for a clearing large enough to hold a pair of duelists. It had begun to rain during the night, and the dawn had come reluctantly, glowing sullen through a cloud-dark sky. The forest whispered to itself, the faint patter of rain on the leaves blending with the subdued rustle and rub of leaf and branches.

The carriage pulled to a stop on the road that led through the Bois, near the last small cluster of ramshackle buildings. I had told the coachman what to do; he swung down from his seat, tethered the horses, and disappeared among the buildings. The folk who lived near the Bois knew what went on there. There could not be that many spots suitable for dueling; those there were would be known.

I sat back and pulled the heavy cloak tighter around me, shivering in the cold of the early dawn. I felt terrible, with the fatigue of a sleepless night dragging at me, and the leaden weight of fear and grief resting in the pit of my stomach. Overlying everything was a seething anger that I tried to push away, lest it interfere with the job at hand.

It kept creeping back, though, bubbling up whenever my guard was down, as it was now. How could he do this? my mind kept muttering, in a cold fury. I shouldn't be here; I should be home, resting quietly by Jamie's side. I shouldn't have to be pursuing him, preventing him, fighting both anger and illness. A nagging pain from the coach ride knotted at the base of my spine. Yes, he might well be upset; I could understand that. But it was a man's *life* at stake, for God's sake. How could his bloody pride be more important than that? And to leave me, with no word of explanation! To leave me to find out from the gossip of neighbors what had happened.

"You promised me, Jamie, damn you, you *promised* me!" I whispered, under my breath. The wood was quiet, dripping and mist-shrouded. Were they here already? Would they be here? Was I wrong in my guess about the place?

The coachman reappeared, accompanied by a young lad, perhaps fourteen, who hopped nimbly up on the seat beside the coachman, and waved his hand, gesturing ahead and to the left. With a brief crack of the whip and a click of the tongue, the coachman urged the horses into a slow trot, and we turned down the road into the shadows of the wakening wood.

We stopped twice, pausing while the lad hopped down and darted into the undergrowth, each time reappearing within a moment or two, shaking his head in negation. The third time, he came tearing back, the excitement on his face so evident that I had the carriage door open before he got near enough to call out to the coachman.

I had money ready in my hand; I thrust it at him, simultaneously clutching at his sleeve, saying, "Show me where! Quickly, quickly!"

I scarcely noticed either the clutching branches that laced across the path, nor the sudden wetness that soaked my clothing as I brushed them. The path was soft with fallen leaves, and neither my shoes nor those of my guide made any sound as I followed the shadow of his ragged, damp-spotted shirt.

I heard them before I saw them; they had started. The clash of metal was muffled by the wet shrubbery, but clear enough, nonetheless. No birds sang in the wet dawn, but the deadly voice of battle rang in my ears.

It was a large clearing, deep in the Bois, but accessible by path and road. Large enough to accommodate the footwork needed for a serious duel. They were stripped to their shirts, fighting in the rain, the wet fabric clinging, showing the outline of shoulder and backbone.

Jamie had said he was the better fighter; he might be, but Jonathan Randall was no mean swordsman, either. He wove and dodged, lithe as a snake, sword striking like a silver fang. Jamie was just as fast, amazing grace in such a tall man, light-footed and sure-handed. I watched, rooted to the ground, afraid to cry out for fear of distracting Jamie's attention. They spun in a tight circle of stroke and parry, feet touching lightly as a dance on the turf.

I stood stock-still, watching. I had come through the fading night to find this, to stop them. And having found them, now I could not intervene, for fear of causing a fatal interruption. All I could do was wait, to see which of my men would die.

Randall had his blade up and in place to deflect the stroke, but not quickly enough to brace it against the savagery that sent his sword flying.

I opened my mouth to scream. I had meant to call Jamie's name, to stop him now, in that moment's grace between the disarming of his opponent and the killing stroke that must come next. I did scream, in fact, but the sound emerged weak and strangled. As I had stood there, watching, the nagging pain in my back had deepened, clenching like a fist. Now I felt a sudden breaking somewhere, as though the fist had torn loose what it held.

I groped wildly, clutching at a nearby branch. I saw Jamie's face, set in a sort of calm exultance, and realized that he could hear nothing through the haze of violence that enveloped him. He would see nothing but his goal, until the fight was ended. Randall, retreating before the inexorable blade, slipped on the wet grass and went down. He arched his back, attempting to rise, but the grass was slippery. The fabric of his stock was torn, and his head was thrown back, dark hair rain-soaked, throat exposed like that of a wolf begging mercy. But vengeance knows no mercy, and it was not the exposed throat that the descending blade sought.

Through a blackening mist, I saw Jamie's sword come down, graceful and deadly, cold as death. The point touched the waist of the doeskin breeches, pierced and cut down in a twisting wrench that darkened the fawn with a sudden flood of black-red blood.

The blood was a hot rush down my thighs, and the chill of my skin moved inward, toward the bone. The bone where my pelvis joined my back was breaking; I could feel the strain as each pain came on, a stroke of lightning flashing down my backbone to explode and flame in the basin of my hips, a stroke of destruction, leaving burnt and blackened fields behind.

My body as well as my senses seemed to fragment. I saw nothing, but could not tell whether my eyes were open or closed; everything was spinning dark, patched now and then with the shifting patterns you see at night as a child, when you press your fists against shut eyelids.

The raindrops beat on my face, on my throat and shoulders. Each heavy drop struck cold, then dissolved into a tiny warm stream, coursing across my chilled skin. The sensation was quite distinct, apart from the wrenching agony that advanced and retreated, lower down. I tried to focus my mind on that, to force my attention from the small, detached voice in the center of my brain, the one saying, as though making notes on a clinical record: "You're having a hemorrhage, of course. Probably a ruptured placenta, judging from the amount of blood. Generally fatal. The loss of blood accounts for the numbness in hands and feet, and the darkened vision. They say that the sense of hearing is the last to go; that seems to be true."

Whether it was the last of my senses to be left to me or not, hearing I still had. And it was voices I heard, most agitated, some striving for calmness, all speaking in French. There was one word I could hear and understand—my own name, shouted over and over, but at a distance. "Claire! Claire!"

"Jamie," I tried to say, but my lips were stiff and numb with cold. Movement of any kind was beyond me. The commotion near me was settling to a steadier level; someone had arrived who was at least willing to act as though they knew what to do.

Perhaps they did. The soaked wad of my skirt was lifted gently from between my thighs, and a thick pad of cloth thrust firmly into place instead. Helpful hands turned me onto my left side, and drew my knees up toward my chest.

"Take her to the Hôpital," suggested one voice near my ear.

"She won't live that long," said another, pessimistically. "Might as well wait a few minutes, then send for the meat wagon."

"No," insisted another. "The bleeding is slowing; she may live. Besides, I know her; I've seen her at L'Hôpital des Anges. Take her to Mother Hildegarde."

I summoned all the strength I had left, and managed to whisper, "Mother." Then I gave up the struggle, and let the darkness take me.

25

Raymond the Heretic

The high, vaulted ceiling over me was supported by ogives, those fourteenth-century architectural features in which four ribs rise from the tops of pillars, to join in double crossing arches.

My bed was set under one of these, gauze curtains drawn around me for privacy. The central point of the ogive was not directly above me, though; my bed had been placed a few feet off-center. This bothered me whenever I glanced upward; I kept wanting to move the bed by force of will, as though being centered beneath the roof would help to center me within myself.

If I had a center any longer. My body felt bruised and tender, as though I had been beaten. My joints ached and felt loose, like teeth undermined by scurvy. Several thick blankets covered me, but they could do no more than trap heat, and I had none to save. The chill of the rainy dawn had settled in my bones.

All these physical symptoms I noted objectively, as though they belonged to someone else; otherwise I felt nothing. The small, cold, logical center of my brain was still there, but the envelope of feeling through which its utterances were usually filtered was gone; dead, or paralyzed, or simply no longer there. I neither knew nor cared. I had been in L'Hôpital des Anges for five days.

Mother Hildegarde's long fingers probed in relentless gentleness through the cotton of the bedgown I wore, probing the depths of my belly, seeking the hard edges of a contracting uterus. The flesh was soft as ripe fruit, though, and tender beneath her fingers. I winced as her fingers sank deep, and she frowned, muttering something under her breath that might have been a prayer.

I caught a name in the murmurings, and asked, "Raymond? You know Master Raymond?" I could think of few less likely pairings than this redoubtable nun and the little gnome of the cavern of skulls.

Mother Hildegarde's thick brows shot up, astonished.

"Master Raymond, you say? That heretical charlatan? *Que Dieu nous en garde!*" May God protect us.

"Oh. I thought I heard you say 'Raymond.' "

"Ah." The fingers had returned to their work, probing the crease of my groin in search of the lumps of enlarged lymph nodes that would signal infection. They were there, I knew; I had felt them myself, moving my hands in restless misery over my empty body. I could feel the fever, an ache and a chill deep in my bones, that would burst into flame when it reached the surface of my skin.

"I was invoking the aid of St. Raymond Nonnatus," Mother Hildegarde explained, wringing out a cloth in cold water. "He is an aid most invaluable in the assistance of expectant mothers."

"Of which I am no longer one." I noticed remotely the brief stab of pain that creased her brows; it disappeared almost at once as she busied herself in mopping my brow, smoothing the cold water briskly over the rounds of my cheeks and down into the hot, damp creases of my neck.

I shivered suddenly at the touch of the cold water, and she stopped at once, laying a considering hand on my forehead.

"St. Raymond is not one to be picky," she said, absently reproving. "I myself take help where it can be found; a course I would recommend to you."

"Mmm." I shut my eyes, retreating into the haven of gray fog. Now there seemed to be faint lights in the fog, brief cracklings like the scatter of sheet lightning on a summer horizon.

I heard the clicking of jet rosary beads as Mother Hildegarde straightened up, and the soft voice of one of the sisters in the doorway, summoning her to another in the day's string of emergencies. She had almost reached the door when a thought struck her. She turned with a swish of heavy skirts, pointing at the foot of my bed with an authoritative finger.

"Bouton!" she said. *"Au pied, reste!"*

The dog, as unhesitating as his mistress, whirled smartly in mid-step and leaped to the foot of the bed. Once there, he took a moment to knead the bedclothes with his paws and turn three times widdershins, as though taking the curse off

his resting place, before lying down at my feet, resting his
nose on his paws with a deep sigh.

Satisfied, Mother Hildegarde murmured, *"Que Dieu vous
bénisse, mon enfant,"* in farewell, and disappeared.

Through the gathering fog and the icy numbness that
wrapped me, I dimly appreciated her gesture. With no child
to lay in my arms, she had given me her own best substitute.

The shaggy weight on my feet was in fact a small bodily
comfort. Bouton lay still as the dogs beneath the feet of the
kings carved on the lids of their tombs at St. Denis, his
warmth denying the marble chill of my feet, his presence an
improvement on either solitude or the company of humans,
as he required nothing of me. Nothing was precisely what I
felt, and all I had to give.

Bouton emitted a small, popping dog-fart and settled
into sleep. I drew the covers over my nose and tried to do
likewise.

I slept, eventually. And I dreamed. Fever dreams of weariness and desolation, of an impossible task done endlessly.
Unceasing painful effort, carried out in a stony, barren place.
Of thick gray fog, through which loss pursued me like a demon in the mist.

I woke, quite suddenly, to find that Bouton was gone, but
I was not alone.

Raymond's hairline was completely level, a flat line
drawn across the wide brow as though with a rule. He wore
his thick, graying hair swept back and hanging straight to the
shoulder, so the massive forehead protruded like a block of
stone, completely overshadowing the rest of his face. It
hovered over me now, looking to my fevered eyes like the
slab of a tombstone.

The lines and furrows moved slightly as he spoke to the
sisters, and I thought they seemed like letters, written just
below the surface of the stone, trying to burrow their way to
the surface so that the name of the dead could be read. I was
convinced that in another moment, my name would be legible
on that white slab, and at that moment, I would truly die. I
arched my back and screamed.

"Now, see there! She doesn't want you, you disgusting
old creature—you're disturbing her rest. Come away at
once!" Mother Hildegarde clutched Raymond imperatively

by the arm, tugging him away from the bed. He resisted, standing rooted like a stone gnome in a lawn, but Sister Celeste added her not inconsiderable efforts to Mother Hildegarde's, and they lifted him clean off his feet and bore him away between them, the clog dropping from one frantically kicking foot as they went.

The clog lay where it had fallen, on its side, square in the center of a scrubbed flagstone. With the intense fixation of fever, I was unable to take my eyes off it. I traced the impossibly smooth curve of the worn edge over and over, each time pulling back my gaze from the impenetrable darkness of the inside. If I let myself enter that blackness, my soul would be sucked out into chaos. As my eyes rested on it, I could hear again the sounds of the time passage through the circle of stones, and I flung out my arms, clutching frantically at the wadded bedding, seeking some anchorage against confusion.

Suddenly an arm shot through the draperies, and a work-reddened hand snatched up the shoe and disappeared. Deprived of focus, my heat-addled mind spun round the grooves of the flags for a time, then, soothed by the geometric regularity, turned inward and wobbled into sleep like a dying top.

There was no stillness in my dreams, though, and I stumbled wearily through mazes of repeating figures, endless loopings and whorls. It was with a sense of profound relief that I saw at last the irregularities of a human face.

And an irregular face it was, to be sure, screwed up as it was in a ferocious frown, lips pursed in adjuration. It was only as I felt the pressure of the hand over my mouth that I realized I was no longer asleep.

The long, lipless mouth of the gargoyle hovered next to my ear.

"Be still, *ma chère*! If they find me here again, I'm done for!" The large, dark eyes darted from side to side, keeping watch for any movement of the drapes.

I nodded slowly, and he released my mouth, his fingers leaving a faint whiff of ammonium and sulfur behind. He had somewhere found—or stolen, I thought dimly—a ragged gray friar's gown to cover the grimy velvet of his apothecary's robe, and the depths of the hood concealed both the telltale silver hair and that monstrous forehead.

The fevered delusions receded slightly, displaced by what

remnants of curiosity remained to me. I was too weak to say more than "What . . ." when he placed a finger once more across my lips, and threw back the sheet covering me.

I watched in some bemusement as he rapidly unknotted the strings of my shift and opened the garment to the waist. His movements were swift and businesslike, completely lacking in lechery. Not that I could imagine anyone capable of trying to ravish a fever-wracked carcass like mine, particularly not within hearing of Mother Hildegarde. But still . . .

I watched with remote fascination as he placed his cupped hands on my breasts. They were broad and almost square, the fingers all of a length, with unusually long and supple thumbs that curved around my breasts with amazing delicacy. Watching them, I had an unusually vivid memory of Marian Jenkinson, a girl with whom I had trained at Pembroke Hospital, telling the rapt inmates of the nurses' quarters that the size and shape of a man's thumbs were a sure indication of the quality of his more intimate appendage.

"And it's true, I swear it," Marian would declare, shaking back her blond hair dramatically. But when pressed for examples, she would only giggle and dimple, rolling her eyes toward Lieutenant Hanley, who strongly resembled a gorilla, opposable—and sizable—thumbs notwithstanding.

The large thumbs were pressing gently but firmly into my flesh, and I could feel my swollen nipples rising against the hard palms, cold by comparison with my own heated skin.

"Jamie," I said, and a shiver passed over me.

"Hush, madonna," said Raymond. His voice was low, kind but somehow abstracted, as though he were paying no attention to me, in spite of what he was doing.

The shiver came back; it was as though the heat passed from me to him, but his hands did not warm. His fingers stayed cool, and I chilled and shook as the fever ebbed and flowed, draining from my bones.

The afternoon light was dim through the thick gauze of the drapes around my bed, and Raymond's hands were dark on the white flesh of my breasts. The shadows between the thick, grimy fingers were not black, though. They were . . . blue, I thought.

I closed my eyes, looking at the particolored swirl of patterns that immediately appeared behind my lids. When I opened them again, it was as though something of the color remained behind, coating Raymond's hands.

As the fever ebbed, leaving my mind clearer, I blinked, trying to raise my head for a better look. Raymond pressed slightly harder, urging me to lie back, and I let my head fall on the pillow, peering slantwise over my chest.

I wasn't imagining it after all—or was I? While Raymond's hands weren't moving themselves, a faint flicker of colored light seemed to move over them, shedding a glow of rose and a pallor of blue across my own white skin.

My breasts were warming now, but warming with the natural heat of health, not the gnawing burn of fever. The draft from the open archway outside found a way through the drapes and lifted the damp hair at my temples, but I wasn't chilled now.

Raymond's head was bent, face hidden by the cowl of his borrowed robe. After what seemed a long time, he moved his hands from my breasts, very slowly over my arms, pausing and squeezing gently at the joints of shoulder and elbow, wrists and fingers. The soreness eased, and I thought I could see briefly a faint blue line within my upper arm, the glowing ghost of the bone.

Always touching, never hurrying, he brought his hands back over the shallow curve of my collarbone and down the meridian of my body, splaying his palms across my ribs.

The oddest thing about all this was that I was not at all astonished. It seemed an infinitely natural thing, and my tortured body relaxed gratefully into the hard mold of his hands, melting and reforming like molded wax. Only the lines of my skeleton held firm.

An odd feeling of warmth now emanated from those broad, square, workman's hands. They moved with painstaking slowness over my body, and I could *feel* the tiny deaths of the bacteria that inhabited my blood, small explosions as each scintilla of infection disappeared. I could feel each interior organ, complete and three-dimensional, and see it as well, as though it sat on a table before me. There the hollow-walled stomach, here the lobed solidity of my liver, and each convolution and twist of intestine, turned in and on and around itself, neatly packed in the shining web of its mesentery membrane. The warmth glowed and spread within each organ, illuminating it like a small sun within me, then died and moved on.

Raymond paused, hands pressed side by side on my swollen belly. I thought he frowned, but it was hard to tell. The cowled head turned, listening, but the usual noises of the hospital continued in the distance, with no warning heeltaps coming our way.

I gasped and moved involuntarily, as one hand moved lower, cupped briefly between my legs. An increase in pressure from the other hand warned me to be silent, and the blunt fingers eased their way inside me.

I closed my eyes and waited, feeling my inner walls adjust to this odd intrusion, the inflammation subsiding bit by bit as he probed gently deeper.

Now he touched the center of my loss, and a spasm of pain contracted the heavy walls of my inflamed uterus. I breathed a small moan, then clamped my lips as he shook his head.

The other hand slid down to rest comfortingly on my belly as the groping fingers of the other touched my womb. He was still then, holding the source of my pain between his two hands as though it were a sphere of crystal, heavy and fragile.

"Now," he said softly. "Call him. Call the red man. Call him."

The pressure of the fingers within and the palm without grew harder, and I pressed my legs against the bed, fighting it. But there was no strength left in me to resist, and the inexorable pressure went on, cracking the crystal sphere, freeing the chaos within.

My mind filled with images, worse than the misery of the fever-dreams, because more real. Grief and loss and fear racked me, and the dusty scent of death and white chalk filled my nostrils. Casting about in the random patterns of my mind for help, I heard the voice still muttering, patiently but firmly, "Call him," and I sought my anchor.

"Jamie! JAMIE!"

A bolt of heat shot through my belly, from one hand to the other, like an arrow through the center of the basin of my bones. The pressing grip relaxed, slid free, and the lightness of harmony filled me.

The bedframe quivered as he ducked beneath it, barely in time.

"Milady! Are you all right?" Sister Angelique shoved through the drapes, round face creased with worry beneath her wimple. The concern in her eyes was underlaid with resignation; the sisters knew I would die soon—if this looked to be my last struggle, she was prepared to summon the priest.

Her small, hard hand rested briefly against my cheek, moved quickly to my brow, then back. The sheet still lay crumpled around my thighs, and my gown lay open. Her hands slid inside it, into my armpits, where they remained for a moment before withdrawing.

"God be praised!" she cried, eyes moistening. "The fever is gone!" She bent close, peering in sudden alarm, to be sure that the disappearance of the fever was not due to the fact that I was dead. I smiled at her weakly.

"I'm all right," I said. "Tell Mother."

She nodded eagerly, and pausing only long enough to draw the sheet modestly over me, she hurried from the room. The drapes had hardly swung closed behind her when Raymond emerged from under the bed.

"I must go," he said. He laid a hand upon my head. "Be well, madonna."

Weak as I was, I rose up, grasping his arm. I slid my hand up the length of forge-tough muscle, seeking, but not finding. The smoothness of his skin was unblemished, clear to the crest of the shoulder. He stared down at me in astonishment.

"What are you doing, madonna?"

"Nothing." I sank back, disappointed. I was too weak and too light-headed to be careful of my words.

"I wanted to see whether you had a vaccination scar."

"Vaccination?" Skilled as I was at reading faces by now, I would have seen the slightest twitch of comprehension, no matter how swiftly it was concealed. But there was none.

"Why do you call me madonna still?" I asked. My hands rested on the slight concavity of my stomach, gently as though not to disturb the shattering emptiness. "I've lost my child."

He looked mildly surprised.

"Ah. I did not call you madonna because you were with child, my lady."

"Why, then?" I didn't really expect him to answer, but he

did. Tired and drained as we both were, it was as though we were suspended together in a place where neither time nor consequence existed; there was room for nothing but truth between us.

He sighed.

"Everyone has a color about them," he said simply. "All around them, like a cloud. Yours is blue, madonna. Like the Virgin's cloak. Like my own."

The gauze curtain fluttered briefly and he was gone.

26

Fontainebleau

or several days, I slept. Whether this was a necessary part of physical recovery, or a stubborn retreat from waking reality, I do not know, but I woke only reluctantly to take a little food, falling at once back into a stupor of oblivion, as though the small, warm weight of broth in my stomach were an anchor that pulled me after it, down through the murky fathoms of sleep.

A few days later I woke to the sound of insistent voices near my ear, and the touch of hands lifting me from the bed. The arms that held me were strong and masculine, and for a moment, I felt afloat in joy. Then I woke all the way, struggling feebly against a wave of tobacco and cheap wine, to find myself in the grasp of Hugo, Louise de La Tour's enormous footman.

"Put me down!" I said, batting at him weakly. He looked startled at this sudden resurrection from the dead, and nearly dropped me, but a high, commanding voice stopped both of us.

"Claire, my dear friend! Do not be afraid, *ma chère*, it's all right. I am taking you to Fontainebleau. The air, and good food—it's what you need. And rest, you need rest . . ."

I blinked against the light like a newborn lamb. Louise's face, round, pink, and anxious, floated nearby like a cherub on a cloud. Mother Hildegarde stood behind her, tall and stern as the angel at the gates of Eden, the heavenly illusion enhanced by the fact that they were both standing in front of the stained-glass window in the vestibule of the Hôpital.

"Yes," she said, her deep voice making the simplest word more emphatic than all Louise's twittering. "It will be good for you. *Au revoir,* my dear."

And with that, I was borne down the steps of the Hôpital and stuffed willy-nilly into Louise's coach, with neither strength nor will to protest.

The bumping of the coach over potholes and ruts kept me awake on the journey to Fontainebleau. That, and Lou-

ise's constant conversation, aimed at reassurance. At first I
made some dazed attempt to respond, but soon realized that
she required no answers, and in fact, talked more easily without them.

After days in the cool gray stone vault of the Hôpital, I
felt like a freshly unwrapped mummy, and shrank from the
assault of so much brightness and color. I found it easier to
deal with if I drew back a bit, and let it all wash past me
without trying to distinguish its elements.

This strategy worked until we reached a small wood just
outside Fontainebleau. The trunks of the oaks were dark and
thick, with low, spreading canopies that shadowed the ground
beneath with shifting light, so that the whole wood seemed to
be moving slightly in the wind. I was vaguely admiring the
effect, when I noticed that some of what I had assumed to be
tree trunks *were* in fact moving, turning very slowly to and fro.

"Louise!" My exclamation and my grip on her arm
stopped her chatter in mid-word.

She lunged heavily across me to see what I was looking
at, then flopped back to her side of the carriage and thrust
her head out of the window, shouting at the coachman.

We came to a slithering, dusty halt just opposite the
wood. There were three of them, two men and a woman.
Louise's high, agitated voice went on, expostulating and questioning, punctuated by the coachman's attempts to explain or
apologize, but I paid no attention.

In spite of their turning and the small fluttering of their
clothing, they were very still, more inert than the trees that
held them. The faces were black with suffocation; Monsieur
Forez wouldn't have approved at all, I thought, through the
haze of shock. An amateur execution, but effective, for all
that. The wind shifted, and a faint, gassy stink blew over us.

Louise shrieked and pounded on the window frame in a
frenzy of indignation, and the carriage started with a jerk that
rocked her back in the seat.

"Merde!" she said, rapidly fanning her flushed face. "The
idiocy of that fool, stopping like that right there! What recklessness! The shock of it is bad for the baby, I am sure, and
you, my poor dear. . . . oh, dear, my poor Claire! I'm so
sorry, I didn't mean to remind you . . . how can you forgive
me, I'm so tactless . . ."

Luckily her agitation at possibly having upset me made her forget her own upset at sight of the bodies, but it was very wearying, trying to stem her apologies. At last, in desperation, I changed the subject back to the hanged ones.

"Who?" The distraction worked; she blinked, and remembering the shock to her *système,* pulled out a bottle of ammoniac spirits and took a hearty sniff that made her sneeze in reflex.

"Hugue . . . choo! Huguenots," she got out, snorting and wheezing. "Protestant heretics. That's what the coachman says."

"They hang them? Still?" Somehow, I had thought such religious persecution a relic of earlier times.

"Well, not just for being Protestants usually, though that's enough," Louise said, sniffing. She dabbed her nose delicately with an embroidered handkerchief, examined the results critically, then reapplied the cloth to her nose and blew it with a satisfying honk.

"Ah, that's better." She tucked the handkerchief back in her pocket and leaned back with a sigh. "Now I am restored. What a shock! If they have to hang them, that's all well, but must they do so by a public thoroughfare, where ladies must be exposed to such disgustingness? Did you *smell* them? Pheew! This is the Comte Medard's land; I'll send him a very nasty letter about it, see if I don't."

"But why did they hang these people?" I asked, interrupting in the brutal manner that was the only possible way of actually conversing with Louise.

"Oh, witchcraft, most likely. There was a woman, you saw. Usually it's witchcraft when the women are involved. If it's only men, most often it's just preaching sedition and heresy, but the women don't preach. Did you see the ugly dark clothes she had on? Horrible! So depressing only to wear dark colors all the time; what kind of religion would make its followers wear such plain clothes all the time? Obviously the Devil's work, anyone can see that. They are afraid of women, that's what it is, so they . . ."

I closed my eyes and leaned back in the seat. I hoped it wasn't very far to Louise's country house.

In addition to the monkey, from whom she would not be parted, Louise's country house contained a number of other decorations of dubious taste. In Paris, her husband's taste and her father's must be consulted, and the rooms of the house there were consequently done richly, but in subdued tones. But Jules seldom came to the country house, being too busy in the city, and so Louise's taste was allowed free rein.

"This is my newest toy; is it not lovely?" she cooed, running her hand lovingly over the carved dark wood of a tiny house that sprouted incongruously from the wall next to a gilt-bronze sconce in the shape of Eurydice.

"That looks like a cuckoo clock," I said disbelievingly.

"You have seen one before? I didn't think there were any to be found anywhere in Paris!" Louise pouted slightly at the thought that her toy might not be unique, but brightened as she twisted the hands of the clock to the next hour. She stood back, beaming proudly as the tiny clockwork bird stuck its head out and emitted several shrill *Cuckoo!*s in succession.

"Isn't it precious?" She touched the bird's head briefly as it disappeared back into its hidey-hole. "Berta, the housekeeper here, got it for me; her brother brought it all the way from Switzerland. Whatever you want to say about the Swiss, they are clever woodcarvers, no?"

I wanted to say no, but instead merely murmured something tactfully admiring.

Louise's grasshopper mind leaped nimbly to a new topic, possibly triggered by thoughts of Swiss servants.

"You know, Claire," she said, with a touch of reproof, "you ought really to come to Mass in the chapel each morning."

"Why?"

She tossed her head in the direction of the doorway, where one of the maids was passing with a tray.

"I don't care at all, myself, but the servants—they're very superstitious out here in the countryside, you know. And one of the footmen from the Paris house was foolish enough to tell the cook all about that silly story of your being La Dame Blanche. I have told them that's all nonsense, of course, and threatened to dismiss anyone I catch spreading such gossip, but . . . well, it might help if you came to Mass. Or at least prayed out loud now and then, so they could hear you."

Unbeliever that I was, I thought daily Mass in the house's chapel might be going a bit far, but with vague amusement, agreed to do what I could to allay the servants' fears; consequently, Louise and I spent the next hour reading psalms aloud to each other, and reciting the Lord's Prayer in unison—loudly. I had no idea what effect this performance might have on the servants, but it did at least exhaust me sufficiently that I went up to my room for a nap, and slept without dreaming until the next morning.

I often had difficulty sleeping, possibly because my waking state was little different from an uneasy doze. I lay awake at night, gazing at the white-gesso ceiling with its furbishes of fruit and flowers. It hung above me like a dim gray shape in the darkness, the personification of the depression that clouded my mind by day. When I did close my eyes at night, I dreamed. I couldn't block the dreams with grayness; they came in vivid colors to assault me in the dark. And so I seldom slept.

There was no word from Jamie—or of him. Whether it was guilt or injury that had kept him from coming to me at the Hôpital, I didn't know. But he hadn't come, nor did he come to Fontainebleau. By now he likely had left for Oviedo.

Sometimes I found myself wondering when—or whether —I would see him again, and what—if anything—we might say to each other. But for the most part, I preferred not to think about it, letting the days come and go, one by one, avoiding thoughts of both the future and the past by living only in the present.

Deprived of his idol, Fergus drooped. Again and again, I saw him from my window, sitting disconsolately beneath a hawthorn bush in the garden, hugging his knees and looking down the road toward Paris. At last, I stirred myself to go out to him, making my way heavily downstairs and down the garden path.

"Can't you find anything to do, Fergus?" I asked him. "Surely one of the stable-lads could use a hand, or something."

"Yes, milady," he agreed doubtfully. He scratched absentmindedly at his buttocks. I observed this behavior with deep suspicion.

"Fergus," I said, folding my arms, "have you got lice?" He snatched his hand back as though burned.

"Oh, no, milady!"

I reached down and pulled him to his feet, sniffed delicately in his general vicinity, and put a finger inside his collar, far enough to reveal the grimy ring around his neck.

"Bath," I said succinctly.

"No!" He jerked away, but I grabbed him by the shoulder. I was surprised by his vehemence; while no fonder of bathing than the normal Parisian—who regarded the prospect of immersion with a repugnance akin to horror—still, I could scarcely reconcile the usually obliging child I knew with the little fury that suddenly squirmed and twisted under my hand.

There was a ripping noise, and he was free, bounding through the blackberry bushes like a rabbit pursued by a weasel. There was a rustle of leaves and a scrabble of stones, and he was gone, over the wall and headed for the outbuildings at the back of the estate.

I made my way through the maze of rickety outbuildings behind the château, cursing under my breath as I skirted mud puddles and heaps of filth. Suddenly, there was a high-pitched whining buzz and a cloud of flies rose from the pile a few feet ahead of me, bodies sparking blue in the sunlight.

I wasn't close enough to have disturbed them; there must have been some movement from the darkened doorway beside the dungheap.

"Aha!" I said out loud. "Got you, you filthy little son of a whatnot! Come out of there this instant!"

No one emerged, but there was an audible stir inside the shed, and I thought I caught a glimpse of white in the shadowed interior. Holding my nose, I stepped over the manure pile into the shed.

There were two gasps of horror; mine, at beholding something that looked like the Wild Man of Borneo flattened against the back wall, and his, at beholding me.

The sunlight trickled through the cracks between the boards, giving enough light for us to see each other clearly, once my eyes had adapted to the relative dark. He wasn't, after all, quite as awful-looking as I'd thought at first, but he wasn't a lot better, either. His beard was as filthy and matted as his hair, flowing past his shoulders onto a shirt ragged as any beggar's. He was barefoot, and if the term *sans-culottes* wasn't yet in common use, it wasn't for lack of trying on his part.

I wasn't afraid of him, because he was so obviously afraid of *me*. He was pressing himself against the wall as though trying to get through it by osmosis.

"It's all right," I said soothingly. "I won't hurt you."

Instead of being soothed, he drew himself abruptly upright, reached into the bosom of his shirt and pulled out a wooden crucifix on a leather thong. He held this out toward me and started praying, in a voice shaking with terror.

"Oh, bother," I said crossly. "Not another one!" I took a deep breath. *"Pater-Noster-qui-es-in-coelis-et-in-terra . . ."* His eyes bugged out, and he kept holding the crucifix, but at least he stopped his own praying in response to this performance.

". . . Amen!" I concluded with a gasp. I held up both hands and waggled them in front of his face. "See? Not a word backward, not a single *quotidianus da nobis hodie* out of place, right? Didn't even have my fingers crossed. So I can't be a witch, can I?"

The man slowly lowered his crucifix and stood gaping at me. "A witch?" he said. He looked as though he thought *I* were crazy, which I felt was a bit thick under the circumstances.

"You didn't think I was a witch?" I said, beginning to feel a trifle foolish.

Something that looked like a smile twitched into existence and out again among the tangles of his beard.

"No, Madame," he said. "I am accustomed to people saying such things of *me*."

"You are?" I eyed him closely. Besides the rags and filth, the man was obviously starving; the wrists that stuck out of his shirt were scrawny as a child's. At the same time, his French was graceful and educated, if oddly accented.

"If you're a witch," I said, "you aren't very successful at it. Who the hell are you?"

At this, the fright came back into his eyes again. He looked from side to side, seeking escape, but the shed was solidly built, if old, with no entrance other than the one in which I was standing. At last, calling on some hidden reserve of courage, he drew himself up to his full height—some three inches below my own—and with great dignity, said "I am the Reverend Walter Laurent, of Geneva."

"You're a *priest*?" I was thunderstruck. I couldn't imagine what might have brought a priest—Swiss or not—to this state.

Father Laurent looked nearly as horror-struck as I.

"A priest?" he echoed. "A papist? Never!"

Suddenly the truth struck me.

"A Huguenot!" I said. "That's it—you're a Protestant, aren't you?" I remembered the bodies I had seen hanging in the forest. That, I thought, explained rather a lot.

His lips quivered, but he pressed them tightly together for a moment before opening them to reply.

"Yes, Madame. I am a pastor; I have been preaching in this district for a month." He licked his lips briefly, eyeing me. "Your pardon, Madame—I think you are not French?"

"I'm English," I said, and he relaxed suddenly, as though someone had taken all the stiffening out of his spine.

"Great Father in Heaven," he said, prayerfully. "You are then a Protestant also?"

"No, I'm a Catholic," I answered. "But I'm not at all vicious about it," I added hastily, seeing the look of alarm spring back into his light-brown eyes. "Don't worry, I won't tell anyone you're here. I suppose you came to try to steal a little food?" I asked sympathetically.

"To steal is a sin!" he said, horrified. "No, Madame. But . . ." He clamped his lips shut, but his glance in the direction of the château gave him away.

"So one of the servants brings you food," I said. "So you let them do the stealing for you. But then I suppose you can absolve them from the sin, so it all works out. Rather thin moral ice you're on, if you ask me," I said reprovingly, "but then it isn't any of my business, I suppose."

A light of hope shone in his eyes. "You mean—you will not have me arrested, Madame?"

"No, of course not. I've a sort of fellow-feeling for fugitives from the law, having come rather close to being burnt at the stake once myself." I didn't know quite why I was being so chatty; the relief of meeting someone who seemed intelligent, I supposed. Louise was sweet, devoted and kind, and had precisely as much brain as the cuckoo clock in her drawing room. Thinking of the Swiss clock, I suddenly realized who Pastor Laurent's secret parishioners must be.

"Look," I said, "if you want to stay here, I'll go up to the château and tell Berta or Maurice that you're here."

The poor man was nothing but skin, bones, and eyes. Everything he thought was reflected in those large, gentle brown orbs. Right now, he was plainly thinking that whoever had tried to burn me at the stake had been on the right track.

"I have heard," he began slowly, reaching for a fresh grip on his crucifix, "of an Englishwoman whom the Parisians call 'La Dame Blanche.' An associate of Raymond the Heretic."

I sighed. "That's me. Though I'm not an associate of Master Raymond's, I don't think. He's just a friend." Seeing him squint doubtfully at me, I inhaled again. *"Pater Noster . . ."*

"No, no, Madame, please." To my surprise, he had lowered the crucifix, and was smiling.

"I also am an acquaintance of Master Raymond's, whom I knew in Geneva. There he was a reputable physician and herbalist. Now, alas, I fear that he has turned to darker pursuits, though of course nothing was proved."

"Proved? About what? And what's all this about Raymond the Heretic?"

"You did not know?" Thin brows lifted over the brown eyes. "Ah. Then you are not associated with Master Raymond's . . . activities." He relaxed noticeably.

"Activity" seemed like a poor description for the way in which Raymond had healed me, so I shook my head.

"No, but I wish you'd tell me. Oh, but I shouldn't be standing here talking; I should go and send Berta with food."

He waved a hand, with some dignity.

"It is of no urgency, Madame. The appetites of the body are of no importance when weighed against the appetites of the soul. And Catholic or not, you have been kind to me. If you are not now associated with Master Raymond's occult activities, then it is right that you should be warned in time."

And ignoring the dirt and the splintered boards of the floor, he folded his legs and sat down against the wall of the shed, gracefully motioning me also to sit. Intrigued, I collapsed opposite him, tucking up the folds of my skirt to keep them from dragging in the manure.

"Have you heard of a man named du Carrefours, Madame?" the Pastor said. "No? Well, his name is well known in Paris, I assure you, but you would do well not to speak it. This man was the organizer and the leader of a ring of unspeakable vice and depravity, in association with the most debased occult practices. I cannot bring myself to mention to you some of the ceremonies that were performed in secret among the nobility. And they call *me* a witch!" he muttered, almost under his breath.

He raised one bony forefinger, as though to forestall my unspoken objection.

"I am aware, Madame, of the sort of gossip that is commonly spread, without reference to fact—who should know it better than we? But the activities of du Carrefours and his followers—these are a matter of common knowledge, for he was tried for them, imprisoned, and eventually burned in the Place de la Bastille as punishment for his crimes."

I remembered Raymond's light remark, *"No one's been burned in Paris in—oh, twenty years at least,"* and shuddered, in spite of the warm weather.

"And you say that Master Raymond was associated with this du Carrefours?"

The Pastor frowned, scratching absently at his matted beard. He likely had both lice and fleas, I thought, and tried to move back imperceptibly.

"Well, it is difficult to say. No one knows where Master Raymond came from; he speaks several tongues, all without noticeable accent. A very mysterious man, Master Raymond, but—I would swear by the name of my God—a good one."

I smiled at him. "I think so, too."

He nodded, smiling, but then grew serious as he resumed his story. "Just so, Madame. Still, he corresponded with du Carrefours from Geneva; I know this, for he told me so himself—he supplied various substances to order: plants, elixirs, the dried skins of animals. Even a sort of fish—a most peculiar and frightening thing, which he told me was brought up from the darkest depths of the sea; a horrible thing, all teeth,

with almost no flesh—but with the most horrifying small . . .
lights . . . like tiny lanterns, beneath its eyes."

"Really," I said, fascinated.

Pastor Laurent shrugged. "All this may be quite innocent, of course, a mere matter of business. But he disappeared from Geneva at the same time that du Carrefours
came at first under suspicion—and within weeks of du Carrefours's execution, I had begun to hear stories that Master
Raymond had established his business in Paris, and that he
had taken over a number of du Carrefours's clandestine activities as well."

"Hmm," I said. I was thinking of Raymond's inner room,
and the cabinet painted with Cabbalistic signs. To keep out
those who believed in them. "Anything else?"

The Reverend Laurent's eyebrows arched skyward.

"No, Madame," he said, rather weakly. "Nothing else, to
my knowledge."

"Well, I'm really not given to that sort of thing myself," I
assured him.

"Oh? Good," he said, hesitantly. He sat silently for a
moment, as though making up his mind about something,
then inclined his head courteously toward me.

"You will pardon me if I intrude, Madame? Berta and
Maurice have told me something of your loss. I am sorry,
Madame."

"Thank you," I said, staring at the stripes of sunlight on
the floor.

There was another silence, then Pastor Laurent said delicately, "Your husband, Madame? He is not here with you?"

"No," I said, still keeping my eyes on the floor. Flies
lighted momentarily, then zoomed off, finding no nourishment. "I don't know where he is."

I didn't mean to say any more, but something made me
look up at the ragged little preacher.

"He cared more for his honor than he did for me or his
child or an innocent man," I said bitterly. "I don't *care* where
he is; I never want to see him again!"

I stopped abruptly, shaken. I had not put it into words
before, even to myself. But it was true. There had been a
great trust between us, and Jamie had broken it, for the sake
of revenge. I understood; I had seen the power of the thing

that drove him, and knew it couldn't be denied forever. But I had asked for a few months' grace, which he had promised me. And then, unable to wait, he had broken his word, and by so doing, sacrificed everything that lay between him and me. Not only that: He had jeopardized the undertaking in which we were engaged. I could understand, but I would not forgive.

Pastor Laurent laid a hand on mine. It was grimy with crusted dirt, and his nails were broken and black-edged, but I didn't draw away. I expected platitudes or a homily, but he didn't speak, either; just held my hand, very gently, for a long time, as the sun moved across the floor and the flies buzzed slow and heavy past our heads.

"You had better go," he said at last, releasing my hand. "You will be missed."

"I suppose so." I drew a deep breath, feeling at least steadier, if not better. I felt in the pocket of my gown; I had a small purse with me.

I hesitated, not wanting to offend him. After all, by his lights I was a heretic, even if not a witch.

"Will you let me give you some money?" I asked carefully.

He thought for a moment, then smiled, the light-brown eyes glowing.

"On one condition, Madame. If you will allow me to pray for you?"

"A bargain," I said, and gave him the purse.

27

An Audience with His Majesty

As the days passed at Fontainebleau, I gradually regained my bodily strength, though my mind continued to drift, my thoughts shying away from any sort of memory or action.

There were few visitors; the country house was a refuge, where the frenetic social life of Paris seemed like one more of the uneasy dreams that haunted me. I was surprised, then, to have a maid summon me to the drawing room to meet a visitor. The thought crossed my mind that it might be Jamie, and I felt a surge of dizzy sickness. But then reason reasserted itself; Jamie must have left for Spain by now; he could not possibly return before late August. And when he did?

I couldn't think of it. I pushed the idea into the back of my mind, but my hands shook as I fastened my laces to go downstairs.

Much to my surprise, the "visitor" was Magnus, the butler from Jared's Paris house.

"Your pardon, Madame," he said, bowing deeply when he saw me. "I did not wish to presume . . . but I could not tell whether perhaps the matter was of importance . . . and with the master gone . . ." Lordly in his own sphere of influence, the old man was badly discomposed by being so far afield. It took some time to extract a coherent story from him, but at length a note was produced, folded and sealed, addressed to me.

"The hand is that of Monsieur Murtagh," Magnus said, in a tone of half-repugnant awe. That explained his hesitance, I thought. The servants in the Paris house all regarded Murtagh with a sort of respectful horror, which had been exaggerated by reports of the events in the Rue du Faubourg St.-Honoré.

It had come to the Paris house two weeks earlier, Magnus explained. Unsure what to do with it, the servants had dithered and conferred, but at length, he had decided that it must be brought to my attention.

"The master being gone," he repeated. This time I paid attention to what he was saying.

"Gone?" I said. The note was crumpled and stained from its journey, light as a leaf in my hand. "You mean Jamie left *before* this note arrived?" I could make no sense of this; this must be Murtagh's note giving the name and sailing date of the ship that would bear Charles Stuart's port from Lisbon. Jamie could not have left for Spain before receiving the information.

As though to verify this, I broke the seal and unfolded the note. It was addressed to me, because Jamie had thought there was less chance of my mail being intercepted than his. From Lisbon, dated nearly a month before, the letter boasted no signature, but didn't need one.

"The *Scalamandre* sails from Lisbon on the 18th of July" was all the note said. I was surprised to see what a small, neat hand Murtagh wrote; somehow I had been expecting a formless scrawl.

I looked up from the paper to see Magnus and Louise exchanging a very odd kind of look.

"What is it?" I said abruptly. "Where's Jamie?" I had put down his absence from L'Hôpital des Anges after the miscarriage to his guilt at the knowledge that his reckless action had killed our child, had killed Frank, and had nearly cost me my life. At that point, I didn't care; I didn't want to see him, either. Now I began to think of another, more sinister explanation for his absence.

It was Louise who spoke at last, squaring her plump shoulders to the task.

"He's in the Bastille," she said, taking a deep breath. "For dueling."

My knees felt watery, and I sat down on the nearest available surface.

"Why in hell didn't you tell me?" I wasn't sure what I felt at this news; shock, or horror—fear? or a small sense of satisfaction?

"I—I didn't want to upset you, *chérie*," Louise stammered, taken aback at my apparent distress. "You were so weak . . . and there was nothing you could do, after all. And you didn't ask," she pointed out.

"But what . . . how . . . how long is the sentence?" I

demanded. Whatever my initial emotion, it was superseded by a sudden rush of urgency. Murtagh's note had arrived at the Rue Trémoulins two weeks ago. Jamie should have left upon its receipt—but he hadn't.

Louise was summoning servants and ordering wine and ammoniac spirits and burnt feathers, all at once; I must have looked rather alarming.

"It is a contravention of the King's order," she said, pausing in her flutter. "He will remain in prison at the King's pleasure."

"Jesus H. Roosevelt Christ," I muttered, wishing I had something stronger to say.

"It is fortunate that *le petit* James did not kill his opponent," Louise hastened to add. "In that case, the penalty would have been much more . . . eek!" She twitched her striped skirts aside just in time to avoid the cascade of chocolate and biscuits as I knocked over the newly arrived refreshments. The tray clanged to the floor unregarded as I stared down at her. My hands were clasped tightly against my ribs, the right protectively curled over the gold ring on my left hand. The thin metal seemed to burn against my skin.

"He isn't dead, then?" I asked, like one in a dream. "Captain Randall . . . he's alive?"

"Why, yes," she said, peering curiously up at me. "You did not know? He is badly wounded, but it is said that he recovers. Are you quite well, Claire? You look . . ." But the rest of what she was saying was lost in the roaring that filled my ears.

"You did too much, too soon," Louise said severely, pulling back the curtains. "I said so, didn't I?"

"I imagine so," I said. I sat up and swung my legs out of bed, checking cautiously for any residual signs of faintness. No swimming of head, ringing of ears, double vision, or inclination to fall on the floor. Vital signs all right.

"I need my yellow gown, and then would you send for the carriage, Louise?" I asked.

Louise looked at me in horror. "You are not meaning to go out? Nonsense! Monsieur Clouseau is coming to attend you! I have sent a messenger to fetch him here at once!"

The news that Monsieur Clouseau, a prominent society physician, was coming from Paris to examine me, would have been sufficient grounds to get me on my feet, had I needed them.

The eighteenth of July was ten days away. With a fast horse, good weather, and a disregard for bodily comfort, the journey from Paris to Oviedo could be made in six. That left me four days to contrive Jamie's release from the Bastille; no time to fiddle about with Monsieur Clouseau.

"Hmm," I said, looking round the room thoughtfully. "Well, call the maid to dress me, at any rate. I don't want Monsieur Clouseau to find me in my shift."

Though she still looked suspicious, this sounded plausible; most ladies of the Court would rise from a deathbed in order to make sure they were dressed appropriately for the occasion.

"All right," she agreed, turning to go. "But you stay in bed until Yvonne arrives, you hear?"

The yellow gown was one of my best, a loose, graceful thing made in the modish sacque style, with a wide rolled collar, full sleeves, and a beaded closure down the front. Powdered, combed, stockinged, and perfumed at last, I surveyed the pair of shoes Yvonne had laid out for me to step into. I turned my head this way and that, frowning appraisingly.

"Mm, no," I said at last. "I don't think so. I'll wear the others, the ones with the red morocco heels, instead."

The maid looked dubiously at my dress, as though mentally assessing the effect of red morocco with yellow moiré silk, but obediently turned to rummage in the foot of the huge armoire.

Tiptoeing silently up behind her in my stockinged feet, I shoved her headfirst into the armoire, and slammed the door on the heaving, shrieking mass beneath the pile of fallen dresses within. Turning the key in the door, I dropped it neatly into my pocket, mentally shaking hands with myself. Neat job, Beauchamp, I thought. All this political intrigue is teaching you things they never dreamt of in nursing school, no doubt about it.

"Don't worry," I told the shaking armoire soothingly. "Someone will be along to let you out soon, I imagine. And you can tell La Princesse that you didn't *let* me go anywhere."

A despairing wail from inside the armoire seemed to be mentioning Monsieur Clouseau's name.

"Tell him to have a look at the monkey," I called over my shoulder, "It's got mange."

The success of my encounter with Yvonne buoyed my mood. Once ensconced in the carriage, rattling back toward Paris, though, my spirits sank appreciably.

While I was no longer quite so angry at Jamie, I still did not wish to see him. My feelings were in complete turmoil, and I had no intention of examining them closely; it hurt too much. Grief was there, and a horrible sense of failure, and over all, the sense of betrayal; his and mine. He should never have gone to the Bois de Boulogne; I should never have gone after him.

But we both did as our natures and our feelings dictated, and together we had—perhaps—caused the death of our child. I had no wish to meet my partner in the crime, still less to expose my grief to him, to match my guilt with his. I fled from anything that reminded me of the dripping morning in the Bois; certainly I fled from any memory of Jamie, caught as I had last seen him, rising from the body of his victim, face glowing with the vengeance that would shortly claim his own family.

I could not think of it even in passing, without a terrible clenching in my stomach, that brought back the ghost of the pain of premature labor. I pressed my fists into the blue velvet of the carriage seat, raising myself to ease the imagined pressure on my back.

I turned to look out the window, hoping to distract myself, but the sights went blindly by, as my mind returned, unbidden, to thoughts of my journey. Whatever my feelings for Jamie, whether we would ever see each other again, what we might be, or not be, to one another—still the fact remained that he was in prison. And I rather thought I knew just what imprisonment might mean to him, with the memories of Wentworth that he carried; the groping hands that fondled him in dreams, the stone walls he hammered in his sleep.

More important, there was the matter of Charles and the

ship from Portugal; the loan from Monsieur Duverney, and Murtagh, about to take ship from Lisbon for a rendezvous off Oviedo. The stakes were too high to allow my own emotions any play. For the sake of the Scottish clans, and the Highlands themselves, for Jamie's family and tenants at Lallybroch, for the thousands who would die at Culloden and in its aftermath—it had to be tried. And to try, Jamie would have to be free; it wasn't something I could undertake myself.

No, there was no question. I would have to do whatever I must to have him released from the Bastille.

And just what could I do?

I watched the beggars scramble and gesture toward the windows as we entered the Rue du Faubourg St.-Honoré. When in doubt, I thought, seek the assistance of a Higher Authority.

I rapped on the panel beside the driver's seat. It slid back with a grating noise, and the mustached face of Louise's coachman peered down at me.

"Madame?"

"Left," I said. "To L'Hôpital des Anges."

Mother Hildegarde tapped her blunt fingers thoughtfully on a sheet of music paper, as though drumming out a troublesome sequence. She sat at the mosaic table in her private office, across from Herr Gerstmann, summoned to join us in urgent council.

"Well, yes," said Herr Gerstmann doubtfully. "Yes, I believe I can arrange a private audience with His Majesty, but . . . you are certain that your husband . . . um . . ." The music master seemed to be having unusual trouble in expressing himself, which made me suspect that petitioning the King for Jamie's release might be just a trifle more complicated than I had thought. Mother Hildegarde verified this suspicion with her own reaction.

"Johannes!" she exclaimed, so agitated as to drop her usual formal manner of address. "She cannot do that! After all, Madame Fraser is not one of the Court ladies—she is a person of virtue!"

"Er, thank you," I said politely. "If you don't mind,

though . . . what, precisely, would my state of virtue have to do with my seeing the King to ask for Jamie's release?"

The nun and the singing-master exchanged looks in which horror at my naiveté was mingled with a general reluctance to remedy it. At last Mother Hildegarde, braver of the two, bit the bullet.

"If you go alone to ask such a favor from the King, he will expect to lie with you," she said bluntly. After all the carry-on over telling me, I was hardly surprised, but I glanced at Herr Gerstmann for confirmation, which he gave in the form of a reluctant nod.

"His Majesty is susceptible to requests from ladies of a certain personal charm," he said delicately, taking a sudden interest in one of the ornaments on the desk.

"But there is a price to such requests," added Mother Hildegarde, not nearly so delicate. "Most of the courtiers are only too pleased when their wives find Royal favor; the gain to them is well worth the sacrifice of their wives' virtue." The wide mouth curled with scorn at the thought, then straightened into its usual grimly humorous line.

"But your husband," she said, "does not appear to me to be the sort who makes a complaisant cuckold." The heavy arched brows supplied the question mark at the end of the sentence, and I shook my head in response.

"I shouldn't think so." In fact, this was one of the grosser understatements I had ever heard. If "complaisant" was not the very last word that came to mind at the thought of Jamie Fraser, it was certainly well down toward the bottom of the list. I tried to imagine just what Jamie would think, say, or do, if he ever learned that I had lain with another man, up to and including the King of France.

The thought made me remember the trust that had existed between us, almost since the day of our marriage, and a sudden feeling of desolation swept over me. I shut my eyes for a moment, fighting illness, but the prospect had to be faced.

"Well," I said, taking a deep breath, "is there another way?"

Mother Hildegarde knitted her brows, frowning at Herr Gerstmann, as though expecting him to produce the answer.

The little music master shrugged, though, frowning in his turn.

"If there were a friend of some importance, who might intercede for your husband with His Majesty?" he asked tentatively.

"Not likely." I had examined all such alternatives myself, in the coach from Fontainebleau, and been forced to conclude that there was no one whom I could reasonably ask to undertake such an ambassage. Owing to the illegal and scandalous nature of the duel—for of course Marie d'Arbanville had spread her gossip all over Paris—none of the Frenchmen of our acquaintance could very well afford to take an interest in it. Monsieur Duverney, who had agreed to see me, had been kind, but discouraging. Wait, had been his advice. In a few months, when the scandal has died down a bit, then His Majesty might be approached. But now . . .

Likewise the Duke of Sandringham, so bound by the delicate proprieties of diplomacy that he had dismissed his private secretary for only the appearance of involvement in scandal, was in no position to petition Louis for a favor of this sort.

I stared down at the inlaid tabletop, scarcely seeing the complex curves of enamel that swept through abstractions of geometry and color. My forefinger traced the loops and whorls before me, providing a precarious anchor for my racing thoughts. If it was indeed necessary for Jamie to be released from prison, in order to prevent the Jacobite invasion of Scotland, then it seemed that I would have to do the releasing, whatever the method, and whatever its consequences.

At last I looked up, meeting the music master's eyes. "I'll have to," I said softly. "There's no other way."

There was a moment of silence. Then Herr Gerstmann glanced at Mother Hildegarde.

"She will stay here," Mother Hildegarde declared firmly. "You may send to tell her the time of the audience, Johannes, once you have arranged it."

She turned to me. "After all, if you are really set upon this course, my dear friend . . ." Her lips pressed tightly together, then opened to say, "It may be a sin to assist you in committing immorality. Still, I will do it. I know that your reasons seem good to you, whatever they may be. And per-

haps the sin will be outweighed by the grace of your friendship." She accepted Claire's proffered note to Jamie.

"Oh, Mother." I thought I might cry if I said more, so
contented myself with merely squeezing the big, work-rough-
ened hand that rested on my shoulder. I had a sudden longing
to fling myself into her arms and bury my face against the
comforting black serge bosom, but her hand left my shoulder
and went to the long jet rosary that clicked among the folds of
her skirt as she walked.

"I will pray for you," she said, smiling what would have
been a tremulous smile on a face less solidly carved. Her
expression changed suddenly to one of deep consideration.
"Though I do wonder," she added meditatively, "exactly *who*
would be the proper patron saint to invoke in the circumstances?"

Mary Magdalene was the name that came to mind as I
raised my hands overhead in a simulation of prayer, to allow
the small wicker dress frame to slip over my shoulders and
settle onto my hips. Or Mata Hari, but I was quite sure *she'd*
never make the Calendar of Saints. I wasn't sure about the
Magdalene, for that matter, but a reformed prostitute
seemed the most likely among the heavenly host to be sympathetic to the venture being now undertaken.

I reflected that the Convent of the Angels had probably
never before seen a robing such as this. While the postulants
about to take their final vows were most splendidly arrayed as
brides of Christ, red silk and rice powder probably didn't
figure heavily in the ceremonies.

Very symbolic, I thought, as the rich scarlet folds slithered over my upturned face. White for purity, and red for
. . . whatever this was. Sister Minèrve, a young sister from a
wealthy noble family, had been selected to assist me in my
toilette; with considerable skill and aplomb, she dressed my
hair, tucking in the merest scrap of ostrich feather trimmed
with seed pearls. She combed my brows carefully, darkening
them with the small lead combs, and painted my lips with a
feather dipped in a pot of rouge. The feel of it on my lips
tickled unbearably, exaggerating my tendency to break into
unhinged giggles. Not hilarity; hysteria.

Sister Minèrve reached for the hand mirror. I stopped her with a gesture; I didn't want to look myself in the eye. I took a deep breath, and nodded.

"I'm ready," I said. "Send for the coach."

I had never been in this part of the palace before. In fact, after the multiple twists and turnings through the candle-lit corridors of mirrors, I was no longer sure exactly how many of me there were, let alone where any of them were going.

The discreet and anonymous Gentleman of the Bed-chamber led me to a small paneled door in an alcove. He rapped once, then bowed to me, whirled, and left without waiting for an answer. The door swung inward, and I entered.

The King still had his breeches on. The realization slowed my heartbeat to something like a tolerable rate, and I ceased feeling as though I might throw up any minute.

I didn't know quite what I had been expecting, but the reality was mildly reassuring. He was informally dressed, in shirt and breeches, with a dressing gown of brown silk draped across his shoulders for warmth. His Majesty smiled, and urged me to rise with a hand under my arm. His palm was warm—I had subconsciously expected his touch to be clammy —and I smiled back, as best I could.

The attempt must not have been altogether successful, for he patted my arm kindly, and said "Don't be afraid of me, *chère* Madame. I don't bite."

"No," I said. "Of course not."

He was a lot more poised than I was. Well, of course he is, I thought to myself, he does this all the time. I took a deep breath and tried to relax.

"You will have a little wine, Madame?" he asked. We were alone; there were no servants, but the wine was already poured, in a pair of goblets that stood on the table, glowing like rubies in the candlelight. The chamber was ornate, but very small, and aside from the table and a pair of oval-backed chairs, held only a luxuriously padded green-velvet chaise longue. I tried to avoid looking at it as I took my goblet, with a murmur of thanks.

"Sit, please." Louis sank down upon one of the chairs,

gesturing to me to take the other. "Now please," he said, smiling at me, "tell me what it is that I may do for you."

"M-my husband," I began, stammering a little from nervousness. "He's in the Bastille."

"Of course," the King murmured. "For dueling. I recall." He took my free hand in his own, fingers resting lightly on my pulse. "What would you have me do, *chère* Madame? You know it is a serious offense; your husband has broken my own decree." One finger stroked the underside of my wrist, sending small tickling sensations up my arm.

"Y-yes, I understand that. But he was . . . provoked." I had an idea. "You know he's a Scot; men of that country are" —I tried to think of a good synonym for "berserk"—"most fierce where questions of their honor are concerned."

Louis nodded, head bent in apparent absorption over the hand he held. I could see the faint greasy shine to his skin, and smell his perfume. Violets. A strong, sweet smell, but not enough to completely mask his own acrid maleness.

He drained his wine in two long swallows and discarded the goblet, the better to clasp my hand in both his own. One short-nailed finger traced the lines of my wedding ring, with its interlaced links and thistle blossoms.

"Quite so," he said, bringing my hand closer, as though to examine the ring. "Quite so, Madame. However . . ."

"I'd be . . . most grateful, Your Majesty," I interrupted. His head rose and I met his eyes, dark and quizzical. My heart was going like a trip-hammer. "Most . . . grateful."

He had thin lips and bad teeth; I could smell his breath, thick with onion and decay. I tried holding my own breath, but this could hardly be more than a temporary expedient.

"Well . . ." he said slowly, as though thinking it over. "I would myself be inclined toward mercy, Madame . . ."

I released my breath in a short gasp, and his fingers tightened on mine in warning. "But you see, there are complications."

"There are?" I said faintly.

He nodded, eyes still fixed on my face. His fingers wandered lightly over the back of my hand, tracing the veins.

"The Englishman who was so unfortunate as to have offended milord Broch Tuarach," he said. "He was in the employ of . . . a certain man—an English noble of some importance."

Sandringham. My heart lurched at the mention of him, indirect as it was.

"This noble is engaged in—shall we say, certain negotiations which entitle him to consideration?" The thin lips smiled, emphasizing the imperious prow of the nose above. "And this nobleman has interested himself in the matter of the duel between your husband and the English Captain Randall. I am afraid that he was most exigent in demanding that your husband suffer the full penalty of his indiscretion, Madame."

Bloody tub of lard, I thought. Of course—since Jamie had refused the bribe of a pardon, what better way to prevent his "involving himself" in the Stuarts' affairs than to ensure Jamie's staying safely jugged in the Bastille for the next few years? Sure, discreet, and inexpensive; a method bound to appeal to the Duke.

On the other hand, Louis was still breathing heavily on my hand, which I took as a sign that all was not necessarily lost. If he wasn't going to grant my request, he could scarcely expect me to go to bed with him—or if he did, he was in for a rude surprise.

I girded my loins for another try.

"And does Your Majesty take orders from the English?" I asked boldly.

Louis's eyes flew open with momentary shock. Then he smiled wryly, seeing what I intended. Still, I had touched a nerve; I saw the small twitch of his shoulders as he resettled his conviction of power like an invisible mantle.

"No, Madame, I do not," he said with some dryness. "I do, however, take account of . . . various factors." The heavy lids drooped over his eyes for a moment, but he still held my hand.

"I have heard that your husband interests himself in the affairs of my cousin," he said.

"Your Majesty is well informed," I said politely. "But since that is so, you will know that my husband does not support the restoration of the Stuarts to the throne of Scotland." I prayed that this was what he wanted to hear.

Apparently it was; he smiled, raised my hand to his lips, and kissed it briefly.

"Ah? I had heard . . . conflicting stories about your husband."

I took a deep breath and resisted the impulse to snatch my hand back.

"Well, it's a matter of business," I said, trying to sound as matter-of-fact as possible. "My husband's cousin, Jared Fraser, is an avowed Jacobite; Jamie—my husband—can't very well go about letting his real views be made public, when he's in partnership with Jared." Seeing the doubt begin to fade from his face, I hurried it along. "Ask Monsieur Duverney," I suggested. "He's well acquainted with my husband's true sympathies."

"I have." Louis paused for a long moment, watching his own fingers, dark and stubby, tracing delicate circles over the back of my hand.

"So very pale," he murmured. "So fine. I believe I could see the blood flow beneath your skin."

He let go of my hand then and sat regarding me. I was extremely good at reading faces, but Louis's was quite impenetrable at the moment. I realized suddenly that he'd been a king since the age of five; the ability to hide his thoughts was as much a part of him as his Bourbon nose or the sleepy brown eyes.

This thought brought another in its wake, with a chill that struck me deep in the pit of the stomach. He was the King. The Citizens of Paris would not rise for forty years or more; until that day, his rule within France was absolute. He could free Jamie with a word—or kill him. He could do with me as he liked; there was no recourse. One nod of his head, and the coffers of France could spill the gold that would launch Charles Stuart, loosing him like a deadly bolt of lightning to strike through the heart of Scotland.

He was the King. He would do as he wished. And I watched his dark eyes, clouded with thought, and waited, trembling, to see what the Royal pleasure might be.

"Tell me, *ma chère* Madame," he said at last, stirring from his introspection. "If I were to grant your request, to free your husband . . ." he paused, considering.

"Yes?"

"He would have to leave France," Louis said, one thick brow raised in warning. "That would be a condition of his release."

"I understand." My heart was pounding so hard that it nearly drowned out his words. Jamie leaving France was, after all, precisely the point. "But he's exiled from Scotland . . ."

"I think that might be arranged."

I hesitated, but there seemed little choice but to agree on Jamie's behalf. "All right."

"Good." The King nodded, pleased. Then his eyes returned to me, rested on my face, glided down my neck, my breasts, my body. "I would ask a small service of you in return, Madame," he said softly.

I met his eyes squarely for one second. Then I bowed my head. "I am at Your Majesty's complete disposal," I said.

"Ah." He rose and threw off the dressing gown, leaving it flung carelessly over the back of his armchair. He smiled and held out a hand to me. "*Très bien, ma chère.* Come with me, then."

I closed my eyes briefly, willing my knees to work. You've been married twice, for heaven's sake, I thought to myself. Quit making such a bloody fuss about it.

I rose to my feet and took his hand. To my surprise, he didn't turn toward the velvet chaise, but instead led me toward the door at the far side of the room.

I had one moment of ice-cold clarity as he let go my hand to open the door.

Damn you, Jamie Fraser, I thought. *Damn you to hell!*

➤

I stood quite still on the threshold, blinking. My meditations on the protocol of Royal disrobing faded into sheer astonishment.

The room was quite dark, lit only by numerous tiny oil-lamps, set in groups of five in alcoves in the wall of the chamber. The room itself was round, and so was the huge table that stood in its center, the dark wood gleaming with pinpoint reflections. There were people sitting at the table, no more than hunched dark blurs against the blackness of the room. There was a murmur at my entrance, quickly stilled at

the King's appearance. As my eyes grew more accustomed to
the murk, I realized with a sense of shock that the people
seated at the table wore hoods; the nearest man turned toward me, and I caught the faint gleam of eyes through holes
in the velvet. It looked like a convention of hangmen.

Apparently I was the guest of honor. I wondered for a
nervous moment just what might be expected of me. From
Raymond's hints, and Marguerite's, I had nightmare visions
of occult ceremonies involving infant sacrifice, ceremonial
rape, and general-purpose satanic rites. It is, however, quite
rare for the supernatural actually to live up to its billing, and I
hoped this occasion would be no exception.

"We have heard of your great skill, Madame, and your
. . . reputation." Louis smiled, but there was a tinge of caution in his eyes as he looked at me, as though not quite certain what I might do. "We should be most obliged, my dear
Madame, should you be willing to give us the benefits of such
skill this evening."

I nodded. Most obliged, eh? Well, that was all to the
good; I wanted him obliged to me. What was he expecting me
to do, though? A servant placed a huge wax candle on the
table and lighted it, shedding a pool of mellow light on the
polished wood. The candle was decorated with symbols like
those I had seen in Master Raymond's secret chamber.

"*Regardez,* Madame." The King's hand was under my
elbow, directing my attention beyond the table. Now that the
candle was lighted, I could see the two figures who stood
silently among the flickering shadows. I started at the sight,
and the King's hand tightened on my arm.

The Comte St. Germain and Master Raymond stood
there, side by side, separated by a distance of six feet or so.
Raymond gave no sign of acknowledgment, but stood quietly,
staring off to one side with the pupil-less black eyes of a frog
in a bottomless well.

The Comte saw me, and his eyes widened in disbelief;
then he scowled at me. He was dressed in his finest, all in
white, as usual; a white stiffened satin coat over cream-
colored silk vest and breeches. A tracery of seed pearls decorated his cuffs and lapels, gleaming in the candlelight. Sartorial splendor aside, the Comte looked rather the worse for

wear, I thought—his face was drawn with strain, and the lace
of his stock was wilted, his collar darkened with sweat.

Raymond, conversely, looked calm as a turbot on ice,
standing stolidly with both hands folded into the sleeves of his
usual scruffy velvet robe, broad, flat face placid and inscrutable.

"These two men stand accused, Madame." said Louis,
with a gesture at Raymond and the Comte. "Of sorcery, of
witchcraft, of the perversion of the legitimate search for
knowledge into an exploration of arcane arts." His voice was
cold and grim. "Such practices flourished during the reign of
my grandfather; but we shall not suffer such wickedness in
our realm."

The King flicked his fingers at one of the hooded figures,
who sat with pen and ink before a sheaf of papers. "Read the
indictments, if you please," he said.

The hooded man rose obediently to his feet and began to
read from one of the papers: charges of bestiality and foul
sacrifice, of the spilling of the blood of innocents, the profa-
nation of the most holy rite of the Mass by desecration of the
Host, the performance of amatory rites upon the altar of God
—I had a quick flash of just what the healing Raymond had
performed on me at L'Hôpital des Anges must have looked
like, and felt profoundly grateful that no one had discovered
him.

I heard the name "du Carrefours" mentioned, and swallowed a sudden rising of bile. What had Pastor Laurent said?
The sorcerer du Carrefours had been burned in Paris, only
twenty years before, on just such charges as those I was hearing: "—the summoning of demons and powers of darkness,
the procurement of illness and death for payment"—I put a
hand to my stomach, in vivid memory of bitter cascara —"the
ill-wishing of members of the Court, the defilement of virgins—" I shot a quick look at the Comte, but his face was
stony, lips pressed tight as he listened.

Raymond stood quite still, silver hair brushing his shoulders, as though listening to something as inconsequential as
the song of a thrush in the bushes. I had seen the Cabbalistic
symbols on his cabinet, but I could hardly reconcile the man I
knew—the compassionate poisoner, the practical apothecary
—with the list of vileness being read.

At last the indictments ceased. The hooded man glanced at the King, and at a signal, sank back into his chair.

"Extensive inquiry has been made," the King said, turning to me. "Evidence has been presented, and the testimony of many witnesses taken. It seems clear"—he turned a cold gaze on the two accused magi—"that both men have undertaken investigations into the writings of ancient philosophers, and have employed the art of divinations, using calculation of the movements of heavenly bodies. Still . . ." He shrugged. "This is not of itself a crime. I am given to understand"—he glanced at a heavyset man in a hood, whom I suspected of being the Bishop of Paris—"that this is not necessarily at variance with the teachings of the Church; even the blessed St. Augustine was known to have made inquiries into the mysteries of astrology."

I rather dimly recalled that St. Augustine had indeed looked into astrology, and had rather scornfully dismissed it as a load of rubbish. Still, I doubted that Louis had read Augustine's *Confessions,* and this line of argument was undoubtedly a good one for an accused sorcerer; star-gazing seemed fairly harmless, by comparison with infant sacrifice and nameless orgies.

I was beginning to wonder, with considerable apprehension, just what I was doing in this assemblage. Had someone seen Master Raymond with me in the Hôpital after all?

"We have no quarrel with the proper use of knowledge, nor the search for wisdom," the King went on in measured tones. "There is much that can be learned from the writings of the ancient philosophers, if they are approached with proper caution and humility of spirit. But it is true that while much good may be found in such writings, so, too, may evil be discovered, and the pure search for wisdom be perverted into the desire for power and wealth—the things of this world."

He glanced back and forth between the two accused sorcerers once more, obviously drawing conclusions as to who might be more inclined to *that* sort of perversion. The Comte was still sweating, damp patches showing dark on the white silk of his coat.

"No, Your Majesty!" he said, shaking back his dark hair and fixing burning eyes on Master Raymond. "It is true that there are dark forces at work in the land—the vileness of which you speak walks among us! But such wickedness does not dwell in the breast of your most loyal subject"—he smote himself on the breast, lest we had missed the point—"no, Your Majesty! For the perversion of knowledge and the use of forbidden arts, you must look beyond your own Court." He didn't accuse Master Raymond directly, but the direction of his pointed gaze was obvious.

The King was unmoved by this outburst. "Such abominations flourished during the reign of my grandfather," he said softly. "We have rooted them out wherever they have been found; destroyed the threat of such evil where it shall exist in our realm. Sorcerers, witches, those who pervert the teachings of the Church . . . Monsieurs, we shall not suffer such wickedness to arise again."

"So." He slapped both palms lightly against the table and straightened himself. Still staring at Raymond and the Comte, he held out a hand in my direction.

"We have brought here a witness," he declared. "An infallible judge of truth, of purity of heart."

I made a small, gurgling noise, which made the King turn to look at me.

"A White Lady," he said softly. "La Dame Blanche cannot lie; she sees the heart and the soul of a man, and may turn that truth to good . . . or to destruction."

The air of unreality that had hung over the evening vanished in a pop. The faint wine-buzz was gone, and I was suddenly stone-cold sober. I opened my mouth, and then shut it, realizing that there was precisely nothing I could say.

Horror snaked down my backbone and coiled in my belly as the King made his dispositions. Two pentagrams were to be drawn on the floor, within which the two sorcerers would stand. Each would then bear witness to his own activities and motives. And the White Lady would judge the truth of what was said.

"Jesus H. Christ," I said, under my breath.

"Monsieur le Comte?" The King gestured to the first pentagram, chalked on the carpet. Only a king would treat a genuine Aubusson with that kind of cavalier disregard.

The Comte brushed close to me as he went to take his place. As he passed me, I caught the faintest whisper: "Be warned, Madame. I do not work alone." He took up his spot and turned to face me with an ironic bow, outwardly composed.

The implication was reasonably clear; I condemned him, and his minions would be round promptly to cut off my nipples and burn Jared's warehouse. I licked dry lips, cursing Louis. Why couldn't he just have wanted my body?

Raymond stepped casually into his own chalk-limned space, and nodded cordially in my direction. No hint of guidance in those round black eyes.

I hadn't the faintest idea what to do next. The King motioned to me to stand opposite him, between the two pentagrams. The hooded men rose to stand behind the King; a blank-faced crowd of menace.

Everything was extremely quiet. Candle smoke hung in a pall near the gilded ceiling, wisps drifting in the languid air currents. All eyes were trained on me. Finally, out of desperation, I turned to the Comte and nodded.

"You may begin, Monsieur le Comte," I said.

He smiled—at least I assumed it was meant to be a smile —and began, starting out with an explication of the foundation of the Cabbala and moving right along to an exegesis on the twenty-three letters of the Hebrew alphabet, and the profound symbolism of it all. It sounded thoroughly scholarly, completely innocuous, and terribly dull. The King yawned, not bothering to cover his mouth.

Meanwhile, I was turning over alternatives in my mind. This man had threatened and attacked me, and tried to have Jamie assassinated—whether for personal or political reasons, it made little difference. He had in all likelihood been the ringleader of the gang of rapists who had waylaid me and Mary. Beyond all this, and beyond the rumors I had heard of his other activities, he was a major threat to the success of our attempt at stopping Charles Stuart. Was I going to let him get away? Let him go on to exert his influence with the King on the Stuarts' behalf, and to go on roaming the darkened streets of Paris with his band of masked bullies?

I could see my nipples, erect with fright, standing out boldly against the silk of my dress. But I drew myself up and glared at him anyway.

"Just one minute," I said. "All that you say so far is true, Monsieur le Comte, but I see a shadow behind your words."

The Comte's mouth fell open. Louis, suddenly interested, ceased slouching against the table and stood upright. I
closed my eyes and laid my fingers against my lids, as though
looking inward.

"I see a name in your mind, Monsieur le Comte," I said.
I sounded breathless and half-choked with fright, but there
was no help for it. I dropped my hands and looked straight at
him. "Les Disciples du Mal," I said. "What have you to do
with Les Disciples, Monsieur le Comte?"

He really wasn't good at hiding his emotions. His eyes
bulged and his face went white, and I felt a small fierce surge
of satisfaction under my fear.

The name of Les Disciples du Mal was familiar to the
King as well; the sleepy dark eyes narrowed suddenly to slits.

The Comte may have been a crook and a charlatan, but
he wasn't a coward. Summoning his resources, he glared at
me and flung back his head.

"This woman lies," he said, sounding as definite as he
had when informing the audience that the letter aleph was
symbolic of the font of Christ's blood. "She is no true White
Lady, but the servant of Satan! In league with her master, the
notorious sorcerer, du Carrefours's apprentice!" He pointed
dramatically at Raymond, who looked mildly surprised.

One of the hooded men crossed himself, and I heard the
soft whisper of a brief prayer among the shadows.

"I can prove what I say," the Comte declared, not letting
anyone else get a word in edgewise. He reached into the
breast of his coat. I remembered the dagger he had produced
from his sleeve on the night of the dinner party, and tensed
myself to duck. It wasn't a knife that he brought out, though.

"The Holy Bible says, 'They shall handle serpents unharmed,' " he thundered. " 'And by such signs shall ye know
the servants of the true God!' "

I thought it was probably a small python. It was nearly
three feet long, a smooth, gleaming length of gold and brown,
slick and sinuous as oiled rope, with a pair of disconcerting
golden eyes.

There was a concerted gasp at its appearance, and two of
the hooded judges took a quick step back. Louis himself was
more than slightly taken aback, and looked hastily about for

his bodyguard, who stood goggle-eyed by the door of the chamber.

The snake flicked its tongue once or twice, tasting the air. Apparently deciding that the mix of candle wax and incense wasn't edible, it turned and made an attempt to burrow back into the warm pocket from which it had been so rudely removed. The Comte caught it expertly behind the head, and shoved it toward me.

"You see?" he said triumphantly. "The woman shrinks away in fear! She is a witch!"

Actually, compared to one judge, who was huddling against the far wall, I was a monument of fortitude, but I must admit that I had taken an involuntary step backward when the snake appeared. Now I stepped forward again, intending to take it away from him. The bloody thing wasn't poisonous, after all. Maybe we'd see how harmless it was if I wrapped it round his neck.

Before I could reach him, though, Master Raymond spoke behind me. What with all the commotion, I'd rather forgotten him.

"That is not all the Bible says, Monsieur le Comte," Raymond observed. He didn't raise his voice, and the wide amphibian face was bland as pudding. Still, the buzz of voices stopped, and the King turned to listen.

"Yes, Monsieur?" he said.

Raymond nodded in polite acknowledgment of having the floor, and reached into his robe with both hands. From one pocket he produced a flask, from the other a small cup.

"'They shall handle serpents unharmed,'" he quoted, "'and if they drink any deadly poison, they shall not die.'" He held the cup out on the palm of his hand, its silver lining gleaming in the candlelight. The flask was poised above it, ready to pour.

"Since both milady Broch Tuarach and myself have been accused," Raymond said, with a quick glance at me, "I would suggest that all three of us partake of this test. With your permission, Your Majesty?"

Louis looked rather stunned by the rapid progress of events, but he nodded, and a thin stream of amber liquid splashed into the cup, which at once turned red and began to bubble, as though the contents were boiling.

"Dragon's blood," Raymond said informatively, waving at the cup. "Entirely harmless to the pure of heart." He smiled a toothless, encouraging smile, and handed me the cup.

There didn't seem much to do but drink it. Dragon's blood appeared to be some form of sodium bicarbonate; it tasted like brandy with seltzer. I took two or three medium-sized swallows and handed it back.

With due ceremony, Raymond drank as well. He lowered the cup, exhibiting pink-stained lips, and turned to the King.

"If La Dame Blanche may be asked to give the cup to Monsieur le Comte?" he said. He gestured to the chalk lines at his feet, to indicate that he might not step outside the protection of the pentagram.

At the King's nod, I took the cup and turned mechanically toward the Comte. Perhaps six feet of carpeting to cross. I took the first step, and then another, knees trembling more violently than they had in the small anteroom, alone with the King.

The White Lady sees a man's true nature. Did I? Did I really know about either of them, Raymond or the Comte?

Could I have stopped it? I asked myself that a hundred times, a thousand times—later. Could I have done otherwise?

I remembered my errant thought on meeting Charles Stuart; how convenient for everyone if he should die. But one cannot kill a man for his beliefs, even if the exercise of those beliefs means the death of innocents—or can one?

I didn't know. I didn't know that the Comte was guilty, I didn't know that Raymond was innocent. I didn't know whether the pursuit of an honorable cause justified the use of dishonorable means. I didn't know what one life was worth— or a thousand. I didn't know the true cost of revenge.

I did know that the cup I held in my hands was death. The white crystal hung around my neck, its weight a reminder of poison. I hadn't seen Raymond add anything to it; no one had, I was sure. But I didn't need to dip the crystal into the bloodred liquid to know what it now contained.

The Comte saw the knowledge in my face; La Dame Blanche cannot lie. He hesitated, looking at the bubbling cup.

"Drink, Monsieur," said the King. The dark eyes were hooded once more, showing nothing. "Or are you afraid?"

The Comte might have a number of things to his discredit, but cowardice wasn't one of them. His face was pale and set, but he met the King's eyes squarely, with a slight smile.

"No, Majesty," he said.

He took the cup from my hand and drained it, his eyes fixed on mine. They stayed fixed, staring into my face, even as they glazed with the knowledge of death. The White Lady may turn a man's nature to good, or to destruction.

The Comte's body hit the floor, writhing, and a chorus of shouts and cries rose from the hooded watchers, drowning any sound he might have made. His heels drummed briefly, silent on the flowered carpet; his body arched, then subsided into limpness. The snake, thoroughly disgruntled, struggled free of the disordered folds of white satin and slithered rapidly away, heading for the sanctuary of Louis's feet.

All was pandemonium.

28

The Coming of the Light

I returned from Paris to Louise's house at Fontainebleau. I didn't want to go to the Rue Trémoulins—or anywhere else that Jamie might find me. He would have little time to look; he would have to leave for Spain virtually at once, or risk the failure of his scheme.

Louise, good friend that she was, forgave my subterfuge, and—to her credit—forbore to ask me where I had gone, or what I had done there. I didn't speak much to anyone, but stayed in my room, eating little, and staring at the fat, naked *putti* that decorated the white ceiling. The sheer necessity of the trip to Paris had roused me for a time, but now there was nothing I must do, no daily routine to support me. Rudderless, I began to drift again.

Still, I tried sometimes to make an effort. Prodded by Louise, I would come down to a social dinner, or join her for tea with a visiting friend. And I tried to pay attention to Fergus, the only person in the world for whom I had still some sense of responsibility.

So, when I heard his voice raised in altercation on the other side of an outbuilding as I dutifully took my afternoon walk, I felt obliged to go and see what was the matter.

He was face to face with one of the stable-lads, a bigger boy with a sullen expression and broad shoulders.

"Shut your mouth, ignorant toad," the stable-lad was saying. "You don't know what you're talking about!"

"I know better than you—you, whose mother mated with a pig!" Fergus put two fingers in his nostrils, pushed his nose up and danced to and fro, shouting "Oink, oink!" repeatedly.

The stable-lad, who did have a rather noticeably upturned proboscis, wasted no time in idle repartee, but waded in with both fists clenched and swinging. Within seconds, the two were rolling on the muddy ground, squalling like cats and ripping at each other's clothes.

While I was still debating whether to interfere, the stable-lad rolled on top of Fergus, got his neck in both hands, and began to bang his head on the ground. On the one hand, I rather considered that Fergus had been inviting some such attention. On the other, his face was turning a dark, dusky red, and I had some reservations about seeing him cut off in his prime. With a certain amount of deliberation, I walked up behind the struggling pair.

The stable-lad was kneeling astride Fergus's body, choking him, and the seat of his breeches was stretched tight before me. I drew back my foot and booted him smartly in the trouser seam. Precariously balanced, he fell forward with a startled cry, atop the body of his erstwhile victim. He rolled to the side and bounced to his feet, fists clenched. Then he saw me, and fled without a word.

"What do you think you're playing at?" I demanded. I yanked Fergus, gasping and spluttering, to his feet, and began to beat his clothes, knocking the worst of the mud clumps and hay wisps off of him.

"Look at that," I said accusingly. "You've torn not only your shirt, but your breeches as well. We'll have to ask Berta to mend them." I turned him around and fingered the torn flap of fabric. The stable-lad had apparently gotten a hand in the waistband of the breeches, and ripped them down the side seam; the buckram fabric drooped from his slender hips, all but baring one buttock.

I stopped talking suddenly, and stared. It wasn't the disgraceful expanse of bare flesh that riveted me, but a small red mark that adorned it. About the size of a halfpenny piece, it was the dark, purplish-red color of a freshly healed burn. Disbelievingly, I touched it, making Fergus start in alarm. The edges of the mark were incised; whatever had made it had sunk into the flesh. I grabbed the boy by the arm to stop him running away, and bent to examine the mark more closely.

At a distance of six inches, the shape of the mark was clear; it was an oval, carrying within it smudged shapes that must have been letters.

"Who did this to you, Fergus?" I asked. My voice sounded queer to my own ears; preternaturally calm and detached.

Fergus yanked, trying to pull away, but I held on.

"Who, Fergus?" I demanded, giving him a little shake.

"It's nothing, Madame; I hurt myself sliding off the fence. It's just a splinter." His large black eyes darted to and fro, seeking a refuge.

"That's not a splinter. I know what it is, Fergus. But I want to know who did it." I had seen something like it only once before, and that wound freshly inflicted, while this had had some time to heal. But the mark of a brand is unmistakable.

Seeing that I meant it, he quit struggling. He licked his lips, hesitating, but his shoulders slumped, and I knew I had him now.

"It was . . . an Englishman, milady. With a ring."

"When?"

"A long time ago, Madame! In May."

I drew a deep breath, calculating. Three months. Three months earlier when Jamie had left the house to visit a brothel, in search of his warehouse foreman. In Fergus's company. Three months since Jamie had encountered Jack Randall in Madame Elise's establishment, and seen something that made all promises null and void, that had formed in him the determination to kill Jack Randall. Three months since he had left—never to return.

It took considerable patience, supplemented by a firm grip on Fergus's upper arm, but I succeeded at last in extracting the story from him.

When they arrived at Madame Elise's establishment, Jamie had told Fergus to wait for him while he went upstairs to make the financial arrangements. Judging from prior experience that this might take some time, Fergus had wandered into the large salon, where a number of young ladies that he knew were "resting," chattering together and fixing each other's hair in anticipation of customers.

"Business is sometimes slow in the mornings," he explained to me. "But on Tuesdays and Fridays, the fishermen come up the Seine to sell their catch at the morning market. Then they have money, and Madame Elise does a fine business, so *les jeunes filles* must be ready right after breakfast."

Most of the "girls" were in fact the older inhabitants of the establishment; fishermen were not considered the choicest of clients, and so went by default to the less desirable prostitutes. Among these were most of Fergus's former friends, though, and he passed an agreeable quarter of an hour in the salon, being petted and teased. A few early clients appeared, made their choice, and departed for the upstairs rooms—Madame Elise's house boasted four narrow stories— without disturbing the conversation of the remaining ladies.

"And then the Englishman came in, with Madame Elise." Fergus stopped and swallowed, the large Adam's apple bobbing uneasily in his skinny throat.

It was obvious to Fergus, who had seen men in every state of inebriation and arousal, that the Captain had been making a night of it. He was flushed and untidy, and his eyes were bloodshot. Ignoring Madame Elise's attempts to guide him toward one of the prostitutes, he had broken away and wandered through the room, restlessly scanning the wares on display. Then his eye had lighted on Fergus.

"He said, 'You. Come along,' and took me by the arm. I held back, Madame—I told him my employer was above, and that I couldn't—but he wouldn't listen. Madame Elise whispered in my ear that I should go with him, and she would split the money with me afterward." Fergus shrugged, and looked at me helplessly. "I knew the ones who like little boys don't usually take very long; I thought he would be finished long before milord was ready to leave."

"Jesus bloody Christ," I said. My fingers relaxed their grip and slid nervelessly down his sleeve. "Do you mean— Fergus, had you done it before?"

He looked as though he wanted to cry. So did I.

"Not very often, Madame," he said, and it was almost a plea for understanding. "There are houses where that is the specialty, and usually the men who like that go there. But sometimes a customer would see me and take a fancy . . ." His nose was starting to run and he wiped it with the back of his hand.

I rummaged in my pocket for a handkerchief and gave it to him. He was beginning to sniffle as he recalled that Friday morning.

"He was much bigger than I thought. I asked him if I could take it in my mouth, but he . . . but he wanted to . . ."

I pulled him to me and pressed his head tight against my shoulder, muffling his voice in the cloth of my gown. The frail blades of his shoulder bones were like a bird's wings under my hand.

"Don't tell me any more," I said. "Don't. It's all right, Fergus; I'm not angry. But don't tell me any more."

This was a futile order; he couldn't stop talking, after so many days of fear and silence.

"But it's all my fault, Madame!" he burst out, pulling away. His lip was trembling, and tears welled in his eyes. "I should have kept quiet; I shouldn't have cried out! But I couldn't help it, and milord heard me, and . . . and he burst in . . . and . . . oh, Madame, I shouldn't have, but I was so glad to see him, and I ran to him, and he put me behind him and hit the Englishman in the face. And then the Englishman came up from the floor with the stool in his hand, and threw it, and I was so afraid, I ran out of the room and hid in the closet at the end of the hall. Then there was so much shouting and banging, and a terrible crash, and more shouting. And then it stopped, and soon milord opened the door of the closet and took me out. He had my clothes, and he dressed me himself, because I couldn't fasten the buttons—my fingers shook."

He grabbed my skirt with both hands, the necessity of making me believe him tightening his face into a monkey mask of grief.

"It's my fault, Madame, but I didn't know! I didn't know he would go to fight the Englishman. And now milord is gone, and he'll never come back, and it's all my fault!"

Wailing now, he fell facedown on the ground at my feet. He was crying so loudly that I didn't think he heard me as I bent to lift him up, but I said it anyway.

"It isn't your fault, Fergus. It isn't mine, either—but you're right; he's gone."

◄───

Following Fergus's revelation, I sank ever deeper into apathy. The gray cloud that had surrounded me since the miscarriage seemed to draw closer, wrapping me in swaddling folds that dimmed the light of the brightest day. Sounds seemed to reach me faintly, like the far-off ringing of a buoy through fog at sea.

Louise stood in front of me, frowning worriedly as she looked down at me.

"You're much too thin," she scolded. "And white as a plate of tripes. Yvonne said you didn't eat any breakfast again!"

I couldn't remember when I had last been hungry. It hardly seemed important. Long before the Bois de Boulogne, long before my trip to Paris. I fixed my gaze on the mantelpiece and drifted off into the curlicues of the rococo carving. Louise's voice went on, but I didn't pay attention; it was only a noise in the room, like the brushing of a tree branch against the stone wall of the château, or the humming of the flies that had been drawn in by the smell of my discarded breakfast.

I watched one of them, rising off the eggs in sudden motion as Louise clapped her hands. It buzzed in short, irritable circles before settling back to its feeding spot. The sound of hurrying footsteps came behind me, there was a sharp order from Louise, a submissive "*Oui,* Madame," and the sudden *thwap!* of a flywhisk as the maid set about removing the flies, one by one. She dropped each small black corpse into her pocket, plucking it off the table and polishing the smear left behind with a corner of her apron.

Louise bent down, thrusting her face suddenly into my field of view.

"I can see all the bones in your face! If you won't eat, at least go outside for a bit!" she said impatiently. "The rain's stopped; come along, and we'll see if there are any muscats left in the arbor. Maybe you'll eat some of those."

Outside or inside was much the same to me; the soft, numbing grayness was still with me, blurring outlines and making every place seem like every other. But it seemed to matter to Louise, so I rose obediently to go with her.

Near the garden door, though, she was waylaid by the cook, with a list of questions and complaints about the menu for dinner. Guests had been invited, with the intention of distracting me, and the bustle of preparation had been causing small explosions of domestic discord all morning.

Louise emitted a martyred sigh, then patted me on the back.

"You go on," she said, urging me toward the door. "I'll send a footman with your cloak."

It was a cool day for August because of the rain that had been coming down since the night before. Pools of water lay in the graveled paths, and the dripping from the drenched trees was nearly as incessant as the rain itself.

The sky was still filled with gray, but it had faded from the angry black of water-logged clouds. I folded my arms around my elbows; it looked as though the sun might come out soon, but it was still cold enough to want a cloak.

When I heard steps behind me on the path, I turned to find François, the second footman, but he carried nothing. He looked oddly hesitant, peering as though to make sure I was the person he was looking for.

"Madame," he said, "there is a visitor for you."

I sighed internally; I didn't want to be bothered with the effort of rousing myself to be civil to company.

"Tell them I'm indisposed, please," I said, turning to continue my walk. "And when they've gone, bring me my cloak."

"But Madame," he said behind me, "it is *le seigneur* Broch Tuarach—your husband."

Startled, I whirled to look at the house. It was true; I could see Jamie's tall figure, already coming around the corner of the house. I turned, pretending I hadn't seen him, and walked off toward the arbor. The shrubbery was thick down there; perhaps I could hide.

"Claire!" Pretending was useless; he had seen me as well, and was coming down the path after me. I walked faster, but I was no match for those long legs. I was puffing before I had covered half the distance to the arbor, and had to slow down; I was in no condition for strenuous exercise.

"Wait, Claire!"

I half-turned; he was almost upon me. The soft gray numbness around me quivered, and I felt a sort of frozen panic at the thought that the sight of him might rip it away from me. If it did, I would die, I thought, like a grub dug up from the soil and tossed onto a rock to shrivel, naked and defenseless in the sun.

"No!" I said. "I don't want to talk to you. Go away." He hesitated for a moment, and I turned away from him and began to walk rapidly down the path toward the arbor. I heard his steps on the gravel of the path behind me, but kept my back turned, and walked faster, almost running.

As I paused to duck under the arbor, he made a sudden lunge forward and grasped my wrist. I tried to pull away from him, but he held on tight.

"Claire!" he said again. I struggled, but kept my face turned away; if I didn't look at him, I could pretend he wasn't there. I could stay safe.

He let go of my wrist, but grabbed me by both shoulders instead, so that I had to lift my head to keep my balance. His face was sunburned and thin, with harsh lines cut beside his mouth, and his eyes above were dark with pain. "Claire," he said more softly, now that he could see me looking at him. "Claire—it was my child, too."

"Yes, it was—and you killed it!" I ripped away from him, flinging myself through the narrow arch. I stopped inside, panting like a terrified dog. I hadn't realized that the arch led into a tiny vine-covered folly. Latticed walls surrounded me on all sides—I was trapped. The light behind me failed as his body blocked the arch.

"Don't touch me." I backed away, staring at the ground. *Go away!* I thought frantically. *Please, for God's sake, leave me in peace!* I could feel my gray wrappings being inexorably stripped away, and small, bright streaks of pain shot through me like lightning bolts piercing clouds.

He stopped, a few feet away. I stumbled blindly toward the latticed wall and half-sat, half-fell onto a wooden bench. I closed my eyes and sat shivering. While it was no longer raining, there was a cold, damp wind coming through the lattice to chill my neck.

He didn't come closer. I could feel him, standing there, looking down at me. I could hear the raggedness of his breathing.

"Claire," he said once more, with something like despair in his voice, "Claire, do ye not see . . . Claire, you must speak to me! For God's sake, Claire, I don't know even was it a girl or a boy!"

I sat frozen, hands gripping the rough wood of the bench. After a moment, there was a heavy, crunching noise on the ground in front of me. I cracked my eyes open, and saw that he had sat down, just as he was, on the wet gravel at my feet. He sat with bowed head, and the rain had left spangles in his damp-darkened hair.

"Will ye make me beg?" he said.

"It was a girl," I said after a moment. My voice sounded funny; hoarse and husky. "Mother Hildegarde baptized her. Faith. Faith Fraser. Mother Hildegarde has a very odd sense of humor."

The bowed head didn't move. After a moment, he said quietly, "Did you see the child?"

My eyes were open all the way now. I stared at my knees, where blown drops of water from the vines behind me were making wet spots on the silk.

"Yes. The *maîtresse sage-femme* said I ought, so they made me." I could hear in memory the low, matter-of-fact tones of Madame Bonheur, most senior and respected of the midwives who gave of their time at L'Hôpital des Anges.

"Give her the child; it's always better if they see. Then they don't imagine things."

So I didn't imagine. I remembered.

"She was perfect," I said softly, as though to myself. "So small. I could cup her head in the palm of my hand. Her ears stuck out just a little—I could see the light shine through them."

The light had shone through her skin as well, glowing in the roundness of cheek and buttock with the light that pearls have; still and cool, with the strange touch of the water world still on them.

"Mother Hildegarde wrapped her in a length of white satin," I said, looking down at my fists, clenched in my lap. "Her eyes were closed. She hadn't any lashes yet, but her eyes were slanted. I said they were like yours, but they said all babies' eyes are like that."

Ten fingers, and ten toes. No nails, but the gleam of tiny joints, kneecaps and fingerbones like opals, like the jeweled bones of the earth itself. Remember man, that thou art dust. . . .

I remembered the far-off clatter of the Hôpital, where life still went on, and the subdued murmur of Mother Hildegarde and Madame Bonheur, closer by, talking of the priest who would say a special Mass at Mother Hildegarde's request. I remembered the look of calm appraisal in Madame Bonheur's eyes as she turned to look me over, seeing my weakness. Perhaps she saw also the telltale brightness of the approaching fever; she had turned again to Mother Hildegarde and her voice had dropped further—perhaps suggesting that they wait; two funerals might be needed.

And unto dust thou shalt return.

But I had come back from the dead. Only Jamie's hold on my body had been strong enough to pull me back from that final barrier, and Master Raymond had known it. I knew that only Jamie himself could pull me back the rest of the way, into the land of the living. That was why I had run from him, done all I could to keep him away, to make sure he would never come near me again. I had no wish to come back, no desire to feel again. I didn't want to know love, only to have it ripped away once more.

But it was too late. I knew that, even as I fought to hold the gray shroud around me. Fighting only hastened its dissolution; it was like grasping shreds of cloud, that vanished in cold mist between my fingers. I could feel the light coming, blinding and searing.

He had risen, was standing over me. His shadow fell across my knees; surely that meant the cloud had broken; a shadow doesn't fall without light.

"Claire," he whispered. "Please. Let me give ye comfort."

"Comfort?" I said. "And how will you do that? Can you give me back my child?"

He sank to his knees before me, but I kept my head down, staring into my upturned hands, laid empty on my lap. I felt his movement as he reached to touch me, hesitated, drew back, reached again.

"No," he said, his voice scarcely audible. "No, I canna do that. But . . . with the grace of God . . . I might give ye another?"

His hand hovered over mine, close enough that I felt the warmth of his skin. I felt other things as well: the grief that he held tight under rein, the anger and the fear that choked him, and the courage that made him speak in spite of it. I gathered my own courage around me, a flimsy substitute for the thick gray shroud. Then I took his hand and lifted my head, and looked full into the face of the sun.

We sat, hands clasped and pressed together on the bench, unmoving, unspeaking, for what seemed like hours, with the cool rain-breeze whispering our thoughts in the grape leaves above. Water drops scattered over us with the passing of the wind, weeping for loss and separation.

"You're cold," Jamie murmured at last, and pulled a fold of his cloak around me, bringing with it the warmth of his skin. I came slowly against him under its shelter, shivering more at the startling solidness, the sudden heat of him, than from the cold.

I laid my hand on his chest, tentative as though the touch of him might burn me in truth, and so we sat for a good while longer, letting the grape leaves talk for us.

"Jamie," I said softly, at last. "Oh, Jamie. Where were you?"

His arm tightened about me, but it was some time before he answered.

"I thought ye were dead, *mo nighean donn*," he said, so softly I could hardly hear him above the rustling of the arbor.

"I saw ye there—on the ground, at the last. God! Ye were so white, and your skirts all soaked wi' blood . . . I tried to go to ye, Claire, so soon as I saw—I ran to ye, but it was then the Guard took me."

He swallowed hard; I could feel the tremor pass down him, through the long curve of his backbone.

"I fought them . . . I fought, and aye I pleaded . . . but they wouldna stay, and they carried me awa' wi' them. And they put me in a cell, and left me there . . . thinking ye were dead, Claire; knowing that I'd killed you."

The fine tremor went on, and I knew he was weeping, though I could not see his face above me. How long had he sat alone in the dark of the Bastille, alone but for the scent of blood and the empty husk of vengeance?

"It's all right," I said, and pressed my hand harder against his chest, as though to still the hasty beating of his heart. "Jamie, it's all right. It . . . it wasn't your fault."

"I tried to bash my head against the wall—only to stop thinking," he said, nearly in a whisper. "So they tied me, hand and foot. And next day, de Rohan found me, and told me that ye lived, though likely not for long."

He was silent then, but I could feel the pain inside him, sharp as crystal spears of ice.

"Claire," he murmured at last. "I am sorry."

I am sorry. The words were those of the note he had left me, before the world shattered. But now I understood them.

"I know," I said. "Jamie, I *know.* Fergus told me. I know why you went."

He drew a deep, shuddering breath.

"Aye, well . . ." he said, and stopped.

I let my hand fall to his thigh; chilled and damp from the rain, his riding breeches were rough under my palm.

"Did they tell you—when they let you go—why you were released?" I tried to keep my own breathing steady, but failed.

His thigh tensed under my hand, but his voice was under better control now.

"No," he said. "Only that it was . . . His Majesty's pleasure." The word "pleasure" was ever so faintly underlined, spoken with a delicate ferocity that made it abundantly clear that he did indeed know the means of his release, whether the warders had told him or not.

I bit my lower lip hard, trying to make up my mind what to tell him now.

"It was Mother Hildegarde," he went on, voice steady. "I went at once to L'Hôpital des Anges, in search of you. And found Mother Hildegarde, and the wee note ye'd left for me. She . . . told me."

"Yes," I said, swallowing. "I went to see the King . . ."

"I know!" His hand tightened on mine, and from the sound of his breathing, I could tell that his teeth were clenched together.

"But Jamie . . . when I went . . ."

"Christ!" he said, and sat up suddenly, turning to face me. "Do ye not know what I . . . Claire." He closed his eyes briefly, and took a deep breath. "I rode all the way to Oviedo, seeing it; seeing his hands on the white of your skin, his lips on your neck, his—his cock—I saw it at the *lever*—I saw the damn filthy, stubby thing sliding up . . . God, Claire! I sat in prison thinking ye dead, and then I rode to Spain, wishing to Christ ye were!"

The knuckles of the hand holding mine were white, and I could feel the small bones of my fingers crackle in his grip.

I jerked my hand free.

"Jamie, listen to me!"

"No!" he said. "No, I dinna want to hear . . ."

"Listen, damn you!"

There was enough force in my voice to shut him up for an instant, and while he was mute, I began rapidly to tell him the story of the King's chamber; the hooded men, and the shadowed room, the sorcerers' duel, and the death of the Comte St. Germain.

As I talked, the high color faded from his wind-brisked cheeks, and his expression softened from anguish and fury to bewilderment, and gradually, to astonished belief.

"Jesus," he breathed at last. "Oh, holy God."

"Didn't know what you were starting with that silly story, did you?" I felt exhausted, but managed a smile. "So . . . so the Comte . . . it's all right, Jamie. He's . . . gone."

He didn't say anything in reply, but drew me gently to him, so my forehead rested on his shoulder, and my tears soaked into the fabric of his shirt. After a minute, though, I sat up, and stared at him, wiping my nose.

"I just thought, Jamie! The port—Charles Stuart's investment! If the Comte is dead . . ."

He shook his head, smiling faintly.

"No, *mo nighean donn.* It's safe."

I felt a flood of relief.

"Oh, thank God. You managed, then? Did the medicines work on Murtagh?"

"Well, no," he said, the smile broadening, "but they did on me."

Relieved at once of fear and anger, I felt light-headed, and half-giddy. The smell of the rain-swept grapes was strong and sweet, and it was a blessed relief to lean against him, feeling his warmth as comfort, not as threat, as I listened to the story of the port-wine piracy.

"There are men that are born to the sea, Sassenach," he began, "but I'm afraid I'm no one of them."

"I know," I said. "Were you sick?"

"I have seldom been sicker," he assured me wryly.

The seas off Oviedo had been rough, and within an hour

it became clear that Jamie was not going to be able to carry
out his original part in the plan.

"I couldna do anything but lie in my hammock and
groan, in any case," he said, shrugging, "so it seemed I might
as well have pox, too."

He and Murtagh had hastily changed roles, and twenty-
four hours off the coast of Spain, the master of the *Scalamandre* had discovered to his horror that plague had broken out
below.

Jamie scratched his neck reflectively, as though still feeling the effects of the nettle juice.

"They thought of throwing me overboard when they
found out," he said, "and I must say it seemed a verra fine
idea to me." He gave me a lopsided grin. "Have ye ever had
seasickness while covered wi' nettle rash, Sassenach?"

"No, thank God." I shuddered at the thought. "Did
Murtagh stop them?"

"Oh, aye. He's verra fierce, is Murtagh. He slept across
the threshold wi' his hand on his dirk, until we came safe to
port at Bilbao."

True to forecast, the *Scalamandre*'s captain, faced with
the unprofitable choice of proceeding to Le Havre and
forfeiting his cargo, or returning to Spain and cooling his
heels while word was sent to Paris, had leaped at the opportunity to dispose of his hold's worth of port to the new purchaser chance had thrown in his way.

"Not that he didna drive a hard bargain," Jamie observed, scratching his forearm. "He haggled for half a day—
and me dying in my hammock, pissing blood and puking my
guts out!"

But the bargain had been concluded, both port and
smallpox patient unloaded with dispatch at Bilbao, and—
aside from a lingering tendency to urinate vermilion—Jamie's
recovery had been rapid.

"We sold the port to a broker there in Bilbao," he said.
"I sent Murtagh at once to Paris, to repay Monsieur
Duverney's loan—and then . . . I came here."

He looked down at his hands, lying quiet in his lap. "I
couldna decide," he said softly. "To come or no. I walked, ye
ken, to give myself time to think. I walked all the way from
Paris to Fontainebleau. And nearly all the way back. I turned

back half a dozen times, thinking myself a murderer and a
fool, not knowing if I would rather kill myself or you . . ."

He sighed then, and looked up at me, eyes dark with
reflections of the fluttering leaves.

"I had to come," he said simply.

I didn't say anything, but laid my hand over his and sat
beside him. Fallen grapes littered the ground under the arbor,
the pungent scent of their fermentation promising the forgetfulness of wine.

The cloud-streaked sun was setting, and a blur of gold
silhouetted the respectful form of Hugo, looming black in the
entrance to the arbor.

"Your pardon, Madame," he said. "My mistress wishes
to know—will *le seigneur* be staying for supper?"

I looked at Jamie. He sat still, waiting, the sun through
the grape leaves streaking his hair with a tiger's blaze, shadows falling across his face.

"I think you'd better," I said. "You're awfully thin."

He looked me over with a half-smile. "So are you, Sassenach."

He rose and offered me his arm. I took it and we went in
together to supper, leaving the grape leaves to their muted
conversation.

I lay next to Jamie, close against him, his hand resting on
my thigh as he slept. I stared upward into the darkness of the
bedroom, listening to the peaceful sigh of his sleeping breath,
breathing myself the fresh-washed scent of the damp night
air, tinged with the smell of wisteria.

The collapse of the Comte St. Germain had been the
end of the evening, so far as all were concerned save Louis.
As the company made to depart, murmuring excitedly among
themselves, he took my arm, and led me out through the
same small door by which I had entered. Good with words
when required, he had no need of them here.

I was led to the green velvet chaise, laid on my back and
my skirts gently lifted before I could speak. He did not kiss
me; he did not desire me. This was the ritual claiming of the
payment agreed upon. Louis was a shrewd bargainer, and not
one to forgive a debt he thought owed to him, whether the

payment had value to him or not. And perhaps it did, after all; there was more than a hint of half-fearful excitement in his preparations—who but a king would dare to take La Dame Blanche in his embrace?

I was closed and dry, unready. Impatient, he seized a flagon of rose-scented oil from the table, and massaged it briefly between my legs. I lay unmoving, soundless, as the hastily probing finger withdrew, replaced at once by a member little larger, and—"suffered" is the wrong word, there was neither pain nor humiliation involved; it was a transaction—I waited, then, through the quick thrusting, and then he was on his feet, face flushed with excitement, hands fumbling to refasten his breeches over the small swelling within. He would not risk the possibility of a half-Royal, half-magic bastard; not with Madame de La Tourelle ready—a good deal readier than I, I hoped—and waiting in her own chambers down the hall.

I had given what was implicitly promised; now he could with honor accede to my request, feeling no *virtu* had gone forth from him. As for me, I met his courteous bow with my own, took my elbow from the grip with which he had gallantly escorted me to the door, and left the audience chamber only a few minutes after entering it, with the King's assurance that the order for Jamie's freedom would be given in the morning.

The Gentleman of the Bedchamber was standing in the hall, waiting. He bowed to me, and I bowed back, then followed him down the Hall of Mirrors, feeling the slipperiness of my oily thighs as they brushed each other, and smelling the strong scent of roses between my legs.

Hearing the gate of the palace shut behind me, I had closed my eyes and thought that I would never see Jamie again. And if by chance I did, I would rub his nose in the scent of roses, until his soul sickened and died.

But now instead I held his hand on my thigh, listening to his breathing, deep and even in the dark beside me. And I let the door close forever on His Majesty's audience.

29

To Grasp the Nettle

"Scotland." I sighed, thinking of the cool brown streams
and dark pines of Lallybroch, Jamie's estate. "Can we
really go home?"

"I expect we'll have to," he answered wryly. "The King's
pardon says I leave France by mid-September, or I'm back in
the Bastille. Presumably, His Majesty has arranged a pardon
as well from the English Crown, so I willna be hanged directly
I get off the ship in Inverness."

"I suppose we could go to Rome, or to Prussia," I
suggested, tentatively. I wanted nothing more than to go
home to Lallybroch, and heal in the quiet peace of the Scottish Highlands. My heart sank at the thought of Royal courts
and intrigue, the constant press of danger and insecurity. But
if Jamie felt we must . . .

He shook his head, red hair falling over his face as he
stooped to pull on his stockings.

"Nay, it's Scotland or the Bastille," he said. "Our passage is already booked, just to make sure." He straightened
and, with a wry smile, brushed the hair out of his eyes. "I
imagine the Duke of Sandringham—and possibly King
George—want me safe at home, where they can keep an eye
on me. Not spying in Rome, or raising money in Prussia.
The three weeks' grace, I gather, is a courtesy to Jared, giving
him time to come home before I leave."

I was sitting in the window seat of my bedroom, looking
out over the tumbled green sea of the Fontainebleau woods.
The hot, languid air of summer seemed to press down, sap-
ping all energy.

"I can't say I'm not glad." I sighed, pressing my cheek
against the glass in search of a moment's coolness. The legacy
of yesterday's chill rain was a blanketing humidity that made
hair and clothes cling to my skin, itching and damp. "Do you
think it's safe, though? I mean, will Charles give up, now that
the Comte is dead, and the money from Manzetti lost?"

Jamie frowned, rubbing his hand along the edge of his jaw to judge the growth of the stubble.

"I wish I knew whether he'd had a letter from Rome in the last two weeks," he said, "and if so, what was in it. But aye, I think we've managed. No banker in Europe will advance anyone of the name of Stuart a brass centime, that's for sure. Philip of Spain has other fish to fry, and Louis—" He shrugged, his mouth twisting wryly. "Between Monsieur Duverney and the Duke of Sandringham, I'd say Charles's expectations in that direction are somewhat less than poor. Shall I shave, d'ye think?"

"Not on my account," I said. The casual intimacy of the question made me suddenly shy. We had shared a bed the night before, but we had both been exhausted, and the delicate web woven between us in the arbor had seemed too fragile to support the stress of attempting to make love. I had spent the night in a terrible consciousness of his warm proximity, but thought I must, under the circumstances, leave the first move to him.

Now I caught the play of light across his shoulders as he turned to find his shirt, and was seized with the desire to touch him; to feel him, smooth and hard and eager against me once more.

His head popped through the neck of his shirt, and his eyes met mine, suddenly and unguarded. He paused for a moment, looking at me, but not speaking. The morning sounds of the château were clearly audible, outside the bubble of silence that surrounded us; the bustling of servants, the high thin sound of Louise's voice, raised in some sort of altercation.

Not here, Jamie's eyes said. *Not in the midst of so many people.*

He looked down, carefully fastening his shirt buttons. "Does Louise keep horses for riding?" he asked, eyes on his task. "There are some cliffs a few miles away; I thought perhaps we might ride there—the air may be cooler."

"I think she does," I said. "I'll ask."

We reached the cliffs just before noon. Not cliffs so much as jutting pillars and ridges of limestone that sat among the yellowing grass of the surrounding hills like the ruins of an ancient city. The pale ridges were split and fissured from time and weather, spattered with thousands of strange, tiny plants that had found a foothold in the merest scrape of eroded soil.

We left the horses hobbled in the grass, and climbed on foot to a wide, flat shelf of limestone covered with tufts of rough grass, just below the highest tumble of stone. There was little shade from the scruffy bushes, but up this high, there was a small breeze.

"God, it's hot!" Jamie said. He flipped loose the buckle of his kilt, so it fell around his feet, and started to wriggle out of his shirt.

"What are you doing, Jamie?" I said, half-laughing.

"Stripping," he replied, matter-of-factly. "Why don't ye do the same, Sassenach? You're more soaked than I am, and there's none here to see."

After a moment's hesitation, I did as he suggested. It was entirely isolated here; too craggy and rocky for sheep, the chance of even a stray shepherd coming upon us was remote. And alone, naked together, away from Louise and her throngs of intrusive servants . . . Jamie spread his plaid on the rough ground as I peeled out of my sweat-clinging garments.

He stretched lazily and settled back, arms behind his head, completely oblivious to curious ants, stray bits of gravel and the stubs of prickly vegetation.

"You must have the hide of a goat," I remarked. "How can you lie on the bare ground like that?" As bare as he, I reposed more comfortably on a thick fold of the plaid he had thoughtfully spread out for me.

He shrugged, eyes closed against the warm afternoon sun. The light gilded him in the hollow where he lay, making him glow red-gold against the dark of the rough grass beneath him.

"It'll do," he said comfortably, and lapsed into silence, the sound of his breathing near enough to reach me over the faint whine of the wind that crossed the ridges above us.

I rolled onto my belly and laid my chin on my crossed forearms, watching him. He was wide at the shoulder and narrow at the hip, with long, powerful haunches slightly dented by muscles held taut even as he relaxed. The small, warm breeze stirred the drying tufts of soft cinnamon hair beneath his arms, and ruffled the copper and gold that waved gently over his wrists, where they braced his head. The slight breeze was welcome, for the early autumn sun was still hot on my shoulders and calves.

"I love you," I said softly, not meaning him to hear me, but only for the pleasure of saying it.

He did hear, though, for the hint of a smile curved the wide mouth. After a moment, he rolled over onto his belly on the plaid beside me. A few blades of grass clung to his back and buttocks. I brushed one lightly away, and his skin shivered briefly at my touch.

I leaned to kiss his shoulder, enjoying the warm scent of his skin and the faint salty taste of him.

Instead of kissing me back, though, he pulled away a bit, and lay propped on one elbow, looking at me. There was something in his expression that I didn't understand, and it made me faintly uneasy.

"Penny for your thoughts," I said, running a finger down the deep groove of his backbone. He moved just far enough to avoid my touch, and took a deep breath.

"Well, I was wondering—" he began, and then stopped. He was looking down, fiddling with a tiny flower that sprang out of the grass.

"You were wondering what?"

"What it was like . . . with Louis."

I thought my heart had stopped for a moment. I knew all the blood had left my face, because I could feel the numbness of my lips as I forced the words out.

"What . . . it . . . was like?"

He looked up then, making only a passing-fair attempt at a lopsided smile.

"Well," he said. "He *is* a king. You'd think it would be . . . different, somehow. You know . . . special, maybe?"

The smile was slipping, and his face had gone as white as my own. He looked down again, avoiding my stricken gaze.

"I suppose all I was wondering," he murmured, "was . . . was he . . . was he different from me?" I saw him bite his lip as though wishing the words unsaid, but it was far too late for that.

"How in hell did you know?" I said. I felt dizzy and exposed, and rolled onto my stomach, pressing myself hard to the short turf.

He shook his head, teeth still clenched in his lower lip. When he finally released it, a deep red mark showed where he had bitten it.

"Claire," he said softly. "Oh, Claire. You gave me all yourself from the first time, and held nothing back from me. You never did. When I asked ye for honesty, I told ye then that it isna in you to lie. When I touched ye so—" His hand moved, cupping my buttock, and I flinched, not expecting it.

"How long have I loved you?" he asked, very quietly. "A year? Since the moment I saw you. And loved your body how often—half a thousand times or more?" One finger touched me then, gently as a moth's foot, tracing the line of arm and shoulder, gliding down my rib cage 'til I shivered at the touch and rolled away, facing him now.

"You never shrank from my touch," he said, eyes intent on the path his finger took, dipping down to follow the curve of my breast. "Not even at the first, when ye might have done so, and no surprise to me if ye had. But you didn't. You gave me everything from the very first time; held nothing back, denied me no part of you."

"But now . . ." he said, drawing back his hand. "I thought at first it was only that you'd lost the child, and maybe were shy of me, or feeling strange after so long apart. But then I knew that wasn't it."

There was a very long silence, then. I could feel the steady, painful thudding of my heart against the cold ground, and hear the conversation of the wind in the pines down below. Small birds called, far away. I wished I were one. Or far away, at any rate.

"Why?" he asked softly. "Why lie to me? When I had come to you thinking I knew, anyway?"

I stared down at my hands, linked beneath my chin, and swallowed.

"If . . . ," I began, and swallowed again. "If I told you that I had let Louis . . . you would have asked about it. I thought you couldn't forget . . . maybe you could forgive me, but you'd never forget, and it would always be there between us." I swallowed once more, hard. My hands were cold despite the heat, and I felt a ball of ice in my stomach. But if I was telling him the truth now, I must tell him all of it.

"If you'd asked—and you did, Jamie, you did! I would have had to talk about it, live it over, and I was afraid . . ." I trailed off, unable to speak, but he wasn't going to let me off.

"Afraid of what?" he prodded.

I turned my head slightly, not meeting his eye, but enough to see his outline dark against the sun, looming through the sun-sparked curtain of my hair.

"Afraid I'd tell you why I did it," I said softly. "Jamie . . . I had to, to get you freed from the Bastille—I would have done worse, if I'd had to. But then . . . and afterward . . . I half-hoped someone would tell you, that you'd find out. I was so angry, Jamie—for the duel, and the baby. And because you'd forced me to do it . . . to go to Louis. I wanted to do something to drive you away, to make sure I never saw you again. I did it . . . partly . . . because I wanted to hurt you," I whispered.

A muscle contracted near the corner of his mouth, but he went on staring downward at his clasped hands. The chasm between us, so perilously bridged, gaped yawning and impassable once more.

"Aye. Well, you did."

His mouth clamped shut in a tight line, and he didn't speak for some time. Finally he turned his head and looked directly at me. I would have liked to avoid his eyes, but couldn't.

"Claire," he said softly. "What did ye feel—when I gave my body to Jack Randall? When I let him take me, at Wentworth?"

A tiny shock ran through me, from scalp to toenails. It was the last question I had expected to hear. I opened and closed my mouth several times before finding an answer.

"I . . . don't know," I said weakly. "I hadn't thought. Angry, of course. I was furious—outraged. And sick. And frightened for you. And . . . sorry for you."

"Were ye jealous? When I told you about it later—that he'd roused me, though I didna want it?"

I drew a deep breath, feeling the grass tickle my breasts.

"No. At least I don't think so; I didn't think so then. After all, it wasn't as though you'd . . . wanted to do it." I bit my lip, looking down. His voice was quiet and matter-of-fact at my shoulder.

"I dinna think you wanted to bed Louis—did you?"

"No!"

"Aye, well," he said. He put his thumbs together on either side of a blade of grass, and concentrated on pulling it up slowly by the roots. "I was angry, too. And sick and sorry." The grass blade came free of its sheath with a tiny squeaking sound.

"When it was me," he went on, almost whispering, "I thought you could not bear the thought of it, and I would not have blamed you. I knew ye must turn from me, and I tried to send you away, so I wouldna have to see the disgust and the hurt in your face." He closed his eyes and raised the grass blade between his thumbs, barely brushing his lips.

"But you wouldna go. You took me to your breast and cherished me. You healed me, instead. You loved me, in spite of it." He took a deep, unsteady breath and turned his head to me again. His eyes were bright with tears, but no wetness escaped to slide down his cheeks.

"I thought, maybe, that I could bring myself to do that for you, as you did it for me. And that is why I came to Fontainebleau, at last."

He blinked once, hard, and his eyes cleared.

"Then when ye told me that nothing had happened—for a bit, I believed you, because I wanted to so much. But then . . . I could tell, Claire. I couldna hide it from myself, and I knew you had lied to me. I thought you wouldna trust me to love you, or . . . that you *had* wanted him, and were afraid to let me see it."

He dropped the grass, and his head sank forward to rest on his knuckles.

"Ye said you wanted to hurt me. Well, the thought of you lying with the King hurt worse than the brand on my breast, or the cut of the lash on my naked back. But the knowledge that ye thought ye couldna trust me to love you is like waking from the hangman's noose to feel the gutting knife sunk in my belly. Claire—" His mouth opened soundlessly, then closed tight for a moment, until he found the strength to go on.

"I do not know if the wound is mortal, but Claire—I do feel my heart's blood leave me, when I look at you."

The silence between us grew and deepened. The small buzz of an insect calling in the rocks vibrated in the air.

Jamie was still as a rock, his face blank as he stared down at the ground below him. I couldn't bear that blank face, and the thought of what must lie concealed behind it. I had seen a hint of his despairing fury in the arbor, and my heart felt hollow at the thought of that rage, mastered at such fearful cost, now held under an iron control that kept in not only rage, but trust and joy.

I wished desperately for some way to break the silence that parted us; some act that could restore the lost truth between us. Jamie sat up then, arms folded tight about his thighs, and turned away as he gazed out over the peaceful valley.

Better violence, I thought, than silence. I reached across the chasm between us and laid a hand on his arm. It was warm from the sun, live to my touch.

"Jamie," I whispered. "Please."

His head turned slowly toward me. His face seemed still calm, though the cat-eyes narrowed further as he looked at me in silence. He reached out, finally, and one hand gripped me by the wrist.

"Do ye wish me to beat you, then?" he said softly. His grasp tightened hard, so that I jerked unconsciously, trying to pull away from him. He pulled back, yanking me across the rough grass, bringing my body against him.

I felt myself trembling, and gooseflesh lifted the hairs on my forearms, but I managed to speak.

"Yes," I said.

His expression was unfathomable. Still holding my eyes with his own, he reached out his free hand, fumbling over the rocks until he touched a bunch of nettles. He drew in his breath as his fingers touched the prickly stems, but his jaw clenched; he closed his fist and ripped the plants up by the roots.

"The peasants of Gascony beat a faithless wife wi' nettles," he said. He lowered the spiky bunch of leaves and brushed the flower heads lightly across one breast. I gasped from the sudden sting, and a faint red blotch appeared as though by magic on my skin.

"Will ye have me do so?" he asked. "Shall I punish you that way?"

"If you . . . if you like." My lips were trembling so hard I could barely get out the words. A few crumbs of earth from the nettles' roots had fallen between my breasts; one rolled down the slope of my ribs, dislodged by my pounding heart, I imagined. The welt on my breast burned like fire. I closed my eyes, imagining in vivid detail exactly what being thrashed with a bunch of nettles would feel like.

Suddenly the viselike grip on my wrist relaxed. I opened my eyes to find Jamie sitting cross-legged by me, the plants thrown aside and scattered on the ground. He had a faint, rueful smile on his lips.

"I beat you once in justice, Sassenach, and ye threatened to disembowel me with my own dirk. Now you'll ask me to whip ye wi' nettles?" He shook his head slowly, wondering, and his hand reached as though by its own volition to cup my cheek. "Is my pride worth so much to you, then?"

"Yes! Yes, it bloody is!" I sat up myself, and grasped him by the shoulders, taking both of us by surprise as I kissed him hard and awkwardly.

I felt his first involuntary start, and then he pulled me to him, arm tight around my back, mouth answering mine. Then he had me pressed flat to the earth, his weight holding me immobile beneath him. His shoulders darkened the bright sky above, and his hands held my arms against my sides, keeping me prisoner.

"All right," he whispered. His eyes bored into mine, daring me to close them, forcing me to hold his gaze. "All right. As ye wish it, I shall punish you." He moved his hips against me in imperious command, and I felt my legs open for him, my gates thrown wide to welcome ravishment.

"Never," he whispered to me. "*Never.* Never another but me! Look at me! Tell me! *Look at me, Claire!*" He moved in me, strongly, and I moaned and would have turned my head, but he held my face between his hands, forcing me to meet his eyes, to see his wide, sweet mouth, twisted in pain.

"Never," he said, more softly. "For you are mine. My wife, my heart, my soul." The weight of him held me still, like a boulder on my chest, but the friction of our flesh made me thrust against him, wanting more. And more.

"My body," he said, gasping for breath as he gave me what I sought. I bucked beneath him as though I wanted to escape, my back arching like a bow, pressing me into him. He lay then at full length on me, scarcely moving, so that our most intimate connection seemed barely closer than the marriage of our skins.

The grass was harsh and prickly under me, the pungence of crushed stems sharp as the smell of the man who took me. My breasts were flattened under him, and I felt the small tickle of the hairs on his chest as we rubbed together, back and forth. I squirmed, urging him to violence, feeling the swell of his thighs as he pressed me down.

"Never," he whispered to me, face only inches from mine.

"Never," I said, and turned my head, closing my eyes to escape the intensity of his gaze.

A gentle, inexorable pressure turned me back to face him, as the small, rhythmic movements went on.

"No, my Sassenach," he said softly. "Open your eyes. Look at me. For that is your punishment, as it is mine. See what you have done to me, as I know what I have done to you. Look at me."

And I looked, held prisoner, bound to him. Looked, as he dropped the last of his masks, and showed me the depths of himself, and the wounds of his soul. I would have wept for his hurt, and for mine, had I been able. But his eyes held mine, tearless and open, boundless as the salt sea. His body held mine captive, driving me before his strength, like the west wind in the sails of a bark.

And I voyaged into him, as he into me, so that when the last small storms of love began to shake me, he cried out, and we rode the waves together as one flesh, and saw ourselves in each other's eyes.

The afternoon sun was hot on the white limestone rocks, casting deep shadows into the clefts and hollows. I found what I was looking for at last, growing from a narrow crack in a giant boulder, in gay defiance of the lack of soil. I broke a

stalk of aloe from its clump, split the fleshy leaf, and spread
the cool green gel inside across the welts on Jamie's palm.

"Better?" I said.

"Much." Jamie flexed his hand, grimacing. "Christ, those
nettles sting!"

"They do." I pulled down the neck of my bodice and
spread a little aloe juice on my breast with a gingerly touch.
The coolness brought relief at once.

"I'm rather glad you didn't take me up on my offer," I
said wryly, with a glance at a nearby bunch of blooming nettle.

He grinned and patted me on the bottom with his good
hand.

"Well, it was a near thing, Sassenach. Ye shouldna tempt
me like that." Then, sobering, he bent and kissed me gently.

"No, *mo nighean donn.* I swore to ye the once, and I was
meaning it. I shallna raise a hand to you in anger, ever. After
all," he added softly, turning away, "I have done enough to
hurt you."

I shrank from the pain of memory, but I owed him justice as well.

"Jamie," I said, lips trembling a bit. "The . . . baby. It
wasn't your fault. I felt as though it was, but it wasn't. I think
. . . I think it would have happened anyway, whether you'd
fought Jack Randall or not."

"Aye? Ah . . . well." His arm was warm and comforting
about me, and he pressed my head into the curve of his shoulder. "It eases me a bit to hear ye say so. It wasna the child so
much as Frank that I meant, though. D'ye think you can forgive me for that?" The blue eyes were troubled as he looked
down at me.

"Frank?" I felt a shock of surprise. "But . . . there's
nothing to forgive." Then a thought struck me; perhaps he
really didn't know that Jack Randall was still alive—after all,
he had been arrested immediately after the duel. But if he
didn't know. . . . I took a deep breath. He would have to
find it out in any case; perhaps better from me.

"You didn't kill Jack Randall, Jamie," I said.

To my puzzlement, he didn't seem shocked or surprised.
He shook his head, the afternoon sun striking sparks from his
hair. Not yet long enough to lace back again, it had grown

considerably in prison, and he had to brush it out of his eyes continuously.

"I know that, Sassenach," he said.

"You do? But . . . what . . ." I was at a loss.

"You . . . dinna know about it?" he said hesitantly.

A cold feeling crept up my arms, despite the heat of the sun.

"Know what?"

He chewed his lower lip, eyeing me reluctantly. At last he took a deep breath and let it out with a sigh.

"No, I didna kill him. But I wounded him."

"Yes, Louise said you wounded him badly. But she said he was recovering." Suddenly, I saw again in memory that last scene in the Bois de Boulogne; the last thing I had seen before the blackness took me. The sharp tip of Jamie's sword, slicing through the rain-spattered doeskin. The sudden red stain that darkened the fabric . . . and the angle of the blade, glinting with the force that drove it downward.

"Jamie!" I said, eyes widening with horror. "You didn't . . . Jamie, what have you done!"

He looked down, rubbing his welted palm against the side of his kilt. He shook his head, wondering at himself.

"I was such a fool, Sassenach. I couldna think myself a man and let him go unpunished for what he'd done to the wee lad, and yet . . . all the time, I kept thinking to myself, 'Ye canna kill the bastard outright, you've promised. Ye canna kill him.' " He smiled faintly, without humor, looking down at the marks on his palm.

"My mind was boiling over like a pot of parritch on the flame, yet I held to that thought. 'Ye canna kill him.' And I didn't. But I was half-mad wi' the fury of the fighting, and the blood singing in my ears—and I didna stop a moment to remember why it was I must not kill him, beyond that I had promised you. And when I had him there on the ground before me, and the memory of Wentworth and Fergus, and the blade live in my hand—" He broke off suddenly.

I felt the blood draining from my head and sat down heavily on a rock outcropping.

"Jamie," I said. He shrugged helplessly.

"Well, Sassenach," he said, still avoiding my gaze, "all I can say is, it's a hell of a place to be wounded."

"Jesus." I sat still, stunned by this revelation. Jamie sat quiet beside me, studying the broad backs of his hands. There was still a small pink mark on the back of the right one. Jack Randall had driven a nail through it, in Wentworth.

"D'ye hate me for it, Claire?" His voice was soft, almost tentative.

I shook my head, eyes closed.

"No." I opened them, and saw his face close by, wearing a troubled frown. "I don't know *what* I think now, Jamie. I really don't. But I don't hate you." I put a hand on his, and squeezed it gently. "Just . . . let me be by myself for a minute, all right?"

Clad once more in my now-dry gown, I spread my hands flat on my thighs. One silver, one gold. Both my wedding rings were still there, and I had no idea what that meant.

Jack Randall would never father a child. Jamie seemed sure of it, and I wasn't inclined to question him. And yet I still wore Frank's ring, I still remembered the man who had been my first husband, could summon at will thoughts and memories of who he had been, what he would do. How was it possible, then, that he would not exist?

I shook my head, thrusting back the wind-dried curls behind my ears. I didn't know. Chances were, I never *would* know. But whether one could change the future or not—and it seemed we had—I was certain that I couldn't change the immediate past. What had been done had been done, and nothing I could do now would alter it. Jack Randall would sire no children.

A stone rolled down the slope behind me, bouncing and setting off small slides of gravel. I turned and glanced up, to where Jamie, dressed once more, was exploring.

The rockfall above was recent. Fresh white surfaces showed where the stained brown of the weathered limestone had fractured, and only the smallest of plants had yet gained a foothold in this tumbled pile of rock, unlike the thick growth of shrubs that blanketed the rest of the hillside.

Jamie inched to one side, absorbed in finding handholds through the intricacies of the fall. I saw him edge around a giant boulder, hugging the rock, and the faint scrape of his dirk against the stone came to me through the still afternoon air.

Then he disappeared. Expecting him to reappear round the other side of the rock, I waited, enjoying the sun on my shoulders. But he didn't come back into sight, and after a few moments, I grew worried. He might have slipped and fallen or banged his head on a rock.

I took what seemed forever to undo the fastenings of my heeled boots again, and still he had not come back. I rucked up my skirts, and started up the hill, bare toes cautious on the rough warm rocks.

"Jamie!"

"Here, Sassenach." He spoke behind me, startling me, and I nearly lost my balance. He caught me by the arm and lifted me down to a small clear space between the jagged fallen stones.

He turned me toward the limestone wall, stained with water rust, and smoke. And something more.

"Look," he said softly.

I looked where he pointed, up across the smooth expanse of the cave wall, and gasped at the sight.

Painted beasts galloped across the rock face above me, hooves spurning the air as they leaped toward the light above. There were bison, and deer, grouped together in tail-raised flight, and at the end of the rock shelf, a tracing of delicate birds, wings spread as they hovered above the charge of the earthbound beasts.

Done in red and black and ochre with a delicate grace that used the lines of the rock itself for emphasis, they thundered soundlessly, haunches rounded with effort, wings taking flight through the crevices of stone. They had lived once in the dark of a cave, lit only by the flames of those who made them. Exposed to the sun by the fall of their sheltering roof, they seemed alive as anything that walked upon the earth.

Lost in contemplation of the massive shoulders that thrust their way from the rock, I didn't miss Jamie until he called me.

"Sassenach! Come here, will ye?" There was something odd about his voice, and I hurried toward him. He stood at the entrance of a small side-cave, looking down.

They lay behind an outcrop of the rock, as though they had sought shelter from the wind that chased the bison.

There were two of them, lying together on the packed earth of the cave floor. Sealed in the dry air of the cave, the bones had endured, though flesh had long since dried to dust. A tiny remnant of brown-parchment skin clung to the round curve of one skull, a strand of hair gone red with age stirring softly in the draft of our presence.

"My God," I said, softly, as though I might disturb them. I moved closer to Jamie, and his hand slid around my waist.

"Do you think . . . were they . . . killed here? A sacrifice, perhaps?"

Jamie shook his head, staring pensively down at the small heap of delicate, friable bones.

"No," he said. He, too, spoke softly, as though in the sanctuary of a church. He turned and lifted a hand to the wall behind us, where the deer leaped and the cranes soared into space beyond the stone.

"No," he said again. "The folk that made such beasts . . . they couldna do such things." He turned again then to the two skeletons, entwined at our feet. He crouched over them, tracing the line of the bones with a gentle finger, careful not to touch the ivory surface.

"See how they lie," he said. "They didna fall here, and no one laid out their bodies. They lay down themselves." His hand glided above the long arm-bones of the larger skeleton, a dark shadow fluttering like a large moth as it crossed the jackstraw pile of ribs.

"He had his arms around her," he said. "He cupped his thighs behind her own, and held her tight to him, and his head is resting on her shoulder."

His hand made passes over the bones, illuminating, indicating, clothing them once more with the flesh of imagination, so I could see them as they had been, embraced for the last time, for always. The small bones of the fingers had fallen apart, but a vestige of gristle still joined the metacarpals of the hands. The tiny phalanges overlay each other; they had linked hands in their last waiting.

Jamie had risen and was surveying the interior of the cavern, the late afternoon sun painting the walls with splashes of crimson and ochre.

"There." He pointed to a spot near the cavern entrance. The rocks there were brown with dust and age, but not rusty with water and erosion, like those deeper in the cave.

"That was the entrance, once," he said. "The rocks fell once before, and sealed this place." He turned back and rested a hand on the rocky outcrop that shielded the lovers from the light.

"They must have felt their way around the cave, hand in hand," I said. "Looking for a way out, in the dust and the dark."

"Aye." He rested his forehead against the stone, eyes closed. "And the light was gone, and the air failed them. And so they lay down in the dark to die." The tears made wet tracks through the dust on his cheeks. I brushed a hand beneath my own eyes, and took his free hand, carefully weaving my fingers with his.

He turned to me, wordless, and the breath rushed from him as he pulled me hard against him. Our hands groped in the dying light of the setting sun, urgent in the touch of warmth, the reassurance of flesh, reminded by the hardness of the invisible bone beneath the skin, how short life is.

PART FIVE

"I Am Come Home"

30

Lallybroch

I t was called Broch Tuarach, for the ancient cylinder of stone, built some hundreds of years before, that poked up from the hillside behind the manor. The people who lived on the estate called it "Lallybroch." Insofar as I could gather, this meant "lazy tower," which made at least as much sense as applying the term "North-facing Tower" to a cylindrical structure.

"How can something that's round face north?" I asked as we made our way slowly down a long slope of heather and granite, leading the horses in single file down the narrow, twisting path the red deer had trampled through the springy growth. "It hasn't *got* a face."

"It has a door," Jamie said reasonably. "The door faces north." He dug in his feet as the slope dropped sharply, hissing through his teeth in signal to the horse he led behind him. The muscular hindquarters in front of me bunched suddenly, as the cautious stride altered to a tentative mincing, each hoof sliding a few inches in the damp earth before another step was risked. The horses, purchased in Inverness, were good-sized, handsome beasts. The wiry little Highland ponies would have made much better work of the steep slope, but these horses, all mares, were meant for breeding, not work.

"All right," I said, stepping carefully over a tiny runnel of water that crossed the deer path. "Good enough. What about 'Lallybroch,' though? Why is it a lazy tower?"

"It leans a bit," Jamie replied. I could see the back of his head, bent in concentration on the footing, a few tendrils of red-gold hair lifting from the crown in the afternoon breeze that blew up the slope. "Ye canna see it much from the house, but if you stand on the west side, you'll see it leans to the north a bit. And if ye look from one of the slits on the top floor over the door, ye canna see the wall beneath you because of the slant."

"Well, I suppose no one had heard of plumb lines in the

thirteenth century," I observed. "It's a wonder it hasn't fallen down by now."

"Oh, it's fallen down a number of times," Jamie said, raising his voice slightly as the wind freshened. "The folk who lived there just put it back up again; that's likely why it leans."

"I see it! I see it!" Fergus's voice, shrill with excitement, came from behind me. He had been allowed to stay on his mount, as his negligible weight was unlikely to cause the horse any great difficulty, bad footing notwithstanding. Glancing back, I could see him kneeling on his saddle, bouncing up and down with excitement. His horse, a patient, good-natured bay mare, gave a grunt at this, but kindly refrained from flinging him off into the heather. Ever since his adventure with the Percheron colt at Argentan, Fergus had seized every chance to get on a horse, and Jamie, amused and sympathetic to a fellow horse-lover, had indulged him, taking him up behind his own saddle when he rode through the Paris streets, allowing him now and then to get up alone on one of Jared's coach horses, large stolid creatures that merely flicked their ears in a puzzled sort of way at Fergus's kicks and shouts.

I shaded my eyes, looking in the direction where he pointed. He was right; from his higher vantage point, he had spotted the dark form of the old stone broch, perched on its hill. The modern manor-house below was harder to see; it was built of white-harled stone, and the sun reflected from its walls as from the surrounding fields. Set in a hollow of sloping barley fields, it was still partly obscured to our view by a row of trees that formed the windbreak at the foot of a field.

I saw Jamie's head rise, and fix as he saw the home farm of Lallybroch below. He stood quite still for a minute, not speaking, but I saw his shoulders lift and set themselves square. The wind caught his hair and the folds of his plaid and lifted them, as though he might rise in the air, joyous as a kite.

It reminded me of the way the sails of the ships had filled, turning past the headland into the shipping roads as they left the harbor of Le Havre. I had stood on the end of the quay, watching the bustle and the comings and goings of shipping and commerce. The gulls dived and shrieked among the masts, their voices raucous as the shouting of the seamen.

Jared Munro Fraser had stood by me, watching benignly the flow of passing seaborne wealth, some of it his. It was one of his ships, the *Portia*, that would carry us to Scotland. Jamie had told me that all Jared's ships were named for his mistresses, the figureheads carved in the likenesses of the ladies in question. I squinted against the wind at the prow of the ship, trying to decide whether Jamie had been teasing me. If not, I concluded, Jared preferred his women well endowed.

"I shall miss you both," Jared said, for the fourth time in half an hour. He looked truly regretful, even his cheerful nose seeming less upturned and optimistic than usual. The trip to Germany had been a success; he sported a large diamond in his stock, and the coat he wore was a rich bottle-green velvet with silver buttons.

"Ah, well," he said, shaking his head. "Much as I should like to keep the laddie with me, I canna grudge him joy of his homecoming. Perhaps I shall come to visit ye someday, my dear; it's been long since I set foot in Scotland."

"We'll miss you, too," I told him, truthfully. There were other people I would miss—Louise, Mother Hildegarde, Herr Gerstmann. Master Raymond most of all. Yet I looked forward to returning to Scotland, to Lallybroch. I had no wish to go back to Paris, and there were people there I most certainly had no desire to see again—Louis of France, for one.

Charles Stuart, for another. Cautious probing amongst the Jacobites in Paris had confirmed Jamie's initial impression; the small burst of optimism fired by Charles's boasting of his "grand venture" had faded, and while the loyal supporters of King James held true to their sovereign, there seemed no chance that this stolid loyalty of stubborn endurance would lead to action.

Let Charles make his own peace with exile, then, I thought. Our own was over. We were going home.

"The baggage is aboard," said a dour Scots voice in my ear. "The master of the ship says come ye along now; we sail wi' the tide."

Jared turned to Murtagh, then glanced right and left down the quay. "Where's the laddie, then?" he asked.

Murtagh jerked his head down the pier. "In the tavern yon. Gettin' stinkin' drunk."

I had wondered just how Jamie had planned to weather

the Channel crossing. He had taken one look at the lowering
red sky of dawn that threatened later storms, excused himself
to Jared, and disappeared. Looking in the direction of Murtagh's nod, I saw Fergus, sitting on a piling near the entrance
to one grogshop, plainly doing sentry duty.

Jared, who had exhibited first disbelief and then hilarity
when informed of his cousin's disability, grinned widely at this
news.

"Oh, aye?" he said. "Well, I hope he's left the last quart
'til we come for him. He'll be hell to carry up the gangplank,
if he hasn't."

"What did he do that for?" I demanded of Murtagh, in
some exasperation. "I told him I had some laudanum for
him." I patted the silk reticule I carried. "It would knock him
out a good deal faster."

Murtagh merely blinked once. "Aye. He said if he was
goin' to have a headache, he'd as soon enjoy the gettin' of it.
And the whisky tastes a good bit better goin' down than yon
filthy black stuff." He nodded at my reticule, then at Jared.
"Come on, then, if ye mean to help me wi' him."

In the forward cabin of the *Portia*, I had sat on the captain's bunk, watching the steady rise and fall of the receding
shoreline, my husband's head cradled on my knees.

One eye opened a slit and looked up at me. I stroked the
heavy damp hair off his brow. The scent of ale and whisky
hung about him like perfume.

"You are going to feel exactly like hell when you wake up
in Scotland," I told him.

The other eye opened, and regarded the dancing waves
of light reflected across the timbered ceiling. Then they fixed
on me, deep pools of limpid blue.

"Between hell now, and hell later, Sassenach," he said,
his speech measured and precise, "I will take later, every
time." His eyes closed. He belched softly, once, and the long
body relaxed, rocked at ease on the cradle of the deep.

◄───

The horses seemed as eager as we; sensing the nearness
of stables and food, they began to push the pace a bit, heads
up and ears cocked forward in anticipation.

I was just reflecting that I could do with a wash and a

bite to eat, myself, when my horse, slightly in the lead, dug in its feet and came to a slithering halt, hooves buried fetlock deep in the reddish dust. The mare shook her head violently from side to side, snorting and whooshing.

"Hey, lass, what's amiss? Got a bee up your nose?" Jamie swung down from his own mount and hurried to grab the gray mare's bridle. Feeling the broad back shiver and twitch beneath me, I slid down as well.

"Whatever is the matter with her?" I gazed curiously at the horse, which was pulling backward against Jamie's grip on the bridle, shaking her mane, with eyes bugging. The other horses, as though infected by her unease, began to stamp and shift as well.

Jamie glanced briefly over his shoulder at the empty road.

"She sees something."

Fergus raised himself in his shortened stirrups and shaded his eyes, staring over the mare's back. Lowering his hand, he looked at me and shrugged.

I shrugged back; there seemed to be nothing whatever to cause the mare's distress—the road and the fields lay vacant all around us, grain-heads ripening and drying in the late summer sun. The nearest grove of trees was more than a hundred yards away, beyond a small heap of stones that might have been the remnants of a tumbled chimneystack. Wolves were almost unheard of in cleared land like this, and surely no fox or badger would disturb a horse at this distance.

Giving up the attempt to coax the mare forward, Jamie led her in a half-circle; she went willingly enough, back in the direction we had come.

He motioned to Murtagh to lead the other horses out of the way, then swung himself into the saddle, and leaning forward, one hand clutched in the mare's mane, urged her slowly forward, speaking softly in her ear. She came hesitantly, but without resistance, until she reached the point of her previous stopping. There she halted again and stood shivering, and nothing would persuade her to move a step farther.

"All right, then," said Jamie, resigned. "Have it your way." He turned the horse's head and led her into the field, the yellow grain-heads brushing the shaggy hairs of her belly. We rustled after them, the horses bending their necks to snatch a mouthful of grain here and there as we passed through the field.

As we rounded a small granite outcrop just below the crest of the hill, I heard a brief warning bark just ahead. We emerged onto the road to find a black and white shepherd dog on guard, head up and tail stiff as he kept a wary eye on us.

He uttered another short yap, and a matching black and white figure shot out of a clump of alders, followed more slowly by a tall, slender figure wrapped in a brown hunting plaid.

"Ian!"

"Jamie!"

Jamie tossed the mare's reins back to me, and met his brother-in-law in the middle of the road, where the two men clutched each other round the shoulders, laughing and pounding each other on the back. Released from suspicion, the dogs frolicked happily around them, tails wagging, darting aside now and then to sniff at the legs of the horses.

"We didna expect ye 'til tomorrow at the earliest," Ian was saying, his long, homely face beaming.

"We had a good wind crossing," Jamie explained. "Or at least Claire tells me we did; I wasna taking much notice, myself." He cast a glance back at me, grinning, and Ian came up to grasp my hand.

"Good-sister," he said in formal greeting. Then he smiled, the warmth of it lighting his soft brown eyes. "Claire." Impulsively, he kissed my fingers, and I squeezed his hand.

"Jenny's gone daft wi' cleaning and cooking," he said, still smiling at me. "You'll be lucky to have a bed to sleep in tonight; she's got all the mattresses outside, being beaten."

"After three nights in the heather, I wouldn't mind sleeping on the floor," I assured him. "Are Jenny and the children all well?"

"Oh, aye. She's breeding again," he added. "Due in February."

"*Again?*" Jamie and I spoke together, and a rich blush rose in Ian's lean cheeks.

"God, man, wee Maggie's less than a year old," Jamie said, with a censorious cock of one brow. "Have ye no sense of restraint?"

"Me?" Ian said indignantly. "Ye think I had anything to do with it?"

"Well, if ye didn't, I should think ye'd be interested in who did," Jamie said, the corner of his mouth twitching.

The blush deepened to a rich rose color, contrasting nicely with Ian's smooth brown hair. "Ye know damn well what I mean," he said. "I slept on the trundle bed wi' Young Jamie for two months, but then Jenny . . ."

"Oh, you're saying my sister's a wanton, eh?"

"I'm saying she's as stubborn as her brother when it comes to getting what she wants," Ian said. He feinted to one side, dodged neatly back and landed a blow in the pit of Jamie's stomach. Jamie doubled over, laughing.

"Just as well I've come home, then," he said. "I'll help ye keep her under control."

"Oh, aye?" Ian said skeptically. "I'll call all the tenants to watch."

"Lost a few sheep, have ye?" Jamie changed the subject with a gesture that took in the dogs and Ian's long crook, dropped in the dust of the roadway.

"Fifteen yows and a ram," Ian said, nodding. "Jenny's own flock of merinos, that she keeps for the special wool. The ram's a right bastard; broke down the gate. I thought they might have been in the grain up here, but nay sign o' them."

"We didn't see them up above," I said.

"Oh, they wouldna be up there," Ian said, waving a dismissive hand. "None o' the beasts will go past the cottage."

"Cottage?" Fergus, growing impatient with this exchange of civilities, had kicked his mount up alongside mine. "I saw no cottage, milord. Only a pile of stones."

"That's all that's left of MacNab's cottage, laddie," said Ian. He squinted up at Fergus, silhouetted against the late afternoon sun. "And ye'd be well-advised to keep away from there yourself."

The hair prickled on the back of my neck, despite the heat of the day. Ronald MacNab was the tenant who had betrayed Jamie to the men of the Watch a year before, the man who had died for his treachery within a day of its being found out. Died, I remembered, among the ashes of his home, burned over his head by the men of Lallybroch. The pile of chimneystones, so innocent when we had passed them a moment ago, had now the grim look of a cairn. I swallowed, forcing back the bitter taste that rose at the back of my throat.

"MacNab?" Jamie said softly. His expression was at once alert. "Ronnie MacNab?"

I had told Jamie of MacNab's betrayal, and his death, but I hadn't told him the means of it.

Ian nodded. "Aye. He died there, the night the English took ye, Jamie. The thatch must ha' caught from a spark, and him too far gone in drink to get out in time." He met Jamie's eyes straight on, all teasing gone.

"Ah? And his wife and child?" Jamie's look was the same as Ian's; cool and inscrutable.

"Safe. Mary MacNab's kitchen-maid at the house, and Rabbie works in the stables." Ian glanced involuntarily over his shoulder in the direction of the ruined cottage. "Mary comes up here now and again; she's the only one on the place will go there."

"Was she fond of him, then?" Jamie had turned to look in the direction of the cottage, so his face was hidden from me, but there was tension in the line of his back.

Ian shrugged. "I shouldna think so. A drunkard, and vicious with it, was Ronnie; not even his auld mother had much use for him. No, I think Mary feels it her duty to pray for his soul—much good it'll do him," he added.

"Ah." Jamie paused a moment as though in thought, then tossed his horse's reins over its neck and turned up the hill.

"Jamie," I said, but he was already walking back up the road, toward the small clearing beside the grove. I handed the reins I was holding to a surprised Fergus.

"Stay here with the horses," I said. "I have to go with him." Ian moved to come with me, but Murtagh stopped him with a shake of the head, and I went on alone, following Jamie up over the crest of the hill.

He had the long, tireless stride of a hill-walker, and had reached the small clearing before I caught him up. He stood at the edge of what had been the outer wall. The square shape of the cottage's earth floor was still barely visible, the new growth that covered it sparser than the nearby barley, greener and wild in the shade of the trees.

There was little trace of the fire left; a few chunks of charred wood poked through the grass near the stone hearth that lay open now, flat and exposed as a tombstone. Careful not to step within the outlines of the vanished walls, Jamie began to walk around the clearing. He circled the hearthstone three times, walking always widdershins, left, and left, and left again, to confound any evil that might follow.

I stood to one side and watched. This was a private confrontation, but I couldn't leave him to face it alone, and though he didn't glance at me, still I knew he was glad of my presence.

At last he stopped by the fallen pile of stones. Reaching out, he laid a hand gingerly on it and closed his eyes for a moment, as though in prayer. Then, stooping, he picked up a stone the size of his fist, and placed it carefully on the pile, as though it might weigh down the uneasy soul of the ghost. He crossed himself, turned and came toward me with a firm, unhurried step.

"Don't look back," he said quietly, taking me by the arm as we turned toward the road.

I didn't.

Jamie, Fergus, and Murtagh went with Ian and the dogs in search of the sheep, leaving me to take the string of horses down to the house alone. I was far from being an accomplished horse-handler, but thought I could manage half a mile, so long as nothing popped out at me unexpectedly.

This was very different from our first homecoming to Lallybroch; then, we had been in flight, both of us. Me from the future, Jamie from his past. Our residence then had been happy, but tenuous and insecure; always there was the chance of discovery, of Jamie's arrest. Now, thanks to the Duke of Sandringham's intervention, Jamie had come to take possession of his birthright, and I, my lawful place beside him as his wife.

Then, we had arrived disheveled, unexpected, a violent disruption in the household. This time, we had come announced, with due ceremony, bearing presents from France. While I was sure our reception would be cordial, I did wonder how Ian and Jamie's sister Jenny would take our permanent return. After all, they had lived as master and mistress of the estate for the last several years, ever since the death of Jamie's father, and the disastrous events that had precipitated him into a life of outlawry and exile.

I topped the last hill without incident, and the manor house and its outbuildings lay below me, slate roofs darkening as the first banks of rain clouds rolled in. Suddenly, my mare started, and so did I, struggling to keep a hold on the reins as she curvetted and plunged in alarm.

Not that I could blame her; from around the corner of the house had emerged two huge, puffy objects, rolling along the ground like overweight clouds.

"Stop that!" I shouted. "Whoa!" All the horses were now swerving and pulling, and I was inches away from a stampede. Fine homecoming, I thought, if I let all Jamie's new breeding stock break their collective legs.

One of the clouds rose slightly, then sank flat to the ground, and Jenny Fraser Murray, released from the burden of the feather mattress she had been carrying, raced for the road, dark curls flying.

Without a moment's hesitation, she leaped for the bridle of the nearest animal, and jerked down, hard.

"Whoa!" she said. The horse, obviously recognizing the voice of authority, did whoa. With a little effort, the other horses were calmed, and by the time I could slide down from my saddle, we had been joined by another woman and a boy of nine or ten, who lent an experienced hand with the remaining beasts.

I recognized young Rabbie MacNab, and deduced that the woman must be his mother, Mary. The bustle and shuffle of horses, bundles and mattresses precluded much conversation, but I had time for a quick hug of greeting with Jenny. She smelled of cinnamon and honey and the clean sweat of exertion, with an undertone of baby-scent, that paradoxical smell composed of spit-up milk, soft feces, and the ultimate cleanliness of fresh, smooth skin.

We clung together for a moment, hugging tight, remembering our last embrace, when we had parted on the edge of a night-dark wood—me to go in search of Jamie, she to return to a newborn daughter.

"How's little Maggie?" I asked, breaking away at last.

Jenny made a face, wryness mingled with pride. "She's just walking, and the terror o' the house." She glanced up the empty road. "Met Ian, did ye?"

"Yes, Jamie, Murtagh, and Fergus went with him to find the sheep."

"Better them than us," she said, with a quick gesture toward the sky. "It's coming on to rain any minute. Let Rabbie stable the horses and you come lend a hand wi' the mattresses, or we'll all sleep wet tonight."

A frenzy of activity ensued, but when the rain came, Jenny and I were snug in the parlor, undoing the parcels we had brought from France, and admiring the size and precocity of wee Maggie, a sprightly miss of some ten months, with round blue eyes and a head of strawberry fuzz, and her elder brother, Young Jamie, a sturdy almost-four-year-old. The impending arrival was no more than a tiny bulge beneath their mother's apron, but I saw her hand rest tenderly there from time to time, and felt a small pang to see it.

"You mentioned Fergus," Jenny said, as we talked. "Who's that?"

"Oh, Fergus? He's—well, he's—" I hesitated, not sure quite how to describe Fergus. A pickpocket's prospects for employment on a farm seemed limited. "He's Jamie's," I said at last.

"Oh, aye? Well, I suppose he can sleep in the stable," said Jenny, resigned. "Speaking of Jamie"—she glanced at the window, where the rain was streaming down—"I hope they find those sheep soon. I've a good dinner planned, and I dinna want it to spoil with keeping."

In fact, darkness had fallen, and Mary MacNab had laid the table before the men returned. I watched her at her work; a small, fine-boned woman with dark-brown hair and a faintly worried look that faded into a smile when Rabbie returned from the stables and went to the kitchen, hungrily asking when dinner would be.

"When the men are back, *mo luaidh*," she said, "Ye know that. Go and wash, so you'll be ready."

When the men finally did appear, they seemed a good deal more in need of a wash than did Rabbie. Rain-soaked, draggled, and muddy to the knees, they trailed slowly into the parlor. Ian unwound the wet plaid from his shoulders and hung it over the firescreen, where it dripped and steamed in the heat of the fire. Fergus, worn out by his abrupt introduction to farm life, simply sat down where he was and stared numbly at the floor between his legs.

Jenny looked up at the brother she had not seen for nearly a year. Glancing from his rain-drenched hair to his mud-crusted feet, she pointed to the door.

"Outside, and off wi' your boots," she said firmly. "And if ye've been in the high field, remember to piss on the doorposts on your way back in. That's how ye keep a ghost from comin' in the house," she explained to me in a lowered tone, with a quick look at the door through which Mary MacNab had disappeared to fetch the dinner.

Jamie, slumped into a chair, opened one eye and gave his sister a dark-blue look.

"I land in Scotland near dead wi' the crossing, ride for four days over the hills to get here, and when I arrive, I canna even come in the house for a drop to wet my parched throat; instead I'm off through the mud, huntin' lost sheep. And once I *do* get here, ye want to send me out in the dark again to piss on doorposts. Tcha!" He closed the eye again, crossed his hands across his stomach, and sank lower in his chair, a study in stubborn negation.

"Jamie, my dearie," his sister said sweetly. "D'ye want your dinner, or shall I feed it to the dogs?"

He remained motionless for a long moment, eyes closed. Then, with a hissing sigh of resignation, he got laboriously to his feet. With a moody twitch of his shoulder, he summoned Ian and the two of them turned, following Murtagh, who was already out the door. As he passed, Jamie reached down a long arm, hauled Fergus to his feet, and dragged the boy sleepily along.

"Welcome home," Jamie said morosely, and with a last wistful glance at fire and whisky, trudged out into the night once more.

31

Mail Call

After this inauspicious homecoming, matters rapidly improved. Lallybroch absorbed Jamie at once, as though he had never left, and I found myself pulled effortlessly into the current of farm life as well. It was an unsettled autumn, with frequent rain, but with fair, bright days that made the blood sing, too. The place bustled with life, everyone hurrying through the harvest time and the preparations that must be made for the coming winter.

Lallybroch was remote, even for a Highland farm. No real roads led there, but the post still reached us by messenger, over the crags and the heather-clad slopes, a connection with the world outside. It was a world that sometimes seemed unreal in memory, as though I had never danced among the mirrors of Versailles. But the letters brought back France, and reading them, I could see the poplar trees along the Rue Trémoulins, or hear the reverberating bong of the cathedral bell that hung above L'Hôpital des Anges.

Louise's child was born safely; a son. Her letters, rife with exclamations and underlinings, overflowed with besotted descriptions of the angelic Henri. Of his father, putative or real, there was no mention.

Charles Stuart's letter, arriving a month later, made no mention of the child, but according to Jamie, was even more incoherent than usual, seething with vague plans and grandiosities.

The Earl of Mar wrote soberly and circumspectly, but his general annoyance with Charles was clear. The Bonnie Prince was not behaving. He was rude and overbearing to his most loyal followers, ignored those who might be of help to him, insulted whom he should not, talked wildly, and—reading between the lines—drank to excess. Given the attitude of the times regarding alcoholic intake on the part of gentlemen, I thought Charles's performance must have been fairly spectacular, to occasion such comment. I supposed the birth of his son had not, in fact, escaped his notice.

Mother Hildegarde wrote from time to time, brief, informative notes squeezed into a few minutes that could be snatched from her daily schedule. Each letter ended with the same words; "Bouton also sends his regards."

Master Raymond did not write, but every so often, a parcel would come addressed to me, unsigned and unmarked, but containing odd things: rare herbs and small, faceted crystals; a collection of stones, each the size of Jamie's thumbnail, smooth and disc-shaped. Each one had a tiny figure carved into one side, some with lettering above or on the reverse. And then there were the bones—a bear's digit, with the great curved claw still attached; the complete vertebrae of a small snake, articulated and strung on a leather thong, so the whole string flexed in a lifelike manner; an assortment of teeth, ranging from a string of round, peglike things that Jamie said came from a seal, through the high-crowned, scythe-cusped teeth of deer, to something that looked suspiciously like a human molar.

From time to time, I carried some of the smooth, carved stones in my pocket, enjoying the feel of them between my fingers. They were old; I knew that much. From Roman times at least; perhaps even earlier. And from the look of some of the creatures on them, whoever had carved them had meant them to be magic. Whether they were like the herbs—having some actual virtue—or only a symbol, like the signs of the Cabbala, I didn't know. They seemed benign, though, and I kept them.

While I enjoyed the daily round of domestic tasks, what I liked best were the long walks to the various cottages on the estate. I always carried a large basket with me on these visits, containing an assortment of things, from small treats for the children to the most commonly needed medicines. These were called for frequently, for poverty and poor hygiene made illness common, and there were no physicians north of Fort William or south of Inverness.

Some ailments I could treat readily, like the bleeding gums and skin eruptions characteristic of mild scurvy. Other things were beyond my power to heal.

I laid a hand on Rabbie MacNab's head. The shaggy hair was damp at his temples, but his jaw hung open, slack, relaxed, and the pulse in his neck beat slowly.

"He's all right now," I said. His mother could see that as well as I could; he lay sprawled in the peaceful abandon of sleep, cheeks flushed from the heat of the nearby fire. Still, she stayed tense and watchful, hovering over the bedstead until I spoke. Once I had given absolution to the evidence of her own eyes, she was willing to believe, though; her bunched shoulders slumped under her shawl.

"Thank the Blessed Mother," Mary MacNab murmured, crossing herself briefly, "and you, my lady."

"I didn't do anything," I protested. This was quite literally true; the only service I had been able to render young Rabbie was to make his mother let him alone. It had, in fact, taken a certain amount of forcefulness to discourage her efforts to feed him bran mixed with cock's blood, wave burning feathers under his nose, or dash cold water over him—none of these remedies being of marked use to someone suffering an epileptic seizure. When I arrived, his mother had been volubly regretting her inability to administer the most effective of remedies: spring water drunk from the skull of a suicide.

"It frichts me so when he's taen like that," Mary MacNab said, gazing longingly at the bed where her son lay. "I had Father MacMurtry to him the last time, and he prayed a terrible long time, and sprinkled holy water on the lad to drive the de'ils out. But noo they've come back." She clasped her hands tight together, as though she wished to touch her son, but couldn't bring herself to do so.

"It isn't devils," I said. "It's only a sickness, and not all that bad a one, at that."

"Aye, my lady, an' ye say so," she murmured, unwilling to contradict me, but plainly unconvinced.

"He'll be all right." I tried to reassure the woman, without raising hopes that couldn't be met. "He always recovers from these fits, doesn't he?" The fits had come on two years ago—probably the result of head injury from beatings administered by his late father, I thought—and while the seizures were infrequent, they were undeniably terrifying to his mother when they occurred.

She nodded reluctantly, plainly unconvinced.

"Aye . . . though he bangs his heid something fearful now and then, thrashin' as he does."

"Yes, that's a risk," I said patiently. "If he does it again, just pull him away from anything hard, and let him alone. I know it looks bad, but really, he'll be quite all right. Just let the fit run its course, and when it's over, put him to bed and let him sleep." I knew that words were of limited value, no matter how true they might be. Something more concrete was needed for reassurance.

As I turned to go, I heard a small click in the deep pocket of my skirt, and had a sudden inspiration. Reaching in, I pulled out two or three of the small smooth charmstones Raymond had sent me. I selected the milky white one—chalcedony, perhaps—with the tiny figure of a writhing man carved into one side. So that's what it's for, I thought.

"Sew this into his pocket," I said, laying the tiny charm ceremoniously in the woman's hand. "It will protect him from . . . from devils." I cleared my throat. "You needn't worry about him, then, even if he has another fit; he'll come out of it all right."

I left then, feeling at once extremely foolish and halfway pleased, amidst an eager flood of relieved thanks. I wasn't sure whether I was becoming a better physician or merely a more practiced charlatan. Still, if I couldn't do much for Rabbie, I could help his mother—or let her help herself, at least. Healing comes from the healed; not from the physician. That much, Raymond had taught me.

I left the house then, to do my errands for the day, calling on two of the cottages near the west end of the farm. All was well at the Kirbys and the Weston Frasers, and I was soon on my way back to the house. At the top of a slope, I sat down under a large beech tree to rest for a moment before the long walk back. The sun was coming down the sky, but hadn't yet reached the row of pines that topped the ridge on the west side of Lallybroch. It was still late afternoon, and the world glowed with the colors of late autumn.

The fallen beechmast was cool and slippery under me, but a good many leaves still clung, yellowed and curling, to the tree above. I leaned back against the smooth-barked trunk and closed my eyes, dimming the bright glare of ripe barley fields to a dark red glow behind my eyelids.

The stifling confines of the crofters' cottages had given me a headache. I leaned my head against the birch's smooth bark and began to breathe slowly and deeply, letting the fresh outdoor air fill my lungs, beginning what I always thought of as "turning in."

This was my own imperfect attempt to duplicate the feeling of the process Master Raymond had shown me in L'Hôpital des Anges; a summoning of the look and feel of each bit of myself, imagining exactly what the various organs and systems looked and felt like when they were functioning properly.

I sat quietly, hands loose in my lap, and listened to the beat of my heart. Beating fast from the exertion of the climb, it slowed quickly to a resting pace. The autumn breeze lifted the tendrils of hair from my neck and cooled my fire-flushed cheeks.

I sat, eyes closed, and traced the path of my blood, from the secret, thick-walled chambers of my heart, blue-purple through the pulmonary artery, reddening swiftly as the sacs of the lungs dumped their burden of oxygen. Then out in a bursting surge through the arch of the aorta, and the tumbling race upward and down and out, through carotids, renals, subclavians. To the smallest capillaries, blooming beneath the surface of the skin, I traced the path of my blood through the systems of my body, remembering the feel of perfection, of health. Of peace.

I sat still, breathing slowly, feeling languorous and heavy as though I had just risen from the act of love. My skin felt thin, my lips slightly swollen, and the pressure of my clothes was like the touch of Jamie's hands. It was no random choice that had invoked his name to cure me. Whether it was health of mind or body, the love of him was necessary to me as breath or blood. My mind reached out for him, sleeping or waking, and finding him, was satisfied. My body flushed and glowed, and as it came to full life, it hungered for his.

The headache was gone. I sat a moment longer, breathing slowly. Then I got to my feet and walked down the hill toward home.

I had never actually had a home. Orphaned at five, I had lived the life of a academic vagabond with my uncle Lamb for the next thirteen years. In tents on a dusty plain, in caves in the hills, in the swept and garnished chambers of an empty pyramid, Quentin Lambert Beauchamp, M.S., Ph.D., F.R.A.S., etc., had set up the series of temporary camps in which he did the archaeological work that would make him famous long before a car crash ended his brother's life and threw me into his. Not one to dither over petty details like an orphaned niece, Uncle Lamb had promptly enrolled me in a boarding school.

Not one to accept the vagaries of fate without a fight, I declined absolutely to go there. And, recognizing something in me that he had himself in abundant measure, Uncle Lamb had shrugged, and on the decision of a heartbeat, had taken me forever from the world of order and routine, of sums, clean sheets, and daily baths, to follow him into vagabondage.

The roving life had continued with Frank, though with a shift from field to universities, as the digging of an historian is usually conducted within walls. So, when the war came in 1939, it was less a disruption to me than to most.

I had moved from our latest hired flat into the junior nurses' quarters at Pembroke Hospital, and from there to a field station in France, and back again to Pembroke before war's end. And then, those few brief months with Frank, before we came to Scotland, seeking to find each other again. Only to lose each other once and for all, when I had walked into a stone circle, through madness, and out the other side, into the past that was my present.

It was strange, then, and rather wonderful, to wake in the upper bedroom at Lallybroch, next to Jamie, and realize, as I watched the dawn touch his sleeping face, that he had been born in this bed. All the sounds of the house, from the creak of the back stair under an early-rising maid's foot, to the drumming rain on the roofslates, were sounds he had heard a thousand times before; heard so often, he didn't hear them anymore. I did.

His mother, Ellen, had planted the late-blooming rose-bush by the door. Its faint, rich scent still wafted up the walls of the house to the bedroom window. It was as though she reached in herself, to touch him lightly in passing. To touch me, too, in welcome.

Beyond the house itself lay Lallybroch; fields and barns and village and crofts. He had fished in the stream that ran down from the hills, climbed the oaks and towering larches, eaten by the hearthstone of every croft. It was his place.

But he, too, had lived with disruption and change. Arrest, and the flight of outlawry; the rootless life of a mercenary soldier. Arrest again, imprisonment and torture, and the flight into exile so recently ended. But he had lived in one place for his first fourteen years. And even at that age, when he had been sent, as was the custom, to foster for two years with his mother's brother, Dougal MacKenzie, it was part and parcel of the life expected for a man who would return to live forever on his land, to care for his tenants and estate, to be a part of a larger organism. Permanence was his destiny.

But there had been that space of absence, and the experience of things beyond the boundaries of Lallybroch, even beyond the rocky coasts of Scotland. Jamie had spoken with kings, had touched law, and commerce, seen adventure and violence and magic. Once the boundaries of home had been transgressed, could destiny be enough to hold him? I wondered.

As I came down from the crest of the hill, I saw him below, heaving boulders into place as he repaired a rift in a drystone dike that bordered one of the smaller fields. Near him on the ground lay a pair of rabbits, neatly gutted but not yet skinned.

" 'Home is the sailor, home from the sea, and the hunter home from the hill,' " I quoted, smiling at him as I came up beside him.

He grinned back, wiped the sweat from his brow, then pretended to shudder.

"Dinna mention the sea to me, Sassenach. I saw two wee laddies sailing a bit of wood in the millpond this morning and nearly heaved up my breakfast at the sight."

I laughed. "You haven't any urge to go back to France, then?"

"God, no. Not even for the brandy." He heaved one last

stone to the top of the wall and settled it into place. "Going back to the house?"

"Yes. Do you want me to take the rabbits?"

He shook his head, and bent to pick them up. "No need; I'm going back myself. Ian needs a hand wi' the new storage cellar for the potatoes."

The first potato crop ever planted on Lallybroch was due for harvest within a few days, and—on my timorous and inexpert advice—a small root-cellar was being dug to house them. I had distinctly mixed feelings, whenever I looked at the potato field. On the one hand, I felt considerable pride in the sprawling, leafy vines that covered it. On the other, I felt complete panic at the thought that sixty families might depend on what lay under those vines for sustenance through the winter. It was on my advice—given hastily a year ago— that a prime barley field had been planted in potatoes, a crop hitherto unknown in the Highlands.

I knew that in the fullness of time, potatoes would become an important staple of life in the Highlands, less susceptible to blight and failure than the crops of oats and barley. Knowing that from a paragraph read in a geography book long ago was a far cry from deliberately taking responsibility for the lives of the people who would eat the crop.

I wondered if the taking of risks for other people got easier with practice. Jamie did it routinely, managing the affairs of the estate and the tenants as though he had been born to it. But, of course, he *had* been born to it.

"Is the cellar nearly ready?" I asked.

"Oh, aye. Ian's got the doors built, and the pit's nearly dug. It's only there's a soft bit of earth near the back, and his peg gets stuck in when he stands there." While Ian managed very well on the wooden peg he wore in substitute for his lower right leg, there were the occasional awkwardnesses such as this.

Jamie glanced thoughtfully up the hill behind us. "We'll need the cellar finished and covered by tonight; it's going to rain again before dawn."

I turned to look in the direction of his gaze. Nothing showed on the slope but grass and heather, a few trees, and the rocky seams of granite that poked bony ridges through the scruffy overgrowth.

"How in hell can you tell that?"

He smiled, pointing uphill with his chin. "See the small oak tree? And the ash nearby?"

I glanced at the trees, baffled. "Yes. What about them?"

"The leaves, Sassenach. See how both trees look lighter than usual? When there's damp in the air, the leaves of an oak or an ash will turn, so ye see the underside. The whole tree looks several shades lighter."

"I suppose it does," I agreed doubtfully. "If you happen to know what color the tree is normally."

Jamie laughed and took my arm. "I may not have an ear for music, Sassenach, but I've eyes in my head. And I've seen those trees maybe ten thousand times, in every weather there is."

It was some way from the field to the farmhouse, and we walked in silence for the most part, enjoying the brief warmth of the afternoon sun on our backs. I sniffed the air, and thought that Jamie was probably right about the coming rain; all the normal autumn smells seemed intensified, from the sharp pine resins to the dusty smell of ripe grain. I thought that I must be learning, myself; becoming attuned to the rhythms and sights and smells of Lallybroch. Maybe in time, I would come to know it as well as Jamie did. I squeezed his arm briefly, and felt the pressure of his hand on mine in response.

"D'ye miss France, Sassenach?" he said suddenly.

"No," I said, startled. "Why?"

He shrugged, not looking at me. "Well, it's only I was thinking, seeing ye come down the hill wi' the basket on your arm, how bonny ye looked wi' the sun on your brown hair. I thought you looked as though ye grew there, like one of the saplings—like ye'd always been a part of this place. And then it struck me, that to you, Lallybroch's maybe a poor wee spot. There's no grand life, like there was in France; not even interesting work, as ye had at the Hôpital." He glanced down at me shyly.

"I suppose I worry you'll grow bored wi' it here—in time."

I paused before answering, though it wasn't something I hadn't thought about.

"In time," I said carefully. "Jamie—I've seen a lot of

things in my life, and been in a lot of places. Where I came from—there were things there that I miss sometimes. I'd like to ride a London omnibus again, or pick up a telephone and talk to someone far away. I'd like to turn a tap, and have hot water, not carry it from the well and heat it in a cauldron. I'd like all that—but I don't need it. As for a grand life, I didn't want it when I had it. Nice clothes are all very well, but if gossip and scheming and worry and silly parties and tiny rules of etiquette go with them . . . no. I'd as soon live in my shift and say what I like."

He laughed at that, and I squeezed his arm once more.

"As for the work . . . there's work for me here." I glanced down into the basket of herbs and medicines on my arm. "I can be useful. And if I miss Mother Hildegarde, or my other friends—well, it isn't as fast as a telephone, but there are always letters."

I stopped, holding his arm, and looked up at him. The sun was setting, and the light gilded one side of his face, throwing the strong bones into relief.

"Jamie . . . I only want to be where you are. Nothing else."

He stood still for a moment, then leaned forward and kissed me very gently on the forehead.

"It's funny," I said as we came over the crest of the last small hill that led down to the house. "I had just been wondering the same kinds of things about *you*. Whether you'd be happy here, after the things you did in France."

He smiled, half-ruefully, and looked toward the house, its three stories of white-harled stone glowing gold and umber in the sunset.

"Well, it's home, Sassenach. It's my place."

I touched him gently on the arm. "And you were born to it, you mean?"

He drew a deep breath, and reached out to rest a hand on the wooden fence-rail that separated this lower field from the grounds near the house.

"Well, in fact I wasna born to it, Sassenach. By rights, it should have been Willie was lairdie here. Had he lived, I expect I would have been a soldier—or maybe a merchant, like Jared."

Willie, Jamie's elder brother, had died of the smallpox at the age of eleven, leaving his small brother, aged six, as the heir to Lallybroch.

He made an odd half-shrugging gesture, as though seeking to ease the pressure of his shirt across his shoulders. It was something he did when feeling awkward or unsure; I hadn't seen him do it in months.

"But Willie died. And so I am laird." He glanced at me, a little shyly, then reached into his sporran and pulled something out. A little cherrywood snake that Willie had carved for him as a birthday gift lay on his palm, head twisted as though surprised to see the tail following it.

Jamie stroked the little snake gently; the wood was shiny and seasoned with handling, the curves of the body gleaming like scales in early twilight.

"I talk to Willie, sometimes, in my mind," Jamie said. He tilted the snake on his palm. "If you'd lived, Brother, if ye'd been laird as you were meant to be, would ye do what I've done? or would ye find a better way?" He glanced down at me, flushing slightly. "Does that sound daft?"

"No." I touched the snake's smooth head with a fingertip. The high clear call of a meadowlark came from the far field, thin as crystal in the evening air.

"I do the same," I said softly, after a moment. "With Uncle Lamb. And my parents. My mother especially. I—I didn't think of her often, when I was young, just every now and then I'd dream about someone soft and warm, with a lovely singing voice. But when I was sick, after . . . Faith— sometimes I imagined she was there. With me." A sudden wave of grief swept over me, remembrance of losses recent and long past.

Jamie touched my face gently, wiping away the tear that had formed at the corner of one eye but not quite fallen.

"I think sometimes the dead cherish us, as we do them," he said softly. "Come on, Sassenach. Let's walk a bit; there's time before dinner."

He linked my arm in his, tight against his side, and we turned along the fence, walking slowly, the dry grass rustling against my skirt.

"I ken what ye mean, Sassenach," Jamie said. "I hear my father's voice sometimes, in the barn, or in the field. When I'm not even thinkin' of him, usually. But all at once I'll turn my head, as though I'd just heard him outside, laughing wi' one of the tenants, or behind me, gentling a horse."

He laughed suddenly, and nodded toward a corner of the pasture before us.

"It's a wonder I dinna hear him here, but I never have."

It was a thoroughly unremarkable spot, a wood-railed gate in the stone fence that paralleled the road.

"Really? What did he used to say here?"

"Usually it was 'If ye're through talkin', Jamie, turn about and bend ower.' "

We laughed, pausing to lean on the fence. I bent closer, squinting at the wood.

"So this is where you got smacked? I don't see any tooth-marks," I said.

"No, it wasna all that bad," he said, laughing. He ran a hand affectionately along the worn ash fence rail.

"We used to get splinters in our fingers, sometimes, Ian and me. We'd go up to the house after, and Mrs. Crook or Jenny would pick them out for us—scolding all the time."

He glanced toward the manor, where all the first-floor windows glowed with light against the gathering night. Dark forms moved briefly past the windows; small, quick-moving shadows in the kitchen windows, where Mrs. Crook and the maids were at the dinner preparations. A larger form, tall and slender as a fence rail, loomed suddenly in one of the drawing room windows. Ian stood a moment, silhouetted in the light as though called by Jamie's reminiscence. Then he drew the curtains and the window dulled to a softer, shrouded glow.

"I was always glad when Ian was with me," Jamie said, still looking toward the house. "When we got caught at some devilry and got thrashed for it, I mean."

"Misery loves company?" I said, smiling.

"A bit. I didna feel quite so wicked when there were the two of us to share the guilt between. But it was more that I could always count on him to make a lot of noise."

"What, to cry out, you mean?"

"Aye. He'd always howl and carry on something awful, and I knew he would do it, so I didna feel so ashamed of my own noise, if I had to cry out." It was too dark to see his face anymore, but I could still see the half-shrugging gesture he made when embarrassed or uncomfortable.

"I always tried not to, of course, but I couldna always manage. If my da thought it worth thrashing me over, he thought it worth doing a proper job. And Ian's father had a right arm like a tree bole."

"You know," I said, glancing down at the house, "I never thought of it particularly before, but why on earth did your father thrash you out here, Jamie? Surely there's enough room in the house—or the barn."

Jamie was silent for a moment, then shrugged again.

"I didna ever ask. But I reckon it was something like the King of France."

"The King of France?" This apparent non sequitur took me aback a bit.

"Aye. I dinna ken," he said dryly, "quite what it's like to have to wash and dress and move your bowels in public, but I can tell ye that it's a verra humbling experience to have to stand there and explain to one of your father's tenants just what ye did that's about to get your arse scalded for ye."

"I imagine it must be," I said, sympathy mingled with the urge to laugh. "Because you were going to be laird, you mean? That's why he made you do it here?"

"I expect so. The tenants would know I understood justice—at least, from the receiving end."

32

Field of Dreams

The field had been plowed in the usual "rigs," high ridges of piled earth, with deep furrows drawn between them. The rigs rose knee-high, so a man walking down the furrows could sow his seed easily by hand along the top of the rig beside him. Designed for the planting of barley or oats, no reason had been seen to alter them for the planting of potatoes.

"It said 'hills,' " Ian said, peering over the leafy expanse of the potato field, "but I thought the rigs would do as well. The point of the hills seemed to be to keep the things from rotting wi' too much water, and an old field wi' high rigs seemed like to do that as well."

"That seems sensible," Jamie agreed. "The top parts seem to be flourishing, anyway. Does the man say how ye ken when to dig the things up, though?"

Charged with the planting of potatoes in a land where no potato had ever been seen, Ian had proceeded with method and logic, sending to Edinburgh both for seed potatoes, and for a book on the subject of planting. In due course, *A Scientific Treatise on Methods of Farming,* by Sir Walter O'Bannion Reilly had made its appearance, with a small section on potato planting as presently practiced in Ireland.

Ian was carrying this substantial volume under one arm —Jenny had told me that he wouldn't go near the potato field without it, lest some knotty question of philosophy or technique occur to him while there—and now flipped it open, bracing it on one forearm as he groped in his sporran for the spectacles he wore when reading. These had belonged to his late father; small circles of glass, set in wire rims, and customarily worn on the end of his nose, they made him look like a very earnest young stork.

"Harvesting of the crop should be undertaken simultaneously with the appearance of the first winter goose," he read, then looked up, squinting accusingly over his spectacles at the potato field, as though expecting an indicative goose to stick its head up among the furrowed rigs.

"Winter goose?" Jamie peered frowning at the book over Ian's shoulder. "What sort of goose does he mean? Greylags? But ye see those all year. That canna be right."

Ian shrugged. "Maybe ye only see them in the winter in Ireland. Or maybe it's some kind of Irish goose he means, and not greylags at all."

Jamie snorted. "Well, the fat lot of good that does us. Does he say anything useful?"

Ian ran a finger down the lines of type, moving his lips silently. We had by now collected a small crowd of cottars, all fascinated by this novel approach to agriculture.

"Ye dinna dig potatoes when it's wet," Ian informed us, eliciting a louder snort from Jamie.

"Hmm," Ian murmured to himself. "Potato rot, potato bugs—we didna ha' any potato bugs, I suppose that's lucky— potato vines . . . umm, no, that's only what to do if the vines wilt. Potato blight—we canna tell if we have that until we see the potatoes. Seed potatoes, potato storage—"

Impatient, Jamie turned away from Ian, hands on his hips.

"Scientific farming, eh?" he demanded. He glared at the field of dark-green, leafy vines. "I suppose it's too damn scientific to explain how ye tell when the bloody things are ready to eat!"

Fergus, who had been tagging along behind Jamie as usual, looked up from a caterpillar, inching its slow and fuzzy way along his forefinger.

"Why don't you just dig one up and see?" he asked.

Jamie stared at Fergus for a moment. His mouth opened, but no sound emerged. He shut it, patted Fergus gently on the head, and went to fetch a pitchfork from its place against the fence.

The cottars, all men who had helped to plant and tend the field under Ian's direction—assisted by Sir Walter—clustered round to see the results of their labor.

Jamie chose a large and flourishing vine near the edge of the field and poised the fork carefully near its roots. Visibly holding his breath, he put a foot on the heel of the fork and pushed. The tines slid slowly into the damp brown dirt.

I was holding my own breath. There was a good deal more depending on this experiment than the reputation of Sir Walter O'Bannion Reilly. Or my own, for that matter.

Jamie and Ian had confirmed that the barley crop this year was smaller than normal, though still sufficient for the needs of the Lallybroch tenants. Another bad year would exhaust the meager reserves of grain, though. For a Highland estate, Lallybroch was prosperous; but that was saying something only by comparison with other Highland farms. Successful potato planting could well make the difference between hunger and plenty for the folk of Lallybroch over the next two years.

Jamie's heel pressed down and he leaned back on the handle of the fork. The earth crumbled and cracked around the vine, and with a sudden, rending *pop* the potato vine lifted up and the earth revealed its bounty.

A collective "Ah!" went up from the spectators, at sight of the myriad brown globules clinging to the roots of the uprooted vine. Ian and I both fell to our knees in the dirt, scrabbling in the loosened soil for potatoes severed from the parent vine.

"It worked!" Ian kept saying as he pulled potato after potato out of the ground. "Look at that! See the size of it?"

"Yes, look at this one!" I exclaimed in delight, brandishing one the size of my two fists held together.

At length, we had the produce of our sample vine laid in a basket; perhaps ten good-sized potatoes, twenty-five or so fist-size specimens, and a number of small things the size of golf balls.

"What d'ye think?" Jamie scrutinized our collection quizzically. "Ought we to leave the rest, so the little ones will grow more? Or take them now, before the cold comes?"

Ian groped absently for his spectacles, then remembered that Sir Walter was over by the fence, and abandoned the effort. He shook his head.

"No, I think this is right," he said. "The book says ye keep the bittie ones for the seed potatoes for next year. We'll want a lot of those." He gave me a grin of relieved delight, his hank of thick, straight brown hair dropping across his forehead. There was a smudge of dirt down the side of his face.

One of the cottars' wives was bending over the basket,

peering at its contents. She reached out a tentative finger and prodded one of the potatoes.

"Ye eat them, ye say?" Her brow creased skeptically. "I dinna see how ye'd ever grind them in a quern for bread or parritch."

"Well, I dinna believe ye grind them, Mistress Murray," Jamie explained courteously.

"Och, aye?" The woman squinted censoriously at the basket. "Well, what d'ye do wi' them, then?"

"Well, you . . ." Jamie started, and then stopped. It occurred to me, as it no doubt had to him, that while he had eaten potatoes in France, he had never seen one prepared for eating. I hid a smile as he stared helplessly at the dirt-crusted potato in his hand. Ian also stared at it; apparently Sir Walter was mute on the subject of potato cooking.

"You roast them." Fergus came to the rescue once more, bobbing up under Jamie's arm. He smacked his lips at the sight of the potatoes. "Put them in the coals of the fire. You eat them with salt. Butter's good, if you have it."

"We have it," said Jamie, with an air of relief. He thrust the potato at Mrs. Murray, as though anxious to be rid of it. "You roast them," he informed her firmly.

"You can boil them, too," I contributed. "Or mash them with milk. Or fry them. Or chop them up and put them in soup. A very versatile vegetable, the potato."

"That's what the book says," Ian murmured, with satisfaction.

Jamie looked at me, the corner of his mouth curling in a smile.

"Ye never told me you could cook, Sassenach."

"I wouldn't call it cooking, exactly," I said, "but I probably can boil a potato."

"Good." Jamie cast an eye at the group of tenants and their wives, who were passing the potatoes from hand to hand, looking them over rather dubiously. He clapped his hands loudly to attract attention.

"We'll be having supper here by the field," he told them. "Let's be fetching a bit of wood for a fire, Tom and Willie, and Mrs. Willie, if ye'd be so kind as to bring your big kettle? Aye, that's good, one of the men will help ye to bring it down. You, Kincaid—" He turned to one of the younger men, and waved off in the direction of the small cluster of cottages under the trees. "Go and tell everyone—it's potatoes for supper!"

And so, with the assistance of Jenny, ten pails of milk from the dairy shed, three chickens caught from the coop, and four dozen large leeks from the kailyard, I presided over the preparation of cock-a-leekie soup and roasted potatoes for the laird and tenants of Lallybroch.

The sun was below the horizon by the time the food was ready, but the sky was still alight, with streaks of red and gold that lanced through the dark branches of the pine grove on the hill. There was a little hesitation when the tenants came face-to-face with the proposed addition to their diet, but the party-like atmosphere—helped along by a judicious keg of home-brewed whisky—overcame any misgivings, and soon the ground near the potato field was littered with the forms of impromptu diners, hunched over bowls held on their knees.

"What d'ye think, Dorcas?" I overheard one woman say to her neighbor. "It's a wee bit queer-tasting, no?"

Dorcas, so addressed, nodded and swallowed before replying.

"Aye, it is. But the laird's eaten six o' the things so far, and they havena kilt him yet."

The response from the men and children was a good deal more enthusiastic, likely owing to the generous quantities of butter supplied with the potatoes.

"Men would eat horse droppings, if ye served them wi' butter," Jenny said, in answer to an observation along these lines. "Men! A full belly, and a place to lie down when they're drunk, and that's all they ask o' life."

"A wonder ye put up wi' Jamie and me," Ian teased, hearing her, "seein' ye've such a low opinion of men."

Jenny waved her soup ladle dismissively at husband and brother, seated side by side on the ground near the kettle.

"Och, you two aren't 'men.' "

Ian's feathery brows shot upward, and Jamie's thicker red ones matched them.

"Oh, we're not? Well, what are we, then?" Ian demanded.

Jenny turned toward him with a smile, white teeth flashing in the firelight. She patted Jamie on the head, and dropped a kiss on Ian's forehead.

"You're mine," she said.

⊱━━━⊰

After supper, one of the men began to sing. Another brought out a wooden flute and accompanied him, the sound thin but piercing in the cold autumn night. The air was chilly, but there was no wind, and it was cozy enough, wrapped in shawls and blankets, huddled in small family clusters round the fire. The blaze had been built up after the cooking, and now made a substantial dent in the darkness.

It was warm, if a trifle active, in our own family huddle. Ian had gone to fetch another armload of wood, and baby Maggie clung to her mother, forcing her elder brother to seek refuge and body warmth elsewhere.

"I'm going to stick ye upside down in yonder kettle, an' ye dinna leave off pokin' me in the balls," Jamie informed his nephew, who was squirming vigorously on his uncle's lap. "What's the matter, then—have ye got ants in your drawers?"

This query was greeted with a gale of giggles and a marked effort to burrow into his host's midsection. Jamie groped in the dark, making deliberately clumsy grabs at his namesake's arms and legs, then wrapped his arms around the boy and rolled suddenly over on top of him, forcing a startled whoop of delight from small Jamie.

Jamie pinned his nephew forcibly to the ground and held him there with one hand while he groped blindly on the ground in the dark. Seizing a handful of wet grass with a grunt of satisfaction, he raised himself enough to jam the grass down the neck of small Jamie's shirt, changing the giggling to a high-pitched squeal, no less delighted.

"There, then," Jamie said, rolling off the small form. "Go plague your auntie for a bit."

Small Jamie obligingly scrambled over to me on hands and knees, still giggling, and nestled on my lap among the folds of my cloak. He sat as still as is possible for an almost four-year-old boy—which is not very still, all things considered—and let me remove the bulk of the grass from his shirt.

"You smell nice, Auntie," he said, buffing my chin affectionately with his mop of black curls. "Like food."

"Well, thank you," I said. "Ought I to take that to mean you're hungry again?"

"Aye. Is there milk?"

"There is." I could just reach the stoneware jug by stretching out my fingers. I shook the bottle, decided there was not enough left to make it worthwhile to fetch a cup, and tilted the jug, holding it for the little boy to drink from.

Temporarily absorbed in the taking of nourishment, he was still, the small, sturdy body heavy on my thigh, back braced against my arm as he wrapped his own pudgy hands around the jug.

The last drops of milk gurgled from the jug. Small Jamie relaxed all at once, and emitted a soft burp of repletion. I could feel the heat glowing from him, with that sudden rise of temperature which presages falling asleep in very young children. I wrapped a fold of the cloak around him, and rocked him slowly back and forth, humming softly to the tune of the song beyond the fire. The small bumps of his vertebrae were round and hard as marbles under my fingers.

"Gone to sleep, has he?" The larger Jamie's bulk loomed near my shoulder, the firelight picking out the hilt of his dirk, and the gleam of copper in his hair.

"Yes," I said. "At least he's not squirming, so he must have. It's rather like holding a large ham."

Jamie laughed, then was still himself. I could feel the hardness of his arm just brushing mine, and the warmth of his body through the folds of plaid and arisaid.

A night breeze brushed a strand of hair across my face. I brushed it back, and discovered that small Jamie was right; my hands smelled of leeks and butter, and the starchy smell of cut potatoes. Asleep, he was a dead weight, and while holding him was comforting, he was cutting off the circulation in my left leg. I twisted a bit, intending to lay him across my lap.

"Don't move, Sassenach," Jamie's voice came softly, next to me. "Just for a moment, *mo nighean donn*—be still."

I obligingly froze, until he touched me on the shoulder.

"That's all right, Sassenach," he said, with a smile in his voice. "It's only that ye looked so beautiful, wi' the fire on your face, and your hair waving in the wind. I wanted to remember it."

I turned to face him, then, and smiled at him, across the body of the child. The night was dark and cold, alive with people all around, but there was nothing where we sat but light and warmth—and each other.

33

Thy Brother's Keeper

Fergus, after an initial period of silent watchfulness from corners, had become a part of the household, taking on the official position of stable-lad, along with young Rabbie MacNab.

While Rabbie was a year or two younger than Fergus, he was as big as the slight French lad, and they quickly became inseparable friends, except on the occasions when they argued—which was two or three times a day—and then attempted to kill each other. After a fight one morning had escalated into a punching, kicking, fist-swinging brawl that rolled through the dairy shed and spilled two pannikins of cream set out to sour, Jamie took a hand.

With an air of long-suffering grimness, he had taken each miscreant by the scruff of a skinny neck, and removed them to the privacy of the barn, where, I assumed, he overcame any lingering scruples he might have had about the administration of physical retribution. He strode out of the barn, shaking his head and buckling his belt back on, and left with Ian to ride up the valley to Broch Mordha. The boys had emerged some time later, substantially subdued and—united in tribulation—once more the best of friends.

Sufficiently subdued, in fact, to allow young Jamie to tag along with them as they did their chores. As I glanced out the window later in the morning, I saw the three of them playing in the dooryard with a ball made of rags. It was a cold, misty day, and the boys' breath rose in soft clouds as they galloped and shouted.

"Nice sturdy little lad you've got there," I remarked to Jenny, who was sorting through her mending basket in search of a button. She glanced up, saw what I was looking at, and smiled.

"Oh, aye, wee Jamie's a dear lad." She came to join me by the window, peering out at the game below.

"He's the spit of his da," she remarked fondly, "but he's going to be a good bit wider through the shoulder, I think.

He'll maybe be the size of his uncle; see those legs?" I thought she was probably right; while small Jamie, nearly four, still had the chunky roundness of a toddler, his legs were long, and the small back was wide and flat with muscle. He had the long, graceful bones of his uncle, and the same air his larger namesake projected, of being composed of something altogether tougher and springier than mere flesh.

I watched the little boy pounce on the ball, scoop it up with a deft snatch, and throw it hard enough to sail past the head of Rabbie MacNab, who raced off, shouting, to retrieve it.

"Something else is like his uncle," I said. "I think he's maybe going to be left-handed, too."

"Oh, God!" said Jenny, brow furrowed as she peered at her offspring. "I hope not, but you're maybe right." She shook her head, sighing.

"Lord, when I think of the trouble poor Jamie had, from being caurry-fisted! Everybody tried to break him of it, from my parents to the schoolmaster, but he always was stubborn as a log, and wouldna budge. Everybody but Ian's father, at least," she added, as an afterthought.

"He didn't think being left-handed was wrong?" I asked curiously, aware that the general opinion of the times was that left-handedness was at the best unlucky, and at the worst, a symptom of demonic possession. Jamie wrote—with difficulty—with his right hand, because he had been beaten regularly at school for picking up the quill with his left.

Jenny shook her head, black curls bobbing under her kertch.

"No, he was a queer man, auld John Murray. He said if the Lord had chosen to strengthen Jamie's left arm so, then 'twould be a sin to spurn the gift. And he was a rare man wi' a sword, auld John, so my father listened, and he let Jamie learn to fight left-handed."

"I thought Dougal MacKenzie taught Jamie to fight left-handed," I said. I rather wondered what Jenny thought of her uncle Dougal.

She nodded, licking the end of a thread before putting it through the eye of her needle with one quick poke.

"Aye, it was, but that was later, when Jamie was grown,

and went to foster wi' Dougal. It was Ian's father taught him
his first strokes." She smiled, eyes on the shirt in her lap.

"I remember, when they were young, auld John told Ian
it was his job to stand to Jamie's right, for he must guard his
chief's weaker side in a fight. And he did—they took it verra
seriously, the two of them. And I suppose auld John was
right, at that," she added, snipping off the excess thread. "After a time, nobody would fight them, not even the MacNab
lads. Jamie and Ian were both fair-sized, and bonny fighters,
and when they stood shoulder to shoulder, there was no one
could take the pair o' them down, even if they were outnumbered."

She laughed suddenly, and smoothed back a lock of hair
behind her ear.

"Watch them sometime, when they're walking the fields
together. I dinna suppose they even realize they do it still, but
they do. Jamie always moves to the left, so Ian can take up his
place on the right, guardin' the weak side."

Jenny gazed out the window, the shirt momentarily forgotten in her lap, and laid a hand over the small swelling of
her stomach.

"I hope it's a boy," she said, looking at her black-haired
son below. "Left-handed or no, it's good for a man to have a
brother to help him." I caught her glance at the picture on
the wall—a very young Jamie, standing between the knees of
his elder brother, Willie. Both young faces were snub-nosed
and solemn; Willie's hand rested protectively on his little
brother's shoulder.

"Jamie's lucky to have Ian," I said.

Jenny looked away from the picture, and blinked once.
She was two years older than Jamie; she would have been
three years younger than William.

"Aye, he is. And so am I," she said softly, picking up the
shirt once more.

I took a child's smock from the mending basket and
turned it inside out, to get at the ripped seam beneath the
armhole. It was too cold out for anyone but small boys at play
or men at work, but it was warm and cozy in the parlor; the
windows fogged over quickly as we worked, isolating us from
the icy world outside.

"Speaking of brothers," I said, squinting as I threaded

my own needle, "did you see Dougal and Colum MacKenzie much, as you were growing up?"

Jenny shook her head. "I've never met Colum. Dougal came here a time or two, bringing Jamie home for Hogmanay or such, but I canna say I know him well." She looked up from her mending, slanted eyes bright with interest. "You'll know them, though. Tell me, what's Colum MacKenzie like? I always wondered, from the bits of things I'd hear from visitors, but my parents never would speak of him." She paused a moment, a crease between her brows.

"No, I'm wrong; my da did say something about him, once. 'Twas just after Dougal had left, to go back to Beannachd wi' Jamie. Da was leaning on the fence outside, watching them ride out o' sight, and I came up to wave to Jamie—it always grieved me sore when he left, for I didna ken how long he'd be gone. Anyway, we watched them over the crest of the hill, and then Da stirred a bit, and grunted, and said, 'God help Dougal MacKenzie when his brother Colum dies.' Then he seemed to remember I was there, for he turned round and smiled at me, and said, 'Well, lassie, what's for our dinner, then?' and wouldna say more about it." The black brows, fine and bold as the strokes of calligraphy, lifted in puzzled inquiry.

"I thought that odd, for I'd heard—who hasn't?—that Colum is sore crippled, and Dougal does the chief's work for him, collecting rents and settling claims—and leading the clan to battle, when needs be."

"He does. But—" I hesitated, unsure how to describe that odd symbiotic relationship. "Well," I said with a smile, "the closest I can come is to tell you that once I overheard them arguing, and Colum said to Dougal, 'I'll tell ye, if the brothers MacKenzie have but one cock and one brain between them, then I'm glad of my half of the bargain!' "

Jenny gave a sudden laugh of surprise, then stared at me, a speculative gleam deep in her blue eyes, so like her brother's.

"Och, so that's the way of it, is it? I did wonder once, hearing Dougal talk about Colum's son, wee Hamish; he seemed a bit fonder than an uncle might be."

"You're quick, Jenny," I said, staring back at her. "Very

quick. It took me a long time to work that out, and I saw them every day for months."

She shrugged modestly, but a small smile played about her lips.

"I listen," she said simply. "To what folk say—and what they don't. And people do gossip something terrible here in the Highlands. So"—she bit off a thread and spat the ends neatly into the palm of her hand—"tell me about Leoch. Folk say it's big, but not so grand as Beauly or Kilravock."

We worked and talked through the morning, moving from mending to winding wool for knitting, to laying out the pattern for a new baby dress for Maggie. The shouts from the boys outside ceased, to be replaced by murmurous noises and banging from the back of the house, suggesting that the younger male element had gotten cold and come to infest the kitchens, instead.

"I wonder will it snow soon?" Jenny said, with a glance at the window. "There's wetness in the air; did ye see the haze over the loch this morning?"

I shook my head. "I hope not. That will make it hard for Jamie and Ian, coming back." The village of Broch Mordha was less than ten miles from Lallybroch, but the way lay over steadily rising hills, with steep and rocky slopes, and the road was little more than a deer track.

In the event, it did snow, soon after noon, and the flakes kept swirling down long past nightfall.

"They'll have stayed in Broch Mordha," Jenny said, pulling her nightcapped head in from an inspection of the cloudy sky, with its snow-pink glow. "Dinna worry for them; they'll be tucked up cozy in someone's cottage for the night." She smiled reassuringly at me as she pulled the shutters to. A sudden wail came from down the hall, and she picked up the skirts of her nightrobe with a muffled exclamation.

"Good night, Claire," she called, already hurrying off on her maternal errand of mercy. "Sleep well."

I usually did sleep well; in spite of the cold, damp climate, the house was tightly constructed, and the goosefeather bed was plentifully supplied with quilts. Tonight, though, I found myself restless without Jamie. The bed seemed vast and clammy, my legs twitchy, and my feet cold.

I tried lying on my back, hands lightly clasped across my

ribs, eyes closed, breathing deep, to summon up a picture of Jamie; if I could imagine him there, breathing deeply in the dark beside me, perhaps I could fall asleep.

The sound of a cock crowing at full blast lifted me off the pillow, as though a stick of dynamite had been touched off beneath the bed.

"Idiot!" I said, every nerve in my body twanging from the shock. I got up and cracked the shutter. It had stopped snowing, but the sky was still pale with cloud, a uniform color from horizon to horizon. The rooster let loose another bellow in the hen-coop below.

"Shut up!" I said. "It's the middle of the night, you feathered bastard!" The avian equivalent of a raspberry echoed through the still night, and down the hall, a child began to cry, followed by a rich but muffled Gaelic expletive in Jenny's voice.

"You," I said to the invisible rooster, "are living on borrowed time." There was no response to this, and after a pause to make certain that the rooster had in fact called it a night, I closed the shutters and did the same.

The commotion had derailed any coherent train of thought. Instead of trying to start another, I decided to try turning inward, in the hopes that physical contemplation would relax me enough to sleep.

It worked. As I began to hover on the edge of sleep, my mind fixed somewhere around my pancreas, I could dimly hear the sounds of small Jamie pattering down the hall to his mother's bedroom—roused from sleep by a full bladder, he seldom had the presence of mind to take the obvious step, and would frequently blunder down the stair from the nursery in search of assistance instead.

I had wondered, coming to Lallybroch, whether I might find it difficult to be near Jenny; if I would be envious of her easy fruitfulness. And I might have been, had I not seen that abundant motherhood had its price as well.

"There's a pot right by your bed, clot-heid," Jenny's exasperated voice came outside my door as she steered small Jamie back to his bed. "Ye must have stepped in it on your way out; why can ye no get it through your heid to use that one? Why have ye got to come use mine, every night in creation?" Her voice faded as she turned up the stair, and I smiled, visualization moving down the sweeping curve of my intestines.

There was another reason I did not envy Jenny. I had at first feared that the birth of Faith had done me some internal damage, but that fear had disappeared with Raymond's touch. As I completed the inventory of my body, and felt my spine go slack on the edge of sleep, I could feel that all was well there. It had happened once, it could happen again. All that was needed was time. And Jamie.

Jenny's footsteps sounded on the boards of the hallway, quickening in response to a sleepy squawk from Maggie, at the far end of the house.

"Bairns are certain joy, but nay sma' care," I murmured to myself, and fell asleep.

Through the next day, we waited, doing our chores and going through the daily routine with one ear cocked for the sound of horses in the dooryard.

"They'll have stayed to do some business," Jenny said, outwardly confident. But I saw her pause every time she passed the window that overlooked the lane leading to the house.

As for me, I had a hard time controlling my imagination. The letter, signed by King George, confirming Jamie's pardon, was locked in the drawer of the desk in the laird's study. Jamie regarded it as a humiliation, and would have burned it, but I had insisted it be kept, just in case. Now, listening for sounds through the rush of winter wind, I kept having visions of it having all been a mistake, or a hoax of some kind—of Jamie once more arrested by red-coated dragoons, taken away again to the misery of prison, and the impending danger of the hangman's noose.

The men returned at last just before nightfall, horses laden with bags containing the salt, needles, pickling spice, and other small items that Lallybroch could not produce for itself.

I heard one of the horses whinny as it came into the stableyard, and ran downstairs, meeting Jenny on her way out through the kitchens.

Relief swept through me as I saw Jamie's tall figure,

shadowed against the barn. I ran through the yard, disregarding the light covering of snow that lingered on the ground, and flung myself into his arms.

"Where the hell have you been?" I demanded.

He took time to kiss me before replying. His face was cold against mine, and his lips tasted faintly and pleasantly of whisky.

"Mm, sausage for supper?" he said approvingly, sniffing at my hair, which smelled of kitchen smoke. "Good, I'm fair starved."

"Bangers and mash," I said. "Where have you been?"

He laughed, shaking out his plaid to get the blown snow off. "Bangers and mash? That's food, is it?"

"Sausages with mashed potatoes," I translated. "A nice traditional English dish, hitherto unknown in the benighted reaches of Scotland. Now, you bloody Scot, where in hell have you been for the last two days? Jenny and I were worried!"

"Well, we had a wee accident—" Jamie began, when he spotted the small figure of Fergus, bearing a lantern. "Och, ye've brought a light, then, Fergus? Good lad. Set it there, where ye won't set fire to the straw, and then take this poor beast into her stall. When ye've got her settled, come along to your own supper. You'll be able to sit to it by now, I expect?" He aimed a friendly cuff at Fergus's ear. The boy dodged and grinned back; apparently whatever had happened in the barn yesterday had left no hard feelings.

"Jamie," I said, in measured tones. "If you don't stop talking about horses and sausages and tell me what sort of accident you had, I am going to kick you in the shins. Which will be very hard on my toes, because I'm only wearing slippers, but I warn you, I'll do it anyway."

"That's a threat, is it?" he said, laughing. "It wasna serious, Sassenach, only that—"

"Ian!" Jenny, delayed momentarily by Maggie, had just arrived, in time to see her husband step into the circle of lanternlight. Startled by the shock in her voice, I turned to see her dart forward and put a hand to Ian's face.

"Whatever happened to ye, man?" she said. Plainly, whatever the accident had been, Ian had borne the brunt of it. One eye was blackened and swollen half-shut, and there was a long, raw scrape down the slope of one cheekbone.

"I'm all right, *mi nighean dubh*," he said, patting Jenny gently as she embraced him, little Maggie squeezed uncomfortably between them. "Only a bit bruised here and there."

"We were comin' down the slope of the hill two miles outside the village, leading the horses because the footing was bad, and Ian stepped in a molehole and broke his leg," Jamie explained.

"The wooden one," Ian amplified. He grinned, a little sheepishly. "The mole had a bit the best o' that encounter."

"So we stayed at a cottage nearby long enough to carve him a new one," Jamie ended the story. "Can we eat? The sides of my belly are flapping together."

We went in without further ado, and Mrs. Crook and I served the supper while Jenny bathed Ian's face with witch hazel and made anxious inquiries about other injuries.

"It's nothing," he assured her. "Only bruises here and there." I had watched him coming into the house, though, and seen that his normal limp was badly exaggerated. I had a few quiet words with Jenny as we cleared away the supper plates, and once we were settled in the parlor, the contents of the saddlebags safely disposed of, she knelt on the rug beside Ian and took hold of the new leg.

"Let's have it off, then," she said firmly. "You've hurt yourself, and I want Claire to look it over. She can maybe help ye more than I can."

The original amputation had been done with some skill, and greater luck; the army surgeon who had taken the lower leg off had been able to save the knee joint. This gave Ian a great deal more flexibility of movement than he might otherwise have had. For the moment, though, the knee joint was more a liability than an advantage.

The fall had twisted his leg cruelly; the end of the stump was blue with bruising, and lacerated where the sharp edge of the cuff had pressed through the skin. It must have been agony to set any weight on it, even had all else been normal. As it was, the knee had twisted, too, and the flesh on the inside of the joint was swollen, red and hot.

Ian's long, good-natured face was nearly as red as the injured joint. While perfectly matter-of-fact about his disability, I knew he hated the occasional helplessness it imposed. His embarrassment at being so exposed now was likely as painful to him as my touching of his leg.

"You've torn a ligament through here," I told him, tracing the swelling inside his knee with a gentle finger. "I can't tell how bad it is, but bad enough. You've got fluid inside the joint; that's why it's swollen."

"Can ye help it, Sassenach?" Jamie was leaning over my shoulder, frowning worriedly at the angry-looking limb.

I shook my head. "Not a lot I can do for it, beyond cold compresses to reduce the swelling." I looked up at Ian, fixing him with my best approximation of a Mother Hildegarde look.

"What *you* can do," I said, "is stay in bed. You can have whisky for the pain tomorrow; tonight, I'll give you laudanum so you can sleep. Keep off it for a week, at least, and we'll see how it does."

"I canna do that!" Ian protested. "There's the stable wall needs mending, two dikes down in the upper field, and the plowshares to be sharpened, and—"

"And a leg to mend, too," said Jamie, firmly. He gave Ian what I privately called his "laird's look," a piercing blue glare that caused most people to leap to his bidding. Ian, who had shared meals, toys, hunting expeditions, fights, and thrashings with Jamie, was a good deal less susceptible than most people.

"The hell I will," he said flatly. His hot brown eyes met Jamie's with a look in which pain and anger mingled with resentment—and something else I didn't recognize. "D'ye think ye can order me?"

Jamie sat back on his heels, flushing as though he'd been slapped. He bit back several obvious retorts, finally saying quietly, "No. I wilna try to order ye. May I ask ye, though—to care for yourself?"

A long look passed between the men, containing some message I couldn't read. At last, Ian's shoulders slumped as he relaxed, and he nodded, with a crooked smile.

"You can ask." He sighed, and rubbed at the scrape on his cheekbone, wincing as he touched the abraded skin. He took a deep breath, steeling himself, then held out a hand to Jamie. "Help me up, then?"

It was an awkward job, getting a man with one leg up two flights of stairs, but it was managed at last. At the bedroom door, Jamie left Ian to Jenny. As he stepped back, Ian said something soft and quick to Jamie in Gaelic. I still was not proficient in the tongue, but I thought he had said, "Be well, brother."

Jamie paused, looking back, and smiled, the candle lighting his eyes with warmth.

"You, too, *mo brathair.*"

I followed Jamie down the hall to our own room. I could tell from the slump of his shoulders that he was tired, but I had a few questions I wanted to ask before he fell asleep.

"It's only bruises here and there," Ian had said, reassuring Jenny. It was. Here and there. Besides the bruises on his face and leg, I had seen the darkened marks that lay half-hidden under the collar of his shirt. No matter how much Ian's intrusion had been resented, I couldn't imagine a mole trying to strangle him in retaliation.

In the event, Jamie didn't want to sleep at once.

"Oh, absence makes the heart grow fonder, does it?" I said. The bed, so vast the night before, now seemed scarcely big enough.

"Mm?" he said, eyes half-closed in content. "Oh, the heart? Aye, that, too. Oh, God, don't stop; that feels wonderful."

"Don't worry, I'll do it some more," I assured him. "Let me put out the candle, though." I rose and blew it out; with the shutters left open, there was plenty of light reflected into the room from the snowy sky, even without the candle's flame. I could see Jamie clearly, the long shape of his body relaxed beneath the quilts, hands curled half-open at his side. I crawled in beside him and took up his right hand, resuming my slow massage of his fingers and palm.

He gave a long sigh, almost a groan, as I rubbed a thumb in firm circles over the pads at the base of his fingers. Stiffened by hours of clenching around his horse's reins, the fingers warmed and relaxed slowly under my touch. The house was quiet, and the room cold, outside the sanctuary of the bed. It was pleasant to feel the length of his body warming the space beside me, and enjoy the intimacy of touch, with no immediate feeling of demand. In time, this touch might token more; it was winter, and the nights were long. He was there; so was I, and content with things as they were for the moment.

"Jamie," I said, after a time, "who hurt Ian?"

He didn't open his eyes, but gave a long sigh before answering. He didn't stiffen in resistance, though; he had been expecting the question.

"I did," he said.

"What?" I dropped his hand in shock. He closed his fist and opened it, testing the movement of his fingers. Then he laid his left hand on the counterpane beside it, showing me the knuckles, slightly puffed by contact with the protuberances of Ian's bony countenance.

"Why?" I said, appalled. I could tell that there was something new and edgy between Jamie and Ian, though it didn't look exactly like hostility. I couldn't imagine what might have made Jamie strike Ian; his brother-in-law was nearly as close to him as was his sister, Jenny.

Jamie's eyes were open now, but not looking at me. He rubbed his knuckles restlessly, looking down at them. Aside from the mild bruising of his knuckles, there were no marks on Jamie; apparently Ian hadn't fought back.

"Well, Ian's been married too long," he said defensively.

"I'd say you'd been out in the sun too long," I remarked, staring at him, "except that there isn't any. Have you got a fever?"

"No," he said, evading my attempts to feel his forehead. "No, it's only—stop that, Sassenach, I'm all right." He pressed his lips together, but then gave up and told me the whole story.

Ian had in fact broken his wooden leg by stepping into a molehole near Broch Mordha.

"It was near evening—we'd had a lot to do in the village —and snowing. And I could see Ian's leg was paining him a lot, even though he kept insisting he could ride. Anyway, there were two or three cottages near, so I got him up on one of the ponies, and brought him up the slope to beg shelter for the night."

With characteristic Highland hospitality, both shelter

and supper were offered with alacrity, and after a warm bowl of brose and fresh oatcake, both visitors had been accommodated with a pallet before the fire.

"There was scarce room to lay a quilt by the hearth, and we were squeezed a bit, but we lay down side by side and made ourselves as comfortable as might be." He drew a deep breath, and looked at me half-shyly.

"Well, I was worn out by the journey, and slept deep, and I suppose Ian did the same. But he's slept every night wi' Jenny for the last five years, and I suppose, havin' a warm body next to him in the bed—well, somewhere in the night, he rolled toward me, put his arm about me and kissed me on the back o' the neck. And I"—he hesitated, and I could see the deep color flood his face, even in the grayish light of the snow-lit room—"I woke from a sound sleep, thinking he was Jack Randall."

I had been holding my breath through this story; now I let it out slowly.

"That must have been the hell of a shock," I said.

One side of Jamie's mouth twitched. "It was the hell of a shock to Ian, I'll tell ye," he said. "I rolled over and punched him in the face, and by the time I came all the way to myself, I was on top of him, throttling him, wi' his tongue sticking out of his head. Hell of a shock to the Murrays in the bed, too," he added reflectively. "I told them I'd had a nightmare—well, I had, in a way—but it caused the hell of a stramash, what wi' the bairns shriekin', and Ian choking in the corner, and Mrs. Murray sittin' bolt upright in bed, sayin' 'Who, who?' like a wee fat owl."

I laughed despite myself at the image.

"Oh God, Jamie. Was Ian all right?"

Jamie shrugged a little. "Well, ye saw him. Everyone went back to sleep, after a time, and I just lay before the fire for the rest of the night, staring at the roof beams." He didn't resist as I picked up his left hand, gently stroking the bruised knuckles. His fingers closed over mine, holding them.

"So when we left the next morning," he went on, "I waited 'til we'd come to a spot where ye can sit and look over the valley below. And then"—he swallowed, and his hand tightened slightly on mine—"I told him. About Randall. And everything that happened."

I began to understand the ambiguity of the look Ian had given Jamie. And I now understood the look of strain on Jamie's face, and the smudges under his eyes. Not knowing what to say, I just squeezed his hands.

"I hadna thought I'd ever tell anyone—anyone but you," he added, returning the squeeze. He smiled briefly, then pulled one hand away to rub his face.

"But Ian . . . well, he's . . ." He groped for the right word. "He *knows* me, d'ye see?"

"I think so. You've known him all your life, haven't you?"

He nodded, looking sightlessly out the window. The swirling snow had begun to fall again, small flakes dancing against the pane, whiter than the sky.

"He's only a year older than me. When I was growing, he was always there. Until I was fourteen, there wasna a day went by when I didna see Ian. And even later, after I'd gone to foster wi' Dougal, and to Leoch, and then later still to Paris, to university—when I'd come back, I'd walk round a corner and there he would be, and it would be like I'd never left. He'd just smile when he saw me, like he always did, and then we'd be walkin' away together, side by side, ower the fields and the streams, talkin' of everything." He sighed deeply, and rubbed a hand through his hair.

"Ian . . . he's the part of me that belongs here, that never left," he said, struggling to explain. "I thought . . . I must tell him; I didna want to feel . . . apart. From Ian. From here." He gestured toward the window, then turned toward me, eyes dark in the dim light. "D'ye see why?"

"I think so," I said again, softly. "Did Ian?"

He made that small, uncomfortable shrugging motion, as though easing a shirt too tight across his back. "Well, I couldna tell. At first, when I began to tell him, he just kept shaking his head, as though he couldna believe me, and then when he did—" He paused and licked his lips, and I had some idea of just how much that confession in the snow had cost him. "I could see he wanted to jump to his feet and stamp back and forth, but he couldn't, because of his leg. His fists were knotted up, and his face was white, and he kept saying 'How? Damn ye, Jamie, *how* could ye let him do it?' "

He shook his head. "I dinna remember what I said. Or

what he said. We shouted at each other, I know that much. And I wanted to hit him, but I couldn't, because of his leg. And he wanted to hit me, but couldn't—because of his leg." He gave a brief snort of laughter. "Christ, we must ha' looked a rare pair of fools, wavin' our arms and shouting at each other. But I shouted longer, and finally he shut up and listened to the end of it.

"Then all of a sudden, I couldna go on talking; it just seemed like no use. And I sat down all at once on a rock, and put my head in my hands. Then after a time, Ian said we'd best be going on. And I nodded, and got up, and helped him on his horse, and we started off again, not speakin' to each other."

Jamie seemed suddenly to realize how tightly he was holding my hand. He released his grip, but continued to hold my hand, turning my wedding ring between his thumb and forefinger.

"We rode for a long time," he said softly. "And then I heard a small sound behind me, and reined up so Ian's horse came alongside, and I could see he'd been weeping—still was, wi' the tears streaming down his face. And he saw me look at him, and shook his head hard, as if he was still angry, but then he held out his hand to me. I took it, and he gave me a squeeze, hard enough to break the bones. Then he let go, and we came on home."

I could feel the tension go out of him, with the ending of the story. "Be well, brother," Ian had said, balanced on his one leg in the bedroom door.

"It's all right, then?" I asked.

"It will be." He relaxed completely now, sinking back into the goose-down pillows. I slid down under the quilts beside him, and lay close, fitted against his side. We watched the snow fall, hissing softly against the glass.

"I'm glad you're safe home," I said.

I woke to the same gray light in the morning. Jamie, already dressed for the day, was standing by the window.

"Oh, you're awake, Sassenach?" he said, seeing me lift my head from the pillow. "That's good. I brought ye a present."

He reached into his sporran and pulled out several copper doits, two or three small rocks, a short stick wrapped with fishline, a crumpled letter, and a tangle of hair ribbons.

"Hair ribbons?" I said. "Thank you; they're lovely."

"No, those aren't for you," he said, frowning as he disentangled the blue strands from the mole's foot he carried as a charm against rheumatism. "They're for wee Maggie." He squinted dubiously at the rocks remaining in his palm. To my astonishment, he picked one up and licked it.

"No, not that one," he muttered, and dived back into his sporran.

"What on earth do you think you're doing?" I inquired with interest, watching this performance. He didn't answer, but came out with another handful of rocks, which he sniffed at, discarding them one by one until he came to a nodule that struck his fancy. This one he licked once, for certainty, then dropped it into my hand, beaming.

"Amber," he said, with satisfaction, as I turned the irregular lump over with a forefinger. It seemed warm to the touch, and I closed my hand over it, almost unconsciously.

"It needs polishing, of course," he explained. "But I thought it would make ye a bonny necklace." He flushed slightly, watching me. "It's . . . it's a gift for our first year of marriage. When I saw it, I was minded of the bit of amber Hugh Munro gave ye, when we wed."

"I still have that," I said softly, caressing the odd little lump of petrified tree sap. Hugh's chunk of amber, one side sheared off and polished into a small window, had a dragonfly embedded in the matrix, suspended in eternal flight. I kept it in my medicine box, the most powerful of my charms.

A gift for our first anniversary. We had married in June, of course, not in December. But on the date of our first anniversary, Jamie had been in the Bastille, and I . . . I had been in the arms of the King of France. No time for a celebration of wedded bliss, that.

"It's nearly Hogmanay," Jamie said, looking out the window at the soft snowfall that blanketed the fields of Lallybroch. "It seems a good time for beginnings, I thought."

"I think so, too." I got out of bed and came to him at the window, putting my arms around his waist. We stayed locked together, not speaking, until my eye suddenly fell on the other small, yellowish lumps that Jamie had removed from his sporran.

"What on earth are those things, Jamie?" I asked, letting go of him long enough to point.

"Och, those? They're honey balls, Sassenach." He picked up one of the objects, dusting at it with his fingers. "Mrs. Gibson in the village gave them to me. Verra good, though they got a bit dusty in my sporran, I'm afraid." He held out his open hand to me, smiling. "Want one?"

34

The Postman Always Rings Twice

I didn't know what—or how much—Ian had told Jenny of his conversation in the snow with Jamie. She behaved toward her brother just as always, matter-of-fact and acerbic, with a slight touch of affectionate teasing. I had known her long enough, though, to realize that one of Jenny's greatest gifts was her ability to see something with utter clarity—and then to look straight through it, as though it wasn't there.

The dynamics of feeling and behavior shifted among the four of us during the months, and settled into a pattern of solid strength, based on friendship and founded in work. Mutual respect and trust were simply a necessity; there was so much to be done.

As Jenny's pregnancy progressed, I took on more and more of the domestic duties, and she deferred to me more often. I would never try to usurp her place; she had been the axis of the household since the death of her mother, and it was to her that the servants or tenants most frequently came. Still, they grew used to me, treating me with a friendly respect which bordered sometimes on acceptance, and sometimes on awe.

The spring was marked first by the planting of an enormous crop of potatoes; over half the available land was given to the new crop—a decision justified within weeks by a hailstorm that flattened the new-sprung barley. The potato vines, creeping low and stolid over the ground, survived.

The second event of the spring was the birth of a second daughter, Katherine Mary, to Jenny and Ian. She arrived with a suddenness that startled everyone, including Jenny. One day Jenny complained of an aching back and went to lie down. Very shortly it became clear what was really happening, and Jamie went posthaste for Mrs. Martins, the midwife. The two of them arrived back just in time to share in a celebratory glass of wine as the thin, high squalls of the new arrival echoed through the halls of the house.

And so the year burgeoned and greened, and I bloomed, the last of my hurts healing in the heart of love and work.

Letters arrived irregularly; sometimes there would be mail once a week, sometimes nothing would come for a month or more. Considering the lengths to which messengers had to go to deliver mail in the Highlands, I thought it incredible that anything ever arrived.

Today, though, there was a large packet of letters and books, wrapped against the weather in a sheet of oiled parchment, tied with twine. Sending the postal messenger to the kitchen for refreshment, Jenny untied the string carefully and thriftily stowed it in her pocket. She thumbed through the small pile of letters, putting aside for the moment an enticing-looking package addressed from Paris.

"A letter for Ian—that'll be the bill for the seed, I expect, and one from Auntie Jocasta—oh, good, we've not heard from her in months, I thought she might be ill, but I see her hand is firm on the pen—"

A letter addressed with bold black strokes fell onto Jenny's pile, followed by a note from one of Jocasta's married daughters. Then another for Ian from Edinburgh, one for Jamie from Jared—I recognized the spidery, half-legible writing—and another, a thick, creamy sheet, sealed with the Royal crest of the House of Stuart. Another of Charles's complaints about the rigors of life in Paris, and the pains of intermittently requited love, I imagined. At least this one looked short; usually he went on for several pages, unburdening his soul to *"cher* James," in a misspelled quadrilingual patois that at least made it clear he sought no secretarial help for his personal letters.

"Ooh, three French novels and a book of poetry from Paris!" Jenny said in excitement, opening the paper-wrapped package. *"C'est un embarras de richesse,* hm? Which shall we read tonight?" She lifted the small stack of books from their wrappings, stroking the soft leather cover of the top one with a forefinger that trembled with delight. Jenny loved books with the same passion her brother reserved for horses. The manor boasted a small library, in fact, and if the evening leisure between work and bed was short, still it usually included at least a few minutes' reading.

"It gives ye something to think on as ye go about your

work," Jenny explained, when I found her one night swaying with weariness, and urged her to go to bed, rather than stay up to read aloud to Ian, Jamie, and myself. She yawned, fist to her mouth. "Even if I'm sae tired I hardly see the words on the page, they'll come back to me next day, churning or spinning or waulkin' wool, and I can turn them over in my mind."

I hid a smile at the mention of wool waulking. Alone among the Highland farms, I was sure, the women of Lallybroch waulked their wool not only to the old traditional chants but also to the rhythms of Molière and Piron.

I had a sudden memory of the waulking shed, where the women sat in two facing rows, barefooted and bare-armed in their oldest clothes, bracing themselves against the walls as they thrust with their feet against the long, sodden worm of woolen cloth, battering it into the tight, felted weave that would repel Highland mists and even light rain, keeping the wearer safe from the chill.

Every so often one woman would rise and go outside, to fetch the kettle of steaming urine from the fire. Skirts kilted high, she would walk spraddle-legged down the center of the shed, drenching the cloth between her legs, and the hot fumes rose fresh and suffocating from the soaking wool, while the waulkers pulled back their feet from random splashes, and made crude jokes.

"Hot piss sets the dye fast," one of the women had explained to me as I blinked, eyes watering, on my first entrance to the shed. The other women had watched at first, to see if I would shrink back from the work, but wool-waulking was no great shock, after the things I had seen and done in France, both in the war of 1944 and the hospital of 1744. Time makes very little difference to the basic realities of life. And smell aside, the waulking shed was a warm, cozy place, where the women of Lallybroch visited and joked between bolts of cloth, and sang together in the working, hands moving rhythmically across a table, or bare feet sinking deep into the steaming fabric as we sat on the floor, thrusting against a partner thrusting back.

I was pulled back from my memories of wool-waulking by the noise of heavy boots in the hallway, and a gust of cool, rainy air as the door opened. Jamie, and Ian with him, talking

together in Gaelic, in the comfortable, unemphatic manner
that meant they were discussing farm matters.

"That field's going to need draining next year," Jamie
was saying as he came past the door. Jenny, seeing them, had
put down the mail and gone to fetch fresh linen towels from
the chest in the hallway.

"Dry yourselves before ye come drip on the rug," she
ordered, handing one to each of the men. "And tak' off your
filthy boots, too. The post's come, Ian—there's a letter for ye
from that man in Perth, the one ye wrote to about the seed
potatoes."

"Oh, aye? I'll come read it, then, but is there aught to eat
while I do it?" Ian asked, rubbing his wet head with the towel
until the thick brown hair stood up in spikes. "I'm famished,
and I can hear Jamie's belly growling from here."

Jamie shook himself like a wet dog, making his sister
emit a small screech as the cold drops flew about the hall. His
shirt was pasted to his shoulders and loose strands of rain-
soaked hair hung in his eyes, the color of rusted iron.

I draped a towel around his neck. "Finish drying off, and
I'll go fetch you something."

I was in the kitchen when I heard him cry out. I had
never heard such a sound from him before. Shock and horror
were in it, and something else—a note of finality, like the cry
of a man who finds himself seized in a tiger's jaws. I was down
the hall and running for the drawing room without conscious
thought, a tray of oatcakes still clutched in my hands.

When I burst through the door, I saw him standing by
the table where Jenny had laid the mail. His face was dead
white, and he swayed slightly where he stood, like a tree cut
through, waiting for someone to shout "Timber" before falling.

"What?" I said, scared to death by the look on his face.
"Jamie, what? What is it?!"

With a visible effort, he picked up one of the letters on
the table and handed it to me.

I set down the oatcakes and took the sheet of paper,
scanning it rapidly. It was from Jared; I recognized the thin,
scrawly handwriting at once. " 'Dear Cousin,' " I read to myself, " '. . . so pleased . . . words cannot express my admiration . . . your boldness and courage will be an inspiration

. . . cannot fail of success . . . my prayers shall be with you . . .' " I looked up from the paper, bewildered. "What on earth is he talking about? What have you done, Jamie?"

The skin was stretched tight across the bones of his face, and he grinned, mirthless as a death's-head, as he picked up another sheet of paper, this one a cheaply printed handbill.

"It's not what *I've* done, Sassenach," he said. The broadsheet was headed by the crest of the Royal House of Stuart. The message beneath was brief, couched in stately language.

It stated that by the ordination of Almighty God, King James, VIII of Scotland and III of England and Ireland asserted herewith his just rights to claim the throne of three kingdoms. And herewith acknowledged the support of these divine rights by the chieftains of the Highland clans, the Jacobite lords, and "various other such loyal subjects of His Majesty, King James, as have subscribed their names upon this Bill of Association in token thereof."

My fingers grew icy as I read, and I was conscious of a feeling of terror so acute that it was a real effort to keep on breathing. My ears rang with pounding blood, and there were dark spots before my eyes.

At the bottom of the sheet were signed the names of the Scottish chieftains who had declared their loyalty to the world, and staked their lives and reputations on the success of Charles Stuart. Clanranald was there, and Glengarry. Stewart of Appin, Alexander MacDonald of Keppoch, Angus MacDonald of Scotus.

And at the bottom of the list was written, "James Alexander Malcolm MacKenzie Fraser, of Broch Tuarach."

"Jesus bloody fucking Christ," I whispered, wishing there were something stronger I could say, as a form of relief. "The filthy bastard's signed your name to it!"

Jamie, still pale and tight-faced, was beginning to recover.

"Aye, he has," he said briefly. His hand snaked out for the unopened letter remaining on the table—a heavy vellum, with the Stuart crest showing plainly in the wax seal. Jamie ripped the letter open impatiently, tearing the paper. He read it quickly, then dropped it on the table as though it burned his hands.

"An apology," he said hoarsely. "For lacking the time to

send me the document, in order that I might sign it myself. And his gratitude, for my loyal support. Jesus, Claire! What am I going to do?"

It was a cry from the heart, and one to which I had no answer. I watched helplessly as he sank onto a hassock and sat staring, rigid, at the fire.

Jenny, transfixed by all this drama, moved now to take up the letters and the broadsheet. She read them over carefully, her lips moving slightly as she did so, then set them gently down on the polished tabletop. She looked at them, frowning, then crossed to her brother, and laid a hand on his shoulder.

"Jamie," she said. Her face was very pale. "There's only the one thing ye *can* do, my dearie. Ye must go and fight for Charles Stuart. Ye must help him win."

The truth of her words penetrated slowly through the layers of shock that wrapped me. The publication of this Bond of Association branded those who signed it as rebels, and as traitors to the English crown. It didn't matter now how Charles had managed, or where he had gotten the funds to begin; he was well and truly launched on the seas of rebellion, and Jamie—and I—were launched with him, willy-nilly. There was, as Jenny had said, no choice.

My eye caught Charles's letter, where it had fallen from Jamie's hand. ". . . Though there be manie who tell me I am foolish to embark in this werk without the support of Louis— or at least of his bankes!—I will entertain no notion at all of returning to that place from whence I come," it read. "Rejoice with me, my deare frend, for I am come Home."

35

Moonlight

s the preparations for leaving went forward, a current of excitement and speculation ran all through the estate. Weapons hoarded since the Rising of '15 were excavated from thatch and hayrick and hearth, burnished and sharpened. Men met in passing and paused to talk in earnest groups, heads together under the hot August sun. And the women grew quiet, watching them.

Jenny shared with her brother the capacity to be opaque, to give no clue of what she was thinking. Transparent as a pane of glass myself, I rather envied this ability. So, when she asked me one morning if I would fetch Jamie to her in the brewhouse, I had no notion of what she might want with him.

Jamie stepped in behind me and stood just within the door of the brewhouse, waiting as his eyes adjusted to the dimness. He took a deep breath, inhaling the bitter, damp pungency with evident enjoyment.

"Ahh," he said, sighing dreamily. "I could get drunk in here just by breathing."

"Weel, hold your breath, then, for a moment, for I need ye sober," his sister advised.

He obligingly inflated his lungs and puffed out his cheeks, waiting. Jenny poked him briskly in the stomach with the handle of her masher, making him double over in an explosion of breath.

"Clown," she said, without rancor. "I wanted to talk to ye about Ian."

Jamie took an empty bucket from the shelf, and up-turning it, sat down on it. A faint glow from the oiled-paper window above him lit his hair with a deep copper gleam.

"What about Ian?" he asked.

Now it was Jenny's turn to take a deep breath. The wide bran tub before her gave off a damp warmth of fermentation, filled with the yeasty aroma of grain, hops, and alcohol.

"I want ye to take Ian with you, when ye go."

Jamie's eyebrows flew up, but he didn't say anything immediately. Jenny's eyes were fixed on the motions of the masher, watching the smooth roil of the mixture. He looked at her thoughtfully, big hands hanging loose between his thighs.

"Tired of marriage, are ye?" he asked conversationally. "Likely it would be easier just for me to take him out in the wood and shoot him for ye." There was a quick flash of blue eyes over the mash tub.

"If I want anyone shot, Jamie Fraser, I'll do it myself. And Ian wouldna be my first choice as target, either."

He snorted briefly, and one corner of his mouth quirked up.

"Oh, aye? Why, then?"

Her shoulders moved in a seamless rhythm, one motion fading into the next.

"Because I'm asking ye."

Jamie spread his right hand out on his knee, absently stroking the jagged scar that zigzagged its way down his middle finger.

"It's dangerous, Jenny," he said quietly.

"I know that."

He shook his head slowly, still gazing down at his hand. It had healed well, and he had good use of it, but the stiff fourth finger and the roughened patch of scar tissue on the back gave it an odd, crooked appearance.

"You think ye know."

"I know, Jamie."

His head came up, then. He looked impatient, but was striving to stay reasonable.

"Aye, I know Ian will ha' told ye stories, about fighting in France, and all. But you've no notion how it really is, Jenny. *Mo chridhe,* it isna a matter of a cattle raid. It's a war, and likely to be a damn bloody shambles of one, too. It's—"

The masher struck the side of the tub with a clack and fell back into the mash.

"Don't tell me I dinna ken what it's like!" Jenny blazed at him. "Stories, is it? Who d'ye think nursed Ian when he came home from France wi' half a leg and a fever that nearly killed him?"

She slapped her hand flat on the bench. The stretched nerves had snapped.

"Don't know? *I* don't know? *I* picked the maggots out of the raw flesh of his stump, because his own mother couldna bring herself to do it! *I* held the hot knife against his leg to seal the wound! *I* smelled his flesh searing like a roasted pig and listened to him scream while I did it! D'ye dare to stand there and tell me I . . . don't . . . KNOW how it is!"

Angry tears ran down her cheeks. She brushed at them, groping in her pocket for a handkerchief.

Lips pressed tight together, Jamie rose, pulled a handkerchief from his sleeve, and handed it to her. He knew better than to touch or try to comfort her. He stood staring at her for a moment as she wiped furiously at her eyes and dripping nose.

"Aye, well, ye know, then," he said. "And yet you want me to take him?"

"I do." She blew her nose and wiped it briskly, then tucked the handkerchief in her pocket.

"He kens well enough that he's crippled, Jamie. Kens it a good bit too well. But he could manage with ye. There's a horse for him; he wouldna have to walk."

He made an impatient gesture with one hand.

"Could he manage is no the question, is it? A man can do what he thinks he must—why do *you* think he must?"

Composed once more, she fished the tool out of the mash and shook it. Brown droplets spattered into the tub.

"He hasna asked ye, has he? Whether ye'll need him or no?"

"No."

She stabbed the masher back into the tub and resumed her work.

"He thinks ye wilna want him because he's lame, and that he'd be no use to ye." She looked up then, troubled dark-blue eyes the twins of her brother's. "Ye knew Ian before, Jamie. He's different now."

He nodded reluctantly, resuming his seat on the bucket.

"Aye. Well, but ye'd expect it, no? And he seems well enough." He looked up at his sister and smiled.

"He's happy wi' ye, Jenny. You and the bairns."

She nodded, black curls bobbing.

"Aye, he is," she said softly. "But that's because he's a whole man to me, and always will be." She looked directly at her brother. "But if he thinks he's of no use to you, he wilna be whole to himself. And that's why I'll have ye take him."

Jamie laced his hands together, elbows braced on his knees, and rested his chin on his linked knuckles.

"This wilna be like France," he said quietly. "Fighting there, ye risk no more than your life in battle. Here . . ." He hesitated, then went on. "Jenny, this is treason. If it goes wrong, those that follow the Stuarts are like to end on a scaffold."

Her normally pale complexion went a shade whiter, but her motions didn't slow.

"There's nay choice for me," he went on, eyes steady on her. "But will ye risk us both? Will ye have Ian look down from the gallows on the fire waiting for his entrails? You'll chance raising your bairns wi'out their father—to save his pride?" His face was nearly as pale as hers, glimmering in the darkness of the brewhouse.

The strokes of the masher were slower now, without the fierce velocity of her earlier movements, but her voice held all the conviction of her slow, inexorable mashing.

"I'll have a whole man," she said steadily. "Or none."

Jamie sat without moving for a long moment, watching his sister's dark head bent over her work.

"All right," he said at last, quietly. She didn't look up or vary her movements, but the white kertch seemed to incline slightly toward him.

He sighed explosively, then rose and turned abruptly to me.

"Come on out of here, Sassenach," he said. "Christ, I *must* be drunk."

"What makes ye think you can order me about?" The vein in Ian's temple throbbed fiercely. Jenny's hand squeezed mine tighter.

Jamie's assertion that Ian would accompany him to join the Stuart army had been met first with incredulity, then with suspicion, and—as Jamie persisted—anger.

"You're a fool," Ian declared flatly. "I'm a cripple, and ye ken it well enough."

"I ken you're a bonny fighter, and there's none I'd rather

have by my side in a battle," Jamie said firmly. His face gave no sign of doubts or hesitation; he had agreed to Jenny's request, and would carry it out, no matter what. "You've fought there often enough; will ye desert me now?"

Ian waved an impatient hand, dismissing this flattery. "That's as may be. If my leg comes off or gives way, there's precious little fighting I'll do—I'll be lyin' on the ground like a worm, waiting for the first Redcoat who comes by to spit me. And beyond that"—he scowled at his brother-in-law—"who d'ye think will mind this place for ye until you come back, and I'm off to the wars with ye?"

"Jenny," Jamie replied promptly. "I shall leave enough men behind that they can be seeing to the work; she can manage the accounts well enough."

Ian's brows shot up, and he said something very rude in Gaelic.

"*Pog ma mahon!* You'll ha' me leave her to run the place alone, wi' three small bairns at her apron, and but half the men needed? Man, ye've taken leave o' your senses!" Flinging up both hands, Ian swung around to the sideboard where the whisky was kept.

Jenny, seated next to me on the sofa with Katherine on her lap, made a small sound under her breath. Her hand sought mine under cover of our mingled skirts, and I squeezed her fingers.

"What makes ye think ye can order me about?"

Jamie eyed his brother-in-law's tense back for a moment, scowling. Suddenly, a muscle at the corner of his mouth twitched.

"Because I'm bigger than you are," he said belligerently, still scowling.

Ian rounded on him, incredulity stamped on his face. Indecision played in his eyes for less than a second. His shoulders squared up and his chin lifted.

"I'm older than you," he answered, with an identical scowl.

"I'm stronger."

"No, you're not!"

"Aye, I am!"

"No, *I* am!"

A vein of dead seriousness underlay the laughter in their

voices; while this little confrontation might be passed off as all in fun, they were as intent on each other as they had ever been in youth or childhood, and the echoes of challenge rang in Jamie's voice as he ripped loose his cuff and jerked back the sleeve of his shirt.

"Prove it," he said. He cleared the chess table with a careless sweep of the hand, sat down and braced his elbow on the inlaid surface, fingers flexed for an offensive. Deep blue eyes glared up into Ian's dark-brown ones, hot with the same anger.

Ian took half a second to appraise the situation, then jerked his head in a brief nod of acceptance, making his heavy sheaf of dark hair flop into his eyes.

With calm deliberation, he brushed it back, unfastened his cuff, and rolled his sleeve to the shoulder, turn by turn, never taking his eyes from his brother-in-law.

From where I stood, I could see Ian's face, a little flushed under his tan, long, narrow chin set in determination. I couldn't see Jamie's face, but the determination was eloquently expressed by the line of back and shoulders.

The two men set their elbows carefully, maneuvering to find a good spot, rubbing back and forth with the point of the elbow to be sure the surface was not slippery.

With due ritual, Jamie spread his fingers, palm toward Ian. Ian carefully placed his own palm against it. The fingers matched, touching for a moment in a mirror image, then shifted, one to the right and one to the left, linked and clasping.

"Ready?" Jamie asked.

"Ready." Ian's voice was calm, but his eyes gleamed under the feathery brows.

The muscles tensed at once, all along the length of the two arms, springing into sharp definition as they shifted in their seats, seeking leverage.

Jenny caught my eye and rolled her eyes heavenward. Whatever she had been expecting of Jamie, it wasn't this.

Both men were focused on the straining knot of fingers, to the exclusion of everything else. Both faces were deep red with exertion, sweat damping the hair on their temples, eyes bulging slightly with effort. Suddenly I saw Jamie's gaze break from its concentration on the clenched fists as he saw Ian's

lips clamp tighter. Ian felt the shift, looked up, met Jamie's
eyes . . . and the two men burst into laughter.

The hands clung for a moment longer, locked in spasm,
then fell apart.

"A draw, then," said Jamie, pushing back a strand of
sweat-damp hair. He shook his head good-naturedly at Ian.

"All right, man. If I could order ye, I wouldna do it. But I
can ask, no? Will ye come with me?"

Ian dabbed at the side of his neck, where a runnel of
sweat dampened his collar. His gaze roamed about the room,
resting for a moment on Jenny. Her face was no paler than
usual, but I could see the hasty pulse, beating just below the
angle of her jaw. Ian stared at her intently as he rolled his
sleeve down again, in careful turns. I could see a deep pink
flush begin to rise from the neck of her gown.

Ian rubbed his jaw as though thinking, then turned toward Jamie and shook his head.

"No, my jo," he said softly. "Ye need me here, and here I
shall stay." His eyes rested on Jenny, with Katherine held
against her shoulder, and on small Maggie, clutching her
mother's skirt with grubby hands. And on me. Ian's long
mouth curled in a slight smile. "I shall stay here," he repeated. "Guardin' your weak side, man."

"Jamie?"

"Aye?" The answer came at once; I knew he hadn't been
asleep, though he lay still as a figure carved on a tomb. It was
moon-bright in the room, and I could see his face when I rose
on my elbow; he was staring upward, as though he could see
beyond the heavy beams to the open night and the stars beyond.

"You aren't going to try to leave me behind, are you?" I
wouldn't have thought of asking were it not for the scene with
Ian, earlier in the evening. For once it was settled that Ian
would stay, Jamie had sat down with him to issue orders—
choosing who would march with the laird to the aid of the
Prince, who would stay behind to tend to animals and pasture
and the maintenance of Lallybroch.

I knew it had been a wrenching process of decision,
though he gave no sign of it, calmly discussing with Ian

whether Ross the smith could be spared to go and deciding
that he could, though the plowshares needed for the spring
must all be in good repair before leaving. Whether Joseph
Fraser Kirby might go, and deciding that he should not, as he
was the main support not only of his own family but that of
his widowed sister. Brendan was the oldest boy of both families, and at nine, ill-prepared to replace his father, should
Joseph not come home.

It was a matter for the most delicate planning. How
many men should go, to have some impact on the course of
the war? For Jenny was right, Jamie had no choice now—no
choice but to help Charles Stuart win. And to that end, as
many men and arms as could possibly be summoned should
be thrown into the cause.

But on the other side was me, and my deadly knowledge
—and lack of it. We had succeeded in preventing Charles
Stuart from getting money to finance his rebellion; and still
the Bonnie Prince, reckless, feckless, and determined to claim
his legacy, had landed to rally the clans at Glenfinnan. From a
further letter from Jared, we had learned that Charles had
crossed the Channel with two small frigates, provided by one
Antoine Walsh, a sometime-slaver with an eye for opportunity. Apparently, he saw Charles's venture as less risky than a
slaving expedition, a gamble in which he might or might not
be justified. One frigate had been waylaid by the English; the
other had landed Charles safe on the isle of Eriskay.

Charles had landed with only seven companions, including the owner of a small bank named Aeneas MacDonald.
Unable to finance an entire expedition, MacDonald had provided the funds for a small stock of broadswords, which constituted Charles's entire armament. Jared sounded simultaneously admiring and horrified by the recklessness of the
venture, but, loyal Jacobite that he was, did his best to swallow his misgivings.

And so far, Charles had succeeded. From the Highland
grapevine, we learned that he had landed at Eriskay, crossed
to Glenfinnan, and there waited, accompanied only by several
large casks of brandywine, to see whether the clans would
answer the call to his standard. And after what must have
been several nerve-racking hours, three hundred men of clan
Cameron had çome down the defiles of the steep green hills,

led not by their chieftain, who was away from his home—but
by his sister, Jenny Cameron.

The Camerons had been the first, but they had been
joined by others, as the Bill of Association showed.

If Charles should now proceed to disaster, despite all
efforts, then how many men of Lallybroch could be spared,
left at home to save something from the wreck?

Ian himself would be safe; that much was sure, and some
balm to Jamie's spirit. But the others—the sixty families who
lived on Lallybroch? Choosing who would go and who would
stay must seem in some lights like choosing men for sacrifice.
I had seen commanders before; the men whom war forced to
make such choices—and I knew what it cost them.

Jamie had done it—he had no choice—but on two matters he had held firm; no women would accompany his troop,
and no lads under eighteen years of age would go. Ian had
looked mildly surprised at this—while most women with
young children would normally stay behind, it was far from
unusual for Highland wives to follow their men to battle,
cooking and caring for them, and sharing the army's rations.
And the lads, who considered themselves men at fourteen,
would be grossly humiliated at being omitted from the tally.
But Jamie had given his orders in a tone that brooked no
argument, and Ian, after a moment's hesitation, had merely
nodded and written them down.

I hadn't wanted to ask him, in the presence of Ian and
Jenny, whether his ban on womenfolk was intended to include me. Because, whether it was or not, I was going with
him, and that, I thought, was bloody all·about it.

"Leave you behind?" he said now, and I saw his mouth
curl into a sideways grin. "D'ye think I'd stand a chance of
it?"

"No," I said, snuggling next to him in sudden relief.
"You wouldn't. But I thought you might think about it."

He gave a small snort, and drew me down, head on his
shoulder. "Oh, aye. And if I thought I could leave ye, I'd
chain ye to the banister; not much else would stop ye." I
could feel his head shake above me, in negation. "No. I must
take ye wi' me, Sassenach, whether I will or no. There are
things you'll maybe know along the way—even if they dinna
seem like anything now, they may later. And you're a rare

fine healer, Sassenach—I canna deny the men your skill, and it be needed."

His hand patted my shoulder, and he sighed. "I would give anything, *mo nighean donn*, could I leave ye here safe, but I cannot. So you will go with me—you and Fergus."

"Fergus?" I was surprised by this. "But I thought you wouldn't take any of the younger lads!"

He sighed again, and I put my hand flat on the center of his chest, where his heart beat beneath the small hollow, slow and steady.

"Well, Fergus is a bit different. The other lads—I wilna take them, because they belong here; if it all goes to smash, they'll be left to keep their families from starving, to work the fields and tend beasts. They'll likely need to grow up fast, if it happens, but at least they'll be here to do it. But Fergus . . . this isna his place, Sassenach. Nor is France, or I would send him back. But he has no place there, either."

"His place is with you," I said softly, understanding. "Like mine."

He was silent for a long time, then his hand squeezed me gently.

"Aye, that's so," he said quietly. "Sleep now, *mo nighean donn*, it's late."

The fretful wail pulled me toward the surface of wakefulness for the third time. Baby Katherine was teething, and didn't care who knew it. From their room down the hall, I heard Ian's sleepy mumble, and Jenny's higher voice, resigned, as she got out of bed and went to soothe the infant.

Then I heard the soft, heavy footfalls in the corridor, and realized that Jamie, still wakeful, was walking barefoot through the house.

"Jenny?" His voice, low-pitched to avoid disturbance, was still plainly audible in the creaking silence of the manor house,

"I heard the wee lassie greetin'," he said. "If she canna sleep, neither can I, but you can. If she's fed and dry, perhaps we can bear each other company for a bit, while you go back to your bed."

Jenny smothered a yawn, and I could hear the smile in her voice.

"Jamie dear, you're a mother's blessing. Aye, she's full as a drum, and a dry clout on her this minute. Take her, and I wish ye joy of each other." A door closed, and I heard the heavy footfall again, heading back toward our room, and the low murmur of Jamie's voice as he muttered soothingly to the baby.

I snuggled deeper into the comfort of the goose-down bed and turned toward sleep again, hearing with half an ear the baby's whining, interspersed with hiccuping sobs, and Jamie's deep, tuneless humming, the sound as comforting as the thought of beehives in the sun.

"Eh, wee Kitty, *ciamar a tha thu? Much, mo naoid-heachan, much.*"

The sound of them went up and down the passage, and I dropped further toward sleep, but kept half-wakeful on purpose to hear them. One day perhaps he would hold his own child so, small round head cradled in the big hands, small solid body cupped and held firm against his shoulder. And thus he would sing to his own daughter, a tuneless song, a warm, soft chant in the dark.

The constant small ache in my heart was submerged in a flood of tenderness. I had conceived once; I could do so again. Faith had given me the gift of that knowledge, Jamie the courage and means to use it. My hands rested lightly on my breasts, cupping the deep swell of them, knowing beyond doubt that one day they would nourish the child of my heart. I drifted into sleep with the sound of Jamie's singing in my ears.

Sometime later I drifted near the surface again, and opened my eyes to the light-filled room. The moon had risen, full and beaming, and all the objects in the room were plainly visible, in that flat, two-dimensional way of things seen without shadow.

The baby had quieted, but I could hear Jamie's voice in the hall, still speaking, but much more quietly, hardly more than a murmur. And the tone of it had changed; it wasn't the rhythmic, half-nonsense way one talks to babies, but the broken, halting speech of a man seeking the way through the wilderness of his own heart.

Curious, I slipped out of bed and crept quietly to the door. I could see them there at the end of the hall. Jamie sat leaning back against the side of the window seat, wearing only his shirt. His bare legs were raised, forming a back against which small Katherine Mary rested as she sat facing him in his lap, her own chubby legs kicking restlessly over his stomach.

The baby's face was blank and light as the moon's, her eyes dark pools absorbing his words. He traced the curve of her cheek with one finger, again and again, whispering with heartbreaking gentleness.

He spoke in Gaelic, and so low that I could not have told what he said, even had I known the words. But the whispering voice was thick, and the moonlight from the casement behind him showed the tracks of the tears that slid unregarded down his own cheeks.

It was not a scene that bore intrusion. I came back to the still-warm bed, holding in my mind the picture of the laird of Lallybroch, half-naked in the moonlight, pouring out his heart to an unknown future, holding in his lap the promise of his blood.

＿＿＞

When I woke in the morning, there was a warm, unfamiliar scent next to me, and something tangled in my hair. I opened my eyes to find Katherine Mary's rosebud lips smacking dreamily an inch from my nose, her fat fingers clutched in the hair above my left ear. I cautiously disengaged myself, and she stirred, but flopped over onto her stomach, drew her knees up and went back to sleep.

Jamie was lying on the other side of the child, face half-buried in his pillow. He opened one eye, clear blue as the morning sky.

"Good morning, Sassenach," he said, speaking quietly so as not to disturb the small sleeper. He smiled at me as I sat up in bed. "Ye looked verra sweet, the two of you, asleep face-to-face like that."

I ran a hand through my tangled hair, and smiled myself at Kitty's upturned bottom, jutting absurdly into the air.

"That doesn't look at all comfortable," I observed. "But

she's still asleep, so it can't be that bad. How late were you up with her last night? I didn't hear you come to bed."

He yawned and ran a hand through his hair, smoothing it away from his face. There were shadows under his eyes, but he seemed peacefully content.

"Oh, some time. Before moonset, at least. I didna want to wake Jenny by taking the wean back to her, so I laid her in the bed between us, and she didna twitch once, the rest of the night."

The baby was kneading the mattress with elbows and knees, rootling in the bedclothes with a low grunting noise. It must be close to time for her morning feed. This supposition was borne out in the next moment, when she raised her head, eyes still tight shut, and let out a healthy howl. I reached hastily for her and picked her up.

"There-there-there," I soothed, patting the straining little back. I swung my legs out of bed, then reached back and patted Jamie on the head. The rough bright hair was warm under my hand.

"I'll take her to Jenny," I said. "It's early yet; you sleep some more."

"I may do that, Sassenach," Jamie said, flinching at the noise. "I'll see ye at breakfast, shall I?" He rolled onto his back, crossed his hands on his chest in his favorite sleeping posture, and was breathing deeply again by the time Katherine Mary and I had reached the door.

The baby squirmed vigorously, rooting for a nipple and squawking in frustration when none was immediately forthcoming. Hurrying along the hall, I met Jenny, hurrying out of her bedroom in response to her offspring's cries, pulling on a green dressing gown as she came. I held out the baby, waving little fists in urgent demand.

"There, *mo mùirninn,* hush now, hush," Jenny soothed. With a cock of the eyebrow in invitation, she took the child from me and turned back into her room.

I followed her in and sat on the rumpled bed as she sat down on a nursing stool by the hearth and hastily bared one breast. The yowling little mouth clamped at once on to a nipple and we all relaxed in relief as sudden silence descended.

"Ah," Jenny sighed. Her shoulders slumped a fraction as

the flow of milk started. "That's better, my wee piggie, no?" She opened her eyes and smiled at me, eyes clear and blue as her brother's.

" 'Twas kind of ye to keep the lassie all night; I slept like the dead."

I shrugged, smiling at the picture of mother and child, relaxed together in total content. The curve of the baby's head exactly echoed the high, round curve of Jenny's breast and small, slurping noises came from the little bundle as her body sagged against her mother's, fitting easily into the curve of Jenny's lap.

"It was Jamie, not me," I said. "He and his niece seem to have got on well together." The picture of them came back to me, Jamie talking in earnest, low tones to the child, tears slipping down his face.

Jenny nodded, watching my face.

"Aye. I thought perhaps they'd comfort each other a bit. He doesna sleep well these days?" Her voice held a question.

"No," I answered softly. "He has a lot on his mind."

"Well he might," she said, glancing at the bed behind me. Ian was gone already, risen at dawn to see to the stock in the barn. The horses that could be spared from the farming—and some that couldn't—needed shoeing, needed harness, in preparation for their journey to rebellion.

"You can talk to a babe, ye ken," she said suddenly, breaking into my thought. "Really talk, I mean. Ye can tell them anything, no matter how foolish it would sound did ye say it to a soul could understand ye."

"Oh. You heard him, then?" I asked. She nodded, eyes on the curve of Katherine's cheek, where the tiny dark lashes lay against the fair skin, eyes closed in ecstasy.

"Aye. Ye shouldna worrit yourself," she added, smiling gently at me. "It isna that he feels he canna talk to you; he knows he can. But it's different to talk to a babe that way. It's a person; ye ken that you're not alone. But they dinna ken your words, and ye don't worry a bit what they'll think of ye, or what they may feel they must do. You can pour out your heart to them wi'out choosing your words, or keeping anything back at all—and that's a comfort to the soul."

She spoke matter-of-factly, as though this were something that everyone knew. I wondered whether she spoke that way often to her child. The generous wide mouth, so like her brother's, lifted slightly at one side.

"It's the way ye talk to them before they're born," she said softly. "You'll know?"

I placed my hands gently over my belly, one atop the other, remembering.

"Yes, I know."

She pressed a thumb against the baby's cheek, breaking the suction, and with a deft movement, shifted the small body to bring the full breast within reach.

"I've thought that perhaps that's why women are so often sad, once the child's born," she said meditatively, as though thinking aloud. "Ye think of them while ye talk, and you have a knowledge of them as they are inside ye, the way you think they are. And then they're born, and they're different—not the way ye thought of them inside, at all. And ye love them, o' course, and get to know them the way they are . . . but still, there's the thought of the child ye once talked to in your heart, and that child is gone. So I think it's the grievin' for the child unborn that ye feel, even as ye hold the born one in your arms." She dipped her head and kissed her daughter's downy skull.

"Yes," I said. "Before . . . it's all possibility. It might be a son, or a daughter. A plain child, a bonny one. And then it's born, and all the things it might have been are gone, because now it *is*."

She rocked gently back and forth, and the small clutching hand that seized the folds of green silk over her breast began to loose its grip.

"And a daughter is born, and the son that she might have been is dead," she said quietly. "And the bonny lad at your breast has killed the wee lassie ye thought ye carried. And ye weep for what you didn't know, that's gone for good, until you know the child you have, and then at last it's as though they could never have been other than they are, and ye feel naught but joy in them. But 'til then, ye weep easy."

"And men . . ." I said, thinking of Jamie, whispering secrets to the unhearing ears of the child.

"Aye. They hold their bairns, and they feel all the things that might be, and the things that will never be. But it isna so easy for a man to weep for the things he doesna ken."

PART SIX

The Flames of
Rebellion

36

Prestonpans

Four days' march found us on the crest of a hill near
Calder. A sizable moor stretched out at the foot of the
hill, but we set up camp within the shelter of the trees
above. There were two small streams cutting through
the moss-covered rock of the hillside, and the crisp weather
of early fall made it seem much more like picnicking than a
march to war.

But it was the seventeenth of September, and if my
sketchy knowledge of Jacobite history was correct, war it
would be, in a matter of days.

"Tell it to me again, Sassenach," Jamie had said, for the
dozenth time, as we made our way along the winding trails
and dirt roads. I rode Donas, while Jamie walked alongside,
but now slid down to walk beside him, to make conversation
easier. While Donas and I had reached an understanding of
sorts, he was the kind of horse that demanded your full concentration to ride; he was all too fond of scraping an unwary
rider off by walking under low branches, for example.

"I told you before, I don't know that much," I said.
"There was very little written about it in the history books,
and I didn't pay a great deal of attention at the time. All I can
tell you is that the battle was fought—er, *will* be fought—near
the town of Preston, and so it's called the Battle of Prestonpans, though the Scots called—call—it the Battle of Gladsmuir, because of an old prophecy that the returning king will
be victorious at Gladsmuir. Heaven knows where the real
Gladsmuir is, if there is one."

"Aye. And?"

I furrowed my brow, trying to recall every last scrap of
information. I could conjure a mental picture of the small,
tattered brown copy of *A Child's History of England,* read by
the flickering light of a kerosene lantern in a mud hut somewhere in Persia. Mentally flicking the pages, I could just recall
the two-page section that was all the author had seen fit to
devote to the second Jacobite Rising, known to historians as

"the '45." And within that two-page section, the single paragraph dealing with the battle we were about to fight.

"The Scots win," I said helpfully.

"Well, that's the important point," he agreed, a bit sarcastically, "but it would be a bit of help to know a little more."

"If you wanted prophecy, you should have gotten a seer," I snapped, then relented. "I'm sorry. It's only that I don't *know* much, and it's very frustrating."

"Aye, it is." He reached down and took my hand, squeezing it as he smiled at me. "Dinna fash yourself, Sassenach. Ye canna say more than ye know, but tell me it all, just once more."

"All right." I squeezed back, and we walked on, hand in hand. "It was a remarkable victory," I began, reading from my mental page, "because the Jacobites were so greatly outnumbered. They surprised General Cope's army at dawn—they charged out of the rising sun, I remember that—and it was a rout. There were hundreds of casualties on the English side, and only a few from the Jacobite side—thirty men, that was it. Only thirty men killed."

Jamie glanced behind us, at the straggling tail of the Lallybroch men, strung out as they walked along the road, chatting and singing in small groups. Thirty men was what we had brought from Lallybroch. It didn't seem that small a number, looking at them. But I had seen the battlefields of Alsace-Lorraine, and the acres of meadowland converted to muddy boneyards by the burial of the thousands slain.

"Taken all in all," I said, feeling faintly apologetic, "I'm afraid it was really rather . . . unimportant, historically speaking."

Jamie blew out his breath through pursed lips, and looked down at me rather bleakly.

"Unimportant. Aye, well."

"I'm sorry," I said.

"Not your fault, Sassenach."

But I couldn't help feeling that it was, somehow.

The men sat around the fire after their supper, lazily enjoying the feeling of full stomachs, exchanging stories and scratching. The scratching was endemic; close quarters and lack of hygiene made body lice so common as to excite no remark when one man detached a representative specimen from a fold of his plaid and tossed it into the fire. The louse flamed for an instant, one among the sparks of the fire, and then was gone.

The young man they called Kincaid—his name was Alexander, but there were so many Alexanders that most of them ended up being called by nicknames or middle names—seemed particularly afflicted with the scourge this evening. He dug viciously under one arm, into his curly brown hair, then—with a quick glance to see whether I was looking in his direction—at his crotch.

"Got 'em bad, have ye, lad?" Ross the smith observed sympathetically.

"Aye," he answered, "the wee buggers are eatin' me alive."

"Bloody hell to get out of your cock hairs," Wallace Fraser observed, scratching himself in sympathy. "Gives me the yeuk to watch ye, laddie."

"D'ye ken the best way to rid yourself o' the wee beasties?" Sorley McClure asked helpfully, and at Kincaid's negative shake of the head, leaned forward and carefully pulled a flaming stick from the fire.

"Lift your kilt a moment, laddie, and I'll smoke 'em out for ye," he offered, to catcalls and jeers of laughter from the men.

"Bloody farmer," Murtagh grumbled. "And what would ye know about it?"

"You know a better way?" Wallace raised thick brows skeptically, wrinkling the tanned skin of his balding forehead.

"O' course." He drew his dirk with a flourish. "The laddie's a soldier now; let him do it like a soldier does."

Kincaid's open face was guileless and eager. "How's that?"

"Weel, verra simple. Ye take your dirk, lift your plaidie, and shave off half the hairs on your crutch." He raised the dirk warningly. "Only half, mind."

"Half? Aye, well . . ." Kincaid looked doubtful, but was paying close attention. I could see the grins of anticipation broadening on the faces of the men around the fire, but no one was laughing yet.

"Then . . ." Murtagh gestured at Sorley and his stick. "*Then,* laddie, ye set the other half on fire, and when the beasties rush out, ye spear them wi' your dirk."

Kincaid blushed hotly enough to be seen even by firelight as the circle of men erupted in hoots and roars. There was a good deal of rude shoving as a couple of the men pretended to try the fire cure on each other, brandishing flaming billets of wood. Just as it seemed that the horseplay was getting out of hand, and likely to lead to blows in earnest, Jamie returned from hobbling the animals. He stepped into the circle, and tossed a stone bottle from under one arm to Kincaid. Another went to Murtagh, and the shoving died down.

"Ye're fools, the lot o' ye," he declared. "The second best way to rid yourself of lice is to pour whisky on them and get them drunk. When they've fallen down snoring, then ye stand up and they'll drop straight off."

"Second best, eh?" said Ross. "And what's the best way, sir, and I might ask?"

Jamie smiled indulgently round the circle, like a parent amused by the antics of his children.

"Why, let your wife pick them off ye, one by one." He cocked an elbow and bowed to me, one eyebrow raised. "If you'd oblige me, my lady?"

While put forward as a joke, individual removal was in fact the only effective method of ridding oneself of lice. I fine-combed my own hair—all of it—morning and evening, washed it with yarrow whenever we paused near water deep enough to bathe in, and had so far avoided any serious infestations. Aware that I would remain louseless only so long as Jamie did, I administered the same treatment to him, whenever I could get him to sit still long enough.

"Baboons do this all the time," I remarked, delicately disentangling a foxtail from his thick red mane. "But I believe they eat the fruits of their labors."

"Dinna let me prevent ye, Sassenach, and ye feel so inclined," he responded. He hunched his shoulders slightly in pleasure as the comb slid through the thick, glossy strands.

The firelight filled my hands with a cascade of sparks and golden streaks of fire. "Mm. Ye wouldna think it felt so nice to have someone comb your hair for ye."

"Wait 'til I get to the rest of it," I said, tweaking him familiarly and making him giggle. "Tempted though I am to try Murtagh's suggestion instead."

"Touch my cock hairs wi' a torch, and you'll get the same treatment," he threatened. "What was it Louise de La Tour says bald lassies are?"

"Erotic." I leaned forward and nipped the upper flange of one ear between my teeth.

"Mmmphm."

"Well, tastes differ," I said. "*Chacun ses goûts,* and all that."

"A bloody French sentiment, and I ever heard one."

"Isn't it, though?"

A loud, rolling growl interrupted my labors. I laid down the comb and peered ostentatiously into the tree-filled shadows.

"Either," I said, "there are bears in this wood, or . . . why haven't you eaten?"

"I was busy wi' the beasts," he answered. "One of the ponies has a cracked hoof and I had to bind it with a poultice. Not that I've so much appetite, what wi' all this talk of eating lice."

"What sort of poultice do you use on a horse's hoof?" I asked, ignoring this remark.

"Different things; fresh dung will do in a pinch. I used chewed vetch leaves mixed wi' honey this time."

The saddlebags had been dumped by our private fire, near the edge of the small clearing where the men had erected my tent. While I would have been willing to sleep under the stars, as they did, I admitted to a certain thankfulness for the small privacy afforded me by the sheet of canvas. And, as Murtagh had pointed out with his customary bluntness, when I thanked him for his assistance in erecting the shelter, the arrangement was not solely for *my* benefit.

"And if he takes his ease between your thighs of a night, there's none will grudge it to him," the little clansman had said, with a jerk of the head toward Jamie, deep in conversation with several of the other men. "But there's nay need to make the lads think ower-much o' things they canna have, now is there?"

"Quite," I said, with an edge to my voice. "Very thoughtful of you."

One of his rare smiles curled the corner of the thin-lipped mouth.

"Och, quite," he said.

A quick rummage through the saddlebags turned up a heel of cheese and several apples. I gave these to Jamie, who examined them dubiously.

"No bread?" he asked.

"There may be some in the other bag. Eat those first, though; they're good for you." He shared the Highlanders' innate suspicion of fresh fruit and vegetables, though his great appetite made him willing to eat almost anything in extremity.

"Mm," he said, taking a bite of one apple. "If ye say so, Sassenach."

"I do say so. Look." I pulled my lips back, baring my teeth. "How many women of my age do you know who still have all their teeth?"

A grin bared his own excellent teeth.

"Well, I'll admit you're verra well preserved, Sassenach, for such an auld crone."

"Well nourished, is what I am," I retorted. "Half the people on your estate are suffering from mild scurvy, and from what I've seen on the road, it's even worse elsewhere. It's vitamin C that prevents scurvy, and apples are full of it."

He took the apple away from his mouth and frowned at it suspiciously.

"They are?"

"Yes, they are," I said firmly. "So are most other kinds of plants—oranges and lemons are best, but of course you can't get those here—but onions, cabbage, apples . . . eat something like that every day, and you won't get scurvy. Even green herbs and meadow grass have vitamin C."

"Mmphm. And that's why deer dinna lose their teeth as they get old?"

"I daresay."

He turned the apple to and fro, examining it critically, then shrugged.

"Aye, well," he said, and took another bite.

I had just turned to fetch the bread when a faint crackling sound drew my attention. I caught sight from the corner
of my eye of shadowy movement in the darkness and the
firelight flashed from something near Jamie's head. I whirled
toward him, shouting, just in time to see him topple backward
off the log and disappear into the void of the night.

There was no moon, and the only clue to what was happening was a tremendous scuffling sound in the dry alder
leaves, and the noise of men locked in effortful but silent
conflict, with grunts, gasps, and the occasional muffled curse.
There was a short, sharp cry, and then complete quiet. It
lasted, I suppose, only a few seconds, though it seemed to go
on forever.

I was still standing by the fire, frozen in my original position, when Jamie reemerged from the Stygian dark of the
forest, a captive before him, one arm twisted behind its back.
Loosing his grip, he whirled the dark figure around and gave
it an abrupt shove that sent it crashing backward into a tree.
The man hit the trunk hard, loosing a shower of leaves and
acorns, and slid slowly down to lie dazed in the leaf-meal.

Attracted by the noise, Murtagh, Ross, and a couple of
the other Fraser men materialized by the fire. Hauling the
intruder to his feet, they pulled him roughly into the circle of
firelight. Murtagh grabbed the captive by the hair and jerked
his head backward, bringing his face into view.

It was a small, fine-boned face, with big, long-lashed eyes
that blinked dazedly at the crowding faces.

"But he's only a boy!" I exclaimed. "He can't be more
than fifteen!"

"Sixteen!" said the boy. He shook his head, senses returning. "Not that that makes any difference," he added
haughtily, in an English accent. Hampshire, I thought. He
was a long way from home.

"It doesn't," Jamie grimly agreed. "Sixteen or sixty, he's
just made a verra creditable attempt at cutting my throat." I
noticed then the reddened handkerchief pressed against the
side of his neck.

"I shan't tell you anything," the boy said. His eyes were
dark pools in the pale face, though the firelight shone on the
gleam of fair hair. He was clutching one arm tightly in front

of him; I thought perhaps it was injured. The boy was clearly making a major effort to stand upright among the men, lips compressed against any wayward expression of fear or pain.

"Some things you don't need to tell me," said Jamie, looking the lad over carefully. "One, you're an Englishman, so likely you've come with troops nearby. And two, you're alone."

The boy seemed startled. "How do you know that?"

Jamie raised his eyebrows. "I suppose that ye'd not have attacked me unless you thought that the lady and I were alone. If you were with someone else who also thought that, they would presumably have come to your assistance just now —is your arm broken, by the way? I thought I felt something snap. If you were with someone else who knew we were not alone, they would ha' stopped ye from trying anything so foolish." Despite this diagnosis, I noticed three of the men fade discreetly into the forest in response to a signal from Jamie, presumably to check for other intruders.

The boy's expression hardened at hearing his act described as foolish. Jamie dabbed at his neck, then inspected the handkerchief critically.

"If you're tryin' to kill someone from behind, laddie, pick a man who's not sitting in a pile of dry leaves," he advised. "And if you're using a knife on someone larger than you, pick a surer spot; throat-cutting's chancy unless your victim will sit still for ye."

"Thank you for the valuable advice," the boy sneered. He was doing a fair job at maintaining his bravado, though his eyes flicked nervously from one threatening, whiskered face to another. None of the Highlanders would have won any beauty prizes in broad daylight; by night, they weren't the sort of thing you wanted to meet in a dark place.

Jamie answered courteously, "You're quite welcome. It's unfortunate that ye won't get the chance to apply it in future. Why *did* you attack me, since I think to ask?"

Men, attracted by the noise, had begun filtering in from the surrounding campsites, sliding wraithlike out of the woods. The boy's glance flickered around the growing circle of men, resting at length on me. He hesitated for a moment, but answered, "I was hoping to release the lady from your custody."

A small stir of suppressed amusement ran around the circle, only to be quelled by a brief gesture from Jamie. "I see," he said noncommittally. "You heard us talking and determined that the lady is English and well-born. Whereas I—"

"Whereas you, sir, are a conscienceless outlaw, with a reputation for thievery and violence!. Your face and description are on broadsheets throughout Hampshire and Sussex! I recognized you at once; you're a rebel and an unprincipled voluptuary!" the boy burst out hotly, face stained a deeper red even than the firelight.

I bit my lip and looked down at my shoes, so as not to meet Jamie's eye.

"Aye, well. Just as ye say," Jamie agreed cordially. "That being the case, perhaps you can advance some reason why I shouldna kill ye immediately?" Drawing the dirk smoothly from its sheath, he twisted it delicately, making the fire jump from the blade.

The blood had faded from the young man's face, leaving him ghostly in the shadows, but he drew himself upright at this, pulling against the captors on either side. "I expected that. I am quite prepared to die," he said, stiffening his shoulders.

Jamie nodded thoughtfully, then, stooping, laid the blade of his dirk in the fire. A plume of smoke rose around the blackening metal, smelling strongly of the forge. We all watched in silent fascination as the flame, spectral blue where it touched the blade, seemed to bring the deadly iron to life in a flush of deep red heat.

Wrapping his hand in the bloodstained cloth, Jamie cautiously pulled the dirk from the fire. He advanced slowly toward the boy, letting the blade fall, as though of its own volition, until it touched the lad's jerkin. There was a strong smell of singed cloth from the handkerchief wrapped around the haft of the knife, which grew stronger as a narrow burnt line traced its way up the front of the jerkin in the dagger's path. The point, darkening as it cooled, stopped just short of the upwardly straining chin. I could see thin lines of sweat shining in the stretched hollows of the slender neck.

"Aye, well, I'm afraid that I'm no prepared to kill ye—

just yet." Jamie's voice was soft, filled with a quiet menace all the more frightening for its control.

"Who d'ye march with?" The question snapped like a whip, making its hearers flinch. The knife point hovered slightly nearer, smoking in the night wind.

"I'll—I'll not tell you!" The boy's lips closed tight on the stammered answer, and a tremor ran down the delicate throat.

"Nor how far away your comrades lie? Nor their number? Nor their direction of march?" The questions were put lightly again, with a finicking touch of the blade along the edge of the boy's jaw. His eyes showed white all around, like a panicked horse, but he shook his head violently, making the golden hair fly. Ross and Kincaid tightened their grip against the pull of the boy's arms.

The darkened blade pressed suddenly flat along its length, hard under the angle of the jaw. There was a thin and breathy scream, and the stink of burning skin.

"Jamie!" I said, shocked beyond bearing. He did not turn to look at me, but kept his eyes fixed on his prisoner, who, released from the grip on his arms, had sunk to his knees in the drift of dead leaves, hand clutched to his neck.

"This is no concern of yours, Madam," he said between his teeth. Reaching down, he grabbed the boy by the shirt-front and jerked him to his feet. Wavering, the knife blade rose between them, and poised itself just under the lad's left eye. Jamie tilted his head in silent question, to receive a minimal but definite negative shake in return.

The boy's voice was no more than a shaky whisper; he had to clear his throat to make himself heard. "N-no," he said. "No. There is nothing you can do to me that will make me tell you anything."

Jamie held him for a moment longer, eye to eye, then let go of the bunched fabric and stepped back. "No," he said slowly, "I dinna suppose there is. Not to you. But what about the lady?"

I didn't at first realize that he meant me, until he grabbed me by the wrist and yanked me to him, making me stumble slightly on the rough ground. I fell toward him, and he twisted my arm roughly behind my back.

"You may be indifferent to your own welfare, but ye

might perhaps have some concern for the lady's honor, since you were at such pains to rescue her." Turning me toward himself, he twined his fingers in my hair, forced my head back and kissed me with a deliberate brutality that made me squirm involuntarily in protest.

Freeing my hair, he pulled me hard against him, facing the boy on the other side of the fire. The boy's eyes were enormous, aghast with reflections of flame in the wide dark pupils.

"Let her go!" he demanded hoarsely. "What are you proposing to do with her?"

Jamie's hands reached to the neck of my gown. With a sudden jerk, he tore the fabric of gown and shift, baring most of my bosom. Reacting instinctively, I kicked him in the shin. The boy made an inarticulate sound and jerked forward, but was stopped short once more by Ross and Kincaid.

"Since you ask," said Jamie's voice pleasantly behind me, "I am proposing to ravish this lady before your eyes. I shall then give her to my men, to do what they will with her. Perhaps ye would like to have a turn before I kill you? A man should no die a virgin, do ye think?"

I was struggling in good earnest now, my arm held in an iron grip behind my back, my protests muffled by Jamie's large, warm palm clapped over my mouth. I sank my teeth hard into the heel of his hand, tasting blood. He took his hand sharply away with a smothered exclamation, but returned it almost immediately, forcing a wadded piece of cloth past my teeth. I made strangled sounds around the gag as Jamie's hands darted to my shoulders, forcing the torn pieces of my gown farther apart. With a rending of linen and fustian, he bared me to the waist, pinning my arms at my sides. I saw Ross glance at me and quickly away, fixing his gaze with dogged intent on the prisoner, a slow flush staining his cheekbones. Kincaid, himself no more than nineteen, stared in shock, his mouth open as a flytrap.

"Stop it!" The boy's voice was trembling, but with outrage now rather than fear. "You—you unspeakable poltroon! How dare you dishonor a lady, you Scottish jackal!" He stood for a moment, chest heaving with emotion, then made up his mind. He raised his jaw and thrust out his chin.

"Very well. I do not see that in honor I have any choice. Release the lady and I will tell you what you want to know."

One of Jamie's hands left my shoulder momentarily. I didn't see his gesture, but Ross released the boy's injured arm and went quickly to fetch my cloak, which had fallen unheeded to the ground during the excitement of the boy's capture. Jamie pulled both my hands behind me, and, yanking off my belt, used it to bind them securely behind my back. Taking the cloak from Ross, he swirled it around my shoulders and fastened it carefully. Stepping back, he bowed ironically to me, then turned to face his captive.

"You have my word that the lady will be safe from my advances," he said. The note in his voice could have been due to the strain of anger and frustrated lust; I recognized it as the agonized restraint of an overwhelming impulse to laugh, and could cheerfully have killed him.

Face like stone, the boy gave the required information, speaking in brief syllables.

His name was William Grey, second son of Viscount Melton. He accompanied a troop of two hundred men, traveling to Dunbar, intending to join there with General Cope's army. His fellows were presently encamped some three miles to the west. He, William, out walking through the forest, had seen the light of our fire, and come to investigate. No, he had no companion with him. Yes, the troop carried heavy armament, sixteen carriage-mounted "galloper" cannon, and two sixteen-inch mortars. Most of the troop were armed with muskets, and there was one company of thirty horse.

The boy was beginning to wilt under the combined strain of the questioning and his injured arm, but refused an offer to be seated. Instead, he leaned against the tree, cradling his elbow in his left palm.

The questions went on for nearly an hour, covering the same ground over and over, pinpointing discrepancies, enlarging details, searching out the telltale omission, the point evaded. Satisfied at last, Jamie sighed deeply and turned from the boy, who slumped in the wavering shadows of the oak. He held out a hand without speaking; Murtagh, as usual divining his intent, handed him a pistol.

He turned back to the prisoner, busying himself in checking the priming and loading of the pistol. The twelve inches of heart-butted metal gleamed dark, the firelight picking out sparks of silver at trigger and priming pin. "Head or heart?" Jamie asked casually, raising his head at last.

"Eh?" The boy's mouth hung open in blank incomprehension.

"I am going to shoot you," Jamie explained patiently. "Spies are usually hanged, but in consideration of your gallantry, I am willing to give you a quick, clean death. Do ye prefer to take the ball in the head, or the heart?"

The boy straightened quickly, squaring his shoulders. "Oh, ah, yes, of course." He licked his lips and swallowed. "I think . . . in the—in the heart. Thank you," he added, as an obvious afterthought. He raised his chin, compressing lips that still held a suggestion of their soft, childish curve.

Nodding, Jamie cocked the pistol with a click that echoed in the silence under the oak trees.

"Wait!" said the prisoner. Jamie looked at him inquiringly, pistol leveled at the thin chest.

"What assurance have I that the lady will remain unmolested after I am—after I have gone?" the boy demanded, looking belligerently around the circle of men. His single working hand was clenched hard, but shook nonetheless. Ross made a sound which he skillfully converted into a sneeze.

Jamie lowered the pistol, and with an iron control, kept his face carefully composed in an expression of solemn gravity.

"Weel," he said, the Scots accent growing broader under the strain, "ye ha' my own word, of course, though I quite see that ye might have some hesitation in accepting the word of a . . ."—his lip twitched despite himself—"of a Scottish poltroon. Perhaps ye would accept the assurances of the lady herself?" He raised an eyebrow in my direction and Kincaid sprang at once to free me, fumbling awkwardly with the gag.

"Jamie!" I exclaimed furiously, mouth freed at last. "This is unconscionable! How could you do such a thing? You —you—"

"Poltroon," he supplied helpfully. "Or jackal, if ye like that better. What d'ye say, Murtagh," turning to his lieutenant, "am I a poltroon or a jackal?"

Murtagh's seam of a mouth twisted sourly. "I'd say ye're dogsmeat, if you untie yon lass wi'out a dirk in yer hand."

Jamie turned apologetically to his prisoner. "I must apologize to my wife for forcing her to take part in this deception. I assure you that her participation was entirely unwilling." He ruefully examined his bitten hand in the light from the fire.

"Your wife!" The boy stared wildly from me to Jamie.

"I'll assure ye likewise that while the lady on occasion honors my bed with her presence, she has never done so under duress. And won't now," he added pointedly, "but let's no untie her just yet, Kincaid."

"James Fraser," I hissed between clenched teeth. "If you touch that boy, you'll certainly never share my bed again!"

Jamie raised one eyebrow. His canines gleamed briefly in the firelight. "Well, that's a serious threat, to an unprincipled voluptuary such as myself, but I dinna suppose I can consider my own interests in such a situation. War's war, after all." The pistol, which had been allowed to fall, began to rise once more.

"Jamie!" I screamed.

He lowered the pistol again, and turned to me with an expression of exaggerated patience. "Yes?"

I took a deep breath, to keep my voice from shaking with rage. I could only guess what he was up to, and hoped I was doing the right thing. Right or not, when this was over . . . I choked off an intensely pleasing vision of Jamie writhing on the ground with my foot on his Adam's apple, in order to concentrate on my present role.

"You haven't any evidence whatever that he's a spy," I said. "He says he stumbled on you by accident. Who wouldn't be curious if they saw a fire out in the woods?"

Jamie nodded, following the argument. "Aye, and what about attempted murder? Spy or no, he tried to kill me, and admits as much." He tenderly fingered the raw scratch at the side of his throat.

"Well, of course he did," I said hotly. "He says he knew you were an outlaw. There's a bloody price on your head, for heaven's sake!"

Jamie rubbed his chin dubiously, at last turning to the prisoner. "Well, it's a point," he said. "William Grey, your advocate makes a good case for ye. It's no the policy either of

His Highness Prince Charles or myself to execute persons unlawfully, enemy or no." He summoned Kincaid with a wave of the hand.

"Kincaid, you and Ross take this man in the direction he says his camp lies. If the information he gave us proves to be true, tie him to a tree a mile from the camp in the line of march. His friends will find him there tomorrow. If what he told us is *not* true . . . "—he paused, cold eyes bent on the prisoner—"cut his throat."

He looked the boy in the face and said, without a shadow of mockery, "I give you your life. I hope ye'll use it well."

Moving behind me, he cut the belt binding my wrists. As I turned furiously, he motioned toward the boy, who had sat down suddenly on the ground beneath the oak. "Perhaps ye'd be good enough to tend the boy's arm before he goes?" The scowl of pretended ferocity had left his face, leaving it blank as a wall. His eyelids were lowered, preventing me from meeting his gaze.

Without a word, I went to the boy and sank to my knees beside him. He seemed dazed, and didn't protest my examination, or the subsequent manipulations, though the handling must have been painful.

The split bodice of my gown kept sliding off my shoulders, and I muttered beneath my breath as I irritably hitched up one side or the other for the dozenth time. The bones of the boy's forearm were light and angular under the skin, hardly thicker than my own. I splinted the arm and slung it, using my own kerchief. "It's a clean break," I told him, keeping my voice impersonal. "Try to keep it still for two weeks, at least." He nodded, not looking at me.

Jamie had been sitting quietly on a log watching my ministrations. My breath coming unevenly, I walked up to him and slapped him as hard as I could. The blow left a white patch on one cheek and made his eyes water, but he didn't move or change expression.

Kincaid pulled the boy to his feet and propelled him to the edge of the clearing with a hand at his back. At the edge of the shadows he halted and turned back. Avoiding looking at me, he spoke only to Jamie.

"I owe you my life," he said formally. "I should greatly prefer not to, but since you have forced the gift upon me, I must regard it as a debt of honor. I shall hope to discharge that debt in the future, and once it is discharged . . ." The boy's voice shook slightly with suppressed hatred, losing all its assumed formality in the utter sincerity of his feelings. ". . . I'll kill you!"

Jamie rose from the log to his full height. His face was calm, free of any taint of amusement. He inclined his head gravely to his departing prisoner. "In that case, sir, I must hope that we do not meet again."

The boy straightened his shoulders and returned the bow stiffly. "A Grey does not forget an obligation, sir," he said, and vanished into the darkness, Kincaid at his elbow.

There was a discreet interval of breathless waiting, as the leaf-shuffling sounds of feet moved off through the darkness. Then the laughter started, first with a soft, fizzing noise through the nostrils of one man, then a tentative chuckle from another. Never raucous, still it gathered volume, spiraling round the circle of men.

Jamie took one step into the circle, face turned toward his men. The laughter stopped abruptly. Glancing down at me, he said briefly, "Go to the tent."

Warned by my expression, he gripped my wrist before I could raise my hand.

"If you're going to slap me again, at least let me turn the other cheek," he said dryly. "Besides, I think I can save ye the trouble. But I'd advise you to go to the tent, just the same."

Dropping my hand, he strode out to the edge of the fire, and with one peremptory jerk of the head, gathered the scattered men into a reluctant, half-wary clump before him. Their faces were big-eyed, orbits scooped with darkness by the shadows.

I didn't understand everything he said, as he spoke in an odd mixture of Gaelic and English, but I gathered sufficient sense to realize that he was inquiring, in a soft, level tone that seemed to turn his listeners to stone, as to the identity of the sentinels on duty for the evening.

There was a furtive glancing to and fro, and uneasy movement among the men, who seemed to clump more strongly together in the face of danger. But then the closed ranks parted, and two men stepped out, glanced up—once—

then hastily down, and stood shoulder to shoulder, eyes on the ground, outside the protection of their fellows.

It was the McClure brothers, George and Sorley. Close in age, somewhere in their thirties, they stood hang-dog near each other, fingers of the work-toughened hands twitching as though longing to link and clasp together, as some small protection before the coming storm.

There was a brief, wordless pause as Jamie looked over the two delinquent sentinels. Then followed five solid minutes of unpleasantness, all conducted in that same soft, level voice. There wasn't a sound from the grouped men, and the McClures, both burly men, seemed to dwindle and shrink under the weight of it. I wiped my sweating palms on my skirt, glad that I didn't understand it all, and beginning to regret not following Jamie's order to return to the tent.

I regretted it still more in the next moment, when Jamie turned suddenly to Murtagh, who, expecting the command, was ready with a leather strip, some two feet long, knotted at one end to provide a rough grip.

"Strip and stand to me, the both of ye." The McClures moved at once, thick fingers fumbling with shirt fastenings, as though eager to obey, relieved that the preliminaries were over and the reckoning arrived.

I thought perhaps I would be sick, though I gathered that the punishment was light enough, by the standards applied to such things. There was no sound in the clearing, save the slap of the lash and an occasional gasp or groan from the man being flogged.

At the last stroke, Jamie let the thong fall to his side. He was sweating heavily, and the grimed linen of his shirt was pasted to his back. He nodded to the McClures in dismissal, and wiped his wet face on his sleeve as one man bent painfully to retrieve the discarded shirts, his brother, shaky himself, bracing him on the other side.

The men in the clearing seemed to have ceased even breathing, during the punishment. Now there was a tremor through the group, as though a collective breath had been released in a sigh of relief.

Jamie eyed them, shaking his head slightly. The night wind was rising, stirring and lifting the hair on his crown.

"We canna afford carelessness, *mo nighean donn,*" he said

softly. "Not from anyone." He took a deep breath and his
mouth twisted wryly. "And that includes me. It was my un-
shielded fire drew the lad to us." Fresh sweat had sprung out
on his brow, and he wiped a hand roughly across his face,
drying it on his kilt. He nodded toward Murtagh, standing
grimly apart from the other men, and held the leather strap
out toward him.

"If ye'll oblige me, sir?"

After a moment's hesitation, Murtagh's gnarled hand
reached out and took the strap. An expression that might
have been amusement flickered in the little clansman's bright
black eyes.

"Wi' pleasure . . . sir."

Jamie turned his back to his men, and began to unfasten
his shirt. His eye caught me, standing frozen between the tree
trunks, and one eyebrow lifted in ironic question. Did I want
to watch? I shook my head frantically, whirled, and blundered
away through the trees, belatedly taking his advice.

In fact, I didn't return to the tent. I couldn't bear the
thought of its stifling enclosure; my chest felt tight and I
needed air.

I found it on the crest of a small rise, just beyond the
tent. I stumbled to a stop in a small open space, flung myself
full-length on the ground, and put both arms over my head. I
didn't want to hear the faintest echo of the drama's final act,
down behind me by the fire.

The rough grass beneath me was cold on bare skin, and I
hunched to wrap the cloak around me. Cocooned and insulated, I lay quiet, listening to the pounding of my heart, waiting for the turmoil inside me to calm.

Sometime later, I heard men passing by in small groups
of four or five, returning to their sleeping spots. Muffled by
folds of cloth, I couldn't distinguish their words, but they
sounded subdued, perhaps a little awed. Some time passed
before I realized that he was there. He didn't speak or make a
noise, but I suddenly knew that he was nearby. When I rolled
over and sat up, I could see his bulk shadowed on a stone,
head resting on forearms, folded across his knees.

Torn between the impulse to stroke his head, and the urge to cave it in with a rock, I did neither.

"Are you all right?" I asked, after a moment's pause, voice neutral as I could make it.

"Aye, I'll do." He unfolded himself slowly, and stretched, moving gingerly, with a deep sigh.

"I'm sorry for your gown," he said, a minute later. I realized that he could see my bare flesh shining dim-white in the darkness, and pulled the edges of my cloak sharply together.

"Oh, for the *gown*?" I said, more than a slight edge to my voice.

He sighed again. "Aye, and for the rest of it, too." He paused, then said, "I thought perhaps ye might be willing to sacrifice your modesty to prevent my havin' to damage the lad, but under the circumstances, I hadna time to ask your permission. If I was wrong, then I'll ask your pardon, lady."

"You mean you would have tortured him further?"

He was irritated, and didn't trouble to hide it. "Torture, forbye! I didna hurt the lad."

I drew the folds of my cloak more tightly around me. "Oh, you don't consider breaking his arm and branding him with a hot knife as hurting him, then?"

"No, I don't." He scooted across the few feet of grass between us, and grasped me by the elbow, pulling me around to face him. "Listen to me. He broke his own silly arm, trying to force his way out of an unbreakable lock. He's brave as any man I've got, but he's no experience at hand-to-hand fighting."

"And the knife?"

Jamie snorted. "Tcha! He's a small sore spot under one ear, that won't pain him much past dinner tomorrow. I expect it hurt a bit, but I meant to scare him, not wound him."

"Oh." I pulled away and turned back to the dark wood, looking for our tent. His voice followed me.

"I could have broken him, Sassenach. It would have been messy, though, and likely permanent. I'd rather not use such means if I dinna have to. Mind ye, Sassenach"—his voice reached me from the shadows, holding a note of warning— "sometime I may have to. I had to know where his fellows were, their arms and the rest of it. I couldna scare him into it; it was trick him or break him."

"He said you couldn't do anything that would make him talk."

Jamie's voice was weary. "Christ, Sassenach, of course I could. Ye can break anyone if you're prepared to hurt them enough. I know that, if anyone does."

"Yes," I said quietly, "I suppose you do."

Neither of us moved for a time, nor spoke. I could hear the murmurs of men bedding down for the night, the occasional stamp of boots on hard earth and the rustle of leaves heaped up as a barrier against the autumn chill. My eyes had adjusted sufficiently to the dark that I could now see the outline of our tent, some thirty feet away in the shelter of a big larch. I could see Jamie, too, his figure black against the lighter darkness of the night.

"All right," I said at last. "All right. Given the choice between what you did, and what you might have done . . . yes, all right."

"Thank you." I couldn't tell whether he was smiling or not, but it sounded like it.

"You were taking the hell of a chance with the rest of it," I said. "If I hadn't given you an excuse for not killing him, what would you have done?"

The large figure stirred and shrugged, and there was a faint chuckle in the shadows.

"I don't know, Sassenach. I reckoned as how you'd think of something. If ye hadn't—well, I suppose I would have had to shoot the lad. Couldna very well disappoint him by just lettin' him go, could I?"

"You bloody Scottish bastard," I said without heat.

He heaved a deep exasperated sigh. "Sassenach, I've been stabbed, bitten, slapped, and whipped since supper—which I didna get to finish. I dinna like to scare children and I dinna like to flog men, and I've had to do both. I've two hundred English camped three miles away, and no idea what to do about them. I'm tired, I'm hungry, and I'm sore. If you've anything like womanly sympathy about ye, I could use a bit!"

He sounded so aggrieved that I laughed in spite of myself. I got up and walked toward him.

"I suppose you could, at that. Come here, and I'll see if I can find a bit for you." He had put his shirt back on loose over his shoulders, not troubling to do it up. I slid my hands under it and over the hot, tender skin of his back. "Didn't cut the skin," I said, feeling gently upward.

"A thong doesn't; it just stings."

I removed the shirt and sat him down to have his back sponged with cold water from the stream.

"Better?" I asked.

"Mmmm." The muscles of his shoulders relaxed, but he flinched slightly as I touched a particularly tender spot.

I turned my attention to the scratch under his ear. "You wouldn't really have shot him, would you?"

"What d'ye take me for, Sassenach?" he said, in mock outrage.

"A Scottish poltroon. Or at best, a conscienceless outlaw. Who knows what a fellow like that would do? Let alone an unprincipled voluptuary."

He laughed with me, and his shoulder shook under my hand. "Turn your head. If you want womanly sympathy, you'll have to keep still while I apply it."

"Mmm." There was a moment of silence. "No," he said at last, "I wouldna have shot him. But I had to save his pride somehow, after making him feel ridiculous over you. He's a brave lad; he deserved to feel he was worth killing."

I shook my head. "I will never understand men," I muttered, smoothing marigold ointment over the scratch.

He reached back for my hands and brought them together under his chin.

"You dinna need to understand me, Sassenach," he said quietly. "So long as ye love me." His head tilted forward and he gently kissed my clasped hands.

"And feed me," he added, releasing them.

"Oh, womanly sympathy, love *and* food?" I said, laughing. "Don't want a lot, do you?"

There were cold bannocks in the saddlebags, cheese, and a bit of cold bacon as well. The tensions and absurdities of the last two hours had been more draining than I realized, and I hungrily joined in the meal.

The sounds of the men surrounding us had now died down, and there was neither sound nor any flicker of an unguarded fire to indicate that we were not a thousand miles from any human soul. Only the wind rattled busily among the leaves, sending the odd twig bouncing down through the branches.

Jamie leaned back against a tree, face dim in the starlight, but body instinct with mischief.

"I gave your champion my word that I'd no molest ye wi' my loathsome advances. I suppose that means unless ye invite me to share your bed, I shall have to go and sleep wi' Murtagh or Kincaid. And Murtagh snores."

"So do you," I said.

I looked at him for a moment, then shrugged, letting half my ruined gown slide off my shoulder. "Well, you've made a good start at ravishing me." I dropped the other shoulder, and the torn cloth fell free to my waist. "You may as well come and finish the job properly."

The warmth of his arms was like heated silk, sliding over my cold skin.

"Aye, well," he murmured into my hair, "war's war, no?"

———➤

"I'm very bad at dates," I said to the star-thick sky sometime later. "Has Miguel de Cervantes been born yet?"

Jamie was lying—perforce—on his stomach next to me, head and shoulders protruding from the tent's shelter. One eye slowly opened, and swiveled toward the eastern horizon. Finding no trace of dawn, it traveled slowly back and rested on my face, with an expression of jaundiced resignation.

"You've a sudden urge to discuss Spanish novels?" he said, a little hoarsely.

"Not particularly," I said. "I just wondered whether perhaps you were familiar with the term 'quixotic.' "

He heaved himself onto his elbows, scrubbed at his scalp with both hands to wake himself fully, then turned toward me, blinking but alert.

"Cervantes was born almost two hundred years ago, Sassenach, and, me having had the benefit of a thorough education, aye, I'm familiar with the gentleman. Ye wouldna be implying anything personal by that last remark, would ye?"

"Does your back hurt?"

He hunched his shoulders experimentally. "Not much. A wee bit bruised, I expect."

"Jamie, *why,* for God's sake?" I burst out.

He rested his chin on his folded forearms, the sidelong turn of his head emphasizing the slant of his eyes. The one I could see narrowed still further with his smile.

"Well, Murtagh enjoyed it. He's owed me a hiding since I was nine and put pieces of honeycomb in his boots while he had them off to cool his feet. He couldna catch me at the time, but I learned a good many interesting new words whilst he was chasing me barefoot. He—"

I put a stop to this by punching him as hard as I could on the point of the shoulder. Surprised, he let the arm collapse under him with a sharp "Oof!" and rolled onto his side, back toward me.

I brought my knees up behind him and wrapped an arm around his waist. His back, wide and smoothly muscled, still gleaming faintly with the moisture of exertion, blotted out the stars. I kissed him between the shoulder blades, then drew back and blew gently, for the pleasure of feeling his skin shiver under my fingertips and the tiny fine hairs stand up in goose bumps down the furrow of his spine.

"Why?" I said again. I rested my face against his warm, damp back. Shadowed by the darkness, the scars were invisible, but I could feel them, faint tough lines hard under my cheek.

He was quiet for a moment, his ribs rising and falling under my arm with each deep, slow breath.

"Aye, well," he said, then fell silent again, thinking.

"I dinna ken exactly, Sassenach," he said finally. "Could be I thought I owed it to you. Or maybe to myself."

I laid a light palm across the width of one shoulder blade, broad and flat, the edges of the bone clear-drawn beneath the skin.

"Not to me."

"Aye? Is it the act of a gentleman to unclothe his wife in the presence of thirty men?" His tone was suddenly bitter, and my hands stilled, pressing against him. "Is it the act of a gallant man to use violence against a captive enemy, and a child to boot? To consider doing worse?"

"Would it have been better to spare me—or him—and

lose half your men in two days' time? You had to know. You couldn't—you *can't* afford to let notions of gentlemanly conduct sway you."

"No," he said softly, "I can't. And so I must ride wi' a man—with the son of my King—whom duty and honor call me to follow—and seek meanwhiles to pervert his cause that I am sworn to uphold. I am forsworn for the lives of those I love—I betray the name of honor that those I honor may survive."

"Honor has killed one bloody hell of a lot of men," I said to the dark groove of his bruised back. "Honor without sense is . . . foolishness. A gallant foolishness, but foolishness nonetheless."

"Aye, it is. And it will change—you've told me. But if I shall be among the first who sacrifice honor for expedience . . . shall I feel nay shame in the doing of it?" He rolled suddenly to face me, eyes troubled in the starlight.

"I wilna turn back—I canna, now—but Sassenach, sometimes I do sorrow for that bit of myself I have left behind."

"It's my fault," I said softly. I touched his face, the thick brows, wide mouth, and the sprouting stubble along the clean, long jaw. "Mine. If I hadn't come . . . and told you what would happen . . ." I felt a true sorrow for his corruption, and shared a sense of loss for the naive, gallant lad he had been. And yet . . . what choice had either of us truly had, being who we were? I had had to tell him, and he had had to act on it. An Old Testament line drifted through my mind: "When I kept silence, my bones waxed old through my roaring all the day long."

As though he had picked up this biblical strain of thought, he smiled faintly.

"Aye, well," he said. "I dinna recall Adam's asking God to take back Eve—and look what she did to *him.*" He leaned forward and kissed my forehead as I laughed, then drew the blanket up over my bare shoulders. "Go to sleep, my wee rib. I shall be needin' a helpmeet in the morning."

An odd metallic noise woke me. I poked my head out of the blanket and blinked in the direction of the noise, to find my nose a foot from Jamie's plaid-covered knee.

"Awake, are ye?" Something silvery and chinking suddenly descended in front of my face, and a heavy weight settled around my neck.

"What on earth is this?" I asked, sitting up in astonishment and peering downward. I seemed to be wearing a necklace composed of a large number of three-inch metal objects, each with a divided shank and a hooped top, strung together on a leather bootlace. Some of the objects were rusted at the tops, others brand-new. All showed scratches along the length of the shanks, as though they had been wrenched by force out of some larger object.

"Trophies of war, Sassenach," said Jamie.

I looked up at him, and uttered a small shriek at the sight.

"Oh," he said, putting a hand to his face. "I forgot. I hadna time to wash it off."

"You scared me to death," I said, hand pressed to my palpitating heart. "What *is* it?"

"Charcoal," he said, voice muffled in the cloth he was rubbing over his face. He let it down and grinned at me. The rubbing had removed some of the blackening from nose, chin and forehead, which glowed pinkish-bronze through the remaining smears, but his eyes were still ringed black as a raccoon's, and charcoal lines bracketed his mouth. It was barely dawn, and in the dim light of the tent, his darkened face and hair tended to fade into the drab background of the canvas wall behind him, giving the distinctly unsettling impression that I was speaking to a headless body.

"It was your idea," he said.

"*My* idea? You look like the end man in a minstrel show," I replied. "What the hell have you been doing?"

His teeth gleamed a brilliant white amid the sooty creases of his face.

"Commando raid," he said, with immense satisfaction. "Commando? Is that the right word?"

"Oh, God," I said. "You've been in the English camp? Christ! Not alone, I hope?"

"I couldna leave my men out of the fun, could I? I left three of them to guard you, and the rest of us had a verra profitable night." He gestured at my necklace with pride.

"Cotter pins from the cannon carriages. We couldna take

the cannon, or damage them without noise, but they'll no be goin' far, wi' no wheels to them. And the hell of a lot of good sixteen gallopers will do General Cope, stranded out on the moor."

I examined my necklace critically.

"That's well and good, but can't they contrive new cotter pins? It looks like you could make something like this from heavy wire."

He nodded, his air of smugness abating not a whit.

"Oh, aye. They could. But nay bit o' good it will do them, wi' no new wheels to put them to." He lifted the tent flap, and gestured down toward the foot of the hill, where I could now see Murtagh, black as a wizened demon, supervising the activities of several similarly decorated subdemons, who were gaily feeding the last of thirty-two large wooden wheels into a roaring fire. The iron rims of the wheels lay in a stack to one side; Fergus, Kincaid, and one of the other young men had improvised a game with one of them, rolling it to and fro with sticks. Ross sat on a log nearby, sipping at a horn cup and idly twirling another round his burly forearm.

I laughed at the sight.

"Jamie, you *are* clever!"

"I may be clever," he replied, "but *you're* half-naked, and we're leaving now. Have ye something to put on? We left the sentinels tied up in an abandoned sheep-pen, but the rest of them will be up by now, and none so far behind us. We'd best be off."

As though to emphasize his words, the tent suddenly shook above me, as someone jerked free the lines on one side. I uttered an alarmed squeak and dived for the saddle-bags as Jamie left to superintend the details of departure.

It was midafternoon before we reached the village of Tranent. Perched on the hills above the seaside, the usually tranquil hamlet was reeling under the impact of the Highland army. The main bulk of the army was visible on the hills beyond, overlooking the small plain that stretched toward the shore. But with the usual disorganized comings and goings, there were as many men in Tranent as out of it, with detachments coming and going in more or less military formation, messengers galloping to and fro—some on ponies, some by shanks' mare—and the wives, children, and camp followers, who overflowed the cottages and sat outside, leaning on stone walls and nursing babies in the intermittent sun, calling to passing messengers for word of the most recent action.

We halted at the edge of this seethe of activity, and Jamie sent Murtagh to discover the whereabouts of Lord George Murray, the army's commander in chief, while he made a hasty toilet in one of the cottages.

My own appearance left a good bit to be desired; while not deliberately covered with charcoal, my face undoubtedly sported a few streaks of grime left as tokens of several nights spent sleeping out-of-doors. The goodwife kindly lent me a towel and a comb, and I was seated at her table, doing battle with my ungovernable locks, when the door opened and Lord George himself burst in without ceremony.

His usually impeccable dress was disheveled, with several buttons of his waistcoat undone, his stock slipped loose, and one garter come untied. His wig had been thrust unceremoniously into his pocket, and his own thinning brown curls stood on end, as though he had been tugging at them in frustration.

"Thank God!" he said. "A sane face, at last!" Then he leaned forward, squinting as he peered at Jamie. Most of the charcoal dust had been rinsed from the blazing hair, but gray rivulets ran down his face and dripped on his shirtfront, and his ears, which had been overlooked in the hastiness of his ablutions, were still coal-black.

"What—" began a startled Lord George, but he broke off, shook his head rapidly once or twice as though to dismiss some figment of his imagination, and resumed his conversation as though he had noticed nothing out of the ordinary.

"How does it go, sir?" said Jamie respectfully, also affecting not to notice the ribboned tail of the periwig which hung out of Lord George's pocket, wagging like the tail of a small dog as His Lordship gestured violently.

"How does it go?" he echoed. "Why, I'll tell you, sir! It goes to the east, and then it goes to the west, and then half of it comes downhill to have luncheon, while the other half marches off to devil-knows-where! *That's* how it goes!"

" '*It*,' " he said, momentarily relieved by his outburst, "being His Highness's loyal Highland army." Somewhat calmer, he began to tell us of the events transpiring since the army's first arrival in Tranent the day before.

Arriving with the army, Lord George had left the bulk of the men in the village and rushed with a small detachment to take possession of the ridge above the plain. Prince Charles, coming along somewhat later, had been displeased with this action and said so—loudly and publicly. His Highness had then taken half the army and marched off westward, the Duke of Perth—nominally the other commander in chief— tamely in tow, presumably to assess the possibilities of attacking through Preston.

With the army divided, and His Lordship occupied in conferring with villagemen who knew the hell of a lot more about the surrounding terrain than did either His Highness *or* His Lordship, O'Sullivan, one of the Prince's Irish confidants, had taken it upon himself to order a contingent of Lochiel's Cameron clansmen to the Tranent churchyard.

"Cope, of course, brought up a pair of galloper guns and bombarded them," Lord George said grimly. "And I've had the devil of a time with Lochiel this afternoon. He was rather understandably upset at having a number of his men wounded for no evident purpose. He asked that they be withdrawn, which request I naturally acceded to. Whereupon here comes His Highness's frog-spawn, O'Sullivan—pest! Simply because he landed at Eriskay with His Highness, the man thinks he—well, anyway, he comes whining that the presence of the Camerons in the churchyard is essential—*essential*, mind you!—if we are to attack from the west. Told him in no uncertain terms that we attack from the east, if at all. Which prospect is exceedingly doubtful at the moment, insofar as we do not presently know exactly where half of our men are— nor His Highness, come to that," he added, in a tone that made it clear that he considered the whereabouts of Prince Charles a matter of academic interest only.

"And the chiefs! Lochiel's Camerons drew the lot that gives them the honor of fighting on the right hand in the battle—if there is one—but the MacDonalds, having agreed to the arrangement, now energetically deny having done any such thing, and insist that they will not fight at all if they're denied their traditional privilege of fighting on the right."

Having started this recitation calmly enough, Lord

George had grown heated again in the telling, and at this point sprang to his feet again, rubbing his scalp energetically with both hands.

"The Camerons have been drilled all day. By now, they've been marched to and fro so much that they can't tell their pricks from their arseholes—saving your presence, mum," he added, with a distracted glance at me, "and Clanranald's men have been having fistfights with Glengarry's." He paused, lower jaw thrust out, face red. "If Glengarry wasn't who he is, I'd . . . ah, well." He dismissed Glengarry with a flip of the hand and resumed his pacing.

"The only saving grace of the matter," he said, "is that the English have been forced to turn themselves about as well, in response to our movements. They've turned Cope's entire force no less than four times, and now he's strung his right flank out nearly to the sea, no doubt wondering what in God's name we'll do next." He bent and peered out the window, as though expecting to see General Cope himself advancing down the main road to inquire.

"Er . . . where exactly *is* your half of the army at present, sir?" Jamie made a move as though to join His Lordship in his random peregrinations about the cottage, but was restrained by my grip on his collar. Armed with a towel and a bowl of warm water, I had occupied myself during His Lordship's exegesis with removing the soot from my husband's ears. They stood out now, glowing pinkly with earnestness.

"On the ridge just south of town."

"We still hold the high ground, then?"

"Yes, it sounds good, doesn't it?" His Lordship smiled bleakly. "However, occupation of the high ground profits us relatively little, in consideration of the fact that the ground just below the ridge is riddled with pools and boggy marsh. God's eyes! There's a six-foot ditch filled with water that runs a hundred feet along the base of that ridge! There's scarce five hundred yards between the armies this moment, and it might as well be five hundred miles, for all we can do." Lord George plunged a hand into his pocket in search of a handkerchief, brought it out, and stood staring blankly at the wig with which he had been about to wipe his face.

I delicately offered him the sooty handkerchief. He

closed his eyes, inhaled strongly through both nostrils, then opened them and bowed to me with his usual courtly manner.

"Your servant, mum." He polished his face thoroughly with the filthy rag, handed it politely back to me, and clapped the tousled wig on his head.

"Damn my liver," he said distinctly, "if I let that fool lose this engagement for us." He turned to Jamie with decision.

"How many men have you, Fraser?"

"Thirty, sir."

"Horses?"

"Six, sir. And four ponies for pack animals."

"Pack animals? Ah. Carrying provisions for your men?"

"Yes, sir. And sixty sacks of meal abstracted from an English detachment last night. Oh, and one sixteen-inch mortar, sir."

Jamie imparted this last bit of information with an air of such perfect offhand casualness that I wanted to cram the handkerchief down his throat. Lord George stared at him for a moment, then one corner of his mouth twitched upward in a smile.

"Ah? Well, come with me, Fraser. You can tell me all about it on the way." He wheeled toward the door, and Jamie, with a wide-eyed glance at me, caught up his hat and followed.

At the cottage door, Lord George stopped suddenly, and turned back. He glanced up at Jamie's towering form, shirt collar undone and coat flung hastily over one arm.

"I may be in a hurry, Fraser, but we have still sufficient time to observe the civilities. Go and kiss your wife goodbye, man. Meet me outside."

Turning on his heel, he made a leg to me, bowing deeply, so that the tail of his wig flopped forward.

"Your servant, mum."

I knew enough about armies to realize that nothing apparent was likely to happen for some time, and sure enough, it didn't. Random parties of men marched up and down the single main street of Tranent. Wives, camp followers, and the displaced citizens of Tranent milled aimlessly, uncertain whether to stay or go. Messengers darted sideways through the crowd, carrying notes.

I had met Lord George before, in Paris. He was not a man to stand on ceremony when action would better suit, though I thought it likely that the fraying of his temper at Prince Charles's actions, and a desire to escape the company of O'Sullivan, were more responsible for his coming in person to meet Jamie than any desire either for expeditiousness or confidentiality. When the total strength of the Highland army stood somewhere between fifteen hundred and two thousand, thirty men were neither to be regarded as a gift from the gods, nor sneered at altogether.

I glanced at Fergus, fidgeting to and fro like a hoptoad with St. Vitus's dance, and decided that I might as well send a few messages myself. There is a saying, "In the kingdom of the blind, the one-eyed man is king." I promptly invented its analogy, based on experience: "When no one knows what to do, anyone with a sensible suggestion is going to be listened to."

There was paper and ink in the saddlebags. I sat down, watched with an almost superstitious awe by the goodwife, who had likely never seen a woman write anything before, and composed a note to Jenny Cameron. It was she who had led three hundred Cameron clansmen across the mountains to join Prince Charles, when he had raised his banner at Glenfinnan on the coast. Her brother Hugh, arriving home belatedly and hearing what had happened, had ridden post-haste to Glenfinnan to take the chieftain's place at the head of his men, but Jenny had declined to go home and miss the fun. She had thoroughly enjoyed the brief stop in Edinburgh, where Charles received the plaudits of his loyal subjects, but she had been equally willing to accompany her Prince on his way to battle.

I hadn't a signet, but Jamie's bonnet was in one of the bags, bearing a badge with the Fraser clan crest and motto. I dug it out and pressed it into the splodge of warm candle wax with which I had sealed the note. It looked very official.

"For the Scottish milady with the freckles," I instructed Fergus, and with satisfaction saw him dart out the door and into the melee in the street. I had no idea where Jenny Cameron was at the moment, but the officers were quartered in

Diana Gabaldon

the manse near the kirk, and that was as good a place to start
as any. At least the search would keep Fergus out of mischief.

That errand out of the way, I turned to the cottage wife.
"Now, then," I said. "What have you got in the way of
blankets, napkins, and petticoats?"

I soon found that I had been correct in my surmise as to
the force of Jenny Cameron's personality. A woman who
could raise three hundred men and lead them across the
mountains to fight for an Italian-accented fop with a taste for
brandywine was bound to have both a low threshold of boredom and a rare talent for bullying people into doing what she
wanted.

"Verra sensible," she said, having heard my plan.
"Cousin Archie's made some arrangements, I expect, but of
course he's wanting to be with the army just now." Her firm
chin stuck out a little farther. "That's where the fun is, after
all," she said wryly.

"I'm surprised you didn't insist on going along," I said.

She laughed, her small, homely face with its undershot
jaw making her look like a good-humored bulldog.

"I would if I could, but I can't," she admitted frankly.
"Now that Hugh's come, he keeps trying to make me go
home. Told him I was"—she glanced around to be sure we
weren't overheard, and lowered her voice conspiratorially—
"*damned* if I'd go home and sit. Not while I can be of use
here."

Standing on the cottage doorstep, she looked thoughtfully up and down the street.

"I didn't think they'd listen to me," I said. "Being English."

"Aye, you're right," she said, "but they will to me. I don't
know how many the wounded will be—pray God not many,"
and she crossed herself unobtrusively. "But we'd best start
with the houses near the manse; it'll be less trouble to carry
water from the well." With decision, she stepped off the doorstep and headed down the street, me following close behind.

We were aided not only by the persuasion of Miss Cameron's position and person but by the fact that sitting and
waiting is one of the most miserable occupations known to

man—not that it usually is known to men; women do it much more often. By the time the sun sank behind Tranent kirk, we had the bare rudiments of a hospital brigade organized.

The leaves were beginning to fall from larch and alder in the nearby wood, lying loose, flat and yellow on the sandy ground. Here and there a leaf had crisped and curled to brown, and took off scudding in the wind like a small boat over rough seas.

One of these spiraled past me, settling gently as its wind current failed. I caught it on my palm and held it for a moment, admiring the perfection of midribs and veins, a lacy skeleton that would remain past the rotting of the blade. There was a sudden puff of wind, and the cup-curled leaf lifted off my hand, to tumble to the ground and go rolling along, down the empty street.

Shading my eyes against the setting sun, I could see the ridge beyond the town where the Highland army was camped. His Highness's half of the army had returned an hour before, sweeping the last stragglers from the village as they marched to join Lord George. At this distance, I could only pick out an occasional tiny figure, black against the graying sky, as here and there a man came over the crest of the ridge. A quarter-mile past the end of the street, I could see the first lighting of the English fires, burning pale in the dying light. The thick smell of burning peat from the cottages joined the sharper scent of the English wood fires, overlying the tang of the nearby sea.

Such preparations as could be made were under way. The wives and families of the Highland soldiers had been welcomed with generous hospitality, and were now mostly housed in the cottages along the main street, sharing their hosts' plain supper of brose and salt herring. My own supper was waiting inside, though I had little appetite.

A small form appeared at my elbow, quiet as the lengthening shadows.

"Will you come and eat, Madame? The goodwife is keeping food for you."

"Oh? Oh, yes, Fergus. Yes, I'll come." I cast a last glance toward the ridge, then turned back to the cottages.

"Are you coming, Fergus?" I asked, seeing him still standing in the street. He was shading his eyes, trying to see the activities on the ridge beyond the town. Firmly ordered by Jamie to stay with me, he was plainly longing to be with the fighting men, preparing for battle on the morrow.

"Uh? Oh, yes, Madame." He turned with a sigh, resigned for the moment to a life of boring peace.

The long days of summer were yielding quickly to darkness, and the lamps were lit well before we had finished our preparations. The night outside was restless with constant movement and the glow of fires on the horizon. Fergus, unable to keep still, flitted in and out of the cottages, carrying messages, collecting rumors and bobbing up out of the shadows periodically like a small, dark ghost, eyes gleaming with excitement.

"Madame," he said, plucking at my sleeve as I ripped linens into strips and threw them into a pile for sterilization. "Madame!"

"What is it this time, Fergus?" I was mildly irritated at the intrusion; I had been in the middle of a lecture to a group of housewives on the importance of washing the hands frequently while treating the wounded.

"A man, Madame. He is wanting to speak with the commander of His Highness's army. He has important information, he says."

"Well, I'm not stopping him, am I?" I tugged at a recalcitrant shirt seam, then used my teeth to wrench loose the end, and yanked. It tore cleanly, with a satisfying ripping sound.

I spit out a thread or two. He was still there, waiting patiently.

"All right," I said, resigned. "What do you—or he— think I can do about it?"

"If you will give me permission, Madame," he said eagerly, "I could guide him to my master. *He* could arrange for the man to speak to the commander."

"He," of course, could do anything, so far as Fergus was concerned; including, no doubt, walking on water, turning water into wine, and inducing Lord George to talk to mysteri-

ous strangers who materialized out of the darkness with important information.

I brushed the hair out of my eyes; I had tied it back under a kertch, but curly strands kept escaping.

"Is this man somewhere nearby?"

That was all the encouragement he needed; he disappeared through the open door, returning momentarily with a thin young man whose eager gaze fastened at once on my face.

"Mrs. Fraser?" He bowed awkwardly at my nod, wiping his hands on his breeches as though he didn't know quite what to do with them, but wanted to be ready if something suggested itself.

"I—I'm Robert Anderson, of Whitburgh."

"Oh? Well, good for you," I said politely. "My servant says you have some valuable information for Lord George Murray."

He nodded, bobbing his head like a water ouzel. "Ye see, Mrs. Fraser, I've lived in these parts all my life. I—I know all of that ground where the armies are, know it like the back o' my hand. And there's a way down from the ridge where the Highland troops are camped—a trail that will lead them past the ditch at the bottom."

"I see." I felt a hollowing of the stomach at these words. If the Highlanders were to charge out of the rising sun next morning, they would have to leave the high ground of the ridge during the night watches. And if a charge was to be successful, plainly that ditch must be crossed or bypassed.

While I *thought* I knew what was to come, I had no certainty at all about it. I had been married to an historian—and the usual faint stab came at the thought of Frank—and knew just how unreliable historical sources often were. For that matter, I had no surety that my own presence couldn't or wouldn't change anything.

For the space of a moment, I wondered wildly what might happen if I tried to keep Robert Anderson from speaking to Lord George. Would the outcome of tomorrow's battle be changed? Would the Highland army—including Jamie and his men—be slaughtered as they ran downhill over boggy ground and into a ditch? Would Lord George come up with another plan that would work? Or would Robert An-

derson merely go off on his own and find a way of speaking to
Lord George himself, regardless of what I did?

It wasn't a risk I cared to take for experiment's sake. I
looked down at Fergus, fidgeting with impatience to be gone.

"Do you think you can find your master? It's black as the
inside of a coal hole up on that ridge. I wouldn't like either of
you to be shot by mistake, traipsing around up there."

"I can find him, Madame," Fergus said confidently. He
probably could, I thought. He seemed to have a sort of radar
where Jamie was concerned.

"All right, then," I conceded. "But for God's sake, be
careful."

"*Oui*, Madame!" In a flash, he was at the door, vibrating
with eagerness to be gone.

It was half an hour after they had left that I noticed the
knife I had left on the table was gone as well. And only then
did I remember, with a sickening lurch of my stomach, that
while I had told Fergus to be careful, I had forgotten altogether to tell him to come back.

The sound of the first cannon came in the lightening
predawn, a dull, booming noise that seemed to echo through
the plank boards on which I slept. My buttocks tightened, the
involuntary flattening of a tail I didn't possess, and my fingers
clasped those of the woman lying under the blanket next to
me. The knowledge that something is going to happen should
be some defense, but somehow it never is.

There was a faint moan from one corner of the cottage,
and the woman next to me muttered, "Mary, Michael, and
Bride preserve us," under her breath. There was a stirring
over the floor as the women began to rise. There was little
talk, as though all ears were pricked to catch the sounds of
battle from the plain below.

I caught sight of one of the Highlanders' wives, a Mrs.
MacPherson, as she folded her blanket next to the graying
window. Her face was blank with fear, and she closed her eyes
with a small shudder as another muffled boom came from
below.

I revised my opinion as to the uselessness of knowledge.
These women had no knowledge of secret trails, sunrise

charges, and surprise routs. All these women knew was that
their husbands and sons were now facing the cannon and
musket fire of an English army four times their number.

Prediction is a risky business at the best of times, and I
knew they would pay me no mind. The best thing I could do
for them was to keep them busy. A fleeting image crossed my
mind, of the rising sun shining bright off blazing hair, making
a perfect target of its owner. A second image followed hard
on its heels; a squirrel-toothed boy, armed with a stolen
butcher knife and a bright-eyed belief in the glories of war. I
closed my own eyes and swallowed hard. Keeping busy was
the best thing I could do for myself.

"Ladies!" I said. "We've done a lot, but there's a lot
more to do. We shall be needing boiling water. Cauldrons for
boiling, cream pans for soaking. Parritch for those who can
eat; milk for those who can't. Tallow and garlic for dressings.
Wood laths for splints. Bottles and jugs, cups and spoons.
Sewing needles and stout thread. Mrs. MacPherson, if you
would be so kind . . ."

I knew little of the battle, except which side was supposed to win, and that the casualties of the Jacobite army
were to be "light." From the far-off, blurry page of the textbook, I again retrieved that tiny bit of information: ". . .
while the Jacobites triumphed, with only thirty casualties."

Casualties. Fatalities, I corrected. Any injury is a casu-
alty, in nursing terms, and there were a good many more than
thirty in my cottage as the sun burned its way upward through
the sea mist toward noon. Slowly, the victors of the battle
were making their way in triumph back toward Tranent, the
sound-of-body helping their wounded comrades.

Oddly enough, His Highness had ordered that the English wounded be retrieved first from the field of battle and
carefully tended. "They are my Father's subjects," he said
firmly, making the capital "F" thoroughly audible, "and I will
have them well cared for." The fact that the Highlanders who
had just won the battle for him were also presumably his
Father's subjects seemed to have escaped his notice for the
moment.

"Given the behavior of the Father and the Son," I muttered to Jenny Cameron on hearing this, "the Highland army had better hope that the Holy Ghost doesn't choose to descend today."

A look of shock at this blasphemous observation crossed the face of Mrs. MacPherson, but Jenny laughed.

The whoops and shrieks of Gaelic celebration overwhelmed the faint groans of the wounded, borne in on makeshift stretchers made of planks or bound-together muskets, or more often, leaning on the arms of friends for support. Some of the casualties staggered in under their own power, beaming and drunk on their own exuberance, the pain of their wounds seeming a minor inconvenience in the face of glorious vindication of their faith. Despite the injuries that brought them here to be tended, the intoxicating knowledge of victory filled the house with a mood of hilarious exhilaration.

"Christ, did ye see 'em scutter like wee mousies wi' a cat on their tails?" said one patient to another, seemingly oblivious of the nasty powder burn that had singed his left arm from knuckles to shoulder.

"And a rare good many of 'em missin' their tails," answered his friend, with a chortle.

Joy was not quite universal; here and there, small parties of subdued Highlanders could be seen making their way across the hills, carrying the still form of a friend, plaid's end covering a face gone blank and empty with heaven's seeing.

It was the first test of my chosen assistants, and they rose to the challenge as well as had the warriors of the field. That is, they balked and complained and made nuisances of themselves, and then, when necessity struck, threw themselves into battle with unparalleled fierceness.

Not that they stopped complaining while they did it.

Mrs. McMurdo returned with yet another full bottle, which she hung in the assigned place on the cottage wall, before stooping to rummage in the tub that held the bottles of honey water. The elderly wife of a Tranent fisherman pressed into army service, she was the waterer on this shift; in charge of going from man to man, urging each to sip as much of the sweetened fluid as could be tolerated—and then making a second round to deal with the results, equipped with two or three empty bottles.

"If ye didna gie them so much to drink, they'd no piss sae much," she complained—not for the first time.

"They need the water," I explained patiently—not for the first time. "It keeps their blood pressure up, and replaces some of the fluids they've lost, and helps avoid shock—well, look, woman, do you see many of them dying?" I demanded, suddenly losing a good deal of my patience in the face of Mrs. McMurdo's continuing dubiousness and complaints; her nearly toothless mouth lent a note of mournfulness to an already dour expression—all is lost, it seemed to say; why trouble further?

"Mphm," she said. Since she took the water and returned to her rounds without further remonstrance, I took this sound for at least temporary assent.

I stepped outside to escape both Mrs. McMurdo and the atmosphere in the cottage. It was thick with smoke, heat, and the fug of unwashed bodies, and I felt a bit dizzy.

The streets were filled with men, drunk, celebrating, laden with plunder from the battlefield. One group of men in the reddish tartan of the MacGillivrays pulled an English cannon, tethered with ropes like a dangerous wild beast. The resemblance was enhanced by the fanciful carvings of crouching wolves that decorated the touch-hole and muzzle. One of General Cope's showpieces, I supposed.

Then I recognized the small black figure riding astride the cannon's muzzle, hair sticking up like a bottle brush. I closed my eyes in momentary thankfulness, then opened them and hastened down the street to drag him off the cannon.

"Wretch!" I said, giving him a shake and then a hug. "What do you mean sneaking off like that? If I weren't so busy, I'd box your ears 'til your head rattled!"

"Madame," he said, blinking stupidly in the afternoon sun. "Madame."

I realized he hadn't heard a word I'd said. "Are you all right?" I asked, more gently.

A look of puzzlement crossed his face, smeared with mud and powder-stains. He nodded, and a sort of dazed smile appeared through the grime.

"I killed an English soldier, Madame."

"Oh?" I was unsure whether he wanted congratulation, or needed comfort. He was ten.

His brow wrinkled, and his face screwed up as though trying very hard to remember something.

"I *think* I killed him. He fell down, and I stuck him with my knife." He looked at me in bewilderment, as though I could supply the answer.

"Come along, Fergus," I said. "We'll find you some food and a place to sleep. Don't think about it anymore."

"*Oui,* Madame." He stumbled obediently along beside me, but within moments, I could see that he was about to fall flat on his face. I picked him up, with some difficulty, and lugged him toward the cottages near the church where I had centered our hospital operation. I had intended to feed him first, but he was sound asleep by the time I reached the spot where O'Sullivan was attempting—with little success—to organize his commissary wagons.

Instead, I left him curled in the box bed in one of the cottages, where a woman was looking after assorted children while their mothers tended wounded men. It seemed the best place for him.

The cottage had filled up with twenty or thirty men by midafternoon, and my two-woman staff was hopping. The house normally held a family of five or six, and the men able to stand were standing on the plaids of those lying down. In the distance across the small flat, I could see officers coming and going to the manse, the minister's residence commandeered by the High Command. I kept an eye on the battered door, which hung constantly ajar, but didn't see Jamie among those arriving to report casualties and receive congratulations.

I batted away the recurrent small gnat of worry, telling myself that I didn't see him among the wounded, either. I had not had time since early on to visit the small tent up the slope, where the dead of the battle were being laid out in orderly rows, as though awaiting a last inspection. But surely he could not be there.

Surely not, I told myself.

The door swung open and Jamie walked in.

I felt my knees give slightly at sight of him, and put out a hand to steady myself on the cottage's wooden chimney. He had been looking for me; his eyes darted around the room before they lighted on me, and a heart-stopping smile lit his face.

He was filthy, grimed with black-powder smoke, splattered with blood, and barefoot, legs and feet caked with mud. But he was whole, and standing. I wasn't inclined to quibble with the details.

Cries of greeting from some of the wounded men on the floor dragged his gaze away from me. He glanced down, smiled at George McClure, who, despite an ear that hung from his head by a sliver of flesh, grinned up at his commander, then looked quickly back at me.

Thank God, his dark-blue eyes said, and *Thank God,* my own echoed back.

There was no time for more; wounded men were still coming in, and every able-bodied nonmilitary person in the village had been pressed into service to care for them. Archie Cameron, Lochiel's doctor brother, bustled back and forth among the cottages, nominally in charge, and actually doing some good here and there.

I had arranged that any Fraser men from Lallybroch should be brought to the cottage where I was conducting my own triage, quickly evaluating the severity of wounds, sending the still-mobile down the street to be dealt with by Jenny Cameron, the dying across to Archie Cameron's headquarters in the church—I did think him competent to dispense laudanum, and the surroundings might provide some consolation.

Serious wounds I dealt with as I could. Broken bones next door, where two surgeons from the Macintosh regiment could apply splints and bandages. Nonfatal chest wounds propped as comfortably as possible against one wall in a half-sitting position to assist breathing; lacking oxygen or facilities for surgical repair, there was little else I could do for them. Serious head wounds were dispatched to the church with the obviously dying; I had nothing to offer them, and they were better off in the hands of God, if not Archie Cameron.

Shattered and missing limbs and abdominal wounds were the worst. There was no possibility of sterility; all I could do was to cleanse my own hands between patients, browbeat

my assistants into doing the same—so long as they were under my direct scrutiny, anyway—and try to ensure that the
dressings we applied had all been boiled before application. I
knew, beyond doubt, that similar precautions were being ignored as a waste of time in the other cottages, despite my
lectures. If I couldn't convince the sisters and physicians of
L'Hôpital des Anges of the existence of germs, I was unlikely
to succeed with a mixed bag of Scottish housewives and army
surgeons who doubled as farriers.

I blocked my mind to the thought of the men with treat-
able injuries who would die from infection. I could give the
men of Lallybroch, and a few more, the benefit of clean
hands and bandages; I couldn't worry about the rest. One
dictum I had learned on the battlefields of France in a far
distant war: You cannot save the world, but you might save
the man in front of you, if you work fast enough.

Jamie stood a moment in the doorway, assessing the situation, then moved to help with the heavy work, shifting patients, lifting cauldrons of hot water, fetching buckets of clean
water from the well in Tranent square. Relieved of fear for
him, and caught up in the whirlwind of work and detail, I
forgot about him for the most part.

The triage station of any field hospital always bears a
strong resemblance to an abattoir, and this was no exception.
The floor was pounded dirt, not a bad surface, insofar as it
absorbed blood and other liquids. On the other hand, saturated spots did become muddy, making the footing hazardous.

Steam billowed from the boiling cauldron over the fire,
adding to the heat of exertion. Everyone streamed with moisture; the workers with the sticky wash of exercise, the
wounded men with the stinking sweat of fear and long-spent
rage. The dissipating fog of black-powder smoke from the
battlefield below drifted through the streets of Tranent and in
through the open doors, its eye-stinging haze threatening the
purity of the freshly boiled linens, hung dripping from the
mackeral-drying rack by the fire.

The flow of the wounded came in waves, washing into
the cottage like surf-scour, churning everything into confusion with the arrival of each fresh surge. We thrashed about,

fighting the pull of the tide, and were left at last, gasping, to deal with the new flotsam left behind as each wave ebbed.

There are lulls, of course, in the most frantic activity. These began to come more frequently in the afternoon, and toward sundown, as the flow of wounded dropped to a trickle, we began to settle into a routine of caring for the patients who remained with us. It was still busy, but there was at last time to draw breath, to stand in one place for a moment and look around.

I was standing by the open door, breathing in the freshening breeze of the offshore wind, when Jamie came back into the cottage, carrying an armload of firewood. Dumping it by the hearth, he came back to stand by me, one hand resting briefly on my shoulder. Trickles of sweat ran down the edge of his jaw, and I reached up to dab them with a corner of my apron.

"Have you been to the other cottages?" I asked.

He nodded, breath beginning to slow. His face was so blotched with smoke and blood that I couldn't tell for sure, but thought he looked pale.

"Aye. There's still looting going on in the field, and a good many men still missing. All of our own wounded are here, though—none elsewhere." He nodded at the far end of the cottage where the three wounded men from Lallybroch lay or sat companionably near the hearth, trading good-natured insults with the other Scots. The few English wounded in this cottage lay by themselves, near the door. They talked much less, content to contemplate the bleak prospects of captivity.

"None bad?" he asked me, looking at the three.

I shook my head. "George McClure might lose the ear; I can't tell. But no; I think they'll be all right."

"Good." He gave me a tired smile, and wiped his hot face on the end of his plaid. I saw he had wrapped it carelessly around his body instead of draping it over one shoulder. Probably to keep it out of the way, but it must have been hot.

Turning to go, he reached for the water bottle hanging from the door peg.

"Not that one!" I said.

"Why not?" he asked, puzzled. He shook the wide-mouthed flask, with a faint sloshing sound. "It's full."

"I know it is," I said. "That's what I've been using as a urinal."

"Oh." Holding the bottle by two fingers, he reached to replace it, but I stopped him.

"No, go ahead and take it," I suggested. "You can empty it outside, and fill this one at the well." I handed him another gray stone bottle, identical with the first.

"Try not to get them mixed up," I said helpfully.

"Mmphm," he replied, giving me a Scottish look to go along with the noise, and turned toward the door.

"Hey!" I said, seeing him clearly from the back. "What's that?"

"What?" he said, startled, trying to peer over one shoulder.

"That!" My fingers traced the muddy shape I had spotted above the sagging plaid, printed on the grubby linen of his shirt with the clarity of a stencil. "It looks like a horseshoe," I said disbelievingly.

"Oh, that," he said, shrugging.

"A *horse* stepped on you?"

"Well, not on purpose," he said, defensive on the horse's behalf. "Horses dinna like to step on people; I suppose it feels a wee bit squashy underfoot."

"I would suppose it does," I agreed, preventing his attempts to escape by holding on to one sleeve. "Stand still. How the hell did this happen?"

"It's no matter," he protested. "The ribs don't feel broken, only a trifle bruised."

"Oh, just a trifle," I agreed sarcastically. I had worked the stained fabric free in back, and could see the clear, sharp imprint of a curved horseshoe, embedded in the fair flesh of his back, just above the waist. "Christ, you can see the horseshoe nails." He winced involuntarily as I ran my finger over the marks.

It had happened during one brief sally by the mounted dragoons, he explained. The Highlanders, mostly unaccustomed to horses other than the small, shaggy Highland ponies, were convinced that the English cavalry horses had been trained to attack them with hooves and teeth. Panicked at the horses' charge, they had dived under the horses' hooves, slashing ferociously at legs and bellies with swords and scythes and axes.

"And you think they aren't?"

"Of course not, Sassenach," he said impatiently. "He wasna trying to attack me. The rider wanted to get away, but he was sealed in on either side. There was noplace to go but over me."

Seeing this realization dawn in the eyes of the horse's rider, a split second before the dragoon applied spurs to his mount's sides, Jamie had flung himself flat on his face, arms over his head.

"Then the next was the breath bursting from my lungs," he explained. "I felt the dunt of it, but it didna hurt. Not then." He reached back and rubbed a hand absently over the mark, grimacing slightly.

"Right," I said, dropping the edge of the shirt. "Have you had a piss since then?"

He stared at me as though I had gone suddenly barmy.

"You've had four-hundredweight of horse step smack on one of your kidneys," I explained, a trifle impatiently. There were wounded men waiting. "I want to know if there's blood in your urine."

"Oh," he said, his expression clearing. "I don't know."

"Well, let's find out, shall we?" I had placed my big medicine box out of the way in one corner; now I rummaged about in it and withdrew one of the small glass urinoscopy cups I had acquired from L'Hôpital des Anges.

"Fill it up and give it back to me." I handed it to him and turned back toward the hearth, where a cauldron full of boiling linens awaited my attention.

I glanced back to find him still regarding the cup with a slightly quizzical expression.

"Need help, lad?" A big English soldier on the floor was peering up from his pallet, grinning at Jamie.

A flash of white teeth showed in the filth of Jamie's face. "Oh, aye," he said. He leaned down, offering the cup to the Englishman. "Here, hold this for me while I aim."

A ripple of mirth passed through the men nearby, distracting them momentarily from their distress.

After a moment's hesitation, the Englishman's big fist closed around the fragile cup. The man had taken a dose of shrapnel in one hip, and his grip was none too steady, but he still smiled, despite the sweat dewing his upper lip.

"Sixpence says you can't make it," he said. He moved the cup, so it stood on the floor three or four feet from Jamie's bare toes. "From where you stand now."

Jamie looked down thoughtfully, rubbing his chin with one hand as he measured the distance. The man whose arm I was dressing had stopped groaning, absorbed in the developing drama.

"Weel, I'll no say it would be easy," Jamie said, letting his Scots broaden on purpose. "But for sixpence? Aye, weel, that's a sum might make it worth the effort, eh?" His eyes, always faintly slanted, turned catlike with his grin.

"Easy money, lad," said the Englishman, breathing heavily but still grinning. "For me."

"Two silver pennies on the lad," called one of the Mac-Donald clansmen in the chimney corner.

An English soldier, coat turned inside-out to denote his prisoner status, fumbled inside the skirts, searching for the opening of his pocket.

"Ha! A pouch of weed against!" he called, triumphantly holding up a small cloth bag of tobacco.

Shouted wagers and rude remarks began to fly through the air as Jamie squatted down and made a great show of estimating the distance to the cup.

"All right," he said at last, standing up and throwing back his shoulders. "Are ye set, then?"

The Englishman on the floor chuckled. "Oh, *I'm* set, lad."

"Well, then."

An expectant hush fell over the room. Men raised on their elbows to watch, ignoring both discomfort and enmity in their interest.

Jamie glanced around the room, nodded at his Lallybroch men, then slowly raised the hem of his kilt and reached beneath it. He frowned in concentration, groping randomly, then let an expression of doubt flit across his countenance.

"I had it when I went out," he said, and the room erupted in laughter.

Grinning at the success of his joke, he raised his kilt

further, grasped his clearly visible weapon and took careful aim. He squinted his eyes, bent his knees slightly, and his fingers tightened their grip.

Nothing happened.

"It's a misfire!" crowed one of the English.

"His powder's wet!" Another hooted.

"No balls to your pistol, lad?" jibed his accomplice on the floor.

Jamie squinted dubiously at his equipment, bringing on a fresh riot of howls and catcalls. Then his face cleared.

"Ha! My chamber's empty, that's all!" He snaked an arm toward the array of bottles on the wall, cocked an eyebrow at me, and when I nodded, took one down and upended it over his open mouth. The water splashed over his chin and onto his shirt, and his Adam's apple bobbed theatrically as he drank.

"Ahhh." He lowered the bottle, swabbed some of the grime from his face with a sleeve, and bowed to his audience.

"Now, then," he began, reaching down. He caught sight of my face, though, and stopped in mid-motion. He couldn't see the open door at his back, nor the man standing in it, but the sudden quiet that fell upon the room must have told him that all bets were off.

———➤

His Highness Prince Charles Edward bent his head under the lintel to enter the cottage. Come to visit the wounded, he was dressed for the occasion in plum velvet breeches with stockings to match, immaculate linen, and—to show solidarity with the troops, no doubt—a coat and waistcoat in Cameron tartan, with a subsidiary plaid looped over one shoulder through a cairngorm brooch. His hair was freshly powdered, and the Order of St. Andrew glittered brilliantly upon his breast.

He stood in the doorway, nobly inspiring everyone in sight and noticeably impeding the entrance of those behind him. He looked slowly about him, taking in the twenty-five men crammed cheek by jowl on the floor, the helpers crouching over them, the mess of bloodied dressings tossed into the corner, the scatter of medicines and instruments across the table, and me, standing behind it.

His Highness didn't care overmuch for women with the army in general, but he was thoroughly grounded in the rules of courtesy. I *was* a woman, despite the smears of blood and vomit that streaked my skirt, and the fact that my hair was shooting out from under my kertch in half a dozen random sprays.

"Madame Fraser," he said, bowing graciously to me.

"Your Highness." I bobbed a curtsy back, hoping he didn't intend to stay long.

"Your labors in our behalf are very much appreciated, Madame," he said, his soft Italian accent stronger than usual.

"Er, thank you," I said. "Mind the blood. It's slippery just there."

The delicate mouth tightened a bit as he skirted the puddle I had pointed out. The doorway freed, Sheridan, O'Sullivan, and Lord Balmerino came in, adding to the congestion in the cottage. Now that the demands of courtesy had been attended to, Charles crouched carefully between two pallets.

He laid a gentle hand on the shoulder of one man.

"What is your name, my brave fellow?"

"Gilbert Munro . . . erm, Your Highness," added the man, hastily, awed at the sight of the Prince.

The manicured fingers touched the bandage and splints that swathed what was left of Gilbert Munro's right arm.

"Your sacrifice was great, Gilbert Munro," Charles said simply. "I promise you it will not be forgotten." The hand brushed across a whiskered cheek, and Munro reddened with embarassed pleasure.

I had a man before me with a scalp wound that needed stitching, but was able to watch from the corner of my eye as Charles made the rounds of the cottage. Moving slowly, he went from bed to bed, missing no one, stopping to inquire each man's name and home, to offer thanks and affection, congratulations, and condolence.

The men were stunned into silence, English and Highlander alike, barely managing to answer His Highness in soft murmurs. At last he stood and stretched, with an audible creaking of ligaments. An end of his plaid had trailed in the mud, but he didn't seem to notice.

"I bring you the blessing and the thanks of my Father,"

he said. "Your deeds of today will always be remembered."
The men on the floor were not in the proper mood to cheer,
but there were smiles, and a general murmur of appreciation.

Turning to go, Charles caught sight of Jamie, standing
out of the way in the corner, so as not to have his bare toes
trampled by Sheridan's boots. His Highness's face lighted
with pleasure.

"Mon cher! I had not seen you today. I feared some
malchance had overtaken you." A look of reproach crossed
the handsome, ruddy face. "Why did you not come to supper
at the manse with the other officers?"

Jamie smiled and bowed respectfully.

"My men are here, Highness."

The Prince's brows shot up at this, and he opened his
mouth as though to say something, but Lord Balmerino
stepped forward and whispered something in his ear.
Charles's expression changed to one of concern.

"But what this is I hear?" he said to Jamie, losing control
of his syntax as he did in moments of emotion. "His Lordship
tells me that you have yourself suffered a wound."

Jamie looked mildly discomfited. He shot a quick glance
my way, to see if I had heard, and seeing that I most certainly
had, jerked his eyes back to the Prince.

"It's nothing, Highness. Only a scratch."

"Show me." It was simply spoken, but unmistakably an
order, and the stained plaid fell away without protest.

The folds of dark tartan were nearly black on the inner
side. His shirt beneath was reddened from armpit to hip, with
stiff brown patches where the blood had begun to dry.

Leaving my head injury to mind himself for a moment, I
stepped forward and opened the shirt, pulling it gently away
from the injured side. Despite the quantity of blood, I knew it
must not be a serious wound; he stood like a rock, and the
blood no longer flowed.

It was a saber-slash, slanting across the ribs. A lucky angle; straight in and it would have gone deep into the intercos-
tal muscles between the ribs. As it was, an eight-inch flap of
skin gaped loose, red beginning to ooze beneath it again with
the release of pressure. It would take a goodly number of
stitches to repair, but aside from the constant danger of infection, the wound was in no way serious.

Turning to report this to His Highness, I halted, stopped by the odd look on his face. For a split second, I thought it was "rookie's tremors," the shock of a person unaccustomed to the sight of wounds and blood. Many a trainee nurse at the combat station had removed a field dressing, taken one look and bolted, to vomit quietly outside before returning to tend the patient. Battle wounds have a peculiarly nasty look to them.

But it couldn't be that. By no means a natural warrior, still Charles had been blooded, like Jamie, at the age of fourteen, in his first battle at Gaeta. No, I decided, even as the momentary expression of shock faded from the soft brown eyes. He would not be startled by blood or wounds.

This wasn't a cottar or a herder that stood before him. Not a nameless subject, whose duty was to fight for the Stuart cause. This was a friend. And I thought that perhaps Jamie's wound had suddenly brought it home to him; that blood was shed on *his* order, men wounded for *his* cause—little wonder if the realization struck him, deep as a sword-cut.

He looked at Jamie's side for a long moment, then looked up to meet his eyes. He grasped Jamie by the hand, and bowed his own head.

"Thank you," he said softly.

And just for that one moment, I thought perhaps he might have made a king, after all.

On a small slope behind the church, a tent had been erected at His Highness's order, for the last shelter of those dead in battle. Given preference in treatment, the English soldiers received none here; the men lay in rows, cloths covering their faces, Highlanders distinguished only by their dress, all awaiting burial on the morrow. MacDonald of Keppoch had brought a French priest with him; the man, shoulders sagging with weariness, purple stole worn incongruously over a stained Highland plaid, moved slowly through the tent, pausing to pray at the foot of each recumbent figure.

"Perpetual rest grant unto him, O Lord, and let perpetual light shine upon him." He crossed himself mechanically, and moved on to another corpse.

I had seen the tent earlier, and—heart in mouth—

counted the bodies of the Highland dead. Twenty-two. Now, as I entered the tent, I found the toll had risen to twenty-six.

A twenty-seventh lay in the nearby church, on the last mile of his journey. Alexander Kincaid Fraser, dying slowly of the wounds that riddled his belly and chest, of a slow internal seepage that couldn't be halted. I had seen him when they brought him in, bleached white from an afternoon of bleeding slowly to death, alone in the field among the bodies of his foes.

He had tried to smile at me, and I had wetted his cracked lips with water and coated them with tallow. To give him a drink was to kill him at once, as the liquid would rush through his perforated intestines and cause fatal shock. I hesitated, seeing the seriousness of his wounds, and thinking that a quick death might be better . . . but then I had stopped. I realized that he would want to see a priest and make his confession, at least. And so I had dispatched him to the church, where Father Benin tended the dying as I tended the living.

Jamie had made short visits to the church every half-hour or so, but Kincaid held his own for an amazingly long time, clinging to life despite the constant ebbing of its substance. But Jamie had not come back from his latest visit. I knew that the fight was ending now at last, and went to see if I could help.

The space under the windows where Kincaid had lain was empty, save for a large, dark stain. He wasn't in the tent of the dead, either, and neither was Jamie anywhere in sight.

I found them at length some distance up the hill behind the church. Jamie was sitting on a rock, the form of Alexander Kincaid cradled in his arms, curly head resting on his shoulder, the long, hairy legs trailing limp to one side. Both were still as the rock on which they sat. Still as death, though only one was dead.

I touched the white, slack hand, to be sure, and rested my hand on the thick brown hair, feeling still so incongruously alive. A man should not die a virgin, but this one did.

"He's gone, Jamie," I whispered.

He didn't move for a moment, but then nodded, opening his eyes as though reluctant to face the realities of the night.

"I know. He died soon after I brought him out, but I didna want to let him go."

I took the shoulders and we lowered him gently to the ground. It was grassy here, and the night wind stirred the stems around him, brushing them lightly across his face, a welcome to the caress of the earth.

"You didn't want him to die under a roof," I said, understanding. The sky swept over us, cozy with cloud, but endless in its promise of refuge.

He nodded slowly, then knelt by the body and kissed the wide, pale forehead.

"I would have someone do the same for me," he said softly. He drew a fold of the plaid up over the brown curls, and murmured something in Gaelic that I didn't understand.

A medical casualties station is no place for tears; there is much too much to be done. I had not wept all day, despite the things I had seen, but now gave way, if only for a moment. I leaned my face against Jamie's shoulder for strength, and he patted me briefly. When I looked up, wiping the tears from my face, I saw him still staring, dry-eyed, at the quiet figure on the ground. He felt me watching him and looked down at me.

"I wept for him while he was still alive to know it, Sassenach," he said quietly. "Now, how is it in the house?"

I sniffed, wiped my nose, and took his arm as we turned back to the cottage.

"I need your help with one."

"Which is it?"

"Hamish MacBeth."

Jamie's face, strained for so many hours, relaxed a bit under the stains and smudges.

"He's back, then? I'm glad. How bad is he, though?"

I rolled my eyes. "You'll see."

MacBeth was one of Jamie's favorites. A massive man with a curly brown beard and a reticent manner, he had been always there within Jamie's call, ready when something was needed on the journey. Seldom speaking, he had a slow, shy smile that blossomed out of his beard like a night-blooming flower, rare but radiant.

I knew the big man's absence after the battle had been worrying Jamie, even among the other details and stresses. As the day wore on and the stragglers came back one by one, I had been keeping an eye out for MacBeth. But sundown came and the fires sprang up amid the army camp, with no Hamish MacBeth, and I had begun to fear we would find him among the dead, too.

But he had come into the casualties station half an hour before, moving slowly, but under his own power. One leg was stained with blood down to the ankle, and he walked with a ginger, spraddled gait, but he would on no account let a "wumman" lay hands on him to see what was the matter.

The big man was lying on a blanket near a lantern, hands clasped across the swell of his belly, eyes fastened patiently on the raftered ceiling. He swiveled his eyes around as Jamie knelt down beside him, but didn't move otherwise. I lingered tactfully in the background, hidden from view by Jamie's broad back.

"All right, then, MacBeth," said Jamie, laying a hand on the thick wrist in greeting. "How is it, man?"

"I'll do, sir," the giant rumbled. "I'll do. Just that it's a bit . . ." He hesitated.

"Well, then, let's have a look at it." MacBeth made no protest as Jamie flipped back the edge of the kilt. Peeking through a crack between Jamie's arm and body, I could see the cause of MacBeth's hesitations.

A sword or pike had caught him high in the groin and ripped its way downward. The scrotum was torn jaggedly on one side, and one testicle hung halfway out, its smooth pink surface shiny as a peeled egg.

Jamie and the two or three other men who saw the wound turned pale, and I saw one of the aides touch himself reflexively, as though to assure that his own parts were unscathed.

Despite the horrid look of the wound, the testicle itself seemed undamaged, and there was no excessive bleeding. I touched Jamie on the shoulder and shook my head to signify that the wound was not serious, no matter what its effect on the male psyche. Catching my gesture with the tail of his eye, Jamie patted MacBeth on the knee.

"Och, it's none so bad, MacBeth. Nay worry, ye'll be a father yet."

The big man had been looking down apprehensively, but

at these words, transferred his gaze to his commander. "Weel, that's no such a consairn to me, sir, me already havin' the six bairns. It's just what my wife'd say, if I . . ." MacBeth blushed crimson as the men surrounding him laughed and hooted.

Casting an eye back at me for confirmation, Jamie suppressed his own grin and said firmly, "That'll be all right, too, MacBeth."

"Thank ye, sir," the man breathed gratefully, with complete trust in his commander's assurance.

"Still," Jamie went on briskly, "it'll need to be stitched up, man. Now, ye've your choice about that."

He reached into the open kit for one of my handmade suture needles. Appalled by the crude objects barber-surgeons customarily used to sew up their customers, I'd made three dozen of my own, by selecting the finest embroidery needles I could get, and heating them in forceps over the flame of an alcohol lamp, bending them gently until I had the proper half-moon curve needed for stitching severed tissues. Likewise, I'd made my own catgut sutures; a messy, disgusting business, but at least I was sure of the sterility of my materials.

The tiny suture needle looked ridiculous, pinched between Jamie's large thumb and index finger. The illusion of medical competence was not furthered by Jamie's cross-eyed attempts to thread the needle.

"Either I'll do it myself," he said, tongue-tip protruding slightly in his concentration, "or—" He broke off as he dropped the needle and fumbled about in the folds of Mac-Beth's plaid for it. "Or," he resumed, holding it up triumphantly before his patient's apprehensive eyes, "my wife can do it for ye." A slight jerk of the head summoned me into view. I did my best to look as matter-of-fact as possible, taking the needle from Jamie's incompetent grasp and threading it neatly with one thrust.

MacBeth's large brown eyes traveled slowly between Jamie's big paws, which he contrived to make look as clumsy as possible by setting the crooked right hand atop the left, and my own small, swift hands. At last he lay back with a dismal sigh, and mumbled his consent to let a "wumman" lay hands on his private parts.

"Dinna worry yourself, man," Jamie said, patting him companionably on the shoulder. "After all, she's had the handling of my own for some time now, and she's not unmanned me yet." Amid the laughter of the aides and nearby patients, he started to rise, but I stopped him by thrusting a small flask into his hands.

"What's this?" he asked.

"Alcohol and water," I said. "Disinfectant solution. If he's not to have fever or pustulence or something worse, the wound will have to be washed out." MacBeth had plainly walked some way from where the injury had occurred, and there were smears of dirt as well as blood near the wound. Grain alcohol was a harsh disinfectant, even cut 50/50 with distilled sterile water as I used it. Still, it was the single most effective tool I had against infection, and I was adamant about its usage, in spite of complaints from the aides and screams of anguish from the patients who were subjected to it.

Jamie glanced from the alcohol flask to the gaping wound and shuddered slightly. He'd had his own dose when I stitched his side, earlier in the evening.

"Weel, MacBeth, better you than me," he said, and, placing his knee firmly in the man's midriff, sloshed the contents of the flask over the exposed tissues.

A dreadful roar shook the walls, and MacBeth writhed like a cut snake. When the noise at last subsided, his face had gone a mottled greenish color, and he made no objection at all as I began the routine, if painful, job of stitching up the scrotum. Most of the patients, even those horribly wounded, were stoic about the primitive treatment to which we subjected them, and MacBeth was no exception. He lay unmoving in hideous embarrassment, eyes fixed on the lantern flame, and didn't move a muscle as I made my repairs. Only the changing colors of his face, from green to white to red and back again, betrayed his emotions.

At the last, however, he went purple. As I finished the stitching, the limp penis began to stiffen slightly, brushed in passing by my hand. Thoroughly rattled by this justification of his faith in Jamie's word, MacBeth snatched down his kilts the instant I was finished, lurched to his feet, and staggered away into the darkness, leaving me giggling over my kit.

I found a corner where a chest of medical supplies made a seat, and leaned against the wall. A surge of pain shot up my calves; the sudden release of tension, and the nerves' reaction to it. I slipped off my shoes and leaned back against the wall, reveling in the smaller spasms that shot up backbone and neck as the strain of standing was relieved.

Every square inch of skin seems newly sensitive in such a state of fatigue; when the necessity of forcing the body to perform is suddenly suspended, the lingering impetus seems to force the blood to the perimeter of the body, as though the nervous system is reluctant to believe what the muscles have already gratefully accepted; you need not move, just now.

The air in the cottage was warm and noisy with breathing; not the healthy racket of snoring men, but the shallow gasps of men for whom breathing hurts, and the moans of those who have found a temporary oblivion that frees them from the manly obligation of suffering in silence.

The men in this cottage were those badly wounded, but in no immediate danger. I knew, though, that death walks at night in the aisles of a sick ward, searching for those whose defenses are lowered, who may stray unwittingly into its path through loneliness and fear. Some of the wounded had wives who slept next to them, to comfort them in the dark, but none in this cottage.

They had me. If I could do little to heal them or stop their pain, I could at least let them know that they didn't lie alone; that someone stood here, between them and the shadow. Beyond anything I could do, it was my job only to be there.

I rose and made my way slowly once again through the pallets on the floor, stooping at each one, murmuring and touching, straightening a blanket, smoothing tangled hair, rubbing the knots that form in cramped limbs. A sip of water here, a change of dressing there, the reading of an attitude of tense embarrassment that meant a urinal was needed, and the matter-of-fact presentation that allowed the man to ease himself, the stone bottle growing warm and heavy in my hand.

I stepped outdoors to empty one of these, and paused for a moment, gathering the cool, rainy night to myself, letting the soft moisture wipe away the touch of coarse, hairy skin and the smell of sweating men.

"Ye dinna sleep much, Sassenach." The soft Scottish voice came from the direction of the road. The other hospital cottages lay in that direction; the officers' quarters, the other way, in the village manse.

"You dinna sleep much, either," I responded dryly. How long had he gone without sleep? I wondered.

"I slept in the field last night, with the men."

"Oh, yes? Very restful," I said, with an edge that made him laugh. Six hours' sleep in a wet field, followed by a battle in which he'd been stepped on by a horse, wounded by a sword, and done God knows what else. Then he had gathered his men, collected the wounded, tended the hurt, mourned his dead, and served his Prince. And through none of it had I seen him pause for food, drink, or rest.

I didn't bother scolding. It wasn't even worth mentioning that he ought to have been among the patients on the floor. It was his job to be here, as well.

"There are other women, Sassenach," he said gently. "Shall I have Archie Cameron send someone down?"

It was a temptation, but one I pushed away before I could think about it too long, for fear that if I acknowledged my fatigue, I would never move again.

I stretched, hands against the small of my back.

"No," I said. "I'll manage 'til the dawn. Then someone else can take over for a time." Somehow I felt that I must get them through the night; at dawn they would be safe.

He didn't scold, either; just laid a hand on my shoulder and drew me to lean against him for a moment. We shared what strength we had, unspeaking.

"I'll stay with ye, then," he said, drawing away at last. "I canna sleep before light, myself."

"The other men from Lallybroch?"

He moved his head toward the fields near the town where the army was camped.

"Murtagh's in charge."

"Oh, well, then. Nothing to worry about," I said, and saw him smile in the light from the window. There was a bench outside the cottage, where the goodwife would sit on sunny days to clean fish or mend clothes. I drew him down to sit beside me, and he sagged back against the wall of the house with a sigh. His patent exhaustion reminded me of Fergus, and the boy's expression of confused bewilderment after the battle.

I reached to caress the back of Jamie's neck, and he turned his head blindly toward me, resting his brow against my own.

"How was it, Jamie?" I asked softly, fingers rubbing hard and slow over the tight-ridged muscles of his neck and shoulders. "What was it like? Tell me."

There was a short silence, then he sighed, and began to talk, haltingly at first, and then faster, as if wanting to get it out.

"We had no fire, for Lord George thought we must move off the ridge before daylight, and wanted no hint of movement to be seen below. We sat in the dark for a time. Couldna even talk, for the sound would carry to the plain. So we sat.

"Then I felt something grab my thigh in the dark, and near jumped out of my skin." He inserted a finger in his mouth and rubbed gingerly. "Nearly bit my tongue off." I felt the shift of his muscles as he smiled, though his face was hidden.

"Fergus?"

The ghost of a laugh floated through the dark.

"Aye, Fergus. Crawled through the grass on his belly, the little bastard, and I thought he was a snake, at that. He whispered to me about Anderson, and I crawled off after him and took Anderson to see Lord George."

His voice was slow and dreamy, talking under the spell of my touch.

"And then the order came that we'd move, following Anderson's trail. And the whole of the army got to its feet, and set off in the dark."

◆──────

The night was clear black and moonless, without the usual cover of cloud that trapped starlight and diffused it toward the earth. As the Highland army made its way in silence down the narrow path behind Robert Anderson, each man could see no farther than the shuffling heels of the man before him, each step widening the trodden path through wet grass.

The army moved almost without noise. Orders were relayed in murmurs from man to man, not shouted. Broadswords and axes were muffled in the folds of their plaids, powder flasks tucked inside shirts against fast-beating hearts.

Once on sound footing, still in total silence, the Highlanders sat down, made themselves as comfortable as was possible without fire, ate what cold rations there were, and composed themselves to rest, wrapped in their plaids, in sight of the enemy's campfires.

"We could hear them talking," Jamie said. His eyes were closed, hands clasped behind his head, as he leaned against the cottage wall. "Odd, to hear men laughing over a jest, or asking for a pinch of salt or a turn at the wineskin—and know that in a few hours, ye may kill them—or them you. Ye can't help wondering, ye ken; what does the face behind that voice look like? Will you know the fellow if ye meet him in the morning?"

Still, the tremors of anticipated battle were no match for sheer fatigue, and the "Black Frasers"—so called for the traces of charcoal that still adorned their features—and their chief had been awake for more than thirty-six hours by then. He had picked a sheaf of marrow-grass for a pillow, tucked the plaid around his shoulders, and lain down in the waving grass beside his men.

During his time with the French army, years before, one of the sergeants had explained to the younger mercenaries the trick of falling asleep the night before a battle.

"Make yourself comfortable, examine your conscience, and make a good Act of Contrition. Father Hugo says that in time of war, even if there is no priest to shrive you, your sins can be forgiven this way. Since you cannot commit sins while asleep—not even *you*, Simenon!—you will awake in a state of grace, ready to fall on the bastards. And with nothing to look forward to but victory or heaven—how can you be afraid?"

While privately noting a few flaws in this argument, Jamie had found it still good advice; freeing the conscience eased the soul, and the comforting repetition of prayer distracted the mind from fearful imaginings and lulled it toward sleep.

He gazed upward into the black vault of the sky, and willed the tightness of neck and shoulders to relax into the ground's hard embrace. The stars were faint and hazy tonight, no match for the nearby glow of the English fires.

His mind reached out to the men around him, resting briefly on each, one by one. The stain of sin was small weight on his conscience, compared with these. Ross, McMurdo, Kincaid, Kent, McClure . . . he paused to give brief thanks that his wife and the boy Fergus at least were safe. His mind lingered on his wife, wanting to bask in the memory of her reassuring smile, the solid, wonderful warmth of her in his arms, pressed tight against him as he had kissed her goodbye that afternoon. Despite his own weariness and the waiting presence of Lord George outside, he had wanted to tumble her onto the waiting mattress right then and take her quickly, at once, without undressing. Strange how the imminence of fighting made him so ready, always. Even now . . .

But he hadn't yet finished his mental roster, and he felt his eyelids closing already, as tiredness sought to pull him under. He dismissed the faint tightening of his testicles that came at thought of her, and resumed his roll call, a shepherd treacherously lulled to sleep by counting the sheep he was leading to slaughter.

But it wouldn't be a slaughter, he tried to reassure himself. Light casualties for the Jacobite side. Thirty men killed. Out of two thousand, only a slim chance that some of the Lallybroch men would be among that number, surely? If she was right.

He shuddered faintly under the plaid, and fought down the momentary doubt that wrenched his bowels. If. God, if. Still he had trouble believing it, though he had seen her by that cursed rock, face dissolving in terror around the panic-wide gold eyes, the very outlines of her body blurring as he, panicked also, had clutched at her, pulling her back, feeling little more than the frail double bone of her forearm under his hand. Perhaps he should have let her go, back to her own place. No, no perhaps. He knew that he should. But he had pulled her back. Given her the choice, but kept her with him by the sheer force of his wanting her. And so she had stayed. And given *him* the choice—to believe her, or not. To act, or to run. And the choice was made now, and no power on earth could stop the dawn from coming.

His heart beat heavily, pulse echoing in wrists and groin and the pit of his stomach. He sought to calm it, resuming his count, one name to each heartbeat. Willie MacNab, Bobby MacNab, Geordie MacNab . . . thank God, young Rabbie MacNab was safe, left at home . . . Will Fraser, Ewan Fraser, Geoffrey McClure . . . McClure . . . had he touched on both George and Sorley? Shifted slightly, smiling faintly, feeling for the soreness left along his ribs. Murtagh. Aye, Murtagh, tough old boot . . . my mind is no troubled on your account, at least. William Murray, Rufus Murray, Geordie, Wallace, Simon . . .

And at last, had closed his eyes, commended all of them to the care of the black sky above, and lost himself in the murmured words that came to him still most naturally in French—*"Mon Dieu, je regrette . . ."*

◆

I made my rounds inside the cottage, changing a blood-soaked dressing on one man's leg. The bleeding should have stopped by now, but it hadn't. Poor nutrition and brittle bones. If the bleeding hadn't stopped before cockcrow, I would have to fetch Archie Cameron or one of the farrier-surgeons to amputate the leg, and cauterize the stump.

I hated the thought of it. Life was sufficiently hard for a man with all his limbs in good working order. Hoping for the best, I coated the new dressing with a light sprinkling of alum and sulfur. If it didn't help, it wouldn't hinder. Likely it *would* hurt, but that couldn't be helped.

"It will burn a bit," I murmured to the man, as I wrapped his leg in the layers of cloth.

"Dinna worry yourself, Mistress," he whispered. He smiled at me, in spite of the sweat that ran down his cheeks, shiny in the light of my candle. "I'll stand it."

"Good." I patted his shoulder, smoothed the hair off his brow, and gave him a drink of water. "I'll check again in an hour, if you can bear it that long."

"I'll stand it," he said again.

◆

Outside once more, I thought Jamie had fallen asleep.
His face rested on his folded forearms, crossed on his knees.
But he looked up at the sound of my step, and took my hand
as I sat beside him.

"I heard the cannon at dawn," I said, thinking of the
man inside, leg broken by a cannonball. "I was afraid for
you."

He laughed softly. "So was I, Sassenach. So were we all."

Quiet as wisps of mist, the Highlanders advanced
through the sea grass, one foot at a time. There was no sense
of darkness lessening, but the feel of the night had changed.
The wind had changed, that was it; it blew from the sea over
the cold dawning land, and the faint thunder of waves on
distant sand could be heard.

Despite his impression of continued dark, the light was
coming. He saw the man at his feet just in time; one more
step and he would have been headlong across the man's
curled body.

Heart pounding from the shock of the near-meeting, he
dropped to his haunches to get a better look. A Redcoat, and
sleeping, not dead or wounded. He squinted hard into the
darkness around them, willing his ears to listen for the
breathing of other sleeping men. Nothing but sea sounds,
grass and wind sounds, the tiny swish of stealthy feet almost
hidden in their muted roar.

He glanced hastily back, licking lips gone dry despite the
moist air. There were men close behind him; he dared not
hesitate long. The next man might not be so careful where he
stepped, and they could risk no outcry.

He set hand to his dirk, but hesitated. War was war, but
it went against the grain to slay a sleeping enemy. The man
seemed to be alone, some distance from his companions. Not
a sentinel; not even the slackest of guards would sleep, knowing the Highlanders to be camped on the ridge above. Perhaps the soldier had gotten up to relieve himself, thoughtfully
come some distance from his fellows to do it, then, losing his
direction in the dark, lain down to sleep where he was.

The metal of his musket was slick from his sweating
palm. He rubbed his hand on his plaid, then stood, grasped
the barrel of the musket, and swung the butt in a vicious arc,
down and around. The shock of impact jolted him to the

shoulder blades; an immobile head is solid. The man's arms
had flown out with the force of the impact, but beyond an
explosion of breath, he had made no noise, and now lay
sprawled on his face, limp as a clout.

Palms tingling, he stooped again and groped beneath the
man's jaw, looking for a pulse. He found one, and reassured,
stood up. There was a muffled cry of startlement from behind, and he swung around, musket already at his shoulder,
to find its barrel poking into the face of one of Keppoch's
MacDonald clansmen.

"Mon Dieu!" the man whispered, crossing himself, and
Jamie clenched his teeth with aggravation. It was Keppoch's
bloody French priest, dressed, at O'Sullivan's suggestion, in
shirt and plaid like the fighting men.

"The man insisted that it was his duty to bring the sacraments to the wounded and dying on the field," Jamie explained to me, hitching his stained plaid higher on his shoulder. The night was growing colder. "O'Sullivan's idea was
that if the English caught him on the battlefield in his cassock, they'd tear him to pieces. As to that, maybe so, maybe
no. But he looked a right fool in a plaid," he added censoriously.

Nor had the priest's behavior done anything to amelio-
rate the impression caused by his attire. Realizing belatedly
that his assailant was a Scot, he had sighed in relief, and then
opened his mouth. Moving quickly, Jamie had clapped a hand
over it before any ill-advised questions could emerge.

"What are ye doing here, Father?" he growled, mouth
pressed to the priest's ear. "You're meant to be behind the
lines."

A widening of the priest's eyes at this told Jamie the
truth—the man of God, lost in the darkness, had thought he
was behind the lines, and the belated realization that he was,
in fact, in the vanguard of the advancing Highlanders, made
him buckle slightly at the knees.

Jamie glanced backward; he didn't dare send the priest
back through the lines. In the misty dark, he could easily
stumble into an advancing Highlander, be mistaken for an
enemy, and be killed on the spot. Gripping the smaller man
by the back of the neck, he pushed him to his knees.

"Lie flat and stay that way until the firing stops," he

hissed into the man's ear. The priest nodded frantically, then suddenly saw the body of the English soldier, lying on the ground a few feet away. He glanced up at Jamie in awed horror, and reached for the bottles of chrism and holy water that he wore at his belt in lieu of a dirk.

Rolling his eyes in exasperation, Jamie made a series of violent motions, meant to indicate that the man was not dead, and thus in no need of the priest's services. These failing to make their point, he bent, seized the priest's hand, and pressed the fingers on the Englishman's neck, as the simplest method of illustrating that the man was not in fact the first victim of the battle. Caught in this ludicrous position, he froze as a voice cut through the mist behind him.

"Halt!" it said. "Who goes there?"

"Have ye got a bit of water, Sassenach?" asked Jamie. "I'm gettin' a bit dry with the talking."

"Bastard!" I said. "You can't stop there! What happened?"

"Water," he said, grinning, "and I'll tell ye."

"All right," I said, handing him a water bottle and watching as he tilted it into his mouth. "What happened then?"

"Nothing," he said, lowering the bottle and wiping his mouth on his sleeve. "What did ye think, I was going to answer him?" He grinned impudently at me and ducked as I aimed a slap at his ear.

"Now, now," he reproved. "No way to treat a man wounded in the service of his King, now is it?"

"Wounded, are you?" I said. "Believe me, Jamie Fraser, a mere saber slash is as nothing compared to what I will do to you if . . ."

"Oh, threats, too, is it? What was that poem ye told me about, 'When pain and anguish wring the brow, a ministering angel' . . . ow!"

"Next time, I twist it right off at the roots," I said, releasing the ear. "Get on with it, I have to go back in a minute."

He rubbed the ear gingerly, but leaned back against the wall and resumed his story.

"Well, we just sat there on our haunches, the padre and I, staring at each other and listening to the sentries six feet away. 'What's that?' says the one, and me thinking can I get up in time to take him with my dirk before he shoots me in the back, and what about his friend? For I canna expect help from the priest, unless maybe it's a last prayer over my body."

There was a long, nerve-racking silence, as the two Jacobites squatted in the grass, hands still clasped, afraid to move enough even to let go.

"Ahhh, yer seein' things," came from the other sentry at last, and Jamie felt the shudder of relief run through the priest, as his damp fingers slid free. "Nothin' up there but furze bushes. Never mind, lad," the sentry said reassuringly, and Jamie heard the clap of a hand on a shoulder and the stamp of booted feet, trying to keep warm. "There's the damn lot of 'em, sure, and in this dark, they could be the whole bloody Highland army, for all you can see." Jamie thought he heard the breath of a smothered laugh from one of the "furze bushes," on the hillside within hearing.

He glanced at the crest of the hill, where the stars were beginning to dim. Less than ten minutes to first light, he judged. At which point, Johnnie Cope's troops would swiftly realize that the Highland army was not, as they thought, an hour's march away in the opposite direction, but already face-to-face with their front lines.

There was a noise to the left, in the direction of the sea. It was faint, and indistinct, but the note of alarm was clear to battle-trained ears. Someone, he supposed, had tripped over a furze bush.

"Hey?" The note of alarm was taken up by one of the sentries nearby. "What's happening?"

The priest would have to take care of himself, he thought. Jamie drew the broadsword as he rose, and with one long step, was within reach. The man was no more than a shape in the darkness, but distinct enough. The merciless blade smashed down with all his strength, and split the man's skull where he stood.

"Highlanders!" The shriek broke from the man's companion, and the second sentry sprang out like a rabbit flushed from a copse, bounding away into the fading dark before Jamie could free his weapon from its gory cleft. He put a foot on the fallen man's back and jerked, gritting his teeth against the unpleasant sensation of slack flesh and grating bone.

Alarm was spreading up and down the English lines; he could feel as much as hear it—an agitation of men rudely wakened, groping blindly for weapons, searching in all directions for the unseen threat.

Clanranald's pipers were behind to the right, but no signal as yet came for the charge. Continue the advance, then, heart pounding and left arm tingling from the death blow, belly muscles clenched and eyes straining through the waning dark, the spray of warm blood across his face going cold and sticky in the chill.

"I could hear them first," he said, staring off into the night as though still searching for the English soldiers. He bent forward, hugging his knees. "Then I could see, too. The English, wriggling over the ground like maggots in meat, and the men behind me. George McClure came up with me, and Wallace and Ross on the other side, and we were walkin' still, one pace at a time, but faster and faster, seein' the *sassenaches* breaking before us."

There was a dull boom off to the right; the firing of a single cannon. A moment later, another, and then, as though this were the signal, a wavering cry rose from the oncoming Highlanders.

"The pipes started then," he said, eyes closed. "I didna remember my musket 'til I heard one fire close behind me; I'd left it in the grass next to the priest. When it's like that, ye dinna see anything but the small bit that's happening round you.

"Ye hear a shout, and of a sudden, you're running. Slow, for a step or two, while ye free your belt, and then your plaid falls free and you're bounding, wi' your feet splashing mud up your legs and the chill of the wet grass on your feet, and your shirttails flying off your bare arse. The wind blows into your shirt and up your belly and out along your arms. . . . Then the noise takes ye and you're screaming, like runnin' down a hill yelling into the wind when you're a bairn, to see can ye lift yourself on the sound."

They rode the waves of their own shrieking onto the plain, and the force of the Highland charge crashed onto the shoals of the English army, smothering them in a boiling surge of blood and terror.

"They ran," he said softly. "One man stood to face me—

all during the fight, only one. The others I took from behind."
He rubbed a grimy hand over his face, and I could feel a fine
tremor start somewhere deep inside him.

"I remember . . . everything," he said, almost whispering. "Every blow. Every face. The man lying on the ground in
front of me who wet himself wi' fear. The horses screaming.
All the stinks—black powder and blood and the smell of my
own sweat. Everything. But it's like I was standin' outside,
watching myself. I wasna really there." He opened his eyes
and looked sidelong at me. He was bent almost double, head
on his knees, the shivering visible now.

"D'ye know?" he asked.

"I know."

While I hadn't fought with sword or knife, I had fought
often enough with hands and will; getting through the chaos
of death only because there is no other choice. And it did
leave behind that odd feeling of detachment; the brain
seemed to rise above the body, coldly judging and directing,
the viscera obediently subdued until the crisis passed. It was
always sometime later that the shaking started.

I hadn't reached that point yet. I slid the cloak from my
shoulders and covered him before going back into the cottage.

The dawn came, and relief with it, in the person of two
village women and an army surgeon. The man with the
wounded leg was pale and shaky, but the bleeding had
stopped. Jamie took me by the arm and led me away, down
the street of Tranent.

O'Sullivan's constant difficulties with the commissary
had been temporarily relieved by the captured wagons, and
there was food in plenty. We ate quickly, scarcely tasting the
hot porridge, aware of food only as a bodily necessity, like
breathing. The feeling of nourishment began to creep
through my body, freeing me to think of the next most pressing need—sleep.

Wounded men were quartered in every house and cottage, the sound-of-body mostly sleeping in the fields outside.
While Jamie could have claimed a place in the manse with
the other officers, he instead took my arm and turned me

aside, heading between the cottages and up a hill, into one of the scattered small groves that lay outside Tranent.

"It's a bit of a walk," he said apologetically, looking down at me, "but I thought perhaps ye'd rather be private."

"I would." While I had been raised under conditions that would strike most people of my time as primitive—often living in tents and mud houses on Uncle Lamb's field expeditions—still, I wasn't used to living crowded cheek by jowl with numbers of other people, as was customary here. People ate, slept, and frequently copulated, crammed into tiny, stifling cottages, lit and warmed by smoky peat fires. The only thing they didn't do together was bathe—largely because they didn't bathe.

Jamie led the way under the drooping limbs of a huge horse chestnut, and into a small clearing, thick with the fallen leaves of ash, alder, and sycamore. The sun was barely up, and it was still cold under the trees, a faint edge of frost rimming some of the yellowed leaves.

He scraped a rough trench in the layer of leaves with one heel, then stood at one end of the hollow, set his hand to the buckle of his belt, and smiled at me.

"It's a bit undignified to get into, but it's verra easy to take off." He jerked the belt loose, and his plaid dropped around his ankles, leaving him clad to mid-thigh in only his shirt. He usually wore the military "little kilt," which buckled about the waist, with the plaid a separate strip of cloth around the shoulders. But now, his own kilt rent and stained from the battle, he had acquired one of the older belted plaids—nothing more than a long strip of cloth, tucked about the waist and held in place with no fastening but a belt.

"How *do* you get into it?" I asked curiously.

"Well, ye lay it out on the ground, like this"—he knelt, spreading the cloth so that it lined the leaf-strewn hollow—"and then ye pleat it every few inches, lie down on it, and roll."

I burst out laughing, and sank to my knees, helping to smooth the thick tartan wool.

"*That,* I want to see," I told him. "Wake me up before you get dressed."

He shook his head good-naturedly, and the sunlight filtering through the leaves glinted off his hair.

"Sassenach, the chances of me wakin' before you do are less than those of a worm in a henyard. I dinna care if another horse steps on me, I'll no be moving 'til tomorrow." He lay down carefully, pushing back the leaves.

"Come lie wi' me." He extended an inviting hand upward. "We'll cover ourselves with your cloak."

The leaves beneath the smooth wool made a surprisingly comfortable mattress, though at this point I would cheerfully have slept on a bed of nails. I relaxed bonelessly against him, reveling in the exquisite delight of simply lying down.

The initial chill faded quickly as our bodies warmed the pocket where we lay. We were far enough from the town that the sounds of its occupation reached us only in wind-borne snatches, and I thought with drowsy satisfaction that it might well *be* tomorrow before anyone looking for Jamie found us.

I had removed my petticoats and torn them up for additional bandages the night before, and there was nothing between us but the thin fabric of skirt and shirt. A hard, solid warmth stirred briefly against my stomach.

"Surely not?" I said, amused despite my tiredness. "Jamie, you must be half-dead."

He laughed tiredly, holding me close with one large, warm hand on the small of my back.

"A lot more than half, Sassenach. I'm knackered, and my cock's the only thing too stupid to know it. I canna lie wi' ye without wanting you, but wanting's all I'm like to do."

I fumbled with the hem of his shirt, then pushed it up and wrapped my hand gently around him. Even warmer than the skin of his belly, his penis was silken under the touch of my stroking thumb, pulsing strongly with each beat of his heart.

He made a small sound of half-painful content, and rolled slowly onto his back, letting his legs sprawl loosely outward, half-covered by my cloak.

The sun had reached our pile of leaves, and my shoulders relaxed under the warming touch of the light. Everything seemed slightly tinged with gold, the mingled result of early autumn and extreme fatigue. I felt languid and vaguely disembodied, watching the small stirrings of his flesh under my fingers. All the terror and the tiredness and the noise of the two days past ebbed slowly away, leaving us alone together.

The haze of fatigue seemed to act as a magnifying glass, exaggerating tiny details and sensations. The tail of his saber wound was visible beneath the rucked-up shirt, crusted black against the fair skin. Two or three small flies buzzed low, investigating, and I waved them away. My ears rang with the silence, the breath of the trees no match for the echoes of the town.

I laid my cheek against him, feeling the hard, smooth curve of his hip bone, close under the skin. His skin was transparent in the crease of his groin, the branching veins blue and delicate as a child's.

His hand rose slowly, floating like the leaves, and rested lightly on my head.

"Claire. I need you," he whispered. "I need ye so."

Without the hampering petticoats, it was easy. I felt as though I were floating myself, rising without volition, drifting my skirts up the length of his body, settling over him like a cloud on a hilltop, sheltering his need.

His eyes were closed, head laid back, the red gold of his hair tumbled coarsely in the leaves. But his hands rose together and settled surely on my waist, resting without weight on the curve of my hips.

My eyes closed as well, and I felt the shapes of his mind, as surely as I felt those of his body under me; exhaustion blocked our every thought and memory; every sensation but the knowledge of each other.

"Not . . . long," he whispered. I nodded, knowing he felt what he did not see, and rose above him, thighs powerful and sure under the stained fabric of my gown.

Once, and twice, and again, and once again, and the tremor rose through him and through me, like the rising of water through the roots of a plant and into its leaves.

The breath left him in a sigh, and I felt his descent into unconsciousness like the dimming of a lamp. I fell beside him, with barely time to draw the heavy folds of the cloak up over us before the darkness filled me, and I lay weighted to the earth by the heavy warmth of his seed in my belly. We slept.

37

Holyrood

Edinburgh, October 1745

The knock on my door surprised me from an inspection of my newly replenished medical boxes. After the stunning victory at Prestonpans, Charles had led his triumphant army back to Edinburgh, to bask in adulation. While he was basking, his generals and chieftains labored, rallying their men and procuring what equipment was to be had, in preparation for whatever was coming next.

Buoyed by early success, Charles talked freely of taking Stirling, then Carlyle, and then, perhaps, of advancing south, even to London itself. I spent my spare time counting suture needles, hoarded willow bark, and stole every spare ounce of alcohol I could find, to be brewed into disinfectant.

"What is it?" I asked, opening the door. The messenger was a young boy, scarcely older than Fergus. He was trying to look grave and deferential, but couldn't suppress his natural curiosity. I saw his eyes dart around the room, resting on the large medicine chest in the corner with fascination. Clearly the rumors concerning me had spread through the palace of Holyrood.

"His Highness has asked for ye, Mistress Fraser," he answered. Bright brown eyes scanned me closely, no doubt looking for signs of supernatural possession. He seemed slightly disappointed at my depressingly normal appearance.

"Oh, has he?" I said. "Well, all right. Where is he, then?"

"In the morning drawing room, Mistress. I'm to take ye. Oh . . ." The thought struck him as he turned, and he swung back before I could close the door. "You're to bring your box of medicines, if ye'd be so kind."

My escort brimmed with self-importance at his mission as he escorted me down the long hallway to the Royal wing of the palace. Plainly someone had been schooling him in the behavior appropriate to a Royal page, but an occasional exuberant skip in his step betrayed his newness to the job.

What on earth did Charles want with me? I wondered.

While he tolerated me on Jamie's account, the story of La Dame Blanche had plainly disconcerted him and made him uneasy. More than once, I had surprised him crossing himself surreptitiously in my presence, or making the quick two-fingered "horns" sign against evil. The idea that he would ask me to treat him medically was unlikely in the extreme.

When the heavy cross-timbered door swung open into the small morning drawing room, it seemed still more unlikely. The Prince, plainly in good health, was leaning on the painted harpsichord, picking out a hesitant tune with one finger. His delicate skin was mildly flushed, but with excitement, not fever, and his eyes were clear and attentive when he looked up at me.

"Mistress Fraser! How kind of you to attend me so shortly!" He was dressed this morning with even more lavishness than usual, bewigged and wearing a new cream-colored silk waistcoat, embroidered with flowers. He must be excited about something, I thought; his English went to pot whenever he became agitated.

"My pleasure, Your Highness," I said demurely, dropping a brief curtsy. He was alone, an unusual state of affairs. Could he want my medical services for himself after all?

He made a quick, nervous gesture toward one of the gold damask chairs, urging me to be seated. A second chair was pulled up, facing it, but he walked up and down in front of me, too restless to sit.

"I need your help," he said abruptly.

"Um?" I made a politely inquiring noise. Gonorrhea? I wondered, scanning him covertly. I hadn't heard of any women since Louise de La Tour, but then, it only took once. He worked his lips in and out, as though searching for some alternative to telling me, but finally gave it up.

"I have a *capo*—a chief, you understand?—here. He thinks of joining my Father's cause, but has still some doubt."

"A clan chieftain, you mean?" He nodded, brow furrowed beneath the careful curls of his wig.

"*Oui*, Madame. He is of course in support of my Father's claims . . ."

"Oh, of course," I murmured.

". . . but he is wishing to speak to you, Madame, before he will commit his men to follow me."

He sounded incredulous, hearing his own words, and I realized that the flush on his cheeks came from a combination of bafflement and suppressed fury.

I was more than a little baffled myself. My imagination promptly visualized a clan chieftain with some dread disease, whose adherence to the cause depended on my performing a miraculous cure.

"You're sure he wants to speak to me?" I said. Surely my reputation hadn't gone *that* far.

Charles inclined his head coldly in my direction. "So he says, Madame."

"But I don't *know* any clan chieftains," I said. "Bar Glengarry and Lochiel, of course. Oh, and Clanranald and Keppoch, of course. But they've all committed themselves to you already. And why on earth . . ."

"Well, he is of the opinion you are knowing him," the Prince interrupted, syntax becoming more mangled with his rising temper. He clenched his hands, obviously forcing himself to speak courteously. "It is of importance—*most* importance, Madame, that he should become convinced to join me. I require . . . I *request* . . . you therefore, that you . . . convince him."

I rubbed my nose thoughtfully, looking at him. One more point of decision. One more opportunity to make events move in the path I chose. And once more, the inability to know what best to do.

He was right; it was important to convince this chieftain to commit his resources to the Jacobite cause. With the Camerons, the various MacDonalds, and the others so far committed, the Jacobite army numbered barely two thousand men, and those the most ill-assorted lot of ragtag and draggletail that any general had ever been lumbered with. And yet, that ragged-arsed lot had taken the city of Edinburgh, routed a greatly superior English force at Preston, and showed every disposition to continue going through the countryside like a dose of salts.

We had been unable to stop Charles; perhaps, as Jamie said, the only way to avert calamity was now to do everything possible to help him. The addition of an important clan chieftain to the roster of supporters would greatly influence the odds of others joining. This might be a turning point, where the Jacobite forces could be increased to the level of a true army, actually capable of the proposed invasion of England. And if so, what in bloody hell would happen then?

I sighed. No matter what I decided to do, I couldn't make any decision until I saw this mysterious person. I glanced down to make sure my gown was suitable for interviewing clan chieftains, infected or otherwise, and rose, tucking the medicine box under my arm.

"I'll try, Your Highness," I said.

The clenched hands relaxed, showing the bitten nails, and his frown lessened.

"Ah, good," he said. He turned toward the door of the larger afternoon drawing room. "Come, I shall take you myself."

The guard at the door jumped back in surprise as Charles flung the door open and strode past him without a glance. On the far side of the long, tapestry-hung room was an enormous marble fireplace, lined with white Delft tiles, painted with Dutch country scenes in shades of blue and mulberry. A small sofa was drawn up before the fire, and a big, broad-shouldered man in Highland dress stood beside it.

In a room less imposing, he would have bulked huge, legs like tree trunks in their checkered stockings beneath the kilt. As it was, in this immense room with its high gessoed ceilings, he was merely big—quite in keeping with the heroic figures of mythology that decorated the tapestries at either end of the room.

I stopped dead at sight of the enormous visitor, the shock of recognition still mingled with absolute incredulity. Charles had kept on, and now glanced back with some impatience, beckoning me to join him before the fire. I nodded to the big man. Then I walked slowly around the end of the sofa and gazed down at the man who lay upon it.

He smiled faintly when he saw me, the dove-gray eyes lighting with a spark of amusement.

"Yes," he said, answering my expression. "I hadn't really expected to meet *you* again, either. One might almost believe we are fated." He turned his head and lifted a hand toward his enormous body-servant.

"Angus. Will ye fetch a drop of the brandy for Mistress Claire? I'm afraid the surprise of seeing me may have somewhat discomposed her."

That, I thought, was putting it mildly. I sank into a splay-footed chair and accepted the crystal goblet Angus Mhor held out to me.

Colum MacKenzie's eyes hadn't changed; neither had his voice. Both held the essence of the man who had led clan MacKenzie for thirty years, despite the disease that had crippled him in his teens. Everything else had changed sadly for the worse, though; the black hair streaked heavily with gray, the lines of his face cut deep into skin that had fallen slack over the sharp outlines of bone. Even the broad chest was sunken and the powerful shoulders hunched, flesh fallen away from the fragile skeleton beneath.

He already held a glass half-filled with amber liquid, glowing in the firelight. He raised himself painfully to a sitting position and lifted the cup in ironic salute.

"You're looking very well . . . niece." From the corner of my eye, I saw Charles's mouth drop open.

"You aren't," I said bluntly.

He glanced dispassionately down at the bowed and twisted legs. In a hundred years' time, they would call this disease after its most famous sufferer—the Toulouse-Lautrec syndrome.

"No," he said. "But then, it's been two years since you saw me last. Mrs. Duncan estimated my survival at less than two years, then."

I took a swallow of the brandy. One of the best. Charles *was* anxious.

"I shouldn't have thought you'd put much stock in a witch's curse," I said.

A smile twitched the fine-cut lips. He had the bold beauty of his brother Dougal, ruined as it was, and when he lifted the veil of detachment from his eyes, the power of the man overshone the wreck of his body.

"Not in curses, no. I had the distinct impression that the lady was dealing in observation, however, not malediction. And I have seldom met a more acute observer than Geillis Duncan—with one exception." He inclined his head gracefully toward me, making his meaning clear.

"Thanks," I said.

Colum glanced up at Charles, who was gaping in bewilderment at these exchanges.

"I thank you for your graciousness in permitting me to use your premises for my meeting with Mrs. Fraser, Your Highness," he said, with a slight bow. The words were sufficiently civil, but the tone made it an obvious dismissal. Charles, who was by no means used to being dismissed, flushed hotly and opened his mouth. Then, recalling himself, he snapped it shut, bowed shortly, and turned on his heel.

"We won't need the guard, either," I called after him. His shoulders hunched and the back of his neck grew red beneath the tail of his wig, but he gestured abruptly, and the guard at the door, with an astonished glance at me, followed him out.

"Hm." Colum cast a brief glance of disapproval at the door, then returned his attention to me.

"I asked to see you because I owe ye an apology," he said, without preamble.

I leaned back in my chair, goblet resting nonchalantly on my stomach.

"Oh, an apology?" I said, with as much sarcasm as could be mustered on short notice. "For trying to have me burnt for witchcraft, I suppose you mean?" I flipped a hand in gracious dismissal. "Pray think nothing of it." I glared at him. *"Apology?!"*

He smiled, not disconcerted in the slightest.

"I suppose it seems a trifle inadequate," he began.

"Inadequate?! For having me arrested and thrown into a thieves' hole for three days without decent food or water? For having me stripped half-naked and whipped before every person in Cranesmuir? For leaving me a hairsbreadth away from a barrel of pitch and a bundle of faggots?" I stopped and took a deep breath. "Now that you mention it," I said, a little more calmly, " 'inadequate' is precisely what I'd call it."

The smile had vanished.

"I beg your pardon for my apparent levity," he said softly. "I had no intent to mock you."

I looked at him, but could see no lingering gleam of amusement in the black-lashed eyes.

"No," I said, with another deep breath. "I don't suppose

you did. I suppose you're going to say that you had no intent to have me arrested for witchcraft, either."

The gray eyes sharpened. "You knew that?"

"Geilie said so. While we were in the thieves' hole. She said it was her you meant to dispose of; I was an accident."

"You were." He looked suddenly very tired. "Had ye been in the castle, I could have protected you. What in the name of God led ye to go down to the village?"

"I was told that Geilie Duncan was ill and asking for me," I replied shortly.

"Ah," he said softly. "You were told. By whom, and I may ask?"

"Laoghaire." Even now, I could not repress a brief spurt of rage at the girl's name. Out of thwarted jealousy over my having married Jamie, she had deliberately tried to have me killed. Considerable depths of malice for a sixteen-year-old girl. And even now, mingled with the rage was that tiny spark of grim satisfaction; he's mine, I thought, almost subconsciously. Mine. You'll never take him from me. Never.

"Ah," Colum said again, staring thoughtfully at my flushed countenance. "I thought perhaps that was the way of it. Tell me," he continued, raising one dark brow, "if a mere apology strikes you as inadequate, will ye have vengeance instead?"

"Vengeance?" I must have looked startled at the idea, for he smiled faintly, though without humor.

"Aye. The lass was wed six months ago, to Hugh Mac-Kenzie of Muldaur, one of my tacksmen. He'll do with her as I say, and ye want her punished. What will ye have me do?"

I blinked, taken aback by his offer. He appeared in no hurry for an answer; he sat quietly, sipping the fresh glass of brandy that Angus Mhor poured for him. He wasn't staring at me, but I got up and moved away toward the windows, wanting to be alone for a moment.

The walls here were five feet thick; by leaning forward into the deep window embrasure I could assure myself of privacy. The bright sun illuminated the fine blond hairs on my forearms as I rested them on the sill. It made me think of the thieves' hole, that damp, reeking pit, and the single bar of sunlight that had shone through an opening above, making

the dark hole below seem that much more like a grave by
contrast.

I had spent my first day there in cold and dirt, full of
stunned disbelief; the second in shivering misery and growing
fear as I discovered the full extent of Geillis Duncan's treachery and Colum's measures against it. And on the third day,
they had taken me to trial. And I had stood, filled with shame
and terror, under the clouds of a lowering autumn sky, feeling
the jaws of Colum's trap close round me, sprung by a word
from the girl Laoghaire.

Laoghaire. Fair-skinned and blue-eyed, with a round,
pretty face, but nothing much to distinguish her from the
other girls at Leoch. I had thought about her—in the pit with
Geillis Duncan, I had had time to think of a lot of things. But
furious and terrified as I had been, furious as I remained, I
couldn't, either then or now, bring myself to see her as intrin-
sically evil.

"She was only sixteen, for God's sake!"

"Old enough to marry," said a sardonic voice behind me,
and I realized that I had spoken aloud.

"Yes, she wanted Jamie," I said, turning around. Colum
was still sitting on the sofa, stumpy legs covered with a rug.
Angus Mhor stood silent behind him, heavy-lidded eyes fixed
on his master. "Perhaps she thought she loved him."

Men were drilling in the courtyard, amid shouts and
clashing of arms. The sun glanced off the metal of swords and
muskets, the brass studding of targes—and off the red-gold of
Jamie's hair, flying in the breeze as he wiped a hand across
his face, flushed and sweating from the exercise, laughing at
one of Murtagh's deadpan remarks.

I had perhaps done Laoghaire an injustice, after all, in
assuming her feelings to be less than my own. Whether she
had acted from immature spite or from a true passion, I could
never know. In either case, she had failed. I had survived.
And Jamie was mine. As I watched, he rucked up his kilt and
casually scratched his bottom, the sunlight catching the reddish-gold fuzz that softened the iron-hard curve of his thigh. I
smiled, and went back to my seat near Colum.

"I'll take the apology," I said.

He nodded, gray eyes thoughtful.

"You've a belief in mercy, then, Mistress?"

"More in justice," I said. "Speaking of which, I don't imagine you traveled all the way from Leoch to Edinburgh merely to apologize to me. It must have been a hellish journey."

"Aye, it was." The huge, silent bulk of Angus Mhor shifted an inch or two behind him, and the massive head bent toward his laird in eloquent witness. Colum sensed the movement and raised a hand briefly—it's all right, the gesture said, I'm all right for the present.

"No," Colum went on. "I did not know ye were in Edinburgh, in fact, until His Highness mentioned Jamie Fraser, and I asked." A sudden smile grew on his face. "His Highness isn't overfond of you, Mistress Claire. But I suppose ye knew that?"

I ignored this. "So you really are considering joining Prince Charles?"

Colum, Dougal, and Jamie all had the capacity for hiding what they were thinking when they chose to, but of the three, Colum was undoubtedly best at it. You'd get more from one of the carved heads on the fountain in the front courtyard, if he was feeling uncommunicative.

"I've come to see him" was all he said.

I sat a moment, wondering what, if anything, I could—or should—say in Charles's behalf. Perhaps I would do better to leave it to Jamie. After all, the fact that Colum felt regret over nearly killing me by accident didn't mean he was necessarily inclined to trust me. And while the fact that I was here, part of Charles's entourage, surely argued against my being an English spy, it wasn't impossible that I was.

I was still debating with myself when Colum suddenly put down his glass of brandy and looked straight at me.

"D'ye know how much of this I've had since morning?"

"No." His hands were steady, calloused and roughened from his disease, but well kept. The reddened lids and slightly bloodshot eyes could as easily be from the rigors of travel as from drink. There was no slurring of speech, and no more than a certain deliberateness of movement to indicate that he wasn't sober as a judge. But I had seen Colum drink before, and had a very respectful idea of his capacity.

He waved away Angus Mhor's hand, hovering above the decanter. "Half a bottle. I'll have finished it by tonight."

"Ah." So that was why I had been asked to bring my medicine box. I reached for it, where I had set it on the floor.

"If you're needing that much brandy, there isn't much that will help you besides some form of opium," I said, flicking through my assortment of vials and jars. "I think I have some laudanum here, but I can get you some—"

"That isn't what I want from you." The tone of authority in his voice stopped me, and I looked up. If he could keep his thoughts to himself, he could also let them show when he chose.

"I could get laudanum easily enough," he said. "I imagine there's an apothecarist in the city who sells it—or poppy syrup, or undiluted opium, for that matter."

I let the lid of the small chest fall shut and rested my hands on top of it. So he didn't mean to waste away in a drugged state, leaving the leadership of the clan uncertain. And if it were not a temporary oblivion he sought from me, what else? A permanent one, perhaps. I knew Colum MacKenzie. And the clear, ruthless mind that had planned Geillis Duncan's destruction would not hesitate over his own.

Now it was clear. He had come to see Charles Stuart, to make the final decision whether to commit the MacKenzies of Leoch to the Jacobite cause. Once committed, it would be Dougal who led the clan. And then . . .

"I was under the impression that suicide was considered a mortal sin," I said.

"I imagine it is," he said, undisturbed. "A sin of pride, at least, that I should choose a clean death at the time of my own devising, as best suits my purpose. I don't, however, expect to suffer unduly for my sin, having put no credence in the existence of God since I was nineteen or so."

It was quiet in the room, beyond the crackle of the fire and the muffled shouts of mock battle from below. I could hear his breathing, a slow and steady sigh.

"Why ask me?" I said. "You're right, you could get laudanum where you liked, so long as you have money—and you do. Surely you know that enough of it will kill you. It's an easy death, at that."

"Too easy." He shook his head. "I have had little to depend on in life, save my wits. I would keep them, even to meet death. As for ease . . ." He shifted slightly on the sofa, making no effort to hide his discomfort. "I shall have enough, presently."

He nodded toward my box. "You shared Mrs. Duncan's knowledge of medicines. I thought it possible that you knew what she used to kill her husband. That seemed quick and certain. And appropriate," he added wryly.

"She used witchcraft, according to the verdict of the court." The court that condemned her to death, in accordance with your plan, I thought. "Or do you not believe in witchcraft?" I asked.

He laughed, a pure, carefree sound in the sunlit room. "A man who doesn't believe in God can scarce credit power to Satan, can he?"

I still hesitated, but he was a man who judged others as shrewdly as he did himself. He had asked my pardon before asking my favor, and satisfied himself that I had a sense of justice—or of mercy. And it was, as he said, appropriate. I opened the box and took out the small vial of cyanide that I kept to kill rats.

"I thank ye, Mistress Claire," he said, formal again, though the smile still lingered in his eyes. "Had my nephew not proved your innocence with such flamboyance at Cranesmuir, still I would never believe you a witch. I have no more notion now than I had at our first meeting, as to who you are, or why you are here, but a witch is not one of the possibilities I've ever considered." He paused, one brow raised. "I don't suppose you'd be inclined to tell me who—or what—you are?"

I hesitated for a moment. But a man with belief in neither God nor Devil was not likely to believe the truth of my presence here, either. I squeezed his fingers lightly and released them.

"Better call me a witch," I said. "It's as close as you're likely to get."

On my way out to the courtyard next morning, I met Lord Balmerino on the stairs.

"Oh, Mistress Fraser!" he greeted me jovially. "Just who I was looking for."

I smiled at him; a chubby, cheerful man, he was one of the refreshing features of life in Holyrood.

"If it isn't fever, flux, or French pox," I said, "can it wait for a moment? My husband and his uncle are giving a demonstration of Highland sword-fighting for the benefit of Don Francisco de la Quintana."

"Oh, really? I must say, I should like to see that myself." Balmerino fell into step beside me, head bobbing cheerfully at the level of my shoulder. "I do like a pretty man with a sword," he said. "And anything that will sweeten the Spaniards has my most devout approval."

"Mine, too." Deeming it too dangerous for Fergus to lift His Highness's correspondence inside Holyrood, Jamie was dependent for information on what he learned from Charles himself. This seemed to be quite a lot, though; Charles considered Jamie one of his intimates—virtually the only Highland chief to be accorded such a mark of favor, small as was his contribution in men and money.

So far as money went, though, Charles had confided that he had high hopes of support from Philip of Spain, whose latest letter to James in Rome had been distinctly encouraging. Don Francisco, while not quite an envoy, was certainly a member of the Spanish Court, and might be relied upon to carry back his report of how matters stood with the Stuart rising. This was Charles's opportunity to see how far his own belief in his destiny would carry him, in convincing Highland chiefs and foreign kings to join him.

"What did you want to see me for?" I asked as we came out onto the walkway that edged the courtyard of Holyrood. A small crowd of spectators was assembling, but neither Don Francisco nor the two combatants were yet in sight.

"Oh!" Reminded, Lord Balmerino groped inside his coat. "Nothing of great importance, my dear lady. I received these from one of my messengers, who obtained them from a kinsman to the South. I thought you might find them amusing."

He handed me a thin sheaf of crudely printed papers. I recognized them as broadsheets, the popular circulars distributed in taverns or that fluttered from doorposts and hedges through towns and villages.

"CHARLES EDWARD STUART, known to all as The

Younge Pretender" read one. "Be it Known to all Present that this Depraved and Dangerous Person, having landed Unlawfully upon the shores of Scotland, hath Incited to Riot the Population of that Country, and hath Unleashed upon Innocent Citizens the Fury of an Unjust War." There was quite a lot more of it, all in the same vein, concluding with an exhortation to the Innocent Citizens reading this indictment "to do all in their Power to Deliver ye this Person to the Justice which he so Richly Deserves." The sheet was decorated at the top with what I supposed was meant as a drawing of Charles; it didn't bear much resemblance to the original, but definitely looked Depraved and Dangerous, which I supposed was the general idea.

"That one's quite fairly restrained," said Balmerino, peering over my elbow. "Some of the others show a most impressive range both of imagination and invective, though; look at this one. That's me," he said, pointing at the paper with evident delight.

The broadsheet showed a rawboned Highlander, thickly bewhiskered, with beetling brows and eyes that glared wildly under the shadow of a Scotch bonnet. I looked askance at Lord Balmerino, clad, as was his habit, in breeches and coat in the best of taste; made of fine stuff, but subdued both in cut and color, to flatter his tubby little form. He stared at the broadsheet, meditatively stroking his round, clean-shaven cheeks.

"I don't know," he said. "The whiskers do lend me a most romantic air, do they not? Still, a beard itches most infernally; I'm not sure I could bear it, even for the sake of being picturesque."

I turned to the next page, and nearly dropped the whole sheaf.

"They did a slightly better job in rendering a likeness of your husband," Balmerino observed, "but of course our dear Jamie does actually look somewhat like the popular English conception of a Highland thug—begging your pardon, my dear, I mean no offense. He *is* large, though, isn't he?"

"Yes," I said faintly, perusing the broadsheet's charges.

"Didn't realize your husband was in the habit of roasting and eating small children, did you?" said Balmerino, chortling. "I always thought his size was due to something special in his diet."

The little earl's irreverent attitude did a good deal to steady me. I could almost smile myself at the ridiculous charges and descriptions, though I wondered just how much credence the readers of the broadsheets placed in them. Rather a lot, I was afraid; people so often seemed not only willing but eager to believe the worst—and the worse, the better.

"It's the last one I thought you'd be interested in." Balmerino interrupted my thoughts, flipping over the next-to-last sheet.

"THE STUART WITCH" proclaimed the heading. A long-nosed female with pinpoint pupils stared back at me, over a text which accused Charles Stuart of invoking "ye Pow'rs of Darkness" in support of his unlawful cause. By retaining among his intimate entourage a well-known witch— one holding power of life and death over men, as well as the more usual power of blighting crops, drying up cattle, and causing blindness—Charles gave evidence of the fact that he had sold his own soul to the devil, and thus would "Frye in Hell Forever!" as the tract gleefully concluded.

"I assume it must be you," Balmerino said. "Though I assure you, my dear, the picture hardly does you justice."

"Very entertaining," I said. I gave the sheaf back to his lordship, restraining the urge to wipe my hand on my skirt. I felt a trifle ill, but did my best to smile at Balmerino. He glanced at me shrewdly, then took my elbow with a reassuring squeeze.

"Don't trouble yourself, my dear," he said. "Once His Majesty has regained his crown, all this nonsense will be forgotten in short order. Yesterday's villain is tomorrow's hero in the eyes of the populace; I've seen it time and again."

"Plus ça change, plus c'est la même chose," I murmured. And if His Majesty King James *didn't* regain his crown . . .

"And if our efforts should by misfortune be unsuccessful," Balmerino said, echoing my thoughts, "what the broadsheets say will be the least of our worries."

"En garde." With the formal French opening, Dougal fell into a classic dueler's stance, side-on to his opponent, sword-arm bent with the blade at the ready, back arm raised in a graceful arc, hand dropping from the wrist in open demonstration that no dagger was held in reserve.

Jamie's blade crossed Dougal's, the metal meeting with the whisper of a clash.

"Je suis prest." Jamie caught my eye, and I could see the flicker of humor cross his face. The customary dueler's response was his own clan motto. *Je suis prest.* "I am ready."

For a moment, I thought he might not be, and gasped involuntarily as Dougal's sword shot out in a lunging flash. But Jamie had seen the motion start, and by the time the blade crossed the place where he had been standing, he was no longer there.

Sidestep, a quick beat of the blade, and a counter-lunge that brought the blades screeching together along their lengths. The two swords held fast together at the hilt for only a second, then the swordsmen broke, stepped back, circled and returned to the attack.

With a clash and a beat, a parry and a lunge in *tierce,* Jamie came within an inch of Dougal's hip, swung adroitly aside with a flare of green kilt. A parry and a dodge and a quick upward beat that knocked the pressing blade aside, and Dougal stepped forward, forcing Jamie back a pace.

I could see Don Francisco, standing on the opposite side of the courtyard with Charles, Sheridan, the elderly Tullibardine, and a few others. A small smile curved the Spaniard's lips under a wisp of waxed mustache, but I couldn't tell whether it was admiration for the fighters, or merely a variation on his normally supercilious expression. Colum was nowhere in sight. I wasn't surprised; aside from his normal reluctance to appear in public, he must have been exhausted by the journey to Edinburgh.

Both gifted swordsmen, and both left-handed, uncle and nephew were putting on a skilled display—a show made more impressive by the fact that they were fighting in accordance with the most exacting rules of French dueling, but using neither the rapier-like smallsword that formed part of a gentleman's *costume,* nor the saber of a soldier. Instead, both men wielded Highland broadswords, each a full yard of tem-

pered steel, with a flat blade that could cleave a man from
crown to neck. They handled the enormous weapons with a
grace and an irony that could not have been managed by
smaller men.

I saw Charles murmur in Don Francisco's ear, and the
Spaniard nod, never taking his eyes off the flash and clang of
the battle in the grass-lined court. Well matched in size and
agility, Jamie and his uncle gave every appearance of intending to kill each other. Dougal had been Jamie's teacher
in the art of swordsmanship, and they had fought back to
back and shoulder to shoulder many times before; each man
knew the subtleties of the other's style as well as he knew his
own—or at least I hoped so.

Dougal pressed his advantage with a double lunge, forcing Jamie back toward the edge of the courtyard. Jamie
stepped quickly to one side, struck Dougal's blade away with
one beat, then slashed back the other way, with a speed that
sent the blade of his broadsword through the cloth of Dougal's right sleeve. There was a loud ripping noise, and a strip
of white linen hung free, fluttering in the breeze.

"Oh, nicely fought, sir!" I turned to see who had spoken,
and found Lord Kilmarnock standing at my shoulder. A serious, plain-faced man in his early thirties, he and his young
son Johnny were also housed in the guest quarters of
Holyrood.

The son was seldom far from his father, and I glanced
around in search of him. I hadn't far to look; he was standing
on the other side of his father, jaw slightly agape as he
watched the swordplay. My eye caught a faint movement
from the far side of a pillar: Fergus, black eyes fixed unblinkingly on Johnny. I lowered my brows and glowered at him
menacingly.

Johnny, rather overconscious of being Kilmarnock's heir,
and still more conscious of his privilege in going to war with
his father at the age of twelve, tended to lord it over the other
lads. In the manner of lads, most of them either avoided
Johnny, or bided their time, waiting for him to step out of his
father's protective shadow.

Fergus most definitely fell into the latter group. Taking
umbrage at a disparaging remark of Johnny's about "bonnet
lairds," which he had—quite accurately—interpreted as an

insult to Jamie, Fergus had been forcibly prevented from assaulting Johnny in the rock garden a few days before. Jamie had administered swift justice on a physical level, and then pointed out to Fergus that while loyalty was an admirable virtue, and highly prized by its recipient, stupidity was not.

"That lad is two years older than you, and two stone heavier," he had said, shaking Fergus gently by the shoulder. "D'ye think you'll help me by getting your own head knocked in? There's times to fight wi'out counting the cost, but there's times ye bite your tongue and bide your time. '*Ne pète pas plus haut que ton cul,*' eh?"

Fergus had nodded, wiping his tear-stained cheeks with the tail of his shirt, but I had my doubts as to whether Jamie's words had made much impression on him. I didn't like the speculative look I saw now in those wide black eyes, and thought that had Johnny been a trifle brighter, he would have been standing between me and his father.

Jamie dropped halfway to one knee, with a murderous jab upward that brought his blade whizzing past Dougal's ear. The MacKenzie jerked back, looking startled for a moment, then grinned with a flash of white teeth, and banged his blade flat on top of Jamie's head, with a resounding *clong*.

I heard the sound of applause from across the square. The fight was degenerating from elegant French duel into Highland brawl, and the spectators were thoroughly enjoying the joke of it.

Lord Kilmarnock, also hearing the sound, looked across the square and grimaced sourly.

"His Highness's advisers are summoned to meet the Spaniard," he observed sarcastically. "O'Sullivan, and that ancient fop Tullibardine. Does he take advice of Lord Elcho? Balmerino, Lochiel, or even my humble self?"

This was plainly a rhetorical question, and I contented myself with a faint murmur of sympathy, keeping my eyes on the fighters. The clash of steel rang off the stones, nearly drowning out Kilmarnock's words. Once having started, though, he seemed unable to contain his bitterness.

"No, indeed!" he said. "O'Sullivan and O'Brien and the rest of the Irish; they risk nothing! If the worst should ever happen, they can plead immunity from prosecution by reason of their nationality. But we—we who are risking property, honor—life itself! We are ignored and treated like common dragoons. I said good morning to His Highness yesterday, and he swept by me, nose in the air, as though I had committed a breach in etiquette by so addressing him!"

Kilmarnock was plainly furious, and with good reason. Ignoring the men whom he had charmed and courted into providing the men and money for his adventure, Charles then had rejected them, turning to the comfort of his old advisers from the Continent—most of whom regarded Scotland as a howling wilderness, and its inhabitants as little more than savages.

There was a whoop of surprise from Dougal, and a wild laugh from Jamie. Dougal's left sleeve hung free from the shoulder, the flesh beneath brown and smooth, unmarred by a scratch or a drop of blood.

"I'll pay ye for that, wee Jamie," Dougal said, grinning. Droplets of sweat ran down his face.

"Will ye, Uncle?" Jamie panted. "With what?" A flash of metal, judged to a nicety, and Dougal's sporran flew jingling across the stones, clipped free from the belt.

I caught a movement from the corner of my eye, and turned my head sharply.

"Fergus!" I said.

Kilmarnock turned in the direction I was looking, and saw Fergus. The boy carried a large stick in one hand, with a casualness so assumed as to be laughable, if it weren't for the implicit threat.

"Don't trouble yourself, my lady Broch Tuarach," said Lord Kilmarnock, after a brief glance. "You may depend upon my son to defend himself honorably, if the occasion demands it." He beamed indulgently at Johnny, then turned back to the swordsmen. I turned back, too, but kept an ear cocked in Johnny's direction. It wasn't that I thought Fergus lacked a sense of honor; I just had the impression that it diverged rather sharply from Lord Kilmarnock's notion of that virtue.

"Gu leoir!" At the cry from Dougal, the fight stopped abruptly. Sweating freely, both swordsmen bowed toward the applause of the Royal party, and stepped forward to accept congratulations and be introduced to Don Francisco.

"Milord!" called a high voice from the pillars. "Please—
la parabole!"

Jamie turned, half-frowning at the interruption, but then
shrugged, smiled, and stepped back into the center of the
courtyard. *La parabole* was the name Fergus had given this
particular trick.

With a quick bow to His Highness, Jamie took the
broadsword carefully by the tip of the blade, stooped slightly,
and with a tremendous heave, sent the blade whirling straight
up into the air. Every eye fixed on the basket-hilted sword,
the tempered length of it glinting in the sun as it turned end
over end over end, with such inertia that it seemed to hang in
the air for a moment before plunging earthward.

The essence of the trick, of course, was to hurl the
weapon so that it buried itself point-first in the earth as it
came down. Jamie's refinement of this was to stand directly
under the arc of descent, stepping back at the last moment to
avoid being skewered by the falling blade.

The sword chunked home at his feet to the accompaniment of a collective "ah!" from the spectators. It was only as
Jamie bent to pull the sword from its grassy sheath that I
noticed the ranks of the spectators had been reduced by two.

One, the twelve-year-old Master of Kilmarnock, lay
facedown on the grassy verge, the swelling bump on his head
already apparent through the lank brown hair. The second
was nowhere visible, but I caught a faint whisper from the
shadows behind me.

"Ne pète pas plus haut que ton cul," it said, with satisfaction. Don't fart above your arsehole.

The weather was unseasonably warm for November, and
the omnipresent clouds had broken, letting a fugitive autumn
sun shine briefly on the grayness of Edinburgh. I had taken
advantage of the transient warmth to be outside, however
briefly, and was crawling on my knees through the rock garden behind Holyrood, much to the amusement of several
Highlanders hanging about the grounds, enjoying the sunshine in their own manner, with a jug of home-brewed
whisky.

"Art huntin' *burras*, Mistress?" called one man.

"Nay, it'll be fairies, surely, not caterpillars," joked another.

"You're more likely to find fairies in that jug than I am under rocks," I called back.

The man held the jug up, closed one eye and squinted theatrically into its depths.

"Aye, well, so long as it isna caterpillars in my jug," he replied, and took a deep swig.

In fact, what I was hunting would make as little—or as much—sense to them as caterpillars, I reflected, shoving one boulder a few inches to the side to expose the orange-brown lichen on its surface. A delicate scraping with the small penknife, and several flakes of the odd symbiont fell into my palm, to be transferred with due care to the cheap tin snuffbox that held my painfully acquired hoard.

Something of the relatively cosmopolitan attitude of Edinburgh had rubbed off on the visiting Highlanders; while in the remote mountain villages, such behavior would have gotten me viewed with suspicion, if not downright hostility, here it seemed no more than a harmless quirk. While the Highlanders treated me with great respect, I was relieved to find that there was no fear mingled with it.

Even my basic Englishness was forgiven, once it was known who my husband was. I supposed I was never going to know more than Jamie had told me about what he had done at the Battle of Prestonpans, but whatever it was, it had mightily impressed the Scots, and "Red Jamie" drew shouts and hails whenever he ventured outside Holyrood.

In fact, a shout from the nearby Highlanders drew my attention at this point, and I looked up to see Red Jamie himself, strolling across the grass, waving absently to the men as he scanned the serried rocks behind the palace.

His face lightened as he saw me, and he came across the grass to where I knelt in the rockery.

"There you are," he said. "Can ye come with me for a bit? And bring your wee basket along, if ye will."

I scrambled to my feet, dusting the dried grass from the knees of my gown, and dropped my scraping knife into the basket.

"All right. Where are we going?"

"Colum's sent word he wishes to speak with us. Both of us."

"Where?" I asked, stretching my steps to keep up with his long stride down the path.

"The kirk in the Canongate."

This was interesting. Whatever Colum wished to see us about, he clearly didn't want the fact that he had spoken with us privately to be known in Holyrood.

Neither did Jamie; hence the basket. Passing arm in arm through the gate, my basket gave an apparent excuse for our venturing up the Royal Mile, whether it were to convey purchases home or distribute medicines to the men and their families quartered in the wynds and closes of Edinburgh.

Edinburgh sloped upward steeply along its one main street. Holyrood sat in dignity at the foot, the creaking Abbey vault alongside conferring a spurious air of gracious security. It loftily ignored the glowering presence of Edinburgh Castle, perched high on the crest of the rocky hill above. In between the two castles, the Royal Mile rose at a rough angle of forty-five degrees. Puffing red-faced at Jamie's side, I wondered how in hell Colum MacKenzie had ever negotiated the quarter-mile of cobbled slope from the palace to the kirk.

We found Colum in the kirkyard, sitting on a stone bench where the late afternoon sun could warm his back. His blackthorn stick lay on the bench beside him, and his short, bowed legs dangled a few inches above the ground. Shoulders hunched and head bowed in thought, at a distance he looked like a gnome, a natural inhabitant of this man-made rock garden, with its tilted stones and creeping lichens. I eyed a prime specimen on a weathered vault, but supposed we had better not stop.

The grass was soundless under our feet, but Colum raised his head while we were still some distance away. There was nothing wrong with his senses, at least.

The shadow under a nearby lime tree moved slightly at our approach. There was nothing wrong with Angus Mhor's senses, either. Satisfied of our identity, the big servant resumed his silent guardianship, becoming again part of the landscape.

Colum nodded in greeting and motioned to the seat beside him. Near at hand, there was no suggestion of the gnomish, despite his twisted body. Face-to-face, you saw nothing but the man within.

Jamie found me a seat on a nearby stone, before taking up the place indicated next to Colum. The marble was surprisingly cold, even through my thick skirts, and I shifted a bit, the carved skull and crossbones atop the memorial lumpy and uncomfortable under me. I saw the epitaph carved below it and grinned:

> *Here lies Martin Elginbrod,*
> *Have mercie on my soul, Lord God,*
> *As I would do were I Lord God,*
> *And thou wert Martin Elginbrod.*

Jamie raised one brow at me in warning, then turned back to Colum. "You asked to see us, Uncle?"

"I've a question for ye, Jamie Fraser," Colum said, without preamble. "D'ye hold me as your kinsman?"

Jamie was silent for a moment, studying his uncle's face. Then he smiled faintly.

"You've my mother's eyes," he said. "Shall I deny that?"

Colum looked startled for a moment. His eyes were the clear, soft gray of a dove's wing, fringed thick with black lashes. For all their beauty, they could gleam cold as steel, and I wondered, not for the first time, just what Jamie's mother had been like.

"You remember your mother? You were no more than a wee laddie when she died."

Jamie's mouth twisted slightly at this, but he answered calmly.

"Old enough. For that matter, my father's house had a looking glass; I'm told I favor her a bit."

Colum laughed shortly. "More than a bit." He peered closely at Jamie, eyes squinting slightly in the bright sun. "Oh, aye, lad; you're Ellen's son, not a doubt of it. That hair, for the one thing . . ." He gestured vaguely toward Jamie's hair, glinting auburn and amber, roan and cinnabar, a thick, wavy mass with a thousand colors of red and gold. ". . . And that mouth." Colum's own mouth rose at one side, as though in reluctant reminiscence. "Wide as a nightjar's, I used to tease her. Ye could catch bugs like a toad, I'd say to her, had ye no but a sticky tongue."

Taken by surprise, Jamie laughed.

"Willie said that once, to me," he said, and then the full lips clamped shut; he spoke rarely of his dead elder brother, and never, I imagined, had he mentioned Willie to Colum before.

If Colum noticed the slip, he gave no sign of it.

"I wrote to her then," he said, looking abstractedly at one of the tilted stones nearby. "When your brother and the babe died of the pox. That was the first time, since she left Leoch."

"Since she wed my father, ye mean."

Colum nodded slowly, still looking away.

"Aye. She was older than me, ye ken, by two years or so; about the same as between your sister and you." The deep-set gray eyes swiveled back and fixed on Jamie.

"I've never met your sister. Were ye close, the two of you?"

Jamie didn't speak, but nodded slightly, studying his uncle closely, as though looking for the answer to a puzzle in the worn face before him.

Colum nodded, too. "It was that way between Ellen and myself. I was a sickly wee thing, and she nursed me often. I remember the sun shining through her hair, and she telling me tales as I lay in bed. Even later"—the fine-cut lips lifted in a slight smile—"when my legs first gave way; she'd come and go, all about Leoch, and stop each morning and night in my chamber, to tell me who she'd seen and what they'd said. We'd talk, about the tenants and the tacksmen, and how things might be arranged. I was married then, but Letitia had no mind for such matters, and less interest." He flipped a hand, dismissing his wife.

"We talked between us—sometimes with Dougal, sometimes alone—of how the fortunes of the clan might best be maintained; how peace might be kept among the septs, which alliances could be made with other clans, how the lands and the timber should be managed. . . . And then she left," he said abruptly, looking down at the broad hands folded on his knee. "With no asking of leave nor word of farewell. She was gone. And I heard of her from others now and then, but from herself—nothing."

"She didn't answer your letter?" I asked softly, not wanting to intrude. He shook his head, still looking down.

"She was ill; she'd lost a child, as well as having the pox. And perhaps she meant to write later; it's an easy task to put off." He smiled briefly, without humor, and then his face relaxed into somberness. "But by Christmas twelvemonth, she was dead."

He looked directly at Jamie, who met his gaze squarely.

"I was a bit surprised, then, when your father wrote to tell me he was taking you to Dougal, and wished ye then to come to me at Leoch for your schooling."

"It was agreed so, when they wed," Jamie answered. "That I should foster with Dougal, and then come to you for a time." The dry twigs of a larch rattled in a passing wind, and he and Colum both hunched their shoulders against the sudden chill of it, their family resemblance exaggerated by the similarity of the gesture.

Colum saw my smile at their resemblance, and one corner of his mouth turned up in answer.

"Oh, aye," he said to Jamie. "But agreements are worth as much as the men who make them, and nay more. And I didna know your father then."

He opened his mouth to go on, but then seemed to reconsider what he had been about to say. The silence of the kirkyard flowed back into the space their conversation had made, filling in the gap as though no word were ever spoken.

It was Jamie, finally, who broke the silence once more.

"What did ye think of my father?" he asked, and I glimpsed in his tone that curiosity of a child who has lost his parents early, seeking clues to the identity of these people known only from a child's restricted point of view. I understood the impulse; what little I knew of my own parents came almost entirely from Uncle Lamb's brief and unsatisfactory answers to my questions—he was not a man given to character analysis.

Colum, on the other hand, was.

"What was he like, d'ye mean?" He looked his nephew over carefully, then gave a short grunt of amusement.

"Look ye in the mirror, lad," he said, a half-grudging

smile lingering on his face. "If it's your mother's face ye see, it's your father looking back at ye through those damned Fraser cat-eyes." He stretched and shifted his position, easing his bones on the lichened stone bench. His lips were pressed tight, by habit, against any exclamation of discomfort, and I could see what had made those deep creases between nose and mouth.

"To answer ye, though," he went on, once more comfortably settled, "I didn't like the man overmuch—nor he me—but I knew him at once for a man of honor." He paused, then said, very softly, "I know you for the same, Jamie MacKenzie Fraser."

Jamie didn't change expression, but there was a faint quiver to his eyelids; only one as familiar with him as I was—or as observant as Colum was—would have noticed.

Colum let out his breath in a long sigh.

"So, lad, that's why I wished to talk with you. I must decide, ye see, whether the MacKenzies of Leoch go for King James or King Geordie." He smiled sourly. "It's a case, I think, of the devil ye know, or the devil ye don't, but it's a choice I must make."

"Dougal—" Jamie began, but his uncle cut him off with a sharp motion of his hand.

"Aye, I know what Dougal thinks—I've had little rest from it, these two years past," he said impatiently. "But I am the MacKenzie of Leoch, and it's mine to decide. Dougal will abide by what I say. I'd know what you'd advise me to do—for the sake of the clan whose blood runs in your veins."

Jamie glanced up, eyes dark blue and impervious, hooded against the afternoon sun that shone in his face.

"I am here, and my men with me," he said. "Surely my choice is plain?"

Colum shifted himself again, head cocked attentively to his nephew, as though to catch any nuances of voice or expression that might give him a clue.

"Is it?" he asked. "Men give their allegiance for any number of reasons, lad, and few of them have much to do with the reasons they speak aloud. I've talked with Lochiel, and Clanranald, and Angus and Alex MacDonald of Scotus. D'ye think they're here only because they feel James Stuart their rightful king? Now I would talk with you—and hear the truth, for the sake of your father's honor."

Seeing Jamie hesitate, Colum went on, still watching his nephew keenly.

"I don't ask for myself; if you've eyes, ye can see that the matter isn't one that will trouble me long. But for Hamish— the lad is your cousin, remember. If there's to be a clan for him to lead, once he's of age—then I must choose rightly, now."

He stopped speaking and sat still, the usual caution now relaxed from his features, the gray eyes open and listening.

Jamie sat as still as Colum, frozen like the marble angel on the tomb behind him. I knew the dilemma that preoccupied him, though no trace of it showed on the stern, chiseled face. It was the same one we had faced before, choosing to come with the men from Lallybroch. Charles's Rising was balanced on a knife edge; the allegiance of a large clan such as the MacKenzies of Leoch might encourage others to join the brash Young Pretender, and lead to his success. But if it ended in failure nonetheless, the MacKenzies of Leoch could well end with it.

At last Jamie turned his head deliberately, and looked at me, blue eyes holding my own. *You have some say in this,* his look said. *What shall I do?*

I could feel Colum's eyes upon me, too, and felt rather than saw the questioning lift of the thick, dark brows above them. But what I saw in my mind's eye was young Hamish, a redheaded ten-year-old who looked enough like Jamie to be his son, rather than his cousin. And what life might be for him, and the rest of his clan, if the MacKenzies of Leoch fell with Charles at Culloden. The men of Lallybroch had Jamie to save them from final slaughter, if it came to that. The men of Leoch would not. And yet the choice could not be mine. I shrugged and bowed my head. Jamie took a deep breath, and made up his mind.

"Go home to Leoch, Uncle," he said. "And keep your men there."

Colum sat motionless for a long minute, looking straight at me. Finally, his mouth curled upward, but the expression was not quite a smile.

"I nearly stopped Ned Gowan, when he went to keep

you from burning," he said to me. "I suppose I'm glad I didn't."

"Thanks," I said, my tone matching his.

He sighed, rubbing the back of his neck with a calloused hand, as though it ached under the weight of leadership.

"Well, then. I shall see His Highness in the morning, and tell him my decision." The hand descended, lying inert on the stone bench, halfway between him and his nephew. "I thank ye, Jamie, for your advice." He hesitated, then added, "And may God go with you."

Jamie leaned forward and laid his hand over Colum's. He smiled his mother's wide, sweet smile and said, "And with you, too, *mo caraidh.*"

The Royal Mile was busy, thronged with people taking advantage of the brief hours of warmth. We walked in silence through the crowd, my hand tucked deep into the crook of Jamie's elbow. Finally he shook his head, muttering something to himself in Gaelic.

"You did right," I said to him, answering the thought rather than the words. "I would have done the same. Whatever happens, at least the MacKenzies will be safe."

"Aye, perhaps." He nodded to a greeting from a passing officer, jostling through the crowd that surrounded the World's End. "But what of the rest—the MacDonalds and MacGillivrays, and the others that have come? Will they be destroyed now, where maybe they wouldn't, had I had the nerve to tell Colum to join them?" He shook his head, face clouded. "There's no knowing, is there, Sassenach?"

"No," I said softly, squeezing his arm. "Never enough. Or maybe too much. But we can't do nothing on that account, surely?"

He gave me a half-smile back, and pressed my hand against his side.

"No, Sassenach. I dinna suppose we can. And it's done now, and naught can change it, so it's no good worrying. The MacKenzies will stay out of it."

The sentry at the gate of Holyrood was a MacDonald, one of Glengarry's men. He recognized Jamie and nodded us into the courtyard, barely looking up from his louse-search-

ing. The warm weather made the vermin active, and as they
left their cozy nests in crotch and armpit, often they could be
surprised while crossing the perilous terrain of shirt or tartan
and removed from the body of their host.

Jamie said something to him in Gaelic, smiling. The man
laughed, picked something from his shirt, and flicked it at
Jamie, who pretended to catch it, eyed the imaginary beastie
critically, then, with a wink at me, popped it into his mouth.

◆————

"Er, how is your son's head, Lord Kilmarnock?" I inquired politely as we stepped out together onto the floor of
Holyrood's Great Gallery. I didn't care greatly, but I thought
as the topic couldn't be avoided altogether, it was perhaps
better to air it in a place where hostility was unlikely to be
openly exhibited.

The Gallery met that criterion, I thought. The long, high-
ceilinged room with its two vast fireplaces and towering windows had been the scene of frequent balls and parties since
Charles's triumphant entry into Edinburgh in September.
Now, crowded with the luminaries of Edinburgh's upper
class, all anxious to do honor to their Prince—once it appeared that he might actually win—the room positively glittered. Don Francisco, the guest of honor, stood at the far end
of the room with Charles, dressed in the depressing Spanish
style, with baggy dark pantaloons, shapeless coat, and even a
small ruff, which seemed to provoke considerable suppressed
amusement among the younger and more fashionable element.

"Oh, well enough, Mistress Fraser," replied Kilmarnock
imperturbably. "A dunt on the skull will not discommode a
lad of that age for long; though his pride may take a bit more
mending," he added, with a sudden humorous twist to his
long mouth.

I smiled at him, relieved to see it.

"You're not angry?"

He shook his head, looking down to be sure that his feet
were clear of my sweeping skirt.

"I have tried to teach John the things he should know as
heir to Kilmarnock. In teaching him humility I seem to have

signally failed; perhaps your servant may have had more success."

"I suppose you didn't whack him outside," I said absently.

"Pardon?"

"Nothing," I said flushing. "Look, is that Lochiel? I thought he was ill."

Dancing required most of my breath, and Lord Kilmarnock appeared not to wish for conversation, so I had time to look around. Charles was not dancing; though he was a good dancer, and the young women of Edinburgh vied for his attentions, tonight he was thoroughly engrossed in the entertainment of his guest. I had seen a small cask with a Portuguese brand-mark burned into its side being rolled into the kitchens in the afternoon, and glasses of the ruby liquid kept reappearing by Don Francisco's left hand as though by magic through the evening.

We crossed the path of Jamie, propelling one of the Misses Williams through the figures of the dance. There were three of them, nearly indistinguishable from one another—young, brown-haired, comely, and all "so terribly interested, Mr. Fraser, in this noble Cause." They made me quite tired, but Jamie, ever the soul of patience, danced with them all, one by one, and answered the same silly questions over and over.

"Well, it's a change for them to get out, poor things," he explained kindly. "And their father's a rich merchant, so His Highness would like to encourage the sympathy of the family."

The Miss Williams with him looked enthralled, and I wondered darkly just how encouraging he was being. Then my attention shifted, as Balmerino danced by with Lord George Murray's wife. I saw the Murrays exchange affectionate glances as they passed, he with another of the Misses Williams, and felt mildly ashamed of my noticing who Jamie danced with.

Not surprisingly, Colum wasn't at the ball. I wondered whether he had had a chance to speak to Charles beforehand, but decided probably not; Charles looked much too cheerful and animated to have been the recipient of bad news anytime recently.

At one side of the Gallery, I caught sight of two stocky
figures, almost identical in uncomfortable and unaccustomed
formal dress. It was John Simpson, Master of the Swordmakers Guild of Glasgow, and his son, also John Simpson.
Arrived earlier in the week to present His Highness with one
of the magnificent basket-hilted broadswords for which they
were famed throughout Scotland, the two artisans had plainly
been invited tonight to show Don Francisco the depth of support that the Stuarts enjoyed.

Both men had thick, dark hair and beards, lightly frosted
with gray. Simpson senior was salt with a sprinkle of pepper,
while Simpson junior gave the impression of a dark hillside
with a rim of snow crusted lightly round its frostline, white
hairs confined to the temples and upper cheeks. As I
watched, the older swordmaker poked his son sharply in the
back and nodded with significance toward one of the merchants' daughters, hovering near the edge of the floor under
her father's protection.

Simpson junior gave his father a skeptical glance, but
then shrugged, stepped out, and offered his arm with a bow
to the third Miss Williams.

I watched with amusement and fascination as they
whirled out into the steps of the dance, for Jamie, who had
met the Simpsons earlier, had told me that Simpson junior
was quite deaf.

"From all the hammering at the forge, I should think,"
he had said, showing me with pride the beautiful sword he
had bought from the artisans. "Deaf as a stone; his father
does the talkin', but the young one sees everything."

I saw the sharp dark eyes flick rapidly across the floor
now, judging to a nicety the distance from one couple to the
next. The young swordmaster trod a little heavily, but kept
the measure of the dance well enough—at least as well as I
did. Closing my eyes, I felt the thrum of the music vibrating
through the wooden floor, from the cellos resting on it, and
assumed that was what he followed. Then, opening my eyes
so as not to crash into anyone, I saw Junior wince at a
screeching miscue among the violins. Perhaps he did hear
some sounds, then.

The circling of the dancers brought Kilmarnock and myself close to the place where Charles and Don Francisco

stood, warming their coattails before the huge, tile-lined fireplace. To my surprise, Charles scowled at me over Don Francisco's shoulder, motioning me away with a surreptitious movement of one hand. Seeing it as we turned, Kilmarnock gave a short laugh.

"So His Highness is afraid to have you introduced to the Spaniard!" he said.

"Really?" I looked back over my shoulder as we whirled away, but Charles had returned to his conversation, waving his hands with expressive Italian gestures as he talked.

"I expect so." Lord Kilmarnock danced skillfully, and I was beginning to relax enough to be able to speak, without worrying incessantly about tripping over my skirts.

"Did you see that silly broadsheet Balmerino was showing everyone?" he asked, and when I nodded, went on, "I imagine His Highness saw it, too. And the Spanish are sufficiently superstitious to be ridiculously sensitive to idiocies of that sort. No person of sense or breeding could take such a thing seriously," he assured me, "but no doubt His Highness thinks it best to be safe. Spanish gold is worth a considerable sacrifice, after all," he added. Apparently including the sacrifice of his own pride; Charles still treated the Scottish earls and the Highland chieftains like beggars at his table, though they had at least been invited to the festivities tonight—no doubt to impress Don Francisco.

"Have you noticed the pictures?" I asked, wanting to change the subject. There were more than a hundred of them lining the walls of the Great Gallery, all portraits, all of kings and queens. And all with a most striking similarity.

"Oh, the nose?" he said, an amused smile replacing the grim expression that had taken possession of his face at sight of Charles and the Spaniard. "Yes, of course. Do you know the story behind it?"

The portraits, it seemed, were all the work of a single painter, one Jacob de Wet, who had been commissioned by Charles II, upon that worthy's restoration, to produce portraits of all the King's ancestors, from the time of Robert the Bruce onward.

"To assure everyone of the ancientness of his lineage, and the entire appropriateness of his restoration," Kilmarnock explained, a wry twist to his mouth. "I wonder if King

James will undertake a similar project when he regains the throne?"

In any case, he continued, De Wet had painted furiously, completing one portrait every two weeks in order to comply with the monarch's demand. The difficulty, of course, was that De Wet had no way of knowing what Charles's ancestors had actually looked like, and had therefore used as sitters anyone he could drag into his studio, merely equipping each portrait with the same prominent nose, by way of ensuring a family resemblance.

"That's King Charles himself," Kilmarnock said, nodding at a full-length portrait, resplendent in red velvet and plumed hat. He cast a critical glance at the younger Charles, whose flushed face gave evidence that he had been hospitably keeping his guest company in his potations.

"A better nose, anyway," the Earl murmured, as though to himself. "His mother was Polish."

It was growing late, and the candles in the silver candelabra were beginning to gutter and go out before the gentlefolk of Edinburgh had had their fill of wine and dancing. Don Francisco, possibly not as accustomed as Charles to unrestrained drinking, was nodding into his ruff.

Jamie, having with an obvious expression of relief restored the last Miss Williams to her father for the journey home, came to join me in the corner where I had found a seat that enabled me to slip off my shoes under cover of my spreading skirts. I hoped I wouldn't have to put them on again in a hurry.

Jamie sat down on a vacant seat beside me, mopping his glowing face with a large white handkerchief. He reached past me to the small table, where a tray with a few leftover cakes was sitting.

"I'm fair starved," he said. "Dancing gives ye a terrible appetite, and the talking's worse." He popped a whole cake into his mouth at once, chewed it briefly, and reached for another.

I saw Prince Charles bend over the slumped form of the guest of honor and shake him by the shoulder, to little effect. The Spanish envoy's head was fallen back and his mouth was slack beneath the drooping mustache. His Highness stood, rather unsteadily, and glanced about for help, but Sheridan and Tullibardine, both elderly gentlemen, had fallen asleep themselves, leaning companionably together like a couple of old village sots in lace and velvet.

"Maybe you'd better give His Highness a hand?" I suggested.

"Mmphm."

Resigned, Jamie swallowed the rest of his cake, but before he could rise, I saw the younger Simpson, who had taken quick note of the situation, nudge his father in the ribs.

Senior advanced and bowed ceremoniously to Prince Charles, then, before the glazed prince could respond, the swordmakers had the Spanish envoy by wrists and ankles. With a heave of forge-toughened muscles, they lifted him from his seat, and bore him away, gently swinging him between them like some specimen of big game. They disappeared through the door at the far end of the hall, followed unsteadily by His Highness.

This rather unceremonious departure signaled the end of the ball.

The other guests began to relax and move about, the ladies disappearing into an anteroom to retrieve shawls and cloaks, the gentlemen standing about in small, impatient knots, exchanging complaints about the time the women were taking to make ready.

As we were housed in Holyrood, we left by the other door, at the north end of the gallery, going through the morning and evening drawing rooms to the main staircase.

The landing and the soaring stairwell were lined with tapestries, their figures dim and silvery in candlelight. And below them stood the giant form of Angus Mhor, his shadow huge on the wall, wavering like one of the tapestry figures as they shimmered in the draft.

"My master is dead," he said.

———➤

"His Highness said," Jamie reported, "that perhaps it was as well." He spoke with a tone of sarcastic bitterness.

"Because of Dougal," he added, seeing my shocked bewilderment at this statement. "Dougal has always been more than willing to join His Highness in the field. Now Colum's gone, Dougal is chief. And so the MacKenzies of Leoch will

march with the Highland army," he said softly, "to victory—
or not."

The lines of grief and weariness were cut deep into his
face, and he didn't resist as I moved behind him and laid my
hands on the broad swell of his shoulders. He made a small
sound of incoherent relief as my fingertips pressed hard into
the muscles at the base of his neck, and let his head fall
forward, resting on his folded arms. He was seated before the
table in our room, and piles of letters and dispatches lay
neatly stacked around him. Amid the documents lay a small
notebook, rather worn, bound in red morocco leather.
Colum's diary, which Jamie had taken from his uncle's rooms
in hopes that it would contain a recent entry confirming
Colum's decision not to support the Jacobite cause.

"Not that it would likely sway Dougal," he had said,
grimly thumbing the close-written pages, "but there's nothing
else to try."

In the event, though, there had been nothing in Colum's
diary for the last three days, save one brief entry, clearly
made upon his return from the churchyard the day before.

*Met with young Jamie and his wife. Have made my peace
with Ellen at last.* And that was, of course, important—to
Colum, to Jamie, and possibly to Ellen—but of little use in
swaying the convictions of Dougal MacKenzie.

Jamie straightened up after a moment and turned to me.
His eyes were dark with worry and resignation.

"What it means is that now we are committed to him,
Claire—to Charles, I mean. There's less choice than there
ever was. We must try to assure his victory."

My mouth felt dry with too much wine. I licked my lips
before answering, to moisten them.

"I suppose so. Damn! Why couldn't Colum have waited
a little longer? Just 'til the morning, when he could have seen
Charles?"

Jamie smiled lopsidedly.

"I dinna suppose he had so much to say about it, Sassenach. Few men get to choose the hour of their death."

"Colum meant to." I had been of two minds whether to
tell Jamie what had passed between me and Colum at our
first meeting in Holyrood, but now there was no point in
keeping Colum's secrets.

Jamie shook his head in disbelief and sighed, his shoulders slumping under the revelation that Colum had meant to take his own life.

"I wonder then," he murmured, half to himself. "Was it a sign, do ye think, Claire?"

"A sign?"

"Colum's death now, before he could do as he meant to and refuse Charles's plea for help. Is it a sign that Charles is destined to win his fight?"

I remembered my last sight of Colum. Death had come for him as he sat in bed, a glass of brandy untouched near his hand. He had met it as he wished, then, clearheaded and alert; his head had fallen back, but his eyes were wide open, dulled to the sights he had left behind. His mouth was pressed tight, the habitual lines carved deep from nose to chin. The pain that was his constant companion had accompanied him as far as it could.

"God knows," I said at last.

"Aye?" he said, voice once more muffled in his arms. "Aye, well. I hope somebody does."

38

A Bargain with the Devil

C atarrh settled on Edinburgh like the cloud of cold
rain that masked the Castle from sight on its hill.
Water ran day and night in the streets, and if the
cobbles were temporarily clean of sewage, the relief from
stench was more than made up for by the splatter of expectorations that slimed every close and wynd, and the choking
cloud of fireplace smoke that filled every room from waist-
height to ceiling.

Cold and miserable as the weather was outside, I found
myself spending a good deal of time walking the grounds of
Holyrood and the Canongate. A faceful of rain seemed preferable to lungfuls of woodsmoke and germ-filled air indoors.
The sounds of coughing and sneezing rang through the Palace, though the constraint of His Highness's genteel presence
caused most hawking sufferers to spit into filthy handkerchiefs
or the Delft-lined fireplaces, rather than on the polished
Scotch oak floors.

The light failed early at this time of year, and I turned
back, halfway up the High Street, in order to reach Holyrood
before dark. I had no fear at all of assault in the darkness;
even had I not been known by now to all the Jacobite troops
occupying the city, the prevailing horror of fresh air kept everyone indoors.

Men still well enough to leave their homes on business
completed their errands with dispatch before diving thankfully into the smoke-filled sanctuary of Jenny Ha's tavern, and
stayed there, nestled cozily into warm airlessness, where the
smell of damp wool, unwashed bodies, whisky, and ale nearly
succeeded in overcoming the reek of the stove.

My only fear was of losing my footing in the dark and
breaking an ankle on the slippery cobbles. The city was lit
only by the feeble lanterns of the town watchmen, and these
had a disconcerting habit of ducking from doorway to doorway, appearing and disappearing like fireflies. And sometimes
disappearing altogether for half an hour at a time, as the

lantern-bearer darted into The World's End at the bottom of the Canongate for a life-saving draught of hot ale.

I eyed the faint glow over the Canongate kirk, estimating how much time remained 'til dark. With luck, I might have time to stop at Mr. Haugh's apothecary's shop. While boasting nothing of the variety to be found in Raymond's Paris emporium, Mr. Haugh did a sound trade in horse chestnuts and slippery-elm bark, and usually was able to provide me with peppermint and barberry, as well. At this time of year, his chief income was derived from the sale of camphor balls, considered a sovereign remedy for colds, catarrh, and consumption. If it was no more effective than modern cold remedies, I reflected, it was no worse, and at least smelled invigoratingly healthy.

Despite the prevalence of red noses and white faces, parties were held at the palace several nights a week, as the noblesse of Edinburgh welcomed their Prince with enthusiasm. Another two hours, and the lanterns of servants accompanying ball-goers would start to flicker in the High Street.

I sighed at the thought of another ball, attended by sneezing gallants, paying compliments in phlegm-thickened voices. Perhaps I'd better add some garlic to the list; worn in a silver pomander-locket about the neck, it was supposed to ward off disease. What it actually did do, I supposed, was to keep disease-ridden companions at a safe distance—equally satisfactory, from my point of view.

The city was occupied by Charles's troops, and the English, while not besieged, were at least sequestered in the Castle above. Still, news—of dubious veracity—tended to leak in both directions. According to Mr. Haugh, the most recent rumor held that the Duke of Cumberland was gathering troops south of Perth, with the intent of marching north almost immediately. I hadn't any idea whether this was true; I doubted it, in fact, recalling no mention of Cumberland's activities much before the spring of 1746, which hadn't arrived. Still, I could hardly ignore the rumor.

The sentry at the gate nodded me in, coughing. The sound was taken up by the guards stationed down the hallways and on the landings. Resisting the impulse to wave my basket of garlic at them like a censer as I passed, I made my way upstairs to the afternoon drawing room, where I was admitted without question.

I found His Highness with Jamie, Aeneas MacDonald, O'Sullivan, His Highness's secretary, and a saturnine man named Francis Townsend, who was lately much in His Highness's good graces. Most of them were red-nosed and sneezing, and splattered phlegm smeared the hearth before the gracious mantel. I cast a sharp look at Jamie, who was slumped wearily in his chair, white-faced and drooping.

Accustomed to my forays into the city, and eager for any intelligence regarding the English movements, the men heard me out with great attention.

"We are indebted greatly to you for your news, Mistress Fraser," said His Highness, with a gracious bow and a smile. "You must tell me if there is some way in which I might repay your generous service."

"There is," I said, seizing the opportunity. "I want to take my husband home to bed. Now."

The Prince's eyes bulged slightly, but he recovered himself quickly. Not so restrained, Aeneas MacDonald broke out into a fit of suspiciously strangled coughing. Jamie's white face blazed suddenly crimson. He sneezed, and buried his countenance in a handkerchief, blue eyes shooting sparks at me over its folds.

"Ah . . . your husband," said Charles, rallying gallantly to the challenge. "Um . . ." A soft pink blush began to tint his cheeks.

"He's ill," I said, with some asperity. "Surely you can see that? I want him to go to bed and rest."

"Oh, *rest*," murmured MacDonald, as though to himself.

I searched for some sufficiently courtly words.

"I should be sorry to deprive Your Highness temporarily of my husband's attendance, but if he isn't allowed to take sufficient rest, he isn't likely to go on attending you much longer."

Charles, recovered from his momentary discomposure, seemed now to be finding Jamie's patent discomfiture entertaining.

"To be sure," he said, eyeing Jamie, whose complexion had faded now into a sort of mottled pallor. "We should dislike exceedingly the contemplation of such a prospect as you describe, Madam." He inclined his head in my direction. "It shall be as you wish, Madam. *Cher* James is excused from attendance upon our person until he shall be recovering. By all means, take your husband to your rooms at once, and, er . . . undertake what cure seems . . . ah . . . fitting." The corner of the Prince's mouth twitched suddenly, and pulling a large handkerchief from his pocket, he followed Jamie's example and buried the lower half of his face, coughing delicately.

"Best take care, Highness," MacDonald advised somewhat caustically. "You may catch Mr. Fraser's ailment."

"One could wish to have *half* Mr. Fraser's complaint," murmured Francis Townsend, with no attempt at concealing the sardonic smile that made him look like a fox in a hen coop.

Jamie, now bearing a strong resemblance to a frostbitten tomato, rose abruptly, bowed to the Prince with a brief "I thank ye, Highness," and headed for the door, clutching me by the arm.

"Let go," I snarled as we swept past the guards in the anteroom. "You're breaking my arm."

"Good," he muttered. "As soon as I've got ye in private, I'm going to break your neck." But I caught sight of the curl of his mouth, and knew the gruffness was only a facade.

Once in our apartment, with the door safely shut, he pulled me to him, leaned against the door and laughed, his cheek pressed to the top of my head.

"Thank ye, Sassenach," he said, wheezing slightly.

"You're not angry?" I asked, voice somewhat muffled in his shirtfront. "I didn't mean to embarrass you."

"Nay, I'm no minding it." he said, releasing me. "God, I wouldna ha' cared if ye'd said ye meant to set me on fire in the Great Gallery, so long as I could leave His Highness and come to rest for a bit. I'm tired to death of the man, and every muscle I've got is aching." A sudden spasm of coughing shook his frame, and he leaned against the door once more, this time for support.

"Are you all right?" I stretched up on tiptoe to feel his forehead. I wasn't surprised, but was somewhat alarmed, to feel how hot his skin was beneath my palm.

"You," I said accusingly, "have a temperature!"

"Aye well, everyone's got a temperature, Sassenach," he said, a bit crossly. "Only some are hotter than others, no?"

"Don't quibble," I said, relieved that he still felt well enough to chop logic. "Take off your clothes. And don't say it," I added crisply, seeing the grin forming as he opened his mouth to reply. "I have no designs whatever on your disease-ridden carcass, beyond getting it into a nightshirt."

"Oh, aye? Ye dinna think I'd benefit from the exercise?" he teased, beginning to unfasten his shirt. "I thought ye said exercise was healthy." His laugh turned suddenly to an attack of hoarse coughing that left him breathless and flushed. He dropped the shirt on the floor, and almost immediately began to shiver with chill.

"Much too healthy for you, my lad." I yanked the thick woolen nightshirt over his head, leaving him to struggle into it as I got him out of kilt, shoes, and stockings. "Christ, your feet are like ice!"

"You could . . . warm them . . . for me." But the words were forced out between chattering teeth, and he made no protest when I steered him toward the bed.

He was shaking too hard to speak by the time I had snatched a hot brick from the fire with tongs, wrapped it in flannel, and thrust it in at his feet.

The chill was hard but brief, and he lay still again by the time I had set a pan of water to steep with a handful of peppermint and black currant.

"What's that?" he asked, suspiciously, sniffing the air as I opened another jar from my basket. "Ye dinna mean me to drink it, I hope? It smells like a duck that's been hung ower-long."

"You're close," I said. "It's goose grease mixed with camphor. I'm going to rub your chest with it."

"No!" He snatched the covers protectively up beneath his chin.

"Yes," I said firmly, advancing with purpose.

In the midst of my labors, I became aware that we had an audience. Fergus stood on the far side of the bed, watching the proceedings with fascination, his nose running freely. I removed my knee from Jamie's abdomen and reached for a handkerchief.

"And what are *you* doing here?" Jamie demanded, trying to yank the front of his nightshirt back into place.

Not noticeably disconcerted by the unfriendly tone of this greeting, Fergus ignored the proffered handkerchief and wiped his nose on his sleeve, meanwhile staring with round-eyed admiration at the broad expanse of muscular, gleaming chest on display.

"The skinny milord sent me to fetch a packet he says you have for him. Do all Scotsmen have such quantities of hair upon their chests, milord?"

"Christ! I forgot all about the dispatches. Wait, I'll take them to Cameron myself." Jamie began to struggle up in bed, a process that brought his nose close to the site of my recent endeavors.

"Phew!" He flapped the nightshirt in an effort to dispel the penetrating aroma, and glared accusingly at me. "How am I to get this reek off me? D'ye expect me to go out in company smellin' like a dead goose, Sassenach?"

"No, I don't," I said. "I expect you to lie quietly in bed and rest, or you'll *be* a dead goose." I uncorked a fairly high-caliber glare of my own.

"I can carry the package, milord," Fergus was assuring him.

"You will do nothing of the kind," I said, noting the boy's flushed cheeks and overbright eyes. I put a hand to his forehead.

"Don't tell me," said Jamie sarcastically. "He's got a temperature?"

"Yes, he has."

"Ha," he said to Fergus with gloomy satisfaction. "Now you're for it. See how *you* like bein' basted."

A short period of intense effort saw Fergus tucked up in his pallet by the fire, goose grease and medicinal hot tea administered lavishly all round, and a clean handkerchief deposited beneath the chin of each sufferer.

"There," I said, fastidiously rinsing my hands in the basin. "Now, *I* will take this precious packet of dispatches across to Mr. Cameron. *You* will both rest, drink hot tea, rest, blow your nose, and rest, in that order. Got it, troops?"

The tip of a long, reddened nose was barely visible above

the bedclothes. It oscillated slowly back and forth as Jamie
shook his head.

"Drunk wi' power," he remarked disapprovingly to the
ceiling. "Verra unwomanly attitude, that."

I dropped a kiss on his hot forehead and swung my cloak
down from its hook.

"How little you know of women, my love," I said.

Ewan Cameron was in charge of what passed for intelligence operations at Holyrood. His quarters were at the end
of the west wing, tucked away near the kitchens. On purpose,
I suspected, having witnessed the man's appetite in action.
Possibly a tapeworm, I thought, viewing the officer's cadaverous countenance as he opened the packet and scanned the
dispatches.

"All in order?" I asked after a moment. I had to repress
the automatic urge to add "sir."

Startled from his train of thought, he jerked his head up
from the dispatches and blinked at me.

"Um? Oh!" Recalled to himself, he smiled and hastened
to make apologies.

"I'm sorry, Mistress Fraser. How impolite of me to forget myself and leave you standing there. Yes, everything appears to be in order—most interesting," he murmured to
himself. Then, snapping back to an awareness of me, "Would
you be so kind as to tell your husband that I wish to discuss
these with him as soon as possible? I understand that he is
unwell," he added delicately, carefully avoiding my eye. Apparently it hadn't taken Aeneas MacDonald long to relay an
account of my interview with the Prince.

"He is," I said unhelpfully. The last thing I wanted was
Jamie leaving his bed and sitting up poring over intelligence
dispatches all night with Cameron and Lochiel. That would
be nearly as bad as staying up dancing all night with the ladies
of Edinburgh. Well, possibly not *quite* as bad, I amended to
myself, recalling the three Misses Williams.

"I'm sure he will attend upon you as soon as he's able," I
said, pulling the edges of the cloak together. "I'll tell him."
And I would—tomorrow. Or possibly the next day. Wherever

the English forces presently were, I was positive they weren't within a hundred miles of Edinburgh.

A quick peek into the bedroom upon my return showed two lumps, immobile beneath the bedclothes, and the sounds of breathing—slow and regular, if a trifle congested—filled the room. Reassured, I removed my cloak and sat down in the sitting room with a preventative cup of hot tea, to which I had added a fair dollop of medicinal brandy.

Sipping slowly, I felt the liquid heat flow down the center of my chest, spread comfortably through my abdomen, and begin working its steady way down toward my toes, quick-frozen after a dash across the courtyard, undertaken in preference to the circuitous inside passage with its endless stairs and turnings.

I held the cup below my chin, inhaling the pleasant, bitter smell, feeling the heated fumes of the brandy clarify my sinuses. Sniffing, it occurred to me to wonder exactly *why,* in a city and a building plagued with colds and influenza, my own sinuses remained unclogged.

In fact, aside from the childbed fever, I had not been ill once since my passage through the stone circle. That *was* odd, I thought; given the standards of hygiene and sanitation, and the crowded conditions in which we frequently lived, I ought surely to have come down at least with a case of sniffles by this time. But I remained as disgustingly healthy as always.

Plainly I was not immune to all diseases, or I would not have had the fever. But the common communicable ones? Some were explainable on the basis of vaccination, of course. I couldn't, for example, catch smallpox, typhus, cholera, or yellow fever. Not that yellow fever was likely, but still. I set down the cup and felt my left arm, through the cloth of the sleeve. The vaccination scar had faded with time, but was still prominent enough to be detectable; a roughly circular patch of pitted skin, perhaps a half-inch in diameter.

I shuddered briefly, reminded again of Geillis Duncan, then pushed the thought away, diving back into a contemplation of my state of health in order to avoid thinking either of the woman who had gone to a death by fire, or of Colum MacKenzie, the man who had sent her there.

The cup was nearly empty, and I rose to refill it, thinking. An acquired immunity, perhaps? I had learned in nurses' training that colds are caused by innumerable viruses, each distinct and ever-evolving. Once exposed to a particular virus, the instructor had explained, you became immune to it. You continued to catch cold as you encountered new and different viruses, but the chances of meeting something you hadn't been exposed to before became smaller as you got older. So, he had said, while children caught an average of six colds per year, people in middle age caught only two, and elderly folk might go for years between colds, only because they had already met most of the common viruses and become immune.

Now there was a possibility, I thought. What if some types of immunity became hereditary, as viruses and people co-evolved? Antibodies to many diseases could be passed from mother to child, I knew that. Via the placenta or the breast milk, so that the child was immune—temporarily—to any disease to which the mother had been exposed. Perhaps I never caught cold because I harbored ancestral antibodies to eighteenth-century viruses—benefiting from the colds caught by all my ancestors for the past two hundred years?

I was pondering this entertaining idea, so caught up in it that I hadn't bothered to sit down, but was sipping my tea standing in the middle of the room, when a soft knock sounded on the door.

I sighed impatiently, annoyed at being distracted. I didn't bother to set the cup down, but came to the door prepared to receive—and repel—the expected inquiries about Jamie's health. Likely Cameron had come across an unclear passage in a dispatch, or His Highness had thought better of his generosity in dismissing Jamie from attendance at the ball. Well, they would get him out of bed tonight only over my dead and trampled body.

I yanked open the door, and the words of greeting died in my throat. Jack Randall stood in the shadows of the doorway.

The wetness of the spilled tea soaking through my skirt brought me to my senses, but he had already stepped inside.

He looked me up and down with his usual air of disdainful appraisal, then glanced at the closed bedroom door.

"You are alone?"

"Yes!"

The hazel glance flickered back and forth between me and the door, assessing my truthfulness. His face was lined from ill health, pale from poor nutrition and a winter spent indoors, but showed no diminution of alertness. The quick, ruthless brain had retreated a bit further back, behind the curtain of those ice-glazed eyes, but it was still there; no doubt of that.

Making his decision, he grasped me by the arm, scooping up my discarded cloak with his other hand.

"Come with me."

I would have allowed him to chop me in pieces before I made a sound that would cause the bedroom door to open.

We were halfway down the corridor outside before I felt it safe to speak. There were no guards stationed within the confines of the staff quarters, but the grounds were heavily patrolled. He couldn't hope to get me through the rockery or the side gates without detection, let alone through the main palace entrance. Therefore, whatever he wanted with me, it must be a business that could be conducted within the precincts of Holyrood.

Murder, perhaps, in revenge for the injury Jamie had done him? Stomach lurching at the thought, I inspected him as closely as I could as we walked swiftly through the pools of light cast from the candleholders on the wall. Not intended for decoration or for graciousness, the candles in this part of the palace were small and widely spaced and the flames feeble, meant only to provide sufficient light to assist visitors returning to their chambers.

He wasn't in uniform, and appeared completely unarmed. He was dressed in nondescript homespun, with a thick coat over plain brown breeks and hose. Nothing but the straightness of his carriage and the arrogant tilt of his unwigged head gave evidence of his identity—he could easily have slipped inside the grounds with one of the parties arriving for the ball, posing as a servant.

No, I decided, glancing warily at him as we passed from dimness to light, he *wasn't* armed, though his hand clamped around my arm was hard as iron. Still, if it was strangling he had in mind, he wouldn't find me an easy victim; I was nearly as tall as he was, and a good deal better nourished.

As though he sensed my thought, he paused near the end of the corridor and turned me to face him, hands tight above my elbows.

"I mean you no harm," he said, low-voiced but firm.

"Tell me another one," I said, estimating the chances of anyone hearing me if I screamed here. I knew there would be a guard at the foot of the stair, but that was on the other side of two doors, a short landing, and a long staircase.

On the other hand, it was stalemate. If he couldn't take me farther, neither could I summon aid where I was. This end of the corridor was sparsely populated, and such residents as there were would undoubtedly be in the other wing now, either attending the ball or serving at it.

He spoke impatiently.

"Don't be idiotic. If I wished to kill you, I could do it here. It would be a great deal safer than taking you outside. For that matter," he added, "if I meant you harm, inside or out, why should I have brought your cloak?" He lifted the garment from his arm in illustration.

"How the hell should I know?" I said, though it seemed a definite point. "Why *did* you bring it?"

"Because I wish you to go outside with me. I have a proposal to make to you, and I will brook no chance of being overheard." He glanced toward the door at the end of the corridor. Like all the others in Holyrood, it was constructed in the cross-and-Book style, the upper four panels arranged to form a cross, the lower two panels standing tall, forming the likeness of an open Bible. Holyrood had once been an Abbey.

"Will you come into the church? We can speak there without fear of interruption." This was true; the church adjoining the palace, part of the original Abbey, was abandoned, rendered unsafe by lack of maintenance over the years. I hesitated, wondering what to do.

"Think, woman!" He gave me a slight shake, then released me and stood back. The candlelight silhouetted him, so that his features were no more than a dark blur facing me. "Why should I take the risk of entering the palace?"

This was a good question. Once he had left the shelter of the Castle in disguise, the streets of Edinburgh were open to him. He could have lurked about the alleys and wynds until he caught sight of me on my daily expeditions, and waylaid me there. The only possible reason not to do so was the one he gave; he needed to speak to me without risk of being overseen or overheard.

He saw conclusion dawn in my face, and his shoulders relaxed slightly. He spread the cloak, holding it for me.

"You have my word that you will return from our conversation unmolested, Madam."

I tried to read his expression, but nothing showed on the thin, chiseled features. The eyes were steady, and told me no more than would my own, seen in a looking glass.

I reached for the cloak.

"All right," I said.

We went out into the dimness of the rock garden, passing the sentry with no more than a nod. He recognized me, and it was not unusual for me to go out at night, to attend to an urgent case of sickness in the city. The guard glanced sharply at Jack Randall—it was usually Murtagh who accompanied me, if Jamie could not—but dressed as he was, there was no hint of the Captain's real identity. He returned the guard's glance with indifference, and the door of the palace closed behind us, leaving us in the chill dark outside.

It had been raining earlier, but the storm was breaking up. Thick clouds shredded and flew overhead, driven by a wind that whipped aside my cloak and plastered my skirt to my legs.

"This way." I clutched the heavy velvet close around me, bent my head against the wind, and followed Jack Randall's lean figure through the path of the rockery.

We emerged at the lower end, and after a pause for a quick look around, crossed rapidly across the grass to the portal of the church.

The door had warped and hung ajar; it had been disused for several years because of structural faults that made the building dangerous, and no one had troubled to repair it. I kicked my way through a barrier of dead leaves and rubbish, ducking from the flickering moonlight of the palace's back garden into the absolute darkness of the church.

Or not quite absolute; as my eyes grew accustomed to the dark, I could see the tall lines of the pillars that marched down each side of the nave, and the delicate stonework of the enormous window at the far end, glass mostly gone.

A movement in the shadows showed me where Randall had gone; I turned between the pillars and found him in a space where a recess once used as a baptismal font had left a stone ledge along the wall. To either side were pale blotches on the walls; the memorial tablets of those buried in the church. Others lay flat, embedded in the floor on either side of the central aisle, the names blurred by the traffic of feet.

"All right," I said. "We can't be overheard now. What do you want of me?"

"Your skill as a physician, and your complete discretion. In exchange for such information as I possess regarding the movements and plans of the Elector's troops," he answered promptly.

That rather took my breath away. Whatever I had been expecting, it wasn't this. He couldn't possibly mean . . .

"You're looking for medical treatment?" I asked, making no effort to disguise the mingled horror and amazement in my voice. "From me? I understood that you . . . er, I mean . . ." With a major effort of will, I stopped myself floundering and said firmly, "Surely you have already received whatever medical treatment is possible? You appear to be in reasonably good condition." Externally, at least. I bit my lip, suppressing an urge toward hysteria.

"I am informed that I am fortunate to be alive, Madam," he answered coldly. "The point is debatable." He set the lantern in a niche in the wall, where the scooped basin of a piscina lay dry and empty in its recess.

"I assume your inquiry to be motivated by medical curiosity rather than concern for my welfare," he went on. The lanternlight, shed at waist height, illuminated him from the ribs downward, leaving head and shoulders hidden. He laid a hand on the waistband of his breeches, turning slightly toward me.

"Do you wish to inspect the injury, in order to judge the effectiveness of treatment?" The shadows hid his face, but the splinters of ice in his voice were tipped with poison.

"Perhaps later," I said, as cool as he. "If not yourself, for whom do you seek my skill?"

He hesitated, but it was far too late for reticence.

"For my brother."

"Your brother?" I couldn't keep the shock from my voice. "Alexander?"

"Since my elder brother Edward is, so far as I know, virtuously engaged in stewardship of the family estates in Sussex, and in need of no assistance," he said dryly. "Yes, my brother Alex."

I spread my hands on the cold stone of a sarcophagus to steady myself.

"Tell me about it," I said.

It was a simple enough story, and a sad one. Had it been anyone other than Jonathan Randall who told it, I might have found myself prey to sympathy.

Deprived of his employment with the Duke of Sandringham because of the scandal over Mary Hawkins, and too frail of health to secure another appointment, Alexander Randall had been forced to seek aid from his brothers.

"Edward sent him two pounds and a letter of earnest exhortations." Jack Randall leaned back against the wall, crossing his ankles. "Edward is a very earnest sort, I'm afraid. But he wasn't prepared to have Alex come home to Sussex. Edward's wife is a bit . . . extreme, shall we say? in her religious opinions." There was a wisp of amusement in his voice that suddenly made me like him for a moment. In different circumstances, might he have been like the great-grandson he resembled?

The sudden thought of Frank so unsettled me that I missed his next remark.

"I'm sorry. What did you say?" I clutched my left hand with my right, fingers pinching tight on my gold wedding ring. Frank was gone. I must stop thinking of him.

"I said that I had procured rooms for Alex near the Castle, so that I might look in on him myself, as my funds did not stretch far enough to allow of employing a proper servant for him."

But the occupation of Edinburgh had of course made

such attendance difficult, and Alex Randall had been left more or less to his own devices for the past month, aside from the intermittent offices of a woman who came in to clean now and then. In ill health to start with, his condition had been worsened by cold weather, poor diet, and squalid conditions until, seriously alarmed, Jack Randall had been moved to seek my help. And to offer for that help, the betrayal of his King.

"Why would you come to me?" I asked at last, turning from the plaque.

He looked faintly surprised.

"Because of who you are." His lips curved in a slight, self-mocking smile. "If one seeks to sell one's soul, is it not proper to go to the powers of darkness?"

"You really think that I'm a power of darkness, do you?" Plainly he did; he was more than capable of mockery, but there had been none in his original proposal.

"Aside from the stories about you in Paris, you told me so yourself," he pointed out. "When I let you go from Wentworth." He turned in the dark, shifting himself on the stone ledge.

"That was a serious mistake," he said softly. "You should never have left that place alive, dangerous creature. And yet I had no choice; your life was the price he set. And I would have paid still higher stakes than that, for what he gave me."

I made a slight hissing noise, which I muffled at once, but too late to stop him hearing me. He half-sat on the ledge, one hip resting on the stone, one leg stretched down to balance him. The moon broke through the scudding clouds outside, backlighting him through the broken window. In the dimness, head half-turned and the lines of cruelty around his mouth erased by darkness, I could mistake him again, as I had once before, for a man I had loved. For Frank.

Yet I had betrayed that man; because of my choice, that man would never be. *For the sins of the fathers shall be visited on the children . . . and thou shalt destroy him, root and branch, so that his name shall no more be known among the tribes of Israel.*

"Did he tell you?" the light, pleasant voice asked from the shadows. "Did he ever tell you all the things that passed between us, him and me, in that small room at Wentworth?"

Through my shock and rage, I noticed that he obeyed Jamie's injunction; not once did he use his name. "He." "Him." Never "Jamie." That was mine.

My teeth were clenched tight, but I forced the words through them.

"He told me. Everything."

He made a small sound, half a sigh.

"Whether the idea pleases you or not, my dear, we are linked, you and I. I cannot say it pleases me, but I admit the truth of it. You know, as I do, the touch of his skin—so warm, is he not? Almost as though he burned from within. You know the smell of his sweat and the roughness of the hairs on his thighs. You know the sound that he makes at the last, when he has lost himself. So do I."

"Be quiet," I said. *"Be still!"* He ignored me, leaning back, speaking thoughtfully, as though to himself. I recognized, with a fresh burst of rage, the impulse that led him to this—not the intention, as I had thought, to upset me, but an overwhelming urge to talk of a beloved; to rehearse aloud and live again vanished details. For after all, to whom might he speak of Jamie in this way, but to me?

"I am leaving!" I said loudly, and whirled on my heel.

"Will you leave?" said the calm voice behind me. "I can deliver General Hawley into your hands. Or you can let him take the Scottish army. Your choice, Madam."

I had the strong urge to reply that General Hawley wasn't worth it. But I thought of the Scottish chieftains now quartered in Holyroodhouse—Kilmarnock and Balmerino and Lochiel, only a few feet away on the other side of the Abbey wall. Of Jamie himself. Of the thousands of clansmen they led. Was the chance of victory worth the sacrifice of my feelings? And was this the turning point, again a place of choice? If I didn't listen, if I didn't accept the bargain Randall proposed, what then?

I turned, slowly. "Talk, then," I said. "If you must." He seemed unmoved by my anger, and unworried by the possibility that I would refuse him. The voice in the dark church was even, controlled as a lecturer's.

"I wonder, you know," he said. "Whether you have had from him as much as I?" He tilted his head to one side, sharp features coming into focus as he moved out of the shadow.

The fugitive light caught him momentarily from the side, lighting the pale hazel of his eyes and making them shine, like those of a beast glimpsed hiding in the bushes.

The note of triumph in his voice was faint, but unmistakable.

"I," he said softly, "I have had him as you could never have him. You are a woman; you cannot understand, even witch as you are. I have held the soul of his manhood, have taken from him what he has taken from me. I know him, as he now knows me. We are bound, he and I, by blood."

I give ye my Body, that we Two may be One . . .

"You choose a very odd way of seeking my help," I said, my voice shaking. My hands were clenched in the folds of my skirt, the fabric cold and bunched between my fingers.

"Do I? I think it best you understand, Madam. I do not beseech your pity, do not call upon your power as a man might seek mercy from a woman, depending upon what people call womanly sympathy. For that cause, you might come to my brother on his own account." A lock of dark hair fell loose across his forehead; he brushed it back with one hand.

"I prefer that it be a straight bargain made between us, Madam; of service rendered and price paid—for realize, Madam, that my feelings toward you are much as yours toward me must be."

That was a shock; while I struggled to find an answer, he went on.

"We are linked, you and I, through the body of one man —through *him*. I would have no such link formed through the body of my brother; I seek your help to heal his body, but I take no risk that his soul shall fall prey to you. Tell me, then; is the price I offer acceptable to you?"

I turned away from him and walked down the center of the echoing nave. I was shaking so hard that my steps felt uncertain, and the shock of the hard stone beneath my soles jolted me. The tracery of the great window over the disused altar stood black against the white of racing clouds, and dim shafts of moonlight lit my path.

At the end of the nave, as far as I could get from him, I stopped and pressed my hands against the wall for support. It was too dark even to see the letters of the marble tablet under my hands, but I could feel the cool, sharp lines of the carving. The curve of a small skull, resting on crossed thigh bones, a pious version of the jolly Roger. I let my head fall forward, forehead to forehead with the invisible skull, smooth as bone against my skin.

I waited, eyes closed, for my gorge to subside, and the heated pulse that throbbed in my temples to cool.

It makes no difference, I told myself. No matter what he is. No matter what he says.

We are linked, you and I, through the body of one man . . . Yes, but not through Jamie. *Not through him!* I insisted, to him, to myself. Yes, you took him, you bastard! But I took him back, I freed him from you. *You have no part of him!* But the sweat that trickled down my ribs and the sound of my own sobbing breath belied my conviction.

Was this the price I must pay for the loss of Frank? A thousand lives that might be saved, perhaps, in compensation for that one loss?

The dark mass of the altar loomed to my right, and I wished with all my heart that there might be some presence there, whatever its nature; something to turn to for an answer. But there was no one here in Holyrood; no one but me. The spirits of the dead kept their own counsel, silent in the stones of wall and floor.

I tried to put Jack Randall out of my mind. If it weren't he, if it were any other man who asked, would I go? There was Alex Randall to be considered, all other things aside. "For that cause, you might come to my brother on his own account," the Captain had said. And of course I would. Whatever I might offer him in the way of healing, could I withhold it because of the man who asked it?

It was a long time before I straightened, pushing myself wearily erect, my hands damp and slick on the curve of the skull. I felt drained and weak, my neck aching and my head heavy, as though the sickness in the city had laid its hand on me after all.

He was still there, patient in the cold dark.

"Yes," I said abruptly, as soon as I came within speaking distance. "All right. I'll come tomorrow, in the forenoon. Where?"

"Ladywalk Wynd," he said. "You know it?"

"Yes." Edinburgh was a small city—no more than the

single High Street, with the tiny, ill-lit wynds and closes opening off it. Ladywalk Wynd was one of the poorer ones.

"I will meet you there," he said. "I shall have the information for you." He slid to his feet and took a step forward,
then stood, waiting for me to move. I saw that he didn't want
to pass close by me, in order to reach the door.

"Afraid of me, are you?" I said, with a humorless laugh.
"Think I'll turn you into a toadstool?"

"No," he said, surveying me calmly. "I do not fear you,
Madam. You cannot have it both ways, you know. You sought
to terrify me at Wentworth, by giving me the day of my death.
But having told me that, you cannot now threaten me, for if I
shall die in April of next year, you cannot harm me now, can
you?"

Had I had a knife with me, I might have shown him
otherwise, in a soul-satisfying moment of impulse. But the
doom of prophecy lay on me, and the weight of a thousand
Scottish lives. He was safe from me.

"I keep my distance, Madam," he said, "merely because
I would prefer to take no chance of touching you."

I laughed once more, this time genuinely.

"And that, Captain," I said, "is an impulse with which I
am entirely in sympathy." I turned and left the church, leaving him to follow as he would.

I had no need to ask or to wonder whether he would
keep his word. He had freed me once from Wentworth, because he had given his word to do so. His word, once given,
was his bond. Jack Randall was a gentleman.

What did you feel, when I gave my body to Jack Randall?
Jamie had asked me.

Rage, I had said. *Sickness. Horror.*

I leaned against the door of the sitting room, feeling
them all again. The fire had died out and the room was cold.
The smell of camphorated goose grease tingled in my nostrils.
It was quiet, save for the heavy rasp of breathing from the
bed, and the faint sound of the wind, passing by the six-foot
walls.

I knelt at the hearth and began to rebuild the fire. It had
gone out completely, and I pushed back the half-burnt log

and brushed the ashes away before breaking the kindling into a small heap in the center of the hearthstone. We had wood fires in Holyrood, not peat. Unfortunate, I thought; a peat fire wouldn't have gone out so easily.

My hands shook a little, and I dropped the flint box twice before I succeeded in striking a spark. The cold, I said to myself. It was very cold in here.

Did he ever tell you all the things that passed between us? said Jack Randall's mocking voice.

"All I need to know," I muttered to myself, touching a paper spill to the tiny flame and carrying it from point to point, setting the tinder aglow in half a dozen spots. One at a time, I added small sticks, poking each one into the flame and holding it there until the fire caught. When the pile of kindling was burning merrily, I reached back and caught the end of the big log, lifting it carefully into the heart of the fire. It was pinewood; green, but with a little sap, bubbling from a split in the wood in a tiny golden bead.

Crystallized and frozen with age, it would make a drop of amber, hard and permanent as gemstone. Now, it glowed for a moment with the sudden heat, popped and exploded in a tiny shower of sparks, gone in an instant.

"All I need to know," I whispered. Fergus's pallet was empty; waking and finding himself cold, he had crawled off in search of a warm haven.

He was curled up in Jamie's bed, the dark head and the red one resting side by side on the pillow, mouths slightly open as they snored peacefully together. I couldn't help smiling at the sight, but I didn't mean to sleep on the floor myself.

"Out you go," I murmured to Fergus, manhandling him to the edge of the bed, and rolling him into my arms. He was light-boned and thin for a ten-year-old, but still awfully heavy. I got him to his pallet without difficulty and plunked him in, still unconscious, then came back to Jamie's bed.

I undressed slowly, standing by the bed, looking down at him. He had turned onto his side and curled himself up against the cold. His lashes lay long and curving against his cheek; they were a deep auburn, nearly black at the tips, but a pale blond near the roots. It gave him an oddly innocent air, despite the long, straight nose and the firm lines of mouth and chin.

Clad in my chemise, I slid into bed behind him, snuggling against the wide, warm back in its woolen nightshirt. He stirred a little, coughing, and I put a hand on the curve of his hip to soothe him. He shifted, curling further and thrusting himself back against me with a small exhalation of awareness. I put my arm around his waist, my hand brushing the soft mass of his testicles. I could rouse him, I knew, sleepy as he was; it took very little to bring him standing, no more than a few firm strokes of my fingers.

I didn't want to disturb his rest, though, and contented myself with gently patting his belly. He reached back a large hand and clumsily patted my thigh in return.

"I love you," he muttered, half-awake.

"I know," I said, and fell asleep at once, holding him.

39

Family Ties

It was not quite a slum, but the next thing to it. I stepped gingerly aside to avoid a substantial puddle of filth, left by the emptying of chamber pots from the windows overhead, awaiting removal by the next hard rain.

Randall caught my elbow to save my slipping on the slimy cobblestones. I stiffened at the touch, and he withdrew his hand at once.

He saw my glance at the crumbling doorpost, and said defensively, "I couldn't afford to move him to better quarters. It isn't so bad inside."

It wasn't—quite. Some effort had been made at furnishing the room comfortably, at least. There was a large bowl and ewer, a sturdy table with a loaf, a cheese, and a bottle of wine upon it, and the bed was equipped with a feather mattress, and several thick quilts.

The man who lay on the mattress had thrown off the quilts, overheated by the effort of coughing, I assumed. He was quite red in the face, and the force of his coughing shook the bed frame, sturdy as it was.

I crossed to the window and threw it up, disregarding Randall's exclamation of protest. Cold air swept into the stifling room, and the stench of unwashed flesh, unclean linen, and overflowing chamber pot lightened a bit.

The coughing gradually eased, and Alexander Randall's flushed countenance faded to a pasty white. His lips were slightly blue, and his chest labored as he fought to recover his breath.

I glanced around the room, but didn't see anything suitable to my purpose. I opened my medical kit and drew out a stiff sheet of parchment. It was a trifle frayed at the edges, but would still serve. I sat down on the edge of the bed, smiling as reassuringly at Alexander as I could manage.

"It was . . . kind of you . . . to come," he said, struggling not to cough between words.

"You'll be better in a moment," I said. "Don't talk, and don't fight the cough. I'll need to hear it."

His shirt was unfastened already; I spread it apart to expose a shockingly sunken chest. It was nearly fleshless; the ribs were clearly visible from abdomen to clavicle. He had always been thin, but the last year's illness had left him emaciated.

I rolled the parchment into a tube and placed one end against his chest, my ear against the other. It was a crude stethoscope, but amazingly effective.

I listened at various spots, instructing him to breathe deeply. I didn't need to tell him to cough, poor boy.

"Roll onto your stomach for a moment." I pulled up the shirt and listened, then tapped gently on his back, testing the resonance over both lungs. The bare flesh was clammy with sweat under my fingers.

"All right. Onto your back again. Just lie still, now, and relax. This won't hurt at all." I kept up the soothing talk as I checked the whites of his eyes, the swollen lymph glands in his neck, the coated tongue and inflamed tonsils.

"You've a touch of catarrh," I said, patting his shoulder. "I'll brew you something that will ease the cough. Meanwhile . . ." I pointed a toe distastefully at the lidded china receptacle under the bed, and glanced at the man who stood waiting by the door, back braced and rigid as though on parade.

"Get rid of that," I ordered. Randall glared at me, but came forward and stooped to obey.

"Not out the window!" I said sharply, as he made a move toward it. "Take it downstairs." He about-faced and left without looking at me.

Alexander drew a shallow breath as the door closed behind his brother. He smiled up at me, hazel eyes glowing in his pale face. The skin was nearly transparent, stretched tight over the bones of his face.

"You'd better hurry, before Johnny comes back. What is it?"

His dark hair was disordered by the coughing; trying to restrain the feelings it roused in me, I smoothed it for him. I didn't want to tell him, but he clearly knew already.

"You have got catarrh. You also have tuberculosis—consumption."

"And?"

"And congestive heart failure," I said, meeting his eyes straight on.

"Ah. I thought . . . something of the kind. It flutters in my chest sometimes . . . like a very small bird." He laid a hand lightly over his heart.

I couldn't bear the look of his chest, heaving under its impossible burden, and I gently closed his shirt and fastened the tie at the neck. One long, white hand grasped mine.

"How long?" he said. His tone was light, almost unconcerned, displaying no more than a mild curiosity.

"I don't know," I said. "That's the truth. I don't know."

"But not long," he said, with certainty.

"No. Not long. Months perhaps, but almost surely less than a year."

"Can you . . . stop the coughing?"

I reached for my kit. "Yes. I can help it, at least. And the heart palpitations; I can make you a digitalin extract that will help." I found the small packet of dried foxglove leaves; it would take a little time to brew them.

"Your brother," I said, not looking at him. "Do you want me—"

"No," he said, definitely. One corner of his mouth curved up, and he looked so like Frank that I wanted momentarily to weep for him.

"No," he said. "He'll know already, I think. We've always . . . known things about each other."

"Have you, then?" I asked, looking directly at him. He didn't turn away from my eyes, but smiled faintly.

"Yes," he said softly. "I know about him. It doesn't matter."

Oh, doesn't it? I thought. Not to you, perhaps. Not trusting either my face or my voice, I turned away and busied myself in lighting the small alcohol lamp I carried.

"He *is* my brother," the soft voice said behind me. I took a deep breath and steadied my hands to measure out the leaves.

"Yes," I said, "at least he's that."

Since news had spread of Cope's amazing defeat at Prestonpans, offers of support, of men and money, poured in from the north. In some cases, these offers even materialized: Lord Ogilvy, the eldest son of the Earl of Airlie, brought six hundred of his father's tenants, while Stewart of Appin appeared at the head of four hundred men from the shires of Aberdeen and Banff. Lord Pitsligo was single-handedly responsible for most of the Highland cavalry, bringing in a large number of gentlemen and their servants from the northeastern counties, all well mounted and well armed—at least by comparison with some of the miscellaneous clansmen, who came armed with claymores saved by their grandsires from the Rising of the '15, rusty axes, and pitchforks lately removed from the more homely tasks of cleaning cow-byres.

They were a motley crew, but none the less dangerous for that, I reflected, making my way through a knot of men gathered round an itinerant knife-grinder, who was sharpening dirks, razors, and scythes with perfect indifference. An English soldier facing them might be risking tetanus rather than instant death, but the results were likely to be the same.

While Lord Lewis Gordon, the Duke of Gordon's younger brother, had come to do homage to Charles in Holyrood, holding out the glittering prospect of raising the whole of clan Gordon, it was a long way from hand-kissing to the actual provisioning of men.

And the Scottish Lowlands, while perfectly willing to cheer loudly at news of Charles's victory, were singularly unwilling to send men to support him; nearly the whole of the Stuart army was composed of Highlanders, and likely to remain so. The Lowlands hadn't been a total washout, though; Lord George Murray had told me that levies of food, goods, and money on the southern burghs had resulted in a very useful sum being contributed to the army's treasury, which might tide them over for a time.

"We've gotten fifty-five hundred pounds from Glasgow, alone. Though it's but a pittance, compared to the promised moneys from France and Spain," His Lordship had confided to Jamie. "But I'm not inclined to turn up my nose at it, particularly as His Highness has had nothing from France but soothing words, and no gold."

Jamie, who knew just how unlikely the French gold was to materialize, had merely nodded.

———➤

"Have ye found out anything more today, *mo nighean donn*?" he asked me as I came in. He had a half-written dispatch in front of him, and stuck his quill into the inkpot to wet it again. I pulled the damp hood off my hair with a crackle of static electricity, nodding.

"There's a rumor that General Hawley is forming cavalry units in the south. He has orders for the formation of eight regiments."

Jamie grunted. Given the Highlanders' aversion to cavalry, this wasn't good news. Absentmindedly, he rubbed his back, where the hoofprint-shaped bruise from Prestonpans had all but faded.

"I'll put it down for Colonel Cameron, then," he said. "How good a rumor do ye think it is, Sassenach?" Almost automatically, he glanced over his shoulder, to be sure we were alone. He called me "Sassenach" now only in privacy, using the formality of "Claire" in public.

"You can take it to the bank," I said. "I mean, it's good."

It wasn't a rumor at all; it was the latest bit of intelligence from Jack Randall, the latest installment payment on the debt he insisted on assuming for my care of his brother.

Jamie knew, of course, that I visited Alex Randall, as well as the sick of the Jacobite army. What he didn't know, and what I could never tell him, was that once a week—sometimes more often—I would meet Jack Randall, to hear what news seeped into Edinburgh Castle from the South.

Sometimes he came to Alex's room when I was there; other times, I would be coming home in the winter twilight, watching my footing on the slippery cobbles of the Royal Mile, when suddenly a stick-straight form in brown homespun would beckon from the mouth of a close, or a quiet voice come out of the mist behind my shoulder. It was unnerving; like being haunted by Frank's ghost.

It would have been simpler in many ways for him to leave a letter for me at Alex's lodging, but he would have nothing put in writing, and I could see his point. If such a letter was ever found, even unsigned, it could implicate not only him but Alex as well. As it was, Edinburgh teemed with strangers; volunteers to King James's standard, curious visitors from south and north, foreign envoys from France and Spain, spies and informers in plenty. The only people not abroad on the streets were the officers and men of the English garrison, who remained mewed up in the Castle. So long as no one heard him speak to me, no one would recognize him for what he was, nor think anything odd of our encounters, even were we seen—and we seldom were, such were his precautions.

For my part, I was just as pleased; I would have had to destroy anything put in writing. While I doubted that Jamie would recognize Randall's hand, I couldn't explain a regular source of information without outright lying. Far better to make it appear that the information he gave me was merely part of the gleanings of my daily rounds.

The drawback, of course, was that by treating Randall's contributions in the same light as the other rumors I collected, they might be discounted or ignored. Still, while I believed that Jack Randall was supplying information in good faith—assuming one could entertain such a concept in conjunction with the man—it didn't necessarily follow that it was always correct. As well to have it regarded skeptically.

I relayed the news of Hawley's new regiments with the usual faint twinge of guilt at my quasi deception. However, I had concluded that while honesty between husband and wife was essential, there was such a thing as carrying it too bloody far. And I saw no reason why the supplying of useful information to the Jacobites should cause Jamie further pain.

"The Duke of Cumberland is still waiting for his troops to return from Flanders," I added. "And the siege of Stirling Castle is getting nowhere."

Jamie grunted, scribbling busily. "That much I knew; Lord George had a dispatch from Francis Townsend two days ago; he holds the town, but the ditches His Highness insisted on are wasting men and time. There's no need for them; they'd do better just to batter the Castle from a distance with cannon fire, and then storm it."

"So why are they digging ditches?"

Jamie waved a hand distractedly, still concentrating on his writing. His ears were pink with frustration.

"Because the Italian army dug ditches when they took Verona Castle, which is the only siege His Highness has seen, so plainly that's how it must be done, aye?"

"Och, aye," I said.

It worked; he looked up at me and laughed, his eyes slanting half-shut with it.

"That's a verra fair try, Sassenach," he said. "What else can ye say?"

"Settle for the Lord's Prayer in Gaelic, would you?" I asked.

"No," he said, scattering sand across his dispatch. He got up, kissed me briefly, and reached for his coat. "But I'll settle for some supper. Come along, Sassenach. We'll find a nice, cozy tavern and I'll teach you a lot of things ye mustn't say in public. They're all fresh in my mind."

Stirling Castle fell at last. The cost had been high, the likelihood of holding it low, and the benefit in keeping it dubious. Still, the effect on Charles was euphoric—and disastrous.

"I have succeeded at last in convincing Murray—such a stubborn fool as he is!" Charles interjected, frowning. Then he remembered his victory, and beamed around the room once more. "I have prevailed, I say, though. We march into England on this day a week, to reclaim *all* of my Father's lands!"

The Scottish chieftains gathered in the morning drawing room glanced at each other, and there was considerable coughing and shifting of weight. The overall mood didn't seem to be one of wild enthusiasm at the news.

"Er, Your Highness," Lord Kilmarnock began, carefully. "Would it not be wiser to consider . . . ?"

They tried. They all tried. Scotland, they pointed out, already belonged to Charles, lock, stock, and barrel. Men were still pouring in from the North, while from the South there seemed little promise of support. And the Scottish lords were all too aware that the Highlanders, while fierce fighters and loyal followers, were also farmers. Fields needed to be tilled for the spring planting; cattle needed to be provisioned for overwintering. Many of the men would resist going deeply into the South in the winter months.

"And these men—they are not my subjects? They go not where I command them? Nonsense," Charles said firmly. And that was that. Almost.

"James, my friend! Wait, I speak with you a moment in private, if you please." His Highness turned from a few sharp words with Lord Pitsligo, his long, stubborn chin softening a bit as he waved a hand at Jamie.

I didn't think I was included in this invitation. I hadn't any intention of leaving, though, and settled more firmly into one of the gold damask chairs as the Jacobite lords and chieftains filed out, muttering to each other.

"Ha!" Charles snapped his fingers contemptuously in the direction of the closing door. "Old women, all of them! They will see. So will my cousin Louis, so will Philip—do I need their help? I show them all." I saw the pale, manicured fingers touch briefly at a spot just over his breast. A faint rectangular outline showed through the silk of his coat. He was carrying Louise's miniature; I had seen it.

"I wish Your Highness every good fortune in the endeavor," Jamie murmured, "but . . ."

"Ah, I thank you, *cher* James! *You* at least believe in me!" Charles threw an arm about Jamie's shoulders, massaging his deltoids affectionately.

"I am desolated that you will not accompany me, that you will not be at my side to receive the applause of my subjects as we march into England," Charles said, squeezing vigorously.

"I won't?" Jamie looked stunned.

"Alas, *mon cher ami,* duty demands of you a great sacrifice. I know how much your great heart yearns for the glories of battle, but I require you for another task."

"You do?" said Jamie.

"What?" I said bluntly.

Charles cast a glance of well-mannered dislike in my direction, then turned back to Jamie and resumed the bonhomie.

"It is a task of the greatest import, my James, and one that only you can do. It is true that men flock to my Father's standard; more come every day. Still, we must not haste to feel secure, no?"

"No," Jamie said, a look of horror dawning on his face.

"But yes," said Charles, with a final squeeze. He swung around to face Jamie, beaming. "You will go to the north, to the land of your fathers, and return to me at the head of the men of clan Fraser!"

40

The Fox's Lair

"Oo you know your grandfather well?" I asked, waving away an unseasonable deerfly that seemed unable to make up its mind whether I or the horse would make a better meal.

Jamie shook his head.

"No. I've heard he acts like a terrible auld monster, but ye shouldna be scairt of him." He smiled at me as I swatted at the deerfly with the end of my shawl. "I'll be with you."

"Oh, crusty old gentlemen don't bother me," I assured him. "I've seen a good many of those in my time. Soft as butter underneath, most of them. I imagine your grandfather's much the same."

"Mm, no," he replied thoughtfully. "He really *is* a terrible auld monster. It's only, if ye act scairt of him, it makes him worse. Like a beast scenting blood, ye ken?"

I cast a look ahead, where the far-off hills that hid Beaufort Castle suddenly loomed in a rather sinister manner. Taking advantage of my momentary lack of attention, the deerfly made a strafing run past my left ear. I squeaked and ducked to the side, and the horse, taken aback by this sudden movement, shied in a startled manner.

"Hey! *Cuir stad*!" Jamie dove sideways to grab my reins, dropping his own. Better schooled than my own mount, his horse snorted, but accommodated this maneuver, merely flicking its ears in a complacently superior way.

Jamie dug his knees into his horse's sides, pulling mine to a stop alongside.

"Now then," he said, narrowed eyes following the zigzag flight of the humming deerfly. "Let him light, Sassenach, and I'll get him." He waited, hands raised at the ready, squinting slightly in the sunlight.

I sat like a mildly nervous statue, half-hypnotized by the menacing buzz. The heavy winged body, deceptively slow, hummed lazily back and forth between the horse's ears and my own. The horse's ears twitched violently, an impulse with which I was in complete sympathy.

"If that thing lands in my ear, Jamie, I'm going to—" I began.

"Shh!" he ordered, leaning forward in anticipation, left hand cupped like a panther about to strike. "Another second, and I'll have him."

Just then I saw the dark blob alight on his shoulder. Another deerfly, seeking a basking place. I opened my mouth again.

"Jamie . . ."

"Hush!" He clapped his hands together triumphantly on my tormentor, a split second before the deerfly on his collar sank its fangs into his neck.

Scottish clansmen fought according to their ancient traditions. Disdaining strategy, tactics, and subtlety, their method of attack was simplicity itself. Spotting the enemy within range, they dropped their plaids, drew their swords, and charged the foe, shrieking at the tops of their lungs. Gaelic shrieking being what it is, this method was more often successful than not. A good many enemies, seeing a mass of hairy, bare-limbed banshees bearing down on them, simply lost all nerve and fled.

Well schooled as it might ordinarily be, nothing had prepared Jamie's horse for a grade-A, number one Gaelic shriek, uttered at top volume from a spot two feet behind its head. Losing all nerve, it laid back its ears and fled as though the devil itself were after it.

My mount and I sat transfixed in the road, watching an outstanding exhibition of Scottish horsemanship as Jamie, both stirrups lost and the reins free, flung half out of his saddle by his horse's abrupt departure, heaved himself desperately forward, grappling for the mane. His plaid fluttered madly about him, stirred by the wind of his passing, and the horse, thoroughly panicked by this time, took the thrashing mass of color as an excuse to run even faster.

One hand tangled in the long mane, Jamie was grimly hauling himself upright, long legs clasping the horse's sides, ignoring the stirrup irons that danced beneath the beast's belly. Scraps of what even my limited Gaelic recognized as extremely bad language floated back on the gentle wind.

A slow, clopping sound made me look behind, to where
Murtagh, leading the pack horse, was coming over the small
rise we had just descended. He made his careful way down
the road to where I waited. He pulled his animal to a leisurely
stop, shaded his eyes, and looked ahead, to the spot where
Jamie and his panicked mount were just vanishing over the
next hilltop.

"A deerfly," I said, in explanation.

"Late for them. Still, I didna think he'd be in such a
hurry to meet his grandsire as to leave ye behind," Murtagh
remarked, with his customary dryness. "Not that I'd say a wife
more or less will make much difference in his reception."

He picked up his reins and booted his pony into reluctant, motion, the packhorse amiably coming along for the
journey. My own mount, cheered by the company and reassured by a temporary absence of flies, stepped out quite gaily
alongside.

"Not even an English wife?" I asked curiously. From the
little I knew, I didn't think Lord Lovat's relations with anything English were much to cheer about.

"English, French, Dutch, or German. It isna like to make
much difference; it'll be the lad's liver the Old Fox will be
eatin' for breakfast, not yours."

"What do you mean by that?" I stared at the dour little
clansman, looking much like one of his own bundles, under
the loose wrapping of plaid and shirt. Somehow every garment that Murtagh put on, no matter how new or how well
tailored, immediately assumed the appearance of something
narrowly salvaged from a rubbish heap.

"What kind of terms is Jamie on with Lord Lovat?"

I caught a sidelong glance from a small, shrewd black
eye, and then his head turned toward Beaufort Castle. He
shrugged, in resignation or anticipation.

"No terms at all, 'til now. The lad's never spoken to his
grandsire in his life."

"But how do you know so much about him if you've
never met him?"

At least I was beginning to understand Jamie's earlier
reluctance to approach his grandfather for help. Reunited

with Jamie and his horse, the latter looking rather chastened, and the former irritable to a degree, Murtagh had gazed speculatively at him, and offered to ride ahead to Beaufort with the pack animal, leaving Jamie and me to enjoy lunch at the side of the road.

Over a restorative ale and oatcake, he had at length told me that his grandfather, Lord Lovat, had not approved of his son's choice of bride, and had not seen fit either to bless the union or to communicate with his son—or his son's children —anytime since the marriage of Brian Fraser and Ellen Mac-Kenzie, more than thirty years before.

"I've heard a good bit about him, one way and another, though." Jamie replied, chewing a bite of cheese. "He's the sort of man that makes an impression on folk, ye ken."

"So I gather." The elderly Tullibardine, one of the Parisian Jacobites, had regaled me with a number of uncensored opinions regarding the leader of clan Fraser, and I thought that perhaps Brian Fraser had not been desolated at his father's inattention. I said as much, and Jamie nodded.

"Oh, aye. I canna recall my father having much good to say of the old man, though he wouldna be disrespectful of him. He just didna speak of him often." He rubbed at the side of his neck, where a red welt from the deerfly bite was beginning to show. The weather was freakishly warm, and he had unfolded his plaid for me to sit on. The deputation to the head of clan Fraser had been thought worth some investment in dignity, and Jamie wore a new kilt, of the buckled military cut, with the plaid a separate strip of cloth. Less enveloping for shelter from the weather than the older, belted plaid, it was a good deal more efficient to put on in a hurry.

"I wondered a bit," he said thoughtfully, "whether my father was the sort of father he was because of the way old Simon treated *him*. I didna realize it at the time, of course, but it's no so common for a man to show his feelings for his sons."

"You've thought about it a lot." I offered him another flask of ale, and he took it with a smile that lingered on me, more warming than the feeble autumn sun.

"Aye, I did. I was wondering, ye see, what sort of father I'd be to my own bairns, and looking back a bit to see, my own father being the best example I had. Yet I knew, from the bits that he said, or that Murtagh told me, that his own father was nothing like him, so I thought as how he must have made up his mind to do it all differently, once he had the chance."

I sighed a bit, setting down my bit of cheese.

"Jamie," I said. "Do you really think we'll ever—"

"I do," he said, with certainty, not letting me finish. He leaned over and kissed my forehead. "I know it, Sassenach, and so do you. You were meant to be a mother, and I surely dinna intend to let anyone else father your children."

"Well, *that's* good," I said. "Neither do I."

He laughed and tilted my chin up to kiss my lips. I kissed him back, then reached up to brush away a breadcrumb that clung to the stubble around his mouth.

"Ought you to shave, do you think?" I asked. "In honor of seeing your grandfather for the first time?"

"Oh, I've seen him the once before," he said casually. "And he's seen me, for that matter. As for what he thinks of my looks now, he can take me as I am, and be damned to him."

"But Murtagh said you'd never met him!"

"Mphm." He brushed the rest of the crumbs from his shirtfront, frowning slightly as if deciding how much to tell me. Finally he shrugged and lay back in the shade of a gorse bush, hands clasped behind his head as he stared at the sky.

"Well, we never have *met,* as ye'd say. Or not exactly. 'Twas like this . . ."

At the age of seventeen, young Jamie Fraser set sail for France, to finish his education at the University of Paris, and to learn further such things as are not taught in books.

"I sailed from the harbor at Beauly," he said, nodding over the next hill, where a narrow slice of gray on the far horizon marked the edge of the Moray Firth. "There were other ports I could have gone by—Inverness would have been most like—but my father booked my passage, and from Beauly it was. He rode with me, to see me off into the world, ye might say."

Brian Fraser had seldom left Lallybroch in the years since his marriage, and took pleasure as they rode in pointing out various spots to his son, where he had hunted or traveled as boy and young man.

"But he grew much quieter as we drew near Beaufort.

He hadna spoken of my grandsire on this trip, and I knew
better than mention him myself. But I kent he had reason for
sending me from Beauly."

A number of small sparrows edged their way cautiously
nearer, popping in and out of the low shrubs, ready to dart
back to safety at the slightest hint of danger. Seeing them,
Jamie reached for a remnant of bread, and tossed it with
considerable accuracy into the middle of the flock, which exploded like shrapnel, all fleeing the sudden intrusion.

"They'll be back," he said, motioning toward the scattered birds. He put an arm across his face as though to shield
it from the sun, and went on with his story.

"There was a sound of horses along the road from the
castle, and when we turned to see, there was a small party
coming down, six horsemen with a wagon, and one of them
held Lovat's banner, so I knew my grandfather was with
them. I looked quick at my father, to see did he mean to do
anything, but he just smiled and squeezed my shoulder quick
and said, 'Let's go aboard, then, lad.'

"I could feel my grandsire's eyes on me as I walked down
the shore, wi' my hair and my height fair shriekin' 'MacKenzie,' and I was glad I had my best clothes on and didna look a
beggar. I didna look round, but I stood as tall as I could, and
was proud that I had half a head's height above the tallest
man there. My father walked by my side, quiet like he was,
and he didna look aside, either, but I could feel him there,
proud that he'd sired me."

He smiled at me, lopsided.

"That was the last time I was sure I'd done well by him,
Sassenach. I wasna so sure times after, but I was glad of that
one day."

He locked his arms around his knees, staring ahead as
though reliving the scene on the quay.

"We stepped aboard the ship, and met the master, then
we stood by the rail, talking a bit about nothing, both of us
careful not to look at the men from Beaufort who were loading the bundles, or glance to the shore where the horsemen
stood. Then the master gave the order to cast off. I kissed my
father, and he jumped over the rail, down to the dock, and
walked to his horse. He didna look back until he was

mounted, and by then the ship had started out into the harbor.

"I waved, and he waved back, then he turned, leading my horse, and started on the road back to Lallybroch. And the party from Beaufort turned then, too, and started back. I could see my grandsire at the head of the party, sitting straight in his saddle. And they rode, my father and grandfather, twenty yards apart, up the hill and over it, out of my sight, and neither one turned to the other, or acted as though the other one was there at all."

He turned his head down the road, as though looking for signs of life from the direction of Beaufort.

"I met his eyes," he said softly. "The once. I waited until Father reached his horse, and then I turned and looked at Lord Lovat, bold as I could. I wanted him to know we'd ask nothing of him, but that I wasna scairt of him." He smiled at me, one-sided. "I was, though."

I put a hand over his, stroking the grooves of his knuckles.

"Was he looking back at you?"

He snorted briefly.

"Aye, he was. Reckon he didna take his eyes off me from the time I came down the hill 'til my ship sailed away; I could feel them borin' into my back like an auger. And when I looked at him, there he was, wi' his eyes black under his brows, starin' into mine."

He fell silent, still looking at the castle, 'til I gently prodded him.

"How did he look, then?"

He pulled his eyes from the dark cloud mass on the far horizon to look down at me, the customary expression of good humor missing from the curve of his mouth, the depths of his eyes.

"Cold as stone, Sassenach," he replied. "Cold as the stone."

We were lucky in the weather; it had been warm all the way from Edinburgh.

"It's no going to last," Jamie predicted, squinting toward the sea ahead. "See the bank of cloud out there? It will be inland by tonight." He sniffed the air, and pulled his plaid across his shoulders. "Smell the air? Ye can feel weather coming."

Not so experienced at olfactory meteorology, I still thought that perhaps I *could* smell it; a dampness in the air, sharpening the usual smells of dried heather and pine resin, with a faint, moist scent of kelp from the distant shore mixed in.

"I wonder if the men have got back to Lallybroch yet," I said.

"I doubt it." Jamie shook his head. "They've less distance to go than we've had, but they're all afoot, and it will ha' been slow getting them all away." He rose in his stirrups, shading his eyes to peer toward the distant cloud bank. "I hope it's just rain; that wilna trouble them overmuch. And it might not be a big storm, in any case. Perhaps it wilna reach so far south."

I pulled my arisaid, a warm tartan shawl, tighter around my own shoulders, in response to the rising breeze. I had thought this few days' stretch of warm weather a good omen; I hoped it hadn't been deceptive.

Jamie had spent an entire night sitting by the window in Holyrood, after receipt of Charles's order. And in the morning, he had gone first to Charles, to tell His Highness that he and I would ride alone to Beauly, accompanied only by Murtagh, to convey His Highness's respects to Lord Lovat, and his request that Lovat honor his promise of men and aid.

Next, Jamie had summoned Ross the smith to our chamber, and given him his orders, in a voice so low that I could not make out the words from my place near the fire. I had seen the burly smith's shoulders rise, though, and set firm, as he absorbed their import.

The Highland army traveled with little discipline, in a ragtag mob that could scarcely be dignified as a "column." In the course of one day's movement, the men of Lallybroch were to drop away, one by one. Stepping aside into the shrubbery as though to rest a moment or relieve themselves, they were not to return to the main body, but to steal quietly away, and make their way, one by one, to a rendezvous with the other men from Lallybroch. And once regathered under the command of Ross the smith, they were to go home.

"I doubt they'll be missed for some time, if at all," Jamie had said, discussing the plan with me beforehand. "Desertion is rife, all through the army. Ewan Cameron told me they'd lost twenty men from his regiment within the last week. It's winter, and men want to be settling their homes and making things ready for the spring planting. In any case, it's sure there's no one to spare to go after them, even should their leavin' be noticed."

"Have you given up, then, Jamie?" I had asked, laying a hand on his arm. He had rubbed a hand tiredly over his face before answering.

"I dinna ken, Sassenach. It may be too late; it may not. I canna tell. It was foolish to go south so near to the winter; and more foolish still to waste time in besieging Stirling. But Charles hasna been defeated, and the chiefs—some of them—are coming in answer to his summons. The MacKenzies, now, and others because of them. He's twice as many men now as we had at Preston. What will that mean?" He flung up his hands, frustrated.

"I dinna ken. There's no opposition; the English are terrified. Well, ye know; you've seen the broadsheets." He smiled without humor. "We spit small children and roast them ower the fire, and dishonor the wives and daughters of honest men." He gave a snort of wry disgust. While such crimes as theft and insubordination were common among the Highland army, rape was virtually unknown.

He sighed, a brief, angry sound. "Cameron's heard a rumor that King Geordie's makin' ready to flee from London, in fear that the Prince's army will take the city soon." He had—a rumor that had reached Cameron through me, from Jack Randall. "And there's Kilmarnock, and Cameron. Lochiel, and Balmerino, and Dougal, with his MacKenzies. Bonny fighters all. And should Lovat send the men he's promised—God, maybe it would be enough. Christ, should we march into London—" He hunched his shoulders, then stretched suddenly, shrugging as though to fight his way out of a strangling shirt.

"But I canna risk it," he said simply. "I canna go to Beauly, and leave my own men here, to be taken God knows where. If I were there to head them—that would be something else. But damned if I'll leave them for Charles or Dougal to throw at the English, and me a hundred miles away at Beauly."

So it was arranged. The Lallybroch men—including Fergus, who had protested vociferously, but been overruled—would desert, and depart inconspicuously for home. Once our business at Beauly was completed, and we had returned to join Charles—well, then it would be time enough to see how matters went.

"That's why I'm takin' Murtagh with us," Jamie had explained. "If it looks all right, then I shall send him to Lallybroch to fetch them back." A brief smile lightened his somber face. "He doesna look much on a horse, but he's a braw rider, is Murtagh. Fast as chain lightning."

He didn't look it at the moment, I reflected, but then, there was no emergency at hand. In fact, he was moving even slower than usual; as we topped one hill, I could see him at the bottom, pulling his horse to a halt. By the time we had reached him, he was off, glaring at the packhorse's saddle.

"What's amiss, then?" Jamie made to get down from his own saddle, but Murtagh waved him irritably off.

"Nay, nay, naught to trouble ye. A binding's snapped, is all. Get ye on."

With no more than a nod of acknowledgment, Jamie reined away, and I followed him.

"Not very canty today, is he?" I remarked, with a flip of the hand back in Murtagh's direction. In fact, the small clansman had grown more testy and irritable with each step in the direction of Beauly. "I take it he's not enchanted with the prospect of visiting Lord Lovat?"

Jamie smiled, with a brief backward glance at the small, dark figure, bent in absorption over the rope he was splicing.

"Nay, Murtagh's no friend of Old Simon. He loved my father dearly"—his mouth quirked to one side—"and my mother, as well. He didna care for Lovat's treatment of them. Or for Lovat's methods of getting wives. Murtagh's got an Irish grandmother, but he's related to Primrose Campbell through his mother's side," he explained, as though this made everything crystal clear.

"Who's Primrose Campbell?" I asked, bewildered.

"Oh." Jamie scratched his nose, considering. The wind

off the sea was rising steadily, and his hair was being whipped from its lacing, ruddy wisps flickering past his face.

"Primrose Campbell was Lovat's third wife—still is, I suppose," he added, "though she's left him some years since and gone back to her father's house."

"Popular with women, is he?" I murmured.

Jamie snorted. "I suppose ye can call it that. He took his first wife by a forced marriage. Snatched the Dowager Lady Lovat from her bed in the middle o' the night, married her then and there, and went straight back to bed with her. Still," he added fairly, "she did later decide she loved him, so maybe he wasna so bad."

"Must have been rather special in bed, at least," I said flippantly. "Runs in the family, I expect."

He cast me a mildly shocked look, which dissolved into a sheepish grin.

"Aye, well," he said. "If he was or no, it didna help him much. The Dowager's maids spoke up against him, and Simon was outlawed and had to flee to France."

Forced marriages and outlawry, hm? I refrained from further remark on family resemblances, but privately trusted that Jamie wouldn't follow in his grandfather's footsteps with regard to subsequent wives. One had apparently been insufficient for Simon.

"He went to visit King James in Rome and swear his fealty to the Stuarts," Jamie went on, "and then turned round and went straight to William of Orange, King of England, who was visiting in France. He got James to promise him his title and estates, should a restoration come about, and then— God knows how—got a full pardon from William, and was able to come home to Scotland."

Now it was my turn for raised eyebrows. Apparently it wasn't just attractiveness to the opposite sex, then.

Simon had continued his adventures by returning later to France, this time to spy on the Jacobites. Being found out, he was thrown into prison, but escaped, returned to Scotland, masterminded the assembling of the clans under the guise of a hunting-party on the Braes of Mar in 1715—and then managed to get full credit with the English Crown for putting down the resultant Rising.

"Proper old twister, isn't he?" I said, completely intrigued. "Though I suppose he can't have been so old then; only in his forties." Having heard that Lord Lovat was now in his middle seventies, I had been expecting something fairly doddering and decrepit, but was rapidly revising my expectations, in view of these stories.

"My grandsire," Jamie observed evenly, "has by all reports got a character that would enable him to hide conveniently behind a spiral staircase. Anyway," he went on, dismissing his grandfather's character with a wave of his hand, "then he married Margaret Grant, the Grant o' Grant's daughter. It was after she died that he married Primrose Campbell. She was maybe eighteen at the time."

"Was Old Simon enough of a catch for her family to force her into it?" I asked sympathetically.

"By no means, Sassenach." He paused to brush the hair out of his face, tucking the stray locks back behind his ears. "He kent well enough that she wouldna have him, no matter if he was rich as Croesus—which he wasn't—so he had her sent a letter, saying her mother was fallen sick in Edinburgh, and giving the house there she was to go to."

Hastening to Edinburgh, the young and beautiful Miss Campbell had found not her mother, but the old and ingenious Simon Fraser, who had informed her that she was in a notorious house of pleasure, and that her only hope of preserving her good name was to marry him immediately.

"She must have been a right gump, to fall for that one," I remarked cynically.

"Well, she was verra young," Jamie said defensively, "and it wasna an idle threat, either; had she refused him, Old Simon would ha' ruined her reputation without a second thought. In any event, she married him—and regretted it."

"Hmph." I was busy doing sums in my head. The encounter with Primrose Campbell had been only a few years ago, he'd said. Then . . . "Was it the Dowager Lady Lovat or Margaret Grant who was your grandmother?" I asked curiously.

The high cheekbones were chapped by sun and wind; now they flushed a sudden, painful red.

"Neither one," he said. He didn't look at me, but kept his gaze fixed straight ahead, in the direction of Beaufort Castle. His lips were pressed tightly together.

"My father was a bastard," he said at last. He sat straight as a sword in the saddle, and his knuckles were white, fist clenched on the reins. "Acknowledged, but a bastard. By one of the Castle Downie maids."

"Oh," I said. There didn't seem a lot to add.

He swallowed hard; I could see the ripple in his throat.

"I should ha' told ye before," he said stiffly. "I'm sorry."

I reached out to touch his arm; it was hard as iron.

"It doesn't matter, Jamie," I said, knowing even as I spoke that nothing I said could make a difference. "I don't mind in the slightest."

"Aye?" he said at last, still staring straight ahead. "Well . . . I do."

The steadily freshening wind off Moray Firth rustled its way through a hillside of dark pines. The country here was an odd combination of mountain slope and seashore. Thick growth of alders, larch, and birch blanketed the ground on both sides of the narrow track we followed, but as we approached the dark bulk of Beaufort Castle, over everything floated the effluvia of mud flats and kelp.

We were in fact expected; the kilted, ax-armed sentries at the gate made no challenge as we rode through. They looked at us curiously enough, but seemingly without enmity. Jamie sat straight as a king in his saddle. He nodded once to the man on his side, and received a similar nod in return. I had the distinct feeling that we entered the castle flying a white flag of truce; how long that state would last was anyone's guess.

We rode unchallenged into the courtyard of Beaufort Castle, a small edifice as castles went, but sufficiently imposing, for all that, built of the native stone. Not so heavily fortified as some of the castles I had seen to the south, it looked still capable of withstanding a certain amount of abrasion. Wide-mouthed gun-holes gaped at intervals along the base of the outer walls, and the keep still boasted a stable opening onto the courtyard.

Several of the small Highland ponies were housed in this, heads poking over the wooden half-door to whicker in welcome to our own mounts. Near the wall lay a number of packs, recently unloaded from the ponies in the stable.

"Lovat's summoned a few men to meet us," Jamie observed grimly, noting the packs. "Relatives, I expect." He shrugged. "At least they'll be friendly enough to start with."

"How do you know?"

He slid to the ground and reached up to help me down. "They've left the broadswords wi' the luggage."

Jamie handed over the reins to an ostler who came out of the stables to meet us, dusting his hands on his breeks.

"Er, now what?" I murmured to Jamie under my breath. There was no sign of chatelaine or majordomo; nothing like the cheery, authoritative figure of Mrs. FitzGibbons that had welcomed us to Castle Leoch two years before.

The few ostlers and stable-lads about glanced at us now and then, but continued about their tasks, as did the servants who crossed the courtyard, lugging baskets of laundry, bundles of peat, and all the other cumbrous paraphernalia that living in a stone castle demanded. I looked approvingly after a burly manservant sweating under the burden of two five-gallon copper cans of water. Whatever its shortcomings in the hospitality department, Beaufort Castle at least boasted a bathtub somewhere.

Jamie stood in the center of the courtyard, arms crossed, surveying the place like a prospective buyer of real estate who harbors black doubts about the drains.

"Now we wait, Sassenach," he said. "The sentries will ha' sent word that we're here. Either someone will come down to us . . . or they won't."

"Um," I said. "Well, I hope they make up their minds about it soon; I'm hungry, and I could do with a wash."

"Aye, ye could," Jamie agreed, with a brief smile as he looked me over. "You've a smut on your nose, and there's teasel-heads caught in your hair. No, leave them," he added, as my hand went to my head in dismay. "It looks bonny, did ye do it on purpose or no."

Definitely no, but I left them. Still, I sidled over to a nearby watering trough, to inspect my appearance and remedy it so far as was possible using nothing but cold water.

It was something of a delicate situation, so far as old Simon Fraser was concerned, I thought, bending over the trough and trying to make out which blotches on my reflected complexion were actual smudges and which caused by floating bits of hay.

On the one hand, Jamie was a formal emissary from the Stuarts. Whether Lovat's promises of support for the cause were honest, or mere lip service, chances were that he would feel obliged to welcome the Prince's representative, if only for the sake of courtesy.

On the other hand, said representative was an illegitimately descended grandson who, if not precisely disowned in his own person, certainly wasn't a bosom member of the family, either. And I knew enough by now of Highland feuds to know that ill feeling of this sort was unlikely to be diminished by the passage of time.

I ran a wet hand across my closed eyes and back across my temples, smoothing down stray wisps of hair. On the whole, I didn't think Lord Lovat would leave us standing in the courtyard. He might, however, leave us there long enough to realize fully the dubious nature of our reception.

After that—well, who knew? We would most likely be received by Lady Frances, one of Jamie's aunts, a widow who —from all we had heard from Tullibardine—managed domestic affairs for her father. Or, if he chose to receive us as a diplomatic ambassage rather than as family connections, I supposed that Lord Lovat himself might appear to receive us, supported by the formal panoply of secretary, guards, and servants.

This last possibility seemed most likely, in view of the time it was taking; after all, you wouldn't keep a full-dress entourage standing about—it would take some time to assemble the necessary personnel. Envisioning the sudden appearance of a fully equipped earl, I had second thoughts about leaving teasel-heads tangled in my hair, and leaned over the trough again.

At this point, I was interrupted by the sound of footsteps in the passageway behind the mangers. A squat-bodied elderly man in open shirt and unbuckled breeks stepped out into the courtyard, shoving aside a plump chestnut mare with a sharp elbow and an irritable "Tcha!" Despite his age, he had a back like a ramrod, and shoulders nearly as broad as Jamie's.

Pausing by the horse trough, he glanced around the courtyard as though looking for someone. His eye passed over me without registering, then suddenly snapped back, clearly startled. He stepped forward and thrust his face pugnaciously forward, an unshaven gray beard bristling like a porcupine's quills.

"Who the hell are you?" he demanded.

"Claire Fraser, er, I mean, Lady Broch Tuarach," I said, belatedly remembering my dignity. I gathered my self-possession, and wiped a drop of water off my chin. "Who the hell are *you*?" I demanded.

A firm hand gripped my elbow from behind, and a resigned voice from somewhere above my head said, "That, Sassenach, is my grandsire. My lord, may I present my wife?"

"Ah?" said Lord Lovat, giving me the benefit of a cold blue eye. "I'd heard you'd married an Englishwoman." His tone made it clear that this act confirmed all his worst suspicions about the grandson he'd never met.

He raised a thick gray brow in my direction, and shifted the gimlet stare to Jamie. "No more sense than your father, it seems."

I could see Jamie's hands twitch slightly, resisting the urge to clench into fists.

"At the least, I had nay need to take a wife by rape or trickery," he observed evenly.

His grandfather grunted, unfazed by the insult. I thought I saw the corner of his wrinkled mouth twitch, but wasn't sure.

"Aye, and ye've gained little enough by the bargain ye struck," he observed. "Though at that, this one's less expensive than that MacKenzie harlot Brian fell prey to. If this *sassenach* wench brings ye naught, at least she looks as though she costs ye little." The slanted blue eyes, so much like Jamie's own, ran over my travel-stained gown, taking in the unstitched hem, the burst seam, and the splashes of mud on the skirt.

I could feel a fine vibration run through Jamie, and wasn't sure whether it was anger or laughter.

"Thanks," I said, with a friendly smile at his lordship. "I

don't eat much, either. But I could use a bit of a wash. Just water; don't bother about the soap, if it comes too dear."

This time I was sure about the twitch.

"Aye, I see," his lordship said. "I shall send a maid to see ye to your rooms, then. *And* provide ye with soap. We shall see ye in the library before supper . . . grandson," he added to Jamie, and turning on his heel, disappeared back under the archway.

"Who's *we*?" I asked.

"Young Simon, I suppose," Jamie answered. "His lordship's heir. A stray cousin or two, maybe. And some of the tacksmen, I should imagine, judging from the horses in the courtyard. If Lovat's going to consider sending troops to join the Stuarts, his tacksmen and tenants may have a bit to say about it."

◆━━

"Ever seen a small worm in a barnyard, in the middle of a flock of chickens?" he murmured as we walked down the hall an hour later behind a servant. "That's me—or us, I should say. Stick close to me, now."

The various connections of clan Fraser were indeed assembled; when we were shown into the Beaufort Castle library, it was to find more than twenty men seated around the room.

Jamie was formally introduced, and gave a formal statement on behalf of the Stuarts, giving the respects of Prince Charles and King James to Lord Lovat and appealing for Lovat's help, to which the old man replied briefly, eloquently and noncommittally. Etiquette attended to, I was then brought forward and introduced, and the general atmosphere became more relaxed.

I was surrounded by a number of Highland gentlemen, who took turns exchanging words of welcome with me as Jamie chatted with someone named Graham, who seemed to be Lord Lovat's cousin. The tacksmen eyed me with a certain amount of reserve, but were all courteous enough—with one exception.

Young Simon, much like his father in squatty outline, but nearly fifty years younger, came forward and bowed over my hand. Straightening up, he looked me over with an attention that seemed just barely this side of rudeness.

"Jamie's wife, hm?" he asked. He had the slanted eyes of his father and half-nephew, but his were brown, muddy as bogwater. "I suppose that means I may call ye 'niece,' does it not?" He was just about Jamie's age, clearly a few years younger than I.

"Ha-ha," I said politely, as he chortled at his own wit. I tried to retrieve my hand, but he wasn't letting go. Instead, he smiled jovially, giving me the once-over again.

"I'd heard of ye, you know," he said. "You've a bit of fame through the Highlands, Mistress."

"Oh, really? How nice." I tugged inconspicuously; in response, his hand tightened around mine in a grip that was nearly painful.

"Oh, aye. I've heard you're verra popular with the men of your husband's command," he said, smiling so hard his eyes narrowed to dark-brown slits. "They call ye *neo-geimnidh meala,* I hear. That means 'Mistress Honeylips,' " he translated, seeing my look of bewilderment at the unfamiliar Gaelic.

"Why, thank you . . ." I began, but got no more than the first words out before Jamie's fist crashed into Simon Junior's jaw and sent his half-uncle reeling into a piecrust table, scattering sweetmeats and serving spoons across the polished slates with a terrific clatter.

He dressed like a gentleman, but he had a brawler's instincts. Young Simon rolled up onto his knees, fists clenched, and froze there. Jamie stood over him, fists doubled but loose, his stillness more menacing than open threat.

"No," he said evenly, "she doesna have much Gaelic. And now that ye've proved it to everyone's satisfaction, ye'll kindly apologize to my wife, before I kick your teeth down your throat." Young Simon glowered up at Jamie, then glanced aside at his father, who nodded imperceptibly, looking impatient at this interruption. The younger Fraser's shaggy black hair had come loose from its lacing, and hung like tree moss about his face. He eyed Jamie warily, but with a strange tinge of what looked like amusement as well, mingled with respect. He wiped the back of his hand across his mouth and, still on his knees, bowed gravely to me.

"Your pardon, Mistress Fraser, and my apologies for any offense ye may have suffered."

I could do no more than nod graciously in return, before Jamie was steering me out into the corridor. We had almost reached the door at the end before I spoke, glancing back to see that we were not overheard.

"*What* on earth does *neo-geimnidh meala* mean?" I said, jerking on his sleeve to slow him. He glanced down, as though I had just been recalled to his wandering attention.

"Ah? Oh, it means honeylips, all right. More or less."

"But—"

"It's no your mouth he was referring to, Sassenach," Jamie said dryly.

"Why, that—" I made as if to turn back to the study, but Jamie tightened his grip on my arm.

"Cluck, cluck, cluck," he murmured in my ear. "Dinna worry, Sassenach. They're only tryin' me. It will be all right."

I was left in the care of Lady Frances, Young Simon's sister, while Jamie returned to the library, shoulders squared for battle. I hoped he wouldn't hit any more of his relatives; while the Frasers were, on the whole, not as sizable as the MacKenzies, they had a sort of tough watchfulness that boded ill for anyone trying something on in their immediate vicinity.

Lady Frances was young, perhaps twenty-two, and inclined to view me with a sort of terrorized fascination, as though I might spring upon her if not incessantly placated with tea and sweetmeats. I exerted myself to be as pleasant and unthreatening as possible, and after a time, she relaxed sufficiently to confess that she had never met an Englishwoman before. "Englishwoman," I gathered, was an exotic and dangerous species.

I was careful to make no sudden moves, and after a bit, she grew comfortable enough to introduce me shyly to her son, a sturdy little chap of three or so, maintained in a state of unnatural cleanliness by the constant watchfulness of a stern-faced maidservant.

I was telling Frances and her younger sister Aline about Jenny and her family, whom they had never met, when there was a sudden crash and a cry in the hallway outside. I sprang to my feet, and reached the sitting-room door in time to see a huddled bundle of cloth struggling to rise to its feet in the stone corridor. The heavy door to the library stood open, and the squat figure of Simon Fraser the elder stood framed in it, malevolent as a toad.

"Ye'll get worse than that, my lass, and ye make no better job of it," he said. His tone was not particularly menacing; only a statement of fact. The bundled figure raised its head, and I saw an odd, angularly pretty face, dark eyes wide over the red blotch deepening on her cheekbone. She saw me, but made no acknowledgment of my presence, only getting to her feet and hurrying away without a word. She was very tall and extremely thin, and moved with the strange, half-clumsy grace of a crane, her shadow following her down the stones.

I stood staring at Old Simon, silhouetted against the firelight from the library behind him. He felt my eyes upon him, and turned his head to look at me. The old blue eyes rested on me, cold as sapphires.

"Good evening, my dear," he said, and closed the door.

I stood looking blankly at the dark wooden door.

"What was *that* all about?" I asked Frances, who had come up behind me.

"Nothing," she said, licking her lips nervously. "Come away, Cousin." I let her pull me away, but resolved to ask Jamie later what had happened in the library.

. We had reached the chamber allotted us for the night, and Jamie graciously dismissed our small guide with a pat on the head.

I sank down on the bed, gazing around helplessly.

"*Now* what do we do?" I asked. Dinner had passed with little to remark, but I had felt the weight of Lovat's eyes on me from time to time.

Jamie shrugged, pulling his shirt over his head.

"Damned if I know, Sassenach," he said. "They asked me the state of the Highland army, the condition of the troops, what I knew of His Highness's plans. I told them. And then they asked it all again. My grandfather's no inclined to think anyone could be giving him a straight answer," he added dryly. "He thinks everyone must be as twisted as himself, wi' a dozen different motives; one for every occasion."

He shook his head and tossed the shirt onto the bed next to me.

"He canna tell whether I might be lying about the state of the Highland army or no. For if I wanted him to join the Stuarts, then I might say as how things were better than they are, where if I didna care personally, one way or the other, then I might tell the truth. And he doesna mean to commit himself one way or the other until he thinks he knows where I stand."

"And just how does he mean to tell whether you *are* telling the truth?" I asked skeptically.

"He has a seer," he replied casually, as though this were one of the normal furnishings of a Highland castle. For all I knew, it was.

"Really?" I sat up on the bed, intrigued. "Is that the odd-looking woman he threw out into the hall?"

"Aye. Her name's Maisri, and she's had the Sight since she was born. But she couldna tell him anything—or wouldn't," he added. "It was clear enough she knows *something,* but she'd do naught but shake her head and say she couldn't see. That's when my grandsire lost patience and struck her."

"Bloody old crumb!" I said, indignant.

"Well, he's no the flower o' gallantry," Jamie agreed.

He poured out a basin of water and began to splash handfuls over his face. He looked up, startled and streaming, at my gasp.

"Hah?"

"Your stomach . . ." I said, pointing. The skin between breastbone and kilt was mottled with a large fresh bruise, spreading like a large, unsightly blossom on his fair skin.

Jamie glanced down, said "Oh, that," dismissively, and returned to his washing.

"Yes, *that,*" I said, coming to take a closer look. "What happened?"

"It's no matter," he said, speech coming thickly through a towel. "I spoke a bit hasty this afternoon, and my grandsire had Young Simon give me a small lesson in respect."

"So he had a couple of minor Frasers hold you while he punched you in the belly?" I said, feeling slightly ill.

Tossing the towel aside, Jamie reached for his nightshirt.

"Verra flattering of you to suppose it took two to hold me," he said, grinning as his head popped through the opening. "Actually, there were three; one was behind, chokin' me."

"Jamie!"

He laughed, shaking his head ruefully as he pulled back the quilt on the bed.

"I don't know what it is about ye, Sassenach, that always makes me want to show off for ye. Get myself killed one of these days, tryin' to impress ye, I expect." He sighed, gingerly smoothing the woolen shirt over his stomach. "It's only play-acting, Sassenach; ye shouldna worry."

"Play-acting! Good God, Jamie!"

"Have ye no seen a strange dog join a pack, Sassenach? The others sniff at him, and nip at his legs, and growl, to see will he cower or growl back at them. And sometimes it comes to biting, and sometimes not, but at the end of it, every dog in the pack knows his place, and who's leader. Old Simon wants to be sure I ken who leads this pack; that's all."

"Oh? And do you?" I lay down, waiting for him to come to bed. He picked up the candle and grinned down at me, the flickering light picking up a blue gleam in his eyes.

"Woof," he said, and blew out the candle.

I saw very little of Jamie for the next two weeks, save at night. During the day, he was always with his grandfather, hunting or riding—for Lovat was a vigorous man, despite his age—or drinking in the study, as the Old Fox slowly drew his conclusions and laid his plans.

I spent most of my time with Frances and the other women. Out of the shadow of her redoubtable old father, Frances gained enough courage to speak her own mind, and proved an intelligent and interesting companion. She had the responsibility for the smooth running of the castle and its staff, but when her father appeared on the scene, she dwindled into insignificance, seldom raising her eyes or speaking above a whisper. I wasn't sure I blamed her.

Two weeks after our arrival, Jamie came to fetch me from the drawing room where I sat with Frances and Aline, saying that Lord Lovat wished to see me.

Old Simon waved a casual hand at the decanters set on
the table by the wall, then sat down in a wide-seated chair of
carved walnut, with crushed padding in well-worn blue velvet.
The chair fitted his short, stocky form as though it had been
built around him; I wondered whether it had in fact been
built to order, or whether, from long use, he had grown into
the shape of the chair.

I sat down quietly in a corner with my glass of port, and
kept quiet while Simon questioned Jamie once again about
Charles Stuart's situation and prospects.

For the twentieth time in a week, Jamie patiently re-
hearsed the number of troops available, the structure of command—insofar as one existed—the armament on hand and its
condition—mostly poor—the prospects of Charles being
joined by Lord Lewis Gordon or the Farquharsons, what
Glengarry had said following Prestonpans, what Cameron
knew or deduced of the movement of English troops, why
Charles had decided to march south, and so on and so forth. I
found myself nodding over the cup in my hand, and jerked
myself into wakefulness, just in time to keep the ruby liquid
from tipping onto my skirt.

". . . and Lord George Murray and Kilmarnock both
think His Highness would be best advised to pull back into
the Highlands for the winter," Jamie concluded, yawning
widely. Cramped on the narrow-backed chair he had been
given, he rose and stretched, his shadow flickering on the pale
hangings that covered the stone walls.

"And what d'ye think, yourself?" Old Simon's eyes glittered under half-fallen lids as he leaned back in his chair. The
fire burned high and bright on the hearth; Frances had
smoored the fire in the main hall, covering it with peats, but
this one had been rekindled at Lovat's order, and with wood,
not peat. The smell of pine resin from the burning wood was
sharp, mingled with the thicker smell of smoke.

The light cast Jamie's shadow high on the wall as he
turned restlessly, not wanting to sit down again. It was close
and dark in the small study, with the window draped against
the night—very different from the open, sunny kirkyard in
which Colum had asked him the same question. And the situation now had shifted; no longer the popular darling to whom
clan chieftains deferred, Charles now was sending to the

chiefs, grimly calling in his obligations. But the shape of the problem was the same—a dark, amorphous shape, hanging like a shadow over us.

"I've told ye what I think—a dozen times or more." Jamie spoke abruptly. He moved his shoulders impatiently, shrugging as though the fit of his coat were too tight.

"Oh, aye. You've told me. But this time I think we shall have the truth." The old man settled more comfortably into his padded chair, hands linked across his belly.

"Will ye, then?" Jamie uttered a short laugh, and turned to face his grandfather. He leaned back against the table, hands braced behind him. Despite the differences in posture and figure, there was a tension between the two men that brought out a fugitive resemblance between them. The one tall and the other squat, but both of them strong, stubborn, and determined to win this encounter.

"Am I not your kinsman? And your chief? I command your loyalty, do I not?"

So that was the point. Colum, so accustomed to physical weakness, had known the secret of turning another man's weakness to his own purposes. Simon Fraser, strong and vigorous even in old age, was accustomed to getting his own way by more direct means. I could see from the sour smile on Jamie's face that he, too, was contrasting Colum's appeal with his grandfather's demand.

"Can ye? I dinna recall that I've sworn ye an oath."

Several long stiff hairs grew out of Simon's eyebrows, in the way of old men. These quivered in the firelight, though I couldn't tell whether with indignation or amusement.

"Oath, is it? And is it not Fraser blood in your veins?"

Jamie's mouth twisted wryly as he answered. "They do say that it's a wise child as kens his own father, no? My mother was a MacKenzie; I know that much."

Simon's face grew dark with blood, and his brows drew together. Then his mouth fell open, and he shouted with laughter. He laughed until he was forced to pull himself up in the chair and bend forward, sputtering and choking. At last, beating one hand on the arm of the chair in helpless mirth, he reached into his mouth with the other and pulled out his false teeth.

"Dod," he sputtered, gasping and wheezing. Face

streaming with tears and saliva, he groped blindly for the small table by his chair, and dropped the teeth onto the cake plate. The gnarled fingers closed on a linen napkin, and he pressed it to his face, still emitting strangled grunts of laughter as he conducted his mopping up.

"Chritht, laddie," he said at last, lisping heavily. "Path me the whithky."

Eyebrows raised, Jamie took the decanter from the table behind him and passed it to his grandfather, who removed the stopper and gulped a substantial amount of the contents without bothering about the formality of a glass.

"You think you're not a Frather?" he said, lowering the decanter and exhaling gustily. "Ha!" He leaned back once more, belly rising and falling rapidly as he caught his breath. He pointed a long, skinny finger at Jamie.

"Your own father thtood right where you're thtanding, laddie, and told me jutht what you did, the day he left Beaufort Cathtle once and for all." The old man was growing calmer now; he coughed several times and wiped his face again.

"Did ye know that I'd tried to thtop your parents' marriage by claiming that Ellen MacKenzie's child wathn't Brian's?"

"Aye, I knew." Jamie was leaning back on the table again, surveying his grandfather through narrowed eyes.

Lord Lovat snorted. "I'll not thay there's been always goodwill atween me and mine, but I know my thons. *And* my grandthons," he added pointedly. "De'il take me and I think any one of 'em could be a cuckold, nay more than I could."

Jamie didn't turn a hair, but I couldn't stop myself from glancing away from the old man. I found myself staring at his discarded teeth, the stained beechwood gleaming wetly amid the cake crumbs. Luckily Lord Lovat hadn't noticed my slight motion.

He went on, serious once more. "Now, then. Dougal MacKenzie of Leoch hath declared for Charles. D'ye call him your chief? Is that what ye're telling me—that ye've given him an oath?"

"No. I havena sworn to anyone."

"Not even Charles?" The old man was fast, pouncing on this like a cat on a mouse. I could almost see his tail twitch as he watched Jamie, slanted eyes deep-set and gleaming under crepey lids.

Jamie's eyes were fixed on the leaping flames, his shadow motionless on the wall behind him.

"He hasna asked me." This was true. Charles had had no need to request an oath from Jamie—having precluded the necessity by signing Jamie's name to his Bond of Association. Still, I knew that the fact that he had not, in fact, given his word to Charles was important to Jamie. If he must betray the man, let it not be as an acknowledged chief. The idea that the entire world thought such an oath existed was a matter of much less concern.

Simon grunted again. Without his false teeth, his nose and chin came close together, making the lower half of his face oddly foreshortened.

"Then nothing hampers you to thwear to me, as chief of your clan," he said quietly. The twitching tail was less visible, but still there. I could almost hear the thoughts in his head, gliding round on padded feet. With Jamie's loyalty sworn to him, rather than Charles, Lovat's power would be increased. As would his wealth, with a share of the income from Lallybroch that he might claim as his chieftain's due. The prospect of a dukedom drew slightly nearer, gleaming through the mist.

"Nothing save my own will," Jamie agreed pleasantly. "But that's some small obstacle, no?" His own eyes creased at the corners as they narrowed further.

"Mmphm." Lovat's eyes were almost closed, and he shook his head slowly from side to side. "Oh, aye, lad, you're your father's thon. Thtubborn as a block, and twith ath thtupid. I thould have known that Brian would thire nothing but fools from that harlot."

Jamie reached forward and plucked the beechwood teeth from the plate. "Ye'd better put these back, ye auld gomerel," he said rudely. "I canna understand a word ye say."

His grandfather's mouth widened in a humorless smile that showed the yellowed stump of a lone broken tooth in the lower jaw.

"No?" he said. "Will ye underthand a bargain?" He shot a quick look at me, seeing nothing more than another counter to be put into play. "Your oath for your wife's honor, how's that?"

Jamie laughed out loud, still holding the teeth in one hand.

"Oh, aye? D'ye mean to force her before my eyes, then, Grandsire?" He lounged back contemptuously, hand on the table. "Go ahead, and when she's done wi' ye, I'll send Aunt Frances up to sweep up the pieces."

His grandfather looked him over calmly. "Not I, lad." One side of the toothless mouth rose in a lopsided smile as he turned his head to look at me. "Though I've taken my pleasure with worthe." The cold malice in the dark eyes made me want to pull my cloak over my breasts in protection; unfortunately, I wasn't wearing one.

"How many men are there in Beaufort, Jamie? How many, who'd be of a mind to put your *thathenach* wench to the only uth thee's good for? You cannot guard her night and day."

Jamie straightened slowly, the great shadow echoing his movements on the wall. He stared down at his grandfather with no expression on his face.

"Oh, I think I needna worry, Grandsire," he said softly. "For my wife's a rare woman. A wisewoman, ye ken. A white lady, like Dame Aliset."

I had never heard of Dame Aliset, but Lord Lovat plainly had; his head jerked round to stare at me, eyes sprung wide with shocked alarm. His mouth drooped open, but before he could speak, Jamie had gone on, an undercurrent of malice clearly audible in his smooth speech.

"The man that takes her in unholy embrace will have his privates blasted like a frostbitten apple," he said, with relish, "and his soul will burn forever in hell." He bared his teeth at his grandfather, and drew back his hand. "Like this." The beechwood teeth landed in the midst of the fire with a plop, and at once began to sizzle.

41

The Seer's Curse

Oost of the Lowland Scots had gone over to Presbyterianism in the two centuries before. Some of the Highland clans had gone with them, but others, like the Frasers and MacKenzies, had kept their Catholic faith. Especially the Frasers, with their strong family ties to Catholic France.

There was a small chapel in Beaufort Castle, to serve the devotional uses of the Earl and his family, but Beauly Priory, ruined as it was, remained the burying place of the Lovats, and the floor of the open-roofed chancel was paved thick with the flat tombstones of those who lay under them.

It was a peaceful place, and I walked there sometimes, in spite of the cold, blustery weather. I had no idea whether Old Simon had meant his threat against me, or whether Jamie's comparing me to Dame Aliset—who turned out to be a legendary "white woman" or healer, the Scottish equivalent of La Dame Blanche—was sufficient to put a stop to that threat. But I thought that no one was likely to accost me among the tombs of extinct Frasers.

One afternoon, a few days after the scene in the study, I walked through a gap in the ruined Priory wall and found that for once, I didn't have it to myself. The tall woman I had seen outside Lovat's study was there, leaning against one of the red-stone tombs, arms folded about her for warmth, long legs thrust out like a stork.

I made to turn aside, but she saw me, and motioned me to join her.

"You'll be my lady Broch Tuarach?" she said, though there was no more than a hint of question in her soft Highland voice.

"I am. And you're . . . Maisri?"

A small smile lit her face. She had a most intriguing face, slightly asymmetrical, like a Modigliani painting, and long black hair that flowed loose around her shoulders, streaked with white, though she was plainly still young. A seer, hm? I thought she looked the part.

"Aye, I have the Sight," she said, the smile widening a bit on her lopsided mouth.

"Do mind-reading, too, do you?" I asked.

She laughed, the sound vanishing on the wind that moaned through the ruined walls.

"No, lady. But I do read faces, and . . ."

"And mine's an open book. I know," I said, resigned.

We stood side by side for a time then, watching tiny spatters of fine sleet dashing against the sandstone and the thick brown grass that overgrew the kirkyard.

"They do say as you're a white lady," Maisri observed suddenly. I could feel her watching me intently, but with none of the nervousness that seemed common to such an observation.

"They do say that," I agreed.

"Ah." She didn't speak again, just stared down at her feet, long and elegant, stockinged in wool and clad in leather sandals. My own toes, rather more sheltered, were growing numb, and I thought hers must be frozen solid, if she'd been here any time.

"What are you doing up here?" I asked. The Priory was a beautiful, peaceful place in good weather, but not much of a roost in the cold winter sleet.

"I come here to think," she said. She gave me a slight smile, but was plainly preoccupied. Whatever she was thinking, her thoughts weren't overly pleasant.

"To think about what?" I asked, hoisting myself up to sit on the tomb beside her. The worn figure of a knight lay on the lid, his claymore clasped to his bosom, the hilt forming a cross over his heart.

"I want to know why!" she burst out. Her thin face was suddenly alight with indignation.

"Why what?"

"Why! Why can I see what will happen, when there's no mortal thing I can be doin' to change it or stop it? What's the good of a gift like that? It's no a gift, come to that—it's a damn curse, though I havena done anything to be cursed like this!"

She turned and glared balefully at Thomas Fraser, serene under his helm, with the hilt of his sword clasped under crossed hands.

"Aye, and maybe it's *your* curse, ye auld gomerel! You and the rest o' your damned family. Did ye ever think that?" she asked suddenly, turning to me. Her brows arched high over brown eyes that sparked with furious intelligence.

"Did ye ever think perhaps that it's no your own fate at all that makes you what ye are? That maybe ye have the Sight or the power only because it's necessary to someone else, and it's nothing to do wi' you at all—except that it's you has it, and has to suffer the having of it. Have you?"

"I don't know," I said slowly. "Or yes, since you say it, I have wondered. Why me? You ask that all the time, of course. But I've never come up with a satisfactory answer. You think perhaps you have the Sight because it's a curse on the Frasers —to know their deaths ahead of time? That's a hell of an idea."

"A hell is right," she agreed bitterly. She leaned back against the sarcophagus of red stone, staring out at the sleet that sprayed across the top of the broken wall.

"What d'ye think?" she asked suddenly. "Do I tell him?"

I was startled.

"Who? Lord Lovat?"

"Aye, his lordship. He asks what I see, and beats me when I tell him there's naught to see. He knows, ye ken; he sees it in my face when I've had the Sight. But that's the only power I've got; the power not to say." The long white fingers snaked out from her cloak, playing nervously with the folds of soaked cloth.

"There's always the chance of it, isn't there?" she said. Her head was bent so that the hood of her cloak shielded her face from my gaze. "There's a chance that my telling would make a difference. It has, now and then, ye know. I told Lachlan Gibbons when I saw his son-in-law wrapped in sea-weed, and the eels stirring beneath his shirt. Lachlan listened; he went out straightaway and stove a hole in his son-in-law's boat." She laughed, remembering. "Lord, there was the kebbie-lebbie to do! But when the great storm came the next week, three men were drowned, and Lachlan's son-in-law was safe at hame, still mending his boat. And when I saw him next, his shirt hung dry on him, and the seaweed was gone from his hair."

"So it can happen," I said softly. "Sometimes."

"Sometimes," she said, nodding, still staring at the ground. Lady Sarah Fraser lay at her feet, the lady's stone surmounted with a skull atop crossed bones. *Hodie mihi cras tibi,* said the inscription. *Sic transit gloria mundi.* My turn today, yours tomorrow. And thus passes away the glory of the world.

"Sometimes not. When I see a man wrapped in his winding sheet, the illness follows—and there's naught to be done about that."

"Perhaps," I said. I looked at my own hands, spread on the stone beside me. Without medicine, without instruments, without knowledge—yes, then illness was fate, and naught to be done. But if a healer was near, and had the things to heal with . . . was it possible that Maisri saw the shadow of a coming illness, as a real—if usually invisible—symptom, much like a fever or a rash? And then only the lack of medical facilities made the reading of such symptoms a sentence of death? I would never know.

"We aren't ever going to know," I said, turning to her. "We can't say. We know things that other people don't know, and we can't say why or how. But we have got it—and you're right, it's a curse. But if you have knowledge, and it *may* prevent harm . . . do you think it could *cause* harm?"

She shook her head.

"I canna say. If you knew ye were to die soon, are there things you'd do? And would they be good things only that ye'd do, or would ye take the last chance ye might have to do harm to your enemies—harm that might otherwise be left alone?"

"Damned if I know." We were quiet for a time, watching the sleet turn to snow, and the blowing flakes whirl up in gusts through the ruined tracery of the Priory wall.

"Sometimes I know there's something there, like," Maisri said suddenly, "but I can block it out of my mind, not look. 'Twas like that with his lordship; I knew there was something, but I'd managed not to see it. But then he bade me look, and say the divining spell to make the vision come clear. And I did." The hood of her cloak slipped back as she tilted

her head, looking up at the wall of the Priory as it soared
above us, ochre and white and red, with the mortar crumbling
between its stones. White-streaked black hair spilled down
her back, free in the wind.

"He was standing there before the fire, but it was daylight, and clear to see. A man stood behind him, still as a tree,
and his face covered in black. And across his lordship's face
there fell the shadow of an ax."

She spoke matter-of-factly, but the shiver ran up my
spine nonetheless. She sighed at last, and turned to me.

"Weel, I will tell him, then, and let him do what he will.
Doom him or save him, that I canna do. It's his choice—and
the Lord Jesus help him."

She turned to go, and I slid off the tomb, landing on the
Lady Sarah's slab.

"Maisri," I said. She turned back to look at me, eyes
black as the shadows among the tombs.

"Aye?"

"What do you see, Maisri?" I asked, and stood waiting,
facing her, hands dropped to my sides.

She stared at me hard, above and below, behind and
beside. At last she smiled faintly, nodding.

"I see naught but you, lady," she said softly. "There's
only you."

She turned and disappeared down the path between the
trees, leaving me among the blowing flakes of snow.

Doom, or save. That I cannot do. For I have no power
beyond that of knowledge, no ability to bend others to my
will, no way to stop them doing what *they* will. There is only
me.

I shook the snow from the folds of my cloak, and turned
to follow Maisri down the path, sharing her bitter knowledge
that there was only me. And I was not enough.

Old Simon's manner was much as usual over the course
of the next two or three weeks, but I imagined that Maisri
had kept her intention of telling him about her visions. While
he had seemed on the verge of summoning the tacksmen and
tenants to march, suddenly he backed off, saying that there
was no hurry, after all. This shilly-shallying infuriated Young

Simon, who was champing at the bit to go to war and cover himself with glory.

"It's not a matter of urgency," Old Simon said, for the dozenth time. He lifted an oatcake, sniffed at it, and set it down again. "Perhaps we'll do best to wait for the spring planting, after all."

"They could be in London before spring!" Young Simon glowered across the dinner table at his father and reached for the butter. "If ye will not go yourself, then let me take the men to join His Highness!"

Lord Lovat grunted. "You've the Devil's own impatience," he said, "but not half his judgment. Will ye never learn to wait?"

"The time for waiting's long since past!" Simon burst out. "The Camerons, the MacDonalds, the MacGillivrays—they've all been there since the first. Are we to come mearchin' along at the finish, to find ourselves beggars, and taking second place to Clanranald and Glengarry? Fat chance you'll have of a dukedom then!"

Lovat had Jamie's wide, expressive mouth; even in old age, it retained some trace of humor and sensuality. Neither was visible at the moment. He pressed his lips tight together, surveying his heir without enthusiasm.

"Marry in haste, repent at leisure," he said. "And it's more true when choosing a laird than a lass. A woman can be got rid of."

Young Simon snorted and looked at Jamie for support. Over the last two months, his initial suspicious hostility had faded into a reluctant respect for his bastard relative's obvious expertise in the art of war.

"Jamie says . . ." he began.

"I ken well enough what he says," Old Simon interrupted. "He's said it often enough. I shall make up my own mind in my own time. But bear it in mind, lad—when it comes to declaring yourself in a war, there's little to be lost by waiting."

"Waiting to see who wins," Jamie murmured, studiously wiping his plate with a bit of bread. The old man looked up sharply, but evidently decided to ignore this contribution.

"Ye gave your word to the Stuarts," Young Simon continued stubbornly, paying no heed to his father's displeasure.

"Ye dinna mean to break it, surely? What will people say of your honor?"

"The same things they said in '15," his father calmly replied. "Most of those who 'said things' then are dead, bankrupt, or paupers in France. But I am still here."

"But . . ." Young Simon was red in the face, the usual result of this sort of conversation with his father.

"That will do," the old Earl interrupted sharply. He shook his head as he glared at his son, lips tight with disapproval. "Christ. Sometimes I could wish that Brian hadna died. He may have been a fool, too, but at least he knew when to stop talking."

Both Young Simon and Jamie flushed with anger, but after a wary glance at each other, turned their attentions to their food.

"And what are you looking at?" Lord Lovat growled, catching my eye on him as he turned away from his son.

"You," I said bluntly. "You don't look at all well." He didn't, even for a man in his seventies. No more than middle-height, slumped and broadened by age, he was normally still a solid-looking man, giving the impression that his barrel chest and rounded paunch were firm and healthy under his linen. Lately he had begun to look flabby, though, as if he had shrunk a bit within his skin. The wrinkled bags beneath his eyes were darkened, and his skin had a sickly pallor to it.

"Mphm," he grunted. "And why not? I get nay rest when I sleep, nor comfort when I'm awake. No wonder if I dinna look like a bridegroom."

"Oh, but ye do, Father," said Young Simon maliciously, seeing a chance to get a bit of his own back. "One at the end of his honeymoon, wi' all the juice sapped out of him."

"Simon!" said Lady Frances. Still, there was a ripple of laughter around the table at this, and even Lord Lovat's mouth twitched slightly.

"Aye?" he said. "Well, I'd sooner suffer soreness from that cause, I'll tell ye, lad." He shifted uncomfortably in his seat, and pushed away the platter of boiled turnips being offered. He reached for his wineglass, raised it to his nose for a sniff, then morosely put it down again.

"It's ill-mannered to stare," he remarked coldly to me.

"Or perhaps the English have different standards of politeness?"

I flushed slightly, but didn't drop my eyes. "I was just wondering—you don't have an appetite, and you don't drink. What other symptoms have you?"

"Going to prove yourself some worth, eh?" Lovat leaned back in his chair, folding his hands across his broad stomach like an elderly frog. "A healer, my grandson says. A white lady, aye?" He flicked a basilisk glance at Jamie, who simply went on eating, ignoring his grandfather. Lovat grunted, and tilted his head ironically in my direction.

"Well, I dinna drink, lady, for I canna piss, and I've little wish to blow up like a pig's bladder. And I dinna rest, for I rise a dozen times a night to make use of my pot, and damn little use it gets. So what have ye to say to that, Dame Aliset?"

"Father," murmured Lady Frances, "really, I don't think you should . . ."

"Could be an infection of the bladder, but it sounds like prostatitis to me," I replied. I picked up my wineglass and took a mouthful, savoring it before letting it slide down my throat. I smiled demurely at his lordship across my glass as I set it down.

"Oh, it does?" he said, eyebrows raised high. "And what's that, pray?"

I pushed back my sleeves and raised my hands, flexing my fingers like a magician about to perform some act of prestidigitation. I held up my left forefinger.

"The prostate gland in males," I said instructively, "encircles the tube of the urethra—which is the passage that leads from the bladder to the outside." I clasped two fingers of my right hand in a circle around my left forefinger, in illustration. "When the prostate becomes inflamed or enlarged—and that's called prostatitis, when it does—it clamps down on the urethra"—I narrowed the circle of my fingers—"cutting off the flow of urine. Very common in older men. Do you see?"

Lady Frances, failing to make any impression on her father with her opinions of proper dinner conversation, was whispering agitatedly to her younger sister, both of them watching me with deeper suspicion than usual.

Lord Lovat watched my little demonstration in fascination.

"Aye, I see," he said. The slanted cat-eyes narrowed, looking speculatively at my fingers. "What's to do about it, then, if ye've so much learning on the subject?"

I thought, frowning as I searched my memory. I had never actually seen—much less treated—a case of prostatitis, as it wasn't a condition that much afflicted young soldiers. Still, I had read medical texts where it was described; I remembered the treatment, because it had caused such hilarity among the student nurses, who had pored in fascinated horror over the rather graphic illustrations in the text.

"Well," I said, "barring surgery, there are really only two things you can do. You can insert a metal rod through the penis and up into the bladder, to force the urethra open"—I jabbed my forefinger through the constricting circle—"or you can massage the prostate itself, to reduce the swelling. Through the rectum," I added helpfully.

I heard a faint choking noise next to me, and glanced up at Jamie. His eyes were still fixed on his plate, but the tide of crimson was creeping upward from his collar, and the tips of his ears blazed red. He quivered slightly. I looked around the table, to find a phalanx of fascinated gazes fixed on me. The Lady Frances, Aline, and the other women were staring at me with varying expressions, ranging from curiosity to disgust, while the men all wore variations of revolted horror.

The exception to the general reaction was Lord Lovat himself, who was rubbing his chin thoughtfully, eyes half-closed.

"Mmphm," he said. "Hell of a choice, there. A stick up the cock, or a finger up the backside, eh?"

"More like two or three," I said. "Repeatedly." I gave him a small, decorous smile.

"Ah." A similar small smile decorated Lord Lovat's mouth, and he slowly lifted his gaze, fixing deep blue eyes on mine with an expression of mockery tinged with challenge.

"That sounds . . . diverting," he observed mildly. The slanted eyes slid down over my hands, assessing.

"You've lovely hands, my dear," he said. "Prettily kept, and such long white slender fingers, aye?"

Jamie brought both his own hands down on the table

with a crash and stood up. He leaned across the table, bringing his face within a foot of his grandfather's.

"And you're needing such attentions, Grandsire," he said. "I'll see to it myself." He spread out his hands on the tabletop, broad and massive, each long finger the rough diameter of a pistol barrel. "It's no pleasure to me to be stickin' my fingers up your hairy auld arse," he informed his grandfather, "but I expect it's my filial duty to save ye from exploding in a shower of piss, no?"

Frances emitted a faint squeak.

Lord Lovat eyed his grandson with considerable disfavor, then rose slowly from his seat.

"Don't trouble yourself," he said shortly. "I'll ha' one of the maidservants do it." He waved a hand at the company, giving notice that we might continue the meal, and left the hall, pausing to look speculatively at a young serving girl coming in with a platter of sliced pheasant. Eyes wide, she turned sideways to edge past him.

There was a dead silence over the dinner table following his lordship's exit. Young Simon looked at me and opened his mouth. Then he glanced at Jamie, and closed it again. He cleared his throat.

"I'll have the salt, if ye please," he said.

". . . and in consequence of the regrettable infirmity that prevents me from personal attendance upon Your Highness, I send by the hand of my son and heir a token of the loyalty—nay, make that 'regard'—a token of the regard in which I have long cherished His Majesty and Your Highness." Lord Lovat paused, frowning at the ceiling.

"What shall we send, Gideon?" he asked the secretary. "Rich-looking, but not so much I can't say it was only a trifling present of no importance."

Gideon sighed and wiped his face with a handkerchief. A stout, middle-aged man with thinning hair and round red cheeks, he plainly found the heat of the bedroom fire oppressive.

"The ring your lordship had from the Earl of Mar?" he suggested, without hope. A drop of sweat fell from his double chin onto the letter he was taking down, and he surreptitiously blotted it with his sleeve.

"Not expensive enough," his lordship judged, "and too many political associations." The mottled fingers tapped pensively on the coverlet as he thought.

Old Simon had done it up brown, I thought. He was wearing his best nightshirt, and was propped up in bed with an impressive panoply of medicines arrayed on the table, attended by his personal physician, Dr. Menzies, a small man with a squint who kept eyeing me with considerable doubt. I supposed the old man simply distrusted Young Simon's powers of imagination, and had staged this elaborate tableau so that his heir might faithfully report Lord Lovat's state of decrepitude when he presented himself to Charles Stuart.

"Ha," said his lordship with satisfaction. "We'll send the gold and sterling picnic set. That's rich enough, but too frivolous to be interpreted as political support. Besides," he added practically, "the spoon's dented. All right then," he said to the secretary, "let's go on with 'As Your Highness is aware . . .'"

I exchanged a glance with Jamie, who hid a smile in response.

"I think you've given him what he needs, Sassenach," he had told me as we undressed after our fateful dinner the week before.

"And what's that?" I asked, "an excuse to molest the maidservants?"

"I doubt he bothers greatly wi' excuses of that sort," Jamie said dryly. "Nay, you've given him a way to walk both sides—as usual. If he's got an impressive-sounding disease that keeps him to his bed, then he canna be blamed for not appearing himself wi' the men he promised. At the same time, if he sends his heir to fight, the Stuarts will credit Lovat with keeping his promise, and if it goes wrong, the Old Fox will claim to the English that he didna intend to give any aid to the Stuarts, but Young Simon went on his own account."

"Spell 'prostatitis' for Gideon, would ye, lass?" Lord Lovat called to me, breaking into my thoughts. "And mind ye write it out carefully, clot," he said to his secretary, "I dinna want His Highness to misread it."

"P-r-o-s-t-a-t-i-t-i-s," I spelled slowly, for Gideon's benefit. "And how is it this morning, anyway?" I asked, coming to stand by his lordship's bedside.

"Greatly improved, I thank ye," the old man said, grinning up at me with a fine display of false teeth. "Want to see me piss?"

"Not just now, thanks," I said politely.

It was a clear, icy day in mid-December when we left Beauly to join Charles Stuart and the Highland army. Against all advice, Charles had pressed on into England, defying weather and common sense, as well as his generals. But at last, in Derby, the generals had prevailed, the Highland chiefs refusing to go farther, and the Highland army was returning northward. An urgent letter from Charles to Jamie had urged us to head south "without delay," to rendezvous with His Highness upon his return to Edinburgh. Young Simon, looking every inch the clan chieftain in his crimson tartan, rode at the head of a column of men. Those men with mounts followed him, while the larger number on foot walked behind.

Being mounted, we rode with Simon at the head of the column, until such time as we would reach Comar. There we would part company, Simon and the Fraser troops to go to Edinburgh, Jamie ostensibly escorting me to Lallybroch before returning to Edinburgh himself. He had, of course, no intention of so returning, but that was none of Simon's business.

At midmorning, I emerged from a small wooded clump by the side of the track, to find Jamie waiting impatiently. Hot ale had been served to the departing men, to hearten them for the journey. And while I had myself found that hot ale made a surprisingly good breakfast, I had also found it had a marked effect on the kidneys.

Jamie snorted. "Women," he said. "How can ye all take such the devil of a time to do such a simple thing as piss? Ye make as much fuss over it as my grandsire."

"Well, you can come along next time and watch," I suggested acerbically. "Perhaps you'll have some helpful suggestions."

He merely snorted again, and turned back to watch the column of men filing past, but he was smiling nonetheless.

The clear, bright day raised everyone's spirits, but Jamie was in a particularly good mood this morning. And no wonder; we were going home. I knew he didn't deceive himself that all would be well; this war would have its price. But if we had failed to stop Charles, it might still be that we could save the small corner of Scotland that lay closest to us—Lallybroch. That much might be still within our power.

I glanced at the trailing column of clansmen.

"Two hundred men make a fair show."

"A hundred and seventy," Jamie corrected absently, reaching for his horse's reins.

"Are you sure?" I asked curiously. "Lord Lovat said he was sending two hundred. I heard him dictating the letter saying so."

"Well, he didn't." Jamie swung into the saddle, then stood up in his stirrups, pointing down the slope ahead, to the distant spot where the Fraser banner with its stag's-head crest fluttered at the head of the column.

"I counted them while I waited for you," he explained. "Thirty cavalry up there wi' Simon, then fifty wi' broadswords and targes—those will be the men from the local Watch—and then the cottars, wi' everything from scythes to hammers at their belts, and there's ninety of those."

"I suppose your grandfather's betting on Prince Charles not counting them personally," I observed cynically. "Trying to get credit for more than he's sent."

"Aye, but the names will be entered on the army rolls when they reach Edinburgh," Jamie said, frowning. "I'd best see."

I followed more sedately. I judged my mount to be approximately twenty years old, and capable of no more than a staid amble. Jamie's mount was a trifle friskier, though still no match for Donas. The huge stallion had been left in Edinburgh, as Prince Charles wished to ride him on public occasions. Jamie had acceded to this request, as he harbored suspicions that Old Simon might well be capable of appropriating the big horse, should Donas come within reach of his rapacious grasp.

Judging from the tableau unfolding before me, Jamie's estimate of his grandfather's character had not been in error. Jamie had first ridden up alongside Young Simon's clerk, and what looked from my vantage point like a heated argument ended when Jamie leaned from his saddle, grabbed the clerk's reins, and dragged the indignant man's horse out of line, onto the verge of the muddy track.

The two men dismounted and stood face-to-face, obviously going at it hammer and tongs. Young Simon, seeing the altercation, reined aside himself, motioning the rest of the column to proceed. A good deal of to and fro then ensued; we were close enough to see Simon's face, flushed red with annoyance, the worried grimace on the clerk's countenance, and a series of rather violent gestures on Jamie's part.

I watched this pantomime in fascination, as the clerk, with a shrug of resignation, unfastened his saddlebag, scrabbled in the depths, and came up with several sheets of parchment. Jamie snatched these and skimmed rapidly through them, forefinger tracing the lines of writing. He seized one sheet, letting the rest drop to the ground, and shook it in Simon Fraser's face. The Young Fox looked taken aback. He took the sheet, peered at it, then looked up in bewilderment. Jamie grabbed back the sheet, and with a sudden effort, ripped the tough parchment down, then across, and stuffed the pieces into his sporran.

I had halted my pony, who took advantage of the recess to nose about among the meager shreds of plant life still to be found. The back of Young Simon's neck was bright red as he turned back to his horse, and I decided to keep out of the way. Jamie, remounted, came trotting back along the verge to join me, red hair flying like a banner in the wind, eyes gleaming with anger over tight-set lips.

"The filthy auld arse-wipe," he said without ceremony.

"What's he done?" I inquired.

"Listed the names of my men on his own rolls," Jamie said. "Claimed them as part of his Fraser regiment. Mozie auld pout-worm!" He glanced back up the track with longing. "Pity we've come such a way; it's too far to go back and proddle the auld mumper."

I resisted the temptation to egg Jamie on to call his grandfather more names, and asked instead, "Why would he do that? Just to make it look as though he were making more of a contribution to the Stuarts?"

Jamie nodded, the tide of fury receding slightly from his cheeks.

"Aye, that. Make himself look better, at no cost. But not only that. The wretched auld nettercap wants my land back—he has, ever since he was forced to give it up when my parents wed. Now he thinks if it all comes right and he's made Duke of Inverness, he can claim Lallybroch has been his all along, and me just his tenant—the proof being that he's raised men from the estate to answer the Stuarts' call to the clans."

"Could he actually get away with something like that?" I asked doubtfully.

Jamie drew in a deep breath and released it, the cloud of vapor rising like dragon smoke from his nostrils. He smiled grimly and patted the sporran at his waist.

"Not now he can't," he said.

It was a two-day trip from Beauly to Lallybroch in good weather, given sound horses and dry ground, pausing for nothing more than the necessities of eating, sleeping, and personal hygiene. As it was, one of the horses went lame six miles out of Beauly, it snowed and sleeted and blew by turns, the boggy ground froze in patches of slippery ice, and what with one thing and another, it was nearly a week before we made our way down the last slope that led to the farmhouse at Lallybroch—cold, tired, hungry, and far from hygienic.

We were alone, just the two of us. Murtagh had been sent to Edinburgh with Young Simon and the Beaufort men-at-arms, to judge how matters stood with the Highland army.

The house stood solid among its outbuildings, white as the snow-streaked fields that surrounded it. I remembered vividly the emotions I had felt when I first saw the place. Granted, I had seen it first in the glow of a fine autumn day, not through sheets of blowing, icy snow, but even then it had seemed a welcoming refuge. The house's impression of strength and serenity was heightened now by the warm lamplight spilling through the lower windows, soft yellow in the deepening gray of early evening.

The feeling of welcome grew even stronger when I followed Jamie through the front door, to be met by the mouth-watering smell of roasting meat and fresh bread.

"Supper," Jamie said, closing his eyes in bliss as he inhaled the fragrant aromas. "God, I could eat a horse." Melting ice dripped from the hem of his cloak, making wet spots on the wooden floor.

"I thought we were going to *have* to eat one of them," I remarked, untying the strings of my cloak and brushing melting snow from my hair. "That poor creature you traded in Kirkinmill could barely hobble."

The sound of our voices carried through the hall, and a door opened overhead, followed by the sound of small running feet and a cry of joy as the younger Jamie spotted his namesake below.

The racket of their reunion attracted the attention of the rest of the household, and before we knew it, we were enveloped in greetings and embraces as Jenny and the baby, little Maggie, Ian, Mrs. Crook, and assorted maidservants all rushed into the hall.

"It's so good to see ye, my dearie!" Jenny said for the third time, standing on tiptoe to kiss Jamie. "Such news as we've heard of the army, we feared it would be months before ye came home."

"Aye," Ian said, "have ye brought any of the men back with ye, or is this only a visit?"

"Brought them back?" Arrested in the act of greeting his elder niece, Jamie stared at his brother-in-law, momentarily forgetting the little girl in his arms. Brought to a realization of her presence by her yanking his hair, he kissed her absently and handed her to me.

"What d'ye mean, Ian?" he demanded. "The men should all ha' returned a month ago. Did some of them not come home?"

I held small Maggie tight, a dreadful feeling of foreboding coming over me as I watched the smile fade from Ian's face.

"None of them came back, Jamie," he said slowly, his long, good-humored face suddenly mirroring the grim expression he saw on Jamie's. "We havena seen hide nor hair of any of them, since they marched awa' with you."

There was a shout from the dooryard outside, where Rabbie MacNab was putting away the horses. Jamie whirled, turned to the door and pushed it open, leaning out into the storm.

Over his shoulder, I could see a rider coming through the blowing snow. Visibility was too poor to make out his face, but that small, wiry figure, clinging monkeylike to the saddle, was unmistakable. "Fast as chain lightning," Jamie had said, and clearly he was right; to make the trip from Beauly to Edinburgh, and then to Lallybroch in a week was a true feat of endurance. The coming rider was Murtagh, and it didn't take Maisri's gift of prophecy to tell us that the news he bore was ill.

42

Reunions

White with rage, Jamie flung back the door of Holyrood's morning drawing room with a crash. Ewan Cameron leaped to his feet, upsetting the inkpot he had been using. Simon Fraser, Master of Lovat, was seated across the table, but merely raised thick black brows at his half-nephew's entrance.

"Damn!" Ewan said, scrabbling in his sleeve for a handkerchief to mop the spreading puddle with. "What's the matter wi' ye, Fraser? Oh, good morning to ye, Mistress Fraser," he added, seeing me behind Jamie.

"Where's His Highness?" Jamie demanded without preamble.

"Stirling Castle," Cameron replied, failing to find the handkerchief he was searching for. "Got a cloth, Fraser?"

"If I did, I'd choke ye with it," Jamie said. He had relaxed slightly, upon finding that Charles Stuart was not in residence, but the corners of his lips were still tight. "Why have ye let my men be kept in the Tolbooth? I've just seen them, kept in a place I wouldna let pigs live! Surely to God you could have done something!"

Cameron flushed at this, but his clear brown eyes met Jamie's steadily.

"I tried," he said. "I told His Highness that I was sure it was a mistake—aye, and the thirty of them ten miles from the army when they were found, some mistake!—and besides, even if they'd really meant to desert, he didna have such a strength of men that he could afford to do without them. That's all that kept him from ordering the lot of them to be hanged on the spot, ye ken," he said, beginning to grow angry as the shock of Jamie's entrance wore off. "God, man, it's treason to desert in time of war!"

"Aye?" Jamie said skeptically. He nodded briefly to Young Simon, and pushed a chair in my direction before sitting down himself. "And have you sent orders to hang the twenty of your men who've gone home, Ewan? Or is it more like forty, now?"

Cameron flushed more deeply and dropped his eyes, concentrating on mopping up the ink with the cloth Simon Fraser handed him.

"They weren't caught," he muttered at last. He glanced up at Jamie, his thin face earnest. "Go to His Highness at Stirling," he advised. "He was furious about the desertion, but after all, it was his orders sent ye to Beauly and left your men untended, aye? And he's always thought well of ye, Jamie, and called ye friend. It might be he'll pardon your men, and ye beg him for their lives."

Picking up the ink-soaked cloth, he looked dubiously at it, then, with a muttered excuse, left to dispose of it outside, obviously eager to get away from Jamie.

Jamie sat sprawled in his chair, breathing through clenched teeth with a small hissing noise, eyes fixed on the small embroidered hanging on the wall that showed the Stuart coat of arms. The two stiff fingers of his right hand tapped slowly on the table. He had been in much the same state ever since Murtagh's arrival at Lallybroch with the news that the thirty men of Jamie's command had been apprehended in the act of desertion and imprisoned in Edinburgh's notorious Tolbooth Prison, under sentence of death.

I didn't myself think that Charles intended to execute the men. As Ewan Cameron pointed out, the Highland army had need of every able-bodied man it could muster. The push into England that Charles had argued for had been costly, and the influx of support he had foreseen from the English countryside had not materialized. Not only that; to execute Jamie's men in his absence would have been an act of political idiocy and personal betrayal too great even for Charles Stuart to contemplate.

No, I imagined that Cameron was right, and the men would be pardoned eventually. Jamie undoubtedly realized it, too, but the realization was poor consolation to him, faced with the matching realization that rather than seeing his men safely removed from the risks of a deteriorating campaign, his orders had landed them in one of the worst prisons in all of Scotland, branded as cowards and sentenced to a shameful death by hanging.

This, coupled with the imminent prospect of leaving the men in their dark, filthy imprisonment, to go to Stirling and face the humiliation of pleading with Charles, was more than sufficient to explain the look on Jamie's face—that of a man who has just breakfasted on broken glass.

Young Simon also was silent, frowning, wide forehead creasing with thought.

"I'll come with ye to His Highness," he said abruptly.

"You will?" Jamie glanced at his half-uncle in surprise, then his eyes narrowed at Simon. "Why?"

Simon gave a half-grin. "Blood's blood, after all. Or do ye think I'd try to claim your men, like Father did?"

"Would you?"

"I might," Simon said frankly, "if I thought there was a chance of it doing me some good. More likely to cause trouble, though, is what I think. I've no wish to fight wi' the Mac-Kenzies—or you, nevvie," he added, the grin widening. "Rich as Lallybroch might be, it's a good long way from Beauly, and likely to be the devil of a fight to get hold of it, either by force or by the courts. I told Father so, but he hears what he wants to."

. The young man shook his head and settled his swordbelt around his hips.

"There's like to be better pickings with the army; certainly there will be with a restored king. And—" he concluded, "if that army's going to fight again like they did at Preston, they'll need every man they can get. I'll go with ye," he repeated firmly.

Jamie nodded, a slow smile dawning on his face. "I thank ye, then, Simon. It will be of help."

Simon nodded. "Aye, well. It wouldna hurt matters any for ye to ask Dougal MacKenzie to come speak for ye, either. He's in Edinburgh just now."

"Dougal MacKenzie?" Jamie's brows rose quizzically. "Aye, I suppose it would do no harm, but . . ."

"Do no harm? Man, did ye no hear? The MacKenzie's Prince Charles's fair-haired boy the noo." Simon lounged back in his seat, looking mockingly at his half-nephew.

"What for?" I asked. "What on earth has he done?" Dougal had brought two hundred and fifty men-at-arms to fight for the Stuart cause, but there were a number of chieftains who had made greater contributions.

"Ten thousand pounds," Simon said, savoring the words as he rolled them around on his tongue. "Ten thousand pounds in fine sterling, Dougal MacKenzie's brought to lay at the feet of his sovereign. And it wilna come amiss, either," he said matter-of-factly, dropping his lounging pose. "Cameron was just telling me that Charles had gone through the last of the Spanish money, and damn little coming in from the English supporters he'd counted on. Dougal's ten thousand will keep the army in weapons and food for a few more weeks, at least, and with luck, by then he'll ha' got more from France." At last, realizing that his reckless cousin was providing him with an excellent distraction for the English, Louis was reluctantly agreeing to cough up a bit of money. It was a long time coming, though.

I stared at Jamie, his face reflecting my own bewilderment. Where on earth would Dougal MacKenzie have gotten ten thousand pounds? Suddenly I remembered where I had heard that sum mentioned once before—in the thieves' hole at Cranesmuir, where I had spent three endless days and nights, awaiting trial on charges of witchcraft.

"Geillis Duncan!" I exclaimed. I felt cold at the memory of that conversation, carried out in the pitch-blackness of a miry pit, my companion no more than a voice in the dark. The drawing-room fire was warm, but I pulled my cloak tighter around me.

"I diverted near on to ten thousand pounds," Geillis had said, boasting of the thefts accomplished by judicious forgery of her late husband's name. Arthur Duncan, whom she had killed by poison, had been the procurator fiscal for the district. "Ten thousand pounds for the Jacobite cause. When it comes to rebellion, I shall know that I helped."

"She stole it," I said, feeling a tremor run up my arms at the thought of Geillis Duncan, convicted of witchcraft, gone to a fiery death beneath the branches of a rowan tree. Geillis Duncan, who had escaped death just long enough to give birth to the child she bore to her lover—Dougal MacKenzie. "She stole it and she gave it to Dougal; or he took it from her, no telling which, now." Agitated, I stood up and paced back and forth before the fire.

"That bastard!" I said. "That's what he was doing in Paris two years ago!"

"What?" Jamie was frowning at me, Simon staring openmouthed.

"Visiting Charles Stuart. He came to see whether Charles was really planning a rebellion. Maybe he promised the money then, maybe that's what encouraged Charles to risk coming to Scotland—the promise of Geillis Duncan's money. But Dougal couldn't give Charles the money openly while Colum was alive—Colum would have asked questions; he was much too honest a man to have used stolen money, no matter who stole it in the first place."

"I see." Jamie nodded, eyes hooded in thought. "But now Colum is dead," he said quietly. "And Dougal MacKenzie is the Prince's favorite."

"Which is all to the good for you, as I've been saying," Simon put in, impatient with talk of people he didn't know and matters he only half-understood. "Go find him; likely he'll be in the World's End at this time o' day."

"Do you think he'll speak to the Prince for you?" I asked Jamie, worried. Dougal had been Jamie's foster father for a time, but the relationship had assuredly had its ups and downs. Dougal might not want to risk his newfound popularity with the Prince by speaking out for a bunch of cowards and deserters.

The Young Fox might lack his father's years, but he had a good bit of his sire's acumen. The heavy black brows quirked upward.

"MacKenzie still wants Lallybroch, no? And if he thinks Father and I might have an eye on reclaiming your land, he'll be more eager to help you get your men back, aye? Cost him a lot more to fight us for it than to deal wi' you, once the war's over." He nodded, happily chewing his upper lip as he contemplated the ramifications of the situation.

"I'll go wave a copy of Father's list under his nose before ye speak to him. You come in and tell him you'll see me in hell before ye let me claim your men, and then we'll all go to Stirling together." He grinned at Jamie complicitously.

"I always thought there was some reason why 'Scot' rhymed with 'plot,' " I remarked.

"What?" Both men looked up, startled.

"Never mind," I said, shaking my head. "Blood will tell."

I stayed in Edinburgh while Jamie and his rival uncles rode to Stirling to straighten out matters with the Prince. Under the circumstances, I couldn't stay at Holyroodhouse, but found lodgings in one of the wynds above the Canongate. It was a small, cold, cramped room, but I wasn't in it much.

The Tolbooth prisoners couldn't come out, but there was nothing barring visitors who wanted to get in. Fergus and I visited the prison daily, and a small amount of discriminating bribery allowed me to pass food and medicine to the men from Lallybroch. Theoretically, I wasn't allowed to talk privately to the prisoners, but here again, the system had a certain amount of slip to it, when suitably greased, and I managed to talk alone with Ross the smith on two or three occasions.

"'Twas my fault, lady," he said at once, the first time I saw him. "I should ha' had the sense to make the men go in small groups of three and four, not altogether like we did. I was afraid of losing some, though; the most of them had never been more than five mile from home before."

"You needn't blame yourself," I assured him. "From what I heard, it was only ill luck that you were caught. Don't worry; Jamie has gone to see the Prince at Stirling; he'll have you out of here in no time."

He nodded, tiredly brushing back a lock of hair. He was filthy and unkempt, and a good bit diminished from the burly, robust craftsman he had been a few months before. Still, he smiled at me, and thanked me for the food.

"It wilna come amiss," he said frankly. "It's little we get but slops. D'ye think . . ." He hesitated. "D'ye think ye might manage a few blankets, my lady? I wouldna ask, only four of the men have the ague, and . . ."

"I'll manage," I said.

I left the prison, wondering exactly *how* I would manage. While the main army had gone south to invade England, Edinburgh was still an occupied city. With soldiers, lords, and hangers-on drifting constantly in and out, goods of all sorts were high-priced and in short supply. Blankets and warm clothes could be found, but they would cost a lot, and I had precisely ten shillings left in my purse.

There was a banker in Edinburgh, a Mr. Waterford, who had in the past handled some of Lallybroch's business and investments, but Jamie had removed all his funds from the bank some months before, fearing that bank-held assets might be seized by the Crown. The money had been converted to gold, some of it sent to Jared in France for safe-keeping, the rest of it hidden in the farmhouse. All of it equally inaccessible to me at the moment.

I paused on the street to think, passersby jostling past me on the cobbles. If I didn't have money, I had still a few things of value. The crystal Raymond had given me in Paris—while the crystal itself was of no particular value, its gold mounting and chain were. My wedding rings—no, I didn't want to part with those, even temporarily. But the pearls . . . I felt inside my pocket, checking to see that the pearl necklace Jamie had given me on our wedding day was still safely sewn into the seam of my skirt.

It was; the small, irregular beads of the freshwater pearls were hard and smooth under my fingers. Not as expensive as oriental pearls, but it was still a fine necklace, with gold pierced-work roundels between the pearls. It had belonged to Jamie's mother, Ellen. I thought she would have liked to see it used to comfort his men.

"Five pounds," I said firmly. "It's worth ten, and I could get six for it, if I cared to walk all the way up the hill to another shop." I had no idea whether this was true or not, but I reached out as though to pick up the necklace from the counter anyway, pretending that I was about to leave the pawnbroker's shop. The pawnbroker, Mr. Samuels, placed a quick hand over the necklace, his eagerness letting me know that I should have asked six pounds to start with.

"Three pound ten, then," he said. "It's beggaring me own family to do it, but for a fine lady like yourself . . ."

The small bell over the shop door chimed behind me as the door opened, and there was the sound of hesitant footsteps on the worn boards of the pawnshop floor.

"Excuse me," began a girl's voice, and I whirled around,

pearl necklace forgotten, to see the shadow of the pawnbroker's balls falling across the face of Mary Hawkins. She
had grown in the last year, and filled out as well. There was a
new maturity and dignity in her manner, but she was still very
young. She blinked once, and then fell on me with a shriek of
joy, her fur collar tickling my nose as she hugged me tight.

"What are you doing here?" I asked, disentangling myself at last.

"Father's sister lives here," she replied. "I'm st-staying
with her. Or do you mean why am I here?" She waved a hand
at the dingy confines of Mr. Samuels's emporium.

"Well, that too," I said. "But that can wait a bit." I
turned to the pawnbroker. "Four pound six, or I'll walk up
the hill," I told him. "Make up your mind, I'm in a hurry."

Grumbling to himself, Mr. Samuels reached beneath his
counter for the cash box, as I turned back to Mary.

"I have to buy some blankets. Can you come with me?"

She glanced outside, to where a small man in a footman's livery stood by the door, clearly waiting for her. "Yes, if
you'll come with me afterward. Oh, Claire, I'm *so* glad to see
you!"

"He sent a message to me," Mary confided, as we walked
down the hill. "Alex. A friend brought me his letter." Her
face glowed as she spoke his name, but there was a small
frown between her brows as well.

"When I found he was in Edinburgh, I m-made Father
send me to visit Aunt Mildred. He didn't mind," she added
bitterly. "It m-made him ill to look at me, after what happened in Paris. He was happy to get me out of his house."

"So you've seen Alex?" I asked. I wondered how the
young curate had fared, since I had last seen him. I also wondered how he had found the courage to write to Mary.

"Yes. He didn't ask me to come," she added quickly. "I
c-came by myself." Her chin lifted in defiance, but there was a
small quiver as she said, "He. . . . he wouldn't have written
to me, but he thought he was d-dying, and he wanted me to
know . . . to know . . ." I put an arm about her shoulders
and turned quickly into one of the closes, standing with her
out of the flow of jostling street traffic.

"It's all right," I said to her, patting her helplessly, knowing that nothing I could do would make it right. "You came, and you've seen him, that's the important thing."

She nodded, speechless, and blew her nose. "Yes," she said thickly, at last. "We've had . . . two months. I k-keep telling myself that that's more than most people ever have, two months of happiness . . . but we lost so much time that we might have h-had, and . . . it's not enough. Claire, it isn't enough!"

"No," I said quietly. "A lifetime isn't enough, for that kind of love." With a sudden pang, I wondered where Jamie was, and how he was faring.

Mary, more composed now, clutched me by the sleeve. "Claire, can you come with me to see him? I know there's n-not much you can do . . ." Her voice faltered, and she steadied it with a visible effort. "But maybe you could . . . help." She caught my look at the footman, who stood stolidly outside the wynd, oblivious to the passing traffic. "I pay him," she said simply. "My aunt thinks I go w-walking every afternoon. Will you come?"

"Yes, of course." I glanced between the towering buildings, judging the level of the sun over the hills outside the city. It would be dark in an hour; I wanted the blankets delivered to the prison before night made the damp stone walls of the Tolbooth still colder. Making a sudden decision, I turned to Fergus, who had been standing patiently next to me, watching Mary with interest. Returned to Edinburgh with the rest of the Lallybroch men, he had escaped imprisonment by virtue of his French citizenship, and had survived hardily by reverting to his customary trade. I had found him faithfully hanging about near the Tolbooth, where he brought bits of food for his imprisoned companions.

"Take this money," I said, handing him my purse, "and find Murtagh. Tell him to get as many blankets as that will buy, and see they're taken to the gaolkeeper at the Tolbooth. He's been bribed already, but keep back a few shillings, just in case."

"But Madame," he protested, "I promised milord I would not let you go alone . . ."

"Milord isn't here," I said firmly, "and I am. Go, Fergus."

He glanced from me to Mary, evidently decided she was

less a threat to me than my temper was to him, and departed, shrugging his shoulders and muttering in French about the stubbornness of women.

The little room at the top of the building had changed considerably since my last visit. It was clean, for one thing, with polish gleaming on every horizontal surface. There was food in the hutch, a down quilt on the bed, and numerous small comforts provided for the patient. Mary had confided on the way that she had been quietly pawning her mother's jewelry, to ensure that Alex Randall was as comfortable as money could make him.

There were limits to what money could manage, but Alex's face glowed like a candle flame when Mary came through the door, temporarily obscuring the ravages of illness.

"I've brought Claire, dearest." Mary dropped her cloak unheeded onto a chair and knelt beside him, taking his thin, blue-veined hands in her own.

"Mrs. Fraser." His voice was light and breathless, though he smiled at me. "It's good to see a friendly face again."

"Yes, it is." I smiled at him, noting half-consciously the rapid, fluttering pulse visible in his throat, and the transparency of his skin. The hazel eyes were soft and warm, holding most of the life left in his frail body.

Lacking medicine, there was nothing I could do for him, but I examined him carefully, and saw him tucked up comfortably afterward, his lips slightly blue from the minor exertion of the examination.

I covered the anxiety I felt at his condition, and promised to come next day with some medicine to help him sleep more easily. He hardly noticed my assurances; all his attention was for Mary, sitting anxiously by him, holding his hand. I saw her glance at the window, where light was fading rapidly, and realized her concern; she would have to return to her aunt's house before nightfall.

"I'll take my leave, then," I told Alex, removing myself as tactfully as I could, to leave them a few precious moments alone together.

He glanced from me to Mary, then smiled back at me in gratitude.

"God bless you, Mrs. Fraser," he said.

"I'll see you tomorrow," I said, and left, hoping that I would.

I was busy over the next few days. The men's arms had been confiscated, of course, when they were arrested, and I did my best to recover what I could, bullying and threatening, bribing and charming where necessary. I pawned two brooches that Jared had given me as a farewell present, and bought enough food to ensure that the men of Lallybroch ate as well as the army in general—poorly as that might be.

I talked my way into the cells of the prison, and spent some time in treating the prisoners' ailments, ranging from scurvy and the more generalized malnutrition common in winter, to chafing sores, chilblains, arthritis, and a variety of respiratory ailments.

I made the rounds of those chieftains and lords still in Edinburgh—not many—who might be helpful to Jamie, if his visit to Stirling should fail. I didn't think it would, but it seemed wise to take precautions.

And among the other activities of my days, I made time to see Alex Randall once a day. I took pains to come in the mornings, so as not to use up his time with Mary. Alex slept little, and that little, ill; consequently, he tended to be tired and drooping in the morning, not wanting to talk, but always smiling in welcome when I arrived. I would give him a light mixture of mint and lavender, with a few drops of poppy syrup stirred in; this would generally allow him a few hours of sleep, so that he could be alert when Mary arrived in the afternoon.

Aside from me and Mary, I had seen no other visitors at the top of the building. I was therefore surprised, coming up the stairs to his room one morning, to hear voices behind the closed door.

I knocked once, briefly, as was our agreed custom, and let myself in. Jonathan Randall was sitting by his brother's bed, clad in his captain's uniform of red and fawn. He rose at my entrance and bowed correctly, face cold.

"Madam," he said.

"Captain," I said. We then stood awkwardly in the middle of the room, staring at each other, each unwilling to go further.

"Johnny," said Alex's hoarse voice from the bed. It had a note of coaxing, as well as one of command, and his brother shrugged irritably when he heard it.

"My brother has summoned me to give you a bit of news," he said, tight-lipped. He wore no wig this morning, and with his dark hair tied back, his resemblance to his brother was startling. Pale and frail as Alex was, he looked like Jonathan's ghost.

"You and Mr. Fraser have been kind to my Mary," Alex said, rolling onto his side to look at me. "And to me as well. I . . . knew of my brother's bargain with you"—the faintest of pinks rose in his cheeks—"but I know, too, what you and your husband did for Mary . . . in Paris." He licked his lips, cracked and dry from the constant heat in the room. "I think you should hear the news Johnny brought from the Castle yesterday."

Jack Randall eyed me with dislike, but he was good as his word.

"Hawley has succeeded Cope, as I told you earlier that he would," he said. "Hawley has little gift for leadership, bar a certain blind confidence in the men under his command. Whether that will stand him in better stead than did Cope's cannon—" He shrugged impatiently.

"Be that as it may, General Hawley has been directed to march north to recover Stirling Castle."

"Has he?" I said. "Do you know how many troops he has?"

Randall nodded shortly. "He has eight thousand troops at the moment, thirteen hundred of them cavalry. He is also in daily expectation of the arrival of six thousand Hessians." He frowned, thinking. "I have heard that the chief of clan Campbell is sending a thousand men to join with Hawley's forces as well, but I cannot say whether that information is reliable; there seems no way of predicting what Scots will do."

"I see." This was serious; the Highland army at this point had between one and two thousand men. Against Hawley, minus his expected reinforcements, they might manage. To wait until his Hessians and Campbells arrived was clearly madness, to say nothing of the fact that the Highlanders' fighting skills were much better suited to attack than defense. This news had best reach Lord George Murray at once.

Jack Randall's voice called me back from my ruminations.

"Good day to you, Madam," he said, formal as ever, and there was no trace of humanity on the hard, handsome features as he bowed to me and took his leave.

"Thank you," I said to Alex Randall, waiting for Jonathan to descend the long, twisting stair before leaving myself. "I appreciate it very much."

He nodded. The shadows under his eyes were pronounced; another bad night.

"You're welcome," he said simply. "I suppose you'll be leaving some of the medicine for me? I imagine it may be some time before I see you again."

I halted, struck by his assumption that I would go myself to Stirling. That was what every fiber of my being urged me to do, but there was the matter of the men in the Tolbooth to be considered.

"I don't know," I said. "But yes; I'll leave the medicine."

I walked slowly back to my lodgings, my mind still spinning. Obviously, I must get word to Jamie immediately. Murtagh would have to go, I supposed. Jamie would believe me, of course, if I wrote him a note. But could he convince Lord George, the Duke of Perth, or the other army commanders?

I couldn't tell him where I had come by this knowledge; would the commanders be willing to believe a woman's unsupported, written word? Even the word of a woman popularly supposed to have supernatural powers? I thought of Maisri suddenly, and shivered. *It's a curse,* she had said. Yes, but what choice was there? *I have no power but the power not to say what I know.* I had that power, too, but dared not risk using it.

To my surprise, the door to my small room was open, and there were clashing, banging noises coming from inside it. I had been storing the recovered arms under my bed, and stacking swords and assorted blades by the hearth once the space under the bed was filled, until there was virtually no floor space left, save the small square of floorboards where Fergus laid his blankets.

I stood on the stair, amazed at the scene visible through the open door above. Murtagh, standing on the bed, was overseeing the handing-out of weaponry to the men who crowded the room to overflowing—the men of Lallybroch.

"Madame!" I turned at the cry, to find Fergus at my elbow, beaming up at me, a square-toothed grin on his sallow face.

"Madame! Is it not wonderful? Milord has received pardon for his men—a messenger came from Stirling this morning, with the order to release them, and we are ordered at once to join milord at Stirling!"

I hugged him, grinning a bit myself. "That *is* wonderful, Fergus." A few of the men had noticed me, and were beginning to turn to me, smiling and plucking at each other's sleeves. An air of exhilaration and excitement filled the small room. Murtagh, perched on the bedstead like the Gnome King on a toadstool, saw me then, and smiled—an expression which rendered him virtually unrecognizable, so much did it transform his face.

"Will Mr. Murtagh take the men to Stirling?" Fergus asked. He had received a whinger, or short sword, as his share of the weaponry, and was practicing drawing and sheathing it as he spoke.

I met Murtagh's eye and shook my head. After all, I thought, if Jenny Cameron could lead her brother's men to Glenfinnan, I could take my husband's troops to Stirling. And just let Lord George and His Highness try to disregard my news, delivered in person.

"No," I said. "I will."

I could feel the men close by, all around me in the dark. There was a piper walking next to me; I could hear the creak of the bag under his arm and see the outline of the drones, poking out behind. They moved as he walked, so that he seemed to be carrying a small, feebly struggling animal.

I knew him, a man named Labhriunn MacIan. The pipers of the clans took it in turns to call the dawn at Stirling, walking to and fro in the encampment with the piper's measured stride, so that the wail of the drones bounced from the flimsy tents, calling all within to the battle of the new day.

Again in the evening a single piper would come out, strolling slow across the yard, and the camp would stop to listen, voices stilling and the glow of the sunset fading from the tents' canvas. The high, whining notes of the pibroch called down the shadows from the moor, and when the piper was done, the night had come.

Evening or morning, Labhriunn MacIan played with his eyes closed, stepping sure and slow across the yard and back, elbow tight on the bag and his fingers lively on the chanters' holes. Despite the cold, I sat sometimes to watch in the evenings, letting the sound drive its spikes through my heart. MacIan paced to and fro, ignoring everything around him, making his turns on the ball of his foot, pouring his being out through his chanter.

There are the small Irish pipes, used indoors for making music, and the Great Northern pipes, used outdoors for reveille, and for calling of clans to order, and the spurring of men to battle. It was the Northern pipes that MacIan played, walking to and fro with his eyes shut tight.

Rising from my seat as he finished one evening, I waited while he pressed the last of the air from his bag with a dying wail, and fell in alongside him as he came in through Stirling's gate with a nod to the guard.

"Good e'en to ye, Mistress," he said. His voice was soft,

and his eyes, now open, softer still with the unbroken spell of his playing still on him.

"Good evening to you, MacIan," I said. "I wondered, MacIan, why do you play with your eyes tight shut?"

He smiled and scratched his head, but answered readily enough.

"I suppose it is because my grandsire taught me, Mistress, and he was blind. I see him always when I play, pacing the shore with his beard flying in the wind and his blind eyes closed against the sting of the sand, hearing the sound of the pipes come down to him off the rocks of the cliffside and knowing from that where he was in his walk."

"So you see him, and you play, too, to the cliffs and the sea? From where do you come, MacIan?" I asked. His speech was low and sibilant, even more than that of most Highlanders.

"It is from the Shetlands, Mistress," he replied, making the last word almost "Zetlands." "A long way from here." He smiled again, and bowed to me as we came to the guest quarters, where I would turn. "But then, I am thinking that you have come farther still, Mistress."

"That's true," I said. "Good night, MacIan."

Later that week, I wondered whether his skill at playing unseeing would help him, here in the dark. A large body of men moving makes a good bit of noise, no matter how quietly they go, but I thought any echoes they created would be drowned in the howl of the rising wind. The night was moonless, but the sky was light with clouds, and an icy sleet was falling, stinging my cheeks.

The men of the Highland army covered the ground in small groups of ten or twenty, moving in uneven bumps and patches, as though the earth thrust up small hillocks here and there, or as though the groves of larch and alder were walking through the dark. My news had not come unsupported; Ewan Cameron's spies had reported Hawley's moves as well, and the Scottish army was now on its way to meet him, somewhere south of Stirling Castle.

Jamie had given up urging me to go back. I had promised to stay out of the way, but if there was a battle to be fought, then the army's physicians must be at hand afterward. I could tell when his attention shifted to his men, and the prospects ahead, by the sudden cock of his head. On Donas, he sat high enough to be visible as a shadow, even in the dark, and when he threw up an arm, two smaller shadows detached themselves from the moving mass and came up beside his stirrup. There was a moment's whispered conversation; then he straightened in his saddle and turned to me.

"The scouts say we've been seen; English guards have gone flying for Callendar House, to warn General Hawley. We shallna wait longer; I'm taking my men and circling beyond Dougal's troops to the far side of Falkirk Hill. We'll come down from behind as the MacKenzies come in from the west. There's a wee kirk up the hill to your left, maybe a quarter-mile. That's your place, Sassenach. Ride there now, and stay." He groped for my arm in the darkness, found it, and squeezed.

"I shall come for ye when I can, or send Murtagh if I can't. If things should go wrong, go into the kirk and claim sanctuary there. It's the best I can think of."

"Don't worry about me," I said. My lips were cold, and I hoped my voice didn't sound as shaky as I felt. I bit back the "Be careful" that would have been my next words, and contented myself with touching him quickly, the cold surface of his cheek hard as metal under my hand, and the brush of a lock of hair, cold and smooth as a deer's pelt.

I reined to the left, picking my way slowly as the oncoming men flowed around me. The gelding was excited by the stir; he tossed his head, snorting, and fidgeted under me. I pulled him up sharply, as Jamie had taught me, and kept a close rein as the ground sloped suddenly up beneath the horse's hooves. I glanced back once, but Jamie had disappeared into the night, and I needed all my attention to find the church in the dark.

It was a tiny building, stone with a thatched roof, crouched in a small depression of the hill, like a cowering animal. I felt a strong feeling of kinship with it. The English watchfires were visible from here, glimmering through the sleet, and I could hear shouting in the distance—Scots or English, I couldn't tell.

Then the pipes began, a thin, eerie scream in the storm.

There were discordant shrieks, rising unearthly from several different places on the hill. Having seen it before at close hand, I could imagine the pipers blowing up their bags, chests inflating with quick gasps and blue lips clamped tight on the chanters' stems, cold-stiff fingers fumbling to guide the blowing into coherence.

I could almost feel the stubborn resistance of the leathern bag, kept warm and flexible under a plaid, but reluctant to be coaxed into fullness, then suddenly springing to life, part of the piper's body, like a third lung, breathing for him when the wind stole his breath, as though the shouting of the clansmen near him filled it.

The shouting was louder, now, and reached me in waves as the wind turned, carrying eddying blasts of sleet. There was no porch to give shelter, or any trees on the hillside to break the wind. My horse turned and put his head down, facing into the wind, and his mane whipped hard against my face, rough with ice.

The church offered sanctuary from the elements, as well as from the English. I pushed the door open and, tugging on the bridle, led the horse inside after me.

It was dark inside, with the single oiled-skin window no more than a dim patch in the blackness over the altar. It seemed warm, by contrast with the weather outside, but the smell of stale sweat made it suffocating. There were no seats for the horse to knock over; nothing save a small shrine set into one wall, and the altar itself. Oppressed by the strong smell of people, the horse stood still, snorting and blowing, but not fidgeting overmuch. Keeping a wary eye on him, I went back to the door and thrust my head out.

No one could tell what was happening on Falkirk Hill. The sparks of gunfire twinkled randomly in the dark. I could hear, faint and intermittent, the ring of metal and the thump of an occasional explosion. Now and then came the scream of a wounded man, high as a bagpipe's screech, different from the Gaelic cries of the warriors. And then the wind would turn, and I would hear nothing, or would imagine I heard voices that were nothing but the shrieking wind.

I had not seen the fight at Prestonpans; subconsciously accustomed to the ponderous movements of huge armies bound to tanks and mortars, I had not realized just how quickly things could happen in a small pitched battle of hand-to-hand fighting and small, light arms.

The first warning I had was a shout from near at hand. *"Tulach Ard!"* Deafened by wind, I hadn't heard them as they came up the hill. *"Tulach Ard!"* It was the battle cry of clan MacKenzie; some of Dougal's troops, forced backward in the direction of my sanctuary. I ducked back inside, but kept the door ajar, so that I could peer out.

They were coming up the hill, a small group of men in flight. Highlanders, both from the sound and the sight of them, plaids and beards and hair flying around them, so they looked like black clouds against the grassy slope, scudding uphill before the wind.

I jumped back into the church as the first of them burst through the door. Dark as it was, I couldn't see his face, but I recognized his voice when he crashed headfirst into my horse.

"Jesus!"

"Willie!" I shouted. "Willie Coulter!"

"Sweet bleeding Jesus! Who's that!"

I hadn't time to answer before the door crashed against the wall, and two more black forms shot into the tiny church. Incensed by this noisy intrusion, my horse reared and whinnied, pawing the air. This gave rise to cries of alarm from the intruders, who clearly had thought the building unoccupied, and were disconcerted to find otherwise.

The entrance of several more men only increased the confusion, and I gave up any idea of trying to subdue the horse. Forced to the rear of the church, I squeezed myself into the small space between altar and wall and waited for things to sort themselves out.

They began to show signs of doing so when one of the confused voices in the darkness rose above the others.

"Be QUIET!" it shouted, in a tone that brooked no opposition. Everyone but the horse obeyed, and as the racket died down, even the horse subsided, backing into a corner and making snorting noises, mixed with querulous squeals of disgust.

"It is MacKenzie of Leoch," said the imperious voice. "Who else bides here?"

"It is Geordie, Dougal, and my brother with me," said a voice nearby, in tones of profound relief. "We've brought Rupert with us, too; he's wounded. Christ, I thought it was the de'il himself in here!"

"Gordon McLeod of Ardsmuir," said another voice I didn't recognize.

"And Ewan Cameron of Kinnoch," said another. "Whose is the horse?"

"Mine," I said, sidling cautiously out from behind the altar. The sound of my voice caused another outbreak, but Dougal put a stop to it once more, raising his own voice above the racket.

"QUIET, damn the lot of ye! Is that you, Claire Fraser?"

"Well, it isn't the Queen," I said testily. "Willie Coulter's in here, too, or he was a minute ago. Hasn't anyone got a flint box?"

"No light!" said Dougal. "Little chance that the English will overlook this place if they follow us, but little sense in drawing their attention to it if they don't."

"All right," I said, biting my lip. "Rupert, can you talk? Say something so I can tell where you are." I didn't know how much I could do for him in the dark; as it was, I couldn't even reach my medicine box. Still, I couldn't leave him to bleed to death on the floor.

There was a nasty-sounding cough from the side of the church opposite me, and a hoarse voice said, "Here, lass," and coughed again.

I felt my way across the floor, cursing under my breath. I could tell merely from the bubbling sound of that cough that it was bad; the sort of bad that my medicine box wasn't likely to help. I crouched and duck-walked the last few feet, waving my arms in a wide swathe to feel what might be in my way.

One hand struck a warm body, and a big hand fastened on to me. It had to be Rupert; I could hear him breathing, a stertorous sound with a faint gurgle behind it.

"I'm here," I said, patting him blindly in what I hoped was a reassuring spot. I supposed it was, because he gave a sort of gasping chuckle and arched his hips, pressing my hand down hard against him.

"Do that again, lass, and I'll forget all about the musket ball," he said.

I grabbed my hand back.

"Perhaps a bit later," I said dryly. I moved my hand up-

ward, skimming over his body in search of his head. The thick
bristle of beard told me I'd reached my goal, and I felt carefully under the dense growth for the pulse in his throat. Fast
and light, but still fairly regular. His forehead was slick with
sweat, though his skin felt clammy to the touch. The tip of his
nose was cold when I brushed it, chilled from the air outside.

"Pity I'm no a dog," he said, a thread of laughter coming
between the gasps for air. "Cold nose . . . would be a good
sign."

"Be a better sign if you'd quit talking," I said. "Where
did the ball take you? No, don't tell me, take my hand and
put it on the wound . . . and if you put it anywhere else,
Rupert MacKenzie, you can die here like a dog, and good
riddance to you."

I could feel the wide chest vibrate with suppressed laughter under my hand. He drew my hand slowly under his plaid,
and I pushed back the obstructing fabric with my other hand.

"All right, I've got it," I whispered. I could feel the small
tear in his shirt, damp with blood around the edges, and I put
both hands to it and ripped it open. I brushed my fingers very
lightly down his side, feeling the ripple of gooseflesh under
them, and then the small hole of the entrance wound. It
seemed a remarkably small hole, compared to the bulk of
Rupert, who was a burly man.

"Did it come out anywhere?" I whispered. The inside of
the church was quiet, except for the horse, who was moving
restlessly in his own corner. With the door closed, the sounds
of battle outside were still audible, but diffuse; it was impossible to tell how close they were.

"No," he said, and coughed again. I could feel his hand
move toward his mouth, and I followed it with a fold of his
plaid. My eyes were as accustomed to the darkness as they
were likely to get, but he was still no more than a hunched
black shape on the floor before me. For some things, though,
touch was enough. There was little bleeding at the site of the
wound, but the cloth I held to his mouth flooded my hand
with sudden damp warmth.

The ball had taken him through one lung at least, possibly both, and his chest was filling with blood. He could last a
few hours in this condition, perhaps a day if one lung remained functional. If the pericardium had been nicked, he

would go faster. But only surgery would save him, and that of a kind I couldn't do.

I could feel a warm presence behind me, and heard normal breathing as someone groped toward me. I reached back and felt my hand gripped tight. Dougal MacKenzie.

He made his way up beside me, and laid a hand on Rupert's supine body.

"How is it, man?" he asked softly. "Can ye walk?" My other hand still on Rupert, I could feel his head shake in answer to Dougal's question. The men in the church behind us had begun to talk among themselves in whispers.

Dougal's hand pressed down on my shoulder.

"What d'ye need to help him? Your wee box? Is it on the horse?" He had risen before I could tell him that there was nothing in the box to help Rupert.

A sudden loud crack from the altar stopped the whispers, and there was a quick movement all around, as men snatched up the weapons they had laid down. Another crack, and a ripping noise, and the oiled-skin covering of the window gave way to a rush of cold, clean air and a few swirling snowflakes.

"Sassenach! Claire! Are ye there?" The low voice from the window brought me to my feet in momentary forgetfulness of Rupert.

"Jamie!" All around me was a collective exhalation, and the clank of falling swords and targes. The new faint light from outdoors was blotted out for a moment by the bulk of Jamie's head and shoulders. He dropped down lightly from the altar, silhouetted against the open window.

"Who's here?" he said softly, looking around. "Dougal, is that you?"

"Aye, it's me, lad. Your wife and a few more. Did ye see the *sassenach* bastards anywhere near outside?"

Jamie uttered a short laugh.

"Why d'ye think I came in through the window? There's maybe twenty of them at the foot of the hill."

Dougal made a displeased noise deep in his throat. "The bastards that cut us off from the main troop, I'll be bound."

"Just so. *Ho, mo chridhe! Ciamar a tha thu*?" Recognizing a familiar voice in the midst of madness, my horse had thrust its nose up with a loud whinny of greeting.

"Hush, ye wee fool!" Dougal said to it violently. "D'ye want the English to hear?"

"I dinna suppose the English would hang *him*," Jamie observed mildly. "As for them telling you're here, they won't need ears, if they've eyes in their heads; the slope's half mud outside, and the prints of all your feet show clear."

"Mmphm." Dougal cast an eye toward the window, but Jamie was already shaking his head.

"No good, Dougal. The main body's to the south, and Lord George Murray's gone to meet them, but there's the few English from the party we met still left on this side. A group of them chased me over the hill; I dodged to the side and crawled up to the church on my belly through the grass, but I'll guess they're still combing the hillside above." He reached out a hand in my direction, and I took it. It was cold and damp from crawling through grass, but I was glad just to touch him, to have him there.

"Crawled in, eh? And how were ye planning to get out again?" Dougal asked.

I could feel Jamie shrug. He tilted his head in the direction of my horse.

"I'd thought I might burst out and ride them down; they'll not know about the horse. That would cause enough kerfuffle maybe for Claire to slip free."

Dougal snorted. "Aye, and they'd pick ye off your horse like a ripe apple."

"It hardly matters," Jamie said dryly. "I canna see the lot of ye to be slipping out quietly with no one noticing, no matter how much fuss I made over it."

As though in confirmation of this, Rupert gave a loud groan by the wall. Dougal and I dropped onto our knees beside him at once, followed more slowly by Jamie.

He wasn't dead, but wasn't doing well, either. His hands were chilly, and his breathing had a wheezing, whining note to it.

"Dougal," he whispered.

"I'm here, Rupert. Be still, man, you'll be all right soon." The MacKenzie chieftain quickly pulled off his own plaid and folded it into a pillow, which he thrust beneath Rupert's head and shoulders. Raised a bit, his breathing seemed easier, but a touch below his beard showed me wet blotches on his shirt.

He still had some strength; he reached out a hand and grasped Dougal's arm.

"If . . . they'll find us anyway . . . give me a light," he said, gasping. "I'd see your face once more, Dougal."

Close as I was to Dougal, I felt the shock run through him at these words and their implication. His head turned sharply toward me, but of course he couldn't see my face. He muttered an order over his shoulder, and after a bit of shuffling and murmuring, someone cut loose a handful of the thatch, which was twisted into a torch and lit with a spark from a flint. It burned fast, but gave enough light for me to examine Rupert while the men worked at chiseling loose a long splinter of wood from the poles of the roof, to serve as a less temporary torch.

He was white as a fish belly, hair matted with sweat, and a faint smear of blood still showed on the flesh of his full lower lip. Dark spots showed on the glossy black beard, but he smiled faintly at me as I bent over him to check his pulse again. Lighter, and very fast, missing beats now and then. I smoothed the hair back from his face, and he touched my hand in thanks.

I felt Dougal's hand on my elbow, and sat back on my heels, turning to face him. I had faced him once like this before, over the body of a man mortally wounded by a boar. He had asked me then, "Can he live?" and I saw the memory of that day cross his face. The same question stood in his eyes again, but this time in eyes glazed with fear of my answer. Rupert was his closest friend, the kinsman who rode and who fought on his right-hand side, as Ian did for Jamie.

This time I didn't answer; Rupert did it for me.

"Dougal," he said, and smiled as his friend bent anxiously over him. He closed his eyes for a moment and breathed as deeply as he could, gathering strength for the moment.

"Dougal," he said again, opening his eyes. "Ye'll no grieve for me, man."

Dougal's face twitched in the torchlight. I could see the denial of death come to his lips, but he bit it back and forced it aside.

"I'm your chief, man," he said, with a quivering half-smile. "Ye'll not order me; I shall grieve ye and I like." He clasped Rupert's hand, where it lay across his chest, and held it tightly.

There was a faint, wheezing chuckle from Rupert, and another coughing spell.

"Weel, grieve for me and ye will, Dougal," he said, when he'd finished. "And I'm glad for it. But ye canna grieve 'til I be deid, can ye? I would die by your hand, *mo caraidh,* not in the hands of the strangers."

Dougal jerked, and Jamie and I exchanged appalled glances behind his back.

"Rupert . . ." Dougal began helplessly, but Rupert interrupted him, clasping his hand and shaking it gently.

"You *are* my chief, man, and it's your duty," he whispered. "Come now. Do it now. This dying hurts me, Dougal, and I would have it over." His eyes moved restlessly, lighting on me.

"Will ye hold my hand while I go, lass?" he asked. "I'd like it so."

There seemed nothing else to do. Moving slowly, feeling that this was all a dream, I took the broad, black-haired hand in both of mine, pressing it as though I might force my own warmth into the cooling flesh.

With a grunt, Rupert heaved himself slightly to one side and glanced up at Jamie, who sat by his head.

"She should ha' married me, lad, when she had the choice," he wheezed. "You're a poor weed, but do your best." One eye squeezed shut in a massive wink. "Gi'e her a good one for me, lad."

The black eyes swiveled back to me, and a final grin spread across his face.

"Goodbye, bonnie lassie," he said softly.

Dougal's dirk took him under the breastbone, hard and straight. The burly body convulsed, turning to the side with a coughing explosion of air and blood, but the brief sound of agony came from Dougal.

The MacKenzie chieftain stayed frozen for a moment, eyes shut, hands clenched on the hilt of the dirk. Then Jamie rose, took him by the shoulders, and turned him away, murmuring something in Gaelic. Jamie glanced at me, and I nodded and held out my arms. He turned Dougal gently toward

me, and I gathered him to me as we both crouched on the
floor, holding him while he wept.

Jamie's own face was streaked with tears, and I could
hear the brief sighs and sobbing breaths of the other men. I
supposed it was better they wept for Rupert than for themselves. If the English did come for us here, all of us stood to
be hanged for treason. It was easier to mourn for Rupert,
who was safely gone, sped on his way by the hand of a friend.

They did not come anytime in the long winter night. We
huddled together against one wall, under plaids and cloaks,
waiting. I dozed fitfully, leaning against Jamie's shoulder,
with Dougal hunched and silent on my other side. I thought
that neither of them slept, but kept watch through the night
over Rupert's corpse, quiet under his own draped plaid across
the church, on the other side of the abyss that separates the
dead from the living.

We spoke little, but I knew what they were thinking.
They were wondering, as I was, whether the English troops
had left, regrouping with the main army at Callendar House
below, or whether they still watched outside, waiting for the
dawn before making a move, lest anyone in the tiny church
escape under cover of darkness.

The matter was settled with the coming of first light.

"Ho, the church! Come out and give yourselves up!" The
call came from the slope below, in a strong English voice.

There was a stir among the men in the church, and the
horse, who had been dozing in his corner, snapped his head
up with a startled snort at the movement nearby. Jamie and
Dougal exchanged a glance, then, as though they had planned
it together, rose and stood, shoulder to shoulder, before the
closed door. A jerk of Jamie's head sent me to the rear of the
church, back to my shelter behind the altar.

Another shout from the outside was met with silence.
Jamie drew the snaphance pistol from his belt and checked
the loading of it, casually, as though there were all the time in
the world. He sank to one knee and braced the pistol, pointing it at the door at the level of a man's head.

Geordie and Willie guarded the window to the rear,
swords and pistols to the ready. But it was likely from the

front that an attack would come; the hill behind the church
sloped steeply up, with barely room between the slope and
the wall of the church for one man to squeeze past.

I heard the squelching of footsteps, approaching the
door through the mud, and the faint clanking of sidearms.
The sounds stopped at a distance, and a voice came again,
closer and louder.

"In the name of His Majesty King George, come out and
surrender! We know you are there!"

Jamie fired. The report inside the tiny church was deaf-
ening. It must have been sufficiently impressive from outside
as well; I could hear the hasty sounds of slipping retreat,
accompanied by muffled curses. There was a small hole in the
door, made by the pistol ball; Dougal sidled up to it and
peered out.

"Damn," he said under his breath. "There's a lot of
them."

Jamie cast a glance at me, then set his lips and turned his
attention to reloading his pistol. Clearly, the Scots had no
intention of surrendering. Just as clearly, the English had no
desire to storm the church, given the easily defended entrances. They couldn't mean to starve us out? Surely the
Highland army would be sending out men to search for the
wounded of the battle from the night before. If they arrived
before the English had opportunity to bring a cannon to bear
on the church, we might be saved.

Unfortunately, there was a thinker outside. The sound of
footsteps came once more, and then a measured English
voice, full of authority.

"You have one minute to come out and give yourselves
up," it said, "or we fire the thatch."

I glanced upward in complete horror. The walls of the
church were stone, but the thatch would burn in short order,
even soaked with rain and sleet, and once well caught, would
send flames and smoking embers raining down to engulf us. I
remembered the awful speed with which the torch of twisted
reed had burned the night before; the charred remnant lay on
the floor near Rupert's shrouded corpse, a grisly token in the
gray dawn light.

"No!" I screamed. "Bloody bastards! This is a church!
Have you never heard of sanctuary?"

"Who is that?" came the sharp voice from outside. "Is that an Englishwoman in there?!"

"Yes!" shouted Dougal, springing to the door. He cracked it ajar and bellowed out at the English soldiers on the hillside below. "Yes! We hold an English lady captive! Fire the thatch, and she dies with us!"

There was an outbreak of voices at the bottom of the hill, and a sudden shifting among the men in the church. Jamie whirled on Dougal with a scowl, saying, "What . . . !"

"It's the only chance!" Dougal hissed back. "Let them take her, in return for our freedom. They'll not harm her if they think she's our hostage, and we'll get her back later, once we're free!"

I came out of my hiding space and went to Jamie, gripping his sleeve.

"Do it!" I said urgently. "Dougal is right, it's the only chance!"

He looked down at me helplessly, rage and fear mingled on his face. And under it all, a trace of humor at the underlying irony of the situation.

"I am a *sassenach*, after all," I said, seeing it.

He touched my face briefly with a rueful smile.

"Aye, *mo nighean donn.* But you're *my sassenach.*" He turned to Dougal, squaring his shoulders. He drew in a deep breath, and nodded.

"All right. Tell them we took her"—he thought quickly, rubbing one hand through his hair—"from Falkirk road, late yesterday."

Dougal nodded, and without waiting for more, slipped out of the church door, a white handkerchief held high overhead in signal of truce.

Jamie turned to me, frowning, glancing at the church door, where the sounds of English voices were still audible, though we couldn't make out words as they talked.

"I don't know what you're to tell them, Claire; perhaps ye'd better pretend to be so shocked that ye canna speak of it. It's maybe better than telling a tale; for if they should realize who you are—" He stopped suddenly and rubbed his hand hard over his face.

If they realized who I was, it would be London, and the Tower—followed quite possibly by swift execution. But while the broadsheets had made much of "the Stuart Witch," no one, so far as I knew, had realized or published the fact that the witch was English.

"Don't worry," I said, realizing just what a silly remark this was, but unable to come up with anything better. I laid a hand on his sleeve, feeling the swift pulse that beat in his wrist. "You'll get me back before they have a chance to realize anything. Do you think they'll take me to Callendar House?"

He nodded, back in control. "Aye, I think so. If ye can, try to be alone near a window, just after nightfall. I'll come for ye then."

There was time for no more. Dougal slipped back through the door, closing it carefully behind him.

"Done," he said, looking from me to Jamie. "We give them the woman, and we'll be allowed to leave unmolested. No pursuit. We keep the horse. We'll need it, for Rupert, ye see," he said to me, half-apologetically.

"It's all right," I told him. I looked at the door, with its small dark spot where the bullet had passed, the same size as the hole in Rupert's side. My mouth was dry and I swallowed hard. I was a cuckoo's egg, about to be laid in the wrong nest. The three of us hesitated before the door, all reluctant to take the final step.

"I'd b-better go," I said, trying hard to control my shaking voice and limbs. "They'll wonder what's keeping us."

Jamie closed his eyes for a moment, nodded, then stepped toward me.

"I think you'd better swoon, Sassenach," he said. "It will be easier that way, maybe." He stooped, picked me up in his arms, and carried me through the door that Dougal held open.

His heart pounded beneath my ear, and I could feel the trembling in his arms as he carried me. After the stuffiness of the church, with its smells of sweat, blood, black powder and horse manure, the cold fresh air of early morning took my breath away, and I huddled against him, shivering. His hands tightened under my knees and shoulders, hard as a promise; he would never let me go.

"God," he said once, under his breath, and then we had

reached them. Sharp questions, mumbled answers, the reluctant loosening of his grip as he laid me on the ground, and then the swish of his feet, going away through wet grass. I was alone, in the hands of the strangers.

44

In Which Quite a Lot of Things Gang Agley

I hunched closer to the fire, holding out my hands to thaw. They were grimy from holding the reins all day, and I wondered briefly whether it was worthwhile walking the distance to the stream to wash them. Maintaining modern standards of hygiene in the absence of all forms of plumbing sometimes seemed a good deal more trouble than it was worth. No bloody wonder if people got ill frequently and died, I thought sourly. They died of simple filth and ignorance more than anything.

The thought of dying in filth was sufficient to get me to my feet, tired as I was. The tiny streamlet that passed by the campsite was boggy near the edges, and my shoes sank deep into the marshy growth. Having traded dirty hands for wet feet, I slogged back to the fire, to find Corporal Rowbotham waiting for me with a bowl of what he said was stew.

"The Captain's compliments, Mum," he said, actually tugging his forelock as he handed me the bowl, "and he says to tell yer as we'll be in Tavistock tomorrow. There's an inn there." He hesitated, his round, homely, middle-aged face concerned, then added, "The Captain's apologies for the lack of accommodation, Mum, but we've fixed a tent for yer for tonight. 'S not much, but mebbe'll keep the rain off yer."

"Thank the Captain for me, Corporal," I said, as graciously as I could manage. "And thank *you*, too," I added, with more warmth. I was entirely aware that Captain Mainwaring considered me a burdensome nuisance, and would have taken no thought at all for my night's shelter. The tent—a spare length of canvas draped carefully over a tree limb and pegged at both sides—was undoubtedly the sole idea of Corporal Rowbotham.

The Corporal went away and I sat by myself, slowly eating scorched potatoes and stringy beef. I'd found a late patch of charlock near the stream, leaves wilting and brown around the edges, and had brought back a handful in my pocket, along with a few juniper berries picked during a stop earlier in the day. The mustard leaves were old and very bitter, but I managed to get them down by wodging them between bites of potato. I finished the meal with the juniper berries, biting each one briefly to avoid choking and then swallowing the tough, flattened berry, seed and all. The oily burst of flavor sent fumes up the back of my throat that made my eyes water, but they did cleanse my tongue of the taste of grease and scorch, and would, with the charlock leaves, maybe be sufficient to ward off scurvy.

I had had a large store of dried fiddleheads, rose hips, dried apples and dill seeds in the larger of my two medicine chests, carefully collected as a defense against nutritional deficiency during the long winter months. I hoped Jamie was eating them.

I put my head down on my knees; I didn't think anyone was looking at me, but I didn't want my face to show when I thought of Jamie.

I had stayed in my pretended swoon on Falkirk Hill as long as I could, but was roused before too long by a British dragoon trying to force brandy from a pocket flask down my throat. Unsure quite what to do with me, my "rescuers" had taken me to Callendar House and turned me over to General Hawley's staff.

So far, all had gone according to plan. Within the hour, though, things had gone rather seriously awry. From sitting in an anteroom and listening to everything that was said around me, I soon learned that what I had thought was a major battle during the night had in fact been no more than a small skirmish between the MacKenzies and a detachment of English troops on their way to join the main body of the army. Said army was even now assembling itself to meet the expected Highland charge on Falkirk Hill; the battle I thought I had lived through had not, in fact, happened yet!

General Hawley himself was overseeing this process, and as no one seemed to have any idea what ought to be done with me, I was consigned to the custody of a young private, along with a letter describing the circumstances of my rescue, and dispatched to a Colonel Campbell's temporary headquarters at Kerse. The young private, a stocky specimen named

Dobbs, was distressingly zealous in his urge to perform his duty, and despite several tries along the way, I had been unable to get away from him.

We had arrived in Kerse, only to find that Colonel Campbell was not there, but had been summoned to Livingston.

"Look," I had suggested to my escorting gaoler, "plainly Colonel Campbell is not going to have time or inclination to talk to me, and there's nothing I could tell him in any case. Why don't I just find lodging in the town here, until I can make some arrangement for continuing my journey to Edinburgh?" For lacking any better idea, I had given the English basically the same story I had given to Colum MacKenzie, two years earlier; that I was a widowed lady from Oxford, traveling to visit a relative in Scotland, when I had been set upon and abducted by Highland brigands.

Private Dobbs shook his head, flushing stubbornly. He couldn't be more than twenty, and he wasn't very bright, but once he got an idea in his head, he hung on to it.

"I can't let you do that, Mrs. Beauchamp," he said—for I had used my own maiden name as an alias—"Captain Bledsoe'll have my liver for it, an' I don't bring you safe to the Colonel."

So to Livingston we had gone, mounted on two of the sorriest-looking nags I had ever seen. I was finally relieved of the attentions of my escort, but with no improvement in my circumstances. Instead, I found myself immured in an upper room in a house in Livingston, telling the story once again, to one Colonel Gordon MacLeish Campbell, a Lowland Scot in command of one of the Elector's regiments.

"Aye, I see," he said, in the sort of tone that suggested that he didn't see at all. He was a small, foxy-faced man, with balding reddish hair brushed back from his temples. He narrowed his eyes still further, glancing down at the crumpled letter on his blotter.

"This says," he said, placing a pair of half-spectacles on his nose in order to peer more closely at the sheet of paper, "that one of your captors, Mistress, was a Fraser clansman, very large, and with red hair. Is this information correct?"

"Yes," I said, wondering what he was getting at.

He tilted his head so the spectacles slid down his nose, the better to fix me with a piercing stare over the tops.

"The men who rescued you near Falkirk gave it as their impression that one of your captors was none other than the notorious Highland chief known as 'Red Jamie.' Now, I am aware, Mrs. Beauchamp, that you were . . . distressed, shall we say?"—his lips pulled back from the word, but it wasn't a smile—"during the period of your captivity, and perhaps in no fit frame of mind to make close observations, but did you notice at any time whether the other men present referred to this man by name?"

"They did. They called him Jamie." I couldn't imagine any harm that could be done by telling him this; the broadsheets I had seen made it abundantly clear that Jamie was a supporter of the Stuart cause. The placing of Jamie at the battle of Falkirk was possibly of interest to the English, but could hardly incriminate him further.

"They canna very well hang me more than once," he'd said. Once would be more than enough. I glanced at the window. Night had fallen half an hour ago, and lanterns glowed in the street below, carried by soldiers passing to and fro. Jamie would be at Callendar House, searching for the window where I should be waiting.

I had the absurd certainty, all of a sudden, that he had followed me, had known somehow where I was going, and would be waiting in the street below, for me to show myself.

I rose abruptly and went to the window. The street below was empty, save for a seller of pickled herrings, seated on a stool with his lantern at his feet, waiting for the possibility of customers. It wasn't Jamie, of course. There was no way for him to find me. No one in the Stuart camp knew where I was; I was entirely alone. I pressed my hands hard against the glass in sudden panic, not caring that I might shatter it.

"Mistress Beauchamp! Are ye well?" The Colonel's voice behind me was sharp with alarm.

I clamped my lips tight together to stop them shaking and took several deep breaths, clouding the glass so the street below vanished in mist. Outwardly calm, I turned back to face the Colonel.

"I'm quite well," I said. "If you've finished asking questions, I'd like to go now."

"Would ye? Mmm." He looked me over with something like doubt, then shook his head decidedly.

"Ye'll stay the night here," he declared. "In the morning, I shall be sendin' ye southward."

I felt a spasm of shock clench my insides. "South! What the hell for?" I blurted.

His fox-fur eyebrows rose in astonishment and his mouth fell open. Then he shook himself slightly, and clamped it shut, opening it only a slit to deliver himself of his next words.

"I have orders to send on any information pertaining to the Highland criminal known as Red Jamie Fraser," he said. "Or any person associated with him."

"I'm not associated with him!" I said. Unless you wanted to count marriage, of course.

Colonel Campbell was oblivious. He turned to his desk and shuffled through a stack of dispatches.

"Aye, here it is. Captain Mainwaring will be the officer who escorts you. He will come to fetch ye here at dawn." He rang a small silver bell shaped like a goblin, and the door opened to reveal the inquiring face of his private orderly. "Garvie, ye'll see the lady to her quarters. Lock the door." He turned to me and bowed perfunctorily. "I think we shall not meet again, Mrs. Beauchamp; I wish ye good rest and God-speed." And that was that.

I didn't know quite how fast God-speed was, but it was likely faster than Captain Mainwaring's detachment had ridden. The Captain was in charge of a supply train of wagons, bound for Lanark. After delivery of these and their drivers, he was then to proceed south with the rest of his detachment, delivering nonvital dispatches as he went. I was apparently in the category of nonurgent intelligence, for we had been more than a week on the road, and no sign of reaching whatever place I was bound for.

"South." Did that mean London? I wondered, for the thousandth time. Captain Mainwaring had not told me my final destination, but I could think of no other possibility.

Lifting my head, I caught one of the dragoons across the fire staring at me. I stared flatly back at him, until he flushed and dropped his eyes to the bowl in his hands. I was accustomed to such looks, though most were less bold about it.

It had started from the beginning, with a certain reserved embarrassment on the part of the young idiot who had taken me to Livingston. It had taken some little time for me to realize that what caused the attitude of distant reserve on the part of the English officers was not suspicion, but a mixture of contempt and horror, mingled with a trace of pity and a sense of official responsibility that kept their true feelings from showing openly.

I had not merely been rescued from a band of the rapacious, marauding Scots. I had been delivered from a captivity during which I had spent an entire night in a single room with a number of men who were, to the certain knowledge of all right-thinking Englishmen, "Little more than Savage Beasts, guilty of Rapine, Robbery, and countless other such Hideous Crimes." Not thinkable, therefore, that a young Englishwoman had passed a night in the company of such beasts and emerged unscathed.

I reflected grimly that Jamie's carrying me out in an apparent swoon might have eased matters originally, but had undoubtedly contributed to the overall impression that he—and the other assorted Scots—had been having their forcible way with me. And thanks to the detailed letter written by the captain of my original band of rescuers, everyone to whom I had later been passed on—and everyone to whom they talked, I imagined—knew about it. Schooled in Paris, I understood the mechanics of gossip very well.

Corporal Rowbotham had certainly heard the stories, but continued to treat me kindly, with none of the smirking speculation I occasionally surprised on the faces of the other soldiers. If I had been inclined to offer up bedtime prayers, I would have included his name therein.

I rose, dusted off my cloak, and went to my tent. Seeing me go, Corporal Rowbotham also rose, and circling the fire discreetly, sat down by his comrades again, his back in direct line with the entrance to my tent. When the soldiers retired to their beds, I knew he would seek a spot at a respectful distance, but still within call of my resting place. He had done this for the past three nights, whether we slept in inn or field.

Three nights earlier I had tried yet another escape. Cap-

tain Mainwaring was well aware that I traveled with him under compulsion, and while he didn't like being burdened with
me, he was too conscientious a soldier to shirk the responsibility. I had two guards, who watched me closely, riding on
each side by day.

At night, the guard was relaxed, the Captain evidently
thinking it unlikely that I would strike out on foot over deserted moors in the dead of winter. The Captain was correct.
I had no interest in committing suicide.

On the night in question, however, we had passed
through a small village about two hours before we stopped
for the night. Even on foot, I was sure I could backtrack and
reach the village before dawn. The village boasted a small
distillery, from which wagons bearing loads of barrels departed for several towns in the surrounding region. I had seen
the distiller's yard, piled high with barrels, and thought I had
a decent chance of hiding there, and leaving with the first
wagon.

So after the camp was quiet, and the soldiers lumped and
snoring in their blankets round the fire, I had crept out of my
own blanket, carefully laid near the edge of a willow grove,
and made my way through the trailing fronds, with no more
sound than the rustle of the wind.

Leaving the grove, I had thought it was the rustle of the
wind behind me, too, until a hand clamped down on my
shoulder.

"Don't scream. Y' don't want the Capting to know yer
out wi'out leave." I didn't scream, only because all the breath
had been startled out of me. The soldier, a tallish man called
"Jessie" by his mates, because of the trouble he took in
combing out his yellow curls, smiled at me, and I smiled a
little uncertainly back at him.

His eyes dropped to my bosom. He sighed, raised his
eyes to mine, and took a step toward me. I took three steps
back, fast.

"It doesn't matter, really, does it, sweet'art?" he said,
still smiling lazily. "Not after what's 'appened already. What's
once more, eh? And I'm an Englishman, too," he coaxed.
"Not a filthy Scot."

"Leave the poor woman alone, Jess," Corporal
Rowbotham said, emerging silently from the screen of willows

behind him. "She's had enough trouble, poor lady." He spoke
softly enough, but Jessie glared at him, then, thinking better
of whatever he'd had in mind, turned without another word
and disappeared under the willow leaves.

The Corporal had waited, unspeaking, for me to gather
up my fallen cloak, and then had followed me back to the
camp. He had gone to pick up his own blanket, motioned to
me to lie down, and placed himself six feet away, sitting up
with his blanket about his shoulders Indian-style. Whenever I
woke during the night, I had seen him still sitting there, staring shortsightedly into the fire.

Tavistock did have an inn. I didn't have much time to
enjoy its amenities, though. We arrived in the village at midday, and Captain Mainwaring set off at once to deliver his
current crop of dispatches. He returned within the hour,
though, and told me to fetch my cloak.

"Why?" I said, bewildered. "Where are we going?"

He glanced at me indifferently and said "To Bellhurst
Manor."

"Right," I said. It sounded a trifle more impressive than
my current surroundings, which featured several soldiers
playing at chuck-a-luck on the floor, a flea-ridden mongrel
asleep by the fire, and a strong smell of hops.

The manor house, without regard to the natural beauty
of its site, stubbornly turned its back on the open meadows
and huddled inland instead, facing the stark cliffside.

The drive was straight, short, and unadorned, unlike the
lovely curving approaches to French manors. But the entrance was equipped with two utilitarian stone pillars, each
bearing the heraldic device of the owner. I stared at it as my
horse clopped past, trying to place it. A cat—perhaps a leopard?—couchant, with a lily in its paw. It was familiar, I knew.
But whose?

There was a stir in the long grass near the gate, and I
caught a quick glimpse of pale blue eyes as a hunched bundle
of rags scuttled into the shadows, away from the churn of the
horses' hooves. Something about the ragged beggar seemed
faintly familiar, too. Perhaps I was merely hallucinating;

grasping at anything that didn't remind me of English soldiers.

The escort waited in the dooryard, not bothering to dismount, while I mounted the steps with Captain Mainwaring, and waited while he hammered at the door, rather wondering what might be on the other side of it.

"Mrs. Beauchamp?" The butler, if that's what he was, looked rather as though he suspected the worst. No doubt he was right.

"Yes," I said. "Er, whose house is this?"

But even as I asked, I raised my eyes and looked into the gloom of the inner hall. A face stared back at me, doe-eyes wide and startled.

Mary Hawkins.

As the girl opened her mouth, I opened mine as well. And screamed as loudly as I could. The butler, taken unprepared, took a step back, tripped on a settee, and fell over sideways like a bowls pin. I could hear the startled noises of the soldiers outside, coming up the steps.

I picked up my skirts, shrieked "A mouse! A mouse!" and fled toward the parlor, yelling like a banshee.

Infected by my apparent hysteria, Mary shrieked as well, and clutched me about the middle as I cannoned into her. I bore her back into the recesses of the parlor with me, and grabbed her by the shoulders.

"Don't tell anyone who I am," I breathed into her ear. "No one! My life depends on it!" I had thought I was being melodramatic, but it occurred to me, as I spoke the words, that I could very well be telling the exact truth. Being married to Red Jamie Fraser was likely a dicey proposition.

Mary had time only to nod in a dazed sort of way, when the door at the far side of the room opened, and a man came in.

"Whatever is all this wretched noise, Mary?" he demanded. A plump, contented-looking man, he had also the firm chin and tightly satisfied lips of the man who is contented because he generally gets his own way.

"N-nothing, Papa," said Mary, stuttering in her nervousness. "Only a m-m-mouse."

The baronet squeezed his eyes shut and inhaled deeply, seeking patience. Having found a simulacrum of that state, he opened them and gazed at his offspring.

"Say it again, child," he ordered. "But straight. I'll not have you mumbling and blithering. Take a deep breath, steady yourself. Now. Again."

Mary obeyed, inhaling 'til the laces of her bodice strained across the budding chest. Her fingers wound themselves in the silk brocade of her skirt, seeking support.

"It w-was a mouse, Papa. Mrs. Fr . . . er, this lady was frightened by a mouse."

Dismissing this attempt as barely satisfactory, the baronet stepped forward, examining me with interest.

"Oh? And who might you be, Madam?"

Captain Mainwaring, arriving belatedly after the search for the mythical mouse, popped up at my elbow and introduced me, handing over the note of introduction from Colonel MacLeish.

"Hum. So, it seems His Grace is to be your host, Madam, at least temporarily." He handed the note to the waiting butler, and took the hat the latter had taken from the nearby rack.

"I regret that our acquaintance should be so short, Mrs. Beauchamp. I was just leaving myself." He glanced over his shoulder, to a short stairway that branched off the hall. The butler, dignity restored, was already mounting it, grubby note reposing on a salver held before him. "I see Walmisley has gone to tell His Grace of your arrival. I must go, or I shall miss the post-coach. *Adieu,* Mrs. Beauchamp."

He turned to Mary, hanging back against the paneled wainscoting.

"Goodbye, daughter. Do try to . . . well." The corners of his mouth turned up in what was meant to be a fatherly smile. "Goodbye, Mary."

"Goodbye, Papa," she murmured, eyes on the ground. I glanced from one to the other. What on earth was Mary Hawkins, of all people, doing here? Plainly she was staying at the house; I supposed the owner must be some connection of her family's.

"Mrs. Beauchamp?" A small, tubby footman was bowing at my elbow. "His Grace will see you now, Madam."

Mary's hands clutched at my sleeve as I turned to follow the footman.

"B-b-b-but . . ." she began. In my keyed-up state, I didn't think I could manage sufficient patience to hear her out. I smiled vaguely and patted her hand.

"Yes, yes," I said. "Don't worry, it will be all right."

"B-but it's my . . ."

The footman bowed and pushed open a door at the end of the corridor. Light within fell on the richness of brocade and polished wood. The chair I could see to one side had a family crest embroidered on its back; a clearer version of the worn stone shield I had seen outside.

A leopard couchant, holding in its paw a bunch of lilies —or were they crocuses? Alarm bells rang in my mind as the chair's occupant rose, his shadow falling across the polished doorsill as he turned. Mary's final anguished word made it out, neck and neck with the footman's announcement.

"My *g-g-godfather*!" she said.

"His Grace, the Duke of Sandringham," said the footman.

"Mrs. . . . Beauchamp?" said the Duke, his mouth dropping open in astonishment.

"Well," I said weakly. "Something like that."

◆━━━

The door of the drawing room closed behind me, leaving me alone with His Grace. My last sight of Mary had been of her standing out in the hall, eyes like saucers, mouth opening and shutting silently like a goldfish.

There were huge Chinese jars flanking the windows, and inlaid tables under them. A bronze Venus posed coquettishly on the mantelpiece, companioned by a pair of gold-rimmed porcelain bowls and silver-gilt candelabra, blazing with beeswax candles. A close-napped carpet that I recognized as a very good Kermanshah covered most of the floor and a spinet crouched in one corner; what little space was left bare was occupied by marquetried furniture and the odd bit of statuary.

"Nice place you have here," I remarked graciously to the Duke, who had been standing before the fire, hands folded beneath his coattail as he watched me, an expression of wary amusement on the broad, florid face.

"Thank you," he said, in the piping tenor that came so oddly from that barrel-chested frame. "Your presence adorns it, my dear." Amusement won out over wariness, and he smiled, a bluff, disarming grin.

"Why Beauchamp?" he asked. "That isn't by chance your real name, is it?"

"My maiden name," I answered, rattled into the truth. His thick blond eyebrows shot up.

"*Are* you French?"

"No. English. I couldn't use Fraser, though, could I?"

"I see." Brows still raised, he nodded at a small brocaded love seat, inviting me to be seated. It was richly carved and beautifully proportioned, a museum piece, like everything else in the room. I swept my sodden skirts to one side as gracefully as I could, ignoring their liberal stains of mud and horsehair, and delicately lowered myself onto the primrose satin.

The Duke paced slowly back and forth before the fire, watching me, still with a slight smile on his features. I fought the growing warmth and comfort that spread through my aching legs, threatening to drag me into the abyss of fatigue that gaped open at my feet. This was no time to let down my guard.

"Which are you?" the Duke inquired suddenly. "An English hostage, a fervent Jacobite, or a French agent?"

I rubbed two fingers over the ache between my eyes. The correct answer was "none of the above," but I didn't think it would get me very far.

"The hospitality of this house seems a trifle lacking by comparison with its appointments," I said, as haughtily as I could manage under the circumstances, which wasn't all that much. Still, Louise's example of great-ladydom had not been entirely in vain.

The Duke laughed, a high, chittering sort of laugh, like a bat that has just heard a good one.

"Your pardon, Madam. You're quite right; I should have thought to offer you refreshment before presuming to question you. *Most* thoughtless of me."

He murmured something to the footman who appeared

in answer to his ring, then waited calmly before the fire for the tray to arrive. I sat in silence, glancing around the room, occasionally stealing a look at my host. Neither of us was interested in making small talk. Despite his outward geniality, this was an armed truce, and both of us knew it.

What I wanted to know was why. No stranger to people wondering who in hell I was, I rather wondered myself where the Duke came into it. Or where he thought *I* did. He had met me before, as Mrs. Fraser, wife of the laird of Lallybroch. Now I had turned up on his doorstep, posing as an English hostage named Beauchamp lately rescued from a gang of Scottish Jacobites. That was enough to make anyone wonder. But his attitude toward me went a long way past simple curiosity.

The tea arrived, complete with scones and cake. The Duke picked up his own cup, motioned to mine with a lift of one brow, and we took tea, still both in silence. Somewhere on the other side of the house, I could hear a muffled banging, as of someone hammering. The soft chime of the Duke's cup against its saucer was the signal for the resumption of hostilities.

"Now, then," he said, with as much firmness as a man who sounded like Mickey Mouse could manage. "Let me begin, Mrs. Fraser—I may call you so? Thank you. Let me begin by saying that I know a great deal about you already. I intend to know more. You will do well to answer me fully and without hesitations. I must say, Mrs. Fraser, that you are amazingly difficult to kill"—he bowed slightly in my direction, that smile still on his lips—"but I feel sure that it could be accomplished, given sufficient determination."

I stared at him, unmoving; not out of any native sangfroid, but from simple dumbfoundedness. Adopting another of Louise's mannerisms, I raised both eyebrows inquiringly, sipped tea, then patted my lips delicately with the monogrammed serviette provided.

"I am afraid you will think me dense, Your Grace," I said politely, "but I haven't the faintest idea what you're talking about."

"Haven't you, my dear?"

The small, jolly blue eyes didn't blink. He reached for the silver-gilt bell on the tray and rang it once.

The man must have been waiting in the next room for the summons, for the door opened immediately. A tall, lean man in the dark habiliments and good linen of an upper servant advanced to the Duke's side and bowed deeply.

"Your Grace?" He spoke English, but the French accent was unmistakable. The face was French, too; long-nosed and white, with thin, tight lips and a pair of ears that stood out from his head like small wings on either side, their tips fiercely red. His lean face grew still paler as he looked up and spotted me, and he took an involuntary step backward.

Sandringham watched this with a frown of irritation, then switched his gaze to me.

"You don't recognize him?" he asked.

I was beginning to shake my head, when the man's right hand twitched suddenly against the cloth of his breeches. As unobtrusively as possible, he was making the sign of the horns, middle fingers folded down, index and little finger pointed at me. I knew, then, and in the next instant had seen the confirmation of my knowledge—the small beauty mark above the fork of his thumb.

I hadn't the slightest doubt; it was the man in the spotted shirt who had attacked me and Mary in Paris. And all too obviously in the Duke's employ.

"You bloody *bastard*!" I said. I leaped to my feet, overturning the tea table, and snatched up the nearest object to hand, a carved alabaster tobacco jar. I hurled it at the man's head, and he turned and fled precipitately, the heavy jar missing him by inches to smash against the door frame.

The door slammed to as I started after him, and I stopped in my tracks, breathing heavily. I glared at Sandringham, hands braced on my hips.

"Who is he?" I demanded.

"My valet," said the Duke calmly. "Albert Danton, by name. A good fellow with neckcloths and stockings, but a trifle excitable, as so many of these Frenchmen are. Incredibly superstitious, too." He frowned disapprovingly at the closed door. "Bloody papists, with all these saints and smells and such. Believe anything at all."

My breathing was slowing, though my heart still banged against the whalebones of my bodice. I had trouble drawing a deep breath.

"You filthy, disgusting, outrageous. . . . *pervert*!"

The Duke seemed bored by this, and nodded negligently.

"Yes, yes, my dear. All that, I'm sure, and more. A trifle unlucky, too, at least on that occasion."

"Unlucky? Is that what you'd call it?" Unsteadily, I moved to the love seat, and sat down. My hands were shaking with nerves, and I clasped them together, hidden in the folds of my skirt.

"On several counts, my dear lady. Just look at it." He spread out both hands in graceful entreaty. "I send Danton to dispose of you. He and his companions decide to entertain themselves a bit first; that's all well and good, but in the process, they get a good look at you, leap unaccountably to the conclusion that you're a witch of some kind, lose their heads entirely and run off. But not before debauching my goddaughter, who is present by accident, thus ruining all chance of the excellent marriage I had painstakingly arranged for her. Consider the irony of it!"

The shocks were coming thick and fast, and I hardly knew which to respond to first. There seemed one particularly striking statement in this speech, though.

"What do you mean 'dispose of me'?" I demanded. "Do you mean to say you actually tried to have me *killed*?" The room seemed to be swaying a bit, and I took a deep gulp of tea as being the nearest thing to a restorative available. It wasn't terribly effective.

"Well, yes," Sandringham said pleasantly. "That was the point I was endeavoring to make. Tell me, my dear, would you care for a cup of sherry?"

I eyed him narrowly for a moment. Having just stated that he'd tried to have me killed, he now expected me to accept a cup of sherry from his hands?

"Brandy," I said. "Lots of it."

He giggled in that high-pitched way again, and made his way to the sideboard, remarking over his shoulder, "Captain Randall said you were a most diverting woman. Quite an encomium from the Captain, you know. He hasn't much use for women ordinarily, though they swarm over him. His looks, I suppose; it can't be his manner."

"So Jack Randall *does* work for you," I said, taking the glass he handed me. I had watched him pour out two glasses, and was sure that both contained nothing but brandy. I took a large and sorely needed swallow.

The Duke matched me, blinking his eyes at the effect of the pungent liquid.

"Of course," he said. "Often the best tool is the most dangerous. One doesn't hesitate to use it on that account; one merely makes sure to take adequate precautions."

"Dangerous, eh? Just how much do you know about Jonathan Randall?" I asked curiously.

The Duke tittered. "Oh, virtually everything, I should think, my dear. Most likely a great deal more than you do, in fact. It doesn't do to employ a man like that without having a means at hand to control him, you know. And money is a good bridle, but a weak rein."

"Unlike blackmail?" I said dryly.

He sat back, hands clasped across his bulging stomach, and regarded me with bland interest.

"Ah. You are thinking that blackmail might work both ways, I suppose?" He shook his head, dislodging a few grains of snuff that floated down onto the silk waistcoat.

"No, my dear. For one thing, there is something of a difference in our stations. While rumor of that sort might affect my reception in some circles of society, that is not a matter of grave concern to me. While for the good Captain—well, the army takes a very dim view of such unnatural predilections. The penalty is often death, in fact. No, not much comparison, really." He cocked his head to one side, so far as the multiple chins allowed.

"But it is neither the promise of wealth nor the threat of exposure that binds Jack Randall to me," he said. The small, watery blue eyes gleamed in their orbits. "He serves me because I can give him what he desires."

I eyed the corpulent frame with unconcealed disgust, making His Grace shake with laughter.

"No, not that," he said. "The Captain's tastes are somewhat more refined than that. Unlike my own."

"What, then?"

"Punishment," he said softly. "But you know that, don't you? Or at least your husband does."

I felt unclean simply from being near him, and rose to get away. The shards of the alabaster tobacco jar lay on the

828

floor, and I kicked one inadvertently, so that it pinged off the wall, ricocheting and spinning off under the love seat, reminding me of the recent Danton.

I wasn't at all sure that I wanted to discuss the subject of my aborted murder with him, but it seemed at the moment preferable to some alternatives.

"What did you want to kill me for?" I asked abruptly, turning to face him. I glanced quickly over the collection of objects on a piecrust table, looking for a suitable weapon of defense, just in case he still felt the urge.

He didn't seem to. Instead, he bent laboriously over and picked up the teapot—miraculously unbroken—and set it upright on the restored tea table.

"It seemed expedient at the time," he said calmly. "I had learned that you and your husband were attempting to thwart a particular affair in which I had interested myself. I considered removing your husband instead, but it seemed too dangerous, what with his close relation to two of the greatest families in Scotland."

"Considered removing him?" A light dawned—one of many that were going off in my skull like fireworks. "Was it you who sent the seamen who attacked Jamie in Paris?"

The Duke nodded in an offhand manner.

"That seemed the simplest method, if a bit crude. But then, Dougal MacKenzie turned up in Paris, and I wondered whether in fact your husband was in fact working *for* the Stuarts. I became unsure where his interests lay."

What I was wondering was just where the *Duke*'s interests lay. This odd speech made it sound very much as though he was a secret Jacobite—and if so, he'd done a really masterly job of keeping his secrets.

"And then," he went on, delicately placing the teapot's lid back in place, "there was your growing friendship with Louis of France. Even had your husband failed with the bankers, Louis could have supplied Charles Stuart with what he needed—provided you kept your pretty nose out of the affair."

He frowned closely at the scone he was holding, flicked a couple of threads off it, then decided against eating it and tossed it onto the table.

"Once it became clear what was really happening, I tried

to lure your husband back to Scotland, with the offer of a pardon; very expensive, that was," he said reflectively. "And all for nothing, too!

"But then I recalled your husband's apparent devotion to you—quite touching," he said, with a benevolent smile that I particularly disliked. "I supposed that your tragic demise might well distract him from the endeavor in which he was engaged without provoking the sort of interest his own murder would have involved."

Suddenly thinking of something, I turned to look at the harpsichord in the corner of the room. Several sheets of music adorned its rack, written in a fine, clear hand. *Fifty thousand pounds, upon the occasion of Your Highness's setting foot in Scotland.* Signed *S.* "S," of course, for Sandringham. The Duke laughed, in apparent delight.

"That was really very clever of you, my dear. It must have been you; I'd heard of your husband's unfortunate inability with music."

"Actually, it wasn't," I replied, turning back from the piano. The table at my side lacked anything useful in the way of letter openers or blunt objects, but I hastily picked up a vase, and buried my face in the mass of hothouse flowers it held. I closed my eyes, feeling the brush of cool petals against my suddenly heated cheeks. I didn't dare to look up, for fear my telltale face would give me away.

For behind the Duke's shoulder, I had seen a round, leathery object, shaped like a pumpkin, framed by the green velvet draperies like one of the Duke's exotic art objects. I opened my eyes, peering cautiously through the petals, and the wide, snaggle-toothed mouth split in a grin like a jack-o'-lantern's.

I was torn between terror and relief. I had been right, then, about the beggar near the gate. It was Hugh Munro, an old companion from Jamie's days as a Highland outlaw. A one-time schoolmaster, he had been captured by the Turks at sea, disfigured by torture, and driven to beggary and poaching —professions he augmented by successful spying. I had heard he was an agent of the Highland army, but hadn't realized his activities had brought him so far south.

How long had he been there, perched like a bird on the ivy outside the second-story window? I didn't dare try to communicate with him; it was all I could do to keep my eyes fixed on a point just above the Duke's shoulder, gazing with apparent indifference into space.

The Duke was regarding me with interest. "Really? Not Gerstmann, surely? I shouldn't have thought he had a sufficiently devious mind."

"And you think I do? I'm flattered." I kept my nose in the flowers, speaking distractedly into a peony.

The figure outside released his grip on the ivy long enough to bring one hand up into view. Deprived of his tongue by his Saracen captors, Hugh Munro's hands spoke for him. Staring intently at me, he pointed deliberately, first at me, then at himself, then off to one side. The broad hand tilted and the first two fingers became a pair of running legs, racing away to the east. A final wink, a clenched fist in salute, and he was gone.

I relaxed, trembling slightly with reaction, and took a deep, restorative breath. I sneezed, and put the flowers down.

"So you're a Jacobite, are you?" I asked.

"Not necessarily," the Duke answered genially. "The question is, my dear—are you?" Completely unselfconscious, he took off his wig and scratched his fair, balding head before putting it back on.

"You tried to stop the effort to restore King James to his throne when you were in Paris. Failing at that, you and your husband appear now to be His Highness's most loyal supporters. Why?" The small blue eyes showed nothing more than a mild interest, but it wasn't a mild interest that had tried to have me killed.

Ever since finding out who my host was, I had been trying as hard as I could to remember what it was that Frank and the Reverend Mr. Wakefield had once said about him. *Was* he a Jacobite? So far as I could recall, the verdict of history—in the persons of Frank and the Reverend—was uncertain. So was I.

"I don't believe I'm going to tell you," I said slowly.

One blond brow arched high, the Duke took a small enameled box from his pocket and abstracted a pinch of the contents.

"Are you sure that's wise, my dear? Danton is still within call, you know."

"Danton wouldn't touch me with a ten-foot pole," I said bluntly. "Neither would you, for that matter. Not," I added hastily, seeing his mouth open, "on that account. But if you want so badly to know which side I'm on, you aren't going to kill me before finding out, now, are you?"

The Duke choked on his pinch of snuff and coughed heavily, thumping himself on the chest of his embroidered waistcoat. I drew myself up and stared coldly down my nose at him as he sneezed and spluttered.

"You're trying to frighten me into telling you things, but it won't work," I said, with a lot more confidence than I felt.

Sandringham dabbed gently at his streaming eyes with a handkerchief. At last he drew a deep breath, and blew it out between plump, pursed lips as he stared at me.

"Very well, then," he said, quite calmly. "I imagine my workmen have finished their alterations to your quarters by now. I shall summon a maid to take you to your room."

I must have gawped foolishly at him, for he smiled derisively as he hoisted himself out of his chair.

"To a point, you know, it doesn't matter," he said. "Whatever else you may be or whatever information you may possess, you have one invaluable attribute as a houseguest."

"And what's that?" I demanded. He paused, hand on the bell, and smiled.

"You're Red Jamie's wife," he said softly. "And he *is* fond of you, my dear, is he not?"

As prisons go, I had seen worse. The room measured perhaps thirty feet in each dimension, and was furnished with a lavishness exceeded only by the sitting room downstairs. The canopied bed stood on a small dais, with baldachins of ostrich feathers sprouting from the corners of its damask drapes, and a pair of matching brocaded chairs squatted comfortably before a huge fireplace.

The maidservant who had accompanied me in set down the basin and ewer she carried, and hurried to light the ready-laid fire. The footman laid his covered supper-tray on the table by the door, then stood stolidly in the doorway, dishing any thoughts I might have had of trying a quick dash down the hall. Not that it would do me much good to try, I thought gloomily; I'd be hopelessly lost in the house after the first turn of the corridor; the bloody place was as big as Buckingham Palace.

"I'm sure His Grace hopes as you'll be comfortable, ma'am," said the servant, curtsying prettily on her way out.

"Oh, I'll bet he does," I said, ungraciously.

The door closed behind her with a depressingly solid thud, and the grating sound of the big key turning seemed to scrape away the last bit of insulation covering my raw nerves.

Shivering in the chill of the vast room, I clutched my elbows and walked to the fire, where I subsided into one of the chairs. My impulse was to take advantage of the solitude to have a nice private little fit of hysterics. On the other hand, I was afraid that if I allowed my tight-reined emotions any play at all, I would never get them in check again. I closed my eyes tight and watched the red flicker of the firelight on my inner eyelids, willing myself to calmness.

After all, I was in no danger for the moment, and Hugh Munro was on his way to Jamie. Even if Jamie had lost my trail over the course of the week's travel, Hugh would find him and lead him right. Hugh knew every cottar and tinker, every farmhouse and manor within four parishes. A message from the speechless man would travel through the network of news and gossip as quickly as the wind-driven clouds passed over the mountains. If he had made it down from his lofty perch in the ivy and safely off the Duke's grounds without being apprehended, that was.

"Don't be ridiculous," I said aloud, "the man's a professional poacher. Of course he made it." The echo of my words against the ornate white-plaster ceiling was somehow comforting.

"And if so," I continued firmly, still talking to hear myself, "then Jamie will come."

Right, I thought suddenly. And Sandringham's men will be waiting for him, when he does. *You're Red Jamie's wife,* the Duke had said. My one invaluable attribute. I was bait.

"I'm a salmon egg!" I exclaimed, sitting up straight in my chair. The sheer indignity of the image summoned up a small but welcome spurt of rage that pushed the fear back a little way. I tried to fan the flames of anger by getting up and striding back and forth, thinking of new names to call the

Duke next time we met. I'd gotten as far in my compositions as "skulking pederast," when a muffled shouting from outside distracted my attention.

Pushing back the heavy velvet drapes from the window, I found that the Duke had been as good as his word. Stout wooden bars crisscrossed the window frame, latticed so closely together that I could scarcely thrust an arm between them. I could see, though.

Dusk had fallen, and the shadows under the park trees were black as ink. The shouting was coming from there, matched by answering cries from the stables, where two or three figures suddenly appeared, bearing lit torches.

The small, dark figures ran toward the wood, the fire of their pine torches streaming backward, flaring orange in the cold, damp wind. As they reached the edge of the park, a knot of vaguely human shapes became visible, tumbling onto the grass before the house. The ground was wet, and the force of their struggle left deep gashes of black in the winter-dead lawn.

I stood on tiptoe, gripping the bars and pressing my head against the wood in an effort to see more. The light of the day had failed utterly, and by the torchlight, I could distinguish no more than the occasional flailing limb in the riot below.

It couldn't be Jamie, I told myself, trying to swallow the lump in my throat that was my heart. Not so soon, not now. And not alone, surely he wouldn't have come alone? For I could see by now that the fight centered on one man, now on his knees, no more than a hunched black shape under the fists and sticks of the Duke's gamekeepers and stable-lads.

Then the hunched figure sprawled flat, and the shouting died, though a few more blows were given for good measure before the small gang of servants stood back. A few words of conversation were exchanged, inaudible from my vantage point, and two of the men stooped and seized the figure beneath the arms. As they passed beneath my third-floor window on their way toward the back of the house, the torchlight illuminated a pair of dragging, sandal-shod feet, and the tatters of a grimy smock. Not Jamie.

One of the stable-lads scampered alongside, triumphantly carrying a thick leather wallet on a strap. I was too far above to hear the clink of the tiny metal ornaments on the strap, but they glittered in the torchlight, and all the strength went from my arms in a rush of horror and despair.

They were coins and buttons, the small metal objects. And gaberlunzies. The tiny lead seals that gave a beggar license to plead his poverty through a given parish. Hugh Munro had four of them, a mark of favor for his trials at the hands of the Turk. Not Jamie, but Hugh.

I was shaking so badly that my legs would hardly carry me, but I ran to the door and pounded on it with all my strength.

"Let me out!" I shrieked. "I have to see the Duke! Let me out, I say!"

There was no response to my continued yelling and pounding, and I dashed back to the window. The scene below was eminently peaceful now; a boy stood holding a torch for one of the gardeners, who was kneeling at the edge of the lawn, tenderly replacing the divots of turf dug up by the fight.

"Hoy!" I roared. Covered as they were by bars, I couldn't crank the casements outward. I ran across the room to fetch one of the heavy silver candlesticks, dashed back, and smashed a pane of glass, heedless of the flying fragments.

"Help! Ahoy, down there! Tell the Duke I want to see him! Now! Help!" I thought one of the figures turned its head toward me, but neither made any motion toward the house, going on with their work as though no more than a night bird's cry disturbed the darkness around them.

Back to the door I ran, hammering and shouting, and back to the window, and back to the door again. I shouted, pleaded, and threatened until my throat was raw and hoarse, and beat upon the unyielding door until my fists were red and bruised, but no one came. I might have been alone in the great house, for all I could hear. The silence in the hallway was as deep as that of the night outside; as silent as the grave. All check on my fear was gone, and I sank at last to my knees before the door, sobbing without restraint.

I woke, chilled and stiff, with a throbbing headache, to feel something wide and solid shoving me across the floor. I came awake with a jerk as the opening edge of the heavy door pinched my thigh against the floor.

"Ow!" I rolled clumsily, then scrabbled to my hands and knees, hair hanging in my face.

"Claire! Oh, do be quiet, p-please! Darling, are you hurt?" With a rustle of starched lawn, Mary dropped to her knees beside me. Behind her, the door swung shut and I heard the click of the lock above.

"Yes—I mean, no. I'm all right," I said dazedly. "But Hugh . . ." I clamped my lips shut and shook my head, trying to clear it. "What in bloody hell are you doing here, Mary?"

"I b-bribed the housekeeper to let me in," she whispered. "Must you talk so loudly?"

"It doesn't matter much," I said, in a normal tone of voice. "That door's so thick, nothing short of a football match could be heard through it."

"A what?"

"Never mind." My mind was beginning to clear, though my eyes were sticky and swollen and my head still throbbed like a drum. I pushed myself to my feet and staggered to the basin, where I splashed cold water over my face.

"You bribed the housekeeper?" I said, wiping my face with a towel. "But we're still locked in, aren't we? I heard the key turn."

Mary was pale in the dimness of the room. The candle had guttered out while I slept on the floor, and there was no light but the deep red glow of the fireplace embers. She bit her lip.

"It was the b-best I could do. Mrs. Gibson was too afraid of the Duke to give me a key. All she would do was agree to lock me in with you, and let me out in the morning. I thought you m-might like company," she added timidly.

"Oh," I said. "Well . . . thank you. It was a kind thought." I took a new candle from the drawer and went to the fireplace to light it. The candlestick was clotted with wax from the burned-out candle; I tipped a small puddle of melted wax onto the tabletop and set the fresh candle in it, heedless of damage to the Duke's intaglio.

"Claire," Mary said. "Are you . . . are you in trouble?"

I bit my lip to prevent a hasty reply. After all, she was only seventeen, and her ignorance of politics was probably

even more profound than her lack of knowledge of men had
been.

"Er, yes," I said. "Rather a lot, I'm afraid." My brain was
starting to work again. Even if Mary was not equipped to be
of much practical help in escaping, she might at least be able
to provide me with information about her godfather and the
doings of his household.

"Did you hear the racket out by the wood earlier?" I
asked. She shook her head. She was beginning to shiver; in
such a large room, the heat of the fire died away long before
it reached the bed dais.

"No, but I heard one of the cookmaids saying the keepers had caught a poacher in the park. It's awfully cold. Can't
we get into b-bed?"

She was already crawling across the coverlet, burrowing
beneath the bolster for the edge of the sheet. Her bottom was
round and neat, childlike under the white nightdress.

"That wasn't a poacher," I said. "Or rather it was, but it
was also a friend. He was on his way to find Jamie, to tell him
I was here. Do you know what happened after the keepers
took him?"

Mary swung around, face a pale blur within the shadows
of the bed hangings. Even in this light, I could see that the
dark eyes had grown huge.

"Oh, Claire! I'm so sorry!"

"Well, so am I," I said impatiently. "Do you know where
the poacher is, though?" If Hugh had been imprisoned somewhere accessible, like the stables, there was a bare chance
that Mary might be able to release him somehow in the
morning.

The trembling of her lips, making her normal stutter
seem comprehensible by comparison, should have warned
me. But the words, once she got them out, struck through my
heart, sharp and sudden as a thrown dirk.

"Th-they h-h-hanged him," she said. "At the p-park
g-gate."

It was some time before I was able to pay attention to my
surroundings. The flood of shock, grief, fear, and shattered
hope washed over me, swamping me utterly. I was dimly con-

scious of Mary's small hand timidly patting my shoulder, and her voice offering handkerchiefs and drinks of water, but remained curled in a ball, not speaking, but shaking, and waiting for the relaxation of the wrenching despair that clenched my stomach like a fist. Finally I exhausted the panic, if not myself, and opened my eyes blearily.

"I'll be all right," I said at last, sitting up and wiping my nose inelegantly on my sleeve. I took the proffered towel and blotted my eyes with it. Mary hovered over me, looking concerned, and I reached out and squeezed her hand reassuringly.

"Really," I said. "I'm all right now. And I'm very glad you're here." A thought struck me, and I dropped the towel, looking curiously at her.

"Come to think of it, why *are* you here?" I asked. "In this house, I mean."

She looked down, blushing, and picked at the coverlet.

"The D-Duke is my godfather, you know."

"Yes, so I gathered," I said. "Somehow I doubt that he merely wanted the pleasure of your company, though."

She smiled a little at the remark. "N-no. But he—the Duke, I mean—he thinks he's found another h-h-husband for me." The effort to get out "husband" left her red-faced. "Papa brought me here to meet him."

I gathered from her demeanor that this wasn't news requiring immediate congratulations. "Do you know the man?"

Only by name, it turned out. A Mr. Isaacs, an importer, of London. Too busy to travel all the way to Edinburgh to meet his intended, he had agreed to come to Bellhurst, where the marriage would take place, all parties being agreeable.

I picked up the silver-backed hairbrush from the bed table and abstractedly began to tidy my hair. So, having failed to secure an alliance with the French nobility, the Duke was intending to sell his goddaughter to a wealthy Jew.

"I have a new trousseau," Mary said, trying to smile. "Forty-three embroidered petticoats—two with g-gold thread." She broke off, her lips pressed tight together, staring down sightlessly at her bare left hand. I put my own hand over it.

"Well." I tried to be encouraging. "Perhaps he'll be a kind man."

"That's what I'm af-fraid of." Avoiding my questioning look, she glanced down, twisting her hands together in her lap.

"They didn't tell Mr. Isaacs—about P-Paris. And they say I mustn't, either." Her face crumpled miserably. "They brought a horrible old woman to tell me how I must act on my w-w-wedding night, to—to pretend it's the first time, but I . . . oh, Claire, how can I do it?" she wailed. "And Alex—I didn't tell him; I couldn't! I was such a coward, I d-didn't even say goodbye!"

She threw herself into my arms, and I patted her back, losing a little of my own grief in the effort to comfort her. At length, she grew calmer, and sat up, hiccuping, to take a little water.

"Are you going to go through with it?" I asked. She looked up at me, her lashes spiked and wet.

"I haven't any choice," she said simply.

"But—" I started, and then stopped, helpless.

She was quite right. Young and female, with no resources, and no man who could come to her rescue, there was simply nothing to do but to accede to her father's and godfather's wishes, and marry the unknown Mr. Isaacs of London.

Heavyhearted, neither of us had any appetite for the food on the tray. We crawled under the covers to keep warm, and Mary, worn out with emotion, was sound asleep within minutes. No less exhausted, I found myself unable to sleep, grieving for Hugh, worried for Jamie, and curious about the Duke.

The sheets were chilly, and my feet seemed like chunks of ice. Avoiding the more distressful things on my mind, I turned my thoughts to Sandringham. What was his place in this affair?

To all appearances, the man was a Jacobite. He had, by his own admission, been willing to do murder—or pay for it, at least—in order to ensure that Charles got the backing he needed to launch his expedition to Scotland. And the evidence of the musical cipher made it all but certain that it was the Duke who had finally induced Charles to set sail in August, with his promise of help.

There were certainly men who took pains to conceal their Jacobite sympathies; given the penalties for treason, it was hardly peculiar. And the Duke had a good deal more to lose than some, should he back a failing cause.

Still, Sandringham hardly struck me as an enthusiastic supporter of the Stuart monarchy. Given his remarks about Danton, clearly he wouldn't be in sympathy with a Catholic ruler. And why wait so long to provide support, when Charles was in desperate need of money now—and had been, in fact, ever since his arrival in Scotland?

I could think of two conceivable reasons for the Duke's behavior, neither particularly creditable to the gentleman, but both well within the bounds of his character.

He could in fact be a Jacobite, willing to countenance an unpalatable Catholic king in return for the future benefits he might anticipate as chief backer of the restored Stuart monarchy. I could see that; "principle" wasn't in the man's vocabulary, whereas "self-interest" clearly was a term he knew well. He might wish to wait until Charles reached England, in order that the money not be wasted before the Highland army's final, crucial push to London. Anyone familiar with Charles Stuart could see the common sense in not entrusting him with too much money at once.

Or, for that matter, he might have wished to ensure that the Stuarts did in fact have some substantial backing for their cause before becoming financially involved himself; after all, contributing to a rebellion is not the same thing as supporting an entire army single-handed.

Contrariwise, I could see a much more sinister reason for the conditions of the Duke's offer. Making support conditional on the Jacobite army reaching English soil ensured that Charles would struggle on against the increasing opposition of his own leaders, dragging his reluctant, straggling army farther and farther south, away from the sheltering mountains in which they might find refuge.

If the Duke could expect benefits from the Stuarts for help in restoring them, what might he expect from the Hanovers, in return for luring Charles Stuart within their reach—and betraying him and his followers into the hands of the English army?

History had not been able to say what the Duke's true leanings had been. That struck me as odd; surely he would have to reveal his true intent sooner or later. Of course, I mused, the Old Fox, Lord Lovat, had managed to play off both sides of the Jacobite Rising last time, simultaneously ingratiating himself with the Hanovers and retaining the favor of the Stuarts. And Jamie had done it himself, for a time. Maybe it wasn't all that difficult to hide one's loyalties, in the constantly shifting morass of Royal politics.

The chill was creeping up my feet, and I moved my legs restlessly, my skin seeming numb as I rubbed my calves together. Legs obviously generated much less friction than dry sticks; no perceptible warmth resulted from this activity.

Lying sleepless, restless and clammy, I suddenly became aware of a tiny, rhythmic popping noise next to me. I turned my head, listening, then raised up on one elbow and peered incredulously at my companion. She was curled on her side, delicate skin flushed with sleep, so that she looked like a hothouse flower in full bloom, thumb tucked securely in the soft pink recesses of her mouth. Her lower lip moved as I watched, in the faintest of sucking motions.

I wasn't sure whether to laugh or cry. In the end, I did neither; merely pulled the thumb gently free and laid the limp hand curled upon her bosom. I blew out the candle and cuddled close to Mary.

Whether it was the innocence of that small gesture, with the far-off memories of trust and safety it provoked, the simple comfort of a warm body nearby, or only the exhaustion of fear and grief, my feet thawed, I relaxed at last, and fell asleep.

Wrapped in a warm cocoon of quilts, I slept deep and dreamlessly. It was all the greater a shock, then, when I was jerked abruptly from the soft, quiet dark of oblivion. It was still dark—black as a coachman's hat, in fact, as the fire had gone out—but the surroundings were neither soft nor quiet. Something heavy had landed suddenly on the bed, striking my arm in the process, and was apparently in the process of murdering Mary.

The bed heaved and the mattress tilted sharply under

me, the bedframe shuddering with the force of the struggle taking place next to me. Agonized grunts and whispered threats came from close at hand, and a flailing hand—Mary's, I thought—struck me in the eye.

I rolled hastily out of bed, tripping on the step of the dais and falling flat on the floor. The sounds of struggle above me intensified, with a horrible, high-pitched squealing noise that I took to be Mary's best effort at a scream while being strangled.

There was a sudden startled exclamation, in a deep male voice, then a further convulsion of bedclothes, and the squealing stopped abruptly. Moving hastily, I found the flint box on the table and struck a light for the candle. Its wavering flame strengthened and rose, revealing what I had suspected from the sound of that vigorous Gaelic expletive—Mary, invisible save for a pair of wildly scrabbling hands, face smothered under a pillow and body flattened by the prostrate form of my large and agitated husband, who despite his advantage of size, appeared to have his hands well and truly full.

Intent on subduing Mary, he hadn't glanced up at the newly lit candle, but went on trying to capture her hands, while simultaneously holding the pillow over her face. Suppressing the urge to laugh hysterically at the spectacle, I instead set down the candle, leaned over the bed, and tapped him on the shoulder.

"Jamie?" I said.

"Jesus!" He leaped like a salmon, springing off the bed and coming to rest on the floor in a crouch, dirk half-drawn. He saw me then, and sagged in relief, closing his eyes for an instant.

"Jesus God, Sassenach! Never do that again, d'ye hear? Be quiet," he said briefly to Mary, who had escaped from the pillow and was now sitting bolt upright in bed, bug-eyed and spluttering. "I didna mean ye harm; I thought ye were my wife." He strode purposefully round the bed, took me by both shoulders and kissed me hard, as though to reassure himself that he'd got the right woman now. He had, and I kissed him back with considerable fervor, reveling in the scrape of his unshaven beard and the warm, pungent scent of him; damp linen and wool, with a strong hint of male sweat.

"Get dressed," he said, letting go. "The damn house is crawling wi' servants. It's like an ant's nest below."

"How did you get in here?" I asked, looking around for my discarded gown.

"Through the door, of course," he said impatiently. "Here." He seized my gown from the back of a chair and tossed it at me. Sure enough, the massive door stood open, a great ring of keys protruding from the lock.

"But how . . ." I began.

"Later," he said brusquely. He spotted Mary, out of bed and struggling into her nightrobe. "Best get back in bed, lassie," he advised. "The floor's cold."

"I'm coming with you." The words were muffled by the folds of cloth, but her determination was evident as her head popped through the neck of the robe and emerged, tousled-haired and defiant.

"The hell you are," Jamie said. He glared at her, and I noticed the fresh, raw scratches down his cheek. Seeing the quiver of her lips, though, he mastered his temper with an effort, and spoke reassuringly. "Dinna mind, lassie. You'll have no trouble over it. I'll lock the door behind us, and ye can tell everyone in the morning what's happened. No one shall hold ye to blame."

Ignoring this, Mary thrust her feet hastily into her slippers and ran toward the door.

"Hey! Where d'ye think you're going?" Startled, Jamie swung around after her, but not soon enough to stop her reaching the door. She stood in the hallway just outside, poised like a deer.

"I'm going with you!" she said fiercely. "If you don't take me, I shall run down the corridor, screaming as loudly as I can. So there!"

Jamie stared at her, his hair gleaming copper in the candlelight and the blood rising in his face, obviously torn between the necessity for silence and the urge to kill her with his bare hands and damn the noise. Mary glared back, one hand holding up her skirts, ready to run. Now dressed and shod, I poked him in the ribs, breaking his concentration.

"Take her," I said briefly. "Let's go."

He gave me a look that was twin to the one he'd been giving Mary, but hesitated no more than a moment. With a short nod, he took my arm and the three of us hurried out into the chill darkness of the corridor.

The house was at once deathly still and full of noises; boards squeaked loud beneath our feet and our garments rustled like leaves in a gale. The walls seemed to breathe with the settlings of wood, and small, half-heard sounds beyond the corridor suggested the secretive burrowings of animals underground. And over all was the deep and frightening silence of a great, dark house, sunk in a sleep that must not be broken.

Mary's hand was tight on my arm, as we crept down the hall behind Jamie. He moved like a shadow, hugging the wall, but quickly, for all his silence.

As we passed one door, I heard the sound of soft footsteps on the other side. Jamie heard them, too, and flattened himself against the wall, motioning Mary and me ahead of him. The plaster of the wall was cold against the palms of my hands, as I tried to press backward into it.

The door opened cautiously, and a head in a puffy white mobcap poked out, peering down the hall in the direction away from us.

"Hullo?" it said in a whisper. "Is that you, Albert?" A tickle of cold sweat ran down my spine. A housemaid, apparently expecting a visitation from the Duke's valet, who seemed to be keeping up the reputation of Frenchmen.

I didn't think she was going to consider an armed Highlander an adequate substitute for her absent lover. I could feel Jamie tense beside me, trying to overcome his scruples against striking a woman. Another instant, and she would turn, see him, and scream the house down.

I stepped out from the wall.

"Er, no," I said apologetically, "I'm afraid it's only me."

The maidservant started convulsively, and I took a swift step past, so that she was facing me, with Jamie still behind her.

"Sorry to alarm you," I said, smiling cheerily. "I couldn't sleep, you see. Thought I'd try a spot of hot milk. Tell me, am I headed right for the kitchens?"

"Eh?" The maid, a plump miss in her early twenties,

gaped unbecomingly, exposing evidence of a distressing lack
of concern for dental hygiene. Luckily, it wasn't the same
maid who had seen me to my room; she might not realize that
I was a prisoner, not a guest.

"I'm a guest in the house," I said, driving the point
home. Continuing on the principle that the best defense is a
good offense, I stared accusingly at her.

"Albert, eh? Does His Grace know that you are in the
habit of entertaining men in your room at night?" I demanded. This seemed to hit a nerve, for the woman paled and
dropped to her knees, clutching at my skirt. The prospect of
exposure was so alarming that she didn't pause to ask exactly
why a guest should be wandering about the halls in the wee
hours of the morning, wearing not only gown and shoes, but a
traveling cloak as well.

"Oh, mum! Please, you won't say nothing to His Grace,
will you? I can see you've a kind face, mum, surely you'd not
want to see me dismissed from my place? Have pity on me,
my lady, I've six brothers and sisters still at home, and I . . ."

"Now, now," I soothed, patting her on the shoulder.
"Don't worry about it. I won't tell the Duke. You just go back
to your bed, and . . ." Talking in the sort of voice one uses
with children and mental patients, I eased her, still volubly
protesting her innocence, back into the small closet of a
room.

I shut the door on her and leaned against it for support.
Jamie's face loomed up from the shadows before me, grinning. He said nothing, but patted me on the head in congratulation, before taking my arm and urging me down the hall
once more.

Mary was waiting under the window on the landing, her
nightrobe glowing white in the moonlight that beamed momentarily through scudding clouds outside. A storm was gathering, from the looks of it, and I wondered whether this
would help or hinder our escape.

Mary clutched at Jamie's plaid as he stepped onto the
landing.

"Shh!" she whispered. "Someone's coming!"

Someone was; I could hear the faint thud of footsteps
coming from below, and the pale wash of a candle lit the
stairwell. Mary and I looked wildly about, but there was abso-

lutely no place to hide. This was a back stair, meant for the servants' use, and the landings were simple squares of flooring, totally unrelieved by furniture or convenient hangings.

Jamie sighed in resignation. Then, motioning me and Mary back into the hallway from which we had come, he drew his dirk and waited, poised in the shadowed corner of the landing.

Mary's fingers clutched and twined with mine, squeezing tight in an agony of apprehension. Jamie had a pistol hanging from his belt, but plainly couldn't use it within the house—and a servant would realize that, making it useless for threat. It would have to be the knife, and my stomach quivered with pity for the hapless servant who was just about to come face-to-face with fifteen stone of keyed-up Scot and the threat of black steel.

I was taking stock of my apparel, and thinking that I could spare one of my petticoats to be used for bindings, when the bowed head of the candle-bearer came in sight. The dark hair was parted down the middle and slicked with a stinkingly sweet pomade that at once brought back the memory of a dark Paris street and the curve of thin, cruel lips beneath a mask.

My gasp of recognition made Danton look up sharply, one step below the landing. The next instant, he was grasped by the neck and flung against the wall of the landing with a force that sent the candlestick flying through the air.

Mary had seen him too.

"That's him!" she exclaimed, in her shock forgetting either to whisper or to stutter. "The man in Paris!"

Jamie had the feebly struggling valet squashed against the wall, held by one muscled forearm pressed across his chest. The man's face, fading in and out as the light ebbed and flooded with the passing clouds, was ghastly pale. It grew paler in the next moment, as Jamie laid the edge of his blade against Danton's throat.

I stepped onto the landing, not sure either what Jamie would do, or what I wanted him to do. Danton let out a strangled moan when he saw me, and made an abortive attempt to cross himself.

"La Dame Blanche!" he whispered, eyes starting in horror.

Jamie moved with sudden violence, grasping the man's hair and jerking his head back so hard that it thumped against the paneling.

"Had I time, *mo garhe,* ye would die slow," he whispered, and his voice lacked nothing in conviction, quiet as it was. "Count it God's mercy I have not." He yanked Danton's head back even further, so I could see the bobbing of his Adam's apple as he swallowed convulsively, his eyes fixed on me in fear.

"You call her 'Dame Blanche,' " Jamie said, between his teeth. "I call her wife! Let her face be the last that ye see, then!"

The knife ripped across the man's throat with a violence that made Jamie grunt with the effort, and a dark sheet of blood sprayed over his shirt. The stench of sudden death filled the landing, with a wheezing, gurgling sound from the crumpled heap on the floor that seemed to go on for a very long time.

The sounds behind me brought me finally to my senses: Mary, being violently sick in the hallway. My first coherent thought was that the servants were going to have the hell of a mess to clean up in the morning. My second was for Jamie, seen in a flash of the fleeting moon. His face was spattered and his hair matted with droplets of blood, and he was breathing heavily. He looked as though he might be going to be sick, too.

I turned toward Mary, and saw, far beyond her down the hall, the crack of light behind an opening door. Someone was coming to investigate the noise. I grabbed the hem of her nightrobe, wiped it roughly across her mouth, and seized her by the arm, tugging her toward the landing.

"Come on!" I said. "Let's get out of here!" Starting from his dazed contemplation of Danton's corpse, Jamie shook himself suddenly, and returning to his senses, turned to the stair.

He seemed to know where we were going, leading us through the darkened corridors without hesitation. Mary stumbled along beside me, puffing, her breath loud as an engine in my ear.

At the scullery door, Jamie came to a sudden halt, and gave a low whistle. This was returned immediately, and the door swung open on a darkness inhabited by indistinct forms. One of these detached itself from the murk and hastened forward. A few muttered words were exchanged, and the man —whichever it was—reached for Mary and pulled her into the shadows. A cold draft told me there was an open door somewhere ahead.

Jamie's hand on my shoulder steered me through the obstacles of the darkened scullery and some smaller chamber that seemed to be a lumber room of some sort; I barked my shin against something, but bit back the exclamation of pain.

Out in the free night at last, the wind seized my cloak and whirled it out in a exuberant balloon. After the nerve-stretching trek through the darkened house, I felt as though I might take wing, and sail for the sky.

The men around me seemed to share the mood of relief; there was a small outbreak of whispered remarks and muffled laughter, quickly shushed by Jamie. One at a time, the men flitted across the open space before the house, no more than shadows under the dancing moon. At my side, Jamie watched as they disappeared into the woods of the park.

"Where's Murtagh?" he muttered, as though to himself, frowning after the last of his men. "Gone to look for Hugh, I suppose," he said, in answer to his own question. "D'ye ken where he might be, Sassenach?"

I swallowed, feeling the wind bite cold beneath my cloak, memory killing the sudden exhilaration of freedom.

"Yes," I said, and told him the bad news, as briefly as I could. His expression darkened under its mask of blood, and by the time I had finished, his face was hard as stone.

"D'ye mean just to stand there all night," inquired a voice behind us, "or ought we to sound an alarm, so they'll know where to look first?"

Jamie's expression lightened slightly as Murtagh appeared from the shadows beside us, quiet as a wraith. He had a cloth-wrapped bundle under one arm; a joint from the kitchens, I thought, seeing the blotch of dark blood on the cloth. This impression was borne out by the large ham he had tucked beneath the other arm, and the strings of sausages about his neck.

Jamie wrinkled his nose, with a faint smile.

"Ye smell like a butcher, man. Can ye no go anywhere without thinkin' of your stomach?"

Murtagh cocked his head to one side, taking in Jamie's blood-spattered appearance.

"Better to look like the butcher than his wares, lad," he said. "Shall we go?"

The trip through the park was dark and frightening. The trees were tall and widely spaced here, but there were saplings left to grow between them that changed abruptly into the menacing shapes of gamekeepers in the uncertain light. The clouds were gathering thicker, at least, and the full moon made fewer appearances, which was something to be grateful for. As we reached the far side of the park, it began to rain.

Three men had been left with the horses. Mary was already mounted before one of Jamie's men. Plainly embarrassed by the necessity of riding astride, she kept tucking the folds of her nightrobe under her thighs, in a vain attempt to hide the fact that she had legs.

More experienced, but still cursing the heavy folds of my skirt, I plucked them up and set a foot in Jamie's offered hand, swinging aboard with a practiced thump. The horse snorted at the impact and set his ears back.

"Sorry, cully," I said without sympathy. "If you think that's bad, just wait 'til *he* gets back on."

Glancing around for the "he" in question, I found him under one of the trees, hand on the shoulder of a strange boy of about fourteen.

"Who's that?" I asked, leaning over to attract the attention of Geordie Paul Fraser, who was busy tightening his girth next to me.

"Eh? Oh, him." He glanced at the boy, then back at his reluctant girth, frowning. "His name's Ewan Gibson. Hugh Munro's eldest stepson. He was wi' his da, seemingly, when the Duke's keepers came on 'em. The lad got awa', and we found him near the edge o' the moor. He brought us here." With a final unnecessary tug, he glared at the girth as though daring it to say something, then looked up at me.

"D'ye ken where the lad's da is?" he asked abruptly.

I nodded, and the answer must have been plain in my

face, for he turned to look at the boy. Jamie was holding the boy, hugged hard against his chest, and patting his back. As we watched, he held the boy away from him, both hands on his shoulders, and said something, looking down intently into his face. I couldn't hear what it was, but after a moment, the boy straightened himself and nodded. Jamie nodded as well, and with a final clap on the shoulder, turned the lad toward one of the horses, where George McClure was already reaching down a hand to him. Jamie strode toward us, head down, and the end of his plaid fluttering free behind him, despite the cold wind and the spattering rain.

Geordie spat on the ground. "Poor bugger," he said, without specifying whom he meant, and swung into his own saddle.

Near the southeast corner of the park we halted, the horses stamping and twitching, while two of the men disappeared back into the trees. It cannot have been more than twenty minutes, but it seemed twice as long before they came back.

The men rode double now, and the second horse bore a long, hunched shape bound across its saddle, wrapped in a Fraser plaid. The horses didn't like it; mine jerked its head, nostrils flaring, as the horse bearing Hugh's corpse came alongside. Jamie yanked the rein and said something angrily in Gaelic, though, and the beast desisted.

I could feel Jamie rise in the stirrups behind me, looking backward as though counting the remaining members of his band. Then his arm came around my waist, and we set off, on our way north.

We rode all night, with only brief stops for rest. During one of these, sheltering under a horse-chestnut tree, Jamie reached to embrace me, then suddenly stopped.

"What is it?" I said, smiling. "Afraid to kiss your wife in front of your men?"

"No," he said, proving it, then stepped back, smiling. "No, I was afraid for a moment ye were going to scream and claw my face." He dabbed gingerly at the marks Mary had left on his cheek.

"Poor thing," I said, laughing. "Not the welcome you expected, was it?"

"Well, by that time, actually it was," he said, grinning. He had taken two sausages from one of Murtagh's strings, and now handed me one. I couldn't remember when I had last eaten, but it must have been quite some time, for not even my fears of botulism kept the fatty, spiced meat from being delicious.

"What do you mean by that? You thought I wouldn't recognize you after only a week?"

He shook his head, still smiling, and swallowed the bite of sausage.

"Nay. It's only, when I got in the house to start, I kent where ye were, more or less, because of the bars on your windows." He arched one brow. "From the looks of them, ye must have made one hell of an impression on His Grace."

"I did," I said shortly, not wanting to think about the Duke. "Go on."

"Well," he said, taking another bite and shifting it expertly to his cheek while he talked, "I kent the room, but I needed the key, didn't I?"

"Oh, yes," I said. "You were going to tell me about that."

He chewed briefly and swallowed.

"I got it from the housekeeper, but not without trouble." He rubbed himself tenderly, a few inches below the belt. "From appearances, I'd say the woman's been waked in her bed a few times before—and didna care for the experience."

"Oh, yes," I said, entertained by the mental picture this provoked. "Well, I daresay you came as rare and refreshing fruit to her."

"I doubt it extremely, Sassenach. She screeched like a banshee and kneed me in the stones, then came altogether too near to braining me wi' a candlestick whilst I was doubled up groaning."

"What did you do?"

"Thumped her a good one—I wasna feeling verra chivalrous just at the moment—and tied her up wi' the strings to her nightcap. Then I put a towel in her mouth to put a stop to the things she was callin' me, and searched her room 'til I found the keys."

"Good work," I said, something occurring to me, "but how did you know where the housekeeper slept?"

"I didn't," he said calmly. "The laundress told me—after I told her who I was, and threatened to gut her and roast her on a spit if she didna tell me what I wanted to know." He gave me a wry smile. "Like I told ye, Sassenach, sometimes it's an advantage to be thought a barbarian. I reckon they've all heard of Red Jamie Fraser by now."

"Well, if they hadn't, they will," I said. I looked him over, as well as I could in the dim light. "What, didn't the laundress get a lick in?"

"She pulled my hair," he said reflectively. "Took a clump of it out by the roots. I'll tell ye, Sassenach; if ever I feel the need to change my manner of employment, I dinna think I'll take up attacking women—it's a bloody hard way to make a living."

It was beginning to sleet heavily near dawn, but we rode for some time before Ewan Gibson dragged his pony uncertainly to a stop, rose up clumsily in the stirrups to look around, then motioned up the hillside that rose to the left.

Dark as it was, it was impossible to ride the horses uphill. We had to descend to the ground and lead them, foot by muddy, slogging foot, along the nearly invisible track that zigzagged through heather and granite. Dawn was beginning to lighten the sky as we paused for breath at the crest of the hill. The horizon was hidden, thick with clouds, but a dull gray of no apparent source began to replace the darker gray of the night. Now I could at least see the cold streamlets that I sank in, ankle-deep, and avoid the worst of the foot-twisting snags of rock and bramble that we encountered on the way down the hill.

At the bottom was a small corrie, with six houses—though "house" was an overdignified word for the rude structures crouched beneath the larch trees there. The thatched roofs came down within a few feet of the ground, leaving only a bit of the stone walls showing.

Outside one bothy, we came to a halt. Ewan looked at Jamie, hesitating as though lost for direction, then at his nod,

ducked and disappeared beneath the low rooftree of the hut.
I drew closer to Jamie, putting my hand on his arm.

"This is Hugh Munro's house," he said to me, low-
voiced. "I've brought him home to his wife. The lad's gone in
to tell her."

I glanced from the dark, low doorway of the hut to the
limp, plaid-draped bundle that two of the men were now un-
strapping from the horse. I felt a small tremor run through
Jamie's arm. He closed his eyes for a moment, and I saw his
lips move; then he stepped forward and held out his arms for
the burden. I drew a deep breath, brushed my hair back from
my face, and followed him, stooping below the lintel of the
door.

It wasn't as bad as I had feared it might be, though bad
enough. The woman, Hugh's widow, was quiet, accepting Jamie's soft Gaelic speech of condolence with bowed head, the
tears slipping down her face like rain. She reached tentatively
for the covering plaid, as though meaning to draw it down,
but then her nerve failed, and she stood, one hand resting
awkwardly on the curve of the shroud, while the other drew a
small child close against her thigh.

There were several children huddled near the fire—
Hugh's stepchildren—and a swaddled mass in the rough cradle nearest the hearth. I felt some small comfort, looking at
the baby; at least this much of Hugh was left. Then the comfort was overwhelmed with a cold fear as I looked at the
children, grimy faces blending with the shadows. Hugh had
been their main support. Ewan was brave and willing, but he
was no more than fourteen, and the next eldest child was a
girl of twelve or so. How would they manage?

The woman's face was worn and lined, nearly toothless. I
realized with a shock that she could be only a few years older
than I was. She nodded toward the single bed, and Jamie laid
the body gently on it. He spoke to her again in Gaelic; she
shook her head hopelessly, still staring down at the long
shape upon her bed.

Jamie knelt down by the bed, bowed his head, and
placed one hand on the corpse. His words were soft, but
clearly spoken, and even my limited Gaelic could follow
them.

"I swear to thee, friend, and may God Almighty bear me

witness. For the sake of your love to me, never shall those that are yours go wanting, while I have aught to give." He knelt unmoving for a long moment, and there was no sound in the cottage but the crackle of the peat on the hearth and the soft patter of rain on the thatch. The wet had darkened Jamie's bowed head; droplets of moisture shone jewel-like in the folds of his plaid. Then his hand tightened once in final farewell, and he rose.

Jamie bowed to Mrs. Munro and turned to take my arm. Before we could leave, though, the cowhide that hung across the low doorway was thrust aside, and I stood back to make way for Mary Hawkins, followed by Murtagh.

Mary looked both bedraggled and bewildered, a damp plaid clasped around her shoulders and her muddy bedroom slippers protruding under the sodden hem of her nightrobe. Spotting me, she pressed close to me as though grateful for my presence.

"I didn't w-want to come in," she whispered to me, glancing shyly at Hugh Munro's widow, "but Mr. Murtagh insisted."

Jamie's brows were raised in inquiry, as Murtagh nodded respectfully to Mrs. Munro and said something to her in Gaelic. The little clansman looked just as he always did, dour and competent, but I thought there was an extra hint of dignity in his demeanor. He carried one of the saddlebags before him, bulging heavily with something. Perhaps a parting gift for Mrs. Munro, I thought.

Murtagh laid the bag on the floor at my feet, then straightened up and looked from me to Mary, to Hugh Munro's widow, and at last to Jamie, who looked as puzzled as I felt. Having thus assured himself of his audience, Murtagh bowed formally to me, a lock of wet dark hair falling free over his brow.

"I bring ye your vengeance, lady," he said, as quietly as I'd ever heard him speak. He straightened and inclined his head in turn to Mary and Mrs. Munro. "And justice for the wrong done to ye."

Mary sneezed, and wiped her nose hastily with a fold of her plaid. She stared at Murtagh, eyes wide and baffled. I gazed down at the bulging saddlebag, feeling a sudden deep

chill that owed nothing to the weather outside. But it was
Hugh Munro's widow who sank to her knees, and with steady
hands opened the bag and drew out the head of the Duke of
Sandringham.

45

Damn All Randalls

It was a torturous trip northward into Scotland. We had to dodge and hide, always afraid of being recognized as Highlanders, unable to buy or beg food, needing to steal small bits from unattended sheds or pluck the few edible roots I could find in the fields.

Slowly, slowly, we made our way north. There was no telling where the Scottish army was by now, except that it lay to the north. With no way of telling where the army was, we decided to make for Edinburgh; there at least there would be news of the campaign. We had been out of touch for several weeks; I knew the relief of Stirling Castle by the English had failed, Jamie knew the Battle of Falkirk had succeeded, ending in victory for the Scots. But what had come after?

When we rode at last into the cobbled gray street of the Royal Mile, Jamie went at once to the army's headquarters, leaving me to go with Mary to Alex Randall's quarters. We hurried up the street together, barely speaking, both too afraid of what we might find.

He was there, and I saw Mary's knees give way as she entered the room and collapsed by his bed. Startled from a doze, he opened his eyes and blinked once, then Alex Randall's face blazed as though he had received a heavenly visitation.

"Oh, God!" he kept muttering brokenly into her hair. "Oh, God. I thought . . . oh, Lord, I had prayed . . . one more sight of you. Just one. Oh, Lord!"

Simply averting my gaze seemed insufficient; I went out onto the landing, and sat on the stairs for half an hour, resting my weary head on my knees.

When it seemed decent to return, I went back into the small room, grown grimy and cheerless again in the weeks of Mary's absence. I examined him, my hands gentle on the wasted flesh. I was surprised that he had lasted so long; it couldn't be much longer.

He saw the truth in my face, and nodded, unsurprised.

"I waited," he said softly, lying back in exhaustion on his pillows. "I hoped . . . she would come once more. I had no reason . . . but I prayed. And now it is answered. I shall die in peace now."

"Alex!" Mary's cry of anguish burst out of her as though his words had struck her a physical blow, but he smiled and pressed her hand.

"We have known it for a long time, my love," he whispered to her. "Don't despair. I will be with you always, watching you, loving you. Don't cry, my dearest." She brushed obediently at her pink-washed cheeks, but could do nothing to stem the tears that came streaming down them. Despite her obvious despair, she had never looked so blooming.

"Mrs. Fraser," Alex said, clearly mustering his strength to ask one more favor. "I must ask . . . tomorrow . . . will you come again, and bring your husband? It is important."

I hesitated for a moment. Whatever Jamie found out, he was going to want to leave Edinburgh immediately, to join the army and find the rest of his men. But surely one more day could make no difference to the outcome of the war—and I could not deny the appeal in the two pairs of eyes that looked at me so hopefully.

"We'll come," I said.

⟶

"I am a fool," Jamie grumbled, climbing the steep, cobbled streets to the wynd where Alex Randall had his lodgings. "We should have left yesterday, at once, as soon as we got back your pearls from the pawnbroker! D'ye no ken how far it is to Inverness? And we wi' little more than nags to get us there?"

"I know," I said impatiently. "But I promised. And if you'd seen him . . . well, you will see him in a moment, and then you'll understand."

"Mphm." But he held the street door for me and followed me up the winding stair of the decrepit building without further complaint.

Mary was half-sitting, half-lying on the bed. Still dressed in her tattered traveling clothes, she was holding Alex, cradling him fiercely against her bosom. She must have stayed with him so all night.

Seeing me, he gently freed himself from her grasp, patting her hands as he laid them aside. He propped himself on one elbow, face paler than the linen sheets on which he lay.

"Mrs. Fraser," he said. He smiled faintly, despite the sheen of unhealthy sweat and the gray pallor that betokened a bad attack.

"It was good of you to come," he said, gasping a little. He glanced beyond me. "Your husband . . . he is with you?"

As though in answer, Jamie stepped into the room behind me. Mary, stirred from her misery by the noise of our entry, glanced from me to Jamie, then rose to her feet, laying a hand timidly on his arm.

"I . . . we . . . n-need you, Lord Tuarach." I thought it was the stammer, more than the use of his title, that touched him. Though he was still grim-faced, some of the tension went out of him. He inclined his head courteously toward her.

"I asked your wife to bring you, my lord. I am dying, as you see." Alex Randall had pushed himself upright, sitting on the edge of the bed. His slender shins gleamed white as bone beneath the frayed hem of his nightshirt. The toes, long, slim, and bloodless, were shadowed with the bluing of poor circulation.

I had seen death often enough before, in all its forms, but this was always the worst—and the best; a man who met death with knowledge and courage, while the healer's futile arts fell aside. Futile or not, I rummaged through the contents of my case for the digitalin I had made for him. I had several infusions, in varying strengths, a spectrum of brown liquids in glass vials. I chose the darkest vial without hesitation; I could hear his breath bubbling through the water in his lungs.

It wasn't digitalin, but his purpose that sustained him now, lighting him with a glow as though a candle burned behind the waxy skin of his face. I had seen that a few times before, too; the man—or woman—whose will was strong enough to override for a time the imperatives of the body.

I thought that was perhaps how some ghosts were made; where a will and a purpose had survived, heedless of the frail flesh that fell by the wayside, unable to sustain life long enough. I didn't much want to be haunted by Alex Randall;

that, among other reasons, was why I had made Jamie come with me today.

Jamie himself appeared to be coming to similar conclusions.

"Aye," he said softly. "I do see. Do ye ask aught of me?"

Alex nodded, closing his eyes briefly. He lifted the vial I handed him and drank, shuddering briefly at the bitter taste. He opened his eyes and smiled at Jamie.

"The indulgence of your presence only. I promise I shall not detain you long. We are waiting for one more person."

While we waited, I did what I could for Alex Randall, which under the circumstances was not much. The foxglove infusion again, and a bit of camphor to help ease his breathing. He seemed a little better after the administration of such medicine as I had, but placing my homemade stethoscope against the sunken chest, I could hear the labored thud of his heart, interrupted by such frequent flutters and palpitations that I expected it to stop at any moment.

Mary held his hand throughout, and he kept his eyes fixed on her, as though memorizing every line of her face. It seemed almost an intrusion to be in the same room with them.

The door opened, and Jack Randall stood on the threshold. He looked uncomprehendingly at me and Mary for a moment, then his gaze lighted on Jamie and he turned to stone. Jamie met his eyes squarely, then turned, nodding toward the bed.

Seeing that haggard face, Jack Randall crossed the room rapidly and fell on his knees beside the bed.

"Alex!" he said. "My God, Alex . . ."

"It's all right," his brother said. He held Jack's face between frail hands and smiled at him, trying to reassure him. "It's all right, Johnny," he said.

I put a hand under Mary's elbow, gently urging her off the bed. Whatever Jack Randall might be, he deserved a few last words in privacy with his brother. Stunned with despair, she didn't resist, but came with me to the far side of the room, where I perched her on a stool. I poured a little water from the ewer and wet my handkerchief. I tried to give it to her to swab her eyes, but she simply sat, clutching it lifelessly.

Sighing, I took it and wiped her face, smoothing her hair as much as I could.

There was a small, choked sound from behind that made me glance toward the bed. Jack, still on his knees, had his face buried in his brother's lap, while Alex stroked his head, holding one of his hands.

"John," he said. "You'll know that I do not ask this lightly. But for the sake of your love for me . . ." He broke off to cough, the effort flushing his cheeks with hectic color.

I felt Jamie's body stiffen still further, if such a thing were possible. Jonathan Randall stiffened, too, as though he felt the force of Jamie's eyes upon him, but didn't look up.

"Alex," he said quietly. He laid a hand on his younger brother's shoulder, as though to quiet the cough. "Don't trouble your mind, Alex. You know you needn't ask; I'll do whatever you wish. Is it the—the girl?" He glanced in Mary's direction, but couldn't quite bring himself to look at her.

Alex nodded, still coughing.

"It's all right," John said. He put both hands on Alex's shoulders, trying to ease him back on the pillow. "I won't let her want for anything. Put your mind at rest."

Jamie looked down at me, eyes wide. I shook my head slowly, feeling the hair prickle from my neck to the base of my spine. Everything made sense now; the bloom on Mary's cheeks, despite her distress, and her apparent willingness to wed the wealthy Jew of London.

"It isn't money," I said. "She's with child. He wants . . ." I stopped, clearing my throat, "I think he wants you to marry her."

Alex nodded, eyes still closed. He breathed heavily for a moment, then opened them, bright pools of hazel, fixed on his brother's stunned and uncomprehending face.

"Yes," he said. "John . . . Johnny, I need you to take care of her for me. I want . . . my child to have the Randall name. You can . . . give them some position in the world— so much more than I could." He reached out a hand, groping, and Mary seized it, clutching it to her bosom as though it were a life preserver. He smiled tenderly at her, and stretched up a hand to touch the shiny, dark ringlets that fell by her cheek, hiding her face.

"Mary. I wish . . . well, you know what I wish, my dear;

so many things. And so many things I am sorry for. But I cannot regret the love between us. Having known such joy, I would die content, save for my fear that you might be exposed to shame and disgrace."

"I don't care!" Mary burst out fiercely. "I don't care who knows!"

"But I care for you," Alex said, softly. He stretched out a hand to his brother, who took it after a moment's hesitation. Then he brought them together, laying Mary's hand in Randall's. Mary's lay inert, and Jack Randall's stiff, like a dead fish on a wooden slab, but Alex pressed his hands tightly around the two, pressing them together.

"I give you to each other, my dear ones," he said softly. He looked from one face to the other, each reflecting the horror of the suggestion, submerged in the overwhelming grief of impending loss.

"But . . ." For the first time in our acquaintance, I saw Jonathan Randall completely at a loss for words.

"Good." It was almost a whisper. Alex opened his eyes and let out the breath he had been holding, smiling at his brother. "There is not much time. I shall marry you myself. Now. That is why I asked Mrs. Fraser to bring her husband—if you will be witness with your wife, sir?" He looked up at Jamie, who, after a moment's stunned immobility, nodded his head like an automation.

I do not believe I have ever seen three people look so entirely wretched.

Alex was so weak that his brother, with a face like stone, had to help him, tying his minister's high white stock about the pallid throat. Jonathan himself looked little better. Gaunt from illness, the lines in his face were carved so deep that he looked years older than his age, and his eyes peered out from deep sockets like caves of bone. Impeccably attired as always, he looked like a badly made tailor's dummy, features carelessly hacked from a block of wood.

As for Mary, she sat miserably on the bed, weeping helplessly into the folds of her cloak, hair disheveled and static with electricity. I did what I could for her, straightening her gown and combing out her hair. She sat drearily sniffling, her eyes fixed on Alex.

Bracing himself with a hand on the bureau, Alex groped

in the drawer, coming out at last with his large *Book of Common Prayer*. It was too heavy for him to hold open before him in the normal fashion. He couldn't stand, but sat heavily on the bed, holding the book open on his knees. He closed his eyes, breathing heavily, and a drop of sweat fell from his face, making a blot on the page.

"Dearly beloved," Alex began, and I hoped for his own sake, as well as everyone else's, that he was using the short form of the ceremony.

Mary had stopped crying, but her nose was red and shiny in her white face, and a small snail track showed on her upper lip. Jonathan saw it, and expressionless, pulled a large square of linen from his sleeve and offered it to her silently.

She took it with a faint nod, not looking at him, and carelessly mopped her face.

"I will," she said, when the time came, as though not caring at all what she said now.

Jack Randall made his promises in a firm voice, but one remote from the scene. It gave me an odd feeling to see a marriage contracted between two people who were quite unaware of each other; the complete attention of both was focused on the man who sat before them, eyes fixed on the pages of his book.

It was done. Congratulations to the bridal pair hardly seemed in order, and there was an awkward silence. Jamie glanced at me questioningly and I shrugged. I had fainted immediately after marrying him, and Mary looked rather as though she meant to follow my example.

The act complete, Alex sat quite still for a moment. He smiled slightly, and looked deliberately round the room, his eyes resting for a moment on each face in turn. Jonathan, Jamie, Mary, and me. I saw the glow in those soft hazel depths as his glance met mine. The candle's stub grew low, but the last of the wick blazed up, for a moment bright and strong.

His gaze lingered on Mary's face, then he closed his eyes briefly, as though he could not stand to look upon her, and I could hear the slow, labored rasp of his breathing. The glow of his skin was blanching and fading, the candle guttering.

Without opening his eyes, he reached up a hand, groping blindly. Jonathan grasped it, caught him behind the shoulders and eased him slowly back, onto the pillows. The long hands, smooth as a boy's, twitched uneasily, whiter than the shirt they lay against.

"Mary." The blue lips moved in a whisper, and she trapped the nervous hands between her own, holding them still against her bosom.

"I'm here, Alex. Oh, Alex, I'm here!" She bent close to him, murmuring in his ear. The movement forced Jonathan Randall back a bit, so that he stepped away from the bed. He stood, staring expressionlessly down.

The heavy, domed lids lifted once more, only halfway this time, seeking a face and finding it.

"Johnny. So . . . good to me. Always, Johnny."

Mary bent over him, the shadow of her fallen hair hiding his face. Jonathan Randall stood, still as one of the stones in a henge, watching his brother and his wife. There was no sound in the room but the whisper of the fire and the soft sobbing of Mary Randall.

I felt a touch on my shoulder, and looked up at Jamie. He nodded in Mary's direction.

"Stay with her," he said quietly. "It wilna be long, will it?"

"No."

He nodded. Then he took a deep breath, let it out slowly, and crossed the room to Jonathan Randall. He took the frozen figure by one arm and turned him gently toward the door.

"Come, man," he said quietly. "I'll see ye safe to your quarters."

The crooked door creaked to as he left, assisting Jack Randall to the place where he would spend his wedding night, alone.

———◄———

I closed the door of our inn room behind me and leaned against it, exhausted. It was first dark outside, and the watchman's cries echoed down the street.

Jamie was by the window, watching for me. He came to me at once, pulling me tight against him before I had even got my cloak off. I sagged against him, grateful for his warmth and solid strength. He scooped me up with an arm beneath my knees and carried me to the window seat.

"Have a bit of a drink, Sassenach," he urged. "Ye look all in, and no wonder." He took the flask from the table and mixed something that appeared to be brandy and water without the water.

I shoved a hand tiredly through my hair. It had been just after breakfast when we went to the room in Ladywalk Wynd; now it was past six o'clock. It seemed as though I had been gone for days.

"It wasn't long, poor chap. It was as though he was only waiting to see her safely taken care of. I sent word to her aunt's house; the aunt and two cousins came to fetch her. They'll take care of . . . him." I sipped gratefully at the brandy. It burned my throat and the fumes rose inside my head like fog on the moors, but I didn't care.

"Well," I said, attempting a smile, "at least we know Frank is safe, after all."

Jamie glowered down at me, ruddy brows nearly touching each other.

"Damn Frank!" he said ferociously. "Damn all Randalls! Damn Jack Randall, and damn Mary Hawkins Randall, and damn Alex Randall—er, God rest his soul, I mean," he amended hastily, crossing himself.

"I thought you didn't begrudge—" I started. He glared at me.

"I lied."

He grabbed me by the shoulders and shook me slightly, holding me at arm's length.

"And damn you, too, Claire Randall Fraser, while I'm at it!" he said. "Damn right I begrudge! I grudge every memory of yours that doesna hold me, and every tear ye've shed for another, and every second you've spent in another man's bed! Damn you!" He knocked the brandy glass from my hand—accidentally, I think—pulled me to him and kissed me hard.

He drew back enough to shake me again.

"You're mine, damn ye, Claire Fraser! Mine, and I wilna share ye, with a man or a memory, or anything whatever, so long as we both shall live. You'll no mention the man's name to me again. D'ye hear?" He kissed me fiercely to emphasize the point. "Did ye hear me?" he asked, breaking off.

"Yes," I said, with some difficulty. "If you'd . . . stop . . . shaking me, I might . . . answer you."

Rather sheepishly, he released his grip on my shoulders.

"I'm sorry, Sassenach. It's only . . . God, why did ye . . . well, aye, I see why . . . but did you have to—" I interrupted this incoherent sputtering by putting my hand behind his head and drawing him down to me.

"Yes," I said firmly, releasing him. "I had to. But it's over now." I loosened the ties of my cloak and let it fall back off my shoulders to the floor. He bent to pick it up, but I stopped him.

"Jamie," I said. "I'm tired. Will you take me to bed?"

He drew a deep breath and let it out slowly, staring down at me, eyes sunk deep with tiredness and strain.

"Aye," he said softly, at last. "Aye, I will."

He was silent, and rough at the start, the edges of his anger sharpening his love.

"Ooh!" I said, at one point.

"Christ, I'm sorry, *mo nighean donn.* I couldna . . ."

"It's all right." I stopped his apologies with my mouth and held him tightly, feeling the wrath ebb away as the tenderness grew between us. He didn't break away from the kiss, but held himself motionless, gently exploring my lips, the tip of his tongue caressing, barely stroking.

I touched his tongue with my own, and held his face between my hands. He hadn't shaved since morning, and the faint red stubble rasped pleasantly beneath my fingertips.

He lowered himself and rolled slightly to one side, so as not to crush me with his weight, and we went on, touching all along our lengths, joined in closeness, speaking in silent tongues.

Alive, and one. We are one, and while we love, death will never touch us. "The grave's a fine and private place / But none, I think, do there embrace." Alex Randall lay cold in his bed, and Mary Randall alone in hers. But we were here together, and no one and nothing mattered beyond that fact.

He grasped my hips, large hands warm on my skin, and pulled me toward him, and the shudder that went through me went through him, as though we shared one flesh.

I woke in the night, still in his arms, and knew he was not asleep.

"Go back to sleep, *mo nighean donn.*" His voice was soft,

low and soothing, but with a catch that made me reach up to feel the wetness on his cheeks.

"What is it, love?" I whispered. "Jamie, I do love you."

"I know it," he said quietly. "I do know it, my own. Let me tell ye in your sleep how much I love you. For there's no so much I can be saying to ye while ye wake, but the same poor words, again and again. While ye sleep in my arms, I can say things to ye that would be daft and silly waking, and your dreams will know the truth of them. Go back to sleep, *mo nighean donn.*"

I turned my head, enough that my lips brushed the base of his throat, where his pulse beat slow beneath the small three-cornered scar. Then I laid my head upon his chest and gave my dreams up to his keeping.

46

Timor Mortis Conturbat Me

There were men and their traces all around, as we made our way north, following the retreat of the Highland army. We passed small groups of men on foot, walking doggedly, heads down against the windy rain. Others lay in the ditches and under the hedgerows, too exhausted to go on. Equipment and weapons had been abandoned along the way; here a wagon lay overturned, its sacks of flour split and ruined in the wet, there a brace of small culverin stood beneath a tree, twin barrels gleaming darkly in the shadows.

The weather had been bad all the way, delaying us. It was April 13, and I rode and walked with a constant, gnawing feeling of dread beneath my heart. Lord George and the clan chieftains, the Prince and his chief advisers—all were at Culloden House, or so we had been told by one of the MacDonalds that we met along the way. He knew little more than that, and we did not detain him; the man stumbled away into the mist, moving like a zombie. Rations had been short when I was captured by the English a month gone; matters had plainly gone from bad to worse. The men we saw moved slowly, many of them staggering with exhaustion and starvation. But they moved stubbornly north, all the same, following their Prince's orders. Moving toward the place the Scots called Drumossie Moor. Toward Culloden.

At one point, the road became too bad for the faltering ponies. They would have to be led around the outer edge of a small wood, through the wet spring heather, to where the road became passable, a half-mile beyond.

"It will be swifter to walk through the wood," Jamie told me, taking the reins from my numbed hand. He nodded toward the small grove of pine and oak, where the sweet, cool smell of wet leaves rose from the soaked ground. "D'ye go that way, Sassenach; we'll meet wi' ye on the other side."

I was too tired to argue. Putting one foot in front of the other was a distinct effort, and the effort would undoubtedly be less on the smooth layer of leaves and fallen pine needles in the wood than through the boggy, treacherous heather.

It was quiet in the wood, the whine of the wind softened by the pine boughs overhead. What rain came through the branches pattered lightly on the layers of leathery fallen oak leaves, rustling and crackled, even when wet.

He lay only a few feet from the far edge of the wood, next to a big gray boulder. The pale green lichens of the rock were the same color as his tartan, and its browns blended with the fallen leaves that had drifted half across him. He seemed so much a part of the wood that I might have stumbled over him, had I not been stopped by the patch of brilliant blue.

Soft as velvet, the strange fungus spread its cloak over the naked, cold white limbs. It followed the curve of bone and sinew, sending up small trembling fronds, like the grasses and trees of a forest, invading barren land.

It was an electric, vivid blue, stark and alien. I had never seen it, but had heard of it, from an old soldier I had nursed, who had fought in the trenches of the first world war.

"We called it corpse-candle," he had told me. "Blue, bright blue. You never see it anywhere but on a battlefield—on dead men." He had looked up at me, old eyes puzzled beneath the white bandage.

"I always wondered where it lives, between wars."

In the air, perhaps, its invisible spores waiting to seize an opportunity, I thought. The color was brilliant, incongruous, bright as the woad with which this man's ancestors had painted themselves before going forth to war.

A breeze passed through the wood, ruffling the man's hair. It stirred and rose, silky and lifelike. There was a crunch of leaves behind me, and I started convulsively from the trance in which I had stood, staring at the corpse.

Jamie stood beside me, looking down. He said nothing; only took me by the elbow and led me from the wood, leaving the dead man behind, clothed in the saprophytic hues of war and sacrifice.

It was mid-morning of April 15 by the time we came to Culloden House, having pushed ourselves and our ponies unmercifully to reach it. We approached it from the south, com-

ing first through a cluster of outbuildings. There was a stir—
almost a frenzy—of men on the road, but the stableyard was
curiously deserted.

Jamie dismounted and handed his reins to Murtagh.

"D'ye wait here a moment," he said. "Something doesna
seem quite right here."

Murtagh glanced at the door of the stables, standing
slightly ajar, and nodded. Fergus, mounted behind the clansman, would have followed Jamie, but Murtagh prevented him
with a curt word.

Stiff from the ride, I slid off my own horse and followed
Jamie, slipping in the mud of the stableyard. There *was* something odd about the stableyard. Only as I followed him
through the door of the stable building did I realize what it
was—it was too quiet.

Everything inside was still; the building was cold and
dim, without the usual warmth and stir of a stable. Still, the
place was not entirely devoid of life; a dark figure stirred in
the gloom, too big to be a rat or a fox.

"Who is that?" Jamie said, stepping forward to put me
behind him automatically. "Alec? Is it you?"

The figure in the hay raised its head slowly, and the plaid
fell back. The Master of Horse of Castle Leoch had but one
eye; the other, lost in an accident many years before, was
patched with black cloth. Normally, one eye sufficed him;
brisk and snapping blue, it was enough to command the obedience of stable-lads and horses, grooms and riders alike.

Now Alec MacMahon MacKenzie's eye was dull as dusty
slate. The broad, once vigorous body was curled in upon itself, and the cheeks of his face were sunk with the apathy of
starvation.

Knowing the old man suffered from arthritis in damp
weather, Jamie squatted beside him to prevent him rising.

"What has been happening?" he asked. "We are newly
come; what is happening here?"

It seemed to take Old Alec a long time to absorb the
question, assimilate it, and form his reply into words; perhaps
it was only the stillness of the empty, shadowed stable that
made his words ring hollow when they finally came.

"It has all gone to pot," he said. "They marched to Nairn
two nights ago, and came fleeing back yesterday. His High-

ness has said they will take a stand on Culloden; Lord George is there now, with what troops he has gathered."

I couldn't repress a small moan at the name of Culloden. It was here, then. Despite everything, it had come to pass, and we were here.

A shiver passed through Jamie, as well; I saw the red hairs standing erect on his forearms, but his voice betrayed nothing of the anxiety he must feel.

"The troops—they are ill-provisioned to fight. Does Lord George not realize they must have rest, and food?"

The creaking sound from Old Alec might have been the shade of a laugh.

"What His Lordship knows makes little difference, lad. His Highness has taken command of the army. And His Highness says we shall stand against the English on Drumossie. As for food—" His old-man's eyebrows were thick and bushy, gone altogether white in the last year, with coarse hairs sprouting from them. One brow raised now, heavily, as though even this small change of expression was an exhaustion. One gnarled hand stirred in his lap, gesturing toward the empty stalls.

"They ate the horses last month," he said, simply. "There's been little else, since."

Jamie stood abruptly, and leaned against the wall, head bowed in shock. I couldn't see his face, but his body was stiff as the boards of the stable.

"Aye," he said at last. "Aye. My men—did they have their fair share of the meat? Donas . . . he was . . . a good-sized horse." He spoke quietly, but I saw from the sudden sharpness of Alec's one-eyed glance that he heard as well as I did the effort that kept Jamie's voice from breaking.

The old man rose slowly from the hay, crippled body moving with painful deliberation. He set one gnarled hand on Jamie's shoulder; the arthritic fingers could not close, but the hand rested there, a comforting blunt weight.

"They didna take Donas," he said quietly. "They kept him—for Prince *Tcharlach* to ride, on his triumphal return to Edinburgh. O'Sullivan said it wouldna be . . . fitting . . . for His Highness to walk."

Jamie covered his face in his hands and stood shaking against the boards of the empty stall.

"I am a fool," he said at last, gasping to recover his breath. "Oh, God, I am a fool." He dropped his hands, showing his face, tears streaking through the grime of travel. He dashed the back of his hand across his cheek, but the moisture continued to overflow from his eyes, as though it were a process quite out of his control.

"The cause is lost, my men are being taken to slaughter, there are dead men rotting in the wood . . . and I am weeping for a horse! Oh, God," he whispered, shaking his head. "I am a fool."

Old Alec heaved a sigh, and his hand slid heavily down Jamie's arm.

"It's as well that ye still can, lad," he said. "I'm past it, myself."

The old man folded one leg awkwardly at the knee and eased himself down once more. Jamie stood for a moment, looking down at Old Alec. The tears still streamed unchecked down his face, but it was like rain washing over a sheet of polished granite. Then he took my elbow, and turned away without a word.

I looked back at Alec when we reached the stable door. He sat quite still, a dark, hunched shape shawled in his plaid, the one blue eye unseeing as the other.

Men sprawled through the house, worn to exhaustion, seeking oblivion from gnawing hunger and the knowledge of certain and imminent disaster. There were no women here; those chiefs whose womenfolk had accompanied them had sent the ladies safely away—the coming doom cast a long shadow.

Jamie left me with a murmured word outside the door that led to the Prince's temporary quarters. My presence would help nothing. I walked softly through the house, murmurous with the heavy breathing of sleeping men, the air thick with the dullness of despair.

At the top of the house, I found a small lumber-room. Crowded with junk and discarded furniture, it was otherwise unoccupied. I crept into this warren of oddities, feeling much like a small rodent, seeking refuge from a world in which huge and mysterious forces were let loose to destruction.

There was one small window, filled with the misty gray morning. I rubbed dirt away from one pane with the corner of my cloak, but there was nothing to be seen but the encompassing mist. I leaned my forehead against the cold glass. Somewhere out there was Culloden Field, but I saw nothing but the dim silhouette of my own reflection.

News of the gruesome and mysterious death of the Duke of Sandringham had reached Prince Charles, I knew; we had heard of it from almost everyone we spoke to as we passed to the north and it became safe for us to show ourselves again. What exactly had we done? I wondered. Had we doomed the Jacobite cause for good and all in that one night's adventure, or had we inadvertently saved Charles Stuart from an English trap? I drew a squeaking finger in a line down the misty glass, chalking up one more thing I would never find out.

It seemed a very long time before I heard a step on the uncarpeted boards of the stair outside my refuge. I came to the door to find Jamie coming onto the landing. One look at his face was enough.

"Alec was right," he said, without preliminaries. The bones of his face were stark beneath the skin, made prominent by hunger, sharpened by anger. "The troops are moving to Culloden—as they can. They havena slept or eaten in two days, there is no ordnance for the cannon—but they are going." The anger erupted suddenly and he slammed his fist down on a rickety table. A cascade of small brass dishes from the pile of household rubble woke the echoes of the attic with an ungodly clatter.

With an impatient gesture, he snatched the dirk from his belt and jabbed it violently into the table, where it stood, quivering with the force of the blow.

"The country folk say that if ye see blood on your dirk, it means death." He drew in his breath with a hiss, fist clenched on the table. "Well, I have seen it! So have they all. They know—Kilmarnock, Lochiel, and the rest. And no bit of good does the seeing of it do!"

He bent his head, hands braced on the table, staring at the dirk. He seemed much too large for the confines of the room, an angry smoldering presence that might break suddenly into flame. Instead, he flung up his hands, and threw himself onto a decrepit settle, where he sat, head buried in his hands.

"Jamie," I said, and swallowed. I could barely speak the next words, but they had to be said. I had known what news he would bring, and I had thought of what might still be done. "Jamie. There's only one thing left—only the one possibility."

His head was bent, forehead resting on his knuckles. He shook his head, not looking at me.

"There is no way," he said. "He's bent on it. Murray has tried to turn him, so has Lochiel. Balmerino. Me. But the men are standing on the plain this hour. Cumberland has set out for Drumossie. There is no way."

The healing arts are powerful ones, and any physician versed in the use of substances that heal knows also the power of those that harm. I had given Colum the cyanide he had not had time to use, and taken back the deadly vial from the table by the bed where his body lay. It was in my box now, the crudely distilled crystals a dull brownish-white, deceptively harmless in appearance.

My mouth was so dry that I couldn't speak at once. There was a little wine left in my flask; I drank it, the acid taste like bile on my tongue.

"There is one way," I said. "Only one."

Jamie's head stayed sunk in his hands. It had been a long ride, and the shock of Alec's news had added depression to his tiredness. We had detoured to find his men, or most of them, a miserable, ragged crew, indistinguishable from the skeletal Frasers of Lovat who surrounded them. The interview with Charles was far beyond the last straw.

"Aye?" he said.

I hesitated, but had to speak. The possibility had to be mentioned; whether he—or I—could bring ourselves to it or not.

"It's Charles Stuart," I said, at last. "It's him—everything. The battle, the war—everything depends on him, do you see?"

"Aye?" Jamie was looking up at me now, bloodshot eyes quizzical.

"If he were dead. . . ." I whispered at last.

Jamie's eyes closed, and the last vestiges of blood drained from his face.

"If he were to die . . . now. Today. Or tonight. Jamie, without Charles, there's nothing to fight for. No one to order the men to Culloden. There wouldn't be a battle."

The long muscles of his throat rippled briefly as he swallowed. He opened his eyes and stared at me, appalled.

"Christ," he whispered. "Christ, ye canna mean it."

My hand closed on the smoky, gold-mounted crystal around my neck.

They had called me to attend the Prince, before Falkirk. O'Sullivan, Tullibardine, and the others. His Highness was ill —an indisposition, they said. I had seen Charles, made him bare his breast and arms, examined his mouth and the whites of his eyes.

It was scurvy, and several of the other diseases of malnutrition. I said as much.

"Nonsense!" said Sheridan, outraged. "His Highness cannot suffer from the yeuk, like a common peasant!"

"He's been eating like one," I retorted. "Or rather worse than one." The "peasants" were forced to eat onions and cabbage, having nothing else. Scorning such poor fare, His Highness and his advisers ate meat—and little else. Looking around the circle of scared, resentful faces, I saw few that didn't show symptoms of the lack of fresh food. Loose and missing teeth, soft, bleeding gums, the pus-filled, itching follicles of "the yeuk" that so lavishly decorated His Highness's white skin.

I was loath to surrender any of my precious supply of rose hips and dried berries, but had offered, reluctantly, to make the Prince a tea of them. The offer had been rejected, with a minimum of courtesy, and I understood that Archie Cameron had been summoned, with his bowl of leeches and his lancet, to see whether a letting of the Royal blood would relieve the Royal itch.

"I could do it," I said. My heart was beating heavily in my chest, making it hard to breathe. "I could mix him a draught. I think I could persuade him to take it."

"And if he should die upon drinking your medicine? Christ, Claire! They would kill ye on the spot!"

I folded my hands beneath my arms, trying to warm them.

"D-does that matter?" I asked, desperately trying to

steady my voice. The truth was that it did. Just at the moment, my own life weighed a good deal more in the balance than did the hundreds I might save. I clenched my fists, shaking with terror, a mouse in the jaws of the trap.

Jamie was at my side in an instant. My legs didn't work very well; he half-carried me to the broken settle and sat down with me, his arms wrapped tight around me.

"You've the courage of a lion, *mo nighean donn*," he murmured in my ear. "Of a bear, a wolf! But you know I wilna let ye do it."

The shivering eased slightly, though I still felt cold, and sick with the horror of what I was saying.

"There might be another way," I said. "There's little food, but what there is goes to the Prince. I think it might not be difficult to add something to his dish without being noticed; things are so disorganized." This was true; all over the house, officers lay sleeping on tables and floors, still clad in their boots, too tired to lay aside their arms. The house was in chaos, with constant comings and goings. It would be a simple matter to distract a servant long enough to add a deadly powder to the evening dish.

The immediate terror had receded slightly, but the awfulness of my suggestion lingered like poison, chilling my own blood. Jamie's arm tightened briefly around my shoulders, then fell away as he contemplated the situation.

The death of Charles Stuart would not end the matter of the Rising; things had gone much too far for that. Lord George Murray, Balmerino, Kilmarnock, Lochiel, Clanranald —all of us were traitors, lives and property forfeit to the Crown. The Highland army was in tatters; without the figurehead of Charles to rally to, it would dissipate like smoke. The English, terrorized and humiliated at Preston and Falkirk, would not hesitate to pursue the fugitives, seeking to retrieve their lost honor and wash out the insult in blood.

There was little chance that Henry of York, Charles's pious younger brother, already bound by churchly vows, would take his brother's place to continue the fight for restoration. There was nothing ahead but catastrophe and wreck, and no possible way to avert it. All that might be salvaged now was the lives of the men who would die on the moor tomorrow.

It was Charles who had chosen to fight at Culloden, Charles whose stubborn, shortsighted autocracy had defied the advice of his own generals and gone to invade England. And whether Sandringham had meant his offer for good or ill, it had died with him. There was no support from the South; such English Jacobites as there were did not rally as expected to the banner of their king. Forced against his will to retreat, Charles had chosen this last stubborn stand, to place ill-armed, exhausted, starving men in a battle line on a rain-soaked moor, to face the wrath of Cumberland's cannon fire. If Charles Stuart were dead, the battle of Culloden might not take place. One life, against two thousand. One life—but that life a Royal one, and taken not in battle, but in cold blood.

The small room where we sat had a hearth, but a fire had not been lit—there was no fuel. Jamie sat gazing at it as though seeking an answer in invisible flames. Murder. Not only murder, but regicide. Not only murder, but the killing of a sometime friend.

And yet—the clansmen of the Highlands shivered already on the open moor, shifting in their serried ranks as the plan of battle was adjusted, rearranged, reordered, as more men drifted to join them. Among them were the MacKenzies of Leoch, the Frasers of Beauly, four hundred men of Jamie's blood. And the thirty men of Lallybroch, his own.

His face was blank, immobile as he thought, but the hands laced together on his knee knotted tight with the struggle. The crippled fingers and the straight strove together, twisting. I sat beside him, scarcely daring to breathe, awaiting his decision.

At last the breath went from him in an almost inaudible sigh, and he turned to me, a look of unutterable sadness in his eyes.

"I cannot," he whispered. His hand touched my face briefly, cupping my cheek. "Would God that I could, Sassenach. I cannot do it."

The wave of relief that washed through me robbed me of speech, but he saw what I felt, and grasped my hands between his own.

"Oh, God, Jamie, I'm glad of it!" I whispered.

He bowed his head over my hands. I turned my head to lay my cheek against his hair, and froze.

In the doorway, watching me with a look of absolute revulsion, was Dougal MacKenzie.

The last months had aged him; Rupert's death, the sleepless nights of fruitless argument, the strains of the hard campaign, and now the bitterness of imminent defeat. There were gray hairs in the russet beard, a gray look to his skin, and deep lines in his face that had not been there in November. With a shock, I realized that he looked like his brother, Colum. He had wanted to lead, Dougal MacKenzie. Now he had inherited the chieftainship, and was paying its price.

"Filthy . . . traitorous . . . whoring . . . *witch*!"

Jamie jerked as though he had been shot, face gone white as the sleet outside. I sprang to my feet, overturning the bench with a clatter that echoed through the room.

Dougal MacKenzie advanced on me slowly, putting aside the folds of his cloak, so that the hilt of his sword was freed to his hand. I hadn't heard the door behind me open; it must have stood ajar. How long had he been on the other side, listening?

"You," he said softly. "I should have known it; from the first I saw ye, I should have known." His eyes were fixed on me, something between horror and fury in the cloudy green depths.

There was a sudden stir in the air beside me; Jamie was there, a hand on my arm, urging me back behind him.

"Dougal," he said. "It isna what ye think, man. It's—"

"No?" Dougal cut in. His gaze left me for a second, and I shrank behind Jamie, grateful for the respite.

"Not what I think?" he said, still speaking softly. "I hear the woman urging ye to foul murder—to the murder of your Prince! Not only vile murder, but treason as well! And ye tell me I havena heard it?" He shook his head, the tangled russet curls lank and greasy on his shoulders. Like the rest of us, he was starving; the bones jutted in his face, but his eyes burned from their shadowy orbits.

"I dinna blame ye, lad," he said. His voice was suddenly weary, and I remembered that he was a man in his fifties. "It isna your fault, Jamie. She's bewitched ye—anyone can see that." His mouth twisted as he looked again at me.

"Aye, I ken weel enough how it's been for ye. She's worked the same sorcery on me, betimes." His eyes raked over me, burning. "A murdering, lying slut, would take a man by the cock and lead him to his doom, wi' her claws sunk deep in his balls. That's the spell that they lay on ye, lad—she and the other witch. Take ye to their beds and steal the soul from you as ye lie sleeping wi' your head on their breasts. They take your soul, and eat your manhood, Jamie."

His tongue darted out and wetted his lips. He was still staring at me, and his hand tightened on the hilt of his sword.

"Stand aside, laddie. I'll free ye of the *sassenach* whore."

Jamie stepped in front of me, momentarily blocking Dougal from my view.

"You're tired, Dougal," he said, speaking calmly, soothingly. "Tired, and hearin' things, man. D'ye go down now. I shall—"

He had no chance to finish. Dougal wasn't listening to him; the deep-set green eyes were fixed on my face, and the MacKenzie chief had drawn the dirk from its sheath at his waist.

"I shall cut your throat," he said to me softly. "I should ha' done it when first I saw ye. It would have saved us all a great grief."

I wasn't sure that he wasn't right, but that didn't mean I intended to let him remedy the matter. I took three quick steps back, and fetched up hard against the table.

"Get back, man!" Jamie thrust himself before me, holding up a shielding forearm as Dougal advanced on me.

The MacKenzie chieftain shook his head, bull-like, red-rimmed eyes fixed on me.

"She's mine," he said hoarsely. "Witch. Traitoress. Step aside, lad. I wouldna harm ye, but by God, if ye shield that woman, I shall kill you, too, foster son or no."

He lunged past Jamie, grabbing my arm. Exhausted, starved, and aging as he was, he was still a formidable man, and his fingers bit deep into my flesh.

I yelped with pain, and kicked frantically at him as he jerked me toward him. He snatched at my hair and caught it, forcing my head hard back. His breath was hot and sour on my face. I shrieked and struck at him, digging my nails into his cheek in an effort to get free.

The air exploded from his lungs as Jamie's fist struck him in the ribs, and his grip on my hair tore loose as Jamie's other fist came down in a numbing blow on the point of his shoulder. Suddenly freed, I fell back against the table, whimpering with shock and pain.

Dougal whirled to face Jamie then, dropping into a fighter's crouch, the dirk held blade upward.

"Let it be, then," he said, breathing heavily. He swayed slightly from side to side, shifting his weight as he sought the advantage. "Blood will tell. Ye damned Fraser spawn. Treachery runs in your blood. Come here to me, fox cub. I'll kill ye quick, for your mother's sake."

There was little room for maneuver in the small attic. No room to draw a sword; with his dirk stuck fast in the tabletop, Jamie was effectively unarmed. He matched Dougal's stance, eyes watchful, fixed on the point of the menacing dirk.

"Put it down, Dougal," he said. "If ye bear my mother in mind, then listen to me, for her sake!"

The MacKenzie made no answer, but jabbed suddenly, a ripping blow aimed upward.

Jamie dodged aside, dodged again the wide-armed sweep that came from the other side. Jamie had the agility of youth on his side—but Dougal held the knife.

Dougal closed with a rush, and the dirk slid up Jamie's side, ripping his shirt, scoring a dark line in his flesh. With a hiss of pain, he jerked back, grabbing for Dougal's wrist, catching it as the blade struck down.

The dull gleam of the blade flashed once, disappeared between the struggling bodies. They strove together, locked like lovers, the air filled with the smell of male sweat and fury. The blade rose again, two hands grappling on its rounded hilt. A shift, and a jerk, a sudden grunt of effort, one of pain. Dougal stepped back, staggering, face congested and pouring sweat, the hilt of the dagger socketed at the base of his throat.

Jamie half-fell, gasping, and leaned against the table. His eyes were dark with shock, and his hair sweat-soaked, the rent edges of his shirt tinged with blood from the scratch.

There was a terrible sound from Dougal, a sound of shock and stifled breath. Jamie caught him as he tottered and fell, Dougal's weight bringing him to his knees. Dougal's head lay on Jamie's shoulder, Jamie's arms locked around his foster father.

I dropped to my knees beside them, reaching to help,

trying to get hold of Dougal. It was too late. The big body went limp, then spasmed, sliding out of Jamie's grasp. Dougal lay crumpled on the floor, muscles jerking with involuntary contractions, struggling like a fish out of water.

His head was pillowed on Jamie's thigh. One heave brought his face into view. It was contorted, and dark red, eyes gone to slits. His mouth moved continuously, saying something, talking with great force—but without sound, save the bubbling rasp from his ruined throat.

Jamie's face was ashen; apparently he could tell what Dougal was saying. He struggled violently, trying to hold the thrashing body still. There was a final spasm, then a dreadful rattling sound, and Dougal MacKenzie lay still, Jamie's hands clenched tight upon his shoulders, as though to prevent his rising again.

"Blessed Michael defend us!" The hoarse whisper came from the doorway. It was Willie Coulter MacKenzie, one of Dougal's men. He stared in stupefied horror at the body of his chief. A small puddle of urine was forming under it, creeping out from under the sprawled plaid. The man crossed himself, still staring.

"Willie." Jamie rose, passing a trembling hand across his face. "Willie." The man seemed struck dumb. He looked at Jamie in complete bewilderment, mouth open.

"I need one hour, man." Jamie had a hand on Willie Coulter's shoulder, easing him into the room. "An hour to see my wife safe. Then I shall come back to answer for this. I give ye my word, on my honor. But I must have an hour free. One hour. Will ye give me one hour, man, before ye speak?"

Willie licked dry lips, looking back and forth between the body of his chief and his chieftain's nephew, clearly frightened out of his wits. At last he nodded, plainly having no idea what to do, choosing to follow this request because no reasonable alternative presented itself.

"Good." Jamie swallowed heavily, and wiped his face on his plaid. He patted Willie on the shoulder. "Stay here, man. Pray for his soul"—he nodded toward the still form on the floor, not looking at it—"and for mine." He leaned past Willie to pry his dirk from the table, then pushed me before him, out the door and down the stairs.

Halfway down, he stopped, leaning against the wall with

his eyes closed. He drew deep, ragged breaths, as though he were about to faint, and I put my hands on his chest, alarmed. His heart was beating like a drum, and he was trembling, but after a moment, he drew himself upright, nodded at me, and took my arm.

"I need Murtagh," he said.

We found the clansman just outside, cowled in his plaid against the sleety rain, sitting in a dry spot beneath the eaves of the house. Fergus was curled up next to him, dozing, tired from the long ride.

Murtagh took one look at Jamie's face, and rose to his feet, dark and dour, ready for anything.

"I've killed Dougal MacKenzie," Jamie said bluntly, without preliminary.

Murtagh's face went quite blank for a moment, then his normal expression of wary grimness reasserted itself.

"Aye," he said. "What's to do, then?"

Jamie groped in his sporran and brought out a folded paper. His hands shook as he tried to unfold it, and I took it from him, spreading it out under the shelter of the eaves.

"Deed of Sasine" it said, at the top of the sheet. It was a short document, laid out in a few black lines, conveying title of the estate known as Broch Tuarach to one James Jacob Fraser Murray, said property to be held in trust and administered by the said James Murray's parents, Janet Fraser Murray and Ian Alastair Robert Murray, until the said James Murray's majority. Jamie's signature was at the bottom, and there were two blank spaces provided below, each with the word "Witness" written alongside. It was dated 1 July, 1745—a month before Charles Stuart had launched his rebellion on the shores of Scotland, and made Jamie Fraser a traitor to the Crown.

"I need ye to sign this, you and Claire," Jamie said, taking the note from me and handing it to Murtagh. "But it means forswearing yourself; I have nay right to ask it."

Murtagh's small black eyes scanned the deed quickly. "No," he said dryly. "No right—nor any need, either." He nudged Fergus with a foot, and the boy sat bolt upright, blinking.

"Nip into the house and fetch your chief ink and a quill, lad," Murtagh said. "And quick about it—go!"

Fergus shook his head once to clear it, glanced at Jamie for a confirming nod—and went.

Water was dripping from the eaves down the back of my neck. I shivered and drew the woolen arisaid closer around my shoulders. I wondered when Jamie had written the document. The false date made it seem the property had been transferred before Jamie became a traitor, with his goods and lands subject to seizure—if it was not questioned, the property would pass safely to small Jamie. Jenny's family at least would be safe, still in possession of land and farmhouse.

Jamie had seen the possible need for this; yet he had not executed the document before we left Lallybroch; he had hoped somehow to return, and claim his own place once again. Now that was impossible, but the estate might still be saved from seizure. There was no one to say when the document had really been signed—save the witnesses, me and Murtagh.

Fergus returned, panting, with a small glass inkpot and a ragged quill. We signed one at a time, leaning against the side of the house, careful to shake the quill first to keep the ink from dripping down. Murtagh went first; his middle name, I saw, was FitzGibbons.

"Will ye have me take it to your sister?" Murtagh asked as I shook the paper carefully to dry it.

Jamie shook his head. The rain made damp, coin-sized splotches on his plaid, and glittered on his lashes like tears.

"No. Fergus will take it."

"Me?" The boy's eyes went round with astonishment.

"You, man." Jamie took the paper from me, folded it, then knelt and tucked it inside Fergus's shirt.

"This must reach my sister—Madam Murray—without fail. It is worth more than my life, man—or yours."

Practically breathless with the enormity of the responsibility entrusted to him, Fergus stood up straight, hands clasped over his middle.

"I will not fail you, milord!"

A faint smile crossed Jamie's lips, and he rested a hand briefly on the smooth cap of Fergus's hair.

"I know that, man, and I am grateful," he said. He twisted the ring off his left hand; the cabochon ruby that had belonged to his father. "Here," he said, handing it to Fergus.

"Go to the stables, and show this to the old man ye'll see there. Tell him I said you are to take Donas. Take the horse, and ride for Lallybroch. Stop for nothing, except as you must, to sleep, and when ye do sleep, hide yourself well."

Fergus was speechless with alarmed excitement, but Murtagh frowned dubiously at him.

"D'ye think the bairn can manage yon wicked beast?" he said.

"Aye, he can," Jamie said firmly. Overcome, Fergus stuttered, then sank to his knees and kissed Jamie's hand fervently. Springing to his feet, he darted away in the direction of the stables, his slight figure disappearing in the mist.

Jamie licked dry lips, and closed his eyes briefly, then turned to Murtagh with decision.

"And you—*mo caraidh*—I need ye to gather the men."

Murtagh's sketchy brows shot up, but he merely nodded.

"Aye," he said. "And when I have?"

Jamie glanced at me, then back at his godfather. "They'll be on the moor now, I think, with Young Simon. Just gather them together, in one place. I shall see my wife safe, and then —" He hesitated, then shrugged. "I will find you. Wait my coming."

Murtagh nodded once more, and turned to go. Then he paused, and turned back to face Jamie. The thin mouth twitched briefly, and he said, "I would ask the one thing of ye, lad—let it be the English. Not your ain folk."

Jamie flinched slightly, but after a moment, he nodded. Then, without speaking, he held out his arms to the older man. They embraced quickly, fiercely, and Murtagh, too, was gone, in a swirl of ragged tartan.

I was the last bit of business on the agenda.

"Come on, Sassenach," he said, seizing me by the arm. "We must go."

No one stopped us; there was so much coming and going by the roads that we were scarcely noticed while we were near the moor. Farther away, when we left the main road, there was no one to see.

Jamie was completely silent, concentrating single-mindedly on the job at hand. I said nothing to him, too occupied with my own shock and dread to wish for conversation.

"I shall see my wife safe." I hadn't known what he meant

by that, but it became obvious within two hours, when he turned the head of his horse farther south, and the steep green hill called Craigh na Dun came in view.

"No!" I said, when I saw it, and realized where we were headed. "Jamie, no! I won't go!"

He didn't answer me, only spurred his horse and galloped ahead, leaving me no option but to follow.

My feelings were in turmoil; beyond the doom of the coming battle and the horror of Dougal's death, now there was the prospect of the stones. That accursed circle, through which I had come here. Plainly Jamie meant to send me back, back to my own time—if such a thing was possible.

He could mean all he liked, I thought, clenching my jaw as I followed him down the narrow trail through the heather. There was no power on earth that could make me leave him now.

We stood together on the hillside, in the small dooryard of the ruined cottage that stood below the crest of the hill. No one had lived there for years; the local folk said the hill was haunted—a fairy's dun.

Jamie had half-urged, half-dragged me up the slope, paying no attention to my protests. At the cottage he had stopped, though, and sunk to the ground, chest heaving as he gasped for breath.

"It's all right," he said at last. "We have a bit of time now; no one will find us here."

He sat on the ground, his plaid wrapped around him for warmth. It had stopped raining for the moment, but the wind blew cold from the mountains nearby, where snow still capped the peaks and choked the passes. He let his head fall forward onto his knees, exhausted by the flight.

I sat close by him, huddled within my cloak, and felt his breathing gradually slow as the panic subsided. We sat in silence for a long time, afraid to move from what seemed a precarious perch above the chaos below. Chaos I felt I had somehow helped create.

"Jamie," I said, at last. I reached out a hand to touch him, but then drew back and let it fall. "Jamie—I'm sorry."

He continued to look out, into the darkening void of the

moor below. For a moment, I thought he hadn't heard me.
He closed his eyes. Then he shook his head very slightly.

"No," he said softly. "There is no need."

"But there is." Grief nearly choked me, but I felt as
though I must say it; must tell him that I knew what I had
done to him.

"I should have gone back. Jamie—if I had gone, then,
when you brought me here from Cranesmuir . . . maybe
then—"

"Aye, maybe," he interrupted. He swung toward me
abruptly, and I could see his eyes fixed on me. There was
longing there, and a grief that matched mine, but no anger,
no reproach.

He shook his head again.

"No," he said once more. "I ken what ye mean, *mo
nighean donn.* But it isna so. Had ye gone then, matters might
still have happened as they have. Maybe so, maybe no. Perhaps
it would have come sooner. Perhaps differently. Perhaps—just
perhaps—not at all. But there are more folk have had a hand
in this than we two, and I wilna have ye take the guilt of it
upon yourself."

His hand touched my hair, smoothing it out of my eyes.
A tear rolled down my cheek, and he caught it on his finger.

"Not that," I said. I flung a hand out toward the dark,
taking in the armies, and Charles, and the starved man in the
wood, and the slaughter to come. "Not that. What I did to
you."

He smiled then, with great tenderness, and smoothed his
palm across my cheek, warm on my spring-chilled skin.

"Aye? And what have I done to you, Sassenach? Taken
ye from your own place, led ye into poverty and outlawry,
taken ye through battlefields and risked your life. D'ye hold it
against me?"

"You know I don't."

He smiled. "Aye, well; neither do I, my Sassenach." The
smile faded from his face as he glanced up at the crest of the
hill above us. The stones were invisible, but I could feel
the menace of them, close at hand.

"I won't go, Jamie," I repeated stubbornly. "I'm staying
with you."

"No." He shook his head. He spoke gently, but his voice

was firm, with no possibility of denial. "I must go back, Claire."

"Jamie, you can't!". I clutched his arm urgently. "Jamie, they will have found Dougal by now! Willie Coulter will have told someone."

"Aye, he will." He put a hand over my arm and patted it. He had reached his decision on the ride to the hill; I could see it in his shadowed face, resignation and determination mingled. There was grief there, and sadness, too, but those had been put aside; he had no time for mourning now.

"We could try to get away to France," I said. "Jamie, we must!" But even as I spoke, I knew I could not turn him from the course he had decided on.

"No," he said again, softly. He turned and lifted a hand, gesturing toward the darkening valley below, the shaded hills beyond. "The country is roused, Sassenach. The ports are closed; O'Brien has been trying for the last three months to bring a ship to rescue the Prince, to take him to safety in France—Dougal told me . . . before." A tremor passed over his face, and a sudden spasm of grief knit his brows. He pushed it aside, though, and went on, explaining in a steady voice.

"It's only the English who are hunting Charles Stuart. It will be the English, and the clans as well, who hunt me. I am a traitor twice over, a rebel and a murderer. Claire . . ." He paused, rubbing a hand across the back of his neck, then said gently, "Claire, I am a dead man."

The tears were freezing on my cheeks, leaving icy trails that burned my skin.

"No," I said again, but to no effect.

"I'm no precisely inconspicuous, ye ken," he said, trying to make a joke of it as he ran a hand through the rusty locks of his hair. "Red Jamie wouldna get far, I think. But you . . ." He touched my mouth, tracing the line of my lips. "I can save you, Claire, and I will. That is the most important thing. But then I shall go back—for my men."

"The men from Lallybroch? But how?"

Jamie frowned, absently fingering the hilt of his sword as he thought.

"I think I can get them away. It will be confused on the moor, wi' men and horses moving to and fro, and orders shouted and contradicted; battles are verra messy affairs. And even if it's known by then what I—what I have done," he continued, with a momentary catch in his voice, "there are none who would stop me then, wi' the English in sight and the battle about to begin. Aye, I can do it," he said. His voice had steadied, and his fists clenched at his sides with determination.

"They will follow me without question—God help them, that's what's brought them here! Murtagh will have gathered them for me; I shall take them and lead them from the field. If anyone tries to stop me, I shall say that I claim the right to lead my own men in battle; not even Young Simon will deny me that."

He drew a deep breath, brows knit as he visualized the scene on the battlefield come morning.

"I shall bring them safely away. The field is broad enough, and there are enough men that no one will realize that we havena but moved to a new position. I shall bring them off the moor, and see them set on the road toward Lallybroch."

He fell silent, as though this were as far as he had thought in his plans.

"And then?" I asked, not wanting to know the answer, but unable to stop myself.

"And then I shall turn back to Culloden," he said, letting out his breath. He gave me an unsteady smile. "I'm no afraid to die, Sassenach." His mouth quirked wryly. "Well . . . not a lot, anyway. But some of the ways of accomplishing the fact . . ." A brief, involuntary shudder ran through him, but he tried to keep smiling.

"I doubt I should be thought worthy of the services of a true professional, but I expect in such a case, both Monsieur Forez and myself might find it . . . awkward. I mean, havin' my heart cut out by someone I've shared wine with . . ."

With a sound of incoherent distress, I flung my arms around him, holding him as tightly as I could.

"It's all right," he whispered into my hair. "It's all right, Sassenach. A musket ball. Maybe a blade. It will be over quickly."

I knew this was a lie; I had seen enough of battle wounds and the deaths of warriors. All that was true was that it was better than waiting for the hangman's noose. The terror that had ridden with me from Sandringham's estate rose now to high tide, choking, drowning me. My ears rang with my own pulsebeat, and my throat closed so tight that I felt I could not breathe.

Then all at once, the fear left me. I could not leave him, and I would not.

"Jamie," I said, into the folds of his plaid. "I'm going back with you."

He started back, staring down at me.

"The hell you are!" he said.

"I am." I felt very calm, with no trace of doubt. "I can make a kilt of my arisaid; there are enough young boys with the army that I can pass for one. You've said yourself it will all be confusion. No one will notice."

"No!" he said. "No, Claire!" His jaw was clenched, and he was glaring at me with a mixture of anger and horror.

"If you're not afraid, I'm not either," I said, firming my own jaw. "It will . . . be over quickly. You said so." My chin was beginning to quiver, despite my determination. "Jamie—I won't . . . I can't . . . I bloody won't live without you, and that's all!"

He opened his mouth, speechless, then closed it, shaking his head. The light over the mountains was failing, painting the clouds with a dull red glow. At last he reached for me, drew me close and held me.

"D'ye think I don't know?" he asked softly. "It's me that has the easy part now. For if ye feel for me as I do for you—then I am asking you to tear out your heart and live without it." His hand stroked my hair, the roughness of his knuckles catching in the blowing strands.

"But ye must do it, *mo nighean donn*. My brave lioness. Ye must."

"Why?" I demanded, pulling back to look up at him. "When you took me from the witch trial at Cranesmuir—you said then that you would have died with me, you would have gone to the stake with me, had it come to that!"

He grasped my hands, fixing me with a steady blue gaze.

"Aye, I would," he said. "But I wasna carrying your child."

The wind had frozen me; it was the cold that made me shake, I told myself. The cold that took my breath away.

"You can't tell," I said, at last. "It's much too soon to be sure."

He snorted briefly, and a tiny flicker of amusement lit his eyes.

"And me a farmer, too! Sassenach, ye havena been a day late in your courses, in all the time since ye first took me to your bed. Ye havena bled now in forty-six days."

"You bastard!" I said, outraged. "You counted! In the middle of a bloody war, you counted!"

"Didn't you?"

"No!" I hadn't; I had been much too afraid to acknowledge the possibility of the thing I had hoped and prayed for so long, come now so horribly too late.

"Besides," I went on, trying still to deny the possibility, "that doesn't mean anything. Starvation could cause that; it often does."

He lifted one brow, and cupped a broad hand gently beneath my breast.

"Aye, you're thin enough; but scrawny as ye are, your breasts are full—and the nipples of them gone the color of Champagne grapes. You forget," he said, "I've seen ye so before. I have no doubt—and neither have you."

I tried to fight down the waves of nausea—so easily attributable to fright and starvation—but I felt the small heaviness, suddenly burning in my womb. I bit my lip hard, but the sickness washed over me.

Jamie let go of my hands, and stood before me, hands at his sides, stark in silhouette against the fading sky.

"Claire," he said quietly. "Tomorrow I will die. This child . . . is all that will be left of me—ever. I ask ye, Claire—I beg you—see it safe."

I stood still, vision blurring, and in that moment, I heard my heart break. It was a small, clean sound, like the snapping of a flower's stem.

At last I bent my head to him, the wind grieving in my ears.

"Yes," I whispered. "Yes. I'll go."

It was nearly dark. He came behind me and held me, leaning back against him as he looked over my shoulder, out over the valley. The lights of watchfires had begun to spring up, small glowing dots in the far distance. We were silent for a long time, as the evening deepened. It was very quiet on the hill; I could hear nothing but Jamie's even breathing, each breath a precious sound.

"I will find you," he whispered in my ear. "I promise. If I must endure two hundred years of purgatory, two hundred years without you—then that is my punishment, which I have earned for my crimes. For I have lied, and killed, and stolen; betrayed and broken trust. But there is the one thing that shall lie in the balance. When I shall stand before God, I shall have one thing to say, to weigh against the rest."

His voice dropped, nearly to a whisper, and his arms tightened around me.

"Lord, ye gave me a rare woman, and God! I loved her well."

He was slow, and careful; so was I. Each touch, each moment must be savored, remembered—treasured as a talisman against a future empty of him.

I touched each soft hollow, the hidden places of his body. Felt the grace and the strength of each curving bone, the marvel of his firm-knit muscles, drawn lean and flexible across the span of his shoulders, smooth and solid down the length of his back, hard as seasoned oakwood in the columns of his thighs.

Tasted the salty sweat in the hollow of his throat, smelled the warm muskiness of the hair between his legs, the sweetness of the soft, wide mouth, tasting faintly of dried apple and the bitter tang of juniper berries.

"You are so beautiful, my own," he whispered to me, touching the slipperiness between my legs, the tender skin of my inner thighs.

His head was no more than a dark blur against the white blur of my breasts. The holes in the roof admitted only the faintest light from the overcast sky; the soft grumble of spring thunder muttered constantly in the hills beyond our fragile walls. He was hard in my hand, so stiff with the wanting that my touch made him groan in a need close to pain.

When he could wait no longer, he took me, a knife to its

scabbard, and we moved hard together, pressing, wanting, needing so urgently that moment of ultimate joining, and fearing to reach it, for the knowledge that beyond it lay eternal separation.

He brought me again and again to the peaks of sensation, holding back himself, stopping, gasping and shuddering on the brink. Until at last I touched his face, twined my fingers in his hair, pressed him tight and arched my back and hips beneath him, urging, forcing.

"Now," I said to him, softly. "Now. Come with me, come to me, now. Now!"

He yielded to me, and I to him, despair lending edge to passion, so the echo of our cries seemed to die away slowly, ringing in the darkness of the cold stone hut.

We lay pressed together, unmoving, his weight a heavy blessing, a shield and reassurance. A body so solid, so filled with heat and life; how could it be possible that he would cease to exist within hours?

"Listen," he said at last, softly. "Do you hear?"

At first I heard nothing but the rushing of the wind, and the trickle of rain, dripping through the holes of the roof. Then I heard it, the steady, slow thump of his heartbeat, pulsing against me, and mine against his, each matching each, in the rhythm of life. The blood coursed through him, and through our fragile link, through me, and back again.

We lay so, warm beneath the makeshift covering of plaid and cloak, on a bed of our clothing, tangled together. Then at last he slipped free, and turning me away from him, cupped his hand across my belly, his breath warm on the nape of my neck.

"Sleep now a bit, *mo nighean donn*," he whispered. "I would sleep once more this way—holding you, holding the babe."

I had thought I could not sleep, but the pull of exhaustion was too much, and I slipped beneath the surface with scarcely a ripple. Near dawn I woke, Jamie's arms still around me, and lay watching the imperceptible bloom of night into day, futilely willing back the friendly shelter of the dark.

I rolled to the side and lifted myself to watch him, to see the light touch the bold shape of his face, innocent in sleep, to see the dawning sun touch his hair with flame—for the last time.

A wave of anguish broke through me, so acute that I must have made some sound, for he opened his eyes. He smiled when he saw me, and his eyes searched my face. I knew that he was memorizing my features, as I was his.

"Jamie," I said. My voice was hoarse with sleep and swallowed tears. "Jamie. I want you to mark me."

"What?" he said, startled.

The tiny *sgian dubh* he carried in his stocking was lying within reach, its handle of carved staghorn dark against the piled clothing. I reached for it and handed it to him.

"Cut me," I said urgently. "Deep enough to leave a scar. I want to take away your touch with me, to have something of you that will stay with me always. I don't care if it hurts; nothing could hurt more than leaving you. At least when I touch it, wherever I am, I can feel your touch on me."

His hand was over mine where it rested on the knife's hilt. After a moment, he squeezed it and nodded. He hesitated for a moment, the razor-sharp blade in his hand, and I offered him my right hand. It was warm beneath our coverings, but his breath came in wisps, visible in the cold air of the room.

He turned my palm upward, examining it carefully, then raised it to his lips. A soft kiss in the well of the palm, then he seized the base of my thumb in a hard, sucking bite. Letting go, he swiftly cut into the numbed flesh. I felt no more than a mild burning sensation, but the blood welled at once. He brought the hand quickly to his mouth again, holding it there until the flow of blood slowed. He bound the wound, now stinging, carefully in a handkerchief, but not before I saw that the cut was in the shape of a small, slightly crooked letter "J."

I looked up to see that he was holding out the tiny knife to me. I took it, and somewhat hesitantly, took the hand he offered me.

He closed his eyes briefly, and set his lips, but a small grunt of pain escaped him as I pressed the tip of the knife into the fleshy pad at the base of his thumb. The Mount of Venus, a palm-reader had told me; indicator of passion and love.

It was only as I completed the small semicircular cut that I realized he had given me his left hand.

"I should have taken the other," I said. "Your sword hilt will press on it."

He smiled faintly.

"I could ask no more than to feel your touch on me in my last fight—wherever it comes."

Unwrapping the blood-spotted handkerchief, I pressed my wounded hand tightly against his, fingers gripped together. The blood was warm and slick, not yet sticky between our hands.

"Blood of my Blood . . ." I whispered.

". . . and Bone of my Bone," he answered softly. Neither of us could finish the vow, "so long as we both shall live," but the unspoken words hung aching between us. Finally he smiled crookedly.

"Longer than that," he said firmly, and pulled me to him once more.

"Frank," he said at last, with a sigh. "Well, I leave it to you what ye shall tell him about me. Likely he'll not want to hear. But if he does, if ye find ye can talk to him of me, as you have to me of him—then tell him . . . I'm grateful. Tell him I trust him, because I must. And tell him—" His hands tightened suddenly on my arms, and he spoke with a mixture of laughter and absolute sincerity. "Tell him I hate him to his guts and the marrow of his bones!"

We were dressed, and the dawn light had strengthened into day. There was no food, nothing with which to break our fast. Nothing left that must be done . . . and nothing left to say.

He would have to leave now, to make it to Drumossie Moor in time. This was our final parting, and we could find no way to say goodbye.

At last, he smiled crookedly, bent, and kissed me gently on the lips.

"They say . . ." he began, and stopped to clear his throat. "They say, in the old days, when a man would go forth to do a great deed—he would find a wisewoman, and ask her to bless him. He would stand looking forth, in the direction he would go, and she would come behind him, to say the words of the prayer over him. When she had finished, he would walk straight out, and not look back, for that was ill-luck to his quest."

He touched my face once, and turned away, facing the open door. The morning sun streamed in, lighting his hair in a thousand flames. He straightened his shoulders, broad beneath his plaid, and drew a deep breath.

"Bless me, then, wisewoman," he said softly, "and go."

I laid a hand on his shoulder, groping for words. Jenny had taught me a few of the ancient Celtic prayers of protection; I tried to summon the words in my mind.

"Jesus, Thou Son of Mary," I started, speaking hoarsely, "I call upon Thy name; and on the name of John the Apostle beloved, And on the names of all the saints in the red domain, To shield thee in the battle to come . . ."

I stopped, interrupted by a sound from the hillside below. The sound of voices, and of footsteps.

Jamie froze for a second, shoulder hard beneath my hand, then whirled, pushing me toward the rear of the cottage, where the wall had fallen away.

"That way!" he said. "They are English! Claire, go!"

I ran toward the opening in the wall, heart in my throat, as he turned back to the doorway, hand on his sword. I stopped, just for a moment, for the last sight of him. He turned his head, caught sight of me, and suddenly he was with me, pushing me hard against the wall in an agony of desperation. He gripped me fiercely to him. I could feel his erection pressing into my stomach and the hilt of his dagger dug into my side.

He spoke hoarsely into my hair. "Once more. I must! But quick!" He pushed me against the wall and I scrabbled up my skirts as he raised his kilts. This was not lovemaking; he took me quickly and powerfully and it was over in seconds. The voices were nearer; only a hundred yards away.

He kissed me once more, hard enough to leave the taste of blood in my mouth. "Name him Brian," he said, "for my father." With a push, he sent me toward the opening. As I ran for it, I glanced back to see him standing in the middle of the doorway, sword half-drawn, dirk ready in his right hand.

The English, unaware that the cottage was occupied, had not thought to send a scout round the back. The slope behind the cottage was deserted as I dashed across it and into the thicket of alders below the hillcrest.

I pushed my way through the brush and the branches, stumbling over rocks, blinded by tears. Behind me I could hear shouts and the clash of steel from the cottage. My thighs were slick and wet with Jamie's seed. The crest of the hill seemed never to grow nearer; surely I would spend the rest of my life fighting my way through the strangling trees!

There was a crashing in the brush behind me. Someone had seen me rush from the cottage. I dashed aside the tears and scrabbled upward, groping on all fours as the ground grew steeper. I was in the clear space now, the shelf of granite I remembered. The small dogwood growing out of the cliff was there, and the tumble of small boulders.

I stopped at the edge of the stone circle, looking down, trying desperately to see what was happening. How many soldiers had come to the cottage? Could Jamie break free of them and reach his hobbled horse below? Without it, he would never reach Culloden in time.

All at once, the brush below me parted with a flash of red. An English soldier. I turned, ran gasping across the turf of the circle, and hurled myself through the cleft in the rock.

PART SEVEN

Hindsight

47

Loose Ends

"He was right, of course. Bloody man, he was almost always right." Claire sounded half-cross as she spoke. A rueful smile crossed her face, then she looked at Brianna, who sat on the hearthrug, gripping her knees, her face completely blank. Only the faint stir of her hair, lifting and moving in the rising heat of the fire, showed any motion at all.

"It was a dangerous pregnancy—again—and a hazardous birth. Had I risked it there, it would almost certainly have killed us both." She spoke directly to her daughter, as though they were alone in the room. Roger, waking slowly from the spell of the past, felt like an intruder.

"The truth, then, all of it. I couldn't bear to leave him," Claire said softly. "Even for you . . . I hated you for a bit, before you were born, because it was for you that he'd made me go. I didn't mind dying—not with him. But to have to go on, to live without him—he was right, I had the worst of the bargain. But I kept it, because I loved him. And we lived, you and I, because he loved you."

Brianna didn't move; didn't take her eyes from her mother's face. Only her lips moved, stiffly, as though unaccustomed to talking.

"How long . . . did you hate me?"

Gold eyes met blue ones, innocent and ruthless as the eyes of a falcon.

"Until you were born. When I held you and nursed you and saw you look up at me with your father's eyes."

Brianna made a faint, strangled sound, but her mother went on, voice softening a little as she looked at the girl at her feet.

"And then I began to know you, something separate from myself or from Jamie. And I loved you for yourself, and not only for the man who fathered you."

There was a blur of motion on the hearthrug, and Brianna shot erect. Her hair bristled out like a lion's mane, and the blue eyes blazed like the heart of the flames behind her.

"Frank Randall was my father!" she said. "He was! I know it!" Fists clenched, she glared at her mother. Her voice trembled with rage.

"I don't know why you're doing this. Maybe you did hate me, maybe you still do!" Tears were beginning to make their way down her cheeks, unbidden, and she dashed them angrily away with the back of one hand.

"Daddy . . . Daddy loved me—he couldn't have, if I weren't his! Why are you trying to make me believe he wasn't my father? Were you jealous of me? Is that it? Did you mind so much that he loved me? He didn't love *you,* I know that!" The blue eyes narrowed, cat-like, blazing in a face gone dead-white.

Roger felt a strong desire to ease behind the door before she noticed his presence and turned that molten wrath on him. But beyond his own discomfort he was conscious of a sense of growing awe. The girl that stood on the hearthrug, hissing and spitting in defense of her paternity, flamed with the wild strength that had brought the Highland warriors down on their enemies like shrieking banshees. Her long, straight nose lengthened still further by the shadows, eyes slitted like a snarling cat's, she was the image of her father—and her father was patently not the dark, quiet scholar whose photo adorned the jacket of the book on the table.

Claire opened her mouth once, but then closed it again, watching her daughter with absorbed fascination. That powerful tension of the body, the flexing arch of the broad, flat cheekbones; Roger thought that she had seen that many times before—but not in Brianna.

With a suddenness that made them both flinch, Brianna spun on her heel, grabbed the yellowed news-clippings from the desk, and thrust them into the fire. She snatched the poker and jabbed it viciously into the tindery mass, heedless of the shower of sparks that flew from the hearth and hissed about her booted feet.

Whirling from the rapidly blackening mass of glowing paper, she stamped one foot on the hearth.

"Bitch!" she shouted at her mother. "You hated me? Well, I hate *you!*" She drew back the arm with the poker, and

Roger's muscles tensed instinctively, ready to lunge for her. But she turned, arm drawn back like a javelin thrower, and hurled the poker through the full-length window, where the panes of night-dark glass reflected the image of a burning woman for one last instant before the crash and shiver into empty black.

The silence in the study was shattering. Roger, who had leaped to his feet in pursuit of Brianna, was left standing in the middle of the room, awkwardly frozen. He looked down at his hands as if not quite sure what to do with them, then at Claire. She sat perfectly still in the sanctuary of the wing chair, like an animal frozen by the passing shadow of a raptor.

After several moments, Roger moved across to the desk and leaned against it.

"I don't know what to say," he said.

Claire's mouth twitched faintly. "Neither do I."

They sat in silence for several minutes. The old house creaked, settling around them, and a faint noise of banging pots came down the hallway from the kitchen, where Fiona was doing something about dinner. Roger's feeling of shock and constrained embarrassment gradually gave way to something else, he wasn't sure what. His hands felt icy, and he rubbed them on his legs, feeling the warm rasp of the corduroy on his palms.

"I . . ." He started to speak, then stopped and shook his head.

Claire drew a deep breath, and he realized that it was the first movement he had seen her make since Brianna had left. Her gaze was clear and direct.

"Do you believe me?" she asked.

Roger looked thoughtfully at her. "I'll be damned if I know," he said at last.

That provoked a slightly wavering smile. "That's what Jamie said," she said, "when I asked him at the first where he thought I'd come from."

"I can't say I blame him." Roger hesitated, then, making up his mind, got off the desk and came across the room to her. "May I?" He knelt and took her unresisting hand in his, turning it to the light. You can tell real ivory from the synthetic, he remembered suddenly, because the real kind feels. warm to the touch. The palm of her hand was a soft pink, but the faint line of the "J" at the base of her thumb was white as bone.

"It doesn't prove anything," she said, watching his face. "It could have been an accident; I could have done it myself."

"But you didn't, did you?" He laid the hand back in her lap very gently, as though it were a fragile artifact.

"No. But I can't prove it. The pearls"—her hand went to the shimmer of the necklace at her throat—"they're authentic; that can be verified. But can I prove where I got them? No."

"And the portrait of Ellen MacKenzie—" he began.

"The same. A coincidence. Something to base my delusion upon. My lies." There was a faintly bitter note in her voice, though she spoke calmly enough. There was a patch of color in each cheek now, and she was losing that utter stillness. It was like watching a statue come to life, he thought.

Roger got to his feet. He paced slowly back and forth, rubbing a hand through his hair.

"But it's important to you, isn't it? It's very important."

"Yes." She rose herself and went to the desk, where the folder of his research sat. She laid a hand on the manila sheeting with reverence, as though it were a gravestone; he supposed to her it was.

"I had to know." There was a faint quaver in her voice, but he saw her chin firm instantly, suppressing it. "I had to know if he'd done it—if he'd saved his men—or if he'd sacrificed himself for nothing. And I had to tell Brianna. Even if she doesn't believe it—if she never believes it. Jamie was her father. I had to tell her."

"Yes, I see that. And you couldn't do it while Dr. Randall—your hus—I mean, Frank," he corrected himself, flushing, "was alive."

She smiled faintly. "It's all right; you can call Frank my husband. He was, after all, for a good many years. And Bree's right, in a way—he was her father, as well as Jamie." She glanced down at her hands, and spread the fingers of both, so the light gleamed from the two rings she wore, silver and gold. Roger was struck by a thought.

"Your ring," he said, coming to stand close by her again.

"The silver one. Is there a maker's mark in it? Some of the eighteenth-century Scottish silversmiths used them. It might not be proof positive, but it's something."

Claire looked startled. Her left hand covered the right protectively, fingers rubbing the wide silver band with its pattern of Highland interlace and thistle blooms.

"I don't know," she said. A faint blush rose in her cheeks. "I haven't seen inside it. I've never taken it off." She twisted the ring slowly over the joint of the knuckle; her fingers were slender, but from long wearing, the ring had left a groove in her flesh.

She squinted at the inside of the ring, then rose and brought it to the table, where she stood next to Roger, tilting the silver circle to catch the light from the table lamp.

"There are words in it," she said wonderingly. "I never realized that he'd . . . Oh, dear God." Her voice broke, and the ring slipped from her fingers, rattling on the table with a tiny metal chime. Roger hurriedly scooped it up, but she had turned away, fists held tight against her middle. He knew she didn't want him to see her face; the control she had kept through the long hours of the day and the scene with Brianna had deserted her now.

He stood for a minute, feeling unbearably awkward and out of place. With a terrible feeling that he was violating a privacy that ran deeper than anything he had ever known, but not knowing what else to do, he lifted the tiny metal circle to the light and read the words inside.

"Da mi basia mille . . ." But it was Claire's voice that spoke the words, not his. Her voice was shaky, and he could tell that she was crying, but it was coming back under her control. She couldn't let go for long; the power of what she held leashed could so easily destroy her.

"It's Catullus. A bit of a love poem. Hugh. . . . Hugh Munro—he gave me the poem for a wedding present, wrapped around a bit of amber with a dragonfly inside it." Her hands, still curled into fists, had now dropped to her sides. "I couldn't say it all, still, but the one bit—I know that much." Her voice was growing steadier as she spoke, but she kept her back turned to Roger. The small silver circle glowed in his palm, still warm with the heat of the finger it had left.

". . . da mi basia mille . . ."

Still turned away, she went on, translating,

> *"Then let amorous kisses dwell*
> *On our lips, begin and tell*
> *A Thousand and a Hundred score*
> *A Hundred, and a Thousand more."*

When she had finished, she stood still a moment, then slowly turned to face him again. Her cheeks were flushed and wet, and her lashes clumped together, but she was superficially calm.

"A hundred, and a thousand more," she said, with a feeble attempt at a smile. "But no maker's mark. So that isn't proof, either."

"Yes, it is." Roger found there seemed to be something sticking in his own throat, and hastily cleared it. "It's absolute proof. To me."

Something lit in the depths of her eyes, and the smile grew real. Then the tears welled up and overflowed as she lost her grip once and for all.

"I'm sorry," she said at last. She was sitting on the sofa, elbows on her knees, face half-buried in one of the Reverend Mr. Wakefield's huge white handkerchiefs. Roger sat close beside her, almost touching. She seemed very small and vulnerable. He wanted to pat the ash-brown curls, but felt too shy to do it.

"I never thought . . . it never occurred to me," she said, blowing her nose again. "I didn't know how much it would mean, to have someone believe me."

"Even if it isn't Brianna?"

She grimaced slightly at his words, brushing back her hair with one hand as she straightened.

"It was a shock," she defended her daughter. "Naturally, she couldn't—she was so fond of her father—of Frank, I mean," she amended hastily. "I knew she might not be able to take it all in at first. But . . . surely when she's had time to think about it, ask questions . . ." Her voice faded, and the shoulders of her white linen suit slumped under the weight of the words.

As though to distract herself, she glanced at the table, where the stack of shiny-covered books still sat, undisturbed.

"It's odd, isn't it? To live twenty years with a Jacobite scholar, and to be so afraid of what I might learn that I could never bear to open one of his books?" She shook her head, still staring at the books. "I don't know what happened to many of them—I couldn't stand to find out. All the men I knew; I couldn't forget them. But I could bury them, keep their memory at bay. For a time."

And that time now was ended, and another begun. Roger picked up the book from the top of the stack, weighing it in his hands, as if it were a responsibility. Perhaps it would take her mind off Brianna, at least.

"Do you want me to tell you?" he asked quietly.

She hesitated for a long moment, but then nodded quickly, as though afraid she would regret the action if she paused to think about it longer.

He licked dry lips, and began to talk. He didn't need to refer to the book; these were facts known to any scholar of the period. Still, he held Frank Randall's book against his chest, solid as a shield.

"Francis Townsend," he began. "The man who held Carlisle for Charles. He was captured. Tried for treason, hanged and disemboweled."

He paused, but the white face was drained of blood already, no further change was possible. She sat across the table from him, motionless as a pillar of salt.

"MacDonald of Keppoch charged the field at Culloden on foot, with his brother Donald. Both of them were cut down by English cannon fire. Lord Kilmarnock fell on the field of battle, but Lord Ancrum, scouting the fallen, recognized him and saved his life from Cumberland's men. No great favor; he was beheaded the next August on Tower Hill, together with Balmerino." He hesitated. "Kilmarnock's young son was lost on the field; his body was never recovered."

"I always liked Balmerino," she murmured. "And the Old Fox? Lord Lovat?" Her voice was little more than a whisper. "The shadow of an ax . . ."

"Yes." Roger's fingers stroked the slick jacket of the book unconsciously, as though reading the words within by

Braille. "He was tried for treason, and condemned to be beheaded. He made a good end. All the accounts say that he
met his death with great dignity."

A scene flashed through Roger's mind; an anecdote from
Hogarth. He recited from memory, as closely as he could.
" 'Carried through the shouts and jeers of an English mob on
his way to the Tower, the old chieftain of clan Fraser appeared nonchalant, indifferent to the missiles that sailed past
his head, and almost good-humored. In reply to a shout from
one elderly woman—"You're going to get your head chopped
off, you old Scotch cur!"—he leaned from his carriage window and shouted jovially back, "I expect I shall, you ugly old
English bitch!" ' "

She was smiling, but the sound she made was a cross
between a laugh and a sob.

"I'll bet he did, the bloody old bastard."

"When he was led to the block," Roger went on cautiously, "he asked to inspect the blade, and instructed the
executioner to do a good job. He told the man, 'Do it right,
for I shall be very angry indeed if you don't.' "

Tears were running down beneath her closed lids, glittering like jewels in the firelight. He made a motion toward
her, but she sensed it and shook her head, eyes still closed.

"I'm all right. Go on."

"There isn't much more. Some of them survived, you
know. Lochiel escaped to France." He carefully refrained
from mention of the chieftain's brother, Archibald Cameron.
The doctor had been hanged, disemboweled, and beheaded
at Tyburn, his heart torn out and given to the flames. She did
not seem to notice the omission.

He finished the list rapidly, watching her. Her tears had
stopped, but she sat with her head hung forward, the thick
curly hair hiding all expression.

He paused for a moment when he had finished speaking,
then got up and took her firmly by the arm.

"Come on," he said. "You need a little air. It's stopped
raining; we'll go outside."

◄━━━►

The air outside was fresh and cool, almost intoxicating
after the stuffiness of the Reverend's study. The heavy rain

had ceased about sunset, and now, in the early evening, only the pit-a-pat dripping of trees and shrubs echoed the earlier downpour.

I felt an almost overwhelming relief at being released from the house. I had feared this for so long, and now it was done. Even if Bree never . . . but no, she would. Even if it took a long time, surely she would recognize the truth. She must; it looked her in the face every morning in the mirror; it ran in the very blood of her veins. For now, I had told her everything, and I felt the lightness of a shriven soul, leaving the confessional, unburdened as yet by thought of the penance ahead.

Rather like giving birth, I thought. A short period of great difficulty and rending pain, and the certain knowledge of sleepless nights and nerve-racking days in future. But for now, for a blessed, peaceful moment, there was nothing but a quiet euphoria that filled the soul and left no room for misgivings. Even the fresh-felt grief for the men I had known was muted out here, softened by the stars that shone through rifts in the shredding cloud.

The night was damp with early spring, and the tires of cars passing on the main road nearby hissed on the wet pavement. Roger led me without speaking down the slope behind the house, up another past a small, mossy glade, and down again, where there was a path that led to the river. A black iron railroad bridge spanned the river here; there was an iron ladder from the path's edge, attached to one of the girders. Someone armed with a can of white spray-paint had inscribed FREE SCOTLAND on the span with random boldness.

In spite of the sadness of memory, I felt at peace, or nearly so. I'd done the hardest part. Bree knew now who she was. I hoped fervently that she would come to believe it in time—not only for her own sake, I knew, but also for mine. More than I could ever have admitted, even to myself, I wanted to have someone with whom to remember Jamie; someone I could talk to about him.

I felt an overwhelming tiredness, one that touched both mind and body. But I straightened my spine just once more, forcing my body past its limits, as I had done so many times before. Soon, I promised my aching joints, my tender mind, my freshly riven heart. Soon, I could rest. I could sit alone in the small, cozy parlor of the bed-and-breakfast, alone by the fire with my ghosts. I could mourn them in peace, letting the weariness slip away with my tears, and go at last to seek the temporary oblivion of sleep, in which I might meet them alive once more.

But not yet. There was one thing more to be done before I slept.

They walked in silence for some time, with no sound but the passing of distant traffic, and the closer lapping of the river at its banks. Roger felt reluctant to start any conversation, lest he risk reminding her of things she wished to forget. But the floodgates had been opened, and there was no way of holding back.

She began to ask him small questions, hesitant and halting. He answered them as best he could, and hesitant in return, asked a few questions of his own. The freedom of talking, suddenly, after so many years of pent-up secrecy, seemed to act on her like a drug, and Roger, listening in fascination, drew her out despite herself. By the time they reached the railroad bridge, she had recovered the vigor and strength of character he had first seen in her.

"He was a fool, and a drunkard, and a weak, silly man," she declared passionately. "They were all fools—Lochiel, Glengarry, and the rest. They drank too much together, and filled themselves with Charlie's foolish dreams. Talk is cheap, and Dougal was right—it's easy to be brave, sitting over a glass of ale in a warm room. Stupid with drink, they were, and then too proud of their bloody honor to back down. They whipped their men and threatened them, bribed them and lured them—took them all to bloody ruin . . . for the sake of honor and glory."

She snorted through her nose, and was silent for a moment. Then, surprisingly, she laughed.

"But do you know what's really funny? That poor, silly sot and his greedy, stupid helpers; and the foolish, honorable men who couldn't bring themselves to turn back . . . they had the one tiny virtue among them; they believed. And the odd thing is, that that's all that's endured of them—all the silliness, the incompetence, the cowardice and drunken vain-glory; that's all gone. All that's left now of Charles Stuart and his men is the glory that they sought for and never found.

"Perhaps Raymond was right," she added in a softer tone; "it's only the essence of a thing that counts. When time strips everything else away, it's only the hardness of the bone that's left."

"I suppose you must feel some bitterness against the historians," Roger ventured. "All the writers who got it wrong— made him out a hero. I mean, you can't go anywhere in the Highlands without seeing the Bonnie Prince on toffee tins and souvenir tourist mugs."

Claire shook her head, gazing off in the distance. The evening mist was growing heavier, the bushes beginning to drip again from the tips of their leaves.

"Not the historians. No, not them. Their greatest crime is that they presume to know what happened, how things come about, when they have only what the past chose to leave behind—for the most part, they think what they were meant to think, and it's a rare one that sees what really happened, behind the smokescreen of artifacts and paper."

There was a faint rumble in the distance. The evening passenger train from London, Roger knew. You could hear the whistle from the manse on clear nights.

"No, the fault lies with the artists," Claire went on. "The writers, the singers, the tellers of tales. It's them that take the past and re-create it to their liking. Them that could take a fool and give you back a hero, take a sot and make him a king."

"Are they all liars, then?" Roger asked. Claire shrugged. In spite of the chilly air, she had taken off the jacket to her suit; the damp molded the cotton shirt to show the fineness of collarbone and shoulder blades.

"Liars?" she asked, "or sorcerers? Do they see the bones in the dust of the earth, see the essence of a thing that was, and clothe it in new flesh, so the plodding beast reemerges as a fabulous monster?"

"And are they wrong to do it, then?" Roger asked. The rail bridge trembled as the Flying Scotsman hit the switch below. The wavering white letters shook with vibration—FREE SCOTLAND.

Claire stared upward at the letters, her face lit by fugitive starlight.

"You still don't understand, do you?" she said. She was irritated, but the husky voice didn't rise above its normal level.

"You don't *know* why," she said. "You don't know, and I don't know, and we never *will* know. Can't you see? You don't know, because you can't say what the end is—there isn't any end. You can't say, 'This particular event' was 'destined' to happen, and therefore all these other things happened. What Charles did to the people of Scotland—was that the 'thing' that had to happen? Or was it 'meant' to happen as it did, and Charles's real purpose was to be what he is now—a figure-head, an icon? Without him, would Scotland have endured two hundred years of union with England, and still—*still* "— she waved a hand at the sprawling letters overhead—"have kept its own identity?"

"I don't know!" said Roger, having to shout as the swinging searchlight lit the trees and track, and the train roared over the bridge above them.

There was a solid minute of clash and roar, earthshaking noise that held them rooted to the spot. Then at last it was past, and the clatter died to a lonely crying wail as the red light of the end car swept out of sight beyond them.

"Well, that's the hell of it, isn't it?" she said, turning away. "You never *know*, but you have to act anyway, don't you?"

She spread her hands suddenly, flexing the strong fingers so her rings flashed in the light.

"You learn it when you become a doctor. Not in school —that isn't where you learn, in any case—but when you lay your hands on people and presume to heal them. There are so many there, beyond your reach. So many you can never touch, so many whose essence you can't find, so many who slip through your fingers. But you can't think about them. The only thing you can do—the *only* thing—is to try for the one who's in front of you. Act as though this one patient is the only person in the world—because to do otherwise is to lose that one, too. One at a time, that's all you can do. And you learn not to despair over all the ones you can't help, but only to do what you can."

She turned back to him, face haggard with fatigue, but eyes glowing with the rain-light, spangles of water caught in the tangles of her hair. Her hand rested on Roger's arm, compelling as the wind that fills a boat's sail and drives it on.

"Let's go back to the manse, Roger," she said. "I have something particular to tell you."

Claire was quiet on the walk back to the manse, avoiding Roger's tentative queries. She refused his proffered arm, walking alone, head down in thought. Not as though she were making up her mind, Roger thought; she had already done that. She was deciding what to say.

Roger himself was wondering. The quiet gave him respite from the turmoil of the day's revelations—enough to wonder precisely why Claire had chosen to include him in them. She could easily have told Brianna alone, had she wished to. Was it only that she had feared what Brianna's reaction to the story might be, and been reluctant to meet it alone? Or had she gambled that he would—as he had—believe her, and thus sought to enlist him as an ally in the cause of truth—her truth, and Brianna's?

His curiosity had reached near boiling point by the time they reached the manse. Still, there was work to do first; together, they unloaded one of the tallest bookshelves, and pushed it in front of the shattered window, shutting out the cold night air.

Flushed from the exertion, Claire sat down on the sofa while he went to pour a pair of whiskies from the small drinks-table in the corner. When Mrs. Graham had been alive, she had always brought drinks on a tray, properly napkined, doilied, and adorned with accompanying biscuits. Fiona, if allowed, would willingly have done the same, but Roger much preferred the simplicity of pouring his own drink in solitude.

Claire thanked him, sipped from the glass, then set it down and looked up at him, tired but composed.

"You'll likely be wondering why I wanted you to hear the whole story," she said, with that unnerving ability to see into his thoughts.

"There were two reasons. I'll tell you the second presently, but as for the first, I thought you had some right to hear it."

"Me? What right?"

The golden eyes were direct, unsettling as a leopard's guileless stare. "The same as Brianna. The right to know who you are." She moved across the room to the far wall. It was cork-lined from floor to ceiling, encrusted with layers of photographs, charts, notes, stray visiting cards, old parish schedules, spare keys, and other bits of rubbish pinned to the cork.

"I remember this wall." Claire smiled, touching a picture of Prize Day at the local grammar school. "Did your father ever take anything off it?"

Roger shook his head, bewildered. "No, I don't believe he did. He always said he could never find things put away in drawers; if it was anything important, he wanted it in plain sight."

"Then it's likely still here. He thought it was important."

Reaching up, she began to thumb lightly through the overlapping layers, gently separating the yellowed papers.

"This one, I think," she murmured, after some riffling back and forth. Reaching far up under the detritus of sermon notes and car-wash tickets, she detached a single sheet of paper and laid it on the desk.

"Why, it's my family tree," Roger said in surprise. "I haven't seen that old thing in years. And never paid any attention to it when I did see it, either," he added. "If you're going to tell me I'm adopted, I already know that."

Claire nodded, intent on the chart. "Oh, yes. That's why your father—Mr. Wakefield, I mean—drew up this chart. He wanted to be sure that you would know your real family, even though he gave you his own name."

Roger sighed, thinking of the Reverend, and the small silver-framed picture on his bureau, with the smiling likeness of an unknown young man, dark-haired in World War II RAF uniform.

"Yes, I know that, too. My family name was MacKenzie. Are you going to tell me I'm connected to some of the Mac-Kenzies you . . . er, knew? I don't see any of those names on this chart."

Claire acted as though she hadn't heard him, tracing a finger down the spidery hand-drawn lines of the genealogy.

"Mr. Wakefield was a terrible stickler for accuracy," she murmured, as though to herself. "He wouldn't want any mistakes." Her finger came to a halt on the page.

"Here," she said. "This is where it happened. Below this point"—her finger swept down the page—"everything is right. These were your parents, and your grandparents, and your great-grandparents, and so on. But not above." The finger swept upward.

Roger bent over the chart, then looked up, moss-green eyes thoughtful.

"This one? William Buccleigh MacKenzie, born 1744, of William John MacKenzie and Sarah Innes. Died 1782."

Claire shook her head. "Died 1744, aged two months, of smallpox." She looked up, and the golden eyes met his with a force that sent a shiver down his spine. "Yours wasn't the first adoption in that family, you know," she said. Her finger tapped the entry. "He needed a wet nurse," she said. "His own mother was dead—so he was given to a family that had lost a baby. They called him by the name of the child they had lost—that was common—and I don't suppose anyone wanted to call attention to his ancestry by recording the new child in the parish register. He would have been baptized at birth, after all; it wasn't necessary to do it again. Colum told me where they placed him."

"Geillis Duncan's son," he said slowly. "The witch's child."

"That's right." She gazed at him appraisingly, head cocked to one side. "I knew it must be, when I saw you. The eyes, you know. They're hers."

Roger sat down, feeling suddenly quite cold, in spite of the bookshelf blocking the draft, and the newly kindled fire on the hearth.

"You're sure of this?" he said, but of course she was sure. Assuming that the whole story was not a fabrication, the elaborate construction of a diseased mind. He glanced up at her, sitting unruffled with her whisky, composed as though about to order cheese straws.

Diseased mind? Dr. Claire Beauchamp-Randall, chief of staff at a large, important hospital? Raving insanity, rampant delusions? Easier to believe himself insane. In fact, he was beginning to believe just that.

He took a deep breath and placed both hands flat on the chart, blotting out the entry for William Buccleigh MacKenzie.

"Well, it's interesting all right, and I suppose I'm glad you told me. But it doesn't really change anything, does it? Except that I suppose I can tear off the top half of this genealogy and throw it away. After all, we don't know where Geillis Duncan came from, nor the man who fathered her child; you seem sure it wasn't poor old Arthur."

Claire shook her head, a distant look in her eyes.

"Oh, no, it wasn't Arthur Duncan. It was Dougal MacKenzie who fathered Geilie's child. That was the real reason she was killed. Not witchcraft. But Colum MacKenzie couldn't let it be known that his brother had had an adulterous affair with the fiscal's wife. And she wanted to marry Dougal; I think perhaps she threatened the MacKenzies with the truth about Hamish."

"Hamish? Oh, Colum's son. Yes, I remember." Roger rubbed his forehead. His head was starting to spin.

"Not Colum's son," Claire corrected. "Dougal's. Colum couldn't sire children, but Dougal could—and did. Hamish was the heir to the chieftainship of clan MacKenzie; Colum would have killed anyone who threatened Hamish—and did."

She drew a deep breath. "And that," she said, "leads to the second reason why I told you the story."

Roger buried both hands in his hair, staring down at the table, where the lines of the genealogical chart seemed to writhe like mocking snakes, forked tongues flickering between the names.

"Geillis Duncan," he said hoarsely. "She had a vaccination scar."

"Yes. It was that, finally, that made me come back to Scotland. When I left with Frank, I swore I would never come back. I knew I could never forget, but I could bury what I knew; I could stay away, and never seek to know what happened after I left. It seemed the least I could do, for both of them, for Frank and Jamie. And for the baby coming." Her lips pressed tightly together for a moment.

"But Geilie saved my life, at the trial in Cranesmuir. Perhaps she was doomed herself in any case; I think she believed so. But she threw away any chance she might have had, in order to save me. And she left me a message. Dougal gave it to me, in a cave in the Highlands, when he brought me the news that Jamie was in prison. There were two pieces to the message. A sentence, 'I do not know if it is possible, but I think so,' and a sequence of four numbers—one, nine, six, and eight.''

"Nineteen sixty-eight," Roger said, with the feeling that this was a dream. Surely he would be waking soon. "This year. What did she mean, she thought it was possible?"

"To go back. Through the stones. She hadn't tried, but she thought I could. And she was right, of course." Claire turned and picked up her whisky from the table. She stared at Roger across the rim of the glass, eyes the same color as the contents. "This is 1968; the year she went back herself. Except that I think she hasn't yet gone."

The glass slipped in Roger's hand, and he barely caught it in time.

"What . . . here? But she . . . why not . . . you can't tell . . ." He was sputtering, thoughts jarred into incoherency.

"I don't *know*," Claire pointed out. "But I think so. I'm fairly sure she was Scots, and the odds are good that she came through somewhere in the Highlands. Granted that there are any number of standing stones, we know that Craigh na Dun *is* a passage—for those that can use it. Besides," she added, with the air of one presenting the final argument, "Fiona's seen her."

"Fiona?" This, Roger felt, was simply too much. The crowning absurdity. Anything else he could manage to believe —time passages, clan treachery, historical revelations—but bringing Fiona into it was more than his reason could be expected to stand. He looked pleadingly at Claire. "Tell me you don't mean that," he begged. "Not Fiona."

Claire's mouth twitched at one corner. "I'm afraid so," she said, not without sympathy. "I asked her—about the Druid group that her grandmother belonged to, you know. She's been sworn to secrecy, of course, but I knew quite a bit about them already, and well . . ." She shrugged, mildly apologetic. "It wasn't too difficult to get her to talk. She told me that there'd been another woman asking questions—a tall, fair-haired woman, with very striking green eyes. Fiona said the woman reminded her of someone," she added delicately, carefully not looking at him, "but she couldn't think who." .

Roger merely groaned, and bending at the waist, collapsed slowly forward until his forehead rested on the table. He closed his eyes, feeling the cool hardness of the wood under his· head.

"Did Fiona know who she was?" he asked, eyes still closed.

"Her name is Gillian Edgars," Claire replied. He heard her rising, crossing the room, adding another tot of whisky to her glass. She came back and stood by the table. He could feel her gaze on the back of his neck.

"I'll leave it to you." Claire said quietly. "It's your right to say. Shall I look for her?"

Roger lifted his head off the table and blinked at her incredulously. "Shall you look for her?" he said. "If this—if it's all true—then we have to find her, don't we? If she's going back to be burned alive? Of course you have to find her!" he burst out. "How could you consider anything else?"

"And if I do find her?" she replied. She placed a slender hand on the grubby chart and raised her eyes to his. "What happens to you?" she asked softly.

He looked around helplessly, at the bright, cluttered study, with the wall of miscellanea, the chipped old teapot on the ancient oak table. Solid as . . . He gripped his thighs, clutching the rough corduroy as though for reassurance that he was as solid as the chair on which he sat.

"But . . . I'm *real*!" he burst out. "I can't just . . . evaporate!"

Claire raised her brows consideringly. "I don't know that you would. I have no idea what would happen. Perhaps you would never have existed? In which case, you oughtn't to be too agitated now. Perhaps the part of you that makes you unique, your soul or whatever you want to call it—perhaps that's fated to exist in any case, and you would still be you, though born of a slightly different lineage. After all, how much of your physical makeup can be due to ancestors six generations back? Half? Ten percent?" She shrugged, and pursed her lips, looking him over carefully.

"Your eyes come from Geilie, as I told you. But I see Dougal in you, too. No specific feature, though you have the MacKenzie cheekbones; Bree has them, too. No, it's something more subtle, something in the way you move; a grace, a suddenness—no . . ." She shook her head. "I can't describe it. But it's there. Is it something you *need*, to be who you are? Could you do without that bit from Dougal?"

She rose heavily, looking her age for the first time since he had met her.

"I've spent more than twenty years looking for answers, Roger, and I can tell you only one thing: There aren't any answers, only choices. I've made a number of them myself, and no one can tell me whether they were right or wrong. Master Raymond perhaps, though I don't suppose he would; he was a man who believed in mysteries.

"I can see the right of it only far enough to know that I must tell you—and leave the choice to you."

He picked up the glass and drained the rest of the whisky.

The Year of our Lord 1968. The year when Geillis Duncan stepped into the circle of standing stones. The year she went to meet her fate beneath the rowan trees in the hills near Leoch. An illegitimate child—and death by fire.

He rose and wandered up and down the rows of books that lined the study. Books filled with history, that mocking and mutable subject.

No answers, only choices.

Restless, he fingered the books on the top shelf. These were the histories of the Jacobite movement, the stories of the Rebellions, the '15 and the '45. Claire had known a number of the men and women described in these books. Had fought and suffered with them, to save a people strange to her. Had lost all she held dear in the effort. And in the end, had failed. But the choice had been hers, as now it was his.

Was there a chance that this was a dream, a delusion of some kind? He stole a glance at Claire. She lay back in her chair, eyes closed, motionless but for the beating of her pulse, barely visible in the hollow of her throat. No. He could, for a moment, convince himself that it was make-believe, but only while he looked away from her. However much he wanted to believe otherwise, he could not look at her and doubt a word of what she said.

He spread his hands flat on the table, then turned them over, seeing the maze of lines that crossed his palms. Was it only his own fate that lay here in his cupped hands, or did he hold an unknown woman's life as well?

No answers. He closed his hands gently, as though holding something small trapped inside his fists, and made his choice.

"Let's find her," he said.

There was no sound from the still figure in the wing chair, and no movement save the rise and fall of the rounded breast. Claire was asleep.

48

Witch-hunt

The old-fashioned buzzer whirred somewhere in the depths of the flat. It wasn't the best part of town, nor was it the worst. Working-class houses, for the most part, some, like this one, divided into two or three flats. A hand-lettered notice under the buzzer read MCHENRY UPSTAIRS —RING TWICE. Roger carefully pressed the buzzer once more, then wiped his hand on his trousers. His palms were sweating, which annoyed him considerably.

There was a trough of yellow jonquils by the doorstep, half-dead for lack of water. The tips of the blade-shaped leaves were brown and curling, and the frilly yellow heads drooped disconsolately near his shoe.

Claire saw them, too. "Perhaps no one's home," she said, stooping to touch the dry soil in the trough. "These haven't been watered in over a week."

Roger felt a mild wave of relief at the thought; whether he believed Geillis Duncan was Gillian Edgars or not, he hadn't been looking forward to this visit. He was turning to go when the door suddenly opened behind him, with a screech of sticking wood that brought his heart into his mouth.

"Aye?" The man who answered the door squinted at them, eyes swollen in a flushed, heavy face shadowed with unshaven beard.

"Er . . . We're sorry to disturb your sleep, sir," said Roger, making an effort to calm himself. His stomach felt slightly hollow. "We're looking for a Miss Gillian Edgars. Is this her residence?"

The man rubbed a stubby, black-furred hand over his head, making the hair stick up in belligerent spikes.

"That's *Mrs.* Edgars to you, jimmy. And what's it you want wi' my wife?" The alcoholic fumes from the man's breath made Roger want to step backward, but he stood his ground.

"We only want to talk with her," he said, as conciliatingly as he could. "Is she at home, please?"

"Is she at home, please?" said the man who must be Mr. Edgars, squinching his mouth in a savage, high-pitched mockery of Roger's Oxford accent. "No, she's not home. Bugger off," he advised, and swung the door to with a crash that left the lace curtain shivering with the vibration.

"I can see why she *isn't* home," Claire observed, standing on tiptoe to peer through the window. "I wouldn't be, either, if that's what was waiting for me."

"Quite," said Roger shortly. "And that would appear to be that. Have you any other suggestions for finding this woman?"

Claire let go of the windowsill.

"He's settled in front of the telly," she reported. "Let's leave him, at least until after the pub's opened. Meanwhile, we can go try this Institute. Fiona said Gillian Edgars took courses there."

The Institute for the Study of Highland Folklore and Antiquities was housed on the top floor of a narrow house just outside the business district. The receptionist, a small, plump woman in a brown cardigan and print dress, seemed delighted to see them; she mustn't get much company up here, Roger reflected.

"Oh, Mrs. *Edgars*," she said, upon hearing their business. Roger thought that a sudden note of doubt had crept into Mrs. Andrews's voice, but she remained bright and cheerful. "Yes," she said, "she's a regular member of the Institute, all paid up for her classes. She's around here quite a bit, is Mrs. Edgars." A lot more than Mrs. Andrews really cared for, from the sound of it.

"She isn't here now, by chance, is she?" Claire asked.

Mrs. Andrews shook her head, making the dozens of gray-streaked pincurls dance on her head.

"Oh, no," she said. "It's a Monday. Only me and Dr. McEwan are here on the Monday. He's the Director, you know." She looked reproachfully at Roger, as though he ought really to have known that. Then, apparently reassured by their evident respectability, she relented slightly.

"If you want to ask about Mrs. Edgars, you should see Dr. McEwan. I'll just go and tell him you're here, shall I?"

As she began to ease out from behind her desk, Claire stopped her, leaning forward.

"Have you perhaps got a photograph of Mrs. Edgars?" she asked bluntly. At Mrs. Andrews's stare of surprise, Claire smiled charmingly, explaining, "We wouldn't want to waste the Director's time, if it's the wrong person, you see."

Mrs. Andrews mouth dropped open slightly, and she blinked in confusion, but she nodded after a moment, and began fussing round her desk, opening drawers and talking to herself.

"I know they're here somewhere. I saw them just yesterday, so they can't have gone far . . . oh, here!" She bobbed up with a folder of eight-by-ten black-and-white photographs in her hand, and sorted rapidly through them.

"There," she said. "That's her, with one of the digging expeditions, out near town, but you can't see her face, can you? Let me see if there's any more . . ."

She resumed her sorting, muttering to herself, as Roger peered interestedly over Claire's shoulder at the photograph Mrs. Andrews had laid on the desk. It showed a small group of people standing near a Land-Rover, with a number of burlap sacks and small tools on the ground beside them. It was an impromptu shot, and several of the people were turned away from the camera. Claire's finger reached out without hesitation, touching the image of a tall girl with long, straight, fair hair hanging halfway down her back. She tapped the photograph and nodded silently to Roger.

"You can't possibly be sure," he muttered to her under his breath.

"What's that, luv?" said Mrs. Andrews, looking up absently over her spectacles. "Oh, you weren't talking to me. That's all right, then, I've found one a little better. It's still not her whole face—she's turned sideways, like—but it's better nor the other." She plopped the new picture down on top of the other with a triumphant little splat.

This one showed an older man with half-spectacles and the same fair-haired girl, bent over a table holding what looked to Roger like a collection of rusted motor parts, but which were undoubtedly valuable artifacts. The girl's hair swung down beside her cheek, and her head was turned toward the older man, but the slant of a short, straight nose, a sweetly rounded chin, and the curve of a beautiful mouth showed clearly. The eye was cast down, hidden under long, thick lashes. Roger repressed the admiring whistle that rose unbidden to his lips. Ancestress or not, she was a real dolly, he thought irreverently.

He glanced at Claire. She nodded, without speaking. She was paler even than usual, and he could see the pulse beating rapidly in her throat, but she thanked Mrs. Andrews with her usual composure.

"Yes, that's the one. I think perhaps we *would* like to talk to the Director, if he's available."

Mrs. Andrews cast a quick glance at the white-paneled door behind her desk.

"Well, I'll go and ask for you, dearie. Could I tell him what it's for, though?"

Roger was opening his mouth, groping for some excuse, when Claire stepped smoothly into the breach.

"We're from Oxford, actually," she said. "Mrs. Edgars has applied for a study grant with the Department of Antiquities, and she'd given the Institute as a reference with the rest of her credentials. So, if you wouldn't mind . . . ?"

"Oh, I see," said Mrs. Andrews, looking impressed. "Oxford. Just think! I'll ask Dr. McEwan if he can see you just now."

As she disappeared behind the white-paneled door, pausing for no more than a perfunctory rap before entering, Roger leaned down to whisper in Claire's ear.

"There is no such thing as a Department of Antiquities at Oxford," he hissed, "and you know it."

"You know that," she replied demurely, "and I, as you so cleverly point out, do too. But there are any number of people in the world who don't, and we've just met one of them."

The white-paneled door was beginning to open.

"Let's hope they're thick on the ground hereabouts," Roger said, wiping his brow, "or that you're a quick liar."

Claire rose, smiling at the beckoning figure of Mrs. Andrews as she spoke out of the side of her mouth.

"I? I, who read souls for the King of France?" She brushed down her skirt and set it swinging. "This will be pie."

Roger bowed ironically, gesturing toward the door. "*Après vous,* Madame."

As she stepped ahead of him, he added, *"Après vous, le déluge,"* under his breath. Her shoulders stiffened, but she didn't turn around.

———◆———

Rather to Roger's surprise, it *was* pie. He wasn't sure whether it was Claire's skill at misrepresentation, or Dr. McEwan's own preoccupation, but their bona fides went unquestioned. It didn't seem to occur to the man that it was highly unlikely for scouting parties from Oxford to penetrate to the wilds of Inverness to make inquiries about the background of a potential graduate student. But then, Roger thought, Dr. McEwan appeared to have something on his mind; perhaps he wasn't thinking as clearly as usual.

"Weeeel . . . yes, Mrs. Edgars unquestionably has a fine mind. Very fine," the Director said, as though convincing himself. He was a tall, spare man, with a long upper lip like a camel's, which wobbled as he searched hesitantly for each new word. "Have you . . . has she . . . that is . . ." He trailed off, lip twitching, then, "Have you ever actually *met* Mrs. Edgars?" he finally burst out.

"No," said Roger, eyeing Dr. McEwan with some austerity. "That's why we're asking about her."

"Is there anything . . ." Claire paused delicately, inviting, "that you think perhaps the committee should know, Dr. McEwan?" She leaned forward, opening her eyes very wide. "You know, inquiries like this are *completely* confidential. But it's so important that we be fully informed; there is a position of trust involved." Her voice dropped suggestively. "The Ministry, you know."

Roger would dearly have loved to strangle her, but Dr. McEwan was nodding sagely, lip wobbling like mad.

"Oh, yes, dear lady. Yes, of course. The Ministry. I completely understand. Yes, yes, Well, I . . . hm, perhaps—I shouldn't like to mislead you in any respect, you know. And it is a wonderful chance, no doubt . . ."

Now Roger wanted to throttle both of them. Claire must have noticed his hands twitching in his lap with irresistible desire, for she put a firm stop to the Director's maundering.

"We're basically interested in two things," she said briskly, opening the notebook she carried and poising it on her knee as if for reference. *Pick up bottle sherry for Mrs. T,* Roger read out of the corner of one eye. *Sliced ham for picnic.*

"We want to know, first, your opinion of Mrs. Edgars's scholarship, and secondly, your opinion of her overall personality. The first we have of course evaluated ourselves"—she made a small tick in the notebook, next to an entry that read *Change traveler's cheques*—"but you have a much more substantial and detailed grasp, of course." Dr. McEwan was nodding away by this time, thoroughly mesmerized.

"Yes, well . . ." He puffed a little, then, with a glance at the door to make sure it was shut, leaned confidentially across his desk. "The quality of her work—well, about that I think I can satisfy you completely. I'll show you a few things she's been working on. And the other . . ." Roger thought he was about to go in for another spot of lip-twitching and leaned forward menacingly.

Dr. McEwan leaned back abruptly, looking startled. "It's nothing very much, really," he said. "It's only . . . well, she's such an *intense* young lady. Perhaps her interest seems at times a trifle . . . obsessive?" His voice went up questioningly. His eyes darted from Roger to Claire, like a trapped rat's.

"Would the direction of this intense interest perhaps be focused on the standing stones? The stone circles?" Claire suggested gently.

"Oh, it showed up in her application materials, then?" The Director hauled a large, grubby handkerchief out of his pocket and mopped his face with it. "Yes, that's it. Of course, a lot of people get quite carried away with them," he offered. "The romance of it, the mystery. Look at those benighted souls out at Stonehenge on Midsummer's Day, in hoods and robes. Chanting . . . all that nonsense. Not that I would compare Gillian Edgars to . . ."

There was quite a lot more of it, but Roger quit listening. It seemed stifling in the narrow office, and his collar was too tight; he could hear his heart beating, a slow, incessant thrumping in both ears that was very irritating.

It simply couldn't be! he thought. *Positively impossible.* True, Claire Randall's story was convincing—quite awfully convincing. But then, look at the effect she was having on this poor old dodderer, who wouldn't know scholarship if it was served up on a plate with piccalilli relish. She could obviously talk a tinker out of his pans. Not that he, Roger, was as susceptible as Dr. McEwan surely, but . . .

Beset with doubt and dripping with sweat, Roger paid little attention as Dr. McEwan fetched a set of keys from his drawer and rose to lead them out through a second door into a long hallway studded with doors.

"Study carrels," the Director explained. He opened one of the doors, revealing a cubicle some four feet on a side, barely big enough to contain a narrow table, a chair, and a small bookshelf. On the table, neatly stacked, were a series of folders in different colors. To the side, Roger saw a large notebook with gray covers, and a neat hand-lettered label on the front—MISCELLANEOUS. For some reason, the sight of the handwriting sent a shiver through him.

This was getting more personal by the moment. First photographs, now the woman's writings. He was assailed by a moment's panic at the thought of actually meeting Geillis Duncan. Gillian Edgars, he meant. *Whoever* the woman was.

The Director was opening various folders, pointing and explaining to Claire, who was putting on a good show of having some idea what he was talking about. Roger peered over her shoulder, nodding and saying, "Um-hm, very interesting," at intervals, but the slanted lines and loops of the script were incomprehensible to him.

She wrote this, he kept thinking. *She's real. Flesh and blood and lips and long eyelashes.* And if she goes back through the stone, she'll burn—crackle and blacken, with her hair lit like a torch in the black dawn. And if she doesn't, then . . . I don't exist.

He shook his head violently.

"You disagree, Mr. Wakefield?" The Director of the Institute was peering at him in puzzlement.

He shook his head again, this time in embarrassment.

"No, no. I mean . . . it's only . . . do you think I could have a drink of water?"

"Of course, of course! Come with me, there's a fountain just round the corner, I'll show you." Dr. McEwan bustled him out of the carrel and down the hall, expressing voluble, disjointed concern for his state of health.

Once away from the claustrophobic confines of the carrel and the proximity of Gillian Edgars's books and folders,
Roger began to feel slightly better. Still, the thought of going
back into that tiny room, where all Claire's words about her
past seemed to echo off the thin partitions . . . no. He made
up his mind. Claire could finish with Dr. McEwan by herself.
He passed the carrel quickly, not looking inside, and went
through the door that led back to the receptionist's desk.

Mrs. Andrews stared at him as he came in, her spectacles
gleaming with concern and curiosity.

"Dear me, Mr. Wakefield. Are ye not feeling just right,
then?" Roger rubbed a hand over his face; he must look really ghastly. He smiled weakly at the plump little secretary.

"No, thanks very much. I just got a bit hot back there;
thought I'd step down for a little fresh air."

"Oh, aye." The receptionist nodded understandingly.
"The radiators." She pronounced it "raddiators." "They get
stuck on, ye know, and won't turn off. I'd best see about it."
She rose from her desk, where the picture of Gillian Edgars
still rested. She glanced down at the picture, then up at
Roger.

"Isn't that odd?" she said conversationally. "I was just
looking at this and wondering what it was about Mrs. Edgars's face that struck me all of a sudden. And I couldn't
think what it was. But she's quite a look of *you*, Mr. Wakefield
—especially round the eyes. Isn't that a coincidence? Mr.
Wakefield?" Mrs. Andrews stared in the direction of the stair,
where the thump of Roger's footsteps echoed from the
wooden risers.

"Taken a bit short, I expect," she said kindly. "Poor lad."

The sun was still above the horizon when Claire rejoined
him on the street, but it was late in the day; people were
going home to their tea, and there was a feeling of general
relaxation in the air—a looking forward to leisured peace
after the long day's work.

Roger himself had no such feeling. He moved to open
the car door for Claire, conscious of such a mix of emotions
that he couldn't decide what to say first. She got in, glancing
up at him sympathetically.

"Rather a jar, isn't it?" was all she said.

The fiendish maze of new one-way streets made getting through the town center a task that demanded all his attention. They were well on their way before he could take his eyes off the road long enough to ask, "What next?"

Claire was leaning back in her seat, eyes closed, the tendrils of her hair coming loose from their clip. She didn't open her eyes at his question, but stretched slightly, easing herself in the seat.

"Why don't you ask Brianna out for supper somewhere?" she said. Supper? Somehow it seemed subtly wrong to stop for supper in the midst of a life-or-death detective endeavor, but on the other hand, Roger was suddenly aware that the hollowness in his stomach wasn't entirely due to the revelations of the last hour.

"Well, all right," he said slowly. "But then tomorrow—"

"Why wait 'til tomorrow?" Claire broke in. She was sitting up now, combing out her hair. It was thick and unruly, and loosed swirling on her shoulders, Roger thought it made her look suddenly very young. "You can go talk to Greg Edgars again after supper, can't you?"

"How do you know his name is Greg?" Roger asked curiously. "And if he wouldn't talk to me this afternoon, why should he tonight?"

Claire looked at Roger as though suddenly doubting his basic intelligence.

"I know his name because I saw it on a letter in his mailbox," she said. "As for why he'll talk to you tonight, he'll talk to you because you're going to take along a bottle of whisky when you come this time."

"And you think that will make him invite us in?"

She lifted one brow. "Did you see the collection of empty bottles in his waste bin? Of course he will. Like a shot." She sat back, fists thrust into the pockets of her coat, and stared out at the passing street.

"You might see if Brianna will go with you," she said casually.

"She said she isn't having anything to do with this," Roger objected.

Claire glanced at him impatiently. The sun was setting behind her, and it made her eyes glow amber, like a wolf's.

"In that case, I suggest you don't tell her what you're up to," she said, in a tone that made Roger remember that she was chief of staff at a large hospital.

His ears burned, but he stubbornly said, "You can't very well hide it, if you and I—"

"Not me," Claire interrupted. "You. I have something else to do."

This was too much, Roger thought. He pulled the car over without signaling and skidded to a stop at the side of the road. He glared at her.

"Something else to do, have you?" he demanded. "I like that! You're landing me with the job of trying to entice a drunken sot who will likely assault me on sight, *and* luring your daughter along to watch! What, do you think she'll be needed to drive me to hospital after Edgars has finished beating me over the head with a bottle?"

"No," Claire said, ignoring his tone. "I think you and Greg Edgars together may succeed where I couldn't, in convincing Bree that Gillian Edgars is the woman I knew as Geillis Duncan. She won't listen to me. She likely won't listen to you, either, if you try to tell her what we found at the Institute today. But she'll listen to Greg Edgars." Her tone was flat and grim, and Roger felt his annoyance ebbing slightly. He started the car once more, and pulled out into the stream of traffic.

"All right, I'll try," he said grudgingly, not looking at her. "And just where are you going to be, while I do this?"

There was a small, shuffling movement alongside as she groped in her pocket again. Then she drew out her hand and opened it. His eye caught the silvery gleam of a small object in the darkness of her palm. A key.

"I'm going to burgle the Institute," she said calmly. "I want that notebook."

After Claire excused herself to run her unspecified "errand"—making Roger shudder only slightly—he and Brianna had driven to the pub, but then decided to wait for their supper, since the evening was unexpectedly fine. They strolled down the narrow walk by the River Ness, and he had forgotten his misgivings about the evening in the pleasure of Brianna's company.

They talked carefully at first, avoiding anything controversial. Then the chat turned to Roger's work, and grew gradually more animated.

"And how do you know so much about it, anyway?" Roger demanded, breaking off in the middle of a sentence.

"My father taught me," she replied. At the word "father," she stiffened a bit, and drew back, as though expecting him to say something. "My *real* father," she added pointedly.

"Well, he certainly knew," Roger replied mildly, leaving the challenge strictly alone. Plenty of time for that later, my girl, he thought cynically. But it isn't going to be me that springs the trap.

Just down the street, Roger could see a light in the window of the Edgars's house. The quarry was denned, then. He felt an unexpected surge of adrenaline at the thought of the coming confrontation.

Adrenaline lost out to the surge of gastric juices that resulted when they stepped into the pub's savory atmosphere, redolent of shepherd's pie. Conversation was general and friendly, with an unspoken agreement to avoid any reference to the scene at the manse the day before. Roger had noticed the coolness between Claire and her daughter, before he had left her at the cab stand on their way to the pub. Seated side by side in the backseat, they had reminded him of two strange cats, ears laid flat and tails twitching, but both avoiding the eye-locking stare that would lead to claws and flying fur.

After dinner, Brianna fetched their coats while he paid the bill.

"What's that for?" she asked, noticing the bottle of whisky in his hand. "Planning a rave-up for later on?"

"Rave-up?" he said, grinning at her. "You *are* getting on, aren't you? And what else have you picked up in your linguistic studies?"

She cast her eyes down in exaggerated demureness.

"Oh, well. There's a dance in the States, called the Shag. I gather I shouldn't ask you to do it with me here, though."

"Not unless you mean it," he said. They both laughed, but he thought the flush on her cheeks had deepened, and he was conscious of a certain stirring at the suggestion that made him keep his coat hung over one arm instead of putting it on.

"Well, after enough of *that* stuff, anything's possible," she said, indicating the whisky bottle with a mildly malicious smile. "Terrible taste, though."

"It's acquired, lassie," Roger informed her, letting his accent broaden. "Only Scots are born wi' it. I'll buy ye a bottle of your own to practice with. This one's a gift, though —something I promised to leave off. Want to come along, or shall I do it later?" he asked. He didn't know whether he wanted her to come or not, but felt a surge of happiness when she nodded and shrugged into her own coat.

"Sure, why not?"

"Good." He reached out and delicately turned down the flap of her collar, so it lay flat on her shoulder. "It's just down the street—let's walk, shall we?"

The neighborhood looked a little better at night. Some of its shabbiness was hidden by the darkness, and the lights glowing from windows into the tiny front gardens gave the street an air of coziness that it lacked during the day.

"This won't take a minute," Roger told Brianna as he pressed the buzzer. He wasn't sure whether to hope he was right or not. His first fear passed as the door opened; someone was home, and still conscious.

Edgars had plainly spent the afternoon in the company of one of the bottles lined up along the edge of the sway-backed buffet visible behind him. Luckily, he appeared not to connect his evening visitors with the intrusion of the afternoon. He squinted at Roger's introduction, composed on the way to the house.

"Gilly's cousin? I didn' know she had a cousin."

"Well, she has," said Roger, boldly taking advantage of this admission. "I'm him." He would deal with Gillian herself when he saw her. If he saw her.

Edgars blinked once or twice, then rubbed an inflamed eye with one fist, as though to get a better look at them. His eyes focused with some difficulty on Brianna, hovering diffidently behind Roger.

"Who's that?" he demanded.

"Er . . . my girlfriend," Roger improvised. Brianna narrowed her eyes at him, but said nothing. Plainly she was beginning to smell a rat, but went ahead of him without protest as Greg Edgars swung the door wider to admit them.

The flat was small and stuffy, overfurnished with second-hand furniture. The air reeked of stale cigarettes and insufficiently taken-out garbage, and the remnants of take-away meals were scattered heedlessly over every horizontal surface in the room. Brianna gave Roger a sidelong look that said *Nice relatives you have,* and he shrugged slightly. *Not my fault.* The woman of the house was plainly not at home, and hadn't been for some time.

Or not in the physical sense, at least. Turning to take the chair Edgars offered him, Roger came face-to-face with a large studio photograph, framed in brass, standing in the center of the tiny mantelpiece. He bit his tongue to stifle a startled exclamation.

The woman seemed to be looking out of the photograph into his face, a slight smile barely creasing the corner of her mouth. Wings of platinum-fair hair fell thick and glossy past her shoulders, framing a perfect heart-shaped face. Eyes deep green as winter moss glowed under thick, dark lashes.

"Good likeness, i'n't?" Greg Edgars looked at the photo, his expression one of mingled hostility and longing.

"Er, yes. Just like her." Roger felt a little breathless, and turned to remove a crumpled fish-and-chips paper from his chair. Brianna was staring at the portrait with interest. She glanced from the photo to Roger and back, clearly drawing comparisons. Cousins, was it?

"I take it Gillian's not here?" Roger started to wave away the bottle Edgars had tilted inquiringly in his direction, then changed his mind and nodded. Perhaps a shared drink would gain Edgars's confidence. If Gillian wasn't here, he needed to find out where she was.

Occupied in removing the excise seal with his teeth, Edgars shook his head, then delicately plucked the bit of wax and paper off his lower lip.

"Not hardly, mate. 'S not quite so much a slum as this when she's here." A sweeping gesture took in the overflowing ashtrays and tumbled paper drinks cups. "Close, maybe, but not quite this bad." He took down three wineglasses from the china cupboard, peering dubiously into each one, as though checking for dust.

He poured the whisky with the exaggerated care of the very drunk, taking the glasses one by one across the room to his guests. Brianna accepted hers with equal care, but declined a chair, instead leaning gracefully against the corner of the china cabinet.

Edgars plumped at last onto the rump-sprung sofa, ignoring the debris, and raised his glass.

"Cheers, mate," he said briefly, and took a long, slurping gulp. "Wotcher say yer name is?" he demanded, emerging abruptly from his immersion. "Oh, Roger, right. Gilly never mentioned ye . . . but then, she wouldn'," he added moodily. "Never knew nothin' about her family, and she wasn' sayin'. Think she was ashamed of 'em all . . . but you don't look such a nelly," he said, generously. "Yer lass is a looker, at least. Aye, that sounds right, eh? 'Yer lass is a looker, at least!' Hear 'at, eh?" He laughed uproariously, spraying whisky droplets.

"Yeah," said Roger. "Thanks." He took a small sip of his drink. Brianna, offended, turned her back on Edgars and affected to be examining the contents of the china closet through the bevel-cut glass doors.

There seemed no point in beating around the bush, Roger decided. Edgars wouldn't recognize subtlety if it bit him on the bum at this point, and there seemed a substantial danger that he might pass out soon, at the rate he was going.

"D'you know where Gillian is?" he asked bluntly. Every time he said her name, it felt strange on his tongue. This time, he couldn't help glancing up at the mantelpiece, where the photo smiled serenely on the debauch below.

Edgars shook his head, swinging it slowly back and forth over his glass like an ox over a corncrib. He was a short, heavyset man, about Roger's age, perhaps, but looking older because of the heavy growth of unshaved beard and disheveled black hair.

"Nah," he said. "Thought maybe you knew. It'll be the Nats or the Roses, likely, but I've no kep' up. I couldn' say who, specially."

"Nats?" Roger's heart began to speed up. "You mean the Scottish Nationalists?"

Edgars's eyelids were beginning to droop, but they blinked open once more.

"Oh, aye. Bloody Nats. 'S where I met Gilly, aye?"

"When was this, Mr. Edgars?"

Roger looked up in surprise at the soft voice from above. It wasn't the photograph that had spoken, though, but Brianna, looking intently down at Greg Edgars. Roger couldn't tell whether she was merely making conversation, or if she suspected something. Her face showed nothing beyond polite interest.

"Dunno . . . maybe two, three years gone. Fun at first, hm? Toss the bloody English out, join the Common Market on our own . . . beer in the pub and a cuddle i' the back of the van comin' home from rallies. Mmm." Edgars shook his head again, dreamy-eyed at the vision. Then the smile faded from his face, and he frowned into his drink. "That's before she went potty."

"Potty?" Roger took another quick glance at the photo. Intense, yes. She looked that. But not barking mad, surely. Or could you tell, from a photo?

"Aye. Society o' the White Rose. Charlie's m' darlin'. Will ye no come back again, and all that rot. Lot of jimmies dressed up in kilts and full rig, wi' swords and all. All right if ye like it, o' course," he added, with a cockeyed attempt at objectivity. "But Gilly'd always take a thing too far. On and on about the Bonnie Prince, and wouldn' it be a thing if he'd won the '45? Blokes in the kitchen 'til all hours, drinking up the beer and arguing why he hadn't. In the Gaelic, too." He rolled his eyes. "Load o' rubbish." He drained his glass to emphasize this opinion.

Roger could feel Brianna's eyes boring into the side of his neck like gimlets. He pulled at his collar to loosen it, though he wasn't wearing a tie and his collar button was undone.

"I don't suppose your wife's also interested in standing stones, is she, Mr. Edgars?" Brianna wasn't bothering a lot with the polite interest anymore; her voice was sharp enough to cut cheese. The effect was largely wasted on Edgars.

"Stones?" He seemed fuddled, and stuck a forefinger into one ear, screwing it in industriously, as though in hopes of improving his hearing.

"The prehistoric stone circles. Like the Clava Cairns," Roger offered, naming one of the more famous local landmarks. In for a penny, in for a pound, he thought, with a mental sigh of resignation. Brianna was plainly never going to speak to him again, so he might as well find out what he could.

"Oh, those." Edgars uttered a short laugh. "Aye, and every other bit o' auld rubbish ye could name. That's the last bit, and the worst. Down at that In-stitewt day an' night, spendin' all my money on courses . . . courses! Make a cat laugh, ay? Fairy tales, they teach 'em there. Ye'll learn nothin' useful in that place, lass, I told her. Whyna learn to type? Get a job, if she's bored. 'S what I tell't her. So she left," he said morosely. "Not seen her in two weeks." He stared into his wineglass as though surprised to find it empty.

"Have another?" he offered, reaching for the bottle, but Brianna shook her head decidedly.

"Thanks, no. We have to be going. *Don't* we, Roger?"

Seeing the dangerous glint in her eye, Roger wasn't at all sure that he wouldn't be better off staying to split the rest of the bottle with Greg Edgars. Still, it was a long walk home, if he let Brianna take the car. He rose with a sigh, and shook Edgars's hand in farewell. It was warm and surprisingly firm in its grip, if a trifle moist.

Edgars followed them to the door, clutching the bottle by the neck. He peered after them through the screen, suddenly calling down the walk, "If ye see Gilly, tell her to come home, eh?"

Roger turned and waved at the blurry figure in the lighted rectangle of the door.

"I'll try," he called, the words sticking in his throat.

They made it to the walk and half down the street toward the pub before she rounded on him.

"What in bloody hell are you up to?" she said. She sounded angry, but not hysterical. "You told me you haven't any family in the Highlands, so what's all this about cousins? Who is that woman in the picture?"

He looked round the darkened street for inspiration, but there was no help for it. He took a deep breath and took her by the arm.

"Geillis Duncan," he said.

She stopped stock-still, and the shock of it jarred up his own arm. With great deliberation, she detached her elbow from his grip. The delicate tissue of the evening had torn down the middle.

"Don't . . . touch . . . me," she said through her teeth. "Is this something Mother thought up?"

Despite his resolve to be understanding, Roger felt himself growing angry in return.

"Look," he said, "can you not think of anyone but yourself in this? I know it's been a shock to you—God, how could it not be? And if you cannot bring yourself even to think about it . . . well, I'll not push you to it. But there's your mother to consider. And there's me, as well."

"You? What have you got to do with it?" It was too dark to see her face, but the surprise in her voice was evident.

He had not meant to complicate matters further by telling her of his involvement, but it was clearly too late for keeping secrets. And no doubt Claire had seen that, when she suggested his taking Brianna out this evening.

In a flash of revelation, he realized for the first time just what Claire had meant. She did have one means of proving her story to Brianna, beyond question. She had Gillian Edgars, who had—perhaps—not yet vanished to meet her fate as Geillis Duncan, tied to a flaming stake beneath the rowan trees of Leoch. The most stubborn cynic would be convinced, he supposed, by the sight of someone disappearing into the past before their eyes. No wonder Claire had wanted to find Gillian Edgars.

In a few words, he told Brianna his relationship with the would-be witch of Cranesmuir.

"And so it looks like being my life or hers," he ended, shrugging, hideously conscious of how ridiculously melodramatic it sounded. "Claire—your mother—she left it to me. But I thought I had to find her, at the least."

Brianna had stopped walking to listen to him. The dim light from a corner shop caught the gleam of her eyes as she stared at him.

"You believe it, then?" she asked. There was no incredulity or scorn in her voice; she was altogether serious.

He sighed and reached for her arm again. She didn't resist, but fell into step beside him.

"Yes," he said. "I had to. You didn't see your mother's face, when she saw the words written inside her ring. That was real—real enough to break my heart."

"You'd better tell me," she said, after a short silence. "What words?"

By the time he had finished the story, they had reached the car-park behind the pub.

"Well . . ." Brianna said hesitantly. "If . . ." She stopped again, looking into his eyes. She was standing near enough for him to feel the warmth of her breasts, close to his chest, but he didn't reach for her. The kirk of St. Kilda was a long way off, and neither of them wanted to remember the grave beneath the yew trees, where the names of her parents were written in stone.

"I don't know, Roger," she said, shaking her head. The neon sign over the pub's back door made purple glints in her hair. "I just can't . . . I can't think about it yet. But . . ." Words failed her, but she lifted a hand and touched his cheek, light as the brush of the evening wind. "I'll think of you," she whispered.

———

When you come right down to it, committing burglary with a key is not really a difficult proposition. The chance that either Mrs. Andrews or Dr. McEwan was going to come back and cop me in the act were vanishingly small. Even if they had, all I would have to do is say that I'd come back to look for a lost pocketbook, and found the door open. I was out of practice, but deception had at one point been second nature to me. Lying was like riding a bicycle, I thought; you don't forget how.

So it wasn't the act of getting hold of Gillian Edgars's notebook that made my heart race and my breath sound loud in my own ears. It was the book itself.

As Master Raymond had told me in Paris, the power and the danger of magic lie in the people who believe it. From the glimpse I had had of the contents earlier, the actual information written in this cardboard notebook was an extraordinary mishmash of fact, speculation, and flat-out fantasy that could be of importance only to the writer. But I felt an almost physical revulsion at touching it. Knowing who had written it,

I knew it for what it likely was: a grimoire, a magician's book of secrets.

Still, if there existed any clue to Geillis Duncan's whereabouts and intentions, it would be here. Suppressing a shudder at the touch of the slick cover, I tucked it under my coat, holding it in place with my elbow for the trip down the stairs.

Safely out on the street, still I kept the book under my elbow, the cover growing clammy with perspiration as I walked. I felt as though I were transporting a bomb, something which must be handled with scrupulous carefulness, in order to prevent an explosion.

I walked for some time, finally turning into the front garden of a small Italian restaurant with a terrace near the river. The night was chilly, but a small electric fire made the terrace tables warm enough for use; I chose one and ordered a glass of Chianti. I sipped at it for some time, the notebook lying on the paper placemat in front of me, in the concealing shadow of a basket of garlic bread.

It was late April. Only a few days until May Day—the Feast of Beltane. That was when I had made my own impromptu voyage into the past. I supposed it was possible that there was something about the date—or just the general time of year? It had been mid-April when I returned—that made that eerie passage possible. Or maybe not; maybe the time of year had nothing to do with it. I ordered another glass of wine.

It could be that only certain people had the ability to penetrate a barrier that was solid to everyone else—something in the genetic makeup? Who knew? Jamie had not been able to enter it, though I could. And Geillis Duncan obviously had—or would. Or wouldn't, depending. I thought of young Roger Wakefield, and felt mildly queasy. I thought perhaps I had better have some food to go with the wine.

The visit to the Institute had convinced me that wherever Gillian/Geillis was, she had not yet made her own fateful passage. Anyone who had studied the legends of the Highlands would know that the Feast of Beltane was approaching; surely anyone planning such an expedition would undertake it then? But I had no idea where she might be, if she wasn't at home; in hiding? Performing some peculiar rite of preparation, picked up from Fiona's group of neo-Druids? The notebook might hold a clue, but God only knew.

God only also knew what my own motives were in this; I had thought I did, but was no longer sure. Had I involved Roger in the search for Geillis because it seemed the only way of convincing Brianna? And yet—even if we found her in time, my own purpose would be served only if Gillian succeeded in going back. And thus, in dying by fire.

When Geillis Duncan had been condemned as a witch, Jamie had said to me, "Dinna grieve for her, Sassenach; she's a wicked woman." And whether she had been wicked or mad, it had made little difference at the time. Should I not have left well enough alone, and left her to find her own fate? Still, I thought, she had once saved my life. In spite of what she was—would be—did I owe it to her to try to save her life? And thus perhaps doom Roger? What right did I have to meddle any further?

It isna a matter of right, Sassenach, I heard Jamie's voice saying, with a tinge of impatience. *It's a question of duty. Of honor.*

"Honor, is it?" I said aloud. "And what's that?" The waiter with my plate of tortellini Portofino looked startled.

"Eh?" he said.

"Never mind," I said, too distracted to care much what he thought of me. "Perhaps you'd better bring the rest of the bottle."

I finished my meal surrounded by ghosts. Finally, fortified by food and wine, I pushed my empty plate aside, and opened Gillian Edgars's gray notebook.

49

Blessed Are Those . . .

There's no place darker than a Highland road in the middle of a moonless night. I could see the flash of passing headlights now and then, silhouetting Roger's head and shoulders in a sudden flare of light. They were hunched forward, as though in defense against oncoming danger. Bree sat hunched as well, curled into the corner of the seat beside me. We were all three self-contained, insulated from each other, sealed in small, individual pockets of silence, inside the larger silence of the car and its rushing flight.

My fists curled in the pockets of my coat, idly scooping up coins and small bits of debris; shredded tissue, a pencil stub, a tiny rubber ball left on the floor of my office by a small patient. My thumb circled and identified the milled edge of an American quarter, the broad embossed face of an English penny, and the serrated edge of a key—the key to Gillian Edgars's carrel, which I had neglected to return to the Institute.

I had tried again to call Greg Edgars, just before we left the old manse. The phone had rung again and again without answer.

I stared at the dark glass of the window beside me, seeing neither my own faint reflection nor the massy shapes of stone walls and scattered trees that rushed by in the night. Instead, I saw the row of books, arranged on the carrel's single shelf in a line as neat as a row of apothecary's jars. And below, the notebook filled with fine cursive script, laying out in strict order conclusion and delusion, mingling myth and science, drawing from learned men and legends, all of it based on the power of dreams. To any casual observer, it could be either a muddle of half-thought-out nonsense or, at best, the outline for a clever-silly novel. Only to me did it have the look of a careful, deliberate plan.

In a parody of the scientific method, the first section of the book was titled "Observations." It contained disjointed references, tidy drawings, and carefully numbered tables.

"The position of sun and moon on the Feast of Beltane" was one, with a list of more than two hundred paired figures laid out beneath. Similar tables existed for Hogmanay and Midsummer's Day, and another for Samhain, the Feast of All Hallows. The ancient feasts of fire and sun, and Beltane's sun would rise tomorrow.

The central section of the notebook was titled "Speculations." That was accurate, at least, I reflected wryly. One page had borne this entry, in neat, slanting script: "The Druids burnt sacrificial victims in wicker cages shaped like men, but individuals were killed by strangling, and the throat slit to drain the body of blood. Was it fire or blood that was the necessary element?" The cold-blooded curiosity of the question brought Geillis Duncan's face before me clearly—not the wide-eyed, straight-haired student whose portrait adorned the Institute, but the secretive, half-smiling fiscal's wife, ten years older, versed in the uses of drugs and the body, who lured men to her purposes, and killed without passion to achieve her ends.

And the last few pages of the book, neatly labeled "Conclusions," which had led us to this dark journey, on the eve of the Feast of Beltane. I curled my fingers around the key, wishing with all my heart that Greg Edgars had answered his phone.

*   ⟶

Roger slowed, turning onto the bumpy dirt lane that led past the base of the hill called Craigh na Dun.

"I don't see anything," he said. He hadn't spoken in so long that the statement came out gruffly, sounding belligerent.

"Well, of course not," Brianna said impatiently. "You can't see the stone circle from here."

Roger grunted in reply, and slowed the car still more. Obviously, Brianna's nerves were stretched, but so were his own. Only Claire seemed calm, unaffected by the growing air of tension in the car.

"She's here," Claire said suddenly. Roger slammed on the brakes so abruptly that both Claire and her daughter pitched forward, thumping into the back of the seat in front of them.

"Be careful, you idiot!" Brianna snapped furiously at Roger. She shoved a hand through her hair, pushing it off her face with a quick, nervous gesture. A swallow ran visibly down her throat as she bent to peer through the dark window.

"Where?" she said.

Claire nodded ahead to the right, keeping her hands shoved deep into her pockets.

"There's a car parked, just behind that thicket."

Roger licked his lips and reached for the door handle.

"It's Edgars's car. I'll go and look; you stay here."

Brianna flung her door open with a squeal of metal from the unoiled hinges. Her silent look of scorn made Roger flush red in the dim glow of the dome light overhead.

She was back almost before Roger had gotten out of the car himself.

"No one there," she reported. She glanced up at the top of the hill. "Do you think . . . ?"

Claire finished buttoning up her coat, and stepped into the darkness without answering her daughter's question.

"The path is this way," she said.

She led the way, perforce, and Roger, watching the pale form drift ghostlike up the hill ahead of him, was forcibly reminded of that earlier trip up a steep hill, to St. Kilda's kirkyard. So was Brianna; she hesitated and he heard her mutter something angrily under her breath, but then her hand reached for his elbow, and gave it a hard squeeze—whether as encouragement or as a plea for support, he couldn't tell. It encouraged *him*, in any case, and he patted the hand and tugged it through the curve of his arm. In spite of his general doubts, and the undeniable eeriness of the whole expedition, he felt a sense of excitement as they approached the crest of the hill.

It was a clear night, moonless and very dark, with no more than the tiny gleams of mica flecks in the starlight serving to distinguish the looming stones of the ancient circle from the night around them. The trio paused on the gently rounded top of the hill, huddling together like a misplaced flock of sheep. Roger's own breath sounded unnaturally loud to himself.

"This," said Brianna through her teeth, "is *silly*!"

"No, it isn't," said Roger. He felt suddenly breathless, as

though a constricting band had squeezed the air from his chest. "There's a light over there."

It was barely there—no more than a flicker that promptly disappeared—but she saw it. He heard the sharp intake of her breath.

Now what? Roger wondered. Ought they to shout? Or would the noise of visitors frighten their quarry into precipitate action? And if so, what action might that be?

He saw Claire shake her head suddenly, as though trying to dismiss a buzzing insect. She took a step back, away from the nearest stone, and blundered into him.

He grabbed her by the arm, murmuring, "Steady, steady there," as one might to a horse. Her face was a dim blur in the starlight, but he could feel the quiver that ran through her, like electricity through a wire. He stood frozen, holding her arm, stiff with indecision.

It was the sudden stink of petrol that jerked him into motion. He was vaguely conscious of Brianna, head flung up as the smell met her nostrils, turning toward the north end of the circle, and then he had dropped Claire's arm, and was through the surrounding bushes and the stones themselves, striding toward the center of the ring, where a hunched black figure made an inkblot on the lighter darkness of the grass.

Claire's voice came from behind him, strong and urgent, shattering the silence.

"Gillian!" she called.

There was a soft, sudden whoosh, and the night lit up in brilliance. Dazzled, Roger fell back a pace, stumbling and dropping to his knees.

For a moment, there was nothing but the sharp pain of light on his retinas, and the blaze of brightness that hid everything behind it. He heard a cry beside him, and felt Brianna's hand on his shoulder. He blinked hard, eyes streaming, and sight began to return.

The slim figure stood between them and the fire, silhouetted like an hourglass. As his sight cleared, he realized that she was dressed in a long, full skirt and tight bodice—the clothes of another time. She had turned at the call, and he had a brief impression of wide eyes and fair, flying hair, lifted and tossed in the hot wind of the fire.

He found time, struggling to his feet, to wonder how she

had dragged a log of that size up here. Then the smell of burned hair and crackled skin hit his face like a blow, and he remembered. Greg Edgars was not at home tonight. Not knowing whether blood or fire was the necessary element, she had chosen both.

He pushed past Brianna, focused only on the tall, slim girl before him, and the image of a face that mirrored his own. She saw him coming, turned and ran like the wind for the cleft stone at the end of the circle. She had a knapsack of rough canvas, slung over one shoulder; he heard her grunt as it swung heavily and struck her in the side.

She paused for an instant, hand outstretched to the rock, and looked back. He could have sworn that her eyes rested on him, met his own and held them, beyond the barrier of the fire's blaze. He opened his mouth in a wordless shout. She whirled then, light as a dancing spark, and vanished in the cleft of the rock.

The fire, the body, the night itself, disappeared abruptly in a shriek of blinding noise. Roger found himself facedown in the grass, clutching at the earth in frantic search of a familiar sensation to which to anchor his sanity. The search was vain; none of his senses seemed to function—even the touch of the ground was insubstantial, amorphous as though he lay on quicksand, not granite.

Blinded by whiteness, deafened by the scream of rending stone, he groped, flailing wildly, out of touch with his own extremities, conscious only of an immense pull and the need to resist it.

There was no sense of time passing; it felt as though he had been struggling in emptiness forever, when he at last became aware of something outside himself. Hands that gripped his arms with desperate strength, and the smothering softness of breasts thrust against his face.

Hearing began gradually to return, and with it the sound of a voice calling his name. Calling *him* names, in fact, panting between phrases.

"You idiot! You . . . jerk! Wake *up*, Roger, you . . . ass!" Her voice was muffled, but the sense of it reached him clearly. With a superhuman effort, he reached up and got hold of her wrists. He rolled, feeling ponderous as the start of an avalanche, and found himself blinking stupidly at the tear-

streaked face of Brianna Randall, eyes dark as caves in the
dying light of the fire.

The smell of petrol and roasting flesh was overwhelming.
He turned aside and gagged, retching heavily into the damp
grass. He was too occupied even to be grateful that his sense
of smell had returned.

He wiped his mouth on his sleeve and groped unsteadily
for Brianna's arm. She was huddled into herself, shaking.

"Oh, God," she said. "Oh, God. I didn't think I could
stop you. You were crawling straight to it. Oh, God."

She didn't resist as he pulled her to him, but neither did
she respond to him. She merely went on shaking, the tears
running from wide, empty eyes, repeating "Oh, God," at intervals, like a broken record.

"Hush," he said, patting her. "It will be all right. Hush."
The spinning sensation in his head was easing, though he still
felt as though he had been split into several pieces and scattered violently among the points of the compass.

There was a faint, crackling *pop* from the darkening object on the ground, but beyond that and Brianna's mechanical
ejaculations, the stillness of the night was returning. He put
his hands to his ears, as though to still the echoes of the
killing noise.

"You heard it, too?" he asked. Brianna went on crying,
but nodded her head, jerky as a puppet.

"Did your—" he began, still laboriously assembling his
thoughts piecemeal, then snapped upright as one came to
him full-formed.

"Your mother!" he exclaimed, gripping Brianna hard by
both arms. "Claire! Where is she?"

Brianna's mouth dropped open in shock, and she scrambled to her feet, wildly scanning the confines of the empty
circle, where the man-high stones loomed stark, half-seen in
the shadows of the dying fire.

"Mother!" she screamed. "Mother, *where are you*?"

◆━━━━➤

"It's all right," Roger said, trying to sound authoritatively reassuring. "She'll be all right now."

In truth, he had no idea whether Claire Randall would

ever be all right. She was alive, at least, and that was all he could vouch for.

They had found her, senseless in the grass near the edge of the circle, white as the rising moon above, with nothing but the slow, dark seep of blood from her abraded palms to testify that her heart still beat. Of the hellish journey down the path to the car, her dead weight slung across his shoulder, bumping awkwardly as stones rolled under his feet and twigs snatched at his clothing, he preferred to remember nothing.

The trip down the cursed hill had exhausted him; it was Brianna, the bones of her face stark with concentration, who had driven them back to the manse, hands clamped to the wheel like vises. Slumped in the seat beside her, Roger had seen in the rearview mirror the last faint glow of the hilltop behind them, where a small, luminous cloud floated like a puff of cannon smoke, mute evidence of battle past.

Brianna hovered now over the sofa where her mother lay, motionless as a tomb figure on a sarcophagus. With a shudder, Roger had avoided the hearth where the banked fire lay sleeping, and had instead pulled up the small electric fire with which the Reverend had warmed his feet on winter nights. Its bars glowed orange and hot, and it made a loud, friendly whirring noise that covered the silence in the study.

Roger sat on a low stool beside the sofa, feeling limp and starchless. With the last remnants of resolve, he reached toward the telephone table, his hand hovering a few inches above the instrument.

"Should we—" He had to stop to clear his throat. "Should we . . . call a doctor? The police?"

"No." Brianna's voice was intent, almost absentminded, as she bent over the still figure on the couch. "She's coming around."

The domed eyelids stirred, tightened briefly in the returning memory of pain, then relaxed and opened. Her eyes were clear and soft as honey. They drifted to and fro, skimmed over Brianna, standing tall and stiff at Roger's side, and fixed on his face.

Claire's lips were bloodless as the rest of her face; it took more than one try to get the words out, in a hoarse whisper. "Did she . . . go back?"

Her fingers were twisted in the fabric of her skirt, and he

saw the faint, dark smear of blood they left behind. His own hands clutched instinctively on his knees, palms tingling. She had held on, too, then, grappling among the grass and gravel for any small hold against the engulfment of the past. He closed his eyes against the memory of that pulling rupture, nodding.

"Yes," he said. "She went."

The clear eyes went at once to her daughter's face, brows above them arched as though in question. But it was Brianna who asked.

"It was true, then?" she asked hesitantly. "Everything was true?"

Roger felt the small shudder that ran through the girl's body, and without thinking about it, reached up to take her hand. He winced involuntarily as she squeezed it, and suddenly in memory heard one of the Reverend's texts: "Blessed are those who have not seen, and have believed." And those who *must* see, in order to believe? The effects of belief wrought by seeing trembled fearful at his side, terrified at what else must now be believed.

Even as the girl tightened, bracing herself to meet a truth she had already seen, the lines of Claire's tensed body on the sofa relaxed. The pale lips curved in the shadow of a smile, and a look of profound peace smoothed the strained white face, and settled glowing in the golden eyes.

"It's true," she said. A tinge of color came back into the pallid cheeks. "Would your mother lie to you?" And she closed her eyes once more.

Roger reached down to switch off the electric fire. The night was cold, but he could stay no longer in the study, his temporary sanctuary. He still felt groggy, but he couldn't delay longer. The decision had to be made.

It had been dawn before the police and the doctor had finished their work the night before, filling in their forms, taking statements and vital signs, doing their best to explain away the truth. "Blessed are they who have not seen," he thought again, devoutly, "but who have believed." Especially in this case.

Finally, they had left, with their forms and badges and

cars with flashing lights, to oversee the removal of Greg Edgars's body from the ring of stone, to issue a warrant for the
arrest of his wife, who, having lured her husband to his death,
had fled the scene. To put it mildly, Roger thought dazedly.

Exhausted in mind and body, Roger had left the Randalls to the care of the doctor and Fiona, and had gone to
bed, not bothering to undress or turn back the quilts, merely
collapsing into a welcome oblivion. Roused near sunset by
gnawing hunger, he had stumbled downstairs to find his
guests, similarly silent, if less disheveled, helping Fiona with
the preparation of supper.

It had been a quiet meal. The atmosphere was not
strained; it was as though communication ran unseen among
the people at the table. Brianna sat close to her mother,
touching her now and then in the passing of food, as though
to reassure herself of her presence. She had glanced occasionally at Roger, shy small looks from beneath her lashes,
but didn't talk to him.

Claire said little, and ate almost nothing, but sat quite
still, quiet and peaceful as a loch in the sun, her thoughts
turned inward. After dinner, she had excused herself and
gone to sit in the deep window seat at the end of the hall,
pleading tiredness. Brianna had cast a quick glance at her
mother, silhouetted in the last glow of the fading sun as she
faced the window, and gone to help Fiona in the kitchen with
the dishes. Roger had gone to the study, Fiona's good meal
heavy in his stomach, to think.

Two hours later, he was still thinking, to remarkably little
effect. Books were stacked untidily on the desk and table, left
half-open on the seats of chairs and the back of the sofa, and
gaping holes in the crowded bookshelves testified to the effort of his haphazard research.

It had taken some time, but he had found it—the short
passage he remembered from his earlier search on Claire
Randall's behalf. Those results had brought her comfort and
peace; this wouldn't—if he told her. And if he were right?
But he must be; it accounted for that misplaced grave, so far
from Culloden.

He rubbed a hand over his face, and felt the rasp of
beard. Not surprising that he had forgotten to shave, what
with everything. When he closed his eyes, he could still smell

smoke and blood; see the blaze of fire on dark rock, and the strands of fair hair, flying just beyond the reach of his fingers. He shuddered at the memory, and felt a sudden surge of resentment. Claire had destroyed his own peace of mind; did he owe her any less? And Brianna—if she knew the truth now, should she not know all of it?

Claire was still there at the end of the hall; feet curled under her on the window seat, staring out at the blank black stretch of the night-filled glass.

"Claire?" His voice felt scratchy from disuse, and he cleared his throat and tried again. "Claire? I . . . have something to tell you."

She turned and looked up at him, no more than the faintest curiosity visible on her features. She wore a look of calm, the look of one who has borne terror, despair, and mourning, and the desperate burden of survival—and has endured. Looking at her, he felt suddenly that he couldn't do it.

But she had told the truth; he must do likewise.

"I found something." He raised the book in a brief, futile gesture. "About . . . Jamie." Speaking that name aloud seemed to brace him, as though the big Scot himself had been conjured by his calling, to stand solid and unmoving in the hallway, between his wife and Roger. Roger took a deep breath in preparation.

"What is it?"

"The last thing he meant to do. I think . . . I think he failed."

Her face paled suddenly, and she glanced wide-eyed at the book.

"His men? But I thought you found—"

"I did," Roger interrupted. "No, I'm fairly sure he succeeded in that. He got the men of Lallybroch out; he saved them from Culloden, and set them on the road home."

"But then . . ."

"He meant to turn back—back to the battle—and I think he did that, too." He was increasingly reluctant, but it had to be said. Finding no words of his own, he flipped the book open, and read aloud:

"After the final battle at Culloden, eighteen Jacobite officers, all wounded, took refuge in the old house and for

two days, their wounds untended, lay in pain; then they were taken out to be shot. One of them, a Fraser of the Master of Lovat's regiment, escaped the slaughter; the others were buried at the edge of the domestic park."

"*One man, a Fraser of the Master of Lovat's regiment, escaped. . . .*" Roger repeated softly. He looked up from the stark page to see her eyes, wide and unseeing as a deer's fixed in the headlights of an oncoming car.

"He meant to die on Culloden Field," Roger whispered. "But he didn't."

Acknowledgments

The author's thanks and best wishes to:

the three Jackies (Jackie Cantor, Jackie LeDonne, and my mother), guardian angels of my books; the four Johns (John Myers, John E. Simpson, Jr., John Woram, and John Stith) for Constant Readership, Scottish miscellanea, and general enthusiasm; Janet McConnaughey, Margaret J. Campbell, Todd Heimarck, Deb and Dennis Parisek, Holly Heinel, and all the other LitForumites who do not begin with the letter J—especially Robert Riffle, for plantago, French epithets, ebony keyboards, and his everdiscerning eye; Paul Solyn, for belated nasturtiums, waltzes, copperplate handwriting, and botanical advice; Margaret Ball, for references, useful suggestions, and great conversation; Fay Zachary, for lunch; Dr. Gary Hoff, for medical advice and consultation (he had nothing to do with the descriptions of how to disembowel someone); the poet Barry Fogden, for translations from the English; Labhriunn MacIan, for Gaelic imprecations and the generous use of his most poetic name; Kathy Allen-Webber, for general assistance with the French (if anything is still in the wrong tense, it's my fault); Vonda N. McIntyre, for sharing tricks of the trade; Michael Lee West, for wonderful comments on the text, and the sort of phone conversations that make my family yell, "Get off the phone! We're starving!"; Michael Lee's mother, for reading the manuscript, looking up periodically to ask her critically acclaimed daughter, "Why don't you write something like this?"; and Elizabeth Buchan, for queries, suggestions, and advice—the effort involved was nearly as enormous as the help provided.

And don't miss the next
installment of the acclaimed
OUTLANDER series . . .

DIANA GABALDON'S

VOYAGER

Available now
from Dell Books!

Read on for a preview. . .

Voyager
On Sale Now

Inverness
May 2, 1968

"Of course he's dead!" Claire's voice was sharp with agitation; it rang loudly in the half-empty study, echoing among the rifled bookshelves. She stood against the cork-lined wall like a prisoner awaiting a firing squad, staring from her daughter to Roger Wakefield and back again.

"I don't think so." Roger felt terribly tired. He rubbed a hand over his face, then picked up the folder from the desk; the one containing all the research he'd done since Claire and her daughter had first come to him, three weeks before, and asked his help.

He opened the folder and thumbed slowly through the contents. The Jacobites of Culloden. The Rising of the '45. The gallant Scots who had rallied to the banner of Bonnie Prince Charlie, and cut through Scotland like a blazing sword—only to come to ruin and defeat against the Duke of Cumberland on the gray moor at Culloden.

"Here," he said, plucking out several sheets clipped together. The archaic writing looked odd, rendered in the black crispness of a photocopy. "This is the muster roll of the Master of Lovat's regiment."

He thrust the thin sheaf of papers at Claire, but it was her daughter, Brianna, who took the sheets from him and began to turn the pages, a slight frown between her reddish brows.

"Read the top sheet," Roger said. "Where it says 'Officers.'"

"All right. 'Officers,' " she read aloud, " 'Simon, Master of Lovat' . . ."

"The Young Fox," Roger interrupted. "Lovat's son. And five more names, right?"

Brianna cocked one brow at him, but went on reading.

" 'William Chisholm Fraser, Lieutenant; George D'Amerd Fraser Shaw, Captain; Duncan Joseph Fraser, Lieutenant; Bayard Murray Fraser, Major,' " she paused, swallowing, before reading the last name, " '. . . James Alexander Malcolm MacKenzie Fraser, Captain.' " She lowered the papers, looking a little pale. "My father."

Claire moved quickly to her daughter's side, squeezing the girl's arm. She was pale, too.

"Yes, she said to Roger. "I know he went to Culloden. When he left me . . . there at the stone circle . . . he meant to go back to Culloden Field, to rescue his men who were with Charles Stuart. And we know he did"—she nodded at the folder on the desk, its manila surface blank and innocent in the lamplight—"you found their names. But . . . but . . . Jamie . . ." Speaking the name aloud seemed to rattle her, and she clamped her lips tight.

Now it was Brianna's turn to support her mother.

"He meant to go back, you said." Her eyes, dark blue and encouraging, were intent on her mother's face. "He meant to take his men away from the field, and then go back to the battle."

Claire nodded, recovering herself slightly.

"He knew he hadn't much chance of getting away; if the English caught him . . . he said he'd rather die in battle. That's what he meant to do." She turned to Roger, her gaze an unsettling amber. Her eyes always reminded him of hawk's eyes, as though she could see a good deal farther than most people. "I can't believe he didn't die there—so many men did, and *he* meant to!"

Almost half the Highland army had died at Culloden, cut down in a blast of cannonfire and searing musketry. But not Jamie Fraser.

"No," Roger said doggedly. "That bit I read you from Linklater's book—" He reached to pick it up, a white volume, entitled *The Prince in the Heather.*

" *'Following the battle,'* " he read, " *'eighteen wounded Jacobite officers took refuge in the farmhouse near the moor. Here they lay in pain, their wounds untended, for two days. At the end of that time, they were taken out and shot. One man, a Fraser of the*

Master of Lovat's regiment, escaped the slaughter. The rest are buried at the edge of the domestic park.'

"See?" he said, laying the book down and looking earnestly at the two women over its pages. "An officer, of the Master of Lovat's regiment." He grabbed up the sheets of the muster roll.

"And here they are! Just six of them. Now, we know the man in the farmhouse can't have been Young Simon; he's a well-known historical figure, and we know very well what happened to him. He retreated from the field—unwounded, mind you—with a group of his men, and fought his way north, eventually making it back to Beaufort Castle, near here." He waved vaguely at the full-length window, through which the nighttime lights of Inverness twinkled faintly.

"Nor was the man who escaped Leanach farmhouse any of the other four officers—William, George, Duncan, or Bayard," Roger said. "Why?" He snatched another paper out of the folder and brandished it, almost triumphantly. "Because they all *did* die at Culloden! All four of them were killed on the field—I found their names listed on a plaque in the church at Beauly."

Claire let out a long breath, then eased herself down into the old leather swivel chair behind the desk.

"Jesus H. Christ," she said. She closed her eyes and leaned forward, elbows on the desk, and her head against her hands, the thick, curly brown hair spilling forward to hide her face. Brianna laid a hand on Claire's back, face troubled as she bent over her mother. She was a tall girl, with large, fine bones, and her long red hair glowed in the warm light of the desk lamp.

"If he didn't die . . ." she began tentatively.

Claire's head snapped up. "But he *is* dead!" she said. Her face was strained, and small lines were visible around her eyes. "For God's sake, it's two hundred years; whether he died at Culloden or not, he's dead now!"

Brianna stepped back from her mother's vehemence, and lowered her head, so the red hair—her father's red hair—swung down beside her cheek.

"I guess so," she whispered. Roger could see she was fighting back tears. And no wonder, he thought. To find out in short order that first, the man you had loved and called "Father" all your life really *wasn't* your father, secondly, that your real father was a Highland Scot who had lived two hundred years ago, and thirdly, to realize that he had likely perished in some horrid fashion, unthinkably far from the wife and child he had sacrificed himself to save . . . enough to rattle one, Roger thought.

He crossed to Brianna and touched her arm. She gave him a brief, distracted glance, and tried to smile. He put his arms around her, even in his pity for her distress thinking how marvelous she felt, all warm and soft and springy at once.

Claire still sat at the desk, motionless. The yellow hawk's eyes had gone a softer color now, remote with memory. They rested sightlessly on the east wall of the study, still covered from floor to ceiling with the notes and memorabilia left by the Reverend Wakefield, Roger's late adoptive father.

Looking at the wall himself, Roger saw the annual meeting notice sent by the Society of the White Rose—those enthusiastic, eccentric souls who still championed the cause of Scottish independence, meeting in nostalgic tribute to Charles Stuart, and the Highland heroes who had followed him.

Roger cleared his throat slightly.

"Er . . . if Jamie Fraser didn't die at Culloden . . ." he said.

"Then he likely died soon afterward." Claire's eyes met Roger's, straight on, the cool look back in the yellow-brown depths. "You have no idea how it was," she said. "There was a famine in the Highlands—none of the men had eaten for days before the battle. He was wounded—we know that. Even if he escaped, there would have been . . . no one to care for him." Her voice caught slightly at that; she was a doctor now, had been a healer even then, twenty years before, when she had stepped through a circle of standing stones, and met destiny with James Alexander Malcolm MacKenzie Fraser.

Roger was conscious of them both; the tall, shaking girl he held in his arms, and the woman at the desk, so still, so poised. She had traveled through the stones, through time; been suspected as a spy, arrested as a witch, snatched by an unimaginable quirk of circumstance from the arms of her first husband, Frank Randall. And three years later, her second husband, James Fraser, had sent her back through the stones, pregnant, in a desperate effort to save her and the unborn child from the onrushing disaster that would soon engulf him.

Surely, he thought to himself, she's been through enough? But Roger was a historian. He had a scholar's insatiable, amoral curiosity, too powerful to be constrained by simple compassion. More than that, he was oddly conscious of the third figure in the family tragedy in which he found himself involved—Jamie Fraser.

"If he didn't die at Culloden," he began again, more firmly, "then perhaps I can find out what did happen to him. Do you want me to try?" He waited, breathless, feeling Brianna's warm breath through his shirt.

Jamie Fraser had had a life, and a death. Roger felt obscurely that it was his duty to find out all the truth; that Jamie Fraser's women deserved to know all they could of him. For Brianna, such knowledge was all she would ever have of the father she had never known. And for Claire—behind the question he had asked was the thought that had plainly not yet struck her, stunned with shock as she was: she had crossed the barrier of time twice before. She could, just possibly, do it again. And if Jamie Fraser had not died at Culloden . . .

He saw awareness flicker in the clouded amber of her eyes, as the thought came to her. She was normally pale; now her face blanched white as the ivory handle of the letter opener before her on the desk. Her fingers closed around it, clenching so the knuckles stood out in knobs of bone.

She didn't speak for a long time. Her gaze fixed on Brianna and lingered there for a moment, then returned to Roger's face.

"Yes," she said, in a whisper so soft he could barely hear her. "Yes. Find out for me. Please. Find out."

T he foot traffic was heavy on the bridge over the River Ness, with folk streaming home to their teas. Roger moved in front of me, his wide shoulders protecting me from the buffets of the crowd around us.

I could feel my heart beating heavily against the stiff cover of the book I was clutching to my chest. It did that whenever I paused to think what we were truly doing. I wasn't sure which of the two possible alternatives was worse; to find that Jamie had died at Culloden, or to find that he hadn't.

The boards of the bridge echoed hollowly underfoot, as we trudged back toward the manse. My arms ached from the weight of the books I carried, and I shifted the load from one side to the other.

"Watch your bloody wheel, man!" Roger shouted, nudging me adroitly to the side, as a workingman on a bicycle plowed head-downward through the bridge traffic, nearly running me against the railing.

"Sorry!" came back the apologetic shout, and the rider gave a wave of the hand over his shoulder, as the bike wove its way between two groups of schoolchildren, coming home for their teas. I glanced back across the bridge, in case Brianna should be visible behind us, but there was no sign of her.

Roger and I had spent the afternoon at the Society for the Preservation of Antiquities. Brianna had gone down to the Highland Clans office, there to collect photocopies of a list of documents Roger had compiled.

"It's very kind of you to take all this trouble, Roger," I said, raising my voice to be heard above the echoing bridge and the river's rush.

"It's all right," he said, a little awkwardly, pausing for me to catch him up. "I'm curious," he added, smiling a little. "You know historians—can't leave a puzzle alone." He shook his head, trying to brush the windblown dark hair out of his eyes without using his hands.

I did know historians. I'd lived with one for twenty years. Frank hadn't wanted to leave this particular puzzle alone, either. But neither had he been willing to solve it. Frank had been dead for two years, though, and now it was my turn—mine and Brianna's.

"Have you heard yet from Dr. Linklater?" I asked, as we came down the arch of the bridge. Late in the afternoon as it was, the sun was still high, so far north as we were. Caught among the leaves of the lime trees on the riverbank, it glowed pink on the granite cenotaph that stood below the bridge.

Roger shook his head, squinting against the wind. "No, but it's been only a week since I wrote. If I don't hear by the Monday, I'll try telephoning. Don't worry"—he smiled sideways at me—"I was very circumspect. I just told him that for purposes of a study I was making, I needed a list—if one existed—of the Jacobite officers who were in Leanach farmhouse after Culloden, and if any information exists as to the survivor of that execution, could he refer me to the original sources?"

"Do you know Linklater?" I asked, easing my left arm by tilting the books sideways against my hip.

"No, but I wrote my request on the Balliol College letterhead, and made tactful reference to Mr. Cheesewright, my old tutor, who *does* know Linklater." Roger winked reassuringly, and I laughed.

His eyes were a brilliant, lucent green, bright against his olive skin. Curiosity might be his stated reason for helping us to find out Jamie's history, but I was well aware that his interest went a good bit deeper—in the direction of Brianna. I also knew that the interest was returned. What I didn't know was whether Roger realized that as well.

Back in the late Reverend Wakefield's study, I dropped my armload of books on the table in relief, and collapsed into the wing chair by the hearth, while Roger went to fetch a glass of lemonade from the manse's kitchen.

My breathing slowed as I sipped the tart sweetness, but my pulse stayed erratic, as I looked over the imposing stack of books we had brought back. Was Jamie in there somewhere? And if he was . . . my hands grew wet on the cold glass, and I choked the thought off. Don't look too far ahead, I cautioned myself. Much better to wait, and see what we might find.

Roger was scanning the shelves in the study, in search of other possibilities. The Reverend Wakefield, Roger's late adoptive father, had been both a good amateur historian, and a terrible pack rat; letters, journals, pamphlets and broadsheets, antique and contemporary volumes—all were crammed cheek by jowl together on the shelves.

Roger hesitated, then his hand fell on a stack of books sitting on the nearby table. They were Frank's books—an impressive achievement, so far as I could tell by reading the encomiums printed on the dust jackets.

"Have you ever read this?" he asked, picking up the volume entitled *The Jacobites*.

"No," I said. I took a restorative gulp of lemonade, and coughed. "No," I said again. "I couldn't." After my return, I had resolutely refused to look at any material dealing with Scotland's past, even though the eighteenth century had been one of Frank's areas of specialty. Knowing Jamie dead, and faced with the necessity of living without him, I avoided anything that might bring him to mind. A useless avoidance—there was no way of keeping him out of my mind, with Brianna's existence a daily reminder of him —but still, I could not read books about the Bonnie Prince—that terrible, futile young man—or his followers.

"I see. I just thought you might know whether there might be something useful in here." Roger paused, the flush deepening over his cheekbones. "Did—er, did your husband—Frank, I mean," he added hastily. "Did you tell him . . . um . . . about . . ." His voice trailed off, choked with embarrassment.

"Well, of course I did!" I said, a little sharply. "What did you think—I'd just stroll back into his office after being gone for three years and say, "Oh, hullo there, darling, and what would you like for supper tonight?'"

"No, of course not," Roger muttered. He turned away, eyes fixed on the bookshelves. The back of his neck was deep red with embarrassment.

"I'm sorry," I said, taking a deep breath. "It's a fair question to ask. It's only that it's—a bit raw, yet." A good deal more than a bit. I was both surprised and appalled to find just how raw the wound still was. I set the glass down on the table at my elbow. If we were going on with this, I was going to need something stronger than lemonade.

"Yes," I said. "I told him. All about the stones—about Jamie. Everything."

Roger didn't reply for a moment. Then he turned, halfway, so that only the strong, sharp lines of his profile were visible. He didn't look at me, but down at the stack of Frank's books, at the back-cover photo of Frank, leanly dark and handsome, smiling for posterity.

"Did he believe you?" Roger asked quietly.

My lips felt sticky from the lemonade, and I licked them before answering.

"No," I said. "Not at first. He thought I was mad; even had me vetted by a psychiatrist." I laughed, shortly, but the memory made me clench my fists with remembered fury.

"Later, then?" Roger turned to face me. The flush had faded from his skin, leaving only an echo of curiosity in his eyes. "What did he think?"

I took a deep breath and closed my eyes. "I don't know."

The tiny hospital in Inverness smelled unfamiliar, like carbolic disinfectant and starch.

I couldn't think, and tried not to feel. The return was much more terrifying than my venture into the past had been, for there, I had been shrouded by a protective layer of doubt and disbelief about where I was and what was happening, and had lived in constant hope of escape. Now I knew only too well where I was, and I knew that there was no escape. Jamie was dead.

The doctors and nurses tried to speak kindly to me, to feed me and bring me things to drink, but there was no room in me for anything but grief and terror. I had told them my name when they asked, but wouldn't speak further.

I lay in the clean white bed, fingers clamped tight together over my vulnerable belly, and kept my eyes shut. I visualized over and over the last things I had seen before I stepped through the stones—the rainy moor and Jamie's face—knowing that if I looked too long at my new surroundings, these sights would fade, replaced by mundane things like the nurses and the vase of flowers by my bed. I pressed one thumb secretly against the base of the other, taking an obscure comfort in the tiny wound there, a small cut in the shape of a J. Jamie had made it, at my demand—the last of his touch on my flesh.

I must have stayed that way for some time; I slept sometimes, dreaming of the last few days of the Jacobite Rising—I saw again the dead man in the wood, asleep beneath a coverlet of bright blue fungus, and Dougal MacKenzie dying on the floor of an attic in Culloden House; the ragged men of the Highland army, asleep in the muddy ditches; their last sleep before the slaughter.

I would wake screaming or moaning, to the scent of disinfectant and the sound of soothing words, incomprehensible against the echoes of Gaelic shouting in my dreams, and fall asleep again, my hurt clutched tight in the palm of my hand.

And then I opened my eyes and Frank was there. He stood in the door, smoothing back his dark hair with one hand, looking uncertain—and no wonder, poor man.

I lay back on the pillows, just watching him, not speaking. He had the look of his ancestors, Jack and Alex Randall; fine, clear, aristocratic features and a well-shaped head, under a spill of straight dark hair. His face had some indefinable difference from theirs, though, beyond the small differences of feature. There was no mark of fear or ruthlessness on him; neither the spirituality of Alex nor the icy arrogance of Jack. His lean face looked intelligent, kind, and slightly tired, unshaven and with smudges beneath his eyes. I knew without being told that he had driven all night to get here.

"Claire?" He came over to the bed, and spoke tentatively, as though not sure that I really was Claire.

I wasn't sure either, but I nodded and said, "Hullo, Frank." My voice was scratchy and rough, unaccustomed to speech.

He took one of my hands, and I let him have it.

"Are you . . . all right?" he said, after a minute. He was frowning slightly as he looked at me.

"I'm pregnant." That seemed the important point, to my disordered mind. I had not thought of what I would say to Frank, if I ever saw him again, but the moment I saw him standing in the door, it seemed to come clear in my mind. I would tell him I was pregnant, he would leave, and I would be alone with my last sight of Jamie's face, and the burning touch of him on my hand.

His face tightened a bit, but he didn't let go of my other hand. *"I know. They told me."* He took a deep breath and let it out. *"Claire—can you tell me what happened to you?"*

I felt quite blank for a moment, but then shrugged.

"I suppose so," I said. I mustered my thoughts wearily; I didn't want to be talking about it, but I had some feeling of obligation to this man. Not guilt, not yet; but obligation nonetheless. I had been married to him.

"Well," I said, *"I fell in love with someone else, and I married him. I'm sorry,"* I added, in response to the look of shock that crossed his face, *"I couldn't help it."*

He hadn't been expecting that. His mouth opened and closed for a bit and he gripped my hand, hard enough to make me wince and jerk it out of his grasp.

"What do you mean?" he said, his voice sharp. *"Where have you been, Claire?"* He stood up suddenly, looming over the bed.

"Do you remember that when I last saw you, I was going up to the stone circle on Craigh na Dun?"

"Yes?" He was staring down at me with an expression somewhere between anger and suspicion.

"Well"—I licked my lips, which had gone quite dry—*"the fact is, I walked through a cleft stone in that circle, and ended up in 1743."*

"Don't be facetious, Claire!"

"You think I'm being funny?" The thought was so absurd that I actually began to laugh, though I felt a good long way from real humor.

"Stop that!"

I quit laughing. Two nurses appeared at the door as though

by magic; they must have been lurking in the hall nearby. Frank leaned over and grabbed my arm.

"Listen to me," he said through his teeth. "You are going to tell me where you've been and what you've been doing!"

"I am telling you! Let go!" I sat up in bed and yanked at my arm, pulling it out of his grasp. "I told you; I walked through a stone and ended up two hundred years ago. And I met your bloody ancestor, Jack Randall, there!"

Frank blinked, entirely taken aback. "Who?"

"Black Jack Randall, and a bloody, filthy, nasty pervert he was, too!"

Frank's mouth hung open, and so did the nurses'. I could hear feet coming down the corridor behind them, and hurried voices.

"I had to marry Jamie Fraser to get away from Jack Randall, but then—Jamie—I couldn't help it, Frank, I loved him and I would have stayed with him if I could, but he sent me back because of Culloden, and the baby, and—" I broke off, as a man in a doctor's uniform pushed past the nurses by the door.

"Frank," I said tiredly, "I'm sorry. I didn't mean it to happen, and I tried all I could to come back—really, I did— but I couldn't. And now it's too late."

Despite myself, tears began to well up in my eyes and roll down my cheeks. Mostly for Jamie, and myself, and the child I carried, but a few for Frank as well. I sniffed hard and swallowed, trying to stop, and pushed myself upright in the bed.

"Look," I said, "I know you won't want to have anything more to do with me, and I don't blame you at all. Just—just go away, will you?"

His face had changed. He didn't look angry anymore, but distressed, and slightly puzzled. He sat down by the bed, ignoring the doctor who had come in and was groping for my pulse.

"I'm not going anywhere," he said, quite gently. He took my hand again, though I tried to pull it away. "This—Jamie. Who was he?"

I took a deep, ragged breath. The doctor had hold of my other hand, still trying to take my pulse, and I felt absurdly panicked, as though I were being held captive between them. I fought down the feeling, though, and tried to speak steadily.

"James Alexander Malcolm MacKenzie Fraser," I said, spacing the words, formally, the way Jamie had spoken them to me when he first told me his full name—on the day of our wedding. The thought made another tear overflow, and I blotted it against my shoulder, my hands being restrained.

"He was a Highlander. He was k-killed at Culloden." It was no use, I was weeping again, the tears no anodyne to the grief that ripped through me, but the only response I had to unendurable pain. I bent forward slightly, trying to encapsulate it, wrapping myself around the tiny, imperceptible life in my belly, the only remnant left to me of Jamie Fraser.

Frank and the doctor exchanged a glance of which I was only half-conscious. Of course, to them, Culloden was part of the distant past. To me, it had happened only two days before.

"Perhaps we should let Mrs. Randall rest for a bit," the doctor suggested. "She seems a wee bit upset just now."

Frank looked uncertainly from the doctor to me. "Well, she certainly does seem upset. But I really want to find out . . . what's this, Claire?" Stroking my hand, he had encountered the silver ring on my fourth finger, and now bent to examine it. It was the ring Jamie had given me for our marriage; a wide silver band in the Highland interlace pattern, the links engraved with tiny, stylized thistle blooms.

"No!" I exclaimed, panicked, as Frank tried to twist it off my finger. I jerked my hand away and cradled it, fisted, beneath my bosom, cupped in my left hand, which still wore Frank's gold wedding band. "No, you can't take it, I won't let you! That's my wedding ring!"

"Now, see here, Claire—" Frank's words were interrupted by the doctor, who had crossed to Frank's side of the bed, and was now bending down to murmur in his ear. I caught a few words— "not trouble your wife just now. The shock"—and then Frank was on his feet once more, being firmly urged away by the doctor, who gave a nod to one of the nurses in passing.

I barely felt the sting of the hypodermic needle, too engulfed in the fresh wave of grief to take notice of anything. I dimly heard Frank's parting words, "All right—but Claire, I will know!" And then the blessed darkness came down, and I slept without dreaming, for a long, long time.

———

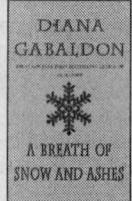

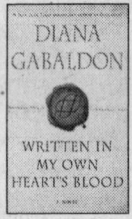

Also by DIANA GABALDON

THE COMPANION VOLUMES

THE OUTLANDER GRAPHIC NOVEL

THE LORD JOHN SERIES

Lord John and the Private Matter
Lord John and the Brotherhood of the Blade
Lord John and the Hand of Devils
The Scottish Prisoner

Continue the saga with original eNovellas,
engrossing tales to complement the Outlander series.

A Plague of Zombies | The Custom of the Army | A Leaf on the Wind of All Hallows | The Space Between

DianaGabaldon.com
🅕 AuthorDianaGabaldon 🐦 @Writer_DG

Random House 🏠 Bantam • Dell • Delacorte • Del Rey

OUTLANDER

SEASON ONE
THE ULTIMATE COLLECTION

THE ULTIMATE COLLECTION comes with:

- A Keepsake Box

- A Collectible Behind-the-Scenes Book

- An Engraved Flask with one of three unique quotes from the series

- A Curated Collection of Photographs and a Frame

- The Complete First Season Blu-ray™ & Soundtrack
  with Three Exclusive Tracks

VOLUMES 1 & 2 ALSO AVAILABLE ON BLU-RAY™

A STARZ ORIGINAL SERIES

OUTLANDER

STARZ

By Diana Gabaldon

DIANA
GABALDON

OUTLANDER

A DELL BOOK

OUTLANDER
A Dell Book

PUBLISHING HISTORY
Dell mass market edition / July 1992
Dell mass market reissue / September 2002
Dell mass market reissue / August 2005

Published by
Bantam Dell
A Division of Random House, Inc.
New York, New York

This is a work of fiction. Names, characters, places, and incidents
either are the product of the author's imagination or are used
fictitiously. Any resemblance to actual persons, living or dead, events,
or locales is entirely coincidental.

Library of Congress Catalog Card Number: 90-019122

ISBN 978-0-440-21256-0

Printed in the United States of America
Published simultaneously in Canada

randomhousebooks.com

OPM   79   78

To the Memory of My Mother,
Who Taught Me to Read—
Jacqueline Sykes Gabaldon

People disappear all the time. Ask any policeman. Better yet, ask a journalist. Disappearances are bread-and-butter to journalists.

Young girls run away from home. Young children stray from their parents and are never seen again. Housewives reach the end of their tether and take the grocery money and a taxi to the station. International financiers change their names and vanish into the smoke of imported cigars.

Many of the lost will be found, eventually, dead or alive. Disappearances, after all, have explanations.

Usually.

PART ONE

Inverness, 1945

1

A New Beginning

It wasn't a very likely place for disappearances, at least at first glance. Mrs. Baird's was like a thousand other Highland bed-and-breakfast establishments in 1945; clean and quiet, with fading floral wallpaper, gleaming floors, and a coin-operated hot-water geyser in the lavatory. Mrs. Baird herself was squat and easygoing, and made no objection to Frank lining her tiny rose-sprigged parlor with the dozens of books and papers with which he always traveled.

I met Mrs. Baird in the front hall on my way out. She stopped me with a pudgy hand on my arm and patted at my hair.

"Dear me, Mrs. Randall, ye canna go out like that! Here, just let me tuck that bit in for ye. There! That's better. Ye know, my cousin was tellin' me about a new perm she tried, comes out beautiful and holds like a dream; perhaps ye should try that kind next time."

I hadn't the heart to tell her that the waywardness of my light brown curls was strictly the fault of nature, and not due to any dereliction on the part of the permanent-wave manufacturers. Her own tightly marceled waves suffered from no such perversity.

"Yes, I'll do that, Mrs. Baird," I lied. "I'm just going down to the village to meet Frank. We'll be back for tea." I ducked out the door and down the path before she could detect any further defects in my undisciplined appearance. After four years as a Royal Army nurse, I was enjoying the escape from uniforms and rationing by indulging in brightly printed light cotton dresses, totally unsuited for rough walking through the heather.

Not that I had originally planned to do a lot of that; my thoughts ran more on the lines of sleeping late in the mornings, and long, lazy afternoons in bed with Frank, not sleeping. However, it was difficult to maintain the proper mood of languorous romance with Mrs. Baird industriously Hoovering away outside our door.

"That must be the dirtiest bit of carpet in the entire Scottish Highlands," Frank had observed that morning as we lay in bed listening to the ferocious roar of the vacuum in the hallway.

"Nearly as dirty as our landlady's mind," I agreed. "Perhaps we should have gone to Brighton after all." We had chosen the Highlands as a place to holiday before Frank took up his appointment as a history professor at Oxford, on the grounds that Scotland had been somewhat less touched by the physical horrors of war than the rest of Britain, and was less susceptible to the frenetic postwar gaiety that infected more popular vacation spots.

And without discussing it, I think we both felt that it was a symbolic place to reestablish our marriage; we had been married and spent a two-day honeymoon in the Highlands, shortly before the outbreak of war seven years before. A peaceful refuge in which to rediscover each other, we thought, not realizing that, while golf and fishing are Scotland's most popular outdoor sports, gossip is the most popular indoor sport. And when it rains as much as it does in Scotland, people spend a lot of time indoors.

"Where are you going?" I asked, as Frank swung his feet out of bed.

"I'd hate the dear old thing to be disappointed in us," he answered. Sitting up on the side of the ancient bed, he bounced gently up and down, creating a piercing rhythmic squeak. The Hoovering in the hall stopped abruptly. After a minute or two of bouncing, he gave a loud, theatrical groan and collapsed backward with a twang of protesting springs. I giggled helplessly into a pillow, so as not to disturb the breathless silence outside.

Frank waggled his eyebrows at me. "You're supposed to moan ecstatically, not giggle," he admonished in a whisper. "She'll think I'm not a good lover."

"You'll have to keep it up for longer than that, if you expect ecstatic moans," I answered. "Two minutes doesn't deserve any more than a giggle."

"Inconsiderate little wench. I came here for a rest, remember?"

"Lazybones. You'll never manage the next branch on your family tree unless you show a bit more industry than that."

Frank's passion for genealogy was yet another reason for choosing the Highlands. According to one of the filthy scraps of paper he lugged to and fro, some tiresome ancestor of his had had something to do with something or other in this region back in the middle of the eighteenth—or was it seventeenth?—century.

"If I end as a childless stub on my family tree, it will undoubtedly be the fault of our untiring hostess out there. After all, we've been married almost eight years. Little Frank Jr. will be quite legitimate without being conceived in the presence of a witness."

"If he's conceived at all," I said pessimistically. We had been disappointed yet again the week before leaving for our Highland retreat.

"With all this bracing fresh air and healthy diet? How could we help but manage here?" Dinner the night before had been herring, fried. Lunch had been herring, pickled. And the pungent scent now wafting up the stairwell strongly intimated that breakfast was to be herring, kippered.

"Unless you're contemplating an encore performance for the edification of Mrs. Baird," I suggested, "you'd better get dressed. Aren't you meeting that parson at ten?" The Rev. Dr. Reginald Wakefield, vicar of the local parish, was to provide some rivetingly fascinating baptismal registers for Frank's inspection, not to mention the glittering prospect that he might have unearthed some moldering army dispatches or somesuch that mentioned the notorious ancestor.

"What's the name of that great-great-great-great-grandfather of yours again?" I asked. "The one that mucked about here during one of the Risings? I can't remember if it was Willy or Walter."

"Actually, it was Jonathan." Frank took my complete disinterest in family history placidly, but remained always on guard, ready to seize the slightest expression of inquisitiveness as an excuse for telling me all facts known to date about the early Randalls and their connections. His eyes assumed the fervid gleam of the fanatic lecturer as he buttoned his shirt.

"Jonathan Wolverton Randall—Wolverton for his mother's uncle, a minor knight from Sussex. He was, however, known by the rather dashing nickname of 'Black Jack,' something he acquired in the army, probably during the time he was stationed here." I flopped facedown on the bed and affected to snore. Ignoring me, Frank went on with his scholarly exegesis.

"He bought his commission in the mid-thirties—1730s, that is—and served as a captain of dragoons. According to those old letters Cousin May sent me, he did quite well in the army. Good choice for a second son, you know; his younger brother followed tradition as well by becoming a curate, but I haven't found out much about him yet. Anyway, Jack Randall was highly commended by the Duke of Sandringham for his activities before and during the '45—the second—Jacobite Rising, you know," he amplified for the benefit of the ignorant amongst his audience, namely me. "You know, Bonnie Prince Charlie and that lot?"

"I'm not entirely sure the Scots realize they lost that one," I interrupted, sitting up and trying to subdue my hair. "I distinctly heard the barman at that pub last night refer to us as Sassenachs."

"Well, why not?" said Frank equably. "It only means 'Englishman,' after all, or at worst, 'outlander,' and we're all of that."

"I know what it means. It was the tone I objected to."

Frank searched through the bureau drawer for a belt. "He was just annoyed because I told him the ale was weak. I told him the true Highland brew requires an old boot to be added to the vat, and the final product to be strained through a well-worn undergarment."

"Ah, that accounts for the amount of the bill."

"Well, I phrased it a little more tactfully than that, but only because the Gaelic language hasn't got a specific word for drawers."

I reached for a pair of my own, intrigued. "Why not? Did the ancient Gaels not wear undergarments?"

Frank leered. "You've never heard that old song about what a Scotsman wears beneath his kilts?"

"Presumably not gents' knee-length step-ins," I said dryly. "Perhaps I'll go out in search of a local kilt-wearer whilst you're cavorting with vicars and ask him."

"Well, do try not to get arrested, Claire. The dean of St. Giles College wouldn't like it at all."

In the event, there were no kilt-wearers loitering about the town square or patronizing the shops that surrounded it. There were a number of other people there, though, mostly housewives of the Mrs. Baird type, doing their daily shopping. They were garrulous and gossipy, and their solid, print-clad presences filled the shops with a cozy warmth; a buttress against the cold mist of the morning outdoors.

With as yet no house of my own to keep, I had little that needed buying, but enjoyed myself in browsing among the newly replenished shelves, for the pure joy of seeing lots of things for sale again. It had been a long time of rationing, of doing without the simple things like soap and eggs, and even longer without the minor luxuries of life, like L'Heure Bleu cologne.

My gaze lingered on a shop window filled with household goods—embroidered tea cloths and cozies, pitchers and glasses, a stack of quite homely pie tins, and a set of three vases.

I had never owned a vase in my life. During the war years, I had, of course, lived in the nurses' quarters, first at Pembroke Hospital, later at the field station in France. But even before that, we had lived nowhere long enough to justify the purchase of such an item. Had I had such a thing, I reflected, Uncle Lamb would have filled it with potsherds long before I could have got near it with a bunch of daisies.

Quentin Lambert Beauchamp. "Q" to his archaeological students and his friends. "Dr. Beauchamp" to the scholarly circles in which he moved and lectured and had his being. But always Uncle Lamb to me.

My father's only brother, and my only living relative at the time, he had been landed with me, aged five, when my parents were killed in a car crash. Poised for a trip to the Middle East at the time, he had paused in his perparations long enough to make the funeral arrangements, dispose of my parents' estates, and enroll me in a proper girls' boarding school. Which I had flatly refused to attend.

Faced with the necessity of prying my chubby fingers off the car's door handle and dragging me by the heels up the steps of the school, Uncle Lamb, who hated personal conflict of any kind, had sighed in exasperation, then finally shrugged and tossed his better judgment out the window along with my newly purchased round straw boater.

"Ruddy thing," he muttered, seeing it rolling merrily away in the rearview mirror as we roared down the drive in high gear. "Always loathed hats on women, anyway." He had glanced down at me, fixing me with a fierce glare.

"One thing," he said, in awful tones. "You are *not* to play dolls with my Persian grave figurines. Anything else, but not that. Got it?"

I had nodded, content. And had gone with him to the Middle East, to South America, to dozens of study sites throughout the world. Had learned to read and write from the drafts of journal articles, to dig latrines and boil water, and to do a number of other things not suitable for a young lady of gentle birth—until I had met the handsome, dark-haired historian who came to consult Uncle Lamb on a point of French philosophy as it related to Egyptian religious practice.

Even after our marriage, Frank and I led the nomadic life of junior faculty, divided between continental conferences and temporary flats, until the outbreak of war had sent him to Officers Training and the Intelligence Unit at MI6, and me to nurses training. Though we had been married nearly eight years, the new house in Oxford would be our first real home.

Tucking my handbag firmly under my arm, I marched into the shop and bought the vases.

I met Frank at the crossing of the High Street and the Gereside Road and we turned up it together. He raised his eyebrows at my purchases.

"Vases?" He smiled. "Wonderful. Perhaps now you'll stop putting flowers in my books."

"They aren't flowers, they're specimens. And it was you who suggested I take up botany. To occupy my mind, now that I've not got nursing to do," I reminded him.

"True." He nodded good-humoredly. "But I didn't realize I'd have bits of greenery dropping out into my lap every time I opened a reference. What was that horrible crumbly brown stuff you put in Tuscum and Banks?"

"Groutweed. Good for hemorrhoids."

"Preparing for my imminent old age, are you? Well, how very thoughtful of you, Claire."

We pushed through the gate, laughing, and Frank stood back to let me go first up the narrow front steps.

Suddenly he caught my arm. "Look out! You don't want to step in it."

I lifted my foot gingerly over a large brownish-red stain on the top step.

"How odd," I said. "Mrs. Baird scrubs the steps down every morning; I've seen her. What do you suppose that can be?"

Frank leaned over the step, sniffing delicately.

"Offhand, I should say that it's blood."

"Blood!" I took a step back into the entryway. "Whose?" I glanced nervously into the house. "Do you suppose Mrs. Baird's had an accident of some kind?" I couldn't imagine our immaculate landlady leaving bloodstains to dry on her doorstep unless some major catastrophe had occurred, and wondered just for a moment whether the parlor might be harboring a crazed ax-murderer, even now preparing to spring out on us with a spine-chilling shriek.

Frank shook his head. He stood on tiptoe to peer over the hedge into the next garden.

"I shouldn't think so. There's a stain like it on the Collinses' doorstep as well."

"Really?" I drew closer to Frank, both to see over the hedge and for moral support. The Highlands hardly seemed a likely spot for a mass murderer, but then I doubted such persons used any sort of logical criteria when picking their sites. "That's rather . . . disagreeable," I observed. There was no sign of life from the next residence. "What do you suppose has happened?"

Frank frowned, thinking, then slapped his hand briefly against his trouser leg in inspiration.

"I think I know! Wait here a moment." He darted out to the gate and set off down the road at a trot, leaving me stranded on the edge of the doorstep.

He was back shortly, beaming with confirmation.

"Yes, that's it, it must be. Every house in the row has had it."

"Had what? A visit from a homicidal maniac?" I spoke a bit sharply, still nervous at having been abruptly abandoned with nothing but a large bloodstain for company.

Frank laughed. "No, a ritual sacrifice. Fascinating!" He was down on his hands and knees in the grass, peering interestedly at the stain.

This hardly sounded better than a homicidal maniac. I squatted beside him, wrinkling my nose at the smell. It was early for flies, but a couple of the big, slow-moving Highland midges circled the stain.

"What do you mean, 'ritual sacrifice'?" I demanded. "Mrs. Baird's a good church-goer, and so are all the neighbors. This isn't Druid's Hill or anything, you know."

He stood, brushing grass-ends from his trousers. "That's all you know, my girl," he said. "There's no place on earth with more of the old superstitions and magic mixed into its daily life than the Scottish Highlands. Church or no church, Mrs. Baird believes in the Old Folk, and so do all the neighbors."

He pointed at the stain with one neatly polished toe. "The blood of a black cock," he explained, looking pleased. "The houses are new, you see. Pre-fabs."

I looked at him coldly. "If you are under the impression that that explains everything, think again. What difference does it make how old the houses are? And where on earth is everybody?"

"Down the pub, I should expect. Let's go along and see, shall we?" Taking my arm, he steered me out the gate and we set off down the Gereside Road.

"In the old days," he explained as we went, "and not so long ago, either, when a house was built, it was customary to kill something and bury it under the foundation, as a propitiation to the local earth spirits. You know, 'He shall lay the foundations thereof in his firstborn and in his youngest son shall he set up the gates of it.' Old as the hills."

I shuddered at the quotation. "In that case, I suppose it's quite modern and enlightened of them to be using chickens instead. You mean, since the houses are fairly new, nothing was buried under them, and the inhabitants are now remedying the omission."

"Yes, exactly." Frank seemed pleased with my progress, and patted me on the back. "According to the vicar, many of the local folk thought the War was due in part to people turning away from their roots and omitting to take proper precautions, such as burying a sacrifice under the foundation, that is, or burning fishes' bones on the hearth—except haddocks, of course," he added, happily distracted. "You never burn a haddock's bones—did you know?—or you'll never catch another. Always bury the bones of a haddock instead."

"I'll bear it in mind," I said. "Tell me what you do in order never to see another herring, and I'll do it forthwith."

He shook his head, absorbed in one of his feats of memory, those brief periods of scholastic rapture where he lost touch with the world around him, absorbed completely in conjuring up knowledge from all its sources.

"I don't know about herring," he said absently. "For mice, though, you hang bunches of Trembling Jock about—'Trembling Jock i' the hoose, and ye'll ne'er see a moose,' you know. Bodies under the foundation, though—that's where a lot of the local ghosts come from. You know Mountgerald, the big house at the end of the High Street? There's a ghost there, a workman on the house who was killed as a sacrifice for the foundation. In the eighteenth century sometime; that's really fairly recent," he added thoughtfully.

"The story goes that by order of the house's owner, one wall was built up first, then a stone block was dropped from the top of it onto one of the workmen—presumably a dislikable fellow was chosen for the sacrifice—and he was buried then in the cellar and the rest of the house built up over him. He haunts the cellar where he was killed, except on the anniversary of his death and the four Old Days."

"Old Days?"

"The ancient feasts," he explained, still lost in his mental notes. "Hogmanay, that's New Year's, Midsummer Day, Beltane and All Hallows'. Druids, Beaker Folk, early Picts, everybody kept the sun feasts and the fire feasts, so far as we know. Anyway, ghosts are freed on the holy days, and can wander about at will, to do harm or good as they please." He rubbed his chin thoughtfully. "It's getting on for Beltane—close to the spring equinox. Best keep an eye out, next time you pass the kirkyard." His eyes twinkled, and I realized the trance had ended.

I laughed. "Are there a number of famous local ghosts, then?"

He shrugged. "Don't know. We'll ask the Vicar, shall we, next time we see him?"

We saw the Vicar quite shortly, in fact. He, along with most of the other inhabitants of the village, was down in the pub, having a lager-and-light in celebration of the houses' new sanctification.

He seemed rather embarrassed at being caught in the act of condoning acts of paganism, as it were, but brushed it off as merely a local observance with historical color, like the Wearing of the Green.

"Really rather fascinating, you know," he confided, and I recognized, with an internal *sigh*, the song of the scholar, as identifying a sound as the *terr-whit!* of a thrush. Harking to the call of a kindred spirit, Frank at once settled down to the mating dance of academe, and they were soon neck-deep in archetypes and the parallels between ancient superstitions and modern religions. I shrugged and made my own way through the crowd to the bar and back, a large brandy-and-splash in each hand.

Knowing from experience how difficult it was to distract Frank's attention from this sort of discussion, I simply picked up his hand, wrapped his fingers about the stem of the glass and left him to his own devices.

I found Mrs. Baird on a deep bench near the window, sharing a companionable pint of bitter with an elderly man whom she introduced to me as Mr. Crook.

"This is the man I tell't ye about, Mrs. Randall," she said, eyes bright with the stimulation of alcohol and company. "The one as knows about plants of all sorts.

"Mrs. Randall's verra much interested in the wee plants," she confided to her companion, who inclined his head in a combination of politeness and deafness. "Presses them in books and such."

"Do ye, indeed?" Mr. Crook asked, one tufted white brow raised in interest. "I've some presses—the real ones, mind— for plants and such. Had them from my nephew, when he come up from university over his holiday. He brought them for me, and I'd not the heart to tell him I never uses such things. Hangin's what's wanted for herbs, ye ken, or maybe to be dried on a frame and put in a bit o' gauze bag or a jar, but whyever you'd be after squashing the wee things flat, I've no idea."

"Well, to look at, maybe," Mrs. Baird interjected kindly. "Mrs. Randall's made some lovely bits out of mallow blossoms, and violets, same as you could put in a frame and hang on the wall, like."

"Mmmphm." Mr. Crook's seamed face seemed to be admitting a dubious possibility to this suggestion. "Weel, if they're of any use to ye, Missus, you can have the presses, and welcome. I didna wish to be throwing them awa', but I must say I've no use for them."

I assured Mr. Crook that I would be delighted to make use

of the plant presses, and still more delighted if he would show me where some of the rarer plants in the area could be found. He eyed me sharply for a moment, head to one side like an elderly kestrel, but appeared finally to decide that my interest was genuine, and we fixed it up that I should meet him in the morning for a tour of the local shrubbery. Frank, I knew, meant to go into Inverness for the day to consult some records in the town hall there, and I was pleased to have an excuse not to accompany him. One record was much like another, so far as I was concerned.

Soon after this, Frank pried himself away from the Vicar, and we walked home in company with Mrs. Baird. I was reluctant to mention the cock's blood on the doorstep, myself, but Frank suffered from no such reticence, and questioned her eagerly as to the background of the custom.

"I suppose it's quite old, then?" he asked, swishing a stick along through the roadside weeds. Lamb's-quarters and cinquefoil were already blooming, and I could see the buds of sweet broom swelling; another week and they'd be in flower.

"Och, aye." Mrs. Baird waddled along at a brisk pace, asking no quarter from our younger limbs. "Older than anyone knows, Mr. Randall. Even back before the days of the giants."

"Giants?" I asked.

"Aye. Fionn and the Feinn, ye ken."

"Gaelic folktales," Frank remarked with interest. "Heroes, you know. Probably from Norse roots. There's a lot of the Norse influence round here, and all the way up the coast to the West. Some of the place names are Norse, you know, not Gaelic at all."

I rolled my eyes, sensing another outburst, but Mrs. Baird smiled kindly and encouraged him, saying that was true, then, she'd been up to the north, and seen the Two Brothers stone, and that was Norse, wasn't it?

"The Norsemen came down on that coast hundreds of times between A.D. 500 and 1300 or so," Frank said, looking dreamily at the horizon, seeing dragon-ships in the windswept cloud. "Vikings, you know. And they brought a lot of their own myths along. It's a good country for myths. Things seem to take root here."

This I could believe. Twilight was coming on, and so was a storm. In the eerie light beneath the clouds, even the thoroughly modern houses along the road looked as ancient and as sinister as the weathered Pictish stone that stood a hundred feet away, guarding the crossroads it had marked for a thousand years. It seemed a good night to be inside with the shutters fastened.

Rather than staying cozily in Mrs. Baird's parlor to be entertained by stereopticon views of Perth Harbor, though, Frank chose to keep his appointment for sherry with Mr. Bainbridge, a solicitor with an interest in local historical records. Bearing in mind my earlier encounter with Mr. Bainbridge, I elected to stay at home with Perth Harbor.

"Try to come back before the storm breaks," I said, kissing Frank goodbye. "And give my regards to Mr. Bainbridge."

"Umm, yes. Yes, of course." Carefully not meeting my eye, Frank shrugged into his overcoat and left, collecting an umbrella from the stand by the door.

I closed the door after him, but left it on the latch so he could get back in. I wandered back toward the parlor, reflecting that Frank would doubtless pretend that he didn't have a wife—a pretense in which Mr. Bainbridge would cheerfully join. Not that I could blame him, particularly.

At first, everything had gone quite well on our visit to Mr. Bainbridge's home the afternoon before. I had been demure, genteel, intelligent but self-effacing, well groomed, and quietly dressed—everything the Perfect Don's Wife should be. Until the tea was served.

I now turned my right hand over, ruefully examining the large blister that ran across the bases of all four fingers. After all, it was not my fault that Mr. Bainbridge, a widower, made do with a cheap tin teapot instead of a proper crockery one. Nor that the solicitor, seeking to be polite, had asked me to pour out. Nor that the potholder he provided had a worn patch that allowed the red-hot handle of the teapot to come into direct contact with my hand when I picked it up.

No, I decided. Dropping the teapot was a perfectly normal reaction. Dropping it into Mr. Bainbridge's lap was merely an accident of placement; I had to drop it somewhere. It was my exclaiming "Bloody fucking hell!" in a voice that topped Mr. Bainbridge's heartcry that had made Frank glare at me across the scones.

Once he recovered from the shock, Mr. Bainbridge had been quite gallant, fussing about my hand and ignoring Frank's attempts to excuse my language on grounds that I had been stationed in a field hospital for the better part of two years. "I'm afraid my wife picked up a number of, er, colorful expressions from the Yanks and such," Frank offered, with a nervous smile.

"True," I said, gritting my teeth as I wrapped a water-soaked napkin about my hand. "Men tend to be very 'colorful' when you're picking shrapnel out of them."

Mr. Bainbridge had tactfully tried to distract the conversation onto neutral historical ground by saying that he had always been interested in the variations of what was considered profane speech through the ages. There was "Gorblimey," for example, a recent corruption of the oath "God blind me."

"Yes, of course," said Frank, gratefully accepting the diversion. "No sugar, thank you, Claire. What about 'Gadzooks'? The 'Gad' part is quite clear, of course, but the 'zook'. . . ."

"Well, you know," the solicitor interjected, "I've sometimes thought it might be a corruption of an old Scots word, in fact—'yeuk.' Means 'itch.' That would make sense, wouldn't it?"

Frank nodded, letting his unscholarly forelock fall across his forehead. He pushed it back automatically. "Interesting," he said, "the whole evolution of profanity."

"Yes, and it's still going on," I said, carefully picking up a lump of sugar with the tongs.

"Oh?" said Mr. Bainbridge politely. "Did you encounter some interesting variations during your, er, war experience?"

"Oh, yes," I said. "My favorite was one I picked up from a Yank. Man named Williamson, from New York, I believe. He said it every time I changed his dressing."

"What was it?"

" 'Jesus H. Roosevelt Christ,' " I said, and dropped the sugar lump neatly into Frank's tea.

After a peaceful and not unpleasant sit with Mrs. Baird, I made my way upstairs, to ready myself before Frank came home. I knew his limit with sherry was two glasses, so I expected him back soon.

The wind was rising, and the very air of the bedroom was prickly with electricity. I drew the brush through my hair, making the curls snap with static and spring into knots and furious tangles. My hair would have to do without its hundred strokes tonight, I decided. I would settle for brushing my teeth, in this sort of weather. Strands of hair adhered stickily to my cheeks, clinging stubbornly as I tried to smooth them back.

No water in the ewer; Frank had used it, tidying himself before setting out for his meeting with Mr. Bainbridge, and I had not bothered to refill it from the lavatory tap. I picked up the bottle of L'Heure Bleu and poured a generous puddle into the palm of my hand. Rubbing my hands briskly together before the scent could evaporate, I smoothed them rapidly through my hair. I poured another dollop onto my hairbrush and swept the curls back behind my ears with it.

Well. That was rather better, I thought, turning my head from side to side to examine the results in the speckled looking glass. The moisture had dissipated the static electricity in my hair, so that it floated in heavy, shining waves about my face. And the evaporating alcohol had left behind a very pleasant scent. Frank would like that, I thought. L'Heure Bleu was his favorite.

There was a sudden flash close at hand, with the crash of thunder following close on its heels, and all the lights went out. Cursing under my breath, I groped in the drawers.

Somewhere I had seen candles and matches; power failure was so frequent an occurrence in the Highlands that candles were a necessary furnishing for all inn and hotel rooms. I had seen them even in the most elegant hotels, where they were scented with honeysuckle, and presented in frosted glass holders with shimmering pendants.

Mrs. Baird's candles were far more utilitarian—plain white

plumber's candles—but there were a lot of them, and three folders of matches as well. I was not inclined to be picky over style at a time like this.

I fitted a candle to the blue ceramic holder on the dressing table by the light of the next flash, then moved about the room, lighting others, 'til the whole room was filled with a soft, wavering radiance. Very romantic, I thought, and with some presence of mind, I pressed down the light switch, so that a sudden return of power shouldn't ruin the mood at some inopportune moment.

The candles had burned no more than a half-inch when the door opened and Frank blew in. Literally, for the draft that followed him up the stairs extinguished three of the candles.

The door closed behind him with a bang that blew out two more, and he peered into the sudden gloom, pushing a hand through his disheveled hair. I got up and relit the candles, making mild remarks about his abrupt methods of entering rooms. It was only when I had finished and turned to ask him whether he'd like a drink, that I saw he was looking rather white and unsettled.

"What's the matter?" I said. "Seen a ghost?"

"Well, you know," he said slowly, "I'm not at all sure that I haven't." Absentmindedly, he picked up my hairbrush and raised it to tidy his hair. When a sudden whiff of L'Heure Bleu reached his nostrils, he wrinkled his nose and set it down again, settling for the attentions of his pocket comb instead.

I glanced through the window, where the elm trees were lashing to and fro like flails. A loose shutter was banging somewhere on the other side of the house, and it occurred to me that we ought perhaps to close our own, though the carry-on outside was rather exciting to watch.

"Bit blustery for a ghost, I'd think," I said. "Don't they like quiet, misty evenings in graveyards?"

Frank laughed a bit sheepishly. "Well, I daresay it's only Bainbridge's stories, plus a bit more of his sherry than I really meant to have. Nothing at all, likely."

Now I was curious. "What exactly did you see?" I asked, settling myself on the dressing-table seat. I motioned to the whisky bottle with a half-lifted brow, and Frank went at once to pour a couple of drinks.

"Well, only a man, really," he began, measuring out a jigger for himself and two for me. "Standing down in the road outside."

"What, outside this house?" I laughed. "Must have been a ghost, then; I can't feature any living person standing about on a night like this."

Frank tilted the ewer over his glass, then looked accusingly at me when no water came out.

"Don't look at me," I said. "You used up all the water. I don't mind it neat, though." I took a sip in illustration.

Frank looked as though he were tempted to nip down to the lavatory for water, but abandoned the idea and went on with his story, sipping cautiously as though his glass contained vitriol, rather than the best Glenfiddich single malt whisky.

"Yes, he was down at the edge of the garden on this side, standing by the fence. I thought"—he hesitated, looking down into his glass—"I rather thought he was looking up at your window."

"My window? How extraordinary!" I couldn't repress a mild shiver, and went across to fasten the shutters, though it seemed a bit late for that. Frank followed me across the room, still talking.

"Yes, I could see you myself from below. You were brushing your hair and cursing a bit because it was standing on end."

"In that case, the fellow was probably enjoying a good laugh," I said tartly. Frank shook his head, though he smiled and smoothed his hands over my hair.

"No, he wasn't laughing. In fact, he seemed terribly unhappy about something. Not that I could see his face well; just something about the way he stood. I came up behind him, and when he didn't move, I asked politely if I could help him with something. He acted at first as though he didn't hear me, and I thought perhaps he didn't, over the noise of the wind, so I repeated myself, and I reached out to tap his shoulder, to get his attention, you know. But before I could touch him, he whirled suddenly round and pushed past me and walked off down the road."

"Sounds a bit rude, but not very ghostly," I observed, draining my glass. "What did he look like?"

"Big chap," said Frank, frowning in recollection. "And a Scot, in complete Highland rig-out, complete to sporran and the most beautiful running-stag brooch on his plaid. I wanted to ask where he'd got it from, but he was off before I could."

I went to the bureau and poured another drink. "Well, not so unusual an appearance for these parts, surely? I've seen men dressed like that in the village now and then."

"Nooo . . ." Frank sounded doubtful. "No, it wasn't his dress that was odd. But when he pushed past me, I could swear he was close enough that I should have felt him brush my sleeve—but I didn't. And I was intrigued enough to turn round and watch him as he walked away. He walked down the Gereside Road, but when he'd almost reached the corner, he . . . disappeared. That's when I began to feel a bit cold down the backbone."

"Perhaps your attention was distracted for a second, and he just stepped aside into the shadows," I suggested. "There are a lot of trees down near that corner."

"I could swear I didn't take my eyes off him for a moment," muttered Frank. He looked up suddenly. "I know! I remember now why I thought he was so odd, though I didn't realize it at the time."

"What?" I was getting a bit tired of the ghost, and wanted to go on to more interesting matters, such as bed.

"The wind was cutting up like billy-o, but his drapes—his kilts and his plaid, you know—they didn't move at all, except to the stir of his walking."

We stared at each other. "Well," I said finally, "that is a bit spooky."

Frank shrugged and smiled suddenly, dismissing it. "At least I'll have something to tell the Vicar next time I see him. Perhaps it's a well-known local ghost, and he can give me its gory history." He glanced at his watch. "But now I'd say it's bedtime."

"So it is," I murmured.

I watched him in the mirror as he removed his shirt and reached for a hanger. Suddenly he paused in mid-button.

"Did you have many Scots in your charge, Claire?" he asked abruptly. "At the field hospital, or at Pembroke?"

"Of course," I replied, somewhat puzzled. "There were quite a few of the Seaforths and Camerons through the field hospital at Amiens, and then a bit later, after Caen, we had a lot of the Gordons. Nice chaps, most of them. Very stoic about things generally, but terrible cowards about injections." I smiled, remembering one in particular.

"We had one—rather a crusty old thing really, a piper from the Third Seaforths—who couldn't stand being stuck, especially not in the hip. He'd go for hours in the most awful discomfort before he'd let anyone near him with a needle, and even then he'd try to get us to give him the injection in the arm, though it's meant to be intramuscular." I laughed at the memory of Corporal Chisholm. "He told me, 'If I'm goin' to lie on my face wi' my buttocks bared, I want the lass *under* me, not behind me wi' a hatpin!' "

Frank smiled, but looked a trifle uneasy, as he often did about my less delicate war stories. "Don't worry," I assured him, seeing the look, "I won't tell that one at tea in the Senior Common Room."

The smile lightened and he came forward to stand behind me as I sat at the dressing table. He pressed a kiss on the top of my head.

"Don't worry," he said. "The Senior Common Room will love you, no matter what stories you tell. Mmmm. Your hair smells wonderful."

"Do you like it then?" His hands slid forward over my shoulders in answer, cupping my breasts in the thin night-dress. I could see his head above mine in the mirror, his chin resting on top of my head.

"I like everything about you," he said huskily. "You look wonderful by candlelight, you know. Your eyes are like sherry in crystal, and your skin glows like ivory. A candlelight witch, you are. Perhaps I should disconnect the lamps permanently."

"Make it hard to read in bed," I said, my heart beginning to speed up.

"I could think of better things to do in bed," he murmured.

"Could you, indeed?" I said, rising and turning to put my arms about his neck. "Like what?"

Sometime later, cuddled close behind bolted shutters, I lifted my head from his shoulder and said, "Why did you ask me that earlier? About whether I'd had to do with any Scots, I mean—you must know I had, there are all sorts of men through those hospitals."

He stirred and ran a hand softly down my back.

"Mmm. Oh, nothing, really. Just, when I saw that chap outside, it occurred to me he might be"—he hesitated, tightening his hold a bit—"er, you know, that he might have been someone you'd nursed, perhaps . . . maybe heard you were staying here, and came along to see . . . something like that."

"In that case," I said practically, "why wouldn't he come in and ask to see me?"

"Well," Frank's voice was very casual, "maybe he didn't want particularly to run into me."

I pushed up onto one elbow, staring at him. We had left one candle burning, and I could see him well enough. He had turned his head, and was looking oh-so-casually off toward the chromolithograph of Bonnie Prince Charlie with which Mrs. Baird had seen fit to decorate our wall.

I grabbed his chin and turned his head to face me. He widened his eyes in simulated surprise.

"Are you implying," I demanded, "that the man you saw outside was some sort of, of . . ." I hesitated, looking for the proper word.

"Liaison?" he suggested helpfully.

"Romantic interest of mine?" I finished.

"No, no, certainly not," he said unconvincingly. He took my hands away from his face, and tried to kiss me, but now it was my turn for head-turning. He settled for pressing me back down to lie beside him.

"It's only. . . ." he began. "Well, you know, Claire, it *was*

six years. And we saw each other only three times, and only
just for the day that last time. It wouldn't be unusual if . . . I
mean, everyone knows doctors and nurses are under tremendous stress during emergencies, and . . . well, I . . . it's
just that . . . well, I'd understand, you know, if anything, er,
of a spontaneous nature . . ."

I interrupted this rambling by jerking free and exploding
out of bed.

"Do you think I've been unfaithful to you?" I demanded.
"Do you? Because if so, you can leave this room this instant.
Leave the house altogether! How dare you imply such a
thing?" I was seething, and Frank, sitting up, reached out to
try to soothe me.

"Don't you touch me!" I snapped. "Just tell me—*do* you
think, on the evidence of a strange man happening to glance
up at my window, that I've had some flaming affair with one
of my patients?"

Frank got out of bed and wrapped his arms around me. I
stayed stiff as Lot's wife, but he persisted, caressing my hair
and rubbing my shoulders in the way he knew I liked.

"No, I don't think any such thing," he said firmly. He
pulled me closer, and I relaxed slightly, though not enough to
put my arms around him.

After a long time, he murmured into my hair, "No, I know
you'd never do such a thing. I only meant to say that even if
you ever did . . . Claire, it would make no difference to me.
I love you so. Nothing you ever did could stop my loving
you." He took my face between his hands—only four inches
taller than I, he could look directly into my eyes without trouble—and said softly, "Forgive me?" His breath, barely
scented with the tang of Glenfiddich, was warm on my face,
and his lips, full and inviting, were disturbingly close.

Another flash from outside heralded the sudden breaking of
the storm, and a thundering rain smashed down on the slates
of the roof.

I slowly put my arms around his waist.

" 'The quality of mercy is not strained,' " I quoted. " 'It
droppeth as the gentle dew from heaven . . .' "

Frank laughed and looked upward; the overlapping stains

on the ceiling boded ill for the prospects of our sleeping dry all night.

"If that's a sample of your mercy," he said, "I'd hate to see your vengeance." The thunder went off like a mortar attack, as though in answer to his words, and we both laughed, at ease again.

It was only later, listening to his regular deep breathing beside me, that I began to wonder. As I had said, there was no evidence whatsoever to imply unfaithfulness on my part. *My* part. But six years, as he'd said, was a long time.

2

Standing Stones

M r. Crook called for me, as arranged, promptly at
seven the next morning.

"So as we'll catch the dew on the buttercups,
eh, lass?" he said, twinkling with elderly gallantry. He had
brought a motorcycle of his own approximate vintage, on
which to transport us into the countryside. The plant presses
were tidily strapped to the sides of this enormous machine,
like bumpers on a tugboat. It was a leisurely ramble through
the quiet countryside, made all the more quiet by contrast
with the thunderous roar of Mr. Crook's cycle, suddenly
throttled into silence. The old man did indeed know a lot
about the local plants, I discovered. Not only where they were
to be found but their medicinal uses, and how to prepare
them. I wished I had brought a notebook to get it all down,
but listened intently to the cracked old voice, and did my best
to commit the information to memory as I stowed our specimens in the heavy plant presses.

We stopped for a packed luncheon near the base of a curious flat-topped hill. Green as most of its neighbors, with the
same rocky juts and crags, it had something different: a well-
worn path leading up one side and disappearing abruptly behind a granite outcrop.

"What's up there?" I asked, gesturing with a ham sandwich. "It seems a difficult place for picnicking."

"Ah." Mr. Crook glanced at the hill. "That's Craigh na
Dun, lass. I'd meant to show ye after our meal."

"Really? Is there something special about it?"

"Oh, aye," he answered, but refused to elaborate further, merely saying that I'd see when I saw.

I had some fears about his ability to climb such a steep path, but these evaporated as I found myself panting in his wake. At last, Mr. Crook extended a gnarled hand and pulled me up over the rim of the hill.

"There 'tis." He waved a hand with a sort of proprietorial gesture.

"Why, it's a henge!" I said, delighted. "A miniature henge!"

Because of the war, it had been several years since I had last visited Salisbury Plain, but Frank and I had seen Stonehenge soon after we were married. Like the other tourists wandering awed among the huge standing stones, we had gaped at the Altar Stone ('w'ere ancient Druid priests performed their dreadful 'uman sacrifices,' announced the sonorous Cockney tour guide accompanying a busload of Italian tourists, who all dutifully took photographs of the rather ordinary-looking stone block).

Out of the same passion for exactness that made Frank adjust his ties on the hanger so that the ends hung precisely even, we had even trekked around the circumference of the circle, pacing off the distance between the Z holes and the Y holes, and counting the lintels in the Sarsen Circle, the outermost ring of monstrous uprights.

Three hours later, we knew how many Y and Z holes there were (fifty-nine, if you care; I didn't), but had no more clue to the purpose of the structure than had the dozens of amateur and professional archaeologists who had crawled over the site for the last five hundred years.

No lack of opinions, of course. Life among academics had taught me that a well-expressed opinion is usually better than a badly expressed fact, so far as professional advancement goes.

A temple. A burial ground. An astronomical observatory. A place of execution (hence the inaptly named "Slaughter Stone" that lies to one side, half sunk in its own pit). An open-air market. I liked this last suggestion, visualizing Megalithic housewives strolling between the lintels, baskets on their arms, critically judging the glaze on the latest shipment of red-clay beakers and listening skeptically to the claims of stone-age bakers and vendors of deer-bone shovels and amber beads.

The only thing I could see against that hypothesis was the presence of bodies under the Altar Stone and cremated remains in the Z holes. Unless these were the hapless remains of merchants accused of short-weighting the customers, it seemed a bit unsanitary to be burying people in the marketplace.

There were no signs of burial in the miniature henge atop the hill. By "miniature," I mean only that the circle of standing stones was smaller than Stonehenge; each stone was still twice my own height, and massive in proportion.

I had heard from another tour-guide at Stonehenge that these stone circles occur all over Britain and Europe—some in better repair than others, some differing slightly in orientation or form, all of purpose and origin unknown.

Mr. Crook stood smiling benignly as I prowled among the stones, pausing now and then to touch one gently, as though my touch could make an impression on the monumental boulders.

Some of the standing stones were brindled, striped with dim colors. Others were speckled with flakes of mica that caught the morning sun with a cheerful shimmer. All of them were remarkably different from the clumps of native stone that thrust out of the bracken all around. Whoever built the stone circles, and for whatever purpose, thought it important enough to have quarried, shaped, and transported special stone blocks for the erection of their testimonial. Shaped—how? Transported—how, and from what unimaginable distance?

"My husband would be fascinated," I told Mr. Crook, stopping to thank him for showing me the place and the plants. "I'll bring him up to see it later." The gnarled old man gallantly offered me an arm at the top of the trail. I took it, deciding after one look down the precipitous decline that in spite of his age, he was likely steadier on his pins than I was.

———

I swung down the road that afternoon toward the village, to fetch Frank from the vicarage. I happily breathed in that heady Highland mix of heather, sage, and broom, spiced here and there with chimney smoke and the tang of fried herring, as I passed the scattered cottages. The village lay nestled in a small declivity at the foot of one of those soaring crags that rise so steeply from the Highland moors. Those cottages near the road were nice. The bloom of postwar prosperity had spread as far as a new coat of paint, and even the manse, which must be at least a hundred years old, sported bright yellow trim around its sagging windowframes.

The vicar's housekeeper answered the door, a tall, stringy woman with three strands of artificial pearls round her neck. Hearing who I was, she welcomed me in and towed me down a long, narrow, dark hallway, lined with sepia engravings of people who may have been famous personages of their time, or cherished relatives of the present vicar, but might as well have been the Royal Family, for all I could see of their features in the gloom.

By contrast, the vicar's study was blinding with light from the enormous windows that ran nearly from ceiling to floor in one wall. An easel near the fireplace, bearing a half-finished oil of black cliffs against the evening sky, showed the reason for the windows, which must have been added long after the house was built.

Frank and a short, tubby man with a clerical dog-collar were cozily poring over a mass of tattered paper on the desk by the far wall. Frank barely looked up in greeting, but the vicar politely left off his explanations and hurried over to clasp my hand, his round face beaming with sociable delight.

"Mrs. Randall!" he said, pumping my hand heartily. "How nice to see you again. And you've come just in time to hear the news!"

"News?" Casting an eye on the grubbiness and typeface of the papers on the desk, I calculated the date of the news in question as being likely around 1750. Not precisely stop-the-presses, then.

"Yes, indeed. We've been tracing your husband's ancestor, Jack Randall, through the army dispatches of the period." The vicar leaned close, speaking out of the side of his mouth like a gangster in an American film. "I've, er, 'borrowed' the original dispatches from the local Historical Society files. You'll be careful not to tell anyone?"

Amused, I agreed that I would not reveal his deadly secret, and looked about for a comfortable chair in which to receive the latest revelations from the eighteenth century. The wing chair nearest the windows looked suitable, but as I reached to turn it toward the desk, I discovered that it was already occupied. The inhabitant, a small boy with a shock of glossy black hair, was curled up in the depths of the chair, sound asleep.

"Roger!" The vicar, coming to assist me, was as surprised as I. The boy, startled out of sleep, shot bolt upright, wide eyes the color of moss.

"Now what are you up to in here, you young scamp?" The vicar was scolding affectionately. "Oh, fell asleep reading the comic papers again?" He scooped up the brightly colored pages and handed them to the lad. "Run along now, Roger, I have business with the Randalls. Oh, wait, I've forgotten to introduce you—Mrs. Randall, this is my son, Roger."

I was a bit surprised. If ever I'd seen a confirmed bachelor, I would have thought the Reverend Wakefield was it. Still, I took the politely proffered paw and shook it warmly, resisting the urge to wipe a certain residual stickiness on my skirt.

The Reverend Wakefield looked fondly after the boy as he trooped off toward the kitchen.

"My niece's son, really," he confided. "Father shot down over the Channel, and mother killed in the Blitz, though, so I've taken him."

"How kind of you," I murmured, thinking of Uncle Lamb. He, too, had died in the Blitz, killed by a hit to the auditorium of the British Museum, where he had been lecturing. Knowing him, I thought his main feeling would have been gratification that the wing of Persian antiquities next door had escaped.

"Not at all, not at all." The vicar flapped a hand in embarrassment. "Nice to have a bit of young life about the house. Now, do have a seat."

Frank began talking even before I had set my handbag down. "The most amazing luck, Claire," he enthused, thumbing through the dog-eared pile. "The vicar's located a whole series of military dispatches that mention Jonathan Randall."

"Well, a good deal of the prominence seems to have been Captain Randall's own doing," the vicar observed, taking some of the papers from Frank. "He was in command of the garrison at Fort William for four years or so, but he seems to have spent quite a bit of his time harassing the Scottish countryside above the Border on behalf of the Crown. This lot"—he gingerly separated a stack of papers and laid them on the desk—"is reports of complaints lodged against the Captain by various families and estate holders, claiming everything from interference with their maidservants by the soldiers of the garrison to outright theft of horses, not to mention assorted instances of 'insult,' unspecified."

I was amused. "So you have the proverbial horse thief in your family tree?" I said to Frank.

He shrugged, unperturbed. "He was what he was, and nothing I can do about it. I only want to find out. The complaints aren't all that odd, for that particular time period; the English in general, and the army in particular, were rather notably unpopular throughout the Highlands. No, what's odd is that nothing ever seems to have come of the complaints, even the serious ones."

The vicar, unable to keep still for long, broke in. "That's right. Not that officers then were held to anything like modern standards; they could do very much as they liked in minor matters. But this is odd. It's not that the complaints are investigated and dismissed; they're just never mentioned again. You know what I suspect, Randall? Your ancestor must have had a patron. Someone who could protect him from the censure of his superiors."

Frank scratched his head, squinting at the dispatches. "You could be right. Had to have been someone quite powerful, though. High up in the army hierarchy, perhaps, or maybe a member of the nobility."

"Yes, or possibly—" The vicar was interrupted in his theories by the entrance of the housekeeper, Mrs. Graham.

"I've brought ye a wee bit of refreshment, gentlemen," she announced, setting the tea tray firmly in the center of the desk, from which the vicar rescued his precious dispatches in the nick of time. She looked me over with a shrewd eye, assessing the twitching limbs and faint glaze over the eyeballs.

"I've brought but the two cups, for I thought perhaps Mrs. Randall would care to join me in the kitchen. I've a bit of—" I didn't wait for the conclusion of her invitation, but leapt to my feet with alacrity. I could hear the theories breaking out again behind me as we pushed through the swinging door that led to the manse's kitchen.

The tea was green, hot and fragrant, with bits of leaf swirling through the liquid.

"Mmm," I said, setting the cup down. "It's been a long time since I tasted oolong."

Mrs. Graham nodded, beaming at my pleasure in her refreshments. She had clearly gone to some trouble, laying out handmade lace mats beneath the eggshell cups and providing thick clotted cream with the scones.

"Aye, I couldna get it during the War, ye know. It's the best for the readings, though. Had a terrible time with that Earl Grey. The leaves fall apart so fast, it's hard to tell anything at all."

"Oh, you read tea leaves?" I asked, mildly amused. Nothing could be farther from the popular conception of the gypsy fortune-teller than Mrs. Graham, with her short, iron-grey perm and triple-stranded pearl choker. A swallow of tea ran visibly down the long, stringy neck and disappeared beneath the gleaming beads.

"Why, certainly I do, my dear. Just as my grandmother taught me, and her grandmother before her. Drink up your cup, and I'll see what you have there."

She was silent for a long time, once in a while tilting the cup to catch the light, or rolling it slowly between lean palms to get a different angle.

She set the cup down carefully, as though afraid it might blow up in her face. The grooves on either side of her mouth had deepened, and her brows pressed together in what looked like puzzlement.

"Well," she said finally. "That's one of the stranger ones I've seen."

"Oh?" I was still amused, but beginning to be curious. "Am I going to meet a tall dark stranger, or journey across the sea?"

"Could be." Mrs. Graham had caught my ironic tone, and echoed it, smiling slightly. "And could not. That's what's odd about your cup, my dear. Everything in it's contradictory. There's the curved leaf for a journey, but it's crossed by the broken one that means staying put. And strangers there are, to be sure, several of them. And one of them's your husband, if I read the leaves aright."

My amusement dissipated somewhat. After six years apart, and six months together, my husband *was* still something of a stranger. Though I failed to see how a tea leaf could know it.

Mrs. Graham's brow was still furrowed. "Let me see your hand, child," she said.

The hand holding mine was bony, but surprisingly warm. A scent of lavender water emanated from the neat part of the grizzled head bent over my palm. She stared into my hand for quite a long time, now and then tracing one of the lines with a finger, as though following a map whose roads all petered out in sandy washes and deserted wastes.

"Well, what is it?" I asked, trying to maintain a light air. "Or is my fate too horrible to be revealed?"

Mrs. Graham raised quizzical eyes and looked thoughtfully at my face, but retained her hold on my hand. She shook her head, pursing her lips.

"Oh, no, my dear. It's not your fate is in your hand. Only the seed of it." The birdlike head cocked to one side, considering. "The lines in your hand change, ye know. At another point in your life, they may be quite different than they are now."

"I didn't know that. I thought you were born with them, and that was that." I was repressing an urge to jerk my hand

away. "What's the point of palm reading, then?" I didn't wish
to sound rude, but I found this scrutiny a bit unsettling, especially following on the heels of that tea-leaf reading. Mrs. Graham smiled unexpectedly, and folded my fingers closed over
my palm.

"Why, the lines of your palm show what ye are, dear. That's
why they change—or should. They don't, in some people;
those unlucky enough never to change in themselves, but
there are few like that." She gave my folded hand a squeeze
and patted it. "I doubt that you're one of those. Your hand
shows quite a lot of change already, for one so young. That
would likely be the War, of course," she said, as though to
herself.

I was curious again, and opened my palm voluntarily.

"What am I, then, according to my hand?"

Mrs. Graham frowned, but did not pick up my hand again.

"I canna just say. It's odd, for most hands have a likeness to
them. Mind, I'd no just say that it's 'see one, you've seen
them all,' but it's often like that—there are patterns, you
know." She smiled suddenly, an oddly engaging grin, displaying very white and patently false teeth.

"That's how a fortune-teller works, you know. I do it for
the church fete every year—or did, before the War; suppose
I'll do it again now. But a girl comes into the tent—and there
am I, done up in a turban with a peacock feather borrowed
from Mr. Donaldson, and 'robes of oriental splendor'—that's
the vicar's dressing gown, all over peacocks it is and yellow as
the sun—anyway, I look her over while I pretend to be watching her hand, and I see she's got her blouse cut down to her
breakfast, cheap scent, and earrings down to her shoulders. I
needn't have a crystal ball to be tellin' her she'll have a child
before the next year's fete." Mrs. Graham, paused, grey eyes
alight with mischief. "Though if the hand you're holding is
bare, it's tactful to predict first that she'll marry soon."

I laughed, and so did she. "So you don't look at their hands
at all, then?" I asked. "Except to check for rings?"

She looked surprised. "Oh, of course you do. It's just that
you know ahead of time what you'll see. Generally." She nodded at my open hand. "But that is not a pattern I've seen

before. The large thumb, now"—she did lean forward then and touch it lightly—"that wouldn't change much. Means you're strong-minded, and have a will not easily crossed." She twinkled at me. "Reckon your husband could have told ye that. Likewise about that one." She pointed to the fleshy mound at the base of the thumb.

"What is it?"

"The Mount of Venus, it's called." She pursed her thin lips primly together, though the corners turned irrepressibly up. "In a man, ye'd say it means he likes the lasses. For a woman, 'tis a bit different. To be polite about it, I'll make a bit of a prediction for you, and say your husband isna like to stray far from your bed." She gave a surprisingly deep and bawdy chuckle, and I blushed slightly.

The elderly housekeeper pored over my hand again, stabbing a pointed forefinger here and there to mark her words.

"Now, there, a well-marked lifeline; you're in good health, and likely to stay so. The lifeline's interrupted, meaning your life's changed markedly—well, that's true of us all, is it not? But yours is more chopped-up, like, than I usually see; all bits and pieces. And your marriage-line, now"—she shook her head again—"it's divided; that's not unusual, means two marriages . . ."

My reaction was slight, and immediately suppressed, but she caught the flicker and looked up at once. I thought she probably was quite a shrewd fortune-teller, at that. The grey head shook reassuringly at me.

"No, no, lass. It doesna mean anything's like to happen to your good man. It's only that if it did," she emphasized the "if" with a slight squeeze of my hand, "you'd not be one to pine away and waste the rest of your life in mourning. What it means is, you're one of those can love again if your first love's lost."

She squinted nearsightedly at my palm, running a short, ridged nail gently down the deep marriage line. "But most divided lines are broken—yours is forked." She looked up with a roguish smile. "Sure you're not a bigamist, on the quiet, like?"

I shook my head, laughing. "No. When would I have the time?" Then I turned my hand, showing the outer edge.

"I've heard that small marks on the side of the hand indicate how many children you'll have?" My tone was casual, I hoped. The edge of my palm was disappointingly smooth.

Mrs. Graham flicked a scornful hand at this idea.

"Pah! After ye've had a bairn or two, ye might show lines there. More like you'd have them on your face. Proves nothing at all beforehand."

"Oh, it doesn't?" I was foolishly relieved to hear this. I was going to ask whether the deep lines across the base of my wrist meant anything (a potential for suicide?), but we were interrupted at that point by the Reverend Wakefield coming into the kitchen bearing the empty tea cups. He set them on the drainboard and began a loud and clumsy fumbling through the cupboard, obviously in hopes of provoking help.

Mrs. Graham sprang to her feet to defend the sanctity of her kitchen, and pushing the Reverend adroitly to one side, set about assembling tea things on a tray for the study. He drew me to one side, safely out of the way.

"Why don't you come to the study and have another cup of tea with me and your husband, Mrs. Randall? We've made really a most gratifying discovery."

I could see that in spite of outward composure, he was bursting with the glee of whatever they had found, like a small boy with a toad in his pocket. Plainly I was going to have to go and read Captain Jonathan Randall's laundry bill, his receipt for boot repairs, or some document of similar fascination.

Frank was so absorbed in the tattered documents that he scarcely looked up when I entered the study. He reluctantly surrendered them to the vicar's podgy hands, and came round to stand behind the Reverend Wakefield and peer over his shoulder, as though he could not bear to let the papers out of his sight for a moment.

"Yes?" I said politely, fingering the dirty bits of paper. "Ummm, yes, very interesting." In fact, the spidery handwriting was so faded and so ornate that it hardly seemed worth the trouble of deciphering it. One sheet, better preserved than the rest, had some sort of crest at the top.

"The Duke of . . . Sandringham, is it?" I asked, peering at the crest, with its faded leopard couchant, and the printing below, more legible than the handwriting.

"Yes, indeed," the vicar said, beaming even more. "An extinct title, now, you know."

I didn't, but nodded intelligently, being no stranger to historians in the manic grip of discovery. It was seldom necessary to do more than nod periodically, saying "Oh, really?" or "How perfectly fascinating!" at appropriate intervals.

After a certain amount of deferring back and forth between Frank and the vicar, the latter won the honor of telling me about their discovery. Evidently, all this rubbish made it appear that Frank's ancestor, the notorious Black Jack Randall, had not been merely a gallant soldier for the Crown, but a trusted—and secret—agent of the Duke of Sandringham.

"Almost an agent provocateur, wouldn't you say, Dr. Randall?" The vicar graciously handed the ball back to Frank, who seized it and ran.

"Yes, indeed. The language is very guarded, of course. . . ." He turned the pages gently with a scrubbed forefinger.

"Oh, really?" I said.

"But it seems from this that Jonathan Randall was entrusted with the job of stirring up Jacobite sentiments, if any existed, among the prominent Scottish families in his area. The point being to smoke out any baronets and clan chieftains who might be harboring secret sympathies in that direction. But that's odd. Wasn't Sandringham a suspected Jacobite himself?" Frank turned to the vicar, a frown of inquiry on his face. The vicar's smooth, bald head creased in an identical frown.

"Why, yes, I believe you're right. But wait, let's check in Cameron"—he made a dive for the bookshelf, crammed with calf-bound volumes—"he's sure to mention Sandringham."

"How perfectly fascinating," I murmured, allowing my attention to wander to the huge corkboard that covered one wall of the study from floor to ceiling.

It was covered with an amazing assortment of things; mostly papers of one sort or another, gas bills, correspondence, notices from the Diocesan Council, loose pages of novels, notes in the vicar's own hand, but also small items like keys, bottle caps, and what appeared to be small car parts, attached with tacks and string.

I browsed idly through the miscellanea, keeping half an ear tuned to the argument going on behind me. (The Duke of Sandringham probably *was* a Jacobite, they decided.) My attention was caught by a genealogical chart, tacked up with special care in a spot by itself, using four tacks, one to a corner. The top of the chart included names dated in the early seventeenth century. But it was the name at the bottom of the chart that had caught my eye: "Roger W. (MacKenzie) Wakefield," it read.

"Excuse me," I said, interrupting a final sputter of dispute as to whether the leopard in the Duke's crest had a lily in its paw, or was it meant to be a crocus? "Is this your son's chart?"

"Eh? Oh, why, yes, yes it is." Distracted, the vicar hurried over, beaming once more. He detached the chart tenderly from the wall and laid it on the table in front of me.

"I didn't want him to forget his own family, you see," he explained. "It's quite an old lineage, back to the sixteen hundreds." His stubby forefinger traced the line of descent almost reverently.

"I gave him my own name because it seemed more suitable, as he lives here, but I didn't want him to forget where he came from." He made an apologetic grimace. "I'm afraid my own family is nothing to boast of, genealogically. Vicars and curates, with the occasional bookseller thrown in for variety, and only traceable back to 1762 or so. Rather poor record-keeping, you know," he said, wagging his head remorsefully over the lethargy of his ancestors.

It was growing late by the time we finally left the vicarage, with the vicar promising to take the letters to town for copying first thing in the morning. Frank babbled happily of spies and Jacobites most of the way back to Mrs. Baird's. Finally, though, he noticed my quietness.

"What is it, love?" he asked, taking my arm solicitously. "Not feeling well?" This was asked with a mingled tone of concern and hope.

"No, I'm quite well. I was only thinking . . ." I hesitated, because we had discussed this matter before. "I was thinking about Roger."

"Roger?"

I gave a sigh of impatience. "Really, Frank! You can be so . . . oblivious! Roger, the Reverend Wakefield's son."

"Oh. Yes, of course," he said vaguely. "Charming child. What about him?"

"Well . . . only that there are a lot of children like that. Orphaned, you know."

He gave me a sharp look, and shook his head.

"No, Claire. Really, I'd like to, but I've told you how I feel about adoption. It's just . . . I couldn't feel properly toward a child that's not . . . well, not of my blood. No doubt that's ridiculous and selfish of me, but there it is. Maybe I'll change my mind in time, but now. . . ." We walked a few steps in a barbed silence. Suddenly he stopped and turned to me, gripping my hands.

"Claire," he said huskily, "I want *our* child. You're the most important thing in the world to me. I want you to be happy, above all else, but I want . . . well, I want to keep you to myself. I'm afraid a child from outside, one we had no real relationship with, would seem an intruder, and I'd resent it. But to be able to give you a child, see it grow in you, see it born . . . then I'd feel as though it were more an . . . extension of you, perhaps. And me. A real part of the family." His eyes were wide, pleading.

"Yes, all right. I understand." I was willing to abandon the topic—for now. I turned to go on walking, but he reached out and took me in his arms.

"Claire. I love you." The tenderness in his voice was overwhelming, and I leaned my head against his jacket, feeling his warmth and the strength of his arms around me.

"I love you too." We stood locked together for a moment, swaying slightly in the wind that swept down the road. Suddenly Frank drew back a bit, smiling down at me.

"Besides," he said softly, smoothing the wind-blown hair back from my face, "we haven't given up yet, have we?"

I smiled back. "No."

He took my hand, tucking it snugly beneath his elbow, and we turned toward our lodgings.

"Game for another try?"

"Yes. Why not?" We strolled, hand in hand, back toward the Gereside Road. It was the sight of the Baragh Mhor, the Pictish stone that stands at the corner of the road there, that made me remember things ancient.

"I forgot!" I exclaimed. "I have something exciting to show you." Frank looked down at me and pulled me closer. He squeezed my hand.

"So have I," he said, grinning. "You can show me yours tomorrow."

When tomorrow came, though, we had other things to do. I had forgotten that we had planned a day trip to the Great Glen of Loch Ness.

It was a long drive through the Glen, and we left early in the morning, before sunup. After the hurry to the waiting car through the freezing dawn, it was cozy to relax under the rug and feel the warmth stealing back into my hands and feet. Along with it came a most delicious drowsiness, and I fell blissfully asleep against Frank's shoulder, my last conscious sight the driver's head in red-rimmed silhouette against the dawning sky.

It was after nine when we arrived, and the guide Frank had called for was awaiting us on the edge of the loch with a small sailing skiff.

"An' it suits ye, sir, I thought we'd take a wee sail down the loch-side to Urquhart Castle. Perhaps we'll sup a bit there, before goin' on." The guide, a dour-looking little man in weather-beaten cotton shirt and twill trousers, stowed the picnic hamper tidily beneath the seat, and offered me a callused hand down into the well of the boat.

It was a beautiful day, with the burgeoning greenery of the steep banks blurring in the ruffled surface of the loch. Our guide, despite his dour appearance, was knowledgeable and talkative, pointing out the islands, castles, and ruins that rimmed the long, narrow loch.

"Yonder, that's Urquhart Castle." He pointed to a smooth-faced wall of stone, barely visible through the trees. "Or what's left of it. 'Twas cursed by the witches of the Glen, and saw one unhappiness after another."

He told us the story of Mary Grant, daughter of the laird of Urquhart Castle, and her lover, Donald Donn, poet son of MacDonald of Bohuntin. Forbidden to meet because of her father's objection to the latter's habits of "lifting" any cattle he came across (an old and honorable Highland profession, the guide assured us), they met anyway. The father got wind of it, Donald was lured to a false rendezvous and thus taken. Condemned to die, he begged to be beheaded like a gentleman, rather than hanged as a felon. This request was granted, and the young man led to the block, repeating "The Devil will take the Laird of Grant out of his shoes, and Donald Donn shall not be hanged." He wasn't, and legend reports that as his severed head rolled from the block, it spoke, saying, "Mary, lift ye my head."

I shuddered, and Frank put an arm around me. "There's a bit of one of his poems left," he said quietly. "Donald Donn's. It goes:

> *"Tomorrow I shall be on a hill, without a head.*
> *Have you no compassion for my sorrowful maiden,*
> *My Mary, the fair and tender-eyed?"*

I took his hand and squeezed it lightly.

As story after story of treachery, murder, and violence were recounted, it seemed as though the loch had earned its sinister reputation.

"What about the monster?" I asked, peering over the side into the murky depths. It seemed entirely appropriate to such a setting.

Our guide shrugged and spat into the water.

"Weel, the loch's queer, and no mistake. There's stories, to be sure, of something old and evil that once lived in the depths. Sacrifices were made to it—kine, and sometimes even wee bairns, flung into the water in withy baskets." He spat again. "And some say the loch's bottomless—got a hole in the center deeper than anything else in Scotland. On the other hand"—the guide's crinkled eyes crinkled a bit more—" 'twas a family here from Lancashire a few years ago, cam' rushin' to the police station in Invermoriston, screamin' as they'd seen the monster come out o' the water and hide in the bracken. Said 'twas a terrible creature, covered wi' red hair and fearsome horns, and chewin' something, wi' the blood all dripping from its mouth." He held up a hand, stemming my horrified exclamation.

"The constable they sent to see cam' back and said, weel, bar the drippin' blood, 'twas a verra accurate description"—he paused for effect—"of a nice Highland cow, chewin' her cud in the bracken!"

We sailed down half the length of the loch before disembarking for a late lunch. We met the car there and motored back through the Glen, observing nothing more sinister than a red fox in the road, who looked up startled, a small animal of some sort hanging limp in its jaws, as we zoomed around a curve. He leapt for the side of the road and swarmed up the bank, swift as a shadow.

It was very late indeed when we finally staggered up the path to Mrs. Baird's, but we clung together on the doorstep as Frank groped for the key, still laughing over the events of the day.

It wasn't until we were undressing for bed that I remembered to mention the miniature henge on Craigh na Dun to Frank. His fatigue vanished at once.

"Really? And you know where it is? How marvelous, Claire!" He beamed and began rattling through his suitcase.

"What are you looking for?"

"The alarm clock," he replied, hauling it out.

"Whatever for?" I asked in astonishment.

"I want to be up in time to see them."

"Who?"

"The witches."

"Witches? Who told you there are witches?"

"The vicar," Frank answered, clearly enjoying the joke. "His housekeeper's one of them."

I thought of the dignified Mrs. Graham and snorted derisively. "Don't be ridiculous!"

"Well, not witches, actually. There have been witches all over Scotland for hundreds of years—they burnt them 'til well into the eighteenth century—but this lot is really meant to be Druids, or something of the sort. I don't suppose it's actually a coven—not devil-worship, I don't mean. But the vicar said there was a local group that still observes rituals on the old sun-feast days. He can't afford to take too much interest in such goings-on, you see, because of his position, but he's much too curious a man to ignore it altogether, either. He didn't know where the ceremonies took place, but if there's a stone circle nearby, that must be it." He rubbed his hands together in anticipation. "What luck!"

Getting up once in the dark to go adventuring is a lark. Twice in two days smacks of masochism.

No nice warm car with rugs and thermoses this time, either. I stumbled sleepily up the hill behind Frank, tripping over roots and stubbing my toes on stones. It was cold and misty, and I dug my hands deeper into the pockets of my cardigan.

One final push up over the crest of the hill, and the henge was before us, the stones barely visible in the somber light of predawn. Frank stood stock-still, admiring them, while I subsided onto a convenient rock, panting.

"Beautiful," he murmured. He crept silently to the outer edge of the ring, his shadowy figure disappearing among the larger shadows of the stones. Beautiful they were, and bloody eerie too. I shivered, and not entirely from the cold. If whoever had made them had meant them to impress, they'd known what they were doing.

Frank was back in a moment. "No one here yet," he whispered suddenly from behind me, making me jump. "Come on, I've found a place we can watch from."

The light was coming up from the east now, just a tinge of paler grey on the horizon, but enough to keep me from stumbling as Frank led me through a gap he had found in some alder bushes near the top of the path. There was a tiny clearing inside the clump of bushes, barely enough for the two of us to stand shoulder to shoulder. The path was clearly visible, though, and so was the interior of the stone circle, no more than twenty feet away. Not for the first time, I wondered just what kind of work Frank had done during the War. He certainly seemed to know a lot about maneuvering soundlessly in the dark.

Drowsy as I was, I wanted nothing more than to curl up under a cozy bush and go back to sleep. There wasn't room for that, though, so I continued to stand, peering down the steep path in search of oncoming Druids. I was getting a crick in my back, and my feet ached, but it couldn't take long; the streak of light in the east had turned a pale pink, and I supposed it was less than half an hour 'til dawn.

The first one moved almost as silently as Frank. There was only the faintest of rattles as her feet dislodged a pebble near the crest of the hill, and then the neat grey head rose silently into sight. Mrs. Graham. So it was true, then. The vicar's housekeeper was sensibly dressed in tweed skirt and woolly coat, with a white bundle under one arm. She disappeared behind one of the standing stones, quiet as a ghost.

They came quite quickly after that, in ones and twos and threes, with subdued giggles and whispers on the path that were quickly shushed as they came into sight of the circle.

I recognized a few. Here came Mrs. Buchanan, the village postmistress, blond hair freshly permed and the scent of Evening in Paris wafting strongly from its waves. I suppressed a laugh. So this was a modern-day Druid!

There were fifteen in all, and all women, ranging in age from Mrs. Graham's sixty-odd years to a young woman in her early twenties, whom I had seen pushing a pram round the shops two days before. All of them were dressed for rough walking, with bundles beneath their arms. With a minimum of chat, they disappeared behind stones or bushes, emerging empty-handed and bare-armed, completely clad in white. I caught the scent of laundry soap as one brushed by our clump of bushes, and recognized the garments as bedsheets, wrapped about the body and knotted at the shoulder.

They assembled outside the ring of stones, in a line from eldest to youngest, and stood in silence, waiting. The light in the east grew stronger.

As the sun edged its way above the horizon, the line of women began to move, walking slowly between two of the stones. The leader took them directly to the center of the circle, and led them round and round, still moving slowly, stately as swans in a circular procession.

The leader suddenly stopped, raised her arms, and stepped into the center of the circle. Raising her face toward the pair of easternmost stones, she called out in a high voice. Not loud, but clear enough to be heard throughout the circle. The still mist caught the words and made them echo, as though they came from all around, from the stones themselves.

Whatever the call was, it was echoed again by the dancers. For dancers they now became. Not touching, but with arms outstretched toward each other, they bobbed and weaved, still moving in a circle. Suddenly the circle split in half. Seven of the dancers moved clockwise, still in a circular motion. The others moved in the opposite direction. The two semicircles passed each other at increasing speeds, sometimes forming a complete circle, sometimes a double line. And in the center, the leader stood stock-still, giving again and again that mournful high-pitched call, in a language long since dead.

They should have been ridiculous, and perhaps they were. A collection of women in bedsheets, many of them stout and far from agile, parading in circles on top of a hill. But the hair prickled on the back of my neck at the sound of their call.

They stopped as one, and turned to face the rising sun, standing in the form of two semicircles, with a path lying clear between the halves of the circle thus formed. As the sun rose above the horizon, its light flooded between the eastern stones, knifed between the halves of the circle, and struck the great split stone on the opposite side of the henge.

The dancers stood for a moment, frozen in the shadows to either side of the beam of light. Then Mrs. Graham said something, in the same strange language, but this time in a speaking voice. She pivoted and walked, back straight, iron-grey waves glinting in the sun, along the path of light. Without a word, the dancers fell in step behind her. They passed one by one through the cleft in the main stone and disappeared in silence.

We crouched in the alders until the women, now laughing and chatting normally, had retrieved their clothes and set off in a group down the hill, headed for coffee at the vicarage.

"Goodness!" I stretched, trying to get the kinks out of my legs and back. "That was quite a sight, wasn't it?"

"Wonderful!" enthused Frank. "I wouldn't have missed it for the world." He slipped out of the bush like a snake, leaving me to disentangle myself while he cast about the interior of the circle, nose to the ground like a bloodhound.

"Whatever are you looking for?" I asked. I entered the circle with some hesitation, but day was fully come, and the stones, while still impressive, had lost a good deal of the brooding menace of dawn light.

"Marks," he replied, crawling about on hands and knees, eyes intent on the short turf. "How did they know where to start and stop?"

"Good question. I don't see anything." Casting an eye over the ground, though, I did see an interesting plant growing near the base of one of the tall stones. Myosotis? No, probably not; this had orange centers to the deep blue flowers. Intrigued, I started toward it. Frank, with keener hearing than I, leapt to his feet and seized my arm, hurrying me out of the circle a moment before one of the morning's dancers entered from the other side.

It was Miss Grant, the tubby little woman who, suitably enough in view of her figure, ran the sweets and pastries shop in the town's High Street. She peered nearsightedly around, then fumbled in her pocket for her spectacles. Jamming these on her nose, she strolled about the circle, at last pouncing on the lost hair-clip for which she had returned. Having restored it to its place in her thick, glossy locks, she seemed in no hurry to return to business. Instead, she seated herself on a boulder, leaned back against one of the stone giants in comradely fashion and lighted a leisurely cigarette.

Frank gave a muted sigh of exasperation beside me. "Well," he said, resigned, "we'd best go. She could sit there all morning, by the looks of her. And I didn't see any obvious markings in any case."

"Perhaps we could come back later," I suggested, still curious about the blue-flowered vine.

"Yes, all right." But he had plainly lost interest in the circle itself, being now absorbed in the details of the ceremony. He quizzed me relentlessly on the way down the path, urging me to remember as closely as I could the exact wording of the calls, and the timing of the dance.

"Norse," he said at last, with satisfaction. "The root words are Ancient Norse, I'm almost sure of it. But the dance," he shook his head, pondering. "No, the dance is very much older. Not that there aren't Viking circle dances," he said, raising his brows censoriously, as though I had suggested there weren't. "But that shifting pattern with the double-line business, that's . . . hmm, it's like . . . well, some of the patterns on the Beaker Folk glazeware show a pattern rather like that, but then again . . . hmm."

He dropped into one of his scholarly trances, muttering to himself from time to time. The trance was broken only when he stumbled unexpectedly over an obstacle near the bottom of the hill. He flung his arms out with a startled cry as his feet went out from under him and he rolled untidily down the last few feet of the path, fetching up in a clump of cow parsley.

I dashed down the hill after him, but found him already sitting up among the quivering stems by the time I reached the bottom.

"Are you all right?" I asked, though I could see that he was.

"I think so." He passed a hand dazedly over his brow, smoothing back the dark hair. "What did I trip over?"

"This." I held up a sardine tin, discarded by some earlier visitor. "One of the menaces of civilization."

"Ah." He took it from me, peered inside, then tossed it over one shoulder. "Pity it's empty. I'm feeling rather hungry after that excursion. Shall we see what Mrs. Baird can provide in the way of a late breakfast?"

"We might," I said, smoothing the last strands of hair for him. "And then again, we might make it an early lunch instead." My eyes met his.

"Ah," he said again, with a completely different tone. He ran a hand slowly up my arm and up the side of my neck, his thumb gently tickling the lobe of my ear. "So we might."

"If you aren't too hungry," I said. The other hand found its way behind my back. Palm spread, it pressed me gently toward him, fingers stroking lower and lower. His mouth opened slightly and he breathed, ever so lightly, down the neck of my dress, his warm breath tickling the tops of my breasts.

He laid me carefully back in the grass, the feathery blossoms of the cow parsley seeming to float in the air around his head. He bent forward and kissed me, softly, and kept on kissing me as he unbuttoned my dress, one button at a time, teasing, pausing to reach a hand inside and play with the swelling tips of my breasts. At last he had the dress laid open from neck to waist.

"Ah," he said again, in yet another tone. "Like white velvet." He spoke hoarsely, and his hair had fallen forward again, but he made no attempt to brush it back.

He sprang the clasp of my brassiere with one accomplished flick of the thumb, and bent to pay a skilled homage to my breasts. Then he drew back, and cupping my breasts with both hands, drew his palms slowly down to meet between the rising mounds, and without stopping, drew them softly outward again, tracing the line of my rib cage clear to the back. Up and again, down and around, until I moaned and turned toward him. He sank his lips onto mine, and pressed me toward him until our hips fitted tightly together. He bent his head to mine, nibbling softly around the rim of my ear.

The hand stroking my back slipped lower and lower, stopping suddenly in surprise. It felt again, then Frank raised his head and looked down at me, grinning.

"What's all this, then?" he asked, in imitation of a village bobby. "Or rather, what's *not* all this?"

"Just being prepared," I said primly. "Nurses are taught to anticipate contingencies."

"Really, Claire," he murmured, sliding his hand under my skirt and up my thigh to the soft, unprotected warmth between my legs, "you are the most terrifyingly practical person I have ever known."

⸻

Frank came up behind me as I sat in the parlor chair that evening, a large book spread out on my lap.

"What are you doing?" he asked. His hands rested gently on my shoulders.

"Looking for that plant," I answered, sticking a finger between the pages to mind my place. "The one I saw in the stone circle. See . . ." I flipped the book open. "It could be in the Campanulaceae, or the Gentianaceae, the Polemoniaceae, the Boraginaceae—that's most likely, I think, forget-me-nots—but it could even be a variant of this one, the *Anemone patens.*" I pointed out a full color illustration of a pasqueflower. "I don't think it was a gentian of any kind; the petals weren't really rounded, but—"

"Well, why not go back and get it?" he suggested. "Mr. Crook would lend you his old banger, perhaps, or—no, I've a better idea. Borrow Mrs. Baird's car, it's safer. It's a short walk from the road to the foot of the hill."

"And then about a thousand yards, straight up," I said. "Why are you so interested in that plant?" I swiveled around to look up at him. The parlor lamp outlined his head with a thin gold line, like a medieval engraving of a saint.

"It's not the plant I care about. But if you're going up there anyway, I wish you'd have a quick look around the outside of the stone circle."

"All right," I said obligingly. "What for?"

"Traces of fire," he said. "In all the things I've been able to read about Beltane, fire is always mentioned in the rituals, yet the women we saw this morning weren't using any. I wondered if perhaps they'd set the Beltane fire the night before, then come back in the morning for the dance. Though historically it's the cow herds who were supposed to set the fire. There wasn't any trace of fire inside the circle," he added. "But we left before I thought of checking the outside."

"All right," I said again, and yawned. Two early risings in two days were taking their toll. I shut the book and stood up. "Provided I don't have to get up before nine."

It was in fact nearly eleven before I reached the stone circle. It was drizzling, and I was soaked through, not having thought to bring a mac. I made a cursory examination of the outside of the circle, but if there had ever been a fire there, someone had taken pains to remove its traces.

The plant was easier to find. It was where I remembered it, near the foot of the tallest stone. I took several clippings of the vine and stowed them temporarily in my handkerchief, meaning to deal with them properly when I got back to Mrs. Baird's tiny car, where I had left the heavy plant presses.

The tallest stone of the circle was cleft, with a vertical split dividing the two massive pieces. Oddly, the pieces had been drawn apart by some means. Though you could see that the facing surfaces matched, they were separated by a gap of two or three feet.

There was a deep humming noise coming from somewhere near at hand. I thought there might be a beehive lodged in some crevice of the rock, and placed a hand on the stone in order to lean into the cleft.

The stone screamed.

I backed away as fast as I could, moving so quickly that I tripped on the short turf and sat down hard. I stared at the stone, sweating.

I had never heard such a sound from anything living. There is no way to describe it, except to say that it was the sort of scream you might expect from a stone. It was horrible.

The other stones began to shout. There was a noise of battle, and the cries of dying men and shattered horses.

I shook my head violently to clear it, but the noise went on. I stumbled to my feet and staggered toward the edge of the circle. The sounds were all around me, making my teeth ache and my head spin. My vision began to blur.

I do not know now whether I went toward the cleft in the main stone, or whether it was accidental, a blind drifting through the fog of noise.

Once, traveling at night, I fell asleep in the passenger seat of a moving car, lulled by the noise and motion into an illusion of serene weightlessness. The driver of the car took a bridge too fast and lost control, and I woke from my floating dream straight into the glare of headlights and the sickening sensation of falling at high speed. That abrupt transition is as close as I can come to describing the feeling I experienced, but it falls woefully short.

I could say that my field of vision contracted to a single dark spot, then disappeared altogether, leaving not darkness, but a bright void. I could say that I felt as though I were spinning, or as though I were being pulled inside out. All these things are true, yet none of them conveys the sense I had of complete disruption, of being slammed very hard against something that wasn't there.

The truth is that nothing moved, nothing changed, nothing whatever appeared to *happen* and yet I experienced a feeling of elemental terror so great that I lost all sense of who, or what, or where I was. I was in the heart of chaos, and no power of mind or body was of use against it.

I cannot really say I lost consciousness, but I was certainly not aware of myself for some time. I "woke," if that's the word, when I stumbled on a rock near the bottom of the hill. I half slid the remaining few feet and fetched up on the thick tufted grass at the foot.

I felt sick and dizzy. I crawled toward a stand of oak saplings and leaned against one to steady myself. There was a confused noise of shouting nearby, which reminded me of the sounds I had heard, and felt, in the stone circle. The ring of inhuman violence was lacking, though; this was the normal sound of human conflict, and I turned toward it.

3

The Man in the Wood

The men were some distance away when I saw them. Two or three, dressed in kilts, running like the dickens across a small clearing. There was a far-off banging noise that I rather dazedly identified as gunshots.

I was quite sure I was still hallucinating when the sound of shots was followed by the appearance of five or six men dressed in red coats and knee breeches, waving muskets. I blinked and stared. I moved my hand before my face and held up two fingers. I saw two fingers, all present and correct. No blurring of vision. I sniffed the air cautiously. The pungent odor of trees in spring and a faint whiff of clover from a clump near my feet. No olfactory delusions.

I felt my head. No soreness anywhere. Concussion unlikely then. Pulse a little fast, but steady.

The sound of distant yelling changed abruptly. There was a thunder of hooves, and several horses came charging in my direction, kilted Scots atop them, yodeling in Gaelic. I dodged out of the way with an agility that seemed to prove I had not been physically damaged, whatever my mental state.

And then it came to me, as one of the redcoats, knocked flat by a fleeing Scot, rose and shook his fist theatrically after the horses. Of course. A film! I shook my head at my own slowness. They were shooting a costume drama of some sort, that was all. One of those Bonnie-Prince-in-the-heather sorts of things, no doubt.

Well. Regardless of artistic merit, the film crew wouldn't

thank me for introducing a note of historic inauthenticity into their shots. I doubled back into the wood, meaning to make a wide circle around the clearing and come out on the road where I had left the car. The going was more difficult than I had expected, though. The wood was a young one, and dense with underbrush that snagged my clothes. I had to go carefully through the spindly saplings, disentangling my skirts from the brambles as I went.

Had he been a snake, I would have stepped on him. He stood so quietly among the saplings as almost to have been one of them, and I did not see him until a hand shot out and gripped me by the arm.

Its companion clapped over my mouth as I was dragged backward into the oak grove, thrashing wildly in panic. My captor, whoever he was, seemed not much taller than I, but rather noticeably strong in the forearms. I smelled a faint flowery scent, as of lavender water, and something more spicy, mingled with the sharper reek of male perspiration. As the leaves whipped back into place in the path of our passage, though, I noticed something familiar about the hand and forearm clasped about my waist.

I shook my head free of the restraint over my mouth.

"Frank!" I burst out. "What in heaven's name are you playing at?" I was torn between relief at finding him here and irritation at the horseplay. Unsettled as I was by my experience among the stones, I was in no mood for rough games.

The hands released me, but even as I turned to him, I sensed something wrong. It was not only the unfamiliar cologne, but something more subtle. I stood stock-still, feeling the hair prickle on my neck.

"You aren't Frank," I whispered.

"I am not," he agreed, surveying me with considerable interest. "Though I've a cousin of that name. I doubt, though, that it's he you have confused me with, madam. We do not resemble one another greatly."

Whatever this man's cousin looked like, the man himself might have been Frank's brother. There was the same lithe, spare build and fine-drawn bones; the same chiseled lines of the face; the level brows and wide hazel eyes; and the same dark hair, curved smooth across the brow.

But this man's hair was long, tied back from his face with a leather thong. And the gypsy skin showed the deep-baked tan of months, no, years, of exposure to the weather, not the light golden color Frank's had attained during our Scottish holiday.

"Just who are you?" I demanded, feeling most uneasy. While Frank had numerous relatives and connections, I thought I knew all the British branch of the family. Certainly, there was no one who looked like this man among them. And surely Frank would have mentioned any near relative living in the Highlands? Not only mentioned him but insisted upon visiting him as well, armed with the usual collection of genealogical charts and notebooks, eager for any tidbits of family history about the famous Black Jack Randall.

The stranger raised his brows at my question.

"Who am I? I might ask the same question, madam, and with considerably more justification." His eyes raked me slowly from head to toe, traveling with a sort of insolent appreciation over the thin peony-sprigged cotton dress I wore, and lingering with an odd look of amusement on my legs. I did not at all understand the look, but it made me extremely nervous, and I backed up a step or two, until I was brought up sharp by bumping into a tree.

The man finally removed his gaze and turned aside. It was as though he had taken a constraining hand off me, and I let out my breath in relief, not realizing until then that I had been holding it.

He had turned to pick up his coat, thrown across the lowest branch of an oak sapling. He brushed some scattered leaves from it and began to put it on.

I must have gasped, because he looked up again. The coat was a deep scarlet, long-tailed and without lapels, frogged down the front. The buff linings of the turned-back cuffs extended a good six inches up the sleeve, and a small coil of gold braid gleamed from one epaulet. It was a dragoon's coat, an officer's coat. Then it occurred to me—of course, he was an actor, from the company I had seen on the other side of the wood. Though the short sword he proceeded to strap on seemed remarkably more realistic than any prop I had ever seen.

I pressed myself against the bark of the tree behind me, and found it reassuringly solid. I crossed my arms protectively in front of me.

"Who the bloody hell are you?" I demanded again. The question this time came out in a croak that sounded frightened even to my ears.

As though not hearing me, he ignored the question, taking his time in the fastening of the frogs down the front of his coat. Only when he finished did he turn his attention to me once more. He bowed sardonically, hand over his heart.

"I am, madam, Jonathan Randall, Esquire, Captain of His Majesty's Eighth Dragoons. At your service, madam."

I broke and ran. My breath rasped in my chest as I tore through the screen of oak and alder, ignoring brambles, nettles, stones, fallen logs, everything in my path. I heard a shout behind me, but was much too panicked to determine its direction.

I fled blindly, branches scratching my face and arms, ankles turning as I stepped in holes and stumbled on rocks. I had no room in my mind for any form of rational thought; I wanted only to get away from him.

A heavy weight struck me hard in the lower back and I pitched forward at full length, landing with a thud that knocked the wind out of me. Rough hands flipped me onto my back, and Captain Jonathan Randall rose to his knees above me. He was breathing heavily and had lost his sword in the chase. He looked disheveled, dirty, and thoroughly annoyed.

"What the devil do you mean by running away like that?" he demanded. A thick lock of dark-brown hair had come loose and curved across his brow, making him look even more disconcertingly like Frank.

He leaned down and grasped me by the arms. Still gasping for breath, I struggled to get free, but succeeded only in dragging him down on top of me.

He lost his balance and collapsed at full length on me, flattening me once more. Surprisingly enough, this seemed to make his annoyance vanish.

"Oh, like that, is it?" he said, with a chuckle. "Well, I'd be most willing to oblige you, Chuckie, but it happens you've chosen a rather inopportune moment." His weight pressed my hips to the ground, and a small rock was digging painfully into the small of my back. I squirmed to dislodge it. He ground his hips hard against mine, and his hands pinned my shoulders to the earth. My mouth fell open in outrage.

"What do you . . ." I began, but he ducked his head and kissed me, cutting short my expostulations. His tongue thrust into my mouth and explored me with a bold familiarity, roving and plunging, retreating and lunging again. Then, just as suddenly as he had begun, he pulled back.

He patted my cheek. "Quite nice, Chuck. Perhaps later, when I've the leisure to attend to you properly."

I had by this time recovered my breath, and I used it. I screamed directly into his earhole, and he jerked as though I had run a hot wire into it. I took advantage of the movement to get my knee up, and jabbed it into his exposed side, sending him sprawling into the leaf mold.

I scrambled awkwardly to my feet. He rolled expertly, and came up alongside me. I glanced wildly around, looking for a way out, but we were flush up against the foot of one of those towering granite cliffs that jut so abruptly from the soil of the Scottish Highlands. He had caught me at a point where the rock face broke inward, forming a shallow stony box. He blocked the entrance to the declivity, arms spread and braced between the rock walls, an expression of mingled anger and curiosity on his handsome dark face.

"Who were you with?" he demanded. "Frank, whoever he is? I've no man by that name among my company. Or is it some man who lives nearby?" He smiled derisively. "You haven't the smell of dung on your skin, so you haven't been with a cottar. For that matter, you look a bit more expensive than the local farmers could afford."

I clenched my fists and set my chin. Whatever this joker had in mind, I was having none of it.

"I haven't the faintest idea what you are talking about, and

I'll thank you to let me pass at once!" I said, adopting my very best ward-sister's tone. This generally had a good effect on recalcitrant orderlies and young interns, but appeared merely to amuse Captain Randall. I was resolutely repressing the feelings of fear and disorientation that were flapping under my ribs like a panicked flock of hens.

He shook his head slowly, examining me once more in detail.

"Not just at present, Chuckie. I'm asking myself," he said, conversationally, "just why a whore abroad in her shift would be wearing her shoes? And quite fine ones, at that," he added, glancing at my plain brown loafers.

"A what!" I exclaimed.

He ignored me completely. His gaze had returned to my face, and he suddenly stepped forward and gripped my chin in his hand. I grabbed his wrist and yanked.

"Let go of me!" He had fingers like steel. Disregarding my efforts to free myself, he turned my face from one side to the other, so the fading afternoon light shone on it.

"The skin of a lady, I'll swear," he murmured to himself. He leaned forward and sniffed. "And a French scent in your hair." He let go then, and I rubbed my jaw indignantly, as though to erase the touch I still felt on my skin.

"The rest might be managed with money from your patron," he mused, "but you've the speech of a lady too."

"Thanks so much!" I snapped. "Get out of my way. My husband is expecting me; if I'm not back in ten minutes, he'll come looking for me."

"Oh, your husband?" The derisively admiring expression retreated somewhat, but did not disappear completely. "And what is your husband's name, pray? Where is he? And why does he allow his wife to wander alone through deserted woods in a state of undress?"

I had been throttling that part of my brain that was beating itself to pieces trying to make sense of the whole afternoon. It now managed to break through long enough to tell me that however absurd I thought its conjectures, giving this man Frank's name, the same as his own, was only likely to lead to further trouble. Disdaining therefore to answer him, I made to push past him. He blocked my passage with a muscular arm, and reached for me with his other hand.

There was a sudden whoosh from above, followed immediately by a blur before my eyes and a dull thud. Captain Randall was on the ground at my feet, under a heaving mass that looked like a bundle of old plaid rags. A brown, rocklike fist rose out of the mass and descended with considerable force, meeting decisively with some bony protuberance, by the sound of the resultant crack. The Captain's struggling legs, shiny in tall brown boots, relaxed quite suddenly.

I found myself staring into a pair of sharp black eyes. The sinewy hand that had temporarily distracted the Captain's unwelcome attentions was attached like a limpet to my forearm.

"And who the hell are you?" I said in astonishment. My rescuer, if I cared to call him that, was some inches shorter than I and sparely built, but the bare arms protruding from the ragged shirt were knotted with muscle and his whole frame gave the impression of being made of some resilient material such as bedsprings. No beauty, either, with a pockmarked skin, low brow, and narrow jaw.

"This way." He jerked on my arm, and I, stupefied by the rush of recent events, obediently followed.

My new companion pushed his way rapidly through a scrim of alder, made an abrupt turn around a large rock, and suddenly we were on a path. Overgrown with gorse and heather, and zigzagging so that it was never visible for more than six feet ahead, it was still unmistakably a path, leading steeply up toward the crest of a hill.

Not until we were picking our way cautiously down the far side of the hill did I gather breath and wit enough to ask where we were going. Receiving no answer from my companion, I repeated "Where on earth are we going?" in a louder tone.

To my considerable surprise, he rounded on me, face contorted, and pushed me off the path. As I opened my mouth to protest, he clapped a hand over it and dragged me to the ground, rolling on top of me.

Not again! I thought, and was heaving desperately to and fro to free myself when I heard what he had heard, and suddenly lay still. Voices called back and forth, accompanied by trampling and splashing sounds. They were unmistakably English voices. I struggled violently to get my mouth free. I sank my teeth into his hand, and had time only to register the fact that he had been eating pickled herring with his fingers, before something crashed against the back of my skull, and everything went dark.

The stone cottage loomed up suddenly through a haze of night mist. The shutters were bolted tight, showing no more than a thread of light. Having no idea how long I had been unconscious, I couldn't tell how far this place was from the hill of Craigh na Dun or the town of Inverness. We were on horseback, myself mounted before my captor, with hands tied to the pommel, but there was no road, so progress was still rather slow.

I thought I had not been out for long; I showed no symptoms of concussion or other ill effects from the blow, save a sore patch on the base of my skull. My captor, a man of few words, had responded to my questions, demands and acerbic remarks alike with the all-purpose Scottish noise that can best be rendered phonetically as "Mmmmphm." Had I been in any doubt as to his nationality, that sound alone would have been sufficient to remove it.

My eyes had gradually adapted to the dwindling light outside as the horse stumbled through the stones and gorse, so it was a shock to step from near-dark into what seemed a blaze of light inside. As the dazzle receded, I could see that in fact the single room was lit only by a fire, several candlesticks, and a dangerously old-fashioned-looking oil lamp.

"What is it ye have there, Murtagh?"

The weasel-faced man grabbed me by the arm and urged me blinking into the firelight.

"A Sassenach wench, Dougal, by her speech." There were several men in the room, all apparently staring at me, some in curiosity, some with unmistakable leers. My dress had been torn in various spots during the afternoon's activities, and I hastily took stock of the damage. Looking down, I could see the curve of one breast clearly through a rip, and I was sure the assembled men could too. I decided that making an attempt to pull the torn edges together would only draw further attention to the prospect; instead I chose a face at random and stared boldly at him, in hopes of distracting either the man or myself.

"Eh, a bonny one, Sassenach or no," said the man, a fat, greasy-looking sort, seated by the fire. He was holding a chunk of bread and didn't bother to set it down as he rose and came over to me. He pushed my chin up with the back of his hand, shoving the hair out of my face. A few breadcrumbs fell down the neck of my dress. The other men clustered close around, a mass of plaid and whiskers, smelling strongly of sweat and alcohol. It was only then that I saw they were all kilted—odd, even for this part of the Highlands. Had I stumbled into the meeting of a clan society, or perhaps a regimental reunion?

"C'mere, lass." A large, dark-bearded man remained seated at the table by the window as he beckoned me. By his air of command, he seemed to be the leader of this pack. The men parted reluctantly as Murtagh pulled me forward, apparently respecting his rights as captor.

The dark man looked me over carefully, no expression on his face. He was good-looking, I thought, and not unfriendly. There were lines of strain between his brows, though, and it wasn't a face one would willingly cross.

"What's your name, lass?" His voice was light for a man of his size, not the deep bass I would have expected from the barrel chest.

"Claire . . . Claire Beauchamp," I said, deciding on the spur of the moment to use my maiden name. If it was ransom they had in mind, I didn't want to help them by giving a name that could lead to Frank. And I wasn't sure I wanted these rough-looking men to know who I was, before I found out who they were. "And just what do you think you're—" The dark man ignored me, establishing a pattern that I was to grow tired of very quickly.

"Beauchamp?" The heavy brows lifted and the general company stirred in surprise. "A French name, it is, surely?"

He had in fact pronounced the name in correct French, though I had given it the common English pronunciation of "Beecham."

"Yes, that's right," I answered, in some surprise.

"Where did ye find this lass?" Dougal demanded, swinging round on Murtagh, who was refreshing himself from a leather flask.

The swarthy little man shrugged. "At the foot o' Craigh na Dun. She was havin' words with a certain captain of dragoons wi' whom I chanced to be acquent'," he added, with a significant lift of his eyebrows. "There seemed to be some question as to whether the lady was or was not a whore."

Dougal looked me over carefully once more, taking in every detail of cotton print dress and walking shoes.

"I see. And what was the lady's position in this discussion?" he inquired, with a sarcastic emphasis on the word "lady" that I didn't particularly care for. I noticed that while his Scots was less pronounced than that of the man called Murtagh, his accent was still broad enough that the word was almost, though not quite, "leddy."

Murtagh seemed grimly amused; at least one corner of the thin mouth turned up. "She said she wasna. The captain himself appeared to be of two minds on the matter, but inclined to put the question to the test."

"We could do the same, come to that." The fat, black-bearded man stepped toward me grinning, hands tugging at his belt. I backed up hastily as far as I could, which was not nearly far enough, given the dimensions of the cottage.

"That will do, Rupert." Dougal was still scowling at me, but his voice held the ring of authority, and Rupert stopped his advances, making a comical face of disappointment.

"I don't hold wi' rape, and we've not the time for it, anyway." I was pleased to hear this statement of policy, dubious as its moral underpinning might be, but remained a bit nervous in the face of the openly lascivious looks on some of the other faces. I felt absurdly as though I had appeared in public in my undergarments. And while I had no idea who or what these Highland bandits were up to, they seemed bloody dangerous. I bit my tongue, repressing a number of more or less injudicious remarks that were bubbling toward the surface.

"What d'ye say, Murtagh?" Dougal demanded of my captor. "She doesna appear to care for Rupert, at least."

"That's no proof," objected a short, balding man. "He didna offer her any siller. Ye canna expect any woman to take on something like Rupert without substantial payment—in advance," he added, to the considerable hilarity of his companions. Dougal stilled the racket with an abrupt gesture, though, and jerked his head toward the door. The balding man, still grinning, obediently slid out into the darkness.

Murtagh, who had not joined in the laughter, was frowning as he looked me over. He shook his head, making the lank fringe across his forehead sway.

"Nay," he said definitely. "I've no idea what she might be —or who—but I'll stake my best shirt she's no a whore." I hoped in that case that his best was not the one he was wearing, which scarcely looked worth the wagering.

"Weel, ye'd know, Murtagh, ye've seen enough o' them," jibed Rupert, but was gruffly hushed by Dougal.

"We'll puzzle it out later," said Dougal brusquely. "We've a good distance to go tonight, and we mun' do something for Jamie first; he canna ride like that."

I shrank back into the shadows near the fireplace, hoping to avoid notice. The man called Murtagh had untied my hands before leading me in here. Perhaps I could slip away while they were busy elsewhere. The men's attention had shifted to a young man crouched on a stool in the corner. He had barely looked up through my appearance and interrogation, but kept his head bent, hand clutching the opposite shoulder, rocking slightly back and forth in pain.

Dougal gently pushed the clutching hand away. One of the men pulled back the young man's plaid, revealing a dirt-smeared linen shirt blotched with blood. A small man with a thick mustache came up behind the lad with a single-bladed knife, and holding the shirt at the collar, slit it across the breast and down the sleeve, so that it fell away from the shoulder.

I gasped, as did several of the men. The shoulder had been

wounded; there was a deep, ragged furrow across the top, and blood was running freely down the young man's breast. But more shocking was the shoulder joint itself. A dreadful hump rose on that side, and the arm hung at an impossible angle.

Dougal grunted. "Mmph. Out o' joint, poor bugger." The young man looked up for the first time. Though drawn with pain and stubbled with red beard, it was a strong, good-humored face.

"Fell wi' my hand out, when the musket ball knocked me off my saddle. I landed with all my weight on the hand, and *crunch!*, there it went."

"Crunch is right." The mustached man, a Scot, and educated, to judge by his accent, was probing the shoulder, making the lad grimace in pain. "The wound's no trouble. The ball went right through, and it's clean—the blood's runnin' free enough." The man picked up a wad of grimy cloth from the table and used it to blot the blood. "I don't know quite what to do about the disjointure, though. We'd need a chirurgeon to put it back in place properly. You canna ride with it that way, can you, Jamie lad?"

Musket ball? I thought blankly. *Chirurgeon?*

The young man shook his head, white-faced. "Hurts bad enough sitting still. I couldna manage a horse." He squeezed his eyes shut and set his teeth hard in his lower lip.

Murtagh spoke impatiently. "Well, we canna leave him behind noo, can we? The lobsterbacks are no great shakes trackin' in the dark, but they'll find this place sooner or later, shutters or no. And Jamie can hardly pass for an innocent cottar, wi' yon great hole in 'im."

"Dinna worrit yourself," Dougal said shortly. "I don't mean to be leaving him behind."

The mustached man sighed. "No help for it, then. We'll have to try and force the joint back. Murtagh, you and Rupert hold him; I'll give it a try."

I watched in sympathy as he picked up the young man's arm by wrist and elbow and began forcing it upward. The angle was quite wrong; it must be causing agonizing pain. Sweat poured down the young man's face, but he made no sound beyond a soft groan. Suddenly he slumped forward, kept from falling on the floor only by the grip of the men holding him.

One unstoppered a leather flask and pressed it to his lips. The reek of the raw spirit reached me where I stood. The young man coughed and gagged, but swallowed nonetheless, dribbling the amber liquid onto the remains of his shirt.

"All right for another go, lad?" the bald man asked. "Or maybe Rupert should have a try," he suggested, turning to the squat, black-bearded ruffian.

Rupert, so invited, flexed his hands as though about to toss a caber, and picked up the young man's wrist, plainly intending to put the joint back by main force; an operation, it was clear, which was likely to snap the arm like a broomstick.

"Don't you dare to do that!" All thought of escape submerged in professional outrage, I started forward, oblivious to the startled looks of the men around me.

"What do you mean?" snapped the bald man, clearly irritated by my intrusion.

"I mean that you'll break his arm if you do it like that," I snapped back. "Stand out of the way, please." I elbowed Rupert back and took hold of the patient's wrist myself. The patient looked as surprised as the rest, but didn't resist. His skin was very warm, but not feverish, I judged.

"You have to get the bone of the upper arm at the proper angle before it will slip back into its joint," I said, grunting as I pulled the wrist up and the elbow in. The young man was sizable; his arm was heavy as lead.

"This is the worst part," I warned the patient. I cupped the elbow, ready to whip it upward and in.

His mouth twitched, not quite a smile. "It canna hurt much worse than it does. Get on wi' it." Sweat was popping out on my own face by now. Resetting a shoulder joint is hard work at the best of times. Done on a large man who had gone hours since the dislocation, his muscles now swollen and pulling on the joint, the job was taking all the strength I had. The fire was dangerously close; I hoped we wouldn't both topple in, if the joint went back with a jerk.

Suddenly the shoulder gave a soft, crunching *pop!* and the

joint was back in place. The patient looked amazed. He put an unbelieving hand up to explore.

"It doesna hurt anymore!" A broad grin of delighted relief spread across his face, and the men broke out in exclamations and applause.

"It will." I was sweating from the exertion, but smugly pleased with the results. "It will be tender for several days. You mustn't extend the joint at all for two or three days; when you do use it again, go very slowly at first. Stop at once if it begins to hurt, and use warm compresses on it daily."

I became aware, in the midst of this advice, that while the patient was listening respectfully, the other men were eyeing me with looks ranging from wonder to outright suspicion.

"I'm a nurse, you see," I explained, feeling somehow defensive.

Dougal's eyes, and Rupert's as well, dropped to my bosom and fastened there with a sort of horrified fascination. They exchanged glances, then Dougal looked back at my face.

"Be that as it may," he said, raising his brows at me. "For a wet nurse, you'd seem to have some skill at healing. Can ye stanch the lad's wound, well enough for him to sit a horse?"

"I can dress the wound, yes," I said with considerable asperity. "Provided you've anything to dress it with. But just what do you mean 'wet nurse'? And why do you suppose I'd want to help you, anyway?"

I was ignored as Dougal turned and spoke in a tongue I dimly recognized as Gaelic to a woman who cowered in the corner. Surrounded by the mass of men, I had not noticed her before. She was dressed oddly, I thought, in a long, ragged skirt and a long-sleeved blouse half-covered by a sort of bodice or jerkin. Everything was rather on the grubby side, including her face. Glancing around, though, I could see that the cottage lacked not only electrification but also indoor plumbing; perhaps there was some excuse for the dirt.

The woman bobbed a quick curtsy, and scuttling past Rupert and Murtagh, she began digging in a painted wooden chest by the hearth, emerging finally with a pile of ratty cloths.

"No, that won't do," I said, fingering them gingerly. "The

wound needs to be disinfected first, then bandaged with a clean cloth, if there are no sterile bandages."

Eyebrows rose all around. "Disinfected?" said the small man, carefully.

"Yes, indeed," I said firmly, thinking him a bit simple-minded, in spite of his educated accent. "All dirt must be removed from the wound and it must be treated with a compound to discourage germs and promote healing."

"Such as?"

"Such as iodine," I said. Seeing no comprehension on the faces before me, I tried again. "Merthiolate? Dilute carbolic?" I suggested. "Or perhaps even just alcohol?" Looks of relief. At last I had found a word they appeared to recognize. Murtagh thrust the leather flask into my hands. I sighed with impatience. I knew the Highlands were primitive, but this was nearly unbelievable.

"Look," I said, as patiently as I could. "Why don't you just take him down into the town? It can't be far, and I'm sure there's a doctor there who could see to him."

The woman gawped at me. "What town?"

The big man called Dougal was ignoring this discussion, peering cautiously into the darkness around the curtain's edge. He let it fall back into place and stepped quietly to the door. The men fell quiet as he vanished into the night.

In a moment he was back, bringing the bald man and the cold, sharp scent of dark pines with him. He shook his head in answer to the men's questioning looks.

"Nay, nothing close. We'll go at once, while it's safe."

Catching sight of me, he stopped for a moment, thinking. Suddenly he nodded at me, decision made.

"She'll come with us," he said. He rummaged in the pile of cloths on the table and came up with a tattered rag; it looked like a neckcloth that had seen better days.

The mustached man seemed disinclined to have me along, wherever they were going.

"Why do ye no just leave her here?"

Dougal cast him an impatient glance, but left it to Murtagh to explain. "Wherever the redcoats are now, they'll be here by dawn, which is no so far off, considering. If this woman's an

English spy, we canna risk leaving her here to tell them which way we've gone. And if she should not be on good terms wi' them"—he looked dubiously at me—"we certainly canna leave a lone woman here in her shift." He brightened a bit, fingering the fabric of my skirt. "She might be worth a bit in the way of ransom, at that; little as she has on, it's fine stuff."

"Besides," Dougal added, interrupting, "she may be useful on the way; she seems to know a bit about doctoring. But we've no time for that now. I'm afraid ye'll have to go without bein' 'disinfected,' Jamie," he said, clapping the younger man on the back. "Can ye ride one-handed?"

"Aye."

"Good lad. Here," he said, tossing the greasy rag at me. "Bind up his wound, quickly. We'll be leaving directly. Do you two get the horses," he said, turning to weasel-face and the fat one called Rupert.

I turned the rag around distastefully.

"I can't use this," I complained. "It's filthy."

Without seeing him move, I found the big man gripping my shoulder, his dark eyes an inch from mine. "Do it," he said.

Freeing me with a push, he strode to the door and disappeared after his two henchmen. Feeling more than a little shaken, I turned to the task of bandaging the bullet wound as best I could. The thought of using the grimy neckrag was something my medical training wouldn't let me contemplate. I tried to bury my confusion and terror in the task of trying to find something more suitable, and, after a quick and futile search through the pile of rags, finally settled on strips of rayon torn from the hem of my slip. While hardly sterile, it was by far the cleanest material at hand.

The linen of my patient's shirt was old and worn, but still surprisingly tough. With a bit of a struggle, I ripped the rest of the sleeve open and used it to improvise a sling. I stepped back to survey the results of my impromptu field dressing, and backed straight into the big man, who had come in quietly to watch.

He looked approvingly at my handiwork. "Good job, lass. Come on, we're ready."

Dougal handed a coin to the woman and hustled me out of the cottage, followed more slowly by Jamie, still a bit white-faced. Unfolded from the low stool, my patient proved to be quite tall; he stood several inches over Dougal, himself a tall man.

The black-bearded Rupert and Murtagh were holding six horses outside, muttering soft Gaelic endearments to them in the dark. It was a moonless night, but the starlight caught the metal bits of the harness in flashes of quicksilver. I looked up and almost gasped in wonder; the night sky was thick with a glory of stars such as I had never seen. Glancing round at the surrounding forest, I understood. With no nearby city to veil the sky with light, the stars here held undisputed dominion over the night.

And then I stopped dead, feeling much colder than the night chill justified. No city lights. "What town?" the woman inside had asked. Accustomed as I was to blackouts and air raids from the war years, the lack of light had not at first disturbed me. But this was peacetime, and the lights of Inverness should have been visible for miles.

The men were shapeless masses in the dark. I thought of trying to slip away into the trees, but Dougal, apparently divining my thought, grabbed my elbow and pulled me toward the horses.

"Jamie, get yourself up," he called. "The lass will ride wi' you." He squeezed my elbow. "You can hold the reins, if Jamie canna manage one-handed, but do ye take care to keep close wi' the rest of us. Should ye try anythin' else, I shall cut your throat. D'ye understand me?"

I nodded, throat too dry to answer. His voice was not particularly threatening, but I believed every word. I was the less tempted to "try anythin'," in that I had no idea what to try. I didn't know where I was, who my companions were, why we were leaving with such urgency, or where we were going, but I lacked any reasonable alternatives to going with them. I was worried about Frank, who must long since have started looking for me, but this didn't seem the time to mention him.

Dougal must have sensed my nod, for he let go of my arm and stooped suddenly beside me. I stood stupidly staring

down at him until he hissed, "Your foot, lass! Give me your
foot! Your *left* foot," he added disgustedly. I hastily took my
misplaced right foot out of his hand and stepped up with my
left. With a slight grunt, he boosted me into the saddle in
front of Jamie, who gathered me in closely with his good arm.

In spite of the general awkwardness of my situation, I was
grateful for the young Scot's warmth. He smelt strongly of
woodsmoke, blood, and unwashed male, but the night chill
bit through my thin dress and I was happy enough to lean
back against him.

With no more than a faint chinking of bridles, we moved
off into the starlit night. There was no conversation among
the men, only a general wary watchfulness. The horses broke
into a trot as soon as we reached the road, and I was jostled
too uncomfortably to want to talk myself, even assuming that
anyone was willing to listen.

My companion seemed to be having little trouble, in spite
of being unable to use his right hand. I could feel his thighs
behind mine, shifting and pressing occasionally to guide the
horse. I clutched the edge of the short saddle in order to stay
seated; I had been on horses before, but was by no means the
horseman this Jamie was.

After a time, we reached a crossroads, where we stopped a
moment while the bald man and the leader conferred in low
tones. Jamie dropped the reins over the horse's neck and let it
wander to the verge to crop grass, while he began twisting and
turning behind me.

"Careful!" I said. "Don't twist like that, or your dressing
will come off! What are you trying to do?"

"Get my plaid loose to cover you," he replied. "You're
shivering. But I canna do it one-handed. Can ye reach the
clasp of my brooch for me?"

With a good deal of tugging and awkward shifting, we got
the plaid loosened. With a surprisingly dexterous swirl, he
twirled the cloth out and let it settle, shawllike, around his
shoulders. He then put the ends over my shoulders and
tucked them neatly under the saddle edge, so that we were
both warmly wrapped.

"There!" he said. "We dinna want ye to freeze before we get there."

"Thank you," I said, grateful for the shelter. "But where are we going?"

I couldn't see his face, behind and above me, but he paused a moment before answering.

At last he laughed shortly. "Tell ye the truth, lassie, I don't know. Reckon we'll both find out when we get there, eh?"

Something seemed faintly familiar about the section of countryside through which we were passing. Surely I knew that large rock formation ahead, the one shaped like a rooster's tail?

"Cocknammon Rock!" I exclaimed.

"Aye, reckon," said my escort, unexcited by this revelation.

"Didn't the English use it for ambushes?" I asked, trying to remember the dreary details of local history Frank had spent hours regaling me with over the last week. "If there is an English patrol in the neighborhood . . ." I hesitated. If there was an English patrol in the neighborhood, perhaps I was wrong to draw attention to it. And yet, in case of an ambush, I would be quite indistinguishable from my companion, shrouded as we were in one plaid. And I thought again of Captain Jonathan Randall, and shuddered involuntarily. Everything I had seen since I had stepped through the cleft stone pointed toward the completely irrational conclusion that the man I had met in the wood was in fact Frank's six-times-great-grandfather. I fought stubbornly against this conclusion, but was unable to formulate another that met the facts.

I had at first imagined that I was merely dreaming more vividly than usual, but Randall's kiss, rudely familiar and immediately physical, had dispelled that impression. Neither did I imagine that I had dreamed being knocked on the head by Murtagh; the soreness on my scalp was being matched by a chafing of my inner thighs against the saddle, which seemed most undreamlike. And the blood; yes, I was familiar enough with blood to have dreamed of it before. But never had I dreamed the scent of blood; that warm, coppery tang that I could still smell on the man behind me.

"Tck." He clucked to our horse and urged it up alongside the leader's, engaging the burly shadow in quiet Gaelic conversation. The horses slowed to a walk.

At a signal from the leader, Jamie, Murtagh, and the small bald man dropped back, while the other two spurred up and galloped toward the rock, a quarter mile ahead to the right. A half-moon had come up, and the light was bright enough to pick out the leaves of the mallow plants growing on the roadside, but the shadows in the clefts of the rock could hide anything.

Just as the galloping shapes passed the rock, a flash of musket fire sparked from a hollow. There was a bloodcurdling shriek from directly behind me, and the horse leapt forward as though jabbed with a sharp stick. We were suddenly racing toward the rock across the heather, Murtagh and the other man alongside, hair-raising screams and bellows splitting the night air.

I hung on to the pommel for dear life. Suddenly reining up next to a large gorse bush, Jamie grabbed me round the waist and unceremoniously dumped me into it. The horse whirled sharply and sprinted off again, circling the rock to come along the south side. I could see the rider crouching low in the saddle as the horse vanished into the rock's shadow. When it emerged, still galloping, the saddle was empty.

The rock surfaces were cratered with shadow; I could hear shouts and occasional musket shots, but couldn't tell if the movements I saw were those of men, or only the shades of the stunted oaks that sprouted from cracks in the rock.

I extricated myself from the bush with some difficulty, picking bits of prickly gorse from my skirt and hair. I licked a scratch on my hand, wondering what on earth I was to do now. I could wait for the battle at the rock to be decided. If the Scots won, or at least survived, I supposed they would come back looking for me. If they did not, I could approach the English, who might well assume that if I was traveling with the Scots I was in league with them. In league to do what, I had no idea, but it was quite plain from the men's behavior at the cottage that they were up to something which they expected the English strongly to disapprove of.

Perhaps it would be better to avoid both sides in this conflict. After all, now that I knew where I was, I stood some chance of getting back to a town or village that I knew, even if I had to walk all the way. I set off with decision toward the road, tripping over innumerable lumps of granite, the bastard offspring of Cocknammon Rock.

The moonlight made walking deceptive; though I could see every detail of the ground, I had no depth perception; flat plants and jagged stones looked the same height, causing me to lift my feet absurdly high over nonexistent obstacles and stub my toes on protruding rocks. I walked as fast as I could, listening for sounds of pursuit behind me.

The noises of battle had faded by the time I reached the road. I realized that I was too visible on the road itself, but I needed to follow it, if I was to find my way to a town. I had no sense of direction in the dark, and had never learned from Frank his trick of navigation by the stars. Thinking of Frank made me want to cry, so I tried to distract myself by trying to make sense of the afternoon's events.

It seemed inconceivable, but all appearances pointed to my being someplace where the customs and politics of the late eighteenth century still held sway. I would have thought the whole thing a fancy-dress show of some type, had it not been for the injuries of the young man they called Jamie. That wound had indeed been made by something very like a musket ball, judging from the evidence it left behind. The behavior of the men in the cottage was not consistent with any sort of play-acting, either. They were serious men, and the dirks and swords were real.

Could it be some secluded enclave, perhaps, where the villagers reenacted part of their history periodically? I had heard of such things in Germany, though never in Scotland. *You've never heard of the actors shooting each other with muskets, either, have you?* jeered the uncomfortably rational part of my mind.

I looked back at the rock to check my position, then ahead to the skyline, and my blood ran cold. There was nothing there but the feathered needles of pine trees, impenetrably black against the spread of stars. Where were the lights of Inverness? If that was Cocknammon Rock behind me, as I knew it was, then Inverness must be less than three miles to the southwest. At this distance, I should be able to see the glow of the town against the sky. If it was there.

I shook myself irritably, hugging my elbows against the chill. Even admitting for a moment the completely implausible idea that I was in another time than my own, Inverness had stood in its present location for some six hundred years. It was there. But, apparently, it had no lights. Under the circumstances, this strongly suggested that there were no electric lights to be had. Yet another piece of evidence, if I needed it. But evidence of what, exactly?

A shape stepped out of the dark so close in front of me that I nearly bumped into it. Stifling a scream, I turned to run, but a large hand gripped my arm, preventing escape.

"Dinna worry, lass. 'Tis me."

"That's what I was afraid of," I said crossly, though in fact I was relieved that it was Jamie. I was not so afraid of him as of the other men, though he looked just as dangerous. Still, he was young, even younger than I, I judged. And it was difficult for me to be afraid of someone I had so recently treated as a patient.

"I hope you haven't been misusing that shoulder," I said in the rebuking voice of a hospital Matron. If I could establish a sufficient tone of authority, perhaps I could persuade him into letting me go.

"Yon wee stramash didna do it any good," he admitted, massaging the shoulder with his free hand.

Just then, he moved into a patch of moonlight, and I saw the huge spread of blood on his shirtfront. Arterial bleeding, I thought at once; but then, why is he still standing?

"You're hurt!" I exclaimed. "Have you broken open your shoulder wound, or is it fresh? Sit down and let me see!" I pushed him toward a pile of boulders, rapidly reviewing procedures for emergency field treatment. No supplies to hand, save what I was wearing. I was reaching for the remains of my slip, intending to use it to stanch the flow, when he laughed.

"Nay, pay it no mind, lass. This lot isna *my* blood. Not much of it, anyway," he added, plucking the soaked fabric gingerly away from his body.

I swallowed, feeling a bit queasy. "Oh," I said weakly.

"Dougal and the others will be waiting by the road. Let's go." He took me by the arm, less as a gallant gesture than a means of forcing me to accompany him. I decided to take a chance and dug in my heels.

"No! I'm not going with you!"

He stopped, surprised at my resistance. "Yes, you are." He didn't seem upset by my refusal; in fact, he seemed slightly amused that I had any objection to being kidnapped again.

"And what if I won't? Are you going to cut my throat?" I demanded, forcing the issue. He considered the alternatives and answered calmly.

"Why, no. You don't look heavy. If ye won't walk, I shall pick you up and sling ye over my shoulder. Do ye want me to do that?" He took a step toward me, and I hastily retreated. I hadn't the slightest doubt he would do it, injury or no.

"No! You can't do that; you'll damage your shoulder again."

His features were indistinct, but the moonlight caught the gleam of teeth as he grinned.

"Well then, since ye don't want me to hurt myself, I suppose that means as you're comin' with me?" I struggled for an answer, but failed to find one in time. He took my arm again, firmly, and we set off toward the road.

Jamie kept a tight hold on my arm, hauling me upright when I stumbled over rocks and plants. He himself walked as though the stubbled heath were a paved road in broad daylight. He has cat blood, I reflected sourly, no doubt that was how he managed to sneak up on me in the darkness.

The other men were, as advertised, waiting with the horses at no great distance; apparently there had been no losses or injuries, for they were all present. Scrambling up in an undignified scuffle, I plopped down in the saddle again. My head gave Jamie's bad shoulder an unintentional thump, and he drew in his breath with a hiss.

I tried to cover my resentment at being recaptured and my

remorse at having hurt him with an air of bullying officiousness.

"Serves you right, brawling round the countryside and chasing through bushes and rocks. I told you not to move that joint; now you've probably got torn muscles as well as bruises."

He seemed amused by my scolding. "Well, it wasna much of a choice. If I'd not moved my shoulder, I wouldna have ever moved anything else again. I can handle a single redcoat wi' one hand—maybe even two of them," he said, a bit boastfully, "but not three."

"Besides," he said, drawing me against his blood-encrusted shirt, "ye can fix it for me again when we get where we're going."

"That's what you think," I said coldly, squirming away from the sticky fabric. He clucked to the horse, and we set off again. The men were in ferocious good spirits after the fight, and there was a good deal of laughter and joking. My minor part in thwarting the ambush was much praised, and toasts were drunk in my honor from the flasks that several of the men carried.

I was offered some of the contents, but declined at first on grounds that I found it hard enough to stay in the saddle sober. From the men's discussion, I gathered it had been a small patrol of some ten English soldiers, armed with muskets and sabers.

Someone passed a flask to Jamie, and I could smell the hot, burnt-smelling liquor as he drank. I wasn't at all thirsty, but the faint scent of honey reminded me that I was starving, and had been for some time. My stomach gave an embarrassingly loud growl, protesting my neglect.

"Hey, then, Jamie-lad! Hungry, are ye? Or have ye a set of bagpipes with ye?" shouted Rupert, mistaking the source of the noise.

"Hungry enough to eat a set of pipes, I reckon," called Jamie, gallantly assuming the blame. A moment later, a hand with a flask came around in front of me again.

"Better have a wee nip," he whispered to me. "It willna fill your belly, but it will make ye forget you're hungry."

And a number of other things as well, I hoped. I tilted the flask and swallowed.

My escort had been correct; the whisky built a small, warm fire that burned comfortably in my stomach, obscuring the hunger pangs. We managed without incident for several miles, taking turns with both reins and whisky flask. Near a ruined cottage, though, the breathing of my escort gradually changed to a ragged gasping. Our precarious balance, heretofore contained in a staid wobble, suddenly became much more erratic. I was confused; if *I* wasn't drunk, it seemed rather unlikely that *he* was.

"Stop! Help!" I yelled. "He's going over!" I remembered my last unrehearsed descent and had no inclination to repeat it.

Dark shapes swirled and crowded around us, with a confused muttering of voices. Jamie slid off headfirst like a sack of stones, luckily landing in someone's arms. The rest of the men were off their horses and had him laid in a field by the time I had scrambled down.

"He's breathin'," said one.

"Well, how very helpful," I snapped, groping frantically for a pulse in the blackness. I found one at last, rapid but fairly strong. Putting a hand on his chest and an ear to his mouth, I could feel a regular rise and fall, with less of that gasping note. I straightened up.

"I think he's just fainted," I said. "Put a saddlebag under his feet and if there's water, bring me some." I was surprised to find that my orders were instantly obeyed. Apparently the young man was important to them. He groaned and opened his eyes, black holes in the starlight. In the faint light his face looked like a skull, white skin stretched tight over the angled bones around the orbits.

"I'm all right," he said, trying to sit up. "Just a bit dizzy is all." I put a hand on his chest and pushed him flat.

"Lie still," I ordered. I carried out a rapid inspection by touch, then rose on my knees and turned to a looming shape that I deduced from its size to be the leader, Dougal.

"The gunshot wound has been bleeding again, and the id-iot's been knifed as well. I think it's not serious, but he's lost quite a lot of blood. His shirt is soaked through, but I don't know how much of it is his. He needs rest and quiet; we should camp here at least until morning." The shape made a negative motion.

"Nay. We're farther than the garrison will venture, but there's still the Watch to be mindful of. We've a good fifteen miles yet to go." The featureless head tilted back, gauging the movement of the stars.

"Five hours, at the least, and more likely seven. We can stay long enough for ye to stop the bleeding and dress the wound again; no much more than that."

I set to work, muttering to myself, while Dougal, with a soft word, dispatched one of the other shadows to stand guard with the horses by the road. The other men relaxed for the moment, drinking from flasks and chatting in low voices. The ferret-faced Murtagh helped me, tearing strips of linen, fetching more water, and lifting the patient up to have the dressing tied on, Jamie being strictly forbidden to move him-self, despite his grumbling that he was perfectly all right.

"You are not all right, and it's no wonder," I snapped, venting my fear and irritation. "What sort of idiot gets himself knifed and doesn't even stop to take care of it? Couldn't you tell how badly you were bleeding? You're lucky you're not dead, tearing around the countryside all night, brawling and fighting and throwing yourself off horses . . . hold still, you bloody fool." The rayon and linen strips I was working with were irritatingly elusive in the dark. They slipped away, elud-ing my grasp, like fish darting away into the depths with a mocking flash of white bellies. Despite the chill, sweat sprang out on my neck. I finally finished tying one end and reached for another, which persisted in slithering away behind the pa-tient's back. "Come back here, you . . . oh, you god-damned bloody bastard!" Jamie had moved and the original end had come untied.

There was a moment of shocked silence. "Christ," said the fat man named Rupert. "I've ne'er heard a woman use such language in me life."

"Then ye've ne'er met my auntie Grisel," said another voice, to laughter.

"Your husband should tan ye, woman," said an austere voice from the blackness under a tree. "St. Paul says 'Let a woman be silent, and—'"

"You can mind your own bloody business," I snarled, sweat dripping behind my ears, "and so can St. Paul." I wiped my forehead with my sleeve. "Turn him to the left. And if you," addressing my patient, "move so much as one single muscle while I'm tying this bandage, I'll throttle you."

"Och, aye," he answered meekly.

I pulled too hard on the last bandage, and the entire dressing scooted off.

"Goddamn it all to hell!" I bellowed, striking my hand on the ground in frustration. There was a moment of shocked silence, then, as I fumbled in the dark for the loose ends of the bandages, further comment on my unwomanly language.

"Perhaps we should send her to Ste. Anne, Dougal," offered one of the blank-faced figures squatting by the road. "I've not heard Jamie swear once since we left the coast, and he used to have a mouth on him would put a sailor to shame. Four months in a monastery must have had some effect. You do not even take the name of the Lord in vain anymore, do ye, lad?"

"You wouldna do so either, if you'd been made to do penance for it by lying for three hours at midnight on the stone floor of a chapel in February, wearing nothin' but your shirt," answered my patient.

The men all laughed, as he continued. "The penance was only for two hours, but it took another to get myself up off the floor afterward; I thought my . . . er, I thought I'd frozen to the flags, but it turned out just to be stiffness."

Apparently he was feeling better. I smiled, despite myself, but spoke firmly nonetheless. "You be quiet," I said, "or I'll hurt you." He gingerly touched the dressing, and I slapped his hand away.

"Oh, threats, is it?" he asked impudently. "And after I shared my drink with ye too!"

The flask completed the circle of men. Kneeling down next

to me, Dougal tilted it carefully for the patient to drink. The pungent, burnt smell of very raw whisky floated up, and I put a restraining hand on the flask.

"No more spirits," I said. "He needs tea, or at worst, water. Not alcohol."

Dougal pulled the flask from my hand, completely disregarding me, and poured a sizable slug of the hot-smelling liquid down the throat of my patient, making him cough. Waiting only long enough for the man on the ground to catch his breath, he reapplied the flask.

"Stop that!" I reached for the whisky again. "Do you want him so drunk he can't stand up?"

I was rudely elbowed aside.

"Feisty wee bitch, is she no?" said my patient, sounding amused.

"Tend to your business, woman," Dougal ordered. "We've a good way to go yet tonight, and he'll need whatever strength the drink can give him."

The instant the bandages were tied, the patient tried to sit up. I pushed him flat and put a knee on his chest to keep him there. "You are *not* to move," I said fiercely. I grabbed the hem of Dougal's kilt and jerked it roughly, urging him back down on his knees next to me.

"Look at that," I ordered, in my best ward-sister voice. I plopped the sopping mass of the discarded shirt into his hand. He dropped it with an exclamation of disgust.

I took his hand and put it on the patient's shoulder. "And look there. He's had a blade of some kind right through the trapezius muscle."

"A bayonet," put in the patient helpfully.

"A bayonet!" I exclaimed. "And why didn't you tell me?"

He shrugged, and stopped short with a mild grunt of pain. "I felt it go in, but I couldna tell how bad it was; it didna hurt that much."

"Is it hurting now?"

"It is," he said, shortly.

"Good," I said, completely provoked. "You deserve it. Maybe that will teach you to go haring round the countryside kidnapping young women and k-killing people, and. . . ." I felt myself ridiculously close to tears and stopped, fighting for control.

Dougal was growing impatient with this conversation. "Well, can ye keep one foot on each side of the horse, man?"

"He can't go anywhere!" I protested indignantly. "He ought to be in hospital! Certainly he can't—"

My protests, as usual, went completely ignored.

"Can ye ride?" Dougal repeated.

"Aye, if ye'll take the lassie off my chest and fetch me a clean shirt."

4

I Come to the Castle

The rest of the journey passed uneventfully, if you consider it uneventful to ride fifteen miles on horseback through rough country at night, frequently without benefit of roads, in company with kilted men armed to the teeth, and sharing a horse with a wounded man. At least we were not set upon by highwaymen, we encountered no wild beasts, and it didn't rain. By the standards I was becoming used to, it was quite dull.

Dawn was coming up in streaks and slashes over the foggy moor. Our destination loomed ahead, a huge bulk of dark stone outlined by the grey light.

The surroundings were no longer quiet and deserted. There was a trickle of rudely dressed people, heading toward the castle. They moved to the side of the narrow road to let the horses trot past, gawking at what they plainly thought my outlandish garb.

Not surprisingly, it was misting heavily, but there was enough light to show a stone bridge, arching over a small stream that ran past the front of the castle, down to a dully gleaming loch a quarter mile away.

The castle itself was blunt and solid. No fanciful turrets or toothed battlements. This was more like an enormous fortified house, with thick stone walls and high, slitted windows. A number of chimney pots smoked over the slick tiles of the roof, adding to the general impression of greyness.

The gated entrance of the castle was wide enough to accommodate two wagons side by side. I say this without fear of contradiction, because it was doing exactly that as we crossed the bridge. One ox-drawn wagon was loaded with barrels, the other with hay. Our little cavalcade huddled on the bridge, waiting impatiently for the wagons to complete their laborious entry.

I risked a question as the horses picked their way over the slippery stones of the wet courtyard. I hadn't spoken to my escort since hastily re-dressing his shoulder by the roadside. He had been silent, too, aside from an occasional grunt of discomfort when a misstep by the horse jolted him.

"Where are we?" I croaked, my voice hoarse from cold and disuse.

"The keep of Leoch," he answered shortly.

Castle Leoch. Well, at least now I knew where I was. When I had known it, Castle Leoch was a picturesque ruin, some thirty miles north of Bargrennan. It was considerably more picturesque now, what with the pigs rooting under the walls of the keep and the pervasive smell of raw sewage. I was beginning to accept the impossible idea that I was, most likely, somewhere in the eighteenth century.

I was sure that such filth and chaos existed nowhere in the Scotland of 1945, bomb craters or no. And we were definitely in Scotland; the accents of the people in the courtyard left no doubt of that.

"Ay, Dougal!" shouted a tattered hostler, running up to grab the halter of the lead horse. "You're early, man; we hadna thought to see ye before the Gathering!"

The leader of our little group swung down from the saddle, leaving the reins to the grubby youth.

"Aye, well, we've had some luck, both good and bad. I'm off to see my brother. Will ye summon Mrs. Fitz to feed the lads? They'll need their breakfasts and their beds."

He beckoned Murtagh and Rupert down to accompany him, and together they disappeared under a pointed archway.

The rest of us dismounted and stood steaming in the wet courtyard for another ten minutes before Mrs. Fitz, whoever she might be, consented to show herself. A cluster of curious children gathered around us, speculating on my possible origins and function. The bolder ones had just begun to get up enough courage to pluck at my skirt when a large, stout lady in dark brown linen and homespun bustled out and shooed them away.

"Willy, my dear!" she cried. "How good to see ye! And Neddie!" She gave the small balding man a hearty buss of welcome that nearly knocked him over. "Ye'll be needin' breakfast, I reckon. Plenty in the kitchen; do ye go and feed yerselves." Turning to me and Jamie, she started back as though bitten by a snake. She looked openmouthed at me, then turned to Jamie for an explanation of this apparition.

"Claire," he said, with a brief tilt of his head toward me. "And Mistress FitzGibbons," he added, with a tilt the other way. "Murtagh found her yesterday, and Dougal said we must bring her along wi' us," he added, making it clear it was no good blaming *him*.

Mistress FitzGibbons closed her mouth and looked me up and down with an air of shrewd evaluation. Apparently she decided that I looked harmless enough, despite my odd and scandalous appearance, for she smiled—kindly, despite several missing teeth—and took me by the arm.

"Well then, Claire. Welcome to ye. Come wi' me and we shall find ye somethin' a bit more . . . mmm." She looked over my short skirt and inadequate shoes, shaking her head.

She was leading me firmly away when I remembered my patient.

"Oh, wait, please! I forgot Jamie!"

Mistress FitzGibbons was surprised. "Why, Jamie can fend for himself. He knows where to get food and someone will find him a bed."

"But he's hurt. He was shot yesterday and stabbed last night. I bandaged the wound for riding, but I didn't have time to clean or dress it properly. I must care for it now, before it gets infected."

"Infected?"

"Yes, that is, I mean, inflamed, you know, with pus and swelling and fever."

"Oh, aye, I know what ye mean. But do ye mean to say as

ye know what to do for that? Are ye a charmer then? A Beaton?"

"Something like that." I had no notion what a Beaton might be, nor any wish to go into my medical qualifications, standing out in the chilly drizzle that had set in. Mistress FitzGibbons seemed of a like mind, for she called back Jamie, who was making off in the opposite direction, and taking him also by an arm, towed us both into the castle.

After a long trip through cold narrow corridors, dimly lit by slitted windows, we came to a fairly large room furnished with a bed, a couple of stools, and most importantly, a fire.

I ignored my patient temporarily in favor of thawing my hands. Mistress FitzGibbons, presumably immune to cold, sat Jamie on a stool by the fire and gently got the remains of his tattered shirt off, replacing it with a warm quilt from the bed. She clucked at the shoulder, which was bruised and swollen, and poked at my clumsy dressing.

I turned from the fire. "I think it will need to be soaked off, and then the wound cleansed with a solution for . . . for preventing fevers."

Mistress FitzGibbons would have made an admirable nurse. "What will ye be needin'?" she asked simply.

I thought hard. What in the name of God had people used for preventing infection before the advent of antibiotics? And of those limited compounds, which might be available to me in a primitive Scottish castle just after dawn?

"Garlic!" I said in triumph. "Garlic, and if you have it, witch hazel. Also I'll need several clean rags and a kettle of water for boiling."

"Aye, well, I think we can manage that; perhaps a bit of comfrey as well. What about a bit o' boneset tea, or chamomile? T'lad looks as though it's been a long night."

The young man was in fact swaying with weariness, too tired to protest our discussing him as though he were an inanimate object.

Mrs. FitzGibbons was soon back, with an apron full of garlic bulbs, gauze bags of dried herbs, and torn strips of old linen. A small black iron kettle hung from one meaty arm, and she held a large demijohn of water as though it were so much goosedown.

"Now then, m' dear, what would ye have me do?" she said cheerfully. I set her to boiling water and peeling the cloves of garlic while I inspected the contents of the herb packets. There was the witch hazel I had asked for, boneset and comfrey for tea, and something I tentatively identified as cherry bark.

"Painkiller," I muttered happily, recollecting Mr. Crook explaining the uses of the barks and herbs we found. Good, we'd need that.

I threw several cloves of peeled garlic into the boiling water with some of the witch hazel, then added the cloth strips to the mixture. The boneset, comfrey, and cherry bark were steeping in a small pan of hot water set by the fire. The preparations had steadied me a bit. If I didn't know for certain where I was, or why I was there, at least I knew what to do for the next quarter of an hour.

"Thank you . . . ah, Mrs. FitzGibbons," I said respectfully. "I can manage now, if you have things to do." The giant dame laughed, breasts heaving.

"Ah, lass! There aye be things for me to do! I'll send a bit o' broth up for ye. Do ye call oot if ye need anything else." She waddled to the door with surprising speed and disappeared on her rounds.

I pulled the bandages off as carefully as I could. Still, the rayon pad stuck to the flesh, coming away with a soft crackling of dried blood. Droplets of fresh blood oozed around the edges of the wound, and I apologized for hurting him, though he hadn't moved or made a sound.

He smiled slightly, with a hint perhaps of flirtation. "No worry, lass. I've been hurt much worse, and by people much less pretty." He bent forward for me to wash the wound with the boiled garlic decoction, and the quilt slipped from his shoulder.

I saw at once that, whether meant as a compliment or not, his remark was a statement of plain fact; he had been hurt much worse. His upper back was covered with a criss-cross of faded white lines. He had been savagely flogged, and more than once. There were small lines of silvery scar tissue in some spots, where the welts had crossed, and irregular patches where several blows had struck the same spot, flaying off skin and gouging the muscle beneath.

I had, of course, seen a great variety of wounds and injuries, doing combat nursing, but there was something about these scars that seemed shockingly brutal. I must have drawn in my breath at the sight, for he turned his head and caught me staring. He shrugged his good shoulder.

"Lobsterbacks. Flogged me twice, in the space of a week. They'd ha' done it twice the same day, I expect, were they not afraid of killing me. No joy in flogging a dead man."

I tried to keep my voice steady while I sponged. "I shouldn't think anyone would do such a thing for joy."

"No? You should ha' seen him."

"Who?"

"The redcoat captain that skinned my back for me. If he was not precisely joyous, he was at least verra pleased with himself. More nor I was," he added wryly. "Randall was the name."

"Randall!" I couldn't keep the shock from my voice. Cold blue eyes fixed on mine.

"You're familiar with the man?" The voice was suddenly suspicious.

"No, no! I used to know a family of that name, a long time, uh, a long time ago." In my nervousness, I dropped the sponge cloth.

"Drat, now that will have to be boiled again." I scooped it off the floor and bustled to the fireplace, trying to hide my confusion in busyness. Could this Captain Randall possibly be Frank's ancestor, the soldier with the sterling record, gallant on the field of battle, recipient of commendations from dukes? And if so, could someone related to my sweet gentle Frank possibly be capable of inflicting the horrifying marks on this lad's back?

I busied myself at the fire, dropping in a few more handfuls of witch hazel and garlic, setting more cloths to soak. When I thought I could control my voice and face, I came back to Jamie, sponge in hand.

"Why were you flogged?" I asked abruptly.

It was hardly tactful, but I badly wanted to know, and was too tired to phrase it more gently.

He sighed, moving his shoulder uneasily under my ministrations. He was tired, too, and I was undoubtedly hurting him, gentle as I tried to be.

"The first time was escape, and the second was theft—or at least that's what the charge-sheet read."

"What were you escaping from?"

"The English," he said, with an ironic lift of his brow. "If ye mean where, Fort William."

"I gathered it was the English," I said, matching the dryness of his tone. "What were you doing in Fort William in the first place?"

He rubbed his brow with his free hand. "Oh, that. I think that was obstruction."

"Obstruction, escape, and theft. You sound a right dangerous character," I said lightly, hoping to distract him from what I was doing.

It worked at least slightly; one corner of the wide mouth turned up, and one dark blue eye glinted back over his shoulder at me.

"Oh, I am that," he said. "A wonder you think yourself safe in the same room wi' me, and you an English lassie."

"Well, you look harmless enough at the moment." This was entirely untrue; shirtless, scarred and blood-smeared, with stubbled cheeks and reddened eyelids from the long night ride, he looked thoroughly disreputable. And tired or not, he looked entirely capable of further mayhem, should the need arise.

He laughed, a surprisingly deep, infectious sound.

"Harmless as a setting dove," he agreed. "I'm too hungry to be a threat to anything but breakfast. Let a stray bannock come within reach, though, and I'll no answer for the consequences. Ooh!"

"Sorry," I muttered. "The stab wound's deep, and it's dirty."

"It's all right." But he had gone pale beneath the coppery stubble of his beard. I tried to lead him back into conversation.

"What exactly is obstruction?" I asked casually. "I must say it doesn't sound a major crime."

He took a deep breath, fixing his eyes resolutely on the carved bedpost as I swabbed deeper.

"Ah. Well, I suppose it's whatever the English say it is. In my case, it meant defending my family and my property, and getting myself half killed in the process." He pressed his lips together, as if to say no more, but after a moment went on, as though seeking to focus his attention on anything other than his shoulder.

"It was near to four years ago. There was a levy put on the manors near Fort William—food for the garrison, horses for transport, and suchlike. I wouldna say many liked it, but most would yield what they had to. Small parties of soldiers would go round with an officer and a wagon or two, collecting the bits of food and things. And one day in October, yon Captain Randall came along to L—" he caught himself quickly, with a glance at me, "to our place."

I nodded encouragingly, eyes on my work.

"We'd thought they'd not come so far; the place is a good distance from the fort, and not easy to get to. But they did."

He closed his eyes briefly. "My father was away—gone to a funeral at the next farm. And I was up in the fields wi' most of the men, for it was close to harvest, and a lot to be done. So my sister was alone in the house, except for two or three of the women servants, and they all rushed upstairs to hide their heads under the bedclothes when they saw the red coats. Thought the soldiers were sent by the devil—and I'll no just say they were wrong."

I laid down my cloth. The nasty part was done; now all we needed was a poultice of some kind—lacking iodine or penicillin, it was the best I could do for infection—and a good tight dressing. Eyes still closed, the young man did not appear to notice.

"I came down toward the house from behind, meaning to

fetch a piece of harness from the barn, and heard the shouting and my sister screaming inside the house."

"Oh?" I tried to make my voice as quiet and unintrusive as I could. I wanted very much to know about this Captain Randall; so far, this story had done little to dispel my original impression of him.

"I went in through the kitchen and found two of 'em riflin' the pantry, stuffin' their sacks wi' flour and bacon. I punched one of them in the head, and threw the other out the window, sack and all. Then I burst into the parlor, where I found two of the redcoats with my sister, Jenny. Her dress was torn a bit, and one of them had a scratched face."

He opened his eyes and smiled, a bit grimly. "I didna stop to ask questions. We were going round and about, and I wasna doing too poorly, for all there were two of them, when Randall came in."

Randall had stopped the fight by the simple expedient of holding a pistol to Jenny's head. Forced to surrender, Jamie had quickly been seized and bound by the two soldiers. Randall had smiled charmingly at his captive and said, "Well, well. Two spitfire scratchcats here, have we? A taste of hard labor'll cure your temper, I trow, and if it doesn't, well, there's another cat you'll meet, name of nine-tails. But there's other cures for other cats, aren't there, my sweet pussy?"

Jamie stopped for a moment, jaw working. "He was holdin' Jenny's arm behind her back, but he let go then, to bring his hand round and put it down her dress, round her breast, like." Remembering the scene, he smiled unexpectedly. "So," he resumed, "Jenny stamped down on his foot and gave him her elbow deep in the belly. And as he was bent over choking, she whirled round and gave him a good root in the stones wi' her knee." He snorted briefly with amusement.

"Weel, at that he dropped the pistol, and she went for it, but one of the dragoons holding me got to it first."

I had finished the bandaging and stood quiet behind him, a hand resting on his good shoulder. It seemed important he should tell me everything, but I was afraid he would stop if he were reminded of my presence.

"When he'd got back enough breath to talk with, Randall

had his men haul us both outside. They stripped off my shirt, bound me to the wagon tongue, and Randall beat me across the back with the flat of his saber. He was in a black fury, but a wee bit the worse for wear, ye might say. It stung me a bit, but he couldna keep it up for long."

The brief spurt of amusement had vanished now, and the shoulder under my hand was hard with tension. "When he stopped, he turned to Jenny—one of the dragoons had hold of her—and asked her did she want to see more, or would she rather go into the house with him, and offer him better entertainment?" The shoulder twitched uneasily.

"I couldna move much, but I shouted to her that I wasna hurt—and I wasn't, too much—and that she was not to go with him, not if they cut my throat before her eyes."

"They were holding her behind me, so I couldna see, but from the sound of it, she spat in his face. She must have done, because next thing I knew, he'd grabbed a handful of my hair, pulled my head back, and set his knife against my throat."

"I've a mind to take you at your suggestion," Randall had said through his teeth, and dug the point just beneath the skin, far enough to draw blood.

"I could see the dagger close to my face," Jamie said, "and the pattern of spots my blood was making in the dust under the wagon." His tone was almost dreamy, and I realized that, from fatigue and pain, he had lapsed into something like a hypnotic state. He might not even remember that I was there.

"I made to call out to my sister, to tell her that I'd much prefer to die than have her dishonor herself wi' such scum. Randall took the dagger from my throat, though, and thrust the blade betwixt my teeth, so I couldna call out." He rubbed at his mouth, as though still tasting bitter steel. He stopped talking, staring straight ahead.

"But what happened then?" I shouldn't have spoken, but I had to know.

He shook himself, like a man rousing from sleep, and rubbed a large hand tiredly across the back of his neck.

"She went with him," he said abruptly. "She thought he would kill me, and perhaps she was right. After that, I dinna ken what happened. One of the dragoons hit me in the head wi' the stock of his musket. When I woke, I was trussed up in the wagon wi' the chickens, jolting down the road toward Fort William."

"I see," I said quietly. "I'm sorry. It must have been terrible for you."

He smiled suddenly, the haze of fatigue gone. "Oh, aye. Chickens are verra poor company, especially on a long journey." Realizing that the dressing was completed, he hunched the shoulder experimentally, wincing as he did so.

"Don't do that!" I said in alarm. "You really mustn't move it. In fact," I glanced at the table, to be sure there were some strips of dry fabric left. "I'm going to strap that arm to your side. Hold still."

He didn't speak further, but relaxed a bit under my hands when he realized that it wasn't going to hurt. I felt an odd sense of intimacy with this young Scottish stranger, due in part, I thought, to the dreadful story he had just told me, and in part to our long ride through the dark, pressed together in drowsy silence. I had not slept with many men other than my husband, but I had noticed before that to sleep, actually *sleep* with someone did give this sense of intimacy, as though your dreams had flowed out of you to mingle with his and fold you both in a blanket of unconscious knowing. A throwback of some kind, I thought. In older, more primitive times (*like these?* asked another part of my mind), it was an act of trust to sleep in the presence of another person. If the trust was mutual, simple sleep could bring you closer together than the joining of bodies.

The strapping finished, I helped him on with the rough linen shirt, easing it over the bad shoulder. He stood up to tuck it one-handed into his kilt, and smiled down at me.

"I thank ye, Claire. You've a good touch." His hand reached out as though to touch my face, but he seemed to think better of it; the hand wavered and dropped to his side. Apparently he had felt that odd surge of intimacy too. I looked hastily away, flipping a hand in a think-nothing-of-it gesture.

My gaze traveled around the room, taking in the smoke-blacked fireplace, the narrow, unglazed windows, and the solid oak furnishings. No electrical fittings. No carpeting. No shiny brass knobs on the bedstead.

It looked, in fact, like an eighteenth-century castle. But what about Frank? The man I had met in the wood looked disturbingly like him, but Jamie's description of Captain Randall was completely foreign to everything I knew about my gentle, peace-loving husband. But then, if it were true—and I was beginning to admit, even to myself, that it might be— then he could in fact be almost anything. A man I knew only from a genealogical chart was not necessarily bound to resemble his descendants in conduct.

But it was Frank himself I was concerned with at the moment. If I was, in fact, in the eighteenth century, where was he? What would he do when I failed to return to Mrs. Baird's? Would I ever see him again? Thinking about Frank was the last straw. Since the moment I stepped into the rock and ordinary life ceased to exist, I had been assaulted, threatened, kidnapped and jostled. I had not eaten or slept properly for more than twenty-four hours. I tried to control myself, but my lip wobbled and my eyes filled in spite of myself.

I turned to the fire to hide my face, but too late. Jamie took my hand, asking in a gentle voice what was wrong. The firelight glinted on my gold wedding band, and I began to sniffle in earnest.

"Oh, I'll . . . I'll be all right, it's all right, really, it's . . . just my . . . my husband . . . I don't—"

"Ah lass, are ye widowed, then?" His voice was so full of sympathetic concern that I lost control entirely.

"No . . . yes . . . I mean, I don't . . . yes, I suppose I am!" Overcome with emotion and tiredness, I collapsed against him, sobbing hysterically.

The lad had nice feelings. Instead of calling for help or retreating in confusion, he sat down, gathered me firmly onto his lap with his good arm and sat rocking me gently, muttering soft Gaelic in my ear and smoothing my hair with one hand. I wept bitterly, surrendering momentarily to my fear and heartbroken confusion, but slowly I began to quiet a bit, as Jamie stroked my neck and back, offering me the comfort of his broad, warm chest. My sobs lessened and I began to calm myself, leaning tiredly into the curve of his shoulder. No wonder he was so good with horses, I thought blearily, feeling his fingers rubbing gently behind my ears, listening to the soothing, incomprehensible speech. If I were a horse, I'd let him ride me anywhere.

This absurd thought coincided unfortunately with my dawning realization that the young man was not completely exhausted after all. In fact, it was becoming embarrassingly obvious to both of us. I coughed and cleared my throat, wiping my eyes with my sleeve as I slid off his lap.

"I'm so sorry . . . that is, I mean, thank you for . . . but I . . ." I was babbling, backing away from him with my face flaming. He was a bit flushed, too, but not disconcerted. He reached for my hand and pulled me back. Careful not to touch me otherwise, he put a hand under my chin and forced my head up to face him.

"Ye need not be scairt of me," he said softly. "Nor of anyone here, so long as I'm with ye." He let go and turned to the fire.

"You need somethin' hot, lass," he said matter-of-factly, "and a bit to eat as well. Something in your belly will help more than anything." I laughed shakily at his attempts to pour broth one-handed, and went to help. He was right; food did help. We sipped broth and ate bread in a companionable silence, sharing the growing comfort of warmth and fullness.

Finally, he stood up, picking up the fallen quilt from the floor. He dropped it back on the bed, and motioned me toward it. "Do ye sleep a bit, Claire. You're worn out, and likely someone will want to talk wi' ye before too long."

This was a sinister reminder of my precarious position, but I was too exhausted to care much. I uttered no more than a pro forma protest at taking the bed; I had never seen anything so enticing. Jamie assured me that he could find a bed elsewhere. I fell headfirst into the pile of quilts and was asleep before he reached the door.

5

The Mackenzie

I woke in a state of complete confusion. I vaguely remembered that something was very wrong, but couldn't remember what. In fact, I had been sleeping so soundly that I couldn't remember for a moment who I was, much less where. I was warm, and the surrounding room was piercingly cold. I tried to burrow back into my cocoon of quilts, but the voice that had wakened me was still nagging.

"Come then, lass! Come now, ye must get up!" The voice was deep and genially hectoring, like the barking of a sheepdog. I pried one reluctant eye open far enough to see the mountain of brown homespun.

Mistress FitzGibbons! The sight of her shocked me back to full consciousness, and memory returned. It was still true, then.

Wrapping a blanket about me against the chill, I staggered out of bed and headed for the fire as fast as possible. Mistress FitzGibbons had a cup of hot broth waiting; I sipped it, feeling like the survivor of some major bombing raid, as she laid out a pile of garments on the bed. There was a long yellowish linen chemise, with a thin edging of lace, a petticoat of fine cotton, two overskirts in shades of brown, and a pale lemon-yellow bodice. Brown-striped stockings of wool and a pair of yellow slippers completed the ensemble.

Brooking no protests, the dame bustled me out of my inadequate garments and oversaw my dressing from the skin out. She stood back, surveying her handiwork with satisfaction.

"The yellow suits ye, lass; I thought it would. Goes well wi' that brown hair, and it brings out the gold in your eyes. Stay, though, ye'll need a wee bit o' ribbon." Turning out a pocket like a gunnysack, she produced a handful of ribbons and bits of jewelry.

Too stunned to resist, I allowed her to dress my hair, tying back the sidelocks with primrose ribbon, clucking over the unfeminine unbecomingness of my shoulder-length bob.

"Goodness, me dear, whatever were ye thinkin', to cut your hair so short? Were ye in disguise, like? I've heard o' some lasses doin' so, to hide their sex when travelin', same as to be safe from the dratted redcoats. 'Tis a fine day, says I, when leddies canna travel the roads in safety." She ran on, patting me here and there, tucking in a curl or arranging a fold. Finally I was arrayed to her satisfaction.

"Weel now, that's verra gude. Now, ye've just time for a wee bite, then I must take you to himself."

"Himself?" I said. I didn't care for the sound of this. Whoever Himself was, he was likely to ask difficult questions.

"Why, the MacKenzie to be sure. Whoever else?"

Who else indeed? Castle Leoch, I dimly recalled, was in the middle of the clan MacKenzie lands. Plainly the clan chieftain was still the MacKenzie. I began to understand why our little band of horsemen had ridden through the night to reach the castle; this would be a place of impregnable safety to men pursued by the Crown's men. No English officer with a grain of sense would lead his men so deeply into the clan lands. To do so was to risk death by ambush at the first clump of trees. And only a good-sized army would come as far as the castle gates. I was trying to remember whether in fact the English army ever had come so far, when I suddenly realized that the eventual fate of the castle was much less relevant than my immediate future.

I had no appetite for the bannocks and parritch that Mrs. FitzGibbons had brought for my breakfast, but crumbled a bit and pretended to eat, in order to gain some time for thought. By the time Mrs. Fitz came back to conduct me to the MacKenzie, I had cobbled together a rough plan.

The laird received me in a room at the top of a flight of stone steps. It was a tower room, round, and rich with paintings and tapestries hung against the sloping walls. While the rest of the castle seemed comfortable enough, if somewhat bare, this room was luxuriously crowded, crammed with furniture, bristling with ornaments, and warmly lit by fire and candle against the drizzle of the day outside. While the outer walls of the castle had only the high slit windows suited to resisting attack, this inner wall had been more recently furnished with long casement windows that let in what daylight there was.

As I entered, my attention was drawn at once by an enormous metal cage, cleverly engineered to fit the curve of the wall from floor to ceiling, filled with dozens of tiny birds: finches, buntings, tits, and several kinds of warblers. Drawing near, my eye was filled with plump smooth bodies and bead-bright eyes, set like jewels in a background of velvet green, darting among the leaves of oak, elm, and chestnut, carefully tended trees rooted in mulched pots set on the floor of the cage. The cheerful racket of conversing birds was punctuated by the whir of wings and rustle of leaves as the inhabitants flitted and hopped about their business.

"Busy wee things, are they no?" A deep, pleasant voice spoke from behind me, and I turned with a smile that froze on my face.

Colum MacKenzie shared the broad planes and high forehead of his brother Dougal, though the vital force that gave Dougal an air of intimidation was here mellowed into something more welcoming, though no less vibrant. Darker, with dove-grey rather than hazel eyes, Colum gave that same impression of intensity, of standing just slightly closer to you than was quite comfortable. At the moment, though, my discomfort arose from the fact that the beautifully modeled head and long torso ended in shockingly bowed and stumpy legs. The man who should have topped six feet came barely to my shoulder.

He kept his eyes on the birds, tactfully allowing me a much-needed moment to gain control of my features. Of course, he must be used to the reactions of people meeting him for the first time. It occurred to me, glancing around the room, to wonder how often he did meet new people. This was clearly a sanctuary; the self-constructed world of a man to whom the outer world was unwelcome—or unavailable.

"I welcome ye, mistress," he said, with a slight bow. "My name is Colum ban Campbell MacKenzie, laird of this castle. I understand from my brother that he, er, encountered you some distance from here."

"He kidnapped me, if you want to know," I said. I would have liked to keep the conversation cordial, but I wanted even more to get away from this castle and back to the hill with the standing stone circle. Whatever had happened to me, the answer lay there—if anywhere.

The laird's thick brows rose slightly, and a smile curved the fine-cut lips.

"Well, perhaps," he agreed. "Dougal is sometimes a wee bit . . . impetuous."

"Well." I waved a hand, indicating gracious dismissal of the matter. "I'm prepared to admit that a misunderstanding might have arisen. But I would greatly appreciate being returned to . . . the place he took me from."

"Mm." Brows still raised, Colum gestured toward a chair. I sat, reluctantly, and he nodded toward one of the attendants, who vanished through the door.

"I've sent for some refreshment, Mistress . . . Beauchamp, was it? I understand that my brother and his men found ye in . . . er, some apparent distress." He seemed to be hiding a smile, and I wondered just how my supposed state of undress had been described to him.

I took a deep breath. Now it was time for the explanation I had devised. Thinking this out, I had recalled Frank's telling me, during his officer's training, about a course he had taken in withstanding interrogation. The basic principle, insofar as I remembered it, was to stick to the truth as much as humanly possible, altering only those details that must be kept secret. Less chance, the instructor explained, of slipping up in the minor aspects of one's cover story. Well, we'd have to see how effective that was.

"Well, yes. I had been attacked, you see."

He nodded, face alight with interest. "Aye? Attacked by whom?"

Tell the truth. "By English soldiers. In particular, by a man named Randall."

The patrician face changed suddenly at the name. Though Colum continued to look interested, there was an increased intensity in the line of the mouth, and a deepening of the creases that bracketed it. Clearly that name was familiar. The MacKenzie chief sat back a bit, and steepled his fingers, regarding me carefully over them.

"Ah?" he said. "Tell me more."

So, God help me, I told him more. I gave him in great detail the story of the confrontation between the Scots and Randall's men, since he would be able to check that with Dougal. I told him the basic facts of my conversation with Randall, since I didn't know how much the man Murtagh had overheard.

He nodded absorbedly, paying close attention.

"Aye," he said. "But how did you come to be there in that spot? It's far off the road to Inverness—you meant to take ship from there, I suppose?" I nodded and took a deep breath.

Now we entered perforce the realm of invention. I wished I had paid closer attention to Frank's remarks on the subject of highwaymen, but I would have to do my best. I was a widowed lady of Oxfordshire, I replied (true, so far as it went), traveling with a manservant en route to distant relatives in France (that seemed safely remote). We had been set upon by highwaymen, and my servant had either been killed or run off. I had myself dashed into the wood on my horse, but been caught some distance from the road. While I had succeeded in escaping from the bandits, I had perforce to abandon my horse and all property thereon. And while wandering in the woods, I had run afoul of Captain Randall and his men.

I sat back a little, pleased with the story. Simple, neat, true in all checkable details. Colum's face expressed no more than a polite attention. He was opening his mouth to ask me a question, when there was a faint rustle at the doorway. A man, one of those I had noticed in the courtyard when we arrived, stood there, holding a small leather box in one hand.

The chief of clan MacKenzie excused himself gracefully and left me studying the birds, with the assurance that he would shortly return to continue our most interesting conversation.

No sooner had the door swung shut behind him than I was at the bookshelf, running my hand along the leather bindings. There were perhaps two dozen books on this shelf; more on the opposite wall. Hurriedly I flipped the opening pages of each volume. Several had no publication dates; those that did were all dated from 1720 to 1742. Colum MacKenzie obviously liked luxury, but the rest of his room gave no particular indication that he was an antiquarian. The bindings were new, with no sign of cracking or foxed pages within.

Quite beyond ordinary scruples by this time, I shamelessly rifled the olivewood desk, keeping an ear out for returning footsteps.

I found what I supposed I had been looking for in the central drawer. A half-finished letter, written in a flowing hand rendered no more legible by the eccentric spelling and total lack of punctuation. The paper was fresh and clean, and the ink crisply black. Legible or not, the date at the top of the page sprang out at me as though written in letters of fire: 20 April, 1743.

When he returned a few moments later, Colum found his guest seated by the casement windows, hands clasped decorously in her lap. Seated, because my legs would no longer hold me up. Hands clasped, to hide the trembling that had made it difficult for me to stuff the letter back into its resting place.

He had brought with him the tray of refreshments; mugs of ale and fresh oatcakes spread with honey. I nibbled sparingly at these; my stomach was churning too vigorously to allow for any appetite.

After a brief apology for his absence, he commiserated with me on my sad misfortune. Then he leaned back, eyed me speculatively, and asked, "But how is it, Mistress Beauchamp, that my brother's men found ye wandering about in your shift? Highwaymen would be reluctant to molest your person, as they'd likely mean to hold ye for ransom. And even with such things as I've heard of Captain Randall, I'd be surprised to hear that an officer in the English army was in the habit of raping stray travelers."

"Oh?" I snapped. "Well, whatever you've heard about him, I assure you he's entirely capable of it." I had overlooked the detail of my clothing when planning my story, and wondered at what point in our encounter the man Murtagh had spotted the Captain and myself.

"Ah, well," said Colum. "Possible, I daresay. The man's a bad reputation, to be sure."

"Possible?" I said. "Why? Don't you believe what I've told you?" For the MacKenzie chieftain's face was showing a faint but definite skepticism.

"I did not say I didn't believe ye, mistress," he answered evenly. "But I've not held the leadership of a large clan for twenty-odd years without learning not to swallow whole every tale I'm told."

"Well, if you don't believe I am who I say, who in bloody hell do you think I am?" I demanded.

He blinked, taken aback by my language. Then the sharp-cut features firmed again.

"That," he said, "remains to be seen. In the meantime, mistress, you're a welcome guest at Leoch." He raised a hand in gracious dismissal, and the ever-present attendant near the door came forward, obviously to escort me back to my quarters.

Colum didn't say the next words, but he might as well have. They hung in the air behind me as clearly as though spoken, as I walked away:

"Until I find out who you really are."

PART TWO

Castle Leoch

6
Colum's Hall

The small boy Mrs. FitzGibbons had referred to as "young Alec" came to fetch me to dinner. This was held in a long, narrow room outfitted with tables down the length of each wall, supplied by a constant stream of servants issuing from archways at either end of the room, laden with trays, trenchers, and jugs. The rays of early summer's late sunlight came through the high, narrow windows; sconces along the walls below held torches to be lighted as the daylight failed.

Banners and tartans hung on the walls between the windows, plaids and heraldry of all descriptions splotching the stones with color. By contrast, most of the people gathered below for dinner were dressed in serviceable shades of grey and brown, or in the soft brown and green plaid of hunting kilts, muted tones suited for hiding in the heather.

I could feel curious glances boring into my back as young Alec led me toward the top of the room, but most of the diners kept their eyes politely upon their plates. There seemed little ceremony here; people ate as they pleased, helping themselves from the serving platters, or taking their wooden plates to the far end of the room, where two young boys turned a sheep's carcass on a spit in the enormous fireplace. There were some forty people set to eat, and perhaps another ten to serve. The air was loud with conversation, most of it in Gaelic.

Colum was already seated at a table at the head of the room, stunted legs tucked out of sight beneath the scarred oak. He nodded graciously at my appearance and waved me to a seat on his left, next to a plump and pretty red-haired woman he introduced as his wife, Letitia.

"And this is my son, Hamish," he said, dropping a hand on the shoulder of a handsome red-haired lad of seven or eight, who took his eyes off the waiting platter just long enough to acknowledge my presence with a quick nod.

I looked at the boy with interest. He looked like all the other MacKenzie males I had seen, with the same broad, flat cheekbones and deep-set eyes. In fact, allowing for the difference in coloring, he might be a smaller version of his uncle Dougal, who sat next to him. The two teenage girls next to Dougal, who giggled and poked each other when introduced to me, were his daughters, Margaret and Eleanor.

Dougal gave me a brief but friendly smile before snatching the platter out from under the reaching spoon of one of his daughters and shoving it toward me.

"Ha' ye no manners, lass?" he scolded. "Guests first!"

I rather hesitantly picked up the large horn spoon offered me. I had not been sure what sort of food was likely to be offered, and was somewhat relieved to find that this platter held a row of homely and completely familiar smoked herrings.

I'd never tried to eat a herring with a spoon, but I saw nothing resembling a fork, and dimly recalled that runcible spoons would not be in general use for quite a few years yet.

Judging from the behavior of eaters at other tables, when a spoon proved impracticable, the ever-handy dirk was employed, for the slicing of meat and removal of bones. Lacking a dirk, I resolved to chew cautiously, and leaned forward to scoop up a herring, only to find the deep blue eyes of young Hamish fixed accusingly on me.

"Ye've not said grace yet," he said severely, small face screwed into a frown. Obviously he considered me a conscienceless heathen, if not downright depraved.

"Er, perhaps you would be so kind as to say it for me?" I ventured.

The cornflower eyes popped open in surprise, but after a moment's consideration, he nodded and folded his hands in a businesslike fashion. He glared round the table to ensure that everyone was in a properly reverential attitude before bowing his own head. Satisfied, he intoned,

> *"Some hae meat that canna eat,*
> *And some could eat that want it.*
> *We hae meat, and we can eat,*
> *And so may God be thankit. Amen."*

Looking up from my respectfully folded hands, I caught Colum's eye, and gave him a smile that acknowledged the sangfroid of his offspring. He suppressed his own smile and nodded gravely at his son.

"Nicely said, lad. Will ye hand round the bread?"

Conversation at table was limited to occasional requests for further food, as everyone settled down to serious eating. I found my own appetite rather lacking, partly owing to the shock of my circumstances, and partly to the fact that I really didn't care for herring, when all was said and done. The mutton was quite good, though, and the bread was delicious, fresh and crusty, with large dollops of fresh unsalted butter.

"I hope Mr. MacTavish is feeling better," I offered, during a momentary pause for breath. "I didn't see him when I came in."

"MacTavish?" Letitia's delicate brows tilted over round blue eyes. I felt, rather than saw Dougal look up beside me.

"Young Jamie," he said briefly, before returning his attention to the mutton bone in his hands.

"Jamie? Why, whatever is the matter wi' the lad?" Her full-cheeked countenance creased with concern.

"Naught but a scratch, my dear," Colum soothed. He glanced across at his brother. "Where is he, though, Dougal?" I imagined perhaps, that the dark eyes held a hint of suspicion.

His brother shrugged, eyes still on his plate. "I sent him down to the stables to help auld Alec wi' the horses. Seemed the best place for him, all things considered." He raised his eyes to meet his brother's gaze. "Or did ye have some other idea?"

Colum seemed dubious. "The stables? Aye, well . . . ye trust him so far?"

Dougal wiped a hand carelessly across his mouth and reached for a loaf of bread. "It's yours to say, Colum, if ye dinna agree wi' my orders."

Colum's lips tightened briefly, but he only said, "Nay, I reckon he'll do well enough there," before returning to his meal.

I had some doubts myself, as to a stable being the proper place for a patient with a gunshot wound, but was reluctant to offer an opinion in this company. I resolved to seek out the young man in question in the morning, just to assure myself that he was as suitably cared for as could be managed.

I refused the pudding and excused myself, pleading tiredness, which was in no way prevarication. I was so exhausted that I scarcely paid attention when Colum said "Good night to ye, then, Mistress Beauchamp. I'll send someone to bring ye to Hall in the morning."

One of the servants, seeing me groping my way along the corridor, kindly lighted me to my chamber. She touched her candle to the one on my table, and a mellow light flickered over the massive stones of the wall, giving me a moment's feeling of entombment. Once she had left, though, I pulled the embroidered hanging away from the window, and the feeling blew away with the inrush of cool air. I tried to think about everything that had happened, but my mind refused to consider anything but sleep. I slid under the quilts, blew out the candle, and fell asleep watching the slow rise of the moon.

It was the massive Mrs. FitzGibbons who arrived again to wake me in the morning, bearing what appeared to be the full array of toiletries available to a well-born Scottish lady. Lead combs to darken the eyebrows and lashes, pots of powdered orrisroot and rice powder, even a stick of what I assumed was kohl, though I had never seen any, and a delicate lidded porcelain cup of French rouge, incised with a row of gilded swans.

Mrs. FitzGibbons also had a striped green overskirt and

bodice of silk, with yellow lisle stockings, as a change from the homespun I had been provided with the day before. Whatever "Hall" involved, it seemed to be an occasion of some consequence. I was tempted to insist on attending in my own clothes, just to be contrary, but the memory of fat Rupert's response to my shift was sufficient to deter me.

Besides, I rather liked Colum, despite the fact that he apparently intended to keep me here for the foreseeable future. Well, we'd just see about *that*, I thought, as I did my best with the rouge. Dougal had said the young man I had doctored was in the stables, hadn't he? And stables presumably had horses, upon which one could ride away. I resolved to go looking for Jamie MacTavish, as soon as Hall was over with.

Hall turned out to be just that: the dining hall where I had eaten the night before. Now it was transformed, though; tables, benches, and stools pushed back against the walls, the head table removed and replaced by a substantial carved chair of dark wood, covered with what I assumed must be the MacKenzie tartan, a plaid of dark green and black, with a faint red and white over-check. Sprigs of holly decorated the walls, and there were fresh rushes strewn on the stone flags.

A young piper was blowing up a set of small pipes behind the empty chair, with numerous sighs and wheezes. Near him were what I assumed must be the intimate members of Colum's staff: a thin-faced man in trews and smocked shirt, who lounged against the wall; a balding little man in a coat of fine brocade, clearly a scribe of some sort, as he was seated at a small table equipped with inkhorn, quills, and paper; two brawny kilted men with the attitude of guards; and to one side, one of the largest men I have ever seen.

I stared at this giant with some awe. Coarse black hair grew far down on his forehead, nearly meeting the beetling eyebrows. Similar mats covered the immense forearms, exposed by the rolled-up sleeves of his shirt. Unlike most of the men I had seen, the giant did not seem to be armed, save for a tiny knife he carried in his stocking-top; I could barely make out the stubby hilt in the thickets of black curls that covered his legs above the gaily checked hose. A broad leather belt circled what must be a forty-inch waist, but carried neither dirk nor sword. In spite of his size, the man had an amiable expression, and seemed to be joking with the thin-faced man, who looked like a marionette in comparison with his huge conversant.

The piper suddenly began to play, with a preliminary belch, followed at once by an ear-splitting screech that eventually settled down into something resembling a tune.

There were some thirty or forty people present, all seeming somewhat better-dressed and groomed than the diners of the night before. All heads turned to the lower end of the hall, where, after a pause for the music to build up steam, Colum entered, followed at a few paces by his brother Dougal.

Both MacKenzies were clearly dressed for ceremony, in dark green kilts and well-cut coats, Colum's of pale green and Dougal's of russet, both with the plaid slung across their chests and secured at one shoulder by a large jeweled brooch. Colum's black hair was loose today, carefully oiled and curled upon his shoulders. Dougal's was still clubbed back in a queue that nearly matched the russet satin of his coat.

Colum walked slowly up the length of the hall, nodding and smiling to faces on either side. Looking across the hall, I could see another archway, near where his chair was placed. Clearly he could have entered the hall by that doorway, instead of the one at the far end of the room. So it was deliberate, this flaunting of his twisted legs and ungainly waddle on the long progress to his seat. Deliberate, too, the contrast with his tall, straight-bodied younger brother, who looked neither to left nor right, but walked straight behind Colum to the wooden chair and took up his station standing close behind.

Colum sat and waited for a moment, then raised one hand. The pipes' wailing died away in a pitiful whine, and "Hall" began.

It quickly became apparent that this was the regular occasion on which the laird of Castle Leoch dispensed justice to his tacksmen and tenants, hearing cases and settling disputes. There was an agenda; the balding scribe read out the names and the various parties came forward in their turn.

While some cases were presented in English, most of the proceedings were held in Gaelic. I had already noticed that the language involved considerable eye-rolling and foot-stamping for emphasis, making it difficult to judge the seriousness of a case by the demeanor of the participants.

Just as I had decided that one man, a rather moth-eaten specimen with an enormous sporran made of an entire badger, was accusing his neighbor of nothing less than murder, arson, and wife-stealing, Colum raised his eyebrows and said something quick in Gaelic that had both complainant and defendant clutching their sides with laughter. Wiping his eyes, the complainant nodded at last, and offered a hand to his opponent, as the scribe scribbled busily, quill scratching like a mouse's feet.

I was fifth on the agenda. A placement, I thought, carefully calculated to indicate to the assembled crowd the importance of my presence in the Castle.

For my benefit, English was spoken during my presentation.

"Mistress Beauchamp, will ye stand forth?" called the scribe.

Urged forward by an unnecessary shove from Mrs. FitzGibbons's meaty hand, I stumbled out into the clear space before Colum, and rather awkwardly curtsied, as I had seen other females do. The shoes I had been given did not distinguish between right foot and left, being in either case only an oblong of formed leather, which made graceful maneuvering difficult. There was a stir of interest through the crowd as Colum paid me the honor of getting up from his chair. He offered me his hand, which I took in order not to fall flat on my face.

Rising from the curtsy, mentally cursing the slippers, I found myself staring at Dougal's chest. As my captor, it was apparently up to him to make formal application for my reception—or captivity, depending how you wanted to look at it. I waited with some interest to see just how the brothers had decided to explain me.

"Sir," began Dougal, bowing formally to Colum, "we pray your indulgence and mercy with regard to a lady in need of succor and safe refuge. Mistress Claire Beauchamp, an English lady of Oxford, finding herself set upon by highwaymen and her servant most traitorously killed, fled into the forests of your lands, where she was discovered and rescued by myself and my men. We beg that Castle Leoch might offer this lady refuge until"—he paused, and a cynical smile twisted his mouth—"her *English* connections may be apprised of her whereabouts and due provision made for her safe transport."

I didn't miss the emphasis laid on "English," and neither did anyone else in the hall, I was sure. So, I was to be tolerated, but held under suspicion. Had he said "French," I would have been considered a friendly, or at worst, neutral intrusion. It might be more difficult than I had expected to get away from the castle.

Colum bowed graciously to me and offered me the unlimited hospitality of his humble hearth, or words to that effect. I curtsied again, with somewhat more success, and retired to the ranks, followed by curious but more or less friendly stares.

Until this point, the cases seemed to have been of interest chiefly to the parties involved. The spectators had chatted quietly among themselves, waiting their turns. My own appearance had been met with an interested murmur of speculation and, I thought, approval.

But now there was an excited stir through the hall. A burly man stepped forward into the clear space, dragging a young girl by the hand. She looked about sixteen, with a pretty, pouting face and long yellow hair tied back with blue ribbon. She stumbled into the space and stood alone, while the man behind her expostulated in Gaelic, waving his arms and occasionally pointing at her in illustration or accusation. Small murmurs ran through the crowd as he talked.

Mrs. FitzGibbons, her bulk resting on a sturdy stool, was craning forward with interest. I leaned forward and whispered in her ear. "What's she done?"

The huge dame replied without moving her lips or taking her eyes from the action. "Her father accuses her of loose behavior; consortin' improperly wi' young men against his orders," muttered Mistress FitzGibbons, leaning her bulk backward on the stool. "Her father wishes the MacKenzie to have her punished for disobedience."

"Punished? How?" I hissed, as quietly as I could.

"Shhh."

In the center, attention now focused on Colum, who was considering the girl and her father. Looking from one to the other, he began to speak. Frowning, he rapped his knuckles sharply on the arm of his chair, and a shiver ran through the crowd.

"He's decided," whispered Mrs. FitzGibbons, unnecessarily. What he had decided was also clear; the giant stirred for the first time, unbuckling his leather belt in a leisurely manner. The two guards took the terrified girl by the arms and turned her so that her back was to Colum and her father. She began to cry, but made no appeal. The crowd was watching with the sort of intent excitement that attends public executions and road accidents. Suddenly a Gaelic voice from the back of the crowd rose, audible over the shuffle and murmur.

Heads turned to locate the speaker. Mrs. FitzGibbons craned, even rising on tiptoe to see. I had no idea what had been said, but I thought I recognized that voice, deep but soft, with a spiky way of clipping the final consonants.

The crowd parted, and Jamie MacTavish came out into the clear space. He inclined his head respectfully to the MacKenzie, then spoke some more. Whatever he said seemed to cause some controversy. Colum, Dougal, the little scribe, and the girl's father all seemed to be getting into the act.

"What is it?" I muttered to Mrs. Fitz. My patient was looking much better than when last seen, though still a bit white-faced, I thought. He'd found a clean shirt somewhere; the empty right sleeve had been folded and tucked into the waist of his kilt.

Mrs. Fitz was watching the proceedings with great interest.

"The lad's offering to take the girl's punishment for her," she said absently, peeking around a spectator in front of us.

"What? But he's injured! Surely they won't let him do something like that!" I spoke as quietly as I could under the hum of the crowd.

Mrs. Fitz shook her head. "I dunno, lass. They're arguin' it now. See, 'tis allowable for a man o' her own clan to offer for her, but the lad is no a MacKenzie."

"He's not?" I was surprised, having naively assumed that all

the men in the group that had captured me came from Castle
Leoch.

"O' course not," said Mrs. Fitz impatiently. "Do ye no see
his tartan?"

Of course I did, once she had pointed it out. While Jamie
also wore a hunting tartan in shades of green and brown, the
colors were different than that of the other men present. It
was a deeper brown, almost a bark color, with a faint blue
stripe.

Apparently Dougal's contribution was the deciding argument. The knot of advisers dispersed and the crowd hushed,
falling back to wait. The two guards released the girl, who ran
back into the crowd, and Jamie stepped forward to take her
place between them. I watched in horror as they moved to
take his arms, but he spoke in Gaelic to the man with the
strap, and the two guards fell back. Amazingly, a wide, impudent grin lighted his face briefly. Stranger still, there was a
quick answering smile on the face of the giant.

"What did he say?" I demanded of my interpreter.

"He chooses fists rather than the strap. A man may choose
so, though a woman may not."

"Fists?" I had no time to question further. The executioner
drew back a fist like a ham and drove it into Jamie's abdomen,
doubling him up and driving his breath out with a gasp. The
man waited for him to straighten up before moving in and
administering a series of sharp jabs to the ribs and arms. Jamie
made no effort to defend himself, merely shifting his balance
to remain upright in the face of the assault.

The next blow was to the face. I winced and shut my eyes
involuntarily as Jamie's head rocked back. The executioner
took his time between blows, careful not to knock his victim
down or strike too many times in one spot. It was a scientific
beating, skillfully engineered to inflict bruising pain, but not
to disable or maim. One of Jamie's eyes was swelling shut and
he was breathing heavily, but otherwise he didn't appear too
badly off.

I was in an agony of apprehension, lest one of the blows
redamage the wounded shoulder. My strapping job was still in
place, but it wouldn't hold for long against this sort of treat-

ment. How long was this going to go on? The room was silent, except for the smacking thud of flesh on flesh and an occasional soft grunt.

"Wee Angus'll stop when blood's drawn," whispered Mrs. Fitz, apparently divining my unasked question. "Usually when the nose is broken."

"That's barbarous," I hissed fiercely. Several people around us looked at me censoriously.

The executioner apparently now decided that the punishment had gone on for the prescribed length of time. He drew back and let fly a massive blow; Jamie staggered and fell to his knees. The two guards hurried forward to pull him to his feet, and as he raised his head, I could see blood welling from his battered mouth. The crowd burst into a hum of relief, and the executioner stepped back, satisfied with the performance of his duty.

One guard held Jamie's arm, supporting him as he shook his head to clear it. The girl had disappeared. Jamie raised his head and looked directly at the towering executioner. Amazingly, he smiled again, as best he could. The bleeding lips moved.

"Thank you," he said, with some difficulty, and bowed formally to the bigger man before turning to go. The attention of the crowd shifted back to the MacKenzie and the next case before him.

I saw Jamie leave the hall by the door in the opposite wall. Having more interest in him now than in the proceedings, I took my leave of Mrs. FitzGibbons with a quick word and pushed my way across the hall to follow him.

I found him in a small side courtyard, leaning against a wellhead and dabbing at his mouth with his shirttail.

"Here, use this," I said, offering him a kerchief from my pocket.

"Unh." He accepted it with a noise that I took for thanks. A pale, watery sun had come out by now, and I looked the young man over carefully by its light. A split lip and badly swollen eye seemed to be the chief injuries, though there were marks along the jaw and neck that would be black bruises soon.

"Is your mouth cut inside too?"

"Unh-huh." He bent down and I pulled down his lower jaw, gently turning down the lip to examine the inside. There was a deep gash in the glistening cheek lining, and a couple of small punctures in the pinkness of the inner lip. Blood mixed with saliva welled up and overflowed.

"Water," he said with some difficulty, blotting the bloody trickle that ran down his chin.

"Right." Luckily there was a bucket and horn cup on the rim of the well. He rinsed his mouth and spat several times, then splashed water over the rest of his face.

"What did you do that for?" I asked curiously.

"What?" he said, straightening up and wiping his face on his sleeve. He felt the split lip gingerly, wincing slightly.

"Offer to take that girl's punishment for her. Do you know her?" I felt a certain diffidence about asking, but I really wanted to know what lay behind that quixotic gesture.

"I ken who she is. Havena spoken to her, though."

"Then why did you do it?"

He shrugged, a movement that also made him wince.

"It would have shamed the lass, to be beaten in Hall. Easier for me."

"Easier?" I echoed incredulously, looking at his smashed face. He was probing his bruised ribs experimentally with his free hand, but looked up and gave me a one-sided grin.

"Aye. She's verra young. She would ha' been shamed before everyone as knows her, and it would take a long time to get over it. I'm sore, but no really damaged; I'll get over it in a day or two."

"But why *you*?" I asked. He looked as though he thought this an odd question.

"Why not me?" he said.

Why *not*? I wanted to say. Because you didn't know her, she was nothing to you. Because you were already hurt. Because it takes something rather special in the way of guts to stand up in front of a crowd and let someone hit you in the face, no matter what your motive.

"Well, a musket ball through the trapezius might be considered a good reason," I said dryly.

He looked amused, fingering the area in question.

"Trapezius, is it? I didna know that."

"Och, here ye are, lad! I see ye've found your healer already; perhaps I won't be needed." Mrs. FitzGibbons waddled through the narrow entrance to the courtyard, squeezing a bit. She held a tray with a few jars, a large bowl, and a clean linen towel.

"I haven't done anything but fetch some water," I said. "I think he's not badly hurt, but I'm not sure what we can do besides wash his face for him."

"Och, now, there's always somethin', always somethin' that can be done," she said comfortably. "That eye, now, lad, let's have a look at that." Jamie sat obligingly on the edge of the well, turning his face toward her. Pudgy fingers pressed gently on the purple swelling, leaving white depressions that faded quickly.

"Still bleedin' under the skin. Leeches will help, then." She lifted the cover from the bowl, revealing several small dark sluglike objects, an inch or two long, covered with a disagreeable-looking liquid. Scooping out two of them, she pressed one to the flesh just under the brow bone and the other just below the eye.

"See," she explained to me, "once a bruise is set, like, leeches do ye no good. But where ye ha' a swellin' like this, as is still comin' up, that means the blood is flowin' under the skin, and leeches can pull it out."

I watched, fascinated and disgusted. "Doesn't that hurt?" I asked Jamie. He shook his head, making the leeches bounce obscenely.

"No. Feels a bit cold, is all." Mrs. Fitz was busy with her jars and bottles.

"Too many folk misuses leeches," she instructed me. "They're verra helpful sometimes, but ye must understand how. When ye use 'em on an old bruise, they just take healthy blood, and it does the bruise no good. Also ye must be careful not to use too many at a time; they'll weaken someone as is verra ill or has lost blood already."

I listened respectfully, absorbing all this information,

though I sincerely hoped I would never be asked to make use of it.

"Now, lad, rinse your mouth wi' this; 'twill cleanse the cuts and ease the pain. Willow-bark tea," she explained in an aside to me, "wi' a bit of ground orrisroot." I nodded; I recalled vaguely from a long-ago botany lecture hearing that willow bark in fact contained salicylic acid, the active ingredient in aspirin.

"Won't the willow bark increase the chance of bleeding?" I asked. Mrs. Fitz nodded approvingly.

"Aye. It do sometimes. That's why ye follow it wi' a good handful of St. John's wort soaked in vinegar; that stops bleedin', if it's gathered under a full moon and ground up well." Jamie obediently swilled his mouth with the astringent solution, eyes watering at the sting of the aromatic vinegar.

The leeches were fully engorged by now, swollen to four times their original size. The dark wrinkled skins were now stretched and shiny; they looked like rounded, polished stones. One leech dropped suddenly off, bouncing to the ground at my feet. Mrs. Fitz scooped it up deftly, bending easily despite her bulk, and dropped it back in the bowl. Grasping the other leech delicately just behind the jaws, she pulled gently, making the head stretch.

"Ye don't want to pull too hard, lass," she said. "Sometimes they burst." I shuddered involuntarily at the idea. "But if they're nearly full, sometimes they'll come off easy. If they don't, just leave 'em be and they'll fall off by themselves." The leech did, in fact, let go easily, leaving a trickle of blood where it had been attached. I blotted the tiny wound with the corner of a towel dipped in the vinegar solution. To my surprise, the leeches had worked; the swelling was substantially reduced, and the eye was at least partially open, though the lid was still puffy. Mrs. Fitz examined it critically and decided against the use of another leech.

"Ye'll be a sight tomorrow, lad, and no mistake," she said, shaking her head, "but at least ye'll be able to see oot o' that eye. What ye want now is a wee bit o' raw meat on it, and a drop o' broth wi' ale in it, for strengthenin' purposes. Come along to the kitchen in a bit, and I'll find some for ye." She scooped up her tray, pausing for a moment.

"What ye did was kindly meant, lad. Laoghaire is my grand-daughter, ye ken; I'll thank ye for her. Though she had better thank ye herself, if she's any manners at all." She patted Jamie's cheek, and padded heavily off.

I examined him carefully; the archaic medical treatment had been surprisingly effective. The eye was still somewhat swollen, but only slightly discolored, and the cut through the lip was now a clean, bloodless line, only slightly darker than the surrounding tissue.

"How do you feel?" I asked.

"Fine." I must have looked askance at this, because he smiled, still careful of his mouth. "It's only bruises, ye know. I'll have to thank ye again, it seems; this makes three times in three days you've doctored me. Ye'll be thinking I'm fair clumsy."

I touched a purple mark on his jaw. "Not clumsy. A little reckless, perhaps." A flutter of movement at the courtyard entrance caught my eye; a flash of yellow and blue. The girl named Laoghaire hung back shyly, seeing me.

"I think someone wants to speak with you alone," I said. "I'll leave you. The bandages on your shoulder can come off tomorrow, though. I'll find you then."

"Aye. Thank ye again." He squeezed my hand lightly in farewell. I went out, looking curiously at the girl as I passed. She was even prettier close up, with soft blue eyes and rose-petal skin. She glowed as she looked at Jamie. I left the court-yard, wondering whether in fact his gallant gesture had been quite so altruistic as I supposed.

Next morning, roused at daylight by the twittering of birds outside and people inside, I dressed and found my way through the drafty corridors to the hall. Restored to its nor-mal identity as a refectory, enormous cauldrons of porridge were being dispensed, together with bannocks baked on the hearth and spread with molasses. The smell of steaming food was almost strong enough to lean against. I felt still off-bal-

ance and confused, but a hot breakfast heartened me enough
to explore a bit.

Finding Mrs. FitzGibbons up to her dimpled elbows in
floured dough, I announced that I wanted to find Jamie, in
order to remove his bandages and inspect the healing of the
gunshot wound. She summoned one of her tiny minions with
the wave of a massive white-smeared hand.

"Young Alec, do ye run and find Jamie, the new horse-
breaker. Tell 'im to come back wi' ye to ha' his shoulder seen
to. We shall be in the herb garden." A sharp fingersnap sent
the lad scampering out to locate my patient.

Turning the kneading over to a maid, Mrs. Fitz rinsed her
hands and turned to me.

"It will take a while yet before they're back. Would ye care
for a look at the herb gardens? It would seem ye've some
knowledge of plants, and if you've a mind to, ye might lend a
hand there in your spare moments."

The herb garden, valuable repository of healing and flavors
that it was, was cradled in an inner courtyard, large enough to
allow for sun, but sheltered from spring winds, with its own
wellhead. Rosemary bushes bordered the garden to the west,
chamomile to the south, and a row of amaranth marked the
north border, with the castle wall itself forming the eastern
edge, an additional shelter from the prevailing winds. I correctly identified the green spikes of late crocus and soft-leaved
French sorrel springing out of the rich dark earth. Mrs. Fitz
pointed out foxglove, purslane, and betony, along with a few I
did not recognize.

Late spring was planting time. The basket on Mrs. Fitz's
arm carried a profusion of garlic cloves, the source of the
summer's crop. The plump dame handed me the basket,
along with a digging stick for planting. Apparently I had lazed
about the castle long enough; until Colum found some use
for me, Mrs. Fitz could always find work for an idle hand.

"Here, m'dear. Do ye set 'em here along the south side,
between the thyme and foxglove." She showed me how to
divide the heads into individual buds without disturbing the
tough casing, then how to plant them. It was simple enough,
just poke each clove into the ground, blunt end down, buried

about an inch and a half below the surface. She got up, dusting her voluminous skirts.

"Keep back a few heads," she advised me. "Divide 'em and plant the buds single, one here and one there, all round the garden. Garlic keeps the wee bugs awa' from the other plants. Onions and yarrow will do the same. And pinch the dead marigold heads, but keep them, they're useful."

Numerous marigolds were scattered throughout the garden, bursting into golden flower. Just then the small lad she had sent in search of Jamie came up, out of breath from the run. He reported that the patient refused to leave his work.

"He says," panted the boy, "as 'e doesna hurt bad enough to need doctorin', but thank ye for yer consairn." Mrs. Fitz shrugged at this not altogether reassuring message.

"Weel, if he won't come, he won't. Ye might go out to the paddock near noontide, though, lass, if ye've a mind to. He may not stop to be doctored, but he'll stop for food, if I ken young men. Young Alec here will come back for ye at noontide and guide ye to the paddock." Leaving me to plant the rest of the garlic, Mrs. Fitz sailed away like a galleon, young Alec bobbing in her wake.

I worked contentedly through the morning, planting garlic, pinching back dead flower heads, digging out weeds and carrying on the gardener's never-ending battle against snails, slugs, and similar pests. Here, though, the battle was waged bare-handed, with no assistance from chemical antipest compounds. I was so absorbed in my work that I didn't notice the reappearance of young Alec until he coughed politely to attract my attention. Not one to waste words, he waited barely long enough for me to rise and dust my skirt before vanishing through the courtyard gate.

The paddock to which he led me was some way from the stables, in a grassy meadow. Three young horses frolicked gaily in the meadow nearby. Another, a clean-looking young bay mare, was tethered to the paddock fence, with a light blanket thrown across her back.

Jamie was sidling cautiously up along one side of the mare, who was watching his approach with considerable suspicion. He placed his one free arm lightly on her back, talking softly, ready to pull back if the mare objected. She rolled her eyes and snorted, but didn't move. Moving slowly, he leaned across the blanket, still muttering to the mare, and very gradually rested his weight on her back. She reared slightly and shuffled, but he persisted, raising his voice just a trifle.

Just then the mare turned her head and saw me and the boy approaching. Scenting some threat, she reared, whinnying, and swung to face us, crushing Jamie against the paddock fence. Snorting and bucking, she leapt and kicked against the restraining tether. Jamie rolled under the fence, out of the way of the flailing hooves. He rose painfully to his feet, swearing in Gaelic, and turned to see what had caused this setback to his work.

When he saw who it was, his thunderous expression changed at once to one of courteous welcome, though I gathered our appearance was still not as opportune as might have been wished. The basket of lunch, thoughtfully provided by Mrs. Fitz, who did in fact know young men, did a good deal to restore his temper.

"Ahh, settle then, ye blasted beastie," he remarked to the mare, still snorting and dancing on her tether. Dismissing young Alec with a friendly cuff, he retrieved the mare's fallen blanket, and shaking off the dust of the paddock, he gallantly spread it for me to sit on.

I tactfully avoided any reference to the recent contretemps with the mare, instead pouring ale and offering chunks of bread and cheese.

He ate with a single-minded concentration that reminded me of his absence from the dining hall the two nights before.

"Slept through it," he said, when I asked him where he had been. "I went to sleep directly I left ye at the castle, and didna wake 'til dawn yesterday. I worked a bit yesterday after Hall, then sat down on a bale of hay to rest a bit before dinner." He laughed. "Woke up this morning still sitting there, wi' a horse nibbling at my ear."

I thought the rest had done him good; the bruises from yesterday's beating were dark, but the skin around them had a good healthy color, and certainly he had a good appetite.

I watched him polish off the last of the meal, tidily dabbing stray crumbs from his shirt with a moistened fingertip and popping them into his mouth.

"You've a healthy appetite," I said, laughing. "I think you'd eat grass if there was nothing else."

"I have," he said in all seriousness. "It doesna taste bad, but it's no verra filling."

I was startled, then thought he must be teasing me. "When?" I asked.

"Winter, year before last. I was livin' rough—ye know, in the woods—with the . . . with a group of lads, raidin' over the Border. We'd had poor luck for a week and more, and no food amongst us left to speak of. We'd get a bit of parritch now and then from a crofter's cottage, but those folk are so poor themselves there's seldom anything to spare. They'll always find something to give a stranger, mind, but twenty strangers is a bit much, even for a Highlander's hospitality."

He grinned suddenly. "Have ye heard—well, no, ye wouldna. I was goin' to say had ye heard the grace they say in the crofts."

"No. How does it go?"

He shook his hair out of his eyes and recited,

> *"Hurley, hurley, round the table,*
> *Eat as muckle as ye're able.*
> *Eat muckle, pooch nane,*
> *Hurley, hurley, Amen."*

"Pooch nane?" I said, diverted. He patted the sporran on his belt.

"Put it in your belly, not your bag," he explained.

He reached out for one of the long-bladed grasses and pulled it smoothly from its sheath. He rolled it slowly between his palms, making the floppy grain-heads fly out from the stem.

"It was a late winter then, and mild, which was lucky, or we'd not have lasted. We could usually snare a few rabbits—ate them raw, sometimes, if we couldna risk a fire—and once in a while some venison, but there'd been no game for days, this time I'm talkin' of.'"

Square white teeth crunched down on the grass stem. I plucked a stem myself and nibbled the end. It was sweet and faintly acid, but there was only an inch or so of stem tender enough to eat; hardly much nourishment there.

Tossing the half-eaten stalk away, Jamie plucked another, and went on with his story.

"There was a light snow a few days before; just a crust under the trees, and mud everywhere else. I was looking for *fungas*, ye know, the big orange things that grow on the trees low down, sometimes—and put my foot through a rind of snow into a patch of grass, growing in an open spot between the trees; reckon a little sun got in there sometimes. Usually the deer find those patches. They paw away the snow and eat the grass down to the roots. They hadn't found this one yet, and I thought if they managed the winter that way, why not me? I was hungry enough I'd ha' boiled my boots and eaten them, did I not need them to walk in, so I ate the grass, down to the roots, like the deer do."

"How long had you been without food?" I asked, fascinated and appalled.

"Three days wi' nothing; a week with naught more than drammach—a handful of oats and a little milk. Aye," he said, reminiscently viewing the grass stalk in his hand, "winter grass is tough, and it's sour—not like this—but I didna pay it much mind." He grinned at me suddenly.

"I didna pay much mind to the thought that a deer's got four stomachs, either, while I had but one. Gave me terrible cramps, and I had wind for days. One of the older men told me later that if you're going to eat grass, ye boil it first, but I didna know that at the time. Wouldn't ha' mattered; I was too hungry to wait." He scrambled to his feet, leaning down to give me a hand up.

"Best get back to work. Thank ye for the food, lass." He handed me the basket, and headed for the horse-sheds, sun glinting on his hair as though on a trove of gold and copper coins.

I made my way slowly back to the castle, thinking about men who lived in cold mud and ate grass. It didn't occur to me until I had reached the courtyard that I had forgotten all about his shoulder.

7

Davie Beaton's Closet

To my surprise, one of Colum's kilted men-at-arms was waiting for me near the gate when I returned to the castle. Himself would be obliged, I was told, if I would wait upon him in his chambers.

The long casements were open in the laird's private sanctum, and the wind swept through the branches of the captive trees with a rush and a murmur that gave the illusion of being outdoors.

The laird himself was writing at his desk when I entered, but stopped at once and rose to greet me. After a few words of inquiry as to my health and well-being, he led me over to the cages against the wall, where we admired the tiny inhabitants as they chirped and hopped through the foliage, excited by the wind.

"Dougal and Mrs. Fitz both say as you've quite some skill as a healer," Colum remarked conversationally, extending a finger through the mesh of the cage. Well accustomed to this, apparently, a small grey bunting swooped down and made a neat landing, tiny claws gripping the finger and wings slightly spread to keep its balance. He stroked its head gently with the callused forefinger of the other hand. I saw the thickened skin around the nail and wondered at it; it hardly seemed likely that he did much manual labor.

I shrugged. "It doesn't take that much skill to dress a superficial wound."

He smiled. "Maybe not, but it takes a bit of skill to do it in the pitch-black dark by the side of a road, eh? And Mrs. Fitz says you've mended one of her wee lads' fingers as was broken, and bound up a kitchen-maid's scalded arm this morning as well."

"That's nothing very difficult, either," I replied, wondering what he was getting at. He gestured to one of the attendants, who quickly fetched a small bowl from one of the drawers of the secretary. Removing the lid, Colum began scattering seed from it through the mesh of the cage. The tiny birds popped down from the branches like so many cricket balls bouncing on a pitch, and the bunting flew down to join its fellows on the ground.

"No connections to clan Beaton, have ye?" he asked. I remembered Mrs. FitzGibbons asking at our first meeting, *Are ye a charmer, then? A Beaton?*

"None. What have the clan Beaton to do with medical treatment?"

Colum eyed me in surprise. "You've not heard of them? The healers of clan Beaton are famous through the Highlands. Traveling healers, many of them. We had one here for a time, in fact."

"Had one? What happened to him?" I asked.

"He died," Colum responded matter-of-factly. "Caught a fever and it carried him off within a week. We've not had a healer since, save Mrs. Fitz."

"She seems very competent," I said, thinking of her efficient treatment of the young man Jamie's injuries. Thinking of that made me think of what had caused them, and I felt a wave of resentment toward Colum. Resentment, and caution as well. This man, I reminded myself, was law, jury, and judge to the people in his domain—and clearly accustomed to having things his own way.

He nodded, still intent on the birds. He scattered the rest of the seed, favoring a late-coming grey-blue warbler with the last handful.

"Oh, aye. She's quite a hand with such matters, but she's more than enough to take care of already, running the whole castle and everyone in it—including me," he said, with a sudden charming grin.

"I was wondering," he said, taking swift advantage of my answering smile, "seeing as how you've not a great deal to occupy your time at present, you might think of having a look at the things Davie Beaton left behind him. You might know the uses of a few of his medicines and such."

"Well . . . I suppose so. Why not?" In fact, I was becoming slightly bored with the round between garden, stillroom, and kitchen. I was curious to see what the late Mr. Beaton had considered useful in the way of paraphernalia.

"Angus or I could show the lady down, sir," the attendant suggested respectfully.

"Don't trouble yourself, John," Colum said, gesturing the man politely away. "I'll show Mistress Beauchamp myself."

His progress down the stair was slow and obviously painful. Just as obviously, he didn't wish for help, and I offered none.

The surgery of the late Beaton proved to be in a remote corner of the castle, tucked out of sight behind the kitchens. It was in close proximity to nothing save the graveyard, in which its late proprietor now rested. In the outer wall of the castle, the narrow, dark room boasted only one of the tiny slit windows, set high in the wall so that a flat plane of sunlight knifed through the air, separating the darkness of the high, vaulted ceiling from the deeper gloom of the floor below.

Peering past Colum into the dim recesses of the room, I made out a tall cabinet, equipped with dozens of tiny drawers, each with a label in curlicue script. Jars, boxes, and vials of all shapes and sizes were neatly stacked on the shelves above a counter where the late Beaton evidently had been in the habit of mixing medicines, judging from the residue of stains and a crusted mortar that rested there.

Colum went ahead of me into the room. Shimmering motes disturbed by his entry swirled upward into the bar of sunlight like dust raised from the breaking of a tomb. He stood for a moment, letting his eyes grow used to the dimness, then walked forward slowly, looking from side to side. I thought perhaps it was the first time he had ever been in this room.

Watching his halting progress as he traversed the narrow room, I said, "You know, massage can help a bit. With the pain, I mean." I caught a flash from the grey eyes, and wished for a moment that I hadn't spoken, but the spark disappeared almost at once, replaced by his usual expression of courteous attention.

"It needs to be done forcefully," I said, "at the base of the spine, especially."

"I know," he said. "Angus Mhor does it for me, at night." He paused, fingering one of the vials. "It would seem you do know a bit about healing, then."

"A bit." I was cautious, hoping he didn't mean to test me by asking what the assorted medicaments were used for. The label on the vial he was holding said PURLES OVIS. Anyone's guess what *that* was. Luckily, he put the vial back, and drew a finger gingerly through the dust on a large chest near the wall.

"Been some time since anyone's been here," he said. "I'll have Mrs. Fitz send some of her wee lassies along to clean up a bit, shall I?"

I opened a cupboard door and coughed at the resulting cloud of dust. "Perhaps you'd better," I agreed. There was a book on the lower shelf of the cupboard, a fat volume bound in blue leather. Lifting it, I discovered a smaller book beneath, this one bound cheaply in black cloth, much worn along the edges.

This second book proved to be Beaton's daily log book, in which he had tidily recorded the names of his patients, details of their ailments, and the course of treatment prescribed. A methodical man, I thought with approval. One entry read: "2nd February, A.D. 1741. Sarah Graham MacKenzie, injury to thumb by reason of catching the appendage on edge of spinning reel. Application of boiled pennyroyal, followed by poultice of: one part each yarrow, [St. John's wort,] ground slaters, and mouse-ear, mixed in a base of fine clay." Slaters? Mouse-ear? Some of the herbs on the shelves, no doubt.

"Did Sarah MacKenzie's thumb heal well?" I asked Colum, shutting the book.

"Sarah? Ah," he said thoughtfully. "No, I believe not."

"Really? I wonder what happened," I said. "Perhaps I could take a look at it later."

He shook his head, and I thought I caught a glimpse of grim amusement showing in the lines of his full, curved lips.

"Why not?" I asked. "Has she left the castle, then?"

"Ye might say so," he answered. The amusement was now apparent. "She's dead."

I stared at him as he picked his way across the dusty stone floor toward the doorway.

"It's to be hoped you'll do somewhat better as a healer than the late Davie Beaton, Mrs. Beauchamp," he said. He turned and paused at the door, regarding me sardonically. The sunbeam held him as though in a spotlight.

"Ye could hardly do worse," he said, and vanished into the dark.

I wandered up and down the narrow little room, looking at everything. Likely most of it was rubbish, but there might be a few useful things to be salvaged. I pulled out one of the tiny drawers in the apothecary's chest, letting loose a gust of camphor. Well, *that* was useful, right enough. I pushed the drawer in again, and rubbed my dusty fingers on my skirt. Perhaps I should wait until Mrs. Fitz's merry maids had had a chance to clean the place before I continued my investigations.

I peered out into the corridor. Deserted. No noises, either. But I was not naive enough to assume that no one was nearby. Whether by order or by tact, they were fairly subtle about it, but I knew that I was being watched. When I went to the garden, someone went with me. When I climbed the stair to my room, I would see someone casually glance up from the foot to see which way I turned. And as we had ridden in, I hadn't failed to note the armed guards sheltering under the overhang from the rain. No, I definitely wasn't going to be allowed simply to walk out of here, let alone be provided with transport and means to leave.

I sighed. At least I was alone for the moment. And solitude was something I very much wanted, at least for a little.

I had tried repeatedly to think about everything that had happened to me since I stepped through the standing stone.

But things moved so rapidly around this place that I had hardly had a moment to myself when I wasn't asleep.

Apparently I had one now, though. I pulled the dusty chest away from the wall and sat down, leaning back against the stones. They were very solid. I reached back and rested my palms against them, thinking about the stone circle, trying to recall every tiny detail of what had happened.

The screaming stones were the last thing I could truly say I remembered. And even that I had doubts about. The screaming had kept up, all the time. It was possible, I thought, that the noise came not from the stones themselves, but from . . . whatever . . . I had stepped into. Were the stones a door of some kind? And into what did they open? There simply were no words for whatever it was. A crack through time, I supposed, because clearly I had been *then,* and I was *now,* and the stones were the only connection.

And the sounds. They had been overwhelming, but looking back from a short distance, I thought they were very similar to the sounds of battle. The field hospital at which I was stationed had been shelled three times. Even knowing that the flimsy walls of our temporary structures would not protect us, still doctors, nurses and orderlies had all dashed inside at the first alarm, huddling together for courage. Courage is in very short supply when there are mortar shells screaming overhead and bombs going off next door. And the kind of terror I had felt then was the closest thing to what I had felt in the stone.

I now realized that I did recall some things about the actual trip through the stone. Very minor things. I remembered a sensation of physical struggle, as though I were caught in a current of some kind. Yes, I had deliberately fought against it, whatever it was. There were images in the current, too, I thought. Not pictures, exactly, more like incomplete thoughts. Some were terrifying and I had fought away from them as I . . . well, as I "passed." Had I fought toward others? I had some consciousness of fighting toward a surface of some kind. Had I actually *chosen* to come to this particular time because it offered some sort of haven from that whirling maelstrom?

I shook my head. I could find no answers by thinking about

it. Nothing was clear, except the fact that I would have go back to the standing stones.

"Mistress?" A soft Scottish voice from the doorway made me look up. Two girls, perhaps sixteen or seventeen, hung back shyly in the corridor. They were roughly dressed, with clogs on their feet and homespun scarves covering their hair. The one who had spoken carried a brush and several folded cloths, while her companion held a steaming pail. Mrs. Fitz's lasses, here to clean the surgery.

"We'll no be disturbin' ye, mistress?" one asked anxiously.

"No, no," I assured them. "I was about to leave anyway."

"You've missed the noon meal," the other informed me. "But Mrs. Fitz said to tell ye as there's food for ye in the kitchens whenever ye like to go there."

I glanced out the window at the end of the corridor. The sun was, in fact, a little past the zenith, and I became conscious of increasing hunger pangs. I smiled at the girls.

"I might just do that. Thank you."

I brought lunch to the fields again, fearing that Jamie might get nothing to eat until dinner otherwise. Seated on the grass, watching him eat, I asked him why he had been living in the rough, raiding cattle and thieving over the Border. I had seen enough by now both of the folk that came and went from the nearby village and of the castle dwellers, to be able to tell that Jamie was both higher born and much better educated than most. It seemed likely that he came from a fairly wealthy family, judging from the brief description he had given me of their farm estate. Why was he so far from home?

"I'm an outlaw," he said, as though surprised that I didn't know. "The English have a price of ten pounds sterling on my head. Not quite so much as a highwayman," he said, deprecatingly, "but a bit more than a pickpocket."

"Just for obstruction?" I said, unbelievingly. Ten pounds sterling here was half the yearly income of a small farm; I couldn't imagine a single escaped prisoner was worth that much to the English government.

"Och, no. Murder." I choked on a mouthful of bread-and-pickle. Jamie pounded me helpfully on the back until I could speak again.

Eyes watering, I asked, "Wh-who did you k-kill?"

He shrugged. "Well, it's a bit odd. I didna actually kill the man whose murder I'm outlawed for. Mind ye, I've done for a few other redcoats along the way, so I suppose it's not un-just."

He paused and shifted his shoulders, as though rubbing against some invisible wall. I had noticed him do it before, on my first morning in the castle, when I had doctored him and seen the marks on his back.

"It was at Fort William. I could hardly move for a day or two, after I'd been flogged the second time, and then I had fever from the wounds. Once I could stand again, though, some . . . friends made shift to get me out of the camp, by means I'd best not go into. Anyhow, there was some ruckus as we left, and an English sergeant-major was shot—by coincidence, it was the man that gave me the first flogging. I'd not ha' shot him, though; I had nothing personal against him, and I was too weak to do more than hang on to the horse, in any case." The wide mouth tightened and thinned. "Though had it been Captain Randall, I expect I'd ha' made the effort." He eased his shoulders again, stretching the rough linen shirt taut across his back, and shrugged.

"There it is, though. That's one reason I do not go far from the castle alone. This far into the Highlands, there's little chance of running into an English patrol, but they do come over the Border quite often. And then there's the Watch, though they'll not come near the castle, either. Colum's not much need of their services, having his own men to hand." He smiled, running a hand through his bright cropped hair 'til it stood on end like porcupine quills.

"I'm no precisely inconspicuous, ye ken. I doubt there's informers in the castle itself, but there might be a few here and there about the countryside as would be glad enough to earn a few pence by letting the English know where I was, did they know I was a wanted man." He smiled at me. "Ye'll have gathered the name's not MacTavish?"

"Does the laird know?"

"That I'm an outlaw? Oh, aye, Colum knows. Most people through this part of the Highlands likely know that; what happened at Fort William caused quite a bit of stir at the time, and news travels fast here. What they won't know is that Jamie MacTavish is the man that's wanted; provided nobody that knows me by my own name sees me." His hair was still sticking up absurdly. I had a sudden impulse to smooth it for him, but resisted.

"Why do you wear your hair cropped?" I asked suddenly, then blushed. "I'm sorry, it's none of my business. I only wondered, since most of the other men I've seen here wear it long. . . ."

He flattened the spiky licks, looking a bit self-conscious.

"I used to wear mine long as well. It's short now because the monks had to shave the back of my head and it's had but a few months to grow again." He bent forward at the waist, inviting me to inspect the back of his head.

"See there, across the back?" I could certainly feel it, and see it as well when I spread the thick hair aside; a six-inch weal of freshly healed scar tissue, still pink and slightly raised. I pressed gently along its length. Cleanly healed, and a nice neat job by whoever had stitched it; a wound like that must have gaped and bled considerably.

"Do you have headaches?" I asked professionally. He sat up, smoothing the hair down over the wound. He nodded.

"Sometimes, though none so bad as it was. I was blind for a month or so after it happened, and my head ached like fury all the time. The headache started to go away when my sight came back." He blinked several times, as though testing his vision.

"Fades a bit sometimes," he explained, "if I'm verra tired. Things get blurry round the edges."

"It's a wonder it didn't kill you," I said. "You must have a good thick skull on you."

"That I have. Solid bone, according to my sister." We both laughed.

"How did it happen?" I asked. He frowned, and a look of uncertainty came over his face.

"Weel, there's just the question," he answered slowly. "I dinna remember anything about it. I was down near Carryarick Pass with a few lads from Loch Laggan. Last I knew, I was pushing my way uphill through a wee thicket; I remember pricking my hand on a hollybush and thinking the blood drops looked just like the berries. And the next thing I remember is waking in France, in the Abbey of Sainte Anne de Beaupré, with my head throbbing like a drum and someone I couldn't see giving me something cool to drink."

He rubbed the back of his head as though it ached yet.

"Sometimes I think I remember little bits of things—a lamp over my head, swinging back and forth, a sort of sweet oily taste on my lips, people saying things to me—but I do not know if any of it's real. I know the monks gave me opium, and I dreamed nearly all the time." He pressed his fingers flat over closed eyelids.

"There was one dream I had over and over. Tree roots growing inside my head, big gnarled things, growing and swelling, pushing out through my eyes, thrusting down my throat to choke me. It went on and on, with the roots twisting and curling and getting bigger all the time. Finally they'd get big enough to burst my skull and I'd wake hearing the sound of the bones popping apart." He grimaced. "Sort of a juicy, cracking noise, like gunshots under water."

"Ugh!"

A shadow fell suddenly over us and a stout boot shot out and nudged Jamie in the ribs.

"Idle young bastard," the newcomer said without heat, "stuffin' yerself while the horses run wild. And when's that filly goin' to be broke, hey, lad?"

"None the sooner for my starving myself, Alec," Jamie replied. "Meanwhile, have a bit; there's plenty." He reached a chunk of cheese up to a hand knotted with arthritis. The fingers, permanently curled in a half-grip, slowly closed on the cheese as their owner sank down on the grass.

With unexpectedly courtly manners, Jamie introduced the visitor; Alec McMahon MacKenzie, Master of Horse of Castle Leoch.

A squat figure in leather breeks and rough shirt, the Master of Horse had an air of authority sufficient, I thought, to quell the most recalcitrant stallion. An "eye like Mars, to threaten or command," the quotation sprang at once to mind. A single eye it was, the other being covered with a black cloth patch. As if to make up for the loss, his eyebrows sprouted profusely from a central point, sporting long grey hairs like insects' antennae that waved threateningly from the basic brown tufts.

After an initial nod of acknowledgment, Old Alec (for so Jamie referred to him, no doubt to distinguish him from the Young Alec who had been my guide) ignored me, dividing his attention instead between the food and the three young horses switching their tails in the meadow below. I rather lost interest during a long discussion involving the parentage of several no doubt distinguished horses not among those present, details of breeding records of the entire stable for several years, and a number of incomprehensible points of equine conformation, dealing with hocks, withers, shoulders, and other items of anatomy. Since the only points I noticed on a horse were nose, tail, and ears, the subtleties were lost on me.

I leaned back on my elbows and basked in the warming spring sun. There was a curious peace in this day, a sense of things working quietly in their proper courses, nothing minding the upsets and turmoils of human concerns. Perhaps it was the peace that one always finds outdoors, far enough away from buildings and clatter. Maybe it was the result of gardening, that quiet sense of pleasure in touching growing things, the satisfaction of helping them thrive. Perhaps just the relief of finally having found work to do, rather than rattling around the castle feeling out of place, conspicuous as an inkblot on parchment.

In spite of the fact that I took no part in the horsey conversation, I didn't feel out of place here at all. Old Alec acted as though I were merely a part of the landscape, and while Jamie cast an occasional glance my way, he, too, gradually ignored me as their conversation segued into the sliding rhythms of Gaelic, sure sign of a Scot's emotional involvement in his subject matter. Since I gathered no sense from the talk, it was as soothing as listening to bees humming in the heather blossoms. Oddly contented and drowsy, I pushed away all thoughts of Colum's suspicions, my own predicament, and other disturbing ideas. "Sufficient unto the day," I thought sleepily, picking up the biblical quotation from some recess of memory.

It may have been the chill from a passing cloud, or the changed tone of the men's conversation that woke me sometime later. The talk had switched back to English, and the tone was serious, no longer the meandering chat of the horse-obsessed.

"It's no but a week 'til the Gathering, laddie," Alec was saying. "Have ye made up your mind what you'll do then?"

There was a long sigh from Jamie. "No, Alec, that I havena. Sometimes I think one way, sometimes the other. Granted that it's good here, working wi' the beasts and with you." There was a smile somewhere in the young man's voice, which disappeared as he went on. "And Colum's promised me to . . . well, you'll not know about that. But kiss the iron and change my name to MacKenzie, and forswear all I'm born to? Nay, I canna make up my mind to it."

"Stubborn as your da, ye are," remarked Alec, though the words held a tone of grudging approval. "You've the look of him about ye sometimes, for all you're tall and fair as your mother's folk."

"Knew him, did ye?" Jamie sounded interested.

"Oh, a bit. And heard more. I've been here at Leoch since before your parents wed, ye ken. And to hear Dougal and Colum speak of Black Brian, ye'd think he was the de'il himself, if not worse. And your ma the Virgin Mary, swept awa' to the Bad Place by him."

Jamie laughed. "And I'm like him, am I?"

"Ye are and all that, laddie. Aye, I see why it'd stick in your craw to be Colum's man, weel enough. But there's considerations the other way, no? If it comes to fighting for the Stuarts, say, and Dougal has his way. Come out on the right side in *that* fight, laddie, and you'll ha' your land back and more besides, whatever Colum does."

Jamie replied with what I had come to think of as a "Scottish noise," that indeterminate sound made low in the throat that can be interpreted to mean almost anything. This particular noise seemed to indicate some doubt as to the likelihood of such a desirable outcome.

"Aye," he said, "and if Dougal doesna get his way, then what? Or if the fight goes against the house of Stuart?"

Alec made a guttural sound of his own. "Then you stay here, laddie. Be Master of Horse in my place; I'll not last so much longer, and there's no better hand I've seen wi' a horse."

Jamie's modest grunt indicated appreciation of the compliment.

The older man went on, disregarding such interruptions. "The MacKenzies are kin to ye, too; it's not a matter of forswearing your blood. And there's other considerations, too" —his voice took on a teasing note—"like Mistress Laoghaire, perhaps?"

He got another noise in response, this one indicating embarrassment and dismissal.

"Hey now, lad, a young feller doesna let himself be beaten for the sake of a lass he cares nothin' for. And ye know her father will no let her wed outside the clan."

"She was verra young, Alec, and I felt sorry for her," said Jamie defensively. "There's nothin' more to it than that." This time it was Alec who made the Scottish noise, a guttural snort full of derisory disbelief.

"Tell that one to the barn door, laddie; it's no more brains than to believe ye. Weel, even if it's no Laoghaire—and ye could do a deal worse, mark me—ye'd be a better prospect for marriage did ye ha' a bit of money and a future; as ye would if ye're next Master. Ye could take yer choice of the lasses—if one doesna choose *you* first!" Alec snorted with the half-choked mirth of a man who seldom laughs. "Flies round a honeypot would be nothin' to it, lad! Penniless and nameless as ye are now, the lasses still sigh after ye—I've seen 'em!" More snorting. "Even this Sassenach wench can no keep away from ye, and her a new widow!"

Wishing to prevent what promised to be a series of increasingly distasteful personal remarks, I decided it was time to be officially awake. Stretching and yawning, I sat up, ostentatiously rubbing my eyes to avoid looking at either of the speakers.

"Mmmm. I seem to have fallen asleep," I said, blinking prettily at them. Jamie, rather red around the ears, was taking an exaggerated interest in packing up the remains of the picnic. Old Alec stared down at me, apparently taking notice of me for the first time.

"Interested in horses, are ye, lass?" he demanded. I could hardly say no, under the circumstances. Agreeing that horses were most interesting, I was treated to a detailed exegesis on the filly in the paddock, now standing drowsily at rest, tail twitching for the occasional fly.

"Ye're welcome to come and watch anytime, lass," Alec concluded, "so long as ye dinna get so close ye distract the horses. They need to work, ye ken." This was plainly intended as a dismissal, but I stood my ground, remembering my original purpose in coming here.

"Yes, I'll be careful next time," I promised. "But before I go back to the castle, I wanted to check Jamie's shoulder and take the dressings off."

Alec nodded slowly, but to my surprise, it was Jamie who refused my attentions, turning away to go back to the paddock.

"Ah, it'll wait awhile, lass," he said, looking away. "There's much to be done yet today; perhaps later, after supper, hey?" This seemed very odd; he hadn't been in any hurry to return to work earlier. But I could hardly force him to submit to my ministrations if he didn't want to. Shrugging, I agreed to meet him after supper, and turned uphill to go back to the castle.

As I made my way back up the hill, I considered the shape of the scar on Jamie's head. It wasn't a straight line, as might be made by an English broadsword. The wound was curved, as though made by a blade with a definite bend. A blade like a Lochaber ax? But so far as I knew, the murderous axes had been—no, were, I corrected myself—carried only by clans-men.

It was only as I walked away that it occurred to me. For a young man on the run, with unknown enemies, Jamie had been remarkably confiding to a stranger.

Leaving the picnic basket in the kitchens, I returned to the late Beaton's surgery, now dustless and pristine after a visita-tion by Mrs. Fitz's energetic assistants. Even the dozens of glass vials in the cupboard gleamed in the dim light from the window.

The cupboard seemed a good place to start, with an inven-tory of the herbs and medicaments already on hand. I had spent a few moments the night before, before sleep overcame me, thumbing through the blue leather-bound book I had taken from the surgery. This proved to be *The Physician's Guide and Handbook,* a listing of recipes for the treatment of assorted symptoms and diseases, the ingredients for which were apparently displayed before me.

The book was divided into several sections: "Centauries, Vomitories, and Electuaries," "Troches and Lodochs," "As-sorted Plasters and Their Virtus," "Decoctions and Theri-acs," and a quite extensive section ominously headed with the single word "Purges."

Reading through a few of the recipes, the reason for the late Davie Beaton's lack of success with his patients became appar-ent. "For headache," read one entry, "take ye one ball of horse dunge, this to be carefully dried, pounded to powder, and the whole drunk, stirred into hot ale." "For convulsions in children, five leeches to be applied behind the ear." And a few pages later, "decoctions made of the roots of celandine, turmeric, and juice of 200 slaters cannot but be of great ser-vice in a case of jaundice." I closed the book, marveling at the large number of the late doctor's patients who, according to his meticulous log, had not only survived the treatment meted out to them but actually recovered from their original ail-ments.

There was a large brown glass jar in the front containing

several suspicious-looking balls, and in view of Beaton's recipes, I had a good idea what it might be. Turning it around, I triumphantly read the hand-lettered label: DUNGE OF HORSES. Reflecting that such a substance likely didn't improve much with keeping, I gingerly set the jar aside without opening it.

Subsequent investigation proved PURLES OVIS to be a latinate version of a similar substance, this time from sheep. MOUSE-EAR also proved to be animal in nature, rather than herbal; I pushed aside the vial of tiny pinkish dried ears with a small shudder.

I had been wondering about the "slaters," spelled variously as "slatters," "sclaters," and "slatears," which seemed to be an important ingredient in a number of medicines, so I was pleased to see a clear cork-stoppered vial with this name on the label. The vial was about half-full of what appeared to be small grey pills. These were no more than a quarter-inch in diameter, and so perfectly round that I marveled at Beaton's dispensing skill. I brought the vial up close to my face, wondering at its lightness. Then I saw the fine striations across each "pill" and the microscopic legs, folded into the central crease. I hastily set the vial down, wiping my hand on my apron, and made another entry in the mental list I had been compiling. For "slaters," read "woodlice."

There were a number of more or less harmless substances in Beaton's jars, as well as several containing dried herbs or extractions that might actually be helpful. I found some of the orrisroot powder and aromatic vinegar that Mrs. Fitz had used to treat Jamie MacTavish's injuries. Also angelica, wormwood, rosemary, and something labeled STINKING ARAG. I opened this one cautiously, but it proved to be nothing more than the tender tips of fir branches, and a pleasant balsamic fragrance floated out of the unsealed bottle. I left the bottle open and set it on the table to perfume the air in the dark little room as I went on with my inventory.

I discarded jars of dried snails; OIL OF EARTHWORMS—which appeared to be exactly that; VINUM MILLEPEDATUM—millipedes, these crushed to pieces and soaked in wine; POWDER OF EYGYPTIANE MUMMIE—an indeterminate-looking dust, whose origin I thought more likely a silty streambank than a pharaoh's tomb;

PIGEONS BLOOD, ant eggs, a number of dried toads painstakingly packed in moss, and HUMAN SKULL, POWDERED. Whose? I wondered.

It took most of the afternoon to finish my inspections of the cupboard and multidrawered cabinet. When I had finished, there was a great heap of discarded bottles, boxes, and flasks set outside the door of the surgery for disposal, and a much smaller collection of possibly useful items stowed back into the cupboard.

I had considered a large packet of cobwebs for some time, hesitating between the piles. Both Beaton's *Guide* and my own dim memories of folk medicine held that spider's web was efficacious in dressing wounds. While my own inclination was to consider such usage unhygienic in the extreme, my experience with linen bandages by the roadside had shown me the desirability of having something with adhesive as well as absorbent properties for dressings. At last, I set the cobwebs back in the cupboard, resolving to see whether there might be a way of sterilizing them. Not boiling, I thought. Maybe steam would cleanse them without destroying the stickiness?

I rubbed my hands against my apron, considering. I had inventoried almost everything now—except the wooden chest against the wall. I flung back the lid, and recoiled at once from the stench that gusted out.

The chest was the repository of the surgical side of Beaton's practice. Within were a number of sinister-looking saws, knives, chisels, and other tools looking more suited to building construction than to use on delicate human tissues. The stench apparently derived from the fact that Davie Beaton had seen no particular benefit to cleaning his instruments between uses. I grimaced in distaste at the sight of the dark stains on some of the blades, and slammed shut the lid.

I dragged the chest toward the door, intending to tell Mrs. Fitz that the instruments, once safely boiled, should be distributed to the castle carpenter, if there were such a personage.

A stir behind alerted me, in time to avoid crashing into the person who had just come in. I turned to see two young men, one supporting the other, who was hopping on one foot. The lame foot was bound up in an untidy bundle of rags, stained with fresh blood.

I glanced around, then gestured at the chest, for lack of anything else. "Sit down," I said. Apparently the new physician of Castle Leoch was now in practice.

8

An Evening's Entertainment

I lay on my bed feeling altogether exhausted. Oddly enough, I had quite enjoyed the rummage through the memorabilia of the late Beaton, and treating those few patients, with however meager a resource, had made me feel truly solid and useful once more. Feeling flesh and bone beneath my fingers, taking pulses, inspecting tongues and eyeballs, all the familiar routine, had done much to settle the feeling of hollow panic that had been with me since my fall through the rock. However strange my circumstances, and however out of place I might be, it was somehow very comforting to realize that these were truly other people. Warm-fleshed and hairy, with hearts that could be felt beating and lungs that breathed audibly. Bad-smelling, louse-ridden, and filthy, some of them, but that was nothing new to me. Certainly no worse than conditions in a field hospital, and the injuries were so far reassuringly minor. It was immensely satisfying to be able once again to relieve a pain, reset a joint, repair damage. To take responsibility for the welfare of others made me feel less victimized by the whims of whatever impossible fate had brought me here, and I was grateful to Colum for suggesting it.

Colum MacKenzie. Now there was a strange man. A cultured man, courteous to a fault, and thoughtful as well, with a reserve that all but hid the steely core within. The steel was much more evident in his brother Dougal. A warrior born, that one. And yet, to see them together, it was clear which was the stronger. Colum was a chieftain, twisted legs and all.

Toulouse-Lautrec syndrome. I had never seen a case before, but I had heard it described. Named for its most famous sufferer (who did not yet exist, I reminded myself), it was a degenerative disease of bone and connective tissue. Victims often appeared normal, if sickly, until their early teens, when the long bones of the legs, under the stress of bearing a body upright, began to crumble and collapse upon themselves.

The pasty skin, with its premature wrinkling, was another outward effect of the poor circulation that characterized the disease. Likewise the dryness and pronounced callusing of fingers and toes that I had already noticed. As the legs twisted and bowed, the spine was put under stress, and often twisted as well, causing immense discomfort to the victim. I mentally read back the textbook description to myself, idly smoothing out the tangles of my hair with my fingers. Low white-cell count, increased susceptibility to infection, liable to early arthritis. Because of the poor circulation and the degeneration of connective tissue, victims were invariably sterile, and often impotent as well.

I stopped suddenly, thinking of Hamish. *My son,* Colum had said, proudly introducing the boy. Mmm, I thought to myself. Perhaps not impotent then. Or perhaps so. But rather fortunate for Letitia that so many of the MacKenzie males resembled each other to such a marked degree.

I was disturbed in these interesting ruminations by a sudden knock on the door. One of the ubiquitous small boys stood without, bearing an invitation from Colum himself. There was to be singing in the Hall, he said, and the MacKenzie would be honored by my presence, if I cared to come down.

I was curious to see Colum again, in light of my recent speculations. So, with a quick glance in the looking glass, and a futile smoothing of my hair, I shut the door behind me and followed my escort through the cold and winding corridors.

The Hall looked different at night, quite festive with pine torches crackling all along the walls, popping with an occasional blue flare of turpentine. The huge fireplace, with its multiple spits and cauldrons, had diminished its activity since the frenzy of supper; now only the one large fire burned on the hearth, sustained by two huge, slow-burning logs, and the spits were folded back into the cavernous chimney.

The tables and benches were still there, but pushed back slightly to allow for a clear space near the hearth; apparently that was to be the center of entertainment, for Colum's large carved chair was placed to one side. Colum himself was seated in it, a warm rug laid across his legs and a small table with decanter and goblets within easy reach.

Seeing me hesitating in the archway, he beckoned me to his side with a friendly gesture, waving me onto a nearby bench.

"I'm pleased you've come down, Mistress Claire," he said, pleasantly informal. "Gwyllyn will be glad of a new ear for his songs, though we're always willing to listen." The MacKenzie chieftain looked rather tired, I thought; the wide shoulders slumped a bit and the premature lines on his face were deeply cut.

I murmured something inconsequential and looked around the hall. People were beginning to drift in, and sometimes out, standing in small groups to chat, gradually taking seats on the benches ranged against the walls.

"I beg your pardon?" I turned, having missed Colum's words in the growing noise, to find him offering me the decanter, a lovely bell-shaped thing of pale green crystal. The liquid within, seen through the glass, seemed green as the sea-depths, but once poured out it proved to be a beautiful pale-rose color, with the most delicious bouquet. The taste was fully up to the promise, and I closed my eyes in bliss, letting the wine fumes tickle the back of my palate before reluctantly allowing each sip of nectar to trickle down my throat.

"Good, isn't it?" The deep voice held a note of amusement, and I opened my eyes to find Colum smiling at me in approval.

I opened my mouth to reply, and found that the smooth delicacy of the taste was deceptive; the wine was strong enough to cause a mild paralysis of the vocal cords.

"Won—wonderful," I managed to get out.

Colum nodded. "Aye, that it is. Rhenish, ye know. You're

not familiar with it?" I shook my head as he tipped the decanter over my goblet, filling the bowl with a pool of glowing rose. He held his own goblet by the stem, turning it before his face so that the firelight lit the contents with dashes of vermilion.

"You know good wine, though," Colum said, tilting the glass to enjoy the rich, fruity scent himself. "But that's natural, I suppose, with your family French. Or half French, I should say," he corrected himself with a quick smile. "What part of France do your folk come from?"

I hesitated a moment, then thought, stick to the truth, so far as you can, and answered, "It's an old connection, and not a close one, but such relatives as I may have there come from the north, near Compiègne." I was mildly startled to realize that at this point, my relatives *were* in fact near Compiègne. Stick to the truth, indeed.

"Ah. Never been there yourself, though?"

I tilted the glass, shaking my head as I did so. I closed my eyes and breathed deeply, inhaling the wine's perfume.

"No," I said, eyes still closed. "I haven't met any of my relatives there, either." I opened my eyes to find him watching me closely. "I told you that."

He nodded, not at all perturbed. "So ye did." His eyes were a beautiful soft grey, thickly lashed with black. A very attractive man, Colum MacKenzie, at least down to the waist. My gaze flickered past him to the group nearest the fire, where I could see his wife, Letitia, part of a group of several ladies, all engaged in animated conversation with Dougal MacKenzie. Also a most attractive man, and a whole one.

I pulled my attention back to Colum and found him gazing abstractedly at one of the wall hangings.

"And as I also told you before," I said abruptly, bringing him out of his momentary inattention, "I'd like to be on my way to France as soon as possible."

"So ye did," he said again, pleasantly, and picked up the decanter with a questioning lift of the brow. I held my goblet steady, gesturing at the halfway point to indicate that I wanted only a little, but he filled the delicate hollow nearly to the rim once more.

"Well, as *I* told *you*, Mistress Beauchamp," he said, eyes fixed on the rising wine, "I think ye must be content to bide here a bit, until suitable arrangements can be made for your transport. No need for haste, after all. It's only the spring of the year, and months before the autumn storms make the Channel crossing chancy." He raised eyes and decanter together, and fixed me with a shrewd look.

"But if ye'd care to give me the names of your kin in France, I might manage to send word ahead—so they'll be fettled against your coming, eh?"

Bluff called, I had little choice but to mutter something of the yes-well-perhaps-later variety, and excuse myself hastily on the pretext of visiting the necessary facilities before the singing should start. Game and set to Colum, but not yet match.

My pretext had not been entirely fictitious, and it took me some time, wandering about the darkened halls of the Castle, to find the place I was seeking. Groping my way back, wineglass still in hand, I found the lighted archway to the Hall, but realized on entering that I had reached the lower entrance, and was now at the opposite end of the Hall from Colum. Under the circumstances, this suited me quite well, and I strolled unobtrusively into the long room, taking pains to merge with small groups of people as I worked my way along the wall toward one of the benches.

Casting a look at the upper end of the Hall, I saw a slender man who must be Gwyllyn the bard, judging from the small harp he carried. At Colum's gesture, a servant hastened up to bring the bard a stool, on which he seated himself and proceeded to tune the harp, plucking lightly at the strings, ear close to the instrument. Colum poured another glass of wine from his own decanter, and with another wave, dispatched it via the servant in the bard's direction.

"Oh, he called for his pipe, and he called for his bowl, and he called for his fiddlers threeee," I sang irreverently under my breath, eliciting an odd look from the girl Laoghaire. She was seated under a tapestry showing a hunter with six elongated and cross-eyed dogs, in erratic pursuit of a single hare.

"Bit of overkill, don't you think?" I said breezily, waving a hand at it and plumping myself down beside her on the bench.

"Oh! er, aye," she answered cautiously, edging away slightly. I tried to engage her in friendly conversation, but she answered mostly in monosyllables, blushing and starting when I spoke to her, and I soon gave it up, my attention drawn by the scene at the end of the room.

Harp tuned to his satisfaction, Gwyllyn had brought out from his coat three wooden flutes of varying sizes, which he laid on a small table, ready to hand.

Suddenly I noticed that Laoghaire was not sharing my interest in the bard and his instruments. She had stiffened slightly and was peering over my shoulder toward the lower archway, simultaneously leaning back into the shadows under the tapestry to avoid detection.

Following the direction of her gaze, I spotted the tall, red-haired figure of Jamie MacTavish, just entering the Hall.

"Ah! The gallant hero! Fancy him, do you?" I asked the girl at my side. She shook her head frantically, but the brilliant blush staining her cheeks was answer enough.

"Well, we'll see what we can do, shall we?" I said, feeling expansive and magnanimous. I stood up and waved cheerily to attract his attention.

Catching my signal, the young man made his way through the crowd, smiling. I didn't know what might have passed between them in the courtyard, but I thought his manner in greeting the girl was warm, if still formal. His bow to me was slightly more relaxed; after the forced intimacy of our relations to date, he could hardly treat me as a stranger.

A few tentative notes from the upper end of the hall signaled an imminent beginning to the entertainment, and we hastily took our places, Jamie seating himself between Laoghaire and myself.

Gwyllyn was an insignificant-looking man, light-boned and mousy-haired, but you didn't see him once he began to sing. He only served as a focus, a place for the eyes to rest while the ears enjoyed themselves. He began with a simple song, something in Gaelic with a strong rhyming chime to the lines, accompanied by the merest touch of his harp strings, so that each plucked string seemed by its vibration to carry the echo of the words from one line to the next. The voice was also deceptively simple. You thought at first there was nothing much to it—pleasant, but without much strength. And then you found that the sound went straight through you, and each syllable was crystal clear, whether you understood it or not, echoing poignantly inside your head.

The song was received with a warm surge of applause, and the singer launched at once into another, this time in Welsh, I thought. It sounded like a very tuneful sort of gargling to me, but those around me seemed to follow well enough; doubtless they had heard it before.

During a brief pause for retuning, I asked Jamie in a low voice, "Has Gwyllyn been at the Castle long?" Then, remembering, I said, "Oh, but you wouldn't know, would you? I'd forgotten you were so new here yourself."

"I've been here before," he answered, turning his attention to me. "Spent a year at Leoch when I was sixteen or so, and Gwyllyn was here then. Colum's fond of his music, ye see. He pays Gwyllyn well to stay. Has to; the Welshman would be welcome at any laird's hearth where he chose to roost."

"I remember when you were here, before." It was Laoghaire, still blushing pinkly, but determined to join the conversation. Jamie turned his head to include her, smiling slightly.

"Do ye, then? You canna have been more than seven or eight yourself. I'd not think I was much to see then, so as to be remembered." Turning politely to me, he said, "Do ye have the Welsh, then?"

"Well, I do remember, though," Laoghaire said, pursuing it. "You were, er, ah . . . I mean . . . do ye not remember me, from then?" Her hands fiddled nervously with the folds of her skirt. She bit her nails, I saw.

Jamie's attention seemed distracted by a group of people across the room, arguing in Gaelic about something.

"Ah?" he said, vaguely. "No, I dinna think so. Still," he said with a smile, pulling his attention suddenly back to her, "I wouldna be likely to. A young burke of sixteen's too taken up wi' his own grand self to pay much heed to what he thinks are naught but a rabble of snot-nosed bairns."

I gathered he had meant this remark to be deprecatory to himself, rather than his listener, but the effect was not what he might have hoped. I thought perhaps a brief pause to let Laoghaire recover her self-possession was in order, and broke in hastily with, "No, I don't know any Welsh at all. Do you have any idea what it is he was saying?"

"Oh, aye." And Jamie launched into what appeared to be a verbatim recitation of the song, translated into English. It was an old ballad, apparently, about a young man who loved a young woman (what else?), but feeling unworthy of her because he was poor, went off to make his fortune at sea. The young man was shipwrecked, met sea serpents who menaced him and mermaids who entranced him, had adventures, found treasure, and came home at last only to find his young woman wed to his best friend, who, if somewhat poorer, also apparently had better sense.

"And which would you do?" I asked, teasing a bit. "Would you be the young man who wouldn't marry without money, or would you take the girl and let the money go hang?" This question seemed to interest Laoghaire as well, who cocked her head to hear the answer, meanwhile pretending great attention to an air on the flute that Gwyllyn had begun.

"Me?" Jamie seemed entertained by the question. "Well, as I've no money to start with, and precious little chance of ever getting any, I suppose I'd count myself lucky to find a lass would wed me without." He shook his head, grinning. "I've no stomach for sea serpents."

He opened his mouth to say something further, but was silenced by Laoghaire, who laid a hand timidly on his arm, then blushing, snatched it back as though he were red-hot.

"Shh," she said. "I mean . . . he's going to tell stories. Do ye not want to hear?"

"Oh, aye." Jamie sat forward a bit in anticipation, then realizing that he blocked my view, insisted that I sit on the other side of him, displacing Laoghaire down the bench. I could see the girl was not best pleased at this arrangement, and I tried to protest that I was all right as I was, but he was firm about it.

"No, you'll see and hear better there. And then, if he speaks in the Gaelic, I can whisper in your ear what he says."

Each part of the bard's performance had been greeted with warm applause, though people chatted quietly while he played, making a deep hum below the high, sweet strains of the harp. But now a sort of expectant hush descended on the hall. Gwyllyn's speaking voice was as clear as his singing, each word pitched to reach the end of the high, drafty hall without strain.

"It was a time, two hundred years ago . . ." He spoke in English, and I felt a sudden sense of déjà vu. It was exactly the way our guide on Loch Ness had spoken, telling legends of the Great Glen.

It was not a story of ghosts or heroes, though, but a tale of the Wee Folk he told.

"There was a clan of the Wee Folk as lived near Dundreggan," he began. "And the hill there is named for the dragon that dwelt there, that Fionn slew and buried where he fell, so the dun is named as it is. And after the passing of Fionn and the Feinn, the Wee Folk that came to dwell in the dun came to want mothers of men to be wet nurses to their own fairy bairns, for a man has something that a fairy has not, and the Wee Folk thought that it might pass through the mothers' milk to their own small ones.

"Now, Ewan MacDonald of Dundreggan was out in the dark, tending his beasts, on the night when his wife bore her firstborn son. A gust of the night wind passed by him, and in the breath of the wind he heard his wife's sighing. She sighed as she sighed before the child was born, and hearing her there, Ewan MacDonald turned and flung his knife into the wind in the name of the Trinity. And his wife dropped safe to the ground beside him."

The story was received with a sort of collective "ah" at the conclusion, and was quickly followed by tales of the cleverness and ingenuity of the Wee Folk, and others about their interactions with the world of men. Some were in Gaelic and some in English, used apparently according to which language best fitted the rhythm of the words, for all of them had a beauty to the speaking, beyond the content of the tale itself. True to his promise, Jamie translated the Gaelic for me in an undertone, so quickly and easily that I thought he must have heard these stories many times before.

There was one I noticed particularly, about the man out late at night upon a fairy hill, who heard the sound of a woman singing "sad and plaintive" from the very rocks of the hill. He listened more closely and heard the words:

> *"I am the wife of the Laird of Balnain*
> *The Folk have stolen me over again."*

So the listener hurried to the house of Balnain and found there the owner gone and his wife and baby son missing. The man hastily sought out a priest and brought him back to the fairy knoll. The priest blessed the rocks of the dun and sprinkled them with holy water. Suddenly the night grew darker and there was a loud noise as of thunder. Then the moon came out from behind a cloud and shone upon the woman, the wife of Balnain, who lay exhausted on the grass with her child in her arms. The woman was tired, as though she had traveled far, but could not tell where she had been, nor how she had come there.

Others in the hall had stories to tell, and Gwyllyn rested on his stool to sip wine as one gave place to another by the fireside, telling stories that held the hall rapt.

Some of these I hardly heard. I was rapt myself, but by my own thoughts, which were tumbling about, forming patterns under the influence of wine, music, and fairy legends.

"It was a time, two hundred years ago . . ."

It's always two hundred years in Highland stories, said the Reverend Wakefield's voice in memory. *The same thing as "Once upon a time,"* you know.

And women trapped in the rocks of fairy duns, traveling far and arriving exhausted, who knew not where they had been, nor how they had come there.

I could feel the hair rising on my forearms, as though with cold, and rubbed them uneasily. Two hundred years. From

1945 to 1743; yes, near enough. And women who traveled through the rocks. Was it always women? I wondered suddenly.

Something else occurred to me. The women came back. Holy water, spell, or knife, *they came back*. So perhaps, just perhaps, it was possible. I must get back to the standing stones on Craigh na Dun. I felt a rising excitement that made me feel a trifle sick, and I reached for the wine goblet to calm myself.

"Be careful!" My groping fingers fumbled the edge of the nearly full crystal goblet which I had carelessly set on the bench beside me. Jamie's long arm shot across my lap, narrowly saving the goblet from disaster. He lifted the glass, holding the stem delicately between two large fingers, and passed it gently back and forth under his nose. He handed it back to me, eyebrows lifted.

"Rhenish," I explained helpfully.

"Aye, I know," he said, still looking quizzical. "Colum's, is it?"

"Why, yes. Would you like to try some? It's very good." I held out the glass, a trifle unsteadily. After a moment's hesitation, he accepted the glass and tried a small sip.

"Aye, it's good," he said, handing the goblet back. "It's also double strength. Colum takes it at night because his legs pain him. How much of it have you had?" he asked, eyeing me narrowly.

"Two, no, three glasses," I said, with some dignity. "Are you implying that I'm intoxicated?"

"No," he said, brows still raised, "I'm impressed that you're not. Most folk that drink wi' Colum are under the table after the second glass." He reached out and took the goblet from me again.

"Still," he added firmly, "I think you'd best drink no more of it, or ye won't get back up the stairs." He tilted the glass and deliberately drained it himself, then handed the empty goblet to Laoghaire without looking at her.

"Take that back, will ye, lass," he said casually. "It's grown late; I believe I'll see Mistress Beauchamp to her chamber." And putting a hand under my elbow, he steered me toward the archway, leaving the girl staring after us with an expression that made me relieved that looks in fact cannot kill.

Jamie followed me up to my chamber, and somewhat to my surprise, came in after me. The surprise vanished when he shut the door and immediately shed his shirt. I had forgotten the dressing, which I had been meaning to remove for the last two days.

"I'll be glad to get this off," he said, rubbing at the rayon and linen harness arrangement under his arm. "It's been chafing me for days."

"I'm surprised you didn't take it off yourself, then," I said, reaching up to untie the knots.

"I was afraid to, after the scolding ye gave me when you put the first one on," he said, grinning impudently down at me. "Thought I'd get my bum smacked if I touched it."

"You'll get it smacked now, if you don't sit down and keep still," I answered, mock-stern. I put both hands on his good shoulder and, a little unsteadily, pulled him down onto the bedroom stool.

I slipped the harness off and carefully probed the shoulder joint. It was still slightly swollen, with some bruising, but thankfully I could find no evidence of torn muscles.

"If you were so anxious to get rid of it, why didn't you let me take it off for you yesterday afternoon?" His behavior at the paddock had puzzled me then, and did so still more, now that I could see the patches of reddened skin where the rough edges of the linen bandages had rubbed him nearly raw. I lifted the dressing cautiously, but all was well beneath.

He glanced sidelong at me, then looked down a bit sheepishly. "Well, it's—ah, it's only that I didna want to take my shirt off before Alec."

"Modest, are you?" I asked dryly, making him raise his arm to test the extension of the joint. He winced slightly at the movement, but smiled at the remark.

"If I were, I should hardly be sittin' half-naked in your chamber, should I? No, it's the marks on my back." Seeing my raised eyebrows, he went on to explain. "Alec knows who I am—I mean, he's heard I was flogged, but he's not seen it. And to know something like that is no the same as seein' it wi' your own eyes." He felt the sore shoulder tentatively, eyes turned away. He frowned at the floor. "It's—maybe you'll not know what I mean. But when you know a man's suffered some harm, it's only one of the things you know about him, and it doesna make much difference to how ye see him. Alec knows I've been flogged, like he knows I've red hair, and it doesna matter to how he treats me." He looked up then, searching for some sign of understanding from me.

"But when you see it yourself, it's like"—he hesitated, looking for words—"it's a bit . . . personal, maybe, is what I mean. I think . . . if he were to see the scars, he couldna see *me* anymore without thinking of my back. And I'd be able to see him thinking of it, and that would make me remember it, and—" He broke off, shrugging.

"Well. That's a poor job of explaining, no? I daresay I'm too tender-minded about it, in any case. After all, I canna see it for myself; perhaps it's not as bad as I think." I had seen wounded men making their way on crutches down the street, and the people passing them with averted eyes, and I thought it was not at all a bad job of explanation.

"You don't mind my seeing your back?"

"No, I don't." He sounded mildly surprised, and paused a moment to think about it. "I suppose . . . it's that ye seem to have a knack for letting me know you're sorry for it, without makin' me feel pitiful about it."

He sat patiently, not moving as I circled behind him and inspected his back. I didn't know how bad he thought it was, but it was bad enough. Even by candlelight and having seen it once before, I was appalled. Before, I had seen only the one shoulder. The scars covered his entire back from shoulders to waist. While many had faded to little more than thin white lines, the worst formed thick silver wedges, cutting across the smooth muscles. I thought with some regret that it must have been quite a beautiful back at one time. His skin was fair and fresh, and the lines of bone and muscle were still solid and graceful, the shoulders flat and square-set and the backbone a smooth, straight groove cut deep between the rounded columns of muscle that rose on either side of it.

Jamie was right too. Looking at this wanton damage, I

could not avoid a mental picture of the process that had caused it. I tried not to imagine the muscular arms raised, spread-eagled and tied, ropes cutting into wrists, the coppery head pressed hard against the post in agony, but the marks brought such images all too readily to mind. Had he screamed when it was done? I pushed the thought hastily away. I had heard the stories that trickled out of postwar Germany, of course, of atrocities much worse than this, but he *was* right; hearing is not at all the same as seeing.

Involuntarily, I reached out, as though I might heal him with a touch and erase the marks with my fingers. He sighed deeply, but didn't move as I traced the deep scars, one by one, as though to show him the extent of the damage he couldn't see. I rested my hands at last lightly on his shoulders in silence, groping for words.

He placed his own hand over mine, and squeezed lightly in acknowledgment of the things I couldn't find to say.

"There's worse has happened to others, lass," he said quietly. Then he let go and the spell was broken.

"It feels as though it's healing well," he said, trying to look sideways at the wound in his shoulder. "It doesna pain me much."

"That's good," I said, clearing my throat of some obstruction that seemed to have lodged there. "It *is* healing well; it's scabbed over nicely, and there's no drainage at all. Just keep it clean, and don't use the arm more than you must for another two or three days." I patted the undamaged shoulder, signifying dismissal. He put his shirt back on without assistance, tucking the long tails down into the kilt.

There was an awkward moment as he paused by the door, seeking something to say in farewell. Finally, he invited me to come to the stable next day and see a newborn foal. I promised that I would, and we said good night, both speaking together. We laughed and nodded absurdly to each other as I shut the door. I went at once to bed and fell asleep in a winey haze, to dream unsettling dreams that I would not recall come morning.

Next day, after a long morning of treating new patients, rummaging the stillroom for useful herbs to replenish the medical supplies cupboard, and—with some ceremony—recording the details in Davie Beaton's black ledger, I left my narrow closet in search of air and exercise.

There was no one about for the moment, and I took the opportunity to explore the upper floors of the castle, poking into empty chambers and winding staircases, mapping the castle in my mind. It was a most irregular floor plan, to say the least. Bits and pieces had been added here and there over the years, until it was difficult to say whether there ever *had* been a plan originally. In this hall, for example, there was an alcove built into the wall by the stairs, apparently serving no purpose but to fill in a blank space too small for a complete room.

The alcove was partly shielded from view by a hanging curtain of striped linen; I would have passed by without stopping, had a sudden flash of white from within not attracted my attention. I stopped just short of the opening and peered inside to see what it was. It was the sleeve of Jamie's shirt, passing around a girl's back, drawing her close for a kiss. She sat on his lap, and her yellow hair caught the sunlight coming through a slit, reflecting light like the surface of a trout stream on a bright morning.

I paused, uncertain what to do. I had no desire to spy on them, but was afraid the sound of my footsteps on the corridor stones would draw their attention. While I hesitated, Jamie broke from the embrace and looked up. His eyes met mine, and his face twitched from alarm to recognition. With a raised eyebrow and a faintly ironic shrug, he settled the girl more firmly on his knee and bent to his work. I shrugged back, and tiptoed away. Not my business. I had little doubt, however, that both Colum and the girl's father would consider this "consorting" highly improper. The next beating might well be on his own account, if they weren't more careful in choosing a meeting place.

Finding him at supper that night with Alec, I sat down opposite them at the long table. Jamie greeted me pleasantly enough, but with a watchful expression in his eyes. Old Alec gave me his usual "Mmphm." Women, as he had explained to me at the paddock, have no natural appreciation for horses, and are therefore difficult to talk to.

"How's the horse-breaking coming along?" I asked, to interrupt the industrious chewing on the other side of the table.

"Well enough," answered Jamie cautiously.

I peered at him across a platter of boiled turnips. "Your mouth looks a bit swollen, Jamie. Get thumped by a horse, did you?" I asked wickedly.

"Aye," he answered, narrowing his eyes. "Swung its head when I wasna looking." He spoke placidly, but I felt a large foot come down on top of mine under the table. It rested lightly at the moment, but the threat was explicit.

"Too bad; those fillies can be dangerous," I said innocently.

The foot pressed down hard as Alec said, "Filly? Ye're no workin' fillies now, are ye, lad?" I used my other foot as a lever; that failing, I used it to kick his ankle sharply. Jamie jerked suddenly.

"What's wrong wi' ye?" Alec demanded.

"Bit my tongue," muttered Jamie, glaring at me over the hand he had clapped to his mouth.

"Clumsy young dolt. No more than I'd expect, though, from an idjit as canna even keep clear of a horse when. . . ." Alec went on for several minutes, accusing his assistant at length of clumsiness, idleness, stupidity, and general ineptitude. Jamie, possibly the least clumsy person I had ever seen in my life, kept his head down and ate stolidly through the diatribe, though his cheeks flushed hotly. I kept my eyes demurely on my plate for the rest of the meal.

Refusing a second helping of stew, Jamie left the table abruptly, putting an end to Alec's tirade. The old horsemaster and I munched silently for a few minutes. Wiping his plate with the last bite of bread, the old man pushed it into his mouth and leaned back, surveying me sardonically with his one blue eye.

"Ye shouldna devil the lad, ye ken," he said conversationally. "If her father or Colum comes to know about it, young Jamie could get summat more than a blackened eye."

"Like a wife?" I said, looking him squarely in the eye. He nodded slowly.

"Could be. And that's not the wife he should have."

"No?" I was a bit surprised at this, after overhearing Alec's remarks in the paddock.

"Nay, he needs a woman, not a girl. And Laoghaire will be a girl when she's fifty." The grim old mouth twisted in something like a smile. "Ye may think I've lived in a stable all my life, but I had a wife as was a woman, and I ken the difference verra weel." The blue eye flashed as he made to get up. "So do you, lass."

I reached out a hand impulsively to stop him. "How did you know—" I began. Old Alec snorted derisively.

"I may ha' but one eye, lass; it doesna mean I'm blind." He creaked off, snorting as he went. I found the stairs and went up to my room, contemplating what, if anything, the old horsemaster had meant by his final remark.

9

The Gathering

My life seemed to be assuming some shape, if not yet a formal routine. Rising at dawn with the rest of the castle inhabitants, I breakfasted in the Great Hall, then, if Mrs. Fitz had no patients for me to see, I went to work in the huge castle gardens. Several other women worked there regularly, with an attending phalanx of lads in varying sizes, who came and went, hauling rubbish, tools, and loads of manure. I generally worked through the day there, sometimes going to the kitchens to help prepare a newly picked crop for eating or preserving, unless some medical emergency called me back to the Skulkery, as I called the late Beaton's closet of horrors.

Once in a while, I would take up Alec's invitation and visit the stables or paddock, enjoying the sight of the horses shedding their shaggy winter coats in clumps, growing strong and glossy with spring grass.

Some evenings I would go to bed immediately after supper, exhausted by the day's work. Other times, when I could keep my eyes open, I would join the gathering in the Great Hall to listen to the evening's entertainment of stories, song, or the music of harp or pipes. I could listen to Gwyllyn the Welsh bard for hours, enthralled in spite of my total ignorance of what he was saying, most times.

As the castle inhabitants grew accustomed to my presence, and I to them, some of the women began to make shy overtures of friendship, and to include me in their conversations.

They were plainly very curious about me, but I replied to all their tentative questions with variations of the story I had told Colum, and after a bit, they accepted that as all they were likely to know. Having found out that I knew something of medicine and healing, though, they grew still more interested in me, and began to ask questions about the ailments of their children, husbands, and beasts, in most cases making little distinction between the latter two in level of importance.

Besides the normal questions and gossip, there was considerable talk of the coming Gathering that I had heard Old Alec mention at the paddock. I concluded that this was an occasion of some importance, and grew more convinced by the extent of the preparations for it. A constant stream of foodstuffs poured into the great kitchens, and more than twenty skinned carcasses hung in the slaughter shed, behind a screen of fragrant smoke that kept the flies away. Hogsheads of ale were delivered by wagon and carted down to the castle cellars, bags of fine flour were brought up from the village mill for baking, and baskets of cherries and apricots were fetched daily from the orchards outside the castle wall.

I was invited to go on one of these fruit-picking expeditions with several of the young women of the castle, and accepted with alacrity, eager to get out from under the forbidding shadow of the stone walls.

It was beautiful in the orchard, and I greatly enjoyed wandering through the cool mist of the Scottish morning, fingering through the damp leaves of the fruit trees for the bright cherries and smooth, plump apricots, squeezing gently to judge the ripeness. We plucked only the best, dropping them into our baskets in juicy heaps, eating as much as we could hold, and carrying back the remainder to be made into tarts and pies. The enormous pantry shelves were nearly filled now with pastries, cordials, hams, and assorted delicacies.

"How many people customarily come to a Gathering?" I asked Magdalen, one of the girls with whom I had become friendly.

She wrinkled a snub, freckled nose in thought. "I dinna ken for sure. The last great Gathering at Leoch was over twenty year past, and then there were oh, maybe ten score of men come then—when old Jacob died, ye ken, and Colum was made laird. Might be more this year; been a good year for the crops and folk will ha' a bit more money put by, so a good many will bring their wives and bairns along."

Visitors were already beginning to arrive at the castle, though I had heard that the official parts of the Gathering, the oath-taking, the tynchal, and the games, would not take place for several days. The more illustrious of Colum's tacksmen and tenants were housed in the castle proper, while the poorer men-at-arms and cottars set up camp on a fallow field below the stream that fed the castle's loch. Roving tinkers, gypsies, and sellers of small goods had set up a sort of impromptu fair near the bridge. The inhabitants of both castle and nearby village had begun to visit the spot in the evenings, when the day's work was done, to buy tools and bits of finery, watch the jugglers and catch up on the latest gossip.

I kept a close eye on the comings and goings, and made a point of paying frequent visits to stable and paddock. There were horses in plenty now, those of the visitors being accommodated in the castle stables. Among the confusion and disturbance of the Gathering, I thought, I should have no difficulty in finding my chance to escape.

It was on one of the fruit-picking expeditions to the orchard that I first met Geillis Duncan. Finding a small patch of *Ascaria* beneath the roots of an alder, I was hunting for more. The scarlet caps grew in tiny clumps, only four or five mushrooms in a group, but there were several clumps scattered through the long grass in this part of the orchard. The voices of the women picking fruit grew fainter as I worked my way toward the edge of the orchard, stooping or dropping on hands and knees to gather the fragile stalks.

"Those kind are poison," said a voice from behind me. I straightened up from the patch of *Ascaria* I had been bending over, thumping my head smartly on a branch of the pine they were growing under.

As my vision cleared, I could see that the peals of laughter were coming from a tall young woman, perhaps a few years older than myself, fair of hair and skin, with the loveliest green eyes I had ever seen.

"I am sorry to be laughing at you," she said, dimpling as she stepped down into the hollow where I stood. "I could not help it."

"I imagine I looked funny," I said rather ungraciously, rubbing the sore spot on top of my head. "And thank you for the warning, but I know those mushrooms are poisonous."

"Och, you know? And who is it you're planning to do away with, then? Your husband, perhaps? Tell me if it works, and I'll try it on mine." Her smile was infectious, and I found myself smiling back.

I explained that though the raw mushroom caps were indeed poisonous, you could prepare a powdered preparation from the dried fungi that was very efficacious in stopping bleeding when applied topically. Or so Mrs. Fitz said; I was more inclined to trust her than Davie Beaton's *Physician's Guide*.

"Fancy that!" she said, still smiling. "And did you know that these"—she stooped and came up with a handful of tiny blue flowers with heart-shaped leaves—"will *start* bleeding?"

"No," I said, startled. "Why would anyone want to start bleeding?"

She looked at me with an expression of exasperated patience. "To get rid of a child ye don't want, I mean. It brings on your flux, but only if ye use it early. Too late, and it can kill you as well as the child."

"You seem to know a lot about it," I remarked, still stung by having appeared stupid.

"A bit. The girls in the village come to me now and again for such things, and sometimes the married women too. They say I'm a witch," she said, widening her brilliant eyes in feigned astonishment. She grinned. "But my husband's the procurator fiscal for the district, so they don't say it too loud."

"Now the young lad ye brought with ye," she went on, nodding in approval, "there's one that's had a few love-philtres bought on his behalf. Is he yours?"

"Mine? Who? You mean, er, Jamie?" I was startled.

The young woman looked amused. She sat down on a log, twirling a lock of fair hair idly around her index finger.

"Och, aye. There's quite a few would settle for a fellow wi' eyes and hair like that, no matter the price on his head or whether he's any money. Their fathers may think differently, o' course.

"Now, me," she went on, looking off into the distance, "I'm a practical sort. I married a man with a fair house, a bit o' money put away, and a good position. As for hair, he hasn't any, and as for eyes, I never noticed, but he doesna trouble me much." She held out the basket she carried for my inspection. Four bulbous roots lay in the bottom.

"Mallow root," she explained. "My husband suffers from a chill on the stomach now and again. Farts like an ox."

I thought it best to stop this line of conversation before things got out of hand. "I haven't introduced myself," I said, extending a hand to help her up from the log. "My name is Claire. Claire Beauchamp."

The hand that took mine was slender, with long, tapering white fingers, though I noticed the tips were stained, probably with the juices of the plants and berries resting alongside the mallow roots in her basket.

"I know who ye are," she said. "The village has been humming with talk of ye, since ye came to the castle. My name is Geillis, Geillis Duncan." She peered into my basket. "If it's *balgan-buachrach* you're looking for, I can show you where they grow best."

I accepted her offer, and we wandered for some time through the small glens near the orchard, poking under rotted logs and crawling around the rim of the sparkling tarns, where the tiny toadstools grew in profusion. Geillis was very knowledgeable about the local plants and their medicinal uses, though she suggested a few usages I thought questionable, to say the least. I thought it very unlikely, for instance, that bloodwort would be effective in making warts grow on a rival's nose, and I strongly doubted whether wood betony was useful in transforming toads into pigeons. She made these explanations with a mischievous glance that suggested she was testing my own knowledge, or perhaps the local suspicion of witchcraft.

Despite the occasional teasing, I found her a pleasant companion, with a ready wit and a cheerful, if cynical, outlook on life. She appeared to know everything there was to know about everyone in village, countryside, and castle, and our explorations were punctuated by rests during which she entertained me with complaints about her husband's stomach trouble, and amusing if somewhat malicious gossip.

"They say young Hamish is not his father's son," she said at one point, referring to Colum's only child, the red-haired lad of eight or so whom I had seen at dinner in the Hall.

I was not particularly startled by this bit of gossip, having formed my own conclusions on the matter. I was only surprised that there was but one child of questionable parentage, surmising that Letitia had been either lucky, or smart enough to seek out someone like Geilie in time. Unwisely, I said as much to Geilie.

She flung back her long, fair hair and laughed. "No, not me. The fair Letitia does not need any help in such matters, believe me. If people are seeking a witch in this neighborhood, they'd do better to look in the castle than the village."

Anxious to change the subject to something safer, I seized on the first thing that came to mind.

"If young Hamish isn't Colum's son, whose is he supposed to be?" I asked, scrambling over a heap of boulders.

"Why, the lad's, of course." She turned to face me, small mouth mocking and green eyes bright with mischief. "Young Jamie."

———

Returning to the orchard alone, I met Magdalen, hair coming loose under her kerchief and wide-eyed with worry.

"Oh, there ye are," she said, heaving a sigh of relief. "We were going back to the castle, when I missed ye."

"It was kind of you to come back for me," I said, picking up the basket of cherries I'd left in the grass. "I know the way, though."

She shook her head. "You should take care, my dearie,

walking alone in the woods, wi' all the tinkers and folk coming for the Gathering. Colum's given orders—'' She stopped abruptly, hand over her mouth.

"That I'm to be watched?" I suggested gently. She nodded reluctantly, clearly afraid I would be offended. I shrugged and tried to smile reassuringly at her.

"Well, that's natural, I suppose," I said. "After all, he's no one's word but my own for who I am or how I came here." Curiosity overcame my better judgment. "Who does he think I am?" I asked. But the girl could only shake her head.

"You're English," was all she said.

I didn't return to the orchard next day. Not because I was ordered to remain in the castle, but because there was a sudden outbreak of food poisoning among the castle inhabitants that demanded my attention as physician. Having done what I could for the sufferers, I set out to track the trouble to its source.

This proved to be a tainted beef carcass from the slaughter shed. I was in the shed next day, giving the chief smoker a piece of my mind regarding proper methods of meat preserving, when the door swung open behind me, sending a thick wave of choking smoke over me.

I turned, eyes watering, to see Dougal MacKenzie looming through the clouds of oakwood smoke.

"Supervising the butchering as well as the physicking, are ye now, mistress?" he asked mockingly. "Soon ye'll have the whole castle under your thumb, and Mrs. Fitz will be seeking employment elsewhere."

"I have no desire to have anything to do with your filthy castle," I snapped, wiping my streaming eyes and coming away with charcoal streaks on my handkerchief. "All I want is to get out of here, as fast as possible."

He inclined his head courteously, still grinning. "Well, I might be in a position to gratify that wish, mistress," he said. "At least temporarily."

I dropped the handkerchief and stared at him. "What do you mean?"

He coughed and waved a hand at the smoke, now drifting

in his direction. He drew me outside the shed and turned in the direction of the stables.

"You were saying yesterday to Colum that ye needed betony and some odd bits of herbs?"

"Yes, to make up some medicines for the people with food poisoning. What of it?" I demanded, still suspicious.

He shrugged good-naturedly. "Only that I'm going down to the smith's in the village, taking three horses to be shod. The fiscal's wife is something of an herb-woman, and has stocks to hand. Doubtless she has the simples that you're needing. And if it please ye, lady, you're welcome to ride one of the horses down wi' me to the village."

"The fiscal's wife? Mrs. Duncan?" I immediately felt happier. The prospect of escaping the castle altogether, even if only for a short time, was irresistible.

I mopped my face hurriedly and tucked the soiled kerchief in my belt.

"Let's go," I said.

—➤

I enjoyed the short ride downhill to the village of Cranesmuir, even though the day was dark and overcast. Dougal himself was in high spirits, and chatted and joked pleasantly as we went along.

We stopped first at the smith's, where he left the three extra horses, taking me up behind him on his saddle for the trip up the High Street to the Duncans' house. This was an imposing half-timbered manor of four stories, the lower two equipped with elegant leaded-glass windows; diamond-shaped panes in watery tones of purple and green.

Geilie greeted us with delight, pleased to have company on such a dreary day.

"How splendid!" she exclaimed. "I've been wanting an excuse to go through the stillroom and sort out some things. Anne!"

A short, middle-aged serving woman with a face like a winter apple popped out of a door I hadn't noticed, concealed as it was in the bend of the chimney.

"Take Mistress Claire up to the stillroom," Geilie ordered,

"and then go and fetch us a bucket of spring water. From the spring, mind, not the well in the square!" She turned to Dougal. "I've the tonic put by that I promised your brother. If you'll come out to the kitchen with me for a moment?"

I followed the serving woman's pumpkin-shaped rear up a set of narrow wooden stairs, emerging unexpectedly into a long, airy loft. Unlike the rest of the house, this room was furnished with casement windows, shut now against the damp, but still providing a great deal more light than had been available in the fashionably gloomy parlor downstairs.

It was clear that Geilie knew her business as an herbalist. The room was equipped with long drying frames netted with gauze, hooks above the small fireplace for heat-drying, and open shelves along the walls, drilled with holes to allow for air circulation. The air was thick with the delicious, spicy scent of drying basil, rosemary, and lavender. A surprisingly modern long counter ran along one side of the room, displaying a remarkable assortment of mortars, pestles, mixing bowls, and spoons, all immaculately clean.

It was some time before Geilie appeared, flushed from climbing the stairs, but smiling in anticipation of a long afternoon of herb-pounding and gossip.

It began to rain lightly, drops spattering the long casements, but a small fire was burning on the stillroom hearth, and it was very cozy. I enjoyed Geilie's company immensely; she had a wry-tongued, cynical viewpoint that was a refreshing contrast to the sweet, shy clanswomen at the castle, and clearly she had been well educated, for a woman in a small village.

She also knew every scandal that had occurred either in village or castle in the last ten years, and she told me endless amusing stories. Oddly enough, she asked me few questions about myself. I thought perhaps that was not her way; she would find out what she wanted to know about me from other people.

For some time, I had been conscious of noises coming from the street outside, but had attributed them to the traffic of villagers coming from Sunday Mass; the kirk was located at the end of the street by the well, and the High Street ran from kirk to square, spreading from there into a fan of tiny lanes and walks.

In fact, I had amused myself on the ride to the smithy by imagining an aerial view of the village as a representation of a skeletal forearm and hand; the High Street was the radius, along which lay the shops and businesses and the residences of the more well-to-do. St. Margaret's Lane was the ulna, a narrower street running parallel with the High, tenanted by smithy, tannery, and the less genteel artisans and businesses. The village square (which, like all village squares I had ever seen, was not square at all, but roughly oblong) formed the carpals and metacarpals of the hand, while the several lanes of cottages made up the phalangeal joints of the fingers.

The Duncans' house stood on the square, as behooved the residence of the procurator fiscal. This was a matter of convenience as well as status; the square could be used for those judicial matters which, by reason of public interest or legal necessity, overflowed the narrow confines of Arthur Duncan's study. And it was, as Dougal explained, convenient to the pillory, a homely wooden contraption that stood on a small stone plinth in the center of the square, adjacent to the wooden stake used—with thrifty economy of purpose—as whipping post, maypole, flagstaff and horse tether, depending upon requirements.

The noise outside was now much louder, and altogether more disorderly than seemed appropriate to people coming soberly home from church to their dinners. Geilie put aside the jars with an exclamation of impatience and threw open the window to see what caused the uproar.

Joining her at the window, I could see a crowd of folk dressed in church-going garb of gown, kirtle, coat, and bonnet, led by the stocky figure of Father Bain, the priest who served both village and castle. He had in his custody a youth, perhaps twelve years old, whose ragged trews and smelly shirt proclaimed him a tanner's lad. The priest had the boy gripped by the nape of the neck, a hold made somewhat difficult to maintain by the fact that the lad was slightly taller than his minatory captor. The crowd followed the pair at a small distance, rumbling with disapproving comment like a passing thunder cloud in the wake of a lightning bolt.

As we watched from the upper window, Father Bain and the boy disappeared beneath us, into the house. The crowd remained outside, muttering and jostling. A few of the bolder souls chinned themselves on the window ledges, attempting to peer within.

Geilie shut the window with a slam, making a break in the anticipatory rumble below.

"Stealing, most like," she said laconically, returning to the herb table. "Usually is, wi' the tanners' lads."

"What will happen to him?" I asked curiously. She shrugged, crumbling dried rosemary between her fingers into the mortar.

"Depends on whether Arthur's dyspeptic this morning, I should reckon. If he's made a good breakfast, the lad might get off with a whipping. But happen he's costive or flatulent" —she made a moue of distaste—"the boy'll lose an ear or a hand, most like."

I was horrified, but hesitant to interfere directly in the matter. I was an outlander, and an Englishwoman to boot, and while I thought I would be treated with some respect as an inhabitant of the castle, I had seen many of the villagers surreptitiously make the sign against evil as I passed. My intercession might easily make things worse for the boy.

"Can't *you* do anything?" I asked Geilie. "Speak to your husband, I mean; ask him to be, er, lenient?"

Geilie looked up from her work, surprised. Clearly the thought of interfering in her husband's affairs had never crossed her mind.

"Why should you care what happens to him?" she asked, but curiously, not with any hostile meaning.

"Of course I care!" I said. "He's only a lad; whatever he did, he doesn't deserve to be mutilated for life!"

She raised pale brows; plainly this argument was unconvincing. Still, she shrugged and handed me the mortar and pestle.

"Anything to oblige a friend," she said, rolling her eyes. She scanned her shelves and selected a bottle of greenish stuff, labeled, in fine cursive script, EXTRACT OF PEPPERMINT.

"I'll go and dose Arthur, and whilst I'm about it, I'll see if aught can be done for the lad. It may be too late, mind," she warned. "And if that poxy priest's got a hand in, he'll want the stiffest sentence he can get. Still, I'll try. You keep after the pounding; rosemary takes forever."

I took up the pestle as she left, and pounded and ground automatically, paying little heed to the results. The shut window blocked the sound both of the rain and the crowd below; the two blended in a soft, pattering susurrus of menace. Like any schoolchild, I had read Dickens. And earlier authors, as well, with their descriptions of the pitiless justice of these times, meted out to all ill-doers, regardless of age or circumstance. But to read, from a cozy distance of one or two hundred years, accounts of child hangings and judicial mutilation, was a far different thing than to sit quietly pounding herbs a few feet above such an occurrence.

Could I bring myself to interfere directly, if the sentence went against the boy? I moved to the window, carrying the mortar with me, and peered out. The crowd had increased, as merchants and housewives, attracted by the gathering, wandered down the High Street to investigate. Newcomers leaned close as the standees excitedly relayed the details, then merged into the body of the crowd, more faces turned expectantly to the door of the house.

Looking down on the assembly, standing patiently in the drizzle awaiting a verdict, I suddenly had a vivid understanding of something. Like so many, I had heard, appalled, the reports that trickled out of postwar Germany: the stories of deportations and mass murder, of concentration camps and burnings. And like so many others had done, and would do, for years to come, I had asked myself, "How could the people have let it happen? They must have known, must have seen the trucks, the coming and going, the fences and smoke. How could they stand by and do nothing?" Well, now I knew.

The stakes were not even life or death in this case. And Colum's patronage would likely prevent any physical attack on me. But my hands grew clammy around the porcelain bowl as I thought of myself stepping out, alone and powerless, to confront that mob of solid and virtuous citizens, avid for the excitement of punishment and blood to alleviate the tedium of existence.

People are gregarious by necessity. Since the days of the first cave dwellers, humans—hairless, weak, and helpless save for cunning—have survived by joining together in groups; knowing, as so many other edible creatures have found, that there is protection in numbers. And that knowledge, bred in the bone, is what lies behind mob rule. Because to step outside the group, let alone to stand against it, was for uncounted thousands of years death to the creature who dared it. To stand against a crowd would take something more than ordinary courage; something that went beyond human instinct. And I feared I did not have it, and fearing, was ashamed.

It seemed forever before the door opened and Geilie stepped in, looking cool and unperturbed as usual, a small stick of charcoal in her hand.

"We'll need to filter it after it's boiled," she remarked, as though going on with our previous conversation. "I think we'll run it through charcoal in muslin; that's best."

"Geilie," I said impatiently. "Don't try me. What about the tanner's boy?"

"Oh, that." She lifted a shoulder dismissively, but a mischievous smile lurked about the corners of her lips. She dropped the facade then, and laughed.

"You should have seen me," she said, giggling. "I was awfully good, an' I say it myself. All wifely solicitude and womanly kindness, with a small dab o' maternal pity mixed in. 'Oh, Arthur,'" she dramatized, "'had our own union been blessed'—not much chance, if I've aught to say about it," she said, dropping the soulful mask for a moment with a tilt of her head toward the herb shelves—"'why, how would ye feel, my darling, should your own son be taken so? Nae doubt it was but hunger made the lad take to thievery. Oh, Arthur, can ye no find it in your heart to be merciful—and you the soul of justice?'" She dropped onto a stool, laughing and pounding her fist lightly against her leg. "What a pity there's no place for acting here!"

The sound of the crowd outside had changed, and I moved

to the window to see what was happening, ignoring Geilie's self-congratulations.

The throng parted, and the tanner's lad came out, walking slowly between priest and judge. Arthur Duncan was swollen with benevolence, bowing and nodding to the more eminent members of the assembly. Father Bain, on the other hand, resembled a sullen potato more than anything else, brown face lumpy with resentment.

The little procession proceeded to the center of the square, where the village locksman, one John MacRae, stepped out of the crowd to meet them. This personage was dressed as befitted his office in the sober elegance of dark breeches and coat and grey velvet hat (removed for the nonce and tenderly sheltered from the rain beneath the tail of his coat). He was not, as I had at first assumed, the village jailer, though in a pinch he did perform such office. His duties were primarily those of constable, customs inspector, and when needed, executioner; his title came from the wooden "lock" or scoop that hung from his belt, with which he was entitled to take a percentage of each bag of grain sold in the Thursday market: the remuneration of his office.

I had found all this out from the locksman himself. He had been to the Castle only a few days before to see whether I could treat a persistent felon on his thumb. I had lanced it with a sterile needle and dressed it with poplar-bud salve, finding MacRae a shy and soft-spoken man with a pleasant smile.

There was no trace of a smile now, though; MacRae's face was suitably stern. Reasonable, I thought; no one wants to see a grinning executioner.

The miscreant was brought to stand on the plinth in the center of the square. The lad looked pale and frightened, but did not move as Arthur Duncan, procurator fiscal for the parish of Cranesmuir, drew his plumpness up into an approximation of dignity and prepared to pronounce sentence.

"The ninny had already confessed by the time I came in," said a voice by my ear. Geilie peered interestedly over my shoulder. "I couldna get him freed entirely. I got him off as light as could be, though; only an hour in the pillory and one ear nailed."

"One ear nailed! Nailed to *what*?"

"Why, the pillory, o' course." She shot me a curious look, but turned back to the window to watch the execution of this light sentence obtained by her merciful intercession.

The crush of bodies around the pillory was so great that little of the miscreant could be seen, but the crowd drew back a bit to allow the locksman free movement for the ear-nailing. The lad, white-faced and small in the jaws of the pillory, had both eyes tight shut and kept them that way, shuddering with fear. He uttered a high, thin scream when the nail was driven in, audible through the closed windows, and I shuddered a bit myself.

We returned to our work, as did most of the spectators in the square, but I could not help rising to glance out from time to time. A few idlers passing by paused to jeer at the victim and throw balls of mud, and now and then a more sober citizen was to be seen, seizing a moment from the round of daily duties to attend to the moral improvement of the delinquent by means of a few well-chosen words of reproval and advice.

It was still an hour to the late spring sunset, and we were drinking tea below in the parlor, when a pounding at the door announced the arrival of a visitor. The day was so dark from the rain that one could hardly tell the level of the sun. The Duncans' house, however, boasted a clock, a magnificent contrivance of walnut panels, brass pendulums, and a face decorated with quiring cherubim, and this instrument pointed to half-past six.

The scullery maid opened the door to the parlor and unceremoniously announced, "In here." Jamie MacTavish ducked automatically as he came through the door, bright hair darkened by the rain to the color of ancient bronze. He wore an elderly and disreputable coat against the wet, and carried a riding cloak of heavy green velvet folded under one arm.

He nodded in acknowledgment as I rose and introduced him to Geilie.

"Mistress Duncan, Mrs. Beauchamp." He waved a hand toward the window. "I see ye've had a wee bit doing this afternoon."

"Is he still there?" I asked, peering out. The boy was only a dark shape, seen through the distortion of the wavering drawing-room panes. "He must be soaked through."

"He is." Jamie spread the cloak and held it for me. "So you'd be as well, Colum thought. I'd business in the village, so he sent along the cloak with me for ye. You're to ride back wi' me."

"That was kind of him." I spoke absently, for my mind was still on the tanner's lad.

"How long must he stay there?" I asked Geilie. "The lad in the pillory," I added impatiently, seeing her blank look.

"Oh, him," she said, frowning slightly at the introduction of such an unimportant topic. "An hour, I told you. The locksman should ha' freed him from the pillory by now."

"He has," Jamie assured her. "I saw him as I was crossing the green. It's only the lad's not got up courage to tear the griss from his lug yet."

My mouth dropped open. "You mean the nail won't be taken out of his ear? He's to *tear* himself loose?"

"Oh, aye." Jamie was cheerfully offhand. "He's still a bit nervous, but I imagine he'll set his mind to it soon. It's wet out, and growing dark as well. We must leave ourselves, or we'll get naught but scraps to our dinner." He bowed to Geilie and turned to go.

"Wait a bit," she said to me. "Since you've a big, strong lad like yon to see ye home, I've a chest of dried marsh cabbage and other simples as I've promised to Mrs. FitzGibbons up at the Castle. Perhaps Mr. MacTavish would be so kind?"

Jamie assenting, she had a manservant fetch down the chest from her workroom, handing over the enormous wrought-iron key for the purpose. While the servant was gone, she busied herself for a moment at a small writing desk in the corner. By the time the chest, a sizable wooden box with brass bands, was brought in, she had finished her note. She hastily sanded it, folded and sealed it with a blob of wax from the candle, and pressed it into my hand.

"There," she said. "That's the bill for it. Will ye give it to Dougal for me? It's him that handles the payments and such. Dinna give it to anyone else, or I'll not be paid for weeks."

"Yes, of course."

She embraced me warmly, and with admonitions about avoiding the chill, saw us to the door.

I stood sheltering beneath the eave of the house, as Jamie tied the box to his horse's saddle. The rain was coming down harder now, and the eaves ran with a ragged sheet of water.

I eyed the broad back and muscular forearms as he lifted the heavy box with little apparent effort. Then I glanced at the plinth, where the tanner's boy, in spite of encouragement from the regathered crowd, was still firmly pinioned. Granted this was not a lovely young girl with moonbeam hair, but Jamie's earlier actions in Colum's Hall of justice made me think that he might not be unsympathetic to the youngster's plight.

"Er, Mr. MacTavish?" I began, hesitantly. There was no response. The comely face did not change expression; the wide mouth stayed relaxed, the blue eyes focused on the strap he was fastening.

"Ah, Jamie?" I tried again, a little louder, and he looked up at once. So it really wasn't MacTavish. I wondered what it was.

"Aye?" he said.

"You're, er, quite sizable, aren't you?" I said. A half-smile curved his lips and he nodded, clearly wondering what I was up to.

"Big enough for most things," he answered.

I was encouraged, and moved casually closer, so as not to be overheard by any stragglers from the square.

"And tolerably strong in the fingers?" I asked.

He flexed one hand and the smile widened. "Aye, that's so. Happen you've a few chestnuts you want cracked?" He looked down at me with a shrewd and merry glint.

I glanced briefly past him to the knot of onlookers in the square.

"More like one to be pulled from the fire, I think." I looked up to meet that questioning blue gaze. "Could you do it?"

He stood looking down at me for a moment, still smiling, then shrugged. "Aye, if the shank's long enough to grip. Can ye draw the crowd away, though? Interference wouldna be looked on kindly, and me a stranger."

I had not anticipated the possibility that my request might put him in any danger, and I hesitated, but he seemed game to try, danger notwithstanding.

"Well, if we both went over for a closer look, and then I were to faint at the sight, do you think—?"

"You being so unused to blood and all?" One brow lifted sardonically and he grinned. "Aye, that'll do. If ye can make shift to fall off the plinth, still better."

I had in fact felt a bit squeamish about looking, but it was not so daunting a sight as I had feared. The ear was pinned firmly through the upper flange, close to the edge, and a full two inches of the nail's square, headless shank was free above the pinioned appendage. There was almost no blood, and it was clear from the boy's face that while he was both frightened and uncomfortable, he was in no great pain. I began to think that Geilie perhaps had been right in considering this a fairly lenient sentence, given the overall state of current Scottish jurisprudence, though this didn't alter by one whit my opinion as to the barbarity of it.

Jamie edged casually through the fringe of lookers-on. He shook his head reprovingly at the boy.

"Na then, lad," he said, clicking his tongue. "Got yourself in a rare swivet, have ye no?" He rested one large, firm hand on the wooden edge of the pillory, under pretext of looking more closely at the ear. "Och, laddie," he said, disparaging, "yon's no job to be making heavy weather of. A wee snatch o' the head and it's over. Here, shall I help ye?" He reached out as though to grasp the lad by the hair and wrench his head free. The boy yelped in fear.

Recognizing my cue, I stepped back, taking care to tread heavily on the toes of the woman behind me, who yipped in anguish as my boot heel crushed her metatarsals.

"I beg your pardon," I gasped. "I'm . . . so dizzy! Please . . ." I turned away from the pillory and took two or three steps, staggering artfully and clutching at the sleeves of those nearby. The edge of the plinth was only six inches away; I took a firm hold on a slightly built girl I had marked out for the purpose and pitched headfirst over the edge, taking her with me.

We rolled on the wet grass in a tangle of skirts and squeals. Letting go of her blouse at last, I relaxed into a dramatically spread-eagled heap, rain pattering down on my upturned face.

I was in truth a trifle winded by the impact—the girl had fallen on top of me—and I fought for breath, listening to the babble of concerned voices gathered around me. Speculations, suggestions, and shocked interjections rained on me, thicker than the drops of water from the sky, but it was a pair of familiar arms that raised me to a sitting position, and a pair of gravely concerned blue eyes that I saw when I opened my own. A faint flicker of the eyelids told me that the mission had been accomplished, and in fact, I could see the tanner's lad, napkin clutched to his ear, making off at speed in the direction of his loft, unnoticed by the crowd that had turned to attend to this new sensation.

The villagers, so lately calling for the lad's blood, were kindness itself to me. I was tenderly gathered up and carried back to the Duncans' house, where I was plied with brandy, tea, warm blankets, and sympathy. I was only allowed to depart at last by Jamie's stating bluntly that we must go, then lifting me bodily off the couch and heading for the door, disregarding the expostulations of my hosts.

Mounted once more in front of him, my own horse led by the rein, I tried to thank him for his help.

"No trouble, lass," he said, dismissing my thanks.

"But it was a risk to you," I said, persisting. "I didn't realize you'd be in danger when I asked you."

"Ah," he said, noncommittally. And a moment later, with a hint of amusement, "Ye wouldna expect me to be less bold than a wee Sassenach lassie, now would ye?"

He urged the horses into a trot as the shadows of dusk gathered by the roadside. We did not speak much on the rest of the journey home. And when we reached the castle, he left me at the gate with no more than a softly mocking, "Good' e'en, Mistress Sassenach." But I felt as though a friendship had been begun that ran a bit deeper than shared gossip under the apple trees.

10

The Oath-taking

There was a terrific stir over the next two days, with comings and goings and preparations of every sort. My medical practice dropped off sharply; the food-poisoning victims were well again, and everyone else seemed to be much too busy to fall sick. Aside from a slight rash of splinters-in-fingers among the boys hauling in wood for the fires, and a similar outbreak of scalds and burns among the busy kitchen maids, there were no accidents either.

I was excited myself. Tonight was the night. Mrs. Fitz had told me that all the fighting men of the MacKenzie clan would be in the hall tonight, to make their oaths of allegiance to Colum. With a ceremony of this importance going on inside, no one would be watching the stables.

During my hours helping in the kitchens and orchards, I had managed to stow away sufficient food to see me provided for several days, I thought. I had no water flask, but had contrived a substitute using one of the heavier glass jugs from the surgery. I had stout boots and a warm cloak, courtesy of Colum. I would have a decent horse; on my afternoon visit to the stables, I had marked out the one I meant to take. I had no money, but my patients had given me a handful of small trinkets, ribbons, and bits of carving or jewelry. If necessary, I might be able to use these to trade for anything else I needed.

I felt bad about abusing Colum's hospitality and the friendship of the castle inhabitants by leaving without a word or a note of farewell, but after all, what could I possibly say? I had pondered the problem for some time, but finally decided just to leave. For one thing, I had no writing paper, and was not willing to take the risk of visiting Colum's quarters in search of any.

An hour past first dark, I approached the stable cautiously, ears alert for any signs of human presence, but it seemed that everyone was up in the Hall, readying themselves for the ceremony. The door stuck, but gave with a slight push, its leather hinges letting it swing silently inward.

The air inside was warm and alive with the faint stirrings of resting horses. It was also black as the inside of an undertaker's hat, as Uncle Lamb used to say. Such few windows as there were for ventilation were narrow slits, too small to admit the faint starlight outside. Hands outstretched, I walked slowly into the main part of the stable, feet shuffling in the straw.

I groped carefully in front of me, looking for the edge of a stall to guide me. My hands found only empty air, but my shins met a solid obstruction resting on the floor, and I pitched headlong with a startled cry that rang in the rafters of the old stone building.

The obstruction rolled over with a startled oath and grasped me hard by the arms. I found myself held against the length of a sizable male body, with someone's breath tickling my ear.

"Who are you?" I gasped, jerking backward. "And what are you doing here?" Hearing my voice, the unseen assailant relaxed his grip.

"I might ask the same of you, Sassenach," said the deep, soft voice of Jamie MacTavish, and I relaxed a little in relief. There was a stirring in the straw, and he sat up.

"Though I suppose I could guess," he added dryly. "How far d'ye think you'd get, lassie, on a dark night and a strange horse, wi' half the MacKenzie clan after ye by morning?"

I was ruffled, in more ways than one.

"They wouldn't be after me. They're all up at the Hall, and if one in five of them is sober enough to stand by morning, let alone ride a horse, I'll be *most* surprised."

He laughed, and standing up, reached down a hand to help

me to my feet. He brushed the straw from the back of my skirt, with somewhat more force than I thought strictly necessary.

"Well, that's verra sound reasoning on your part, Sassenach," he said, sounding mildly surprised that I was capable of reason. "Or would be," he added, "did Colum not have guards posted all round the castle and scattered through the woods. He'd hardly leave the castle unprotected, and the fighting men of the whole clan inside it. Granted that stone doesna burn so well as wood . . ."

I gathered he was referring to the infamous Glencoe Massacre, when one John Campbell, on government orders, had put thirty-eight members of the MacDonald clan to the sword and burned the house above them. I calculated rapidly. That would have been only fifty-some years before; recent enough to justify any defensive precautions on Colum's part.

"In any case, ye could scarcely have chosen a worse night to try to escape," MacTavish went on. He seemed entirely unconcerned with the fact that I *had* meant to escape, only with the reasons why it wouldn't work, which struck me as a little odd. "Besides the guards, and the fact that every good horseman for miles around is here, the way to the castle will be filled wi' folk coming from the countryside for the tynchal and the games."

"Tynchal?"

"A hunt. Usually stags, maybe a boar this time; one of the stable lads told Old Alec there's a large one in the east wood." He put a large hand in the center of my back and turned me toward the faint oblong of the open door.

"Come along," he said. "I'll take ye back up to the castle."

I pulled away from him. "Don't bother," I said ungraciously. "I can find my own way."

He took my elbow with considerable firmness. "I daresay ye can. But you'll not want to meet any of Colum's guards alone."

"And why not?" I snapped. "I'm not doing anything wrong; there's no law against walking outside the castle, is there?"

"No. I doubt they'd mean to ye harm," he said, peering

thoughtfully into the shadows. "But it's far from unusual for a man to take a flask along to keep him company when he stands guard. And the drink may be a boon companion, but it's no a verra good adviser as to suitable behavior, when a small, sweet lass comes on ye alone in the dark."

"I came on *you* in the dark, alone," I reminded him, with some boldness. "And I'm neither particularly small, nor very sweet, at least at present."

"Aye, well, I was asleep, not drunk," he responded briefly. "And questions of your temper aside, you're a good bit smaller than most of Colum's guards."

I put that aside as an unproductive line of argument, and tried another tack. "And why *were* you asleep in the stable?" I asked. "Haven't you a bed somewhere?" We were in the outer reaches of the kitchen gardens by now, and I could see his face in the faint light. He was intent, checking the stone arches carefully as we went, but he glanced sharply aside at this.

"Aye," he said. He continued to stride forward, still gripping me by the elbow, but went on after a moment, "I thought I'd be better out of the way."

"Because you don't mean to swear allegiance to Colum MacKenzie?" I guessed. "And you don't want to stand any racket about it?"

He glanced at me, amused at my words. "Something like that," he admitted.

One of the side gates had been left welcomingly ajar, and a lantern perched atop the stone ledge next to it shed a yellow glow on the path. We had almost reached this beacon when a hand suddenly descended on my mouth from behind and I was jerked abruptly off my feet.

I struggled and bit, but my captor was heavily gloved, and, as Jamie had said, a good deal larger than I.

Jamie himself seemed to be having minor difficulties, judging from the sound of it. The grunting and muffled cursing ceased abruptly with a thud and a rich Gaelic expletive.

The struggle in the dark stopped, and there was an unfamiliar laugh.

"God's eyes, if it's no the young lad, Colum's nephew.

Come late to the oath-taking, are ye not, lad? And who's that wi' ye?"

"It's a lassie," replied the man holding me. "And a sweet, juicy one, too, by the heft of her." The hand left my mouth and administered a hearty squeeze elsewhere. I squeaked in indignation, reached over my shoulder, got hold of his nose and yanked. The man set me down with a quick oath of his own, less formal than those about to be taken within the hall. I stepped back from the blast of whisky fumes, feeling a sudden surge of appreciation for Jamie's presence. Perhaps his accompanying me had been prudent, after all.

He appeared to be thinking otherwise, as he made a vain attempt to remove the clinging grip of the two men-at-arms who had attached themselves to him. There was nothing hostile about their actions, but there was a considerable amount of firmness. They began to move purposefully toward the open gate, their captive in tow.

"Nay, let me go and change first, man," he protested. "I'm no decent to be going into the oath-taking like this."

His attempt at graceful escape was foiled by the sudden appearance of Rupert, fatly resplendent in ruffled shirt and gold-laced coat, who popped out of the narrow gate like a cork from a bottle.

"Dinna worrit yourself about that, laddie," he said, surveying Jamie with a gleaming eye. "We'll outfit ye proper—inside." He jerked his head toward the gate, and Jamie disappeared within, under compulsion. A meaty hand gripped my own elbow, and I followed, willy-nilly.

Rupert appeared to be in very high spirits, as did the other men I saw inside the castle. There were perhaps sixty or seventy men, all dressed in their best, festooned with dirks, swords, pistols, and sporrans, milling about in the courtyard nearest the entrance to the Great Hall. Rupert gestured to a door set in the wall, and the men hustled Jamie into a small lighted room. It was one apparently used for storage; odds and ends of all kinds littered the tables and shelves with which it was furnished.

Rupert surveyed Jamie critically, with an eye to the oatstraws in his hair and the stains on his shirt. I saw his glance flicker to the oatstraws in my own hair, and a cynical grin split his face.

"No wonder ye're late, laddie," he said, digging Jamie in the ribs. "Dinna blame ye a bit."

"Willie!" he called to one of the men outside. "We need some clothes, here. Something suitable for the laird's nephew. See to it, man, and hurry!"

Jamie looked around, thin-lipped, at the men surrounding him. Six clansmen, all in tearing high spirits at the prospect of the oath-taking and brimming over with a fierce MacKenzie pride. The spirits had plainly been assisted by an ample intake from the tub of ale I had seen in the yard. Jamie's eye lighted on me, his expression still grim. This was *my* doing, his face seemed to say.

He could, of course, announce that he did not mean to swear his oath to Colum, and head back to his warm bed in the stables. If he wanted a serious beating or his throat cut, that is. He raised an eyebrow at me, shrugged, and submitted with a fair show of grace to Willie, who rushed up with a pile of snowy linen in his arms and a hairbrush in one hand. The pile was topped by a flat blue bonnet of velvet, adorned with a metal badge that held a sprig of holly. I picked up the bonnet to examine it, as Jamie fought his way into the clean shirt and brushed his hair with suppressed savagery.

The badge was round and the engraving surprisingly fine. It showed five volcanos in the center, spouting most realistic flames. And on the border was a motto, *Luceo non Uro*.

"I shine, not burn," I translated aloud.

"Aye, lassie; the MacKenzie motto," said Willie, nodding approvingly at me. He snatched the bonnet from my hands and pushed it into Jamie's, before dashing off in search of further clothing.

"Er . . . I'm sorry," I said in a low voice, taking advantage of Willie's absence to move closer. "I didn't mean—"

Jamie, who had been viewing the badge on the bonnet with disfavor, glanced down at me, and the grim line of his mouth relaxed.

"Ah, dinna worrit yourself on my account, Sassenach. It would ha' come to it sooner or later." He twisted the badge loose from the bonnet and smiled sourly at it, weighing it speculatively in his hand.

"D'ye ken my own motto, lass?" he asked. "My clan's, I mean?"

"No," I answered, startled. "What is it?"

He flipped the badge once in the air, caught it, and dropped it neatly into his sporran. He looked rather bleakly toward the open archway, where the MacKenzie clansmen were massing in untidy lines.

"Je suis prest," he replied, in surprisingly good French. He glanced back, to see Rupert and another large MacKenzie I didn't know, faces flushed with high spirits and spirits of another kind, advancing with solid purpose. Rupert held a huge length of MacKenzie tartan cloth.

Without preliminaries, the other man reached for the buckle of Jamie's kilt.

"Best leave, Sassenach," Jamie advised briefly. "It's no place for women."

"So I see," I responded dryly, and was rewarded with a wry smile as his hips were swathed in the new kilt, and the old one yanked deftly away beneath it, modesty preserved. Rupert and friend took him firmly by the arms and hustled him toward the archway.

I turned without delay and made my way back toward the stair to the minstrels' gallery, carefully avoiding the eye of any clansman I passed. Once around the corner, I paused, shrinking back against the wall to avoid notice. I waited for a moment, until the corridor was temporarily deserted, then nipped inside the gallery door and pulled it quickly to behind me, before anyone else could come around the corner and see where I had gone. The stairs were dimly lit by the glow from above, and I had no trouble keeping my footing on the worn flags. I climbed toward the noise and light, thinking of that last brief exchange.

"Je suis prest." I am ready. I hoped he was.

The gallery was lit by pine torches, brilliant flares that rose straight up in their sockets, outlined in black by the soot their predecessors had left on the walls. Several faces turned, blinking, to look at me as I came out of the hangings at the back of the gallery; from the looks of it, all the women of the castle were up here. I recognized the girl Laoghaire, Magdalen and some of the other women I had met in the kitchens, and, of course, the stout form of Mrs. FitzGibbons, in a position of honor near the balustrade.

Seeing me, she beckoned in a friendly manner, and the women squeezed against each other to let me pass. When I reached the front, I could see the whole Hall spread out beneath.

The walls were decked with myrtle branches, yew and holly, and the fragrance of the evergreens rose up into the gallery, mingled with the smoke of fires and the harsh reek of men. There were dozens of them, coming, going, standing talking in small groups scattered throughout the hall, and all clad in some version of the clan tartan, be it only a plaid or a tartan bonnet worn above ordinary working shirt and tattered breeches. The actual patterns varied wildly, but the colors were mostly the same—dark greens and white.

Most of them were completely dressed as Jamie now was, kilt, plaid, bonnet, and—in most cases—badges. I caught a glimpse of him standing near the wall, still looking grim. Rupert had disappeared into the throng, but two more burly MacKenzies flanked Jamie, obviously guards.

The confusion in the hall was gradually becoming organized, as the castle residents pushed and led the newcomers into place at the lower end.

Tonight was plainly special; the young lad who played the pipes at Hall had been augmented by two other pipers, one a man whose bearing and ivory-mounted pipes proclaimed him a master piper. This man nodded to the other two, and soon the hall was filled with the fierce drone of pipe music. Much smaller than the great Northern pipes used in battle, these versions made a most effective racket.

The chanters laid a trill above the drones that made the blood itch. The women stirred around me, and I thought of a line from "Maggie Lauder" :

> *"Oh, they call me Rab the Ranter,*
> *and the lassies all go daft,*
> *When I blow up my chanter."*

If not daft, the women around me were fully appreciative, and there were many murmurs of admiration as they hung over the rail, pointing out one man or another, striding about the Hall decked in his finery. One girl spotted Jamie, and with a muffled exclamation, beckoned her friends to see. There was considerable whispering and murmuring over his appearance.

Some of it was admiration for his fine looks, but more was speculation about his presence at the oath-taking. I noticed that Laoghaire, in particular, glowed like a candle as she watched him, and I remembered what Alec had said in the paddock—*Ye know her father will no' let her wed outside the clan.* And Colum's nephew, was he? The lad might be quite a catch, at that. Bar the minor matter of outlawry, of course.

The pipe music rose to a fervent pitch, and then abruptly ceased. In the dead silence of the Hall, Colum MacKenzie stepped out from the upper archway, and strode purposefully to a small platform that had been erected at the head of the room. If he made no effort to hide his disability, he did not flaunt it now either. He was splendid in an azure-blue coat, heavily laced with gold, buttoned with silver, and with rose silk cuffs that turned back almost to the elbow. A tartan kilt in fine wool hung past his knees, covering most of his legs and the checked stockings on them. His bonnet was blue, but the silver badge held plumes, not holly. The entire Hall held its breath as he took center stage. Whatever else he was, Colum MacKenzie was a showman.

He turned to face the assembled clansmen, raised his arms and greeted them with a ringing shout.

"Tulach Ard!"

"Tulach Ard!" the clansmen gave back in a roar. The woman next to me shivered.

There was a short speech next, given in Gaelic. This was greeted with periodic roars of approval, and then the oath-taking proper commenced.

Dougal MacKenzie was the first man to advance to Colum's

platform. The small rostrum gave Colum enough height that the brothers met face to face. Dougal was richly dressed, but in plain chestnut velvet with no gold lace, so as not to distract attention from Colum's magnificence.

Dougal drew his dirk with a flourish and sank to one knee, holding the dirk upright by the blade. His voice was less powerful than Colum's, but loud enough so that every word rang through the hall.

"I swear by the cross of our Lord Jesus Christ, and by the holy iron that I hold, to give ye my fealty and pledge ye my loyalty to the name of the clan MacKenzie. If ever my hand shall be raised against ye in rebellion, I ask that this holy iron shall pierce my heart."

He lowered the dirk, kissed it at the juncture of haft and tang, and thrust it home in its sheath. Still kneeling, he offered both hands clasped to Colum, who took them between his own and lifted them to his lips in acceptance of the oath so offered. Then he raised Dougal to his feet.

Turning, Colum picked up a silver quaich from its place on the tartan-covered table behind him. He lifted the heavy eared cup with both hands, drank from it, and offered it to Dougal. Dougal took a healthy swallow and handed back the cup. Then, with a final bow to the laird of the clan MacKenzie, he stepped to one side, to make room for the next man in line.

This same process was repeated over and over, from vow to ceremonial drink. Viewing the number of men in the line, I was impressed anew at Colum's capacity. I was trying to work out how many pints of spirit he would have consumed by the end of the evening, given one swallow per oath-taker, when I saw Jamie approach the head of the line.

Dougal, his own oath completed, had taken up a station to Colum's rear. He saw Jamie before Colum, who was occupied with another man, and I saw his sudden start of surprise. He stepped close to his brother and muttered something. Colum kept his eyes fixed on the man before him, but I saw him stiffen slightly. He was surprised, too, and, I thought, not altogether pleased.

The level of feeling in the hall, high to start with, had risen through the ceremony. If Jamie were to refuse his oath at this point, I thought he could easily be torn to shreds by the overwrought clansmen around him. I wiped my palms surreptitiously against my skirt, feeling guilty at having brought him into such a precarious situation.

He seemed composed. Hot as the hall was, he wasn't sweating. He waited patiently in line, showing no signs of realizing that he was surrounded by a hundred men, armed to the teeth, who would be quick to resent any insult offered to the MacKenzie and the clan. *Je suis prest,* indeed. Or perhaps he had decided after all to take Alec's advice?

My nails were digging into my palms by the time it came his turn.

He went gracefully to one knee and bowed deeply before Colum. But instead of drawing his knife for the oath, he rose to his feet and looked Colum in the face. Fully erect, he stood head and shoulders over most of the men in the hall, and he topped Colum on his rostrum by several inches. I glanced at the girl Laoghaire. She had gone pale when he rose to his feet, and I saw that she also had her fists clenched tight.

Every eye in the hall was on him, but he spoke as though to Colum alone. His voice was as deep as Colum's, and every word was clearly audible.

"Colum MacKenzie, I come to you as kinsman and as ally. I give ye no vow, for my oath is pledged to the name that I bear." There was a low, ominous growl from the crowd, but he ignored it and went on. "But I give ye freely the things that I have; my help and my goodwill, wherever ye should find need of them. I give ye my obedience, as kinsman and as laird, and I hold myself bound by your word, so long as my feet rest on the lands of clan MacKenzie."

He stopped speaking and stood, tall and erect, hands relaxed at his sides. Ball now in Colum's court, I thought. One word from him, one sign, and they'd be scrubbing the young man's blood off the flags come morning.

Colum stood unmoving for a moment, then smiled and held out his hands. After an instant's hesitation, Jamie placed his own hands lightly on Colum's palms.

"We are honored by your offer of friendship and goodwill," said Colum clearly. "We accept your obedience and hold you in good faith as an ally of the clan MacKenzie."

There was a lessening of the tension over the hall, and almost an audible sigh of relief in the gallery as Colum drank from the quaich and offered it to Jamie. The young man accepted it with a smile. Instead of the customary ceremonial sip, however, he carefully raised the nearly full vessel, tilted it and drank. And kept on drinking. There was a gasp of mingled respect and amusement from the spectators, as the powerful throat muscles kept moving. Surely he'd have to breathe soon, I thought, but no. He drained the heavy cup to the last drop, lowered it with an explosive gasp for air, and handed it back to Colum.

"The honor is mine," he said, a little hoarsely, "to be allied with a clan whose taste in whisky is so fine."

There was an uproar at this, and he made his way toward the archway, much impeded by congratulatory handshakes and thumps on the back as he passed. Apparently Colum Mac-Kenzie was not the only member of the family with a knack for good theater.

The heat in the gallery was stifling, and the rising smoke was making my head ache before the oath-taking finally came to an end, with what I assumed were a few stirring words by Colum. Unaffected by six shared quaichs of spirit, the strong voice still reverberated off the stones of the hall. At least his legs wouldn't pain him tonight, I thought, in spite of all the standing.

There was a massive shout from the floor below, an outbreak of skirling pipes, and the solemn scene dissolved into a heaving surge of riotous yelling. An even louder shout greeted the tubs of ale and whisky that now appeared on trestles, accompanied by platters of steaming oatcakes, haggis, and meat. Mrs. Fitz, who must have organized this part of the proceedings, leaned precariously across the balustrade, keeping a sharp eye on the behavior of the stewards, mostly lads too young to swear a formal oath.

"And where's the pheasants got to, then?" she muttered under her breath, surveying the incoming platters. "Or the stuffed eels, either? Drat that Mungo Grant, I'll skin him if he's burnt the eels!" Making up her mind, she turned and began to squeeze toward the back of the gallery, plainly unwilling to leave administration of something so critical as the feasting in the untried hands of Mungo Grant.

Seizing the opportunity, I pushed along behind her, taking advantage of the sizable wake she left through the crowd. Others, clearly thankful for a reason to leave, joined me in the exodus.

Mrs. Fitz, turning at the bottom, saw the flock of women above and scowled ferociously.

"You wee lassies clear off to your rooms right sharp," she commanded. "If you'll not stay up there safe out o' sight, ye'd best scamper awa' to your own places. But no lingering in the corridors, nor peeping round the corners. There's not a man in the place who's not half in his cups already, and they'll be far gone in an hour. 'Tis no place for lasses tonight."

Pushing the door ajar, she peered cautiously into the corridor. The coast apparently clear, she shooed the women out the door, one at a time, sending them hurriedly on their way to their sleeping quarters on the upper floors.

"Do you need any help?" I asked as I came even with her. "In the kitchens, I mean?"

She shook her head, but smiled at the offer. "Nay, there's no need, lass. Get along wi' ye now, you're no safer than the rest." And a kindly shove in the small of the back sent me hurtling out into the dim passage.

I was inclined to take her advice, after the encounter with the guard outside. The men in the Hall were rioting, dancing, and drinking, with no thought of restraint or control. No place for a woman, I agreed.

Finding my way back to my room was another matter altogether. I was in an unfamiliar part of the castle, and while I knew the next floor had a breezeway that connected it to the corridor leading to my room, I couldn't find anything resembling stairs.

I came around a corner, and smack into a group of clansmen. These were men I didn't know, come from the outlying clan lands, and unused to the genteel manners of a castle. Or so I deduced from the fact that one man, apparently in search of the latrines, gave it up and chose to relieve himself in a corner of the hallway as I came upon them.

I whirled at once, intending to go back the way I had come, stairs or no stairs. Several hands reached to stop me, though, and I found myself pressed against the wall of the corridor, surrounded by bearded Highlanders with whisky on their breath and rape on their minds.

Seeing no point in preliminaries, the man in front of me grabbed me by the waist and plunged his other hand into my bodice. He leaned close, rubbing his bearded cheek against my ear. "And how about a sweet kiss, now, for the brave lads of the clan MacKenzie? Tulach Ard!"

"Erin go bragh," I said rudely, and pushed with all my strength. Unsteady with drink, he staggered backward into one of his companions. I dodged to the side and fled, kicking off my clumsy shoes as I ran.

Another shape loomed in front of me, and I hesitated. There seemed to be only one in front of me, though, and at least ten behind me, catching up fast despite their cargo of drink. I raced forward, intending to dodge around him. He stepped sharply in front of me, though, and I came to a halt, so fast that I had to put my hands on his chest to avoid crashing into him. It was Dougal MacKenzie.

"What in hell—" he began, then saw the men after me. He pulled me behind him and barked something at my pursuers in Gaelic. They protested in the same language, but after a short exchange like the snarling of wolves, they gave it up and went off in search of better entertainment.

"Thank you," I said, a little dazed. "Thank you. I'll . . . I'll go. I shouldn't be down here." Dougal glanced down at me, and took my arm, pulling me around to face him. He was disheveled and clearly had been joining in the roistering in the Hall.

"True enough, lass," he said. "Ye shouldna be here. Since ye are, weel, you'll have to pay the penalty for that," he murmured, eyes gleaming in the half-dark. And without warning, he pulled me hard against him and kissed me. Kissed me hard enough to bruise my lips and force them apart. His tongue flicked against mine, the taste of whisky sharp in my mouth.

His hands gripped me firmly by the bottom and pressed me against him, making me feel the rigid hardness under his kilt through my layers of skirts and petticoats.

He released me as suddenly as he had seized me. He nodded and gestured down the hall, breathing a little unsteadily. A lock of russet hair hung loose over his forehead and he brushed it back with one hand.

"Get ye gone, lassie," he said. "Before ye pay a greater price."

I went, barefoot.

———

Given the carryings-on of the night before, I had expected most inhabitants of the castle to lie late the next morning, possibly staggering down for a restorative mug of ale when the sun was high—assuming that it chose to come out at all, of course. But the Highland Scots of clan MacKenzie were a tougher bunch than I had reckoned with, for the castle was a buzzing hive long before dawn, with rowdy voices calling up and down the corridors, and a great clanking of armory and thudding of boots as men prepared for the tynchal.

It was cold and foggy, but Rupert, whom I met in the courtyard on my way to the hall, assured me that this was the best sort of weather in which to hunt boar.

"The beasts ha' such a thick coat, the cold's no hindrance to them," he explained, sharpening a spearpoint with enthusiasm against a foot-driven grindstone, "and they feel safe wi' the mist so heavy all round them—canna see the men coming toward them, ye ken."

I forbore to point out that this meant the hunting men would not be able to see the boar they were approaching, either, until they were upon it.

As the sun began to streak the mist with blood and gold, the hunting party assembled in the forecourt, spangled with damp and bright-eyed with anticipation. I was glad to see that the women were not expected to participate, but contented themselves with offering bannocks and drafts of ale to the departing heroes. Seeing the large number of men who set out for the east wood, armed to the teeth with boar spears, axes, bows, quivers, and daggers, I felt a bit sorry for the boar.

This attitude was revised to one of awed respect an hour later, when I was hastily summoned to the forest's edge to dress the wounds of a man who had, as I surmised, stumbled over the beast unawares in the fog.

"Bloody Christ!" I said, examining a gaping, jagged wound that ran from knee to ankle. "An *animal* did this? What's it got, stainless steel teeth?"

"Eh?" The victim was white with shock, and too shaken to answer me, but one of the fellows who had assisted him from the wood gave me a curious look.

"Never mind," I said, and yanked tight the compression bandage I had wound about the injured calf. "Take him up to the castle and we'll have Mrs. Fitz give him hot broth and blankets. That'll have to be stitched, and I've no tools for it here."

The rhythmic shouts of the same beaters still echoed in the mists of the hillside. Suddenly there was a piercing scream that rose high above fog and tree, and a startled pheasant broke from its hiding place nearby with a frightening rattle of wings.

"Dear God in heaven, what now?" Seizing an armful of bandages, I abandoned my patient to his caretakers and headed into the forest at a dead run.

The fog was thicker under the branches, and I could see no more than a few feet ahead, but the sound of excited shouting and thrashing underbrush guided me in the right direction.

It brushed past me from behind. Intent on the shouting, I didn't hear it, and I didn't see it until it had passed, a dark mass moving at incredible speed, the absurdly tiny cloven hooves almost silent on the sodden leaves.

I was so stunned by the suddenness of the apparition that it didn't occur to me at first to be frightened. I simply stared into the mist where the bristling black thing had vanished. Then, raising my hand to brush back the ringlets that were curling damply around my face, I saw the blotched red streak across it. Looking down, I found a matching streak on my skirt. The beast was wounded. Had the scream come from the boar, perhaps?

I thought not; I knew the sound of mortal wounding. And the pig was moving well under its own power when it had passed me. I took a deep breath and went on into the wall of mist, in search of a wounded man.

I found him at the bottom of a small slope, surrounded by kilted men. They had spread their plaids over him to keep him warm, but the cloth covering his legs was ominously dark with wetness. A wide scrape of black mud showed where he had tumbled down the length of the slope, and a scrabble of muddied leaves and churned earth, where he had met the boar. I sank to my knees beside the man, pulled back the cloth and set to work.

I had scarcely begun when the shouts of the men around us made me turn, to see the nightmare shape appear, once more soundless, out of the trees.

This time I had time to see the dagger hilt protruding from the beast's side, perhaps the work of the man on the ground before me. And the wicked yellow ivory, stained red as the mad little eyes.

The men around me, as stunned as I was, began to stir and reach for weapons. Faster than the rest, a tall man seized a boar-spear from the hands of a companion who stood frozen, and stepped out into the clearing.

It was Dougal MacKenzie. He walked almost casually, carrying the spear low, braced in both hands, as though about to lift a spadeful of dirt. He was intent on the beast, speaking to it in an undertone, murmuring in Gaelic as though to coax the beast from the shelter of the tree it stood beside.

The first charge was sudden as an explosion. The beast shot past, so closely that the brown hunting tartan flapped in the breeze of its passing. It spun at once and came back, a blur of muscular rage. Dougal leapt aside like a bull-fighter, jabbing at it with his spear. Back, forth, and again. It was less a rampage than a dance, both adversaries rooted in strength, but so nimble they seemed to float above the ground.

The whole thing lasted only a minute or so, though it seemed much longer. It ended when Dougal, whirling aside from the slashing tusks, raised the point of the short, stout spear and drove it straight down between the beast's sloping shoulders. There was the thunk of the spear and a shrill squealing noise that made the hairs stand up along my forearms. The small, piggy eyes cast to and fro, veering wildly in search of nemesis, and the dainty hooves sank deep in mud as the boar staggered and lurched. The squealing went on, rising to an inhuman pitch as the heavy body toppled to one side, driving the protruding dagger hilt-deep in the hairy flesh. The delicate hooves spurned the ground, churning up thick clods of damp earth.

The squeal stopped abruptly. There was silence for a moment, and then a thoroughly piggish grunt, and the bulk was still.

Dougal had not waited to make sure of the kill, but had circled the twitching animal and made his way back to the injured man. He sank to his knees and put an arm behind the victim's shoulders, taking the place of the man who had been supporting him. A fine spray of blood had spattered the high cheekbones, and drying droplets matted his hair on one side.

"Now then, Geordie," he said, rough voice suddenly gentle. "Now then. I've got him, man. It's all right."

"Dougal? Is't you, man?" The wounded man turned his head in Dougal's direction, struggling to open his eyes.

I was surprised, listening as I rapidly checked the man's pulse and vital signs. Dougal the fierce, Dougal the ruthless, was speaking to the man in a low voice, repeating words of comfort, hugging the man hard against him, stroking the tumbled hair.

I sat back on my heels, and reached again toward the pile of cloths on the ground beside me. There was a deep wound, running at least eight inches from the groin down the length of the thigh, from which the blood was gushing in a steady flow. It wasn't spurting, though; the femoral artery wasn't cut, which meant there was a good chance of stopping it.

What couldn't be stopped was the ooze from the man's belly, where the ripping tushes had laid open skin, muscles, mesentery, and gut alike. There were no large vessels severed there, but the intestine was punctured; I could see it plainly, through the jagged rent in the man's skin. This sort of abdominal wound was frequently fatal, even with a modern op-

erating room, sutures, and antibiotics readily to hand. The
contents of the ruptured gut, spilling out into the body cavity,
simply contaminated the whole area and made infection a
deadly certainty. And here, with nothing but cloves of garlic
and yarrow flowers to treat it with . . .

My gaze met Dougal's as he also looked down at the hideous wound. His lips moved, mouthing soundlessly over the
man's head the words, "Can he live?"

I shook my head mutely. He paused for a moment, holding
Geordie, then reached forward and deliberately untied the
emergency tourniquet I had placed around the man's thigh.
He looked at me, challenging me to protest, but I made no
move save a small nod. I could stanch the bleeding, and allow
the man to be transported by litter back to the castle. Back to
the castle, there to linger in increasing agony as the belly
wound festered, until the corruption spread far enough finally
to kill him, wallowing perhaps for days in long-drawn-out
pain. A better death, perhaps, was what Dougal was giving
him—to die cleanly under the sky, his heart's blood staining
the same leaves, dyed by the blood of the beast that killed
him. I crawled over the damp leaves to Geordie's head, and
took half his weight on my own arm.

"It will be better soon," I said, and my voice was steady, as
it always was, as it had been trained to be. "The pain will be
better soon."

"Aye. It's better . . . now. I canna feel my leg anymore
. . . nor my hands . . . Dougal . . . are ye there? Are ye
there, man?" The numb hands were blindly flailing before the
man's face. Dougal grasped them firmly between his own and
leaned close, murmuring in the man's ear.

Geordie's back arched suddenly, and his heels dug deeply
into the muddy ground, his body in violent protest at what his
mind had begun already to accept. He gasped deeply from
time to time, as a man who is bleeding to death gulps for air,
hungry for the oxygen that his body is starving for.

The forest was very quiet. No birds sang in the mist, and
the men who waited patiently hunkered in the shadow of the
trees, were silent as the trees themselves. Dougal and I leaned
close together over the struggling body, murmuring and

comforting, sharing the messy, heartrending, and necessary task of helping a man to die.

The trip up the hill to the castle was silent. I walked beside the dead man, borne on a makeshift litter of pine boughs. Behind us, borne in precisely similar fashion, came the body of his foe. Dougal walked ahead, alone.

As we entered the gate to the main courtyard, I caught sight of the tubby little figure of Father Bain, the village priest, hurrying belatedly to the aid of his fallen parishioner.

Dougal paused, reaching out to stay me as I turned toward the stair leading to the surgery. The bearers with Geordie's plaid-shrouded body on its litter passed on, heading toward the chapel, leaving us together in the deserted corridor. Dougal held me by the wrist, looking me over intently.

"You've seen men die before," he said flatly. "By violence." Not a question, almost an accusation.

"Many of them," I said, just as flatly. And pulling myself free, I left him standing there and went to tend my living patient.

The death of Geordie, hideous as it was, put only a momentary damper on the celebrations. A lavish funeral Mass was said over him that afternoon in the castle chapel, and the games began the next morning.

I saw little of them, being occupied in patching up the participants. All I could say for sure of authentic Highland games is that they were played for keeps. I bound up some fumble-foot who had managed to slash himself trying to dance between swords, I set the broken leg of a hapless victim who'd got in the way of a carelessly thrown hammer, and I doled out castor oil and nasturtium syrup to countless children who had overindulged in sweeties. By late afternoon, I was near exhaustion.

I climbed up on the surgery table in order to poke my head out of the tiny window for some air. The shouts and laughter and music from the field where the games were held had ceased. Good. No more new patients, then, at least not until tomorrow. What had Rupert said they were going to do next?

Archery? Hmm. I checked the supply of bandages, and wearily closed the surgery door behind me.

Leaving the castle, I trailed downhill toward the stables. I could do with some good nonhuman, nonspeaking, non-bleeding company. I also had in mind that I might find Jamie, whatever his last name was, and try again to apologize for involving him in the oath-taking. True, he had brought it off well, but clearly he would not have been there at all, left to his own devices. As to the gossip Rupert might now be spreading about our supposed amorous dalliance, I preferred not to think.

As to my own predicament, I preferred not to think about that, either, but I would have to, sooner or later. Having so spectacularly failed to escape at the beginning of the Gathering, I wondered whether the chances might be better at the end. True, most of the horses would be leaving, along with the visitors. But there would be a number of castle horses still available. And with luck, the disappearance of one would be put down to random thievery; there were plenty of villainous-looking scoundrels hanging about the fairground and the games. And in the confusion of leaving, it might be some time before anyone discovered that I was gone.

I scuffed along the paddock fence, pondering escape routes. The difficulty was that I had only the vaguest idea where I was, with reference to where I wanted to go. And since I was now known to virtually every MacKenzie between Leoch and the Border, thanks to my doctoring at the games, I would not be able to ask directions.

I wondered suddenly whether Jamie had told Colum or Dougal of my abortive attempt to escape on the night of the oath-taking. Neither of them had mentioned it to me, so per-haps not.

There were no horses out in the paddock. I pushed open the stable door, and my heart skipped a beat to see both Jamie and Dougal seated side by side on a bale of hay. They looked almost as startled at my appearance as I was at theirs, but gallantly rose and invited me to sit down.

"That's all right," I said, backing toward the door. "I didn't mean to intrude on your conversation."

"Nay, lass," said Dougal, "what I've just been saying to young Jamie here concerns you too."

I cast a quick look at Jamie, who responded with a trace of a headshake. So he hadn't told Dougal about my attempted escape.

I sat down, a bit wary of Dougal. I remembered that little scene in the corridor on the night of the oath-taking, though he had not referred to it since by word or gesture.

"I'm leaving in two days' time," he said abruptly. "And I'm taking the two of you with me."

"Taking us where?" I asked, startled. My heart began to beat faster.

"Through the MacKenzie lands. Colum doesna travel, so visiting the tenants and tacksmen that canna come to the Gathering—that's left to me. And to take care of the bits of business here and there. . . ." He waved a hand, dismissing these as trivial.

"But why me? Why us, I mean?" I demanded.

He considered for a moment before answering. "Why, Jamie's a handy lad wi' the horses. And as to you, lass, Colum thought it wise I should take ye along as far as Fort William. The commander there might be able to . . . assist ye in finding your family in France." Or to assist *you*, I thought, in determining who I really am. And how much else are you not telling me? Dougal stared down at me, obviously wondering how I would take this news.

"All right," I said tranquilly. "That sounds a good idea." Outwardly tranquil, inwardly I was rejoicing. What luck! Now I wouldn't have to try to escape from the castle. Dougal would take me most of the way himself. And from Fort William, I thought I could find my own way without much difficulty. To Craigh na Dun. To the circle of standing stones. And with luck, back home.

PART THREE

On the Road

11

Conversations with a
Lawyer

We rode out of the gates of Castle Leoch two days later, just before dawn. In twos and threes and fours, to the sound of shouted farewells and the calls of wild geese on the loch, the horses stepped their way carefully over the stone bridge. I glanced behind from time to time, until the bulk of the castle disappeared at last behind a curtain of shimmering mist. The thought that I would never again see that grim pile of stone or its inhabitants gave me an odd feeling of regret.

The noise of the horses' hooves seemed muffled in the fog. Voices carried strangely through the damp air, so that calls from one end of the long string were sometimes heard easily at the other, while the sounds of nearby conversations were lost in broken murmurs. It was like riding through a vapor peopled by ghosts. Disembodied voices floated in the air, speaking far away, then remarkably near at hand.

My place fell in the middle of the party, flanked on the one side by a man-at-arms whose name I did not know, and on the other by Ned Gowan, the little scribe I had seen at work in Colum's hall. He was something more than a scribe, I found, as we fell into conversation on the road.

Ned Gowan was a solicitor. Born, bred, and educated in Edinburgh, he looked the part thoroughly. A small, elderly man of neat, precise habits, he wore a coat of fine broadcloth, fine woolen hose, a linen shirt whose stock bore the merest suggestion of lace, and breeches of a fabric that was a nicely judged compromise between the rigors of travel and the status of his calling. A small pair of gold-rimmed half-spectacles, a neat hair-ribbon and a bicorne of blue felt completed the picture. He was so perfectly the quintessential man of law that I couldn't look at him without smiling.

He rode alongside me on a quiet mare whose saddle was burdened with two enormous bags of worn leather. He explained that one held the tools of his trade; inkhorn, quills, and papers.

"And what's the other for?" I asked, eyeing it. While the first bag was plump with its contents, the second seemed nearly empty.

"Oh, that's for his lairdship's rents," the lawyer replied, patting the limp bag.

"He must be expecting rather a lot, then," I suggested. Mr. Gowan shrugged good-naturedly.

"Not so much as all that, m'dear. But the most of it will be in doits and pence and other small coins. And such, unfortunately, take up more room than the larger denominations of currency." He smiled, a quick curve of thin, dry lips. "At that, a weighty mass of copper and silver is still easier of transport than the bulk of his lairdship's income."

He turned to direct a piercing look over his shoulder at the two large mule-drawn wagons that accompanied the party.

"Bags of grain and bunches of turnips have at least the benefit of lack of motion. Fowl, if suitably trussed and caged, I have nae argument with. Nor with goats, though they prove some inconvenience in terms of their omnivorous habits; one ate a handkerchief of mine last year, though I admit the fault was mine in allowin' the fabric to protrude injudiciously from my coat-pocket." The thin lips set in a determined line. "I have given explicit directions this year, though. We shall *not* accept live pigs."

The necessity of protecting Mr. Gowan's saddlebags and the two wagons explained the presence of the twenty or so men who made up the rest of the rent-collecting party, I supposed. All were armed and mounted, and there were a number of pack animals, bearing what I assumed were supplies for the sustenance of the party. Mrs. Fitz, among her farewells and exhortations, had told me that accommodations would be primitive or nonexistent, with many nights spent encamped along the road.

I was quite curious to know what had led a man of Mr. Gowan's obvious qualifications to take up a post in the remote Scottish Highlands, far from the amenities of civilized life to which he must be accustomed.

"Well, as to that," he said, in answer to my questions, "as a young man, I had a small practice in Edinburgh. With lace curtains in the window, and a shiny brass plate by the door, with my name inscribed upon it. But I grew rather tired of making wills and drawing up conveyances, and seeing the same faces in the street, day after day. So I left," he said simply.

He had purchased a horse and some supplies and set off, with no idea where he was going, or what to do once he got there.

"Ye see, I must confess," he said, dabbing his nose primly with a monogrammed handkerchief, "to something of a taste for . . . adventure. However, neither my stature nor my family background had fitted me for the life of highwayman or seafarer, which were the most adventurous occupations I could envision at the time. As an alternative, I determined that my best path lay upward, into the Highlands. I thought that in time I might perhaps induce some clan chieftain to, well, to allow me to serve him in some way."

And in the course of his travels, he had in fact encountered such a chieftain.

"Jacob MacKenzie," he said, with a fond, reminiscent smile. "And a wicked, red auld rascal he was." Mr. Gowan nodded toward the front of the line, where Jamie MacTavish's bright hair blazed in the mist. "His grandson's verra like him, ye ken. We met first at the point of a pistol, Jacob and I, as he was robbing me. I yielded my horse and my bags with good grace, having little other choice. But I believe he was a bit taken aback when I insisted upon accompanying him, on foot if necessary."

"Jacob MacKenzie. That would be Colum and Dougal's father?" I asked.

The elderly lawyer nodded. "Aye. Of course, he was not laird then. That happened a few years later . . . with a very small bit of assistance from me," he added modestly. "Things were less . . . civilized then," he said nostalgically.

"Oh, were they?" I said politely. "And Colum, er, inherited you, so to speak?"

"Something of the kind," Mr. Gowan said. "There was a wee bit o' confusion when Jacob died, d'ye see. Colum was heir to Leoch, to be sure, but he . . ." The lawyer paused, looking ahead and behind to see that no one was close enough to listen. The man-at-arms had ridden forward, though, to catch up with some of his mates, and a good four lengths separated us from the wagon-driver behind.

"Colum was a whole man to the age of eighteen or so," he resumed his story, "and gave promise to be a fine leader. He took Letitia to wife as part of an alliance with the Camerons— I drew up the marriage contract," he added, as a footnote, "but soon after the marriage he had a bad fall, during a raid. Broke the long bone of his thigh, and it mended poorly."

I nodded. It would have, of course.

"And then," Mr. Gowan went on with a sigh, "he rose from his bed too soon, and took a tumble down the stairs that broke the other leg. He lay in his bed close on a year, but it soon became clear that the damage was permanent. And that was when Jacob died, unfortunately."

The little man paused to marshal his thoughts. He glanced ahead again, as though looking for someone. Failing to find them, he settled back into the saddle.

"That was about the time there was all the fuss about his sister's marriage too," he said. "And Dougal . . . well, I'm afraid Dougal did not acquit himself so verra weel over that affair. Otherwise, d'ye see, Dougal might have been made chief at the time, but 'twas felt he'd not the judgment for it yet." He shook his head. "Oh, there was a great stramash about it all. There were cousins and uncles and tacksmen, and a great Gathering to decide the matter."

"But they did choose Colum, after all?" I said. I marveled

once again at the force of personality of Colum MacKenzie. And, casting an eye at the withered little man who rode at my side, I rather thought Colum had also had some luck in choosing his allies.

"They did, but only because the brothers stood firm together. There was nae doubt, ye see, of Colum's courage, nor yet of his mind, but only of his body. 'Twas clear he'd never be able to lead his men into battle again. But there was Dougal, sound and whole, if a bit reckless and hot-headed. And he stood behind his brother's chair and vowed to follow Colum's word and be his legs and his sword-arm in the field. So a suggestion was made that Colum be allowed to become laird, as he should in the ordinary way, and Dougal be made war chieftain, to lead the clan in time of battle. It was a situation not without precedent," he added primly.

The modesty with which he had said "A suggestion was made . . ." made it clear just whose suggestion it had been.

"And whose man are you?" I asked. "Colum's or Dougal's?"

"My interests must lie with the MacKenzie clan as a whole," Mr. Gowan said circumspectly. "But as a matter of form, I have sworn my oath to Colum."

A matter of form, my foot, I thought. I had seen that oathtaking, though I did not recall the small form of the lawyer specifically among so many men. No man could have been present at that ceremony and remained unmoved, not even a born solicitor. And the little man on the bay mare, dry as his bones might be, and steeped to the marrow in the law, had by his own testimony the soul of a romantic.

"He must find you a great help," I said diplomatically.

"Oh, I do a bit from time to time," he said, "in a small way. As I do for others. Should ye find yourself in need of advice, m'dear," he said, beaming genially, "do feel free to call upon me. My discretion may be relied upon, I do assure you." He bowed quaintly from his saddle.

"To the same extent as your loyalty to Colum MacKenzie?" I said, arching my brows. The small brown eyes met mine full on, and I saw both the cleverness and the humor that lurked in their faded depths.

"Ah, weel," he said, without apology. "Worth a try."

"I suppose so," I said, more amused than angered. "But I assure *you*, Mr. Gowan, that I have no need of your discretion, at least at present." It's catching, I thought, hearing myself. I sound just like him.

"I am an English lady," I added firmly, "and nothing more. Colum is wasting his time—and yours—in trying to extract secrets from me that don't exist." Or that do exist, but are untellable, I thought. Mr. Gowan's discretion might be limitless, but not his belief.

"He didn't send you along just to coerce me into damaging revelations, did he?" I demanded, suddenly struck by the thought.

"Oh, no." Mr. Gowan gave a short laugh at the idea. "No, indeed, m'dear. I fulfill an essential function, in managing the records and receipts for Dougal, and performing such small legal requirements that the clansmen in the more distant areas may have. And I am afraid that even at my advanced age, I have not entirely outgrown the urge to seek adventure. Things are much more settled now than they used to be"—he heaved a sigh that might have been one of regret—"but there is always the possibility of robbery along the road, or attack near the borders."

He patted the second bag on his saddle. "This bag is not entirely empty, ye ken." He turned back the flap long enough for me to see the gleaming grips of a pair of scroll-handled pistols, snugly set in twin loops that kept them within easy reach.

He surveyed me with a glance that took in every detail of my costume and appearance.

"Ye should really be armed yourself, m'dear," he said in a tone of mild reproof. "Though I suppose Dougal thought it would not be suitable . . . still. I'll speak to him about it," he promised.

We passed the rest of the day in pleasant conversation, wandering among his reminiscences of the dear departed days when men were men, and the pernicious weed of civilization was less rampant upon the bonny wild face of the Highlands.

At nightfall, we made camp in a clearing beside the road. I

had a blanket, rolled and tied behind my saddle, and with this I prepared to spend my first night of freedom from the castle. As I left the fire and made my way to a spot behind the trees, though, I was conscious of the glances that followed me. Even in the open air, it seemed, freedom had definite limits.

We reached the first stopping-place near noon of the second day. It was no more than a cluster of three or four huts, set off the road at the foot of a small glen. A stool was brought out from one of the cottages for Dougal's use, and a plank—thoughtfully brought along in one of the wagons—laid across two others to serve as a writing surface for Mr. Gowan.

He withdrew an enormous square of starched linen from the tailpocket of his coat and laid it neatly over a stump, temporarily withdrawn from its usual function as chopping block. He seated himself upon this and began to lay out inkhorn, ledgers, and receipt-book, as composed in his manner as though he were still behind his lace curtains in Edinburgh.

One by one, the men from the nearby crofts appeared, to conduct their annual business with the laird's representative. This was a leisurely affair, and conducted with a good deal less formality than the goings-on in the Hall of Castle Leoch. Each man came, fresh from field or shed, and drawing up a vacant stool, sat alongside Dougal in apparent equality, explaining, complaining, or merely chatting.

Some were accompanied by a sturdy son or two, bearing bags of grain or wool. At the conclusion of each conversation, the indefatigable Ned Gowan would write out a receipt for the payment of the year's rent, record the transaction neatly in his ledger, and flick a finger to one of the drovers, who would obligingly heave the payment onto a wagon. Less frequently, a small heap of coins would disappear into the depths of his leather bag with a faint chinking sound. Meanwhile, the men-at-arms lounged beneath the trees or disappeared up the wooded bank—to hunt, I supposed.

Variations of this scene were repeated over the next few days. Now and then I would be invited into a cottage for cider or milk, and all of the women would crowd into the small single room to talk with me. Sometimes a cluster of rude huts would be large enough to support a tavern or even an inn, which became Dougal's headquarters for the day.

Once in a while, the rents would include a horse, a sheep, or other livestock. These were generally traded to someone in the neighborhood for something more portable, or, if Jamie declared a horse fit for inclusion in the castle stables, it would be added to our string.

I wondered about Jamie's presence in the party. While the young man clearly knew horses well, so did most of the men in the party, including Dougal himself. Considering also that horses were both a rare sort of payment, and usually nothing special in the way of breeding, I wondered why it had been thought necessary to bring an expert along. It was a week after we had set out, in a village with an unpronounceable name, that I found out the real reason why Dougal had wanted Jamie.

The village, though small, was large enough to boast a tavern with two or three tables and several rickety stools. Here Dougal held his hearings and collected his rents. And after a rather indigestible luncheon of salt beef and turnips, he held court, buying ale for the tenants and cottars who had lingered after their transactions, and a few villagers who drifted in when their daily work was completed, to gawk at the strangers and hear such news as we carried.

I sat quietly on a settle in the corner, sipping sour ale and enjoying the respite from horseback. I was paying little attention to Dougal's talk, which shifted back and forth between Gaelic and English, ranging from bits of gossip and farming talk to what sounded like vulgar jokes and meandering stories.

I was wondering idly how long, at this rate, it might take to reach Fort William. And once there, exactly how I might best part company with the Scots of Castle Leoch without becoming equally entangled with the English army garrison. Lost in my own thoughts, I had not noticed that Dougal had been speaking for some time alone, as though making a speech of some kind. His hearers were following him intently, with occasional brief interjections and exclamations. Coming gradually back to an awareness of my surroundings, I realized that he was skillfully rousing his audience to a high pitch of excitement about *something*.

I glanced around. Fat Rupert and the little lawyer, Ned Gowan, sat against the wall behind Dougal, tankards of ale forgotten on the bench beside them as they listened intently. Jamie, frowning into his own tankard, leaned forward with his elbows on the table. Whatever Dougal was saying, he didn't seem to care for it.

With no warning, Dougal stood, seized Jamie's collar and pulled. Old, and shabbily made to begin with, the shirt tore cleanly down the seams. Taken completely by surprise, Jamie froze. His eyes narrowed, and I saw his jaw set tightly, but he didn't move as Dougal spread aside the ripped flaps of cloth to display his back to the onlookers.

There was a general gasp at sight of the scarred back, then a buzz of excited indignation. I opened my mouth, then caught the word "Sassenach," spoken with no kindly intonation, and shut it again.

Jamie, with a face like stone, stood and stepped back from the small crowd clustering around him. He carefully peeled off the remnants of his shirt, wadding the cloth into a ball. An elderly little woman, who reached the level of his elbow, was shaking her head and patting his back gingerly, making what I assumed were comforting remarks in Gaelic. If so, they were clearly not having the hoped-for effect.

He replied tersely to a few questions from the men present. The two or three young girls who had come in to fetch their families' dinner ale were clustered together against the far wall, whispering intently to each other, with frequent big-eyed glances across the room.

With a look at Dougal that should by rights have turned the older man to stone, Jamie tossed the ruins of his shirt into a corner of the hearth and left the room in three long strides, shaking off the sympathetic murmurs of the crowd.

Deprived of spectacle, their attentions turned back to Dougal. I didn't understand most of the comment, though the bits I caught seemed to be highly anti-English in nature. I was torn between wanting to follow Jamie outside, and staying inconspicuously where I was. I doubted that he wanted any company, though, so I shrank back into my corner and kept my head down, studying my blurry, pale reflection in the surface of my tankard.

The clink of metal made me look up. One of the men, a sturdy-looking crofter in leather trews, had tossed a few coins on the table in front of Dougal, and seemed to be making a short speech of his own. He stood back, thumbs braced in his belt, as though daring the rest to something. After an uncertain pause, one or two bold souls followed suit, and then a few more, digging copper doits and pence out of purse and sporran. Dougal thanked them heartily, waving a hand at the landlord for another round of ale. I noticed that the lawyer Ned Gowan was tidily stowing the new contributions in a separate pouch from that used for the MacKenzie rents bound for Colum's coffers, and I realized what the purpose of Dougal's little performance must be.

Rebellions, like most other business propositions, require capital. The raising and provisioning of an army takes gold, as does the maintenance of its leaders. And from the little I remembered of Bonnie Prince Charlie, the Young Pretender to the throne, part of his support had come from France, but part of the finances behind his unsuccessful rising had come from the shallow, threadbare pockets of the people he proposed to rule. So Colum, or Dougal, or both, were Jacobites; supporters of the Young Pretender against the lawful occupant of the throne of England, George II.

Finally, the last of the cottars and tenants drifted away to their dinners, and Dougal stood up and stretched, looking moderately satisfied, like a cat that has dined at least on milk, if not cream. He weighed the smaller pouch, and tossed it back to Ned Gowan for safekeeping.

"Aye, well enough," he remarked. "Canna expect a great deal from such a small place. But manage enough of the same, and it will be a respectable sum."

" 'Respectable' is not quite the word I'd use," I said, rising stiffly from my lurking place.

Dougal turned, as though noticing me for the first time.

"No?" he said, mouth curling in amusement. "Why not?

Have ye an objection to loyal subjects contributing their mite in support of their sovereign?"

"None," I said, meeting his stare. "No matter which sovereign it is. It's your collection methods I don't care for."

Dougal studied me carefully, as though my features might tell him something. "No matter which sovereign it is?" he repeated softly. "I thought ye had no Gaelic."

"I haven't," I said shortly. "But I've the sense I was born with, and two ears in good working order. And whatever 'King George's health' may be in Gaelic, I doubt very much that it sounds like 'Bragh Stuart.' "

He tossed back his head and laughed. "That it doesna," he agreed. "I'd tell ye the proper Gaelic for your liege lord and ruler, but it isna a word suitable for the lips of a lady, Sassenach or no."

Stooping, he plucked the balled-up shirt out of the ashes of the hearth and shook the worst of the soot off it.

"Since ye dinna care for my methods, perhaps ye'd wish to remedy them," he suggested, thrusting the ruined shirt into my hands. "Get a needle from the lady of the house and mend it."

"Mend it yourself!" I shoved it back into his arms and turned to leave.

"Suit yourself," Dougal said pleasantly from behind me. "Jamie can mend his own shirt, then, if you're not disposed to help."

I stopped, then turned reluctantly, hand out.

"All right," I began, but was interrupted by a large hand that snaked over my shoulder and snatched the shirt from Dougal's grasp. Dividing an opaque glance evenly between us, Jamie tucked the shirt under his arm and left the room as silently as he had entered it.

We found accommodation for the night at a crofter's cottage. Or I should say I did. The men slept outside, disposed in various haystacks, wagon-beds and patches of bracken. In deference to my sex or my status as semicaptive, I was provided with a pallet on the floor inside, near the hearth.

While my pallet seemed vastly preferable to the single bed-stead in which the entire family of six was sleeping, I rather envied the men their open-air sleeping arrangements. The fire was not put out, only damped for the night, and the air in the cottage was stifling with warmth and the scents and sounds of the tossing, turning, groaning, snoring, sweating, farting in-habitants.

After some time, I gave up any thought of sleeping in that smothered atmosphere. I rose and stole quietly outside, tak-ing a blanket with me. The air outside was so fresh by contrast with the congestion in the cottage that I leaned against the stone wall, gulping in enormous lungfuls of the delicious cool stuff.

There was a guard, sitting in quiet watchfulness under a tree by the path, but he merely glanced at me. Apparently deciding that I was not going far in my shift, he went back to whittling at a small object in his hands. The moon was bright, and the blade of the tiny *sgian dhu* flickered in the leafy shad-ows.

I walked around the cottage, and a little way up the hill behind it, careful to watch for slumbering forms in the grass. I found a pleasant private spot between two large boulders and made a comfortable nest for myself from heaped grass and the blanket. Stretched at length on the ground, I watched the full moon on its slow voyage across the sky.

Just so had I watched the moon rise from the window of Castle Leoch, on my first night as Colum's unwilling guest. A month, then, since my calamitous passage through the circle of standing stones. At least I now thought I knew why the stones had been placed there.

Likely of no particular importance in themselves, they were markers. Just as a signpost warns of rockfalls near a cliff-edge, the standing stones were meant to mark a spot of danger. A spot where . . . what? Where the crust of time was thin? Where a gate of some sort stood ajar? Not that the makers of the circles would have known what it was they were marking. To them, the spot would have been one of terrible mystery and powerful magic; a spot where people disappeared without warning. Or appeared, perhaps, out of thin air.

That was a thought. What would have happened, I wondered, had anyone been present on the hill of Craigh na Dun when I made my abrupt appearance? I supposed it might depend on the time one entered. Here, had a cottar encountered me under such circumstances, I would doubtless have been thought a witch or a fairy. More likely a fairy, popping into existence on that particular hill, with its reputation.

And that might well be where its reputation came from, I thought. If people through the years had suddenly disappeared, or just as suddenly appeared from nowhere at a certain spot, it might with good reason acquire a name for enchantment.

I poked a foot out from under the blanket and waggled my long toes in the moonlight. Most unfairylike, I decided critically. At five foot six, I was quite a tall woman for these times; as tall as many men. Since I could hardly pass as one of the Wee Folk, then, I would likely have been thought a witch or an evil spirit of some kind. From the little I knew of current methods for dealing with such manifestations, I could only be grateful that no one, in fact, had seen me appear.

I wondered idly what would happen if it worked the other way. What if someone disappeared from this time, and popped up in my own? That, after all, was precisely what I was intending to do, if there were any possible way of managing it. How would a modern-day Scot, like Mrs. Buchanan, the postmistress, react if someone like Murtagh, for instance, were suddenly to spring from the earth beneath her feet?

The most likely reaction, I thought, would be to run, to summon the police, or perhaps to do nothing at all, beyond telling one's friends and neighbors about the most extraordinary thing that happened the other day. . . .

As for the visitor? Well, he might manage to fit into the new time without arousing excessive attention, if he was cautious and lucky. After all, I was managing to pass with some success as a normal resident of this time and place, though my appearance and language had certainly aroused plenty of suspicion.

What if a displaced person were *too* different, though, or went about loudly proclaiming what had happened to him? If the exit were in primitive times, likely a conspicuous stranger would simply have been killed on the spot without further inquiry. And in more enlightened times, they would most likely be considered mad and tidied away into an institution somewhere, if they didn't quiet down.

This sort of thing could have been going on as long the earth itself, I reflected. Even when it happened in front of witnesses, there would be no clues at all; nothing to tell what had happened, because the only person who knew would be gone. And as for the disappeared, they'd likely keep their mouths shut at the other end.

Deep in my thoughts, I hadn't noticed the faint murmur of voices or the stirrings of footsteps through the grass, and I was quite startled to hear a voice speak only a few yards away.

"Devil take ye, Dougal MacKenzie," it said. "Kinsman or no, I dinna owe ye that." The voice was pitched low, but tight with anger.

"Do ye no?" said another voice, faintly amused. "I seem to recall a certain oath, giving your obedience. 'So long as my feet rest on the lands of clan MacKenzie,' I believe was the way of it." There was a soft thud, as of a foot stamping packed earth. "And MacKenzie land it is, laddie."

"I gave my word to Colum, not to you." So it was young Jamie MacTavish, and precisely three guesses as to what he was upset about.

"One and the same, man, and ye ken it well." There was the sound of a light slap, as of a hand against a cheek. "Your obedience is to the chieftain of the clan, and outside of Leoch, I am Colum's head and arms and hands as well as his legs."

"And never saw I a better case of the right hand not knowin' what the left is up to," came the quick rejoinder. Despite the bitterness of the tone, there was a lurking wit that enjoyed this clash of wills. "What d'ye think the right is going to say about the left collecting gold for the Stuarts?"

There was a brief pause before Dougal replied, "MacKenzies and MacBeolains and MacVinichs; they're free men all. None can force them to give against their will, and none can stop them, either. And who knows? It may happen that Colum will give more for Prince Charles Edward than all o' them put together, in the end."

"It may," the deeper voice agreed. "It may rain straight up tomorrow instead of down, as well. That doesna mean I'll stand waiting at the stairhead wi' my wee bucket turned upside down."

"No? You've more to gain from a Stuart throne than I have, laddie. And naught from the English, save a noose. If ye dinna care for your own silly neck—"

"My neck is my own concern," Jamie interrupted savagely. "And so is my back."

"Not while ye travel with me, sweet lad," said his uncle's mocking voice. "If ye wish to hear what Horrocks may tell ye, you'll do as you're told, yourself. And wise to do it, at that; a fine hand ye may be wi' a needle, but you've no but the one clean shirt."

There was a shifting, as of someone rising from his seat on a rock, and the soft passage of footsteps through the grass. Only one set of footsteps, though, I thought. I sat up as quietly as I could, and peered cautiously around the edge of one of the boulders that hid me.

Jamie was still there, sitting hunched on a rock a few feet away, elbows braced on his knees, chin sunk on his locked hands. His back was mostly to me. I started to ease backward, not wishing to intrude on his solitude, when he suddenly spoke.

"I know you're there," he said. "Come out, if ye like." From his tone, it was a matter of complete indifference to him. I rose and started to come out, when I realized I had been lying in my shift. Reflecting that he had enough to worry about without needing to blush for me as well, I tactfully wrapped myself in the blanket before emerging.

I sat down near him and leaned back against a rock, watching him a little diffidently. Beyond a brief nod of acknowledgment, he ignored me, completely occupied with inward thoughts of no very pleasant form, to judge from the dark frown on his face. One foot tapped restlessly against the rock he sat on, and he twisted his fingers together, clenching, then spreading them with a force that made several knuckles pop with soft crackling sounds.

It was the popping knuckles that reminded me of Captain

Manson. The supply officer for the field hospital where I had worked, Captain Manson suffered shortages, missed deliveries, and the endless idiocies of the army bureaucracy as his own personal slings and arrows. Normally a mild and pleasant-spoken man, when the frustrations became too great, he would retire briefly into his private office and punch the wall behind the door with all the force he could muster. Visitors in the outer reception area would watch in fascination as the flimsy wallboard quivered under the force of the blows. A few moments later, Captain Manson would reemerge, bruised of knuckle but once more calm of spirit, to deal with the current crisis. By the time he was transferred to another unit, the wall behind his door was pocked with dozens of fist-sized holes.

Watching the young man on the rock trying to disjoint his own fingers, I was forcibly reminded of the captain, facing some insoluble problem of supply.

"You need to hit something," I said.

"Eh?" He looked up in surprise, apparently having forgotten I was there.

"Hit something," I advised. "You'll feel better for it."

His mouth quirked as though about to say something, but instead he rose from his rock, headed decisively for a sturdy-looking cherry tree, and dealt it a solid blow. Apparently finding this some palliative to his feelings, he smashed the quivering trunk several times more, causing a delirious shower of pale-pink petals to rain down upon his head.

Sucking a grazed knuckle, he came back a moment later.

"Thank ye," he said, with a wry smile. "Perhaps I'll sleep tonight after all."

"Did you hurt your hand?" I rose to examine it, but he shook his head, rubbing the knuckles gently with the palm of the other hand.

"Nay, it's nothing."

We stood a moment in awkward silence. I didn't want to refer to the scene I had overheard, or to the earlier events of the evening. I broke the silence finally by saying, "I didn't know you were a lefty."

"A lefty? Oh, cack-handed, ye mean. Aye, always have been.

The schoolmaster used to tie that one to my belt behind my back, to make me write wi' the other."

"Can you? Write with the other, I mean?"

He nodded, reapplying the injured hand to his mouth. "Aye. Makes my head ache to do it, though."

"Do you fight left-handed too?" I asked, wanting to distract him. "With a sword, I mean?" He was wearing no arms at the moment except his dirk and *sgian dhu*, but during the day he customarily wore both sword and pistols, as did most of the men in the party.

"No, I use a sword well enough in either hand. A left-handed swordsman's at a disadvantage, ye ken, wi' a small-sword, for ye fight wi' your left side turned to the enemy, and your heart's on that side, d'ye see?"

Too filled with nervous energy to keep still, he had begun to stride about the grassy clearing, making illustrative gestures with an imaginary sword. "It makes little difference wi' a broadsword," he said. He extended both arms straight out, hands together and swept them in a flat, graceful arc through the air. "Ye use both hands, usually," he explained.

"Or if you're close enough to use only one, it doesna matter much which, for you come down from above and cleave the man through the shoulder. Not the head," he added instructively, "for the blade may slip off easy. Catch him clean in the notch, though"—he chopped the edge of his hand at the juncture of neck and shoulder—"and he's dead. And if it's not a clean cut, still the man will no fight again that day—or ever, likely," he added.

His left hand dropped to his belt and he drew the dirk in a motion like water pouring from a glass.

"Now, to fight wi' sword and dirk together," he said, "if ye have no targe to shelter your dirk hand, then you favor the right side, wi' the small-sword in that hand, and come up from underneath wi' the dirk if ye fight in close. But if the dirk hand is well shielded, ye can come from either side, and twist your body about"—he ducked and weaved, illustrating—"to keep the enemy's blade away, and use the dirk only if ye lose the sword or the use of the sword arm."

He dropped low and brought the blade up in a swift, murderous jab that stopped an inch short of my breast. I stepped back involuntarily, and at once he stood upright, sheathing the dirk with an apologetic smile.

"I'm sorry. I'm showin' off. I didna mean to startle ye."

"You're awfully good," I said, with sincerity. "Who taught you to fight?" I asked. "I'd think you'd need another left-handed fighter to show you."

"Aye, it was a left-handed fighter. The best I've ever seen." He smiled briefly, without humor. "Dougal MacKenzie."

Most of the cherry blossoms had fallen from his head by now; only a few pink petals clung to his shoulders, and I reached out to brush them away. The seam of his shirt had been mended neatly, I saw, if without artistry. Even a rip through the fabric had been catch-stitched together.

"He'll do it again?" I said abruptly, unable to stop myself.

He paused before answering, but there was no pretense of not understanding what I meant.

"Oh, aye," he said at last, nodding. "It gets him what he wants, ye see."

"And you'll let him do it? Let him use you that way?"

He looked past me, down the hill toward the tavern, where a single light still showed through chinks in the timbers. His face was smooth and blank as a wall.

"For now."

—

We continued on our rounds, moving no more than a few miles a day, often stopping for Dougal to conduct business at a crossroads or a cottage, where several tenants would gather with their bags of grain and bits of carefully hoarded money. All was recorded in ledgers by the quick-moving pen of Ned Gowan, and such receipts as were needed dispensed from his scrap-bag of parchment and papers.

And when we reached a hamlet or village large enough to boast an inn or tavern, Dougal would once more do his turn, standing drinks, telling stories, making speeches, and finally, if he judged the prospects good enough, he would force Jamie to his feet to show his scars. And a few more coins would be added to the second bag, the purse bound for France and the court of the Pretender.

I tried to judge such scenes as they developed, and step outside before the climax, public crucifixion never having been much to my taste. While the initial reaction to the sight of Jamie's back was horrified pity, followed by bursts of invective against the English army and King George, often there was a slight flavor of contempt that even I could pick up. On one occasion I heard one man remark softly to a friend in English, "An awfu' sight, man, is it no? Christ, I'd die in my blood before I let a whey-faced Sassenach to use me so."

Angry and miserable to start with, Jamie grew more wretched each day. He would shrug back into his shirt as soon as possible, avoiding questions and commiseration, and seek an excuse to leave the gathering, avoiding everyone until we took horse the following morning.

The breaking point came a few days later, in a small village called Tunnaig. This time, Dougal was still exhorting the crowd, a hand on Jamie's bare shoulder, when one of the onlookers, a young lout with long, dirty brown hair, made some personal remark to Jamie. I couldn't tell what was said, but the effect was instantaneous. Jamie wrenched out of Dougal's grasp and hit the lad in the stomach, knocking him flat.

I was slowly learning to put a few words of Gaelic together, though I could in no way be said to understand the language yet. However, I had noticed that I often could tell what was being said from the attitude of the speaker, whether I understood the words or not.

"Get up and say that again," *looks* the same said in any schoolyard, pub, or alley in the world.

So does "Right you are, mate," and "Get him, lads!"

Jamie disappeared under an avalanche of grimy work clothes as the rents-table went over with a crash beneath the weight of brown-hair and two of his friends. Innocent bystanders pressed back against the walls of the tavern and prepared to enjoy the spectacle. I sidled closer to Ned and Murtagh, eyeing the heaving mass of limbs uneasily. A lonely flash of red hair showed occasionally in the twisting sea of arms and legs.

"Shouldn't you help him?" I murmured to Murtagh, out of the corner of my mouth. He looked surprised at the idea. "No, why?"

"He'll call for help if he needs it," said Ned Gowan, tranquilly watching from my other side.

"Whatever you say." I subsided doubtfully.

I wasn't at all sure Jamie would be able to call for help if he needed it; at the moment he was being throttled by a stout lad in green. My personal opinion was that Dougal would soon be short one prime exhibit, but he didn't seem concerned. In fact, none of the watchers seemed at all bothered by the mayhem taking place on the floor at our feet. A few bets were being taken, but the overall air was one of quiet enjoyment of the entertainment.

I was glad to notice that Rupert drifted casually across the path of a couple of men who seemed to be contemplating joining the action. As they took a step toward the fray, he bumbled absentmindedly into their way, hand lightly resting on his dirk. They fell back, deciding to leave well enough alone.

The general feeling appeared to be that three to one was reasonable odds. Given that the one was quite large, an accomplished fighter, and obviously in the grip of a berserk fury, that might be true.

The contest seemed to be evening out with the abrupt retirement of the stout party in green, dripping blood as the result of a well-placed elbow to the nose.

It went on for several minutes more, but the conclusion became more and more obvious, as a second fighter fell by the wayside and rolled under a table, moaning and clutching his groin. Jamie and his original antagonist were still hammering each other earnestly in the middle of the floor, but the Jamie-backers amongst the spectators were already collecting their winnings. A forearm across the windpipe, accompanied by a vicious kidney punch, decided brown-hair that discretion was the better part of valor.

I added a mental translation of "That's enough, I give up," to my growing Gaelic/English word list.

Jamie rose slowly off the body of his last opponent to the

cheers of the crowd. Nodding breathlessly in acknowledgment, he staggered to one of the few benches still standing, and flopped down, streaming sweat and blood, to accept a tankard of ale from the publican. Gulping it down, he set the empty tankard on the bench and leaned forward, gasping for breath, elbows on his knees and the scars on his back defiantly displayed.

For once he was in no hurry to resume his shirt; in spite of the chill in the pub, he remained half-naked, only putting on his shirt to go outside when it was time to seek our lodging for the night. He left to a chorus of respectful good nights, looking more relaxed than he had in days, in spite of the pain from scrapes, cuts, and assorted contusions.

"One scraped shin, one cut eyebrow, one split lip, one bloody nose, *six* smashed knuckles, one sprained thumb, and two loosened teeth. Plus more contusions than I care to count." I completed my inventory with a sigh. "How do you feel?" We were alone, in the small shed behind the inn where I had taken him to administer first aid.

"Fine," he said, grinning. He started to stand up, but froze halfway, grimacing. "Aye, well. Perhaps the ribs hurt a bit."

"Of course they hurt. You're black and blue—again. Why do you do such things? What in God's name do you think you're made of? Iron?" I demanded irritably.

He grinned ruefully and touched his swollen nose.

"No. I wish I were."

I sighed again and prodded him gently around the middle.

"I don't think they're cracked; it's only bruises. I'll strap them, though, in case. Stand up straight, roll up your shirt, and hold your arms out from your sides." I began to tear strips from an old shawl I'd got from the innkeeper's wife. Muttering under my breath about sticking plaster and other amenities of civilized life, I improvised a strap dressing, pulling it tight and fastening it with the ring-brooch off his plaid.

"I can't breathe," he complained.

"If you breathe, it will hurt. Don't move. Where did you learn to fight like that? Dougal, again?"

"No." he winced away from the vinegar I was applying to the cut eyebrow. "My father taught me."

"Really? What was your father, the local boxing champion?"

"What's boxing? No, he was a farmer. Bred horses too." Jamie sucked in his breath as I continued the vinegar application on his barked shin.

"When I was nine or ten, he said he thought I was going to be big as my mother's folk, so I'd have to learn to fight." He was breathing more easily now, and held out a hand to let me rub marigold ointment into the knuckles.

"He said, 'If you're sizable, half the men ye meet will fear ye, and the other half will want to try ye. Knock one down,' he said, 'and the rest will let ye be. But learn to do it fast and clean, or you'll be fightin' all your life.' So he'd take me to the barn and knock me into the straw until I learned to hit back. Ow! That stings."

"Fingernail gouges are nasty wounds," I said, swabbing busily at his neck. "Especially if the gouger doesn't wash regularly. And I doubt that greasy-haired lad bathes once a year. 'Fast and clean' isn't quite how I'd describe what you did tonight, but it *was* impressive. Your father would be proud of you."

I spoke with some sarcasm, and was surprised to see a shadow pass across his face.

"My father's dead," he said flatly.

"I'm sorry." I finished the swabbing, then said softly, "But I meant it. He *would* be proud of you."

He didn't answer, but gave me a half-smile in reply. He suddenly seemed very young, and I wondered just how old he was. I was about to ask when a raspy cough from behind announced a visitor to the shed.

It was the stringy little man named Murtagh. He eyed Jamie's strapped-up ribs with some amusement, and lobbed a small wash leather bag through the air. Jamie put up a large hand and caught it easily, with a small clinking sound.

"And what's this?" he asked.

Murtagh raised one sketchy brow. "Your share o' the wagers, what else?"

Jamie shook his head and made to toss the bag back.

"I didna wager anything."

Murtagh raised a hand to stop him. "You did the work. You're a verra popular fellow at the moment, at least wi' those that backed ye."

"But not with Dougal, I don't suppose," I interjected.

Murtagh was one of those men who always looked a bit startled to find that women had voices, but he nodded politely enough.

"Aye, that's true. Still, I dinna see as that should trouble ye," he said to Jamie.

"No?" A glance passed between the two men, with a message I didn't understand. Jamie blew his breath out softly through his teeth, nodding slowly to himself.

"When?" he asked.

"A week. Ten days, perhaps. Near a place called Lag Cruime. You'll know it?"

Jamie nodded again, looking more content than I had seen him in some time. "I know it."

I looked from one face to the other, both closed and secretive. So Murtagh had found out something. Something to do with the mysterious "Horrocks" perhaps? I shrugged. Whatever the cause, it appeared that Jamie's days as an exhibition were over.

"I suppose Dougal can always tap-dance instead," I said.

"Eh?" The secretive looks changed to looks of startlement.

"Never mind. Sleep well." I picked up my box of medical supplies and went to find my own rest.

12

The Garrison Commander

We were drawing nearer to Fort William, and I began to ponder seriously what my plan of action should be, once we had arrived there.

It depended, I thought, upon what the garrison commander was likely to do. If he believed that I was a gentlewoman in distress, he might provide me with temporary escort toward the coast and my putative embarkation for France.

But he might be suspicious of me, turning up in the company of the MacKenzies. Still, I was patently not a Scot myself; surely he would not be inclined to think me a spy of some sort? That was evidently what Colum and Dougal thought—that I was an English spy.

Which made me wonder what I was meant to be spying on? Well, unpatriotic activities, I supposed; of which, collecting money for the support of Prince Charles Edward Stuart, pretender to the throne, was definitely one.

But in that case, why had Dougal allowed me to see him do it? He could easily enough have sent me outside before that part of the proceedings. Of course, the proceedings had all been held in Gaelic, I argued with myself.

Perhaps that was the point, though. I remembered the odd gleam in his eyes and his question, "I thought ye had no Gaelic?" Perhaps it was a test, to see whether I really was ignorant of the language. For an English spy scarcely would have been sent into the Highlands, unable to speak with more than half the people there.

But no, the conversation I had overheard between Jamie and Dougal would seem to indicate that Dougal was indeed a Jacobite, though Colum apparently was not—yet.

My head was beginning to buzz with all these suppositions, and I was glad to see that we were approaching a fairly large village. Likely that meant a good inn, as well, and a decent supper.

The inn was in fact commodious, by the standards I had grown accustomed to. If the bed was apparently designed for midgets—and flea-bitten ones, at that—at least it was in a chamber to itself. In several of the smaller inns, I had slept on a settle in the common room, surrounded by snoring male forms and the humped shadows of plaid-wrapped shapes.

Customarily I fell asleep immediately, whatever the sleeping conditions, worn out by a day in the saddle and an evening of Dougal's politicizing. The first evening in an inn, though, I had remained awake for a good half-hour, fascinated by the remarkable variety of noises the male respiratory apparatus could produce. An entire dormitory full of student nurses couldn't come close.

It occurred to me, listening to the chorus, that men in a hospital ward seldom really snore. Breathe heavily, yes. They gasp, groan occasionally, and sometimes sob or cry out in sleep. But there was no comparison to this healthy racket. Perhaps it was that sick or injured men could not sleep deeply enough to relax into that sort of din.

If my observations were sound, then my companions were plainly in the most robust health. They certainly looked it, limbs casually asprawl, faces slack and glowing in the firelight. The complete abandon of their sleep on hard boards was the satisfying of an appetite as hearty as the one they had brought to dinner. Obscurely comforted by the cacophony, I had pulled my traveling cloak around my shoulders and went to sleep myself.

By comparison, I found myself now rather lonely here in the solitary splendor of my tiny, smelly attic. Despite having removed the bedclothes and beaten the mattress to discourage unwelcome co-habitants, I had some difficulty in sleeping, so silent and dark did the chamber seem after I had blown out the candle.

There were a few faint echoes from the common room two floors below, and a brief flurry of noise and movement, but this served only to emphasize my own isolation. It was the first time I had been left so completely alone since my arrival at the castle, and I was not at all sure I liked it.

I was hovering uneasily on the verge of sleep, when my ears picked up an ominous creaking of floorboards in the hall outside. The step was slow and halting, as though the intruder hesitated in his path, picking the soundest-appearing of the boards for each next step. I sat bolt upright, groping for the candle and flint box by the bed.

My hand, blindly searching, struck the flint box and knocked it to the floor with a soft thump. I froze, and the steps outside did likewise.

There was a soft scratching at the door, as of someone groping for the latch. I knew the door was unbolted; though it was fitted with brackets for a bolt, I had searched unavailingly for the bolt itself before retiring. I grabbed the candlestick, yanked the stub of the candle out, and slid out of bed as quietly as I could, clutching the heavy pottery.

The door squeaked slightly on its hinges as it gave. The room's only window was tightly shuttered against both elements and light; nonetheless I could just make out the dim outline of the door as it opened. The outline grew, then to my surprise, it shrank and disappeared as the door shut again. Everything was quiet once more.

I stayed pressed against the wall for what seemed like ages, holding my breath and trying to hear through the noise of my pounding heart. At last I inched toward the door, edging carefully around the room next to the wall, thinking the floorboards must surely be more solid here. I eased my foot down at each step, gradually trusting my weight to it, then pausing and groping with bare toes for the seam between two boards, before setting the other foot as solidly as I could judge.

Once the door was reached, I paused, ear pressed to the

thin panels, hands braced on the frame, on guard against a sudden bursting inward. I thought perhaps I heard slight sounds, but wasn't sure. Was it only the sounds of the activity down below, or was it the stifled breathing of someone on the other side of the panel?

The constant flow of adrenaline was making me slightly sick. Tiring at last of this nonsense, I took a firm grip of my candlestick, yanked open the door, and rushed into the hallway.

I say "rushed"; in actuality, I took two steps, trod heavily on something soft, and fell headlong into the passageway, skinning my knuckles and banging my head quite painfully on something solid.

I sat up, clutching my brow with both hands, completely uncaring that I might be assassinated at any moment.

The person I had stepped on was swearing in a rather breathless manner. Through the haze of pain, I was dimly aware that he (I assumed from the size and the smell of sweat that my visitor was male) had risen and was groping for the fastening of the shutters in the wall above us.

A sudden inrush of fresh air made me wince and shut my eyes. When I opened them, there was enough light from the night sky for me to see the intruder.

"What are *you* doing here?" I asked accusingly.

At the same time Jamie asked, in a similarly accusatory tone, "How much do ye weigh, Sassenach?"

Still a bit addled, I actually replied "Nine stone," before thinking to ask "Why?"

"Ye nearly crushed my liver," he answered, gingerly prodding the affected area. "Not to mention scaring living hell out of me." He reached a hand down and hauled me to my feet. "Are ye all right?"

"No, I bumped my head." Rubbing the spot, I looked dazedly around the bare hallway. "What did I bang it on?" I demanded ungrammatically.

"*My* head," he said, rather grumpily, I thought.

"Serves you right," I said nastily. "What were you doing, sneaking about outside my door?"

He gave me a testy look.

"I wasna 'sneaking about,' for God's sake. I was sleeping— or trying to." He rubbed what appeared to be a knot forming on his temple.

"Sleeping? *Here?*" I looked up and down the cold, bare, filthy hallway with exaggerated amazement. "You do pick the oddest places; first stables, now this."

"It may interest ye to know that there's a small party of English dragoons stopped in to the taproom below," he informed me coldly. "They're a bit gone in drink, and disporting themselves a bit reckless with two women from the town. Since there's but the two lasses, and five men, some of the soldiers seemed a bit inclined to venture upward in search of . . . ah, partners. I didna think you'd care overmuch for such attentions." He flipped his plaid back over his shoulder and turned in the direction of the stairway. "If I was mistaken in that impression, then I apologize. I'd no intention of disturbin' your rest. Good e'en to ye."

"Wait a minute." He stopped, but did not turn back, forcing me to walk around him. He looked down at me, polite but distant.

"Thank you," I said. "It was very kind of you. I'm sorry I stepped on you."

He smiled then, his face changing from a forbidding mask to its usual expression of good humor.

"No harm done, Sassenach," he said. "As soon as the headache goes away and the cracked rib heals, I'll be good as new."

He turned back and pushed open the door of my room, which had swung shut in the wake of my hasty exit, owing to the fact that the builder had apparently constructed the inn without benefit of a plumb line. There wasn't a right angle in the place.

"Go back to bed, then," he suggested. "I'll be here."

I looked at the floor. Besides its essential hardness and coldness, the oaken boards were blotched with expectorations, spills, and forms of filth I didn't wish even to contemplate. The builder's mark in the door lintel had said 1732, and that was plainly the last time the boards had been cleaned.

"You can't sleep out here," I said. "Come in; at least the floor in the room isn't quite this bad."

Jamie froze, hand on the doorframe.

"Sleep in your room with ye?" He sounded truly shocked. "I couldna do that! Your reputation would be ruined!"

He really meant it. I started to laugh, but converted it into a tactful coughing fit. Given the exigencies of road travel, the crowded state of the inns, and the crudity or complete lack of sanitary facilities, I was on terms of such physical intimacy with these men, Jamie included, that I found the idea of such prudery hilarious.

"You've slept in the same room with me before," I pointed out, when I had recovered a bit. "You and twenty other men."

He sputtered a bit. "That isna at all the same thing! I mean, it was a quite public room, and . . ." He paused as an awful thought struck him. "You didna think I meant that you were suggesting anything improper?" he asked anxiously. "I assure ye, I—"

"No, no. Not at all." I made haste to reassure him that I had taken no offense.

Seeing that he could not be persuaded, I insisted that at the least he must take the blankets from my bed to lie upon. He agreed to this reluctantly, and only upon my repeated assurances that I would not use them myself in any case, but intended to sleep as usual in the cover of my thick traveling cloak.

I tried to thank him again, as I paused by the makeshift pallet before returning to my fetid sanctuary, but he waved away my appreciation with a gracious hand.

"It isna entirely disinterested kindness on my part, ye ken," he observed. "I'd as soon avoid notice myself."

I had forgotten that he had his own reasons for keeping away from English soldiery. It did not escape me, however, that this could have been much better accomplished, not to say more comfortably, by his sleeping in the warm and airy stables, rather than on the floor before my door.

"But if anyone *does* come up here," I protested, "they'll find you then."

He reached a long arm out to grasp the swinging shutter and pulled it to. The hall was plunged in blackness, and Jamie appeared as no more than a shapeless bulk.

"They canna see my face," he pointed out. "And in the condition they're in, my name would be of no interest to them, either, even were I to give them the right one, which I dinna mean to do."

"That's true," I said, doubtfully. "Won't they wonder, though, what you're doing up here in the dark?" I could see nothing of his face, but the tone of his voice told me he was smiling.

"Not at all, Sassenach. They'll just think I'm waiting my turn."

I laughed and went in then. I curled myself on the bed and went to sleep, marveling at the mind that could make such ribald jokes even as it recoiled at the thought of sleeping in the same room with me.

When I awoke, Jamie was gone. Going down to breakfast, I met Dougal at the foot of the stairs, waiting for me.

"Eat up quickly, lass," he said. "You and I are riding to Brockton."

He declined to tell me anything further, but he seemed a bit uneasy, I thought. I ate quickly, and we soon found ourselves trotting through the misty early morning. Birds were busy in the shrubbery, and the air gave promise of a warm summer day to come.

"Who are we going to see?" I asked. "You may as well tell me, since if I don't know, I'll be surprised, and if I do, I'm intelligent enough to act surprised, anyway."

Dougal cocked an eye at me, considering, but decided that my argument was sound.

"The garrison commander from Fort William," he said.

I felt a minor shock. I wasn't quite ready for this. I had thought we had three days yet until we reached the Fort.

"But we're nowhere near Fort William!" I exclaimed.

"Mmphm."

Apparently this garrison commander was an energetic sort.

Not content to stay at home minding his garrison, he was out inspecting the countryside with a party of dragoons. The soldiers who had come to our inn the night before were part of this group, and had told Dougal that the commander was presently in residence at the inn at Brockton.

This presented a problem, and I was silent for the rest of the ride, contemplating it. I had counted on being able to extract myself from Dougal's company at Fort William, which I thought to be within a day's travel of the hill of Craigh na Dun. Even unprepared for camping, and lacking food or other resources, I thought I could cover that much ground alone, and find my way to the stone circle. As to what would happen then—well, there was no way to tell except by going there.

But this development threw an unexpected spanner into my plans. If I parted company with Dougal here, as I well might, I would be four days' ride from the hill, not one. And I did not have sufficient faith in my sense of direction, let alone my endurance, to risk it alone on foot among the wild crags and moors. The last weeks of rugged travel had given me a wary respect for the jagged rocks and crashing burns of the Highlands, let alone the occasional wild beast. I had no particular desire to meet a boar, for example, face-to-face in some deserted glen.

We reached Brockton at midmorning. The mist had burned away, and the day was sunny enough to give me a sense of optimism. Perhaps it would be a simple matter, after all, to persuade the garrison commander to provide me with a small escort who could see me to the hill.

I could see why the commander had chosen Brockton as his temporary headquarters. The village was large enough to boast two taverns, one of them an imposing three-story edifice with attached stable. Here we stopped, turning our horses over to the attention of a hostler, who moved so slowly as to seem ossified. He had barely succeeded in reaching the stable door by the time we were inside and Dougal was ordering refreshment from the innkeeper.

I was left below, contemplating a plate of rather stale-looking oatcakes, while Dougal mounted the stair to the commander's sanctum. It felt a bit strange to see him go. There were three or four English soldiers in the taproom, who eyed me speculatively, chatting to each other in low voices. After a month among the Scots of clan MacKenzie, the presence of English dragoons made me unaccountably nervous. I told myself I was being silly. After all, they were my own country-men, out of time or not.

Still, I found myself missing the congenial company of Mr. Gowan and the pleasant familiarity of Jamie whatever-his-name-was. I was feeling rather sorry that I had had no chance to bid farewell to anyone before leaving that morning, when I heard Dougal's voice calling from the stair behind me. He was standing at the top, beckoning me upward.

He looked somewhat more grim than usual, I thought, as he stood aside without speaking and gestured me into the room. The garrison commander stood by the open window, his slim, straight figure silhouetted by the light. He gave a short laugh when he saw me.

"Yes, I thought so. It had to be you, from MacKenzie's description." The door closed behind me, and I was alone with Captain Jonathan Randall of His Majesty's Eighth Dragoons.

He was dressed this time in a clean red-and-fawn uniform, with a lace-trimmed stock and a neatly curled and powdered wig. But the face was the same—Frank's face. My breath caught in my throat. This time, though, I noticed the small lines of ruthlessness around his mouth, and the touch of arro-gance in the set of his shoulders. Still, he smiled affably enough, and invited me to sit down.

The room was plainly furnished, with no more than a desk and chair, a long deal table, and a few stools. Captain Randall motioned to a young corporal who stood to attention near the door, and a mug of ale was clumsily poured and set before me.

The Captain waved the corporal back and poured his own ale, then sank gracefully onto a stool across the table from me.

"All right," he said pleasantly. "Why don't you tell me who you are, and how you come to find yourself here?"

Having little choice at this point, I told him the same story

I had given Colum, omitting only the less tactful references to his own behavior, which he knew about in any case. I had no idea how much Dougal had told him, and didn't wish to risk being tripped up.

The captain appeared polite but skeptical throughout my recital. He took less trouble to hide it than Colum had, I reflected. He rocked back on his stool, considering.

"Oxfordshire, you say? There are no Beauchamps in Oxfordshire that I know of."

"How would you know?" I snapped. "You're from Sussex yourself."

His eyes popped open in surprise. I could have bitten my tongue.

"And may I ask just how you know *that*?" he asked.

"Er, your voice. Yes, it's your accent," I said hastily. "Clearly Sussex."

The graceful dark brows nearly touched the curls of his wig.

"Neither my tutors nor my parents would be much obliged to hear that my speech so clearly reflects my birthplace, Madam," he said dryly. "They having gone to considerable trouble and expense to remedy it. But, being the expert at local speech patterns that you are"—he turned to the man standing against the wall—"no doubt you can also identify my corporal's place of origin. Corporal Hawkins, would you oblige me by reciting something? Anything at all will do," he added, seeing the confusion on the man's face. "Some popular verse, perhaps?"

The corporal, a young man with a stupid, beefy face and broad shoulders, glanced wildly about the room seeking inspiration, then drew himself up to attention and intoned,

> *Buxom Meg, she washed my clothes,*
> *And took them all away.*
> *I waited thus in sore distress,*
> *And then I made her pay.*

"Er, that will do, Corporal, thank you." Randall made a dismissive motion, and the corporal subsided against the wall, sweating freely.

"Well?" Randall turned to me, questioning.

"Er, Cheshire," I guessed.

"Close. Lancashire." He eyed me narrowly. Putting his hands together behind his back, he strolled over to the window and peered out. Checking to see whether Dougal had brought any men with him? I wondered.

Suddenly he whirled back to me with an abrupt *"Parlez-vous français?"*

"Très bien," I promptly replied. "What of it?"

Head to one side, he looked me over carefully.

"Damme if I think you're French," he said, as though to himself. "Could be, I suppose, but I've yet to meet a Frenchie could tell a Cockney from a Cornishman."

His neatly manicured fingers tapped the wood of the table-top. "What was your maiden name, Mrs. Beauchamp?"

"Look, Captain," I said, smiling as charmingly as I could, "entertaining as it is to play Twenty Questions with you, I should really like to conclude these preliminaries and arrange for the continuation of my journey. I've already been delayed for some time, and—"

"You do not help your case by adopting this frivolous attitude, Madam," he interrupted, narrowing his eyes. I had seen Frank do that when displeased about something, and I felt a little weak in the knees. I put my hands on my thighs to brace myself.

"I have no case to help," I said, as boldly as I could. "I'm making no claims on you, the garrison, or for that matter, on the MacKenzies. All I want is to be allowed to resume my journey in peace. And I see no reason why you ought to have any objection to that."

He glared at me, lips pressed tight together in irritation.

"Oh, you don't? Well, consider my position for a moment, Madam, and perhaps my objections will become clearer. A month ago I was, with my men, in hot pursuit of a band of unidentified Scottish bandits who had absconded with a small herd of cattle from an estate near the border, when—"

"Oh, so that's what they were doing!" I exclaimed. "I wondered," I added lamely.

Captain Randall breathed heavily, then decided against

whatever he had been going to say, in favor of continuing his story.

"In the midst of this lawful pursuit," he went on, in measured tones, "I encounter a half-dressed Englishwoman—in a place where no Englishwoman should be, even with a proper escort—who resists my inquiries, assaults my person—"

"You assaulted mine first!" I said hotly.

"Whose accomplice renders me unconscious by a cowardly attack, and who then flees the area, plainly with some assistance. My men and I searched that area most thoroughly, and I assure you, Madam, there was no trace of your murdered servant, your plundered baggage, your discarded gown, nor the merest sign that there is the slightest truth to your story!"

"Oh?" I said, a little weakly.

"Yes. Furthermore, there have been no reports of bandits in that area within the last four months. And *now*, Madam, you turn up in company with the war chieftain of clan MacKenzie, who tells me that his brother Colum is convinced you are a spy, presumably working for *me*!"

"Well, I'm not, am I?" I said, reasonably. "You know that, at least."

"Yes, I know that," he said with exaggerated patience. "What I don't know is who the devil you are! But I mean to find out, Madam, have no doubts as to that. I am the commander of this garrison. As such, I am empowered to take certain steps in order to secure the safety of this area against traitors, spies, and any other persons whose behavior I consider suspicious. And those steps, Madam, I am fully prepared to take."

"And just what might those steps be?" I inquired. I honestly wanted to know, though I suppose the tone of my question must have sounded rather baiting.

He stood up, looked down at me consideringly for a moment, then walked around the table, extended his hand, and drew me to my feet.

"Corporal Hawkins," he said, still staring at me, "I shall require your assistance for a moment."

The youth by the wall looked profoundly uneasy, but sidled over to us.

"Stand behind the lady, please, Corporal," Randall said, sounding bored. "And take her firmly by both elbows."

He drew back his arm and hit me in the pit of the stomach.

I made no noise, because I had no breath. I sat on the floor, doubled over, struggling to draw air into my lungs. I was shocked far beyond the actual pain of the blow, which was beginning to make itself felt, along with a wave of giddy sickness. In a fairly eventful life, no one had ever purposely struck me before.

The Captain squatted down in front of me. His wig was slightly awry, but aside from that and a certain brightness to his eyes, he showed no change from his normal controlled elegance.

"I trust you are not with child, Madam," he said in a conversational tone, "because if you are, you won't be for long."

I was beginning to make a rather odd wheezing noise, as the first wisps of oxygen found their way painfully into my throat. I rolled onto my hands and knees and groped feebly for the edge of the table. The corporal, after a nervous glance at the captain, reached down to help me up.

Waves of blackness seemed to ripple over the room. I sank onto the stool and closed my eyes.

"Look at me." The voice was as light and calm as though he were about to offer me tea. I opened my eyes and looked up at him through a slight fog. His hands were braced on his exquisitely tailored hips.

"Have you anything to say to me now, Madam?" he demanded.

"Your wig is crooked," I said, and closed my eyes again.

13
A Marriage Is
Announced

I sat at a table in the taproom below, gazing into a cup of milk and fighting off waves of nausea.

Dougal had taken one look at my face as I came downstairs, supported by the beefy young corporal, and strode purposefully past me, up the stairs to Randall's room. The floors and doors of the inn were stout and well constructed, but I could still hear the sound of raised voices upstairs.

I raised the cup of milk, but my hands were still shaking too badly to drink it.

I was gradually recovering from the physical effects of the blow, but not from the shock of it. I *knew* the man was not my husband, but the resemblance was so strong and my habits so ingrained, that I had been half-inclined to trust him, and had spoken to him as I would have to Frank, expecting civility, if not active sympathy. To have those feelings abruptly turned inside out by his vicious attack was what was making me ill now.

Ill, and frightened as well. I had seen his eyes as he crouched next to me on the floor. Something had moved in their depths, just for a moment. It was gone in a flash, but I did not want ever to see it again.

The sound of a door opening above brought me out of my reverie. The thud of heavy footsteps was succeeded by the rapid appearance of Dougal, followed closely by Captain Randall. So closely indeed, that the Captain appeared to be in pursuit of the Scot, and was brought up short when Dougal, catching sight of me, halted suddenly at the foot of the stairs.

With a glare over his shoulder at Captain Randall, Dougal came swiftly over to where I was seated, tossed a small coin on the table in payment, and jerked me to my feet without a word. He was hustling me out the door before I had time to do more than register the extraordinary look of speculative acquisitiveness on the face of the redcoat officer.

We were mounted and moving before I had even tucked the voluminous skirts around my legs, and the material billowed around me like a settling parachute. Dougal was silent, but the horses seemed to pick up his sense of urgency; we were all but galloping by the time we hit the main road.

Near a crossroads marked with a Pictish cross, Dougal abruptly reined to a halt. Dismounting, he seized the bridles of both horses and tied them loosely to a sapling. He helped me down, then abruptly disappeared into the bushes, beckoning me to follow.

I followed the swing of his kilt up the hillside, ducking as the branches he pushed out of the way snapped back across the path over my head. The hillside was overgrown with oak and scrubby pine. I could hear titmice in the copse to the left, and a flock of jays calling out to each other as they fed, further on. The grass was the fresh green of early summer, clumps of sturdy growth shooting out of the rocks and furring the ground under the oaks. Nothing grew under the pines, of course; the needles lay inches thick, affording protection for the small crawling things that hid there from sunlight and predators.

The sharp scents made my throat ache. I had been up such hillsides before, and smelled these same spring scents. But then the pine and grass scent had been diluted with the smell of petrol fumes from the road below and the voices of day trippers replaced those of the jays. Last time I walked such a path, the ground was littered with sandwich wrappers and cigarette butts instead of mallow blossoms and violets. Sandwich wrappers seemed a reasonable enough price to pay, I supposed, for such blessings of civilization as antibiotics and telephones, but just for the moment, I was willing to settle for the violets. I badly needed a little peace, and I felt it here.

Dougal turned suddenly aside just below the crest of the hill and disappeared into a thick growth of broom. Shoving my way in after him with some difficulty, I found him seated on the flat stone edging of a small pool. A weathered block of stone stood askew behind him, with a dim and vaguely human figure etched into the stained surface. It must be a saint's pool, I realized. These small shrines to one saint or another dotted the Highlands, and were often to be found in such secluded spots, though even up here, tattered remnants of fabric flapped from the branches of a rowan tree that overhung the water; pledges from visitors who petitioned the saint, for health or a safe journey, perhaps.

Dougal greeted my appearance with a nod. He crossed himself, bent his head, and scooped up a double handful of water. The water had an odd dark color, and a worse smell—likely a sulfur spring, I thought. The day was hot and I was thirsty, though, so I followed Dougal's example. The water was faintly bitter, but cold, and not unpalatable. I drank some, then splashed my face. The road had been dusty.

I looked up, face dripping, to find him watching me with a very odd expression. Something between curiosity and calculation, I thought.

"Bit of a climb for a drink, isn't it?" I asked lightly. There were water bottles on the horses. And I doubted that Dougal meant to petition the patron of the spring for our safe journey back to the inn. He struck me as a believer in more worldly methods.

"How well d'ye know the Captain?" he asked abruptly.

"Less well than you," I snapped back. "I've met him once before today, and that by accident. We didn't get on."

Surprisingly, the stern face lightened a bit.

"Well," he admitted, "I canna say as I care for the man much myself." He drummed his fingers on the well coping, considering something. "He's well-thought of by some, though," he said, eyeing me. "A brave soldier and a bonny fighter, by what I hear."

I raised my eyebrows. "Not being an English general, I am

not impressed." He laughed, showing startlingly white teeth. The sound disturbed three rooks in the tree overhead, who flapped off, full of hoarse complaint.

"Are ye a spy for the English or the French?" he asked, with another bewildering change of subject. At least he was being direct, for a change.

"Certainly not," I said crossly. "I'm plain Claire Beauchamp, and nothing more." I soaked my handkerchief in the water and used it to wipe my neck. Small refreshing trickles ran down my back under the grey serge of my traveling gown. I pressed the wet cloth to my bosom and squeezed, producing a similar effect.

Dougal was silent for several minutes, watching me intently as I conducted my haphazard ablutions.

"You've seen Jamie's back," he said suddenly.

"I could hardly help doing so," I said a little coldly. I had given up wondering what he was up to with these disconnected questions. Presumably he would tell me when he was ready.

"You mean did I know Randall did it, then? Or did you know that yourself?"

"Aye, *I* kent it well enough," he answered, calmly appraising me, "but I wasna aware that *you* did."

I shrugged, implying that what I knew and what I didn't were hardly his concern.

"I was there, ye ken," he said, casually.

"Where?"

"At Fort William. I had a bit of business there, with the garrison. The clerk there knew Jamie was some kin to me, and sent me word when they arrested him. So I went along to see could aught be done for him."

"Apparently you weren't very successful," I said, with an edge.

Dougal shrugged. "Unfortunately not. Had it been the regular sergeant-major in charge, I might ha' saved Jamie at least the second go-round, but as it was, Randall was new in command. He didna know me, and was indisposed to listen much to what I said. I thought at the time, it was only he meant to make an example of Jamie, to show everyone at the start that there'd be no softness from him." He tapped the short sword he wore at his belt. "It's a sound enough principle, when you're in command of men. Earn their respect before ye do aught else. And if you canna do that, earn their fear."

I remembered the expression on the face of Randall's corporal, and thought I knew which route the captain had taken.

Dougal's deep-set eyes were on my face, interested.

"You knew it was Randall. Did Jamie tell ye about it?"

"A bit," I said cautiously.

"He must think well of ye," he said musingly. "He doesna generally speak of it to anyone."

"I can't imagine why not," I said, provoked. I still held my breath each time we came to a new tavern or inn, until it was clear that the company had settled for an evening of drinking and gossip by the fire. Dougal smiled sardonically, clearly knowing what was in my mind.

"Well, it wasna necessary to tell me, was it? Since I kent it already." He swished a hand idly through the strange dark water, stirring up brimstone fumes.

"I'd not know how it goes in Oxfordshire," he said, with a sarcastic emphasis that made me squirm slightly, "but hereabouts, ladies are generally not exposed to such sights as floggings. Have ye ever seen one?"

"No, nor do I much want to," I responded sharply. "I can imagine what it would take to make marks like the ones on Jamie's back, though."

Dougal shook his head, flipping water out of the pool at a curious jay that ventured close.

"Now, there you're wrong, lass, and you'll pardon my saying so. Imagination is all verra well, but it isna equal to the sight of a man having his back laid open. A verra nasty thing— it's meant to break a man, and most often it succeeds."

"Not with Jamie." I spoke rather more sharply than I had intended. Jamie was my patient, and to some extent, my friend as well. I had no wish to discuss his personal history with Dougal, though I would, if pressed, admit to a certain morbid curiosity. I had never met anyone more open and at the same time more mysterious than the tall young MacTavish.

Dougal laughed shortly and wiped his wet hand through his hair, pasting back the strands that had escaped during our flight—for so I thought of it—from the tavern.

"Weel, Jamie's as stubborn as the rest of his family—like rocks, the lot of them, and he's the worst." But there was a definite tone of respect in his voice, grudging though it was.

"Jamie told ye he was flogged for escape?"

"Yes."

"Aye, he went over the wall of the camp just after dark, same day as the dragoons brought him in. That was a fairly frequent occurrence there, the prisoners' accommodations not bein' as secure as might be wished, so the English ran patrols near the walls every night. The garrison clerk told me Jamie put up a good fight, from the look of him when he came back, but it was six against one, and the six all wi' muskets, so it didna last long. Jamie spent the night in chains, and went to the whipping post first thing in the morning." He paused, checking me for signs of faintness or nausea, I supposed.

"Floggings were done right after assembly, so as to start everyone off in the proper frame of mind for the day. There were three to be flogged that day, and Jamie was the last of them."

"You actually *saw* it?"

"Oh, aye. And I'll tell ye, lass, watchin' men bein' flogged is not pleasant. I've had the good fortune never to experience it, but I expect bein' flogged is not verra pleasant, either. Watching it happen to someone else while waitin' for it yourself is probably least pleasant of all."

"I don't doubt it," I murmured.

Dougal nodded. "Jamie looked grim enough, but he didna turn a hair, even listening to the screams and the other noises —did ye know ye can *hear* the flesh being torn?"

"Ugh!"

"So I thought myself, lass," he said, grimacing in memory of it. "To say nothing of the blood and bruises. Ech!" He spat, carefully avoiding the pool and its coping. "Turned my stomach to see, and I'm no a squeamish man by any means."

Dougal went on with his ghastly story.

"Come Jamie's turn, he walks up to the post—some men have to be dragged, but not him—and holds out his hands so the corporal can unlock the manacles he's wearing. The corporal goes to pull his arm, like, to haul him into place, but Jamie shakes him off and steps back a pace. I was half expectin' him to make a dash for it, but instead he just pulls off his shirt. It's torn here and there and filthy as a clout, but he folds it up careful like it was his Sunday best, and lays it on the ground. Then he walks over to the post steady as a soldier and puts his hands up to be bound."

Dougal shook his head, marveling. The sunlight filtering through the rowan leaves dappled him with lacy shadows, so he looked like a man seen through a doily. I smiled at the thought, and he nodded approvingly at me, thinking my response due to his story.

"Aye, lass, courage like that is uncommon rare. It wasna ignorance, mind; he'd just seen two men flogged and he knew the same was coming to him. It's just he had made up his mind there was no help for it. Boldness in battle is nothing out of the way for a Scotsman, ye ken, but to face down fear in cold blood is rare in any man. He was but nineteen at the time," Dougal added as an afterthought.

"Must have been rather gruesome to watch," I said ironically. "I wonder you weren't sick."

Dougal saw the irony, and let it lie. "I nearly was, lass," he said, lifting his dark brows. "The first lash drew blood, and the lad's back was half red and half blue within a minute. He didna scream, though, or beg for mercy, or twist round to try and save himself. He just set his forehead hard against the post and stood there. He flinched when the lash hit, of course, but nothin' more. I doubt I could do that," he admitted, "nor are there many that could. He fainted half through it, and they roused him wi' water from a jug and finished it."

"Very nasty indeed," I observed. "Why are you telling me about it?"

"I havena finished telling ye about it." Dougal pulled the

dirk from his belt and began to clean his fingernails with the point. He was a fastidious man, in spite of the difficulties of keeping clean on the road.

"Jamie was slumped in the ropes, with the blood running down and staining his kilt. I dinna think he'd fainted, he was just too wambly to stand for the moment. But just then Captain Randall came down into the yard. I don't know why he'd not been there to begin with; had business that delayed him, perhaps. Anyway, Jamie saw him coming, and had the presence o' mind left to close his eyes and let his head flop, like as if he were unconscious."

Dougal knitted his brows, concentrating fiercely on a recalcitrant hangnail.

"The Captain was fair put out that they'd flogged Jamie already; seems that was a pleasure he'd meant to have for himself. Still, not much to be done about it at the moment. But then he thought to make inquiries about how Jamie came to escape in the first place."

He held up the dirk, examining it for nicks, then began to sharpen the edge against the stone he sat on. "Had several soldiers shaking in their boots before he was done—the man's a way wi' words, I'll say that for him."

"That he has," I said dryly.

The dirk scraped rhythmically against the stone. Every so often, a faint spark leapt from the metal as it struck a rough patch in the rock.

"Weel, in the course of this inquiry, it came out that Jamie'd had the heel of a loaf and a bit of cheese with him when they caught him—taken it along when he went over the wall. Whereupon the Captain thinks for a moment, then smiles a smile I should hate to see on my grandmother's face. He declares that theft bein' a serious offense, the penalty should be commensurate, and sentences Jamie on the spot to another hundred lashes."

I flinched in spite of myself. "That would kill him!"

Dougal nodded. "Aye, that's what the garrison doctor said. He said as he'd permit no such thing; in good conscience, the prisoner must be allowed a week to heal before receiving the second flogging."

"Well, how humanitarian of him," I said. "Good conscience, my aunt Fanny! And what did Captain Randall think of this?"

"He was none too pleased at first, but he reconciled himself. Once he did, the sergeant-major, who knew a real faint when he saw one, had Jamie untied. The lad staggered a bit, but he kept to his feet, and a few of the men there cheered, which didna go ower a treat wi' the Captain. He wasna best pleased when the sergeant picked up Jamie's shirt and handed it back to the lad, either, though it was quite a popular move with the men."

Dougal twisted the blade back and forth, examining it critically. Then he laid it across his knee and gave me a direct look.

"Ye know, lass, it's fairly easy to be brave, sittin' in a warm tavern ower a glass of ale. 'Tis not so easy, squatting in a cold field, wi' musket balls going past your head and heather ticklin' your arse. And it's still less easy when you're standing face to face wi' your enemy, wi' your own blood running down your legs."

"I wouldn't suppose so," I said. I did feel a little faint, in spite of everything. I plunged both hands into the water, letting the dark liquid chill my wrists.

"I did go back to see Randall, later in the week," Dougal said defensively, as though he felt some need to justify the action. "We talked a good bit, and I even offered him compensation—"

"Oh, I *am* impressed," I murmured, but desisted in the face of his glare. "No, I mean it. It was kind of you. I gather Randall declined your offer, though?"

"Aye, he did. And I still dinna ken why, for I've not found English officers on the whole to be ower-scrupulous when it comes to their purses, and clothes such as the Captain's come a bit dear."

"Perhaps he has—other sources of income," I suggested.

"He does, for a fact," Dougal confirmed, but with a sharp glance at me. "Still . . ." he hesitated, then proceeded, more slowly.

"I went back, then, to be there for Jamie when he came up

again, though there wasna much I could do for him at that point, poor lad."

The second time, Jamie had been the only prisoner up for flogging. The guards had removed his shirt before bringing him out, just after sunup on a cold October morning.

"I could see the lad was dead scairt," said Dougal, "though he was walking by himself and wouldna let the guard touch him. I could see him shaking, as much wi' the cold as wi' nerves, and the gooseflesh thick on his arms and chest, but the sweat was standing on his face as well."

A few minutes later, Randall came out, the whip tucked under his arm, and the lead plummets at the tips of the lashes clicking softly together as he walked. He had surveyed Jamie coolly, then motioned to the sergeant-major to turn the prisoner around to show his back.

Dougal grimaced. "A pitiful sight, it was, too—still raw, no more than half-healed, wi' the weals turned black and the rest yellow wi' bruises. The thought of a whip comin' down on that soreness was enough to make me blench, along wi' most of those watching."

Randall then turned to the sergeant-major and said, "A pretty job, Sergeant Wilkes. I must see if I can do as well." With considerable punctilio, he then called for the garrison doctor, and had him certify officially that Jamie was fit enough to be flogged.

"You've seen a cat play wi' a wee mousie?" Dougal asked. " 'Twas like that. Randall strolled round the lad, making one kind of remark and another, none of them what ye'd call pleasant. And Jamie stood there like an oak tree, sayin' nothing and keeping his eyes fixed on the post, not lookin' at Randall at all. I could see the lad was hugging his elbows to try to stop the shivering, and ye could tell Randall saw it too.

"His mouth tightened up and he says, 'I thought this was the young man who only a week past was shouting that he wasn't afraid to die. Surely a man who's not afraid to die isn't afraid of a few lashes?' and he gives Jamie a poke in the belly wi' the handle of the whip.

"Jamie met Randall's eye straight on then, and said, 'No, but I'm afraid I'll freeze stiff before ye're done talking.' "

Dougal sighed. "Well. It was a braw speech, but damn reckless, for a' that. Now, scourging a man is never a pretty business, but there's ways to make it worse than it might be; strikin' sideways to cut deep, or steppin' in wi' a hard blow ower the kidneys, for instance." He shook his head. "Verra ugly."

He frowned, choosing his words slowly.

"Randall's face was—intent, I suppose ye'd say—and sort o' lighted up, like when a man is lookin' at a lass he's soft on, if ye know what I mean. 'Twas as though he were doin' somethin' much worse to Jamie than just skinning him alive. The blood was running down the lad's legs by the fifteenth stroke, and the tears running down his face wi' the sweat."

I swayed a little, and put out a hand to the stone of the coping.

Well," he said abruptly, catching sight of my expression, "I'll say no more except that he lived through it. When the corporal untied his hands, he nearly fell, but the corporal and sergeant-major each caught him by an arm and kind o' steadied him 'til he could keep his feet. He was shakin' worse than ever from shock and cold, but his head was up and his eyes blazin'—I could see it from twenty feet away. He keeps his eyes fixed on Randall while they help him off the platform, leavin' bloody footprints—it's like watchin' Randall is the only thing keeping him on his feet. Randall's face was almost as white as Jamie's, and his eyes were locked wi' the lad's—as though either of them would fall if he took his eyes away." Dougal's own eyes were fixed, still seeing the eerie scene.

Everything was quiet in the small glade except for the faint rush of wind through the leaves of the rowan tree. I closed my eyes and listened to it for some time.

"Why?" I asked finally, eyes still closed. "Why did you tell me?"

Dougal was watching me intently when I opened my eyes. I dipped a hand in the spring again, and applied the cool water to my temples.

"I thought it might serve as what ye may call a character illustration," he said.

"Of Randall?" I uttered a short, mirthless laugh. "I don't need any further evidence as to his character, thank you."

"Of Randall," he agreed, "and Jamie too."

I looked at him, suddenly ill at ease.

"Ye see, I have *orders,*" he emphasized the word sarcastically, "from the good captain."

"Orders to do what?" I asked, the agitated feeling increasing.

"To produce the person of an English subject, one Claire Beauchamp by name, at Fort William on Monday, the 18th of June. For questioning."

I must have looked truly alarming, for he jumped to his feet and came over to me.

"Put your head between your knees, lass," he instructed, pushing on the back of my neck, " 'til the faintness passes off."

"I know what to do," I said irritably, doing it nonetheless. I closed my eyes, feeling the ebbing blood begin to throb in my temples again. The clammy sensation around my face and ears began to disappear, though my hands were still icy. I concentrated on breathing properly, counting *in* -one-two-three-four, *out* -one-two, *in* -one-two-three-four. . . .

At length I sat up, feeling more or less in possession of all my faculties. Dougal had resumed his seat on the stone coping, and was waiting patiently, watching to be sure that I didn't fall backward into the spring.

"There's a way out of it," he said abruptly. "The only one I can see."

"Lead me to it," I said, with an unconvincing attempt at a smile.

"Verra well, then." He sat forward, leaning toward me to explain. "Randall's the right to take ye for questioning because you're a subject of the English crown. Well, then, we must change that."

I stared at him, uncomprehending. "What do you mean? You're a subject of the crown as well, aren't you? How would you change such a thing?"

"Scots law and English law are verra similar," he said,

frowning, "but no the same. And an English officer canna compel the person of a Scot, unless he's firm evidence of a crime committed, or grounds for serious suspicions. Even with suspicion, he could no remove a Scottish subject from clan lands without the permission of the laird concerned."

"You've been talking to Ned Gowan," I said, beginning to feel a little dizzy again.

He nodded. "Aye, I have. I thought it might come to this, ye ken. And what he told me is what I thought myself; the only way I can legally refuse to give ye to Randall is to change ye from an Englishwoman into a Scot."

"Into a Scot?" I said, the dazed feeling quickly being replaced by a horrible suspicion.

This was confirmed by his next words.

"Aye," he said, nodding at my expression. "Ye must marry a Scot. Young Jamie."

"I couldn't do that!"

"Weel," he frowned, considering. "I suppose ye could take Rupert, instead. He's a widower, and he's the lease of a small farm. Still, he's a good bit older, and—"

"I don't want to marry Rupert, either! That's the . . . the most absurd . . ." Words failed me. Springing to my feet in agitation, I paced around the small clearing, fallen rowan berries crunching under my feet.

"Jamie's a goodly lad," Dougal argued, still sitting on the coping. "He's not much in the way of property just now, true, but he's a kind-hearted lad. He'd not be cruel to ye. And he's a bonny fighter, with verra good reason to hate Randall. Nay, marry him, and he'll fight to his last breath to protect ye."

"But . . . but I *can't* marry anyone!" I burst out.

Dougal's eyes were suddenly sharp. "Why not, lass? Do ye have a husband living still?"

"No. It's just . . . it's ridiculous! Such things don't happen!"

Dougal had relaxed when I said "No." Now he glanced up at the sun and rose to go.

"Best get moving, lass. There are things we'll have to attend to. There'll have to be a special dispensation," he murmured, as though to himself. "But Ned can manage that."

He took my arm, still muttering to himself. I wrenched it away.

"I will not marry anyone," I said firmly.

He seemed undisturbed by this, merely raising his brows.

"You *want* me to take you to Randall?"

"No!" Something occurred to me. "So at least you believe me when I say I'm not an English spy?"

"I do *now*." He spoke with some emphasis.

"Why now and not before?"

He nodded at the spring, and at the worn figure etched in the rock. It must be hundreds of years old, much older even than the giant rowan tree that shaded the spring and cast its white flowers into the black water.

"St. Ninian's spring. Ye drank the water before I asked ye."

I was thoroughly bewildered by this time.

"What does that have to do with it?"

He looked surprised, then his mouth twisted in a smile. "Ye didna know? They call it the liar's spring, as well. The water smells o' the fumes of hell. Anyone who drinks the water and then tells untruth will ha' the gizzard burnt out of him."

"I see." I spoke between my teeth. "Well, my gizzard is quite intact. So you can believe me when I say I'm not a spy, English *or* French. And you can believe something else, Dougal MacKenzie. I'm not marrying anyone!"

He wasn't listening. In fact, he had already pushed his way through the bushes that screened the spring. Only a quivering oak branch marked his passage. Seething, I followed him.

I remonstrated at some length further on the ride back to the inn. Dougal advised me finally to save my breath to cool my parritch with, and after that we rode in silence.

Reaching the inn, I flung my reins to the ground and stamped upstairs to the refuge of my room.

The whole idea was not only outrageous, but unthinkable. I paced around and around the narrow room, feeling increasingly like a rat in a trap. Why in hell hadn't I had the nerve to steal away from the Scots earlier, whatever the risk?

I sat down on the bed and tried to think calmly. Considered strictly from Dougal's point of view, no doubt the idea had merit. If he refused point-blank to hand me over to Randall, with no excuse, the Captain might easily try to take me by force. And whether he believed me or not, Dougal might understandably not want to engage in a skirmish with a lot of English dragoons for my sake.

And, viewed in cold blood, the idea had some merit from my side as well. If I were married to a Scot, I would presumably no longer be watched and guarded. It would be that much easier to get away when the time came. And if it were Jamie—well, he liked me, clearly. And he knew the Highlands like the backs of his hands. He would perhaps take me to Craigh na Dun, or at least in the general direction. Yes, possibly marriage was the best way to gain my goal.

That was the cold-blooded way to look at it. My blood, however, was anything but cold. I was hot with fury and agitation, and could not keep still, pacing and fuming, looking for a way out. Any way. After an hour of this, my face was flushed and my head throbbing. I got up and threw open the shutters, sticking my head out into the cooling breeze.

There was a peremptory rap on the door behind me. Dougal entered as I pulled my head in. He bore a sheaf of stiff paper like a salver and was followed by Rupert and the immaculate Ned Gowan, bringing up the rear like royal equerries.

"Please do come in," I said courteously.

Ignoring me as usual, Dougal removed a chamber pot from its resting place on the table and fanned the sheets of paper out ceremoniously on the rough oak surface.

"All done," he said, with the pride of one who has shepherded a difficult project to a successful conclusion. "Ned's drawn up the papers; nothing like a lawyer—so long as he's on your side, eh, Ned?"

The men all laughed, evidently in good humor.

"Not really difficult, ye ken," Ned said modestly. "It's but a simple contract." He riffled the pages with a proprietary forefinger, then paused, wrinkling his brow at a sudden thought.

"You've no property in France, have ye?" he asked, peering worriedly at me over the half-spectacles he wore for close work. I shook my head, and he relaxed, shuffling the papers back into a pile and tapping the edges neatly together.

"That's that, then. You'll only need to sign here at the foot, and Dougal and Rupert to witness."

The lawyer set down the inkpot he had brought in, and whipping a clean quill from his pocket, presented it ceremoniously to me.

"And just what is this?" I asked. This was in the nature of a rhetorical question, for the top page of the bundle said CONTRACT OF MARRIAGE in a clear calligraphic hand, the letters two inches high and starkly black across the page.

Dougal suppressed a sigh of impatience at my recalcitrance.

"Ye ken quite weel what it is," he said shortly. "And unless you've had another bright thought for keeping yourself out of Randall's hands, you'll sign it and have done with it. Time's short."

Bright thoughts were in particularly short supply at the moment, despite the hour I had spent hammering away at the problem. It really began to seem that this incredible alternative was the best I could do, struggle as I might.

"But I don't *want* to marry!" I said stubbornly. It occurred to me as well that mine was not the only point of view involved. I remembered the girl with blond hair I had seen kissing Jamie in the alcove at the castle.

"And maybe Jamie doesn't want to marry me!" I said. "What about that?" Dougal dismissed this as unimportant.

"Jamie's a soldier; he'll do as he's told. So will you," he said pointedly, "unless, of course, ye'd prefer an English prison."

I glared at him, breathing heavily. I had been in a stir ever since our abrupt removal from Randall's office, and my level of agitation had now increased substantially, confronted with the choice in black and white, as it were.

"I want to talk to him," I said abruptly. Dougal's eyebrows shot up.

"Jamie? Why?"

"*Why?* Because you're forcing me to marry him, and so far as I can see, you haven't even told him!"

Plainly this was an irrelevancy, as far as Dougal was concerned, but he eventually gave in and, accompanied by his minions, went to fetch Jamie from the taproom below.

Jamie appeared shortly, looking understandably bewildered.

"Did you know that Dougal wants us to marry?" I demanded bluntly.

His expression cleared. "Oh, aye. I knew that."

"But surely," I said, "a young man like yourself; I mean, isn't there anyone else you're, ah, interested in?" He looked blank for a moment, then understanding dawned.

"Oh, am I promised? Nay, I'm no much of a prospect for a girl." He hurried on, as though feeling this might sound insulting. "I mean, I've no property to speak of, and nothing more than a soldier's pay to live on."

He rubbed his chin, eyeing me dubiously. "Then there's the minor difficulty that I've a price on my head. No father much wants his daughter married to a man as may be arrested and hanged any time. Did ye think of that?"

I flapped my hand, dismissing the matter of outlawry as a minor consideration, compared to the whole monstrous idea. I had one last try.

"Does it bother you that I'm not a virgin?" He hesitated a moment before answering.

"Well, no," he said slowly, "so long as it doesna bother you that I am." He grinned at my drop-jawed expression, and backed toward the door.

"Reckon one of us should know what they're doing," he said. The door closed softly behind him; clearly the courtship was over.

⟶

The papers duly signed, I made my way cautiously down the inn's steep stairs and over to the bar table in the taproom.

"Whisky," I said to the rumpled old creature behind it. He glared rheumily, but a nod from Dougal made him oblige with a bottle and glass. The latter was thick and greenish, a bit smeared, with a chip out of the rim, but it had a hole in the top, and that was all that mattered at the moment.

Once the searing effect of swallowing the stuff had passed, it did induce a certain spurious calmness. I felt detached, noticing details of my surroundings with a peculiar intensity: the small stained-glass inset over the bar, casting colored shadows over the ruffianly proprietor and his wares, the curve of the handle on a copper-bottomed dipper that hung on the wall next to me, a green-bellied fly struggling on the edges of a sticky puddle on the table. With a certain amount of fellow-feeling, I nudged it out of danger with the edge of my glass.

I gradually became aware of raised voices behind the closed door on the far side of the room. Dougal had disappeared there after the conclusion of his business with me, presumably to firm up arrangements with the other contracting party. I was pleased to hear that, judging from the sound of it, my intended bridegroom was cutting up rough, despite his apparent lack of objection earlier. Perhaps he hadn't wanted to offend me.

"Stick to it, lad," I murmured, and took another gulp.

Sometime later, I was dimly conscious of a hand prying my fingers open in order to remove the greenish glass. Another hand was steadyingly under my elbow.

"Christ, she's drunk as an auld besom in a bothy," said a voice in my ear. The voice rasped unpleasantly, I thought, as though its owner had been eating sandpaper. I giggled softly at the thought.

"Quiet yerself, woman!" said the unpleasant rasping voice. It grew fainter as the owner turned to talk to someone else. "Drunk as a laird and screechin' like a parrot—what do ye expect—"

Another voice interrupted the first, but I couldn't tell what it said; the words were blurred and indistinguishable. It was a pleasanter sound, though, deep and somehow reassuring. It came nearer, and I could make out a few words. I made an effort to focus, but my attention had begun to wander again.

The fly had found its way back to the puddle, and was floundering in the middle, hopelessly mired. The light from the stained-glass window fell on it, glittering like sparks on the straining green belly. My gaze fixed on the tiny green spot, which seemed to pulsate as the fly twitched and struggled.

"Brother . . . you haven't a shance," I said, and the spark went out.

14

A Marriage Takes Place

There was a low, beamed ceiling over me when I woke, and a thick quilt tucked tidily under my chin. I seemed to be clad only in my shift. I started to sit up to look for my clothes, but thought better of it halfway up. I eased myself very carefully back down, closed my eyes and held on to my head to prevent it from rolling off the pillow and bouncing on the floor.

I woke again, sometime later, when the door of the room opened. I cracked one eye cautiously. A wavering outline resolved itself into the dour figure of Murtagh, staring disapprovingly down at me from the foot of the bed. I closed the eye. I heard a muffled Scottish noise, presumably indicating appalled disgust, but when I looked again he was gone.

I was just sinking thankfully back into unconsciousness when the door opened again, this time to reveal a middle-aged woman I took to be the publican's wife, carrying a ewer and basin. She bustled cheerily into the room and banged the shutters open with a crash that reverberated through my head like a tank collision. Advancing on the bed like a Panzer division, she ripped the quilt from my feeble grasp and tossed it aside, leaving me quaking and exposed.

"Come along then, me love," she said. "We mun get ye ready now." She put a hefty forearm behind my shoulders and levered me into a sitting position. I clutched my head with one hand, my stomach with the other.

"Ready?" I said, through a mouth filled with decayed moss.

The woman began briskly washing my face. "Och, aye," she said. "Ye dinna want to miss yer own wedding, now, do ye?"

"Yes," I said, but was ignored as she unceremoniously stripped off my shift and stood me in the middle of the floor for further intimate attentions.

A bit later I sat on the bed, fully dressed, feeling dazed and belligerent, but thanks to a glass of port supplied by the goodwife, at least functional. I sipped carefully at a second glass, as the woman tugged a comb through the thickets of my hair.

I jumped and shuddered, spilling the port, as the door crashed open once more. One damn thing after another, I thought balefully. This time it was a double visitation, Murtagh and Ned Gowan, wearing similar looks of disapprobation. I exchanged glares with Ned while Murtagh came into the room and walked slowly around the bed, surveying me from every angle. He returned to Ned and muttered something in a tone too low for me to hear. With a final glance of despair in my direction, he pulled the door shut behind them.

At last my hair was dressed to the woman's satisfaction, swept back and pulled high in a knot at the crown, curls picked loose to tumble to the back, and ringlets in front of my ears. It felt as though my scalp were going to pop off from the tension of the strained-back hair, but the effect in the looking glass the woman provided was undeniably becoming. I began to feel slightly more human, and even brought myself to thank her for her efforts. She left me the looking glass, and departed, remarking that it was so lucky to be married in summer, wasn't it, as I'd have plenty of flowers for my hair.

"We who are about to die," I said to my reflection, sketching a salute in the glass. I collapsed on the bed, plastered a wet cloth over my face, and went back to sleep.

I was having a rather nice dream, something to do with grassy fields and wildflowers, when I became aware that what I had thought a playful breeze tugging at my sleeves was a pair of none-too-gentle hands. I sat up with a jerk, blindly flailing.

When I got my eyes open, I saw that my small chamber now resembled a Tube station, with faces wall-to-wall: Ned Gowan, Murtagh, the innkeeper, the innkeeper's wife, and a lanky young man, who turned out to be the innkeeper's son, with his arms full of assorted flowers, which accounted for the scents in my dream. There was also a young woman, armed with a round wicker basket, who smiled amiably at me, displaying the lack of several rather important teeth.

This person, it developed, was the village sempstress, recruited to repair the deficiencies of my wardrobe by adjusting the fit of a dress, obtained on short notice from some local connection of the innkeeper's. Ned was carrying the dress in question, hanging from one hand like a dead animal. Smoothed out on the bed, it proved to be a low-necked gown of heavy cream-colored satin, with a separate bodice that buttoned with dozens of tiny cloth-covered buttons, each embroidered with a gold fleur-de-lis. The neckline and the belled sleeves were heavily ruched with lace, as was the embroidered overskirt of chocolate-brown velvet. The innkeeper was half-buried in the petticoats he carried, his bristling whiskers barely visible over the foamy layers.

I looked at the port-wine stain on my grey serge skirt and vanity won out. If I were in fact to be married, I didn't want to do it looking like the village drudge.

After a short spell of frenetic activity, with me standing like a dressmaker's dummy and everyone else racing about fetching, carrying, criticizing, and tripping over each other, the final product was ready, complete to white asters and yellow roses pinned in my hair and a heart pounding madly away beneath the lacy bodice. The fit was not quite perfect, and the gown smelled rather strongly of its previous owner, but the satin was weighty and swished rather fascinatingly about my feet, over the layers of petticoats. I felt quite regal, and not a little lovely.

"You can't make me do this, you know," I hissed threateningly at Murtagh's back as I followed him downstairs, but he and I both knew my words were empty bravado. If I had ever had the strength of character to defy Dougal and take my chances with the English, it had drained away with the whisky.

Dougal, Ned, and the rest were in the main taproom at the foot of the stair, drinking and exchanging pleasantries with a few villagers who seemed to have nothing better to do with their afternoon than hang about getting sloshed.

Dougal caught sight of me slowly descending, and abruptly stopped talking. The others fell silent as well, and I floated down in a most gratifying cloud of reverent admiration. Dougal's deep-set eyes covered me slowly from head to foot and returned to my face with a completely ungrudging nod of acknowledgment.

What with one thing and another, it was some time since a man had looked at me that way, and I nodded quite graciously back.

After the first silence, the rest of those in the taproom became vocal in their admiration, and even Murtagh allowed himself a small smile, nodding in satisfaction at the results of his efforts. *And who appointed* you *fashion editor?* I thought disagreeably. Still, I had to admit that he was responsible for my not marrying in grey serge.

Marrying. Oh, God. Buoyed temporarily by port wine and cream lace, I had momentarily managed to ignore the significance of the occasion. I gripped the banister as fresh realization hit like a blow in the stomach.

Looking over the throng, though, I noticed one glaring omission. My groom was nowhere in sight. Heartened by the thought that he might have succeeded in escaping out of a window, and be miles away by now, I accepted a parting cup of wine from the innkeeper before following Dougal outside.

Ned and Rupert went to fetch the horses. Murtagh had disappeared somewhere, perhaps to search for traces of Jamie.

Dougal held me by one arm; ostensibly to support me lest I stumble in my satin slippers, in reality to prevent any last-minute breaks for freedom.

It was a "warm" Scottish day, meaning that the mist wasn't quite heavy enough to qualify as a drizzle, but not far off, either. Suddenly the inn door opened, and the sun came out, in the person of James. If I was a radiant bride, the groom was positively resplendent. My mouth fell open and stayed that way.

A Highlander in full regalia is an impressive sight—any Highlander, no matter how old, ill-favored, or crabbed in appearance. A tall, straight-bodied, and by no means ill-favored young Highlander at close range is breath-taking.

The thick red-gold hair had been brushed to a smooth gleam that swept the collar of a fine lawn shirt with tucked front, belled sleeves, and lace-trimmed wrist frills that matched the cascade of the starched jabot at the throat, decorated with a ruby stickpin.

His tartan was a brilliant crimson and black that blazed among the more sedate MacKenzies in their green and white. The flaming wool, fastened by a circular silver brooch, fell from his right shoulder in a graceful drape, caught by a silver-studded sword belt before continuing its sweep past neat calves clothed in woolen hose and stopping just short of the silver-buckled black leather boots. Sword, dirk, and badger-skin sporran completed the ensemble.

Well over six feet tall, broad in proportion, and striking of feature, he was a far cry from the grubby horse-handler I was accustomed to—and he knew it. Making a leg in courtly fashion, he swept me a bow of impeccable grace, murmuring "Your servant, ma'am," eyes glinting with mischief.

"Oh," I said faintly.

I had seldom seen the taciturn Dougal at a loss for words before. Thick brows knotted over a suffused face, he seemed in his way as taken aback by this apparition as I was.

"Are ye mad, man?" he said at last. "What if someone's to see ye!"

Jamie cocked a sardonic eyebrow at the older man. "Why, uncle," he said. "Insults? And on my wedding day too. You wouldna have me shame my wife, now, would ye? Besides," he added, with a malicious gleam, "I hardly think it would be legal, did I not marry in my own name. And you do want it legal, now, don't you?"

With an apparent effort, Dougal recovered his self-possession. "If ye're quite finished, Jamie, we'll get on wi' it," he said.

But Jamie was not quite finished, it seemed. Ignoring Dougal's fuming, he drew a short string of white beads from his sporran. He stepped forward and fastened the necklace around my neck. Looking down, I could see it was a string of small baroque pearls, those irregularly shaped productions of freshwater mussels, interspersed with tiny pierced-work gold roundels. Smaller pearls dangled from the gold beads.

"They're only Scotch pearls," he said, apologetically, "but they look bonny on you." His fingers lingered a moment on my neck.

"Those were your mother's pearls!" said Dougal, glowering at the necklace.

"Aye," said Jamie calmly, "and now they're my wife's. Shall we go?"

→

Wherever we were going, it was some distance from the village. We made a rather morose wedding party, the bridal pair encircled by the others like convicts being escorted toward some distant prison. The only conversation was a muted apology from Jamie for being late, explaining that there had been some difficulty in finding a clean shirt and coat large enough to fit him.

"I think this one belongs to the local squire's son," he said, flipping the lacy jabot. "Bit of a dandy, it looks like."

We dismounted and left the horses at the foot of a small hill. A footpath led upward through the heather.

"Ye've made the arrangements?" I heard Dougal say in an undertone to Rupert, as they tethered the beasts.

"Och, aye." There was a flash of teeth in the black beard. "Was a bit o' trouble to persuade the padre, but we showed him the special license." He patted his sporran, which clinked musically, giving me some idea of the nature of the special license.

Through the drizzle and mist, I saw the chapel jutting out of the heather. With a sense of complete disbelief, I saw the round-shouldered roof and the odd little many-paned windows, which I had last seen on the bright sunny morning of my marriage to Frank Randall.

"No!" I exclaimed. "Not here! I can't!"

"Hst, now, hst. Dinna worry, lass, dinna worry. It will be

all right." Dougal put a large paw on my shoulder, making soothing Scottish noises, as if I were a skittish horse. " 'Tis natural to be a bit nervous," he said, to all of us. A firm hand in the small of my back urged me on up the path. My shoes sank moistly in the damp layer of fallen leaves.

Jamie and Dougal walked close on either side of me, preventing escape. Their looming plaid presences were unnerving, and I felt a mounting sense of hysteria. Two hundred years ahead, more or less, I had been married in this chapel, charmed then by its ancient picturesqueness. The chapel now was creaking with newness, its boards not yet settled into charm, and I was about to marry a twenty-three-year-old Scottish Catholic virgin with a price on his head, whose—

I turned to Jamie in sudden panic. "I can't marry you! I don't even know your last name!"

He looked down at me and cocked a ruddy eyebrow. "Oh. It's Fraser. James Alexander Malcolm MacKenzie Fraser." He pronounced it formally, each name slow and distinct.

Completely flustered, I said "Claire Elizabeth Beauchamp," and stuck out my hand idiotically. Apparently taking this as a plea for support, he took the hand and tucked it firmly into the crook of his elbow. Thus inescapably pinioned, I squelched up the path to my wedding.

Rupert and Murtagh were waiting for us in the chapel, keeping guard over a captive cleric, a spindly young priest with a red nose and a justifiably terrified expression. Rupert was idly slicing a willow twig with a large knife, and while he had laid aside his horn-handled pistols on entering the church, they remained in easy reach on the rim of the baptismal font.

The other men also disarmed, as was suitable in the house of God, leaving an impressively bristling pile of lethality in the back pew. Only Jamie kept his dagger and sword, presumably as a ceremonial part of his dress.

We knelt before the wooden altar, Murtagh and Dougal took their places as witnesses, and the ceremony began.

The form of the Catholic marriage service has not changed appreciably in several hundred years, and the words linking me with the redheaded young stranger at my side were much the same as those that had consecrated my wedding to Frank.

I felt like a cold, hollow shell. The young priest's stammering words echoed somewhere in the empty pit of my stomach.

I stood automatically when it came time for the vows, watching in a sort of numbed fascination as my chilly fingers disappeared into my bridegroom's substantial grasp. His fingers were as cold as my own, and it occurred to me for the first time that despite his outwardly cool demeanor, he might be as nervous as I was.

I had so far avoided looking at him, but now glanced up to find him staring down at me. His face was white and carefully expressionless; he looked as he had when I dressed the wound in his shoulder. I tried to smile at him, but the corners of my mouth wobbled precariously. The pressure of his fingers on mine increased. I had the impression that we were holding each other up; if either of us let go or looked away, we would both fall down. Oddly, the feeling was mildly reassuring. Whatever we were in for, at least there were two of us.

"I take thee, Claire, to be my wife . . ." His voice didn't shake, but his hand did. I tightened my grip. Our stiff fingers clenched together like boards in a vise. ". . . to love, honor and protect . . . for better and for worse . . ." The words came from far away. The blood was draining from my head. The boned bodice was infernally tight, and though I felt cold, sweat ran down my sides beneath the satin. I hoped I wouldn't faint.

There was a small stained-glass window set high in the wall at the side of the sanctuary, a crude rendering of John the Baptist in his bearskin. Green and blue shadows flowed over my sleeve, reminding me of the tavern's public room, and I wished fervently for a drink.

My turn. I stuttered slightly, to my fury. "I t-take thee, James . . ." I stiffened my spine. Jamie had got through his half creditably enough; I could try to do as well. ". . . to have and to hold, from this day forth . . ." My voice came stronger now.

" 'Til death us do part." The words rang out in the quiet chapel with a startling finality. Everything was still, as though in suspended animation. Then the priest asked for the ring.

There was a sudden stir of agitation and I caught a glimpse

of Murtagh's stricken face. I barely registered the fact that someone had forgotten to provide for the ring, when Jamie released my hand long enough to twist a ring from his own finger.

I still wore Frank's ring on my left hand. The fingers of my right looked frozen, pallid and stiff in a pool of blue light, as the large metal circlet passed over the fourth finger. It hung loose on the digit and would have slid off, had Jamie not folded my fingers around it and enclosed my fist once more in his own.

More mumbling from the priest, and Jamie bent to kiss me. It was clear that he intended only a brief and ceremonial touching of lips, but his mouth was soft and warm and I moved instinctively toward him. I was vaguely conscious of noises, Scottish whoops of enthusiasm and encouragement from the spectators, but really noticed nothing beyond the enfolding warm solidness. Sanctuary.

We drew apart, both a little steadier, and smiled nervously. I saw Dougal draw Jamie's dirk from its sheath and wondered why. Still looking at me, Jamie held out his right hand, palm up. I gasped as the point of the dirk scored deeply across his wrist, leaving a dark line of welling blood. There was not time to jerk away before my own hand was seized and I felt the burning slice of the blade. Swiftly, Dougal pressed my wrist to Jamie's and bound the two together with a strip of white linen.

I must have swayed a bit, because Jamie gripped my elbow with his free left hand.

"Bear up, lass," he urged softly. "It's not long now. Say the words after me." It was a short bit of Gaelic, two or three sentences. The words meant nothing to me, but I obediently repeated them after Jamie, stumbling on the slippery vowels. The linen was untied, the wounds blotted clean, and we were married.

There was a general air of relief and exhilaration on the way back down the footpath. It might have been any merry wedding party, albeit a small one, and one composed entirely of men, save the bride.

We were nearly at the bottom when lack of food, the remnants of a hangover, and the general stresses of the day caught up with me. I came to lying on damp leaves, my head in my new husband's lap. He put down the wet cloth with which he had been wiping my face.

"That bad, was it?" He grinned down at me, but his eyes held an uncertain expression that rather touched me, in spite of everything. I smiled shakily back.

"It's not you," I assured him. "It's just . . . I don't think I've had anything at all to eat since breakfast yesterday—and rather a lot to drink, I'm afraid."

His mouth twitched. "So I heard. Well, that I can remedy. I've not a lot to offer a wife, as I said, but I do promise I'll keep ye fed." He smiled and shyly pushed a stray curl off my face with a forefinger.

I started to sit up and grimaced at a slight burning in one wrist. I had forgotten that last bit of the ceremony. The cut had come open, no doubt as a result of the fall I had taken. I took the cloth from Jamie and wrapped it awkwardly around the wrist.

"I thought it might have been that that made ye faint," he said, watching. "I should have thought to warn ye about it; I didna realize you weren't expecting it until I saw your face."

"What was it, exactly?" I asked, trying to tuck in the ends of the cloth.

"It's a bit pagan, but it's customary hereabouts to have a blood vow, along with the regular marriage service. Some priests won't have it, but I don't suppose this one was likely to object to anything. He looked almost as scared as I felt," he said, smiling.

"A blood vow? What do the words mean?"

Jamie took my right hand and gently tucked in the last end of the makeshift bandage.

"It rhymes, more or less, when ye say it in English. It says:

> *'Ye are Blood of my Blood, and Bone of my Bone.*
> *I give ye my Body, that we Two might be One.*
> *I give ye my Spirit, 'til our Life shall be Done.'* "

He shrugged. "About the same as the regular vows, just a bit more . . . ah, primitive."

I gazed down at my bound wrist. "Yes, you could say that."

I glanced about; we were alone on the path, under an aspen tree. The round dead leaves lay on the ground, gleaming in the wet like rusted coins. It was very quiet, save for the occasional splat of water droplets falling from the trees.

"Where are the others? Did they go back to the inn?"

Jamie grimaced. "No. I made them go away so I could tend ye, but they'll be waitin' for us just over there." He gestured with his chin, in the countryman's manner. "They're no going to trust us alone 'til everything's official."

"Isn't it?" I said blankly. "We're married, aren't we?"

He seemed embarrassed, turning away and elaborately brushing dead leaves from his kilts.

"Mmmphm. Aye, we're married, right enough. But it's no legally binding, ye know, until it's been consummated." A slow, fierce blush burned its way up from the lacy jabot.

"Mmmphm," I said. "Let's go and find something to eat."

15

Revelations of the Bridal Chamber

At the inn, food was readily available, in the form of a modest wedding feast, including wine, fresh bread, and roast beef.

Dougal took me by the arm as I started for the stairs to freshen myself before eating.

"I want this marriage consummated, wi' no uncertainty whatsoever," Dougal instructed me firmly in an undertone. "There's to be no question of it bein' a legal union, and no way open for annulment, or we're all riskin' our necks."

"Seems to me you're doing that anyway," I remarked crossly. "Mine, especially."

Dougal patted me firmly on the rump.

"Dinna ye worry about that; ye just do your part." He looked me over critically, as though judging my capacity to perform my role adequately.

"I kent Jamie's father. If the lad's much like him, ye'll have no trouble at all. Ah, Jamie lad!" He hurried across the room, to where Jamie had come in from stabling the horses. From the look on Jamie's face, he was getting his orders as well.

How in the name of God did this happen? I asked myself sometime later. Six weeks ago, I had been innocently collecting wildflowers on a Scottish hill to take home to my husband. I was now shut in the room of a rural inn, awaiting a completely different husband, whom I scarcely knew, with firm orders to consummate a forced marriage, at risk of my life and liberty.

I sat on the bed, stiff and terrified in my borrowed finery. There was a faint noise as the heavy door of the room swung open, then shut.

Jamie leaned against the door, watching me. The air of embarrassment between us deepened. It was Jamie who broke the silence finally.

"You dinna need to be afraid of me," he said softly. "I wasna going to jump on ye." I laughed in spite of myself.

"Well, I didn't think you would." In fact, I didn't think he would touch me, until and unless I invited him to; the fact remained that I was going to have to invite him to do considerably more than that, and soon.

I eyed him dubiously. I supposed it would be harder if I found him unattractive; in fact, the opposite was true. Still, I had not slept with any man but Frank in over eight years. Not only that, this young man, by his own acknowledgment, was completely inexperienced. I had never deflowered anyone before. Even dismissing my objections to the whole arrangement, and considering matters from a completely practical standpoint, how on earth were we to start? At this rate, we would still be standing here, staring at each other, three or four days hence.

I cleared my throat and patted the bed beside me.

"Ah, would you like to sit down?"

"Aye." He came across the room, moving like a big cat. Instead of sitting beside me, though, he pulled up a stool and sat down facing me. Somewhat tentatively, he reached out and took my hands between his own. They were large, blunt-fingered, and very warm, the backs lightly furred with reddish hairs. I felt a slight shock at the touch, and thought of an Old Testament passage—"For Jacob's skin was smooth, while his brother Esau was a hairy man." Frank's hands were long and slender, nearly hairless and aristocratic-looking. I had always loved watching them as he lectured.

"Tell me about your husband," said Jamie, as though he

had been reading my mind. I almost jerked my hands away in shock.

"What?"

"Look ye, lass. We have three or four days together here. While I dinna pretend to know all there is to know, I've lived a good bit of my life on a farm, and unless people are verra different from other animals, it isna going to take that long to do what we have to. We have a bit of time to talk, and get over being scairt of each other." This blunt appraisal of our situation relaxed me a little bit.

"Are you scared of me?" He didn't look it. Perhaps he was nervous, though. Even though he was no timid sixteen-year-old lad, this *was* the first time. He looked into my eyes and smiled.

"Aye. More scairt than you, I expect. That's why I'm holdin' your hands; to keep my own from shaking." I didn't believe this, but squeezed his hands tightly in appreciation.

"It's a good idea. It feels a little easier to talk while we're touching. Why did you ask about my husband, though?" I wondered a bit wildly if he wanted me to tell him about my sex life with Frank, so as to know what I expected of him.

"Well, I knew ye must be thinking of him. Ye could hardly not, under the circumstances. I do not want ye ever to feel as though ye canna talk of him to me. Even though I'm your husband now—that feels verra strange to say—it isna right that ye should forget him, or even try to. If ye loved him, he must ha' been a good man."

"Yes, he . . . was." My voice trembled, and Jamie stroked the backs of my hands with his thumbs.

"Then I shall do my best to honor his spirit by serving his wife." He raised my hands and kissed each one formally.

I cleared my throat. "That was a very gallant speech, Jamie."

He grinned suddenly. "Aye. I made it up while Dougal was making toasts downstairs."

I took a deep breath. "I have questions," I said.

He looked down, hiding a smile. "I'd suppose ye do," he agreed. "I imagine you're entitled to a bit of curiosity, under the circumstances. What is it ye want to know?" He looked up suddenly, blue eyes bright with mischief in the lamplight. "Why I'm a virgin yet?"

"Er, I should say that that was more or less your own business," I murmured. It seemed to be getting rather warm suddenly, and I pulled one hand free to grope for my handkerchief. As I did so, I felt something hard in the pocket of the gown.

"Oh, I forgot! I still have your ring." I drew it out and gave it back to him. It was a heavy gold circlet, set with a cabochon ruby. Instead of replacing it on his finger, he opened his sporran to put it inside.

"It was my father's wedding ring," he explained. "I dinna wear it customarily, but I . . . well, I wished to do ye honor today by looking as well as I might." He flushed slightly at this admission, and busied himself with refastening the sporran.

"You did do me great honor," I said, smiling in spite of myself. Adding a ruby ring to the blazing splendor of his costume was coals to Newcastle, but I was touched by the anxious thought behind it.

"I'll get one that fits ye, so soon as I may," he promised.

"It's not important," I said, feeling slightly uncomfortable. I meant, after all, to be gone soon.

"Er, I have one main question," I said, calling the meeting to order. "If you don't mind telling me. Why did you agree to marry me?"

"Ah." He let go of my hands and sat back a bit. He paused for a moment before answering, smoothing the woolen cloth over his thighs. I could see the long line of muscle taut under the drape of the heavy fabric.

"Well, I would ha' missed talking to ye, for one thing," he said, smiling.

"No, I mean it," I insisted. "Why?"

He sobered then. "Before I tell ye, Claire, there's the one thing I'd ask of you," he said slowly.

"What's that?"

"Honesty."

I must have flinched uncomfortably, for he leaned forward earnestly, hands on his knees.

"I know there are things ye'd not wish to tell me, Claire. Perhaps things that ye *can't* tell me."

You don't know just how right you are, I thought.

"I'll not press you, ever, or insist on knowin' things that are your own concern," he said seriously. He looked down at his hands, now pressed together, palm to palm.

"There are things that I canna tell *you,* at least not yet. And I'll ask nothing of ye that ye canna give me. But what I would ask of ye—when you do tell me something, let it be the truth. And I'll promise ye the same. We have nothing now between us, save—respect, perhaps. And I think that respect has maybe room for secrets, but not for lies. Do ye agree?" He spread his hands out, palms up, inviting me. I could see the dark line of the blood vow across his wrist. I placed my own hands lightly on his palms.

"Yes, I agree. I'll give you honesty." His fingers closed lightly about mine.

"And I shall give ye the same. Now," he drew a deep breath, "you asked why I wed ye."

"I *am* just the slightest bit curious," I said.

He smiled, the wide mouth taking up the humor that lurked in his eyes. "Well, I canna say I blame ye. I had several reasons. And in fact, there's one—maybe two—that I canna tell ye yet, though I will in time. The main reason, though, is the same reason you wed me, I imagine; to keep ye safe from the hands of Jack Randall."

I shuddered a bit at the memory of the Captain, and Jamie's hands tightened on mine.

"You *are* safe," he said firmly. "You have my name and my family, my clan, and if necessary, the protection of my body as well. The man willna lay hands on ye again, while I live."

"Thank you," I said. Looking at that strong, young, determined face, with its broad cheekbones and solid jaw, I felt for the first time that this preposterous scheme of Dougal's might actually have been a reasonable suggestion.

The protection of my body. The phrase struck with particular impact, looking at him—the resolute set of the wide shoulders and the memory of his graceful ferocity, "showing off" at swordplay in the moonlight. He meant it; and young as he was, he knew what he meant, and bore the scars to prove it. He was no older than many of the pilots and the infantrymen I had nursed, and he knew as well as they the price of commitment. It was no romantic pledge he had made me, but the blunt promise to guard my safety at the cost of his own. I hoped only that I could offer him something in return.

"That's *most* gallant of you," I said, with absolute sincerity. "But was it worth, well, worth marriage?"

"It was," he said, nodding. He smiled again, a little grimly this time. "I've good reason to know the man, ye ken. I wouldna see a dog given into his keeping if I could prevent it, let alone a helpless woman."

"How flattering," I remarked wryly, and he laughed. He stood up and went to the table near the window. Someone—perhaps the landlady—had supplied a bouquet of wildflowers, set in water in a whisky tumbler. Behind this stood two wineglasses and a bottle.

Jamie poured out two glasses and came back, handing me one as he resumed his seat.

"Not quite so good as Colum's private stock," he said with a smile, "but none so bad, either." He raised his glass briefly. "To Mrs. Fraser," he said softly, and I felt a thump of panic again. I quelled it firmly and raised my own glass.

"To honesty," I said, and we both drank.

"Well, that's one reason," I said, lowering my glass. "Are there others you can tell me?"

He studied his wineglass with some care. "Perhaps it's just that I want to bed you." He looked up abruptly. "Did ye think of that?"

If he meant to disconcert me, he was succeeding nicely, but I resolved not to show it.

"Well, do you?" I asked boldly.

"If I'm bein' honest, yes, I do." The blue eyes were steady over the rim of the glass.

"You wouldn't necessarily have had to marry me for that," I objected.

He appeared honestly scandalized. "You do not think I would take ye without offering you marriage!"

"Many men would," I said, amused at his innocence.

He sputtered a bit, at a momentary loss. Then regaining his composure, said with formal dignity, "Perhaps I am pretentious in saying so, but I would like to think that I am not 'many men,' and that I dinna necessarily place my behavior at the lowest common denominator."

Rather touched by this speech, I assured him that I had so far found his behavior both gallant and gentlemanly, and apologized for any doubt I might inadvertently have cast on his motives.

On this precariously diplomatic note, we paused while he refilled our empty glasses.

We sipped in silence for a time, both feeling a bit shy after the frankness of that last exchange. So, apparently there *was* something I could offer him. I couldn't, in fairness, say the thought had not entered my mind, even before the absurd situation in which we found ourselves arose. He was a very engaging young man. And there had been that moment, right after my arrival at the castle, when he had held me on his lap, and—

I tilted my wineglass back and drained the contents. I patted the bed beside me again.

"Sit down here with me," I said. "And"—I cast about for some neutral topic of conversation to ease us over the awkwardness of close proximity—"and tell me about your family. Where did you grow up?"

The bed sank noticeably under his weight, and I braced myself not to roll against him. He sat closely enough that the sleeve of his shirt brushed my arm. I let my hand lie open on my thigh, relaxed. He took it naturally as he sat, and we leaned against the wall, neither of us looking down, but as conscious of the link as though we had been welded together.

"Well, now, where shall I start?" He put his rather large feet up on the stool and crossed them at the ankles. With some amusement, I recognized the Highlander settling back for a leisurely dissection of that tangle of family and clan relationships which forms the background of almost any event of significance in the Scottish Highlands. Frank and I had spent one evening in the village pub, enthralled by a conversation between two old codgers, in which the responsibility for the recent destruction of an ancient barn was traced back through the intricacies of a local feud dating, so far as I could tell, from about 1790. With the sort of minor shock to which I was becoming accustomed, I realized that that particular feud, whose origins I had thought shrouded in the mists of time, had not yet begun. Suppressing the mental turmoil this realization caused, I forced my attention to what Jamie was saying.

"My father was a Fraser, of course; a younger half-brother to the present Master of Lovat. My mother was a MacKenzie, though. Ye'll know that Dougal and Colum are my uncles?" I nodded. The resemblance was clear enough, despite the difference in coloring. The broad cheekbones and long, straight, knife-edged nose were plainly a MacKenzie inheritance.

"Aye, well, my mother was their sister, and there were two more sisters, besides. My auntie Janet is dead, like my mother, but my auntie Jocasta married a cousin of Rupert's, and lives up near the edge of Loch Eilean. Auntie Janet had six children, four boys and two girls, Auntie Jocasta has three, all girls, Dougal's got the four girls, Colum has little Hamish only, and my parents had me and my sister, who's named for my Auntie Janet, but we called her Jenny always."

"Rupert's a MacKenzie, too?" I asked, already struggling to keep everyone straight.

"Aye. He's—" Jamie paused a moment considering, "he's Dougal, Colum, and Jocasta's first cousin, which makes him my second cousin. Rupert's father and my grandfather Jacob were brothers, along with—"

"Wait a minute. Don't let's go back any farther than we have to, or I shall be getting hopelessly muddled. We haven't even got to the Frasers yet, and I've already lost track of your cousins."

He rubbed his chin, calculating. "Hmm. Well, on the Fraser side it's a bit more complicated, because my grandfather Simon married three times, so my father had two sets of half-brothers and half-sisters. Let's leave it for now that I've six

Fraser uncles and three aunts still living, and we'll leave out all the cousins from that lot."

"Yes, let's." I leaned forward and poured another glass of wine for each of us.

The clan territories of MacKenzie and Fraser, it turned out, adjoined each other for some distance along their inner borders, running side by side from the seacoast past the lower end of Loch Ness. This shared border, as borders tend to be, was an unmapped and most uncertain line, shifting to and fro in accordance with time, custom and alliance. Along this border, at the southern end of the Fraser clan lands, lay the small estate of Broch Tuarach, the property of Brian Fraser, Jamie's father.

"It's a fairly rich bit of ground, and there's decent fishing and a good patch of forest for hunting. It maybe supports sixty crofts, and the small village—Broch Mordha, it's called. Then there's the manor house, of course—that's modern," he said, with some pride, "and the old broch that we use now for the beasts and the grain.

"Dougal and Colum were not at all pleased to have their sister marrying a Fraser, and they insisted that she not be a tenant on Fraser land, but live on a freehold. So, Lallybroch— that's what the folk that live there call it—was deeded to my father, but there was a clause in the deed stating that the land was to pass to my mother, Ellen's, issue only. If she died without children, the land would go back to Lord Lovat after my father's death, whether Father had children by another wife or no. But he didn't remarry, and I am my mother's son. So Lallybroch's mine, for what that's worth."

"I thought you were telling me yesterday that you didn't have any property." I sipped the wine, finding it rather good; it seemed to be getting better, the more I drank of it. I thought perhaps I had better stop soon.

Jamie wagged his head from side to side. "Well, it belongs to me, right enough. The thing is, though, it doesna do me much good at present, as I can't go there." He looked apologetic. "There's the minor matter of the price on my head, ye see."

After his escape from Fort William, he had been taken to

Dougal's house, Beannachd (means "Blessed," he explained), to recover from his wounds and the consequent fever. From there, he had gone to France, where he had spent two years fighting with the French army, around the Spanish border.

"You spent two years in the French army and stayed a virgin?" I blurted out incredulously. I had had a number of Frenchmen in my care, and I doubted very much that the Gallic attitude toward women had changed appreciably in two hundred years.

One corner of Jamie's mouth twitched, and he looked down at me sideways.

"If ye had seen the harlots that service the French army, Sassenach, ye'd wonder I've the nerve even to touch a woman, let alone bed one."

I choked, spluttering wine and coughing until he was obliged to pound me on the back. I subsided, breathless and red-faced, and urged him to go on with his story.

He had returned to Scotland a year or so ago, and spent six months alone or with a gang of "broken men"—men without clans—living hand to mouth in the forest, or raiding cattle from the borderlands.

"And then, someone hit me in the head wi' an ax or something o' the sort," he said, shrugging. "And I've to take Dougal's word for what happened during the next two months, as I wasna taking much notice of things myself."

Dougal had been on a nearby estate at the time of the attack. Summoned by Jamie's friends, he had somehow managed to transport his nephew to France.

"Why France?" I asked. "Surely it was taking a frightful risk to move you so far."

"More of a risk to leave me where I was. There were English patrols all over the district—we'd been fairly active thereabouts, ye see, me and the lads—and I suppose Dougal didna want them to find me lying senseless in some cottar's hut."

"Or in his own house?" I said, a little cynically.

"I imagine he'd ha' taken me there, but for two things," Jamie replied. "For one, he'd an English visitor at the time. For the second, he thought from the look of me I was going to die in any case, so he sent me to the abbey."

The Abbey of Ste. Anne de Beaupré, on the French coast, was the domain, it seemed, of the erstwhile Alexander Fraser, now abbot of that sanctuary of learning and worship. One of Jamie's six Fraser uncles.

"He and Dougal do not get on, particularly," Jamie explained, "but Dougal could see there was little to be done for me here, while if there was aught to help me, it might be found there."

And it was. Assisted by the monks' medical knowledge and his own strong constitution, Jamie had survived and gradually mended, under the care of the holy brothers of St. Dominic.

"Once I was well again, I came back," he explained. "Dougal and his men met me at the coast, and we were headed for the MacKenzie lands when we, er, met with you."

"Captain Randall said you were stealing cattle," I said.

He smiled, undisturbed by the accusation. "Well, Dougal isna the man to overlook an opportunity of turning a bit of a profit," he observed. "We came on a nice bunch of beasts, grazing in a field, and no one about. So . . ." He shrugged, with a fatalistic acceptance of the inevitabilities of life.

Apparently I had come upon the end of the confrontation between Dougal's men and Randall's dragoons. Spotting the English bearing down on them, Dougal had sent half his men around a thicket, driving the cattle before them, while the rest of the Scots had hidden among the saplings, ready to ambush the English as they came by.

"Worked verra well too," Jamie said in approval. "We popped out at them and rode straight through them, yelling. They took after us, of course, and we led them a canty chase uphill and through burns and over rocks and such; and all the while the rest of Dougal's men were making off over the border wi' the kine. We lost the lobsterbacks, then, and denned up at the cottage where I first saw ye, waiting for darkness to slip out."

"I see," I said. "Why did you come back to Scotland in the first place, though? I should have thought you'd be much safer in France."

He opened his mouth to reply, then reconsidered, sipping

wine. Apparently I was getting near the edge of his own area of secrecy.

"Well, that's a long story, Sassenach," he said, avoiding the issue. "I'll tell it ye later, but for now, what about you? Will ye tell me about your own family? If ye feel ye can, of course," he added hastily.

I thought for a moment, but there really seemed little risk in telling him about my parents and Uncle Lamb. There was, after all, some advantage to Uncle Lamb's choice of profession. A scholar of antiquities made as much—or as little—sense in the eighteenth century as in the twentieth.

So I told him, omitting only such minor details as automobiles and airplanes, and of course, the war. As I talked, he listened intently, asking questions now and then, expressing sympathy at my parents' death, and interest in Uncle Lamb and his discoveries.

"And then I met Frank," I finished up. I paused, not sure how much more I could say, without getting into dangerous territory. Luckily Jamie saved me.

"And ye'd as soon not talk about him right now," he said understandingly. I nodded, wordless, my vision blurring a little. Jamie let go of the hand he had been holding, and putting an arm around me, pulled my head gently down on his shoulder.

"It's all right," he said, softly stroking my hair. "Are ye tired, lass? Shall I leave ye to your sleep?"

I was tempted for a moment to say yes, but I felt that that would be both unfair and cowardly. I cleared my throat and sat up, shaking my head.

"No," I said, taking a deep breath. He smelled faintly of soap and wine. "I'm all right. Tell me—tell me what games you used to play, when you were a boy."

The room was furnished with a thick twelve-hour candle, rings of dark wax marking the hours. We talked through three of the rings, only letting go of each other's hands to pour wine or get up to visit the privy stool behind the curtain in the corner. Returning from one of these trips, Jamie yawned and stretched.

"It is awfully late," I said, getting up too. "Maybe we should go to bed."

"All right," he said, rubbing the back of his neck. "To bed? Or to sleep?" He cocked a quizzical eyebrow and the corner of his mouth twitched.

In truth, I had been feeling so comfortable with him that I had almost forgotten why we were there. At his words, I suddenly felt a hollow panic. "Well—" I said, faintly.

"Either way, you're no intending to sleep in your gown, are ye?" he asked, in his usual practical manner.

"Well, no, I suppose not." In fact, during the rush of events, I had not even thought about a sleeping garment—which I did not possess, in any case. I had been sleeping in my chemise or nothing, depending on the weather.

Jamie had nothing but the clothes he wore; he was plainly going to sleep in his shirt or naked, a state of affairs which was likely to bring matters rapidly to a head.

"Well, then, come here and I'll help ye wi' the laces and such."

His hands did in fact tremble briefly as he began to undress me. He lost some of his self-consciousness, though, in the struggle with the dozens of tiny hooks that attached the bodice.

"Ha!" he said in triumph as the last one came loose, and we laughed together.

"Now let me do you," I said, deciding that there was no point in further delay. I reached up and unfastened his shirt, sliding my hands inside and across his shoulders. I brought my palms slowly down across his chest, feeling the springy hair and the soft indentations around his nipples. He stood still, hardly breathing, as I knelt down to unbuckle the studded belt around his hips.

If it must be sometime, it may as well be now, I thought, and deliberately ran my hands up the length of his thighs, hard and lean under his kilt. Though by this time I knew perfectly well what most Scotsmen wore beneath their kilts—nothing—it was still something of a shock to find only Jamie.

He lifted me to my feet then, and bent his head to kiss me. It went on a long while, and his hands roamed downward, finding the fastening of my petticoat. It fell to the floor in a billow of starched flounces, leaving me in my chemise.

"Where did you learn to kiss like that?" I said, a little breathless. He grinned and pulled me close again.

"I said I was a virgin, not a monk," he said, kissing me again. "If I find I need guidance, I'll ask."

He pressed me firmly to him, and I could feel that he was more than ready to get on with the business at hand. With some surprise, I realized that I was ready too. In fact, whether it was the result of the late hour, the wine, his own attractiveness, or simple deprivation, I wanted him quite badly.

I pulled his shirt loose at the waist and ran my hands up over his chest, circling his nipples with my thumbs. They grew hard in a second, and he crushed me suddenly against his chest.

"Oof!" I said, struggling for breath. He let go, apologizing.

"No, don't worry; kiss me again." He did, this time slipping the straps of the chemise down over my shoulders. He drew back slightly, cupping my breasts and rubbing my nipples as I had done his. I fumbled with the buckle that held his kilt; his fingers guided mine and the clasp sprang free.

Suddenly he lifted me in his arms and sat down on the bed, holding me on his lap. He spoke a little hoarsely.

"Tell me if I'm too rough, or tell me to stop altogether, if ye wish. Anytime until we are joined; I dinna think I can stop after that."

In answer, I put my hands behind his neck and pulled him down on top of me. I guided him to the slippery cleft between my legs.

"Holy God," said James Fraser, who never took the name of his Lord in vain.

"Don't stop now," I said.

Lying together afterward, it seemed natural for him to cradle my head on his chest. We fitted well together, and most of our original constraint was gone, lost in shared excitement and the novelty of exploring each other. "Was it like you thought it would be?" I asked curiously. He chuckled, making a deep rumble under my ear.

"Almost; I had thought—nay, never mind."

"No, tell me. What did you think?"

"I'm no goin' to tell ye; ye'll laugh at me."

"I promise not to laugh. Tell me." He caressed my hair, smoothing the curls back from my ear.

"Oh, all right. I didna realize that ye did it face to face. I thought ye must do it the back way, like; like horses, ye know."

It was a struggle to keep my promise, but I didn't laugh.

"I know that sounds silly," he said defensively. "It's just . . . well, ye know how you get ideas in your head when you're young, and then somehow they just stick there?"

"You've never seen *people* make love?" I was surprised at this, having seen the crofters' cottages, where the whole family shared a single room. Granted that Jamie's family were not crofters, still it must be the rare Scottish child who had never waked to find his elders coupling nearby.

"Of course I have, but generally under the bedclothes, ye know. I couldna tell anything except the man was on top. *That* much I knew."

"Mm. I noticed."

"Did I squash you?" he asked, a little anxiously.

"Not much. Really, though, is that what you thought?" I didn't laugh, but couldn't help grinning broadly. He turned slightly pink around the ears.

"Aye. I saw a man take a woman plain, once, out in the open. But that . . . well, it was a rape, was what it was, and he took her from the back. It made some impression on me, and as I say, it's just the idea stuck."

He continued to hold me, using his horse-gentling techniques again. These gradually changed, though, to a more determined exploration.

"I want to ask ye something," he said, running a hand down the length of my back.

"What's that?"

"Did ye like it?" he said, a little shyly.

"Yes, I did," I said, quite honestly.

"Oh. I thought ye did, though Murtagh told me that women generally do not care for it, so I should finish as soon as I could."

"What would Murtagh know about it?" I said indignantly. "The slower the better, as far as most women are concerned." Jamie chuckled again.

"Well, you'd know better than Murtagh. I had considerable good advice offered me on the subject last night, from Murtagh and Rupert and Ned. A good bit of it sounded verra unlikely to me, though, so I thought I'd best use my own judgment."

"It hasn't led you wrong yet," I said, curling one of his chest hairs around my finger. "What other sage bits of advice did they give you?" His skin was a ruddy gold in the candle-light; to my amusement, it grew still redder in embarrassment.

"I could no repeat most of it. As I said, I think it's likely wrong, anyway. I've seen a good many kinds of animals mate with each other, and most seem to manage it without any advice at all. I would suppose people could do the same."

I was privately entertained by the notion of someone picking up pointers on sexual technique from barnyard and forest, rather than locker rooms and dirty magazines.

"What kinds of animals have you seen mating?"

"Oh, all kinds. Our farm was near the forest, ye see, and I spent a good deal of time there, hunting, or seeking cows as had got out and suchlike. I've seen horses and cows, of course, pigs, chickens, doves, dogs, cats, red deer, squirrels, rabbits, wild boar, oh, and once even a pair of snakes."

"Snakes!?"

"Aye. Did ye know that snakes have two cocks?—male snakes, I mean."

"No, I didn't. Are you sure about that?"

"Aye, and both of 'em forked, like this." He spread his second and third fingers apart in illustration.

"That sounds terribly uncomfortable for the female snake," I said, giggling.

"Well, she appeared to be enjoying herself," said Jamie.

"Near as I could tell; snakes havena got much expression on their faces."

I buried my face in his chest, snorting with mirth. His pleasant musky smell mingled with the harsh scent of linen.

"Take off your shirt," I said, sitting up and pulling at the hem of the garment.

"Why?" he asked, but sat up and obliged. I knelt in front of him, admiring his naked body.

"Because I want to look at you," I said. He was beautifully made, with long, graceful bones and flat muscles that flowed smoothly from the curves of chest and shoulder to the slight concavities of belly and thigh. He raised his eyebrows.

"Well then, fair's fair. Take off yours, then." He reached out and helped me squirm out of the wrinkled chemise, pushing it down over my hips. Once it was off, he held me by the waist, studying me with intense interest. I grew almost embarrassed as he looked me over.

"Haven't you ever seen a naked woman before?" I asked.

"Aye, but not one so close." His face broke into a broad grin. "And not one that's mine." He stroked my hips with both hands. "You have good wide hips; ye'd be a good breeder, I expect."

"What!" I drew away indignantly, but he pulled me back and collapsed on the bed with me on top of him. He held me until I stopped struggling, then raised me enough to meet his lips again.

"I know once is enough to make it legal, but . . ." He paused shyly.

"You want to do it again?"

"Would ye mind verra much?"

I didn't laugh this time either, but I felt my ribs creak under the strain.

"No," I said gravely. "I wouldn't mind."

———

"Are you hungry?" I asked softly, sometime later.

"Famished." He bent his head to bite my breast softly, then looked up with a grin. "But I need food too." He rolled to the edge of the bed. "There's cold beef and bread in the kitchen, I expect, and likely wine as well. I'll go and bring us some supper."

"No, don't you get up. I'll fetch it." I jumped off the bed and headed for the door, pulling a shawl over my shift against the chill of the corridor.

"Wait, Claire!" Jamie called. "Ye'd better let me—" but I had already opened the door.

My appearance at the door was greeted by a raucous cheer from some fifteen men, lounging around the fireplace of the main room below, drinking, eating and tossing dice. I stood nonplussed on the balcony for a moment, fifteen leering faces flickering out of the firelit shadows at me.

"Hey, lass!" shouted Rupert, one of the loungers. "Ye're still able t' walk! Isn't Jamie doin' his duty by ye, then?"

This sally was greeted with gales of laughter and a number of even cruder remarks regarding Jamie's prowess.

"If ye've worn Jamie out a'ready, I'll be happy t' take 'is place!" offered a short dark-haired youth.

"Nay, nay, 'e's no good, lass, take me!" shouted another.

"She'll ha' none o' ye, lads!" yelled Murtagh, uproariously drunk. "After Jamie, she'll need somethin' like this to satisfy 'er!" He waved a huge mutton bone overhead, causing the room to rock with laughter.

I whirled back into the room, slammed the door and stood with my back to it, glaring at Jamie, who lay naked on the bed, shaking with laughter.

"I tried to warn ye," he said, gasping. "You should see your face!"

"Just what," I hissed, "are all those men doing out there?"

Jamie slid gracefully off our wedding couch and began rummaging on his knees through the pile of discarded clothing on the floor. "Witnesses," he said briefly. "Dougal is no takin' any chances of this marriage bein' annulled." He straightened with his kilt in his hands, grinning at me as he wrapped it around his loins. "I'm afraid your reputation's compromised beyond repair, Sassenach."

He started shirtless for the door. "Don't go out there!" I said, in sudden panic. He turned to smile reassuringly, hand on the latch. "Dinna worry, lass. If they're witnesses, they may as well have somethin' to see. Besides, I'm no intendin' to starve for the next three days for fear of a wee bit o' chaff."

He stepped out of the room to a chorus of bawdy applause, leaving the door slightly ajar. I could hear his progress toward the kitchen, marked by shouted congratulations and ribald questions and advice.

"How was yer first time, Jamie? Did ye bleed?" shouted Rupert's easily recognized gravel-pit voice.

"Nay, but ye will, ye auld bugger, if ye dinna clapper yer face," came Jamie's spiked tones in broad Scots reply. Howls of delight greeted this sally, and the raillery continued, following Jamie down the hall to the kitchen and back up the stairs.

I pushed open the door a crack to admit Jamie, face red as the fire below and hands piled high with food and drink. He sidled in, followed by a final burst of hilarity from below. I choked it off with a decisive slam of the door, and shot the bolt to.

"I brought enough we'll no need to go out again for a bit," Jamie said, laying out dishes on the table, carefully not looking at me. "Will ye have a bite?"

I reached past him for the bottle of wine. "Not just yet. What I need is a drink."

◄━━━

There was a powerful urgency in him that roused me to response despite his awkwardness. Not wanting to lecture nor yet to highlight my own experience, I let him do what he would, only offering an occasional suggestion, such as that he might carry his weight on his elbows and not my chest.

As yet too hungry and too clumsy for tenderness, still he made love with a sort of unflagging joy that made me think that male virginity might be a highly underrated commodity. He exhibited a concern for my safety, though, that I found at once endearing and irritating.

Sometime in our third encounter, I arched tightly against him and cried out. He drew back at once, startled and apologetic.

"I'm sorry," he said. "I didna mean to hurt ye."

"You didn't." I stretched languorously, feeling dreamily wonderful.

"Are you sure?" he said, inspecting me for damage. Suddenly it dawned on me that a few of the finer points had likely been left out of his hasty education at the hands of Murtagh and Rupert.

"Does it happen every time?" he asked, fascinated, once I had enlightened him. I felt rather like the Wife of Bath, or a Japanese geisha. I had never envisioned myself as an instructress in the arts of love, but I had to admit to myself that the role held certain attractions.

"No, not every time," I said, amused. "Only if the man is a good lover."

"Oh." His ears turned faintly pink. I was slightly alarmed to see the look of frank interest being replaced with one of growing determination.

"Will you tell me what I should do next time?" he asked.

"You don't need to do anything special," I assured him. "Just go slowly and pay attention. Why wait, though? You're still ready."

He was surprised. "You don't need to wait? I canna do it again right away after—"

"Well, women are different."

"Aye, I noticed," he muttered.

He circled my wrist with thumb and index finger. "It's just . . . you're so small; I'm afraid I'm going to hurt you."

"You are not going to hurt me," I said impatiently. "And if you did, I wouldn't mind." Seeing puzzled incomprehension on his face, I decided to show him what I meant.

"What are you doing?" he asked, shocked.

"Just what it looks like. Hold still." After a few moments, I began to use my teeth, pressing progressively harder until he drew in his breath with a sharp hiss. I stopped.

"Did I hurt you?" I asked.

"Yes. A little." He sounded half-strangled.

"Do you want me to stop?"

"No!"

I went on, being deliberately rough, until he suddenly convulsed, with a groan that sounded as though I had torn his heart out by the roots. He lay back, quivering and breathing heavily. He muttered something in Gaelic, eyes closed.

"What did you say?"

"I said," he answered, opening his eyes, "I thought my heart was going to burst."

I grinned, pleased with myself. "Oh, Murtagh and company didn't tell you about that, either?"

"Aye, they did. That was one of the things I didn't believe."

I laughed. "In that case, maybe you'd better not tell me what else they told you. Do you see what I meant, though, about not minding if you're rough?"

"Aye." He drew a deep breath and blew it out slowly. "If I did that to you, would it feel the same?"

"Well, you know," I said, slowly, "I don't really know." I had been doing my best to keep my thoughts of Frank at bay, feeling that there should really be no more than two people in a marriage bed, regardless of how they got there. Jamie was very different from Frank, both in body and mind, but there are in fact only a limited number of ways in which two bodies can meet, and we had not yet established that territory of intimacy in which the act of love takes on infinite variety. The echoes of the flesh were unavoidable, but there were a few territories still unexplored.

Jamie's brows were tilted in an expression of mocking threat. "Oh, so there's something you don't know? Well, we'll find out then, won't we? As soon as I've the strength for it." He closed his eyes again. "Next week, sometime."

I woke in the hours before dawn, shivering and rigid with terror. I could not recall the dream that woke me, but the abrupt plunge into reality was equally frightening. It had been possible to forget my situation for a time the night before, lost in the pleasures of newfound intimacy. Now I was alone, next to a sleeping stranger with whom my life was inextricably linked, adrift in a place filled with unseen threat.

I must have made some sound of distress, for there was a sudden upheaval of bedclothes as the stranger in my bed vaulted to the floor with the heart-stopping suddenness of a pheasant rising underfoot. He came to rest in a crouch near the door of the chamber, barely visible in the pre-dawn light.

Pausing to listen carefully at the door, he made a rapid inspection of the room, gliding soundlessly from door to window to bed. The angle of his arm told me that he held a weapon of some sort, though I could not see what it was in the darkness. Sitting down next to me, satisfied that all was secure, he slid the knife or whatever it was back into its hiding place above the headboard.

"Are you all right?" he whispered. His fingers brushed my wet cheek.

"Yes. I'm sorry to wake you. I had a nightmare. What on earth—" I started to ask what it was that had made him spring so abruptly to the alert.

A large, warm hand ran down my bare arm, interrupting my question. "No wonder; you're frozen." The hand urged me under the pile of quilts and into the warm space recently vacated. "My fault," he murmured. "I've taken all the quilts. I'm afraid I'm no accustomed yet to share a bed." He wrapped the quilts comfortably around us and lay back beside me. A moment later, he reached again to touch my face.

"Is it me?" he asked quietly. "Can ye not bear me?"

I gave a short, hiccupping laugh, not quite a sob. "No, it isn't you." I reached out in the dark, groping for a hand to press reassuringly. My fingers met a tangle of quilts and warm flesh, but at last I found the hand I had been seeking. We lay side by side, looking up at the low, beamed ceiling.

"What if I said I couldn't bear you?" I asked suddenly. "What on earth could you do?" The bed creaked as he shrugged.

"Tell Dougal you wanted an annulment on grounds of nonconsummation, I suppose."

This time I laughed outright. "Nonconsummation! With all those witnesses?"

The room was growing light enough to see the smile on the face turned toward me. "Aye well, witnesses or no, it's only you and me that can say for sure, isn't it? And I'd rather be embarrassed than wed to someone that hated me."

I turned toward him. "I don't hate you."

"I don't hate you, either. And there's many good marriages have started wi' less than that." Gently, he turned me away from him and fitted himself to my back so we lay nested together. His hand cupped my breast, not in invitation or demand, but because it seemed to belong there.

"Don't be afraid," he whispered into my hair. "There's the two of us now." I felt warm, soothed, and safe for the first time in many days. It was only as I drifted into sleep under the first rays of daylight that I remembered the knife above my head, and wondered again, what threat would make a man sleep armed and watchful in his bridal chamber?

16

One Fine Day

The hard-won intimacy of the night seemed to have evaporated with the dew, and there was considerable constraint between us in the morning. After a mostly silent breakfast taken in our room, we climbed the small hillock behind the inn, exchanging rather strained politenesses from time to time.

At the crest, I settled on a log to rest, while Jamie sat on the ground, back against a pine sapling, a few feet away. Some bird was active in the bush behind me, a siskin, I supposed, or possibly a thrush. I listened to its dilatory rustlings, watched the small fluffy clouds float by, and pondered the etiquette of the situation.

The silence was becoming really too heavy to bear, when Jamie suddenly said, "I hope—" then stopped and blushed. Though I rather felt it should be me blushing, I was glad that at least one of us was able to do it.

"What?" I said as encouragingly as possible.

He shook his head, still pink. "It doesna matter."

"Go ahead." I reached out a foot and nudged his leg with a tentative toe. "Honesty, remember?" It was unfair, but I really couldn't stand any more nervous throat-clearing and eye-twitching.

His clasped hands tightened around his knees, and he rocked back a bit, but fixed his gaze directly on me.

"I was going to say," he said softly, "that I hoped the man who had the honor to lie first wi' you was as generous as you were with me." He smiled, a little shyly. "But on second thought, that didna sound quite right. What I meant . . . well, all I wanted was to say thank you."

"Generosity had nothing to do with it!" I snapped, looking down and brushing energetically at a nonexistent spot on my dress. A large boot pushed into my downcast field of vision and nudged my ankle.

"Honesty, is it?" he echoed, and I looked up to meet a derisively raised pair of eyebrows above a wide grin.

"Well," I said defensively, "not after the first time, anyway." He laughed, and I discovered to my horror that I was not beyond blushing after all.

A cool shadow fell over my heated face and a large pair of hands took firm hold of mine and pulled me to my feet. Jamie took my place on the log, and patted his knee invitingly.

"Sit," he said.

I reluctantly obliged, keeping my face turned away. He settled me comfortably against his chest and wrapped his arms about my waist. I felt the steady thump of his heart against my back.

"Now then," he said. "If we canna talk easy yet without touching, we'll touch for a bit. Tell me when you're accustomed to me again." He leaned back so that we were in the shade of an oak, and held me close without speaking, just breathing slowly, so that I felt the rise and fall of his chest and the stir of his breath in my hair.

"All right," I said after a moment.

"Good." He loosened his grip and turned me to face him. At close range, I could see the bristle of auburn stubble on cheek and chin. I brushed my fingers across it; it was like the plush on an old-fashioned sofa, stiff and soft at the same time.

"I'm sorry," he said, "I couldna shave this morning. Dougal gave me a razor before the wedding yesterday, but he took it back—in case I cut my throat after the wedding night, I expect." He grinned down at me and I smiled back.

The reference to Dougal reminded me of our conversation of the night before.

"I wondered . . ." I said. "Last night, you said Dougal and his men met you at the coast when you came back from

France. Why did you come back with him, instead of going to your own home, or the Fraser lands? I mean, the way Dougal's treated you . . ." I trailed off, hesitant.

"Oh," he said, shifting his legs to bear my weight more evenly. I could almost hear him thinking to himself. He made up his mind quite quickly.

"Well, it's something ye should know, I suppose." He frowned to himself. "I told ye why I'm outlawed. Well, for a time after—after I left the Fort, I didna care much . . . about anything. My father died about that time, and my sister . . ." He paused again, and I sensed some kind of struggle going on inside him. I twisted around to look at him. The normally cheerful face was shadowed with some strong emotion.

"Dougal told me," he said slowly, "Dougal told me that—that my sister was wi' child. By Randall."

"Oh, dear."

He glanced sideways at me, then away. His eyes were bright as sapphires and he blinked hastily once or twice.

"I . . . I couldna bring myself to go back," he said, low-voiced. "To see her again, after what happened. And too"—he sighed, then set his lips firmly—"Dougal told me that she . . . that after the child was born, she . . . well, of course, she couldna help it; she was alone—damn it, I *left* her alone! He said she had taken up wi' another English soldier, someone from the garrison, he didna know which one."

He swallowed heavily, then went on more firmly. "I sent back what money I could, of course, but I could not . . . well, I couldna bring myself to write to her. What could I say?" He shrugged helplessly.

"Anyway, after a time I grew tired of soldiering in France. And I heard through my uncle Alex that he'd had word of an English deserter, named Horrocks. The man had left the army and taken service wi' Francis MacLean o' Dunweary. He was in his cups one day and let out that he'd been stationed wi' the garrison at Fort William when I escaped. And he'd seen the man who shot the sergeant-major that day."

"So he could prove that it wasn't you!" This sounded good news, and I said so. Jamie nodded.

"Well, yes. Though the word of a deserter would likely not count for much. Still, it's a start. At least I'd know myself who it was. And while I . . . well, I dinna see how I can go back to Lallybroch; still it would be as well if I could walk the soil of Scotland without the risk of being hanged."

"Yes, that seems a good idea," I said dryly. "But where do the MacKenzies come into it?"

There followed a certain amount of complicated analysis of family relationships and clan alliances, but when the smoke cleared away, it appeared that Francis MacLean was some connection with the MacKenzie side, and had sent word of Horrocks to Colum, who had sent Dougal to make contact with Jamie.

"Which is how he came to be nearby when I was wounded," Jamie finished up. He paused, squinting into the sun. "I wondered, afterward, ye know, whether perhaps he'd done it."

"Hit you with an ax? Your own uncle? Why on earth?"

He frowned as though weighing how much to tell me, then shrugged.

"I dinna ken how much ye know about the clan MacKenzie," he said, "though I imagine ye canna have ridden wi' old Ned Gowan for days without hearin' something of it. He canna keep off the subject for long."

He nodded at my answering smile. "Well, you've seen Colum for yourself. Anyone can see that he'll not make old bones. And wee Hamish is barely eight; he'll no be able to lead a clan for ten years yet. So what happens if Colum dies before Hamish is ready?" He looked at me, prompting.

"Well, Dougal would be laird, I suppose," I said slowly, "at least until Hamish is old enough."

"Aye, that's true." Jamie nodded. "But Dougal's not the man Colum is, and there are those in the clan that wouldna follow him so gladly—if there were an alternative."

"I see," I said slowly, "and you are the alternative."

I looked him over carefully, and had to admit that there was a certain amount of possibility there. He was old Jacob's grandson; a MacKenzie by blood, if only on his mother's side. A big, comely, well-made lad, plainly intelligent, and with the family knack for managing people. He had fought in France and proved his ability to lead men in battle; an important consideration. Even the price on his head might not be an insurmountable obstacle—if he were laird.

The English had enough trouble in the Highlands, between the constant small rebellions, the border raids and the warring clans, not to risk a major uprising by accusing the chieftain of a major clan of murder—which would seem no murder at all to the clansmen.

To hang an unimportant Fraser clansman was one thing; to storm Castle Leoch and drag out the laird of the clan Mac-Kenzie to face English justice was something else again.

"Do you mean to be laird, if Colum dies?" It was one way out of his difficulties, after all, though I suspected it was a way hedged with its own considerable obstacles.

He smiled briefly at the thought. "No. Even if I felt myself entitled to it—which I don't—it would split the clan, Dougal's men against those that might follow me. I havena the taste for power at the cost of other men's blood. But Dougal and Colum couldna be sure of that, could they? So they might think it safer just to kill me than to take the risk."

My brow was furrowed, thinking it all out. "But surely you could tell Dougal and Colum that you don't intend . . . oh." I looked up at him with considerable respect. "But you did. At the oath-taking."

I had thought already how well he had handled a dangerous situation there; now I saw just *how* dangerous it had been. The clansmen had certainly wanted him to take his oath; just as certainly Colum had not. To swear such an oath was to declare himself a member of the clan MacKenzie, and as such, a potential candidate for chieftain of the clan. He risked open violence or death for refusal; he risked the same—more privately—for compliance.

Seeing the danger, he had taken the prudent course of staying away from the ceremony. And when I, by my botched escape attempt, had led him straight back to the edge of the abyss, he had set a sure and certain foot on a very narrow tightrope, and walked it to the other side. *Je suis prest*, indeed.

He nodded, seeing the thoughts cross my face.

"Aye. If I had sworn my oath that night, chances are I wouldna have seen the dawn."

I felt a little shaky at the thought, as well as at the knowledge that I had unwittingly exposed him to such danger. The knife over his bed suddenly seemed nothing more than a sensible precaution. I wondered how many nights he had slept armed at Leoch, expecting death to come visiting.

"I always sleep armed, Sassenach," he said, though I had not spoken. "Except for the monastery, last night is the first time in months I've not slept wi' my dirk in my fist." He grinned, plainly remembering what *had* been in his fist, instead.

"How the bloody hell did you know what I was thinking?" I demanded, ignoring the grin. He shook his head good-naturedly.

"You'd make a verra poor spy, Sassenach. Everything ye think shows on your face, plain as day. You looked at my dirk and then ye blushed." He studied me appraisingly, bright head on one side. "I asked ye for honesty last night, but it wasna really necessary; it isna in you to lie."

"Just as well, since I'm apparently so bad at it," I observed with some asperity. "Am I to take it that at least *you* don't think I'm a spy, then?"

He didn't answer. He was looking over my shoulder toward the inn, body suddenly tense as a bowstring. I was startled for a moment, but then heard the sounds that had attracted his attention. The thud of hooves and jangle of harness; a large group of mounted men was coming down the road toward the inn.

Moving cautiously, Jamie crouched behind the screen of bushes, at a spot commanding a view of the road. I tucked my skirts up and crawled after him as silently as I could.

The road hooked sharply past a rocky outcrop, then curved more gently down to the hollow where the inn lay. The morning breeze carried the sounds of the approaching group in our direction, but it was a minute or two before the first horse poked its nose into sight.

It was a group of some twenty or thirty men, mostly wearing leather trews and tartan-clad, but in a variety of colors and patterns. All, without exception, were well armed. Each horse bore at least one musket strapped to the saddle, and there was an abundance of pistols, dirks, and swords on view, plus whatever further armament might be concealed in the capacious saddlebags of the four packhorses. Six of the men also led extra mounts, unburdened and saddleless.

Despite their warlike accoutrements, the men seemed relaxed; they were chatting and laughing in small groups as they rode, though here and there a head raised, watchful of the surroundings. I fought back the urge to duck as one man's gaze passed over the spot where we lay hidden; it seemed as though that searching look must surely discover some random movement or the gleam of the sun off Jamie's hair.

Glancing up at this thought, I discovered that it had occurred to him as well; he had pulled a fold of his plaid up over his head and shoulders, so that the dull hunting pattern made him effectively part of the shrubbery. As the last of the men wound down into the innyard, Jamie dropped the plaid and motioned back toward the path up the hill.

"Do you know who they are?" I panted, as I followed him up into the heather.

"Oh, aye." Jamie took the steep path like a mountain goat, with no loss of breath or composure. Glancing back, he noticed my labored progress and stopped, reaching down a hand to help me.

"It's the Watch," he said, nodding back in the direction of the inn. "We're safe enough, but I thought we'd as soon be a bit further away."

I had heard of the famous Black Watch, that informal police force that kept order in the Highlands, and heard also that there were other Watches, each patrolling its own area, collecting "subscriptions" from clients for the safeguarding of cattle and property. Clients in arrears might well wake one morning to find their livestock vanished in the night, and none to tell where they had gone—certainly not the men of the Watch. I was seized by a sudden irrational terror.

"They're not looking for you, are they?"

Startled, he looked back as though expecting to see men scrambling up the hill in pursuit, but there was no one, and he

looked back at me with a relieved smile and put an arm about
my waist to help me along.

"Nay, I doubt it. Ten pound sterling is not enough to make
me worth the hunting by a pack like that. And if they kent I
was at the inn, they wouldna have come as they did, traipsing
up to the door all of a piece." He shook his head decisively.
"No, were they hunting anyone, they'd send men to guard
the back and the windows before coming in the front door.
They've but stopped there for refreshment, likely."

We continued to climb, past the spot where the rude path
petered out in clumps of gorse and heather. We were among
foothills here, and the granite rocks rose higher than Jamie's
head, reminding me uncomfortably of the standing stones of
Craigh na Dun.

We emerged then, onto the top of a small dun, and the hills
sloped away in a breathtaking fall of rocks and green on all
sides. Most places in the Highlands gave me a feeling of being
surrounded by trees or rocks or mountains, but here we were
exposed to the fresh drafts of the wind and the rays of the sun,
which had come out as though in celebration of our unorthodox marriage.

I experienced a heady sense of freedom at being out from
under Dougal's influence and the claustrophobic company of
so many men. I was tempted to urge Jamie to run away, and
to take me with him, but common sense prevailed. We had
neither of us any money nor any food beyond the bit of lunch
that he carried in his sporran. We would certainly be pursued
if we did not return to the inn by sundown. And while Jamie
could plainly climb rocks all day without breaking a sweat or
getting out of breath, I was in no such training. Noticing my
red face, he led me to a rock and sat beside me, contentedly
gazing out over the hills while he waited for me to regain my
breath. We were certainly safe here.

Thinking of the Watch, I laid a hand impulsively on Jamie's
arm.

"I'm awfully glad you're not worth very much," I said.

He regarded me for a moment, rubbing his nose, which
was beginning to redden.

"Well, I might take that several ways, Sassenach, but under the circumstances," he said, "thank you."

"I should thank *you*," I said, "for marrying me. I must say that I'd rather be here than in Fort William."

"I thank ye for the compliment, lady," he said, with a slight bow. "So would I. And while we're busy thanking each other," he added, "I should thank you for marrying *me*, as well."

"Er, well . . ." I blushed once more.

"Not only for that, Sassenach," he said, his grin widening. "Though certainly for that as well. But I imagine you've also saved my life for me, at least so far as the MacKenzies are concerned."

"Whatever do you mean?"

"Being half MacKenzie is one thing," he explained. "Being half MacKenzie wi' an English wife is quite another. There isna much chance of a Sassenach wench ever becoming lady of Leoch, whatever the clansmen might think of me alone. That's why Dougal picked me to wed ye to, ye ken."

He lifted one brow, reddish-gold in the morning sun. "I hope ye wouldna have preferred Rupert, after all?"

"No, I wouldn't," I said with emphasis.

He laughed and got up, brushing pine needles from his kilts.

"Well, my mother told me I'd be some lassie's choice one fine day." He reached down a hand and helped me up.

"I told her," he continued, "that I thought it was the man's part to choose."

"And what did she say to that?" I asked.

"She rolled her eyes and said 'You'll find out, my fine wee cockerel, you'll find out.' " He laughed. "And so I have."

He looked upward, to where the sun was now seeping through the pine needles in lemon threads.

"And it is a fine day, at that. Come along, Sassenach. I'll take ye fishin'."

We went further up into the hills. This time Jamie turned to the north, and over a jumble of stone and through a crevice, into the head of a tiny glen, rock-walled and leafy, filled with the gurgling of water from the burn that spilled from a dozen wee falls among the rocks and plunged roistering down the length of the canyon into a series of rills and pools below.

We dangled our feet in the water, moving from shade to sun and back to shade as we grew too warm, talking of this and that and not much of anything, both aware of each other's smallest movement, both content to wait until chance should bring us to that moment when a glance should linger, and a touch should signal more.

Above one dark speckled pool, Jamie showed me how to tickle trout. Crouched to avoid the low-growing branches overhead, he duck-walked along an overhanging ledge, arms outstretched for balance. Halfway along, he turned carefully on the rock and stretched out his hand, urging me to follow.

I had my skirts tucked up already, for walking through rough country, and managed well enough. We stretched full-length on the cool rock, head to head, peering down into the water, willow branches brushing our backs.

"All it is," he said, "is to pick a good spot, and then wait." He dipped one hand below the surface, smoothly, no splashing, and let it lie on the sandy bottom, just outside the line of shadow made by the rocky overhang. The long fingers curled delicately toward the palm, distorted by the water so that they seemed to wave gently to and fro in unison, like the leaves of a water plant, though I saw from the still muscling of his forearm that he was not moving his hand at all. The column of his arm bent abruptly at the surface, seeming as disjointed as it had been when I had met him, little more than a month—my God, only a month?—before.

Met one month, married one day. Bound by vows and by blood. And by friendship as well. When the time came to leave, I hoped that I would not hurt him too badly. I found myself glad that for the moment, I need not think about it; we were far from Craigh na Dun, and not a chance in the world of escape from Dougal for the present.

"There he is." Jamie's voice was low, hardly more than a breath; he had told me that trout have sensitive ears.

From my angle of view, the trout was little more than a stirring of the speckled sand. Deep in the rock shadow, there was no telltale gleam of scales. Speckles moved on speckles, shifted by the fanning of transparent fins, invisible but for their motion. The minnows that had gathered to pluck curiously at the hairs on Jamie's wrist fled away into the brightness of the pool.

One finger bent slowly, so slowly it was hard to see the movement. I could tell it moved only by its changing position, relative to the other fingers. Another finger, slowly bent. And after a long, long moment, another.

I scarcely dared breathe, and my heart beat against the cold rock with a rhythm faster than the breathing of the fish. Sluggishly the fingers bent back, lying open, one by one, and the slow hypnotic wave began again, one finger, one finger, one finger more, the movement a smooth ripple like the edge of a fish's fin.

As though drawn by the slow-motion beckoning, the trout's nose pressed outward, a delicate gasping of mouth and gills, busy in the rhythm of breathing, pink lining showing, not showing, showing, not showing, as the opercula beat like a heart.

The chewing mouth groped and bit water. Most of the body was clear of the rock now, hanging weightless in the water, still in the shadow. I could see one eye, twitching to and fro in a blank, directionless stare.

An inch more would bring the flapping gill-covers right over the treacherous beckoning fingers. I found that I was gripping the rock with both hands, pressing my cheek hard against the granite, as though I could make myself still more inconspicuous.

There was a sudden explosion of motion. Everything happened so fast I couldn't see what actually *did* take place. There was a heavy splatter of water that sluiced across the rock an inch from my face, and a flurry of plaid as Jamie rolled across the rock above me, and a heavy splat as the fish's body sailed through the air and struck the leaf-strewn bank.

Jamie surged off the ledge and into the shallows of the side pool, splashing across to retrieve his prize before the stunned fish could succeed in flapping its way back to the sanctuary of the water. Seizing it by the tail, he slapped it expertly against a rock, killing it at once, then waded back to show it to me.

"A good size," he said proudly, holding out a solid four-teen-incher. "Do nicely for breakfast." He grinned up at me, wet to the thighs, hair hanging in his face, shirt splotched with water and dead leaves. "I told you I'd not let ye go hungry."

He wrapped the trout in layers of burdock leaves and cool mud. Then he rinsed his fingers in the cold water of the burn, and clambering up onto the rock, handed me the neatly wrapped parcel.

"An odd wedding present, maybe," he nodded at the trout, "but not without precedent, as Ned Gowan might say."

"There are precedents for giving a new wife a fish?" I asked, entertained.

He stripped off his stockings to dry and laid them on the rock to lie in the sun. His long, bare toes wiggled in enjoyment of the warmth.

"It's an old love song, from the Isles. D'ye want to hear it?"

"Yes, of course. Er, in English, if you can," I added.

"Oh, aye. I've no voice for music, but I'll give you the words." And fingering the hair back out of his eyes, he recited,

> *"Thou daughter of the King of bright-lit mansions*
> *On the night that our wedding is on us,*
> *If living man I be in Duntulm,*
> *I will go bounding to thee with gifts.*
> *Thou wilt get a hundred badgers, dwellers in banks,*
> *A hundred brown otters, natives of streams,*
> *A hundred silver trout, rising from their pools . . ."*

And on through a remarkable list of the flora and fauna of the Isles. I had time, watching him declaim, to reflect on the oddity of sitting on a rock in a Scottish pool, listening to Gaelic love songs, with a large dead fish in my lap. And the greater oddity that I was enjoying myself very much indeed.

When he finished, I applauded, keeping hold of the trout by gripping it between my knees.

"Oh, I like that one! Especially the 'I will go bounding to thee with gifts.' He sounds a most enthusiastic lover."

Eyes closed against the sun, Jamie laughed. "I suppose I could add a line for myself—'I will leap into pools for thy sake.' "

We both laughed, and then were quiet for a time, basking in the warm sun of the early summer. It was very peaceful there, with no sound but the rushing of water beyond our still pool. Jamie's breathing had calmed. I was very conscious of the slow rise and fall of his breast, and the slow beat of the pulse in his neck. He had a small triangular scar, just there at the base of his throat.

I could feel the shyness and constraint beginning to creep back. I reached out a hand and grasped his tightly, hoping that the touch would reestablish the ease between us as it had before. He slid an arm about my shoulders, but it only made me aware of the hard lines of his body beneath the thin shirt. I pulled away, under the pretext of plucking a bunch of pink-flowered storksbill that grew from a crack in the rock.

"Good for headache," I explained, tucking them into my belt.

"It troubles you," he said, tilting his head to look at me intently. "Not headache, I don't mean. Frank. You're thinking of him, and so it troubles you when I touch you, because ye canna hold us both in your mind. Is that it?"

"You're very perceptive," I said, surprised. He smiled, but made no move to touch me again.

"No great task to puzzle that out, lass. I knew when we married that you couldna help but have him often in your mind, did ye want to or no."

I didn't, at the moment, but he was right; I couldn't help it.

"Am I much like him?" he asked suddenly.

"No."

In fact, it would be difficult to imagine a greater contrast. Frank was slender, lithe and dark, where Jamie was large, powerful and fair as a ruddy sunbeam. While both men had the compact grace of athletes, Frank's was the build of a tennis player, Jamie's the body of a warrior, shaped—and battered—by the abrasion of sheer physical adversity. Frank stood a scant four inches above my own five foot six. Face-to-face with Jamie, my nose fitted comfortably into the small hollow in the center of his chest, and his chin could rest easily on top of my head.

Nor was the physical the only dimension where the two men varied. There was nearly fifteen years' difference in their ages, for one thing, which likely accounted for some of the difference between Frank's urbane reserve and Jamie's frank openness. As a lover, Frank was polished, sophisticated, considerate, and skilled. Lacking experience or the pretense of it, Jamie simply gave me all of himself, without reservation. And the depth of my response to that unsettled me completely.

Jamie was watching my struggle, not without sympathy.

"Well, then, it would seem I have two choices in the matter," he said. "I can let you brood about it, or . . ."

He leaned down and gently fitted his mouth over mine. I had kissed my share of men, particularly during the war years, when flirtation and instant romance were the light-minded companions of death and uncertainty. Jamie, though, was something different. His extreme gentleness was in no way tentative; rather it was a promise of power known and held in leash; a challenge and a provocation the more remarkable for its lack of demand. I am yours, it said. And if you will have me, then . . .

I would, and my mouth opened beneath his, wholeheartedly accepting both promise and challenge without consulting me. After a long moment, he lifted his head and smiled down at me.

"Or, I can try to distract ye from your thoughts," he finished.

He pressed my head against his shoulder, stroking my hair and smoothing the leaping curls around my ears.

"I do not know if it will help," he said, quietly, "but I will tell you this: it is a gift and a wonder to me, to know that I can please you—that your body can rouse to mine. I hadna thought of such a thing—beforehand."

I drew a long breath before replying. "Yes," I said. "It helps. I think."

We were silent again for what seemed a long time. At last Jamie drew away and looked down at me, smiling.

"I told ye I've neither money nor property, Sassenach?"

I nodded, wondering what he intended.

"I should have warned ye before that we'd likely end up sleeping in haystacks, wi' naught but heather ale and drammach for food."

"I don't mind," I said.

He nodded toward an opening in the trees, not taking his eyes off me.

"I havena got a haystack about me, but there's a fair patch of fresh bracken yonder. If ye'd care to practice, just to get the way of it . . . ?"

A little later, I stroked his back, damp with exertion and the juice of crushed ferns.

"If you say 'thank you' once more, I will slap you," I said.

Instead, I was answered with a gentle snore. An overhanging fern brushed his cheek, and an inquisitive ant crawled across his hand, making the long fingers twitch in his sleep.

I brushed it away and leaned back on one elbow, watching him. His lashes were long, seen thus with his eyes closed, and thick. Oddly colored, though; dark auburn at the tips, they were very light, almost blond at the roots.

The firm line of his mouth had relaxed in sleep. While it kept a faintly humorous curl at the corner, his lower lip now eased into a fuller curve that seemed both sensual and innocent.

"Damn," I said softly to myself.

I had been fighting it for some time. Even before this ridiculous marriage, I had been more than conscious of his attraction. It had happened before, as it doubtless happens to almost everyone. A sudden sensitivity to the presence, the appearance, of a particular man—or woman, I suppose. The urge to follow him with my eyes, to arrange for small "inadvertent" meetings, to watch him unawares as he went about his work, an exquisite sensitivity to the small details of his body—the shoulder-blades beneath the cloth of his shirt, the lumpy bones of his wrists, the soft place underneath his jaw, where the first prickles of his beard begin to show.

Infatuation. It was common, among the nurses and the

doctors, the nurses and the patients, among any gathering of people thrown for long periods into one another's company.

Some acted on it, and brief, intense affairs were frequent. If they were lucky, the affair flamed out within a few months and nothing resulted from it. If they were not . . . well. Pregnancy, divorce, here and there the odd case of venereal disease. Dangerous thing, infatuation.

I had felt it, several times, but had had the good sense not to act on it. And as it always does, after a time the attraction had lessened, and the man lost his golden aura and resumed his usual place in my life, with no harm done to him, to me, or to Frank.

And now. Now I had been forced to act on it. And God only knew what harm might be done by that action. But there was no turning back from this point.

He lay at ease, sprawled on his stomach. The sun glinted off his red mane and lit the tiny soft hairs that crested his spine, running down to the reddish-gold fuzz that dusted his buttocks and thighs, and deepened into the thicket of soft auburn curls that showed briefly between his spread legs.

I sat up, admiring the long legs, with the smooth line of muscling that indented the thigh from hip to knee, and another that ran from knee to long, elegant foot. The bottoms of his feet were smooth and pink, slightly callused from going barefoot.

My fingers ached, wanting to trace the line of his small, neat ear and the blunt angle of his jaw. Well, I thought, the action *had* been taken, and it was far past the time for restraint. Nothing I did now could make matters worse, for either of us. I reached out and gently touched him.

He slept very lightly. With a suddenness that made me jump, he flipped over, bracing himself on his elbows as though to leap to his feet. Seeing me, he relaxed, smiling.

"Madam, you have me at a disadvantage."

He made a very creditable courtly bow, for a man stretched at full length in a patch of ferns, wearing nothing but a few dappled splotches of sunlight, and I laughed. The smile stayed on his face, but it altered as he looked at me, naked in the ferns. His voice was suddenly husky.

"In fact, Madam, you have me at your mercy."

"Have I, then?" I said softly.

He didn't move, as I reached out once more and drew my hand slowly down his cheek and neck, over the gleaming slope of his shoulder, and down. He didn't move, but he closed his eyes.

"Dear Holy Lord," he said.

He drew his breath in sharply.

"Don't worry," I said. "It doesn't *have* to be rough."

"Thank God for small mercies."

"Keep still."

His fingers dug deeply into the crumbling earth, but he obeyed.

"Please," he said after a time. Glancing up, I could see that his eyes were open now.

"No," I said, enjoying myself. He closed his eyes again.

"You'll pay for this," he said a short time later. A fine dew of sweat shone on the straight bridge of his nose.

"Really?" I said. "What are you going to do?"

The tendons stood out in his forearms as he pressed his palms against the earth, and he spoke with an effort, as though his teeth were clenched.

"I don't know, but . . . by Christ and St. Agnes . . . I will . . . th-think of s-something! God! Please!"

"All right," I said, releasing him.

And I uttered a small shriek as he rolled onto me, pinning me against the ferns.

"Your turn," he said, with considerable satisfaction.

We returned to the inn at sunset, pausing at the top of the hill to be sure that the horses of the Watch were no longer hobbled outside.

The inn looked welcoming, light already shining through the small windows, and through the chinks in the walls. The last of the sun glowed behind us as well, so that everything on the hillside threw a double shadow. The breeze rose with the cooling of the day, and the fluttering leaves of the trees made the multiple shadows dance on the grass. I could easily imagine that there were fairies on the hill, dancing with those shadows, threading their way through the slender trunks to blend into the depths of the wood.

"Dougal's not back yet, either," I observed as we came down the hill. The large black gelding he customarily rode was not in the inn's small paddock. Several other beasts were missing as well; Ned Gowan's for one.

"No, he shouldna come back for another day at least—maybe two." Jamie offered me his arm and we descended the hill slowly, careful of the many rocks that poked through the short grass.

"Where on earth has he gone?" Caught in the rush of recent events, I had not thought to question his absence—or even to notice it.

Jamie handed me over the stile at the back of the inn.

"To do his business wi' the cottars nearby. He's got but a day or two before he's supposed to produce you at the Fort, ye ken." He squeezed my arm reassuringly. "Captain Randall willna be best pleased when Dougal tells him he's not to have ye, and Dougal would as soon not linger in the area afterward."

"Sensible of him," I observed. "Also kind of him to leave us here to, er . . . get acquainted with each other."

Jamie snorted. "Not kindness. That was one of the conditions I set for takin' ye. I said I'd wed if I must, but damned if I'd consummate my marriage under a bush, wi' twenty clansmen lookin' on and offering advice."

I stopped, staring at him. So that was what the shouting had been about.

"*One* of the conditions?" I said, slowly. "And what were the others?"

It was growing too dark to see his face clearly, but I thought he seemed embarrassed.

"Only two others," he said finally.

"Which were?"

"Well," he said, kicking a pebble diffidently out of the way, "I said ye must wed me proper, in kirk, before a priest. Not just by contract. As for the other—he must find ye a suitable gown to be wed in." He looked away, avoiding my gaze, and his voice was so soft I could scarcely hear him.

"I—I knew ye didna wish to wed. I wanted to make it . . . as pleasant as might be for you. I thought ye might feel a bit less . . . well, I wanted ye to have a decent dress, is all."

I opened my mouth to say something, but he turned away, toward the inn.

"Come along, Sassenach," he said gruffly. "I'm hungry."

The price of food was company, as was obvious from the moment of our appearance at the door of the inn's main room. We were greeted by raucous cheers, and hurriedly pushed into seats at the table, where a hearty supper was already in progress.

Having been somewhat prepared this time, I didn't mind the rough jests and crude remarks at our expense. For once, I was pleased to be modestly self-effacing, scrunching back into the corner and leaving Jamie to deal with the rough teasing and bawdy speculations about what we had been doing all day.

"Sleeping," said Jamie, in answer to one question of this sort. "Didna catch a wink last night." The roars of laughter that greeted this were topped by louder ones as he added in confidential tones, "She snores, ye ken."

I obligingly cuffed his ear, and he gathered me to him and kissed me soundly, to general applause.

After supper there was dancing, to the accompaniment of the landlord's fiddle. I had never been much of a dancer, being rather prone to trip over my own feet in times of stress. I scarcely expected that I would do better, attired in long skirts and clumsy footgear. Once I had shed the clogs, though, I was surprised to find that I danced with no difficulty and great enjoyment.

Women being in short supply, the innkeeper's wife and I tucked up our skirts and danced jigs and reels and strathspeys without ceasing, until I had to stop and lean against the settle, red-faced and gasping for breath.

The men were absolutely indefatigable, whirling about like

plaid tops, by themselves or with each other. Finally, they stood back against the wall, watching, cheering and clapping, as Jamie took both my hands and led me through something fast and frantic called "The Cock o' the North."

Ending up by forethought near the stair, we swirled to a close with his arm about my waist. Here we paused, and he made a short speech, mixed in Gaelic and English, which was received with further applause, particularly when he reached into his sporran and tossed a small wash-leather bag to the landlord, instructing that worthy to serve whisky so long as it lasted. I recognized it as his share of the wagers from his fight at Tunnaig. Likely all the money he had in the world; I thought it could not have been better spent.

We had made it up to the balcony, followed by a hail of indelicate good wishes, when a voice louder than the others called Jamie's name.

Turning, I saw Rupert's broad face, redder than usual above its bush of black beard, grinning up from below.

"No good, Rupert," called Jamie. "She's mine."

"Wasted on ye, lad," said Rupert, mopping his face with his sleeve. "She'll ha' ye on the floor in an hour. No stayin' power, these young lads," he called to me. "Ye want a man who doesna waste his time sleepin', lass, let me know. In the meantime . . ." He flung something upward.

A fat little bag clanked on the floor at my feet.

"A wedding present," he called. "Courtesy of the men of the Shimi Bogil Watch."

"Eh?" Jamie stooped to pick it up.

"*Some* of us dinna spend our day idlin' about the grassy banks, lad," he said reprovingly, rolling his eyes lewdly at me. "That money was hard earned."

"Oh, aye," said Jamie, grinning. "Dice or cards?"

"Both." A raffish grin split the black beard. "Skint 'em to the bone, lad. To the bone!"

Jamie opened his mouth, but Rupert held up a broad, callused palm.

"Nay, lad, nay need o' thanks. Just give her a good one for me, eh?"

I pressed my fingers to my lips and blew him a kiss. Slap-

ping a hand to his face as though struck, he staggered back
with an exclamation and reeled off into the taproom, weaving
as though drunk, which he wasn't.

After all the hilarity below, the room seemed a haven of
peace and quiet. Jamie, still laughing quietly to himself,
sprawled out on the bed to recover his breath.

I loosened my bodice, which was uncomfortably tight, and
sat down to comb the tangles out of my dance-disordered
hair.

"You've the loveliest hair," said Jamie, watching me.

"What? *This?*" I raised a hand self-consciously to my locks,
which as usual, could be politely described as higgledy-piggledy.

He laughed. "Well, I like the other too," he said, deliberately straight-faced, "but yes, I meant that."

"But it's so . . . curly," I said, blushing a little.

"Aye, of course." He looked surprised. "I heard one of
Dougal's girls say to a friend at the Castle that it would take
three hours with the hot tongs to make hers look like that.
She said she'd like to scratch your eyes out for looking like
that and not lifting a hand to do so." He sat up and tugged
gently on one curl, stretching it down so that, uncurled, it
reached nearly to my breast. "My sister Jenny's hair is curly,
too, but not so much as yours."

"Is your sister's hair red, like yours?" I asked, trying to
envision what the mysterious Jenny might look like. She
seemed to be often in Jamie's mind.

He shook his head, still twisting curls in and out between
his fingers. "No. Jenny's hair is black. Black as night. I'm red
like my mother, and Jenny takes after Father. Brian Dhu, they
called him, 'Black Brian,' for his hair and his beard."

"I've heard that Captain Randall is called 'Black Jack,' " I
ventured. Jamie laughed humorlessly.

"Oh, aye. But that's with reference to the color of his soul,
not his hair." His gaze sharpened as he looked down at me.
"You're not worrying about him, are ye, lass? Ye shouldna
do so." His hands left my hair and tightened possessively on
my shoulders.

"I meant it, ye know," he said softly. "I will protect you.

From him, or anyone else. To the last drop of my blood, *mo duinne.*"

"*Mo duinne?*" I asked, a little disturbed by the intensity of this speech. I didn't want to be responsible for *any* of his blood being spilt, last drop or first.

"It means 'my brown one.' " He raised a lock of hair to his lips and smiled, with a look in his eyes that started all the drops of my own blood chasing each other through my veins. "*Mo duinne,*" he repeated, softly. "I have been longing to say that to you."

"Rather a dull color, brown, I've always thought," I said practically, trying to delay things a bit. I kept having the feeling of being whirled along much faster than I intended.

Jamie shook his head, still smiling.

"No, I'd not say that, Sassenach. Not dull at all." He lifted the mass of my hair with both hands and fanned it out. "It's like the water in a burn, where it ruffles over the stones. Dark in the wavy spots, with bits of silver on the surface where the sun catches it."

Nervous and a little breathless, I pulled away in order to pick up the comb I had dropped on the floor. I came up to find Jamie eyeing me steadily.

"I said I wouldna ask for anything you did not wish to tell me," he said, "and I won't, but I draw my own conclusions. Colum thought perhaps you were an English spy, though he couldna imagine in that case why you'd no Gaelic. Dougal thinks you're likely a French spy, maybe looking for support for King James. But in that case, *he* canna imagine why you were alone."

"And what about you?" I asked, pulling hard at a stubborn tangle. "What do you think I am?"

He tilted his head appraisingly, looking me over carefully.

"To look at, you could be French. You've that fine-boned look through the face that some of the Angevin ladies have. Frenchwomen are usually sallow-faced, though, and you have skin like an opal." He traced a finger slowly across the curve of my collarbone, and I felt the skin glow beneath his touch.

The finger moved to my face, drawing from temple to cheek, smoothing the hair back behind my ear. I remained immobile under his scrutiny, trying not to move as his hand passed behind my neck, thumb gently stroking my earlobe.

"Golden eyes; I've seen a pair like that once before—on a leopard." He shook his head. "Nay, lass. Ye could be French, but you're not."

"How do you know?"

"I've talked with you a good deal; and listened to you besides. Dougal thinks you're French because you speak French well—verra well."

"Thank you," I said sarcastically. "And the fact that I speak French well proves I'm not French?"

He smiled and tightened his grip on my neck. *"Vous parlez très bien*—but not quite as well as I do," he added, dropping back into English. He released me suddenly. "I spent a year in France, after I left the castle, and two more later on with the army. I know a native speaker of French when I hear one. And French is not your mother tongue." He shook his head slowly.

"Spanish? Perhaps, but why? Spain's no interests in the Highlands. German? Surely not." He shrugged. "Whoever you are, the English would want to find out. They canna afford to have unknown quantities at large, with the clans restless and Prince Charlie waiting to set sail from France. And their methods of finding out are not very gentle. I've reason to know."

"And how do you know I'm not an *English* spy, then? Dougal thought I was, you said so."

"It's possible, though your spoken English is more than a little odd too. If you were, though, why would you choose to wed me, rather than go back to your own folk? That was another reason for Dougal's makin' ye wed me—to see would ye bolt last night, when it came to the point."

"And I didn't bolt. So what does that prove?"

He laughed and lay back down on the bed, an arm over his eyes to shield them from the lamp.

"Damned if I know, Sassenach. *Damned* if I know. There isna any reasonable explanation I can think of for you. You might be one of the Wee Folk, for all I know"—he peeked sideways from under his arm—"no, I suppose not. You're too big."

"Aren't you afraid I might kill you in your sleep some night, if you don't know who I am?"

He didn't answer, but took his arm away from his eyes, and his smile widened. His eyes must be from the Fraser side, I thought. Not deep-set like the MacKenzies', they were set at an odd angle, so that the high cheekbones made them look almost slanted.

Without troubling to lift his head, he opened the front of his shirt and spread the cloth aside, laying his chest bare to the waist. He drew the dirk from its sheath and tossed it toward me. It thunked on the boards at my feet.

He put his arm back over his eyes and stretched his head back, showing the place where the dark stubble of his sprouting beard stopped abruptly, just below the jaw.

"Straight up, just under the breastbone," he advised. "Quick and neat, though it takes a bit of strength. The throat-cutting's easier, but it's verra messy."

I bent to pick up the dirk.

"Serve you right if I did," I remarked. "Cocky bastard."

The grin visible beneath the crook of his arm widened still further.

"Sassenach?"

I stopped, dirk still in my hand.

"What?"

"I'll die a happy man."

17

We Meet a Beggar

We slept fairly late the next morning, and the sun was high as we left the inn, heading south this time. Most of the horses were gone from the paddock, and none of the men from our party seemed to be about. I wondered aloud where they had gone.

Jamie grinned. "I canna say for sure, but I could guess. The Watch went *that* way yesterday"—he pointed west—"so I should say Rupert and the others have gone *that* way." Pointing east.

"Cattle," he explained, seeing that I still didn't understand. "The estate-holders and tacksmen pay the Watch to keep an eye out, and get back their cattle, if they're stolen in a raid. But if the Watch is riding west toward Lag Cruime, any herds to the east are helpless—for a bit, anyway. It's the Grants' lands down that way, and Rupert's one of the best cattle-lifters I've ever seen. Beasts will follow him anywhere, wi' scarcely a bleat amongst them. And since there's no more entertainment to be had here, most likely he's got restless."

Jamie himself seemed rather restless, and set a good pace. There was a deer trail through the heather, and the going was fairly easy, so I kept up with no difficulty. After a bit, we came out onto a stretch of moorland, where we could walk side by side.

"What about Horrocks?" I asked suddenly. Hearing him mention the town of Lag Cruime, I had remembered the

English deserter and his possible news. "You were supposed to meet him in Lag Cruime, weren't you?"

He nodded. "Aye. But I canna go there now, wi' both Randall and the Watch headed that way. Too dangerous."

"Could someone go for you? Or do you trust anyone enough?"

He glanced down at me and smiled. "Well, there's you. Since ye didna kill me last night after all, I suppose I may trust you. But I'm afraid you couldna go to Lag Cruime alone. No, if necessary, Murtagh will go for me. But I may be able to arrange something else—we'll see."

"You trust Murtagh?" I asked curiously. I had no very friendly feelings toward the scruffy little man, since he was more or less responsible for my present predicament, having kidnapped me in the first place. Still, there was clearly a friendship of some kind between him and Jamie.

"Oh, aye." He glanced at me, surprised. "Murtagh's known me all my life—a second cousin of my father's, I think. His father was my—"

"He's a Fraser, you mean," I interrupted hastily. "I thought he was one of the MacKenzies. He was with Dougal when I met you."

Jamie nodded. "Aye. When I decided to come over from France I sent word to him, asking him to meet me at the coast." He smiled wryly. "I didna ken, ye see, whether it was Dougal had tried to kill me earlier. And I did not quite like the idea of meeting several MacKenzies alone, just in case. Didna want to end up washing about in the surf off Skye, if that's what they had in mind."

"I see. So Dougal isn't the only one who believes in witnesses."

He nodded. "Very handy things, witnesses."

On the other side of the moorland was a stretch of twisted rocks, pitted and gouged by the advance and retreat of glaciers long gone. Rainwater filled the deeper pits, and thistle and tansy and meadowsweet surrounded these tarns with thick growth, the flowers reflected in the still water.

Sterile and fishless, these pools dotted the landscape and formed traps for unwary travelers, who might easily stumble into one in darkness and be forced to spend a wet and uncomfortable night on the moor. We sat down beside one pool to eat our morning meal of bread and cheese.

This tarn at least had birds; swallows dipped low over the water to drink, and plovers and curlews poked long bills into the muddy earth at its edges, digging for insects.

I tossed crumbs of bread onto the mud for the birds. A curlew eyed one suspiciously, but while it was still making up its mind, a quick swallow zoomed in under its bill and made off with the treat. The curlew ruffled its feathers and went back to its industrious digging.

Jamie called my attention to a plover, calling and dragging a seemingly broken wing near us.

"She's a nest somewhere near," I said.

"Over there." He had to point it out several times before I finally spotted it; a shallow depression, quite out in the open, but with its four spotted eggs so close in appearance to the leaf-speckled bank that when I blinked I lost sight of the nest again.

Picking up a stick, Jamie gently poked the nest, pushing one egg out of place. The mother plover, excited, ran up almost in front of him. He sat on his heels, quite motionless, letting the bird dart back and forth, squalling. There was a flash of movement and he held the bird in his hand, suddenly still.

He spoke to the bird in Gaelic, a quiet, hissing sort of speech, as he stroked the soft, mottled plumage with one finger. The bird crouched in his hand, completely motionless, even the reflections frozen in its round black eyes.

He set it gently on the ground, but the bird did not move away until he said a few more words, and waved his hand slowly back and forth behind it. It gave a short jerk and darted away into the weeds. He watched it go, and, quite unconscious, crossed himself.

"Why did you do that?" I asked, curious.

"What?" He was momentarily startled; I think he had forgotten I was there.

"You crossed yourself when the bird flew off; I wondered why."

He shrugged, mildly embarrassed.

"Ah, well. It's an old tale, is all. Why plovers cry as they do, and run keening about their nests like that." He motioned to the far side of the tarn, where another plover was doing exactly that. He watched the bird for a few moments, abstracted.

"Plovers have the souls of young mothers dead in childbirth," he said. He glanced aside at me, shyly. "The story goes that they cry and run about their nests because they canna believe the young are safe hatched; they're mourning always for the lost one—or looking for a child left behind." He squatted by the nest and nudged the oblong egg with his stick, turning it bit by bit until the pointed end faced in, like the others. He stayed squatting, even after the egg had been replaced, balancing the stick across his thighs, staring out over the still waters of the tarn.

"It's only habit, I suppose," he said. "I did it first when I was much younger, when I first heard that story. I didna really believe they have souls, of course, even then, but, ye ken, just as a bit of respect . . ." He looked up at me and smiled suddenly. "Done it so often now, I'd not even notice. There's quite a few plovers in Scotland, ye ken." He rose and tossed the stick aside. "Let's go on, now; there's a place I want to show you, near the top of the hill yon." He took my elbow to help me out of the declivity, and we set off up the slope.

I had heard what he said to the plover he released. Though I had only a few words of Gaelic, I had heard the old salutation often enough to be familiar with it. 'God go with ye, Mother,' he had said.

A young mother, dead in childbirth. And a child left behind. I touched his arm and he looked down at me.

"How old were you?" I asked.

He gave me a half-smile. "Eight," he answered. "Weaned, at least."

He spoke no more, but led me uphill. We were in sloping foothills, now, thick with heather. Just beyond, the countryside changed abruptly, with huge heaps of granite rearing up from the earth, surrounded by clusters of sycamore and larch.

We came over the crest of the hill, and left the plovers crying by the tarns behind us.

⎯⎯

The sun was growing hot, and after an hour of shoving through thick foliage—even with Jamie doing most of the shoving—I was ready for a rest.

We found a shady spot at the foot of one of the granite outcrops. The spot reminded me a bit of the place where I had first met Murtagh—and parted company with Captain Randall. Still, it was pleasant here. Jamie told me that we were alone, because of the constant birdsong all around. If anyone came near, most birds would stop singing, though the jays and the jackdaws would screech and call in alarm.

"Always hide in a forest, Sassenach," he advised me. "If ye dinna move too much yourself, the birds will tell you in plenty of time if anyone's near."

Looking back from pointing out a squawking jay in the tree overhead, his eyes caught mine. And we sat as though frozen, within hand's reach but not touching, barely breathing. After a time, the jay grew bored with us and left. It was Jamie who looked away first, with an almost imperceptible shiver, as though he were cold.

The heads of shaggy-cap mushrooms poked whitely through the mold beneath the ferns. Jamie's blunt forefinger flipped one off its stem, and traced the spokes of the basidium as he marshaled his next words. When he spoke carefully, as now, he all but lost the slight Scots accent that usually marked his speech.

"I do not wish to . . . that is. . . . I do not mean to imply. . . ." He looked up suddenly and smiled, with a helpless gesture. "I dinna want to insult you by sounding as though I think you've a vast experience of men, is all. But it would be foolish to pretend that ye don't know more than I do about such matters. What I meant to ask is, is this . . . usual? What it is between us, when I touch you, when you . . . lie with me? Is it always so between a man and a woman?"

In spite of his difficulties, I knew exactly what he meant.

His gaze was direct, holding my eyes as he waited my answer. I wanted to look away, but couldn't.

"There's often something like it," I said, and had to stop and clear my throat. "But no. No, it isn't—usual. I have no idea why, but no. This is . . . different."

He relaxed a bit, as though I had confirmed something about which he had been anxious.

"I thought perhaps not. I've not lain with a woman before, but I've . . . ah, had my hands on a few." He smiled shyly, and shook his head. "It wasna the same. I mean, I've held women in my arms before, and kissed them, and . . . well." He waved a hand, dismissing the *and*. "It was verra pleasant indeed. Made my heart pound and my breath come short, and all that. But it wasna at all as it is when I take you in my arms and kiss you." His eyes, I thought, were the color of lakes and skies, and as fathomless as either.

He reached out and touched my lower lip, barely brushing the edge. "It starts out the same, but then, after a moment," he said, speaking softly, "suddenly it's as though I've a living flame in my arms." His touch grew firmer, outlining my lips and caressing the line of my jaw. "And I want only to throw myself into it and be consumed."

I thought of telling him that his own touch seared my skin and filled my veins with fire. But I was already alight and glowing like a brand. I closed my eyes and felt the kindling touch move to cheek and temple, ear and neck, and shuddered as his hands dropped to my waist and drew me close.

Jamie seemed to have a definite idea where we were going. At length he stopped at the foot of a huge rock, some twenty feet high, warty with lumps and jagged cracks. Tansy and eglantine had taken root in the cracks, and waved in precarious yellow flags against the stone. He took my hand and nodded at the rock face before us.

"D'ye see the steps, there, Sassenach? Think ye can manage it?" There were, in fact, faintly marked protuberances in the stone, rising at an angle across the face of the rock. Some were bona fide ledges, and others merely a foothold for lichens. I couldn't tell whether they were natural, or perhaps had known some assistance in their forming, but I thought it might just be possible to climb them, even in a full-length skirt and tight bodice.

With some slippages and scares, and with Jamie pushing helpfully from the rear on occasion, I made it to the top of the rock, and paused to look around. The view was spectacular. The dark bulk of a mountain rose to the east, while far below to the south the foothills ran out into a vast, barren moorland. The top of the rock sloped inward from all sides, forming a shallow dish. In the center of the dish was a blackened circle, with the sooty remnants of charred sticks. We were not the first visitors, then.

"You knew this place?" Jamie stood to one side a little, observing me and taking pleasure in my raptness. He shrugged, deprecating.

"Oh, aye. I know most places through this part of the Highlands. Come here, there's a spot ye can sit, and see down to where the road comes past the hill." The inn also was visible from here, reduced from doll-house to child's building-block by the distance. A few tethered horses were clustered under the trees by the road, small blobs of brown and black from here.

No trees grew on the top of the rock, and the sun was hot on my back. We sat side by side, legs dangling over the edge, and companionably shared one of the bottles of ale that Jamie had thoughtfully lifted from the well in the inn yard as we left.

There were no trees atop the rock, but the smaller plants, the ones that could gain a foothold in the precarious cracks and root themselves in meager soil, sprouted here and there, raising their faces bravely to the hot spring sun. There was a small clump of daisies sheltering in the lee of an outcrop near my hand, and I reached to pluck one.

There was a faint whir, and the daisy leapt off its stem and landed on my knee. I stared stupidly, my mind unable to make sense of this bizarre behavior. Jamie, a good deal faster than I in his apprehensions, had flung himself flat on the rock.

"Get *down*!" he said. A large hand fastened on my elbow and jerked me flat beside him. As I hit the spongy moss, I saw the shaft of the arrow, still quivering above my face, where it had struck home in a cleft of the outcrop.

I froze, afraid even to look around, and tried to press myself still flatter against the ground. Jamie was motionless at my side, so still that he might have been a stone himself. Even the birds and insects seemed to have paused in their song, and the air hung breathless and waiting. Suddenly Jamie began to laugh.

He sat up, and grasping the arrow by the shaft, twisted it carefully out of the rock. It was fletched with the split tail-feathers of a woodpecker, I saw, and banded with blue thread, wrapped in a line half an inch wide below the quills.

Laying the arrow aside, Jamie cupped his hands around his mouth and gave a remarkably good imitation of the call of a green woodpecker. He lowered his hands and waited. In a moment, the call was answered from the grove below, and a broad smile spread across his face.

"A friend of yours?" I guessed. He nodded, eyes intent on the narrow path up the rock-face.

"Hugh Munro, unless someone else has taken to making arrows in his style."

We waited a moment longer, but no one appeared on the path below.

"Ah," said Jamie softly, and whirled around, just in time to confront a head, rising slowly above the edge of the rock behind us.

The head burst into a jack-o'-lantern grin, snaggle-toothed and jolly, beaming with pleasure at surprising us. The head itself was roughly pumpkin-shaped, the impression enhanced by the orange-brown, leathery skin that covered not only the face but the round, bald crown of the head as well. Few pumpkins, however, could boast such a luxuriant growth of beard, nor such a pair of bright blue eyes. Stubby hands with filthy nails planted themselves beneath the beard and swiftly hoisted the remainder of the jack-o'-lantern up into view.

The body rather matched the head, having a distinct look of the Halloween goblin about it. The shoulders were very broad, but hunched and slanted, one being considerably higher than the other. One leg, too, seemed somewhat shorter than its fellow, giving the man a rather hopping, hitching sort of gait.

Munro, if this was indeed Jamie's friend, was clad in what appeared to be multiple layers of rags, the faded colors of berry-dyed fabric peeking out through rents in a shapeless garment that might once have been a woman's smock.

He carried no sporran at his belt—which was in any case no more than a frayed length of rope, from which two furry carcasses swung, head-down. Instead, he had a fat leather wallet slung across his chest, of surprisingly good quality, considering the rest of his outfit. A collection of small metal oddments dangled from the strap of the wallet: religious medals, military decorations, what looked to be old uniform buttons, worn coins, pierced and sewn on, and three or four small rectangular bits of metal, dull grey and with cryptic marks incised in their surfaces.

Jamie rose as the creature hopped nimbly over the intervening protrusions of rock, and the two men embraced warmly, thumping each other hard on the back in the odd fashion of manly greeting.

"And how goes it then, with the house of Munro?" inquired Jamie, standing back at length and surveying his old companion.

Munro ducked his head and made an odd gobbling noise, grinning. Then, raising his eyebrows, he nodded in my direction and waved his stubby hands in a strangely graceful interrogatory gesture.

"My wife," said Jamie, reddening slightly with a mixture of shyness and pride at the new introduction. "Married but the two days."

Munro smiled more broadly still at this information, and executed a remarkably complex and graceful bow, involving the rapid touching of head, heart, and lips and ending up in a near-horizontal position on the ground at my feet. Having executed this striking maneuver, he sprang to his feet with the grace of an acrobat and thumped Jamie again, this time in apparent congratulation.

Munro then began an extraordinary ballet of the hands, motioning to himself, away down toward the forest, at me, and back to himself, with such an array of gestures and wavings that I could hardly follow his flying hands. I had seen deaf-mute talk before, but never executed so swiftly and gracefully.

"Is that so, then?" Jamie exclaimed. It was his turn to buffet the other man in congratulation. No wonder men got impervious to superficial pain, I thought. It came from this habit of hammering each other incessantly.

"He's married as well," Jamie explained, turning to me. "Six months since, to a widow—oh, all right, to a *fat* widow," he amended, in response to an emphatic gesture from Munro, "with six children, down in the village of Dubhlairn."

"How nice," I said politely. "It looks as though they'll eat well, at least." I motioned to the rabbits hanging from his belt.

Munro at once unfastened one of the corpses and handed it to me, with such an expression of beaming goodwill that I felt obliged to accept it, smiling back and hoping privately that it didn't harbor fleas.

"A wedding gift," said Jamie. "And most welcome, Munro. Ye must allow us to return the favor." With which, he extracted one of the bottles of ale from its mossy bed and handed it across.

The courtesies attended to in this manner, we all sat down again to a companionable sharing of the third bottle. Jamie and Munro carried on an exchange of news, gossip, and conversation which seemed no less free for the fact that only one of them spoke.

I took little part in the conversation, being unable to read Munro's hand-signs, though Jamie did his best to include me by translation and reference.

At one point, Jamie jabbed a thumb at the rectangular bits of lead that adorned Munro's strap.

"Gone official, have ye?" he asked. "Or is that just for when the game is scarce?" Munro bobbed his head and nodded like a jack-in-the-box.

"What are they?" I asked curiously.

"Gaberlunzies."

"Oh, to be sure," I said. "Pardon my asking."

"A gaberlunzie is a license to beg, Sassenach," Jamie explained. "It's good within the borders of the parish, and only on the one day a week when begging's allowed. Each parish has its own, so the beggars from one parish canna take overmuch advantage of the charity of the next."

"A system with a certain amount of elasticity, I see," I said, eyeing Munro's stock of four lead seals.

"Ah, well, Munro's a special case, d'ye see. He was captured by the Turks at sea. Spent a good many years rowing up and down in a galley, and a few more as a slave in Algiers. That's where he lost his tongue."

"They . . . cut it out?" I felt a bit faint.

Jamie seemed undisturbed by the thought, but then he had apparently known Munro for some time.

"Oh, aye. And broke his leg for him, as well. The back, too, Munro? No," he amended, at a series of signs from Munro, "the back was an accident, something that happened jumping off a wall in Alexandria. The feet, though; that was the Turks' doing."

I didn't really want to know, but both Munro and Jamie seemed dying to tell me. "All right," I said, resigned. "What happened to his feet?"

With something approaching pride, Munro stripped off his battered clogs and hose, exposing broad, splayed feet on which the skin was thickened and roughened, white shiny patches alternating with angry red areas.

"Boiling oil," said Jamie. "It's how they force captive Christians to convert to the Mussulman religion."

"It looks a very effective means of persuasion," I said. "So that's why several parishes will give him leave to beg? To make up for his trials on behalf of Christendom?"

"Aye, exactly." Jamie was evidently pleased with my swift appreciation of the situation. Munro also expressed his admiration with another deep salaam, followed by a very expressive if indelicate sequence of hand movements which I gathered were meant to be praising my physical appearance as well.

"Thank ye, man. Aye, she'll do me proud, I reckon." Jamie, seeing my uplifted brows, tactfully turned Munro so that his back was to me and the flying fingers hidden. "Now, tell me what's doing in the villages?"

The two men drew closer together, continuing their lop-sided conversation with an increased intensity. Since Jamie's part seemed to be limited mainly to grunts and exclamations of interest, I could glean little of the content, and busied myself instead with a survey of the strange little rock plants sprouting from the surfaces of our perch.

I had collected a pocketful of eyebright and dittany by the time they finished talking and Hugh Munro rose to go. With a final bow to me and a thump on the back for Jamie, he shuffled to the edge of the rock and disappeared as quickly as one of the rabbits he poached might vanish into its hole.

"What fascinating friends you have," I said.

"Oh, aye. Nice fellow, Hugh. I hunted wi' him and some others, last year. He's on his own, now that he's an official beggar, but his work keeps him moving about the parishes; he'll know everything that goes on within the borders of Ardagh and Chesthill."

"Including the whereabouts of Horrocks?" I guessed.

Jamie nodded. "Aye. And he'll carry a message for me, to change the meeting place."

"Which foxes Dougal rather neatly," I observed. "If he had any ideas about holding you to ransom over Horrocks."

He nodded, and a smile creased one corner of his mouth.

"Aye, there's that about it."

➤

It was near supper-time again as we reached the inn. This time, though, Dougal's big black and its five companions were standing in the inn yard, contentedly munching hay.

Dougal himself was inside, washing the road dust from his throat with sour ale. He nodded to me and swung round to greet his nephew. Instead of speaking, though, he just stood there, head on one side, eyeing Jamie quizzically.

"Ah, that's it," he said finally, in the satisfied tones of a man who has solved a difficult puzzle. "Now I know what ye mind me of, lad." He turned to me.

"Ever seen a red stag near the end of the rutting season,

lass?" he said confidentially. "The poor beasts dinna sleep nor eat for several weeks, because they canna spare the time, between fightin' off the other stags and serving the does. By the end o' the season, they're naught but skin and bones. Their eyes are deep-sunk in their heads, and the only part o' them that doesna shake wi' palsy is their—"

The last of this was lost in a chorus of laughter as Jamie pulled me up the stairs. We did not come down to supper.

◄—

Much later, on the edge of sleep, I felt Jamie's arm around my waist, and felt his breath warm against my neck.

"Does it ever stop? The wanting you?" His hand came around to caress my breast. "Even when I've just left ye, I want you so much my chest feels tight and my fingers ache with wanting to touch ye again."

He cupped my face in the dark, thumbs stroking the arcs of my eyebrows. "When I hold ye between my two hands and feel you quiver like that, waitin' for me to take you . . . Lord, I want to pleasure you 'til ye cry out under me and open yourself to me. And when I take my own pleasure from you, I feel as though I've given ye my soul along with my cock."

He rolled above me and I opened my legs, wincing slightly as he entered me. He laughed softly. "Aye, I'm a bit sore, too. Do ye want me to stop?" I wrapped my legs around his hips in answer and pulled him closer.

"*Would* you stop?" I asked.

"No. I can't."

We laughed together, and rocked slowly, lips and fingers exploring in the dark.

"I see why the Church says it is a sacrament," Jamie said dreamily.

"This?" I said, startled. "Why?"

"Or at least holy," he said. "I feel like God Himself when I'm in you."

I laughed so hard he nearly came out. He stopped and gripped my shoulders to steady me.

"What's so funny?"

"It's hard to imagine God doing this."

Jamie resumed his movements. "Well, if God made man in His own image, I should imagine He's got a cock." He started to laugh as well, losing his rhythm again. "Though ye dinna remind me much of the Blessed Virgin, Sassenach."

We shook in each other's arms, laughing until we came uncoupled and rolled apart.

Recovering, Jamie slapped my hip. "Get on your knees, Sassenach."

"Why?"

"If you'll not let me be spiritual about it, you'll have to put up wi' my baser nature. I'm going to be a beast." He bit my neck. "Do ye want me to be a horse, a bear, or a dog?"

"A hedgehog."

"A hedgehog? And just how does a hedgehog make love?" he demanded.

No, I thought. I won't. I will *not*. But I did. "*Very* carefully," I replied, giggling helplessly. So now we know just how old *that* one is, I thought.

Jamie collapsed in a ball, wheezing with laughter. At last he rolled over and got to his knees, groping for the flint box on the table. He glowed like red amber against the room's darkness as the wick caught and the light swelled behind him.

He flopped back on the foot of the bed, grinning down at me, where I still shook on the pillow with spasms of giggles. He rubbed the back of his hand across his face and assumed a mock-stern expression.

"All right, woman. I see the time has come when I shall have to exert my authority as your husband."

"Oh, you will?"

"Aye." He dived forward, grabbing my thighs and spreading them. I squeaked and tried to wriggle upward.

"No, don't do that!"

"Why not?" He lay full-length between my legs, squinting up at me. He kept a firm hold on my thighs, preventing my struggles to close them.

"Tell me, Sassenach. Why don't ye want me to do that?" He rubbed his cheek against the inside of one thigh, ferocious young beard rasping the tender skin. "Be honest. Why not?"

He rasped the other side, making me kick and squirm wildly to get away, to no avail.

I turned my face into the pillow, which felt cool against my flushed cheek. "Well, if you must know," I muttered, "I don't think—well, I'm afraid that it doesn't—I mean, the smell . . ." My voice faded off into an embarrassed silence. There was a sudden movement between my legs, as Jamie heaved himself up. He put his arms around my hips, laid his cheek on my thigh, and laughed until the tears ran down his cheeks.

"Jesus God, Sassenach," he said at last, snorting with mirth, "don't ye know what's the first thing you do when you're getting acquainted with a new horse?"

"No," I said, completely baffled.

He raised one arm, displaying a soft tuft of cinnamon-colored hair. "You rub your oxter over the beast's nose a few times, to give him your scent and get him accustomed to you, so he won't be nervous of ye." He raised himself on his elbows, peering up over the slope of belly and breast.

"That's what you should have done wi' me, Sassenach. You should ha' rubbed my face between your legs first thing. Then I wouldn't have been skittish."

"Skittish!"

He lowered his face and rubbed it deliberately back and forth, snorting and blowing in imitation of a nuzzling horse. I writhed and kicked him in the ribs, with exactly as much effect as kicking a brick wall. Finally he pressed my thighs flat again and looked up.

"Now," he said, in a tone that brooked no opposition, "lie still."

I felt exposed, invaded, helpless—and as though I were about to disintegrate. Jamie's breath was alternately warm and cool on my skin.

"Please," I said, not knowing whether I meant "please stop" or "please go on." It didn't matter; he didn't mean to stop.

Consciousness fragmented into a number of small separate sensations: the roughness of the linen pillow, nubbled with embroidered flowers; the oily reek of the lamp, mingled with the fainter scent of roast beef and ale and the still fainter wisps of freshness from the wilting flowers in the glass; the cool timber of the wall against my left foot, the firm hands on my hips. The sensations swirled and coalesced behind my closed eyelids into a glowing sun that swelled and shrank and finally exploded with a soundless *pop* that left me in a warm and pulsing darkness.

Dimly, from a long way away, I heard Jamie sit up.

"Well, that's a bit better," said a voice, gasping between words. "Takes a bit of effort to make *you* properly submissive, doesn't it?" The bed creaked with a shifting of weight and I felt my knees being nudged further apart.

"Not as dead as you look, I hope?" said the voice, coming nearer. I arched upward with an inarticulate sound as exquisitely sensitive tissues were firmly parted in a fresh assault.

"Jesus Christ," I said. There was a faint chuckle near my ear.

"I only said I *felt* like God, Sassenach," he murmured, "I never said I *was*."

And later, as the rising sun began to dim the glow of the lamp, I roused from a drifting sleep to hear Jamie murmur once more, "Does it ever stop, Claire? The wanting?"

My head fell back onto his shoulder. "I don't know, Jamie. I really don't."

18

Raiders in the Rocks

"What did Captain Randall say?" I asked.

With Dougal on one side and Jamie on the other, there was barely room for the three horses to ride abreast down the narrow road. Here and there, one or both of my companions would have to drop back or spur up, in order to avoid becoming entangled in the overgrowth that threatened to reclaim the crude track.

Dougal glanced at me, then back at the road, in order to guide his horse around a large rock. A wicked grin spread slowly across his features.

"He wasna best pleased about it," he said circumspectly. "Though I am not sure I should tell ye what he actually *said;* there's likely limits even to *your* tolerance for bad language, Mistress Fraser."

I overlooked his sardonic use of my new title, as well as the implied insult, though I saw Jamie stiffen in his saddle.

"I, er, don't suppose he means to take any steps about it?" I asked. Despite Jamie's assurances, I had visions of scarlet-coated dragoons bursting out of the bushes, slaughtering the Scots and dragging me away to Randall's lair for questioning. I had an uneasy feeling that Randall's ideas of interrogation might be creative, to say the least.

"Shouldn't think so," Dougal answered casually. "He's more to worry about than one stray Sassenach wench, no matter how pretty." He raised an eyebrow and half-bowed toward me, as though the compliment were meant in apology.

"He's also better sense than to rile Colum by kidnapping his niece," he said, more matter-of-factly.

Niece. I felt a small shiver run down my spine, in spite of the warm weather. Niece to the MacKenzie chieftain. Not to mention to the war chieftain of clan MacKenzie, riding so nonchalantly by my side. And on the other side, I was now presumably linked with Lord Lovat, chief of clan Fraser, with the abbot of a powerful French abbey, and with who knew how many other assorted Frasers. No, perhaps Jonathan Randall *wouldn't* think it worthwhile to pursue me. And that, after all, had been the point of this ridiculous arrangement.

I stole a glance at Jamie, riding ahead now. His back was straight as an alder sapling and his hair shone under the sun like a helmet of burnished metal.

Dougal followed my glance.

"Could have been worse, no?" he said, with an ironic lift of his brow.

Two nights later, we were encamped on a stretch of moorland, near one of those strange outcroppings of glacier-pocked granite. It had been a long day's travel, with only a hasty meal eaten in the saddle, and everyone was pleased to stop for a cooked dinner. I had tried early on to assist with the cooking, but my help had been more or less politely rejected by the taciturn clansman whose job it apparently was.

One of the men had killed a deer that morning, and a portion of the fresh meat, cooked with turnips, onions, and whatever else he could find, had made a delicious dinner. Bursting with food and contentment, we all sprawled around the fire, listening to stories and songs. Surprisingly enough, little Murtagh, who seldom opened his mouth to speak, had a beautiful, clear tenor voice. While it was difficult to persuade him to sing, the results were worth it.

I nestled closer to Jamie, trying to find a comfortable spot to sit on the hard granite. We had camped at the edge of the rocky outcrop, where a broad shelf of reddish granite gave us a natural hearth, and the towering jumble of rocks behind made a place to hide the horses. When I asked why we did not sleep more comfortably on the springy grass of the moor, Ned Gowan had informed me that we were now near the southern border of the MacKenzie lands. And thus near the territory of both Grants and Chisholms.

"Dougal's scouts say there's no sign of anyone nearabouts," he had said, standing on a large boulder to peer into the sunset himself, "but ye can never tell. Better safe than sorry, ye ken."

When Murtagh called it quits, Rupert began to tell stories. While he lacked Gwyllyn's elegant way with words, he had an inexhaustible fund of stories, about fairies, ghosts, the *tannasg* or evil spirits, and other inhabitants of the Highlands, such as the waterhorses. These beings, I was given to understand, inhabited almost all bodies of water, being especially common at fords and crossings, though many lived in the depths of the lochs.

"There's a spot at the eastern end of Loch Garve, ye ken," he said, rolling his eyes around the gathering to be sure everyone was listening, "that never freezes. It's always black water there, even when the rest o' the loch is frozen solid, for that's the waterhorse's chimney."

The waterhorse of Loch Garve, like so many of his kind, had stolen a young girl who came to the loch to draw water, and carried her away to live in the depths of the loch and be his wife. Woe betide any maiden, or any man, for that matter, who met a fine horse by the water's side and thought to ride upon him, for a rider once mounted could not dismount, and the horse would step into the water, turn into a fish, and swim to his home with the hapless rider still stuck fast to his back.

"Now, a waterhorse beneath the waves has but fish's teeth," said Rupert, wiggling his palm like an undulating fish, "and feeds on snails and waterweeds and cold, wet things. His blood runs cold as the water, and he's no need of fire, d'ye ken, but a human woman's a wee bit warmer than that." Here he winked at me and leered outrageously, to the enjoyment of the listeners.

"So the waterhorse's wife was sad and cold and hungry in her new home beneath the waves, not caring owermuch for snails and waterweed for her supper. So, the waterhorse being a kindly sort, takes himself to the bank of the loch near the house of a man with the reputation of a builder. And when the man came down to the river, and saw the fine golden horse with his silver bridle, shining in the sun, he couldna resist seizing the bridle and mounting."

"Sure enough, the waterhorse carries him straight into the water, and down through the depths to his own cold, fishy home. And there he tells the builder if he would be free, he must build a fine hearth, and a chimney as well, that the waterhorse's wife might have a fire to warm her hands and fry her fish."

I had been resting my head on Jamie's shoulder, feeling pleasantly drowsy and looking forward to bed, even if that was only a blanket spread over granite. Suddenly I felt his body tense. He put a hand on my neck, warning me to keep still. I looked around the campsite, and could see nothing amiss, but I caught the air of tension, running from man to man as though transmitted by wireless.

Looking in Rupert's direction, I saw him nod fractionally as he caught Dougal's eye, though he went on with the story imperturbably.

"So the builder, havin' little choice, did as he was bid. And so the waterhorse kept his word, and returned the man to the bank near his home. And the waterhorse's wife was warm, then, and happy, and full of the fish she fried for her supper. And the water never freezes over the east end of Loch Garve because the heat from the waterhorse's chimney melts the ice."

Rupert was seated on a rock, his right side toward me. As he spoke, he bent down as though casually to scratch his leg. Without the slightest hitch in his movements, he grasped the knife that lay on the ground near his foot and transferred it smoothly to his lap, where it lay hidden in the folds of his kilt.

I wriggled closer and pulled Jamie's head down as though overcome by amorousness. "What is it?" I whispered in his ear.

He seized my earlobe between his teeth and whispered back. "The horses are restless. Someone's near."

One man got up and strolled to the edge of the rock to

relieve himself. When he returned, he sat down in a new spot, next to one of the drovers. Another man rose and peered into the cook-pot, helping himself to a morsel of venison. All around the campsite, there was a subtle shifting and moving, while Rupert kept on talking.

Watching carefully, with Jamie's arm tight around me, I finally realized that the men were moving closer to wherever their weapons had been placed. All of them slept with their dirks, but generally left swords, pistols, and the round leather shields called targes in small, neat heaps near the edge of the campsite. Jamie's own pair of pistols lay on the ground with his sword, just a few feet away.

I could see the firelight dancing on the damascened blade. While his pistols were no more than the customary horn-handled "dags" worn by most of the men, both broadsword and claymore were something special. He had showed them to me with pride at one of our stops, turning the gleaming blades over lovingly in his hands.

The claymore was wrapped inside his blanket roll; I could see the enormous T-shaped hilt, the grip roughened for battle by careful sanding. I had lifted it, and nearly dropped it. It weighed close to fifteen pounds, Jamie told me.

If the claymore was somber and lethal-looking, the broadsword was beautiful. Two-thirds the weight of the larger weapon, it was a deadly, gleaming thing with Islamic tracery snaking its way up the blue steel blade to the spiraled basket hilt, enameled in reds and blues. I had seen Jamie use it in playful practice, first right-handed with one of the men-at-arms, later left-handed with Dougal. He was a glory to watch under those conditions, swift and sure, with a grace made the more impressive by his size. But my mouth grew dry at the thought of seeing that skill used in earnest.

He bent toward me, planting a tender kiss under the edge of my jaw, and taking the opportunity to turn me slightly, so that I faced one of the jumbled piles of rocks.

"Soon, I think," he murmured, kissing me industriously. "D'ye see the small opening in the rock?" I did; a space less than three feet high, formed by two large slabs fallen together.

He clasped my face and nuzzled me lovingly. "When I say go, get into it and stay there. Have ye the dirk?"

He had insisted I keep the dirk he had tossed to me that night at the inn, despite my own insistence that I had neither the skill nor the inclination to use it. And when it came to insisting, Dougal had been right; Jamie *was* stubborn.

Consequently, the dirk was in one of the deep pockets of my gown. After a day of uncomfortable awareness of its weight against my thigh, I had grown almost oblivious to it. He ran a hand playfully down my leg, checking to make certain of its presence.

He lifted his head then, like a cat scenting the breeze. Looking up, I could see him glance at Murtagh, then down at me. The little man gave no outward sign, but rose and stretched himself thoroughly. When he sat down again, he was several feet nearer to me.

A horse whickered nervously behind us. As though it had been a signal, they came screaming over the rocks. Not English, as I had feared, nor bandits. Highlanders, shrieking like banshees. Grants, I supposed. Or Campbells.

On hands and knees, I made for the rocks. I banged my head and scraped my knees, but managed to wedge myself into the small crevice. Heart hammering, I fumbled for the dirk in my pocket, almost jabbing myself in the process. I had no idea what to do with the long, wicked knife, but felt slightly better for having it. There was a moonstone set in the hilt and it was comforting to feel the small bulge against my palm; at least I knew I had hold of the right end in the darkness.

The fighting was so confused that at first I had no idea what was going on. The small clearing was filled with yelling bodies, heaving to and fro, rolling on the ground, and running back and forth. My sanctuary was luckily to one side of the main combat, so I was in no danger for the moment. Glancing around, I saw a small, crouching figure close by, pressed against my rock in the shadow. I took a firmer grip on my dirk, but realized almost at once that it was Murtagh.

So that was the purpose of Jamie's glance. Murtagh had been told off to guard me. I couldn't see Jamie himself anywhere. Most of the fighting was taking place in the rocks and shadows near the wagons.

Of course, that must be the object of the raid; the wagons and the horses. The attackers were an organized band, well armed and decently fed, from the little I could see of them in the light of the dying fire. If these were Grants, then, perhaps they were seeking either booty or revenge for the cattle Rupert and friends had pilfered a few days before. Confronted with the results of that impromptu raid, Dougal had been mildly annoyed—not with the fact of the raid, but only concerned that the cattle would slow our progress. He had managed to dispose of them almost at once, though, at a small market in one of the villages.

It was soon clear that the attackers were not much concerned with inflicting harm on our party; only with getting to the horses and wagons. One or two succeeded. I crouched low as a barebacked horse leapt the fire and disappeared into the darkness of the moor, a caterwauling man clinging to its mane.

Two or three more raced away on foot, clutching bags of Colum's grain, pursued by furious MacKenzies shouting Gaelic imprecations. From the sound of it, the raid was dying down. Then a large group of men staggered out into the firelight and the action picked up again.

This seemed to be serious fighting, an impression borne out by the flashing of blades and the fact that the participants were grunting a good deal, but not yelling. At length I got it sorted out. Jamie and Dougal were at the center of it, fighting back to back. Each of them held his broadsword in the left hand, dirk in the right, and both of them were putting the arms to good use, so far as I could see.

They were surrounded by four men—or five; I lost count in the shadows—armed with short swords, though one man had a broadsword hung on his belt and at least two more carried undrawn pistols.

It must be Dougal, or Jamie, or both, that they wanted. Alive, for preference. For ransom, I supposed. Thus the deliberate use of smallswords, which might merely wound, rather than the more lethal broadsword or pistols.

Dougal and Jamie suffered from no such scruples, and were attending to business with considerable grim efficiency. Back to back, they formed a complete circle of threat, each man covering the other's weaker side. When Dougal drove his dirk hand upward with considerable force, I thought that "weaker" might not be precisely the term.

The whole roiling, grunting, cursing mess was staggering toward me. I pressed myself back as far as I could, but the crevice was barely two feet deep. I caught a stir of movement from the corner of my eye. Murtagh had decided to take a more active part in affairs.

I could scarcely pull my horrified gaze away from Jamie, but saw the little clansman draw his pistol, so far unfired, in a leisurely manner. He checked the firing mechanism carefully, rubbed the weapon on his sleeve, braced it on his forearm and waited.

And waited. I was shivering with fear for Jamie, who had given up finesse and was slashing savagely from side to side, beating back the two men who now faced him with sheer bloody-mindedness. Why in hell didn't the man fire? I thought furiously. And then I realized why not. Both Jamie and Dougal were in the line of fire. I seemed to recall that flintlock pistols sometimes lacked a bit in the way of accuracy.

This supposition was borne out in the next minute, as an unexpected lunge by one of Dougal's opponents caught him at the wrist. The blade ripped up the length of his forearm and he sank to one knee. Feeling his uncle fall, Jamie pulled back his own blade and took two quick steps backward. This put his back near a rock face, Dougal crouched to one side, within reach of the protection of his single blade. It also brought the attackers side-on to my hiding-place and Murtagh's pistol.

Close at hand, the report of the pistol was startlingly loud. It took the attackers by surprise, particularly the one who was hit. The man stood still for a moment, shook his head in a confused way, then very slowly sat down, fell limply backward, and rolled down a slight decline into the dying embers of the fire.

Taking advantage of the surprise, Jamie knocked the sword from the hand of one attacker. Dougal was on his feet again, and Jamie moved to the side to give him room for swordplay. One of the fighters had abandoned the fray and run down the hill to drag his wounded companion out of the hot ashes. Still, that left three of the raiders, and Dougal wounded. I could see dark drops splashing against the rock face as he wielded the sword.

They were close enough now that I could see Jamie's face, calm and intent, absorbed with the exultancy of battle. Suddenly Dougal shouted something to him. Jamie tore his eyes from his opponent's face for a split second and glanced down. Glancing back just in time to avoid being skewered, he ducked to one side and *threw* his sword.

His opponent gazed in considerable surprise at the sword sticking in his leg. He touched the blade in some bemusement, then grasped it and pulled. From the ease with which it came out, I assumed the wound was not deep. The man still seemed slightly bewildered, and glanced up as though to ask the purpose of this unorthodox behavior.

He uttered a scream, dropped the sword, and ran, limping heavily. Startled by the noise, the other two attackers looked over, turned, and likewise fled, pursued by Jamie, moving like an avalanche. He had succeeded in yanking the huge claymore out of the blanket roll, and was swinging it in a murderous, two-handed arc. Backing him up came Murtagh, shouting something highly uncomplimentary in Gaelic and brandishing both sword and reloaded pistol.

Things mopped up quite quickly after that, and it was only a quarter of an hour or so before the MacKenzie party had reassembled and assessed its damages.

These had been slight; two horses had been taken, and three bags of grain, but the drovers, who slept with their loads, had prevented further depredations on the wagons, while the men-at-arms had succeeded in driving off the would-be horse thieves. The major loss seemed to be one of the men.

I thought when he was missed at first that he must have been wounded or killed in the scrimmage, but a thorough search of the area failed to turn him up.

"Kidnapped," said Dougal grimly. "Blast, he'll cost me a month's income in ransom."

"Could ha' been worse, Dougal," said Jamie, mopping his face on his sleeve. "Think what Colum would say if they'd taken *you*!"

"If they'd taken *you*, lad, I'd ha' let them keep ye, and ye could change your name to Grant," Dougal retorted, but the mood of the party lightened substantially.

I unearthed the small box of medical supplies I had packed, and lined up the injured in order of severity. Nothing really bad, I was pleased to see. The wound on Dougal's arm was likely the worst.

Ned Gowan was bright-eyed and fizzing with vitality, apparently so intoxicated with the thrill of the fight as hardly to notice the tooth that had been knocked out by an ill-aimed dagger hilt. He had, however, retained sufficient presence of mind to keep it carefully held under his tongue.

"Just on the off-chance, d'ye see," he explained, spitting it into the palm of his hand. The root was not broken, and the socket still bled slightly, so I took the chance and pressed the tooth firmly back into place. The little man went quite white, but didn't utter a sound. He gratefully swished his mouth with whisky for disinfectant purposes, though, and thriftily swallowed it.

I had bound Dougal's wound at once with a pressure bandage, and was glad to see that the bleeding had all but stopped by the time I unwrapped it. It was a clean slash, but a deep one. A tiny rim of yellow fat showed at the edge of the gaping cut, which went at least an inch deep into the muscle. No major vessels severed, thank goodness, but it would have to be stitched.

The only needle available turned out to be a sturdy thing like a slender awl, used by the drovers to mend harness. I eyed it dubiously, but Dougal merely held out his arm and looked away.

"I dinna mind blood in general," he explained, "but I've some objection to seein' my own." He sat on a rock as I worked, teeth clenched hard enough to make his jaw muscles quiver. The night was turning cold, but sweat stood out on the high forehead in beads. At one point, he asked me politely to stop for a moment, turned aside and was neatly sick behind a rock, then turned back and braced his arm on his knee again.

By good luck, one tavern owner had chosen to remit his rent this quarter in the form of a small keg of whisky, and it came in quite handily. I used it to disinfect some of the open wounds, and then let my patients self-medicate as they liked. I even accepted a cupful myself, at the conclusion of the doctoring. I drained it with pleasure and sank thankfully onto my blanket. The moon was sinking, and I was shivering, half with reaction and half with cold. It was a wonderful feeling to have Jamie lie down and firmly gather me in, next to his large, warm body.

"Will they come back, do you think?" I asked, but he shook his head.

"Nay, it was Malcolm Grant and his two boys—it was the oldest I stuck in the leg. They'll be home in their own beds by now," he replied. He stroked my hair and said, in softer tones, "Ye did a braw bit o' work tonight, lass. I was proud of ye."

I rolled over and put my arms about his neck.

"Not as proud as I was. You were wonderful, Jamie. I've never seen anything like that."

He snorted deprecatingly, but I thought he was pleased, nonetheless.

"Only a raid, Sassenach. I've been doin' that since I was fourteen. It's only in fun, ye see; it's different when you're up against someone who really means to kill ye."

"Fun," I said, a little faintly. "Yes, quite."

His arms tightened around me, and one of the stroking hands dipped lower, beginning to inch my skirt upward. Clearly the thrill of the fight was being transmuted into a different kind of excitement.

"Jamie! Not here!" I said, squirming away and pushing my skirt down again.

"Are ye tired, Sassenach?" he asked with concern. "Dinna worry, I won't take long." Now both hands were at it, rucking the heavy fabric up in front.

"No!" I replied, all too mindful of the twenty men lying a

few feet away. "I'm not tired, it's just—" I gasped as his groping hand found its way between my legs.

"Lord," he said softly. "It's slippery as waterweed."

"Jamie! There are twenty men sleeping right next to us!" I shouted in a whisper.

"They wilna be sleeping long, if you keep talking." He rolled on top of me, pinning me to the rock. His knee wedged between my thighs and began to work gently back and forth. Despite myself, my legs were beginning to loosen. Twenty-seven years of propriety were no match for several hundred thousand years of instinct. While my mind might object to being taken on a bare rock next to several sleeping soldiers, my body plainly considered itself the spoils of war and was eager to complete the formalities of surrender. He kissed me, long and deep, his tongue sweet and restless in my mouth.

"Jamie," I panted. He pushed his kilt out of the way and pressed my hand against him.

"Bloody Christ," I said, impressed despite myself. My sense of propriety slipped another notch.

"Fighting gives ye a terrible cockstand, after. Ye want me, do ye no?" he said, pulling back a little to look at me. It seemed pointless to deny it, what with all the evidence to hand. He was hard as a brass rod against my bared thigh.

"Er . . . yes . . . but . . ."

He took a firm grip on my shoulders with both hands.

"Be quiet, Sassenach," he said with authority. "It isna going to take verra long."

It didn't. I began to climax with the first powerful thrust, in long, racking spasms. I dug my fingers hard into his back and held on, biting the fabric of his shirt to muffle any sounds. In less than a dozen strokes, I felt his testicles contract, tight against his body, and the warm flood of his own release. He lowered himself slowly to the side and lay trembling.

The blood was still beating heavily in my ears, echoing the fading pulse between my legs. Jamie's hand lay on my breast, limp and heavy. Turning my head, I could see the dim figure of the sentry, leaning against a rock on the far side of the fire. He had his back tactfully turned. I was mildly shocked to realize that I was not even embarrassed. I wondered rather

dimly whether I would be in the morning, and then wondered
no more.

———

In the morning, everyone behaved as usual, if moving a
little more stiffly from the effects of fighting and sleeping on
rocks. Everyone was in a cheerful humor, even those with
minor wounds.

The general humor was improved still further when Dougal
announced that we would travel only as far as the clump of
woods we could see from the edge of our rocky platform.
There we could water and graze the horses, and rest a bit
ourselves. I wondered whether this change of plan would affect Jamie's rendezvous with the mysterious Horrocks, but he
seemed undisturbed at the announcement.

The day was overcast but not drizzling, and the air was
warm. Once the new camp was made, the horses taken care
of, and the wounded all rechecked, everyone was left to his
own devices, to sleep in the grass, to hunt or fish, or merely to
stretch legs after several days in the saddle.

I was sitting under a tree talking to Jamie and Ned Gowan,
when one of the men-at-arms came up and flipped something
into Jamie's lap. It was the dirk with the moonstone hilt.

"Yours, lad?" he asked. "Found it in the rocks this morning."

"I must have dropped it, in all the excitement," I said.
"Just as well; I've no idea what to do with it. I'd likely have
stabbed myself if I'd tried to use it."

Ned eyed Jamie censoriously over his half-spectacles.

"Ye gave her a knife and didn't teach her to use it?"

"There wasna time, under the circumstances," Jamie defended himself. "But Ned's right, Sassenach. Ye should learn
how to handle arms. There's no tellin' what may happen on
the road, as ye saw last night."

So I was marched out into the center of a clearing and the
lessons began. Seeing the activity, several of the MacKenzie
men came by to investigate, and stayed to offer advice. In no
time, I had half a dozen instructors, all arguing the fine points
of technique. After a good deal of amiable discussion, they

agreed that Rupert was likely the best among them at dirks, and he took over the lesson.

He found a reasonably flat spot, free of rocks and pine cones, in which to demonstrate the art of dagger-wielding.

"Look, lass," he said. He held the dagger balanced on his middle finger, resting an inch or so below the haft. "The balance point, that's where ye want to hold it, so it fits comfortable in yer hand." I tried it with my dagger. When I had it comfortably fitted, he showed me the difference between an overhand strike and an underhanded stab.

"Generally, ye want to use the underhand; overhand is only good when ye're comin' down on someone wi' a considerable force from above." He eyed me speculatively, then shook his head.

"Nay, you're tall for a woman, but even if ye could reach as high as the neck, ye wouldna have the force to penetrate, unless he's sittin'. Best stick to underhand." He pulled up his shirt, revealing a substantial furry paunch, already glistening with sweat.

"Now, here," he said, pointing to the center, just under the breastbone, "is the spot to aim for, if ye're killin' face to face. Aim straight up and in, as hard as ye can. That'll go into the heart, and it kills wi'in a minute or two. The only problem is to avoid the breastbone; it goes down lower than ye think, and if ye get yer knife stuck in that soft bit on the tip, it will hardly harm yer victim at all, but ye'll be wi'out a knife, and he'll ha' you. Murtagh! Ye ha' a skinny back; come 'ere and we'll show the lass how to stick from the back." Spinning a reluctant Murtagh around, he yanked up the grubby shirt to show a knobbly spine and prominent ribs. He poked a blunt forefinger under the lower rib on the right, making Murtagh squeak in surprise.

"This is the spot in back—either side. See, wi' all the ribs and such, 'tis verra difficult to hit anythin' vital when ye stab in the back. *If* ye can slip the knife between the ribs, that's one thing, but that's harder to do than ye might think. But here, under the last rib, ye stab upward into the kidney. Get him straight up, and he'll drop like a stone."

Rupert then set me to try stabbing in various positions and

postures. As he grew winded, all the men took it in turns to act as victim, obviously finding my efforts hilarious. They obligingly lay on the grass or turned their backs so I could ambush them, or leapt at me from behind, or pretended to choke me so I could try to stab them in the belly.

The spectators urged me on with cries of encouragement, and Rupert instructed me firmly not to pull back at the last moment.

"Thrust as though ye meant it, lass," he said. "Ye canna pull back if it's in earnest. And if any o' these laggards canna get themselves out of the way in time, they deserve what they get."

I was timid and extremely clumsy at first, but Rupert was a good teacher, very patient and good about demonstrating moves, over and over. He rolled his eyes in mock lewdness when he moved behind me and put his arm about my waist, but he was quite businesslike about taking hold of my wrist to show me the way of ripping an enemy across the eyes.

Dougal sat under a tree, minding his wounded arm and making sardonic comments on the training as it progressed. It was he, though, who suggested the dummy.

"Give her something she can sink her dirk into," he said, when I had begun to show some facility at lunging and jabbing. "It's a shock, the first time."

"So it is," Jamie agreed. "Rest a bit, Sassenach, while I manage something."

He went off to the wagons with two of the men-at-arms, and I could see them standing heads together, gesticulating and pulling bits of things from the wagon bed. Thoroughly winded, I collapsed under the tree next to Dougal.

He nodded, a slight smile on his face. Like most of the men, he had not bothered to shave while traveling, and a heavy growth of dark brown beard framed his mouth, accentuating the full lower lip.

"How is it, then?" he asked, not meaning my skill with small arms.

"Well enough," I answered warily, not meaning knives either. Dougal's gaze flicked toward Jamie, busy with something by the wagons.

"Marriage seems to suit the lad," he observed.

"Rather healthy for him—under the circumstances," I agreed, somewhat coldly. His lips curved at my tone.

"And you, lass, as well. A good arrangement for everyone, it seems."

"Particularly for you and your brother. And speaking of him, just what do you think Colum's going to say when he hears about it?"

The smile widened. "Colum? Ah, well. I should think he'd be only too pleased to welcome such a niece to the family."

The dummy was ready, and I went back into training. It proved to be a large bag of wool, about the size of a man's torso, with a piece of tanned bull's hide wrapped around it, secured with rope. This I was to practice stabbing, first as it was tied to a tree at man-height, later as it was thrown or rolled past me.

What Jamie hadn't mentioned was that they had inserted several flat pieces of wood between the wool sack and the hide; to simulate bones, as he later explained.

The first few stabs were uneventful, though it took several tries to get through the bull-hide. It was tougher than it looked. So is the skin on a man's belly, I was informed. On the next try, I tried a direct overhand strike, and hit one of the wood pieces.

I thought for a moment that my arm had suddenly fallen off. The shock of impact reverberated all the way to my shoulder, and the dirk dropped from my nerveless fingers. Everything below the elbow was numb, but an ominous tingling warned me that it wouldn't be for long.

"Jesus H. Roosevelt Christ," I said. I stood gripping my elbow and listening to the general hilarity. Finally Jamie took me by the shoulder and massaged some feeling back into the arm, pressing the tendon at the back of the elbow, and digging his thumb into the hollow at the base of my wrist.

"All right," I said through my teeth, gingerly flexing my tingling right hand. "What do you do when you hit a bone and lose your knife? *Is* there a standard operating procedure for that?"

"Oh, aye," said Rupert, grinning. "Draw your pistol wi'

the left hand and shoot the bastard dead." This resulted in more howls of laughter, which I ignored.

"All right," I said, more or less calmly. I gestured at the long, claw-handled pistol Jamie wore on his left hip. "Are you going to show me how to load and shoot that, then?"

"I am not." He was firm.

I bristled a bit at this. "Why not?"

"Because you're a woman, Sassenach."

I felt my face flush at this. "Oh?" I said sarcastically. "You think women aren't bright enough to understand the workings of a gun?"

He looked levelly at me, mouth twisting a bit as he thought over various replies.

"I've a mind to let ye try it," he said at last. "It would serve ye right."

Rupert clicked his tongue in annoyance at us both. "Dinna be daft, Jamie. As for you, lass," turning to me, "it's not that women are stupid, though sure enough some o' 'em are; it's that they're small."

"Eh?" I gaped stupidly at him for a moment. Jamie snorted and drew the pistol from its loop. Seen up close, it was enormous; a full eighteen inches of silvered weapon measured from stock to muzzle.

"Look," he said, holding it in front of me. "Ye hold it here, ye brace it on your forearm, and ye sight along here. And when ye pull the trigger, it kicks like a mule. I'm near a foot taller than you, four stone heavier, and I know what I'm doin'. It gives *me* a wicked bruise when I fire it; it might knock *you* flat on your back, if it didna catch ye in the face." He twirled the pistol and slid it back into its loop.

"I'd let ye see for yourself," he said, raising one eyebrow, "but I like ye better wi' all of your teeth. You've a nice smile, Sassenach, even if ye *are* a bit feisty."

Slightly chastened by this episode, I accepted without argument the men's judgment that even the lighter smallsword was too heavy for me to wield efficiently. The tiny *sgian dhu*, the sock dagger, was deemed acceptable, and I was provided with one of those, a wicked-looking, needle-sharp piece of black iron about three inches long, with a short hilt. I practiced drawing it from its place of concealment over and over while the men watched critically, until I could sweep up my skirt, grab the knife from its place and come up in the proper crouch all in one smooth move, ending up with the knife held underhand, ready to slash across an adversary's throat.

Finally I was passed as a novice knife-wielder, and allowed to sit down to dinner, amid general congratulations—with one exception. Murtagh shook his head dubiously.

"I still say the only good weapon for a woman is poison."

"Perhaps," replied Dougal, "but it has its deficiencies in face-to-face combat."

19

The Waterhorse

We camped the next night on the banks above Loch Ness. It gave me an odd feeling to see the place again; so little had changed. Or would change, I should say. The larches and alders were a deeper green, because it was now midsummer, not late spring. The flowers had changed from the fragile pinks and whites of May blossom and violets to the warmer golds and yellows of gorse and broom. The sky above was a deeper blue, but the surface of the loch was the same; a flat blue-black that caught the reflections from the bank above and held them trapped, colors muted under smoked glass.

There were even a few sailboats visible, far up the loch. Though when one drew near, I saw it was a coracle, a rough half-shell of tanned leather on a frame, not the sleek wooden shape I was used to.

The same pungent scent that pervades all watercourses was there; a sharp mix of tangy greenness and rotted leaf, fresh water, dead fish, and warm mud. Above all, there was that same feeling of lurking strangeness about the place. The men as well as the horses seemed to feel it, and the air of the camp was subdued.

Having found a comfortable place for my own bedroll and Jamie's, I wandered down to the edge of the loch to wash my face and hands before supper.

The bank sloped sharply down until it broke in a jumble of large rock slabs that formed a sort of irregular jetty. It was very peaceful under the bank, out of sight and sound of the camp, and I sat down beneath a tree to enjoy a moment's privacy. Since my hasty marriage to Jamie, I was no longer followed every moment; that much had been accomplished.

I was idly plucking the clusters of winged seeds from a low-hanging branch and tossing them out into the loch when I noticed the tiny waves against the rocks growing stronger, as though pushed by an oncoming wind.

A great flat head broke the surface not ten feet away. I could see the water purling away from keeled scales that ran in a crest down the sinuous neck. The water was agitated for some considerable distance, and I caught a glimpse here and there of dark and massive movement beneath the surface of the loch, though the head itself stayed relatively still.

I stood quite still myself. Oddly enough, I was not really afraid. I felt some faint kinship with it, a creature further from its own time than I, the flat eyes old as its ancient Eocene seas, eyes grown dim in the murky depths of its shrunken refuge. And there was a sense of familiarity mingled with its unreality. The sleek skin was a smooth, deep blue, with a vivid slash of green shining with brilliant iridescence beneath the jaw. And the strange, pupilless eyes were a deep and glowing amber. So very beautiful.

And so very different from the smaller, mud-colored replica I remembered, adorning the fifth-floor diorama in the British Museum. But the shape was unmistakable. The colors of living things begin to fade with the last breath, and the soft, springy skin and supple muscle rot within weeks. But the bones sometimes remain, faithful echoes of the shape, to bear some last faint witness to the glory of what was.

Valved nostrils opened suddenly with a startling hiss of breath; a moment of suspended motion, and the creature sank again, a churning roil of waters the only testimony to its passage.

I had risen to my feet when it appeared. And unconsciously I must have moved closer in order to watch it, for I found myself standing on one of the rock slabs that jutted out into the water, watching the dying waves fall back into the smoothness of the loch.

I stood there for a moment, looking out across the fathomless loch. "Goodbye," I said at last to the empty water. I
shook myself and turned back to the bank.

A man was standing at the top of the slope. I was startled at
first, then recognized him as one of the drovers from our
party. His name was Peter, I recalled, and the bucket in his
hand gave the reason for his presence. I was about to ask him
whether he had seen the beast, but the expression on his face
as I drew near was more than sufficient answer. His face was
paler than the daisies at his feet, and tiny droplets of sweat
trickled down into his beard. His eyes showed white all
around like those of a terrified horse, and his hand shook so
that the bucket bumped against his leg.

"It's all right," I said, as I came up to him. "It's gone."

Instead of finding this statement reassuring, it seemed occasion for fresh alarm. He dropped the bucket, fell to his knees
before me and crossed himself.

"Ha-have mercy, lady," he stammered. To my extreme embarrassment, he then flung himself flat on his face and
clutched at the hem of my dress.

"Don't be ridiculous," I said with some asperity. "Get up."
I prodded him gently with my toe, but he only quivered and
stayed pressed to the ground like a flattened fungus. "Get
up," I repeated. "Stupid man, it's only a . . ." I paused,
trying to think. Telling him its Latin name was unlikely to
help.

"It's only a wee monster," I said at last, and grabbing his
hand, tugged him to his feet. I had to fill the bucket, as he
would (not unreasonably) not go near the water's edge again.
He followed me back to the camp, keeping a careful distance,
and scuttled off at once to tend to his mules, casting apprehensive glances over his shoulder at me as he went.

As he seemed undisposed to mention the creature to anyone else, I thought perhaps I should keep quiet as well. While
Dougal, Jamie, and Ned were educated men, the rest were
largely illiterate Highlanders from the remote crags and glens
of the MacKenzie lands. They were courageous fighters and

dauntless warriors, but they were also as superstitious as any primitive tribesmen from Africa or the Middle East.

So I ate my supper quietly and went to bed, conscious all the time of the wary gaze of the drover Peter.

20

Deserted Glades

Two days after the raid, we turned again to the north. We were drawing closer to the rendezvous with Horrocks, and Jamie seemed abstracted from time to time, perhaps considering what importance the English deserter's news might have.

I had not seen Hugh Munro again, but I had wakened in darkness the night before to find Jamie gone from the blanket beside me. I tried to stay awake, waiting for him to return, but fell asleep as the moon began to sink. In the morning, he was sound asleep beside me, and on my blanket rested a small parcel, done up in a sheet of thin paper, fastened with the tail-feather of a woodpecker thrust through the sheet. Unfolding it carefully, I found a large chunk of rough amber. One face of the chunk had been smoothed off and polished, and in this window could be seen the delicate dark form of a tiny dragon-fly, suspended in eternal flight.

I smoothed out the wrapping. A message was incised on the grimy white surface, written in small and surprisingly elegant lettering.

"What does it say?" I asked Jamie, squinting at the odd letters and marks. "I think it's in Gaelic."

He raised up on one elbow, squinting at the paper.

"Not Gaelic. Latin. Munro was a schoolmaster once, before the Turks took him. It's a bit from Catullus," he said.

> *. . . da mi basia mille, diende centum,*
> *dein mille altera, dein secunda centum . . .*

A faint blush pinkened his earlobes as he translated:

> *Then let amorous kisses dwell*
> *On our lips, begin and tell*
> *A Thousand and a Hundred score*
> *A Hundred, and a Thousand more.*

"Well, that's a bit more high-class than your usual fortune cookie," I observed, amused.

"What?" Jamie looked startled.

"Never mind," I said hastily. "Did Munro find Horrocks for you?"

"Oh, aye. It's arranged. I'll meet him in a small place I know in the hills, a mile or two above Lag Cruime. In four days' time, if nothing goes wrong meanwhile."

The mention of things going wrong made me a bit nervous.

"Do you think it's safe? I mean, do you trust Horrocks?"

He sat up, rubbing the remnants of sleep from his eyes and blinking.

"An English deserter? God, no. I imagine he'd sell me to Randall as soon as he'd spit, except that he canna very well go to the English himself. They hang deserters. No, I dinna trust him. That's why I came wi' Dougal on this journey, instead of seeking out Horrocks alone. If the man's up to anything, at least I'll have company."

"Oh." I wasn't sure that Dougal's presence was all that reassuring, given the apparent state of affairs between Jamie and his two scheming uncles.

"Well, if you think so," I said doubtfully. "I don't suppose Dougal would take the opportunity to shoot you, at least."

"He did shoot me," Jamie said cheerfully, buttoning his shirt. "You should know, ye dressed the wound."

I dropped the comb I had been using.

"Dougal! I thought the English shot you!"

"Well, the English shot *at* me," he corrected. "And I

shouldna say it was Dougal shot me; in fact, it was probably Rupert—he's the best marksman among Dougal's men. No, when we were running from the English, I realized we were near the edge of the Fraser lands, and I thought I'd take my chances there. So I spurred up and cut to the left, around Dougal and the rest. There was a good deal of shooting goin' on, mind ye, but the ball that hit me came from behind. Dougal, Rupert, and Murtagh were back of me then. And the English were all in front—in fact, when I fell off the horse, I rolled down the hill and ended almost in their laps." He bent over the bucket of water I had brought, splashing cold handfuls over his face. He shook his head to clear his eyes, then blinked at me, grinning, glistening drops clinging to his thick lashes and brows.

"Come to that, Dougal had a sore fight to get me back. I was lyin' on the ground, not fit for much, and he was standing over me, pulling on my belt with one hand to get me up and his sword in the other, going hand-to-hand with a dragoon who thought he had a certain cure for my ills. Dougal killed the man and got me on his own horse." He shook his head. "Everything was a bit dim to me then; all I could think of was how hard it must be on the horse, tryin' to make it up a hill like that with four hundred pounds on his back."

I sat back, a little stunned.

"But . . . if he'd wanted to, Dougal could have killed you then."

Jamie shook his head, taking out the straight razor he had borrowed from Dougal. He moved the bucket slightly, so the surface formed a reflecting pool, and pulling his face into the tortuous grimace men use when they shave, began to scrape his cheeks.

"No, not in front of the men. Besides, Dougal and Colum didna necessarily want me dead—especially not Dougal."

"But—" My head was beginning to whirl again, as it seemed to do whenever I encountered the complexities of Scottish family life.

Jamie's words were a little muffled, as he stuck out his chin, tilting his head to reach the bit of stubble beneath his jaw.

"It's Lallybroch," he explained, feeling with his free hand

for stray whiskers. "Besides being a rich bit of ground, the estate sits at the head of a mountain pass, d'ye see. The only good pass into the Highlands for ten miles in either direction. Come to another Rising, it would be a valuable bit of land to control. And if I were to die before wedding, chances are the land would go back to the Frasers."

He grinned, stroking his neck. "No, I'm a pretty problem to the brothers MacKenzie. On the one hand, if I'm a threat to young Hamish's chieftainship, they want me safely dead. On the other, if I'm not, they want me—and my property—securely on their side if it comes to war—not wi' the Frasers. That's why they're willing to help me wi' Horrocks, ye see. I canna do that much wi' Lallybroch while I'm outlawed, even though the land's still mine."

I rolled up the blankets, shaking my head in bewilderment over the intricate—and dangerous—circumstances through which Jamie seemed to move so nonchalantly. And it struck me suddenly that not only Jamie was involved now. I looked up.

"You said that if you died before wedding, the land would go back to the Frasers," I said. "But you're married now. So who—"

"That's right," he said, nodding at me with a lopsided grin. The morning sun lit his hair with flames of gold and copper. "If I'm killed now, Sassenach, Lallybroch is yours."

It was a beautiful sunny morning, once the mist had risen. Birds were busy in the heather, and the road was wide here, for a change, and softly dusty under the horses' hooves.

Jamie rode up close beside me as we crested a small hill. He nodded to the right.

"See that wee glade down below there?"

"Yes." It was a small green patchwork of pines, oaks, and aspens, set back some distance from the road.

"There's a spring with a pool there, under the trees, and smooth grass. A very bonny place."

I looked over at him quizzically.

"A little early for lunch, isn't it?"

"That's not precisely what I had in mind." Jamie, I had found out by accident a few days previously, had never mastered the art of winking one eye. Instead, he blinked solemnly, like a large red owl.

"And just what *did* you have in mind?" I inquired. My suspicious look met an innocent, childlike gaze of blue.

"I was just wondering what you'd look like . . . on the grass . . . under the trees . . . by the water . . . with your skirts up around your ears."

"Er—" I said.

"I'll tell Dougal we're going to fetch water." He spurred up ahead, returning in a moment with the water bottles from the other horses. I heard Rupert shout something after us in Gaelic as we rode down the hill, but couldn't make out the words.

I reached the glade first. Sliding down, I relaxed on the grass and shut my eyes against the glare of the sun. Jamie reined up beside me a moment later, and swung down from the saddle. He slapped the horse and sent it away, reins dangling, to graze with mine, before dropping to his knees on the grass. I reached up and pulled him down to me.

It was a warm day, redolent with grass and flower scents. Jamie himself smelled like a fresh-plucked grass blade, sharp and sweet.

"We'll have to be quick," I said. "They'll be wondering why it's taking so long to get water."

"They won't wonder," he said, undoing my laces with a practiced ease. "They know."

"What do you mean?"

"Did ye no hear what Rupert said as we left?"

"I heard him, but I couldn't tell what he said." My Gaelic was improving to the point that I could understand the more common words, but conversation was still far beyond me.

"Good. It wasna fit for your ears." Having freed my breasts, he buried his face in them, sucking and biting gently until I could stand it no more and slid down beneath him, tucking my skirts up out of the way. Feeling absurdly self-conscious after that fierce and primitive encounter on the rock, I had been shy about letting him make love to me near the camp, and the woods were too thick to safely move very far from the campsite. Both of us were feeling the mild and pleasant strain of abstinence, and now, safely removed from curious eyes and ears, we came together with an impact that made my lips and fingers tingle with a rush of blood.

We were both nearing the end when Jamie froze abruptly. Opening my eyes, I saw his face dark against the sun, wearing a perfectly indescribable expression. There was something black pressed against his head. My eyes at last adjusting to the glare, I saw it was a musket barrel.

"Get up, you rutting bastard." The barrel moved sharply, jarring against Jamie's temple. Very slowly, he rose to his feet. A drop of blood began to well from the graze, dark against his white face.

There were two of them; Redcoat deserters from the look of their ragtag remnants of uniform. Both were armed with muskets and pistols, and looked very much amused by what chance had delivered into their hands. Jamie stood with his hands raised, the barrel of a musket pressed against his chest, face carefully expressionless.

"You might ha' let 'im finish, 'Arry," said one of the men. He grinned broadly, with a fine display of rotting teeth. "Stoppin' in the middle like that's bad for a man's 'ealth."

His fellow prodded Jamie in the chest with the musket.

" 'Is 'ealth's no concern o' mine. An' it won't be any concern to 'im for much longer. I've a mind to take a piece o' that," he nodded briefly in my direction, "an' I don't care to come second to any man, let alone a Scottish whoreson like this."

Rotten-teeth laughed. "I bain't so bloody particular. Kill 'im, then, and get on wi' it."

Harry, a short, stout man with a squint, considered a moment, eyeing me speculatively. I still sat on the ground, knees drawn up and skirts pressed firmly around my ankles. I had made some effort to close my bodice, but a good deal was still exposed. Finally the short man laughed and beckoned to his companion.

"No, let 'im watch. Come ower 'ere, Arnold, and 'old your musket on 'im." Arnold obeyed, still grinning widely. Harry set his musket down on the ground and dropped his pistol belt beside it in preparation.

Pressing my skirts down, I became aware of a hard object in the right-hand pocket. The dagger Jamie had given me. Could I bring myself to use it? Yes, I decided, looking at Harry's pimpled, leering face, I definitely could.

I would have to wait 'til the last possible second, though, and I had my doubts as to whether Jamie could control himself that long. I could see the urge to kill marked strong on his features; soon consideration of the consequences would no longer be enough to hold him back.

I didn't dare let too much show on my face, but narrowed my eyes and glared at him as hard as I could, willing him not to move. The cords stood out in his neck, and his face was suffused with dark blood, but I saw an infinitesimal nod in acknowledgment of my message.

I struggled as Harry pressed me to the ground and tried to pull up my skirts, more in order to get my hand on the dagger hilt than in actual resistance. He slapped me hard across the face, ordering me to be still. My cheek burned and my eyes watered, but the dagger was now in my hand, concealed under the folds of my skirt.

I lay back, breathing heavily. I concentrated on my objective, trying to erase everything else from my mind. It would have to be in the back; the quarters were too close to try for the throat.

The filthy fingers were digging into my thighs now, wrenching them apart. In my mind, I could see Rupert's blunt finger stabbing at Murtagh's ribs, and hear his voice, "Here, lass, up under the lowest ribs, close to the backbone. Stab hard, upward into the kidney, and he'll drop like a stone."

It was almost time; Harry's foul breath was disgustingly warm on my face, and he was fumbling between my bared legs, intent on his goal.

"Take a good look, laddie-buck, and see how it's done," he panted, "I'll 'ave your slut moaning for more before—"

I whipped my left arm around his neck to hold him close; holding the knife hand high, I plunged it in as hard as I could.

The shock of impact reverberated up my arm, and I nearly lost my hold on the dagger. Harry yelped and squirmed, twisting to get away. Unable to see, I had aimed too high, and the knife had skittered off a rib.

I couldn't let go now. Luckily, my legs were free of the entangling skirts. I wrapped them tightly around Harry's sweating hips, holding him down for the precious seconds I needed for another try. I stabbed again, with a desperate strength, and this time found the spot.

Rupert had been right. Harry bucked in a hideous parody of the act of love, then collapsed without a sound in a limp heap on top of me, blood jetting in diminishing spurts from the wound in his back.

Arnold's attention had been distracted for an instant by the spectacle on the ground, and an instant was more than long enough for the maddened Scotsman he held at bay. By the time I had gathered my wits sufficiently to wriggle out from under the defunct Harry, Arnold had joined his companion in death, throat neatly cut from ear to ear by the *sgian dhu* that Jamie carried in his stocking.

Jamie knelt beside me, pulling me out from under the corpse. We were both shaking with nerves and shock, and we clung together without speaking for minutes. Still without speaking, he picked me up and carried me away from the two bodies, to a grassy space behind a screen of aspen.

He lowered me to the ground and sat down awkwardly beside me, collapsing as though his knees had suddenly given way. I felt a chilly isolation, as though the winter wind blew through my bones, and reached for him. He raised his head from his knees, face haggard, and stared at me as though he had never seen me before. When I put my hands on his shoulders, he pulled me hard against his chest with a sound midway between a groan and a sob.

We took each other then, in a savage, urgent silence, thrusting fiercely and finishing within moments, driven by a compulsion I didn't understand, but knew we must obey, or be lost to each other forever. It was not an act of love, but one of necessity, as though we knew that left alone, neither of us could stand. Our only strength lay in fusion, drowning the memories of death and near-rape in the flooding of the senses.

We clung together on the grass then, disheveled, blood-stained, and shivering in the sunshine. Jamie muttered something, his voice so low that I caught only the word "sorry."

"Not your fault," I muttered, stroking his hair. "It's all right, we're both all right." I felt dreamlike, as though nothing whatever was real around me, and I dimly recognized the symptoms of delayed shock.

"Not that," he said. "Not that. It *was* my fault. . . . So foolish to come here without taking proper heed. And to let you be . . . I didna mean that, though. I meant . . . I'm sorry for using ye as I did just now. To take you like that, so soon after . . . like some sort of animal. I'm sorry, Claire . . . I don't know what . . . I couldna help it, but . . . Lord, you're so cold, *mo duinne,* your hands are ice. Come then, let me warm ye."

Shock, too, I thought fuzzily. Funny how it takes some people in talk. Others just shake quietly. Like me. I pressed his mouth against my shoulder to quiet him.

"It's all right," I said, over and over. "It's all right."

Suddenly a shadow fell across us, making us both jump. Dougal stood glowering down at us, arms folded. He courteously averted his eyes while I hastily did up my laces, frowning instead at Jamie.

"Now look ye, lad, takin' your pleasure wi' your wife is all verra weel, but when it comes to leavin' us all waiting for more than an hour, and being so taen up wi' each other that ye dinna even hear me comin'—that kind o' behavior will get ye in trouble one day, laddie. Why, someone could come up behind ye and clap a pistol to your head before ye knew—"

He stopped in his tirade to stare incredulously at me, rolling on the grass in hysterics. Jamie, red as a beetroot, led Dougal to the other side of the aspen screen, explaining in a subdued voice. I continued to whoop and giggle uncontrollably, finally stuffing a handkerchief in my mouth to muffle the noise. The sudden release of emotions, coupled with Dougal's words, had evoked a picture of Jamie's face, caught in the act as it were, that I found totally hilarious in my unhinged state.

I laughed and moaned until my sides ached. Finally, I sat up, wiping my eyes on my kerchief, to see Dougal and Jamie standing over me, wearing identical expressions of disapproval. Jamie hoisted me to my feet and led me, still hiccuping and snorting occasionally, to where the rest of the men were waiting with the horses.

Except for a lingering tendency to laugh hysterically over nothing, I seemed to suffer no ill effects from our encounter with the deserters, though I became very cautious about leaving the campsite. Dougal assured me that bandits were not, in fact, that common on the Highland roads, only because there were not many travelers worth robbing, but I found myself starting nervously at sounds in the wood, and hastening back from routine chores like fetching wood and water, eager for the sight and sound of the MacKenzie men. I also found new reassurance in the sound of their snoring around me at night, and lost whatever self-consciousness I might have had about the discreet writhings that took place under our blankets.

I was still somewhat fearful of being alone when, a few days later, the time for the meeting with Horrocks arrived.

"Stay here?" I said in disbelief. "No! I'm going with you."

"You can't," said Jamie patiently, once more. "The bulk of the men will go on to Lag Cruime wi' Ned, to collect the rents as expected. Dougal and a few of the others are coming wi' me to the meeting, in case of any treachery by Horrocks. You can't be seen in the open near Lag Cruime, though; Randall's men may be about, and I wouldna put it past him to take ye by force. And as for the meeting wi' Horrocks, I've no idea what may happen. No, there's a small copse near the bend of the road—it's thick and grassy, and there's water nearby. You'll be comfortable there, until I come back for ye."

"No," I said stubbornly. "I'm coming with you." Some sense of pride made me unwilling to tell him that I was frightened of being away from him. But I was willing to tell him that I was frightened *for* him.

"You said yourself you don't know what will happen with

Horrocks," I argued. "I don't want to wait here, wondering all day what's happening to you. Let me come with you," I coaxed. "I promise I'll stay out of sight during the meeting. But I don't want to stay here alone, worrying all day."

He sighed impatiently, but didn't argue further. When we reached the copse, though, he leaned over and seized my horse's bridle, forcing me off the road into the grass. He slid off his horse, tying both sets of reins to a bush. Ignoring my vociferous objections, he disappeared into the trees. Stubbornly, I refused to dismount. He couldn't *make* me stay, I thought.

He came down at last to the road. The others had gone on before, but Jamie, mindful of our last experience with deserted glades, wouldn't leave until he had thoroughly searched the copse, quartering methodically through the trees and swishing the tall grass with a stick. Coming back, he untied the horses, and swung up into his saddle.

"It's safe," he said. "Ride up well into the thicket, Claire, and hide yourself and the horse. I'll be back for ye, as soon as our business is done. I canna tell how long, but surely by sunset."

"No! I'm coming with you." I couldn't stand the thought of stewing in a forest, not knowing what was happening. I would far rather be in active danger than be left for anxious hours, waiting and wondering. And alone.

Jamie curbed his impatience to be gone. He reached over and grasped my shoulder.

"Did ye no promise to obey me?" he asked, shaking me gently.

"Yes, but—" But only because I had to, I was going to say, but he was already urging my horse's head around toward the thicket.

"It's verra dangerous, and I'll not have ye there, Claire. I shall be busy, and if it comes to it, I can't fight and protect you at the same time." Seeing my mutinous look, he dropped his hand to the saddlebag and began rummaging.

"What are you looking for?"

"Rope. If ye wilna do as I say, I shall tie ye to a tree until I come back."

"You wouldn't!"

"Aye, I would!" Plainly he meant it. I gave in with bad grace, and reluctantly reined in my horse. Jamie leaned to kiss me glancingly on the cheek, already turning to go.

"Take care, Sassenach. You've your dirk? Good. I shall come back as soon as I can. Oh, one more thing."

"What's that?" I said sullenly.

"If you leave that copse before I come for ye, I'll tan your bare arse wi' my sword belt. Ye wouldna enjoy walking all the way to Bargrennan. Remember," he said, pinching my cheek gently, "I dinna make idle threats." He didn't, either. I rode slowly toward the grove, looking back to watch him racing away, bent low over the saddle, one with the horse, the ends of his plaid flying behind.

It was cool under the trees; the horse and I both exhaled with relief as we entered the shade. It was one of those rare hot days in Scotland, when the sun blazes out of a bleached muslin sky and the early haze is burnt away by eight o'clock. The copse was loud with birds; a gang of titmice was foraging in the oak clump to the left, and I could hear what I thought was a thrasher in the near distance.

I had always been an enthusiastic amateur birder. If I were marooned here 'til it suited my overbearing, domineering, pig-headed jackass of a husband to finish risking his stupid neck, I'd use the time to see what I could spot.

I hobbled the gelding and turned him loose to graze in the lush grass at the edge of the copse, knowing he wouldn't go far. The grass ceased abruptly a few feet from the trees, smothered by the encroaching heather.

It was a glade of mixed conifers and oak saplings, perfect for bird-watching. I wandered through it, still mentally fuming at Jamie, but growing gradually calmer as I listened for the distinctive *tsee* of a flycatcher and the harsh chatter of the mistle thrush.

The glade ended quite suddenly on the far side, on the edge of a small precipice. I thrust my way through the saplings and the sound of bird song was drowned in rushing water. I stood on the lip of a small burn, a steep rocky canyon with waterfalls bounding down the jagged walls to splash in the brown and

silver pools below. I sat down on the edge of the bank and let
my feet dangle over the water, enjoying the sun on my face.

A crow shot past overhead, closely pursued by a pair of
redstarts. The bulky black body zigzagged through the air,
trying to avoid the tiny dive-bombers. I smiled, watching the
furious small parents chivying the crow to and fro, and wondered whether crows, left to their own devices, really did fly in
a straight line. That one, if it kept to a straight path, would
head straight for . . .

I stopped dead.

I had been so intent on arguing with Jamie that it had not
until this minute dawned on me that the situation I had been
vainly trying to bring about for two months had finally occurred. I was alone. And I knew where I was.

Looking across the burn, my eyes were dazzled by the
morning sun blazing through the red ash trees on the far
bank. So that was east. My heart began to beat faster. East was
over there, Lag Cruime was directly behind me. Lag Cruime
was four miles to the north of Fort William. And Fort William
was no more than three miles due west of the hill of Craigh na
Dun.

So, for the first time since my meeting with Murtagh, I
knew approximately where I was—no more than seven miles
from that bloody hill and its accursed stone circle. Seven miles
—perhaps—from home. From Frank.

I started back into the copse, but changed my mind. I dared
not take the road. This close to Fort William and the several
small villages that surrounded it, there was too much risk of
meeting someone. And I could not take a horse down the
precipitous course of the burn. In fact, I had some doubt that
it could be managed on foot; the rock walls were sheer in
some spots, plunging directly into the foaming water of the
stream, with no real footing save the tops of scattered rocks
sticking out of the rushing water.

But it was by far the most direct path in the direction I
wanted. And I did not dare to take too circuitous a route; I
might easily lose my way in the wild growth or be overtaken
by Jamie and Dougal, returning.

My stomach gave a sudden lurch as I thought of Jamie.

God, how could I do it? Leave him without a word of explanation or apology? Disappear without a trace, after what he
had done for me?

With that thought I finally decided to leave the horse. At
least he would think I had not left him willingly; he might
believe I had been killed by wild beasts—I touched the dagger
in my pocket—or possibly kidnapped by outlaws. And finding
no trace of me, eventually he would forget me, and wed again.
Perhaps the lovely young Laoghaire, back at Leoch.

Absurdly enough, I found that the thought of Jamie sharing Laoghaire's bed upset me as much as the thought of leaving him. I cursed myself for idiocy, but I couldn't help imagining her sweet round face, flushed with ardent longing, and
his big hands burying themselves in that moonbeam hair . . .

I unclenched my teeth and resolutely wiped the tears off my
cheeks. I hadn't time or energy for senseless reflections. I
must go, and now, while I could. It might be the best chance
I would get. I hoped that Jamie would forget me. I knew that
I would never be able to forget him. But for now, I must put
him out of my mind, or I wouldn't be able to concentrate on
the job at hand, which was tricky enough.

Cautiously, I picked my way down the steep bank to the
edge of the water. The noise of the rushing stream drowned
out the birds in the copse above. The going was rough, but
there was at least room to walk by the water's edge here. The
bank was muddy, and strewn with rocks, but passable. Further
down, I saw that I would have to step out actually into the
water, and make my way precariously from rock to rock, balancing above the flood, until the bank widened enough to go
ashore again.

I picked my way painfully along, estimating how much time
I might have. Jamie had said only that they would return
before sundown. Three or four miles to Lag Cruime, but I
had no way of knowing what the roads were like, nor how
long the business with Horrocks might take. If he was there.
But he would be, I argued with myself. Hugh Munro had said
so, and outlandish as that grotesque figure had been, Jamie
plainly considered him a reliable source of information.

My foot slipped off the first rock in the stream, plunging

me into icy water to the knee and soaking my skirt. I withdrew to the bank, tucked my skirts as high as I could and removed both shoes and stockings. I slipped these into the pocket made by my tucked-up skirt and set my foot again on the rock.

I found that by gripping with my toes, I could manage to step from rock to rock without slipping. The bunches of my skirt made it difficult to see where I was going to step next, though, and more than once I found myself sliding into the water. My legs were chilled, and as my feet grew numb, it got harder to maintain my grip.

Luckily the bank widened again, and I stepped gratefully ashore into warm, sticky mud. Short periods of more or less comfortable squelching alternated with much longer periods of precarious rock-hopping through the freezing rapids, and I found to my relief that I was much too busy to think very much about Jamie.

After a time, I had the routine worked out. Step, grip, pause, look around, locate next step. Step, grip, pause, and so on. I must have become over-confident, or perhaps only tired, because I got careless, and undershot my goal. My foot skidded helplessly down the near side of the slime-coated rock. I waved my arms wildly, trying to move back to the rock I had been on, but my balance had shifted too far. Skirts, petticoats, dagger and all, I plunged into the water.

And kept on plunging. While the stream overall was only a foot or two deep, there were intermittent deep pools, where the scouring water had scooped out deep depressions in the rock. The one on which I'd lost my footing was perched on the edge of one such pool, and when I hit the water, I sank like a rock myself.

I was so stunned by the shock of the icy water rushing into my nose and mouth that I didn't cry out. Silvery bubbles shot out of the bodice of my dress and rushed past my face toward the surface above. The cotton fabric soaked through almost at once, and the freezing grip of the water paralyzed my breathing.

I began almost at once to fight my way up to the surface, but the weight of my garments pulled me down. I yanked frantically at the laces of my bodice, but there was no hope of getting everything off before I drowned. I made a number of savage and uncharitable silent observations about dressmakers, women's fashions, and the stupidity of long skirts, while kicking frenziedly to keep the entangling folds away from my legs.

The water was crystal clear. My fingers brushed the rock wall, sliding through the dark, slick streamers of duckweed and algae. Slippery as waterweed, that's what Jamie said about my . . .

The thought jarred me out of my panic. Suddenly I realized that I shouldn't be exhausting myself trying to kick to the surface. The pool couldn't be more than eight or nine feet deep; what I needed to do was relax, float down to the bottom, brace my feet and spring upward. With luck, that would get my head clear for a breath, and even if I went down again, I could continue bouncing off the bottom until I worked my way close enough to the edge to get a decent grip on a rock.

The descent was agonizingly slow. As I was no longer fighting upward, my skirts rose round me in billows, floating in front of my face. I batted them away; I must keep my face clear. My lungs were bursting and there were dark spots behind my eyes by the time my feet touched the smooth bottom of the pool. I let my knees bend slightly, pressing my skirts down around me, then shoved upward with all my might.

It worked, just barely. My face broke the surface at the top of my leap, and I had just time for the briefest of life-saving gulps before the water closed over me again. But it was enough. I knew I could do it again. I pressed my arms down to my sides to streamline myself and make the descent more rapid. Once more, Beauchamp, I thought. Bend your knees, brace yourself, jump!

I shot upward, arms extended overhead. I had seen a flash of red overhead when I broke water last; there must be a rowan tree overhanging the water. Perhaps I could get hold of a branch.

As my face broke water, something seized my outstretched hand. Something hard, warm, and reassuringly solid. Another hand.

Coughing and spluttering, I groped blindly with my free hand, too glad of rescue to regret the interruption of my escape attempt. Glad, at least until, wiping the hair out of my eyes, I looked up into the beefy, anxious Lancashire face of young Corporal Hawkins.

21

Un Mauvais Quart d'Heure After Another

I delicately removed a strand of still-damp waterweed from my sleeve and placed it squarely in the center of the blotter. Then, seeing the inkstand handy, I picked up the weed and dipped it in, using the result to paint interesting patterns on the thick blotting paper. Getting fully into the spirit of the thing, I finished off my masterpiece with a rude word, carefully sprinkled it with sand and blotted it before propping it up against the bank of pigeon-holes.

I stepped back to admire the effect, then looked around for any other diversions that might take my mind off the impending advent of Captain Randall.

Not bad for the private office of a captain, I thought, eyeing the paintings on the wall, the silver desk fittings, and the thick carpet on the floor. I moved back onto the carpet, in order to drip more effectively. The ride to Fort William had dried my outer garments fairly well, but the underlying layers of petticoat were still wringing wet.

I opened a small cupboard behind the desk and discovered the Captain's spare wig, neatly bestowed on one of a pair of wrought-iron stands, with a matched silver-backed set of looking glass, military brushes, and tortoiseshell comb laid out in orderly ranks before it. Carrying the wig stand over to the desk, I gently sifted the remaining contents of the sander over it before replacing it in the cupboard.

I was seated behind the desk, comb in hand, studying my reflection in the looking glass, when the Captain came in. He gave me a glance that took in my disheveled appearance, the rifled cupboard, and the disfigured blotter.

Without blinking, he drew up a chair and sat down across from me, lounging casually with one booted foot resting on the opposite knee. A riding crop dangled from one fine, aristocratic hand. I watched the braided tip, black and scarlet, as it swung slowly back and forth over the carpet.

"The idea has its attractions," he said, watching my eyes follow the sweep of the whip. "But I could probably think of something better, given a few moments to collect myself."

"I daresay you could," I said, fingering a thick sheaf of hair out of my eyes. "But you aren't allowed to flog women, are you?"

"Only under certain circumstances," he said politely. "Which your situation doesn't meet—yet. That's rather public, though. I had thought we might get better acquainted in private, first." He reached to the sideboard behind him for a decanter.

We sipped the claret in silence, eyeing each other over the wine.

"I had forgotten to offer you felicitations on your marriage," he said suddenly. "Forgive my lack of manners."

"Think nothing of it," I said graciously. "I'm sure my husband's family will be most obliged to you for offering me hospitality."

"Oh, I rather doubt it," he said, with an engaging smile. "But then, I didn't think I'd tell them you were here."

"What makes you think they don't know?" I asked, beginning to feel rather hollow, despite my earlier resolve to brazen it out. I cast a quick glance at the window, but it was on the wrong side of the building. The sun wasn't visible, but the light looked yellow; perhaps mid-afternoon? How long before Jamie found my abandoned horse? And how long after that before he followed my trail into the stream—and promptly lost it? Disappearing without a trace had its drawbacks. In fact, unless Randall decided to send word of my whereabouts to Dougal, there was no way on earth the Scots could know where I had gone.

"If they knew," the Captain said, arching one elegantly shaped brow, "they would presumably be calling on me already. Considering the sorts of names Dougal MacKenzie applied to me on the occasion of our last meeting, I scarcely think he feels me a suitable chaperon for a kinswoman. And the clan MacKenzie seems to think you're of such value that they'd rather adopt you as one of their own than see you fall into my hands. I can hardly imagine they would allow you to languish in durance vile here."

He looked me over disapprovingly, taking in every detail of my waterlogged costume, unkempt hair, and generally disheveled appearance.

"Damned if I know what they want you for," he observed. "Or, if you're so valuable to them, why the devil they let you wander about the countryside by yourself. I thought even barbarians took better care of their womenfolk than that." A sudden gleam came into his eyes. "Or have you perhaps decided to part company with them?" He sat back, intrigued by this new speculation.

"The wedding night was more of a trial than you anticipated?" he inquired. "I must confess, I was somewhat put out to hear that you preferred the alternative of bedding one of those hairy, half-naked savages to further discussions with me. That argues a high devotion to duty, Madam, and I must congratulate whomever employs you on their ability to inspire it. But," he leaned still further back in his chair, balancing the claret cup on his knee, "I am afraid I still must insist on the name of your employer. If you have indeed parted company with the MacKenzies, the most likely supposition is that you're a French agent. But whose?"

He stared at me intently, like a snake hoping to fascinate a bird. By now I had had enough claret to fill part of the hollow space inside me, though, and I stared back.

"Oh," I said, elaborately polite, "I'm included in this conversation, am I? I thought you were doing quite well by yourself. Pray continue."

The graceful line of his mouth tightened a bit, and the deep crease at the corner grew deeper, but he didn't say anything. Setting his glass aside, he rose, and taking off his wig, went to the cupboard, where he placed it on an empty stand. I saw him pause for a moment, as he saw the dark grains of sand adorning his other wig, but his expression didn't change noticeably.

Unwigged, his hair was dark, thick, fine-textured, and shiny. It was also disturbingly familiar-looking, though it was shoulder-length and tied back with a blue silk ribbon. He removed this, plucked the comb from the desk and tidied the hair flattened by the wig, then retied the ribbon with some care. I helpfully held up the looking glass, so that he could judge the final effect. He took it from me in a marked manner and restored it to its place, shutting the cupboard door with what was almost a slam.

I couldn't tell whether this delay was in hopes of unnerving me—in which case, it was working—or merely because he couldn't decide what to do next.

The tension was slightly relieved by the entrance of an orderly, bearing a tray of tea things. Still silent, Randall poured out and offered me a cup. We sipped some more.

"Don't tell me," I said finally. "Let me guess. It's a new form of persuasion you've invented—torture by bladder. You ply me with drinkables until I promise to tell you anything in exchange for five minutes with a chamber pot."

He was so taken by surprise that he actually laughed. It quite transformed his face, and I had no difficulty seeing why there were so many scented envelopes with feminine handwriting in the bottom left-hand drawer of his desk. Having let the facade crack, he didn't stifle the laugh, but let it go. Finished, he stared at me again, a half-smile lingering on his mouth.

"Whatever else you may be, Madam, at least you're a diversion," he remarked. He yanked at a bellpull hanging by the door, and when the orderly reappeared, instructed him to convey me to the necessary facilities.

"But take care not to lose her on the way, Thompson," he added, opening the door for me with a sardonic bow.

I leaned weakly against the door of the privy to which I was shown. Being out of his presence was a relief, but a short-lived one. I had had ample opportunity to judge Randall's true character, both from the stories I had heard and from personal experience. But there were those damnable flashes of Frank that kept showing through the gleaming, ruthless exterior. It had been a mistake to make him laugh, I thought.

I sat down, ignoring the stench in my concentration on the problem at hand. Escape seemed unlikely. The vigilant Thompson aside, Randall's office was in a building located near the center of the compound. And while the fort itself was no more than a stone stockade, the walls were ten feet high and the double gates well guarded.

I thought of feigning illness and remaining in my refuge, but dismissed it—and not only because of the unpleasantness of the surroundings. The unpalatable truth was that there was little point in delaying tactics, unless I had something to delay for, and I didn't. No one knew where I was, and Randall didn't mean to tell anyone. I was his, for as long as he cared to amuse himself with me. Once again, I regretted making him laugh. A sadist with a sense of humor was particularly dangerous.

Thinking frantically in search of something useful I might know about the Captain, I latched on to a name. Half-heard and carelessly remembered, I hoped I had it right. It was a pitifully small card to play, but the only one I had. I drew a deep breath, hastily let it out again, and stepped out of my sanctuary.

Back in the office, I added sugar to my tea and stirred it carefully. Then cream. Having drawn out the ceremony as long as I could, I was forced to look at Randall. He was sitting back in his favorite pose, cup elegantly suspended in midair, the better to look at me over.

"Well?" I said. "You needn't worry about spoiling my appetite, since I haven't got one. What do you mean to do about me?"

He smiled and took a careful sip of the scalding tea before replying.

"Nothing."

"Really?" I lifted my brows in surprise. "Invention failed you, has it?"

"I shouldn't care to think so," he said, polite as usual. His eyes traveled over me once more, far from polite.

"No," he said, his gaze lingering on the edge of my bodice, where the tucked kerchief left the upper swell of my breasts visible, "much as I would like to give you a badly needed lesson in manners, I am afraid the pleasure must be postponed indefinitely. I'm sending you to Edinburgh with the next posting of dispatches. And I shouldn't care to have you arrive damaged in any visible way; my superiors might consider it careless of me."

"Edinburgh?" I couldn't hide my surprise.

"Yes. You've heard of the Tolbooth, I imagine?"

I had. One of the most noisome and notorious prisons of the period, it was famous for filth, crime, disease, and darkness. A good many of the prisoners held there died before they could be brought to trial. I swallowed hard, forcing down the bitter bile that had risen at the back of my throat, mingling with the swallow of sweet tea.

Randall sipped his own tea, pleased with himself.

"You should feel quite cozy there. After all, you seem to prefer a certain dank squalor in your surroundings." He cast a condemning glance at the soggy hem of my petticoat, sagging below my gown. "Should be quite homelike, after Castle Leoch."

I rather doubted that the cuisine at the Tolbooth was as good as that to be had at Colum's board. And general questions of amenities aside, I couldn't—*could not*—allow him to send me to Edinburgh. Once immured in the Tolbooth, I would never get back to the stone circle.

The time to play my card had arrived. Now or never. I raised my own cup.

"Just as you like," I said calmly. "What do you suppose the Duke of Sandringham will have to say about it?"

He upset the hot tea on his doeskin lap and made several very gratifying noises.

"*Tsk,*" I said, reprovingly.

He subsided, glaring. The teacup lay on its side, its brown

contents soaking into the pale green carpet, but he made no move toward the bellpull. A small muscle jumped in the side of his neck.

I had already found the pile of starched handkerchiefs in the upper left-hand drawer of the desk, alongside an enameled snuffbox. I pulled one out and handed it to him.

"I do hope it doesn't stain," I said sweetly.

"No," he said, ignoring the handkerchief. He eyed me closely. "No, it isn't possible."

"Why not?" I asked, affecting nonchalance, wondering *what* wasn't possible.

"I would have been told. And if *you* were working for Sandringham, why the devil would you act in such a damned ridiculous manner?"

"Perhaps the Duke is testing your loyalty," I suggested at random, preparing to leap to my feet if necessary. His fists were bunched at his side, and the discarded riding crop was within much too easy a reach on the desk nearby.

He snorted in response to this suggestion.

"*You* may be testing my gullibility. Or my tolerance to irritation. Both, Madam, are extremely low." His eyes narrowed speculatively, and I braced myself for a quick dash.

He lunged, and I flung myself to one side. Getting hold of the teapot, I threw it at him. He dodged, and it hit the door with a satisfying crash. The orderly, who must have been lingering just outside, poked a startled head in.

Breathing heavily, the Captain motioned him impatiently into the room.

"Hold her," he ordered brusquely, crossing toward the desk. I began to breathe deeply, both in hopes of calming myself and in anticipation of not being able to do it in a moment.

Instead of hitting me, though, he merely pulled out the lower right-hand drawer, which I had not had time to investigate, and pulled out a long strand of thin rope.

"What kind of gentleman keeps rope in his desk drawers?" I inquired indignantly.

"A prepared one, Madam," he murmured, tying my wrists securely behind me.

"Go," he said impatiently to the orderly, jerking his head toward the door. "And don't come back, no matter what you hear."

This sounded distinctly ominous, and my forebodings were abundantly justified as he reached into the drawer once more.

There is something unnerving about a knife. Men who are fearless in personal combat will shrink from a naked blade. I shrank myself, until my bound hands collided with the white-washed wall. The wicked gleaming point lowered and pressed between my breasts.

"Now," he said pleasantly, "you are going to tell me everything you know about the Duke of Sandringham." The blade pressed a little harder, making a dent in the fabric of my gown. "Take as long as you like about it, my dear. I am in no hurry whatsoever." There was a small *pop!* as the point punctured the fabric. I felt it, cold as fear, a tiny spot directly over my heart.

Randall slowly drew the knife in a semicircle under one breast. The homespun came free and fell away with a flutter of white chemise, and my breast sprang out. Randall seemed to have been holding his breath; he exhaled slowly now, his eyes fixed on mine.

I sidled away from him, but there was very little room to maneuver. I ended up pressed against the desk, bound hands gripping the edge. If he came close enough, I thought, I might be able to rock backward on my hands and kick the knife out of his hand. I doubted that he meant to kill me; certainly not until he had found out just what I knew about his relations with the Duke. Somehow that conclusion was of relatively little comfort.

He smiled, with that unnerving resemblance to Frank's smile; that lovely smile which I had seen charm students and melt the stoniest college administrator. Possibly under other circumstances, I would have found this man charming, but just at present . . . no.

He moved in fast, thrusting a knee between my thighs and pushing my shoulders back. Unable to keep my balance, I fell heavily backward on the desk, crying out as I landed painfully on my bound wrists. He pressed himself between my legs, scrabbling with one hand to raise my skirts while the other fastened on my bared breast, rolling and pinching. I kicked frantically, but my skirts got in the way. He grasped my foot and ran a hand up my leg, pushing damp petticoats, skirt, and chemise out of the way, tossing them up above my waist. His hand dropped to his breeches.

Shades of Harry the deserter, I thought furiously. What in God's name is the British army coming to? Glorious traditions, my aunt Fanny.

In the midst of an English garrison, screaming was unlikely to attract any helpful attention, but I filled my lungs and had a try, more as a pro forma protest than anything else. I had expected a slap or shake in return, to shut me up. Instead, unexpectedly, he appeared to like it.

"Go ahead and scream, sweeting," he murmured, busy with his flies. "I'll enjoy it much more if you scream."

I looked him straight in the eye and snapped "Get stuffed!" with perfect clarity and terrible inaptness.

A lock of dark hair came loose and fell across his forehead in rakish disarray. He looked so like his six-times-great grandson that I was seized by a horrible impulse to open my legs and respond to him. He twisted my breast savagely and the impulse disappeared at once.

I was furiously angry, disgusted, humiliated, and revolted, but curiously not very frightened. I felt a heavy, flopping movement against my leg and suddenly realized why. He wasn't going to enjoy it *unless* I screamed—and possibly not then.

"Oh, like that, is it?" I said, and was rewarded at once with a sharp slap across the face. I shut my mouth grimly and turned my head away lest I be tempted into any more injudicious remarks. I realized that rape or not, I was in considerable danger from his unstable temper. Looking away from the sight of Randall, I caught a sudden flicker of movement at the window.

"I'll thank ye," said a cool, level voice, "to take your hands off my wife." Randall froze with a hand still on my breast. Jamie was crouched in the window frame, a large, brass-handled pistol braced across one forearm.

Randall stood frozen for a second, as though unable to believe his ears. As his head turned slowly toward the window, his right hand, shielded from Jamie's view, left my breast, sliding stealthily toward the knife, which he had laid on the desk next to my head.

"*What* did you say?" he said, incredulously. As his hand fastened on the knife, he turned far enough to see who had spoken. He stopped again for a moment, staring, then began to laugh.

"Lord help us, it's the young Scottish wildcat! I thought I'd dealt with you once and for all! Back healed after all, did it? And this is *your* wife, you say? Quite a tasty little wench, she is, quite like your sister."

Still shielded by his partly turned body, Randall's knife-hand swiveled; the blade was now pointed at my throat. I could see Jamie over his shoulder, braced in the window like a cat about to spring. The pistol barrel didn't waver, nor did he change expression. The only clue to his emotions was the dusky red creeping up his throat; his collar was unbuttoned and the small scar on his neck flamed crimson.

Almost casually, Randall slowly raised the knife into view, point almost touching my throat. He half turned toward Jamie.

"Perhaps you'd better toss that pistol over here—unless you're weary of married life. If you'd prefer to be a widower, of course . . ." Their eyes locked tight as a lover's embrace, neither man moved for a long minute. Finally, Jamie's body relaxed its springlike tension. He let out his breath in a long sigh of resignation and tossed the pistol into the room. It hit the floor with a clunk and slid almost to Randall's feet.

Randall bent and scooped up the gun in a quicksilver motion. As soon as the knife left my throat, I tried to sit up, but he placed a hand on my chest and shoved me flat again. He held me down with one hand, using the other to aim the pistol at Jamie. The discarded knife lay somewhere on the floor near my feet, I thought. Now, if only I had prehensile toes. . . . The dirk in my pocket was as unreachable as if it were on Mars.

The smile had not left Randall's features since Jamie's appearance. Now it broadened, enough to show the pointed dog teeth.

"Well, that's a bit better." The pressing hand left my chest to return to the swelling flies of his breeches. "I was engaged when you arrived, my dear fellow. You'll forgive me if I get on with what I was doing before I attend to you."

The red color had spread completely over Jamie's face, but he stood motionless, the gun pointed at his middle. As Randall finished his maneuvers, Jamie launched himself at the open mouth of the pistol. I tried to scream, to stop him, but my mouth was dry with terror. Randall's knuckles whitened as he squeezed the trigger.

The hammer clicked on an empty chamber, and Jamie's fist drove into Randall's stomach. There was a dull, crunching sound as his other fist splintered the officer's nose, and a fine spray of blood spattered my skirt. Randall's eyes rolled up in his head, and he dropped to the floor like a stone.

Jamie was behind me, pulling me up, sawing at the rope around my wrists.

"You bluffed your way in here with an *empty* gun?" I croaked hysterically.

"If it were loaded, I would ha' just shot him in the first place, wouldn't I?!" Jamie hissed.

Feet were coming down the corridor toward the office. The rope came free and Jamie yanked me to the window. It was an eight-foot drop to the ground, but the footsteps were almost to the door. We jumped together.

I landed with a bone-shaking jar and rolled in a tumble of skirts and petticoats. Jamie jerked me to my feet and pressed me against the wall of the building. Feet were passing the corner of the building; six soldiers came into view, but didn't look in our direction.

As soon as they were safely past, Jamie took my hand and motioned toward the other corner. We sidled along the building, stopping short of the corner. I could see where we were now. About twenty feet away, a ladder led up to a sort of catwalk that ran along the inside of the fort's outer wall. He nodded toward it; this was our objective.

He brought his head close to mine and whispered, "When

ye hear an explosion, run like hell and get up that ladder. I'll be behind ye."

I nodded understanding. My heart was going like a trip-hammer; glancing down, I saw that one breast was still exposed. Not much to be done about it just at present. I rucked up my skirts, ready to run.

There was an almighty roar from the other side of the building, like a mortar explosion. Jamie gave me a shove and I was off, running as fast as I could go. I jumped for the ladder, caught it and scrambled up; I felt the wood jerk and tremble as Jamie's weight hit the ladder below me.

Turning at the top of the ladder, I had a bird's-eye view of the fort. Black smoke was billowing up from a small building near the back wall, and men were running toward it from every direction.

Jamie popped up beside me. "This way." He ran crouching along the catwalk, and I followed. We stopped near the flag staff set in the wall. The ensign flapped heavily above us, halyard beating a rhythmic tattoo against the pole. Jamie was peering over the wall, looking for something.

I looked back over the camp. The men were clustering at the small building, milling and shouting. Off to one side, I spotted a small wooden platform, set three or four feet high, with steps leading up. A heavy wooden post rose out of the center, cross-beamed, with rope manacles dangling from the arms of the cross.

Suddenly Jamie gave a whistle; looking over the wall, I saw Rupert, mounted and leading Jamie's horse. He looked up at the sound of the whistle and maneuvered the horses close to the wall below us.

Jamie was cutting the halyard from the flagpole. The heavy red and blue folds of the flag drooped and slid down, landing with a swishing thud next to me. Twisting a rope end rapidly around one of the struts, Jamie tossed the rest down the outside of the wall.

"Come on!" he said. "Hold tight with both hands, brace your feet against the wall! Go!" I went, bracing my feet and paying out rope; the thin cordage slipped and burned in my hands. I dropped next to the horses and hurried to mount.

Jamie vaulted into the saddle behind me a moment later, and we took off at a gallop.

We slowed our pace a mile or two from the camp, when it became apparent that we had lost any pursuers. After a short conference, Dougal decided that we had better make for the border of the Mackintosh lands, as being the closest safe clan territory.

"Doonesbury's within riding distance by tonight, and likely to be safe enough. There'll be word out on us tomorrow, but we'll be across the border before it reaches there." It was mid-afternoon by then; we set off at a steady pace, our horse with its double load lagging slightly behind the others. My horse, I supposed, was still happily eating grass in the copse, waiting to be led home by whoever was lucky enough to find it.

"How did you find me?" I asked. I was beginning to shake in reaction, and folded my arms around myself to still the quivering. My clothes had dried completely by this time, but I felt a chill that went bone-deep.

"I thought better of leaving ye alone, and sent a man back to stay wi' ye. He didna see ye leave, but he saw the English soldiers cross the ford, and you wi' them." Jamie's voice was cold. I couldn't blame him, I supposed. My teeth were beginning to chatter.

"I'm s-surprised that you didn't just think I was an English spy and l-leave me there."

"Dougal wanted to. But the man who saw ye with the soldiers said you were struggling. I had to go and see, at least." He glanced down at me, not changing expression.

"You're lucky, Sassenach, that I saw what I did in that room. At least Dougal must admit that you're not in league wi' the English."

"D-Dougal, eh? And what about you? Wh-what do *you* think?" I demanded.

He did not reply, but only snorted briefly. He did at last take pity on me to the extent of jerking off his plaid and flinging it over my shoulders, but he would not put his arm around me nor touch me more than strictly necessary. He rode in grim silence, handling the reins with an angry jerkiness quite unlike his usual smooth grace.

Upset and unsettled myself, I was in no frame of mind to put up with moods.

"Well, what is it, then? What's the matter?" I asked impatiently. "Don't sulk, for heaven's sake!" I spoke more sharply than I intended, and I felt him stiffen still further. Suddenly he turned the horse's head aside and reined up at the side of the road. Before I knew what was happening, he had dismounted and jerked me from the saddle as well. I landed awkwardly, staggering to keep my balance as my feet hit the ground.

Dougal and the others paused, seeing us stop. Jamie made a short, sharp gesture, sending them on, and Dougal waved in acknowledgment. "Don't take too long," he called, and they set off again.

Jamie waited until they were out of earshot. Then he yanked me around to face him. He was clearly furious, on the verge of explosion. I felt my own wrath rising; what right did he have to treat me like this?

"Sulking!" he said. "Sulking, is it? I'm using all the self-control I've got, to keep from shakin' ye 'til your teeth rattle, and you tell me not to sulk!"

"What in the name of God is the matter with you?" I asked angrily. I tried to shake off his grip, but his fingers dug into my upper arms like the teeth of a trap.

"What's the matter wi' me? I'll tell ye what the matter is, since ye want to know!" he said through clenched teeth. "I'm tired of having to prove over and over that you're no an English spy. I'm tired of having to watch ye very minute, for fear of what foolishness you'll try next. And I'm *verra* tired of people trying to make me watch while they rape you! I dinna enjoy it a bit!"

"And you think *I* enjoy it?" I yelled. "Are you trying to make out it's *my* fault?!" At this, he did shake me slightly.

"It *is* your fault! Did ye stay put where I ordered ye to stay this mornin', this would never have happened! But no, ye won't listen to me, I'm no but your husband, why mind *me*? You take it into your mind to do as ye damn please, and next I ken, I find ye flat on your back wi' your skirts up, an' the worst scum in the land between your legs, on the point of takin' ye before my eyes!" His Scots accent, usually slight, was growing broader by the second, sure sign that he was upset, had I needed any further indication.

We were almost nose to nose by this time, shouting into each other's face. Jamie was flushed with fury, and I felt the blood rising in my own face.

"It's your own fault, for ignoring me and suspecting me all the time! I told you the truth about who I am! And I told you there was no danger in my going with you, but would you listen to *me*? No! I'm only a woman, why should you pay any attention to what I say? Women are only fit to do as they're told, and follow orders, and sit meekly around with their hands folded, waiting for the *men* to come back and tell them what to do!"

He shook me again, unable to control himself.

"And if ye'd done that, we wouldna be on the run, with a hundred Redcoats on our tail! God, woman, I dinna know whether to strangle ye or throw ye on the ground and hammer ye senseless, but by Jesus, I want to do *something* to you."

At this, I made a determined effort to kick him in the balls. He dodged, and jammed his own knee between my legs, effectively preventing any further attempts.

"Try that again and I'll slap you 'til your ears ring," he growled.

"You're a brute and a fool," I panted, struggling to escape his grip on my shoulders. "Do you think I went out and got captured by the English on purpose?"

"I do think ye did it on purpose, to get back at me for what happened in the glade!"

My mouth fell open.

"In the glade? With the English deserters?"

"Aye! Ye think I should ha' been able to protect ye there, an' you're right. But I couldna do it; you had to do it yourself, and now you're tryin' to make me pay for it by deliberately putting yourself, *my* wife, in the hands of a man that's shed my blood!"

"*Your* wife! *Your* wife! You don't care a thing about me! I'm just your property; it only matters to you because you think I belong to you, and you can't stand to have someone take something that belongs to you!"

"Ye *do* belong to me," he roared, digging his fingers into my shoulders like spikes. "And you *are* my wife, whether ye like it or no!"

"I don't like it! I don't like it a bit! But that doesn't matter either, does it? As long as I'm there to warm your bed, you don't care what I think or how I feel! That's all a wife is to you—something to stick your cock into when you feel the urge!"

At this, his face went dead white and he began to shake me in earnest. My head jerked violently and my teeth clacked together, making me bite my tongue painfully.

"Let go of me!" I shouted. "Let go, you"—I deliberately used the words of Harry the deserter, trying to hurt him— "you rutting bastard!" He did let go, and fell back a pace, eyes blazing.

"Ye foul-tongued bitch! Ye'll no speak to me that way!"

"I'll speak any way I want to! You can't tell me what to do!"

"Seems I can't! Ye'll do as ye wish, no matter who ye hurt by it, won't ye? Ye selfish, willful—"

"It's your bloody pride that's hurt!" I shouted. "I saved us both from those deserters in the glade, and you can't stand it, can you? You just stood there! If I hadn't had a knife, we'd both be dead now!"

Until I spoke the words, I had had no idea that I had been angry with him for failing to protect me from the English deserters. In a more rational mood, the thought would never have entered my mind. It wasn't his fault, I would have said. It was just luck that I had the knife, I would have said. But now I realized that fair or not, rational or not, I *did* somehow feel that it was his responsibility to protect me, and that he had failed me. Perhaps because *he* so clearly felt that way.

He stood glaring at me, panting with emotion. When he spoke again, his voice was low and ragged with passion.

"You saw that post in the yard of the fort?" I nodded shortly.

"Well, I was tied to that post, tied like an animal, and whipped 'til my blood ran! I'll carry the scars from it 'til I die. If I'd not been lucky as the devil this afternoon, that's the least as would have happened to me. Likely they'd have flogged me, then hanged me." He swallowed hard, and went on.

"I knew that, and I didna hesitate for one second to go into that place after you, even thinking that Dougal might be right! Do ye know where I got the gun I used?" I shook my head numbly, my own anger beginning to fade. "I killed a guard near the wall. He fired at me; that's why it was empty. He missed and I killed him wi' my dirk; left it sticking in his wishbone when I heard you cry out. I would have killed a dozen men to get to you, Claire." His voice cracked.

"And when ye screamed, I went to you, armed wi' nothing but an empty gun and my two hands." Jamie was speaking a little more calmly now, but his eyes were still wild with pain and rage. I was silent. Unsettled by the horror of my encounter with Randall, I had not at all appreciated the desperate courage it had taken for him to come into the fort after me.

He turned away suddenly, shoulders slumping.

"You're right," he said quietly. "Aye, you're quite right." Suddenly the rage was gone from his voice, replaced by a tone I had never heard in him before, even in the extremities of physical pain.

"My pride is hurt. And my pride is about all I've got left to me." He leaned his forearms against a rough-barked pine and let his head drop onto them, exhausted. His voice was so low I could barely hear him.

"You're tearin' my guts out, Claire."

Something very similar was happening to my own. Tentatively, I came up behind him. He didn't move, even when I slipped my arms around his waist. I rested my cheek on his bowed back. His shirt was damp, sweated through with the intensity of his passion, and he was trembling.

"I'm sorry," I said, simply. "Please forgive me." He turned then, to hold me tightly. I felt his trembling ease bit by bit.

"Forgiven, lass," he murmured at last into my hair. Releasing me, he looked down at me, sober and formal.

"I'm sorry too," he said. "I'll ask your pardon for what I said; I was sore, and I said more nor I meant. Will ye forgive me too?" After his last speech, I hardly felt that there was anything for me to forgive, but I nodded and pressed his hands.

"Forgiven."

In an easier silence, we mounted again. The road was straight for a long way here, and far ahead I could see a small cloud of dust that must be Dougal and the other men.

Jamie was back with me again; he held me with one arm as we rode, and I felt safer. But there was still a vague sense of injury and constraint; things were not yet healed between us. We had forgiven each other, but our words still hung in memory, not to be forgotten.

22

Reckonings

We reached Doonesbury well after dark. It was a fair-sized coach-stop with an inn, fortunately. Dougal closed his eyes briefly in pain as he paid the innkeeper; it would take quite a bit of extra silver to ensure his silence as to our presence.

The silver, however, also insured a hearty supper, with plenty of ale. Despite the food, supper was a grim affair, eaten mostly in silence. Sitting there in my ruined gown, modestly covered by Jamie's extra shirt, I was plainly in disgrace. Except for Jamie, the men behaved as though I were completely invisible, and even Jamie did no more than shove bread and meat in my direction from time to time. It was a relief at last to go up to our chamber, small and cramped though it was.

I sank on the bed with a sigh, disregarding the state of the bedclothes.

"I'm done in. It's been a long day."

"Aye, it has that." Jamie unfastened his collar and cuffs and unbuckled his sword belt, but made no move to undress further. He pulled the strap from the scabbard and doubled it, flexing the leather meditatively.

"Come to bed, Jamie. What are you waiting for?"

He came to stand by the bed, swinging the belt gently back and forth.

"Well, lass, I'm afraid we've a matter still to settle between us before we sleep tonight." I felt a sudden stab of apprehension.

"What is it?"

He didn't answer at once. Deliberately not sitting down on the bed by me, he pulled up a stool and sat facing me instead.

"Do ye realize, Claire," he said quietly, "that all of us came close to bein' killed this afternoon?"

I looked down at the quilt, shamefaced. "Yes, I know. My fault. I'm sorry."

"Aye, so ye realize," he said. "Do ye know that if a man among us had done such a thing, to put the rest in danger, he would ha' likely had his ears cropped, or been flogged, if not killed outright?" I blanched at this.

"No, I didn't know."

"Well, I know as you're not yet familiar wi' our ways, and it's some excuse. Still, I did tell ye to stay hid, and had ye done so, it would never have happened. Now the English will be lookin' high and low for us; we shall have to lie hid during the days and travel at night now."

He paused. "And as for Captain Randall . . . aye, that's something else again."

"He'll be looking for you especially, you mean, now that he knows you're here?" He nodded absently, looking off into the fire.

"Aye. He . . . it's personal, with him, ye know?"

"I'm so sorry, Jamie," I said. Jamie dismissed this with a wave of the hand.

"Eh, if it were only me ye'd hurt by it, I wouldna say more about it. Though since we're talkin'," he shot me a sharp glance, "I'll tell ye that it near killed me to see that animal with his hands on you." He looked off into the fire, grim-faced, as though reliving the afternoon's events.

I thought of telling him about Randall's . . . difficulties, but was afraid it would do more harm than good. I desperately wanted to hold Jamie and beg him to forgive me, but I didn't dare to touch him. After a long moment of silence, he sighed and stood up, slapping the belt lightly against his thigh.

"Well, then," he said. "Best get on wi' it. You've done considerable damage by crossing my orders, and I'm going to punish ye for it, Claire. Ye'll recall what I told ye when I left ye this morning?" I recalled all right, and I hastily flung myself across the bed so my back was pressed to the wall.

"What do you mean?"

"Ye know quite well what I mean," he said firmly. "Kneel down by the bed and lift your skirts, lass."

"I'll do no such thing!" I took a good hold on the bedpost with both hands and wormed my way further into the corner.

Jamie watched me through narrowed eyes for a moment, debating what to do next. It occurred to me that there was nothing whatever to stop him doing anything he liked to me; he outweighed me by a good five stone. He at last decided on talk rather than action, though, and carefully laid the strap aside before crawling over the bedclothes to sit beside me.

"Now, Claire—" he began.

"I've said I'm sorry!" I burst out. "And I am. I'll never do such a thing again!"

"Well, that's the point," he said slowly. "Ye might. And it's because ye dinna take things as serious as they are. Ye come from a place where things are easier, I think. 'Tis not a matter of life or death where ye come from, to disobey orders or take matters into your own hands. At worst, ye might cause someone discomfort, or be a bit of a nuisance, but it isna likely to get someone killed." I watched his fingers pleating the brownish plaid of his kilt as he arranged his thoughts.

"It's the hard truth that a light action can have verra serious consequences in places and times like these—especially for a man like me." He patted my shoulder, seeing that I was close to tears.

"I know ye would never endanger me or anyone else on purpose. But ye might easily do so without meanin' it, like ye did today, because ye do not really believe me yet when I tell ye that some things are dangerous. You're accustomed to think for yourself, and I know," he glanced sidewise at me, "that you're not accustomed to lettin' a man tell ye what to do. But you must learn to do so, for all our sakes."

"All right," I said slowly. "I understand. You're right, of course. All right; I'll follow your orders, even if I don't agree with them."

"Good." He stood up, and picked up the belt. "Now then, get off the bed, and we'll get it over with."

My mouth dropped open in outrage. "What! I *said* I'd follow your orders!"

He sighed, exasperated, then sat down again on the stool. He looked at me levelly.

"Now, listen. Ye understand me, ye say, and I believe it. But there's a difference between understandin' something with your mind and really knowing it, deep down." I nodded, reluctantly.

"All right. Now, I will have to punish you, and for two reasons: first, so that ye *will* know." He smiled suddenly. "I can tell ye from my own experience that a good hiding makes ye consider things in a more serious light." I took a tighter hold on the bedpost.

"The other reason," he went on, "is because of the other men. Ye'll have noticed how they were tonight?" I had; it had been so uncomfortable at dinner that I was glad to escape to the room.

"There's such a thing as justice, Claire. You've done wrong to them all, and you'll have to suffer for it." He took a deep breath. "I'm your husband; it's my duty to attend to it, and I mean to do it."

I had strong objections to this proposal on several levels. Whatever the justice of the situation—and I had to admit that at least some of it lay on his side—my sense of amour-propre was deeply offended at the thought of being beaten, by whomever and for whatever reason.

I felt deeply betrayed that the man I depended on as friend, protector, and lover intended to do such a thing to me. And my sense of self-preservation was quietly terrified at the thought of submitting myself to the mercies of someone who handled a fifteen-pound claymore as though it were a flywhisk.

"I will not allow you to beat me," I said firmly, keeping a tight hold on the bedpost.

"Oh, you won't?" He raised sandy brows. "Well, I'll tell ye, lass, I doubt you've much to say about it. You're my wife, like it or not. Did I want to break your arm, or feed ye naught but bread and water, or lock ye in a closet for days—and don't think ye don't tempt me, either—I could do that, let alone warm your bum for you."

"I'll scream!"

"Likely. If not before, certainly during. I expect they'll hear ye at the next farm; you've got good lungs." He grinned odiously and came across the bed after me.

He pried my fingers loose with some difficulty, and pulled firmly, hauling me to the side of the bed. I kicked him in the shins, but did no damage, not having shoes on. Grunting slightly, he managed to turn me facedown on the bed, twisting my arm to hold me there.

"I mean to do it, Claire! Now, if you'll cooperate wi' me, we'll call the account square with a dozen strokes."

"And if not?" I quavered. He picked up the strap and slapped it against his leg with a nasty thwapping sound.

"Then I shall put a knee in your back and beat you 'til my arm tires, and I warn ye, you'll tire of it long before I do."

I bounced off the bed and whirled to face him, fists clenched.

"You barbarian! You . . . you sadist!" I hissed furiously. "You're doing this for your own pleasure! I'll never forgive you for this!" Jamie paused, twisting the belt.

He replied levelly, "I dinna know what's a sadist. And if I forgive you for this afternoon, I reckon you'll forgive me, too, as soon as ye can sit down again."

"As for my pleasure . . ." His lip twitched. "I said I would have to punish you. I did *not* say I wasna going to enjoy it." He crooked a finger at me.

"Come here."

⟡

I was reluctant to leave the sanctuary of the room next morning, and fiddled about, tying and untying ribbons and brushing my hair. I had not spoken to Jamie since the night before, but he noticed my hesitation and urged me to come out with him to breakfast.

"You dinna need to fear meetin' the others, Claire. They'll chaff ye a bit, likely, but it won't be bad. Chin up." He chucked me under the chin, and I bit his hand, sharply but not deep.

"Ooh!" He snatched his fingers back. "Be careful, lass; you don't know where they've been." He left me, chuckling, and went in to breakfast.

He might well be in a good mood, I thought bitterly. If it was revenge he'd wanted the night before, he'd had it.

It had been a most unpleasant night. My reluctant acquiescence had lasted precisely as far as the first searing crack of leather on flesh. This was followed by a short, violent struggle, which left Jamie with a bloody nose, three lovely gouges down one cheek, and a deeply bitten wrist. Not surprisingly, it left me half smothered in the greasy quilts with a knee in my back, being beaten within an inch of my life.

Jamie, damn his black Scottish soul, turned out to be right. The men were restrained in their greetings, but friendly enough; the hostility and contempt of the night before had vanished.

As I was dishing eggs at the sideboard, Dougal came up and slipped a fatherly arm around my shoulders. His beard tickled my ear as he spoke in a confidential rumble.

"I hope Jamie wasna too harsh wi' ye last night, lass. It sounded as though ye were bein' murderrt, at least."

I flushed hotly and turned away so he wouldn't see it. After Jamie's obnoxious remarks, I had resolved to keep my mouth firmly shut through the whole ordeal. However, when it came to the event, I would have challenged the Sphinx itself to keep a shut mouth while on the receiving end of a strap wielded by Jamie Fraser.

Dougal turned to call to Jamie, seated at the table eating bread and cheese. "Hey now, Jamie, it wasna necessary to half-kill the lass. A gentle reminder would ha' sufficed." He patted me firmly on the posterior in illustration, making me wince. I glowered at him.

"A blistered bum never did anyone no permanent harm," said Murtagh, through a mouthful of bread.

"No, indeed," said Ned, grinning. "Come have a seat, lassie."

"I'll stand, thank you," I said with dignity, making them all roar with laughter. Jamie was careful not to meet my eyes, as he studiously cut up a bit of cheese.

There was a bit more good-natured chaff during the day, and each of the men made some excuse to pat my rump in mock sympathy. On the whole, though, it was bearable, and I grudgingly began to consider that Jamie might have been right, though I still wanted to strangle him.

Since sitting down was completely out of the question, I busied myself during the morning with small chores such as hemming and button-sewing, which could be done at the windowsill, with the excuse of needing the light to sew by. After lunch, which I ate standing, we all went to our rooms to rest. Dougal had decided that we would wait 'til full dark to set out for Bargrennan, the next stop on our journey. Jamie followed me to our room, but I shut the door firmly in his face. Let him sleep on the floor again.

He had been fairly tactful last night, buckling his belt back on and leaving the room without speaking immediately after he'd finished. He had come back an hour later, after I'd put out the light and gone to bed, but had had sense enough not to try to come into bed with me. After peering into the darkness where I lay unmoving, he had sighed deeply, wrapped himself in his plaid, and gone to sleep on the floor near the door.

Too angry, upset, and physically uncomfortable to sleep, I had lain awake most of the night, alternately thinking over what Jamie had said with wanting to get up and kick him in some sensitive spot.

Were I being objective, which I was in no mood to be, I might admit that he was right when he said that I didn't take things with the proper seriousness. He was wrong, though, when he said it was because things were less precarious in my own place—wherever that was. In fact, I thought, it was more likely the opposite was true.

This time was in many ways still unreal to me; something from a play or a fancy-dress pageant. Compared to the sights of mechanized mass warfare I had come from, the small, pitched battles I had seen—a few men armed with swords and muskets—seemed picturesque rather than threatening to me.

I was having trouble with the scale of things. A man killed with a musket was just as dead as one killed with a mortar. It was just that the mortar killed impersonally, destroying dozens of men, while the musket was fired by one man who could see the eyes of the one he killed. That made it murder, it seemed to me, not war. How many men to make a war? Enough, perhaps, so they didn't really have to see each other? And yet this plainly was war—or serious business at least—to Dougal, Jamie, Rupert, and Ned. Even little rat-faced Murtagh had a reason for violence beyond his natural inclinations.

And what about those reasons? One king rather than another? Hanovers and Stuarts? To me, these were still no more than names on a chart on the schoolroom wall. What were they, compared with an unthinkable evil like Hitler's Reich? It made a difference to those who lived under the kings, I supposed, though the differences might seem trivial to me. Still, when had the right to live as one wished ever been considered trivial? Was a struggle to choose one's own destiny less worthwhile than the necessity to stop a great evil? I shifted irritably, gingerly rubbing my sore bottom. I glared at Jamie, curled into a ball by the door. He was breathing evenly, but lightly; perhaps he couldn't sleep either. I hoped not.

I had been inclined at first to take this whole remarkable misadventure as melodrama; such things just did not happen in real life. I had had many shocks since I stepped through the rock, but the worst to date had been this afternoon.

Jack Randall, so like and so horribly unlike Frank. His touch on my breasts had suddenly forged a link between my old life and this one, bringing my separate realities together with a bang like a thunderclap. And then there was Jamie: his face, stark with fear in the window of Randall's room, contorted with rage by the roadside, tight with pain at my insults.

Jamie. Jamie was real, all right, more real than anything had ever been to me, even Frank and my life in 1945. Jamie, tender lover and perfidious blackguard.

Perhaps that was part of the problem. Jamie filled my senses so completely that his surroundings seemed almost irrelevant. But I could no longer afford to ignore them. My recklessness had almost killed him this afternoon, and my stomach turned over at the thought of losing him. I sat up suddenly, intending to go and wake him to tell him to come to bed with me. As my weight fell full on the results of his handiwork, I just as suddenly changed my mind and flounced angrily back onto my stomach.

A night spent thus torn between fits of rage and philosophy had left me worn out. I slept all afternoon, and stumbled blearily down for a light supper when Rupert roused me just before dark.

Dougal, no doubt writhing at the expense, had procured another horse for me. A sound beast, if inelegantly built, with a kindly eye and a short, bristly mane; at once I named it Thistle.

I had not reckoned on the effects of a long horseback ride following a severe beating. I eyed Thistle's hard saddle dubiously, suddenly realizing what I was in for. A thick cloak plopped across the saddle, and Murtagh's shiny black rat-eye winked conspiratorially at me from the opposite side. I determined that I would at least suffer in dignified silence, and grimly set my jaw as I hoisted myself into the saddle.

There seemed to be an unspoken conspiracy of gallantry among the men; they took turns stopping at frequent intervals to relieve themselves, allowing me to dismount for a few minutes and surreptitiously rub my aching fundament. Now and again, one would suggest stopping for a drink, which necessitated my stopping as well, since Thistle carried the water bottles.

We jolted along for a couple of hours in this manner, but the pain grew steadily worse, keeping me shifting in the saddle incessantly. Finally I decided to hell with dignified suffering, I simply must get off for a while.

"Whoa!" I said to Thistle, and swung down. I pretended to examine her front left foot, as the other horses came to a milling stop around us.

"I'm afraid she's had a stone in her shoe," I lied. "I've got it out, but I'd better walk her a bit; don't want her to go lame."

"No, we can't have that," said Dougal. "All right, walk for a bit, then, but someone must stay wi' ye. 'Tis a quiet enough road, but I canna have ye walkin' alone." Jamie immediately swung down.

"I'll walk with her," he said quietly.

"Good. Dinna tarry too long; we must be in Bargrennan before dawn. The sign of the Red Boar; landlord's a friend." With a wave, he gathered the others and they set off at a brisk trot, leaving us in the dust.

Several hours of torture by saddle had not improved my temper. Let him walk with me. I was damned if I'd speak to him, the sadistic, violent brute.

He didn't look particularly brutish in the light of the half-moon rising, but I hardened my heart and limped along, carefully not looking at him.

My abused muscles at first protested the unaccustomed exercise, but after a half hour or so I began to move much more easily.

"You'll feel much better by tomorrow," Jamie observed casually. "Though you won't sit easy 'til the next day."

"And what makes you such an expert?" I flared at him. "Do you beat people all that frequently?"

"Well, no," he said, undisturbed by my attitude. "This is the first time I've tried it. I've considerable experience on the other end, though."

"You?" I gaped at him. The thought of anyone taking a strap to this towering mass of muscle and sinew was completely untenable.

He laughed at my expression. "When I was a bit smaller, Sassenach. I've had my backside leathered more times than I could count, between the ages of eight and thirteen. That's when I got taller than my father, and it got unhandy for him to bend me over a fence rail."

"Your father beat you?"

"Aye, mostly. The schoolmaster, too, of course, and Dougal or one of the other uncles now and then, depending on where I was and what I'd been doing."

I was growing interested, in spite of my determination to ignore him.

"What *did* you do?"

He laughed again, a quiet but infectious sound in the still night air.

"Well, I canna remember everything. I will say I generally deserved it. I don't think my da ever beat me unfairly, at least." He paced without speaking for a minute, thinking.

"Mm. Let's see, there was once for stoning the chickens, and once for riding the cows and getting them too excited for milking, and then for eating all of the jam out of the cakes and leaving the cakes behind. Ah, and letting the horses out of the barn by leaving the gate unlatched, and setting the thatch of the dovecote on fire—that was an accident, I didna do it on purpose—and losing my schoolbooks—I did do that on purpose—and . . ." He broke off, shrugging, as I laughed despite myself.

"The usual sorts of things. Most often, though, it was for opening my mouth when I should ha' kept it closed."

He snorted at some memory. "Once my sister Jenny broke a pitcher; I made her angry, teasing, and she lost her temper and threw it at me. When my da came in and demanded to know who'd done it, she was too scared to speak up, and she just looked at me, with her eyes all wide and frightened—she's got blue eyes, like mine, but prettier, wi' black lashes all around." Jamie shrugged again. "Anyway, I told my father I'd done it."

"That was very noble of you," I said, sarcastically. "Your sister must have been grateful."

"Aye, well, she might have been. Only my father'd been on the other side of the open door all along, and he'd seen what really happened. So she got whipped for losing her temper and breaking the pitcher, and I got whipped twice; once for teasing her and again for lying."

"That's not fair!" I said indignantly.

"My father wasna always gentle, but he was usually fair," Jamie said imperturbably. "He said the truth is the truth, and people should take responsibility for their own actions, which is right." He shot me a sidelong glance.

"But he said it was good-hearted of me to take the blame, so while he'd have to punish me, I could take my choice between being thrashed or going to bed without my supper." He laughed ruefully, shaking his head. "Father knew me pretty well. I took the thrashing with no questions."

"You're nothing but a walking appetite, Jamie," I said.

"Aye," he agreed without rancor, "always have been. You too, glutton," he said to his mount. "Wait a bit, 'til we stop for a rest." He twitched the rein, pulling his horse's questing nose from the tempting tufts of grass along the roadside.

"Aye, Father was fair," he went on, "and considerate about it, though I certainly didna appreciate that at the time. He wouldn't make me wait for a beating; if I did something wrong, I got punished at once—or as soon as he found out about it. He always made sure I knew what I was about to get walloped for, and if I wanted to argue my side of it, I could."

Oh, so that's what you're up to, I thought. You disarming schemer. I doubted he could charm me out of my set intention of disemboweling him at the first opportunity, but he was welcome to try.

"Did you ever win an argument?" I asked.

"No. It was generally a straightforward-enough case, with the accused convicted out of his own mouth. But sometimes I got the sentence reduced a bit." He rubbed his nose.

"Once I told him I thought beating your son was a most uncivilized method of getting your own way. He said I'd about as much sense as the post I was standing next to, if as much. He said respect for your elders was one of the cornerstones of civilized behavior, and until I learned that, I'd better get used to looking at my toes while one of my barbaric elders thrashed my arse off."

This time I laughed along with him. It was peaceful on the road, with that sort of absolute quiet that comes when you are miles from any other person. The sort of quiet so hard to come by in my own more crowded time, when machines spread the influence of man, so that a single person could make as much noise as a crowd. The only sounds here were the stirrings of plants, the occasional *skreek* of a nightbird, and the soft thudding steps of the horses.

I was walking a little easier now, as my cramped muscles began to stretch freely with the exercise. My prickly feelings began to relax a little, too, listening to Jamie's stories, all humorous and self-deprecating.

"I didna like being beaten at all, of course, but if I had a choice, I'd rather my da than the schoolmaster. We'd mostly get it across the palm of the hand with a tawse, in the school-house, instead of on the backside. Father said if he whipped me on the hand, I'd not be able to do any work, whereas if he whipped my arse, I'd at least not be tempted to sit down and be idle.

"We had a different schoolmaster each year, usually; they didna last long—usually turned farmer or moved on to richer parts. Schoolmasters are paid so little, they're always skinny and starving. Had a fat one once, and I could never believe he was a real schoolmaster; he looked like a parson in disguise." I thought of plump little Father Bain and smiled in agreement.

"One I remember especially, because he'd make ye stand out in the front of the schoolroom with your hand out, and then he'd lecture ye at great length about your faults before he started, and again in between strokes. I'd stand there wi' my hand out, smarting, just praying he'd stop yammering and get on with the job before I lost all my courage and started crying."

"I imagine that's what he wanted you to do," I said, feeling some sympathy in spite of myself.

"Oh, aye," he replied matter-of-factly. "It took some time for me to realize that, though. And once I did, as usual I couldna keep my mouth shut." He sighed.

"What happened?" I had all but forgotten to be furious by this time.

"Well, he had me up one day—I got it a lot because I couldna write properly with my right hand, kept doing it with my left. He'd smacked me three times—takin' nearly five minutes to do it, the bastard—and he was goin' on at me for being a stupid, idle, stubborn young lout before givin' me the next. My hand burned something fierce, because it was the second time that day, and I was scared because I knew I'd get an awful thrashing when I got home—that was the rule; if I got a beating at school, I'd get another directly I came home, for my father thought schooling important—anyway, I lost

my temper." His left hand curled involuntarily around the
rein, as though protecting the sensitive palm.

He paused and glanced at me. "I seldom lose my temper,
Sassenach, and generally regret it when I do." And that, I
thought, was likely to be as close to an apology as I'd get.

"Did you regret it that time?"

"Well, I doubled up my fists and glared up at him—he was
a tall, scrawny fellow, maybe twenty, I suppose, though he
looked quite old to me—and I said 'I'm not afraid o' you, and
ye can't make me cry, no matter how hard you hit me!' " He
drew a deep breath and blew it out slowly. "I suppose it was a
bit of a mistake in judgment to tell him that while he was still
holding the strap."

"Don't tell me," I said. "He tried to prove you were
wrong?"

"Oh, aye, he tried." Jamie nodded, head dark against the
cloud-lit sky. His voice held a certain grim satisfaction on the
word "tried."

"He didn't succeed, then?"

The shaggy head shook back and forth. "No. At least he
couldna make me cry. He surely made me regret not keeping
quiet, though."

He paused for a moment, turning his own face toward me.
The cloud cover had parted for a moment and the light
touched the edges of jaw and cheek, making him look gilded,
like one of Donatello's archangels.

"When Dougal was describing my character to ye, before
we wed, did he by chance mention that I'm sometimes a bit
stubborn?" The slanted eyes glinted, much more Lucifer than
Michael.

I laughed. "That's putting it mildly. As I recall, what he
said is that all the Frasers are stubborn as rocks, and you're the
worst of the lot. Actually," I said, a little dryly, "I'd noticed
something of the kind myself."

He smiled as he reined the horse around a deep puddle in
the road, leading mine by the checkrein after him.

"Mmph, well, I'll no just say Dougal's wrong," he said,
once the hazard had been negotiated. "But if I'm stubborn, I
come by it honest. My father was just the same, and we'd get

in wrangles from time to time that we couldna get out of without the application of force, usually wi' me bent over the fence rail."

Suddenly, he put out a hand to grab my horse's rein, as the beast reared and snorted. "Hey now! Hush! *Stad, mo dhu!*" His own, less spooked, only jerked and tossed its head nervously.

"What is it?" I could see nothing, despite the patches of moonlight that mottled road and field. There was a pine grove up ahead, and the horses seemed disinclined to go any nearer to it.

"I don't know. Stay here and keep quiet. Mount your horse and hold mine. If I call to ye, drop the checkrein and run for it." Jamie's voice was low and casual, calming me as well as the horses. With a muttered *"Sguir!"* to the horse and a slap on the neck to urge it closer to me, he faded into the heather, hand on his dirk.

I strained eyes and ears to discern whatever it was still troubling the horses; they shifted and stamped, ears and tails twitching in agitation. The clouds by now had shredded and flown on the nightwind, leaving only scattered trails across the face of a brilliant half moon. In spite of the brightness, I could see nothing on the road ahead, or in the menacing grove.

It seemed a late hour and an unprofitable road for highwaymen, scarce as these were anywhere in the Highlands; there were too few travelers to make an ambush worthwhile.

The grove was dark, but not still. The pines roared softly to themselves, millions of needles scouring in the wind. Very ancient trees, pines, and eerie in the gloom. Gymnosperms, cone-bearers, winged-seed scatterers, older and sterner by far than the soft-leaved, frail-limbed oaks and aspens. A suitable home for Rupert's ghosts and evil spirits.

Only you, I thought crossly to myself, could work yourself up into being afraid of a lot of trees. Where was Jamie, though?

The hand gripping my thigh made me squeak like a startled bat; a natural consequence of trying to scream with your heart in your mouth. With the unreasonable fury of the irrationally afraid, I struck out at him, kicking him in the chest.

"Don't sneak up on me like that!"

"Hush," he said, "come with me." Tugging me unceremoniously from the saddle, he swung me down and hastily tethered the horses, who whickered uneasily after us as he led me into the tall grass.

"What is it?" I hissed, stumbling blindly over roots and rocks.

"Quiet. Don't speak. Look down and watch my feet. Step where I step, and stop when I touch you."

Slowly and more or less silently, we made our way into the edges of the pine grove. It was dark under the trees, with only crumbs of light falling through to the needle litter underfoot. Even Jamie couldn't walk silently on that, but the rustle of dry needles was lost in that of the green ones overhead.

There was a rift in the litter, a mass of granite rising from the forest floor. Here Jamie put me in front of him, guiding my hands and feet to climb the sloping crumble of the mound. At the top, there was enough room to lie belly-flat, side by side. Jamie put his mouth next to my ear, barely breathing. "Thirty feet ahead, to the right. In the clearing. See them?"

Once I saw them, I could hear as well. Wolves, a small pack, eight or ten animals, perhaps. No howling, not these. The kill lay in the shadow, a blob of dark with an upthrust leg, stick-thin and vibrating under the impact of teeth yanking at the carcass. There was only the occasional soft growl and yip as a cub was batted away from an adult's morsel, and the contented sounds of feeding, crunching, and the crack of a bone.

As my eyes grew more accustomed to the moon-flecked scene, I could pick out several shaggy forms stretched under the trees, glutted and peaceful. Bits of grey fur shone here and there, as those still at the carcass pushed and rooted for tender bits overlooked by the earlier diners.

A broad, yellow-eyed head thrust suddenly up into a blotch of light, ears pricked. The wolf made a soft, urgent noise, something between a whine and a growl, and there was a sudden stillness under the trees below.

The saffron eyes seemed fixed on my own. There was no fear in the animal's posture, nor curiosity, only a wary acknowledgment. Jamie's hand on my back warned me not to move, though I felt no desire to run. I could have stayed locked in the wolf's eyes for hours, I think, but she—I was sure it was a female, though I didn't know how I knew— flicked her ears once, as though dismissing me, and bent once more to her meal.

We watched them for a few minutes, peaceful in the scattered light. At last, Jamie signaled that it was time to go, with a touch on my arm.

He kept the hand on my arm to support me as we made our way back through the trees to the road. It was the first time I had willingly allowed him to touch me since he had rescued me from Fort William. Still charmed by the sight of the wolves, we did not speak much, but began to feel comfortable with each other again.

As we walked, considering the stories he had told me, I couldn't help but admire the job he had done. Without one word of direct explanation or apology, he had given me the message he intended. I gave you justice, it said, as I was taught it. And I gave you mercy, too, so far as I could. While I could not spare you pain and humiliation, I make you a gift of my own pains and humiliations, that yours might be easier to bear.

"Did you mind a lot?" I said abruptly. "Being beaten, I mean. Did you get over it easily?"

He squeezed my hand lightly before letting it go.

"Mostly I forgot it as soon as it was over. Except for the last time; that took a while."

"Why?"

"Ah, well. I was sixteen, for one thing, and a man grown . . . I thought. For another, it hurt like hell."

"You don't have to tell me about it if you don't want to," I said, sensing his hesitation. "Is it a painful story?"

"Not nearly as painful as the beating," he said, laughing. "No, I don't mind tellin' ye. It's a long story, is all."

"It's a long way to Bargrennan yet."

"So it is. Well, then. You recall I told ye I spent a year at Castle Leoch when I was sixteen? It was an agreement between Colum and my father—so I'd be familiar wi' my mother's clan. I fostered wi' Dougal for two years, and then went to the Castle for a year, to learn manners, and Latin and such."

"Oh. I wondered how you'd come to be there."

"Aye, that was the way of it. I was big for my age, or tall at least; a good swordsman even then, and a better horseman than most."

"Modest, too," I said.

"Not very. Cocky as hell, and even faster with my tongue than I am now."

"The mind boggles," I said, amused.

"Well it might, Sassenach. I found I could make people laugh wi' my remarks, and I made them more frequent, without carin' much what I said, or to whom. I was cruel sometimes, to the other lads, not meanin' it, just not able to resist if I thought of something clever to say."

He looked up at the sky, to gauge the time. Blacker still, now that the moon had gone down. I recognized Orion floating near the horizon, and was strangely comforted by the familiar sight.

"So, one day I went too far. I was with a couple of the other lads, going down a corridor when I saw Mistress Fitz-Gibbons at the other end. She was carryin' a big basket, near as big as she was, and bumping to and fro as she walked. You know what she looks like now; she wasna much smaller then." He rubbed his nose, embarrassed.

"Well, I made a number of ungallant remarks concerning her appearance. Funny, but most ungallant. They amused my companions considerably. I didna realize she could hear me as well."

I recalled the massive dame of Castle Leoch. While I had never seen her other than good-humored, she did not appear to be the sort of person to be insulted with impunity.

"What did she do?"

"Nothing—then. I didna know she'd heard, until she got up at the Hall gathering next day and told Colum all about it."

"Oh, dear." I knew how highly Colum regarded Mrs. Fitz,

and didn't think he would take any irreverence directed at her lightly. "What happened?"

"The same thing that happened to Laoghaire—or almost." He chuckled.

"I got verra bold though, and I stood up and said I chose to take my beating wi' fists. I was tryin' to be verra calm and grown-up about it all, though my heart was going like a blacksmith's hammer, and I felt a bit sick when I looked at Angus's hands; they looked like stones, and big ones at that. There were a few laughs from the folk gathered in the Hall; I wasna so tall then as I am now, and I weighed less than half as much. Wee Angus could ha' torn my head off with one blow.

"Anyway, Colum and Dougal both frowned at me, though I thought they were really a bit pleased I'd had the nerve to ask it. Then Colum said no, if I was goin' to behave like a child, I'd to be punished like one. He gave a nod, and before I could move, Angus bent me across his knee, turned up the edge of my kilt and blistered me with his strap, in front of the entire Hall."

"Oh, Jamie!"

"Mmmphm. You'll have noticed Angus is verra professional about his work? He gave me fifteen strokes, and to this day I could tell ye exactly where each one landed." He shuddered reminiscently. "I had the marks for a week."

He reached out and broke a clump of pine needles from the nearest tree, spreading them like a fan between thumb and fingers. The scent of turpentine was suddenly sharper.

"Well, I wasna allowed just to go quietly away and tend to my wounds, either. When Angus finished wi' me, Dougal took me by the scruff of the neck and marched me to the far end of the Hall. Then I was made to come all the way back on my knees, across the stones. I had to kneel before Colum's seat and beg Mrs. Fitz's pardon, then Colum's, then apologize to everyone in the Hall for my rudeness, and finally, I'd to thank Angus for the strapping. I nearly choked over that, but he was verra gracious about it; he reached down and gave me a hand to get up. Then I was plunked down on a stool next to Colum, and bid to sit there 'til Hall was ended."

He hunched his shoulders protectively. "That was the

worst hour I ever had. My face was on fire, and so was my arse, my knees were skinned and I couldna look anywhere but at my feet, but the worst of it was that I had to piss something awful. I almost died; I'd ha' burst before I wet myself in front of everyone on top of it all, but it was a near thing. I sweated right through my shirt."

I suppressed my urge to laugh. "Couldn't you have told Colum what was the matter?" I asked.

"He knew perfectly well what was the matter; so did everyone else in the Hall, the way I was squirming on that stool. People were making wagers as to whether I'd last or not." He shrugged.

"Colum would have let me go, if I'd asked. But—well, I got stubborn about it." He grinned a bit sheepishly, teeth white in a dark face. "Thought I'd rather die than ask, and nearly did. When at last Colum said I could go, I made it out of the Hall, but only as far as the nearest door. Threw myself behind the wall and spurted streams; I thought I'd never stop.

"So," he spread his hands deprecatingly, dropping the clump of pine needles, "now you know the worst thing that ever happened to me."

I couldn't help it; I laughed until I had to sit down at the side of the road. Jamie waited patiently for a minute, then sank down on his knees.

"What are you laughing for?" he demanded. "It wasna funny at all." But he was smiling himself.

I shook my head, still laughing. "No, it isn't. It's an awful story. It's just . . . I can see you sitting there, being stubborn about it, with your jaw clenched and steam coming out of your ears."

Jamie snorted, but laughed a little too. "Aye. It's no verra easy to be sixteen, is it?"

"So you did help that girl Laoghaire because you felt sorry for her," I said, when I had recovered my composure. "You knew what it was like."

He was surprised. "Aye, I said so. It's a lot easier to get punched in the face at three-and-twenty than to have your bum strapped in public at sixteen. Bruised pride hurts worse than anything, and it bruises easy then."

"I wondered. I'd never seen anyone grin in anticipation of being punched in the mouth."

"Couldna very well do it afterward."

"Mmh." I nodded agreement. "I thought—" I said, then stopped in embarrassment.

"Ye thought what? Oh, about me and Laoghaire, ye mean," he said, divining my thought. "You and Alec and everyone else, including Laoghaire. I'd have done the same if she'd been plain." He nudged me in the ribs. "Though I dinna expect you'll believe that."

"Well, I did see you together that day in the alcove," I defended myself, "and *somebody* certainly taught you how to kiss."

Jamie shuffled his feet in the dust, embarrassed. He ducked his head shyly. "Well now, Sassenach, I'm no better than most men. Sometimes I try, but I dinna always manage. Ye know that bit in St. Paul, where he says 'tis better to marry than burn? Well, I was burnin' quite badly there."

I laughed again, feeling light-hearted as a sixteen-year-old myself. "So you married me," I teased, "to avoid the occasion of sin?"

"Aye. That's what marriage is good for; it makes a sacrament out of things ye'd otherwise have to confess."

I collapsed again.

"Oh, Jamie, I do love you!"

This time it was his turn to laugh. He doubled over, then sat down at the roadside, fizzing with mirth. He slowly fell over backward and lay in the long grass, wheezing and choking.

"What on earth is the matter with you?" I demanded, staring at him. At long last, he sat up, wiping his streaming eyes. He shook his head, gasping.

"Murtagh was right about women. Sassenach, I risked my life for ye, committing theft, arson, assault, and murder into the bargain. In return for which ye call me names, insult my manhood, kick me in the ballocks and claw my face. Then I beat you half to death and tell ye all the most humiliating things have ever happened to me, and you say ye love me." He laid his head on his knees and laughed some more. Finally he rose and held out a hand to me, wiping his eyes with the other.

"You're no verra sensible, Sassenach, but I like ye fine. Let's go."

It was getting late—or early, depending on your viewpoint, and it was necessary to ride, if we were to make Bargrennan by dawn. I was enough recovered by this time to bear sitting, though the effects were still noticeable.

We rode in a companionable silence for some way. Left to my own thoughts, I considered for the first time at leisure what would happen if and when I ever managed to find my way back to the circle of standing stones. Married to him by coercion and dependent on him from necessity, I had undeniably grown very fond of Jamie.

More to the point, perhaps, were his feelings about me. Linked at first by circumstance, then by friendship, and finally by a startlingly deep bodily passion, still he had never made even a casual statement to me about his feelings. And yet.

He had risked his life for me. That much he might do for the sake of his marriage vow; he would, he said, protect me to the last drop of his blood, and I believed he meant it.

I was more touched by the events of the last twenty-four hours, when he had suddenly admitted me to his emotions and his personal life, warts and all. If he felt as much for me as I thought perhaps he did, what would he feel if I suddenly disappeared? The remnants of physical discomfort receded as I grappled with these uncomfortable thoughts.

We were within three miles of Bargrennan when Jamie suddenly broke the silence.

"I havena told you how my father died," he said abruptly.

"Dougal said he had a stroke—an apoplexy, I mean," I said, startled. I supposed that Jamie, alone with his thoughts as well, had found them dwelling on his father as a result of our earlier conversation, but I could not imagine what led him to this particular subject.

"That's right. But it . . . he . . ." He paused, considering his words, then shrugged, abandoning carefulness. He drew a deep breath and let it out. "You should know about it. It's to do with . . . things." The road here was wide enough to ride easily abreast, provided only that we kept a sharp eye out for protruding rocks; my excuse to Dougal about my horse had not been chosen at random.

"It was at the Fort," Jamie said, picking his way around a bad patch, "where we were yesterday. Where Randall and his men took me from Lallybroch. Where they flogged me. Two days after the first time, Randall summoned me to his office—two soldiers came for me, and took me from the cells up to his room—the same where I found you; it's how I knew where to go."

"Just outside, we met my father in the courtyard. He'd found out where they'd taken me, and come to see if he could get me out some way—or at least to see for himself that I was all right."

Jamie kicked a heel gently into his horse's ribs, urging it on with a soft click of his tongue. There was no trace of daylight yet, but the look of the night had changed. Dawn could be no more than an hour away.

"I hadna realized until I saw him just how alone I'd felt there—or how scairt. The soldiers would not give us any time alone together, but at least they let me greet him." He swallowed and went on.

"I told him I was sorry—about Jenny, I meant, and the whole sorry mess. He told me to hush, though, and hugged me tight to him. He asked me was I hurt badly—he knew about the flogging—and I said I'd be all right. The soldiers said I must go then, so he squeezed my arms tight, and told me to remember to pray. He said he would stand by me, no matter what happened, and I must just keep my head up and try not to worrit myself. He kissed my cheek and the soldiers took me away. That was the last time I ever saw him."

His voice was steady, but a little thick. My own throat felt tight, and I would have touched him if I could, but the road narrowed through a small glen and I was forced to fall back behind him for a moment. By the time I came alongside again he had composed himself.

"So," he said, taking a deep breath, "I went in to see Captain Randall. He sent the soldiers out, so we were alone, and offered me a stool. He said my father had offered security for my bond, to have me released, but that my charge was a serious one, and I could not be bonded without a written clearance signed by the Duke of Argyll, whose boundaries we were under. I reckoned that was where my father was headed, then, to see Argyll.

"In the meantime, Randall went on, there was the matter of this second flogging I was sentenced to." He stopped a minute, as though uncertain how to go on.

"He . . . was strange in his manner, I thought. Verra cordial, but with something under it I didna understand. He kept watching me, as though he expected me to do something, though I was just sitting still.

"He half-apologized to me, saying he was sorry that our relations had been so difficult to the present, and that he wished the circumstances had been different, and so on." Jamie shook his head. "I couldna imagine what he was talking about; two days earlier, he'd been trying his best to beat me to death. When he finally got down to it, though, he was blunt enough."

"What did he want, then?" I asked. Jamie glanced at me, then away. The dark hid his features, but I thought he seemed embarrassed.

"Me," he said baldly.

I started so violently that the horse tossed its head and whickered reproachfully. Jamie shrugged again.

"He was quite plain about it. If I would . . . ah, make him free of my body, he'd cancel the second flogging. If I would not—then I'd wish I'd never been born, he said."

I felt quite sick.

"I was already wishing something of the sort," he said, with a glint of humor. "My belly felt as though I'd swallowed broken glass, and if I hadna been sitting, my knees would have knocked together."

"But what . . ." My voice was hoarse, and I cleared my throat and started over. "But what did you do?"

He sighed. "Well, I'll no lie to ye, Sassenach. I considered it. The first stripes were still so raw on my back I could scarce bear a shirt, and I felt giddy whenever I stood up. The thought of going through that again—being bound and help-less, waiting for the next lash . . ." He shuddered involuntarily.

"I'd no real idea," he said wryly, "but I rather thought being buggered would be at least a bit less painful. Men have died under the lash sometimes, Sassenach, and from the look on his face, I thought he meant me to be one of them, were that my choice." He sighed again.

"But . . . well, I could still feel my father's kiss on my cheek, and thought of what he'd say, and . . . well, I couldna do it, that's all. I did not stop to think what my death might mean to my father." He snorted, as though finding something faintly amusing. "Then, too, I thought, the man's already raped my sister—damned if he'll have me too."

I didn't find this amusing. I was seeing Jack Randall again, in a new and revolting light. Jamie rubbed the back of his neck, then dropped his hand to the pommel.

"So, I took what little courage I had left by then, and said no. I said it loud, too, and added whatever filthy names I could think of to call him, all at the top of my lungs."

He grimaced. "I was afraid I'd change my mind if I thought about it; I wanted to make sure there was no chance of going back. Though I dinna suppose," he added thought-fully, "that there's any really tactful way to refuse an offer like that."

"No," I agreed dryly. "I don't suppose he'd have been pleased, no matter what you said."

"He wasn't. He backhanded me across the mouth, to shut me up. I fell down—I was still a bit weak—and he stood over me, just staring down at me. I'd better sense than to try and get up, so I just lay there until he called the soldiers to take me back to my cell." He shook his head. "He didna change expression at all; just said as I left, 'I'll see you on Friday,' as though we had an appointment to discuss business or somesuch."

The soldiers had not returned Jamie to the cell he had shared with three other prisoners. Instead, he was put into a small room by himself, to await Friday's reckoning with no distractions save the daily visit of the garrison's physician, who came to dress his back.

"He wasna much of a doctor," Jamie said, "but he was kindly enough. The second day he came, along wi' the goose grease and charcoal, he brought me a small Bible that belonged to a prisoner who'd died. Said he understood I was a Papist, and whether I found the word of God any comfort or not, at least I could compare my troubles with Job's." He laughed.

"Oddly enough, it *was* some comfort. Our Lord had to put up wi' being scourged too; and I could reflect that at least I wasna going to be hauled out and crucified afterward. On the other hand," he said judiciously, "Our Lord wasna forced to listen to indecent proposals from Pontius Pilate, either."

Jamie had kept the small Bible. He rummaged in his saddlebag, and handed it across now for me to look at. It was a worn, leather-covered volume, about five inches long, printed on paper so flimsy the print showed through from one side of each page to the other. On the flyleaf was written ALEXANDER WILLIAM RODERICK MACGREGOR, 1733. The ink was faded and blurred, and the covers warped as though the book had gotten wet on more than one occasion.

I turned the little book over curiously. Small as it was, it must have cost something in effort to keep it by him, through the travels and adventures of the last four years.

"I've never seen you read it." I handed it back.

"No, that's not why I keep it," he said. He tucked it away, stroking the edge of the worn cover with a thumb as he did so. He patted the saddlebag absently.

"There's a debt owing to Alex MacGregor; I mean to collect it sometime.

"Anyway," he continued, returning to his story, "Friday came at last, and I don't know whether I was glad or sorry to see it. The waiting and the fear were almost worse than I thought the pain would be. When it came, though . . ." He made that odd half-shrugging gesture of his, easing the shirt across his back. "Well, you've seen the marks. You know what it was like."

"Only because Dougal told me. He said he was there."

Jamie nodded. "Aye, he was there. And my father as well, though I didna know it at the time. I'd no mind for anything much beyond my own problems, then."

"Oh," I said slowly, "and your father—"

"Mmm. That's when it happened. Some of the men there told me after that they thought I was dead, halfway through, and I reckon my father thought so too." He hesitated, and his voice was thick when he resumed. "When I fell, Dougal told me, my father made a small sound and put his hand to his head. Then he dropped like a rock. And did not get up again."

The birds were moving in the heather, trilling and calling from the still-dark leaves of the trees. Jamie's head was bowed, face still invisible.

"I did not know he was dead," he said softly. "They didna tell me until a month later—when they thought I was strong enough to bear it. So I did not bury him, as his son should have done. And I have never seen his grave—because I am afraid to go home."

"Jamie," I said. "Oh, Jamie, dear."

After what seemed a long silence, I said, "But you don't— you *can't*—feel responsible. Jamie, there was nothing you could have done; or done differently."

"No?" he said. "No, maybe not; though I wonder would it still have happened, had I chosen the other way. But to know that does not much help the way I feel—and I feel as though I had done him to death with my own hands."

"Jamie—" I said again, and stopped, helpless. He rode silently for a bit, then straightened up and squared his shoulders once more.

"I've not told anyone about it," he said abruptly. "But I thought that now ye should know—about Randall, I mean. You've a right to know what it is that lies between him and me."

What it is that lies between him and me. The life of a good man, the honor of a girl, and an indecent lust that found its vent in blood and fear. And, I supposed, with a lurch of the stomach, that there was now one more item weighting the scales. Me. For the first time, I began to realize what Jamie had felt, crouching in the window of Randall's room, with an empty gun in his hand. And I began to forgive him for what he had done to me.

As though reading my mind, he said, not looking at me, "Do you know . . . I mean, can ye understand, maybe, why I thought it needful to beat you?"

I waited a moment before answering. I understood, all right, but that was not quite all there was to it.

"I understand," I said. "And so far as that goes, I forgive you. What I can't forgive," I said, my voice rising slightly in spite of myself, "is that you enjoyed it!"

He bent forward in the saddle, clasping the pommel, and laughed for a long time. He reveled in the release of tension before finally tossing his head back and turning to me. The sky was noticeably lighter now, and I could see his face, lined with exhaustion, strain, and mirth. The scratches down his cheek were black in the dim light.

"Enjoyed it! Sassenach," he said, gasping, "you don't know just how much I enjoyed it. You were so . . . God, you looked lovely. I was so angry, and you fought me so fierce. I hated to hurt you, but I wanted to do it at the same time . . . Jesus," he said, breaking off and wiping his nose, "yes. Yes, I did enjoy it.

"Though come to that," he said, "you might give me some credit for exercising restraint."

I was getting rather angry again. I could feel my cheeks flushing hotly against the cool dawn air.

"Restraint, was it? I was under the impression that what you were exercising was your good left arm. You almost crippled me, you arrogant Scottish bastard!"

"Did I want to cripple ye, Sassenach, you'd know it," he answered dryly. "I meant afterward. I slept on the floor, if ye recall."

I eyed him narrowly, breathing through my nose. "Oh, so that was restraint, was it?"

"Well, I didna think it right to roger you in that state, however fierce I wanted to. And I did want to," he added, laughing again. "Terrible strain on my natural instincts."

"Roger me?" I said, diverted by the expression.

"I would hardly call it 'love-making' under the circumstances, would you?"

"Whatever you might call it," I said evenly, "it's a good thing you didn't try it, or you'd now be missing a few valued bits of your anatomy."

"That thought occurred to me."

"And if you think you deserve applause for nobly refraining from committing rape on top of assault—" I choked on my choler.

We rode a half-mile or so in silence. Then he heaved a sigh. "I can see I should not have started this conversation. What I was tryin' to do was to work up to asking ye would you allow me to share your bed again, once we get to Bargrennan." He paused shyly. "It's a bit cold on the floor."

I rode for a good five minutes before answering. When I had decided what to say, I reined in, turning across the road, so as to force Jamie to stop as well. Bargrennan was in sight, rooftops just visible in the dawning light.

I urged my horse parallel with the other, so that I was no more than a foot away from Jamie. I looked him in the eye for a minute before speaking.

"Will you do me the honor of sharing my bed, O lord and master?" I asked politely.

Obviously suspecting something, he considered a moment, then nodded, just as formally. "I will. Thank you." He was raising the reins to go when I stopped him.

"There's just one more thing, master," I said, still polite.

"Aye?"

I whipped my hand from the concealed pocket in my skirt, and the dawn light struck sparks from the blade of the dagger pressed against his chest.

"If," I said through my teeth, "you ever raise a hand to me again, James Fraser, I'll cut out your heart and fry it for breakfast!"

There was a long silence, broken only by the shiftings and creakings of horses and harness. Then he held out his hand, palm up.

"Give it to me." When I hesitated, he said impatiently, "I'm no going to use it on ye. Give it to me!"

He held the dirk by the blade, upright so that the rising sun caught the moonstone in the hilt and made it glow. Holding the dagger like a crucifix, he recited something in Gaelic. I recognized it from the oath-taking ceremony in Colum's hall, but he followed it with the English translation for my benefit:

"I swear on the cross of my Lord Jesus, and by the holy iron which I hold, that I give ye my fealty and pledge ye my loyalty. If ever my hand is raised against you in rebellion or in anger, then I ask that this holy iron may pierce my heart." He kissed the dirk at the juncture of haft and tang, and handed it back to me.

"I don't make idle threats, Sassenach," he said, raising one brow, "and I don't take frivolous vows. Now, can we go to bed?"

23

Return to Leoch

dougal was waiting for us at the sign of the Red Boar, impatiently pacing to and fro outside.

"Made it, did ye?" he asked, watching with approval as I dismounted without assistance, staggering only slightly. "Gallant lass—ten miles without a whimper. Get up to your bed then; ye've earned it. Jamie and I will stable the horses." He patted me, very gently, on the rump in dismissal. I was only too glad to follow his suggestion, and was asleep almost before my head touched the pillow.

I didn't stir when Jamie crawled in beside me, but woke suddenly in the late afternoon, convinced that there was something important I had forgotten.

"Horrocks!" I exclaimed suddenly, sitting bolt upright in bed.

"Hah?" Jamie, startled out of a sound sleep, shot sideways out of bed, ending on the floor in a crouch, hand on the dirk he had left on top of his piled clothes. "What?" he demanded, staring wildly around the room. "What is it?"

I stifled a giggle at the sight of him, crouched naked on the floor, red hair standing on end like quills.

"You look like a fretful porpentine," I said.

He gave me a dirty look and rose to his feet, replacing the dirk on the stool that held his clothes.

"You couldna wait 'til I woke to tell me that?" he inquired.

"You thought it would make more impression if ye woke me out of a sound sleep by shouting 'Hedgehog!' in my ear?"

"Not 'hedgehog,' " I explained. "Horrocks. I remembered all at once that I'd forgotten to ask you about him. Did you find him?"

He sat down on the bed and sank his head in his hands. He rubbed his face vigorously, as though to restore circulation.

"Oh, aye," he said through the muffling fingers. "Aye, I found him."

I could tell from the tone of voice that the deserter's information had not been good.

"Would he not tell you anything after all?" I asked sympathetically. That had always been a possibility, though Jamie had gone prepared to part with not only his own money, and some provided by Dougal and Colum, but even his father's ring if necessary.

Jamie lay back on the bed beside me, staring up at the ceiling.

"No," he said. "No, he told me all right. And at a reasonable price."

I rolled up onto an elbow in order to look down at his face.

"Well, then?" I demanded. "Who *did* shoot the sergeant-major?"

He looked up at me and smiled, a trifle grimly.

"Randall," he said, and shut his eyes.

"Randall?" I said blankly. "But why?"

"I don't know," he said, eyes still shut. "I could guess, perhaps, but it doesna much matter. Damn-all chance of proving it."

I had to agree that this was true. I sank back on the bed beside him and stared up at the black oak beams of the low ceiling.

"What can you do then?" I asked. "Go to France? Or perhaps"—a bright thought occurred to me—"perhaps to America? You could likely do well in the New World."

"Across the ocean?" A brief shudder ran through him. "No. No, I couldna do that."

"Well, what then?" I demanded, turning my head to look

at him. He opened one eye enough to give me a jaundiced look.

"I'd thought for a start that I might get another hour's sleep," he said, "but apparently not." Resigned, he pulled himself up in bed, leaning against the wall. I had been too tired to pull the bedclothes off before retiring, and there was a suspicious black spot on the quilt near his knee. I kept a wary eye on it as he talked.

"You're right," he agreed, "we could go to France." I started, having momentarily forgotten that whatever he decided to do, I was now included in the decision.

"But there isna that much for me there," he said, idly scratching his thigh. "Only soldiering, and that's no life for you. Or to Rome, to join King James's court. That might be managed; I've some Fraser uncles and cousins with a foot in that camp, who would help me. I've no great taste for politics, and less for princes, but aye, it's a possibility. I'd rather try first to clear myself in Scotland, though. If I did, at the worst I might end up as a small crofter in the Fraser lands; at best, I might be able to go back to Lallybroch." His face clouded, and I knew he was thinking of his sister. "For myself," he said softly, "I wouldna go, but it isn't only me anymore."

He looked down at me and smiled, his hand gently smoothing my hair. "I forget sometimes, that there's you now, Sassenach," he said.

I felt extraordinarily uncomfortable. I felt like a traitor, in fact. Here he was, making plans that would affect his entire life, taking my comfort and safety into account, when I had been doing my best to abandon him completely, dragging him into substantial danger in the process. I had meant none of it, but the fact remained. Even now, I was thinking that I should try to talk him out of going to France, as that would carry me farther away from my own goal: the stone circle.

"Is there any way to stay in Scotland, though?" I asked, looking away from him. I thought the black spot on the quilt had moved, but I wasn't sure. I fixed my eyes on it, staring hard.

Jamie's hand traveled under my hair and began idly to fondle my neck.

"Aye," he said thoughtfully. "There may be. That's why Dougal waited up for me; he's had some news."

"Really? What sort?" I turned my head to look up at him again; the movement brought my ear within reach of his fingers, and he began to stroke lightly around it, making me want to arch my neck and purr like a cat. I repressed the impulse, though, in favor of finding out what he meant to do.

"A messenger from Colum," he said. "He didna think to find us here, but he passed Dougal on the road by accident. Dougal's to return at once to Leoch, and leave Ned Gowan to manage the rest of the rents. Dougal's suggested we should go with him."

"Back to Leoch?" It wasn't France, but it wasn't a lot better. "Why?"

"There's a visitor expected shortly, an English noble that's had dealings wi' Colum before. He's a powerful man, and it might be he could be persuaded to do something for me. I've not been tried or condemned on the charge of murder. He might be able to have it dismissed, or arrange to have me pardoned." He grinned wryly. "It goes a bit against the grain to be pardoned for something I've not done, but it's better than being hanged."

"Yes, that's true." The spot *was* moving. I squinted, trying to focus on it. "Which English noble is it?"

"The Duke of Sandringham."

I jerked upright with an exclamation.

"What is it, Sassenach?" Jamie asked, alarmed.

I pointed a trembling finger at the black spot, which was now proceeding up his leg at a slow but determined pace.

"What's that?!" I said.

He glanced at it, and casually flicked it off with a fingernail.

"Oh, that? It's only a bedbug, Sassenach. Nothing to—"

He was interrupted by my abrupt exit. At the word "bedbug," I had shot out from under the covers, and stood pressed against the wall, as far away as possible from the teeming nest of vermin I now envisioned as our bed.

Jamie eyed me appreciatively.

"Fretful porpentine, was it?" he asked. He tilted his head, examining me inquisitively. "Mmm," he said, running a hand over his head to smooth down his own hair. "Fretful, at least. You're a fuzzy wee thing when ye wake, to be sure." He rolled over toward me, reaching out a hand.

"Come here, my wee milkweed. We'll not leave before sunset. If we're not going to sleep . . ."

In the end, we did sleep a bit more, peacefully entangled on the floor, atop a hard but bugless bed composed of my cloak and Jamie's kilt.

It was a good thing that we had slept while we had the chance. Anxious to reach Castle Leoch before the Duke of Sandringham, Dougal kept to a fast pace and a grueling schedule. Traveling without the wagons, we made much better time, despite bad roads. Dougal pushed us, though, stopping only for the briefest of rests.

By the time we rode once more through the gates of Leoch, we were nearly as bedraggled as the first time we had arrived there, and certainly as tired.

I slid off my horse in the courtyard, then had to catch the stirrup to keep from falling. Jamie caught my elbow, then realizing that I couldn't stand, swung me up into his arms. He carried me through the archway, leaving the horses to the grooms and stableboys.

"Are ye hungry, Sassenach?" he asked, pausing in the corridor. The kitchens lay in one direction, the stairs to the bedchambers in the other. I groaned, struggling to keep my eyes open. I *was* hungry, but knew I would end up facedown in the soup if I tried to eat before sleeping.

There was a stir to one side and I groggily opened my eyes to see the massive form of Mrs. FitzGibbons, looming disbelievingly alongside.

"Why, what's the matter wi' the poor child?" she demanded of Jamie. "Has she had an accident o' some sort?"

"No, it's only she's married me," he said, "though if ye care to call it an accident, ye may." He moved to one side, to push through what proved to be an increasing throng of kitchen-maids, grooms, cooks, gardeners, men-at-arms, and assorted castle inhabitants, all inquisitively drawn to the scene by Mrs. Fitz's loud questions.

Making up his mind, Jamie pressed to the right, toward the stairs, making disjointed explanations to the hail of questions from every side. Blinking owlishly against his chest, I could do no more than nod to the surrounding welcomers, though most of the faces seemed friendly as well as curious.

As we came around a corner of the hallway, I saw one face that seemed a good deal friendlier than the rest. It was the girl Laoghaire, face shining and radiant as she heard Jamie's voice. Her eyes grew wide and the rosebud mouth dropped unbecomingly open, though, as she saw what he carried.

There was no time for her to ask questions, though, before the stir and bustle around us halted abruptly. Jamie stopped too. Raising my head, I saw Colum, whose startled face was now on a level with mine.

"What—" he began.

"They're married," said Mrs. Fitz, beaming. "How sweet! You can give them your blessing, sir, while I get a room ready." She turned and made off for the stairs, leaving a substantial gap in the crowd, through which I could see the now pasty-white face of the girl Laoghaire.

Colum and Jamie were both talking together, questions and explanations colliding in midair. I was beginning to wake up, though it would have been overstating matters to say I was entirely myself.

"Well," Colum was saying, not altogether approvingly, "if you're married, you're married. I'll have to talk to Dougal and Ned Gowan—there'll be legal matters to attend to. There are a few things you're entitled to when ye wed, by the terms of your mother's dower contract."

I felt Jamie straighten slightly.

"Since ye mention it," he said casually, "I believe that's true. And one of the things I'm entitled to is a share of the quarterly rents from the MacKenzie lands. Dougal's brought back what he'd collected so far; perhaps you'll tell him to leave aside my share when he does the reckoning? Now, if ye'll excuse me, Uncle, my wife is tired." And hoisting me into a more solid position, he turned to the stairs.

◄━━

I staggered across the room, still wobbly-legged, and collapsed gratefully on the huge tester bed our newly married
status apparently entitled us to. It was soft, inviting, and—
thanks to the ever-vigilant Mrs. Fitz—clean. I wondered
whether it was worth the effort to get up and wash my face
before succumbing to the urge to sleep.

I had just about decided that I might get up for Gabriel's
Trump, but not much else, when I saw that Jamie, who had
not only washed face and hands but combed his hair to boot,
was headed toward the door.

"Aren't you going to sleep?" I called. I thought he must be
at least as tired as I, if less saddle sore.

"In a bit, Sassenach. I've a small errand to do, first." He
went out, leaving me staring at the oaken door with a very
unpleasant sensation in the pit of my stomach. I was remembering the look of gay anticipation on Laoghaire's face as she
came around the corner, hearing Jamie's voice, and the look
of angry shock that replaced it when she saw me cradled in his
arms. I remembered the momentary tightening of his joints as
he saw her, and wished most fervently that I had been able to
see his face at that moment. I thought it likely he had gone
now, unrested but washed and combed, to find the girl and
break the news of his marriage. Had I seen his face, I would at
least have some idea what he meant to say to her.

Absorbed in the events of the last month, I had forgotten
the girl entirely—and what she might mean to Jamie, or he to
her. Granted, I had thought of her when the question of our
abrupt marriage first occurred, and Jamie then had given no
sign that she constituted an impediment so far as he was concerned.

But, of course, if her father would not allow her to marry an
outlaw—and if Jamie needed a wife, in order to collect his
share of the MacKenzie rents . . . well, one wife would do as
well as another, in that case, and doubtless he would take
what he could get. I thought I knew Jamie well enough now
to see that practicality with him went deep—as it must, with a
man who had spent the last few years of his life on the run. He

would not, I thought, be swayed in his decisions by sentiment or the attraction of rose-leaf cheeks and hair like liquid gold. But that didn't mean that neither sentiment nor attraction existed.

There was, after all, the little scene I had witnessed in the alcove, Jamie holding the girl on his knee and kissing her ardently *(I've held women in my arms before,* his voice came back to me, *and they've made my heart pound and my breath come short . . .).* I found that my hands were clenched, making bunched ridges in the green and yellow quilt. I released it and wiped my hands over my skirt, realizing in the process just how filthy they were, grimed with the dirt of two days of holding reins, with no respite in between for washing.

I rose and went to the basin, forgetting my tiredness. I found, a bit to my surprise, that I strongly disliked the memory of Jamie kissing Laoghaire. I remembered what he had said about that, too—*'Tis better to marry than burn, and I was burning badly then.* I burned a bit myself, flushing strongly as I remembered the effect of Jamie's kisses on my own lips. Burning, indeed.

I splashed water on my face, spluttering, trying to dissipate the feeling. I had no claim on Jamie's affections, I reminded myself firmly. I had married him from necessity. And he had married me for his own reasons, one of them being the frankly stated desire to alter his virginal state.

Another reason apparently being that he needed a wife in order to collect his income, and could not induce a girl of his own kind to marry him. A reason much less flattering than the first, if no more lofty.

Quite awake by now, I slowly changed from my stained traveling garments into a fresh shift, provided, as was the basin and ewer, by Mrs. Fitz's minions. How she had managed to make accommodation for two newlyweds in the time between Jamie's abrupt announcement to Colum and the time we had mounted the stairs was one of the mysteries of the ages. Mrs. Fitz, I reflected, would have done quite well in charge of the Waldorf-Astoria or the London Ritz.

Such reflections made me suddenly more lonely for my own world than I had been in many days. *What am I doing here?* I asked myself for the thousandth time. Here, in this strange place, unreachable distances from everything familiar, from home and husband and friends, adrift and alone among what amounted to savages? I had begun to feel safe and even inter- mittently happy during the last weeks with Jamie. But now I realized that the happiness was likely an illusion, even if the safety was not.

I had no doubt that he would abide by what he conceived to be his responsibilities, and continue to protect me from any harm that threatened. But here, returned from the dreamlike isolation of our days among the wild hills and dusty roads, the filthy inns and fragrant haystacks, he must surely feel the pull of his old associations, as I felt mine. We had grown very close in the month of our marriage, but I had felt that closeness crack under the strains of the last few days, and thought it might now shatter completely, back among the practical reali- ties of life at Castle Leoch.

I leaned my head against the stone of the window case- ment, looking out across the courtyard. Alec McMahon and two of his stable lads were visible at the far side, rubbing down the horses we had ridden in. The beasts, fed and watered adequately for the first time in two days, exuded con- tentment as willing hands curried the glossy sides and cleansed the dirt from hock and fetlock with twists of straw. A stable- boy led away my fat little Thistle, who followed him happily toward the well-earned rest of her stable.

And with her, I thought, went my hopes of any imminent escape and return to my own place. Oh, Frank. I closed my eyes, letting a tear slide down the side of my nose. I opened my eyes wide on the courtyard then, blinked and shut them tight, trying frantically to recall Frank's features. Just for a moment, when I closed my eyes, I had seen not my beloved husband, but his ancestor, Jack Randall, full lips curved in a mocking smile. And shying mentally from that image, my mind had summoned at once a picture of Jamie, face set in fear and anger, as I had seen him in the window of Randall's private office. Try as I might, I could not bring back Frank's remembered image with any certainty.

I felt suddenly quite cold with panic, and clasped my hands

about my elbows. And what if I had succeeded in escaping and finding my way back to the circle of stone? I thought. What then? Jamie would, I hoped, soon find solace—with Laoghaire, perhaps. I had worried before about his reaction to finding me gone. But aside from that hasty moment of regret on the edge of the burn, it had not before occurred to me to wonder how I would feel to part with him.

I fiddled idly with the ribbon drawstring that gathered the neck of my shift, tying and untying it. If I meant to leave, as I did, I was doing neither of us a favor by allowing the bond between us to strengthen any further. I should not allow him to fall in love with me.

If he meant to do any such thing, I thought, remembering once more Laoghaire and the conversation with Colum. If he had married me so cold-bloodedly as it seemed, perhaps his emotions were safer than mine.

Between fatigue, hunger, disappointment, and uncertainty, I had by this time succeeded in reducing myself to such a state of confused misery that I could neither sleep or sit still. Instead, I roamed unhappily about the room, picking up objects and putting them down at random.

The draft from the opening door upset the delicate equilibrium of the comb I had been balancing on its end, heralding Jamie's return. He looked faintly flushed and oddly excited.

"Oh, you're awake," he said, obviously surprised and disconcerted to find me so.

"Yes," I said unkindly, "were you hoping I'd be asleep so you could go back to her?"

His brows drew together for a moment, then raised in inquiry. "Her? To Laoghaire, ye mean?"

Hearing her name spoken in that casual Highland lilt—"L'heer"—suddenly made me irrationally angry.

"Oh, so you *have* been with her!" I snapped.

Jamie looked puzzled and wary, and slightly annoyed. "Aye," he said. "I met her by the stair as I went out. Are ye well, Sassenach? Ye look a bit fashed, all in all." He eyed me appraisingly. I picked up the looking glass, and found that my hair was standing out in a bushy mane round my head and there were dark circles under my eyes. I put it down again with a thump.

"No, I'm perfectly all right," I said, with an effort at controlling myself. "And how is Laoghaire?" I asked, assuming casualness.

"Oh, quite bonny," he said. He leaned back against the door, arms crossed, watching me speculatively. "A bit surprised to hear we were married, I reckon."

"Bonny," I said, and took a deep breath. I looked up to find him grinning at me.

"You'd not worrit yourself over the lassie, would ye now, Sassenach?" he asked shrewdly. "She's naught to you—or me," he added.

"Oh, no? She wouldn't—or couldn't—marry you. You had to have someone, so you took me when the chance offered. I don't blame you for that"—not much I didn't—"but I—"

He crossed the room in two steps and took me by the hands, interrupting me. He put a finger under my chin and forced my gaze up.

"Claire," he said evenly, "I shall tell ye in my own time why I've wed ye—or I won't. I asked honesty of you, and I've given ye the same. And I give it to you now. The girl has no claim on me beyond that of courtesy." He squeezed my chin lightly. "But that claim she has, and I'll honor it." He released my chin and chucked me softly under it. "D'ye hear me, Sassenach?"

"Oh, I hear!" I jerked free, rubbing my chin resentfully. "And I'm sure you'll be very courteous to her. But next time draw the drapes of the alcove—I don't want to see it."

The coppery brows shot up, and his face reddened slightly.

"Are ye suggesting I've played ye false?" he said, unbelievingly. "We've been back to the Castle less than an hour, I'm covered wi' the sweat and dust of two days in the saddle, and so tired my knees wabble, and yet ye think I've gone straight out to seduce a maid of sixteen?" He shook his head, looking stunned. "I canna tell whether ye mean to compliment my virility, Sassenach, or insult my morals, but I dinna care much for either suggestion. Murtagh told me women were unreasonable, but Jesus God!" He ran a large hand through his hair, making the short ends stick up wildly.

"Of course I don't mean I think you've been seducing her," I said, struggling to inject an air of calmness into my tone. "All I mean . . ." It occurred to me that Frank had handled this kind of thing much more gracefully than I was managing to do, and yet I had been angry then too. Likely there was no good way to suggest such a possibility to one's mate.

"I simply mean that . . . that I realize that you married me for your own reasons—and those reasons are your own business," I added hastily, "and that I have no claim at all on you. You're at perfect liberty to behave as you wish. If you . . . if there's an attraction elsewhere . . . I mean . . . I won't stand in your way," I finished lamely. The blood was hot in my cheeks and I could feel my ears burning.

Looking up, I found that Jamie's ears were burning as well, visibly, and so was the rest of him from the neck up. Even his eyes, bloodshot from lack of sleep, seemed to be flaming slightly.

"No claim on me!" he exclaimed. "And what d'ye think a wedding vow is, lassie? Just words in a church?" He brought one big fist down on the chest with a crash that shook the porcelain ewer. "No claim," he muttered, as though to himself. "At liberty to behave as I wish. And you'll not stand in my way?!"

He bent to pull off his boots, then picked up them up and threw them, one after the other, as hard as he could at the wall. I winced as each one thudded off the stones and bounced to the floor. He yanked off his plaid and tossed it heedlessly behind him. Then he started toward me, glaring.

"So you've no claim on me, Sassenach? You'll free me to take my pleasure where I like, is that it? Well, is it?" he demanded.

"Er, well, yes," I said, taking a step backward despite myself. "That's what I meant." He grabbed my arms, and I found the combustion had spread to his hands as well. His callused palms were so hot on my skin that I jerked involuntarily.

"Well, if you've no claim on me, Sassenach," he said, "I've one on you! Come here." He took my face in his hands and set his mouth on mine. There was nothing either gentle or undemanding about that kiss, and I fought against it, trying to pull back from him.

He bent and scooped me up with an arm under my knees, ignoring my attempts to get down. I hadn't realized just how bloody strong he really was.

"Let go of me!" I said. "What do you think you're doing?"

"Well, I should ha' thought that was reasonably clear, Sassenach," he said through his teeth. He lowered his head, the clear gaze piercing me like a hot iron. "Though if ye want telling," he said, "I mean to take ye to bed. Now. And keep ye there until you've learned just what claim I have on you." And he kissed me again, deliberately hard, cutting off my protest.

"I don't want to sleep with you!" I said, when at last he freed my mouth.

"I dinna intend to sleep, Sassenach," he replied evenly. "Not just yet." He reached the bed and set me carefully on the rose-patterned quilt.

"You know bloody well what I mean!" I rolled, meaning to escape from the other side, but was stopped by a solid grip on my shoulder that flipped me back to face him. "I don't want to make love with you, either!"

Blue eyes blazed down at me from close range, and my breath came thick in my throat.

"I didna ask your preferences in the matter, Sassenach," he answered, voice dangerously low. "You are my wife, as I've told ye often enough. If ye didna wish to wed me, still ye chose to. And if ye didna happen to notice at the time, your part of the proceedings included the word 'obey.' You're my wife, and if I want ye, woman, then I'll have you, and be damned to ye!" His voice rose throughout, until he was near shouting.

I rose to my knees, fists balled at my sides, and shouted back at him. The contained misery of the last hour had reached explosion point and I let him have it, point-blank.

"I *will* be damned if I'll have *you,* you bullying swine! You think you can order me to your bed? Use me like a whore when you feel like it? Well, you can't, you fucking bastard! Do that, and you're no better than your precious Captain Randall!"

He glared at me for a moment, then stood abruptly aside. "Leave, then," he said, jerking his head toward the door. "If that's what ye think of me, go! I'll not hinder ye."

I hesitated for a moment, watching him. His jaw was clenched with anger and he was looming over me like the Colossus of Rhodes. His temper this time was under tight rein, though he was as angry now as he had been by the roadside near Doonesbury. But he meant it. If I chose to leave, he wouldn't stop me.

I lifted my chin, my own jaw clenched as tightly as his. "No," I said. "No. I don't run away from things. And I'm not afraid of you."

His gaze fastened on my throat, where my pulse was going at a frantic rate.

"Aye, I see," he said. He stared down at me, and his face gradually relaxed into a look of grudging acquiescence. He sat down gingerly on the bed, keeping a good distance between us, and I sat back warily. He breathed deeply several times before speaking, his face fading a bit toward its natural ruddy bronze.

"I don't run either, Sassenach," he said gruffly. "Now, then. What does 'fucking' mean?"

My surprise must have shown plainly, for he said irritably, "If ye must call me names, that's one thing. But I dinna care to be called things I can't answer. I know it's a damn filthy word, from the way ye said it, but what does it mean?"

Taken off guard, I laughed, a little shakily. "It . . . it means . . . what you were about to do to me."

One brow lifted, and he looked sourly amused. "Oh, swiving? Then I was right; it is a damn filthy word. And what's a sadist? Ye called me that the other day."

I suppressed the urge to laugh. "It's, er, it's a person who . . . who, er, gets sexual pleasure from hurting someone." My face was crimsoning, but I couldn't stop the corners of my mouth from turning up slightly.

Jamie snorted briefly. "Well, ye dinna flatter me over-much," he said, "but I canna fault your observations." He took a deep breath and leaned back, unclenching his hands. He stretched his fingers deliberately, then laid his hands flat on his knees and looked directly at me.

"What is it, then? Why are ye doing this? The girl? I've told ye the plain truth there. But it's not a matter for proof. It's a question of whether ye believe me or no. Do ye believe me?"

"Yes, I believe you," I admitted grudgingly. "But that's not it. Or not all of it," I added, in an attempt at honesty. "It's . . . I think it's finding that you married me for the money you'd get." I looked down, tracing the pattern of the quilt with my finger. "I know I've no right to complain—I married you for selfish reasons, too, but"—I bit my lip and swallowed to steady my voice—"but I have a small bit of pride, too, you know."

I stole a glance at him, and found him staring at me with an expression of complete dumbfoundedness.

"Money?" he said blankly.

"Yes, money!" I blazed, angered at his pretense of igno-rance. "When we came back, you couldn't wait to tell Colum you were married and collect your share of the MacKenzie rents!"

He stared at me for a moment longer, mouth opening gradually as though to say something. Instead, he began to shake his head slowly back and forth, and then began to laugh. He threw his head back and roared, in fact, then sank his head between his hands, still laughing hysterically. I flung myself back on the pillows in indignation. Funny, was it?

Still shaking his head and wheezing intermittently, he stood up and set hands to the buckle of his belt. I flinched involun-tarily as he did so, and he saw it.

Face still flushed with a mixture of anger and laughter, he looked down at me in total exasperation. "No," he said dryly, "I dinna mean to beat you. I gave ye my word I'd not do so again—though I didna think I'd regret it quite so soon." He laid the belt aside, groping in the sporran attached to it.

"My share of the MacKenzie rents comes to about twenty pounds a quarter, Sassenach," he said, digging through the oddments inside the badgerskin. "And that's Scots, not sterling. About the price of half a cow."

"That's . . . that's all?" I said stupidly. "But—"

"That's all," he confirmed. "And all I ever will have from the MacKenzies. Ye'll have noticed Dougal's a thrifty man, and Colum's twice as tight-fisted wi' his coin. But even the princely sum of twenty pound a quarter is hardly worth marrying to get, I should think," he added sarcastically, eyeing me.

"I wouldna have asked for it straightaway, at that," he added, bringing out a small paper-wrapped parcel, "but there was something I wanted to buy with it. That's where my errand took me; meeting Laoghaire was an accident."

"And what did you want to buy so much?" I asked suspiciously.

He sighed and hesitated for a moment, then tossed the small package lightly into my lap.

"A wedding ring, Sassenach," he said. "I got it from Ewen the armorer; he makes such things in his own time."

"Oh," I said in a small voice.

"Go ahead," he said, a moment later. "Open it. It's yours."

The outlines of the little package blurred under my fingers. I blinked and sniffed, but made no move to open it. "I'm sorry," I said.

"Well, so ye should be, Sassenach," he said, but his voice was no longer angry. Reaching, he took the package from my lap and tore away the wrapping, revealing a wide silver band, decorated in the Highland interlace style, a small and delicate Jacobean thistle bloom carved in the center of each link.

So much I saw, and then my eyes blurred again.

I found a handkerchief thrust into my hand, and did my best to stanch the flow with it. "It's . . . beautiful," I said, clearing my throat and dabbling at my eyes.

"Will ye wear it, Claire?" His voice was gentle now, and his use of my name, mostly reserved for occasions of formality or tenderness, nearly made me break down again.

"You needna do so," he said, looking at me seriously over his cupped palm. "The marriage contract between us is satisfied—it's legal. You're protected, safe from anything much save a warrant, and even from that, so long as you're at Leoch. If ye wish, we may live apart—if that's what ye were trying to say wi' all yon rubbish about Laoghaire. You need have little more to do wi' me, if that's your honest choice." He sat motionless, waiting, holding the tiny circlet near his heart.

So he was giving me the choice I had started out to give him. Forced on me by circumstance, he would force himself on me no longer, if I chose to reject him. And there was the alternative, of course: to accept the ring, and all that went with it.

The sun was setting. The last rays of light shone through a blue glass flagon that stood on the table, streaking the wall with a shaft of brilliant lapis. I felt as fragile and as brilliant as the glass, as though I would shatter with a touch, and fall in glittering fragments to the floor. If I had meant to spare either Jamie's emotions or my own, it seemed I was very much too late.

I couldn't speak, but held out my right hand to him, fingers trembling. The ring slipped cool and bright over my knuckle and rested snug at the base of my finger—a good fit. Jamie held my hand a moment, looking at it, then suddenly pressed my knuckles hard against his mouth. He raised his head, and I saw his face for an instant, fierce and urgent, before he pulled me roughly onto his lap.

He held me hard against him then, without speaking, and I could feel the pulsebeat in his throat, hammering like my own. His hands went to my bare shoulders, and he held me slightly away, so that I was looking upward into his face. His hands were large and very warm, and I felt slightly dizzy.

"I want ye, Claire," he said, sounding choked. He paused a moment, as though unsure what to say next. "I want ye so much—I can scarcely breathe. Will—" He swallowed, then cleared his throat. "Will ye have me?"

By now I had found my voice. It squeaked and wobbled, but it worked.

"Yes," I said. "Yes, I'll have you."

"I think . . ." he began, then stopped. He fumbled loose the buckle of his kilt, but then looked up at me, bunching his hands at his sides. He spoke with difficulty, controlling something so powerful that his hands shook with the effort. "I'll not . . . I can't . . . Claire, I canna be gentle about it."

I had time only to nod once, in acknowledgment or permission, before he bore me back before him, his weight pinning me to the bed.

He did not pause to undress further. I could smell the road dust in his shirt, and taste the sun and sweat of travel on his skin. He held me, arms outstretched, wrists pinioned. One hand brushed the wall, and I felt the tiny scrape of one wedding ring chiming against the stone. One ring for each hand, one silver, one gold. And the thin metal suddenly heavy as the bonds of matrimony, as though the rings were tiny shackles, fastening me spread-eagled to the bed, stretched forever between two poles, held in bondage like Prometheus on his lonely rock, divided love the vulture that tore at my heart.

He spread my thighs with his knee and sheathed himself to the root in a single thrust that made me gasp. He made a sound that was almost a groan, and gripped me tighter.

"You're mine, *mo duinne*," he said softly, pressing himself into my depths. "Mine alone, now and forever. Mine, whether ye will it or no." I pulled against his grip, and sucked in my breath with a faint "ah" as he pressed even deeper.

"Aye, I mean to use ye hard, my Sassenach," he whispered. "I want to own you, to possess you, body and soul." I struggled slightly and he pressed me down, hammering me, a solid, inexorable pounding that reached my womb with each stroke. "I mean to make ye call me 'master,' Sassenach." His soft voice was a threat of revenge for the agonies of the last minutes. "I mean to make you mine."

I quivered and moaned then, my flesh clutching in spasms at the invading, battering presence. The movement went on, disregarding, on and on for minutes, striking me over and over with an impact on the edge between pleasure and pain. I felt dissolved, as though I existed only at the point of the assault, being forced to the edge of some total surrender.

"No!" I gasped. "Stop, please, you're hurting me!" Beads of sweat ran down his face and dropped on the pillow and on my breasts. Our flesh met now with the smack of a blow that was fast crossing the edge into pain. My thighs were bruising with the repeated impact, and my wrists felt as though they would break, but his grip was inexorable.

"Aye, beg me for mercy, Sassenach. Ye shallna have it, though; not yet." His breath came hot and fast, but he showed no signs of tiring. My entire body convulsed, legs rising to wrap around him, seeking to contain the sensation.

I could feel the jolt of each stroke deep in my belly, and cringed from it, even as my hips rose traitorously to welcome it. He felt my response, and redoubled his assault, pressing now on my shoulders to keep me pinned under him.

There was no beginning and no end to my response, only a continuous shudder that rose to a peak with each thrust. The hammering was a question, repeated over and over in my flesh, demanding my answer. He pushed my legs flat again, and bore me down past pain and into pure sensation, over the edge of surrender.

"Yes!" I cried. "Oh God, Jamie, yes!" He gripped my hair and forced my head back to meet his eyes, glowing with furious triumph.

"Aye, Sassenach," he muttered, answering my movements rather than my words. "Ride ye I will!" His hands dropped to my breasts, squeezing and stroking, then slid down my sides. His whole weight rested on me now as he cupped and raised me for still greater penetration. I screamed then and he stopped my mouth with his, not a kiss, but another attack, forcing my mouth open, bruising my lips and rasping my face with bearded stubble. He thrust harder and faster, as though he would force my soul as he forced my body. In body or soul, somewhere he struck a spark, and an answering fury of passion and need sprang from the ashes of surrender. I arched upward to meet him, blow for blow. I bit his lip and tasted blood.

I felt his teeth then on my neck and dug my nails into his back. I raked him from nape to buttocks, spurring him to rear and scream in his turn. We savaged each other in desperate need, biting and clawing, trying to draw blood, trying each to pull the other into ourselves, tearing each other's flesh in the consuming desire to be one. My cry mingled with his, and we lost ourselves finally in each other in that last moment of dissolution and completion.

━━━

I returned only slowly to myself, lying half on Jamie's breast, sweated bodies still glued together, thigh to thigh. He breathed heavily, eyes closed. I could hear his heart under my ear, beating with the preternaturally slow and powerful rhythm that follows climax.

He felt me wake, and drew me close, as though to preserve a moment longer the union we had reached in those last seconds of our perilous joining. I curled beside him, putting my arms around him.

He opened his eyes then and sighed, the long mouth curling in a faint smile as his glance met mine. I raised my brows in silent question.

"Oh, aye, Sassenach," he answered a bit ruefully. "I am your master . . . and you're mine. Seems I canna possess your soul without losing my own." He turned me on my side and curled his body around me. The room was cooling in the evening breeze from the window, and he reached to draw a quilt over us. You're too quick by half, lad, I thought drowsily to myself. Frank never did find that out. I fell asleep with his arms locked hard around me and his breathing warm in my ear.

━━━

I was lame and sore in every muscle when I woke next morning. I shuffled to the privy closet, then to the wash basin. My innards felt like churned butter. It felt as though I had been beaten with a blunt object, I reflected, then thought that that was very near the truth. The blunt object in question was visible as I came back to bed, looking now relatively harmless. Its possessor woke as I sat down next to him, and examined me with something that looked very much like male smugness.

"Looks as though it was a hard ride, Sassenach," he said, lightly touching a blue bruise on my inner thigh. "A bit saddle-sore, are ye?"

I narrowed my eyes and traced a deep bite-mark on his shoulder with my finger.

"You look a bit ragged around the edges yourself, my lad."

"Ah, weel," he said in broad Scots, "if ye bed wi' a vixen, ye must expect to get bit." He reached up and grasped me behind the neck, pulling me down to him. "Come here to me, vixen. Bite me some more."

"Oh, no, you don't," I said, pulling back. "I can't possibly; I'm too sore."

James Fraser was not a man to take no for an answer.

"I'll be verra gentle," he wheedled, dragging me inexorably under the quilt. And he was gentle, as only big men can be, cradling me like a quail's egg, paying me court with a humble patience that I recognized as reparation—and a gentle insistence that I knew was a continuation of the lesson so brutally begun the night before. Gentle he would be, denied he would not.

He shook in my arms at his own finish, shuddering with the effort not to move, not to hurt me by thrusting, letting the moment shatter him as it would.

Afterward, still joined, he traced the fading bruises his fingers had left on my shoulders by the roadside two days before.

"I'm sorry for those, *mo duinne,*" he said, gently kissing each one. "I was in a rare temper when I did it, but it's no excuse. It's shameful to hurt a woman, in a rage or no. I'll not do it again."

I laughed a bit ironically. "You're apologizing for *those?* What about the rest? I'm a mass of bruises, from head to toe!"

"Och?" He drew back to look me over judiciously. "Well now, these I've apologized for," touching my shoulder, *"those,"* slapping my rear lightly, "ye deserved, and I'll not say I'm sorry for it, because I'm not."

"As for these," he said, stroking my thigh, "I'll not apologize for that, either. Ye paid me full measure already." He rubbed his shoulder, grimacing. "Ye drew blood in at least two places, Sassenach, and my back stings like holy hell."

"Well, bed with a vixen . . ." I said, grinning. "You won't

get an apology for that." He laughed in response and pulled me on top of him.

"I didna say I wanted an apology, did I? If I recall aright, what I said was 'Bite me again.' "

PART FOUR

A Whiff of Brimstone

24

By the Pricking of
My Thumbs

The hubbub occasioned by our sudden arrival and the announcement of our marriage was overshadowed almost at once by an event of greater importance.

We were sitting at supper in the Great Hall the next day, accepting the toasts and good wishes being offered in our honor.

"Buidheachas, mo caraid." Jamie bowed gracefully to the latest toaster, and sat down amid the increasingly sporadic applause. The wooden bench shook under his weight, and he closed his eyes briefly.

"Getting a bit much for you?" I whispered. He had borne the brunt of the toasting, matching each cup drained on our behalf, while I had so far escaped with no more than token sips, accompanied by bright smiles at the incomprehensible Gaelic toasts.

He opened his eyes and looked down at me, smiling himself.

"Am I drunk, do ye mean? Nay, I could drink this stuff all night."

"You practically have," I said, peering at the array of empty wine bottles and stone ale-jars lined up on the board in front of us. "It's getting rather late." The candles on Colum's table burned low in their holders, and the guttered wax glowed gold, the light marking the MacKenzie brothers with odd patches of shadow and glinting flesh as they leaned together, talking in low voices. They could have joined the company of carved gnomic heads that edged the huge fireplace, and I wondered how many of those caricatured figures had in fact been drawn from the patronizing features of earlier MacKenzie lairds—perhaps by a carver with a sense of humor . . . or a strong family connection.

Jamie stretched slightly in his seat, grimacing in mild discomfort.

"On the other hand," he said, "my bladder's going to burst in another moment or two. I'll be back shortly." He put his hands on the bench and hopped nimbly up and over it, disappearing through the lower archway.

I turned my attention to my other side, where Geillis Duncan sat, demurely sipping at a silver cup of ale. Her husband, Arthur, sat at the next table with Colum, as befitted the procurator fiscal of the district, but Geilie had insisted on sitting next to me, saying that she had no wish to be wearied by hearing man-talk all through supper.

Arthur's deep-set eyes were half-closed, blue-pouched and sunk with wine and fatigue. He leaned heavily on his forearms, face slack, ignoring the conversation of the MacKenzies next to him. While the light threw the sharp-cut features of the laird and his brother into a high relief, it merely made Arthur Duncan look fat and ill.

"Your husband isn't looking very well," I observed. "Has his stomach trouble got worse?" The symptoms were rather puzzling; not like ulcer, I thought, nor cancer—not with that much flesh still on his bones—perhaps just chronic gastritis, as Geilie insisted.

She cast the briefest of glances at her spouse before turning back to me with a shrug.

"Oh, he's well enough," she said. "No worse, at any rate. But what about *your* husband?"

"Er, what about him?" I replied cautiously.

She dug me familiarly in the ribs with a rather sharp elbow, and I realized that there were a fair number of bottles at her end of the table as well.

"Well, what d'ye think? Does he look as nice out of his sark as he does in it?"

"Um . . ." I groped for an answer as she craned her neck toward the entryway.

"And you claiming you didna care a bit for him! Cleverboots. Half the girls in the castle would like to tear your hair out by the roots—I'd be careful what I ate, if I were you."

"What I eat?" I looked down in bafflement at the wooden platter before me, empty but for a smear of grease and a forlorn boiled onion.

"Poison," she hissed dramatically in my ear, along with a considerable wafting of brandy fumes.

"Nonsense," I said, rather coldly, drawing away from her. "No one would want to poison me simply because I . . . well, because . . ." I was floundering a bit, and it occurred to me that I might have had a few sips more than I had realized.

"Now, really, Geilie. This marriage . . . I didn't plan it, you know. I didn't *want* it!" No lie there. "It was merely a . . . sort of . . . necessary business arrangement," I said, hoping the candlelight hid my blushes.

"Ha," she said cynically. "I ken the look of a lass that's been well bedded." She glanced toward the archway where Jamie had disappeared. "And damned if I think those are midge bites on the laddie's neck, either." She raised one silver brow at me. "If it was a business arrangement, I'd say ye got your money's worth."

She leaned close again.

"Is it true?" she whispered. "About the thumbs?"

"Thumbs? Geilie, what in God's name are you babbling about?"

She looked down her small, straight nose at me, frowning in concentration. The beautiful grey eyes were slightly unfocused, and I hoped she wouldn't fall over.

"Surely ye know that? Everyone knows! A man's thumbs tell ye the size of his cock. Great toes, too, of course," she added judiciously, "but those are harder to judge, usually, what wi' the shoon and all. Yon wee fox-cub," she nodded toward the archway, where Jamie had just reappeared, "he could cup a good-sized marrow in those hands of his. Or a good-sized arse, hm?" she added, nudging me once more.

"Geillis Duncan, will . . . you . . . shut . . . up!" I hissed, face flaming. "Someone will hear you!"

"Oh, no one who—" she began, but stopped, staring. Jamie had passed right by our table, as though he didn't see us. His face was pale, and his lips set firmly, as though bent on some unpleasant duty.

"Whatever ails him?" Geilie asked. "He looks like Arthur after he's eaten raw turnips."

"I don't know." I pushed back the bench, hesitating. He was heading for Colum's table. Should I follow him? Plainly something had happened.

Geilie, peering back down the room, suddenly tugged at my sleeve, pointing in the direction from which Jamie had appeared.

A man stood just within the archway, hesitating even as I was. His clothes were stained with mud and dust; a traveler of some sort. A messenger. And whatever the message, he had passed it on to Jamie, who was even now bending to whisper it in Colum's ear.

No, not Colum. Dougal. The red head bent low between the two dark ones, the broad handsome features of the three faces taking on an unearthly similarity in the light of the dying candles. And as I watched, I realized that the similarity was due not so much to the inheritance of bone and sinew that they shared, but to the expression of shocked grief that they now held in common.

Geilie's hand was digging into the flesh of my forearm.

"Bad news," she said, unnecessarily.

◆━━━

"Twenty-four years," I said softly. "It seems a long time to be married."

"Aye, it does," Jamie agreed. A warm wind stirred the branches of the tree above us, lifting the hair from my shoulders to tickle my face. "Longer than I've been alive."

I glanced at him leaning on the paddock fence, all lanky

grace and strong bones. I tended to forget how young he really was; he seemed so self-assured and capable.

"Still," he said, flicking a straw into the churned mud of the paddock, "I doubt Dougal spent more than three years of that with her. He was generally here, ye ken, at the Castle—or here and there about the lands, doing Colum's business for him."

Dougal's wife, Maura, had died at their estate of Beannachd. A sudden fever. Dougal himself had left at dawn, in company with Ned Gowan and the messenger who had brought the news the night before, to arrange the funeral and dispose of his wife's property.

"Not a close marriage, then?" I asked curiously.

Jamie shrugged.

"As close as most, I should reckon. She had the children and the running of the house to keep her busy; I doubt she missed him greatly, though she seemed glad enough to see him when he came home."

"That's right, you lived with them for a time, didn't you?" I was quiet, thinking. I wondered whether this was Jamie's idea of marriage; separate lives, joining only infrequently for the breeding of children. Yet, from the little he had said, his own parents' marriage had been a close and loving one.

With that uncanny trick of reading my thoughts, he said, "It was different wi' my own folk, ye ken. Dougal's was an arranged marriage, like Colum's, and a matter more of lands and business than the wanting of each other. But my parents —well, they wed for love, against the wishes of both families, and so we were . . . not cut off, exactly; but more by ourselves at Lallybroch. My parents didna go often to visit relatives or do business outside, and so I think they turned more to each other than husband and wife usually do."

He laid a hand low on my back and urged me closer to him. He bent his head and brushed his lips across the top of my ear.

"It was an arrangement between us," he said softly. "Still, I would hope . . . perhaps one day—" He broke off awkwardly, with a crooked smile and a gesture of dismissal.

Not wanting to encourage him in that direction, I smiled

back as neutrally as I could, and turned toward the paddock. I could feel him there beside me, not quite touching, big hands gripping the top rail of the fence. I gripped the rail myself, to keep from taking his hand. I wanted more than anything to turn to him, offer him comfort, assure him with body and words that what lay between us *was* more than a business arrangement. It was the truth of it that stopped me.

What it is between us, he had said. *When I lie with you, when you touch me.* No, it wasn't usual at all. It wasn't a simple infatuation, either, as I had first thought. Nothing could be less simple.

The fact remained that I was bound, by vows and loyalty and law, to another man. And by love as well.

I could not, could *not* tell Jamie what I felt for him. To do that and then to leave, as I must, would be the height of cruelty. Neither could I lie to him.

"Claire." He had turned to me, was looking down at me; I could feel it. I didn't speak, but raised my face to him as he bent to kiss me. I couldn't lie to him that way either, and didn't. After all, I thought dimly, I had promised him honesty.

We were interrupted by a loud "Ahem!" from behind the paddock fence. Jamie, startled, whirled toward the sound, instinctively thrusting me behind him. Then he stopped and grinned, seeing Old Alec MacMahon standing there in his filthy trews, viewing us sardonically with his one bright blue eye.

The old man held a wicked-looking pair of gelding shears, which he raised in ironic salute.

"I was goin' to use these on Mahomet," he remarked. "Perhaps they could be put to better use here, eh?" He snicked the thick blades invitingly. "It'd keep your mind on your work, and off your cock, laddie."

"Don't even jest about it, man," said Jamie, grinning. "Wanting me, were ye?"

Alec waggled an eyebrow like a woolly caterpillar.

"No, what gives ye to think that? I thought I'd like to try gelding a blooded two-year-old all by mysel', for the joy of it." He wheezed briefly at his own wit, then waved the shears toward the Castle.

"Off wi' ye, lassie. Ye can have him back at supper—for what good he'll be to ye by then."

Apparently not trusting the nature of this last remark, Jamie reached out a long arm and neatly snagged the shears.

"I'll feel safer if *I've* got these," he said, cocking an eyebrow at Old Alec. "Go along, Sassenach. When I've finished doing all of Alec's work for him, I'll come and find ye."

He leaned down to kiss my cheek, and whispered in my ear, "The stables. When the sun's mid-sky."

The stables of Castle Leoch were better built than many of the cottages I had seen on our journey with Dougal. Stone floored and stone walled, the only openings were the narrow windows at one end, the door at the other, and the narrow slits under the thick thatched roof, intended for the convenience of the owls who kept down the mice in the hay. They let in plenty of air, though, and enough light that the stables were pleasantly dim rather than gloomy.

Up in the hayloft, just under the roof, the light was even better, striping the piled hay with yellow bars and lighting the drifting dust motes like showers of gold dust. The air came in through the chinks in warm drafts, scented with stock and sweet william and garlic from the gardens outside, and the pleasant animal smell of the horses wafted up from below.

Jamie stirred under my hand and sat up, the movement bringing his head from the shadow into a blaze of sunlight like the lighting of a candle.

"What is it?" I asked sleepily, turning my head in the direction he was looking.

"Wee Hamish," he said softly, peering over the edge of the loft into the stable below. "Wants his pony, I expect."

I rolled awkwardly onto my stomach beside him, dragging the folds of my shift over me for modesty's sake; a silly thought, as no one below could see more than the top of my head.

Colum's son Hamish was walking slowly down the aisle of

the stable between the stalls. He seemed to hesitate near some stalls, though he ignored the curious heads of chestnut and sorrel poking out to inspect him. Clearly he was looking for something, and it wasn't his fat brown pony, placidly munching straw in its stall near the stable door.

"Holy God, he's going for Donas!" Jamie seized his kilt and wrapped it hurriedly about himself before swinging down from the edge of the loft. Not bothering with the ladder, he hung by his hands and then dropped to the floor. He landed lightly on the straw-scattered stones, but with enough of a thud to make Hamish whirl around with a startled gasp.

The small freckled face relaxed somewhat as he realized who it was, but the blue eyes stayed wary.

"Needing a bit of help, coz?" Jamie inquired pleasantly. He moved toward the stalls and leaned against one of the uprights, managing to insert himself between Hamish and the stall the boy had been heading for.

Hamish hesitated, but then drew himself up, small chin thrust out.

"I'm going to ride Donas," he said, in a tone that tried for determination, but fell somewhat short.

Donas—his name meant "demon," and was in no way meant as flattery—was in a horse-box to himself at the far end of the stable, safely separated by an empty stall from the nearest neighboring horses. A huge, evil-tempered sorrel stallion, he was ridable by no one, and only Old Alec and Jamie dared go near him. There was an irritable squeal from the shadows of his stall, and an enormous copper head shot suddenly out, huge yellow teeth clacking together as the horse made a vain attempt to bite the bare shoulder so temptingly displayed.

Jamie stayed motionless, knowing that the stallion couldn't reach him. Hamish jumped back with a squeak, clearly scared speechless by the sudden appearance of that monstrous shimmering head, with its rolling, bloodshot eyes and flaring nostrils.

"I dinna think so," observed Jamie mildly. He reached down and took his small cousin by the shoulder, steering him away from the horse, who kicked his stall in protest. Hamish shuddered in concert with the boards of the stall as the lethal hooves crashed against the wood.

Jamie turned the boy around to face him and stood looking down at him, hands on his kilted hips.

"Now then," he said firmly. "What's this all about? Why are ye wanting aught to do wi' Donas?"

Hamish's jaw was set stubbornly, but Jamie's face was both encouraging and adamant. He punched the boy gently on the shoulder, getting a tiny smile in response.

"Come on, *duine*," Jamie said, softly. "Ye know I wilna tell anyone. Have ye done something foolish?"

A faint flush came up on the boy's fair skin.

"No. At least . . . no. Well, maybe a bit foolish."

After a bit more encouragement, the story came out, reluctantly at first, then in a tumbling flood of confession.

He had been out on his pony, riding with some of the other boys the day before. Several of the older lads had started competing, to see who could jump his horse over a higher obstacle. Jealously admiring them, Hamish's better judgment was finally overcome by bravado, and he had tried to force his fat little pony over a stone fence. Lacking both ability and interest, the pony had come to a dead stop at the fence, tossing young Hamish over his head, over the fence, and ignominiously into a nettle patch on the other side. Stung both by nettles and by the hoots of his comrades, Hamish was determined to come out today on "a proper horse," as he put it.

"They wouldna laugh if I came out on Donas," he said, envisioning the scene with grim relish.

"No, they wouldna laugh," Jamie agreed. "They'd be too busy picking up the pieces."

He eyed his cousin, shaking his head slowly. "I'll tell ye, lad. It takes courage and sense to make a good rider. You've the courage, but the sense is a wee bit lacking, yet." He put a consoling arm round Hamish's shoulders, drawing him down toward the end of the stable.

"Come along, man. Help me fork the hay, and we'll get ye acquainted wi' Cobhar. You're right; ye should have a better horse if you're ready, but it isna necessary to kill yourself to prove it."

Glancing up into the loft as he passed, he raised his eyebrows and shrugged helplessly. I smiled and waved down at him, telling him to go ahead, it was all right. I watched them as Jamie took an apple from the basket of windfalls kept near the door. Fetching a pitchfork from the corner, he led Hamish back to one of the center stalls.

"Here, coz," he said, pausing. He whistled softly through his teeth and a wide-browed bay horse put its head out, blowing through its nostrils. The dark eyes were large and kind, and the ears had a slight forward cock that gave the horse an expression of friendly alertness.

"Now then, Cobhar, *ciamar a tha thu?*" Jamie patted the sleek neck firmly, and scratched the cocked ears.

"Come on up," he said, motioning to his small cousin. "That's it, next to me. Near enough he can smell ye. Horses like to smell ye."

"*I* know." Hamish's high voice was scornful. He barely reached the horse's nose, but reached up and patted. He stood his ground as the big head came down and sniffed interestedly around his ear, whuffling in his hair.

"Give me an apple," he said to Jamie, who obliged. The soft velvet lips plucked the fruit delicately out of Hamish's palm, and flicked it back between the huge molars, where it vanished with a juicy crunch. Jamie watched approvingly.

"Aye. You'll get on fine. Go on and make friends, then, while I finish feeding the others, then ye can take him out to ride."

"By myself?" Hamish asked eagerly. Cobhar, whose name meant "foam," was good-tempered, but a sound, spirited 14-hand gelding, nonetheless, and a far cry from the brown pony.

"Twice round the paddock wi' me watchin' ye, and if ye dinna fall off or jerk his mouth, ye can take him by yourself. No jumping him 'til I say, though." The long back bent, gleaming in the warm dusk of the stable, as Jamie caught up a forkful of hay from the pile in one corner and carried it to one of the stalls.

He straightened and smiled at his cousin. "Gi' me one of those, will ye?" He leaned the fork against a stall and bit into the proffered fruit. The two stood companionably eating, leaning side by side against the stable wall. When he finished, Jamie handed the core to a nuzzling sorrel and fetched his fork again. Hamish followed him down the aisle, chewing slowly.

"I've heard my father was a good rider," Hamish offered tentatively, after a moment's silence. "Before—before he couldn't anymore."

Jamie shot a swift glance at his cousin, but finished pitching hay into the sorrel's stall before speaking. When he did, he answered the thought, rather than the words.

"I never saw him ride, but I'll tell ye, lad, I hope never to need as much courage as Colum has."

I saw Hamish's gaze rest curiously on Jamie's scarred back, but he said nothing. After a second apple, his thoughts appeared to have shifted to another topic.

"Rupert said ye had to get married," he remarked, through a mouthful of apple.

"I *wanted* to get married," Jamie said firmly, replacing the pitchfork against the wall.

"Oh. Well . . . good," Hamish said uncertainly, as though disconcerted by this novel idea. "I only wondered . . . do ye mind?"

"Mind what?" Seeing that this conversation might take a while, Jamie sat down on a bale of hay.

Hamish's feet did not quite reach the floor, or he might have shuffled them. Instead, he drummed his heels lightly against the firm-packed hay.

"Do ye mind being married," he said, staring at his cousin. "Getting into bed every night with a lady, I mean."

"No," said Jamie. "No, in fact, it's verra pleasant."

Hamish looked doubtful.

"I dinna think I should like it much. But then all the girls I know are skinny as sticks, and they smell o' barley water. The lady Claire—your lady, I mean," he added hastily, as though wishing to avoid confusion, "she's, er, she looks as though she'd be nicer to sleep with. Soft, I mean."

Jamie nodded. "Aye, that's true. Smells all right, too," he offered. Even in the dim light, I could see a small muscle twitching near the corner of his mouth, and knew he didn't dare look up in the direction of the loft.

There was a long pause.

"How d'ye know?" Hamish said.

"Know what?"

"Which is the right lady to get married to," the boy said impatiently.

"Oh." Jamie rocked back and settled himself against the stone wall, hands behind his head.

"I asked my own da that, once," he said. "He said ye just ken. And if ye dinna ken, then she's no the right lassie."

"Mmmphm." This seemed a less than satisfactory explanation, to judge from the expression on the small freckle-spattered face. Hamish sat back, consciously aping Jamie's posture. His stockinged feet stuck out over the edge of the hay bale. Small as he was, his sturdy frame gave promise of someday matching his cousin's. The set of the square shoulders, and the tilt of the solid, graceful skull were nearly identical.

"Where's your shoon, then?" Jamie asked accusingly. "You'll no ha' left them in the pasture again? Your mother will box your ears for ye if ye've lost them."

Hamish shrugged this off as a threat of no consequence. Clearly there was something of more importance on his mind.

"John—" he started, wrinkling his sandy brows in thought, "John says—"

"John the stable-lad, John the cook-boy, or John Cameron?" Jamie asked.

"The stable-lad." Hamish waved a hand, pushing away the distraction. "He said, er, about getting married . . ."

"Mmm?" Jamie made an encouraging noise, keeping his face tactfully turned away. Rolling his eyes upward, his glance met mine, as I peered over the edge. I grinned down at him, causing him to bite his lip to keep from grinning back.

Hamish drew a deep breath, and let it out in a rush, propelling his words like a burst of birdshot. "He-said-ye-must-serve - a - lass - like - a - stallion - does - a - mare - and - I - didna-believe-him-but-is-it-true?"

I bit my finger hard to keep from laughing out loud. Not so fortunately placed, Jamie dug his fingers into the fleshy part of his leg, turning as red in the face as Hamish. They looked like two tomatoes, set side by side on a hay bale for judging at a county vegetable show.

"Er, aye . . . weel, in a way . . ." he said, sounding strangled. Then he got a grip on himself.

"Yes," he said firmly, "yes, ye do."

Hamish cast a half-horrified glance into the nearby stall, where the bay gelding was relaxing, a foot or so of reproductive equipment protruding from its sheath. He glanced doubtfully down into his lap then, and I stuffed a handful of fabric into my mouth as far as it would go.

"There's some difference, ye ken," Jamie went on. The rich color was beginning to fade from his face, though there was still an ominous quiver around his mouth. "For one thing, it's . . . more gentle."

"Ye dinna bite them on the neck, then?" Hamish had the serious, intent expression of one taking careful notes. "To make them keep still?"

"Er . . . no. Not customarily, anyway." Exercising his not inconsiderable willpower, Jamie faced up manfully to the responsibilities of enlightenment.

"There's another difference, as well," he said, carefully not looking upward. "Ye may do it face to face, instead of from the back. As the lady prefers."

"The lady?" Hamish seemed dubious about this. "I think *I'd* rather do it from the back. I dinna think I'd like to have anyone lookin' at me while I did something like that. Is it hard," he inquired, "is it hard to keep from laughing?"

I was still thinking about Jamie and Hamish when I came to bed that night. I turned down the thick quilts, smiling to myself. There was a cool draft from the window, and I looked forward to crawling under the quilts and nestling against Jamie's warmth. Impervious to cold, he seemed to carry a small furnace within himself, and his skin was always warm; sometimes almost hot, as though he burned more fiercely in answer to my own cool touch.

I was still a stranger and an outlander, but no longer a guest at the Castle. While the married women seemed somewhat friendlier, now that I was one of them, the younger girls seemed strongly to resent the fact that I had removed an eligible young bachelor from circulation. In fact, noting the number of cold glances and behind-the-hand remarks, I rather wondered just how many of the Castle maidens had found their way into a secluded alcove with Jamie MacTavish during his short residency.

MacTavish no longer, of course. Most of the Castle inhabitants had always known who he was, and whether I was an English spy or not, I now knew of necessity as well. So he became Fraser publicly, and so did I. It was as Mistress Fraser that I was welcomed into the room above the kitchens where the married women did their sewing and rocked their babies, exchanging bits of mother-lore and eyeing my own waistline with frank appraisal.

Because of my earlier difficulties in conceiving, I had not considered the possibility of pregnancy when I agreed to marry Jamie, and I waited in some apprehension until my monthly occurred on time. My feelings this time were entirely of relief, with none of the sadness that usually accompanied it. My life was more than complicated enough at the moment, without introducing a baby into it. I thought that Jamie perhaps felt a small twinge of regret, though he also professed himself relieved. Fatherhood was a luxury that a man in his position could ill afford.

The door opened and he came in, still rubbing his head with a linen towel, water droplets from his wet hair darkening his shirt.

"Where have you been?" I asked in astonishment. Luxurious as Leoch might be in contrast to the residences of village and croft, it didn't boast any bathing facilities beyond a copper tub that Colum used to soak his aching legs, and a slightly larger one used by such ladies as thought the labor involved in filling it worth the privacy. All other washing was done either in bits, using basin and ewer, or outside, either in the loch or in a small, stone-floored chamber off the garden, where the young women were accustomed to stand naked and let their friends throw buckets of water over them.

"In the loch," he answered, hanging the damp towel neatly over the windowsill. *"Someone,"* he said grimly, "left the stall door ajar, and the stable door as well, and Cobhar had a wee swim in the twilight."

"Oh, so that's why you weren't at supper. But horses don't like to swim, do they?" I asked.

He shook his head, running his fingers through his hair to dry it.

"No, they don't. But they're just like folk, ye ken; all different. And Cobhar is fond of the young water plants. He was down nibbling by the water's edge when a pack of dogs from the village came along and chased him into the loch. I had to run them off and then go in after him. Wait 'til I get my hands on wee Hamish," he said, with grim intent. "I'll teach him to leave gates ajar."

"Are you going to tell Colum about it?" I asked, feeling a qualm of sympathy for the culprit.

Jamie shook his head, groping in his sporran. He drew out a roll and a chunk of cheese, apparently filched from the kitchens on his way up to the chamber.

"No," he said. "Colum's fair strict wi' the lad. If he heard he'd been so careless, he'd not let him ride for a month—not that he could, after the thrashing he'd get. Lord, I'm starving." He bit ferociously into the roll, scattering crumbs.

"Don't get into bed with that," I said, sliding under the quilts myself. "What are you planning to do to Hamish, then?"

He swallowed the remainder of the roll and smiled at me. "Dinna worry. I'm going to row him out on the loch just before supper tomorrow and toss him in. By the time he makes it to shore and dries off, supper will be over." He finished the cheese in three bites and unashamedly licked his fingers. "Let *him* go to bed wet and hungry and see how he likes it," he concluded darkly.

He peered hopefully in the drawer of the desk where I sometimes kept apples or other small bits of food. There was nothing there tonight, though, and he shut the drawer with a sigh.

"I suppose I'll live 'til breakfast," he said philosophically.

He stripped rapidly and crawled in next to me, shivering. Though his extremities were chilled from his swim in the icy loch, his body was still blissfully warm.

"Mm, you're nice to croodle wi'," he murmured, doing what I assumed was croodling. "You smell different; been digging plants today?"

"No," I said, surprised. "I thought it was you—the smell, I mean." It was a tangy, herbal smell, not unpleasant, but unfamiliar.

"*I* smell like fish," he observed, sniffing the back of his hand. "And wet horse. No," he leaned closer, inhaling. "No, it isna you, either. But it's close by."

He slid out of bed and turned back the quilts, searching. We found it under my pillow.

"What on earth . . . ?" I picked it up, and promptly dropped it. "Ouch! It has thorns!"

It was a small bundle of plants, plucked up roughly by the roots, and bound together with a bit of black thread. The plants were wilted, but a pungent smell still rose from the drooping leaves. There was one flower in the bouquet, a crushed primrose, whose thorny stem had pricked my thumb.

I sucked the offended digit, turning the bundle over more cautiously with my other hand. Jamie stood still, staring down at it for a moment. Then he suddenly picked it up, and crossing to the open window, flung it out into the night. Returning to the bed, he energetically brushed the crumbs of earth from the plants' roots into the palm of his hand and threw them out after the bundle. He closed the window with a slam and came back, dusting his palms.

"It's gone," he said, unnecessarily. He climbed back into bed. "Come back to bed, Sassenach."

"What was it?" I asked, climbing in beside him.

"A joke, reckon," he said. "A nasty one, but only a joke." He raised himself on one elbow and blew out the candle. "Come here, *mo duinne*," he said. "I'm cold."

———

Despite the unsettling ill-wish, I slept well, secure in the dual protection of a bolted door and Jamie's arms. Toward dawn, I dreamed of grassy meadows filled with butterflies. Yellow, brown, white, and orange, they swirled around me like autumn leaves, lighting on my head and shoulders, sliding down my body like rain, the tiny feet tickling on my skin and the velvet wings beating like faint echoes of my own heart.

I floated gently to the surface of reality, and found that the butterfly feet against my stomach were the flaming tendrils of Jamie's soft red thatch, and the butterfly trapped between my thighs was his tongue.

"Mmm," I said, sometime later. "Well, that's all very well for me, but what about you?"

"About three-quarters of a minute, if you keep on in that fashion," he said, putting my hand away with a grin. "But I'd rather take my time over it—I'm a slow and canny man by nature, d'ye see. Might I ask the favor of your company for this evening, mistress?"

"You might," I said. I put my arms behind my head, and fixed him with a half-lidded look of challenge. "If you mean to tell me that you're so decrepit you can't manage more than once in a day anymore."

He regarded me narrowly from his seat on the edge of the bed. There was a sudden flash of white as he lunged, and I found myself pressed deep into the featherbed.

"Aye, well," he said into the tangles of my hair, "you'll no say I didna warn ye."

Two and a half minutes later, he groaned and opened his eyes. He scrubbed his face and head vigorously with both hands, making the shorter ends stick up like quills. Then, with a muffled Gaelic oath, he slid reluctantly out from under the blankets and began to dress, shivering in the chilly morning air.

"I don't suppose," I asked hopefully, "that you could tell Alec you're sick, and come back to bed?"

He laughed and bent to kiss me before groping under the bed for his stockings. "Would that I could, Sassenach. I doubt much short of pox, plague, or grievous bodily harm would answer as an excuse, though. If I weren't bleeding, old Alec would be up here in a trice, dragging me off my deathbed to help wi' the worming."

I eyed his graceful long calves as he pulled a stocking up neatly and folded the top. " 'Grievous bodily harm,' eh? I might manage something along those lines," I said darkly.

He grunted as he reached across for the other stocking. "Well, watch where ye toss your elf-darts, Sassenach." He tried a lewd wink, but wound up squinting at me instead. "Aim too high, and I'll be no good to *you*, either."

I arched one eyebrow and snuggled back under the quilts. "Not to worry. Nothing above the knee, I promise."

He patted one of my rounder bulges and left for the stables, singing rather loudly the air from "Up Among the Heather." The refrain floated back from the stairwell:

> *"Sittin' wi' a wee girl, holdin' on my knee—*
> *When a bumblebee stung me, weel above the kneeeee—*
> *Up among the heather, at the head o' Bendikee!"*

He was right, I decided; he *didn't* have any ear for music.

I relapsed temporarily into a state of satisfied somnolence, but roused myself shortly to go down for breakfast. Most of the castle inhabitants had eaten and gone to their work already; those still in the hall greeted me pleasantly enough. There were no sidelong looks, no expressions of veiled hostility, of someone wondering how well their nasty little trick had worked. But I watched the faces, nonetheless.

The morning was spent alone in the garden and fields with my basket and digging stick. I was running short of some of the most popular herbs. Generally the village people went to Geillis Duncan for help, but there had been several patients from the village turning up of late in my dispensary, and the traffic in nostrums had been heavy. Maybe her husband's illness was keeping her too busy to care for her regular customers.

I spent the latter part of the afternoon in my dispensary. There were few patients to be seen; only a case of persistent eczema, a dislocated thumb, and a kitchen boy who had spilled a pot of hot soup down one leg. Having dispensed ointment of yawroot and blue flag and reset and bound the thumb, I settled down to the task of pounding some very aptly named stoneroot in one of the late Beaton's smaller mortars.

It was tedious work, but well suited to this sort of lazy afternoon. The weather was fair, and I could see blue shadows lengthening under the elms to the west when I stood on my table to peer out.

Inside, the glass bottles gleamed in orderly ranks, neat stacks of bandages and compresses in the cupboards next to them. The apothecary's cabinet had been thoroughly cleaned and disinfected, and now held stores of dried leaves, roots, and fungi, neatly packed in cotton-gauze bags. I took a deep breath of the sharp, spicy odors of my sanctum and let it out in a sigh of contentment.

Then I stopped pounding and set the pestle down. I *was* contented, I realized with a shock. Despite the myriad uncertainties of life here, despite the unpleasantness of the ill-wish, despite the small, constant ache of missing Frank, I was in fact not unhappy. Quite the contrary.

I felt immediately ashamed and disloyal. How *could* I bring myself to be happy, when Frank must be demented with worry? Assuming that time was in fact continuing without me —and I couldn't see why it wouldn't—I must have gone missing for upwards of four months. I imagined him searching the Scottish countryside, calling the police, waiting for some sign, some word of me. By now, he must nearly have given up hope and be waiting, instead, for word that my body had been found.

I set down the mortar and paced up and down the length of my narrow room, rubbing my hands on my apron in a spasm of guilty sorrow and regret. I should have got away sooner. I should have tried harder to return. But I had, I reminded myself. I had tried repeatedly. And look what had happened.

Yes, look. I was married to a Scottish outlaw, the both of us hunted by a sadistic captain of dragoons, and living with a lot of barbarians, who would as soon kill Jamie as look at him, if they thought him a threat to their precious clan succession. And the worst of it all was that I was happy.

I sat down, staring helplessly at the array of jars and bottles. I had been living day to day since our return to Leoch, delib-

erately suppressing the memories of my earlier life. Deep
down, I knew that I must soon make some kind of decision,
but I had delayed, putting off the necessity from day to day
and hour to hour, burying my uncertainties in the pleasures of
Jamie's company—and his arms.

There was a sudden bumping and cursing out in the corridor, and I rose hastily and went to the door, just in time to see
Jamie himself stumble in, supported by the bowed form of
Old Alec McMahon on one side, and the earnest but spindly
efforts of one of the stable lads on the other. He sank onto my
stool, left foot outstretched, and grimaced unpleasantly at it.
The grimace seemed to be more of annoyance than pain, so I
knelt to examine the offending appendage with relatively little
concern.

"Mild strain," I said, after a cursory inspection. "What did
you do?"

"Fell off," Jamie said succinctly.

"Off the fence?" I asked, teasing. He glowered.

"No. Off Donas."

"You were *riding* that thing?" I asked incredulously. "In
that case, you're lucky to get off with a strained ankle." I
fetched a length of bandage and began to wrap the joint.

"Weel, it wasna sae bad as a' that," said Old Alec judiciously. "In fact, lad, ye were doin' quite weel wi' him for a
bit."

"I know I was," snapped Jamie, gritting his teeth as I
pulled the bandage tight. "A bee stung him."

The bushy brows lifted. "Oh, that was it? Beast acted like
he'd been struck wi' an elf-dart," he confided to me. "Went
straight up in the air on all fours, and came down again, then
went stark, staring mad—all over the pen like a bumblebee in
a jar. Yon wee laddie stuck on too," he said, nodding at Jamie,
who invented a new unpleasant expression in response, "until
the big yellow fiend went ower the fence."

"Over the fence? Where is he now?" I asked, standing up
and dusting my hands.

"Halfway back to hell, I expect," said Jamie, putting his
foot down and trying his weight gingerly on it. "And welcome to stay there." Wincing, he sat back.

"I doubt the de'il's got much use for a half-broke stallion," observed Alec. "Bein' able to turn himself into a horse when needed."

"Perhaps that's who Donas really is," I suggested, amused.

"I wouldna doubt it," said Jamie, still smarting, but beginning to recover his usual good humor. "The de'il's customarily a black stallion, though, is he no?"

"Oh, aye," said Alec. "A great black stallion, that travels as fast as the thought between a man and a maid."

He grinned genially at Jamie and rose to go.

"And speakin' of that," he said, with a wink at me, "I'll no expect ye in the stables tomorrow. Keep to your bed, laddie, and, er . . . rest."

"Why is it," I demanded, looking after the crusty old horsemaster, "that everyone seems to assume we've no more on our minds than to get into bed with each other?"

Jamie tried his weight on the foot again, bracing himself on the counter.

"For one thing, we've been married less than a month," he observed. "For another—" He looked up and grinned, shaking his head. "I've told ye before, Sassenach. Everything ye think shows on your face."

"Bloody hell," I said.

Aside from a quick trip to the dispensary to check for emergencies, I spent the next morning ministering to the rather demanding needs of my solitary patient.

"You are supposed to be resting," I said reprovingly, at one point.

"I am. Well, my ankle is resting, at least. See?"

A long, unstockinged shin thrust up into the air, and a bony, slender foot waggled back and forth. It stopped abruptly in mid-waggle with a muffled "ouch" from its owner. He lowered it and tenderly massaged the still-puffy ankle.

"That'll teach you," I said, swinging my own legs out from under the blankets. "Come along now. You've been frowsting in bed quite long enough. You need fresh air."

He sat up, hair falling over his face.

"I thought ye said it was rest I needed."

"You can rest in the fresh air. Get up. I'm making up the bed."

Amid complaints about my general unfeelingness and lack of consideration for a gravely injured man, he got dressed and sat long enough for me to bind up the weak ankle before his natural exuberance asserted itself.

"It's a bit saft out," he said, with a glance through the casement, where the mild drizzle had just decided to buckle down to it and become a major downpour. "Let's go up to the roof."

"The roof? Oh, to be sure. I couldn't think of a better prescription for a strained ankle than climbing six flights of stairs."

"Five. Besides, I've a stick." He produced the stick in question, an aged hawthorn club, from behind the door with a triumphant flourish.

"Wherever did you get that?" I inquired, examining it. At closer range, it was even more battered, a three-foot length of chipped hardwood, age-hardened as a diamond.

"Alec lent it me. He uses it on the mules; raps them twixt the eyes wi' it to make them pay attention."

"Sounds very effective," I said, eyeing the scuffed wood. "I must try it sometime. On you."

We emerged at last in a small sheltered spot, just under the overhang of the slate roof. A low parapet guarded the edge of this small lookout.

"Oh, it's beautiful!" Despite the gusty rain, the view from the roof was magnificent; we could see the broad silver sweep of the loch and the towering crags beyond, thrusting into the solid grey of the sky like ridged black fists.

Jamie leaned on the parapet, taking the weight from his injured foot.

"Aye, it is. I used to come up here sometimes, when I was at the Castle before."

He pointed across the loch, dimpling under the beat of the rain.

"D'ye see the notch there, between those two *craigs*?"

"In the mountains? Yes."

"That's the way to Lallybroch. When I'd feel lonely for my home, sometimes I'd come up here and look that way. I'd imagine flying like a corbie across that pass, and the look of the hills and the fields, falling down the other side of the mountain, and the manor house at the end of the valley."

I touched him gently on the arm.

"Do you want to go back, Jamie?"

He turned his head and smiled down at me.

"Well, I've been thinking of it. I don't know if I want to, precisely, but I think we must. I canna say what we'll find there, Sassenach. But . . . aye. I'm wed now. You're lady of Broch Tuarach. Outlaw or no, I need to go back, even if just long enough to set things straight."

I felt a thrill, compounded of relief and apprehension, at the thought of leaving Leoch and its assorted intrigues.

"When will we go?"

He frowned, drumming his fingers on the parapet. The stone was dark and slick with rain.

"Well, I think we must wait for the Duke to come. It's possible that he might see his way to doing Colum a favor by taking up my case. If he cannot get me cleared, he might be able to arrange a pardon. There'd be a good deal less danger in going back to Lallybroch, then, ye see."

"Well, yes, but . . ." He glanced sharply at me as I hesitated.

"What is it, Sassenach?"

I took a deep breath. "Jamie . . . if I tell you something will you promise not to ask me how I know?"

He took me by both arms, looking down into my face. The rain misted his hair and small droplets ran down the sides of his face. He smiled at me.

"I told you that I wouldna ask for anything that ye dinna wish to tell me. Yes, I promise."

"Let's sit down. You shouldn't be standing on that foot so long."

We made our way to the wall where the overhanging slates of the roof sheltered a small dry patch of pavement, and settled ourselves comfortably, backs against the wall.

"All right, Sassenach. What is it?" Jamie asked.

"The Duke of Sandringham," I said. I bit my lip. "Jamie, don't trust him. I don't know everything about him myself, but I do know—there's something about him. Something wrong."

"You know about that?" He looked surprised.

Now it was my turn to stare.

"You mean *you* know about him already? Have you met him?" I was relieved. Perhaps the mysterious links between Sandringham and the Jacobite cause were much better known than Frank and the vicar had thought.

"Oh, aye. He was here, visiting, when I was sixteen. When I . . . left."

"Why did you leave?" I was curious, remembering suddenly what Geillis Duncan had said when first I'd met her in the wood. The odd rumor that Jamie was the real father of Colum's son Hamish. I knew myself that he wasn't, couldn't have been—but I was quite possibly the only person in the Castle who *did* know. A suspicion of that sort could easily have led to Dougal's earlier attempt on Jamie's life—if in fact that's what the attack at Carryarick had been.

"It wasn't because of . . . the lady Letitia, was it?" I asked with some hesitation.

"Letitia?" His startled astonishment was plain, and something inside me that I hadn't known was clenched suddenly relaxed. I hadn't *really* thought there was anything to Geilie's supposition, but still. . . .

"What on earth makes ye mention Letitia?" Jamie asked curiously. "I lived at the Castle for a year, and had speech of her maybe once that I remember, when she called me to her chamber and gave me the raw side of her tongue for leading a game of shinty through her rose garden."

I told him what Geilie had said, and he laughed, breath misting in the cool, rainy air.

"God," he said, "as though I'd have the nerve!"

"You don't think Colum suspected any such thing, do you?" I asked.

He shook his head decidedly.

"No, I don't, Sassenach. If he had any inkling of such a

thing, I wouldna have lived to be seventeen, let alone achieve the ripe old age of three-and-twenty."

This more or less confirmed my own impression of Colum, but I was relieved, nonetheless. Jamie's expression had grown thoughtful, blue eyes suddenly remote.

"Come to think on it, though, I don't know that Colum *does* know why I left the Castle so sudden, then. And if Geillis Duncan is goin' about the place spreading such rumors—that woman's a troublemaker, Sassenach; a gossip and a scold, if not the witch folk say she is—well, I'd best see that he finds out, then."

He glanced up at the sheet of water pouring from the eaves.

"Perhaps we'd best go down, Sassenach. It's getting a wee bit damp out."

We took a different way down, crossing the roof to an outer stairway that led down to the kitchen gardens, where I wanted to pull a bit of borage, if the downpour would let me. We sheltered under the wall of the Castle, one of the jutting window ledges diverting the rain above.

"What do ye do wi' borage, Sassenach?" Jamie asked with interest, looking out at the straggly vines and plants, beaten to the earth by the rain.

"When it's green, nothing. First you dry it, and then—"

I was interrupted by a terrific noise of barking and shouting, coming from outside the garden wall. I raced through the downpour toward the wall, followed more slowly by Jamie, limping.

Father Bain, the village priest, was running up the path, puddles exploding under his feet, pursued by a yelping pack of dogs. Hampered by his voluminous soutane, the priest tripped and fell, water and mud flying in spatters all around him. In a moment, the dogs were upon him, growling and snapping.

A blur of plaid vaulted over the wall next to me, and Jamie was among them, laying about with his stick and shouting in Gaelic, adding his voice to the general racket. If the shouts and curses had little effect, the stick had more. There were sharp yelps as the club struck hairy flesh, and gradually the pack retreated, finally turning and galloping off in the direction of the village.

Jamie wiped the hair out of his eyes, panting.

"Bad as wolves," he said. "I'd told Colum about that pack already; they're the ones that chased Cobhar into the loch two days ago. Best he has them shot before they kill someone." He looked down at me as I knelt next to the fallen priest, inspecting. The rain dripped from the ends of my hair, and I could feel my shawl growing sodden.

"They haven't yet," I said. "Bar a few toothmarks, he's basically all right."

Father Bain's soutane was ripped down one side, showing an expanse of hairless white thigh with an ugly gash and several puncture marks beginning to ooze blood. The priest, pasty-white with shock, was struggling to his feet; plainly he wasn't too badly injured.

"If you'll come to the surgery with me, Father, I'll cleanse those cuts for you," I offered, suppressing a smile at the spectacle the fat little priest presented, soutane flapping and argyle socks revealed.

At the best of times, Father Bain's face resembled a clenched fist. This similarity was made more pronounced at the moment by the red mottling that streaked his jowls and emphasized the vertical creases between cheeks and mouth. He glared at me as though I had suggested that he commit some public indecency.

Apparently I had, for his next words were "What, a man o' God to expose his pairsonal parts to the handling of a wumman? Weel, I'll tell ye, madam, I've no notion what sorts of immorality are practiced in the circles you're accustomed to move in, but I'll ha'e ye to ken that such'll no be tolerated here—not sae long as I've the cure of the souls in this parish!" With that, he turned and stumped off, limping rather badly and trying unsuccessfully to hold up the torn side of his robe.

"Suit yourself," I called after him. "If you don't let me cleanse it, it will fester!"

The priest did not respond, but hunched his round shoulders and hitched his way up the garden stair a step at a time, like a penguin hopping up an ice floe.

"That man doesn't care overmuch for women, does he?" I remarked to Jamie.

"Considering his occupation, I imagine that's as well," he replied. "Let's go and eat."

After lunch, I sent my patient back to bed to rest—alone, this time, in spite of his protestations—and went down to the surgery. The heavy rain seemed to have made business slack; people tended to stay safely inside, rather than running over their feet with ploughshares or falling off roofs.

I passed the time pleasantly enough, bringing the records in Davie Beaton's book up to date. Just as I finished, though, a visitor darkened my door.

He literally darkened it, his bulk filling it from side to side. Squinting in the semidarkness, I made out the form of Alec MacMahon, swathed in an extraordinary get-up of coats, shawls, and odd bits of horse-blanket.

He advanced with a slowness that reminded me of Colum's first visit to the surgery with me, and gave me a clue to his problem.

"Rheumatism, is it?" I asked with sympathy, as he subsided stiffly into my single chair with a stifled groan.

"Aye. The damp settles in my bones," he said. "Aught to be done about it?" He laid his huge, gnarled hands on the table, letting the fingers relax. The hands opened slowly, like a night-blooming flower, to show the callused palms within. I picked up one of the knotted appendages and turned it gently to and fro, stretching the fingers and massaging the horny palm. The seamed old face above the hand contorted for a moment as I did it, but then relaxed as the first twinges passed.

"Like wood," I said. "A good slug of whisky and a deep massage is the best I can recommend. Tansy tea will do only so much."

He laughed, shawls slipping off his shoulder.

"Whisky, eh? I had my doubts, lassie, but I see ye've the makings of a fine physician."

I reached into the back of my medicine cupboard and

pulled out the anonymous brown bottle that held my supply from the Leoch distillery. I plunked it on the table before him, with a horn cup.

"Drink up," I said, "then get stripped off as far as you think decent and lie on the table. I'll make up the fire so it will be warm enough."

The blue eye surveyed the bottle with appreciation, and a crooked hand reached slowly for the neck.

"Best have a nip yourself, lassie," he advised. "It'll be a big job."

He groaned, with a cross between pain and contentment, as I leaned hard on his left shoulder to loosen it, then lifted from underneath and rotated the whole quarter of his body.

"My wife used to iron my back for me," he remarked, "for the lumbago. But this is even better. Ye've a good strong pair of hands, lassie. Make a good stable-lad, ye would."

"I'll assume that's a compliment," I said dryly, pouring more of the heated oil-and-tallow mixture into my palm and spreading it over the broad white expanse of his back. There was a sharp line of demarcation between the weathered, mottled brown skin of his arms, where the rolled-up sleeves of his shirt stopped, and the milk-white skin of his shoulders and back.

"Well, you were a fine, fair laddie at one time," I remarked. "The skin of your back's as white as mine."

A deep chuckle shook the flesh under my hands.

"Never know now, would ye? Aye, Ellen MacKenzie once saw me wi' my sark off, birthin' a foal, and told me it looked like the good Lord had put the wrong head to my body— should have had a bag of milk-pudding on my shoulders, instead of a face from the altarpiece."

I gathered he was referring to the rood screen in the chapel, which featured a number of extremely unattractive demons, engaged in torturing sinners.

"Ellen MacKenzie sounds as though she was rather free with her opinions," I observed. I was more than slightly curious about Jamie's mother. From the small things he said now and then, I had some picture of his father Brian, but he had never mentioned his mother, and I knew nothing about her, other than that she had died young, in childbed.

"Oh, she had a tongue on her, did Ellen, and a mind of her own to go wi' it." Untying the garters of his trews, I tucked them up out of the way and began operations on the muscular calves of his legs. "But enough sweetness with it that no one minded much, other than her brothers. And she wasna one to pay much heed to Colum or Dougal."

"Mm. So I heard. Eloped, didn't she?" I dug my thumbs into the tendons behind his knee, and he let out a sound that would have been a squeak in anyone less dignified.

"Oh, aye. Ellen was the eldest o' the six MacKenzie bairns —a year or two older than Colum, and the apple of auld Jacob's eye. That's why she'd gone so long unwed; wouldna ha' aught to do wi' John Cameron or Malcolm Grant, or any of the others she might have gone to, and her father wouldna force her against her will."

When old Jacob died, though, Colum had less patience with his sister's foibles. Struggling desperately to consolidate his shaky hold on the clan, he had sought an alliance with Munro to the north, or Grant to the south. Both clans had young chieftains, who would make useful brothers-in-law. Young Jocasta, only fifteen, had obligingly accepted the suit of John Cameron, and gone north. Ellen, on the verge of spinsterhood at twenty-two, had been a good deal less cooperative.

"I take it Malcolm Grant's suit was rather firmly rejected, judging from his behavior two weeks ago," I observed.

Old Alec laughed, the laugh turning to a satisfied groan as I pressed deeper.

"Aye. I never heard exactly what she said to him, but I expect it stung. It was at the big Gathering, ye ken, that they met. Out in the rose garden they went, in the evening, and everyone waiting to see would she tak' him or no. And it grew dark, and they still waiting. And darker still, and the lanterns all lit, and the singing begun, and no sign yet of Ellen or Malcolm Grant."

"Goodness. It must have been quite a conversation." I

poured another dollop of the liniment between his shoulder blades, and he grunted with the warm pleasure of it.

"So it seemed. But time went on, and they didna come back, and Colum began to fear as Grant had eloped wi' her; taken her by force, ye see. And it seemed as that must be the way of it, for they found the rose garden empty. And when he sent down to the stables for me, sure enough—I told him Grant's men had come for the horses, and the whole boiling of 'em gone awa' without a word of farewell."

Furious, eighteen-year-old Dougal had mounted his horse at once and set out on the track of Malcolm Grant, not waiting either for company nor for conference with Colum.

"When Colum heard as Dougal had gone after Grant, he sent me and some others helter-skelter after him, Colum being well acquent wi' Dougal's temper and not wishing to have his new brother-in-law slain in the road before the banns were called. For he reckoned as how Malcolm Grant, not being able to talk Ellen into wedding him, must ha' taken her away in order to have his way wi' her and force her into marriage that way."

Alec paused meditatively. "All Dougal could see was the insult, of course. But I dinna think Colum was that upset about it, to tell the truth, insult or no. It would ha' solved his problem—and Grant would likely have had to take Ellen wi'out her dower and pay reparation to Colum as well."

Alec snorted cynically. "Colum is no the man to let an opportunity pass by him. He's quick, and he's ruthless, is Colum." The single ice-blue eye swiveled back to regard me over one humped shoulder. "Ye'd be wise to bear that in mind, lassie."

"I'm not likely to forget it," I assured him, with some grimness. I remembered Jamie's story of his punishment at Colum's order, and wondered how much of that had been in revenge for his mother's rebellion.

Still, Colum had had no chance to seize the opportunity of marrying his sister to the laird of clan Grant. Toward dawn, Dougal had found Malcolm Grant camped along the main road with his followers, asleep under a gorse bush, wrapped in his plaid.

And when Alec and the others had come pelting along the road sometime later, they had been stopped in their tracks by the sight of Dougal MacKenzie and Malcolm Grant, both stripped to the waist and scarred with the marks of battle, swaying and staggering up and down the roadway, still exchanging random blows whenever they got within reach of each other. Grant's retainers were perched along the roadway like a row of owls, heads turning one way and then the other, as the waning fight meandered up and down in the dripping dawn.

"They were both of them puffing like blown horses, and the steam rising off their bodies in the chill. Grant's nose was swelled to twice its size, and Dougal could scarce see out o' either eye, and both wi' their blood dripping down and dried ower their breasts."

Upon the appearance of Colum's men, Grant's tacksmen had all sprung to their feet, hands upon their swords, and the meeting would likely have resulted in serious bloodshed, had some sharp-eyed lad among the MacKenzies not noted the rather important fact that Ellen MacKenzie was nowhere to be seen among the Grants.

"Weel, after they'd poured water on Malcolm Grant and brought him to his senses, he managed to tell them what Dougal wouldna pause to hear—that Ellen had spent but a quarter-hour wi' him in the rose garden. He wouldna say what had passed between them, but whatever it was, he'd been so offended as to wish to take his leave at once, without showing his face in the Hall. And he'd left her there, and seen her no more, nor did he wish ever to hear the name of Ellen MacKenzie spoken in his presence again. And wi' that, he mounted his horse—a bit unsteady, still—and rode awa'. And been no friend since, to anyone of the clan MacKenzie."

I listened, fascinated. "And where *was* Ellen all this time?"

Old Alec laughed, with the sound of a stable door hinge creaking.

"Ower the hills and far away. But they didna find it out for some time yet. We turned about and pelted home again, to find Ellen still missing and Colum standing white-faced in the courtyard, leanin' on Angus Mhor."

There followed more confusion still, for with all the guests, the rooms of the Castle were full, as were all the lofts and cubbyholes, the kitchens and closets. It seemed hopeless to tell which of all the folk in the Castle might also be missing, but Colum called all of the servants, and went doggedly down the lists of the invited, asking who had been seen the evening before, and where, and when. And finally he found a kitchen-maid who recalled seeing a man in a back passage, just before the supper was served.

She had noticed him only because he was so handsome; tall and sturdy, she said, with hair like a black silkie's and eyes like a cat. She had watched him down the passage, admiring him, and seen him meet someone at the outer door—a woman dressed in black from head to toe, and shrouded in a hooded cloak.

"What's a silkie?" I asked.

Alec's eye slanted toward me, crinkling at the corners.

"Ye call them seals in English. For quite a bit after that, even after they knew the truth of it, folk in the village would tell the tale to each other that Ellen MacKenzie was taken to the sea, to live among the seals. Did ye know that the silkies put aside their skins when they come ashore, and walk like men? And if ye find a silkie's skin and hide it, he—or she—" he added, fairly, "canna go into the sea again, but must stay with ye on the land. It's thought good to take a seal-wife that way, for they're very good cooks, and most devoted mothers.

"Still," he said judiciously, "Colum wasna inclined to believe his sister'd gone off wi' a seal, and said so. So he called the guests down, one by one, and asked them all who knew a man of that description. And at long last, they worked it out that his name was Brian, but no one knew his clan or his surname; he'd been at the Games, but there they only called him Brian Dhu."

So there the matter seemed to rest for a time, for the searchers had no idea in which direction to look. Still, even the best of hunters must stop at a cottage now and then, to ask for a handful of salt or a pannikin of milk. And eventually word of the pair reached Leoch, for Ellen MacKenzie was a maid of no ordinary appearance.

"Hair like fire," Alec said dreamily, enjoying the warmth of the oil on his back. "And eyes like Colum's—grey, and fringed wi' black lashes—verra pretty, but the kind would go through ye like a bolt. A tall woman; even taller than you. And sae fair it would hurt the eyes to see her.

"I heard tell later as they'd met at the Gathering, taken one look and decided on the spot as there could be none other for either one o' them. So they laid their plans and they stole awa', under the noses of Colum MacKenzie and three hundred guests."

He laughed suddenly, remembering. "Dougal finally found them, living in a crofter's cottage on the edge of the Fraser lands. They'd decided the only way to manage was to hide until Ellen was wi' child, and big enough that there'd be no question whose it was. Then Colum would have to give his blessing to the marriage, like it or no—and he didn't."

Alec grinned. "Whiles ye were on the road, did ye chance to see a scar Dougal carries, running down his breast?"

I had; a thin white line that crossed his heart and ran from shoulder to ribs.

"Did Brian do that?" I asked.

"No, Ellen," he replied, grinning at my expression. "To stop him cutting Brian's throat, which he was about to do. I wouldna mention it to Dougal, if I were you."

"No, I don't suppose I will."

Luckily, the plan had worked, and Ellen was five months gone with child by the time that Dougal found them.

"There was the great to-do about it all, and a lot of verra nasty letters exchanged between Leoch and Beauly, but they settled it in the end, and Ellen and Brian took up house at Lallybroch the week before the child was born. They were married in the dooryard," he added, as an afterthought, "so he could carry her over the threshold for the first time as a wife. He said after as he nearly ruptured himself, lifting her."

"You talk as though you knew them well," I said. Finishing my ministrations, I wiped the slippery ointment off my hands with a towel.

"Oh, a bit," Alec said, drowsy with warmth. The lid drooped over his single eye, and the lines of his old face had relaxed from the expression of mild discomfort that normally made him look so fierce.

"I kent Ellen weel, of course. Then Brian I met years later, when he brought the lad to stay—we got on. A good man wi' a horse." His voice trailed off, and the lid fell shut.

I drew a blanket up over the old man's prostrate form, and tiptoed away, leaving him dreaming by the fire.

———

Leaving Alec asleep, I had gone up to our chamber, only to find Jamie in the same condition. There are a limited number of activities suitable for indoor amusement on a dark, rainy day, and assuming that I didn't wish either to rouse Jamie or to join him in oblivion, that seemed to leave reading or needlework. Given the worse-than-mediocre state of my abilities in the latter direction, I had decided to borrow a book from Colum's library.

In accordance with the peculiar architectural principles governing the construction of Leoch—based on a general abhorrence of straight lines—the stair leading to Colum's suite had two right-angle bends in it, each marked by a small landing. An attendant usually stood on the second landing, ready to run errands or lend assistance to the laird, but he wasn't at his station today. I could hear the rumble of voices from above; perhaps the attendant was with Colum. I paused outside the door, uncertain whether to interrupt.

"I've always known ye to be a fool, Dougal, but I didna think ye *quite* such an idiot." Accustomed to the company of tutors since youth, and unused to venturing out as his brother did among fighting men and common people, Colum's voice normally lacked the broad Scots that marked Dougal's speech. The cultured accent had slipped a bit now, though, and the two voices were nearly indistinguishable, both thickened by anger. "I might have expected such behavior from ye when ye were in your twenties, but for God's sake, man, you're five-and-forty!"

"Well, it isna a matter *you'd* know owermuch about, now, is it?" Dougal's voice held an ugly sneer.

"No." Colum's response came in a cutting tone. "And

while I've seldom found cause to thank the Lord, perhaps
He's done better by me than I've thought. I've heard it said
often enough that a man's brain stops workin' when his cock's
standin', and now I think maybe I believe it." There was a
loud scrape as chair legs were pushed back across the stone
flooring. "If the brothers MacKenzie have but one cock and
one brain between the two of them, then I'm glad of my half
of the bargain!"

I decided that a third participant in this particular conversation would be decidedly unwelcome, and stepped softly back
from the door, turning to go down the stair.

The sound of rustling skirts from the first landing made me
stop in my tracks. I didn't wish to be discovered eavesdropping outside the laird's study, and turned back toward the
door. The landing here was wide, and a tapestry covered one
wall almost from floor to ceiling. My feet would show, but it
couldn't be helped.

Lurking like a rat behind the arras, I heard the steps from
below slow as they approached the door, and stop at the far
side of the landing, as the unseen visitor realized, as I had, the
private nature of the brothers' conversation.

"No," Colum was saying, calmer now. "No, of course not.
The woman's a witch, or next thing to it."

"Aye, but—" Dougal's response was cut short by his
brother's impatient tones.

"I've said I'll attend to it, man. Don't worry yourself over
it, little brother; I'll see she's done rightly by." A note of
grudging affection had crept into Colum's voice.

"I'll tell ye, man. I've written the Duke as he may have
leave to hunt the lands above Erlick—he's keen to have a shot
at the stags there. I mean to send Jamie along wi' him; may be
as he still has some feeling for the lad—"

Dougal interrupted with something in Gaelic, evidently a
coarse remark, for Colum laughed and said, "Nay, I reckon
Jamie's big enough to have a care for himself. But if the
Duke's a mind to intercede for him with His Royal Majesty,
it's the lad's best chance for a pardon. If ye will, I'll tell His
Grace you'll go as well. You can aid Jamie as ye may, and
you'll be out of the way while I settle matters here."

There was a muffled thump from the far side of the landing, and I risked peeping out. It was the girl Laoghaire, pale as the plastered wall behind her. She was holding a tray with a decanter; a pewter cup had fallen from the tray to the carpeted floor, making the sound I had heard.

"What's that?" Colum's voice, suddenly sharp, spoke from inside the study. Laoghaire dropped the tray on the table next to the door, almost upsetting the decanter in her haste, and turning, fled precipitately.

I could hear Dougal's footsteps approaching the door, and knew I would never make it down the stairs without discovery. I barely had time to wriggle out of my hiding place and pick up the fallen cup, before the door opened.

"Oh, it's you." Dougal sounded mildly surprised. "Is that the stuff Mrs. Fitz sent for Colum's raw throat?"

"Yes," I said glibly. "She says she hopes he'll be better presently."

"I'll do." Moving more slowly, Colum came into view in the open door. He smiled at me. "Thank Mrs. Fitz for me. And my thanks to you, my dear, for bringing it. Will ye sit a moment while I drink it?"

The conversation I had overheard had effectually made me forget my original purpose, but I now remembered my intention of borrowing a book. Dougal excused himself, and I followed Colum slowly into his library, where he offered me the run of his shelves.

Colum's color was still high, the quarrel with his brother still fresh in his mind, but he answered my questions about the books with a good approximation of his usual poise. Only the brightness of his eyes and a certain tenseness of posture betrayed his thoughts.

I found one or two herbals that looked interesting and put them aside while I browsed a novel.

Colum crossed to the birds' cage, no doubt intending to soothe himself as per his usual custom by watching the beautiful little self-absorbed creatures hop about amongst the branches, each a world unto itself.

The sound of shouts from outside attracted my attention. From this high point, the fields behind the castle were visible, all the way to the loch. A small group of horsemen was sweeping around the end of the loch, shouting with exhilaration, as the rain pelted them on.

As they drew nearer, I could see that they weren't men after all, but boys, mostly teenagers, but with a younger lad here and there on a pony, pressing hard to stay up with the older youths. I wondered if Hamish was with them, and quickly found the telltale spot of bright hair, gleaming wildly from Cobhar's back in the middle of the pack.

The gang came charging toward the castle, headed for one of the innumerable stone walls that separated one field from another. One, two, three, four, the older boys on their mounts popped over the wall with the careless ease born of experience.

It was doubtless my imagination that made the bay seem to hang back a moment, for Cobhar followed the other horses with apparent eagerness. He charged the fence, set himself, braced and leapt.

He seemed to do it just as the others had, and yet something happened. Perhaps a hesitation by his rider, a too-hard pulling on the reins, or a not-quite-firm seat. For the front hooves struck the wall just a few inches too low, and horse, rider and all, somersaulted over the wall in the most spectacular parabola of doom I had ever seen.

"Oh!"

Drawn by my exclamation, Colum turned his head to the window in time to see Cobhar land heavily on his side, the small figure of Hamish pinned beneath. Crippled as he was, Colum moved with speed. He was by my side, leaning out of the window, before the horse had even begun to struggle to his feet.

The wind and rain beat in, soaking the velvet of Colum's coat. Peering anxiously over his shoulder, I saw a cluster of lads, pushing and shoving each other in their eagerness to help. It seemed a long time before the crowd parted, and we saw the small, sturdy figure stumble out of the press, clutching his stomach. He shook his head to the many offers of help, and staggered purposefully to the wall, where he leaned over and vomited profusely. Then he slid down the wall and sat in the wet grass, legs sprawled, face upturned to the rain. When I saw him stick out his tongue to catch the falling drops, I laid a hand on Colum's shoulder.

"He's all right," I said. "Only had the wind knocked out of him."

Colum closed his eyes and let his breath out, body sagging suddenly with the release of tension. I watched him with sympathy.

"You care for him as though he were your own, don't you?" I asked.

The grey eyes blazed suddenly into mine with the most extraordinary expression of alarm. For an instant, there was no sound in the study but the ticking of the glass clock on the shelf. Then a drop of water rolled down Colum's nose, to hang glimmering from the tip. I reached involuntarily to blot it with my handkerchief, and the tension in his face broke.

"Yes," he said simply.

In the end I told Jamie only about Colum's plan to send him hunting with the Duke. I was convinced by now that his feelings for Laoghaire were only those of a chivalrous friendship, but I didn't know what he might do if he knew that his uncle had seduced the girl and got her with child. Apparently Colum didn't mean to procure the services of Geilie Duncan in the emergency; I wondered if the girl would be wed to Dougal, or if Colum would find her another husband before the child began to show. In any case, if Jamie and Dougal were going to be shut up together in a hunting lodge for days on end, I thought it might be as well if the shade of Laoghaire were not one of the party.

"Hm," he said thoughtfully. "Worth a try. Ye get verra friendly wi' each other, hunting all day and coming back to drink whisky by the fire." He finished fastening my gown up the back and bent to kiss my shoulder briefly.

"I'd be sorry to leave ye, Sassenach, but it might be best."

"Don't mind for me," I said. I hadn't realized before that his departure would necessarily leave me alone at the Castle, and the thought made me more than slightly nervous. Still, I was resolved to manage, if it might help him.

"Are you ready for supper?" I asked. His hand lingered on my waist, and I turned toward him.

"Mmm," he said a moment later. "I'd be willing to go hungry."

"Well, *I* wouldn't," I said. "You'll just have to wait."

I glanced down the dinner table and across the room. By now I knew most of the faces, some intimately. And a motley crew they were, I reflected. Frank would have been fascinated by the gathering—so many different facial types.

Thinking about Frank was rather like touching a sore tooth; my inclination was to shy away. But the time was coming when I would be able to delay no longer, and I forced my mind back, carefully drawing him in my mind, tracing the long, smooth arcs of his brows with my thoughts as I had once traced them with my fingers. No matter that my fingers tingled suddenly with the memory of rougher, thicker brows, and the deep blue of the eyes beneath them.

I hastily turned toward the nearest face, as an antidote to such disturbing thoughts. It happened to be Murtagh's. Well, at least he looked like neither of the men who haunted my thoughts.

Short, slightly built but sinewy as a gibbon, with long arms that reinforced the simian resemblance, he had a low brow and narrow jaw that for some reason made me think of cave dwellers and pictures of Early Man shown in some of Frank's texts. Not a Neanderthal, though. A Pict. That was it. There was something very durable about the small clansman that reminded me of the weathered, patterned stones, ancient even now, that stood their implacable guard over crossroads and burial grounds.

Amused at the idea, I looked over the other diners with an eye to spotting ethnic types. That man near the hearth, for example, John Cameron, his name was, was a Norman if I'd ever seen one—not that I had—high cheekbones and a high, narrow brow, long upper lip, and the dark skin of a Gaul.

The odd fair Saxon here and there . . . ah, Laoghaire, the perfect exemplar. Pale-skinned, blue-eyed, and just the tiniest bit plump . . . I repressed the uncharitable observation. She carefully avoided looking at either me or Jamie, chattering animatedly with her friends at one of the lower tables.

I looked in the opposite direction, toward the next table, where Dougal MacKenzie sat, apart from Colum for once. A bloody Viking, that one. With his impressive height and those broad, flat cheekbones, I could easily imagine him in command of a dragon ship, deep-sunk eyes gleaming with avarice and lust as he peered through the fog at some rocky coastal village.

A large hand, wrist lightly haired with copper, reached past me to take a small loaf of oat-bread from the tray. Another Norseman, Jamie. He reminded me of Mrs. Baird's legends of the race of giants who once walked Scotland and laid their long bones in the earth of the north.

The conversation was general, as it usually was, small groups buzzing between mouthfuls. But my ears suddenly caught a familiar name, spoken at a nearby table. Sandringham. I thought the voice was Murtagh's, and turned around to see. He was seated next to Ned Gowan, munching industriously.

"Sandringham? Ah, old Willie the arse-bandit," said Ned, meditatively.

"What?!" said one of the younger men-at-arms, choking on his ale.

"Our revered duke has something of a taste for boys, or so I understand," Ned explained.

"Mmm," agreed Rupert, his mouth full. Swallowing, he added, "Had a wee bit of a taste for young Jamie here, last time he visited these parts, if I remember rightly. That were when, Dougal? Thirty-eight? Thirty-nine?"

"Thirty-seven," Dougal answered from the next table. He narrowed his eyes at his nephew. "Ye were rather a pretty lad at sixteen, Jamie."

Jamie nodded, chewing. "Aye. Fast, too."

When the laughter had died down, Dougal began to tease Jamie.

"I didna ken ye were a favorite, Jamie, lad. There's several about the Duke as ha' traded a sore arse for lands and offices."

"Ye'll notice I havena got either one," responded Jamie with a grin, to further roars of laughter.

"What? Never even got close?" said Rupert, chewing noisily.

"A good bit closer than I would have liked, truth be known."

"Ah, but how close would ye ha' liked it, hey, lad?" The shout came from further down the table, from a tall, brownbearded man I didn't recognize, and was greeted with more laughter and ribald remarks. Jamie smiled tranquilly and reached for another loaf, undisturbed by the teasing.

"Is that why ye left the Castle so sudden and went back to your father?" asked Rupert.

"Aye."

"Why, Jamie, lad, ye should ha' told me ye were having trouble that way," said Dougal, with mock concern. Jamie made a low Scottish noise in his throat.

"And if I'd told ye about it, you old rogue, ye would have slipped a bit of poppy juice in my ale some evening, and left me in His Grace's bed as a wee gift."

The table roared, and Jamie dodged as Dougal hurled an onion at him.

Rupert squinted across at Jamie. "Seems to me, lad, I saw ye, soon before ye left, goin' into the Duke's chambers near nightfall. Ye're sure ye're not holdin' back on us?" Jamie grabbed another onion and threw it at him. It missed and rolled away into the rushes.

"Nay," Jamie said, laughing, "I'm a maiden still—that way, at least. But if ye must know all about it before you can sleep, Rupert, I'll tell ye, and welcome."

Amid shouts of "Tell! Tell!" he deliberately poured a mug of ale and sat back in the classic storyteller's posture. I could see Colum at the head table, head cocked forward to hear, as attentive as the ostlers and fighting-men at our table.

"Well," he began, "it's true enough what Ned says; His Grace had something of an eye for me, though being the innocent I was at sixteen—" Here he was interrupted by a number of cynical remarks, and raised his voice to go on. "Bein', as I say, innocent of such carryings on, I'd no idea what he meant, though it seemed a bit strange to me, the way His Grace was always wanting to pat me like a wee dog and was so interested in what I might ha' in my sporran." ("Or under it!" shouted a drunken voice.)

"I thought it stranger still," he went on, "when he found me washing myself at the river and wanted to wash my back for me. When he finished my back and went on wi' the rest, I began to get a wee bit nervous, and when he put his hand under my kilts, I began to get the general idea. I may have been an innocent, but no a complete fool, ye ken.

"I got out of that particular situation by diving into the water, kilts and all, and swimming across to the other side; His Grace being not of a mind to risk his costly clothes in the mud and water. Anyway, after that I was verra wary of being alone with him. He caught me once or twice in the garden or the courtyard, but there was room to get away, wi' no more harm than him kissing my ear. The only other bad time was when he came on me alone in the stables."

"In *my* stables?" Old Alec looked aghast. He half-rose to his feet and called across the room to the head table. "Colum, ye'll see that man stays oot o' my sheds! I'll not have him frightening my horses, duke or no! Or troubling the boys, neither!" he added, as an obvious afterthought.

Jamie went on with his story, unperturbed by the interruption. Dougal's two teenaged daughters were listening raptly, mouths slightly agape.

"I was in a horsebox, ye ken, and there wasna room to maneuver much. I was bendin' over [more ribald remarks]— bendin' over the manger, I say, muckin' up husks from the bottom, when I hear a sound behind me, and before I can straighten up, my kilts are tossed up round my waist, and there's something hard pressed against my arse."

He waved a hand to still the tumult before going on. "Weel, I didna care much for the thought of being buggered in a horsebox, but I didna see much way out at that point, either. I was just gritting my teeth and hoping it wouldn't hurt too much, when the horse—it was that big black gelding, Ned, the one ye got at Brocklebury—you know, the one Colum sold to Breadalbin—anyway, the horse took an objection to the noise His Grace was making. Now, most horses like ye to talk to them, and so did that one, but he had a peculiar aversion to verra high voices; I couldna take him in the yard when there were small bairns about, because he'd get nervous at their squeaks, and start pawing and stamping.

"His Grace, ye might recall, has a rather high-pitched voice, and it was a bit higher than usual on this occasion, him bein' a trifle excited. Weel, as I say, the horse didna care for it—nor did I, I must say—and he starts stamping, and snorting, and swings his body round and squashes His Grace flat against the side of the box. As soon as the Duke let go of me, I jumped into the manger and eased away round the other side of the horse, leavin' His Grace to get out as best he might."

Jamie paused for breath and a sip of ale. He had the attention of the whole room by this time, faces turned toward him, gleaming in the light of the torchères. Here and there might have been discerned a frown at these revelations concerning a most puissant noble of the English Crown, but the overriding reaction was an untrammeled delight in the scandal. I gathered that the Duke was not a particularly popular personage at Castle Leoch.

"Havin' been so close, as ye might say, His Grace made up his mind as he'd have me, come what might. So next day he tells the MacKenzie that his body servant's fallen ill, and can he borrow me to help him wash and dress." Colum covered his face in mock dismay, to the amusement of the crowd. Jamie nodded to Rupert.

"That's why ye saw me go to His Grace's room in the evening. Under orders, ye might say."

"You could have told me, Jamie. I'd not have made you go," Colum called, with a look of reproach.

Jamie shrugged and grinned. "I was prevented by my natural modesty, Uncle. Besides, I knew ye were trying to deal with the man; I thought it might impair your negotiations a bit if you were forced to tell His Grace to keep his hands off your nephew's bum."

"Very thoughtful of you, Jamie," said Colum dryly. "So you sacrificed yourself for my interests, did you?"

Jamie raised his mug in a mock-toast. "Your interests are always foremost in my mind, Uncle," he said, and I thought that in spite of the teasing tone, there was a sharp undercurrent of truth to this, one that Colum perceived as well as I.

He drained the mug and set it down. "But, no," he said, wiping his mouth, "in this case, I didna feel that family duty required quite that much of me. I went to the Duke's rooms, because you told me to, but that was all."

"And ye came out again wi' yer arse-hole unstretched?" Rupert sounded skeptical.

Jamie grinned. "Aye, I did. Ye see, directly I heard about it, I went to Mrs. Fitz, and told her I was in desperate need of a dose of syrup of figs. When she gave it to me, I saw where she put the bottle, and I came back quiet a bit later, and drank the whole lot."

The room rocked with laughter, including Mrs. Fitz, who turned so red in the face I thought she might have a seizure. She rose ceremoniously from her place, waddled round the table and cuffed Jamie good-naturedly on the ear.

"So that's what became of my good physick, ye young wretch!" Hands on her hips, she wagged her head, making the green ear-bobbles wink like dragonflies. "The best lot I ever made too!"

"Oh, it was most effective," he assured her, laughing up at the massive dame.

"I should think so! When I think what that much physick must have done to your innards, lad, I hope it was worth it to ye. Ye canna have been much good to yourself for days after."

He shook his head, still laughing.

"I wasn't, but then, I wasna much good for what His Grace had in mind, either. He did not seem to mind at all when I begged leave to remove myself from his presence. But I knew I couldna do it twice, so as soon as the cramps eased up, I got a horse from the stables and lit out. It took a long time to get home, since I had to stop every ten minutes or so, but I made it by supper next day."

Dougal beckoned for a new jug of ale, which he passed down the board hand-to-hand to Jamie.

"Aye, your father sent word he thought perhaps you'd learned enough of castle life for the present," he said, smiling ruefully. "I thought there was a tone to his letter I did not quite understand at the time."

"Weel, I hope ye've laid up a new batch of fig syrup, Mrs. Fitz," Rupert interrupted, poking her familiarly in the ribs. "His Grace is like to be here in a day or two. Or are ye counting on your new wife to guard ye this time, Jamie?" He leered at me. "From all accounts, ye may need to guard *her*. I hear the Duke's servant does not share His Grace's preferences, though he's every bit as active."

Jamie pushed back the bench and rose from the table, handing me out. He put an arm around my shoulders and smiled back at Rupert.

"Well, then, I suppose the two of us will just have to fight it out back to back."

Rupert's eyes flew open in horrified dismay.

"Back to back!?" he exclaimed. "I knew we'd forgot to tell ye something before your wedding, lad! No wonder you've not got her with child yet!"

Jamie's hand tightened on my shoulder, turning me toward the archway, and we made our escape, pelted by a hail of laughter and bawdy advice.

In the dark hall outside, Jamie leaned against the stones, doubled over. Unable to stand, I sank to the ground at his feet and giggled helplessly.

"You didn't tell him, did you?" Jamie gasped at last.

I shook my head. "No, of course not." Still wheezing, I groped for his hand, and he hauled me upright. I collapsed against his chest.

"Let me see if I've got it right, now." He cupped my face between his hands and pressed his forehead to mine, face so close that his eyes blurred into one large blue orb and his breath was warm on my chin.

"Face to face. Is that it?" The fizz of laughter was dying down in my blood, replaced by something else just as potent.

I touched my tongue against his lips, while my hands busied themselves lower down.

"Faces are not the essential parts. But you're learning."

⟶

Next day, I was in my surgery, listening patiently to an elderly lady from the village, some relation to the soup cook, who was rather garrulously detailing her daughter-in-law's bout with the morbid sore throat which theoretically had something to do with her current complaint of quinsy, though I couldn't at the moment see the connection. A shadow fell across the doorway, interrupting the old lady's catalog of symptoms.

I looked up, startled, to see Jamie rush in, followed by Old Alec, both men looking worried and excited. Jamie unceremoniously removed the makeshift tongue depressor I was holding and pulled me to my feet, clasping both hands between his own.

"What—" I began, but was interrupted by Alec, peering over Jamie's shoulder at my hands, which Jamie was displaying to him.

"Aye, that's verra weel, but the arms, man? Has she the arm for it?"

"Look." Jamie grasped one of my hands and stretched my arm out straight, measuring it along one of his.

"Weel," said Alec, examining it doubtfully, "could do. Aye, it could."

"Would you care to tell me what you think you're doing?" I inquired, but before I could finish, I was being hustled down the stairs between the two men, leaving my aged patient to gape after us in perplexity.

A few moments later, I was dubiously eyeing the large, shiny, brown hind-quarters of a horse, located some six inches from my face. The problem had been made clear on the way to the stables, Jamie explaining and Old Alec -chiming in with remarks, imprecations, and interjections.

Losgann, customarily a good foaler, and a prize member of Colum's stable, was having trouble. This much I could see for myself; the mare lay on her side and periodically the shining on flanks heaved and the enormous body seemed to shiver. Down on hands and knees at the rear of the horse, I could see the lips of the vagina gape slightly with each contraction, but nothing further happened; no sight of tiny hoof or delicate wet nose appeared at the opening. The foal, a late one, was evidently presenting side-on or backward. Alec thought side-on, Jamie thought backward, and they paused to argue about it for a moment, until I impatiently called the meeting to order to ask what they expected me to do about it, in either case.

Jamie looked at me as though I were a bit simple. "Turn the foal, of course," he said patiently. "Bring the forelegs round so it can get out."

"Oh, is *that* all?" I looked at the horse. Losgann, whose elegant name actually meant "frog," was delicately boned for a horse, but bloody big for all that.

"Er, reach inside, you mean?" I glanced covertly at my hand. It probably would fit—the opening was big enough—but what then?

Both men's hands were clearly too big for the job. And Roderick, the stable lad who was usually pressed into service in such delicate situations, was, of course, immobilized with a splint and sling of my devising on his right arm—he had broken his arm two days before. Willie, the other stable lad, had gone to fetch Roderick, nonetheless, to give advice and moral encouragement. At this juncture, he arrived, clad in nothing but a pair of ragged breeches, thin chest glimmering whitely in the dim stable.

"It's hard work," he said dubiously, apprised of the situation and the suggestion that I substitute for him. "Tricky, ye ken. There's a knack to it, but it takes a bit of strength as well."

"Nay worry," said Jamie confidently. "Claire's stronger by far than you, ye poor weed. If you'll but tell her what to feel for and what to do, she'll have it round in no time."

I appreciated the vote of confidence, but was in no way so sanguine myself. Telling myself firmly that this was no worse than assisting at abdominal surgery, I retired to a stall to change my gown for breeches and a rough smock of sacking, and lathered my hand and arm up to the shoulder with greasy tallow soap.

"Well, over the top," I muttered under my breath, and slid my hand inside.

There was very little room to maneuver, and at first I couldn't tell what I was feeling. I closed my eyes to concentrate better, though, and groped cautiously. There were smooth expanses, and bumpy bits. The smooth parts would be body and the bumps legs or head. It was legs I wanted—forelegs, to be specific. Gradually I became accustomed to the feel of things, and the necessity for keeping quite still when a contraction came on; the amazingly powerful muscles of the uterus clamped down on my hand and arm like a vise, grinding my own bones very painfully until the constriction eased, and I could resume my groping.

At last, my fumbling fingers encountered something I was sure of.

"I've got my fingers in its nose!" I cried triumphantly. "I've found the head!"

"Good lass, good! Dinna let go!" Alec crouched anxiously alongside, patting the mare reassuringly as another contraction set in. I gritted my teeth and leaned my forehead against the shining rump as my wrist was crushed by the force. It eased, though, and I kept my grip. Feeling cautiously upward, I found the curve of eyesocket and brow, and the small ridge of the folded ear. Waiting through one more contraction, I followed the curve of the neck down to the shoulder.

"It's got its head turned back on its shoulder," I reported. "The head's pointing the right way, at least."

"Good." Jamie, at the horse's head, ran his hand soothingly down the sweating chestnut neck. "Likely the legs will be folded under the chest. See can you get a hand on one knee."

So it went on, feeling, fumbling, up to my shoulder in the warm darkness of the horse, feeling the awful force of the birth pangs and their grateful easing, struggling blindly to reach my goal. I felt rather as though I were giving birth myself, and bloody hard work it was, too.

At last I had my hand on a hoof; I could feel the rounded

surface, and the sharp edge of the yet-unused curve. Following the anxious, often contradictory instructions of my guides as best I could, I alternately pulled and pushed, easing the unwieldy mass of the foal around, bringing one foot forward, pushing another back, sweating and groaning along with the mare.

And then suddenly everything worked. A contraction eased, and all at once, everything slid smoothly into place. I waited, not moving, for the next contraction. It came, and a small wet nose popped suddenly out, pushing my hand out with it. The tiny nostrils flared briefly, as though interested in this new sensation, then the nose vanished.

"Next one will do it!" Alec was almost dancing in ecstasy, his arthritic form capering up and down in the hay. "Come on, Losgann. Come on, my sweet wee froggie!"

As though in answer, there was a convulsive grunt from the mare. Her hindquarters flexed sharply and the foal slid smoothly onto the clean hay in a slither of knobbly legs and big ears.

I sat back on the hay, grinning idiotically. I was covered with soap and slime and blood, exhausted and aching, and smelt strongly of the less pleasant aspects of horse. I was euphoric.

I sat watching as Willy and the one-handed Roderick tended the new arrival, wiping him down with wisps of straw. And cheered with the rest when Losgann turned and licked him, butting him gently and nosing him to stand at last on his huge, wobbly feet.

"A damn good job, lassie! *Damn* good!" Alec was exuberant, pumping my unslimed hand in congratulation. Suddenly realizing that I was swaying on my perch, and much less than presentable, he turned and barked at one of the lads to bring some water. Then he circled behind me and set his horny old hands on my shoulders. With an amazingly deft and gentle touch, he pressed and stroked, easing the strain in my shoulders, relaxing the knots in my neck.

"There, lassie," he said at last. "Hard work, no?" He smiled down at me, then beamed adoringly at the new colt.

"Bonny laddie," he crooned. "Who's a sweet lad, then?"

Jamie helped me to clean up and change. My fingers were too stiff to manage the buttons of my bodice, and I knew my entire arm would be blue with bruising by morning, but I felt thoroughly peaceful and contented.

───────

The rain seemed to have lasted forever, so that when a day finally dawned bright and fair, I squinted in the daylight like a newly emerged mole.

"Your skin is so fine I can see the blood moving beneath it," Jamie said, tracing the path of a sunbeam across my bare stomach. "I could follow the veins from your hand to your heart." He drew his finger gently up my wrist to the bend of the elbow, up the inner side of my upper arm, and across the slope below my collarbone.

"That's the subclavian vein," I remarked, looking down my nose at the path of his tracking finger.

"Is it? Oh, aye, because it's below your clavicle. Tell me some more." The finger moved slowly downward. "I like to hear the Latin names for things; I never dreamed it would be so pleasant to make love to a physician."

"That," I said primly, "is an areola, and you know it, because I told you last week."

"So ye did," he murmured. "And there's another one, fancy that." The bright head dipped to let his tongue replace the finger, then traveled lower.

"Umbilicus," I said with a short gasp.

"Um," he said, muffled lips stretching in a smile against my transparent skin. "And what's this, then?"

"You tell me," I said, clutching his head. But he was incapable of speech.

Later I lounged in my surgery chair, basking dreamily in memories of awaking in a bed of sunbeams, sheets tumbled in blinding shoals of white like the sands of a beach. One hand rested on my breast, and I toyed idly with the nipple, enjoying the feel of it rising against my palm beneath the thin calico of my bodice.

"Enjoying yourself?"

The sarcastic voice from the door brought me upright so quickly that I bumped my head on a shelf.

"Oh," I said, rather grumpily. "Geilie. Who else? What are you doing here?"

She glided into the surgery, moving as though on wheels. I knew she had feet; I'd seen them. What I couldn't figure out was where she put them when she walked.

"I came to bring Mrs. Fitz some saffron from Spain; she was wanting it against the Duke's coming."

"More spices?" I said, beginning to recover my good humor. "If the man eats half the things she's fixing for him, they'll need to roll him home."

"They could do that now. He's a wee round ball of a fellow, I've heard." Dismissing the Duke and his physique, she asked whether I'd like to join her for an expedition to the nearby foothills.

"I'm needing a bit of moss," she explained. She waved her long, boneless hands gracefully to and fro. "Makes a wonderful lotion for the hands, boiled in milk with a bit of sheep's wool."

I cast a look up at my slit window, where the dust motes were going mad in the golden light. A faint scent of ripe fruit and fresh-cut hay floated on the breeze.

"Why not?"

Waiting as I gathered my baskets and bottles together, Geilie strolled about my surgery, picking things up and putting them down at random. She stopped at a small table and picked up the object that lay there, frowning.

"What's this?"

I stopped what I was doing, and came to stand beside her. She was holding a small bundle of dried plants, tied with three twisted threads; black, white, and red.

"Jamie says it's an ill-wish."

"He's right. Where did ye come to get it?"

I told her about the finding of the small bundle in my bed.

"I went and found it under the window next day, where Jamie threw it. I meant to bring it round to your house and ask if you knew anything about it, but I forgot."

She stood tapping a fingernail thoughtfully against her front teeth, shaking her head.

"No, I canna say that I do. But there might be a way of finding out who left it for ye."

"Really?"

"Aye. Come to my house in the morning tomorrow, and I'll tell ye then."

Refusing to say more, she whirled about in a swirl of green cloak, leaving me to follow as I would.

She led me well up into the foothills, galloping when there was road enough to do so, walking when there wasn't. An hour's ride from the village, she stopped near a small brook, overhung by willows.

We forded the brook and wandered up into the foothills, gathering such late summer plants as still lingered, together with the ripening berries of early autumn and the thick yellow shelf fungus that sprouted from the trunks of trees in the small shady glens.

Geilie's figure disappeared into the bracken above me, as I paused to scrape a bit of aspen bark into my basket. The globules of dried sap on the papery bark looked like frozen drops of blood, the deep crimson refulgent with trapped sunlight.

A sound startled me out of my reverie, and I looked up the hill, in the direction it seemed to come from.

I heard the sound again; a high-pitched, mewling cry. It seemed to come from above, from a rocky notch near the crest of the hill. I set my basket down and began to climb.

"Geilie!" I shouted. "Come up here! Someone's left a baby!"

The sound of scrabbling and muttered imprecations preceded her up the hill, as she fought her way through the entangling bushes on the slope. Her fair face was flushed and cross and she had twigs in her hair.

"What in God's name—" she began, and then darted forward. "Christ's blood! Put it down!" She hastily snatched the baby from my arms, then laid it back where I had found it, in a small depression in the rock. The smooth, bowl-shaped hollow was less than a yard across. At one side of the hollow was a shallow wooden bowl, half-full of fresh milk, and at the baby's feet was a small bouquet of wildflowers, tied with a bit of red twine.

"But it's sick!" I protested, stooping toward the child again. "Who would leave a sick child up here by itself?"

The baby was plainly very ill; the small pinched face was greenish, with dark hollows under the eyes, and the little fists waved weakly under the blanket. The child had hung slack in my arms when I picked it up; I wondered that it had had the strength to cry.

"Its parents," Geilie said briefly, restraining me with a hand on my arm. "Leave it. Let's get out of here."

"Its parents?" I said indignantly. "But—"

"It's a changeling," she said impatiently. "Leave it and come. Now!"

Dragging me with her, she dodged back into the undergrowth. Protesting, I followed her down the slope until we arrived, breathless and red faced, at the bottom, where I forced her to stop.

"What is this?" I demanded. "We can't just abandon a sick child, out in the open like that. And what do you mean, it's a changeling?"

"A changeling," she said impatiently. "Surely you know what a changeling is? When the fairies steal a human child away, they leave one of their own in its place. You know it's a changeling because it cries and fusses all the time and doesn't thrive or grow."

"Of course I know what it is," I said. "But you don't believe that nonsense, do you?"

She shot me a sudden strange look, full of wary suspicion. Then the lines of her face relaxed into their normal expression of half-amused cynicism.

"No, I don't," she admitted. "But the folk here do." She glanced nervously up the slope, but no further sound came from the rocky notch. "The family will be somewhere near about. Let's go."

Reluctantly, I allowed her to tow me away in the direction of the village.

"Why did they put it up there?" I asked, sitting on a rock to remove my stockings before wading across a small stream.

"Do they hope the Wee Folk will come and cure it?" I was still bothered about the child; it seemed desperately ill. I didn't know what was wrong with it, but perhaps I could help.

Maybe I could leave Geilie in the village, then come back for the child. It would have to be soon, though; I glanced up at the eastern sky, where soft grey rain clouds were swiftly darkening into purple dusk. A pink glow still showed to the west, but there could be no more than half an hour's light left.

Geilie looped the twisted withy handle of her basket over her neck, picked up her skirt and stepped into the stream, shivering at the cold water.

"No," she said. "Or rather, yes. That's one of the fairies' hills, and it's dangerous to sleep there. If ye leave a changeling out overnight in such a place, the Folk will come and take it back, and leave the human child they've stolen in its place."

"But they won't, because it isn't a changeling," I said, sucking in my breath at the touch of the melted snow water. "It's only a sick child. It might very well not survive a night in the open!"

"It won't," she said briefly. "It will be dead by morning. And I hope to God no one saw us near it."

I stopped abruptly in the midst of putting on my shoes.

"Dead! Geilie, I'm going back for it. I can't leave it there." I turned and started back across the stream.

She caught me from behind and pushed me flat on my face into the shallow water. Floundering and gasping, I managed to rise to my knees, sloshing water in all directions. Geilie stood calf-deep in the stream, skirts soaked, glaring down at me.

"You bloody pig-headed English ass!" she shouted at me. "There's nothing ye can do! Do ye hear me? Nothing! That child's as good as dead! I'll not stand here and let ye risk your own life and mine for some crack-brained notion of yours!" Snorting and grumbling under her breath, she reached down and got me under the arms with both hands, lugging me to my feet.

"Claire," she said urgently, shaking me by the arms. "Listen to me. If ye go near that child and it dies—and it will, believe me, I've seen them like that—then the family will blame you for it. Do ye no see the danger of it? Don't ye know what they say about you in the village?"

I stood shivering in the cold breeze of sunset, torn between her obvious panic for my safety, and the thought of a helpless child, slowly dying alone in the dark, with wildflowers at its feet.

"No," I said, shaking the wet hair out of my face. "Geilie, no, I can't. I'll be careful, I promise, but I have to go." I pulled myself out of her grasp and turned toward the far bank, stumbling and splashing in the uncertain shadows of the streambed.

There was a muffled cry of exasperation from behind me, then a frenzied sploshing in the opposite direction. Well, at least she wouldn't hamper me further.

It was growing dark fast, and I pushed through the bushes and weeds as quickly as I could. I wasn't sure that I could find the right hill if it grew dark before I reached it; there were several nearby, all about the same height. And fairies or not, the thought of wandering about alone out here in the dark was not one I cared for. The question of how I was going to make it back to the Castle with a sick baby was something I would deal with when the time came.

I found the hill, finally, by spotting the stand of young larches I remembered at the base. It was nearly full dark by this time, a moonless night, and I stumbled and fell frequently. The larches stood huddled together, talking quietly in the evening breeze with clicks and creaks and rustling sighs.

Bloody place *is* haunted, I thought, listening to the leafy conversation overhead as I threaded my way through the slender trunks. I wouldn't be surprised to meet a ghost behind the next tree.

I *was* surprised, though. Actually, I was scared out of my wits when the shadowy figure slid out and grabbed me. I let out a piercing shriek and struck at it.

"Jesus Christ," I said, "what are you doing here?" I crumpled for a moment against Jamie's chest, relieved to see him, in spite of the fright he had given me.

He took me by the arm and turned to lead me out of the wood.

"Came for you," he said, low voiced. "I was coming to meet you because night was comin' on; I met Geillis Duncan near St. John's brook and she told me where you were."

"But the baby—" I began, turning back toward the hill.

"The child's dead," he said briefly, tugging me back. "I went up there first, to see."

I followed him then without demur, distressed over the child's death, but relieved that I would not, after all, have to face the climb to the fairies' crest or the long journey back alone. Oppressed by the dark and the whispering trees, I didn't speak until we had crossed the brook again. Still damp from the previous immersion, I didn't bother removing my stockings, but sloshed across regardless. Jamie, still dry, stayed that way by leaping from the bank to a central boulder that stood above the current, then vaulted to my bank like a broad-jumper.

"Have ye any idea how dangerous it is to be out alone at night like that, Sassenach?" he inquired. He didn't seem angry, just curious.

"No . . . I mean yes. I'm sorry if I worried you. But I *couldn't* leave a child out there, I just couldn't."

"Aye, I know." He hugged me briefly. "You've a kind heart, Sassenach. But you've no idea what you're dealing with, here."

"Fairies, hm?" I was tired, and disturbed over the incident, but covered it with flippancy. "I'm not afraid of superstitions." A thought struck me. "Do *you* believe in fairies, and changelings, and all that?"

He hesitated for a moment before answering.

"No. No, I dinna believe in such things, though damned if I'd care to sleep all night on a fairies' hill, for a' that. But I'm an educated man, Sassenach. I had a German tutor at Dougal's house, a good one, who taught me Latin and Greek and such, and later when I went to France at eighteen—well, I studied history and philosophy and I saw that there was a good deal more to the world than the glens and the moors, and the waterhorses in the lochs. But these people . . ." He waved an arm, taking in the darkness behind us.

"They've ne'er been more than a day's walk from the place they were born, except for a great thing like a clan Gathering, and that might happen twice in a lifetime. They live among the glens and the lochs, and they hear no more of the world than what Father Bain tells them in kirk of a Sunday. That and the old stories."

He held aside an alder branch and I stooped under it. We were on the deer trail Geilie and I had followed earlier, and I was heartened by this fresh evidence that he could find his way, even in the dark. Away from the fairies' hill, he spoke in his normal voice, only pausing occasionally to brush away some tangling growth from his path.

"Those tales are naught but entertainment in Gwyllyn's hands, when ye sit in the Hall drinking Rhenish wine." He preceded me down the path, and his voice floated back to me, soft and emphatic in the cool night air.

"Out here, though, and even in the village—nay, that's something else. Folk live by them. I suppose there's some truth behind some of them."

I thought of the amber eyes of the waterhorse, and wondered which others were true.

"And others . . . well," his voice grew softer, and I had to strain to hear him. "For the parents of that child, maybe it will ease them a bit to believe it is the changeling who died, and think of their own child, healthy and well, living forever with the fairies."

We reached the horses then, and within half an hour the lights of Castle Leoch shone through the darkness to welcome us. I had never thought I would consider that bleak edifice an outpost of advanced civilization, but just now the lights seemed those of a beacon of enlightenment.

It was not until we drew closer that I realized the impression of light was due to the string of lanterns blazing along the parapet of the bridge.

"Something's happened," I said, turning to Jamie. And seeing him for the first time in the light, I realized that he was not wearing his usual worn shirt and grubby kilt. His snowy

linen shone in the lantern light, and his best—his only—velvet
coat lay across his saddle.

"Aye," he nodded. "That's why I came to get you. The
Duke's come at last."

———

The Duke was something of a surprise. I don't know quite
what I had been expecting, but it wasn't the bluff, hearty, red-
faced sportsman I met in Leoch's hall. He had a pleasantly
blunt, weatherbeaten face, with light blue eyes that always
squinted slightly, as though looking into the sun after the
flight of a pheasant.

I wondered for a moment whether that earlier bit of theatrics regarding the Duke might have been overstated. Looking
around the hall, though, I noticed that every boy under eighteen wore a slightly wary expression, keeping his eyes fixed on
the Duke as he laughed and talked animatedly with Colum
and Dougal. Not merely theatrics, then; they had been
warned.

When I was presented to the Duke, I had some difficulty in
keeping a straight face. He was a big man, fit and solid, the
sort you so often see booming out their opinions in pubs,
bearing down the opposition by dint of loudness and repetition. I had been warned, of course, by Jamie's story, but the
physical impression was so overwhelming that when the Duke
bowed low over my hand and said, "But how charming to
find a countrywoman in this remote spot, mistress," in a voice
like an overwrought mouse, I had to bite the inside of my
cheek to keep from disgracing myself in public.

Worn out from travel, the Duke and his party retired early
to bed. The next night, though, there was music and conversation after dinner, and Jamie and I joined Colum, Dougal,
and the Duke. Sandringham grew expansive over Colum's
Rhenish wine, and talked volubly, expounding equally upon
the horrors of travel in the Highlands and the beauties of the
countryside. We listened politely, and I tried not to catch Jamie's eye as the Duke squeaked out the story of his travails.

"Broke an axle-tree outside of Stirling, and we were be-
calmed three days—*in* the pouring rain, mind you—before

my footman could find a blacksmith to come and repair the blasted thing. And not half a day later, we bounced into the most tremendous pothole I've ever seen and broke the damn thing again! And then one horse threw a shoe, and we had to unload the coach and walk beside it—*in* the mud—leading the lame nag. And *then* . . ." As the tale went on, from misfortune to misfortune, I felt an increasing urge to giggle, and attempted to drown it with more wine—possibly an error in judgment.

"But the game, MacKenzie, the game!" the Duke exclaimed at one point, rolling his eyes in ecstasy. "I could scarce believe it. No wonder you set such a table." He gently patted his large, solid stomach. "I swear I'd give my eyeteeth for a try at a stag like the one we saw two days ago; splendid beast, simply splendid. Leapt out of the brush right in front of the coach, m'dear," he confided to me. "Startled the horses so we near as a toucher went off the road *again*!"

Colum raised the bell-shaped decanter, with an inquiring cock of one dark brow. As he poured to the proffered glasses, he said, "Well, perhaps we might arrange a hunt for ye, Your Grace. My nephew's a bonny huntsman." He glanced sharply from under his brows at Jamie; there was a scarcely perceptible nod in response.

Colum sat back, replacing the decanter, and said casually, "Aye, that'll do well, then. Perhaps early next week. It's too early for pheasant, but the stag hunting will be fine." He turned to Dougal, lounging in a padded chair to one side. "My brother might go along; if you have it in mind to travel northwards, he can show ye the lands we were discussing earlier."

"Capital, capital!" The Duke was delighted. He patted Jamie on the leg; I saw the muscles tighten, but Jamie didn't move. He smiled tranquilly, and the Duke let his hand linger just a moment too long. Then His Grace caught my eye on him, and smiled jovially at me, his expression saying "Worth a try, eh?" Despite myself, I smiled back. Much to my surprise, I quite liked the man.

In the excitement of the Duke's arrival, I had forgotten Geilie's offer to help me discover the sender of the ill-wish. And after the unpleasant scene with the changeling child on the fairies' hill, I wasn't sure that I wanted to try anything she might suggest.

Still, curiosity overcame suspicion, and when Colum asked Jamie to ride down and escort the Duncans to the castle for the Duke's banquet two days later, I went with him.

Thus it was that Thursday found me and Jamie in the Duncans' parlor, being entertained with a sort of awkward friendliness by the fiscal, while his wife finished her dressing upstairs. Largely recovered from the effects of his last gastric attack, Arthur still did not look terribly healthy. Like many fat men who lose too much weight abruptly, the weight had gone from his face, rather than his stomach. His paunch still swelled the green silk of his waistcoat, while the skin of his face drooped in flabby folds.

"Perhaps I could slip upstairs and help Geilie with her hair or something," I suggested. "I've brought her a new ribbon." Foreseeing the possible need of an excuse for talking to Geilie alone, I had brought a small package with me. Producing it as an excuse, I was through the door and up the stairs before Arthur could protest.

She was ready for me.

"Come on," she said, "we'll go up to my private room for this. We'll have to hurry, but it won't take too long."

I followed Geilie up the narrow, twisting stair. The steps were irregular heights; some of the risers were so high I had to lift my skirts to avoid tripping on the way up. I concluded that seventeenth-century carpenters either had faulty methods of measuring or rich senses of humor.

Geilie's private sanctum was at the top of the house, in one of the remote attics above the servants' quarters. It was guarded by a locked door, opened by a truly formidable key that Geilie produced from her apron pocket; it must have been at least six inches long, with a broad fretwork head ornamented with a vine-and-flower pattern. The key must have weighed nearly a pound; held by the barrel, it would have made a good weapon. Both lock and hinges were well oiled, and the thick door swung inward silently.

The attic room was small, cramped by the gabled dormers that cut across the front of the house. Shelves lined every inch of wall space, holding jars, bottles, flasks, vials, and beakers. Bunches of drying herbs, carefully tied with threads of different colors, hung neatly in rows from the rafters overhead, brushing my hair with a fragrant dust as we passed beneath.

This was nothing like the clean, businesslike order of the herb room downstairs, though. It was crowded, almost cluttered, and dark in spite of the dormer windows.

One shelf held books, mostly old and crumbling, the spines unmarked. I ran a curious finger over the row of leather bindings. Most were calf, but there were two or three bound in something different; something soft, but unpleasantly oily to the touch. And one that to all appearances was bound in fish skin. I pulled a volume out and opened it gingerly. It was handwritten in a mixture of archaic French, and even more obsolete Latin, but I could make out the title. *L'Grimoire d'le Comte St. Germain.*

I closed the book and set it back on the shelf, feeling a slight shock. A grimoire. A handbook of magic. I could feel Geilie's gaze boring into my back, and turned to meet a mixture of mischief and wary speculation. What would I do, now that I knew?

"So it isn't a rumor, then, is it?" I said, smiling. "You really are a witch." I wondered just how far it went, and whether she believed it herself, or whether these were merely the trappings of an elaborate make-believe that she used to alleviate the boredom of marriage to Arthur. I also wondered just what sort of magic she practiced—or thought she practiced.

"Oh, white," she said, grinning. "Definitely white magic."

I thought ruefully that Jamie must be right about my face—*everyone* seemed to be able to tell what I was thinking.

"Well, that's good," I said. "I'm really not much of a one for dancing round bonfires at midnight and riding brooms, let alone kissing the devil's arse."

Geilie tossed back her hair and laughed delightedly.

"Ye don't kiss anyone's much, that I can see," she said.

"Nor do I. Though if I had a sweet fiery devil like yours in my bed, I'll not say I might not come to it in time."

"That reminds me—" I began, but she had already turned away, and was about her preparations, murmuring to herself.

Checking first to see that the door was securely locked behind us, Geilie crossed to the gabled window and rummaged in a chest built into the window seat. She pulled out a large, shallow pan and a tall white candle stuck in a pottery holder. A further foray produced a worn quilt, which she spread on the floor as protection against dust and splinters.

"What exactly is it you're planning to do, Geilie?" I asked, examining the preparations suspiciously. Off-hand, I couldn't see much sinister intent in a pan, a candle, and a quilt, but then I was a novice magician, to say the least.

"Summoning," she said, tugging the corners of the quilt around so that the sides lay straight with the boards of the floor.

"Summoning whom?" I asked. Or what.

She stood and brushed her hair back. Baby-fine and slippery, it was coming down from its fastenings. Muttering, she yanked the pins from her hair and let it fall down in a straight, shiny curtain, the color of heavy cream.

"Oh, ghosts, spirits, visions. Anything ye might have need of," she said. "It starts the same in any case, but the herbs and the words are different for each thing. What we want now is a vision—to see who it is who's ill-wished ye. Then we can turn the ill-wish back upon them."

"Er, well . . ." I really had no wish to be vindictive, but I *was* curious—both to see what summoning was like, and to know who had left me the ill-wish.

Setting the pan in the middle of the quilt, she poured water into it from a jug, explaining, "You can use any vessel big enough to make a good reflection, though the grimoire says to use a silver *bassin.* Even a pond or a puddle of water outside will do for some kinds of summoning, though it must be secluded. Ye need peace and quiet to do this."

She passed rapidly from window to window, drawing the heavy black curtains until virtually all the light in the room was extinguished. I could barely see Geilie's slender form flitting through the gloom, until she lit the candle. The wavering flame lit her face as she carried it back to the quilt, throwing wedge-shaped shadows under the bold nose and chiseled jaw.

She set the candle next to the pan of water, on the side away from me. She filled the pan very carefully, so full that the water bulged slightly above the rim, kept from spilling by its surface tension. Leaning over, I could see that the surface of the water provided an excellent reflection, far better than that obtainable in any of the Castle's looking glasses. As though mind reading again, Geilie explained that in addition to its use in summoning spirits, the reflecting pan was an excellent accessory for dressing the hair.

"Don't bump into it, or you'll get soaked," she advised, frowning in concentration as she lit the candle. Something about the practical tone of the remark, so prosaic in the midst of these supernatural preparations, reminded me of someone. Looking up at the slender, pallid figure, stooping elegantly over the tinderbox, I couldn't think at first of whom she reminded me. But of course. While no one could be less like that dowdy figure athwart the teapot in Reverend Wakefield's study, the tone of voice had been that of Mrs. Graham, exactly.

Perhaps it was an attitude they shared, a pragmatism that regarded the occult as merely a collection of phenomena like the weather. Something to be approached with cautious respect, of course—much as one would take care in using a sharp kitchen knife—but certainly nothing to avoid or fear.

Or it might have been the smell of lavender water. Geilie's loose, flowing gowns smelled always of the essences she distilled: marigold, chamomile, bay leaf, spikenard, mint, marjoram. Today, though, it was lavender that drifted from the folds of the white dress. The same scent that permeated Mrs. Graham's practical blue cotton and wafted from the corrugations of her bony chest.

If Geilie's chest was likewise underlaid by such skeletal supports, there was no hint of it visible, in spite of her robe's low neckline. It was the first time I had seen Geilie Duncan *en déshabillé;* customarily she wore the severe and voluminous gowns, buttoned high at the neck, that were suitable to the wife of a fiscal. The swelling opulence now revealed was a surprise, a creamy abundance almost the same shade as the dress she wore, and gave me some idea why a man like Arthur Duncan might have married a penniless girl of no family. My eye went involuntarily to the line of neatly labeled jars along the wall, looking for saltpeter.

Geilie selected three of the jars from the shelf, pouring a small quantity from each into the bowl of a tiny metal brazier. She lit the layer of charcoal underneath from the candle flame, and blew on the dawning flame to encourage it. A fragrant smoke began to rise as the spark took hold.

The air in the attic was so still that the greyish smoke rose straight up without diffusing, forming a column that echoed the shape of the tall white candle. Geilie sat between the two columns like a priestess in her temple, legs folded gracefully under her.

"Well then, that will do nicely, I think." Briskly dusting crumbs of rosemary from her fingers, Geilie surveyed the scene with satisfaction. The black drapes, with their mystic symbols, shut out all intrusive beams of sunlight, and left the candle as the only source of direct illumination. The flame was reflected and diffused through the pan of still water, which seemed to glow as though it, too, were a source rather than a reflection of light.

"What now?" I inquired.

The large grey eyes glowed like the water, alight with anticipation. She waved her hands across the surface of the water, then folded them between her legs.

"Just sit quiet for a moment," she said. "Listen to your heartbeat. Do you hear it? Breathe easy, slow and deep." In spite of the liveliness of her expression, her voice was calm and slow, a distinct contrast to her usual sprightly conversation.

I obediently did as she instructed, feeling my heart slow as my breathing steadied to an even rhythm. I recognized the scent of rosemary in the smoke, but I wasn't sure of the other two herbs; foxglove, perhaps, or cinquefoil? I had thought the purple flowers were those of nightshade, but surely that couldn't be. Whatever they were, the slowness of my breathing did not seem to be attributable only to the power of

Geilie's suggestion. I felt as though a weight were pressing against my breastbone, slowing my breathing without my having to will it.

Geilie herself sat perfectly still, watching me with unblinking eyes. She nodded, once, and I looked down obediently into the still surface of the water.

She began to talk, in an even, conversational way that reminded me again of Mrs. Graham, calling down the sun in the circle of stones.

The words were not English, and yet not quite *not* English, either. It was a strange tongue, but one I felt that I should know, as though the words were spoken just below the level of my hearing.

I felt my hands begin to go numb, and wanted to move them from their folded position in my lap, but they wouldn't move. Her even voice went on, soft and persuading. Now I *knew* that I understood what was being said, but still could not summon the words to the surface of my mind.

I realized dimly that I was either being hypnotized, or under the influence of some drug, and my mind took some last foothold on the edge of conscious thought, resisting the pull of the sweet-scented smoke. I could see my reflection in the water, pupils shrunk to pinpoints, eyes wide as a sun-blind owl's. The word "opium" drifted through my fading thoughts.

"Who are you?" I couldn't tell which of us had asked the question, but I felt my own throat move as I answered, "Claire."

"Who sent you here?"

"I came."

"Why did you come?"

"I can't tell."

"Why can't you tell?"

"Because no one will believe me."

The voice in my head grew still more soothing, friendly, beguiling.

"I will believe you. Believe me. Who are you?"

"Claire."

A sudden loud noise broke the spell. Geilie started and her

knee bumped the bassin, startling the reflection back into the water.

"Geillis? My dear?" A voice called through the door, tentative yet commanding. "We must be going, my dear. The horses are ready, and you're not yet gowned."

Muttering something rude under her breath, Geilie rose and flung open the window, so that the fresh air rushed into my face, making me blink and dispelling some of the fog in my head.

She stood looking down at me speculatively, then stooped to help me up.

"Come along, then," she said. "Come over a bit queer, have you? Sometimes it takes folk that way. You'd best lie down on my bed while I dress."

I lay flat on the coverlet in her bedroom below, eyes closed, listening to the small rustling noises Geilie made in her privy closet, wondering what the hell *that* had been all about. Nothing to do with the ill-wish or its sender, clearly. Only with my identity. With sharpness returning gradually to my wits, it occurred to me to wonder whether Geilie perhaps was a spy for Colum. Placed as she was, she heard the business and the secrets of the whole district. And who, other than Colum, would be so interested in my origins?

What would have happened, I wondered, had Arthur not interrupted the summoning? Would I have heard, somewhere in the scented fog, the standard hypnotist's injunction, "When you wake, you will remember nothing"? But I did remember, and I wondered.

In the event, however, there was no chance to ask Geilie about it. The bedroom door flew open, and Arthur Duncan came in. Crossing to the door of the privy closet, he knocked once, hastily, and went in.

There was a small startled scream from within, and then dead silence.

Arthur Duncan reappeared in the door, eyes wide and staring-blind, face so white that I thought perhaps he was suffering an attack of some sort. I leapt to my feet and hurried toward him as he leaned heavily against the door jamb.

Before I reached him, though, he pushed himself away

from the door and went out of the room, staggering slightly, pushing past me as though he didn't see me.

I knocked on the door myself.

"Geilie! Are you all right?"

There was a moment's silence, then a perfectly composed voice said, "Aye, of course. I'll be out in a moment."

When we at length descended the stairs, we found Arthur, apparently somewhat recovered, sipping brandy with Jamie. He seemed a bit abstracted, as though he were thinking of something, but greeted his wife with a mild compliment on her appearance, before sending the groom for the horses.

The banquet was just beginning as we arrived, and the fiscal and his wife were shown to their places of honor at the head table. Jamie and I, somewhat lower in status, took our places at a table with Rupert and Ned Gowan.

Mrs. Fitz had surpassed herself, and beamed in gratification at the compliments heaped upon the food, the drink, and other preparations.

It was in fact delicious. I had never tasted roast pheasant stuffed with honeyed chestnuts, and was helping myself to a third slice, when Ned Gowan, watching in some amusement at my appetite, asked whether I had yet tried the suckling pig.

My reply was interrupted by a stir at the far end of the Hall. Colum had risen from his table, and was headed toward me, accompanied by Old Alec MacMahon.

"I see there is no end to your talents, Mistress Fraser," Colum remarked, bowing slightly. A broad smile marked the arresting features.

"From dressing wounds and healing the sick to delivering foals. We shall be calling upon you to raise the dead before long, I suppose." There was a general chuckle at this, though I noticed one or two men glancing nervously in the direction of Father Bain, in attendance this evening, who was methodically stuffing himself with roast mutton in the corner.

"In any case," Colum continued, reaching into his coat pocket, "you must allow me to present you with a small token of my gratitude." He handed me a small wooden box, lid carved with the MacKenzie badge. I hadn't realized just how valuable a horse Losgann was, and mentally thanked whatever benign spirits presided over such events that nothing had gone wrong.

"Nonsense," I said, trying to give it back. "I didn't do anything out of the way. It was only luck that I have small hands."

"Nevertheless." Colum was firm. "If you prefer, consider it a small wedding gift, but I wish you to have it."

At a nod from Jamie, I reluctantly accepted the box and opened it. It contained a beautiful rosary of jet, each bead intricately carved, and the crucifix inlaid with silver.

"It's lovely," I said sincerely. And it was, though I had no notion what I might do with it. Though nominally a Catholic, I had been raised by Uncle Lamb, the completest of agnostics, and had only the vaguest idea of the significance of a rosary. Nonetheless, I thanked Colum warmly, and gave the rosary to Jamie to keep for me in his sporran.

I curtsied to Colum, gratified to find that I was mastering the art of doing so without falling on my face. He opened his mouth to take a gracious leave, but was interrupted by a sudden crash that came from behind me. Turning, I could see nothing but backs and heads, as people leapt from their benches to gather round whatever had caused the uproar. Colum made his way with some difficulty around the table, clearing aside the crowd with an impatient wave of the hand. As people stepped respectfully out of his way, I could see the rotund form of Arthur Duncan on the floor, limbs flailing convulsively, batting away the helpful hands of would-be assistants. His wife pushed her way through the muttering throng, dropped to the floor beside him, and made a vain attempt to cradle his head in her lap. The stricken man dug his heels into the floor and arched his back, making gargling, choking noises.

Glancing up, Geilie's green eyes anxiously scanned the crowd as though looking for someone. Assuming that I was the one she was looking for, I took the path of least resistance, dodging under the table and crawling across on hands and knees.

Reaching Geilie's side, I grabbed her husband's face between my hands and tried to pry his jaws open. I thought, from the sounds he was making, that he had perhaps choked on a piece of meat, which might still be lodged in his wind-pipe.

His jaws were clamped and rigid, though, lips blue and flecked with a foamy spittle that didn't seem consistent with choking. Choking he surely was, though; the plump chest heaved vainly, fighting for breath.

"Quickly, turn him on his side," I said. Several hands reached out at once to help, and the heavy body was deftly turned, broad black-serge back toward me. I drove the heel of my hand hard between the shoulder-blades, smacking him repeatedly with a dull thumping noise. The massive back quivered slightly with the blows, but there was no answering jerk as of an obstruction suddenly released.

I gripped a meaty shoulder and pulled him onto his back once more. Geilie bent close over the staring face, calling his name, massaging his mottled throat. The eyes were rolled back now, and the drumming heels began to slacken their beat. The hands, clawed in agony, suddenly flung wide, smacking an anxiously crouching onlooker in the face.

The sputtering noises abruptly ceased, and the stout body went limp, lying inert as a sack of barley on the stone flags. I felt frantically for a pulse in one slack wrist, noticing with half an eye that Geilie was doing the same, pulling up the round, shaven chin and pressing her fingertips hard into the flesh under the angle of the jaw in search of the carotid artery.

Both searches were futile. Arthur Duncan's heart, already taxed by the necessity of pumping blood through that massive frame for so many years, had given up the struggle.

I tried all the resuscitative techniques at my disposal, useless though I knew them now to be: arm-flapping, chest-massage, even mouth-to-mouth breathing, distasteful as that was, but with the expected result. Arthur Duncan was dead as a door-nail.

I straightened wearily and stood back, as Father Bain, with a nasty glare at me, dropped to his knees by the fiscal's side and began hastily to administer the final rites. My back and arms ached, and my face felt oddly numb. The hubbub around me seemed strangely remote, as though a curtain separated me from the crowded hall. I closed my eyes and rubbed a hand across my tingling lips, trying to erase the taste of death.

———

Despite the death of the fiscal, and the subsequent formalities of obsequies and burial, the Duke's stag hunt was delayed by no more than a week.

The realization of Jamie's imminent departure was deeply depressing; I suddenly realized just how much I looked forward to seeing him at dinner after the day's work, how my heart would leap when I saw him unexpectedly at odd moments during the day, and how much I depended on his company and his solid, reassuring presence amid the complexities of life in the castle. And, to be perfectly honest, how much I liked the smooth, warm strength of him in my bed each night, and waking to his tousled, smiling kisses in the mornings. The prospect of his absence was bleak.

He held me closely, my head snuggled under his chin.

"I'll miss you, Jamie," I said softly.

He hugged me tighter, and gave a rueful chuckle.

"So will I, Sassenach. I hadna expected it, to tell the truth —but it will hurt me to leave ye." He stroked my back gently, fingers tracing the bumps of the vertebrae.

"Jamie . . . you'll be careful?"

I could feel the deep rumble of amusement in his chest as he answered.

"Of the Duke or the horse?" He was, much to my apprehension, intending to ride Donas on the stag hunt. I had visions of the huge sorrel beast plunging over a cliff out of sheer wrong-headedness, or trampling Jamie under those lethal hooves.

"Both," I said dryly. "If the horse throws you and you break a leg, you'll be at the Duke's mercy."

"True. Dougal will be there, though."

I snorted. "He'll break the other leg."

He laughed and bent his head to kiss me.

"I'll careful, *mo duinne*. Will ye give me the same promise?"

"Yes," I said, meaning it. "Do you mean whoever left the ill-wish?"

The momentary amusement was gone now.

"Perhaps. I dinna think you're in any danger, or I wouldna leave ye. But still . . . oh, and stay away from Geillis Duncan."

"What? Why?" I drew back a little to look up at him. It was a dark night and his face was invisible, but his tone was altogether serious.

"The woman's known as a witch, and the stories about her —well, they've got a deal worse since her husband died. I dinna want ye anywhere near her, Sassenach."

"Do you honestly think she's a witch?" I demanded. His strong hands cupped my bottom and scooped me in close to him. I put my arms around him, enjoying the feel of his smooth, solid torso.

"No," he said finally. "But it isna what *I* think that could be a danger to ye. Will ye promise?"

"All right." In truth, I had little reluctance to give the promise; since the incidents of the changeling and the summoning, I had not felt much desire to visit Geilie. I put my mouth on Jamie's nipple, flicking it lightly with my tongue. He made a small sound deep in his throat and pulled me nearer.

"Open your legs," he whispered. "I mean to be sure you'll remember me while I'm gone."

Sometime later, I woke feeling cold. Groping sleepily for the quilt, I couldn't find it. Suddenly it came up over me of its own accord. Surprised, I raised up on one elbow to look.

"I'm sorry," Jamie said. "I didna mean to wake ye, lass."

"What are you doing? Why are you awake?" I squinted over my shoulder at him. It was still dark, but my eyes were so accustomed that I could see the faintly sheepish expression on his face. He was wide awake, sitting on a stool by the side of the bed, his plaid flung around him for warmth.

"It's only . . . well, I dreamed you were lost, and I couldna find ye. It woke me, and . . . I wanted to look at ye, is all. To fix ye in my mind, to remember while I'm gone. I turned back the quilt; I'm sorry you were chilled."

"It's all right." The night was cold, and very quiet, as though we were the only two souls in the world. "Come into bed. You must be chilled too."

He slid in next to me and curled himself against my back. His hands stroked me from neck to shoulder, waist to hip, tracing the lines of my back, the curves of my body.

"Mo duinne," he said softly. "But now I should say *mo airgeadach.* My silver one. Your hair is silver-gilt and your skin is white velvet. *Calman geal.* White dove."

I pressed my hips back against him, inviting, and settled against him with a sigh as his solid hardness filled me. He held me against his chest and moved with me, slowly, deeply. I gasped a little and he slackened his hold.

"I'm sorry," he murmured. "I didna mean to hurt ye. But I do want to be in you, to stay in you, so deep. I want to leave the feel of me deep inside ye with my seed. I want to hold ye so and stay wi' you 'til dawn, and leave you sleeping and go, with the shapes of you warm in my hands."

I pressed firmly back against him.

"You won't hurt me."

After Jamie's departure, I moped about the castle. I saw patients in the surgery, I occupied myself as much as I could in the gardens, and I tried to distract myself by browsing in Colum's library, but still time hung heavy on my hands.

I had been alone nearly two weeks, when I met the girl Laoghaire in the corridor outside the kitchens. I had watched her covertly now and then, since the day when I had seen her on the landing outside Colum's study. She seemed blooming enough, but there was an air of tenseness about her that was easily discernible. She seemed distracted and moody—and little wonder, poor girl, I thought kindly.

Today, though, she looked somewhat excited.

"Mrs. Fraser!" she said. "I've a message for you." The widow Duncan, she said, had sent word that she was ill, and requested me to come and tend her.

I hesitated, remembering Jamie's injunctions, but the twin forces of compassion and boredom were sufficient to set me on the road to the village within the hour, my medicine box strapped behind me on the horse's saddle.

The Duncans' house when I arrived had an air of neglected abandon, a sense of disorder that extended through the house itself. There was no answer to my knock, and when I pushed the door open, I found the entry hall and parlor scattered with books and dirty glasses, mats askew and dust thick on the furniture. My calls produced no maidservant, and the kitchen proved to be as empty and disordered as the rest of the house.

Increasingly anxious, I went upstairs. The bedroom in front also was vacant, but I heard a faint shuffling noise from the stillroom across the landing.

Pushing open the door, I saw Geilie, sitting in a comfortable chair, feet propped on the counter. She had been drinking; there was a glass and decanter on the counter, and the room smelled strongly of brandy.

She was startled to see me, but struggled to her feet, smiling. Her eyes were slightly out of focus, I thought, but she certainly seemed well enough.

"What's the matter?" I asked. "Aren't you ill?"

She goggled at me in amazement. "Ill? Me? No. The servants have all left, and there's no food in the house, but there's plenty of brandy. Will ye have a drop?" She turned back toward the decanter. I grabbed her sleeve.

"You didn't send for me?"

"No." She stared at me, wide-eyed.

"Then why—" My question was interrupted by a noise from outside. A far-off, rumbling, muttering sort of noise. I had heard it before, from this room, and my palms had grown sweaty then at the thought of confronting the mob that made it.

I wiped my hands on the skirts of my dress. The rumbling was nearer, and there was neither need nor time for questions.

25

Thou Shalt Not Suffer a Witch to Live

The drab-clad shoulders ahead of me parted on darkness. My elbow struck wood with a bone-numbing thump as I was shoved roughly over a threshold of some sort, and I fell headlong into a black stench, alive and wriggling with unseen forms. I shrieked and thrashed, trying to free myself from entanglement with innumerable scrabbling tiny feet and an attack by something larger, that squealed and struck me a hard blow on the thigh.

I succeeded in rolling away, though only a foot or two before I hit an earthen wall that sent a shower of dirt cascading down on my head. I huddled as close to it as I could get, trying to suppress my own gasping breath so that I could hear whatever was trapped in this reeking pit with me. Whatever it was, was large, and breathing hoarsely, but not growling. A pig, perhaps?

"Who's there?" came a voice from the Stygian black, sounding scared but defiantly loud. "Claire, is it you?"

"Geilie!" I gasped and groped toward her, meeting her hands likewise searching. We clasped each other tightly, rocking slightly back and forth in the gloom.

"Is there anything else in here besides us?" I asked, glancing cautiously around. Even with my eyes now accustomed to the dark, there was precious little to be seen. There were faint streaks of light coming from somewhere above, but the tene-

brous shadows were shoulder-high here below; I could barely
make out Geilie's face, level with my own and only a few
inches away.

She laughed, a little shakily. "Several mice, I think, and
other vermin. And a smell that would knock a ferret over."

"I noticed the smell. Where in God's name are we?"

"The thieves' hole. Stand back!"

There was a grating sound from overhead and a sudden
shaft of light. I pressed myself against the wall, barely in time
to avoid a shower of mud and filth that cascaded through a
small opening in the roof of our prison. A single soft plop
followed the deluge. Geilie bent and picked up something
from the floor. The opening above remained, and I could see
that what she held was a small loaf, stale and smeared with
assorted muck. She dusted it gingerly with a fold of her skirt.

"Dinner," she said. "Hungry, are you?"

◄━━

The hole above remained open, and empty, save for the
occasional missile flung by a passerby. The drizzle came in,
and a searching wind. It was cold, damp, and thoroughly miserable. Suitable, I supposed, for the malefactors it was meant
to house. Thieves, vagrants, blasphemers, adulterers . . . and
suspected witches.

Geilie and I huddled together for warmth against one wall,
not speaking much. There was little to say, and precious little
either of us could do for ourselves, beyond possess our souls
in patience.

The hole above grew gradually darker as the night came on,
until it faded into the black all around.

◄━━

"How long do you think they mean to keep us here?"

Geilie shifted, stretching her legs so that the small oblong
of morning light from above shone on the striped linen of her
skirt. Originally a fresh pink and white, it was now considerably the worse for wear.

"Not too long," she said. "They'll be waiting for the ecclesiastical examiners. Arthur had letters last month, arranging

for it. The second week of October, it was. They should be here any time."

She rubbed her hands together to warm them, then put them on her knees, in the little square of sunlight.

"Tell me about the examiners," I said. "What will happen, exactly?"

"I canna say, exactly. I've ne'er seen a witch trial, though I've heard of them, of course." She paused a moment, considering. "They'll not be expecting a witch trial, since they were coming to try some land disputes. So they'll not have a witch-pricker, at least."

"A what?"

"Witches canna feel pain," Geilie explained. "Nor do they bleed when they're pricked." The witch-pricker, equipped with a variety of pins, lancets, and other pointed implements, was charged with testing for this condition. I vaguely recalled something of this from Frank's books, but had thought it a practice common to the seventeenth century, not this one. On the other hand, I thought wryly, Cranesmuir was not exactly a hotbed of civilization.

"In that case, it's too bad there won't be one," I said, though recoiling slightly at the thought of being stabbed repeatedly. "We could pass that test with no difficulty. Or I could," I added caustically. "I imagine they'd get ice water, not blood, when they tried it on you."

"I'd not be too sure," she said reflectively, overlooking the insult. "I've heard of witch-prickers with special pins—made to collapse when they're pressed against the skin, so it looks as though they don't go in."

"But why? Why try to prove someone a witch on purpose?"

The sun was on the decline now, but the afternoon light was enough to suffuse our hutch with a dim glow. The elegant oval of Geilie's face showed only pity for my innocence.

"Ye still dinna understand, do ye?" she said. "They mean to kill us. And it doesna matter much what the charge is, or what the evidence shows. We'll burn, all the same."

The night before, I had been too shocked from the mob's attack and the misery of our surroundings to do more than huddle with Geilie and wait for the dawn. With the light, though, what remained of my spirit was beginning to awake.

"Why, Geilie?" I asked, feeling rather breathless. "Do you know?" The atmosphere in the hole was thick with the stench of rot, filth, and damp soil, and I felt as though the impenetrable earthen walls were about to cave in upon me like the sides of an ill-dug grave.

I felt rather than saw her shrug; the shaft of light from above had moved with the sun, and now struck the wall of our prison, leaving us in cold dark below.

"If it's much comfort to ye," she said dryly, "I misdoubt ye were meant to be taken. It's a matter between me and Colum —you had the ill-luck to be with me when the townsfolk came. Had ye been wi' Colum, you'd likely have been safe enough, Sassenach or no."

The term "Sassenach," spoken in its usual derogatory sense, suddenly struck me with a sense of desperate longing for the man who called me so in affection. I wrapped my arms around my body, hugging myself to contain the lonely panic that threatened to envelop me.

"Why did you come to my house?" Geilie asked curiously.

"I thought you had sent for me. One of the girls at the castle brought me a message—from you, she said."

"Ah," she said thoughtfully. "Laoghaire, was it?"

I sat down and rested my back against the earth wall, despite my revulsion for the muddy, stinking surface. Feeling my movement, Geilie shifted closer. Friends or enemies, we were each other's only source of warmth in the hole; we huddled together perforce.

"How did you know it was Laoghaire?" I asked, shivering.

" 'Twas her that left the ill-wish in your bed," Geilie replied. "I told ye at the first there were those minded your taking the red-haired laddie. I suppose she thought if ye were gone, she'd have a chance at him again."

I was struck dumb at this, and it took a moment to find my voice.

"But she couldn't!"

Geilie's laugh was hoarsened by cold and thirst, but still held that edge of silver.

"Anyone seein' the way the lad looks at ye would know that. But I dinna suppose she's seen enough o' the world to ken such things. Let her lie wi' a man once or twice, and she'll know, but not now."

"That's not what I meant!" I burst out. "It isn't Jamie she wants; the girl's with child by Dougal MacKenzie."

"What?!" She was genuinely shocked for a moment, and her fingers bit into the flesh of my arm. "How d'ye come to think that?"

I told her of seeing Laoghaire on the stair below Colum's study, and the conclusions I had come to.

Geilie snorted.

"Pah! She heard Colum and Dougal talking about me; that's what made her blench—she'd think Colum had heard she'd been to me for the ill-wish. He'd have her whipped to bleeding for that; he doesna allow any truck wi' such arts."

"*You* gave her the ill-wish?" I was staggered.

Geilie drew herself sharply away at this.

"I didn't *give* it to her, no. I sold it to her."

I stared, trying to meet her eyes through the gathering darkness.

"There's a difference?"

"Of course there is." She spoke impatiently. "It was a matter of business, was all. And I don't give away my customers' secrets. Besides, she didna tell me who it was meant for. And you'll remember that I did try to warn ye."

"Thanks," I said with some sarcasm. "But . . ." my brain was churning, trying to rearrange my ideas in light of this new information. "But if she put the ill-wish in my bed, then it was Jamie she wanted. That *would* explain her sending me to your house. But what about Dougal?"

Geilie hesitated for a moment, then seemed to come to some decision.

"The girl's no more wi' child by Dougal MacKenzie than you are."

"How can you be so sure?"

She groped for my hand in the darkness. Finding it, she

drew it close and placed it squarely on the swelling bulge beneath her gown.

"Because I am," she said simply.

"Not Laoghaire then," I said. "You."

"Me." She spoke quite simply, without any of her usual affectation. "What was it Colum said—'I'll see that she's done rightly by'? Well, I suppose this is his idea of a suitable disposal of the problem."

I was silent for a long time, mulling things over.

"Geilie," I said at last, "that stomach trouble of your husband's . . ."

She sighed. "White arsenic," she said. "I thought it would finish him before the child began to show too much, but he hung on longer than I thought possible."

I remembered the look of mingled horror and realization on Arthur Duncan's face as he burst out of his wife's closet on the last day of his life.

"I see," I said. "He didn't know you were with child until he saw you half-dressed, the day of the Duke's banquet. And when he found out . . . I suppose he had good reason to know it wasn't his?"

There was a faint laugh from the far corner.

"The saltpeter came dear, but it was worth every farthing."

I shuddered slightly, hunched against the wall.

"But that's why you had to risk killing him in public, at the banquet. He would have denounced you as an adulteress— and a poisoner. Or do you think he realized about the arsenic?"

"Oh, Arthur knew," she said. "He wouldna admit it, to be sure—not even to himself. But he knew. We'd sit across the board from each other at supper, and I'd ask, 'Will ye have a bit more o' the cullen skink, my dear?' or 'A sup of ale, my own?' And him watching me, with those eyes like boiled eggs, and he'd say no, he didna feel himself with an appetite just then. And he'd push his plate back, and later I'd hear him in the kitchen, secret-like, gobbling his food standing by the hutch, thinking himself safe, because he ate no food that came from my hand."

Her voice was light and amused as though she had been recounting some bit of juicy gossip. I shuddered again, drawing away from the thing that shared the darkness with me.

"He didna guess it was in the tonic he took. He'd take no medicine I made; ordered a patent tonic from London—cost the earth too." Her voice was resentful at the extravagance. "The stuff had arsenic in it to start; he didna notice any difference in the taste when I added a bit more."

I had always heard that vanity was the besetting weakness of murderers; it seemed this was true, for she went on, ignoring our situation in the pride of recounting her accomplishments.

"It was a bit risky, to kill him before the whole company like that, but I had to manage something quickly." Not arsenic, either, to kill like that. I remembered the fiscal's hard blue lips and the numbness of my own where they had touched him. A quick and deadly poison.

And here I had thought that Dougal was confessing to an affair with Laoghaire. But in that case, while Colum might be disapproving, there would have been nothing to prevent Dougal marrying the girl. He was a widower, and free.

But an adulterous affair, with the wife of the fiscal? That was a different kettle of fish for all concerned. I seemed to recall that the penalties for adultery were severe. Colum could hardly smooth over an affair of that magnitude, but I couldn't see him condemning his brother to public whipping or banishment. And Geilie might well consider murder a reasonable alternative to being burnt on the face with a hot iron and shut up for several years in a prison, pounding hemp for twelve hours a day.

So she had taken her preventive measures, and Colum had taken his. And here was I, caught up in the middle.

"The child, though?" I asked. "Surely . . ."

There was a grim chuckle in the blackness. "Accidents happen, my friend. To the best of us. And once it happened . . ." I felt rather than saw her shrug. "I meant to get rid of it, but then I thought it might be a way to make him marry me, once Arthur was dead."

A horrible suspicion struck me.

"But Dougal's wife was still alive, then. Geillis, did you—?"

Her dress rustled as she shook her head, and I caught a faint gleam from her hair.

"I meant to," she said. "But God saved me the trouble. I rather thought that was a sign, you know. And it might all have worked nicely, too, if not for Colum MacKenzie."

I hugged my elbows against the cold. I was talking now only for distraction.

"Was it Dougal you wanted, or only his position and money?"

"Oh, I had plenty of money," she said, with a note of satisfaction. "I knew where Arthur kept the key to all his papers and notes, ye ken. And the man wrote a fair hand, I'll say that for him—'twas simple enough to forge his signature. I'd managed to divert near on to ten thousand pound over the last two years."

"But what for?" I asked, completely startled.

"For Scotland."

"What?" For a moment, I thought I had misheard. Then I decided that one of us was possibly a trifle unbalanced. And going on the evidence to hand, it wasn't me.

"What do you mean, Scotland?" I asked cautiously, drawing away a bit. I wasn't sure just how unstable she was; perhaps pregnancy had unhinged her mind.

"Ye needna fear; I'm not mad." The cynical amusement in her voice made me flush, grateful for the darkness.

"Oh, no?" I said, stung. "By your own admission, you've committed fraud, theft, and murder. It might be charitable to consider that you're mad, because if you're not—"

"Neither mad nor depraved," she said, decisively. "I'm a patriot."

The light dawned. I let out the breath I had been holding in expectation of a deranged attack.

"A Jacobite," I said. "Holy Christ, you're a bloody Jacobite!"

She was. And that explained quite a bit. Why Dougal, generally the mirror of his brother's opinions, should have shown such initiative in raising money for the House of Stuart. And why Geillis Duncan, so well equipped to lead any man she wanted to the altar, had chosen two such dissimilar specimens as Arthur Duncan and Dougal MacKenzie. The one for his money and position, the other for his power to influence public opinion.

"Colum would have been better," she continued. "A pity. His misfortune is my own, as well. It's him would have been the one I should have had; the only man I've seen could be my proper match. Together, we could . . . well, no help for it. The one man I'd want, and the one man in the world I couldn't touch with the weapon I had."

"So you took Dougal, instead."

"Oh, aye," she said, deep in her own thoughts. "A strong man, and with some power. A bit of property. The ear of the people. But really, he's no more than the legs, and the cock" —she laughed briefly—"of Colum MacKenzie. It's Colum has the strength. Almost as much as I have."

Her boastful tone annoyed me.

"Colum has a few small things that you haven't, so far as I can see. Such as a sense of compassion."

"Ah, yes. 'Bowels of mercy and compassion,' is it?" She spoke ironically. "Much good it may do him. Death sits on his shoulder; ye can see it with half an eye. The man may live two years past Hogmanay; not much longer than that."

"And how much longer will *you* live?" I asked.

The irony turned inward, but the silver voice stayed steady.

"A bit less than that, I expect. No great matter. I've managed a good deal in the time I had; ten thousand pounds diverted to France, and the district roused for Prince Charles. Come the Rising, I shall know I helped. If I live so long."

She stood nearly under the hole in the roof. My eyes were sufficiently accustomed to the darkness that she showed as a pale shape in the murk, a premature and unlaid ghost. She turned abruptly toward me.

"Whatever happens with the examiners, I have no regrets, Claire."

"I regret only that I have but one life to give for my country?" I asked ironically.

"That's nicely put," she said.

"Isn't it, just?"

We fell silent as it grew darker. The black of the hole seemed a tangible force, pressing cold and heavy on my chest, clogging my lungs with the scent of death. At last I huddled into as close a ball as I could, put my head on my knees, and gave up the fight, lapsing into an uneasy doze on the edge between cold and panic.

"Do ye love the man, then?" Geilie asked suddenly.

I raised my head from my knees, startled. I had no idea what time it was; one faint star shone overhead, but shed no light into the hole.

"Who, Jamie?"

"Who else?" she said dryly. "It's his name ye call out in your sleep."

"I didn't know I did that."

"Well, do ye?" The cold encouraged a sort of deadly drowsiness, but Geilie's prodding voice dragged me a bit further out of my stupor.

I hugged my knees, rocking slightly back and forth. The light from the hole above had faded away to the soft dark of early night. The examiners would arrive within the next day or so. It was getting a bit late for prevarications, either to myself or anyone else. While I still found it difficult to admit that I might be in serious danger of death, I was beginning to understand the instinct that made condemned prisoners seek shriving on the eve of execution.

"Really love him, I mean," Geilie persisted. "Not just want to bed him; I know you want that, and he does too. They all do. But do you love him?"

Did I love him? Beyond the urges of the flesh? The hole had the dark anonymity of the confessional, and a soul on the verge of death had no time for lies.

"Yes," I said, and laid my head back on my knees.

It was silent in the hole for some time, and I hovered once more on the verge of sleep, when I heard her speak once more, as though to herself.

"So it's possible," she said thoughtfully.

The examiners arrived a day later. From the dankness of the thieves' hole, we could hear the stir of their arrival; the shouts of the villagers, and the clopping of horses on the stone of the High Street. The bustle grew fainter as the procession passed down the street toward the distant square.

"They've come," said Geilie, listening to the excitement above.

We clasped hands reflexively, enmities buried in fear.

"Well," I said, with attempted bravado, "I suppose being burned is better than freezing to death."

In the event, we continued to freeze. It was not until noon of the next day that the door of our prison slid abruptly back, and we were pulled out of the pit to be taken to trial.

No doubt to accommodate the crowd of spectators, the session was held in the square, before the Duncans' house. I saw Geilie glance up briefly at the diamond-paned windows of her parlor, then turn away, expressionless.

There were two ecclesiastical examiners, seated on padded stools behind a table that had been erected in the square. One judge was abnormally tall and thin, the other short and stout. They reminded me irresistibly of an American comic-paper I had once seen; not knowing their names, I mentally christened the tall one Mutt and the other Jeff.

Most of the village was there. Looking about, I could see a good many of my former patients. But the inhabitants of the Castle were notably absent.

It was John MacRae, locksman of the village of Cranesmuir, who read out the dittay, or indictment, against the persons of one Geillis Duncan and one Claire Fraser, both accused before the Church's court of the crime of witchcraft.

"Stating in evidence whereof the accused did cause the death of Arthur Duncan, by means of witchcraft," MacRae read, in a firm, steady voice. "And whereas they did procure the death of the unborn child of Janet Robinson, did cause the boat of Thomas MacKenzie to sink, did bring upon the village of Cranesmuir a wasting sickness of the bowels . . ."

It went on for some time. Colum had been thorough in his preparations.

After the reading of the dittay, the witnesses were called.

Most of them were villagers I didn't recognize; none of my own patients were among them, a fact for which I was grateful.

While the testimony of many of the witnesses was simply absurd, and other witnesses had plainly been paid for their services, some had a clear ring of truth to their words. Janet Robinson, for example, who was haled before the court by her father, pale and trembling, with a purple bruise on her cheek, to confess that she had conceived a child by a married man, and sought to rid herself of it, through the offices of Geillis Duncan.

"She gave me a draft to drink, and a charm to say three times, at the rising o' the moon," the girl mumbled, glancing fearfully from Geillis to her father, unsure which one posed the greater threat. "She said 'twould bring my courses on."

"And did it?" Jeff asked with interest.

"Not at the first, your honor," the girl answered, bobbing her head nervously. "But I took the draft again, at the waning o' the moon, and then it started."

"Started?! The lassie near bled to death!" An elderly lady, plainly the girl's mother, broke in. " 'Twas only because she felt herself to be dyin' as she told me the truth o' the matter." More than willing to add to the gory details, Mrs. Robinson was shut up with some difficulty, in order to make way for the succeeding witnesses.

There seemed to be no one with anything in particular to say about me, aside from the vague accusation that since I had been present at Arthur Duncan's death, and had laid hands on him before he died, clearly I must have had something to do with it. I began to think that Geilie was right; I had not been Colum's target. That being so, I thought it possible that I would escape. Or at least I thought so until the hill woman appeared.

When she came forward, a thin, bowed woman with a yellow shawl, I sensed that we were in serious trouble. She was not one of the villagers; no one I had ever seen before. Her feet were bare, stained with the dust of the road she had walked to come here.

"Have ye a charge to make against either o' the women here?" asked the tall, thin judge.

The woman was afraid; she wouldn't raise her eyes to look at the judges. She bobbed her head briefly, though, and the crowd quieted its murmur to hear her.

Her voice was low, and Mutt had to ask her to repeat herself.

She and her husband had an ailing child, born healthy but then turned puny and unthrifty. Finally deciding that the child was a fairy changeling, they had placed it in the Fairy's Seat on the hill of Croich Gorm. Keeping watch so as to recover their own child when the fairies should return it, they had seen the two ladies standing here go to the Fairy's Seat, pick up the child and speak strange spells over it.

The woman twisted her thin hands together, working them under her apron.

"We watched through the nicht, sirs. And when the dark came, soon after there cam' a great demon, a huge black shape comin' through the shadows wi' no sound, to lean ower the spot where we'd laid the babe."

There was an awed murmur from the crowd, and I felt the hair on the back of my neck stir slightly, even knowing as I did that the "great demon" had been Jamie, gone to see whether the child still lived. I braced myself, knowing what was coming next.

"And when the sun rose, my man and I went to see. And there we found the changeling babe, dead on the hill, and no sign of our own wee bairn." At this, she broke, and threw her apron over her face to hide her weeping.

As though the mother of the changeling had been a signal of some sort, the crowd parted and the figure of Peter the drover came out. I groaned inwardly when I saw him. I had felt the emotions of the crowd turn against me as the woman spoke; all I needed now was for this man to tell the court about the waterhorse.

Enjoying his moment of celebrity, the drover drew himself up and pointed dramatically at me.

" 'Tis right ye are to call her witch, my lords! Wi' my own eyes I saw this woman call up a waterhorse from the waters of the Evil Loch, to do her bidding! A great fearsome creature, sirs, tall as a pine tree, wi' a neck like a great blue snake, an' eyes big as apples, wi' a look in them as would steal the soul from a man."

The judges appeared impressed with his testimony, and whispered between themselves for several minutes, while Peter glared defiantly at me, with a "that'll show *you*!" sort of look.

At length, the fat judge broke from the conference and beckoned imperiously to John MacRae, who stood to one side, alert for trouble.

"Locksman!" he said. He turned and pointed at the drover.

"Tak' that man away and shut him up in the pillory for public drunkenness. This is a solemn coort o' law; we'll no ha' the time of the examiners wasted by frivolous accusations from a sot who sees waterhorses when he's taken too much whisky!"

Peter the drover was so astonished that he did not even resist as the locksman strode firmly forward and took him by the arm. Mouth hanging open, he glared back wildly in my direction as he was led away. I couldn't resist fluttering my fingers in a tiny salute after him.

After this slight break in the tension of the proceedings, though, things got rapidly worse. There was a procession of girls and women to swear that they had bought charms and philtres from Geillis Duncan, for purposes such as causing illness, ridding oneself of an unwanted babe, or casting spells of love upon some man. All, without exception, swore that the charms had worked—an enviable record for a general practitioner, I thought cynically. While no one claimed such results for me, there were several to say—truthfully—that they had seen me often in Mrs. Duncan's herb room, mixing medicines and grinding herbs.

Still, that might not have been fatal; there were an equal number of people to claim that I had healed them, using nothing more than ordinary medicines, with nothing in the way of spells, charms, or general hocus-pocus. Given the force of public opinion, it took some nerve for these people to step forward to testify in my behalf, and I was grateful.

My feet were aching from standing so long; while the judges sat in relative comfort, no stools were provided for the prisoners. But when the next witness appeared, I entirely forgot my feet.

With an instinct for drama that rivaled Colum's, Father Bain flung wide the door of the kirk and emerged into the square, limping heavily on an oaken crutch. He advanced slowly to the center of the square, inclined his head to the judges, then turned and surveyed the crowd, until his steely glare had reduced the noise to a low, uneasy muttering. When he spoke, his voice lashed out like the crack of a whip.

"It's a judgment on ye, ye folk o' Cranesmuir! 'Before him went the pestilence, and burning coals went forth with his feet.' Aye, ye've allowed yerselves to be seduced from the paths o' righteousness! Ye've sown the wind, and the whirlwind's amongst ye now!"

I stared, somewhat taken aback by this unsuspected gift for rhetoric. Or perhaps he was capable of such flights of oratory only under the stimulus of crisis. The florid voice thundered on.

"The pestilence will come upon ye, and ye shall die o' your sins, unless ye be cleansed! Ye've welcomed the whore of Babylon into yer midst"—That was me, I assumed, from the glare he shot at me—"Ye've sold your soul to your enemies, ye've taken the English viper to your bosom, and now the vengeance o' the Lord God Almighty is on ye. 'Deliver thee from the strange woman, even from the stranger that flattereth with her words. For her house inclineth unto death, and her paths unto the dead.' Repent, people, before it's too late! Fall to your knees, I say, and pray for forgiveness! Cast out the English whore, and renounce your bargain wi' the spawn o' Satan!" He snatched the rosary from his belt and brandished the large wooden crucifix in my direction.

Entertaining as this all was, I could see Mutt becoming rather restive. Professional jealousy, perhaps.

"Er, your Reverence," the judge said, with a slight bow in Father Bain's direction, "have ye evidence to bring as to the charge regarding these women?"

"That I have." The first explosion of oratory spent, the

little priest was calm now. He leveled a menacing forefinger in my direction and I had to brace myself to keep from taking a step backward.

"At noonday on a Tuesday, two weeks past, I met this woman in the gardens of Castle Leoch. Using unnatural powers, she called down a pack of hounds upon me, such that I fell before them, and was in mortal peril. Bein' wounded grievously in the leg, I made to leave her presence. The woman tried to lure me wi' her sinfulness, to go awa' in private with her, and when I resisted her wiles, she cast a curse upon me."

"What bloody nonsense!" I said indignantly. "That's the most ridiculous exaggeration I've ever heard!"

Father Bain's eye, dark and glittering as with fever, swiveled from the examiners and fixed on me.

"Do ye deny, woman, that ye said these words to me? 'Come with me now, priest, or your wound shall fester and go putrid'?"

"Well, tone it down a bit, but something to that effect, perhaps," I admitted.

Jaw clenched in triumph, the priest whipped aside the skirts of his soutane. A bandage stained with dried blood and wet with yellow pus encircled his thigh. The pale flesh of the leg puffed above and below the bandage, with ominous red streaks extending up from the hidden wound.

"Jesus Christ, man!" I said, shocked at the sight. "You've got blood poisoning. You need it tended, and right now, or you'll die!"

There was a deep murmur of shock from the crowd. Even Mutt and Jeff seemed a bit stunned.

Father Bain shook his head slowly.

"You hear?" he demanded. "The temerity of the woman kens nae bounds. She curses me wi' death, a man of God, before the judgment seat of the kirk itself!"

The excited murmuring of the crowd grew louder. Father Bain spoke again, raising his voice slightly in order to be heard over the noise.

"I leave ye, gentlemen, wi' the judgment o' your own

senses, and the injunction o' the Lord—'Ye shallna suffer a witch to live!' "

Father Bain's dramatic evidence put a stop to the testimony. Presumably no one was prepared to top *that* performance. The judges called a short recess and were brought refreshments from the inn. No such amenities were forthcoming for the accused.

I braced myself and pulled experimentally against my bonds. The leather of the straps creaked a bit, but didn't give an inch. This, I thought cynically, trying to still my panic, was surely where the dashing young hero was meant to ride through the crowd, beating back the cringing townspeople and scooping the fainting heroine up onto his saddle.

But my own dashing young hero was out in the forest somewhere, swilling ale with an aging poofter of noble blood and slaughtering innocent deer. It was rather unlikely, I thought, gritting my teeth, that Jamie would return in time even to gather up my ashes for ceremonial disposal, before I was scattered to the four winds.

Preoccupied with my growing fear, I didn't at first hear the hoofbeats. It was only as the faint murmurs and head-turnings of the crowd attracted my attention that I noticed the rhythmic clopping, ringing from the stones of the High Street.

The murmurs of surprise grew louder, and the fringes of the crowd began to draw apart to admit the rider, still beyond the range of my sight. Despite my earlier despair, I began to feel a faint flicker of illogical hope. What if Jamie had come back early? Perhaps the Duke's advances had been too pressing, or the deer too few and far between. Whatever it might be, I strained on tiptoe to see the face of the approaching rider.

The ranks of the crowd parted reluctantly as the horse, a strong bay, poked its long nose between two sets of shoulders. Before the astonished eyes of everyone—including me—the sticklike figure of Ned Gowan spryly dismounted.

Jeff surveyed the spare, neat form before him with some astonishment.

"And you are, sir?" No doubt his tone of reluctant courtesy was a result of the visitor's silver shoe-buckles and velvet coat —employment with the laird of clan MacKenzie was not without its compensations.

"My name is Edward Gowan, your lordship," he said precisely. "Solicitor."

Mutt hunched his shoulders and wriggled a bit; the stool he had been provided had no back, and his lengthy torso was no doubt feeling the strain. I stared hard at him, wishing him a herniated lumbar disk. If I were about to be burnt for having an evil eye, I thought, let it count for something.

"Solicitor?" he rumbled. "What brings you here, then?"

Ned Gowan's grey peruke inclined itself in the most precise of formal bows.

"I have come to offer my humble services in the support of Mistress Fraser, your lordships," he said, "a most gracious lady, whom I know of my own witness to be as kind and beneficial in the administration of the healing arts as she is knowledgeable in their application."

Very nice, I thought approvingly. Get a blow in for our side first thing. Looking across the square, I could see Geilie's mouth quirk up in a half-admiring, half-derisive smile. While Ned Gowan wouldn't be everyone's choice as Prince Charming, I was not inclined to be picky at a time like this. I would take my champions as they came.

With a bow to the judges and another, no less formal, to myself, Mr. Gowan drew himself still straighter than his normal upright posture, braced both thumbs in the waist of his breeks, and prepared with all the romanticism of his aged, gallant heart to do battle, fighting with the law's chosen weapon of excruciating boredom.

Boring he most certainly was. With the deadly precision of an automated mincing machine, he arranged each charge of the dittay on the slab of his scrutiny and diced it ruthlessly into shreds with the blade of statute and the cleaver of precedent.

It was a noble performance. He talked. And he talked. And he talked some more, seeming occasionally to pause respectfully for instruction from the bench, but in fact only drawing breath for another onslaught of verbiage.

With my life hanging in the balance, and my future entirely dependent on the eloquence of this skinny little man, I should have hung rapt on his every word. Instead, I found myself yawning appallingly, unable to cover my gaping mouth, and shifting from foot to aching foot, wishing fervently that they would burn me at once and end this torture.

The crowd appeared to feel much the same, and as the high excitement of the morning faded into ennui, Mr. Gowan's small, tidy voice went on and on and on. People began to drift away, suddenly mindful of beasts that needed milking and floors that wanted sweeping, secure in the surety that nothing of any interest could possibly happen while that deadly voice droned on.

When Ned Gowan finally finished his initial defense, evening had set in; and the squatty judge I had named Jeff announced that the court would reconvene in the morning.

After a short, muttering conference amongst Ned Gowan, Jeff, and John MacRae the locksman, I was led off toward the inn between two burly townsmen. Casting a glance over my shoulder, I saw Geilie being moved away in the opposite direction, back straight, refusing to be hurried, or for that matter, to acknowledge her surroundings in any way.

In the dark back room of the inn, my bonds were at last removed, and a candle brought. Then Ned Gowan arrived, bearing a bottle of ale and a plate of meat and bread.

"I've but the few minutes with ye, my dear, and that hard-won, so listen closely." The little man leaned nearer, conspiratorial in the flickering candlelight. His eyes were bright, and save a slight disarrangement of his peruke, he gave no hint of exertion or fatigue.

"Mr. Gowan, I am so glad to see you," I said sincerely.

"Yes, yes, my dear," he said, "but there's no time for that now." He patted my hand in a kindly but perfunctory fashion.

"I've succeeded in getting them to consider your case as separate from that of Mrs. Duncan, and that may be of help. It would appear that there was no original intent to arrest you, but that you were taken because of your association with the w——with Mrs. Duncan."

"Still," he continued briskly, "there is some danger to ye, and I'll not hide it from you. The climate of opinion in the village is none too favorable to ye at present. What possessed ye," he demanded, with uncharacteristic heatedness, "to touch that child?"

I opened my mouth to reply, but he waved the question aside impatiently.

"Ah, well, it's of no matter now. What we must do is to play upon the fact of your Englishness—and hence your ignorance, ye ken, not your strangeness—and draw matters out so long as we may. Time is on our side, ye see, for the worst of these trials take place in a climate of hysteria, when the soundness of evidence may be disregarded for the sake of satisfyin' blood-hunger."

Blood-hunger. That captured completely the feeling of the emotion I had felt emanating from the faces of the mob. Here and there I saw some traces of doubt or sympathy, but it was a rare soul who would stand against a crowd, and Cranesmuir was rather lacking in characters of that stamp. Or no, I corrected myself. There was one—this dry little Edinburgh lawyer, tough as the old boot he so strongly resembled.

"The longer we go on," Mr. Gowan continued matter-of-factly, "the less inclined anyone will be to take hasty action. So," he said, hands on his knees, "your part on the morrow is only to keep silent. I shall do all the talkin', and pray God it will be to some effect."

"That seems sound enough," I said, with a weary attempt at a smile. I glanced at the door to the front of the inn, where voices were being raised. Catching my look, Mr. Gowan nodded.

"Aye, I'll have to leave ye momentarily. I've arranged that you'll spend the night here." He glanced around dubiously. A small shed tacked on to the inn, and used mostly for the storage of oddments and spare supplies, it was cold and dark, but an improvement of several-fold over the thieves' hole.

The door to the shed opened, silhouetting the form of the inn-keeper, peering into the dark behind the pale waver of a candle flame. Mr. Gowan rose to go, but I gripped him by the sleeve. There was one thing I needed to know.

"Mr. Gowan—did Colum send you to help me?" He hesitated in his reply, but within the limits of his profession, he was a man of irreproachable honesty.

"No," he said bluntly. A look almost of embarrassment flitted over his withered features, and he added, "I came for . . . for myself." He clapped his hat upon his head and turned to the door, wishing me a brief "Good e'en," before disappearing into the light and bustle of the inn.

There had been little preparation for my accommodation, but a small jug of wine and a loaf of bread—clean, this time—sat on one of the hogsheads, and there was an old blanket folded on the ground at its foot.

I wrapped myself in the blanket and sat down on one of the smaller casks to dine, musing as I munched the sparse fare.

So Colum had not sent the lawyer. Had he known, even, that Mr. Gowan intended to come? Chances were that Colum had forbidden anyone to come down to the village, for fear of being caught up in the witch-hunt. The waves of fear and hysteria that swept over the village were palpable; I could feel them beating against the walls of my flimsy shelter.

A noisy outburst from the nearby taproom distracted me from my thoughts. Perhaps it was only deathwatch plus one. But on the edge of destruction, even an extra hour was cause for thanks. I rolled myself up in the blanket, pulled it over my head to shut out the noises from the inn, and tried very hard to feel nothing but gratitude.

After an exceedingly restless night, I was roused soon after dawn and marched back out to the square, though the judges didn't arrive for another hour.

Fine, fat, and full of breakfast, they buckled straight down to work. Jeff turned to John MacRae, who had returned to his station behind the accused.

"We find ourselves unable to determine guilt solely on the basis of the evidence presented." There was a burst of outrage from the regathered crowd, which had made its own determi-

nation, but this was quelled by Mutt, who turned a pair of
eyes like gimlets on the young workmen in the front row,
quieting their yapping like dogs doused with cold water. Order restored, he turned his angular face back to the locksman.

"Conduct the prisoners to the loch side, if ye please."
There was a pleased sound of expectation at this that roused
all my worst suspicions. John MacRae took me by one arm
and Geilie by the other, to steer us along, but he had plenty of
help. Vicious hands tore at my gown, pinching and pushing as
I was yanked along. Some idiot had a drum, and was beating
out a ragged tattoo. The crowd was chanting in a rough
rhythm to the tuck of the drum, something that I didn't catch
among the random shouts and cries. I didn't think I wanted
to know what they were saying.

The procession flowed down the meadow to the edge of
the loch, where a small wooden quay projected into the water.
We were pulled out to the end of this, where the two judges
had taken up their posts, one at either side of the quay. Jeff
turned to the crowd waiting onshore.

"Bring out the cords!" There was a general mutter and
expectant looking around from one to another, until someone
ran up hastily with a length of thin rope. MacRae took it and
approached me rather hesitantly. He stole a glance at the examiners, though, which seemed to harden his resolve.

"Please be so kind as to remove your shoon, ma'am," he
ordered.

"What the he—what for?" I demanded, crossing my arms.

He blinked, plainly unprepared for resistance, but one of
the judges forestalled his reply.

"'Tis the proper procedure for trial by water. The suspected witch shall have the right thumb bound by a cord of
hemp to the great toe of the left foot. Likewise, the left thumb
shall be bound to the right great toe. And then . . ." He cast
an eloquent glance at the waters of the loch. Two fishermen
stood barefooted in the mud of the shore, trews rolled above
their knees and tied with twine. Grinning insinuatingly at me,
one of them picked up a small stone and heaved it out across
the steely surface. It skipped once and sank.

"Upon entering the water," the short judge chimed in, "a

guilty witch will float, as the purity of the water rejects her tainted person. An innocent woman will sink."

"So I've the choice of being condemned as a witch or being found innocent but drowned, have I?" I snapped. "No thank you!" I hugged my elbows harder, trying to still the shiver that seemed to have become a permanent part of my flesh.

The short judge puffed himself up like a threatened toad.

"You'll nae speak before this court without leave, woman! Do ye dare to refuse lawful examination?"

"Do I dare refuse to be drowned? Too right I do!" Too late I caught sight of Geilie, frantically shaking her head, so that the fair hair swirled around her face.

The judge turned to MacRae.

"Strip her and skelp her," he said flatly.

Through a daze of disbelief, I heard a collective inhalation, presumably of shocked dismay—in truth, of anticipatory enjoyment. And I realized just what hate really meant. Not theirs. Mine.

They didn't bother taking me back to the village square. So far as I was now concerned, I had little left to lose, and I didn't make it easy for them.

Rough hands jerked me forward, yanking at the edges of blouse and bodice.

"Let go of me, you bloody lout!" I yelled, and kicked one man-handler squarely where it would do most good. He crumpled with a groan, but his doubled form was quickly lost in a boiling eruption of shouting, spitting, glaring faces. More hands seized my arms and hustled me stumbling onward, half-lifting me over bodies fallen in the crush, pushing me bodily through gaps too small to walk through.

Someone hit me in the stomach, and I lost my breath. My bodice was virtually in shreds by this time, so it was with no great difficulty that the remainder was stripped off. I had never suffered from excessive modesty, but standing half-naked before the jeers of that crowd of ill-wishers, with the prints of sweaty hands on my bare breasts, filled me with a hatred and humiliation I could not even have imagined.

John MacRae bound my hands before me, looping a woven rope about my wrists, leaving a length of several feet. He had the grace to look ashamed as he did it, but would not raise his eyes to mine, and it was clear I could expect neither help nor lenience from that quarter; he was as much at the mercy of the crowd as I was.

Geilie was there, no doubt similarly treated; I caught a glimpse of her platinum hair, flying in a sudden breeze. My arms stretched high above my head as the rope was thrown over the branch of a large oak and hauled tight. I gritted my teeth and held tight to my fury; it was the only thing I had to combat my fear. There was an air of breathless expectancy, punctuated by the excited murmurs and shouts from the crowd of watchers.

"Give it 'er, John!" one shouted. "Get on wi' it!"

John MacRae, sensitive to the theatrical responsibilities of his profession, paused, scourge held level at waist height, and surveyed the crowd. He walked forward and gently adjusted my position, so that I faced the trunk of the tree, almost touching the rough bark. Then he drew back two paces, raised the whip and let it fall.

The shock of it was worse than the pain. In fact, it was only after several blows that I realized the locksman was doing his level best to spare me what he could. Still, one or two blows were hard enough to break the skin; I felt the sharp tingle in the wake of the impact.

I had my eyes shut tight, cheek pressed hard against the wood, trying for all I was worth to be somewhere else. Suddenly, though, I heard something that recalled me at once to the here and now.

"Claire!"

There was a little slack in the rope that bound my wrists; enough to let me make a lunge that brought me clear around, facing the mob. My sudden escape disconcerted the locksman, who brought his lash down on empty air, stumbled forward off-balance, and knocked his head against a limb. This had a very good effect on the mob, who roared insults and started jeering at him.

My hair was in my eyes, stuck to my face with sweat, tears, and the filth of confinement. I shook my head to free it, and managed at least a sidelong glance that confirmed what my ears had heard.

Jamie was shoving his way through the hindering crowd, face like thunder, ruthlessly taking advantage of his size and muscle.

I felt very much like General MacAuliffe at Bastogne, sighting Patton's Third Army in the offing. In spite of the horrible danger to Geilie, to me, and now to Jamie himself, I had never been so happy to see anyone.

"The witch's man!" "Her husband, it is!" "Stinkin' Fraser! Crowner!" and similar epithets began to be heard among the more general abuse aimed at me and Geilie. "Take him too!" "Burn 'em! Burn 'em all!" The crowd's hysteria, temporarily dispersed by the locksman's accident, was rising to fever pitch once more.

Hampered by the clinging forms of the locksman's assistants, who were trying to restrain him, Jamie had come to a dead halt. A man hanging from each arm, he struggled to force his hand toward his belt. Thinking him reaching for a knife, one man punched him hard in the belly.

Jamie doubled slightly, then came up, smashing an elbow to the nose of the man who'd hit him. One arm temporarily freed, he ignored the frantic pawings of the man on the other side. He dipped a hand into his sporran, raised his arm and threw. His shout reached me as the object left his hand.

"Claire! Stand *still*!"

Not much place for me to go, I thought dazedly. There was a dark blur headed straight for my face, and I started to flinch backward, but stopped in time. The blur struck my face with a clattering sting and the black beads fell on my shoulders as the jet rosary, flung bola-style, neatly ringed my neck. Or not quite neatly; the strand had caught on my right ear. I shook my head, eyes watering from the blow, and the circlet settled into place, crucifix swinging jauntily between my naked breasts.

The faces in the front row were staring at it in a kind of horrified bemusement. Their sudden silence affected those further back, and the roaring seethe of noise subsided. Jamie's voice, customarily soft-spoken, even in anger, rang out in the silence. There was nothing soft about it now.

"Cut her down!"

The hangers-on had dropped away, and the waves of the crowd parted before him as he strode forward. The locksman watched him come, standing gape-jawed and frozen.

"I said, cut her down! Now!" The locksman, freed from his trance by the apocalyptic vision of red-haired death bearing down on him, stirred himself and fumbled hastily for his dirk. The rope, sawn through, let go with a shuddering snap and my arms dropped like bolsters, aching with released strain. I staggered and would have fallen, but a strong, familiar hand caught my elbow and pulled me upright. Then my face was against Jamie's chest, and nothing mattered to me anymore.

I may have lost consciousness for a few moments, or only been so overcome with relief that it seemed that way. Jamie's arm was hard around my waist, holding me up, and his plaid had been thrown over me, hiding me at last from the stare of the villagers. There was a confusion of voices all around, but it was no longer the crazed and gleeful blood-lust of the mob.

The voice of Mutt—or was it Jeff?—cut through the confusion.

"Who are you? How dare ye to interfere wi' the investigations of the court?"

I could feel, rather than see, the crowd pushing forward. Jamie was large, and he was armed, but he was only one man. I cowered against him under the folds of the plaid. His right arm tightened around me, but his left hand went to the sheath on his hip. The silver-blue blade hissed with menace as it came half out of its scabbard, and those in the forefront of the crowd came to a sudden stop.

The judges were made of somewhat tougher fabric. Peering out from my hiding place, I could see Jeff glaring at Jamie. Mutt appeared more bemused than annoyed at this sudden intrusion.

"Do ye dare to draw arms against the justice of God?" snapped the tubby little judge.

Jamie drew the sword completely, with a flash of steel, then thrust it point-first into the ground, leaving the hilt quivering with the force of the blow.

"I draw it in defense of this woman, and the truth," he said. "If any here be against those two, they'll answer to me, and then God, in that order."

The judge blinked once or twice, as though unable to credit this behavior, then surged to the attack once more.

"You have no place in the workings o' this court, sir! I'll demand that ye surrender the prisoner at once. Your own behavior will be dealt with presently!"

Jamie looked the judges over coolly. I could feel his heart hammering beneath my cheek as I clung to him, but his hands were rock-steady, one resting on the hilt of his sword, the other on the dirk at his belt.

"As to that, sir, I swore an oath before the altar of God to protect this woman. And if you're tellin' me that ye consider your own authority to be greater than that of the Almighty, then I must inform ye that I'm no of that opinion, myself."

The silence that followed this was broken by an embarrassed titter, echoed here and there by a nervous laugh. While the sympathies of the crowd had not shifted to our side, still the momentum carrying us to disaster had been broken.

Jamie turned me with a hand on my shoulder. I couldn't bear to face the crowd, but I knew I must. I kept my chin as high as I could, and my eyes focused beyond the faces, to a small boat in the center of the loch. I stared at it 'til my eyes watered.

Jamie turned back the plaid, holding it around me, but letting it drop far enough to show my neck and shoulders. He touched the black rosary and set it swinging gently to and fro.

"Jet will burn a witch's skin, no?" he demanded of the judges. "Still more, I should think, would the cross of Our Lord. But look." He dipped a finger under the beads and lifted up the crucifix. My skin beneath was pure white, unmarked save for the smudges of captivity, and there was a gasp and murmur from the crowd.

Raw courage, an ice-cold presence of mind, and that instinct for showmanship. Colum MacKenzie had been right to be apprehensive of Jamie's ambitions. And given his fear that I might reveal Hamish's parentage, or what he thought I knew of it, what he had done to me was understandable too. Understandable, but not forgivable.

The mood of the crowd now swayed to and fro, uncertain. The bloodlust that had driven it earlier was dissipating, but it might still tilt like a cresting wave and crush us. Mutt and Jeff glanced at each other, undecided; taken aback by this last development, the judges had momentarily lost control of the situation.

Geillis Duncan stepped forward into the breach. I do not know whether there was hope for her at that point or not. In any case, she now tossed her fair hair defiantly over one shoulder, and threw her life away.

"This woman is no witch," she said simply. "But I am."

Jamie's show, good as it was, was no match for this. The resulting uproar drowned completely the voices of the judges, questioning and exclaiming.

There was no clue to what she thought or felt, no more than there ever was; her high white brow was clear, the big green eyes gleaming in what might be amusement. She stood straight in her ragged garments, daubed with filth, and stared down her accusers. When the tumult had quieted a bit, she began to speak, not deigning to raise her voice, but forcing them to quiet themselves to hear her.

"I, Geillis Duncan, do confess that I am a witch, and the mistress of Satan." This caused another outcry, and she waited again with perfect patience for them to quiet.

"In obedience to my Master, I do confess that I killed my husband, Arthur Duncan, by means of witchcraft." At this, she glanced aside, catching my eye, and the hint of a smile touched her lips. Her eyes rested on the woman in the yellow shawl, but did not soften. "Of malice, I placed a spell upon the changeling child, that it might die, and the human child it replaced remain with the fairies." She turned and gestured in my direction.

"I took advantage of the ignorance of Claire Fraser, using her for my purposes. But she had neither part nor knowledge in my doings, nor does she serve my Master."

The crowd was muttering again, people jostling to get a

better look, pushing nearer. She stretched out both hands toward them, palm outward.

"Stay back!" The clear voice cracked like a whip, to much the same effect. She tilted back her head to the skies and froze, like one listening.

"Hear!" she said. "Hear the wind of his coming! Beware, ye people of Cranesmuir! For my Master comes on the wings o' the wind!" She lowered her head and screamed, a high, eerie sound of triumph. The large green eyes were fixed and staring, trancelike.

The wind *was* rising; I could see the clouds of the storm rolling across the far side of the loch. People began to look uneasily around; a few souls dropped back from the edge of the crowd.

Geilie began to spin, twirling round and round, hair whipping in the wind, hand gracefully overhead like a maypole dancer's. I watched her in stunned disbelief.

As she turned, her hair hid her face. On the last turn, though, she snapped her head to throw the fair mane to one side and I saw her face clearly, looking at me. The mask of trance had vanished momentarily, and her mouth formed a single word. Then her turn took her around to face the crowd once more, and she began her eerie screaming again.

The word had been "Run!"

She stopped her spinning suddenly, and with a look of mad exultation, gripped the remnants of her bodice with both hands and tore it down the front. Tore it far enough to show the crowd the secret I had learned, huddled close beside her in the cold filth of the thieves' hole. The secret Arthur Duncan had learned, in the hour before his death. The secret for which he had died. The shreds of her loose gown dropped away, exposing the swelling bulge of a six-month pregnancy.

I still stood like a rock, staring. Jamie had no such hesitations. Seizing me with one hand and his sword with the other, he flung himself into the crowd, knocking people out of the way with elbows, knees, and sword hilt, bulling his way toward the edge of the loch. He let out a piercing whistle through his teeth.

Intent on the spectacle under the oak, few people at first

realized what was happening. Then, as individuals began to shout and grab at us, there was the sound of galloping hooves on the hard-packed dirt above the shore.

Donas still didn't care much for people, and was all too willing to show it. He bit the first hand reaching for his bridle, and a man dropped back, crying out and dripping blood. The horse reared, squealing and pawing the air, and the few bold souls still intent on stopping him suddenly lost interest.

Jamie flung me over the saddle like a sack of meal and swung up himself in one fluid motion. Clearing a path with vicious swipes of his sword, he turned Donas through the hindering mass of the crowd. As people fell back from the onslaught of teeth, hooves, and blade, we picked up speed, leaving the loch, the village, and Leoch behind. Breath knocked out of me by the impact, I struggled to speak, to scream to Jamie.

For I hadn't stood frozen at the revelation of Geilie's pregnancy. It was something else I had seen that chilled me to the marrow of my bones. As Geilie had spun, white arms stretched aloft, I saw what she had seen when my own clothes were stripped away. A mark on one arm like the one I bore. Here, in this time, the mark of sorcery, the mark of a magus. The small, homely scar of a smallpox vaccination.

Rain pattered on the water, soothing my swollen face and the rope burns on my wrists. I dipped a handful of water from the stream and sipped it slowly, feeling the cold liquid trickle down my throat with gratitude.

Jamie disappeared for a few minutes. He came back with a handful of dark green oblate leaves, chewing something. He spat a glob of macerated green into the palm of his hand, stuffed another wad of leaves into his mouth and turned me away from him. He rubbed the chewed leaves gently over my back, and the stinging eased considerably.

"What is that?" I asked, making an effort to control myself. I was still shaky and snuffling, but the helpless tears were beginning to ebb.

"Watercress," he answered, voice slightly muffled by the

leaves in his mouth. He spat them out and applied them to my back. "You're no the only one knows a bit about grass-cures, Sassenach," he said, a bit clearer.

"How—how does it taste?" I asked, gulping back the sobs.

"Fair nasty," he replied laconically. He finished his application and laid the plaid softly back across my shoulders.

"It won't—" he began, then hesitated, "I mean, the cuts are not deep. I—I think you'll no be . . . marked." He spoke gruffly, but his touch was very gentle, and reduced me to tears once more.

"I'm sorry," I mumbled, dabbling my nose on a corner of the plaid. "I—I don't know what's wrong with me. I don't know why I can't stop crying."

He shrugged. "I dinna suppose anyone's tried to hurt ye on purpose before, Sassenach," he said. "It's likely the shock of that, so much as the pain." He paused, picking up a plaid-end.

"I did just the same, lass," he said matter-of-factly. "Puked after, and cried while they cleansed the cuts. Then I shook." He wiped my face carefully with the plaid, then put a hand under my chin and tilted my face up to his.

"And when I stopped shaking, Sassenach," he said quietly, "I thanked God for the pain, because it meant I was still alive." He let go, nodding at me. "When ye get to that point, lassie, tell me; for I've a thing or two I want to be sayin' to ye then."

He got up and went down to the edge of the burn, to wash out the blood-stained handkerchief in cold water.

"What brought you back?" I asked, when he returned. I had managed to stop crying, but I still shook, and huddled deeper into the folds of the plaid.

"Alec MacMahon," he said, smiling. "I told him to watch over ye while I was gone. When the villagers took you and Mrs. Duncan, he rode all night and the next day to find me. And then I rode like the devil himself comin' back. Lord, that's a good horse." He looked approvingly up the slope to Donas, tethered to a tree at the top of the bank, his wet coat gleaming like copper.

"I'll have to move him," he said, thoughtfully. "I doubt

anyone will follow, but it isna that far from Cranesmuir. Can ye walk now?"

I followed him up the steep slope with some difficulty, small rocks rolling under my feet and bracken and bramble catching my shift. Near the top of the slope was a grove of young alders, grown so close together that the lower branches interlaced, forming a green roof over the bracken beneath. Jamie shoved the branches up far enough for me to crawl into the narrow space, then carefully rearranged the crushed bracken before the entrance. He stood back and surveyed the hiding place critically, nodding in satisfaction.

"Aye, that's good. No one will find ye there." He turned to go, then turned back. "Try to sleep, if ye can, and don't worry if I'm not back at once. I'll hunt a bit on the way back; we've no food with us, and I dinna want to attract attention by stopping at a croft. Pull the tartan up over your head, and make sure it covers your shift; the white shows for a long way."

Food seemed irrelevant; I felt as though I would never want to eat again. Sleep was something else again. My back and arms still ached, the rope burns on my wrists were raw, and I felt sore and bruised all over; but worn out with fear, pain, and simple exhaustion, I fell asleep almost at once, the pungent scent of ferns rising around me like incense.

I awoke with something gripping my foot. Startled, I sat up straight, crashing into the springy branches overhead. Leaves and sticks showered down around me, and I flailed my arms wildly, trying to disentangle my hair from the snagging twigs. Scratched, disheveled, and irritated, I crawled out of my sanctuary to find an amused Jamie squatting nearby, watching my emergence. It was near sunset; the sun had dropped below the lip of the burn, leaving the rocky canyon in shadow. The smell of roasting meat rose from a small fire burning among the rocks near the stream, where two rabbits browned on a makeshift spit made of sharpened green sticks.

Jamie held out a hand to help me down the slope. I haughtily declined and swept down myself, tripping only once on the trailing ends of the plaid. My earlier nausea had vanished, and I fell ravenously on the meat.

"We'll move up into the forest after supper, Sassenach," Jamie said, tearing a joint from the rabbit carcass. "I dinna want to sleep near the burn; I canna hear anyone coming over the noise of the water."

There was not much conversation as we ate. The horror of the morning, and the thought of what we had left behind, oppressed us both. And for me there was a profound sense of mourning. I had lost not only the chance of finding out more about the why and wherefore of my presence here, but a friend as well. My only friend. I was often in doubt as to Geilie's motives, but I had no doubt at all that she had saved my life that morning. Knowing herself doomed, she had done her best to give me a chance of escape. The fire, almost invisible in daylight, was growing brighter now as darkness filled the burn. I looked into the flames, seeing the crisp skin and browned bones of the rabbits on their spits. A drop of blood from a broken bone fell into the fire, hissing into nothing. Suddenly the meat stuck in my throat. I set it down hastily and turned away, retching.

Still without speaking much, we moved out of the burn and found a comfortable place near the edge of a clearing in the forest. Hills rose in undulant mounds all around us, but Jamie had chosen a high spot, with a good view of the road from the village. The dusk momentarily heightened all the colors of the countryside, lighting the land with jewels; a glowing emerald in the hollows, a lovely shadowed amethyst among the clumps of heather, and burning rubies on the red-berried rowan trees that crowned the hills. Rowan berries, a specific against witchcraft. Far in the distance, the outline of Castle Leoch was still visible at the foot of Ben Aden. It faded quickly as the light died.

Jamie made a fire in a sheltered spot, and sat down next to it. The rain had eased to a faint drizzle that misted the air and spangled my eyelashes with rainbows when I looked at the flames.

He sat staring into the fire for a long time. Finally he looked up at me, hands clasped around his knees.

"I said before that I'd not ask ye things ye had no wish to

tell me. And I'd not ask ye now; but I must know, for your safety as well as mine." He paused, hesitating.

"Claire, if you've never been honest wi' me, be so now, for I must know the truth. Claire, are ye a witch?"

I gaped at him. "A witch? You—you can really ask that?" I thought he must be joking. He wasn't.

He took me by the shoulders and gripped me hard, staring into my eyes as though willing me to answer him.

"I *must* ask it, Claire! And you must tell me!"

"And if I were?" I asked through dry lips. "If you had thought I were a witch? Would you still have fought for me?"

"I would have gone to the stake with you!" he said violently. "And to hell beyond, if I must. But may the Lord Jesus have mercy on my soul and on yours, tell me the truth!"

The strain of it all caught up with me. I tore myself out of his grasp and ran across the clearing. Not far, only to the edge of the trees; I could not bear the exposure of the open space. I clutched a tree; put my arms around it and dug my fingers hard into the bark, pressed my face to it and shrieked with hysterical laughter.

Jamie's face, white and shocked, loomed up on the other side of the tree. With the dim realization that what I was doing must sound unnervingly like cackling, I made a terrific effort and stopped. Panting, I stared at him for a moment.

"Yes," I said, backing away, still heaving with gasps of unhinged laughter. "Yes, I am a witch! To you, I must be. I've never had smallpox, but I can walk through a room full of dying men and never catch it. I can nurse the sick and breathe their air and touch their bodies, and the sickness can't touch me. I can't catch cholera, either, or lockjaw, or the morbid sore throat. And you must think it's an enchantment, because you've never heard of vaccine, and there's no other way you can explain it."

"The things I know—" I stopped backing away and stood still, breathing heavily, trying to control myself. "I know about Jonathan Randall because I was told about him. I know when he was born and when he'll die, I know about what he's done and what he'll do, I know about Sandringham because . . . because Frank told me. He knew about Randall because he . . . he . . . oh, God!" I felt as though I might be sick, and closed my eyes to shut out the spinning stars overhead.

"And Colum . . . he thinks I'm a witch, because I know Hamish isn't his own son. I know . . . he can't sire children. But he thought I knew who Hamish's father is . . . I thought maybe it was you, but then I knew it couldn't be, and . . ." I was talking faster and faster, trying to keep the vertigo at bay with the sound of my own voice.

"Everything I've ever told you about myself was true," I said, nodding madly as though to reassure myself. "Everything. I haven't any people, I haven't any history, because I haven't happened yet.

"Do you know when I was born?" I asked, looking up. I knew my hair was wild and my eyes staring, and I didn't care. "On the twentieth of October, in the Year of Our Lord nineteen hundred and eighteen. Do you hear me?" I demanded, for he was blinking at me unmoving, as though paying no attention to a word I said. "I said nineteen eighteen! Nearly two hundred years from now! Do you hear?"

I was shouting now, and he nodded slowly.

"I hear," he said softly.

"Yes, you hear!" I blazed. "And you think I'm raving mad. Don't you? Admit it! That's what you think. You have to think so, there isn't any other way you can explain me to yourself. You *can't* believe me, you can't dare to. Oh, Jamie . . ." I felt my face start to crumple. All this time spent hiding the truth, realizing that I could never tell anyone, and now I realized that I could tell Jamie, my beloved husband, the man I trusted beyond all others, and he wouldn't—he *couldn't* believe me either.

"It was the rocks—the fairy hill. The standing stones. Merlin's stones. That's where I came through." I was gasping, half-sobbing, becoming less coherent by the second. "Once upon a time, but it's really two hundred years. It's always two hundred years, in the stories. . . . But in the stories, the people always get back. I couldn't get back." I turned away, staggering, grasping for support. I sank down on a rock, shoulders slumped, and put my head in my hands. There was a long silence in the wood. It went on long enough for the small night birds to recover their courage and start their noises once again, calling to each other with a thin, high *zeek!* as they hawked for the last insects of the summer.

I looked up at last, thinking that perhaps he had simply risen and left me, overcome by my revelations. He was still there, though, still sitting, hands braced on his knees, head bowed as though in thought.

The hairs on his arms shone stiff as copper wires in the firelight, though, and I realized that they stood erect, like the bristles on a dog. He was afraid of me.

"Jamie," I said, feeling my heart break with absolute loneliness. "Oh, Jamie."

I sat down and curled myself into a ball, trying to roll myself around the core of my pain. Nothing mattered any longer, and I sobbed my heart out.

His hands on my shoulders raised me, enough to see his face. Through the haze of tears, I saw the look he wore in battle, of struggle that had passed the point of strain and become calm certainty.

"I believe you," he said firmly. "I dinna understand it a bit —not yet—but I believe you. Claire, I believe you! Listen to me! There's the truth between us, you and I, and whatever ye tell me, I shall believe it." He gave me a gentle shake.

"It doesna matter what it is. You've told me. That's enough for now. Be still, *mo duinne.* Lay your head and rest. You'll tell me the rest of it later. And I'll believe you."

I was still sobbing, unable to grasp what he was telling me. I struggled, trying to pull away, but he gathered me up and held me tightly against himself, pushing my head into the folds of his plaid, and repeating over and over again, "I believe you."

At last, from sheer exhaustion, I grew calm enough to look up and say, "But you *can't* believe me."

He smiled down at me. His mouth trembled slightly, but he smiled.

"Ye'll no tell *me* what I canna do, Sassenach." He paused a moment. "How old are ye?" he asked curiously. "I never thought to ask."

The question seemed so preposterous that it took me a minute to think.

"I'm twenty-seven . . . or maybe twenty-eight," I added. That rattled him for a moment. At twenty-eight, women in this time were usually on the verge of middle-age.

"Oh," he said. He took a deep breath. "I thought ye were about my age—or younger."

He didn't move for a second. But then he looked down and smiled faintly at me. "Happy birthday, Sassenach," he said.

It took me completely by surprise and I just stared stupidly at him for a moment. "What?" I managed at last.

"I said 'Happy birthday.' It's the twentieth of October to-day."

"Is it?" I said dumbly. "I'd lost track." I was shaking again, from cold and shock and the force of my tirade. He drew me close against him and held me, smoothing his big hands lightly over my hair, cradling my head against his chest. I began to cry again, but this time with relief. In my state of upheaval, it seemed logical that if he knew my real age and still wanted me, then everything would be all right.

Jamie picked me up, and holding me carefully against his shoulder, carried me to the side of the fire, where he had laid the horse's saddle. He sat down, leaning against the saddle, and held me, light and close.

A long time later, he spoke.

"All right. Tell me now."

I told him. Told him everything, haltingly but coherently. I felt numb from exhaustion, but content, like a rabbit that has outrun a fox, and found temporary shelter under a log. It isn't sanctuary, but at least it is respite. And I told him about Frank.

"Frank," he said softly. "Then he isna dead, after all."

"He isn't *born*." I felt another small wave of hysteria break against my ribs, but managed to keep myself under control. "Neither am I."

He stroked and patted me back into silence, making his small murmuring Gaelic sounds.

"When I took ye from Randall at Fort William," he said

suddenly, "you were trying to get back. Back to the stones. And . . . Frank. That's why ye left the grove."

"Yes."

"And I beat you for it." His voice was soft with regret.

"You couldn't know. I couldn't tell you." I was beginning to feel very drowsy indeed.

"No, I dinna suppose ye could." He pulled the plaid closer around me, tucking it gently around my shoulders. "Do ye sleep now, *mo duinne*. No one shall harm ye; I'm here."

I burrowed into the warm curve of his shoulder, letting my tired mind fall through the layers of oblivion. I forced myself to the surface long enough to ask, "Do you really believe me, Jamie?"

He sighed, and smiled ruefully down at me.

"Aye, I believe ye, Sassenach. But it would ha' been a good deal easier if you'd only been a witch."

___

I slept like the dead, awakening sometime after dawn with a terrible headache, stiff in every muscle. Jamie had a few hand-fuls of oats in a small bag in his sporran, and forced me to eat drammach—oats mixed with cold water. It stuck in my throat, but I choked it down.

He was slow and gentle with me, but spoke very little. After breakfast, he quickly packed up the small campsite and sad-dled Donas.

Numb with the shock of recent events, I didn't even ask where we were going. Mounted behind him, I was content to rest my face against the broad slope of his back, feeling the motion of the horse rock me into a state of mindless trance.

We came down from the braes near Loch Madoch, pressing through the chilly dawn mist to the edge of a still sheet of grey. Wild ducks began to rise from the reeds in untidy flocks that circled the marshes, quacking and calling to rouse late sleepers below. By contrast, a well-disciplined wedge of geese passed over us, calling of heartbreak and desolation.

The grey fog lifted near midday on the second day, and a weak sun lighted the meadows filled with yellow gorse and broom. A few miles past the loch, we came out onto a narrow road and turned northwest. The way took us up again, rising into low, rolling hills that gave way gradually to granite tors and crags. We met few travelers on the road, and prudently turned aside into the brush whenever hoofbeats were heard ahead.

The vegetation turned to pine forest. I sniffed deeply, enjoying the crisp, resinous air, though it was turning chill toward dusk. We stopped for the night in a small clearing some way from the path. We scooped together a nestlike wallow of pine needles and blankets and huddled close together for warmth, covered by Jamie's plaid and blanket.

He woke me sometime in the darkness and made love to me, slowly and tenderly, not speaking. I watched stars winking through the lattice of black branches overhead, and fell asleep again with his comforting weight still warm on top of me.

In the morning Jamie seemed more cheerful, or at least more peaceful, as though a difficult decision had been reached. He promised me hot tea for supper, which was small comfort then in the frigid air. Sleepily I followed him back to the path, brushing pine needles and small spiders from my skirt. The narrow path faded during the morning to no more than a faint trace through rough sheep's fescue, zigzagging around the more prominent rocks.

I had been paying little attention to our surroundings, as I dreamily enjoyed the growing warmth of the sun, but suddenly my eye struck a familiar rock formation and I started out of my torpor. I knew where we were. And why.

"Jamie!"

He turned at my exclamation.

"You didna know?" he asked curiously.

"That we were coming here? No, of course not." I felt mildly sick. The hill of Craigh na Dun was no more than a mile away; I could see the hump-backed shape of it through the last shreds of the morning mist.

I swallowed hard. I had tried for nearly six months to reach this place. Now that I was here at last, I wanted to be anywhere else. The standing stones on the hilltop were invisible from below, but they seemed to emanate a subtle terror that reached out for me.

Well below the summit, the footing grew too uncertain for Donas. We dismounted and tethered him to a scrubby pine, continuing on foot.

I was panting and sweating by the time we reached the granite ledge; Jamie showed no signs of exertion, save a faint flush rising from the neck of his shirt. It was quiet here above the pines, but with a steady wind whining faintly in the crevices of the rock. Swallows shot past the ledge, rising abruptly on the air currents in pursuit of insects, dropping like dive bombers, slender wings outspread.

Jamie took my hand to pull me up the last step to the wide flat ledge at the base of the cleft rock. He didn't release it, but drew me close, looking carefully at me, as though memorizing my features. "Why—?" I began, gasping for breath.

"It's your place," he said roughly. "Isn't it?"

"Yes." I stared as though hypnotized at the stone circle. "It looks just the same."

Jamie followed me into the circle. Taking me by the arm, he marched firmly up to the split rock.

"Is it this one?" he demanded.

"Yes." I tried to pull away. "Careful! Don't go too near it!" He glanced from me to the rock, clearly skeptical. Perhaps he was right to be. I felt suddenly doubtful of the truth of my own story.

"I—I don't know anything about it. Perhaps the . . . whatever it is . . . closed behind me. Maybe it only works at certain times of the year. It was near Beltane when I came through last."

Jamie glanced over his shoulder at the sun, a flat disc hanging in mid-sky behind a thin screen of cloud.

"It's almost Samhain now," he said. "All Hallows' Eve. Seems suitable, no?" He shivered involuntarily, in spite of the joke. "When you . . . came through. What did ye do?"

I tried to remember. I felt ice-cold, and I folded my hands under my armpits.

"I walked round the circle, looking at things. Just randomly, though; there was no pattern. And then I came near to the split rock, and I heard a buzzing, like bees—"

It was still like bees. I drew back as though it had been the rattle of a snake.

"It's still here!" I reared in panic, throwing my arms around Jamie, but he set me firmly away from him, his face white, and turned me once again toward the stone.

"What then?" The keening wind was sharp in my ears, but his voice was sharper still.

"I put my hand on the rock."

"Do it, then." He pushed me closer, and when I did not respond, he grasped my wrist and planted my hand firmly against the brindled surface.

Chaos reached out and grabbed me.

The sun stopped whirling behind my eyes at last, and the shriek faded out of my ears. There was another persistent noise, Jamie calling my name.

I felt too sick to sit up or open my eyes, but I flapped my hand weakly, to let him know I was still alive.

"I'm all right," I said.

"Are ye then? Oh, God, Claire!" He clasped me against his chest then, holding me tightly. "Jesus, Claire. I thought ye were dead, sure. You . . . you began to . . . go, somehow. You had the most awful look on your face, like ye were frightened to death. I—I pulled ye back from the stone. I stopped ye. I shouldna have done so—I'm sorry, lassie."

My eyes were open enough now to see his face above me, shocked and frightened.

"It's all right." It was still an effort to speak, and I felt heavy and disoriented, but things were coming clearer. I tried to smile, but felt nothing more than a twitch.

"At least . . . we know . . . it still works."

"Oh, God. Aye, it works." He cast a glance of fearful loathing at the stone.

He left me long enough to wet a kerchief in a puddle of rainwater that stood in one of the stony depressions. He wet my face, still muttering reassurances and apologies. At last I felt well enough to sit up.

"You didn't believe me after all, did you?" Groggy as I was, I felt somehow vindicated. "It's true, though."

"Aye, it's true." He sat next to me, staring at the stone for several minutes. I rubbed the wet cloth over my face, feeling still faint and dizzy. Suddenly he sprang to his feet, walked to the rock and slapped his hand against it.

Nothing whatsoever happened, and after a minute his shoulders slumped and he came back to me.

"Maybe it's only women it works on," I said fuzzily. "It's always women in the legends. Or maybe it's only me."

"Well, it isna me," he said. "Better make sure, though."

"Jamie! Be careful!" I shouted, to no avail. He marched to the stone, slapped it again, threw himself against it, walked through the split and back again, but it remained no more than a solid stone monolith. As for myself, I shuddered at the thought of even approaching that door to madness once again.

And yet. Yet when I had begun to pass into the realm of chaos this time, I had been thinking of Frank. And I had *felt* him, I was sure of it. Somewhere in the void had been a tiny pinprick of light, and he was in it. I knew. I knew also that there had been another point of light, one that sat still beside me, staring at the stone, cheeks gleaming with sweat in spite of the chill of the day.

At last he turned to me and grasped both my hands. He raised them to his lips and kissed each one formally.

"My lady," he said softly. "My . . . Claire. It's no use in waiting. I must part wi' ye now."

My lips were too stiff to speak, but the expression on my face must have been as easily readable as usual.

"Claire," he said urgently, "it's your own time on the other side of . . . that thing. You've a home there, a place. The things that you're used to. And . . . and Frank."

"Yes," I said, "there's Frank."

Jamie caught me by the shoulders, pulling me to my feet and shaking me gently in supplication.

"There's nothing for ye on this side, lass! Nothing save violence and danger. Go!" He pushed me slightly, turning me toward the stone circle. I turned back to him, catching his hands.

"Is there really nothing for me here, Jamie?" I held his eyes, not letting him turn away from me.

He pulled himself gently from my grasp without answering and stood back, suddenly a figure from another time, seen in relief upon a background of hazy hills, the life in his face a trick of the shadowing rock, as if flattened beneath layers of paint, an artist's reminiscence of forgotten places and passions turned to dust.

I looked into his eyes, filled with pain and yearning, and he was flesh again, real and immediate, lover, husband, man.

The anguish I felt must have been reflected in my face, for he hesitated, then turned to the east and pointed down the slope. "Do ye see behind the small clump of oak down there? About halfway."

I saw the clump, and saw what he was pointing at, the half-ruined crofter's cottage, abandoned on the haunted hill.

"I shall go down to the house, and I shall stay there 'til the evening. To make sure—to be sure that you're safe." He looked at me, but made no move to touch me. He closed his eyes, as though he could no longer bear to look at me.

"Goodbye," he said, and turned to go.

I watched him, numb, and then remembered. There was something that I had to tell him. I called after him.

"Jamie!"

He stopped and stood motionless for a moment, fighting to control his face. It was white and strained and his lips were bloodless when he turned back to me.

"Aye?"

"There's something . . . I mean, I have to tell you something before . . . before I go."

He closed his eyes briefly, and I thought he swayed, but it might have been only the wind tugging at his kilts.

"There's no need," he said. "No. Do ye go, lass. Ye shouldna tarry. Go." He made to turn away, but I clutched him by the sleeve.

"Jamie, listen to me! You must!" He shook his head helplessly, lifting a hand as though to push me away.

"Claire . . . no. I can't." The wind was bringing the moisture to his eyes.

"It's the Rising," I said urgently, shaking his arm. "Jamie, listen. Prince Charlie—his army. Colum is right! Do you hear me, Jamie? Colum is right, not Dougal."

"Eh? What d'ye mean, lass?" I had his attention now. He rubbed his sleeve across his face and the eyes that looked down at me were sharp and clear. The wind sang in my ears.

"Prince Charlie. There will be a Rising, Dougal's right about that, but it won't succeed. Charlie's army will do well for a bit, but it will end in slaughter. At Culloden, that's where it will end. The—the clans . . ." In my mind's eye I saw the clan stones, the grey boulders that would lie scattered on the field, each stone bearing the single clan name of the butchered men who lay under it. I took a breath and gripped his hand to steady myself. It was cold as a corpse's. I shuddered and closed my eyes to concentrate on what I was saying.

"The Highlanders—all the clans that follow Charlie—will be wiped out. Hundreds and hundreds of the clansmen will die at Culloden; those that are left will be hunted and killed. The clans will be crushed . . . and they'll not rise again. Not in your time—not even in mine."

I opened my eyes to find him staring at me, expressionless.

"Jamie, stay out of it!" I begged him. "Keep your people out of it if you can, but for the Lord's sake . . . Jamie, if you—" I broke off. I had been going to say "Jamie, if you love me." But I couldn't. I was going to lose him forever, and if I could not speak of love to him before, I could not do it now.

"Don't go to France," I said, softly. "Go to America, or to Spain, to Italy. But for the sake of the people who love you, Jamie, don't set foot on Culloden Field."

He went on staring at me. I wondered if he had heard.

"Jamie? Did you hear me? Do you understand?"

After a moment, he nodded numbly.

"Aye," he said quietly, so quietly I could hardly hear him, beneath the whining of the wind. "Aye, I hear." He dropped my hand.

"Go wi' God . . . *mo duinne.*"

He stepped off the ledge and made his way down the steep incline, bracing his feet against tufts of grass, catching at branches to keep his balance, not looking back. I watched him until he disappeared into the oak clump, walking slowly, like a man wounded, who knows he must keep moving, but feels his life ebbing slowly away through the fingers he has clenched over the wound.

My knees were trembling. Slowly, I lowered myself to the granite shelf and sat cross-legged, watching the swallows about their business. Below, I could just see the roof of the cottage that now held my past. At my back loomed the cleft stone. And my future.

I sat without moving through the afternoon. I tried to force all emotion from my mind and use reason. Jamie certainly had logic on his side when he argued that I should go back: home, safety, Frank; even the small amenities of life that I sorely missed from time to time, like hot baths and indoor plumbing, to say nothing of larger considerations such as proper medical care and convenient travel.

And yet, while I would certainly admit the inconveniences and outright dangers of this place, I would have also to admit that I had enjoyed many aspects of it. If travel was inconvenient, there were no enormous stretches of concrete blanketing the countryside, nor any noisy, stinking autos—contrivances with their own dangers, I reminded myself. Life was much simpler, and so were the people. Not less intelligent, but much more direct—with a few sterling exceptions like Colum ban Campbell MacKenzie, I thought grimly.

Because of Uncle Lamb's work, I had lived in a great many places, many even cruder and more lacking in amenities than this one. I adapted quite easily to rough conditions, and did not really miss "civilization" when away from it, though I adapted just as easily to the presence of niceties like electric cookers and hot-water geysers. I shivered in the cold wind, hugging myself as I stared at the rock.

Rationality did not appear to be helping much. I turned to emotion, and began, shrinking from the task, to reconstruct the details of my married lives—first with Frank, then with

Jamie. The only result of this was to leave me shattered and weeping, the tears forming icy trails on my face.

Well, if not reason nor emotion, what of duty? I had given Frank a wedding vow, and had meant it with all my heart. I had given Jamie the same, meaning to betray it as soon as possible. And which of them would I betray now? I continued to sit, as the sun sank lower in the sky and the swallows disappeared to their nests.

As the evening star began to glow among the black pines' branches, I concluded that in this situation reason was of little use. I would have to rely on something else; just what, I wasn't sure. I turned toward the split rock and took a step, then another, and another. Pausing, I faced around and tried it in the other direction. A step, then another, and another, and before I even knew that I had decided, I was halfway down the slope, scrabbling wildly at grass clumps, slipping and falling through the patches of granite scree.

When I reached the cottage, breathless with fear lest he had left already, I was reassured to see Donas hobbled and grazing nearby. The horse raised his head and eyed me unpleasantly. Walking softly, I pushed the door open.

He was in the front room, asleep on a narrow oak settle. He slept on his back, as he usually did, hands crossed on his stomach, mouth slightly open. The last rays of daylight from the window behind me limned his face like a metal mask; the silver tracks of dried tears glinted on golden skin, and the copper stubble of his beard gleamed dully.

I stood watching him for a moment, filled with an unutterable tenderness. Moving as quietly as I could, I lay down beside him on the narrow settle and nestled close. He turned to me in sleep as he so often did, gathering me spoon-fashion against his chest and resting his cheek against my hair. Half-conscious, he reached to smooth my hair away from his nose; I felt the sudden jerk as he came awake to realize that I was there, and then we overbalanced and crashed together onto the floor, Jamie on top of me.

I didn't have the slightest doubt that he was solid flesh. I pushed a knee into his abdomen, grunting.

"Get off! I can't breathe!"

Instead, he aggravated my breathless condition by kissing me thoroughly. I ignored the lack of oxygen temporarily in order to concentrate on more important things.

We held each other for a long time without speaking. At last he murmured "Why?"—his mouth muffled in my hair.

I kissed his cheek, damp and salty. I could feel his heart beating against my ribs, and wanted nothing more than to stay there forever, not moving, not making love, just breathing the same air.

"I had to," I said. I laughed, a little shakily. "You don't know how close it was. The hot baths nearly won." And I wept then, and shook a little, because the choice was so freshly made, and because my joy for the man I held in my arms was mingled with a tearing grief for the man I would never see again.

Jamie held me tightly, pressing me down with his weight, as though to protect me, to save me from being swept away by the roaring pull of the stone circle. At length my tears were spent, and I lay exhausted, head against his comforting chest. It had grown altogether dark by this time, but still he held me, murmuring softly as though I were a child afraid of the night. We clung to each other, unwilling to let go even long enough to start a fire or light a candle.

At length Jamie rose, and picking me up, carried me to the settle, where he sat with me cradled on his lap. The door of the cottage still hung open, and we could see the stars beginning to burn over the valley below.

"Do you know," I said drowsily, "that it takes thousands and thousands of years for the light of those stars to reach us? In fact, some of the stars we see may be dead by now, but we won't know it, because we still see the light."

"Is that so?" he answered, stroking my back. "I didna know that."

I must have fallen asleep, head on his shoulder, but roused briefly when he laid me gently on the floor, on a makeshift bed of blankets from the horse's saddleroll. He lay down beside me, and drew me close again.

"Lay your head, lass," he whispered. "In the morning, I'll take ye home."

We rose just before dawn, and were on the downward trail when the sun rose, eager to leave Craigh na Dun.

"Where are we going, Jamie?" I asked, rejoicing that I could look forward into a future that held him, even as I left behind the last chance of returning to the man who had—who would? once love me.

Jamie reined in the horse, pausing to look over his shoulder for a moment. The forbidding circle of standing stones was invisible from here, but the rocky hillside seemed to rise impassable behind us, bristling with boulders and gorse bushes. From here, the crumbling husk of the cottage looked like one more crag, a bony knuckle jutting from the granite fist of the hill.

"I wish I could have fought him for you," he said abruptly, looking back at me. His blue eyes were dark and earnest.

I smiled at him, touched.

"It wasn't your fight, it was mine. But you won it anyway." I reached out a hand, and he squeezed it.

"Aye, but that's not what I meant. If I'd fought him man to man and won, ye'd not need to feel any regret over it." He hesitated. "If ever—"

"There aren't any more ifs," I said firmly. "I thought of every one of them yesterday, and here I still am."

"Thank God," he said, smiling, "and God help you." Then he added, "Though I'll never understand why."

I put my arms around his waist and held on as the horse slithered down the last steep slope.

"Because," I said, "I bloody well can't do without you, Jamie Fraser, and that's all about it. Now, where are you taking me?"

Jamie twisted in his saddle, to look back up the slope.

"I prayed all the way up that hill yesterday," he said softly. "Not for you to stay; I didna think that would be right. I prayed I'd be strong enough to send ye away." He shook his head, still gazing up the hill, a faraway look in his eyes.

"I said 'Lord, if I've never had courage in my life before, let me have it now. Let me be brave enough not to fall on my knees and beg her to stay.' " He pulled his eyes away from the cottage and smiled briefly at me.

"Hardest thing I ever did, Sassenach." He turned in the saddle, and reined the horse's head toward the east. It was a rare bright morning, and the early sun gilded everything, drawing a thin line of fire along the edge of the reins, the curve of the horse's neck, and the broad planes of Jamie's face and shoulders.

He took a deep breath and nodded across the moor, toward a distant pass between two crags.

"So now I suppose I can do the second-hardest thing." He kicked the horse gently, clicking his tongue. "We're going home, Sassenach. To Lallybroch."

PART FIVE

Lallybroch

26

The Laird's Return

At first, we were so happy only to be with each other and away from Leoch that we didn't talk much. Across the flat of the moor, Donas could carry us both without strain, and I rode with my arms about Jamie's waist, glorying in the feel of the sun-warmed muscle shifting under my cheek. Whatever problems we might be facing—and I knew there were plenty—we were together. Forever. And that was enough.

As the first shock of happiness mellowed into the glow of companionship, we began to talk again. About the countryside through which we were passing, at first. Then, cautiously, about me, and where I had come from. He was fascinated by my descriptions of modern life, though I could tell that most of my stories seemed like fairy tales to him. He loved especially the descriptions of automobiles, tanks, and airplanes, and made me describe them over and over, as minutely as I could. By tacit agreement, we avoided any mention of Frank.

As we covered more countryside, the conversation turned back to our present time; Colum, the Castle, then the stag hunt and the Duke.

"He seems a nice chap," Jamie remarked. As the going became rougher, he had dismounted and walked alongside, which made conversation easier.

"I thought so too," I answered. "But—"

"Oh, aye, ye canna put too much faith in what a man seems these days," he agreed. "Still, we got on, he and I. We'd sit together and talk of an evening, round the fire in the hunting lodge. He's a good bit brighter than he seems, for the one thing; he knows how that voice makes him seem, and I think he uses it to make himself look a bit of a fool, while all the time the mind is there, workin' behind his eyes."

"Mmm. That's what I'm afraid of. Did you . . . tell him?"

He shrugged. "A bit. He knew my name, of course, from that time before, at the castle."

I laughed at the memory of his account of that time. "Did you, er, reminisce about old times?"

He grinned, the ends of his hair floating about his face in the autumn breeze.

"Oh, just a bit. He asked me once whether I still suffered from stomach trouble. I kept my face straight and answered that as a rule, no, but I thought perhaps I felt a bit of griping coming on just now. He laughed, and said he hoped it did not discommode my beautiful wife."

I laughed myself. Right now, what the Duke might or mightn't do didn't seem of overwhelming importance. Nevertheless, he might one day be of use.

"I told him a little," Jamie went on. "That I was outlawed, but not guilty of the charge, though I'd have precious little chance of proving it. He seemed sympathetic, but I was cautious about telling him the circumstances—let alone the fact that there's a price on my head. I hadna yet made up my mind whether to trust him with the rest of it, when . . . well, when Old Alec came tearing into the camp like the devil himself was on his tail, and Murtagh and I left the same way."

This reminded me. "Where *is* Murtagh?" I asked. "He came back with you to Leoch?" I hoped the little clansman hadn't fallen afoul of either Colum or the villagers of Cranesmuir.

"He started back wi' me, but the beast he was riding was no match for Donas. Aye, a bonny wee lad ye are, Donas *mo buidheag*." He slapped the shimmering sorrel neck, and Donas snorted and ruffled his mane. Jamie glanced up at me and smiled.

"Dinna worry for Murtagh. There's a canty wee bird can mind for himself."

"Canty? Murtagh?" I knew the word meant "cheerful," which seemed incongruous to a degree. "I don't think I've ever seen him smile. Have you?"

"Oh, aye. At least twice."

"How long have you known him?"

"Twenty-three years. He's my godfather."

"Oh. Well, *that* explains a bit. I didn't think he'd bother on my account."

Jamie patted my leg. "Of course he would. He likes you."

"I'll take your word for it."

Having thus approached the subject of recent events, I took a deep breath and asked something I badly wanted to know.

"Jamie?"

"Aye?"

"Geillis Duncan. Will they . . . will they really burn her?" He glanced up at me, frowning slightly, and nodded.

"I expect so. Not 'til after the child is born, though. Is that what troubles ye?"

"One of the things. Jamie, look at this." I tried to push up the voluminous sleeve, failed, and settled for pulling the neck of the shirt off my shoulder to display my vaccination scar.

"God in heaven," he said slowly, after I had explained. He looked sharply at me. "So that's why . . . is she from your own time then?"

I shrugged helplessly. "I don't know. All I can say is that she was likely born sometime after 1920; that's when public inoculation came in." I looked over my shoulder, but low-lying clouds hid the crags that now separated us from Leoch. "I don't suppose I ever will know . . . now."

Jamie took Donas's reins and led him aside, under a small pine grove, on the banks of a small stream. He grasped me around the waist and lifted me down.

"Dinna grieve for her," he said firmly, holding me. "She's a wicked woman; a murderer, if not a witch. She did kill her husband, no?"

"Yes," I said, with a shudder, remembering Arthur Duncan's glazed eyes.

"I still dinna understand why she should kill him, though,"

he said, shaking his head in puzzlement. "He had money, a good position. And I doubt he beat her."

I looked at him in exasperated amazement.

"And that's your definition of a good husband?"

"Well . . . yes," he said, frowning. "What else might she want?"

"What *else*?" I was so taken aback, I just looked at him for a moment, then slid down on the grass and started to laugh.

"What's funny? I thought this was murder." He smiled, though, and put an arm around me.

"I was just thinking," I said, still snorting a bit, "if your definition of a good husband is one with money and position who doesn't beat his wife . . . what does that make *you*?"

"Oh," he said. He grinned. "Well, Sassenach, I never said I was a good husband. Neither did you. 'Sadist,' I think ye called me, and a few other things that I wouldna repeat for the sake of decency. But not a good husband."

"Good. Then I won't feel obliged to poison you with cyanide."

"Cyanide?" He looked down curiously at me. "What's that?"

"The thing that killed Arthur Duncan. It's a bloody fast, powerful poison. Fairly common in my time, but not here." I licked my lips meditatively.

"I tasted it on his lips, and just that tiny bit was enough to make my whole face go numb. It acts almost instantly, as you saw. I should have known then—about Geilie, I mean. I imagine she made it from crushed peach pits or cherry stones, though it must have been the devil of a job."

"Did she tell ye why she did it, then?"

I sighed and rubbed my feet. My shoes had been lost in the struggle at the loch, and I tended to pick up stickers and cockleburs, my feet not being hardened as Jamie's were.

"That and a good deal more. If there's anything to eat in your saddlebags, why don't you fetch it, and I'll tell you all about it."

We entered the valley of Broch Tuarach the next day. As we came down out of the foothills, I spotted a solitary rider, some distance away, heading roughly in our direction. He was the first person I had seen since we had left Cranesmuir.

The man approaching us was stout and prosperous-looking, with a snowy stock showing at the neck of a serviceable grey serge coat, its long tails covering all but an inch or two of his breeches.

We had been traveling for the best part of a week, sleeping out-of-doors, washing in the cold, fresh water of the burns, and living quite well off such rabbits and fish as Jamie could catch, and such edible plants and berries as I could find. Between our efforts, our diet was better than that in the Castle, fresher, and certainly more varied, if a little unpredictable.

But if nutrition was well served by an outdoor life, appearance was another thing, and I took hasty stock of our looks as the gentleman on horseback hesitated, frowning, then changed direction and trotted slowly toward us to investigate.

Jamie, who had insisted on walking most of the way to spare the horse, was a disreputable sight indeed, hose stained to the knees with reddish dust, spare shirt torn by brambles and a week's growth of beard bristling fiercely from cheek and jaw.

His hair had grown long enough in the last months to reach his shoulders. Usually clubbed into a queue or laced back, it was free now, thick and unruly, with small bits of leaf and stick caught in the disordered coppery locks. Face burned a deep ruddy bronze, boots cracked from walking, dirk and sword thrust through his belt, he looked a wild Highlander indeed.

I was hardly better. Covered modestly enough in the billows of Jamie's best shirt and the remnants of my shift, barefoot, and shawled in his plaid, I looked a right ragamuffin. Encouraged by the misty dampness and lacking any restraint in the form of comb or brush, my hair rioted all over my head. It had grown as well during my sojourn at the Castle, and floated in clouds and tangles about my shoulders, drifting into my eyes whenever the wind was behind us, as it was now.

Shoving the wayward locks out of my eyes, I watched the cautious approach of the gentleman in grey. Jamie, seeing him, brought our own horse to a stop and waited for him to draw near enough for speech.

"It's Jock Graham," he said to me, "from up the way at Murch Nardagh."

The man came within a few yards, reined up and sat looking us over carefully. His eyes, pouched with fat, crinkled and rested suspiciously on Jamie, then suddenly sprang wide.

"Lallybroch?" he said unbelievingly.

Jamie nodded benignly. With a completely unfounded air of proprietorial pride, he laid a hand on my thigh and said, "and my lady Lallybroch."

Jock Graham's mouth dropped an inch or two, then was hastily drawn up again into an expression of flustered respect.

"Ah . . . my . . . lady," he said, belatedly doffing his hat and bowing in my direction. "You'll be, er, going home, then?" he asked, trying to keep his fascinated gaze from resting on my leg, bared to the knee by a rent in my shift, and stained with elderberry juice.

"Aye." Jamie glanced over his shoulder, toward the rift in the hill he had told me was the entrance to Broch Tuarach. "You'll have been there lately, Jock?"

Graham pulled his eyes away from me and looked at Jamie. "Och? Oh, aye. Aye, I've been there. They're all well. Be pleased to see ye, I expect. Go well, then, Fraser." And with a hasty dig into his horse's ribs, he turned aside and headed up the valley.

We watched him go. Suddenly, a hundred yards away, he paused. Turning in the saddle, he rose in his stirrups and cupped his mouth to shout. The sound, borne by the wind, reached us thin but distinct.

"Welcome home!"

And he disappeared over a rise.

Broch Tuarach means "the north-facing tower." From the side of the mountain above, the broch that gave the small estate its name was no more than another mound of rocks, much like those that lay at the foot of the hills we had been traveling through.

We came down through a narrow, rocky gap between two crags, leading the horse between boulders. Then the going was easier, the land sloping more gently down through the fields and scattered cottages, until at last we struck a small winding road that led to the house.

It was larger than I had expected; a handsome three-story manor of harled white stone, windows outlined in the natural grey stone, a high slate roof with multiple chimneys, and several smaller whitewashed buildings clustered about it, like chicks about a hen. The old stone broch, situated on a small rise to the rear of the house, rose sixty feet above the ground, cone-topped like a witch's hat, girdled with three rows of tiny arrow-slits.

As we drew near, there was a sudden terrible racket from the direction of the outbuildings, and Donas shied and reared. No horseman, I promptly fell off, landing ignominiously in the dusty road. With an eye for the relative importance of things, Jamie leapt for the plunging horse's bridle, leaving me to fend for myself.

The dogs were almost upon me, baying and growling, by the time I found my feet. To my panicked eyes, there seemed to be at least a dozen of them, all with teeth bared and wicked. There was a shout from Jamie.

"Bran! Luke! *Sheas!*"

The dogs skidded to a halt within a few feet of me, confused. They milled, growling uncertainly, until he spoke again.

"*Sheas, mo maise!* Stand, ye wee heathen!" They did, and the largest dog's tail began gradually to wag, once, and then twice, questioningly.

"Claire. Come take the horse. He'll not let them close, and it's me they want. Walk slowly; they'll no harm ye." He spoke casually, not to alarm either horse or dogs further. I was not so sanguine, but edged carefully toward him. Donas jerked his head and rolled his eyes as I took the bridle, but I was in no mood to put up with tantrums, and I yanked the rein firmly down and grabbed the headstall.

The thick velvet lips writhed back from his teeth, but I

jerked harder. I put my face close to the big, glaring golden eye and glared back.

"Don't try it!" I warned, "or you'll end up as dogsmeat, and I won't lift a hand to save you!"

Jamie meanwhile was slowly walking toward the dogs, one hand held out fistlike toward them. What had seemed a large pack was only four dogs: a small brownish rat-terrier, two ruffed and spotted shepherds, and a huge black and tan monster that could have stood in for the Hound of the Baskervilles with no questions asked.

This slavering creature stretched out a neck thicker than my waist and sniffed gently at the proffered knuckles. A tail like a ship's cable beat back and forth with increasing fervor. Then it flung back its enormous head, baying with joy, and leapt on its master, knocking him flat in the road.

" 'In which Odysseus returns from the Trojan War and is recognized by his faithful hound,' " I remarked to Donas, who snorted briefly, giving his opinion either of Homer, or of the undignified display of emotion going on in the roadway.

Jamie, laughing, was ruffling the fur and pulling the ears of the dogs, who were all trying to lick his face at once. Finally he beat them back sufficiently to rise, keeping his feet with difficulty against their ecstatic demonstrations.

"Well, *someone's* glad to see me, at any rate," he said, grinning, as he patted the beast's head. "That's Luke—" he pointed to the terrier, "and Elphin and Mars. Brothers, they are, and bonny sheep-dogs. And this," he laid an affectionate hand on the enormous black head, which slobbered in appreciation, "is Bran."

"I'll take your word for it," I said, cautiously extending a knuckle to be sniffed. "*What* is he?"

"A staghound." He scratched the pricked ears, quoting

> "Thus Fingal chose his hounds:
> Eye like sloe, ear like leaf,
> Chest like horse, hough like sickle
> And the tail joint far from the head."

"If those are the qualifications, then you're right," I said, inspecting Bran. "If his tail joint were any further from his head, you could ride him."

"I used to, when I was small—not Bran, I don't mean, but his grandfather, Nairn."

He gave the hound a final pat and straightened, gazing toward the house. He took the restive Donas's bridle and turned him downhill.

"In which Odysseus returns to his home, disguised as a beggar, . . ." he quoted in Greek, having picked up my earlier remark. "And now," he said, straightening his collar with some grimness, "I suppose it's time to go and deal with Penelope and her suitors."

When we reached the double doors, the dogs panting at our heels, Jamie hesitated.

"Should we knock?" I asked, a bit nervous. He looked at me in astonishment.

"It's my home," he said, and pushed the door open.

He led me through the house, ignoring the few startled servants we passed, past the entrance hall and through a small gun room, into the drawing room. It boasted a wide hearth with a polished mantel, and bits of silver and glass gleamed here and there, capturing the late-afternoon sun. For a moment, I thought the room was empty. Then I saw a faint movement in one corner near the hearth.

She was smaller than I had expected. With a brother like Jamie, I had imagined her at least my height, or even taller, but the woman by the fire barely reached five feet. Her back was to us as she reached for something on the shelf of the china cabinet, and the ends of her dress sash dipped close to the floor.

Jamie froze when he saw her.

"Jenny," he said.

The woman turned and I caught an impression of brows black as ink-squills, and blue eyes wide in a white face before she launched herself at her brother.

"Jamie!" Small as she was, she jarred him with the impact of her embrace. His arms went about her shoulders in reflex and they clung for a moment, her face tight against his shirtfront, his hand tender on the nape of her neck. On his face was an expression of such mingled uncertainty and yearning joy that I felt almost an intruder.

Then she pressed herself closer to him, murmuring something in Gaelic, and his expression dissolved in shock. He grasped her by the arms and held her away from him, looking down.

The faces were much alike; the same oddly slanted dark blue eyes and broad cheekbones. The same thin, blade-bridged nose, just a trifle too long. But she was dark where Jamie was fair, with cascades of black curly hair, bound back with green ribbon.

She was beautiful, with clear-drawn features and alabaster skin. She was also clearly in a state of advanced pregnancy.

Jamie had gone white at the lips. "Jenny," he whispered, shaking his head. "Oh, Jenny. *Mo cridh.*"

Her attention was distracted just then by the appearance of a small child in the doorway, and she pulled away from her brother without noticing his discomposure. She took the little boy's hand and led him into the room, murmuring encouragement. He hung back a little, thumb in mouth for comfort, peering up at the strangers from behind his mother's skirts.

For his mother she plainly was. He had her mop of thick, curly black hair and the square set of her shoulders, though the face was not hers.

"This is wee Jamie," she said, looking proudly down at the lad. "And this is your uncle Jamie, *mo cridh,* the one you're named for."

"For me? You named him for me?" Jamie looked like a fighter who has just been punched very hard in the stomach. He backed away from mother and child until he blundered into a chair, and sank into it as though the strength had gone from his legs. He hid his face in his hands.

His sister by this time was aware that something was amiss. She touched him tentatively on the shoulder.

"Jamie? What is it, my dearie? Are ye ill?"

He looked up at her then, and I could see his eyes were full of tears.

"Did ye have to do that, Jenny? Do ye think that I've not

suffered enough for what happened—for what I let happen—that ye must name Randall's bastard for me, to be a reproach to me so long as I live?"

Jenny's face, normally pale, lost all vestiges of color.

"Randall's bastard?" she said blankly. "John Randall, ye mean? The Redcoat captain?"

"Aye, the Redcoat captain. Who else would I mean, for God's sake! You'll remember him, I suppose?" Jamie was recovering enough of his customary poise for sarcasm.

Jenny eyed her brother closely, one arched brow lifted in suspicion.

"Have ye lost your senses, man?" she inquired. "Or have ye taken a drop too much along the way?"

"I should never have come back," he muttered. He rose then, stumbling slightly and tried to pass without touching her. She stood her ground, however, and gripped him by the arm.

"Correct me, brother, if I'm wrong," Jenny said slowly, "but I've the strong impression you're saying I've played the whore to Captain Randall, and what I'm askin' myself is what maggots you've got in your brain to make ye say so?"

"Maggots, is it?" Jamie turned to her, mouth twisted with bitterness. "I wish it were so; I'd rather I was dead and in my grave than to see my sister brought to such a pass." He seized her by the shoulders, and shook her slightly, crying out, "Why, Jenny, why? To have ye ruin yourself for me was shame enough to kill me. But this . . ." He dropped his hands then, with a gesture of despair that took in the protruding belly, swelling accusingly under the light smocking.

He turned abruptly toward the door, and an elderly woman, who had been listening avidly with the child clinging to her skirts, drew back in alarm.

"I should not have come. I'll go."

"You'll do no such thing, Jamie Fraser," his sister said sharply. "Not before you've listened to me. Sit yourself down, then, and I'll tell ye about Captain Randall, since ye want to know."

"I *don't* want to know! I don't want to hear it!" As she advanced toward him, he turned sharply away to the window that looked out over the yard. She followed him, saying "Jamie . . ." but he repelled her with a violent gesture.

"No! Don't talk to me! I've said I canna bear to hear it!"

"Och, is that a fact?" She eyed her brother, standing at the window with his legs braced wide apart, hands on the sill and back stubbornly set against her. She bit her lip and a calculating look came over her face. Quick as lightning, she stooped and her hand shot under his kilt like a striking snake.

Jamie let out a roar of sheer outrage and stood bolt upright with shock. He tried to turn, then froze as she apparently tightened her grip.

"There's men as are sensible," she said to me, with a wicked smile, "and beasts as are biddable. Others ye'll do nothing with, unless ye have 'em by the ballocks. Now, ye can listen to me in a civil way," she said to her brother, "or I can twist a bit. Hey?"

He stood still, red-faced, breathing heavily through clenched teeth. "I'll listen," he said, "and then I'll wring your wee neck, Janet! Let me go!"

No sooner did she oblige than he whirled on her.

"What in hell d'ye think you're doing?" he demanded. "Tryin' to shame me before my own wife?" Jenny was not fazed by his outrage. She rocked back on her heels, viewing her brother and me sardonically.

"Weel, and if she's your wife, I expect she's more familiar wi' your balls than what I am. I havena seen them myself since ye got old enough to wash alone. Grown a bit, no?"

Jamie's face went through several alarming transformations, as the dictates of civilized behavior struggled with the primitive impulse of a younger brother to clout his sister over the head. Civilization at length won out, and he said through his teeth, with what dignity he could summon, "Leave my balls out of it. And then, since you'll not rest 'til ye make me hear it, *tell* me about Randall. Tell me why ye disobeyed my orders and chose to dishonor yourself and your family instead."

Jenny put her hands on her hips and drew herself to her full height, ready for combat. Slower than he to lose her temper; still she had one, no doubt of that.

"Oh, disobey your orders, is it? That's what eats at ye, Jamie, isn't it? You know best, and we'll all do as ye say, or we'll come to rack and ruin, nae doubt." She flounced angrily. "And if I'd done as *you* said, that day, you'd ha' been dead in the dooryard, Faither hanged or in prison for killing Randall, and the lands gone forfeit to the Crown. To say nothing of me, wi' my home and family gone, needing to beg in the byroads to live."

Not pale at all now, Jamie was flushed with anger.

"Aye, so ye chose to sell yourself rather than beg! I'd sooner have died in my blood and seen Faither and the lands in hell along with me, and well ye know it!"

"Aye, I know it! You're a ninny, Jamie, and always have been!" his sister returned in exasperation.

"Fine thing for *you* to say! You're not content wi' ruining your good name and my own, ye must go on with the scandal, and flaunt your shame to the whole neighborhood!"

"You'll not speak to me in that way, James Fraser, brother or no! What d'ye mean, 'my shame'? Ye great fool, you—"

"What I *mean*? When you're goin' about swelled out to here like a mad toad?" He mimicked her belly with a contemptuous swipe of the hand.

She took one step back, drew back her hand and slapped him with all the force she could muster. The impact jarred his head back and left a white outline of her fingers printed on his cheek. He slowly raised a hand to the mark, staring at his sister. Her eyes were glittering dangerously and her bosom heaved. The words spilled out in a torrent between clenched white teeth.

"Toad, is it? Stinking coward—ye've no more courage than to leave me here, thinking ye dead or imprisoned, wi' no word from one day to the next, and then ye come strolling in one fine day—with a wife, no less—and sit in my drawing room calling me toad and harlot and—"

"I didna call ye harlot, but I should! How can ye—"

Despite the differences in their heights, brother and sister were almost nose to nose, hissing at one another in an effort to keep their carrying voices from ringing through the old manor house. The effort was largely wasted, judging from the glimpses I caught of various interested faces peeping discreetly from kitchen, hall, and window. The laird of Broch Tuarach was having an interesting homecoming, to be sure.

I thought it best to let them have it out without my presence, and so I stepped quietly into the hall, with an awkward nod to the elderly woman, and continued into the yard. There was a small arbor there with a bench, on which I seated myself, looking about with interest.

Besides the arbor, there was a small walled garden, blooming with the last of the summer roses. Beyond it was what Jamie referred to as "the doocot"; or so I assumed, from the assorted pigeons that were fluttering in and out of the pierced-work opening at the top of the building.

I knew there was a barn and a shed for silage; these must be to the other side of the house, with the farm's granary and the henyard, kailyard, and disused chapel. Which still left a small stone building on this side unaccounted for. The light autumn wind was from that direction; I sniffed deeply, and was rewarded with the rich smell of hops and yeast. That was the brewhouse, then, where the beer and ale for the estate were made.

The road past the gate led up and over a small hill. As I looked, a small group of men appeared at the crest, silhouetted in the evening light. They seemed to hover a moment, as though taking leave of each other. This appeared to be the case, for only one came down the hill toward the house, the others striking off through the fields toward a clump of cottages in the distance.

As the single man came down the hill, I could see that he limped badly. When he came through the gate, the reason for it was apparent. The right leg was missing below the knee, and he wore a wooden peg in replacement.

In spite of the limp, he moved youthfully. In fact, as he drew near to the arbor, I could see that he was only in his twenties. He was tall, nearly as tall as Jamie, but much narrower through the shoulder, thin, in fact, nearly to the point of skinniness.

He paused at the entrance to the arbor, leaning heavily on the lattice, and looked in at me with interest. Thick brown hair fell smoothly over a high brow, and deep-set brown eyes held a look of patient good humor.

The voices of Jamie and his sister had risen while I waited outside. The windows were open to the warm weather, and the disputants were quite audible from the arbor, though not all the words were clear.

"Interfering, nosy bitch!" came Jamie's voice, loud on the soft evening air.

"Havena the decency to . . ." His sister's reply was lost in a sudden breeze.

The newcomer nodded easily toward the house.

"Ah, Jamie's home, then."

I nodded in reply, not sure whether I should introduce myself. It didn't matter, for the young man smiled and inclined his head to me.

"I'm Ian Murray, Jenny's husband. And I imagine ye'll be . . . ah . . ."

"The Sassenach wench Jamie's married," I finished for him. "My name is Claire. Did you know about it, then?" I asked, as he laughed. My mind was racing. Jenny's *husband*?

"Oh, aye. We heard from Joe Orr, who'd got it from a tinker in Ardraigh. Ye canna keep anything secret long in the Highlands. You should know that, even if you've been wed as little as a month. Jenny's been wondering for weeks what you'd be like."

"Whore!" Jamie bellowed from inside the house. Jenny's husband didn't turn a hair, but went on examining me with friendly curiosity.

"You're a bonny lass," he said, looking me over frankly. "Are ye fond of Jamie?"

"Well . . . yes. Yes, I am," I answered, a bit taken aback. I was becoming accustomed to the directness that characterized most Highlanders, but it still took me unawares from time to time.

He pursed his lips and nodded as though satisfied, and sat down beside me on the bench.

"Better let them have a few minutes longer," he said, with a wave at the house, where the shouting had now turned to Gaelic. He seemed completely unconcerned as to the cause of the battle. "Frasers dinna listen to anything when they've their dander up. When they've shouted themselves out, sometimes ye can make them see reason, but not 'til then."

"Yes, I noticed," I said dryly, and he laughed.

"So you've been wed long enough to find that out, eh? We heard as how Dougal made Jamie wed ye," he said, ignoring the battle and concentrating his attention on me. "But Jenny said it would take more than Dougal MacKenzie to make Jamie do something he didna care to. Now that I see ye, of course I can see why he did it." He lifted his brows, inviting further explanation, but politely not forcing it.

"I imagine he had his reasons," I said, my attention divided between my companion and the house, where the sounds of combat continued. "I don't want . . . I mean, I hope . . ." Ian correctly interpreted my hesitations and my glance toward the drawing-room windows.

"Oh, I expect you've something to do with it. But she'd take it out of him whether you were here or not. She loves Jamie something fierce, ye know, and she worried a lot while he was gone, especially with her father goin' so sudden. Ye'll know about that?" The brown eyes were sharp and observant, as though to gauge the depth of confidence between me and Jamie.

"Yes, Jamie told me."

"Ah." He nodded toward the house. "Then, of course, she's wi' child."

"Yes, I noticed that too," I said.

"Hard to miss, is it no?" Ian answered with a grin, and we both laughed. "Makes her frachetty," he explained, "not that I'd blame her. But it would take a braver man than me to cross words wi' a woman in her ninth month." He leaned back, stretching his wooden leg out in front of him.

"Lost it at Daumier with Fergus nic Leodhas," he explained. "Grape shot. Aches a wee bit toward the end of the day." He rubbed the flesh just above the leather cuff that attached the peg to his stump.

"Have you tried rubbing it with balm of Gilead?" I asked. "Water-pepper or stewed rue might help too."

"I've not tried the water-pepper," he answered, interested. "I'll ask Jenny does she know how to make it."

"Oh, I'd be glad to make it for you," I said, liking him. I looked toward the house again. "If we stay long enough," I added doubtfully. We chatted inconsequentially for a little, both listening with one ear to the confrontation going on beyond the window, until Ian hitched forward, carefully settling his artificial limb under him before rising.

"I imagine we should go in now. If either of them stops shouting long enough to hear the other, they'll be hurting each other's feelings."

"I hope that's all they hurt."

Ian chuckled. "Oh, I dinna think Jamie would strike her. He's used to forbearance in the face of provocation. As for Jenny, she might slap his face, but that's all."

"She already did that."

"Weel, the guns are locked up, and all the knives are in the kitchen, except what Jamie's wearing. And I don't suppose he'll let her close enough to get his dirk away from him. Nay, they're safe enough." He paused at the door. "Now, as for you and me . . ." He winked solemnly. "That's a different matter."

⟡

Inside, the maids started and flitted nervously away at Ian's approach. The housekeeper, though, was still hovering by the drawing room door in fascination, drinking in the scene within, Jamie's namesake cradled against her capacious bosom. Such was her concentration that when Ian spoke to her, she jumped as though he had run a hatpin into her, and put a hand to her palpitating heart.

Ian nodded politely to her, took the little boy in his arms, and led the way into the drawing room. We paused just inside the door to survey the scene. Brother and sister had paused for breath, both still bristling and glaring like a pair of angry cats.

Small Jamie, spotting his mother, struggled and kicked to get down from Ian's arms, and once on the floor, made for her like a homing pigeon. "Mama!" he cried. "Up! Jamie up!" Turning, she scooped up the little boy and held him like a weapon against her shoulder.

"Can ye tell your uncle how old ye are, sweetheart?" she asked him, throttling her voice down to a coo—under which the sound of clashing steel was still all too apparent. The boy heard it; he turned and burrowed his face into his mother's neck. She patted his back mechanically, still glaring at her brother.

"Since he'll not tell ye, I will. He's two, come last August. And if you're bright enough to count—which I take leave to doubt—you'll see he was conceived six months past the time I last saw yon Randall, which was in our own dooryard, beating the living daylight out of my brother with a saber."

"That's so, is it?" Jamie glowered at his sister. "I've heard a bit differently. It's common knowledge you've taken the man to your bed; not the once, but as your lover. That child's his." He nodded contemptuously at his namesake, who had turned to peer under his mother's chin at this big, loud stranger. "I believe ye when ye say the new bastard you're carrying is not; Randall was in France 'til this March. So you're not only a whore, but an unchoosy one too. Who fathered this last devil's-spawn on ye?"

The tall young man beside me coughed apologetically, breaking the tension in the room.

"I did," he said mildly. "That one too." Advancing stiffly on his wooden leg, he took the little boy from his fuming wife and set him in the crook of his arm. "Favors me a bit, some say."

In fact, seen side by side, the faces of man and boy were nearly identical, allowing for the round cheeks of the one and the crooked nose of the other. The same high brow and narrow lips. The same feathery brows arched over the same deep, liquid-brown eyes. Jamie, staring at the pair of them, looked rather as though he'd been hit in the small of the back with a sandbag. He closed his mouth and swallowed once, clearly having no idea what to do next.

"Ian," he said, a little weakly. "You're married, then?"

"Oh, aye," his brother-in-law said cheerfully. "Wouldn't do, otherwise, would it?"

"I see," Jamie murmured. He cleared his throat and bobbed his head at his newly discovered brother-in-law. "It's, er, it's kind of ye, Ian. To take her, I mean. Most kind."

Feeling that he might be in need of some moral support at this point, I moved to Jamie's side, and touched his arm. His sister's eyes lingered on me speculatively, but she said nothing. Jamie looked around and seemed startled to find me there, as though he had forgotten my existence. And no wonder if he had, I thought. But he seemed relieved by the interruption, at least, and put out a hand to draw me forward.

"My wife," he said, rather abruptly. He nodded toward Jenny and Ian. "My sister, and, her, ah . . ." he trailed off, as Ian and I exchanged polite smiles.

Jenny was not to be distracted by social niceties.

"What d'ye mean, it's kind of him to take me?" she demanded, ignoring the introductions. "As if I didna ken!" Ian looked inquiringly at her, and she waved a disdainful hand at Jamie. "He means it was kind of ye to wed me in my soiled condition!" She gave a snort that would have done credit to someone twice her size. "Bletherer!"

"Soiled condition?" Ian looked startled, and Jamie suddenly leaned forward and grasped his sister hard about the upper arm.

"Did ye not tell him about Randall?" He sounded truly shocked. "Jenny, how could ye do such a thing?"

Only Ian's hand on Jenny's other arm restrained her from flying at her brother's throat. Ian drew her firmly behind him, and turning, set small Jamie in her arms, so that she was forced to grasp the child to save him falling. Then Ian put an arm about Jamie's shoulders and tactfully steered him a safe distance away.

"It's hardly a matter for the drawing room," he said, low-voiced and deprecating, "but ye might be interested to know that your sister was virgin on her wedding night. I was, after all, in a position to say."

Jenny's wrath was now more or less evenly divided between brother and husband.

"How dare ye to say such things in my presence, Ian Murray!?" she flamed. "Or out of it, either! My wedding night's no one's business but mine and yours—sure it's not *his*! Next you'll be showing him the sheets from my bridal bed!"

"Weel, if I did now, it would shut him up, no?" said Ian soothingly. "Come now, *mi dhu*, ye shouldna worrit yourself, it's bad for the babe. And the shouting troubles wee Jamie too." He reached out for his son, who was whimpering, not sure yet whether the situation required tears. Ian jerked his head at me and rolled an eye in Jamie's direction.

Taking my cue, I grabbed Jamie by the arm and dragged him to an armchair in a neutral corner. Ian had Jenny likewise installed on the loveseat, a firm arm across her shoulders to keep her in place.

"Now, then." In spite of his unassuming manner, Ian Murray had an undeniable authority. I had my hand on Jamie's shoulder, and could feel the tension begin to go out of it.

I thought that the room looked a bit like the ring of a boxing match, with the fighters twitching restlessly in the corners, each awaiting the signal for action under the soothing hand of a manager.

Ian nodded at his brother-in-law, smiling. "Jamie. It's good to see ye, man. We're pleased you're home, and your wife with ye. Are we not, *mi dhu*?" he demanded of Jenny, his fingers tightening perceptibly on her shoulder.

She was not one to be forced into anything. Her lips compressed into a thin tight line, as though forming a seal, then opened reluctantly to let one word escape.

"Depends," she said, and shut them tight again.

Jamie rubbed a hand over his face, then raised his head, ready for a fresh round.

"I saw ye go into the house with Randall," he said stubbornly. "And from things he said to me later—how comes he to know you've a mole on your breast, then?"

She snorted violently. "Do ye remember all that went on that day, or did the Captain beat it out of ye wi' his saber?"

"Of course I remember! I'm no likely to forget it!"

"Then perhaps you'll remember that I gave the Captain a fair jolt in the crutch wi' my knee at one point in the proceedings?"

Jamie hunched his shoulders, wary. "Aye, I remember."

Jenny smiled in a superior manner.

"Weel then, if your wife here—ye could tell me her name at least, Jamie, I swear you've no manners at all—anyway, if she was to give ye similar treatment—and richly you deserve it, I might add—d'ye think you'd be able to perform your husbandly duties a few minutes later?"

Jamie, who had been opening his mouth to speak, suddenly shut it. He stared at his sister for a long moment, then one corner of his mouth twitched slightly.

"Depends," he said. The mouth twitched again. He had been sitting hunched forward in his chair, but sat back now, looking at her with the half-skeptical expression of a younger brother listening to a sister's fairy tales, feeling himself too old to be amazed, but half-believing still against his will.

"Really?" he said.

Jenny turned to Ian. "Go and fetch the sheets, Ian," she ordered.

Jamie raised both hands in surrender. "No. No, I believe ye. It's just, the way he acted after . . ."

Jenny sat back, relaxed in the curve of Ian's arm, her son cuddling as close as the bulk of her belly would permit, gracious in victory.

"Weel, after all he'd said outside, he could hardly admit in front of his own men to being incapable, now could he? He'd have to seem as though he'd done as he promised, no? And," she admitted, "I'll have to say the man was verra unpleasant about it all; he did strike me and tear my gown. In fact, he knocked me half-senseless trying, and by the time I'd come to myself and got decently covered again, the English had gone, taking you along with them."

Jamie gave a long sigh and closed his eyes briefly. His broad hands rested on his knees, and I covered one of them with a gentle squeeze. He took my hand and opened his eyes, giving me a faint smile of acknowledgment before turning back to his sister.

"All right," he said. "But I want to know, Jenny; did ye know when ye went with him that he'd not harm you?"

She was silent for a moment, but her gaze was steady on her

brother's face, and at last she shook her head, a slight smile on her lips.

She put out a hand to stop Jamie's protest, and the gull-winged brows rose in a graceful arc of inquiry. "And if your life is a suitable exchange for my honor, tell me why my honor is not a suitable exchange for your life?" The brows drew together in a scowl, the twin of the one adorning her brother's face. "Or are you telling me that I may not love you as much as you love me? Because if ye are, Jamie Fraser, I'll tell ye right now, it's not true!"

Opening his mouth to reply before she was finished, Jamie was taken suddenly at a loss by this conclusion. He closed his mouth abruptly as his sister pressed her advantage.

"Because I do love ye, for all you're a thick-headed, slack-witted, lack-brained gomerel. And I'll no have ye dead in the road at my feet just because you're too stubborn to keep your mouth shut for the once in your life!"

Blue eyes glared into blue eyes, shooting sparks in all directions. Swallowing the insults with difficulty, Jamie struggled for a rational reply. He seemed to be making up his mind to something. Finally he squared his shoulders, resigned to it.

"All right, then, I'm sorry," he said. "I was wrong, and I'll beg your pardon."

He and his sister sat staring at each other for a long moment, but whatever pardon he was expecting from her was not forthcoming. She examined him closely, biting her lip, but said nothing. Finally he grew impatient.

"I've said I'm sorry! What more d'ye want of me?" he demanded. "Do ye want me to go on my knees to ye? I'll do it if I must, but tell me!"

She shook her head slowly, lip still caught between her teeth.

"No," she said at last, "I'll not have ye on your knees in your own house. Stand up, though."

Jamie stood, and she set the child down on the loveseat and crossed the room to stand in front of him.

"Take off your shirt," she ordered.

"I'll not!"

She jerked the shirttail out of his kilt and reached for the buttons. Short of forcible resistance, clearly he was going to obey or submit to being undressed. Retaining as much dignity as he could, he backed away from her, and tight-lipped, removed the disputed garment.

She circled behind him and surveyed his back, her face displaying the same carefully blank expression I had seen Jamie adopt when concealing some strong emotion. She nodded, as though confirming something long suspected.

"Weel, and if you've been a fool, Jamie, it seems you've paid for it." She laid her hand gently on his back, covering the worst of the scars.

"It looks as though it hurt."

"It did."

"Did you cry?"

His fists clenched involuntarily at his sides. "Yes!"

Jenny walked back around to face him, pointed chin lifted and slanted eyes wide and bright. "So did I," she said softly. "Every day since they took ye away."

The broad-cheeked faces were once more mirrors of each other, but the expression that they wore was such that I rose and stepped quietly through the kitchen door to leave them alone. As the door swung to behind me, I saw Jamie catch hold of his sister's hands and say something huskily in Gaelic. She stepped into his embrace, and the rough, bright head bent to the dark.

27

The Last Reason

We ate like wolves at dinner, retired to a large, airy bedroom, and slept like logs. The sun would have been high by the time we rose in the morning, save that the sky was covered in clouds. I could tell it was late by the bustling feel of the house, as of people going cheerfully about their business, and by the tempting aromas that drifted up the stairs.

After breakfast the men prepared to go out, visiting tenants, inspecting fences, mending wagons, and generally enjoying themselves. As they paused in the hall to don their coats, Ian spotted Jenny's large basket resting on the table beneath the hall mirror.

"Shall I fetch home some apples from the orchard, Jenny? 'Twould save ye walking so far."

"Good idea," said Jamie, casting an appraising eye at his sister's expansive frontage. "We dinna want her to drop it in the road."

"I'll drop *you* where ye stand, Jamie Fraser," she retorted, calmly holding up the coat for Ian to shrug into. "Be useful for the once, and take this wee fiend outside wi' ye. Mrs. Crook's in the washhouse; ye can leave him there." She moved her foot, dislodging small Jamie, who was clinging to her skirts, chanting "up, up" monotonously.

His uncle obediently grabbed the wee fiend around the middle and swept him out the door, upside down and shrieking with delight. "Ah," Jenny sighed contentedly, bending to inspect her appearance in the gold-framed mirror. She wet a finger and smoothed her brows, then finished doing up the buttons at her throat. "Nice to finish dressing wi'out someone clinging to your skirts or wrapped round your knees. Some days I can scarce go to the privy alone, or speak a single sentence wi'out being interrupted."

Her cheeks were slightly flushed, and her dark hair gleamed against the blue silk of her dress. Ian smiled at her, warm brown eyes glowing at the blooming picture she presented.

"Weel, you'll have time to talk wi' Claire, perhaps," he suggested. He cocked one eyebrow in my direction. "I expect she's mannerly enough to listen, but for God's sake, dinna tell her any of your poems, or she'll be on the next coach to London before Jamie and I get back."

Jenny snapped her fingers under his nose, unperturbed by the teasing.

"I'm none too worried, man. There's no coach going before next April, and I reckon she'll be used to us by that time. Get on wi' ye; Jamie's waiting."

While the men went about their business, Jenny and I spent the day in the parlor, she stitching, I winding up stray bits of yarn and sorting the colored silks.

Outwardly friendly, we circled each other cautiously in conversation, watching each other from the corners of our eyes. Jamie's sister, Jamie's wife; Jamie was the central point, unspoken, about which our thoughts revolved.

Their shared childhood linked them forever, like the warp and the weft of a single fabric, but the patterns of their weave had been loosened, by absence and suspicion, then by marriage. Ian's thread had been present in their weaving since the beginning, mine was a new one. How would the tensions pull in this new pattern, one thread against another?

Our conversation ran on casual lines, but with the words unspoken clearly heard beneath.

"You've run the house here alone since your mother died?"

"Oh, aye. Since I was ten."

I had the nurturing and the loving of him as a boy. What will you do with the man I helped make?

"Jamie says as you're a rare fine healer."

"I mended his shoulder for him when we first met."

Yes, I am capable, and kind. I will care for him.

"I hear ye married very quickly."

Did you wed my brother for his land and money?

"Yes, it was quick. I didn't even know Jamie's true surname until just before the ceremony."

I didn't know he was laird of this place; I can only have married him for himself.

And so it went through the morning, a light luncheon, and into the hours of the afternoon, as we exchanged small talk, tidbits of information, opinions, small and hesitant jokes, taking each other's measure. A woman who had run a large household since the age of ten, who had managed the estate since her father's death and her brother's disappearance, was not a person to be lightly esteemed. I did wonder what she thought of me, but she seemed as capable as her brother of hiding her thoughts when she chose to.

As the clock on the mantelpiece began to strike five, Jenny yawned and stretched, and the garment she had been mending slid down the rounded slope of her belly onto the floor.

She began clumsily to reach for it, but I dropped to my knees beside her.

"No, I'll get it."

"Thank ye . . . Claire." Her first use of my name was accompanied by a shy smile, and I returned it.

Before we could return to our conversation, we were interrupted by the arrival of Mrs. Crook, the housekeeper, who poked a long nose into the parlor and inquired worriedly whether we had seen wee Master Jamie.

Jenny laid aside her sewing with a sigh.

"Got away again, has he? Nay worry, Lizzie. He's likely gone wi' his da or his uncle. We'll go and see, shall we, Claire? I could use a breath of air before supper."

She rose heavily to her feet and pressed her hands against the small of her back. She groaned and gave me a wry smile.

"Three weeks, about. I canna wait."

We walked slowly through the grounds outside, Jenny pointing out the brewhouse and the chapel, explaining the history of the estate, and when the different bits had been built.

As we approached the corner of the dovecote, we heard voices in the arbor.

"There he is, the wee rascal!" Jenny exclaimed. "Wait 'til I lay hands on him!"

"Wait a minute." I laid a hand on her arm, recognizing the deeper voice that underlaid the little boy's.

"Dinna worrit yourself, man," said Jamie's voice. "You'll learn. It's a bit difficult, isn't it, when your cock doesna stick out any further than your belly button?"

I stuck my head around the corner, to find him seated on a chopping block, engaged in converse with his namesake, who was struggling manfully with the folds of his smock.

"What are you doing with the child?" I inquired cautiously.

"I'm teachin' young James here the fine art of not pissing on his feet," he explained. "Seems the least his uncle could do for him."

I raised one eyebrow. "Talk is cheap. Seems the least his uncle could do is show him."

He grinned. "Well, we've had a few practical demonstrations. Had a wee accident last time, though." He exchanged accusatory looks with his nephew. "Dinna look at *me*," he said to the boy. "It was all your fault. I *told* ye to keep still."

"Ahem," said Jenny dryly, with a look at her brother and a matching one at her son. The smaller Jamie responded by pulling the front of his smock up over his head, but the larger one, unabashed, grinned cheerfully and rose from his seat, brushing dirt from his breeks. He set a hand on his nephew's swathed head, and turned the little boy toward the house.

" 'To everything there is a season,' " he quoted, " 'and a time for every purpose under heaven.' First we work, wee James, and then we wash. And *then*—thank God—it's time for supper."

The most pressing matters of business attended to, Jamie took time the next afternoon to show me over the house. Built in 1702, it was indeed modern for its time, with such innovations as porcelain stoves for heating, and a great brick oven built into the kitchen wall, so that bread was no longer baked in the ashes of the hearth. The ground floor hallway, the stairwell, and the drawing room walls were lined with pictures. Here and there was a pastoral landscape, or an animal study, but most were of the family and their connections.

I paused before a picture of Jenny as a young girl. She sat on the garden wall, a red-leaved vine behind her. Lined up in front of her along the top of the wall was a row of birds; sparrows, a thrush, a lark, and even a pheasant, all jostling and sidling for position before their laughing mistress. It was quite unlike most of the formally posed pictures, in which one ancestor or another glared out of their frames as though their collars were choking them.

"My mother painted that," Jamie said, noting my interest. "She did quite a few of the ones in the stairwell, but there are only two of hers in here. She always liked that one best herself." A large, blunt finger touched the surface of the canvas gently, tracing the line of the red-leaved vine. "Those were Jenny's tame birds. Anytime there was a bird found wi' a lame leg or a broken wing, whoever found it would bring it along, and in days she'd have it healed, and eatin' from her hand. That one always reminded me of Ian." The finger tapped above the pheasant, wings spread to keep its balance, gazing at its mistress with dark, adoring eyes.

"You're awful, Jamie," I said, laughing. "Is there one of you?"

"Oh, aye." He led me to the opposite wall, near the window.

Two red-haired, tartan-clad little boys stared solemnly out of the frame, seated with an enormous staghound. That must be Nairn, Bran's grandfather, Jamie, and his older brother Willie, who had died of the smallpox at eleven. Jamie could not have been more than two when it was painted, I thought; he stood between his elder brother's knees, one hand resting on the dog's head.

Jamie had told me about Willie during our journey from Leoch, one night by the fire at the bottom of a lonely glen. I remembered the small snake, carved of cherrywood, that he had drawn from his sporran to show me.

"Willie gave it me for my fifth birthday," he had said, finger gently stroking the sinuous curves. It was a comical little snake, body writhing artistically, and its head turned back to peer over what would have been its shoulder, if snakes had shoulders.

Jamie handed me the little wooden object, and I turned it over curiously.

"What's this scratched on the underside? S-a-w-n-y. Sawny?"

"That's me," Jamie said, ducking his head as though mildly embarrassed. "It's a pet name, like, a play on my second name, Alexander. It's what Willie used to call me."

The faces in the picture were very much alike; all the Fraser children had that forthright look that dared you to take them at less than their own valuation of themselves. In this portrait, though, Jamie's cheeks were rounded and his nose still snubbed with babyhood, while his brother's strong bones had begun to show the promise of the man within, a promise never kept.

"Were you very fond of him?" I asked softly, laying a hand on his arm. He nodded, looking away into the flames on the hearth.

"Oh, aye," he said with a faint smile. "He was five years older than I, and I thought he was God, or at least Christ. Used to follow him everywhere; or everywhere he'd let me, at least."

He turned away and wandered toward the bookshelves. Wanting to give him a moment alone, I stayed, looking out of the window.

From this side of the house I could see dimly through the rain the outline of a rocky, grass-topped hill in the distance. It reminded me of the fairies' dun where I had stepped through a rock and emerged from a rabbit hole. Only six months. But it seemed like a very long time ago.

Jamie had come to stand beside me at the window. Staring absently out at the driving rain, he said, "There was another reason. The main one."

"Reason?" I said stupidly.

"Why I married you."

"Which was?" I don't know what I expected him to say, perhaps some further revelation of his family's contorted affairs. What he did say was more of a shock, in its way.

"Because I wanted you." He turned from the window to face me. "More than I ever wanted anything in my life," he added softly.

I continued staring at him, dumbstruck. Whatever I had been expecting, it wasn't this. Seeing my openmouthed expression, he continued lightly. "When I asked my da how ye knew which was the right woman, he told me when the time came, I'd have no doubt. And I didn't. When I woke in the dark under that tree on the road to Leoch, with you sitting on my chest, cursing me for bleeding to death, I said to myself, 'Jamie Fraser, for all ye canna see what she looks like, and for all she weighs as much as a good draft horse, this is the woman.' "

I started toward him, and he backed away, talking rapidly. "I said to myself, 'She's mended ye twice in as many hours, me lad; life amongst the MacKenzies being what it is, it might be as well to wed a woman as can stanch a wound and set broken bones.' And I said to myself, 'Jamie, lad, if her touch feels so bonny on your collarbone, imagine what it might feel like lower down . . .' "

He dodged around a chair. "Of course, I thought it might ha' just been the effects of spending four months in a monastery, without benefit of female companionship, but then that ride through the dark together"—he paused to sigh theatrically, neatly evading my grab at his sleeve—"with that lovely broad arse wedged between my thighs"—he ducked a blow aimed at his left ear and sidestepped, getting a low table between us—"and that rock-solid head thumping me in the chest"—a small metal ornament bounced off his own head and went clanging to the floor—"I said to myself . . ."

He was laughing so hard at this point that he had to gasp for breath between phrases. "Jamie . . . I said . . . for all she's a Sassenach bitch . . . with a tongue like an adder's

. . . with a bum like that . . . what does it matter if she's a f-face like a sh-sh-sheep?"

I tripped him neatly and landed on his stomach with both knees as he hit the floor with a crash that shook the house.

"You mean to tell me that you married me out of love?" I demanded. He raised his eyebrows, struggling to draw in breath.

"Have I not . . . just been . . . saying so?"

Grabbing me round the shoulders with one arm, he wormed the other hand under my skirt and proceeded to inflict a series of merciless pinches on that part of my anatomy he had just been praising.

Returning to pick up her embroidery basket, Jenny sailed in at this point and stood eyeing her brother with some amusement. "And what are *you* up to, young Jamie me lad?" she inquired, one eyebrow up.

"I'm makin' love to my wife," he panted, breathless between giggling and fighting.

"Well, ye could find a more suitable place for it," she said, raising the other eyebrow. "That floor'll give ye splinters in your arse."

If Lallybroch was a peaceful place, it was also a busy one. Everyone in it seemed to stir into immediate life at cockcrow, and the farm then spun and whirred like a complicated bit of clockwork until after sunset, when one by one the cogs and wheels that made it run began to fall away, rolling off into the dark to seek supper and bed, only to reappear like magic in their proper places in the morning.

So essential did every last man, woman, and child seem to the running of the place that I could not imagine how it had fared these last few years, lacking its master. Now not only Jamie's hands, but mine as well, were pressed into full employment. For the first time, I understood the stern Scotch strictures against idleness that had seemed like mere quaintness before—or after, as the case might be. Idleness would have seemed not only a sign of moral decay, but an affront to the natural order of things.

There were moments, of course. Those small spaces of time, too soon gone, when everything seems to stand still, and existence is balanced on a perfect point, like the moment of change between the dark and the light, when both and neither surround you.

I was enjoying such a moment on the evening of the second or third day following our arrival at the farmhouse. Sitting on the fence behind the house, I could see tawny fields to the edge of the cliff past the broch, and the mesh of trees on the far side of the pass, dimming to black before the pearly glow of the sky. Objects near and far away seemed to be at the same distance, as their long shadows melted into the dusk.

The air was chilly with a hint of the coming frost, and I thought I must go in soon, though I was reluctant to leave the still beauty of the place. I wasn't aware of Jamie approaching until he slid the heavy folds of a cloak around my shoulders. I hadn't realized quite how cold it was until I felt the contrasting warmth of the thick wool.

Jamie's arms came around me with the cloak, and I nestled back against him, shivering slightly.

"I could see ye shivering from the house," he said, taking my hands in his. "Catch a chill, if you're not careful."

"And what about you?" I twisted about to look at him. Despite the increasing bite of the air, he looked completely comfortable in nothing but shirt and kilt, with no more than a slight reddening of the nose to show it was not the balmiest of spring evenings.

"Ah, well, I'm used to it. Scotsmen are none so thin-blooded as ye blue-nosed Southrons." He tilted my chin up and kissed my nose, smiling. I took him by the ears and adjusted his aim downward.

It lasted long enough for our temperatures to have equalized by the time he released me, and the warm blood sang in my ears as I leaned back, balancing on the fence rail. The breeze blew from behind me, fluttering strands of hair across my face. He brushed them off my shoulders, spreading the ruffled locks out with his fingers, so the setting sun shone through the strands.

"You look like you've a halo, with the light behind ye that way," he said, softly. "An angel crowned with gold."

"And you," I answered softly, tracing the edge of his jaw where the amber light sparked from his sprouting beard. "Why didn't you tell me before?"

He knew what I meant. One eyebrow went up, and he smiled, half his face lit by the glowing sun, the other half in shadow.

"Well, I knew ye didna want to wed me. I'd no wish to burden you or make myself foolish by telling you then, when it was plain you'd lie with me only to honor vows you'd rather not have made." He grinned, teeth white in the shadow, forestalling my protest. "The first time, at least. I've my pride, woman."

I reached out and drew him to me, pulling him close, so that he stood between my legs as I sat on the fence. Feeling the faint chill of his skin, I wrapped my legs around his hips and enfolded him with the wings of my cloak. Under the sheltering fabric, his arms came tight around me, pressing my cheek against the smudged cambric of his shirt.

"My love," he whispered. "Oh, my love. I do want ye so."

"Not the same thing, is it?" I said. "Loving and wanting, I mean."

He laughed, a little huskily. "Damn close, Sassenach, for me, at least." I could feel the strength of his wanting, hard and urgent. He stepped back suddenly, and stooping, lifted me from the fence.

"Where are we going?" We were headed away from the house, toward the cluster of sheds in the shadow of the elm grove.

"To find a haystack."

28

Kisses and Drawers

I gradually found my own place in the running of the estate. As Jenny could no longer manage the long walk to the tenants' cottages, I took to visiting them myself, accompanied sometimes by a stable lad, sometimes by Jamie or Ian. I took food and medicines with me, treated the sick as best I could, and made suggestions as to the improvement of health and hygiene, which were received with varying degrees of grace.

At Lallybroch itself, I poked about the house and grounds, making myself useful wherever I could, mostly in the gardens. Besides the lovely little ornamental garden, the manor had a small herb garden and an immense kitchen garden or kailyard that supplied turnips, cabbages, and vegetable marrows.

Jamie was everywhere; in the study with the account books, in the fields with the tenants, in the horse barn with Ian, making up for lost time. There was something more than duty or interest in it, too, I thought. We would have to leave soon; he wanted to set things running in a path that would continue while he was gone, until he—until *we*—could return for good.

I knew we would have to leave, yet surrounded by the peaceful house and grounds of Lallybroch and the cheerful company of Jenny, Ian, and small Jamie, I felt as though I had come home at last.

After breakfast one morning, Jamie rose from the table, announcing that he thought he would go as far as the head of the valley, to see a horse that Martin Mack had for sale.

Jenny turned from the sideboard, brows drawn together.

"D'ye think it safe, Jamie? There's been English patrols all through the district the last month or so."

He shrugged, taking his coat from the chair where he had laid it.

"I'll be careful."

"Oh, Jamie," said Ian, coming in with an armful of firewood for the hearth. "I meant to ask—can ye gang up to the mill this morning? Jock was up yestere'en to say something's gone amiss wi' the wheel. I had a quick look, but he and I together couldna shift it. I think there's a bit o' rubbish stuck in the works outside, but it's well under the water."

He stamped his wooden leg lightly, smiling at me.

"I can still walk, thank God, and ride as well, but I canna swim. I just thrash about, and gang in circles like a doodle-bug."

Jamie laid the coat back on the chair with a smile at his brother-in-law's description.

"None so bad, Ian, if it keeps ye from havin' to spend the morning in a freezing millpond. Aye, I'll go." He turned to me.

"Care to walk up wi' me, Sassenach? It's a fine morning, and ye can bring your wee basket." He cocked an ironic eye at the enormous withy basket I used for gathering. "I'll go and change my sark. Be wi' ye in a moment." He headed for the staircase and bounded athletically up the steps, three at a time.

Ian and I exchanged smiles. If there was any regret that such feats were now beyond him, it was hidden beneath his pleasure in seeing Jamie's exuberance.

"It's good to have him back," he said.

"I only wish we could stay," I said, with regret.

The soft brown eyes filled with alarm. "Ye'll no be going at once, surely?"

I shook my head. "No, not at once. But we'll need to leave well before the snow comes." Jamie had decided that our best course was to go to Beauly, seat of clan Fraser. Perhaps his grandfather, Lord Lovat, could be of help; if not, he might at least arrange us passage to France.

Ian nodded, reassured. "Oh, aye. But you've a few weeks yet."

―――

It was a beautiful bright autumn day, with air like cider and a sky so blue you could drown in it. We walked slowly so that I could keep an eye out for late-blooming eglantine and teasel heads, chatting casually.

"It's Quarter Day next week," Jamie remarked. "Will your new gown be ready then?"

"I expect so. Why, is it an occasion?"

He smiled down at me, taking the basket while I stooped to pull up a stalk of tansy.

"Oh, in a way. Nothing like Colum's great affairs, to be sure, but all the Lallybroch tenants will come to pay their rents—and their respects to the new Lady Lallybroch."

"I expect they'll be surprised you've married an English-woman."

"I reckon there are a few fathers might be disappointed at that; I'd courted a lass or two hereabouts before I got arrested and taken to Fort William."

"Sorry you didn't wed a local girl?" I asked coquettishly.

"If ye think I'm going to say 'yes,' and you standin' there holding a pruning knife," he remarked, "you've less opinion of my good sense than I thought."

I dropped the pruning knife, which I'd taken to dig with, stretched my arms out, and stood waiting. When he released me at last, I stooped to pick up the knife again, saying teasingly, "I always wondered how it was you stayed a virgin so long. Are the girls in Lallybroch all plain, then?"

"No," he said, squinting up into the morning sun. "It was mostly my father was responsible for that. We'd stroll over the fields in the evenings, sometimes, he and I, and talk about things. And once I got old enough for such a thing to be a possibility, he told me that a man must be responsible for any seed he sows, for it's his duty to take care of a woman and protect her. And if I wasna prepared to do that, then I'd no right to burden a woman with the consequences of my own actions."

He glanced behind us, toward the house. And toward the small family graveyard, near the foot of the broch, where his parents were buried.

"He said the greatest thing in a man's life is to lie wi' a woman he loves," he said softly. He smiled at me, eyes blue as the sky overhead. "He was right."

I touched his face lightly, tracing the broad sweep downward from cheek to jaw.

"Rather hard on you, though, if he expected you to wait so long to marry," I said.

Jamie grinned, kilt flapping round his knees in the brisk autumn breeze.

"Well, the Church does teach that self-abuse is a sin, but my father said he thought that if it cáme to a choice between abusin' yourself or some poor woman, a decent man might choose to make the sacrifice."

When I stopped laughing, I shook my head and said, "No. No, I won't ask. You did stay a virgin, though."

"Strictly by the grace of God and my father, Sassenach. I dinna think I thought much about anything but the lasses, once I turned fourteen or so. But that was when I was sent to foster wi' Dougal at Beannachd."

"No girls there?" I asked. "I thought Dougal had daughters."

"Aye, he has. Four. The two younger are no much to look at, but the eldest was a verra handsome lassie. A year or two older than me, Molly was. And not much flattered by my attention, I dinna think. I used to stare at her across the supper table, and she'd look down her nose at me and ask did I have the catarrh? Because if so, I should go to bed, and if not, she would be much obliged if I'd close my mouth, as she didna care to look at my tonsils while she was eating."

"I begin to see how you stayed a virgin," I said, hiking my skirts to climb a stile. "But they can't all have been like that."

"No," he said reflectively, giving me a hand over the stile. "No, they weren't. Molly's younger sister, Tabitha, was a bit friendlier." He smiled reminiscently.

"Tibby was the first girl I kissed. Or perhaps I should say the first girl who kissed me. I was carrying two pails of milk for her, from the barn to the dairy, plotting all the way how I'd get her behind the door, where there wasna room to get away, and kiss her there. But my hands were full, and she had to open the door for me to go through. So it was me ended up behind the door, and Tib who walked up to me, took me by both ears and kissed me. Spilled the milk, too," he added.

"Sounds a memorable first experience," I said, laughing.

"I doubt I was *her* first," he said, grinning. "She knew a lot more about it than I did. But we didna get much practice; a day or two later, her mother caught us in the pantry. She didna do more than give me a sharpish look and tell Tibby to go and set the table for dinner, but she must have told Dougal about it."

If Dougal MacKenzie had been quick to resent an insult to his sister's honor, I could only imagine what he might have done in defense of his daughter's.

"I shudder to think," I said, grinning.

"So do I," said Jamie, shuddering. He shot me a sidelong glance, looking shy.

"You'll know that young men in the morning, sometimes they wake up with . . . well, with—" He was blushing.

"Yes, I know," I said. "So do old men of twenty-three. You think I don't notice? You've brought it to my attention often enough."

"Mmmphm. Well, the morning after Tib's mother caught us, I woke up just at dawn. I'd been dreaming about her— Tib, I mean, not her mother—and I wasna surprised to feel a hand on my cock. What was surprising was that it wasn't mine."

"Surely it wasn't Tibby's?"

"Well, no, it wasna. It was her father's."

"Dougal! Whatever—"

"Well, I opened my eyes wide and he smiled down at me, verra pleasant. And then he sat on the bed and we had a nice little chat, uncle and nephew, foster-father to foster-son. He said how much he was enjoying my being there, him not having a son of his own, and all that. And how his family was all so fond of me, and all. And how he would hate to think that there might be any advantage taken of such fine, innocent feelings as his daughters might have toward me, but how of course he was so pleased that he could trust me as he would his own son."

"And all the time he was talking and me lying there, he had his one hand on his dirk, and the other resting on my fine young balls. So I said yes, Uncle, and no, Uncle, and when he left, I rolled myself up in the quilt and dreamed about pigs. And I didna kiss a girl again until I was sixteen, and went to Leoch."

He looked over at me, smiling. His hair was laced back with a leather thong, but the shorter ends were sticking up at the crown as usual, glimmering red and gold in the brisk, clear air. His skin had darkened to a golden bronze during our journey from Leoch and Craigh na Dun, and he looked like an autumn leaf, swirling joyfully wind-borne.

"And what of you, my bonny Sassenach?" he asked, grinning. "Did ye have the wee laddies panting at your heels, or were ye shy and maidenly?"

"A bit less than you," I said circumspectly. "I was eight."

"Jezebel. Who was the lucky lad?"

"The dragoman's son. That was in Egypt. He was nine."

"Och, well, you're no to blame then. Led astray by an older man. And a bloody heathen, no less."

The mill came into sight below, picture-pretty, with a deep-red vine glowing up the side of the yellow plaster wall, and shutters standing open to the daylight, tidy in spite of the worn green paint. The water gushed happily down the sluice under the idle water-wheel into the millpond. There were even ducks on the pond, teal and goldeneye paused for a rest on their southern flight.

"Look," I said, pausing at the top of the hill, putting a hand on Jamie's arm to stop him. "Isn't it lovely?"

"Be a sight more lovely if the water-wheel were turnin'," he said practically. Then he glanced down at me and smiled.

"Aye, Sassenach. It's a bonny place. I used to swim here when I was a lad—there's a wide pool round the bend of the stream."

A little further down the hill, the pool became visible through the screen of willows. So did the boys. There were four of them, sporting and splashing and yelling, all naked as jays.

"Brrr," I said, watching them. The weather was fine for autumn, but there was enough of a nip in the air to make me glad of the shawl I'd brought. "It makes my blood run cold, just to see them."

"Och?" Jamie said. "Well, let me warm it for ye then."

With a glance down at the boys in the stream, he stepped back into the shade of a big horse chestnut tree. He put his hands about my waist and drew me into the shadow after him.

"Ye werena the first lass I kissed," he said softly. "But I swear you'll be the last." And he bent his head to my up-turned face.

*

Once the miller had emerged from his lair, and hasty introductions were made, I retired to the bank of the millpond, while Jamie spent several minutes listening to an explanation of the problem. As the miller went back into the millhouse, to try turning the stone from within, Jamie stood a moment, staring into the dark, weedy depths of the millpond. Finally, with a shrug of resignation, he began to strip off his clothes.

"No help for it," he remarked to me. "Ian's right; there's something stuck in the wheel under the sluice. I'll have to go down and—" Stopped by my gasp, he turned around to where I sat on the bank with my basket.

"And what's amiss wi' *you*?" he demanded. "Have ye no seen a man in his drawers before?"

"Not . . . not like . . . *that*!" I managed to get out, between sputters. Anticipating possible submergence, he had donned beneath his kilt a short garment of incredible elderliness, originally of red flannel, now patched with a dazzling array of colors and textures. Obviously, this pair of drawers had originally belonged to someone who measured several inches more around the middle than Jamie. They hung precariously from his hipbones, the folds drooping in V's over his flat belly.

"Your grandfather's?" I guessed, making a highly unsuccessful effort to suppress my giggling. "Or your grand-mother's?"

"My father's," he said coldly, looking down his nose at me. "Ye dinna expect me to be swimming bare as an egg before my wife and my tenants, do ye?"

With considerable dignity, he gathered the excess material up in one hand and waded into the millpond. Treading water near the wheel, he took his bearings, then with a deep breath, upended and submerged, my last sight of him the ballooning bottom of the red flannel drawers. The miller, leaning out of the millhouse window, shouted encouragement and directions whenever the sleek wet head broke the surface for air.

The edge of the pond bank was thick with water plants, and I foraged with my digging stick for mallow root and the small, fine-leaved dropwort. I had half the basket filled when I heard a polite cough behind me.

She was a very old lady indeed, or at least she looked it. She leaned on a hawthorn stick, enveloped in garments she must have worn twenty years before, now much too voluminous for the shrunken frame inside them.

"Good morn to ye," she said, nodding a head like a bobbin. She wore a starched white kertch that hid most of her hair, but a few wisps of iron-grey peeped out beside cheeks like withered apples.

"Good morning," I said, and started to scramble up, but she advanced a few steps and sank down beside me with surprising grace. I hoped she could get up again.

"I'm—" I started, but had barely opened my mouth when she interrupted.

"Ye'll be the new lady, o' course. I'm Mrs. MacNab—Grannie MacNab, they call me, along o' my daughters-in-law all bein' Mrs. MacNabs as weel." She reached out a skinny hand and pulled my basket toward her, peering into it.

"Mallow root—ah, that's good for cough. But ye dinna want to use that one, lassie." She poked at a small brownish tuber. "Looks like lily root, but it isna that."

"What is it?" I asked.

"Adder's-tongue. Eat that one, lassie, and ye'll be rollin' round the room wi' your heels behind yer head." She plucked the tuber from the basket and threw it into the pond with a splash. She pulled the basket onto her lap and pawed expertly through the remaining plants, while I watched with a mixture of amusement and irritation. At last, satisfied, she handed it back.

"Weel, you're none sae foolish, for a Sassenach lassie," she remarked. "Ye ken betony from lamb's-quarters, at least." She cast a glance toward the pond, where Jamie's head appeared briefly, sleek as a seal, before disappearing once again beneath the millhouse. "I see his lairdship didna wed ye for your face alone."

"Thank you," I said, choosing to construe this as a compliment. The old lady's eyes, sharp as needles, were fastened on my midsection.

"Not wi' child yet?" she demanded. "Raspberry leaves, that's the thing. Steep a handful wi' rosehips and drink it when the moon's waxing, from the quarter to the full. Then when it wanes from the full to the half, take a bit o' barberry to purge your womb."

"Oh," I said, "well—"

"I'd a bit of a favor to ask his lairdship," the old lady went on. "But as I see he's a bit occupied at present, I'll tell *you* about it."

"All right," I agreed weakly, not seeing how I could stop her anyway.

"It's my grandson," she said, fixing me with small grey eyes the size and shininess of marbles. "My grandson Rabbie, that is; I've sixteen altogether, and the three o' them named Robert, but the one's Bob and t'other Rob, and the wee one's Rabbie."

"Congratulations," I said politely.

"I want his lairdship to take the lad on as stable lad," she went on.

"Well, I can't say—"

"It's his father, ye ken," she said, leaning forward confidentially. "Not as I'll say there's aught wrong wi' a bit o' firmness; spare the rod and spoil the child, I've said often enough, and the good Lord kens weel enough that boys were meant to be smacked, or He'd not ha' filled 'em sae full o' the de'il. But when it comes to layin' a child out on the hearth, and a bruise on his face the size o' my hand, and for naught more than takin' an extra bannock from the platter, then—"

"Rabbie's father beats him, you mean?" I interrupted.

The old lady nodded, pleased with my ready intelligence. "To be sure. Is that no what I've been sayin'?" She held up a hand. "Now, in the regular way, o' course I'd not interfere. A man's son's his ain to do as he sees fit wi', but . . . weel, Rabbie's a bit of a favorite o' mine. And it's no the lad's fault as his father's a drunken sot, shameful as 'tis for his own mither to say such a thing."

She raised an admonitory finger like a stick. "Not but what Ronald's father didna take a drop too much from time to time. But lay a hand on me or the bairns he never did—not after the first time, at any rate," she added thoughtfully. She twinkled suddenly at me, little cheeks round and firm as summer apples, so I could see what a very lively and attractive girl she must have been.

"He struck me the once," she confided, "and I snatched the girdle off the fire and crowned him wi' it." She rocked back and forth, laughing. "Thought I'd kilt him for sure, and me wailin' and holdin' of his heid in my lap, thinkin' what would I do, a widow wi' twa bairns to feed? But he came round," she said matter-of-factly, "and ne'er laid a hand on me or the bairnies again. I bore thirteen, ye ken," she said proudly. "And raised ten."

"Congratulations," I said, meaning it.

"Raspberry leaves," she said, laying a confiding hand on my knee. "Mark me, lassie, raspberry leaves will do it. And if not, come to see me, and I'll make ye a bittie drink o' coneflower and marrow seed, wi' a raw egg beaten up in it. That'll draw yer man's seed straight up into the womb, ye ken, and you'll be swellin' like a pumpkin by Easter."

I coughed, growing a bit red in the face. "Mmmphm. And you want Jamie, er, his lairdship I mean, to take your grandson into his house as stable lad, to get him away from his father?"

"Aye, that's it. Now he's a brankie wee worker, is Rabbie, and his lairdship will no be—"

The old lady's face froze in the midst of her animated conversation. I turned to look over my shoulder, and froze as well. Redcoats. Dragoons, six of them, on horseback, making their way carefully down the hill toward the millhouse.

With admirable presence of mind, Mrs. MacNab stood up and sat down again on top of Jamie's discarded clothes, her spreading skirts hiding everything.

There was a splash and an explosive gasp from the millpond behind me as Jamie surfaced again. I was afraid to call out or move, for fear of attracting the dragoons' attention to the pond, but the sudden dead silence behind me told me he had seen them. The silence was broken by a single word traveling across the water, softly spoken, but heartfelt in its sincerity.

"Merde," he said.

The old lady and I sat unmoving, stone-faced, watching the soldiers come down the hill. At the last moment, as they made the final turn around the mill-house path, she turned swiftly to me and laid a stick-straight finger across her withered lips. I mustn't speak and let them hear that I was English. I didn't have time even to nod in acknowledgment before the mud-caked hooves came to a halt a few feet away.

"Good morrow to you, ladies," said the leader. He was a corporal, but not, I was pleased to see, Corporal Hawkins. A quick glance showed me that none of the men were among those I had seen at Fort William, and I relaxed my grip on the handle of my basket just a fraction.

"We saw the mill from above," the dragoon said, "and thought perhaps to purchase a sack of meal?" He divided a bow between us, not sure who to address.

Mrs. MacNab was frosty, but polite.

"Good morrow," she said, inclining her head. "But if ye've come for meal, I fear me ye'll be sair disappointit. The mill wheel's nae workin' just now. Perhaps next time ye come this way."

"Oh? What's amiss, then?" The corporal, a short young man with a fresh complexion, seemed interested. He walked down to the edge of the pond to peer at the wheel. The miller, popping up in the mill to report the latest progress with the millstone, saw him and hastily popped back down out of sight.

The corporal called to one of his men. Climbing up the slope, he gestured to the other soldier, who obligingly stooped to let the corporal climb on his back. Reaching up, he managed to catch the edge of the roof with both hands, and squirmed up onto the thatch. Standing, he could barely reach the edge of the great wheel. He reached out and rocked it with both hands. Bending down, he shouted through the window to the miller to try turning the millstone by hand.

I willed myself to keep my eyes away from the bottom of the sluice. I wasn't sufficiently familiar with the workings of waterwheels to know for sure, but I was afraid that if the wheel gave way suddenly, anything near the underwater works might be crushed. Apparently this was no idle fear, for Mrs. MacNab spoke sharply to one of the soldiers near us.

"Ye should ca' your master doon now, laddie. He'll do no good tae the mill or himsel'. Ye shouldna meddle wi' things as ye dinna understand."

"Oh, you've no cause for worry, missus," said the soldier casually. "Corporal Silvers's father has a wheat mill in Hampshire. What the Corporal doesn't know about waterwheels would fit in me shoe."

Mrs. MacNab and I exchanged looks of alarm. The corporal, after a bit more clambering up and down and exploratory rockings and pokings, came down to where we sat. He was perspiring freely, and wiped his red face with a large, grubby handkerchief before addressing us.

"I can't move it from above, and that fool of a miller doesn't seem to speak any English at all." He glanced at Mrs. MacNab's sturdy stick and gnarled limbs; then at me. "Perhaps the young lady could come and talk to him for me?"

Mrs. MacNab stretched out a protective hand, gripping me by the sleeve.

"Ye'll hae to pardon my daughter-in-law, sorr. She's gone sair saft in the heid, ever syne her last babe was stillborn. Hasna spoke a word in ower a year, puir lassie. And I canna leave her for a minute, for fear she'll throw hersel' intae the water in her grief."

I did my best to look soft-headed, no great effort in my present state of mind.

The corporal looked disconcerted. "Oh," he said. "Well . . ." He wandered down to the edge of the pond and stood frowning into the water. He looked just as Jamie had an hour before, and apparently for the same reason.

"No help for it, Collins," he said to the old trooper. "I'll have to go under and see what's holding it." He took off his scarlet coat and began to unfasten the cuffs of his shirt. I exchanged looks of horror with Mrs. MacNab. While there might be sufficient air under the millhouse for survival, certainly there was not room to hide very effectively.

I was considering, not very optimistically, the chances of throwing a convincing epileptic fit, when the great wheel suddenly creaked overhead. With a sound like a tree being murdered, the big arc made a swooping half-turn, stuck for a moment, then rolled into a steady revolution, scoops merrily pouring bright streamlets into the sluice.

The corporal paused in his undressing, admiring the arc of the wheel.

"Look at that, Collins! Wonder what was stuck in it?"

As though in answer, something came into sight at the top of the wheel. It hung from one of the scoops, sodden red folds dripping. The scoop hit the stream now churning down the sluice, the object came loose, and Jamie's father's erstwhile drawers floated majestically out onto the waters of the millpond.

The elderly trooper fished them out with a stick, presenting them gingerly to his commander, who plucked them off the stick like a man obliged to pick up a dead fish.

"Hm," he said, holding up the garment critically. "Wonder where on earth *that* came from? Must have been caught around the shaft. Curious that something like that could cause so much trouble, isn't it, Collins?"

"Yessir." The trooper plainly did not consider the interior workings of a Scottish mill wheel to be of absorbing interest, but answered politely.

After turning the cloth over a time or two, the corporal shrugged, and used it to wipe the dirt from his hands.

"Decent bit of flannel," he said, wringing out the sopping cloth. "It'll do to polish tack, at least. Something of a souvenir, eh, Collins?" And with a polite bow to Mrs. MacNab and me, he turned to his horse.

The dragoons had barely disappeared from sight over the brow of the hill when a splashing from the millpond heralded the rising from the depths of the resident water sprite.

He was the bloodless white, blue-tinged, of Carrara marble, and his teeth chattered so hard that I could barely make out his first words, which were, in any case, in Gaelic.

Mrs. MacNab had no trouble making them out, and her ancient jaw dropped. She snapped it shut, though, and made a low reverence toward the emergent laird. Seeing her, he stopped his progress toward the shore, the water still lapping modestly about his hips. He took a deep breath, clenching his teeth to stop the chattering, and plucked a streamer of duckweed off his shoulder.

"Mrs. MacNab," he said, bowing to his elderly tenant.

"Sir," she said, bowing back once again. "A fine day, is it no?"

"A bit b-brisk," he said, casting an eye at me. I shrugged helplessly.

"We're pleased to see ye back in yer home, sir, and it's our hope, the lads and mysel', as you'll soon be back to stay."

"Mine too, Mrs. MacNab," Jamie said courteously. He jerked his head at me, glaring. I smiled blandly.

The old lady, ignoring this byplay, folded her gnarled hands in her lap and settled back with dignity.

"I've a wee favor I was wishin' to ask of your lairdship," she began, "havin' tae do wi'—"

"Grannie MacNab," Jamie interrupted, advancing a menacing half-step through the water, "whatever your wish is, I'll do it. Provided only that ye'll give me back my shirt before my parts fall off wi' cold."

29

More Honesty

I n the evenings, when supper was cleared away, we generally sat in the drawing room with Jenny and Ian, talking companionably of this and that, or listening to Jenny's stories.

Tonight, though, it was my turn, and I held Jenny and Ian rapt as I told them about Mrs. MacNab and the Redcoats.

"God kens well enough that boys need to be smacked, or he'd no fill them sae full o' the de'il." My imitation of Grannie MacNab brought down the house.

Jenny wiped tears of laughter from her eyes.

"Lord, it's true enough. And she'd know it too. What has she got, Ian, eight boys?"

Ian nodded. "Aye, at least. I canna even remember all their names; seemed like there was always a couple of MacNabs about to hunt or fish or swim with, when Jamie and I were younger."

"You grew up together?" I asked. Jamie and Ian exchanged wide, complicitous grins.

"Oh, aye, we're familiar," Jamie said, laughing. "Ian's father was the factor for Lallybroch, like Ian is now. On a number of occasions during my reckless youth, I've found myself standing elbow to elbow with Mr. Murray there, explaining to one or other of our respective fathers how appearances can be deceiving, or failing that, why circumstances alter cases."

"And failin' *that*," said Ian, "I've found myself on the same number of occasions, bent over a fence rail alongside Mr. Fra-

ser there, listenin' to him yell his heid off while waitin' for my
own turn."

"Never!" replied Jamie indignantly. "I never yelled."

"Ye call it what ye like, Jamie," his friend answered, "but ye
were awful loud."

"Ye could hear the both of ye for miles," Jenny interjected.
"And not only the yelling. Ye could hear Jamie arguing all the
time, right up to the fence."

"Aye, ye should ha' been a lawyer, Jamie. But I dinna ken
why I always let you do the talking," said Ian, shaking his
head. "You always got us in worse trouble than we started."

Jamie began to laugh again. "You mean the broch?"

"I do." Ian turned to me, motioning toward the west,
where the ancient stone tower rose from the hill behind the
house.

"One of Jamie's better arguments, that was," he said, rolling his eyes upward. "He told Brian it was uncivilized to use
physical force in order to make your point of view prevail.
Corporal punishment was barbarous, he said, and old-fashioned, to boot. Thrashing someone just because they had
committed an act with whose ram-ramifications, that was it—
with whose ramifications ye didn't agree was not at a' a constructive form of punishment. . . ."

All of us were laughing by this time.

"Did Brian listen to all of this?" I asked.

"Oh, aye." Ian nodded. "I just stood there wi' Jamie, nodding whenever he'd stop for breath. When Jamie finally ran
out of words, his father sort of coughed a bit and said 'I see.'
Then he turned and looked out of the window for a little,
swinging the strap and nodding his head, as though he were
thinking. We were standing there, elbow to elbow like Jamie
said, sweating. At last Brian turned about and told us to follow him to the stables."

"He gave us each a broom, a brush, and a bucket, and
pointed us in the direction of the broch," said Jamie, taking
up the story. "Said I'd convinced him of my point, so he'd
decided on a more 'constructive' form of punishment."

Ian's eyes rolled slowly up, as though following the rough
stones of the broch upward.

"That tower rises sixty feet from the ground," he told me, "and it's thirty feet in diameter, wi' three floors." He heaved a sigh. "We swept it from the top to the bottom," he said, "and scrubbed it from the bottom to the top. It took five days, and I can taste rotted oat-straw when I cough, even now."

"And you tried to kill me on the third day," said Jamie, "for getting us into that." He touched his head gingerly. "I had a wicked gash over my ear, where ye hit me wi' the broom."

"Oh, weel," Ian said comfortably, "that was when ye broke my nose the second time, so we were even."

"Trust a Murray to keep score," Jamie said, shaking his head.

"Let's see," I said, counting on my fingers. "According to you, Frasers are stubborn, Campbells are sneaky, MacKenzies are charming but sly, and Grahams are stupid. What's the Murrays' distinguishing characteristic?"

"Ye can count on them in a fight," said Jamie and Ian together, then laughed.

"Ye can too," said Jamie, recovering. "You just hope they're on your side." And both men went off into fits again.

Jenny shook her head disapprovingly at spouse and brother.

"And we havena even had any wine yet," she said. She put down her sewing and heaved herself to her feet. "Come wi' me, Claire; we'll see has Mrs. Crook made any biscuits to have wi' the port."

Coming back down the hall a quarter of an hour later with trays of refreshments, I heard Ian say, "You'll not mind then, Jamie?"

"Mind what?"

"That we wed without your consent—me and Jenny, I mean."

Jenny, walking ahead of me, came to a sudden stop outside the drawing room door.

There was a brief snort from the love seat where Jamie lay sprawled, feet propped on a hassock. "Since I didna tell ye where I was, and ye had no notion when—if ever—I'd come back, I can hardly blame ye for not waiting."

I could see Ian in profile, leaning over the log basket. His long, good-natured face wore a slight frown.

"Weel, I didna think it right, especially wi' me being crippled . . ."

There was a louder snort.

"Jenny couldna have a better husband, if you'd lost both legs and your arms as well," Jamie said gruffly. Ian's pale skin flushed slightly in embarrassment. Jamie coughed and swung his legs down from the hassock, leaning over to pick up a scrap of kindling that had fallen from the basket.

"How did ye come to wed anyway, given your scruples?" he asked, one side of his mouth curling up.

"Gracious, man," Ian protested, "ye think I had any choice in the matter? Up against a Fraser?" He shook his head, grinning at his friend.

"She came up to me out in the field one day, while I was tryin' to mend a wagon that sprang its wheel. I crawled out, all covered wi' muck, and found her standin' there looking like a bush covered wi' butterflies. She looks me up and down and she says—" He paused and scratched his head. "Weel, I don't know exactly *what* she said, but it ended with her kissing me, muck notwithstanding, and saying, 'Fine, then, we'll be married on St. Martin's Day.' " He spread his hands in comic resignation. "I was still explaining why we couldna do any such thing, when I found myself in front of a priest, saying, 'I take thee, Janet' . . . and swearing to a lot of verra improbable statements."

Jamie rocked back in his seat, laughing.

"Aye, I ken the feeling," he said. "Makes ye feel a bit hollow, no?"

Ian smiled, embarrassment forgotten. "It does and all. I still get that feeling, ye know, when I see Jenny sudden, standing against the sun on the hill, or holding wee Jamie, not lookin' at me. I see her, and I think, 'God, man, she can't be yours, not really.' " He shook his head, brown hair flopping over his brow. "And then she turns and smiles at me . . ." He looked up at his brother-in-law, grinning.

"Weel, ye know yourself. I can see it's the same wi' you and your Claire. She's . . . something special, no?"

Jamie nodded. The smile didn't leave his face, but altered somehow.

"Aye," he said softly. "Aye, she is that."

Over the port and biscuits, Jamie and Ian reminisced further about their shared boyhood, and their fathers. Ian's father, William, had died just the past spring, leaving Ian to run the estate alone.

"You remember when your father came on us down by the spring, and made us go wi' him to the smithy to see how to fix a wagon-tree?"

"Aye, and he couldna understand why we kept squirming and shifting about—"

"And he kept asking ye did ye need to go to the privy—"

Both men were laughing too hard to finish the story, so I looked at Jenny.

"Toads," she said succinctly. "The two o' them each had five or six toads inside his shirt."

"Oh, Lord," said Ian. "When the one crawled up your neck and hopped out of your shirt into the forge, I thought I'd die."

"I cannot imagine why my father didna wring my neck on several occasions," said Jamie, shaking his head. "It's a wonder I ever grew up."

Ian looked consideringly at his own offspring, industriously engaged in piling wooden blocks on top of each other by the hearth. "I don't quite know how I'm goin' to manage it, when the time comes I have to beat my own son. I mean . . . he's, well, he's so *small*." He gestured helplessly at the sturdy little figure, tender neck bent to his task.

Jamie eyed his small namesake cynically. "Aye, he'll be as much a devil as you or I, give him time. After all, I suppose even *I* must ha' looked small and innocent at one point."

"You did," said Jenny unexpectedly, coming to set a pewter cup of cider in her husband's hand. She patted her brother on the head.

"You were verra sweet as a baby, Jamie. I remember standing over your cot. Ye canna ha' been more than two, asleep wi' your thumb in your mouth, and we agreed we'd never seen a prettier lad. You had fat round cheeks and the dearest red curls."

The pretty lad turned an interesting shade of rose, and drained his cider at one gulp, avoiding my glance.

"Didna last long, though," Jenny said, flashing white teeth in a mildly malicious smile at her brother. "How old were ye when ye got your first thrashing, Jamie? Seven?"

"No, eight," Jamie said, thrusting a new log into the smoldering pile of kindling. "Christ, that hurt. Twelve strokes full across the bum, and he didna let up a bit, beginning to end. He never did." He sat back on his heels, rubbing his nose with the knuckles of one hand. His cheeks were flushed and his eyes bright from the exertion.

"Once it was over, Father went off a bit and sat down on a rock while I settled myself. Then when I'd quit howling and got down to a sort of wet snuffle, he called me over to him. Now that I think of it, I can remember just what he said. Maybe you can use it on young Jamie, Ian, when the time comes." Jamie closed his eyes, recalling.

"He stood me between his knees and made me look him in the face, and said, 'That's the first time, Jamie. I'll have to do it again, maybe a hundred times, before you're grown to a man.' He laughed a bit then and said, 'My father did it to me at least that often, and you're as stubborn and cockle-headed as ever I was.'

"He said, 'Sometimes I daresay I'll enjoy thrashing you, depending on what you've done to deserve it. Mostly I won't. But I'll do it nonetheless. So remember it, lad. If your head thinks up mischief, your backside's going to pay for it.' Then he gave me a hug and said, 'You're a braw lad, Jamie. Go away to the house now and let your mother comfort ye.' I opened my mouth to say something to that, and he said, quick-like, 'No, I know you don't need it, but *she* does. Get on wi' ye.' So I came down and Mother fed me bread with jam on it."

Jenny suddenly started to laugh. "I just remembered," she said, "Da used to tell that story about you, Jamie, about thrashing you, and what he said to you. He said when he sent ye back to the house after, you came halfway down, then all of a sudden stopped and waited for him.

"When he came down to ye, you looked up at him and said, 'I just wanted to ask, Faither—did ye enjoy it this time?' And when he said 'no,' you nodded and said, 'Good. I didna like it much either.' "

We all laughed for a minute together, then Jenny looked up at her brother, shaking her head. "He loved to tell that story. Da always said you'd be the death of him, Jamie."

The merriment died out of Jamie's face, and he looked down at the big hands resting on his knees.

"Aye," he said quietly. "Well, and I was, then, wasn't I?"

Jenny and Ian exchanged glances of dismay, and I looked down at my own lap, not knowing what to say. There was no sound for a moment but the crackling of the fire. Then Jenny, with a quick look at Ian, set down her glass and touched her brother on the knee.

"Jamie," she said. "It wasna your fault."

He looked up at her and smiled, a little bleakly.

"No? Who else's, then?"

She took a deep breath and said, "Mine."

"What?" He stared at her in blank astonishment.

She had gone a little paler even than usual, but remained composed.

"I said it was my fault, as much as anyone's. For—for what happened to you, Jamie. And Father."

He covered her hand with his own and rubbed it gently.

"Dinna talk daft, lass," he said. "Ye did what ye did to try to save me; you're right, if ye'd not gone wi' Randall, he'd likely have killed me here."

She studied her brother's face, a troubled frown wrinkling her rounded brow.

"No, I dinna regret taking Randall to the house—not even if he'd . . . well, no. But that wasn't it." She drew a deep breath again, steeling herself.

"When I took him inside, I brought him up to my room. I —I didna ken quite what to expect—I'd not . . . been wi' a man. He seemed verra nervous, though, all flushed and as though he were not certain himself, which seemed strange to me. He pushed me onto the bed, and then he stood there, rubbing himself. I thought at first I'd really damaged him wi' my knee, though I knew I hadna struck him so hard, really." The color was creeping up her cheeks, and she stole a sidelong glance at Ian before looking hastily back at her lap.

"I ken now that he was trying to—to make himself ready. I didna mean to let him know I was frightened, so I sat up straight on the bed and stared at him. That seemed to anger him, and he ordered me to turn round. I wouldna do it, though, and just kept looking at him."

Her face was the color of one of the roses by the doorstep. "He . . . unbuttoned himself, and I . . . well, I laughed at him."

"You did what?" Jamie said incredulously.

"I laughed. I mean—" Her eyes met her brother's with some defiance. "I kent well enough how a man's made. I'd seen you naked often enough, and Willy and Ian as well. But he—" A tiny smile appeared on her lips, despite her apparent efforts to suppress it. He looked so funny, all red in the face, and rubbing himself so frantic, and yet still only half—"

There was a choked sound from Ian, and she bit her lip, but went on bravely.

"He didna like it when I laughed, and I could see it, so I laughed some more. That's when he lunged at me and tore my dress half off me. I smacked him in the face, and he struck me across the jaw, hard enough to make me see stars. Then he grunted a bit, as though that pleased him, and started to climb onto the bed wi' me. I had just about sense enough left to laugh again. I struggled up onto my knees, and I—I taunted him. I told him I kent he was no a real man, and couldna manage wi' a woman. I—"

She bent her head still further, so the dark curls swung down past her flaming cheeks. Her words were very low, almost a whisper.

"I . . . spread the pieces of my gown apart, and I . . . taunted him wi' my breasts. I told him I knew he was afraid o' me, because he wasna fit to touch a woman, but only to sport wi' beasts and young lads . . ."

"Jenny," said Jamie, shaking his head helplessly.

Her head came up to look at him. "Weel, I did then," she said. "It was all I could think of, and I could see that he was fair off his head, but it was plain too that he . . . couldn't. And I stared right at his breeches and I laughed again. And then he got his hands round my throat, throttling me, and I cracked my head against the bedpost, and . . . and when I woke he'd gone, and you wi' him."

There were tears standing in her lovely blue eyes as she grasped Jamie's hands.

"Jamie, will ye forgive me? I know if I'd not angered him that way he wouldna have treated you as he did, and then Faither—"

"Oh, Jenny, love, *mo cridh,* don't." He was kneeling beside her, pulling her face into his shoulder. Ian, on her other side, looked as though he had been turned to stone.

Jamie rocked her gently as she sobbed. "Hush, little dove. Ye did right, Jenny. It wasna your fault, and maybe not mine either." He stroked her back.

"Listen, *mo cridh.* He came here to do damage, under orders. And it would ha' made no difference who he'd found here, or what you or I might have done. He meant to cause trouble, to rouse the countryside against the English, for his own purposes—and those of the man that hired him."

Jenny stopped crying and sat up, looking at him in amazement.

"To rouse folk against the English? But why?"

Jamie made an impatient gesture with one hand. "To find out the folk that might support Prince Charles, should it come to another Rising. But I dinna ken yet which side Randall's employer is on—if he wants to know so those that follow the Prince can be watched, and maybe have their property seized, or if it's that he—Randall's employer—means to go wi' the Prince himself, and wants the Highlands roused and ready for war when the time comes. I dinna ken, and it isna important now." He touched his sister's hair, smoothing it back from her brow.

"All that's important is that you're not harmed, and I am home. Soon I'll come back to stay, *mo cridh.* I promise."

She raised his hand to her lips and kissed it, her face glowing. She fumbled in her pocket for a handkerchief and blew her nose. Then she looked at Ian, still frozen by her side, a look of hurt anger in his eyes.

She touched him gently on the shoulder.

"You think I should ha' told you."

He didn't move, but went on looking at her. "Aye," he said quietly. "I do."

She put the handkerchief down in her lap and took him by both hands.

"Ian, man, I didna tell ye because I didna wish to lose you too. My brother was gone, and my father. I didna mean to lose my own heart's blood as well. For you are dearer to me even than home and family, love." She cast a lopsided smile at Jamie. "And that's saying quite a bit."

She looked into Ian's eyes, pleading, and I could see love and hurt pride struggling for mastery on his face. Jamie rose then and touched me on the shoulder. We left the room quietly, leaving them together before the dying fire.

◆━━

It was a clear night, and the moonlight fell in floods through the tall casements. I could not fall asleep myself, and I thought perhaps it was the light also that kept Jamie awake; he lay quite still, but I could tell by his breathing that he was not asleep. He turned onto his back, and I heard him chuckle softly under his breath.

"What's funny?" I asked quietly.

He turned his head toward me. "Oh, did I wake ye, Sassenach? I'm sorry. I was only remembering about things."

"I wasn't asleep." I scooted closer. The bed had obviously been made for the days when a whole family slept together on one mattress; the gigantic feather-bed must have consumed the entire productivity of hundreds of geese, and navigating through the drifts was like crossing the Alps without a compass. "What were you remembering?" I asked, once I had safely reached his side.

"Oh, about my father, mostly. Things he said."

He folded his arms behind his head, staring musingly at the

thick beams that crossed the low ceiling. "It's strange," he said, "when he was alive, I didna pay him much heed. But once he was dead, the things he'd told me had a good deal more influence." He chuckled briefly again. "What I was thinking about was the last time he thrashed me."

"Funny, was it?" I said. "Anyone ever told you that you have a very peculiar sense of humor, Jamie?" I fumbled through the quilts for his hand, then gave up and pushed them back. He began to stroke my back, and I snuggled next to him, making small noises of pleasure.

"Didn't your uncle beat you, then, when you needed it?" he asked curiously. I smothered a laugh at the thought.

"Lord, no! He would have been horrified at the thought. Uncle Lamb didn't believe in beating children—he thought they should be reasoned with, like adults." Jamie made a Scottish noise in his throat, indicating derision at this ludicrous idea.

"That accounts for the defects in your character, no doubt," he said, patting my bottom. "Insufficient discipline in your youth."

"What defects in my character?" I demanded. The moonlight was bright enough for me to see his grin.

"Ye want me to list them all?"

"No." I dug an elbow into his ribs. "Tell me about your father. How old were you then?" I asked.

"Oh, thirteen—fourteen maybe. Tall and skinny, with spots. I canna remember why I was being thrashed; at that point, it was more often something I'd said than something I'd done. All I remember is we were both of us boiling mad about it. That was one of the times he enjoyed beating me." He pulled me to him and settled me closer against his shoulder, his arm around me. I stroked his flat belly, toying with his navel.

"Stop that, it tickles. D'ye want to hear, or no?"

"Oh, I want to hear. What are we going to do if we ever have children—reason with them, or beat them?" My heart raced a little at the thought, though there was no sign that this would ever be more than an academic question. His hand trapped mine, holding it still over his belly.

"That's simple. You reason with them, and when you're through, I'll take them out and thrash them."

"I thought you *liked* children."

"I do. My father liked *me,* when I wasna being an idiot. And he loved me, too—enough to beat the daylights out of me when I *was* being an idiot."

I flopped onto my stomach. "All right, then. Tell me about it."

Jamie sat up and wadded the pillows more comfortably before lying back down, folded arms behind his head again.

"Well, he sent me up to the fence, as usual—he always made me go up first, so I could experience the proper mixture of terror and remorse while I waited for him, he said—but he was so angry, he was right behind me. I was bent over and taking it, then, gritting my teeth and determined I'd make no noise about it—damned if I'd let him know how much it hurt. I was digging my fingers into the wood of the fence rail as hard as I could—hard enough to leave splinters behind—and I could feel my face turnin' red from holding my breath." He drew a deep breath, as though making up for it, and let it out slowly.

"Usually I'd know when it was going to be over, but this time he didn't stop. It was all I could do to keep my mouth shut; I was grunting wi' each stroke and I could feel the tears starting, no matter how much I blinked, but I held on for dear life." He was uncovered to the waist, almost glowing in the moonlight, frosted with tiny silver hairs. I could see the pulse beat just below his breastbone, a steady throb just under my hand.

"I don't know how long it went on," he continued. "Not that long, likely, but it seemed like a long time to me. At last he stopped a moment and shouted at me. He was beside himself wi' fury, and I was so furious myself I could barely make out what he said at first, but then I could.

"He roared 'Damn you, Jamie! Can ye no cry out? You're grown now, and I dinna mean to beat you ever again, but I want one good yelp out of ye, lad, before I quit, just so I'll think I've made some impression on ye at last!'" Jamie laughed, disturbing the even movement of his pulsebeat.

"I was so upset at that, I straightened up and whirled round and yelled at him, 'Weel, why did ye no say so in the first place, ye auld fool! *OUCH!!'*

"Next thing I knew I was on the ground, wi' my ears ringing and a pain in my jaw, where he'd clouted me. He was standing over me, panting, and wi' his hair and his beard all on end. He reached down and got my hand and hauled me up.

"Then he patted my jaw, and said, still breathing hard, 'That's for calling your father a fool. It may be true, but it's disrespectful. Come on, we'll wash for supper.' And he never struck me again. He still shouted at me, but I shouted back, and it was mostly man to man, after that."

He laughed comfortably, and I smiled into the warmth of his shoulder.

"I wish I'd known your father," I said. "Or maybe it's better not," I said, struck by a thought. "He might not have liked you marrying an Englishwoman."

Jamie hugged me closer and pulled the quilts up over my bare shoulders. "He'd have thought I'd got some sense at last." He stroked my hair. "He'd have respected my choice, whoever it was, but you"—he turned his head and kissed my brow gently—"he would have liked you verra much, my Sassenach." And I recognized it for the accolade it was.

30

Conversations by the Hearth

hatever rift Jenny's revelations had caused between her and Ian, it seemed to have healed. We sat for a short time after dinner in the parlor next evening, Ian and Jamie talking over the farm's business in the corner, accompanied by a decanter of elderberry wine, while Jenny relaxed at last with her swollen ankles propped on a hassock. I tried to write down some of the receipts she had tossed over her shoulder at me as we whizzed through the day's work, consulting her for details as I scribbled.

TO TREAT CARBUNCLES, I headed one sheet.

Three iron nails, to be soaked for one week in sour ale. Add one handful of cedarwood shavings, allow to set. When shavings have sunk to the bottom, mixture is ready. Apply three times daily, beginning on the first day of a quarter moon.

BEESWAX CANDLES began another sheet.

Drain honey from the comb. Remove dead bees, so far as possible. Melt comb with a small amount of water in a large cauldron. Skim bees, wings, and other impurities from surface of water. Drain water, replace. Stir frequently for half an hour, then allow to settle. Drain wa-

ter, keep for use in sweetening. Purify with water twice more.

My hand was getting tired, and I had not even gotten to the making of candle molds, the twisting of wicks, and the hanging of candles to dry.

"Jenny," I called, "how long does it take to make candles, counting everything?"

She laid the small shirt she was stitching in her lap, considering.

"Half a day to gather the combs, two to drain the honey— one if it's hot—one day to purify the wax, unless there's a lot or it's verra dirty—then two. Half a day to make the wicks, one or two to make the molds, half a day to melt the wax, pour the molds and hang them to dry. Say a week altogether."

The dim lamplight and the sputtering quill were too much to contend with after the day's labors. I sat down next to Jenny and admired the tiny garment she was embroidering with nearly invisible stitches.

Her rounded stomach suddenly heaved, as the inhabitant shifted position. I watched, fascinated. I had never been close to someone pregnant for a prolonged period, and hadn't realized the amount of activity that went on inside.

"Would you like to feel it?" Jenny offered, seeing me staring at her middle.

"Well . . ." She took my hand and placed it firmly on her mound.

"Right there. Just wait a moment; he'll kick again soon. They don't like ye lying back like this, ye know. It makes them restless and they start to squirm."

Sure enough, a surprisingly vigorous push raised my hand by several inches.

"Goodness! He's strong!" I exclaimed.

"Aye." Jenny patted her stomach with a touch of pride. "He'll be bonny, like his brother and his da." She smiled across at Ian, whose attention had momentarily wandered from the breeding records of horses to his wife and child-to-be.

"Or even like his good-for-nothing red-heided uncle," she added, raising her voice slightly and nudging me.

"Hey?" Jamie looked up, distracted from his accounts. "Were ye speaking to me?"

"I wonder was it the 'red-heided' or the 'good-for-nothing' that caught his attention," Jenny said to me, sotto voce, with another nudge.

To Jamie she said sweetly, "Nothing at all, *mo cridh*. We were just speculating on the possibility that the new one would have the misfortune to resemble its uncle."

The uncle in question grinned and came across to sit on the hassock, Jenny amiably moving her feet, then replacing them in his lap.

"Rub them for me, Jamie," she begged. "You're better at it than Ian."

He obliged, and Jenny leaned back and closed her eyes in bliss. She dropped the tiny shirt on her central mound, which continued to heave as though in protest. Jamie stared entranced at the movements, just as I had.

"Isn't it uncomfortable?" he asked. "Havin' someone turn somersaults in your belly?"

Jenny opened her eyes and grimaced as a long swell arced across her stomach.

"Mmm. Sometimes I feel my liver's black and blue from bein' kicked. But mostly it's a good feeling, instead. It's like . . ." She hesitated, then grinned at her brother. "It's hard to describe to a man, you not having the proper parts. I don't suppose I could tell ye what carrying a child feels like, no more than you could tell me what it's like to be kicked in the ballocks."

"Oh, I could tell ye that." He promptly doubled up, clasping himself, and rolled his eyes back in his head with a hideous gurgling groan.

"Is that not right, Ian?" he asked, turning his head toward the stool where Ian sat laughing, wooden leg propped on the hearth.

His sister put a delicate foot on his chest and pushed him upright. "All right then, clown. In that case, I'm glad I havena got any."

Jamie straightened up and brushed the hair out of his eyes. "No, really," he said, interested, "is it just that the parts are different? Could you describe it to Claire? After all, she's a woman, though she's not borne a child yet."

Jenny eyed my midriff appraisingly, and I felt that small pang once more.

"Mmm, perhaps." She spoke slowly, thinking. "You feel as though your skin is verra thin all over. You feel everything that touches you, even the rubbing of your clothes, and not just on your belly, but over your legs and flanks and breasts." Her hands went to them unconsciously, curving the lawn under the swelling rounds. "They feel heavy and full . . . and they're verra sensitive just at the tips." The small, blunt thumbs slowly circled the breasts and I saw the nipples rise against the cloth.

"And of course you're big and you're clumsy," Jenny smiled ruefully, rubbing the spot on her hip where she had banged against the table earlier. "You take up more room than you're used to."

"Here, though"—her hands rose protectively to the top of her stomach—"that's where you feel things most, of course." She caressed the rounded bulge as though it were her child's skin she stroked, rather than her own. Ian's eyes followed her hands as they moved from top to bottom of the curving hillock, over and over, smoothing the fabric again and again.

"In the early days, it's a bit like belly-gas," she said, laughing. She poked a toe into her brother's midsection. "Just there—like little bubbles rippling through your belly. But then later, you feel the child move, and it's like a fish on your line and then gone—like a quick tug, but so soon past you're not sure you felt it." As though in protest at this description, her unseen companion heaved to and fro, making her stomach bulge on one side, then the other.

"I imagine you're sure, by this time," Jamie remarked, following the movement with fascination.

"Oh, aye." She placed a hand on one bulge, as though to quiet it. "They sleep, ye know, for hours at a time. Sometimes ye fear they've died, when there's no movement for a long time. Then you try to wake them"—her hand pushed in sharply at the side, and was rewarded immediately by a strong push in the opposite direction—"and you're happy when they kick again. But it's not just the babe itself. You feel swollen all over, near the end. Not painful . . . just so ripe you could burst. It's as though you need to be touched, verra lightly, all over." Jenny was no longer looking at me. Her eyes held her husband's, and I knew she was no longer aware of me or her brother. There was an air of intimacy between her and Ian, as though this were a story often told, but one of which they never tired.

Her voice was lower now, and her hands rose again to her breasts, heavy and compelling under the light bodice.

"And in the last month or so, the milk begins to come in. You feel yourself filling, just a wee bit at a time, a little each time the child moves. And then suddenly, everything comes up hard and round." She cupped her stomach again. "There's no pain, then, just a breathless feeling, and then your breasts tingle as though they'll explode if they're not suckled." She closed her eyes and leaned back, stroking her massive belly, over and over, with a rhythm like the invocation of a spell. It came to me, watching her, that if ever there were such a thing as a witch, then Janet Fraser was one.

The smoky air was filled with the trance over the room; the feeling that lies at the root of lust, the terrible yearning need to join, and create. I could have counted every hair on Jamie's body without looking at him, and knew each one stood erect.

Jenny opened her eyes, dark in the shadows, and smiled at her husband, a slow, rich curve of infinite promise.

"And late in bearing, when the child moves a lot, sometimes there's a feeling like when you've your man inside ye, when he comes to ye deep and pours himself into you. Then, then when that throbbing starts deep inside ye along with him, it's like that, but it's much bigger; it ripples all through the walls of your womb and fills all of you. The child's quiet then, and it's as though it's him you've taken inside you instead."

Suddenly she turned to me, and the spell was broken. "That's what they want sometimes, ye know," she said quietly, smiling into my eyes. "They want to come back."

Some time later, Jenny rose, floating toward the door with a glance back that pulled Ian after her like iron to true north. She paused near the door for him, looking back at her brother, who sat still by the fire hearth.

"You'll see to the fire, Jamie?" She stretched, arching her back, and the curve of her spine echoed the strangely sinuous curve of her belly. Ian's knuckles pressed hard along the length of her back, and ground into the base of her spine, making her groan. And then they were gone.

I stretched too, arms upward, feeling the pleasant pull of tired muscles. Jamie's hands ran down my sides and rested on the swell of my hips. I leaned back into him, drawing his hands forward, imagining them cupping the gentle curve of an unborn child.

As I turned my head to kiss him, I noticed the small form curled in the corner of the settle.

"Look. They've forgotten small Jamie." The little boy customarily slept on a trundle in his parents' room. Tonight he had fallen asleep by the fire while we sat talking over the wine, but no one had remembered to carry him up to his bed. My own Jamie turned me to face him, smoothing my hair away from his nose.

"Jenny never forgets anything," he said. "I expect she and Ian do not care for company just now." His hands went to the fastening at the back of my skirt. "He'll do where he is for the present."

"But what if he wakes up?"

The roving hands came up under the now-loose edge of the bodice. Jamie cocked an eyebrow at the recumbent form of his small nephew.

"Aye well. He'll have to learn his job sometime, won't he? Ye don't want him to be as ignorant as his uncle was." He tossed several cushions to the floor before the fire and lowered himself, carrying me with him.

The firelight gleamed on the silvery scars on his back, as though he were in fact the iron man I had once accused him of being, the metal core showing through rents in the fragile skin. I traced the lashmarks one by one, and he shivered under my touch.

"Do you think Jenny's right?" I asked later. "Do men really want to come back inside? Is that why you make love to us?" A breath of laughter stirred the hair by my ear.

"Well, it's no usually the first thing in my mind when I take ye to bed, Sassenach. Far from it. But then . . ." His hands cupped my breasts softly, and his lips closed on one nipple. "I'd no just say she was completely wrong either. Sometimes . . . aye, sometimes it would be good, to be inside again, safe and . . . one. Knowing we cannot, I suppose, is what makes us want to beget. If we cannot go back ourselves, the best we can do is to give that precious gift to our sons, at least for a little while . . ." He shook himself suddenly, like a dog flinging water from its coat.

"Pay me no mind, Sassenach," he murmured. "I get verra maudlin, drinking elderberry wine."

31

Quarter Day

There was a light knock on the door, and Jenny stepped in, carrying a folded blue garment over her arm and a hat in one hand. She looked her brother over critically, then nodded.

"Aye, the shirt's well enough. And I've let out your best coat for ye; you've grown a bit through the shoulders since I saw ye last." She cocked her head to one side, considering. "Ye've done a braw job of it today—up to the neck, at least. Sit ye down over there, and I'll tend to your hair." She pointed to the stool by the window.

"My hair? What's wrong wi' my hair?" Jamie demanded, putting a hand up to check. Grown nearly to shoulder-length, he had as usual laced it back with a leather thong to keep it out of his face.

Wasting no time on chat, his sister pushed him down onto the stool, yanked the thong loose and began to brush him vigorously with the tortoiseshell brushes.

"What's wrong wi' your hair?" she asked rhetorically. "Weel, now. There's cockleburs in it, for one thing." She plucked a small brown object delicately from his head and dropped it on the dresser. "And bits of oak leaf. Where *were* ye yesterday—rootling under the trees like a hog? And more tangles than a skein of washed yarn—"

"Ouch!"

"Be still, *roy*." Frowning with concentration, she picked up a comb and teased out the tangles, leaving a smooth, shining mass of auburn, copper, cinnamon, and gold, all gleaming together in the morning sun from the window. Jenny spread it in her hands, shaking her head over it.

"I canna think why the good Lord should waste hair like that on a man," she remarked. "Like a red-deer's pelt, in places."

"It is wonderful isn't it?" I agreed. "Look, where the sun's bleached it on top, he's got those lovely blond streaks." The object of our admiration glowered up at us.

"If ye both dinna stop it, I shall shave my head." He stretched out a threatening hand toward the dresser, where his razor rested. His sister, deft in spite of the enormous bulge of pregnancy, reached out and smacked his wrist with the hairbrush. He yelped, then yelped again as she yanked the hair back into a fistful.

"Keep still," she ordered. She began to separate the hair into three thick strands. "I'll make ye a proper cockernonny," she declared with satisfaction. "I'll no have ye goin' down to your tenants looking like a savage."

Jamie muttered something rebellious under his breath, but subsided under his sister's ministrations. Dexterously tucking in stray bits here and there, she plaited the hair into a thick formal queue, tucking the ends under and binding them securely with thread. Then she reached into her pocket, pulled out a blue silk ribbon and triumphantly tied it in a bow.

"There!" she said. "Bonny, no?" She turned to me for confirmation, and I had to admit it. The closely bound hair set off the shape of his head and the bold modeling of his face. Clean and orderly, in snowy linen and grey breeches, he cut a wonderful figure.

"Especially the ribbon," I said, suppressing an urge to laugh. "The same color as his eyes."

Jamie glared at his sister.

"No," he said shortly. "No ribbons. This isna France, nor yet King Geordie's court! I dinna care if it's the color of the Virgin's cloak—no ribbons, Janet!"

"Oh, all right, then, fusspot. There." She pulled the ribbon loose and stood back.

"Aye, ye'll do," she said, with satisfaction. Then she turned her penetrating blue eyes on me.

"Hm," she said, tapping her foot thoughtfully.

As I had arrived more or less in rags, it had been necessary to make me two new gowns as quickly as possible; one of homespun for daily use, and one of silk for occasions of state such as this. Better at stitching wounds than cloth, I had helped with the cutting and pinning, but been obliged to leave the design and sewing to Jenny and Mrs. Crook.

They had done a beautiful job, and the primrose yellow silk fitted my torso like a glove, with deep folds rolling back over the shoulders and falling behind in panels that flowed into the luxuriant drape of the full skirt. Bowing reluctantly to my absolute refusal to wear corsets, they had instead ingeniously reinforced the upper bodice with whale-bone stays ruthlessly stripped from an old corset.

Jenny's eyes traveled slowly upward from my feet to my head, where they lingered. With a sigh, she reached for the hairbrush.

"You, too," she said.

I sat, face burning, avoiding Jamie's eyes, as she carefully removed small twigs and bits of oak leaf from my curls, depositing them on the dresser next to those seined from her brother's hair. Eventually my hair was combed out and pinned up, and she reached into her pocket and pulled out a small lace cap.

"There," she said, pinning it firmly to the top of my pile of curls. "Kertch and all. Verra respectable ye look, Claire."

I assumed this was meant as a compliment, and murmured something in reply.

"Have ye any jewelry, though?" Jenny asked.

I shook my head. "No, I'm afraid not. All I had were the pearls Jamie gave me for our wedding, and those—" Under the circumstances of our departure from Leoch, pearls had been the last thing on my mind.

"Oh!" Jamie exclaimed, suddenly reminded. He dug in the sporran resting on the dresser, and triumphantly pulled out the string of pearls.

"Where on earth did you get those?" I asked in amazement.

"Murtagh brought them, early this morning," he answered. "He went back to Leoch during the trial and got everything he could carry—thinking that we'd need it if we got away. He looked for us on the road here, but of course we'd gone to . . . to the hill, first."

"Is he still here?" I asked.

Jamie stood behind me to fasten the necklace.

"Oh, aye. He's downstairs eating everything in the kitchen and deviling Mrs. Crook."

Aside from his songs, I had heard the wiry little man say less than three dozen words throughout the course of our acquaintanceship, and the thought of his "deviling" anyone was incongruous. He must feel remarkably at home at Lallybroch, I thought.

"Who *is* Murtagh?" I asked. "I mean, is he a relation of yours?"

Jamie and Jenny both looked surprised.

"Oh, aye," the latter replied. She turned to her brother. "He's—what, Jamie?—Father's second cousin's uncle?"

"Nephew," he corrected. "Ye dinna remember? Old Leo had the two boys, and then—"

I put my hands over my ears in a marked manner. This seemed to remind Jenny of something, for she clapped her hands together.

"Earbobs!" she exclaimed. "I think I've some pearl ones that will just do with that necklace! I'll fetch them directly." She vanished with her usual light speed.

"Why does your sister call you Roy?" I asked curiously, watching as he tied his stock before the looking glass. He wore the customary expression of a man doing battle with a mortal enemy, common to all men adjusting their neckwear, but he unclamped his lips to grin at me.

"Och, that. It isna the English name Roy. It's a pet name in Gaelic; the color of my hair. The word's *'ruadh'*—means 'red.'" He had to spell the word and say it over several times before I could catch any difference.

"Sounds the same to me, roy," I said, shaking my head.

Jamie picked up his sporran and began tucking in the loose bits of things that had come out when he pulled out the pearls. Finding a tangled length of fishing line, he upended the bag over the bed, dumping everything in a pile. He began to sort through it, painstakingly winding up the bits of line and string, finding loose fish hooks and firmly re-imbedding them in the piece of cork where they normally rested. I moved over to the bed and inspected the array.

"I've never seen so much rubbish in my life," I observed. "You're a regular jackdaw, Jamie."

"It isna rubbish," he said, stung. "I've uses for all these things."

"Well, the fish lines, and the hooks, yes. And the string for snares. Even, stretching a point, the pistol wadding and the balls—you do carry a pistol now and again. And the little snake Willie gave you, I understand that. But the stones? And a snail shell? And a piece of glass? And . . ." I bent closer to peer at a dark, furry mass of *something.*

"What is—it isn't, is it? Jamie, why on earth are you carrying a dried mole's foot in your sporran?"

"Against rheumatism, of course." He snatched the object from under my nose and stuffed it back in the badger skin.

"Oh, of course," I agreed, surveying him with interest. His face was mildly flushed with embarrassment. "It must work; you don't creak anywhere." I picked a small Bible out of the remaining rubble and thumbed through it, while he stowed away the rest of his valuable equipment.

"Alexander William Roderick MacGregor." I read aloud the name on the flyleaf. "You said there was a debt owing him, Jamie. What did you mean by that?"

"Oh, that." He sat down beside me on the bed, took the small book from me and gently flipped the pages.

"I told ye this belonged to a prisoner who'd died at Fort William, no?"

"Yes."

"I didna know the lad myself; he died a month before I came there. But the doctor who gave it to me told me about him, while he tended my back. I think he needed to tell someone about it, and he couldna speak to anyone in the garrison." He closed the book, holding it on his knee, and stared out the window at the gay October sunshine.

Alex MacGregor, a lad of eighteen or so, had been arrested for the common offense of cattle-lifting. A fair, quiet lad, he had seemed likely to serve his sentence and be released without incident. A week before his release, though, he had been found hanging in the horseshed.

"There was no doubt he'd done it himself, the doctor said." Jamie caressed the leather cover of the small book, drawing one large thumb along the binding. "And he did not exactly *say* what he thought, himself. But he did say that Captain Randall had had a private conversation with the lad a week before."

I swallowed, suddenly cold despite the sunshine.

"And you think—"

"No." His voice was soft and certain. "I dinna think. I *know,* and so did the doctor. And I imagine the sergeant-major knew for certain, and that's why he died." He spread his hands flat on his knees, looking down at the long joints of his fingers. Large, strong and capable; the hands of a farmer, the hands of a warrior. He picked up the small Bible and put it into the sporran.

"I'll tell ye this, *mo duinne.* One day Jack Randall will die at my hands. And when he is dead, I shall send back that book to the mother of Alex MacGregor, with word that her son is avenged."

The air of tension was broken by the sudden reappearance of Jenny, now resplendent in blue silk and her own lace kertch, holding a large box of worn red morocco leather.

"Jamie, the Currans are come, and Willie Murray and the Jeffries. You'd best go down and have a second breakfast with them—I've put out fresh bannocks and salt herring, and Mrs. Crook's doing fresh jam cakes."

"Oh, aye. Claire, come down when you're ready." Rising hastily, he paused long enough to gather me up for a brief but thorough kiss, and disappeared. His footsteps clattered down the first flight of stairs, slowing on the second to the more sedate pace suitable to a laird's entrance, as he neared the ground floor.

Jenny smiled after him, then turned her attention to me. Placing the box on the bed, she threw back the lid, revealing a jumbled array of jewels and baubles. I was surprised to see it; it seemed unlike the neat, orderly Jenny Murray whose iron hand kept the household running smoothly from dawn to dusk.

She stirred a finger through the bright clutter, then as though picking up my thought, looked up and smiled at me.

"I keep thinking I must sort all these things one day. But when I was small, my mother would let me rummage in her box sometimes, and it was like finding magic treasure—I never knew what I'd pick up next. I suppose I think if it were all orderly, the magic would go, somehow. Daft, no?"

"No," I said, smiling back at her. "No, it isn't."

We rummaged slowly through the box, holding the cherished bits and pieces of four generations of women.

"That was my grandmother Fraser's," Jenny said, holding up a silver brooch. It was in the shape of a fret-worked crescent moon, a small single diamond shining above the tip like a star.

"And this—" She pulled out a slender gold band, with a ruby surrounded by brilliants. "That's my wedding ring. Ian spent half a year's salary on it, though I told him he was foolish to do it." The fond look on her face suggested that Ian had been anything but foolish. She polished the stone on the bosom of her dress and admired it once more before replacing it in the box.

"I'll be happy once the babe is born," she said, patting her bulge with a grimace. "My fingers are so swollen in the mornings I can scarcely do up my laces, let alone wear my rings."

I caught a strange nonmetallic gleam in the depths of the box, and pointed. "What's that?"

"Oh, those," she said, dipping into the box again. "I've never worn them; they don't suit me. But you could wear them—you're tall and queenly, like my mother was. They were hers, ye ken."

They were a pair of bracelets. Each made from the curving, almost-circular tusk of a wild boar, polished to a deep ivory

glow, the ends capped with silver tappets, etched with flowered tracery.

"Lord, they're gorgeous! I've never seen anything so . . .
so wonderfully barbaric."

Jenny was amused. "Aye, that they are. Someone gave them
to Mother as a wedding gift, but she never would say who.
My father used to tease her now and then about her admirer,
but she wouldna tell him, either, just smiled like a cat that's
had cream to its supper. Here, try them."

The ivory was cool and heavy on my arm. I couldn't resist
stroking the deep yellow surface, grained with age.

"Aye, they suit ye," Jenny declared. "And they go wi' that
yellow gown, as well. Here are the earbobs—put these on,
and we'll go down."

Murtagh was seated at the kitchen table, industriously eating ham off the end of his dirk. Passing behind him with a
platter, Mrs. Crook dexterously bent and slid three fresh hot
bannocks onto his plate, hardly breaking her stride.

Jenny was bustling to and fro, preparing and overseeing.
Pausing in her progress, she peered over Murtagh's shoulder
at his rapidly emptying plate.

"Don't stint yourself, man," she remarked. "There's another hog in the pen, after all."

"Begrudge a kinsman a bite, do ye?" he asked, not interrupting his chewing.

"Me?" Jenny put both hands on her hips. "Heavens, no!
After all, ye've only had the four helpings so far. Mrs. Crook,"
she turned to call to the departing housekeeper, "when
you've done wi' the bannocks, fix this starveling man a bowl
of parritch to fill in the chinks with. We dinna want him fainting on the doorstep, ye ken."

When Murtagh saw me standing in the doorway, he
promptly choked on a bite of ham.

"Mmmphm," he said, by way of greeting, after Jenny had
pounded him helpfully on the back.

"Nice to see you too," I replied, sitting down opposite
him. "Thank you, by the way."

"Mmphm?" The question was muffled by half a bannock, spread with honey.

"For fetching my things from the Castle."

"Mmp." He dismissed any notion of thanks with a wave that ended in a reach for the butter dish.

"I brought your wee bits of plant and such as well," he said, with a jerk of the head at the window. "Out in the yard, in my saddlebags."

"You've brought my medicine box? That's wonderful!" I was delighted. Some of the medicinal plants were rare, and had taken no little trouble to find and prepare properly.

"But how did you manage?" I asked. Once I had recovered from the horror of the witchcraft trial, I often wondered how the occupants of the Castle had taken my sudden arrest and escape. "I hope you didn't have any difficulty."

"Och, no." He took another healthy bite, but waited until it had made its leisurely way down his throat before replying further.

"Mrs. Fitz had them put away, like, packed up in a box already. I went to her at the first, ye ken, for I wasna sure what reception I'd get."

"Very sensible. I don't imagine Mrs. Fitz would scream at sight of you," I agreed. The bannocks were steaming gently in the cool air, and smelt heavenly. I reached for one, the heavy boar's-tooth bracelets clinking together on my wrist. I saw Murtagh's eyes on them and adjusted them so he could see the engraved silver end pieces.

"Aren't they lovely?" I said. "Jenny said they were her mother's."

Murtagh's eyes dropped to the bowl of parritch that Mrs. Crook had thrust unceremoniously under his nose.

"They suit ye," he mumbled. Then, returning suddenly to the earlier subject, he said, "No, she wouldna summon help against me. I was well acquent' wi' Glenna FitzGibbons, some time ago."

"Oh, a long-lost love of yours, was she?" I teased, enjoying the incongruous thought of him entwined in amorous embrace with the ample Mrs. Fitz.

Murtagh glanced up coldly from his parritch.

"That she wasna, and I'll thank ye to keep a civil tongue when ye speak of the lady. Her husband was my mother's brother. And she was sore grieved for ye, I'll ha' ye to know."

I lowered my eyes, abashed, and reached for the honey to cover my embarrassment. The stone jar had been set in a pot of boiling water to liquefy the contents, and it was comfortingly warm to the touch.

"I'm sorry," I said, drizzling the sweet golden fluid over the bannock, watching carefully so as not to spill it. "I wondered, you know, what she felt like, when . . . when I . . ."

"They didna realize at the first ye were gone," the little man said matter-of-factly, ignoring my apology. "When ye didna come in to dinner, they thought maybe you'd stayed late in the fields and gone up to your bed without eating; your door was closed. And the next day, when there was all the outcry over the taking of Mistress Duncan, no one thought to look for ye. There was no mention of you, only of her, when the news came, and in all the excitement, no one thought to look for ye."

I nodded thoughtfully. No one would have missed me, save those seeking medical treatment; I had spent most of my time in Colum's library while Jamie was away.

"What about Colum?" I asked. I was more than idly curious; had he really planned it, as Geilie thought?

Murtagh shrugged. He scanned the table for further victuals, apparently spotted nothing to his liking, and leaned back, folding his hands comfortably over his lean midriff.

"When he had the news from the village, he had the gates closed at once, and forbade anyone from the Castle to go down, for fear of being caught up in the moil." He leaned further back, eyeing me speculatively.

"Mrs. Fitz thought to find ye, the second day. She said that she asked all the maids if they'd laid eyes on ye. No one had, but one of the girls said she thought perhaps ye'd gone to the village—maybe you'd taken shelter in a house there." One of the girls, I thought cynically. The one that knew bloody well where I was.

He belched softly, not bothering to stifle the sound.

"I heard Mrs. Fitz turned the Castle upside down, then,

and made Colum send down a man to the village, once she was sure ye werena to be found. And when they learned what had happened. . . ." A faint look of amusement lighted the dark face.

"She didna tell me everything, but I gathered she made himself's life more of a misery to him than it usually is, naggin' at him to send down and free ye by force of arms—and not the least bit of use, him arguin' that it had gone well beyond the point where he could do that, and now it was in the hands o' the examiners, and one thing and another. It must ha' been something to see," he said reflectively, "twa wills like that, set one against the other."

And in the end, it seemed, neither had either triumphed nor given way. Ned Gowan, with his lawyer's gift for compromise, had found the way between them, by offering to go himself to the trial, not as representative of the laird, but as an independent advocate.

"Did she think I might be a witch?" I asked curiously. Murtagh snorted briefly.

"I've yet to see the auld woman believes in witches, nor the young one, neither. It's men think there must be ill-wishes and magic in women, when it's only the natural way of the creatures."

"I begin to see why you've never married," I said.

"Do ye, then?" He pushed back his chair abruptly and rose, pulling the plaid forward over his shoulders.

"I'll be off. Gie my respects to the laird," he said to Jenny, who reappeared from the front hall, where she had been greeting tenants. "He'll be busy, I've nae doubt."

Jenny handed him a large cloth sack, tied in a knot at the mouth, and plainly holding enough provisions for a week.

"A wee bite for the journey home," she said, dimpling at him. "Might last ye at least out of sight o' the house."

He tucked the knot of the sack snugly into his belt and nodded briefly, turning toward the door.

"Aye," he said, "and if not, ye'll see the corbies gatherin' just beyond the rise, come to pick my bones."

"A lot of good they'd get from it," she answered cynically,

eyeing his scrawny frame. "I've seen more sound flesh on a broomstick."

Murtagh's dour face remained unchanged, but a faint gleam showed in his eye, nonetheless.

"Oh, aye?" he said. "Weel, I'll tell ye, lass . . ." The voices passed down the hall, mingling in amiable insult and argument, vanishing at last in the echoes of the front hall.

I sat at the table for a moment longer, idly caressing the warm ivory of Ellen MacKenzie's bracelets. At the far-off slam of the door, I shook myself and stood up to take my place as the Lady of Lallybroch.

Usually a busy place, on Quarter Day the manor house simply bristled with activity. Tenants came and went all day. Many came only long enough to pay their rents; some stayed all day, wandering about the estate, visiting with friends, taking refreshment in the parlor. Jenny, blooming in blue silk, and Mrs. Crook, starched in white linen, flitted back and forth between kitchen and parlor, overseeing the two maidservants, who staggered to and fro under enormous platters of oatcake, fruitcake, "crumbly," and other sweets.

Jamie, having introduced me with ceremony to the tenants present in dining room and parlor, then retired into his study with Ian, to receive the tenants singly, to confer with them over the needs of the spring planting, to consult over the sale of wool and grain, to note the activities of the estate, and to set things in order for the next quarter of the year.

I puttered cheerfully about the place, visiting with tenants, lending a hand with the refreshments when needed, sometimes just drifting into the background to watch the comings and goings.

Recalling Jamie's promise to the old woman by the mill-pond, I waited with some curiosity for the arrival of Ronald MacNab.

He came shortly past noon, riding a tall, slip-jointed mule, with a small boy clinging to his belt behind. I viewed them covertly from the parlor door, wondering just how accurate his mother's assessment had been.

I decided that while "drunken sot" might be overstating things slightly, Grannie MacNab's general perceptions were acute. Ronald MacNab's hair was long and greasy, carelessly tied back with twine, and his collar and cuffs were grey with dirt. While surely a year or two younger than Jamie, he looked at least fifteen years older, the bones of his face submerged in bloat, small grey eyes dulled and bloodshot.

As for the child, he also was scruffy and dirty. Worse, so far as I was concerned, he slunk along behind his father, keeping his eyes on the floor, cringing when Ronald turned and spoke sharply to him. Jamie, who had come to the door of his study, saw it too, and I saw him exchange a sharp look with Jenny, bringing a fresh decanter in answer to his call.

She nodded imperceptibly and handed over the decanter. Then, taking the child firmly by the hand, she towed him toward the kitchen, saying, "Come along wi' me now, laddie. I believe we've a crumbly or two going wantin'. Or what about a slice of fruitcake?"

Jamie nodded formally to Ronald MacNab, standing aside as the man went into the study. Reaching out to shut the door, Jamie caught my eye and nodded toward the kitchen. I nodded back and turned to follow Jenny and young Rabbie.

I found them engaged in pleasant converse with Mrs. Crook, who was ladling punch from the big cauldron into a crystal bowl. She tipped a bit into a wooden cup and offered it to the lad, who hung back, eyeing her suspiciously, before finally accepting it. Jenny went on chatting casually to the lad as she loaded platters, receiving little more than grunts in return. Still, the half-wild little creature seemed to be relaxing a bit.

"Your sark's a bit grubby, lad," she observed, leaning forward to turn back the collar. "Take it off, and I'll give it a bit of a wash before ye go." "Grubby" was a gross understatement, but the boy pulled back defensively. I was behind him, though, and at a gesture from Jenny, grabbed him by the arms before he could dart away.

He kicked and yowled, but Jenny and Mrs. Crook closed in on him as well, and between the three of us, we peeled the filthy shirt off his back.

"Ah." Jenny drew in her breath sharply. She was holding the boy's head firmly under one arm, and the scrawny back was fully exposed. Welts and scabs scored the flesh on either side of the knobby backbone, some freshly healed, some so old as to be only faded shadows lapping the prominent ribs. Jenny took a good grip on the back of the boy's neck, speaking soothingly to him as she released his head. She jerked her head in the direction of the hall, looking at me.

"You'd better tell him."

I knocked tentatively at the study door, holding a plate of honeyed oatcakes as excuse. At Jamie's muffled bidding, I opened the door and went in.

My face as I served MacNab must have been sufficient, for I didn't have to ask to speak privately with Jamie. He stared meditatively at me for a moment, then turned back to his tenant.

"Well then, Ronnie, that will do for the grain allotment. There's the one other thing I meant to speak wi' you about, though. You've a likely lad named Rabbie, I understand, and I'm needing a boy of that size to help in the stables. Would ye be willing for him to come?" Jamie's long fingers played with a goose-quill on the desk. Ian, seated at a smaller table to one side, propped his chin on his fists, staring at MacNab with frank interest.

MacNab glowered belligerently. I thought he had the irritable resentment of a man who isn't drunk but wishes he were.

"No, I've need of the lad," he said curtly.

"Mm." Jamie lounged back in his chair, hands folded across his middle. "I'd pay ye for his services, of course."

The man grunted and shifted in his chair.

"My mother's been at ye, eh? I said no, and I meant no. The lad's my son, and I'll deal wi' him as I see fit. And I see fit to keep him to hame."

Jamie eyed MacNab thoughtfully, but turned his attention back to the ledgers without further argument.

Late in the afternoon, as the tenants repaired to the warmer reaches of pantry and parlor for refreshment before departing,

I spotted Jamie from the window, strolling in leisurely fashion toward the pigshed, arm slung about the scruffy MacNab in comradely style. The pair disappeared behind the shed, presumably to inspect something of agricultural interest, and reappeared within a minute or two, coming toward the house.

Jamie's arm was still about the shorter man's shoulders, but seemed now to be supporting him. MacNab's face was an unhealthy grey, slicked with sweat, and he walked very slowly, seeming unable to straighten up all the way.

"Weel, that's good, then," Jamie remarked cheerfully as they came within earshot. "Reckon your missus will be glad of the extra money, eh, Ronald? Ah, here's your animal for you —fine-looking beast, is he no?" The moth-eaten mule that had brought the MacNabs to the farm shambled out of the yard where it had been enjoying the hospitality of the estate. A wisp of hay still protruded from the corners of its mouth, jerking irregularly as the beast chewed.

Jamie gave MacNab a hand under the foot to assist him to his seat; much-needed help, by the look of it. MacNab did not speak or wave in response to Jamie's voluble "Godspeeds" and "safe journeys," but only nodded in a dazed way as he left the yard at a walk, seemingly intent on some secret trouble that absorbed his attention.

Jamie stood leaning on the fence, exchanging pleasantries as other tenants wended their ways homeward, until the untidy figure of MacNab was out of sight over the crest of the hill. He straightened, gazing down the road, then turned and gave a whistle. A small figure in a torn but clean smock and stained kilt crept out from under the haywagon.

"Weel, then, young Rabbie," said Jamie genially. "Looks as though your father's given his permission for ye to be a stable lad after all. I'm sure as you'll be a hard worker and a credit to him, eh?" Round, bloodshot eyes stared up dumbly out of the dirty face, and the boy made no response at all, until Jamie reached out, and grasping him gently by the shoulder, turned him toward the horse trough.

"There'll be some supper waiting ye in the kitchen, laddie. Go and wash a bit first, though; Mrs. Crook's a picky woman. Oh, and Rabbie"—he leaned down to whisper to the lad—

"mind your ears, or she'll do 'em for ye. She scrubbed mine for me this morning." He put his hands behind his ears and flapped them solemnly at the boy, who broke into a shy smile and fled toward the trough.

"I'm glad you managed it," I said, taking Jamie's arm to go in to supper. "With little Rabbie MacNab, I mean. How did you do it, though?"

He shrugged. "Took Ronald back of the brewhouse and fisted him once or twice in the soft parts. Asked him did he want to part wi' his son or his liver." He glanced down at me, frowning.

"It wasna right, but I couldn't think what else to do. And I didna want the lad to go back wi' him. It wasn't only I'd promised his grannie, either. Jenny told me about the lad's back." He hesitated. "I'll tell ye, Sassenach. My father whipped me as often as he thought I needed it, and a lot oftener than I thought I did. But I didna cower when he spoke to me. And I dinna think young Rabbie will lie in bed with his wife one day and laugh about it."

He hunched his shoulders, with that odd half-shrug, something I hadn't seen him do in months.

"He's right; the lad's his own son, he can do as he likes. And I'm not God; only the laird, and that's a good bit lower down. Still . . ." He looked down at me with a crooked half-smile.

"It's a damn thin line between justice and brutality, Sassenach. I only hope I've come down on the right side of it."

I put an arm around his waist and hugged him.

"You did right, Jamie."

"Ye think so?"

"Yes."

We strolled back toward the house, arms about each other. The whitewashed farm buildings glowed amber in the setting sun. Instead of going into the house, though, Jamie steered me up the slight rise behind the manor. Here, sitting on the top rail of a fenced field, we could see the whole of the home farm laid out before us.

I laid my head on Jamie's shoulder and sighed. He squeezed me gently in response.

"This is what you were born to do, isn't it, Jamie?"

"Perhaps, Sassenach." He looked out over the fields and buildings, the crofts and the roads, then looked down, a smile suddenly curving the wide mouth.

"And you, my Sassenach? What were you born for? To be lady of a manor, or to sleep in the fields like a gypsy? To be a healer, or a don's wife, or an outlaw's lady?"

"I was born for you," I said simply, and held out my arms to him.

"Ye know," he observed, letting go at last, "you've never said it."

"Neither have you."

"I have. The day after we came. I said I wanted you more than anything."

"And *I* said that loving and wanting weren't necessarily the same thing," I countered.

He laughed. "Perhaps you're right, Sassenach." He smoothed the hair from my face and kissed my brow. "I wanted ye from the first I saw ye—but I loved ye when you wept in my arms and let me comfort you, that first time at Leoch."

The sun sank below the line of black pines, and the first stars of the evening came out. It was mid-November, and the evening air was cold, though the days still kept fine. Standing on the opposite side of the fence, Jamie bent his head, putting his forehead against mine.

"You first."

"No, you."

"Why?"

"I'm afraid."

"Of what, my Sassenach?" The darkness was rolling in over the fields, filling the land and rising up to meet the night. The light of the new crescent moon marked the ridges of brow and nose, crossing his face with light.

"I'm afraid if I start I shall never stop."

He cast a glance at the horizon, where the sickle moon hung low and rising. "It's nearly winter, and the nights are long, *mo duinne*." He leaned across the fence, reaching, and I stepped into his arms, feeling the heat of his body and the beat of his heart.

"I love you."

32

Hard Labor

A few days later, near sunset, I was on the hill behind the house, digging up the tubers of a small patch of corydalis I had found. Hearing the rustle of footsteps approaching through the grass, I turned, expecting to see Jenny or Mrs. Crook come to call me to supper. Instead it was Jamie, hair spiked with dampness from his predinner ablutions, still in his shirt, knotted together between his legs for working in the fields. He came up behind me and put his arms around me, resting his chin on my shoulder. Together we watched the sun sinking behind the pines, robed in gold and purple glory. The landscape faded quietly around us, but we stayed where we were, wrapped in contentment. Finally, as it began to grow dark, I could hear Jenny calling from the house below.

"We'd better go in," I said, reluctantly stirring.

"Mmm." Jamie didn't move, but merely tightened his hold, still gazing into the deepening shadows, as though trying to fix each stone and blade of grass in memory.

I turned to him and slipped my arms around his neck.

"What is it?" I asked quietly. "Must we leave soon?" My heart sank at the prospect of leaving Lallybroch, but I knew that it was dangerous for us to stay too much longer; another visit from the redcoats could happen at any time, with much more sinister results.

"Aye. Tomorrow, or the day after, at latest. There are English at Knockchoilum; it's twenty miles from here, but that's only two days' ride in fine weather." I started to slither off the fence, but Jamie slid an arm under my knees and lifted me, holding me against his chest.

I could feel the heat of the sun still in his skin, and smell the warm dusty scent of sweat and oat grass. He had been helping with the last of the harvesting, and the smell reminded me of a supper the week before, when I knew that Jenny, always friendly and polite, had finally accepted me fully as a member of the family.

Harvesting was grueling work, and Ian and Jamie were often nodding by the end of supper. On one occasion, I had left the table to fetch a brose pudding for dessert, and returned to find both of them sound asleep, and Jenny laughing quietly to herself amid the remains of supper. Ian lay slumped in his chair, chin resting on his chest, breathing heavily. Jamie had laid his cheek on his folded arms and sprawled forward across the table, snoring peacefully between the platter and the peppermill.

Jenny took the pudding from me and served us both, shaking her head at the slumbering men.

"They were yawning so much I wondered, ye know," she said, "what would happen if I stopped talking. So I kept quiet, and sure enough, two minutes later they were out, the both of them." She smoothed Ian's hair tenderly off his forehead.

"That's why there're so few babies born in July here," she said, with a wicked cock of the eyebrow at me. "The men can't keep awake long enough in November to start one." It was true enough, and I laughed. Jamie stirred and snorted next to me, and I laid a hand on the back of his neck to soothe him. His lips curved at once in a soft, reflexive smile, then relaxed into sleep once more.

Jenny, watching him, said, "That's funny, that is. I've not seen him do that since he was quite small."

"Do what?"

She nodded. "Smile in his sleep. He used always to do it, if ye came by and petted him in his cradle, or even later, in his trundle. Sometimes Mother and I would take it in turns to stroke his head and see could we make him smile; he always would."

"That's odd, isn't it?" I experimented, running a hand gently down the back of his head and neck. Sure enough, I was rewarded at once by a singularly sweet smile that lingered for a moment before the lines of his face relaxed once more into the rather stern expression he presented when asleep.

"I wonder why he does that," I said, watching him in fascination. Jenny shrugged and grinned at me.

"I imagine it means he's happy."

In the event, we did not leave next day. In the middle of the night, I was wakened by low conversation in the room. Rolling over, I saw Ian bending over the bed, holding a candle.

"The babe's on its way," said Jamie, seeing me awake. He sat up, yawning. "A bit early, Ian?"

"Ye never know. Small Jamie was late. Better early than late, I reckon." Ian's smile was quick and nervous.

"Sassenach, can ye deliver a child? Or had I best go for the midwife?" Jamie turned to me, questioning. I didn't hesitate in my answer.

I shook my head. "Get the midwife." I had seen only three births during my training; all conducted in a sterile operating room, the patient draped and anesthetized, nothing visible save the grotesquely swelling perineum and the suddenly emergent head.

Having seen Jamie on his way to fetch the midwife, Mrs. Martins, I followed Ian up the stairs.

Jenny was sitting in a chair near the window, leaning comfortably back. She had put on an old nightgown, stripped the bed and spread an aged quilt over the feather mattress, and was now just sitting. Waiting.

Ian hovered nervously over her. Jenny smiled too, but with a distracted, inward look, as though listening to something far off, which only she could hear. Ian, fully dressed, fidgeted about the room, picking things up and putting them down, until Jenny at last ordered him to leave.

"Go downstairs and rouse Mrs. Crook, Ian," she said, smiling to ease the dismissal. "Tell her to get things ready for Mrs. Martins. She'll ken what to do." She drew in her breath sharply then, and put both hands on her distended abdomen. I stared, seeing her belly draw up suddenly tight and round. She bit her lip and breathed heavily for a moment, then relaxed. Her belly had resumed its normal shape, a slightly pendant teardrop, rounded at both ends.

Ian put a hand hesitantly on her shoulder, and she covered it with her own, smiling up at him.

"Then tell her to feed ye, man. You and Jamie will be needing a bit to eat. They say the second babe comes faster than the first; maybe by the time you're done wi' breakfast, I'll be ready for a bite myself."

He squeezed her shoulder tightly, and kissed her, murmuring something in her ear before turning to go. He hesitated in the doorway, looking back, but she waved him firmly away.

It seemed a very long time before Jamie arrived with the midwife, and I grew more nervous as the contractions grew stronger. Second babies *were* said to be faster, as a rule. What if this one decided to arrive before Mrs. Martins?

At first, Jenny carried on light conversation with me, only pausing to bend forward slightly, holding her stomach, as the contractions tightened their grip. But she quickly lost the urge to talk, and lay back, resting quietly in between the increasingly powerful pains. Finally, after one that almost bent her double in her chair, she rose to her feet, staggering.

"Help me walk a bit, Claire," she said. Unsure what was the proper procedure, I did as she said, grasping her tightly under the arm to help her stand upright. We made several slow circuits of the room, pausing when a contraction struck, going on when it eased. Shortly before the midwife arrived, Jenny made her way to the bed and lay down.

Mrs. Martins was a reassuring-looking person; tallish and thin, she had wide shoulders and muscular forearms, and the sort of kind, down-to-earth expression that invited confidence. Two vertical creases between her iron-grey brows, always visible, deepened when she was concentrating.

They stayed shallow as she made her preliminary examination. Everything normal so far, then. Mrs. Crook had produced a pile of clean, ironed sheets for our use, and Mrs. Martins took one of these, still folded, and pushed it under Jenny. I was startled to see the dark stain of blood between her thighs, as she raised herself slightly.

Seeing my look, Mrs. Martins nodded reassuringly.

"Aye. Bloody show, it's called. It's all right. It's only when the blood is bright red, and a terrible lot all at once, that ye worry. There's nothing wrong."

We all settled down to wait. Mrs. Martins talked quietly and comfortingly to Jenny, rubbing the small of her back, pressing hard during the contractions. As the pains became more frequent, Jenny began to clamp her lips together and snort heavily through her nose. Often, there was a deep, faint groan as the full force of the pain came on.

Jenny's hair was soaked with perspiration by this time, and her face bright red with the strain. Watching her, I realized fully why it was called "labor." Giving birth was bloody hard work.

Over the next two hours, little progress appeared to be made, except that the pains grew obviously stronger. Able at first to answer questions, Jenny quit responding, lying panting at the end of each contraction, face fading from red to white in a matter of seconds.

She clamped her lips through the next one, beckoning me to her side as it eased.

"If the child lives . . ." she said, gasping for air, "and it's a girl . . . her name is Margaret. Tell Ian . . . name her Margaret Ellen."

"Yes, of course," I soothed. "But you'll be able to tell him yourself. It won't be long, now."

She only shook her head in determined negation, and clenched her teeth as the next pain came. Mrs. Martins took me by the arm, steering me away.

"Dinna mind it, lassie," she said matter-of-factly. "They always think they're goin' to die about now."

"Oh," I said, mildly relieved.

"Mind ye," she said, in a lower voice, "sometimes they do."

Even Mrs. Martins seemed a trifle worried as the pains went

on, with no appreciable progress. Jenny was tiring badly; as each pain eased, her body went slack, and she even dozed off, as though seeking escape in small intervals of sleep. Then, as the remorseless fist grasped her once again, she would wake fighting and groaning with effort, writhing to the side to curl protectively over the rigid lump of the unborn child.

"Could the child be . . . backward?" I asked, in a low voice, shy about suggesting such a thing to an experienced midwife. Mrs. Martins seemed not at all offended by the suggestion, though; the lines between her brows merely deepened as she looked at the straining woman.

When the next pain eased, Mrs. Martins flung back the sheet and nightgown, and went rapidly to work, pressing here and there on the huge mound with quick, skilled fingers. It took several tries, as the probing seemed to incite the pains, and examination was impossible during the relentlessly powerful contractions.

At last she drew back, thinking, tapping one foot abstractedly as she watched Jenny writhe through two more of the spine-wrenching pains. As she jerked on the sheets, one of the strained linens parted suddenly with a rending tear.

As though this had been a signal, Mrs. Martins started forward with decision, beckoning to me.

"Lean her back a bit, lass," Mrs. Martins instructed me, not at all disconcerted by Jenny's cries. I supposed she had heard her share of screaming.

At the next relaxation, Mrs. Martins plunged into action. Grasping the child through the momentarily flaccid walls of the womb, she heaved, trying to turn it. Jenny screamed and jerked my arms as another contraction started.

Mrs. Martins tried again. And again. And again. Unable to keep from pushing, Jenny was wearing herself far past the point of exhaustion, her body struggling past the bounds of ordinary strength as it strove to force the child into the world.

Then it worked. There was a sudden strange fluid shifting, and the amorphous bulk of the child turned under Mrs. Martins's hands. All at once, the shape of Jenny's belly was altered, and there was an immediate sense of getting down to business.

"Now push." She did, and Mrs. Martins dropped to her knees beside the bed. Apparently she saw some sign of progress, for she rose and hastily snatched a small bottle from the table where she had put it when she came in. She poured a small amount of what looked like oil on her fingertips, and began to rub it gently between Jenny's legs.

Jenny made a deep and vicious sound of protest at being touched as the next pain came on, and Mrs. Martins took her hand away. Jenny sagged into inertness and the midwife resumed her gentle massage, crooning to her patient, telling her everything was well, just to rest, and now . . . push!

During the next contraction, Mrs. Martins put her hand on top of Jenny's belly and pushed down strongly. Jenny shrieked, but the midwife kept pushing until the contraction eased.

"Push with me on the next one," the midwife said. "It's almost here."

I put my hands above Mrs. Martins's on Jenny's belly, and at her signal, all three of us pushed together. There was a deep, victorious grunt from Jenny, and a slimy blob swelled suddenly between her thighs. She straightened her legs against the mattress and pushed once more, and Margaret Ellen Murray shot into the world like a greased pig.

A little later, I straightened from wiping Jenny's smiling face with a damp rag and glanced out the window. It was nearly sunset.

"I'm all right," Jenny said. "Quite all right." The broad grin of delight with which she had greeted the delivery of her daughter had turned into a small, permanent smile of deep contentment. She reached up with an unsteady hand and touched my sleeve.

"Go tell Ian," she said. "He'll be worrit."

To my cynical eyes, it didn't look it. The scene in the study, where Ian and Jamie had taken refuge, strongly resembled a premature celebratory debauch. An empty decanter stood on the sideboard, accompanied by several bottles, and a strong alcoholic fume hung over the room like a cloud.

The proud father appeared to have passed out, head resting on the laird's desk. The laird himself was still conscious, but bleary-eyed, leaning back against the paneling and blinking like an owl.

Outraged, I stamped over to the desk and gripped Ian by the shoulder, shaking him roughly and ignoring Jamie, who pushed himself upright, saying, "Sassenach, wait . . ."

Ian was not quite unconscious. His head came up reluctantly, and he looked at me with a set, rigid face, eyes bleak and pleading holes. I realized suddenly that he thought I had come to tell him that Jenny was dead.

I relaxed my grip and patted him gently instead.

"She's all right," I said, softly. "You have a daughter."

He laid his head down on his arms again, and I left him, his thin shoulders shaking as Jamie patted his back.

The survivors now revived and cleaned up, the Murray-Fraser families gathered in Jenny's room for a celebratory supper. Little Margaret, tidied for inspection and swaddled in a small blanket, was given to her father, who received his new offspring with an expression of beatific reverence.

"Hello, wee Maggie," he whispered, touching the tiny button of a nose with one fingertip.

His new daughter, unimpressed by the introduction, closed her eyes in concentration, stiffened, and urinated on her father's shirt.

During the brief bustle of hilarity and repair occasioned by this lapse of good manners, small Jamie succeeded in escaping from the clutches of Mrs. Crook and flung himself onto Jenny's bed. She grunted slightly in discomfort, but put out a hand and gathered him in, waving at Mrs. Crook to let him be.

"*My* mama!" he declared, burrowing into Jenny's side.

"Well, who else?" she asked reasonably. "Here, laddie." She hugged him, and kissed the top of his head, and he relaxed, reassured, and snuggled against her. She gently pushed his head down, stroking his hair.

"Lay your head then, man," she said. "Past your bedtime. Lay your head." Comforted by her presence, he put a thumb in his mouth and fell asleep.

Given a turn to hold the baby, Jamie proved remarkably competent, cupping the small fuzzy skull in the palm of one hand like a tennis ball. He seemed reluctant to hand the child back to Jenny, who cuddled her against her breasts, crooning soft endearments.

At last we made our way to our own room, which seemed silent and empty in contrast to the warm family scene we had just left, Ian kneeling by his wife's bed, hand resting on small Jamie as Jenny nursed the new baby. I was conscious for the first time of just how tired I was; it was nearly twenty-four hours since Ian had roused me.

Jamie closed the door quietly behind him. Without speaking, he came behind me and undid the fastenings of my gown. His hands reached around me and I lay back gratefully against his chest. Then he bent his head to kiss me and I turned, putting my own arms around his neck. I felt not only very tired, but very tender, and not a little sad.

"Perhaps it's as well," Jamie said slowly, as though to himself.

"What's as well?"

"That you're barren." He couldn't see my face, buried in his chest, but he must have felt me stiffen.

"Aye, I knew that long ago. Geillis Duncan told me, soon after we wed." He stroked my back gently. "I regretted it a bit at first, but then I began to think it was as well; living as we must, it would be verra difficult if you were to get with child. And now"—he shivered slightly—"now I think I am glad of it; I wouldna want ye to suffer that way."

"I wouldn't mind," I said, after a long while, thinking of the rounded, fuzzy head and tiny fingers.

"I would." He kissed the top of my head. "I saw Ian's face; it was like his own flesh was being torn, each time Jenny screamed." My arms were around him, stroking the ridged scars on his back. "I can bear pain, myself," he said softly, "but I couldna bear yours. That would take more strength than I have."

33

The Watch

Jenny recovered rapidly after Margaret's birth, insisting on coming downstairs the day following the delivery. At the combined insistence of Ian and Jamie, she reluctantly refrained from doing any work, only supervising from the sofa in the parlor where she reclined, baby Margaret sleeping in her cradle alongside.

Not content to sit idle, though, within a day or two she had ventured as far as the kitchen, and then the back garden. Sitting on the wall, the well-wrapped baby in a carrying sling, she was keeping me company as I simultaneously pulled dead vines and kept an eye on the enormous cauldron in which the household's laundry was boiled. Mrs. Crook and the maids had already removed the clean wash to be hung and dried; now I was waiting for the water to cool sufficiently to be dumped out.

Small Jamie was "helping" me, yanking out plants with mad abandon and flinging bits of stick in all directions. I called a warning as he ventured too near the cauldron, then raced after him as he ignored me. Luckily the pot had cooled quickly; the water was no more than warm. Warning him to keep back with his mother, I grasped the pot and tilted it away from the iron contrivance that held it and kept it from falling.

I sprang back out of the way as the dirty water cascaded over the lip of the pot, steaming in the chilly air. Young Jamie, squatting beside me on his heels, splatted his hands joyfully in the warm mud, and black droplets flew all over my skirts.

His mother slid down from the wall, yanked him up by the collar and dealt him a smart clout on the backside.

"Have ye no sense, *gille*? Look at ye! There's your shirt'll have to go and be washed again! And look what ye've done to your auntie's skirt, ye wee heathen!"

"It doesn't matter," I protested, seeing the miscreant's lower lip quiver.

"Weel, it matters to me," said Jenny, giving her offspring the benefit of a gimlet eye. "Say 'sorry' to your auntie, laddie, then get ye into the house and have Mrs. Crook give ye a bit of a wash." She patted his bottom, gently this time, and gave him a push in the direction of the house.

We were turning back to the mass of sodden clothes, when the sound of hoofbeats came from the road.

"That'll be Jamie back, I expect," I said, listening. "He's early, though."

Jenny shook her head, peering intently toward the road. "Not his horse."

The horse, when it appeared at the crest of a hill, was not one she knew, to judge from her frown. The man aboard, though, was no stranger. She stiffened beside me, then began to run toward the gate, wrapping both arms around the baby to hold it steady.

"It's Ian!" she called to me.

He was tattered and dusty and bruised about the face, as he slid off his horse. One bruise on his forehead was swollen, with a nasty split that went through the eyebrow. Jenny caught him under the arm as he hit the ground, and it was only then I saw that his wooden leg was gone.

"Jamie," he gasped. "We met the Watch near the mill. Waiting for us. They knew we were coming."

My stomach lurched. "Is he alive?"

He nodded, panting for breath. "Aye. Not wounded, either. They took him to the west, toward Killin."

Jenny's fingers were exploring his face.

"Are ye bad hurt, man?"

He shook his head. "No. They took my horse and my leg; they didna need to kill me to stop me following."

Jenny glanced at the horizon, where the sun lay just above the trees. Maybe four o'clock, I estimated. Ian followed her gaze and anticipated her question.

"We met them near midday. It took me over two hours to get to a place that had a horse."

She stood still, for a moment, calculating, then turned to me with decision.

"Claire. Help Ian to the house, will ye, and if he needs aught in the way of doctoring, do it as fast as ye can. I'll give the babe to Mrs. Crook and fetch the horses."

She was gone before either of us could protest.

"Does she mean . . . but she can't!" I exclaimed. "She can't mean to leave the baby!"

Ian was leaning heavily on my shoulder as we made our way slowly up the path to the house. He shook his head.

"Maybe not. But I dinna think she means to let the English hang her brother, either."

It was growing dark by the time we reached the spot where Jamie and Ian had been ambushed. Jenny slid off her horse and cast about through the bushes like a small terrier, pushing branches out of her way and muttering things under her breath that sounded suspiciously like some of her brother's better curses.

"East," she said, finally coming out of the trees, scratched and dirty. She beat dead leaves from her skirt, and took her horse's reins from my numbed hands. "We canna follow in the dark, but at least I know which way to go, come the dawn."

We made a simple camp, hobbling the horses and building a small fire. I admired the efficiency with which Jenny had done it, and she smiled.

"I used to make Jamie and Ian show me things, when they were young. How to build fires, and climb trees—even how to skin things. And how to track." She glanced again in the direction taken by the Watch.

"Dinna worry, Claire." She smiled at me and sat down by the fire. "Twenty horses canna go far through the brush, but two can. The Watch will be taking the road toward Eskadale, by the looks of it. We can cut over the hills and meet them near Midmains."

Her nimble fingers were tugging at the bodice of her gown. I stared in amazement as she spread the folds of cloth and pulled down the top of her underblouse to show her breasts. They were very large, and looked hard, swollen with milk. In my ignorance, I had not thought to wonder what a nursing mother does if deprived of her nursling.

"I canna leave the babe for long," she said in answer to my thoughts, grimacing as she cupped one breast from beneath. "I'll burst." In response to the touch, milk had begun to drip from the engorged nipple, thin and bluish. Pulling a large kerchief from her pocket, Jenny tucked it beneath her breast. There was a small pewter cup on the ground beside her, one she had taken from the saddlebag. Pressing the lip of the cup just below the nipple, she gently stroked the breast between two fingers, squeezing gently toward the nipple. The milk dripped faster in response, then suddenly the areole around the nipple contracted and the milk spurted out in a tiny jet of surprising force.

"I didn't know it did that!" I blurted, staring in fascination.

Jenny moved the cup to catch the stream, and nodded. "Oh, aye. The babe's sucking starts it, but once the milk lets down, all the child need do is swallow. Oh, that feels better." She closed her eyes briefly in relief.

She emptied the cup onto the ground, remarking, "Shame to waste it, but there isna much to do wi' it, is there?" Switching hands, she placed the cup again and repeated the process with the other breast.

"It's a nuisance," she said, looking up to see me still watching. "Everything to do wi' bairns is a nuisance, almost. Still, ye'd never choose not to have them."

"No," I answered softly. "You wouldn't choose that."

She looked across the fire at me, face kind and concerned.

"It isna your time yet," she said. "But you'll have bairns of your own one day."

I laughed a little shakily. "First we'd better find the father."

She emptied the second cup and began readjusting her dress.

"Oh, we'll find them. Tomorrow. We have to, for I canna stay away from wee Maggie much longer than that."

"And once we've found them?" I asked. "What then?"

She shrugged and reached for the blanket rolls.

"That depends on Jamie. And on how much he's made them hurt him."

———————

Jenny was right; we did find the Watch the next day. We left our campsite before full day, pausing only long enough for her to express more milk. She seemed to be able to find trails where none existed, and I followed her without question into a heavily wooded area. Quick travel was impossible through the brushy undergrowth, but she assured me that we were taking a much more direct route than the one the Watch would have to follow, bound as they were to roads by the size of their group.

We came on them near noon. I heard the jingle of harness and the casual voices I had heard once before, and put out a hand to stop Jenny, who was following me for the moment.

"There's a ford in the stream below," she whispered to me. "It sounds as though they've stopped there to water the horses." Sliding down, she took both sets of reins and tethered our own horses, then, beckoning to me to follow, she slid into the undergrowth like a snake.

From the vantage point to which she led me, on a small ledge overlooking the ford, we could see almost all of the men of the Watch, mostly dismounted and talking in casual groups, some sitting on the ground eating, some leading the horses in groups of two and three to the water. What we couldn't see was Jamie.

"Do you suppose they've killed him?" I whispered in panic. I had counted every man twice, to be sure I had missed no one. There were twenty men and twenty-six horses; all in plain view, so far as I could see. But no hint of a prisoner, and no telltale gleam of sun on red hair.

"I doubt it," Jenny answered. "But there's only one way to find out." She began to squirm backward from the ledge.

"What's that?"

"Ask."

The road narrowed as it left the ford, becoming little more than a dusty trail through dense stands of pine and alder on either side. The trail was not wide enough for the Watch to ride two abreast; each man would have to pass down it in single file.

As the last man in the line approached a bend in the trail, Jenny Murray stepped suddenly out in the road ahead of him. His horse shied, and the man struggled to rein it in, cursing. As he opened his mouth to demand indignantly what she meant by this behavior, I stepped out of the bush behind, and whacked him solidly behind the ear with a fallen branch.

Taken completely by surprise, he lost his balance as the horse shied again, and fell off into the roadway. He wasn't stunned; the blow had only knocked him over. Jenny remedied this deficiency with the assistance of a good-sized rock.

She grabbed the horse's reins and gestured violently to me.

"Come on!" she whispered. "Get him off the road before they notice he's gone."

So it was that when Robert MacDonald of the Glen Elrive Watch recovered consciousness, it was to find himself securely tied to a tree, looking down the barrel of a pistol held by the steely-eyed sister of his erstwhile prisoner.

"What have ye done wi' Jamie Fraser?" she demanded.

MacDonald shook his head dazedly, obviously thinking her a figment of his imagination. An attempt to move put paid to this notion, and after an allowance for the statutory amount of cursing and threatening, he at last reconciled himself to the idea that the only way to get loose was to tell us what we wanted to know.

"He's dead," MacDonald said sullenly. Then, as Jenny's finger tightened ominously on the trigger, he added in sudden panic, "It wasna me! It was his own fault!"

Jamie, he said, had been mounted double, arms bound with a leather strap, behind one of the Watch, riding between two other men. He had seemed docile enough, and they had taken no particular precautions when fording the river six miles from the mill.

"Damn fool threw himself off the horse and into the deep water," said MacDonald, shrugging as well as he could with his hands tied behind him. "We fired at him. Must have hit him, for he didna come up again. But the stream's swift just below the ford, and it's deep. We searched a bit, but no body. Must ha' been carried downstream. Now, for God's sake, ladies, will ye no untie me!"

After repeated threats from Jenny had elicited no further details or changes in his story, we decided to accept it as true. Declining to free MacDonald altogether, Jenny did at least loosen his bonds, so that given time, he might struggle out of them. Then we ran.

"Do you think he's dead?" I puffed, as we reached the tethered horse.

"I don't. Jamie swims like a fish, and I've seen him hold his breath for three minutes at a time. Come on. We're going to search the riverbank."

We cast up and down the banks of the river, stumbling on rocks, splashing in the shallows, scratching our hands and faces on the willows that trawled their branches in the pools.

At last Jenny gave a triumphant shout, and I splashed my way across, balancing precariously on the mossy rocks that lined the bottom of the burn, shallow at this spot.

She was holding a leather strap, still fastened in a circle. A smear of blood discolored one side.

"Wiggled out of it here," she said, bending the circlet between her hands. She looked back in the direction we had come, down that jagged fall of tangled rocks, deep pools and foaming rapids, and shook her head.

"How ever did ye manage, Jamie?" she said, half to herself.

We found an area of flattened grass, not far from the verge, where he had evidently lain to rest. I found a small brownish smudge on the bark of an aspen nearby.

"He's hurt," I said.

"Aye, but he's moving," Jenny answered, looking at the ground as she paced back and forth.

"Are you good at tracking?" I asked hopefully.

"I'm no much of a hunter," she replied, setting off with me close behind, "but if I canna follow something the size of Jamie Fraser through dry bracken, then I'm daft as well as blind."

Sure enough, a broad track of crushed brown fern led up the side of the hill and disappeared into a thick clump of heather. Circling around this point turned up no further evidence, nor did calling produce any answer.

"He'll be gone," Jenny said, sitting down on a log and fanning herself. I thought she looked pale, and realized that kidnapping and threatening armed men was no pursuit for a woman who had given birth less than a week before.

"Jenny," I said, "you have to go back. Besides, he might go back to Lallybroch."

She shook her head. "No, that he wouldna. Whatever Mac-Donald told us, they're no likely to give up so easy, not with a reward at hand. If they havena hunted him down yet, it's because they couldn't. But they'll have sent someone back to keep an eye on the farm, just in case. No, that's the one place he wouldna go." She pulled at the neck of her gown. The day was cold, but she was sweating slightly, and I could see growing dark stains on the bosom of her dress, from leaking milk.

She saw me looking and nodded. "Aye, I'll have to go back soon. Mrs. Crook's nursing the lassie wi' goat's milk and sugar water, but she canna do without me much longer, nor me without her. I hate to leave ye alone, though."

I didn't much care for the thought of having to hunt alone through the Scottish Highlands for a man who might be anywhere, either, but I put a bold face on it.

"I'll manage," I said. "It could be worse. At least he's alive."

"True." She glanced at the sun, low over the horizon. "I'll stay wi' ye through the night, at least."

Huddled around the fire at night, we didn't talk much. Jenny was preoccupied with thoughts of her abandoned child, me with thoughts of just how I was to proceed on my own, alone with no real knowledge of geography or Gaelic.

Suddenly Jenny's head snapped up, listening. I sat up and listened myself, but heard nothing. I peered into the dark woods in the direction Jenny was looking, but saw no gleaming eyes in the depths, thank God.

When I turned back to the fire, Murtagh was sitting on the other side, calmly warming his hands at the blaze. Jenny snapped round at my exclamation, and uttered a short laugh of surprise.

"I could ha' cut both your throats before ye ever looked in the right direction," the little man observed.

"Oh, could ye then?" Jenny was sitting with her knees drawn up, hands clasped near her ankles. With a lightning dart, her hand went under her skirt and the blade of a *sgian dhu* flashed in the firelight.

"None sae bad," Murtagh agreed, nodding sagely. "Is the wee Sassenach that good?"

"No," said Jenny, restoring her blade to her stocking. "So it's good you'll be with her. Ian sent for ye, I expect?"

The little man nodded. "Aye. Did ye find the Watch yet?"

We told him of our progress to date. At the news that Jamie had escaped, I could have sworn that a muscle twitched near the corner of his mouth, but it would have been stretching matters to call it a smile.

At length, Jenny rose, folding her blanket.

"Where are you going?" I asked in surprise.

"Home." She nodded at Murtagh. "He'll be wi' ye now; you don't need me, and there's others that do."

Murtagh looked up at the sky. The waning moon was faintly visible behind a haze of cloud, and a soft spatter of rain whispered in the pine boughs above us.

"The morning will do. The wind's risin', and no one will move far tonight."

Jenny shook her head and went on tucking her hair beneath her kerchief. "I know my way. And if none will move tonight, there's none will hinder me on the road, no?"

Murtagh sighed impatiently. "You're stubborn as your ox of a brother, beggin' your pardon. Little reason to hurry back, so far as I can see—I doubt your good man will ha' taken a doxy to his bed in the time ye've been gone."

"You see as far as the end o' your nose, *duine,* and that's short enough," Jenny answered sharply. "And if ye've lived so long without knowing better than to stand between a nursing mother and a hungry child, you've not sense enough to hunt hogs, let alone find a man in the heather."

Murtagh raised his hands in surrender. "Oh, aye, ye'll take your own way. I didna ken I was tryin' to talk sense to a wild sow. Get a tush through the leg for my trouble, I expect."

Jenny laughed unexpectedly, dimpling. "I expect ye might at that, ye auld rogue." She bent and heaved the heavy saddle up on her knee. "See that ye take care with my good-sister, then, and send word when ye've found Jamie."

As she turned to saddle the horse, Murtagh added, "By the bye, ye'll reckon to find a new kitchen maid when ye reach home."

She paused and eyed him, then slowly set the saddle on the ground. "And who might that be?" she asked.

"The Widow MacNab," he replied, with deliberation.

She was still for a moment, nothing moving but the kerchief and cloak that stirred in the rising wind.

"How?" she asked at last.

Murtagh bent to pick up the saddle. He heaved it up and secured the girth with what seemed like one effortless motion.

"Fire," he said, giving a final tug to the stirrup leather. "Watch your way as ye pass the high field; the ashes will still be warm."

He cupped his hands to give her a foot up, but she shook her head and took the reins instead, beckoning to me.

"Walk wi' me to the top of the hill, Claire, if ye will."

The air was cold and heavy, away from the fire. My skirts were damp from sitting on the ground, and clung to my legs as I walked. Jenny's head was bent against the wind, but I could see her profile, lips pale and set with chill.

"It was MacNab that gave Jamie to the Watch?" I asked at last. She nodded slowly.

"Aye. Ian will have found out, or one of the other men; it doesna matter which."

It was late November, well past Guy Fawkes Day, but I had a sudden vision of a bonfire, flames leaping up timbered walls and sprouting in the thatch like the tongues of the Holy Ghost, while the fire within roared its prayers for the damned.

And inside, the guy, an effigy crouched in ash on his own hearthstone, ready to fall into black dust at the next blast of cold wind to sweep through the shell of his home. *There is a fine line sometimes, between justice and brutality.*

I realized Jenny was looking full at me, questioning, and I returned her gaze with a nod. We stood together, in this case at least, on the same side of that grim and arbitrary line.

We paused at the top of the hill, Murtagh a dark speck by the fire below. Jenny rummaged for a moment in the side pocket of her skirt, then pressed a small wash leather bag into my hand.

"The rents from quarter day," she said. "Ye might need it."

I tried to give the money back, insisting that Jamie would not want to take money that was needed for the running of the estate, but she would have none of it. And while Janet Fraser was half her brother's size, she more than matched his stubbornness.

Outclassed, I gave up at last, and tucked the money safely away in the recesses of my own costume. At Jenny's insistence, I took also the small *sgian dhu* she pressed upon me.

"It's Ian's, but he has another," she said. "Put it into your stocking top, and hold it with your garter. Don't leave it off, even when ye sleep."

She paused a moment, as though there were something else she meant to say. Apparently there was.

"Jamie said," she said carefully, "that ye might . . . tell me things sometimes. And he said that if ye did, I was to do as ye said. Is there . . . anything ye wish to tell me?"

Jamie and I had discussed the necessity for preparing Lallybroch and its inhabitants against the coming disasters of the Rising. But we had thought then that there was time. Now I had no time, or most a few minutes, in which to give this new sister I held dear enough information to guard Lallybroch against the coming storm.

Being a prophet was a very uncomfortable occupation, I thought, not for the first time. I felt considerable sympathy with Jeremiah and his Lamentations. I also realized exactly why Cassandra was so unpopular. Still, there was no help for it. On the crest of a Scottish hill, the night wind of an autumn storm whipping my hair and skirts like the sheets of a banshee, I turned my face to the shadowed skies and prepared to prophesy.

"Plant potatoes," I said.

Jenny's mouth dropped slightly open, then she firmed her jaw and nodded briskly. "Potatoes. Aye. There's none closer than Edinburgh, but I'll send for them. How many?"

"As many as you can. They're not planted in the Highlands now, but they will be. They're a root crop that will keep for a long time, and the yield is better than wheat. Put as much ground as you can into crops that can be stored. There's going to be a famine, a bad one, in two years. If there's land or property that's not productive now, sell it, for gold. There's going to be war, and slaughter. Men will be hunted, here and everywhere through the Highlands." I thought for a moment. "Is there a priest-hole in the house?"

"No, it was built well after the Protector's time."

"Make one then, or some safe place to hide. I hope Jamie won't need it," I swallowed hard at the thought, "but someone may."

"All right. Is that all?" Her face was serious and intent in the half-light. I blessed Jamie for his forethought in warning her, and her for her trust in her brother. She didn't ask me how, or why, but only took careful note of what I said, and I knew my hasty instructions would be followed.

"That's all. All I can think of just now, anyway." I tried to smile, but the effort seemed unconvincing, even to me.

Hers was better. She touched my cheek briefly in farewell.

"God go wi' ye, Claire. We'll meet again—when ye bring my brother home."

PART SIX

The Search

34

Dougal's Story

Whatever the disadvantages of civilization, I reflected grimly, the benefits were undeniable. Take telephones, for example. For that matter, take newspapers, which were popular in such metropolitan centers as Edinburgh or even Perth, but completely unknown in the wilderness of the Scottish Highlands.

With no such methods of mass communication, news spread from one person to the next at the speed of a man's stride. People generally found out what they needed to know, but with a delay of several weeks. Consequently, faced with the problem of finding exactly where Jamie was, there was little to rely on except the possibility of someone encountering him and sending word back to Lallybroch. That was a process that might take weeks. And the winter would set in shortly, making travel to Beauly impossible. I sat feeding sticks to the fire, pondering the possibilities.

Which way would Jamie have gone from the point of his escape? Not back to Lallybroch, to be sure, and almost certainly not north, into the MacKenzie lands. South to the Border lands, where he might meet again with Hugh Munro or some of his earlier rough companions? No, most likely northeast, toward Beauly. But if I could figure that out, so could the men of the Watch.

Murtagh returned from his gathering, dumping an armload of sticks on the ground. He sat down cross-legged on a fold of his plaid, wrapping the rest around himself to keep out the chill. He cast an eye toward the sky, where the moon glowed behind racing clouds.

"It wilna snow just yet," he said, frowning. "Another week, maybe two. We might reach Beauly before then." Well, nice to have confirmation of my deductions, I supposed.

"You think he'll be there?"

The little clansman shrugged, hunching his plaid higher around his shoulders.

"No tellin'. The travel will no be as easy for him, lyin' hid during the day, and staying off the roads. And he hasna got a horse." He scratched his stubbled chin thoughtfully. "We canna find him; we'd best let him find us."

"How? Send up flares?" I suggested sarcastically. One thing about Murtagh; no matter what incongruous thing I said, he could be counted on to behave as though I hadn't spoken.

"I've brought your wee packet of medicines," he said, nodding toward the saddlebags on the ground. "And you've enough of a reputation near Lallybroch; you'll be known as a healer through most of the countryside near." He nodded to himself. "Aye, that'll do well enough." And without further explanations, he lay down, rolled up in his plaid and went calmly to sleep, ignoring the wind in the trees, the light patter of rain, and me.

I found out soon enough what he meant. Traveling openly —and slowly—along the main roads, we stopped at every croft and village and hamlet we came to. There he would make a quick survey of the local populace, round up anyone suffering from illness or injury, and bring them to me for treatment. Physicians being few and far between in these parts, there was always someone ailing to attend to.

While I was occupied with my tonics and salves, he would chat idly with the friends and relatives of the afflicted, taking care to describe the path of our journey toward Beauly. If by chance there were no patients to be seen in a place, we would pause nonetheless for the night, seeking shelter at a cottage or tavern. In these places, Murtagh would sing to entertain our hosts and earn our supper, stubbornly insisting that I preserve all the money I had with me, in case it should be needed when we found Jamie.

Not naturally inclined toward conversation, he taught me some of his songs, to pass the time as we plodded on from place to place.

"Ye've a decent voice," he observed, one day, after a moderately successful attempt at "The Dowie Dens of Yarrow." "Not well-trained, but strong and true enough. Try it once more and ye'll sing it wi' me tonight. There's a wee tavern at Limraigh."

"Do you really think this will work?" I asked. "What we're doing, I mean?"

He shifted about in the saddle before answering. No natural horseman, he always looked like a monkey trained to ride a horse, but still managed to dismount fresh as a daisy at day's end, while I could barely manage to hobble my horse before staggering off to collapse.

"Oh, aye," he said, at last. "Sooner or later. You're seein' more sick folk these days, no?"

This was true, and I admitted as much.

"Well, then," he said, proving his point, "that means word o' your skill is spreading. And that's what we want. But we could maybe do better. That's why you'll sing tonight. And perhaps . . ." He hesitated, as though reluctant to suggest something.

"Perhaps what?"

"Know anything about fortune-telling, do ye?" he asked warily. I understood the reason for his hesitancy; he had seen the frenzy of the witch-hunt at Cranesmuir.

I smiled. "A bit. You want me to try it?"

"Aye. The more we can offer, the more folk will come to see us—and go back to tell others. And word will spread about us, 'til the lad hears of us. And that's when we'll find him. Game to try, are ye?"

I shrugged. "If it will help, why not?"

I made my debut as singer and fortune-teller that night at Limraigh, with considerable success. I found that Mrs. Graham had been right in what she had told me—it was the faces, not the hands, that gave you the necessary clues.

Our fame spread, little by little, until by the next week, people were running out of their cottages to greet us as we rode into a village, and showering us with pennies and small gifts as we rode away.

"You know, we could really make something of this," I remarked one evening, stowing the night's takings away. "Too bad there's no theater anywhere near—we could do a proper music-hall turn: Magical Murtagh and His Glamorous Assistant, Gladys."

Murtagh treated this remark with his usual taciturn indifference, but it was true; we really did quite well together. Perhaps it was because we were united in our quest, despite our very basic personality differences.

The weather grew increasingly bad, and our pace even slower, but there was as yet no word from Jamie. Outside Belladrum one night, in a driving rain, we met with a band of real Gypsies.

I blinked disbelievingly at the tiny cluster of painted caravans in the clearing near the road. It looked exactly like a camp of the Gypsy bands that came to Hampstead Down every year.

The people looked the same, too; swarthy, cheerful, loud, and welcoming. Hearing the jingle of our harness, a woman's head poked out of the window of one caravan. She looked us over for a moment, then gave a shout, and the ground under the trees was suddenly alive with grinning brown faces.

"Gie me your purse for safekeeping," said Murtagh, unsmiling, watching the young man swaggering toward us with a gay disregard of the rain soaking his colorful shirt. "And dinna turn your back on anyone."

I was cautious, but we were welcomed with expansive motions, and invited to share the Gypsies' dinner. It smelt delicious—some sort of stew—and I eagerly accepted the invitation, ignoring Murtagh's dour speculations as to the basic nature of the beast that had provided the stewmeat.

They spoke little English, and less Gaelic; we conversed largely in gestures, and a sort of bastard tongue that owed its parentage largely to French. It was warm and companionable in the caravan where we ate; men and women and children all ate casually from bowls, sitting wherever they could find space, dipping the succulent stew up with chunks of bread. It was the best food I had had in weeks, and I ate until my sides creaked. I could barely muster breath to sing, but did my best, humming along in the difficult spots, and leaving Murtagh to carry the tunes.

Our performance was greeted with rapturous applause, and the Gypsies reciprocated, a young man singing some sort of wailing lament to the accompaniment of an ancient fiddle. His performance was punctuated by the crashing of a tambourine, wielded with some gravity by a little girl of about eight.

While Murtagh had been circumspect in his inquiries in the villages and crofts we visited, with the Gypsies he was entirely open. To my surprise, he told them bluntly who we sought; a big man, with hair like fire, and eyes like the summer skies. The Gypsies exchanged glances up and down the aisle of the caravan, but there was a unanimous shaking of regretful heads. No, they had not seen him. But . . . and here the leader, the purple-shirted young man who had welcomed us, pantomimed the sending of a messenger, should they happen across the man we sought.

I bowed, smiling, and Murtagh in turn pantomimed the handing across of money for information received. This bit of business was greeted with smiles, but also with gazes of speculation. I was glad when Murtagh declared that we could not stay the night, but must be on our way, thank ye just the same. He shook out a few coins from his sporran, taking care to exhibit the fact that it held only a small handful of coppers. Distributing these by way of thanks for the supper, we made our exit, followed by voluble protestations of farewell, gratitude, and good wishes—at least that's what I assumed they were.

They might actually have been promising to follow us and cut our throats, and Murtagh behaved rather as though this had been the case, leading the horses at a gallop to the crossroads two miles distant, then ducking aside into the vegetation for a substantial detour before reemerging onto the road again.

Murtagh glanced up and down the road, empty in the fading, rain-soaked dusk.

"Do you really think they followed us?" I asked curiously.

"I dinna ken, but since there's twelve o' them, and no but the twa o' us, I thought we'd best act as though they did." This seemed sound reasoning, and I followed him without question through several more evasive maneuvers, arriving at last in Rossmoor, where we found shelter in a barn.

Snow fell the next day. Only a light fall, enough to dust the ground with a white like the flour on the millhouse floor, but it worried me. I didn't like to think of Jamie, alone and un-sheltered in the heather, braving winter's storms in nothing but the shirt and plaid he had been wearing at his capture by the Watch.

Two days later, the messenger came.

The sun was still above the horizon, but it was evening already in the rock-walled glens. The shadows lay so deep under the leafless trees that the path—what there was of one —was nearly invisible. Fearful of losing the messenger in the gathering dark, I walked so closely behind him that once or twice I actually trod on the trailing hem of his cloak. At last, with an impatient grunt, he turned and thrust me ahead of him, steering me through the dusk with a heavy hand on my shoulder.

It felt as though we had been walking for a long time. I had long since lost track of our turnings amid the towering boulders and thick dead undergrowth. I could only hope that Murtagh was somewhere behind, keeping within earshot if not within sight. The man who had come to the tavern to fetch me, a middle-aged Gypsy with no English, had flatly refused to have anyone but me accompany him, pointing em-phatically first at Murtagh and then the ground, to indicate that he must stay put.

The night chill came on fast at this time of year, and my heavy cloak was barely enough protection against the sudden gusts of icy wind that met us in the open spaces of the clear-ings. I was torn between dismay at the thought of Jamie lying through the cold, wet nights of autumn without shelter, and excitement at the thought of seeing him again. A shiver ran up my spine that had nothing to do with the cold.

At last my guide pulled me to a halt, and with a precautionary squeeze of my shoulder, stepped off the path and disappeared. I stood, as patiently as could be managed, hands folded under my arms for warmth. I was sure my guide—or someone—would return; I hadn't paid him, for one thing. Still, the wind rattled through the dead brambles like the passing of a deer's ghost, still in panic-stricken flight from the hunter. And the damp was seeping through the seams of my boots; the otter-fat waterproofing had worn away, and I'd had no chance to reapply it.

My guide reappeared as suddenly as he had left, making me bite my tongue as I stifled a squeak of surprise. With a jerk of his head, he bade me follow him, and pressed aside a screen of dead alders for me to pass.

The cave entrance was narrow. There was a lantern burning on a ledge, silhouetting the tall figure that turned toward the entrance to meet me.

I flung myself forward, realizing even before I touched him that it was not Jamie. Disappointment struck me like a blow in the stomach, and I had to step back and swallow several times to choke back the heavy bile that rose in my throat.

I clenched my hands at my sides, digging my fists into my thighs until I felt calm enough to speak.

"Rather out of your territory, aren't you?" I said, in a voice that surprised me by its coolness.

Dougal MacKenzie had watched my struggle for control, not without some sympathy on his dark face. Now he took my elbow and led me farther into the cave. There were a number of bundles piled against the far side, many more than a single horse could carry. He wasn't alone, then. And whatever he and his men carried, it was something he preferred not to expose to the curious gaze of innkeepers and hostlers.

"Smuggling, I suppose?" I said, with a nod toward the bundle. Then I thought better and answered my own question. "No, not exactly smuggling—goods for Prince Charles, hm?"

He didn't bother to answer me, but sat down on a boulder opposite me, hands on his knees.

"I've news," he said abruptly.

I took a deep breath, bracing myself. News, and not good news, from the expression on his face. I took another breath, swallowed hard, and nodded.

"Tell me."

"He's alive," he said, and the largest of the ice lumps in my stomach dissolved. Dougal cocked his head to one side, watching intently. To see whether I were going to faint? I wondered dimly. It didn't matter; I wasn't.

"He was taken near Kiltorlity, two weeks ago," Dougal said, still watching me. "Not his fault; poor luck. He met six dragoons face-to-face round a turn in the path, and one recognized him."

"Was he hurt?" My voice was still calm, but my hands were beginning to shake. I pressed them flat against my legs to still them.

Dougal shook his head. "Not as I heard." He paused a moment. "He's in Wentworth Prison," he said reluctantly.

"Wentworth," I repeated mechanically. Wentworth Prison. Originally one of the mighty Border fortresses, it had been built sometime in the late sixteenth century, and added to at intervals over the next hundred and fifty years. The sprawling pile of rock now covered nearly two acres of ground, sealed behind three-foot walls of weathered granite. But even granite walls have gates, I thought. I looked up to ask a question, and saw the reluctance still stamped on Dougal's features.

"What else?" I demanded. The hazel eyes met mine, unflinching.

"He stood his trial three days ago," Dougal said. "And was condemned to hang."

The ice lump was back, with company. I closed my eyes.

"How long?" I asked. My voice seemed rather far-off to my own ears and I opened my eyes again, blinking to refocus them in the flickering lantern light. Dougal was shaking his head.

"I dinna ken. Not long, though."

My breath was coming a little easier now, and I was able to unclench my fists.

"We'd better hurry, then," I said, still calmly. "How many men are with you?"

Instead of answering, Dougal rose and came over to me. Reaching down, he took my hands and pulled me to my feet. The look of sympathy was back, and a deep grief lurking in his eyes frightened me more than anything he'd said so far. He shook his head slowly.

"Nay, lass," he said gently. "There's nothing we can do."

Panicked, I tore my hands away from him.

"There is!" I said. "There must be! You said he was still alive!"

"And I said 'Not long'!" he retorted sharply. "The lad's in Wentworth Prison, not the thieves' hole at Cranesmuir! They may hang him today, or tomorrow, or not 'til next week, for all I know o' the matter, but there is no way on earth that ten men can force a way into Wentworth Prison!"

"Oh, no?" I was trembling again, but with rage this time. "You don't know that—you don't know what might be done! You're just not willing to risk your skin, or your miserable . . . profit!" I flung an arm accusingly at the piled bundles.

Dougal grappled with me, seizing my flailing arms. I hammered his chest in a frenzy of grief and rage. He ignored the blows and put his arms around me, pulling me tight against him and holding me until I ceased struggling.

"Claire." It was the first time he had ever used my first name, and it frightened me still further.

"Claire," he said again, loosening his grip so that I could look up at him, "do ye not think I'd do all I could to free the lad, did I think there was the slightest chance? Damn it, he's my own foster-son! But there is no chance—none!" He shook me slightly, to emphasize his words.

"Jamie wouldna have me throw away good men's lives in a vain venture. Ye know that as well as I do."

I could keep back the tears no longer. They burned down my icy cheeks as I pushed against him, seeking to free myself. He held me tighter, though, trying to force my head against his shoulder.

"Claire, my dear," he said, voice gentler. "My heart's sore for the lad—and for you. D'ye come away wi' me. I'll take ye safe. To my own house," he added hastily, feeling me stiffen. "Not to Leoch."

"To your house?" I said slowly. A horrible suspicion was beginning to form in my mind.

"Aye," he said. "Ye dinna think I'd take ye back to Cranesmuir, surely?" He smiled briefly before the stern features relaxed back into seriousness. "Nay. I'll take ye to Beannachd. You'll be safe there."

"Safe?" I said, "or helpless?" His arms dropped away at the tone of my voice.

"What d'ye mean?" The pleasant voice was suddenly cold.

I felt rather cold myself, and pulled my cloak together as I moved away from him.

"You kept Jamie away from his home by telling him his sister had borne a child to Randall," I said, "so that you and that precious brother of yours would have a chance to lure him into your camp. But now the English have him, you've lost any chance of controlling the property through Jamie." I backed up another step, swallowing.

"You were party to your sister's marriage contract. It was by your insistence—yours and Colum's—that Broch Tuarach might be held by a woman. You think that if Jamie dies, Broch Tuarach will belong to me—or to you, if you can seduce or force me into marrying you."

"What?!" His voice was incredulous. "Ye think . . . ye think this is all some plot? Saint Agnes! Do ye think I'm lying to ye?"

I shook my head, keeping my distance. I didn't trust him an inch.

"No, I believe you. If Jamie weren't in prison, you'd never dare to tell me he was. It's too easy to check that. Nor do I think you betrayed him to the English—not even you could do something like that to your own blood. Besides, if you had, and word of it ever reached your men, they'd turn on you in a second. They'd tolerate a lot in you, but not treachery against your own kinsman." As I spoke I was reminded of something.

"Was it you who attacked Jamie near the Border last year?" The heavy brows rose with surprise.

"Me? No! I found the lad near death, and saved him! Does that sound as though I meant him harm?"

Under cover of my cloak, I ran my hand down my thigh, feeling for the comforting bulk of my dagger.

"If it wasn't you, who was it?"

"I dinna ken." The handsome face was wary, but not hiding anything. " 'Twas one of three men—broken men, outlaws—that hunted wi' Jamie then. All of them accused each other, and there was no way of findin' out the truth o' the matter, not then." He shrugged, the traveling cloak falling back from one broad shoulder.

"It doesna matter much now; twa of the men are dead, and the third in prison. Over another matter, but it makes little difference, do ye think?"

"No, I don't suppose so." It was in a way a relief to find that he wasn't a murderer, whatever else he might be. He had no reason to lie to me now; so far as he knew, I was completely helpless. Alone, he could compel me to do whatever he wished. Or at least he likely thought so. I took a grip on the handle of my dirk.

The light was poor in the cave, but I was watching carefully, and I could see indecision flicker momentarily across his face as he chose his next move. He stepped toward me, hand out, but stopped when he saw me flinch away.

"Claire. My sweet Claire." The voice was soft now, and he ran an insinuating hand lightly down my arm. So he had decided to try seduction rather than compulsion.

"I know why ye talk so cold to me, and why ye think ill of me. You know that I burn for ye, Claire. And it's true—I've wanted ye since the night of the Gathering, when I kissed your sweet lips." He had two fingers resting lightly on my shoulder, inching toward my neck. "If I'd been a free man when Randall threatened ye, I'd ha' wed ye myself on the spot, and sent the man to the devil for ye." He was moving his body gradually closer, crowding me against the stone wall of the cavern. His fingertips moved to my throat, tracing the line of my cloak-fastening.

He must have seen my face then, for he stopped his advance, though he left his hand where it was, resting lightly above the rapid pulse that beat in my throat.

"Even so," he said, "even feeling as I do—for I'll hide it

from ye no longer—even so, ye couldna imagine I'd abandon Jamie if there were any hope of saving him? Jamie Fraser is the closest thing I've got to a son!"

"Not quite," I said. "There's your real son. Or perhaps two, by now?" The fingers on my throat increased their pressure, just for a second, then dropped away.

"What d'ye mean?" And this time all pretense, all games, were dispensed with. The hazel eyes were intent and the full lips a grim line in the russet beard. He was very large, and very close to me. But I had gone too far already for caution.

"It means I know who Hamish's father really is," I said. He had been half-expecting it, and had his face well under control, but the last month spent telling fortunes had not been in vain. I saw the tiny flicker of shock that widened his eyes and the sudden panic, swiftly quelled, that tightened the corners of his mouth.

Bull's-eye. In spite of the danger, I knew a moment's fierce exultation. I had been right, then, and the knowledge might just possibly be the weapon I needed.

"Do ye, then?" he said softly.

"Yes," I said, "and I imagine Colum knows as well."

That stopped him for a moment. The hazel eyes narrowed, and I wondered for an instant whether he was armed.

"He thought it was Jamie for a time, I think," I said, staring directly into his eyes. "Because of the rumors. You must have started those, feeding them to Geillis Duncan. Why? Because Colum got suspicious of Jamie and started to question Letitia? She couldn't hold out for long against him. Or was it that Geilie thought you were Letitia's lover, and you told her it was Jamie to quiet her suspicions? She's a jealous woman, but she can't have any reason to protect you now."

Dougal smiled cruelly. The ice never left his eyes.

"No, she can't," he agreed, still speaking softly. "The witch is dead."

"Dead!" The shock must have shown as plainly on my face as in my voice. His smile broadened.

"Oh, aye," he said. "Burnt. Stuck feet first in a barrel of pitch and heaped about with dry peats. Bound to a stake and lit like a torch. Sent to the devil in a pillar of flame, under the branches of a rowan tree."

I thought at first this merciless recitation of detail was meant to impress me, but I was wrong. I shifted to one side, and as the light shone fresh on his face, I could see the lines of grief etched around his eyes. It wasn't a catalog of horror, then, but a lashing of himself. I felt no pity for him, under the circumstances.

"So you were fond of her," I said coldly. "Much good it did her. Or the child. What did you do with that?"

He shrugged. "Saw it placed in a good home. A son, and a healthy babe, for all its mother was a witch and an adulteress."

"And its father an adulterer and a betrayer," I snapped. "Your wife, your mistress, your nephew, your brother—is there anyone you haven't betrayed and deceived? You . . . you . . ." I choked on the words, quite sick with loathing. "I don't know why I'm surprised," I said, trying to speak calmly. "If you've no loyalty to your king, I suppose there's no reason to think you'd feel it for your nephew or your brother, either."

His head snapped round and he glared at me. He raised his thick dark brows, the same shape as Colum's, as Jamie's, as Hamish's. The deep-set eyes, the broad cheekbones, the beautifully shaped skull. Old Jacob MacKenzie's legacy was a strong one.

A big hand clamped hard on my shoulder.

"My brother? You think I'd betray my brother?" For some reason, that had stung him; his face was dark with anger.

"You've just admitted that you did!" And then I realized.

"The both of you," I said slowly. "You did it together, you and Colum. Together, as you've always done things." I pulled his hand off my shoulder and flung it back at him.

"Colum couldn't be chieftain, unless you would go to war for him. He couldn't hold the clan together, without you to travel for him, to collect the rents and settle the claims. He couldn't ride, he couldn't travel. And he couldn't father a son, to pass the chieftainship on to. And you had no son by Maura. You swore to be his arms and legs"—I was beginning to feel a little hysterical by this time—"why shouldn't you be his cock, as well?"

Dougal had lost his anger; he stood watching me speculatively for a moment. Deciding that I was going nowhere, he sat down on one of the bales of goods and waited for me to finish.

"So you did it with Colum's knowledge. Was Letitia willing?" Knowing by now just what sort of ruthlessness they possessed, I wouldn't put it past the brothers MacKenzie to have forced her.

Dougal nodded. His anger had evaporated.

"Oh, aye, willing enough. She didna fancy me particularly, but she wanted a child—enough to take me to her bed for the three months it took to start Hamish. A boring damn job it was too," Dougal added reflectively, scraping a bit of mud from his boot heel. "I'd as soon swive a warm bowl of milk pudding."

"And did you tell Colum that?" I asked. Hearing the edge in my voice, he looked up. He regarded me levelly for a moment, then a faint smile lightened his face.

"No," he said quietly. "No, I didna tell him that." He looked down at his hands, turning them over as though looking for some secret hidden in the lines of his palms.

"I told him," he said softly, not looking at me, "that she was tender and sweet as a ripe peach, and all that a man could want in a woman."

He closed his hands abruptly and looked up at me, that momentary glimpse of Colum's brother submerged once more in the sardonic eyes of Dougal MacKenzie.

"Tender and sweet is not precisely what I'd say of *you*," he observed. "But all that a man could want . . ." The deep-set hazel eyes traveled slowly downward over my body, lingering on the roundness of breast and hip that showed through my open cloak. One hand moved unconsciously back and forth, stroking lightly across the muscles of his thigh as he watched me.

"Who knows?" he said, as though to himself. "I might have yet another son—legitimate, this time. True"—he tilted his head appraisingly, looking at my midsection—"it hasna happened yet wi' Jamie. You may be barren. But I'll take the chance. The property is worth it, at any rate."

He stood suddenly and took a step toward me.

"Who knows?" he said again, very softly. "If I were to plow that pretty brown-haired furrow and seed it deep each day . . ." The shadows on the cavern wall shifted suddenly as he took another step toward me.

"Well, you took your bloody time about it," I said crossly.

A look of incredulous shock spread across his features before he realized that I was looking beyond him, toward the cave mouth.

"It didna seem mannerly to interrupt," said Murtagh, advancing into the cave behind a loaded pair of flintlock pistols. He held one trained on Dougal, using the other to gesture with.

"Unless ye mean to accept that last proposal here and now, I'd suggest ye leave. And if ye *do* mean to accept it, then *I'll* leave."

"Nobody's leaving yet," I said shortly. "Sit down," I said to Dougal. He was still standing, staring at Murtagh as though at an apparition.

"Where's Rupert?" he demanded, finding his voice.

"Oh, Rupert." Murtagh scratched his chin thoughtfully with the muzzle of one pistol. "He's likely made it to Belladrum by now. Should be back before dawn," he added helpfully, "wi' the keg of rum he thinks ye sent him to fetch. The rest o' your men are still asleep in Quinbrough."

Dougal had the grace to laugh, if a little grudgingly. He sat down again, hands on his knees, and glanced from me to Murtagh and back again. There was a momentary silence.

"Well?" Dougal inquired. "Now what?"

That, I realized, was rather a good question. Surprised at finding Dougal instead of Jamie, shocked by his revelations, and infuriated at his consequent proposals, I had had no time to think of what ought to be done. Luckily, Murtagh was better prepared. Well, after all, *he* hadn't been occupied in fighting off lecherous advances.

"We'll need money," he said promptly. "And men." He cast an eye appraisingly over the bundles stacked against the wall. "Nay," he said thoughtfully. "That'll be for King James. But we'll take what ye've got on your person." The small black eyes swiveled back to Dougal and the muzzle of one pistol gestured gently in the vicinity of his sporran.

One thing to be said for life in the Highlands was that it apparently gave one a certain fatalistic attitude. With a sigh, Dougal reached into the sporran and tossed a small purse at my feet.

"Twenty gold pieces and thirty-odd shillings," he said, lifting one brow in my direction. "Take it and welcome."

Seeing my look of skepticism, he shook his head.

"Nay, I mean it. Think what ye like of me. Jamie's my sister's son, and if ye can free him, then God be wi' ye. But ye can't." His tone was final.

He looked at Murtagh, still holding his pistols steady.

"As to the men, no. If you and the lass mean to commit suicide, I canna stop ye. I'll even offer to bury ye, one on either side of Jamie. But you'll not take my men to hell with ye, pistols or no." He crossed his arms and leaned back against the cavern wall, calmly watching us.

Murtagh's hands didn't waver from his aim. His eyes flickered toward me, though. Did I wish him to shoot?

"I'll make you a bargain," I said.

Dougal raised one brow.

"You're in a bit better position to bargain than I am at present," he said. "What's your offer?"

"Let me talk to your men," I said. "And if they'll come with me of their own accord, then let them. If not, we'll go as we came—and we'll hand back your purse, as well."

One side of his mouth came up in a lopsided smile. He looked me over carefully, as though assessing my persuasiveness and my skills as an orator. Then he sat back, hands on his knees. He nodded once.

"Done," he said.

───

In the event, we left the glen of the cave with Dougal's purse and five men, in addition to Murtagh and myself: Rupert, John Whitlow, Willie MacMurtry, and the twin brothers, Rufus and Geordie Coulter. It was Rupert's decision that swayed the others; I could still see—with a feeling of grim satisfaction—the look on Dougal's face when his squat, black-bearded lieutenant eyed me speculatively, then patted the dags at his belt and said, "Aye, lass, why not?"

Wentworth Prison was thirty-five miles away. A half-hour's ride in a fast car over good roads. Two days' hard slog over half-frozen mud by horseback. *Not long.* Dougal's words echoed in my ears, and kept me in my saddle long past the point where I might have dropped from fatigue.

My body was pushed to its limits to keep to the saddle through the long weary miles, but my mind was free to worry. To keep it from thoughts of Jamie, I spent the time remembering my interview in the cave with Dougal.

And the last thing he had said to me. Standing outside the small cave, waiting as Rupert and his companions brought their horses down from a hiding place higher up the glen, Dougal had turned to me abruptly.

"I've a message for ye," he had said. "From the witch."

"From Geilie?" To say I was startled was the least of it.

I couldn't make out his face in the dark, but I saw his head tilt in affirmation.

"I saw her the once," he said softly, "when I came to take the child." Under other circumstances, I might have felt some sympathy for him, parting for the last time from his mistress, who was condemned to the stake, holding the child they had made together, a son whom he could never acknowledge. As it was, my voice was icy.

"What did she say?"

He paused; I wasn't sure if it was merely the disinclination to reveal information, or if he was trying to make sure of his words. Apparently it was the latter, for he spoke carefully.

"She said if ever I saw you again, I was to tell you two things, just as she told them to me. The first was, "I think it is possible, but I do not know." And the second—the second was just numbers. She made me say them over, to be sure I had them right, for I was to tell them to you in a certain order. The numbers were one, nine, six, and seven." The tall figure turned toward me in the dark, inquiring.

"Mean anything to ye?"

"No," I said, and turned away to my horse. But it did, of course, mean something to me.

"I think it is possible." There was only one thing she could mean by that. She thought, though she did not know, that it was possible to go back, through the circle of stone, to my proper place. Clearly she hadn't tried it herself, but had chosen—to her cost—to stay. Likely she had had her own reasons. Dougal, perhaps?

As for the numbers, I thought I knew what those meant, too. She had told them to him separately, for the sake of a secrecy which must have gone bone-deep in her by that time, but they were all part of one number, really. One, nine, six, seven. Nineteen sixty-seven. The year of *her* disappearance into the past.

I felt a small thrill of curiosity, and deep regret. What a pity that I had not seen the vaccination mark on her arm until it was too late! And yet, had I seen it sooner, would I have gone back to the circle of stone, perhaps with her help, and left Jamie.

Jamie. The thought of him was a leaden weight in my mind, a pendulum swinging slowly at the end of a rope. *Not long.* The road stretched endless and dreary before us, sometimes petering out altogether into frozen marshes or open sheets of water that had once been meadows and moors. In a freezing drizzle that would soon turn to snow, we reached our goal near evening of the second day.

The building loomed up black against the overcast sky. Built in the shape of a gigantic cube, four hundred feet on a side, with a tower on each corner, it could house three hundred prisoners, plus the forty soldiers of the garrison and their commander, the civilian governor and his staff, and the four dozen cooks, orderlies, grooms, and other menials necessary for the running of the establishment. Wentworth Prison.

I looked up at the menacing walls of greenish Argyll granite, two feet thick at the base. Tiny windows pierced the walls here and there. A few were beginning to wink with light. Others, serving what I assumed were the prisoners' cells, stayed dark. I swallowed. Seeing the massive edifice, with its impenetrable walls, its monumental gate, and its red-coated guards, I began to have doubts.

"What if"—my mouth was dry and I had to stop and lick my lips—"what if we can't do it?"

Murtagh's expression was the same as always: grim-mouthed and dour, narrow chin receding into the grimy neck of his shirt. It didn't alter as he turned to me.

"Then Dougal will bury us wi' him, one on either side," he answered. "Come on, there's work to be done."

PART SEVEN

Sanctuary

35

Wentworth Prison

Sir Fletcher Gordon was a short and portly man, whose striped silk waistcoat fitted him like a second skin. Slope-shouldered and paunch-bellied, he looked rather like a large ham seated in the governor's wheel-backed chair.

The bald head and rich pinkish color of his complexion did little to dispel this impression, though few hams boasted such bright blue eyes. He turned over the sheaf of papers on his desk with a slow, deliberate forefinger.

"Yes, here it is," he said, after an interminable pause to read a page. "Fraser, James. Convicted of murder. Sentenced to hang. Now, where's the Warrant of Execution?" He paused again, shuffling nearsightedly through the papers. I dug my fingers deep into the satin of my reticule, willing my face to remain expressionless.

"Oh, yes. Date of execution, December 23. Yes, we still have him."

I swallowed, relaxing my hold on my bag, torn between exultation and panic. He was still alive, then. For another two days. And he was nearby, somewhere in the same building with me. The knowledge surged through my veins with a rush of adrenaline and my hands trembled.

I sat forward in the visitor's chair, trying to look winsomely appealing.

"May I see him, Sir Fletcher? Just for a moment, in case he . . . he might wish me to convey a message to his family?"

In the guise of an English friend of the Fraser family, I had found it reasonably easy to gain admittance to Wentworth, and to the office of Sir Fletcher, civilian governor of the prison. It was dangerous to ask to see Jamie; not knowing my cover story, he might well give me away if he saw me suddenly without warning. For that matter, I might give myself away; I was not at all sure that I could maintain my precarious self-control if I saw him. But the next step was clearly to find out where he was; in this huge stone rabbit warren, the chances of finding him without direction were almost nil.

Sir Fletcher frowned, considering. Plainly he considered this request from a mere family acquaintance a nuisance, but he was not an unfeeling man. Finally he shook his head reluctantly.

"No, my dear. No, I'm afraid I really cannot allow that. We are rather crowded at present, and haven't sufficient facilities to permit private interviews. And the man is presently in"—he consulted his pile of papers again—"in one of the large cells in the west block, with several other condemned felons. It would be extremely perilous for you to visit him there—or at all. The man is a dangerous prisoner, you understand; I see here that we have been keeping him in chains since his arrival."

I gripped my bag again; this time to keep from striking him.

He shook his head again, plump chest rising and falling with his labored breathing. "No, if you were an immediate member of his family, perhaps . . ." He looked up, blinking. I clamped my jaw tightly, determined to give nothing away. Surely a slight show of agitation was reasonable, under the circumstances.

"But perhaps, my dear . . ." He seemed struck by sudden inspiration. He got ponderously to his feet and went to an inner door, where a uniformed soldier stood on guard. He murmured to the man, who nodded once and vanished.

Sir Fletcher came back to his desk, pausing on the way to retrieve a decanter and glasses from the top of a cabinet. I accepted his offer of claret; I needed it.

We were both halfway through the second glass by the time the guard returned. He marched in without invitation, placed a wooden box on the desk at Sir Fletcher's elbow, and turned to march out again. I caught his eye lingering on me and modestly lowered my own gaze. I was wearing a gown borrowed from a lady of Rupert's acquaintance in the nearby town, and from the scent that saturated the dress and its matching reticule, I had a reasonably good idea just what this particular lady's profession was. I hoped the guard didn't recognize the gown.

Draining his cup, Sir Fletcher set it down and pulled the box toward him. It was a plain, square box of unfinished wood, with a sliding lid. There were letters chalked on the lid. I could read them, even upside down. FRAYSER, they read.

Sir Fletcher slid back the lid, peered inside for a moment, then closed the box and pushed it toward me.

"The prisoner's personal effects," he explained. "Customarily, we send them to whomever the prisoner designates as next of kin, after execution. This man, though"—he shook his head—"has refused altogether to say anything about his family. Some estrangement, no doubt. Not unusual, of course, but regrettable under the circumstances. I hesitate to make the request, Mrs. Beauchamp, but I thought that perhaps, since you are acquainted with the family, you would consider taking it upon yourself to convey his effects to the appropriate person?"

I didn't trust myself to speak, but nodded and buried my nose in my cup of claret.

Sir Fletcher seemed relieved, whether at disposing of the box, or at the thought of my imminent departure. He sat back, wheezing slightly, and smiled expansively at me.

"That is very kind of you, Mrs. Beauchamp. I know such a thing cannot but be a painful duty to a young woman of feeling, and I am most sensible of your kindness in undertaking it, I do assure you."

"N-not at all," I stammered. I managed to stand up, and to gather up the box. It measured about eight inches by six, and was four or five inches deep. A small, light box, to hold the remains of a man's life.

I knew the things it held. Three fishing lines, neatly coiled; a cork stuck with fishhooks; a flint and steel; a small piece of broken glass, edges blunt with wear; various small stones that looked interesting or had a good feel between the fingers; a dried mole's foot, carried as a charm against rheumatism. A Bible—or perhaps they had let him keep that? I hoped so. A ruby ring, if it hadn't been stolen. And a small wooden snake, carved of cherry wood, with the name SAWNY scratched on its underside.

I paused at the door, gripping the frame with my fingers to steady myself.

Sir Fletcher, following courteously to see me out, was at my side in a moment.

"Mrs. Beauchamp! Are you feeling faint, my dear? Guard, a chair!"

I could feel the prickles of a cold sweat breaking out along the sides of my face, but I managed to smile and wave away the proffered chair. I wanted more than anything to get out of there—I needed fresh air, in large quantities. And I needed to be alone to cry.

"No, I'm quite all right," I said, trying to sound convincing. "It's only . . . a bit close in here, perhaps. No, I shall be perfectly all right. My groom is waiting outside, in any case."

Forcing myself to stand up straight and smile, I had a thought. It might not help, but it couldn't hurt.

"Oh, Sir Fletcher . . ."

Still worried by my appearance, he was all gallantry and attention.

"Yes, my dear?"

"It occurred to me. . . . How sad for a young man in this situation to be estranged from his family. I thought perhaps . . . if he wished to write to them—a letter of reconciliation, perhaps? I would be pleased to deliver it to—to his mother."

"You are thoughtfulness itself, my dear." Sir Fletcher was jovial, now that it seemed I was not going to collapse on his carpet after all. "Of course. I will inquire. Where are you staying, my dear? If there is a letter, I shall have it sent to you."

"Well," I was doing better with the smile, though it felt pasted on my face. "That is rather uncertain at the moment. I have several relatives and close acquaintances in the town, with whom I fear I shall be obliged to stay in turn, in order to avoid offending anyone, you see." I managed a small laugh.

"So if it does not disturb you too much, perhaps my groom could call to inquire for the letter?"

"Of course, of course. That will do excellently, my dear. Excellently!"

And with a quick glance back at his decanter, he took my arm to escort me to the gate.

———

"Better, lassie?" Rupert pushed back the curtain of my hair to peer at my face. "Ye look like an ill-cured pork belly. Here, better have a bit more."

I shook my head at the proffered whisky flask and sat up, wiping the damp rag he had brought across my face.

"No, I'm all right now." Escorted by Murtagh, who was disguised as my groom, I had barely made it out of sight of the prison before sliding off my horse and being sick in the snow. There I remained, weeping, with Jamie's box clutched to my bosom, until Murtagh had gathered me up bodily, forced me to mount, and led me to the small inn in Wentworth town where Rupert had found lodgings. We were in an upper room, from which the bulk of the prison was barely visible in the gathering dusk.

"Is the lad dead then?" Rupert's broad face, half-obscured by his beard, was grave and kind, lacking any of its usual clowning.

I shook my head and took a deep breath. "Not yet."

After hearing my story, Rupert paced slowly around the room, pushing his lips in and out as he thought. Murtagh sat still, as usual, no sign of agitation on his features. He would have made a wonderful poker player, I thought.

Rupert returned, sinking down on the bed beside me with a sigh.

"Weel, he's alive still, and that's the most important thing. Damned if I see what to do next, though. We've no way to get into the place."

"Aye, we have," Murtagh said, suddenly. "Thanks to the wee lassie's thought about the letter."

"Mmmphm. One man, though. And only so far as the governor's office. But aye, it's a start." Rupert drew his dirk and idly scratched his thick beard with the point. "It's a damn big place to search."

"I know where he is," I said, feeling better with the planning, and the knowledge that my companions weren't giving up, no matter how hopeless our enterprise seemed. "At least I know which wing he's in."

"Do ye, then? Hmm." He replaced the dirk and resumed his pacing, stopping to demand, "How much money have ye, lass?"

I fumbled in the pocket of my gown. I had Dougal's purse, the money Jenny had forced me to take, and my string of pearls. Rupert rejected the pearls, but took the purse, pouring a stream of coins into the palm of one capacious hand.

"That'll do," he said, jingling them experimentally. He cocked an eye at the Coulter twins. "You twa laddies and Willie—come wi' me. John and Murtagh can stay here wi' the lassie."

"Where are you going?" I asked.

He poured the coins into his sporran, keeping back one, which he tossed meditatively in the air.

"Och," he said vaguely. "Happen there's another inn, the other side of the town. The guards from the prison go there when they're off duty, for it's closer, and the drink's a penny cheaper." He flipped the coin with his thumb, and turning his hand, caught it between two knuckles.

I watched it, with a growing idea of what he intended.

"Is that so?" I said. "I wouldn't suppose they play cards there, too, would you?"

"I wouldna ken, lassie, wouldna ken," he answered. He tossed the coin once more and clapped his hands together, trapping it, then spread his hands apart, to show nothing but thin air. He smiled, teeth white in the black beard.

"But we might go and see, no?" He snapped his fingers, and the coin appeared once more between them.

Shortly past one o'clock on the following afternoon, I passed again beneath the spiked portcullis that had guarded the gate of Wentworth since its construction in the late sixteenth century. It had lost very little of its forbidding aspect in the succeeding two hundred years, and I touched the dagger in my pocket for courage.

Sir Fletcher should now be well dug in at his midday repast, according to the information Rupert and his assistant spies had extracted from the prison guards during their foray the evening before. They had staggered in, red-eyed and reeking of ale, just before dawn. All Rupert would say in response to my questions was "Och, lassie, all it takes to win is luck. It takes *skill* to lose!" He curled up in the corner then and went soundly to sleep, leaving me to pace the floor in frustration, as I had been doing all night.

He woke an hour later, though, clear-eyed and clear-headed, and laid out the rudiments of the plan I was about to put into execution.

"Sir Fletcher doesna allow anyone or anything to disturb his meals," he said. "Anyone wantin' him then must just go on wantin' until he's done wi' his food and drink. And after the midday meal, it's his habit to retire to his quarters for a wee sleep."

Murtagh, in the character of my groom, had arrived a quarter of an hour previously, and been admitted without difficulty. Presumably, he would be shown to Sir Fletcher's office and asked to wait. While there, he was to search the office, first for a plan of the west wing, and then, on the off-chance, for keys that might open the cells.

I hung back a bit, glancing at the sky to judge the time. If I arrived before he had sat down, I might be invited to join Sir Fletcher for luncheon, which would be highly inconvenient. But Rupert's card-playing acquaintances among the guards had assured him that the governor's habits were invariable; the bell for dinner was rung promptly at one, and the soup served five minutes later.

The guard on duty at the entrance was the same as the day before. He looked surprised, but greeted me courteously.

"So vexing," I said, "I had meant my groom to bring a small present for Sir Fletcher, as some return for his kindness to me yesterday. But I found that the silly man had ridden off without it, and so I was obliged to follow with it myself,

hoping to catch him up. Has he arrived already?" I displayed
the small package I carried and smiled, thinking that it would
help if I had dimples. Since I hadn't, I settled for a brilliant
display of teeth.

It seemed to be sufficient. I was admitted and led through
the corridors of the prison toward the governor's office.
Though this part of the castle was decently furnished, there
was little mistaking the place for anything other than a prison.
There was a smell about the place, which I imagined as the
smell of misery and fear, though I supposed it was no more
than the niff of ancient squalor and an absence of drains.

The guard allowed me to precede him down the hall, following discreetly so as not to step on my cloak. And a damn
good thing he did, for I rounded the corner toward Sir
Fletcher's office a few feet ahead of him, just in time to see
Murtagh through the open door, dragging the unconscious
form of the office guard behind the enormous desk.

I took one step back and dropped my package onto the
stone floor. There was a shattering of glass, and the air was
filled with the smothering aroma of peach brandy.

"Oh, dear," I said, "what *have* I done?"

While the guard was calling for a prisoner to clear up the
mess, I tactfully murmured something about waiting for Sir
Fletcher in his private office, slipped in, and hastily shut the
door behind me.

"What the bloody hell have you done?" I snapped at Murtagh. He looked up from his rummaging of the body, unconcerned at my tone.

"Sir Fletcher doesna keep keys in his office," he informed
me in a low voice, "but *this* wee laddie has a set." He pulled
the huge ring free of the man's coat, careful to keep the keys
from jingling.

I dropped to my knees behind him. "Oh, good show!" I
said. I cast an eye over the prostrate soldier; still breathing, at
least. "What about a plan of the prison?"

He shook his head. "Not that either, but my friend here
told me a bit while we waited. The condemned cells are on
the same floor as this, in the middle of the west corridor.

There're three cells, though, and I couldna ask more than that —he was a bit suspicious as it was."

"It's enough—I hope. All right, give me the keys and get out."

"Me? It's *you* should leave, lassie, and right smart too." He glanced at the door, but there was no sound on the other side.

"No, it has to be me," I said, reaching again for the keys. "Listen," I said impatiently. "If they find you wandering round the prison with a bunch of keys, and the guard here laid out like a mackerel, we're both done for, because why didn't I cry out for help?" I snatched the keys and crammed them in my pocket, with some difficulty.

Murtagh was still skeptical, but had risen to his feet.

"And if *you're* caught?" he demanded.

"I swoon," I said crisply. "And when I recover—eventually —I say that I saw you apparently murdering the guard and fled in terror, with no idea where I was going. I lost my way looking for help."

He nodded slowly. "Aye, all right." He moved toward the door, then stopped.

"But why did I—oh." He crossed swiftly to the desk and pulled out one drawer after another, stirring the contents with one hand and tossing items onto the floor with the other.

"Theft," he explained, coming back to the door. He opened it a crack, looking out.

"If it's theft, shouldn't you take something?" I suggested, looking about for something small and portable. I picked up an enameled snuffbox. "This, perhaps?"

He made an impatient gesture to me to put it down, still peering through the crack.

"Nay, lass! If I'm found wi' Sir Fletcher's property, that's a hanging offense. Attempted theft is only flogging or mutilation."

"Oh." I put the snuffbox down hastily and stood behind him, peering over his shoulder. The hall seemed empty.

"I go first," he said. "If I meet anyone, I'll draw 'em off. Wait to the count of thirty, then follow. We'll meet ye in the small wood to the north." He opened the door, then paused and turned back.

"If you're caught, mind ye throw the keys awa'." Before I could speak, he was through the door like an eel and down the corridor, moving silently as a shadow.

It seemed to take an eternity to find the west wing, dodging through the corridors of the old castle, peering around corners and hiding behind columns. I saw only one guard on my way, though, and managed to avoid him by diving back around a corner, pressing myself to the wall with hammering heart until he passed.

Once I found the west wing, though, I had little doubt that I was in the right place. There were three large doors in the corridor, each with a tiny barred window from which I could catch no more than a frustrating glimpse of the room behind it.

"Eenie, meenie, minie, mo," I muttered to myself, and headed for the center cell. The keys on the ring were unlabeled, but of different sizes. Clearly only one of three big ones would fit the lock before me. Naturally, it was the third one. I took a deep breath as the lock clicked, then wiped my sweating hands on my skirt and shoved the door open.

I sorted frantically through the stinking mass of men in the cell, stepping over outstretched feet and legs, pushing past heavy bodies that moved with maddening sluggishness out of my way. The stir occasioned by my abrupt entrance had spread; those who had been asleep amid the filth on the floor began to sit up, roused by the rippling murmur of astonishment. Some were manacled to the walls; the chains grated and clanked in the half-light as they moved. I grabbed one of the standing men, a brown-bearded clansman in ragged yellow-and-green tartan. The bones of his arm under my hand were frighteningly near the skin; the English wasted little extra food on their prisoners.

"James Fraser! A big, redheaded man! Is he in this cell? Where is he?"

He was already moving toward the door with the others who were not chained, but paused a moment to glance down at me. The prisoners by now had seized the idea, and were pouring through the open door in a shuffling flood, peering and murmuring to each other.

"Who? Fraser? Och, they took him awa' this mornin'." The man shrugged, and pushed at my hands, trying to shake me off.

I took hold of his belt with a grip that halted him in his tracks. "Where did they take him? Who took him?"

"I dinna ken where; was yon Captain Randall took 'im—a pinch-faced snark, he is." With an impatient wrench, he freed himself and headed for the door with a step born of long-nourished purpose.

Randall. I stood stunned for a moment, jostled by the escaping men, deaf to the shouts of the chained. Finally I shook myself from my stupor and tried to think. Geordie had watched the castle since dawn. No one had left in the morning save a small kitchen party going to fetch supplies. So they were still here, somewhere.

Randall was a captain; likely no one ranked higher in a prison garrison, save Sir Fletcher himself. Presumably Randall could thus command the castle's resources so as to provide him with some suitable spot in which to torture a prisoner at his leisure.

And torture it surely was. Even if it was meant to end in hanging, the man I had seen at Fort William was a cat by nature. He could no more resist the chance to play with this particular mouse than he could alter his height or the color of his eyes.

I took a deep breath, resolutely shoving aside thoughts of what might have happened since morning, and charged out the door myself, colliding full force with an English Redcoat rushing in. The man reeled backward, staggering with tiny running steps to keep his balance. Thrown off balance myself, I crashed heavily into the doorjamb, numbing my left side and banging my head. I clutched the doorpost for support, the ringing in my ears chiming with the echoes of Rupert's voice: *Ye have a moment of surprise, lass. Use it!*

It was open to question, I thought dizzily, who was more surprised. I groped madly for the pocket that held my dagger, cursing my stupidity for not having entered the cell with it already drawn.

The English soldier, balance recovered, was staring at me with his mouth agape, but I could feel my precious moment of surprise already slipping away. Abandoning the elusive pocket, I stooped and drew the dagger from my stocking in a move that continued upward with all the force I could muster. The knifepoint took the advancing soldier just under the chin as he reached for his belt. His hands rose halfway to his throat, then, with a look of surprise, he staggered back against the wall, and slid down it in slow motion, as the life drained away from him. Like me, he had come to investigate without bothering to draw his weapon first, and that small oversight had just cost him his life. The grace of God had saved me from this mistake; I could afford no more. Feeling very cold, I stepped over the twitching body, careful not to look.

I dashed back the way I had come, as far as the turning by the stairs. There was a spot here by the wall where I would be sheltered from view from both directions. I leaned against the wall and indulged myself in a moment of trembling nausea.

Wiping my sweaty hands on my skirt, I dredged the dirk from its hidden pocket. It was now my only weapon; I had neither time nor stomach enough to retrieve my sock-knife. Perhaps that was as well, I thought, rubbing my fingers on my bodice; there had been surprisingly little blood, and I shrank from the thought of the gush that would follow if I pulled the knife free.

Dagger now safely in hand, I peered cautiously out into the corridor. The prisoners I had inadvertently released had gone to the left. I had no idea what they were set on doing, but they would likely occupy the English while they were doing it. With no reason to pick one direction over another for my search, it made sense to move away from whatever commotion they caused.

The light from the high slit windows fell aslant behind me; this was the west side of the castle, then. I must keep my bearings as I moved, since Rupert would be waiting for me near the south gate.

Stairs. I forced my numbed mind to think, trying to reason

my way to the spot I was looking for. If you wanted to torture someone, presumably you wanted both privacy and sound-proofing. Both considerations pointed to an isolated dungeon as the most likely spot. And the dungeons in castles such as this were customarily underground, where tons of earth muffled any cries, and darkness hid all cruelty from the eyes of those responsible.

The wall rounded into a curve at the end of the corridor; I had reached one of the four corner towers—and the towers had stairs.

The spiral stair opened around another curve, the wedge-shaped steps plunging down in dizzying flights that deceived the eye and twisted the ankles. The plunge from the relative light of the corridor into the gloom of the stairwell made it even harder to judge the distance from one stair to the next, and I slipped several times, barking my knuckles and skinning my palms on the stone walls as I caught myself.

The stairway yielded one benefit. From a narrow window let in to save the stairwell from total darkness, I could see the main courtyard. At least I could now orient myself. A small group of soldiers was drawn up in neat red lines for inspection, but not, apparently, to witness the summary punishment of a Scottish rebel. There was a gibbet in the courtyard, black and foreboding, but unoccupied. The sight of it was like a blow in the stomach. Tomorrow morning. I clattered down the stairs, heedless of scraped elbows and stubbed toes.

Hitting the bottom in a swish of skirts, I stopped to listen. Dead silence all around, but at least this part of the castle was in use; there were torches in the wall sconces, dyeing the granite blocks in pools of flickering red, each pool ebbing into darkness at its edges before the pool of the next torch leached into light again. Smoke from the torches hung in grey swirls along the vaulted roof of the corridor.

There was only one way to go from this point. I went, dagger still gripped at the ready. It was eerie to be pacing softly down this corridor. I had seen similar dungeons before, as a day-tripper, visiting historic castles with Frank. But then the massive granite blocks had been stripped of their menace by the glare of fluorescent tubes hung from the arches of the cavernous ceiling. I remembered recoiling from the small, dank chambers, even in those days, when they had been in disuse for over a century. Seeing the remnants of old and horrible ways, the thick doors and the rusting manacles on the wall, I had been able, I thought, to imagine the torments of those imprisoned in these forbidding cells. I would have laughed now at my naivete. There were some things, as Dougal said, that the imagination was simply not equal to.

I tiptoed past bolted doors three inches thick; thick enough to smother any sound from inside. Bending close to the floor, I checked for a strip of light at the base of each door. Prisoners might be left to rot in darkness, but Randall would need to see what he was doing. The floor here was gummy with ancient dirt, covered with a thick layer of loose dust. Apparently this part of the prison was not in current use. But the torches showed that *someone* was down here.

The fourth door in the corridor showed the light I was looking for. I listened, kneeling on the floor with my ear pressed against the crack, but heard nothing more than the thin crackle of a fire.

The door was unlocked. I pushed it open a small crack and peered cautiously within. Jamie was there, sitting on the floor against one wall, curled into himself with his head between his knees. He was alone.

The room was small, but well lit, with a rather homely looking brazier in which burned a cheery fire. For a dungeon, it was remarkably cozy; the stone flags were halfway clean, and a small camp bed leaned against one wall. The room was further furnished with two chairs and a table, on which sat a number of objects, including a large pewter flask and horn cups. It was an astonishing sight, after my visions of dripping walls and scuttling rats. It occurred to me that perhaps the garrison officers had furnished this snuggery as a refuge in which to entertain such female companionship as they could induce to visit them within the prison; clearly it had the advantage of privacy over the barracks.

"Jamie!" I called softly. He didn't raise his head or answer me, and I felt a thrill of fear. Pausing only long enough to shut the door behind me, I crossed rapidly to him and touched his shoulder.

"Jamie!"

He looked up then; his face was dead-white, unshaven and sheened with a cold sweat that had soaked his hair and shirt. The room stank of fear and vomit.

"Claire!" he said, speaking hoarsely through lips cracked with dryness. "How did you—ye must get out of here at once. He'll be back soon."

"Don't be ridiculous." I was assessing the situation as rapidly as I could, hoping that concentration on the job at hand would ease the choking sensation and help melt the large ball of ice in the pit of my stomach.

He was chained by the ankle to a bolt in the wall, but otherwise unfettered. A coil of rope among the rubble of objects on the table had plainly been used, though; there were raw marks on his wrists and elbows.

I was puzzled by his condition. He was clearly dazed and every line of his body was eloquent with pain, but I could see no obvious damage. There was no blood and no wound visible. I dropped to my knees and began methodically to try the keys of my ring on the manacle around his ankle.

"What has he done to you?" I asked, keeping my voice low for fear of Randall's return.

Jamie swayed where he sat, eyes closed, the sweat beading in hundreds of tiny pearls on his skin. Plainly he was near to fainting, but opened his eyes for a moment at my voice. Moving with exquisite care, he used his left hand to lift the object he had been cradling in his lap. It was his right hand, almost unrecognizable as a human appendage. Grotesquely swollen, it was now a bloated bag, blotched with red and purple, the fingers dangling at crazy angles. A white shard of bone poked through the torn skin of the middle finger, and a trickle of blood stained the knuckles, puffed into shapeless dimples.

The human hand is a delicate marvel of engineering, an intricate system of joints and pulleys, served and controlled by a network of millions of tiny nerves, exquisitely sensitive to touch. A single broken finger is enough to sink a strong man to his knees with nauseated pain.

"Payment," Jamie said, "for his nose—with interest." I stared at the sight for a moment, then said in a voice that I didn't recognize as mine, "I'm going to kill him for this."

Jamie's mouth twitched slightly as a flicker of humor forced its way through the mask of pain and dizziness. "I'll hold your cloak, Sassenach," he whispered. His eyes closed again and he sagged against the wall, too far gone to protest my presence further.

I went back to work on the lock, glad to see that my hands were no longer shaking. The fear was gone, replaced by a glorious rage.

I had gone through the complete ring of keys twice, and still found none that would turn the lock. My hands were growing sweaty and the keys slid through my fingers like minnows as I began to try the most likely ones again. My muttered cursing roused Jamie from his stupor, and he leaned down slowly to look at what I was doing.

"Ye needn't find a key will turn it," he said, bracing a shoulder on the wall to keep upright. "If one will fit to the length of the barrel, you can spring the lock wi' a good bash on the head of it."

"You've seen this kind of lock before?" I wanted to keep him awake and talking; he was going to have to walk if we were to leave here.

"I've been in one. When they brought me here, they chained me in a big cell with a lot of others. A lad named Reilly was chained next to me; a Leinsterman—said he'd been in most of the jails in Ireland and decided to try Scotland for a change o' scenery." Jamie was struggling to talk; he realized as well as I that he must rouse himself. He managed a feeble smile. "He told me a good bit about locks and such, and showed me how we could break the ones we were wearing, *if* we'd had a spare bit of straight metal, which we didn't."

"Tell me, then." The effort of talking was making him sweat freely, but he seemed more alert. Concentrating on the problem of the lock seemed to help.

Following his directions, I found a suitable key and thrust it in as far as it would go. According to Reilly, a solid blow straight in on the end of the key would force the other end hard against the tumblers and spring them loose. I looked around for a suitable instrument for bashing.

"Use the mallet on the table, Sassenach," said Jamie. Caught by a grim note in his voice, I glanced from his face to the table, where a medium-sized wooden mallet lay, the handle wrapped with tarred twine.

"Is that what—" I began, aghast.

"Aye. Brace the manacle against the wall, lass, before ye hit it."

Grasping the handle gingerly, I picked up the mallet. It was awkward to get the iron manacle correctly positioned so that one side was braced by the wall, as this required that Jamie cross the manacled leg under the other and press his knee to the wall on the far side.

My first two blows were too weak and timorous. Gathering determination about me like a cloak, I smashed the rounded end of the key as hard as I could. The mallet slipped off the key and caught Jamie a glancing but hard blow on the ankle. Recoiling, he lost his precarious balance and fell, instinctively reaching out his right hand to save himself. He let out an unearthly moan as his right arm crumpled beneath him and his shoulder hit the floor.

"Oh, damn," I said wearily. Jamie had fainted, not that I could blame him. Taking advantage of his momentary immobility, I turned his ankle so that the manacle was well braced, and banged doggedly on the embedded key, with little apparent effect. I was thinking grim thoughts about Irish locksmiths, when the door beside me swung suddenly open.

Randall's face, like Frank's, seldom showed what he was thinking, presenting instead a bland and impenetrable facade. At the moment, though, the Captain's customary poise had deserted him, and he stood in the doorway with his jaw agape, looking not unlike the man who accompanied him. A very large man in a stained and ragged uniform, this assistant had the sloping brow, flat nose, and loose prominent lips characteristic of some types of mental retardation. His expression did not change as he peered over Randall's shoulder, showing no particular interest either in me or the unconscious man on the floor.

Recovering, Randall walked into the room and reached down to prod the manacle around Jamie's ankle. "Been damaging the Crown's property, I see, my girl. That's an offense punishable by law, you know. To say nothing of attempting to aid a dangerous prisoner in escaping." His pale grey eyes held a spark of amusement. "We'll have to arrange something suitable for you. In the meantime . . ." He jerked me to my feet and pulled my arms behind me, twisting his stock around my wrists.

Struggle was plainly fruitless, but I stamped on his toes as hard as I could, purely to vent some of my own frustration.

"Ouch!" He turned me and gave me a hard shove, so that my legs hit the bed and I fell, half-lying on the rough blankets. Randall surveyed me with grim satisfaction, rubbing the scuffed toe of his boot with a linen handkerchief. I glared back at him, and he gave a short laugh.

"You're no coward, I'll give you that. In fact, you're a fit match for him," he nodded at Jamie, who was beginning to stir a bit, "and I can't give you a better compliment than that." He tenderly fingered his throat, where a darkening bruise showed in the open neck of his shirt. "He tried to kill me, one-handed, when I untied him. And damned near managed it too. Pity I didn't realize he was left-handed."

"How unreasonable of him," I said.

"Quite," said Randall, with a nod. "I don't suppose you'd be so impolite, do you? Still, on the off-chance . . ." He turned to the large servant, who was simply standing in the doorframe, shoulders sloped, waiting for orders.

"Marley," said Randall, "come here and search this woman for weapons." He watched with some amusement as the man groped clumsily about my person, eventually coming upon and extracting my dirk.

"You don't care for Marley?" asked the Captain, watching me try to avoid the thick fingers that prodded me all too intimately. "Rather a pity; I'm sure he's quite taken with you."

"Poor Marley hasn't much luck with women," the Captain went on, a malicious gleam in his eye. "Have you, Marley? Even the whores won't have him." He fixed me with a de-

signing sort of look, smiling wolfishly. "Too big, they say."
He raised one eyebrow. "Which is quite a judgment, coming
from a whore, is it not?" He raised the other brow, making
his meaning quite clear.

Marley, who had begun to pant rather heavily during the
search, stopped and wiped a thread of saliva from the side of
his mouth. I moved as far away as I could manage, disgusted.

Randall, watching me, said, "I imagine Marley would like
to entertain you privately in his quarters, once we've finished
our conversation. Of course, he might decide later on to share
his good fortune with his friends, but that's up to him."

"Oh, you don't want to watch?" I asked sarcastically.

Randall laughed, truly amused.

"I may have what are called 'unnatural tastes' myself, as I
imagine you know by this time. But give me credit for some
aesthetic principles." He glanced at the immense orderly,
slouched in his filthy clothes, paunch straining over his belt.
The loose, blubbery lips chewed and mumbled constantly, as
though seeking some fragment of food, and the short, thick
fingers worked nervously against the crotch of the stained
breeches. Randall shuddered delicately.

"No," he said. "You're a very lovely woman, shrewish
tongue notwithstanding. To see you with Marley—no, I don't
believe I want to watch that. Appearance aside, Marley's personal
habits leave quite a lot to be desired."

"So do yours," I said.

"That's as may be. At any rate, they'll not concern you
much longer." He paused, looking down at me. "I would still
like to know who you are, you know. A Jacobite, plainly, but
whose? Marischal's? Seaforth's? Lovat's, most likely, since
you're with the Frasers." Randall nudged Jamie gently with a
polished boot-toe, but he still lay inert. I could see his chest
rising and falling regularly; perhaps he had merely slipped
from unconsciousness into sleep. The smudges under his eyes
gave evidence that he had had little rest of late.

"I've even heard from some that you're a witch," the Captain
went on. His tone was light, but he watched me closely,
as though I might suddenly turn myself into an owl and flap
away. "There was some kind of trouble at Cranesmuir, wasn't

there? A death of some kind? But no doubt that's all superstitious nonsense."

Randall eyed me speculatively. "I might be persuaded to make a bargain with you," he said abruptly. He leaned back, half-sitting on the table, inviting me.

I laughed bitterly. "I can't say I'm in either a position or a mood to bargain at the moment. What can you offer me?"

Randall glanced at Marley. The idiot's eyes were fixed on me, and he was mumbling under his breath.

"A choice, at least. Tell me—and convince me—who you are and who sent you to Scotland. What you're doing and what information you've sent to whom. Tell me that, and I'll take you to Sir Fletcher, instead of giving you to Marley."

I kept my eyes firmly away from Marley. I had seen the rotting stumps of teeth embedded in pustulant gums, and the thought of him kissing me, let alone—I choked the thought off. Randall was right; I wasn't a coward. But neither was I a fool.

"You can't take me to Sir Fletcher," I said, "and I know it as well as you do. Take me to him and risk my telling him about *this?*" My nod took in the snug little room, the cozy fire, the bed I sat on, and Jamie lying at my feet. "Whatever his own shortcomings, I don't imagine Sir Fletcher would stand, officially, for his officers torturing prisoners. Even the English army must have *some* standards."

Randall raised both eyebrows. "Torture? Oh, that." He waved negligently at Jamie's hand. "An accident. He fell in his cell and was trampled by the other prisoners. It's rather crowded in those cells, you know." He smiled derisively.

I was silent. While Sir Fletcher might or might not believe the damage to Jamie's hand was an accident, he was most unlikely to believe anything *I* said, once I was unmasked as an English spy.

Randall was watching me, eyes alert for any signs of weakening. "Well? The choice is yours."

I sighed and closed my eyes, tired of looking at him. The choice *wasn't* mine, but I could hardly tell him why not.

"It doesn't matter," I said wearily. "I can't tell you anything."

"Think it over for a moment." He stood up, and stepped carefully over Jamie's unconscious form, taking a key from his pocket. "I may need Marley's help for a bit, but then I'll send him back to his quarters—and you with him, if you don't mean to cooperate." He stooped, unlocked the manacle, and heaved the inert body up with an impressive display of strength for one so slightly built. The muscles of his forearms ridged the cloth of his snowy shirt as he carried Jamie, head lolling, to a stool in the corner. He nodded at the bucket standing nearby.

"Rouse him," he directed the silent hulk curtly. Cold water splashed from the stones in the corner and puddled on the floor, making a filthy pool underneath. "Once more," Randall said, inspecting Jamie, who was moaning slightly, head stirring against the stones of the wall. He flinched and coughed under the second drenching shower.

Randall strode forward and took him by the hair, yanking his head back, shaking it like a drowned animal, so that drops of fetid water spattered the walls. Jamie's eyes were dull slits. Randall threw Jamie's head back in disgust, wiping his hand down the side of his trousers as he turned away. His eye must have caught the flicker of movement, because he began to turn back, but not in time to brace himself against the big Scot's sudden lunge.

Jamie's arms went around Randall's neck. Lacking the use of his right hand, he gripped his right wrist with the able left and pulled, forearm braced on the Englishman's windpipe. As Randall turned purple and began to sag, he let go his left hand long enough to drive it into the captain's kidney. Even weakened as Jamie was, the blow was enough to make Randall give at the knees.

Dropping the limp captain, Jamie whirled to face the hulking orderly, who had been watching events so far without the slightest flicker of interest on his slack-jawed face. Although his expression remained rather inert, he did move, picking up the mallet from the table as Jamie came toward him, holding the stool by one leg in his good left hand. A certain dull wariness came into the orderly's face as the two men circled each other slowly, looking for an opening.

Better-armed, Marley tried first, swinging the mallet at Jamie's ribs. Jamie whirled away and feinted with the stool, forcing the orderly back toward the door. The next attempt, a murderous blow downward, would have split Jamie's skull had it landed on target. As it was, the stool split instead, one leg and the seat sheared away.

Impatiently, Jamie smashed the stool against the wall with his next swing, reducing it to a smaller but more manageable club; a two-foot length of wood with a ragged, splintered end.

The air in the cell, made stifling with smoke from the torches, was still except for the gasping breath of the two men and the occasional bruising thud of wood on flesh. Afraid to speak for fear of disturbing Jamie's precarious concentration, I pulled my feet up onto the bed and shrank back against the wall, trying to stay out of the way.

It was plain to me—and by his faint smile of anticipation, to the orderly also—that Jamie was tiring rapidly. Amazing enough that he was on his feet at all, let alone fighting. It was clear to all three of us that the fight couldn't last much longer; if he was to have any chance at all, he must move soon. With short, hard jabs of the stool-leg, he advanced cautiously on Marley, forcing the bigger man into the corner where the arc of his swing would be restricted. Realizing this by some instinct, the orderly came out with a vicious horizontal swing, expecting to force Jamie back.

Instead of stepping back, Jamie stepped forward into the swing, taking the full brunt of the blow in the left side as he brought his club down full-force on Marley's temple. Intent on the scene before me, I had paid no attention to Randall's prone body on the floor near the door. But as the orderly tottered, eyes glazing, I heard the scraping sounds of boots on stone, and a labored breathing rasped in my ear.

"Nicely fought, Fraser." Randall's voice was hoarse from the choking, but as composed as ever. "Cost you a few ribs, though, didn't it?"

Jamie leaned against the wall, breathing in sobbing gasps, still holding the club, elbow pressed hard to his side. His eyes dropped to the floor, measuring the distance.

"Don't try it, Fraser." The light voice was bland. "She'll be dead before you get two steps." The thin, cool knife blade slid past my ear; I could feel the point gently pricking the corner of my jaw.

Jamie surveyed the scene with dispassionate eyes for a moment, still braced by the wall. With a sudden effort, he straightened painfully and stood swaying. The club clanked hollowly on the stone floor. The knifepoint pricked infinitesimally harder, but otherwise Randall stood motionless as Jamie slowly crossed the few feet to the table, stooping carefully on the way to pick up the twine-wrapped mallet. He held it dangling in two fingers in front of him, his nonoffensive intent apparent.

The mallet clattered on the table in front of me, the handle spinning hard enough to carry the weighty head nearly to the edge. It lay dark and heavy on the oak, a homely, solid tool. A reed basket of ha'penny nails to go with it lay in the jumble of objects at the far end of the table; something perhaps left behind by the carpenters who had furnished the room. Jamie's good hand, the fine straight fingers rimmed with gold in the light, gripped the table-edge hard. With an effort I could only guess at, he lowered himself slowly into a chair and deliberately spread both hands flat before him on the scarred wood surface, the mallet within easy reach.

His gaze had been locked with Randall's during the painful trip across the room, and did not waver now. He nodded briefly in my direction without looking at me and said, "Let her go."

The knife-hand seemed to relax a trifle. Randall's voice was amused and curious. "Why should I?"

Jamie seemed now in complete command of himself, despite his white face and the sweat that ran unregarded down his face like tears.

"You cannot hold a knife on two people at once. Kill the woman or leave her side, and I'll kill you." He spoke softly, a steely thread beneath the quiet Scots accent.

"And what's to stop me killing both of you, one at a time?"

I would have called the expression on Jamie's face a smile only because his teeth were showing. "What, and cheat the hangsman? Bit hard to explain, come morning, no?" He nodded briefly at the unconscious hulk on the floor. "You'll recall that ye had to have your wee helper bind me wi' rope before ye broke my hand."

"So?" The knife stayed steady at my ear.

"Your helper is no going to be much good to ye awhile yet." This was undeniably true; the monstrous orderly was lying on his face in the corner, breathing in ragged, stertorous snores. Severe concussion, I thought, mechanically. Possible cerebral hemorrhage. I couldn't care less if he died before my eyes.

"You can't take me alone, one-handed or no." Jamie shook his head slowly, appraising Randall's size and strength. "No. I'm bigger, and far the better fighter, hand to hand. Did ye not have the woman there, I would take that wee knife from ye and cram it down your throat. And you know it, which is why you've not harmed her."

"But I do have her. You could leave yourself, of course. There's a way out, quite near. That would leave your wife— you did say she's your wife?—to die, of course."

Jamie shrugged. "And myself as well. I'd not get far, with the whole garrison hunting me. To be shot in the open might be preferable to being hanged in here, but not enough to make a difference." A brief grimace of pain crossed his face and he held his breath for a moment. When he breathed again, it was in shallow, panting gulps. Whatever shock had been protecting him from the worst of the pain, it was apparently wearing off.

"So we seem to be at an impasse." Randall's well-bred English tones were casual. "Unless you have a suggestion?"

"I have. You want me." The cool Scottish voice was matter-of-fact. "Let the woman go, and ye can have me." The knifepoint moved slightly, nicking my ear. I felt a sting and the warm ooze of blood.

"Do what ye wish to me. I'll not struggle, though I'll allow you to bind me if ye think it needful. And I'll not speak of it, come tomorrow. But first you'll see the woman safe from the prison." My eyes were on Jamie's ruined hand. A small pool of blood under the middle finger was growing, and I realized with a shock that he was deliberately pressing the finger into the table, using the pain as a spur to stay conscious. He was bargaining for my life using the only thing he had left—himself. If he fainted now, that single chance was gone.

Randall had relaxed completely; the knife lay carelessly on my right shoulder as he thought it through. I was there before him. Jamie was meant to hang in the morning. Sooner or later, he would be missed, and the Castle would be searched. While a certain amount of brutality might be tolerated among officers and gentlemen—I was sure it would extend to a broken hand or a flayed back—Randall's other inclinations were not so likely to be overlooked. No matter what Jamie's status as a condemned prisoner, if he stood at the foot of the gallows come morning and claimed abuse at the hands of Randall, his claims would be investigated. And if physical examination proved them true, Randall's career was at an end, and possibly his life as well. But with Jamie sworn to silence. . . .

"You'll give me your word?"

Jamie's eyes were like blue matchflames in the parchment of his face. After a moment, he nodded slowly. "In return for yours."

The attraction of a victim at once completely unwilling and completely compliant was irresistible.

"Done." The knife left my shoulder and I heard the susurrus of sheathed metal. Randall walked slowly past me, around the table, picking up the mallet as he went. He held it up, ironically questioning. "You'll allow me a brief test of your sincerity?"

"Aye." Jamie's voice was as steady as his hands, flat and motionless on the table. I tried to speak, to utter some protest, but my throat had dried to a sticky silence.

Moving without haste, Randall leaned past Jamie to pluck a ha'penny nail delicately from the reed basket. He positioned the point with care and brought the mallet down, driving the nail through Jamie's right hand into the table with four solid blows. The broken fingers twitched and sprang straight, like the legs of a spider pinned to a collection board.

Jamie groaned, his eyes wide and blank with shock. Randall set the mallet down with care. He took Jamie's chin in his hand and turned his face up. "Now kiss me," he said softly, and lowered his head to Jamie's unresisting mouth.

Randall's face when he rose was dreamy, eyes gentle and faraway, long mouth quirked in a smile. Once upon a time, I had loved a smile like that, and that dreamy look had roused me in anticipation. Now it sickened me. Tears ran into the corner of my mouth, though I didn't remember starting to cry. Randall stood a moment in his trance, gazing down at Jamie. Then he stirred, remembering, and drew the knife once more from its sheath.

The blade slashed carelessly through the binding around my wrists, grazing the skin. I hardly had time to rub the circulation back into my hands before he was urging me up with a hand beneath my elbow, pushing me toward the door.

"Wait!" Jamie spoke behind us, and Randall turned impatiently.

"You'll allow me to say goodbye?" It was a statement more than a question, and Randall hesitated only briefly before nodding and giving me a shove back toward the motionless figure at the table.

Jamie's good arm was tight around my shoulders and my wet face was buried in his neck.

"You can't," I whispered. "You can't. I won't let you."

His mouth was warm against my ear. "Claire, I'm to hang in the morning. What happens to me between now and then doesna matter to anyone." I drew back and stared at him.

"It matters to me!" The strained lips quivered in what was almost a smile, and he raised his free hand and laid it against my wet cheek.

"I know it does, *mo duinne*. And that's why you'll go now. So I'll know there is someone still who minds for me." He drew me close again, kissed me gently and whispered in Gaelic, "He will let you go because he thinks you are helpless. I know you are not." Releasing me, he said in English, "I love you. Go now."

Randall paused as he ushered me out the door. "I'll be back very shortly." It was the voice of a man taking reluctant leave of his lover, and my stomach heaved.

Silhouetted in red by the torch behind him, Jamie inclined

his head gracefully toward the pinioned hand. "I expect you'll find me here."

Black Jack. A common name for rogues and scoundrels in the eighteenth century. A staple of romantic fiction, the name conjured up charming highwaymen, dashing blades in plumed hats. The reality walked at my side.

One never stops to think what underlies romance. Tragedy and terror, transmuted by time. Add a little art in the telling, and voilà! a stirring romance, to make the blood run fast and maidens sigh. My blood was running fast, all right, and never maiden sighed like Jamie, cradling his mangled hand.

"This way." It was the first time Randall had spoken since we had left the cell. He indicated a narrow alcove in the wall, unlighted by torches. The way out, of which he had spoken to Jamie.

By now I had sufficient command of myself to speak, and I did so. I stepped back a pace, so that the torchlight fell full on me, for I wanted him to remember my face.

"You asked me, Captain, if I were a witch," I said, my voice low and steady. "I'll answer you now. Witch I am. Witch, and I curse you. You will marry, Captain, and your wife will bear a child, but you shall not live to see your firstborn. I curse you with knowledge, Jack Randall—I give you the hour of your death."

His face was in shadow, but the gleam of his eyes told me he believed me. And why should he not? For I spoke the truth, and I knew it. I could see the lines of Frank's genealogical chart as though they were drawn on the mortar lines between the stones of the wall, and the names listed by them. "Jonathan Wolverton Randall," I said softly, reading it from the stones. "Born, September the 3rd, 1705. Died—" He made a convulsive movement toward me, but not fast enough to prevent me from speaking.

A narrow door at the back of the alcove crashed open with a squeal of hinges. Expecting further darkness, my eyes were dazzled by a blinding flash of light on snow. A quick shove from behind sent me staggering headlong into the drifts, and the door slammed to behind me.

I was lying in a ditch of sorts, behind the prison. The drifts around me covered heaps of something—the prison's refuse, most likely. There was something hard beneath the drift I had fallen into; wood, perhaps. Looking up at the sheering wall above me, I could see streaks and runnels down the stone, marking the path of garbage tipped from a sliding door forty feet above. That must be the kitchen quarters.

I rolled over, bracing myself to rise, and found myself looking into a pair of wide blue eyes. The face was nearly as blue as the eyes, and hard as the log of wood I had mistaken him for. I stumbled to my feet, choking, and staggered back against the prison wall.

Head down, breathe deep, I told myself firmly. You are *not* going to faint, you have seen dead men before, lots of them, you are not going to faint—God, he has blue eyes like—*you are not going to faint, damn it!*

My breathing slowed at last, and with it my racing pulse. As the panic receded, I forced myself back to that pathetic figure, wiping my hands convulsively on my skirt. I don't know whether it was pity, curiosity, or simple shock that made me look again. Seen without the suddenness of surprise, there was nothing frightening about the dead man; there never is. No matter how ugly the manner in which a man dies, it's only the presence of a suffering human soul that is horrifying; once gone, what is left is only an object.

The blue-eyed stranger had been hanged. He was not the only inhabitant of the ditch. I didn't bother to excavate the drift, but now that I knew what it contained, I could plainly see the outline of frozen limbs and the softly rounded heads under the snow. At least a dozen men lay here, waiting either for a thaw that would make their burial easier, or for a cruder disposal by the beasts of the nearby forest.

The thought startled me out of my pensive immobility. I had no time to waste in graveside meditation, or one more pair of blue eyes would stare sightless up into falling snow.

I had to find Murtagh and Rupert. That hidden postern door could be used, perhaps. Clearly it was not fortified or guarded like the main gates and other entrances to the prison. But I needed help, and I needed it quickly.

I glanced up at the rim of the ditch. The sun was quite low, burning through a haze of cloud just above the treetops. The air felt heavy with moisture. Likely it would snow again by nightfall; the haze was thick across the sky in the east. There was perhaps an hour of light left.

I began to follow the ditch, not wanting to climb the steep rocky sides until I had to. The ravine curved away from the prison quite soon, and looked as though it would lead down toward the river; presumably the runoff of melting snow carried the prison's refuse away. I was nearly to the corner of the soaring wall when I heard a faint sound behind me. I whirled. The sound had been made by a rock falling from the lip of the ditch, dislodged by the foot of a large grey wolf.

As an alternative to the items under the snow, I had certain desirable characteristics, from a wolf's point of view. On the one hand, I was mobile, harder to catch, and posed the possibility of resistance. On the other, I was slow, clumsy, and above all, not frozen stiff, thus offering no danger of broken teeth. I also smelled of fresh blood, temptingly warm in this frozen waste. Were I a wolf, I thought, I wouldn't hesitate. The animal made up its mind at the same time I came to my own decision regarding our future relations.

There had been a Yank at Pembroke Hospital, name of Charlie Marshall. He was a pleasant chap, friendly as all the Yanks were, and most entertaining on his pet subject. His pet subject was dogs; Charlie was a sergeant in the K-9 Corps. He had been blown up, along with two of his dogs, by an antipersonnel mine outside a small village near Arles. He grieved for his dogs, and often told me stories about them when I would sit with him during the odd slack moments in my shift.

More to the immediate point, he had also once told me what to do, and not do, should I ever be attacked by a dog. I felt it was stretching a point to call the eerie creature picking its delicate way down the rocks a dog, but hoped that it might yet share a few basic character traits with its tame descendants.

"Bad dog," I said firmly, staring it in one yellow eyeball. "In fact," I said, backing very slowly toward the prison wall, "you are a perfectly horrible dog." *(Speak firmly and loudly,* I heard Charlie saying.) "Probably the worst I've ever seen," I said, firmly and loudly. I continued to back up, one hand feeling behind me for the stones of the wall, and once there, I sidled toward the corner, some ten yards away.

I pulled the ties at my throat and began to fumble at the brooch fastening my cloak, still telling the wolf firmly and loudly what I thought of him, his ancestors, and his immediate family. The beast seemed interested in the diatribe, tongue lolling in a doggy grin. He was in no hurry; he limped slightly, I could see, as he drew nearer, and was thin and mangy. Perhaps he had trouble hunting, and infirmity was what drew him to the prison midden to scavenge. I certainly hoped so; the more infirm, the better.

I found my leather gloves in the pocket of my cloak and put them on. Then I wrapped the heavy cloak several times around my right forearm, blessing the weight of the velvet. "They'll go for the throat," Charlie had instructed me, "unless their trainer tells them otherwise. Keep looking him in the eye; you'll see it when he makes up his mind to jump. That's your moment."

I could see a number of things in that wicked yellow orb, including hunger, curiosity, and speculation, but not yet a decision to leap.

"You disgusting creature," I told it, "don't you *dare* leap at my throat!" I had other ideas. I had wrapped the cloak in several loose folds about my right arm, leaving the bulk of it dangling, but providing enough padding, I hoped, to keep the beast's teeth from sinking through.

The wolf was thin, but not emaciated. I judged it to weigh perhaps eighty or ninety pounds; less than me, but not enough to give me any great advantage. The leverage was definitely in the animal's favor; four legs against two gave better balance on the slippery crust of snow. I hoped bracing my back against the wall would help.

A certain feeling of emptiness at my back told me I had reached the corner. The wolf was some twenty feet away. This was it. I scraped enough snow from under my feet to give good footing and waited.

I didn't even see the wolf leave the ground. I could swear I had been watching its eyes, but if the decision to leap had registered there, it had been followed by action too swiftly to note. It was instinct, not thought, that raised my arm as a whitish-grey blur hurtled toward me.

The teeth sank into the padding with a force that bruised my arm. It was heavier than I thought; I was unprepared for the weight, and my arm sagged. I had planned to try to throw the beast against the wall, perhaps stunning it. Instead, I heaved myself at the wall, squashing the wolf between the stone blocks and my hip. I struggled to wrap the loose cloak around it. Claws shredded my skirt and scraped my thigh. I drove a knee viciously into its chest, eliciting a strangled yelp. Only then did I realize that the odd, growling whimpers were coming from me and not the wolf.

Strangely enough, I was not at all frightened now, though I had been terrified watching the wolf stalk me. There was room in my mind for only one thought: I would kill this animal, or it would kill me. Therefore, I was going to kill it.

There comes a turning point in intense physical struggle where one abandons oneself to a profligate usage of strength and bodily resource, ignoring the costs until the struggle is over. Women find this point in childbirth; men in battle.

Past that certain point, you lose all fear of pain or injury. Life becomes very simple at that point; you will do what you are trying to do, or die in the attempt, and it does not really matter much which.

I had seen this sort of struggle during my training on the wards, but never had I experienced it before. Now all my concentration was focused on the jaws locked around my forearm and the writhing demon tearing at my body.

I managed to bang the beast's head against the wall, but not hard enough to do much good. I was growing tired rapidly; had the wolf been in good condition, I would have had no chance. I hadn't much now, but took what there was. I fell on the animal, pinning it under me and knocking the wind from it in a gust of carrion breath. It recovered almost immediately and began squirming beneath me, but the second's relaxation enabled me to get it off my arm, one hand clamped under its wet muzzle.

By forcing my fingers back into the corners of its mouth, I managed to keep them out from between the scissoring car- nassial teeth. Saliva drizzled down my arm. I was lying flat on top of the wolf. The corner of the prison wall was perhaps eighteen inches ahead of me. Somehow I must get there, without releasing the fury that heaved and squirmed under me.

Scrabbling with my feet, pressing down with all my might, I pushed myself forward inch by inch, constantly straining to keep the fangs from my throat. It cannot have taken more than a few minutes to move those eighteen inches, but it seemed I had lain there most of my life, locked in battle with this beast whose hind claws raked my legs, seeking a good ripping purchase in my belly.

At last I could see around the corner. The blunt angle of stone was directly in front of my face. Now was the tricky part. I must maneuver the wolf's body to allow me to get both hands under the muzzle; I would never be able to exert the necessary force with one.

I rolled abruptly away, and the wolf slithered at once into the small clear space between my body and the wall. Before it could rise to its feet, I brought my knee up as hard as I could. The wolf grunted as my knee drove into its side, pinning it, however fleetingly, against the wall.

I had both hands beneath its jaw now. The fingers of one hand were actually in its mouth. I could feel a crushing sting across my gloved knuckles, but ignored it as I forced the hairy head back, and back, and back again, using the angle of the wall as a fulcrum for the lever of the beast's body. I thought my arms would break, but this was the only chance.

There was no audible noise, but I *felt* the reverberation through the whole body as the neck snapped. The straining limbs—and the bladder—at once relaxed. The intolerable strain on my arms now released, I dropped, as limp as the dying wolf. I could feel the beast's heart fibrillating beneath my cheek, the only part still capable of a death struggle. The stringy fur stank of ammonia and soggy hair. I wanted to move away, but could not.

I think I must have slept for a moment, odd as that sounds, cheek pillowed on the corpse. I opened my eyes to see the greenish stone of the prison a few inches in front of my nose. Only the thought of what was transpiring on the other side of that wall got me to my feet.

I stumbled down the ditch, cloak dragged over one shoulder, tripping on stones hidden in the snow, banging my shins painfully on half-buried tree branches. Subconsciously, I must have been aware that wolves usually run in packs, because I do not recall being surprised by the howl that wavered out of the forest above and behind me. If I felt anything, it was black rage at what seemed a conspiracy to thwart and delay me.

Wearily I turned to see where the sound had come from. I was in the open away from the prison by this time; no wall to brace my back against, and no weapon to hand. It had been luck as much as anything that helped me with the first wolf; there was not a chance in a thousand that I could kill another animal bare-handed—and how many more might there be? The pack I had seen feeding in the moonlight in the summer had had at least ten wolves. I could hear in memory the sounds of their teeth scraping, and the crack of breaking bones. The only question now was whether I bothered to fight at all, or whether I would rather just lie down in the snow and give up. That option seemed remarkably attractive, all things considered.

Still, Jamie had given up his life, and considerably more than that, to get me out of the prison. I owed it to him at least to try.

Once more I backed slowly away, moving farther down the ditch. The light was fading; soon the ravine would be filled with shadow. I doubted that that would help me. The wolves undoubtedly had better night-sight than I did.

The first of the hunters appeared on the rim of the ditch as the other had; a shaggy figure, standing motionless and alert. It was with something of a shock that I realized two more were already in the ravine with me, trotting slowly, almost in step with each other. They were almost the same color as the snow in the twilight—dirty grey—and almost invisible, though they moved with no attempt at concealment.

I stopped moving. Flight was clearly useless. Bending, I freed a dead pine branch from the snow. The bark was black with the wet, and rough even through my gloves. I waved the branch around my head and shouted. The animals stopped moving toward me, but did not retreat. The closest one flattened its ears, as though objecting to the noise.

"Don't like it?" I screeched. "Too bloody bad! Back off, you fucking sod!" Scooping up a half-buried rock, I hurled it at the wolf. It missed, but the beast scooted to one side. Encouraged, I began to fling missiles wildly; rocks, twigs, handfuls of snow, anything I could grab one-handed. I shrieked until my throat was raw with cold air, howling like the wolves themselves.

At first I thought one of my missiles had scored a hit. The nearest wolf yelped and seemed to convulse. The second arrow passed within a foot of me and I caught the tiny blur of motion before it thudded home in the chest of the second wolf. That animal died where it stood. The first, struck less vitally, kicked and struggled in the snow, no more than a heaving lump in the growing dusk.

I stood stupidly staring at it for some time, then looked up by instinct to the lip of the ravine. The third wolf, wisely choosing discretion, had vanished back into the trees, from whence a shivering howl went up.

I was still looking up at the dark trees when a hand clutched my elbow. I whirled with a gasp to find myself looking up into the face of a stranger. Narrow-jawed and with a weak chin illdisguised by a scabby beard, he was a stranger indeed, but his plaid and his dirk marked him a Scot.

"Help," I said, and fell forward into his arms.

36

MacRannoch

It was dark in the cottage and there was a bear in the corner of the room. In panic, I recoiled against my escort, wanting nothing more to do with wild beasts. He shoved me strongly forward, into the cottage. As I staggered toward the fire, the hulking shape turned toward me, and I realized belatedly that it was merely a large man in a bearskin.

A bearskin cloak, to be exact, fastened at the neck with a silver-gilt brooch as large as the palm of my hand. It was made in the shape of two leaping stags, backs arched and heads meeting to form a circle. The locking pin was a short, tapered fan, the head of it shaped like the tail of a fleeing deer.

I noticed the brooch in detail because it was directly in front of my nose. Looking up, I briefly considered the possibility that I had been wrong; perhaps it really *was* a bear.

Still, bears presumably did not wear brooches or have eyes like blueberries; small, round, and a dark, shiny blue. They were sunk in heavy cheeks whose lower slopes were forested with silver-shot black hair. Similar hair cascaded over thick-set shoulders to mingle with the hair of the cloak, which, in spite of its new use, was still pungently redolent of its former owner.

The shrewd little eyes flickered over me, evaluating both the bedraggled state of my attire, and the good basic quality of it, including the two wedding rings, gold and silver. The bear's address was formulated accordingly.

"You seem to have had some difficulty, mistress," he said

formally, inclining a massive head still spangled with melting snow. "Perhaps we might assist ye?"

I hesitated over what to say. I desperately needed this man's help, yet I would be suspect immediately my speech revealed me to be English. The archer who had brought me here forestalled me.

"Found her near Wentworth," he said laconically. "Fightin' wolves. An English lassie," he added, with an emphasis that made my host's blueberry eyes fix on me with a rather unpleasant speculation in their depths. I pulled myself up to my full height and summoned as much of the Matron attitude as I could.

"English by birth, Scots by marriage," I said firmly. "My name is Claire Fraser. My husband is a prisoner in Wentworth."

"I see," said the bear, slowly. "Weel, my own name is MacRannoch, and ye're presently on my land. I can see by your dress as you're a woman of some family; how come ye to be alone in Eldridge Wood on a winter night?"

I caught at the opening; here was some chance to establish my bona fides, as well as to find Murtagh and Rupert.

"I came to Wentworth with some clansmen of my husband's. As I was English, we thought I could gain entrance to the prison, and perhaps find some way of, er, removing him. However, I—I left the prison by another way. I was looking for my friends when I was set upon by wolves—from which this gentleman kindly rescued me." I tried a grateful smile on the raw-boned archer, who received it in stony silence.

"Ye've certainly met *something* wi' teeth," MacRannoch agreed, eyeing the gaping rents in my skirt. Suspicion yielded temporarily to the demands of hospitality.

"Are ye hurt, then? Just a bit scratched? Weel, you're cold, nae doubt, and a wee bit shaken, I imagine. Sit here by the fire. Hector will fetch ye a sup of something, and then ye can tell me a bit more about these friends of yours." He pulled a rough three-legged stool up with one foot, and sat me firmly on it with a massive hand on my shoulder.

Peat fires give little light but are comfortingly hot. I shuddered involuntarily as the blood started to flow back into my frozen hands. A couple of gulps from the leather flask grudg-ingly provided by Hector started the blood flowing internally again as well.

I explained my situation as well as I could, which was not particularly well. My brief description of my exit from the prison and subsequent hand-to-hand encounter with the wolf was received with particular skepticism.

"Given that ye did manage to get into Wentworth, it doesna seem likely that Sir Fletcher would allow ye to wander about the place. Nor if this Captain Randall had found ye in the dungeons, he would merely ha' shown ye the back door."

"He—he had reasons for letting me go."

"Which were?" The blueberry eyes were implacable.

I gave up and put the matter baldly; I was much too tired for delicacy or circumlocutions.

MacRannoch appeared semiconvinced, but still reluctant to take any action.

"Aye, I see your concern," he argued, "still, that may not be so bad."

"Not so bad!" I sprang to my feet in outrage.

He shook his head as though plagued by deerflies. "What I mean," he explained, "is that if it's the lad's arse he's after, he's none so likely to hurt him badly. And, savin' your pres-ence, ma'am"—he cocked a bushy eyebrow in my direction—"bein' buggered has seldom killed anyone." He held up pla-cating hands the size of soup plates.

"Now, I'm no sayin' he'll enjoy it, mind, but I do say it's not worth a major set-to with Sir Fletcher Gordon, just to save the lad a sore arse. I've a precarious position here, ye know, verra precarious." And he puffed out his cheeks and beetled his brows at me.

Not for the first time, I regretted the fact that there were no real witches. Had I been one, I would have turned him into a toad on the spot. A big fat one, with warts.

I choked down my rage and tried reason yet again.

"I rather think his arse is beyond saving by this time; it's his neck I'm concerned with. The English mean to hang him in the morning."

MacRannoch was muttering to himself, twisting back and

forth like a bear in a too-small cage. He stopped abruptly in front of me and thrust his nose to within an inch of my own. I would have recoiled, had I not been so exhausted. As it was, I merely blinked.

"And if I said I'd help ye, what good would that do?" he roared. He resumed his turning and pacing, two steps to one wall, hurling around in a fling of fur, and two steps to the other. He spoke as he paced, words keeping time to the steps, pausing to puff as he turned.

"If I were to go to Sir Fletcher myself, what would I say? Ye've a captain on your staff who's engaged in torturin' the prisoners in his spare time? And when he asks how I know that, I tell him 'a stray Sassenach wench my men found wanderin' in the dark told me this man's been makin' indecent advances to her husband, who's an outlaw wi' a price on his head, and a condemned murderer, to boot?"

MacRannoch stopped and thumped one paw on the flimsy table. "And as for takin' men into the place! If, and mind ye, I say *if* we could get in—"

"You could get in," I interrupted. "I can show you the way."

"Mmmphm. That's as may be. *If* we could get in, what happens when Sir Fletcher finds my men wanderin' about his fortress? He sends Captain Randall round next mornin' with a brace of cannon and levels Eldridge Hall to the ground, that's what!" He shook his head again, making the black locks fly.

"Nay, lass, I canna see—"

He was interrupted by the sudden flinging open of the cottage door to admit another bowman, this one pushing Murtagh in front of him at knife-point. MacRannoch stopped and stared in amazement.

"What *is* this?" he demanded. "Ye'd think 'twas May Day, and the lads and lassies all out gatherin' flowers in the wood, not the dead o' winter and snow comin' on!"

"This is my husband's clansman," I said. "As I told you—"

Murtagh, undisturbed by the less than cordial greeting, was eyeing the bear-clad figure closely, as though mentally stripping hair and years away.

"MacRannoch, is it no?" he said, in a tone almost accusing.

"Ye'll have been at a Gathering, I think, some time ago at Castle Leoch?"

MacRannoch was more than startled. "Some time ago, I should say! Why, that must ha' been near on thirty year ago. How d'ye know that, man?"

Murtagh nodded, satisfied. "Och, I thought so. I was there. And I remember that Gathering, likely for the same reason ye do yourself."

MacRannoch was studying the wizened little man, trying to subtract thirty years from the seamed countenance.

"Aye, I know ye," he said at last. "Or not the name, but you. Ye killed a wounded boar single-handed with a dagger, during the tynchal. A gallant beast too. That's right, the Mac-Kenzie gave ye the tushes—a bonny set, almost a complete double curve. Lovely work that, man." A look perilously close to gratification creased Murtagh's pitted cheek momentarily.

I started, remembering the magnificent, barbaric bracelets I had seen at Lallybroch. *My mother's,* Jenny had said, *given to her by an admirer.* I stared at Murtagh in disbelief. Even allowing for the passage of thirty years, he did not seem a likely candidate for the tender passion.

Thinking of Ellen MacKenzie, I remembered her pearls, which I was still carrying, sewn into the seam of my pocket. I groped for the free end, pulling them out into the firelight.

"I can pay you," I said. "I wouldn't expect your men to risk themselves for nothing."

Moving a good deal faster than I would have thought possible, he snatched the pearls from my hand. He stared at them disbelievingly.

"Where did ye get these, woman?" he demanded. "Fraser, did ye say your name is?"

"Yes." Tired as I was, I drew myself up straight. "And the pearls are mine. My husband gave them to me on our wedding day."

"Did he, then?" The hoarse voice was suddenly hushed. He turned to Murtagh, still holding the pearls.

"Ellen's son? Is this lass's husband Ellen's son?"

"Aye," Murtagh said, unemphatic as ever. "As ye'd ken at once if ye saw him; he's the spit of her."

Mindful at last of the pearls he was clutching, MacRannoch unfolded his hand and gently stroked the shining gems.

"I gave these to Ellen MacKenzie," he said. "For a wedding gift. I would ha' given them to her as my wife, but as she'd chosen elsewhere—well, I'd thought of them so often, around her bonny throat, I told her I couldna see them elsewhere. So I bade her keep them, and only think of me when she wore them. Hm!" He snorted briefly at some memory, then handed the pearls carefully back to me.

"So they're yours now. Well, wear them in good health, lassie."

"I'll stand a much better chance of doing so," I said, trying to control my impatience at these sentimental displays, "if you'll help me to get my husband back."

The small rosy mouth, which had been smiling slightly at its owner's thought, tightened suddenly.

"Ah," said Sir Marcus, pulling at his beard. "I see. But I've told ye, lassie, I canna see how it can be done. I've a wife and three weans at home. Aye, I'd do a bit for Ellen's lad. But it's a bit much ye're askin'."

Suddenly my legs gave way altogether, and I sat down with a thump, letting my shoulders sag and my head droop. Despair dragged at me like an anchor, pulling me down. I closed my eyes and retreated to some dim place within, where there was nothing but an aching grey blankness, and where the sound of Murtagh's voice, still arguing, was no more than a faint yapping.

It was the bawling of cattle that roused me from my stupor. I looked up to see MacRannoch swirl out of the cottage. As he opened the door, a blast of winter air came in, thick with the lowing of cattle and yelling of men. The door thumped shut behind the vast hairy figure, and I turned to ask Murtagh what he thought we should do next.

The look on his face stopped me, wordless. I had seldom seen him with anything more than a sort of patient dourness showing on his features, but now he positively glowed with suppressed excitement.

I caught at his arm. "What is it? Tell me quickly!"

He had time only to say, "The kine! They're MacRannoch's!" before MacRannoch himself plunged back into the cottage, pushing a lanky young man before him.

With a last shove, he brought the young man flat up against the plastered wall of the cottage. Apparently MacRannoch found confrontation effective; he tried the same nose-to-nose technique he had used on me earlier. Less poised, or less tired, than I, the young man hunched nervously back against the wall as far as he could go.

MacRannoch started out being sweetly reasonable. "Absalom, man, I sent ye out three hours ago to bring in forty head of cattle. I told ye it was important to find them, because there's about to be a damn awfu' snowstorm." The nicely modulated voice was rising. "And when I heard the sound of kine bellowin' outside, I said to meself, Ah, Marcus, there's Absalom gone and found all the cattle, what a good lad, now we can all go home and thaw ourselves by the fire, with the kine safe in their barns."

One ham-fist had fastened itself onto Absalom's jacket. The material, gathered between those stubby fingers, began to twist.

"And then I go out to congratulate you on a good job done, and begin to count the beasts. And how many do I count, Absalom, me bonny wee lad?" The voice had risen to a full-powered roar. While not possessed of a particularly deep voice, Marcus MacRannoch had enough lung-power for three ordinary-sized men.

"Fifteen!" he shouted, jerking the unfortunate Absalom to his tiptoes. "Fifteen beasts he finds, out of forty! And where are the rest o' them? Where? Out loose in the snow, to freeze to death!"

Murtagh had faded quietly back into the shadows in the corner while all this was going on. I was watching his face, though, and saw the sudden gleam of amusement in his eyes at these words. Suddenly I realized what he had started to tell me, and I knew where Rupert was now. Or, if not precisely where he was, at least what he was doing. And I began to hope a little.

It was full dark. The prison's lights below shone weakly through the snow like the lamps of a drowned ship. Waiting under the trees with my two companions, I mentally reviewed for the thousandth time everything that could go wrong.

Would MacRannoch carry out his part of the bargain? He'd have to, if he expected to get his prized purebred Highland cattle back. Would Sir Fletcher believe MacRannoch and order a search of the basement dungeons at once? Likely—the baronet wasn't a man to be taken lightly.

I had seen the cattle disappear, one shaggy beast at a time, down the ditch that led to the hidden postern door, under the expert driving of Rupert and his men. But would they be able to force the cattle through that door, singly or not? And if so, what would they do once inside; half-wild cattle, trapped suddenly in a stone corridor lit with glaring torchlight? Well, perhaps it would work. The corridor itself would be not unlike their stone-floored barn, including torches and the scent of humans. If they got so far, the plan might succeed. Randall himself was unlikely to call for help in the face of the invasion, for fear of having his own little games uncovered.

The handlers were to get away from the prison as fast as possible, once the beasts were well and truly launched on their chaotic path, and then to ride hell-for-leather for the Mac-Kenzie lands. Randall didn't matter; what could he do alone, in the circumstances? But what if the noise attracted the rest of the prison garrison too soon? If Dougal had been reluctant to try to break his nephew *out* of Wentworth, I could imagine his choler if several MacKenzies were arrested for breaking *into* the place. I didn't want to be responsible for that, either, though Rupert had been more than willing to take the risk. I bit my thumb and tried to comfort myself, thinking of the tons of solid, sound-muffling granite that separated the dungeons from the prison quarters above.

Most worrying of all, of course, was the fear that everything might work, and might be still too late. Waiting hangsman or no, Randall might go too far. I knew too well, from stories told by returning soldiers from POW camps, that nothing is easier than for a prisoner to die by "accident," and the body be conveniently disposed of before embarrassing official questions can be asked. Even if questions *were* asked, and Randall found out, it would be small comfort to me—and to Jamie.

I had been resolutely keeping myself from imagining the possible uses of the homely objects on the table of that room. But I could not keep from seeing over and over the bone-ends of that shattered finger pressing into the table. I rubbed my own knuckles hard against the saddle leather, trying to erase the image. I felt a slight burning, and pulled off the glove to examine the grazes left across my hand by the wolf's teeth. Not bad, no more than a few scratches, with one small puncture where a cusp had penetrated the leather. I licked the wound absently. It was little use telling myself that I had done my best. I had done the only possible thing, but knowing it didn't make the waiting easier.

At last, we heard a faint, confused shouting from the direction of the prison. One of the MacRannoch men put a hand on the bridle of my horse and motioned toward the shelter of the trees. The snow was much lighter on the ground and the flurries diminished under the interlaced branches of the grove, thin lines of snow stark and sudden on the rocky leaf-strewn ground. While the snow fell less thickly in here, visibility was still so poor that tree trunks a few feet away loomed surprisingly as I walked my horse restlessly around the small clearing, trunks springing up black in the pinkish light.

Muffled by the heavy snow, the approaching hoofbeats were almost upon us before we heard them. The two MacRannoch men drew their pistols and reined their horses up close to the trees, waiting, but I had picked up the dull lowing of cattle, and spurred my horse forward out of the grove.

Sir Marcus MacRannoch, distinguishable by his piebald mount and his bearskin cloak, was leading the way up the slope, snow spurting in small explosions from under the hooves of his horse. He was followed by several men, all in high good humor, from the sound of it. More of his men rode further back, chivvying the milling herd of cattle from behind, driving the band of bewildered beasts around the base of the hill, toward their well-earned shelter in the MacRannoch barns.

MacRannoch reined up beside me, laughing heartily. "I've to thank ye, Mistress Fraser," he shouted through the snow, "for a most entertaining evening." His earlier suspicion had vanished, and he greeted me with the utmost geniality. His eyebrows and mustache coated with snow, he looked like Father Christmas on a spree. Taking my bridle, he led my horse back into the quieter air of the grove. He waved my two companions down the hill to help with the cattle, then dismounted and swung me down from my saddle, still laughing to himself.

"Ye should ha' seen it!" he chortled, hugging himself in ecstasy. "Sir Fletcher went red as a robin's breast when I pushed in in the midst of his dinner, shouting that he was concealing stolen property on his premises. And then when we got below-stairs and he heard the beasts bellowin' like thunder, I thought he'd dirtied his breeches. He—" I shook his arm impatiently.

"Never mind Sir Fletcher's breeches. Did you find my husband?"

MacRannoch sobered a bit, wiping his eyes with his sleeve. "Oh, aye. We found him."

"Is he all right?" I spoke calmly, though I wanted to scream.

MacRannoch nodded toward the trees behind me, and I whirled to see a rider making his way carefully through the branches, a bulky cloth-covered shape draped across the saddlebow in front of him. I dashed forward, followed by MacRannoch, explaining helpfully.

"He's no deid, or at least he wasn't when we found him. Been mistreated a good bit, though, poor laddie." I had pushed aside the cloth over Jamie's head, and was anxiously examining him as best I could, with the horse fidgeting from the excitement of the cold ride and the extra burden. I could see dark bruises and feel stiff patches of blood in the rumpled hair, but could tell little more in the dim light. I thought I could feel a pulse in the icy neck, but wasn't sure.

MacRannoch caught my elbow and pulled me away. "We'll do best to get him inside quick, lass. Come with me. Hector will bring him along to the house."

In the main drawing room of Eldridge Manor, MacRannoch's home, Hector humped his burden onto the rug before the fire. Seizing one corner of the blanket, he unrolled it carefully, and a limp, naked figure flopped out onto the pink and yellow flowers of Lady Annabelle MacRannoch's pride and joy.

To do the Lady Annabelle credit, she didn't seem to notice the blood soaking into her expensive Aubusson rug. A birdlike woman in her early forties, arrayed like a goldfinch in a sunburst of yellow silk dressing gown, she had servants bustling in all directions with a brisk clap of her hands, and blankets, linen, hot water, and whisky appeared at my elbow almost before I had got my cloak off.

"Best turn him on his belly," advised Sir Marcus, pouring out two large whiskies. "He's had his back flayed, and it must feel fierce to lie on it. Not that he looks like he feels anything, much," he added, peering closely at Jamie's ashen face and sealed, bluish eyelids. "You're sure he's still alive?"

"Yes," I answered shortly, hoping I was right. I struggled to pull Jamie over. Unconsciousness seemed to have tripled his weight. MacRannoch lent a hand, and we got him positioned on a blanket, back to the fire.

A rapid triage having established that he was in fact alive, missing no body parts, and not in immediate danger of bleeding to death, I could afford to make a less hurried inventory of the damage.

"I can send for a physician," said Lady Annabelle, looking dubiously at the corpselike figure on her hearth, "but I doubt he can get here under an hour; it's snowing something fierce out." The reluctance in her tone was only partly on account of the snow, I thought. A physician would make one more dangerous witness to the presence of an escaped criminal in her home.

"Don't bother," I said absently, "I am a physician." Disregarding the looks of surprise from both MacRannochs, I knelt beside what was left of my husband, covered him with blankets and began to apply cloths soaked in hot water to the outlying parts. My chief concern was to get him warm; the blood from his back was a slow ooze, which could be dealt with later.

Lady Annabelle faded into the distance, her high gold-finch's voice summoning, beckoning, and arranging. Her spouse sank down on his haunches beside me, and began to rub Jamie's frozen feet in a businesslike way between large blunt-fingered hands, pausing occasionally to sip his whisky.

Turning back the blankets in bits, I surveyed the damage. He had been finely striped from nape to knees with something like a coachwhip, the weals crisscrossing neatly like hem-stitching. The sheer orderliness of the damage, speaking as it did of a deliberation that reveled in each punishing stroke, made me feel sick with rage.

Something heavier, perhaps a cane, had been used with less restraint across his shoulders, cutting so deeply in spots that a gleam of bone showed over one shoulderblade. I pressed a thick pad of lint gently over the worst of the mess and went on with the examination.

The spot on his left side where the mallet had struck was an ugly contused swelling, a black and purple patch bigger than Sir Marcus's hand. Broken ribs there for sure, but those too could wait. My attention was caught by the livid patches on neck and breast, where the skin was puckered, reddened and blistered. The edges of one such patch were charred, rimmed with white ash.

"What in hell did that?" Sir Marcus had completed his min-istrations and was looking over my shoulder with deep inter-est.

"A hot poker." The voice was weak and indistinct; it was a moment before I realized that it was Jamie who had spoken. He raised his head with an effort, showing the reason for his difficult speech; the lower lip was badly bitten on one side and puffed like a beesting.

With considerable presence of mind, Sir Marcus put a hand behind Jamie's neck and pressed the beaker of whisky to his lips. Jamie winced as the spirit stung his torn mouth, but drained the beaker before laying his head down again. His eyes slanted up at me, slightly filmed with pain and whisky, but alight with amusement nonetheless. "Cows?" he asked, "Was it really cows, or was I dreaming?"

"Well, it was all I could manage in the time," I said, beaming in my relief at seeing him alive and conscious. I placed a hand on his head, turning it to inspect a large bruise over the cheekbone. "You look bloody awful. How do you feel?" I asked, from force of long-held habit.

"Alive." He struggled up onto one elbow to accept with a nod a second beaker of whisky from Sir Marcus.

"Do you think you should drink so much all at once?" I asked, trying to examine his pupils for signs of concussion. He foiled me by closing his eyes and tilting his head back.

"Yes," he said, handing back the empty beaker to Sir Marcus, who bore it back in the direction of the decanter.

"Now, that'll be enough for the present, Marcus." Lady Annabelle, reappearing like the sun in the east, stopped her husband with a commanding chirp. "The lad needs hot strong tea, not more whisky." The tea followed her processionally in a silver pot, borne by a maidservant whose air of natural superiority was unimpaired by the fact that she was still attired in her nightdress.

"Hot strong tea with plenty of sugar in it," I amended.

"And perhaps a wee tot of whisky as well," said Sir Marcus, neatly removing the lid of the teapot as it passed and adding a generous dollop from his decanter. Accepting the steaming cup gratefully, Jamie raised it in mute tribute to Sir Marcus before cautiously bringing the hot liquid to his mouth. His hand shook badly, and I wrapped my own around his fingers to guide the cup.

More servants were bringing in a portable camp bed, a mattress, more blankets, more bandages and hot water, and a large wooden chest containing the household's medical supplies.

"I thought we had best work here before the fire," Lady Annabelle explained in her charming bird-voice. "There's more light, and it's far the warmest place in the house."

At her direction, two of the larger menservants each seized an end of the blanket under Jamie and transferred it smoothly, contents and all, to the camp bed, now set up before the fire, where another servant was industriously poking the night-banked coals and feeding the growing blaze. The maid who had brought in the tea was efficiently lighting the wax tapers in the branched candelabra on the sideboard. Despite her songbird appearance, the Lady Annabelle plainly had the soul of a master-sergeant.

"Yes, now that he's awake, the sooner the better," I said. "Have you a flat board about two feet long," I asked, "a stout strap, and perhaps some small, straight, flat sticks, about so long?" I held my fingers apart, measuring a length of four inches or so. One of the servants disappeared into the shadows, flicking out of sight like a djinn to do my bidding.

The whole house seemed magical, perhaps because of the contrast between the howling cold outside and the luxurious warmth within, or maybe only because of the relief of seeing Jamie safe, after so many hours of fear and worry.

Heavy dark furniture gleamed with polish in the lamp light, silver shone on the sideboard, and a collection of delicate glass and china ornamented the mantelpiece, in bizarre contrast to the bloody, bedraggled figure before it.

No questions were asked. We were Sir Marcus's guests, and Lady Annabelle behaved as though it were an everyday occurrence to have people come and bleed on the carpet at midnight. It occurred to me for the first time that such a visit might have happened before.

"Verra nasty," said Sir Marcus, examining the smashed hand with an expertise born of the battlefield. "And wretched painful, too, I expect. Still, it's no going to kill ye, is it?" He straightened up and addressed me in confidential tones.

"I thought it might be worse than this, given what ye told me. Except the ribs and hand, there's no bones broken, and the rest will heal fine. I'd say maybe ye were lucky, lad."

There was a faint snort from the recumbent figure on the bed.

"I suppose ye could call it luck. They meant to be hanging me in the morning." He moved his head restlessly on the pillow, trying to look up at Sir Marcus. "Did ye know that . . . sir?" he added, catching sight of Sir Marcus's embroidered waistcoat, with its coat of arms worked in silver stitchery among the pigeons and roses.

MacRannoch waved a hand, dismissing this minor detail.

"Weel, if he meant to be keepin' ye presentable for the hangsman, he went a bit far on your back, then," Sir Marcus remarked, removing the soaked lint and replacing it with a fresh pad.

"Aye. He lost his head a bit when . . . when he . . ." Jamie struggled to get the words out, then gave it up as a bad job and turned his face to the fire, eyes closed. "God, I'm tired," he said.

We let him rest until the manservant materialized by my elbow with the splints I had requested. Then I carefully picked up the smashed right hand, bringing it into the candlelight for examination.

It would have to be set, and as soon as possible. The injured muscles were already clawing the fingers inward. I felt hopeless as I saw the full extent of the damage. But if he was ever to have any use of the hand again, it would have to be attempted.

Lady Annabelle had hung back during my examination, watching interestedly. When I set the hand down, she stepped forward and opened the small chest of medical supplies.

"I suppose you'll be wanting the boneset, and perhaps the cherry bark. I don't know . . ." She eyed Jamie doubtfully. "Leeches, do you think?" Her well-kept hand hovered over a small lidded jar filled with murky liquid.

I shuddered and shook my head. "No, I don't think so; not just now. What I could really use . . . do you by chance have any sort of opiate?" I sank to my knees beside her to pore over the contents of the box.

"Oh, yes!" Her hand went unerringly to a small green flask. "Flowers of laudanum," she read from the label. "Will that do?"

"Perfect." I accepted the flask gratefully.

"All right, then," I said briskly to Jamie, pouring a small amount of the odorous liquid into a glass, "you'll need to sit up just long enough to swallow this. Then you'll go to sleep and stay that way for a good long time." In fact, I had some doubts as to the advisability of administering laudanum on top of such a quantity of whisky, but the alternative—reconstructing that hand while he was conscious—was unthinkable. I tipped the bottle to pour a bit more.

Jamie's good hand on my arm stopped me.

"I don't want drugs," he said firmly. "Just perhaps a wee drop more of whisky"—he hesitated, tongue touching the bitten lip—"and maybe something to bite down on."

Sir Marcus, hearing this, crossed to the lovely glowing Sheraton desk in the corner and began to rummage. He returned in a moment with a small piece of well-worn leather. Looking more closely, I could see the dozens of overlapping semicircular indentations in the thick leather—toothmarks, I realized with a shock.

"Here," Sir Marcus said helpfully. "I used this myself at St. Simone; got me through it while I had a musket ball dug out of my leg."

I looked on, open-mouthed, as Jamie took the leather with a nod of thanks, smoothing his thumb over the marks. I spoke slowly, stunned. "You actually expect me to set nine broken bones while you're *awake*?"

"Yes," he said briefly, placing the leather between his teeth and biting down experimentally. He shifted it back and forth, seeking a comfortable grip.

Overcome by the sheer theatricality of it, the precarious control I had been hoarding suddenly snapped.

"Will you stop being such a goddamned frigging hero!" I blazed at Jamie. "We all know what you've done, you don't have to prove how much you can stand! Or do you think we'll all fall apart if you're not in charge, telling everyone what to do every minute? Who in bloody hell do you think you are, frigging John Wayne!"

There was an awkward silence. Jamie looked at me, openmouthed. Finally he spoke.

"Claire," he said softly, "we're perhaps two miles from Wentworth Prison. I'm meant to hang in the morning. No matter what's happened to Randall, the English are going to notice I'm gone soon."

I bit my lip. What he said was true. My inadvertent release

of the other prisoners might confuse the issue for a time, but eventually a tally would be made, and a search begun. And thanks to the flamboyant method of escape I had chosen, attention was bound to be focused on Eldridge Manor in short order.

"If we're lucky," the quiet voice continued, "the snow will delay a search 'til we've gone. If not . . ." He shrugged, staring into the flames. "Claire, I'll not let them take me back. And to be drugged, to lie here helpless if they come, and maybe wake up chained in a cell again. . . . Claire, I couldna bear it."

There were tears blurring on my lower lashes. I stared wide-eyed at him, not wanting to blink and let them run down my cheeks.

He closed his eyes against the fire's heat. The glow lent a spurious look of ruddy health to the white cheeks. I could see the long muscles in his throat work as he swallowed.

"Don't cry, Sassenach," he said, so softly I could hardly hear him. He reached out and patted my leg with his good hand, trying to be reassuring. "I imagine we're safe enough, lass. If I thought likely we'd be captured, I'd certainly no waste one of my last hours having you mend a hand I'd not be going to need. Go and fetch Murtagh for me. Then bring me a drink and we'll get on wi' it."

Busy at the table with the medical preparations, I couldn't hear what he said to Murtagh, but I saw the two heads close together for a moment, then Murtagh's sinewy hand gently touch the younger man's ear—one of the few uninjured spots available.

With a brief nod of farewell, Murtagh sidled toward the door. Like a rat, I thought, darting along the wainscoting, not to be noticed. I was behind him as he went out into the hall, and grabbed him by the plaid just before he escaped altogether through the front door.

"What did he tell you?" I demanded fiercely. "Where are you going?"

The dark, stringy little man hesitated for a moment, but answered evenly, "I'm to go wi' young Absalom toward Wentworth and keep watch in that direction. If any Redcoats are headin' this way, I'm to beat them here, and if there's time, I'm to see you and him both hidden, then ride off with three horses, to draw followers away from the Manor. There's a cellar; it might do for hiding, if the search isna too thorough."

"And if there isn't time to hide?" I eyed him narrowly, daring him not to answer.

"Then I'm to kill him, and take you wi' me," he answered promptly. "Willing or no," he added, with an evil grin, and turned to go.

"Just a minute!" I spoke sharply and he stopped. "Do you have an extra dirk?"

His scruffy brows shot upward, but his hand went to his belt without hesitation.

"Do ye need one? Here?" His glance took in the opulence and serenity of the entrance hall, with its painted Adam ceiling and linenfold paneling.

My dagger-pocket was shredded beyond use. I took the proffered dagger, and slid it between kirtle and bodice in the back, as I had seen the Gypsy women do.

"One never knows, does one?" I said evenly.

—————

Preparations complete, I probed as gently as possible, assessing harm, deciding what must be done. Jamie drew in his breath sharply when I touched an especially bad spot, but kept his eyes closed as I felt my way slowly along each separate bone and joint, noting the position of each fracture and dislocation. "Sorry," I murmured.

I took his good hand as well, and felt carefully down each finger of both the good hand and the injured, making comparisons. With neither X rays nor experience to guide me, I would have to depend on my own sensitivity to find and realign the smashed bones.

The first joint was all right, but the second phalange was cracked, I thought. I pressed harder to determine the length and direction of the crack. The damaged hand stayed motionless in my fingers, but the good one made a small, involuntary clenching gesture.

"I'm sorry," I murmured once more.

The good hand pulled suddenly out of my grasp as Jamie raised himself on one elbow. Spitting out the leather gag, he regarded me with an expression between amusement and exasperation.

"Sassenach," he said, "if you apologize each time ye hurt me, it's going to be a verra long night—and it's lasted some time already."

I must have looked stricken, because he started to reach toward me, then stopped, wincing at the movement. He controlled the pain, though, and spoke firmly. "I know you dinna wish to hurt me. But you've no more choice about it than I have, and there's no need for more than one of us to suffer for it. You do what's needed, and I'll scream if I have to."

Replacing the leather strip, he bared his clenched teeth ferociously at me, then slowly and deliberately crossed his eyes. This made him look so like an addlepated tiger that I burst into half-hysterical laughter before I could stop myself.

I clapped my hands over my mouth, cheeks flaming as I saw the astonished looks on the faces of Lady Annabelle and the servants, who, standing behind Jamie, naturally could see nothing of his face. Sir Marcus, who had caught a brief glimpse from his seat at the bedside, grinned in his spade-shaped beard.

"Besides," said Jamie, spitting out the leather once more, "if the English turn up after *this,* I expect I'll beg them to take me back."

I picked up the leather, put it between his teeth and pushed his head down again.

"Clown," I said. "Know-all. Sodding hero." But he had relieved me of a burden, and I worked more calmly. If I still noticed every twitch and grimace, at least I no longer felt it as badly.

I began to lose myself in the concentration of the job, directing all my awareness to my fingertips, assessing each point of damage and deciding how best to draw the smashed bones back into alignment. Luckily the thumb had suffered least; only a simple fracture of the first joint. That would heal clean. The second knuckle on the fourth finger was completely gone; I felt only a pulpy grating of bone chips when I rolled it gently between my own thumb and forefinger, making Jamie groan. Nothing could be done about that, save splint the joint and hope for the best.

The compound fracture of the middle finger was the worst to contemplate. The finger would have to be pulled straight, drawing the protruding bone back through the torn flesh. I had seen this done before—under general anesthesia, with the guidance of X rays.

To this point, it had been more a mechanical problem than a real one, deciding how to reconstruct a smashed, disembodied hand. I was now smack up against the reason that physicians seldom treat members of their own families. Some jobs in medicine require a certain ruthlessness to complete successfully; detachment is necessary to inflict pain in the process of effecting a healing.

Quietly, Sir Marcus had brought up a stool by the side of the bed. He settled his bulk comfortably as I finished the strapping, and gripped Jamie's good hand with his own.

"Squeeze all ye like, lad," he said.

Divested of the bearskin, and with his grizzled locks neatly clubbed and laced back, MacRannoch was no longer the intimidating wildman of the forest, but appeared as a soberly clad man of late middle age, with a neatly trimmed spade-beard and a military bearing. Nervous at what I was about to attempt, I found his solid presence comforting.

I drew a deep breath and prayed for detachment.

It was a long, horrible, nerve-wracking job, though not without its fascination. Some parts, such as the splinting of the two fingers with simple fractures, went quite easily. Others did not. Jamie did scream—loudly—when I set his middle finger, exerting the considerable force necessary to draw the ends of splintered bone back through the skin. I hesitated for an instant, unnerved, but "Go on, lass!" Sir Marcus said with quiet urgency.

I remembered suddenly what Jamie had said to me, the night Jenny's baby was born: *I can bear pain, myself, but I could not bear yours. That would take more strength than I have.* He was right; it did take strength; I hoped that each of us had enough.

Jamie's face was turned away from me, but I could see the jaw muscles bunch as he clenched his teeth harder on the leather strip. I clenched my own teeth and did go on; the sharp bone end slowly disappeared back through the skin and the finger straightened with agonizing reluctance, leaving us both trembling.

As I worked, I began to lose consciousness of anything outside the job I was doing. Jamie groaned occasionally, and we had to stop twice briefly in order for him to be sick, retching up mostly whisky, as he had taken little food in prison. For the most part, though, he kept up a low, constant muttering in Gaelic, forehead pressed hard against Sir Marcus's knees. I couldn't tell through the leather gag whether he was cursing or praying.

All five fingers eventually lay straight as new pins, stiff as sticks in their bandaged splints. I was afraid of infection, particularly from the torn middle finger, but otherwise was fairly sure they would heal well. By good luck, only the one joint had been badly damaged. It would likely leave him with a stiff ring finger, but the others might function normally—in time. There was nothing I could do about the cracked metacarpal bones or the puncture wound except apply an antiseptic wash and a poultice and pray against a tetanus infection. I stepped back, shaking in every limb from the strain of the night, my bodice soaked with sweat from the fire's heat at my back.

Lady Annabelle was at my side at once, guiding me to a chair and pressing a cup of tea, laced with whisky, into my shaking hands. Sir Marcus, as good an operating-room assistant as any physician could have, was unfastening Jamie's captive arm and rubbing the marks where the strap had bitten deep into straining flesh. The older man's hand was red, I saw, where Jamie had gripped it.

I was not aware of having nodded off, but suddenly jerked, my head snapping on my neck. Lady Annabelle was urging me upward, soft hand under my elbow. "Come along, my dear.

You're all in; you must have your own hurts seen to, and sleep a bit."

I shook her off as politely as possible. "No, I can't. I must finish . . ." My words trailed off into the fuzziness of my mind, as Sir Marcus smoothly took the vinegar bottle and rag from my hand.

"I'll take care of the rest," he said. "I've some experience wi' field dressing, ye understand." Flipping back the blankets, he began to swab the blood from the whip cuts, moving with a brisk gentleness that was impressive. Catching my eye, he grinned, beard tilted jauntily. "I've cleansed a good many stripes in my time," he said. "And applied a few too. These are naught, lass; they'll heal in a few days." Knowing he was right, I walked up to the head of the cot. Jamie was awake, grimacing slightly at the sting of the antiseptic solution on the raw cuts, but his eyelids were heavy and the blue eyes darkened with pain and weariness.

"Go and sleep, Sassenach. I'll do."

Whether he would or not, I didn't know. It was clear, however, that I wouldn't do, or not for much longer. I was swaying with exhaustion and the scratches on my legs were beginning to burn and ache. Absalom had cleansed them for me at the cottage, but they needed salving.

I nodded numbly and turned in response to Lady Annabelle's gently insistent pressure on my elbow.

Halfway up the stairs, I remembered that I had forgotten to tell Sir Marcus how to bandage the cuts. The deep wounds over the shoulders would have to be bound and padded, to allow for wearing a shirt over them when we made our escape. But the lighter lash-marks should be left in the open air to scab over. I took a quick look at the guestroom Lady Annabelle showed me, then excused myself with a word and stumbled back down the stairs toward the drawing room.

I paused in the shadowed doorway, Lady Annabelle behind me. Jamie's eyes were closed; apparently he had fallen into a doze brought on by whisky and fatigue. The blankets were thrown back, rendered unnecessary by the heat of the fire. Sir Marcus casually rested a hand on Jamie's bare rump as he reached across the bed for a rag. The effect was electric. Ja-

mie's back arched sharply, the muscles of his buttocks
clenched tightly and he let out an involuntary sound of protest, flinging himself backward in spite of the shattered ribs, to
glare up at Sir Marcus with startled, dazed eyes. Startled himself, Sir Marcus stood stock-still for a second, then leaned
forward and took Jamie by the arm, gently settling him
facedown once more. Thoughtfully he drew a finger very gingerly across Jamie's flesh. He rubbed his fingers together,
leaving an oily sheen visible in the firelight.

"Oh," he said matter-of-factly. The old soldier drew the
blanket up to Jamie's waist, and I saw the tense shoulders
relax slightly under their dressing.

Sir Marcus seated himself companionably near Jamie's head
and poured another pair of whiskies. "At least he had the
consideration to grease ye a bit beforehand," he observed,
handing one beaker to Jamie, who heaved himself laboriously
up on his elbows to accept it.

"Aye, well. I dinna think it was so much for *my* convenience," he said dryly.

Sir Marcus took a gulp of his drink and smacked his lips
meditatively. There was no sound for a moment save the
crackle of flames, but neither Lady Annabelle nor I made any
motion to enter the room.

"If it's any comfort to ye," Sir Marcus said suddenly, eyes
fixed on the decanter, "he's dead."

"You're sure?" Jamie's tone was unreadable.

"I dinna see how anybody could live after bein' trampled
flat by thirty half-ton beasts. He peeked out into the corridor
to see what was causin' the noise, then tried to go back when
he saw. A horn caught him by the sleeve and pulled him out,
and I saw him go down next to the wall. Sir Fletcher an' I
were on the stair, keepin' out o' the way. O' course Sir
Fletcher was rare excited, and sent some men after 'im, but
they couldna get anywhere near, with all the horns pokin' and
beasts shovin', and the torches shook down from the wall wi'
the ruckus. Christ, man, ye should ha' seen it!" Sir Marcus
hooted at the memory, clutching the decanter by the neck.
"Your wife's a rare lass, and no mistake, lad!" Snorting, he

poured out another glass and gulped, choking a bit as the laugh interfered with the swallow.

"Anyway," he resumed, pounding himself on the chest, "by the time we'd cleared the cattle out, there was no much left but a rag doll rolled in blood. Sir Fletcher's men carried him awa', but if he was still livin' then, he didna last long. A bit more, lad?"

"Aye, thanks."

There was a short silence, broken by Jamie. "No, I canna say it's much comfort to me, but thank ye for tellin' me." Sir Marcus looked at him shrewdly.

"Mmphm. Ye're no goin' to forget it," he said abruptly. "Don't bother to try. If ye can, let it heal like the rest o' your wounds. Don't pick at it, and it'll mend clean." The old warrior held up a knotted forearm, from which the sleeve had been pushed back during his ministrations, to show the scar of a jagged tear running from elbow to wrist. "Scars are nothin' to trouble ye."

"Aye, well. Some scars, maybe." Apparently reminded of something, Jamie struggled to turn onto his side. Sir Marcus set down his glass with an exclamation.

"Here, lad, be careful! Ye'll get a rib-end through the lung, next thing." He helped Jamie balance on his right elbow, wadding a blanket behind to prop him there.

"I need a wee knife," said Jamie, breathing heavily. "A sharp one, if it's handy." Without question, Sir Marcus lumbered to the gleaming French walnut sideboard and rummaged through the drawers with a prodigious clatter, emerging at last with a pearl-handled fruit knife. He thrust it into Jamie's sound left hand and sat down again with a grunt, resuming his glass.

"Ye don't think ye have enough scars?" he inquired. "Going to add a few more?"

"Just one." Jamie balanced precariously on one elbow, chin pressed on his chest as he awkwardly aimed the razor-sharp knife under his left breast. Sir Marcus's hand shot out, a bit unsteadily, and gripped Jamie's wrist.

"Best let me help ye, man. Ye'll fall on it in a moment." After a moment's pause, Jamie reluctantly surrendered the knife and lay back against the wadded blanket. He touched his chest an inch or two below the nipple.

"There." Sir Marcus reached to the sideboard and snagged a lamp, setting it on the stool he had vacated. At this distance, I couldn't see what he was peering at; it looked like a small red burn, roughly circular in shape. He took another deliberate pull at his whisky glass, then set it down next to the lamp and pressed the tip of the knife against Jamie's chest. I must have made an involuntary movement, because the Lady Annabelle clutched my sleeve with a murmured caution. The knife point pressed in and twisted suddenly, flicking away in the motion one uses to cut a bad spot out of a ripe peach. Jamie grunted, once, and a thin stream of red ran down the slope of his belly to stain the blanket. He rolled onto his stomach, stanching the wound against the mattress.

Sir Marcus laid down the fruit knife. "As soon as ye're able, man," he advised, "take your wife to bed, and let her comfort ye. Women like to do that," he said, grinning toward the shadowed doorway, "God knows why."

Lady Annabelle said softly, "Come away now, dear. He's better alone for a bit." I decided that Sir Marcus could manage the bandaging by himself, and stumbled after her up the narrow stair to my room.

I woke with a start from a dream of endless winding stairs, with horror lurking at the bottom. Tiredness dragged at my back and my legs ached, but I sat up in my borrowed nightdress and groped for the candle and flintbox. I felt uneasy, so far from Jamie. What if he needed me? Worse, what if the English did come, while he was alone below, unarmed? I pressed my face against the cold casement, reassured by the steady hiss of snow against the panes. While the storm continued, we were likely safe. I pulled on a bedgown, and picking up candle and dirk, made my way to the stair.

The house was quiet, save for the fire's crackle. Jamie was asleep, or at least had his eyes closed, face turned to the fire. I sat down on the hearthrug, quietly, so as not to wake him. This was the first time we had been alone together since those few desperate minutes in the dungeon of Wentworth Prison. It felt as though that were many years ago. I studied Jamie carefully, as though inspecting a stranger.

He seemed not too bad physically, all things considered, but I worried nonetheless. He had had enough whisky during the surgery to fell a draft horse, and a good bit of it was plainly still inside him, despite the retching.

Jamie was not my first hero. The men moved too quickly through the field hospital, as a rule, for the nurses to become well acquainted with them, but now and again you would see a man who talked too little or joked too much, who held himself more stiffly than pain and loneliness would account for.

And I knew, roughly, what could be done for them. If there was time, and if they were the kind who talked to keep the dark at bay, you sat with them and listened. If they were silent, you touched them often in passing, and watched for the unguarded moment, when you might draw them outside of themselves and hold them while they exorcised their demons. If there was time. And if there wasn't, then you jabbed them with morphine, and hoped they would manage to find someone else to listen, while you passed on to a man whose wounds were visible.

Jamie would talk to someone, sooner or later. There was time. But I hoped it wouldn't be me.

He was uncovered to the waist, and I leaned forward to examine his back. It was a remarkable sight. Barely a hand's thickness separated the welted cuts, inflicted with a regularity that boggled the mind. He must have stood like a guardsman while it was done. I stole a quick glance at his wrists—unmarked. He had kept his word then, not to struggle. And had stood unmoving through the ordeal, paying the ransom agreed on for my life.

I rubbed my eyes on my sleeve. He wouldn't thank me, I thought, for blubbering over his prostrate form. I shifted my weight with a soft rustle of skirts. He opened his eyes at the sound, but did not seem particularly haunted. He gave me a smile, faint and tired, but a real one. I opened my mouth, and suddenly realized I had no idea what to say to him. Thanks were impossible. "How do you feel?" was ridiculous; obviously he felt like hell. While I considered, he spoke first.

"Claire? Are you all right, love?"

"Am *I* all right? My God, Jamie!" Tears stung my eyelids and I blinked hard, sniffing. He raised his good hand slowly, as though it were weighted with chains, and stroked my hair. He drew me toward him, but I pulled away, conscious for the first time what I must look like, face scratched and covered with tree sap, hair stiff with blotches of various unmentionable substances.

"Come here," he said. "I want to hold ye a moment."

"But I'm covered with blood and vomit," I protested, making a vain effort to tidy my hair.

He wheezed, the faint exhalation that was all his broken ribs would permit in the way of laughter. "Mother of God, Sassenach, it's my blood and my vomit. Come here."

His arm was comforting around my shoulders. I rested my head on the pillow next to his, and we sat in silence by the fire, drawing strength and peace from one another. His fingers gently touched the small wound under my jaw.

"I did not think ever to see ye again, Sassenach." His voice was low and a bit hoarse from whisky and screaming. "I'm glad you're here."

I sat up. "Not see me again! Why? Did you think I wouldn't get you out?"

He smiled, one-sided. "Weel, no, I didn't expect ye would. I thought if I said so, though, ye might get stubborn and refuse to go."

"*Me* get stubborn!" I said indignantly. "Look who's talking!"

There was a pause, which grew slightly awkward. There were things I should ask, necessary from the medical point of view, but rather touchy from the personal aspect. Finally, I settled for "How do you feel?"

His eyes were closed, shadowed and sunken in the candlelight, but the lines of the broad back were tense under the bandages. The wide, bruised mouth twitched, somewhere between a smile and a grimace.

"I don't know, Sassenach. I've never felt like this. I seem to want to do a number of things, all at once, but my mind's at war wi' me, and my body's turned traitor. I want to get out of here at once, and run as fast and as far as I can. I want to hit someone. God, I want to hit someone! I want to burn Wentworth Prison to the ground. I want to sleep."

"Stone doesn't burn," I said practically. "Maybe you'd better sleep, instead."

His good hand groped for mine, and found it, and the mouth relaxed somewhat, though his eyes stayed closed.

"I want to hold you hard to me and kiss you, and never let you go. I want to take you to my bed and use you like a whore, 'til I forget that I exist. And I want to put my head in your lap and weep like a child."

The mouth turned up at one corner, and a blue eye opened slitwise.

"Unfortunately," he said, "I can't do any but the last of those without fainting or being sick again."

"Well, then, I suppose you'll just have to settle for that, and put the rest under the heading of future business," I said, laughing a little.

It took a bit of shifting, and he nearly was sick again, but at last I was seated on his cot, my back against the wall, and his head resting on my thigh.

"What was it Sir Marcus cut from your breast?" I asked. "A brand?" I said softly, as he gave me no reply. The bright head moved slightly in affirmation.

"A signet, with his initials." Jamie laughed shortly. "It's enough I'll carry his marks for the rest of my life, without letting him sign me, like a bloody painting."

His head lay heavy on my thigh and his breathing eased at last in drowsy exhalations. The white bandages on his hand were ghostly against the dark blanket. I gently traced a burn mark on his shoulder, gleaming faintly with sweet oil.

"Jamie?"

"Mmm?"

"Are you badly hurt?" Awake, he glanced from his bandaged hand to my face. His eyes closed and he began to shake. Alarmed, I thought I had triggered some unbearable memory, until I realized that he was laughing, hard enough to force tears from the corners of his eyes.

"Sassenach," he said at length, gasping, "I've maybe six square inches of skin left that are not bruised, burned, or cut. Am I *hurt*?" And he shook again, making the felted mattress rustle and squeak.

Somewhat crossly, I said, "I *meant*—" but he stopped me by putting his good hand over mine and bringing it to his lips.

"I know what ye meant, Sassenach," he said, turning his head to look up at me. "Never worry, the six inches that are left are all between my legs."

I appreciated the effort it took to make the joke, feeble as it was. I slapped his mouth lightly. "You're drunk, James Fraser," I said. I paused a moment. "Six, eh?"

"Aye, well. Maybe seven, then. Oh, God, Sassenach, dinna make me laugh again, my ribs won't stand it." I wiped his eyes with a fold of my skirt and fed him a sip of water, holding his head up with my knee.

"That isn't what I meant, anyway," I said.

Serious then, he reached for my hand again and squeezed it.

"I know," he said. "Ye needna be delicate about it." He drew a cautious breath, and winced at the results. "I was right, it did hurt less than flogging." He closed his eyes. "But it was much less enjoyable." A quick flash of bitter humor stirred one corner of his mouth. "At least I'll not be costive for a bit." I flinched, and he gritted his teeth, breathing in short, reedy gasps.

"I'm sorry, Sassenach. I . . . didna think I'd mind it so much. What you mean—that—it's all right. I'm not damaged."

I made an effort to keep my own voice steady and matter-of-fact. "You don't have to tell me about it, if you don't want to. If it might ease you, though . . ." My voice trailed off in embarrassed silence.

"I don't *want* to." His voice was suddenly bitter and emphatic. "I don't want ever to think about it again, but short of cutting my throat, I think I have not got a choice about it. Nay, lass, I dinna want to tell ye about it, any more than ye want to hear it . . . but I think I am going to have to drag it all out before it chokes me." The words came out now in a burst of bitterness.

"He wanted me to crawl and beg, and by Christ, I did so. I told ye once, Sassenach, ye can break anyone if you're willing to hurt them enough. Well, he was willing. He made me crawl, and he made me beg; he made me do worse things than that, and before the end he made me want verra badly to be dead."

He was silent for a long moment, looking into the fire, then heaved a deep sigh, grimacing at the pain.

"I wish ye could ease me, Sassenach, I do wish it most fervently, for I've little of ease in me now. But it's not like a poisoned thorn, where if ye found the right grip, ye could draw it clean out." His good hand rested on my knee. He flexed the fingers and spread them flat, ruddy in the firelight. "It's not even like a brokenness anywhere. If ye could mend it bit by bit, like ye did my hand, I'd stand the pain gladly." He bunched the fingers into a fist and rested it on my leg, frowning at it.

"It's . . . difficult to explain. It's . . . it's like . . . I think it's as though everyone has a small place inside themselves, maybe, a private bit that they keep to themselves. It's like a little fortress, where the most private part of you lives— maybe it's your soul, maybe just that bit that makes you yourself and not anyone else." His tongue probed his swollen lip unconsciously as he thought.

"You don't show that bit of yourself to anyone, usually, unless sometimes to someone that ye love greatly." The hand relaxed, curling around my knee. Jamie's eyes were closed again, lids sealed against the light.

"Now, it's like . . . like my own fortress has been blown up with gunpowder—there's nothing left of it but ashes and a smoking rooftree, and the little naked thing that lived there once is out in the open, squeaking and whimpering in fear, tryin' to hide itself under a blade of grass or a bit o' leaf, but . . . but not . . . makin' m-much of a job of it." His voice broke, and he turned his head so that his face was hidden in my skirt. Helpless, I could do nothing but stroke his hair.

He suddenly raised his head, face strained as though it

would break apart along the seams of the bones. "I've been close to death a few times, Claire, but I've never really *wanted* to die. This time I did. I . . ." His voice cracked and he stopped speaking, clutching my knee hard. When he spoke again, his voice was high and oddly breathless, as though he had been running a long way.

"Claire, will you—I just—Claire, hold on to me. If I start to shake again now, I canna stop it. Claire, hold me!" He was in fact beginning to tremble violently, the shivering making him moan as it caught the splintered ribs. I was afraid to hurt him, but more afraid to let the shaking go on.

I crouched over him, wrapped my arms around his shoulders and held on as tightly as I could, rocking to and fro as though the comforting rhythm might break the racking spasms. I got one hand on the back of his neck and dug my fingers deep into the pillared muscles, willing the clenching to relax as I massaged the deep groove at the base of the skull. Finally the trembling eased, and his head fell forward onto my thigh, exhausted.

"I'm sorry," he said a minute later, in his normal voice. "I didna mean to go on so. The truth is I do hurt verra bad, and I am most awfully damn drunk. I'm no in much control of mysel'." For a Scot to admit, even privately, to being drunk, was some indication, I thought, of just how badly he did hurt.

"You need sleep," I said softly, still rubbing the back of his neck. "You need it badly." I used my fingers as best I could, gentling and pressing as Old Alec had showed me, and managed to ease him back into drowsiness.

"I'm cold," he murmured. There was a good fire, and several blankets on the bed, but his fingers were chilly to the touch.

"You're in shock," I said practically. "You've lost the hell of a lot of blood." I looked around, but MacRannochs and servants alike had all disappeared to their own beds. Murtagh, I assumed, was still out in the snow, keeping an eye out in the direction of Wentworth in case of pursuit. With a mental shrug for anyone's opinion of the proprieties, I stood up, stripped off the nightdress, and crawled under the blankets.

As gently as possible, I eased against him, giving him my

warmth. He turned his face into my shoulder like a small boy. I stroked his hair, gentling him, rubbing the ridged columns of muscle at the back of his neck, avoiding the raw places. "Lay your head, then, man," I said, remembering Jenny and her boy.

Jamie gave a small grunt of amusement. "That's what my mother used to say to me," he murmured. "When I was a bairn."

"Sassenach," he said against my shoulder, a moment later.

"Mm?"

"Who in God's name is John Wayne?"

"You are," I said. "Go to sleep."

37

Escape

his color was better in the morning, though the bruises had darkened through the night and now mottled a good part of his face. He sighed deeply, then stiffened with a groan and let his breath out much more cautiously.

"How do you feel?" I laid a hand on his head. Cool and damp. No fever, thank God.

He grimaced, eyes still closed. "Sassenach, if I've got one, it hurts." He extended his good hand, groping. "Help me up; I'm stiff as pudding."

The snow stopped at mid-morning. The sky was still grey as wool, threatening further flurries, but the threat of search from Wentworth was greater yet, so we set out from Eldridge Manor just before noon, heavily cloaked against the weather. Murtagh and Jamie bristled with arms beneath their cloaks. I carried nothing but my dagger, and that well hidden. Much against my own will, I was to pose as a kidnapped English hostage, should the worst happen.

"But they've seen me at the prison," I had argued. "Sir Fletcher already knows who I am."

"Aye." Murtagh was carefully loading the pistols, an array of balls, wadding, powder, patches, rods, and pouches neatly spread on Lady Annabelle's polished table, but looked up to nail me with a black glance. "That's just the point, lass. We must keep ye out o' Wentworth, no matter what. Do no one any good to have ye in there along wi' us."

He rammed a short rod down the mouth of a scroll-butted dag, punching the wad into place with hard, economical strokes. "Sir Fletcher willna be doin' his own huntin', not on a day like this. Any Redcoats we meet will likely not know ye. If we're found out, ye mun say we forced ye along wi' us unwillin', and convince the Redcoats ye've nothin' to do wi' a pair o' Scottish scalawags like me an' yon ragtag." He nodded at Jamie, balancing gingerly on a stool with a bowl of warm bread and milk.

Sir Marcus and I had padded Jamie's hips and thighs as thickly as we could with linen bandages under a pair of worn breeches and hose, dark in color to hide any telltale blood spots that might seep through. Lady Annabelle had split one of her husband's shirts down the back to accommodate the breadth of Jamie's shoulders and the thickness of the bandage across them. Even so, the shirt would not meet across the front, and the ends of the strapping around his chest peeked through. He had refused to comb his hair, on grounds that even his scalp was sore, and he looked a wild and woolly sight, red spikes sticking up above a swollen purple face with one eye squeezed disreputably shut.

"If ye're taken," Sir Marcus chipped in, "tell them ye're a guest of mine, kidnapped while riding near the estate. Make them bring ye to Eldridge for me to identify. That should convince 'em. We'll tell 'em you're a friend of Annabelle's, from London."

"And then get you safely out of here before Sir Fletcher comes round to offer his regards," Annabelle added, practically.

Sir Marcus had offered us Hector and Absalom as escorts, but Murtagh pointed out that this would certainly implicate Eldridge, should we meet any English soldiers. So there were only the three of us, bundled against the cold, on the road toward Dingwall. I carried a fat purse and a note from the Master of Eldridge, one or both of which should ensure our passage across the Channel.

It was hard going through the snow. Less than a foot deep,

the treacherous white stuff hid rocks, holes, and other obstacles, making footing for the horses slippery and dangerous.
Clods of snow and mud flew up with each step, spattering
bellies and hocks, and clouds of horse-breath vanished steaming into the frozen air.

Murtagh led the way, following the faint depression that
marked the road. I rode beside Jamie, to help if he should lose
consciousness, though he was, at his own insistence, tied to
his horse. Only his left hand was free, resting on the pistol
looped to the saddle bow, concealed under his cloak.

We passed a few scattered bothies, smoke rising from the
thatched roofs, but the inhabitants and their beasts seemed all
within, secured against the cold. Here and there a lone man
passed from cot to shed, carrying buckets or hay, but the road
was deserted for the most part.

Two miles from Eldridge we passed under the shadow of
Wentworth Castle, a grim bulk set in the hillside. The road
was trampled here; traffic in and out did not cease even in the
worst of weathers.

Our passage had been timed to coincide with the midday
meal, in hopes that the sentries would be immersed in their
pasties and ale. We plodded slowly past the short road that led
to the gate, just a party of travelers with the ill-luck to be
abroad on such a miserable day.

Once past the prison, we paused to rest the horses for a
moment, in the shelter of a small pine grove. Murtagh bent to
peer under the slouch hat that masked Jamie's telltale hair.

"All right, lad? Ye're quiet."

Jamie lifted his head. His face was pale, and trickles of sweat
ran down his neck, despite the icy wind, but he managed a
half-hearted grin.

"I'll do."

"How do you feel?" I asked, anxious. He sat slumped in
the saddle, without much sign of his usual erect grace. I got
the other half of the grin.

"I've been trying to decide which hurts worst—my ribs, my
hand, or my arse. Tryin' to choose among them keeps my
mind off my back." He took a deep pull from the flask that Sir
Marcus had thoughtfully provided, shuddered, and passed it

to me. It was a good deal better than the raw spirit I had drunk on the road to Leoch, but every bit as potent. We rode on, a small cheerful fire burning in my stomach.

The horses were laboring up a modest slope, snow spurting from their hooves, when I saw Murtagh's head jerk up. Following the direction of his gaze, I saw the Redcoat soldiers, four of them, mounted, at the top of the slope.

There was no help for it. We had been seen, and a shouted challenge echoed down the hill. There was no place to run. We were going to have to try to bluff it out. Without a backward glance, Murtagh spurred forward to meet them.

The corporal with the group was a middle-aged career soldier, erect in his winter greatcoat. He bowed politely to me, then turned his attention to Jamie.

"Your pardon, sir, madam. We have orders to stop all parties traveling this road, to inquire for details of prisoners lately escaped from Wentworth Prison."

Prisoners. So I *had* managed to release more than Jamie yesterday. I was glad of it, on various grounds. For one, they would dilute the search somewhat. Four against three was better odds than we might have expected.

Jamie didn't reply, but slouched farther forward, letting his head loll. I could see the gleam of his eyes beneath the hat brim; he wasn't unconscious. These must be men he knew; his voice would be recognized. Murtagh was edging his horse forward, between me and the soldiers.

"Aye, the master's a bit the worse for illness, sir, as ye can see," he said, obsequiously tugging his forelock. "Perhaps ye could point out the road toward Ballagh to me? I'm no convinced that we're headed right."

I wondered what on earth he was up to, until I caught his eye. His glance flickered back and down, then back to the soldier, so fast that the soldier would assume him to have been listening with rapt attention all the time. Was Jamie in danger of falling from the saddle? Pretending to adjust my bonnet, I glanced casually over my shoulder in the direction he had indicated, and nearly froze with shock.

Jamie was sitting upright, head bent to shadow his face. But blood was dripping gently from the tip of the stirrup under his foot, pocking the snow with gently steaming red pits.

Murtagh, pretending vast stupidity, had succeeded in drawing the soldiers ahead to the crest of the hill, so that they could point out that the road to Dingwall was the only road in sight, which ran down the other side of the hill. It ran through Ballagh, and straight toward the coast, still three miles away.

I slid hastily to the ground, yanking feverishly at my horse's girth strap. Floundering through the drifts, I kicked enough snow under the belly of Jamie's horse to obliterate the telltale drops. A quick look showed the soldiers apparently still engaged in argument with Murtagh, though one of them glanced down the hill at us, as though to ensure that we had not wandered off. I gave a cheery wave, then as soon as the soldier turned his head, stooped and ripped off one of the three petticoats I was wearing. I whipped Jamie's cloak aside and stuffed the wadded petticoat under his thigh, ignoring his exclamation of pain. The cloak flipped back in place just in time for me to dash back to my own horse and be discovered fiddling with the girth when Murtagh and the Englishmen arrived.

"It seems to have worked its way loose," I explained guilelessly, batting my eyes at the nearest redcoat.

"Oh? And why are you not helping the lady?" he said to Jamie.

"My husband's not well," I said. "I can manage it myself, thank you."

The corporal seemed interested. "Sick, eh? What's the matter with you, then?" He urged his beast forward, staring closely under the slouch hat at Jamie's pale face. "Don't look well, I'll say that much. Take your hat off, fellow. What's the matter with your face?"

Jamie shot him through the folds of his cloak. The redcoat was no more than six feet away, and he toppled sideways out of the saddle before the stain on his chest grew bigger than my hand.

Murtagh had a pistol in each hand before the corporal hit the ground. One bullet went wild as his horse shied away

from the sudden noise and movement. The second found its
mark, ripping through a soldier's upper arm leaving a tuft of
shredded fabric flapping from a rapidly reddening sleeve. The
man kept his saddle, though, and was tugging at his saber,
one-handed, as Murtagh plunged beneath his cloak for fresh
weapons.

One of the two remaining soldiers turned his horse, slipping in the snow, and spurred away, back toward the prison,
presumably in search of help.

"Claire!" The shout came from above. I looked up, startled, to see Jamie waving after the fleeing figure. "Stop him!"
He had time to toss me a second pistol, then turned back,
drawing his sword to meet the charge of the fourth soldier.

My horse was battle-trained; his ears were laid flat against
his head and he stamped and pawed at the noise, but he
hadn't run at the sound of gunshots, and he stood his ground
as I groped for the saddle iron. Glad to be leaving the fight
behind, he dug in as soon as I was mounted, and we made off
at good speed after the fleeing figure.

The snow hampered our going nearly as much as his, but
mine was the better horse, and we had the advantage of the
rough path the soldier's flight had plowed through the fresh
snow. We gained slowly on him, but I could see that it
wouldn't be enough. He had a rise ahead of him, though; if I
cut to the right, perhaps I could make better time on the flat
and meet him coming down the other side. I jerked the rein
and leaned hard to keep my seat as the horse slithered into a
messy turn, found his feet and plunged ahead.

I didn't quite catch him up, but I had cut the distance
between us to no more than ten yards. Given unlimited distance, I could likely catch him, but I didn't have that luxury;
the prison wall loomed less than a mile ahead. Much closer,
and we would be seen from the walls.

I pulled up and slid off. Battle-trained or not, I didn't know
what the horse would do if I fired a pistol from his back. Even
if he stood like a statue, I didn't think my own aim was up to
it. I knelt in the snow, bracing my elbow on my knee, the gun
across my forearm as Jamie had shown me. "Brace it here, aim
there, fire it *here*," he had said. I did.

Much to my amazement, I hit the fleeing horse. It went into a skid, went to one knee and rolled in a flurry of snow and legs. My arm was numb from the pistol's recoil; I stood rubbing it, watching the fallen soldier.

He was injured; he struggled to rise, then fell back in the snow. His horse, bleeding from the shoulder, stumbled away, reins dangling.

I didn't realize until later what I had been thinking, but I knew when I approached him that I could not let him live. Near as we were to the prison, and with other patrols out seeking escaped prisoners, he was sure to be found before too long. And if he were found alive, he could not only describe us—so much for our hostage story in that case!—but tell which way we were traveling. We had still three miles to go to the coast; two hours' travel in the heavy snow. And a boat to find, once there. I simply could not take the chance of allowing him to tell anyone about us.

He struggled to his elbows as I approached. His eyes widened in surprise as he saw me, then relaxed. I was a woman. He wasn't afraid of me.

A more experienced man might have been apprehensive, my sex notwithstanding, but this was a boy. No more than sixteen, I thought, with a sense of sick shock. His spotty cheeks still held the last round curves of childhood, though his upper lip sported the fuzz of a hopeful mustache.

He opened his mouth, but only groaned in pain. He pressed his hand to his side, and I could see blood soaking through his tunic and coat. Internal injuries, then; the horse must have rolled on him.

It was possible, I thought, that he would die in any case. But that wasn't something I could count on.

The dirk in my right hand was hidden under my cloak. I laid my left hand on his head. Just so I had touched the heads of hundreds of men, comforting, examining, steadying them for whatever lay ahead. And they had looked up at me much as this boy did; with hope and trust.

I couldn't cut his throat. I sank to my knees beside him, and turned his head gently away from me. Rupert's techniques for swift killing had all assumed resistance. There was no resistance as I bent his head forward, as far as I could, and plunged the dirk into his neck at the base of his skull.

I left him lying facedown in the snow and went to join the others.

———

Our unwieldy cargo stowed under blankets on a bench below, Murtagh and I met on the *Cristabel*'s deck to survey the storm-tossed skies.

"Looks like a fair, steady wind," I said hopefully, holding a wet finger aloft.

Murtagh gloomily scanned the clouds, hanging black-bellied over the harbor, their freight of snow wastefully melting into the frigid waves. "Aye, well. We'll hope for a smooth crossing. If not, we'll likely get there wi' a corpse on our hands."

Half an hour later, launched on the choppy waters of the English Channel, I discovered what he had meant by this remark.

"Seasick?" I said incredulously. "Scotsmen aren't seasick!"

Murtagh was testy. "Then mayhap he's a red-heided Hottentot. All I know is he's green as a rotten fish and pukin' his guts out. Are ye goin' to come down and help me stop him puttin' his ribs out through his chest?"

"Damn it," I said to Murtagh, as we hung over the rail for fresh air during a brief hiatus in the unpleasantness belowdecks, "if he knows he's seasick, why in the name of God did he insist on a boat?"

The basilisk stare was unwinking. "Because he knows bluidy well we'd never make it overland wi' him in the state he's in, and he'd no stay at Eldridge for fear o' bringin' the English down on MacRannoch."

"So he's going to kill himself quietly at sea, instead," I said bitterly.

"Aye. He figures this way he'll only kill himself, and no take anyone else along wi' him. Unselfish, see. Nothin' quiet about it, though," added Murtagh, heading for the companionway in response to unmistakable sounds from below.

"Congratulations," I said to Jamie an hour or two later,

pushing dank wisps away from my cheeks and forehead. "I believe you're going to make medical history by being the only documented person ever actually to die of seasickness."

"Oh, good," he mumbled into the wreck of pillows and blankets, "I'd hate to think it was all a waste." He heaved himself suddenly to one side. "God, here it comes again." Murtagh and I sprang once more to our stations. The job of holding a large man immobile while he succumbs to merciless spasms of retching is not one for the weak.

Afterward, I took his pulse yet again, and rested a hand briefly on the clammy forehead. Murtagh read my face, and followed me unspeaking up the gangway to the top deck. "He's no doin' verra weel, is he?" he said quietly.

"I don't know," I said helplessly, shaking out my sweat-drenched hair in the sharp wind. "I've honestly never heard of anyone dying of seasickness, but he's bringing up blood now." The little man's hands tightened on the rail, knuckles knifing through the sun-speckled skin. "I don't know if he's damaged himself internally with the sharp rib ends, or if it's just that his stomach is raw with the vomiting. Either way, it's not a good sign. And his pulse is much weaker, and irregular. It's a strain on his heart, you know."

"He's a heart like a lion." It was quietly said, and I wasn't sure I'd heard it at first. It might only have been the salt wind making the tears stand in his eyes. He turned abruptly to me. "And a heid like an ox. Have ye any o' that laudanum left that Lady Annabelle gave ye?"

"Yes, all of it. He wouldn't take it; doesn't want to sleep, he said."

"Aye, well. For most folk, what they want and what they get are no the same thing; I dinna see why he should be any different. Come on."

I followed him anxiously back belowdecks. "I don't think he can keep it down."

"Leave that to me. Get the bottle and help me sit him up."

Jamie was half-unconscious as it was, an unwieldy burden who protested being manhandled upright against the bulkhead. "I'm going to die," he said weakly but precisely, "and the sooner the better. Go away and let me do it in peace."

Taking firm hold of Jamie's blazing hair, Murtagh forced his head up and applied the flask to his lips. "Swallow this, me bonny wee dormouse, or I'll break yer neck. And forbye ye'll keep it down, too. I'm goin' to hold shut yer nose and yer mouth; if ye bring it up, it comes out yer ears."

By the concerted force of our wills, we transferred the contents of the flask slowly but inexorably into the young laird of Lallybroch. Choking and gagging, Jamie manfully drank as much as he could manage before subsiding, green-faced and gasping, against the bulkhead. Murtagh forestalled each threatened explosion of nausea by vicious nose-pinching, an expedient not uniformly successful, but one which allowed a gradual accumulation of the opiate in the patient's bloodstream. At length we laid him slack on the bed, the vivid flames of hair, brows, and lashes the only color on the pillow.

Murtagh came up beside me on deck a bit later. "Look," I said pointing. The dim light of sunset, shining in fugitive rays beneath the clouds, gilded the rocks of the French coast ahead. "The master says we'll be ashore in three or four hours."

"And not before time," said my companion, wiping lank brown hair out of his eyes. He turned to me, and gave me the closest thing I had ever seen to a smile on his dour countenance.

And so at length, following the prostrate body of our charge, laid on a board between two stout monks, we passed through the looming gates of the Abbey of Ste. Anne de Beaupré.

38

The Abbey

The abbey was an enormous twelfth-century edifice, walled to resist both the smashing of sea storms and the onslaughts of land-based invaders. Now, in more peaceful times, its gates stood open to allow easy traffic with the nearby village, and the small stone cells of its guest wing had been softened by the addition of tapestries and comfortable furniture.

I rose from the padded chair in my own chamber, not sure exactly how one greeted an abbot; did one kneel and kiss his ring, or was that only for Popes? I settled for a respectful curtsy.

Jamie's slanted cat-eyes *did* come from the Fraser side. Likewise the solid jaw, though the one facing me was somewhat obscured by black beard.

Abbot Alexander had his nephew's wide mouth as well, though he looked as though he smiled somewhat less with it. The slanted blue eyes remained cool and speculative as he greeted me with a pleasant, warm smile. He was a good deal shorter than Jamie, about my height, and stocky. He wore the robe of a priest, but walked with a warrior's stride. I thought it likely he had been both in his time.

"You are welcome, *ma nièce*," he said, inclining his head. I was a little startled at the greeting, but bowed back.

"I'm grateful for your hospitality," I said, meaning it. "Have—have you seen Jamie?" The monks had taken Jamie away to be bathed, a process in which I thought I had better not assist.

The Abbot nodded. "Oh, aye," he said, a faint Scots accent showing through the cultured English. "I've seen him. I've set Brother Ambrose to tend his wounds." I must have looked dubious at this, for he said, a bit dryly, "Do not worry, madame; Brother Ambrose is most competent." He looked me over with an air of frank appraisal disturbingly like that of his nephew.

"Murtagh said that you are an accomplished physician yourself."

"I am," I said bluntly.

This provoked a real smile. "I see that you do not suffer from the sin of false modesty," he observed.

"I have others," I said, smiling back.

"So do we all," he said. "Brother Ambrose will be eager to converse with you, I'm sure."

"Has Murtagh told you . . . what happened?" I asked hesitantly.

The wide mouth tightened. "He has. So far as he *knows* what happened." He waited, as though expecting further contributions from me, but I stayed silent.

It was clear that he would have liked to ask questions, but he was kind enough not to press me. Instead, he raised his hand in a gesture of benediction and dismissal.

"You are welcome," he said once more. "I will send a serving brother to bring you some food." He looked me over once more. "And some facilities for washing." He made the sign of the Cross over me, in farewell or possibly as an exorcism of filth, and left in a swirl of brown skirts.

Suddenly realizing how tired I was, I sank down on the bed, wondering whether I could stay awake long enough to both eat *and* wash. I was still wondering when my head hit the pillow.

◆

I was having a dreadful nightmare. Jamie was on the other side of a solid stone wall without a door. I could hear him screaming, over and over, but couldn't reach him. I pounded desperately on the wall, only to see my hands sink into the stone as if it were water.

"Ouch!" I sat up in the narrow cot, clutching the hand I had smashed against the unyielding wall next to my bed. I rocked back and forth, squeezing the throbbing hand between my thighs, then realized that the screaming was still going on.

It stopped abruptly as I ran into the hall. The door to Jamie's room was open, flickering lamplight flooding the corridor.

A monk I had not seen before was with Jamie, holding him tightly. A seepage of fresh blood stained the bandages on Jamie's back, and his shoulders shook as though with chill.

"A nightmare," the monk said in explanation, seeing me in the doorway. He relinquished Jamie into my arms, and went to the table for a cloth and the water jug.

Jamie was still trembling, and his face was glossy with sweat. His eyes were closed, and he breathed heavily, with a hoarse, gasping sound. The monk sat down beside me and began to swab his face with a gentle hand, smoothing the heavy, wet hair away from his temples.

"You would be his wife, of course," he said to me. "I think he'll be better presently."

The trembling did begin to ease within a minute or two, and Jamie opened his eyes with a sigh.

"I'm all right," he said. "Claire, I'm all right, now. But for God's sake, get rid of that stink!"

It was only then that I consciously noticed the scent in the room—a light, spicy, floral smell, so common a perfume that I had thought nothing of it. Lavender. A scent for soaps and toilet waters. I had last smelled it in the dungeons of Wentworth Prison, where it anointed the linen or the person of Captain Jonathan Randall.

The source of the scent was a small metal cup filled with herb-scented oil, suspended from a heavy, rose-bossed iron base and hung over a candle flame.

Meant to soothe the mind, its effects were plainly not as intended. Jamie was breathing more easily, sitting up by himself and holding the cup of water the monk had given him.

But his face was still white, and the corner of his mouth twitched uneasily.

I nodded at the Franciscan to do as he said, and the monk quickly muffled the hot cup of oil in a folded towel, then carried it away down the hall.

Jamie heaved a long sigh of relief, then winced, ribs hurting.

"You've opened up your back a bit," I said, turning him slightly to get at the bandages. "Not bad, though."

"I know. I must have rolled onto my back in my sleep." The thick wedge of folded blanket meant to keep him propped on one side had slipped to the floor. I retrieved it and laid it on the bed beside him.

"That's what made me dream, I think. I dreamt of being flogged." He shuddered, took a sip of the water, then handed me the cup. "I need something a bit stronger, if it's handy."

As though on cue, our helpful visitor came through the door with a jug of wine in one hand and a small flask of poppy syrup in the other.

"Alcohol or opium?" he asked Jamie with a smile, holding up the two flasks. "You may have your choice of oblivions."

"I'll have the wine, if ye please. I've had enough of dreams for one night," Jamie said, with a lopsided answering smile. He drank the wine slowly, as the Franciscan helped me to change the stained bandages, smoothing fresh marigold ointment over the wounds. Not until I had resettled Jamie for sleep, back firmly propped and coverlet drawn up, did the visitor turn to go.

Passing the bed, he bent over Jamie and sketched the sign of the Cross above his head. "Rest well," he said.

"Thank ye, Father." Jamie answered drowsily, clearly half-asleep already. Seeing that Jamie would likely not need me now until morning, I touched him on the shoulder in farewell and followed the visitor out into the corridor.

"Thank you," I said. "I'm most grateful for your help."

The monk waved a graceful hand, dismissing my thanks.

"I was pleased to be able to assist you," he said, and I noticed that he spoke excellent English, though with a faint

French accent. "I was passing through the guest wing on my way to the chapel of St. Giles when I heard the screaming."

I winced at the memory of that screaming, hoarse and dreadful, and hoped I would not hear it again. Glancing at the window at the end of the corridor, I saw no sign of dawn behind the shutter.

"To the chapel?" I said, surprised. "But I thought Matins were sung in the main church. And it's surely a bit early, in any case."

The Franciscan smiled. He was fairly young, perhaps in his early thirties, but his silky brown hair was threaded with grey. It was short and neatly tonsured and he had a brown beard, finely trimmed to a point that just skimmed the deep rolled collar of his habit.

"Very early, for Matins," he agreed. "I was on my way to the chapel because it is my turn for the perpetual adoration of the Blessed Sacrament at this hour." He glanced back into Jamie's room, where a clock candle marked the time as half past two.

"I'm very late," he said. "Brother Bartolome will be wanting his bed." Raising his hand, he quickly blessed me, turned on a sandaled heel, and was through the swinging door at the end of the corridor before I could muster wits enough to ask his name.

I stepped into the room and bent to check Jamie. He was asleep again, breathing lightly, with a slight frown creasing his brow. Experimentally, I ran my hand lightly over his hair. The frown eased a bit, and then resumed. I sighed and tucked the blankets more securely around him.

◆

I felt much better in the morning, but Jamie was holloweyed and queasy after the broken night. He emphatically rejected any suggestion of caudle or broth for breakfast, and snapped irritably at me when I tried to check the dressings on his hand.

"For Christ's sake, Claire, will ye no leave me alone! I dinna want to be poked at anymore!"

He yanked his hand away, scowling. I turned away without

speaking and went to busy myself with tidying the small pots and packets of medicines on the side table. I arranged them into small groups, sorted by function: marigold ointment and poplar balm for soothing, willowbark, cherry bark and chamomile for teas, St. John's wort, garlic, and yarrow for disinfection.

"Claire." I turned back, to find him sitting on the bed, looking at me with a shamefaced smile.

"I'm sorry, Sassenach. My bowels are griping, and I've a damn evil temper this morning. But I've no call to snarl at ye. D'ye forgive me?"

I crossed to him swiftly and hugged him lightly.

"You know there's nothing to forgive. But what do you mean, your bowels are griping?" Not for the first time, I reflected that intimacy and romance are not synonymous.

He grimaced, bending forward slightly and folding his arms over his abdomen. "It means," he said, "that I'd like ye to leave me to myself for a bit. If ye dinna mind?" I hastily complied with his request, and went to find my own breakfast.

Returning from the refectory a bit later, I spotted a trim figure in the black robes of a Franciscan, crossing the courtyard toward the cloister. I hurried to catch up with him.

"Father!" I called, and he turned, smiling when he saw me.

"Good morning," he said. "Madame Fraser; is that the name? And how is your husband this morning?"

"Better," I said, hoping it was true. "I wanted to thank you again for last night. You left before I could even ask your name."

Clear hazel eyes sparkled as he bowed to me, hand over his heart. "François Anselm Mericoeur d'Armagnac, madame," he said. "Or so I was born. Known now only as Father Anselm."

"Anselm of the Merry Heart?" I asked, smiling. He shrugged, a completely Gallic gesture, unchanged for centuries.

"One tries," he said, with an ironic twist of the mouth.

"I don't wish to keep you," I said, glancing toward the cloister. "I only wanted to thank you for your help."

"You do not detain me in the least, madame. I was delaying

going to my work, in fact; indulging most sinfully in idleness."

"What is your work?" I asked, intrigued. Plainly this man was a visitor to the monastery, his black Franciscan robes conspicuous as an inkblot among the brown of the Benedictines. There were several such visitors, or so Brother Polydore, one of the serving brothers, had told me. Most of them were scholars, here to consult the works stored in the abbey's renowned library. Anselm, it seemed, was one of these. He was, as he had been for several months, engaged in the translation of several works by Herodotus.

"Have you seen the library?" he asked. "Come, then," he said, seeing me shake my head. "It is really most impressive, and I am sure the Abbot your uncle would have no objection."

I was both curious to see the library, and reluctant to go back at once to the isolation of the guest wing, so I followed him without hesitation.

The library was beautiful, high-roofed, with soaring Gothic columns that joined in ogives in the multichambered roof. Full-length windows filled the spaces between columns, letting an abundance of light into the library. Most were of clear glass, but some had deceptively simple-looking stained-glass parables. Tiptoeing past the bent forms of studying monks, I paused to admire one of the Flight into Egypt.

Some of the bookshelves looked like those I was used to, the books nestling side by side. Other shelves held the books laid flat, to protect the ancient covers. There was even one glass-fronted bookshelf holding a number of rolled parchments. Overall, the library held a hushed exultation, as though the cherished volumes were all singing soundlessly within their covers. I left the library feeling soothed, and strolled slowly across the main courtyard with Father Anselm.

I tried again to thank him for his help the night before, but he shrugged off my thanks.

"Think nothing of it, my child. I hope that your husband is better today?"

"So do I," I said. Not wanting to dwell on that subject, I

asked, "What exactly is perpetual adoration? You said that was where you were going last night."

"You are not a Catholic?" he asked in surprise. "Ah, but I forgot, you are English. So of course, I suppose you would be Protestant."

"I'm not sure that I'm either one, in terms of belief," I said. "But technically, at least, I suppose I am a Catholic."

"Technically?" The smooth eyebrows shot up in astonishment. I hesitated, cautious after my experiences with Father Bain, but this man did not seem the sort to start waving crucifixes in my face.

"Well," I said, bending to pull a small weed from between the paving stones, "I was baptized as a Catholic. But my parents died when I was five, and I went to live with an uncle. Uncle Lambert was . . ." I paused, recalling Uncle Lambert's voracious appetite for knowledge, and that cheerfully objective cynicism that regarded all religion merely as one of the earmarks by which a culture could be cataloged. "Well, he was everything and nothing, I suppose, in terms of faith," I concluded. "Knew them all, believed in none. So nothing further was ever done about my religious training. And my . . . first husband was Catholic, but not very observant, I'm afraid. So I suppose I'm really rather a heathen."

I eyed him warily, but rather than being shocked by this revelation, he laughed heartily.

"Everything and nothing," he said, savoring the phrase. "I like that very much. But as for you, I am afraid not. Once a member of Holy Mother Church, you are eternally marked as her child. However little you know about your faith, you are as much a Catholic as our Holy Father the Pope." He glanced at the sky. It was cloudy, but the leaves of the alder bushes near the church hung still.

"The wind has dropped. I was going for a short stroll to clear my brain in the fresh air. Why do you not accompany me? You need air and exercise, and I can perhaps make the occasion spiritually beneficial as well, by enlightening you as to the ritual of Perpetual Adoration as we go."

"Three birds with one stone, eh?" I said dryly. But the

prospect of air, if not light, was enticing, and I went to fetch my cloak without demur.

With a glance at the form within, head bent in prayer, Anselm led me past the quiet darkness of the chapel entrance and down the cloister, out to the edge of the garden.

Beyond the possibility of disturbing the monks within the chapel, he said, "It's a very simple idea. You recall the Bible, and the story of Gethsemane, where Our Lord waited out the hours before His trial and crucifixion, and His friends, who should have borne Him company, all fell fast asleep?"

"Oh," I said, understanding all at once. "And He said 'Can you not watch with me one hour?' So that's what you're doing—watching with Him for that hour—to make up for it." I liked the idea, and the darkness of the chapel suddenly seemed inhabited and comforting.

"Oui, madame," he agreed. "Very simple. We take it in turns to watch, and the Blessed Sacrament on the altar here is never left alone."

"Isn't it difficult, staying awake?" I asked curiously. "Or do you always watch at night?"

He nodded, a light breeze lifting the silky brown hair. The patch of his tonsure needed shaving; short bristly hairs covered it like moss.

"Each watcher chooses the time that suits him best. For me, that is two o'clock in the morning." He glanced at me, hesitating, as though wondering how I would take what he was about to say.

"For me, in that moment . . ." He paused. "It's as though time has stopped. All the humors of the body, all the blood and bile and vapors that make a man; it's as though just at once all of them are working in perfect harmony." He smiled. His teeth were slightly crooked, the only defect in his otherwise perfect appearance.

"Or as though they've stopped altogether. I often wonder whether that moment is the same as the moment of birth, or of death. I know that its timing is different for each man . . . or woman, I suppose," he added, with a courteous nod to me.

"But just then, for that fraction of time, it seems as though all things are possible. You can look across the limitations of your own life, and see that they are really nothing. In that moment when time stops, it is as though you know you could undertake any venture, complete it and come back to yourself, to find the world unchanged, and everything just as you left it a moment before. And it's as though . . ." He hesitated for a moment, carefully choosing words.

"As though, knowing that everything is possible, suddenly nothing is necessary."

"But . . . do you actually *do* anything?" I asked. "Er, pray, I mean?"

"I? Well," he said slowly, "I sit, and I look at Him." A wide smile stretched the fine-drawn lips. ""And He looks at me."

—◆—

Jamie was sitting up when I returned to the room, and essayed a short trip up and down the hall, leaning on my shoulder. But the effort left him pale and sweating, and he lay down without protest when I turned back the coverlet for him.

I offered him a little broth and milk, but he shook his head wearily. "I've no appetite, Sassenach. If I take anything, I think I shall be sick again."

I didn't press the matter, but took the broth away in silence.

At dinner I was more insistent, and succeeded in persuading him to try a few spoonfuls of soup. He managed quite a bit of it, but didn't manage to keep it down.

"I'm sorry, Sassenach," he said, afterward. "I'm disgusting."

"It doesn't matter, Jamie, and you are not disgusting." I set the basin outside the door and sat down beside him, smoothing back the tumbled hair from his brow.

"Don't worry. It's only that your stomach is still irritated from the seasickness. Perhaps I've pushed you too fast to eat. Let it rest and heal."

He closed his eyes, sighing under my hand.

"I'll be all right," he said, without interest. "What did ye do today, Sassenach?"

He was obviously restless and uncomfortable, but eased a bit as I told him about my explorations of the day; the library, the chapel, the winepress, and finally, the herb garden, where I had at last met the famous Brother Ambrose.

"He's amazing," I said enthusiastically. "Oh, but I forgot, you've met him." Brother Ambrose was tall—even taller than Jamie—and cadaverous, with the long, drooping face of a basset hound. And ten long, skinny fingers, every one of them bright green.

"He seems to be able to make *anything* grow," I said. "He's got all the normal herbs there, and a greenhouse so tiny that he can't even stand up straight inside it, with things that shouldn't grow at this season, or shouldn't grow in this part of the world, or just shouldn't grow. Not to mention the imported spices and drugs."

The mention of drugs reminded me of the night before, and I glanced out the window. The winter twilight set in early, and it was already full dark outside, the lanterns of the monks who tended the stables and outdoor work bobbing to and fro as they passed on their rounds.

"It's getting dark. Do you think you can sleep by yourself? Brother Ambrose has a few things that might help."

His eyes were smudged with tiredness, but he shook his head.

"No, Sassenach. I dinna want anything. If I fall asleep . . . no, I think I'll read for a bit." Anselm had brought him a selection of philosophical and historical works from the library, and he stretched out a hand for a copy of Tacitus that lay on the table.

"You need sleep, Jamie," I said gently, watching him. He opened the book before him, propped on the pillow, but continued to stare at the wall above it.

"I didna tell ye what I dreamed," he said suddenly.

"You said you dreamed of being flogged." I didn't like the look on his face; already pale under the bruises, it was lightly sheened with dampness.

"That's right. I could look up and see the ropes, cutting into my wrists. My hands had gone almost black, and the rope scraped bone when I moved. I had my face pressed against the post. Then I could feel the lead plummets at the ends of the lashes, cutting through the flesh of my shoulders.

"The lashes kept coming, long past when they should have stopped, and I realized that he didn't mean to stop. The tips of the cords were biting out small chunks of my flesh. The blood . . . my blood was running down my sides and my back, soaking into my kilt. I was very cold.

"Then I looked up again, and I could see that the flesh had begun to fall away from my hands, and the bones of my fingers were scrabbling at the wood, leaving long, raw scratches behind. The bones of my arms were bare, and only the ropes were holding them together. I think that's when I began to scream.

"I could hear a strange rattling noise when he hit me, and after a time I realized what it was. He'd stripped all the flesh off my bones, and the plummets of the whip were rattling on my dry rib bones. And I knew that I was dead, but it didn't matter. He would go on and on, and it would never stop, he would go on until I began to fall to pieces and crumble away from the post, and it would never stop, and . . ."

I moved to take hold of him and make him hush, but he had already stopped himself, gripping the edge of the book with his good hand. His teeth were set hard in the torn flesh of his lower lip.

"Jamie, I'll stay with you tonight," I said. "I can lay a pallet on the floor."

"No." Weak as he was, there was no mistaking the basic stubbornness. "I'll do best alone. And I'm not sleepy now. Do ye go and find your own supper, Sassenach. I'll . . . just read for a bit." He bent his head over the page. After a minute of helplessly watching him, I did as he said, and left.

◆───

I was becoming more and more worried by Jamie's condition. The nausea lingered; he ate almost nothing, and what he did eat seldom stayed with him. He grew paler and more listless, showing little interest in anything. He slept a great deal in the daytime, because of sleeping so little at night. Still, whatever his fears of dreaming, he would not allow me to share his chamber, so that his wakefulness need not impair my own rest.

Not wishing to hover over him, even if he would have allowed it, I spent much of my time in the herbarium or the drying shed with Brother Ambrose, or wandering idly through the Abbey's grounds, engaged in conversation with Father Anselm. He took the opportunity to engage in a gentle catechism, trying to instruct me in the basics of Catholicism, though I had assured him over and over of my basic agnosticism.

"Ma chère," he said at last, "do you recall the conditions necessary for the commission of sin that I told you yesterday?"

There was nothing wrong with my memory, whatever my moral shortcomings might be.

"First, that it be wrong, and secondly, that you give full consent to it," I parroted.

"That you give full consent to it," he repeated. "And that, *ma chère,* is the condition for grace to occur, as well." We were leaning on the fence of the abbey pigsty, watching several large brown hogs huddling together in the weak winter sun. He turned his head, resting his face on his forearms, folded on the fence rail.

"I don't see how I can," I protested. "Surely grace is something you have or you don't. I mean"—I hesitated, not wishing to seem rude—"to you, the thing on the altar in the chapel is God. To me, it's a bit of bread, no matter how lovely the holder it's in."

He sighed with impatience and straightened up, stretching his back.

"I have observed, on my way to my nightly watch, that your husband does not sleep well," he said. "And consequently, neither do you. Since you are not asleep in any case, I invite you to come with me tonight. Join me in the chapel for an hour."

I eyed him narrowly. "Why?"

He shrugged. "Why not?"

I had no difficulty in waking up for my appointment with Anselm, largely because I had not been asleep. Neither had Jamie. Whenever I poked my head out into the corridor, I could see the flicker of candlelight from the half-open door of his room, and hear the flip of pages and the occasional grunt of discomfort as he shifted his position.

Unable to rest, I had not bothered to undress, and so was ready when a tap at my door announced Anselm's presence.

The monastery was quiet, in the way that all large institutions grow quiet at night; the rapid pulse of the day's activities has dropped, but the heartbeat goes on, slower, softer, but unending. There is always someone awake, moving quietly through the halls, keeping watch, keeping things alive. And now it was my turn to join the watch.

The chapel was dark except for the burning of the red sanctuary lamp and a few of the clear white votive candles, flames rising straight in still air before the shadowed shrines of saints.

I followed Anselm down the short center aisle, genuflecting in his wake. The slight figure of Brother Bartolome knelt toward the front, head bowed. He didn't turn at the faint noise of our entrance, but stayed motionless, bent in adoration.

The Sacrament itself was almost obscured by the magnificence of its container. The huge monstrance, a sunburst of gold more than a foot across, sat serenely on the altar, guarding the humble bit of bread at its center.

Feeling somewhat awkward, I took the seat Anselm indicated, near the front of the chapel. The seats, ornately carved with angels, flowers, and demons, folded up against the wooden panels of the backing to allow easy passage in and out. I heard the faint creak of a lowered seat behind me, as Anselm found his place.

"But what shall I do?" I had asked him, voice lowered in respect of night and silence as we had approached the chapel.

"Nothing, *ma chère*," he had replied, simply. "Only be."

So I sat, listening to my own breathing, and the tiny sounds of a silent place; the inaudible things normally hidden in other sounds. The settling of stone, the creak of wood. The hissing of the tiny, unquenchable flames. A faint skitter of some small creature, wandered from its place into the home of majesty.

It was a peaceful place, I would grant Anselm that. In spite of my own fatigue and my worry over Jamie, I gradually felt myself relaxing, the tightness of my mind gently unwinding, like the relaxation of a clock spring. Strangely, I didn't feel at all sleepy, despite the lateness of the hour and the strains of the last few days and weeks.

After all, I thought, what were days and weeks in the presence of eternity? And that's what this was, to Anselm and Bartolome, to Ambrose, to all the monks, up to and including the formidable Abbot Alexander.

It was in a way a comforting idea; if there was all the time in the world, then the happenings of a given moment became less important. I could see, perhaps, how one could draw back a little, seek some respite in the contemplation of an endless Being, whatever one conceived its nature to be.

The red of the sanctuary lamp burned steadily, reflected in the smooth gold. The flames of the white candles before the statues of St. Giles and the Blessed Mother flickered and jumped occasionally, as the burning wicks yielded an occasional imperfection, a momentary sputter of wax or moisture. But the red lamp burned serene, with no unseemly waver to betray its light.

And if there was eternity, or even the idea of it, then perhaps Anselm was right; all things were possible. And all love? I wondered. I had loved Frank; I still did. And I loved Jamie, more than my own life. But bound in the limits of time and flesh, I could not keep them both. Beyond, perhaps? Was there a place where time no longer existed, or where it stopped? Anselm thought so. A place where all things were possible. And none were necessary.

And was there love there? Beyond the limits of flesh and time, was all love possible? Was it necessary?

The voice of my thoughts seemed to be Uncle Lamb's. My family, and all I knew of love as a child. A man who had never spoken love to me, who had never needed to, for I knew he loved me, as surely as I knew I lived. For where all love is, the speaking is unnecessary. It is all. It is undying. And it is enough.

Time passed without my awareness of it, and I was startled

by the sudden appearance of Anselm before me, coming through the small door near the altar. Surely he had been sitting behind me? I glanced behind, to see one of the young monks whose name I didn't know genuflecting near the rear entrance. Anselm bowed low before the altar, then motioned to me with a nod toward the door.

"You left?" I said, once outside the chapel. "But I thought you weren't supposed to leave the, er, the Sacrament, alone?"

He smiled tranquilly. "I didn't, *ma chère*. You were there."

I repressed the urge to argue that I didn't count. After all, I supposed, there was no such thing as a Qualified Official Adorer. You only had to be human, and I imagined I was still that, though I barely felt it at times.

Jamie's candle still burned as I passed his door, and I caught the rustle of turning pages. I would have stopped, but Anselm went on, to leave me at the door of my own chamber. I paused there to bid him good night, and to thank him for taking me to the chapel.

"It was . . . restful," I said, struggling to find the right word.

He nodded, watching me. "Oui, madame. It is." As I turned to go, he said, "I told you that the Blessed Sacrament was not alone, for you were there. But what of you, *ma chère*? Were you alone?"

I stopped, and looked at him for a moment before answering.

"No," I said. "I wasn't."

39

To Ransom a Man's Soul

In the morning, I went as usual to check Jamie, hoping that he had managed some breakfast. Just short of his room, Murtagh slid out of a wall alcove, barring my way.

"What is it?" I said abruptly. "What's wrong?" My heart began to beat faster and my palms were suddenly wet.

My panic must have been obvious, for Murtagh shook his head in reassurance. "Nay, he's all right." He shrugged, "Or as much all right as he's been." He turned me with a light hand under the elbow and began to walk me back down the corridor. I thought with a moment's shock that this was the first time Murtagh had ever deliberately touched me; his hand on my arm was light and strong as a pelican's wing.

"What's the matter with him?" I demanded. The little man's seamed face was as expressionless as usual, but the crinkled eyelids twitched at the corners.

"He doesna want to see ye just yet," he said.

I stopped dead and pulled my arm from his grasp.

"Why not?" I demanded.

Murtagh hesitated, as though choosing his words carefully. "Weel, it's just . . . he's decided as it would be best for ye to leave him here and go back to Scotland. He—"

The rest of what he was saying was lost as I pushed my way rudely past him.

The heavy door swung shut with a soft thump behind me.

Jamie was dozing, facedown on the bed. He was uncovered, clad only in a novice's short gown; the charcoal brazier in the corner made the room comfortably warm, if smoky.

He started violently when I touched him. His eyes, still glazed with sleep, were sunk deep and his face was haunted by dreams. I took his hand between both of mine, but he wrenched it away. With a look of near-despair, he shut his eyes and buried his face in the pillow.

Trying not to exhibit any outward sign of disturbance, I quietly pulled up a stool and sat down near his head. "I won't touch you," I said, "but you must talk to me." I waited for several minutes while he lay unmoving, shoulders hunched defensively. At last he sighed and sat up, moving slowly and painfully, swinging his legs over the edge of the cot.

"Aye," he said flatly, not looking at me, "aye, I suppose I must. I should have done so before . . . but I was coward enough to hope I need not." His voice was bitter and he kept his head bowed, hands clasped loosely around his knees. "I didna used to think myself a coward, but I am. I should have made Randall kill me, but I did not. I had no reason to live, but I was not brave enough to die." His voice dropped, and he spoke so softly I could hardly hear him. "And I knew I would have to see you one last time . . . to tell you . . . but . . . Claire, my love . . . oh, my love."

He picked up the pillow from the bed and hugged it to him as though for protection, a substitute for the comfort he could not seek from me. He rested his forehead on it for a moment, gathering strength.

"When ye left me there at Wentworth, Claire," he said quietly, head still bowed, "I listened to your footsteps, going away on the flags outside; and I said to myself, I'll think of her now. I'll remember her; the feel of her skin and the scent of her hair and the touch of her mouth on mine. I'll think of her until that door opens again. And I'll think of her tomorrow, when I stand on the gallows, to give me courage at the last. Between the time the door opens, and the time I leave this place to die"—the big hands clenched briefly and relaxed—"I will not think at all," he finished softly.

In the small dungeon room, he had closed his eyes and sat

waiting. The pain was not bad, so long as he sat still, but he knew it would grow worse soon. Fearing pain, still he had dealt with it often before. He knew it and his own response to it well enough that he was resigned to endurance, hoping only that it would not exceed his strength too soon. The prospect of physical violation, too, was only a matter of mild revulsion now. Despair was in its own way an anesthetic.

There was no window in the room by which to judge the time. It had been late afternoon when he was brought to the dungeon, but his sense of time was unreliable. How many hours could it be until dawn? Six, eight, ten? Until the end of everything. He thought with grim humor that Randall at least had done him the favor of rendering death welcome.

When the door opened, he had looked up, expecting— what? There was only a man, slightly built, handsome, and a little disheveled, linen shirt torn and hair disarranged, leaning against the wood of the door, watching him.

After a moment, Randall had crossed the room unspeaking and stood beside him. He rested a hand briefly on Jamie's neck, then bent and freed the trapped hand with a jerk of the nail that brought Jamie to the edge of fainting. A glass of brandy was set before him, and a firm hand raised his head and helped him to drink it.

"He lifted my face then, between his hands, and he licked the drops of brandy from my lips. I wanted to pull back from him, but I'd given my word, so I just sat still."

Randall had held Jamie's head for a moment, looking searchingly into his eyes, then released him and sat down on the table next to him.

"He sat there for quite a time, not saying anything, just swinging one leg back and forth. I had no idea what he wanted, and wasn't disposed to guess. I was tired and feeling a bit sick from the pain in my hand. So after a time I just laid my head down on my arms and turned my face away." He sighed heavily.

"After a moment, I could feel a hand on my head, but I didn't move. He began to stroke my hair, very gently, over and over. There wasn't any sound but the big fellow's hoarse

breathing and the crackle of the fire in the brazier, and I think
. . . I think I went to sleep for a few moments."

When he woke, Randall was standing in front of him.

"Are you feeling a bit better?" Randall had asked in a remote, courteous tone.

Wordless, Jamie had nodded, and stood up. Randall had
stripped him, careful of the wounded hand, and led him to the
bed.

"I'd given my word not to struggle, but I did not mean to
help, either, so I just stood, as though I were made of wood. I
thought I would let him do as he liked, but I'd take no part in
it—I would keep a distance from him, in my mind at least."
Randall had smiled then, and gripped Jamie's right hand, hard
enough to make him sink onto the bed, sick and dizzy with
the sudden stab of pain. Randall had knelt then on the floor
before him, and taught him, in a few shattering minutes, that
distance is an illusion.

"When he rose up, he took the knife and drew it across my
chest, from one side to the other. It was not a deep cut, but it
bled a bit. He watched my face a moment, then reached out a
finger and dipped it in the blood." Jamie's voice was unsteady, tripping and stammering from time to time. "He
licked my blood off his finger, with little flicks of his tongue,
like a c-cat washing itself. He smiled a bit, then—very kind,
like—and bent his head to my chest. I was not bound at all,
but I could not have moved. I just . . . sat there, while he
used his tongue to . . . It did not hurt, precisely, but it felt
verra queer. After a time, he stood up and cleaned himself
careful with a towel."

I watched Jamie's hand. With his face turned away, it was
the best indicator of his feelings. It clenched convulsively on
the edge of the cot as he went on.

"He—he told me that. . . . I was delicious. The cut had
almost stopped bleeding, but he took the towel and scrubbed
it hard over my chest to open the wound again." The knuckles of the clenched hand were knobs of bloodless bone. "He
unbuttoned his breeches then, and smeared the fresh blood
on himself, and said it was my turn now."

Afterward, Randall held his head and helped him to be sick,

wiped his face gently with a wet cloth, and gave him brandy to cleanse his mouth of foulness. And so, by turns vicious and tender, bit by bit, using pain as his weapon, he had destroyed all barriers of mind and body.

I wanted to stop Jamie, to tell him that he didn't need to go on, must not go on, but I bit my lip hard to keep from speaking and clasped my own hands tight together to keep from touching him.

He told me the rest of it, then; the slow and deliberate whipstrokes, interspersed with kisses. The shocking pain of burns, administered to drag him from the brink of a desperately sought unconsciousness to face further degradations. He told me everything, with hesitations, sometimes with tears, much more than I could bear to hear, but I heard him out, silent as a confessor. He glanced quickly up at me, then away.

"I could have stood being hurt, no matter how bad it was. I expected to be . . . used, and I thought I could stand that too. But I couldn't . . . I . . . he . . ." I dug my nails fiercely into my palms in the struggle to keep quiet. He shook soundlessly for a time, then his voice came again, thick, but desperately steady.

"He did not just hurt me, or use me. He made love to me, Claire. He hurt me—hurt me badly—while he did it, but it was an act of love to him. And he made me answer him— damn his soul! He made me rouse to him!" The hand bunched into a fist and struck the bedframe with an impotent rage that made the whole bed tremble.

"The . . . first time, he was verra careful with me. He used oil, and took a long time, rubbing it all over me . . . touchin' me gentle in all my parts. I could no more stop myself rising to his touch than I could stop myself bleeding when he cut me." Jamie's voice was weary and wretched with despair. He paused, and looked directly at me for the first time since I had come in.

"Claire, I did not want to think of you. I couldna bear to be there, naked, and . . . like that . . . and to remember loving you. It was blasphemy. I meant to wipe you from my mind, and only to . . . exist, so long as I must. But he would not allow it." Wetness shone on his cheeks, but he was not crying now.

"He talked. All during it, he talked to me. Partly it was threats, and partly it was love talk, but often it was you."

"Me?" My voice, unused for so long, came out of my strained throat as little more than a croak. He nodded, looking down at the pillow again.

"Aye. He was most terribly jealous of you, you know."

"No. No, I didn't know."

He nodded again. "Oh, yes. He would ask me—while he touched me—he would ask, 'Does *she* do this for you? Can your woman r-rouse you like this?' " His voice trembled. "I wouldna answer him—I couldn't. And then, he'd ask how I thought you would feel to see me . . . to see me . . ." He bit his lip hard, unable to go on for a moment.

"He'd hurt me a bit, then stop and love me 'til I began to rouse . . . and then he'd hurt me fierce and take me in the midst of the hurting. And all the time, he would talk of you, and keep you before my eyes. I fought, in my mind . . . I tried to keep myself from him, to keep my mind apart from my body, but the pain broke through, again and again, past every barrier I could put up. I tried, Claire—God, I tried so hard, but . . ."

He sank his head in his hands, fingers digging hard into his temples. He spoke abruptly. "I know why young Alex Mac-Gregor hanged himself. I'd do the same, did I not know it to be mortal sin. If he's damned me in life, he'll not do so in heaven." There was a moment's silence while he struggled to control himself. I noticed automatically that the pillow on his knees was blotched with dampness, and wanted to get up and change it for him. He shook his head slowly, still gazing down at his feet.

"The . . . it's all linked for me now. I canna think of you, Claire, even of kissing you or touching your hand, without feeling the fear and the pain and the sickness come back. I lie here feeling that I will die without your touch, but when you touch me, I feel as though I will vomit with shame and loathing of myself. I canna even see you now without . . ." His forehead rested on knotted fists, knuckles dug hard into his eye-sockets. The tendons of his neck were sharply etched with strain, and his voice came half-muffled.

"Claire, I want you to leave me. Go back to Scotland, to Craigh na Dun. Go back to your place, to your . . . husband. Murtagh will take you safe, I've told him." He was silent for a moment, and I did not move.

He looked up again with desperate bravery, and spoke very simply.

"I will love you as long as I live, but I cannot be your husband any longer. And I will not be less to you." His face began to break apart. "Claire, I want you so badly that my bones shake in my body, but God help me, I am afraid to touch you!"

I started up to go to him, but he stopped me with a sudden motion of his hand. He was half doubled up, face contorted with internal struggle, and his voice was strangled and breathless.

"Claire . . . please. Please go. I'm going to be verra sick, and I don't want you to see it. Please."

I heard the pleading in his voice and knew I must spare him this one indignity, at least. I rose, and for the first time in my professional life, left a sick man to his own devices, helpless and alone.

I left his chamber, numbed, and leaned against the white stone wall outside, cooling my flushed cheek against the unyielding blocks, ignoring the stares of Murtagh and Brother William. *God help me,* he had said. *God help me, I am afraid to touch you.*

I straightened and stood alone. Well, why not? Surely there was no one else.

At the hour when time began to slow, I genuflected in the aisle of the chapel of St. Giles. Anselm was there, elegant shoulders straight beneath his habit, but no other. He neither moved nor looked around, but the living silence of the chapel embraced me.

I remained on my knees for a moment, reaching out to the quiet darkness, staying my mind from its hurry. Only when I felt my heart slow to the rhythms of the night did I slide into a seat near the back.

I sat rigid, lacking the form and ritual, the liturgical courtesies that eased the brothers into the depths of their sacred conversation. I did not know how to begin. Finally, I said, silently, bluntly, I need help. Please.

And then I let the silence fall back in waves around me, lapping me like the folds of a cloak, comforting against the cold. And I waited, as Anselm had told me, and the minutes passed by uncounted.

There was a small table at the back of the chapel, covered with a linen cloth, bearing the stoup of holy water, and beside it, a Bible and two or three other inspirational works. For use by adorers for whom the silence was too much, I supposed.

It was becoming too much for me, and I rose and got the Bible, bringing it back to the prie-dieu with me. I was hardly the first person to have recourse to the sortes Virgilianae in time of confusion or trouble. There was sufficient light from the candles for me to read, turning the flimsy pages carefully and squinting over the lines of fine black type.

". . . and he smote them with emerods, and they were very sore." No doubt they were, I thought. What in hell were emerods? Try Psalms, instead.

"But I am a worm, and no man . . . I am poured out like water, and all my bones are out of joint: my heart is like wax; it is melted in the midst of my bowels." Well, yes, a competent diagnosis, I thought, with some impatience. But was there some treatment?

"But be not thou far from me, O Lord: O my strength, haste thee to help me. Deliver my soul from the sword; my darling from the power of the dog." Hmm.

I turned to the Book of Job, Jamie's favorite. Surely if anyone was in a position to offer helpful advice. . . .

"But his flesh upon him shall have pain, and his soul within him shall mourn." Mmm, yes, I thought, and turned the page.

"He is chastened also with pain upon his bed, and the multitude of his bones with strong pain. . . . His flesh is consumed away, that it cannot be seen; and his bones that were not seen stick out." Spot on, I thought. What next?

"Yea, his soul draweth near unto the grave, and his life to the destroyers." Not so good, but the next bit was more heartening. "If there be a messenger with him, an interpreter, one among a thousand, to shew unto man his uprightness: Then he is gracious unto him, and saith, Deliver him from going down to the pit: I have found a ransom. His flesh shall be fresher than a child's: he shall return to the days of his youth." And what was the ransom, then, that would buy a man's soul, and deliver my darling from the power of the dog?

I closed the book and my eyes. The words muddled together, blurring with my urgent need. An overriding misery struck me when I spoke Jamie's name. And yet there was some small peace there, a lessening of tension when I said, as I did over and over again, "O Lord, into thy hands I commend the soul of your servant James."

The thought came to me that perhaps Jamie would be better off dead; he had said he wanted to die. I was morally sure that if I left him as he wished, he would be dead soon, whether from the aftereffects of torture and illness, from hanging, or in some battle. And I was in no doubt that he knew it as well. Ought I to do as he said? Damned if I will, I said to myself. *Damned* if I will, I said fiercely to the sunburst on the altar and opened the book again.

It was some time before I became aware that my thread of petition was no longer a monologue. In fact, I knew it only when I realized that I had just answered a question I had no memory of asking. In my trance of sleepless misery, something had been asked of me, I wasn't sure just what, and I had answered without thinking, "Yes, I will."

I stopped all thought abruptly, listening to the ringing silence. And then, more cautiously, repeated, voiceless, "Yes. Yes, I will," and thought fleetingly, *The conditions of sin are these: first, you must give your full consent to it. . . . And the conditions of grace as well,* came an echo of Anselm's quiet voice.

There was a feeling, not sudden, but complete, as though I

had been given a small object to hold unseen in my hands. Precious as opal, smooth as jade, weighty as a river stone, more fragile than a bird's egg. Infinitely still, live as the root of Creation. Not a gift, but a trust. Fiercely to cherish, softly to guard. The words spoke themselves and disappeared into the groined shadows of the roof.

I genuflected to the Presence then, and left the chapel, never doubting, in the eternity of the moment when time stops, that I had an answer, but having no idea what that answer was. I knew only that what I held was a human soul; my own or another's, I could not tell.

It did not appear to be an answer to prayer, when I woke to the resumption of ordinary time in the morning to find a lay brother standing over me, telling me that Jamie was burning with fever.

"How long has he been like this?" I asked, laying a practiced hand on brow and back, armpit and groin. No trace of relieving sweat; only the dry stretched skin of persistent parching, fiery with heat. He was awake, but heavy-eyed and groggy. The source of the fever was plain. The shattered right hand was puffy, with a foul-smelling ooze soaking the bandages. Ominous red streaks ran up the wrist. A bloody infection, I thought to myself. A filthy, suppurating, blood poisoning, life-threatening infection.

"I found him so when I came to look in on him after Matins," replied the serving brother who had come to fetch me. "I gave him water, but he began to vomit just after dawn."

"You should have fetched me at once," I said. "Still, never mind. Bring me hot water, raspberry leaves, and Brother Polydore, as quickly as possible." He left with the assurance that he would see some breakfast was brought for me as well, but I waved such amenities aside, reaching for the pewter jug of water.

By the time Brother Polydore appeared, I had tried the internal application of water, only to have it violently rejected, and was applying it externally instead, soaking the sheets and wrapping them loosely over the hot skin.

Simultaneously, I set the infected hand to soak in fresh-boiled water, as hot as could be stood without burning the skin. Without sulfa drugs or modern antibiotics, heat was the only defense against a bacterial infection. The patient's body was doing its best to supply that heat by means of high fever, but the fever itself posed a serious danger, wasting muscle and damaging brain cells. The trick was to apply sufficient local heat to destroy the infection, while keeping the rest of the body cool enough to prevent damage, and sufficiently hydrated to maintain its normal functions. A bloody three-tier balancing act, I thought bleakly.

Neither Jamie's state of mind nor his physical discomfort were relevant any longer. It was a straightforward struggle to keep him alive until the infection and the fever ran their course; nothing else mattered.

In the afternoon of the second day, he began to hallucinate. We tied him to the bed with soft rags to prevent his hurling himself to the floor. Finally, as a desperate measure to break the fever, I sent one of the lay brothers out to bring in a bushel basket of snow, which we packed around him. This resulted in a violent shivering fit that left him drained and exhausted, but did briefly bring his temperature down.

Unfortunately, the treatment had to be repeated at hourly intervals. By sunset, the room looked like a swamp, with puddles of melted snow standing on the floor, tussocks of sodden sheeting mounded among them, and steam like marsh gas rising from the brazier in the corner. Brother Polydore and myself were sodden, too, soaked with sweat, chilled with snow water, and near to exhaustion, in spite of the helpful assistance of Anselm and the lay brothers. Febrifuges such as coneflower, goldenseal, catnip, and hyssop had been tried, without effect. Willowbark tea, which might have helped with its content of salicylic acid, could not be consumed in amounts large enough to matter.

In one of his increasingly rare lucid intervals, Jamie asked me to let him die. I answered curtly, as I had the night before, "Damned if I will," and went on with what I was doing.

As the sun went down, there was a stir of approaching men in the corridor. The door opened and the abbot, Jamie's un-

cle Alex, came in, accompanied by Brother Anselm and three
other monks, one carrying a small cedarwood box. The abbot
came over to me and blessed me briefly, then took one of my
hands in his.

"We are going to anoint the lad," he said, his deep voice
kind. "Do not be frightened."

He turned toward the bed and I looked wildly to Anselm
for explanation.

"The sacrament of Extreme Unction," he explained, moving close so that his low tones would not disturb the monks
gathered around the bed. "The Last Anointing."

"Last Anointing! That's for people who are dying!"

"Shh." He drew me farther away from the bed. "It might
more properly be called anointing of the sick, though in fact it
is usually reserved for those in danger of death." The monks
had turned Jamie gently onto his back, arranging him tenderly
so that he might lie with the least hurt to his raw shoulders.

"The purpose of the sacrament is twofold," Anselm went
on, murmuring in my ear as the preparations went on. "First,
it is intended as a sacrament of healing; we pray that the sufferer may be restored to health, if that be God's will for him.
The chrism, the consecrated oil, is used as a symbol of life and
healing."

"And the second purpose?" I asked, already knowing.

Anselm nodded. "If it is not God's will that he should recover, then he is given absolution of sins, and we commend
him to God, that his soul may depart in peace." He saw me
tighten in protest, and laid a warning hand on my arm.

"These are the last rites of the Church. He is entitled to
them, and to whatever peace they may bring him."

The preparations were complete. Jamie lay on his back, a
cloth modestly draped across his loins, with lighted candles at
the head and the foot of the bed that reminded me most
unpleasantly of grave lights. Abbot Alexander sat at the bedside, accompanied by a monk who held a tray with a covered
ciborium, two small silver bottles containing holy water and
chrism, and a white cloth draped across both forearms. Like a
bloody wine steward, I thought crossly. The whole procedure
unnerved me.

The rites were conducted in Latin, the soft antiphonal murmuring soothing to the ear, though I did not understand the meaning. Anselm whispered softly to me the meaning of some parts of the service; others were self-explanatory. At one point, the Abbot motioned to Polydore, who stepped forward and held a small vial under Jamie's nose. It must have contained spirits of ammonia or some other stimulant, because he jerked and turned his head away sharply, eyes still closed.

"Why are they trying to wake him?" I whispered.

"If possible, the person should be conscious in order to give assent to the statement that he is sorry for any sins committed during his life. Also, if he is capable of receiving it, the Abbot will give him the Blessed Sacrament."

The Abbot stroked Jamie's cheek softly, turning his head back to the vial, speaking quietly to him. He had dropped from Latin into the broad Scots of their family, and his voice was gentle.

"Jamie! Jamie, lad! It's Alex, lad. I'm here wi' ye. Ye must wake a bit now, only for a bit. I shall be givin' ye the absolution now, and then the Blessed Sacrament of Our Lord. Take a wee sup, now, so ye can answer me when ye must." The monk called Polydore held the cup against Jamie's lips, carefully pouring the water a drop at a time, until the parched tongue and throat could take more. His eyes were open, still heavy with fever, but alert enough.

The Abbot went on then, the questions in English, but pitched so low that I could scarcely catch them. "Do ye renounce Satan and all his works?" "Do ye believe in the Resurrection of Our Lord Jesus Christ?" and so on. To each one, Jamie answered "Aye," in a scratchy whisper.

Once the sacrament had been given, Jamie lay back with a sigh, closing his eyes once more. I could see his ribs as the deep-sprung chest moved with his breathing. He had wasted dreadfully, between the sickness and the fever. The Abbot, taking the vials of holy water and chrism in turn, made the sign of the Cross on his body, anointing forehead, lips, nose, ears, and eyelids. Then, in turn, he made the sign of the Cross with the holy oil in the hollow of the chest over the heart, on the palm of each hand, and the arch of each foot. He lifted the injured hand with infinite care, brushing the oil across the wound lightly and laying the hand back on Jamie's chest, where it lay below the livid slash of the knife scar.

The anointing was quick and immeasurably gentle, a feather touch by the Abbot's rapidly moving thumb. "Superstitious magic," said the rational side of my brain, but I was deeply moved by the love on the faces of the monks as they prayed. Jamie's eyes were open once more, but very calm, and his face was peaceful for the first time since we had left Lallybroch.

The ceremony concluded with a brief prayer in Latin. Laying his hand on Jamie's head, the Abbot said in English, "Lord, into Thy hands we commend the soul of Thy servant, James. Heal him, we pray, if that be Thy will, and strengthen his soul, that he may be filled with grace, and know Thy peace throughout eternity."

"Amen," replied the other monks. And so did I.

By dark, the patient had lapsed into semiconsciousness again. As Jamie's strength waned, it was all we could do to rouse him for the sips of water that were keeping him alive. His lips were cracked and peeling, and he could no longer talk, though he would still open glazed eyes when shaken roughly. He no longer recognized us; his eyes stared fixedly, then gradually closed as he turned his head away, moaning.

I stood by the bed looking down at him, so exhausted from the rigors of the day that I felt no more than a sort of dull despair. Brother Polydore touched me gently, bringing me out of my daze.

"You cannot do any more for him now," he said, leading me firmly away. "You must go and rest."

"But—" I began, then stopped. He was right, I realized. We had done everything possible. Either the fever would break soon of itself, or Jamie would die. Even the strongest body could not endure the consuming ravages of high fever for more than a day or two, and Jamie had little strength left to see him through such a siege.

"I will stay with him," Polydore said. "Go to your bed. I'll summon you if . . ." He didn't finish the sentence, but waved me gently in the direction of my own chamber.

I lay sleepless on my cot, staring at the beamed ceiling. My eyes were dry and hot, and my throat ached, as though I were coming down with a fever as well. Was this the answer to my prayer, that we would die here together?

At last I rose, and took up the jug and basin from the table by the door. I set the heavy pottery dish in the center of the floor and filled it carefully, letting the water swell up over the thickened rim into a trembling bubble.

I had made a short detour to Brother Ambrose's stillroom on the way to my chamber. I undid the small packets of herbs and scattered the contents into my brazier, where the myrrh leaves gave off a fragrant smoke, and the crumbs of camphor flamed with tiny blue tongues between the red glow of the charcoal sticks.

I set the candlestick behind my reflecting pool, took my place before it, and sat down to summon a ghost.

➤

The stone corridor was cold and dark, lit at intervals by dimly flickering oil lamps hung from the ceiling. My shadow stretched forward under my feet as I passed beneath each one, lengthening until it seemed to dive headfirst and disappear into the dark ahead.

In spite of the cold, I was barefoot and wearing only a coarse white cotton nightrobe. A small envelope of warmth moved with me under the robe, but the chill from the stones crept up my feet and legs.

I knocked once, softly, and pushed open the heavy door without waiting for an answer.

Brother Roger was with him, sitting by the bed, telling beads with bowed head. The wooden rosary rattled as he looked up, but his lips continued to move silently for a few seconds, finishing the Ave Maria before acknowledging my presence.

He met me near the door, speaking quietly, though it was clear that he could have shouted without disturbing the motionless figure on the bed.

"No change. I've just put fresh water in the hand bath." A few drops gleamed on the sides of the small pewter kettle on the brazier, freshly filled.

I nodded and put a hand on his arm in thanks. It was startlingly solid and warm after the imaginations of the last hour, and somehow comforting.

"I'd like to stay with him alone, if you don't mind."

"Of course. I'll go to the chapel—or should I stay near in case . . ." His voice trailed off, hesitant.

"No." I tried to smile reassuringly. "Go to the chapel. Or better yet, go to bed. I can't sleep; I'll stay here 'til morning. If I need help, I'll send for you."

Still dubious, he glanced back at the bed. But it was very late, and he was tired; there were shadows under the kind brown eyes.

The heavy door squeaked on its hinges, and I was alone with Jamie. Alone and afraid, and very, very doubtful about what I proposed to do.

I stood at the foot of the bed, watching him for a moment. The room was dimly lit by the glow of the brazier and by two enormous candlesticks, each nearly three feet tall, that stood on the table at the side of the room. He was naked, and the faint light seemed to accentuate the hollows left by the wasting fever. The multicolored bruise over the ribs stained the skin like a spreading fungus.

A dying man takes on a faint greenish tinge. At first just a touch at the edge of the jaw, this pallor spreads gradually, over the face and down the chest as the force of life begins to ebb. I had seen it many times. A few times, I had seen that deadly progress arrested and reversed, the skin flush with blood once more, and the man live. More often . . . I shook myself vigorously and turned away.

I brought my hand out of the folds of my robe and laid on the table the objects I had collected in a surreptitious visit to Brother Ambrose's darkened workshop. A vial of spirits of ammonia. A packet of dried lavender. Another of valerian. A small metal incense burner, shaped like an open blossom. Two pellets of opium, sweet scented and sticky with resin. And a knife.

The room was close and stuffy with smoke from the brazier. The only window was covered with a heavy tapestry, one showing the execution of Saint Sebastian. I eyed the saint's upturned face and arrow-punctured torso, wondering afresh at the mentality of the person who had chosen this particular decoration for a sickroom.

Indifferently rendered as it was, the tapestry was of heavy silk and wool, and excluded all but the strongest drafts. I lifted the lower edge and flapped it, urging the charcoal smoke out through the stone arch. The cold, damp air that streamed in was refreshing, and did something to calm the throbbing that had started in my temples as I stared into the reflecting water, remembering.

There was a faint moan behind me, and Jamie stirred in the draft. Good. He was not deeply unconscious, then.

Letting the tapestry fall back over the window, I next took up the incense burner. I fixed one of the opium pellets on the spike and lighted it with one of the wax tapers for the candlesticks. I placed it on the small table near Jamie's head, careful not to inhale the sickly fumes myself.

There was not much time. I must finish my preparations quickly, before the opium smoke drove him too far under to be roused.

I unlaced the front of my robe and rubbed my body quickly with handfuls of the lavender and valerian. It was a pleasant, spicy smell, distinctive and richly evocative. A smell that, to me, conjured the shade of the man who wore its perfume, and the shade of the man behind him; shades that evoked confusing images of present terror and lost love. A smell that, to Jamie, must recall the hours of pain and rage spent wrapped in its waves. I rubbed the last of it vigorously between my palms and dropped the fragrant shreds on the floor.

With a deep breath for courage, I picked up the vial of ammoniacal spirits. I stood by the bed a moment holding it, looking down at the gaunt, stubbled face. At most he might last a day; at the least, only a few more hours.

"All right, you bloody Scottish bastard," I said softly. "Let's see how stubborn you really are." I lifted the injured hand, dripping, from the water and set the soaking dish aside.

I opened the vial and waved it closely under his nose. He snorted and tried to turn his head away, but didn't open his eyes. I dug my fingers into the hair on the back of his head to prevent his turning away, and brought the vial back to his face. He shook his head slowly, swinging it from side to side like an ox roused from slumber, and his eyes came open just a crack.

"Not done yet, Fraser," I whispered in his ear, trying as best I could to catch the rhythm of Randall's clipped consonants.

Jamie moaned and hunched his shoulders. I grasped him by both shoulders and shook him roughly. His skin was so hot I nearly let go.

"Wake up, you Scottish bastard! I'm not done with you yet!" He began to struggle up onto his elbows with a pitiful effort at obedience that nearly broke my heart. His head was still shaking back and forth, and the cracked lips were muttering something that sounded like "please not yet" over and over again.

Strength failing, he rolled to one side and collapsed facedown on the pillow again. The room was beginning to fill with opium smoke and I felt mildly dizzy.

I gritted my teeth and plunged my hand between his buttocks, gripping one curving round. He screamed, a high breathy sound, and rolled painfully sideways, curling into a ball with his hands clasped between his legs.

I had spent the hour in my chamber, hovering over my pool of reflection, conjuring memories. Of Black Jack Randall and of Frank, his six-times-great-grandson. Such very different men, but with such startling physical similarities.

It tore me to think of Frank, to recall his face and voice, his mannerisms, his style of lovemaking. I had tried to obliterate him from my mind, once my choice was made in the circle of stone, but he was always there, a shadowy figure in the recesses of my mind.

I felt sick with betrayal of him, but in the extremity I had forced my mind to clear as Geilie had shown me, concentrating on the flame of the candle, breathing the astringency of the herbs, calming myself until I could bring him from the shadows, see the lines of his face, feel once more the touch of his hand without weeping.

There was another man in the shadows, with the same hands, the same face. Eyes filled with the candle flame, I had brought him forward, too, listening, watching, seeing the likenesses and the differences, building a—a what? A simulacrum, a persona, an impression, a masquerade. A shaded face, a whispered voice, and a loving touch that I might bring to deceive a mind adrift in delirium. And I left my chamber at last, with a prayer for the soul of the witch Geillis Duncan.

Jamie was on his back now, writhing slightly against the pain of his wounds. His eyes were fixed and staring, with no sign of recognition.

I caressed him in the way I knew so well, tracing the line of his ribs from breastbone to back, lightly as Frank would have done, pressing hard on the aching bruise, as I was sure the other would have. I leaned forward and ran my tongue slowly around his ear, tasting and probing, and whispered, "Fight me! Fight back, you filthy scut!"

His muscles tightened and his jaw clenched, but he continued to stare upward. No choice, then. I would have to use the knife after all. I knew the risk I was taking in this, but better to kill him myself, I thought, than to sit quietly by and let him die.

I took the knife from the table and drew it firmly across his chest, along the path of the freshly healed scar. He gasped with the shock of it, and arched his back. Seizing a towel, I scrubbed it briskly over the wound. Before I could falter, I forced myself to run my fingers over his chest, scooping up a gout of blood which I rubbed savagely over his lips. There was one phrase that I didn't have to invent, having heard it myself. Bending low over him, I whispered, "Now kiss me."

I was not at all prepared for it. He hurled me half across the room as he came up off the bed. I staggered and fell against the table, making the giant candlesticks sway. The shadows darted and swung as the wicks flared and went out.

The edge of the table had struck me hard across the back, but I recovered in time to dodge away as he lunged for me.

With an inarticulate growl, he came after me, hands out-stretched.

He was both faster and stronger than I expected, though he staggered awkwardly, bumping into things. He cornered me for a moment between the brazier and the table, and I could hear his breath rasping harshly in his throat as he grabbed for me. He smashed his left hand toward my face; had his strength and reflexes been anything like normal, the blow would have killed me. Instead, I jerked to one side, and his fist glanced off my forehead, knocking me to the floor, mildly stunned.

I crawled under the table. Reaching for me, he lost his balance and fell against the brazier. Glowing coals scattered across the stone floor of the chamber. He howled as his knee crunched heavily into a patch of hot coal. I seized a pillow from the bed and beat out a smoldering nest of sparks in the trailing bedcover. Preoccupied with this, I didn't notice his approach, until a solid clout across the head knocked me sprawling.

The cot overturned as I tried to pull myself up with a hand on the frame. I lay sheltering behind it for a moment, trying to get my senses back. I could hear Jamie hunting me in the semidarkness, breath rasping between incoherent phrases of Gaelic cursing. Suddenly he caught sight of me and flung himself over the bed, eyes mad in the dim light.

It is difficult to describe in detail what happened next, if only because everything happened a number of times, and the times all overlap in my memory. It seems as though Jamie's burning hands closed on my neck only once, but that once went on forever. In fact, it happened dozens of times. Each time I managed to break his grip and throw him off, to retreat once more, dodging and ducking around the wrecked furniture. And once again he would follow, a man pulled by rage from the edge of death, swearing and sobbing, staggering and flailing wildly.

Deprived of the sheltering brazier, the coals died quickly, leaving the room black as pitch and peopled with demons. In the last flickers of light, I saw him crouched against the wall, maned in fire and mantled in blood, penis stiff against the matted hair of his belly, eyes blue murder in a skull-white face. A Viking berserker. Like the Northern devils who burst from their dragon-ships into the mists of the ancient Scottish coast, to kill and plunder and burn. Men who would kill with the last ounce of their strength. Who would use that last strength to rape and sow their violent seed in the bellies of the conquered. The tiny incense burner gave no light, but the sickly smell of opium clogged my lungs. Though the coals were out, I saw lights in the darkness, colored lights that floated at the edge of my vision.

Movement was becoming harder; I felt as though I were wading through water thigh-deep, pursued by monstrous fish. I lifted my knees high, running in slow motion, feeling the water splash against my face.

I shook off the dream, to realize that there was in fact wetness on my face and hands. Not tears, but blood, and the sweat of the nightmare creature I grappled with in the dark.

Sweat. There was something I should remember about sweat, but I couldn't recall it. A hand tightened on my upper arm and I pulled away, a slick film left on my skin.

Around and around the mulberry bush, the monkey chased the weasel. But something was wrong, it was the weasel chasing me, a weasel with sharp white teeth that pierced my forearm. I hit out at it and the teeth let go, but the claws . . . around and around the mulberry bush . . .

The demon had me up against the wall; I could feel stone behind my head and stone beneath my grasping fingers, and a stone-hard body pressing hard against me, bony knee between my own, stone and bone, between my own . . . legs, more stony hardness . . . ah. A softness amidst the hardness of life, pleasant coolness in the heat, comfort in the midst of woe . . .

We fell locked together to the floor, rolling over and over, tangled in the folds of the fallen tapestry, washed in the drafts of cold air from the window. The mists of madness began to recede.

We bashed into some piece of furniture and both lay still. Jamie's hands were locked on my breasts, fingers digging bruisingly into the flesh. I felt the plop of dampness on my

face, sweat or tears, I couldn't tell, but opened my eyes to see.
Jamie was looking down at me, face blank in the moony light,
eyes wide, unfocused. His hands relaxed. One finger gently
traced the outline of my breast, from slope to tip, over and
over. His hand moved to cup the breast, fingers spread like a
starfish, soft as the grip of a nursing child.

"M-mother?" he said. The hair stood up on the back of my
neck. It was the high, pure voice of a young boy. "Mother?"

The cold air laved us, whirling the unhealthy smoke away in
a drift of snowflakes. I reached up and laid the palm of my
hand along his cold cheek.

"Jamie, love," I said, whispering through a bruised throat,
"Come then, come lay your head, man." The mask trembled
then and broke, and I held the big body hard against me, the
two of us shaking with the force of his sobbing.

———

It was, by considerable good luck, the unflappable Brother
William who found us in the morning. I woke groggily to the
sound of the door opening, and snapped to full consciousness
when I heard him clear his throat emphatically before saying
"Good morning to ye," in his soft Yorkshire drawl.

The heavy weight on my chest was Jamie. His hair had
dried in bronze streaks and whorled over my breasts like the
petals of a Chinese chrysanthemum. The cheek pressed
against my sternum was warm and slightly sticky with sweat,
but the back and arms I could touch were as cold as my
thighs, chilled by the winter air gusting in on us.

Daylight streaming through the uncurtained window revealed the full extent of the wreckage I had only dimly realized the night before; smashed furniture and crockery littered
the room, and the massive paired candlesticks lay like fallen
logs in the midst of a tangle of torn hangings and scattered
bedclothes. From the pattern of indentations impressing itself
painfully into my back, I thought I must be lying on the
indifferently executed tapestry of St. Sebastian the Human
Pincushion; no great loss to the monastery, if so.

Brother William stood motionless in the doorway, jug and
basin in hand. With great precision, he fixed his eyes on Ja-

mie's left eyebrow and inquired, "And how do you feel this morning?"

There was a rather long pause, during which Jamie considerately remained in place, blanketing most of me from view. At last, in the hoarse tones of one to whom a revelation has been vouchsafed, he replied, "Hungry."

"Oh, good," said Brother William, still staring hard at the eyebrow, "I'll go and tell Brother Josef." The door closed soundlessly behind him.

"Nice of you not to move," I remarked. "I shouldn't like us to be responsible for giving Brother William impure thoughts."

Dense blue eyes stared down at me. "Aye, well," he said judiciously, "a view of *my* arse is no going to corrupt anyone's Holy Orders; not in its present condition. Yours, though . . ." He paused to clear his throat.

"What *about* mine?" I demanded.

The bright head lowered slowly to plant a kiss on my shoulder. "Yours," he said, "would compromise a bishop."

"Mmmphm." I was, I felt, getting rather good at Scottish noises myself. "Be that as it may, perhaps you should move now. I don't suppose even Brother William's tact is infinite."

Jamie lowered his head next to mine with some care, laying it on a fold of tapestry, from which he peered sideways at me. "I dinna know how much of last night I dreamed and how much was real." His hand unconsciously strayed to the scratch across his chest. "But if half what I thought happened really happened, I should be dead now."

"You're not. I looked." With some hesitation, I asked, "Do you want to be?"

He smiled slowly, eyes half-closing. "No, Sassenach, I don't." His face was gaunt and shadowed with illness and fatigue, but peaceful, the lines around his mouth smoothed out and the blue eyes clear. "But I'm damned close to it, want to or not. The only reason I think I'm not dying now is that I'm hungry. I wouldna be hungry if I were about to die, do ye think? Seems a waste." One eye closed altogether, but the other stayed half-open, fixed on my face with a quizzical expression.

"You can't stand up?"

He considered carefully. "If my life depended on it, I might possibly lift my head again. But stand up? No."

With a sigh, I wriggled out from under him and righted the bed before trying to lever him into a vertical position. He managed to stand for only a few seconds before his eyes rolled back and he fell across the bed. I groped frantically for the pulse in his neck, and found it, slow and strong, just below the three-cornered scar at the base of his throat. Simple exhaustion. After a month of imprisonment and a week of intense physical and mental stress, starvation, injury, sickness and high fever, even that vigorous frame had finally come to the end of its resources.

"The heart of a lion," I said, shaking my head, "and the head of an ox. Too bad you haven't also got the hide of a rhinoceros." I touched a freshly bloodied weal on his shoulder.

He opened one eye. "What's a rhinoceros?"

"I thought you were unconscious!"

"I was. I am. My head's spinning like a top."

I drew a blanket up over him. "What you need now are food and rest."

"What *you* need now," he said, "are clothes." And shutting the eye again, he fell promptly asleep.

40

Absolution

I had no memory of finding my way to bed, but I must have done so, because I woke up there. Anselm was sitting by the window, reading.

I sat bolt upright in bed.

"Jamie?" I croaked.

"Asleep," he said, putting the book aside. He glanced at the hour-candle on the table. "Like you. You have been with the angels for the last thirty-six hours, *ma belle*." He filled a cup from the earthenware jug and held it to my lips. At one time I would have considered drinking wine in bed before brushing one's teeth to be the last word in decadence. Performed in a monastery, in company with a robed Franciscan, the act seemed somewhat less degenerate. And the wine did cut through the mossy feeling in my mouth.

I swung my feet over the side of the bed, and sat swaying. Anselm caught me by the arm and eased me back onto the pillow. He seemed suddenly to have four eyes, and altogether more noses and mouths than strictly necessary.

"I'm a bit dizzy," I said, closing my eyes. I opened one. Somewhat better. At least there was only one of him, if a trifle blurry around the edges.

Anselm bent over me, concerned.

"Shall I fetch Brother Ambrose or Brother Polydore, madame? I have little skill in medicine, unfortunately."

"No, I don't need anything. I just sat up too suddenly." I tried again, more slowly. This time the room and its contents stayed relatively still. I became aware of numerous bruises and sore spots earlier submerged in the dizziness. I tried to clear my throat and discovered that it hurt. I grimaced.

"Really, *ma chère,* I think perhaps . . ." Anselm was poised by the door, ready to fetch assistance. He looked quite alarmed. I reached for the looking glass on the table and then changed my mind. I really wasn't ready for that. I grasped the wine jug instead.

Anselm came slowly back into the room and stood watching me. Once convinced that I wasn't going to collapse after all, he sat down again. I sipped the wine slowly as my head cleared, trying to shake off the aftereffects of opium-induced dreams. So we were alive, after all. Both of us.

My dreams had been chaotic, filled with violence and blood. I had dreamed over and over that Jamie was dead or dying. And somewhere in the fog had been the image of the boy in the snow, his surprised round face overlying the image of Jamie's bruised and battered one. Sometimes the pathetic, fuzzy mustache seemed to appear on Frank's face. I distinctly remembered killing all three of them. I felt as though I had spent the night in stabbing and butchery, and I ached in every muscle with a sort of dull depression.

Anselm was still there, patiently watching me, hands on his knees.

"There is something you could do for me, Father," I said.

He rose at once, eager to help, reaching for the jug.

"Of course? More wine?"

I smiled wanly.

"Yes, but later. Right now, I want you to hear my confession."

He was startled, but quickly gathered his professional self-possession around him like his robes.

"But of course, *chère madame,* if you wish it. But really, would it not be better to fetch Father Gerard? He is well known as a confessor, while I"—he gave a Gallic shrug—"I am allowed to hear confessions, of course, but in truth I seldom do so, being only a poor scholar."

"I want you," I said firmly. "And I want to do it now."

He sighed in resignation and went to fetch his stola. Arranging it about his neck so that the purple silk lay straight and shimmering down the black front of his habit, he took a seat on the stool, blessed me briefly and sat back, waiting.

And I told him. Everything. Who I was and how I came there. About Frank, and about Jamie. And about the young English dragoon with the pale, spotty face, dying against the snow.

He showed no change of expression while I spoke, except that the round brown eyes grew rounder still. When I finished, he blinked once or twice, opened his mouth as though to speak, closed it again, and shook his head as though to clear it.

"No," I said patiently. I cleared my throat again; I croaked like a bullfrog. "You haven't been hearing things. And you're not imagining it, either. Now you see why I wanted you to hear it under the seal of confession?"

He nodded, a bit abstractedly.

"Yes. Yes, to be sure. If . . . but yes. Of course, you wished me to tell no one. And also, since you tell it to me under the seal of the sacrament, then you expect that I must believe it. But . . ." He scratched his head, then looked up at me. A wide smile spread slowly across his countenance.

"But how marvelous!" he exclaimed softly. "How extraordinary, and how wonderful!"

" 'Wonderful' isn't precisely the word I would have chosen," I said dryly, "but 'extraordinary' is all right." I coughed and reached for more wine.

"But it is . . . a miracle," he said, as though to himself.

"If you insist," I said, sighing. "But what I want to know—what ought I to do? Am I guilty of murder? Or adultery, for that matter? Not that there's much to be done about it in either case, but I'd like to know. And since I *am* here, how ought I to act? Can I—*should* I, I mean—use what I know to . . . change things? I don't even know if such a thing is possible. But if it is, have I the right?"

He rocked back on his stool, considering. Slowly he raised both index fingers, placed them tip to tip and stared at them for a long time. Finally, he shook his head and smiled at me.

"I don't know, *ma bonne amie*. It is not, you will appreciate, a situation one is prepared to encounter in the confessional. I will have to think, and to pray. Yes, assuredly to pray. Tonight I will contemplate your situation when I hold my watch before the Blessed Sacrament. And tomorrow perhaps I can advise you."

He motioned me gently to kneel.

"But for now, my child, I will absolve you. Whatever your sins might be, have faith that they will be forgiven."

He lifted one hand in blessing, placing the other on my head. *"Te absolvo, in nomine Patri, et Filii, . . ."*

Rising, he lifted me to my feet.

"Thank you, Father," I said. Unbeliever that I was, I had used confession only to force him to take me seriously, and was somewhat surprised to feel a lightening of the burden on my spirits. Perhaps it was only the relief of telling someone the truth.

He waved a hand in dismissal. "I will see you tomorrow, *chère madame*. For now, you should rest more, if you can."

He headed for the door, winding his stola up neatly into a square. At the doorway, he paused for a moment, turning to smile at me. A childlike excitement lighted his eyes.

"And perhaps tomorrow . . ." he said, "perhaps you could . . . tell me what it is like?"

I smiled back.

"Yes, Father. I'll tell you."

After he left, I staggered down the hall to see Jamie. I had seen any number of corpses in much better condition, but his chest rose and fell regularly, and the sinister green tinge had faded from his skin.

"I've been waking him every few hours, just long enough to swallow a few spoonfuls of broth." Brother Roger was at my elbow, speaking softly. He moved his gaze from the patient to me, and recoiled noticeably at my appearance. I should probably have combed my hair. "Er, perhaps you would . . . like some?"

"No, thank you. I think . . . I think perhaps I will sleep a bit more, after all." I no longer felt weighed down by guilt and depression, but a drowsy, contented heaviness was spreading through my limbs. Whether it was due to the effects of confession or of wine, I found to my surprise that I was looking forward to bed and to oblivion.

I leaned forward to touch Jamie. He was warm, but with no trace of fever. I gently stroked his head, smoothing the tumbled red hair. The corner of his mouth stirred briefly and fell back into place. But it had turned up. I was sure of it.

The sky was cold and damp, filling the horizon with a grey blankness that blended into the grey mist of the hills and the grimy cover of last week's snow, so that the abbey seemed wrapped inside a ball of dirty cotton. Even inside the cloister, the winter's silence weighed on the inhabitants. The chanting from the Hours of Praise in the chapel was muted, and the thick stone walls seemed to absorb all sound, swaddling the bustle of daily activity.

Jamie slept for nearly two days, waking only to take a little broth or wine. Once awake, he began to heal in the usual fashion of a normally healthy young man, suddenly deprived of the strength and independence usually taken for granted. In other words, he enjoyed the cosseting for approximately twenty-four hours and then became in turn restive, restless, testy, irritable, cranky, fractious, and extremely bad tempered.

The cuts on his shoulders ached. The scars on his legs itched. He was sick of lying on his belly. The room was too hot. His hand hurt. The smoke from the brazier made his eyes burn so that he could not read. He was sick of broth, posset, and milk. He wanted meat.

I recognized the symptoms of returning health, and was glad of them, but was prepared to put up with only so much of this. I opened the window, changed his sheets, applied marigold salve to his back and rubbed his legs with aloe juice. Then I summoned a serving brother and ordered more broth.

"I don't want any more of this slop! I need food!" He pushed the tray irritably away, making the broth splash onto the napkin cradling the bowl.

I folded my arms and stared down at him. Imperious blue eyes stared right back. He was thin as a rail, the lines of jaw and cheekbone bold against the skin. Though he was mending well, the raw nerves of his stomach would take a little longer to heal. He still could not always keep down the broth and milk.

"You'll get food when I say you can have it," I informed him, "and not before."

"I'll have it now! D'ye think you can tell me what I'm to eat?"

"Yes, I bloody well do! I'm the doctor here, if you've forgotten."

He swung his feet over the edge of the bed, clearly intending to take steps. I put a hand on his chest and shoved him back.

"Your job is to stay in that bed and do as you're told, for once in your life," I snapped. "You're not fit to be up, and you're not fit for solid foot yet. Brother Roger said you vomited again this morning."

"Brother Roger can mind his own business, and so can you," he said through his teeth, struggling back up. He reached out and got a hold on the table edge. With considerable effort, he made it to his feet, and stood there, swaying.

"Get back in bed! You're going to fall down!" He was alarmingly pale, and even the small effort of standing had made him break out in a cold sweat.

"I'll not," he said. "And if I do, it's my own concern."

I was really angry by this time.

"Oh, is it! And who do you think saved your miserable life for you, anyway? Did it all by yourself, did you?" I grabbed his arm to steer him back to bed, but he jerked it away.

"I didna ask ye to, did I? I told ye to leave me, no? And I canna see why ye bothered to save my life, anyway, if it's only to starve me to death—unless ye enjoy watching it!"

This was altogether too much.

"Bloody ingrate!"

"Shrew!"

I drew myself to my full height, and pointed menacingly at the cot. With all the authority learned in years of nursing, I said, "Get back in that bed this instant, you stubborn, mulish, idiotic—"

"Scot," he finished for me, succinctly. He took a step toward the door, and would have fallen, had he not caught hold of a stool. He plumped heavily down on it and sat swaying, his eyes a little unfocused with dizziness. I clenched my fists and glared at him.

"Fine," I said. "Bloody fine! I'll order bread and meat for you, and after you vomit on the floor, you can just get down on your hands and knees and clean it up yourself! I won't do it, and if Brother Roger does, I'll skin him alive!"

I stormed into the hall and slammed the door behind me, just before the porcelain washbasin crashed into it from the other side. I turned to find an interested audience, no doubt attracted by the racket, standing in the hall. Brother Roger and Murtagh stood side by side, staring at my flushed face and heaving bosom. Roger looked disconcerted, but a slow smile spread over Murtagh's craggy countenance as he listened to the string of Gaelic obscenities going on behind the door.

"He's feeling better, then," he said contentedly. I leaned against the corridor wall, and felt an answering smile spread slowly across my own face.

"Well, yes," I said, "he is."

On my way back to the main building from a morning spent in the herbary, I met Anselm coming from the cloister near the library. His face lighted when he saw me, and he hurried to join me in the courtyard. We walked together through the abbey grounds, talking.

"Yours is an interesting problem, to be sure," he said, breaking a stick from a bush near the wall. He examined the winter-tight buds critically, then tossed it aside, and glanced up at the sky, where a feeble sun poked its way through the light cloud layer.

"Warmer, but a good way to go until the spring," he observed. "Still, the carp should be lively today—let us go down to the fish pools."

Far from being the delicate ornamental structures I had imagined them to be, the fish pools were little more than utilitarian rock-lined troughs, placed conveniently near to the kitchens. Stocked with carp, they provided the necessary food for Fridays and fast days, when the weather was too rough to permit ocean fishing for the more customary haddock, herring, and flounder.

True to Anselm's word, the fish were lively, the fat fusiform bodies gliding past each other, white scales reflecting the clouds overhead, the vigor of their movements occasionally stirring up small waves that sloshed against the sides of their rocky prison. As our shadows fell on the water, the carp turned toward us like compass needles surging toward the north.

"They expect to be fed, when they see people," Anselm explained. "It would be a shame to disappoint them. One moment, *chère madame.*"

He darted into the kitchens, returning shortly with two loaves of stale bread. We stood on the lip of the pool, tearing crumbs from the loaves and tossing them to the endlessly hungry mouths below.

"You know, there are two aspects to this curious situation of yours," Anselm said, absorbed in tearing bread. He glanced aside at me, a sudden smile lighting his face. He shook his head in wonderment. "I can scarcely believe it still, you know. Such a marvel! Truly, God has been good, to show me such things."

"Well, that's nice," I said, a bit dryly, "I don't know whether He's been quite so obliging to me."

"Really? *I* think so." Anselm sank down on his haunches, crumbling bread between his fingers. "True," he said, "the situation has caused you no little personal inconvenience—"

"That's one way of putting it," I muttered.

"But it may also be regarded as a signal mark of God's favor," he went on, disregarding my interruption. The bright brown eyes regarded me speculatively.

"I prayed for guidance, kneeling before the Blessed Sacrament," he went on, "and as I sat in the silence of the chapel, I seemed to see you as a shipwrecked traveler. And it seems to me that that is a good parallel to your present situation, is it not? Imagine such a soul, madame, suddenly cast away in a strange land, bereft of friends and familiarity, without resources save what the new land can provide. Such a happening is disaster, truly, and yet may be the opening for great opportunity and blessings. What if the new land shall be rich? New friends may be made, and a new life begun."

"Yes, but—" I began.

"So"—he said authoritatively, holding up a finger to hush me—"if you have been deprived of your earlier life, perhaps it is only that God has seen fit to bless you with another, that may be richer and fuller."

"Oh, it's full, all right," I agreed. "But—"

"Now, from the standpoint of canon law," he said frowning, "there is no difficulty regarding your marriages. Both were valid marriages, consecrated by the church. And strictly speaking, your marriage to the young chevalier in there antedates your marriage to Monsieur Randall."

"Yes, 'strictly speaking,'" I agreed, getting to finish a sentence for once. "But not in *my* time. I don't believe canon law was constructed with such contingencies in mind."

Anselm laughed, the pointed end of his beard quivering in the slight breeze.

"More than true, *ma chère,* more than true. All that I meant was that, considered from a strictly legal standpoint, you have committed neither sin nor crime in what you have done regarding these two men. Those were the two aspects of your situation, of which I spoke earlier: what you have done, and what you *will* do." He reached up a hand and took mine, tugging me down to sit beside him, so our eyes were on a level.

"That is what you asked me when I heard your confession, is it not? What have I done? And what shall I do?"

"Yes, that's it. And you're telling me that I haven't done anything wrong? But I've—"

He was, I thought, nearly as bad as Dougal MacKenzie for interrupting.

"No, you have not," he said firmly. "It is possible to act in strict accordance with God's law and with one's conscience, you comprehend, and still to encounter difficulties and tragedy. It is the painful truth that we still do not know why *le bon Dieu* allows evil to exist, but we have His word for it that this is true. 'I created good,' He says in the Bible, 'and I created evil.' Consequently, even good people sometimes, I think, *especially* good people," he added meditatively, "may encounter great confusion and difficulties in their lives. For example, take the young boy you were obliged to kill. No," he said, raising a hand against my interruption, "make no mistake. You were obliged to kill him, given the exigencies of your situation. Even Holy Mother Church, which teaches the sanctity of life, recognizes the need for defense of oneself and of one's family. And having seen the earlier condition of your husband"—he cast a look back at the guests' wing—"I have no doubt that you were obliged to take the path of violence. That being so, you have nothing with which to reproach yourself. You do, of course, feel pity and regret for the action, for you are, madame, a person of great sympathy and feeling." He gently patted the hand that rested on my drawn-up knees.

"Sometimes our best actions result in things that are most regrettable. And yet you could not have acted otherwise. We do not know what God's plan for the young man was—perhaps it was His will that the boy should join Him in heaven at that time. But you are not God, and there are limits to what you can expect of yourself."

I shivered briefly as a cold wind came round the corner, and drew my shawl closer. Anselm saw it, and motioned toward the pool.

"The water is warm, madame. Perhaps you would care to soak your feet?"

"Warm?" I gaped incredulously at the water. I hadn't noticed before, but there were no broken sheets of ice in the corners of the trough, as there were on the holy water fonts outside the church, and small green plants floated in the water, sprouting from the cracks between the rocks that lined the pool.

In illustration, Anselm slipped off his own leather sandals. Cultured as his face and voice were, he had the square, sturdy hands and feet of a Normandy peasant. Hiking the skirt of his habit to his knees, he dipped his feet into the pool. The carp dashed away, turning almost at once to nose curiously at this new intrusion.

"They don't bite, do they?" I asked, viewing the myriad voracious mouths suspiciously.

"Not flesh, no," he assured me. "They have no teeth to speak of."

I shed my own sandals and gingerly inserted my feet into the water. To my surprise, it was pleasantly warm. Not hot, but a delightful contrast to the damp, chilly air.

"Oh, that's nice!" I wiggled my toes with pleasure, causing considerable consternation among the carp.

"There are several mineral springs near the abbey," Anselm explained. "They bubble hot from the earth, and the waters hold great healing powers." He pointed to the far end of the trough, where I could see a small opening in the rocks, half obscured by the drifting water plants.

"A small amount of the hot mineral water is piped here from the nearest spring. That is what enables the cook to maintain live fish for the table at all seasons; normally the winter weather would be too bitter for them."

We paddled our feet in congenial silence for a time, the heavy bodies of the fish flicking past, occasionally bumping into our legs with a surprisingly weighty impact. The sun came out again, bathing us in a weak but perceptible warmth. Anselm closed his eyes, letting the light wash over his face. He spoke again without opening them.

"Your first husband—Frank was his name?—he, too, I think, must be commended to God as one of the regrettable things that you can do nothing about."

"But I could have done something," I argued. "I could have gone back—perhaps."

He opened one eye and regarded me skeptically.

"Yes, 'perhaps,'" he agreed. "And perhaps not. You need not reproach yourself for hesitating to risk your life."

"It wasn't the risk," I said, flicking my toes at a big black-and-white splotched carp. "Or not entirely. It was—well, it was partly fear, but mostly it was that I—I couldn't leave Jamie." I shrugged helplessly. "I—simply couldn't."

Anselm smiled, opening both eyes.

"A good marriage is one of the most precious gifts from God," he observed. "If you had the good sense to recognize and accept the gift, it is no reproach to you. And consider . . ." He tilted his head to one side, like a brown sparrow.

"You have been gone from your place for nearly a year. Your first husband will have begun to reconcile himself to your loss. Much as he may have loved you, loss is common to all men, and we are given means of overcoming it for our good. He will have started, perhaps, to build a new life. Would it do good for you to desert the man who needs you so deeply, and whom you love, to whom you are united in the bonds of holy matrimony, to return and disrupt this new life? And in particular, if you were to go back from a sense of duty, but feeling that your heart is given elsewhere—no." He shook his head decisively.

"No man can serve two masters, and no more can a woman. Now, if that were your only valid marriage, and this"—he nodded again toward the guest wing—"merely an irregular attachment, then your duty might lie elsewhere. But you were bound by God, and I think you may honor your duty to the chevalier.

"Now, as to the other aspect—what you shall do. That may require some discussion." He pulled his feet from the water, and dried them on the skirt of his habit.

"Let us adjourn this meeting to the abbey kitchens, where perhaps Brother Eulogius may be persuaded to provide us with a warming drink."

Finding a stray bit of bread on the ground, I tossed it to the carp and stooped to put my sandals on.

"I can't tell you what a relief it is to talk to someone about it," I said. "And I still can't get over the fact that you really do believe me."

He shrugged, gallantly offering me an arm to hold while I slipped the rough straps of the sandal over my instep.

"*Ma chère,* I serve a man who multiplied the loaves and fishes"—he smiled, nodding at the pool, where the swirls of the carps' feeding were still subsiding—"who healed the sick and raised the dead. Shall I be astonished that the master of eternity has brought a young woman through the stones of the earth to do His will?"

Well, I reflected, it was better than being denounced as the whore of Babylon.

The kitchens of the abbey were warm and cavelike, the arching roof blackened with centuries of grease-filled smoke. Brother Eulogius, up to his elbows in a vat of dough, nodded a greeting to Anselm and called in French to one of the lay brothers to come and serve us. We found a seat out of the bustle, and sat down with two cups of ale and a plate containing a hot pastry of some kind. I pushed the plate toward Anselm, too preoccupied to be interested in food.

"Let me put it this way," I said, choosing my words carefully. "If I knew that some harm was going to occur to a group of people, should I feel obliged to try to avert it?"

Anselm rubbed his nose reflectively on his sleeve; the heat of the kitchen was beginning to make it run.

"In principle, yes," he agreed. "But it would depend also upon a number of other things—what is the risk to yourself, and what are your other obligations? Also what is the chance of your success?"

"I haven't the faintest idea. Of any of those things. Except obligation, of course—I mean, there's Jamie. But he's one of the group who might be hurt."

He broke off a piece of pastry and passed it to me, steaming. I ignored it, studying the surface of my ale. "The two men I killed," I said, "either of them might have had children, if I hadn't killed them. They might have done—" I made a helpless gesture with the cup, "—who knows what they might have done? I may have affected the future . . . no, I *have* affected the future. And I don't know how, and that's what frightens me so much."

"Um." Anselm grunted thoughtfully, and motioned to a passing lay brother, who hastened over with a fresh pasty and more ale. He refilled both cups before speaking.

"If you have taken life, you have also preserved it. How many of the sick you have treated would have died without your intervention? They also will affect the future. What if a person you have saved should commit an act of great evil? Is that your fault? Should you on that account have let that person die? Of course not." He rapped his pewter mug on the table for emphasis.

"You say that you are afraid to take any actions here for fear of affecting the future. This is illogical, madame. *Everyone's* actions affect the future. Had you remained in your own place, your actions would still have affected what was to happen, no less than they will now. You have still the same responsibilities that you would have had then—that any man has at any time. The only difference is that you may be in a position to see more exactly what effects your actions have—and then again, you may not." He shook his head, looking steadily across the table.

"The ways of the Lord are hidden to us, and no doubt for good reason. You are right, *ma chère;* the laws of the Church were not formulated with situations such as yours in mind, and therefore you have little guidance other than your own conscience and the hand of God. I cannot tell you what you should do, or not do.

"You have free choice; so have all the others in this world. And history, I believe, is the cumulation of all those actions. Some individuals are chosen by God to affect the destinies of many. Perhaps you are one of those. Perhaps not. I do not know why you are here. You do not know. It is likely that neither of us will ever know." He rolled his eyes, comically. "Sometimes I don't even know why *I* am here!" I laughed and he smiled in return. He leaned toward me across the rough planks of the table, intense.

"Your knowledge of the future is a tool, given to you as a shipwrecked castaway might find himself in possession of a knife or a fishing line. It is not immoral to use it, so long as you do so in accordance with the dictates of God's law, to the best of your ability."

He paused, drew a deep breath, and blew it out in an explosive sigh that ruffled his silky mustache. He smiled.

"And that, *ma chère madame,* is all I can tell you—no more than I can tell any troubled soul who comes to me for advice: put your trust in God, and pray for guidance."

He shoved the fresh pastry toward me.

"But whatever you are to do, you will require strength for it. So take one last bit of advice: when in doubt, eat."

When I came into Jamie's room in the evening, he was asleep, head pillowed on his forearms. The empty broth bowl sat virtuously on the tray, the untouched platter of bread and meat beside it. I looked from the innocent, dreaming face to the platter and back. I touched the bread. My finger left a slight depression in the moist surface. Fresh.

I left him asleep and went in search of Brother Roger, who I found in the buttery.

"Did he eat the bread and meat?" I demanded, without preliminaries.

Brother Roger smiled in his fluffy beard. "Yes."

"Did he keep it down?"

"No."

I eyed him narrowly. "You didn't clean up after him, I hope."

He was amused, the round cheeks pink above his beard. "Would I dare? No, he took the precaution of having a basin ready, in case."

"Damn wily Scot," I said, laughing despite myself. I returned to his chamber and kissed him lightly on the forehead. He stirred, but didn't wake. Heeding Father Anselm's advice, I took the platter of fresh bread and meat back to my chamber for my own supper.

Thinking I would give Jamie time to recover, both from pique and indigestion, I stayed in my own room most of the next day, reading an herbal Brother Ambrose had provided me. After lunch I went to check on my recalcitrant patient. Instead of Jamie, though, I found Murtagh, sitting on a stool tilted back against the wall, wearing a bemused expression.

"Where is he?" I said, looking blankly around the room.

Murtagh jerked a thumb toward the window. It was a cold, dark day, and the lamps were lit. The window was uncovered and the chilly draft set the little flame fluttering in its dish.

"He went *out*?" I asked incredulously. "Where? Why? And what on earth is he wearing?" Jamie had remained largely naked over the last several days, since the room was warm and any pressure on his healing wounds was painful. He had worn a monk's outer robe when leaving his room on necessary short excursions, with the support of Brother Roger, but the robe was still present, neatly folded at the foot of the bed.

Murtagh rocked his stool forward and regarded me owlishly.

"How many questions is that? Four?" He held up one hand, index finger pointing up.

"One: Aye, he went out." The middle finger rose. "Two: Where? Damned if I know." The fourth finger joined its companions. "Three: Why? He said he was tired of bein' cooped up indoors." The little finger waggled briefly. "Four: Also damned if I know. He wasna wearin' anything at all last time I saw him."

Murtagh folded all four fingers and stuck out his thumb.

"Ye didna ask me, but he's been gone an hour or so."

I fumed, at a loss as to what to do. Since the offender wasn't available, I snapped at Murtagh instead.

"Don't you know it's near freezing out there, and snow coming on? Why didn't you stop him? And what do you mean he isn't wearing anything?"

The diminutive clansman was tranquil. "Aye, I know it. Reckon he does, too, not bein' blind. As for stoppin' him, I tried." He nodded at the robe on the bed.

"When he said he was goin' out, I said he wasna fit for it, and you'd have my head, did I let him go. I snatched up his gown and set my back against the door, and told him he wasna leavin', unless he was prepared to go through me."

Murtagh paused, then said irrelevantly, "Ellen MacKenzie had the sweetest smile I ever saw; would warm a man to the backbone just to see it."

"So you let her fat-headed son go out and freeze to death," I said impatiently. "What's his mother's smile to do with it?"

Murtagh rubbed his nose meditatively. "Weel, when I said I wouldna let him pass, young Jamie just looked at me for a moment. Then he gave me a smile looked just like his ma's, and stepped out of the window in naught but his skin. By the time I got to the window, he was gone."

I rolled my eyes heavenward.

"Reckoned I should let ye know where he'd gone," Murtagh continued, "so ye'd no be worrit for him."

"So I'd no be worrit for him!" I muttered under my breath as I strode toward the stables. "*He'd* better be 'worrit,' when I catch up to him!"

There was only the one main road heading inland. I rode along it at a good pace, keeping an eye on the fields as I passed. This part of France was a rich farming area, and luckily most of the forest had been cleared; wolves and bears would not be as much a danger as they might be further inland.

As it happened, I found him barely a mile beyond the gates of the monastery, sitting on one of the ancient Roman mile-markers that dotted the roads.

He was barefoot, but otherwise clad in a short jerkin and thin breeches, the property of one of the stable lads, to judge from the stains on them.

I reined up and stared at him for a moment, leaning on the pommel. "Your nose is blue," I remarked conversationally. I glanced downward. "And so are your feet."

He grinned and wiped his nose on the back of his hand.

"So are my balls. Want to warm them for me?" Cold or not, he was plainly in good spirits. I slid off the horse and stood in front of him, shaking my head.

"It's no use at all, is it?" I asked.

"What isn't?" He rubbed his hand on the ragged breeches.

"Being angry with you. You don't care a bit whether you give yourself pneumonia, or get eaten by bears, or worry me half to death, do you?"

"Well, I'm no much worrit about the bears. They sleep in the winter, ye know."

I lost my temper and swung my hand at him, intending to slap his ear through the side of his head. He caught my wrist and held it without difficulty, laughing at me. After a moment's fruitless struggle, I gave up and laughed too.

"Are you coming back, now?" I asked. "Or have you got anything else to prove?"

He gestured back along the road with his chin. "Take the horse back to that big oak tree and wait for me there. I'll walk that far. Alone."

I bit my tongue to repress the several remarks I felt bubbling to the surface, and mounted. At the oak tree, I got off and looked down the road. After a moment, though, I found I couldn't bear to watch his labored progress. When he fell the first time, I clutched the reins tight in my gloved hands, then resolutely turned my back, and waited.

We barely made it back to the guests' wing, but managed, staggering through the corridor, his arm looped over my shoulder for support. I spotted Brother Roger, anxiously lurking in the hall, and sent him scampering for a warming pan, while I steered my awkward burden into the chamber and dumped him onto the bed. He grunted at the impact, but lay still, eyes closed, as I proceeded to strip the filthy rags off him.

"All right; in you get."

He rolled obediently under the covers I held back for him. I thrust the warming pan hastily between the sheets at the foot of the bed and shoved it back and forth. When I removed it, he stretched his long legs down and relaxed with a blissful sigh as his feet reached the pocket of warmth.

I went quietly about the room, picking up the discarded clothes, straightening the trifling disorder on the table, putting fresh charcoal in the brazier, adding a pinch of elecampane to sweeten the smoke. I thought he was asleep, and was startled when he spoke behind me.

"Claire."

"Yes?"

"I love you."

"Oh." I was mildly surprised, but undeniably pleased. "I love you too."

He sighed, and opened his eyes halfway.

"Randall," he said. "Toward the end. That's what he wanted." I was even more startled by this, and replied cautiously.

"Oh?"

"Aye." His eyes were fixed on the open window, where the snow clouds filled the space with a deep, even grey.

"I was lying on the floor, and he was lying next to me. He was naked by then, too, and both of us were smeared with blood—and other things. I remember trying to lift my head, and feeling my cheek stuck to the stone of the floor with dried blood." He frowned, a distant look in his eyes as he conjured the memory.

"I was far gone by then; so far that I didna even feel much pain—I was just terribly tired, and everything seemed far away and not very real."

"Just as well," I said, with some asperity, and he smiled briefly.

"Aye, just as well. I was drifting a bit, half-fainted, I expect, so I don't know how long we both lay there, but I came awake to find him holding me and pressing himself against me." He hesitated, as though the next part were difficult to say.

"I'd not fought him 'til then. But I was so tired, and I thought I couldna bear it again. . . . anyway, I started to squirm away from him, not really fighting, just pulling back. He had his arms round my neck, and he pulled on me, and buried his face in my shoulder, and I could feel he was crying. I couldna tell what he was saying for a bit, and then I could; he was saying 'I love you, I love you,' over and over, with his tears and his spittle running down my chest." Jamie shuddered briefly, from cold or memory. He blew out a long breath, disturbing the cloud of fragrant smoke that swirled near the ceiling.

"I canna think why I did it. But I put my arms about him, and we just lay still for a bit. He stopped crying, finally, and kissed me and stroked me. Then he whispered to me, 'Tell me that you love me.'" He paused in the recital, smiling faintly.

"I would not do it. I dinna know why. By then I would ha' licked his boots and called him the King of Scotland, if he'd wanted it. But I wouldna tell him that. I don't even remember thinking about it; I just—wouldn't." He sighed and his good hand twitched, gripping the coverlet.

"He used me again—hard. And he kept on saying it: 'Tell me that you love me, Alex. Say that you love me.'"

"He called you Alex?" I interrupted, not able to hold back.

"Aye. I remember I wondered how he knew my second name. Did not occur to me to wonder why he'd use it, even if he knew." He shrugged.

"Anyway, I didna move or say a word, and when he'd finished, he jumped up as though he'd gone mad, and started to beat me with something—I could not see what—cursing and shouting at me, saying 'You know you love me! Tell me so! I know it's true!' I got my arms up over my head to protect it, and after a bit I must have fainted again, because the pain in my shoulders was the last I remember, except for sort of a dream about bellowing kine. Then I woke, jouncing along belly-down on a horse for a few moments, and then nothing again 'til I came round on the hearthside at Eldridge, with you looking down on me." He closed his eyes again. His tone was dreamy, almost unconcerned.

"I think . . . if I had told him that . . . he would have killed me."

Some people have nightmares peopled by monsters. I dreamed of genealogical charts, thin black branches, bearing clusters of dates on every stem. The lines like snakes, with death between the brackets of their jaws. Once again I heard Frank's voice, saying *He became a soldier, a good choice for a second son. There was a third brother who became a curate, but I don't know much about him* . . . I didn't know much about him, either. Only his name. There were the three sons listed on that chart; the sons of Joseph and Mary Randall. I had seen it many times: the oldest, William; and the second, Jonathan; and the third, Alexander.

Jamie spoke again, summoning me from my thoughts.

"Sassenach?"

"Yes?"

"Ye know the fortress I told ye of, the one inside me?"

"I remember."

He smiled without opening his eyes, and reached out a hand for me.

"Well, I've a lean-to built, at least. And a roof to keep out the rain."

I went to bed tired but peaceful, and wondering. Jamie would recover. When that had been in doubt, I had looked no further than the next hour, the next meal, the next administration of medicine. But now I needed to look further.

The abbey was a sanctuary, but only a temporary one. We could not stay here indefinitely, no matter how hospitable the monks. Scotland and England were too dangerous by far; unless Lord Lovat could help—a remote contingency, under the circumstances. Our future must lie on this side of the channel. Knowing what I now knew about Jamie's seasickness, I understood his reluctance to consider emigration to America—three months of nausea was a daunting prospect to anyone. So what was left?

France was the most likely. We both spoke French fluently. While Jamie could do as well in Spanish, German, or Italian, I was not so linguistically blessed. Also, the Fraser family was rich in connections here; perhaps we could find a place on an estate owned by a relative or friend, and live peacefully in the country. The idea held considerable attractions.

But there remained, as always, the question of time. It was the beginning of 1744—the New Year was but two weeks past. And in 1745, Bonnie Prince Charlie would take ship from France to Scotland, the Young Pretender come to claim his father's throne. With him would come disaster; war and slaughter, the crushing of the Highland clans, and with them, the butchery of all that Jamie—and I—held dear.

And between now and then, there lay one year. One year, when things might happen. When steps might be taken to prevent disaster. How, and by what means? I had no idea, but neither had I any doubts about the consequences of inaction.

Could events be changed? Perhaps. My fingers stole to my left hand and idly caressed the gold ring on my fourth finger. I thought of what I had said to Jonathan Randall, burning with rage and horror in the dungeons under Wentworth Prison.

"I curse you," I had said, "with the hour of your death." And I had told him when he would die. Had told him the date written on the genealogical chart, in Frank's fine black calligraphic script—April 16, 1745. Jonathan Randall was to die at the battle of Culloden, caught up in the slaughter that the English would create. But he didn't. He had died instead a few hours later, trampled beneath the hooves of my revenge.

And he had died a childless bachelor. Or at least I thought so. The chart—that cursed chart!—had given the date of his marriage, sometime in 1744. And the birth of his son, Frank's five-times-great-grandfather, soon after. If Jack Randall was dead and childless, how would Frank be born? And yet his ring was still upon my hand. He had existed, would exist. I comforted myself with the thought, rubbing the ring in the darkness, as though it contained a jinni that could advise me.

I woke out of a sound sleep sometime later with a half-scream.

"Shh. 'Tis only me." The large hand lifted from my mouth. With the candle out, the room was pitch-black. I groped blindly until my hand struck something solid.

"You shouldn't be out of bed!" I exclaimed, still groggy with sleep. My fingers slid over smooth, cold flesh. "You're freezing!"

"Well, of course I am," he said, somewhat crossly. "I havena got any clothes on, and it's perishing in the corridor. Will ye let me in bed?"

I wriggled as far over as I could in the narrow cot, and he slid in naked beside me, clutching me for warmth. His breathing was uneven, and I thought his trembling was from weakness as much as from cold.

"God, you're warm." He snuggled closer, sighing. "It feels good to hold ye, Sassenach."

I didn't bother asking what he was doing there; that was becoming quite plain. Nor did I ask whether he was sure. I had my own doubts, but would not voice them for fear of making self-fulfilling prophecies. I rolled to face him, mindful of the injured hand.

There was that sudden, startling moment of joining, that quick, gliding strangeness that at once becomes familiar. Jamie sighed deeply, with satisfaction and, perhaps, relief. We lay still for a moment, as though afraid to disturb our fragile link by moving. Jamie's good hand caressed me slowly, feeling its way in the dark, fingers spread like a cat's whiskers, sensitive to vibration. He moved against me, once, as though asking a question, and I answered him in the same language.

We began a delicate game of slow movements, a balancing act between his desire and his weakness, between pain and the growing pleasure of the body. Somewhere in the dark, I thought to myself that I must tell Anselm that there was another way to make time stop, but then thought perhaps not, as it was not a way open to a priest.

I held Jamie steady, with a light hand on his scarred back. He set our rhythm, but let me carry the force of our movement. We were both silent save our breathing, until the end. Feeling him tiring, I grasped him firmly and pulled him to me, rocking my hips to take him deeper, forcing him toward the climax. "Now," I said softly, "come to me. Now!" He put his forehead hard against mine and yielded himself to me with a quivering sigh.

The Victorians called it "the little death," and with good reason. He lay so limp and heavy that I would have thought him dead, if not for the slow thump of his heart against my ribs. It seemed a long time before he stirred and mumbled something against my shoulder.

"What did you say?"

He turned his head so his mouth was just below my ear. I felt warm breath on my neck. "I said," he answered softly, "my hand doesna hurt at all just now."

The good hand gently explored my face, smoothing away the wetness on my cheeks.

"Were ye afraid for me?" he asked.

"Yes," I said. "I thought it was too soon."

He laughed softly in the dark. "It was; I almost killed myself. Aye, I was afraid too. But I woke with my hand painin' me and couldna go back to sleep. I was tossing about, feeling lonely for ye. The more I thought about ye, the more I wanted ye, and I was halfway down the corridor before I thought to worry about what I was going to do when I got here. And once I thought . . ." He paused, stroking my cheek. "Well, I'm no verra good, Sassenach, but I'm maybe not a coward, after all."

I turned my head to meet his kiss. His stomach rumbled loudly.

"Don't laugh, you," he grumbled. "It's your fault, starving me. It's a wonder I could manage at all, on nothing but beef broth and ale."

"All right," I said, still laughing. "You win. You can have an egg for your breakfast tomorrow."

"Ha," he said, in tones of deep satisfaction. "I knew ye'd feed me, if I offered ye a suitable inducement."

We fell asleep face to face, locked in each other's arms.

41

From the Womb of
the Earth

Over the next two weeks, Jamie continued to heal, and I continued to wonder. Some days I would feel that we must go to Rome, where the Pretender's court held sway, and do . . . what? Other times, I wanted with all my heart only to find a safe and isolated spot, to live our lives in peace.

It was a warm, bright day, and the icicles hanging from the gargoyles' noses dripped incessantly, leaving deep, ragged pits in the snow beneath the eaves. The door of Jamie's room had been left ajar and the window uncovered, to clear out some of the lingering vapors of smoke and illness.

I poked my head cautiously around the jamb, not wishing to wake him if he was asleep, but the narrow cot was empty. He was seated by the open window, turned half away from the door so that his face was mostly hidden.

He was desperately thin still, but the shoulders were broad and straight beneath the rough fabric of the novice's habit, and the grace of his strength was returning; he sat solidly without a tremor, back straight and legs curled back beneath the stool, the lines of his body firm and harmonious. He was holding his right wrist with his sound left hand, slowly turning the right hand in the sunlight.

There was a small pile of cloth strips on the table. He had removed the bandages from the injured hand and was examining it closely. I stood in the doorway, not moving. From here, I could see the hand clearly as he turned it back and forth, probing gingerly.

The stigma of the nail wound in the palm of the hand was quite small, and well healed, I was glad to see; no more than a small pink knot of scar tissue that would gradually fade. On the back of the hand, the situation was not so favorable. Eroded by infection, the wound there covered an area the size of sixpence, still patched with scabs and the rawness of a new scar.

The middle finger, too, showed a jagged ridge of pink scar tissue, running from just below the first joint almost to the knuckle. Released from their splints, the thumb and index finger were straight, but the little finger was badly twisted; that one had had three separate fractures, I remembered, and apparently I had not been able to set them all properly. The ring finger was set oddly, so that it protruded slightly upward when he laid the hand flat on the table, as he did now.

Turning the hand palm upward, he began to manipulate the fingers gently. None would bend more than an inch or two; the ring finger not at all. As I had feared, the second joint was likely permanently frozen.

He turned the hand to and fro, holding it before his face, watching the stiff, twisted fingers and the ugly scars, mercilessly vivid in the sunlight. Then he suddenly bent his head, clutching the injured hand to his chest, covering it protectively with the sound one. He made no sound, but the wide shoulders trembled briefly.

"Jamie." I crossed the room swiftly and knelt beside him, putting my hand softly on his knee.

"Jamie, I'm sorry," I said. "I did the best I could."

He looked down at me in astonishment. The thick auburn lashes sparkled with tears in the sunlight, and he dashed them hastily away with the back of his hand.

"What?" he said, gulping, clearly taken aback by my sudden appearance. "Sorry? For what, Sassenach?"

"Your hand." I reached out and took it, lightly tracing the crooked lines of the fingers, touching the sunken scar on the back.

"It will get better," I assured him anxiously. "Really it will. I know it seems stiff and useless right now, but that's only because it's been splinted so long, and the bones haven't fully knitted yet. I can show you how to exercise, and massage. You'll get back a good deal of the use of it, honestly—"

He stopped me by laying his good hand along my cheek.

"Did you mean . . . ?" He started, then stopped, shaking his head in disbelief. "You thought . . . ?" He stopped once more and started over.

"Sassenach," he said, "ye didna think that I was grieving for a stiff finger and a few more scars?" He smiled, a little crookedly. "I'm a vain man, maybe, but it doesna go that deep, I hope."

"But you—" I began. He took both my hands in both of his and stood up, drawing me to my feet. I reached up and smoothed away the single tear that had rolled down his cheek. The tiny smear of moisture was warm on my thumb.

"I was crying for joy, my Sassenach," he said softly. He reached out slowly and took my face between his hands. "And thanking God that I have two hands. That I have two hands to hold you with. To serve you with, to love you with. Thanking God that I am a whole man still, because of you."

I put my own hands up, cupping his.

"But why wouldn't you be?" I asked. And then I remembered the butcherous assortment of saws and knives I had seen among Beaton's implements at Leoch, and I knew. Knew what I had forgotten when I had been faced with the emergency. That in the days before antibiotics, the usual—the only —cure for an infected extremity was amputation of the limb.

"Oh, Jamie," I said. I was weak-kneed at the thought, and sat down on the stool rather abruptly.

"I never thought of it," I said, still stunned. "I honestly never thought of it." I looked up at him. "Jamie. If I'd thought of it, I probably would have done it. To save your life."

"It's not how . . . they don't do it that way, then, in . . . your time?"

I shook my head. "No. There are drugs to stop infections.

So I didn't even think of it," I marveled. I looked up suddenly. "Did you?"

He nodded. "I was expecting it. It's why I asked you to let me die, that once. I was thinking of it, in between the bouts of muzzy-headedness, and—just for that one moment—I didna think I could bear to live like that. It's what happened to Ian, ye know."

"No, really?" I was shocked. "He told me he'd lost it by grape shot, but I didn't think to ask about the details."

"Aye, a grape-shot wound in the leg went bad. The surgeons took it off to keep it from poisoning his blood." He paused.

"Ian does verra well, all things considered. But"—he hesitated, pulling on the stiff ring finger—"I knew him before. He's as good as he is only because of Jenny. She . . . keeps him whole." He smiled sheepishly at me. "As ye did for me. I canna think why women bother."

"Well," I said softly, "women like to do that."

He laughed quietly and drew me close. "Aye. God knows why."

We stood entwined for a bit, not moving. My forehead rested on his chest, my arms around his back, and I could feel his heart beating, slow and strong. Finally he stirred and released me.

"I've something to show ye," he said. He turned and opened the small drawer of the table, removing a folded letter which he handed to me.

It was a letter of introduction, from Abbot Alexander, commending his nephew, James Fraser, to the attention of the Chevalier-St. George—otherwise known as His Majesty King James of Scotland—as a most proficient linguist and translator.

"It's a place," Jamie said, watching as I folded the letter. "And we'll need a place to go, soon. But what ye told me on the hill at Craigh na Dun—that was true, no?"

I took a deep breath and nodded. "It's true."

He took the letter from me and tapped it thoughtfully on his knee.

"Then this"—he waved the letter—"is not without a bit of danger."

"It could be."

He tossed the parchment into the drawer and sat staring after it for a moment. Then he looked up and the dark blue eyes held mine. He laid a hand along my cheek.

"I meant it, Claire," he said quietly. "My life is yours. And it's yours to decide what we shall do, where we go next. To France, to Italy, even back to Scotland. My heart has been yours since first I saw ye, and you've held my soul and body between your two hands here, and kept them safe. We shall go as ye say."

There was a light knock at the door, and we sprang apart like guilty lovers. I dabbed hastily at my hair, thinking that a monastery, while an excellent convalescent home, lacked something as a romantic retreat.

A lay brother came in at Jamie's bidding, and dumped a large leather saddlebag on the table. "From MacRannoch of Eldridge Manor," he said with a grin. "For my lady Broch Tuarach." He bowed then and left, leaving a faint breath of seawater and cold air behind.

I unbuckled the leather straps, curious to see what MacRannoch might have sent. Inside were three things: a note, unaddressed and unsigned, a small package addressed to Jamie, and the cured skin of a wolf, smelling strongly of the tanner's arts.

The note read: "For a virtuous woman is a pearl of great price, and her value is greater than rubies."

Jamie had opened the other parcel. He held something small and glimmering in one hand and was quizzically regarding the wolf pelt.

"A bit odd, that. Sir Marcus has sent ye a wolf pelt, Sassenach, and me a pearl bracelet. Perhaps he's got his labels mixed?"

The bracelet was a lovely thing, a single row of large baroque pearls, set between twisted gold chains.

"No," I said, admiring it. "He's got it right. The bracelet goes with the necklace you gave me when we wed. He gave that to your mother; did you know?"

"No, I didn't," he answered softly, touching the pearls.

"Father gave them to me for my wife, whoever she was to be"
—and a quick smile tugged at his mouth—"but he didna tell
me where they came from."

I remembered Sir Marcus's help on the night we had burst
so unceremoniously into his house, and the look on his face
when we had left him next day. I could see from Jamie's face
that he also was remembering the baronet who might have
been his father. He reached out and took my hand, fastening
the bracelet about my wrist.

"But it's not for me!" I protested.

"Aye, it is," he said firmly. "It isna suitable for a man to
send jewelry to a respectable married woman, so he gave it to
me. But clearly it's for you." He looked at me and grinned.
"For one thing, it won't go round my wrist, even scrawny as I
am."

He turned to the bundled wolfskin and shook it out.

"Whyever did MacRannoch send ye this, though?" He
draped the shaggy wolfhide about his shoulders and I recoiled
with a sharp cry. The head had been carefully skinned and
cured as well, and equipped with a pair of yellow glass eyes, it
was glaring nastily at me from Jamie's left shoulder.

"Ugh!" I said. "It looks just like it did when it was alive!"

Jamie, following the direction of my glance, turned his head
and found himself suddenly face-to-face with the snarling
countenance. With a startled exclamation, he jerked the skin
off and flung it across the room.

"Jesus God," he said, and crossed himself. The skin lay on
the floor, glowering balefully in the candlelight.

"What d'ye mean, 'when it was alive,' Sassenach? A personal friend, was it?" Jamie asked, eyeing it narrowly.

I told him then the things I had had no chance to tell him;
about the wolf, and the other wolves, and Hector, and the
snow, and the cottage with the bear, and the argument with
Sir Marcus, and the appearance of Murtagh, and the cattle,
and the long wait on the hillside in the pink mist of the snow-
swept night, waiting to see whether he was dead or alive.

Thin or not, his chest was broad and his arms warm and
strong. He pressed my face into his shoulder and rocked me
while I sobbed. I tried for a bit to control myself, but he only

hugged me harder, and said small and gentle things into the cloud of my hair, and I finally gave up and cried with the complete abandon of a child, until I was worn to utter limpness and hiccupping exhaustion.

"Come to think of it, I've a wee giftie for ye, myself, Sassenach," he said, smoothing my hair. I sniffed and wiped my nose on my skirt, having nothing else handy.

"I'm sorry I haven't got anything to give you," I said, watching as he stood up and began to dig through the tumbled bedclothes. Probably looking for a handkerchief, I thought, sniffing some more.

"Aside from such minor gifts as my life, my manhood, and my right hand?" he asked dryly. "They'll do nicely, *mo duinne.*" He straightened up with a novice's robe in one hand. "Undress."

My mouth fell open. "What?"

"Undress, Sassenach, and put this on." He handed me the robe, grinning. "Or do ye want me to turn my back first?"

Clutching the rough homespun around me, I followed Jamie down yet another flight of dark stairs. This was the third, and the narrowest yet; the lantern he held lit the stone blocks of walls no more than eighteen inches apart. It felt rather like being swallowed up into the earth, as we went further and further down the narrow black shaft.

"Are you sure you know where you're going?" I asked. My voice echoed in the stairwell, but with a curiously muffled sound, as though I were speaking underwater.

"Well, there's no much chance of taking the wrong turning, now is there?"

We had reached another landing, but true enough, the way ahead lay in only one direction—down.

At the bottom of this flight of steps, though, we came to a door. There was a small landing, carved out of the solid side of a mountain, from the looks of it, and a wide, low door made of oak planks and brass hinging. The planks were grey with age, but still solid, and the landing swept clean. Plainly this part of the monastery was still in use, then. The wine cellar perhaps?

There was a sconce near the door that held a torch, half-burnt from previous use. Jamie paused to light it with a paper spill from the pile that lay ready nearby, then pushed open the unlocked door and ducked beneath the lintel, leaving me to follow.

At first, I could see nothing at all inside but the glow of Jamie's lantern. Everything was black. The lantern bobbed along, moving away from me. I stood still, following the blob of light with my eyes. Every few feet he would stop, then continue, and a slow flame would rise up in his wake to burn in a small red glow. As my eyes slowly accustomed themselves, the flames became a row of lanterns, situated on rock pillars, shining into the black like beacons.

It was a cave. At first I thought it was a cave of crystals, because of the odd black shimmer beyond the lanterns. But I stepped forward to the first pillar and looked beyond, and then I saw it.

A clear black lake. Transparent water, shimmering like glass over fine black volcanic sand, giving off red reflections in the lantern light. The air was damp and warm, humid with the steam that condensed on the cool cavern walls, running down the ribbed columns of rock.

A hot spring. The faint scent of sulfur bit at my nostrils. A hot mineral spring, then. I remembered Anselm's mentioning the springs that bubbled up from the ground near the abbey, renowned for their healing powers.

Jamie stood behind me, looking out over the gently steaming expanse of jet and rubies.

"A hot bath," he said proudly. "Do ye like it?"

"Jesus H. Roosevelt Christ," I said.

"Oh, ye do," he said, grinning at the success of his surprise. "Come in, then."

He dropped his own robe and stood glowing dimly in the darkness, patched with red in the glimmering reflections off the water. The arched ceiling of the cave seemed to swallow the light of the lanterns, so that the glow reached only a few feet before being engulfed.

A little hesitantly, I let the novice's robe drop from my arms.

"How hot is it?" I asked.

"Hot enough," he answered. "Dinna worry, it won't burn ye. But stay over an hour or so, and it might cook the flesh off your bones like soupmeat."

"What an appealing idea," I said, discarding the robe.

Following his straight, slender figure, I stepped cautiously into the water. There were steps cut in the stone, leading down underwater, with a knotted rope fastened along the wall to provide handholds.

The water flowed up over my hips, and the flesh of my belly shivered in delight as the heat swirled through me. At the bottom of the steps, I stood on clean black sand, the water just below the level of my shoulders, my breasts floating like glass fisher-floats. My skin was flushed with the heat, and small prickles of perspiration were starting on the back of my neck, under the heavy hair. It was pure bliss.

The surface of the spring was smooth and waveless, but the water wasn't still; I could feel small stirrings, currents running through the body of the pool like nerve impulses. It was that, I suppose, added to the incredible soothing heat, that gave me the momentary illusion that the spring was alive—a warm, welcoming entity that reached out to soothe and embrace. Anselm had said that the springs had healing powers, and I wasn't disposed to doubt it.

Jamie came up behind me, tiny wavelets marking his passage through the water. He reached around me to cup my breasts, softly smoothing the hot water over the upper slopes.

"Do ye like it, *mo duinne*?" He bent forward and planted a kiss on my shoulder.

I let my feet float out from under me, resting against him.

"It's wonderful! It's the first time I've been warm all the way through since August." He began to tow me, backing slowly through the water; my legs streamed out in the wake of our passage, the amazing warmth passing down my limbs like caressing hands.

He stopped, swung me around, and lowered me gently onto hard wood. Half-visible in the shadowy underwater light, I could see planks set into a rocky niche. He sat down on the bench beside me, stretching his arms out on the rocky ledge behind us.

"Brother Ambrose brought me down here the other day to soak," he said. "To soften the scars a bit. It does feel good, doesn't it?"

"More than good." The water was so buoyant that I felt I might float away if I loosed my hold on the bench. I looked upward into the black shadows of the roof.

"Does anything live in this cave? Bats, I mean? Or fish?"

He shook his head. "Nothing but the spirit of the spring, Sassenach. The water bubbles up from the earth through a narrow crack back there"—he nodded toward the Stygian blackness at the back of the cave—"and trickles out through a dozen tiny openings in the rock. But there's no real opening to the outside, save the door into the monastery."

"Spirit of the spring?" I said, amused. "Sounds rather pagan, to be hiding under a monastery."

He stretched luxuriously, long legs wavering under the glassy surface like the stems of water plants.

"Well, whatever ye wish to call it, it's been here a good deal longer than the monastery."

"Yes, I can see that."

The walls of the cave were of smooth, dark volcanic rock, almost like black glass, slick with the moisture of the spring. The whole chamber looked like a gigantic bubble, half-filled with that curiously alive but sterile water. I felt as though we were cradled in the womblike center of the earth, and that if I pressed my ear to the rock, I would hear the infinitely slow beat of a great heart nearby.

We were very quiet for a long time then, half-floating, half-dreaming, brushing now and then against each other as we drifted in the unseen currents of the cave.

When I spoke at last, my voice seemed slow and drugged. "I've decided."

"Ah. Will it be Rome, then?" Jamie's voice seemed to come from a long way away.

"Yes. I don't know, once there—"

"It doesna matter. We shall do what we can." His hand

reached for me, moving so slowly I thought it would never touch me.

He drew me close, until the sensitive tips of my breasts rubbed across his chest. The water was not only warm but heavy, almost oily to the touch, and his hands floated down my back to cup my buttocks and lift me.

The intrusion was startling. Hot and slippery as our skins were, we drifted over each other with barely a sensation of touching or pressure, but his presence within me was solid and intimate, a fixed point in a watery world, like an umbilical cord in the random driftings of the womb. I made a brief sound of surprise at the small inrush of hot water that accompanied his entrance, then settled firmly onto my fixed point of reference with a little sigh of pleasure.

"Oh, I like that one," he said appreciatively.

"Like what?" I asked.

"That sound that ye made. The little squeak."

It wasn't possible to blush; my skin was already as flushed as it could get. I let my hair swing forward to cover my face, the curls relaxing as they dragged the surface of the water.

"I'm sorry; I didn't mean to be noisy."

He laughed, the deep sound echoing softly in the columns of the roof.

"I said I like it. And I do. It's one of the things I like the best about bedding ye, Sassenach, the small noises that ye make."

He pulled me closer, so my forehead rested against his neck. Moisture sprang up at once between us, slick as the sulfur-laden water. He made a slight movement with his hips, and I drew in my breath in a half-stifled gasp.

"Yes, like that," he said softly. "Or . . . like that?"

"Urk," I said. He laughed again, but kept doing it.

"That's what I thought most about," he said, drawing his hands slowly up and down my back, cupping, curving, tracing the swell of my hips. "In prison at night, chained in a room with a dozen other men, listening to the snoring and farting and groaning. I thought of those small, tender sounds that ye make when I love you, and I could feel ye there next to me in the dark, breathing soft and then faster, and the little grunt that ye give when I first take you, as though ye were settling yourself to your job."

My breathing was definitely coming faster. Supported by the dense, mineral-saturated water, I was buoyant as an oiled feather, kept from floating away only by my grip on the curved muscles of his shoulders, and the snug, firm clasp I kept of him lower down.

"Even better," his voice was a hot murmur in my ear, "when I come to ye fierce and wanting, and ye whimper under me, and struggle as though you wanted to get away, and I know it's only that you're struggling to come closer, and I'm fighting the same fight."

His hands were exploring, gently, slowly as tickling a trout, sliding deep into the rift of my buttocks, gliding lower, groping, caressing the stretched and yearning point of our joining. I quivered and the breath went from me in an unwilled gasp.

"Or when I come to you needing, and ye take me into you with a sigh and that quiet hum like a hive of bees in the sun, and ye carry me wi' you into peace with a little moaning sound."

"Jamie," I said hoarsely, my voice echoing off the water. "Jamie, please."

"Not yet, *mo duinne*." His hands came hard around my waist, settling and slowing me, pressing me down until I did groan.

"Not yet. We've time. And I mean to hear ye groan like that again. And to moan and sob, even though you dinna wish to, for ye canna help it. I mean to make you sigh as though your heart would break, and scream with the wanting, and at last to cry out in my arms, and I shall know that I've served ye well."

The rush began between my thighs, shooting like a dart into the depths of my belly, loosening my joints so that my hands slipped limp and helpless off his shoulders. My back arched and the slippery, firm roundness of my breasts pressed flat against his chest. I shuddered in hot darkness, Jamie's steadying hands all that kept me from drowning.

Resting against him, I felt boneless as a jellyfish. I didn't know—or care—what sort of sounds I had been making, but I felt incapable of coherent speech. Until he began to move again, strong as a shark under the dark water.

"No," I said. "Jamie, no. I can't bear it like that again." The blood was still pounding in my fingertips and his movement within me was an exquisite torture.

"You can, for I love ye." His voice was half-muffled in my soaking hair. "And you will, for I want ye. But this time, I go wi' you."

He held my hips firm against him, carrying me beyond myself with the force of an undertow. I crashed formless against him, like breakers on a rock, and he met me with the brutal force of granite, my anchor in the pounding chaos.

Boneless and liquid as the water around us, contained only by the frame of his hands, I cried out, the soft, bubbling half-choked cry of a sailor sucked beneath the waves. And heard his own cry, helpless in return, and knew I had served him well.

We struggled upward, out of the womb of the world, damp and steaming, rubber-limbed with wine and heat. I fell to my knees at the first landing, and Jamie, trying to help me, fell down next to me in an untidy heap of robes and bare legs. Giggling helplessly, drunk more with love than with wine, we made our way side by side, on hands and knees up the second flight of steps, hindering each other more than helping, jostling and caroming softly off each other in the narrow space, until we collapsed at last in each other's arms on the second landing.

Here an ancient oriel window opened glassless to the sky, and the light of the hunter's moon washed us in silver. We lay clasped together, damp skins cooling in the winter air, waiting for our racing hearts to slow and breath to return to our heaving bodies.

The moon above was a Christmas moon, so large as almost to fill the empty window. It seemed no wonder that the tides of sea and woman should be subject to the pull of that stately orb, so close and so commanding.

But my own tides moved no longer to that chaste and sterile summons, and the knowledge of my freedom raced like danger through my blood.

"I have a gift for you too," I said suddenly to Jamie. He turned toward me and his hand slid, large and sure, over the plane of my still-flat stomach.

"Have you, now?" he said.

And the world was all around us, new with possibility.

ACKNOWLEDGMENTS

The author would like to thank:

Jackie Cantor, *Editor par excellence, whose consistent enthusiasm had so much to do with getting this story between covers;* Perry Knowlton, *Agent of impeccable judgment, who said,* "Go ahead and tell the story the way it should be told; we'll worry about cutting it later"; *my husband,* Doug Watkins, *who, despite occasionally standing behind my chair, saying,* "If it's set in Scotland, why doesn't anybody say 'Hoot, mon?' " *also spent a good deal of time chasing children and saying,* "Mommy is writing! Leave her alone!"; *my daughter* Laura, *for loftily informing a friend,* "My mother writes books!"; *my son* Samuel, *who, when asked what Mommy does for a living, replied cautiously,* "Well, she watches her computer a lot"; *my daughter* Jennifer, *who says,* "Move over, Mommy; it's my turn to type!"; Jerry O'Neill, *First Reader and Head Cheerleader, and the rest of my personal Gang of Four—* Janet McConnaughey, Margaret J. Campbell, *and* John L. Myers *—who read everything I write, and thereby keep me writing;* Dr. Gary Hoff, *for verifying the medical details and kindly explaining the proper way to reset a dislocated shoulder;* T. Lawrence Tuohy, *for details of military history and costuming;* Robert Riffle, *for explaining the difference between betony and bryony, listing every kind of forget-me-not known to man, and verifying that aspens really do grow in Scotland;* Virginia Kidd, *for reading early parts of the manuscript and encouraging me to go on with it;* Alex Krislov, *for co-hosting with other systems operators the most extraordinary electronic literary cocktail-party-cum-writers'-incubator in the world, the CompuServe Literary Forum; and the many members of LitForum—* John Stith, John Simpson, John L. Myers, Judson Jerome, Angelia Dorman, Zilgia Quafay, *and the rest—for Scottish folk songs, Latin love poetry, and for laughing (and crying) in the right places.*

And don't miss the next
installment of the acclaimed
OUTLANDER series . . .

DIANA GABALDON'S

DRAGONFLY
IN AMBER

Available now
from Dell Books!

Read on for a preview. . . .

DRAGONFLY IN AMBER

On Sale Now

"**B**read," I muttered feebly, keeping my eyes tightly closed. There was no response from the large, warm object next to me, other than the faint sigh of his breathing.

"Bread!" I said, a little louder. There was a sudden startled heave of the bedclothes, and I grasped the edge of the mattress and tightened all my muscles, hoping to stabilize the pitch and yaw of my internal organs.

Fumbling noises came from the far side of the bed, followed by the sliding of a drawer, a muffled exclamation in Gaelic, the soft thud of a bare foot stamping planks, and then the sinking of the mattress under the weight of a heavy body.

"Here, Sassenach," said an anxious voice, and I felt the touch of a dry bread crust against my lower lip. Groping blindly without opening my eyes, I grasped it and began to chew gingerly, forcing each choking bite down a parched throat. I knew better than to ask for water.

The desiccated wads of bread crumbs gradually made their way down my throat and took up residence in my stomach, where they lay like small heaps of ballast. The nauseating roll of my inner waves slowly calmed, and at last my innards lay at anchor. I opened my eyes, to see the anxious face of Jamie Fraser hovering a few inches above me.

"Ak!" I said, startled.

"All right, then?" he asked. When I nodded and feebly began to sit up, he put an arm around my back to help me. Sitting down beside me on the rough inn bed, he pulled me gently against him and stroked my sleep-tousled hair.

"Poor love," he said. "Would a bit of wine help? There's a flask of hock in my saddlebag."

"No. No, thank you." I shuddered briefly at the thought of drinking hock—I seemed to smell the dark, fruity fumes, just at the mention of it—and pushed myself upright.

"I'll be fine in a moment," I said, with forced cheerfulness. "Don't worry, it's quite normal for pregnant women to feel sick in the morning."

With a dubious look at me, Jamie rose and went to retrieve his clothes from the stool near the window. France in February is cold as hell frozen over, and the bubbled-glass panes of the window were coated thick with frost.

He was naked, and a ripple of gooseflesh brushed his shoulders and raised the red-gold hairs on his arms and legs. Accustomed to cold, though, he neither shivered nor hurried as he pulled on stockings and shirt. Pausing in his dressing, he came back to the bed and hugged me briefly.

"Go back to bed," he suggested. "I'll send up the chambermaid to light the fire. Perhaps ye can rest a bit, now you've eaten. You won't be sick now?" I wasn't entirely sure, but nodded reassuringly.

"I don't think so." I cast an eye back at the bed; the quilts, like most coverings supplied by public inns, were none too clean. Still, the silver in Jamie's purse had procured us the best room in the inn, and the narrow bed was stuffed with goose feathers rather than with chaff or wool.

"Um, perhaps I *will* just lie down a moment," I murmured, pulling my feet off the freezing floor and thrusting them under the quilts, in search of the last remnants of warmth. My stomach seemed to have settled sufficiently to risk a sip of water, and I poured a cupful from the cracked bedroom ewer.

"What were you stamping on?" I asked, sipping carefully. "There aren't spiders up here, are there?"

Fastening his kilt about his waist, Jamie shook his head.

"Och, no," he said. Hands busy, he tilted his head toward the table. "Just a rat. After the bread, I expect."

Glancing down, I saw the limp gray form on the floor, a small pearl of blood glistening on the snout. I made it out of bed just in time.

"It's all right," I said faintly, a bit later. "There isn't anything left to throw up."

"Rinse your mouth, Sassenach, but don't swallow, for God's sake." Jamie held the cup for me, wiped my mouth with a cloth as though I were a small and messy child, then lifted me and laid me carefully back in the bed. He frowned worriedly down at me.

"Perhaps I'd better stay here," he said. "I could send word."

"No, no, I'm all right," I said. And I was. Fight as I would to keep from vomiting in the mornings, I could hold nothing down for long. Yet once the bout was over, I felt entirely restored. Aside from a sour taste in my mouth, and a slight soreness in the abdominal muscles, I felt quite my normal self. I threw back the covers and stood up, to demonstrate.

"See? I'll be fine. And you have to go; it wouldn't do to keep your cousin waiting, after all."

I was beginning to feel cheerful again, despite the chilly air rushing under the door and beneath the folds of my nightgown. Jamie was still hesitating, reluctant to leave me, and I went to him and hugged him tightly, both in reassurance and because he was delightfully warm.

"Brrr," I said. "How on earth can you be warm as toast, dressed in nothing but a kilt?"

"I've a shirt on as well," he protested, smiling down at me.

We clung together for a bit, enjoying each other's warmth in the quiet cold of the early French morning. In the corridor, the clash and shuffle of the chambermaid with her scuttle of kindling grew nearer.

Jamie shifted a bit, pressing against me. Because of the difficulties of traveling in the winter, we had been nearly a week on the road from Ste. Anne to Le Havre. And between the late arrivals at dismal inns, wet, filthy, and shivering with fatigue and cold, and the increasingly unsettled wakenings as my morning sickness got worse, we had scarcely touched each other since our last night at the Abbey.

"Come to bed with me?" I invited, softly.

He hesitated. The strength of his desire was obvious through the fabric of his kilt, and his hands were warm on the cool flesh of my own, but he didn't move to take me in his arms.

"Well . . ." he said doubtfully.

"You want to, don't you?" I said, sliding a chilly hand under his kilt to make sure.

"Oh! er . . . aye. Aye, I do." The evidence at hand bore out this statement. He groaned faintly as I cupped my hand between his legs. "Oh, Lord. Don't do that, Sassenach; I canna keep my hands from ye."

He did hug me then, wrapping long arms about me and pulling my face into the snowy tucks of his shirt, smelling faintly of the laundry starch Brother Alfonse used at the Abbey.

"Why should you?" I said, muffled in his linen. "You've a bit of time to spare, surely? It's only a short ride to the docks."

"It isna that," he said, smoothing my riotous hair.

"Oh, I'm too fat?" In fact, my stomach was still nearly flat, and I was thinner than usual because of the sickness. "Or is it . . . ?"

"No," he said, smiling. "Ye talk too much." He bent and kissed me, then scooped me up and sat down on the bed, holding me on his lap. I lay down and pulled him determinedly down on top of me.

"Claire, no!" he protested as I started unbuckling his kilt.

I stared at him. "Whyever not?"

"Well," he said awkwardly, blushing a bit. "The child . . . I mean, I dinna want to hurt it."

I laughed.

"Jamie, you can't hurt it. It's no bigger than the tip of my finger yet." I held up a finger in illustration, then used it to trace the full, curving line of his lower lip. He seized my hand and bent to kiss me abruptly, as though to erase the tickle of my touch.

"You're sure?" he asked. "I mean . . . I keep thinking he wouldna like being jounced about . . ."

"He'll never notice," I assured him, hands once more busy with the buckle of his kilt.

"Well . . . if you're sure of it."

There was a peremptory rap at the door, and with impeccable Gallic timing, the chambermaid pushed her way in backward, carelessly gouging the door with a billet of wood as she turned. From the scarred surfaces of door and jamb, it appeared that this was her usual method of operations.

"*Bonjour*, Monsieur, Madame," she muttered, with a curt nod toward the bed as she shuffled toward the hearth. All right for *some* people, said her attitude, louder than words. Used by this time to the matter-of-factness with which servants treated the sight of inn patrons in any form of dishabille, I merely murmured "*Bonjour*, Mademoiselle," in return and let it go at that. I also let go of Jamie's kilt, and slid under the covers, pulling the quilt up to hide my scarlet cheeks.

Possessed of somewhat greater sang-froid, Jamie placed one of the bolsters strategically across his lap, parked his elbows on it, rested his chin on upturned palms, and made pleasant conversation with the maid, praising the cuisine of the house.

"And from where do you procure the wine, Mademoiselle?" he asked politely.

"From here, from there." She shrugged, stuffing kindling rapidly under the sticks with a practiced hand. "Wherever it's cheapest." The woman's plump face creased slightly as she gave Jamie a sidelong look from the hearth.

"I gathered as much," he said, grinning at her, and she gave a brief snort of amusement.

"I'll wager I can match the price you're getting, and double the quality," he offered. "Tell your mistress."

One eyebrow rose skeptically. "And what's your own price, Monsieur?"

He made an altogether Gallic gesture of self-abnegation. "Nothing, Mademoiselle. I go to call upon a kinsman who sells wine. Perhaps I can bring him some new business to ensure my welcome, no?"

She nodded, seeing the wisdom of this, and grunted as she rose from her knees.

"Well enough, Monsieur. I'll speak to the *patronne*."

The door thumped to behind the maid, aided by a skillful swing of her hip in passing. Putting the bolster aside, Jamie stood up and began to rebuckle his kilt.

"Where do you think you're going?" I protested.

He glanced down at me, and a reluctant smile curved the wide mouth.

"Oh. Well . . . you're sure you're up to it, Sassenach?"

"I am if you are," I said, unable to resist.

He eyed me austerely.

"Just for that, I should go at once," he said. "Still, I've heard that ye ought to humor expectant mothers." He let the kilt fall to the floor and sat down beside me in his shirt, the bed creaking beneath his weight.

His breath rose in a faint cloud as he turned back the quilt and spread the front of the nightdress to expose my breasts. Bending his head, he kissed each one, touching the nipple delicately with his tongue, so it rose as though by magic, a swelling dark pink against the white skin of my breast.

"God, they're so lovely," he murmured, repeating the process on the other side. He cupped both breasts, admiring them.

"They're heavier," he said, "just a bit. And the nipples are darker, too." One forefinger traced the springing curve of a single fine hair that rose near the dark areola, silver in the frosted light of the morning.

Lifting the quilt, he rolled next to me and I turned into his arms, clasping the solid curves of his back, letting my hands cup the firm rounds of his buttocks. His bare flesh was chilled by the morning air, but the goose bumps smoothed away under the warmth of my touch.

I tried to bring him to me at once, but he resisted me gently, forcing me down onto the pillow as he nibbled the edges of neck and ear. One hand slid up my thigh, the thin material of the nightgown gliding in waves before it.

His head dipped lower, and his hands gently spread my thighs apart. I shivered momentarily as the cold air hit the bare skin of my legs, then relaxed completely into the warm demand of his mouth.

His hair was loose, not yet laced back for the day, and the soft red tickle of it brushed my thighs. The solid weight of his body rested comfortably between my legs, broad hands cupped on the roundness of my hips.

"Mmmm?" came an interrogative sound from below.

I arched my hips slightly in response, and a brief chuckle grazed my skin with warmth.

The hands slid beneath my hips and raised me, and I relaxed into deliquescence as the tiny shudder grew and spread, rising in seconds to a fulfillment that left me limp and gasping, Jamie's head resting on my thigh. He waited a moment for me to recover, caressing the slope of my leg, before returning to his self-appointed task.

I smoothed the tumbled hair back, caressing those ears, so incongruously small and neat for such a large, blunt man. The upper curve glowed with a faint, translucent pink, and I ran my thumb along the edge of the curve.

"They're pointed at the tips," I said. "Just a bit. Like a faun's."

"Oh, aye?" he said, interrupting his labors for a moment. "Like a small deer, ye mean, or the things ye see in classical paintings wi' goat's legs, chasing naked women?"

I lifted my head and peered down across the roil of bed-clothes, nightgown, and naked flesh, to the deep blue cat-eyes, gleaming above damp curls of brown hair.

"If the shoe fits," I said, "wear it." And let my head fall back on the pillow as the resultant muffled laugh vibrated against my all too sensitive flesh.

"Oh," I said, straining upward. "Oh, my. Jamie, come here."

"Not yet," he said, doing something with the tip of his tongue that made me squirm uncontrollably.

"Now," I said.

He didn't bother to reply, and I had no more breath to speak with.

"Oh," I said, a bit later. "That's . . ."

"Mmmm?"

"Good," I murmured. "Come here."

"No, I'll do," he said, face invisible behind the tangle of roan and cinnamon. "Would ye like it if I . . ."

"Jamie," I said. "I want you. Come *here.*"

Sighing in resignation, he rose to his knees and let me pull him upward, settling at last with his weight balanced on his elbows, but comfortingly solid on top of me, belly to belly and lips to lips. He opened his mouth to protest further, but I promptly kissed him, and he slid between my thighs before he could stop himself. He moaned slightly in involuntary pleasure as he entered me, muscles tensing as he gripped my shoulders.

He was gentle and slow, pausing now and then to kiss me deeply, moving again only at my silent urging. I ran my hands softly down the slope of his back, careful not to press on the healing ridges of the fresh scars. The long muscles of his thigh trembled briefly against my own, but he held back, unwilling to move as quickly as he needed to.

I moved my hips against him, to bring him deeper.

He closed his eyes, and his brow furrowed slightly in concentration. His mouth was open, and his breath came hard.

"I can't . . ." he said. "Oh, God, I canna help it." His buttocks clenched suddenly, taut beneath my hands.

I sighed with deep satisfaction, and pulled him hard against me.

"You're all right?" he asked, a few moments later.

"I won't break, you know," I said, smiling into his eyes.

He laughed huskily. "Maybe not, Sassenach, but *I* may." He gathered me close against him, his cheek pressed against my hair. I flipped the quilt up and tucked it around his shoulders, sealing us in a pocket of warmth. The heat of the fire had not yet reached the bed, but the ice on the window was thawing, the crusted edge of the rime melted into glowing diamonds.

We lay quiet for a time, listening to the occasional crack of the burning applewood in the hearth and the faint sounds of the inn as the guests stirred to life. There were callings to and fro from the balconies across the courtyard, the swish and clop of hooves on the slushy stones outside, and the odd squeal now and then from below, from the piglets the land-lady was raising in the kitchen behind the stove.

"Très français, n'est-ce pas?" I said, smiling at the sounds of an altercation drifting up through the floorboards, an ami-able settling of accounts between the innkeeper's wife and the local vintner.

"Diseased son of a pox-ridden whore," the female voice remarked. "The brandy from last week tasted like horse-piss."

I didn't need to see the reply to imagine the one-shoul-dered shrug that went with it.

"How would you know, Madame? After the sixth glass, it all tastes the same, is it not so?"

The bed shook slightly as Jamie laughed with me. He lifted his head from the pillow and sniffed appreciatively at the scent of frying ham that filtered through the drafty chinks of the floorboards.

"Aye, it's France," he agreed. "Food, and drink—and love." He patted my bare hip before tugging the wrinkled gown down over it.

"Jamie," I said softly, "are you happy about it? About the baby?" Outlawed in Scotland, barred from his own home, and with only vague prospects in France, he could pardonably have been less than enthused about acquiring an additional obligation.

He was silent for a moment, only hugging me harder, then sighed briefly before answering.

"Aye, Sassenach." His hand strayed downward, gently rubbing my belly. "I'm happy. And proud as a stallion. But I am most awfully afraid, too."

"About the birth? I'll be all right." I could hardly blame him for apprehension; his own mother had died in childbirth, and birth and its complications were the leading cause of death for women in these times. Still, I knew a thing or two myself, and I had no intention whatever of exposing myself to what passed for medical care here.

"Aye, that—and everything," he said softly. "I want to protect ye, Sassenach—spread myself over ye like a cloak and shield you and the child wi' my body." His voice was soft and husky, with a slight catch in it. "I would do anything for ye . . . and yet . . . there's nothing I *can* do. It doesna matter how strong I am, or how willing; I canna go with you where ye must go . . . nor even help ye at all. And to think of the things that might happen, and me helpless to stop them . . . aye, I'm afraid, Sassenach.

"And yet"—he turned me toward him, hand closing gently over one breast—"yet when I think of you wi' my child at your breast . . . then I feel as though I've gone hollow as a soap bubble, and perhaps I shall burst with joy."

He pressed me tight against his chest, and I hugged him with all my might.

"Oh, Claire, ye do break my heart wi' loving you."

I slept for some time, and woke slowly, hearing the clang of a church bell ringing in the nearby square. Fresh from the Abbey of Ste. Anne, where all the day's activities took place to the rhythm of bells, I automatically glanced at the window, to gauge the intensity of the light and guess the time of day. Bright, clear light, and a window free of ice. The bells rang for the Angelusthen, and it was noon.

I stretched, enjoying the blissful knowledge that I needn't get up at once. Early pregnancy made me tired, and the strain of travel had added to my fatigue, making the long rest doubly welcome.

It had rained and snowed unceasingly on the journey as the winter storms battered the French coast. Still, it could have been worse. We had originally intended to go to Rome, not Le Havre. That would have been three or four weeks' travel, in this weather.

Faced with the prospect of earning a living abroad, Jamie had obtained a recommendation as a translator to James Francis Edward Stuart, exiled King of Scotland—or merely the Chevalier St. George, Pretender to the Throne, depending on your loyalties—and we had determined to join the Pretender's court near Rome.

It had been a near thing, at that; we had been on the point of leaving for Italy, when Jamie's uncle Alexander, Abbot of Ste. Anne's, had summoned us to his study.

"I have heard from His Majesty," he announced without preamble.

"Which one?" Jamie asked. The slight family resemblance between the two men was exaggerated by their posture —both sat bolt upright in their chairs, shoulders squared. On the abbot's part, the posture was due to natural asceticism; on Jamie's, to reluctance to let the newly healed scars on his back contact the wood of the chair.

"His Majesty King James," his uncle replied, frowning slightly at me. I was careful to keep my face blank; my presence in Abbot Alexander's study was a mark of trust, and I didn't want to do anything to jeopardize it. He had known me a bare six weeks, since the day after Christmas, when I had appeared at his gate with Jamie, who was near death from torture and imprisonment. Subsequent acquaintance had presumably given the abbot some confidence in me. On the other hand, I was still English. And the English King's name was George, not James.

"Aye? Is he not in need of a translator, then?" Jamie was still thin, but he had been working outdoors with the Brothers who minded the stables and fields of the Abbey, and his face was regaining tinges of its normal healthy color.

"He is in need of a loyal servant—and a friend." Abbot Alexander tapped his fingers on a folded letter that lay on his desk, the crested seal broken. He pursed his lips, glancing from me to his nephew and back.

"What I tell you now must not be repeated," he said sternly. "It will be common knowledge soon, but for now—" I had tried to look trustworthy and close-mouthed; Jamie merely nodded, with a touch of impatience.

"His Highness, Prince Charles Edward, has left Rome, and will arrive in France within the week," the Abbot said, leaning slightly forward as though to emphasize the importance of what he was saying.

And it was important. James Stuart had mounted an abortive attempt to regain his throne in 1715—an ill-considered military operation that had failed almost immediately for lack of support. Since then—according to Alexander—the exiled James of Scotland had worked tirelessly, writing ceaselessly to his fellow monarchs, and particularly to his cousin, Louis of France, reiterating the legitimacy of his claim to the throne of Scotland and England, and the position of his son, Prince Charles, as heir to that throne.

"His royal cousin Louis has been distressingly deaf to these entirely proper claims," the Abbot had said, frowning at the letter as though it were Louis. "If he's now come to a realization of his responsibilities in the matter, it's cause for great rejoicing among those who hold dear the sacred right of kingship."

Among the Jacobites, that was, James's supporters. Of whom Abbot Alexander of the Abbey of Ste. Anne—born Alexander Fraser of Scotland—was one. Jamie had told me that Alexander was one of the exiled King's most frequent correspondents, in touch with all that touched the Stuart cause.

"He's well placed for it," Jamie had explained to me, discussing the endeavor on which we were about to embark. "The papal messenger system crosses Italy, France, and Spain faster than almost any other. And the papal messengers canna be interfered with by government customs officers, so the letters they carry are less likely to be intercepted."

James of Scotland, exiled in Rome, was supported in large part by the Pope, in whose interest it very much was to have a Catholic monarchy restored to England and Scotland. Therefore, the largest part of James's private mail was carried by papal messenger—and passed through the hands of loyal supporters within the Church hierarchy, like Abbot Alexander of Ste. Anne de Beaupré, who could be depended on to communicate with the King's supporters in Scotland, with less risk than sending letters openly from Rome to Edinburgh and the Highlands.

I watched Alexander with interest, as he expounded the importance of Prince Charles's visit to France. A stocky man of about my own height, he was dark, and considerably shorter than his nephew, but shared with him the faintly slanted eyes, the sharp intelligence, and the talent for discerning hidden motive that seemed to characterize the Frasers I had met.

"So," he finished, stroking his full, dark-brown beard, "I cannot say whether His Highness is in France at Louis's invitation, or has come uninvited, on behalf of his father."

"It makes a wee bit of difference," Jamie remarked, raising one eyebrow skeptically.

His uncle nodded, and a wry smile showed briefly in the thicket of his beard.

"True, lad," he said, letting a faint hint of his native Scots emerge from his usual formal English. "Very true. And that's where you and your wife may be of service, if ye will."

The proposal was simple; His Majesty King James would provide travel expenses and a small stipend, if the nephew of his most loyal and most esteemed friend Alexander would agree to travel to Paris, there to assist his son, His Highness Prince Charles Edward, in whatever ways the latter might require.

I was stunned. We had meant originally to go to Rome because that seemed the best place to embark on our quest: the prevention of the second Jacobite Rising—the '45. From my own knowledge of history, I knew that the Rising, financed from France and carried out by Charles Edward Stuart, would go much farther than had his father's attempt in 1715—but not nearly far enough. If matters progressed as I thought they would, then the troops under Bonnie Prince

Charlie would meet with disastrous defeat at Culloden in 1746, and the people of the Highlands would suffer the repercussions of defeat for two centuries thereafter.

Now, in 1744, apparently Charles himself was just beginning his search for support in France. Where better to try to stop a rebellion, than at the side of its leader?

I glanced at Jamie, who was looking over his uncle's shoulder at a small shrine set into the wall. His eyes rested on the gilded figure of Ste. Anne herself and the small sheaf of hothouse flowers laid at her feet, while his thoughts worked behind an expressionless face. At last he blinked once, and smiled at his uncle.

"Whatever assistance His Highness might require? Aye," he said quietly, "I think I can do that. We'll go."

And we had. Instead of proceeding directly to Paris, though, we had come down the coast from Ste. Anne to Le Havre, to meet first with Jamie's cousin, Jared Fraser.

A prosperous Scottish émigré, Jared was an importer of wines and spirits, with a small warehouse and large town house in Paris, and a very large warehouse indeed here in Le Havre, where he had asked Jamie to meet him, when Jamie had written to say we were en route to Paris.

Sufficiently rested by now, I was beginning to feel hungry. There was food on the table; Jamie must have told the chambermaid to bring it while I slept.

I had no dressing gown, but my heavy velvet traveling cloak was handy; I sat up and pulled the warm weight of it over my shoulders before rising to relieve myself, add another stick of wood to the fire, and sit down to my late breakfast.

I chewed hard rolls and baked ham contentedly, washing them down with the jug of milk provided. I hoped Jamie was being adequately fed as well; he insisted that Jared was a good friend, but I had my doubts about the hospitality of some of Jamie's relatives, having met a few of them by now. True, Abbot Alexander had welcomed us—insofar as a man in the abbot's position could be said to welcome having an outlaw nephew with a suspect wife descend upon him unexpectedly. But our sojourn with Jamie's mother's people, the MacKenzies of Leoch, had come within inches of killing me the autumn before, when I had been arrested and tried as a witch.

"Granted," I'd said, "this Jared's a Fraser, and they seem a trifle safer than your MacKenzie relatives. But have you actually met him before?"

"I lived with him for a time when I was eighteen," he told me, dribbling candle-wax onto his reply and pressing his father's wedding ring on the resultant greenish-gray puddle. A small cabochon ruby, its mount was engraved with the Fraser clan motto, *je suis prest:* "I am ready."

"He had me to stay with him when I came to Paris to finish my schooling, and learn a bit of the world. He was verra kind to me; a good friend of my father's. And there's no one knows more about Parisian society than the man who sells it drink," he added, cracking the ring loose from the hardened wax. "I want to talk to Jared before I walk into Louis's court by the side of Charles Stuart; I should like to feel that I have some chance of getting out again," he finished wryly.

"Why? Do you think there'll be trouble?" I asked. "Whatever assistance His Highness might require" seemed to offer quite a bit of latitude.

He smiled at my worried look.

"No, I dinna expect any difficulty. But what is it the Bible says, Sassenach? 'Put not your trust in princes'?" He rose and kissed me quickly on the brow, tucking the ring back in his sporran. "Who am I to ignore the word of God, eh?"

I spent the afternoon in reading one of the herbals that my friend Brother Ambrose had pressed upon me as a parting gift, then in necessary repairs with needle and thread. Neither of us owned many clothes, and while there were advantages in traveling light, it meant that holey socks and undone hems demanded immediate attention. My needlecase was nearly as precious to me as the small chest in which I carried herbs and medicines.

The needle dipped in and out of the fabric, winking in the light from the window. I wondered how Jamie's visit with Jared was going. I wondered still more what Prince Charles would be like. He would be the first historically famous person I had met, and while I knew better than to believe all the legends that had (not had, *would,* I reminded myself) sprung up around him, the reality of the man was a mystery. The

Rising of the '45 would depend almost entirely on the personality of this one young man—its failure or success. Whether it took place at all might depend upon the efforts of another young man—Jamie Fraser. And me.

I was still absorbed in my mending and my thoughts, when heavy footsteps in the corridor aroused me to the realization that it was late in the day; the drip of water from the eaves had slowed as the temperature dropped, and the flames of the sinking sun glowed in the ice spears hanging from the roof. The door opened, and Jamie came in.

He smiled vaguely in my direction, then stopped dead by the table, face absorbed as though he were trying to remember something. He took his cloak off, folded it, and hung it neatly over the foot of the bed, straightened, marched over to the other stool, sat down on it with great precision, and closed his eyes.

I sat still, my mending forgotten in my lap, watching this performance with considerable interest. After a moment, he opened his eyes and smiled at me, but didn't say anything. He leaned forward, studying my face with great attention, as though he hadn't seen me in weeks. At last, an expression of profound revelation passed over his face, and he relaxed, shoulders slumping as he rested his elbows on his knees.

"Whisky," he said, with immense satisfaction.

"I see," I said cautiously. "A lot of it?"

He shook his head slowly from side to side, as though it were very heavy. I could almost hear the contents sloshing.

"Not me," he said, very distinctly. "You."

"Me?" I said indignantly.

"Your eyes," he said. He smiled beatifically. His own eyes were soft and dreamy, cloudy as a trout pool in the rain.

"My eyes? What have my eyes got to do with . . ."

"They're the color of verra fine whisky, wi' the sun shining through them from behind. I thought this morning they looked like sherry, but I was wrong. Not sherry. Not brandy. It's whisky. That's what it is." He looked so gratified as he said this that I couldn't help laughing.

"Jamie, you're terribly drunk. What have you been doing?"

His expression altered to a slight frown.

"I'm not drunk."

"Oh, no?" I laid the mending aside and came over to lay a hand on his forehead. It was cool and damp, though his face was flushed. He at once put his arms about my waist and pulled me close, nuzzling affectionately at my bosom. The smell of mingled spirits rose from him like a fog, so thick as almost to be visible.

"Come here to me, Sassenach," he murmured. "My whisky-eyed lass, my love. Let me take ye to bed."

I thought it a debatable point as to who was likely to be taking whom to bed, but didn't argue. It didn't matter why he thought he was going to bed, after all, provided he got there. I bent and got a shoulder under his armpit to help him up, but he leaned away, rising slowly and majestically under his own power.

"I dinna need help," he said, reaching for the cord at the neck of his shirt. "I told ye, I'm not drunk."

"You're right," I said. "'Drunk' isn't anywhere near sufficient to describe your current state. Jamie, you're completely pissed."

His eyes traveled down the front of his kilt, across the floor, and up the front of my gown.

"No, I'm not," he said, with great dignity. "I did that outside." He took a step toward me, glowing with ardor. "Come here to me, Sassenach; I'm ready."

I thought "ready" was a bit of an overstatement in one regard; he'd gotten his buttons half undone, and his shirt hung askew on his shoulders, but that was as far as he was likely to make it unaided.

In other respects, though . . . the broad expanse of his chest was exposed, showing the small hollow in the center where I was accustomed to rest my chin, and the small curly hairs sprang up joyous around his nipples. He saw me looking at him, and reached for one of my hands, clasping it to his breast. He was startlingly warm, and I moved instinctively toward him. The other arm swept round me and he bent to kiss me. He made such a thorough job of it that I felt mildly intoxicated, merely from sharing his breath.

"All right," I said, laughing. "If you're ready, so am I. Let me undress you first, though—I've had enough mending today."

He stood still as I stripped him, scarcely moving. He

didn't move, either, as I attended to my own clothes and turned down the bed.

I climbed in and turned to look at him, ruddy and magnificent in the sunset glow. He was finely made as a Greek statue, long-nosed and high-cheeked as a profile on a Roman coin. The wide, soft mouth was set in a dreamy smile, and the slanted eyes looked far away. He was perfectly immobile.

I viewed him with some concern.

"Jamie," I said, "how, exactly, do you decide whether you're drunk?"

Aroused by my voice, he swayed alarmingly to one side, but caught himself on the edge of the mantelpiece. His eyes drifted around the room, then fixed on my face. For an instant, they blazed clear and pellucid with intelligence.

"Och, easy, Sassenach. If ye can stand up, you're not drunk." He let go of the mantelpiece, took a step toward me, and crumpled slowly onto the hearth, eyes blank, and a wide, sweet smile on his dreaming face.

"Oh," I said.

The yodeling of roosters outside and the clashing of pots below woke me just after dawn the next morning. The figure next to me jerked, waking abruptly, then froze as the sudden movement jarred his head.

I raised up on one elbow to examine the remains. Not too bad, I thought critically. His eyes were screwed tightly shut against stray beams of sunlight, and his hair stuck out in all directions like a hedgehog's spines, but his skin was pale and clear, and the hands clutching the coverlet were steady.

I pried up one eyelid, peered within, and said playfully, "Anybody home?"

The twin to the eye I was looking at opened slowly, to add its baleful glare to the first. I dropped my hand and smiled charmingly at him.

"Good morning."

"That, Sassenach, is entirely a matter of opinion," he said, and closed both eyes again.

"Have you got any idea how much you weigh?" I asked conversationally.

"No."

The abruptness of the reply suggested that he not only didn't know, he didn't care, but I persisted in my efforts.

"Something around fifteen stone, I make it. About as much as a good-sized boar. Unfortunately, I didn't have any beaters to hang you upside down from a spear and carry you home to the smoking shed."

One eye opened again, and looked consideringly at me, then at the hearthstone on the far side of the room. One corner of his mouth lifted in a reluctant smile.

"How did you get me in bed?"

"I didn't. I couldn't budge you, so I just laid a quilt over you and left you on the hearth. You came to life and crawled in under your own power, somewhere in the middle of the night."

He seemed surprised, and opened the other eye again.

"I did?"

I nodded and tried to smooth down the hair that spiked out over his left ear.

"Oh, yes. Very single-minded, you were."

"Single-minded?" He frowned, thinking, and stretched, thrusting his arms up over his head. Then he looked startled.

"No. I couldn't have."

"Yes, you could. Twice."

He squinted down his chest, as though looking for confirmation of this improbable statement, then looked back at me.

"Really? Well, that's hardly fair; I dinna remember a thing about it." He hesitated for a moment, looking shy. "Was it all right, then? I didna do anything foolish?"

I flopped down next to him and snuggled my head into the curve of his shoulder.

"No, I wouldn't call it foolish. You weren't very conversational, though."

"Thank the Lord for small blessings," he said, and a small chuckle rumbled through his chest.

"Mm. You'd forgotten how to say anything except "I love you,' but you said that a lot."

The chuckle came back, louder this time. "Oh, aye? Well, could have been worse, I suppose."

He drew in his breath, then paused. He turned his head and sniffed suspiciously at the soft tuft of cinnamon under his raised arm.

"Christ!" he said. He tried to push me away. "Ye dinna want to put your head near my oxter, Sassenach. I smell like a boar that's been dead a week."

"And pickled in brandy after," I agreed, snuggling closer. "How on earth did you get so—ahem—stinking drunk, anyway?"

"Jared's hospitality." He settled himself in the pillows with a deep sigh, arm round my shoulder.

"He took me down to show me his warehouse at the docks. And the storeroom there where he keeps the rare vintages and the Portuguese brandy and the Jamaican rum." He grimaced slightly, recalling. "The wine wasna so bad, for that you just taste, and spit it on the floor when you've done wi' a mouthful. But neither of us could see wasting the brandy that way. Besides, Jared said ye need to let it trickle down the back of your throat, to appreciate it fully."

"How much of it did you appreciate?" I asked curiously.

"I lost count in the middle of the second bottle." Just then, a church bell started to ring nearby; the summons to early Mass. Jamie sat bolt upright, staring at the windowpane, bright with sun.

"Christ, Sassenach! What time is it?"

"About six, I suppose," I said, puzzled. "Why?"

He relaxed slightly, though he stayed sitting up.

"Oh, that's all right, then. I was afraid it was the Angelus bell. I'd lost all track of time."

"I'd say so. Does it matter?"

In a burst of energy, he threw back the quilts and stood up. He staggered a moment, but kept his balance, though both hands went to his head, to make sure it was still attached.

"Aye," he said, gasping a bit. "We've an appointment this morning down at the docks, at Jared's warehouse. The two of us."

"Really?" I clambered out of bed myself, and groped for the chamber pot under the bed. "If he's planning to finish the job, I shouldn't think he'd want witnesses."

Jamie's head popped through the neck of his shirt, eyebrows raised.

"Finish the job?"

"Well, most of your other relatives seem to want to kill

you or me; why not Jared? He's made a good start at poisoning you, seems to me."

"Verra funny, Sassenach," he said dryly. "Have ye something decent to wear?"

I had been wearing a serviceable gray serge gown on our travels, acquired through the good offices of the almoner at the Abbey of Ste. Anne, but I did also have the gown in which I had escaped from Scotland, a gift from Lady Annabelle MacRannoch. A pretty leaf-green velvet, it made me look rather pale, but was stylish enough.

"I think so, if there aren't too many saltwater stains on it."

I knelt by the small traveling chest, unfolding the green velvet. Kneeling next to me, Jamie flipped back the lid of my medicine box, studying the layers of bottles and boxes and bits of gauze-wrapped herbs.

"Have ye got anything in here for a verra vicious headache, Sassenach?"

I peered over his shoulder, then reached in and touched one bottle.

"Horehound might help, though it's not the best. And willow-bark tea with sow fennel works fairly well, but it takes some time to brew. Tell you what—why don't I make you up a recipe for hobnailed liver? Wonderful hangover cure."

He bent a suspicious blue eye on me.

"That sounds nasty."

"It is," I said cheerfully. "But you'll feel lots better after you throw up."

"Mphm." He stood up and nudged the chamber pot toward me with one toe.

"Vomiting in the morning is *your* job, Sassenach," he said. "Get it over with and get dressed. I'll stand the headache."

Jared Munro Fraser was a small, spare, black-eyed man, who bore more than a passing resemblance to his distant cousin Murtagh, the Fraser clansman who had accompanied us to Le Havre. When I first saw Jared, standing majestically in the gaping doors of his warehouse, so that streams of longshoremen carrying casks were forced to go around him, the resemblance was strong enough that I blinked and rubbed my eyes. Murtagh, so far as I knew, was still at the inn, attending a lame horse.

Jared had the same lank, dark hair and piercing eyes; the same sinewy, monkey-like frame. But there all resemblance stopped, and as we drew closer, Jamie gallantly clearing a path for me through the mob with elbows and shoulders, I could see the differences as well. Jared's face was oblong, rather than hatchet-shaped, with a cheerful snub nose that effectively ruined the dignified air conferred at a distance by his excellent tailoring and upright carriage.

A successful merchant rather than a cattle-raider, he also knew how to smile—unlike Murtagh, whose natural expression was one of unrelieved dourness—and a broad grin of welcome broke out on his face as we were jostled and shoved up the ramp into his presence.

"My dear!" he exclaimed, clutching me by the arm and yanking me deftly out of the way of two burly stevedores rolling a gigantic cask through the huge door. "So pleased to see you at last!" The cask bumped noisily on the boards of the ramp, and I could hear the rolling slosh of its contents as it passed me.

"You can treat rum like that," Jared observed, watching the ungainly progress of the enormous barrel through the obstructions of the warehouse, "but not port. I always fetch that up myself, along with the bottled wines. In fact, I was just setting off to see to a new shipment of Belle Rouge port. Would you perhaps be interested in accompanying me?"

I glanced at Jamie, who nodded, and we set off at once in Jared's wake, sidestepping the rumbling traffic of casks and hogsheads, carts and barrows, and men and boys of all descriptions carrying bolts of fabric, boxes of grain and foodstuffs, rolls of hammered copper, sacks of flour, and anything else that could be transported by ship.

Le Havre was an important center of shipping traffic, and the docks were the heart of the city. A long, solid wharf ran nearly a quarter-mile round the edge of the harbor, with smaller docks protruding from it, along which were anchored three-masted barks and brigantines, dories and small galleys; a full range of the ships that provisioned France.

Jamie kept a firm hold on my elbow, the better to yank

me out of the way of oncoming handcarts, rolling casks, and careless merchants and seamen, who were inclined not to look where they were going but rather to depend on sheer momentum to see them through the scrum of the docks.

As we made our way down the quay, Jared shouted genteelly into my ear on the other side, pointing out objects of interest as we passed, and explaining the history and ownership of the various ships in a staccato, disjointed manner. The *Arianna*, which we were on our way to see, was in fact one of Jared's own ships. Ships, I gathered, might belong to a single owner, more often to a company of merchants who owned them collectively, or, occasionally, to a captain who contracted his vessel, crew, and services for a voyage. Seeing the number of company-owned vessels, compared to the relatively few owned by individuals, I began to form a very respectful idea of Jared's worth.

The *Arianna* was in the middle of the anchored row, near a large warehouse with the name FRASER painted on it in sloping, whitewashed letters. Seeing the name gave me an odd little thrill, a sudden feeling of alliance and belonging, with the realization that I shared that name, and with it, an acknowledged kinship with those who bore it.

The *Arianna* was a three-masted ship, perhaps sixty feet long, with a wide bow. There were two cannon on the side of the ship that faced the dock; in case of robbery on the high seas, I supposed. Men were swarming all over the deck with what I assumed was some purpose, though it looked like nothing so much as an ant's nest under attack.

All sails were reefed and tied, but the rising tide shifted the vessel slightly, swinging the bowsprit toward us. It was decorated with a rather grim-visaged figurehead; with her formidable bare bosom and tangled curls all spangled with salt, the lady looked as though she didn't enjoy sea air allthat much.

"Sweet little beauty, is she not?" Jared asked, waving a hand expansively. I assumed he meant the ship, not the figurehead.

"Verra nice," said Jamie politely. I caught his uneasy glance at the boat's waterline, where the small waves lapped dark gray against the hull. I could see that he was hoping we would not be obliged to go on board. A gallant warrior, brilliant, bold, and courageous in battle, Jamie Fraser was also a landlubber.

Definitely not one of the hardy, seafaring Scots who hunted whales from Tarwathie or voyaged the world in search of wealth, he suffered from a seasickness so acute that our journey across the Channel in December had nearly killed him, weakened as he then was by the effects of torture and imprisonment. And while yesterday's drinking orgy with Jared wasn't in the same league, it wasn't likely to have made him any more seaworthy.

I could see dark memories crossing his face as he listened to his cousin extolling the sturdiness and speed of the *Arianna,* and drew near enough to whisper to him.

"Surely not while it's at anchor?"

"I don't know, Sassenach," he replied, with a look at the ship in which loathing and resignation were nicely mingled. "But I suppose we'll find out." Jared was already halfway up the gangplank, greeting the captain with loud cries of welcome. "If I turn green, can ye pretend to faint or something? It will make a poor impression if I vomit on Jared's shoes."

I patted his arm reassuringly. "Don't worry. I have faith in you."

"It isna *me,*" he said, with a last, lingering glance at terra firma, "it's my stomach."

The ship stayed comfortingly level under our shoes, however, and both Jamie and his stomach acquitted themselves nobly—assisted, perhaps, by the brandy poured out for us by the captain.

"A nice make," Jamie said, passing the glass briefly under his nose and closing his eyes in approval of the rich, aromatic fumes. "Portuguese, isn't it?"

Jared laughed delightedly and nudged the captain.

"You see, Portis? I told you he had a natural palate! He's only tasted it once before!"

I bit the inside of my cheek and avoided Jamie's eye. The captain, a large, scruffy-looking specimen, looked bored, but grimaced politely in Jamie's direction, exhibiting three gold teeth. A man who liked to keep his wealth portable.

"Ung," he said. "This the lad's going to keep your bilges dry, is it?"

Jared looked suddenly embarrassed, a slight flush rising

under the leathery skin of his face. I noticed with fascination that one ear was pierced for an earring, and wondered just what sort of background had led to his present success.

"Aye, well," he said, betraying for the first time a hint of Scots accent, "that's to be seen yet. But I think—" He glanced through the port at the activity taking place on the dock, then back at the captain's glass, drained in three gulps while the rest of us were sipping. "Um, I say, Portis, would you allow me to use your cabin for a moment? I should like to confer with my nephew and his wife—and I see that the aft hold seems to be having a bit of trouble with the cargo nets, from the sound of it." This craftily added observation was enough to send Captain Portis out of the cabin like a charging boar, hoarse voice uplifted in a Spanish-French patois that I luckily didn't understand.

Jared stepped delicately to the door and closed it firmly after the captain's bulky form, cutting down the noise level substantially. He returned to the tiny captain's table and ceremoniously refilled all our glasses before speaking. Then he looked from Jamie to me and smiled once more, in charming deprecation.

"It's a bit more precipitous than I'd meant to make such a request," he said. "But I see the good captain has rather given away my hand. The truth of the matter is"—he raised his glass so the watery reflections from the port shivered through the brandy, striking patches of wavering light from the brass fittings of the cabin—"I need a man." He tipped the cup in Jamie's direction, then brought it to his lips and drank.

"A good man," he amplified, lowering the glass. "You see, my dear," bowing to me, "I have the opportunity of making an exceptional investment in a new winery in the Moselle region. But the evaluation of it is not one I should feel comfortable in entrusting to a subordinate; I should need to see the facilities myself, and advise in their development. The undertaking would require several months."

He gazed thoughtfully into his glass, gently swirling the fragrant brown liquid so its perfume filled the tiny cabin. I had drunk no more than a few sips from my own glass, but began to feel slightly giddy, more from a rising excitement than from drink.

"It's too good a chance to be missed," Jared said. "And

there's the chance of making several good contracts with the wineries along the Rhône; the products there are excellent, but relatively rare in Paris. God, they'd sell among the nobility like snow in summer!" His shrewd black eyes gleamed momentarily with visions of avarice, then sparkled with humor as he looked at me.

"But—" he said.

"But," I finished for him, "you can't leave your business here without a guiding hand."

"Intelligence as well as beauty and charm. I congratulate you, Cousin." He tilted a well-groomed head toward Jamie, one eyebrow cocked in humorous approval.

"I confess that I was at something of a loss to see how I was to proceed," he said, setting the glass down on the small table with the air of a man putting aside social frivolity for the sake of serious business. "But when you wrote from Ste. Anne, saying you intended to visit Paris . . ." He hesitated a moment, then smiled at Jamie, with an odd little flutter of the hands.

"Knowing that you, my lad"—he nodded to Jamie— "have a head for figures, I was strongly inclined to consider your arrival an answer to prayer. Still, I thought that perhaps we should meet and become reacquainted before I took the step of making you a definite proposal."

You mean you thought you'd better see how presentable *I* was, I thought cynically, but smiled at him nonetheless. I caught Jamie's eye, and one of his brows twitched upward. This was our week for proposals, evidently. For a dispossessed outlaw and a suspected English spy, our services seemed to be rather in demand.

Jared's proposal was more than generous; in return for Jamie's running the French end of the business during the next six months, Jared would not only pay him a salary but would leave his Paris town house, complete with staff, at our disposal.

"Not at all, not at all," he said, when Jamie tried to protest this provision. He pressed a finger on the end of his nose, grinning charmingly at me. "A pretty woman to host dinner parties is a great asset in the wine business, Cousin. You have no idea how much wine you can sell, if you let the customers taste it first." He shook his head decidedly. "No, it will be a great service to me, if your wife would allow herself to be troubled by entertaining."

The thought of hosting supper parties for Parisian society was in fact a trifle daunting. Jamie looked at me, eyebrows raised in question, but I swallowed hard and smiled, nodding. It was a good offer; if he felt competent to take over the running of an importing business, the least I could do was order dinner and brush up my sprightly conversational French.

"Not at all," I murmured, but Jared had taken my agreement for granted, and was going on, intent black eyes fixed on Jamie.

"And then, I thought perhaps you'd be needing an establishment of sorts—for the benefit of the other interests which bring you to Paris."

Jamie smiled noncommittally, at which Jared uttered a short laugh and picked up his brandy glass. We had each been provided a glass of water as well, for cleansing the palate between sips, and he pulled one of these close with the other hand.

"Well, a toast!" he exclaimed. "To our association, Cousin—and to His Majesty!" He lifted the brandy glass in salute, then passed it ostentatiously over the glass of water and brought it to his lips.

I watched this odd behavior in surprise, but it apparently meant something to Jamie, for he smiled at Jared, picked up his own glass and passed it over the water.

"To His Majesty," he repeated. Then, seeing me staring at him in bewilderment, he smiled and explained, "To His Majesty—over the water, Sassenach."

"Oh?" I said, then, realization dawning, "oh!" The king over the water—King James. Which did a bit to explain this sudden urge on the part of everyone to see Jamie and myself established in Paris, which would otherwise have seemed an improbable coincidence.

If Jared were also a Jacobite, then his correspondence with Abbot Alexander was very likely more than coincidental; chances were that Jamie's letter announcing our arrival had come together with one from Alexander, explaining the commission from King James. And if our presence in Paris fitted in with Jared's own plans—then so much the better. With a sudden appreciation for the complexities of the Jacobite network,

I raised my own glass, and drank to His Majesty across the water—and our new partnership with Jared.

Jared and Jamie then settled down to a discussion of the business, and were soon head to head, bent over inky sheets of paper, evidently manifests and bills of lading. The tiny cabin reeked of tobacco, brandy fumes, and unwashed sailor, and I began to feel a trifle queasy again. Seeing that I wouldn't be needed for a while, I stood up quietly and found my way out on deck.

I was careful to avoid the altercation still going on around the rear cargo hatch, and picked my way through coils of rope, objects which I assumed to be belaying pins, and tumbled piles of sail fabric, to a quiet spot in the bow. From here, I had an unobstructed view over the harbor.

I sat on a chest against the taffrail, enjoying the salty breeze and the tarry, fishy smells of ships and harbor. It was still cold, but with my cloak pulled tight around me, I was warm enough. The ship rocked slowly, rising on the incoming tide; I could see the beards of algae on nearby dock pilings lifting and swirling, obscuring the shiny black patches of mussels between them.

The thought of mussels reminded me of the steamed mussels with butter I had had for dinner the night before, and I was suddenly starving. The absurd contrasts of pregnancy seemed to keep me always conscious of my digestion; if I wasn't vomiting, I was ravenously hungry. The thought of food led me to the thought of menus, which led back to a contemplation of the entertaining Jared had mentioned. Dinner parties, hm? It seemed an odd way to begin the job of saving Scotland, but then, I couldn't really think of anything better.

At least if I had Charles Stuart across a dinner table from me, I could keep an eye on him, I thought, smiling to myself at the joke. If he showed signs of hopping a ship for Scotland, maybe I could slip something into his soup.

Perhaps that wasn't so funny, after all. The thought reminded me of Geillis Duncan, and my smile faded. Wife of the procurator fiscal in Cranesmuir, she had murdered her husband by dropping powdered cyanide into his food at a banquet. Accused as a witch soon afterward, she had been arrested while I was with her, and I had been taken to trial myself; a trial from which Jamie had rescued me. The memories of several days spent in the cold dark of the thieves' hole at Cranesmuir were all too fresh, and the wind seemed suddenly very cold.

I shivered, but not altogether from chill. I could not think of Geillis Duncan without that cold finger down my spine. Not so much because of what she had done, but because of who she had been. A Jacobite, too; one whose support of the Stuart cause had been more than slightly tinged with madness. Worse than that, she was what I was—a traveler through the standing stones.

I didn't know whether she had come to the past as I had, by accident, or whether her journey had been deliberate. Neither did I know precisely *where* she had come from. But my last vision of her, screaming defiance at the judges who would condemn her to burn, was of a tall, fair woman, arms stretched high, showing on one arm the telltale round of a vaccination scar. I felt automatically for the small patch of roughened skin on my own upper arm, beneath the comforting folds of my cloak, and shuddered when I found it.

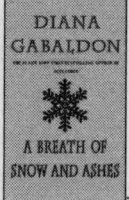

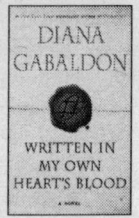

Also by DIANA GABALDON

THE COMPANION
VOLUME

THE OUTLANDER
GRAPHIC NOVEL

THE
LORD JOHN
SERIES

Lord John and the Private Matter
Lord John and the Brotherhood of the Blade
Lord John and the Hand of Devils
The Scottish Prisoner

Continue the saga with original eNovellas,
engrossing tales to complement the Outlander series.

A Plague of Zombies   *The Custom of*   *A Leaf on the Wind*   *The Space Between*
               the Army   *of All Hallows*

DianaGabaldon.com
AuthorDianaGabaldon @Writer_DG

Random House Bantam • Dell • Delacorte • Del Rey

By Diana Gabaldon

(in chronological order)
Outlander
Dragonfly in Amber
Voyager
Drums of Autumn
The Fiery Cross
A Breath of Snow and Ashes
An Echo in the Bone
Written in My Own Heart's Blood

The Outlandish Companion
(nonfiction)

The Exile
(graphic novel)

The Outlandish Companion, Volume Two
(nonfiction)

(in chronological order)
Lord John and the Hellfire Club (novella)
Lord John and the Private Matter
Lord John and the Succubus (novella)
Lord John and the Brotherhood of the Blade
Lord John and the Haunted Soldier (novella)
The Custom of the Army (novella)
Lord John and the Hand of Devils (collected novellas)
The Scottish Prisoner
A Plague of Zombies (novella)

Other Outlander-related novellas
A Leaf on the Wind of All Hallows
The Space Between

DIANA
GABALDON

DRUMS OF
AUTUMN

A DELL BOOK

Published by
Dell Publishing
a division of
Random House, Inc.

Copyright © 1997 by Diana Gabaldon
Excerpt from *The Fiery Cross* by Diana Gabaldon copyright © 2001
by Diana Gabaldon
Cover design by Marietta Anastassatos

LIBRARY OF CONGRESS CATALOG CARD NUMBER:
96-014035

ISBN 978-0-440-22425-9

Reprinted by arrangement with Delacorte Press

MANUFACTURED IN THE UNITED STATES OF AMERICA

Published simultaneously in Canada

Dell mass market edition/December 1997
Dell reissue/September 2002

38 39 37

OPM

*This book turned out to
have a lot to do with fathers,
and so it's for my own father,
Tony Gabaldon,
who also tells stories.*

Acknowledgments

The author's grateful thanks to:

My editor, Jackie Cantor, who said, when informed that there was (ahem) actually another book in this series, "Why am I not surprised to hear this?"

Susan Schwartz and her loyal minions—the copyeditors, typesetters, and book designers—without whom this book would not exist; I hope they eventually recover from the experience.

My husband, Doug Watkins, who said, "I don't know how you go on getting away with this; you don't know *anything* about men!"

My daughter Laura, who generously allowed me to steal two lines of her eighth-grade essay for my Prologue; my son Samuel, who said, "Aren't you *ever* going to finish writing that book?" and (without pausing for breath), "Since you're still busy writing, can we have McDonald's again?" and my daughter Jennifer, who said, "You *are* going to change clothes before you come talk to my class, aren't you? Don't worry, Mommy, I have an outfit all picked out for you."

The anonymous sixth grader who handed back a sample chapter passed around during a talk at his school and said, "That was kind of gross, but really interesting. People don't really *do* that, do they?"

Iain MacKinnon Taylor and his brother Hamish, for Gaelic translations, idioms, and colorful invective. Nancy Bushey, for Gaelic tapes. Karl Hagen, for general advice on Latin grammar. Susan Martin and Reid Snider, for Greek epigrams and rotting pythons. Sylvia Petter, Elise Skidmore, Janet Kieffer Kelly, and Karen Pershing for help with the French bits.

Janet MacConnaughey and Keith Sheppard, for Latin love poetry, macaronics, and the original lyrics of "To Anacreon in Heaven."

Mary Campbell Toerner and Ruby Vincent, for the loan of an

unpublished historical manuscript about the Highlanders of the Cape Fear. Claire Nelson for the loan of the Encyclopaedia Britannica, 1771 edition. Esther and Bill Schindler, for the loan of the books on Eastern forests.

Ron Wodaski, Karl Hagen, Bruce Woods, Rich Hamper, Eldon Garlock, Dean Quarrel, and several other gentlemen members of the CompuServe Writers Forum, for expert opinions on what it feels like to be kicked in the testicles.

Marte Brengle, for detailed descriptions of sweat lodge ceremonials and suggestions on sports cars. Merrill Cornish, for his stunning description of redbuds in bloom. Arlene and Joe McCrea, for saints' names and descriptions of plowing with a mule. Ken Brown, for details of the Presbyterian Baptismal rite (much abridged in the text). David Stanley, Scotland's next great writer, for advice on anoraks, jackets, and the difference between them.

Barbara Schnell, for German translations, error-checking, and sympathetic reading.

Dr. Ellen Mandell, for medical opinions, close reading, and useful suggestions for dealing with inguinal hernias, abortion, and other forms of harrowing bodily trauma.

Dr. Rosina Lippi-Green, for details of Mohawk life and customs, and notes on Scots linguistics and German grammar.

Mac Beckett, for his notion of new and ancient spirits.

Jack Whyte, for his memoirs of life as a Scottish folksinger, including the proper response to kilt jokes.

Susan Davis, for friendship, boundless enthusiasm, dozens of books, descriptions of pulling ticks off her kids—and the strawberries.

Walt Hawn and Gordon Fenwick, for telling me how long is a furlong. John Ravenscroft and miscellaneous members of the UKForum, for a riveting discussion of the RAF's underpants, circa WWII. Eve Ackerman and helpful members of the CompuServe SFLIT Forum, for the publication dates of Conan the Barbarian.

Barbara Raisbeck and Mary M. Robbins, for their helpful references on herbs and early pharmacology.

My anonymous library friend, for the *reams* of useful references.

Arnold Wagner and Steven Lopata, for discussions of high and low explosives and general advice on how to blow things up.

Margaret Campbell and other online residents of North Carolina, for miscellaneous descriptions of their fair state.

John L. Myers, both for telling me about his ghosts, and for generously allowing me to incorporate certain elements of his physique and persona into the formidable John Quincy Myers, Mountain Man. The hernia is fictitious.

As always, thanks also to the many members of the CompuServe Literary Forum and Writers Forum whose names have escaped my memory, for their helpful suggestions and convivial conversation, and to the AOL folder-folk for their stimulating discussions.

A special thanks to Rosana Madrid Gatti, for her labor of love in constructing and maintaining the award-winning Official Diana Gabaldon Web Page (http://www.cco.caltech.edu/~gatti/gabaldon/gabaldon.html).

And thanks to Lori Musser, Dawn Van Winkle, Kaera Hallahan, Virginia Clough, Elaine Faxon, Ellen Stanton, Elaine Smith, Cathy Kravitz, Hanneke (whose last name remains unfortunately illegible), Judith MacDonald, Susan Hunt and her sister Holly, the Boise gang, and many others, for their thoughtful gifts of wine, drawings, rosaries, chocolate, Celtic music, soap, statuary, pressed heather from Culloden, handkerchiefs with echidnas, Maori pens, English teas, garden trowels, and other miscellanea meant to boost my spirits and keep me writing far past the point of exhaustion. It worked.

And lastly to my mother, who touches me in passing.

Diana Gabaldon
dgabaldon@aol.com
76530,523@compuserve.com
[Section Leader, Research and the Craft of Writing, CompuServe Writers Forum]

Prologue

I 've never been afraid of ghosts. I live with them daily, after all. When I look in a mirror, my mother's eyes look back at me; my mouth curls with the smile that lured my great-grandfather to the fate that was me.

No, how should I fear the touch of those vanished hands, laid on me in love unknowing? How could I be afraid of those that molded my flesh, leaving their remnants to live long past the grave?

Still less could I be afraid of those ghosts who touch my thoughts in passing. Any library is filled with them. I can take a book from dusty shelves, and be haunted by the thoughts of one long dead, still lively as ever in their winding sheet of words.

Of course it isn't these homely and accustomed ghosts that trouble sleep and curdle wakefulness. Look back, hold a torch to light the recesses of the dark. Listen to the footsteps that echo behind, when you walk alone.

All the time the ghosts flit past and through us, hiding in the future. We look in the mirror and see the shades of other faces looking back through the years; we see the shape of memory, standing solid in an empty doorway. By blood and by choice, we make our ghosts; we haunt ourselves.

Each ghost comes unbidden from the misty grounds of dream and silence.

Our rational minds say, "No, it isn't."

But another part, an older part, echoes always softly in the dark, "Yes, but it *could* be."

We come and go from mystery and, in between, we try to forget. But a breeze passing in a still room stirs my hair now and then in soft affection. I think it is my mother.

PART ONE

O Brave New World

1

A Hanging in Eden

Charleston, June 1767

I heard the drums long before they came in sight. The beating echoed in the pit of my stomach, as though I too were hollow. The sound traveled through the crowd, a harsh military rhythm meant to be heard over speech or gunfire. I saw heads turn as the people fell silent, looking up the stretch of East Bay Street, where it ran from the half-built skeleton of the new Customs House toward White Point Gardens.

It was a hot day, even for Charleston in June. The best places were on the seawall, where the air moved; here below, it was like being roasted alive. My shift was soaked through, and the cotton bodice clung between my breasts. I wiped my face for the tenth time in as many minutes and lifted the heavy coil of my hair, hoping vainly for a cooling breeze upon my neck.

I was morbidly aware of necks at the moment. Unobtrusively, I put my hand up to the base of my throat, letting my fingers circle it. I could feel the pulse beat in my carotid arteries, along with the drums, and when I breathed, the hot wet air clogged my throat as though I were choking.

I quickly took my hand down, and drew in a breath as deep as I could manage. That was a mistake. The man in front of me hadn't bathed in a month or more; the edge of the stock about his thick neck was dark with grime and his clothes smelled sour and musty, pungent even amid the sweaty reek of the crowd. The smell of hot bread and frying pig fat from the food vendors' stalls lay heavy over a musk of rotting seagrass from the marsh, only slightly relieved by a whiff of salt-breeze from the harbor.

There were several children in front of me, craning and gawking, running out from under the oaks and palmettos to look up the street, being called back by anxious parents. The girl nearest me had a neck like the white part of a grass stalk, slender and succulent.

There was a ripple of excitement through the crowd; the gallows procession was in sight at the far end of the street. The drums grew louder.

"Where is he?" Fergus muttered beside me, craning his own neck to see. "I knew I should have gone with him!"

"He'll be here." I wanted to stand on tiptoe, but didn't, feeling that this would be undignified. I did glance around, though, searching. I could always spot Jamie in a crowd; he stood head and shoulders above most men, and his hair caught the light in a blaze of reddish gold. There was no sign of him yet, only a bobbing sea of bonnets and tricornes, sheltering from the heat those citizens come too late to find a place in the shade.

The flags came first, fluttering above the heads of the excited crowd, the banners of Great Britain and of the Royal Colony of South Carolina. And another, bearing the family arms of the Lord Governor of the colony.

Then came the drummers, walking two by two in step, their sticks an alternate beat and blur. It was a slow march, grimly inexorable. A dead march, I thought they called that particular cadence; very suitable under the circumstances. All other noises were drowned by the rattle of the drums.

Then came the platoon of red-coated soldiers and in their midst, the prisoners.

There were three of them, hands bound before them, linked together by a chain that ran through rings on the iron collars about their necks. The first man was small and elderly, ragged and disreputable, a shambling wreck who lurched and staggered so that the dark-suited clergyman who walked beside the prisoners was obliged to grasp his arm to keep him from falling.

"Is that Gavin Hayes? He looks sick," I murmured to Fergus.

"He's drunk." The soft voice came from behind me, and I whirled, to find Jamie standing at my shoulder, eyes fixed on the pitiful procession.

The small man's disequilibrium was disrupting the progress of the parade, as his stumbling forced the two men chained to him to zig and zag abruptly in order to keep their feet. The general impression was of three inebriates rolling home from the local tavern; grossly at odds with the solemnity of the occasion. I could hear the rustle of laughter over the drums, and shouts and jeers from the crowds on the wrought-iron balconies of the houses on East Bay Street.

"Your doing?" I spoke quietly, so as not to attract notice, but I could have shouted and waved my arms; no one had eyes for anything but the scene before us.

I felt rather than saw Jamie's shrug, as he moved forward to stand beside me.

"It was what he asked of me," he said. "And the best I could manage for him."

"Brandy or whisky?" asked Fergus, evaluating Hayes' appearance with a practiced eye.

"The man's a Scot, wee Fergus." Jamie's voice was as calm as his face, but I heard the small note of strain in it. "Whisky's what he wanted."

"A wise choice. With luck, he won't even notice when they hang him," Fergus muttered. The small man had slipped from the preacher's grasp and fallen flat on his face in the sandy road, pulling one of his companions to his knees; the last prisoner, a tall young man, stayed on his feet but swayed wildly from side to side, trying desperately to keep his balance. The crowd on the point roared with glee.

The captain of the guard glowed crimson between the white of his wig and the metal of his gorget, flushed with fury as much as with sun. He barked an order as the drums continued their somber roll, and a soldier scrambled hastily to remove the chain that bound the prisoners together. Hayes was jerked unceremoniously to his feet, a soldier grasping each arm, and the procession resumed, in better order.

There was no laughter by the time they reached the gallows—a mule-drawn cart placed beneath the limbs of a huge live oak. I could feel the drums beating through the soles of my feet. I felt slightly sick from the sun and the smells. The drums stopped abruptly, and my ears rang in the silence.

"Ye dinna need to watch it, Sassenach," Jamie whispered to me. "Go back to the wagon." His own eyes were fixed unblinkingly on Hayes, who swayed and mumbled in the soldiers' grasp, looking blearily around.

The last thing I wanted was to watch. But neither could I leave Jamie to see it through alone. He had come for Gavin Hayes; I had come for him. I touched his hand.

"I'll stay."

Jamie drew himself straighter, squaring his shoulders. He moved a pace forward, making sure that he was visible in the crowd. If Hayes was still sober enough to see anything, the last thing he saw on earth would be the face of a friend.

He could see; Hayes glared to and fro as they lifted him into the cart, twisting his neck, desperately looking.

"Gabhainn! A charaid!" Jamie shouted suddenly. Hayes' eyes found him at once, and he ceased struggling.

The little man stood swaying slightly as the charge was read: theft in the amount of six pounds, ten shillings. He was covered in reddish dust, and pearls of sweat clung trembling to the gray stubble of his beard. The preacher was leaning close, murmuring urgently in his ear.

Then the drums began again, in a steady roll. The hangman guided the noose over the balding head and fixed it tight, knot positioned precisely, just under the ear. The captain of the guard stood poised, saber raised.

Suddenly, the condemned man drew himself up straight. Eyes on Jamie, he opened his mouth, as though to speak.

The saber flashed in the morning sun, and the drums stopped, with a final *thunk!*

I looked at Jamie; he was white to the lips, eyes fixed wide. From the corner of my eye, I could see the twitching rope, and the faint, reflexive jerk of the dangling sack of clothes. A sharp stink of urine and feces struck through the thick air.

On my other side, Fergus watched dispassionately.

"I suppose he noticed, after all," he murmured, with regret.

The body swung slightly, a dead weight oscillating like a plumb-bob on its string. There was a sigh from the crowd, of awe and release. Terns squawked from the burning sky, and the harbor sounds came faint and smothered through the heavy air, but the point was wrapped in silence. From where I stood, I could hear the small *plit . . . plat . . . plit* of the drops that fell from the toe of the corpse's dangling shoe.

I hadn't known Gavin Hayes, and felt no personal grief for his death, but I was glad it had been quick. I stole a glance at him, with an odd feeling of intrusion. It was a most public way of accomplishing a most private act, and I felt vaguely embarrassed to be looking.

The hangman had known his business; there had been no undignified struggle, no staring eyes, no protruding tongue; Gavin's small round head tilted sharply to the side, neck grotesquely stretched but cleanly broken.

It was a clean break in more ways than one. The captain of the guard, satisfied that Hayes was dead, motioned with his saber for the next man to be brought to the gibbet. I saw his eyes travel down the red-clad file, and then widen in outrage.

At the same moment, there was a cry from the crowd, and a ripple of excitement that quickly spread. Heads turned and people pushed each against his neighbor, striving to see where there was nothing to be seen.

"He's gone!"

"There he goes!"

"Stop him!"

It was the third prisoner, the tall young man, who had seized the moment of Gavin's death to run for his life, sliding past the guard who should have been watching him, but who had been unable to resist the gallows' fascination.

I saw a flicker of movement behind a vendor's stall, a flash of dirty blond hair. Some of the soldiers saw it, too, and ran in that direction, but many more were rushing in other directions, and among the collisions and confusion, nothing was accomplished.

The captain of the guard was shouting, face purple, his voice barely audible over the uproar. The remaining prisoner, looking stunned, was seized and hustled back in the direction of the Court of Guard as the redcoats began hastily to sort themselves back into order under the lash of their captain's voice.

Jamie snaked an arm around my waist and dragged me out of the way of an oncoming wave of humanity. The crowd fell back before the advance of squads of soldiers, who formed up and marched briskly off to quarter the area, under the grim and furious direction of their sergeant.

"We'd best find Ian," Jamie said, fending off a group of excited apprentices. He glanced at Fergus, and jerked his head toward the gibbet and its melancholy burden. "Claim the body, aye? We'll meet at the Willow Tree later."

"Do you think they'll catch him?" I asked, as we pushed through the ebbing crowd, threading our way down a cobbled lane toward the merchants' wharves.

"I expect so. Where can he go?" He spoke abstractedly, a narrow line visible between his brows. Plainly the dead man was still on his mind, and he had little attention to spare for the living.

"Did Hayes have any family?" I asked. He shook his head.

"I asked him that, when I brought him the whisky. He thought he might have a brother left alive, but no notion where. The brother was transported soon after the Rising—to Virginia, Hayes thought, but he'd heard nothing since.''

Not surprising if he hadn't; an indentured laborer would have had no facilities for communicating with kin left behind in Scotland, unless the bondsman's employer was kind enough to send a letter on his behalf. And kind or not, it was unlikely that a letter would have found Gavin Hayes, who had spent ten years in Ardsmuir prison before being transported in his turn.

"Duncan!" Jamie called out, and a tall, thin man turned and raised a hand in acknowledgment. He made his way through the crowd in a corkscrew fashion, his single arm swinging in a wide arc that fended off the passersby.

"Mac Dubh," he said, bobbing his head in greeting to Jamie. "Mrs. Claire." His long, narrow face was furrowed with sadness. He too had once been a prisoner at Ardsmuir, with Hayes and with Jamie. Only the loss of his arm to a blood infection had prevented his being transported with the others. Unfit to be sold for labor, he had instead been pardoned and set free to starve—until Jamie had found him.

"God rest poor Gavin," Duncan said, shaking his head dolorously.

Jamie muttered something in response in Gaelic, and crossed himself. Then he straightened, casting off the oppression of the day with a visible effort.

"Aye, well. I must go to the docks and arrange about Ian's passage, and then we'll think of burying Gavin. But I must have the lad settled first."

We struggled through the crowd toward the docks, squeezing our way between knots of excited gossipers, eluding the drays and barrows that came and went through the press with the ponderous indifference of trade.

A file of red-coated soldiers came at the quick-march from the other end of the quay, splitting the crowd like vinegar dropped on mayonnaise. The sun glittered hot on the line of bayonet points and the rhythm of their tramping beat through the noise of the crowd like a muffled drum. Even the rumbling sledges and handcarts stopped abruptly to let them pass by.

"Mind your pocket, Sassenach," Jamie murmured in my ear, ushering me through a narrow space between a turban-clad slave clutching two small children and a street preacher perched on a box. He was shouting sin and repentance, but with only one word in three audible through the noise.

"I sewed it shut," I assured him, nonetheless reaching to touch the small weight that swung against my thigh. "What about yours?"

He grinned and tilted his hat forward, dark blue eyes narrowing against the bright sunlight.

"It's where my sporran would be, did I have one. So long as I dinna meet with a quick-fingered harlot, I'm safe."

I glanced at the slightly bulging front of his breeches, and then up at him. Broad-shouldered and tall, with bold, clean features and a Highlander's proud carriage, he drew the glance of every woman he passed, even with his bright hair covered by a sober blue tricorne. The breeches, which were borrowed, were substantially too tight, and did nothing whatever to detract from the general effect—an effect enhanced by the fact that he himself was totally ignorant of it.

"You're a walking inducement to harlots," I said. "Stick by me; I'll protect you."

He laughed and took my arm as we emerged into a small clear space.

"Ian!" he shouted, catching sight of his nephew over the heads of the crowd. A moment later, a tall, stringy gawk of a boy popped out of the crowd, pushing a thatch of brown hair out of his eyes and grinning widely.

"I thought I should never find ye, Uncle!" he exclaimed. "Christ, there are more folk here than at the Lawnmarket in Edinburgh!" He wiped a coat sleeve across his long, half-homely face, leaving a streak of grime down one cheek.

Jamie eyed his nephew askance.

"Ye're lookin' indecently cheerful, Ian, for having just seen a man go to his death."

Ian hastily altered his expression into an attempt at decent solemnity.

"Oh, no, Uncle Jamie," he said. "I didna see the hanging." Duncan raised one brow and Ian blushed slightly. "I—I wasna afraid to see; it was only I had . . . something else I wanted to do."

Jamie smiled slightly and patted his nephew on the back.

"Don't trouble yourself, Ian; I'd as soon not have seen it myself, only that Gavin was a friend."

"I know, Uncle. I'm sorry for it." A flash of sympathy showed in the boy's large brown eyes, the only feature of his face with any claim to beauty. He glanced at me. "Was it awful, Auntie?"

"Yes," I said. "It's over, though." I pulled the damp handkerchief out of my bosom and stood on tiptoe to rub away the smudge on his cheek.

Duncan Innes shook his head sorrowfully. "Aye, poor Gavin. Still, it's a quicker death than starving, and there was little left for him but that."

"Let's go," Jamie interrupted, unwilling to spend time in useless lamenting. "The *Bonnie Mary* should be near the far end of the quay." I saw Ian glance at Jamie and draw himself up as though about to speak, but Jamie had already turned toward the harbor and was shoving his way through the crowd. Ian glanced at me, shrugged, and offered me an arm.

We followed Jamie behind the warehouses that lined the docks, sidestepping sailors, loaders, slaves, passengers, customers and merchants of all sorts. Charleston was a major shipping port, and business was booming, with as many as a hundred ships a month coming and going from Europe in the season.

The *Bonnie Mary* belonged to a friend of Jamie's cousin Jared Fraser, who had gone to France to make his fortune in the wine business and succeeded brilliantly. With luck, the *Bonnie Mary*'s captain might be persuaded for Jared's sake to take Ian with him back to Edinburgh, allowing the boy to work his passage as a cabin lad.

Ian was not enthused at the prospect, but Jamie was determined to ship his errant nephew back to Scotland at the earliest opportunity. It was—among other concerns—news of the *Bonnie Mary*'s presence in Charleston that had brought us here from Georgia, where we had first set foot in America—by accident—two months before.

As we passed a tavern, a slatternly barmaid came out with a bowl of slops. She caught sight of Jamie and stood, bowl braced against her hip, giving him a slanted brow and a pouting smile. He passed without a glance, intent on his goal. She tossed her head, flung the slops to the pig who slept by the step, and flounced back inside.

He paused, shading his eyes to look down the row of towering ships' masts, and I came up beside him. He twitched unconsciously at the front of his breeches, easing the fit, and I took his arm.

"Family jewels still safe, are they?" I murmured.

"Uncomfortable, but safe," he assured me. He plucked at the

lacing of his flies, grimacing. "I would ha' done better to hide them up my bum, I think."

"Better you than me, mate," I said, smiling. "I'd rather risk robbery, myself."

The family jewels were just that. We had been driven ashore on the coast of Georgia by a hurricane, arriving soaked, ragged, and destitute—save for a handful of large and valuable gemstones.

I hoped the captain of the *Bonnie Mary* thought highly enough of Jared Fraser to accept Ian as a cabin boy, because if not, we were going to have a spot of difficulty about the passage.

In theory, Jamie's pouch and my pocket contained a sizable fortune. In practice, the stones might have been beach pebbles so far as the good they were to us. While gems were an easy, compact way of transporting wealth, the problem was changing them back into money.

Most trade in the southern colonies was conducted by means of barter—what wasn't, was handled by the exchange of scrip or bills written on a wealthy merchant or banker. And wealthy bankers were thin on the ground in Georgia; those willing to tie up their available capital in gemstones rarer still. The prosperous rice farmer with whom we had stayed in Savannah had assured us that he himself could scarcely lay his hand on two pounds sterling in cash—indeed, there was likely not ten pounds in gold and silver to be had in the whole colony.

Nor was there any chance of selling one of the stones in the endless stretches of salt marsh and pine forest through which we had passed on our journey north. Charleston was the first city we had reached of sufficient size to harbor merchants and bankers who might help to liquidate a portion of our frozen assets.

Not that anything was likely to stay frozen long in Charleston in summer, I reflected. Rivulets of sweat were running down my neck and the linen shift under my bodice was soaked and crumpled against my skin. Even so close to the harbor, there was no wind at this time of day, and the smells of hot tar, dead fish, and sweating laborers were nearly overwhelming.

Despite their protestations, Jamie had insisted on giving one of our gemstones to Mr. and Mrs. Olivier, the kindly people who had taken us in when we were shipwrecked virtually on their doorstep, as some token of thanks for their hospitality. In return, they had provided us with a wagon, two horses, fresh clothes for traveling, food for the journey north, and a small amount of money.

Of this, six shillings and threepence remained in my pocket, constituting the entirety of our disposable fortune.

"This way, Uncle Jamie," Ian said, turning and beckoning his uncle eagerly. "I've got something to show ye."

"What is it?" Jamie asked, threading his way through a throng of sweating slaves, who were loading dusty bricks of dried indigo into an anchored cargo ship. "And how did ye get whatever it is? Ye havena got any money, have you?"

"No, I won it, dicing." Ian's voice floated back, his body invisible as he skipped around a cartload of corn.

"Dicing! Ian, for God's sake, ye canna be gambling when ye've not a penny to bless yourself with!" Holding my arm, Jamie shoved a way through the crowd to catch up to his nephew.

"You do it all the time, Uncle Jamie," the boy pointed out, pausing to wait for us. "Ye've been doing it in every tavern and inn where we've stayed."

"My God, Ian, that's cards, not dice! And I know what I'm doing!"

"So do I," said Ian, looking smug. "I won, no?"

Jamie rolled his eyes toward heaven, imploring patience.

"Jesus, Ian, but I'm glad you're going home before ye get your head beaten in. Promise me ye willna be gambling wi' the sailors, aye? Ye canna get away from them on a ship."

Ian was paying no attention; he had come to a half-crumbled piling, around which was tied a stout rope. Here he stopped and turned to face us, gesturing at an object by his feet.

"See? It's a dog," Ian said proudly.

I took a quick half-step behind Jamie, grabbing his arm.

"Ian," I said, "that is not a dog. It's a wolf. It's a bloody *big* wolf, and I think you ought to get away from it before it takes a bite out of your arse."

The wolf twitched one ear negligently in my direction, dismissed me, and twitched it back. It continued to sit, panting with the heat, its big yellow eyes fixed on Ian with an intensity that might have been taken for devotion by someone who hadn't met a wolf before. I had.

"Those things are dangerous," I said. "They'd bite you as soon as look at you."

Disregarding this, Jamie stooped to inspect the beast.

"It's not quite a wolf, is it?" Sounding interested, he held out a loose fist to the so-called dog, inviting it to smell his knuckles. I closed my eyes, expecting the imminent amputation of his hand.

Hearing no shrieks, I opened them again to find him squatting on the ground, peering up the animal's nostrils.

"He's a handsome creature, Ian," he said, scratching the thing familiarly under the chin. The yellow eyes narrowed slightly, either in pleasure at the attention or—more likely, I thought—in anticipation of biting off Jamie's nose. "Bigger than a wolf, though; it's broader through the head and chest, and a deal longer in the leg."

"His mother was an Irish wolfhound." Ian was hunkered down by Jamie, eagerly explaining as he stroked the enormous gray-brown back. "She got out in heat, into the woods, and when she came back in whelp—"

"Oh, aye, I see." Now Jamie was crooning in Gaelic to the monster while he picked up its huge foot and fondled its hairy toes. The curved black claws were a good two inches long. The thing half closed its eyes, the faint breeze ruffling the thick fur at its neck.

I glanced at Duncan, who arched his eyebrows at me, shrugged slightly, and sighed. Duncan didn't care for dogs.

"Jamie—" I said.

"*Balach Boidheach,*" Jamie said to the wolf. "Are ye no the bonny laddie, then?"

"What would he eat?" I asked, somewhat more loudly than necessary.

Jamie stopped caressing the beast.

"Oh," he said. He looked at the yellow-eyed thing with some regret. "Well." He rose to his feet, shaking his head reluctantly. "I'm afraid your auntie's right, Ian. How are we to feed him?"

"Oh, that's no trouble, Uncle Jamie," Ian assured him. "He hunts for himself."

"Here?" I glanced around at the warehouses, and the stuccoed row of shops beyond. "What does he hunt, small children?"

Ian looked mildly hurt.

"Of course not, Auntie. Fish."

Seeing three skeptical faces surrounding him, Ian dropped to his knees and grabbed the beast's muzzle in both hands, prying his mouth open.

"He does! I swear, Uncle Jamie! Here, just smell his breath!"

Jamie cast a dubious glance at the double row of impressively gleaming fangs on display, and rubbed his chin.

"I—ah, I shall take your word for it, Ian. But even so—for Christ's sake, be careful of your fingers, lad!" Ian's grip had loosened, and the massive jaws clashed shut, spraying droplets of saliva over the stone quay.

"I'm all right, Uncle," Ian said cheerfully, wiping his hand on his breeks. "He wouldn't bite me, I'm sure. His name is Rollo."

Jamie rubbed his knuckles across his upper lip.

"Mmphm. Well, whatever his name is, and whatever he eats, I dinna think the captain of the *Bonnie Mary* will take kindly to his presence in the crew's quarters."

Ian didn't say anything, but the look of happiness on his face didn't diminish. In fact, it grew. Jamie glanced at him, caught sight of his glowing face, and stiffened.

"No," he said, in horror. "Oh, no."

"Yes," said Ian. A wide smile of delight split his bony face. "She sailed three days ago, Uncle. We're too late."

Jamie said something in Gaelic that I didn't understand. Duncan looked scandalized.

"Damn!" Jamie said, reverting to English. "Bloody damn!" Jamie took off his hat and rubbed a hand over his face, hard. He looked hot, disheveled, and thoroughly disgruntled. He opened his mouth, thought better of whatever he had been going to say, closed it, and ran his fingers roughly through his hair, jerking loose the ribbon that tied it back.

Ian looked abashed.

"I'm sorry, Uncle. I'll try not to be a worry to ye, truly I will. And I can work; I'll earn enough for my food."

Jamie's face softened as he looked at his nephew. He sighed deeply, and patted Ian's shoulder.

"It's not that I dinna want ye, Ian. You know I should like nothing better than to keep ye with me. But what in hell will your mother say?"

The glow returned to Ian's face.

"I dinna ken, Uncle," he said, "but she'll be saying it in Scotland, won't she? And we're here." He put his arms around Rollo and hugged him. The wolf seemed mildly taken aback by the gesture, but after a moment, put out a long pink tongue and daintily licked Ian's ear. Testing him for flavor, I thought cynically.

"Besides," the boy added, "she kens well enough that I'm safe; you wrote from Georgia to say I was with you."

Jamie summoned a wry smile.

"I canna say that that particular bit of knowledge will be ower-comforting to her, Ian. She's known me a long time, aye?"

He sighed and clapped the hat back on his head, and turned to me.

"I badly need a drink, Sassenach," he said. "Let's find that tavern."

The Willow Tree was dark, and might have been cool, had there been fewer people in it. As it was, the benches and tables were crowded with sightseers from the hanging and sailors from the docks, and the atmosphere was like a sweatbath. I inhaled as I stepped into the taproom, then let my breath out, fast. It was like breathing through a wad of soiled laundry, soaked in beer.

Rollo at once proved his worth, parting the crowd like the Red Sea as he stalked through the taproom, lips drawn back from his teeth in a constant, inaudible growl. He was evidently no stranger to taverns. Having satisfactorily cleared out a corner bench, he curled up under the table and appeared to go to sleep.

Out of the sun, with a large pewter mug of dark ale foaming gently in front of him, Jamie quickly regained his normal self-possession.

"We've the two choices," he said, brushing back the sweat-soaked hair from his temples. "We can stay in Charleston long enough to maybe find a buyer for one of the stones, and perhaps book passage for Ian to Scotland on another ship. Or we can make our way north to Cape Fear, and maybe find a ship for him out of Wilmington or New Bern."

"I say north," Duncan said, without hesitation. "Ye've kin in Cape Fear, no? I mislike the thought of staying ower-long among strangers. And your kinsman would see we were not cheated nor robbed. Here—" He lifted one shoulder in eloquent indication of the un-Scottish—and thus patently dishonest—persons surrounding us.

"Oh, do let's go north, Uncle!" Ian said quickly, before Jamie could reply to this. He wiped away a small mustache of ale foam with his sleeve. "The journey might be dangerous; you'll need an extra man along for protection, aye?"

Jamie buried his expression in his own cup, but I was seated close enough to feel a subterranean quiver go through him. Jamie was indeed very fond of his nephew. The fact remained that Ian was the sort of person to whom things happened. Usually through no fault of his own, but still, they happened.

The boy had been kidnapped by pirates the year before, and it was the necessity of rescuing him that had brought us by circuitous and often dangerous means to America. Nothing had happened recently, but I knew Jamie was anxious to get his fifteen-year-old nephew back to Scotland and his mother before something did.

"Ah . . . to be sure, Ian," Jamie said, lowering his cup. He carefully avoided meeting my gaze, but I could see the corner of his mouth twitching. "Ye'd be a great help, I'm sure, but . . ."

"We might meet with Red Indians!" Ian said, eyes wide. His face, already a rosy brown from the sun, glowed with a flush of pleasurable anticipation. "Or wild beasts! Dr. Stern told me that the wilderness of Carolina is alive wi' fierce creatures—bears and wildcats and wicked panthers—and a great foul thing the Indians call a skunk!"

I choked on my ale.

"Are ye all right, Auntie?" Ian leaned anxiously across the table.

"Fine," I wheezed, wiping my streaming face with my kerchief. I blotted the drops of spilled ale off my bosom, pulling the fabric of my bodice discreetly away from my flesh in hopes of admitting a little air.

Then I caught a glimpse of Jamie's face, on which the expression of suppressed amusement had given way to a small frown of concern.

"Skunks aren't dangerous," I murmured, laying a hand on his knee. A skilled and fearless hunter in his native Highlands, Jamie was inclined to regard the unfamiliar fauna of the New World with caution.

"Mmphm." The frown eased, but a narrow line remained between his brows. "Maybe so, but what of the other things? I canna say I wish to be meeting a bear or a pack o' savages, wi' only this to hand." He touched the large sheathed knife that hung from his belt.

Our lack of weapons had worried Jamie considerably on the trip from Georgia, and Ian's remarks about Indians and wild animals had brought the concern to the forefront of his mind once more. Besides Jamie's knife, Fergus bore a smaller blade, suitable for cutting rope and trimming twigs for kindling. That was the full extent of our armory—the Oliviers had had neither guns nor swords to spare.

On the journey from Georgia to Charleston, we had had the company of a group of rice and indigo farmers—all bristling with knives, pistols, and muskets—bringing their produce to the port to be shipped north to Pennsylvania and New York. If we left for Cape Fear now, we would be alone, unarmed, and essentially defenseless against anything that might emerge from the thick forests.

At the same time, there were pressing reasons to travel north, our lack of available capital being one. Cape Fear was the largest settlement of Scottish Highlanders in the American Colonies, boasting several towns whose inhabitants had emigrated from Scotland during the last twenty years, following the upheaval after Culloden. And among these emigrants were Jamie's kin, who I knew would willingly offer us refuge: a roof, a bed, and time to establish ourselves in this new world.

Jamie took another drink and nodded at Duncan.

"I must say I'm of your mind, Duncan." He leaned back against the wall of the tavern, glancing casually around the crowded room. "D'ye no feel the eyes on your back?"

A chill ran down my own back, despite the trickle of sweat doing likewise. Duncan's eyes widened fractionally, then narrowed, but he didn't turn around.

"Ah," he said.

"*Whose* eyes?" I asked, looking rather nervously around. I didn't see anyone taking particular notice of us, though anyone might be watching surreptitiously; the tavern was seething with alcohol-soaked humanity, and the babble of voices was loud enough to drown out all but the closest conversation.

"Anyone's, Sassenach," Jamie answered. He glanced sideways at me, and smiled. "Dinna look so scairt about it, aye? We're in no danger. Not here."

"Not yet," Innes said. He leaned forward to pour another cup of ale. "*Mac Dubh* called out to Gavin on the gallows, d'ye see? There will be those who took notice—*Mac Dubh* bein' the bittie wee fellow he is," he added dryly.

"And the farmers who came with us from Georgia will have sold their stores by now, and be takin' their ease in places like this," Jamie said, evidently absorbed in studying the pattern of his cup. "All of them are honest men—but they'll talk, Sassenach. It makes a good story, no? The folk cast away by the hurricane? And what are the chances that at least one of them kens a bit about what we carry?"

"I see," I murmured, and did. We had attracted public interest by our association with a criminal, and could no longer pass as inconspicuous travelers. If finding a buyer took some time, as was likely, we risked inviting robbery from unscrupulous persons, or scrutiny from the English authorities. Neither prospect was appealing.

Jamie lifted his cup and drank deeply, then set it down with a sigh.

"No. I think it's perhaps not wise to linger in the city. We'll see Gavin buried decently, and then we'll find a safe spot in the woods outside the town to sleep. Tomorrow we can decide whether to stay or go."

The thought of spending several more nights in the woods—with or without skunks—was not appealing. I hadn't taken my dress off in eight days, merely rinsing the outlying portions of my anatomy whenever we paused in the vicinity of a stream.

I had been looking forward to a real bed, even if flea-infested, and a chance to scrub off the grime of the last week's travel. Still, he had a point. I sighed, ruefully eyeing the hem of my sleeve, gray and grubby with wear.

The tavern door flung suddenly open at this point, distracting me from my contemplation, and four red-coated soldiers shoved their way into the crowded room. They wore full uniform, held muskets with bayonets fixed, and were obviously not in pursuit of ale or dice.

Two of the soldiers made a rapid circuit of the room, glancing under tables, while another disappeared into the kitchen beyond. The fourth remained on watch by the door, pale eyes flicking over the crowd. His gaze lighted on our table, and rested on us for a moment, full of speculation, but then passed on, restlessly seeking.

Jamie was outwardly tranquil, sipping his ale in apparent obliviousness, but I saw the hand in his lap clench slowly into a fist. Duncan, less able to control his feelings, bent his head to hide his expression. Neither man would ever feel at ease in the presence of a red coat, and for good reason.

No one else appeared much perturbed by the soldiers' presence. The little knot of singers in the chimney corner went on with an interminable version of "Fill Every Glass," and a loud argument broke out between the barmaid and a pair of apprentices.

The soldier returned from the kitchen, having evidently found nothing. Stepping rudely through a dice game on the hearth, he rejoined his fellows by the door. As the soldiers shoved their way out of the tavern, Fergus's slight figure squeezed in, pressing against the doorjamb to avoid swinging elbows and musket butts.

I saw one soldier's eyes catch the glint of metal and fasten with interest on the hook Fergus wore in replacement of his missing left hand. He glanced sharply at Fergus, but then shouldered his musket and hurried after his companions.

Fergus shoved through the crowd and plopped down on the bench beside Ian. He looked hot and irritated.

"Blood-sucking *salaud*," he said, without preamble.

Jamie's brows went up.

"The priest," Fergus elaborated. He took the mug Ian pushed in his direction and drained it, lean throat glugging until the cup was empty. He lowered it, exhaled heavily, and sat blinking, looking noticeably happier. He sighed and wiped his mouth.

"He wants ten shillings to bury the man in the churchyard," he said. "An Anglican church, of course; there are no Catholic churches here. Wretched usurer! He knows we have no choice about it. The body will scarcely keep till sunset, as it is." He ran a finger inside his stock, pulling the sweat-wilted cotton away from his neck, then banged his fist several times on the table to attract the attention of the servingmaid, who was being run off her feet by the press of patrons.

"I told the super-fatted son of a pig that you would decide whether to pay or not. We could just bury him in the wood, after all. Though we should have to purchase a shovel," he added, frowning. "These grasping townsfolk know we are strangers; they'll take our last coin if they can."

Last coin was perilously close to the truth. I had enough to pay for a decent meal here and to buy food for the journey north; perhaps enough to pay for a couple of nights' lodging. That was all. I saw Jamie's eyes flick round the room, assessing the possibilities of picking up a little money at hazard or loo.

Soldiers and sailors were the best prospects for gambling, but there were few of either in the taproom—likely most of the garrison was still searching the town for the fugitive. In one corner, a small group of men was being loudly convivial over several pitchers of brandywine; two of them were singing, or trying to, their attempts causing great hilarity among their comrades. Jamie gave an almost imperceptible nod at sight of them, and turned back to Fergus.

"What have ye done with Gavin for the time being?" Jamie asked. Fergus hunched one shoulder.

"Put him in the wagon. I traded the clothes he was wearing to a ragwoman for a shroud, and she agreed to wash the body as part of the bargain." He gave Jamie a faint smile. "Don't worry, milord; he's seemly. For now," he added, lifting the fresh mug of ale to his lips.

"Poor Gavin." Duncan Innes lifted his own mug in a half salute to his fallen comrade.

"*Slàinte*," Jamie replied, and lifted his own mug in reply. He set it down and sighed.

"He wouldna like being buried in the wood," he said.

"Why not?" I asked, curious. "I shouldn't think it would matter to him one way or the other."

"Oh, no, we couldna do that, Mrs. Claire." Duncan was shaking his head emphatically. Duncan was normally a most reserved man, and I was surprised at so much apparent feeling.

"He was afraid of the dark," Jamie said softly. I turned to stare at him, and he gave me a lopsided smile. "I lived wi' Gavin Hayes nearly as long as I've lived with you, Sassenach—and in much closer quarters. I kent him well."

"Aye, he was afraid of being alone in the dark," Duncan chimed in. "He was most mortally scairt of *tannagach*—of spirits, aye?"

His long, mournful face bore an inward look, and I knew he was seeing in memory the prison cell that he and Jamie had shared with Gavin Hayes—and with forty other men—for three long years. "D'ye recall, *Mac Dubh*, how he told us one night of the *tannasq* he met?"

"I do, Duncan, and could wish I did not." Jamie shuddered despite the heat. "I kept awake myself half the night after he told us that one."

"What was it, Uncle?" Ian was leaning over his cup of ale, round-eyed. His cheeks were flushed and streaming, and his stock crumpled with sweat.

Jamie rubbed a hand across his mouth, thinking.

"Ah. Well, it was a time in the late, cold autumn in the Highlands, just when the season turns, and the feel of the air tells ye the ground will be shivered wi' frost come dawn," he said. He settled himself in his seat and sat back, alecup in hand. He smiled wryly, plucking at his own throat. "Not like now, aye?

"Well, Gavin's son brought back the kine that night, but there was one beast missing—the lad had hunted up the hills and down the corries, but couldna find it anywhere. So Gavin set the lad to milk the two others, and set out himself to look for the lost cow.''

He rolled the pewter cup slowly between his hands, staring down into the dark ale as though seeing in it the bulk of the night-black Scottish peaks and the mist that floats in the autumn glens.

"He went some distance, and the cot behind him disappeared. When he looked back, he couldna see the light from the window anymore, and there was no sound but the keening of the wind. It was cold, but he went on, tramping through the mud and the heather, hearing the crackle of ice under his boots.

"He saw a small grove through the mist, and thinking the cow might have taken shelter beneath the trees, he went toward it. He said the trees were birches, standing there all leafless, but with their branches grown together so he must bend his head to squeeze beneath the boughs.

"He came into the grove and saw it was not a grove at all, but a circle of trees. There were great tall trees, spaced verra evenly, all around him, and smaller ones, saplings, grown up between to make a wall of branches. And in the center of the circle stood a cairn.''

Hot as it was in the tavern, I felt as though a sliver of ice had slid melting down my spine. I had seen ancient cairns in the Highlands myself, and found them eerie enough in the broad light of day.

Jamie took a sip of ale, and wiped away a trickle of sweat that ran down his temple.

"He felt quite queer, did Gavin. For he kent the place—everyone did, and kept well away from it. It was a strange place. And it seemed even worse in the dark and the cold, from what it did in the light of day. It was an auld cairn, the kind laid wi' slabs of rock, all heaped round with stones, and he could see before him the black opening of the tomb.

"He knew it was a place no man should come, and he without a powerful charm. Gavin had naught but a wooden cross about his neck. So he crossed himself with it and turned to go.''

Jamie paused to sip his ale.

"But as Gavin went from the grove," he said softly, "he heard footsteps behind him."

I saw the Adam's apple bob in Ian's throat as he swallowed. He reached mechanically for his own cup, eyes fixed on his uncle.

"He didna turn to see," Jamie went on, "but kept walking. And the steps kept pace wi' him, step by step, always following.

And he came through the peat where the water seeps up, and it was crusted with ice, the weather bein' so cold. He could hear the peat crackle under his feet, and behind him the crack! crack! of breaking ice.

"He walked and he walked, through the cold, dark night, watching ahead for the light of his own window, where his wife had set the candle. But the light never showed, and he began to fear he had lost his way among the heather and the dark hills. And all the time, the steps kept pace with him, loud in his ears.

"At last he could bear it no more, and seizing hold of the crucifix he wore round his neck, he swung about wi' a great cry to face whatever followed."

"What did he see?" Ian's pupils were dilated, dark with drink and wonder. Jamie glanced at the boy, and then at Duncan, nodding at him to take up the story.

"He said it was a figure like a man, but with no body," Duncan said quietly. "All white, like as it might have been made of the mist. But wi' great holes where its eyes should be, and empty black, fit to draw the soul from his body with dread."

"But Gavin held up his cross before his face, and he prayed aloud to the Blessed Virgin." Jamie took up the story, leaning forward intently, the dim firelight outlining his profile in gold. "And the thing came no nearer, but stayed there, watching him.

"And so he began to walk backward, not daring to face round again. He walked backward, stumbling and slipping, fearing every moment as he might tumble into a burn or down a cliff and break his neck, but fearing worse to turn his back on the cold thing.

"He couldna tell how long he'd walked, only that his legs were trembling wi' weariness, when at last he caught a glimpse of light through the mist, and there was his own cottage, wi' the candle in the window. He cried out in joy, and turned to his door, but the cold thing was quick, and slippit past him, to stand betwixt him and the door.

"His wife had been watching out for him, and when she heard him cry out, she came at once to the door. Gavin shouted to her not to come out, but for God's sake to fetch a charm to drive away the *tannasq*. Quick as thought, she snatched the pot from beneath her bed, and a twig of myrtle bound wi' red thread and black, that she'd made to bless the cows. She dashed the water against the doorposts, and the cold thing leapt upward, astride the lintel. Gavin rushed in beneath and barred the door, and stayed inside in his wife's arms until the dawn. They let the candle burn all the night, and Gavin Hayes never again left his house past sunset—until he went to fight for Prince *Tearlach*.''

Even Duncan, who knew the tale, sighed as Jamie finished speaking. Ian crossed himself, then looked about self-consciously, but no one seemed to have noticed.

"So, now Gavin has gone into the dark," Jamie said softly. "But we willna let him lie in unconsecrated ground."

"Did they find the cow?" Fergus asked, with his usual practicality. Jamie quirked one eyebrow at Duncan, who answered.

"Oh, aye, they did. The next morning they found the poor beast, wi' her hooves all clogged wi' mud and stones, staring mad and lathered about the muzzle, and her sides heavin' fit to burst.'' He glanced from me to Ian and back to Fergus. "Gavin did say," he said precisely, "that she looked as though she'd been ridden to Hell and back."

"Jesus." Ian took a deep gulp of his ale, and I did the same. In the corner, the drinking society was making attempts on a round of "Captain Thunder," breaking down each time in helpless laughter.

Ian put down his cup on the table.

"What happened to them?" he asked, his face troubled. "To Gavin's wife, and his son?"

Jamie's eyes met mine, and his hand touched my thigh. I knew, without being told, what had happened to the Hayes family. Without Jamie's own courage and intransigence, the same thing would likely have happened to me and to our daughter Brianna.

"Gavin never knew," Jamie said quietly. "He never heard aught of his wife—she will have been starved, maybe, or driven out to die of the cold. His son took the field beside him at Culloden. Whenever a man who had fought there came into our cell, Gavin would ask—'Have ye maybe seen a bold lad named Archie Hayes, about so tall?' '' He measured automatically, five feet from the floor, capturing Hayes' gesture. " 'A lad about fourteen,' he'd say, 'wi' a green plaidie and a small gilt brooch.' But no one ever came who had seen him for sure—either seen him fall or seen him run away safe."

Jamie took a sip of the ale, his eyes fixed on a pair of British officers who had come in and settled in the corner. It had grown dark outside, and they were plainly off duty. Their leather stocks were unfastened on account of the heat, and they wore only sidearms, glinting under their coats; nearly black in the dim light save where the firelight touched them with red.

"Sometimes he hoped the lad might have been captured and transported," he said. "Like his brother."

"Surely that would be somewhere in the records?" I said. "Did they—do they—keep lists?"

"They did," Jamie said, still watching the soldiers. A small, bitter smile touched the corner of his mouth. "It was such a list that saved me, after Culloden, when they asked my name before shooting me, so as to add it to their roll. But a man like Gavin would have no way to see the English dead-lists. And if he could have found out, I think he would not." He glanced at me. "Would you choose to know for sure, and it was your child?"

I shook my head, and he gave me a faint smile and squeezed my hand. Our child was safe, after all. He picked up his cup and drained it, then beckoned to the serving maid.

The girl brought the food, skirting the table widely in order to avoid Rollo. The beast lay motionless under the table, his head protruding into the room and his great hairy tail lying heavily across my feet, but his yellow eyes were wide open, watching everything. They followed the girl intently, and she backed nervously away, keeping an eye on him until she was safely out of biting distance.

Seeing this, Jamie cast a dubious look at the so-called dog.

"Is he hungry? Must I ask for a fish for him?"

"Oh, no, Uncle," Ian reassured him. "Rollo catches his own fish."

Jamie's eyebrows shot up, but he only nodded, and with a wary glance at Rollo, took a platter of roasted oysters from the tray.

"Ah, the pity of it." Duncan Innes was quite drunk by now. He sat slumped against the wall, his armless shoulder riding higher than the other, giving him a strange, hunchbacked appearance. "That a dear man like Gavin should come to such an end!" He shook his head lugubriously, swinging it back and forth over his alecup like the clapper of a funeral bell.

"No family left to mourn him, cast alone into a savage land—hanged as a felon, and to be buried in an unconsecrated grave. Not even a proper lament to be sung for him!" He picked up the cup, and with some difficulty, found his mouth with it. He drank deep and set it down with a muffled clang.

"Well, he *shall* have a *caithris*!" He glared belligerently from Jamie to Fergus to Ian. "Why not?"

Jamie wasn't drunk, but he wasn't completely sober either. He grinned at Duncan and lifted his own cup in salute.

"Why not, indeed?" he said. "Only it will have to be you singin' it, Duncan. None of the rest knew Gavin, and I'm no singer. I'll shout along wi' ye, though."

Duncan nodded magisterially, bloodshot eyes surveying us. Without warning, he flung back his head and emitted a terrible howl. I jumped in my seat, spilling half a cup of ale into my lap. Ian and Fergus, who had evidently heard Gaelic laments before, didn't turn a hair.

All over the room, benches were shoved back, as men leapt to their feet in alarm, reaching for their pistols. The barmaid leaned out of the serving hatch, eyes big. Rollo came awake with an explosive *"Woof!"* and glared round wildly, teeth bared.

"Tha sinn cruinn a chaoidh ar caraid, Gabhainn Hayes," Duncan thundered, in a ragged baritone. I had just about enough Gaelic to translate this as "We are met to weep and cry out to heaven for the loss of our friend, Gavin Hayes!"

"Eisd ris!" Jamie chimed in.

"Rugadh e do Sheumas Immanuel Hayes agus Louisa N'ic a Liallainn an am baile Chill-Mhartainn, ann an sgire Dhun Domhnuill, anns a bhliadhnaseachd ceud deug agus a haon!" He was born of Seaumais Emmanuel Hayes and of Louisa Maclellan, in the village of Kilmartin in the parish of Dodanil, in the year of our Lord seventeen hundred and one!

"Eisd ris!" This time Fergus and Ian joined in on the chorus, which I translated roughly as "Hear him!"

Rollo appeared not to care for either verse or refrain; his ears lay flat against his skull, and his yellow eyes narrowed to slits. Ian scratched his head in reassurance, and he lay down again, muttering wolf curses under his breath.

The audience, having caught on to it that no actual violence threatened, and no doubt bored with the inferior vocal efforts of the drinking society in the corner, settled down to enjoy the show. By the time Duncan had worked his way into an accounting of the names of the sheep Gavin Hayes had owned before leaving his croft to follow his laird to Culloden, many of those at the surrounding tables were joining enthusiastically in the chorus, shouting *"Eisd ris!"* and banging their mugs on the tables, in perfect ignorance of what was being said, and a good thing too.

Duncan, drunker than ever, fixed the soldiers at the next table with a baleful glare, sweat pouring down his face.

"A Shasunnaich na galladh, 's olc a thig e dhuibh fanaid air bàs gasgaich. Gun toireadh an diabhul fhein leis anns a bhàs

sibh, direach do Fhirinn!!'' Wicked Sassenach dogs, eaters of
dead flesh! Ill does it become you to laugh and rejoice at the death
of a gallant man! May the devil himself seize upon you in the
hour of your death and take you straight to hell!

Ian blanched slightly at this, and Jamie cast Duncan a narrow
look, but they stoutly shouted *''Eisd ris!''* along with the rest of
the crowd.

Fergus, seized by inspiration, got up and passed his hat among
the crowd, who, carried away by ale and excitement, happily flung
coppers into it for the privilege of joining in their own denunciation.

I had as good a head for drink as most men, but a much smaller
bladder. Head spinning from the noise and fumes as much as
from alcohol, I got up and edged my way out from behind the
table, through the mob, and into the fresh air of the early evening.

It was still hot and sultry, though the sun was long since down.
Still, there was a lot more air out here, and a lot fewer people
sharing it.

Having relieved the internal pressure, I sat down on the tavern's
chopping block with my pewter mug, breathing deeply. The night
was clear, with a bright half-moon peeping silver over the harbor's edge. Our wagon stood nearby, no more than its outline
visible in the light from the tavern windows. Presumably, Gavin
Hayes' decently shrouded body lay within. I trusted he had enjoyed his *caithris*.

Inside, Duncan's chanting had come to an end. A clear tenor
voice, wobbly with drink, but sweet nonetheless, was singing a
familiar tune, audible over the babble of talk.

> *''To Anacreon in heav'n, where he sat in full glee,*
> *A few sons of harmony sent a petition,*
> *That he their inspirer and patron would be!*
> *When this answer arrived from the jolly old Grecian:*
> *'Voice, fiddle, and flute,*
> > *No longer be mute!*
> > *I'll lend you my name and inspire you to boot.' ''*

The singer's voice cracked painfully on ''voice, fiddle, and
flute,'' but he sang stoutly on, despite the laughter from his audience. I smiled wryly to myself as he hit the final couplet,

" 'And, besides, I'll instruct you like me to entwine,
The Myrtle of Venus with Bacchus's vine!' "

I lifted my cup in salute to the wheeled coffin, softly echoing
the melody of the singer's last lines.

"Oh, say, does that star-spangled banner yet wave
O'er the land of the free and the home of the brave?"

I drained my cup and sat still, waiting for the men to come out.

In Which We Meet a Ghost

"Ten, eleven, twelve . . . and two, and six . . . one pound, eight shillings, sixpence, two farthings!" Fergus dropped the last coin ceremoniously into the cloth pocket, pulled tight the drawstrings, and handed it to Jamie. "And three buttons," he added, "but I have kept those," and patted the side of his coat.

"Ye've settled with the landlord for our meal?" Jamie asked me, weighing the little bag.

"Yes," I assured him. "I have four shillings and sixpence left, plus what Fergus collected."

Fergus smiled modestly, square white teeth gleaming in the faint light from the tavern's window.

"We have the necessary money for the burial, then," he said. "Will we take Monsieur Hayes to the priest now, or wait till morning?"

Jamie frowned at the wagon, standing silent at the edge of the inn yard.

"I shouldna think the priest will be awake at this hour," he said, with a glance at the rising moon. "Still—"

"I'd just as soon not take him with us," I said. "Not to be rude," I added apologetically to the wagon. "But if we're going to sleep out in the woods, the . . . er . . . scent . . ." It wasn't overpowering, but once away from the smoky reek of the tavern, a distinct odor was noticeable in the vicinity of the wagon. It hadn't been a gentle death, and it *had* been a hot day.

"Auntie Claire is right," Ian said, brushing his knuckles inconspicuously under his nose. "We dinna want to be attracting wild animals."

"We canna be leaving Gavin here, surely!" Duncan protested, scandalized at the thought. "What, leave him lying on the step o' the inn in his shroud, like a foundling wrapped in swaddling clothes?'' He swayed alarmingly, his alcoholic intake affecting his always precarious balance.

I saw Jamie's wide mouth twitch with amusement, the moon shining white on the knife-edged bridge of his nose.

''No,'' he said. ''We willna be leaving him here.'' He tossed the little bag from hand to hand with a faint chinking sound, then, making his decision, thrust it into his coat.

''We'll bury him ourselves,'' he said. ''Fergus, will ye be stepping into the stable yonder and see can ye buy a spade verra cheap?''

The short journey to the church through the quiet streets of Charleston was somewhat less dignified than the usual funeral cortege, marked as it was by Duncan's insistence on repeating the more interesting portions of his lament as a processional.

Jamie drove slowly, shouting occasional encouragement to the horses; Duncan staggered beside the team, chanting hoarsely and clutching one animal by its headstall, while Ian held the other to prevent bolting. Fergus and I brought up the rear in staid respectability, Fergus holding his newly purchased shovel at port-arms, and muttering dire predictions as to the likelihood of us all spending the night in gaol for disturbing the peace of Charleston.

As it was, the church stood by itself in a quiet street, some distance from the nearest house. This was all to the good, in terms of avoiding notice, but it did mean that the churchyard was dauntingly dark, with no glow of torch or candle to pierce the blackness.

Great magnolia trees overhung the gate, leathery leaves drooping in the heat, and a border of pines, meant to provide shade and respite in the day, served at night to block all traces of moon and starlight, leaving the churchyard itself black as a . . . well, as a crypt.

Walking through the air felt like pushing aside curtains of black velvet, perfumed with an incense of turpentine from the sun-heated pines; endless layers of soft, pungent smothering. Nothing could have been farther from the cold purity of the Highlands than this stifling southern atmosphere. Still, faint patches of mist hung under the dark brick walls, and I could have wished not to recall Jamie's story of the *tannasq* quite so vividly.

''We'll find a place. Do you stay and hold the horses, Duncan.'' Jamie slid down from the wagon's seat and took me by the arm.

"We'll find a nice wee spot by the wall, perhaps," he said, guiding me toward the gate. "Ian and I will dig while you hold the light, and Fergus can stand guard."

"What about Duncan?" I asked, with a backward glance. "Will he be all right?" The Scotsman was invisible, his tall, lanky form having faded into the larger blot comprising horses and wagon, but he was still clearly audible.

"He'll be chief mourner," Jamie said, with a hint of a smile in his voice. "Mind your head, Sassenach." I ducked automatically beneath a low magnolia branch; I didn't know whether Jamie could actually see in total darkness, or merely felt things by instinct, but I had never seen him stumble, no matter how dark the surroundings.

"Don't you think someone's going to notice a fresh grave?" It was not completely black in the churchyard, after all; once out from under the magnolias, I could make out the dim forms of gravestones, looking insubstantial but sinister in the dark, a faint mist rising from the thick grass about their feet.

The soles of my own feet tingled as we picked a ginger way through the stones. I seemed to feel silent waves of reproach at this unseemly intrusion wafting up from below. I barked my shin on a tombstone and bit my lip, stifling an urge to apologize to its owner.

"I expect they might." Jamie let go of my arm to rummage in his coat. "But if the priest wanted money to bury Gavin, I shouldna think he'd trouble to dig him up again for nothing, aye?"

Young Ian materialized out of the darkness at my elbow, startling me.

"There's open space by the north wall, Uncle Jamie," he said, speaking softly in spite of the obvious fact that there was no one to hear. He paused, and drew slightly closer to me.

"It's verra dark in here, no?" The boy sounded uneasy. He had had nearly as much to drink as Jamie or Fergus, but while the alcohol had imbued the older men with grim humor, it had clearly had a more depressing effect on Ian's spirits.

"It is, aye. I've the bit of a candle I took from the tavern, though; wait a bit." Faint rustlings announced Jamie's search for flint and tinderbox.

The encompassing dark made me feel disembodied, like a ghost myself. I looked upward and saw stars, so faintly visible through the thick air that they shed no light upon the ground, but only gave a feeling of immense distance and infinite remoteness.

"It's like the vigil of Easter." Jamie's voice came softly, accompanied by the small scratching sounds of a striking flint. "I saw the service once, at Notre Dame in Paris. Watch yourself, Ian, there's a stone just there!" A thud and a stifled grunt announced that Ian had belatedly discovered the stone for himself.

"The church was all dark," Jamie continued, "but the folk coming for the service would buy small tapers from the crones at the doors. It was something like this"—I felt, rather than saw, his motion at the sky above—"a great space above, all ringing wi' the silence, and folk packed in on every side." Hot as it was, I gave an involuntary shiver at these words, which conjured up a vision of the dead around us, crowding silently side by side, in anticipation of an imminent resurrection.

"And then, just when I thought I couldna bear the silence and the crowd, there came the priest's voice from the door. *'Lumen Christi!'* he called out, and the acolytes lit the great candle that he carried. Then from it they took the flame to their own tapers, and scampered up and down the aisles, passing the fire to the candles o' the faithful."

I could see his hands, lit faintly by the tiny sparks from his flint.

"Then the church came alive wi' a thousand small flames, but it was that first candle that broke the dark."

The scratching sounds ceased, and he took away the cupped hand that had shielded the newborn flame. The flame strengthened and lit his face from below, gilding the planes of high cheekbones and forehead, and shadowing the deep-set orbits of his eyes.

He lifted the candle, surveying the looming grave markers, eerie as a circle of standing stones.

"Lumen Christi," he said softly, inclining his head toward a granite pillar surmounted with a cross, *"et requiescat in pace, amice."* The half-mocking note had left his voice; he spoke with complete seriousness, and I felt at once oddly comforted, as though some watchful presence had withdrawn.

He smiled at me then, and handed me the candle.

"See can ye find a bit of wood for a torch, Sassenach," he said. "Ian and I will take it in turns to dig."

I was no longer nervous, but still felt like a grave robber, standing under a pine tree with my torch, watching Young Ian and Jamie take their turns in the deepening pit, their naked backs gleaming with sweat in the torchlight.

"Medical students used to pay men to steal fresh bodies from churchyards," I said, handing my soiled kerchief to Jamie as he hauled himself out of the hole, grunting with effort. "That was the only way they could practice dissection."

"Did they?" Jamie said. He wiped the sweat from his face and gave me a quick, wry glance. "Or do they?"

Luckily, it was too dark for Ian to notice my flush, despite the torchlight. It wasn't the first slip I had made, nor was it likely to be the last, but most such inadvertencies resulted in nothing more than a quizzical glance, were they noticed at all. The truth simply was not a possibility that would occur to anyone.

"I imagine they do it now," I admitted. I shivered slightly at the thought of confronting a freshly exhumed and unpreserved body, still smeared with the dirt of its desecrated grave. Cadavers embalmed and laid on a stainless steel surface were not particularly pleasant either, but the formality of their presentation served to keep the corruptive realities of death at some small distance.

I exhaled strongly through my nose, trying to rid myself of odors, imagined and remembered. When I breathed in, my nostrils were filled with the smell of damp earth and hot pitch from my pine torch, and the fainter, cooler echo of live scent from the pines overhead.

"They take paupers and criminals from the prisons, too." Young Ian, who had evidently heard the exchange, if not understood it, took the opportunity to stop for a moment, wiping his brow as he leaned on the shovel.

"Da told me about one time he was arrested, when they took him to Edinburgh, and kept him in the Tolbooth. He was in a cell wi' three other men, and one of them a fellow with the consumption, who coughed something dreadful, keeping the rest awake all night and all day. Then one night the coughing stopped, and they kent he was dead. But Da said they were so tired, they couldna do more than say a Pater Noster for his soul, and fall asleep."

The boy paused and rubbed an itching nose.

"Da said he woke quite sudden wi' someone clutching his legs and another someone takin' him by the arms, liftin' him up. He kicked and cried out, and the one who had his arms screeched and dropped him, so that he cracked his head on the stones. He sat up rubbin' his pate and found himself staring at a doctor from the hospital and two fellows he'd brought along to carry awa' the corpse to the dissecting room.''

Ian grinned broadly at the recollection, wiping his sweat-soaked hair out of his face.

"Da said he wasna sure who was most horrified, him or the fellows who'd got the wrong body. He did say as the doctor seemed regretful, though—said Da would have made a more interesting specimen, what wi' his leg stump and all.''

Jamie laughed, stretching his arms to ease his shoulders. With face and torso streaked with red dirt, and his hair bound back with a kerchief round his forehead, he looked disreputable as any grave robber.

"Aye, I mind that story,'' he said. "Ian did say after that as all doctors were ghouls, and wouldna have a thing to do with them.'' He grinned at me; I had been a doctor—a surgeon—in my own time, but here I passed as nothing more than a wisewoman, skilled in the use of herbs.

"Fortunately, I'm no afraid of wee ghoulies, myself,'' he said, and leaned down to kiss me briefly. His lips were warm, tasting of ale. I could see droplets of sweat caught in the curly hairs of his chest, and his nipples, dark buds in the dim light. A tremor that had nothing to do either with cold or with the eeriness of our surroundings ran down my spine. He saw it and his eyes met mine. He took a deep breath, and all at once I was conscious of the close fit of my bodice, and the weight of my breasts in the sweat-soaked fabric.

Jamie shifted himself slightly, plucking to ease the fit of his breeches.

"Damn,'' he said softly. He lowered his eyes and turned away, mouth barely touched by a rueful smile.

I hadn't expected it, but I recognized it, all right. A sudden surge of lust was a common, if peculiar, response to the presence of death. Soldiers feel it in the lull after battle; so do healers who deal in blood and struggle. Perhaps Ian had been more right than I thought about the ghoulishness of doctors.

Jamie's hand touched my back and I started, showering sparks from the blazing torch. He took it from me and nodded toward a nearby gravestone.

"Sit down, Sassenach,'' he said. "Ye shouldna be standing so long.'' I had cracked the tibia of my left leg in the shipwreck, and while it had healed quickly, the leg still ached sometimes.

"I'm all right." Still, I moved toward the stone, brushing against him as I passed. He radiated heat, but his naked flesh was cool to the touch, the sweat evaporating on his skin. I could smell him.

I glanced at him, and saw goose bumps rise on the fair flesh where I'd touched him. I swallowed, fighting back a sudden vision of tumbling in the dark, to a fierce blind coupling amid crushed grass and raw earth.

His hand lingered on my elbow as he helped me to a seat on the stone. Rollo was lying by its side, drops of saliva gleaming in the torchlight as he panted. The slanted yellow eyes narrowed at me.

"Don't even think about it," I said, narrowing my own eyes back at him. "Bite me, and I'll cram my shoe down your throat so far you'll choke."

"*Wuff!*" Rollo said, quite softly. He laid his muzzle on his paws, but the hairy ears were pricked, turned to catch the slightest sound.

The spade chunked softly into the earth at Ian's feet, and he straightened up, slicking sweat off his face with a palm swipe that left black smears along his jaw. He blew out a deep breath and glanced up at Jamie, miming exhaustion, tongue lolling from the corner of his mouth.

"Aye, I expect it's deep enough." Jamie answered the wordless plea with a nod. "I'll fetch Gavin along, then."

Fergus frowned uneasily, his features sharp in the torchlight.

"Will you not need help to carry the corpse?" His reluctance was evident; still, he had offered. Jamie gave him a faint, wry smile.

"I'll manage well enough," he said. "Gavin was a wee man. Still, ye might bring the torch to see by."

"I'll come too, Uncle!" Young Ian scrambled hastily out of the pit, skinny shoulders gleaming with sweat. "Just in case you need help," he added breathlessly.

"Afraid to be left in the dark?" Fergus asked sarcastically. I thought that the surroundings must be making him uneasy; though he occasionally teased Ian, whom he regarded as a younger brother, he was seldom cruel about it.

"Aye, I am," Ian said simply. "Aren't you?"

Fergus opened his mouth, brows arched skyward, then shut it again and turned without a word toward the black opening of the lych-gate, whence Jamie had disappeared.

"D'ye not think this is a terrible place, Auntie?" Ian murmured uneasily at my elbow, sticking close as we made our way through the looming stones, following the flicker of Fergus's torch. "I keep thinking of that story Uncle Jamie told. And thinking now Gavin's dead, maybe the cold thing . . . I mean, do you think would it maybe . . . come for him?" There was an audible swallow punctuating this question, and I felt an icy finger touch me, just at the base of my spine.

"No," I said, a little too loudly. I grabbed Ian's arm, less for support than for the reassurance of his solidity. "Certainly not."

His skin was clammy with evaporating sweat, but the skinny muscularity of the arm under my hand was comforting. His half-visible presence reminded me faintly of Jamie; he was nearly as tall as his uncle, and very nearly as strong, though still lean and gangling with adolescence.

We emerged with gratitude into the little pool of light thrown by Fergus's torch. The flickering light shone through the wagon wheels, throwing shadows that lay like spiderwebs in the dust. It was as hot in the road as it was in the churchyard, but the air seemed somehow freer, easier to breathe, out from under the suffocating trees.

Rather to my surprise, Duncan was still awake, perched drooping on the wagon's seat like a sleepy owl, shoulders hunched about his ears. He was crooning under his breath, but stopped when he saw us. The long wait seemed to have sobered him a bit; he got down from the seat steadily enough and came round to the rear of the wagon to help Jamie.

I smothered a yawn. I would be glad to be done with this melancholy duty and on our way to rest, even if the only bed to look forward to was one of piled leaves.

"Ifrinn an Diabhuil! A Dhia, thoir cobhair!"

"Sacrée Vierge!"

My head snapped up. Everyone was shouting, and the horses, startled, were neighing and jerking frantically against their hobbles, making the wagon hop and lurch like a drunken beetle.

"Wuff!" Rollo said next to me.

"Jesus!" said Ian, goggling at the wagon. "Jesus *Christ*!"

I swung in the direction he was looking, and screamed. A pale figure loomed out of the wagon bed, swaying with the wagon's jerking. I had no time to see more before all hell broke loose.

Rollo bunched his hindquarters and launched himself through the dark with a roar, to the accompaniment of shouts from Jamie and Ian, and a terrible scream from the ghost. Behind me, I could hear the sound of French cursing as Fergus ran back into the churchyard, stumbling and crashing over tombstones in the dark.

Jamie had dropped the torch; it flickered and hissed on the dusty road, threatening to go out. I fell to my knees and grabbed it, blowing on it, desperate to keep it alight.

The chorus of shouts and growling grew to a crescendo, and I rose up, torch in hand, to find Ian struggling with Rollo, trying to keep him away from the dim figures wrestling together in a cloud of dust.

"Arrêtes, espèce de cochon!" Fergus galloped out of the dark, brandishing the spade he had gone to fetch. Finding his injunction disregarded, he stepped forward and brought it down one-handed on the intruder's head with a dull *clong!* Then he swung toward Ian and Rollo.

"You be quiet, too!" Fergus said to the dog, threatening him with the shovel. "Shut up this minute, foul beast, or I brain you!"

Rollo snarled, with a show of impressive teeth that I interpreted roughly to mean "You and who else?" but was prevented from mayhem by Ian, who wrapped his arm about the dog's throat and choked off any further remarks.

"Where did *he* come from?" Ian asked in amazement. He craned his neck, trying to get a look at the fallen figure without letting go of Rollo.

"From hell," Fergus said briefly. "And I invite him to go back there at once." He was trembling with shock and exertion; the light gleamed dully from his hook as he brushed a thick lock of black hair out of his eyes.

"Not from hell; from the gallows. Do ye not know him?"

Jamie rose slowly to his feet, dusting his breeches. He was breathing heavily, and smeared with dirt, but seemed unhurt. He picked up his fallen kerchief and glanced about, wiping his face. "Where's Duncan?"

"Here, *Mac Dubh*," said a gruff voice from the front of the wagon. "The beasts werena likin' Gavin much to start with, and they're proper upset to think he was a-resurrectin'. Not," he added fairly, "but what I was a wee bit startled myself." He eyed the figure on the ground with disfavor, and patted one skittish horse firmly on the neck. "Ah, it's no but a silly bugger, *luaidh,* hush your noise now, aye?"

I had handed Ian the torch and knelt to inspect the damage to our visitor. This seemed to be slight; the man was already stirring. Jamie was right; it was the man who had escaped hanging earlier in the day. He was young, about thirty, muscular and powerfully built, his fair hair matted with sweat and stiff with filth. He reeked of prison, and the musky-sharp smell of prolonged fear. Little wonder.

I got a hand under his arm and helped him to sit up. He grunted and put his hand to his head, squinting in the torchlight.

"Are you all right?" I asked.

"Thankin' ye kindly, ma'am, I will have been better." He had a faint Irish accent and a soft, deep voice.

Rollo, upper lip lifted just enough to show a menacing eye-tooth, shoved his nose into the visitor's armpit, sniffed, then jerked back his head and sneezed explosively. A small tremor of laughter ran round the circle, and the tension relaxed momentarily.

"How long have ye been in the wagon?" Duncan demanded.

"Since midafternoon." The man rose awkwardly onto his knees, swaying a bit from the effects of the blow. He touched his head again and winced. "Oh, Jaysus! I crawled in there just after the Frenchie loaded up poor old Gavin."

"Where were you before that?" Ian asked.

"Hidin' under the gallows cart. It was the only place I thought they wouldn't be looking." He rose laboriously to his feet, closed his eyes to get his balance, then opened them. They were a pale green in the torchlight, the color of shallow seas. I saw them flick from face to face, then settle on Jamie. The man bowed, careful of his head.

"Stephen Bonnet. Your servant, sir." He made no move to extend a hand in greeting, nor did Jamie.

"Mr. Bonnet." Jamie nodded back, face carefully blank. I didn't know quite how he contrived to look commanding, wearing nothing but a pair of damp and dirt-stained breeks, but he managed it. He looked the visitor over, taking in every detail of his appearance.

Bonnet was what country people called "well set up," with a tall, powerful frame and a barrel chest, his features heavy-boned but coarsely handsome. A few inches shorter than Jamie, he stood easy, balanced on the balls of his feet, fists half closed in readiness.

No stranger to a fight, judging by the slight crookedness of his nose and a small scar by the corner of his mouth. The small imperfections did nothing to mar the overall impression of animal magnetism; he was the sort of man who attracted women easily. Some women, I amended, as he cast a speculative glance at me.

"For what crime were ye condemned, Mr. Bonnet?" Jamie asked. He himself stood easy, but with a look of watchfulness that reminded me forcibly of Bonnet himself. It was the ears-back look male dogs give each other before deciding whether to fight.

"Smuggling," Bonnet said.

Jamie didn't reply, but tilted his head slightly. One brow rose in inquiry.

"And piracy." A muscle twitched near Bonnet's mouth; a poor attempt at a smile, or an involuntary quiver of fear?

"And will ye have killed anyone in the commission of your crimes, Mr. Bonnet?" Jamie's face was blank, save for the watchful eyes. *Think twice,* his eyes said plainly. *Or maybe three times.*

"None that were not tryin' to kill me first," Bonnet replied. The words were easy, the tone almost flippant, but belied by the hand that closed tight into a fist by his side.

It dawned on me that Bonnet must feel he was facing judge and jury, as surely as he had faced them once before. He had no way of knowing that we were nearly as reluctant to go near the garrison soldiers as he was.

Jamie looked at Bonnet for a long moment, peering closely at him in the flickering torchlight, then nodded and took a half step back.

"Go, then," he said quietly. "We will not hinder ye."

Bonnet took an audible breath; I could see the big frame relax, shoulders slumping under the cheap linen shirt.

"Thank you," he said. He wiped a hand across his face, and took another deep breath. The green eyes darted from me to Fergus to Duncan. "But will ye help me, maybe?"

Duncan, who had relaxed at Jamie's words, gave a grunt of surprise.

"Help you? A thief?"

Bonnet's head swiveled in Duncan's direction. The iron collar was a dark line about his neck, giving the eerie impression that his severed head floated several inches above his shoulders.

"Help me," he repeated. "There will be soldiers on the roads tonight—huntin' me." He gestured toward the wagon. "You could take me safely past them—if ye will." He turned back to Jamie, and straightened his back, shoulders stiff. "I am begging for your help, sir, in the name of Gavin Hayes, who was my friend as well as yours—and a thief, as I am."

The men studied him in silence for a moment, digesting this. Fergus glanced inquiringly at Jamie; the decision was his.

But Jamie, after a long, considering look at Bonnet, turned to Duncan.

"What say ye, Duncan?" Duncan gave Bonnet the same kind of look that Jamie himself had used, and finally nodded.

"For Gavin's sake," he said, and turned away toward the lych-gate.

"All right, then," Jamie said. He sighed and pushed a loose lock of hair behind his ear.

"Help us to bury Gavin," he said to our new guest, "and then we'll go."

An hour later, Gavin's grave was a blank rectangle of fresh-turned earth, stark among the gray hues of the surrounding grass.

"He must have his name to mark him by," Jamie said. Painstakingly, he scratched the letters of Gavin's name and his dates upon a piece of smooth beach-stone, using the point of his knife. I rubbed soot from the torch into the incised letters, making a crude but readable grave marker, and Ian set this solidly into a small cairn of gathered pebbles. Atop the tiny monument, Jamie gently set the stub of candle that he had taken from the tavern.

Everyone stood awkwardly about the grave for a moment, not knowing how to take farewell. Jamie and Duncan stood close together, looking down. They would have taken final leave of many such comrades since Culloden, if often with less ceremony.

Finally Jamie nodded to Fergus, who took a dry pine twig, and lighting it from my torch, bent and touched it to the candle's wick.

"Requiem aeternam dona ei, et lux perpetua luceat ei. . . ." Jamie said quietly.

"Eternal rest grant unto him, O God—and let perpetual light shine upon him." Young Ian echoed it softly, his face solemn in the torchlight.

Without a word, we turned and left the churchyard. Behind us, the candle burned without a flicker in the still, heavy air, like the sanctuary lamp in an empty church.

The moon was high in the sky by the time we reached the military checkpoint outside the city walls. It was only a half-moon, but shed enough light for us to see the trampled dirt track of the wagon road that ran before us, wide enough for two wagons to travel abreast.

We had encountered several such points on the road between Savannah and Charleston, mostly manned by bored soldiers who waved us through without bothering to check the passes we had obtained in Georgia. The checkpoints were mostly concerned with the interception of smuggled goods, and with the capture of the odd bondservant or slave, escaped from his master.

Even filthy and unkempt, we passed notice for the most part; few travelers were in better case. Fergus and Duncan could not be indentured men, maimed as they were, and Jamie's presence transcended his clothes; shabby coat or not, no man would take him for a servant.

Tonight was different, though. There were eight soldiers at the checkpoint, not the usual two, and all were armed and alert. Musket barrels flashed in the moonlight as the shout of "Halt! Your name and your business!" came from the dark. A lantern was hoisted up six inches from my face, blinding me for a moment.

"James Fraser, bound for Wilmington, with my family and servants." Jamie's voice was calm, and his hands were steady as he handed me the reins before reaching for the passes in his coat.

I kept my head down, trying to look tired and indifferent. I was tired, all right—I could have lain down in the road and slept—but far from indifferent. What did they do to you for aiding the escape of a fugitive from the gallows? I wondered. A single drop of sweat snaked its way down the back of my neck.

"Have you seen anyone along the road as you passed, sir?" The "sir" came a little reluctantly; the dilapidation of Jamie's coat and my gown were obvious in the pool of yellow lantern light.

"A carriage that passed us from the town; I suppose you will have seen that yourselves," Jamie answered. The sergeant replied with a grunt, checking the passes carefully, then squinting into the dark to count and see that the attendant bodies matched.

"What goods do you carry?" He handed back the passes, motioning to one of his subordinates to search the wagon. I twitched the reins inadvertently, and the horses snorted and shook their heads. Jamie's foot nudged mine, but he didn't look at me.

"Small household goods," he answered, still calm. "A half of venison and a bag of salt, for provision. And a body."

The soldier who had been reaching for the wagon covering stopped abruptly. The sergeant looked up sharply.

"A what?"

Jamie took the reins from me and wrapped them casually about his wrist. From the corner of my eye, I saw Duncan edge toward the darkness of the wood; Fergus, with his pickpocket's skill, had already faded from view.

"The corpse of the man who was hanged this afternoon. He was known to me; I asked permission of Colonel Franklin to take him to his kinsmen in the north. That is why we travel by night," he added delicately.

"I see." The sergeant motioned a lantern bearer closer. He gave Jamie a long thoughtful look, eyes narrowed, and nodded. "I remember you," he said. "You called out to him at the last. A friend, was he?"

"I knew him once. Some years ago," he added. The sergeant nodded to his subordinate, not taking his eyes off Jamie.

"Have a look, Griswold."

Griswold, who was perhaps fourteen, betrayed a notable lack of enthusiasm for the order, but dutifully lifted the canvas cover and raised his lantern to peer into the wagon bed. With an effort, I kept myself from turning to look.

The near horse snorted and tossed its head. If we did have to bolt, it would take several seconds for the horses to get the wagon moving. I heard Ian shift behind me, getting his hand on the club of hickory wood stowed behind the seat.

"Yes, sir, it's a body," Griswold reported. "In a shroud." He dropped the canvas with an air of relief, and exhaled strongly through his nostrils.

"Fix your bayonet and give it a jab," the sergeant said, eyes still on Jamie. I must have made a small noise, for the sergeant's glance shifted to me.

"You'll soil my wagon," Jamie objected. "The man's fair ripe, after a day in the sun, aye?"

The sergeant snorted impatiently. "Jab it in the leg, then. Get on, Griswold!"

With a marked air of reluctance, Griswold affixed his bayonet, and standing on tiptoe, began to poke gingerly about in the wagon bed. Behind me, Ian had begun to whistle softly. A Gaelic tune whose title translated to "In the Morn We Die," which I thought very tasteless of him.

"No, sir, he's dead all right." Griswold dropped back on his heels, sounding relieved. "I poked right hard, but not a twitch."

"All right, then." Dismissing the young soldier with a jerk of his hand, the sergeant nodded to Jamie. "Drive on then, Mr. Fraser. But I'd advise you to choose your friends more carefully in future."

I saw Jamie's knuckles whiten on the reins, but he only drew himself up straight and settled his hat more firmly on his head. He clicked his tongue and the horses set off sharply, leaving puffs of pale dust floating in the lantern light.

The darkness seemed engulfing after the light; despite the moon, I could see almost nothing. The night enfolded us. I felt the relief of a hunted animal that finds safe refuge, and in spite of the oppressive heat, I breathed more freely.

We covered a distance of nearly a quarter mile before anyone spoke.

"Are ye wounded, Mr. Bonnet?" Ian spoke in a loud whisper, just audible over the rattle of the wagon.

"Yes, he's pinked me in the thigh, damn the puppy." Bonnet's voice was low, but calm. "Thank Christ he left off before the blood soaked through the shroud. Dead men don't bleed."

"Are you hurt badly? Shall I come back and have a look at it?" I twisted around. Bonnet had pushed back the canvas cover and was sitting up, a vague pale shape in the darkness.

"No, I thank ye, ma'am. I've my stocking wound round it and 'twill serve well enough, I expect." My night vision was returning; I could see the gleam of fair hair as he bent his head to his task.

"Can ye walk, do ye think?" Jamie slowed the horses to a walk, and twisted round to inspect our guest. While his tone was not inhospitable, it was clear that he would prefer to be rid of our dangerous cargo as soon as possible.

"Not easily, no. I'm that sorry, sir." Bonnet was aware of Jamie's eagerness to be rid of him, too. With some difficulty, he hoisted himself up in the wagon bed, rising onto his good knee behind the seat. His lower half was invisible in darkness, but I could smell the blood on him, a sharper scent than the lingering faint reek of Gavin's shroud.

"A suggestion, Mr. Fraser. In three miles, we'll come to the Ferry Trail road. A mile past the crossroads, another road leads toward the coast. It's little more than a pair of ruts, but passable. That will take us to the edge of a creek with an outlet to the sea.

Some associates of mine will be puttin' in to anchor there within the week; if ye would grant me some small stock of provisions, I can await them in reasonable safety, and you can be on your way, free o' the taint of my company."

"Associates? Ye mean pirates?" Ian's voice held a certain amount of wariness. Having been abducted from Scotland by pirates, he invested such persons with none of the romanticism normal to a fifteen-year-old.

"That would depend upon your perspective, lad." Bonnet sounded amused. "Certainly the governors of the Carolinas would call them so; the merchants of Wilmington and Charleston perhaps regard them otherwise."

Jamie gave a brief snort. "Smugglers, aye? And what might these associates of yours be dealing in, then?"

"Whatever will fetch a price to make it worth the risk of carrying." The amusement had not left Bonnet's voice, but was now tinged with cynicism. "Will you be wanting some reward for your assistance? That can be managed."

"I do not." Jamie's voice was cold. "I saved you for Gavin Hayes' sake, and for my own. I wouldna seek reward for such service."

"I meant no offense to ye, sir." Bonnet's head inclined slightly toward us.

"None taken," Jamie answered shortly. He shook out the reins and wrapped them afresh, changing hands.

Conversation lapsed after this small clash, though Bonnet continued to ride kneeling behind us, peering over my shoulder at the dark road ahead. There were no more soldiers, though; nothing moved, not even a breath of wind in the leaves. Nothing disturbed the silence of the summer night save the occasional thin *zeek* of a passing night bird, or the hooting of an owl.

The soft rhythmic thump of the horses' hooves in the dust and the squeak and rattle of the wagon began to lull me to sleep. I tried to keep upright, watching the black shadows of the trees along the road, but found myself gradually inclining toward Jamie, my eyes falling shut despite my best efforts.

Jamie transferred the reins to his left hand, and putting his right arm around me, drew me down to rest against his shoulder. As always, I felt safe when I touched him. I went limp, cheek pressed against the dusty serge of his coat, and fell at once into that uneasy doze that is the consequence of a combination of utter exhaustion and the inability to lie down.

I opened my eyes once to see the tall, lean figure of Duncan Innes, pacing alongside the wagon with his tireless hillman's stride, head bowed as though in deep thought. Then I closed them again, and drifted into a doze in which memories of the day mingled with inchoate fragments of dreams. I dreamt of a giant skunk sleeping under a tavern's table, waking to join in a chorus of "The Star-Spangled Banner," and then of a swinging corpse that raised its lolling head and grinned with empty eyes . . . I came awake to find Jamie gently shaking me.

"Ye'd best crawl into the back and lie down, Sassenach," he said. "You're craicklin' in your sleep. You'll be slippin' into the road, next thing."

Blearily assenting, I clambered awkwardly over the seat back, changing places with Bonnet, and found a place in the wagonbed next to the slumbering form of Young Ian.

It smelt musty—and worse—in the wagon bed. Ian had his head pillowed on a packet of roughly butchered venison, wrapped in the untanned skin of the deer. Rollo had done somewhat better, his hairy muzzle resting comfortably on Ian's stomach. For myself, I took the leathern bag of salt. The smooth leather was hard under my cheek, but odorless.

The jolting boards of the wagon bed couldn't by any stretch of the imagination be called comfortable, but the relief of being able to stretch out at full length was so overwhelming that I scarcely noticed the bumps and jolts. I rolled onto my back and looked up into the hazy immensity of the southern sky, studded thick with blazing stars. *Lumen Christi,* I thought, and comforted by the thought of Gavin Hayes finding his way safe home by the lights of heaven, fell once more fast asleep.

I could not tell how long I slept, wrapped in a drugged blanket of heat and exhaustion. I woke when the pace of the wagon changed, swimming toward the surface of consciousness, drenched with sweat.

Bonnet and Jamie were talking, in the low, easy tones of men who had found their way past the early awkwardness of first acquaintance.

"You said that ye saved me for Gavin Hayes' sake—and for your own," Bonnet was saying. His voice was soft, barely audible above the rumble of the wheels. "What did ye mean by that, sir, and ye'll pardon my asking—?"

Jamie didn't answer at once; I nearly fell asleep again before he spoke, but at last his answer came, floating disembodied in the warm, dark air.

"Ye wilna have slept much last night, I think? Knowing what was to come to ye with the day?"

There was a low laugh from Bonnet, not entirely amused.

"Too right," he said. "I doubt I shall forget it in a hurry."

"Nor will I." Jamie said something soft in Gaelic to the horses, and they slowed in response. "I once lived through such a night, knowing I would hang, come morning. And yet I lived, through the grace of one who risked much to save me."

"I see," Bonnet said softly. "So you are an *asgina ageli*, are you?"

"Aye? And what will that be?"

There was a sound of scraping and brushing leaves against the side of the wagon, and the spicy sap-scent of the trees grew suddenly stronger. Something light touched my face—leaves, falling from above. The horses slowed, and the rhythm of the wagon changed markedly, the wheels finding an uneven surface. We had turned into the small road that led to Bonnet's creek.

"*Asgina ageli* is a term that the red savages employ—the Cherokee of the mountains; I heard it from one I had as guide one time. It means 'half-ghost,' one who should have died by right, but yet remains on the earth; a woman who survives a mortal illness, a man fallen into his enemies' hands who escapes. They say an *asgina ageli* has one foot on the earth and the other in the spirit world. He can talk to the spirits, and see the Nunnahee—the Little People."

"Little People? Will that be like the faeries?" Jamie sounded surprised.

"Something of the kind." Bonnet shifted his weight and the seat creaked as he stretched. "The Indians do say that the Nunnahee live inside the rocks of the mountains, and come out to help their people in time of war or other evil."

"Is that so? It will be something like the tales they tell in the Highlands of Scotland, then—of the Auld Folk."

"Indeed." Bonnet sounded amused. "Well, from what I have heard of the Scotch Highlanders, there is little to choose between them and the red men for barbarous conduct."

"Nonsense," said Jamie, sounding not the least offended. "The red savages eat the hearts of their enemies, or so I have heard. I prefer a good dish of oatmeal parritch, myself."

Bonnet made a noise, hastily stifled.

"You are a Highlander? Well, I will say that for a barbarian, I have found ye passing civil, sir," he assured Jamie, the laughter quivering in his voice.

"I am exceedingly obliged for your kind opinion, sir," Jamie replied, with equal politeness.

Their voices faded into the rhythmic squeaking of the wheels, and I was asleep again before I could hear more.

The moon hung low over the trees by the time we came to a halt. I was roused by the movements of Young Ian, clambering sleepily over the wagon's edge to help Jamie tend to the horses. I poked my head up to see a broad stretch of water flowing past shelving banks of clay and silt, the stream a shiny black glittering with silver where riffles purled on the rocks near shore. Bonnet, with customary New World understatement, might call it a creek, but it would pass for a decent river among most boatmen, I thought.

The men moved to and fro in the shadows, carrying out their tasks with no more than an occasional muttered word. They moved with unaccustomed slowness, seeming to fade into the night, made insubstantial by fatigue.

"Do ye go and find a place to sleep, Sassenach," Jamie said, pausing to steady me as I dropped down from the wagon. "I must just see our guest provisioned and set on his way, and the beasts wiped down and put to grass."

The temperature had dropped scarcely at all since nightfall, but the air seemed fresher here near the water, and I found myself reviving somewhat.

"I can't sleep until I've bathed," I said, pulling the soaked bodice of my gown away from my breasts. "I feel terrible." My hair was pasted to my temples with sweat, and my flesh felt grimed and itchy. The dark water looked cool and inviting. Jamie cast a longing look at it, plucking at his crumpled stock.

"I canna say I blame ye. Go careful, though; Bonnet says the channel in midstream is deep enough to float a ketch, and it's a tide-creek; there'll be a strong current."

"I'll stay near the shore." I pointed downstream, where a small point of land marked a bend in the river, its willows shining dusky silver in the moonlight. "See that little point? There should be an eddy pool there."

"Aye. Go careful, then," he said again, and squeezed my elbow in farewell. As I turned to go, a large pale shape loomed up before me; our erstwhile guest, one leg of his breeches stained dark with dried blood.

"Your servant, ma'am," he said, making me a creditable bow, despite the injured leg. "Do I bid you now adieu?" He was standing a bit closer to me than I quite liked, and I repressed the urge to step backward.

"You do," I said, and nodded to him, brushing back a dangling lock of hair. "Good luck, Mr. Bonnet."

"I thank ye for your kind wishes, ma'am," he answered softly. "But I have found that a man most often makes his own luck. Good night to ye, ma'am." He bowed once more and turned away, limping heavily, like the ghost of a crippled bear.

The creek's rushing masked most of the ordinary night sounds. I saw a bat blink through a patch of moonlight over the water, in pursuit of insects too small to see, and vanish into the night. If anything else lurked in the dark, it was quiet.

Jamie grunted softly to himself.

"Well, I've my doubts of the man," he said, as though answering a question I hadn't asked. "I must hope I've only been softhearted, and not softheaded, by helpin' him."

"You couldn't leave him to hang, after all," I said.

"Oh, aye, I could," he said, surprising me. He saw me look up at him, and smiled, the wry twist of his mouth barely visible in the dark.

"The Crown doesna *always* pick the wrong man to hang, Sassenach," he said. "More often than not, the man on the end of a rope deserves to be there. And I shouldna like to think I've helped a villain to go free." He shrugged, and shoved his hair back out of his face.

"Aye, well, it's done. Go and have your bath, Sassenach; I'll come to ye so soon as I may."

I stood on tiptoe to kiss him, and felt him smile as I did so. My tongue touched his mouth in delicate invitation, and he bit my lower lip gently, in answer.

"Can ye stay awake a wee bit longer, Sassenach?"

"As long as it takes," I assured him. "But do hurry, won't you?"

There was a patch of thick grass edging the point below the willows. I undressed slowly, enjoying the feel of the water-borne breeze through the damp cloth of shift and stockings, and the final freedom as the last bits of clothing fell to the ground, leaving me naked to the night.

I stepped gingerly into the water. It was surprisingly cool—cold, by contrast to the hot night air. The bottom under my feet was mostly silt, but it yielded to fine sand within a yard of shore.

Though it was a tidal creek, we were far enough upstream that the water was fresh and sweet. I drank and splashed my face, washing away the dust in throat and nose.

I waded in up to mid-thigh, mindful of Jamie's cautions about channels and currents. After the staggering heat of the day and the smothering embrace of the night, the sensation of coolness on bare skin was an overwhelming relief. I cupped handfuls of cold water and splashed them on my face and breasts; the droplets ran down my stomach and tickled coldly between my legs.

I could feel the slight push of the tide coming in, shoving gently against my calves, urging me toward shore. I wasn't ready to come in yet, though. I had no soap, but knelt and rinsed my hair over and over in the clear dark water, and scrubbed my body with handfuls of fine sand, until my skin felt thin and glowing.

Finally, I climbed out onto a rocky shelf and lay languid as a mermaid in the moonlight, the heat of the air and the sun-warmed stone now a comfort to my chilled body. I combed out my thick curly hair with my fingers, scattering drops of water. The wet stone smelled like rain, dusty and tingling.

I felt very tired, but at the same time, very much alive, in that state of half consciousness where thought is slowed and small physical sensations magnified. I moved my bare foot slowly over the sandstone rock, enjoying the slight friction, and ran a hand lightly down the inside of my thigh, a ripple of goose bumps rising in the wake of my touch.

My breasts rose in the moonlight, cool white domes spangled with clear droplets. I brushed one nipple and watched it slowly stiffen by itself, rising as if by magic.

Quite a magical place at that, I thought. The night was quiet and still, but with a languid atmosphere that was like floating in a warm sea. So near the coast, the sky was clear, and the stars shone overhead like diamonds, burning with a fierce, bright light.

A faint splash made me look toward the stream. Nothing moved on the surface but faint coruscations of starlight, caught like fireflies in a spider's web.

As I watched, a great head broke water in the middle of the

stream, water purling back from the pointed snout. There was a fish struggling in Rollo's jaws; the flap and gleam of its scales showed briefly as he shook his head violently to break its back. The huge dog swam slowly to the shore, shook his coat briefly, and stalked away, his evening meal dangling limp and shimmering from his jaws.

He paused for a moment on the far edge of the creek, looking at me, the ruff of his hackles a dark shadow framing yellow eyes and gleaming fish. Like a primitive painting, I thought; something from Rousseau, with its contrast of utter wildness and complete stillness.

Then the dog was gone, and there was nothing on the far shore but the trees, hiding whatever might lie behind them. And what did? I wondered. More trees, answered the logical part of my mind.

"A *lot* more," I murmured, looking into the mysterious dark. Civilization—even of the primitive kind I had grown used to— was no more than a thin crescent on the edge of the continent. Two hundred miles from the coast, you were beyond the ken of city and farm. And, past that point lay three thousand miles . . . of what? Wilderness, surely, and danger. Adventure, too—and freedom.

It was a new world, after all, free of fear and filled with joy, for now Jamie and I were together, for all of our lives before us. Parting and sorrow lay behind us. Even the thought of Brianna caused no dreadful regret—I missed her greatly, and thought of her constantly, but I knew she was safe in her own time, and that knowledge made her absence easier to bear.

I lay back on the rock, the trapped heat of the day radiating from its surface into my body, happy only to be alive. The drops of water were drying on my breasts as I watched, vanishing to a film of moistness and then disappearing altogether.

Small clouds of gnats hovered over the water; I couldn't see them, but I knew they were there by the occasional splash of leaping fish, rising to snatch them from the air.

The bugs had been a ubiquitous plague. I inspected Jamie's skin minutely every morning, picking voracious ticks and wood fleas from his crevices, and anointed all of the men liberally with the juice of crushed pennyroyal and tobacco leaves. This kept them from being devoured alive by the clouds of mosquitoes, gnats, and carnivorous midges that hung in the sun-tinged shadows of the woods, but it didn't prevent the hordes of inquisitive

bugs from driving them mad with a constant tickling inquiry into
ears, eyes, noses, and mouths.

Oddly enough, the majority of insects left me strictly alone. Ian
joked that the strong scent of herbs that hung about me must repel
them, but I thought it went further than that—even when I was
freshly bathed, the insects showed no desire to bother me.

I thought it might be a manifestation of the evolutionary oddity
that—I surmised—protected me from colds and minor illness
here. Bloodthirsty bugs, like microbes, evolved very closely with
humans, and were sensitive to the subtle chemical signals of their
hosts. Coming from another time, I no longer had precisely the
same signals, and consequently the bugs no longer perceived me
as prey.

"Or maybe Ian's right, and I just smell awful," I said aloud. I
dipped my fingers in the water and flicked a spray of drops at a
dragonfly resting on my rock, no more than a transparent shadow,
its colors drained by darkness.

I hoped Jamie would hurry. Riding for days on the wagon seat
next to him, watching the subtle shifts of his body as he drove,
seeing the changing light on the angles of his face as he talked
and smiled, was enough to make my palms tingle with the urge to
touch him. We had not made love in several days, owing to our
hurry to reach Charleston, and my inhibitions about intimacy
within earshot of a dozen men.

A breath of warm breeze slipped past me, and all the tiny down
hairs on my body prickled with its passing. No hurry now, and no
one to hear. I drew a hand down the soft curve of my belly and the
softer skin inside my thighs, where the blood pulsed slowly to the
beat of my heart. I cupped my hand, feeling the swollen moist
ache of urgent desire.

I closed my eyes, rubbing lightly, enjoying the feeling of increasing urgency.

"And where the hell are *you,* Jamie Fraser?" I murmured.

"Here," came a husky answer.

Startled, my eyes popped open. He was standing in the stream,
six feet away, thigh-deep in the water, his genitals stiff and dark
against the pallid glow of his body. His hair lay loose around his
shoulders, framing a face white as bone, eyes unblinking and
intent as those of the wolf-dog. Utter wildness, utter stillness.

Then he stirred and came toward me, still intent, but still no
longer. His thighs were cold as water when he touched me, but
within seconds he warmed and grew hot. Sweat sprang up at once

where his hands touched my skin, and a flush of hot moisture dampened my breasts once more, making them round and slick against the hardness of his chest.

Then his mouth moved to mine and I melted—almost literally —into him. I didn't care how hot it was, or whether the dampness on my skin was my sweat or his. Even the clouds of insects faded into insignificance. I raised my hips and he slid home, slick and solid, the last faint coolness of him quenched by my heat, like the cold metal of a sword, slaked in hot blood.

My hands glided on a film of moisture over the curves of his back, and my breasts wobbled against his chest, a rivulet trickling between them to oil the friction of belly and thigh.

"Christ, your mouth is slick and salty as your quim," he muttered, and his tongue darted out to taste the tiny beads of salt on my face, butterfly wings on temple and eyelids.

I was vaguely conscious of the hard rock under me. The stored heat of the day rose up and through me, and the rough surface scraped my back and buttocks, but I didn't care.

"I can't wait," he said in my ear, breathless.

"Don't," I said, and wrapped my legs tight around his hips, flesh bonded to flesh in the brief madness of dissolution.

"I have heard of melting with passion," I said, gasping slightly, "but this is ridiculous."

He lifted his head from my breast with a faint sticky sound as his cheek came away. He laughed and slid slowly sideways.

"God, it's hot!" he said. He pushed back the sweat-soaked hair from his forehead and blew out his breath, chest still heaving from exertion. "How do folk do that when it's like this?"

"The same way we just did," I pointed out. I was breathing heavily myself.

"They can't," he said with certainty. "Not all the time; they'd die."

"Well, maybe they do it slower," I said. "Or underwater. Or wait until the autumn."

"Autumn?" he said. "Perhaps I dinna want to live in the south, after all. Is it hot in Boston?"

"It is at this time of year," I assured him. "And beastly cold in the winter. I'm sure you'll get used to the heat. And the bugs."

He brushed a questing mosquito off his shoulder and glanced from me to the nearby creek.

"Maybe so," he said, "and maybe no, but for now . . ." He wrapped his arms firmly around me, and rolled. With the ponderous grace of a rolling log, we fell off the edge of the rocky shelf, and into the water.

We lay damp and cool on the rock, barely touching, the last drops of water evaporating on our skins. Across the creek, the willows trailed their leaves in the water, crowns ruffled black against the setting moon. Beyond the willows lay acre upon acre and mile upon mile of the virgin forest, civilization for now no more than a foothold on the edge of the continent.

Jamie saw the direction of my glance and divined my thought.

"It will be a good bit different now than when ye last kent it, I expect?" He nodded toward the leafy dark.

"Oh, a bit." I linked my hand with his, my thumb idly caressing his big, bony knuckles. "The roads will be paved then; not cobbled, covered with a hard, smooth stuff—invented by a Scotsman called MacAdam, in fact."

He grunted slightly with amusement.

"So there will be Scots in America, then? That's good."

I ignored him and went on, staring into the wavering shadows as though I could conjure the burgeoning cities that would one day rise there.

"There will be a lot of everyone in America, then. All the land will be settled, from here to the far west coast, to a place called California. But for now"—I shivered slightly, in spite of the warm, humid air—"it's three thousand miles of wilderness. There's nothing there at all."

"Aye, well, nothing save thousands of bloodthirsty savages," he said practically. "And the odd vicious beast, to be sure."

"Well, yes," I agreed. "I suppose they are." The thought was unsettling; I had of course known, in a vague, academic way, that the woods were inhabited by Indians, bears, and other forest denizens, but this general notion had suddenly been replaced by a particular and most acute awareness that we might easily—and unexpectedly—meet any one of these denizens, face-to-face.

"What happens to them? To the wild Indians?" Jamie asked curiously, peering into the dark as I was, as though trying to divine the future among the shifting shadows. "They'll be defeated and driven back, will they?"

Another small shiver passed over me, and my toes curled.

"Yes, they will," I said. "Killed, a lot of them. A good many taken prisoner, locked up."

"Well, that's good."

"I expect that depends a lot on your point of view," I said, rather dryly. "I don't suppose the Indians will think so."

"I daresay," he said. "But when a bloody fiend's tryin' his best to chop off the top of my head, I'm no so much concerned with his point of view, Sassenach."

"Well, you can't really blame them," I protested.

"I most certainly can," he assured me. "If one of the brutes scalps ye, I shall blame him a great deal."

"Ah . . . hmm," I said. I cleared my throat and had another stab at it. "Well, what if a bunch of strangers came round and tried to kill you and shove you off the land you'd always lived on?"

"They have," he said, very dryly indeed. "If they hadna, I should still be in Scotland, aye?"

"Well . . ." I said, floundering. "But all I mean is—you'd fight, too, under those circumstances, wouldn't you?"

He drew a deep breath and exhaled strongly through his nose.

"If an English dragoon came round to my house and began to worry me," he said precisely, "I should certainly fight him. I would also have not the slightest hesitation in killing him. I would *not* cut off his hair and wave it about, and I wouldna be eating his private parts, either. I am not a savage, Sassenach."

"I didn't say you were," I protested. "All I said was—"

"Besides," he added with inexorable logic, "I dinna mean to be killing any Indians. If they keep to themselves, I shallna be worrying them a bit."

"I'm sure they'll be relieved to know that," I murmured, giving up for the present.

We lay cradled close together in the hollow of the rock, lightly glued with sweat, watching the stars. I felt at once shatteringly happy and mildly apprehensive. Could this state of exaltation possibly last? Once I had taken "forever" for granted between us, but I was younger, then.

Soon, God willing, we would settle; find a place to make a home and a life. I wanted nothing more, and yet at the same time, I worried. We had known each other only a few months since my return. Each touch, each word was still at once tinged with memory and new with rediscovery. What would happen when we were thoroughly accustomed to each other, living day by day in a routine of mundane tasks?

"Will ye grow tired of me, do ye think?" he murmured. "Once we're settled?"

"I was just wondering the same thing about you."

"No," he said, and I could hear the smile in his voice. "That I willna, Sassenach."

"How do you know?" I asked.

"I didn't," he pointed out. "Before. We were wed three years, and I wanted ye as much on the last day as the first. More, maybe," he added softly, thinking, as I was, of the last time we had made love before he sent me through the stones.

I leaned down and kissed him. He tasted clean and fresh, faintly scented with the pungency of sex.

"I did, too."

"Then dinna trouble yourself about it, Sassenach, and neither will I." He stroked my hair, smoothing damp curls off my forehead. "I could know ye all my life, I think, and always love you. And often as I've lain wi' you, ye still surprise me mightily sometimes, like ye did tonight."

"I do? Why, what have I done?" I stared down at him, surprised myself.

"Oh . . . well. I didna mean . . . that is—"

He sounded suddenly shy, and there was an unaccustomed stiffness in his body.

"Mm?" I kissed the tip of his ear.

"Ah . . . when I came upon you . . . what ye were doing . . . I mean—were ye doing what I thought?"

I smiled against his shoulder in the darkness.

"I suppose that depends what you thought, doesn't it?"

He lifted up on one elbow, his skin coming away from mine with a small sucking noise. The damp spot where he had adhered was suddenly cool. He rolled onto his side and grinned at me.

"Ye ken verra well what I thought, Sassenach."

I touched his chin, shadowed with sprouting whiskers.

"I do. And you know perfectly well what I was doing, too, so why are you asking?"

"Well, I—I didna think women did that, is all."

The moon was bright enough for me to see his half-cocked eyebrow.

"Well, men do," I pointed out. "Or you do, at least. You told me so—when you were in prison, you said you—"

"That was different!" I could see his mouth twist as he tried to decide what to say. "I—that is to say, there wasna any help for it then. After all, I couldna be—"

"Haven't you done it other times?" I sat up and fluffed out my damp hair, glancing sidelong at him over my shoulder. A blush didn't show in the moonlight, but I thought he had gone pink.

"Aye, well," he muttered. "I suppose I have, yes." A sudden thought struck him and his eyes widened, looking at me. "Do you —have ye done that—often?" The last word emerged in a croak, and he was obliged to stop and clear his throat.

"I suppose it depends on what you mean by 'often,' " I said, allowing a bit of acerbity to creep into my tone. "I was widowed for two years, you know."

He rubbed a knuckle over his lips, eyeing me with interest.

"Aye, that's so. It's only—well, I hadna thought of women doing such a thing, is all." Growing fascination was overcoming his surprise. "You can—finish? Without a man, I mean?"

That made me laugh out loud, and soft reverberations sounded from the trees around us, echoed by the stream.

"Yes, but it's much nicer with a man," I assured him. I reached out and touched his chest. I could see the goose bumps ripple over his chest and shoulders, and he shivered slightly as I drew a fingertip in a gentle circle round one nipple. "Much," I said softly.

"Oh," he said, sounding happy. "Well, that's good, aye?"

He was hot—even hotter than the liquid air—and my first instinct was to draw back, but I didn't follow it. Sweat sprang up at once where his hands rested on my skin, and trickles of sweat ran down my neck.

"I've never made love to ye before like this," he said. "Like eels, aye? Wi' your body sliding through my hands, all slippery as seaweed." Both hands passed slowly down my back, his thumbs pressing the groove of my spine, making the tiny hairs at the base of my neck prickle with pleasure.

"Mm. That's because it's too cold in Scotland to sweat like pigs," I said. "Though come to that, do pigs really sweat? I've always wondered."

"I couldna say; I've never made love to a pig." His head ducked down and his tongue touched my breast. "But ye do taste a bit like a trout, Sassenach."

"I taste like a *what*?"

"Fresh and sweet, wi' a bit of salt," he explained, lifting his head for a moment. He put it back down, and resumed his downward course.

"That tickles," I said, quivering under his tongue, but making no effort to escape.

"Well, I mean it to," he answered, lifting his wet face for a breath before returning to his work. "I shouldna like to think ye could do without me entirely."

"I can't," I assured him. "Oh!"

"Ah?" came a thick interrogative. I lay back on the rock, my back arching as the stars spun dizzily overhead.

"I said . . . 'oh,' " I said faintly. And then didn't say anything coherent for some time, until he lay panting, chin resting lightly on my pubic bone. I reached down and stroked the sweat-drenched hair away from his face, and he turned his head to kiss my palm.

"I feel like Eve," I said softly, watching the moon set behind him, over the dark of the forest. "Just on the edge of the Garden of Eden."

There was a small snort of laughter from the vicinity of my navel.

"Aye, and I suppose I'm Adam," Jamie said. "In the gateway to Paradise." He turned his head to look wistfully across the creek toward the vast unknown, resting his cheek on the slope of my belly. "I only wish I knew was I coming in, or going out?"

I laughed myself, startling him. I took him by both ears then, urging him gently up across the slippery expanse of my naked flesh.

"In," I said. "I don't see an angel with a fiery sword, after all."

He lowered himself upon me, his own flesh heated as with fever, and I shivered under him.

"No?" he murmured. "Aye, well, you'll no be looking close enough, I suppose."

Then the fiery sword severed me from consciousness and set fire to my body. We blazed up together, bright as stars in the summer night, and then sank back burnt and limbless, ashes dissolved in a primordial sea of warm salt, stirring with the nascent throbbings of life.

PART TWO

Past Imperfect

3

The Minister's Cat

Boston, Massachusetts, June 1969

"Brianna?"

"Ha?" She sat bolt upright, heart pounding, the sound of her name ringing in her ear. "Who—wha'?"

"You were asleep. Damn, I knew I'd got the time wrong! Sorry, shall I ring off?"

It was the faint hint of a burr in his voice that belatedly made the scrambled connections of her nervous system fall into place. Phone. Ringing phone. She'd snatched it by reflex, deep in her dream.

"Roger!" The rush of adrenaline from being startled awake was fading, but her heart was still beating fast. "No, don't hang up! It's all right, I'm awake." She scrubbed a hand over her face, trying at once to disentangle the phone cord and straighten the rumpled bedclothes.

"Aye? You're sure? What time is it there?"

"I don't know; it's too dark to see the clock," she said, still sleep-addled. A reluctant deep chuckle answered her.

"I *am* sorry; I tried to calculate the time difference, but must've got it backward. Didn't mean to wake you."

"That's okay, I had to wake up to answer the phone anyway," she assured him, and laughed.

"Aye. Well . . ." She could hear the answering smile in his voice, and eased herself back against the pillows, shoving tangles of hair out of her eyes, slowly adjusting to the here and now. The feel of her dream was still with her, more real than the dark-shrouded shapes of her bedroom.

"It's good to hear your voice, Roger," she said softly. She was surprised at just *how* good it was. His voice was far away and yet seemed much more immediate than the far-off whines of sirens, and the *whish!* of tires on wet pavement outside.

"Yours, too." He sounded a little shy. "Look—I've got the

chance of a conference next month, in Boston. I thought of coming, if—damn, there's no good way to say this. Do you want to see me?''

Her hand squeezed tight on the receiver, and her heart jumped.

"I'm sorry," he said at once, before she could reply. "That's putting you on the spot, isn't it? I—look—just say straight out if you'd rather not."

"I do. Of course I want to see you!"

"Ah. You don't mind, then? Only . . . you didn't answer my letter. I thought maybe I'd done something—"

"No, you didn't. I'm sorry. It was just—"

"It's fine, I didn't mean—"

Their sentences collided, and they both stopped, stricken with shyness.

"I didn't want to push—"

"I didn't mean to be—"

It happened again, and this time he laughed, a low sound of Scottish amusement coming over the vast distance of space and time, comforting as though he'd touched her.

"It's all right, then," he said firmly. "I do understand, aye?"

She didn't answer, but closed her eyes, an indefinable sensation of relief sweeping over her. Roger Wakefield was likely the only person in the world who *could* understand; what she hadn't fully realized before was how important that understanding might be.

"I was dreaming," she said. "When the phone rang."

"Mmphm?"

"About my father." Her throat tightened, just a little, whenever she spoke the word. The same thing happened when she said "mother," too. She could still smell the sun-warmed pines of her dream, and feel the crunch of pine needles under her boots.

"I couldn't see his face. I was walking with him, in the woods somewhere. I was following him up a trail, and he was talking to me, but I couldn't hear what he was saying—I kept hurrying, trying to catch up, so I could hear, but I couldn't quite manage."

"But you knew the man was your father?"

"Yes—but maybe I only thought so because of hiking in the mountains. I used to do that with Dad."

"Did you? I used to do that with my dad, as well. If you come back to Scotland ever, I'll take ye Munro bagging."

"You'll take me *what*?"

He laughed, and she had a sudden memory of him, brushing back the thick black hair that he didn't cut often enough, moss-green eyes creased half-shut by his smile. She found she was rubbing the tip of her thumb slowly across her lower lip, and stopped herself. He'd kissed her when they parted.

"A Munro is any Scottish peak more than three thousand feet. There are so many of them, it's a sport to see how many you can climb. Folk collect them, like stamps, or matchbooks."

"Where are you now—Scotland or England?" she said, then interrupted before he could answer. "No, let me see if I can guess. It's . . . Scotland. You're in Inverness."

"That's right." The surprise was evident in his voice. "How did you know that?"

She stretched, scissoring her long legs slowly under the sheets.

"You roll your r's when you've been talking to other Scots," she said. "You don't when you talk to English people. I noticed when we—went to London." There was no more than a faint catch in her voice; it was getting easier, she thought.

"And herrrrre I was beginning to think ye were psychic," he said, and laughed.

"I wish you were here now," she said impulsively.

"You do?" He sounded surprised, and suddenly shy. "Oh. Well . . . that's good, isn't it?"

"Roger—why I didn't write—"

"You're not to trouble about it," he said quickly. "I'll be there in a month; we can talk, then. Bree, I—"

"Yes?"

She heard him draw breath, and had a vivid memory of the feel of his chest rising and falling as he breathed, warm and solid under her hand.

"I'm glad you said yes."

She couldn't go back to sleep after hanging up; restless, she swung her feet out of bed and padded out to the kitchen of the small apartment for a glass of milk. It was only after several minutes of staring blankly into the recesses of the refrigerator that she realized she wasn't seeing ranks of ketchup bottles and half-used cans. She was seeing standing stones, black against a pale dawn sky.

She straightened up with a small exclamation of impatience, and shut the door with a slam. She shivered slightly, and rubbed her arms, chilled by the draft of the air conditioner. Impulsively, she reached up and clicked it off, then went to the window and raised the sash, letting in the warm mugginess of the rainy summer night.

She should have written. In fact, she *had* written—several times, all half-finished attempts thrown away in frustration.

She knew why, or thought she did. Explaining it coherently to Roger was something else.

Part of it was the simple instinct of a wounded animal; the urge to run away and hide from hurt. What had happened the year before was in no way Roger's fault, but he was inextricably wrapped up in it.

He'd been so tender, and so kind afterward, treating her like one freshly bereaved—which she was. But such a strange bereavement! Her mother gone for good, but certainly—she hoped—not dead. And yet it was in some ways just as it had been when her father died; like believing in a blessed afterlife, ardently hoping that your loved one was safe and happy—and being forced to suffer the pangs of loss and loneliness nonetheless.

An ambulance went by, across the park, red light pulsing in the dark, its siren muted by distance.

She crossed herself from habit, and murmured *"Miserere nobis"* under her breath. Sister Marie Romaine had told the fifth grade that the dead and dying needed their prayers; so strongly had she inculcated the notion in her class that none of the children had ever been able to pass the scene of an emergency without sending a small silent prayer upward, to succor the souls of the imminently heaven-bound.

She prayed for them every day, her mother and her father—her fathers. That was the other part of it. Uncle Joe knew the truth of her paternity, too, but only Roger could truly understand what had happened; only Roger could hear the stones, too.

No one could pass through an experience like that and not be marked by it. Not him, not her. He'd wanted her to stay, after Claire had gone, but she couldn't.

There were things to do here, she'd told him, things to be attended to, her schooling to finish. That was true. More importantly, she'd had to get away—get clear away from Scotland and stone circles, back to a place where she might heal, might begin to rebuild her life.

If she'd stayed with Roger, there was no way to forget what had happened, even for a moment. And that was the last part of it, the final piece in her three-sided puzzle.

He had protected her, had cherished her. Her mother had confided her into his care, and he'd kept that trust well. But had he done it to keep his promise to Claire—or because he truly cared? Either way, it wasn't any basis for a shared future, with the crushing weight of obligation on both sides.

If there might be a future for them . . . and that was what she couldn't write to him, because how could she say it without sounding both presumptuous and idiotic?

"Go away, so you can come back and do it right," she murmured, and made a face at the words. The rain was still pattering down, cooling the air enough to breathe comfortably. It was just before dawn, she thought, but the air was still warm enough that moisture condensed on the cool skin of her face; small beads of water formed and slid tickling down her neck one by one, dampening the cotton T-shirt she slept in.

She'd wanted to put the events of last November well behind them; make a clean break. Then, when enough time had passed, perhaps they could come to each other again. Not as supporting players in the drama of her parents' life, but this time as the actors in a play of their own choosing.

No, if anything was to happen between her and Roger Wakefield, it would definitely be by choice. It looked as though she was going to get the chance to choose now, and the prospect gave her a small, excited flutter in the pit of her stomach.

She wiped a hand over her face, slicking off the rain-wet, wiping it casually through her hair to tame the floating strands. If she wasn't going to sleep, she might as well work.

She left the window open, careless of the rain puddling on the floor. She felt too restless to be sealed in, chilled by artificial air.

Clicking on the lamp on the desk, she pulled out her calculus book and opened it. One small and unexpected bonus of her change of study was her belated discovery of the soothing effects of mathematics.

When she had come back to Boston, alone, and back to school, engineering had seemed a much safer choice than history; solid, fact-bound, reassuringly immutable. Above all, controllable. She picked up a pencil, sharpened it slowly, enjoying the preparation, then bent her head and read the first problem.

Slowly, as it always did, the calm inexorable logic of the figures built its web inside her head, trapping all the random thoughts, wrapping the distracting emotions up in silken threads like so many flies. Round the central axis of the problem, logic spun her web, orderly and beautiful as an orb-weaver's jeweled confection.

Only the one small thought stayed free of its strands, hovering in her mind like a bright, tiny butterfly.

I'm glad you said yes, he'd said. So was she.

July 1969

"Does he talk like the Beatles? Oh, I'll just die if he sounds like John Lennon! You know how he says, 'It's me grandfather?' That just knocks me out!"

"He doesn't sound anything like John Lennon, for God's sake!" Brianna hissed. She peered cautiously around a concrete pillar, but the International Arrivals gate was still empty. "Can't you tell the difference between a Liverpudlian and a Scot?"

"No," her friend Gayle said blithely, fluffing out her blond hair. "All Englishmen sound the same to me. I could listen to them forever!"

"He's not an Englishman! I told you, he's a Scot!"

Gayle gave Brianna a look, clearly suggesting that her friend was crazed.

"Scotland's part of England; I looked on the map."

"Scotland's part of Great Britain, not England."

"What's the difference?" Gayle stuck her head out and craned around the pillar. "Why are we standing back here? He'll never see us."

Brianna ran a hand over her hair to smooth it. They were standing behind a pillar because she wasn't sure she *wanted* him to see them. Not much help for it, though; disheveled passengers were beginning to trickle through the double doors, burdened with luggage.

She let Gayle tow her out into the main reception area, still babbling. Her friend's tongue led a double life; though Gayle was capable of cool and reasoned discourse in class, her chief social skill was babbling on cue. That was why Bree had asked Gayle to come with her to the airport to pick up Roger; no chance of any awkward pauses in the conversation.

"Have you done it with him already?"

She jerked toward Gayle, startled.

"Have I done *what*?"

Gayle rolled her eyes.

"Played tiddlywinks. Honestly, Bree!"

"No. Of course not." She felt the blood rising in her cheeks.

"Well, are you *going* to?"

"Gayle!"

"Well, I mean, you have your own apartment and everything, and nobody's going to—"

At this awkward moment, Roger Wakefield appeared. He wore a white shirt and scruffy jeans, and Brianna must have stiffened at the sight of him. Gayle's head whipped round to see where Brianna was looking.

"Ooh," she said in delight. "Is that him? He looks like a *pirate*!"

He did, and Brianna felt the bottom of her stomach drop another inch or two. Roger was what her mother called a Black Celt, with clear olive skin and black hair, and "eyes put in with a sooty thumb"—thick black lashes round eyes you expected to be blue but that were instead a surprising deep green. With his hair worn long enough to brush his collar, disheveled and beard-stubbled, he looked not only rakish but mildly dangerous.

Alarm tingled up her spine at the sight of him, and she wiped sweating palms on the sides of her embroidered jeans. She shouldn't have let him come.

Then he saw her, and his face lit like a candle. In spite of herself, she felt a huge, idiotic smile break out on her own face in answer, and without stopping to think of misgivings, she ran across the room, dodging stray children and luggage carts.

He met her halfway and swept her almost off her feet, hugging her hard enough to crack her ribs. He kissed her, stopped, and kissed her again, the stubble of his beard scraping her face. He smelled of soap and sweat and he tasted like Scotch whisky and she didn't want him to stop.

Then he did and let go, both of them half breathless.

"A-hem," said a loud voice near Brianna's elbow. She swung away from Roger, revealing Gayle, who smiled angelically up at him under blond bangs, and waved like a child going bye-bye.

"Hell-ooo," she said. "You must be Roger, because if you're not, Roger's sure in for a shock when he shows up, isn't he?"

She looked him up and down with obvious approval.

"All that, and you play the guitar, too?"

Brianna hadn't even noticed the case he had dropped. He stooped and picked it up, swinging it over his shoulder.

"Well, that's my bread and butter, this trip," he said, with a smile at Gayle, who clutched a hand to her heart in simulated ecstasy.

"Ooh, say that again!" she begged.

"Say what?" Roger looked puzzled.

"Bread and butter," Brianna told him, hoisting one of his bags onto her shoulder. "She wants to hear you roll the r's again. Gayle has a thing about British accents. Oh—that's Gayle." She gestured at her friend in resignation.

"Yes, I gathered. Er . . ." He cleared his throat, fixed Gayle with a piercing stare, and dropped his voice an octave. "Arround the rrrugggged rrrock, the rrragged rrrascals rran. That do you for a bit?"

"Would you stop that?" Brianna looked crossly at her friend, who had swooned dramatically into one of the plastic seats. "Ignore her," she advised Roger, turning toward the door. With a cautious glance at Gayle, he took her advice, and picking up a large box tied with string, followed her into the concourse.

"What did you mean about your bread and butter?" she asked, looking for some way to return the conversation to a sane footing.

He laughed, a little self-consciously.

"Well, the historical conference is paying the airfare, but they couldn't manage expenses. So I called round, and wangled a bit of a job to take care of that end."

"A job playing the guitar?"

"By day, mild-mannered historian Roger Wakefield is a harmless Oxford academic. But at night, he dons his secret tartan rrregalia and becomes the dashing—Roger MacKenzie!"

"Who?"

He smiled at her surprise. "Well, I do a bit of Scottish folksinging, for festivals and *ceilidhs*—Highland Games and the like. I'm on to do a turn at a Celtic festival up in the mountains at the end of the week, is all."

"Scottish singing? Do you wear a kilt when you sing?" Gayle had popped up on Roger's other side.

"I do indeed. How else would they know I was a Scotsman?"

"I just love fuzzy knees," Gayle said dreamily. "Now, tell me, is it true about what a Scotsman—"

"Go get the car," Brianna ordered, hastily thrusting her keys at Gayle.

Gayle perched her chin on the windowsill of the car, watching Roger make his way into the hotel. "Gee, I hope he doesn't shave before he meets us for dinner. I just love the way men look when they haven't shaved for a while. What do you think's in that big box?''

''His bodhran. I asked.''

''His *what*?''

''It's a Celtic war drum. He plays it with some of his songs.''

Gayle's lips formed a small circle of speculation.

''I don't suppose you want me to drive him to this festival thing, do you? I mean, you must have lots of things to do, and—''

''Ha ha. You think I'd let you anywhere around him in a kilt?''

Gayle sighed wistfully, and pulled her head in as Brianna started the car.

''Well, maybe there'd be other men there in kilts.''

''I think that's pretty likely.''

''I bet they don't have Celtic war drums, though.''

''Maybe not.''

Gayle leaned back in her seat, and glanced at her friend.

''So, are you going to do it?''

''How should I know?'' But the blood bloomed under her skin, and her clothes felt too tight.

''Well, if you don't,'' Gayle said positively, ''you're crazy.''

''The Minister's cat is an . . . androgynous cat.''

''The Minister's cat is an . . . alagruous cat.''

Bree gave him a lifted brow, taking her eyes briefly off the road.

''Scots again?''

''It's a Scottish game,'' Roger said. ''Alagruous—'grim or woebegone.' Your turn. Letter 'B.' ''

She squinted through the windshield at the narrow mountain road. The morning sun was toward them, filling the car with light.

''The Minister's cat is a brindled cat.''

''The Minister's cat is a bonnie cat.''

''Well, that's a soft pitch for both of us. Draw. Okay, the Minister's cat is a . . .'' He could see the wheels turning in her mind, then the gleam in her narrowed blue eyes as inspiration struck. ''. . . coccygodynious cat.''

Roger narrowed his own eyes, trying to work that one out.

''A cat with a wide backside?''

She laughed, braking slightly as the car hit a switchback curve.

''A cat that's a pain in the ass.''

''That's a real word, is it?''

"Uh-huh." She accelerated neatly out of the turn. "One of Mama's medical terms. Coccygodynia is a pain in the region of the tailbone. She used to call the hospital administration coccygodynians, all the time."

"And here I thought it was one of your engineering terms. All right, then . . . the Minister's cat is a camstairy cat." He grinned at her lifted eyebrow. "Quarrelsome. Coccygodynians are camstairy by nature."

"Okay, I'll call that one a draw. The Minister's cat is . . ."

"Wait," Roger interrupted, pointing. "There's the turn."

Slowing, she pulled off the narrow highway and onto a still narrower road, indicated by a small red-and-white-arrowed sign that read CELTIC FESTIVAL.

"You're a love to bring to me all the way up here," Roger said. "I didn't realize how far it was, or I'd never have asked."

She gave him a brief glance of amusement.

"It's not that far."

"It's a hundred and fifty miles!"

She smiled, but with a wry edge to it.

"My father always said that was the difference between an American and an Englishman. An Englishman thinks a hundred miles is a long way; an American thinks a hundred years is a long time."

Roger laughed, taken by surprise.

"Too right. You'll be an American, then, I suppose?"

"I suppose." But her smile had faded.

So had the conversation; they drove in silence for a few minutes, with no sound but the rush of tires and wind. It was a beautiful hot summer's day, the mugginess of Boston left far below as they snaked their way upward, into the clearer air of the mountains.

"The Minister's cat is a distant cat," Roger said at last, softly. "Have I said something wrong?"

She flashed him a quick blue glance, and a half-curled mouth.

"The Minister's cat is a daydreaming cat. No, it's not you." Her lips compressed as she slowed behind another car, then relaxed. "No, that's not right—it *is* you, but it's not your fault."

Roger shifted, turning in his seat to face her.

"The Minister's cat is an enigmatic cat."

"The Minister's cat is an embarrassed cat—I shouldn't have said anything, sorry."

Roger was wise enough not to press her. Instead, he leaned

forward and dug under the seat for the thermos of hot tea with lemon.

"Want some?" He offered her the cup, but she made a small face and shook her head.

"No thanks. I hate tea."

"Definitely not an Englishwoman, then," he said, and wished he hadn't; her hands squeezed tight on the wheel. She didn't say anything, though, and he drank the tea in silence, watching her.

She didn't look English, her parentage and coloring notwithstanding. He couldn't tell whether the difference was more than a matter of clothes, but he thought so. Americans seemed so much more . . . what? Vibrant? Intense? Bigger? Just *more.* Brianna Randall was definitely more.

The traffic grew thicker, slowing to a crawling line of cars as they reached the entrance to the resort where the festival was being held.

"Look," Brianna said abruptly. She didn't turn toward him, but stared out through the windshield at the New Jersey license plate of the car in front of them. "I have to explain."

"Not to me."

She flicked one red eyebrow in brief irritation.

"To who else?" She pressed her lips together and sighed. "Yeah, all right, me too. But I do."

Roger could taste the acid from the tea, bitter in the back of his throat. Was this where she told him it had been a mistake for him to come? He'd thought so himself, all the way across the Atlantic, twitching and cramped in the tiny airline seat. Then he'd seen her across the airport lobby, and all doubt had vanished on the instant.

It hadn't come back during the intervening week, either; he'd seen her at least briefly every day—even managed a baseball game with her at Fenway Park on Thursday afternoon. He'd found the game itself baffling, but Brianna's enthusiasm for it enchanting. He found himself counting the hours left before he'd have to leave, and looking forward nonetheless to this—the only whole day they'd have together.

That didn't mean she felt the same. He glanced quickly over the line of cars; the gate was visible, but still a quarter-mile off. He had maybe three minutes to convince her.

"In Scotland," she was saying, "when all—that—happened with my mother. You were great, Roger—really wonderful." She didn't look at him, but he could see a shimmer of moisture just above the thick auburn lashes.

"It was no great thing to do," he said. He curled his hands into fists to keep from touching her. "I was interested."

She laughed shortly.

"Yeah, I bet you were." She slowed, and turned her head to look at him, full-on. Even wide open, her eyes had a faint catlike slant to them.

"Have you been back to the stone circle? To Craigh na Dun?"

"No," he said shortly. Then coughed and added, as if casually, "I don't go up to Inverness all that often; it's been term time at College."

"It isn't that the Minister's cat is a fraidycat?" she asked, but she smiled slightly when she said it.

"The Minister's cat is scared stiff of that place," he said frankly. "He wouldn't set foot up there if it were knee-deep in sardines." She laughed outright, and the tension between them eased noticeably.

"Me too," she said, and took a deep breath. "But I remember. All the trouble you went to, to help—and then, when it—when she—when Mama went through—" Her teeth clamped savagely on her lower lip, and she hit the brake, harder than necessary.

"Do you see?" she said, in a small voice. "I can't be around you more than half an hour, and it all comes back. I haven't talked about my parents in more than six months, and no sooner do we start playing that silly game than I've mentioned both of them in less than a minute. It's been happening all week."

She thumbed a loose strand of red hair off her shoulder. She went a lovely pink when she was excited or upset, and the color was burning high in her cheeks.

"I thought it might be something like that—when you didn't answer my letter."

"It wasn't only that." She caught her lower lip between her teeth, as though to bite back the words, but it was too late. A brilliant tide of red washed up out of the V of her white T-shirt, turning her the color of the tomato sauce she insisted on eating with chips.

He reached across the seat and gently brushed the veil of hair back from her face.

"I had a terrible crush on you," she blurted, staring straight ahead through the windshield. "But I didn't know whether you were just being nice to me because Mama asked you to, or whether—"

"Whether," he interrupted, and smiled as she risked a tiny look at him. "Definitely whether."

"Oh." She relaxed fractionally, loosening her stranglehold on the wheel. "Well. Good."

He wanted to take her hand, but didn't want to pry it off the wheel and cause an accident. Instead, he laid his arm across the back of the seat, letting his fingers brush her shoulder.

"Anyway. I didn't think—I thought—well, it was either throw myself into your arms or get the hell out of Dodge. So I did, but I couldn't figure out how to explain without looking like an idiot, and then when you wrote, it was worse—well, see, I *do* look like an idiot!"

Roger flipped open the catch of his seat belt.

"Will you drive into that car in front of us if I kiss you?"

"No."

"Good." He slid across the seat, took her chin in one hand, and kissed her, fast. They bumped sedately over the dirt road and into the parking lot.

She was breathing easier, and her color had receded a little. She pulled neatly into a parking slot, killed the motor, and sat for a moment, looking straight ahead. Then she opened her seat belt and turned to him.

It wasn't until they got out of the car several minutes later that it occurred to Roger that she had mentioned her parents more than once—but the real problem had likely more to do with the parent she so carefully *hadn't* mentioned.

Great, he thought, absently admiring her backside as she bent to open the trunk. *She's trying not to think of Jamie Fraser, and where the hell do* you *bring her?* He glanced at the entrance to the resort, where the Union Jack and the Saltire of Scotland snapped in the summer breeze. From the mountainside beyond came the mournful sound of bagpipes playing.

4

A Blast from the Past

U sed as he was to changing in the back of someone's horse
van or in the Gents' facilities of a pub, the small backstage
cubicle allotted to Roger's personal use seemed remarkably luxurious. It was clean, it had hooks for his street clothes,
and there were no drunken patrons snoring on the threshold. Of
course, this was America, he reflected, unbuttoning his jeans and
dropping them on the floor. Different standards, at least with regard to material comforts.

He yanked the bell-sleeved shirt over his head, wondering just
what level of comfort Brianna was accustomed to. He was no
judge of women's clothing—how expensive could blue jeans possibly be?—but he knew a bit about cars. Hers was a brand-new
blue Mustang that made him itch to take the wheel.

Plainly her parents had left her enough to live on; he could trust
Claire Randall to have seen to that. He only hoped it wasn't so
much that she might think him interested on that account. Reminded of her parents, he glanced at the brown envelope; should
he give it to her, after all?

The Minister's cat had nearly jumped out of her skin when
they'd walked through the performers' entrance and come face-
to-face with the 78th Fraser Highlanders' pipe-band from Canada,
practicing at full blast behind the dressing rooms. She'd actually
gone pale when he'd introduced her to the pipe major, an old
acquaintance. Not that Bill Livingstone was intimidating on his
own; it was the Fraser clan badge on his chest that had done it.

Je suis prest, it said. *I am ready.* Not nearly ready enough,
Roger thought, and wanted to kick himself for bringing her.

Still, she had assured him she'd be all right exploring on her
own while he dressed and got himself up for his turn.

And he'd best turn his mind to that, too, he thought, snugging
the buckles of his kilt at waist and hip, and reaching for the long

woolen stockings. He was on in the early afternoon, for forty-five minutes, then a shorter solo turn at the evening *ceilidh*. He had a rough lineup of songs in mind, but you always had to take the crowd into account. Lots of women, the ballads went well; more men, more of the martial—"Killiecrankie" and "Montrose," "Guns and Drums." The bawdy songs did best when the audience was well warmed up—preferably after a bit of beer.

He turned the stocking tops down neatly, and slid the antler-handled *sgian dhu* inside, tight against his right calf. He laced the buskins quickly, hurrying a little. He wanted to find Brianna again, have a little time to walk round with her, get her something to eat, see she had a good seat for the performances.

He flung the plaid over one shoulder, fastened his brooch, belted on dirk and sporran, and was ready. Or not quite. He halted, halfway to the door.

The ancient olive-drab drawers were military issue, circa World War II—one of Roger's few mementos of his father. He didn't bother with pants much in the normal course, but included these with his kilt sometimes as a defensive measure against the amazing boldness of some female spectators. He'd been warned by other performers, but wouldn't have believed it, had he not experienced it firsthand. German ladies were the worst, but he'd known a few American women run them a close second for taking liberties in close quarters.

He didn't think he'd need such measures here; the crowd sounded civil, and he'd seen that the stage was safely out of reach. Besides, offstage he'd have Brianna with him, and if she should choose to take any liberties of her own . . . He dropped the pants back in his bag, on top of the brown envelope.

"Wish me luck, Dad," he whispered, and went to find her.

◄━━━

"Wow!" She walked round him in a circle, goggling. "Roger, you are *gorgeous*!" She smiled, a trifle lopsided. "My mother always said men in kilts were irresistible. I guess she was right."

He saw her swallow hard, and wanted to hug her for her bravery, but she had already turned away, gesturing toward the main food area.

"Are you hungry? I had a look while you were changing. We've got our choice between octopus-on-a-stick, Baja fish tacos, Polish dogs—"

He took her arm and pulled her round to face him.

"Hey," he said softly. "I'm sorry; I wouldn't have brought you if I'd known it would be a shock."

"It's all right." Her smile was better this time. "It's—I'm glad you brought me."

"Truly?"

"Yeah. Really. It's—" She waved helplessly at the tartan swirl of noise and color all around them. "It's so—Scottish."

He wanted to laugh at that; nothing could be less like Scotland than this mix of tourist claptrap and the bald-faced selling of half-faked traditions. At the same time, she was right, it *was* uniquely Scottish; an example of the Scots' age-old talent for survival—the ability to adapt to anything, and make a profit from it.

He did hug her, then. Her hair smelled clean, like fresh grass, and he could feel her heart beating through the white T-shirt she wore.

"You're Scots, too, you know," he said in her ear, and let go. Her eyes were still bright, but with a different emotion now, he thought.

"I guess you're right," she said, and smiled again, a good one. "That doesn't mean I have to eat haggis, does it? I saw some over there, and I think I'd even rather try the octopus-on-a-stick."

He'd thought she was joking, but she wasn't. The resort's sole business, it seemed, was "ethnic fairs," as one of the food vendors explained.

"Polacks dancin' polkas, Swiss yodelers—Jeez, they musta had ten million cuckoo clocks here! Spanish, Italian, Japanese cherry blossom festivals—you wouldn't believe all the cameras them Japs have, you just wouldn't believe it." He shook his head in bemusement, sliding across two paper plates filled with hamburgers and french fries.

"Anyways, it's something different, every two weeks. Never a dull moment. But us food vendors, we just stay in business, no matter what kinda food it is." The man eyed Roger's kilt with some interest.

"So, you Scotch, or you just like wearing a skirt?"

Having heard several dozen variations of that pleasantry, Roger gave the man a bland look.

"Well, as my auld grand-da used to say," he said, thickening his accent atrociously, "when ye put on yer kilt, laddie, ye ken for sure yer a man!"

The man doubled up appreciatively, and Brianna rolled her eyes.

"Kilt jokes," she muttered. "God, if you start telling kilt jokes, I'll drive off and leave you, I swear I will."

Roger grinned at her.

"Och, now, ye wouldna do that, would ye, lass? Go off and leave a man, only because he'll tell ye what's worn under the kilt, if ye like?"

Her eyes narrowed into blue triangles.

"Oh, I'd bet nothing at all's worn under *that* kilt," she said, with a nod at Roger's sporran. "Why, I'll bet everything under there is in pairrrrrfect operrrating condition, no?"

Roger choked on a french fry.

"You're s'posed to say 'Give us your hand, lassie, and I'll show you,' " the food vendor prompted. "Boy, if I've heard that one once, I've heard it a hunderd times this week."

"If he says it now," Brianna put in darkly, "I'll drive off and leave him marooned on this mountain. He can stay here and eat octopus, for all I care."

Roger took a gulp of Coca-Cola and wisely kept quiet.

There was time for a wander up and down the aisles of the vendors' stalls, selling everything from tartan ties to penny whistles, silver jewelry, clan maps of Scotland, butterscotch and shortbread, letter openers in the shape of claymores, lead Highlander figures, books, records, and every imaginable small item on which a clan badge or motto could be imprinted.

Roger attracted no more than a brief glance of curiosity; while of better quality than most, his costume was no oddity here. Still, most of the crowd were tourists, dressed in shorts and jeans, but breaking out here and there in bits of tartan, like a rash.

"Why MacKenzie?" Brianna asked, pausing by one display of clan-marked keychains. She fingered one of the silver disks that read *Luceo non uro,* the Latin motto curved around a depiction of what looked like a volcano. "Didn't Wakefield sound Scottish enough? Or did you think the people at Oxford wouldn't like you doing—this?" She waved at the venue around them.

Roger shrugged.

"Partly that. But it's my family name, as well. Both my parents were killed during the war, and my great-uncle adopted me. He gave me his own name—but I was christened Roger Jeremiah MacKenzie."

"Jeremiah?" She didn't laugh out loud, but the end of her nose pinkened as though she was trying not to. "Like the Old Testament prophet?"

"Don't laugh," he said, taking her arm. "I was named for my father—they called him Jerry. My Mum called me Jemmy when I was small. Old family name. It could have been worse, after all; I might have been christened Ambrose or Conan."

The laughter fizzed out of her like Coke bubbles.

"Conan?"

"Perfectly good Celtic name, before the fantasists got hold of it. Anyway, Jeremiah seems to have been the pick of the lot for good cause."

"Why's that?"

They turned and headed slowly back toward the stage, where a gang of solemnly starched little girls were doing the Highland fling in perfect unison, every pleat and bow in place.

"Oh, it's one of the stories Dad—the Reverend, I always called him Dad—used to tell me, going down my family tree and pointing out the folk on it."

Ambrose MacKenzie, that's your great-grandfather, Rog. He'll have been a boatwright in Dingwall. And there's Mary Oliphant —I knew your great-grandma Oliphant, did I tell you? Lived to be ninety-seven, and sharp as a tack to her last breath; wonderful woman.

She was married six times—all died of natural causes, too, she assured me—but I've only put Jeremiah MacKenzie here, since he was your ancestor. The only one she had children by, I did wonder about that.

I asked her, and she closed one eye and nodded at me, and said, "Is fhearr an giomach na 'bhi gun fear tighe." It's an old Gaelic proverb—"Better a lobster than no husband." She said some would do for marrying, but Jeremiah was the only lad bonny enough to take to her bed every night.

"I wonder what she told the others," Brianna said, meditatively.

"Well, she didn't say she didn't sleep with them now and then," Roger pointed out. "Just not every night."

"Once is enough to get pregnant," Brianna said. "Or so my mother assured my high school health class. She'd draw pictures of sperm on the blackboard, all racing toward this huge egg with leers on their faces." She'd gone pink again, but evidently from amusement rather than distressed memory.

Arm in arm, he could feel the heat of her through the thin

T-shirt, and a stirring under his kilt that made him think leaving the pants off had been a mistake.

"Putting aside the question of whether sperm have faces, what has that particular subject got to do with health?"

"Health is an American euphemism for anything to do with sex," she explained. "They teach girls and boys separately; the girls' class is The Mysteries of Life, and Ten Ways to Say No to a Boy."

"And the boys' class?"

"Well, I don't know for sure, because I didn't have any brothers to tell me. Some of my friends had brothers, though—one of them said they learned eighteen different synonyms for penile erection."

"Really useful, that," Roger said, wondering why anyone required more than one. Luckily, a sporran covered a multitude of sins.

"I suppose it might keep the conversation going—under certain circumstances."

Her cheeks were red. He could feel the heat creeping up his own throat, and imagined that they were beginning to attract curious glances from passersby. He hadn't let a girl embarrass him in public since he was seventeen, but she was doing nicely. She'd started it, though—let her finish it, then.

"Mmphm. I hadn't noticed much conversation, under those particular circumstances."

"I imagine you'd know." It wasn't quite a question. Rather late, he realized what she was up to. He tightened his arm, pulling her closer.

"If you mean have I, yes. If you mean am I, no."

"Are you, what?" Her lips were quivering slightly, holding back the urge to laugh.

"You're asking if I've got a girl in England, right?"

"Am I?"

"I don't. Or rather I do, but nothing serious." They were outside the door to the dressing rooms; nearly time to fetch his instruments. He stopped and turned to look at her. "Have you? Got a bloke, I mean."

She was tall enough to look him in the eye, and close enough that her breasts grazed his forearm when she turned to face him.

"What was it your great-grandmother said? *'Is fhearr an giomach . . .'?"*

"*'. . . na 'bhi gun fear tighe.'* "

"Uh-huh. Well, better a lobster than no boyfriend." She lifted a hand and touched his brooch. "So yes, there are people I go out with. But I don't have a bonny lad—yet."

He caught her fingers and brought them to his mouth.

"Give it time, lass," he said, and kissed them.

The audience was amazingly quiet; not at all like a rock concert. Of course, they couldn't be noisy, she thought; there weren't any electric guitars or amplifiers, only a small microphone on a stand. But then, some things didn't need amplifying. Her heart, for one, hammering in her ears.

"Here," he'd said, appearing abruptly out of the dressing room with guitar and drum. He'd handed her a small brown envelope. "I found these, going through my dad's old bumf in Inverness. I thought you'd maybe want them."

She could tell it was photographs, but she hadn't looked at them right away. She'd sat with them burning a hole on her knee, listening to Roger's set.

He was good—even distracted, she could tell he was good. He had a surprisingly rich deep baritone voice, and he knew what to do with it. Not just in terms of tone and melody; he had the true performer's ability to pull aside the curtain between singer and audience, to look out into the crowd, meet someone's eyes, and let them see what lay behind both words and music.

He'd got them going with "The Road to the Isles," a quick and lively clap-along song with a rousing chorus, and when they'd subsided from that, kept them going with "The Gallowa' Hills," and a sweet slide into "The Lewis Bridal Song," with a lovely, lilting chorus in Gaelic.

He let the last note die away on "Vhair Me Oh," and smiled, directly at her, she thought.

"And here's one from the '45," he said. "This one is from the famous battle of Prestonpans, at which the Highland Army of Charles Stuart routed a much greater English force, under the command of General Jonathan Cope."

There was an appreciative murmur from the crowd, for many of whom the song was plainly an old favorite, quickly shushed as Roger's fingers plucked out the marching line.

> *"Cope sent a challenge from Dunbar*
> *Sayin' 'Charlie, meet me, and ye daur*

> *An' I'll learn ye the art o' war*
> *If ye'll meet me in the mornin'.' "*

He bent his head over the strings, nodding to the crowd to join in the jeering chorus.

> *"Hey, Johnnie Cope, are ye walkin' yet?*
> *And are your drums a-beatin' yet?*
> *If ye were walkin', I would wait*
> *Tae gang tae the coals in the mornin'!"*

Brianna felt a sudden prickle at the roots of her hair that had nothing to do with singer or crowd, but with the song itself.

> *"When Charlie looked the letter upon,*
> *He drew his sword the scabbard from,*
> *Come, follow me, my merry men,*
> *And we'll meet Johnnie Cope in the morning!"*

"No," she whispered, her fingers cold on the smooth brown envelope. *Come follow me, my merry men . . .* They'd been there—both her parents. It was her father who had charged the field at Preston, his broadsword and his targe in his hands.

> *". . . For it will be a bluidie morning!"*

> *"Hey, Johnnie Cope, are ye walkin' yet?*
> *And are your drums a-beatin' yet? . . ."*

The voices rose around her in a roar of approbation as they joined in the chorus. She had a moment of rising panic, when she would have fled away like Johnnie Cope, but it passed, leaving her buffeted by emotion as much as by the music.

> *"In faith, quo Johnnie, I got sic flegs,*
> *Wi' their claymores an' philabegs,*
> *Gin I face them again, de'il brak my legs,*
> *So I wish you a' good morning!*
>
> *Hey, Johnnie Cope, are ye walkin' yet? . . ."*

Yes, he was. And he would be, as long as that song lasted. Some people tried to preserve the past; others, to escape it. And that was by far the greatest gulf between herself and Roger. Why hadn't she seen it before?

She didn't know whether Roger had seen her momentary distress, but he abandoned the dangerous territory of the Jacobites and went into "MacPherson's Lament," sung with no more than an occasional touch of the strings. The woman next to Brianna let out a long sigh and looked doe-eyed at the stage.

> *"Sae rantingly, sae wantonly, sae dauntingly gaed he,*
> *He played a tune and he danced it roond . . . alow the*
>   *gallows tree!"*

She picked up the envelope, weighing it on her fingers. She ought to wait, maybe, until she got home. But curiosity was warring with reluctance. Roger hadn't been sure he should give it to her; she'd seen that in his eyes.

". . . a bodhran," Roger was saying. The drum was no more than a wooden hoop, a few inches wide, with a skin head stretched over it, some eighteen inches across. He held the drum balanced on the fingers of one hand, a small double-headed stick in the other. "One of the oldest known instruments, this is the drum with which the Celtic tribes scared the bejesus out of Julius Caesar's troops in 52 BC." The audience tittered, and he touched the wide drumhead with the stick, back and forth in a soft, quick rhythm like a heartbeat.

"And here's 'The Sheriffmuir Fight,' from the first Jacobite Rising, in 1715."

The drumhead shifted and the beat dropped in pitch, became martial in tone, a thundering behind the words. The audience was still well-behaved, but now sat up and leaned forward, hanging on the chant that described the battle of Sheriffmuir, and all the clans who had fought in it.

> *". . . then on they rushed, and blood out-gushed, and many a*
>   *puke did fall, man . . .*
> *They hacked and hashed, while broadswords clashed . . ."*

As the song ended she put her fingers inside the envelope and pulled out a set of photographs. Old snapshots, black-and-white faded to tones of brown. Her parents. Frank and Claire Randall, both looking absurdly young—and terribly happy.

They were in a garden somewhere; there were lawn chairs, and a table with drinks in a background dappled with the scattered light of tree leaves. The faces showed clearly, though—laughing, faces alight with youth, eyes only for each other.

Posing formally, arm in arm, mocking their own formality. Laughing, Claire half bent over with hilarity at something Frank had said, holding down a wide skirt flying in the wind, her curly hair suffering no such restraint. Frank handing Claire a cup, she looking up into his face as she took it, with such a look of hope and trust that Brianna's heart squeezed tight to see it.

Then she looked at the last of the pictures, and realized what she was looking at. The two of them stood by the table, hands together on a knife, laughing as they cut into an obviously home-made cake. A wedding cake.

"And for the last, an old favorite that you'll know. This song is said to have been sent by a Jacobite prisoner, on his way to London to be hanged, to his wife in the Highlands . . ."

She spread her hands out flat on top of the pictures, as though to keep anyone from seeing them. An icy shock went through her. Wedding pictures. Snapshots of their wedding day. Of course; they'd been married in Scotland. The Reverend Wakefield wouldn't have done the ceremony, not being a Catholic priest, but he was one of her father's oldest friends; the reception must have been held at the manse.

Yes. Peeking through her fingers, she could make out familiar bits of the old house in the background. Then, reluctantly sliding her hand aside, she looked again at her mother's young face.

Eighteen. Claire had married Frank Randall at eighteen—perhaps that explained it. How could anyone know their mind so young?

> *"By yon bonnie banks, and by yon bonnie braes,*
> *Where the sun shines bright on Loch Lomond,*
> *Where me and my true love were ever wont to gae . . ."*

But Claire had been sure—or she'd thought so. The broad clear brow and delicate mouth admitted of no doubt; the big, luminous eyes were fixed on her new husband with no sign of reservation or misgiving. And yet—

> *"But me and my true love will never meet again*
> *On the bonnie, bonnie banks of Loch Lomond."*

Oblivious of the toes she stepped on, Brianna blundered out of the row and fled, before anyone should see the tears.

"I can stay with you through part of the calling of the clans," Roger said, "but I've a bit to do at the end of it, so I'll have to leave you. Will you be all right?"

"Yes, of course," she said firmly. "I'm fine. Don't worry."

He looked at her a little anxiously, but let it pass. Neither of them had mentioned her precipitous departure earlier; by the time he had made his way through the congratulatory well-wishers and gone to find her, she had had time to find a Ladies' and get herself under control with cold water.

They had spent the rest of the afternoon strolling through the festival, shopping a bit, going outside to watch the pipe-bands' competition, coming in half deafened to see a young man dance between two swords crossed on the ground. The photographs stayed safely out of sight in her handbag.

It was nearly dark now; people were leaving the eating area and heading for the open stands outside, at the foot of the mountain.

She had thought the families with young children would leave, and some did, but there were small bodies and sleepy heads drooping among the older people in the stands. A tiny girl lay limp, sound asleep on her father's shoulder as they made their way into one of the upper rows of the stands. There was a clear, flat space in front of the bleachers, in which a huge heap of wood had been piled.

"What's the calling of the clans?" she heard a woman ask her companion in the row ahead. The companion shrugged, and Brianna looked at Roger for enlightenment, but he only smiled.

"You'll see," he said.

It was full dark, and the moon not risen; the bulk of the mountainside rose up as a darker black against the star-flecked sky. There was an exclamation from somewhere in the crowd, a scattering of more, and then the notes of a single bagpipe came faintly through the air, silencing everything else.

A pinpoint of light appeared near the top of the mountain. As they watched, it moved down, and another sprang up behind it. The music grew stronger, and another light came over the top of the mountain. For nearly ten minutes, the anticipation grew, as the music grew louder, and the string of lights grew longer, a blazing chain down the mountainside.

Near the bottom of the slope, a trail came out from the trees above; she had seen it during her earlier exploration. Now a man stepped out of the trees into sight, holding a blazing torch above his head. Behind him was the piper, and the sound now was strong enough to drown even the oohs and ahhs of the crowd.

As the two moved down the trail and toward the cleared space in front of the bleachers, Brianna could see that there were more men behind them; a long line of men, each with a torch, all dressed in the finery of the Highland chieftains. They were barbarous and splendid, decked in grouse feathers, the silver of swords and dirks gleaming red by the torchlight, picked out amid the folds of tartan cloth.

The pipes stopped abruptly, and the first of the men strode into the clearing and stopped before the stands. He raised his torch above his head and shouted, "The Camerons are here!"

Loud whoops of delight rang out from the stands, and he threw the torch into the kerosene-soaked wood, which went up with a roar, in a pillar of fire ten feet high.

Against the blinding sheet of flame, another man stepped out, and called, "The MacDonalds are here!"

Screams and yelps from those in the crowd that claimed kinship with clan MacDonald, and then—

"The MacLachlans are here!"

"The MacGillivrays are here!"

She was so entranced by the spectacle that she was only dimly aware of Roger. Then another man stepped out and cried, "The MacKenzies are here!"

"Tulach Ard!" bellowed Roger, making her jump.

"What was *that*?" she asked.

"That," he said, grinning, "is the war cry of clan MacKenzie."

"Sounded like it."

"The Campbells are here!" There must have been a lot of Campbells; the response shook the bleachers. As though that was the signal he had been waiting for, Roger stood up and flung his plaid over his shoulder.

"I'll meet you afterward by the dressing rooms, all right?" She nodded, and he bent suddenly and kissed her.

"Just in case," he said. "The Frasers' cry is *Caisteal Dhuni*!"

She watched him go, climbing down the bleachers like a mountain goat. The smell of woodsmoke filled the night air, mixing with the smaller fragrance of tobacco from cigarettes in the crowd.

"The MacKays are here!"

"The MacLeods are here!"

"The Farquarsons are here!"

Her chest felt tight, from the smoke and from emotion. The clans had died at Culloden—or had they? Yes, they had; this was no more than memory, than the calling up of ghosts; none of the people shouting so enthusiastically owed kinship to each other, none of them lived any longer by the claims of laird and land, but . . .

"The Frasers are here!"

Sheer panic gripped her, and her hand closed tight on the clasp of her bag.

No, she thought. *Oh, no. I'm not.*

Then the moment passed, and she could breathe again, but jolts of adrenaline still thrilled through her blood.

"The Grahams are here!"

"The Inneses are here!"

The Ogilvys, the Lindsays, the Gordons . . . and then finally, the echoes of the last shout died. Brianna held the bag on her lap, gripped tight, as though to keep its contents from escaping like the jinn from a lamp.

How could she? she thought, and then, seeing Roger come into the light, fire on his head and his bodhran in his hand, thought again, *How could she help it?*

5

Two Hundred Years from Yesterday

"**Y**ou didn't wear your kilt!" Gayle's mouth turned down in disappointment.

"Wrong century," Roger said, smiling down at her. "Drafty for a moonwalk."

"You have to teach me to do that." She bounced on her toes, leaning toward him.

"Do what?"

"Roll your r's like that." She puckered her brows and made an earnest attempt, sounding like a motorboat in low gear.

"Verra nice," he said, trying not to laugh. "Keep it up. Prractice makes perfect."

"Well, did you bring your guitar, at least?" She stood on tiptoes, trying to look behind him. "Or that groovy drum?"

"It's in the car," Brianna said, putting away her keys as she came up beside Roger. "We're going to the airport from here."

"Oh, too bad; I thought we could hang around and have a hootenanny afterward, to celebrate. Do you know 'This Land Is Your Land,' Roger? Or are you more into protest songs? But I guess you wouldn't be, since you're English—oops, I mean Scotch. You guys don't have anything to protest about, do you?"

Brianna gave her friend a look of mild exasperation. "Where's Uncle Joe?"

"In the living room, kicking the TV," Gayle said. "Shall I entertain Roger while you find him?" She linked one arm cosily through Roger's, batting her eyelashes.

"We got half the doggone MIT College of Engineering here, and nobody who can fix a doggone *television*?" Dr. Joseph Abernathy glared accusingly at the clusters of young people scattered around his living room.

"That's *electrical* engineering, Pop," his son told him loftily. "We're all mechanical engineers. Ask a mechanical engineer to fix your color TV, that's like asking an Ob-Gyn to look at the sore on your di—ow!''

"Oh, sorry," said his father, peering blandly over gold-rimmed glasses. "That your foot, Lenny?"

Lenny hopped storklike around the room to general laughter, clutching one large sneaker-clad foot in exaggerated agony.

"Bree, honey!" The doctor spotted her and abandoned the television, beaming. He hugged her enthusiastically, disregarding the fact that she topped him by four inches or so, then let go and looked at Roger, his features rearranged in a look of wary cordiality.

"This the boyfriend?"

"This is Roger Wakefield," Brianna said, narrowing her eyes slightly at the doctor. "Roger, Joe Abernathy."

"Dr. Abernathy."

"Call me Joe."

They shook hands in mutual assessment. The doctor looked him over with quick brown eyes, no less shrewd for their warmth.

"Bree, honey, you want to go lay hands on that piece of junk, see can you bring it back to life?" He jerked a thumb at the twenty-four-inch RCA sitting in mute defiance on its wire stand. "It was working fine last night, then today . . . pffft!"

Brianna looked dubiously at the big color TV, and groped in the pocket of her jeans, coming out with a Swiss Army knife.

"Well, I can check the connections, I guess." She flicked out the screwdriver blade. "How much time do we have?"

"Half hour, maybe," called a crew-cut student from the kitchen doorway. He glanced at the crowd clustered around the small black-and-white set on the table. "We're still with Mission Control in Houston—ETA thirty-four minutes." The muted excitement of the TV commentator came in bursts through the more vivid excitement of the spectators.

"Good, good," said Dr. Abernathy. He laid a hand on Roger's shoulder. "Plenty of time for a drink, then. You a Scotch man, Mr. Wakefield?"

"Call me Roger."

Abernathy poured a generous measure of amber nectar and handed it over.

"Don't imagine you take water, do you, Roger?"

"No." It was Lagavulin; astonishing to find it in Boston. He sipped appreciatively, and the doctor smiled.

"Claire gave it to me—Bree's mama. Now, there was a woman

with a taste for fine whisky.'' He shook his head nostalgically, and raised his glass in tribute.

"*Slàinte,*" Roger said quietly, and tipped his own glass before drinking.

Abernathy closed his eyes in silent appreciation—whether of the whisky or the woman, Roger couldn't tell.

"Water of life, huh? I do believe that particular stuff could raise the dead.'' He set the bottle back in the liquor cabinet with reverent hands.

How much had Claire told Abernathy? Enough, Roger supposed. The doctor picked up his tumbler and gave him a long look of assessment.

"Since Bree's daddy is dead, I guess I get to do the honors. Reckon we got time for the third degree before they land, or shall we keep it short?''

Roger raised one eyebrow.

"Your intentions,'' the doctor elaborated.

"Oh. Strictly honorable.''

"Yeah? I called Bree last night, to see if she was coming tonight. No answer.''

"We'd gone to a Celtic festival, up in the mountains.''

"Uh-huh. I called again, eleven p.m. And midnight. No answer.'' The doctor's eyes were still shrewd, but a good deal less warm. He set his glass down with a small click.

"Bree's alone,'' he said. "And she's lonely. And she's lovely. I wouldn't like to see anybody take advantage of that, Mr. Wakefield.''

"Neither would I—Dr. Abernathy.'' Roger drained his glass and set it down hard. Warmth burned in his cheeks, and it wasn't due to the Lagavulin. "If you think that I—''

"THIS IS HOUSTON,'' boomed the television. "TRANQUILITY BASE, WE HAVE TOUCH-DOWN IN TWENTY MINUTES.''

The inhabitants of the kitchen came pouring out, waving Coke bottles and cheering. Brianna, flushed with her labors, was laughing and brushing off their congratulations as she put away her knife. Abernathy put a hand on Roger's arm, to keep him.

"Mind me, Mr. Wakefield,'' Abernathy said, his voice low enough not to be heard over the crowd. "I don't want to hear that you've made that girl unhappy. Ever.''

Roger carefully released his arm from the other's grip.

"D'ye think she looks unhappy?" he asked, as politely as he could.

"No-oo," said Abernathy, rocking back on his heels and squinting hard at him. "On the contrary. It's the way she looks tonight that makes me think I should maybe punch you in the nose, on her daddy's behalf."

Roger couldn't help turning to look at her himself; it was true. She had dark circles under her eyes, wisps of hair were coming down from her ponytail, and her skin was glowing like the wax of a lighted candle. She looked like a woman who'd had a long night —and enjoyed it.

As though by radar, her head turned and her eyes fixed on him, over Gayle's head. She went on talking to Gayle, but her eyes spoke straight to him.

The doctor cleared his throat loudly. Roger jerked his attention away from her, to find Abernathy looking up at him, his expression thoughtful.

"Oh," the doctor said, in a changed tone. "Like that, is it?"

Roger's collar was unbuttoned, but he felt as though he were wearing a tie tied too tight. He met the doctor's eyes straight on.

"Yeah," he said. "Like that."

Dr. Abernathy reached for the bottle of Lagavulin, and filled both glasses.

"Claire did say she liked you," he said in resignation. He lifted one glass. "Okay. *Slàinte.*"

"Turn it the other way—Walter Cronkite's orange!" Lenny Abernathy obligingly twirled the knob, turning the commentator green. Unaffected by his sudden change of complexion, Cronkite went on talking.

"In approximately two minutes, Commander Neil Armstrong and the crew of the Apollo 11 will make history in the first manned landing on the moon . . ."

The living room was darkened and packed with people, everyone's attention riveted on the big TV as the footage shifted to a replay of the Apollo's launch.

"I'm impressed," Roger said in Brianna's ear. "How did you fix it?" He leaned against the end of a bookshelf, and pulled her snug against him, his hands on the swell of her hips, his chin on her shoulder.

Her eyes were on the television, but he felt her cheek move against his own.

"Somebody kicked the plug out of the wall," she said. "I just plugged it back in."

He laughed and kissed the side of her neck. It was hot in the room, even with the air conditioner humming, and her skin tasted moist and salty.

"You've got the roundest arse in the world," he whispered. She didn't answer, but deliberately nestled her bottom against him.

A buzz of voices from the screen and pictures of the flag the astronauts would plant on the moon.

He glanced across the room, but Joe Abernathy was as hypnotized as any of them, face rapt in the glow of the television screen. Safe in the darkness, he wrapped his arms around Brianna, and felt the soft weight of her breasts on his forearm. She sighed deeply and relaxed against him, putting her hand over his and squeezing tight.

They would both be less bold if there were any danger to it. But he was leaving in two hours; there was no chance of it going further. The night before, they had known they were playing with dynamite, and been more cautious. He wondered if Abernathy would actually have punched him, had he admitted that Brianna had spent the night in his bed?

He had driven them down the mountain, torn between trying to stay on the right side of the road, and the excitement of Brianna's soft weight, pressed against him. They'd stopped for coffee, talked long past midnight, touching constantly, hands, thighs, heads close together. Driven on to Boston in the wee hours, the conversation dying, Brianna's head heavy on his shoulder.

Unable to keep awake long enough to find his way through the maze of unfamiliar streets to her apartment, he had driven to his hotel, smuggled her upstairs, and laid her on his bed, where she had fallen asleep in seconds.

He had himself spent the rest of the night on the chaste hardness of the floor, Brianna's woolly cardigan across his shoulders for warmth. With the dawn, he'd got up and sat in the chair, wrapped in her scent, silently watching the light spread across her sleeping face.

Yeah, it was like that.

"Tranquility Base . . . the Eagle has landed." The silence in the room was broken by a deep collective sigh, and Roger felt the hair rise on the back of his neck.

"One . . . small . . . step for man," said the tinny voice, *"one giant leap . . . for mankind."* The picture was fuzzy, but not through any fault of the television. Heads strained forward, avid to see the bulky figure making its ginger way down the ladder, setting foot for the first time on the lunar soil. Tears gleamed on one girl's cheeks, silver in the glow.

Even Brianna had forgotten everything else; her hand had fallen from his arm and she was leaning forward, caught up in the moment.

It was a fine day to be an American.

He had a momentary qualm, seeing them all so fiercely intent, so fervently proud, and she so much a part of it. It *was* a different century, two hundred years from yesterday.

Might there be common ground for them, a historian and an engineer? He facing backward to the mysteries of the past, she to the future and its dazzling gleam?

Then the room relaxed in cheers and babbling, and she turned in his arms to kiss him hard and cling to him, and he thought perhaps it didn't matter that they faced in opposite directions—so long as they faced each other.

PART THREE

Pirates

6

I Encounter a Hernia

June 1767

"I hate boats," Jamie said through clenched teeth. "I loathe boats. I view boats with the most profound abhorrence."

Jamie's uncle, Hector Cameron, lived on a plantation called River Run, just above Cross Creek. Cross Creek in turn lay some way upriver from Wilmington; some two hundred miles, in fact. At this time of year, we were told, the trip might take four days to a week by boat, depending on wind. If we chose rather to travel overland, the journey could take two weeks or more, depending on such things as washed-out roads, mud, and broken axles.

"Rivers do not have waves," I said. "And I view the notion of trudging on foot for two hundred miles through the mud with a lot more than abhorrrence." Ian grinned broadly, but quickly exchanged the grin for an expression of bland detachment as Jamie's glare moved in his direction.

"Besides," I said to Jamie, "if you get seasick, I still have my needles." I patted the pocket where my tiny set of gold acupuncture needles rested in their ivory case.

Jamie exhaled strongly through his nose, but said no more. That little matter settled, the major problem remaining was to manage the boat-fare.

We were not rich, but did have a little money, as the result of a spot of good fortune on the road. Gypsying our way north from Charleston, and camping well off the road at night, we had discovered an abandoned homestead in the wood, its clearing nearly obliterated by new growth.

Cottonwood saplings shot like spears through the beams of the fallen roof, and a hollybush sprouted through a large crack in the hearthstone. The walls were half collapsed, black with rot and furred with green moss and rusty fungus. There was no telling how long the place had been abandoned, but it was clear that both cabin and clearing would be swallowed by the wilderness within a few years, nothing left to mark its existence save a tumbled cairn of chimney stones.

However, flourishing incongruously among the invading trees were the remains of a small peach orchard, the fruit of it burstingly ripe and swarming with bees. We had eaten as much as we could, slept in the shelter of the ruins, then risen before dawn and loaded the wagon with heaping mounds of smooth gold fruit, all juice and velvet.

We had sold it as we went, and consequently had arrived in Wilmington with sticky hands, a bag of coins—mostly pennies—and a pervasive scent of fermentation that clung to hair, clothes, and skin, as though we had all been dipped in peach brandy.

"You take this," Jamie advised me, handing me the small leather sack containing our fortune. "Buy what ye can for provisions—dinna buy any peaches, aye?—and perhaps a few bits and pieces so we dinna look *quite* such beggars when we come to my kinsman. A needle and thread, maybe?" He raised a brow and nodded at the large rent in Fergus's coat, incurred while falling out of a peach tree.

"Duncan and I will go about and see can we sell the wagon and horses, and inquire for a boat. And if there's such a thing as a goldsmith here, I'll maybe see what he'd offer for one of the stones."

"Be careful, Uncle," Ian advised, frowning at the motley crew of humanity coming and going from the harbor nearby. "Ye dinna want to be taken advantage of, nor yet be robbed in the street."

Jamie, gravely straight-faced, assured his nephew that he would take due precaution.

"Take Rollo," Ian urged him. "He'll protect ye."

Jamie glanced down at Rollo, who was surveying the passing crowds with a look of panting alertness that suggested not so much social interest as barely restrained appetite.

"Oh, aye," he said. "Come along then, wee dog." He glanced at me as he turned to go. "Perhaps ye'd best buy a few dried fish, as well."

Wilmington was a small town, but because of its fortuitous situation as a seaport at the mouth of a navigable river, it boasted not only a farmer's market and a shipping dock, but several shops that stocked imported luxuries from Europe, as well as the home-grown necessities of daily life.

"Beans, all right," Fergus said. "I like beans, even in large quantities." He shifted the burlap sack on his shoulder, balancing its unwieldy weight. "And bread, of course we must have bread—and flour and salt and lard. Salt beef, dried cherries, fresh apples, all well and good. Fish, to be sure. Needles and thread I see also are certainly necessary. Even the hairbrush," he added, with a sidelong glance at my hair, which, inspired by the humidity, was making mad efforts to escape the confinement of my broad-brimmed hat. "And the medicines from the apothecary, naturally. But *lace*?"

"Lace," I said firmly. I tucked the small paper packet containing three yards of Brussels lace into the large basket he was carrying. "Likewise ribbons. One yard each of wide silk ribbon," I told the perspiring young girl behind the counter. "Red—that's yours, Fergus, so don't complain—green for Ian, yellow for Duncan, and the very dark blue for Jamie. And no, it isn't an extravagance; Jamie doesn't want us to look like ragamuffins when we meet his uncle and aunt."

"What about you, Auntie?" Ian said, grinning. "Surely ye willna let us men be dandies, and you go plain as a sparrow?"

Fergus blew air between his lips, in mingled exasperation and amusement.

"That one," he said, pointing to a wide roll of dark pink.

"That's a color for a young girl," I protested.

"Women are never too old to wear pink," Fergus replied firmly. "I have heard *les mesdames* say so, many times." I had heard *les mesdames'* opinions before; Fergus's early life had been spent in a brothel, and judging from his reminiscences, not a little of his later life, too. I rather hoped that he could overcome the habit now that he was married to Jamie's stepdaughter, but with Marsali still in Jamaica awaiting the birth of their first child, I had my doubts. Fergus was a Frenchman born, after all.

"I suppose the Madams would know," I said. "All right, the pink, too."

Burdened with baskets and bags of provisions, we made our way out into the street. It was hot and thickly humid, but there was a breeze from the river, and after the stifling confines of the shop, the air seemed sweet and refreshing. I glanced toward the harbor, where the masts of several small ships poked up, swaying gently to the rocking of the current, and saw Jamie's tall figure stride out between two buildings, Rollo pacing close behind.

Ian hallooed and waved, and Rollo came bounding down the street, tail wagging madly at sight of his master. There were few people out at this time of day; those with business in the narrow street prudently flattened themselves against the nearest wall to avoid the rapturous reunion.

"My Gawd," said a drawling voice somewhere above me. "That'll be the biggest dawg I believe I've *ever* seen." I turned to see a gentleman detach himself from the front of a tavern, and lift his hat politely to me. "Your servant, ma'am. He ain't partial to human flesh, I do sincerely hope?"

I looked up at the man addressing me—and up. I refrained from expressing the opinion that he, of all people, could scarcely find Rollo a threat.

My interlocutor was one of the tallest men I'd ever seen; taller by several inches even than Jamie. Lanky and rawboned with it, his huge hands dangled at the level of my elbows, and the ornately beaded leather belt about his midriff came to my chest. I could have pressed my nose into his navel, had the urge struck me, which fortunately it didn't.

"No, he eats fish," I assured my new acquaintance. Seeing me craning my neck, he courteously dropped to his haunches, his knee joints popping like rifle shots as he did so. His face thus coming into view, I found his features still obscured by a bushy black beard. An incongruous snub nose poked out of the undergrowth, surmounted by a pair of wide and gentle hazel eyes.

"Well, I'm surely obliged to hear that. Wouldn't care to have a chunk taken out my leg, so early in the day." He removed a disreputable slouch hat with a ragged turkey feather thrust through the brim, and bowed to me, loose snaky black locks falling forward on his shoulders. "John Quincy Myers, your servant, ma'am."

"Claire Fraser," I said, offering him a hand in fascination. He squinted at it a moment, brought my fingers to his nose and sniffed them, then looked up and broke into a broad smile, nonetheless charming for missing half its teeth.

"Why, you'll maybe be a yarb-woman, won't you?"

"I will?"

He turned my hand gently over, tracing the chlorophyll stains around my cuticles.

"A green-fingered lady might just be tendin' her roses, but a lady whose hands smell of sassafras root and Jesuit bark is like to know more than how to make flowers bloom. Don't you reckon that's so?'' he asked, turning a friendly gaze on Ian, who was viewing Mr. Myers with unconcealed interest.

''Oh, aye,'' Ian assured him. ''Auntie Claire's a famous healer. A wisewoman!'' He glanced proudly at me.

''That so, boy? Well, now.'' Mr. Myers's eyes went round with interest, and swiveled back to focus on me. ''Smite me if this ain't Lucifer's own luck! And me thinkin' I'd have to wait till I come to the mountains and find me a *shaman* to take care of it.''

''Are you ill, Mr. Myers?'' I asked. He didn't look it, but it was hard to tell, what with the beard, the hair, and a thin layer of greasy brown dirt that seemed to cover everything not concealed by his ragged buckskins. The sole exception was his forehead; normally protected from the sun by the black felt hat, it was now exposed to view, a wide flat slab of purest white.

''Not to say ill, I don't reckon,'' he replied. He suddenly stood up, and began to fumble up the tail of his buckskin shirt. ''It ain't the clap or the French pox, anyhow, 'cause I seen those before.'' What I had thought were trousers were in fact long buckskin leggings, surmounted by a breechclout. Still talking, Mr. Myers had hold of the leather thong holding up this latter garment, and was fumbling with the knot.

''Damnedest thing, though; all of a sudden this great big swelling come up just along behind of my balls. Purely inconvenient, as you may imagine, though it don't hurt me none to speak of, save on horseback. Might be you could take a peep and tell me what I best do for it, hm?''

''Ah. . . .'' I said, with a frantic glance at Fergus, who merely shifted his sack of beans and looked amused, blast him.

''Would I have the pleasure to make the acquaintance of Mr. John Myers?'' said a polite Scottish voice over my shoulder.

Mr. Myers ceased fumbling with his breechclout and glanced up inquiringly.

''Can't say whether it's a pleasure to you or not, sir,'' he replied courteously. ''But be you lookin' for Myers, you've found him.''

Jamie stepped up beside me, tactfully inserting his body between me and Mr. Myers's breechclout. He bowed formally, hat under his arm.

''James Fraser, your servant, sir. I was told to offer the name of Mr. Hector Cameron by way of introduction.''

Mr. Myers looked at Jamie's red hair with interest.

"Scotch, are you? Be you one of them Highlander fellows?"

"I am a Scotsman, aye, and a Highlander."

"Be you kin to Old Hector Cameron?"

"He is my uncle by marriage, sir, though I have not met him myself. I was told that he was well known to you, and that you might consent to guide my party to his plantation."

The two men were frankly sizing each other up, eyes flicking head to toe as they talked, appraising bearing, dress, and armament. Jamie's eyes rested approvingly on the long sheath-knife at the woodsman's belt, while Mr. Myers's nostrils flared wide with interest.

"Comme deux chiens," Fergus remarked softly behind me. Like two dogs. *". . . aux culs."* Next thing you know, they will be smelling each other's backside.

Mr. Myers darted a glance at Fergus, and I saw a quick flash of amusement in the hazel depths before he returned to his assessment of Jamie. Uncultured the woodsman might be, but he plainly had some working knowledge of French.

Given Mr. Myers's olfactory inclinations and lack of self-consciousness, I might not have been surprised to see him drop to all fours and perform in the manner Fergus had suggested. As it was, he contented himself with a careful inspection that took in not only Jamie but Ian, Fergus, myself, and Rollo.

"Nice dawg," he said casually, holding out a set of massive knuckles to the latter. Rollo, thus invited, instituted his own inspection, sniffing industriously from moccasins to breechclout as the conversation went on.

"Your uncle, eh? Does he know you're coming?"

Jamie shook his head.

"I canna say. I sent a letter from Georgia, a month ago, but I've no way to tell whether he's had it yet."

"I shouldn't think so," Myers said thoughtfully. His eyes lingered on Jamie's face, then passed swiftly over the rest of us.

"I've met your wife. This'll be your son?" He nodded at Ian.

"My nephew, Ian. My foster son, Fergus." Jamie made the introductions with a wave of his hand. "And a friend, Duncan Innes, who'll be along presently."

Myers grunted, nodding, and made up his mind.

"Well, I should reckon I can get you to Cameron's all right. Wanted to be sure you was kin, but you got the look of the widder Cameron, in the face. The boy some, too."

Jamie's head jerked up sharply.

"The *widow* Cameron?"

A sly smile flitted through the thicket of beard.

"Old Hector caught the morbid sore throat, up and died late last winter. Don't figure they get much mail, wherever he is now."

Abandoning the Camerons for matters of more immediate personal interest, Myers resumed his interrupted excavations.

"Big purple thing," he explained to me, fumbling his loosened thong. "Almost as big as one o' my balls. You don't think it might could be as I've decided sudden-like to grow an extry, do you?"

"Well, no," I said, biting my lip. "I really doubt it." He moved very slowly, but had almost got the knot in his thong undone; people in the street were beginning to pause, staring.

"Please don't trouble yourself," I said. "I do believe I know what that is—it's an inguinal hernia."

The wide hazel eyes got wider.

"It is?" He seemed impressed, and not at all displeased by the news.

"I'd have to look—somewhere indoors, that is," I added hastily "—to be sure, but it sounds like it. It's quite easy to repair surgically, but . . ." I hesitated, looking up at the Colossus. "I really couldn't—I mean, you'd need to be asleep. Unconscious," I amplified. "I'd have to cut you, and sew you up again, you see. Perhaps a truss—a brace—might be better, though."

Myers scratched slowly at his jaw, meditating.

"No, I done tried that, 'twon't do. Cuttin', though . . . You folks be staying here in the town for a spell before you head up to Cameron's?"

"Not long," Jamie interrupted firmly. "We shall be sailing upriver to my aunt's estate, as soon as passage can be arranged."

"Oh." The giant pondered this for a moment, then nodded, beaming.

"I know the very man for you, sir. I'll go this minute and fetch Josh Freeman out the Sailor's Rest. Sun's still high, he'll be not too drunk to do business yet." He swept me a bow, battered hat to his middle. "And then could be your wife might have the kindness to meet me in yonder tavern—it's a mite more genteel than the Sailor's—and have a look at this . . . this . . ." I saw his lips try to form themselves around "inguinal hernia," then give up the effort and relax. "This yere obstruction."

He clapped the hat back on his head, and with a nod to Jamie, was off.

Jamie watched the mountain man's stiff-legged retreat down the street, slowed by cordial greetings to all he passed.

"What is it about ye, Sassenach, I wonder?" he said conversationally, eyes still fixed on Myers.

"What is *what* about me?"

He turned then, and gave me a narrow eye.

"What it is that makes every man ye meet want to take off his breeks within five minutes of meetin' ye."

Fergus choked slightly, and Ian went pink. I looked as demure as possible.

"Well, if you don't know, my dear," I said, "no one does. *I* seem to have found us a boat. And what have *you* been up to this morning?"

Industrious as always, Jamie had found us a potential gem-buyer. And not only a buyer, but an invitation to dinner with the Governor.

"Governor Tryon's in the town just now," he explained. "Staying at the house of a Mr. Lillington. I talked this morning wi' a merchant named MacEachern, who put me on to a man named MacLeod, who—"

"Who introduced you to MacNeil, who took you to drink with MacGregor, who told you all about his nephew Bethune, who's the second cousin half removed of the boy who cleans the Governor's boots," I suggested, familiar by this time with the Byzantine pathways of Scottish business dealings.

Put two Highland Scots in a room together, and within ten minutes they would know each other's family histories for the last two hundred years, and have discovered a helpful number of mutual relatives and acquaintances.

Jamie grinned.

"It was the Governor's wife's secretary," he corrected, "and his name's Murray. That'll be your Da's cousin Maggie's eldest boy from Loch Linnhe," he added, to Ian. "His father emigrated after the Rising." Ian nodded casually, doubtless docketing the information in his own version of the genetic encyclopedia, stored against the day it would prove useful.

Edwin Murray, the Governor's wife's secretary, had welcomed Jamie warmly as a kinsman—if only by marriage—and had obtained an invitation for us to dine at Lillington's that night, there ostensibly to acquaint the Governor with matters of trade in the Indies. In reality, we were intending to acquaint ourselves with Baron Penzler—a well-to-do German nobleman who would be dining there as well. The Baron was a man not only of wealth but of taste, with a reputation as a collector of fine objects.

"Well, it sounds a good idea," I said dubiously. "But I think you'd better go alone. I can't be dining with governors looking like *this.*"

"Ah, ye look f—" His voice faded as he actually looked at me. His eye roamed slowly over me, taking in my grimy, bedraggled gown, wild hair and ragged bonnet.

He frowned at me. "No, I want ye there, Sassenach; I may need a distraction."

"Speaking of distraction, how many pints did it take you to wangle an invitation to dinner?" I asked, mindful of our dwindling finances. Jamie didn't blink, but took my arm, turning me toward the row of shops.

"Six, but he paid half. Come along, Sassenach; dinner's at seven, and we must find ye something decent to wear."

"But we can't afford—"

"It's an investment," he said firmly. "And besides, Cousin Edwin has advanced me a bit against the sale of a stone."

The gown was two years out of fashion by the cosmopolitan standards of Jamaica but it was clean, which was the main thing so far as I was concerned.

"You're dripping, madame." The sempstress's voice was cold. A small, spare woman of middle age, she was the preeminent dressmaker in Wilmington and—I gathered—accustomed to having her fashion dictates obeyed without question. My rejection of a frilled cap in favor of freshly washed hair had been received with bad grace and predictions of pleurisy, and the pins she held in her mouth bristled like porcupine quills at my insistence on replacing the normal heavy corsetry with light boning, scalloped at the top to lift the breasts without pinching them.

"Sorry." I tucked up the offending wet lock inside the linen towel that wrapped my head.

The guest quarters of Mr. Lillington's great house being fully occupied by the Governor's party, I had been relegated to Cousin Edwin's tiny attic over the stable block, and the fitting of my gown was being accomplished to the accompaniment of muffled stampings and chewings from below, punctuated by the monotonous strains of the groom's whistling as he mucked out the stalls.

Still, I was not inclined to complain; Mr. Lillington's stables were a deal cleaner than the inn where Jamie and I had left our companions, and Mrs. Lillington had very graciously seen me provided with a large basin of hot water and a ball of lavender-scented soap—a consideration more important even than the fresh dress. I hoped never to see another peach.

I rose slightly on my toes, trying to see out of the window in case Jamie should be coming, but desisted at a grunt of protest from the sempstress, who was trying to adjust the hem of my skirt.

The gown itself was not at all bad; it was of cream silk, half-sleeved and very simple, but with panniers of wine-striped silk over the hips, and a ruching of claret-colored silk piping that ran in two rows from waist to bosom. With the Brussels lace I had purchased sewn around the sleeves, I thought it would do, even if the cloth was not quite of the first quality.

I had at first been surprised at the price, which was remarkably low, but now observed that the fabric of the dress was coarser than usual, with occasional slubs of thickened thread that caught the light in shimmers. Curious, I rubbed it between my fingers. I was no great judge of silk, but a Chinese acquaintance had spent most of one idle afternoon on board a ship explaining to me the lore of silkworms, and the subtle variation of their output.

"Where does this silk come from?" I asked. "It isn't China silk; is it French?"

The sempstress looked up, her crossness temporarily relieved by interest.

"No, indeed it's not. That's made in South Carolina, that is. There's a lady, Mrs. Pinckney by name, has gone and put half her land to mulberry trees, and went to raising silkworms on 'em. The cloth's maybe not quite so fine as the China," she acknowledged reluctantly, "but 'tisn't but half the cost, either."

She squinted up at me, nodding slowly.

"It'll do for fit, and the bit o' piping's good; brings out the color in your cheeks. But begging your pardon, madame, you do need something above the neck, not to look too bare. If you won't have a cap nor a wig, might be you'd have a ribbon?"

"Oh, ribbon!" I said, remembering. "Yes, what a good idea.

Do look in my basket over there, and you'll find a length that might just do.''

Between us we managed to get my hair piled up, loosely bound with the length of dark pink ribbon, damp curly tendrils coming down—I couldn't stop them—around my ears and brow.

"Not too much mutton dressed as lamb, is it?" I asked, suddenly worried. I smoothed a hand down the front of the bodice, but it fit snugly—and trimly—around my waist.

"Oh, no, madame," the sempstress assured me. "Quite appropriate, and I say it myself." She frowned at me, calculating. "Only it is a bit *bare* over the bosom, still. You haven't any jewelry, at all?"

"Just this." We turned in surprise as Jamie ducked his head to come in the door; neither of us had heard him coming.

He had somewhere managed to have a bath and procure a clean shirt and neckcloth; beyond that, someone had combed and plaited his hair into a smooth queue, bound with the new blue silk ribbon. His serviceable coat had not only been brushed, but improved by the application of a set of silver-gilt buttons, each delicately engraved with a small flower in the center.

"Very nice," I said, touching one.

"Rented from the goldsmith," he said. "But they'll do. So will this, I think." He drew out a filthy handkerchief from his pocket, from the folds of which he produced a slender gold chain.

"He hadna time for any but the simplest mount," he said, frowning in concentration as he fastened the chain around my neck. "But I think that's best, don't you?"

The ruby hung glinting just above the hollow of my breasts, casting a pale rosy glow against my white skin.

"I'm glad you picked that one," I said, touching the stone gently. It was warm from his body. "Goes much better with the dress than the sapphire or the emerald would." The sempstress's jaw hung slightly open. She glanced from me to Jamie, her impression of our social position evidently going up by leaps and bounds.

Jamie had finally taken time to notice the rest of my costume. His eyes traveled slowly over me from head to hem, and a smile spread across his face.

"Ye make a verra ornamental jewel box, Sassenach," he said. "A fine distraction, aye?"

He glanced out the window, where a pale peach color stained a hazy evening sky, then turned to me, bowed and made a leg. "Might I claim the pleasure of your company for dinner, madame?"

7

Great Prospects
Fraught with Peril

While I was familiar with the eighteenth-century willingness to eat anything that could be physically overpowered and dragged to the table, I did not subscribe to the mania for presenting wild dishes as though they had not in fact undergone the intermediary processes of being killed and cooked before making their appearance at dinner.

I thus viewed the large sturgeon with which I sat eyeball-to-eyeball with a marked lack of appetite. Complete not only with eyes but with scales, fins, and tail, the three-foot fish rode majestically on waves of roe in aspic, decorated with a vast quantity of tiny spiced crabs, which had been boiled whole and scattered artistically over the platter.

I took another large sip of wine and turned to my dinner companion, trying to keep my eyes off the bulging glare of the sturgeon by my elbow.

". . . the most impertinent fellow!" Mr. Stanhope was saying, by way of describing a gentleman he had encountered in a posthouse whilst on his way to Wilmington from his property near New Bern.

"Why, in the very midst of our refreshment, he began to speak of his piles, and what torment they caused him with the coach's continual bouncing. And then damme if the crude fellow did not pull his kerchief out of his pocket, all spotted with blood, to show the company by way of evidence! Quite destroyed my appetite, ma'am, I assure you," he assured me, forking up a substantial mouthful of chicken fricassee. He chewed it slowly, regarding me with pale, bulging eyes that reminded me uncomfortably of the sturgeon's.

Across the table, Phillip Wylie's long mouth twitched with amusement.

"Take care your conversation doesn't incur a similar effect,

Stanhope," he said, with a nod at my untouched plate. "Though a certain crudeness of company is one of the perils of public transport, I do admit."

Stanhope sniffed, brushing crumbs from the folds of his neck-cloth.

"Needn't put on airs, Wylie. It's not everyone can afford to keep a coachman, 'specially not with all these fresh taxes. New one stuck on every time one turns around, I do declare!" He waved his fork indignantly. "Tobacco, wine, brandy, all very well, but a tax upon *newspapers,* have you heard the like? Why, my sister's oldest boy was awarded a degree from Yale University a year past"—he puffed his chest unconsciously, speaking just slightly louder than usual—"and damned if she was not required to pay half a shilling, merely to have his diploma officially stamped!"

"But that is no longer the case at present," Cousin Edwin said patiently. "Since the repeal of the Stamp Act—"

Stanhope plucked one of the tiny crabs from the platter and brandished it at Edwin in accusation.

"Get rid of one tax, and another pops up in its place directly. Just like mushrooms!" He popped the crab into his mouth and was heard to mumble something indistinctly about taxing the air next, he shouldn't wonder.

"You are come but recently from the Indies, I understand, Madame Fraser?" Baron Penzler, on my other side, seized the momentary opportunity to interrupt. "I doubt you will be familiar with such provincial matters—or interested in them," he added, with a nod of benevolent dismissal at Stanhope.

"Oh, surely everyone is interested in taxes," I said, turning slightly sideways so as to display my bosom to best effect. "Or don't you believe that taxes are what we pay for a civilized society? Though having heard Mr. Stanhope's story"—I nodded to my other side—"perhaps he would agree that the level of civilization isn't quite equal to the level of taxation?"

"Ha ha!" Stanhope choked on his bread, spewing crumbs. "Oh, very good! Not equal to—ha ha, no, certainly not!"

Phillip Wylie gave me a look of sardonic acknowledgment.

"You must try not to be so amusing, Mrs. Fraser," he said. "It may be the death of poor Stanhope."

"Er . . . what is the current rate of taxation, do you think?" I asked, tactfully drawing attention away from Stanhope's spluttering.

Wylie pursed his lips, considering. A dandy, he wore the latest in modish wigs, and a small patch in the shape of a star beside his mouth. Under the powder, though, I thought I detected both a good-looking face and a very shrewd brain.

"Oh, considering all incidentals, I should say it can amount to as much as two per centum of all income, if one was to include the taxes on slaves. Add taxes on lands and crops, and it amounts to a bit more, perhaps."

"Two percent!" Stanhope choked, pounding himself on the chest. "Iniquitous! Simply iniquitous!"

With vivid memories of the last IRS form I had signed, I agreed sympathetically that a two percent tax rate was a positive outrage, wondering to myself just what had become of the fiery spirit of American taxpayers over the intervening two hundred years.

"But perhaps we should change the subject," I said, seeing that heads were beginning to turn in our direction from the upper end of the table. "After all, speaking of taxes at the Governor's table is rather like talking of rope in the house of the hanged, isn't it?"

At this, Mr. Stanhope swallowed a crab whole, and choked in good earnest.

His partner on the other side pounded him helpfully on the back, and the small black boy who had been occupied in swatting flies near the open windows was sent hastily to fetch water. I marked out a sharp, slender knife by the fish platter, just in case, though I hoped I shouldn't be compelled to perform a tracheotomy on the spot; it wasn't the kind of attention I was hoping to attract.

Luckily such drastic measures weren't required; the crab was disgorged by a fortunate slap, leaving the victim empurpled and gasping, but otherwise unharmed.

"Someone had mentioned newspapers," I said, once Mr. Stanhope had been thus rescued from his excesses. "We've been here so short a time that I haven't seen any; is there a regular paper printed in Wilmington?"

I had ulterior motives for asking this, beyond a desire to allow Mr. Stanhope time to recover himself. Among the few worldly goods Jamie possessed was a printing press, presently in storage in Edinburgh.

Wilmington, it appeared, had two printers in residence, but only one of these gentlemen—a Mr. Jonathan Gillette—produced a regular newspaper.

"And it may soon cease to be so regular," Stanhope said

darkly. "I hear that Mr. Gillette has received a warning from the Committee of Safety, that—ah!" He gave a brief exclamation, his plump face creased in pained surprise.

"Have you a particular interest, Mrs. Fraser?" Wylie inquired politely, darting a look under his brows at his friend. "I had heard that your husband had some connection with the printing trade in Edinburgh."

"Why, yes," I said, rather surprised that he should know so much about us. "Jamie owned a printing establishment there, though he didn't issue a newspaper—books and pamphlets and plays and the like."

Wylie's finely arched brow twitched up.

"No political leanings, then, your husband? So often printers find their skills suborned by those whose passions seek outlet in print—but then, such passions are not necessarily shared by the printer."

That rang numerous alarm bells; did Wylie actually know anything about Jamie's political connections in Edinburgh—most of whom had been thoroughly seditious—or was this only normal dinner table conversation? Judging from Stanhope's remarks, newspapers and politics were evidently connected in people's minds—and little wonder, given the times.

Jamie, at the far end of the table, had caught his name and now turned his head slightly to smile at me, before returning to an earnest conversation with the Governor, at whose right hand he sat. I wasn't sure whether this placement was the work of Mr. Lillington, who sat on the Governor's left, following the conversation with the intelligent, slightly mournful expression of a basset hound, or of Cousin Edwin, consigned to the seat opposite me, between Phillip Wylie and Wylie's sister, Judith.

"Oh, a tradesman," this lady now remarked, in a meaningful tone of voice. She smiled at me, careful not to expose her teeth. Likely decayed, I thought. "And is this"—she gave a vague wave at her head, comparing my ribbon to the towering confection of her wig—"the style in Edinburgh, Mrs. Fraser? How . . . charming."

Her brother gave her a narrowed eye.

"I believe I have also heard that Mr. Fraser is the nephew of Mrs. Cameron of River Run," he said pleasantly. "Have I been correctly informed, Mrs. Fraser?"

Cousin Edwin, who had undoubtedly been the source of this information, buttered his roll with sedulous concentration. Cousin

Edwin looked very little like a secretary, being a tall and prepossessing young man with a pair of lively brown eyes—one of which now gave me the merest suggestion of a wink.

The Baron, as bored with newspapers as with taxes, perked up a bit at hearing the name Cameron.

"River Run?" he said. "You have relations with Mrs. Jocasta Cameron?"

"She's my husband's aunt," I replied. "Do you know her?"

"Oh, indeed! A charming woman, most charming!" A broad smile lifted the Baron's pendulous cheeks. "Since many years, I am the dear friend of Mrs. Cameron and her husband, unfortunately dead."

The Baron launched into an enthusiastic recounting of the delights of River Run, and I took advantage of the lull to accept a small wedge of fish pie, full not only of fish, but of oysters and shrimps in a creamy sauce. Mr. Lillington had certainly spared no effort to impress the Governor.

As I leaned back for the footman to ladle more sauce onto my plate, I caught Judith Wylie's eyes on me, narrowed in a look of dislike that she didn't trouble to disguise. I smiled pleasantly at her, displaying my own excellent teeth, and turned back to the Baron, newly confident.

There had been no looking glass in Edwin's quarters, and while Jamie had assured me that I looked all right, his standards were rather different from those of fashion. I had received any number of admiring compliments from the gentlemen at table, true, but this might be no more than customary politeness; extravagant gallantry was common among upper-class men.

But Miss Wylie was twenty-five years my junior, fashionably gowned and jeweled, and if no great beauty, not plain, either. Her jealousy was a better reflection of my appearance, I thought, than any looking glass.

"Such a beautiful stone, Mrs. Fraser—you will permit me to look more closely?" The Baron bent toward me, pudgy fingers delicately poised above my cleavage.

"Oh, certainly," I said with alacrity, and quickly unclasped the chain, dropping the ruby into his broad, moist palm. The Baron looked slightly disappointed not to have been allowed to examine the stone *in situ,* but lifted his hand, squinting at the glinting droplet with the air of a connoisseur—which he evidently was, for he reached into his watch pocket and withdrew a small gadget that proved to be a combination of optical lenses, including both a magnifying glass and a jeweler's loupe.

I relaxed, seeing this, and accepted a helping of something hot and savory-smelling from a glass dish being passed by the butler. What possessed people to serve hot food when the temperature in the room must be at least in the nineties?

"Beautiful," murmured the Baron, rolling the stone gently in his palm. *"Sehr schön."*

There were not many things about which I would have trusted Geillis Duncan, but I was sure of her taste in jewels. "It must be a stone of the first class," she had said to me, explaining her theory of time travel via gems. "Large, and completely flawless."

The ruby was large, all right; nearly the size of the pickled quail's eggs surrounding the fully plumed pheasant on the sideboard. As to its flawlessness, I felt no doubt. Geilie had trusted this stone to carry her into the future; I thought it would probably get us as far as Cross Creek. I took a bite of the food on my plate; some sort of ragout, I thought, very tender and flavorful.

"How delicious this is," I said to Mr. Stanhope, lifting another forkful. "What is this dish, do you know?"

"Oh, it is one of my particular favorites, ma'am," he said, inhaling beatifically over his own plate. "Soused hog's face. Delectable, is it not?"

I shut the door of Cousin Edwin's room behind me and leaned against it, letting my jaw hang open in sheer relief at no longer being required to smile. Now I could take off the clinging dress, undo the tight corset, slip off the sweaty shoes.

Peace, solitude, nakedness, and silence. I couldn't think of anything else required to make my life complete for the moment, save a little fresh air. I stripped off, and attired in nothing but my shift, went to open the window.

The air outside was so thick, I thought I could have stepped out and floated down through it, like a pebble dropped in a jar of molasses. The bugs came at once to the flame of my candle, light-crazed and blood-hungry. I blew it out and sat on the window seat in the dark, letting the soft, warm air move over me.

The ruby still hung at my neck, black as a blood drop against my skin. I touched it, set it swinging gently between my breasts; the stone was warm as my own blood, too.

Outside, the guests were beginning to depart; a line of waiting carriages was drawn up on the drive. The sounds of goodbyes, conversations, and soft laughter drifted up to me in snatches.

". . . quite clever, I thought," came up in Phillip Wylie's cultured drawl.

"Oh, *clever,* certainly it was *clever!*" His sister's higher-pitched tones made it quite clear what she thought of cleverness as a social attribute.

"Well, cleverness in a woman can be tolerated, my dear, so long as she is also pleasant to look upon. By the same token, a woman who has beauty may perhaps dispense with wit, so long as she has sense enough to conceal the lack by keeping her mouth shut."

Miss Wylie might not be accused of cleverness, but had certainly adequate sensibility to perceive the barb in this. She gave a rather unladylike snort.

"She is a thousand years old, at least," she replied. "Pleasant to look at, indeed. Though I will say it was a handsome trinket about her neck," she added grudgingly.

"Oh, quite," said a deeper voice that I recognized as Lloyd Stanhope's. "Though in my own opinion, it was the setting rather than the jewel that was striking."

"Setting?" Miss Wylie sounded blank. "There was no setting; the jewel merely rested upon her bosom."

"Really?" Stanhope said blandly. "I hadn't noticed." Wylie burst out laughing, breaking off abruptly as the door opened to release more guests.

"Well, if you didn't, old man, there were others who did," he said with sly intonation. "Come, here's the carriage."

I touched the ruby again, watching the Wylies' handsome grays drive off. Yes, others had noticed. I could still feel the Baron's eyes on my bosom, knowingly avaricious. I rather thought he was a connoisseur of more than gems.

The stone was warm in my hand; it felt warmer even than my skin, though that must be illusion. I did not normally wear jewelry beyond my wedding rings; had never cared much for it. It would be a relief to be rid of at least part of our dangerous treasure. And still I sat there holding the stone, cradling it in my hand, till I almost thought I could feel it beating like a small separate heart, in time with my blood.

There was only one carriage left, its driver standing by the horses' heads. Some twenty minutes later, the occupant came out, adding to his goodbyes a good-humored *"Gute Nacht"* as he

stepped into his coach. The Baron. He had waited till last, and
was leaving in a good mood; that seemed a good sign.

One of the footmen, stripped of his livery coat, was extinguishing the torches at the foot of the drive. I could see the pale blur of
his shirt as he walked back to the house through the dark, and the
sudden flare of light onto the terrace as a door opened to admit
him below. Then that too was gone, and a night silence settled on
the grounds.

I had expected Jamie to come up at once, but the minutes
dragged on with no sound of his step. I glanced at the bed, but felt
no desire to lie down.

At last I stood up and slipped the dress back on, not bothering
with shoes or stockings. I left the room, walking quietly down the
hallway in my bare feet, down the stair, through the breezeway to
the main house, and in through the side entrance from the garden.
It was dark, save the pale squares of moonlight that came through
the casements; most of the servants must have retired, along with
household and guests. There was light glowing through the stairwell's banister, though; the sconces were still alight in the dining
room beyond.

I could hear the murmur of masculine voices as I tiptoed past
the polished stair, Jamie's deep soft Scots alternating with the
Governor's English tones, in the intimate cadences of a
tête-à-tête.

The candles had burnt low in their sconces. The air was sweet
with melted beeswax, and low clouds of fragrant cigar smoke
hung heavy outside the dining room doors.

Moving quietly, I stopped just short of the door. From this
vantage point I could see the Governor, back to me, neck
stretched forward as he lit a fresh cigar from the candlestick on
the table.

If Jamie saw me, he gave no hint of it. His face bore its usual
expression of calm good humor, but the recent lines of strain
around eyes and mouth had eased, and I could tell from the slope
of his shoulders that he was relaxed and at peace. My heart lightened at once; he had been successful then.

"A place called River Run," he was saying to the Governor.
"Well up in the hills past Cross Creek."

"I know the place," Governor Tryon remarked, a little surprised. "My wife and I passed several days in Cross Creek last
year; we made a tour of the colony, upon the occasion of my

taking office. River Run is well up in the foothills, though, not in the town—why, it is halfway to the mountains, I believe.''

Jamie smiled and sipped his brandy.

"Aye, well," he said, "my family are Highlanders, sir; the mountains will be home to us.''

"Indeed." A small puff of smoke rose over the Governor's shoulder. Then he took the cigar from his mouth and leaned confidentially toward Jamie.

"Since we are alone, Mr. Fraser, there is another matter I wished to put before you. A glass with you, sir?'' He picked up the decanter without waiting for an answer, and poured more brandy.

"I thank ye, sir.''

The Governor puffed fiercely for a moment, sending up blue clouds, then having got his weed well alight, sat back, cigar fuming negligently in one hand.

"You are very newly come to the Colonies, young Edwin tells me. Are you familiar with conditions here?''

Jamie shrugged slightly.

"I have made it my business to learn what I could, sir," he replied. "To which conditions might ye refer?''

"North Carolina is a land of considerable richness," the Governor answered, "and yet it has not reached the same level of prosperity as have its neighbors—owing mostly to a lack of laborers to take advantage of its opportunities. We have no great harbor for a seaport, you see; thus slaves must be brought overland at great cost from South Carolina or Virginia—and we cannot hope to compete with Boston and Philadelphia for indentured labor.

"It has long been the policy both of the Crown and of myself, Mr. Fraser, to encourage the settlement of land in the Colony of North Carolina by intelligent, industrious and godly families, to the furtherance of the prosperity and security of all.'' He lifted his cigar, took a deep lungful and exhaled slowly, pausing to cough.

"To this end, sir, there is established a system of land grants whereby a large acreage may be given to a gentleman of means, who will undertake to persuade a number of emigrants to come and settle upon a part of it under his sponsorship. This policy has been blessed with success over the last thirty years; a good many Highlanders and families from the Isles of Scotland have been induced to come and take up residence here. Why, when I arrived, I was astonished to find the banks of the Cape Fear River quite thick with MacNeills, Buchanans, Grahams, and Campbells!''

The Governor tasted his cigar again, but this time the barest nip; he was anxious to make his point.

"Yet there remains a great deal of desirable land to be settled, further inland toward the mountains. It is somewhat remote, and yet, as you say, for men accustomed to the far reaches of the Scottish Highlands—"

"I did hear mention of such grants, sir," Jamie interrupted. "Yet is not the wording that persons holding such grants shall be white males, Protestant, and above thirty years of age? And this statement holds the force of law?"

"That is the official wording of the Act, yes." Mr. Tryon turned so that I saw him now in profile, tapping the ash from his cigar into a small porcelain bowl. The corner of his mouth was turned up in anticipation; the face of a fisherman who feels the first twitch on his line.

"The offer is one of considerable interest," Jamie said formally. "I must point out, however, that I am not a Protestant, nor are most of my kinsmen."

The Governor pursed his lips in deprecation, lifting one brow.

"You are neither a Jew nor a Negro. I may speak as one gentleman to another, may I not? In all frankness, Mr. Fraser, there is the law, and then there is what is done." He raised his glass with a small smile, setting the hook. "And I am convinced that you understand that as well as I do."

"Possibly better," Jamie murmured, with a polite smile.

The Governor shot him a sharp look, but then uttered a quick bark of laughter. He raised his brandy glass in acknowledgment, and took a sip.

"We understand each other, Mr. Fraser," he said, nodding with satisfaction. Jamie inclined his head a fraction of an inch.

"There would be no difficulties raised, then, regarding the personal qualifications of those who might be persuaded to take up your offer?"

"None at all," said the Governor, setting down his glass with a small thump. "Provided only that they are able-bodied men, capable of working the land, I ask nothing more. And what is not asked need not be told, eh?" One thin brow flicked up in query.

Jamie turned the glass in his hands, as though admiring the deep color of the liquid.

"Not all who passed through the Stuart Rising were so fortunate as myself, Your Excellency," he said. "My foster son suffered the loss of his hand; another of my companions has but one arm. Yet they are men of good character and industry. I could not in conscience partake of a proposal which did not offer them some part."

The Governor dismissed this with an expansive wave of the hand.

"Provided that they are able to earn their bread and will not prove a burden upon the community, they are welcome." Then, as though fearing he had been incautious in his generosity, he sat up straight, leaving the cigar to burn, propped on the edge of the bowl.

"Since you mention Jacobites—these men will be required to swear an oath of loyalty to the Crown, if they have not already done so. If I might presume to ask, sir, as you imply you are Papist . . . you, yourself . . ."

Jamie's eyes might have narrowed only against the sting of the smoke, but I didn't think so. Neither did Governor Tryon, who was only in his thirties but no mean judge of men. He swiveled to face the table again, so that I saw only his back, but I could tell that he was gazing intently at Jamie, eyes tracing the swift movements of the trout beneath the water.

"I do not seek to remind you of past indignity," he said quietly. "Nor yet to offend present honor. Still, you will understand that it is my duty to ask."

Jamie smiled, quite without humor.

"And mine to answer, I expect," he said. "Yes, I am a pardoned Jacobite. And aye, I have sworn the oath—like the others who paid that price for their lives."

Quite abruptly, he set down his still-full glass and pushed back the heavy chair. He stood and bowed to the Governor.

"It grows late, Your Excellency. I must beg to take my leave."

The Governor sat back in his chair, and lifted the cigar slowly to his lips. He drew heavily on it, making the tip glow bright, as he gazed up at Jamie. Then, he nodded, letting a thin plume of smoke drift from his pursed lips.

"Good night, Mr. Fraser. Do consider my offer, will you not?"

I didn't wait to hear the answer—I didn't need to. I skimmed down the hall in a rustle of skirts, startling a footman dozing in a dark corner.

I made it back to our borrowed room in the stable block without meeting anyone else, and collapsed. My heart was pounding; not only from the dash up the stairs but from what I had heard.

Jamie would consider the Governor's offer, all right. And what an offer! To regain in one swoop all that he had lost in Scotland—and more.

Jamie had not been born a laird, but the death of his elder brother had left him heir to Lallybroch, and from the age of eight he had been raised to take responsibility for an estate, to see to the welfare of land and tenants, to place that welfare above his own. Then had come Charles Stuart, and his mad march to glory; a fiery cross leading his followers to shambles and destruction.

Jamie had never spoken bitterly of the Stuarts; had never spoken of Charles Stuart at all. Nor had he often spoken of what that venture had cost him personally.

But now . . . to have that back. New lands, cultivable and rich with game, and settled by families under his sponsorship and protection. It was rather like the Book of Job, I thought—all those sons and daughters and camels and houses, destroyed so casually, and then replaced with such extravagant largesse.

I had always viewed that bit of the Bible with some doubt, myself. One camel was much like another, but children seemed a different proposition. And while Job might have regarded the replacement of his children as simple justice, I couldn't help thinking that the dead children's mother might possibly have been of another mind about it.

Unable to sit, I went again to the window, gazing out unseeingly at the dark garden.

It wasn't simply excitement that was making my heart beat fast and my hands perspire; it was fear. With matters as they were in Scotland—as they had been since the Rising—it would be no difficult matter to find willing emigrants.

I had seen ships come into port in the Indies and in Georgia, disgorging their cargos of emigrants, so emaciated and worn by their passage that they reminded me of nothing so much as concentration camp victims—skeletal as living corpses, white as maggots from two months in the darkness belowdecks.

Despite the expense and difficulty of the journey, despite the pain of parting from friends and family and homeland forever, the immigrants poured in, in hundreds and in thousands, carrying their children—those who survived the voyage—and their possessions in small, ragged bundles; fleeing poverty and hopelessness, seeking not fortune but only a small foothold on life. Only a chance.

I had spent only a short time at Lallybroch the winter before, but I knew there were tenants there who survived only by the goodwill of Ian and Young Jamie, their crofts not yielding enough to live on. While such goodwill was invariably given, it was not inexhaustible; I knew that the estate's slender resources were often stretched to the maximum.

Beyond Lallybroch, there were the smugglers Jamie had known in Edinburgh, and the illegal distillers of Highland whisky—any number of men, in fact, who had been forced to turn to lawlessness to feed their families. No, finding willing emigrants would be no problem at all for Jamie.

The problem was that in order to recruit suitable men for the purpose, he would have to go to Scotland. And in my mind was the sight of a granite gravestone in a Scottish kirkyard, on a hill high above the moors and sea.

JAMES ALEXANDER MALCOLM MACKENZIE FRASER, it read, and below that, my own name was carved—*Beloved husband of Claire.*

I would bury him in Scotland. But there had been no date on the stone when I saw it, two hundred years hence; no notion when the blow would fall.

"Not yet," I whispered, clenching my fists in the silk of my petticoat. "I've only had him for a little while—oh, God, please, not yet!"

As though in answer, the door swung open, and James Alexander Malcolm MacKenzie Fraser came in, carrying a candle.

He smiled at me, loosening his stock.

"You're verra light on your feet, Sassenach. I see I must teach ye to hunt one day, and you such a fine stalker."

I made no apology for eavesdropping, but came to help him with his waistcoat buttons. In spite of the late hour and the brandy, he was clear-eyed and alert, his body tautly alive when I touched him.

"You'd best put out the candle," I said. "The bugs will eat you alive." I pinched a mosquito off his neck by way of illustration, the fragile body crushed to a smear of blood between my fingers.

Among the scents of brandy and cigar smoke, I could smell the night on him, and the faint musky spice of nicotiana; he had been walking, then, amid the flowers in the garden. He did that when he was either distressed or excited—and he didn't seem distressed.

He sighed and flexed his shoulders as I took his coat; his shirt was damp with sweat underneath, and he plucked it away from his skin with a mild grunt of distaste.

"I canna tell how folk live in such heat, dressed like this. It makes the savages look quite sensible, to be goin' about in loin-cloths and aprons."

"It would be a lot cheaper," I agreed, "if less aesthetically appealing. Imagine Baron Penzler in a loincloth, I mean." The Baron weighed perhaps eighteen stone, with a pasty complexion.

He laughed, the sound muffled in his shirt as he pulled it over his head.

"You, on the other hand . . ." I sat down on the window seat, admiring the view as he stripped off his breeches, standing on one leg to roll down his stocking.

With the candle extinguished, it was dark in the room, but with my eyes adapted, I could still make him out, long limbs pale against the velvet night.

"And speaking of the Baron—" I prodded.

"Three hundred pounds sterling," he replied, in tones of extreme satisfaction. He straightened up and tossed the rolled stockings onto a stool, then bent and kissed me. "Which is in large part due to you, Sassenach."

"For my value as an ornamental setting, you mean?" I asked dryly, recalling the Wylies' conversation.

"No," he said, rather shortly. "For keeping Wylie and his friends occupied at dinner, while I talked wi' the Governor. Ornamental setting . . . tcha! Stanhope nearly dropped his eyeballs into your bosom, the filthy lecher; I'd a mind to call him out for it, but—"

"Discretion is the better part of valor," I said, standing up and kissing him back. "Not that I've ever met a Scot who seemed to think so."

"Aye, well, there was my grandsire, Old Simon. I suppose ye could say it was discretion that did for him, in the end." I could hear both the smile and the edge in his voice. If he seldom spoke of the Jacobites and the events of the Rising, it didn't mean he had forgotten; his conversation with the Governor had obviously brought them close to the surface of his mind tonight.

"I'd say that discretion and deceit are not necessarily the same things. And your grandfather had been asking for it for fifty years, at least," I replied tartly. Simon Fraser, Lord Lovat, had died by beheading on Tower Hill—at the age of seventy-eight, after a lifetime of unparalleled chicanery, both personal and political. For all of that, I quite regretted the old rogue's passing.

"Mmphm." Jamie didn't argue with me, but moved to stand

beside me at the window. He breathed in deeply, as though smelling the thick perfume of the night.

I could see his face quite clearly in the dim glow of starlight. It was calm and smooth, but with an inward look, as though his eyes didn't see what was before them, but something else entirely. The past? I wondered. Or the future?

"What did it say?" I asked suddenly. "The oath you swore."

I felt rather than saw the movement of his shoulders, not quite a shrug.

" 'I, James Alexander Malcolm MacKenzie Fraser, do swear, and as I shall answer to God at the great day of judgment, I have not, nor shall have, in my possession any gun, sword, pistol, or arm whatsoever, and never use tartan, plaid, or any part of the Highland garb; and if I do so, may I be cursed in my undertakings, family, and property.' " He took a deep breath, and went on, speaking precisely.

" 'May I never see my wife and children, father, mother or relations. May I be killed in battle as a coward, and lie without Christian burial, in a strange land, far from the graves of my forefathers and kindred; may all this come across me if I break my oath.' "

"And did you mind a lot?" I said, after a moment.

"No," he said softly, still looking out at the night. "Not then. There are things worth dying or starving for—but not words."

"Maybe not those words."

He turned to look at me, features dim in starlight, but the hint of a smile visible on his mouth.

"Ye know of words that are?"

The gravestone had his name, but no date. I could stop him going back to Scotland, I thought. If I would.

I turned to face him, leaning back against the window frame.

"What about—'I love you'?"

He reached out a hand and touched my face. A breath of air stirred past us, and I saw the small hairs rise along his arm.

"Aye," he whispered. "That'll do."

There was a bird calling somewhere close at hand. A few clear notes, succeeded by an answer; a brief twitter, and then silence. The sky outside was still thick black, but the stars were less brilliant than before.

I turned over restlessly; I was naked, covered only by a linen sheet, but even in the small hours of the night, the air was warm and smothering, and the small depression in which I lay was damp.

I had tried to sleep, and could not. Even lovemaking, which normally could relax me into a bonelessly contented stupor, had this time left me only restless and sticky. At once excited and worried by the possibilities of the future—and unable to confide my disturbed feelings—I had felt separate from Jamie; estranged and detached, despite the closeness of our bodies.

I turned again, this time toward Jamie. He lay in his usual position, on his back, the sheet crumpled about his hips, hands gently folded over a flat stomach. His head was turned slightly on the pillow, his face relaxed in sleep. With the wide mouth gentled by slumber and the dark lashes long on his cheeks, in this dim light he looked about fourteen.

I wanted to touch him, though I wasn't sure whether I meant to caress or to poke him. While he had given me physical release, he had taken my peace of mind, and I was irrationally envious of his effortless repose.

I did neither, though, and merely turned onto my back, where I lay with my eyes shut, grimly counting sheep—who disobliged me by being Scottish sheep, cantering merrily through a kirkyard, leaping the gravestones with gay abandon.

"Is something troubling ye, Sassenach?" said a sleepy voice at my shoulder.

My eyes popped open.

"No," I said, trying to sound equally drowsy. "I'm fine."

There was a faint snort and a rustling of the chaff-filled mattress as he turned over.

"You're a terrible liar, Sassenach. Ye're thinking so loudly, I can hear ye from here."

"You can't hear people think!"

"Aye, I can. You, at least." He chuckled and reached out a hand, which rested lazily on my thigh. "What is it—has the spiced crab given ye flatulence?"

"It has not!" I tried to twitch my leg away, but his hand clung like a limpet.

"Oh, good. What is it, then—ye've finally thought of a witty riposte to Mr. Wylie's remarks about oysters?"

"No," I said irritably. "If you must know, I was thinking about the offer Governor Tryon made you. Will you let go of my leg?"

"Ah," he said, not letting go but sounding less sleepy. "Well, come to that, I was thinking on the matter a bit myself."

"What *do* you think about it?" I gave up trying to detach his hand and rolled onto my elbow, facing him. The window was still dark, but the stars had dimmed visibly, faded by the distant approach of day.

"I wonder why he made it, for the one thing."

"Really? But I thought he told you why."

He gave a brief grunt.

"Well, he's no offering me land for the sake of my bonny blue eyes, I'll tell ye that." He opened the eyes in question and cocked one brow at me. "Before I make a bargain, Sassenach, I want to know what's on both sides of it, aye?"

"You don't think he's telling the truth? About Crown grants to help settle the land? But he said it's been going on for thirty years," I protested. "He couldn't lie about something like that, surely."

"No, that's the truth," he agreed. "So far as it goes. But bees that hae honey in their mouths hae stings in their tails, aye?" He scratched at his head and smoothed the loose hair out of his face, sighing.

"Ask yourself this, Sassenach," he said. "Why me?"

"Well—because he wants a gentleman of substance and authority," I said slowly. "He needs a good leader, which Cousin Edwin has obviously told him you are, and a fairly wealthy man—"

"Which I am not."

"He doesn't know that, though," I protested.

"Doesn't he?" he said cynically. "Cousin Edwin will ha' told him as much as he knows—and the Governor kens well I was a Jacobite. True, there are a few who mended their fortunes in the Indies after the Rising, and I might be one o' those—but he has nae reason to think so."

"He knows you have *some* money," I pointed out.

"Because of Penzler? Aye," he said thoughtfully. "What else does he know about me?"

"Only what you told him at dinner, so far as I know. And he can't have heard much about you from anyone else; after all, you've been in town less than a—what, you mean that's it?" My voice rose in incredulity, and he smiled, a little grimly. The light was still far off, but moving closer, and his features were clearcut in the dimness.

"Aye, that's it. I've connections to the Camerons, who are not only wealthy but well respected in the colony. But at the same time, I'm an incomer, wi' few ties and no known loyalties here."

"Except, perhaps, to the Governor who's offering you a large tract of land," I said slowly.

He didn't reply at once, but rolled onto his back, still keeping a grip on my leg. His eyes were fastened on the dim whiteness of the plaster ceiling above, with its clouded garlands and ghostly cupids.

"I've known a German or two in my time, Sassenach," he said, musing. His thumb began to move slowly, back and forth upon the tender flesh of my inner thigh. "I havena found them careless wi' their money, be they Jew or Gentile. And while ye looked bonny as a white rose this evening, I canna think it was entirely your charms that made the gentleman offer me a hundred pounds more than the goldsmith did."

He glanced at me. "Tryon is a soldier. He'll ken me for one, too. And there was that wee bit of trouble with the Regulators two year past."

My mind was so diverted by the possibilities intrinsic in this speech, that I was nearly unconscious of the increasing familiarity of the hand between my thighs.

"Who?"

"Oh, I forgot; ye wouldna have heard that part of the conversation—bein' otherwise occupied with your host of admirers."

I let that one pass in favor of finding out about the Regulators. These, it appeared, were a loose association of men, mostly from the rough backcountry of the colony, who had taken offense at what they perceived as capricious and inequitable—and now and then downright illegal—behavior on the part of the Crown's appointed officials, the sheriffs, justices, tax collectors, and so on.

Feeling that their complaints were not sufficiently addressed by the Governor and Assembly, they had taken matters into their own hands. Sheriff's deputies had been assaulted, justices of the peace marched from their houses by mobs and forced to resign.

A committee of Regulators had written to the Governor, imploring him to address the iniquities under which they suffered, and Tryon—a man of action and diplomacy—had replied soothingly, going so far as to replace one or two of the most corrupt sheriffs, and issue an official letter to the court officers, regarding seizure of effects.

"Stanhope said something about a Committee of Safety," I said, interested. "But it sounded quite recent."

"The trouble is damped down but not settled," Jamie said, shrugging. "And damp powder may smolder for a long time, Sassenach, but once it catches, it goes off with an almighty bang."

Would Tryon think it worth the investment, to buy the loyalty and obligation of an experienced soldier, himself in turn commanding the loyalty and service of the men under his sponsorship, all settled in a remote and troublesome area of the colony?

I would myself have called the prospect cheap, at the cost of a hundred pounds and a few measly acres of the King's land. His Majesty had quite a lot of it, after all.

"So you're thinking about it." We were by this time facing each other, and my hand lay over his, not in restraint, but in acknowledgment.

He smiled lazily.

"I havena lived so long by believing everything I'm told, Sassenach. So perhaps I'll take up the Governor's kind offer, and perhaps I will not—but I want to know the hell of a lot more about it before I say, one way or the other."

"Yes, it does seem a little odd—his making you such an offer on short acquaintance."

"I should be surprised to hear I am the only gentleman he's so approached," Jamie said. "And it's no great risk, now, is it? Ye overheard me telling him I am a Catholic? It was no surprise to him to hear it."

"Yes. He didn't seem to think that was a problem, though."

"Oh, I daresay it wouldna be—unless the Governor chose to make it one."

"My goodness." My evaluation of Governor Tryon was rapidly changing, though I wasn't sure whether for the better or not. "So if things didn't work out as he liked, all he would have to do is let it be known that you're a Catholic, and a court would take back the land on those grounds. Whereas if he chooses to keep quiet—"

"And if I choose to do as he likes, aye."

"He's much sneakier than I thought," I said, not without admiration. "Practically Scottish."

He laughed at that, and brushed the loose hair out of his face.

The long curtains at the window, hitherto hanging limp, suddenly puffed inward, letting in a breath of air that smelt of sandy mud, river water, and the far-off hint of fresh pines. Dawn was coming, borne on the wind.

As though this had been a signal, Jamie's hand cupped itself, and a slight shiver communicated itself from him to me, as the coolness struck his bare back.

"I didna really do myself credit earlier," he said softly. "But if you're sure there's nothing troubling your mind just now . . ."

"Nothing," I said, watching the glow from the window touch the line of his head and neck with gold. His mouth was still wide and gentle, but he didn't look fourteen any longer.

"Not a thing, just now."

Man of Worth

"God, I hate boats!"

With this heart-felt valediction ringing in my ears, we swung slowly out into the waters of Wilmington harbor.

Two days of purchases and preparations found us now bound for Cross Creek. With money from the sale of the ruby in hand, there had been no need to sell the horses; Duncan had been sent with the wagon and the heavier goods, with Myers aboard to guide him, the rest of us to take a quicker, more comfortable passage with Captain Freeman, aboard the *Sally Ann*.

A craft of singular and indescribable type, the *Sally Ann* was square-beamed, long, low-sided, and blunt-prowed. She boasted a tiny cabin that measured roughly six feet square, leaving a scant two feet on either side for passage, and a somewhat greater area of deck fore and aft, this now partially obscured by bundles, bags, and barrels.

With a single sail mounted on a mast and boom above the cabin, the *Sally Ann* looked from a distance like a crab on a shingle, waving a flag of truce. The peaty brown waters of the Cape Fear lapped a scant four inches below the rail, and the boards of the bottom were perpetually damp with slow leakage.

Still, I was happy. Cramped conditions or no, it was good to be on the water, away—if only temporarily—from the Governor's siren song.

Jamie wasn't happy. He did indeed hate boats, with a profound and undying passion, and suffered from a seasickness so acute that watching the swirl of water in a glass could turn him green.

"It's dead calm," I observed. "Maybe you won't be sick."

Jamie squinted suspiciously at the chocolate-brown water around us, then clamped his eyes shut as the wake from another boat struck the *Sally Ann* broadside, rocking her violently.

"Maybe not," he said, in tones indicating that while the suggestion was a hopeful one, he also thought the possibility remote.

"Do you want the needles? It's better if I put them in before you vomit." Resigned, I groped in the pocket of my skirt, where I had placed the small box containing the Chinese acupuncture needles that had saved his life on our Atlantic crossing.

He shuddered briefly and opened his eyes.

"No," he said. "I'll maybe do. Talk to me, Sassenach—take my mind off my stomach, aye?"

"All right," I said obligingly. "What is your Aunt Jocasta like?"

"I havena seen her since I was two years old, so my impressions are a bit lacking," he replied absently, eyes fixed on a large raft coming down the river, set on an apparent collision course with us. "D'ye think that Negro can manage? Perhaps I ought to give him a bit of help."

"Perhaps you shouldn't," I said, eyeing the oncoming raft warily. "He seems to know what he's doing." Besides the captain —a disreputable old wreck who reeked of tobacco—the *Sally Ann* had a single hand, an elderly black freedman who was dealing alone with the steerage of our craft, by means of a large pole.

The man's lean muscles flexed and bulged in easy rhythm. Grizzled head bowed in effort, he took no apparent notice of the oncoming barge, but plunged and lifted in a liquid motion that made the long pole seem like a third limb.

"Let him alone. I suppose you don't know much about your aunt, then?" I added, in hopes of distracting him. The raft was moving ponderously and inexorably toward us.

Some forty feet from end to end, it rode low in the water, weighed down with barrels and stacks of hides, tied down under netting. A pungent wave of odor preceded it, of musk and blood and rancid fat, strong enough to overpower temporarily all the other smells of the river.

"No; she wed the Cameron of Erracht and left Leoch the year before my mother married my father." He spoke abstractedly, not looking at me; his attention was all on the oncoming barge. His knuckles whitened; I could feel his urge to leap forward, snatch the pole away from the deckhand, and stave off the raft. I laid a restraining hand on his arm.

"And she never came to visit at Lallybroch?"

I could see the gleam of sun on dull iron, where it struck cleats along the edge of the raft, and the half-naked forms of the three deckhands, sweating even in the early morning. One of them waved his hat and grinned, shouting something that sounded like, "Hah, *you*!" as they came on.

"Well, John Cameron died of a flux, and she wed his cousin, Black Hugh Cameron of Aberfeldy, and then—" He shut his eyes reflexively as the raft shot past, its hull no more than six inches from our own, amid a hail of good-natured jeers and shouts from its crew. Rollo, front paws perched on the low cabin roof, barked madly, until Ian cuffed him and told him to stop.

Jamie opened one eye, then seeing that the danger was past, opened the other and relaxed, letting go his grip on the roof.

"Aye, well, Black Hugh—they called him so for a great black wen on his knee—he was killed hunting, and so then she wed Hector Mor Cameron, of Loch Eilean—"

"She seems to have had quite a taste for Camerons," I said, fascinated. "Is there something special about them as a clan—beyond being accident-prone, I mean?"

"They've a way wi' words, I suppose," he said, with a sudden wry grin. "The Camerons are poets—and jesters. Sometimes both. Ye'll remember Lochiel, aye?"

I smiled, sharing his bittersweet recollection of Donald Cameron of Lochiel, one of the chiefs of clan Cameron at the time of the Rising. A handsome man with a soulful gaze, Lochiel's gentle-eyed demeanor and elegant manners hid a truly great talent for the creation of vulgar doggerel, with which, *sotto voce,* he had not infrequently entertained me at balls in Edinburgh, during the brief heyday of Charles Stuart's coup.

Jamie was leaning on the roof of the boat's tiny cabin, watching the river traffic with a wary eye. We had not yet cleared Wilmington's harbor, and small pirettas and sculls darted past like water bugs, whipping in and out between the larger, slower-moving craft. He was pale, but not green yet.

I leaned my elbows on the cabin roof as well, and stretched my back. Hot as it was, the heavy sunshine was comforting to the sore muscles caused by impromptu sleeping arrangements; I had spent the last night curled up on a hard oak settle in the taproom of a riverside tavern, sleeping with my head on Jamie's knee as he completed the arrangements for our passage.

I groaned and stretched.

"Was Hector Cameron a poet, or a joker?"

"Neither one at the moment," Jamie replied, automatically

gripping the back of my neck and massaging it with one hand. "He's dead, aye?"

"That's wonderful," I said, groaning with ecstasy as his thumb sank into a particularly tender spot. "What you're doing, I mean, not that your uncle's dead. Ooh, don't stop. How did he get to North Carolina?"

Jamie snorted with amusement, and moved behind me so he could use both hands on my neck and shoulders. I nestled my bottom against him and sighed in bliss.

"You're a verra noisy woman, Sassenach," he said, leaning forward to whisper in my ear. "Ye make the same kind of sounds when I rub your neck as ye do when I—" He thrust his pelvis against me in a discreet but explicit motion that made it quite clear what he meant. "Mm?"

"Mmmm," I replied, and kicked him—discreetly—in the shin. "Fine. If anyone hears me behind closed doors, they'll assume you're rubbing my neck—which is about all you're likely to do until we get off this floating plank. Now, what about your late uncle?"

"Oh, him." His fingers dug in on either side of my backbone, rubbing slowly up and down as he unraveled yet another strand in the tangled web of his family history. At least it was keeping his mind off his stomach.

Luckier—and either more perceptive or more cynical—than his famous kinsman, Hector Mor Cameron had cannily prepared himself against the eventuality of a Stuart disaster. He had escaped Culloden unwounded and made for home, where he had promptly loaded wife, servant, and portable assets into a coach, in which they fled to Edinburgh and thence by ship to North Carolina, narrowly escaping the Crown's pursuit.

Once arrived in the New World, Hector had purchased a large tract of land, cleared the forest, built a house and a sawmill, bought slaves to work the place, planted his land in tobacco and indigo, and—no doubt worn out by so much industry—succumbed to the morbid sore throat at the ripe old age of seventy-three.

Having evidently decided that three times was enough, Jocasta MacKenzie Cameron Cameron Cameron had—so far as Myers knew—declined to wed again, but stayed on alone as mistress of River Run.

"Do you think the messenger with your letter will get there before we do?"

"He'd get there before we do if he crawled on his hands and knees," Young Ian said, appearing suddenly beside us. He glanced in mild disgust at the patient deckhand, plunging and lifting his dripping pole. "It will be *weeks* before we get there, at this rate. I told ye it would have been best to ride, Uncle Jamie."

"Dinna fret yourself, Ian," his uncle assured him, letting go of my neck. He grinned at his nephew. "You'll have a turn at the pole yourself before long—and I expect ye'll have us in Cross Creek before nightfall, aye?"

Ian gave his uncle a dirty look and wandered off to pester Captain Freeman with questions about Red Indians and wild animals.

"I hope the Captain doesn't put Ian overboard," I said, observing Freeman's scrawny shoulders draw defensively toward his ears as Ian approached. My own neck and shoulders glowed from the attention; so did portions further south. "Thanks for the rub," I said, lifting one eyebrow at him.

"I'll let ye return the favor, Sassenach—after dark." He made an unsuccessful attempt at a leer. Unable to close one eye at a time, his ability to wink lewdly was substantially impaired, but he managed to convey his meaning nonetheless.

"Indeed," I said. I fluttered my lashes at him. "And just what is it you'd like rubbed after dark?"

"After dark?" Ian asked, popping up again like a jack-in-the-box before his uncle could answer. "What happens after dark?"

"That's when I drown ye and cut ye up for fish bait," his uncle informed him. "God's sake, can ye not settle, Ian? Ye're bumpin' about like a bumblebee in a bottle. Go and sleep in the sun, like your beast—there's a sensible dog." He nodded at Rollo, sprawled like a rug on the cabin roof with his eyes half-closed, twitching an occasional ear against the flies.

"Sleep?" Ian looked at his uncle in amazement. *"Sleep?"*

"It's what normal people do when they're tired," I told him, stifling a yawn. The growing heat and the boat's slow movement were highly soporific, after the short night—we had been up before dawn. Unfortunately, the narrow benches and rough deck planks of the *Sally Ann* didn't look any more inviting than the tavern's settle had been.

"Oh, I'm not a scrap tired, Auntie!" Ian assured me. "I dinna think I'll sleep for days!"

Jamie eyed his nephew.

"We'll see if ye still think so, after a turn at the pole. In the meantime, perhaps I can find something to occupy your mind. Wait a bit—'' He broke off, and ducked into the low cabin, where I heard him rootling through the baggage.

"God, it's hot!" said Ian, fanning himself. "What's Uncle Jamie after, then?"

"God knows," I said. Jamie had brought aboard a large crate, about the contents of which he had been most evasive. He had been playing cards when I had fallen asleep the night before, and my best guess was that he had acquired some embarrassing object in the course of gambling, which he was reluctant to expose to Ian's teasing.

Ian was right; it *was* hot. I could only hope that there would be a breeze later; for the moment, the sail above hung limp as a dishcloth, and the fabric of my shift clung damp against my legs. With a murmured word to Ian, I edged past and sidled toward the bow, where the water barrel stood.

Fergus was standing in the prow, arms crossed, giving a splendid impression of a noble figurehead, with his sternly handsome profile pointed upriver, thick, dark hair flowing back from his brow.

"Ah, milady!" He greeted me with a sudden dazzle of white teeth. "Is this not a splendid country?"

What I could see at the moment was not particularly splendid, the landscape consisting of an extensive mudflat, reeking in the sun, and a large collection of gulls and seabirds, all raucously excited about something smelly they had found near the water's edge.

"Milord tells me that any man may enter a claim for fifty acres of land, so long as he builds a house upon it, and promises to work it for a period of ten years. Imagine—fifty acres!" He rolled the words around in his mouth, savoring them with a kind of awe. A French peasant might think himself well blessed with five.

"Well, yes," I said, a little doubtfully. "I think you ought to pick your fifty acres carefully, though. Some parts of this place aren't much good for farming." I didn't hazard a guess as to how difficult Fergus might find it to carve a farm and homestead out of a howling wilderness with one hand, no matter how fertile the ground.

He wasn't paying attention in any case, his eyes shiny with dreams.

"I might perhaps have a small house built by Hogmanay," he murmured to himself. "Then I could send for Marsali and the child in the spring." His hand went automatically to the vacant spot on his chest, where the greenish medal of St. Dismas had hung since his childhood.

He had come to join us in Georgia, leaving his young and pregnant wife behind in Jamaica, under the care of friends. He assured me that he had no fear for her safety, however, for he had left her also under the protection of his patron saint, with strict instructions not to remove the battered medal from around her neck until she was safely delivered.

I wouldn't myself have thought that mothers and babies fell into the sphere of influence of the patron saint of thieves, but Fergus had lived as a pickpocket for all his early life, and his trust in Dismas was absolute.

"Will you call the baby Dismas, if it's a boy?" I asked, joking.

"No," he said in all seriousness. "I shall call him Germaine. Germaine James Ian Aloysius Fraser—James Ian for Milord and Monsieur," he explained, for so he always referred to Jamie and his brother-in-law, Ian Murray.

"Marsali liked Aloysius," he added dismissively, making it clear that he had had nothing to do with the choice of so undistinguished a name.

"And what if it's a girl?" I asked, with a sudden vivid memory. Twenty-odd years before, Jamie had sent me back through the stones, pregnant. And the last thing he had said to me, convinced the child I carried was a boy, was, "Name him Brian, for my father."

"Oh." Fergus had clearly not considered this possibility, either, for he looked vaguely disconcerted. Then his features cleared.

"Genevieve," he said firmly. "For Madame," by this meaning Jenny Murray, Jamie's sister. "Genevieve Claire, I think," he added, with another dazzling smile.

"Oh," I said, flustered and oddly flattered. "Well. Thank you. Are you sure that you ought not to go back to Jamaica to be with Marsali, Fergus?" I asked, changing the subject.

He shook his head decidedly.

"Milord may have need of me," he said. "And I am of more use here than I should be there. Babies are women's work, and who knows what dangers we may encounter in this strange place?"

As though in answer to this rhetorical question, the gulls rose in a squawking cloud, wheeling out over the river and mudflats, revealing the object of their appetite.

A stout pine stake had been driven into the mud of the bank, the top of it a foot below the dark, weedy line that marked the upper reaches of the incoming tide. The tide was still low; it had reached no higher than halfway up the stake. Above the lapping waves of silty water hung the figure of a man, fastened to the stake by a chain around his chest. Or what had once been his chest.

I couldn't tell how long he had been there, but quite long enough, from the looks of him. A narrow gash of white showed the curve of skull where skin and hair had been stripped off. Impossible to say what he had looked like; the birds had been busy.

Beside me, Fergus said something very obscene in French, softly under his breath.

"Pirate," said Captain Freeman laconically, coming up beside me and pausing long enough to spit a brown stream of tobacco juice into the river. "If they ain't taken to Charleston for hangin', sometimes they stake 'em out at low tide and let the river have 'em."

"Are—are there a lot of them?" Ian had seen it, too; he was much too old to reach for my hand, but he stood close beside me, his face pale under its tan.

"Not so much, no more. The Navy does a good job keepin' 'em down. But go back a few years, why, you could see four or five pirates out here at a time. Folk would pay to come out by boat, to sit and watch 'em drown. Real pretty out here when the tide comes in at sunset," he said, jaws moving in a slow, nostalgic rhythm. "Turns the water red."

"Look!" Ian, forgetting his dignity, clutched me by the arm. There was a movement near the riverbank, and we saw what had startled the birds away.

It slid into the water, a long, scaly form some five or six feet long, carving a deep groove in the soft mud of the bank. On the far side of the boat, the deckhand muttered something under his breath, but didn't stop his poling.

"It is a crocodile," Fergus said, and made the sign of the horns in distaste.

"No, I dinna think so." Jamie spoke behind me, and I swung around to see him peering over the cabin roof, at the still figure in the water and the V-shaped wake moving toward it. He held a book in his hand, thumb between the pages to hold his place, and now bent his head to consult the volume.

"I believe it is an alligator. They dine upon carrion, it says here, and willna eat fresh meat. When they take a man or a sheep, they pull the victim beneath the water to drown it, but then drag it to their den below ground and leave it there until it has rotted enough to suit their fancy. Of course," he added, with a bleak glance at the bank, "they're sometimes fortunate enough to find a meal prepared."

The figure on the stake seemed to tremble briefly, as something bumped it from below, and Ian made a small choking noise beside me.

"Where did you get that book?" I asked, not taking my eyes off the stake. The top of the wooden pole was vibrating, as though something under the waves was worrying at it. Then the pole was still, and the V-shaped wake could be seen again, traveling back toward the riverbank. I turned away before it could emerge.

Jamie handed me the book, his eyes still fixed on the black mudflat and its cloud of screeching birds.

"The Governor gave it to me. He said he thought it might be of interest on our journey."

I glanced down at the book. Bound in plain buckram, the title was stamped on the spine in gold leaf—*The Natural History of North Carolina.*

"Eeugh!" said Ian beside me, watching the scene on shore in horror. "That's the most awful thing I've ever—"

"Of interest," I echoed, eyes fixed firmly on the book. "Yes, I expect it will be."

Fergus, impervious to squeamishness of any kind, was watching the reptile's progress up the mudbank with interest.

"An alligator, you say. Still, it is much the same thing as a crocodile, is it not?"

"Yes," I said, shuddering despite the heat. I turned my back on the shore. I had met a crocodile at close range in the Indies, and wasn't anxious to improve my acquaintance with any of its relatives.

Fergus wiped sweat from his upper lip, dark eyes intent on the gruesome thing.

"Dr. Stern once told Milord and myself about the travels of a Frenchman named Sonnini, who visited Egypt and wrote much of the sights he had witnessed and the customs he was told of. He said that in that country, the crocodiles copulate upon the muddy banks of the rivers, the female being laid upon her back, and in that position, incapable of rising without the assistance of the male.''

"Oh, aye?" Ian was all ears.

"Indeed. He said that some men there, hurried on by the impulses of depravity, would take advantage of this forced situation of the female, and hunt away the male, whereupon they would take his place and enjoy the inhuman embrace of the reptile, which is said to be a most powerful charm for the procurement of rank and riches.''

Ian's mouth sagged open.

"You're no serious, man?" he demanded of Fergus, incredulous. He turned to Jamie. "Uncle?"

Jamie shrugged, amused.

"I should rather live poor but virtuous, myself." He cocked an eyebrow at me. "Besides, I think your auntie wouldna like it much if I was to forsake her embraces for a reptile's.''

The black man, listening to this from his position in the bow, shook his head and spoke without looking round.

"Any man what gone frig with an alligator to get rich, he's done earnt it, you ask me."

"I rather think you're right," I said, with a vivid memory of the Governor's charming, toothy smile. I glanced at Jamie, but he was no longer paying attention. His eyes were fixed upriver, intent on possibility, both book and alligator forgotten for the moment. At least he'd forgotten to be sick.

The tidal surge caught us a mile above Wilmington, allaying Ian's fears for our speed. The Cape Fear was a tidal river, whose daily surge carried up two-thirds of its length, nearly as far as Cross Creek.

I felt the river quicken under us, the boat rising an inch or two, then beginning slowly to pick up speed as the power of the incoming tide was funneled up the harbor and into the river's narrow channel. The slave sighed with relief and hoisted the dripping pole free of the water.

There would be no need for poling until the surge ran out, in five or six hours. Then we would either anchor for the night and catch the fresh surge of the next incoming tide, or use the sail for further progress, wind allowing. Poling, I was given to understand, was necessary only in case of sandbars or windless days.

A sense of peaceful somnolence settled over the craft. Fergus and Ian curled up in the bow to sleep, while Rollo kept guard on the roof above, tongue dripping as he panted, eyes half closed against the sun. The Captain and his hand—commonly addressed as "you, Troklus," but whose name was actually Eutroclus—disappeared into the tiny cabin, from which I could hear the musical sound of liquid being poured.

Jamie was in the cabin, too, having gone to fetch something from his mysterious crate. I hoped it was drinkable; even sitting still on the stern transom with my feet dangling in the water, and with the small breeze of movement stirring the hair on my neck, I could feel sweat forming wherever skin touched skin.

There were indistinct murmurs in the cabin, and laughter. Jamie came out and turned toward the stern, stepping delicately through the piles of goods like a Clydesdale stallion in a field of frogs, a large wooden box held in his arms.

He set this gently on my lap, shucked off his shoes and stockings, and sat down beside me, putting his feet in the water with a sigh of pleasure at the coolness.

"What's this?" I ran my hand curiously over the box.

"Oh, only a wee present." He didn't look at me, but the tips of his ears were pink. "Open it, hm?"

It was a heavy box, both wide and deep. Carved of a dense, fine-grained dark wood, it bore the marks of heavy use—nicks and dents that had seasoned but not impaired its polished beauty. It was hasped for a lock, but there was none; the lid rose easily on oiled brass hinges, and a whiff of camphor floated out, vaporous as a jinn.

The instruments gleamed under the smoky sun, bright despite a hazing of disuse. Each had its own pocket, carefully fitted and lined in green velvet.

A small, heavy-toothed saw; scissors, three scalpels—round-bladed, straight-bladed, scoop-bladed; the silver blade of a tongue depressor, a tenaculum . . .

"Jamie!" Delighted, I lifted out a short ebony rod, to the end of which was affixed a ball of worsted, wrapped in rather moth-eaten velvet. I'd seen one before, at Versailles; the eighteenth-century version of a reflex hammer. "Oh, Jamie! How wonderful!"

He wiggled his feet, pleased.

"Oh, ye like it?"

"I love it! Oh, look—there's more in the lid, under this flap—"

I stared for a moment at the disjointed tubes, screws, platforms
and mirrors, until my mind's eye shuffled them and presented me
with the neatly assembled vision. "A microscope!" I touched it
reverently. "My God, a microscope."

"There's more," he pointed out, eager to show me. "The front
opens and there are wee drawers inside."

There were—containing, among other things, a miniature balance and set of brass weights, a tile for rolling pills, and a stained
marble mortar, its pestle wrapped in cloth to prevent its being
cracked in transit. Inside the front, above the drawers, were row
upon row of small, corked bottles made of stone or glass.

"Oh, they're beautiful!" I said, handling the small scalpel with
reverence. The polished wood of the handle fit my hand as though
it had been made for me, the blade weighted to an exquisite balance. "Oh, Jamie, thank you!"

"Ye like them, then?" His ears had gone bright red with pleasure. "I thought they'd maybe do. I've no notion what they're
meant for, but I could see they were finely made."

I had no notion what some of the pieces were meant for, but all
of them were beautiful in themselves; made by or for a man who
loved his tools and what they did.

"Who did they belong to, I wonder?" I breathed heavily on the
rounded surface of a lenticular and brought it to a soft gleam with
a fold of my skirt.

"The woman who sold it to me didna ken; he left behind his
doctor's book, though, and I took that, as well—perhaps it will
give his name."

Lifting the top tray of instruments, he revealed another, shal-
lower tray, from which he drew out a fat square-bound book,
some eight inches wide, covered in scuffed black leather.

"I thought ye might be wanting a book, too, like the one ye
kept in France," he explained. "The one where ye kept the pictures and the notes of the people ye saw at L'Hôpital. He's written
a bit in this one, but there's a deal of blank pages left at the
back."

Perhaps a quarter of the book had been used; the pages were
covered with a closely written, fine black script, interspersed with
drawings that took my eye with their clinical familiarity: an ulcer-
ated toe, a shattered kneecap, the skin neatly peeled aside; the
grotesque swelling of advanced goiter, and a dissection of the calf
muscles, each neatly labeled.

I turned back to the inside cover; sure enough, his name was written on the first page, adorned with a small, gentlemanly flourish: *Dr. Daniel Rawlings, Esq.*

"What happened to Dr. Rawlings, I wonder? Did the woman who had the box say?"

Jamie nodded, his brow slightly creased.

"The Doctor lodged with her for a night. He said he'd come from Virginia, where his home was, bound upon some errand, and his case with him. He was looking for a man named Garver—she thought that was the name, at least. But that night after supper he went out—and never came back."

I stared at him.

"Never came back? Did she find out what happened to him?"

Jamie shook his head, batting away a small cloud of midges. The sun was sinking, painting the surface of the water gold and orange, and bugs were beginning to gather as the afternoon cooled into evening.

"No. She went to the sheriff, and to the justice, and the constable searched high and low—but there was nay sign of the man. They looked for a week, and then gave up. He had never told his landlady which town it was in Virginia, so they couldna trace him further."

"How very odd." I wiped a droplet of moisture off my chin. "When did the Doctor disappear?"

"A year past, she said." He looked at me, a little anxious. "Ye dinna mind? Using his things, I mean?"

"No." I closed the lid and stroked it gently, the dark wood warm and smooth under my fingers. "If it were me—I'd want someone to use them."

I remembered vividly the feel of my own doctor's bag—cordovan leather, with my initials stamped in gilt on the handle. Originally stamped in gilt on the handle, that is; they had long since worn off, the leather gone smooth and shiny, rich with handling. Frank had given me the bag when I graduated from medical school; I had given it to my friend Joe Abernathy, wanting it to be used by someone who would treasure it as I had.

He saw the shadow drift across my face—I saw the reflection of it darken his—but I took his hand and smiled as I squeezed it.

"It's a wonderful gift. However did you find it?"

He smiled then, in return. The sun blazed low, a brilliant orange ball glimpsed briefly through dark treetops.

"I'd seen the box when I went to the goldsmith's shop—it was the goldsmith's wife who'd kept it. Then I went back yesterday, meaning to buy ye a bit of jewelry—maybe a brooch—and whilst the goodwife was showing me the gauds, we happened to speak of this and that, and she told me of the Doctor, and—'' He shrugged.

"Why did you want to buy me jewelry?'' I looked at him, puzzled. The sale of the ruby had left us with a bit of money, but extravagance was not at all like him, and under the circumstances—

"Oh! To make up for sending all that money to Laoghaire? I didn't mind; I said I didn't.''

He had—with some reluctance—arranged to send the bulk of the proceeds from the sale of the stone to Scotland, in payment of a promise made to Laoghaire MacKenzie—damn her eyes—Fraser, whom he had married at his sister's persuasion while under the rather logical impression that if I was not dead, I was at least not coming back. My apparent resurrection from the dead had caused any amount of complications, Laoghaire not least among them.

"Aye, ye said so,'' he said, openly cynical.

"I meant it—more or less,'' I said, and laughed. "You couldn't very well let the beastly woman starve to death, appealing as the idea is.''

He smiled, faintly.

"No. I shouldna like to have that on my conscience; there's enough without. But that's not why I wished to buy ye a present.''

"Why, then?'' The box was heavy; a gracious, substantial, satisfying weight across my legs, its wood a delight under my hands. He turned his head to look full at me, then, his hair fire-struck with the setting sun, face dark in silhouette.

"Twenty-four years ago today, I married ye, Sassenach,'' he said softly. "I hope ye willna have cause yet to regret it.''

The river's edge was settled, rimmed with plantations from Wilmington to Cross Creek. Still, the banks were thickly forested, with only the occasional glimpse of fields where a break in the trees showed plantings, or every so often, a wooden dock, half-hidden in the foliage.

We proceeded slowly upriver, following the tidal surge so long as it lasted, tying up for the night when it ran out. We ate dinner by a small fire on shore, but slept on the boat, Eutroclus having casually mentioned the prevalence of water moccasins, who—he said—inhabited dens beneath the riverbank but were much inclined to come and warm their cold blood next to the bodies of unwary sleepers.

I awoke soon before dawn, stiff and sore from sleeping on boards, hearing the soft rush of a vessel passing on the river nearby, feeling the push of its wake against our hull. Jamie stirred in his sleep when he felt me move, turned over, and clasped me to his bosom.

I could feel his body curled behind mine, in its paradoxical morning state of sleep and arousal. He made a drowsy noise and moved against me in inquiry, his hand fumbling at the hem of my rumpled shift.

"Stop," I said under my breath, batting his hand away. "Remember where we are, for God's sake!"

I could hear the shouts and barking of Ian and Rollo, galumphing to and fro on the shore, and small stirrings in the cabin, featuring hawking and spitting noises, indicating the imminent emergence of Captain Freeman.

"Oh," said Jamie, coming to the surface of consciousness. "Oh, aye. A pity, that." He reached up, squeezed my breasts with both hands, and stretched his body with voluptuous slowness against me, giving me a detailed idea of what I was missing.

"Ah, well," he said, relaxing reluctantly, but not yet letting go. "*Foeda est in coitu,* um?"

"It what?"

" '*Foeda est in coitu et breois voluptas,* ' " he recited obligingly. " '*Et taedat Veneiis statim peractae.* Doing, a filthy pleasure is—and short. And done, we straight repent us of the sport.' "

I glanced down at the stained boards under us. "Well, perhaps 'filthy' isn't altogether the wrong word," I began, "but—"

"It's not the filthiness that troubles me, Sassenach," he interrupted, scowling at Ian, who was hanging over the side of the boat, shouting encouragement to Rollo as he swam. "It's the short."

He glanced at me, scowl changing to a look of approval as he took in my state of dishevelment. "I mean to take my time about it, aye?"

This classical start to the day seemed to have had some lasting influence on Jamie's mind. I could hear them at it as I sat in the afternoon sun, thumbing through Daniel Rawlings's casebook—at once entertained, enlightened, and appalled at the things recorded there.

I could hear Jamie's voice in the ordered rise and fall of ancient Greek. I had heard that bit before—a passage from the *Odyssey*. He paused, with an expectant rise.

"Ah . . ." said Ian.

"What comes next, Ian?"

"Er . . ."

"Once more," said Jamie, with a slight edge to his voice. "Pay attention, man. I'm no talkin' for the pleasure of hearin' myself, aye?" He began again, the elegant, formal verse warming to life as he spoke.

He might not take pleasure in hearing himself, but I did. I had no Greek myself, but the rise and fall of syllables in that soft, deep voice was as soothing as the lap of water against the hull.

Reluctantly accepting his nephew's continued presence, Jamie took his guardianship of Ian with due seriousness, and had been tutoring the lad as we traveled, seizing odd moments of leisure to teach—or attempt to teach—the lad the rudiments of Greek and Latin grammar, and to improve his mathematics and conversational French.

Fortunately, Ian had the same quick grasp of mathematical principles as his uncle; the side of the small cabin beside me was covered with elegant Euclidean proofs, carried out in burnt stick. When the subject turned to languages, though, they found less common ground.

Jamie was a natural polygogue; he acquired languages and dialects with no visible effort, picking up idioms as a dog picks up foxtails in a romp through the fields. In addition, he had been schooled in the Classics at the *Université* in Paris, and—while disagreeing now and then with some of the Roman philosophers —regarded both Homer and Virgil as personal friends.

Ian spoke the Gaelic and English with which he had been raised, and a sort of low French patois acquired from Fergus, and felt this quite sufficient to his needs. True, he had an impressive repertoire of swear words in six or seven other languages—acquired from exposure to a number of disreputable influences in the recent past, not least of these being his uncle—but he had no more than a vague apprehension of the mysteries of Latin conjugation.

Still less did he have an appreciation for the necessity of learning languages that to him were not only dead, but—he clearly thought—long decayed beyond any possibility of usefulness. Homer couldn't compete with the excitement of this new country, adventure reaching out from both shores with beckoning green hands.

Jamie finished his Greek passage, and with a sigh clearly audible to me where I sat, directed Ian to take out the Latin book he had borrowed from Governor Tryon's library. With no recitation to distract me, I returned to my perusal of Dr. Rawlings's casebook.

Like myself, the Doctor had plainly had some Latin, but preferred English for the bulk of his notes, dropping into Latin only for an occasional formal entry.

Bled Mr. Beddoes of a pt. Note distinct lessening of the bilious humor, his complexion much improved of the yellowness and pustules which have afflicted him. Administered black draught to assist purifying of the blood.

"Ass," I muttered—not for the first time. "Can't you see the man's got liver disease?" Probably a mild cirrhosis; Rawlings had noted a slight enlargement and hardening of the liver—though he attributed this to excessive production of bile. Most likely alcohol poisoning; the pustules on face and chest were characteristic of a nutritional deficiency that I saw commonly associated with excessive alcohol consumption—and God knew, *that* was epidemic.

Beddoes, if he were still alive—a prospect I considered doubtful—was likely drinking anything up to a quart of mixed spirit daily and hadn't so much as smelled a green vegetable in months. The pustules on whose disappearance Rawlings was congratulating himself had likely diminished because he had used turnip leaves as a coloring agent in his special recipe for "black draught."

Absorbed in my reading, I half heard Ian's stumbling rendition of Plautus's *Vertue* from the other side of the cabin, interrupted in every other line by Jamie's deeper voice, prompting and correcting.

"'*Virtus praemium est optimus . . .*'"

"*Optimum.*"

"'. . . *est optimum. Virtus omnibus rebus*' and . . . ah . . . and . . ."

"*Anteit.*"

"Thank ye, Uncle. *'Virtus omnibus rebus anteit . . . profectus'?''*

"*Profecto.''*

"Oh, aye, *profecto*. Um . . . *'Virtus'?''*

"*Libertas. 'Libertas salus vita res et parentes, patria et prognati . . .'* d'ye recall what is meant by *'vita,'* Ian?"

"Life," came Ian's voice, seizing gratefully on this buoyant object in a flounderous sea.

"Aye, that's good, but it's more than life. In Latin, it means not only being alive but it's also a man's substance, what he's made of. See, then it goes on, *' . . . libertas salus vita res et parentes, patria et prognati tutantur, servantur; virtus omnia in sese habet, omnia adsunt bona quem penest virtus.'* Now, what is he sayin' there, d'ye think?"

"Ah . . . virtue is a good thing?" Ian ventured.

There was a momentary silence, during which I could almost hear Jamie's blood pressure rising. A hiss of indrawn breath, then, as he thought better of whatever he had been about to say, a long-suffering exhalation.

"Mmphm. Look ye, Ian. *'Tutantur, servantur.'* What does he mean by using those two together, instead of putting it as . . .''

My attention faded, drawn back to the book, wherein Dr. Rawlings now gave account of a duel and its consequences.

May 15. Was called from my bed at dawn to attend a gentleman staying at the Red Dog. Found him in sad case, with a wound to his hand, occasioned by the misfire of a pistol, the thumb and index fingers of the hand being blown off altogether by the explosion, the middle finger badly mangled and two-thirds of the hand so lacerated that it was scarce recognizable as a human appendage.

Determining that only prompt amputation would serve, I sent for the landlord and requested a pannikin of brandy, linen for bandages, and the help of two strong men. These being rapidly provided and the patient suitably restrained, I proceeded to take the hand—it was the right, to the misfortune of the patient—off just above the wrist. Successfully ligated two arteries, but the anterior interosseus escaped me, being retracted into the flesh after I sawed through the bones. Was forced to loosen the tourniquet in order to find it, so bleeding was considerable—a fortunate accident, as the copious outpouring of blood rendered the patient

*insensible and thus put an end for the moment to his agony, as
well as to his struggles, which were greatly hampering my work.*

*The amputation being successfully concluded, the gentleman
was put to bed, but I stayed near at hand, lest he regain consciousness abruptly and in random movement do hurt to my stitching.*

This fascinating narrative was interrupted by a sudden outburst
from Jamie, who had evidently reached the end of his patience.

"Ian, your Latin would disgrace a dog! And as for the rest, ye
havena got enough understanding of Greek to tell the difference
between water and wine!"

"If they're drinkin' it, it's not water," Ian muttered, sounding
rebellious.

I closed the book and got hastily to my feet. It sounded rather
as though the services of a referee might shortly be called for. Ian
was making small Scottish noises of discontent as I rounded the
cabin.

"Aye, mphm, but I dinna care so much—"

"Aye, ye don't care! That's the true pity of it—that ye havena
the grace even to feel shame for your ignorance!"

There was a charged silence after this, broken only by the soft
splash of Troklus's pole in the bow. I peeked around the corner,
to see Jamie glaring at his nephew, who looked abashed. Ian
glanced at me, coughed and cleared his throat.

"Well, I'll tell ye, Uncle Jamie, if I thought shame would help,
I wouldna scruple to blush."

He looked so apologetically hangdog that I couldn't help laughing. Jamie turned, hearing me, and his scowl faded slightly.

"Ye're not a bit of help, Sassenach," he said. "You've the
Latin, have ye not? Being a physician, ye must. Perhaps I should
leave his Latin schooling to you, aye?"

I shook my head. While it was more or less true that I could
read Latin—badly and laboriously—I didn't fancy trying to cram
the ragbag remnants of my education into Ian's head.

"All I remember is *Arma virumque cano*." I glanced at Ian and
translated, grinning. "My arm got bit off by a dog."

Ian burst into giggles, and Jamie gave me a look of profound
disillusion.

He sighed and ran a hand through his hair. While Jamie and Ian
didn't resemble each other in any physical respect beyond height,
both had thick hair and the habit of running a hand through it

when agitated or thoughtful. It looked to have been a stressful lesson—both of them looked as though they'd been pulled backward through a hedgerow.

Jamie smiled wryly at me, then turned back to Ian, shaking his head.

"Ah, well. I'm sorry to bark at ye, Ian, truly. But ye've a fine mind, and I shouldna like to see ye waste it. God, man, at your age, I was in Paris, already starting in to study at the *Université*!"

Ian stood looking down into the water that swirled past the side of the ship in smooth brown riffles. His hands rested on the rail; big hands, broad-backed and browned by the sun.

"Aye," he said. "And at my age, my own father was in France, too. Fighting."

I was a bit startled to hear this. I had known that the elder Ian had soldiered in France for a time, but not that he had gone so early for a soldier—nor stayed so long. Young Ian was just fifteen. The elder Ian had served as a foreign mercenary from that age, then, until the age of twenty-two; when a cannon blast had left him with a leg so badly shattered by grapeshot that it had been amputated just below the knee—and he had come home for good.

Jamie looked at his nephew for a moment, frowning slightly. Then he came to stand beside Ian, leaning backward, hands on the rail to balance himself.

"I ken that, aye?" Jamie said quietly. "For I followed him, four years later, when I was outlawed."

Ian looked up at that, startled.

"Ye were together there in France?"

There was a slight breeze caused by our movement, but it was still a hot day. Perhaps the temperature decided him that it was better to let the subject of higher learning drop for a moment, for Jamie nodded, lifting the thick tail of his hair to cool his neck.

"In Flanders. For more than a year, before Ian was wounded and sent home. We fought wi' a regiment of Scots mercenaries then—under Fergus mac Leodhas."

Ian's eyes were alight with interest.

"Is that where Fergus—our Fergus—got his name, then?"

His uncle smiled.

"Aye, I named him for mac Leodhas; a bonny man, and a great soldier, forbye. He thought weel o' Ian. Did your Da never speak to you of him?"

Ian shook his head, his brow slightly clouded.

"He's never said a thing to me. I—I kent he'd lost his leg

fighting in France—Mam told me that, when I asked—but he wouldna say a word about it, himself.''

With Dr. Rawlings's description of amputation vivid in my mind, I thought it likely that the elder Ian hadn't wanted to recall the occasion.

Jamie shrugged, plucking the sweat-damp shirt away from his chest.

"Aye, well. I suppose he meant to put that time behind him, once he'd come home and settled at Lallybroch. And then . . ." He hesitated, but Ian was insistent.

"And then what, Uncle Jamie?"

Jamie glanced at his nephew, and one side of his mouth curled up.

"Well, I think he didna want to tell too many tales of war and fighting, lest you lads get thinking on it and set yourselves to go for soldiers, too. He and your mother will ha' wanted better for you, aye?"

I thought the elder Ian had been wise; it was clear from the look on his face that the younger Ian couldn't think of a much more exciting prospect than war and fighting.

"That will ha' been my Mam's doing," Ian said, with an air of disgust. "She'd have me wrapped in wool and tied to her apron strings, did I let her."

Jamie grinned.

"Oh, let her, is it? And d'ye think she'd wrap ye in wool and smother ye wi' kisses if ye were home this minute?"

Ian dropped the pose of disdain.

"Well, no," he admitted. "I think she'd skelp me raw."

Jamie laughed.

"Ye know a bit about women, Ian, if not so much as ye think."

Ian glanced skeptically from his uncle to me, and back.

"And you'll ken all about them, I suppose, Uncle?"

I raised one eyebrow, inviting an answer to this, but Jamie merely laughed.

"It's a wise man who kens the limits of his knowledge, Ian." He bent and kissed my damp forehead, then turned back to his nephew, adding, "Though I could wish your own limits went a bit further."

Ian shrugged, looking bored.

"I dinna mean to set up for a gentleman," he said. "After all, Young Jamie and Michael dinna read Greek; they do well enough!"

Jamie rubbed his nose, considering his nephew thoughtfully.

"Young Jamie has Lallybroch. And wee Michael does well wi' Jared in Paris. They'll be settled. We did as best we might for the two o' them, but there was precious little money to pay for travel or schooling when they came to manhood. There wasna much choice for them, aye?"

He pushed himself off the rail and stood upright.

"But your parents dinna want that for you, Ian, if better might be managed. They'd have ye grow to be a man of learning and influence; *duine uasal,* perhaps." It was a Gaelic expression I had heard before, literally "a man of worth." It was the term for tacksmen and lairds, the men of property and followers who ranked only below chieftains in the Highland clans.

Such a man as Jamie himself had been, before the Rising. But not now.

"Mmphm. And did ye do as your parents wanted for ye, then, Uncle Jamie?" Ian looked blandly at his uncle, with only a wary twitch of the eye to show he knew he was treading on shaky ground. Jamie had been meant to be *duine uasal,* indeed; Lallybroch had been his by right. It was only in an effort to save the property from confiscation by the Crown that he had made it over legally to Young Jamie, instead.

Jamie stared at him for a moment, then rubbed a knuckle across his upper lip before replying.

"I did say ye'd a fine mind, no?" he answered dryly. "Though since ye ask . . . I was raised to do two things, Ian. To mind my land and people, and to care for my family. I've done those two things, as best I might—and I shall go on doing them as best I can."

Young Ian had the grace to look abashed at this.

"Aye, well, I didna mean . . ." he mumbled, looking at his feet.

"Dinna fash, laddie," Jamie interrupted, clapping him on the shoulder. He grinned wryly at his nephew. "Ye'll amount to something for your mother's sake—if it kills us both. And now I think it will be my turn at the pole."

He glanced forward, to where Troklus's shoulders gleamed like oily copper, snake-muscled with long labor. Jamie untied his breeches—unlike the other men, he would not take off his shirt for poling, but stripped his breeks for coolness and worked with his shirt knotted between his thighs, in the Highland style—and nodded to Ian.

''You think about it, laddie. Youngest son or no, your life's not meant to be wasted.''

He smiled at me then, with a sudden heart-stopping brilliance, and handed me his shed breeks. Then, still holding my hand in his, he stood upright and, hand over heart, declaimed,

> *''Amo, amas, I love a lass,*
> *As cedar tall and slender;*
> *Sweet cowslip's grace*
> *Is her nominative case,*
> *And she's o' the feminine gender.''*

He nodded graciously to Ian, who had dissolved in giggles, and lifted my hand to his lips, blue eyes aslant with mischief.

> *''Can I decline a nymph so divine?*
> *Her voice like a flute is dulcis;*
> *Her oculus bright, her manus white*
> *And soft, when I tacto, her pulse is.*
>
> *O how bella, my puella*
> *I'll kiss in secula seculorum;*
> *If I've luck, sir, she's my uxor,*
> *O dies benedictorum.''*

He made a courtly leg to me, blinked solemnly in his version of a wink, and strode off in his shirt.

9

Two-thirds of a Ghost

The surface of the river gleamed like oil, the water moving gently past without a ripple. There was a single lantern hung from the starboard bow; sitting on a low stool perched on the forward deck, I could see the light below, not so much reflected in the water as trapped under it, moving slowly side by side with the boat.

The moon was a faint sickle, making its feeble sweep through the treetops. Beyond the thick trees that lined the river, the ground fell away in broad sweeps of darkness, over the rice plantations and tobacco fields. The heat of the day was sucked down into the earth, glowing with unseen energy beneath the surface of the soil, the rich, fertile flatlands simmering in black heat behind the screen of pines and sweetgum trees, working the alchemy of water and trapped sun.

To move at all was to break a sweat. The air was tangible, each tiny ripple of warmth a caress against my face and arms.

There was a soft rustle in the dark behind me, and I reached up a hand, not turning to look. Jamie's big hand closed gently over mine, squeezed and let go. Even that brief touch left my fingers damp with perspiration.

He eased himself down next to me with a sigh, plucking at the collar of his shirt.

"I dinna think I've breathed air since we left Georgia," he said. "Every time I take a breath, I think I'll maybe drown."

I laughed, feeling a trickle of sweat snake down between my breasts.

"It will be cooler in Cross Creek; everyone says so." I took a deep breath myself, just to prove I could. "Doesn't it smell wonderful, though?" The darkness released all the pungent green scents of the trees and plants along the water's edge, mingling with the damp mud of the riverbank and the scent of sun-warmed wood from the deck of the boat.

''Ye'd have made a good dog, Sassenach.'' He leaned back against the wall of the cabin with a sigh. ''It's no wonder yon beast admires ye so.''

The click of toenails on deckboards announced the arrival of Rollo, who advanced cautiously toward the rail, stopped a careful foot short of it, and lowered himself gingerly to the deck. He laid his nose on his paws and sighed deeply. Rollo disapproved almost as strongly of boats as Jamie did.

''Hullo there,'' I said. I extended a hand for him to sniff, and he politely condescended to let me scratch his ears. ''And where's your master, eh?''

''In the cabin, bein' taught new ways to cheat at cards,'' Jamie said wryly. ''God kens best what will happen to the lad; if he's not shot or knocked on the head in some tavern, he'll likely come home wi' an ostrich he's won at faro next.''

''Surely they haven't either ostriches or faro games up in the mountains? If there aren't any towns to speak of, surely there aren't many taverns, either.''

''Well, I shouldna think so,'' he admitted. ''But if a man's bound to go to the devil, he'll find a way to do it, no matter where ye set him down.''

''I'm sure Ian isn't going to the devil,'' I replied soothingly. ''He's a fine boy.''

''He's a man,'' Jamie corrected. He cocked an ear toward the cabin, where I could hear muffled laughter and the occasional comfortable obscenity. ''A damn young one, though, and fat-heided with it.'' He looked at me, a rueful smile visible in the lantern light.

''If he were a wee lad yet, I could keep some rein on him. As it is—'' He shrugged. ''He's old enough to mind his own business, and he'll not thank me for sticking my nose in.''

''He always listens to you,'' I protested.

''Mmphm. Wait till I tell him something he doesna want to hear.'' He leaned his head against the wall, closing his eyes. Sweat gleamed across the high cheekbones, and a small trickle ran down the side of his neck.

I put out a finger and delicately flicked the tiny drop away, before it further dampened his shirt.

''You've been telling him for two months that he has to go home to Scotland; he doesn't want to hear that, I don't think.''

Jamie opened one eye and surveyed me cynically.

"Is he in Scotland?"

"Well . . ."

"Mmphm," he said, and closed the eye again.

I sat quietly for a bit, blotting the perspiration off my face with a fold of my skirt. The river had narrowed here; the near bank was no more than ten feet away. I caught a rustle of movement among the shrubs, and a pair of eyes gleamed briefly red with reflected light from our lantern.

Rollo lifted his head with a sudden low *Woof,* ears pricked to attention. Jamie opened his eyes and glanced at the bank, then sat up abruptly.

"Christ! That's the biggest rat I've ever seen!"

I laughed.

"It's not a rat; it's a possum. See the babies on her back?"

Jamie and Rollo regarded the possum with identical looks of calculation, assessing its plumpness and possible speed. Four small possums stared solemnly back, pointed noses twitching over their mother's humped, indifferent back. Obviously thinking the boat no threat, the mother possum finished lapping water, turned, and trundled slowly into the brush, the tip of her naked thick pink tail disappearing as the lantern light faded.

The two hunters let out identical sighs, and relaxed again.

"Myers did say as they're fine eating," Jamie remarked wistfully. With a small sigh of my own, I groped in the pocket of my gown and handed him a cloth bag.

"What's this?" He peered interestedly into the bag, then poured the small, lumpy brown objects out into the palm of his hand.

"Roasted peanuts," I said. "They grow underground hereabouts. I found a farmer selling them for hogfood, and had the inn-wife roast some for me. You take off the shells before you eat them." I grinned at him, enjoying the novel sensation of for once knowing more about our surroundings than he did.

He gave me a mildly dirty look, and crushed a shell between thumb and forefinger, yielding three nuts.

"I'm ignorant, Sassenach," he said. "Not a fool. There's a difference, aye?" He put a peanut in his mouth and bit down gingerly. His skeptical look changed to one of pleased surprise, and he chewed with increasing enthusiasm, tossing the other nuts into his mouth.

"Like them?" I smiled, enjoying his pleasure. "I'll make you peanut butter for your bread, once we're settled and I have my new mortar unpacked.''

He smiled back and swallowed before cracking another nut.

"I will say that if it's a swampish place, at least it's fine soil. I've never seen so many things grow so easily.''

He tossed another nut into his mouth.

"I have been thinking, Sassenach," he said, looking down into the palm of his hand. "What would ye think of maybe settling here?''

The question wasn't entirely unexpected. I had seen him eyeing the black fields and lush crops with a farmer's glittering eye, and caught his wistful expression when he admired the Governor's horses.

We couldn't go back to Scotland immediately, in any case. Young Ian, yes, but not Jamie or me, owing to certain complications—not the least of these being a complication by the name of Laoghaire MacKenzie.

"I don't know," I said slowly. "Indians and wild animals quite aside—''

"Och, well," he interrupted, mildly embarrassed. "Myers told me they were no difficulty at all, and ye keep clear of the mountains.''

I forbore from pointing out that the Governor's offer would take us into the precincts of precisely those mountains.

"Yes, but you do remember what I told you, don't you? About the Revolution? This is 1767, and you heard the conversation at the Governor's table. Nine years, Jamie, and all hell breaks loose.'' We had both lived through war, and neither of us took the thought lightly. I laid a hand on his arm, forcing him to look at me.

"I was right, you know—before.'' I had known what would happen at Culloden; had told him the fate of Charles Stuart and his men. And neither my knowing nor his had been enough to save us. Twenty aching years of separation, and the ghost of a daughter he would never see lay behind that knowing.

He nodded slowly, and lifted a hand to touch my cheek. The soft glow of the small lantern overhead attracted clouds of tiny gnats; they swirled suddenly, disturbed by his movement.

"Aye, ye were," he said softly. "But then—we thought we must change things. Or try, at the least. But here—'' He turned, waving an arm at the vast land that lay unseen beyond the trees.

"I shouldna think it my business," he said simply. "Either to help or to hinder much."

I waved the gnats away from my face.

"It might *be* our business, if we lived here."

He rubbed a finger below his lower lip, thinking. His beard was sprouting, a glimmer of red stubble sparked with silver in the lantern light. He was a big man, handsome and strong in the prime of his life, but no longer a young one, and I realized that with sudden gratitude.

Highland men were bred to fight; Highland boys became men when they could lift their swords and go to battle. Jamie had never been reckless, but he had been a warrior and a soldier most of his life. As a young man in his twenties, nothing could have kept him from a fight, whether it was his own or not. Now, in his forties, sense might temper passion—or at least I hoped so.

And it was true; beyond this aunt whom he didn't know, he had no family here, no ties that might compel involvement. Perhaps, knowing what was coming, we might contrive to stay clear of the worst?

"It's a verra big place, Sassenach." He looked out over the prow of the boat, into the vast black sweep of invisible land. "Only since we left Georgia, we have traveled farther than the whole length of Scotland and England both."

"That's true," I admitted. In Scotland, even among the high crags of the Highlands, there had been no way to escape the ravages of war. Not so here; should we seek our place carefully, we might indeed escape the roving eye of Mars.

He tilted his head to one side, smiling up at me.

"I could see ye as a planter's lady, Sassenach. If the Governor will find me a buyer for the other stones, then I shall have enough, I think, to send Laoghaire all the money I promised her, and still have enough over to buy a good place—one where we might prosper."

He took my right hand in his, his thumb gently stroking my silver wedding ring.

"Perhaps one day I shall deck ye in laces and jewels," he said softly. "I havena been able to give ye much, ever, save a wee silver ring, and my mother's pearls."

"You've given me a lot more than that," I said. I wrapped my fingers around his thumb and squeezed. "Brianna, for one."

He smiled faintly, looking down at the deck.

"Aye, that's true. She's maybe the real reason—for staying, I mean."

I pulled him toward me, and he rested his head against my knee.

"This is her place, no?" he said quietly. He lifted a hand, gesturing toward the river, the trees and the sky. "She will be born here, she'll live here."

"That's right," I said softly. I stroked his hair, smoothing the thick strands that were so much like Brianna's. "This will be her country." Hers, in a way it could never be mine or his, no matter how long we might live here.

He nodded, beard rasping gently against my skirt.

"I dinna wish to fight, or have ye ever in danger, Sassenach, but if there is a bit I can do . . . to build, maybe, to make it safe, and a good land for her . . ." He shrugged. "It would please me," he finished softly.

We sat silently for a bit, close together, watching the dull shine of the water and the slow progress of the sunken lantern.

"I left the pearls for her," I said at last. "That seemed right; they were an heirloom, after all." I drew my ringed hand, curved, across his lips. "And the ring is all I need."

He took both my hands in his, then, and kissed them—the left, which still bore the gold ring of my marriage to Frank, and then the right, with his own silver ring.

"Da mi basia mille," he whispered, smiling. Give me a thousand kisses. It was the inscription inside my ring, a brief quotation from a love song by Catullus. I bent and gave him one back.

"Dein mille altera," I said. Then a thousand more.

It was near midnight when we tied up near a brushy grove to rest. The weather had changed; still hot and muggy, now the air held the hint of thunder, and the undergrowth stirred with small movements—random air currents, or the scurryings of tiny night things hastening for home before the storm.

We were nearly at the end of the tidal surge; from here it would be a matter of sail and pole, and Captain Freeman had hopes of catching a good breeze on the wings of a storm. It would pay us to rest while we could. I curled into our nest on the stern, but was unable to fall asleep at once, late as it was.

By the Captain's estimation, we might make Cross Creek by evening tomorrow—certainly by the day after. I was surprised to realize how eagerly I was looking forward to our arrival; two months of living hand-to-mouth on the road had given me an urgent longing for some haven, no matter how temporary.

Familiar as I was with Highland notions of hospitality and kinship, I had no fears regarding our welcome. Jamie plainly did not consider the fact that he hadn't met this particular aunt in forty-odd years to be any bar to our cordial reception, and I was quite sure he was right. At the same time, I couldn't help entertaining considerable curiosity about Jocasta Cameron.

There had been five MacKenzie siblings, the children of old Red Jacob, who had built Castle Leoch. Jamie's mother, Ellen, had been the eldest, Jocasta the youngest. Janet, the other sister, had died, like Ellen, well before I met Jamie, but I had known the two brothers, Colum and Dougal, quite well indeed, and from that knowledge, couldn't help speculating as to what this last Mac-Kenzie of Leoch might be like.

Tall, I thought, with a glance at Jamie, curled up peacefully on the deck beside me. Tall, and maybe red-haired. They were all tall —even Colum, victim of a crippling degenerative disease, had been tall to begin with—fair-skinned Vikings, the lot of them, with a ruddy blaze to their coloring that shimmered from Jamie's fiery red through his uncle Dougal's deep russet. Only Colum had been truly dark.

Remembering Colum and Dougal, I felt a sudden stir of unease. Colum had died before Culloden, killed by his disease. Dougal had died on the eve of the battle—killed by Jamie. It had been a matter of self-defense—*my* self, in fact—and only one of so many deaths in that bloody April. Still, I did wonder whether Jamie had given any thought as to what he might say, when the greetings were past at River Run, and the casual family chat got round to "Oh, and when did you last see So-and-so?"

Jamie sighed and stretched in his sleep. He could—and did—sleep well on any surface, accustomed as he had been to sleeping in conditions that ranged from wet heather to musty caves to the cold stone floors of prison cells. I supposed the wooden decking under us must be thoroughly comfortable by contrast.

I was neither so elastic nor so hardened, myself, but gradually weariness overwhelmed me, and even the prick of curiosity about the future was unable to keep me awake.

I woke to confusion. It was still dark, and there was noise all around, shouting and barking, and the deck beneath me trembled with the vibration of stamping feet. I jerked upright, half thinking myself aboard a sailing ship, convinced that we had been boarded by pirates.

Then my mind cleared, along with my foggy vision, and I discovered that we *had* been boarded by pirates. Strange voices shouted oaths and orders, and booted feet were heavy on the deck. Jamie was gone.

I scrabbled onto my hands and feet, taking no heed for clothes or anything else. It was near dawn; the sky was dark, but light enough that the cabin showed as a darker blotch against it. As I struggled upright, clinging to the cabin roof for support, I was nearly knocked flat by flying bodies hurling themselves across it.

There was a confused blur of fur and white faces, a shout and a shot and a terrible thud, and Ian was crouching ashen on the deck, over Rollo's heaving form. A strange man, hatless and disheveled, pushed himself to his feet.

"Damn! He nearly got me!" Unhinged by the near miss, the robber's hand trembled as he fumbled with the spare pistol at his belt. He pointed it at the dog, face drawing down in an ugly squint.

"Take that, arse-bite!"

A taller man appeared from nowhere, his hand knocking down the pistol before the flint could strike.

"Don't waste the shot, fool." He gestured to Troklus and Captain Freeman—the latter volubly incensed—being herded toward me. "How d'you mean to hold them with an empty gun?"

The shorter man cast an evil look at Rollo, but swung his pistol to bear on Freeman's midriff instead.

Rollo was making an odd noise, a low growling mixed with whimpers of pain, and I could see a wet, dark stain on the boards under his twitching body. Ian bent low over him, hands stroking his head helplessly. He looked up, and tears shone wet on his cheeks.

"Help me, Auntie," he said. "Please help!"

I moved impulsively, and the tall man stepped forward, thrusting out an arm to stop me.

"I want to help the dog," I said.

"What?" said the short robber, in tones of outrage.

The tall man was masked—they all were, I realized, my eyes adjusting to the growing half-light. How many were there? It was impossible to tell under the mask, but I had the distinct impression that the tall man was smiling. He didn't answer, but gave a short jerk of his pistol, giving me leave.

"Hullo, old boy," I said under my breath, dropping to my knees next to the dog. "Don't bite, there's a good doggie. Where is he hurt, Ian, do you know?"

Ian shook his head, sniffing back the tears.

"It's under him; I can't get him to turn over."

I wasn't about to try to heave the dog's huge carcass over either. I felt quickly for a pulse in the neck, but my fingers sank into Rollo's thick ruff, prodding uselessly. Seized by inspiration, I instead picked up a front leg and felt up its length, getting my fingers into the hollow where the leg met the body.

Sure enough, there it was; a steady pulse, throbbing reassuringly under my fingers. I began by habit to count, but quickly abandoned the effort, as I had no idea what a dog's normal pulse rate should be. It *was* steady, though; no fluttering, no arrhythmia, no weakness. That was a very good sign.

Another was that Rollo hadn't lost consciousness; the great leg I held tucked under my elbow had the tension of coiled spring, not the limp dangle of shock. The dog made a long, high-pitched noise, halfway between a whine and a howl, and began to scrabble with his claws, pulling his leg out of my grasp in an effort to right himself.

"I don't think it's very bad, Ian," I said in relief. "Look, he's turning over."

Rollo stood up, swaying. He shook his head violently, shaggy coat twitching from head to tail, and a shower of blood drops flew over the deck with a sound like pattering rain. The big yellow eyes fixed on the short man with a look that was clear to the meanest intelligence.

"Here! You stop him, or I swear I'll shoot him dead!" Panic and sincerity rang out in the robber's voice, as the muzzle of the pistol drifted uncertainly between the little group of prisoners and Rollo's lip-curled snarl.

Ian, who had been frantically undoing his shirt, whipped the garment off and over Rollo's head, temporarily blinding the dog, who shook his head madly, making growling noises inside the restraint. Blood stained the yellow linen—I could see now, though, that it came from a shallow gash in the dog's shoulder; evidently, the bullet had only grazed him.

Ian hung on grimly, forcing Rollo back on his haunches, muttering orders to the dog's swaddled head.

"How many aboard?" The taller man's sharp eyes flicked toward Captain Freeman, whose mouth was pressed so tightly together, it looked no more than a purse seam in the gray fur of his face, then toward me.

I knew him; knew the voice. The knowledge must have shown in my face, for he paused for a moment, then jerked his head and let the masking kerchief fall from his face.

"How many?" Stephen Bonnet asked again.

"Six," I said. There was no reason not to answer; I could see Fergus on the shore, hands raised as a third pirate herded him at gunpoint toward the boat; Jamie had materialized out of the darkness beside me, looking grim.

"Mr. Fraser," Bonnet said pleasantly, at sight of him. "A pleasure to be renewing our acquaintance. But did ye not have another companion, sir? The one-armed gentleman?"

"Not here," Jamie replied shortly.

"I'll have a look," the short robber muttered, turning, but Bonnet stopped him with a gesture.

"Ah, now, and would ye be doubting the word of a gentleman like Mr. Fraser? No, you'll be after guarding these fine folk here, Roberts; I'll be having the look around." With a nod to his companion, he vanished.

Looking after Rollo had distracted me momentarily from the commotion going on elsewhere on the boat. Sounds of breakage came from inside the cabin, and I leapt to my feet, reminded of my medicine box.

"Here! Where you going? Stop! I'll shoot!" The robber's voice held a desperate note, but an uncertain one, as well. I didn't stop to look at him, but dived into the cabin, cannoning into a fourth robber, who was indeed rummaging through my medicine chest.

I staggered back from the collision, then clutched his arm, with a cry of outrage. He had been carelessly opening boxes and bottles, shaking out the contents, and tossing them on the floor; a litter of bottles, many of them broken, lay amid the scattered remnants of Dr. Rawlings's selection of medicines.

"Don't you *dare* touch those!" I said, and snatching the nearest vial from the chest, I popped out the cork and flung the contents in his face.

Like most of Rawlings's mixtures, it contained a high proportion of alcohol. He gasped as the liquid hit, and reeled backward, eyes streaming.

I pressed my advantage by seizing a stone ale bottle from the wreckage and hitting him on the head with it. It hit with a satisfying *thunk!* but I hadn't hit him quite hard enough; he staggered but stayed upright, lurching as he grabbed at me.

I drew back my arm for another swing, but my wrist was seized from behind by a grip like iron.

"Beggin' your pardon, Mrs. Fraser dear," said a polite, familiar Irish voice. "But I really cannot allow ye to crack his head. It's not very ornamental, sure, but he needs it to hold up his hat."

"Frigging bitch! She *hit* me!" The man I had hit was clutching his head, his features screwed up in pain.

Bonnet hauled me out onto the deck, my arm twisted painfully behind my back. It was nearly light by now; the river glowed like flat silver. I stared hard at our assailants; I meant to know them again, if I saw them, masks or no masks.

Unfortunately, the improved light allowed the robbers better vision as well. The man I had hit, who seemed to be bearing a distinct grudge, seized my hand and wrenched at my ring.

"Here, let's have that!"

I yanked my hand away and made to slap him, but was stopped by a meaningful cough from Bonnet, who had stepped close to Ian and was holding his pistol an inch from the boy's left ear.

"Best hand them over, Mrs. Fraser," he said politely. "I fear Mr. Roberts requires some compensation for the damage ye've caused him."

I twisted my gold ring off, hands trembling both with fear and rage. The silver one was harder; it stuck on my knuckle as though reluctant to part from me. Both rings were damp and slippery with sweat, the metal warmer than my suddenly chilled fingers.

"Give 'em up." The man poked me roughly in the shoulder, then turned up a broad, grubby palm for the rings. I reached toward him, reluctantly, rings cupped in my hand—and then, with an impulse I didn't stop to examine, clapped my hand to my mouth instead.

My head hit the cabin wall with a thud as the man knocked me backward. His callused fingers jabbed my cheeks and poked into my mouth, probing roughly in search of the rings. I twisted and gulped hard, mouth filling with saliva and a silver taste that might have been either metal or blood.

I bit down and he jerked back with a cry; one ring must have flown out of my mouth, for I heard a faint, metallic *ping* somewhere, and then I gagged and choked, the second ring sliding into my gullet, hard and round.

"Bitch! I'll slit your friggin' throat! You'll go to hell without your rings, you cheating whore!'' I saw the man's face, contorted in rage, and the sudden glitter of a knife blade drawn. Then something hit me hard and knocked me over, and I found myself crushed to the deck, flattened under Jamie's body.

I was too stunned to move, though I couldn't have moved in any case; Jamie's chest was pressing on the back of my head, squashing my face into the deck. There was a lot of shouting and confusion, muffled by the folds of damp linen around my head. There was a soft *thunk!* and I felt Jamie jerk and grunt.

Oh, God, they've stabbed him! I thought, in an agony of terror. Another *thump* and a louder grunt, though, indicated only a kick in the ribs. Jamie didn't move; just pressed himself harder against the deck, flattening me like the filling of a sandwich.

''Leave off! Roberts! I said leave him!'' Bonnet's voice rang out in tones of authority, sharp enough to penetrate the muffling cloth.

''But she—'' Roberts began, but his querulous whine was stopped abruptly with a sharp, meaty smack.

''Raise yourself, Mr. Fraser. Your wife is safe—not that she deserves to be.'' Bonnet's husky baritone held mingled tones of amusement and irritation.

Jamie's weight lifted slowly off me, and I sat up, feeling dizzy and mildly sick from the blow on the head. Stephen Bonnet stood looking down at me, examining me with faint distaste, as though I were a mangy deerhide he'd been offered for sale. Next to him, Roberts glared malevolently, dabbing at a smear of blood at his hairline.

Bonnet blinked finally, and switched his gaze to Jamie, who had regained his feet.

''A foolish woman,'' Bonnet said dispassionately, ''but I suppose you don't mind that.'' He nodded, a faint smile showing. ''I am obliged for the opportunity to repay my debt to ye, sir. A life for a life, as the Good Book says.''

''Repay us?'' Ian said angrily. ''After what we've done for ye, ye'll rob and spoil us, lay violent hands upon my aunt and my dog, and then ye'll ha' the gall to speak of repayment?''

Bonnet's pale eyes fixed on Ian's face; they were green, the color of peeled grapes. He had a deep dimple in one cheek, as though God had pressed a thumb there in his making, but the eyes were cold as river water at dawn.

''Why, were ye never after learning your Scripture, lad?'' Bonnet shook his head reprovingly, with a click of the tongue. ''A virtuous woman is prized above rubies; her price is greater than pearls.''

He opened his hand, still smiling, and the lantern light glittered off three gems: emerald, sapphire, and the dark fire of a black diamond.

''I'm sure Mr. Fraser would agree, would ye not, sir?'' He slipped the hand into his coat, then brought it out empty.

''And after all,'' he said, cold eyes swiveling once more toward Ian, ''there are repayments of different kinds.'' He smiled, not very pleasantly. ''Though I should not suppose you can be old enough to know that yet. Be glad I've no mind to give ye a lesson.''

He turned away, beckoning to his comrades.

''We have what we came for,'' he said abruptly. ''Come.'' He stepped up onto the rail and jumped, landing with a grunt on the muddy riverbank. His henchmen followed, Roberts casting an evil look at me before splashing awkwardly into the shallows and ashore.

The four men disappeared at once into the brush, and I heard the high-pitched greeting whinny of a horse, somewhere in the darkness. Aboard, all was silence.

The sky was the color of charcoal, and thunder grumbled faintly in the distance, sheet lightning flickering just above the far horizon.

''Bastards.''

Captain Freeman spat in valediction over the side, and turned to his mate.

''Fetch the poles, you, Troklus,'' he said, and shambled toward the tiller, hitching his breeks upward as he went.

Slowly, the others stirred and came to life. Fergus, with a glance at Jamie, lit the lantern and then disappeared into the cabin, where I heard him beginning to set things to rights. Ian sat huddled on the deck, his dark head bent over Rollo as he dabbed at the dog's neck with his wadded shirt.

I didn't want to look at Jamie. I rolled onto my hands and knees and crawled slowly over to Young Ian. Rollo watched me, yellow eyes wary, but made no objection to my presence.

''How is he?'' I said, rather hoarsely. I could feel the ring in my throat, an uncomfortable obstruction, and swallowed heavily several times.

Young Ian looked up at once; his face was white and set, but his eyes were alert.

"He's all right, I think," he said softly. "Auntie—are ye all right? Ye're no hurt, are ye?"

"No," I said, and tried to smile reassuringly. "I'm fine." There was a sore spot on the back of my skull and my ears still rang slightly; the yellow halo of light around the lantern seemed to oscillate, to swell and shrink in rhythm with the beating of my heart. One cheek was scraped, I had a bruised elbow and a large splinter in one hand, but I seemed to be fundamentally sound, physically. Otherwise, I had my doubts.

I didn't look around at Jamie, some six feet behind me, but I could feel his presence, ominous as a thundercloud. Ian, who plainly *could* see him over my shoulder, looked faintly apprehensive.

There was a slight creaking of the deck, and Ian's expression eased. I heard Jamie's voice inside the cabin, outwardly casual as he asked Fergus a question, then it faded, lost in the sounds of bumping and shuffling as the men righted furniture and repiled the scattered goods. I let my breath out slowly.

"Dinna fash, Auntie," Ian said, in an attempt at comfort. "Uncle Jamie's no the sort to lay hands on ye, I dinna think."

I wasn't at all sure of that, given the vibrations coming from Jamie's direction, but I hoped he was right.

"Is he terribly angry, do you think?" I asked in a low voice. Ian shrugged uneasily.

"Well, last time I saw him look at *me* that way, he took me back o' the house and knocked me flat. He wouldna serve you that way, though, I'm sure," he added hastily.

"I don't suppose so," I said, a little bleakly. I wasn't sure I wouldn't prefer it if he did.

"It's no verra nice to get the rough side o' Uncle Jamie's tongue, either," Ian said, shaking his head sympathetically. "I'd rather a thrashing, myself."

I gave Ian a quelling look and leaned over the dog.

"Sufficient to the day is the evil thereof. Has the bleeding stopped?"

It had; disregarding the blood-matted fur, there was surprisingly little damage; no more than a deep nick in the skin and muscle near the shoulder. Rollo flattened his ears and showed his teeth as I examined him, but made no audible protest.

"Good dog," I murmured. Had I any way to numb the skin, I would have stitched the wound, but we would have to do without such niceties. "He should have a little ointment there, to keep the flies out."

"I'll get it, Auntie; I ken where your wee box is." Ian gently edged Rollo's nose off his knee and got to his feet. "It'll be the green stuff ye put on Fergus's toe?" At my nod, he disappeared into the cabin, leaving me to deal with my quivering stomach, sore head, and congested throat. I swallowed several times, but with no great result. I touched my throat gingerly, wondering which ring I still had.

Eutroclus came round the corner of the cabin, carrying a long thick pole of white wood, deeply stained at one end, the marks testifying to the frequent necessity of its use. Stabbing the pole firmly down off the side, he leaned his weight against it, heaving with a long, sustained effort.

I jumped, as Jamie came out of the shadows, a similar pole in his hand. I hadn't heard him, above the miscellaneous thumpings and shouts. He didn't look at me, but shed his shirt, and at the deckhand's indication, stabbed down his pole.

On the fourth try, I felt the vibration of the hull, a small judder as something shifted. Encouraged, Jamie and the hand shoved harder, and all of sudden, the hull slid free, with a muted *bwong!* of resonant wood that made Rollo lift his head with a startled *Wuff!*

Eutroclus nodded to Jamie, face beaming under a shiny layer of sweat, and took the pole from him. Jamie nodded back, smiling, and picking up his shirt from the deck, turned toward me.

I stiffened, and Rollo twitched his ears to full alert, but Jamie showed no immediate disposition either to berate me or to toss me overboard. Instead, he leaned down, frowning as he peered at me in the wavering lantern light.

"How d'ye feel, Sassenach? I canna tell if you're really green, or is it only the light."

"I'm all right. A bit shaky, perhaps." More than a bit; my hands were still clammy, and I knew my trembling knees wouldn't hold me if I tried to stand. I swallowed hard, coughed, and thumped myself on the chest.

"It's probably my imagination, but it feels like the ring is caught in my throat."

He squinted thoughtfully at me, then turned to Fergus, who had appeared from the cabin and was hovering nearby.

"Ask the captain might I see his pipe for a moment, Fergus."

He turned away, pulling his shirt over his head, and disappeared aft himself, returning moments later with a cup of water.

I reached gratefully for it, but he held it out of my reach.

"Not just yet, Sassenach," he said. "Got it? Aye, thanks, Fergus. Fetch an empty bucket, now, will ye?" Taking the filthy pipe from a puzzled Fergus, he inserted his thumb into the stained bowl and began to scrape at the burnt, gummy residue that lined it.

Turning the pipe upside down, he tapped it over the cup of water, causing a small shower of brown crusts and moist crumbs of half-burnt tobacco, which he stirred into the water with his blackened thumb. Finished with these preparations, he looked up at me over the rim of the cup in a distinctly sinister fashion.

"No," I said. "Oh, no."

"Oh, yes," he said. "Come along, Sassenach; it'll cure what ails ye."

"I'll just . . . wait," I said. I folded my arms across my chest. "Thanks anyway."

Fergus had by this time reappeared with the bucket, eyebrows raised high. Jamie took it from him and plunked it on the deck next to me.

"I've done it that way, Sassenach," he informed me, "and it's a good deal messier than ye might think. It's also not a pleasant thing to do on a boat, in close company, aye?" He put a hand on the back of my head and pressed the cup against my lower lip. "This will be quick. Come on, now; a wee sip is all."

I pressed my lips tightly together; the smell from the cup was enough to make my stomach turn over, combining as it did the stale reek of tobacco, the sight of the noisome brown surface of the liquid, crusts swimming below the surface, and the memory of Captain Freeman's blobs of brown-tinged spittle sliding down the deck.

Jamie didn't bother with argument or persuasion. He simply let go of my head, pinched my nose shut, and when I opened my mouth to breathe, tipped in the foul-smelling contents of the cup.

"Mmmfff!"

"Swallow," he said, clapping a hand tightly across my mouth and ignoring both my frenzied squirming and the muffled sounds of protest I was making. He was a lot stronger than I was, and he didn't mean to let go. It was swallow or strangle.

I swallowed.

"Good as new." Jamie finished polishing the silver ring on his shirttail and held it up, admiring it in the glow of the lantern.

"That is somewhat better than can be said of me," I replied coldly. I lay in a crumpled heap on the deck, which in spite of the placid current, seemed still to be heaving very slightly under me. "You are a grade-A, double-dyed, sadistic fucking bastard, Jamie Fraser!"

He bent over me and smoothed the damp hair off my face.

"I expect so. If ye feel well enough to call me names, Sassenach, you'll do. Rest a bit, aye?" He kissed me gently on the forehead and sat back.

Excitement over and order restored to the ravaged decks, the other men had gone back to the cabin to restore themselves with the aid of a bottle of applejack that Captain Freeman had contrived to save from the pirates by dropping it into the water barrel. A small cup of this beverage rested on the deck near my head; I was still too queasy to countenance swallowing anything, but the warm, fruity smell was mildly comforting.

We were under sail; everyone was eager to get away, as though some danger still lingered over the place of the attack. We were moving faster, now; the usual small cloud of insects that hovered near the lanterns had dispersed, reduced to no more than a few lacewings resting on the beam above, their delicate green bodies casting tiny streaks of shadow. Inside the cabin, there was a small burst of laughter, and an answering growl from Rollo on the side deck—things were returning to normal.

A small, welcome breeze played across the deck, evaporating the clammy sweat on my face and lifting the ends of Jamie's hair, drifting them across his face. I could see the small vertical line between his brows and the tilt of his head that indicated deep thought.

Little wonder if he was thinking. In one stroke, we had gone from riches—potential riches, at least—to rags, our well-equipped expedition reduced to a sack of beans and a used medicine chest. So much for his desire not to appear as beggars at Jocasta Cameron's door—we were little more than that now.

My throat ached for him, pity replacing irritation. Beyond the question of his immediate pride, there was now a terrifying void in that unknown territory marked "The Future." The future had been well open to question before, but the sharp edges of all such questions had been buffered by the comforting knowledge that we would have money to help accomplish our aims—whatever those turned out to be.

Even our penurious trip north had felt like an adventure, with the certain knowledge that we possessed a fortune, whether it was spendable or not. I had never before considered myself a person who placed much value on money, but having the certainty of security ripped away in this violent fashion had given me a sudden and quite unexpected attack of vertigo, as though I were falling down a long, dark well, powerless to stop.

What had it done to Jamie, who felt not only his danger and mine but the crushing responsibility of so many other lives? Ian, Fergus, Marsali, Duncan, the inhabitants of Lallybroch—even that bloody nuisance Laoghaire. I wasn't sure whether to laugh or cry, thinking of the money Jamie had sent her; the vengeful creature was a good deal better off at present than we were.

At the thought of vengeance, I felt a new stab that displaced all lesser fears. While Jamie was not markedly vengeful—for a Scot —no Highlander would suffer a loss such as this with silent resignation; a loss not only of fortune but of honor. What might he feel compelled to do about it?

Jamie stared fixedly into the dark water, his mouth set; was he seeing once again the graveyard where, swayed by Duncan's intoxicated sentimentality, he had agreed to help Bonnet escape?

It belatedly occurred to me that the financial aspects of the disaster likely had not yet entered Jamie's mind—he was occupied in more bitter reflection; it was he who had helped Bonnet escape the hangman's rope, and set him free to prey on the innocent. How many besides us would suffer because of that?

"You're not to blame," I said, touching his knee.

"Who else?" he said quietly, not looking at me. "I kent the man for what he was. I could have left him to the fate he'd earned —but I did not. I was a fool."

"You were kind. It's not the same thing."

"Near enough."

He breathed in deeply; the air was freshening with the scent of ozone; the rain was near. He reached for the cup of applejack and drank, then looked at me for the first time, holding up the cup inquiringly.

"Yes, thanks." I struggled to sit up, but Jamie took me by the shoulders and lifted me to lean against him. He held the cup for me to drink, the blood-warm liquid sliding soft across my tongue, then taking fire as it slid down my throat, burning away the traces of sickness and tobacco, leaving in their place rum's lingering taste of burning sugarcane.

"Better?"

I nodded, and held up my right hand. He slid the ring onto my finger, the metal warm from his hand. Then, folding down my fingers, he squeezed my fist hard in his own and held it, tight.

"Had he been following us since Charleston?" I wondered aloud.

Jamie shook his head. His hair was still loose, heavy waves falling forward to hide his face.

"I dinna think so. If he'd kent we had the jewels, he would have set upon us on the road before we reached Wilmington. No, I expect he learned it from one of Lillington's servants. I thought we'd be safe enough, for we'd be away to Cross Creek before anyone heard of the gems. Someone talked, though—a footman; perhaps the sempstress who sewed your gown."

His face was outwardly calm, but it always was, when he was hiding strong emotions. A sudden gust of hot wind shot sideways across the deck; the rain was getting closer. It whipped the loose ends of his hair across his cheek, and he wiped them back, running his fingers through the thick mass.

"I'm sorry for your other ring," he said, after a moment.

"Oh. It's—" I started to say "It's all right," but the words stuck in my throat, choked by the sudden realization of loss.

I had worn that gold ring for nearly thirty years; token of vows taken, forsaken, renewed, and at last absolved. A token of marriage, of family; of a large part of my life. And the last trace of Frank—whom, in spite of everything, I had loved.

Jamie didn't say anything, but he took my left hand in his own and held it, lightly stroking my knuckles with his thumb. I didn't speak either. I sighed deeply and turned my face toward the stern; the trees along the shore were shivering in a rising wind of anticipation, leaves rustling loudly enough to drown the sound of the vessel's passage.

A small drop struck my cheek, but I didn't move. My hand lay limp and white in his, looking unaccustomedly frail; it was something of a shock to see it that way.

I was used to paying a great deal of attention to my hands, one way and another. They were my tools, my channel of touch, mingling the delicacy and strength by which I healed. They had a certain beauty, which I admired in a detached sort of way, but it was the beauty of strength and competence, the assurance of power that made its form admirable.

It was the same hand now, pale and long-fingered, the knuckles slightly bony—oddly bare without my ring, but recognizably my hand. Yet it lay in a hand so much larger and rougher that it seemed small, and fragile by comparison.

His other hand squeezed tighter, pressing the metal of the silver ring into my flesh, reminding me of what remained. I lifted his fist and pressed it hard against my heart in answer. The rain began to fall, in large, wet drops, but neither of us moved.

It came in a rush, dropping a veil over boat and shore, pattering noisily on leaves and deck and water, lending a temporary illusion of concealment. It washed cool and soft across my skin, momentary balm on the wounds of fear and loss.

I felt at once horribly vulnerable and yet completely safe. But then—I had always felt that way with Jamie Fraser.

PART FOUR

River Run

Cross Creek, North Carolina, June 1767

River Run stood by the edge of the Cape Fear, just above the confluence that gave Cross Creek its name. Cross Creek itself was good-sized, with a busy public wharf and several large warehouses lining the water's edge. As the *Sally Ann* made her way slowly through the shipping lane, a strong, resinous smell hung over town and river, trapped by the hot, sticky air.

"Jesus, it's like breathin' turpentine," Ian wheezed as a fresh wave of the stultifying reek washed over us.

"You *is* breathin' turpentine, man." Eutroclus's rare smile flashed white and disappeared. He nodded toward a barge tethered to a piling by one of the wharfs. It was stacked with barrels, some of which showed a thick black ooze through split seams. Other, larger barrels bore the brandmarks of their owners, with a large "T" burned into the pinewood below.

" 'At's right," Captain Freeman agreed. He squinted in the bright sunlight, waving one hand slowly in front of his nose, as though this might dispel the stink. "This time o' year's when the pitch-bilers come down from the backcountry. Pitch, turpentine, tar—bring it all down by barge t' Wilmington, then send it on south to the shipyards at Charleston."

"I shouldna think it's *all* turpentine," Jamie said. He mopped the back of his neck with a handkerchief and nodded toward the largest of the warehouses, its door flanked by red-coated soldiers. "Smell it, Sassenach?"

I inhaled, cautiously. There *was* something else in the air here; a hot, familiar scent.

"Rum?" I said.

"And brandywine. And a bit of port, as well." Jamie's long nose twitched, sensitive as a mongoose's. I looked at him in amusement.

"You haven't lost it, have you?" Twenty years before, he had managed his cousin Jared's wine business in Paris, and his nose and palate had been the awe of the winery tasting rooms.

He grinned.

"Oh, I expect I could still tell Moselle from horse piss, if ye held it right under my nose. But telling rum from turpentine is no great feat, is it?"

Ian drew a huge lungful of air and let it out, coughing.

"It all smells the same to me," he said, shaking his head.

"Good," said Jamie, "I'll give ye turpentine next time I stand ye a drink. It'll be a good deal cheaper.

"Turpentine's just about what I could afford now," he added under cover of the laughter this remark caused. He straightened, brushing down the skirts of his coat. "We'll be there soon. Do I look a terrible beggar, Sassenach?"

Seen with the sun glowing on his neatly ribboned hair, his darkened profile coin-stamped against the light, I privately thought he looked dazzling, but I had caught the faint tone of anxiety in his voice, and knew well enough what he meant. Penniless he might be, but he didn't mean to look it.

I was well aware that the notion of appearing at his aunt's door as a poor relation come a-begging stung his pride considerably. The fact that he had been forced into precisely that role didn't make it any easier to bear.

I looked him over carefully. The coat and waistcoat were not spectacular, but quite acceptable, courtesy of Cousin Edwin; a quiet gray broadcloth with a good hand and an excellent fit, buttons not silver, but not of wood or bone either—a sober pewter, like a prosperous Quaker.

Not that the rest of him bore the slightest resemblance to a Quaker, I thought. The linen shirt was rather grubby, but as long as he kept his coat on, no one would notice, and the missing button on the waistcoat was hidden by the graceful fall of his lace jabot, the sole extravagance he had permitted himself in the way of wardrobe.

The stockings were all right; pale blue silk, no visible holes. The white linen breeches were tight, but not—not quite—indecent, and reasonably clean.

The shoes were the only real flaw in his ensemble; there had been no time to have any made. His were sound, and I had done my best to hide the scuff-marks with a mixture of soot and dripping, but they were clearly a farmer's footwear, not a gentleman's; thick-soled, made of rough leather, and with buckles of lowly horn. Still, I doubted that his aunt Jocasta would be looking at his feet first thing.

I stood on tiptoe to straighten his jabot, and brushed a floating down-feather off his shoulder.

"It will be all right," I whispered back, smiling up at him. "You're beautiful."

He looked startled; then the expression of grim aloofness relaxed into a smile.

"*You're* beautiful, Sassenach." He leaned over and kissed me on the forehead. "You're flushed as a wee apple; verra bonny." He straightened up, glanced at Ian, and sighed.

"As for Ian, perhaps I can pass him off as a bondsman I've taken on to be swineherd."

Ian was one of those people whose clothes, no matter what their original quality, immediately look as though they had been salvaged from a rubbish tip. Half his hair had escaped from its green ribbon, and one bony elbow protruded from a rip in his new shirt, whose cuffs were already noticeably gray round the wrists.

"Captain Freeman says we'll be there in no time!" he exclaimed, eyes shining with excitement as he leaned over the side, peering upriver in order to be first to sight our destination. "What d'ye think we'll get for supper?"

Jamie surveyed his nephew with a marked lack of favor.

"I expect you'll get table scraps, wi' the dogs. Do ye not own a coat, Ian? Or a comb?"

"Oh, aye," Ian said, glancing round vaguely, as though expecting one of these objects to materialize in front of him. "I've a coat here. Somewhere. I think."

The coat was finally located under one of the benches, and extracted with some difficulty from the possession of Rollo, who had made a comfortable bed of it. After a quick brush to remove at least some of the dog hairs from the garment, Ian was forcibly inserted into it, and sat firmly down to have his hair combed and plaited while Jamie gave him a quick refresher course in manners, this consisting solely of the advice to keep his mouth shut as much as possible.

Ian nodded amiably.

"Will ye tell Great-auntie Jocasta about the pirates yourself, then?" he inquired.

Jamie glanced briefly at Captain Freeman's scrawny back. It was futile to expect that such a story would not be told in every tavern in Cross Creek, as soon as they had left us. It would be a matter of days—hours perhaps—before it spread to River Run plantation.

"Aye, I'll tell her," he said. "But not just on the instant, Ian. Let her get accustomed to us, first."

The mooring for River Run was some distance above Cross Creek, separated from the noise and reek of the town by several miles of tranquil tree-thick river. Having seen Jamie, Ian, and Fergus all rendered as handsome as water, comb, and ribbons could make them, I retired to the cabin, changed out of my grubby muslin, sponged myself hastily, and slipped into the cream silk I had worn to dinner with the Governor.

The soft fabric was light and cool against my skin. Perhaps a bit more formal than was usual for afternoon, but it was important to Jamie that we must look decent—especially now, after our encounter with the pirates—and my only alternatives were the filthy muslin or a clean but threadbare camlet gown that had traveled with me from Georgia.

There wasn't a great deal to be done with my hair; I gave it a cursory stab with a comb, then tied it back off my neck, letting the ends curl up as they would. I needn't trouble about jewelry, I thought ruefully, and rubbed my silver wedding ring to make it shine. I still avoided looking at my left hand, so nakedly bare; if I didn't look, I could still feel the imaginary weight of the gold upon it.

By the time I emerged from the cabin, the mooring was in sight. By contrast to the rickety fittings of most plantation moorings we had passed, River Run boasted a substantial and well-built wooden dock. A small black boy was sitting on the end of it, swinging bare legs in boredom. When he saw the *Sally Ann*'s approach, he leapt to his feet and tore off, presumably to announce our arrival.

Our homely craft bumped to a stop against the dock. From the screen of trees near the river, a brick walk swept up through a broad array of formal lawns and gardens, splitting in two to circle paired marble statues that stood in their own beds of flowers, then joining again and fanning out in a broad piazza in front of an imposing two-storied house, colonnaded and multi-chimneyed. At one side of the flower beds stood a miniature building, made of white marble—a mausoleum of some kind, I thought. I revised my opinions as to the suitability of the cream silk dress, and touched nervously at my hair.

I found her at once, among the people hurrying out of the house and down the walk. I would have known her for a MacKenzie, even if I hadn't known who she was. She had the bold bones, the broad Viking cheekbones and high, smooth brow of her brothers, Colum and Dougal. And like her nephew, like her great-niece, she had the extraordinary height that marked them all as descendants of one blood.

A head higher than the bevy of black servants who surrounded her, she floated down the path from the house, hand on the arm of her butler, though a woman less in need of support I had seldom seen.

She was tall and she was quick, with a firm step at odds with the white of her hair. She might once have been as red as Jamie; her hair still held a tinge of ruddiness, having gone that rich soft white that redheads do, with the buttery patina of an old gold spoon.

There was a cry from one of the little boys in the vanguard, and two of them broke loose, galloping down the path toward the mooring, where they circled us, yapping like puppies. At first I couldn't make out a word—it was only as Ian replied jocularly to them that I realized they were shouting in Gaelic.

I didn't know whether Jamie had thought what to say or to do upon this first meeting, but in the event, he simply stepped forward, went up to Jocasta MacKenzie, and embraced her, saying, "Aunt—it's Jamie."

It was only as he released her and stepped back that I saw his face, with an expression I had never seen before; something between eagerness, joy, and awe. It occurred to me, with a small jolt of shock, that Jocasta MacKenzie must look very much like her elder sister—Jamie's mother.

I thought she might have his deep blue eyes, though I couldn't tell; they were blurred as she laughed through her tears, holding him by the sleeve, reaching up to touch his cheek, to smooth nonexistent strands of hair from his face.

"Jamie!" she said, over and over. "Jamie, wee Jamie! Oh, I'm glad ye've come, lad!" She reached up once more, and touched his hair, a look of amazement on her face.

"Blessed Bride, but he's a giant! You'll be as tall as my brother Dougal was, at least!"

The expression of happiness on his face faded slightly at that, but he kept his smile, turning her with him so she faced me.

"Auntie, may I present my wife? This is Claire."

She put out a hand at once, beaming, and I took it between my own, feeling a small pang of recognition at the long, strong fingers; though her knuckles were slightly knobbed with age, her skin was soft and the feel of her grip was unnervingly like Brianna's.

"I am so glad to meet ye, my dear," she said, and drew me close to kiss my cheek. The scent of mint and verbena wafted strongly from her dress, and I felt oddly moved, as though I had suddenly come under the protection of some beneficent deity.

"So beautiful!" she said admiringly, long fingers stroking the sleeve of my dress.

"Thank you," I said, but Ian and Fergus were coming up to be introduced in their turn. She greeted them both with embraces and endearments, laughing as Fergus kissed her hand in his best French manner.

"Come," she said, breaking away at last, and wiping at her wet cheeks with the back of a hand. "Do come in, my dearies, and take a dish of tea, and some food. Ye'll be famished, no doubt, after such a journey. Ulysses!" She turned, seeking, and her butler stepped forward, bowing low.

"Madame," he said to me, and "Sir," to Jamie. "Everything is ready, Miss Jo," he said softly to his mistress, and offered her his arm.

As they started up the brick walk, Fergus turned to Ian and bowed, mimicking the butler's courtly manner, then offered an arm in mockery. Ian kicked him neatly in the backside, and walked up the path, head turning from side to side to take in everything. His green ribbon had come undone, and was dangling halfway down his back.

Jamie snorted at the horseplay, but smiled nonetheless.

"Madame?" He put out an arm to me, and I took it, sweeping rather grandly up the path to the doors of River Run, flung wide to greet us.

The house was spacious and airy inside, with high ceilings and wide French doors in all the downstairs rooms. I caught a glimpse of silver and crystal as we passed a large formal dining room, and thought that on the evidence, Hector Cameron must have been a very successful planter indeed.

Jocasta led us to her private parlor, a smaller, more intimate room no less well furnished than the larger rooms, but which sported homely touches among the gleam of polished furniture and the glitter of ornaments. A large knitting basket full of yarn balls sat on a small table of polished wood, beside a glass vase spilling summer flowers and a small, ornate silver bell; a spinning wheel turned slowly by itself in the breeze from the open French doors.

The butler escorted us into the room, saw his mistress seated, then turned to a sideboard that held a collection of jugs and bottles.

"Ye'll have a dram to celebrate your coming, Jamie?" Jocasta waved a long, slim hand in the direction of the sideboard. "I shouldna think ye'll have tasted decent whisky since ye left Scotland, aye?"

Jamie laughed, sitting down opposite her.

"Indeed not, Aunt. And how d'ye come by it here?"

She shrugged and smiled, looking complacent.

"Your uncle had the luck to lay down a good stock, some years agone. He took half a shipload of wine and liquor in trade for a warehouse of tobacco, meaning to sell it—but then the Parliament passed an Act making it illegal for any but the Crown to sell any liquor stronger than ale in the Colonies, and so we ended with two hundred bottles o' the stuff in the wine cellar!"

She stretched out her hand toward the table by her chair, not bothering to look. She didn't need to; the butler set down a crystal tumbler softly, just where her fingers would touch it. Her hand closed around it, and she lifted it, passing it under her nose and sniffing, eyes closed in sensual delight.

"There's a good bit left of it yet. A great deal more than I can guzzle by myself, I'll tell ye!" She opened her eyes and smiled, lifting the tumbler toward us. "To you, nephew, and your dear wife—may ye find this house home! *Slàinte!*"

"*Slàinte mhar!*" Jamie answered, and we all drank.

It *was* good whisky; smooth as buttered silk and heartening as sunshine. I could feel it hit the pit of my stomach, take root, and spread up my backbone.

It seemed to have a similar effect on Jamie; I could see the slight frown between his brows ease, as his face relaxed.

"I shall have Ulysses write this night, to tell your sister that

ye've come safe here," Jocasta was saying. "She'll have been
sair worrit for her wee laddie, I'm sure, thinking of all the misfor-
tunes that might have beset ye along the way."

Jamie set down his glass and cleared his throat, steeling himself
for the ordeal of confession.

"As to misfortune, Aunt, I am afraid I must tell ye . . ."

I looked away, not wanting to increase his discomfort by watching as he explained concisely the dismal state of our fortunes.
Jocasta listened with close attention, uttering small noises of dismay at his account of our meeting with the pirates. "Wicked, ah,
wicked!" she exclaimed. "To repay your kindness in such fashion! The man should be hangit!"

"Well, there's none to blame save myself, Aunt," Jamie said
ruefully. "He would have *been* hangit, if not for me. And since I
did ken the man for a villain to start, I canna be much surprised to
see him commit villainy at the end."

"Mmphm." Jocasta drew herself up taller in her seat, looking a
bit over Jamie's left shoulder as she spoke.

"Be that as it may, nephew. I said ye must consider River Run
as your home; I did mean it. You and yours are welcome here.
And I am sure we shall contrive a way to mend your fortunes."

"I thank ye, Aunt," Jamie murmured, but he didn't want to
meet her eyes, either. He looked down at the floor, and I could see
the hand around his whisky glass clenched tight enough to leave
the knuckles white.

The conversation fortunately moved on to talk of Jenny and her
family at Lallybroch, and Jamie's embarrassment eased a bit.
Dinner had been ordered; I could smell brief tantalizing whiffs of
roasting meat from the cookhouse, borne on the evening breeze
that wafted across the lawns and flower beds.

Fergus got up and tactfully excused himself, while Ian wandered around the room, picking things up and putting them down.
Rollo, bored with the indoors, sniffed his way industriously along
the doorsill, watched with open dislike by the fastidious butler.

The house and all its furnishings were simple but well crafted,
beautiful, and arranged with something more than just taste. I
realized what lay behind the elegant proportions and graceful arrangements, when Ian stopped abruptly by a large painting on the
wall.

"Auntie Jocasta!" he exclaimed, turning eagerly to face her.
"Did you paint this? It's got your name on it."

I thought a sudden shadow crossed her face, but then she smiled again.

"The view o' the mountains? Aye, I always loved the sight of them. I'd go with Hector, when he went up into the backcountry to trade for hides. We'd camp in the mountains, and set up a great blaze of a bonfire, wi' the servants keeping it going day and night, as a signal. And within a few days, the red savages would come down through the forest, and sit by the fire to talk and to drink whisky and trade—and I, I would sit by the hour wi' my sketchbook and my charcoals, drawing everything I could see."

She turned, nodding toward the far end of the room.

"Go and look at that one in the corner, laddie. See can ye find the Indian I put in it, hiding in the trees."

Jocasta finished her whisky and set down her glass. The butler offered to refill it, but she waved him away without looking at him. He set down the decanter and vanished quietly into the hall.

"Aye, I loved the sight o' the mountains," Jocasta said again, softly. "They're none so black and barren as Scotland, but the sun on the rocks and the mist in the trees did remind me of Leoch, now and then."

She shook her head then, and smiled a bit too brightly at Jamie.

"But this has been home for a long time now, nephew—and I hope ye will consider it yours as well."

We had little other choice, but Jamie bobbed his head, murmuring something dutifully appreciative in reply. He was interrupted, though, by Rollo, who raised his head with a startled *Wuff!*

"What is it, dog?" said Ian, coming to stand by the big wolf-dog. "D'ye smell something?" Rollo was whining, staring out into the shadowy flower border and twitching his thick ruff with unease.

Jocasta turned her head toward the open door and sniffed audibly, fine nostrils flaring.

"It's a skunk," she said.

"A skunk!" Ian whirled to stare at her, appalled. "They come so close to the house?"

Jamie had got up in a hurry, and gone to peer out into the evening.

"I dinna see it yet," he said. His hand groped automatically at his belt, but of course he wasn't wearing a dirk with his good suit. He turned to Jocasta. "Have ye any weapons in the house, Aunt?"

Jocasta's mouth hung open.

"Aye," she said. "Plenty. But—"

"Jamie," I said. "A skunk isn't—"

Before either of us could finish, there was a sudden disturbance among the snapdragons in the herbaceous border, the tall stalks waving back and forth. Rollo snarled, and the hackles stood up on his neck.

"Rollo!" Ian glanced round for a makeshift weapon, seized the poker from the fireplace, and brandishing it above his head, made for the door.

"Wait, Ian!" Jamie grabbed his nephew's upraised arm. "Look." A wide grin spread across his face, and he pointed to the border. The snapdragons parted, and a fine, fat skunk strolled into view, handsomely striped in black and white, and obviously feeling that all was right with his personal world.

"*That's* a skunk?" Ian asked incredulously. "Why, that's no but a bittie wee stinkard like a polecat!" He wrinkled his nose, with an expression between amusement and disgust. "Phew! And here I thought it was a dangerous huge beastie!"

The skunk's satisfied insouciance was too much for Rollo, who pounced forward, uttering a short, sharp bark. He feinted to and fro on the terrace, growling and making short lunges at the skunk, who looked annoyed at the racket.

"Ian," I said, taking refuge behind Jamie. "Call off your dog. Skunks *are* dangerous."

"They are?" Jamie turned a look of puzzlement on me. "But what—"

"Polecats only stink," I explained. "Skunks—Ian, no! Let it alone, and come inside!" Ian, curious, had reached out and prodded the skunk with his poker. The skunk, offended at this unwarranted intimacy, stamped its feet and elevated its tail.

I heard the noise of a chair sliding back, and glanced behind me. Jocasta had stood up and was looking alarmed, but made no move to come to the door.

"What is it?" she said. "What are they doing?" To my surprise, she was staring into the room, turning her head from one side to the other, as though trying to locate someone in the dark.

Suddenly, the truth dawned on me: her hand on the butler's arm, her touching Jamie's face in greeting, the glass put ready for her grasp, and the shadow on her face when Ian talked of her painting. Jocasta Cameron was blind.

A strangled cry and a piercing yelp jerked me back to more pressing issues on the terrace. A tidal wave of acrid scent cas-

caded into the room, hit the floor, and boiled up around me like a
mushroom cloud.

Choking and gasping, eyes watering from the reek, I groped
blindly for Jamie, who was making breathless remarks in Gaelic.
Above the cacophony of groaning and piteous yowling outside, I
barely heard the small *ting!* of Jocasta's bell behind me.

"Ulysses?" she said, sounding resigned. "Ye'd best tell Cook
the dinner will be late."

"It was luck that it's summer, at least," Jocasta said at breakfast next day. "Think if it had been winter and we had to keep the
doors closed!" She laughed, showing teeth in surprisingly good
condition for her age.

"Oh, aye," Ian murmured. "Please, may I have more toast,
ma'am?"

He and Rollo had been first soused in the river, then rubbed
with tomatoes from the burgeoning vines that overgrew the necessary house out back. The odor-reducing properties of these fruits
worked as well on skunk oil as on the lesser stinks of human
waste, but in neither case was the neutralizing effect complete. Ian
sat by himself at one end of the long table, next to an open French
door, but I saw the maid who brought his toast to him wrinkle her
nose unobtrusively as she set the plate before him.

Perhaps inspired by Ian's proximity and a desire for open air,
Jocasta suggested that we might ride out to the turpentine works
in the forest above River Run.

"It's a day's journey there and back, but I think the weather
will keep fine." She turned toward the open French window,
where bees hummed over a herbaceous border of goldenrod and
phlox. "Hear them?" she said, turning her slightly off-kilter
smile toward Jamie. "The bees do say it will be hot and fair."

"You have keen ears, Madame Cameron," Fergus said politely.
"If I may be permitted to borrow a horse from your stable,
though, I should prefer to go into the town, myself." I knew he
was dying to send word to Marsali in Jamaica; I had helped him
to write a long letter the night before, describing our adventures
and safe arrival. Rather than wait for a slave to take it with the
week's mail, he would much rather post it with his own hands.

"Indeed and ye may, Mr. Fergus," Jocasta said graciously. She
smiled round the table generally. "As I said, ye must all consider
River Run as ye would your own home."

Jocasta plainly meant to accompany us on the ride; she came down dressed in a habit of dark green muslin, the girl named Phaedre coming behind, carrying a hat trimmed to match with velvet ribbon. She paused in the hall, but instead of putting on the hat at once, she stood while Phaedre tied a strip of white linen firmly round her head, covering her eyes.

"I can see nothing but light," she explained. "I canna make out objects at all. Still, the light of the sun causes me pain, so I must shield my eyes when venturing out. Are you ready, my dears?"

That answered some of my speculations concerning her blindness, though didn't entirely assuage them. Retinitis pigmentosum? I wondered with interest, as I followed her down the wide front hall. Or perhaps macular degeneration, though glaucoma was perhaps the most likely possibility. Not for the first time—or the last, I was sure—my fingers curved around the handle of an invisible ophthalmoscope, itching to see what could not be seen with eyes alone.

To my surprise, when we went out to the stable block, a mare was standing ready saddled for Jocasta, rather than the carriage I had expected. The gift of charming horses ran strong in the MacKenzie line; the mare lifted her head and whickered at sight of her mistress, and Jocasta went to the horse at once, her face alight with pleasure.

"Ciamar a tha tu?" she said, stroking the soft Roman nose. "This will be my sweet Corinna. Is she not a dear lassie?" Reaching in her pocket, she pulled out a small green apple, which the horse accepted with delicate pleasure.

"And have they seen to your knee, *mo chridhe*?" Stooping, Jocasta ran a hand down the horse's shoulder and leg to just inside the knee, finding and exploring a healing scar with expert fingers. "What say ye, nephew? Is she sound? Can she stand a day's ride?"

Jamie clicked his tongue, and Corinna obligingly took a step toward him, clearly recognizing someone who spoke her language. He took a look at her leg, took her bridle in hand and with a word or two in soft Gaelic, urged her to walk. Then he pulled her to a halt, swung into the saddle, and trotted gently twice round the stableyard, coming to a stop by the waiting Jocasta.

"Aye," he said, stepping down. "She's canty enough, Aunt. What did her the injury?"

"Happen as it was a snake, sir," said the groom, a young black man who had stood back, intently watching Jamie with the horse.

"Not a snakebite, surely?" I said, surprised. "It looks like a tear—as though she'd caught her leg on something."

He looked at me with raised brows, but nodded with respect.

"Aye, mum, that it was. 'Twas a month past, I heard the lass let out a rare skelloch, and such a kebbie-lebbie o' bangin' and crashin', as ye'd think the whole stable was comin' doon aboot my head. When I rushed to see the trouble, I found the bloody corpse of a great poison snake lyin' crushed in the straw beneath the manger. The manger was dashit all to pieces, and the wee lassie quiverin' in the corner, the blood streamin' doon her leg from a splinter where she'd caught herself." He glanced at the horse with obvious pride. "Och, such a brave wee creature as ye are, lass!"

"The 'great poison snake' was perhaps a foot long," Jocasta said to me in an dry undertone. "And a simple green garden-snake, forbye. But the foolish thing's got a morbid dread o' snakes. Let her see one, and she loses her head entirely." She cocked her head in the direction of the young groom and smiled. "Wee Josh is none so fond o' them, either, is he?"

The groom grinned in answer.

"No, ma'am," he said. "I canna thole the creatures, nay more than my lassie."

Ian, who had been listening to this exchange, couldn't hold back his curiosity any longer.

"Where d'ye come from, man?" he asked the groom, peering at the young man in fascination.

Josh wrinkled his brow.

"Come from? I dinna come—oh, aye, I tak' your meaning now. I was born upriver, on Mr. George Burnett's place. Miss Jo bought me twa year past, at Eastertide."

"And I think we may assume that Mr. Burnett himself was conceived within crow's flight of Aberdeen," Jamie said softly to me. "Aye?"

River Run took in quite a large territory, including not only its prime riverfront acreage but a substantial chunk of the longleaf pine forest that covered a third of the colony. In addition, Hector Cameron had cannily acquired land containing a wide creek, one of many that flowed into Cape Fear.

Thus provided not only with the valuable commodities of timber, pitch, and turpentine but with a convenient means of getting them to market, it was little wonder that River Run had prospered, even though it produced only modest quantities of tobacco and indigo—though the fragrant fields of green tobacco through which we rode looked more than modest to me.

"There's a wee mill," Jocasta was explaining, as we rode. "Just above the joining of the creek and the river. The sawing and shaping are done there, and then the boards and barrels are sent downriver by barge to Wilmington. It's no great distance from the house to the mill by water, if ye choose to row upstream, but I thought to show ye a bit of the country instead." She breathed the pine-scented air with pleasure. "It's been a time since I was out, myself."

It *was* pleasant country. Once in the pine forest, it was much cooler, the sun blocked out by the clustered needles overhead. Far overhead the trunks of the trees soared upward for twenty or thirty feet before branching out—no great surprise to hear that the largest part of the mill's output was masts and spars, made for the Royal Navy.

River Run did a great deal of business with the navy, it seemed, judging from Jocasta's conversation; masts, spars, laths, timbers, pitch, turpentine, and tar. Jamie rode close by her side, listening intently as she explained everything in detail, leaving me and Ian to trail behind. Evidently, she had worked closely with her husband in building River Run; I wondered how she managed the place by herself, now that he was gone.

"Look!" Ian said, pointing. "What's that?"

I pulled up and walked my horse, along with his, to the tree he had pointed out. A great slab of bark had been taken off, exposing the inner wood for a stretch of four feet or more on one side. Within this area, the yellow-white wood was crosshatched in a sort of herringbone pattern, as though it had been slashed back and forth with a knife.

"We're near," Jocasta said. Jamie had seen us stop, and they had ridden back to join us. "That will be a turpentine tree you're seeing; I smell it."

We all could; the scent of cut wood and pungent resin was so strong that even *I* could have found the tree blindfolded. Now that we had stopped, I could hear noises in the distance; the rumblings and thumps of men at work, the chunk of an ax and voices calling back and forth. Breathing in, I also caught a whiff of something burning.

Jocasta edged Corinna close to the cut tree.

"Here," she said, touching the bottom of the cut, where a rough hollow had been chiseled out of the wood. "We call it the box; that's where the sap and the raw turpentine drip down and collect. This one is nearly full; there'll be a slave along soon to dip it out."

No sooner had she spoken than a man appeared through the trees; a slave dressed in no more than a loincloth, leading a large white mule with a broad strap slung across its back, a barrel suspended on either side. The mule stopped dead when he saw us, flung back his head, and brayed hysterically.

"That will be Clarence," Jocasta said, loudly enough to be heard above the noise. "He likes to see folk. And who is that with him? Is it you, Pompey?"

"Yah'm. S'me." The slave gripped the mule by the upper lip and gave it a vicious twist. "Lea'f, vassar!" As I made the mental translation of this expression into "Leave off, you bastard!" the man turned toward us, and I saw that his slurred speech was caused by the fact that the lower left half of his jaw was gone; his face below the cheekbone simply fell away into a deep depression filled with white scar tissue.

Jocasta must have heard my gasp of shock—or only have expected such a response—for she turned her blindfold toward me.

"It was a pitch explosion—fortunate he was not killed. Come, we're near the works." Without waiting for her groom, she turned her horse's head expertly, and made off through the trees, toward the scent of burning.

The contrast of the turpentine works with the quiet of the forest was amazing; a large clearing full of people, all in a hum of activity. Most were slaves, dressed in the minimum of clothing, limbs and bodies smudged with charcoal.

"Is anyone at the sheds?" Jocasta turned her head toward me.

I rose in my stirrups to look; at the far side of the clearing, near a row of ramshackle sheds, I caught a flash of color; three men in the uniform of the British Navy, and another in a bottle-green coat.

"That will be my particular friend," Jocasta said, smiling in satisfaction at my description. "Mr. Farquard Campbell. Come, Nephew; I should like ye to meet him."

Seen up close, Campbell proved to be a man of sixty or so, no more than middle height, but with that particular brand of leathery toughness that some Scotsmen exhibit as they age—not so much a weathering as a tanning process that results in a surface like a leather targe, capable of turning the sharpest blade.

Campbell greeted Jocasta with pleasure, bowed courteously to me, acknowledged Ian with the flick of a brow, then turned the full force of his shrewd gray eyes on Jamie.

"It's verra pleased I am that you're here, Mr. Fraser," he said, extending his hand. "Verra pleased, indeed. I've heard a deal about ye, ever since your aunt learned of your intentions to visit River Run."

He appeared sincerely delighted to meet Jamie, which struck me as odd. Not that most people weren't happy to meet Jamie— he was quite a prepossessing man, if I did say so—but there was an air almost of relief in Campbell's effusive greeting, which seemed unusual for someone whose outward appearance was entirely one of reserve and taciturnity.

If Jamie noticed anything odd, he hid his puzzlement behind a facade of courtesy.

"I'm flattered that ye should have spared a moment's thought to me, Mr. Campbell." Jamie smiled pleasantly, and bowed toward the naval officers. "Gentlemen? I am pleased to make your acquaintance, as well."

Thus given an opening, a chubby, frowning little person named Lieutenant Wolff and his two ensigns made their introductions, and after perfunctory bows, dismissed me and Jocasta from mind and conversation, turning their attention at once to a discussion of board feet and gallons.

Jamie lifted one eyebrow at me, with a slight nod toward Jocasta, suggesting in marital shorthand that I take his aunt and bugger off while business was conducted.

Jocasta, however, showed not the slightest inclination to remove herself.

"Do go on, my dear," she urged me. "Josh will show ye everything. I'll just wait in the shade whilst the gentlemen conduct their business; the heat's a bit much for me, I'm afraid."

The men had sat down to discuss business inside an open-fronted shed that boasted a crude table with a number of stools; presumably this was where the slaves took their meals, suffering the blackflies for the sake of air. Another shed served for storage; the third, which was enclosed, I deduced must be the sleeping quarters.

Beyond the sheds, toward the center of the clearing, were two or three large fires, over which huge kettles steamed in the sunshine, suspended from tripods.

"They'll be cookin' doon the turpentine, a-boilin' it intae pitch," Josh explained, taking me within eyeshot of one of the kettles. "Some is put intae the barrels as is"—he nodded toward the sheds, where a wagon was parked, piled high with barrels—"but the rest is made intae pitch. The naval gentlemen will be sayin' how much they'll be needin', so as we'll know."

A small boy of seven or eight was perched on a high, rickety stool, stirring the pot with a long stick; a taller youth stood by with an enormous ladle, with which he removed the lighter layer of purified turpentine at the top of the kettle, depositing this in a barrel to one side.

As I watched them, a slave came out of the forest, leading a mule, and headed for the kettle. Another man came to help, and together they unloaded the barrels—plainly heavy—from the mule, and upended them into the kettle, one at a time, with a great whoosh of pungent yellowish pinesap.

"Och, ye'll want to stand back a bit, mum," Josh said, taking my arm to draw me away from the fire. "The stuff does splash a bit, and happen it should take fire, ye wouldna want to be burnt."

Having seen the man in the forest, I most certainly didn't want to be burned. I drew away, and glanced back at the sheds. Jamie, Mr. Campbell, and the naval men were sitting on stools around a table inside one hut, sharing something from a bottle and poking at a sheaf of papers on the table.

Standing pressed against the shed wall, out of sight of the men within, was Jocasta Cameron. Having abandoned her pretense of exhaustion, she was plainly listening for all she was worth.

Josh caught the expression of surprise on my face, and turned to see what I was looking at.

"Miss Jo does hate not to have the charge o' things," he murmured regretfully. "I havena haird her myself, but yon lass Phaedre did say as how Mistress takes on when she canna manage something—a'rantin' dreadful, she says, and stampin' something fierce."

"That must be quite a remarkable spectacle," I murmured. "What is she not able to manage, though?" From all appearances, Jocasta Cameron had her house, fields, and people well in hand, blind or not.

Now it was his turn to look surprised.

"Och, it's the bluidy Navy. Did she not say why we came today?"

Before I could go into the fascinating question of why Jocasta Cameron should wish to manage the British Navy, today or any other day, we were interrupted by a cry of alarm from the far side of the clearing. I turned to look, and was nearly trampled by several half-naked men running in panic toward the sheds.

At the far side of the clearing a peculiar sort of mound rose up out of the ground; I had noticed it earlier but had had no chance to ask about it yet. While the floor of the clearing was mostly dirt, the mound was covered with grass—but grass of a peculiar, patchy sort; part was green, part gone yellow, and here and there was an oblong of grass that was stark, dead brown.

Just as I realized that this effect was the result of the mound's being covered in cut turves, the whole thing blew up. There was no sound of explosion, just a sort of muffled noise like a huge sneeze, and a faint wave of concussion in the air that brushed my cheek.

If it didn't sound like an explosion, it certainly looked like one; pieces of turf and bits of burnt wood began to rain down all over the clearing. There was a lot of shouting, and Jamie and his companions came rocketing out of the shed like a flock of startled pheasants.

"Are ye all right, Sassenach?" He grasped my arm, looking anxious.

"Yes, fine," I said, rather confused. "What on earth just happened?"

"Damned if I ken," he said briefly, already looking round the clearing. "Where's Ian?"

"I don't know. You don't think he had anything to do with this, do you?" I brushed at several floating specks of charcoal that had landed on my bosom. With black streaks ornamenting my décolletage, I followed Jamie into the small knot of slaves, all babbling in a confusing mixture of Gaelic, English, and bits of various African tongues.

We found Ian with one of the young naval ensigns. They were peering interestedly into the blackened pit that now occupied the spot where the mound had stood.

"It happens often, I understand," the ensign was saying as we arrived. "I hadn't seen it before, though—amazing powerful blast, wasn't it?"

"*What* happens often?" I asked, peering around Ian. The pit was filled with a crisscross jumble of blackened pine logs, all tossed higgledy-piggledy by the force of the explosion. The base of the mound was still there, rising up around the pit like the rim of a pie shell.

"A pitch explosion," the ensign explained, turning to me. He was small and ruddy-cheeked, about Ian's age. "They lay a charcoal fire, d'ye see, ma'am, below a great pot of pitch, and cover it all over with earth and cut turves, to keep in the heat, but allow enough air through the cracks to keep the fire burning. The pitch boils down, and flows out through a hollowed log into the tar barrel—see?" He pointed. A split log dangled over the remains of a shattered barrel oozing sticky black. The reek of burnt wood and thick tar filled the air, and I tried to breathe only through my mouth.

"The difficulty lies in regulating the flow of air," the little ensign went on, preening himself a bit on his knowledge. "Too little air, and the fire goes out; too much, and it burns with such energy that it cannot be contained, and is like to ignite the fumes from the pitch and burst its bonds. As you see, ma'am." He gestured importantly toward a nearby tree, where one of the turves had been thrown with such force as to wrap itself around the trunk like some shaggy yellow fungus.

"It is a matter of the nicest adjustment," he said, and stood on tiptoe, looking around with interest. "Where is the slave whose task it is to manage the fire? I do hope the poor fellow has not been killed."

He hadn't. I had been checking carefully through the crowd as we talked, looking for any injuries, but everyone seemed to have escaped intact—this time.

"Aunt!" Jamie exclaimed, suddenly recalling Jocasta. He whirled toward the sheds, but then stopped, relaxing. She was there, clearly visible in her green dress, standing rigid by the shed.

Rigid with fury, as we discovered when we reached her. Forgotten by everyone in the flurry of the explosion, she had been unable to move, sightless as she was, and was thus left to stand helpless, hearing the turmoil but unable to do anything.

I recalled what Josh had said about Jocasta's temper, but she was too much the lady to stamp and rant in public, however angry she might be. Josh himself apologized in profuse Aberdonian for not having been by her side to aid her, but she dismissed this with kind, if brusque, impatience.

"Clapper your tongue, lad; ye did as I bade ye." She turned her head restlessly from side to side, as though trying to see through her blindfold.

"Farquard, where are you?"

Mr. Campbell moved to her and put her hand through his arm, patting it briefly.

"There's no great harm done, my dear," he assured her. "No one hurt, and only the one barrel of tar destroyed."

"Good," she said, the tension in her tall figure relaxing slightly. "But where is Byrnes?" she inquired. "I do not hear his voice."

"The overseer?" Lieutenant Wolff mopped several smuts from his sweating face with a large linen kerchief. "I had wondered that myself. We found no one here to greet us this morning. Fortunately, Mr. Campbell arrived soon thereafter."

Farquard Campbell made a small noise in his throat, deprecating his own involvement.

"Byrnes will be at the mill, I expect," he said. "One of the slaves here told me there had been some trouble wi' the main blade of the saw. Doubtless he will be attending to that."

Wolff looked puff-faced, as though he considered defective saw blades a poor excuse for not having been appropriately received. From the tight line of Jocasta's lips, so did she.

Jamie coughed, reached over and plucked a small clump of grass out of my hair.

"I do believe that I saw a basket of luncheon packed, did I not, Aunt? Perhaps ye might help the Lieutenant to a wee bit of refreshment, whilst I tidy up matters here?"

It was the right suggestion. Jocasta's lips eased a bit, and Wolff looked distinctly happier at the mention of lunch.

"Indeed, Nephew." She drew herself upright, her air of command restored, and nodded in the general direction of Wolff's voice. "Lieutenant, will ye be so kind as to join me?"

➤

Over lunch, I gathered that the Lieutenant's visit to the turpentine works was a quarterly affair, during which a contract was drawn up for the purchase and delivery of assorted naval stores. It was the Lieutenant's business to make and review similar arrangements with plantation owners from Cross Creek to the Virginia border, and Lieutenant Wolff made it plain which end of the colony he preferred.

"If there is one area of endeavor at which I will admit the

Scotch excel,'' the Lieutenant proclaimed rather pompously, taking a good-sized swallow of his third cup of whisky, "it is in the production of drink."

Farquard Campbell, who had been taking appreciative sips from his own pewter cup, gave a small, dry smile and said nothing. Jocasta sat beside him on a rickety bench. Her fingers rested lightly on his arm, sensitive as a seismograph, feeling for subterranean clues.

Wolff made an unsuccessful attempt to stifle a belch, and belatedly turned what he appeared to consider his charm on me.

"In most other respects," he went on, leaning toward me confidentially, "they are as a race both lazy and stubborn, a pair of traits which renders them unfit for—" At this point, the youngest ensign, red with embarrassment, knocked over a bowl of apples, creating enough of a diversion to prevent the completion of the Lieutenant's thought—though not, unfortunately, sufficient to deflect its train altogether.

The Lieutenant dabbed at the sweat leaking from under his wig, and peered at me through bloodshot eyes.

"But I collect that you are not Scotch, ma'am? Your voice is most melodious and well-bred, and I may say so. You have no trace of a barbarous accent, in spite of your associations."

"Ah . . . thank you," I murmured, wondering what trick of administrative incompetence had sent the Lieutenant to conduct the Navy's business in the Cape Fear River Valley, possibly the single largest collection of Scottish Highlanders to be found in the New World. I began to see what Josh had meant by "Och, the bluidy Navy!"

Jocasta's smile might have been stitched on. Mr. Campbell, beside her, gave me the barest flick of gray eyebrow, and looked austere. Evidently, stabbing the Lieutenant through the heart with a fruit knife wasn't on—at least not until he had signed the requisition order—so I did the next best thing I could think of; I picked up the whisky bottle and refilled his cup to the brim.

"It's terribly good, isn't it? Won't you have a bit more, Lieutenant?"

It *was* good; smooth and warm. Also very expensive. I turned to the youngest ensign, smiled warmly at him, and left the Lieutenant to find his own way to the bottom of the bottle.

Conversation proceeded jerkily but without further incident, though the two ensigns kept a wary eye on the Drunkard's Progress going on across the table. No wonder; it would be their responsibility to get the Lieutenant on a horse and back to Cross Creek in one piece. I began to see why there were two of them.

"Mr. Fraser seems to be managing most creditably," the older ensign murmured, nodding outside in a feeble attempt to restart the stalled conversation. "Do you not think, sir?"

"Oh? Ah. No doubt." Wolff had lost interest in anything much beyond the bottom of his cup, but it was true enough. While the rest of us sat over our lunch, Jamie—with Ian's aid—had managed to restore order to the clearing, set the pitch boilers and sap gatherers back to work, and collect the debris of the explosion. At present he was on the far side of the clearing, stripped to shirt and breeches, helping to heave half-burned logs back into the tar pit. I rather envied him; it looked to be much more pleasant work than lunching with Lieutenant Wolff.

"Aye, he's done well." Farquard Campbell's quick eyes flicked over the clearing, then returned to the table. He assessed the Lieutenant's condition, and gave Jocasta's hand a brief squeeze. Without turning her head, she spoke to Josh, who had been lurking quietly in the corner.

"Do ye put that second bottle into the Lieutenant's saddlebag, laddie," she said. "I should not want it to be going to waste." She gave the Lieutenant a charming smile, rendered the more convincing as he couldn't see her eyes.

Mr. Campbell cleared his throat.

"Since ye will so soon be leaving us, sir, perhaps we might settle the matter of your requisitions now?"

Wolff seemed vaguely surprised to hear that he had been about to leave, but his ensigns sprang to their feet with alacrity, and began to gather up papers and saddlebags. One snatched out a traveling inkwell and a sharpened quill and set them down in front of the Lieutenant; Mr. Campbell whipped out a folded quire of paper from his coat and laid it down, ready for signature.

Wolff frowned at the paper, and swayed a little.

"Just there, sir," murmured the elder ensign, putting the quill into his senior's slack hand and pointing at the paper.

Wolff picked up his cup, tilted back his head, and drained the last drops. Setting the cup down with a bang, he smiled vacantly around, his eyes unfocused. The youngest ensign closed his eyes in resignation.

"Oh, why not?" the Lieutenant said recklessly, and dipped his quill.

"Will ye not wish to wash and change your clothes at once, Nephew?" Jocasta's nostrils flared delicately. "Ye stink most dreadfully of tar and charcoal."

I thought it just as well she couldn't see him. It went a long way beyond stinking; his hands were black, his new shirt reduced to a filthy rag, and his face so begrimed that he looked as though he had been cleaning chimneys. Such portions of him as weren't black, were red. He had left off his hat while working in the midday sun, and the bridge of his nose was the color of cooked lobster. I didn't think the color was due entirely to the sun, though.

"My ablutions can wait," he said. "First, I wish to know the meaning of yon wee charade." He fixed Mr. Campbell with a dark blue look.

"I am lured to the forest upon the pretext of smelling turpentine, and before I ken where I am, I'm sitting wi' the British Navy, saying aye and nay to matters I ken nothing of, wi' yon wee mannie kickin' my shins under the table like a trained monkey!"

Jocasta smiled at that.

Campbell sighed. In spite of the exertions of the day, his neat coat showed no signs of dust, and his old-fashioned peruke sat squarely on his head.

"You have my apologies, Mr. Fraser, for what must seem a monstrous imposition upon your good nature. As it is, your arrival was fortuitous in the extreme, but did not allow sufficient time for communications to be made. I was in Averasboro until last evening, and by the time I received word of your arrival, it was much too late for me to ride here to acquaint you with the circumstances."

"Indeed? Well, as I perceive we have a bit of time at present, I invite ye to do so now," Jamie said, with a slight click as his teeth closed on the "now."

"Will ye not sit down first, Nephew?" Jocasta put in, with a graceful wave of her hand. "It will take a bit of talk to explain, and ye've had a tiring day of it, no?" Ulysses had materialized out of the ether with a linen sheet over his arm; he spread this over a chair with a flourish, and gestured to Jamie to sit down.

Jamie eyed the butler narrowly, but it *had* been a tiring day; I could see blisters amid the soot on his hands, and sweat had made clear runnels in the filth on face and neck. He sank slowly into the proffered chair, and allowed a silver cup to be put into his hand.

A similar cup appeared as if by magic in my own hand, and I smiled in gratitude at the butler; I hadn't been hoiking logs about, but the long, hot ride had worn *me* out. I took a deep, appreciative sip; a lovely cool rough cider, that bit the tongue and slaked the thirst at once.

Jamie took a deep draught, and looked a little calmer.

"Well, then, Mr. Campbell?"

"It is a matter of the Navy," Campbell began, and Jocasta snorted.

"A matter of Lieutenant Wolff, ye mean," she corrected.

"For your purposes the same, Jo, and well ye know it," Mr. Campbell said, a little sharply. He turned back to Jamie to explain.

The majority of River Run's revenues were, as Jocasta had told us, derived from the sale of its timber and turpentine products, the largest and most profitable customer being the British Navy.

"But the Navy's not what it was," Mr. Campbell said, shaking his head regretfully. "During the war wi' the French, they could scarce keep the fleet supplied, and any man with a working sawmill was rich. But for the last ten years, it's been peaceful, and the ships left to rot—the Admiralty's not laid a new keel in five years." He sighed at the unfortunate economic consequences of peace.

The Navy did still require such stores as pitch and turpentine and spars—with a leaky fleet to keep afloat, tar would always find a market. However, the market had shrunk severely, and the Navy now could pick and choose those landowners with whom they did business.

The Navy requiring dependability above all things, their covetable contracts were renewed quarterly, upon inspection and approval by a senior naval officer—in this case, Wolff. Always difficult to deal with, Wolff had nonetheless been adroitly managed by Hector Cameron, until the latter's death.

"Hector drank with him," Jocasta put in bluntly. "And when he left, there'd be a bottle in his saddlebag, and a bit besides." The death of Hector Cameron, though, had severely affected the business of the estate.

"And not only because there's less for bribes," Campbell said, with a sidelong glance at Jocasta. He cleared his throat primly.

Lieutenant Wolff, it seemed, had come to give his condolences to the widow Cameron upon the death of her husband, properly uniformed, attended by his ensigns. He had come back again the next day, alone—with a proposal of marriage.

Jamie, caught mid-swallow, choked on his drink.

"It wasna my person the man was interested in," Jocasta said, sharply, hearing this. "It was my land."

Jamie wisely decided not to comment, merely eyeing his aunt with new interest.

Having heard the background, I thought she was likely right—Wolff's interest was in acquiring a profitable plantation, which could be rendered still more profitable by means of the naval contracts his influence could assure. At the same time, the person of Jocasta Cameron was no small added inducement.

Blind or not, she was a striking woman. Beyond the simple beauty of flesh and bone, though, she exuded a sensual vitality that caused even such a dry stick as Farquard Campbell to ignite when she was near.

"I suppose that explains the Lieutenant's offensive behavior at lunch," I said, interested. "Hell hath no fury like a woman scorned, but the blokes don't like it, either."

Jocasta turned her head toward me, startled—I think she had forgotten I was there—but Farquard Campbell laughed.

"Indeed they don't, Mrs. Fraser," he assured me, eyes twinkling. "We're fragile things, we poor men; ye trifle with our affections at your peril."

Jocasta gave an unladylike snort at this.

"Affections, forbye!" she said. "The man has nay affection for anything that doesna come in a bottle."

Jamie was eyeing Mr. Campbell with a certain amount of interest.

"Since ye raise the matter of affections, Aunt," he said, with a small edge, "might I inquire as to the interests of your particular friend?"

Mr. Campbell returned the stare.

"I've a wife at home, sir," he said dryly, "and eight weans, the eldest of whom is perhaps a few years older than yourself. But I kent Hector Cameron for more than thirty years, and I'll do my best by his wife for the sake of his friendship—and hers."

Jocasta laid a hand on his arm, and turned her head toward him. If she could no longer use her eyes for impression, she still knew the effect of downswept lashes.

"Farquard has been a great help to me, Jamie," she said, with a touch of reproof. "I couldna have managed, without his assistance, after poor Hector died."

"Oh, aye," Jamie said, with no more than a hint of skepticism. "And I'm sure I must be as grateful to ye as is my aunt, sir. But I am still wondering just a bit where I come into this tale?"

Campbell coughed discreetly and went on with his story.

Jocasta had put off the Lieutenant, feigning collapse from the stress of bereavement and had herself carried to her bedroom, from which she did not emerge until he had concluded his business in Cross Creek and left for Wilmington.

"Byrnes managed the contracts that time, and a fine mess he made of them," Jocasta put in.

"Ah, Mr. Byrnes, the invisible overseer. And where was he this morning?"

A maid had appeared with a bowl of warm perfumed water, and a towel. Without asking, she knelt by Jamie's chair, took one of his hands, and began gently to wash the soot away. Jamie looked slightly taken aback by this attention, but was too occupied by the conversation to send her away.

A slight wry smile crossed Campbell's face.

"I'm afraid Mr. Byrnes, though usually a competent overseer, shares one small weakness wi' the Lieutenant. I sent to the sawmill for him, first thing, but the slave came back and told me Byrnes was insensible in his quarters, reekin' of drink, and could not be roused."

Jocasta made another unladylike noise, which caused Campbell to glance at her with affection before turning back to Jamie.

"Your aunt is more than capable of managing the business of the estate with Ulysses to assist her in the documentary aspects. However, as ye will have seen yourself"—he gestured delicately at the bowl of water, which now resembled a bowl of ink—"there are physical concerns to the running of it, as well."

"That was the point that Lieutenant Wolff put to me," Jocasta said, lips thinning at the memory. "That I could not expect to manage my property alone, and me not only a woman, but sightless as well. I could not, he said, depend upon Byrnes, unable as I am to go to the forest and the mill to see what the man is doing. Or not doing." Her mouth shut firmly on the thought.

"Which is true enough," Campbell put in ruefully. "It is a proverb amongst us—'Happiness is a son old enough to be factor.' For when it's a matter of money or slaves, ye cannot trust anyone save your kin."

I drew a deep breath and glanced at Jamie, who nodded. At last we'd got to it.

"And that," I said, "is where Jamie comes in. Am I right?"

Jocasta had already enlisted Farquard Campbell to deal with Lieutenant Wolff upon his next visit, intending that Campbell should keep Byrnes from committing folly with the contracts. When we had so opportunely arrived, though, Jocasta had hit upon a better plan.

"I sent word to Farquard that he should inform the Lieutenant that my nephew had come to take up the management of River Run. That would cause him to go cautiously," she explained. "For he would not dare to press me, with a kinsman who had an interest standing by."

"I see." Despite himself, Jamie was beginning to look amused. "So the Lieutenant would think his attempt at a good down-setting here was usurped by my arrival. No wonder the man seemed to take such a mislike to me. I thought it was perhaps a general disgust of Scotsmen that he had, from what he said."

"I should imagine that he has—now," Campbell said, dabbing his lips circumspectly with his napkin.

Jocasta reached across the table, groping, and Jamie put out his hand instinctively to hers.

"You will forgive me, Nephew?" she said. With his hand to guide her, she could look toward his face; one would not have known her blind, by the expression of pleading in her beautiful blue eyes.

"I knew nothing of your character, d'ye see, before ye came. I could not risk that you would refuse a part in the deception, did I tell ye of it first. Do say that ye hold no grudge toward me, Jamie, if only for sweet Ellen's sake."

Jamie squeezed her hand gently, assuring her that he held no grudge. Indeed, he was pleased to have come in time to help, and his aunt might count upon his assistance, in any way she chose to call upon him.

Mr. Campbell beamed and rang the bell; Ulysses brought in the special whisky, with a tray of crystal goblets and a plate of savories, and we drank confusion to the British Navy.

Looking at that fine-boned face, so full of blind eloquence, though, I couldn't help recalling the brief synopsis Jamie had once given me of the outstanding characteristics of the members of his family.

"Frasers are stubborn as rocks," he'd said. "And MacKenzies are charming as larks in the field—but sly as foxes, with it."

"And where have *you* been?" Jamie asked, giving Fergus a hard up-and-down. "I didna think ye'd money enough for what it looks as though ye've been doing."

Fergus smoothed his disheveled hair, and sat down, radiating offended dignity.

"I met with a pair of French fur-traders in the town. They speaking little English, and myself being fluent, I could not but agree to assist them in their transactions. If they should then choose to invite me to share a small supper at their inn . . ." He lifted one shoulder in Gallic dismissal of the matter, and turned to more immediate concerns, reaching inside his shirt for a letter.

"This had arrived in Cross Creek for you," he said, handing it to Jamie. "The postmaster asked me to bring it."

It was a thick packet of paper, with a battered seal, and looked in little better condition than did Fergus. Jamie's face lighted when he saw it, though he opened it with some trepidation. Three letters fell out; one in what I recognized as his sister's writing, the other two plainly addressed by someone else.

Jamie picked up the letter from his sister, eyed it as though it might contain something explosive, and set it gently down by the fruit bowl on the table.

"I'll start wi' Ian," he said, picking up the second letter with a grin. "I'm not sure I want to be reading Jenny's without a glass of whisky in my hand."

He prised off the seal with the tip of the silver fruit knife, and opened the letter, scanning the first page. "I wonder if he . . ." His voice faded off as he began to read.

Curious, I got up and stood behind his chair, looking over his shoulder. Ian Murray wrote a clear, large hand, and it was easy to read, even at a distance.

Dear Brother—

All here are well, and give thanks to God for the news of your safe arrival in the Colonies. I send this missive in care of Jocasta Cameron; should it find you in her company, Jenny bids you to give her kindest regards to her Aunt.

You will see from the enclosed that you are restored to my wife's good graces; she has quite ceased to talk of you in the same breath with Auld Scratch, and I have heard no recent references to Emasculation, which may relieve your mind.

To put aside jesting—her Heart is much lightened by news of Young Ian's safety, as is my own. You will know the depth of our gratitude at his Deliverance, I think; therefore I will not Weary you with Repetitions, though in all truth, I could write a Novel upon that theme.

We manage to keep all here fed, though the barley suffered much from hail, and there is a flux abroad in the village which has claimed two children this month, to their parents' sorrow. It will be Annie Fraser and Alasdair Kirby we have lost, may God have mercy on their innocence.

On a happier note, we have had word from Michael in Paris; he continues to prosper in the wine business, and thinks of marrying soon.

I take joy in acquainting you with news of the birth of my newest grandson, Anthony Brian Montgomery Lyle. I shall content myself with this announcement, leaving a fuller description to Jenny; she is besotted of him, as are we all, he is a Dear Lad. His father, Paul—Maggie's husband—is a soldier, so Maggie and wee Anthony bide here at Lallybroch. Paul is in France at present; we pray nightly he may be left there, in relative peace, and not sent to the dangers of the Colonies nor the wilds of Canada.

We have had visitors this week; Simon, Lord Lovat, and his companions. He has come a-gathering again, seeking recruits for the Highland regiment he commands. You will perhaps hear of them in the Colonies, where I understand they have established some small reputation. Simon tells great tales of their bravery against the Indians and the wicked French, some of which are doubtless true.

Jamie grinned at this, and turned the page over.

He quite enthralled Henry and Matthew by his stories, and the girls as well. Josephine ("Kitty's eldest," Jamie observed in an aside to me) *was so inspired, indeed, as to engineer a raid upon the chicken-coop, wherefrom she and her Cousins all emerged bedecked with feathers, mud from the kail-yard being employed in lieu of war-paint.*

As all wished to play Savage, Young Jamie, Kitty's husband Geordie and myself were pressed into service as the Highland regiment, and obliged to suffer attack by Tomahawk (kitchen spoons and ladles) and other forms of enthusiastic assault, we essaying meanwhile a valiant defense with our broadswords (pieces of lath and willow twigs).

I put a stop to the Suggestion that the thatch of the dove-cote be set afire with flaming arrows, but was obliged in the end to submit to being Scalped. I flatter myself that I survived this Operation in better case than did the chickens.

The letter continued in this vein, giving more news of family, but dealing more often with the business of the farm, and reports of events in the district. Emigration, Ian wrote, was "become epidemic," with virtually all of the inhabitants of the village of Shewglie having decided upon this expedient.

Jamie finished the letter and put it down. He was smiling, his eyes faintly dreamy, as though he saw the cool mists and stones of Lallybroch rather than the humid, vivid jungle that surrounded us.

The second letter was also addressed in Ian's hand, but marked *Private* below the blue wax seal.

"And what will this be, I wonder?" Jamie murmured, breaking the seal and unfolding it. It began without salutation, obviously meant as continuation to the larger letter.

Now, Brother, I have a matter of some concern to put to you, upon which I write separately, so that you might share my larger letter with Ian, without disclosing this matter.

Your last letter spoke of putting Ian aboard ship in Charleston. Should this have occurred, we will of course welcome his coming with joy. However, if by chance he has not yet quitted your company, it is our wish that he remain with you, should this obligation be not unpleasing to you and to Claire.

"Not unpleasing to me," Jamie muttered, nostrils flaring slightly as he glanced from the page to the window. Ian and Rollo were wrestling on the grass with two young slaves, rolling over and over in a giggling tangle of limbs and cloth and wagging tail. "Mmphm." He turned his back to the window and resumed reading.

I mentioned Simon Fraser to you, and the cause of his presence here. The regimental levies have been a matter of concern to us for some time, though the matter has not often been pressing, our location being fortunately remote and difficult of travel.

Lovat finds little trouble in inducing lads to take the King's shilling; what is there for them here? Poverty and want, with no hope of betterment. Why should they remain here, where they have nothing to inherit, where they are forbidden the plaid or the right to carry a man's weapons? Why should they not seize the chance of reclaiming the notion of manhood—even should it mean they wear the tartan and carry a sword in the service of a German usurper?

I think sometimes this is the worst of it; not only that murder and injustice have been loosed unchecked upon us, without hope of cure or recourse—but that our young men, our hope and future, should be thus piped away, squandered for the profit of the conqueror, and paid in the small coin of their pride.

Jamie looked up at me, one brow raised.

"Ye wouldna think to look at him that Ian had such poesy in him, aye?"

There was a break in the text here. When it resumed, toward the bottom of the page, the writing, which had sprawled above into an angry scrawl with frequent blots and scratches, was once more controlled and tidy.

I must beg pardon for the passion of my words. I had not meant to say so much, but the temptation to open my heart to you as I always have is overwhelming. These are things I would not say to Jenny, though I imagine she knows them.

To the point, then; I grow garrulous. Young Jamie and Michael are well enough for the present—at least we have no fear that either of them will be tempted by a soldier's life.

The same is not true of Ian; you know the lad, and his spirit of adventure, so similar to your own. There is no real work for him here, yet he has not the mind of a scholar or a head for business. How shall he fare, in a world where he must choose between beggary and the profession of war? For there is little else.

We would have him stay with you, if you will have him. It may be that there is a greater opportunity in the New World for him than might be found here. Even if this should not be so, his mother will at least be spared the sight of her son marching away with his regiment.

I could ask no better Guardian or example for him than Your-

*self. I know I ask a great Favour of you in this Matter. Still, I hope
the situation will not be entirely without benefit to you, beyond the
presumed Great Pleasure of Ian's company.*

"Not only a poet, but an ironist, too," Jamie observed, with
another glance at the boys on the lawn.

Here there was another break in the text, before the writing
resumed, this time with a freshly sharpened quill, the words written carefully, reflecting the thought behind them.

*I had left off writing, Brother, wishing my thoughts to be clear
and unmazed by weariness before addressing this concern. I have
in fact taken up my pen and put it down a dozen times, unsure
whether to speak at all—I fear to offend you, in the same breath I
ask your favour. And yet I must speak.*

*I wrote of Simon Fraser, earlier. He is a man of honour, though
his father's son—but he is a bloody man. I have known him since
all of us were lads (sometimes that seems but yesterday; and then
again, a gulf of years), and there is a hardness in him now, a
glimpse of steel at the back of his eyes, that was not there before
Culloden.*

*What troubles me—and the knowledge you bear of my love
toward you is all that emboldens me to say this—is that I have
seen that steel in your own eyes, Brother.*

*I know too well the sights that freeze a man's heart, to harden
his eyes in that fashion. I trust that you will forgive my frankness,
but I have feared for your soul, many times since Culloden.*

*I have not spoken of the matter to Jenny, but she has seen it,
too. She is a woman, forbye, and will know you in ways I cannot.
It will be that fear, I think, that caused her to throw Laoghaire at
your head. I did think the match ill-made, but* (here a large, deliberate blotch obscured several lines). *You are fortunate in Claire.*

"Mmphm," Jamie said at this, giving me an eye. I squeezed
his shoulder, and leaned forward to read the rest.

*It is late, and I ramble. I spoke of Simon—care for his men is
now his sole link with humanity. He has neither wife nor child, he
lives without root or hearth, his patrimony hostage to the conqueror he serves. There is a burning fire in such a man, but no
heart. I hope never to say the same of you—or of Young Ian.*

Thus I give you to each other, and may God's blessing—and mine—be with you both.

Write as soon as you may. We hunger for News of you, and for your accounts of the exotic precincts in which you now Abide.

Your Most Affectionate Brother,
      Ian Murray

Jamie carefully folded the letter, and put it into his coat. "Mmphm," he said.

11

The Law of Bloodshed

July 1767

I became gradually accustomed to the rhythm of life at River Run. The presence of the slaves disturbed me, but there was little I could do about that, save to call upon their services as little as I could, fetching and carrying for myself whenever possible.

River Run boasted a "simples" room, essentially a small closet in which dried herbs and medicines were kept. There was not much there—no more than a few jars of dandelion root and willow bark, and a few patent poultices, dusty from disuse. Jocasta professed herself delighted that I should want to use the space—she had herself no talent for medicinals, she said with a shrug, nor had any of the slaves.

"There is a new woman who may show some skill in that direction," she said, long fingers drawing out the line of wool from the spindle as the spinning wheel whirred round.

"She is not a house slave, though; she was fresh come from Africa only a few months past, and has neither speech nor manners. I had thought to train her, perhaps, but since you are here . . . ah, now the thread's grown too thin, d'ye see?"

While I spent some time each day chatting with Jocasta and attempting to learn from her the art of spinning wool, Jamie spent an hour or two with the butler, Ulysses, who in addition to serving as Jocasta's eyes and as major domo of the house, had evidently also been managing the accounts of the plantation since Hector Cameron's death.

"And doing a fair job of it, too," Jamie told me privately, after one such session. "If he were a white man, my aunt would have no difficulty in handling her affairs. As it is, though—" He shrugged.

"As it is, it's lucky for her that you're here," I said, leaning close to sniff at him. He had spent the day in Cross Creek, arranging a complicated exchange involving indigo blocks, lumber, three pairs of mules, five tons of rice, and a warehouse receipt for a gilded clock, and as a result, a fascinating variety of scents clung to his coat and hair.

"It's the least I can do," he said, his eyes on the boots he was brushing. His lips tightened briefly. "Not as though I were otherwise occupied, is it?"

"A dinner party," Jocasta declared, a few days later. "I must have a proper festival, to introduce the two of ye to the folk of the county."

"There's no need of it, Aunt," Jamie said mildly, looking up from his book. "I think I shall have met most of the county at the stock-buying last week. Or the masculine part of it, at least," he added, smiling at me. "Come to think on it, though, perhaps it would suit Claire to be acquainted wi' the ladies of the district."

"I wouldn't mind knowing a few more people," I admitted. "Not that I don't find ample occupation here," I assured Jocasta, "but—"

"But not of a sort that interests you," she answered, though with enough of a smile to take the sting out of the remark. "Ye've no great fondness for needlework, I think." Her hand went to the big basket of colored wools and plucked out a ball of green, to be attached to the shawl she was knitting.

The balls of wool were carefully arranged each morning by one of the maids, in a spiral spectrum, so that by counting, Jocasta could pick up a ball of the right color.

"Aye, well, not *that* sort of needlework," Jamie put in, closing his book and smiling at me. "It's more the stitching of severed flesh that appeals to Claire. I expect she'll be getting restless these days, wi' no more than a cracked head or a case of piles to be dealing with."

"Ha ha," I said tartly, but in fact he was quite right. While I was pleased to find that the inhabitants of River Run were on the whole healthy and well nourished, there was not a great deal of scope for a physician. While I certainly wished no ill to anyone, there was no denying that I *was* getting restless. So was Jamie, but I thought that was a matter better left unremarked for the moment.

"I do hope Marsali's quite well," I said, changing the subject. Convinced at last that Jamie would not require his aid for a little while, Fergus had left the day before, bound downriver for Wilmington, thence to take ship for Jamaica. If all went well, he would return in the springtime with Marsali and—God willing—their new child.

"So do I," said Jamie. "I told Fergus that—"

Jocasta turned her head sharply toward the door.

"What is it, Ulysses?"

Absorbed by the conversation, I hadn't noticed footsteps in the hallway. Not for the first time, I was struck by the acuteness of Jocasta's hearing.

"Mr. Farquard Campbell," the butler said quietly, and stood back against the wall.

It was an indication of Farquard Campbell's familiarity with the household, I thought, that he should not have waited for Ulysses to return with an invitation for him to enter. He came into the drawing room on the butler's heels, hat carelessly thrust beneath one arm.

"Jo, Mrs. Fraser," he said with a quick bow to Jocasta and me, and "Your servant, sir," to Jamie. Mr. Campbell had been riding, and riding hard; the skirts of his coat were thick with dust, and sweat streamed down his face beneath a wig crammed on askew.

"What is it, Farquard? Has something happened?" Jocasta sat forward on the edge of her chair, her face reflecting his obvious anxiety.

"Yes," he said abruptly. "An accident at the sawmill. I've come to ask Mrs. Fraser—"

"Yes, of course. Let me get my box. Ulysses, will you have someone fetch a horse?" I rose hastily, searching for the slippers I had kicked off. I wasn't dressed for riding, but from Campbell's look, there wasn't time to change. "Is it serious?"

He put out a hand to stop me, as I stooped to pull my slippers on.

"Aye, bad enough. But you needn't come, Mrs. Fraser. If your husband might fetch along some of your medicines and such, though—"

"Of course I'll come," I said.

"No!" He spoke abruptly, and we all stared at him. His eyes sought Jamie's, and he grimaced, lips tight.

"It's not a matter for the ladies," he said. "But I should be most grateful for your company, Mr. Fraser."

Jocasta was on her feet before I could protest, gripping Campbell's arm.

"What is it?" she said sharply. "Is it one of my Negroes? Has Byrnes done something?"

She was taller than he by an inch or two; he had to look up to answer her. I could see the lines of strain in his face, and she plainly sensed it as well; her fingers tightened on the gray serge of his coat sleeve.

He glanced at Ulysses, then back at Jocasta. As though he had received a direct order, the butler turned and left the room, soft-footed as ever.

"It is a matter of bloodshed, Jo," he said to her quietly. "I do not know who, nor how, nor even how bad the injury may be. MacNeill's boy came for me. But for the other—" He hesitated, then shrugged. "It is the law."

"And you're a judge!" she burst out. "For God's sake, can you not do something?" Her head moved jerkily, blind eyes trying to fix him, bend him to her will.

"No!" he said sharply, and then, more gently, repeated, "No." He lifted her hand from his sleeve and held it tightly.

"You know I cannot," he said. "If I could . . ."

"If you could, you would not," she said bitterly. She pulled her hand out of his grasp and stood back, fists clenched at her sides. "Go on, then. They've called ye to be judge; go and give them their judgment." She whirled on her heel and left the room, her skirts rustling with angry futility.

He stared after her, then, as the sound of a slammed door came from down the passage, blew out his breath with a wry grimace and turned to Jamie.

"I hesitate to request such a favor of you, Mr. Fraser, upon such short acquaintance as we have had. But I would greatly appreciate your accompanying me upon my errand. Since Mrs. Cameron herself cannot be present, to have you there as her representative in the matter—"

"What *is* this matter, Mr. Campbell?" Jamie interrupted.

Campbell glanced at me, plainly wishing me to leave. Since I made no move to do so, he shrugged, and pulling a handkerchief from his pocket, wiped his face.

"It is the law of this colony, sir, that if a Negro shall assault a white person and in so doing, cause blood to be shed, then he shall die for his crime." He paused, reluctant. "Such occurrences are most thankfully rare. But when they occur—"

He stopped, lips pressed together. Then he sighed, and with a final pat of his flushed cheeks, put the handkerchief away.

"I must go. Will you come, Mr. Fraser?"

Jamie stood for a moment longer, his eyes searching Campbell's face.

"I will," he said abruptly. He went to the sideboard and pulled open the upper drawer, where the late Hector Cameron's dueling pistols were kept.

Seeing this, I turned to Campbell.

"Is there some danger?"

"I cannot say, Mrs. Fraser." Campbell hunched his shoulders, "Donald MacNeill told me only that there had been an altercation of some kind at the sawmill, and that it was a matter of the law of bloodshed. He asked me to come at once to render judgment and oversee the execution, and then left to summon the other estate owners before I could obtain any particulars."

He looked unhappy, but resigned.

"Execution? Do you mean to say you intend to execute a man without even knowing what he's done?" In my agitation, I had knocked Jocasta's basket of yarn over. Little balls of colored wool ran everywhere, bouncing on the carpet.

"I do know what he's done, Mrs. Fraser!" Campbell lifted his chin, his color high, but with an obvious effort, swallowed his impatience.

"Your pardon, ma'am. I know you are newly come here; you will find some of our ways difficult and even barbarous, but—"

"Too right I find them barbarous! What kind of law is it that condemns a man—"

"A slave—"

"A man! Condemns him without a trial, without even an investigation? What sort of law is that?"

"A bad one, madame!" he snapped. "But it is still the law, and I am charged with its fulfillment. Mr. Fraser, are you ready?" He clapped the hat on his head, and turned to Jamie.

"I am." Jamie finished stowing the pistols and ammunition in the deep pockets of his coat, and straightened, smoothing the skirts down across his thighs. "Sassenach, will ye go and—"

I had crossed to him and grabbed him by the arm before he could finish.

"Jamie, please! Don't go; you can't be part of this!"

"Hush." He laid his hand on mine and squeezed hard. His eyes held mine, and kept me from speaking.

"I am already part of it," he said quietly. "It is my aunt's property, her men involved. Mr. Campbell is right; I am her kinsman. It will be my duty to go—to see, at least. To be there." He hesitated then, as though he might say more, but instead merely squeezed my hand again and let me go.

"Then I'm going with you." I spoke quite calmly, with that eerie sense of detachment that comes with awareness of impending disaster.

His wide mouth twitched briefly.

"I did expect ye would, Sassenach. Go and fetch your wee box, aye? I'll have the horses brought round."

I didn't wait to hear Mr. Campbell's expostulations, but fled toward the stillroom, my slippers pattering on the tiles like the beat of an anxious heart.

We met Andrew MacNeill on the road, resting his horse in the shade of a chestnut tree. He had been waiting for us; he stepped out of the shadows at the sound of our hoofbeats. He nodded to Campbell as we halted by him, but his eyes were on me, frowning.

"Did you not tell him, Campbell?" he said, and turned the frown on Jamie. "It will be no affair for a woman, Mr. Fraser."

"Ye called it a matter of bloodshed, did ye no?" Jamie said, a marked edge in his voice. "My wife is *ban-lighiche;* she has seen war wi' me, and more. If ye wish me there, she will go with me."

MacNeill's lips pressed tight together, but he didn't argue further. He turned abruptly and swung into his saddle.

"Acquaint us, MacNeill, with the history of this unfortunate affair." Campbell urged his mare's nose past the withers of Jamie's horse, skillfully edging between MacNeill and Jamie. "Mr. Fraser is newly come, as you know, and your lad said only to me that it was bloodshed. I have no particulars."

MacNeill's burly shoulders rose slightly, shrugging toward the iron-gray pigtail that bisected his collar. His hat was jammed down on his head, set square with the shoulders, as though he had used a carpenter's level to even it. A square, blunt man, MacNeill, in words as well as appearance.

Told in brief bursts as we trotted, it was a simple story. The sawmill's overseer, Byrnes, had had an altercation with one of the turpentine slaves. This man, being armed with the large slash-knife appropriate to his occupation, had attempted to settle the matter by removing Byrnes' head. Missing his aim, he had succeeded only in depriving the overseer of an ear.

"Barked him like a pine tree," MacNeill said, a certain grim satisfaction apparent in his voice. "Took his lug and a wee bit o' the side of his face, as well. Not that it will ha' impaired his beauty ower-much, the ugly wee pusbag."

I glanced toward Jamie, who lifted one eyebrow in response. Evidently Byrnes was no favorite with the local planters.

The overseer had shrieked for help, and with the assistance of two customers and several of their slaves, had succeeded in subduing his assailant. The wound stanched and the slave locked in a shed, young Donald MacNeill—who had come to have a saw blade set and found himself unexpectedly in the midst of drama—had been dispatched at once to spread the word to the plantation owners nearby.

"You'll not know," Campbell explained, twisting in his saddle to speak to Jamie. "When a slave must be executed, the slaves from those plantations nearby are brought to watch; a deterrent, aye? against future ill-considered action."

"Indeed," Jamie said politely. "I believe that was the Crown's notion in executing my grandsire on Tower Hill after the Rising. Verra effective, too; all my relations have been quite well behaved since."

I had lived long enough among Scots to appreciate the effects of that little jab. Jamie might have come at Campbell's request, but the grandson of the Old Fox did no man's bidding lightly— nor necessarily held English law in high regard.

MacNeill had got the message, all right; the back of his neck flushed turkey-red, but Farquard Campbell looked amused. He uttered a short, dry laugh before turning round.

"Which slave is it, d'ye know?" he asked the older man. MacNeill shook his head.

"Young Donald didna say. But ye ken as well as I do; it'll be that bugger Rufus."

Campbell's shoulders slumped in acknowledgment.

"Jo will be sore pained to hear it," he murmured, shaking his head regretfully.

"It's her ain fault," MacNeill said, brutally thwacking a horsefly that had settled on his leg above the boot. "Yon Byrnes isna fit to mind pigs, let alone run Negroes. I've told her often enough; so've you."

"Aye, but Hector hired the man, not Jo," Campbell protested mildly. "And she couldna well dismiss him out of hand. What's she to do, then, come and manage the place herself?"

The answer was a grunt as MacNeill shifted his broad buttocks in the saddle. I glanced at Jamie, and found him poker-faced, eyes hidden in the shadow under the brim of his hat.

"There's little worse than a willful woman," MacNeill said, a trifle louder than strictly necessary. "They've none to blame save themselves if harm comes to them."

"Whereas," I chipped in, leaning forward and raising my own voice enough to be heard over the clop and creak of the horses, "if harm comes to them because of some man, the satisfaction of blaming him will be adequate compensation?"

Jamie snorted briefly with amusement; Campbell cackled out loud and poked MacNeill in the ribs with his crop.

"Got ye there, Andrew!" he said.

MacNeill did not reply, but his neck grew even redder. We rode in silence after that, MacNeill's shoulders hunched just under his ears.

While mildly satisfying, this exchange did nothing to settle my nerves; my stomach was knotted in dread of what might happen when we reached the mill. Despite their dislike of Byrnes and the obvious assumption that whatever had happened had likely been the overseer's fault, there wasn't the slightest suggestion that this would alter the slave's fate in any way.

"A bad law," Campbell had called it—but the law nonetheless. Still, it was neither outrage nor horror at the thought of judicial atrocity that made my hands tremble and the leather reins slick with sweat; it was wondering what Jamie would do.

I could tell nothing from his face. He rode relaxed, left hand on the reins, the right curled loosely on his thigh, near the bulge of the pistol in his coat.

I was not even sure whether I could take comfort in the fact that he had allowed me to come with him. That might mean that he didn't expect to commit violence—but in that case, did it mean he would stand by and let the execution happen?

And if he did . . . ? My mouth was dry, my nose and throat choked with the soft brown dust that rose in clouds from the horses' hooves.

I am already part of it. Part of what, though? Of clan and family, yes—but of *this*? Highlanders would fight to the death for any cause that touched their honor or stirred their blood, but they were for the most part indifferent to outside matters. Centuries of isolation in their mountain fastnesses had left them disinclined to meddle in the affairs of others—but woe to any who meddled in theirs!

Plainly Campbell and MacNeill saw this as Jamie's affair—but did he? Jamie was not an isolated Highlander, I assured myself. He was well traveled, well educated, a cultured man. And he knew damn well what *I* thought of present matters. I had the terrible feeling, though, that my opinion would count for very little in the reckoning of this day.

It was a hot and windless afternoon, with cicadas buzzing loudly in the weeds along the road, but my fingers were cold, and stiff on the reins. We had passed one or two other parties; small groups of slaves, moving on foot in the direction of the sawmill. They didn't look up as we passed, but melted aside into the bushes, making room as we cantered past.

Jamie's hat flew off, knocked by a low branch; he caught it deftly and clapped it back on his head, but not before I had caught a glimpse of his face, unguarded for a moment, the lines of it tense with anxiety. With a small shock, it occurred to me that *he* didn't know what he was going to do either. And that frightened me more than anything else so far.

We were suddenly in the pine forest; the yellow-green flicker of hickory and alder leaves gave way abruptly to the darker light of cool deep green, like moving from the surface of the ocean into the calmer depths.

I reached back to touch the wooden case strapped on behind my saddle, trying to avoid thinking of what might lie ahead, by making mental preparations for the only role I might reasonably play in this incipient disaster. I likely could not prevent damage; but I could try to repair what had happened already. Disinfection and cleansing—I had a bottle of distilled alcohol, and a wash made from pressed garlic juice and mint. Then dress the wound—yes, I had linen bandages—but surely it would need stitching first?

In the midst of wondering what had been done with Byrnes' detached ear, I stopped. The buzzing in my own ears was not from cicadas. Campbell, in the lead, reined up sharply, listening, and the rest of us halted behind him.

Voices in the distance, lots of voices, in a deep, angry buzz, like a hive of bees turned upside down and shaken. Then there was the faint sound of shouts and screams, and the sudden loud report of a shot.

We galloped down the last slope, dodging trees, and thundered into the sawmill's clearing. The open ground was filled with people; slaves and bondsmen, women and children, milling in panic through the stacks of sawn lumber, like termites exposed by the swing of an ax.

Then I lost all consciousness of the crowd. All my attention was fixed at the side of the mill, where a crane hoist was rigged, with a huge curved hook for raising logs to the level of the saw bed.

Impaled on the hook was the body of a black man, twisting in horrid imitation of a worm. The smell of blood struck sweet and hot through the air; there was a pool of it on the platform below the hoist.

My horse stopped, fidgeting, obstructed by the crowd. The shouts had died away into moans and small, disconnected screams from women in the crowd. I saw Jamie slide off in front of me, and force his way through the press of bodies toward the platform. Campbell and MacNeill were with him, shoving grimly through the mob. MacNeill's hat fell off, unregarded, to be trampled underfoot.

I sat frozen in my saddle, unable to move. There were other men on the platform near the hoist; a small man whose head was wound grotesquely round with bandages, splotched with blood all down one side; several other men, white and mulatto, armed with clubs and muskets, making occasional threatening jabs at the crowd.

Not that there seemed any urge to rush the platform; to the contrary, there seemed a general urge to get away. The faces around me were stamped with expressions ranging from fear to shocked dismay, with only here and there a flash of anger—or satisfaction.

Farquard Campbell emerged from the press, boosted onto the platform by MacNeill's sturdy shoulder, and advanced at once on the men with clubs, waving his arms and shouting something I couldn't hear, though the screams and moans around me were dying away into the silence of shock. Jamie seized the edge of the platform and lifted himself up after Campbell, pausing to give a hand to MacNeill.

Campbell was face-to-face with Byrnes, his lean cheeks convulsed with fury.

". . . unspeakable brutality!" he was shouting. His words came unevenly, half swallowed in the shuffle and murmur around me, but I saw him jab a finger emphatically at the hoist and its grisly burden. The slave had stopped struggling; he hung inert.

The overseer's face was invisible, but his body was stiff with outrage and defiance. One or two of his friends moved slowly toward him, plainly meaning to offer support.

I saw Jamie stand for a moment, assessing events. He drew both pistols from his coat, and coolly checked the priming. Then he stepped forward, and clapped one to Byrnes' bandaged head. The overseer went rigid with surprise.

"Bring him down," Jamie said to the nearest thug, loudly enough to be audible over the dying grumbles of the crowd. "Or I blow off what's left o' your friend's face. And then—" He raised the second pistol and aimed it squarely at the man's chest. The expression on Jamie's own face made further threats unnecessary.

The man moved reluctantly, narrowed eyes fixed on the pistol. He took hold of the brake-handle of the winch that controlled the hoist, and pulled it back. The hook descended slowly, its cable taut with the strain of its burden. There was a massive sigh from the spectators as the limp body touched the earth.

I had managed to urge my horse forward through the crowd, till I was within a foot or two of the end of the platform. The horse shied and stamped, tossing his head and snorting at the strong smell of blood, but was well trained enough not to bolt. I slid off, ordering a man nearby to bring my box.

The boards of the platform felt strange underfoot, heaving like the dry land does when one steps off a ship. It was no more than a few steps to where the slave lay; by the time I reached him, that cold clarity of mind that is the surgeon's chief resource had come upon me. I paid no heed to the heated arguments behind me, or to the presence of the remaining spectators.

He was alive; his chest moved in small, jerky gasps. The hook had pierced the stomach, passing through the lower rib cage, emerging from the back at about the level of the kidneys. The man's skin was an unearthly shade of dark blue-gray, his lips blanched to the color of clay.

"Hush," I said softly, though there was no sound from the slave save the small hiss of his breath. His eyes were pools of incomprehension, pupils dilated, swamped with darkness.

There was no blood from his mouth; the lungs were not punctured. The breathing was shallow, but rhythmic; the diaphragm had not been pierced. My hands moved gently over him, my mind trying to follow the path of the damage. Blood oozed from both wounds, flowed in a black slick over the ridged muscles of back and stomach, shone red as rubies on the polished steel. No spurting; they had somehow missed both abdominal aorta and the renal artery.

Behind me, a heated argument had broken out; some small, detached portion of my mind noted that Byrnes' companions were his fellow overseers from two neighboring plantations, presently being rebuked with vigor by Farquard Campbell.

". . . blatant disregard of the law! You shall answer for it in court, gentlemen, be assured that you shall!''

"What does it matter?'' came a sullen rumble from someone. "It's bloodshed—and mutilation! Byrnes has his rights!''

"Rights no for the likes of you to decide.'' MacNeill's deep growl joined in. "Rabble, that's what ye are, no better than the—''

"And where d'you get off, old man, stickin' your long Scotch nose in where it's not wanted, eh?''

"What will ye need, Sassenach?''

I hadn't heard him come up beside me, but he was there. Jamie crouched next to me, my box open on the boards beside him. He held a loaded pistol still in one hand, his attention mostly on the group behind me.

"I don't know,'' I said. I could hear the argument going on in the background, but the words blurred into meaninglessness. The only reality was under my hands.

It was slowly dawning on me that the man I touched was possibly not fatally wounded, in spite of his horrible injury. From everything I could sense and feel, I thought that the curve of the hook had gone upward through the liver. Likely the right kidney was damaged, and the jejunum or gallbladder might be nicked— but none of those would kill him immediately.

It was shock that might do for him, if he was to die quickly. But I could see a pulse throbbing in the sweat-slick abdomen, just above the piercing steel. It was fast, but steady as a drumbeat; I could feel it echo in the tips of my fingers when I placed a hand on it. He had lost blood—the scent of it was thick, overpowering the smell of sweat and fear—but not so much as to doom him.

An unsettling thought came to me—I might be able to keep this man alive. Likely not; in the wake of the thought came a flood of all the things that could go wrong—hemorrhage when I removed the hook being only the most immediate. Internal bleeding, de- layed shock, perforated intestine, peritonitis—and yet.

At Prestonpans, I had seen a man pierced through the body with a sword, the location of the wound very much like this. He had received no treatment beyond a bandage wrapped around his body—and yet he had recovered.

"Lawlessness!" Campbell was saying, his voice rising over the babble of argument. "It cannot be tolerated, no matter the provocation. I shall have you all taken in charge, be sure of it!"

No one was paying any attention to the true object of the discussion. Only seconds had passed—but I had only seconds more to act. I placed a hand on Jamie's arm, pulling his attention away from the debate.

"If I save him, will they let him live?" I asked him, under my breath.

His eyes flicked from one to another of the men behind me, weighing the possibilities.

"No," he said softly. His eyes met mine, dark with understanding. His shoulders straightened slightly, and he laid the pistol across his thigh. I could not help him make his choice; he could not help with mine—but he would defend me, whichever choice I made.

"Give me the third bottle from the left, top row," I said, with a nod at the lid of the box, where three rows of clear glass bottles, firmly corked, held a variety of medicines.

I had two bottles of pure alcohol, another of brandy. I poured a good dose of the brownish powdered root into the brandy, and shook it briskly, then crawled to the man's head and pressed it to his lips.

His eyes were glazed; I tried to look into them, to make him see me. Why? I wondered, even as I leaned close and called his name. I couldn't ask if this would be his choice—I had made it for him. And having made it, could not ask for either approval or forgiveness.

He swallowed. Once. Twice. The muscles near his blanched mouth quivered; drops of brandy ran across his skin. Once more a deep convulsive gulp, and then his straining neck relaxed, his head heavy on my arm.

I sat with my eyes closed, supporting his head, my fingers on the pulse under his ear. It jumped; skipped a beat and resumed. A shiver ran over his body, the blotched skin twitching as though a thousand ants ran over it.

The textbook description ran through my mind:

Numbness. Tingling. A sensation of the skin crawling, as though affected by insects. Nausea, epigastric pain. Labored breathing, skin cold and clammy, features bloodless. Pulse feeble and irregular, yet the mind remains clear.

None of the visible symptoms were discernible from those he already showed. Epigastric pain, forsooth.

One-fiftieth grain will kill a sparrow in a few seconds. One-tenth grain, a rabbit in five minutes. Aconite was said to be the poison in the cup Medea prepared for Theseus.

I tried to hear nothing, feel nothing, know nothing but the jerky beat beneath my fingers. I tried with all my might to shut out the voices overhead, the murmur nearby, the heat and dust and stink of blood, to forget where I was, and what I was doing.

Yet the mind remains clear.

Oh, God, I thought. It did.

12

The Return of John Quincy Myers

Deeply shaken by the events at the sawmill, Jocasta nonetheless declared her intention of carrying on with the party she had planned.

"It will distract our minds from the sadness," she said firmly. She turned to me, and reaching out, critically fingered the muslin cloth of my sleeve.

"I'll call Phaedre to begin a new gown for ye," she said. "The girl's a fine sempstress."

I rather thought it would take more than a new gown and a dinner party to distract *my* mind, but I caught a warning glance from Jamie and shut my mouth hard to keep the words inside.

In the event, given the shortness of time and a lack of suitable fabric, Jocasta decided to have one of her gowns remade for me.

"How does it look, Phaedre?" Jocasta frowned in my direction, as though she could summon vision by pure will. "Will it do?"

"Do fine," the maid answered around a mouthful of pins. She thrust in three in quick succession, squinted at me, pinched up a fold of fabric at the waistline and stabbed in two more.

"Be just fine," she elaborated, mouth now clear. "She shorter than you, Miss Jo, and a bit thinner in the waist. Some bigger in the bosom, though," Phadre added in an undertone, grinning at me.

"Yes, I know that." Jocasta spoke tartly, having caught the whisper. "Slash the bodice; we can fill it with Valenciennes lace over a field of green silk—take a scrap from that old dressing gown of my husband's; it will be the right color to complement this." She touched the sleeve, with its brilliant green striping. "Band the slash with the green silk, too; it will show off her bosom." The long pale fingers indicated the line of alteration, drifting across the tops of my breasts almost absentmindedly. The touch was cool, impersonal and barely felt, but I narrowly prevented myself jerking back.

"You have a most remarkable memory for color," I said, surprised and slightly unnerved.

"Oh, I remember this dress very well," she said. She touched the full sleeve lightly. "A gentleman once told me I reminded him of Persephone in it; springtime incarnate, he said." A faint smile of memory lit her face, then was erased as she lifted her head toward me.

"What color is your hair, my dear? I hadna thought to ask. You sound a bit blond, somehow, but I've no notion whether that may be actually the case. Pray, do not tell me ye're black-haired and sallow!" She smiled, but the joke sounded somehow like a command.

"It's more or less brown," I said, touching my hair self-consciously. "Faded a bit, though; it's gone light in streaks."

She frowned at this, seeming to consider whether brown was quite suitable. Unable to settle the question for herself, she turned to the maid.

"How does she look, Phaedre?"

The woman took a step back and squinted at me. I realized that she must—as the other house servants were—be in the habit of giving careful descriptions to her mistress. The dark eyes passed swiftly over me, pausing on my face for a long moment of assessment. She took two pins from her mouth before replying.

"Just fine, Miss Jo," Phaedre said. She nodded once, slowly. "Just fine," she said again. "She got white skin, white as skim milk; looks real fine with that bright green."

"Mm. But the underskirt is ivory; if she is too fair, will she not look washed out?"

I disliked being discussed as though I were an objet d'art—and a possibly defective one, at that—but swallowed my objections.

Phaedre was shaking her head, definitely.

"Oh, no, ma'am," she said. "She ain't washed out. She got them bones as makes shadows. And brown eyes, but don't be thinkin' they's mud-color. You recall that book you got, the one with the pictures of all them strange animals?"

"If you mean *Accounts of an Exploration of the Indian Subcontinent,*" Jocasta said, "yes, I recall it. Ulysses read it to me only last month. You mean that Mrs. Fraser reminds you of one of the illustrations?" She laughed, amused.

"Mm-hm." Phaedre hadn't taken her eyes off me. "She look

like that big cat,'' she said softly, staring at me. ''Like that there tiger, a-lookin' out from the leaves.''

An expression of startlement showed briefly on Jocasta's face. ''Indeed,'' she said, and laughed. But she didn't touch me again.

I stood in the lower hall, smoothing the green-striped silk over my bosom. Phaedre's reputation as a sempstress was well founded; the dress fit like a glove, and the bold bands of emerald satin glowed against the paler shades of ivory and leaf.

Proud of her own thick hair, Jocasta did not wear wigs, so there was fortunately no suggestion that I adopt one. Phaedre had tried to powder my hair with rice flour instead, an attempt I had firmly resisted. Inadequately concealing her opinion of my lack of fashionable instinct, she had settled for snaring the mass of curls in a white silk ribbon and pinning them high to the back of my head.

I wasn't sure quite why I had resisted the array of baubles with which she had tried to further bedizen me; perhaps it was mere dislike of fussiness. Or perhaps it was a more subtle objection to being made an object, to be adorned and displayed to Jocasta's purpose. At any rate, I had refused. I wore no ornament save my wedding ring, a small pair of pearl earbobs, and a green velvet ribbon round the stalk of my neck.

Ulysses came down the stairs above me, impeccable in his livery. I moved, and he turned his head, catching the flicker of my skirts.

His eyes widened in a look of frank appreciation as he saw me, and I looked down, smiling a bit, as one does when being admired. Then I heard him gasp and jerked my head up to see his eyes still wide, but now with fear; his hand so tight on the banister that the knuckles shone.

''Your pardon, madame,'' he said, sounding strangled, and rushed down the stairs and past me, head down, leaving the door to the cookhouse breezeway swinging in his wake.

''What on earth . . . ?'' I said aloud, and then I remembered where—and when—we were.

Alone for so long, in a house with a blind mistress and no master, he had grown careless. He had momentarily forgotten that most basic and essential protection—the only true protection a slave had: the blank, bland face that hid all thoughts.

No wonder he had been terrorized when he realized what he

had done. If it had been any woman other than myself to have intercepted that unguarded look . . . my hands grew cold and sweaty, and I swallowed, the remembered scent of blood and turpentine sharp in my throat.

But it had been me, I reminded myself, and no one else had seen. The butler might be afraid, but he was safe. I would behave as though nothing had happened—nothing *had*—and things would be . . . well, things would be what they were. The sound of footsteps on the gallery above interrupted my thoughts. I glanced upward, and gasped, all other thoughts driven at once from my mind.

A Highlander in full regalia is an impressive sight—any Highlander, no matter how old, ill-favored, or crabbed in appearance. A tall, straight-bodied, and by no means ill-favored Highlander in the prime of his life is breathtaking.

He hadn't worn the kilt since Culloden, but his body had not forgotten the way of it.

"Oh!" I said.

He saw me then, and white teeth flashed as he made me a leg, silver shoe-buckles gleaming. He straightened and turned on his heel to set his plaid swinging, then came down slowly, eyes fixed on my face.

For a moment, I saw him as he had looked the morning I married him. The sett of his tartan was nearly the same now as then; black check on a crimson ground, plaid caught at his shoulder with a silver brooch, dipping to the calf of a neat, stockinged leg.

His linen was finer now, as was his coat; the dirk he wore at his waist had bands of gold across the haft. *Duine uasal* was what he looked, a man of worth.

But the bold face above the lace was the same, older now, but wiser with it—yet the tilt of his shining head and the set of the wide, firm mouth, the slanted clear cat-eyes that looked into my own, were just the same. Here was a man who had always known his worth.

"Your servant, ma'am," he said. And then burst into a facesplitting smile as he descended the last few stairs.

"You look wonderful," I said, hardly able to swallow the lump in my throat.

"It's none so bad," he agreed, with no trace of false modesty. He arranged a fold over his shoulder with care. "Of course, that's the advantage of a plaid—there's no trouble about the fit of it."

"It's Hector Cameron's?" I felt ridiculously shy of touching him, garbed so splendidly. Instead, I touched the hilt of the dirk; it was topped with a small knurl of gold, roughly shaped like a bird in flight.

Jamie drew a deep breath.

"It's mine, now. Ulysses brought it to me—with my aunt's compliments." I caught an odd undertone in his voice, and glanced up at him. Despite his obvious deep pleasure at wearing the kilt again, something was troubling him. I touched his hand.

"What's wrong?"

He gave me half a smile, but his brows were drawn together in concern.

"I wouldna say anything's wrong, exactly. It's only—"

The sound of feet on the stairs interrupted him, and he drew me to one side, out of the way of a hurrying slave with a pile of linens. The house was humming with last-minute preparations; even now, I could hear the sound of wheels on the gravel at the back of the house, and savory smells floated through the air as platters were brought in at a gallop from the kitchen.

"We canna talk here," he muttered. "Sassenach, will ye stand ready at dinner? If I should signal to ye"—and he tugged at his earlobe—"will ye make a diversion, right then? It doesna matter what—spill wine, swoon away, stab your dinner partner with a fork—" He grinned at me, and I took heart from that; whatever was worrying him wasn't a matter of life and death, then.

"I can do that," I assured him. "But what—"

A door opened onto the gallery above, and Jocasta's voice floated down, giving last-minute orders to Phaedre. Hearing it, Jamie stooped quickly and kissed me, then whirled away in a swirl of crimson plaid and silver shoe-buckles, disappearing neatly between two slaves bringing trays of crystal goblets toward the drawing room. I stared after him in astonishment, barely getting out of the way in time to avoid being trampled by the servants.

"Is that you, sweet Claire?" Jocasta paused on the bottom step, head turned toward me, eyes trained just over my shoulder. She was quite uncanny.

"It is," I said, and touched her arm to let her know more precisely where I was.

"I smelt the camphor from the dress," she said in answer to my unspoken question, tucking her hand in the crook of my elbow. "I thought I heard Jamie's voice; is he nearby?"

"No," I said, quite truthfully, "I believe he's gone out to greet the guests."

"Ah." Her hand tightened on my arm, and she sighed, somewhere between satisfaction and impatience. "I am not one to lament what cannot be mended, but I swear I should give one of my eyes, could the sight of the other be restored long enough to see the lad in his plaidie this night!"

She shook her head, dismissing it, and the diamonds in her ears flared with light. She wore dark blue silk, a foil to her shining white hair. The cloth was embroidered with dragonflies that seemed to dart among the folds as she moved under the lights of the wall sconces and candle-heavy chandeliers.

"Ah, well. Where is Ulysses?"

"Here, madame." He had come back so quietly that I hadn't heard him, appearing on her other side.

"Come then," she said, and took his arm. I didn't know if the order applied to him or me, but followed obediently in her shimmering wake, dodging to avoid two kitchen boys bearing in the centerpiece—a whole roasted boar, tusked head intact and fiercely glaring, succulent backside gleaming fatly, ready for the knife. It smelled divine.

I smoothed my hair and prepared to meet Jocasta's guests, feeling rather as though I, too, were being presented on a silver platter, with an apple in my mouth.

The guest list would have read like the *Who's Who* of Cape Fear River gentry, had there been such a thing. Campbell, Maxwell, Buchanan, MacNeill, MacEachern . . . names from the Highlands, names from the Isles. MacNeill of Barra Meadows, MacLeod of Islay . . . many of the plantation names carried the flavor of their owners' origins, as did their speech; the high plastered ceiling echoed with the lilt of spoken Gaelic.

Several of the men came kilted, or with plaids wrapped over their coats and silk breeches, but I saw none as striking as Jamie —who was conspicuous by his absence. I heard Jocasta murmur something to Ulysses; he summoned a small serving girl with a clap of his hands and sent her zooming off into the lanterned half-dark of the gardens, presumably in search of him.

Nearly as conspicuous were the few guests who were not Scots; a broad-shouldered, gently smiling Quaker by the picturesque name of Hermon Husband, a tall, rawboned gentleman named

Hunter, and—much to my surprise—Phillip Wylie, immaculately suited, wigged and powdered.

"So we meet again, Mrs. Fraser," he remarked, holding on to my hand much longer than was socially correct. "I confess that I am ravished with enchantment to behold you again!"

"What are you doing here?" I said, rather rudely.

He grinned impudently.

"I was brought by mine host, the noble and puissant Mr. Mac-Neill of Barra Meadows, from whom I have just purchased an excellent pair of grays. Speaking of which, wild horses would have proved insufficient to restrain me from attendance this evening, upon my hearing that this occasion is held in your honor." His eyes wandered slowly over me, with the detached air of a connoisseur appreciating some rare work of art.

"May I observe, ma'am, how most becoming is that shade of green?"

"I don't suppose I can stop you."

"To say nothing of the effect of candlelight upon your skin. 'Thy neck is as a tower of ivory,' " he quoted, drawing a thumb insinuatingly over my palm, " 'thine eyes like the fishpools in Heshbon.' "

" 'Thy nose is as the tower of Lebanon, which looketh toward Damascus,' " I said, with a pointed look at his aristocratically pronounced proboscis.

He burst out laughing, but didn't let go. I stole a glance at Jocasta, who stood only a few feet away; she seemed engrossed in conversation with a new arrival, but experience had taught me just how sharp her ears were.

"How old are you?" I asked, narrowing my eyes at him and trying to retrieve my hand without unseemly struggle.

"Five-and-twenty, ma'am," he answered, rather surprised. He patted at the star-shaped patch near his mouth with a finger of his free hand. "Am I looking indecently haggard?"

"No. I merely wished to be sure I was telling you the truth in informing you that I am old enough to be your mother!"

This news appeared not to distress him in the slightest. Instead he raised my hand to his lips and pressed them fervently upon it.

"I am enchanted," he breathed. "May I call you *Maman*?"

Ulysses stood behind Jocasta, dark eyes intent on the guests coming up the lighted walk from the river—he leaned forward now and then to whisper in her ear. I removed my hand from

Wylie's grasp by main force, and used it to tap the butler on the shoulder.

"Ulysses," I said, smiling charmingly at Wylie, "would you be so kind as to ensure that Mr. Wylie is seated near me at dinner?"

"Indeed, madame; I will attend to it," he assured me, and returned at once to his surveillance.

Mr. Wylie bowed extravagantly, professing undying gratitude, and allowed himself to be propelled into the house by one of the footmen. I waved pleasantly after him, thinking how much I should enjoy sticking a fork into him, when the time came.

I couldn't tell whether it was the luck of the draw, or considerate planning, but I found myself between Mr. Wylie and the Quaker, Mr. Husband, with Mr. Hunter—the other non-Gaelic speaker—across the table from me. We formed a small island of English in the midst of a sea of swirling Scots.

Jamie had appeared at the last moment, and was now seated at the head of the table, with Jocasta at his right hand. For the dozenth time, I wondered what was going on. I kept a sharp eye on him, a clean fork by my plate, ready for action, but we had reached the third course with no untoward occurrence.

"I am surprised to find a gentleman of your persuasion in attendance at such an occasion, Mr. Husband. Does not such frivolity offend you?" Having failed to divert my attention to himself during the first two courses, Wylie now resorted to leaning across me, the action bringing his thigh casually into contact with mine.

Hermon Husband smiled. "Even Quakers must eat, Friend Wylie. And I have had the honor to enjoy Mrs. Cameron's hospitality on many occasions; I should not think to refuse it now, only because she extends it to others." He switched his attention back to me, resuming our interrupted conversation.

"Thou asked of the Regulators, Mrs. Fraser?" He nodded across the table. "I should recommend thy questions to Mr. Hunter, for if the Regulators might be said to enjoy the benefits of leadership, it is to this gentleman that they look."

Mr. Hunter bowed at the compliment. A tall, lantern-jawed individual, he was more plainly dressed than most of those in attendance, though not a Quaker. He and Mr. Husband were traveling together, both returning from Wilmington to their homes in the backcountry. With Governor Tryon's offer in mind, I wanted to find out whatever I could about matters in that area.

"We are but a loose assembly," he said modestly, putting down his wineglass. "In truth, I should be reluctant to claim any title whatever; it is only that I am fortunate enough to have a homestead so situated that it is a convenient meeting place."

"One hears that the Regulators are mere rabble." Wylie dabbed at his lips, careful not to dislodge his patch. "Lawless, and inclined to violence against the duly authorized deputies of the Crown."

"Indeed we are not," Mr. Husband put in, still mildly. I was surprised to hear him claim association with the Regulators; perhaps the movement wasn't quite so violent and lawless as Wylie implied. "We seek only justice, and that is not a quantity that can be obtained by means of violence, for where violence enters in, justice must surely flee."

Wylie laughed, a surprisingly deep and masculine sound, given his foppery.

"Justice apparently *should* flee! That is certainly the impression I was given by Mr. Justice Dodgson when I spoke with him last week. Or perhaps he was mistaken, sir, in his identification of the ruffians who invaded his chambers, knocked him down, and dragged him by the heels into the street?" He smiled engagingly at Hunter, who flushed dark red beneath his weathered tan. His fingers tightened about the stem of his wineglass. I glanced hopefully at Jamie. No sign of a signal.

"Mr. Justice Dodgson," Hunter said precisely, "is a userer, a thief, a disgrace to the profession of law, and—"

I had for some little time been hearing noises outside, but had put these down to some crisis in the cookhouse, which was separated from the main house by a breezeway. The noises became clearer now, though, and I caught a familiar voice that quite distracted me from Mr. Hunter's denunciations.

"Duncan!" I half rose from my seat, and heads nearby turned inquiringly.

There was a sudden confusion of movement out on the terrace, with shadows jerking past the open French windows, and voices calling, arguing and exhorting.

Conversation in the dining room fell silent, and everyone looked to see what was happening. I saw Jamie push back his chair, but before he could rise, an apparition appeared in the doorway.

It was John Quincy Myers, the mountain man, who filled the open double door from top to bottom and side to side, resplendent in the same costume in which I had first met him. He leaned heavily upon the doorframe, surveying the assemblage through bloodshot eyes. His face was flushed, his breathing stertorous, and in one hand he held a long glass bottle.

His eyes lit upon me, and his face contorted into a fearful grimace of gratification.

"THERE ye are," he said, in tones of the deepest satisfaction. "Said sho. Duncan wudd'n havit. Said yesh, Mishess Claire said gotter be drunk afore she cuts me. Sho I'm drunk. Drunk—" He paused, swaying dangerously, and raised his bottle high. "As a SKUNK!" he ended triumphantly. He took a step into the room, fell flat on his face, and didn't move.

Duncan appeared in the doorway, looking a good deal the worse for wear himself. His shirt was ripped, his coat hung off his shoulder, and he had the beginnings of what looked like a black eye.

He glanced down at the prostrate form at his feet, then looked apologetically at Jamie.

"I did try to stop him, *Mac Dubh*."

I extricated myself from my seat, and reached the body at the same time as Jamie, followed by a tidal wave of curious guests. Jamie glanced at me, eyebrows raised.

"Well, ye did say he must be unconscious," he observed. He bent over the mountain man and thumbed back an eyelid, showing a slice of blank white eyeball. "I'd say he's made a good job of it, myself."

"Yes, but I didn't mean dead drunk!" I squatted by the insensible form, and put a ginger two fingers over the carotid pulse. Nice and strong. Still . . .

"Alcohol isn't a good anesthetic at all," I said, shaking my head. "It's a poison. It depresses the central nervous system. Put the shock of operating on top of alcohol intoxication, and it could kill him, easily."

"No great loss," said someone among the guests, but this caustic opinion was drowned in a flood of reproachful shushing.

"Shame to waste so much brandy," someone else said, to general laughter. It was Phillip Wylie; I saw his powdered face loom over Jamie's shoulder, smiling wickedly.

"We've heard a great deal of your skill, Mistress Fraser. Now's your chance of proving yourself—before witnesses!" He waved a graceful hand at the crowd clustered round us.

"Oh, bugger off," I said crossly.

"Ooh, hear her!" Someone murmured behind me, not without admiration. Wylie blinked, taken aback, but then grinned more broadly than ever.

"Your wish is my command, ma'am," he murmured, and bowed himself back into the crowd.

I stood up, racked with doubt. It might work. It was a technically simple operation, and shouldn't take more than a few minutes—if I encountered no complications. It was a small incision—but it did involve going into the peritoneum, with all the attendant risk of infection *that* implied.

Still, I was unlikely to encounter better conditions than I had here—plenty of alcohol for disinfection, plenty of willing assistants. There was no other means of anesthesia available, and I could under no circumstances do it with a conscious patient. Above all, Myers had asked me to do it.

I sought Jamie's face, wanting advice. He was there, standing beside me, and saw the question in my eyes. Well, he'd wanted a diversion, damn it.

"Best do it, Sassenach." Jamie eyed the prostrate form. "He may ne'er have either the courage or the money to get that drunk again." I stooped and checked his pulse again—strong and steady as a carthorse.

Jocasta's stately head appeared among the curious faces looming over MacNeill's shoulder.

"Bring him into the salon," she said briefly. Her head withdrew, and the decision was made for me.

I had operated under odd conditions before, I thought, rinsing my hands hastily in vinegar brought from the kitchen, but none odder than this.

Relieved of his nether garb, Myers lay tastefully displayed on the mahogany table, boneless as a roasted pheasant, and nearly as ornamental. In lieu of platter, he lay upon a stable blanket, a gaudy centerpiece in his quilled shirt and bear's-claw necklace, surrounded by a garnish of bottles, rags, and bandages.

There was no time to change my own clothes; a leather butchering apron was fetched from the smoke shed to cover my dress, and Phaedre pinned up my long, frilled sleeves to leave my forearms bare.

Extra candles had been brought to give me light; candelabra blazed from sideboard and chandelier in a reckless expenditure of fragrant beeswax. Not nearly as fragrant as Myers, though; without hesitation, I took the decanter from the sideboard, and sloshed several shillings' worth of fine brandy over the curly dark-haired crotch.

"Expensive way to kill lice," someone remarked critically behind me, observing the hasty exodus of miscellaneous small forms of life in the wake of the flood.

"Ah, but they'll die happy," said a voice I recognized as Ian's. "I brought your wee box, Auntie." He set the surgical chest by my elbow, and opened it for me.

I snatched out my precious blue bottle of distilled alcohol, and the straight-edged scalpel. Holding the blade over a bowl, I poured alcohol over it, meanwhile scanning the crowd for appropriate assistants. There wouldn't be any shortage of volunteers; the spectators were boiling with suppressed laughter and murmured comment, interrupted dinner forgotten in a rush of anticipation.

Two sturdy carriage drivers were summoned from the kitchen to hold the patient's legs, Andrew MacNeill and Farquard Campbell volunteering to hold the arms, and Young Ian was set in place by my side, holding a large candlestick to cast additional light. Jamie took up his position as chief anesthetist by the patient's head, a glass full of whisky poised near the slack and snoring mouth.

I checked that my supplies and suture needles were ready, took a deep breath, and nodded to my troops.

"Let's go."

Myers's penis, embarrassed by the attention, had already retreated, peeping shyly out of the bushes. With the patient's long legs raised and spread, Ulysses himself delicately cupping the baggy scrotum away, the hernia was clearly revealed, a smooth swelling the size of a hen's egg, its curve a deep purple where it pressed against the taut inguinal skin.

"Jesus, Lord!" said one of the drivers, eyes bulging at the sight. "It's true—he's got three balls!"

A collective gasp and giggle ensued from the spectators, but I was too busy to correct misapprehensions. I swabbed the perineum thoroughly with pure alcohol, dipped my scalpel in the liquid, passed the blade back and forth through the flame of a candle by way of final sterilization, and made a swift cut.

Not large, not deep. Just enough to open the skin, and see the loop of gleaming pinkish-gray intestine bulging down through the tear in the muscle layer. Blood welled, a thin, dark line, then dribbled down staining the blanket.

I extended the incision, swished my fingers thoroughly in the disinfecting bowl, then put two fingers on the loop and pushed it gently upward. Myers moved in a sudden convulsion, nearly dislodging me, and just as suddenly relaxed. He tightened again, buttocks rising, and my assistants nearly lost their grip on his legs.

"He's waking up!" I shouted to Jamie, above the various cries of alarm. "Give him more, quick!" All my doubts about the use of alcohol as an anesthetic were being borne out, but it was too late to change my mind now.

Jamie grasped the mountain man's jaw, and squeezing open his mouth, dribbled whisky into it. Myers choked and spluttered and made noises like a drowning buffalo, but enough of the alcohol made it down his throat—the huge body relaxed. The mountain man subsided into mumbling immobility and then into long, wet, snuffling snores.

I had managed to keep my fingers in place; there was more bleeding than I would have liked, but his struggles had not brought the herniated loop back down. I snatched a clean cloth soaked in brandy and blotted the site; yes, I could see the edge of the muscle layer; scrawny as Myers was, a thin layer of yellow fat lay under the skin, separating it from the dark red fibers below.

I could feel the movement of his intestines as he breathed, the dark wet warmth of his body surrounding my gloveless fingers in that strange one-sided intimacy that is the surgeon's realm. I closed my eyes and let all sense of urgency, all consciousness of the watching crowd drop away.

I breathed in slowly, matched my rhythm to the audible snores. Above the reek of brandy and the faintly nauseating aromas of food, I could smell the earthy odors of his body; stale sweat, grimed skin, a small tang of urine and the copper scent of blood. To another, they would have been offensive, but not to me, not now.

This body *was*. No good, no bad, it simply was. I knew it, now; it was mine.

They were all mine; the unconscious body in my hands, its secrets open to me; the men who held it, their eyes on me. It didn't always happen, but when it did, the sensation was unforgettable; a synthesis of minds into a single organism. And as I took control of this organism, I became part of it, and lost myself.

Time stopped. I was acutely aware of each movement, each breath, the tug and pull of the catgut sutures as I tightened the inguinal ring, but my hands did not belong to me. My voice was high and clear, giving directions instantly obeyed, and somewhere far away, a small watcher in my brain observed the progress of the operation with a remote sense of interest.

Then it was done, and time began again. I took a step back, breaking the link, and feeling slightly dizzy at the unaccustomed solitude.

"Done," I said, and the hum from the spectators erupted into loud applause. Still feeling intoxicated—had I caught drunkenness by osmosis from Myers?—I turned on one heel and sank into an extravagant low curtsy, facing the dinner guests.

An hour later, I was drunk on my own merits, the victim of a dozen toasts in my honor. I managed to escape briefly, on the excuse of checking on my patient, and staggered upstairs to the guest room where he lay.

I paused on the gallery, clinging to the banister while I steadied myself. There was a loud hum of conversation and laughter from below; the party was still going strong, but had dissolved into small groups scattered over the parquet of the foyer and salon. From this perspective, it looked like a honeycomb, fuzzy wigged heads and gauze-winged dresses bobbing to and fro across the six-sided tiles, buzzing busily over glasses filled with the nectar of brandywine and porter.

If Jamie had wanted a diversion, I thought muzzily, he couldn't have asked for better. Whatever had been going to happen had been effectively forestalled. But what was it—and for how long could it be prevented? I shook my head to clear it—with indifferent results—and went in to see my patient.

Myers was still blissfully and deeply asleep, breathing in long, slow exhalations that made the cotton bed-drapes quiver. The slave Betty nodded at me, smiling.

"He's fine, Mrs. Claire," she whispered. "Couldn't wake that man with a gun, I don't think."

I didn't need to check his heart; his head was turned, and I could see the huge vein that ran down the side of his neck, throbbing with a pulse slow and heavy as a hammer blow. I touched him, feeling his skin cool and damp. No fever, no signs of shock. The whole of his enormous person radiated peace and well-being.

"How is he?" Had I been less drunk, I would have been startled. As it was, I merely swayed round on my axis, to find Jamie standing behind me.

"He's fine," I said. "You couldn't kill him with a cannon. Like you," I said, and found myself leaning against him, arms around his waist, my flushed face buried in the cool folds of his linen. "Indestructible."

He kissed the top of my head, smoothing back a few curls that had escaped from their dressing during the operation.

"Ye did well, Sassenach," he whispered. "Verra well, bonnie lassie."

He smelt of wine and candlewax, of herbs and Highland wool. I slid my hands lower, feeling the curves of his buttocks, smooth and free under his kilt. He moved slightly, the length of his thigh pressing briefly against mine.

"Ye need a bit of air, Sassenach—and we must talk. Can ye leave him for a time?"

I glanced at the bed and its stertorous occupant.

"Yes. As long as Betty will keep sitting with him to be sure he doesn't vomit in his sleep and choke?" I glanced at the slave, who looked surprised that I should ask, but nodded willingly.

"Meet me by the herb garden—and take care not to fall down the stairs and break your neck, aye?" Lifting my chin, he kissed me quick and deep, and left me dizzy, feeling at once more sober and more drunk than before.

13

An Examination of Conscience

Something dark landed on the path in front of us with a soft *plop!* and I stopped abruptly, clutching his arm.

"Frog," Jamie said, unperturbed. "D'ye hear them singing?"

"Singing" wasn't the word that would have struck me about the chorus of croaks and grunts from the reedbeds near the river. On the other hand, Jamie was tone deaf, and made no bones about it.

He extended the toe of his shoe and gently prodded the squat dark shape.

" 'Brekekekex, ko-ax, ko-ax,' " he quoted. " 'Brekekekex, ko-ax!' " The shape hopped away and disappeared into the moist plants by the path.

"I always knew you had a gift for tongues," I said, amused. "Didn't know you spoke frog, though."

"Well, I'm no ways fluent," he said modestly. "Though I've a fine accent, and I say it myself."

I laughed, and he squeezed my hand and let it go. The brief spark of the joke faded, failing to kindle conversation, and we walked on, physically together but miles apart in thought.

I should have been exhausted, but adrenaline was still coursing through my veins. I felt the exultation that comes with the completion of a successful bit of surgery, to say nothing of a little standard alcoholic intoxication. The effect of it all was to make me slightly wobbly on my pins, but with an acute and vivid awareness of everything around me.

There was an ornamental seat under the trees near the dock, and it was to this that Jamie led me, into the shadows. He sank onto the marble bench with a deep sigh, reminding me that I wasn't the only one for whom it had been an eventful evening.

I looked around with exaggerated attention, then sat down beside him.

"We're alone and unobserved," I said. "Do you want to tell me what the hell is going on now?"

"Oh, aye." He straightened, stretching his back. "I should have said something to ye sooner, only I didna quite expect she would do such a thing." He reached out and found my hand in the dark.

"It's not anything wrong, exactly, as I told ye. It's only that when Ulysses brought me the plaid and dirk and the brooch, he told me that Jocasta meant to make an announcement at the dinner tonight—to tell everyone that she meant to make me heir to . . . this."

His gesture took in the house and fields behind us—and everything else: the river mooring, the orchard, the gardens, the stables, the endless acres of resinous pines, the sawmill and the turpentine camp—and the forty slaves who worked them.

I could see the whole thing unfolding as Jocasta had no doubt envisioned it; Jamie sitting at the head of the table, dressed in Hector Cameron's tartan, wearing his blade and his brooch—that brooch with the Camerons' unsubtle clan adjuration "Unite!"—surrounded by Hector's old colleagues and comrades, all eager to welcome their friend's younger kinsman into his place.

Let her make such an announcement, in that company of loyal Scots, well lubricated with the late Hector's fine whisky, and they would have acclaimed him on the spot as the master of River Run, anointed him with boar's fat and crowned him with beeswax candles.

It had been a thoroughly MacKenzie-like plan, I thought; audacious, dramatic—and taking no account of the wishes of the persons involved.

"And if she had," he said, echoing my thoughts with uncanny precision, "I should have found it verra awkward to decline the honor."

"Yes, very."

He sprang suddenly to his feet, too restless to stay still. Without speaking, he held out a hand to me; I rose beside him and we turned back into the orchard path, circling the formal gardens. The lanterns lit for the party had been removed; their candles thriftily snuffed for later use.

"Why did Ulysses tell you?" I wondered aloud.

"Ask yourself, Sassenach," he said. "Who is master now, at River Run?"

"Oh?" I said, and then, "Oh!"

"Oh, indeed," he said dryly. "My aunt is blind; who has the keeping of the accounts, the running of the household? She may decide what things should be done—but who is to say whether they *are* done? Who is always at her hand to tell her aught that happens, whose words are in her ear, whose judgment does she trust above all others?"

"I see." I stared down at the ground, thinking. "You don't suppose he's been fiddling the accounts or anything sordid like that?" I hoped not; I liked Jocasta's butler very much, and had thought there was both fondness and respect between them; I didn't like to think of his cold-bloodedly cheating her.

Jamie shook his head.

"He is not. I've been over the ledgers and accounts, and everything is in order—verra good order indeed. I'm sure he is an honest man and a faithful servant—but he wouldna be human, to welcome giving up his place to a stranger."

He snorted briefly.

"My aunt may be blind, but yon black man sees clear enough. He didna say a word to prevent me, or persuade me of anything: only told me what my aunt meant to do, and then left it to me what *I* should do. Or not."

"You think he knew that you wouldn't—" I stopped there, because I wasn't sure myself that he wouldn't. Pride, caution, or both might have caused him to want to thwart Jocasta's plan, but that didn't mean he meant to reject her offer, either.

He didn't reply, and a small cold chill ran through me. I shivered, in spite of the warm summer air, and took his arm as we walked, seeking reassurance in the solid feel of his flesh beneath my fingers.

It was late July, and the scent of ripening fruit from the orchard was sweet, so heavy on the air that I could almost taste the clean, crisp tang of new apples. I thought of temptation—and the worm that lay hidden beneath a shining skin.

Temptation not only for him, but for me. For him, the chance to be what he was made for by nature, what fate had denied him. He was born and bred to this: the stewardship of a large estate, the care of the people on it, a place of respect among men of substance, his peers. More importantly, the restoration of clan and family. *I am already part of it,* he'd said.

He cared nothing for wealth, of itself; I knew that. Neither did I think he wanted power; if he did, knowing what I knew about the future's shape, he would have chosen to go north, to seek a place among the founders of a nation.

But he had been a laird once. He had told me very little of his time in prison, but one thing he had said rang in my memory. Of the men who shared his confinement, he said—*They were mine. And the having of them kept me alive.* And I remembered what Ian had said of Simon Fraser: *"Care for his men is now his only link with humanity."*

Yes, Jamie needed men. Men to lead, to care for, to defend and to fight with. But not to own.

Past the orchard, still in silence, and down the long walk of herbaceous borders, with the scents of lily and lavender, anemone and roses, so pungent and heady that simply to walk through the hot, heavy air was like throwing oneself headlong onto a bed of fragrant petals.

Oh, River Run was a garden of earthly delight, all right . . . but I had called a black man friend, and left my daughter in his care.

Thinking of Joe Abernathy, and Brianna, gave me a strange sense of dislocated double vision, of existing in two places at once. I could see their faces in my mind, hear their voices in my inner ear. And yet reality was the man beside me, kilt swinging with his stride, head bent in anxious thought.

And that was my temptation: Jamie. Not the inconsequentials of soft beds or gracious rooms, silk gowns or social deference. Jamie.

If he did not take Jocasta's offer, he must do something else. And "something else" was most likely William Tryon's dangerous lure of land and men. Better than Jocasta's generous offer, in its way; what he built would be his own, the legacy he wanted to leave for Brianna. If he lived to build it.

I was still living on two planes. In this one, I could hear the whisper of his kilt where it brushed my skirt, feel the humid warmth of his body, warmer even than the heated air. I could smell the musky scent of him that made me want to pull him from his thoughts into the border, unbelt him and let the plaid fall from his shoulders, pull down my bodice and press my breasts against him, take him down half-naked and wholly roused among the damp green plants, and force him from his thoughts to mine.

But on the plane of memory, I smelled yew trees and the wind from the sea, and under my fingers was no warm man, but the cold, smooth granite of a tombstone with his name.

I didn't speak. Neither did he.

We had made a complete circle by now, and come back to the river's edge, where gray stone steps led down and disappeared under a lapping sheen of water; even so far upstream, the faint echoes of the tide could be felt.

There was a boat moored there; a small rowboat, fit for solitary fishing or a leisurely excursion.

"Will ye come for a row?"

"Yes, why not?" I thought he must feel the same desire I had —to get away from the house and Jocasta, to get enough distance in which to think clearly, without danger of interruption.

I came down, putting my hand on his arm for balance. Before I could step into the boat, though, he turned toward me. Pulling me to him, he kissed me, gently, once, then held me against his body, his chin resting on my head.

"I don't know," he said quietly, in answer to my unspoken questions. He stepped into the boat and offered me a hand.

He was silent while we made our way out onto the river. It was a dark, moonless night, but the reflections of starlight from the surface of the river gave enough light to see, once my eyes had adapted to the shifting glimmer of water and tree-shadow.

"Ye dinna mean to say anything?" he asked abruptly, at last.

"It's not my choice to make," I said, feeling a tightness in my chest that had nothing to do with stays.

"No?"

"She's your aunt. It's your life. It has to be your choice."

"And you'll be a spectator, will you?" He grunted as he spoke, digging with the oars as he pulled upstream. "Is it not *your* life? Or do ye not mean to stay with me, after all?"

"What do you mean, not stay?" I sat up, startled.

"Perhaps it will be too much for you." His head was bent over the oars; I couldn't see his face.

"If you mean what happened at the sawmill—"

"No, not that." He heaved back on the oars, shoulders broadening under his linen, and gave me a crooked smile. "Death and disaster wouldna trouble ye ower-much, Sassenach. But the small things, day by day . . . I see ye flinch, when the black maid combs your hair, or when the boy takes your shoes away to clean.

And the slaves who work in the turpentine camp. That troubles ye, no?''

"Yes. It does. I'm—I can't own slaves. I've told you—"

"Aye, ye have." He rested on the oars for a moment, brushing a lock of hair out of his face. His eyes met mine squarely.

"And if I chose to do this, Sassenach . . . could ye stay by me, and watch, and do nothing—for there is nothing that could be done, until my aunt should die. Perhaps not even then.''

"What do you mean?''

"She will not free her slaves—how should she? I could not, while she lived.''

"But once you had inherited the place . . ." I hesitated. Beyond the ghoulish aspects of discussing Jocasta's death, there was the more concrete consideration that that event was unlikely to occur for some time; Jocasta was little more than sixty, and aside from her blindness, in vigorous health.

I suddenly saw what he meant; could I bring myself to live, day after day, month after month, year after year, as an owner of slaves? I could not pretend otherwise, could take no refuge in the notion that I was only a guest, an outsider.

I bit my lip, in order not to cry out instant denial.

"Even then," he said, answering my partial argument. "Did ye not know that a slave owner cannot free his slaves without the written permission of the Assembly?''

"He what?" I stared blankly at him. "Whyever not?''

"The plantation owners go in fear of an armed insurrection of Negroes," he said. "And d'ye blame them?" he added sardonically.

"Slaves are forbidden to carry weapons, save tools such as tree knives, and there are the bloodshed laws to prevent their use.'' He shook his head. "Nay, the last thing the Assembly would allow is a large group of free blacks let loose upon the countryside. Even if a man wishes to manumit one of his slaves, and is given permission to do so, the freed slave is required to leave the colony within a short time—or he may be captured and enslaved by anyone who chooses to take him.''

"You've thought about it," I said slowly.

"Haven't you?''

I didn't answer. I trailed my hand in the water, a little wave purling up my wrist. No, I hadn't thought about the prospect. Not consciously, because I hadn't wanted to face the choice that was now being laid before me.

"I suppose it would be a great chance," I said, my voice sounding strained and unnatural to my ears. "You'd be in charge of everything . . ."

"My aunt is not a fool," he interrupted, with a slight edge to his voice. "She would make me heir, but not owner in her place. She would use me to do those things she cannot—but I would be no more than her cat's-paw. True, she would ask my opinion, listen to my advice; but nothing would be done, and she didna wish it so."

He shook his head.

"Her husband is dead. Whether she was fond of him or no, she is mistress here now, with none to answer to. And she enjoys the taste of power too well to spit it out."

He was plainly correct in this assessment of Jocasta Cameron's character, and therein lay the key to her plan. She needed a man; someone to go into those places she could not go, to deal with the Navy, to handle the chores of a large estate that she could not manage because of her blindness.

At the same time, she patently did *not* want a husband; someone who would usurp her power and dictate to her. Had he not been a slave, Ulysses could have acted for her—but while he could be her eyes and ears, he could not be her hands.

No, Jamie was the perfect choice; a strong, competent man, able to command respect among peers, compel obedience in subordinates. One knowledgeable in the management of land and men. Furthermore, a man bound to her by kinship and obligation, there to do her bidding—but essentially powerless. He would be held in thrall by dependence upon her bounty, and by the rich bribe of River Run itself; a debt that need not be paid until the matter was no longer of any earthly concern to Jocasta Cameron.

There was an increasing lump in my throat as I sought for words. I couldn't, I thought. I couldn't manage it. But I couldn't face the alternative, either; I couldn't urge him to reject Jocasta's offer, knowing it would send him to Scotland, to meet an unknown death.

"I can't say what you should do," I finally said, my voice barely audible above the regular lap of the oars.

There was an eddy pool, where a large tree had fallen into the water, its branches forming a trap for all the debris that drifted downstream. Jamie made for this, backing the rowboat neatly into quiet water. He let down the oars, and wiped a sleeve across his forehead, breathing heavily from exertion.

The night was quiet around us, with little sound but the lapping of water, and the occasional scrape of submerged tree branches against the hull. At last he reached out and touched my chin.

"Your face is my heart, Sassenach," he said softly, "and love of you is my soul. But you're right; ye canna be my conscience."

In spite of everything, I felt a lightening of spirit, as though some indefinable burden had dropped away.

"Oh, I'm glad," I said, adding impulsively, "it would be a terrible strain."

"Oh, aye?" He looked mildly startled. "Ye think me verra wicked, then?"

"You're the best man I've ever met," I said. "I only meant . . . it's such a strain, to try to live for two people. To try to make them fit your ideas of what's right . . . you do it for a child, of course, you have to, but even then, it's dreadfully hard work. I couldn't do it for you—it would be wrong even to try."

I'd taken him back more than a little. He sat for some moments, his face half turned away.

"Do ye really think me a good man?" he said at last. There was a queer note in his voice, that I couldn't quite decipher.

"Yes," I said, with no hesitation. Then added, half jokingly, "Don't you?"

After a long pause, he said, quite seriously, "No, I shouldna think so."

I looked at him, speechless, no doubt with my mouth hanging open.

"I am a violent man, and I ken it well," he said quietly. He spread his hands out on his knees; big hands, which could wield sword and dagger with ease, or choke the life from a man. "So do you—or ye should."

"You've never done anything you weren't forced to do!"

"No?"

"I don't think so," I said, but even as I spoke, a shadow of doubt clouded my words. Even when done from the most urgent necessity, did such things not leave a mark on the soul?

"Ye wouldna hold me in the same estimation as, say, a man like Stephen Bonnet? He might well say he acted from necessity."

"If you think you have the slightest thing in common with Stephen Bonnet, you're dead wrong," I said firmly.

He shrugged, half impatient, and shifted restlessly on the narrow bench.

"There's nay much to choose between Bonnet and me, save

that I have a sense of honor that he lacks. What else keeps me from turning thief?'' he demanded. ''From plundering those whom I might? It is in me to do it—my one grandsire built Leoch on the gold of those he robbed in the Highland passes; the other built his fortune on the bodies of women whom he forced for their wealth and titles.''

He stretched himself, powerful shoulders rising dark against the shimmer of the water behind him. Then he suddenly took hold of the oars across his knees and flung them into the bottom of the boat, with a crash that made me jump.

''I am more than five-and-forty!'' he said. ''A man should be settled at that age, no? He should have a house, and some land to grow his food, and a bit of money put away to see him through his auld age, at the least.''

He took a deep breath; I could see the white bosom of his shirt rise with his swelling chest.

''Well, I dinna have a house. Or land. Or money. Not a croft, not a tattie-plot, not a cow or a sheep or a pig or a goat! I havena got a rooftree or a bedstead, or a pot to piss in!''

He slammed his fist down on the thwart, making the wooden seat vibrate under me.

''I dinna own the clothes I stand up in!''

There was a long silence, broken only by the thin song of crickets.

''You have me,'' I said, in a small voice. It didn't seem a lot.

He made a small sound in his throat that might have been either a laugh or a sob.

''Aye, I have,'' he said. His voice was quivering a bit, though whether with passion or amusement, I couldn't tell. ''That's the hell of it, aye?''

''It is?''

He threw up his hand in a gesture of profound impatience.

''If it was only me, what would it matter? I could live like Myers; go to the woods, hunt and fish for my living, and when I was too old, lie down under a peaceful tree and die, and let the foxes gnaw my bones. Who would care?''

He shrugged his shoulders with irritable violence, as though his shirt was too tight.

''But it's *not* only me,'' he said. ''It's you, and it's Ian and it's Duncan and it's Fergus and it's Marsali—God help me, there's even Laoghaire to think of!''

''Oh, let's don't,'' I said.

"Do ye not understand?" he said, in near desperation. "I would lay the world at your feet, Claire—and I have nothing to give ye!"

He honestly thought it mattered.

I sat looking at him, searching for words. He was half turned away, shoulders slumped in despair.

Within an hour, I had gone from anguish at the thought of losing him in Scotland, to a strong desire to bed him in the herbaceous borders, and from that to a pronounced urge to hit him on the head with an oar. Now I was back to tenderness.

At last I took one big, callused hand and slid forward so I knelt on the boards between his knees. I laid my head against his chest, and felt his breath stir my hair. I had no words, but I had made my choice.

" 'Whither thou goest,' " I said, " 'I will go; and where thou lodgest, I will lodge: thy people shall be my people, and thy God my God: Where thou diest, will I die, and there will I be buried.' " Be it Scottish hill or southern forest. "You do what you have to; I'll be there."

The water ran fast and shallow near the middle of the creek; I could see the boulders black just beneath the glinting surface. Jamie saw them, too, and pulled strongly for the far side, bringing us to rest against a shelving gravel bank, in a pool formed by the roots of a weeping willow. I leaned out and caught a branch of the willow, and wrapped the painter round it.

I had thought we would return to River Run, but evidently this expedition had some point beyond respite. We had continued upriver instead, Jamie pulling strongly against the slow current.

Left alone with my thoughts, I could only listen to the faint hiss of his breath, and wonder what he would do. If he chose to stay . . . well, it might not be as difficult as he thought. I didn't underrate Jocasta Cameron, but neither did I underestimate Jamie Fraser. Both Colum and Dougal MacKenzie had tried to bend him to their will—and both had failed.

I had a moment's qualm at the memory of my last sight of Dougal MacKenzie, mouthing soundless curses as he drowned in his own blood, Jamie's dirk socketed at the base of his throat. *I am a violent man,* he'd said, *you know it.*

But he was still wrong; there was a difference between this man and Stephen Bonnet, I thought, watching the flex of his body on the oars, the grace and power of the sweep of his arms. He had several things beyond the honor that he claimed: kindness, courage . . . and a conscience.

I realized where we were going, as he backed with one oar, steering across the current toward the mouth of a wide creek, overhung with aspens. I had never approached by water before, but Jocasta had said it was not far.

I should not have been surprised; if he had come out tonight to confront his demons, it was a most appropriate place.

A little way above the creek mouth, the mill loomed dark and silent. There was a dim glow behind its bulk; light from the slave shanties near the woods. We were surrounded by the usual night noises, but the place seemed strangely quiet, in spite of the racket made by trees and frogs and water. Though it was night, the huge building seemed to cast a shadow—though this was plainly no more than my imagination.

"Places that are very busy in the daytime always seem particularly spooky at night," I said, in an effort to break the mill's silence.

"Do they?" Jamie sounded abstracted. "I didna much like that one in the daylight."

I shuddered at the memory.

"Neither did I. I only meant—"

"Byrnes is dead." He didn't look at me; his face was turned toward the mill, half-hidden by the willow's shadow.

I dropped the end of the tie rope.

"The overseer? When?" I said, shocked more by the abruptness than the revelation. "And how?"

"This afternoon. Campbell's youngest lad brought the news just before sunset."

"How?" I asked again. I gripped my knees, a double handful of ivory silk twisted in my fingers.

"It was the lockjaw." His voice was casual, unemphatic. "A verra nasty way to die."

He was right about that. I had never actually seen anyone die of tetanus myself, but I knew the symptoms well enough: restlessness and difficulty swallowing, developing into a progressive stiffening as the muscles of arms and legs and neck began to spasm. The spasms increased in severity and duration until the patient's body was hard as wood, arched in an agony that came on and receded, came on again, went off, and at last came on in an endless tetany that could not be relaxed by anything save death.

"He died grinnin'," Ronnie Campbell said. But I shouldna think it was a happy death, forbye." It was a grim joke, but there was little humor in his voice.

I sat up quite straight, feeling cold all down my spine in spite of the warmth of the night.

"It isn't a quick death, either," I said. Suspicion spread cold tentacles through my mind. "It takes days to die of tetanus."

"It took Davie Byrnes five days, first to last." If there had been any trace of humor in his voice to start with, it was gone now.

"You saw him," I said, a small flicker of anger beginning to thaw the internal chill. "You saw him! And you didn't tell me?"

I had dressed Byrnes's injury—hideous, but not life-threatening—and had been told that he would be kept somewhere "safe" until the disturbance over the lynching had died down. Heartsick as I was over the matter, I had made no effort to inquire further after the overseer's whereabouts or welfare; it was my own guilt at this neglect that made me angry, and I knew it—but the knowledge didn't help.

"Could ye have done anything? I thought ye told me that the lockjaw was one of the things that couldna be helped, even in your time." He wasn't looking at me; I could see his profile turned toward the mill, head stamped in darker black against the lighter shadow of pale leaves.

I forced myself to let go of my skirt. I smoothed the crumpled patches over my knee, thinking dimly that Phaedre would have a terrible time ironing it.

"No," I said, with a little effort. "No, I couldn't have saved him. But I should have seen him; I might have eased him a little."

Now he did look at me; I saw his head turn, and felt the shifting of his weight in the boat.

"You might," he said evenly.

"And you wouldn't let me—" I stopped, remembering his absences this past week, and his evasive replies when I had asked him where he'd been. I could imagine the scene all too well; the tiny, stifling attic room in Farquard Campbell's house where I had dressed Byrnes's injury. The racked figure on the bed, dying by inches under the cold eyes of those the law had made his unwilling allies, knowing that he died despised. The sense of cold came back, raising gooseflesh on my arms.

"No, I wouldna let Campbell send for you," he said softly. "There's the law, Sassenach—and there is justice. I ken the difference well enough."

"There's such a thing as mercy, too." And had anyone asked, I would have called Jamie Fraser a merciful man. He had been, once. But the years between now and then had been hard ones—and compassion was a soft emotion, easily eroded by circumstance. I had thought he still had his kindness, though; and felt a queer pain at the thought of its loss. *I shouldna think so, no.* Had that been no more than honesty?

The boat had drifted halfway round, so that the drooping branch hung now between us. There was a small snort from the darkness behind the leaves.

"Blessed are the merciful," he said, "for they shall find mercy. Byrnes wasn't, and he didn't. And as for me, once God had made his opinion of the man known, I didna think it right to interfere."

"You think *God* gave him tetanus?"

"I canna think anyone else would have the imagination for it. Besides," he went on, logically, "where else would ye look for justice?"

I searched for words, and failed to find any. Giving up, I returned to the only possible point of argument. I felt a little sick.

"You ought to have told me. Even if you didn't think I could help, it wasn't your business to decide—"

"I didna want ye to go." His voice was still quiet, but there was a note of steel in it now.

"I know you didn't! But it doesn't matter whether you thought Byrnes deserved to suffer or—"

"Not for him!" The boat rocked suddenly as he moved, and I grasped the sides to keep my balance. He spoke violently.

"I didna care a fig whether Byrnes died easy or hard, but I'm no a monster of cruelty! I didna keep you from him to make him suffer; I kept ye away to protect you."

I was relieved to hear this, but increasingly angry as the truth of what he'd done dawned on me.

"It wasn't your business to decide that. If I'm not your conscience, it isn't up to you to be mine!" I brushed angrily at the screen of willow fronds between us, trying to see him.

Suddenly a hand shot through the leaves and grabbed my wrist.

"It's up to me to keep ye safe!"

I tried to jerk away, but he had a tight grip on me, and he wasn't letting go.

"I am not a young girl who needs protection, nor yet an idiot! If there's some reason for me not to do something, then tell me and I'll listen. But you can't decide what I'm to do and where I'm to go without even consulting me—I won't stand for that, and you bloody well know it!''

The boat lurched, and with a huge rustling of leaves, he popped his head through the willow, glaring.

"I am not trying to say where ye'll go!"

"You decided where I *mustn't* go, and that's just as bad!" The willow leaves slid back over his shoulders as the boat moved, jarred by his violence, and we revolved slowly, coming out of the tree's shadow.

He loomed in front of me, massive as the mill, his head and shoulders blotting out a good bit of the scenery behind him. The long, straight nose was an inch from mine, and his eyes had gone narrow. They were a dark enough blue to be black in this light, and looking into them at close range was most unnerving.

I blinked. He didn't.

He had let go of my wrist when he came through the leaves. Now he took hold of my upper arms. I could feel the heat of his grip through the cloth. His hands were very big and very hard, making me suddenly aware of the fragility of my own bones in contrast. *I am a violent man.*

He'd shaken me a time or two before, and I hadn't liked it. In case he had something of the sort in mind just now, I inserted a foot between his legs, and prepared to give him a swift knee where it would do most good.

"I was wrong," he said.

Tensed for violence, I had actually started to jerk my foot up, when I heard what he had said. Before I could stop, he had clamped his legs tight together, trapping my knee between his thighs.

"I *said* I was wrong, Sassenach," he repeated, a touch of impatience in his voice. "D'ye mind?"

"Ah . . . no," I said, feeling a trifle sheepish. I wiggled my knee tentatively, but he kept his thighs squeezed tight together.

"You wouldn't consider letting go of me, would you?" I said politely. My heart was still pounding.

"No, I wouldn't. Are ye going to listen to me now?"

"I suppose so," I said, still polite. "It doesn't look as though I'm very busy at the moment."

I was close enough to see his mouth twitch. His thighs squeezed tighter for a moment, then relaxed.

"This is a verra foolish quarrel, and you know that as well as I do."

"No, I don't." My anger had faded somewhat, but I wasn't about to let him dismiss it altogether. "It's maybe not important to you, but it is to me. It isn't foolish. And you know it, or you wouldn't be admitting you're wrong."

The twitch was more pronounced this time. He took a deep breath, and dropped his hands from my shoulders.

"Well, then. I should maybe have told ye about Byrnes; I admit it. But if I had, ye would have gone to him, even if I'd said it was the lockjaw—and I kent it was, I've seen it before. Even if there was nothing ye could do, you'd still go? No?"

"Yes. Even if—yes, I would have gone."

In fact, there was nothing I could have done for Byrnes. Myers's anesthetic wouldn't have helped a case of tetanus. Nothing short of injectable curare would ease those spasms. I could have given him nothing more than the comfort of my presence, and it was doubtful that he would have appreciated that—or even noticed it. Still, I would have felt bound to offer it.

"I would have had to go," I said, more gently. "I'm a doctor. Don't you see?"

"Of course I do," he said gruffly. "D'ye think I dinna ken ye at all, Sassenach?"

Without waiting for an answer, he went on.

"There was talk about what happened at the mill—there would be, aye? But with the man dying under your hands as he did—well, no one's said straight out that ye might have killed him on purpose . . . but it's easy to see folk thinkin' it. Not thinkin' that ye killed him, even—but only that ye might have thought to let him die on purpose, so as to save him from the rope."

I stared at my hands, spread out on my knees, nearly as pale as the ivory satin under them.

"I did think of it."

"I ken that fine, aye?" he said dryly. "I saw your face, Sassenach."

I drew a deep breath, if only to assure myself that the air was no longer thick with the smell of blood. There was nothing but the turpentine scent of the pine forest, clean and astringent in my nostrils. I had a sudden vivid memory of the hospital, of the smell of pine-scented disinfectant that hung in the air, that overlaid but could not banish the underlying smell of sickness.

I took another cleansing breath, and raised my head to look at Jamie.

"And did *you* wonder if I'd killed him?"

He looked faintly surprised.

"Ye would have done as ye thought best." He dismissed the minor question of whether I'd killed a man, in favor of the point at issue.

"But it didna seem wise for ye to preside over both deaths, if ye take my meaning."

I did, and not for the first time I was aware of the subtle networks of which he was a part, in a way I could never be. This place in its way was as strange to him as it was to me; and yet he knew not only what people were saying—anyone could find that out, who cared to haunt tavern and market—but what they were thinking.

What was more irritating was that he knew what *I* was thinking.

"So ye see," he said, watching me. "I kent Byrnes was sure to die, and ye couldna help. Yet if ye knew his trouble, ye'd surely go to him. And then he would die, and folk would maybe not say how strange it was, that both men had died under your hand, so to speak—but—"

"But they'd be thinking it," I finished for him.

The twitch grew into a crooked smile.

"Folk notice you, Sassenach."

I bit my lip. For good or for ill, they did, and the noticing had come close to killing me more than once.

He rose, and taking hold of a branch for balance, stepped out on the gravel and pulled the plaid up over his shoulder.

"I told Mrs. Byrnes I would fetch away her husband's things from the mill," he said. "Ye needna come, if ye dinna wish."

The mill loomed against the star-spattered sky. It couldn't have looked more sinister if it had tried. *Whither thou goest, I will go.*

I thought I knew now what he was doing. He had wanted to see it all, before making up his mind; see it with the knowledge that it might be his. Walking through the gardens and orchards, rowing past the acres of thick pines, visiting the mill—he was surveying the domain he was offered, weighing and evaluating, deciding what complications must be dealt with, and whether he could or would accept the challenge.

After all, I thought sourly, the Devil had insisted on showing Jesus everything He was passing up, taking Him up to the top of the Temple to gaze on the cities of the world. The only difficulty was that if Jamie decided to fling himself off, there wasn't a legion of angels standing by to stop him dashing his foot—and everything else—against a slab of Scottish granite.

Only me.

"Wait," I said, clambering out of the boat. "I'm coming, too."

The lumber was still stacked in the millyard; no one had moved any of it since the last time I had been here. The dark took away all sense of perspective; the stacks of fresh timber were pale rectangles that seemed to float above an invisible ground, first distant, then suddenly looming close enough to brush my skirts. The air smelt of pinesap and sawdust.

I couldn't see the ground under my own feet, for that matter, obscured as it was both by darkness and by my billowing ivory skirt. Jamie held my arm to keep me from stumbling. He never stumbled, of course. Perhaps living all his life without even the thought of light outside after sunset had given him some sort of radar, I thought; like a bat.

There was a fire burning, somewhere among the slave huts. It was very late; most would be sleeping. In the Indies, there would have been the nightlong sound of drums and keening; the slaves would have made lamentations for a fellow's death, a festival of mourning to last the week. Here, there was nothing. No sound save the pine trees' soughing, no flicker of movement save the faint light at the forest's edge.

"They are afraid," Jamie said softly, pausing to listen to the silence, as I did.

"Little wonder," I said, half under my breath. "So am I."

He made a small huffing sound that might have been amusement.

"So am I," he muttered, "but not of ghosts." He took my arm and pushed open the small man-door at the side of the mill before I could ask what he *was* afraid of.

The silence inside had a body to it. At first I thought it like the eerie quiet of dead battlefields, but then I realized the difference. This silence was alive. And whatever lived in the silence here, it wasn't lying quiet. I thought I could still smell the blood, thick on the air.

Then I breathed deeply and thought again, cold horror rippling up my spine. I *could* smell blood. Fresh blood.

I gripped Jamie's arm, but he had smelled it himself; his arm had gone hard under my hand, muscles tensed in wariness. Without a word, he detached himself from my grip, and vanished.

For a moment, I thought he truly *had* vanished, and nearly

panicked, groping for him, my hand closing on the empty air where he'd stood. Then I realized that he had merely flung the dark plaid over his head, instantly hiding the paleness of face and linen shirt. I heard his step, quick and light on the dirt floor, and then that was gone too.

The air was hot and still, and thick with blood. A rank, sweet smell, with a metal taste on the back of the tongue. Exactly the same as it had been a week ago, conjuring hallucination. Still in the grip of a cold grue, I swung around and strained my eyes toward the far side of the cavernous room, half expecting to see the scene engraved on my memory materialize again out of darkness. The rope stretched tight from the lumber crane, the huge hook swaying with its groaning burden . . .

A groan rent the air, and I nearly bit my lip in two. My throat swelled with a swallowed scream; only the fear of drawing something to me kept me silent.

Where was Jamie? I longed to call out for him, but didn't dare. My eyes had grown enough accustomed to the dark to make out the shadow of the saw blade, an amorphous blob ten feet away, but the far side of the room was a wall of blackness. I strained my eyes to see, realizing belatedly that in my pale dress, I was undoubtedly visible to anyone in the room with me.

The groan came again, and I started convulsively. My palms were sweating. *It's not!* I told myself fiercely. *It isn't, it can't be!*

I was paralyzed with fear, and it took some moments for me to realize what my ears had told me. The sound hadn't come from the blackness across the room, where the crane stood with its hook. It had come from somewhere behind me.

I whirled. The door we had come through was still open, a pale rectangle in the pitch-black. Nothing showed, nothing moved between me and the door. I took a quick step toward it and stopped. Every muscle in my legs strained to run like hell—but I couldn't leave Jamie.

Again the sound, that same sobbing gasp of physical anguish; pain past the point of crying out. With it, a new thought popped into my mind; what if it was Jamie making the sound?

Shocked out of caution, I turned toward the sound and shouted his name, raising echoes from the roof high above.

"Jamie!" I cried again. "Where *are* you?"

"Here, Sassenach." Jamie's muffled voice came from somewhere to my left, calm but somehow urgent. "Come to me, will ye?"

It wasn't him. Nearly shaking with relief at the sound of his voice, I blundered through the dark, not caring now what had made the sound, as long as it wasn't Jamie.

My hand struck a wooden wall, groped blindly, and finally found a door, standing open. He was inside the overseer's quarters.

I stepped through the door, and felt the change at once. The air was even closer, and much hotter, than that in the mill proper. The floor here was of wood, but there was no echo to my step; the air was dead still, suffocating. And the smell of blood was even stronger.

"Where are you?" I called again, low-voiced this time.

"Here," came the reply, startlingly near at hand. "By the bed. Come and help me; it's a lass."

He was in the tiny bedroom. The small room was windowless, and lightless too. I found them by feel, Jamie kneeling on the wooden floor beside a narrow bed, and in the bed, a body.

It was a female, as he'd said; touch told me that at once. Touch told me also that she was exsanguinating. The cheek I brushed was cool and clammy. Everything else I touched was warm and wet; her clothing, the bedclothes, the mattress beneath her. I could feel wetness soaking through my skirt where I knelt on the floor.

I felt for a pulse in the throat and couldn't find it. The chest moved slightly under my hand, the only sign of life beyond the faint sigh that went with it.

"It's all right now," I heard myself saying, and my voice was soothing, all trace of panic gone, though in truth there was more reason for it now. "We're here, you're not alone. What's happened to you, can you tell me?"

All the time my hands were darting over head and throat and chest and stomach, pushing sodden clothes aside, searching blindly, frantically, for a wound to stanch. Nothing, no spurt of artery, no raw gash. And all the time, there was a faint but steady *pit-a-pat, pit-a-pat,* like the sound of tiny feet running.

"Tell . . ." It was not so much a word as the articulation of a sigh. Then a catch, a sobbing breath indrawn.

"Who has done this to ye, lass?" Jamie's disembodied voice came low and urgent. "Tell me, who?"

"Tell . . ."

I touched all the places where the great vessels lie close beneath the skin and found them whole. Seized her by an unresisting arm and lifted, thrust a hand beneath to feel her back. All the heat of her body was there; the bodice was damp with sweat, but not blood-soaked.

"It will be all right," I said again. "You're not alone. Jamie, hold her hand." Hopelessness came down on me; I knew what it must be.

"I already have it," he said to me, and "Dinna trouble, lass," to her. "It will be all right, d'ye hear me?" *Pit-a-pat, pit-a-pat.* The tiny feet were slowing.

"Tell . . ."

I could not help, but nonetheless slid my hand beneath her skirt again, this time letting my fingers curve between the limp splayed thighs. She was still warm here, very warm. Blood flowed gently over my hand and through my fingers, hot and wet as the air around us, unstoppable as the water that flowed down the mill's sluice.

"I . . . die . . ."

"I think ye are murdered, lass," Jamie said to her, very gently. "Will ye not say who has killed you?"

Her breath came louder now, a soft rattle in her throat. *Pit. Pat. Pit. Pat.* The feet were tiptoeing softly now.

"Ser . . . geant. Tell . . . him . . ."

I drew my hand out from between her thighs and took her other hand in mine, heedless of the blood. It scarcely mattered now, after all.

". . . *tell* . . ." came with sudden intensity, and then silence. A long silence, and then, another long, sighing breath. A silence, even longer. And a breath.

"I will," said Jamie. His voice was no more than a whisper in the dark. "I will do it. I promise ye."

Pit.

Pat.

They called it the "death drop," in the Highlands; the sound of dripping water, heard in a house when one of the inhabitants was about to die. Not water dripping here, but a sure sign, nonetheless.

There was no more sound from the darkness. I couldn't see Jamie, but felt the slight movement of the bed against my thighs as he leaned forward.

"God will forgive ye," he whispered to the silence. "Go in peace."

I could hear the buzzing the moment we stepped into the over-seer's quarters the next morning. In the huge, dusty silence of the mill, everything had been muffled in space and sawdust. But in this small, partitioned area the walls caught every sound and threw it back; our footsteps echoed from wooden floor to wooden ceiling. I felt like a fly sealed inside a snare drum, and suffered a moment's claustrophobia, trapped as I was in the narrow passage between the two men.

There were only two rooms, separated by a short passage that led from the outdoors into the mill proper. On our right lay the larger room that had served the Byrneses for living and cooking, and on the left, the smaller bedroom, from which the noise was coming. Jamie took a deep breath, clasped his plaid to his face, and pulled open the bedroom door.

It looked like a blanket covering the bed, a blanket of gunmetal blue sparked with green. Then Jamie took a step into the room and the flies rose buzzing from their clotted meal in a swarm of gluttonous protest.

I bit back a cry of abhorrence and ducked, flailing at them. Bloated, slow-moving bodies hit my face and arms and bounced away, circling lazily through the thick air. Farquard Campbell made a Scottish noise of overpowering disgust that sounded like "Heuch!" then lowered his head and pushed past me, eyes slitted and lips pressed tight together, nostrils pinched to whiteness.

The tiny bedroom was hardly bigger than the coffin it had become. There were no windows, only cracks between the boards that let in a dim uncertain light. The atmosphere was hot and humid as a tropical greenhouse, thick with the rotting-sweet smell of death. I could feel the sweat snaking down my sides, ticklish as flies' feet, and tried to breathe only through my mouth.

She had not been large; her body made only the slightest mound beneath the blanket we had laid over her the night before, for decency's sake. Her head seemed big by contrast to the shrunken body, like a child's stick figure with a round ball stuck on toothpick limbs.

Brushing away several flies too glutted to move, Jamie pulled back the blanket. The blanket, like everything else, was blotched and crusted, sodden at the foot. The human body, on average, contains eight pints of blood, but it seems a lot more when you spread it around.

I had seen her face briefly the night before, dead features lent an artificial glow by the light of the pine splinter Jamie held above her. Now she lay pallid and dank as a mushroom, blunt features emerging from a web of fine brown hair. It was impossible to tell her age, save that she was not old. Neither could I tell whether she had been attractive; there was no beauty of bone, but animation might have flushed the round cheeks and lent her deepset eyes a sparkle men might have found pretty. One man had, I thought. Pretty enough, anyway.

The men were murmuring together, bent over the still form. Mr. Campbell turned now to me, wearing a slight frown beneath his formal wig.

"You are reasonably sure, Mrs. Fraser, of the cause of death?"

"Yes." Trying not to breathe the fetid air, I picked up the edge of the blanket, and turned it back, exposing the corpse's legs. The feet were faintly blue and beginning to swell.

"I drew her skirt down, but I left everything else as it was," I explained, pulling it up again.

My stomach muscles tightened automatically as I touched her. I had seen dead bodies before, and this was far from the most gruesome, but the hot climate and closed atmosphere had prevented the body from cooling much; the flesh of her thigh was as warm as mine, but unpleasantly flaccid.

I had left it where we found it, in the bed between her legs. A kitchen skewer, more than a foot long. It was covered in dried blood as well, but clearly visible.

"I . . . um . . . found no wound on the body," I said, putting it as delicately as possible.

"Aye, I see." Mr. Campbell's frown seemed to lessen slightly. "Ah, well, at least 'tis likely not a case of deliberate murder, then."

I opened my mouth to reply, but caught a warning look from Jamie. Not noticing, Mr. Campbell went on.

"The question remains whether the poor woman will have done it herself, or met her death by the agency of another. What think ye, Mistress Fraser?"

Jamie narrowed his eyes at me over Campbell's shoulder, but the warning was unnecessary; we had discussed the matter last night, and come to our own conclusions—also to the conclusion that our opinions need not be shared with the forces of law and order in Cross Creek; not just yet. I pinched my nose slightly under pretext of the smell, in order to disguise any telltale alteration of my expression. I was a very bad liar.

"I'm sure she did it by herself," I said firmly. "It takes very little time to bleed to death in this manner, and as Jamie told you, she was still alive when we found her. We were outside the mill, talking, for some time before we came in; no one would have been able to leave without our seeing them.''

On the other hand, a person might quite easily have hidden in the other room, and crept out quietly in the dark while we were occupied in comforting the dying woman. If this possibility did not occur to Mr. Campbell, I saw no reason to draw it to his attention.

Jamie had rearranged his features into an expression of gravity suitable to the occasion by the time Mr. Campbell turned back to him. The older man shook his head in regret.

''Ah, poor unfortunate lass! I suppose we can but be relieved that no one else has shared her sin.''

''What about the man who fathered the child she was trying to get rid of?'' I said, with a certain amount of acidity. Mr. Campbell looked startled, but pulled himself quickly back together.

''Um . . . quite so,'' he said, and coughed. ''Though we do not know whether she were married—''

''So ye do not know the woman yourself, sir?'' Jamie butted in before I could make any further injudicious remarks.

Campbell shook his head.

''She is not the servant of Mr. Buchanan or the MacNeills, I am sure. Nor Judge Alderdyce. Those are the only plantations near enough from which she might have walked. Though it does occur to me to wonder why she should have come to this particular place to perform such a desperate act . . .''

It had occurred to Jamie and me, too. To prevent Mr. Campbell's taking the next step in this line of inquiry, Jamie intervened again.

''She said verra little, but she did mention a 'Sergeant.' 'Tell the Sergeant' were her words. Do ye perhaps have a thought whom she might mean by that, sir?''

''I think there is an army sergeant in charge of the guard on the royal warehouse. Yes, I am sure of it.'' Mr. Campbell brightened slightly. ''Ah! Nay doubt the woman was attached in some way to the military establishment. Depend upon it, that is the explanation. Though I still wonder why she—''

''Mr. Campbell, do pardon me—I'm afraid I'm feeling a bit faint,'' I interrupted, laying a hand on his sleeve. This was no lie; I hadn't slept or eaten. I felt light-headed from the heat and the smell, and I knew I must look pale.

"Will ye see my wife outside, sir?" Jamie said. He gestured toward the bed and its pathetic burden. "I'll bring the poor lass along as I may."

"Pray do not trouble yourself, Mr. Fraser," Campbell protested, already turning to usher me out. "My servant can fetch out the body."

"It is my aunt's mill, sir, and thus my concern." Jamie spoke politely, but firmly. "I shall attend to it."

Phaedre was waiting outside, by the wagon.

"I told you that place got haints," she said, surveying me with an air of grim satisfaction. "You white as ary sheet, ma'am." She handed me a flask of spiced wine, wrinkling her nose delicately in my direction.

"You smellin' worse than what you was last night, and you look like you come from a pig-killin' then. Sit you down in the shade here and drink that up; fix you up peart." She glanced over my shoulder. I looked back as well, and saw that Campbell had reached the shade of the sycamores by the creek bank, and was deep in conversation with his servant.

"Found her," Phaedre said at once, dropping her voice. Her eyes cut sideways, toward the small cluster of slave huts, barely visible from this side of the mill.

"You're sure? You didn't have much time." I took a mouthful of wine and held it, glad of the sharp bouquet that rose up the back of my throat, cleansing my palate of the taste of death.

Phaedre nodded, her glance moving to the men under the trees.

"Didn't need much. Walked down by them houses, saw one door hangin' open, little bits of trash scattered round like somebody done left in a hurry. I find a picanin' and ask him who livin' there, he tell me Pollyanne live there, but she gone now, he don't know where. Ask him when she leave, he say she there for supper last night, this mornin' she gone, nobody see her." Her eyes met mine, dark with questions. "Now you know, what you mean to do?"

A bloody good question, and one for which I had no answer at all. I swallowed the wine, and along with it, a rising sense of panic.

"All the slaves here must know she's gone; how long before anyone else finds out? Whose business will it be to know such things, now that Byrnes is dead?"

Phaedre raised one shoulder in a graceful shrug.

"Anybody come askin' find out right quick. But whose business it be to ask—" She nodded toward the mill. We had left the small door to the living quarters open; Jamie was coming out, a blanket-wrapped burden cradled in his arms.

"Reckon it's his," she said.

I am already part of it. He had known, even before the interrupted dinner party. With no formal announcement, with neither invitation nor acceptance of the role, he fit the place, the part, like a piece slipping into a jigsaw puzzle. Already he was the master of River Run—if he wanted to be.

Campbell's servant had come to help with the body; Jamie sank to one knee by the edge of the mill flume, surrendering his burden gently to the earth. I gave Phaedre back the flask, with a nod of thanks.

"Will you fetch the things from the wagon?"

Without a word, Phaedre went to get the things I had brought— a blanket, a bucket, clean rags, and a jar of herbs—while I went to join Jamie.

He was kneeling by the creek, washing his hands, a little way upstream from where the body lay. It was foolish to wash in preparation for what I was about to do, but habit was strong; I knelt beside him and dipped my hands as well, letting the cold fresh rush of water carry away the touch of clammy flesh.

"I was right," I said to him, low-voiced. "It was a woman called Pollyanne; she's run away in the night."

He grimaced, rubbing his palms briskly together, and glanced over his shoulder. Campbell was standing over the corpse now, a slight frown of distaste still on his face.

Jamie scowled in concentration, gaze returning to his hands. "Well, that'll put a cocked hat on it, aye?" He bent and splashed his face, then shook his head violently, flinging drops like a wet dog. Then he gave me a nod, and stood up, wiping his face with the end of his stained plaid.

"See to the lassie, aye, Sassenach?" He stalked purposefully toward Mr. Campbell, plaid swinging.

There was no use saving any of her clothes; I cut them off. Undressed, she looked to be in her twenties. Undernourished; ribs countable, arms and legs slender and pale as stripped branches. For all that, she was still surprisingly heavy, and the remnants of rigor mortis made her hard to handle. Phaedre and I were both sweating heavily before we finished, and strands of hair were escaping from the knot at my neck and pasting themselves to my flushed cheeks.

At least the heavy labor kept conversation to a minimum, leaving me in peace with my thoughts. Not that my thoughts were particularly peaceful.

A woman seeking to "slip a bairn," as Jamie put it, would do it in her own room, her own bed, if she were doing it alone. The only reason for the stranger to have come to a remote place such as this was to meet the person who would do the office for her—a person who could not come to her.

We must look for a slave in the mill quarters, I had told him, one maybe with the reputation of a midwife, someone women would talk about among themselves, would recommend in whispers.

The fact that I had apparently been proved right gave me no satisfaction. The abortionist had fled, fearing that the woman would have told us who had done the deed. If she had stayed put and said nothing, Farquard Campbell might have taken my word for it that the woman must have done it herself—he could hardly prove otherwise. If anyone else found that the slave Pollyanne had run, though—and of course they would find out!—and she were caught and questioned, the whole matter would no doubt come out at once. And then what?

I shuddered, despite the heat. Did the law of bloodshed apply in this case? It certainly ought, I thought, grimly sluicing yet another bucket of water over the splayed white limbs, if quantity counted for anything.

Damn the woman, I thought, using irritation to cover a useless pity. I could do nothing for her now save try to tidy up the mess she had left—in every sense of the word. And perhaps try to save the other player in this tragedy; the hapless woman who had done murder unmeaning, in the guise of help, and who stood now to pay for that mistake with her own life.

Jamie had gotten the wine flask, I saw; he was passing it back and forth with Farquard Campbell, the two talking intently, occasionally turning to gesture at the mill or back toward the river or the town.

"You got anything I can comb her out with, ma'am?"

Phaedre's question pulled my attention back to the job at hand.

She was squatting by the body, fingering the tangled hair critically.

"Wouldn't like to put her in the ground lookin' like this, poor child," she said, shaking her head.

I thought Phaedre was likely not much older than the dead woman—and in any case, it scarcely mattered that the corpse should go to its grave well-groomed. Still, I groped in my pocket and came up with a small ivory comb, with which Phaedre set to work, humming under her breath.

Mr. Campbell was taking his leave. I heard the creak of his team's harness, and their small stamping of anticipation as the groom settled himself. Mr. Campbell saw me and bowed deeply, hat held low. I sketched him a curtsy in return, and watched with relief as he drove away.

Phaedre, too, had stopped her work and was gazing after the departing carriage.

She said something under her breath, and spat in the dust. It was done without apparent malice; a charm against evil that I'd seen before. She looked up at me.

"Mister Jamie best find that Pollyanne afore sunset. Be wild animals in the piney wood, and Mister Ulysses say that woman worth two hundred pound when Miss Jocasta buy her. She don't know the woods, that Pollyanne; she be come straight from Africa, no more'n a year agone."

Without further comment, she bent her head over her task, fingers moving dark and quick as a spider among the fine silk of our corpse's hair.

I bent to my work as well, realizing with something of a shock that the web of circumstance that enmeshed Jamie had touched me, too. I did not stand outside, as I had thought, and could not if I wanted to.

Phaedre had helped me to find Pollyanne not because she trusted or liked me—but because I was the master's wife. Pollyanne must be found and hidden. And Jamie, she thought, would of course find Pollyanne and hide her—she was his property; or Jocasta's, which in Phaedre's eyes would amount to the same thing.

At last, the stranger lay clean, on the worn linen sheet I had brought for a shroud. Phaedre had combed her hair and braided it; I took up the big stone jar of herbs. I had brought them as much from habit as from reason, but now was glad of them; not so

much for aid against the progress of decomposition, but as the
sole—and necessary—touch of ceremony.

It was difficult to reconcile this clumsy, reeking lump of clay
with the small, cold hand that had grasped mine; with the anguished whisper that had breathed "Tell . . ." in the smothering
dark. And yet there was the memory of her, of the last of her
living blood spilling hot in my hand, more vivid in my mind than
this sight of her empty flesh, naked in the hands of strangers.

There was no minister nearer than Halifax; she would be buried
without rites—and yet, what need had she of rites? Funeral rituals
are for the comfort of the bereaved. It was unlikely that she had
left anyone behind to grieve, I thought; for if she had had anyone
so close to her—family, husband, or even lover—I thought she
would not now be dead.

I had not known her, would not miss her—but I grieved her; her
and her child. And so for myself, rather than for her, I knelt by her
body and scattered herbs: fragrant and bitter, leaves of rue and
hyssop flowers, rosemary, thyme and lavender. A bouquet from
the living to the dead—small token of remembrance.

Phaedre watched in silence, kneeling. Then she reached out and
with gentle fingers, laid the shroud across the girl's dead face.
Jamie had come to watch. Without a word, he stooped and picked
her up, and bore her to the wagon.

He didn't speak until I had climbed up and settled myself on
the seat beside him. He snapped the reins on the horses' backs,
and clicked his tongue.

"Let us go and find the Sergeant," he said.

There were, of course, a few things to be attended to first. We
returned to River Run to leave Phaedre, and Jamie disappeared to
find Duncan and change his stained clothing, while I went to
check on my patient and to acquaint Jocasta with the morning's
events.

I needn't have troubled on either account; Farquard Campbell
was sitting in the morning room sipping tea with Jocasta. John
Myers, his loins swathed in a Cameron plaid, was lounging at full
length upon the green velvet chaise, cheerfully munching scones.
Judging from the unaccustomed cleanliness of the bare legs and
feet extending from the tartan, someone had taken advantage of
his temporary state of unconsciousness the night before to administer a bath.

"My dear." Jocasta's head turned at my step, and she smiled, though I saw the twin lines of concern etched between her brows. "Sit you down, child, and take some nourishment; ye will have had no rest last night—and a dreadful morning, it seems."

I might ordinarily have found it either amusing or insulting to be called "child"; under the circumstances, it was oddly comforting. I sank gratefully into an armchair, and let Ulysses pour me a cup of tea, wondering meanwhile just how much Farquard had told Jocasta—and how much he knew.

"How are you this morning?" I asked my patient. He appeared to be in amazingly good condition, considering his alcoholic intake of the night before. His color was good, and so was his appetite, judging from the quantity of crumbs on the plate by his side.

He nodded cordially at me, jaws champing, and swallowed with some effort.

"Astounding fine, ma'am, I thank ye kindly. A mite sore round the privates"—he tenderly patted the area in question—"but a sweeter job of stitchin' I've not been privileged to see. Mr. Ulysses was kind enough to fetch me a lookin' glass," he explained. He shook his head in some awe. "Never seen my own behind before; as much hair as I got back there, ye'd think my daddy'd been a bear!"

He laughed heartily at this, and Farquard Campbell buried a smile in his teacup. Ulysses turned away with the tray, but I saw the corner of his mouth twitch.

Jocasta laughed out loud, blind eyes crinkling in amusement.

"They do say it's a wise bairn that kens its father, John Quincy. But I kent your mother weel, and I'll say I think it unlikely."

Myers shook his head, but his eyes twinkled over the thick growth of beard.

"Well, my mama did admire a hairy man. Said it was a rare comfort on a cold winter's night." He peered down the open neck of his shirt, viewing the underbrush on display with some satisfaction. "Might be so, at that. The Indian lassies seem to like it—though it's maybe only the novelty, come to think on it. Their own men scarcely got fuzz on their balls, let alone their backsides."

Mr. Campbell inhaled a fragment of scone, and coughed heavily into his napkin. I smiled to myself and took a deep swallow of tea. It was a strong and fragrant Indian blend, and despite the oppressive heat of the morning, more than welcome. A light dew of sweat broke out on my face as I drank, but the warmth settled comfortingly into my uneasy stomach, the perfume of the tea driving the stench of blood and excreta from my nose, even as the cheerful conversation banished the morbid scenes of the morning from my mind.

I eyed the hearth rug wistfully. I felt as though I could lie down there peacefully and sleep for a week. No rest for the weary, though.

Jamie came in, freshly shaved and combed, dressed in sober coat and clean linen. He nodded to Farquard Campbell with no apparent surprise; he must have heard his voice from the hallway.

"Auntie." He bent and kissed Jocasta's cheek in greeting, then smiled at Myers.

"How is it, *a charaid*? Or shall I say, how are they?"

"Right as rain," Myers assured him. He cupped a hand consideringly between his legs. "Think I might wait a day or two before I climb back on a horse, though."

"I would," Jamie assured him. He turned back to Jocasta. "Have ye maybe seen Duncan this morning, Auntie?"

"Oh, aye. He's gone a small errand for me, he and the laddie." She smiled and reached for him; I saw her fingers wrap tight around his wrist. "Such a dear man, Mr. Innes. So helpful. And such a quick, canny man; a real pleasure to talk to. Do ye not find him so, Nephew?"

Jamie glanced at her curiously, then his gaze flicked to Farquard Campbell. The older man avoided his eye, sipping at his tea as he affected to study the large painting that hung above the mantel.

"Indeed," Jamie said dryly. "A useful man, is Duncan. And Young Ian's gone with him?"

"To fetch a bittie package for me," his aunt said placidly. "Did ye need Duncan directly?"

"No," Jamie said slowly, staring down at her. "It can wait."

Her fingers slipped free of his sleeve, and she reached for her teacup. The delicate handle was angled precisely toward her, ready for her hand.

"That's good," she said. "Ye'll have a bite of breakfast, then? And Farquard—another scone?"

"Ah, no, *Cha ghabh mi 'n còrr, tapa leibh.* I've business in the town, and best I be about it." Campbell set down his cup and got to his feet, bowing to me and to Jocasta in turn. "Your servant, ladies. Mr. Fraser," he added, with a lift of one brow, and bowing, he followed Ulysses out.

Jamie sat down, his own brows raised, and reached for a piece of toast.

"Your errand, Aunt—Duncan's gone to find the slave woman?"

"He has." Jocasta turned her blind eyes toward him, frowning. "You'll not mind, Jamie? I ken Duncan's your man, but it seemed an urgent matter; and I couldna be sure when you'd come."

"What did Campbell tell ye?" I could tell what Jamie was thinking; it seemed out of character for the upright and rigid Mr. Campbell, justice of the district, who would not stir a hand to prevent a gruesome lynching, to conspire for the protection of a female slave, and an abortionist to boot. And yet—perhaps he meant it as compensation for what he had not been able to prevent before.

The handsome shoulders moved in the slightest of shrugs, and a muscle dipped near the corner of her mouth.

"I've kent Farquard Campbell these twenty years, *a mhic mo pheathar*. I hear what he doesna say better than what he does."

Myers had been following this exchange with interest.

"Couldn't say as my own ears are that good," he observed mildly. "All I heard him say was how some poor woman kilt herself by accident, up to the mill, tryin' to rid herself of a burden. He said he didn't know her, himself." He smiled blandly at me.

"And that alone tells me the lass is a stranger," Jocasta observed. "Farquard knows the folk on the river and in the town as well as I ken my own folk. She is no one's daughter, no one's servant."

She set down her cup and leaned back in her chair with a sigh.

"It will be all right," she said. "Eat up your food, lad; ye must be starving."

Jamie stared at her for a moment, the piece of toast uneaten in his hand. He leaned forward and dropped it back on the plate.

"I canna say I've much appetite just now, Auntie. Dead lassies curdle my wame a bit." He stood up, brushing down the skirts of his coat.

"She's maybe no one's daughter or servant—but she's lyin' in the yard just now, drawing flies. I'd have a name for her before I bury her." He turned on his heel and stalked out.

I drained the last of my tea and set the cup back with a faint chime of bone china.

"Sorry," I said apologetically. "I don't believe I'm hungry, either."

Jocasta neither moved nor changed expression. As I left the room I saw Myers lean over from his chaise and neatly snag the last of the scones.

It was nearly noon before we reached the Crown's warehouse at the end of Hay Street. It stood on the north side of the river, with its own pier for loading, a little way above the town itself. There seemed little necessity for a guard at the moment; nothing moved in the vicinity of the building save a few sulphur butterflies who, unaffected by the smothering heat, were diligently laboring among the flowering bushes that grew thick along the shore.

"What do they keep here?" I asked Jamie, looking curiously up at the massive structure. The huge double doors were shut and bolted, the single red-coated sentry motionless as a tin soldier in front of them. A smaller building beside the warehouse sported an English flag, drooping limply in the heat; presumably this was the lair of the sergeant we were seeking.

Jamie shrugged and brushed a questing fly away from his eyebrow. We had been attracting more and more of them as the heat of the day increased, despite the movement of the wagon. I sniffed discreetly, but could smell only a faint hint of thyme.

"Whatever the Crown thinks valuable. Furs from the backcountry, naval stores—pitch and turpentine. But the guard is because of the liquor."

While every inn brewed its own beer, and every household had its receipts for applejack and cherry wine, the more potent spirits were the province of the Crown: brandy, whisky, and rum were imported to the colony in small quantities under heavy guard, and sold at great cost under the Crown's seal.

"I should say they haven't got much in stock right now," I said, nodding at the single guard.

"No, the shipments of liquor come upstream from Wilmington once a month. Campbell says they choose a different day each time, so as to run less risk of robbery."

He spoke abstractedly, a small frown lingering between his eyebrows.

"Did Campbell believe us, do you think? About her doing it herself?" Without really meaning to, I cast a half glance into the wagon behind me.

Jamie made a derisory Scottish noise in the back of his throat.

"Of course not, Sassenach; the man's no a fool. But he's a good friend to my aunt; he'll not make trouble if he doesn't have to. Let's hope the woman had no one who'll make a fuss."

"Rather a cold-blooded hope," I said quietly. "I thought you felt differently, in your aunt's drawing room. You're probably right, though; if she'd had someone, she wouldn't be dead now."

He heard the bitterness in my voice, and looked down at me.

"I dinna mean to be callous, Sassenach," he said gently. "But the poor lassie *is* dead. I canna do more for her than see her decently into the ground; it's the living I must take heed for, aye?"

I heaved a sigh and squeezed his arm briefly. My feelings were a good deal too complex to try to explain; I had known the girl no more than minutes before her death, and could in no way have prevented it—but she had died under my hands, and I felt the physician's futile rage in such circumstances; the feeling that somehow I had failed, had been outwitted by the Dark Angel. And beyond rage and pity, was an echo of unspoken guilt; the girl was near Brianna's age—Brianna, who in like circumstances would also have no one.

"I know. It's only . . . I suppose I feel responsible for her, in a way."

"So do I," he said. "Never fear, Sassenach; we'll see she's done rightly by." He reined the horses in under a chestnut tree, and swung down, offering me a hand.

There were no barracks; Campbell had told Jamie that the warehouse guard's ten men were quartered in various houses in the town. Upon inquiry of the clerk laboring in the office, we were directed across the street to the sign of the Golden Goose, wherein the Sergeant might presently be found at his luncheon.

I saw the Sergeant in question at once as I entered the tavern; he was sitting at a table by the window, his white leather stock undone and his tunic unbuttoned, looking thoroughly relaxed over a mug of ale and the remains of a Cornish pasty. Jamie came in behind me, his shadow momentarily blocking the light from the open door, and the Sergeant looked up.

Dim as it was in the taproom, I could see the man's face go blank with shock. Jamie came to an abrupt halt behind me. He said something in Gaelic under his breath that I recognized as a vicious obscenity, but then he was moving forward past me, with no sign of hesitation in his manner.

"Sergeant Murchison," he said, in tones of mild surprise, as one might greet a casual acquaintance. "I hadna thought to lay eyes on you again—not in this world, at least."

The Sergeant's expression strongly suggested that the feeling had been mutual. Also that any meeting this side of heaven was too soon. Blood flooded his beefy, pockmarked cheeks with red, and he shoved back his bench with a screech of wood on the sanded floor.

"You!" he said.

Jamie took off his hat and inclined his head politely.

"Your servant, sir," he said. I could see his face now, outwardly pleasant, but with a wariness that creased the corners of his eyes. He showed it a good deal less, but the Sergeant wasn't the only one to be taken aback.

Murchison was regaining his self-possession; the look of shock was replaced by a faint sneer.

"Fraser. Oh, beg pardon, *Mr.* Fraser, it will be now, won't it?"

"It will." Jamie kept his voice neutral, despite the insulting tone of this. Whatever past conflict lay between them, the last thing he wanted now was trouble. Not with what lay in the wagon outside. I wiped my sweaty palms surreptitiously on my skirt.

The Sergeant had begun to do up his tunic buttons, slowly, not taking his eyes off Jamie.

"I had heard there was a man called Fraser, come to leech off Mistress Cameron at River Run," he said, with an unpleasant twist of thick lips. "That'll be you, will it?"

The wariness in Jamie's eyes froze into a blue as cold as glacier ice, though his lips stayed curved in a pleasant smile.

"Mistress Cameron will be my kinswoman. It is on her behalf that I have come now."

The Sergeant tilted back his head and scratched voluptuously at his throat. There was a deep, hard-edged red crease across the expanse of fat pale flesh, as though someone had tried unsuccessfully to garrote the man.

"Your kinswoman. Well, easy to say so, ain't it? The lady's blind as a bat, I hear. No husband, no sons; fair prey for any sharpster comes a-calling, claiming family." The sergeant lowered his head and smirked at me, his self-possession fully restored.

"And this'll be your doxy, will it?" It was gratuitous malice, a shot at random; the man had scarcely glanced at me.

"This will be my wife, Mistress Fraser."

I could see the two stiff fingers of Jamie's right hand twitch once against the skirt of his coat, the only outward sign of his feelings. He tilted his head back an inch and raised his brows, considering the Sergeant with an air of dispassionate interest.

"And which one are you, sir? I beg pardon for my imperfect recollection, but I confess that I cannot tell you from your brother."

The Sergeant stopped as though he had been shot, frozen in the act of fastening his stock.

"Damn you!" he said, choking on the words. His face had gone an unhealthy shade of plum, and I thought that he ought really to mind his blood pressure. I didn't say so, though.

At this point, the Sergeant seemed to notice that everyone in the taproom was staring at him with great interest. He glared ferociously around him, snatched up his hat, and stamped toward the door, pushing past me as he went, so that I staggered back a pace.

Jamie grabbed my arm to steady me, then ducked beneath the lintel himself. I followed, in time to see him call after the Sergeant.

"Murchison! A word with you!"

The soldier whirled on his heel, hands fisted against the skirts of his scarlet coat. He was a good-sized man, thick through torso and shoulder, and the uniform became him. His eyes glittered with menace, but he had gained possession of himself again.

"A word, is it?" he said. "And what might you have to say to me, *Mister* Fraser?"

"A word in your professional capacity, Sergeant," Jamie said coolly. He nodded toward the wagon, which we had left beneath a nearby tree. "We've brought ye a corpse."

For the second time, the Sergeant's face went blank. He glanced at the wagon; flies and gnats had begun to gather in small clouds, circling lazily over the open bed.

"Indeed." He *was* a professional; while the hostility of his manner was undiminished, the hot blood faded from his face, and the clenched fists relaxed.

"A corpse? Whose?"

"I have no idea, sir. It was my hope that you might be able to tell us. Will ye look?" He nodded toward the wagon, and after a moment's hesitation, the Sergeant nodded briefly back, and strode toward the wagon.

I hurried after Jamie, and was in time to see the Sergeant's face as he drew back the corner of the makeshift shroud. He had no skill at all in hiding his feelings—perhaps in his profession it wasn't necessary. Shock flickered over his face like summer lightning.

Jamie could see the Sergeant's face as well as I.

"Ye'll know her, then?" he said.

"I—she—that is . . . yes, I know her." The Sergeant's mouth snapped shut abruptly, as though he was afraid to let any more words out. He continued to stare at the girl's dead face, his own tightening, freezing out all feeling.

A few men had followed us out of the tavern. While they stayed at a discreet distance, two or three were craning their necks with curiosity. It wasn't going to be long before the whole district knew what had happened at the mill. I hoped Duncan and Ian were well on their way.

"What has happened to her?" the Sergeant asked, staring down at the fixed white face. His own was nearly as pale.

Jamie was watching him intently, and making no pretense otherwise.

"You'll know her, then?" he said again.

"She is—she was—a laundress. Lissa—Lissa Garver is her name." The Sergeant spoke mechanically, still looking down into the wagon as though unable to tear his eyes away. His face was expressionless but his lips were white, and his hands were clenched into fists at his sides. "What happened?"

"Has she people in the town? A husband, maybe?"

It was a reasonable question, but Murchison's head jerked up as though Jamie had stabbed him with it.

"None of your concern, is it?" he said. He stared at Jamie, a thin rim of white visible around the iris of his eye. He bared his teeth in what might have been politeness, but wasn't. "Tell me what happened to her."

Jamie's eyes met the Sergeant's without blinking.

"She meant to slip a bairn, and it went wrong," he said quietly. "If she has a husband, he must be told. If not—if she has no people—I will see her decently buried."

Murchison turned his head to look down into the wagon once more.

"She has someone," he said shortly. "You need not trouble yourself." He turned away, and rubbed a hand over his face, scrubbing violently as though to wipe away all feeling. "Go to my office," he said, voice half muffled. "You must make a statement —see the clerk. Go!"

The office was empty, the clerk no doubt gone in search of his own luncheon. I sat down to wait, but Jamie prowled restlessly around the small room, eyes flitting from the regimental banners on the wall to the drawered cabinet in the corner behind the desk.

"Damn the luck," he said, half to himself. "It would have to be Murchison."

"I take it you know the Sergeant well?"

He glanced at me with a wry quirk of the lips.

"Well enough. He was in the garrison at Ardsmuir prison."

"I see." No love lost between them, then. It was close in the little office; I blotted a trickle of sweat that ran down between my breasts. "What do you suppose he's doing here?"

"That much I ken; he was sent in charge of the prisoners when they were transported to be sold. I imagine the Crown saw no good reason to bring him back to England, when there was need of soldiers here—that would have been during the war wi' the French, aye?"

"What was that business about his brother?"

He snorted, a brief, humorless sound.

"There were two o' them—twins. Wee Billy and Wee Bobby, we called them. Alike as peas, and not only in looks."

He paused, marshaling memories. He didn't often speak of his time in Ardsmuir, and I could see the shadows of it pass across his face.

"Ye'll maybe know the sort of man is decent enough on his own, but get him wi' others like him, and they might as well be wolves?"

"Bit hard on the wolves," I said, smiling. "Think of Rollo. But yes, I know what you mean."

"Pigs, then. But beasts, when they're together. There's no lack of such men in any army; it's why armies work—men will do terrible things in a mob, that they wouldna dream of on their own."

"And the Murchisons were never on their own?" I asked slowly.

He gave me a slight nod of acknowledgment.

"Aye, that's it. There were the two of them, always. And what one might scruple at, the other would not. And of course, when it came to trouble—why, there was no saying which was to blame, was there?"

He was still prowling, restless as a caged panther. He paused by the window, looking out.

"I—the prisoners—we might complain of ill-treatment, but the officers couldna discipline both for the sins of one, and a man seldom knew which Murchison it was that had him on the ground wi' a boot in the ribs, or which it was that hung him from a hook by his fetters and left him so until he'd soil himself for the amusement of the garrison."

His eyes were fixed on something outside, his expression unguarded. He'd spoken of beasts; I could see that the memories had roused one. His eyes caught the light from the window, gemblue and unblinking.

"Are both of them here?" I asked, as much to break that unnerving stare as because I wanted to know.

It worked; he turned abruptly from the window.

"No," he said, shortly. "This is Billy. Wee Bobby died at Ardsmuir." His two stiff fingers twitched against the fabric of his kilt.

It had occurred to me briefly to wonder why he had worn his kilt this morning, instead of changing to breeks; the crimson tartan might be quite literally a red flag to a bull, flaunted thus before an English soldier. Now I knew.

They'd taken it from him once before, thinking to take with it pride and manhood. They had failed in that attempt, and he meant to underscore that failure, whether it was sense to do so or not. Sense had little to do with the sort of stubborn pride that could survive years of such insult—and while he had more than his share of both, I could see that pride was well in the ascendancy at present.

"From the Sergeant's reactions, I suppose we may assume it wasn't natural causes?" I asked.

"No," he said. He sighed and shrugged his shoulders slightly, easing them inside the tight coat.

"They marched us out to the stone quarry each morning, and back again at twilight, wi' two or three guards to each wagon. One day, Wee Bobby Murchison was the sergeant in charge. He came out wi' us in the morning—but he didna come back with us at night." He glanced once more at the window. "There was a verra deep pool at the bottom of the quarry."

His matter-of-fact tone was nearly as chilling as the content of this bald account. I felt a small shiver pass up my spine, in spite of the stifling heat.

"Did you—" I began, but he put a finger to his lips, jerking his head toward the door. A moment later, I heard the footsteps that his keener ears had picked up.

It was the Sergeant, not his clerk. He had been perspiring heavily; streaks of sweat ran down his face beneath his wig, and his whole countenance was the unhealthy color of fresh beef liver.

He glanced at the vacant desk, and made a small, vicious noise in his throat. I felt a qualm on behalf of the absent clerk. The Sergeant shoved aside the clutter on the desk with a sweep of his arm that sent paper cascading onto the floor.

He snatched a pewter inkwell and a sheet of foolscap from the rubble, and banged them down on the desk.

"Write it down," he ordered. "Where you found her, what happened." He thrust a spattered goose-quill at Jamie. "Sign it, date it."

Jamie stared at him, eyes narrowed, but made no move to take the quill. I felt a sudden sinking in my belly.

Jamie was left-handed but had been taught forcibly to write with his right hand, and then had that right hand crippled. Writing, for him, was a slow, laborious business that left the pages blotted, sweat-stained, and crumpled, and the writer himself in no better case. There was no power on earth that would make him humiliate himself in that fashion before the Sergeant.

"Write. It. Down." The Sergeant bit off the words between his teeth.

Jamie's eyes narrowed further, but before he could speak, I reached out and snatched the pen from the Sergeant's grasp.

"I was there; let me do it."

Jamie's hand closed on mine before I could dip the quill in the inkwell. He plucked the pen from my fingers and dropped it in the center of the desk.

"Your clerk can wait upon me later, at my aunt's house," he said briefly to Murchison. "Come with me, Claire."

Not waiting for an answer from the Sergeant, he grasped my elbow and all but pulled me to my feet. We were outside before I knew what had happened. The wagon still stood under the tree, but now it was empty.

"Well, she's safe for the moment, *Mac Dubh,* but what in hell shall we do with the woman?" Duncan scratched at the stubble on his chin; he and Ian had spent three days in the forest, searching, before finding the slave Pollyanne.

"She'll no be easy to move," Ian put in, snaring a piece of bacon off the breakfast table. He broke it in half, and handed one piece to Rollo. "The poor lady near died of terror when Rollo sniffed her out, and we had God's own time gettin' her on her feet. We couldna get her on a horse at all; I had to walk with my arm around her, to keep her from fallin' down."

"We must get her clear away, somehow." Jocasta frowned, blank eyes half hooded in thought. "Yon Murchison was at the mill again yesterday morning, making a nuisance of himself, and last night, Farquard Campbell sent to tell me that the man has declared it was murder, and he's called for men to search the district for the slave who did it. Farquard's sae hot under his collar, I thought his head would burst into flame."

"Do ye think she *could* have done it?" Chewing, Ian looked from Jamie to me. "By accident, I mean?"

In spite of the hot morning, I shuddered, feeling in memory the unyielding stiffness of the metal skewer in my hand.

"You have three possibilities: accident, murder, or suicide," I said. "There are *lots* easier ways of committing suicide, believe me. And no motive for murder, that we know of."

"Be that as it may," Jamie said, neatly fielding the conversation, "if Murchison takes the slave woman, he'll have her hanged or flogged to death within a day. He's no need of trial. No, we must take her clear out of the district. I've arranged it with our friend Myers."

"You've arranged *what* with Myers?" Jocasta asked sharply, her voice cutting through the babble of exclamations and questions that greeted this announcement.

Jamie finished buttering the piece of toast that he held, and handed it to Duncan before speaking.

"We shall take the woman into the mountains," he said. "Myers says she'll be welcome among the Indians; he kens a good place for her, he says. And she'll be safe there from Wee Billy Murchison."

"We?" I asked politely. "And who's *we?"*

He grinned at me in reply.

"Myers and myself, Sassenach. I need to go to the backcountry to have a look before the cold weather comes, and this will be a good chance. Myers is the best guide I could have."

He carefully refrained from noting that it might be as well for *him* to be temporarily out of Sergeant Murchison's sphere of influence, but the implication was not lost on me.

"Ye'll take me, will ye not, Uncle?" Ian brushed the matted hair out of his face, looking eager. "Ye'll need help wi' that woman, believe me—she's the size of a molasses barrel."

Jamie smiled at his nephew.

"Aye, Ian. I expect we can use another man along."

"Ahem," I said, giving him an evil stare.

"To keep an eye on your auntie, if nothing else," Jamie continued, giving the stare back to me. "We leave in three days, Sassenach—if Myers can sit a horse by then."

Three days didn't allow much time, but with the assistance of Myers and Phaedre, my preparations were completed with hours to spare. I had a small traveling box of medicines and tools, and the saddlebags were packed with food, blankets, and cooking implements. The only small matter remaining was that of attire.

I recrossed the ends of the long silk strip across my chest, tied the ends in a jaunty knot between my breasts, and examined the results in the looking glass.

Not bad. I extended my arms and jiggled my torso from side to side, testing. Yes, that would do. Though perhaps if I took one more turn around my chest before crossing the ends . . .

"What, exactly, are ye doing, Sassenach? And what in the name of God are ye wearing?" Jamie, arms crossed, was leaning against the door, watching me with both brows raised.

"I am improvising a brassiere," I said with dignity. "I don't mean to ride sidesaddle through the mountains wearing a dress, and if I'm not wearing stays, I don't mean my breasts to be joggling all the way, either. Most uncomfortable, joggling."

"I daresay." He edged into the room and circled me at a cautious distance, eyeing my nether limbs with interest. "And what are *those*?"

"Like them?" I put my hands on my hips, modeling the drawstring leather trousers that Phaedre had constructed for me—laughing hysterically as she did so—from soft buckskin provided by one of Myers's friends in Cross Creek.

"No," he said bluntly. "Ye canna be going about in—in—" He waved at them, speechless.

"Trousers," I said. "And of course I can. I wore trousers all the time, back in Boston. They're very practical."

He looked at me in silence for a moment. Then, very slowly, he walked around me. At last, his voice came from behind me.

"Ye wore them outside?" he said, in tones of incredulity. "Where folk could see ye?"

"I did," I said crossly. "So did most other women. Why not?"

"Why *not*?" he said, scandalized. "I can see the whole shape of your buttocks, for God's sake, and the cleft between!"

"I can see yours, too," I pointed out, turning around to face him. "I've been looking at your backside in breeks every day for months, but only occasionally does the sight move me to make indecent advances on your person."

His mouth twitched, undecided whether to laugh or not. Taking advantage of the indecision, I took a step forward and put my arms around his waist, firmly cupping his backside.

"Actually, it's your kilt that makes me want to fling you to the floor and commit ravishment," I told him. "But you don't look at all bad in your breeks."

He did laugh then, and bending, kissed me thoroughly, his hands carefully exploring the outlines of my rear, snugly confined in buckskin. He squeezed gently, making me squirm against him.

"Take them off," he said, pausing for air.

"But I—"

"Take them off," he repeated firmly. He stepped back and tugged loose the lacing of his flies. "Ye can put them back on again after, Sassenach, but if there's flinging and ravishing to be done, it'll be me that does it, aye?"

PART FIVE

Strawberry Fields Forever

14

Flee from Wrath to Come

They had hidden the woman in a tobacco shed on the edge
of Farquard Campbell's furthest fields. There was little
chance of anyone noticing—other than Campbell's slaves,
who already knew—but we took care to arrive just after dark,
when the lavender sky had faded nearly to gray, barely outlining
the dark bulk of the drying shed.

The woman slid out like a ghost, cloaked and hooded, and was
hoisted onto the extra horse, bundled hastily aboard like the package of contraband she was. She drew up her legs and clung to the
saddle with both hands, doubled up in a ball of panic; evidently
she'd never been on a horse before.

Myers tried to hand her the reins, but she paid no attention,
only clung tight and moaned in a sort of melodic agony of terror.
The men were becoming restive, glancing over their shoulders
into the empty fields, as though expecting the imminent arrival of
Sergeant Murchison and his minions.

"Let her ride with me," I suggested. "Maybe she'll feel safer
that way."

The woman was detached from her mount with some difficulty
and set down on the horse's rump behind my saddle. She smelt
strongly of fresh tobacco leaves, pungently narcotic, and something else, a little muskier. She at once flung her arms around my
waist, holding on for dear life. I patted one of the hands clutched
about my middle, and she squeezed tighter, but made no other
move or sound.

Little wonder if she was terrified, I thought, turning my horse's
head to follow Myers's. She might not know about the hullabaloo
Murchison was raising in the district, but she could have no illusions about what might happen if she was caught; she had certainly been among the crowd at the sawmill two weeks earlier.

As an alternative to certain death, flight into the arms of red

savages might be slightly preferable, but not by much, to judge
from her trembling; the weather was far from cold, but she shook
as though with chill.

She nearly squeezed the stuffings out of me when Rollo appeared, stalking out of the bushes like some demon of the forest.
My horse didn't like the look of him, either, and backed up,
snorting and stamping, trying to jerk the reins away from me.

I had to admit that Rollo was reasonably fearsome, even when
he was in an amiable mood, which he was, at the moment—Rollo
loved expeditions. Still, he undoubtedly presented a sinister aspect; all his teeth were showing in a grin of delight, his slitted
eyes half closed as he whiffed the air. Add to that the way the
grays and blacks of his coat faded into the shadows, and one was
left with the queer and unsettling illusion that he had materialized
out of the substance of the night, Appetite incarnate.

He trotted directly past us, no more than a foot away, and the
woman gasped, her breath hot on my neck. I patted her hand
again, and spoke to her, but she made no answer. Duncan had said
she was Africa-born and spoke little English, but surely she must
understand a few words.

"It will be all right," I said again. "Don't be afraid."

Occupied with horse and passenger, I hadn't noticed Jamie,
until he appeared suddenly by my stirrup, light-footed as Rollo.

"All right, Sassenach?" he asked softly, putting a hand on my
thigh.

"I think so," I said. I nodded at the death-grip round my middle. "If I don't die of suffocation."

He looked, and smiled.

"Well, she's in no danger of fallin' off, at least."

"I wish I knew something to say to her; poor thing, she's so
afraid. Do you suppose she even knows where we're taking her?"

"I shouldna think so—*I* dinna ken where we're going." He
wore breeks for riding, but had his plaid belted over them, the free
end slung across the shoulder of his coat. The dark tartan blended
into the shadows of the forest as well as it had the shades of the
Scottish heather; all I could see of him was a white blotch of
shirt-front and the pale oval of his face.

"Do you know any useful *taki-taki* to say to her?" I asked. "Of
course, she might not know that, either, if she wasn't brought
through the Indies."

He turned his head and looked up at my passenger, considering.

"Ah," he said. "Well, there's the one thing they'll all know, no matter where they've come." He reached out and squeezed the woman's foot firmly.

"Freedom," he said, and paused. "*Saorsa*. D'ye ken what I say?"

She didn't loosen her grip, but her breath went out in a shuddering sigh, and I thought I felt her nod.

The horses followed each other in single file, Myers in the lead. The rough track was not even a wagon trail, only a sort of flattening of undergrowth, but it did at least provide clear passage through the trees.

I doubted that Sergeant Murchison's vengeance would pursue us so far—if he pursued us at all—but the sense of escape was too strong to ignore. We shared an unspoken but pervasive sense of urgency, and with no particular discussion, agreed to ride on as far as possible.

My passenger was either losing her fear or simply becoming too tired to care anymore; after a midnight stop for refreshment she allowed Ian and Myers to boost her back on the horse without protest, and while she never released her hold on my waist, she did seem to doze now and then, her forehead pressed against my shoulder.

The fatigue of long riding crept over me, too, aided by the hypnotic soft thudding of the horses' feet, and the unending susurrus of the pines overhead. We were still in the longleaf forest, and the tall, straight trunks surrounded us like the masts of long-sunk ships.

Lines of an ancient Scottish song drifted through my mind—*"How many strawberries grow in the salt sea; how many ships sail in the forest?"*—and I wondered muzzily whether the composer had walked through a place like this, unearthly in half-moon and starlight, so dreamlike that the borders between the elements were lost; we might as well be afloat as earthbound, the heave and fall beneath me the rise of planking, and the sound of the pines the wind in our sails.

We stopped at dawn, unsaddled the horses, hobbled them, and left them to feed in the long grass of a small meadow. I found Jamie, and curled up at once into a nest of grass beside him, the horses' peaceful champing the last thing I heard.

We slept heavily through the heat of the day, and awoke near sunset, stiff, thirsty, and covered with ticks. I was profoundly thankful that the ticks seemed to share the mosquitoes' general distaste for my flesh, but I had learned on our trip north to check Jamie and the others every time we slept; there were always outriders.

"Ick," I said, examining a particularly juicy specimen, the size of a grape, nestling amid the soft cinnamon hair of Jamie's underarm. "Damn, I'm afraid to pull that one; it's so full it'll likely burst."

He shrugged, busy exploring his scalp with the other hand, in search of further intruders.

"Leave it while ye deal with the rest," he suggested. "Perhaps it will fall off of its own accord."

"I suppose I'd better," I agreed reluctantly. I hadn't any objection to the tick's bursting, but not while its jaws were still embedded in Jamie's flesh. I'd seen infections caused by forcibly interrupted ticks, and they weren't anything I wanted to deal with in the middle of a forest. I had only a rudimentary medical kit with me—though this luckily included a very fine pair of small tweezer-pointed forceps from Dr. Rawlings's box.

Myers and Ian seemed to be managing all right; both stripped to the waist, Myers was crouched over the boy like a huge black baboon, fingers busy in Ian's hair.

"Here's a wee one," Jamie said, bending over and pushing his own hair aside so I could reach the small dark bleb behind his ear. I was engaged in gently maneuvering the creature out, when I became aware of a presence near my elbow.

I had been too tired to take much notice of our fugitive when we made camp, rightly assuming that she wasn't going to wander off into the wilderness by herself. She had wandered as far as a nearby stream, though, returning with a bucket of water.

She set this on the ground, dipped up a handful of water and funneled it into her mouth. She chewed vigorously for a moment, cheeks puffed out. Then she motioned me aside and, lifting a surprised Jamie's arm, spat forcefully and profusely into his armpit.

She reached into the dripping hollow, and with delicate fingers appeared to tickle the parasite. She certainly tickled Jamie, who was very sensitive in that particular region. He turned pink in the face and flinched at her touch, all the muscles in his torso quivering.

She held tight to his wrist, though, and within seconds, the bulging tick dropped off into the palm of her hand. She flicked it disdainfully away, and turned to me, with a small air of satisfaction.

I had thought she resembled a ball, muffled in her cloak. Seen without it, she still did. She was very short, no more than four feet, and nearly as wide, with a close-cropped head like a cannonball, her cheeks so round that her eyes were slanted above them.

She looked like nothing so much as one of the carved African fertility images I had seen in the Indies; massive of bosom, heavy of haunch, and the rich, burnt-coffee color of a Congolese, with skin so flawless that it looked like polished stone under its thin layer of sweat. She held out her hand to me, showing me a few small objects in her palm, the general size and shape of dried lima beans.

"Paw-paw," she said, in a voice so deep that even Myers turned his head toward her, startled. It was a huge, rich voice, reverberant as a drum. Seeing my reaction to it, she smiled a little shyly, and said something I didn't quite understand, though I knew it was Gaelic.

"She says ye must not swallow the seeds, for they're poison," Jamie translated, eyeing her rather warily as he wiped his armpit with the end of his plaid.

"Hau," Pollyanne agreed, nodding vigorously. "Poi-zin." She stooped over the bucket for another handful of water, washed it round her mouth, and spat it at a rock with a noise like a gunshot.

"You could be dangerous with that," I told her. I didn't know whether she understood me, but she gathered from my smile that I meant to be cordial; she smiled back, popped two more of the paw-paw seeds into her mouth, and beckoned to Myers, already chewing, the seeds making little crunching pops as she pulverized them between her teeth.

By the time we had eaten supper and were ready to leave, she was nervously willing to try riding alone. Jamie coaxed her to the horse, and showed her how to let the beast smell her. She trembled as the big nose nudged her, but then the horse snorted; she jumped, giggled in a voice like honey poured out of a jug, and allowed Jamie and Ian between them to boost her aboard.

Pollyanne remained shy of the men, but she soon gained enough confidence to talk to me, in a polyglot mixture of Gaelic, English, and her own language. I couldn't have translated it, but both her face and body were so expressive that I could often gather the sense of what she was saying, even though I understood only one word in ten. I could only regret that I was not equally fluent in body language; she didn't understand most of my questions and remarks, so I had to wait until we made camp, when I could prevail on Jamie or Ian to help me with bits of Gaelic.

Freed—at least temporarily—from the constraint of terror, and becoming cautiously secure in our company, a naturally effervescent personality emerged, and she talked with abandon as we rode side by side, regardless of my comprehension, laughing now and then with a low hooting noise like wind blowing across the mouth of a cave.

She became subdued only once: when we passed through a large clearing where the grass rose in strange undulant mounds, as though a great serpent lay buried underneath. Pollyanne went silent when she saw them, and in an effort to hurry her horse, instead succeeded only in pulling on the reins and stopping it dead. I rode back to help her.

"Droch àite," she murmured, glancing out of the corner of her eye at the silent mounds. A bad place. *"Djudju."* She scowled, and made a small, quick gesture with her hand, some sign against evil, I thought.

"Is it a graveyard?" I asked Myers, who had circled back to see why we had stopped. The mounds were not evenly spaced, but were distributed around the edge of the clearing in a pattern that didn't look like any natural formation. The mounds seemed too large to be graves, though—unless they were cairns, such as the ancient Scots built, or mass graves, I thought, uneasy at the memory of Culloden.

"Not to say graveyard," he replied, pushing his hat back on his head. " 'Twas a village once. Tuscarora, I expect. Those rises there"—he waved a hand—"those are houses, fallen down. The big 'un to the side, that will have been the chief's longhouse. It be taken no time atall, the grasses come over it. From the looks, though, this 'un will have been buried a time back."

"What happened to it?" Ian and Jamie had stopped, too, and come back to look over the small clearing.

Myers scratched thoughtfully at his beard.

"I couldn't be sayin', not for certain sure. Might be as sickness drove 'em out, might be as they were put to rout by the Cherokee or the Creek, though we be a mite north of the Cherokee land. Most likely as it happened during the war, though." He dug fiercely into his beard, twisted, and flicked away the remnants of a lingering tick. "Can't say as it's a place I'd tarry by choice."

Pollyanne being plainly of the same mind, we rode on. By evening, we had passed entirely out of the pines and scrubby oakland of the foothills. We were climbing in good earnest now, and the trees began to change; small groves of chestnut trees, large patches of oak and hickory, with scattered dogwood and persimmon, chinkapin and poplar, surrounded us in waves of feathery green.

The smell and feel of the air changed, too, as we rose. The overwhelming hot resins of the pine trees gave way to lighter, more varied scents, tree leaves mingled with whiffs of the shrubs and flowers that grew from every crevice of the craggy rocks. It was still damp and humid, but not so hot; the air no longer seemed a smothering blanket, but something we might breathe— and breathe with pleasure, filled as it was with the perfumes of leaf mold, sun-warmed leaves, and damp moss.

By sunset of the sixth day, we were well into the mountains, and the air was full of the sound of running water. Streams crisscrossed the valleys, spilling off ridges and trickling down the steep rock faces, trailing mist and moss like a delicate green fringe. When we rounded the side of one steep hill, I stopped in amazement; from the side of a distant mountain, a waterfall leapt into the air, arching a good eighty feet in its fall to the gorge far below.

"Will ye look at that, now?" Ian was openmouthed with awe.

" 'Tis right pretty," Myers allowed, with the smug complacence of a proprietor. "Ain't the biggest falls I've seen, but it's nice enough."

Ian turned his head, eyes wide.

"There are bigger ones?"

Myers laughed, a mountain man's quiet laugh, no more than a breath of sound.

"Boy, you ain't seen nothin' yet."

We camped for the night in a hollow near a good-sized creek— one big enough for trout. Jamie and Ian waded into this with enthusiasm, harrying the finny denizens with whippy rods cut from black willow. I hoped they would have some luck; our fresh provisions were running low, though we still had plenty of cornmeal left.

Pollyanne came scrambling up the bank, bringing a bucket of water with which to make a new batch of corn dodgers. These were small oblongs of rough cornmeal biscuit made for traveling; tasty when fresh and hot, and at least edible the next day. They became steadily less appetizing with time, resembling nothing so much as small chunks of cement by the fourth day. Still, they were portable, and not prone to mold, and thus were popular traveling fare, along with dried beef and salt pork.

Pollyanne's natural ebullience seemed a trifle subdued, her round face shadowed. Her eyebrows were so sketchy as to be almost nonexistent, which had the paradoxical effect of increasing the expressiveness of her face in motion, and wiping all expression from it in repose. She could be as impassive as a ball bearing when she wanted to; a useful skill for a slave.

I supposed that her preoccupation was at least in part because this was the last night on which we would all be together. We had reached the backcountry, the limits of the King's land; tomorrow, Myers would turn to the north, taking her across the spine of the mountains into the Indian lands, to find what safety and what life she might there.

Her round dark head was bent over the wooden bowl, stubby fingers mixing cornmeal with water and lard. I crouched across from her, feeding small sticks to the infant fire, the black iron girdle standing ready-greased beside it. Myers had gone off to smoke a pipe; I could hear Jamie call to Ian somewhere downstream, and a faint answering laugh.

It was deep twilight by now; our hollow was ringed by brooding mountains, and darkness seemed to fill the shallow bowl, creeping up the trunks of the trees around us. I had no notion of the place she had come from, whether it might be forest or jungle, seashore or desert, but I thought it unlikely to be much like this.

What could she be thinking? She had survived the journey from Africa, and slavery; I supposed whatever lay ahead couldn't be much worse. It was an unknown future, though—going into a wilderness so vast and absolute that I felt every moment as though I might vanish into it, consumed without a trace. Our fire seemed the merest spark against the vastness of the night.

Rollo strolled into the light of the fire and shook himself, spraying water in all directions, making the fire hiss and spit. He had joined in the fishing, I saw.

"Go away, horrible dog," I said. He didn't, of course; simply came up and nosed me rudely, to be sure I was still who he thought I was, then turned to give Pollyanne the same treatment.

With no particular expression, she turned her head and spat in his eye. He yelped, backed up, and stood shaking his head, looking thoroughly surprised. She looked up at me and grinned, her teeth very white in her face.

I laughed, and decided not to worry too much; anyone capable of spitting in a wolf's eye would likely cope with Indians, wilderness, and anything else that came along.

The bowl was nearly empty, a neat row of corn dodgers laid on the girdle. Pollyanne wiped her fingers on a handful of grass, watching the yellow cornmeal begin to sizzle and turn brown as the lard melted. A warm, comforting smell rose from the fire, mingled with the scent of burning wood, and my belly rumbled softly in anticipation. The fire seemed more substantial now, the scent of cooking food spreading its warmth in a wider circle, keeping the night at bay.

Had it been this way where she came from? Had fires and food held back a jungle darkness, kept away leopards instead of bears? Had light and company given comfort, and the illusion of safety? For illusion it had surely been—fire was no protection against men, or the darkness that had overtaken her. I had no words to ask.

"I have never seen such fishing, never," Jamie repeated for the fourth time, a look of dreamy bliss on his face as he broke open a steaming trout fried in cornmeal. "They were *swarming* in the water, were they not, Ian?"

Ian nodded, a similar look of reverence on his own homely features.

"My Da would give his other leg to ha' seen it," he said. "They jumped on the hook, Auntie, truly!"

"The Indians don't generally bother with hook and line," Myers put in, neatly spearing his own share of fish with his knife. "They build snares and fish traps, or sometimes they'll put some sticks and rubbish crost the creek to prevent the fish, then stand above with a sharp stick, just spearin' them from the water."

That was enough for Ian; any mention of Indians and their ways provoked a rash of eager questions. Having exhausted the methods of fish-catching, he asked again about the abandoned village we had seen earlier in our journey.

"Ye said it might have happened in the war," Ian said, lifting the bones from a steaming trout, then shaking his fingers to cool them. He passed a section of the boneless flesh to Rollo, who swallowed it in a single gulp, temperature notwithstanding. "Will

that ha' been the war wi' the French, then? I didna ken there was
any fighting so far south.''

Myers shook his head, chewing and swallowing before he answered.

"Oh, no. It'll be the Tuscarora War I was meanin'; that's how
they call it on the white side, at least.''

The Tuscarora War, he explained, had been a short-lived but
brutal conflict some forty years before, brought on by an attack
upon some backcountry settlers. The then governor of the colony
had sent troops into the Tuscarora villages in retaliation, and the
upshot was a series of pitched battles that the colonists, much
better armed, had won handily—to the devastation of the Tuscarora nation.

Myers nodded toward the darkness.

"Ain't no more than seven villages o' the Tuscarora left, now
—and not above fifty or a hundred souls in any but the biggest
one." So sadly diminished, the Tuscarora would quickly have
fallen prey to surrounding tribes and disappeared altogether, had
they not been formally adopted by the Mohawk, and thus become
part of the powerful Iroquois League.

Jamie came back to the fire with a bottle from his saddlebag. It
was Scotch whisky, a parting present from Jocasta. He poured out
a small cupful, then offered the half-full bottle to Myers.

"Is the Mohawk country not a verra great distance to the
north?" he asked. "How can they offer protection to their fellows
here, and they with hostile tribes all round?''

Myers took a gulp of whisky and washed it pleasurably around
his mouth before answering.

"Mmm. That's fine stuff, friend James. Oh, the Mohawk are a
good ways off, aye. But the Nations of the Iroquois are a name to
reckon with—and of all the Six Nations, the Mohawk are the
fiercest. Ain't no one—red *or* white—goin' to mess with the Mohawk 'thout good cause, nossir.''

I was fascinated by this. I was also pleased to hear that the
Mohawk territory was a good long way away from us.

"Why did the Mohawk want to adopt the Tuscarora, then?"
Jamie asked, lifting one brow. "It doesna seem they'd be needing
allies, and they so fierce as ye say.''

Myers's hazel eyes had gone to dreamy half-slits under the
influence of good whisky.

"Oh, they're fierce, all right—but they're mortal," he said,
"Indians are men o' blood, and none more than the Mohawk.

They're men of honor, mind"—he raised a thick finger in admonition—"but there's a sight of things they'll kill for, some reasonable, some not. They raid, d'ye see, amongst themselves, and they'll kill for revenge—ain't nothin' will stop a Mohawk bent on revenge, save you kill him. And even then, his brother or his son or his nephew will come after you."

He licked his lips in slow meditation, savoring the slick of whisky on his skin.

"Sometimes Indians don't kill for any reason a man would say mattered; specially when liquor's involved."

"Sounds very much like the Scots," I murmured to Jamie, who gave me a cold look in return.

Myers picked up the whisky bottle and rolled it slowly between his palms.

"Any man might take a drop too much and be the worse in his actions for it, but with the Indians, the first drop's too much. I've heard of more than one massacre that might not have been, save for the men bein' mad with drink."

He shook his head, recalling himself to his subject.

"Be so as it may, it's a hard life, and a bloody one. Some tribes are wiped out altogether, and none have men to spare. So they adopt folk into the tribe, to replace those as are killed or die of sickness. They take prisoners, sometimes—take 'em into a family, treat 'em as their own. That's what they'll do with Mrs. Polly, there." He nodded at Pollyanne, who sat quietly by the fire, paying no attention to his speech.

"So happen back fifty years, the Mohawk took and adopted the whole tribe of the Tuscarora. Don't many tribes speak exactly the same language," Myers explained. "But some are closer than others. Tuscarora's more like the Mohawk than 'tis like the Creek or the Cherokee."

"Can ye speak Mohawk yourself, Mr. Myers?" Ian's ears had been flapping all through the explanation. Fascinated by every rock, tree, and bird on our journey, Ian was still more fascinated by any mention of Indians.

"Oh, a good bit." Myers shrugged modestly. "Any trader picks up a few words here and there. Shoo, dawg." Rollo, who had inched his nose within sniffing distance of Myers's last trout, twitched his ears at the admonition but didn't withdraw the nose.

"Will it be the Tuscarora ye mean to take Mistress Polly to?" Jamie asked, crumbling a corn dodger into edible chunks.

Myers nodded, chewing carefully; with as few natural teeth as he had left, even fresh corn dodgers were a hazardous undertaking.

"Aye. Be four, five days ride still," he explained. He turned to me and gave me a reassuring smile. "I'll see her settled fine, Mrs. Claire, you'll not be worried for her."

"What will the Indians think of her, I wonder?" Ian asked. He glanced at Pollyanne, interested. "Will they have seen a black woman before?"

Myers laughed at that.

"Lad, there's a many of the Tuscarora ain't seen a *white* person before. Mrs. Polly won't come as any more a shock than your auntie might." Myers took a vast swig of water and swished it around his mouth, eyeing Pollyanne thoughtfully. She felt his eyes on her, and returned his stare, unblinking.

"I should say they'd find her handsome, though; they do like a woman as is sweetly plump." It was moderately obvious that Myers shared this admiration; his eyes drifted over Pollyanne with an appreciation touched with innocent lasciviousness.

She saw it, and an extraordinary change came over her. She seemed scarcely to move, and yet all at once, her whole person was focused on Myers. No white showed around her eyes; they were black and fathomless, shining in the firelight. She was still short and heavy, but with only the slightest change of posture, depth of bosom and width of hip were emphasized, suddenly curved in a promise of lewd abundance.

Myers swallowed, audibly.

I glanced away from this little byplay to see Jamie watching, too, with an expression somewhere between amusement and concern. I poked him unobtrusively, and squinted hard, in an expression that said as explicitly as I could manage—"Do something!"

He narrowed one eye.

I widened both mine and gave him a good stare, which translated to, "I don't know, but do something!"

"Mmphm."

Jamie cleared his throat, leaned forward, and laid a hand on Myers's arm, jarring the mountain man out of his momentary trance.

"I shouldna like to think the woman will be misused in any way," he said, politely, but with an edge of Scottish innuendo on "misused" that implied the possibility of unlimited impropriety. He squeezed a little. "Will ye undertake to guarantee her safety, Mr. Myers?"

Myers shot him a look of incomprehension, which slowly cleared, cognizance coming into the bloodshot hazel eyes. The mountain man slowly pulled his arm free, then picked up his cup, gulped the last mouthful of whisky, coughed and wiped his mouth. He might have been blushing, but it was impossible to tell behind the beard.

"Oh, yes. That is, I mean to say, oh, no. No, indeed. The Mohawk and the Tuscarora both, their women choose who they bed with, even who they marry. No such thing as rape among 'em. Oh, no. No, sir; she won't be misused, I can promise that."

"Well, and I'm glad to hear it." Jamie sat back, at ease, and gave me an I-trust-you're-satisfied glare out of the corner of his eye. I smiled demurely.

Ian might be not quite sixteen, but he was far too observant to have missed all these exchanges. He coughed, in a meaningful Scottish manner.

"Uncle, Mr. Myers has been kind enough to invite me to go with him and Mrs. Polly, to see the Indian village. I shall be sure to see that she finds good treatment there."

"You—" Jamie started, then broke off. He gave his nephew a long, hard look across the fire. I could see the thoughts racing through his mind.

Ian hadn't asked permission to go; he'd announced he was going. If Jamie forbade him, he must give grounds—and he could scarcely say that it was too dangerous, as this would mean admitting both that he was willing to send the slave woman into danger and that he didn't trust Myers and his relations with the local Indians. Jamie was trapped, and very neatly too.

He breathed in strongly through his nose. Ian grinned.

I looked back across the fire. Pollyanne was still sitting as she had been, not moving. Her eyes were still fixed on Myers, but a slight smile curved her lips in invitation. One hand rose slowly, cupping a massive breast, almost absently.

Myers was staring back, dazed as a deer with a hunter's light in its eyes.

And would I do differently? I thought later, listening to the discreet rustling noises and small groans from the direction of Myers's blankets. If I knew that my life depended on a man? Would I not do anything I could to ensure he would protect me, in the face of unknown danger?

There was a snapping and crackling in the bushes, not far away. It was loud, and I stiffened. So did Jamie. He slid his hand out from under my shirt, reaching for his dirk, then relaxing, as the reassuring scent of skunk reached our nostrils.

He put his hand back under my shirt, squeezed my breast and fell back asleep, his breath warm on my neck.

No great difference at all, perhaps. Was my future any more certain than hers? And did I not depend for my life upon a man bound to me—at least in part—by desire of my body?

A faint wind breathed through the trees, and I hitched the blanket higher on my shoulder. The fire had burned to embers, and so high in the mountains, it was cool at night. The moon had set, but it was very clear; the stars blazed close, a net of light cast over the mountains' peaks.

No, there were differences. However unknown my future, it would be shared, and the bond between my man and me went much deeper than the flesh. Beyond all this was the one great difference, though—I had chosen to be there.

15

Noble Savages

We took our leave of the others in the morning, Jamie and Myers taking pains over the arrangement for a rendezvous in ten days time. Looking around me at the bewildering immensity of forest and mountain, I couldn't imagine how anyone could be sure of finding a specific place again; I could only trust in Jamie's sense of navigation.

They turned to the north, we to the southwest, making our way along the course of the stream we had camped by. It seemed very quiet at first, and strangely lonely, with only the two of us. Within a short time, though, I had grown accustomed to the solitude and began to relax, taking a keen interest in our surroundings. This might, after all, be our home.

The thought was a rather daunting one; it was a place of amazing beauty and richness, but so wild, it hardly seemed that people could live in it. I didn't voice this thought, however; only followed Jamie's horse as he led us deeper and deeper into the mountains, stopping finally in the late afternoon to make a small camp and catch fish for dinner.

The light faded slowly, retreating through the trees. The thick mossy trunks grew dense with shadow, edges still rimmed with a fugitive light that hid among the leaves, green shadows shifting with the sunset breeze.

A tiny glow lit suddenly in the grass a few feet away, cool and bright. I saw another, and another, and then the edge of the wood was full of them, lazily falling, then blinking out, cold sparks drifting in the growing dark.

"You know, I never saw fireflies until I came to live in Boston," I said, filled with pleasure at sight of them, glowing emerald and topaz in the grass. "They don't have fireflies in Scotland, do they?"

Jamie shook his head, reclining lazily on the grass, one arm hooked behind his head.

"Bonny wee things," he observed, and sighed with content. "This is my favorite time of the day, I think. When I lived in the cave, after Culloden, I would come out near evening, and sit on a stone, waiting for the dark."

His eyes were half closed, watching the fireflies. The shadows faded upward as night rose from the earth to the sky. A moment before, light through the oak leaves had mottled him like a fawn; now the brightness had faded, so he lay in a sort of dim green glow, the lines of his body at once solid and insubstantial.

"All the wee bugs come out just now—the moths and the midges; all the bittie things that hang about in clouds over the water. Ye see the swallows come for them, and then the bats, swooping down. And the salmon, rising to the evening hatch and making rings on the water."

His eyes were open now, fixed on the waving sea of grass on the hillside, but I knew he saw instead the surface of the tiny loch near Lallybroch, alive with fleeting ripples.

"It's only a moment, but ye feel as though it will last forever. Strange, is it no?" he said thoughtfully. "Ye can almost see the light go as ye watch—and yet there's no time ye can look and say 'Now! Now it's night.' " He gestured at the opening between the oak trees, and the valley below, its hollows filling with dark.

"No." I lay back in the grass beside him, feeling the warm damp of the grass mold the buckskin to my body. The air was thick and cool under the trees, like the air in a church, dim and fragrant with remembered incense.

"Do you remember Father Anselm at the abbey?" I looked up; the color was going from the oak leaves overhead, leaving the soft silver undersides gray as mouse fur. "He said there was always an hour in the day when time seems to stop—but that it was different for everyone. He thought it might be the hour when one was born."

I turned my head to look at him.

"Do you know when you were born?" I asked. "The time of day, I mean?"

He glanced at me and smiled, rolling over to face me.

"Aye, I do. Perhaps he was right, then, for I was born at suppertime—just at twilight on the first of May." He brushed away a floating firefly and grinned at me.

"Have I never told ye that story? How my mother had put on a pot of brose to cook, and then her pains came on so fast she'd no time to think of it, and no one else remembered either until they smelled the burning, and it ruined the supper and the pot as well? There was nothing else in the house to eat save a great gooseberry pie. So they all ate that, but there was a new kitchenmaid and the gooseberries were green, and all of them—except my mother and me, of course—spent the night writhing wi' the indigestion."

He shook his head, still smiling. "My father said it was months before he could look at me without feeling his bowels cramp."

I laughed, and he reached to pick a last-year's leaf from my hair.

"And what hour were you born, Sassenach?"

"I don't know," I said, with the usual pang of faint regret for my vanished family. "It wasn't on my birth certificate, and if Uncle Lamb knew, he never told me. I know when Brianna was born, though," I added, more cheerfully. "She was born at three minutes past three in the morning. There was a huge clock on the wall of the delivery room, and I saw it."

Dim as the light was, I could see his look of surprise clearly.

"You were awake? I thought ye told me women are drugged then, so as not to feel the pain."

"They mostly were, then. I wouldn't let them give me anything, though." I stared upward. The shadows were thick around us now, but the sky was still clear and light above, a soft, brilliant blue.

"Why the hell not?" he demanded, incredulous. "I've never seen a woman give birth, but I've *heard* it more than once, I'll tell ye. And damned if I can see why a woman in her right mind would do it, and there was any choice about it."

"Well . . ." I paused, not wanting to seem melodramatic. It was the truth, though. "Well," I said, rather defiantly, "I thought I was going to die, and I didn't want to die in my sleep."

He wasn't shocked. He only raised one brow, and snorted faintly with amusement.

"Would ye no?"

"No, would you?" I twisted my head to look at him. He rubbed the bridge of his nose, still amused at the question.

"Aye, well, perhaps. I've come close to death by hanging, and I didna like the waiting a bit. I've nearly been killed in battle a few times; I canna say I was much concerned about the dying then, though, bein' too busy to think of it. And then I've nearly died of wounds and fever, and that was misery enough that I was looking forward verra keenly to being dead. But on the whole, given my choice about it, I think perhaps I wouldna mind dying in my sleep, no.''

He leaned over and kissed me lightly. "Preferably in bed, next to you. At a verra advanced age, mind." He touched his tongue delicately to my lips, then rose to his feet, brushing dried oak leaves from his breeks.

"Best make a fire while there's light enough to strike a flint," he said. "Ye'll fetch the wee fish?"

I left him to deal with flints and kindling while I went down the little hill to the stream, where we had left the fresh-caught trout dangling from stringers in the icy current. As I came back up the hill it had grown dark enough that I could see him only in outline, crouched over a tiny pile of smoldering kindling. A wisp of smoke rose up like incense, pale between his hands.

I set the gutted fish down in the long grass and sat back on my heels beside him, watching as he laid fresh sticks on the fire, building it patiently, a barricade against the coming night.

"What do you think it will be like?" I asked suddenly. "To die."

He stared into the fire, thinking. A burning twig snapped with heat, spurting sparks into the air, which drifted down, blinking out before they touched the ground.

" 'Man is like the grass that withers and is thrown into the fire; he is like the sparks that fly upward . . . and his place will know him no more,' " I quoted softly. "Is there nothing after, do you think?"

He shook his head, looking into the fire. I saw his eyes shift beyond it, to where the cool bright sparks of the fireflies blinked in and out among the dark stems.

"I canna say," he said at last, softly. His shoulder touched mine and I leaned my head toward him. "There's what the Church says, but—" His eyes were still fixed on the fireflies, winking through the grass stems, their light unquenchable. "No, I canna say. But I think it will maybe be all right."

He tilted his head, pressing his cheek against my hair for a moment, then stood up, reaching for his dirk.

"The fire's well started now."

The heavy air of the afternoon had lifted with the coming of twilight, and a soft evening breeze blew the damp tendrils of hair off my face. I sat with my face lifted, eyes closed, enjoying the coolness after the sweaty heat of the day.

I could hear Jamie rustling around the fire, and the quick, soft *whisht* of his knife as he skinned green oak twigs for broiling the fish.

I think it will maybe be all right. I thought so, too. There was no telling what lay on the other side of life, but I had sat many times through an hour where time stops, empty of thought, soothed of soul, looking into . . . what? Into something that had neither name nor face, but which seemed good to me, and full of peace. If death lay there . . .

Jamie's hand touched my shoulder lightly in passing, and I smiled, not opening my eyes.

"Ouch!" he muttered, on the other side of the fire. "Nicked myself, clumsy clot."

I opened my eyes. He was a good eight feet away, head bent as he sucked a small cut on the knuckle of his thumb. A ripple of gooseflesh rose straight up my back.

"Jamie," I said. My voice sounded peculiar, even to me. I felt a small round cold spot, centered like a target on the back of my neck.

"Aye?"

"Is there—" I swallowed, feeling the hair rise on my forearms. "Jamie, is there . . . someone . . . behind me?"

His eyes shifted to the shadows over my shoulder, and sprang wide. I didn't wait to look round, but flung myself flat on the ground, an action that likely saved my life.

There was a loud *whuff!* and a sudden strong smell of ammonia and fish. Something struck me in the back with an impact that knocked the breath out of me, and then stepped heavily on my head, driving my face into the ground.

I jerked up, gasping for breath, shaking leaf mold out of my eyes. A large black bear, squalling like a cat, was lurching round the clearing, its feet scattering burning sticks.

For a moment, half blinded by dirt, I couldn't see Jamie at all. Then I spotted him. He was under the bear, one arm locked around its neck, his head tucked into the joint of the shoulder just under the drooling jaws.

One foot shot out from under the bear, kicking frantically, stabbing at the ground for traction. He had taken his boots and stockings off when we made camp; I gasped as one bare foot slewed through the remnants of the fire, raising showers of sparks.

His forearm was ridged with effort, half buried in thick fur. His free arm thrust and jabbed; he had kept hold of his dirk, at least.

At the same time, he hauled with all his strength on the bear's neck, pulling it down.

The bear was lunging, batting with one paw, trying to shake off the clinging weight around its neck. It seemed to lose its balance, and fell heavily forward, with a loud squall of rage. I heard a muffled *whoof!* that didn't seem to come from the bear, and looked frantically around for something to use as a weapon.

The bear struggled back to its feet, shaking itself violently.

I caught a brief glimpse of Jamie's face, contorted with effort. One bulging eye widened at sight of me, and he shook his mouth clear of the bristling fur.

"Run!" he shouted. Then the bear fell on him again, and he disappeared under three hundred pounds of hair and muscle.

With vague thoughts of Mowgli and the Red Flower, I scrabbled madly over the damp earth in the clearing, finding nothing but small pieces of charred stick and glowing embers that blistered my fingers but were too small to grip.

I had always thought that bears roared when annoyed. This one was making a lot of noise, but it sounded more like a very large pig, with piercing squeals and blatting noises interspersed with hair-raising growls. Jamie was making a lot of noise, too, which was reassuring under the circumstances.

My hand fell on something cold and clammy; the fish, tossed aside at the edge of the fire clearing.

"To hell with the Red Flower," I muttered. I seized one of the trout by the tail, ran forward, and belted the bear across the nose with it as hard as I could.

The bear shut its mouth and looked surprised. Then its head slewed toward me and it lunged, moving faster than I would have thought possible. I fell backward, landing on my bottom, and essayed a final, valiant blow with my fish before the bear charged me, Jamie still clinging to its neck like grim death.

It was like being caught in a meat grinder; a brief moment of total chaos, punctuated by random hard blows to the body and the sensation of being suffocated in a large, reeking hairy blanket. Then it was gone, leaving me lying bruised in the grass on my back, smelling strongly of bear piss and blinking up at the evening star, which was shining serenely overhead.

Things were a good deal less serene on the ground. I rolled onto all fours, shouting "Jamie!" at the trees, where a large, amorphous mass rolled to and fro, smashing down the oak saplings and emitting a cacophony of growls and Gaelic screeches.

It was full dark on the ground by now, but there was enough light from the sky for me to make things out. The bear had fallen over again, but instead of rising and lunging, this time was rolling on its back, hind feet churning in an effort to gain a ripping purchase. One front paw landed in a heavy, rending slap and there was an explosive grunt that didn't sound like the bear's. The smell of blood was heavy on the air.

"Jamie!" I shrieked.

There was no answer, but the writhing pile rolled and tilted slowly sideways into the deeper black shadows under the trees. The mingled noises subsided to heavy grunts and gasps, punctuated by small whimpering moans.

"JAMIE!"

The thrashing and branch-cracking died away into softer rustlings. Something was moving under the branches, swaying heavily from side to side, on all fours.

Very slowly, breathing in gasps with a catch and a groan, Jamie crawled out into the clearing.

Disregarding my own bruises, I ran to him, and dropped to my knees beside him.

"God, Jamie! Are you all right?"

"No," he said shortly, and collapsed on the ground, wheezing gently.

His face was no more than a pale blotch in the starlight; the rest of his body was so dark as to be nearly invisible. I found out why as I ran my hands swiftly over him. His clothes were so soaked with blood that they stuck to his body, his hunting shirt coming away from his chest with a nasty little sucking sound as I pulled at it.

"You smell like a slaughterhouse," I said, feeling under his chin for a pulse. It was fast—no great surprise—but strong, and a wave of relief washed over me. "Is that your blood, or the bear's?"

"If it was mine, Sassenach, I'd be dead," he said testily, opening his eyes. "No credit to you that I'm not, mind." He rolled painfully onto his side and slowly got to his hands and knees, groaning. "What possessed ye, woman, to hit me in the heid wi' a fish whilst I was fighting for my life?"

"Hold still, for heaven's sake!" He couldn't be too badly hurt if he was trying to get away. I clutched him by the hips to stop him, and kneeling behind him, felt my way gingerly up his sides. "Broken ribs?" I said.

"No. But if ye tickle me, Sassenach, I willna like it a bit," he said, gasping between words.

"I won't," I assured him. I ran my hands gently over the arch of his ribs, pressing lightly. No splintered ends protruding through the skin, no sinister depressions or soft spots; cracked maybe, but he was right, nothing broken. He yelped and twitched under my hand. "Bad spot there?"

"It is," he said between his teeth. He was beginning to shiver, and I hurried to fetch his plaid, which I wrapped about his shoulders.

"I'm fine, Sassenach," he said, waving away my attempts to help him to a seat. "Go see to the horses; they'll be upset." They were. We had hobbled the horses a little way from the clearing; they had made it a good deal farther under the impetus of terror, judging from the muffled stamping and whinnying I could hear in the distance.

There were still small wheezing groans coming from the deep shadows under the trees; the sound was so human that the hair prickled on the back of my neck. Carefully skirting the sounds, I went and found the horses, cowering in a birch grove a few hundred yards away. They whickered when they scented me, delighted to see me, bear piss and all.

By the time I had soothed the horses and coaxed them back in the direction of the clearing, the pitiful noises from the shadows had ceased. There was a small glow in the clearing; Jamie had managed to get the fire started again.

He was crouched next to the tiny blaze, still shivering under his plaid. I fed in enough sticks to make sure it wouldn't go out, then turned my attention to him once more.

"You're really not badly damaged?" I asked, still worried.

He gave me a lopsided smile.

"I'll do. It caught me a good one across the back, but I dinna think it's verra bad. Have a look?" He straightened up, wincing, and felt his side gingerly as I crossed behind him.

"What made it do that, I wonder?" he said, twisting his head toward where the bear's carcass lay. "Myers said the black bears dinna often attack ye, without ye provoke them some way."

"Maybe somebody else provoked it," I suggested. "And then had the sense to get out of the way." I lifted the plaid, and whistled under my breath.

The back of his shirt hung in shreds, smeared with dirt and ash, splotched with blood. His blood this time, not the bear's, but luckily not much. I gently pulled the tattered pieces of the shirt apart, exposing the long bow of his back. Four long claw-marks ran from shoulder blade to armpit; deep, wicked gouges that tapered to superficial red welts.

"Ooh!" I said, in sympathy.

"Well, it's no as though my back was much to look at, anyway," he joked feebly. "Really, is it bad?" He twisted around, trying to see, then stopped, grunting as the movement strained his bruised ribs.

"No. Dirty, though; I'll need to wash it out." The blood had already begun to clot; the wounds would need to be cleansed at once. I put the plaid back and set on a pan of water to boil, thinking what else I might use.

"I saw some arrowhead plant down near the stream," I said. "I think I can find it again from memory." I handed him the bottle of ale I'd brought from the saddlebags, and took his dirk.

"Will you be all right?" I paused and looked at him; he was very pale, and still shivering. The fire glimmered red on his brows, throwing the lines of his face into strong relief.

"Aye, I will." He mustered a faint grin. "Dinna worry, Sassenach; the thought of dyin' asleep in my bed seems even better to me now than it did an hour ago."

A sickle-moon was rising, bright over the trees, and I had little trouble finding the place I remembered. The stream ran cold and silver in the moonlight, chilling my hands and feet as I stood calf-deep in the water, groping for tubers of the arrowhead plant.

Small frogs sang all around me, and the stiff leaves of cattails rustled softly in the evening breeze. It was very, very peaceful, and all of a sudden I found myself shaking so hard that I had to sit down on the stream bank.

Anytime. It could happen anytime, and just this fast. I wasn't sure which seemed most unreal; the bear's attack, or this, the soft summer night, alive with promise.

I rested my head on my knees, letting the sickness, the residue of shock, drain away. It didn't matter, I told myself. Not only anytime, but anywhere. Disease, car wreck, random bullet. There was no true refuge for anyone, but like most people, I managed not to think of that most of the time.

I shuddered, thinking of the claw marks on Jamie's back. Had he been slower to react, not as strong . . . had the wounds been slightly deeper . . . for that matter, infection was still a major threat. But at least against that danger, I could fight.

The thought brought me back to myself, the squashed leaves and roots cool and wet in my hand. I splashed cold water over my face, and started up the hill toward the campfire, feeling somewhat better.

I could see Jamie through the thin scrim of saplings, sitting upright, outlined against the fire. Sitting bolt upright, in a way that must surely have been painful, considering his wounds.

I stopped, suddenly wary, just as he spoke.

"Claire?" He didn't turn around, and his voice was calm. He didn't wait for me to answer, but went on, voice cool and steady.

"Walk up behind me, Sassenach, and put your knife into my left hand. Then stay behind me."

Heart hammering, I took the three steps that brought me high enough to see over his shoulder. On the far side of the clearing, just within the light of the fire, stood three Indians, heavily armed. Evidently the bear *had* been provoked.

◆

The Indians looked us over with a lively interest that was more than returned. There were three of them; an older man, whose feathered topknot was liberally streaked with gray, and two younger, perhaps in their twenties. Father and sons, I thought—there was a certain similarity among them, more of body than of face; all three were fairly short, broad-shouldered and bowlegged, with long, powerful arms.

I eyed their weapons covertly. The older man cradled a gun in the curve of his arm; it was an ancient French wheellock, the hexagonal barrel rimed with rust. It looked as though it would explode in his face if he fired it, but I hoped he wouldn't try.

One of the younger men carried a bow to hand, arrow casually nocked. All three had sinister-looking tomahawks and skinning knives slung in their belts. Long as it was, Jamie's dirk seemed rather inadequate by comparison.

Evidently coming to the same conclusion, he leaned forward and placed the dirk carefully on the ground at his feet. Sitting back, he spread his empty hands and shrugged.

The Indians giggled. It was such an unwarlike noise that I found myself half smiling in response, even though my stomach, less easily disarmed, stayed knotted with tension.

I saw Jamie's shoulders relax their rigid line, and felt slightly reassured.

"Bonsoir, messieurs," he said. *"Parlez-vous français?"*

The Indians giggled again, glancing at each other shyly. The older man took a tentative step forward and ducked his head at us, setting the beads in his hair swinging.

"No . . . Fransh," he said.

"English?" I said hopefully. He glanced at me with interest, but shook his head. He said something over one shoulder to one of his sons, who replied in the same unintelligible tongue. The older man turned back to Jamie and asked something, raising his brows in question.

Jamie shook his head in incomprehension, and one of the young men stepped into the firelight. Bending his knees and letting his shoulders slump, he thrust his head forward and swayed from side to side, peering nearsightedly in such perfect imitation of a bear that Jamie laughed out loud. The other Indians grinned.

The young man straightened up and pointed at the blood-soaked sleeve of Jamie's shirt, with an interrogatory noise.

"Oh, aye, it's over there," Jamie said, gesturing toward the darkness under the trees.

Without further ado, all three men disappeared into the dark, from which excited exclamations and murmurings soon emerged.

"It's all right, Sassenach," Jamie said. "They willna harm us. They're only hunters." He closed his eyes briefly, and I saw the faint sheen of sweat on his face. "And a good thing, too, because I think I'm maybe going to swoon."

"Don't even think about it. Don't you *dare* faint and leave me alone with them!" No matter what the savages' possible intentions, the thought of facing them alone over Jamie's unconscious body was enough to reknot my intestines with panic. I put my hand on the back of his neck and forced his head down between his knees.

"Breathe," I said, squeezing cold water from my handkerchief down the back of his neck. "You can faint later."

"Can I puke?" he asked, his voice muffled in his kilt. I recognized the note of wry jest in it, and let my own breath out with relief.

"No," I said. "Sit up; they're coming back."

They were, dragging the bear's carcass with them. Jamie sat up and mopped his face with the wet handkerchief. Warm as the night was, he was shivering slightly from shock, but he sat steadily enough.

The older man came over to us, and pointed with raised brows;

first to the knife that lay at Jamie's feet, then to the dead bear. Jamie nodded modestly.

"It wasna easy, mind," he said.

The Indian's brows rose higher. Then he ducked his head, hands spread in a gesture of respect. He beckoned to one of the younger men, who came over, untying a pouch from his belt.

Shoving me unceremoniously to one side, the younger man ripped open the throat of Jamie's shirt, pulled it off his shoulder, and squinted at the injury. He poured a handful of a lumpy, half-powdery substance into his hand, spat copiously into it, stirred it into a foul-smelling paste, and smeared it liberally over the wounds.

"Now I really am going to puke," Jamie murmured, wincing under the ungentle ministrations. "What is that stuff?"

"At a guess, it's dried trillium mixed with very rancid bear grease," I said, trying not to inhale the pungent fumes. "I don't suppose it will kill you; at least I hope not."

"That's two of us, then," he said under his breath. "No, I'll do now, thank ye kindly." He waved away further ministrations, smiling politely at his would-be doctor.

Joking or not, his lips were white, even in the dimness of the firelight. I put a hand on his good shoulder, and felt the muscles clenched tight with strain.

"Get the whisky, Sassenach. I need it badly."

One of the Indians made a grab at the bottle as I pulled it from the bag, but I pushed him rudely away. He grunted with surprise, but didn't follow me. Instead, he picked up the bag and began rooting through it like a hog hunting truffles. I didn't try to stop him, but hurried back to Jamie with the whisky.

He took a small sip, then a larger one, shuddered once, and opened his eyes. He breathed deeply once or twice, drank again, then wiped his mouth and held out the bottle in invitation to the older man.

"Do you think that's wise?" I muttered, recalling Myers's lurid stories about massacres, and the effects of firewater on Indians.

"I can give it to them or let them take it, Sassenach," he said, a little testily. "There are three of them, aye?"

The older man passed the mouth of the bottle under his nose, nostrils flaring as though in appreciation of a rare bouquet. I could smell the liquor from where I stood, and was surprised that it didn't sear the lining of his nose.

A smile of beatific content spread across the man's craggy face.
He said something to his sons that sounded like *"Haroo!"* and
the one who had been rifling our bag came at once to join his
brother, a couple of corn dodgers clutched in his fist.

The older man stood up with the bottle in his hand, but instead
of drinking, took it over to where the bear's carcass lay, black as
an inkblot on the ground. With great deliberation, he poured a
small amount of whisky into the palm of his hand, bent, and
dribbled the liquid into the bear's half-open mouth. Then he
turned slowly in a circle, shaking drops of whisky ceremoniously
from his fingers. The drops flew gold and amber where they
caught the light, hitting the fire with tiny, sizzling pops.

Jamie sat up straight, dizziness forgotten in his interest.

"Will ye look at that, now?" he said.

"At what?" I said, but he didn't answer, absorbed by the Indians' behavior.

One of the younger men had taken out a small beaded pouch
that held tobacco. Carefully packing the bowl of a small stone
pipe, he lit it with a dry twig dipped into the flames of our fire,
and drew strongly on the barrel. The tobacco leaf sparked and
fumed, spreading its rich aroma over the clearing.

Jamie was leaning against me, his back against my thighs. I had
my hand on his unwounded shoulder again, and could feel the
shiver in his flesh start to ease as the warmth of the whisky began
to spread in his belly. He wasn't badly hurt, but the strain of the
fight and the continued effort to stay alert were taking their toll on
him.

The older man took the pipe and drew several deep, leisurely
mouthfuls, which he exhaled with evident pleasure. Then he
knelt, and taking another deep lungful of smoke, carefully blew it
up the nostrils of the dead bear. He repeated this process several
times, muttering something under his breath as he exhaled.

Then he rose, with no sign of stiffness, and extended the pipe to
Jamie.

Jamie smoked as the Indians had done—one or two long, cere-
monious mouthfuls—and then lifted the pipe, turning to hand it to
me.

I lifted the pipe and drew cautiously. Burning smoke filled my
eyes and nose at once, and my throat constricted with an overwhelming urge to cough. I choked it back, and hastily gave Jamie
the pipe, feeling my face turn red as the smoke curled lazily

through my chest, tickling and burning as it searched its way through the channels of my lungs.

"Ye dinna *breathe* it, Sassenach," he murmured. "Just let it rise up the back of your nose."

"Now . . . you . . . tell me," I said, trying not to strangle.

The Indians watched me in round-eyed interest. The older man put his head on one side, frowning as though trying to puzzle something out. He popped up onto his feet and came round the fire, crouching to peer curiously at me, close enough for me to catch the odd, smoky scent of his skin. He wore nothing but a breechclout and a sort of short leather apron, though his chest was covered by a large, ornate necklace featuring seashells, stones, and the teeth of some large animal.

With no warning, he suddenly reached out and squeezed my breast. There was nothing even faintly lascivious about the gesture, but I jumped. So did Jamie, hand darting for his knife.

The Indian sat back calmly on his heels, waving his hand in dismissal. He clapped his hand flat on his breast, then made a cupping motion and pointed at me. He had meant nothing; he had only wanted to assure himself that I was indeed female. He pointed from me to Jamie, and raised one brow.

"Aye, she's mine." Jamie nodded and lowered his dirk, but kept a hold on it, frowning at the Indian. "Mind your manners, eh?"

Uninterested in this byplay, one of the younger Indians said something, and gestured impatiently at the carcass on the ground. The older man, who had paid no attention to Jamie's annoyance, replied, drawing his skinning knife from his belt as he turned.

"Here—that's mine to do."

The Indians turned in surprise as Jamie rose to his feet. He gestured with his dirk to the bear, and then pointed the tip firmly at his own chest.

Not waiting for any response, he knelt on the ground beside the carcass, crossed himself, and said something in Gaelic, knife raised above the still body. I didn't know all the words, but I had seen him do it once before, when he had killed a deer on the road from Georgia.

It was the gralloch prayer he had been taught as a boy, learning to hunt in the Highlands of Scotland. It was old, he had told me; so old that some of the words were no longer in common use, so it sounded unfamiliar. But it must be said for any animal slain that was larger than a hare, before the throat was cut or the bellyskin split.

Without hesitation, he made a shallow slash across the chest—no need to bleed the carcass; the heart was long since still—and ripped the skin between the legs, so the pale swell of the intestines bulged up from the narrow, black-furred slit, gleaming in the light.

It took both strength and considerable skill to split and peel back the heavy skin without penetrating the mesenteric membrane that held the visceral sac enclosed. I, who had opened softer human bodies, recognized surgical competence when I saw it. So did the Indians, who were watching the proceedings with critical interest.

Jamie's skill at skinning wasn't what had fixed their attention, though—that was surely a common enough ability here. No, it was the gralloch prayer—I had seen the older man's eyes widen, and his glance at his sons as Jamie knelt over the carcass. They might not know what he was saying, but it was plain from their expressions that they knew exactly what he was doing—and were both surprised, and favorably impressed.

A small trickle of sweat ran down behind Jamie's ear, clear red in the firelight. Skinning a large animal is heavy work, and small spots of fresh blood were showing through the grimy cloth of his shirt.

Before I could offer to take the knife, though, he sat back on his heels and offered the dirk hilt-first to one of the younger Indians.

"Go ahead," he said, gesturing at the bear's half-butchered bulk in invitation. "Ye dinna think I'm going to eat it all myself, I hope."

The man took the knife without hesitation, and kneeling, took over the skinning. The two others glanced at Jamie, and seeing his nod, joined in the work.

He let me sit him on the log once more and covertly clean and dress his shoulder, while he watched the Indians make quick work of the skinning and butchering.

"What was it he did with the whisky?" I asked quietly. "Do you know?"

He nodded, eyes fixed absently on the bloody work by the fire.

"It's a charm. Ye scatter holy water to the four airs of the earth, to preserve yourself from evil. And I suppose whisky is a verra reasonable substitute for holy water, in the circumstances."

I glanced at the Indians, stained to the elbows with the bear's blood, talking casually among themselves. One of them was building a small platform near the fire, a crude layer of sticks laid across rocks set in a square. Another was cutting chunks of meat and stringing them on a peeled green stick for cooking.

"From evil? Do you mean they're afraid of *us*?"

He smiled.

"I shouldna think we're so fearsome, Sassenach; no, from spirits."

Frightened as I had been by the Indians' appearance, it would never have occurred to me that they might have been similarly unnerved by ours. But glancing up at Jamie now, I thought they might pardonably have been excused for nervousness.

Used to him as I was, I was seldom aware anymore of how he appeared to others. But even tired and wounded, he was formidable; straight-backed and wide-shouldered, with slanted eyes that caught the fire in a glitter as blue as the flame's heart.

He sat easily now, relaxed, big hands loose between his thighs. But it was the stillness of a great cat, eyes always watchful behind the calm. Beyond size and quickness, there was undeniably an air of savagery about him; he was as much at home in these woods as the bear had been.

The English had always thought the Scottish Highlanders barbarians; I had never before considered the possibility that others might feel likewise. But these men had seen a ferocious savage, and approached him with due caution, arms at the ready. And Jamie, horrified beforehand at the thought of savage Red Indians, had seen their rituals—so like his own—and known them at once for fellow hunters; civilized men.

Even now, he was speaking to them quite naturally, explaining with broad gestures how the bear had come upon us and how he had killed it. They followed him with avid attention, exclaiming in appreciation in all the right places. When he picked up the remains of the mangled fish and demonstrated my role in the proceedings, they all looked at me and giggled hilariously.

I glared at all four of them.

"Dinner," I said loudly, "is served."

We shared a meal of half-roasted meat, corn dodgers, and whisky, watched throughout by the head of the bear, which perched ceremonially on its platform, dead eyes gone dull and gummy.

Feeling mildly glazed, I leaned against the fallen log, listening with half an ear to the conversation. Not that I understood much that was actually said. One of the sons, an accomplished mimic, was giving a spirited rendition of Great Hunts of the Past, alternately playing the parts of hunter and prey, and doing it well enough that even I had no difficulty in telling a deer from a panther.

We had got so far in our acquaintance as an exchange of names. Mine came out in their tongue as "Klah," which they seemed to find very funny. "Klah," they said, pointing at me, "Klah-Klah-Klah-Klah-Klah!" Then they all laughed uproariously, their humor fueled by whisky. I might have been tempted to reply in kind, save that I wasn't sure I could pronounce "Nacognaweto" once, let alone repeatedly.

They were—or so Jamie informed me—Tuscarora. With his gift of tongues, he was already pointing at objects and essaying the Indian names for them. No doubt by dawn he would be exchanging improper stories with them, I thought blearily; they were already telling him jokes.

"Here," I said, tugging on the edge of Jamie's plaid. "Are you all right? Because I can't stay awake to look after you. Are you going to faint and fall headfirst into the fire?"

Jamie patted me absently on the head.

"I'll be fine now, Sassenach," he said. Restored by food and whisky, he seemed to be suffering no lingering ill effects from his battle with the bear. What he'd feel like in the morning was another question, I thought.

I was beyond worrying about that, or anything else, though; my head was spinning from the effects of adrenaline, whisky and tobacco, and I crawled off to fetch my blanket. Curled up by Jamie's feet, I drifted drowsily off to sleep, surrounded by the sacred fumes of smoke and liquor, and watched by the dull, sticky eyes of the bear.

"Know just how you feel," I told it, and then was gone.

16

The First Law of Thermodynamics

I was awakened abruptly just after dawn by a tiny stinging sensation on top of my head. I blinked and put up a hand to investigate. The movement startled a large gray jay who had been pulling hairs out of my head, and he shot up into a nearby pine tree, screeching hysterically.

"Serve you right, mate," I muttered, rubbing the top of my head, but couldn't help smiling. I had been told often enough that my hair looked like a bird's nest first thing in the morning; perhaps there was something to it, after all.

The Indians were gone. Luckily, the bear's head had gone with them. I felt my own head with ginger fingers, but aside from the small sting of the jay's depredations, it seemed intact. Either it had been remarkably good whisky, or my sense of intoxication had been due more to the effects of adrenaline and tobacco than to alcohol.

My comb was in the small deerskin pouch where I kept personal necessities and those few medicines I thought might be useful on the trail. I sat up carefully, so as not to wake Jamie. He lay a short distance away on his back, hands crossed, peaceful as the carved effigy on a sarcophagus.

A lot more colorful, though. He lay in the shade, a creeping patch of sunshine sneaking up on him, barely touching the ends of his hair. In the fresh, cool light, he looked like Adam, newly touched by his Creator's hand.

Rather a battered Adam, though; on closer inspection, this was a snap taken well after the Fall. Not the fragile perfection of a child born of clay, nor yet the unused beauty of the youth God loved. No, this one was a man full-formed and powerful; each line of face and body marked with strength and struggle, made to take hold of the world he would wake to, and subdue it.

I moved very quietly, reaching for my pouch. I didn't want to wake him; the opportunity to watch him sleep came rarely. He slept like a cat, ready to spring up at any intimation of threat, and he normally rose from his bed at first light, while I was still floating on the surface of my dreams. Either he had drunk more than I thought last night, or he was in the deep sleep of healing, letting his body mend itself as he lay still.

The horn comb slid soothingly through my hair. For once, I wasn't in a hurry. There was no baby to feed, no child to rouse and dress for school, no work waiting. No patients to see, no paperwork to do.

Nothing could be farther from the sterile confines of a hospital than this place, I thought. Early birds in search of worms were making a cheerful racket in the forest, and a cool, soft breeze blew through the clearing. I smelt a faint whiff of dried blood, and the stale ashes from last night's fire.

Perhaps it was the scent of blood that had made me remember the hospital. From the moment I first walked into one, I had known it to be my sphere, my natural place. And yet I was not out of place, here in the wildwood. I thought that odd.

The ends of my hair brushed my naked shoulder blades with a pleasant, tickling feel, and the air was cool enough that the small breeze made my skin ripple with gooseflesh, my nipples standing up in tiny puckers. So I hadn't imagined it, I thought, with an inward smile. I certainly hadn't taken my own clothes off before retiring.

I pushed back the thick linen blanket, and saw the flecks of dried blood, smears on my thighs and belly. I felt dampness ooze between my legs, and drew a finger between them. Milky, with a musky scent not my own.

That was enough to bring back the shadow of the dream—or what I had thought must be one; the great bulk of the bear looming over me, darker than the night and reeking of blood, a rush of terror that kept my dream-heavy limbs from moving. My lying limp, pretending death, as he nudged and nuzzled, breath hot on my skin, fur soft on my breasts, gentleness amazing for a beast.

Then that one sharp moment of consciousness; of cold, then hot, as bare skin, not bearskin, touched my own, and then the dizzy slide back into drunken dreaming, the slow and forceful coupling, climax fading into sleep . . . with a soft Scottish growling in my ear.

I looked down and saw the strawberry crescent of a bite mark on my shoulder.

"No *wonder* you're still asleep," I said in accusation. The sun had touched the curve of his cheek, lighting the eyebrow on that side like a match touched to kindling. He didn't open his eyes, but a slow, sweet smile spread across his face in answer.

The Indians had left us a portion of the bear meat, tidily wrapped in oiled skin and hung from the branches of a nearby tree to discourage the attentions of skunks and raccoons. After breakfast and a hasty bath in the creek, Jamie took his bearings by sun and mountain.

"That way," he said, nodding toward a distant blue peak. "See where it makes a notch wi' the shorter one? On the other side, it's the Indians' land; the new Treaty Line follows that ridge."

"Someone actually *surveyed* through there?" I peered unbelievingly at the vista of saw-toothed mountain ranges rising from valleys filled with morning mist. The mountains rose ahead of us like an endless series of floating mirages, fading from black-green to blue to purple, the farthest peaks etched black and needle-sharp against a crystal sky.

"Oh, aye." He swung up into his saddle, turning his horse's head so the sun fell over his shoulder. "They had to, to say for sure which land could be taken for settling. I made sure of the boundary before we left Wilmington, and Myers said the same— this side of the highest ridge. I did think to ask the fellows who dined with us last night, though, only to be sure *they* thought so, too." He grinned down at me. "Ready, Sassenach?"

"As I'll ever be," I assured him, and turned my horse to follow.

He had rinsed out his shirt—or what was left of it—in the stream. The stained rag of linen was spread out to dry behind his saddle, leaving him half-naked in leather riding breeks, his plaid wrapped carelessly round his waist. The long scratches left by the bear's attack were black across his fair skin, but there was no visible inflammation, and from the ease with which he moved in the saddle, the wounds seemed not to trouble him.

Neither did anything else, so far as I could see. The tinge of wariness he always bore was still with him; it had been part of him since boyhood—but some weight had lifted in the night. I thought perhaps it was our meeting with the three hunters; this first encounter with savages had been vastly reassuring to us both,

and seemed substantially to have eased Jamie's visions of toma-
hawk-wielding cannibals behind every tree.

Or it might be the trees themselves—or the mountains. His
spirits had grown lighter with every foot upward from the coastal
plain. I couldn't help sharing his apparent joy—but at the same
time, felt a growing dread of what that joy might lead to.

By midmorning the slopes had grown too thickly forested to
ride any farther. Looking up a nearly vertical rock face into a
dizzying tangle of dark branches, sparked with gold and green
and brown, I was inclined to think the horses were lucky to be
stopping at the bottom. We hobbled them near a stream, thick
with grass along its edge, and plunged in on foot, onward and
upward, ever deeper into the bloody Forest Primeval.

Towering pines and hemlocks, was it? I thought, clambering
over the burled knots of a fallen tree. The monstrous trunks rose
so high that the lowest limbs started twenty feet above my head.
Longfellow had no idea.

The air was damp, cool but fecund, and my moccasins sank
soundlessly into centuries-thick black leaf mold. My own footprint in the soft mud of a stream bank seemed strange and sudden
as a dinosaur's track.

We reached the top of a ridge, only to find another before us,
and another beyond. I did not know what we might be looking for,
or how we would know if we found it. Jamie covered miles with
his tireless hill-walker's stride, taking in everything. I tagged behind, enjoying the scenery, pausing now and then to gather some
fascinating plant or root, stowing my treasures in the bag at my
belt.

We made our way along the back of one ridge, only to find our
way blocked by a great heath bald: a patch of mountain laurel that
looked from a distance like a shiny bare patch among the dark
conifers, but closer to, proved to be an impenetrable thicket, its
springy branches interwoven like a basket.

We backtracked, and turned downward, out from under the
huge fragrant firs, across slopes of wild timothy and muhly grass
that had gone bright yellow in the sun, and at last back into the
soothing green of oak and hickory, on a wooded bluff that overlooked a small and nameless river.

It was cool under the trees' sudden shade, and I sighed in relief,
lifting the hair off my neck to admit a breath of air. Jamie heard
me and turned, smiling, holding back a limber branch so that I
could follow him.

We didn't talk much; aside from the breath required for climbing, the mountain itself seemed to inhibit speech; full of secret green places, it was a vivid offspring of the ancient Scottish mountains, thick with forest, and twice the height of those barren black parental crags. Still, its air held the same injunction to silence, the same promise of enchantment.

The ground here was covered in a foot-deep layer of fallen leaves, soft and spongy underfoot, and the spaces between the trees seemed illusionary, as though to pass between those huge, lichened trunks might transport one suddenly to another dimension of reality.

Jamie's hair sparked in the occasional shafts of sunlight, a torch to follow through the shadows of the wood. It had darkened somewhat over the years, to a deep, rich auburn, but the long days of riding and walking in the sun had bleached his crown to copper fire. He had lost the thong that bound his hair; he paused, and brushed the thick damp locks back from his face, so that I saw the startling streak of white just above one temple. Normally hidden among the darker red, it showed rarely—a legacy of the bullet wound received in the cave of Abandawe.

Despite the warmth of the day, I shivered slightly in recollection. I would greatly have preferred to forget Haiti and its savage mysteries altogether, but there was little hope of that. Sometimes, on the verge of sleep, I would hear the voice of the cave-wind, and the nagging echo of the thought that came in its wake: *Where else?*

We climbed a granite ledge, thick with moss and lichen, wet with the omnipresent flow of water, then followed the path of a descending freshet, brushing aside long grass that pulled at our legs, dodging the drooping branches of mountain laurel and the thick-leaved rhododendrons.

Wonders sprang up by my feet, small orchids and brilliant fungi, trembling and shiny as jellies, shimmering red and black on fallen tree trunks. Dragonflies hung over the water, jewels immobile in the air, vanishing in mist.

I felt dazed with abundance, ravished by beauty. Jamie's face bore the dream-stunned look of a man who knows himself sleeping, but does not wish to wake. Paradoxically, the better I felt, the worse I felt, too; desperately happy—and desperately afraid. This was his place, and surely he felt it as well as I.

In early afternoon we stopped to rest and drink from a small spring at the edge of a natural clearing. The ground beneath the maple trees was covered with a thick carpet of dark green leaves, among which I caught a sudden telltale flash of red.

"Wild strawberries!" I said with delight.

The berries were dark red and tiny, about the size of my thumb joint. By the standards of modern horticulture, they would have been too tart, nearly bitter, but eaten with a meal consisting of half-cooked cold bear meat and rock-hard corn dodgers, they were delicious—fresh explosions of flavor in my mouth; pinpricks of sweetness on my tongue.

I gathered handfuls in my cloak, not caring for stains—what was a little strawberry juice among the stains of pine pitch, soot, leaf smudges and simple dirt? By the time I had finished, my fingers were sticky and pungent with juice, my stomach was comfortably full, and the inside of my mouth felt as though it had been sandpapered, from the tartly acid taste of the berries. Still, I couldn't resist reaching for just one more.

Jamie leaned his back against a sycamore, eyelids half lowered against the dazzle of afternoon sun. The little clearing held light like a cup, still and limpid.

"What d'ye think of this place, Sassenach?" he asked.

"I think it's beautiful. Don't you?"

He nodded, looking down between the trees, where a gentle slope full of wild hay and timothy fell away and rose again in a line of willows that fringed the distant river.

"I am thinking," Jamie said, a little awkwardly. "There is the spring here in the wood. That meadow below—" He waved a hand toward the scrim of alders that screened the ridge from the grassy slope. "It would do for a few beasts at first, and then the land nearer the river might be cleared and put in crops. The rise of the land here is good for drainage. And here, see . . ." Caught by visions, he rose to his feet, pointing.

I looked carefully; to me, the place seemed little different from any of the steep wooded slopes and grassy coves through which we had wandered for the last couple of days. But to Jamie, with his farmer's eye, houses and stock pens and fields sprang up like fairy mushrooms in the shadows of the trees.

Happiness was sticking out all over him, like porcupine quills. My heart felt like lead in my chest.

"You're thinking we might settle here, then? Take the Governor's offer?"

He looked at me, stopping abruptly in his speculations.

"We might," he said. "If—"

He broke off and looked sideways at me. Sun-reddened as he was, I couldn't tell whether he was flushed with sun or shyness.

"D'ye believe in signs at all, Sassenach?"

"What sorts of signs?" I asked guardedly.

In answer, he bent, plucked a sprig from the ground, and dropped it into my hand—the dark green leaves like small round Chinese fans, a pure white flower on a slender stem, and on another a half-ripe berry, its shoulders pale with shade, blushing crimson at the tip.

"This. It's ours, d'ye see?" he said.

"Ours?"

"The Frasers', I mean," he explained. One large, blunt finger gently prodded the berry. "Strawberries ha' always been the emblem of the clan—it's what the name meant, to start with, when a Monsieur Fréselière came across from France wi' King William that was—and took hold of land in the Scottish mountains for his trouble."

King William that was. William the Conqueror, that was. Perhaps not the oldest of the Highland clans, the Frasers had still a distinguished heritage.

"Warriors from the start, were you?"

"And farmers, too." The doubt in his eyes was fading into a smile.

I didn't say what I was thinking, but I knew well enough that the thought must lie in his mind as well. There was no more of clan Fraser save scattered fragments, those who had survived by flight, by stratagem or luck. The clans had been smashed at Culloden, their chieftains slaughtered in battle or murdered by law.

Yet here he stood, tall and straight in his plaid, the dark steel of a Highland dirk by his side. Warrior and farmer both. And if the soil beneath his feet was not that of Scotland, it was free air that he breathed—and a mountain wind that stirred his hair, lifting copper strands to the summer sun.

I smiled up at him, fighting back my growing dismay.

"Fréselière, eh? Mr. Strawberry? He grew them, did he, or was he only fond of eating them?"

"Either or both," he said dryly, "or it was maybe only that he was redheided, aye?"

I laughed, and he hunkered down beside me, unpinning his plaid.

"It's a rare plant," he said, touching the sprig in my open hand. "Flowers, fruit and leaves all together at the one time. The white flowers are for honor, and red fruit for courage—and the green leaves are for constancy.''

My throat felt tight as I looked at him.

''They got that one right,'' I said.

He caught my hand in his own, squeezing my fingers around the tiny stem.

''And the fruit is the shape of a heart,'' he said softly, and bent to kiss me.

The tears were near the surface; at least I had a good excuse for the one that oozed free. He dabbed it away, then stood up and pulled his belt loose, letting the plaid fall in folds around his feet. Then he stripped off shirt and breeks and smiled down at me, naked.

''There's no one here,'' he said. ''No one but us.''

I would have said this seemed no reason, but I felt what it was he meant. We had been for days surrounded by vastness and threat, the wilderness no farther away than the pale circle of our fire. Yet here, we were alone together, part and parcel of the place, with no need in broad daylight to hold the wilderness at bay.

''In the old days, men would do this, to give fertility to the fields,'' he said, giving me a hand to rise.

''I don't see any fields.'' And wasn't sure whether to hope I never would. Nonetheless, I skimmed off my buckskin shirt, and pulled loose the knot of my makeshift brassiere. He eyed me with appreciation.

''Well, no doubt I shall have to cut down a few trees first, but that can wait, aye?''

We made a bed of plaid and cloaks, and lay down upon it naked, skin to skin among the yellow grasses and the scent of balsam and wild strawberries.

We touched each other for what might have been a very long time or no time at all, together in the garden of earthly delight. I forced away the thoughts that had plagued me up the mountain, determined only to share his joy for as long as it lasted. I grasped him tight and he breathed in deep and pressed himself hard into my hand.

''And what would Eden be without a serpent?'' I murmured, fingers stroking.

His eyes creased into blue triangles, so close I could see the black of his pupils.

''And will ye eat wi' me, then, *mo chridhe?* Of the fruit of the tree of the knowledge of Good and Evil?''

I put out the tip of my tongue and drew it along his lower lip in answer. He shivered under my fingers, though the air was warm and sweet.

"Je suis prèst," I said. *"Monsieur Fréselière."*

His head bent and his mouth fastened on my nipple, swollen as one of the tiny ripe berries.

"Madame Fréselière," he whispered back. *"Je suis à votre service."*

And then we shared the fruit and flowers, and the green leaves covering all.

We lay tangled in drowsiness, stirring only to bat away inquisitive insects, until the first shadows touched our feet. Jamie rose quietly, and covered me with a cloak, thinking me asleep. I heard the stealthy rustle as he dressed himself, and then the soft swish of his passage through the grass.

I rolled over, and saw him a little distance away, standing at the edge of the wood, looking out over the fall of land toward the river.

He wore nothing but his plaid, crumpled and blood-stained, belted round his waist. With his hair unbound and tangled round his shoulders, he looked the wild Highlander he was. What I had thought a trap for him—his family, his clan—was his strength. And what I had thought my strength—my solitude, my lack of ties —was my weakness.

Having known closeness, both its good and its bad, he had the strength to leave it, to step away from all notions of safety and venture out alone. And I—so proud of self-sufficiency at one time —could not bear the thought of loneliness again.

I had resolved to say nothing, to live in the moment, to accept whatever came. But the moment was here, and I could not accept it. I saw his head lift in decision, and at the same moment, saw his name carved in cold stone. Terror and despair washed over me.

As though he had heard the echo of my unspoken cry, he turned his head toward me. Whatever he saw in my face brought him swiftly to my side.

"What is it, Sassenach?"

There was no point in lying; not when he could see me.

"I'm afraid," I blurted out.

He glanced quickly round for danger, one hand reaching for his knife, but I stopped him with a hand on his arm.

"Not that. Jamie—hold me. Please."

He gathered me close against him, wrapping the cloak around me. I was shivering, though the air was still warm.

"It's all right, *a nighean donn,*" he murmured. "I'm here. What's frightened ye, then?"

"You," I said, and clung tight. His heart thumped just under my ear, strong and steady. "Here. It makes me afraid to think of you here, of us coming here—"

"Afraid?" he asked. "Of what, Sassenach?" His arms tightened around me. "I did say when we were wed that I would always see ye fed, no?" He pulled me closer, tucking my head into the curve of his shoulder.

"I gave ye three things that day," he said softly. "My name, my family, and the protection of my body. You'll have those things always, Sassenach—so long as we both shall live. No matter where we may be. I willna let ye go hungry or cold; I'll let nothing harm ye, ever."

"I'm not afraid of any of that," I blurted out. "I'm afraid you'll die, and I can't stand it if you do, Jamie, I really can't!"

He jerked back a little, surprised, and looked down into my face.

"Well, I'll do my best to oblige ye, Sassenach," he said, "but ye ken I may not have all the say in the matter." His face was serious, but one corner of his mouth curled up irrepressibly.

The sight did me in utterly.

"Don't you laugh!" I said furiously. "Don't you *dare* laugh!"

"Oh, I'm not," he assured me, trying to straighten his face.

"You are!" I punched him in the chest. Now he *was* laughing. I punched him again, harder, and before I knew it, was hammering him in earnest, my fists making small dull thumps against his plaid. He grabbed for my hand, but I ducked my head and bit him on the thumb. He let out a cry and jerked his hand away.

He examined the toothmarks for a moment, then looked at me, one eyebrow raised. The humor lingered in his eyes, but at least he'd stopped laughing, the bastard.

"Sassenach, ye've seen me damn near dead a dozen times, and not turned a hair. Whyever are ye takin' on so now, and me not even ill?"

"Never turned a hair?" I gawked at him in furious amazement. "You think I wasn't *upset*?"

He rubbed a knuckle across his upper lip, eyeing me in some amusement.

"Oh. Well, I did think ye cared, of course. But I never thought of it in just that way, I admit."

"Of course you didn't! And if you had, it wouldn't make any difference. You—you—Scot!" It was the worst thing I could think of to call him. Finding no more words, I turned and stomped away.

Unfortunately, stomping has relatively little effect when executed in bare feet on a grassy meadow. I stepped on something sharp, uttered a small cry, and limped a few more steps before having to stop.

I had stepped on some sort of cocklebur; half a dozen vicious caltrops were stuck in my bare sole, blood drops welling from the tiny punctures. Precariously balanced on one foot, I tried to pick them out, cursing under my breath.

I wobbled and nearly fell. A strong hand caught me under the elbow and steadied me. I set my teeth and finished jerking out the spiny burs. I pulled my elbow out of his grasp and turning on my heel, walked—with a good deal more care—back to where I had left my clothing.

Dropping the cloak on the ground, I proceeded to dress, with what dignity was possible. Jamie stood, arms folded, watching me without comment.

"When God threw Adam out of Paradise, at least Eve went with him," I said, talking to my fingers as I fastened the draw-string of my trousers.

"Aye, that's true," he agreed, after a cautious pause. He gave me a sidelong glance, to see whether I was about to hit him again.

"Ah—ye havena been eating any o' the plants ye picked this morning, have ye, Sassenach? No, I didna think so," he added hastily, seeing my expression. "I only wondered. Myers says some things here give ye the nightmare something fierce."

"I am not having nightmares," I said, with more force than strictly necessary had I been telling the truth. I *was* having waking nightmares, though ingestion of hallucinogenic plant substances had nothing to do with it.

He sighed.

"D'ye mean to tell me straight out what ye're talkin' about, Sassenach, or do ye mean me to suffer a bit first?"

I glared at him, caught as usual between the urge to laugh and the urge to hit him with a blunt object. Then a wave of despair overcame both laughter and anger. My shoulders slumped in surrender.

"I'm talking about you," I said.

"Me? Why?"

"Because you're a bloody Highlander, and you're all about honor and courage and constancy, and I know you can't help it, and I wouldn't want you to, only—only damn it, it's going to take you to Scotland and get you killed, and there's nothing I can do about it!"

He gave me a look of incredulity.

"Scotland?" he said, as though I'd said something completely mad.

"Scotland! Where your bloody grave is!"

He rubbed a hand slowly through his hair, looking down the bridge of his nose at me.

"Oh," he said at last. "I see, then. Ye think if I go to Scotland, I must die there, since that's where I'll be buried. Is that it?"

I nodded, too upset to speak.

"Mmphm. And just why is it ye think I'm going to Scotland?" he asked carefully.

I glared at him in exasperation, and waved an arm at the expanse of wilderness around us.

"Where the hell else are you going to get settlers for this land? Of course you're going to Scotland!"

He looked at me, exasperated in turn.

"How in the name of God d'ye think I should do that, Sassenach? I might have, when I had the gems, but now? I've maybe ten pound to my name, and that's borrowed. Shall I fly to Scotland like a bird, then? And lead folk back behind me, walkin' on the water?"

"You'll think of something," I said miserably. "You always do."

He gave me a queer look, then looked away and paused for several moments before answering.

"I hadna realized ye thought I was God Almighty, Sassenach," he said at last.

"I don't," I said. "Moses, maybe." The words were facetious, but neither one of us was joking.

He walked away a bit, hands clasped behind his back.

"Watch out for the burs," I called after him, seeing him heading for the location of my recent mishap. He altered his path in response, but said nothing. He walked to and fro across the clearing, head bent in thought. At last he came back, to stand in front of me.

"I canna do it alone," he said quietly. "You're right about that. But I dinna think I need go to Scotland for my settlers."

"What else?"

"My men—the men who were wi' me in Ardsmuir," he said. "They're here already."

"But you haven't any idea where they are," I protested. "And besides, they were transported years ago! They'll be settled; they won't want to pull up stakes and come to the ends of the bloody earth with you!"

He smiled, a little wryly.

"You did, Sassenach."

I took a deep breath. The nagging weight of fear that had burdened my heart for the last weeks had eased. With that concern lifted, though, there was now room in my mind to contemplate the staggering difficulty of the task he was setting himself. Track down men scattered over three colonies, persuade them to come with him, and simultaneously find sufficient capital to finance the clearing of land and planting of crops. To say nothing of the sheer enormity of labor involved in carving some small foothold out of this virgin wilderness . . .

"I'll think of something," he said, smiling slightly as he watched doubts and uncertainties flit across my face. "I always do, aye?"

All of my breath went out in a long sigh.

"You do," I said. "Jamie—are you sure? Your aunt Jocasta—"

He dismissed that possibility with a flick of his hand.

"No," he said. "Never."

I still hesitated, feeling guilty.

"You wouldn't—it's not just because of me? What I said about keeping slaves?"

"No," he said. He paused, and I saw the two twisted fingers of his right hand twitch. He saw it, too, and stopped the movement abruptly.

"I have lived as a slave, Claire," he said quietly, head bent. "And I couldna live, knowing there was a man on earth who felt toward me as I have felt toward those who thought they owned me."

I reached out and covered his crippled hand with my own. Tears ran down my cheeks, warm and soothing as summer rain.

"You won't leave me?" I asked at last. "You won't die?"

He shook his head, and squeezed my hand tight.

"You are my courage, as I am your conscience," he whispered.

"You are my heart—and I your compassion. We are neither of us whole, alone. Do ye not know that, Sassenach?"

"I do know that," I said, and my voice shook. "That's why I'm so afraid. I don't want to be half a person again, I can't bear it."

He thumbed a lock of hair off my wet cheek, and pulled me into his arms, so close that I could feel the rise and fall of his chest as he breathed. He was so solid, so alive, ruddy hair curling gold against bare skin. And yet I had held him so before—and lost him.

His hand touched my cheek, warm despite the dampness of my skin.

"But do ye not see how verra small a thing is the notion of death, between us two, Claire?" he whispered.

My hands curled into fists against his chest. No, I didn't think it a small thing at all.

"All the time after ye left me, after Culloden—I was dead then, was I not?"

"I thought you were. That's why I—oh." I took a deep, tremulous breath, and he nodded.

"Two hundred years from now, I shall most certainly *be* dead, Sassenach," he said. He smiled crookedly. "Be it Indians, wild beasts, a plague, the hangman's rope, or only the blessing of auld age—I will be dead."

"Yes."

"And while ye were there—in your own time—I *was* dead, no?"

I nodded, wordless. Even now, I could look back and see the abyss of despair into which that parting had dropped me, and from which I had climbed, one painful inch at a time.

Now I stood with him again upon the summit of life, and could not contemplate descent. He reached down and plucked a stalk of grass, spreading the soft green beards between his fingers.

" 'Man is like the grass of the field,' " he quoted softly, brushing the slender stem over my knuckles, where they rested against his chest. " 'Today it blooms; tomorrow it withers and is cast into the oven.' "

He lifted the silky green tuft to his lips and kissed it, then touched it gently to my mouth.

"I was dead, my Sassenach—and yet all that time, I loved you."

I closed my eyes, feeling the tickle of the grass on my lips, light as the touch of sun and air.

"I loved you, too," I whispered. "I always will."

The grass fell away. Eyes still closed, I felt him lean toward me, and his mouth on mine, warm as sun, light as air.

"So long as my body lives, and yours—we are one flesh," he whispered. His fingers touched me, hair and chin and neck and breast, and I breathed his breath and felt him solid under my hand. Then I lay with my head on his shoulder, the strength of him supporting me, the words deep and soft in his chest.

"And when my body shall cease, my soul will still be yours. Claire—I swear by my hope of heaven, I will not be parted from you."

The wind stirred the leaves of the chestnut trees nearby, and the scents of late summer rose up rich around us; pine and grass and strawberries, sun-warmed stone and cool water, and the sharp, musky smell of his body next to mine.

"Nothing is lost, Sassenach; only changed."

"That's the first law of thermodynamics," I said, wiping my nose.

"No," he said. "That's faith."

PART SIX

Je T'aime

17

Home for the Holidays

Inverness, Scotland, December 23, 1969

H e checked the train schedule for the dozenth time, then
prowled around the manse's living room, too restless to
settle. An hour yet to wait.

The room was half dismantled, with piles of cartons lying higgledy-piggledy on every surface. He'd promised to have the place
cleared out by the New Year, except for the pieces Fiona wanted
to keep.

He wandered down the hall and into the kitchen, stood staring
into the ancient refrigerator for a moment, decided he wasn't
hungry and closed the door.

He wished that Mrs. Graham and the Reverend could have met
Brianna, and she them. He smiled at the empty kitchen table,
remembering an adolescent conversation with the two elderly
people, when he, in the grip of a mad—and unrequited—lust for
the tobacconist's daughter, had asked how to know if one was
truly in love.

"If ye have to ask yourself if you're in love, laddie—then ye
aren't," Mrs. Graham had assured him, tapping her spoon on the
edge of her mixing bowl for emphasis. "And keep your paws off
wee Mavis MacDowell, or her Da will murder ye."

"When you're in love, Rog, you'll know it with no telling," the
Reverend had chimed in, dipping a finger in the cake batter. He
ducked in mock alarm as Mrs. Graham raised a threatening
spoon, and laughed. "And do mind yourself with young Mavis,
lad; I'm not old enough to be a grandfather."

Well, they'd been right. He knew, with no telling—had known
since he'd met Brianna Randall. What he didn't know for sure
was whether Brianna felt the same.

He couldn't wait any longer. He slapped his pocket to be sure
of his keys, ran down the stairs and out into the winter rain that

had begun to pelt down just after breakfast. They did say a cold shower was the thing. Hadn't worked with Mavis, though.

December 24, 1969

"Now, the plum pudding's in the warming oven, and the hard sauce in the wee pan to the back," Fiona instructed him, pulling on her fuzzy woolen hat. It was red, Fiona was short, and in it she looked like a garden gnome.

"Don't turn up the flame too high, mind. And dinna turn it out altogether, either, or you'll never get it lit again. And here, I've the directions for the birds for tomorrow all written out, they're stuffed in their pan, and I've left the veg already chopped to go along in the big yellow bowl in the fridge, and . . ." She fumbled in the pocket of her jeans and withdrew a handwritten slip of paper, which she thrust into his hand.

He patted her on the head.

"Don't worry, Fiona," he assured her. "We won't burn the place down. Nor starve, either."

She frowned dubiously, hesitating at the door. Her fiancé, sitting in his car outside, revved his engine in an impatient sort of way.

"Aye, well. You're sure the two of ye won't come with us? Ernie's Mam wouldna mind it a bit, and I'm sure she'd not think it right, just the two of ye left here by yourselves to keep Christmas . . ."

"Don't worry, Fiona," he said, edging her gently backward out the door. "We'll manage fine. You have a nice holiday with Ernie, and don't bother about us."

She sighed, giving in reluctantly. "Aye, I suppose you'll do." A short, irritable *beep!* from behind made her turn and glare at the car.

"Well, I'm *coming* then, aren't I?" she demanded. Turning back, she beamed suddenly at Roger, threw her arms about him, and standing on tiptoe, kissed him firmly on the lips.

She drew back and winked conspiratorially, screwing up her small, round face. "*That'll* sort our Ernie out," she whispered. "Happy Christmas, Rog!" she said loudly, and with a gay wave, hopped off the porch and strolled in leisurely fashion toward the car, hips swinging just a bit.

Its engine roaring in protest, the car shot off with a squeal of tires before the door had quite shut behind Fiona. Roger stood on the porch waving, pleased that Ernie wasn't an especially massive bloke.

The door opened behind him and Brianna poked her head out.

"What are you doing out here with no coat on?" she inquired. "It's freezing!"

He hesitated, tempted to tell her. After all, it had evidently worked on Ernie. But it was Christmas Eve, he reminded himself. In spite of the lowering sky and plummeting temperature, he felt warm and tingling all over. He smiled at her.

"Just seeing Fiona off," he said, pulling back the door. "Shall we see if we can make lunch without blowing up the kitchen?"

They managed sandwiches without incident, and returned after lunch to the study. The room was nearly empty now; only a few shelves of books remained to be sorted and packed.

On the one hand, Roger felt immense relief that the job was nearly done. On the other, it was sad to see the warm, cluttered study reduced to such a shell of its former self.

The Reverend's big desk had been emptied and removed to the garage for storage, the floor-to-ceiling shelves denuded of their huge burden of books, the cork-lined wall stripped of its many layers of fluttering papers. This process reminded Roger uncomfortably of chicken-plucking, the result being a stark and pathetic bareness that made him want to avert his eyes.

There was one square of paper still pinned to the cork. He'd take that down last.

"What about these?" Brianna waved a feather duster inquiringly at a small stack of books that sat on the table before her. An array of boxes gaped on the floor at her feet, half filled with books destined for various fates: libraries, antiquarian societies, friends of the Reverend's, Roger's personal use.

"They're autographed, but not inscribed to anybody," she said, handing him the top one. "You've got the set he inscribed to your father, but do you want these, too? They're first editions."

Roger turned the book over in his hands. It was one of Frank Randall's, a lovely book, beautifully typeset and bound to match the elegance of its scholarly content.

"You should have them, shouldn't you?" he said. Without waiting for an answer, he set the book gently into a small box that rested on the seat of an armchair. "Your dad's work, after all."

"I've got some," she protested. "Tons. Boxes and boxes."

"Not autographed, though?"

"Well, no." She picked up another of the books and flipped it open to the flyleaf, where *Tempora mutantur nos et mutamur in illis—F. W. Randall* was written in a strong, slanting hand. She rubbed a finger gently over the signature, and her wide mouth softened.

"*The times are changing, and we with them.* You're sure you don't want them, Roger?"

"Sure," he said, and smiled. He waved a wry hand at their book-strewn surroundings. "Don't worry, you won't leave me short."

She laughed and put the books in her own box, then went back to her work, dusting and wiping the stacked and sorted books before packing them. Most hadn't been cleaned in forty years, and she was liberally smudged herself by this time, long fingers grimy and the cuffs of her white shirt nearly black with filth.

"Won't you miss this place?" she asked. She wiped a strand of hair out of her eyes and gestured at the spacious room. "You grew up here, didn't you?"

"Yes, and yes," he answered, heaving another full carton onto the pile to be shipped to the university library. "Not much choice, though."

"I guess you couldn't live here," she agreed regretfully. "Since you have to be in Oxford most of the time. But do you have to sell it?"

"I *can't* sell it. It's not mine." He stooped to get a grip on an extra-large carton, and rose slowly to his feet, grunting with effort. He staggered across the room and dropped it onto the stack, with a thud that raised small puffs of dust from the boxes beneath it.

"Whew!" He blew out his breath, grinning at her. "God help the antiquarians when they pick that one up."

"What do you mean, it's not yours?"

"What I said," he replied matter-of-factly. "It isn't mine. The house and land belong to the church; Dad lived here for near fifty years, but he didn't own it. It belongs to the Parish Council. The new minister doesn't want it—he's got money of his own, and a wife who likes mod cons—so the Council's putting it to let. Fiona and her Ernie are taking it, heaven help them."

"Just the two of them?"

"It's cheap. For good reason," he added wryly. "She wants

lots of kids, though—be room for an army of them here, I can tell you.'' Designed in Victorian times for ministers with numerous families, the manse had twelve rooms—not counting one unmodernized and highly inconvenient bath.

''The wedding's in February, so that's why I've got to finish the clearing up over Christmas, to give time for the cleaners and painters to come in. Shame to make you work on your holiday, though. Maybe we'll drive down to Fort William Monday?''

Brianna picked up another book, but didn't put it in the box right away.

''So your home's gone for good,'' she said, slowly. ''It doesn't seem right—though I'm glad Fiona will have it.''

Roger shrugged.

''Not as though I meant to settle in Inverness,'' he said. ''And it's not as though it were an ancestral seat or anything.'' He waved at the cracked linoleum, the grubby enamel paint, and the ancient glass-bowl light fixture overhead. ''Can't put it on the National Trust and charge people two quid each to tour the place.''

She smiled at that, and returned to her sorting. She seemed pensive, though, a small frown visible between her thick red brows. Finally she put the last book in the box, stretched and sighed.

''The Reverend had nearly as many books as my parents,'' she said. ''Between Mama's medical books and Daddy's historical stuff, they left enough to supply a whole library. It'll probably take six months to sort it all out, when I get ho—when I go back.'' She bit her lip lightly, and turned to pick up a roll of packing tape, picking at it with a fingernail. ''I told the real estate agent she could list the house for sale by summer.''

''That's what's been bothering you?'' he said slowly, realization dawning as he watched her face. ''Thinking about taking apart the house you grew up in—having your home gone for good?''

One shoulder lifted slightly, her eyes still fixed on the recalcitrant tape.

''If you can stand it, I guess I can. Besides,'' she went on, ''it's not that bad. Mama took care of almost everything—she found a tenant and had the house leased for a year, so I could have time to decide what to do, without worrying about it just sitting there vacant. But it's silly to keep it; it's way too big for me to live in alone.''

"You might get married." He blurted it out without thinking.

"Guess I might," she said. She glanced at him sidelong, and the corner of her mouth twitched in what might have been amusement. "Someday. But what if my husband didn't want to live in Boston?"

It occurred to him quite suddenly that her concern over his losing the manse might—just possibly—have been that she envisioned herself living in it.

"D'you want kids?" he asked abruptly. He hadn't thought to ask before, but hoped like hell she did.

She looked momentarily startled, but then laughed.

"Only children usually want big families, don't they?"

"Couldn't say," he said. "But I do." He leaned across the boxes and kissed her suddenly.

"Me too," she said. Her eyes went slanted when she smiled. She didn't look away, but a faint blush made her look like a spring-ripe apricot.

He wanted kids, all right; just at the moment, he wanted to do what led to kids a lot more.

"But maybe we should finish clearing up, first?"

"What?" The sense of her words penetrated only vaguely. "Oh. Yeah. Right, guess we should."

He bent his head and kissed her again, slowly this time. She had the most wonderful mouth; wide and full-lipped, almost too big for her face—but not quite.

He had her round the waist, his other hand tangled in silky hair. The nape of her neck was smooth and warm under his hand; he gripped it and she shivered slightly, mouth opening in a small sign of submission that made him want to lean her backward over his arm, carry her down to the hearth rug, and . . .

A brisk rapping made him jerk his head up, startled out of the embrace.

"Who's *that*?" Brianna exclaimed, hand to her heart.

The study was lined on one side by floor-to-ceiling windows—the Reverend had been a painter—and a square, whiskered face was pressed against one of these, nose nearly flattened with interest.

"That," said Roger through his teeth, "is the postman, Mac-Beth. What the hell is the old bugger doing out there?"

As though hearing this inquiry, Mr. MacBeth stepped back a pace, drew a letter out of his bag and brandished it jovially at the occupants of the study.

"A letter," he mouthed elaborately, looking at Brianna. He cut his eyes toward Roger and beetled his brows in a knowing leer.

By the time Roger reached the front door, Mr. MacBeth was standing on the porch, holding the letter.

"Why did you not put it in the letter slot, for God's sake?" Roger demanded. "Give it here, then."

Mr. MacBeth held the letter out of reach and assumed an air of injured dignity, somewhat impaired by his attempts to see Brianna over Roger's shoulder.

"Thought it might be important, didn't I? From the States, i'nt it? And it's for the young lady, not you, lad." Screwing up his face into a massive and indelicate wink, he oiled past Roger, arm extended toward Brianna.

"Ma'am," he said, simpering through his whiskers. "With the compliments of Her Majesty's Mail."

"Thank you." Brianna was still rosily flushed, but she'd smoothed her hair, and smiled at MacBeth with every evidence of self-possession. She took the letter and glanced at it, but made no move to open it. The envelope was handwritten, Roger saw, with red postal-forwarding marks, but the distance was too far to make out the return address.

"Visiting, are ye, ma'am?" MacBeth asked heartily. "Just the two of ye here, all on your ownie-o?" He was giving Brianna a rolling eye, looking her up and down with frank interest.

"Oh, no," Brianna said, straight-faced. She folded the letter in half and stuffed it into the back pocket of her jeans. "Uncle Angus is staying with us; he's asleep upstairs."

Roger bit the inside of his cheek. Uncle Angus was a moth-eaten stuffed Scottie, a remnant of his own youth, unearthed during the cleaning of the house. Brianna, charmed with him, had dusted off his plaid bonnet and placed him on her own bed in the guest room.

The postman's heavy brows rose.

"Oh," he said, rather blankly. "Aye, I see. He'll be an American, too, then, your uncle Angus?"

"No, he's from Aberdeen." Other than a slight pinkening at the end of her nose, Brianna's face showed nothing but the most open guilelessness.

Mr. MacBeth was enchanted.

"Oh, you've a wee bit of Scots in your family, then! Well, and I should have known it, now, you wi' that hair. A bonnie, bonnie lass, and no mistake." He shook his head in admiration, lechery replaced by a pseudoavuncular air that Roger found only slightly less objectionable.

"Yes, well." Roger cleared his throat meaningfully. "I'm sure we don't want to keep you from your work, MacBeth."

"Oh, it's no trouble, no trouble at all," the postman assured him, craning to catch a last glimpse of Brianna as he turned to go. "Nay rest for the weary, is there, my dear?"

"That's 'no rest for the *wicked*,' " Roger said, with some emphasis, opening the door. "Good day to you, MacBeth."

MacBeth glanced at him, the shadow of a leer back on his face.

"A good day to *you*, Mr. Wakefield." He leaned close, dug Roger in the ribs with an elbow, and whispered hoarsely, "And a better night, if her uncle sleeps sound!"

"Here, going to read your letter?" He plucked it from the table where she had dropped it, and held it out to her.

She flushed slightly and took it from him.

"It's not important. I'll look at it later."

"I'll go to the kitchen, if it's private."

The flush deepened.

"It's not. It's nothing."

He raised one eyebrow. She shrugged impatiently, and ripped open the flap, pulling out a single sheet of paper.

"See for yourself, then. I told you, it's nothing important."

Oh, isn't it? he thought, but didn't say anything aloud. He took the proffered sheet and glanced at it.

It was in fact nothing much; a notification forwarded from the library at her university, to the effect that a specific reference she had requested was unfortunately not obtainable via interlibrary loan, but could be viewed in the private collection of the Stuart Papers, held in the Royal Annexe of Edinburgh University.

She was watching him when he looked up, arms folded, her eyes shiny and lips tight, daring him to say something.

"You should have told me you were looking for him," he said quietly. "I could have helped."

She shrugged slightly, and he saw her throat move as she swallowed.

"I know how to do historical research. I used to help my fa—" She broke off, lower lip caught between her teeth.

"Yeah, I see," he said, and did. He took her by the arm and

steered her down the hall to the kitchen, where he plunked her in a chair at the battered old table.

"I'll put the kettle on."

"I don't like tea," she protested.

"You *need* tea," Roger said firmly, and lit the gas with a fiery *whoosh*. He turned to the cupboard and took down cups and saucers, and—as an afterthought—the bottle of whisky from the top shelf.

"And I *really* don't like whisky," Brianna said, eyeing it. She started to push herself away from the table, but Roger stopped her with a hand on her arm.

"I like whisky," he said. "But I hate to drink alone. You'll keep me company, aye?" He smiled at her, willing her to smile back. At last she did, grudgingly, and relaxed in her seat.

He sat down opposite her, and filled his cup halfway with the pungent amber liquid. He breathed in the fumes with pleasure, and sipped slowly, letting the fine strong stuff roll down his throat.

"Ah," he breathed. "Glen Morangie. Sure you won't join me? A wee splash in your tea, maybe?"

She shook her head silently, but when the kettle began to whistle, she got up to take it off the fire and pour the hot water into the waiting pot. Roger got up and came behind her, slipping his arms around her waist.

"It's nothing to be ashamed of," he said softly. "You've a right to know, if you can. Jamie Fraser was your father, after all."

"But he wasn't—not really." Her head was bent; he could see the neat whorl of a cowlick at her crown, an echo of the one in the center of her forehead, that lifted her hair in a soft wave off her face.

"I *had* a father," she said, sounding a little choked. "Daddy—Frank Randall—he *was* my father, and I love—loved him. It doesn't seem right to—to go looking for something else, like he wasn't enough, like—"

"That's not it, then, and you know it." He turned her round and lifted her chin with a finger.

"It's nothing to do with Frank Randall or how you feel about him—aye, he *was* your father, and there's not a thing will ever change that. But it's natural to be curious, to want to know."

"Did *you* ever want to know?" Her hand came up and brushed his away—but she clung to his fingers, holding on.

He took a deep breath, finding comfort in the whisky.

"Yeah. Yes, I did. You need to, I think." His fingers tightened around hers, drawing her toward the table. "Come sit down; I'll tell you."

He knew what missing a father felt like, especially an unknown father. For a time, just after he'd started school, he'd pored obsessively over his father's medals, carried the little velvet case about in his pocket, boasted to his friends about his father's heroism.

"Told stories about him, all made up," he said, looking down into the aromatic depths of his teacup. "Got bashed for being a nuisance, got smacked at school for lying." He looked up at her, and smiled, a little painfully.

"I had to make him real, see?"

She nodded, eyes dark with understanding.

He took another deep gulp of the whisky, not bothering to savor it.

"Luckily Dad—the Reverend—he seemed to know the trouble. He began to tell me stories about my father; the real ones. Nothing special, nothing heroic—he was a hero, all right, Jerry Mac-Kenzie, got shot down and all, but the stories Dad told were all about what he was like as a kid—how he made a martin house, but made the hole too big and a cuckoo got in; what he liked to eat when he'd come here on holiday and they'd go into town for a treat; how he filled his pockets with winkles off the rocks and forgot about them and ruined his trousers with the stink—" He broke off, and smiled at her, his throat still tight at the memory.

"He made my father real to me. And I missed him more than ever, because then I knew a bit about what I *was* missing—but I had to know."

"Some people would say you can't miss what you never had— that it's better not to know at all." Brianna lifted her cup, blue eyes steady over the rim.

"Some people are fools. Or cowards."

He poured another tot of whisky into his cup, tilted the bottle toward her with a lifted brow. She held out her cup without comment, and he splashed whisky into it. She drank from it, and set it down.

"What about your mother?" she asked.

"I had a few real memories of her; I was nearly five when she died. And there are the boxes in the garage—" He tilted his head toward the window. "All her things, her letters. It's like Dad said, 'Everybody needs a history.' Mine was out there; I knew if I ever needed to, I could find out more."

He studied her for a long moment.

"You miss her a lot?" he said. "Claire?"

She glanced at him, nodded briefly, and drank, then held out her empty cup for more.

"I'm—I was—afraid to look," she said, eyes fixed on the stream of whisky.

"It's not just him—it's her, too. I mean, I know his stories, Jamie Fraser's; she told me a lot about him. A lot more than I'll ever find in historical records," she added with a feeble attempt at a smile. She took a deep breath.

"But Mama—at first I tried to pretend she was only gone, like on a trip. And then when I couldn't do that anymore, I tried to believe she was dead." Her nose was running, from emotion, whisky, or the heat of the tea. Roger reached for the tea towel hanging by the stove and shoved it across the table to her.

"She *isn't,* though." She picked up the towel and wiped angrily at her nose. "That's the trouble! I have to miss her all the time, and know that I'll never see her again, but she isn't even *dead!* How can I mourn for her, when I think—when I hope—she's happy where she is, when I *made* her go?"

She gulped the rest of her cup, choked slightly, and got her breath. She fixed Roger with a dark blue glare, as though he were to blame for the situation.

"So I want to find out, all right? I want to find her—find them. See if she's all right. But I keep thinking maybe I *don't* want to find out, because what if I find out she's not all right, what if I find out something horrible? What if I find out she's dead, or he is —well, that wouldn't matter so much, maybe, because he already is dead anyway, or he was, or—but I *have* to, I know I have to!"

She banged her cup down on the table in front of him.

"More."

He opened his mouth to say that she'd had a good bit more than she needed already, but a glance at her face changed his mind. He shut his mouth and poured.

She didn't wait for him to add tea, but raised the cup to her mouth and took a large swallow, and another. She coughed, sputtered, and set the cup down, eyes watering.

"So I'm looking. Or I was. When I saw Daddy's books, and his handwriting, though . . . it all seemed wrong, then. Do you think I'm wrong?" she asked, peering woefully at him through tear-clogged lashes.

"No, hen," he said gently. "It's not wrong. You're right,

you've got to know. I'll help you." He stood up and, taking her under the arms, hoisted her to her feet. "But right now, I think you should maybe have a bit of a lie-down, hm?"

He got her up the stairs and halfway down the hall, when she suddenly broke free and darted into the bathroom. He leaned against the wall outside, waiting patiently until she staggered out again, her face the color of the aged plaster above the wainscoting.

"Waste of Glen Morangie, that," he said, taking her by the shoulders and steering her into the bedroom. "If I'd known I was dealing with a sot, I'd have given you the cheap stuff."

She collapsed on the bed, and allowed him to take off her shoes and socks. She rolled onto her stomach, Uncle Angus cradled in the crook of her arm.

"I *told* you I didn't like tea," she mumbled, and was asleep in seconds.

Roger worked for an hour or two by himself, sorting books and tying cartons. It was a quiet, dark afternoon, with no sound but a soft patter of rain and the occasional *whoosh* of a car's tires on the street outside. When the light began to fail, he turned on the lamps and went down the hall to the kitchen, to wash the book grime from his hands.

A huge pot of milky cock-a-leekie soup was burbling on the back of the cooker. What had Fiona said to do about that? Turn it up? Turn it off? Throw things into it? He peered dubiously into the pot and decided to leave well enough alone.

He tidied up the remains of their impromptu tea—rinsed the cups and dried them, hung them carefully from their hooks in the cupboard. They were remnants of the old willow pattern set the Reverend had had for as long as Roger could remember, the blue-and-white Chinese trees and pagodas augmented by odd bits of ill-assorted crockery acquired from jumble sales.

Fiona would have all new, of course. She'd forced them to look at magazine pictures of china and crystal and flatware. Brianna had made suitable admiring noises; Roger's eyes had gone glassy from boredom. He supposed the old stuff would all end up at the jumble sale—at least it might still be useful to someone.

On impulse, he took down the two cups he'd washed, wrapped them in a clean tea towel, and took them to the study, where he tucked them into the box he'd set aside for himself. He felt thoroughly foolish, but at the same time, somewhat better.

He looked around the echoing study, quite bare now save for the single sheet of paper on the cork-lined wall.

So your home's gone for good. Well, he'd left home some time ago, hadn't he?

Yeah, it bothered him. A lot more than he'd let on to Brianna, in fact. That was why it had taken so bloody long to finish clearing out the manse, if he was honest about it. True, it was a monster task, true, he had his own job to do at Oxford, and true, the thousands of books had had to be sorted with care—but he could have done it faster. If he'd wanted.

With the house standing vacant, he might never have got the job finished. But with the impetus of Fiona behind, and the lure of Brianna before . . . he smiled at the thought of the two of them: little dark, curly-headed wren, and tall fire-haired Viking. Likely it took women to get men to do anything much.

Time to finish up, though.

With a sense of somber ceremony, he unpinned the corners of the yellowed sheet of paper and took it down from the cork. It was his family tree, a genealogical chart made out in the Reverend's neat round hand.

MacKenzies and more MacKenzies, generations of them. He'd thought lately of taking back the name permanently, not just for the singing. After all, with Dad gone he didn't mean to come back much more to Inverness, where folk would know him as Wakefield. That had been the point of the genealogy, after all; that Roger shouldn't forget who he was.

Dad had known a few individual stories, but no more than the names for most of the people on the list. And he hadn't known even that, for the most important one—the woman whose green eyes Roger saw each morning in the mirror. *She* was nowhere on this list, for good reason.

Roger's finger stopped near the top of the chart. There he was, the changeling—William Buccleigh MacKenzie. Given to foster parents to raise, the illegitimate offspring of the war chieftain of clan MacKenzie, and of a witch condemned to burning. Dougal MacKenzie and the witch Geillis Duncan.

Not a witch at all, of course, but something just as dangerous. He had her eyes—or so Claire said. Had he inherited something more from her as well? Was the terrifying ability to travel through the stones passed down unsuspected through generations of respectable boatwrights and herdsmen?

He thought of it each time he saw the chart now—and for that reason, tried not to look. He appreciated Brianna's ambivalence; he understood all too well the razor's edge between fear and curiosity, the pull between the need to know and the fear of finding out.

Well, he could help Brianna find out. And for himself . . .

Roger slipped the chart into a folder, and put it in the box. He closed the top of the carton, and added an "X" of sticky tape across the flap for good measure.

"That's that, then," he said aloud, and left the empty room.

He stopped at the head of the stairs, taken by surprise.

Brianna had been bathing, braving the ancient geyser with its cracked enamel and rumbling flame. Now she stepped into the hall, wearing nothing but a towel.

She turned down the hall, not seeing him. Roger stood very still, listening to the thud of his heart, feeling his palm slick on the polished banister.

She was modestly covered; he had seen more of her in the halters and shorts she had worn in the summer. It was the fragility of her covering that roused him; the knowledge that he could undress her with one quick tug. That, and the knowledge that they were quite alone in the house.

Dynamite.

He took a step after her, and stopped. She had heard him; she stopped, too, but it was a long moment before she turned around. Her feet were bare, high-arched and long-toed; the slender curves of her wet footprints were dark on the worn runner that covered the floor of the hallway.

She didn't say anything. Just looked at him straight-on, her eyes dark and slanting. She stood against the tall window at the end of the hall, her swaddled figure black against the pale gray light of the rainy day outside.

If he should touch her, he knew how she would feel. Her skin would be still hot from the bath, damp in the crevices of knee and thigh and elbow. He could smell her, the minglings of shampoo and soap and powder, the smell of her flesh masked by the ghosts of flowers.

Her footprints on the runner stretched before him, a fragile chain of footsteps linking them. He kicked off his sandals and planted a bare foot on one of the prints she had left; it was cool on his skin.

There were drops of water on her shoulders, matching the droplets on the windowpane behind her, as though she had stepped through it out of the rain. She lifted her head as he came toward her, and with a shake, let the towel wrapped round her head fall off.

The bronze snakes of her hair fell gleaming, brushed his cheek with wet. Not a Gorgon's beauty, but a water spirit's, changing shape from serpent-maned horse to magic woman.

"Kelpie," he whispered against the flushed curve of her cheek. "You look like you've come straight out of a Highland burn." She put her arms around his neck, let go of the towel; only the pressure of their bodies held it between them.

Her back was bare. Cold air from the window raised the hair on his forearm, even as her skin warmed his palm. He wanted at once to pull the towel about her, shelter her, cover her from the cold; at the same time, to strip both her and himself, take her heat to himself and give her his own, right there in the damp and drafty hallway.

"Steam," he whispered. "God, you're steaming."

Her mouth curved against his.

"That makes two of us, and you haven't had a bath. Roger—" Her hand was on the back of his neck, fingers cool. She opened her mouth to say something more, but he kissed her, feeling hot damp seep through the fabric of his shirt.

Her breasts rose against him and her mouth opened under his. The muffling terry cloth hid the outlines of her breasts from his hands but not his imagination; he could see them in his mind's eye, round and smooth, with that faint, enchanting wobble of full flesh.

His hand drifted lower, grasping the swell of bare buttock. She shied, lost her balance, and the two of them collapsed awkwardly, grappling with each other in an effort to stay upright.

Roger's knees hit the floor, and he dragged her down with him. She tilted and sprawled, landing laughing on her back.

"Hey!" She grabbed for her towel, then abandoned it as he lunged over her, kissing her again.

He'd been right about her breasts. The one under his hand was bare now, full and soft, the nipple hard in the center of his palm.

Dynamite, and the fuse was lit.

His other hand rested at the top of her thigh under the towel, close enough that he could feel the damp curls brush his finger. God, what color was it? Deep auburn, as he'd imagined? Copper and bronze, like the hair of her head?

Despite himself, his hand slid farther, dying to cup the soft slippery fullness he could sense, so close. With an effort that made him dizzy, he stopped.

Her hand was on his arm, pulling him back down.

"Please," she whispered. "Please, I want you to."

He felt hollow as a bell; his heartbeat echoed in head and chest and painfully hard between his legs. He closed his eyes, breathing, pressing his hands against the rough fiber of the rug, trying to erase the feel of her skin, lest he grab at her again.

"No," he said, and his voice sounded queer, hoarse to his own ear. "No, not here, not like this."

She was sitting up, rising out of the dark blue towel that puddled around her hips, like a mermaid from the waves. She had cooled; her flesh was pale as marble in the gray light, but goose bumps stippled the smoothness of arms and breasts and shoulders.

He touched her, rough skin and smooth, and drew his fingers over her lips, her broad mouth. The taste of her was still on his lips, clean skin and toothpaste—and a sweet, soft tongue.

"Better," he whispered. "I want it to be better . . . the first time."

They knelt staring at each other, the air between them crackling with unsaid things. The fuse was still burning, but a slow match now. Roger felt rooted to the spot; perhaps it was the Gorgon, after all.

Then the smell of scorching milk rose up the stair, and both of them started up at once.

"Something's burning!" Brianna said, and made a dart toward the stair, her towel clumsily back in place.

He caught her by the arm as she passed him. She was cold to the touch, chilled by the drafty hallway.

"I'll do it," he said. "You go and get dressed."

She shot him a quick blue glance and turned, disappearing into the spare bedroom. The door clicked shut behind her and he dashed down the hall, clattering down the stair toward the smell of disaster, feeling his palm burn where he had touched her.

Downstairs, Roger dealt with the spilled and scalded soup, berating himself. Where did he get off, lunging at her like a crazed salmon en route to the spawning grounds? Ripping off her towel and grappling her to the floor—Christ, she must think him next door to a rapist!

At the same time, the hot feeling that suffused his chest wasn't due either to shame or to heat from the cooker. It was the latent heat from her skin, still warming him. *I want you to,* she'd said, and she'd meant it.

He was familiar enough with the language of the body to know desire and surrender when he touched them. But what he'd felt in that brief moment when her body came alive to his went a great deal farther. The universe had shifted, with a small, decisive click; he could still hear its echo in his bones.

He wanted her. He wanted all of her; not just bed, not just body. Everything, always. Suddenly the biblical injunction, *one flesh,* seemed something immediate, and very real. They'd nearly been just that, on the floor of the hallway, and stopping as he had made him feel suddenly and peculiarly vulnerable—he wasn't a whole person any longer, but only half of something not yet made.

He dumped the ruined remains of the soup into the sink. No matter; they'd have supper at the pub. Best to get out of the house and away from temptation.

Supper, casual chat, and maybe a walk by the river. She'd wanted to go to the Christmas Eve services. After that . . .

After that, he would ask her, make it formal. She would say yes, he knew. And then . . .

Why, then, they would come home, to a house dark and private. With themselves alone, on a night of sacrament and secret, with love newly come into the world. And he would lift her in his arms and carry her upstairs, on a night when virginity's sacrifice was no loss of purity, but rather the birth of everlasting joy.

Roger switched out the light and left the kitchen. Behind him, forgotten, the gas flame burned blue and yellow in the dark, ardent and steady as the fires of love.

18

Unseemly Lust

The Reverend Wakefield had been a kindly and ecumenical man, tolerant of all shades of religious opinion, and willing to entertain doctrines his flock would have found outrageous, if not downright blasphemous.

Still, a lifetime of exposure to the stern face of Scottish Presbyterianism and its abiding suspicion of anything "Romish" had left Roger with a certain residual uneasiness upon entering a Catholic church—as though he might be seized at the door and forcibly baptized by outlandishly dressed minions of the True Cross.

No such violence offered as he followed Brianna into the small stone building. There was a boy in a long white robe visible at the far end of the nave, but he was peaceably engaged in lighting two pairs of tall white candles that decorated the altar. A faint, unfamiliar scent hung in the air. Roger inhaled, trying to be unobtrusive about it. Incense?

Beside him, Brianna stopped, rummaging in her purse. She took out a small circle of black lacy stuff, and bobby-pinned it to the top of her head.

"What's that?" he asked.

"I don't know what you call it," she said. "It's what you wear in church if you don't want to wear a hat or a veil. You don't really *have* to do it anymore, but I grew up doing it—it used to be that women couldn't go into a Catholic church with their heads uncovered, you know."

"No, I didn't," he said, interested. "Why not?"

"Saint Paul, probably," she said, whipping a comb from her purse to tidy the ends of her hair. "He thought women ought to keep their hair covered all the time, so as not to be objects of unseemly lust. Cranky old crab," she added, stuffing the comb back into the purse. "Mama always said he was afraid of women. Thought they were dangerous," she said, with a wide grin.

"They are." Impulsively, he leaned forward and kissed her, ignoring the stares of the people nearby.

She looked surprised, but then rocked forward on her toes and kissed him back, soft and quick. Roger heard a faint "Mmphm" of disapproval somewhere nearby, but paid no attention.

"In *kirk*, and on Christmas Eve, too!" came a hoarse whisper from behind.

"Well, it's no the kirk exactly, Annie, it's only the vestibule, aye?"

"And him the meenister's lad and all!"

"Well, ye ken the saying, Annie, as the cobbler's bairns go barefoot. I daresay it's a' the same wi' a preacher's lad that's gone to the deil. Come along in, now."

The voices receded into the church, to the prim tap of Cuban heels and a man's softer shuffle accompanying. Brianna pulled back a little and looked up at him, mouth quivering with laughter.

"Have you gone to the devil?"

He smiled down at her, and touched her glowing face. She wore her grandmother's necklace, in honor of Christmas, and her skin reflected the luster of the freshwater pearls.

"If the devil will have me."

Before she could answer, they were interrupted by a gust of foggy air as the church door opened.

"Mr. Wakefield, is it yourself?" He turned, to meet two pairs of bright, inquisitive eyes beaming up at him. A pair of elderly women, each about four foot six, stood arm in arm in their winter coats, gray hair puffed out under small felt hats, looking like a matched set of doorstops.

"Mrs. McMurdo, Mrs. Hayes! Happy Christmas to you!" He nodded to them, smiling. Mrs. McMurdo lived two doors down from the manse, and walked to church every Sunday with her friend Mrs. Hayes. Roger had known them all his life.

"Come over to Rome then, have ye, Mr. Wakefield?" Chrissie McMurdo asked. Jessie Hayes giggled at her friend's wit, the red cherries bouncing on her hat.

"Maybe not just yet awhile," Roger said, still smiling. "I'm only seeing a friend to the services, aye? You'll know Miss Randall?" He brought Brianna forward and made the introductions, grinning inwardly as the two little old ladies looked her over with a frankly avid curiosity.

To Mrs. McMurdo and Mrs. Hayes, his presence here was as overt a declaration of his intentions as if he'd taken out a full-page ad in the evening newspaper. Too bad Brianna was unaware of it.

Or was she? She glanced at him with a half-hidden smile, and he felt the pressure of her fingers on his arm, just for a moment.

"Och, there's the wee laddie comin' wi' the censer!" cried Mrs. Hayes, spotting another white-robed boy emerging from the sanctuary. "Best get in quick, Chrissie, or we'll never have a seat!"

"Such a pleasure to meet ye, my dear," Mrs. McMurdo told Brianna, head tilted back so far that her hat was in danger of falling off. "My, such a bonny tall lass!" She glanced at Roger, twinkling. "Lucky to have found a lad to match ye, eh?"

"Chrissie!"

"Just coming, Jessie, just coming. Dinna fash, there's time." Straightening her hat, trimmed with a small bunch of grouse's feathers, Mrs. McMurdo turned in leisurely fashion to join her friend.

The bell above began to clang again, and Roger took Brianna's arm. Just in front of them, he saw Jessie Hayes glance back, eyes bright with speculation, her smile half sly with knowing.

Brianna dipped her fingers in a small stone basin set in the wall by the door, and crossed herself. Roger found the gesture suddenly and oddly familiar, despite its Romanness.

Years ago, hill-walking with the Reverend, they had come upon a saint's pool, hidden in a grove. There was a flat stone standing on end beside the tiny spring, the remnants of carving on it worn nearly to smoothness, no more than the shadow of a human figure.

A sense of mystery hung about the small, dark pool; he and the Reverend had stood there for some time, not speaking. Then the Reverend had bent, scooped up a handful of water, and poured it out at the foot of the stone in silent ceremony, scooped up another and splashed it over his face. Only then had they knelt by the spring to drink the cold, sweet water.

Above the Reverend's bowed back, Roger had seen the tattered knots of fabric tied to tree branches above the spring. Pledges; reminders of prayer, left by whoever still visited the ancient shrine.

For how many thousands of years had men thus blessed themselves with water before seeking their heart's desire? Roger dabbed his fingers in the water and awkwardly touched both head and heart, with something that might have been a prayer.

They found seats in the east transept, crowded shoulder to shoulder with a murmuring family, busily engaged in settling belongings and sleepy children, passing coats and handbags and baby bottles to and fro, while a small, wheezy organ played "O Little Town of Bethlehem" somewhere just out of sight.

Then the music stopped. There was a silence of expectation, and then it burst out once more, in a loud rendition of "O Come, All Ye Faithful."

Roger rose with the congregation as the procession came down the center aisle. There were several of the white-robed acolytes, one with a swinging censer that sent puffs of fragrant smoke into the crowd. Another bore a book, and a third a tall crucifix, the gruesome figure on it blatant, daubed with red paint whose bloody echoes shimmered in the priest's vestment of gold and crimson.

Despite himself, Roger felt a slight sense of shocked distaste; the mixture of barbaric pageantry and the undulations of sung Latin were quite foreign to what he subconsciously felt was proper in church.

Still, as the Mass went on, things seemed more normal; there were Bible readings, quite familiar, and then the accustomed descent into the vaguely pleasant boredom of a sermon, in which the inevitable Christmas annunciations of "peace," "goodwill," and "love" rose to the surface of his mind, tranquil as white lilies floating on a pond of words.

By the time the congregation rose again, Roger had lost all sense of strangeness. Surrounded by a warm, familiar church fug composed of floor polish, damp wool, naphtha fumes, and a faint whiff of the whisky with which some worshipers had fortified themselves for the long service, he scarcely noticed the sweet, musky scent of frankincense. Breathing deeply, he thought he caught the hint of fresh grass from Brianna's hair.

It shone in the dim light of the transept, thick and soft against the dark violet of her jumper. Its copper sparks muted by the dimness, it was the deep rufous color of a red deer's pelt, and it gave him the same sense of helpless yearning he had felt when surprised by a deer on a Highland path—the strong urge to touch it, stroke the wild thing and keep it somehow with him, coupled with the sure knowledge that a finger's move would send it flying.

Whatever one thought of Saint Paul, he thought, the man had known what he was on about with respect to women's hair. Unseemly lust, was it? He had a sudden memory of the bare hallway and the steam rising from Brianna's body, the wet snakes of her hair cold on his skin. He looked away, trying to concentrate on the goings-on at the altar, where the priest was raising a large flat disk of bread, while a small boy madly shook a chime of bells.

He watched her when she went up to take Communion, and became aware with a slight start that he was praying wordlessly.

He relaxed just a bit when he realized the content of his prayer; it wasn't the ignoble "Let me have her" he might have expected. It was the more humble—and acceptable, he hoped—"Let me be worthy of her, let me love her rightly; let me take care of her." He nodded toward the altar, then caught the curious eye of the man next to him, and straightened up, clearing his throat, embarrassed as though he had been surprised in private conversation.

She came back, eyes wide-open and fixed on something deep inside, a small dreaming smile on her wide sweet mouth. She knelt, and he beside her.

She had a tender look at the moment, but it was not a gentle face. Straight-nosed and severe, with thick red brows redeemed from heaviness only by the grace of their arch. The cleanness of jaw and cheek might have been cut from white marble; it was the mouth that could change in a moment, from soft generosity to the mouth of a medieval abbess, lips sealed in cool stone celibacy.

The thick Glaswegian voice beside him bawling "We Three Kings" brought him to with a start, in time to see the priest sweep down the aisle, surrounded by his acolytes, in clouds of triumphant smoke.

" 'We Three Kings of Orient Are,' " Brianna sang quietly as they made their way down River Walk, " 'Going to smoke a rubber cigar . . . It was loaded, and explo-oo-ded'—you *did* turn out the gas, didn't you?"

"Yes," he assured her. "Not to worry; between the cooker and the bathroom geyser, if the manse hasn't gone up in flames yet, it must be proof of divine protection."

She laughed.

"Do Presbyterians believe in guardian angels?"

"Certainly not. Popish superstition, aye?"

"Well, I hope I haven't damned you to perdition by making you go to Mass with me. Or do Presbyterians believe in hell?"

"Oh, that we do," he assured her. "As much as heaven, if not more."

It was even foggier, here by the river. Roger was glad they hadn't driven; you couldn't see more than five feet or so in the thick white murk.

They walked arm in arm beside the River Ness, footsteps muffled. Swaddled by the fog, the unseen city around them might not have existed. They had left the other churchgoers behind; they were alone.

Roger felt strangely exposed, chilled and vulnerable, stripped of the warmth and assurance he had felt in the church. Only nerves, he thought, and took a firmer grip of Brianna's arm. It was time. He took a deep breath, cool fog filling his chest.

"Brianna." He had her by the arm, turned to face him before she had stopped walking, so her hair swung heavy through the dim arc from the streetlamp overhead.

Water droplets gleamed in a fine mist on her skin, glowed like pearls and diamonds in her hair, and through the padding of her jacket, he felt in memory her bare skin, cool as fog to his fingers, flesh-hot in his hand.

Her eyes were wide and dark as a loch, with secrets moving, half seen, half sensed, under rippling water. A kelpie for sure. *Each urisge,* a water horse, mane flowing, skin glowing. And the man who touches such a creature is lost, bound to it forever, taken down and drowned in the loch that gives it home.

He felt suddenly afraid, not for himself but for her; as though something might materialize from that water world to snatch her back, away from him. He grasped her by the hand, as if to prevent her. Her fingers were cold and damp, a shock against the warmth of his palm.

"I want you, Brianna," he said softly. "I cannot be saying it plainer than that. I love you. Will you marry me?"

She didn't say anything, but her face changed, like water when a stone is thrown into it. He could see it plainly as his own reflection in the bleakness of a tarn.

"You didn't want me to say that." The fog had settled in his chest; he was breathing ice, crystal needles piercing heart and lungs. "You didn't want to hear it, did you?"

She shook her head, wordless.

"Aye. Well." With an effort, he let go her hand. "That's all right," he said, surprised at the calmness in his voice. "You'll not be worried about it, aye?"

He was turning to walk on when she stopped him, hand on his sleeve.

"Roger."

It was a great effort to turn and face her; he had no wish for empty comfort, no desire to hear a feeble offer to "be friends." He didn't think he could bear even to look at her, so crushing was his sense of loss. But he turned nonetheless and then she was against him, her hands cold on his ears as she gripped his head and pushed her mouth hard onto his, not so much a kiss as blind frenzy, awkward with desperation.

He gripped her hands and pulled them down, pushing her away.

"What in God's name are you playing at?" Anger was better than emptiness, and he shouted at her in the empty street.

"I'm not playing! You said you wanted me." She gulped air. "I want you, too, don't you know that? Didn't I say so in the hall this afternoon?"

"I thought you did." He stared at her. "What in hell do you mean?"

"I mean—I mean I want to go to bed with you," she blurted.

"But you don't want to marry me?"

She shook her head, white as a sheet. Something between sickness and fury stirred in his gut, and then erupted.

"So you'll not marry me, but you'll fuck me? How can ye say such a thing?"

"Don't use that sort of language to me!"

"Language? You can suggest such a thing, but I must not say the word? I have never been so offended, never!"

She was trembling, strands of hair sticking to her face with the damp.

"I didn't mean to insult you. I thought you wanted to—to—"

He grabbed her arms and jerked her toward him.

"If all I wanted was to fuck you, I would have had ye on your back a dozen times last summer!"

"Like hell you would!" She wrenched loose one arm and slapped him hard across the jaw, surprising him.

He grabbed her hand, pulled her toward him and kissed her, a good deal harder and a good deal longer than he ever had before. She was tall and strong and angry—but he was taller, stronger, and much angrier. She kicked and struggled, and he kissed her until he was good and ready to stop.

"The hell I would," he said, gasping for air as he let her go. He wiped his mouth and stood back, shaking. There was blood on his hand; she'd bitten him and he hadn't felt a thing.

She was shaking, too. Her face was white, lips pressed so tight together that nothing showed in her face but dark eyes, blazing.

"But I didn't," he said, breathing slower. "That wasn't what I wanted; it's not what I want now." He wiped his bloody hand against his shirt. "But if you don't care enough to marry me, then I don't care enough to have ye in my bed!"

"I do care!"

"Like hell."

"I care too damn much to marry you, you bastard!"

"You *what*?"

"Because when I marry you—when I marry anybody—it's going to last, do you hear me? If I make a vow like that, I'll keep it, no matter what it costs me!"

Tears were running down her face. He groped in his pocket for a handkerchief and gave it to her.

"Blow your nose, wipe your face, and then tell me what the bloody hell ye think you're talking about, aye?"

She did as he said, sniffing and brushing back her damp hair with one hand. Her foolish little veil had fallen off; it was hanging by its bobby pin. He plucked it off, crumpling it in his hand.

"Your Scottish accent comes out when you get upset," she said, with a feeble attempt at a smile as she handed back the wadded hanky.

"I shouldn't wonder," Roger said in exasperation. "Now tell me what you mean, and do it plainly, before ye drive me all the way to the Gaelic."

"You can speak Gaelic?" She was gradually getting possession of herself.

"I can," he said, "and if you don't want to learn a good many coarse expressions right swiftly . . . talk. What d'ye mean by making me such an offer—and you a nice Catholic girl, straight out of Mass! I thought ye were a virgin."

"I am! What does that have to do with it?"

Before he could answer this piece of outrageousness, she followed it up with another.

"Don't you tell me you haven't had girls, I know you have!"

"Aye, I have! I didn't want to marry them, and they didn't want to marry me. I didn't love them, they didn't love me. I do love you, damn it!"

She leaned against the lamppost, hands behind her, and met his eyes directly. "I think I love you, too."

He didn't realize he had been holding his breath until he let it out.

"Ah. You do." The water had condensed in his hair, and icy trickles were running down his neck. "Mmphm. Aye, and is the operative word there 'think,' then, or is it 'love'?"

She relaxed, just a little, and swallowed.

"Both."

She held up a hand as he started to speak.

"I do—I think. But—but I can't help thinking what happened to my mother. I don't want that to happen to me."

"Your mother?" Simple astonishment was succeeded by a fresh burst of outrage. "What? You're thinking of bloody Jamie Fraser? Ye think ye cannot be satisfied with a boring historian— ye must have a—a—great passion, as she did for him, and you think I'll maybe not measure up?"

"No! I'm not thinking of Jamie Fraser! I'm thinking of my father!" She shoved her hands deep in the pockets of her jacket, and swallowed hard. She'd stopped crying, but there were tears on her lashes, clotting them in spikes.

"She meant it when she married him—I could see it, in those pictures you gave me. She said 'better or worse, richer, poorer'— and she *meant* it. And then . . . and then she met Jamie Fraser, and she didn't mean it anymore."

Her mouth worked silently for a moment, looking for words.

"I—I don't blame her, not really, not after I thought about it. She couldn't help it, and I—when she talked about him, I could see how much she loved him—but don't you see, Roger? She loved my father, too—but then something happened. She didn't expect it, and it wasn't her fault—but it made her break her word. I won't do that, not for anything."

She wiped a hand under her nose, and he gave her back the handkerchief, silently. She blinked back the tears and looked at him, straight.

"It's more than a year before we can be together. You can't leave Oxford; I can't leave Boston, not till I've got my degree."

He wanted to say that he'd resign, that she should quit her schooling—but kept quiet. She was right; neither of them would be happy with such a solution.

"So what if I say yes now, and something happens? What if— if I met somebody else, or you did?" Tears welled again, and one ran down her cheek. "I won't take the chance of hurting you. I won't."

"But you love me now?" He touched a finger gently to her cheek. "Bree, do ye love me?"

She took a step forward, and without speaking, reached to undo the fastenings of her coat.

"What the hell are you doing?" Blank astonishment was added to the mix of other emotions, succeeded by something else as her long pale fingers grasped the zip of his jacket and pulled it down.

The sudden whiff of cold was obliterated by the warmth of her body, pressed against his from throat to knees.

His arms went around her padded back by reflex; she was holding him tight, arms locked round him under his jacket. Her hair smelled cold and sweet, with the last traces of incense trapped in the heavy strands, blending with the fragrance of grass and jasmine flowers. He caught the gleam of a hairpin, bronze metal in the copper loops of her hair.

She didn't say a thing, nor did he. He could feel her body through the thin layers of cloth between them, and a jolt of desire shot up the backs of his legs, as though he were standing on an electric grid. He tilted up her chin, and set his mouth on hers.

". . . see that Jackie Martin, and her with a new fur collar to her coat?"

"Och, and where's she found the money for such a thing, wi' her husband oot o' his work this six month past? I tell ye, Jessie, yon woman . . . ooh!"

The click of French-heeled shoes on the pavement halted, to be succeeded by the sound of a throat being cleared with sufficient resonance to wake the dead.

Roger tightened his grip on Brianna, and didn't move. She tightened her arms around him in response, and he felt the curve of her mouth under his.

"MMPHM!"

"Ah, now, Chrissie," came a hissed whisper from behind him. "Let them be, aye? Can ye not see they're getting engaged?"

"Mmphm" came again, but in a lower tone. "Hmp. They'll be getting something else, and they go on wi' that much longer. Still . . ." A long sigh, tinged with nostalgia. "Ah, weel, it's nice to be young, isn't it?"

The twin tap of heels came on, much slower, passed them, and faded inaudibly into the fog.

He stood for a minute, willing himself to let go of her. But once a man has touched the mane of a water horse, it's no simple matter to let go. An old kelpie-rhyme ran through his head,

> *And sit weel, Janetie*
> *And ride weel, Davie.*
> *And your first stop will be*
> *The bottom of Loch Cavie.*

"I'll wait," he said, and let her go. He held her hands and looked into her eyes, now soft and clear as rain pools.

"Hear me, though," he said softly. "I will have you all—or not at all."

Let me love her rightly, he had said in wordless prayer. And hadn't he been told often enough by Mrs. Graham—"Be careful what ye ask for, laddie, for ye just might get it?"

He cupped her breast, soft through her jumper.

"It's not only your body that I want—though God knows, I want it badly. But I'll have you as my wife . . . or I will not have you. Your choice."

She reached up and touched him, brushed the hair off his brow with fingers so cold, they burned like dry ice.

"I understand," she whispered.

The wind off the river was cold, and he reached to do up the zip of her jacket. In doing so, his hand brushed his own pocket, and he felt the small package lying there. He'd meant to give it to her over supper.

"Here," he said, handing it to her. "Happy Christmas."

"I bought it last summer," he said, watching her cold fingers fumble at the holly-printed paper. "Looks like prescience, now, doesn't it?"

She held a silver circle, a bracelet, a flat silver band, with words etched round it. He took it from her and slipped it over her hand, onto her wrist. She turned it slowly, reading the words.

"Je t'aime . . . un peu . . . beaucoup . . . passionnément . . . pas du tout. I love you . . . a little . . . a lot . . . passionately . . . not at all."

He gave the band a quarter turn more, completing the circle.

"Je t'aime," he said, and then with a twist of fingers, sent it spinning on her wrist. She laid a hand on it, stopping it.

"Moi aussi," she said softly, looking not at the band but at him. *"Joyeux Noël."*

PART SEVEN

On the Mountain

19

Hearth Blessing

September 1767

Sleeping under the moon and stars in the arms of a naked lover, the two of you cradled by furs and soft leaves, lulled by the gentle murmur of the chestnut trees and the far-off rumble of a waterfall, is terribly romantic. Sleeping under a crude lean-to, squashed into a soggy mass between a large, wet husband and an equally large, equally wet nephew, listening to rain thrump on the branches overhead while fending off the advances of a immense and thoroughly saturated dog, is slightly less so.

"Air," I said, struggling feebly into a sitting position and brushing Rollo's tail out of my face for the hundredth time. "I can't breathe." The smell of confined male animals was overpowering; a sort of musky, rancid smell, garnished with the scent of wet wool and fish.

I rolled onto my hands and knees and made my way out, trying not to step on anyone. Jamie grunted in his sleep, compensating for the loss of my body heat by curling himself neatly into a plaid-wrapped ball. Ian and Rollo were inextricably entangled in a mass of fur and cloth, their mingled exhalations forming a faint fog around them in the predawn chill.

It *was* chilly outside, but the air was fresh; so fresh I nearly coughed when I took a good lungful of it. The rain had stopped, but the trees were still dripping, and the air was composed of equal parts water vapor and pure oxygen, spiced with pungent green scents from every plant on the mountainside.

I had been sleeping in Jamie's spare shirt, my buckskins put away in a saddlebag to avoid soaking. I was dappled with goose-flesh and shivering by the time I pulled them on, but the stiff leather warmed enough to shape itself to my body within a few minutes.

Barefooted and cold-toed, I made my way carefully down to the stream to wash, kettle under my arm. It wasn't yet dawn, and the forest was filled with mist and gray-blue light; crepuscle, the mysterious half-light that comes at both ends of the day, when the small secret things come out to feed.

There was an occasional tentative chirp from the canopy overhead, but nothing like the usual raucous chorus. The birds were late in starting today because of the rain; the sky was still lowering, with clouds that ranged from black in the west to a pale slate-blue in the dawning east. I felt a small rush of pleasure at the thought that I knew already the normal hour when the birds should sing, and had noticed the difference.

Jamie had been right, I thought, when he had suggested that we stay on the mountain, instead of returning to Cross Creek. It was the beginning of September; by Myers's estimation, we would have two months of good weather—relatively good weather, I amended, looking up at the clouds—before the cold made shelter imperative. Time enough—maybe—to build a small cabin, to hunt for meat, to supply ourselves for the winter ahead.

"It will be gey hard work," Jamie had said. I stood between his knees as he sat perched high on a large rock, looking over the valley below. "And some danger to it; we may fail if the snow is early, or if I canna hunt meat enough. I willna do it, if ye say nay, Sassenach. Would ye be afraid?"

Afraid was putting it mildly. The thought made the bottom of my stomach drop alarmingly. When I had agreed to settle on the ridge, I had thought we would return to Cross Creek to spend the winter.

We could have gathered both supplies and settlers in a leisurely manner, and returned in the spring in caravan, to clear land and raise houses communally. Instead, we would be completely alone, several days travel from the nearest tiny settlement of Europeans. Alone in a wilderness, alone through the winter.

We had virtually nothing with us in the way of tools or supplies, save a felling ax, a couple of knives, a camp kettle and girdle, and my smaller medicine box. What if something happened, if Ian or Jamie fell ill or was hurt in an accident? If we starved or froze? And while Jamie was sure that our Indian acquaintances had no objection to our intent, I wasn't so sanguine about any others who might happen along.

Yes, I bloody well *would* be afraid. On the other hand, I'd lived long enough to realize that fear wasn't usually fatal—at least not by itself. Add in the odd bear or savage, and I wasn't saying, mind.

For the first time, I looked back with some longing at River Run, at hot water and warm beds and regular food, at order, cleanliness . . . and safety.

I could see well enough why Jamie didn't want to go back; living on Jocasta's bounty for several months more would sink him that much further in obligation, make it that much harder to reject her blandishments.

He also knew—even better than I—that Jocasta Cameron was born a MacKenzie. I had seen enough of her brothers, Dougal and Colum, to have a decent wariness of that heritage; the MacKenzies of Leoch didn't give up a purpose lightly, and were certainly not above plotting and manipulation to achieve their ends. And a blind spider might weave her webs that much more surely, for depending solely on a sense of touch.

There were also really excellent reasons for staying the hell away from the vicinity of Sergeant Murchison, who seemed definitely the type to bear a grudge. And then there was Farquard Campbell and the whole waiting web of planters and Regulators, slaves and politics . . . No, I could see quite well why Jamie mightn't want to go back to such entanglement and complication, to say nothing of the looming fact of the coming war. At the same time, I was fairly sure that none of those reasons accounted for his decision.

"It's not just that you don't want to go back to River Run, is it?" I leaned back against him, feeling his warmth as a contrast to the coolness of the evening breeze. The season had not yet turned; it was still late summer, and the air was rich with the sun-roused scents of leaf and berry, but so high in the mountains, the nights turned cold.

I felt the small rumble of a laugh in his chest, and warm breath brushed my ear.

"Is it so plain, then?"

"Plain enough." I turned in his arms, and rested my forehead against his, so our eyes were inches apart. His were a very deep blue, the same color as the evening sky in the notch of the mountains.

"Owl," I said.

He laughed, startled, and blinked as he pulled back, long auburn lashes sweeping briefly down.

"What?"

"You lose," I explained. "It's a game called 'owl.' First person to blink loses."

"Oh." He took hold of my ears by the lobes and drew me gently back, forehead to forehead. "Owl, then. Ye do have eyes like an owl, have ye noticed?"

"No," I said. "Can't say I have."

"All clear and gold—and verra wise."

I didn't blink.

"Tell me then—why we're staying."

He didn't blink either, but I felt his chest rise under my hand, as he took a deep breath.

"How shall I tell ye what it is, to feel the need of a place?" he said softly. "The need of snow beneath my shoon. The breath of the mountains, breathing their own breath in my nostrils as God gave breath to Adam. The scrape of rock under my hand, climbing, and the sight of the lichens on it, enduring in the sun and the wind."

His breath was gone and he breathed again, taking mine. His hands were linked behind my head, holding me, face-to-face.

"If I am to live as a man, I must have a mountain," he said simply. His eyes were open wide, searching mine for understanding.

"Will ye trust me, Sassenach?" he said. His nose pressed against mine, but his eyes didn't blink. Neither did mine.

"With my life," I said.

I felt his lips smile, an inch from mine.

"And with your heart?"

"Always," I whispered, closed my eyes, and kissed him.

❧

And so it was arranged. Myers would go back to Cross Creek, deliver Jamie's instructions to Duncan, assure Jocasta of our welfare, and procure as much in the way of stores as the remnants of our money would finance. If there was time before the first snowfall, he would return with supplies; if not, in the spring. Ian would stay; his help would be needed to build the cabin, and to help with the hunting.

Give us this day our daily bread, I thought, pushing through the wet bushes that edged the creek, *and deliver us not into temptation.*

We were reasonably safe from temptation, though; for good or ill, we wouldn't see River Run again for at least a year. As for the daily bread, that had been coming through as dependably as manna, so far; at this time of year, there was an abundance of ripe nuts, fruits and berries, which I collected as industriously as any squirrel. In two months, though, when the trees grew bare and the streams froze, I hoped God might still hear us, above the howl of the winter wind.

The stream was noticeably swelled by the rain, the water maybe a foot higher than it had been yesterday. I knelt, groaning slightly as my back unkinked; sleeping on the ground exaggerated all the normal small morning stiffnesses. I splashed cold water on my face, swished it through my mouth, drank from cupped hands, and splashed again, blood tingling through my cheeks and fingers.

When I looked up, face dripping, I saw two deer drinking from a pool on the other side, a little way upstream from me. I stayed very still, not to disturb them, but they showed no alarm at my presence. In the shadow of the birches, they were the same soft blue as the rocks and trees, little more than shadows themselves, but each line of their bodies etched in perfect delicacy, like a Japanese painting done in ink.

Then all of a sudden, they were gone. I blinked, and blinked again. I hadn't seen them turn or run—and in spite of their ethereal beauty, I was sure I hadn't been imagining them; I could see the dark imprints of their hooves in the mud of the far bank. But they were gone.

I didn't see or hear a thing, but the hair rose suddenly on my body, instinct rippling up arms and neck like electric current. I froze, nothing moving but my eyes. Where was it, what was it?

The sun was up; the tops of the trees were visibly green, and the rocks began to glow as their colors warmed to life. But the birds were silent; nothing moved, save the water.

It was no more than six feet away from me, half visible behind a bush. The sound of its lapping was lost in the noise of the stream. Then the broad head lifted, and a tufted ear swiveled toward me, though I had made no noise. Could it hear me breathing?

The sun had reached it, lit it into tawny life, glowed in gold eyes that stared into mine with a preternatural calm. The breeze had shifted; I could smell it now; a faint acrid cat-tang, and the stronger scent of blood. Ignoring me, it lifted a dark-blotched paw and licked fastidiously, eyes slitted in hygienic preoccupation.

It rubbed the paw several times over its ear, then stretched luxuriously in the patch of new sun—my God, it must be six feet long!—and sauntered off, full belly swaying.

I hadn't consciously been afraid; pure instinct had frozen me in place, and sheer amazement—at the cat's beauty, as well as its nearness—had kept me that way. With its going, though, my central nervous system thawed out at once, and promptly went to pieces. I didn't gibber, but did shake considerably; it was several minutes before I managed to get off my knees and stand up.

My hands shook so that I dropped the kettle three times in filling it. Trust him, he'd said, did I trust him? Yes, I did—and a fat lot of good that would do, unless he happened to be standing directly in front of me next time.

But for this time—I was alive. I stood still, eyes closed, breathing in the pure morning air. I could feel every single atom of my body, blood racing to carry round the sweet fresh stuff to every cell and muscle fiber. The sun touched my face, and warmed the cold skin to a lovely glow.

I opened my eyes to a dazzle of green and yellow and blue; day had broken. All the birds were singing now.

I went up the path toward the clearing, resisting the impulse to look behind me.

Jamie and Ian had felled several tall, slender pines the day before, cut them into twelve-foot lengths, and rolled and wrestled and tumbled the logs downhill. Now they lay stacked at the edge of the small clearing, rough bark glistening black with wet.

Jamie was pacing out a line, stamping down the wet grass, when I came back with the kettle filled with water. Ian had a fire started on the top of a large flat stone—he having learned from Jamie the canny trick of keeping a handful of dry kindling always in one's sporran, along with flint and steel.

"This will be a wee shed," Jamie was saying, frowning at the ground in concentration. "We'll build this first, for we can sleep in it, if it should rain again, but it needna be so well built as the cabin—it'll give us something to practice on, eh, Ian?"

"What is it for—beyond practice?" I asked. He looked up and smiled at me.

"Good morning, Sassenach. Did ye sleep well?"

"Of course not," I said. "What's the shed for?"

"Meat," he said. "We'll dig a shallow pit at the back, and fill it wi' embers, to smoke what we can for keeping. And make a rack for drying—Ian's seen the Indians do it, to make what they call jerky. We must have a safe place where beasts canna get at our food."

This seemed a sound idea; particularly in view of the sort of beasts in the area. My only doubts were regarding the smoking. I'd seen it done in Scotland, and knew that smoking meat required a certain amount of attention; someone had to be at hand to keep the fire from burning too high or going out altogether, had to turn the meat regularly, and baste it with fat to avoid scorching and drying.

I had no difficulty in seeing who was going to be nominated for this task. The only trouble was that if I didn't manage to do it right, we'd all die of ptomaine poisoning.

"Right," I said, without enthusiasm. Jamie caught my tone and grinned at me.

"That's the first shed, Sassenach," he said. "The second one's yours."

"Mine?" I perked up a bit at that.

"For your wee herbs and bits of plants. They do take up a bit of room, as I recall." He pointed across the clearing, the light of builder's mania in his eye. "And just there—that's where the cabin will be; where we'll live through the winter."

Rather to my surprise, they had the walls of the first shed erected by the end of the second day, crudely roofed with cut branches until time should permit the cutting of shingles for a proper roof. The walls were made of slender notched logs, still with the bark on, and with noticeable chinks and gaps between them. Still, it was large enough to sleep the three of us and Rollo comfortably, and with a fire burning in a stone-lined pit at one end, it was quite cozy inside.

Enough branches had been removed from the roof to leave a smoke hole; I could see the evening stars, as I cuddled against Jamie and listened to him criticize his workmanship.

"Look at that," he said crossly, lifting his chin at the far corner. "I've gone and laid in a crooked pole, and it's put the whole of that line off the straight."

"I don't imagine the deer carcasses will care," I murmured. "Here, let's see that hand."

"And the rooftree's a good six inches lower at the one end than the other," he went on, ignoring me, but letting me have his left hand. Both hands were smoothly callused, but I could feel the new roughnesses of scrapes and cuts, and so many small splinters that his palm was prickly to the touch.

"You feel like a porcupine," I said, brushing my hand over his fingers. "Here, move closer to the fire, so I can see to pull them out."

He moved obligingly, crawling around Ian, who—freshly de-splintered himself—had fallen asleep with his head pillowed on Rollo's furry side. Unfortunately, the change of position exposed new weaknesses of construction to Jamie's critical eye.

"You've never built a shed out of logs before, have you?" I interrupted his denunciation of the doorway, neatly tweaking a large splinter out of his thumb with my tweezers.

"Ow! No, but—"

"And you built the bloody thing in two days, with nothing but a felling ax and a knife, for God's sake! There's not a nail in it! Why ought you to expect it to look like Buckingham Palace?"

"I've never seen Buckingham Palace," he said, rather mildly. He paused. "I do take your point, though, Sassenach."

"Good." I bent closely over his palm, squinting to make out the small dark streaks of splinters, trapped beneath the skin.

"I suppose it willna fall down, at least," he said, after a longer pause.

"Shouldn't think so." I dabbed a cloth to the neck of the brandy bottle, swabbed his hand with it, then turned my attention to his right hand.

He didn't speak for a time. The fire crackled softly to itself, flaring up now and then as a draft reached in between the logs to tickle it.

"The house is going to be on the high ridge," he said suddenly. "Where the strawberries grow."

"Will it?" I murmured. "The cabin, you mean? I thought that was going to be at the side of the clearing." I'd taken out as many splinters as I could; those that were left were so deeply embedded that I would have to wait for them to work their way nearer the surface.

"No, not the cabin. A fine house," he said softly. He leaned back against the rough logs, looking across the fire, out through the chinks to the darkness beyond. "Wi' a staircase, and glass windows."

"That will be grand." I laid the tweezers back in their slot, and closed the box.

"Wi' high ceilings, and a doorway high enough I shall never bump my heid going in."

"That will be lovely." I leaned back beside him, and rested my head on his shoulder. Somewhere in the far distance, a wolf howled. Rollo lifted his head with a soft *wuff!*, listened for a moment, then lay down again with a sigh.

"With a stillroom for you, and a study for me, lined with shelves for my books."

"Mmmm." At the moment, he possessed one book—*The Natural History of North Carolina,* published 1733, brought along as guide and reference.

The fire was burning low again, but neither of us moved to add more wood. The embers would warm us through the night, to be rekindled with the dawn.

Jamie put an arm around my shoulders, and tilting sideways, took me with him to lie curled together on the thick layer of fallen leaves that was our couch.

"And a bed," I said. "You could build a bed, I expect?"

"As fine as any in Buckingham Palace," he said.

Myers, bless his kindly heart and faithful nature, did return within the month—bringing not only three pack-mules laden with tools, small furnishings, and necessities such as salt, but also Duncan Innes.

"Here?" Innes looked interestedly over the tiny homestead that had begun to take shape on the strawberry-covered ridge. We had two sturdy sheds now, plus a split-railed penfold in which to keep the horses and any other stock we might acquire.

At the moment, our total stock consisted of a small white piglet, which Jamie had obtained from a Moravian settlement thirty miles away, exchanging for it a bag of sweet yams I had gathered and a bundle of willow-twig brooms I had made. Rather too small for the penfold, it had so far been living in the shed with us, where it had become fast friends with Rollo. I wasn't quite so fond of it myself.

"Aye. It's decent land, with plenty of water; there are springs in the wood, and the creek all through."

Jamie guided Duncan to a spot from which the western slopes below the ridge were visible; there were natural breaks, or "coves" in the forest, now overgrown with tangles of wild grass, but ultimately suitable for cultivation.

"D'ye see?" He gestured over the slope, which ran down gently from the ridge to a small bluff, where a line of sycamores marked the distant river's edge. "There's room there for at least thirty homesteads, to start. We'd need to clear a deal of forest, but there's space enough to begin. Any crofter worth his salt could feed his family from a garden plot, the soil's so rich.''

Duncan had been a fisherman, not a farmer, but he nodded obediently, eyes fixed on the vista as Jamie peopled it with future houses.

"I've paced it out," Jamie was saying, "though it will have to be surveyed properly as soon as may be. But I've the description of it in my head—did ye by chance bring ink and paper?"

"Aye, we did. And a few other things, as well." Duncan smiled at me, his long, rather melancholy face transformed by the expression. "Miss Jo's sent a feather bed, which she thought might not come amiss."

"A feather bed? Really? How wonderful!" I immediately dismissed any ungenerous thoughts I had ever harbored about Jocasta Cameron. While Jamie had built us an excellent, sturdy bedstead framed in oakwood, with the bottom ingeniously made of laced rope, I had had nothing to lay on it save cedar branches, which were fragrant but unpleasantly lumpy.

My thoughts of luxuriant wallowing were interrupted by the emergence from the woods of Ian and Myers, the latter with a brace of squirrels hung from his belt. Ian proudly presented me with an enormous black object, which on closer inspection proved to be a turkey, fat from gorging on the autumn grains.

"Boy's got a nice eye, Mrs. Claire," said Myers, nodding approvingly. "Those be wily birds, turkeys. Even the Indians don't take 'em easy."

It was early for Thanksgiving, but I was delighted with the bird, which would be the first substantial item in our larder. So was Jamie, though his pleasure lay more in the thing's tail feathers, which would provide him with a good supply of quills.

"I must write to the Governor," he explained over dinner, "to say that I shall be taking up his offer, and to give the particulars of the land." He picked up a chunk of cake and bit into it absently.

"Do watch out for nutshells," I said, a little nervously. "You don't want to break a tooth."

Dinner consisted of trout grilled over the fire, yams baked in it, wild plums, and a very crude cake made of flour from hickory nuts, ground up in my mortar. We had been living mostly on fish and what edible vegetation I could scrounge, Ian and Jamie having been too busy with the building to take time to hunt. I rather hoped that Myers would see fit to stay for a bit—long enough to bag a deer or some other nice large source of protein. A winter of dried fish seemed a little daunting.

"Dinna fash, Sassenach," Jamie murmured through a mouthful of cake, and smiled at me. "It's good." He turned his attention to Duncan.

"When we've done with eating, Duncan, you'll maybe walk wi' me to the river, and choose your place?"

Innes's face went blank, then flushed with a mixture of pleasure and dismay.

"My place? Land, ye mean, *Mac Dubh*?" Involuntarily, he hunched the shoulder on the side with the missing arm.

"Aye, land." Jamie speared a hot yam with a sharpened stick, and began to peel it carefully with his fingers, not looking at Innes. "I shall be needing you to act as my agent, Duncan—if ye will. It's only right ye should be paid. Now, what I am thinking— if ye should find it fair, mind—is that I shall make the claim for a homestead in your name, but as ye willna be here to work it, Ian and I will see to putting a bit of your land to corn, and to building a wee croft there. Then come time, you shall have a place to settle, if ye like, and a bit of corn put by. Will that suit ye, do ye think?"

Duncan's face had been going through an array of emotions as Jamie spoke, from dismay to amazement to a cautious sort of excitement. The last thing that would ever have occurred to him was that he might own land. Penniless, and unable to work with his hands, in Scotland he would have lived as a beggar—if he had lived at all.

"Why—" he began, then stopped and swallowed, knobbly Adam's apple bobbing. "Aye, *Mac Dubh*. That will suit fine." A small, incredulous smile had formed on his face as Jamie spoke, and stayed there, as though Duncan were unaware of it.

"Agent." He swallowed again, and reached for one of the bottles of ale he had brought. "What will ye have me to do for ye, *Mac Dubh*?"

"The two things, Duncan, and ye will. First is to find me settlers." Jamie waved a hand at the beginnings of our new cabin, which so far consisted entirely of a fieldstone foundation, the framing of the floor, and a wide slab of dark slate selected for the hearthstone, presently leaning against the foundation.

"I canna be leaving here just at present, myself. What I want ye to do is to find as many as ye can of the men who were transported from Ardsmuir. They'll have been scattered, but they came

through Wilmington; a many of them will be in North or South
Carolina. Find as many as ye can, tell them what I'm about here—
and bring as many as are willing here in the spring.''

Duncan was nodding slowly, lips pursed beneath his drooping
mustache. Few men wore such facial adornment, but it suited him,
making him look like a thin but benevolent walrus.

''Verra well,'' he said. ''And the second?''

Jamie glanced at me, then at Duncan.

''My aunt,'' he said. ''Will ye undertake to help her, Duncan?
She's great need of an honest man, who can deal wi' the naval
bastards and speak for her in business.''

Duncan had showed no hesitation in agreeing to comb several
hundred miles of colony in search of settlers for our enterprise,
but the notion of dealing with naval bastards struck him with
profound uneasiness.

''Business? But I dinna ken aught of—''

''Dinna fash,'' Jamie said, smiling at his friend, and the adjuration worked on Duncan as well as it did on me; I could see the
mounting uneasiness in Duncan's eyes begin to recede. For
roughly the ten-thousandth time, I wondered how he did it.

''It'll be little trouble to ye,'' Jamie said soothingly. ''My aunt
kens well enough what's to be done; she can tell ye what to say
and what to do—it's only she needs a man for the saying and
doing of it. I shall write a letter to her, for ye to take back,
explaining that ye'll be pleased to act for her.''

During the latter part of this conversation, Ian had been digging
about in the packs that had been unloaded from the mules. Now
he withdrew a flat piece of metal, and squinted at it curiously.

''What's this?'' he asked, of no one in particular. He held it out
for us to see; a flat piece of dark metal, pointed at one end like a
knife, with rudimentary crosspieces. It looked like a small dirk
that had been run over by a steamroller.

''Iron for your hearth.'' Duncan reached for the piece, and
handed it, handle-first, to Jamie. ''It was Miss Jo's thought.''

''Was it? That was kind.'' Jamie's face was weathered to deep
bronze by long days in the open, but I saw the faint flush of pink
on the side of his neck. His thumb stroked the smooth surface of
the iron, and then he handed it to me.

''Keep it safe, Sassenach,'' he said. ''We'll bless our hearth
before Duncan leaves.''

I could see that he was deeply touched by the gift, but didn't
understand entirely why, until Ian had explained to me that one

buries iron beneath a new hearth, to ensure blessing and prosperity on the house.

It was Jocasta's blessing on our venture; her acceptance of Jamie's decision—and forgiveness for what must have seemed his abandonment. It was more than generosity, and I folded the small piece of iron carefully into my handkerchief, and put it in my pocket for safekeeping.

We blessed the hearth two days later, standing in the wall-less cabin. Myers had removed his hat, from respect, and Ian had washed his face. Rollo was present, too, as was the small white pig, who was required to attend as the personification of our "flocks," despite her objections; the pig saw no point in being removed from her meal of acorns to participate in a ritual so notably lacking in food.

Ignoring piercing pig-screams of annoyance, Jamie held the small iron knife upright by its tip, so that it formed a cross, and said quietly,

> *"God, bless the world and all that is therein.*
> *God, bless my spouse and my children,*
> *God, bless the eye that is in my head,*
> *And bless, God, the handling of my hand,*
> *What time I rise in the morning early,*
> *What time I lie down late in bed,*
> > *Bless my rising in the morning early,*
> > *And my lying down late in bed."*

He reached out and touched first me, then Ian—and with a grin, Rollo and the pig—with the iron, before going on:

> *"God, protect the house, and the household,*
> *God, consecrate the children of the motherhood,*
> *God, encompass the flocks and the young,*
> *Be Thou after them and tending them,*
> *What time the flocks ascend hill and wold,*
> *What time I lie down to sleep.*
> *What time the flocks ascend hill and wold,*
> *What time I lie down in peace to sleep.*

> *"Let the fire of thy blessing burn forever upon us, O God."*

He knelt then by the hearth and placed the iron into the small hole dug for it, covered it over, and tamped the dirt flat. Then he and I took the ends of the big hearthstone, and laid it carefully into place.

I should have felt quite ridiculous, standing in a house with no walls, attended by a wolf and a pig, surrounded by wilderness and mocked by mockingbirds, engaged in a ritual more than half pagan. I didn't.

Jamie stood in front of the new hearth, stretched out a hand to me, and drew me to stand by the hearthstone beside him. Looking down at the slate before us, I suddenly thought of the abandoned homestead we had found on our journey north; the fallen timbers of the roof, and the cracked hearthstone, from which a hollybush had sprouted. Had the unknown founders of that place thought to bless their hearth—and failed anyway? Jamie's hand tightened on mine, in unconscious reassurance.

On a flat rock outside the cabin, Duncan kindled a small fire, Myers holding the steel for him to strike. Once begun, the fire was coaxed into brightness, and a brand taken from it. Duncan held this in his one hand, and walked sunwise around the cabin's foundation, chanting in loud Gaelic. Jamie translated for me as he sang:

> *"The safeguard of Fionn mac Cumhall be yours,*
> *The safeguard of Cormac the shapely be yours,*
> *The safeguard of Conn and Cumhall be yours,*
> *From wolf and from bird-flock*
> *From wolf and from bird-flock."*

He paused in his chanting as he came to each point of the compass, and bowing to the "four airts," swept his brand in a blazing arc before him. Rollo, plainly disapproving of these pyromaniac goings-on, growled deep in his throat, but was firmly shushed by Ian.

> *"The shield of the King of Fiann be yours,*
> *The shield of the king of the sun be yours,*
> *The shield of the king of the stars be yours,*
> *In jeopardy and distress*
> *In jeopardy and distress."*

There were a good many verses; Duncan circled the house three times. It was only as he reached the final point, next to the freshly laid hearthstone, that I realized Jamie had laid out the cabin so that the hearth lay to the north; the morning sun fell warm on my left shoulder and threw our mingled shadows to the west.

> *"The sheltering of the king of kings be yours,*
> *The sheltering of Jesus Christ be yours,*
> *The sheltering of the spirit of Healing be yours,*
> *From evil deed and quarrel,*
> *From evil dog and red dog."*

With a look down his nose at Rollo, Duncan stopped by the hearth, and gave the brand to Jamie, who stooped in turn and set alight the waiting pile of kindling. Ian gave a Gaelic whoop as the flame blazed up, and there was general applause.

Later, we saw Duncan and Myers off. They were bound not for Cross Creek but, rather, for Mount Helicon, where the Scots of the region held a yearly Gathering in the autumn, to give thanks for successful harvests, to exchange news and transact business, to celebrate marriages and christenings, to keep the far-flung elements of clan and family in touch.

Jocasta and her household would be there; so would Farquard Campbell and Andrew MacNeill. It was the best place for Duncan to begin his task of finding the scattered men of Ardsmuir; Mount Helicon was the largest of the Gatherings; Scots would come there from as far away as South Carolina and Virginia.

"I shall be here come spring, *Mac Dubh*," Duncan promised Jamie as he mounted. "With as many men as I can fetch to ye. And I shall hand on your letters without fail." He patted the pouch by his saddle, and tugged his hat down to shade his eyes from the rich September sun. "Will ye have a word for your aunt?"

Jamie paused for a moment, thinking. He had written to Jocasta already; was there anything to add?

"Tell my aunt I shall not see her at the Gathering this year, or perhaps at the next. But the one after that, I shall be there without fail—and my people with me. Godspeed, Duncan!"

He slapped Duncan's horse on the rump, and stood by me waving as the two horses dropped over the edge of the ridge and out of sight. The parting gave me an odd feeling of desolation; Duncan was our last and only link with civilization. Now we were truly alone.

Well, not quite alone, I amended. We had Ian. To say nothing of Rollo, the pig, three horses, and two mules that Duncan had left us, to manage the spring plowing. Quite a little establishment, in fact. My spirits rose in contemplation; within the month, the cabin would be finished, and we would have a solid roof over our heads. And then——

"Bad news, Auntie," said Ian's voice in my ear. "The pig's eaten the rest of your nutmeal."

20

The White Raven

" 'Body, soul, and mind,' " Jamie said, translating as he bent to seize the end of another trimmed log. " 'The body for sensation, the soul for the springs of action, the mind for principles. Yet the capacity for sensation belongs also to the stalled ox; there is no wild beast or degenerate but obeys the twitchings of impulse; and even men who deny the gods, or betray their country, or'—careful, man!''

Ian, thus warned, stepped neatly backward over the ax handle, and turned to the left, steering his end of the burden carefully round the corner of the half-built log wall.

" '—or perpetrate all manner of villainy behind locked doors, have minds to guide them to the clear path of duty,' '' Jamie resumed Marcus Aurelius's *Meditations*. " 'Seeing then'—step up. Aye, good, that's got it—'seeing then that all else is in common heritage of such types, the good man's only singularity lies in his approving welcome to every experience the looms of fate may weave for him, his refusal to soil the divinity seated in his breast or perturb it with disorderly impressions . . .' All right now, one, and two, and . . . *ergh*!''

His face went scarlet with effort as they reached the proper position and, in concert, hoisted the squared log to shoulder height. Too occupied to go on with the meditations of Marcus Aurelius, Jamie directed his nephew's movements with jerks of the head and breathless one-word commands, as they maneuvered the unwieldy chunk of wood into the notches of the cross-pieces below it.

"Och, the twitchings of impulse, is it?" Ian shouldered a lock of hair out of his sweating face. "I feel a wee twitch in the direction of my wame. Is that degenerate, then?"

"I believe that would be an acceptable bodily sensation at this

time o' day," Jamie allowed, grunting slightly as they maneuvered the log the last inch into place. "A bit to the left, Ian."

The log dropped into its notches, and both men stepped back
with a shared sigh of relieved accomplishment. Ian grinned at his
uncle.

"Meanin' ye're hungry yourself, aye?"

Jamie grinned back, but before he could reply, Rollo lifted his
head, ears perking, and a low growl rumbled in his chest. Seeing
this, Ian turned his head to look, and stopped in the act of mopping his face with his shirttail.

"Here's company, Uncle," he said, nodding toward the forest.
Jamie stiffened. Before he could turn or reach for a weapon,
though, I had made out what Rollo and Ian had seen among the
shifting leaf-light.

"Not to worry," I said, amused. "It's your erstwhile drinking
companion—dressed for visiting. A little something the looms of
fate have woven for your approving welcome, I expect."

Nacognaweto waited politely in the shade of the chestnut grove
until he was sure we had seen him. Then he advanced slowly out
of the forest, followed this time not by his sons but by three
women, two of them carrying large bundles on their backs.

One was a young girl, no more than thirteen or so, and the
second, in her thirties, plainly the girl's mother. The third woman
who accompanied them was much older—not the grandmother, I
thought, seeing her bent form and white hair—perhaps the great-
grandmother.

They had indeed come dressed for visiting; Nacognaweto was
bare-legged, with leather buskins on his feet, but he wore muslin
breeches, loose at the knee, and a shirt of dyed pink linen over
them, belted splendidly with a girdle studded with porcupine
quills and bits of white and lavender shell. Over it all he had a
leather vest with beaded trim, and a sort of loose turban in blue
calico over his unbound hair, with two crow's feathers dangling
down beside one ear. Jewelry of shell and silver—an earring,
several necklaces, a belt buckle and small ornaments tied to his
hair—completed the picture.

The women were somewhat less gorgeously arrayed, but still
plainly in their Sunday best, in long loose dresses that reached
their knees, soft boots and leather leggings showing beneath.
They were girdled with deer-leather aprons decorated with
painted patterns, and the two younger women wore ornamental

vests as well. They advanced in single file, halfway across the clearing, then stopped.

"My God," Jamie murmured, "it's an ambassage." He wiped a sleeve across his face, and nudged Ian in the ribs. "Make my curtsies, Ian; I'll be back."

Ian, looking a trifle bewildered, advanced to meet the Indians, waving a large hand in a ceremonial gesture of welcome. Jamie grabbed me by the arm and hustled me round the corner, into the half-built house.

"What—" I began, bewildered.

"Get dressed," he interrupted, shoving the clothes box in my direction. "Put on your gaudiest things, aye? It wouldna be respectful, else."

"Gaudy" was going a bit far in the description of any item of my current wardrobe, but I did my best, hastily tying a yellow linen skirt around my waist and replacing my plain white kerchief with one Jocasta had sent me, embroidered with cherries. I thought that would do—after all, it was obviously the males of the species who were on display here.

Jamie, having flung off his breeks and belted his crimson plaid in record time, fastened it with a small bronze brooch, snatched a bottle out from under the bedframe, and was out through the open side of the house before I had finished tidying my hair. Giving up that attempt as a lost cause, I hurried out after him.

The women watched me with the same fascination I had for them, but they hung back as Jamie and Nacognaweto conducted the necessary greetings involving the ceremonial pouring and sharing of the brandy, Ian being included in this ritual. Only then did the second woman come forward at Nacognaweto's gesture, ducking her head in shy acknowledgment.

"Bonjour, messieurs, madame," she said softly, looking from one to another of us. Her eyes rested on me with frank curiosity, taking in every detail of my appearance, so I felt no compunction in staring at her, likewise. Mixed blood, I thought, perhaps French?

"Je suis sa femme," she said, with a graceful inclination of her head toward Nacognaweto, the words verifying my guess as to her heritage. *"Je m'appelle Gabrielle."*

"Um . . . *je m'appelle* Claire," I said, with a slightly less graceful gesture at myself. *"S'il vous plaît . . ."* I waved at the pile of waiting logs, inviting them to sit down, while mentally wondering whether there was enough of the squirrel stew to go round.

Jamie, meanwhile, was eyeing Nacognaweto with a mixture of amusement and irritation.

"Oh, 'no Franch,' is it?" he said. "Not a word, I dinna suppose!" The Indian gave him a look of profound blandness, and nodded to his wife to continue with the introductions.

The elder lady was Nayawenne, not Gabrielle's grandmother as I had thought but, rather Nacognaweto's. This lady was light-boned, thin, and bent with rheumatism, but bright-eyed as the sparrow she so strongly resembled. She wore a small leather bag tied round her neck, ornamented with a rough green stone pierced through for stringing, and the spotted tail feathers of a woodpecker. She had a larger bag, this one of cloth, tied at her waist. She saw me looking at the green stains on the rough cloth, and smiled, showing two prominent yellow front teeth.

The girl was, as I had surmised, Gabrielle's daughter—but not, I thought, Nacognaweto's; she had no resemblance to him, and behaved shyly toward him. Her rather incongruous name was Berthe, and the effects of mixed blood were even more apparent in her than in her mother; her hair was dark and silky, but a deep brown rather than ebony, and her round face was ruddy, with the fresh complexion of a European, though her eyes had the Indian's epicanthic fold.

Once the official introductions were over, Nacognaweto motioned to Berthe, who obediently brought out the large bundle she had carried, and opened it at my feet, displaying a large basket of orange and green-striped squash, a string of dried fish, a smaller basket of yams, and a huge pile of Indian corn, shucked and dried on the cob.

"My God," I murmured. "The return of Squanto!"

Everyone gave me a blank look, and I hastened to smile and make exclamations—thoroughly heartfelt—of joy and pleasure over the gifts. It might not get us through the whole winter, but it was enough to augment our diet for a good two months.

Nacognaweto explained through Gabrielle that this was a small and insignificant return for Jamie's gift of the bear, which had been received with delight by his village, where Jamie's courageous exploit (here the women cut their eyes at me and tittered, having evidently heard all about the episode of the fish) had been the subject of great talk and admiration.

Jamie, thoroughly accustomed to this sort of diplomatic exchange, modestly disclaimed any pretention to prowess, dismissing the encounter as the merest accident.

While Gabrielle was employed in translation, the old lady ignored the mutual compliments, and sidled crabwise over to me. Without the least sense of offense, she patted me familiarly all over, fingering my clothes and lifting the hem of my dress to examine my shoes, keeping up a running commentary to herself in a soft, hoarse murmur.

The murmur grew louder and took on a tone of astonishment when she got to my hair. I obligingly took out the pins and shook it down over my shoulders. She pulled out a curl, drew it taut, then let it spring back, and laughed like a drain.

The men glanced in our direction, but by this time Jamie had moved on to showing Nacognaweto the construction of the house. The chimney was complete, built of fieldstone like the foundation, and the floor had been laid, but the walls, built of solid squared logs each some eight inches in diameter, rose only shoulder-high. Jamie was urging Ian to a demonstration of the debarking of logs, in which he chopped his way steadily backward as he walked along the top of the log, narrowly missing his toes with each stroke.

This form of male conversation requiring no translation, Gabrielle was left free to come and chat with me; though her French was peculiarly accented and full of strange idioms, we had no trouble understanding each other.

In fairly short order, I discovered that Gabrielle was the daughter of a French fur trader and a Huron woman, and the second wife of Nacognaweto, who in turn was her second husband—the first, Berthe's father, had been a Frenchman, killed in the French and Indian War ten years before.

They lived in a village called Anna Ooka (I bit the inside of my cheek to keep a straight face; no doubt "New Bern" would have sounded peculiar to them), some two days travel to the northwest —Gabrielle indicated the direction with a graceful inclination of her head.

While I talked with Gabrielle and Berthe, augmenting the conversation by means of hand-waving, I slowly became conscious that another sort of communication was taking place, with the old lady.

She said nothing to me directly—though she murmured now and then to Berthe, plainly demanding to know what I had said— but her bright dark eyes stayed fixed on me, and I was peculiarly

aware of her regard. I had the odd feeling that she was talking to
me—and I to her—without the exchange of a single spoken word.

I saw Jamie, across the clearing, offering Nacognaweto the rest
of the bottle of brandy; clearly it was time to offer gifts in return. I
gave Gabrielle the embroidered kerchief, and Berthe, a hairpin
ornamented with paste brilliants, over which gifts they exclaimed
in pleasure. For Nayawenne, though, I had something different.

I had been fortunate enough to find four large ginseng roots the
week before. I fetched all four from my medicine chest and
pressed them into her hands, smiling. She looked back at me, then
grinned, and untying the cloth bag from her belt, thrust it at me. I
didn't have to open it; I could feel the four long, lumpy shapes
through the cloth.

I laughed in return; yes, we definitely spoke the same language!

Moved by curiosity, and by an impulse that I couldn't describe,
I asked Gabrielle about the old lady's amulet, hoping that this
wasn't an insufferable breach of good manners.

"*Grandmère est . . .*" She hesitated, looking for the right
French word, but I already knew.

"*Pas docteur,*" I said, "*et pas sorcière, magicienne. Elle
est . . .*" I hesitated too; there really wasn't a suitable word for it
in French, after all.

"We say she is a singer," Berthe put in shyly, in French. "We
call it *shaman;* her name, it means 'It may be; it will happen.' "

The old lady said something, nodding at me, and the two
younger women looked startled. Nayawenne bent her head,
slipped the thong off her neck, and placed the little bag in my
hand.

It was so heavy that my wrist sagged, and I nearly dropped it.
Astonished, I closed my hand over it. The worn leather was warm
from her body, the rounded contours fitting smoothly into my
palm. For just a moment, I had the remarkable impression that
something in the bag was alive.

My face must have shown my startlement, for the old lady
doubled up laughing. She held out her hand and I gave her back
the amulet, with a fair amount of haste. Gabrielle conveyed politely that her husband's grandmother would be pleased to show
me the useful plants that grew nearby, if I would like to walk with
her?

I accepted this invitation with alacrity, and the old lady set off
up the path with a sure-footed spryness that belied her years. I
watched her feet, tiny in soft leather boots, and hoped that when I

was her age, I might be capable of walking for two days through the woods, and then wanting to go exploring.

We wandered along the stream for some way, followed at a respectful distance by Gabrielle and Berthe, who came up beside us only if summoned to interpret.

"Each of the plants holds the cure to a sickness," the old lady explained through Gabrielle. She plucked a twig from a bush by the path and handed it to me with a wry look. "If we only knew what they all were!"

For the most part, we managed fairly well by means of gesture, but when we reached the big pool where Jamie and Ian fished trout, Nayawenne stopped and waved, bringing Gabrielle to us again. She said something to the woman, who turned to me, a faint look of surprise on her face.

"My husband's grandmother says that she had a dream about you, on the night of the full moon, two moons ago."

"About me?"

Gabrielle nodded. Nayawenne put a hand on my arm and looked up intently into my face, as though to see the impact of Gabrielle's words.

"She told us about the dream; that she had seen a woman with—" Her lips twitched, then hastily straightened themselves, and she delicately touched the ends of her own long, straight hair. "Three days later, my husband and his sons returned, to tell of meeting you and the Bear Killer in the forest."

Berthe was watching me with frank interest, too, twining a lock of her own dark-brown hair around the end of an index finger.

"She who heals said at once that she must see you, and so when we heard that you were here . . ."

That gave me a small start; I had had no sensation of being watched, and yet plainly someone had taken note of our presence on the mountain, and conveyed the news to Nacognaweto.

Impatient with these irrelevancies, Nayawenne poked her granddaughter-in-law and said something, then pointed firmly at the water by our feet.

"My husband's grandmother says that when she dreamed of you, it was here." Gabrielle gestured over the pool, and looked back at me with great seriousness.

"She met you here, at night. The moon was in the water. You became a white raven; you flew over the water and swallowed the moon."

"Oh?" I hoped this wasn't a sinister thing for me to have done.

"The white raven flew back, and laid an egg in the palm of her hand. The egg split open, and there was a shining stone inside. My husband's grandmother knew this was great magic, that the stone could heal sickness."

Nayawenne nodded her head several times, and taking the amulet bag from her neck, reached into it.

"On the day after the dream, my husband's grandmother went to dig *kinnea* root, and on the way, she saw something blue, sticking in the clay of the riverbank."

Nayawenne drew out a small, lumpy object, and dropped it into my hand. It was a pebble; rough, but undeniably a gemstone. Bits of stony matrix clung to it, but the heart of the rock was a deep, soft blue.

"My goodness—it's a sapphire, isn't it?"

"Sapphire?" Gabrielle turned the word over in her mouth, tasting it. "We call it . . ." She hesitated, looking for the proper French translation. *". . . pierre sans peur."*

"Pierre sans peur?" A fearless stone?

Nayawenne nodded, talking again. Berthe butted in with the translation, before her mother could speak.

"My father's grandmother says a stone like this, it keeps people from being afraid, and so it makes their spirit strong, so they will be healed more easily. Already, this stone has healed two people of fever, and cured a soreness of the eyes that my younger brother had."

"My husband's grandmother wishes to thank you for this gift." Gabrielle neatly took back the conversation.

"Ah . . . do tell her she's quite welcome." I nodded cordially at the old lady, and gave her back the blue stone. She popped it into the bag and drew the string tight about its neck. Then she peered closely at me, and reaching out, drew down a curl of my hair, talking as she rubbed the lock between her fingers.

"My husband's grandmother says that you have medicine now, but you will have more. When your hair is white like hers, that is when you will find your full power."

The old lady dropped the lock of hair, and looked into my eyes for a moment. I thought I saw an expression of great sadness in the faded depths, and reached involuntarily to touch her.

She stepped back and said something else. Gabrielle looked at me queerly.

"She says you must not be troubled; sickness is sent from the gods. It won't be your fault."

I looked at Nayawenne, startled, but she had already turned away.

"What won't be my fault?" I asked, but the old lady refused to say more.

21

Night on a Snowy Mountain

December 1767

The winter held off for some time, but snow began to fall in the night on November 28, and we woke to find the world transformed. Every needle on the great blue spruce behind the cabin was frosted, and ragged fringes of ice dripped from the tangle of wild raspberry canes.

The snow wasn't deep, but its coming changed the shape of daily life. I no longer foraged during the day, save for short trips to the stream for water, and for lingering bits of green cress salvaged from the icy slush along the banks. Jamie and Ian ceased their work of log felling and field clearing, and turned to roof shingling. The winter drew in on us, and we in turn withdrew from the cold, turning inward.

We had no candles; only grease lamps and rushlights, and the light of the fire that burned constantly on the hearth, blackening the roof beams. We therefore rose at first light, and lay down after supper, in the same rhythm as the creatures of the forest around us.

We had no sheep yet, and thus no wool to card or spin, no cloth to weave or dye. We had no beehives yet, and thus no wax to boil, no candles to dip. There was no stock to care for, save the horses and mules and the piglet, who had grown considerably in both size and irascibility, and in consequence been exiled to a private compartment in the corner of the crude stable Jamie had built—this itself no more than a large open-fronted shelter with a branch-covered roof.

Myers had brought a small but useful selection of tools, the iron parts clanking in a bag, to be supplied with wooden handles from the forest close at hand: a barking ax and another felling ax, a plowshare for the spring planting, augers, planes and chisels, a small grass scythe, two hammers and a handsaw, a peculiar thing called a "twibil" that Jamie said was for cutting mortises, a "drawknife"—a curved blade with handles at either end, used to smooth and taper wood—two small sharp knives, a hatchet-adze, something that looked like a medieval torture device but was really a nail-header, and a froe for splitting shingles.

Between them, Jamie and Ian had succeeded in getting a roof on the cabin before snow fell, but the sheds were less important. A block of wood sat constantly by the fire, the froe stuck through it, ready for anyone with an idle moment to strike off a few more shingles. That corner of the hearth was in fact devoted to wood carving; Ian had made a rough but serviceable stool, which sat under one of the windows for good light, and the shavings could all be tossed thriftily into the fire, which burned day and night.

Myers had brought a few woman's tools for me, as well: a huge sewing basket, well supplied with needles, pins, scissors, and balls of thread, and lengths of linen, muslin, and woven wool. While sewing was not my favorite occupation, I was nonetheless delighted to see these, since owing to Jamie and Ian's constantly lurching through thickets and crawling about on the roofs, the knees, elbows, and shoulders of all their garments were in constant disrepair.

"Another one!" Jamie sat bolt upright in bed beside me.

"Another what?" I asked sleepily, opening one eye. It was very dark in the cabin, the fire burnt to coals on the hearth.

"Another bloody leak! It hit me in the ear, damn it!" He sprang out of bed, went to the fire and thrust in a stick of wood. Once it was alight, he brought it back and stood on the bedstead, thrusting his torch upward as he glowered at the roof in search of the fiendish leak.

"Urmg?" Ian, who slept on a low trundle bed, rolled over and groaned inquiringly. Rollo, who insisted on sharing it with him, emitted a brief *"uff,"* relapsed into a heap of gray fur, and resumed his loud snoring.

"A leak," I told Ian, keeping a narrow eye on Jamie's torch. I wasn't having my precious feather bed set alight by stray sparks.

"Oh." Ian lay with an arm across his face. "Has it snowed again?"

"It must have." The windows were covered with squares of oiled deerhide, tacked down, and there was no sound from outside, but the air had the peculiar muffled quality that came with snow.

Snow came silently, and mounded on the roof, then, beginning to melt from the warmth of the shingles underneath, would drip down the slope of the roof, to leave a gleaming portcullis of icicles along the eaves. Now and then, though, the roaming water found a split in a shingle, or a join where the overlapping edges had warped, and drips poked their icy fingers through the roof.

Jamie regarded all such intrusions as a personal affront, and brooked no delay in dealing with them.

"Look!" he exclaimed. "There it is. See it?"

I shifted my glassy gaze from the hairy ankles in front of my nose, to the roof overhead. Sure enough, the torchlight revealed the black line of a split in one shingle, with a spreading dark patch of dampness on the underside. As I watched, a clear drop formed, glistening red in the torchlight, and fell with a plop onto the pillow beside me.

"We could shift the bed a bit," I suggested, though with no particular hope. I had been through this before. All suggestions that repair work could wait till daylight were met with astonished refusal; no proper man, I was given to understand, would countenance such a thing.

Jamie stepped down off the bedstead and prodded Ian in the ribs with his foot.

"Get up and knock at the spot where the split is, Ian. I'll deal with it on the outside." Seizing a fresh shingle, a hammer, a hatchet, and a bag of nails, he headed for the door.

"Don't you go up on the roof in that!" I exclaimed, sitting up abruptly. "That's your good woolen shirt!"

He halted by the door, glared briefly at me, then, with the rebuking expression of an early Christian martyr, laid down his tools, stripped off the shirt, dropped it on the floor, picked up the tools, and strode majestically out to deal with the leak, buttocks clenched with determined zeal.

I rubbed a hand over my sleep-puffed face and moaned softly to myself.

"He'll be all right, Auntie," Ian assured me. He yawned widely, not bothering to cover his mouth, and reluctantly rolled out of his own warm bed.

Thumps on the roof that were definitely not the feet of eight tiny reindeer announced that Jamie was in place. I rolled out of the way and got up, resigned, as Ian mounted the bedstead and jabbed a stick of firewood upward into the damp patch, jarring the shingles enough for Jamie to locate the leak on the outside.

A short period of rending and banging followed, as the defective shingle was yanked loose and replaced, and the leak was summarily extinguished, leaving no more evidence of its existence than the small heap of snow that had fallen in through the hole left by the removed shingle.

Back in bed, Jamie curled his freezing body around me, clasped me to his icy bosom, and fell promptly asleep, full of the righteous satisfaction of a man who has defended hearth and home against all threat.

It was a fragile and tenuous foothold that we had upon the mountain—but a foothold, for all that. We had not much meat—there had been little time for hunting, beyond squirrel and rabbit, and those useful rodents had gone to their winter rest by now—but a fair amount of dried vegetables, from yams to squash to wild onions and garlic, plus a bushel or two of nuts, and the small stock of herbs I had managed to gather and dry. It made for a sparse diet, but with careful management, we could survive till spring.

With few chores to do outside, there was time to talk, to tell stories, and to dream. Between the useful objects like spoons and bowls, Jamie took time to carve the pieces of a wooden chess set, and spent a good deal of his time trying to inveigle me or Ian into playing with him.

Ian and Rollo, who both suffered badly from cabin fever, took to visiting Anna Ooka frequently, sometimes going on extended hunting trips with young men from the village, who were pleased to have the benefit of his and Rollo's company.

"The lad speaks the Indian tongue a great deal better than he does Greek or Latin," Jamie observed with some dourness, watching Ian exchanging cordial insults with an Indian companion as they left on one such excursion.

"Well, if Marcus Aurelius had written about tracking porcupines, I expect he'd have found a more eager audience," I replied soothingly.

Dearly as I loved Ian, I was myself not displeased by his frequent absence. There were definitely times when three was a crowd.

There is nothing more delightful in life than a feather bed and an open fire—except a feather bed with a warm and tender lover in it. When Ian was gone, we would not trouble with rushlights but would go to bed with the dark, and lie curled together in shared warmth, talking late into the night, laughing and telling stories, sharing our pasts, planning our future, and somewhere in the midst of the talking, pausing to enjoy the wordless pleasures of the present.

"Tell me about Brianna." These were Jamie's favorite stories; the tales of Brianna as a child. What she had said and worn and done; how she had looked, all her accomplishments and her tastes.

"Did I tell you about the time I was invited to her school, to talk about being a doctor?"

"No." He shifted to make himself more comfortable, rolling onto his side and fitting himself to my shape behind. "Why should you do that?"

"It was what they called Career Day; the schoolteachers invited a lot of people with different jobs to come and explain what they did, so the children would have some idea of what a lawyer does, for instance, or a firefighter—"

"I should think that one would be fairly obvious."

"Hush. Or a veterinarian—that's a doctor who treats animals— or a dentist, that's a special doctor who deals only with teeth—"

"With *teeth*? What can ye do to a tooth, besides pull it?"

"You'd be surprised." I brushed the hair out of my face and up off my neck. "Anyway, they'd always ask me to come, because it wasn't at all common for a woman to be a doctor then."

"Ye think it's common *now*?" He laughed, and I kicked him lightly in the shin.

"Well, it got more common rather soon after that. But at the time, it wasn't. And when I'd got done speaking and asked if there were any questions, an obnoxious little boy piped up and said that *his* mother said women who worked were no better than prostitutes, and they ought to be home minding their families, instead of taking jobs away from men."

"I shouldna think his mother can have met many prostitutes."

"No, I don't imagine. Nor all that many women with jobs, either. But when he said that, Brianna stood up and said in a very loud voice, 'Well, you'd better be glad my mama's a doctor, because you're going to *need* one!' Then she hit him on the head with her arithmetic book, and when he lost his balance and fell down, she jumped on his stomach and punched him in the mouth."

I could feel his chest and stomach quivering against my back.

"Oh, braw lassie! Did the schoolmaster not tawse her for it, though?"

"They don't beat children in school. She had to write a letter of apology to the little beast, but then, he had to write one to *me,* and she thought that was a fair exchange. The more embarrassing part was that it turned out his father was a doctor too; one of my colleagues at the hospital."

"I wouldna suppose you'd taken a job he'd wanted?"

"How did you guess?"

"Mmm." His breath was warm and ticklish on the back of my neck. I reached back and stroked the length of a long, hairy thigh, enjoying the hollow and swell of the muscle.

"Ye said she was at a university, and studying history, like Frank Randall. Did she never want to be a doctor, like you?" A large hand cupped my bottom and began to knead it gently.

"Oh, she did when she was little—I used to take her to the hospital now and then, and she was fascinated by all the equipment; she loved to play with my stethoscope and the otoscope—a thing you look in ears with—but then she changed her mind. She changed it a dozen times, at least; most children do."

"They do?" This was a novel thought to him. Most children of the time would simply adopt the professions of their parents—or perhaps be apprenticed to learn one chosen for them.

"Oh, yes. Let me see . . . she wanted to be a ballerina for a while, like most little girls. That's a dancer who dances on her toes," I explained, and he laughed in surprise. "Then she wanted to be a garbageman—that was after our garbageman gave her a ride in his truck—and then a deep-sea diver, and a mailman, and—"

"What in God's name is a deep-sea diver? Let alone a garbageman?"

By the time I had finished a brief catalog of twentieth-century occupations, we were facing each other, our legs twined comfortably together, and I was admiring the way his nipple stiffened to a tiny bump under the ball of my thumb.

"I never was sure whether she really wanted to read history, or whether she did it mostly to please Frank. She loved him so much —and he was so proud of her." I paused, thinking, as his hand played down the length of my back.

"She started taking history classes at the university when she was still in high school—I told you how the school system works? And then when Frank died . . . I rather think she went ahead with history because she thought he would have wanted it."

"That's loyal."

"Yes." I ran my hand up through his hair, feeling the solid, rounded bones of his skull, and his scalp under my fingers. "Can't think where she got that particular trait from."

He snorted briefly and gathered me closer.

"Can't you?" Without waiting for an answer, he went on, "If she goes on wi' the history—d'ye think she'll find us? Written down somewhere, I mean."

The thought had honestly not occurred to me, and for a moment I lay quite still. Then I stretched a bit, and laid my head on his shoulder with a small laugh, not altogether humorous.

"I shouldn't think so. Not unless we were to do something newsworthy." I gestured vaguely toward the cabin wall, and the endless wilderness outside. "Not much chance of that here, I don't imagine. And she'd have to be deliberately looking, in any case."

"Would she?"

I was silent for a moment, breathing the musky, deep scent of him.

"I hope not," I said quietly, at last. "She should have her own life—not spend her time looking back."

He didn't respond directly to this, but took my hand and eased it between us, sighing as I took hold of him.

"Ye're a verra intelligent woman, Sassenach, but shortsighted, forbye. Though perhaps it's only modesty."

"And what makes you say that?" I asked, mildly piqued.

"The lassie's loyal, ye said. She'll have loved her father enough to shape her life to do as he would have wanted, even after he's dead. D'ye think she loved you less?"

I turned my head, and let the piled hair fall down over my face.

"No," I said at last, voice muffled in the pillow.

"Well, then." He took me by the hips and turned me, rolling slowly on top of me. We didn't speak anymore, then, as the melting boundaries of our bodies disappeared.

It was slow, dreamy and peaceful, his body mine as much as mine was his, so that I curled my foot round his leg and felt both smooth sole and hairy shin, felt callused palm and tender flesh, was knife and sheath together, the rhythm of our movement that of one heart beating.

The fire crackled softly to itself, casting red and yellow highlights on the wooden walls of our snug refuge, and we lay in quiet peace, not bothering to sort out whose limbs were whose. On the very verge of sleep, I felt Jamie's breath, warm on my neck.

"She'll look," he said, with certainty.

There was a brief thaw two days later, and Jamie—suffering slightly from cabin fever himself—decided to take advantage of it to go hunting. There was still snow on the ground, but it was thin and patchy; the going would be easy enough on the slopes, he thought.

I wasn't so sure as I scooped snow into a basket for melting, later in the morning. The snow under the bushes still lay thick, though it had indeed melted on the exposed ground. I hoped he was right, though—our food supplies were low, and we had had no meat at all for more than a week; even the snares Jamie kept set had been buried under the snow.

I took my snow inside and tipped it into the large cauldron, feeling, as I always did, rather like a witch.

" 'Double, double, toil and trouble' " I muttered, watching the white clumps hiss and fade into the roiling liquid.

I had one large cauldron, filled with water, which bubbled constantly on the fire. This was not only the basic supply for washing but the means of cooking everything that could not be grilled, fried, or roasted. Stews and things to be boiled were put into hollow gourds or stoneware jars, sealed, and lowered on strings into the bubbling depths, to be hauled out at intervals for checking. By this means, I could cook an entire meal in the one pot, and have hot water for washing afterward.

I dumped a second basket of snow into a wooden bowl and left it to melt more slowly; drinking water for the day. Then, with nothing of great urgency to do, I sat down to read Daniel Rawlings's casebook and mend stockings, my toes comfortably toasting by the fire.

At first, I didn't worry when Jamie didn't come back. That is, I did worry—I always worried when he was gone for long—but in a small and secret way that I succeeded for the most part in hiding from myself. When the shadows on the snow turned violet with the sinking sun, though, I began to listen for him with an increasing intensity.

I went about my work in constant expectation of the crunch of his footsteps, listening for a shout, ready to run out and lend a hand if he had brought back a turkey for plucking or some more or less edible thing in need of cleaning. I fed and watered the mules and horses, looking always up the mountain. As the afternoon light died around me, though, the expectation faded into hope.

It was growing chilly in the cabin, and I went out for more wood. It couldn't be much past four o'clock, I thought, and yet the shadows under the huckleberry bushes were already cold and blue. Another hour, and it would be dusk; it would be full dark in two.

The woodpile was dusted with snow, the outer logs damp. By pulling a chunk of hickory from the side, though, I could reach inside and extract dry splits—being always mindful of snakes, skunks, and anything else that might have sought shelter in the hollow thus provided.

I sniffed, then bent and peered cautiously inside, and as a final precaution poked a long stick inside and stirred it briefly round. Hearing no scuffles, slitherings, or other sounds of alarm, I reached inside with confidence, and groped until my fingers encountered the deep-ridged grain of a chunk of fat pine. I wanted a hot, quick-burning fire tonight; after a full day spent hunting in snow, Jamie would be chilled through.

Fat pine for the heart of the fire, then, and three small chunks of slower-burning hickory from the wet outer layer of the woodpile. I could stack those inside the hearth to dry, while I finished the supper making; then when we went to bed, I'd smoor the fire with the damp hickory, which would burn more slowly, smoldering till morning.

The shadows went to indigo and faded into the gray winter dusk. The sky was lavender with thick cloud; snow clouds. I could breathe the cold wetness in the air; when the temperature fell after dark, so would the snow.

"Bloody man," I said aloud. "What have you done, shot a moose?" My voice sounded small in the muffled air, but the thought made me feel better. If he had in fact bagged something large near the end of the day, he might well have chosen to camp by the carcass; butchering a large animal was exhausting, lengthy work, and meat was too hard come by to leave it to the mercies of predators.

My vegetable stew was bubbling, and the cabin was filled with the savory scent of onions and wild garlic, but I had no appetite. I pushed the kettle on its hook to the back of the hearth—easy enough to heat again when he came. A tiny flash of green caught

my eye, and I stooped to look. A tiny salamander, frightened out
of its winter refuge in a crack of the wood.

It was green and black, vivid as a tiny jewel; I scooped him up
before he could panic and run into the fire, and carried the damp
little thing outside, wriggling madly against my palm. I put him
back in the woodpile, safely near the bottom.

"Watch out," I said to him, "you might not be so lucky next
time!"

I paused before going back inside. It had gone dark now, but I
could still make out the trunks of the trees around the clearing,
chalk and gray against the looming black bulk of the mountain
beyond. Nothing stirred among the trees, but a few fat wet flakes
of snow began to fall from the soft pink sky, melting at once on
the bare ground of the dooryard.

I barred the door, ate some supper without tasting it, smoored
the fire with damp hickory, and lay down to sleep. He might have
met some men from Anna Ooka and be camped with them.

The scent of hickory smoke floated in the air, wisps of white
curling up over the hearth. The beams above were already black
with soot, though fires had burned here for no more than two
months now. Fresh resin still oozed from the timber by my head,
in small gold droplets that glowed like honey and smelled of
turpentine, sharp and clean. The ax strokes in the wood showed in
the firelight, and I had a sudden, vivid memory of Jamie's broad
back, sheened with sweat as he swung the ax, over and over in
strokes like clockwork, the ax blade coming down in a flash of
metal inches from his foot as he worked his way along the
squared rough timber.

It was awfully easy to misjudge the stroke of an ax or hatchet.
He might have cut wood for his fire and missed his stroke, caught
an arm or leg. My imagination, always eager to help out, promptly
supplied a crystal-clear vision of arterial blood spurting onto
white snow in a crimson spray.

I flounced over onto my side. He knew how to live outdoors.
He'd spent seven years in a cave, for heaven's sake!

In Scotland, said my imagination, cynically. Where the biggest
carnivore was a wildcat the size of a house cat. Where the biggest
human threat was English soldiers.

"Fiddlesticks!" I said, and rolled onto my back. "He's a
grown man and he's armed to the teeth and he certainly knows
what to do if it's snowing!"

What *would* he do? I wondered. Find or make shelter, I supposed. I recalled the crude lean-to he'd built for us when we first camped on the ridge, and felt a little reassured. If he hadn't hurt himself, he probably wouldn't freeze to death.

If he hadn't hurt himself. If something else hadn't hurt him. The bears were presumably fat and fast asleep, but the wolves still hunted in winter, and the catamounts; I recalled the one I had met by the stream, and shivered in spite of the feather bed.

I rolled onto my stomach, the quilts drawn up around my shoulders. It was warm in the cabin, warmer in the bed, but my hands and feet were still icy. I longed for Jamie, in a visceral way that had nothing to do with thought or reason. To be alone with Jamie was bliss, adventure, and absorption. To be alone without him was . . . to be alone.

I could hear the whisper of snow against the oiled hide that covered the window near my head. If it kept up, his tracks would be covered by morning. And if anything *had* happened to him . . .

I flung back the quilts and got up. I dressed quickly, without thinking too much about what I was doing; I'd thought too much already. I put on my woolen cutty sark for insulation beneath my buckskins, and two pairs of stockings. I thanked God that my boots were freshly greased with otter fat; they smelt very fishy, but would keep the damp out for a good while.

He had taken the hatchet; I had to split another piece of fat pine with a mallet and wedge, cursing my slowness as I did so. Having now decided on action, every small delay seemed an unbearable irritation. The long-grained wood split easily, though; I had five decent faggots, four of which I bound with a leather strap. I thrust the end of the fifth deep into the smoky embers of the fire, and waited till the end was well caught.

Then I tied a small medicine bag about my waist, checked to be sure I had the pouch of flints and kindling, put on my cloak, took up my bundle and my torch, and set out into the falling snow.

It was not as cold as I had feared; once I began moving, I was quite warm inside my wrappings. It was very quiet; there was no wind, and the whisper of the snowfall drowned all the usual noises of the night.

He had meant to walk his trapline, that much I knew. If he came across promising sign en route, though, he would have followed it. The previous snow lay thin and patchy on the ground, but the earth was soaked, and Jamie was a big man; I was fairly sure I could follow his track, if I came across it. And if I came across *him,* denned up for the night near his kill, so much the better. Two slept much better than one in the cold.

Past the bare chestnuts that ringed our clearing to the west, I turned uphill. I had no great sense of direction, but could certainly tell up from down. Jamie had also carefully taught me to navigate using large, immutable landmarks. I glanced toward the falls, their white cascade no more than a blur in the distance. I couldn't hear them; what wind there was must be away from me.

"When you're hunting, ye want the wind toward ye," Jamie had explained. "So the stag or the hare wilna scent ye."

I wondered uncomfortably what might be out in the dark, scenting *me* on the snowborne air. I wasn't armed, save for my torch. The light glittered red on the crust of packed snow, and shattered from the ice that coated every twig. If I got within a quarter-mile of him, he'd see me.

The first snare was set in a small dell no more than two hundred yards uphill from the cabin, amid a grove of spruce and hemlock. I had been with him when he set it, but that had been in daylight; even with the torch, everything looked strange and unfamiliar by night.

I cast to and fro, bending close to bring my light near the ground. It took several journeys back and forth across the little dell before I finally spotted what I was looking for—the dark indentation of a foot in a patch of snow between two spruce trees. A little more looking and I found the snare, still set. Either it had caught nothing, or he had removed the catch and reset it.

The footprints led out of the clearing and upward again, then disappeared in a bare patch of matted dead leaves. A moment's panic as I crisscrossed the patch, looking for a scuffled place that might be a footprint. Nothing showed; the leaves must be a foot thick here, spongy and resilient. But there! Yes, there was a log overturned; I could see the dark, wet furrow where it had lain, and the scuffed moss on its side. Ian had told me that squirrels and chipmunks sometimes hibernated in the cavities under logs.

Very slowly, constantly losing the trail and having to circle and backtrack to find it again, I followed him from one snare to another. The snow was falling thicker and faster, and I felt some uneasiness. If it covered his tracks before I found him, how would I find my way back to the cabin?

I looked back, but could see nothing behind me but a long, treacherous slope of unbroken snow that fell to the dark line of an unfamiliar brook below, its rocks poking up like teeth. No sign of

the cheerful plume of smoke and sparks from our chimney. I
turned slowly round in a circle, but I could no longer see the falls,
either.

"Fine," I muttered to myself. "You're lost. *Now* what?" I
sternly quelled an incipient attack of panic, and stood still to
think. I wasn't totally lost. I didn't know where I was, but that
wasn't quite the same thing. I still had Jamie's trail to guide me—
or would have, until the snow covered it. And if I could find him,
he presumably could find the cabin.

My torch was burning dangerously low; I could feel the heat of
it, blistering on my hand. I extracted another of the dry faggots
from under my cloak, and lit it from the stub of the first, dropping
the ember just before it burned my fingers.

Was I going farther from the cabin, I wondered, or walking
parallel to it? I knew that the trapline described a rough circle, but
had no idea precisely how many snares there were. I had found
three so far, all empty and waiting.

The fourth one wasn't empty. My torch caught the glitter of ice
crystals, fringing the fur of a large hare, stretched out under a
frozen bush. I touched it, picked it up and disentangled the noose
from its neck. It was stiff, whether from cold or rigor mortis. Been
dead a while, then—and what did that tell me about Jamie's
whereabouts?

I tried to think logically, ignoring the increasing cold seeping
through my boots and the growing numbness of face and fingers.
The hare lay in snow; I could see the indentations of its pawprints,
and the flurry of its death struggle. I couldn't see any of Jamie's
footprints, though. All right; he hadn't visited this snare, then.

I stood still, my breath forming small white clouds around my
head. I could feel ice forming inside my nostrils; it was getting
colder. Somewhere between the last snare and this one, he had left
his path, then. Where? And where had he gone?

Urgently, I backtracked, looking for the last footprint I was sure
of. It took a long time to find; the snow had nearly covered all the
bare ground with a thin dusting of glitter. My second torch was
half burned through before I found it again. There it was, a featureless blur in the mud on the edge of a stream. I had found the
snare with the rabbit only by going in the direction I thought this
footprint pointed—but evidently it didn't. He had stepped out of
the mud, and gone . . . where?

"Jamie!" I shouted. I called several times, but the snow

seemed to swallow my voice. I listened, but heard nothing save the gurgle of the ice-rimmed water by my feet.

He wasn't behind me, he wasn't in front of me. Left, then, or right?

"Eeny, meeny, miney, mo," I muttered, and turned downhill because the walking was easier, shouting now and then.

I stopped to listen. Was there an answering shout? I called again, but couldn't make out a reply. The wind was coming up, rattling the tree limbs overhead.

I took another step, landed on an icy rock, and my foot slid out from under me. I slipped and skidded, floundering down a short, muddy slope, hit a screen of dog-hobble, burst through and clutched a handful of icy twigs, heart pounding.

At my feet was the edge of a rocky outcrop, ending in thin air. Clinging to the bush to keep from slipping, I edged my way closer, and looked over.

It was not a cliff, as I'd thought; the drop was no more than five feet. It was not this that made my heart leap into my throat, though, but rather the sight that met my eyes in the leaf-filled hollow below.

There was a flurry of tossed and scuffled leaves, reminding me unpleasantly of the death marks left by the limp rabbit that hung at my belt. Something large had struggled on the ground here—and then been dragged away. A wide furrow plowed through the leaves, disappearing into the darkness beyond.

Heedless of my footing, I scrabbled my way down the side of the outcrop and rushed toward the furrow, following it under the overhanging low branches of hemlock and balsam. In the uncertain light of my flickering torch, I followed its path around a pile of rocks, through a clump of wintergreen, and . . .

He was lying near the foot of a large split boulder, half covered in leaves, as though something had tried to bury him. He wasn't curled for warmth, but lay flat on his face, and deathly still. The snow lay thick on the folds of his cloak, dusted the heels of his muddy boots.

I dropped my torch and flung myself on his body with a cry of horror.

He let out a bloodcurdling groan and convulsed under me. I jerked back, torn between relief and terror. He wasn't dead, but he *was* hurt. Where, how badly?

"Where?" I demanded, wrenching at his cloak, which was tangled round his body. "Where are you hurt? Are you bleeding, have you broken something?"

I couldn't see any large patches of blood, but I had dropped my torch, which had promptly extinguished itself in the wet leaves that covered him. The pink sky and falling snow shed a luminous glow over everything, but the light was much too dim to make out details.

He was frighteningly cold; his flesh felt chilly even to my snow-numbed hands, and he stirred sluggishly, subsiding into small moans and grunts. I thought I heard him mumble, "Back," though, and once I got his cloak out of the way, I tore at his shirt, yanking it ruthlessly out of his breeks.

This made him groan loudly, and I thrust my hands under the cloth in a panic, looking for the bullet hole. He must have been shot in the back; the entrance wound wouldn't bleed much, but where had it come out? Had the ball gone clean through? A small piece of my mind found leisure to wonder who'd shot him, and whether they were still nearby.

Nothing. I found nothing; my groping hands encountered nothing but bare, clean flesh; cold as a slab of marble and webbed with old scars, but completely unperforated. I tried again, forcing myself to slow down, feeling with mind as well as fingers, running my palms slowly over his back from nape to small. Nothing.

Lower? There were dark smudges on the seat of his breeks; I'd thought them mud. I thrust a hand under him and groped for his laces, jerked them loose and yanked down his breeches.

It *was* mud; his buttocks glowed before me, white, firm, and perfect in their roundness, unmarred beneath a silver fuzz. I clutched a handful of his flesh, unbelieving.

"Is that you, Sassenach?" he asked, rather drowsily.

"Yes, it's me! What happened to you?" I demanded, frenzy giving way to indignation. "You said you'd been shot in the back!"

"No, I didn't. I couldna, for I haven't been," he pointed out logically. He sounded calm and still rather sleepy, his speech slightly slurred. "There's a verra cold wind whistlin' up my backside, Sassenach; d'ye think ye could maybe cover me?"

I jerked up his breeches, making him grunt again.

"What the hell is the matter with you?" I said.

He was waking up a bit; he twisted his head to look round at me, moving laboriously.

"Aye, well. No real matter. It's only that I canna move much."
I stared at him.

"Why not? Have you twisted your foot? Broken your leg?"

"Ah . . . no." He sounded a trifle sheepish. "I . . . ah . . .
I've put my back out of joint."

"You *what*?"

"I've done it once before," he assured me. "It doesna last
more than a day or two."

"I suppose it didn't occur to you that *you* wouldn't last more
than a day or two, lying out here on the ground, covered with
snow?"

"It did," he said, still drowsy, "but there didna seem much I
could do about it."

It was rapidly dawning on me that there might not be that much
I could do about it, either. He outweighed me by a good sixty
pounds; I couldn't carry him. I couldn't even drag him very far
over slopes and rocks and gullies. It was too steep for a horse; I
might possibly persuade one of the mules to come up here—if I
could first find my way back to the cabin in the dark, and then find
my way back up the mountain, also in the dark—and in the middle of what looked like becoming a blizzard. Or perhaps I could
build a toboggan of tree branches, I thought wildly, and career
down the snowy slopes astride his body.

"Oh, do get a grip, Beauchamp," I said aloud. I wiped at my
running nose with a fold of cloak, and tried to think what to do
next.

It was a sheltered spot, I realized; looking upward, I could see
the snowflakes whirling past the top of the big rock at whose foot
we crouched, but there was no wind where we sat, and only a few
heavy flakes floated down onto my upturned face.

Jamie's hair and shoulders were lightly dusted with snow, and
flakes were settling on the exposed backs of his legs. I pulled the
hem of his cloak down, then brushed the snow away from his
face. His cheek was nearly the same color as the big wet flakes,
and his flesh felt stiff when I touched it.

Fresh alarm surged through me as I realized that he might be a
lot closer to freezing already than I had thought. His eyes were
half closed, and cold as it was, he didn't seem to be shivering
much. That was *bloody* dangerous; with no movement, his muscles were generating no heat, and what warmth he had was leaching slowly from his body. His cloak was already heavy with

damp; if I allowed his clothes to become soaked through, he might very well die of hypothermia right in front of me.

"Wake up!" I said, shaking him urgently by the shoulder. He opened his eyes and smiled drowsily at me.

"Move!" I said. "Jamie, you've got to move!"

"I can't," he said calmly. "I told ye that." He shut his eyes again.

I grabbed him by the ear and dug my fingernails into the tender lobe. He grunted and jerked his head away.

"Wake up," I said peremptorily. "Do you hear me? Wake up this moment! Move, damn you! Give me your hand."

I didn't wait for him to comply, but dug under the cloak and seized his hand, which I chafed madly between my own. He opened his eyes again and frowned at me.

"I'm all right," he said. "But I'm gey tired, aye?"

"Move your arms," I ordered, flinging the hand at him. "Flap them, up and down. Can you move your legs at all?"

He sighed wearily, as though dragging himself out of a sticky bog, and muttered something under his breath in Gaelic, but very slowly he began to move his arms back and forth. With more prodding, he succeeded in flexing his ankles—though any further movement caused instant spasms in his back—and with great reluctance, began to waggle his feet.

He looked rather like a frog trying to fly, but I wasn't in any mood to laugh. I didn't know whether he was actually in danger of freezing or not, but I wasn't taking any chances. By dint of constant exhortation, aided by judicious pokings, I kept him at this exercise until I had got him altogether awake and shivering. In a thoroughly bad temper, too, but I didn't mind that.

"Keep moving," I advised him. I got up with some difficulty, having grown quite stiff from crouching over him so long. "Move, I say!" I added sharply, as he showed symptoms of flagging. "Stop and I'll step square on your back, I swear I will!"

I glanced around, a little blearily. The snow was still falling, and it was difficult to see more than a few feet. We needed shelter —more than the rock alone could provide.

"Hemlock," he said between his teeth. I glanced down at him, and he jerked his head toward a clump of trees nearby. "Take the hatchet. Big . . . branches. Six feet. C-cut four." He was breathing heavily, and there was a tinge of color visible in his face, despite the dim light. He'd stopped moving in spite of my threats, but his teeth were clenched because they were chattering; a sign I rejoiced to see.

I stooped and groped beneath his cloak again, this time searching for the hatchet belted round his waist. I couldn't resist sliding a hand under him, inside the neck of his fringed woolen hunting shirt. Warm! Thank God, he was still warm; his chest felt superficially chilled from its contact with the wet ground, but it was still warmer than my fingers.

"Right," I said, taking my hand away and standing up with the hatchet. "Hemlock. Six-foot branches, do you mean?"

He nodded, shivering violently, and I set off at once for the trees he indicated.

Inside the silent grove, the fragrance of hemlock and cedar enfolded me at once in a mist of resins and turpenes, the odor cold and sharp, clean and invigorating. Many of the trees were enormous, with the lower branches well above my head, but there were smaller ones scattered here and there. I saw at once the virtues of this particular tree—no snow fell under them; the fanlike boughs caught the falling snow like umbrellas.

I hacked at the lower branches, torn between the need for haste and the very real fear of chopping off a few fingers by accident; my hands were numb and awkward with the cold.

The wood was green and elastic and it took forever to chop through the tough, springy fibers. At last, though, I had four good-sized branches, sporting multiple fans of dense needles. They looked soft and black against the new snow, like big fans of feathers; it was almost a surprise to touch them and feel the hard, cold prick of the needles.

I dragged them back to the rock, and found that Jamie had managed to scoop more leaves together; he was almost invisible, submerged in a huge drift of black and gray against the foot of the rock.

Under his terse direction I leaned the hemlock branches fan-up against the face of the rock, the chopped butt ends stuck into the earth at an angle, so as to form a small triangular refuge underneath. Then I took the hatchet again and chopped small pine and spruce branches, pulled up big clumps of dried grass, and piled it all against and over the hemlock screen. Then at last, panting with exertion, I crawled into the shelter beside him.

I nestled down in the leaves between his body and the rock, wrapped my cloak around both of us, put my arms around his body, and held on hard. Then I found the leisure to shake a bit. Not from cold—not yet—but from a mixture of relief and fear.

He felt me shivering, and reached awkwardly back to pat me in reassurance.

"It will be all right, Sassenach," he said. "With the two of us, it will be all right."

"I know," I said, and put my forehead against his shoulder blade. It was a long time before I stopped shaking, though.

"How long have you been out here?" I asked finally. "On the ground, I mean?"

He started to shrug, then stopped abruptly, groaning.

"A good time. It was just past noon when I jumped off a wee crop of rock. It wasna more than a few feet high, but when I landed on one foot, my back went click! and next I knew, I was on my face in the dirt, feelin' as though someone had stabbed me in the spine wi' a dirk."

It wasn't warm in our snug, by any means; the damp from the leaves was seeping in and the rock at my back seemed to radiate coldness, like some sort of reverse furnace. Still, it was noticeably less cold than it was outside. I began shivering again, for purely physical reasons.

Jamie felt me, and groped at his throat.

"Can ye get my cloak unfastened, Sassenach? Put it over ye."

It took some maneuvering, and the cost of a few muffled oaths from Jamie as he tried to shift his weight, but I got it loose at last, and spread it over the two of us. I reached down and laid a cautious hand on his back, gently rucking up his shirt to put my hand on cool, bare flesh.

"Tell me where it hurts," I said. I hoped to hell he hadn't slipped a disc; hideous thoughts of his being permanently crippled raced through my mind, along with pragmatic considerations of how I was to get him off the mountain, even if he wasn't. Would I have to leave him here, and fetch food up to him daily until he recovered?

"Right there," he said, with a hiss of indrawn breath. "Aye, that's it. A wicked stab just there, and if I move, it runs straight down the back o' my leg, like a red-hot wire."

I felt very carefully, with both hands now, probing and pressing, urging him to try to lift one leg, right, now the other knee . . . no?

"No," he assured me. "Dinna be worrit, though, Sassenach. It's the same as before. It gets better."

"Yes, you said it happened before. When was that?"

He stirred briefly and settled, pressing back against my palms with a small groan.

"Och! Damn, that hurts. At the prison."

"Pain in the same place?"

"Aye."

I could feel a hard knot in the muscle on his right side, just below the kidney, and a bunching in the erector spinae, the long muscles near the spine. From his description of the prior occurrence, I was fairly sure it was only severe muscle spasm. For which the proper prescription was warmth, rest, and anti-inflammatory medication.

Couldn't get much further away from those conditions, I thought with some grimness.

"I suppose I could try acupuncture," I said, thinking aloud. "I've got Mr. Willoughby's needles in my pouch, and—"

"Sassenach," he said, in measured tones. "I can stand fine bein' hurt, cold, and hungry. I wilna put up wi' being stabbed in the back by my own wife. Can ye not offer a bit of sympathy and comfort instead?"

I laughed, and slid an arm around him, pressing close against his back. I let my hand slide down and rest in delicate suggestion, well below his navel.

"Er . . . what sort of comfort did you have in mind?"

He hastily grasped my hand, to prevent further intrusions.

"Not that," he said.

"Might take your mind off the pain." I wiggled my fingers invitingly, and he tightened his grip.

"I daresay," he said dryly. "Well, I'll tell ye, Sassenach; once we've got home, and I've a warm bed to lie in and a hot supper in my belly, that notion might have a good bit of appeal. As it is, the thought of—for Christ's sake, have ye not the slightest idea how cold your hands are, woman?"

I laid my cheek against his back and laughed. I could feel the quiver of his own mirth, though he couldn't laugh aloud without hurting his back.

At last we lay silent, listening to the whisper of falling snow. It was dark under the hemlock boughs, but my eyes were adapted enough to be able to see patches of the oddly glowing snow-light through the screen of needles overhead. Tiny flakes came through the open patches; I could see it in some places, as a thin cloud of white mist, and I could feel the cold tingle as it struck my face.

Jamie himself was no more than a humped dark shape in front of me, though as my eyes became accustomed to the murk, I could see the paler stalk where his neck emerged between his shirt and his queued hair. The queue itself lay cool and smooth against my face; by turning my head only a bit, I could brush it with my lips.

"What time do you think it is?" I asked. I had no idea, myself; I had left the house well after dark, and spent what seemed an eternity looking for him on the mountain.

"Late," he said. "It will be a long time before the dawn, though," he added, answering my real question. "It's just past the solstice, aye? It's one of the longest nights of the year."

"Oh, lovely," I said, in dismay. I wasn't warm, by any means —I still couldn't feel my toes—but I had stopped shivering. A dreadful lethargy was stealing over me, my muscles yielding to fatigue and cold. I had visions of the two of us freezing peacefully together, curled up like hedgehogs in the leaves. They did say it was a comfortable death, but that didn't make the prospect any more appealing.

Jamie's breathing was getting slower and deeper.

"Don't go to sleep!" I said urgently, poking him in the armpit.

"Agh!" He pressed his arm tight to his side, recoiling. "Why not?"

"We mustn't sleep; we'll freeze to death."

"No, we won't," he said crossly. "It's snowing outside; we'll be covered over soon."

"I know that," I said, rather cross in my turn. "What's that got to do with it?"

He tried to turn his head to look at me, but couldn't, quite.

"Snow's cold if ye touch it," he explained, striving for patience, "but it keeps the cold out, aye? Like a blanket. It's a great deal warmer in a house that's covered wi' snow than one that's standing clean in the wind. How d'ye think bears manage? They sleep in the winter, and they dinna freeze."

"They have layers of fat," I protested. "I thought that kept them warm."

"Ha ha," he said, and reaching back with some effort, grabbed me firmly by the bottom. "Well, then, ye needna worry a bit, eh?"

With great deliberation I pulled down his collar, stretched my head up, and licked the back of his neck, in a lingering swipe from nape to hairline.

"Aaah!" He shuddered violently, making a sprinkle of snow fall from the branches above us. He let go of my bottom to scrub at the back of his neck.

"That was a *terrible* thing to do!" he said, reproachful. "And me lyin' here helpless as a log!"

"Bah, humbug," I said. I nestled closer, feeling somewhat reassured. "You're sure we aren't going to freeze to death, then?"

"No," he said. "But I shouldna think it likely."

"Hm," I said, feeling somewhat less reassured. "Well, perhaps we'd better stay awake for a bit, then, just in case?"

"I wilna wave my arms about anymore," he said definitely. "There's no room. And if ye stick your icy wee paws in my breeks, I swear I'll throttle ye, bad back or no."

"All right, all right," I said. "What if I tell you a story, instead?"

Highlanders loved stories, and Jamie was no exception.

"Oh, aye," he said, sounding much happier. "What sort of story is it?"

"A Christmas story," I said, settling myself along the curve of his body. "About a miser named Ebenezer Scrooge."

"An Englishman, I daresay?"

"Yes," I said. "Be quiet and listen."

I could see my own breath as I talked, white in the dim, cold air. The snow was falling heavily outside our shelter; when I paused in the story, I could hear the whisper of flakes against the hemlock branches, and the far-off whine of wind in the trees.

I knew the story very well; it had been part of our Christmas ritual, Frank's and Brianna's and mine. From the time Bree was five or six, we had read *A Christmas Carol* every year, starting a week or two before Christmas, Frank and I taking it in turns to read to her each night before bed.

"And the specter said, 'I am the Ghost of Christmas Past . . .' "

I might not be freezing to death, but the cold had a strange, hypnotic effect nonetheless. I had gone past the phase of acute discomfort and felt now slightly disembodied. I knew my hands and feet were icy, and my body chilled half through, but it didn't seem to matter anymore. I floated in a peaceful white mist, seeing the words swirl round my head like snowflakes as I spoke them.

". . . and there was dear old Fezziwig, among the lights and music . . ."

I couldn't tell whether I was gradually thawing or becoming

colder. I was conscious of an overall feeling of relaxation, and an altogether peculiar sense of déjà vu, as though I had once before been entombed, insulated in snow, snug despite desolation outside.

As Bob Cratchit bought his meager bird, I remembered. I went on talking automatically, the flow of the story coming from somewhere well below the level of consciousness, but my memory was in the front seat of a stalled 1956 Oldsmobile, its windscreen caked with snow.

We had been on our way to visit an elderly relative of Frank's, somewhere in upstate New York. The snow came on hard, halfway there, howling down across the icy roads with gusts of wind. Before we knew where we were, we had skidded off the road and halfway into a ditch, the windscreen wipers slashing futilely at the pelting snow.

There was nothing to be done but wait for morning, and rescue. We had had a picnic hamper and some old blankets; we brought Brianna up into the front seat between us, and huddled all together under coats and blankets, sipping lukewarm cocoa from the thermos and making jokes to keep her from being frightened.

As it grew later, and colder, we huddled closer, and to distract Brianna, Frank began to tell her Dickens's story from memory, counting on me to supply the missing bits. Neither of us could have done it alone, but between us, we managed well. By the time the sinister Ghost of Christmas Yet to Come had made his appearance, Brianna was snuggled sound asleep under the coats, a warm, boneless weight against my side.

There was no need to finish the story, but we did, talking to each other below the words, hands touching below the layers of blankets. I remembered Frank's hands, warm and strong on mine, thumb stroking my palm, outlining my fingers. Frank had always loved my hands.

The car had filled with the mist of our breathing, and drops of water ran down inside the white-choked windows. Frank's head had been a dark cameo, dim against the white. He had leaned toward me at the last, nose and cheeks chilled, lips warm on mine as he whispered the last words of the story.

" 'God bless us, every one,' " I ended, and lay silent, a small needle of grief like an ice splinter through my heart. It was quiet inside the shelter, and seemed darker; snow had covered over all the openings.

Jamie reached back and touched my leg.

"Put your hands inside my shirt, Sassenach," he said softly. I slid one hand up under his shirt in front, to rest against his chest, the other up his back. The faded whip marks felt like threads under his skin.

He laid his hand against mine, pressing it tight against his chest. He was very warm, and his heart beat slow and strong under my fingers.

"Sleep, *a nighean donn,*" he said. "I wilna let ye freeze."

I woke abruptly from a chilly doze, with Jamie's hand squeezing my thigh.

"Hush," he said softly. Our tiny shelter was still dim, but the quality of the light had changed. It was morning; we were covered over with a thick blanket of snow that blocked the daylight, but the faint otherworldly quality of the night's darkness had vanished.

The silence had vanished, too. Sounds from outside were muffled, but audible. I heard what Jamie had heard—a faint echo of voices—and jerked up in excitement.

"Hush!" he said again, in a fierce whisper, and squeezed my leg harder.

The voices were drawing closer, and it became almost possible to pick out words. Almost. Strain as I might, I could make no sense of what was being said. Then I realized that it was because they were not speaking any language I recognized.

Indians. It was an Indian tongue. But I thought the language was not Tuscarora, even though I couldn't yet make out words; the rise and fall was similar, but the rhythm was somehow different. I brushed the hair out of my eyes, feeling torn in two directions.

Here was the help we so badly needed—by the sound of it, there were several men in the party, enough to move Jamie safely. On the other hand, did we really want to attract the attention of a band of unfamiliar Indians who might be raiders?

Rather plainly we didn't, judging from Jamie's attitude. He had managed to lift himself on one elbow, and he had his knife drawn, ready in his right hand. He scratched his stubbled chin absently with the point as he tilted his head to listen more intently to the approaching voices.

A clump of snow fell from the framework of our cage, landing on my head with a little *plop!* and making me start. The movement loosened more snow, which poured inward in a glittering cascade, dusting Jamie's head and shoulders with fine white powder.

His fingers were gripping my leg hard enough to leave bruises, but I didn't move or make a sound. A patch of snow had fallen from the latticework of hemlock branches, leaving numerous small spaces through which I could see out between the needles, peering over Jamie's shoulder.

The ground sloped a little away from us, falling a few feet to the level of the grove where I had cut branches the night before. Everything was thick with snow; a good four inches must have fallen during the night. It was just past dawn, and the rising sun painted the black trees with coruscations of red and gold, striking white glare from the icy sweep of snow below. The wind had come up in the wake of the storm; loose snow blew off the branches in drifting clouds, like smoke.

The Indians were on the other side of the grove; I could hear the voices plainly now; arguing about something, from the sound of it. A sudden thought raised gooseflesh on my arms; if they came through the grove, they might see the hacked branches where I had chopped limbs from the hemlocks. I hadn't been neat; there would be needles and bits of bark scattered all over the ground. Would enough snow have trickled through the branches to cover my awkward spoor?

A flash of movement showed in the trees, then another, and suddenly they were there, materializing out of the hemlock grove like dragon's teeth sprung from the snow.

They were dressed for winter travel, in fur and leather, some with cloaks or cloth coats atop their leggings and soft boots. They all carried bundles of blankets and provisions, had headpieces made of fur, and most had snowshoes slung across their shoulders; evidently the snow here was not deep enough to render them necessary.

They were armed; I could see a few muskets, and tomahawks or war clubs hung at every belt. Six, seven, eight . . . I counted silently as they came out of the trees in single file, each man treading in the prints of the one before him. One near the back called out something, half laughing, and a man near the front replied over his shoulder, his words lost in the blowing veil of snow and wind.

I drew a deep breath. I could smell Jamie's scent, a sharp tinge of fresh sweat above his normal musky sleep-smell. I was sweating, too, in spite of the cold. Did they have dogs? Could they sniff us out, hidden as we were beneath the sharp reek of spruce and hemlock?

Then I realized that the wind must be toward us, carrying the sound of their voices. No, even dogs wouldn't scent us. But would they see the branches that framed our den? Even as I wondered this, a large patch of snow slid off with a rush, landing with a soft *flump!* outside.

Jamie drew in his breath sharply, and I leaned over his shoulder, staring. The last man had come out of the gap in the trees, an arm across his face to shield it from the blowing snow.

He was a Jesuit. He wore a short cape of bearskin over his habit, leather leggings and moccasins under it—but he had black skirts, kilted up for walking in the snow, and a wide, flat black priest's hat, held on with one hand against the wind. His face, when he showed it, was blond-bearded, and so fair-skinned that I could see the redness of his cheeks and nose even at such a distance.

"Call them!" I whispered, leaning close to Jamie's ear. "They're Christians, they must be, to have a priest with them. They won't hurt us."

He shook his head slowly, not taking his eyes off the file of men, now vanishing from our view behind a snow-topped outcropping.

"No," he said, half under his breath. "No. Christians they may be, but . . ." He shook his head again, more decidedly. "No."

There was no use arguing with him. I rolled my eyes in mingled frustration and resignation.

"How's your back?"

He stretched gingerly, and halted abruptly in mid-motion, with a strangled cry as though he'd been skewered.

"Not so good, hm?" I said, sympathy well laced with sarcasm. He gave me a dirty look, eased himself very slowly back into his bed of crushed leaves, and shut his eyes with a sigh.

"You have of course thought of some ingenious way of getting down the mountain, I imagine?" I said politely.

He opened one eye.

"No," he said, and shut it again. He breathed quietly, his chest rising and falling gently under his fringed hunting shirt, giving a brilliant impression of a man with nothing on his mind but his hair.

It was a cold day, but a bright one, and the sun was jabbing brilliant fingers of light into our erstwhile sanctum, making little blobs of snow drop like falling sugarplums around us. I scooped up one of these and gently decanted it into the neck of his shirt.

He drew in his breath through his teeth with a sharp hiss, opened his eyes, and regarded me coldly.

"I was thinking," he informed me.

"Oh. Sorry to interrupt, then." I eased myself down beside him, pulling the tangled cloaks up over us. The wind was beginning to lace through the holes in our shelter, and it occurred to me that he'd been quite right about the sheltering effects of snow. Only there wasn't going to be any snow falling tonight, I didn't think.

Then there was the little matter of food to be considered. My stomach had been making subdued protests for some time, and Jamie's now voiced its much louder objections. He squinted censoriously down his long, straight nose at the offender.

"Hush," he said reprovingly in Gaelic, and cast his eyes upward. At last he sighed and looked at me.

"Well, then," he said. "Ye'd best wait a bit, to be sure yon savages are well away. Then ye'll go down to the cabin—"

"I don't know where it is."

He made a small noise of exasperation.

"How did ye find me?"

"Tracked you," I said, with a certain amount of pride. I glanced through the needles at the blowing wilderness outside. "I don't suppose I can do it in reverse, though."

"Oh." He looked mildly impressed. "Well, that was verra resourceful of ye, Sassenach. Dinna worry, though; I can tell ye how to go, to find your way back."

"Right. And then what?"

He shrugged one shoulder. The bit of snow had melted, running down his chest, dampening his shirt and leaving a tiny pool of clear water standing in the hollow of his throat.

"Bring me back a bit of food, and a blanket. I should be able to move in a few days."

"Leave you *here*?" I glared at him, my turn to be exasperated.

"I'll be all right," he said mildly.

"You'll be eaten by wolves!"

"Oh, I shouldna think so," he said casually. "They'll be busy with the elk, most likely."

"What elk?"

He nodded toward the hemlock grove.

"The one I shot yesterday. I took it in the neck, but the shot didna quite kill it at once. It ran through there. I was following it, when I hurt myself." He rubbed a hand over the copper and silver bristles on his chin.

"I canna think it went far. I suppose the snow must have covered the carcass, else our wee friends would have seen it, coming from that direction."

"So you've shot an elk, which is going to draw wolves like flies, and you propose to lie here in the freezing cold waiting for them? I suppose you think by the time they get round to the second course, you'll be so numb you won't notice when they start gnawing on your feet?"

"Don't shout," he said. "The savages might not be so far away, yet."

I was drawing breath for further remarks on the subject, when he stopped me, putting his hand up to caress my cheek.

"Claire," he said gently. "Ye canna move me. There's nothing else to do."

"There is," I said, repressing a quaver in my voice. "I'll stay with you. I'll bring you blankets and food, but I'm not leaving you up here alone. I'll bring wood, and we'll make a fire."

"There's no need. I can manage," he insisted.

"*I* can't," I said, between my teeth. I remembered all too well what it had been like in the cabin, during those empty, suffocating hours of waiting. Freezing my arse off in the snow for several days wasn't at all an appealing prospect, but it was better than the alternative.

He saw I meant it, and smiled.

"Well, then. Ye might bring some whisky, too, if there's any left."

"There's half a bottle," I said, feeling happier. "I'll bring it."

He got an arm around me, and pulled me into the curve of his shoulder. In spite of the howling wind outside, it was actually reasonably cozy under the cloaks, snuggled tight against him. His skin smelled warm and slightly salty, and I couldn't resist raising my head and putting my lips to the damp hollow of his throat.

"Aah," he said, shivering. "Don't *do* that!"

"You don't like it?"

"No, I dinna like it! How could I? It makes my skin crawl!"

"Well, *I* like it," I protested.

He looked at me in amazement.

"You do?"

"Oh, yes," I assured him. "I dearly love to have you nibble on my neck."

He narrowed one eye and squinted dubiously at me. Then he reached up, took me delicately by the ear, and drew my head down, turning my face to the side. He flicked his tongue gently at the base of my throat, then lifted his head and set his teeth very softly in the tender flesh at the side of my neck.

"Eeeee," I said, and shivered uncontrollably.

He let go, looking at me in astonishment.

"I will be damned," he said. "Ye *do* like it; ye've gone all gooseflesh and your nipples are hard as spring cherries." He passed a hand lightly over my breast; I hadn't bothered with my makeshift brassiere when I dressed for my impromptu expedition.

"Told you," I said, blushing slightly. "I suppose one of my ancestresses was bitten by a vampire or something."

"A what?" He looked quite blank.

There was time to kill, so I gave him a thumbnail sketch of the life and times of Count Dracula. He looked bemused and appalled, but his hand carried on with its machinations, having now moved under my buckskin shirt and found its way beneath the cutty sark as well. His fingers were chilly, but I didn't mind.

"Some people find the notion terribly erotic," I ended.

"That's the most disgusting thing I've ever heard!"

"I don't care," I said, stretching out at full length beside him and putting my head back, throat invitingly exposed. "Do it some more."

He muttered something under his breath in Gaelic, but managed to get onto one elbow and roll toward me.

His mouth was warm and soft, and whether he approved of what he was doing or not, he did it awfully well.

"Ooooh," I said, and shuddered ecstatically as his teeth sank delicately into my earlobe.

"Oh, well, if it's like *that*," he said in resignation, and taking my hand, pressed it firmly between his thighs.

"Gracious," I said. "And here I thought the cold . . ."

"It'll be warm enough soon," he assured me. "Get them off, aye?"

It was rather awkward, given the cramped quarters, the difficulty of staying covered in order not to suffer frostbite in any exposed portions, and the fact that Jamie was able to lend only the most basic assistance, but we managed quite satisfactorily nonetheless.

What with one thing and another, I was rather preoccupied, though, and it was only during a temporary lull in the activities that I became aware of an uneasy sensation, as though I was being watched. I lifted myself on my hands and glanced out through the screen of hemlock, but saw nothing beyond the grove and the snow-covered slope below.

Jamie gave a low groan.

"Don't stop," he murmured, eyes half closed. "What is it?"

"I thought I heard something," I said, lowering myself onto his chest again.

At this, I *did* hear something; a laugh, low but distinct, directly above my head.

I rolled off in a tangle of cloaks and discarded buckskins, while Jamie cursed and snatched for his pistol.

He flung aside the branches with a swoosh, pointing the pistol upward.

From the top of the rock above, several heads peered over, all grinning. Ian, and four companions from Anna Ooka. The Indians murmured and snickered among themselves, seeming to find something immoderately funny.

Jamie laid the pistol down, scowling up at his nephew.

"And what the devil are you doin' here, Ian?"

"Why, I was on my way home to keep Christmas with ye, Uncle," Ian said, grinning hugely.

Jamie eyed his nephew with marked disfavor.

"Christmas," he said. "Bah, humbug."

The elk carcass had frozen in the night. The sight of ice crystals frosting its blank eyes made me shudder—not at the sight of death; that was quite beautiful, with the great dark body so still, crusted with snow—but at the thought that had I not yielded to my sense of uneasiness and gone out into the night searching for Jamie, the stark still life before my eyes might well have been entitled "Dead Scotsman in Snow" rather than "Frozen Elk with Arguing Indians."

The discussion at last concluded to their satisfaction, Ian informed me that they had decided to return to Anna Ooka, but would see us safely home, in return for a share of the elk meat.

The carcass had not frozen solidly through; they eviscerated it, leaving the cooling entrails in a heap of blue-gray coils, splotched with black blood. After chopping off the head to further lessen the

weight, two of the men slung the body upside down from a pole,
its legs tied together. Jamie eyed them darkly, obviously suspecting that they meant to give him the same treatment, but Ian
assured him that they could manage a *travois;* the men were afoot,
but they had brought one sturdy pack mule to carry any skins they
took.

The weather had improved; the snow had melted altogether
from the exposed ground, and while the air was still crisp and
cold, the sky was a blinding blue, and the forest coldly pungent
with the scents of spruce and balsam fir.

It was the smell of hemlock, as we passed through one grove,
that reminded me of the beginning of this hegira, and the mysterious band of Indians we had seen.

"Ian," I said, catching up to him. "Just before you and your
friends found us on the mountainside, we saw a band of Indians,
with a Jesuit priest. They weren't from Anna Ooka, I don't think
—do you have any idea who they might have been?"

"Oh, aye, Auntie. I ken all about them." He wiped a mittened
hand under his red-tipped nose. "We were following them, when
we found you."

The strange Indians, he said, were Mohawk, come from far
north. The Tuscarora had been adopted by the Iroquois League
some fifty years before, and there was a close association with the
Mohawk, with frequent exchanges of visits between the two, both
formal and informal.

The present visit held elements of both—it was a party of
young Mohawk men, in search of wives. Their own village having
a shortage of marriageable young women, they had determined to
come south, to see if suitable mates might be found among the
Tuscarora.

"See, a woman must belong to the proper clan," Ian explained.
"If she is the wrong clan, they canna be marrit."

"Like MacDonalds and Campbells, aye?" Jamie chimed in,
interested.

"Aye, a bit," Ian said, grinning. "But that's why they brought
the priest wi' them—if they found women, they could be married
at once, and not have to sleep in a cold bed all the way home."

"They're Christians, then?"

Ian shrugged.

"Some of them. The Jesuits have been among them for some
time, and a good many of the Huron are converts. Not so many
among the Mohawk, though."

"So they'd been to Anna Ooka?" I asked, curious. "Why were you and your friends following them?"

Ian snorted, and tightened the muffler of squirrel skins around his neck.

"They may be allies, Auntie, but it doesna mean Nacognaweto and his braves trust them. Even the other Nations of the Iroquois League are afraid of the Mohawk—Christian or no."

It was near sunset when we came in sight of the cabin. I was cold and tired, but my heart lifted inexpressibly at the sight of the tiny homestead. One of the mules in the penfold, a light gray creature named Clarence, saw us and brayed enthusiastically in welcome, making the rest of the horses crowd up next to the rails, eager for food.

"The horses look fine." Jamie, with a stockman's eye, looked first to the animals' welfare. I was rather more concerned with our own; getting inside, getting warm, and getting fed, as soon as possible.

We invited Ian's friends to stay, but they declined, unloading Jamie in the dooryard and vanishing quickly to resume their vigilance over the departing Mohawk.

"They dinna like to stay in a white person's house, Auntie," Ian explained. "They think we smell bad."

"Oh, really?" I said in pique, thinking of a certain elderly gentleman I had met in Anna Ooka, who appeared to have smeared himself with bear grease and then had himself sewn into his clothes for the winter. The pot calling the kettle black, if you asked me.

Much later, Christmas properly kept with a dram—or two—of whisky all round, we lay at last in our own bed, watching the flames of the newly kindled fire, and listening to Ian's peaceful snores.

"It's good to be home again," I said softly.

"It is." Jamie sighed and pulled me closer, my head tucked into the curve of his shoulder. "I did have the strangest dreams, sleeping in the cold."

"You did?" I stretched, luxuriating in the soft yielding of the feather-stuffed mattress. "What did you dream about?"

"All kinds of things." He sounded a bit shy. "I dreamt of Brianna, now and again."

"Really?" That was a little startling; I too had dreamt of Brianna in our icy shelter—something I seldom did.

"I did wonder . . ." Jamie hesitated for a moment. "Has she a birthmark, Sassenach? And if so, did ye tell me of it?"

"She does," I said slowly, thinking. "I don't *think* I ever told you about it, though; it isn't visible most of the time, so it's been years since I noticed it, myself. It's a—"

His hand tightening on my shoulder stopped me.

"It's a wee brown mark, shaped like a diamond," he said. "Just behind her left ear. Isn't it?"

"Yes, it is." It was warm and cozy in bed, but a small coolness on the back of my neck made me shiver suddenly. "Did you see that in your dream?"

"I kissed her there," he said softly.

22

Spark of an Ancient Flame

Oxford, September 1970

"Oh, Jesus." Roger stared at the page in front of him until the letters lost their meaning and became no more than curlicues. No such trick would erase the meaning of the words themselves; those were already carved into his mind.

"Oh, God, no!" he said out loud. The girl in the next carrel jerked in irritation at the noise, scraping the legs of her chair against the floor.

He leaned over the book, covering it with his forearms, eyes closed. He felt sick, and the palms of his hands were cold and sweaty.

He sat that way for several minutes, fighting the truth. It wasn't going to go away, though. Christ, it had already happened, hadn't it? A long time ago. And you couldn't change the past.

Finally he swallowed the taste of bile in the back of his throat and looked again. It was still there. A small notice from a newspaper, printed on February 13, 1776, in the American Colony of North Carolina, in the town of Wilmington.

It is with grief that the news is received of the deaths by fire of James MacKenzie Fraser and his wife, Claire Fraser, in a conflagration that destroyed their house in the settlement of Fraser's Ridge, on the night of January 21 last. Mr. Fraser, a nephew of the late Hector Cameron of River Run plantation, was born at Broch Tuarach in Scotland. He was widely known in the colony and deeply respected; he leaves no surviving children.

Except that he did.

Roger grasped for a moment at the dim hope that it wasn't them; there were, after all, any number of James Frasers, it was a fairly common name. But not James *MacKenzie* Fraser, not with a wife named Claire. Not born in Broch Tuarach, Scotland.

No, it was them; the sick certainty filled his chest and squeezed his throat with grief. His eyes stung and the ornate eighteenth-century typeface blurred again.

So she had found him, Claire. Found her gallant Highlander, and enjoyed at least a few years with him. He hoped they had been good years. He had liked Claire Randall very much—no, that was to damn her with faint praise. If he were truthful, he had loved her, and for her own sake as well as her daughter's.

More than that. He had wanted badly for her to find her Jamie Fraser, to live happily ever after with him. The knowledge—or more accurately, the hope—that she had done so had been a small talisman to him; a witness that enduring love was possible, a love strong enough to withstand separation and hardship, strong enough to outlast time. And yet all flesh was mortal; no love could outlast that fact.

He gripped the edge of the table, trying to get himself under control. Foolish, he told himself. Thoroughly foolish. And yet he felt as bereft as he had when the Reverend had died; as though he were himself newly orphaned.

Realization came as a fresh blow. He couldn't show this to Bree, he couldn't. She'd known the risk, of course, but—no. She wouldn't have imagined anything like this.

It was the purest chance that had led him to find it. He had been looking for the lyrics of old ballads to add to his repertoire, thumbing through a book of country songs. An illustration had shown the original newspaper page on which one ballad had first been published, and Roger, idly browsing, had glanced at the archaic notices posted on the same newspaper page, his eye caught by the name "Fraser."

The shock was beginning to wear off a little, though grief had settled in the pit of his stomach, nagging as the pain of an ulcer. He was a scholar and the son of a scholar; he had grown up surrounded by books, imbued since childhood with the sanctity of the printed word. He felt like a murderer as he groped for his penknife and stealthily opened it, glancing around to be sure he was unobserved.

It was instinct more than reason; the instinct that leads a man to want to clear up the remains of an accident, to lay a decent covering over the bodies, to obliterate the visible traces of disaster, even though the tragedy itself remains.

With the folded page lying hidden in his pocket like a severed thumb, he left the library, to walk the rainy streets of Oxford.

The walking calmed him, made it possible to think rationally again, to force his own feelings back long enough to plan what he must do, how to protect Brianna from a grief that would be more profound and longer felt than his own.

He had checked the bibliographic information in the front of the book; published in 1906 by a small British press. It wouldn't be widely available, then; but still something Brianna might stumble over in her own researches.

It wasn't a logical place to look for information of the sort she was seeking, but the book was titled *Songs and Ballads of the Eighteenth Century.* He knew well enough that historian's curiosity that led to impulsive pokings in unlikely places; she would know enough to do that too. Still more, he knew the child's hunger for knowledge—any knowledge—that might lead her to look at anything dealing with the period, in an effort to imagine her parents' surroundings, to build a vision of lives she could neither see nor share.

Long odds, but not long enough. Someone jostled him in passing, and he realized that he had been leaning on the bridge railing for several minutes, watching raindrops patter on the surface of the river without seeing them. Slowly, he turned down the street, oblivious of the shops and the mushroom herds of umbrellas.

There was no way to ensure that she would never see a copy of that book; this might be the only copy, or there might be hundreds, lying like time bombs in libraries all over the U.S.

The ache in his guts was getting worse. He was soaked through by now, and freezing. Inside, he felt a deeper cold spreading from a new thought: What might Brianna do, if she found out?

She would be devastated, grief-stricken. But then? He was himself convinced that the past could not be changed; the things Claire had told him had made him sure of it. She and Jamie Fraser had tried to avert the slaughter at Culloden, to no avail. She had tried to save her future husband, Frank, by saving his ancestor, Jack Randall—and failed, only to find that Jack had never been Frank's ancestor after all, but had married his younger brother's pregnant lover in order to legitimize the child when the brother died.

No, the past might twist on itself like a writhing snake, but it could not be changed. He wasn't at all sure that Brianna shared his conviction, though.

How do you mourn a time-traveler? she'd asked him. If he showed her the notice, she could mourn truly; she would know.

The knowledge would wound her terribly, but she would heal, and could put the past behind her. If.

If it wasn't for the stones on Craigh na Dun. The stone circle and its dreadful promise of possibility.

Claire had gone through the stones of Craigh na Dun on the ancient fire feast of Samhain, on the first day of November, nearly two years before.

Roger shivered, and not from the cold. The hairs stood up on the back of his neck whenever he thought of it. It had been a clear, mild fall morning, that dawn of the Feast of All Saints, with nothing to disturb the grassy peace of the hill where the circle of stones stood sentinel. Nothing until Claire had touched the great cleft stone, and vanished into the past.

Then the earth had seemed to dissolve under his own feet, and the air had ripped away with a roar that echoed inside his head like cannon fire. He had gone blind in a blast of light and dark; only his memories of the last time had kept him from utter panic.

He'd had hold of Brianna's hand. Reflex closed his grip, even as all senses disappeared. It was like being dropped from a thousand feet into ice-cold water; terrible vertigo and a shock so intense, he could feel no sensation but the shock itself. Blind and deaf, bereft of sense and senses, he had been conscious of two last thoughts, the remnants of his consciousness flicking out like a candleflame in a hurricane. *I'm dying,* he had thought, with great calmness. And then, *Don't let go.*

The dawning sun had fallen in a bright path through the cleft stone; Claire had walked along it. When Roger stirred at last and raised his head, the sun of late afternoon glowed gold and lavender behind the great stone, leaving it black against the sky.

He was lying on Brianna, sheltering her with his body. She was unconscious but breathing, her face desperately pale against the dark red of her hair. Weak as he was, there was no question of his being able to carry her down the steep hillside to the car below; her father's daughter, she was nearly six feet tall, only a few inches shorter than Roger himself.

He had huddled over her, holding her head in his lap, stroking her face and shivering, until just before sunset. She had opened her eyes then, as dark a blue as the fading sky, and whispered, "She's gone?"

"It's all right," Roger had whispered back. He bent and kissed her cold forehead. "It's all right; I'll take care of you."

He'd meant it. But how?

It was getting dark by the time he returned to his rooms. He could hear a clatter from the dining hall as he passed, and he smelled boiled ham and baked beans, but supper was the farthest thing from his mind.

He squelched up to his rooms and dropped his wet things in a heap on the floor. He dried himself, then sat naked on the bed, towel forgotten in his hand, staring at the desk and at the wooden box that held Brianna's letters.

He would do anything to save her from grief. He would do much more to save her from the threat of the stones.

Claire had gone back—he hoped—from 1968 to 1766. And then died in 1776. Now it was 1970. A person going back now would—might—end in 1768. There would be time. That was the hell of it; there would be time.

Even if Brianna thought as he did—or if he could convince her —that the past could not be changed, could she live through the next seven years, knowing that the window of opportunity was closing, that her only chance ever to know her father, see her mother again, was disappearing day by day? It was one thing to let them go, not knowing where they were or what had happened to them; it was another to know explicitly, and to do nothing.

He had known Brianna for more than two years, yet been with her for only a few months of that time. And yet, they knew each other very well in some respects. How could they not, having shared such an experience? Then there had been the letters— dozens, two or three or four each week—and the rare brief holidays, spent between enchantment and frustration, that left him aching with need of her.

Yes, he knew her. She was quiet, but possessed of a fierce determination that he thought would not submit to grief without a fight. And while she was cautious, once her mind was made up, she acted with hair-raising dispatch. If she decided to risk the passage, he couldn't stop her.

His hands closed tight on the wadded towel, and his stomach dropped, remembering the chasm of the circle and the void that had nearly swallowed them. The only thing more terrifying was the thought of losing Brianna before he had ever truly had her.

He'd never lied to her. But the impact of shock and grief was slowly receding as the rudiments of a plan formed in his mind. He stood up and wrapped the towel around his waist.

One letter wouldn't do it. It would have to be slow, a process of suggestion, of gentle discouragement. He thought it wouldn't be difficult; he had found almost nothing in a year of searching in Scotland, beyond the report of the burning of Fraser's print shop in Edinburgh—he shuddered involuntarily at the thought of flames. Now he knew why, of course; they must have emigrated soon after, though he had found no trace of them on the ship's rolls he had searched.

Time to give up, he would suggest. Let the past rest—and the dead bury the dead. To keep on looking, in the face of no evidence, would border on obsession. He would suggest, very subtly, that it was unhealthy, this looking back—now it was time to look forward, lest she waste her life in futile searching. Neither of her parents would have wanted that.

The room was chilly, but he barely noticed.

I'll take care of you, he'd said, and meant it. Was suppressing a dangerous truth the same as lying? Well, if it was, then he'd lie. To give consent to do wrong was a sin, he'd heard that from his early days. That was all right, he'd risk his soul for her, and willingly.

He rummaged in the drawer for a pen. Then he stopped, bent, and reached two fingers into the pocket of his sopping jeans. The paper was frayed and soggy, half disintegrating already. With steady fingers, he tore it into tiny pieces, disregarding the cold sweat that ran in trickles from his face.

23

The Skull Beneath the Skin

I had told Jamie that I didn't mind being far from civilization; wherever there were people, there would be work for a healer. Duncan had been good as his word, returning in the spring of 1768 with eight former Ardsmuir men and their families, ready to take up homesteading on Fraser's Ridge, as the place was now known. With some thirty souls to hand, there was an immediate call on my mildly rusty services, to stitch up wounds and treat fevers, to lance abscessed boils and scrape infected gums. Two of the women were pregnant, and it was my joy to deliver healthy children, a boy and a girl, both born in early spring.

My fame—if that's the word—as a healer soon spread outside our tiny settlement, and I found myself called farther and farther afield, to tend the ills of folk on isolated hill farms scattered over thirty miles of wild mountain terrain. In addition, I made rare visits with Ian to Anna Ooka to see Nayawenne, returning with baskets and jars of useful herbs.

At first, Jamie had insisted that he or Ian must go with me to the farther places, but it was soon apparent that neither of them could be spared; it was time for the first planting, with ground to break and harrow, corn and barley to be planted, to say nothing of the usual chores required to keep a small farm running. In addition to the horses and mules, we had acquired a small flock of chickens, a depraved-looking black boar to meet the social needs of the pig, and—luxury of luxuries—a milch goat, all of whom required to be fed and watered and generally kept from killing themselves or being eaten by bears or panthers.

So more and more often I went alone when some stranger appeared suddenly in the dooryard, asking for healer or midwife. Daniel Rawlings's casebook began to acquire new entries, and the larder was enriched by the gifts of hams and venison haunches, bags of grain and bushels of apples, with which my patients repaid my attentions. I never asked for payment, but something was always offered—and poor as we were, anything at all was welcome.

My backcountry patients came from many places, and many spoke neither English nor French; there were German Lutherans, Quakers, Scots and Scotch-Irish, and a large settlement of Moravian brethren at Salem, who spoke a peculiar dialect of what I *thought* was Czechoslovakian. I usually managed, though; in most cases, someone could interpret for me, and at the worst, I could fall back on the language of hand and body—"Where does it hurt?" is easy to understand in any tongue.

August 1768

I was chilled to the bone. Despite my best efforts to keep the cloak wrapped tightly round me, the wind ripped it from my body, and sent it billowing like sail canvas. It beat round the head of the boy walking next to me, and jerked me sideways in my saddle with the force of the gale. The rain drove in beneath the flapping folds like frozen needles, and I was soaked through gown and petticoats before we reached Mueller's Creek.

The creek itself was boiling past, uprooted saplings, rocks and drowned branches bubbling briefly to the surface.

Tommy Mueller peered at the torrent, shoulders hunched nearly to the brim of the slouch hat he wore pulled down over his ears. I could see doubt etched in every line of his body, and bent close to shout in his ear.

"Stay here!" I bellowed, pitching my voice below the shriek of the wind.

He shook his head, mouthing something at me, but I couldn't hear. I shook my own head vigorously, and pointed up the bank; the muddy soil was crumbly here; I could see small chunks of the black dirt melt away even as I watched.

"Get back!" I shouted.

He pointed emphatically himself—back in the direction of the farmhouse—and reached for my reins. Clearly he thought it was too dangerous; he wanted me to come back to the house, to wait out the storm.

He definitely had a point. On the other hand, I could see the stream widening, even as I watched, the ravenous water eating away the soft bank in gobbets and chunks. Wait much longer, and no one could cross—neither would it be safe for days after; floods like this kept the water high for as long as a week, as the rains from higher up the mountain trickled down to feed the torrents.

The thought of being cooped up in a four-room house for a week with all ten Muellers was enough to spur me to recklessness. Pulling the reins from Tommy's grasp, I wheeled about, the horse tossing its head against the rain, stepping carefully on the slick mud.

We reached the upper slopes of the bank, where a layer of thick dead leaves gave better footing. I turned the horse, motioned Tommy back out of the way, and leaned forward like a steeplechaser, elbows digging into the bag of barley bound over the saddle in front of me—my payment for services rendered.

The shift of my weight was enough; the horse was no more anxious to hang about here than I was. I felt the sudden thrust as the hindquarters dropped and bunched, and then we were flying down the slope like a runaway toboggan. A jolt and a moment of giddy freefall, then a resounding splash, and I was up past my thighs in freezing water.

My hands were so cold, they might as well have been welded to the reins, but I had nothing useful to offer in terms of guidance. I let my arms go slack, giving the horse his head. I could feel huge muscles moving rhythmically under my legs as it swam, and the even more powerful shove of the water rushing past us. It dragged at my skirts, threatening to pull me off into the surge.

Then came the jar and scrabble of hooves against the stream bottom, and we were out, pouring water like a colander. I turned in the saddle, to see Tommy Mueller on the other side, his jaw hanging open under his hat. I couldn't let go of the reins to wave, but bowed toward him ceremoniously, then nudged the horse with my heels and turned toward home.

The hood of my cloak had fallen back when we jumped, but it made no great difference; I couldn't get much wetter. I knuckled a wet strand of hair out of my eyes and turned the horse's head toward the upland trail, relieved to be headed home, rain or no.

I had been at the Muellers' cabin for three days, seeing eighteen-year-old Petronella through her first labor. It would be her last, too, according to Petronella. Her seventeen-year-old husband, peeking tentatively into the room in the middle of the second day, had received a burst of German invective from Petronella that sent him stumping back to the men's refuge in the barn, ears bright red with mortification.

Still, a few hours later, I had seen Freddy—looking much younger than seventeen—kneel tentatively by his wife's bedside, face whiter than her shift as he reached a hesitant, scrubbed finger to push aside the blanket covering his daughter.

He stared dumbly at the round head, furred with soft black, then looked at his wife, as though in need of prompting.

"Ist sie nicht wunderschön?" Petronella said softly.

He nodded, slowly, then laid his head on her lap and began to cry. The women had all smiled kindly, and gone back to fixing dinner.

It had been a good dinner, too; the food was one of the benefits of house calls to the Muellers. Even now, my stomach was comfortably distended with dumplings and fried *Blutwurst,* and the lingering taste of buttered eggs in my mouth provided some small distraction from the general discomfort of my present situation.

I hoped that Jamie and Ian had managed something adequate to eat in my absence. This being the end of summer but not yet harvest time, the pantry shelves were nowhere near the height of what I hoped would be their autumn bounty, but still there were cheeses on the shelf, a huge stoneware crock of salted fish on the floor, and sacks of flour, corn, rice, beans, barley, and oatmeal.

Jamie *could* in fact cook—at least so far as dressing game and roasting it over a fire—and I had done my best to initiate Ian into the mysteries of making oatmeal parritch, but, they being men, I suspected that they hadn't bothered, choosing instead to survive on raw onions and dried meat.

I couldn't tell whether it was simply that after a day spent in the manly pursuits of chopping down trees, plowing fields, and carrying deer carcasses over mountains, they honestly were too exhausted to think of assembling a proper meal, or whether they did it on purpose, so that I would feel necessary.

The wind had dropped, now that I was in the shelter of the ridge, but the rain was still pelting down, and the footing was treacherous, as the mud of the trail had liquified, leaving a layer of fallen leaves floating on top, deceptive as quicksand. I could feel the horse's discomfort as its hooves slipped with each step.

"Good boy," I said soothingly. "Keep it up, that's a good fellow." The horse's ears pricked slightly, but he kept his head down, stepping carefully.

"Slewfoot?" I said. "How's that?"

The horse had no name at the moment—or rather he did, but I didn't know what it was. The man from whom Jamie had bought him had called him by a German word that Jamie said was not at all suitable for a lady's horse. When I had asked him to translate the word, he had merely compressed his lips and looked Scottish, from which I deduced that it must be pretty bad. I had meant to ask old Mrs. Mueller what it meant, but had forgotten, in the haste of leaving.

In any case, Jamie's theory was that the horse would reveal his true—or at least speakable—name in the course of time, and so we were all watching the animal, in hopes of discerning its character. On the basis of a trial ride, Ian had suggested Coney, but Jamie had merely shaken his head and said, no, that wasn't it.

"Twinkletoes?" I suggested. "Lightfoot? Damn!"

The horse had come to a full stop, for obvious reasons. A small freshet gurgled merrily down the hill, bounding from rock to rock with gay abandon. It was beautiful, the rushing water clear as crystal over dark rock and green leaves. Unfortunately, it was also bounding over the remains of the trail, which, unequal to the force of events, had slithered off the face of the hill into the valley below.

I sat still, dripping. There wasn't any way around. The hill rose nearly perpendicularly on my right, shrubs and saplings poking out of a cracked rock face, and declined so precipitously to the left that going down would have amounted to suicide. Swearing under my breath, I backed the nameless horse and turned around.

If it hadn't been for the flooded creek, I would have gone back to the Muellers and let Jamie and Ian fend for themselves a bit longer. As it was, I had no choice; it was find another way home or stay here and drown.

Wearily, we retraced our slogging steps. Less than a quarter-mile from the washout, though, I found a spot where the hillside fell away into a small saddle, a depression between two "horns" of granite. Such formations were common; there was a big one on a nearby mountain, which had gained it the name of Devil's Peak. If I could cross the saddle to the other side of the hill, and pick my way along it, I would in time come back to the trail where it crossed the ridge to the south.

From the saddle I had a momentary clear view of the foothills, and the blue hollow of the valley beyond. On the other side, though, clouds hid the tops of the mountains, black with rain, suffused with an occasional flicker of hidden lightning.

The wind had dropped, now that the leading edge of the storm had passed. The rain was coming down even more heavily, if such a thing was possible, and I stopped long enough to pry my cold fingers off the reins and put up the hood of my cloak.

The footing on this side of the hill was fair, the ground being rocky but not too steep. We picked our way through small groves of red-berried mountain ash and larger stands of oak. I noted the location of a huge blackberry bramble for future reference, but didn't stop. I would be lucky to get home by dark as it was.

To distract myself from the cold trickles running down my neck, I began a mental inventory of the pantry. What could I make for dinner, once I arrived?

Something quick, I thought, shivering, and something hot. Stew would take too long; so would soup. If there was squirrel or rabbit, we might have it fried, rolled in egg and cornmeal batter. Or if not that, perhaps brose with a little bacon for flavoring, and a couple of scrambled eggs with green onions.

I ducked, wincing. Despite the hood and the thickness of my hair, the raindrops were beating on my scalp like hail pellets.

Then I realized that they *were* hail pellets. Tiny white spheres pinged off the horse's back, and rattled through the oak leaves. Within seconds, the pellets were bigger, the size of marbles, and the hail had grown heavy enough that its popping sounded like machine-gun fire on the wet mats of leaves in the clearings.

The horse flung up its head, shaking its mane vigorously in an effort to escape the stinging pellets. Hastily, I reined in and guided it into the semi-shelter of a huge chestnut tree. Underneath, it was noisy, but the hail slid off the thick canopy of leaves, leaving us protected.

"Right," I said. With some difficulty, I pried one hand off the reins and gave the horse a reassuring pat. "Easy, then. We'll be all right, as long as we don't get struck by lightning."

Evidently this statement had jogged someone's memory; a silent fork of dazzling light split the black sky beyond Roan Mountain. A few moments later, the dull rumble of thunder came booming up the hollow, drowning out the rasp of hail on the leaves overhead.

Sheet lightning shimmered far away, across the mountains. Then more bolts, sizzling across the sky, each succeeded by a louder roll of thunder. The hailstorm passed, and the rain resumed, pelting down as hard as ever. The valley below disappeared in cloud and mist, but the lightning lit the stark mountain ridges like bones on an X ray.

"One hippopotamus, two hippopotamus, three hippopotamus,

four hippopot—'' BWOOOM! The horse jerked its head and stamped nervously.

"I know just how you feel," I told it, peering down the valley. "Steady, though, steady." There it went again, a flash that lit the dark ridge and left the silhouette of the horse's pricked ears imprinted on my retinas.

"One hippopotamus, two hippo—" I could have sworn the ground shook. The horse let out a high-pitched scream and reared against my pull on the reins, hooves thrashing in the leaves. The air reeked of ozone.

Flash.

"One," I said through my teeth. "Damn you, whoa! One hip—"

Flash.

"One—"

Flash.

"Whoa! WHOA!"

I wasn't conscious of the fall at all; nor even the landing. One moment I was sawing at the reins, a thousand pounds of panicked horse going to pieces under me, shying in all directions. The next, I was lying on my back, blinking up at a spinning black sky, trying to will my diaphragm to work.

Echoes of the shock of impact wavered through my flesh, and I tried frantically to fit myself back into my body. Then I drew breath, a painful gasp, and found myself shaking, the shock turning to the first intimations of damage.

I lay still, eyes closed, concentrating on breathing, conducting an inventory. The rain was still pounding down onto my face, puddling in my eye sockets and running down into my ears. My face and hands were numb. My arms moved. I could breathe a little easier now.

My legs. The left one hurt, but not in any threatening way; only a bruised knee. I rolled heavily onto my side, impeded by my wet, bulky garments. Still, it was the heavy clothing that had saved me from serious damage.

Above me came an uncertain whinny, audible amid the booming thunder. I looked up, dizzy, and saw the horse's head, protruding from a thicket of buckbrush some thirty feet overhead. Below the thicket, a steep, rocky slope fell away; a long scrape mark toward the bottom showed where I had struck and rolled before ending up in my present position.

We had been standing virtually on the edge of this small precipice without my seeing it, screened as it was by the heavy growth of shrubs. The horse's panic had sent it to the edge, but evidently it had sensed the danger and caught itself before going over—not before letting me slide off into space, though.

"You bloody bugger!" I said. And wondered whether the unknown German name meant something similar. "I could have broken my neck!" I wiped the mud from my face with a hand that still shook, and looked about me for a way back up.

There wasn't one. Behind me, the rocky cliff face continued, merging into one of the granite horns. Before me, it ended abruptly, in a plunge straight downward into a small hollow. The slope I stood on declined into this hollow as well, rolling down through clumps of yellow-wood and sumac to the banks of a small creek some sixty feet below.

I stood quite still, trying to think. No one knew where I was. *I* didn't know exactly where I was, come to that. Worse, no one would be looking for me for some time. Jamie would think I was still at Muellers' because of the rain. The Muellers would of course have no reason to think I hadn't made it safely home; even if they had doubts, they couldn't follow me, because of the flooded creek. And by the time anyone found the washed-out trail, any traces of my passage would long since have been obliterated by the rain.

I was uninjured, that was something. I was also afoot, alone, without food, moderately lost, and thoroughly wet. About the only certainty was that I wasn't going to die of thirst.

The lightning was still glancing to and fro like dueling pitchforks in the sky above, though the thunder had faded to a dull rumble in the distance. I had no particular fear of being struck by lightning now—not with so many better candidates standing about, in the form of gigantic trees—but finding shelter seemed a very good idea nonetheless.

It was still raining; drops rolled off the end of my nose with monotonous regularity. Limping on my bruised knee and swearing quite a bit, I made my way down the slippery slope to the edge of the stream.

This creek, too, was swollen by the rain; I could see the tops of drowned bushes sticking out of the water, leaves trailing limply in the rushing current. There was no bank to speak of; I fought my way through the grasping claws of holly and red-cedar toward the rocky cliff-face to the south; perhaps there would be a cave or hollow there that would offer shelter of a sort.

I found nothing but tumbled rocks, black with wet and hard to navigate. Some distance beyond, though, I saw something else that offered a small possibility of shelter.

A huge red cedar tree had fallen across the stream, its roots undermined as the water ate away the soil in which it stood. It had fallen away from me and struck the cliff, so that the thick crown sprawled into the water and over the rocks, the trunk canted across the stream at a shallow angle; on my side, I could see the huge mat of its exposed roots, a bulwark of cracked earth and small bushes heaved up about them. The cavity under them might not be complete shelter, but it looked better than standing in the open or crouching in the bushes.

I hadn't even paused to think that the shelter might have attracted bears, catamounts, or other unfriendly fauna. Fortunately, it hadn't.

It was a space about five feet long and five wide, dank, dark, and clammy. The ceiling was composed of the tree's great gnarled roots, packed with sandy earth, like the roof of a badger's sett. But it was a solid ceiling, for all that; the floor of churned earth was damp but not muddy, and for the first time in hours rain was not drumming on my skull.

Exhausted, I crawled into the farthest corner, set my wet shoes beside me, and went to sleep. The cold of my wet clothes made me dream vividly, in jumbled visions of blood and childbirth, trees and rocks and rain, and I woke frequently, in that half-conscious way of utter tiredness, falling asleep again in seconds.

I dreamt that I was giving birth. I felt no pain, but saw the emerging head as though I stood between my own thighs, midwife and mother both together. I took the naked child in my arms, still smeared with the blood that came from both of us, and gave her to her father. I gave her to Frank, but it was Jamie who took the caul from her face and said, "She's beautiful."

Then I woke and slept, finding my way among boulders and waterfalls, urgently seeking something I had lost. Woke and slept, pursued through woods by something fearsome and unknown. Woke and slept, a knife in my hand, red with blood—but whose, I did not know.

I woke all the way to the smell of burning, and sat bolt upright. The rain had stopped; it was the silence that wakened me, I thought. The smell of smoke was still strong in my nostrils, though—it wasn't part of the dream.

I poked my head out of my burrow like a snail cautiously

emerging from its shell. The sky was a pale purple-gray, shot with streaks of orange over the mountains. The woods around me were still, and dripping. It was nearly sundown, and darkness was gathering in the hollows.

I crawled out all the way, and looked around. The creek at my back rushed past in full spate, its gurgling the only sound. The ground rose in front of me to a small ridge. At the top of this stood a large balsam poplar tree, the source of the smoke. The tree had been struck by lightning; half of it still bore green leaves, the canopy bushy against the pale sky. The other half was blackened and charred all down one side of the massive trunk. Wisps of white smoke rose from it like ghosts escaping an enchanter's bondage, and red lines of fire showed fleetingly, glowing beneath the blackened shell.

I looked about for my shoes, but couldn't find them in the shadows. Not bothering, I made my way up the ridge toward the blasted tree, panting with effort. All my muscles were stiffened with sleep and cold; I felt like a tree come awkwardly to life myself, stumping uphill on gnarled and clumsy roots.

It was warm near the tree. Blissfully, wonderfully warm. The air smelled of ash and burnt soot, but it was warm. I stood as close as I dared, spreading my cloak out wide, and stood still, steaming.

For some time I didn't even try to think; just stood there, feeling my chilled flesh thaw and soften again into something resembling humanity. But as my blood began to flow again, my bruises began to ache, and I felt the deeper ache of hunger as well; it had been a long time since breakfast.

Likely to be a lot longer time till supper, I thought grimly. The dark was creeping up from the hollow, and I was still lost. I glanced across to the opposite ridge; not a sign of the bloody horse.

"Traitor," I muttered. "Probably gone off to join a herd of elk or something."

I chafed my hands together; my clothes were halfway dry, but the temperature was dropping; it would be a chilly night. Would it be better to spend the night here, in the open, near the blasted tree, or ought I to return to my burrow while I could still see to do so?

A snapping in the brush behind me decided me. The tree had cooled now; though the charred wood was still hot to the touch, the fire had burned out. It would be no deterrent to prowling night hunters. Lacking fire or weapons, my only defense was that of the hunted; lie hidden through the dark hours, like the mice and rabbits. Well, I had to go back to fetch my shoes anyway.

Reluctantly leaving the last vestiges of warmth, I made my way back down to the fallen tree. Crawling in, I saw a pale blur against the darker earth in the corner. I set my hand on it, and found not the softness of my buckskin moccasins, but something hard and smooth.

My instincts had grasped the reality of the object before my brain could retrieve the word, and I snatched my hand away. I sat for a moment, my heart pounding. Then curiosity overcame atavistic fear, and I began to scoop away the sandy loam around it.

It was indeed a skull, complete with lower jaw, though the mandible was attached only by the remnants of dried ligament. A fragment of broken vertebra rattled in the foramen magnum.

" 'How long will a man lie i' the earth ere he rot?' " I murmured, turning the skull over in my hands. The bone was cold and damp, slightly roughened by exposure to the damp. The light was too dim to see details, but I could feel the heavy ridges over the brows, and the slickness of smooth enamel on the canines. Likely a man, and not an old one; most of the teeth were present, and not unduly worn—at least insofar as I could tell with a groping thumb.

How long? Eight or nine year, the grave-digger said to Hamlet. I had no notion whether Shakespeare knew anything about forensics, but it seemed a reasonable estimate to me. Longer than nine years, then.

How had he come here? By violence, my instincts answered, though my brain was not far behind. An explorer might die of disease, hunger or exposure—I firmly suppressed that line of thought, trying to ignore my growling stomach and damp clothes —but he wouldn't end up buried under a tree.

The Cherokee and Tuscarora buried their dead, all right, but not like this, alone in a hollow. And not in fragments, either. It was that broken bit of vertebra that had told me the story at once; the edges were compressed, the broken face sheared clean, not shattered.

"Somebody took a real dislike to you, didn't they?" I said. "Didn't stop with a scalp; they took your whole head."

Which made me wonder—was the rest of him here, too? I rubbed a hand across my face, thinking, but after all, I had nothing better to do; I wasn't going anywhere before daylight, and the likelihood of sleep had grown remote with the discovery of my companion. I set the skull carefully to one side, and began to dig.

It was fully night by now, but even the darkest of nights outdoors is seldom completely without light. The sky was still covered with cloud, which reflected considerable light, even in my shallow burrow.

The sandy earth was soft, and easy to dig in, but after a few minutes of scratching, my knuckles and fingertips were rubbed raw, and I crawled outside, long enough to find a stick to dig with. A little more probing yielded me something hard; not bone, I thought, and not metal, either. Stone, I decided, fingering the dark oval. Just a river stone? I thought not; the surface was very smooth, but with something incised in it; a glyph of some kind, though my touch was not sufficiently sensitive to tell me what it was.

More digging yielded nothing. Either the rest of Yorick wasn't here, or it was buried so far down that I had no chance of discovering it. I put the stone in my pocket, sat back on my heels, and rubbed my sandy hands on my skirts. At least the exercise had warmed me again.

I sat down again and picked up the skull, holding it in my lap. Gruesome as it was, it was the semblance of company, some distraction from my own plight. And I was quite aware that all my actions of the last hour or so had been distractions; designed to fight off the panic that I could feel submerged below the surface of my mind, waiting to erupt like the sharp end of a drowned tree branch. It was going to be a long night.

"Right," I said aloud to the skull. "Read any good books lately? No, I suppose you don't get round much anymore. Poetry, maybe?" I cleared my throat and started in on Keats, warming up with "Written in Disgust of Vulgar Superstition" and going on with "Ode on a Grecian Urn."

" '. . . *Forever wilt thou love, and she be fair!*' " I declaimed. "There's more of that one, but I forget. Not too bad, though, was it? Want to try a little Shelley? 'Ode to the West Wind' is good— you'd like that one, I think."

It occurred to me to wonder why I thought so; I had no particular reason to think Yorick was an Indian rather than a European, but I realized that I did think so—perhaps it was the stone I had found with him. Shrugging, I set in again, trusting that the repellent effect of great English poetry would be the equal of a campfire, so far as the bears and panthers were concerned.

"Make me thy lyre, even as the forest is:
What if my leaves are falling like its own!
The tumult of thy mighty harmonies
Will take from both a deep, autumnal tone,
Sweet though in sadness. Be thou, Spirit fierce,
My spirit! Be thou me, impetuous one!

"Drive my dead thoughts over the universe
Like wither'd leaves to quicken a new birth;
And, by the incantation of this verse,

"Scatter, as from an unextinguish'd hearth
Ashes and sparks, my words among mankind!
Be through my lips to unawaken'd earth

"The trumpet of a prophecy! O Wind . . ."

The final stanza faded on my lips. There was a light on the
ridge. A small spark, growing to a flame. At first I thought it was
the lightning-blasted tree, some smoldering ember come to life—
but then it moved. It glided slowly down the hill toward me,
floating just above the bushes.

I sprang to my feet, realizing only then that I had no shoes on.
Frantically, I groped about the floor, covering the small space
again and again. But it was no use. My shoes were gone.

I seized the skull and stood barefoot, turning to face the light.

I watched the light come nearer, drifting down the hill like a
milkweed puff. One thought floated in my paralyzed mind—a
random line of Shelley's: *Fiend, I defy thee! with a calm, fixed
mind.* Somewhere in the dimmer recesses of my consciousness,
something observed that Shelley had had much better nerves than
I. I clutched the skull closer. It wasn't much of a weapon—but
somehow I didn't think that whatever was coming would be deterred by knives or pistols, either.

It wasn't only that the wet surroundings made it seem grossly
improbable that anyone was strolling through the woods with a
blazing torch. The light didn't burn like a pine torch or oil lantern.
It didn't flicker, but burned with a soft, steady glow.

It floated a few feet above the ground, just about where someone would hold a torch they carried before them. It drew slowly

nearer, at the pace of a man walking. I could see it bob slightly, moving to the rhythm of a steady stride.

I cowered in my burrow, half hidden by the bank of earth and severed roots. I was freezing cold, but sweat ran down my sides and I could smell the reek of my own fear. My numb toes curled in the dirt, wanting to run.

I had seen St. Elmo's fire before, at sea. Eerie as that was, its liquid blue crackle didn't resemble at all the pale light approaching. This had neither spark nor color; only a spectral glow. Marsh gas, people in Cross Creek said when the mountain lights were mentioned.

Ha, I said to myself, though soundlessly. Marsh gas my left foot!

The light moved through a small thicket of alders, and out into the clearing before me. It wasn't marsh gas.

He was tall, and he was naked. Beyond a breechclout, he wore nothing but paint; long stripes of red down arms and legs and torso, and his face was solid black, from chin to forehead. His hair was greased and dressed in a crest, from which two turkey feathers stiffly pointed.

I was invisible, completely hidden in the darkness of my refuge, while the torch he held washed him in soft light, gleaming off his hairless chest and shoulders, shadowing the orbits of his eyes. But he knew I was there.

I didn't dare to move. My breath sounded painfully loud in my ears. He simply stood there, perhaps a dozen feet away, and looked straight into the dark where I was, as though it were the broadest day. And the light of his torch burned steady and soundless, pallid as a corpse candle, the wood of it not consumed.

I don't know how long I had been standing there before it occurred to me that I was no longer afraid. I was still cold, but my heart had slowed to its normal pace, and my bare toes had uncurled.

"Whatever do you want?" I said, and only then realized that we had been in some sort of communication for some time. Whatever this was, it had no words. Nothing coherent passed between us—but something passed, nonetheless.

The clouds had lifted, shredding away before a light wind, and dark streaks of starlit sky showed through rents in the racing cirrus. The wood was quiet, but in the usual way of a drenched night-wood; the creaks and sighs of tall trees moving, the rustle of shrubs brushed by the wind's restless edge, and in the background the constant rush of invisible water, echoing the turbulence of the air above.

I breathed deeply, feeling suddenly very much alive. The air was thick and sweet with the breath of green plants, the tang of herbs and musk of dead leaves, overlaid and interlaced with the scents of the storm—wet rock, damp earth, and rising mist, and a sharp hint of ozone, sudden as the lightning that had struck the tree.

Earth and air, I thought suddenly, and fire and water too. And here I stood with all the elements; in their midst and at their mercy.

"What do you want?" I said again, feeling helpless. "I can't do anything for you. I know you're there; I can see you. But that's all."

Nothing moved, no words were spoken. But quite clearly the thought formed in my mind, in a voice that was not my own.

That's enough, it said.

Without haste, he turned and walked away. By the time he had gone two dozen paces, the light of his torch disappeared, fading into nonexistence like the final glow of twilight into night.

"Oh," I said, a little blankly. "Goodness." My legs were trembling, and I sat down, the skull—which I had almost forgotten—cradled in my lap.

I sat there for a long time, watching and listening, but nothing further happened. The mountains surrounded me, dark and impenetrable. Perhaps in the morning, I could find my way back to the trail, but for now, wandering about in darkness could lead to nothing but disaster.

I was no longer afraid; my fear had left me during my encounter with—whatever it was. I was still cold, though, and very, very hungry. I put down the skull and curled myself up beside it, pulling my damp cloak around me. It took a long time to fall asleep, and I lay in my chilly burrow watching the evening stars wheel overhead through rifts in the cloud.

I tried to make sense of the last half hour, but there was really nothing to make sense *of;* nothing, really, had happened. And yet it had; he had been there. The sense of him remained with me, somehow vaguely comforting, and at last I fell asleep, cheek pillowed on a clump of dead leaves.

I dreamt uneasily, because of cold and hunger; a procession of disjoint images. Lightning-blasted trees, blazing like torches.

Trees uprooted from the earth, walking on their roots with a dreadful lurching gait.

Lying in the rain with my throat cut, warm blood pulsing down across my chest, a queer comfort to my chilling flesh. My fingers numb, unable to move. The rain striking my skin like hail, each cold drop a hammer blow, and then the rain itself seemed warm, and soft upon my face. Buried alive, black soil showering down into open eyes.

I woke, heart pounding. Lay silent. It was deep night now; the sky stretched clear and endless overhead, and I lay in a bowl of darkness. After a time, I slept again, pursued by dreams.

Wolves howling in the distance. Fleeing panicked through a forest of white aspen that stood in snow, the trees' red sap glowing like bloody jewels on white-paper trunks. A man standing in the bleeding trees with his head plucked bald, save a standing crest of black, greased hair. He had deep eyes and a shattered smile, and the blood on his breast was brighter than the tree sap.

Wolves, much closer. Howling and barking and the scent of blood hot in my own nose, running with the pack, running from the pack. Running. Harefooted, white-toothed, and the ghost of blood a taste in my mouth, a tingle in my nose. Hunger. Chase and catch and kill and blood. Heart hammering, blood racing, sheer panic of the hunted.

I felt my armbone crack with a noise like a dry branch snapping, and tasted marrow warm and salty, slippery on my tongue.

Something brushed my face and I opened my eyes. Great yellow eyes stared into mine, from the dark ruff of a white-toothed wolf. I screamed and struck at it and the beast started back with a startled *"Woof!"*

I floundered to my knees and crouched there, gibbering. It had just gone daybreak. The dawning light was new and tender, and showed me plainly the huge black outline of . . . Rollo.

"Oh, Jesus God, what the bloody *hell* are you doing here, frigging bloody horrible . . . filthy beast!" I might eventually have gotten a grip on myself, but Jamie got one first.

Big hands pulled me up and out of my hiding place, held me tight and patted me anxiously, checking for damage. The wool of his plaid was soft against my face; it smelt of wet and lye soap and his own male scent and I breathed it in like oxygen.

"Are ye all right? For God's sake, Sassenach, are ye all right?"

"No," I said. "Yes," I said, and started to cry.

It didn't last long; it was no more than the shock of relief. I tried to say as much, but Jamie wasn't listening. He scooped me up in his arms, filthy as I was, and began to carry me toward the small stream.

"Hush, then," he said, squeezing me tightly against him. "Hush, *mo chridhe*. It's all right now; you're safe."

I was still fuddled with cold and dreams. Alone so long with no voice but my own, his sounded odd, unreal and hard to understand. The warm solidity of his grasp was real, though.

"Wait," I said, tugging feebly at his shirt. "Wait, I forgot. I have to—"

"Jesus, Uncle Jamie, look at this!"

Jamie turned, holding me. Young Ian was standing in the mouth of my refuge, framed in dangling roots, holding up the skull.

I felt Jamie's muscles tighten as he saw it.

"Holy God, Sassenach, what's that?"

"Who, you mean," I said. "I don't know. Nice chap, though. Don't let Rollo at him; he wouldn't like it." Rollo was sniffing the skull with intense concentration, wet black nostrils flaring with interest.

Jamie peered down into my face, frowning slightly.

"Are ye sure you're quite all right, Sassenach?"

"No," I said, though in fact my wits were coming back as I woke up all the way. "I'm cold and I'm starving. You didn't happen to bring any breakfast, did you?" I asked longingly. "I could murder a plateful of eggs."

"No," he said, setting me down while he groped in his sporran. "I hadna time to trouble for food, but I've got some brandywine. Here, Sassenach; it'll do you good. And then," he added, raising one eyebrow, "you can tell me how the devil ye came to be out in the middle of nowhere, aye?"

I collapsed on a rock and sipped the brandywine gratefully. The flask trembled in my hands, but the shivering began to ease as the dark amber stuff made its way directly through the walls of my empty stomach and into my bloodstream.

Jamie stood behind me, his hand on my shoulder.

"How long have ye been here, Sassenach?" he asked, his voice gentle.

"All night," I said, shivering again. "Since just before noon yesterday, when the bloody horse—I think his name's Judas—dropped me off that ledge up there."

I nodded at the ledge. The middle of nowhere was a good description of the place, I thought. It could have been any of a

thousand anonymous hollows in these hills. A thought struck me
—one that should have occurred to me long before, had I not been
so chilled and groggy.

"How the hell did you find me?" I asked. "Did one of the
Muellers follow me, or—don't tell me the bloody horse led you to
me, like Lassie?"

"It's a gelding, Auntie," Ian put in reprovingly. "No a lassie.
But we havena seen your horse at all. No, Rollo led us to ye." He
beamed proudly at the dog, who contrived to look blandly dignified, as though he did this sort of thing all the time.

"But if you haven't seen the horse," I began, bewildered,
"how did you even know I'd left Muellers'? And how could
Rollo—" I broke off, seeing the two men eyeing each other.

Ian shrugged slightly and nodded, yielding to Jamie. Jamie
hunkered down on the ground beside me, and lifting the hem of
my dress, took my bare feet into his big, warm hands.

"Your feet are frozen, Sassenach," he said quietly. "Where did
ye lose your shoes?"

"Back there," I said, with a nod toward the uprooted tree.
"They must still be there. I took them off to cross a stream, then
put them down and couldn't find them in the dark."

"They're not there, Auntie," said Ian. He sounded so queer
that I looked up at him in surprise. He was still holding the skull,
turning it gingerly over in his hands.

"No, they're not." Jamie's head was bent as he chafed my feet,
and I could see the early light glint copper off his hair, which lay
tumbled loose over his shoulders, disheveled as though he had just
risen from his bed.

"I was in bed, asleep," he said, echoing my thought. "When
yon beast suddenly went mad." He jerked his chin at Rollo, without looking up. "Barking and howling and flingin' his carcass at
the door as though the Devil was outside."

"I shouted at him, and tried to get hold of his scruff and shake
him quiet," Ian put in, "but he wouldna stop, no matter what I
did."

"Aye, he carried on so that the spittle flew from his jaws and I
was sure he'd gone truly mad. I thought he'd do us an injury, so I
bade Ian unbolt the door and let him be gone." Jamie sat back on
his heels and frowned at my foot, then picked a dead leaf off my
instep.

"Well, and *was* the Devil outside?" I asked flippantly.

Jamie shook his head.

"We searched the clearing, from the penfold to the spring, and didna find a thing—except these." He reached into his sporran and drew out my shoes. He looked up into my face, his own quite expressionless.

"They were sitting on the doorstep, side by side."

Every hair on my body rose. I lifted the flask and drained the last of the brandywine.

"Rollo tore off, bayin' like a hound," Ian said, eagerly taking up the story. "But then he came back a moment later, and began to sniff at your shoes and whinge and cry."

"I felt rather like doing that myself, aye?" Jamie's mouth lifted slightly at one corner, but I could see the fear still dark in his eyes.

I swallowed, but my mouth was too dry to talk, despite the brandywine.

Jamie slipped one shoe onto my foot, and then the other. They were damp, but faintly warm from his body.

"I did think ye were maybe dead, Cinderella," he said softly, head bent to hide his face.

Ian didn't notice, caught up in the enthusiasm of the story.

"My clever wee dog was for dashing off, the same as when he's smelt a rabbit, so we caught up our plaids and came away after him, only stopping to snatch a brand from the hearth and smoor the fire. He led us a good chase, too, did ye no, laddie?" He rubbed Rollo's ears with affectionate pride. "And here ye were!"

The brandywine was buzzing in my ears, swaddling my wits in a warm, sweet blanket, but I had enough sense left to tell me that for Rollo to have followed a trail back to me . . . someone had walked all that way in my shoes.

I had recovered some remnants of my voice by this time, and managed to talk with only a little hoarseness.

"Did you—see anything—along the way?" I asked.

"No, Auntie," Ian said, suddenly sober. "Did you?"

Jamie lifted his head, and I could see how worry and exhaustion had hollowed his face, leaving the broad cheekbones sharp beneath his skin. I wasn't the only one who had had a long, hard night.

"Yes," I said, "but I'll tell you later. Right now, I believe I've turned into a pumpkin. Let's go home."

Jamie had brought horses, but there was no way to get them down into the hollow; we were forced to make our way down the banks of the flooded stream, splashing through the shallows, then to clamber laboriously up a rocky slope to the ledge above, where the animals were tethered. Rubber-legged and flimsy after my ordeal, I wasn't a great deal of help in this endeavor, but Jamie and Ian coped matter-of-factly, boosting me over obstructions and handing me back and forth like a large, unwieldy package.

"You really aren't supposed to give alcohol to people suffering from hypothermia," I said feebly as Jamie put the flask to my lips again during one pause for rest.

"I dinna care what you're suffering from, you'll feel it less with the drink in your belly," he said. It was still chilly from the rain, but his face was flushed from the climb. "Besides," he added, mopping his brow with a fold of his plaid, "if ye pass out, you'll be less trouble to hoik about. Christ, it's like hauling a newborn calf out of a bog."

"Sorry," I said. I lay flat on the ground and closed my eyes, hoping I wouldn't throw up. The sky was spinning in one direction, my stomach in the other.

"Away, dog!" Ian said.

I opened one eye to see what was going on, and saw Ian firmly shooing Rollo away from the skull, which I had insisted he bring with us.

Seen in daylight, it was hardly a prepossessing object. Stained and discolored by the soil in which it had been buried, from a distance it resembled a smooth stone, scooped and gouged by wind and weather. Several of the teeth had been chipped or broken, though the skull showed no other damage.

"Just what do ye mean to do wi' Prince Charming there?" Jamie asked, eyeing my acquisition rather critically. His color had faded, and he had got his breath back. He glanced down at me, reached over and smoothed the hair out of my eyes, smiling.

"All right, Sassenach?"

"Better," I assured him, sitting up. The countryside had not quite stopped moving round me, but the brandy sloshing through my veins now gave the movement a rather pleasant quality, like the soothing rush of trees past the window of a railway carriage.

"I suppose we ought to take him home and give him Christian burial, at least?" Ian eyed the skull dubiously.

"I shouldn't think he'd appreciate it; I don't believe he was a Christian." I fought back a vivid recollection of the man I had seen in the hollow. While it was true that some Indians had been converted by missionaries, this particular naked gentleman, with his black-painted face and feathered hair, had given me the impression that he was about as pagan as they come.

I fumbled in the pocket of my skirt, my fingers numb and stiff.

"This was buried with him."

I drew out the flat stone I had unearthed. It was dirty brown in color, an irregular oval half the size of my palm. It was flattened on one side, rounded on the other, and smooth as though it had come from a streambed. I turned it over on my palm and gasped.

The flattened face was indeed incised with a carving, as I had thought. It was a glyph in the shape of a spiral, coiling in on itself. But it wasn't the carving that brought both Jamie and Ian to peer into my hand, heads nearly touching.

Where the smooth surface had been chipped away, the rock within glowed with a lambent fire, little flames of green and orange and red all fighting fiercely for the light.

"My God, what is it?" Ian asked, sounding awed.

"It's an opal—and a damned big one, at that," Jamie said. He poked the stone with a large, blunt forefinger, as though checking to ensure that it was real. It was.

He rubbed a hand through his hair, thinking, then glanced at me.

"They do say that opals are unlucky stones, Sassenach." I thought he was joking, but he looked uneasy. A widely traveled, well-educated man, still he had been born a Highlander, and I knew he had a deeply superstitious streak, though it didn't often show.

Ha, I thought to myself. You've spent the night with a ghost and you think *he's* superstitious?

"Nonsense," I said, with rather more conviction than I felt. "It's only a rock."

"Well, it's no so much they're unlucky, Uncle Jamie," Ian put in. "My Mam has a wee opal ring her mother left her—though it's nothing like this!" Ian touched the stone reverently. "She did say as how an opal takes on something of its owner, though—so if ye had an opal that belonged to a good person before ye, then all was well, and you'd have good luck of it. But if not—" He shrugged.

"Aye, well," Jamie said dryly. He jerked his head toward the skull, pointing with his chin. "If it belonged to this fellow, it doesna seem as if it was ower-lucky for him."

"At least we know nobody killed him for it," I pointed out.

"Perhaps they didna want it because they kent it was bad luck," Ian suggested. He was frowning at the stone, a worried line between his eyes. "Maybe we should put it back, Auntie."

I rubbed my nose and looked at Jamie.

"It's probably rather valuable," I said.

"Ah." The two of them stood in contemplation for a moment, torn between superstition and pragmatism.

"Aye well," Jamie said finally, "I suppose it will do no harm to keep it for a bit." One side of his mouth lifted in a smile. "Let me carry it, Sassenach; if I'm struck by lightning on the way home, ye can put it back."

I got awkwardly to my feet, holding on to Jamie's arm to keep my balance. I blinked and swayed, but stayed upright. Jamie took the stone from my hand and slipped it back into his sporran.

"I'll show it to Nayawenne," I said. "She might know what the carving means, at least."

"A good thought, Sassenach," Jamie approved. "And if Prince Charming should be her kinsman, she can have him, with my blessing." He nodded toward a small stand of maple trees a hundred yards away, their green barely tinged with yellow.

"The horses are tied just yonder. Can ye walk, Sassenach?"

I looked down at my feet, considering. They seemed a lot farther away than I was used to.

"I'm not sure," I said, "I think I'm really rather drunk."

"Och, no, Auntie," Ian assured me kindly. "My Da says you're never drunk, so long as ye can hold on to the floor."

Jamie laughed at this, and threw the end of his plaid over his shoulder.

"*My* Da used to say ye werena drunk, so long as ye could find your arse with both hands." He eyed my backside with a lifted brow, but wisely thought better of whatever else he might have been going to say.

Ian choked on a giggle and coughed, recovering himself.

"Aye, well. It's no much farther, Auntie. Are ye sure ye canna walk?"

"Well, I'm no going to pick her up again, I'll tell ye," Jamie said, not waiting for my answer. "I dinna want to rupture my back." He took the skull from Ian, holding it between the tips of his fingers, and placed it delicately in my lap. "Wait here wi' your wee friend, Sassenach," he said. "Ian and I will fetch the horses."

By the time we reached Fraser's Ridge, it was early afternoon. I had been cold, wet, and without food for nearly two days, and was feeling distinctly light-headed; a feeling exaggerated both by more infusions of brandywine and by my efforts to explain the events of the night before to Ian and Jamie. Viewed in the light of day, the entire night seemed unreal.

But then, almost everything seemed unreal, viewed through a haze of exhaustion, hunger, and mild drunkenness. Consequently, when we turned into the clearing, I thought at first that the smoke from the chimney was a hallucination—until the tang of burning hickory wood struck my nose.

"I thought you said you smoored the fire," I said to Jamie. "Lucky you didn't burn down the house." Such accidents were common; I had heard of more than one wooden cabin burned to the ground as the result of a poorly tended hearth.

"I did smoor it," he said briefly, swinging down from the saddle. "Someone's here. D'ye ken the horse, Ian?"

Ian stood in his stirrups to look down into the penfold.

"Why, it's Auntie's wicked beast!" he said in surprise. "And a big dapple with him!"

Sure enough, the newly named Judas was standing in the penfold, unsaddled, companionably switching flies head to tail with a thick-barreled gray gelding.

"Do you know who owns him?" I asked. I hadn't got down yet; small waves of dizziness had been washing over me every few minutes, forcing me to cling to the saddle. The ground under the horse seemed to be heaving gently up and down, like ocean billows.

"No, but it's a friend," Jamie said. "He's fed my beasts for me, and milked the goat." He nodded from the horses' hay-filled manger to the door, where a pail of milk stood on the bench, neatly covered with a square of cloth to prevent flies falling in.

"Come along, Sassenach." He reached up and took me by the waist. "We'll tuck ye in bed and brew ye a dish of tea."

Our arrival had been heard; the door of the cabin opened, and Duncan Innes looked out.

"Ah, you're there, *Mac Dubh,*" he said. "What's amiss, then? Your goat was carryin' on fit to wake the dead, wi' her bag like to burst, when I came up the trail this morning." Then he saw me, and his long, mournful face went blank with surprise.

"Mrs. Claire!" he said, taking in my mud-stained and battered appearance. "Ye'll have had an accident, then? I was a bit worrit when I found the horse loose on the mountainside as I came up, and your wee box on the saddle. I looked about and called for ye, but I couldna find any sign of ye, so I brought the beast along to the house."

"Yes, I had an accident," I said, trying to stand upright by myself and not succeeding very well. "I'm all right, though." I wasn't altogether sure about that. My head felt three times its normal size.

"Bed," Jamie said firmly, grabbing me by the arms before I could fall over. "Now."

"Bath," I said. "First."

He glanced in the direction of the creek.

"You'll freeze or drown. Or both. For God's sake, Sassenach, eat and go to bed; ye can wash tomorrow."

"Now. Hot water. Kettle." I hadn't the energy to waste on prolonged argument, but I was determined. I wasn't going to bed dirty, and I wasn't going to wash filthy sheets later.

Jamie looked at me in exasperation, then rolled his eyes in surrender.

"Hot water, kettle, now, then," he said. "Ian, fetch some wood, and then take Duncan and see to the pigs. I'm going to scrub your auntie."

"I can scrub myself!"

"The hell ye can."

He was right; my fingers were so stiff, they couldn't undo the hooks of my bodice. He undressed me as though I were a small child, tossing the ripped skirt and mud-caked petticoats carelessly into the corner, and stripping off the chemise and stays, worn so long that the cloth folds had made deep red ridges in my flesh. I groaned with a voluptuous combination of pain and pleasure, rubbing the red marks as blood coursed back through my constricted torso.

"Sit," he said, pushing a stool under me as I collapsed. He wrapped a quilt around my shoulders, put a plate containing one and a half stale bannocks in front of me, and went to rootle in the cupboard after soap, washcloth, and linen towels.

"Find the green bottle, please," I said, nibbling at the dry oatcake. "I'll need to wash my hair."

"Mmphm." More clinking, and he emerged at last with his hands full of things, including a towel and the bottle full of the shampoo I had made—not wishing to wash my hair with lye soap —from soaproot, lupin oil, walnut leaves and calendula flowers. He set these on the table, along with my largest mixing bowl, and carefully filled it with hot water from the cauldron.

Leaving this to cool a bit, Jamie dipped a rag into the water, and knelt down to wash my feet.

The feeling of warmth on my sore, half-frozen feet was as close to ecstasy as I expected to get this side of heaven. Tired and half-drunk as I was, I felt as though I were dissolving from the feet up, as he gently but thoroughly washed me from toe to head.

"Where did ye get this, Sassenach?" Recalled from a state as close to sleep as to waking, I glanced down muzzily at my left knee. It was swollen, and the inner side had gone the deep purplish-blue of a gentian.

"Oh . . . that happened when I fell off the horse."

"That was verra careless," he said sharply. "Have I not told ye time and again to be careful, especially with a new horse? Ye canna trust them at all until ye've known them a good while. And you're not strong enough to deal with one that's headstrong or skittish."

"It wasn't a matter of trusting him," I said. I rather dimly admired the broad spread of his bent shoulders, flexing smoothly under his linen shirt as he sponged my bruised knee. "The lightning scared him, and I fell off a thirty-foot ledge."

"Ye could have broken your neck!"

"Thought I had, for a bit." I closed my eyes, swaying slightly.

"Ye should have taken better thought, Sassenach; ye should never have been on that side of the ridge to begin with, let alone—"

"I couldn't help it," I said, opening my eyes. "The trail was washed out; I had to go around."

He was glaring at me, slanted eyes narrowed into dark blue slits.

"Ye ought not to have left the Muellers' in the first place, and it raining like that! Did ye not have sense enough to know what the ground would be like?"

I straightened up with some effort, holding the quilt against my breasts. It occurred to me, with a faint sense of surprise, that he was more than slightly annoyed.

"Well . . . no," I said, trying to marshal what wits I had. "How could I know something like that? Besides—"

He interrupted me by slapping the washrag into the bowl, spattering water all over the table.

"Be quiet!" he said. "I dinna mean to argue with you!"

I stared up at him.

"What the hell *do* you mean to do? And where do you get off shouting at me? I haven't done anything wrong!"

He inhaled strongly through his nose. Then he stood up, picked the rag from the bowl, and carefully wrung it out. He let out his breath, knelt down in front of me, and deftly swabbed my face clean.

"No. Ye haven't," he agreed. One corner of his long mouth quirked wryly. "But ye scairt hell out of me, Sassenach, and it makes me want to give ye a terrible scolding, whether ye deserve it or no."

"Oh," I said. I wanted at first to laugh, but felt a stab of remorse as I saw how drawn his face was. His shirt sleeve was daubed with mud, and there were burrs and foxtails in his stockings, left from a night of searching for me through the dark mountains, not knowing where I was; if I were alive or dead. I *had* scared hell out of him, whether I meant to or not.

I groped for some means of apology, finding my tongue nearly as thick as my wits. Finally I reached out and picked a fuzzy yellow catkin from his hair.

"Why don't you scold me in Gaelic?" I said. "It will ease your feelings just as much, and I'll only understand half of what you say."

He made a Scottish noise of derision, and shoved my head into the bowl with a firm hand on my neck. When I reemerged, dripping, though, he dropped a towel on my head and started in, rubbing my hair with large, firm hands and speaking in the formally menacing tones of a minister denouncing sin from the pulpit.

"Silly woman," he said in Gaelic. "You have not the brain of a fly!" I caught the words for "foolish," and "clumsy," in the subsequent remarks, but quickly stopped listening. I closed my eyes and lost myself instead in the dreamy pleasure of having my hair rubbed dry and then combed out.

He had a sure and gentle touch, probably gained from handling horses' tails. I had seen him talk to horses while he groomed them, much as he was talking to me now, the Gaelic a soothing descant to the whisk of curry comb or brush. I imagined he was more complimentary to the horses, though.

His hands touched my neck, my bare back, and shoulders as he worked; fleeting touches that brought my newly thawed flesh to life. I shivered, but let the quilt fall to my lap. The fire was still burning high, flames dancing on the side of the kettle, and the room had grown quite warm.

He was now describing, in a pleasantly conversational tone, various things he would have liked to do to me, beginning with beating me black and blue with a stick, and going on from there. Gaelic is a rich language, and Jamie was far from unimaginative in matters of either violence or sex. Whether he meant it or not, I thought it was probably a good thing that I didn't understand everything he said.

I could feel the heat of the fire on my breasts; Jamie's warmth against my back. The loose fabric of his shirt brushed my skin as he leaned across to reach a bottle on the shelf, and I shivered again. He noticed this, and interrupted his tirade for a moment.

"Cold?"

"No."

"Good." The sharp smell of camphor stung my nose, and before I could move, one large hand had seized my shoulder, holding me in place, while the other rubbed slippery oil firmly into my chest.

"Stop! That tickles! Stop, I say!"

He didn't stop. I squirmed madly, trying to escape, but he was a lot bigger than I was.

"Be still," he said, inexorable fingers rubbing deep between my ticklish ribs, under my collarbone, around and under my tender breasts, greasing me as thoroughly as a suckling pig bound for the spit.

"You *bastard*!" I said when he let me go, breathless from struggling and giggling. I reeked of peppermint and camphor, and my skin glowed with heat from chin to belly.

He grinned at me, revenged and thoroughly unrepentant.

"You do it to *me* when I've got an ague," he pointed out, wiping his hands on the towel. "Grease for the gander is grease for the goose, aye?"

"I have not got an ague! Not even a sniffle!"

"I expect ye will have, out all night and sleepin' in wet clothes." He clicked his tongue disapprovingly, like a Scottish housewife.

"And you've never done that, have you? How many times have

you caught cold from sleeping rough?'' I demanded. ''Good heavens, you lived in a *cave* for seven years!''

''And spent three of them sneezing. Besides, I'm a man,'' he added, with total illogic. ''Had ye not better put on your night rail, Sassenach? Ye havena got a stitch on.''

''I noticed. Wet clothes and being cold do not cause sickness,'' I informed him, hunting about under the table for the fallen quilt.

He raised both eyebrows.

''Oh, they don't?''

''No, they don't.'' I backed out from under the table, clutching the quilt. ''I've told you before, it's germs that cause sickness. If I haven't been exposed to any germs, I won't get sick.''

''Ah, gerrrrms,'' he said, rolling it like a marble in his mouth. ''God, ye've got a fine, fat arse! Why do folk have more illness in the winter than the springtime, then? The germs breed in the cold, I expect?''

''Not exactly.'' Feeling absurdly self-conscious, I spread the quilt, meaning to fold it around my shoulders again. Before I could wrap myself in it, though, he had grabbed me by the arm and pulled me toward him.

''Come here,'' he said, unnecessarily. Before I could say anything, he had smacked my bare backside smartly, turned me around and kissed me, hard.

He let go, and I almost fell down. I flung my arms around him, and he grabbed my waist, steadying me.

''I dinna care whether it's the germs or the night air or Billy-be-damned,'' he said, looking sternly down his nose. ''I willna have ye fallin' ill, and that's all about it. Now, hop yourself directly into your gown, and to bed with ye!''

He felt awfully good in my arms. The smooth linen of his shirtfront was cool against the heated glow of my greased breasts, and while the wool of his kilt was much scratchier against my naked thighs and belly, the sensation was by no means unpleasant. I rubbed myself slowly against him, like a cat against a post.

''Bed,'' he said again, sounding a trifle less stern.

''Mmmm,'' I said, making it reasonably obvious that I didn't mean to go there alone.

''No,'' he said, squirming slightly. I supposed that he meant to get away, but since I didn't let go, the movement merely exacerbated the situation between us.

''Mm-hmm,'' I said, holding on tight. Intoxicated as I was, it hadn't escaped me that Duncan would undoubtedly be spending the night on the hearth rug, Ian on the trundle. And while I was feeling somewhat uninhibited at the moment, the feeling didn't extend quite *that* far.

"My father told me never to take advantage of a woman who was the worse for drink," he said. He had stopped squirming, but now started again, slower, as though he couldn't help himself.

"I'm not worse, I'm better," I assured him. "Besides—" I executed a slow, sinuous squirm of my own. "I thought he said you weren't drunk if you could find your arse with both hands."

He eyed me appraisingly.

"I hate to tell ye, Sassenach, but it's not your arse ye've got hold of—it's mine."

"That's all right," I assured him. "We're married. Share and share alike. One flesh; the priest said so."

"Perhaps it was a mistake to put that grease on ye," he muttered, half to himself. "It never does this to *me*!"

"Well, you're a man."

He had one last gallant try.

"Should ye not eat a bit more, lass? You must be starving."

"Mm-hm," I said. I buried my face in his shirt and bit him, lightly. "Ravenous."

———

There is a story told of the Earl of Montrose—that after one battle, he was found lying on the field, half dead of cold and starvation, by a young woman. The young woman whipped off her shoe, mixed barley with cold water in it, and fed the resulting mess to the prostrate earl, thus saving his life.

The cup now thrust under my nose appeared to contain a portion of this same life-giving substance, with the minor difference that mine was warm.

"What is this?" I asked, eyeing the pale grains floating belly-up on the surface of a watery liquid. It looked like a cup full of drowned maggots.

"Barley crowdie," Ian said, gazing proudly at the cup as though it were his firstborn child. "I made it myself, from the bag ye brought from Muellers'."

"Thank you," I said, and took a cautious sip. I didn't *think* he had mixed it in his shoe, despite the musty aroma. "Very good," I said. "How kind of you, Ian."

He went pink with gratification.

"Och, it was nothing," he said. "There's plenty more, Auntie.

Or shall I fetch ye a bit of cheese? I could cut the green bits off for ye.''

"No, no—this will be fine," I said hastily. "Ah . . . why don't you take your gun out, Ian, and see if you can bag a squirrel or a rabbit? I'm sure I'll be well enough to cook supper.''

He beamed, the smile transforming his long, bony face.

"I'm glad to hear it, Auntie," he said. "Ye should *see* what Uncle Jamie and I have been eatin' while ye've been gone!''

He left me lying on my pillows, wondering what to do with the cup of crowdie. I didn't want to drink it, but I felt like a puddle of warm butter—soft and creamy, nearly liquid—and the idea of getting up seemed unthinkably energetic.

Jamie, making no further protests, had taken me to bed, where he had completed the business of thawing me out with thoroughness and dispatch. I thought it was a good thing he wasn't going hunting with Ian. He reeked of camphor as much as I did; the animals would scent him a mile away.

Tucking me tenderly under the quilts, he had left me to sleep while he went to greet Duncan more formally and offer him the hospitality of the house. I could hear the deep murmur of their voices outside now; they were sitting on the bench beside the door, enjoying the last of the afternoon sunshine—long, pale beams slanted through the window, lighting a warm glow of pewter and wood within.

The sun touched the skull, too. This stood on my writing table across the room, composing a cozily domestic still life with a clay jug filled with flowers and my casebook.

It was sight of the casebook that roused me from torpor. The birth I had attended at the Muellers' farm now seemed vague and insubstantial in my mind; I thought I had better record the details while I still recalled them at all.

Thus prompted by the stirrings of professional duty, I stretched, groaned, and sat up. I still felt mildly dizzy and my ears rang from the aftereffects of brandywine. I was also faintly sore almost everywhere—more in some spots than others—but generally speaking, I was in decent working order. Beginning to be hungry, though.

I did hope Ian would come back with meat for the pot; I knew better than to gorge my shriveled stomach on cheese and salt fish, but a nice, strengthening squirrel broth, flavored with spring onions and dried mushrooms, would be just what the doctor ordered.

Speaking of broth—I slid reluctantly out of bed and stumbled across the floor to the hearth, where I poured the cold barley soup back into the pot. Ian had made enough for a regiment—always supposing the regiment to be composed of Scots. Living in a country normally barren of much that was edible, they were capable of relishing glutinous masses of cereal, untouched by any redeeming hint of spice or flavor. From a feebler race myself, I didn't feel quite up to it.

The opened bag of barley stood beside the hearth, the burlap sack still visibly damp. I would have to spread the grain to dry, or it would rot. My bruised knee protesting a bit, I went and got a large flat tray-basket made of plaited reeds, and knelt to spread the damp grain in a thin layer over it.

"Will he have a soft mouth, then, Duncan?" Jamie's voice came clearly through the window; the hide covering was rolled up, to let in air, and I caught the faint tang of tobacco from Duncan's pipe. "He's a big, strong brute, but he's got a kind eye."

"Oh, he's a bonny wee fellow," Duncan said, the note of pride in his voice unmistakable. "And a nice soft mouth, aye. Miss Jo had her stableman pick him from the market in Wilmington; said he must find a horse could be managed well wi' one hand."

"Mmphm. Aye, well, he's a lovely creature." The wooden bench creaked as one of the men shifted his weight. I understood the equivocation behind Jamie's compliment, and wondered whether Duncan did, as well.

Part of it was simple condescension; Jamie had been raised on horseback, and as a born horseman, would scorn the notion that hands were necessary at all; I had seen him maneuver a horse by the shifting pressure of knees and thighs alone, or set his mount at a gallop across a crowded field, the reins knotted on the horse's neck, to leave Jamie's hands free for sword and pistol.

But Duncan was neither a horseman nor a soldier; he had lived as a fisherman near Ardrossan, until the Rising had plucked him, like so many others, from his nets and his boat, and sent him to Culloden and disaster.

Jamie wouldn't be so untactful as to point up an inexperience of which Duncan was more than aware already; he *would,* though, mean to point up something else. Had Duncan caught it?

"It's you she means to help, *Mac Dubh,* and well ye ken it, too." Duncan's tones were very dry; he'd taken Jamie's point, all right.

"I havena said otherwise, Duncan." Jamie's voice was even.

"Mmphm."

I smiled, despite the air of edginess between them. Duncan was every bit as good as Jamie at the Highland art of inarticulate eloquence. This particular noise captured both mild insult at Jamie's implication that it was improper for Duncan to be accepting the gift of a horse from Jocasta, and a willingness to accept the likewise implied apology for the insult.

"Have ye thought, then?" The bench creaked as Duncan abruptly changed the subject. "Will it be Sinclair, or Geordie Chisholm?"

Without giving Jamie time to reply, he went on, but in a way that made it clear that he had said all this before. I wondered whether he was trying to convince Jamie, or himself—or only assist them both in coming to a decision by repeating the facts of the matter.

"It's true Sinclair's a cooper, but Geordie's a good fellow; a thrifty worker, and he's the two wee sons, besides. Sinclair isna marrit, so he wouldna need so much in the way of setting up, but—"

"He'd need lathes and tools, and iron and seasoned wood," Jamie broke in. "He could sleep in his shop, aye, but he'll need the shop to sleep in. And it will cost verra dear, I think, to buy all that's needed for a cooperage. Geordie would need a bit of food for his family, but we can provide that from the place here; beyond that, he'll need no more to begin than a few wee tools—he'll have an ax, aye?"

"Aye, he'll have that from his indenture, but it's the planting season *now*, *Mac Dubh*. With the clearing—"

"I ken that weel enough," Jamie said, a bit testily. "It's me that put five acres in corn a month ago. *And* cleared them, first." While Duncan had been taking his ease at River Run, chatting in taverns and breaking in his new horse. I heard it, and so did Duncan; there was a distinct silence that spoke as loud as words.

A creak from the bench, and then Duncan spoke again, mildly.

"Your auntie Jo's sent a wee gift for ye."

"Oh, has she?" The edge in his voice was even more perceptible. I hoped Duncan had sense enough to heed it.

"A bottle of whisky." There was a smile in Duncan's voice, answered by a reluctant laugh from Jamie.

"Oh, has she?" he said again, in quite a different tone. "That's verra kind."

"She means to be." There was a substantial creak and shuffle as Duncan got to his feet. "Come wi' mè and fetch it, then, *Mac Dubh*. A wee drink wouldna do your temper any harm."

"No, it wouldn't." Jamie sounded rueful. "I've not slept the night, and I'm cranky as a rutting boar. Ye'll forgive my manners, Duncan."

"Och, dinna speak of it." There was a soft sound, as of a hand clapping a shoulder, and I heard them walk off across the yard together. I moved to the window and watched them, Jamie's hair gleaming dark bronze in the setting sun, as he tilted his head to listen to something Duncan was telling him, the shorter man gesturing in explanation. The movements of Duncan's single arm threw off the rhythm of his stride, so he walked with jerky movements, like a large puppet.

What would have become of him, I wondered, had Jamie not found him—and found a place for him? There was no place in Scotland for a one-armed fisherman. There would have been nothing for him but beggary, surely. Starvation, perhaps. Or theft to live, and death at the end of a rope, like Gavin Hayes.

But this was the New World, and if life was chancy here, well, it meant a chance at life, at least. No wonder that Jamie should worry over who should have the best chance. Sinclair the cooper, or Chisholm the farmer?

A cooper would be valuable to have at hand; it would save the men on the ridge the long trip into Cross Creek or Averasboro to fetch the barrels needed for pitch and turpentine, for salted meat and cider. But it would be expensive to set up a cooper's shop, even with the bare rudiments the trade required. And then there was the unknown Chisholm's wife and small children to be considered—how were they living now, and what might become of them without help?

Duncan had so far located thirty of the men of Ardsmuir; Gavin Hayes was the first, and we had done for him all that could be done; seen him safe into heaven's keeping. Two more were known dead, one of fever, one of drowning. Three had completed their terms of indenture, and—armed only with the ax and suit of clothes that were a bondsman's final pay—had managed to find a foothold for themselves, claiming backcountry land and carving out small homesteads there.

Of the remainder, we had brought twenty so far to settle on good land near the river, under Jamie's sponsorship. Another was feebleminded but worked for one of the others as a hired man, and so earned his keep. It had taken all of our resources to do it, using all our small quantity of cash, notes against the value of as yet nonexistent crops—and one hair-raising trip into Cross Creek.

Jamie had called upon all his acquaintance there, borrowing small amounts from each, and had then taken this money to the riverside taverns, where in three sleepless nights of play, he had managed to quadruple his stake—narrowly avoiding being knifed in the process, as I learned much later.

I was speechless, looking at the long, jagged rent in the bosom of his coat.

"What—?" I croaked at last.

He shrugged briefly, looking suddenly very tired.

"It doesna matter," he said. "It's over."

He had then shaved, washed, and gone round to all the plantation owners again, returning each man's money with thanks and a small payment of interest, leaving us with enough to manage seed corn for planting, an extra mule for plowing, a goat and some pigs.

I didn't ask him anything else; only mended the coat, and saw him safely into bed when he came back from repaying the money lent. I sat by him for a long time, though, watching the lines of exhaustion in his face ease a little as he slept.

Only a little. I had lifted his hand, limp and heavy with sleep, and traced the deep lines of his smooth, callused palm, over and over. The lines of head and heart and life ran long and deep. How many lives lay in those creases now?

My own. His settlers. Fergus and Marsali, who had just arrived from Jamaica, in the custody of Germaine, a chubby blond charmer who had his besotted father in the palm of *his* fat little hand.

I glanced involuntarily through the window at the thought. Ian and Jamie had helped to build them a small cabin only a mile from our own, and sometimes Marsali would walk over in the evenings to visit, bringing the baby. I could do with seeing him, I thought wistfully. Lonely as I sometimes was for Bree, little Germaine was a substitute for the grandchild I would never hold.

I sighed, and shrugged away the thought.

Jamie and Duncan had come back with the whisky; I could hear them talking by the paddock, their voices relaxed, all tension between them eased—for the moment.

I finished spreading out a thin layer of the wet barley and set it in the corner of the hearth to dry, then went to the writing table, uncapped the inkwell, and opened my casebook. It didn't take long to record the details of the newest Mueller's arrival into the world; it had been a long labor but otherwise quite normal. The birth itself had presented no complications; the only unusual feature had been the child's caul . . .

I stopped writing and shook my head. Still distracted by thoughts of Jamie, I had let my attention wander. Petronella's child had not been born with a caul. I had a clear memory of the top of the skull crowning, the pudendum a shiny red ring stretched tight around a small patch of black hair. I had touched it, felt the tiny pulse throbbing there, just under the skin. I remembered vividly the sensation of the wet down against my fingers, like the damp skin of a new-hatched chick.

It was the dream, I thought. I had dreamed in my burrow, mingling the events of the two births together—this one, and Brianna's. It was Brianna who had been born with a caul.

A "silly hoo," the Scots called it; a lucky hood. A fortunate portent, a caul offered—they said—protection from drowning in later life. And some children born with a caul were blessed with second sight—though having met one or two of those who saw with the third eye, I took leave to doubt that such a blessing was unmixed.

Whether lucky or not, Brianna had never showed any signs of that strange Celtic "knowing," and I thought it just as well. I knew enough of my own peculiar form of second sight—the certain knowledge of things to come—not to wish its complications on anyone else.

I looked at the page before me. Only half noticing, I had sketched the rough outline of a girl's head. A curving thick line of swirling hair, the bare suggestion of a long, straight nose. Beyond that, she was faceless.

I was no artist. I had learned to make clean clinical drawings, accurate pictures of limbs and bodies, but I lacked Brianna's gift of bringing lines to life. The sketch as it stood was no more than an aide-mémoire; I could look at it and paint her face in memory. To try to do more—to conjure flesh out of the paper—would be to ruin that, and risk losing the image I held of her in my heart.

And would I conjure her in the flesh, if I could do it? No. That I would not; I would a thousand times rather think of her in the safety and comfort of her own time than wish her here amid the harshness and dangers of this one. But it didn't mean that I didn't miss her.

For the first time, I felt some small sympathy for Jocasta Cameron and her desire for an heir; someone to remain behind, to take her place; testimony that her life had not been lived in vain.

Twilight was rising beyond the window, from field and wood and river. People spoke of night falling, but it didn't, really. Darkness rose, filling first the hollows, then shadowing the slopes, creeping imperceptibly up tree trunks and fenceposts as night swallowed the ground and rose up to join the greater dark of the star-spread sky above.

I sat staring out the window, watching the light change on the horses in the paddock; not so much fading as altering, so that everything—arched necks, round rumps, even single blades of grass—stood stark and clean, reality freed for one brief moment from the day's illusions of sun and shadow.

Unseeing, I traced the line of the drawing with my finger, over and over, as the dark rose up around me and the realities of my heart stood clear in the dusky light. No, I would not wish Brianna here. But that didn't mean I didn't miss her.

I finished my notes eventually, and sat quietly for a moment. I should go and begin making supper, I knew, but the weariness of my ordeal still dragged at me, making me unwilling to move. All my muscles ached, and the bruise on my knee throbbed. All I really wanted to do was to crawl back into bed.

Instead, I picked up the skull, which I had set down next to my casebook on the table. I ran my finger gently over the rounded cranium. It was a thoroughly macabre desk ornament, I would admit that, but I felt rather attached to it, nonetheless. I had always found bones beautiful, of man or beast; stark and graceful remnants of life reduced to its foundations.

I thought suddenly of something I had not remembered in many years; a small dark closet of a room in Paris, hidden behind an apothecary's shop. The walls covered with a honeycomb of shelves, each cell holding a polished skull. Animals of many kinds, from shrews to wolves, mice to bears.

And with my hand on the head of my unknown friend, I heard Master Raymond's voice, as clear in memory as though he stood beside me.

"Sympathy?" he had said as I touched the high curve of a polished elk's skull. "It is an unusual emotion to feel for a bone, madonna."

But he had known what I meant. I knew he did, for when I

asked him why he kept these skulls, he had smiled and said, "They are company, of a sort."

I knew what he meant, too; for surely the gentleman whose skull I kept had been company for me, in a very dark and lonely place. Not for the first time, I wondered whether he had in fact had anything to do with the apparition I had seen on the mountain; the Indian with his face painted black.

The ghost—if that is what he was—had not smiled or spoken aloud. I hadn't seen his teeth, which would be my only point of comparison with the skull I held—for I found that I was holding it, rubbing a thumb over the jagged edge of a cracked incisor. I lifted the skull to the light, examining it closely by the soft sunset light.

The teeth on the one side had been shattered; cracked and splintered as though he had been struck violently in the mouth, perhaps by a rock or a club—the stock of a gun? On the other side they were whole; in very good condition, actually. I was no expert but thought the skull was that of a mature man; one in his late thirties or early forties. A man of that age should show a good bit of wear to his teeth, given the Indians' diet of ground corn, which —owing to the manner of preparation, pounded between flat stones—contained quite a bit of ground stone as well.

The incisors and canine on the good side were scarcely worn at all, though. I turned the skull over, to judge the abrasion of the molars, and stopped cold.

Very cold, in spite of the fire at my back. As cold as I had been in the lost, fireless dark, alone on the mountain with a dead man's head. For the late sun now struck sparks from my hands: from the silver band of my wedding ring—and from the silver fillings in my late companion's mouth.

I sat staring for a moment, then turned the skull over and set it gently down on the desk, careful as though it were made of glass.

"My God," I said, all tiredness forgotten. "My God," I said, to the empty eyes and the lopsided grin. "Who *were* you?"

"Who do ye think he can have been?" Jamie touched the skull gingerly. We had no more than moments; Duncan had gone to the privy, Ian to feed the pig. I couldn't bring myself to wait, though —I had had to tell someone at once.

"I haven't the faintest idea. Except, of course, that he has to

have been someone . . . like me.'' A violent shiver ran over me.
Jamie glanced at me, and frowned.

"Ye havena take a chill, have ye, Sassenach?"

"No." I smiled weakly up at him. "Goose walking on my
grave, I expect."

He plucked my shawl from the hook by the door and swung it
around me. His hands stayed on my shoulders, warm and comforting.

"It means the one thing else, doesn't it?" he asked quietly. "It
means there is another . . . place. Perhaps nearby."

Another stone circle—or something like it. I had thought of
that, too, and the notion made me shudder once again. Jamie
looked thoughtfully at the skull, then drew the handkerchief from
his sleeve and draped it gently over the empty eyes.

"I'll bury him after supper," he said.

"Oh, supper." I pushed my hair behind my ear, trying to get
my scattered thoughts to focus on food. "Yes, I'll see if I can find
some eggs. That will be quick."

"Dinna trouble yourself, Sassenach." Jamie peered into the pot
on the hearth. "We can eat this."

This time, the shudder was purely one of fastidiousness.

"Ugh," I said. Jamie grinned at me.

"Nothing wrong wi' good barley crowdie, is there?"

"Assuming there is such a thing," I replied, looking into the
pot with distaste. "This smells more like distiller's mash." Made
with wet grain, insufficiently cooked and left standing, the cold,
scummy soup was already giving off a yeasty whiff of fermentation.

"Speaking of which," I said, giving the opened sack of damp
barley a poke with my toe, "this needs to be spread to dry, before
it starts to mold, if it hasn't already."

Jamie was staring at the disgusting soup, brows furrowed in
thought.

"Aye?" he said absently, then, coming to consciousness, "Oh,
aye. I'll do it." He twisted shut the top of the bag, and heaved it
onto his shoulder. On the way out the door, he paused, looking at
the shrouded skull.

"You said ye didna think him Christian," he said, and glanced
curiously at me. "Why was that, Sassenach?"

I hesitated, but there was no time to tell him about my dream—

if that's what it had been. I could hear Duncan and Ian in conversation, coming toward the house.

"No particular reason," I said, with a shrug.

"Aye, well," he said. "We'll give him the benefit o' the doubt."

24

Letter-Writing:
The Great Art o' Love

Oxford, March 1971

R oger supposed that it must rain as much in Inverness as it did in Oxford, but somehow he had never minded the northern rain. The cold Scottish wind sweeping in off the Moray Firth was exhilarating and the drenching rain both stimulation and refreshment to the spirit.

But that had been Scotland, when Brianna was with him. Now she was in America, he in England, and Oxford was cold and dull, all its streets and buildings gray as the ash of dead fires. Rain pattered on the shoulders of his scholar's gown as he dashed across the quad, shielding an armload of papers under the poplin folds. Once in the shelter of the porter's lodge, he stopped to shake himself, doglike, flinging droplets over the stone passage.

"Any letters?" he asked.

"Think so, Mr. Wakefield. Just a sec." Martin disappeared into his inner sanctum, leaving Roger to read the names of the College's war dead, carved on the stone tablet inside the entry.

George Vanlandingham, Esq. The Honorable Phillip Menzies. Joseph William Roscoe. Not for the first time, Roger found himself wondering about those dead heroes and what they had been like. Since meeting Brianna and her mother, he'd found that the past too often wore a disturbingly human face.

"Here you are, Mr. Wakefield." Martin leaned beaming across the counter, holding out a thin sheaf of letters. "One from the States today," he added, with a broad wink.

Roger felt an answering grin break out on his face, and a warm glow spread at once from his chest through his limbs, dispelling the chill of the rainy day.

"Will we be seeing your young woman up soon, Mr. Wakefield?" Martin craned his neck, peering frankly at the letter with its U.S. stamps. The porter had met Brianna when she had come down with Roger just before Christmas, and had fallen under her spell.

"I hope so. Perhaps in the summer. Thanks!"

He turned toward his staircase, tucking the letters carefully into the sleeve of his gown while he groped for his key. He felt a mingled sense of elation and dismay at thought of the summer. She'd said she'd come in July—but July was still four months away. In some moods, he didn't think he'd last four days.

Roger folded the letter again and tucked it into his inside pocket, next to his heart. She wrote every few days, from brief notes to long screeds, and each of her letters left him with a small warm glow that lasted usually until the next arrived.

At the same time, her letters were faintly unsatisfactory these days. Still warmly affectionate, always signed "Love," always saying she missed him and wanted him with her. No longer the sort of thing that burned the page, though.

Perhaps it was natural; a normal progression as they knew each other longer; no one could go on writing passionate missives day after day, not with any honesty.

No doubt it was only his imagination that Brianna seemed to hold back a bit in her letters. He could do without the excesses of one friend's girl, who had clipped bits of her pubic hair and included them in a letter—though he rather admired the sentiment behind the gesture.

He took a bite of his sandwich and chewed absentmindedly, thinking of the latest article Fiona had showed him. Now married, Fiona considered herself an expert on matters matrimonial, and took a sisterly interest in the bumpy course of Roger's love affair.

She was constantly clipping helpful tips from women's magazines and mailing them to him. The latest had been a piece from *My Weekly,* entitled "How to Intrigue a Man." *Sauce for the gander,* Fiona had written pointedly in the margin.

"Share his interests," one tip advised. "If you think football's a loss, but he's dead keen, sit down beside him and ask about Arsenal's chances the week. If football's boring, *he* isn't."

Roger smiled a little grimly. He'd been sharing Brianna's interests, all right, if tracking her bloody parents through their hair-raising history counted as a pastime. Damn little of that he could share with her, though.

"Be coy," said another of the magazine's tips. "Nothing

piques a man's interest more than an air of reserve. Don't let him get too close, too soon."

It occurred to Roger to wonder whether Brianna had been reading similar advice in American magazines, but he dismissed the thought. She wasn't above reading fashion magazines—he had seen her do it on occasion—but Brianna Randall was as incapable of playing that sort of silly game as he was himself.

No, she wouldn't put him off just to raise his interest in her; what would be the point? Surely she knew just how much he cared about her.

Did she, though? With a qualm of uneasiness, Roger recalled another of *My Weekly*'s tips to the lovelorn.

"Don't assume he can read your mind," the article said. "Give him a hint of how you feel."

Roger took a random bite of the sandwich and chewed, oblivious to its contents. Well, he'd hinted, all right. Come out and bared his bloody soul. And she'd promptly leapt into a plane and buggered off to Boston.

"Don't be too aggressive," he murmured, quoting Tip #14, and snorted. The woman don next to him edged slightly away.

Roger sighed and deposited the bitten sandwich distastefully on the plastic tray. He picked up the cup of what the dining hall was pleased to call coffee, but didn't drink it, merely sat with it between his hands, absorbing its meager warmth.

The trouble was that while he thought he had succeeded in deflecting Brianna's attention from the past, he had been unable to ignore it himself. Claire and that bloody Highlander of hers obsessed him; they might as well have been his own family, for the fascination they held.

"Always be honest." Tip #3. If he had been, if he'd helped her to find out everything, perhaps the ghost of Jamie Fraser would be laid now—and so would Roger.

"Oh, bugger!" he muttered to himself.

The woman next to him crashed her coffee cup onto her tray and stood up suddenly.

"Go bugger *yourself*!" she said crisply, and walked off.

Roger stared after her for a moment.

"No fear," he said. "I think maybe I already have."

25

Enter a Serpent

October 1768

In principle, I had no objection to snakes. They ate rats, which was laudable of them, some were ornamental, and most of them were wise enough to keep out of my way. Live and let live was my basic attitude.

On the other hand, that was theory. In practice, I had any number of objections to the huge snake curled up on the seat of the privy. Beyond the fact that he was gravely discommoding me at present, he wasn't usefully eating rats and he wasn't aesthetically pleasing, either, being a sort of drab gray with darker splotches.

My major objection to him, though, was the fact that he was a rattlesnake. I supposed that in a way it was fortunate that he was; it was only the heartstopping buzz of his rattles that had prevented me sitting on him in the dawn's early light.

The first sound froze me in place, just inside the tiny privy. I extended one foot behind me, groping gingerly for the doorsill. The snake didn't like that; I froze again as the warning buzz increased in volume. I could see the vibrating tip of his tail, sticking up like a thick yellow finger, rudely pointing from the heap of coils.

My mouth had gone dry as paper; I bit the inside of my cheek, trying to summon a little saliva.

How long was he? I seemed to recall Brianna's telling me— from her Girl Scout handbook—that rattlesnakes were capable of striking at a distance up to one-third their own body length. No more than two feet separated my nightgown-covered thighs from the nasty flat head with its lidless eyes.

Was he six feet long? It was impossible to tell, but the squirm of coils looked unpleasantly massive, the rounded body thick with scaled muscle. He was a bloody big snake, and the fear of being ignominiously bitten in the crotch if I moved was enough to make me stand still.

I couldn't stand still forever, though. Other considerations aside, the shock of seeing the snake hadn't decreased the urgency of my bodily functions in the slightest.

I had some vague notion that snakes were deaf; perhaps I could shout for help. But what if they weren't? There was that Sherlock Holmes story about the snake who responded to a whistle. Perhaps the snake would find whistling inoffensive, at least. Cautiously, I pursed my lips and blew. Nothing came out but a thin stream of air.

"Claire?" said a puzzled voice behind me. "What the hell are ye doing?"

I jumped at the sound, and so did the snake—or at least it moved suddenly, flexing its coils in what appeared to be imminent attack.

I froze to the doorframe and the snake quit moving, except for the chronic whirr of its rattles, like the annoying buzz of an alarm clock that wouldn't shut off.

"There's a fucking snake in here," I said through my teeth, trying not to move even my lips.

"Well, why are ye standing there? Move aside and I'll pitch it out." I could hear Jamie's footsteps, coming close.

The snake heard him too—obviously it *wasn't* deaf—and revved up its rattling.

"Ah," Jamie said, in a different tone of voice. I heard a rustle as he stooped behind me. "Stand still, Sassenach."

I hadn't time to respond to this piece of gratuitous advice before a heavy stone whizzed past my hip and struck the snake amidships. It sprang into something resembling a Gordian knot, squirmed, writhed—and fell into the privy, where it landed with a nasty sort of hollow *thwuck*!

I didn't wait to congratulate the victorious warrior, but instead turned and ran for the nearest patch of woods, the dew-wet hem of my nightgown slapping round my ankles.

Returning a few minutes later in a more settled frame of mind, I found Jamie and Young Ian squeezed into the privy together—a tight fit, considering their sizes—the latter squatting on the bench with a pine-knot torch as the former bent over the hole, peering into the depths beneath.

"Can they swim?" Ian was asking, trying to see past Jamie's head without setting his uncle's hair on fire.

"I dinna ken," Jamie replied dubiously. "I think maybe so. What I want to know is, can they jump?"

Ian jerked back, then laughed a little nervously, not altogether sure that Jamie was joking.

"Here, I canna see a thing; hand me the light." Jamie reached up to take the splinter of pine from Ian, and lowered it gingerly into the hole.

"If the stink doesna put the flame out, belike we'll burn down the privy," he muttered, bending low. "Now, then, where the devil—"

"There it is! I see it!" Ian cried.

Both heads jerked, and cracked together with the sound of splitting melons. Jamie dropped the torch, which fell into the hole and was promptly extinguished. A thin wisp of smoke drifted up from the rim of the hole, like incense.

Jamie staggered out of the privy, hands clutching his forehead, eyes squeezed shut with pain. Young Ian leaned against the inside wall, hands pressed tightly over the crown of his head, making abrupt and breathless remarks in Gaelic.

"Is it still alive?" I asked anxiously, peering toward the privy.

Jamie opened one eye and regarded me under the clutching fingers.

"Oh, my head's fine, thanks," he said. "I expect my ears will ha' quit ringing by next week, sometime."

"Now, now," I said soothingly. "It would take a sledge-hammer to dent your skull. Let me look, though." I pushed his fingers aside and pulled his head down, feeling gently through the thick hair. There was a small bruised spot just above the hairline, but no blood.

I kissed the spot perfunctorily and patted him on the head.

"You won't die," I said. "Not from that, anyway."

"Oh, good," he said dryly. "I'd much rather die of snakebite next time I sit down to my business."

"It's a poisonous serpent, is it?" Ian asked, letting go of his head and coming out of the privy. He inhaled deeply, filling his thin chest with fresh air.

"Venomous," Jamie corrected him. "If it bites you and makes ye sick, it's venomous; if you bite *it* and it makes ye sick, it's poisonous."

"Oh, aye," Ian said, dismissing this pedantry. "It's a wicked snake, though?"

"Very wicked," I said, with a slight shudder. "What are you going to do about it?" I asked, turning to Jamie.

He raised one eyebrow.

"Me? Why ought I to do anything about it?" he asked.

"You can't just let him stay in there!"

"Why not?" he said, raising the other brow.

Ian scratched his head absently, winced as he encountered the lump left by his collision with Jamie, and stopped.

"Well, I dinna ken, Uncle Jamie," he said dubiously. "If ye want to let your balls hang over a pit wi' a deadly viper in it, that's your concern, but the notion makes my flesh creep a bit. How big's the thing?"

"Fair-sized, I'll admit." Jamie flexed his wrist, showing his forearm by way of comparison.

"Eeugh!" said Ian.

"You don't *know* they don't jump," I put in helpfully.

"Aye, I do." Jamie eyed me cynically. "Still, I grant ye, the thought's enough to make one a bit costive. How d'ye mean to get him out, though?"

"I could shoot him wi' your pistol," Ian offered, brightening at the thought of getting his hands on Jamie's treasured pistols. "We needn't get him out if we can kill him."

"Is he . . . ah . . . visible?" I put in delicately.

Jamie rubbed his chin dubiously. He hadn't shaved yet, and the dark red bristles rasped under his thumb.

"Not very. There's no more than a few inches o' filth in the pit, but I shouldna think ye could see him well enough to aim, and I hate to waste the shot."

"We could invite all of the Hansens for dinner, serve beer, and drown him," I suggested facetiously, naming a nearby—and very numerous—Quaker family.

Ian erupted in giggles. Jamie gave me an austere sort of look, and turned toward the woods.

"I'll think of something," he said. "After my breakfast."

Breakfast was luckily no great problem, as the hens had helpfully provided me with nine eggs and the bread had risen satisfactorily. The butter was still immured in the back of the pantry, under the baleful guard of the newly farrowed sow, but Ian had managed to lean in and snatch a pot of jam from the shelf as I stood by with the broom, jabbing it into the sow's gnashing jaws as she made little darting charges at Ian's legs.

"I'll have to have a new broom," I remarked, eyeing the tattered remains as I dished up the eggs. "Perhaps I'll go up to the willow grove by the stream this morning."

"Mmphm." Jamie reached out a hand and patted absently around on the table, searching for the bread plate. His attention was wholly focused on the book he was reading, Bricknell's *Natural History of North Carolina.*

"Here it is," he said. "I knew I'd seen a bit about rattlesnakes." Locating the bread by feel, he took a piece and used it to scoop a healthy portion of egg into his mouth. Having engulfed this, he read aloud, holding the book in one hand while groping over the tabletop with the other.

" 'The Indians frequently pull out the snakes' Teeth, so that they never afterwards can do any Mischief by biting; this may be easily done, by tying a bit of red Wollen Cloth to the upper end of a long hollow Cane, and so provoking the Rattle-Snake to bite, and suddenly pulling it away from him, by which means the Teeth stick fast in the Cloath, which are plainly to be seen by those present.' "

"Have we any red cloth, Auntie?" Ian asked, washing down his own share of the eggs with chicory coffee.

I shook my head, and speared the last of the sausages before Jamie's groping hand reached it.

"Blue, green, yellow, drab, white, and brown. No red."

"That's a fine wee book, Uncle Jamie," Ian said, with approval. "Does it say more about the snakes?" He looked hungrily over the expanse of table, in search of more food. Without comment, I reached into the hutch and brought out a plate of spoonbread, which I set before him. He sighed happily and waded in, as Jamie turned the page.

"Well, here's a bit about how the rattlesnakes charm squirrels and rabbits." Jamie touched his plate, but encountered nothing save bare surface. I pushed the muffins toward him.

" 'It is surprizing to observe how these Snakes will allure and charm Squirrels, Hedge-Conneys, Partridges and many other small Beasts and Birds to them, which they quickly devour. The Sympathy is so strong between these, that you shall see the Squirrel or Partridge (as they have espied this Snake) leap or fly from Bough to Bough, until at last they run or leap directly into its Mouth, not having power to avoid their Enemy, who never stirs out of the Posture or Quoil until he obtains his Prey.' "

His hand, blindly groping after sustenance, encountered the

muffins. He picked one up and glanced up at me. "Damned if I've ever seen that, myself. D'ye think it likely?"

"No," I said, pushing the curls back off my forehead. "Does that book have any helpful suggestions for dealing with vicious pigs?"

He waved absently at me with the remnants of his muffin.

"Dinna fash," he murmured. "I'll manage the pig." He took his eyes off the book long enough to glance over the table at the empty dishes. "Are there no more eggs?"

"There are, but I'm taking them up to our guest at the corn-crib." I added two slices of bread to the small basket I was packing, and took up the bottle of infusion I had left steeping overnight. The brew of goldenrod, bee-balm, and wild bergamot was a blackish green, and smelled like burnt fields, but it might help. It couldn't hurt. On impulse, I picked up the tied-feather amulet old Nayawenne had given me; perhaps it would reassure the sick man. Like the medicine, it couldn't hurt.

Our impromptu guest was a stranger; a Tuscarora from a northern village. He had come to the farm several days before, as part of a hunting party from Anna Ooka, on the trail of bear.

We had offered food and drink—several of the hunters were Ian's friends—but in the course of the meal I had noticed this man gazing glassy-eyed into his cup. Close examination had showed him to be suffering from what I was convinced was measles, an alarming disease in these days.

He had insisted on leaving with his companions, but two of them had brought him back a few hours later, stumbling and delirious.

He was plainly—and alarmingly—contagious. I had made him a comfortable bed in the newly built and so-far empty corncrib, and forced his companions to go and wash in the creek, a proceeding which they plainly found senseless, but in which they humored me before departing, leaving their comrade in my hands.

The Indian was lying on his side, curled under his blanket. He didn't turn to look at me, though he must have heard my footsteps on the path. I could hear him, all right; no need for my makeshift stethoscope—the rales in his lungs were clearly audible at six paces.

"*Comment ça va?*" I said, kneeling down by him. He didn't answer; it was unnecessary, in any case. I didn't need anything beyond the rattling wheeze to diagnose pneumonia, and the look of him merely confirmed it—eyes sunken and dull, the flesh of his face fallen away, consumed to the bone by the fierce blaze of fever.

I tried to persuade him to eat—he desperately needed nourishment—but he would not even bother to turn away his face. The water bottle by his side was empty; I had brought more but didn't give it to him right away, thinking he might swallow the infusion from sheer thirst.

He did take a few mouthfuls, but then stopped swallowing, merely allowing the greenish-black liquid to run out of the corners of his mouth. I tried coaxing in French, but he was having none of it; he didn't even acknowledge my presence, just stared past my shoulder at the morning sky.

His thin body sagged with despair; plainly he thought himself abandoned, left to die in the hands of strangers. I felt a gnawing anxiety that he might be right—surely he *would* die if he would take nothing.

He would take water, at least. He drank thirstily, draining the bottle, and I went to the stream to fill it again. When I came back, I drew the amulet from my basket and held it up in front of his face. I thought I saw a flicker of surprise behind the half-closed lids—nothing so strong as to be called hope, but he did at least take conscious notice of me for the first time.

Seized by inspiration, I sank slowly down onto my knees. I had no notion at all of the proper ceremony to employ, but I had been a doctor long enough to know that while the power of suggestion was no substitute for antibiotics, it was certainly better than nothing.

I held up the raven's-feather amulet, turned my face skyward, and solemnly intoned the most sonorous thing I could remember, which happened to be Dr. Rawlings's receipt for the treatment of syphilis, rendered in Latin.

I poured a small bit of lavender oil into my hand, dipped the feather in it, and anointed his temples and throat, while singing "Blow the Man Down," in a low, sinister voice. It might help the headache. His eyes were following the feather's movements; I felt rather like a rattlesnake charming away in its "Quoil," waiting for a squirrel to run down my throat.

I picked up his hand, laid the oil-drabbled amulet across his palm, and closed his fingers round it. Then I took the jar of mentholated bear grease and painted mystic patterns on his chest, being careful to rub it well in with the balls of my thumbs. The reek cleared *my* sinuses; I could only hope it would help the patient's thick congestion.

I completed my ritual by solemnly blessing the bottle of infusion with *"In nomine Patri, et Filii, et Spiritu Sancti, Amen."* and presenting it to my patient's lips. Looking mildly hypnotized, he opened his mouth and obediently drank the rest.

I drew the blanket up around his shoulders, put the food I had brought down beside him, and left him, with mixed feelings of hope and fraudulence.

I walked slowly beside the stream, eyes alert as always for anything useful. It was too early in the year for most medicinals; for medicine, the older and tougher the plant, the better; several seasons of fighting off insects ensured a higher concentration of the active principles in their roots and stems.

Also, with many plants, it was the flower, fruit, or seed that yielded a useful substance, and while I'd spotted clumps of turtlehead and lobelia sprouting in the mud along the path, those had long since gone to seed. I marked the locations carefully in my mind for future reference, and went on hunting.

Watercress was abundant; patches of it floated among the rocks all along the margin of the stream, and a huge mat of the spicy dark green leaves lay temptingly just ahead. A nice patch of scouring rushes, too! I had come down barefoot, knowing I'd be wading before long; I tucked up my skirts and ventured cautiously out into the stream, cutting knife in hand and basket over my arm, breath sucked in against the freezing chill.

My feet lost all feeling within moments—but I didn't care. I quite forgot the snake in the privy, the pig in the pantry, and the Indian in the corncrib, absorbed in the rush of water past my legs, the wet, cold touch of stems and the breath of aromatic leaves.

Dragonflies hung in the patches of sunshine on the shallows, and minnows darted past, snatching gnats too small for me to see. A kingfisher called in a loud, dry rattle from somewhere upstream, but he was after larger prey. The minnows scattered at my intrusion but then swarmed back, gray and silver, green and gold, black marked with white, all insubstantial as the shadows from last year's leaves, floating on the water. Brownian motion, I thought, seeing puffs of silt float up and swirl around my ankles, obscuring the fish.

Everything moving, all of the time, down to the smallest molecule—but in its movement, giving the paradoxical impression of stillness, small local chaos giving way to the illusion of a greater order overall.

I moved, too, taking my part in the stream's bright dance, feeling light and shadow change across my shoulders, toes searching for footholds among the slippery, half-seen rocks. My hands and feet were numb from the water; I felt as though I were half made of wood, yet intensely alive, like the silver birch that glowed above me, or the willows that trailed wet leaves in the pool below.

Perhaps the legends of green men and the myths of transformed nymphs began this way, I thought: not with trees come alive and walking, nor yet with women turned to wood—but with submersion of warm human flesh into the colder sensations of the plants, chilled to slow awareness.

I could feel my heart beat slowly, and the half-painful throb of blood in my fingers. Sap rising. I moved with the rhythms of water and of wind, without haste or conscious thought, part of the slow and perfect order of the universe.

I had forgotten the bit about small local chaos.

Just as I came to the willows' bend, there was a loud shriek from beyond the trees. I'd heard similar noises from a variety of animals, from catamounts to hunting eagles, but I knew a human voice when I heard one.

Blundering out of the stream, I shoved my way through the tangled branches, and burst through into the clear space beyond. A boy was dancing on the bank above me, slapping madly at his legs and howling as he hopped to and fro.

"What—?" I began, and he glanced up at me, blue eyes wide with startlement at my sudden appearance.

He wasn't nearly as startled as I was. He was eleven or twelve; tall and thin as a pine sapling, with a mad tangle of thick russet hair. Slanted blue eyes stared at me from either side of a knife-bridged nose, familiar to me as the back of my own hand, though I knew I had never seen this child before.

My heart was somewhere in the vicinity of my tonsils, and the chill had shot up from my feet into the pit of my stomach. Trained to react in spite of shock, I managed to take in the rest of his appearance—shirt and breeches of good quality, though splashed with water, and long pale shins blobbed with black clots like bits of mud.

"Leeches," I said, professional calm descending by habit over personal tumult. *It couldn't be,* I was telling myself, at the same time that I knew it damn well *was*. "It's only leeches. They won't hurt you."

"I know what they are!" he said. "Get them off me!" He swatted at his calf, shuddering with dislike. "They're vile!"

"Oh, not so terribly vile," I said, beginning to get a grip on myself. "They have their uses."

"I don't care what use they are!" he bellowed, stamping in frustration. "I hate them, get them off me!"

"Well, stop whacking at them," I said sharply. "Sit you down and I'll take care of it."

He hesitated, glaring at me suspiciously, but reluctantly sat down on a rock, thrusting his leech-spattered legs out in front of him.

"Get them off *now*!" he demanded.

"In good time," I said. "Where did you come from?"

He stared blankly at me.

"You don't live near here," I said, with complete certainty. "Where did you come from?"

He made an obvious effort to collect himself.

"Ah . . . we slept in a place called Salem, three nights past. That was the last town I saw." He wiggled his legs hard. "Get them off, I say!"

There were assorted methods of getting leeches off, most of them somewhat more damaging than the leeches themselves. I had a look; he'd picked up four on one leg, three on the other. One of the fat little beasts was already near bloat, gone plump and shiny with stretching. I edged a thumbnail under its head and it popped off into my hand, round as a pebble and heavy with blood.

The boy stared it, pale under his tan, and shuddered.

"Don't want to waste it," I said casually, and went to retrieve the basket I had dropped under the branches as I pushed my way through the trees.

Nearby, I saw his coat on the ground, discarded shoes and stockings with it. Simple buckles on the shoes, but silver, not pewter. Good broadcloth, not showy but cut with a deal more style than one saw anywhere north of Charleston. I hadn't really needed confirmation, but there it was.

I scooped up a handful of mud, pressed the leech gently into it and wrapped the gooey blob in wet leaves, only then noticing that my hands were trembling. The idiot! The deceitful, wicked, conniving . . . what in *hell* had made him come here? And God, what would Jamie do?

I came back to the boy, who was bent double, peering at the remaining leeches with a look of disgusted loathing. One more was close to dropping; as I knelt in front of him, it fell off, bouncing slightly on the damp ground.

"Augh!" he said.

"Where's your stepfather?" I asked abruptly. Few things could have taken his attention off his legs, but that did. His head jerked up and he stared at me in astonishment.

It was a cool day, but a light dew of sweat shone on his face. It was narrower through cheek and temple, I thought, and the mouth was quite unlike; perhaps the resemblance was not really so pronounced as I thought.

"How do you know me?" he asked, drawing himself up with an air of hauteur that would have been extremely funny under other circumstances.

"All I know about you is that your given name is William. Am I right?" My hands curled at my sides, and I hoped I was wrong. If he *was* William, that wasn't quite all I knew about him, but it was plenty to be going on with.

A hot flush rose into his cheeks, and his eyes raked over me, his attention temporarily distracted from the leeches by being so familiarly addressed by what—I suddenly realized—appeared to be a disheveled beldame with her skirts round her thighs. Either he had good manners, or the disparity between my voice and my appearance made him cautious, because he swallowed the instant retort that came to his lips.

"Yes, it is," he said shortly, instead. "William, Viscount Ashness, ninth Earl of Ellesmere."

"All that?" I said politely. "Gracious." I took hold of one leech between thumb and forefinger and pulled gently. The thing stretched out like a thick rubber band, but declined to let go. The boy's pale flesh pulled out, too, and he made a small choking sound.

"Let go!" he said. "It'll break, you'll break it!"

"Could do," I admitted. I got to my feet and shook down my skirts, putting myself in better order.

"Come along," I said, offering him a hand. "I'll take you to the house. If I sprinkle a bit of salt on them, they'll drop off at once."

He refused the hand, but got to his feet, a little shakily. He glanced around, as though looking for someone.

"Papa," he explained, seeing my expression. "We missed the

way, and he told me to wait by the stream while he made sure of our direction. I shouldn't like him to take alarm if I am not here when he returns.''

"I shouldn't worry," I said. "I imagine he'll have found the house himself by this time; it isn't far." A fair guess, as it was the only house in some distance, and at the end of a well-marked trail. Lord John had plainly left the boy while he went ahead, to find Jamie—and warn him. Very thoughtful. My lips tightened involuntarily.

"Will that be Frasers'?" the boy asked. He took a ginger step, spraddling so as not to allow his legs to rub together. "We had come to see a James Fraser."

"I'm Mrs. Fraser," I said, and smiled at him. *Your stepmother,* I might have added—but didn't. "Come along."

He followed me through the scrim of trees toward the house, almost treading on my heels in his haste. I kept tripping over tree roots and half-buried stones, not watching where I was going, fighting the overwhelming urge to turn around and stare at him. If William, Viscount Ashness, ninth Earl of Ellesmere, was not the very last person I had ever expected to see in the backwoods of North Carolina, he was certainly next to the last—King George was a trifle less likely to turn up on the doorstep, I supposed.

What had possessed that . . . that . . . I groped about, trying to choose among several discreditable epithets to apply to Lord John Grey, and gave up the struggle, in favor of trying to think what in heaven's name to do. I gave that up, too; there wasn't a thing I *could* do.

William, Viscount Ashness, ninth Earl of Ellesmere. Or he thought he was. *And just what do you propose to do,* I thought silently and savagely toward Lord John Grey, *when he finds out that he's really the bastard son of a pardoned Scottish criminal? And more important—what's the Scottish criminal going to do? or feel?*

I stopped, causing the boy to stumble as he tried to avoid crashing into me.

"Sorry," I murmured. "Thought I saw a snake," and went on, the thought that had stopped me in my tracks still knotting my midsection like a dose of bitter apples. Could Lord John have brought the boy on purpose to reveal his parentage? Did he mean to leave him here, with Jamie—with us?

Alarming as I found the notion, I couldn't reconcile it with the man I had met in Jamaica. I might have sound reasons for disliking John Grey—always difficult to feel a warm sense of goodwill toward a man with a professed homosexual passion for one's husband, after all—but I had to admit that I had seen no trace of either recklessness or cruelty in his character. On the contrary, he had struck me as a sensitive, kindly, and honorable man—or at least he had, before I'd found out about his predilections toward Jamie.

Could something have happened? Some threat to the boy that made Lord John fear for his safety? Surely no one could have found out the truth about William—no one knew, save Lord John and Jamie. And me, of course, I added as an afterthought. Without the evidence of the resemblance—again I repressed the urge to turn round and stare at him—there was no reason for anyone ever to suspect.

But see them side by side, and—well, I shortly *would* see them side by side. The thought gave me a queer hollowness beneath the breastbone, half fright and half anticipation. Was it really as strong as I thought, that resemblance?

I took a deliberate quick detour, through a clump of low-hanging dogwood, making an excuse to turn and wait for him. He came through after me, ducking awkwardly to retrieve the silver-buckled shoe he had dropped.

No, I thought, watching covertly as he straightened up, face flushed from bending. It wasn't as strong as I'd thought at first. He had the promise of Jamie's bones, but it wasn't all there yet—he had the outlines, but not yet the substance. He would be very tall—that was obvious—but now he was about my height, gawky and slender, his limbs very long, and thin enough to seem almost delicate.

He was much darker than Jamie, too; while his hair glinted red in the shafts of sunlight that came through the branches, it was a deep chestnut, nothing like Jamie's bright red-gold, and his skin had turned a soft golden brown in the sun, not at all like Jamie's half-burnt bronze.

He had the Frasers' slanted cat-eyes, though, and there was something about the set of his head, the cock of the slender shoulders, that made me think of—

Bree. It hit me with a small shock, like a spark of electricity. He did look quite a bit like Jamie, but it was my memories of Brianna that had caused that jolt of instant recognition when I saw him. Only ten years her junior, the childish outlines of his face were much more similar to hers than to Jamie's.

He had paused to disentangle a long strand of hair from a grappling dogwood branch; now he came up with me, one brow raised inquiringly.

"Is it far?" he asked. The color had come back to his face with the exertion of walking, but he still looked a trifle sick, and kept his eyes averted from his legs.

"No," I said. I motioned toward the chestnut grove. "Just there. Look; you can see the smoke from the chimney."

He didn't wait to be led, but set off with dogged speed, anxious to be rid of the leeches.

I followed him quickly, not wanting him to reach the cabin ahead of me. I was prey to a mixture of the most disquieting sensations; uppermost was anxiety for Jamie, a little lower, anger at John Grey. Below that, an intense curiosity. And at the bottom, far enough down that I could almost pretend it wasn't there, was a pang of sharp longing for my daughter, whose face I had never thought to see again.

Jamie and Lord John were sitting on the bench by the door; at the sound of our steps, Jamie rose and looked toward the wood. He'd had time to prepare himself; his glance passed casually over the boy as he turned to me.

"Oh, Claire. Ye've found the other of our visitors, then. I'd sent Ian down to find ye. Ye'll recall Lord John, I expect?"

"How could I forget?" I said, giving his lordship a particularly bright smile. His mouth twitched slightly, but he kept a straight face as he bowed deeply in my direction. How did a man stay so impeccably groomed after several days on horseback, sleeping in the woods?

"Your servant, Mrs. Fraser." He glanced at the boy, frowning slightly at his state of undress. "May I present my stepson, Lord Ellesmere? And William, as I see you have made the acquaintance of our gracious hostess, will you also make your compliments to our host, Captain Fraser?"

The boy was shifting from foot to foot, nearly dancing on his toes. At this prompting, though, he jerked a quick bow in Jamie's direction.

"Your servant, Captain," he said, then cast an agonized glance at me, plainly conscious of nothing but the fact that more of his blood was being sucked out by the second.

"You'll excuse us?" I said politely, and taking the boy by the

arm, led him into the cabin and shut the door firmly in the astonished faces of the men. William sat immediately on the stool I
pointed out, and thrust out his legs, trembling.

"Hurry!" he said. "Oh, please, do hurry!"

There was no salt ground; I took my digging knife and chipped
a piece from the block with reckless haste, dropped it into my
mortar, and smashed it into granules with a few quick jabs of the
pestle. Crumbling the grains between my fingers, I scattered the
salt thickly on each leech.

"Rather hard on the poor old leeches," I said, seeing the first
draw itself slowly up into a ball. "Still, it does the trick." The
leech let go its grip and tumbled off William's leg, followed in
similar fashion by its fellows, who writhed in slow-motion agony
on the floor.

I scooped up the tiny bodies and flung them into the fire, then
knelt in front of him, tactfully keeping my head bent while he got
control of his face.

"Here, let me take care of the bites." Tiny streams of blood ran
down his legs; I dabbed them with a clean cloth, then washed the
small wounds with vinegar and St.-John's-wort to stop the bleeding.

He let out a deep and tremulous sigh of relief as I dried his
shins. "It's not that I'm afraid of—of blood," he said, in a tone
of bravado that made it apparent that that was precisely what he
was afraid of. "It's only they're such filthy creatures."

"Nasty little things," I agreed. I stood up, took a clean cloth,
dipped it in water, and matter-of-factly wiped his smudged face.
Then, without asking, I picked up my hairbrush and began to
comb out the snarls of his hair.

He looked utterly startled at this familiarity, but beyond an
initial stiffening of his spine, made no protest, and as I began to
order his hair, he let out another small sigh, and let his shoulders
slump a little.

His skin had a pleasant animal heat, and my fingers, still chilly
from the stream, warmed comfortably as I ordered the soft strands
of silky chestnut hair. It was very thick, and slightly wavy. On the
crown of his head was a cowlick, a delicate whorl that gave me
mild vertigo to see; Jamie had the same cowlick, in the same
place.

"I've lost my ribbon," he said, looking vaguely round, as
though one might materialize from bread hutch or inkwell.

"That's all right; I'll lend you one." I finished plaiting his hair and tied it with a scrap of yellow ribbon, feeling as I did so an odd sense of protectiveness.

I had learned of his existence only a few years earlier, and if I had thought of him in the meantime at all, had felt no more than a minor sense of curiosity tinged with resentment. But now something—be it his resemblance to my own child, his resemblance to Jamie, or simply the fact that I had taken care of him in some small way—had given me a strange feeling of almost proprietary concern for him.

I could hear the rumble of voices outside; the sound of a sudden laugh, and my annoyance at John Grey came back with a rush. How dare he risk both Jamie and William—and for what? Why was the bloody man *here,* in a wilderness as blatantly unsuited to someone of his sort as a—

The door opened, and Jamie poked his head in.

"Will ye be all right?" he asked. His eyes rested on the boy, an expression of polite concern on his face, but I saw his hand, curled tight as it rested on the door frame, and the line of tension that ran through leg and shoulder. He was strung like a harp; if I had touched him, he would have given off a low twanging noise.

"Quite all right," I said pleasantly. "Would Lord John care for some refreshment, do you think?"

I put the kettle on to boil for tea, and—with an inner sigh—took out the last loaf of bread, which I had meant to use for my next round of penicillin experiments. Feeling that the emergency justified it, I brought out the last bottle of brandy as well. Then I put the jampot on the table, explaining that the butter was unfortunately in the custody of the pig at the moment.

"Pig?" said William, looking confused.

"In the pantry," I said, with a nod at the closed door.

"Why do you keep—" he started, then sat up sharply and closed his mouth, having obviously been kicked under the table by his stepfather, who was smiling pleasantly over his cup.

"It is very kind of you to receive us, Mrs. Fraser," Lord John interjected, giving his stepson a warning eye. "I do apologize for our unexpected arrival; I hope we do not discommode you too greatly."

"Not at all," I said, wondering just where we were going to put them to sleep. William could go to the shed with Ian, I supposed; it was no worse than sleeping rough, as he had been doing. But the thought of sharing a bed with Jamie, with Lord John on the trundle an arm's-length away . . .

Ian, with his usual instinct for mealtimes, appeared at this delicate point in the proceedings, and was introduced all round, with such a confusion of explanations and reciprocal bowing in cramped quarters that the teapot was knocked over.

Using this minor disaster as an excuse, I sent Ian off to show William the attractions of wood and stream, with a packet of jam sandwiches and a bottle of cider to share between them. Then, free of their inhibiting presences, I filled the cups with brandy, sat down again, and fixed John Grey with a narrow eye.

"What are you doing here?" I said, without preamble.

He opened his light blue eyes very wide, then lowered his very long lashes and batted them deliberately at me.

"I did not come with the intention of seducing your husband, I assure you," he said.

"John!" Jamie's fist struck the table with a force that rattled the teacups. His cheekbones were flushed dark red, and he was scowling with embarrassed fury.

"Sorry." Grey, by contrast, had gone white, though he remained otherwise visibly unruffled. It occurred to me for the first time that he might possibly be as unnerved as Jamie by this meeting.

"My apologies, ma'am," he said, with a curt nod in my direction. "That was unforgivable. I would point out, however, that you have been looking at me since we met as though you had encountered me lying in the gutter outside some notorious mollyhouse." A light flush burned over his face now, too.

"Sorry," I breathed. "Give me a bit more notice next time, and I'll take care to adjust my features."

He stood up suddenly and went to the window, where he stood with his back to the room, hands braced on the sill. There was an exceedingly awkward silence. I didn't want to look at Jamie; instead I affected great interest in a bottle of fennel seeds that stood on the table.

"My wife has died," he said abruptly. "On the ship between England and Jamaica. She was coming to join me there."

"I am sorry to hear of it," Jamie said quietly. "The lad will have been with her?"

"Yes." Lord John turned back, leaning against the sill, so that the spring sunlight silhouetted his neat head and gave him a gleaming halo. "Willie was—very close to Isobel. She was the only mother he'd known since his birth."

Willie's true mother, Geneva Dunsany, had died in giving birth to him; his presumed father, the Earl of Ellesmere, had died the same day, in an accident. So much, Jamie had already told me. Likewise, that Geneva's sister, Isobel, had taken care of the orphaned boy, and that John Grey had married Isobel when Willie was six or so—at the time Jamie had left the Dunsanys' employ.

"I'm very sorry," I said, sincerely, and didn't mean only the death of his wife.

Grey glanced at me, and gave me the shadow of a nod in acknowledgment.

"My appointment as governor was nearly at an end; I had intended perhaps to take up residence on the island, should the climate suit my family. As it was . . ." He shrugged.

"Willie was grief-stricken by the loss of his mother; it seemed advisable to seek to distract his mind by whatever means I could. An opportunity presented itself almost at once; my wife's estate includes a large property in Virginia, which she had bequeathed to William. Upon her death, I received inquiries from the factor of the plantation, asking for instruction."

He moved away from the window, coming slowly back toward the table where we sat.

"I could not well decide what to do with the property without seeing it, and evaluating the conditions that obtain here. So I determined that we should sail to Charleston, and from there, travel overland to Virginia. I trusted to the novelty of the experience to divert William from his grief—which I am pleased to observe, it seems to have done. He has been much more cheerful these past weeks."

I opened my mouth to say that Fraser's Ridge seemed a bit out of his way, regardless, but then thought better of it.

He appeared to guess what I was thinking, for he gave me a brief wry smile. I really would have to do something about my face, I thought. Having Jamie read my thoughts was one thing, and not at all unpleasant, on the whole. Having total strangers walk in and out of my mind at will was something else.

"Where is the plantation?" Jamie asked, with somewhat more tact but the same implication.

"The nearest town of any sort is called Lynchburg—on the James River." Lord John looked at me, still wry, but apparent good humor restored. "It is in fact no more than a few days deviation in our journey to come here, in spite of the remoteness of your aerie."

He switched his attention to Jamie, frowning slightly.

"I told Willie that you are an old acquaintance of mine, from my soldiering days—I trust you do not object to the deception?"

Jamie shook his head, one side of his mouth turning up a bit. "Deception, is it? I shouldna think I could well mind what ye called me, under the circumstances. And so far as that bit goes, it's true enough."

"You don't think he'll remember you?" I asked Jamie. He had been a groom on Willie's home estate; a prisoner of war following the Jacobite Rising.

He hesitated, but then shook his head.

"I dinna think so. He was barely six when I left Helwater; that will be half a lifetime ago, to a lad—and a world away. And there's no reason he should think to recall a groom named Mac-Kenzie, let alone connect the name wi' me."

Willie hadn't recognized Jamie on sight, certainly, but then he had been too concerned with the leeches to take much notice of anyone. A thought struck me, and I turned to Lord John, who was fiddling with a snuffbox he had taken from his pocket.

"Tell me," I said, moved by a sudden impulse. "I don't mean to distress you—but . . . do you know how your wife died?"

"How?" He looked startled at the question, but collected himself at once. "She died of a bloody flux, so her maid said." His mouth twisted slightly. "It was . . . not a pleasant death, I believe." Bloody flux, eh? That was the standard description for anything from amebic dysentery to cholera.

"Was there a doctor? Someone on board who took care of her?"

"There was," he said, a little sharply. "What do you imply, ma'am?"

"Nothing," I said. "It's only that I wondered whether perhaps that was where Willie saw leeches used."

A flicker of understanding crossed his face.

"Oh, I see. I hadn't thought—"

At this point, I noticed Ian, who was hovering in the doorway, obviously reluctant to interrupt but with a marked look of urgency on his face.

"Did you want something, Ian?" I asked, interrupting Lord John.

He shook his head, brown hair flying.

"No, I thank ye, Auntie. It's only—" He cast a helpless glance at Jamie. "Well, I'm sorry, Uncle, I ken I shouldna ha' let him do it, but—"

"What?" Alarmed by Ian's tone of voice, Jamie was already on his feet. "What have ye done?"

The lad twisted his big hands together, cracking his knuckles in embarrassment.

"Well, ye see, his Lordship asked for the privy, and so I told him about the snake, and that he'd best go into the wood instead. So he did, but then he wanted to see the snake, and . . . and . . ."

"He's not bitten?" Jamie asked anxiously. Lord John, who had obviously been about to ask the same thing, gave him a glance.

"Oh, no!" Ian looked surprised. "We couldna see it to start with, because it was too dark below. So we lifted off the benchtop to get more light. We could see the serpent fine, then, and we poked at it a bit wi' a long branch, so it was lashin' to and fro like the wee book said, but it didna seem inclined to bite itself. And—and—" He darted a glance at Lord John, and swallowed audibly.

"It was my fault," he said, nobly squaring his shoulders, the better to accept blame. "I said as how I'd thought to shoot it earlier, but we didna want to waste the powder. And so his Lordship said as how he would fetch his papa's pistol from the saddlebag and deal with the thing at once. And so—"

"Ian," said Jamie between his teeth. "Stop blethering this instant and tell me straight what ye've done wi' the lad. Ye've not shot him by mistake, I hope?"

Ian looked offended at this slur upon his marksmanship.

"Of course not!" he said.

Lord John coughed politely, forestalling further recriminations.

"Perhaps you would be good enough to tell me the whereabouts of my son at this moment?"

Ian took a deep breath and visibly commended his soul to God.

"He's in the bottom of the privy," he said. "Have ye got a bit o' rope, Uncle Jamie?"

With an admirable economy of both words and motion, Jamie reached the door in two strides and disappeared, closely followed by Lord John.

"Is he in there *with* the snake?" I asked, hastily scrabbling through the washbasket for something to use as a tourniquet, just in case.

"Oh, no, Auntie," Ian assured me. "Ye dinna think I'd have left him, and the serpent was still there? Maybe I'd best go help," he added, and disappeared as well.

I hurried after him, to find Jamie and Lord John standing shoulder to shoulder in the doorway of the privy, conversing with the depths. Standing on tiptoe to peer over Lord John's shoulder, I saw the torn butt end of a long, slender hickory branch protruding a few inches above the edge of the oblong hole. I held my breath; Lord Ellesmere's struggles had stirred up the contents of the privy, and the reek was enough to sear the cilia off my nasal membranes.

"He says he's not hurt," Jamie assured me, turning away from the hole and unlimbering a coil of rope from his shoulder.

"Good," I said. "Where's the snake, though?" I peeked nervously into the outhouse, but couldn't see anything beyond the silvery cedar boards and the dark recesses of the pit.

"It went that way," Ian said, gesturing vaguely down the path by which I had come. "The laddie couldna quite get a clear shot, so I gave the thing a wee snoove wi' the stick, and damned if the bugger didna turn and come at me, right up the branch! It scairt me so I let out a skelloch and let go, and I bumped the lad, and—well, that's how it happened," he ended lamely.

Trying to avoid Jamie's eye, he sidled toward the pit and, leaning over, yelled awkwardly, "Hey! I'm glad ye didna break your neck!"

Jamie gave him a look that said rather plainly that if necks were to be broken . . . but forbore further remarks in the interests of extracting William promptly from his oubliette. This procedure was carried out without further incident, and the would-be marksman was lifted out, clinging to the rope like a caterpillar on a string.

There had luckily been enough sewage in the bottom of the pit to break his fall. From appearances, the ninth Earl of Ellesmere had landed facedown. Lord John stood for a moment on the path, wiping his hands on his breeches and surveying the encrusted object before him. He rubbed the back of a hand over his mouth, trying either to hide a smile or to stifle his sense of smell.

Then his shoulders started to shake.

"What news from the Underworld, Persephone?" he said, unable to keep the quaver of laughter out of his voice.

A pair of slanted eyes looked blue murder out of the mask of filth obscuring his Lordship's features. It was a thoroughly Fraser expression, and I felt a qualm go through me at the sight. By my side, Ian gave a sudden start. He glanced quickly from the Earl to Jamie and back, then he caught my eye and his own face went perfectly and unnaturally blank.

Jamie was saying something in Greek, to which Lord John replied in the same language, whereupon both men laughed like loons. Trying to ignore Ian, I bent an eye in Jamie's direction. Shoulders still shaking with suppressed mirth, he saw fit to enlighten me.

"Epicharmus," he explained. "At the Oracle of Delphi, seekers after enlightenment would throw down a dead python into the pit, and then hang about, breathing in the fumes as it decayed."

Lord John declaimed, gesturing grandly. " 'The spirit toward the heavens, the body to the earth.' "

William exhaled strongly through his nose, precisely as Jamie did when tried beyond bearing. Ian twitched beside me. Good grief, I thought, freshly unnerved. Does the boy have nothing from his mother?

"And have you attained any spiritual insights as a result of your recent m-mystical experience, William?" Lord John asked, making a poor attempt at self-control. He and Jamie were both flushed, with a laughter that I thought due as much to the release of nervous tension as to brandy or hilarity.

His Lordship, glowering, pulled off his neckcloth and flung it on the path with a soggy splat. Now Ian was giggling nervously, too, unable to help himself. My own belly muscles were quivering under the strain, but I could see that the patches of exposed flesh above William's collar were the color of the ripe tomatoes by the privy. Knowing all too well what usually happened to a Fraser who reached that particular level of incandescence, I thought the time had come to break up the party.

"Er-hem," I said, clearing my throat. "If you will allow me, gentlemen? Unlearned as I am in Greek philosophy, there is one small epigram I know by heart."

I handed William the jar of lye soap I had brought in lieu of a tourniquet.

"Pindar," I said. " 'Water is best.' "

A small flash of what might have been gratitude showed through the muck. His Lordship bowed to me, with utmost correctness, then turned, gave Ian a fishy stare, and stomped off through the grass toward the creek, dripping. He seemed to have lost his shoes.

"Puir clarty bugger," Ian said, shaking his head mournfully. "It'll be days before he gets the stink off."

"No doubt." Lord John's lips were still twitching, but the urge to declaim Greek poetry seemed to have left him, replaced by less elevated concerns. "Do you know what has become of my pistol, by the way? The one William was using before his unfortunate accident?"

"Oh." Ian looked uncomfortable. He lifted his chin in the direction of the privy. "I . . . ah . . . well, I'm verra much afraid—"

"I see." Lord John rubbed his own immaculately barbered chin.

Jamie fixed Ian with a long stare.

"Ah . . ." said Ian, backing up a pace or two.

"Get it," said Jamie, in a tone that brooked no contradiction.

"But—" said Ian.

"Now," said his uncle, and dropped the slimy rope at his feet.

Ian's Adam's apple bobbed, once. He looked at me, wide-eyed as a rabbit.

"Take your clothes off first," I said helpfully. "We don't want to have to burn them, do we?"

26

Plague and Pestilence

I left the house just before sunset, to check on my patient in the corncrib. He was no better, but neither was he visibly worse; the same labored breathing and burning fever. This time, though, the sunken eyes met mine when I entered the shed, and stayed on my face as I examined him.

He still had the raven's-feather amulet, clutched in his hand. I touched it and smiled at him, then gave him a drink. He still would take no food but had a little milk, and swallowed without protest another dose of my febrifuge. He lay motionless through examination and feeding, but as I was wringing out a hot cloth to poultice his chest, he suddenly reached out a hand and grabbed my arm.

He thumped his chest with his other hand, and made an odd humming noise. This puzzled me for a moment, until I realized that he *was* humming.

"Really?" I said. I reached for the packet of poulticing herbs and folded them into the cloth. "Well, all right then. Let me think."

I settled on "Onward, Christian Soldiers," which he appeared to like—I was obliged to sing it through three times before he seemed satisfied and sank back on his blanket with a small spate of coughing, wrapped in camphor fumes.

I paused outside the house, cleansing my hands carefully with the bottle of alcohol I carried. I was sure I was safe from contagion—I had had measles as a child—but wanted to take no chance of infecting anyone else.

"There was talk of an outbreak of the red measle in Cross Creek," Lord John remarked, upon my reporting to Jamie the condition of our guest. "Is it true, Mrs. Fraser, that the savage is congenitally less able to withstand infection than are Europeans, while African slaves are yet more hardy than their masters?"

"Depends on the infection," I said, peering into the cauldron and giving the stew bottle a cautious poke. "The Indians are a lot more resistant to the parasitic diseases—malaria, say—caused by organisms here, and the Africans deal better with things like dengue fever—which came with them from Africa, after all. But the Indians haven't much resistance to European plagues like smallpox and syphilis, no."

Lord John looked a bit taken aback, which gave me a small sense of satisfaction; evidently he had only asked out of courtesy —he hadn't actually expected me to know anything.

"How fascinating," he said, though, sounding truly interested. "You refer to organisms? Do you then subscribe to Mister Evan Hunter's theory of miasmatical creatures?"

Now it was my turn to be taken aback.

"Er . . . not precisely, no," I said, and changed the subject.

We passed a pleasant enough evening, Jamie and Lord John exchanging anecdotes of hunting and fishing, with remarks on the amazing abundance of the countryside, while I darned stockings.

Willie and Ian had a game of chess, which the latter won, to his evident satisfaction. His Lordship yawned hugely, then catching his father's minatory eye, made a belated attempt to cover his mouth. He relaxed into a sleepy smile of contentment, brought on by repletion; he and Ian between them had demolished an entire currant cake, following their huge supper.

Jamie saw it, and cocked a brow at Ian, who obligingly rose and towed his Lordship away to share his pallet in the herb shed. Two down, I thought, keeping my eyes resolutely away from the bed— and three to go.

In the event, the delicate problem of bedtime was solved by my retiring, cloaked in modesty—or at least in my nightgown—while Jamie and Lord John took over the chess table, drinking the last of the brandy by firelight.

Lord John was a much better chess player than I—or so I deduced from the fact that the game took them a good hour. Jamie could normally beat me in twenty minutes flat. The play was mostly silent, though with brief spurts of conversation.

At last Lord John made a move, sat back and stretched, as though concluding something.

"I collect you will not see much disturbance in the political way, here in your mountain refuge?" he said casually. He squinted at the board, considering.

"I do envy you, Jamie, removed from such petty difficulties as afflict the merchants and gentry of the lowlands. If your life has its hardships—as cannot help but be the case—you have the not inconsiderable consolation of knowing your struggles to be significant and heroic.''

Jamie snorted briefly.

"Oh, aye. Verra heroic, to be sure. At the moment, my most heroic struggle is like to be with the pig in my pantry.'' He nodded toward the board, one eyebrow raised. "Ye really mean to make that move?''

Grey narrowed his eyes at Jamie, then looked down, studying the board with pursed lips.

"Yes, I do,'' he answered firmly.

"Damn,'' said Jamie, and with a grin, reached out and tipped over his king in resignation.

Grey laughed, and reached for the brandy bottle.

"Damn!'' he said in turn, finding it empty. Jamie laughed, and rising, went to the cupboard.

"Try a bit of this,'' he said, and I heard the musical glug of liquid into a cup.

Grey lifted the cup to his nose, inhaled and sneezed explosively, scattering droplets over the table.

"It's not wine, John,'' Jamie observed mildly. "Ye're meant to drink it, aye? not savor the bouquet.''

"So I noticed. Christ, what is it?'' Grey sniffed again, more cautiously, and essayed a trial sip. He choked, but swallowed gamely.

"Christ,'' he said again. His voice was hoarse. He coughed, cleared his throat, and set the cup gingerly on the table, eyeing it as though it might explode.

"Don't tell me,'' he said. "Let me guess. It's meant to be Scotch whisky?''

"In ten years or so, it might be,'' Jamie answered, pouring a small cupful for himself. He took a small sip, rolled it around his mouth and swallowed, shaking his head. "At the moment, it's alcohol, and that's as much as I'd say for it.''

"Yes, it's that,'' Grey agreed, taking another very small sip. "Where did you get it?''

"I made it,'' said Jamie, with the modest pride of a master brewer. "I've twelve barrels of the stuff.''

Grey's fair brows shot up at that.

"Assuming that you don't mean to clean your boots with it, may I ask what you intend doing with twelve barrels of *this*?''

Jamie laughed.

"Trade it," he said. "Sell it, when I can. Customs tax and a license to brew spirits being one of the petty political concerns wi' which I am not afflicted, owing to our remoteness," he added ironically.

Lord John grunted, tried another sip, and set the cup down.

"Well, you may well escape the Customs, I'll grant you—the nearest agent is in Cross Creek. But I cannot say I think it a safe practice on that account. To whom, may I ask, are you selling this remarkable concoction? Not to the savages, I trust?"

Jamie shrugged.

"Only verra small amounts—a flask or two at a time, as a gift or in trade. Never more than would make one man drunk."

"Very wise. You'll have heard the stories, I expect. I spoke with one man who'd survived the massacre at Michilimackinac, during the war with the French. That was caused—in part, at least —by a great quantity of drink falling into the hands of a large gathering of Indians at the fort."

"I've heard about it, too," Jamie assured him dryly. "But we are on good terms wi' the Indians nearby, and there are none so many of them as all that. And I'm careful, as I say."

"Mm." He essayed another sip, and grimaced. "I expect you risk more by poisoning one of them than by intoxicating a mob." He set the glass down and changed the subject.

"I have heard talk in Wilmington of an unruly group of men called Regulators, who terrorize the backcountry and cause disruption by means of riot. Have you encountered anything of such nature here?"

Jamie snorted briefly.

"Terrorize what? Squirrels? There is the backcountry, John, and then there is the wilderness. Surely ye will have remarked the lack of human habitation on your journey here."

"I did notice something of the kind," Lord John agreed. "And yet I had heard certain rumors regarding your presence here—that it was in part meant as a quelling influence upon the growth of lawlessness."

Jamie laughed.

"I think it will be some time before there is much lawlessness for me to quell. Though I did go so far as to knock down an old German farmer who was abusing a young woman at the grain mill on the river. He had it in mind she had given him short weight—

which she had not—and I couldna convince him otherwise. But that is my only attempt so far at maintaining public order."

Grey laughed, and picked up the fallen king.

"I am relieved to hear it. Will you redeem your honor with another game? I cannot expect the same trick to work twice, after all."

I rolled onto my side, facing the wall, and stared sleeplessly at the timbers. The firelight glimmered on the wing-shaped marks of the ax, running along the length of each log, regular as sand ripples on a beach.

I tried to ignore the conversation going on behind me, to lose myself instead in the memory of Jamie hewing bark and squaring logs, of sleeping in his arms under the shelter of a half-built wall, feeling the house rise up around me, enclosing me in warmth and safety, the permanent embodiment of his embrace. I always felt safe and soothed by this vision, even when I was alone on the mountain, knowing I was protected by the house he had built for me. Tonight, though, it wasn't working.

I lay still, wondering exactly what was the matter with me. Or rather, not what, but *why.* I knew by now what it was, all right; it was jealousy.

I was indeed jealous; an emotion I hadn't felt for some years, and was appalled to feel now. I rolled onto my back and closed my eyes, trying to shut out the murmur of conversation.

Lord John had been nothing but courtesy itself to me. More than that, he had been intelligent, thoughtful—thoroughly charming, in fact. And listening to him making intelligent, thoughtful, charming conversation with Jamie knotted my insides and made me clench my hands under cover of the quilt.

You are an idiot, I told myself savagely. *What is the matter with you?* I tried to relax, breathing deeply through my nose, eyes closed.

Part of it was Willie, of course. Jamie was very careful, but I had seen his expression when he looked at the boy in unguarded moments. His whole body was suffused with shy joy, pride mingled with diffidence; and it smote me to the heart to see it.

He would never look at Brianna, his firstborn, that way. Would never see her at all. That was hardly his fault—and yet it seemed so unfair. At the same time, I could scarcely begrudge him his joy in his son—and didn't, I told myself firmly. The fact that it gave me a terrible pang of longing to look at the boy, with that bold, handsome face that mirrored his sister's, was simply my problem.

Nothing to do with Jamie, or with Willie. Or with John Grey, who'd brought the boy here.

What for? That was what I'd been thinking ever since I had recovered from the first shock of their appearance, and that was still what I was thinking. What in *hell* was the man up to?

The story about the estate in Virginia might be true—or only an excuse. Even if it was true, it was a considerable detour to come to Fraser's Ridge. Why had he taken so much trouble to bring the boy here? And so much risk; Willie was clearly oblivious to the resemblance that even Ian had noticed, but what if he hadn't been? Had it been so important to Grey, to restate his claim on Jamie's obligation to him?

I rolled onto my other side and cracked an eyelid, watching them over the chessboard, redhead and fair head, bent together in absorption. Grey moved a knight and sat back, rubbing the back of his neck, smiling to himself at the effect of his move. He was a good-looking man; slight and fine-boned, but with a strong, clear-cut face and a beautiful, sensitive mouth that many a woman had no doubt envied.

Grey was even better at guarding his face than Jamie was; I hadn't yet seen an incriminating look from him. I'd seen one once, though, in Jamaica, and wasn't in any doubt about the nature of his feelings for Jamie.

On the other hand, I wasn't in any doubt about Jamie's feelings in that regard, either. The knot under my heart eased a bit, and I took a deeper breath. No matter how late they sat up over the board, drinking and talking, it would be *my* bed Jamie came to.

I unclenched my fists, and it was then, as I rubbed my palms covertly against my thighs, that I realized with a shock just why Lord John affected me so strongly.

My fingernails had dug small crescents in my palms, a small line of throbbing half-moons. For years, I had rubbed away those crescents after every dinner party, every late night when Frank had "worked at the office." For years, I had lain intermittently alone in a double bed, wide-awake in the darkness, nails digging into my hands, waiting for him to come back.

And he had. To his credit, he always did return before dawn. Sometimes to a back curled against him in cold reproach, sometimes to the furious challenge of a body thrust against him in demand, urging him wordlessly to deny it, to prove his innocence with his body—trial by combat. More often than not, he accepted the challenge. But it didn't help.

Yet neither of us spoke of such things in the daylight. I could not; I had no right. Frank did not; he had revenge.

Sometimes it would be months—even a year or more—between episodes, and we would live in peace together. But then it would happen again; the silent phone calls, the too-excused absences, the late nights. Never anything so overt as another woman's perfume, or lipstick on his collar—he had discretion. But I always felt the ghost of the other woman, whoever she was; some faceless, indistinguishable She.

I knew it didn't matter who it was—there were several of them. The only important thing was that She was not me. And I would lie awake and clench my fists, the marks of my nails a small crucifixion.

The murmur of conversation by the fire had mostly ceased; the only sound the small click of the chessmen as they moved.

"Do you feel yourself content?" Lord John asked suddenly.

Jamie paused for a moment.

"I have all that man could want," he said quietly. "A place, and honorable work. My wife at my side. The knowledge that my son is safe and well cared for." He looked up then, at Grey. "And a good friend." He reached over, clasped Lord John's hand, and let it go. "I want no more."

I shut my eyes resolutely, and began to count sheep.

I was awakened just before dawn by Ian, crouching by my bedside.

"Auntie," he said softly, a hand on my shoulder. "Best ye come; the man in the corncrib's verra poorly."

I was on my feet by reflex, wrapped in my cloak and moving bare-footed after Ian before my mind had even begun to function consciously. Not that any great diagnostic skill was needed; I could hear the deep, rattling respirations from ten feet away.

The Earl hovered by the doorway, his thin face pale and scared in the gray light.

"Go away," I told him sharply. "You mustn't be near him; nor you, Ian—the two of you go to the house, fetch me hot water from the cauldron, my box, and clean rags."

Willie moved at once, eager to be away from the frightening sounds coming from the shed. Ian lingered, though, his face troubled.

"I dinna think ye can help him, Auntie," he said quietly. His eyes met mine straight on, with an adult depth of understanding.

"Very likely not," I said, answering him in the same terms. "But I can't do nothing."

He took a deep breath, nodded.

"Aye. But I think . . ." He hesitated, then went on as I nodded, "I think ye shouldna torment him wi' medicine. He's fixed to die, Auntie; we heard an owl in the night—he will have heard it, too. It is a sign of death to them."

I glanced at the dark oblong of the door, biting my lip. The breaths were shallow and wheezing, with alarmingly long pauses between them. I looked back at Ian.

"What do the Indians do, when someone is dying? Do you know?"

"Sing," he said promptly. "The *shaman* puts paint upon her face, and sings the soul away to safety, so the demons dinna take it."

I hesitated, my instincts to do *something* at war with my conviction that action would be futile. Had I any right to deprive this man of peace in his dying? Worse, to alarm him into fear that his soul would be lost by my interference?

Ian hadn't waited for the results of my dithering. He stooped and scraped up a small clot of earth, spat in it and stirred it to mud. Without comment, he dipped his forefinger into the puddle, and drew a line from my forehead down the bridge of my nose.

"Ian!"

"Shh," he murmured, frowning in concentration. "Like this, I think." He added two lines across each cheekbone, and a rough zigzag down the left side of my jawbone. "That's as near as I remember the proper way of it. I've only seen it the once, and from a distance."

"Ian, this isn't—"

"Shhh," he said again, laying a hand on my arm to quell protest. "Go to him, Auntie. Ye willna frighten him; he's accustomed to ye, no?"

I rubbed away a drip from the end of my nose, feeling thoroughly idiotic. There was no time to argue, though. Ian gave me a small push, and I turned to the door. I stepped into the darkness of the corncrib, bent and laid a hand on the man. His skin was hot and dry, his hand limp as worn leather.

"Ian, can you talk to him? Say his name, tell him it's all right?"

"Ye must not say his name, Auntie; it will call demons."

Ian cleared his throat, and said a few words in soft clicking gutterals. The hand in mine twitched slightly. My eyes had adjusted now, I could see the man's face, marked with a faint look of surprise as he saw my mud paint.

"Sing, Auntie," Ian urged, low-voiced. *"Tantum ergo,* maybe; it sounded a wee bit like that."

There was nothing else I could do, after all. Rather helplessly, I began.

"Tantum ergo, sacramentum . . ."

Within a few seconds, my voice steadied, and I sat back on my bare heels, singing slowly, holding his hand. The heavy brows relaxed, and a look of what I thought might be calm came into the sunken eyes.

I had been present at a good many deaths, from accident, warfare, illness, or natural causes, and had seen men meet death in many ways, from philosophical acceptance to violent protest. But I had never seen one die quite this way.

He simply waited, eyes on mine, until I had come to the end of the song. Then he turned his face toward the door, and as the rising sun struck him, he left his body, without the twitch of a muscle or the drawing of a final breath.

I sat quite still, holding the limp hand, until it occurred to me that I was holding my breath, too.

The air around me seemed queerly still, as though time had stopped for a moment. But of course it had, I thought, and forced myself to draw breath. It had stopped for him, forever.

"What are we to do with him?"

There was nothing further to be done *for* our guest; the only question at the moment was how we might best deal with his mortal remains.

I had had a quiet word with Lord John, and he had taken Willie to gather late strawberries on the ridge. While the Indian's death had had nothing even faintly gruesome about it, I could wish Willie hadn't seen it; it wasn't a sight for a child who had seen his mother die no more than a few months before. Lord John had seemed upset himself—perhaps a little sunshine and fresh air would help both of them.

Jamie frowned and rubbed a hand over his face. He hadn't shaved yet, and the stubble made a rasping sound.

"We must give him decent burial, surely?"

"Well, I don't suppose we can leave him lying about in the corncrib, but would his people mind if we buried him here? Do you know anything about how they treat their dead, Ian?"

Ian was still a little pale, but surprisingly self-possessed. He shook his head, and took a drink of milk.

"I dinna ken a great deal, Auntie. But I have seen one man die, as I told ye. They wrapped him in a deerskin and had a procession round the village, singing, then took the body a ways into the wood and put it up on a platform, above the ground, and left it there to dry."

Jamie seemed less than enthralled at the prospect of having mummified bodies perched in the trees near the farm. "I should think it best maybe to wrap the body decently and carry it to the village, then, so his own folk can deal with him properly."

"No, you can't do that." I slid the pan of newly baked muffins out of the Dutch oven, plucked a broomtwig and stuck it into one plump brown cake. It came out clean, so I set the pan on the table, then sat down myself. I frowned abstractedly at the jug of honey, glowing gold in the late morning sun.

"The trouble is that the body is almost certainly still infectious. You didn't touch him at all, did you, Ian?" I glanced at Ian, who shook his head, looking sober.

"No, Auntie. Not after he fell sick here; before that, I dinna recall. We were all together, hunting."

"And you haven't had measles. Drat." I rubbed a hand through my hair. "Have you?" I asked Jamie. To my relief, he nodded.

"Aye, when I was five or so. And you say a person canna have the same sickness twice. So it willna injure me to touch the body?"

"No, nor me either; I've had them too. The thing is, we can't take him to the village. I don't know at all how long the measles virus—that's a sort of germ—can live on clothes or in a body, but how could we explain to his people that they mustn't touch him or go near him? And we can't risk letting them be infected."

"What troubles me," Ian put in unexpectedly, "is that he isna a man from Anna Ooka—he's from a village further north. If we bury him here in the usual way, his folk may hear of it and think we had done him to death in some fashion, then buried him to hide it."

That was a sinister possibility that hadn't occurred to me, and I felt as though a cold hand had been laid on the back of my neck.

"You don't think they would, surely?"

Ian shrugged, broke open a hot muffin, and drizzled honey over the steaming insides.

"Nacognaweto's folk trust us, but Myers did say there were plenty who would not. They've reason to be suspicious, aye?"

Considering that the bulk of the Tuscarora had been exterminated in a vicious war with the North Carolina settlers no more than fifty years before, I rather thought they had a point. It didn't help with the present problem, though.

Jamie swallowed the last of his muffin and sat back with a sigh.

"Well, then. I think best we wrap the poor man in a shroud of sorts, and put him in the wee cave in the hill above the house. I've set the posts for a stable across the opening already; those will keep the beasts off. Then Ian or I should go to Anna Ooka and explain matters to Nacognaweto. Perhaps he will send someone back who can look at the body and assure the man's people that he met with no violence from us—and then we can bury him."

Before I could reply to this suggestion, I heard footsteps, running across the dooryard. I had left the door ajar, to let in light and air. As I turned toward it, Willie's face appeared in the opening, pale and distraught.

"Mrs. Fraser! Please, will you come? Papa's ill."

"Has he got it from the Indian?" Jamie frowned at Lord John, whom we had stripped to his shirt and put to bed. His face was by turns flushed and pale—the symptoms I had put down earlier to emotional distress.

"No, he can't have. The incubation period is one to two weeks. Where were you—" I turned to Willie, then shrugged, dismissing the question. They had been traveling; there was no conceivable way of telling where or when Grey had encountered the virus. Travelers normally slept several to a bed in inns, and the blankets were seldom changed; it would be easy to lie down in one and get up in the morning with the germs of anything from measles to hepatitis.

"You did say there was an epidemic of measles in Cross Creek?" I put a hand on Grey's forehead. Adept as I was at reading fevers by touch, I would have put his near a hundred and three; quite high enough.

"Yes," he said hoarsely, and coughed. "Have I got the measles? You must keep Willie away."

"Ian—take Willie outside, will you, please?" I wrung out a cloth wetted with elderflower water, and wiped Grey's face and neck. There was no rash yet on his face, but when I made him open his mouth, the small whitish Koplik's spots on the lining were clear enough.

"Yes, you have got the measles," I said. "How long have you been feeling ill?"

"I felt somewhat light-headed when I retired last night," he said, and coughed again. "I woke with a bad headache, sometime in the night, but I thought it only the result of Jamie's so-called whisky." He smiled faintly at Jamie. "Then this morning . . ." He sneezed, and I hastily groped for a fresh handkerchief.

"Yes, quite. Well, try to rest a bit. I've put some willow bark to steep; that will help the headache." I stood up and raised a brow at Jamie, who followed me outside.

"We can't let Willie be near him," I said, low-voiced so as not to be overheard; Willie and Ian were by the penfold, forking hay into the horses' manger. "Or Ian. He's very infectious."

Jamie frowned.

"Aye. What ye said, though, about incubation—"

"Yes. Ian might have been exposed through the dead man, Willie might have been exposed to the same source as Lord John. Either one of them might have it now, but show no sign yet." I turned to look at the two boys, both of them outwardly as healthy as the horses they were feeding.

"I think," I said, hesitating as I formed a vague plan, "that perhaps you had better camp outside with the boys tonight—you could sleep in the herb shed, or camp in the grove. Wait a day or so; if Willie's infected—if he got it from the same source as Lord John—he'll likely be showing signs by then. If not, then he's likely all right. If he *is* all right, then you and he could go to Anna Ooka to tell Nacognaweto about the dead man. That would keep Willie safely out of danger."

"And Ian could stay here to take care of you?" He frowned, considering, then nodded. "Aye, I expect that will do."

He turned to glance at Willie. Impassive as he could be when he wanted to, I knew him well enough to detect the flicker of emotion across his face.

There was worry in the tilt of his brows—concern for John Grey, and perhaps for me or Ian. But beyond that was something quite different—interest tinged with apprehension, I thought, at the prospect of spending several days alone with the boy.

"If he hasn't noticed it yet, he isn't going to," I said softly, putting my hand on his arm.

"No," he muttered, turning his back on the boy. "I suppose it's safe enough."

"They do say it's an ill wind that blows nobody good," I said. "You'll be able to talk to him without it seeming odd." I paused. "There's just the one thing, before you go."

He put his hand over mine where it lay on his arm, and smiled down at me.

"Aye, and what's that?"

"Do get that pig out of the pantry, please."

27

Trout Fishing in America

The journey began inauspiciously. It was raining, for one thing. For another, he disliked leaving Claire, especially in such difficult circumstances. For a third, he was badly worried for John; he hadn't liked the look of the man at all when he took leave of him, barely half conscious and wheezing like a grampus, his features so blotched with rash as to be unrecognizable.

And for a fourth, the ninth Earl of Ellesmere had just punched him in the jaw. He took a firm hold on the youngster's scruff and shook him, hard enough to make his teeth clack painfully together.

"Now, then," he said, letting go. The boy staggered, and sat down suddenly as he lost his balance. He glared down at the lad, sitting in the mud by the penfold. They had been having this argument, on and off, for the last twenty-four hours, and he had had enough of it.

"I ken well enough what ye said. But what *I* said is that ye're coming with me. I've told ye why, and that's all about it."

The boy's face drew down in a ferocious scowl. He wasn't easily cowed, but then Jamie supposed that earls weren't used to folk trying, either.

"I am *not* leaving!" the boy repeated. "You can't make me!" He got to his feet, jaw clenched, and turned back toward the cabin.

Jamie snaked out an arm, grabbed the lad's collar, and hauled him back. Seeing the boy draw back his foot for a kick, he closed his fist and punched the boy neatly in the pit of the stomach. William's eyes bulged and he doubled over, holding his middle.

"Don't kick," Jamie said mildly. "It's ill-mannered. And as for makin' you, of course I can."

The Earl's face was bright red and his mouth was opening and closing like a startled goldfish's. His hat had fallen off, and the rain was pasting strands of dark hair to his head.

"It's verra loyal of ye to want to stay by your stepfather," Jamie went on, wiping the water out of his own face, "but ye canna help him, and you may do yourself damage by staying. So ye're not." From the corner of his eye, he caught a glimpse of movement as the oiled hide over the cabin's window moved aside, then fell. Claire, no doubt wondering why they were not already long gone.

Jamie took the Earl by an unresisting arm, and led him to one of the saddled horses.

"Up," he said, and had the satisfaction of seeing the boy stick a reluctant foot in the stirrup and swing aboard. Jamie tossed the boy's hat up to him, donned his own, and mounted himself. As a precaution, though, he kept hold of both sets of reins as they set off.

"You, sir," said a breathless, enraged voice behind him, "are a lout!"

He was torn between irritation and an urge to laugh, but gave way to neither. He cast a look back over his shoulder, to see William also turned, and leaning perilously to the side, half off his saddle.

"Don't try it," he advised the boy, who straightened up abruptly and glared at him. "I wouldna like to tie your feet in your stirrups, but I'll do it, make no mistake."

The boy's eyes narrowed into bright blue triangles, but he evidently took Jamie at his word. His jaw stayed clenched, but his shoulders slumped a little in temporary defeat.

They rode in silence for most of the morning, rain drizzling down their necks and weighting the shoulders of their cloaks. Willie might have accepted defeat, but not graciously. He was still sullen when they dismounted to eat, but did at least fetch water without protest, and pack up the remains of their meal while Jamie watered the horses.

Jamie eyed him covertly, but there was no sign of measles. The Earl's face was frowning but rashless, and while the tip of his nose was dripping, this appeared to be due solely to the effects of the weather.

"How far is it?" It was midafternoon before William's curiosity overcame his stubbornness. Jamie had long since relinquished the boy's reins to him—there was no danger of the lad's trying to make his way back alone now.

"Two days, perhaps." In such mountainous terrain as lay between the Ridge and Anna Ooka, they would make little better speed on horseback than on foot. Having horses, though, allowed them to bring a few small conveniences, such as a kettle, extra food, and a pair of carved fishing rods. And a number of small gifts for the Indians, including a keg of home-brewed whisky to help cushion the bad news they bore.

There was no reason to hurry, and some to delay—Claire had told him firmly not to bring Willie back for at least six days. By then, John would no longer be infectious. He would be well on the way to recovery—or dead.

Claire had been outwardly confident, assuring Willie that his stepfather would be quite all right, but he'd seen the mist of worry in her eyes. It gave him a feeling of hollowness just below the ribs. It was perhaps as well that he was leaving; he could be of no help, and sickness always left him with a helpless feeling that made him at once afraid and angry.

"These Indians—they *are* friendly?" He could hear the tone of doubt in Willie's voice.

"Yes." He felt Willie waiting for him to add "my lord," and took a small, perverse satisfaction in not doing it. He guided his horse's head to the side and slowed his pace, an invitation for Willie to ride up next to him. He smiled at the boy as he did so.

"We have known them more than a year, and been guests in their longhouses—aye, the people of Anna Ooka are more courteous and hospitable than most folk I've met in England."

"You have lived in England?" The boy shot him a surprised look, and he cursed his carelessness, but luckily the lad was a great deal more interested in Red Indians than in the personal history of James Fraser, and the question passed with no more than a vague reply.

He was glad to see the boy abandon his sullen preoccupation and begin to take some interest in their surroundings. He did his best to encourage it, telling stories of the Indians and pointing out animal sign as they went, and he was glad to see the boy thaw into civility, if nothing more, as they rode.

He welcomed the distraction of conversation himself; his mind was a good deal too busy to make silence comfortable. If the worst should happen—if John should die—what then became of Willie? He would doubtless return to England and his grandmother—and Jamie would hear no more of him.

John was the only other person, besides Claire, who knew the truth of Willie's paternity without doubt. It was possible that Willie's grandmother at least suspected the truth, but she would never, under any circumstances, admit that her grandson might be the bastard of a Jacobite traitor rather than the legitimate issue of the late Earl.

He said a small prayer to Saint Bride for the welfare of John Grey, and tried to dismiss the nagging worry from his mind. In spite of his apprehensions, he was beginning to enjoy the trip. The rain had lessened to no more than a light spattering, and the forest was fragrant with the scents of wet, fresh leaves and fecund dark leaf mold.

"D'ye see those scratches down the trunk of that tree?" He pointed with his chin at a large hickory whose bark hung in shreds, showing a number of long, parallel white slashes, some six feet from the ground.

"Yes." Willie took off his hat and slapped it against his thigh to knock the water off, then leaned forward to look more closely. "An animal did that?"

"A bear," Jamie said. "Fresh, too—see the sap's not dried yet in the cuts."

"Is it nearby?" Willie glanced around, seeming more curious than alarmed.

"Not close," Jamie said, "or the horses would be carryin' on. But near enough, aye. Keep an eye out; we'll likely see its dung or its prints."

No, if John died, his tenuous link with William would be broken. He had long since resigned himself to the situation, and accepted the necessity without complaint—but he would feel bereft indeed if the measles robbed him not only of his closest friend but of all connection with his son.

It had stopped raining. As they rounded the flank of a mountain and came out above a valley, Willie gave a small exclamation of surprised delight, and sat up straight in his saddle. Against a backdrop of rain-dark clouds, a rainbow arced from the slope of a distant mountain, falling in a perfect shimmer of light to the floor of the valley far below.

"Oh, it's glorious!" Willie said. He turned a wide smile on Jamie, their differences forgotten. "Have you ever seen such a thing before, sir?"

"Never," said Jamie, smiling back. It occurred to him, with a small shock, that these few days in the wilderness might conceivably be the last he would see or hear of William. He hoped that he wouldn't have to hit the boy again.

He always slept lightly in the wood, and the sound woke him at once. He lay quite still for a moment, unsure what it was. Then he heard the small, choked noise, and recognized the sound of stifled weeping.

He checked his instant urge to turn and lay a hand on the boy in comfort. The lad was making every effort not to be heard; he deserved to keep his pride. He lay still, looking up into the sweep of the vast night sky above, and listening.

Not fright; William had shown no fear of sleeping in dark woods, and had there been a large animal nearby, the boy would not be keeping quiet about it. Was the lad unwell? The sounds were little more than thickened breathing, caught in the throat—perhaps the boy was in pain and too proud to say. It was that fear that decided him to speak; if the measles had caught them up, there was no time to waste; he must carry the boy back to Claire at once.

"My lord?" he said softly.

The sobbing ceased abruptly. He heard the audible sound of a swallow and the rasp of cloth on skin as the lad wiped a sleeve across his face.

"Yes?" the Earl said, with a creditable attempt at coolness, marred only by the thickness in his voice.

"Are ye unwell, my lord?" He could tell already that it wasn't that, but it would do for a pretext. "Have ye maybe taken a touch of the cramp? Sometimes dried apples take a man amiss."

A deep breath came from the far side of the fire, and a snuffle as an attempt was made to clear a running nose unobtrusively. The fire had burned down to nothing more than embers; still, he could see the dark shape that squirmed into a sitting position, crouched on the far side of the fire.

"I—ah—yes, I think perhaps I have got . . . something of the sort."

Jamie sat up himself, the plaid falling away from his shoulders.

"It's no great matter," he said, soothingly. "I've a potion that will cure all manner of ills of the stomach. Do ye rest easy for a moment, my lord; I'll fetch water."

He got to his feet and went away, careful not to look at the boy. By the time he came back from the stream with the kettle filled,

Willie had got his nose blown and his face wiped, and was sitting with his knees drawn up, his head resting on them.

He couldn't keep himself from touching the boy's head as he passed. Familiarity be damned. The dark hair was soft to his touch, warm and slightly damp with sweat.

"A griping in your guts, is it?" he said pleasantly, kneeling and putting the kettle to boil.

"Mm-hm." Willie's voice was muffled in the blanket over his knees.

"That passes soon enough," he said. He reached for his sporran, and sorted through the proliferation of small items in it, coming up eventually with the small cloth bag that held the dried mixture of leaves and flowers Claire had given him. He didn't know how she'd known it would be needed, but he was long past the point of questioning anything she did in the way of healing— whether of heart or of body.

He felt a moment's passionate gratitude to her. He'd seen her look at the boy, and knew how she must feel. She'd known about the lad, of course, but seeing the flesh-and-blood proof that her husband had shared another woman's bed wasn't something a wife should be asked to put up with. Little wonder if she was inclined to stick pins in John, him pushing the lad under her nose as he had.

"It willna take more than a moment to brew up," he assured the boy, rubbing the fragrant mixture between his hands into a wooden cup, as he'd seen Claire do.

She'd not reproached him. Not with *that* at least, he thought, suddenly remembering how she'd acted when she'd found out about Laoghaire. She'd gone for him like a fiend, then, and yet when later she'd learned about Geneva Dunsany . . . perhaps it was only that the boy's mother was dead?

The realization went through him like a sword thrust. The boy's mother was dead. Not just his real mother, who'd died the same day he was born—but the woman he'd called mother all his life since. And now his father—or the man he called father, Jamie thought with an unconscious twist of his mouth—was lying sick of an illness that had killed another man before the lad's eyes no more than days before.

No, it wasn't fright that made the lad greet by himself in the dark. It was grief, and Jamie Fraser, who'd lost a mother in childhood himself, ought to have known that from the beginning.

It wasn't stubbornness, nor even loyalty, that had made Willie insist on staying at the Ridge. It was love of John Grey, and fear of his loss. And it was the same love that made the boy weep in the night, desperate with worry for his father.

An unaccustomed weed of jealousy sprang up in Jamie's heart, stinging like nettles. He stamped firmly on it; he was fortunate indeed to know that his son enjoyed a loving relationship with his stepfather. There, that was the weed stamped out. The stamping, though, seemed to have left a small bruised spot on his heart; he could feel it when he breathed.

The water was beginning to rumble in the kettle. He poured it carefully over the herb mixture, and a sweet fragrance rose up in the steam. Valerian, she'd said, and catmint. The root of a passionflower, soaked in honey and finely ground. And the sweet, half-musky smell of lavender, coming as an afterscent.

"Don't drink it yourself," she'd said, casual in giving it to him. "There's lavender in it."

In fact, it didn't trouble him, if he was warned of it. It was only that now and then a whiff of lavender took him unawares, and sent a sudden surge of sickness through his wame. Claire had seen the effects on him once too often to be unwary of it.

"Here." He leaned forward and handed the cup to the boy, wondering whether forever after, the lad too would feel troubled by the scent of lavender, or if he would find in it a memory of comfort. That, he supposed, might well depend on whether John Grey lived or died.

The respite had given Willie back his outward composure, but his face was still marked with grief. Jamie smiled at the boy, hiding his own concern. Knowing both John and Claire as he did, he was less fearful than the boy—but the dread was still there, persistent as a thorn in the sole of his foot.

"That will ease ye," he said, nodding at the cup. "My wife made it; she's a verra fine healer."

"Is she?" The boy took a deep, trembling breath of the steam, and touched a cautious tongue to the hot liquid. "I saw her—do things. With the Indian who died." The accusation there was clear; she'd done things, and the man had died anyway.

Neither Claire nor Ian had spoken much of that, nor had he been able to ask her what had happened—she had given him a lifted brow and a brief gold look, to say that he should not speak of it before Willie, who had come back with her from the corncrib, white-faced and clammy.

"Aye?" he said curiously. "What sort of—things?"

What the hell had she done? he wondered. Nothing to cause the man's death, surely; he would have seen that in her at once. Nor did she feel herself at fault, or helpless—he had held her in his arms more than once, comforting her as she wept for those she could not save. This time she had been quiet, subdued—as had Ian—but not deeply upset. She had seemed vaguely puzzled.

"She had mud on her face. And she sang to him. I think she was singing a Papist song; it was in Latin, and it had something to do with sacraments."

"Indeed?" Jamie suppressed his own astonishment at this description. "Aye, well. Perhaps she meant only to give the man a bit of comfort, if she saw she couldna save him. The Indians are much more sensible of the effects of measles, ye ken; an infection that will kill one of them wouldna cause a white man to blink twice. I've had the measle myself, as a wee lad, and took no harm from it at all." He smiled and stretched, demonstrating his evident health.

The tense lines of the boy's face relaxed a little, and he took a cautious sip of the hot tea.

"That's what Mrs. Fraser said. She said Papa would be all right. She—she gave me her word upon it."

"Then ye may depend upon it that he will," Jamie said firmly. "Mrs. Fraser is an honorable woman." He coughed, and hitched the plaid up around his shoulders; it wasn't a cold night, but there was a breeze coming down the hill. "Is the drink helping a bit?"

Willie looked blank, then looked down at the cup in his hand.

"Oh! Yes. Yes, thank you; it's very good. I feel very much improved. Perhaps it was not the dried apples, after all."

"Perhaps not," Jamie agreed, bending his head to hide a smile. "Still, I think we'll manage better for our supper tomorrow; if luck is with us, we'll have trout."

This attempt at distraction was successful; Willie's head popped up from his cup, an expression of deep interest on his face.

"Trout? We can fish?"

"Have ye done much fishing in England? I canna think that the trout streams would compare with these, but I know there is good fishing to be had in the Lake District—or so your father tells me."

He held his breath. What in God's name had made him ask that? He had himself taken a five-year-old William fishing for char on the lake near Ellesmere, when he had served his indenture there. Did he *want* the boy to remember?

"Oh . . . yes. It's pleasant on the lakes, surely—but nothing like *this*." Willie waved in the vague direction of the creek. The lines in the boy's face had smoothed themselves, and a small flicker of life had come back into his eyes. "I have never seen such a place. It's not at all like England!"

"That it is not," Jamie agreed, amused. "Will ye not miss England, though?"

Willie thought about it for a moment, as he slurped the rest of his tea.

"I don't think so," he said, with a decided shake of his head. "I miss Grandmamma sometimes, and my horses, but nothing else. It was all tutors and dancing lessons and Latin and Greek— ugh!" He wrinkled his nose, and Jamie laughed.

"Ye dinna care for the dancing, then?"

"No. You have to do it with girls." He shot Jamie a look under his fine, dark brows. "Do you care for music, Mr. Fraser?"

"No," Jamie said, smiling. "I like the girls fine, though." The girls were going to like this wee laddie just fine, too, he thought, covertly noting the youngster's breadth of shoulder and long shanks, and the long, dark lashes that hid his bonny blue eyes.

"Yes. Well, Mrs. Fraser is very pretty," the Earl said politely. His mouth curled suddenly up on one side. "Though she did look funny, with the mud on her face."

"I daresay. Will ye have another cup, my lord?"

Claire had said the mixture was for calming; it seemed to be working. As they talked desultorily of the Indians and their strange beliefs, William's eyelids began to droop, and he yawned more than once. At last, Jamie reached over and took the empty cup from his unresisting hand.

"The night is cold, my lord," he said. "Will ye choose to lie next to me, that we may share our coverings?"

The night was chilly, but a long way from cold. He had guessed right, though; Willie seized the excuse with alacrity. He could not take a lord in his arms to comfort him, nor could a young earl admit to wanting such comfort. Two men could lie close together without shame, though, for the sake of warmth.

Willie fell asleep at once, nestled close against his side. Jamie lay awake for a long time, one arm laid lightly across the sleeping body of his son.

"Now the wee speckled one. Just on top, and hold it with your finger, aye?" He wrapped the thread tightly around the tiny roll of white wool, just missing Willie's finger but catching the end of the woodpecker's down feather, so the fluffy barbs rose up pertly, quivering in the light air.

"You see? It looks like a wee bug taking flight."

Willie nodded, intent on the fly. Two tiny yellow tail feathers lay smooth under the down feather, simulating the spread wing casings of a beetle.

"I see. Is it the color that matters, or the shape?"

"Both, but more the shape, I think." Jamie smiled at the boy. "What matters most is how hungry the fish are. Choose your time right, and they'll strike anything—even a bare hook. Choose it wrong, and ye might as well be fishing wi' lint from your navel. Dinna tell that to a fly fisherman, though; they'll be taking all the credit, and none left to the fish."

Willie didn't laugh—the boy didn't laugh much—but he smiled and took the willow pole with its newly tied fly.

"Is it the right time, now, do you think, Mr. Fraser?" He shaded his eyes and looked out over the water. They stood in the cool shadow of a grove of black willow, but the sun was still above the horizon, and the water of the stream glittered like metal.

"Aye, trout feed at sunset. D'ye see the prickles on the water? This pool's waking."

The surface of the pool was restless; the water itself lay calm, but dozens of tiny ripples spread and overlapped, rings of light and shadow spreading and breaking in endless profusion.

"The rings? Yes. Is that fish?"

"Not yet. It's the hatching; midges and gnats hatch from their cases and burst through the surface to the air—the trout will see them and come to feed."

Without warning, a silver streak shot into the air and fell back with a splash. Willie gasped.

"That's a fish," Jamie said, unnecessarily. He quickly threaded his line through the carved guides, tied a fly to his line, and stepped forward. "Watch now."

He drew back his arm and rocked his wrist, back and forth, feeding more line with each circle of his forearm, until with a snap of the wrist, he sent the line sailing out in a great lazy loop, the fly floating down like a circling gnat. He felt the boy's eyes on him, and was glad the cast had been good.

He let the fly float for a moment, watching—it was hard to see, in the sparkling brightness—then began slowly to pull the line in. Quick as thought, the fly went under. The ring of its disappearance had not even begun to spread before he had jerked the line hard and felt the answering savage tug in reply.

"You've got one! You've got one!" He could hear Willie, dancing on the bank behind him with excitement, but had no attention to spare for anything save the fish.

He had no reel; only the twig that held his spare line. He pulled the tip of the rod far back, let it fall forward and gathered in the loose line with a snatch of the hand. Once more, line in, and then a desperate rush that took out all the line gained, and more.

He could see nothing amid the flashing sparks of light, but the tug and pull through his arms was as good as sight; a quiver as live as the trout itself, as though he held the thing in his hands, squirming and wriggling, fighting . . .

Free. The line went limp, and he stood for a moment, the vibrations of struggle dying away along the muscles of his arms, breathing in the air he had forgotten to take in the heat of battle.

"He got away! Oh, bad luck, sir!" Willie scampered down the bank, pole in hand, face open in sympathy.

"Good luck for the fish." Still exhilarated from the fight, Jamie grinned and wiped a wet hand over his face. "Will ye try, lad?" Too late, he remembered that he must call the boy "lord," but Willie was too eager to have noticed the omission.

Face fixed in a scowl of determination, Willie drew back his arm, squinted at the water, and snapped his wrist with a mighty jerk. The rod sailed from his fingers and flew gracefully into the pond.

The boy gaped after it, then turned an expression of utter dismay on Jamie, who made no effort at all to keep back his laughter. The young lord looked thoroughly taken aback, and not very pleased, but after a moment, one corner of his wide mouth curved up in wry acknowledgment. He gestured at the rod, floating some ten feet from the bank.

"Will it not frighten all the fish, if I go in after it?"

"It will. Take mine; I'll fetch that one back later."

Willie licked his lips and set his jaw in concentration, taking a firm grip on the new rod, testing it with little whips and jerks. Turning to the pool, he rocked his arm back and forth, then snapped his wrist hard. He froze, the tip of the rod extended in a perfect line with his arm. The loose line wrapped itself around the rod and draped over Willie's head.

"A verra pretty cast, my lord," Jamie said, rubbing a knuckle hard over his mouth. "But I think we must put on a new fly first, aye?"

"Oh." Slowly, Willie relaxed his rigid posture, and looked sheepishly at Jamie. "I didn't think of that."

Slightly chastened by these misadventures, the Earl allowed Jamie to fasten a fresh fly in place, and then to take him by the wrist to demonstrate the proper way of casting.

Standing behind the boy, he took Willie's right wrist in his own, marveling both at the slenderness of the arm and at the knobby wristbones that gave promise of both size and strength to come. The boy's skin was cool with perspiration, and the feel of his arm much like the tingle of the trout on the line, live and muscular, vivid to his touch. Then Willie twisted free, and he felt a moment's confusion, and a peculiar sense of loss at the breaking of their brief contact.

"That's not right," Willie was saying, turning to look up at him. "You cast with the left hand. I saw you."

"Aye, but I'm cack-handed, my lord. Most men would cast with the right."

"Cack-handed?" Willie's mouth curved up again.

"I find my left hand more convenient to most purposes than is the right, my lord."

"That's what I thought it meant. I'm the same." Willie looked at once rather pleased and mildly shamefaced at this statement. "My—my mother said it wasn't proper, and that I must learn to use the other, as a gentleman ought. But Papa said no, and made them let me write with my left hand. He said it didn't matter so much if I should look awkward with a quill; when it came to fighting with a sword, I should be at an advantage."

"Your father is a wise man." His heart twisted, with something between jealousy and gratitude—but gratitude was far the uppermost.

"Papa was a soldier." Willie drew himself up a little, straightening his shoulders with unconscious pride. "He fought in Scotland, in the Ris— oh." He coughed, and his face went a dull red as he caught sight of Jamie's kilt and realized that he was quite possibly talking to a defeated warrior of that particular fight. He fiddled with the rod, not knowing where to look.

"Aye, I know. That's where I met him, first." Jamie was careful to keep any hint of amusement from his voice. He was tempted to tell the boy the circumstances of that first meeting, but that would be poor repayment to John for his priceless gift, these precious few days with his son.

"He was a verra gallant soldier, indeed," Jamie agreed, straight-faced. "And right about the hands, as well. Have ye begun your schooling with the sword, then?"

"Just a little." Willie was forgetting his embarrassment in enthusiasm for the new topic. "I've had a little whinger since I was eight, and learnt feint and parry. Papa says I shall have a proper sword when we reach Virginia, now I am tall enough for the reach of tierce and longé."

"Ah. Well, then, if ye've been handling a sword in your left hand, I think ye'll have nay great trouble in mastering a rod that way. Here, let us try again, or we'll have no supper."

On the third try, the fly settled sweetly, to float for no more than a second before a small but hungry trout roared to the surface and engulfed it. Willie let out a shriek of excitement, and yanked the rod so hard that the astounded trout flew through the air and past his head, to land with a splat on the bank beyond.

"I did it! I did it! I caught a fish!" Willie waved his rod and ran around in little circles whooping, forgetting the dignity of both age and title.

"Indeed ye did." Jamie picked up the trout, which measured perhaps six inches from nose to tail, and clapped the capering Earl on the back in congratulations. "Well done, lad! It looks as though they're biting well the e'en; let's have another cast or two, aye?"

The trout were indeed biting well. By the time the sun had sunk below the rim of the distant black mountains, and the silver water faded to dull pewter, they had each a respectable string of fish. They were also both wet to the eyebrows, exhausted, half blind from the glare, and thoroughly happy.

"I have never tasted anything half so delicious," Willie said dreamily. "Never." He was naked, wrapped in a blanket, his shirt, breeches and stockings draped on a tree limb to dry. He lay back with a contented sigh, and belched slightly.

Jamie rearranged his damp plaid on a bush and laid another chunk of wood on the fire. The weather was fine, God be thanked, but it was chilly with the sun down, the night wind rising, and a wet sark on his back. He stood close to the edge of the fire and let the heated air rise up under his shirt. The warmth of it ran up his thighs and touched his chest and belly, comforting as Claire's hands on the chilly flesh between his legs.

He stood quietly for a time, watching the boy without seeming to look at him. Putting vanity aside and judging fairly, he thought William a handsome child. Thinner than he should be; every rib showed—but with a wiry muscularity of limb and well formed in all his parts.

The boy had turned his head, gazing into the fire, and he could look more openly. Sap in the pinewood cracked and popped, flooding Willie's face for a moment with golden light.

Jamie stood quite still, feeling his heart beat, watching. It was one of those strange moments that came to him rarely, but never left. A moment that stamped itself on heart and brain, instantly recallable in every detail, for all of his life.

There was no telling what made these moments different from any other, though he knew them when they came. He had seen sights more gruesome and more beautiful by far, and been left with no more than a fleeting muddle of their memory. But these—the still moments, as he called them to himself—they came with no warning, to print a random image of the most common things inside his brain, indelible. They were like the photographs that Claire had brought him, save that the moments carried with them more than vision.

He had one of his father, smeared and muddy, sitting on the wall of a cow byre, a cold Scottish wind lifting his dark hair. He could call that one up and smell the dry hay and the scent of manure, feel his own fingers chilled by the wind, and his heart warmed by the light in his father's eyes.

He had such glimpses of Claire, of his sister, of Ian . . . small moments clipped out of time and perfectly preserved by some odd alchemy of memory, fixed in his mind like an insect in amber. And now he had another.

For so long as he lived, he could recall this moment. He could feel the cold wind on his face, and the crackling feel of the hair on his thighs, half singed by the fire. He could smell the rich odor of trout fried in cornmeal, and feel the tiny prick of a swallowed bone, hair-thin in his throat.

He could hear the dark quiet of the forest behind, and the soft rush of the stream nearby. And forever now he would remember the firelight golden on the sweet bold face of his son.

"Deo gratias," he murmured, and realized that he had spoken aloud only when the boy turned toward him, startled.

"What?"

"Nothing." To cover the moment, he turned away and took down his half-dry plaid from the bush. Even soaking wet, Highland wool would keep in a man's heat, and shelter him from cold.

"Ye should sleep, my lord," he said, sitting down and arranging the damp folds of plaid around himself. "It will be a long day tomorrow."

"I'm not sleepy." As though to prove it, Willie sat up and scrubbed his hands vigorously through his hair, making the thick russet mass stand out like a mane round his head.

Jamie felt a stab of alarm; he recognized the gesture only too well as one of his. In fact, he had been just about to do precisely the same thing, and it was with an effort that he kept his hands still.

He swallowed the heart that had risen into his throat, and reached for his sporran. No. Surely the lad would never think—a boy of that age paid little heed to anything his elders said or did, let alone thought to look at them closely. Still, it had been the hell of a risk for all of them to take; the look on Claire's face had been enough to tell him just how striking the resemblance was.

He took a deep breath, and began to take out the small cloth bundles that contained his fly-tying materials. They had used all his made flies, and if he meant to fish for their breakfast, a few more should be got ready.

"Can I help?" Willie didn't wait for permission, but scooted around the fire, to sit beside him. Without comment, he pushed the small wooden box of birds' feathers toward the boy, and picked a fishhook from the piece of cork that held them.

They worked in silence for a time, stopping only to admire a completed Silver Doctor or Broom-eye, or for Jamie to lend a word of advice or help in tying. Willie soon tired of the exacting work, though, and laid down his half-done Green Whisker, asking numerous questions about fishing, hunting, the forest, the Red Indians they were going to see.

"No," Jamie said in answer to one such. "I've never seen a scalp in the village. They're verra kindly folk, for the most part. Do one some injury, mind, and they'll not be slow to take revenge for it." He smiled wryly. "They do remind me a bit of Highlanders in that regard."

"Grandmamma says the Scots breed l—" The casually begun

statement choked off abruptly. Jamie looked up to see Willie concentrating fiercely on the half-made fly between his fingers, his face redder than the firelight accounted for.

"Like rabbits?" Jamie let both irony and smile show in his voice. Willie flicked a cautious sideways glance in his direction.

"Scottish families are sometimes large, aye." Jamie plucked a wren's down feather from the small box and laid it delicately against the shank of his hook. "We think children a blessing."

The bright color was fading from Willie's cheeks. He sat up a little straighter.

"I see. Have you got a lot of children yourself, Mr. Fraser?" Jamie dropped the down feather.

"No, not a great many," he said, eyes fixed on the mottled leaves.

"I'm sorry—I didn't think—that is . . ." Jamie glanced up to see Willie gone red again, one hand crushing the half-tied fly.

"Think what?" he said, puzzled.

Willie took a deep breath.

"Well—the . . . the . . . sickness; the measles. I didn't see any children, but I didn't think when I said that . . . I mean . . . that maybe you had some, but they . . ."

"Och, no." Jamie smiled at him reassuringly. "My daughter's grown; she'll be living far away in Boston this long while."

"Oh." Willie let out his breath, tremendously relieved. "That's all?"

The fallen down-feather moved in a breath of wind, betraying its presence in the shadows. Jamie pinched it between thumb and forefinger and lifted it gently from the ground.

"No, I've a son, too," he said, eyes on the hook that had somehow embedded its barb in his thumb. A tiny drop of blood welled up around the shining metal. "A bonny lad, and I love him weel, though he's away from home just now."

28

Heated Conversation

B y evening, Ian was glassy-eyed and hot to the touch. He sat up on his pallet to greet me, but swayed alarmingly, his eyes unfocused. I didn't have the slightest doubt, but looked in his mouth for confirmation; sure enough, the small diagnostic Koplik's spots showed white against the dark pink mucous membrane. Though the skin of his neck was still fair and childlike under his hair, it showed a harmless-looking stipple of small pink spots.

"Right," I said, resigned. "You've got it. You'd best come up to the house so I can take care of you more easily."

"I've got the measle? Am I going to die, then?" he asked. He seemed only mildly interested, his attention concentrated on some interior vision.

"No," I said matter-of-factly, trusting that I was right. "Feeling pretty bad, though, are you?"

"My head hurts a bit," he said. I could see that it did; his brows were drawn together, and he squinted at even so dim a light as that provided by my candle.

Still, he could walk, and a good thing, too, I thought as I watched him make his unsteady way down the ladder from the loft. Scrawny and storklike as he looked, he was a good eight inches taller than I, and outweighed me by at least thirty pounds.

It was no more than twenty yards to the cabin, but Ian was trembling from exertion by the time I got him inside. Lord John sat up as we came in, and made to get out of bed, but I waved him back.

"Stay there," I said, depositing Ian heavily on a stool. "I can manage."

I had been sleeping on the trundle bed; it was already made up with sheets, quilt, and pillow. I peeled Ian out of his breeks and stockings, and tucked him up at once. He was flushed and clammy-cheeked, and looked much sicker than he had done in the dimness of his loft.

The willow-bark brew I had left steeping was dark and aromatic; ready to drink. I poured it off carefully into a cup, glancing as I did so at Lord John.

"I'd meant this for you," I said. "But if you could stand to wait . . ."

"By all means give it to the lad," he said, with a dismissive wave. "I can wait easily. Can I not assist you, though?"

I thought of suggesting that if he really wanted to be helpful, he could walk to the privy rather than use the chamber pot—which I would have to empty—but I could see that he wasn't yet in any condition to be wandering round outside at night by himself. I didn't want to be explaining to young William that I had allowed his remaining parent—or what he thought was his remaining parent—to be eaten by bears, let alone take pneumonia.

So I merely shook my head politely, and knelt by the trundle to administer the brew to Ian. He felt well enough to make faces and complain about the taste, which I found reassuring. Still, the headache was obviously very bad; the line between his brows was fixed and sharp as though it had been carved there with a knife.

I sat on the trundle and took his head onto my lap, gently rubbing his temples. Then I put my thumbs just into the sockets of his eyes, pressing firmly upward on the ridge of his brows. He made a low sound of discomfort, but then relaxed, his head heavy on my thigh.

"Just breathe," I said. "Don't worry if it's a bit tender at first, it means I've got the right spot."

" 'S all right," he murmured, his words a little slurred. His hand drifted up and closed on my wrist, big and very warm. "That's the Chinaman's way, no?"

"That's right. He means Yi Tien Cho—Mr. Willoughby," I explained to Lord John, who was watching the proceedings with a puzzled frown. "It's a way of relieving pain by putting pressure on some points of the body. This one is good for headache. The Chinaman taught me to do it."

I felt some reluctance to mention the little Chinese to Lord John, seeing that the last time we had met, on Jamaica, Lord John had had some four hundred soldiers and sailors combing the island in pursuit of Mr. Willoughby, then suspected of a particularly atrocious murder.

"He didn't do it, you know," I felt compelled to add. Lord John raised one eyebrow at me.

"That's as well," he said dryly, "since we never caught him."

"Oh, I'm glad." I looked down at Ian, and moved my thumbs a quarter of an inch outward, pressing again. His face was still tight with pain, but I thought the whiteness at the corners of his mouth was lessening a bit.

"I . . . ah . . . don't suppose you know who *did* kill Mrs. Alcott?" Lord John's voice was casual. I glanced up at him, but his face betrayed nothing beyond simple curiosity and a large number of spots.

"I do, yes," I said hesitantly, "but—"

"You do? A murder? Who was it? What happened, Auntie? Ooch!" Ian's eyelids popped open under my fingers, wide with interest, then snapped shut in a grimace of pain as the firelight struck them.

"You be still," I said, and dug my thumbs into the muscles in front of his ears. "You're ill."

"Argk!" he said, but subsided obediently into limpness, the corn-shuck mattress rustling loudly under his thin body. "All right, Auntie, but who? Ye canna be telling wee bits o' things like that, and expect me to sleep without knowing the rest of it. Can she, then?" He opened one eye in a slitted appeal toward Lord John, who smiled in reply.

"I bear no further responsibility in the matter," Lord John assured me. "However"—he spoke more firmly to Ian—"you might stop to think that perhaps the story incriminates someone your aunt prefers to shield. It would be discourteous to insist upon details, in that case."

"Och, no, it's never that," Ian assured him, eyes tight closed. "Uncle Jamie wouldna murder anybody, save he had good reason."

From the corner of my eye, I saw Lord John jerk, slightly startled. Plainly, it had never occurred to him that it *could* have been Jamie.

"No," I assured him, seeing the fair brows draw together. "It wasn't."

"Well, and it wasna me, either," Ian said smugly. "And who else would Auntie be protecting?"

"You flatter yourself, Ian," I said dryly. "But since you insist . . ."

My hesitancy had in fact been in the interests of protecting

Young Ian. No one else could be harmed by the story—the murderer was dead and, for all I knew, Mr. Willoughby, too, perished in the hidden jungles of the Jamaican hills, though I sincerely hoped not.

But the story involved someone else, as well; the woman I had first known as Geillis Duncan and known later as Geillis Abernathy, at whose behest Ian had been kidnapped from Scotland, imprisoned on Jamaica, and had suffered things that he had only lately begun to tell us.

Still, there seemed no way out of it now—Ian was fractious as a child insisting on a bedtime story, and Lord John was sitting up in bed like a chipmunk waiting for nuts, eyes bright with interest.

And so, with the macabre urge to begin with "Once upon a time . . ." I leaned back against the wall, and with Ian's head still in my lap, began the story of Rose Hall and its mistress, the witch Geillis Duncan; of the Reverend Archibald Campbell and his strange sister, Margaret, of the Edinburgh Fiend and the Fraser prophecy; and of a night of fire and crocodile's blood, when the slaves of six plantations along the Yallahs River had risen and slain their masters, roused by the *houngan* Ishmael.

Of later events in the cave of Abandawe on Haiti, I said nothing. Ian, after all, had been there. And those happenings had nothing to do with the murder of Mina Alcott.

"A crocodile," Ian murmured. His eyes were closed, and his face had grown more relaxed under my fingers, despite the gruesome nature of my story. "Ye really saw it, Auntie?"

"I not only saw it, I stepped on it," I assured him. "Or rather, I stepped on it, and *then* I saw it. If I'd seen it first, I'd have bloody run the other way."

There was a low laugh from the bed. Lord John scratched at his arm, smiling.

"You must find life here rather dull, Mrs. Fraser, after your adventures in the Indies."

"I could do with a spot of dullness now and then," I said, rather wistfully.

Involuntarily, I glanced at the bolted door, where I had propped Ian's musket, brought back from the storehouse when I had fetched him. Jamie had taken his own gun, but his pistols lay on the sideboard, loaded and primed as he had left them for me, bullet case and powder horn neatly arranged beside them.

It was cozy in the cabin, with the fire flickering gold and red on the rough-barked walls, and the air filled with the warm, lingering scents of squirrel stew and pumpkin bread, spiced with the bitter tang of willow tea. I brushed my fingers over Ian's jaw. No rash yet, but the skin was tight and hot—very hot still, in spite of the willow bark.

Talking about Jamaica had at least distracted me a bit from my worry over Ian. Headache was not an unusual symptom for someone with measles; severe and prolonged headache was. Meningitis and encephalitis were dangerous—and all too possible—complications of the disease.

"How's the head?" I asked.

"A bit better," he said. He coughed, eyes squinching shut as the spasms jarred his head. He stopped and opened them slightly, dark slits that glowed with fever. "I'm awfully hot, Auntie."

I slid off the trundle and went to wring out a cloth in cool water. Ian stirred slightly as I wiped his face, his eyes closed once more.

"Mrs. Abernathy gave me amethysts to drink for the headache," he murmured drowsily.

"Amethysts?" I was startled, but kept my voice low and soothing. "You drank amethysts?"

"Ground up in vinegar," he said. "And pearls in sweet wine, but that was for the bedding, she said." His face looked red and swollen, and he turned his cheek against the cool pillow, seeking relief. "She was a great one for the stones, yon woman. She burned powdered emeralds in the flame of a black candle, and she rubbed my cock wi' a diamond—to keep it hard, she said."

There was a faint sound from the bed, and I looked up to see Lord John, raised up on one elbow, eyes wide.

"And did the amethysts work?" I wiped Ian's face gently with the cloth.

"The diamond did." He made a feeble attempt at an adolescent's bawdy laugh, but it faded into a harsh, rasping cough.

"No amethysts here, I'm afraid," I said. "But there's wine, if you want it." He did, and I helped him to drink it—well diluted with water—then eased him back on the pillow, flushed and heavy-eyed.

Lord John had lain down, too, and lay watching, his thick blond hair unbound, spread out on the pillow behind him.

"That's what she wanted wi' the lads, ye ken," Ian said. His eyes were shut tight against the light, but he could clearly see *something*, if only in the mists of memory. He licked his lips; they were beginning to dry and crack, and his nose was beginning to run.

"She said the stone grew in a lad's innards—the one she wanted. She said it must be a laddie who'd never gone wi' a lass, though, that was important. If he had, the stone wouldna be right, somehow. If he h-huh-had one." He paused to cough, and ended breathless, nose dripping. I held a handkerchief for him to blow.

"What did she want the stone for?" Lord John's face bore a look of sympathy—he knew only too well what Ian felt like at the moment—but curiosity compelled the question. I didn't object; I wanted to know too.

Ian started to shake his head, then stopped with a groan.

"Ah! Oh, God, my head will split surely! I dinna ken, man. She didna say. Only that it was needful; she must have it to be s-sure." He barely got out the last word before dissolving into a coughing attack that was the worst yet; he sounded like a barking dog.

"You'd better stop talk—" I began, but was interrupted by a soft thump at the door.

Instantly I froze, wet cloth still in my hand. Lord John leaned swiftly from the bed and took a pistol from inside one of his high cavalry boots on the floor. A finger to his lips to enjoin silence, he nodded toward Jamie's pistols. I moved silently to the sideboard and grasped one, reassured by the smooth, solid heft of it in my hand.

"Who is there?" Lord John called, in a surprisingly strong voice.

There was no answer save a sort of scratching, and a faint whine. I sighed and laid the pistol down, torn between irritation, relief and amusement.

"It's your blasted dog, Ian."

"Are you sure?" Lord John spoke in a low voice, pistol still aimed unwaveringly at the door. "It might be an Indian trick."

Ian rolled over with an effort, facing the door.

"Rollo!" he shouted, his voice hoarse and cracking.

Hoarse or not, Rollo knew his master's voice; there was a deep, joyful "WARF!" from outside, succeeding by frantic scratching, at a height some four feet from the ground.

"Beastly dog," I said, hurrying to open the door. "Stop that, or I'll make you into a rug, or a coat, or something!"

Giving this threat the attention it deserved, Rollo bounded past me into the room. Exuberant with joy, he launched his hundred and fifty pounds from the middle of the floor and landed directly on the trundle bed, making it sway dangerously, joints screeching in protest. Ignoring a strangled cry from the bed's occupant, he proceeded to lick Ian madly about the face and forearms—the latter being flung up as a wholly inadequate defense to the slobbering onslaught.

"Bad dog," Ian said, making ineffectual efforts to push Rollo off his chest, giggling helplessly in spite of his discomfort. "Bad dog, I say—down, sir!"

"Down, sir!" Lord John echoed sternly. Rollo, interrupted in his demonstrations of affection, rounded on Lord John, his ears laid back. He curled his lip, and gave his lordship a good look at the condition of his back teeth. Lord John started, and raised his pistol convulsively.

"Down, *a dhiobhuil*!" Ian said, prodding Rollo in the hindquarters. "Take your hairy arse out o' my face, ye wicked beast!"

Rollo instantly dismissed Lord John from consideration, and padded around on top of the trundle, turning three times and kneading the bedding with his paws before collapsing next to his master's body. He licked Ian's ear, and with a deep sigh, laid his nose between his large muddy paws on the pillow.

"Would you like me to get him off, Ian?" I offered, eyeing the paws. I wasn't quite sure how I might move a dog of Rollo's size and temperament, bar shooting him with Jamie's pistol and dragging his carcass off the bed, so was rather relieved when Ian shook his head.

"No, let him stay, Auntie," he said, croaking slightly. "He's a good fellow. Are ye no, *a charaid*?" He laid a hand on the dog's neck, and turned his head so his cheek lay pillowed against Rollo's thick ruff.

"All right, then." Moving slowly, with a wary glance at the unblinking yellow eyes, I approached the bed and smoothed Ian's hair. His forehead was still hot, but I thought the fever was a bit lower. If it broke in the night, as it well might, it was likely to be succeeded by a fit of violent shivering—when Ian might well find Rollo's warm hairy bulk a comfort.

"Sleep well."

"Oidhche mhath." He was half asleep already, drifting into the vivid dreams of fever, and his "good-night" was barely more than a murmur.

I moved quietly about the room, tidying away the results of the day's labors; a basket of fresh-gathered peanuts to be washed,

dried and stored; a pan of dried reeds laid flat and covered with a
layer of bacon grease to make rushlights. A trip to the pantry,
where I stirred the beer mash fermenting in its tub, squeezed out
the curds of the soft cheese a-making, and punched down the
slow-rising salt bread, ready to be made into loaves and baked in
the morning, when the small Dutch oven built into the side of the
hearth would be heated through by the night's low fire.

Ian was sound asleep when I came back into the main room;
Rollo's eyes were closed as well, though one yellow slit cracked
open at my entrance. I glanced at Lord John; he was awake, but
did not look round.

I sat down on the settle by the fire, and brought out the big wool
basket with its green and black Indian pattern—Sun-eater,
Gabrielle had called the design.

Two days since Jamie and Willie had left. Two days to the
Tuscarora village. Two days back. If nothing happened to stop
them.

"Nonsense," I muttered, under my breath. Nothing would stop
them. They would be home soon.

The basket was full of dyed skeins of wool and linen thread.
Some I had been given by Jocasta, some I had spun myself. The
difference was obvious, but even the lumpy, awkward-looking
strands I produced could be used for something. Not stockings or
jerseys; perhaps I could knit a tea cozy—that seemed sufficiently
shapeless to disguise all my deficiencies.

Jamie had been simultaneously shocked and amused to find that
I didn't know how to knit. The question had never arisen at Lallybroch, where Jenny and the female servants kept everyone in
knitted goods. I had taken on the chores of stillroom and garden,
and never dealt with needlework beyond the simplest mending.

"Ye canna clickit at all?" he said incredulously. "And what
did ye do for your winter stockings in Boston, then?"

"Bought them," I said.

He had looked elaborately around the clearing where we had
been sitting, admiring the half-finished cabin.

"Since I dinna see any shops about, I suppose ye'd best learn,
aye?"

"I suppose so." I dubiously eyed the knitting basket Jocasta
had given me. It was well equipped, with three long circular wire
needles in different sizes, and a sinister-looking set of four
double-ended ivory ones, slender as stilettos, which I knew were
used in some mysterious fashion to turn the heels of stockings.

"I'll ask Jocasta to show me, next time we go down to River Run. Next year perhaps."

Jamie snorted briefly and picked up a needle and a ball of yarn.

"It's no verra difficult, Sassenach. Look—this is how ye cast up your row." Drawing the thread out through his closed fist, he made a loop round his thumb, slipped it onto the needle, and with a quick economy of motion, cast on a long row of stitches in a matter of seconds. Then he handed me the other needle and another ball of yarn. "There—you try."

I looked at him in complete amazement.

"*You* can knit?"

"Well, of course I can," he said, staring at me in puzzlement. "I've known how to clickit wi' needles since I was seven years old. Do they not teach bairns *anything* in your time?"

"Well," I said, feeling mildly foolish, "they sometimes teach little girls to do needlework, but not boys."

"They didna teach you, did they? Besides, it's no fine needlework, Sassenach, it's only plain knitting. Here, take your thumb and dip it, so . . ."

And so he and Ian—who, it turned out, could also knit and was prostrated by mirth at my lack of knowledge—had taught me the simple basics of knit and purl, explaining, between snorts of derision over my efforts, that in the Highlands all boys were routinely taught to knit, that being a useful occupation well suited to the long idle hours of herding sheep or cattle on the shielings.

"Once a man's grown and has a wife to do for him, and a lad of his own to mind the sheep, he maybe doesna make his own stockings anymore," Ian had said, deftly executing the turn of a heel before handing me back the stocking, "but even wee laddies ken how, Auntie."

I cast an eye at my current project, some ten inches of a wooly shawl, which lay in a small crumpled heap at the bottom of the basket. I had learned the basics, but knitting for me was still a pitched battle with knotted thread and slippery needles, not the soothing, dreamy exercise that Jamie and Ian made of it, needles clicketing away in their big hands by the fire, comforting as the sound of crickets on the hearth.

Not tonight, I thought. I wasn't up to it. Something mindless, like winding up the balls of yarn. That I could do. I laid aside a half-finished pair of stockings Jamie was making for himself—striped, the show-off—and pulled out a heavy skein of fresh-dyed blue wool, still redolent with the heavy scents of its dyeing.

Normally I liked the smell of fresh yarn, with its faint oily
whiff of sheep, the earthy smell of indigo, and the sharp tang of
the vinegar used to set the dye. Tonight it seemed smothering,
added as it was to woodsmoke and candle wax, to the close, acrid
smells of male bodies and the reek of illness—a mingled scent of
sweaty sheets and used chamber pots—all trapped together in the
room's stale air.

I let the skein lie on my lap, and closed my eyes for a moment. I
wanted nothing so much as to undress and sponge myself with
cool water, then slip naked between the clean linen sheets of my
bed and lie still, letting the fresh cool air blow through the open
window across my face while I floated into oblivion.

But there was a sweating Englishman in one of my beds, and a
filthy dog in the other, to say nothing of a teenage boy who was
obviously in for a hard night. The sheets had not been washed in
days, and when they were, it would be a backbreaking business of
boiling, lifting and wringing. My bed for the night—assuming
that I got to sleep in it—would be a pallet made of a folded quilt,
with my pillow a sack of carded wool. I would breathe sheep all
night.

Nursing is hard work, and all of a sudden I was bloody tired of
it. For a moment of intense longing, I wanted them all just to go
away. I opened my eyes, looking at Lord John with resentment.
My little burst of self-pity faded, though, as I looked at him. He
lay on his back, one arm behind his head, gazing somberly up at
the ceiling. It might have been only a trick of the fire, but his face
seemed marked by anxiety and grief, eyes shadowed with dark
loss.

At once I felt ashamed of my ill temper. Granted, I hadn't
wanted him here. I was annoyed at his intrusion into my life and
the burden of obligation his illness had placed upon me. His very
presence made me uneasy—to say nothing of William's. But they
would go, soon. Jamie would be home, Ian would recover, and I
would have back my peace, my happiness, and my clean sheets.
What had happened to him was permanent.

John Grey had lost a wife—however he might have regarded
her. It had taken courage of more than one kind to bring William
here, and to send him off with Jamie. And I didn't suppose the
bloody man could help having caught the measles.

I laid the wool aside for the moment and got up to put the kettle
on. A nice cup of tea all round seemed called for. As I straight-

ened up from the hearth, I saw Lord John turn his head, my movement drawing his attention from his inward thoughts.

"Tea," I said, embarrassed to meet his eyes after my uncharitable thoughts. I made a small, awkward gesture of interrogation toward the kettle.

He smiled faintly and nodded.

"I thank you, Mrs. Fraser."

I took down the tea box from the cupboard, and laid out two cups and spoons, adding the sugar bowl as an afterthought; no molasses tonight.

When I had got the tea made, I sat down near the bed to drink it. We sipped in silence for a few moments, an odd air of shyness hovering between us.

At last, I set down my cup and cleared my throat.

"I'm sorry; I had meant to offer you my condolences on the loss of your wife," I said, rather formally.

He looked surprised for a moment, then bowed his head in acknowledgment, matching my formality.

"It is a coincidence that you should say so at the moment," he said. "I had just been thinking of her."

Used as I was to having other people take one look at my face and discern instantly what I was thinking, it was oddly gratifying to be able to do it to someone else.

"Do you miss her greatly—your wife?" I felt a bit hesitant about asking, but he didn't seem to find the question intrusive. I might almost have thought that he had been asking it himself, for he answered readily, if thoughtfully.

"I don't really know," he said. He glanced at me, one eyebrow raised. "Does that sound unfeeling?"

"I couldn't say," I said, a little tartly. "Surely you'd know better than I whether you had feelings for her or not."

"I did, yes." He let his head fall back on the pillow, his thick fair hair loose about his shoulders. "Or I do, perhaps. That's why I came, do you see?"

"No, I can't say that I do."

I heard Ian cough, and rose to look, but he had only turned over in his sleep; he lay on his stomach, one long arm drooping from the trundle bed. I picked up his hand—it was still hot, but not dangerously so—and put it on the pillow near his face. His hair had fallen in his eyes; I brushed it gently back.

"You are very good with him; have you children of your own?"

Startled, I looked up to see Lord John watching me, chin propped on his fist.

"I—we—have a daughter," I said.

His eyes widened.

"We?" he said sharply. "The girl is Jamie's?"

"Don't call her 'the girl,' " I said, unreasonably irritated. "Her name is Brianna, and yes, she's Jamie's."

"My apologies," he said, rather stiffly.

"I meant no offense," he added a moment later, in a softer tone. "I was surprised."

I looked at him directly. I was too tired to be tactful.

"And a bit jealous, perhaps?"

He had a diplomat's face; almost anything could have been going on behind that facade of handsome amiability. I went on staring at him, though, and he let the mask drop—a flash of knowledge lit the light blue eyes, tinged with grudging humor.

"So. One more thing that we have in common." I was startled by his acuity, though I shouldn't have been. It's always discomfiting to find that feelings you thought safely hidden are in fact sitting out in the open for anyone to look at.

"Don't tell me you didn't think of that when you decided to come here." The tea was finished; I set the cup aside and took up my skein of wool again.

He studied me for a moment, eyes narrowed.

"I thought of it, yes," he said finally. He let his head fall back on the pillow, eyes fixed on the low beamed ceiling. "Still, if I was human enough—or petty enough—to consider that I might offend you by bringing William here, I would ask you to believe that such offense was not my motive in coming."

I laid the finished ball of yarn in the basket and took up another skein, stretching it across the back of a split-willow chair.

"I believe you," I said, my eyes fixed on the skein. "If only because it seems rather a lot of trouble to go to. What *was* your motive, though?"

I sensed the movement as he shrugged, rustling the sheets.

"The obvious—to allow Jamie to see the boy."

"And the other obvious—to allow you to see Jamie."

There was a marked silence from the bed. I kept my eyes on the yarn, turning the ball as I wrapped the strand, over and under, back and forth, an intricate crisscross that would in the end yield a perfect sphere.

"You are a rather remarkable woman," he said at last, in a level tone.

"Indeed," I said, not looking up. "In what way?"

He leaned back; I heard the rustle of his bedding.

"You are neither circumspect nor circuitous. In fact, I don't believe I have ever met anyone more devastatingly straightforward —male *or* female."

"Well, it's not by choice," I said. I came to the end of the thread and tucked it neatly into the ball. "I was born that way."

"So was I," he said, very softly.

I didn't answer; I didn't think he had spoken to be heard.

I rose and went to the cupboard. I took down three jars: catmint, valerian, and wild ginger. I took down the marble mortar and tipped the dried leaves and root chunks into it. A drop of water fell from the kettle, hissing into steam.

"What are you doing?" Lord John asked.

"Making an infusion for Ian," I said, with a nod toward the trundle. "The same I gave you four days ago."

"Ah. We heard of you as we traveled from Wilmington," Grey said. His voice was casual now, making conversation. "You are well known in the countryside for your skills, it would appear."

"Mm." I pounded and ground, and the deep, musky smell of wild ginger filled the room.

"They say you are a conjure-woman. What is that, do you know?"

"Anything from a midwife to a physician to a caster of spells or a fortune-teller," I said. "Depending on who's talking."

He made a sound that might have been a laugh, and then was silent for a bit.

"You think they will be safe." It was a statement, but he was asking.

"Yes. Jamie wouldn't have taken the boy if he thought there'd be any danger. Surely you know that, if you know him at all?" I added, glancing at him.

"I know him," he said.

"Do you indeed," I said.

He was quiet for a moment, bar the sound of scratching.

"I know him well enough—or think I do—to risk sending William away with him, alone. And to be sure he will not tell William the truth."

I poured the green and yellow powder into a small square of cotton gauze and tied it neatly into a tiny bag.

"No, he won't, you're right about that."

"Will you?"

I looked up, startled.

"You really think I would?" He studied my face carefully for a moment, then smiled.

"No," he said quietly. "Thank you."

I snorted briefly and dropped the medicine bag into the teapot. I put back the jars of herbs, and sat down with my blasted wool again.

"It was generous of you—to let Willie go with Jamie. Rather brave," I added, somewhat grudgingly. I looked up; he was staring at the dark oblong of the hide-covered window, as though he could look beyond it to see the two figures, side by side in the forest.

"Jamie has held my life in his hands for a good many years now," he answered softly. "I will trust him with William's."

"And what if Willie remembers a groom named MacKenzie better than you think? Or happens to take a good look at his own face and Jamie's?"

"Twelve-year-old boys are not remarkable for their acute perception," Grey said dryly. "And I think that if a boy has lived all his life in the secure belief that he is the ninth Earl of Ellesmere, the notion that he might actually be the illegitimate offspring of a Scottish groom is not one that would enter his head—or be long entertained there, if it did."

I wound wool in silence, listening to the crackle of the fire. Ian was coughing again, but didn't wake. The dog had moved, and was now curled up by his legs, a dark heap of fur.

I finished the second ball of yarn and began another. One more, and the infusion would have finished steeping. If Ian didn't need me yet, I would lie down then.

Grey had been silent for so long that I was surprised when he started to speak again. When I glanced at him, he wasn't looking at me, but was staring upward, seeking visions once again among the smoke-stained beams.

"I told you I had feelings for my wife," he said softly. "I did. Affection. Familiarity. Loyalty. We had known each other all her life; our fathers had been friends; I had known her brother. She might well have been my sister."

"And was she satisfied with that—to be your sister?"

He gave me a glance somewhere between anger and interest.

"You cannot be at all a comfortable woman to live with." He

shut his mouth, but couldn't leave it there. He shrugged impatiently. "Yes, I believe she was satisfied with the life she led. She never said that she was not."

I didn't reply to this, though I exhaled rather strongly through my nose. He shrugged uncomfortably, and scratched his collarbone.

"I was an adequate husband to her," he said defensively. "That we had no children of our own—that was not my—"

"I really don't want to hear about it!"

"Oh, don't you?" His voice was still low, not to wake Ian, but it had lost the smooth modulations of diplomacy; the anger was rough in it.

"You asked me why I came; you questioned my motives; you accused me of jealousy. Perhaps you *don't* want to know, because if you did, you could not keep thinking of me as you choose to."

"And how the hell do you know what I choose to think of you?"

His mouth twisted in an expression that might have been a sneer on a less handsome face.

"Don't I?"

I looked him full in the face for a minute, not troubling to hide anything at all.

"You did mention jealousy," he said quietly, after a moment.

"So I did. So did you."

He turned his head away, but continued after a moment.

"When I heard that Isobel was dead . . . it meant nothing to me. We had lived together for years, though we had not seen each other for nearly two years. We shared a bed; we shared a life, I thought. I should have cared. But I didn't."

He took a deep breath; I saw the bedclothes stir as he settled himself.

"You mentioned generosity. It wasn't that. I came to see . . . whether I can still feel," he said. His head was still turned away, staring at the hide-covered window, grown dark with the night. "Whether it is my own feelings that have died, or only Isobel."

"*Only* Isobel?" I echoed.

He lay quite still for a moment, facing away.

"I can still feel shame, at least," he said, very softly.

I could tell by the feel of the night that it was very late; the fire had burned low, and the aching of my muscles told me that it was well past my bedtime.

Ian was getting restless; he stirred in his sleep, moaning, and

Rollo got up and nuzzled him, making small whimpering noises. I
went to him and wiped his face again, plumped his pillow and
straightened his sheets, making comforting murmurs. He was no
more than half awake; I held his head and fed him a cup of the
warm infusion, sip by sip.

"You'll feel better in the morning." There were spots visible in
the open neck of his shirt—only a few as yet—but the fever was
less, and the line between his brows had eased.

I wiped his face once more and eased him back on his pillow,
where he turned a cheek to the cool linen and fell asleep again at
once.

There was plenty of the infusion left. I poured another cup and
held it out to Lord John. Surprised, he sat upright and took it from
me.

"And now that you've come, and seen him—do you still have
feelings?" I said.

He stared at me for a moment, eyes unblinking in the candlelight.

"I do, yes." Hand steady as a rock, he picked up the cup and
drank. "God help me," he added, so casual as almost to sound
offhand.

Ian passed a bad night but dropped off into a fitful doze near
dawn. I seized the chance of a little rest myself, and managed a
few hours of delectable sleep on the floor before being roused by
the the loud braying of Clarence the mule.

A sociable creature, Clarence was utterly delighted by the approach of anything he regarded as a friend—this category embracing virtually anything on four legs. He gave tongue to his joy in a
voice that rang off the mountainside. Rollo, affronted at being
thus upstaged in the watchdog department, leapt off Ian's bed,
soared over me, and out through the open window, baying like a
werewolf.

Thus startled out of slumber, I staggered to my feet. Lord John,
who was sitting in his shirt at the table, looked startled too,
though whether at the racket or at my appearance, I couldn't tell. I
went outside, running my fingers hastily through my disheveled
locks, heart beating faster in the hope that it might be Jamie
returning.

My heart fell as I saw that it wasn't Jamie and Willie, but my
disappointment was quickly replaced by astonishment when I saw

who the visitor was—Pastor Gottfried, leader of the Lutheran church in Salem. I had met the Pastor now and then, in the homes of parishioners where I had been paying medical calls, but I was more than surprised to find him so far afield.

It was nearly two days ride from Salem to the Ridge, and the nearest German Lutheran farm was at least fifteen miles away, over rough country. The Pastor was no natural horseman—I could see the mud and dust of repeated falls splashed over his black coat — and I thought that it must be a dire emergency indeed that brought him so far up the mountain.

"Down, wicked dog!" I said sharply to Rollo, who was baring his teeth and growling at the new arrival, much to the displeasure of the Pastor's horse. "Be quiet, I say!"

Rollo gave me a yellow-eyed look and subsided with an air of offended dignity, as though to suggest that if I wished to welcome obvious malefactors onto the premises, *he* wouldn't answer for the consequences.

The Pastor was a tubby little man with a huge, curly gray beard that surrounded his face like a storm cloud, through which his normally beaming face peered like the breaking sun. He wasn't beaming this morning, though; his round cheeks were the color of suet, puffy lips pale, and his eyes red-rimmed with fatigue.

"Meine Dame," he greeted me, doffing his broad-brimmed hat and bowing deeply from the waist. *"Ist Euer Mann hier?"*

I spoke no more than a few words of crude German, but could easily make out that he was looking for Jamie. I shook my head, gesturing vaguely toward the woods, to indicate Jamie's absence.

The Pastor looked even more dismayed than before, nearly wringing his hands in his distress. He said several urgent things in German, then seeing that I didn't understand him, repeated himself, speaking slower and louder, his stubby body straining for expression, trying by sheer force of will to make me understand.

I was still shaking my head helplessly when a voice spoke sharply from behind me.

"Was ist los?" demanded Lord John, emerging into the dooryard. *"Was habt Ihr gesagt?"* He had put on his breeches, I was glad to see, though he was still barefoot, with his fair hair streaming loose on his shoulders.

The Pastor gave me a scandalized look, plainly thinking The Worst, but this expression was wiped off his face at once by a further machine-gun rattle of German from Lord John. The Pastor bobbed in apology to me, then turned eagerly to the Englishman, waving his arms and stammering in his haste to tell his story.

"What?" I said, having failed to pluck more than a word or two from the Teutonic flood. "What on earth is he saying?"

Grey turned a grim face toward me.

"Do you know a family named Mueller?"

"Yes," I said, immediate alarm flaring at the name. "I delivered a child to Petronella Mueller, three weeks ago."

"Ah." Grey licked dry lips and glanced at the ground; he didn't want to tell me. "The—the child is dead, I am afraid. So is the mother."

"Oh, no." I sank down on the bench by the door, swept by a feeling of absolute denial. "No. They can't be."

Grey rubbed a hand over his mouth, nodding as the Pastor went on, waving his small, fat hands in agitation.

"He says it was *Masern;* I think that would be what we call the measle. *Flecken, so ähnlich wie diese?*" he demanded of the Pastor, pointing at the remnants of rash still visible on his face.

The Pastor nodded emphatically, repeating *"Flecken, Masern, ja!"* and patting his own cheeks.

"But what does he want Jamie for?" I asked, bewilderment added to distress.

"Apparently he believes Jamie might be able to reason with the man—with Herr Mueller. Are they friends?"

"Not exactly, no. Jamie hit Gerhard Mueller in the mouth and knocked him down in front of the mill last spring."

A muscle twitched in Lord John's scabbed cheek.

"I see. I suppose he's using the term 'reason with' rather loosely, then."

"Mueller can't be reasoned with by any means more sophisticated than an ax handle," I said. "But what is he being unreasonable about?"

Grey frowned—he didn't recognize my use of "sophisticated," I realized, though he understood what I meant. He hesitated, then turned back to the small minister and asked something else, listening intently to the resulting torrent of *Deutsch.*

Little by little, with constant interruptions and much gesticulation, the story emerged in translation.

There was, as Lord John had told us earlier, an epidemic of measles in Cross Creek. This had evidently spread into the backcountry; several households in Salem were afflicted, but the

Muellers, isolated as they were, had not suffered infection until recently.

However, the day before the first sign of measles appeared, a small band of Indians had stopped at the Mueller farm asking for food and drink. Mueller, with whose opinions of Indians I was thoroughly well acquainted, had driven them off with considerable abuse. The Indians, offended, had made—said Mueller—mysterious signs toward his house as they left.

When measles broke out among the family the next day, Mueller was positive that the disease had been brought upon them by means of a hex, placed on his house by the Indians he had rebuffed. He had at once painted antihexing symbols upon his walls, and summoned the Pastor from Salem to perform an exorcism . . . "I think that is what he said," Lord John added doubtfully. "Though I am not sure whether he means by that . . ."

"Never mind," I said impatiently. "Go on!"

None of these precautions availed Mueller, though, and when Petronella and the new baby succumbed to the disease, the old man had lost what little mind he had. Vowing revenge upon the savages who had brought such devastation to his household, he had forced his sons and sons-in-law to accompany him, and ridden off into the woods.

From this expedition they had returned three days ago, the sons white-faced and silent, the old man burning with cold satisfaction.

"Ich war dort. Ich habe ihn geschen," said Herr Gottfried, sweat trickling down his cheeks at the recollection. I was there. I saw.

Summoned by a hysterical message from the women, the Pastor had ridden into the stableyard, to find two long tails of dark hair hanging from the barn door, stirring gently in the wind above the crudely painted legend *Rache.*

"That means 'revenge,' " Lord John translated for me.

"I know," I said, my mouth so dry I could barely speak. "I've read Sherlock Holmes. You mean he . . ."

"Evidently so."

The Pastor was still speaking; he seized me by the arm and shook it, trying to communicate his urgency. Grey's look sharpened at whatever the minister was saying, and he broke in with an abrupt question, answered by frenzied noddings.

"He's coming here. Mueller." Grey swung round to me, his face set in alarm.

Terribly upset by the scalps, the Pastor had gone in search of
Herr Mueller, only to find that the patriarch had nailed his grisly
trophies to the barn and then left the farm, bound—he had said—
for Fraser's Ridge, to see me.

If I hadn't been sitting down already, I might have collapsed at
this. I could feel the blood draining from my cheeks, and was sure
I looked as pale as Pastor Gottfried.

"Why?" I said. "Is he—he couldn't! He couldn't think I had
done anything to Petronella or the baby. Could he?" I turned in
appeal toward the Pastor, who pushed a pudgy, trembling hand
through his gray-streaked hair, disordering its carefully larded
strands.

"The clerical gentleman doesn't know what Mueller thinks, or
what his purpose is in coming here," said Lord John. He cast an
interested eye over the pastor's unprepossessing form. "Much to
his credit, he set off alone, hell-for-leather after Mueller, and
found him two hours later—insensible by the side of the road."

The huge old farmer had evidently gone for days without food
on his hunt for revenge. Intemperance was not a common failing
among the Lutherans, but under the stimulus of fatigue and emotion, Mueller had drunk deeply upon his return, and the enormous
draughts of beer he had consumed had been too much for him.
Overcome, he had contrived to hobble his mule, but then had
wrapped himself in his coat and fallen asleep among the trailing
arbutus by the road.

The Pastor had made no attempt to rouse Mueller, being well
acquainted with the man's temper and feeling it would not be
improved by drink. Instead, Gottfried had mounted his own horse
and ridden as quickly as he could, trusting to Providence to bring
him here in time to warn us.

He had had no doubt that my *Mann* would be competent to deal
with Mueller, no matter what his state or intentions, but with
Jamie gone . . .

Pastor Gottfried looked helplessly from me to Lord John, and
back again.

"Vielleicht solten Sie gehen?" he suggested, making his meaning clear with a jerk of his head toward the paddock.

"I can't leave," I said, and gestured toward the house. *"Mein*
—Christ, what's nephew?—*Mein junger Mann ist nicht gut."*

"Ihr Neffe ist krank," Lord John corrected briskly. *"Haben Sie
jemals Masern gehabt?"*

The Pastor shook his head, distress altering to alarm.

"He hasn't had the measles," Lord John said, turning to me. "He mustn't stay here, then, or he will put himself in danger of contracting the disease, is that so?"

"Yes." The shock was beginning to recede slightly, and I was starting to pull myself together. "Yes, he should go at once. It's safe for him to be near you, you aren't contagious any longer. Ian is, though." I made a vain attempt at smoothing my hair, which was standing on end—little wonder if it was, I thought. Then I thought of the scalps on Mueller's barn door and my hair actually *did* stand on end, my own scalp rippling with horror.

Lord John was speaking authoritatively to the little Pastor, urging him toward his horse by means of a grip on his sleeve. Gottfried was making protests, but increasingly weak ones. He glanced back at me, round face full of trouble.

I tried to smile reassuringly at him, though I felt as distressed as he did.

"Danke," I said. "Tell him it will be all right, will you?" I said to Lord John. "He won't go, otherwise." He nodded briefly.

"I have. I told him I am a soldier; that I will not let any harm come to you."

The Pastor stood for a moment, hand on his horse's bridle, talking earnestly to Lord John. Then he dropped the bridle, turned with decision and crossed the dooryard to me. Reaching up, he laid a hand gently on my tousled head.

"Seid gesegnet," he said. *"Benedicite."*

"He said—" began Lord John.

"I understand."

We stood silently in the dooryard, watching Gottfried make his way through the chestnut grove. It seemed incongruously peaceful out here, with a soft autumn sun warm on my shoulders, and birds going about their business overhead. I heard the far-off knocking of a woodpecker, and the liquid duet of the mockingbirds that lived in the big blue spruce. No owls, but naturally there would be no owls now; it was midmorning.

Who? I wondered, as another aspect of the tragedy belatedly occurred to me. Who had been the target of Mueller's blind revenge? The Mueller farm was several days ride from the mountain line that separated Indian territory from the settlements, but he could have reached several Tuscarora or Cherokee villages, depending on his direction.

Had he entered a village? If so, what carnage had he and his sons left behind? Worse, what carnage might ensue?

I shuddered, cold in spite of the sun. Mueller was not the only man who believed in revenge. The family, the clan, the village of whomever he had murdered—they would seek vengeance for their slain, as well; and they might not stop with the Muellers—if they even knew the identity of the killers.

And if they did not, but only knew the murderers to be white . . . I shuddered again. I had heard enough massacre stories to realize that the victims very seldom did anything to provoke their fate; they only had the misfortune of being in the wrong place at the wrong time. Fraser's Ridge lay directly between Mueller's farm and the Indian villages—which at the moment seemed distinctly the wrong place to be.

"Oh, God, I wish Jamie were here." I wasn't aware that I had spoken aloud, until Lord John replied.

"So do I," he said. "Though I begin to think that William may be far safer with him than the boy might be here—and not only by reason of the illness."

I glanced at him, realizing suddenly how weak he still was; this was the first time he had been out of bed in a week. He was white-faced under the remnants of his rash, and he was gripping the doorjamb for support, to keep from falling down.

"You shouldn't even be up!" I exclaimed, and grasped him by the arm. "Go in and lie down at once."

"I am quite all right," he said irritably, but he didn't jerk away, or protest when I insisted he get back into bed.

I knelt to check Ian, who was tossing restlessly on the trundle, blazing with fever. His eyes were shut, his features swollen and disfigured with the emergent rash, the glands in his neck round and hard as eggs.

Rollo poked an inquiring nose under my elbow, nudged his master gently and whined.

"He'll be all right," I said firmly. "Why don't you go outside and keep an eye out for visitors, hm?"

Rollo ignored this advice, though, and instead sat patiently watching as I wrung out a rag in cool water and bathed Ian. I nudged him half awake, brushed his hair, gave him the chamber pot, and coaxed bee-balm syrup into him—all the time listening for the sound of hooves, and Clarence's joyful announcement that company was coming.

It was a long day. After several hours of starting at every sound and looking over my shoulder at every step, I finally settled into the day's work. I nursed Ian, who was feverish and miserable, fed the stock, weeded the garden, picked tender young cucumbers for pickling, and set Lord John, who was disposed to be helpful, to work shelling beans.

I looked into the woods with longing, on my way from privy to goat-pen. I would have given a lot simply to walk away into those cool green depths. It wouldn't have been the first time I'd had such an impulse. But the autumn sun beat down on the Ridge, and the hours wore on in tranquil peace, without a sign of Gerhard Mueller.

"Tell me about this Mueller," Lord John said. His appetite was coming back; he'd finished his helping of fried mush, though he pushed aside the salad of dandelion greens and pokeweed.

I plucked a tender stalk of pokeweed from the bowl and nibbled it myself, enjoying the sharp taste.

"He's the head of a large family; German Lutherans, as you no doubt gathered. They live about fifteen miles from here, down in the river valley."

"Yes?"

"Gerhard is big, and he's stubborn, as you no doubt gathered. Speaks a few words of English, but not much. He's old, but my God, he's strong!" I could still see the old man, shoulders corded with stringy muscle, tossing fifty-pound sacks of flour into his wagon like so many sacks of feathers.

"This fight he had with Jamie—did he appear the sort to hold a grudge?"

"He's very definitely the sort to hold a grudge, but not about that. It wasn't really a fight. It—" I shook my head, searching for a way to describe it. "Do you know anything about mules?"

His fair brows lifted and he smiled.

"A bit, yes."

"Well, Gerhard Mueller is a mule. He's not really bad-tempered, and he isn't precisely stupid—but he doesn't pay a great deal of attention to anything other than what's in his head, and it takes a good deal of force to switch his attention to anything else."

I had not been present at the altercation in the mill, but had had it described to me by Ian. The old man had got it firmly stuck into his head that Felicia Woolam, one of the mill owner's three daughters, had given him short weight and owed him another sack of flour.

In vain, Felicia protested that he had brought her five bags of wheat; she had ground them, and filled four bags with the resulting flour. The difference, she insisted, was due to the chaff and hulls removed from the grain. Five bags of wheat equalled four bags of flour.

"Fünf!" Mueller had said, waving his open hand in her face. *"Es gibt fünf!"* He would not be persuaded otherwise, and began to curse volubly in German, glowering and backing the girl into a corner.

Ian, having tried without success to distract the old man's attention, had dashed outside to fetch Jamie from his conversation with Mr. Woolam. Both men had come hurriedly inside, but had no more success than Ian in changing Mueller's conviction that he had been cheated.

Ignoring their exhortations, he had advanced on Felicia, clearly intent on taking by force an extra bag of flour from the stack behind her.

"At that point, Jamie gave up trying to reason with him, and hit him," I said.

He had at first been reluctant to do so, Mueller being nearly seventy, but rapidly changed his mind when his first blow bounced off Mueller's jaw as though it had been made of seasoned oakwood.

The old man had turned on him like a cornered boar, whereupon Jamie had struck him first in the stomach, and then in the mouth as hard as possible, knocking Mueller down and splitting his own knuckles on the old man's teeth.

With a word to Woolam—who was a Quaker and thus opposed to violence—he had then seized Mueller by the legs and dragged the dazed farmer outside, where one of the Mueller sons was waiting patiently in the wagon. Hauling the old man up by the collar, Jamie had pinned him against the wagon and held him there, talking pleasantly in German, until Mr. Woolam—having hastily rebagged the flour—came out and loaded *five* sacks into the wagon, under the gimlet eye of the old man.

Mueller had counted them twice, carefully, then turned to Jamie, and said with dignity, *"Danke, mein Herr."* He had then climbed into the wagon beside his bemused son, and driven away.

Grey scratched at the remnants of his rash, smiling.

"I see. So he appeared to hold no ill will?"

I shook my head, chewing, then swallowed.

"Not at all. He was kindness itself to me, when I went to the farm to help with Petronella's baby." My throat closed suddenly on the renewed realization that they were gone, and I choked on the bitter taste of the dandelion leaves, bile rising in my throat.

"Here." Grey pushed the pot of ale across the table toward me.

I drank deeply, the cool sourness soothing for a moment the deeper bitterness of spirit. I set the pot down and sat for a moment, eyes closed. There was a fresh-smelling breeze from the window, but the sun was warm on the tabletop under my hands. All the tiny joys of physical existence were still mine, and I was the more acutely aware of them, for the knowledge that they had been so abruptly taken from others—from those who had barely tasted them.

"Thank you," I said, opening my eyes.

Grey was watching me, with an expression of deep sympathy.

"You'd think it wouldn't be such a shock," I said, needing suddenly to try to explain. "They die here so easily. The young ones, especially. It isn't as though I haven't seen it before. And there's so seldom anything I can do."

I felt something warm on my cheek, and was surprised to find it was a tear. He reached into his sleeve, pulled out a handkerchief and handed it to me. It wasn't especially clean, but I didn't mind.

"I did sometimes wonder what he saw in you," he said, his tone deliberately light. "Jamie."

"Oh, you did? How flattering." I sniffed, and blew my nose.

"When he began to speak of you, both of us thought you dead," he pointed out. "And while you are undoubtedly a handsome woman, it was never of your looks that he spoke."

To my surprise, he picked up my hand and held it lightly.

"You have his courage," he said.

That made me laugh, if only halfheartedly.

"If you only knew," I said.

He didn't reply to that, but smiled faintly. His thumb ran lightly over the knuckles of my hand, his touch light and warm.

"He doesn't hold back for fear of skinned knuckles," he said. "Neither do you, I think."

"I can't." I took a deep breath and wiped my nose; the tears had stopped. "I'm a doctor."

"So you are," he said quietly, and paused. "I have not thanked you for my life."

"It wasn't me. There isn't really anything much I can do, for something like a disease. All I can do is to . . . be there."

"A little more than that," he said dryly, and released my hand. "Will you have more ale?"

I was beginning to see quite clearly what Jamie saw in John Grey.

The afternoon passed quietly. Ian tossed and moaned, but by late afternoon, the rash was fully developed, and his fever seemed to drop a little. He wouldn't be wanting food, but perhaps I could induce him to take a little milk broth. The thought reminded me that it was nearly milking time, and I stood up, with a murmured word to Lord John, and put aside my mending.

I opened the cabin door and stepped out, directly in front of Gerhard Mueller, who was standing in the dooryard.

Mueller's eyes were a reddish brown, and seemed always to be burning with an inner intensity. They burned more brightly now, for the bruised frailty of the flesh surrounding them. The deep-set eyes fixed on me, and he nodded, once, and then again.

Mueller had shrunk since I had last seen him. All his flesh had fallen away; still a huge man, he was more bone than muscle now, cadaverous and ancient. His eyes were fixed on mine, the only spark of life in a face like crumpled paper.

"Herr Mueller," I said. My voice sounded calm to my own ears; I hoped it sounded the same to him. *"Wie geht es Euch?"*

The old man stood swaying in front of me, as though the evening breeze might knock him down. I didn't know if he had lost his mount, or left it down below the ridge, but there was no sign of horse or mule.

He took a step toward me, and I took one back, involuntarily.

"Frau Klara," he said, and there was a note of pleading in his voice.

I stopped, wanting to call out to Lord John, but hesitant. He wouldn't call me by my first name if he meant to do me harm.

"They are dead," he said. *"Mein Mädchen. Mein Kind."* Tears welled suddenly in the bloodshot eyes, and ran slowly down the weather-beaten grooves of his face. The misery in his eyes was so acute that I reached out and took his huge, work-scarred old hand in mine.

"I know," I said. "I'm sorry."

He nodded again, his old mouth working. He let me lead him to the bench by the door, where he sat down quite suddenly, as though all the strength had gone out of his legs.

The door opened, and John Grey came out. He had his pistol in his hand, but when I shook my head at him, he slid it at once into his shirt. The old man had not let go of my hand; he pulled, forcing me to sit down beside him.

"*Gnädige Frau,*" he said, and suddenly turned and embraced me, hugging me tight against his filthy coat. He shook with soundless crying, and even knowing what he had done, I put my own arms around him.

He smelled dreadful, sour and reeking with old age and sorrow, with beer and sweat and filth, and somewhere under all the other odors was the fetor of dried blood. I shuddered, caught in a web of pity, horror, and revulsion, but could not pull away.

He let go, finally, and seemed suddenly to see John Grey, who was hovering nearby, not sure whether to intervene or not. The old man started at sight of him.

"*Mein Gott!*" he exclaimed, in tones of horror. "*Er hat Masern!*" The sun was sinking fast, bathing the dooryard in bloody light. It struck Grey full in the face, highlighting the darkened spots on his face, flushing his skin with red.

Mueller turned to me, and frantically seized my face between his huge, horny paws. His thumbs scraped across my cheeks, and an expression of relief came into his sunken eyes, as he saw that my skin was still clear.

"*Gott sei dank',*" he said, and letting go of my face, began to rummage in his coat, saying something in German so urgent and so mumbled that I could make out no more than the occasional word.

"He says he was afraid he would be too late, and is glad that he was not," Grey said, seeing my bewilderment. He eyed the old farmer with suspicious dislike. "He says he's brought you something—a charm of some kind. It will ward off the curse, and keep you safe from the illness."

The old man withdrew an object wrapped in cloth from the recesses of his coat, and laid it in my lap, still babbling in German.

"He thanks you for all your help to his family—he thinks you are a fine woman, as dear to him as one of his daughters-in-law—he says that . . ." Mueller unfolded the cloth with shaking hands, and the words died in Grey's throat.

I opened my mouth, but made no sound. I must have made some involuntary movement, for the cloth slipped suddenly to the ground, spilling out the sheaf of white-streaked hair to which a small silver ornament still clung. With it was the leather pouch, the woodpecker's feathers draggled with blood.

Mueller was still speaking, and Grey was trying to, but I was only dimly aware of their words. Inside my ears echoed the words I had heard a year before, down by the stream, in Gabrielle's soft voice, translating for Nayawenne.

Her name meant "It may be; it will happen." Now it had, and all that was left me for consolation was her words: "She says you must not be troubled; sickness is sent from the gods. It won't be your fault."

29

Charnel Houses

Jamie smelled the smoke long before the village came in sight. Willie saw him stiffen, and tensed in his own saddle, glancing warily around them.

"What?" the boy whispered. "What is it?"

"I dinna ken." He kept his own voice low, though there was no evidence that anyone was near enough to hear them. He swung down from his horse and handed the reins to Willie, nodding toward a vine-covered cliff face whose foot was shrouded in brush.

"Take the horses behind the cliff, lad," he said. "There's a deer path there, that leads up to a spruce grove. Get well in among the trees, and wait there for me." He hesitated, not wanting to scare the boy, but there was no help for it.

"If I should not come back by dark," he said, "leave at once. Dinna wait for the morning; go back to the wee stream we just crossed, turn to your left, and follow it to a place where there's a waterfall—you'll hear it, even in the dark. Behind the falls there's a wee cave; the Indians use it when they're hunting."

A small rim of white showed all the way around the lad's blue irises. Jamie took a firm grip of the boy's leg, just above the knee, to impress the directions upon him, and felt a quiver run through the long muscle of the thigh.

"Stay there till the morning," he said, "and if I havena caught ye up by then—go home. Keep the sun on your left in the morning, on your right after noon, and in two days give your horse his head; you'll be near enough home for him to find the way, I think."

He took a deep breath, wondering what else to say, but there was nothing.

"God go with ye, lad." He gave Willie as reassuring a smile as he could muster, clapped the horse on the rump to start it, and turned toward the scent of burning.

It wasn't the normal smell of village fires; not even of the big ceremonial fires that Ian had told him of, when they burned whole trees in the firepit in the center of the village. Those were the size of Beltane fires, Ian said, and he knew the crackle and size of such a blaze. This was much bigger.

With great caution he made a wide circle, at last coming to a small hill from which he knew that he could gain a view of the village. As soon as he emerged from the forest's shelter, though, he saw it. Rolling plumes of gray smoke were rising from the smoldering remnants of every longhouse in the village.

A thick brownish pall of smoke hung over the forest as far as he could see. He took a quick breath, coughed, and hastily drew a fold of his plaid across his nose and mouth, crossing himself with his free hand. He had smelled burning flesh before, and a sudden cold sweat bathed him at the memory of the funeral pyres of Culloden.

His soul misgave him at the sight of the desolation below, but he searched carefully, squinting through the eye-stinging haze for any sign of life among the ruins. Nothing moved save the wavering smoke, its wraiths gliding silent, wind-driven through the blackened houses. Had it been the Cherokee or the Creek, raiding up from the south? Or one of the remnant Algonkian tribes to the north, the Nanticokes or the Tuteloes?

A gust of wind smote him full in the face with the stink of charred flesh. He bent and vomited, trying to rid himself of his bone-deep knowledge of burnt crofts and murdered families. As he straightened up, wiping his mouth on his sleeve, he heard a dog bark in the distance.

He turned and went quickly downhill toward the sound, his heart beating faster. Raiders would not bring dogs. If there were survivors of the massacre, the dogs would be with them.

Still, he went as silently as possible, not daring to call out. That fire had been burning for less than a day; half the walls were still standing. Whoever had set it was still nearby, without a doubt.

It was a dog that met him; a big yellow mongrel, one that he recognized as belonging to Ian's friend Onakara. Off its normal territory, the dog neither barked nor rushed him, but stood its ground in the shadow of a pine tree, ears laid back and growling softly. He walked toward it slowly, holding out his closed fist.

"Balach math," he murmured to it. "Hold. Where are your people, then?"

The dog extended its muzzle, still growling, and sniffed at the proffered hand. Its nostrils twitched, and it relaxed a little, nosing closer in recognition.

He felt rather than saw a human presence, and looked up into the face of the dog's owner. Onakara's face was painted, with white streaks that ran from hair to chin, and behind the pale bars of paint, his eyes were dead.

"What enemy has done this?" Jamie asked, in his halting Tuscaroran. "Does your uncle still live?"

Onakara didn't answer, but turned and went back into the forest, followed by his dog. Jamie came after them, and within a half-hour's walk emerged into a small clearing where the survivors had made a temporary camp.

As he passed through the camp, he saw faces he knew. Some of them registered awareness of his presence; others stared sightlessly into a distance he knew too well—the infinite prospect of sorrow and despair. All too many were missing.

He had seen this before, and the ghosts of war and murder dragged at his footsteps as he passed. He had seen a young woman in the Highlands, sitting on the doorstep of her smoking house with her husband's body at her feet; she had worn the same stunned look as the young Indian woman by the sycamore tree.

Slowly, though, he became aware that something was different here. Wigwam shelters dotted the clearing; bundles lay piled near the edges of the clearing, and horses and ponies were tethered among the trees. This was no hasty exodus of people plundered and fleeing for their lives—it was an orderly retreat, with most of their worldly goods neatly packed and brought along. What in God's name had happened in Anna Ooka this day?

Nacognaweto was in a wigwam at the far side of the clearing. Onakara lifted the flap and silently nodded Jamie in.

A sudden spark leapt in the older man's eyes as he entered, but then died at once as Nacognaweto saw his face, with the shadow of reflected grief on it. The chieftain closed his eyes for a moment, and reopened them, composed.

"You have not met with her who heals, nor with the woman whose longhouse I dwelt in?"

Used to the Indian notion that it was rude to speak a person's name aloud save for the sake of ceremony, Jamie knew he must refer to Gabrielle and old Nayawenne. He shook his head, knowing that that gesture must destroy the last flicker of hope the other had held. It was no consolation, but he took the flask of brandy from his belt, and offered that in mute apology for his failure to bring good news.

Nacognaweto accepted it, and with a tilt of his head, summoned a woman, who dug about in one of the bundles by the hide wall and produced a gourd cup. The Indian poured a quantity of spirit that would flatten a Scotsman, and drank deeply before handing the gourd to Jamie.

He took a small sip for the sake of politeness, and handed back the gourd. It wasn't polite to come to the point of a visit at once, but he had no time for palaver and he could see that the other had no heart for it.

"What has happened?" he asked bluntly.

"Sickness," Nacognaweto answered softly. His eyes shone wetly, watering from the fumes of brandy. "We are cursed."

Haltingly, the story emerged, between the swallows of brandy. Measles had broken out in the village and swept through it like fire. Within the first week, a quarter of the people lay dead; now, at the end, there were no more than a quarter left alive.

When the sickness had begun, Nayawenne had sung over the victims. When more fell sick, she had gone out into the forest in search of . . . Jamie's grasp of Tuscarora was not sufficient to interpret the words. A charm, he thought it was—some plant? Or perhaps she looked for a vision that would tell them what to do, how to make amends for whatever evil had brought the sickness on them, or the name of the enemy who had cursed them. Gabrielle and Berthe had gone with her, because she was old and should not go alone—and none of the three had come back.

Nacognaweto was swaying very slightly as he sat, the gourd cup clasped in his hands. The woman bent over him, trying to take it away, but he shrugged her aside, and she let him be.

They had searched for the women, but there was no sign. Perhaps they had been taken by raiders, perhaps they too had fallen ill, and died in the forest. But the village had no *shaman* to speak for them, and the gods had not listened.

"We are cursed."

Nacognaweto's words were slurred, and the cup tilted dangerously in his hands. The woman knelt behind him and put her hands on his shoulders, to steady him.

"We left the dead in the houses, and set fire to them," she said to Jamie. Her eyes were black with sadness, too, but some life still lurked within them. "Now we will go north, to Oglanethaka." Her hands tightened on Nacognaweto's shoulders, and she nodded to Jamie. "You go now."

He went, the grief of the place clinging to him like the smoke that permeated clothes and hair. And within his charred heart as he left the camp sprang a small green shoot of selfishness, relief that the grief was—for this time—not his own. His woman still lived. His children were safe.

He looked up at the sky and saw the dull glow of the sinking sun reflected in the pall of smoke. He lengthened his stride to a hill-walker's lope that ate the miles. There was not much time; night was coming fast.

PART EIGHT

Beaucoup

30

Into Thin Air

"No," he said positively. Roger swung round to peer out the window at the soggy sky, holding the phone to his ear. "Not a chance. I'm off to Scotland next week, I've told you."

"Oh, now, Rog," coaxed the Dean's voice. "It's just your sort of thing. And it wouldn't put you off your schedule by a lot; you could be in the Hielands a-chasin' the deer this time a month—and you told me yourself your girrrl's not due till July."

Roger gritted his teeth at the Dean's put-on Scots accent, and opened his mouth to say no again, but wasn't quite fast enough.

"It's Americans, too, Rog," she said. "You're so *good* with Americans. Speaking of girrls," she added, with a brief chortle.

"Now, look, Edwina," he said, summoning patience, "I've things to do this holiday. And they don't include herding American tourists round the museums in London."

"No, no," she assured him. "We've paid minders to do the touristy bits; all you'd need to be concerned with is the conference itself."

"Yes, but—"

"Money, Rog," she purred down the phone, pulling out her secret weapon. "It's Americans, I said. You know what *that* means." She paused pregnantly, to allow him to contemplate the fee for running a week-long conference for a gang of visiting American scholars whose official minder had fallen ill. By comparison to his normal salary, it was an astronomical sum.

"Ah . . ." He could feel himself weakening.

"I hear you're thinking of getting married one of these days, Rog. Buy an extra haggis for the wedding, wouldn't it?"

"Anyone ever tell you how subtle you are, Edwina?" he demanded.

"Never." She chortled again briefly, then snapped into executive mode. "Right, then, see you Monday week for the plans meeting," and hung up.

He resisted the futile impulse to slam the receiver down, and dropped it on the hook instead.

Maybe it wasn't a bad thing after all, he thought bleakly. He didn't care about the money, in all truth, but having a conference to run might keep his mind off things. He picked up the much crumpled letter that lay next to the phone, and smoothed it out, his eye traveling over the paragraphs of apology without really reading them.

So sorry, she'd said. Special invitation to engineering conference in Sri Lanka (God, did all Americans go to conferences in the summer?) valuable contacts, job interviews (*job* interviews? Christ, he knew it, she was never coming back!)—couldn't pass it up. Desperately sorry. See you in September. I'll write. Love.

"Yeah, right," he said. "Love."

He balled up the sheet again and threw it at the dresser. It bounced off the edge of the silver picture frame and fell to the carpet.

"You could have told me straight," he said aloud. "So you did find someone else; you were right then, weren't you? You were wise, and me the fool. But could you not be honest, ye lying wee bitch?"

He was trying to work up a good rage; anything to fill the emptiness in the pit of his stomach. It wasn't helping.

He took the picture in its silver frame, wanting to break it to bits, wanting to clutch it to his heart. In the end, he only stood looking at it for a long time, then put it down gently, on its face.

"So sorry," he said. "Yeah, so am I."

May 1971

The boxes were waiting for him at the porter's lodge when he returned to college on the last day of the conference, hot, tired, and thoroughly fed up with Americans. There were five of them, large wooden crates plastered with the bright stickers of international shipping.

"What's this?" Roger juggled the clipboard the deliveryman handed him, groping in his pocket with the other hand for a tip.

"Well, I dunno, do I?" The man, truculent and sweating from

the trip through the courtyard to the porter's lodge, dropped the last crate on top of the others with a bang. "All yours, mate."

Roger gave the top box an experimental shove. If it wasn't books, it was lead. The push had shown him the edge of an envelope taped securely to the box below, though. With some difficulty, he pried it loose and ripped it open.

You told me once that your father said that everyone needs a history, the note inside read. *This is mine. Will you keep it with yours?* There was neither salutation nor closing; only the single letter "B," written in bold angular strokes.

He stared at it for a moment, then folded the note and put it in his shirt pocket. Squatting carefully, he got hold of the top crate and lifted it in his arms. Christ, it must weigh sixty pounds at least!

Sweating, Roger dropped the crate on the floor of his sitting room and went through to the tiny bedroom, where he scrabbled through a drawer. Armed with a screwdriver and a bottle of beer, he came back to deal with the box. He tried to damp down his rising feelings of excitement, but couldn't. *Will you keep it with yours?* Did a girl send half her belongings to a bloke she meant to break off with?

"History, eh?" he muttered. "Museum quality, by the way you packed it." The contents had been double-boxed, with a layer of excelsior between, and the inner box, once opened, revealed a mysterious array of lumpy, newspaper-wrapped bundles and smaller boxes.

He picked up a sturdy shoe box and peeked inside. Photographs; old ones with scalloped edges, and newer ones, glossy and colored. The edge of a large studio portrait showed, and he pulled it out.

It was Claire Randall, much as he had last seen her; amber eyes warm and startling under a tumble of brown-silk curls, a slight smile on the lush, delicate mouth. He shoved it back in the box, feeling like a murderer.

What emerged from the layers of newsprint was a very aptly named Raggedy Ann doll, its painted face so faded that only the shoe-button eyes remained, fixed in a blank and challenging stare. Its dress was torn but had been carefully mended, the soft cloth body stained but clean.

The next bundle yielded a tattered Mickey Mouse hat, with a tiny pink foam-rubber bow still fixed between its perky ears. A cheap music box, that played "Over the Rainbow" when he opened it. A stuffed dog, synthetic fur worn away in patches. A faded red sweatshirt, a man's size Medium. It might have fit Brianna, but somehow Roger knew it had been Frank's. A ragged dressing gown in quilted maroon silk. On an impulse, he pressed it to his nose. Claire. Her scent brought her vividly to life, a faint smell of musk and green things, and he dropped the garment, shaken.

Under the layer of trivia there was more substantial treasure. The weight of the crate was caused mostly by three large flat chests at the bottom, each containing a silver dinner service, carefully wrapped in gray antitarnishing cloth. Each chest had a typewritten note tucked inside, giving the provenance and history of the silver.

A French silver-gilt service, with rope-knot borders, maker's mark DG. Acquired by William S. Randall, 1842. A George III Old English pattern, acquired 1776 Edward K. Randall, Esq. Husk Shell pattern, by Charles Boyton, acquired 1903 by Quentin Lambert Beauchamp, given as a wedding present to Franklin Randall and Claire Beauchamp. The family silver.

With a growing puzzlement, Roger went on, laying each item carefully on the floor beside him, the objects of vertu and objects of use that comprised Brianna Randall's history. History. Jesus, why had she called it that?

Alarm pricked the puzzlement as another thought occurred to him, and he grabbed the lid, checking the address label. Oxford. Yes, she *had* sent them here. Why here, when she'd known—or thought—that he meant to be in Scotland all summer? He would have been, if not for the last-minute conference—and he hadn't told her about that.

Tucked in the last corner was a jewelry box, a small but substantial container. Inside were several rings, brooches, and sets of earrings. The cairngorm brooch he had given her for her birthday was there. Necklaces and chains. Two things weren't.

The silver bracelet he had given her—and her grandmother's pearls.

"Jesus bloody Christ." He looked again, just to be sure, dumping out the glittering junk and spreading it on his counterpane. No pearls. Certainly no string of baroque Scottish pearls, spaced with antique gold roundels.

She couldn't be wearing them, not to an engineering conference in Sri Lanka. The pearls were an heirloom to her, not an ornament. She seldom wore them. They were her link with—

"You didn't," he said aloud. "God, tell me you didn't do it!"

He dropped the jewel box on the bed, and thundered down the stairs to the telephone room.

It took forever to get the international operator on the line, and a longer time yet of vague electronic poppings and buzzings, before he heard the click of connection, followed by a faint ringing. One ring, two, then a click, and his heart leapt. She was home!

"We're sorry," said a woman's pleasant, impersonal voice, *"that number has been disconnected, or is no longer in service."*

God, she *couldn't* have! Could she? Yes, she bloody could, the reckless wee coof! Where in *hell* was she?

He drummed his fingers restlessly against his thigh, fuming, as the transatlantic phone line clicked and hummed, while connections were made, while he dealt with the endless delays and stupidities of hospital switchboards and secretaries. But at last he heard a familiar voice in his ear, deep and resonant.

"Joseph Abernathy."

"Dr. Abernathy? This will be Roger Wakefield here. Do you know where Brianna is?" he demanded without preliminary.

The deep voice rose slightly in surprise.

"With you. Isn't she?"

A cold chill washed over Roger, and he gripped the receiver harder, as though he could force it to give him the answer he wanted.

"She is not," he made himself say, as calmly as he could. "She meant to come in the fall, after she took her degree and went to some conference."

"No. No, that's not right. She finished her coursework the end of April—I took her to dinner to celebrate—and she said she was going straight out to Scotland, without waiting for commencement. Wait, let me think . . . yeah, that's right; my son Lenny drove her to the airport . . . when? Yeah, Tuesday . . . the 27th. You mean to say she didn't get there?" Dr. Abernathy's voice rose in agitation.

"I don't know whether she got here or not." Roger's free hand was clenched into a fist. "She didn't tell me she was coming." He forced himself to take a deep breath. "Where was she flying to—which city, do you know? London? Edinburgh?" She *might* have meant to surprise him with a sudden, unexpected arrival.

He'd been surprised, all right, but he doubted that was her intention.

Visions of kidnapping, assault, IRA bombings, drifted through his mind. Almost anything might have happened to a girl traveling alone in a large city—and almost anything that could have happened would be preferable to what his gut was telling him *had* happened. *Damn* the woman!

"Inverness," Dr. Abernathy's voice was saying in his ear. "Boston to Edinburgh, then the train to Inverness."

"Oh, Jesus." It was both a curse and a prayer. If she had left Boston on Tuesday, she would likely have made Inverness sometime on the Thursday. And Friday was the thirtieth day of April—the eve of Beltane, the ancient fire feast, when the hilltops of old Scotland had blazed with the flames of purification and fertility. When—perhaps—the door to the fairies' hill of Craigh na Dun lay widest open.

Abernathy's voice quacked in his ear, urgently demanding. He forced his attention to focus on it.

"No," he said, with some difficulty. "No, she didn't. I'm still in Oxford. I had no idea."

The empty air between them vibrated, the silence filled with dread. He had to ask. He took another breath—he seemed to be taking them one at a time, each one a conscious effort—and changed his grip on the receiver, wiping his cramped and sweaty palm on the leg of his trousers.

"Dr. Abernathy," he said carefully. "It's just possible that Brianna's gone to her mother—to Claire. Tell me—do you know where she is?"

The silence this time was charged with wariness.

"Ah . . . no." Abernathy's voice came slowly, reluctant with caution. "No, afraid I don't. Not exactly."

Not exactly. Great way to put it. Roger rubbed a hand over his face, feeling the stubble rasp under his palm.

"Let me ask you this," Roger said carefully. "Have you ever heard the name Jamie Fraser?"

The line was utterly silent in his hand. Then there came a deep sigh in his ear.

"Oh, Jesus Christ on a piece of toast," Dr. Abernathy said. "She did it."

Wouldn't you?

That was what Joe Abernathy had said to him, at the conclusion of their lengthy conversation, and the question lingered in his mind as he drove north, barely noticing the road signs that whizzed past, blurred by the rain.

Wouldn't you?

"I would," Abernathy had said. "If you didn't know your dad, never *had* known him—and all of a sudden, you found out where he was? Wouldn't you want to meet him, find out what he was really like? I'd be kind of curious, myself."

"You don't understand," Roger had said, rubbing a hand across his forehead in frustration. "It's not like someone who's adopted, finding out her real father's name and then just popping up on his doorstep."

"Seems to me that's just what it's like." The deep voice was cool. "Bree *was* adopted, right? I think she'd have gone before, if she hadn't felt it was disloyal to Frank."

Roger shook his head, disregarding the fact that Abernathy couldn't see him.

"It's not that—it's the popping-up-on-the-doorstep part. That —the way through—how she went—look, did Claire tell you—?"

"Yeah, she did," Abernathy broke in. His tone was bemused. "Yeah, she did say it wasn't quite like walking through a revolving door."

"To put it mildly." The mere thought of the standing stone circle on Craigh na Dun gave Roger a cold grue.

"To put it mildly—you *know* what it's like?" The far-off voice sharpened with interest.

"Yes, damn it, I do!" He took a long, deep breath. "Sorry. Look, it's not—I can't explain it, I don't think anyone could. Those stones . . . not everyone hears them, obviously. But Claire did. Bree does, and—and I do. And for us . . ."

Claire had gone through the stones of Craigh na Dun on the ancient fire feast of Samhain, on the first day of November, two and a half years before. Roger shivered, and not from cold. The hairs stood up on the back of his neck whenever he thought of it.

"So not everybody can go through—but you can." Abernathy's voice was filled with curiosity—and what sounded vaguely like envy.

"I don't know." Roger rubbed a hand through his hair. His eyes were burning, as though he'd sat up all night. "I might.

"The thing is . . ." He spoke slowly, trying to control his

voice, and with it, his fear. "The thing is—even if she *has* gone through, there's no way of telling whether, or where, she came out again."

"I see." The deep American voice had lost its jauntiness. "And you don't know about Claire either, then. Whether she made it?"

He shook his head, his vision of Joe Abernathy so clear that he forgot again that the man couldn't see him. Dr. Abernathy was no more than average size, a thickset black man in gold-rimmed spectacles, but with such an air of authority that his simple presence gave one confidence and compelled calm. Roger was surprised to find that this presence transferred itself over the phone lines—but he was more than grateful for it.

"No," he said aloud. Leave it at that, for now. He wasn't about to go into everything now, on the phone with a near stranger. "She's a woman; there wasn't that much public notice of what individual women were doing, then—not unless they did something spectacular, like get burned for witchcraft, or hanged for murder. Or *be* murdered."

"Ha ha," said Abernathy, but he wasn't laughing. "She did make it, though, at least once. She went—and she came back."

"Aye, she did." Roger had been trying to take comfort in that fact himself, but there were too many other possibilities forcing themselves upon his consciousness. "But we don't know that Brianna went back as far—or farther. And even if she did survive the stones and come out in the right time . . . have you any idea how dangerous a place the eighteenth century *was*?"

"No," Abernathy said dryly. "Though I gather you do. But Claire seemed to manage all right there."

"She survived," Roger agreed. "Not much of a sell for a vacation spot, is it, though—'If your luck's in, you'll come back alive?' " Once, at least.

Abernathy did laugh at that, though with a nervous undertone. He coughed then, and cleared his throat.

"Yeah. Well. The point is—Bree's gone *someplace*. And I think you're probably right about where. I mean, if it was me, I'd have gone. Wouldn't you?"

Wouldn't you? He pulled to the left, passed a lorry with its headlights on, plodding its way through the gathering fog.

I would. Abernathy's confident voice rang in his ear.

INVERNESS, 30, read the sign, and he swung the tiny Morris abruptly to the right, skidding on wet pavement. The rain was drumming down on the tarmac, hard enough to raise a mist above the grass on the verge.

Wouldn't you? He touched the breast pocket of his shirt, where the squarish shape of Brianna's photo lay stiff over his heart. His fingers touched the small round hardness of his mother's locket, snatched at the last moment, brought along for luck.

"Yeah, maybe I would," he muttered, squinting through the rain streaming over the windscreen. "But I would have told you I was going to do it. In the name of God, woman—why did you not tell *me*?"

31

Return to Inverness

The fumes of furniture polish, floor wax, fresh paint, and air freshener hung in throat-clutching clouds in the hallway. Not even these olfactory evidences of Fiona's domestic zeal were able to compete with the delectable aromas floating out of the kitchen, though.

"Eat your heart out, Tom Wolfe," Roger murmured, inhaling deeply as he set down his bag in the hall. Granted, the old manse was definitely under new management, but even its transformation from manse to bed-and-breakfast had been unable to alter its basic character.

Welcomed with enthusiasm by Fiona—and somewhat less by Ernie—he settled into his old room at the top of the stairs, and embarked at once on his job of detection. It wasn't that difficult; beyond the normal Highland inquisitiveness about strangers, a six-feet-tall woman with waist-length red hair tended to attract notice.

She'd come to Inverness from Edinburgh. He knew that much for a fact; she'd been seen at the station. Also for a fact he knew that a tall red-haired woman had hired a car and told the driver to take her out into the country. The driver had no real notion where they had gone; just that all of a sudden, the woman had said, "Here, this is the place, let me off here."

"Said she meant to meet her friends for a walking tour across the moors," the driver had said, shrugging. "She had a haversack with her, and she was dressed for walking, sure enough. A damn wet day for a walk on the moors, but ye know what loons these American tourists are."

Well, he knew what kind of a loon *that* one was, at least. Curse her thick head and fiendish stubbornness, if she thought she had to do it, why in *hell* hadn't she told him? Because she didn't want you to know, sport, he thought grimly. And he didn't want to think about why not.

So far he had gotten. And only one way of following her any farther.

Claire had speculated that the whatever-it-was stood widest open on the ancient sun feasts and fire feasts. It seemed to work—she had herself gone through the first time on Beltane, May 1, the second time on Samhain, the first of November. And now Brianna had evidently followed in her mother's footsteps, going on Beltane.

Well, he wasn't going to wait till November—God only knew what could happen to her in five months! Beltane and Samhain were fire feasts, though; there was a sunfeast between.

Midsummer's Eve, the summer solstice; that would be next. June 20, four weeks away. He ground his teeth at the thought of waiting—his impulse was to go *now* and damn the danger—but it wouldn't help Brianna if his impulse to rush chivalrously after her killed him. He was under no illusions about the nature of the stone circle, not after what he'd seen and heard so far.

Very quietly, he began to make what preparations he could. And in the evenings, when the fog rolled in off the river, he sought distraction from his thoughts, playing draughts with Fiona, going to the pub with Ernie, and—as a last resort—having another bash at the dozens of boxes that still crammed the old garage.

The garage had an air of sinister miracle about it; the boxes seemed to multiply like the loaves and fishes—every time he opened the door, there were more of them. He'd probably finish the job of sorting his late father's effects just before being carried out feetfirst himself, he thought. Still, for the moment, the boring work was a godsend, dulling his mind enough to keep him from fretting himself to pieces in the waiting. Some nights, he even slept.

"You've got a picture on your desk." Fiona didn't look at him, but kept her attention riveted on the dishes she was clearing.

"Lots of them." Roger took a cautious mouthful of tea; hot and fresh, but not scalding. How did she do that? "Is there one you want? I know there are a few snaps of your grannie—you're more than welcome, though I'd like one to keep."

She did look up at that, mildly startled.

"Oh. Of Grannie? Aye, our Da'll like to see those. But it's the big one I meant."

"Big one?" Roger tried to think which photo she could mean; most of them were black-and-white snapshots taken with the Reverend's ancient Brownie, but there were a couple of the larger cabinet photos—one of his parents, another of the Reverend's grandmother, looking like a pterodactyl in black bombazine, taken on the occasion of that lady's hundredth birthday. Fiona couldn't possibly mean those.

"Of her that kilt her husband and went away." Fiona's mouth compressed.

"Her that—oh." Roger took a deep gulp of tea. "You mean Gillian Edgars."

"Her," Fiona repeated stubbornly. "Why've you got a photo of her?"

Roger set the cup down and picked up the morning paper, affecting casualness as he wondered what to say.

"Oh—someone gave it to me."

"Who?"

Fiona was normally persistent, but seldom so direct. What was troubling her?

"Mrs. Randall—Dr. Randall, I mean. Why?"

Fiona didn't reply, but pressed her lips tight shut.

Roger had by now abandoned all interest in the paper. He laid it down carefully.

"Did you know her?" he said. "Gillian Edgars?"

Fiona didn't answer directly, but turned aside, fiddling with the tea cozy.

"You've been up to the standing stones on Craigh na Dun; Joycie said her Albert saw ye comin' down when he was drivin' to Drumnadrochit Thursday."

"I have, yes. No crime in that, is there?" He tried to make a joke of it, but Fiona wasn't having any.

"Ye know it's a queer place, all circles are. And don't be tellin' me ye went up there to admire the view."

"I wouldn't tell you that."

He sat back in his chair, looking up at her. Her curly dark hair was standing on end; she rumpled her hands through it when she was agitated, and agitated she surely was.

"You *do* know her. That's right; Claire said you'd met her." The small flicker of curiosity he had felt at the mention of Gillian Edgars was growing into a clear flame of excitement.

"I canna be knowing her, now, can I? She's dead." Fiona scooped up the empty egg cup, eyes fixed on the discarded fragments of shell. "Isn't she?"

Roger reached out and stopped her with a hand on her arm. "Is she?"

"It's what everyone thinks. The police havena found a trace of her." The word came out "polis" in her soft Highland accent.

"Perhaps they're not looking in the right place."

All the blood drained out of her flushed, fair face. Roger tightened his grip, though she wasn't trying to pull away. She knew, dammit, she knew! But *what* did she know?

"Tell me, Fiona," he said. "Please—tell me. What do you know about Gillian Edgars—and the stones?"

She did pull away from him then, but didn't leave, just stood there, turning the egg cup over and over in her hands, as if it were a miniature hourglass. Roger stood up, and she shied back, glancing fearfully up at him.

"A bargain, then," he said, trying to keep his voice calm, so as not to frighten her further. "Tell me what you know, and I'll tell you why Dr. Randall gave me that picture—and why I was up on Craigh na Dun."

"I've got to think." Swiftly she bent and snatched up the tray of dirty crockery. She was out the door before he could speak a word to stop her.

Slowly he sat down again. It had been a good breakfast—all Fiona's meals were delicious—but it lay in his stomach like a bag of marbles, heavy and indigestible.

He shouldn't be so eager, he told himself. It was courting disappointment. What could Fiona know, after all? Still, any mention of the woman who had called herself Gillian—and later Geillis—was enough to rivet his attention.

He picked up his neglected teacup and swallowed, not tasting it. What if he kept the bargain, and told her everything? Not only about Claire Randall and Gillian, but about himself—and Brianna.

The thought of Bree was like a rock dropped into the pool of his heart, sending ripples of fear in all directions. *She's dead.* Fiona had said of Gillian. *Isn't she?*

Is she? he had answered, the picture of a woman vivid in his mind, green eyes wide and fair hair flying in the hot wind of a fire, poised to flee through the doors of time. No, she hadn't died. Not then, at least, because Claire had met her—would meet her? Earlier? Later? She hadn't died, but was she dead? She must be now, mustn't she, and yet—damn this twistiness! How could he even think about it coherently?

Too unsettled to stay in one place, he got up and walked down the hall. He paused in the doorway of the kitchen. Fiona was standing at the sink, staring out of the window. She heard him and turned around, an unused dishcloth clutched in her hand.

Her face was red, but determined.

"I'm not to tell, but I will, I've got to." She took a deep breath and squared her chin, looking like a Pekingese facing up to a lion.

"Bree's Mam—that nice Dr. Randall—she asked me about my grannie. She kent Grannie'd been a—a—dancer."

"Dancer? What, you mean in the stones?" Roger felt faintly startled. Claire had told him, when he'd first met her, but he had never quite believed it—not that the staid Mrs. Graham performed arcane ceremonies on green hilltops in the May dawn.

Fiona let out a long breath.

"So ye do know. I thought so."

"No, I don't know. All I know is what Claire—Dr. Randall—told me. She and her husband saw women dancing in the stone circle one Beltane dawn, and your grannie was one of them."

Fiona shook her head.

"Not just one o' them, no. Grannie was the caller."

Roger moved into the kitchen and took the dishcloth from her unresisting hand.

"Come and sit down," he said, leading her to the table. "And tell me, what's a caller?"

"The one who calls down the sun." She sat, unresisting. She had made up her mind, he saw; she was going to tell him.

"It's one of the auld tongues, the sun-song; some of the words are a bit like the Gaelic, but not all of it. First we dance, in the circle, then the caller stops and faces the split stone, and—it's no singing, really, but it's no quite talking, either; more like the minister at kirk. You've to begin at just the right moment, when the light first shows over the sea, so just as ye finish, the sun comes through the stone."

"Do you remember any of the words?" The scholar in Roger stirred briefly, curiosity rearing its head through his confusion.

Fiona didn't much resemble her grandmother, but she gave him a look that reminded him suddenly of Mrs. Graham in its directness.

"I know them all," she said. "I'm the caller now."

He realized that his mouth was hanging open, and closed it. She reached for the biscuit tin and plunked it in front of him.

"That's no what ye need to know, though," she said matter-of-factly, "and so I won't tell ye. You want to know about Mrs. Edgars."

Fiona had met Gillian Edgars, all right; Gillian had been one of the dancers, though quite a new one. Gillian had asked questions of the older women, eager to learn all she could. She'd wanted to learn the sun-song, too, but that was secret; only the caller and her successor had that. Some of the older women would know some of it—those who had heard the chant every year for a long time—but not all of it, and not the secrets of when to begin and how to time the song to coincide with the rising of the sun.

Fiona paused, looking down at her folded hands.

"It's women; only women. The men havena got a part in it, and we do not tell them. Not ever."

He laid a hand over hers.

"You're right to tell me, Fiona," he said, very softly. "Tell me the rest, please. I've got to know."

She drew a deep, quivering breath and pulled her hand out from under his. She looked directly at him. "D'ye know where she's gone? Brianna?"

"I think so. She's gone where Gillian went, hasn't she?"

Fiona didn't reply, but went on looking at him. The unreality of the situation swept over him all of a sudden. He couldn't be sitting here, in the comfortable, shabby kitchen he'd known since boyhood, sipping tea from a mug with the Queen's face painted on the side, discussing sacred stones and time-flight with Fiona. Not *Fiona*, for God's sake, whose interests were confined to Ernie and the domestic economy of her kitchen!

Or so he'd thought. He picked up the mug, drained it, and set it down with a soft thump.

"I have to go after her, Fiona—if I can. Can I?"

She shook her head, clearly afraid.

"I canna say. It's only women I know about; maybe it's only women who can."

Roger's hand clenched round the saltshaker. That's what he was afraid of—or one of the things he was afraid of.

"Only one way to find out, isn't there?" he said, outwardly casual. In the back of his mind, unbidden, a tall cleft stone rose up black, stark as a threat against a soft dawn sky.

"I have her wee book," Fiona blurted.

"What—whose? Gillian's? She wrote something?"

"Aye, she did. There's a place—" She darted a look at him, and licked her lips. "We keep our things there, ready beforehand. She'd put the book there, and—and—I took it, after." After Gillian's husband had been found murdered in the circle, Roger thought she meant.

"I kent the polis should maybe have it," Fiona went on, "but it —well, I didna like to give it to them, and yet I was thinkin' what if it's to do with the killing? And I couldna keep it back if it was to be important, and yet—" She looked up at Roger in a plea for understanding. "It was her own book, ye see, her writing. And if she'd left it in that place . . ."

"It was secret." Roger nodded.

Fiona nodded, and drew a deep breath.

"So I read it."

"And that's how you know where she's gone," Roger said softly.

Fiona let out a shuddering sigh and gave him a wan smile.

"Well, the book's no going to help the polis, that's for sure."

"Could it help me?"

"I hope so," she said simply, and turning to the sideboard, pulled open a drawer and withdrew a small book, bound in green cloth.

32

Grimoire

*T*his is the grimoire of the witch, Geillis. It is a witch's name, and I take it for my own; what I was born does not matter, only what I will make of myself, only what I will become.

And what is that? I cannot yet say, for only in the making will I find what I have made. Mine is the path of power.

Absolute power corrupts absolutely, yes—and how? Why, in the assumption that power can be absolute, for it never can. For we are mortal, you and I. Watch the flesh shrink and wither on your bones, feel the lines of your skull, pushing through the skin, your teeth behind soft lips a grin of grim acknowledgment.

And yet within the bounds of flesh, many things are possible. Whether such things are possible beyond those bounds—that is the realm of others, not mine. And that is the difference between them and me, those others who have gone before to explore the Black Realm, those who seek power in magic and the summoning of demons.

I go in the body, not the soul. And by denying my soul, I give no power to any force but those I control. I do not seek favor from devil or god; I deny them. For if there is no soul, no death to contemplate, then neither god nor devil rules—their battle is of no consequence, to one who lives in the flesh alone.

We rule for a moment, and yet for all time. A fragile web woven to snare both earth and space. Only one life is given to us—and yet its years may be spent in many times—how many times?

If you will wield power, you must choose both your time and your place, for only when the shadow of the stone falls at your feet is the door of destiny truly open.

"A nutcase for sure," Roger murmured. "Horrible prose style, too." The kitchen was empty; he was talking to reassure himself. It wasn't helping.

He turned the pages carefully, skimming down the lines of clear, round writing.

After the first bit, there was a section titled "Sun Feasts and Fire Feasts," with a listing after—Imbolc, Alban Eilir, Beltane, Litha, Lughnassadh, Alban Elfed, Samhain, Alban Arthuan—with a paragraph of notes following each name, and a series of small crosses inscribed alongside. What the hell was that for?

Samhain caught his eye, with six crosses by it.

> *This is the first of the feasts of the dead. Long before Christ and his Resurrection, on the night of Samhain, the souls of heroes rose from their graves. They are rare, these heroes. Who is born when the stars are right? Not all who are born to it have the courage to take hold of the power that is their right.*

Even in what was plainly raving madness, she had method and organization—a queer admixture of cool observation and poetic flight. The center section of the book was labeled "Case Studies," and if the first section had raised the hair on Roger's neck, the second was enough to freeze the blood in his veins.

It was a careful listing, by date and by place, of bodies found in the vicinity of stone circles. The appearance of each was noted, and below each description were a few words of speculation.

> *August 14, 1931. Sur-le-Meine, Brittany. Body of a male, unidentified. Age, mid-40s. Found near north end of standing stone circle. No evident cause of death, but deep burns on arms and legs. Clothing described only as "rags." No photograph.*
> *Possible cause of failure: (1) male, (2) wrong date—23 days from nearest sun feast.*

> *April 2, 1650. Castlerigg, Scotland. Body of female, unidentified. Age, about 15. Found outside circle. Substantial mutilation noted, may have been dragged from circle by wolves. Clothing not described.*
> *Possible cause of failure: (1) wrong date—28 days prior to fire feast. (2) lack of preparation.*

February 5, 1953. Callanish, Isle of Lewis. Body of male, identified as John MacLeod, lobsterman, age 26. Cause of death diagnosed as massive cerebral hemorrhage, coroner's inquest held owing to appearance of body—second-degree burns on skin of face and extremities, and scorched look of clothing. Coroner's verdict, death by lightning—possible, but not likely. Possible cause of failure: (1) male. (2) very close to Imbolc, but perhaps not close enough? (3) improper preparation–N.B. newspaper photograph shows victim, shirt open; there is a burnt spot on the chest which appears to be in shape of Bridhe's Cross, but too indistinct to say for sure.

May 1, 1963. Tomnahurich, Scotland. Body of female, identified as Mary Walker Willis. Coroner's inquest, substantial scorching of body and clothing, death due to heart failure—rupture of aorta. Inquest notes Miss Walker dressed in "odd" clothing, details unspecified.

Failure—this one knew what she was doing, but didn't make it. Failure likely due to omission of proper sacrifice.

The list went on, chilling Roger more with each name. She had found twenty-two, altogether, reported over a period from the mid-1600s to the mid-1900s, from sites scattered over Scotland, northern England, and Brittany, all sites showing some evidence of prehistoric building. Some had been obvious accidents, he thought—people who'd walked into a circle all unsuspecting and had no notion what had hit them.

A few—only two or three—seemed to have known; they'd made some preparation of clothing. Perhaps they had passed through before, and tried again—but this time it hadn't worked. His stomach curled into a small, cold snail. Claire had been right; it wasn't like stepping through a revolving door.

Then there were the disappearances . . . these were in a separate section, neatly docketed by date, sex, and age, with as much noted of the circumstances as was recorded. Ah—that was the meaning of the crosses; how many people had disappeared near each feast. There were more of the disappeared than of the dead, but there was of necessity less data. Most bore question marks— Roger supposed because there was no telling whether disappearance in the vicinity of a circle was necessarily connected with it.

He turned over a page, and stopped, feeling as though he'd been punched in the stomach.

May 1, 1945. Craigh na Dun, Inverness-shire, Scotland. Claire Randall, age 27, housewife. Seen last in early morning, having declared intention to visit the circle in search of unusual plant specimens, did not return by dark. Car found parked at foot of hill. No traces in circle, no signs of foul play.

He turned the page gingerly, as though expecting it to blow up in his hand. So Claire had inadvertently given Gillian Edgars part of the evidence that had led to her own experiment. Had Geilie found the reports of Claire's return, three years later?

No, evidently not, he concluded, after flipping back and forth through those pages—or if she had, she hadn't recorded it here.

Fiona had brought him more tea and a plate of fresh ginger nut biscuits, which had sat untouched since he had begun reading. A sense of obligation rather than hunger made him pick up a biscuit and take a bite, but the sharp-flavored crumbs caught in his throat and made him cough.

The last section of the book bore the heading "Techniques and Preparations." It began,

Something lies here, older than man, and the stones keep its power. The old spells speak of "the lines of the earth," and the power that flows through them. The purpose of the stones is to do with those lines, I am sure. But do the stones warp the lines of power, or are they only markers?

The bite of biscuit seemed permanently stuck in his throat, no matter how much tea he drank. He found himself reading faster, skimming, skipping pages, and finally sat back and shut the book. He would read the rest later—and more than once. But for now, he had to get out, into the fresh air. No wonder the book had upset Fiona.

He walked fast down the street, heading for the river, oblivious of the light rain falling. It was late; there was a churchbell ringing for evensong, and the evening foot traffic to the pubs was picking up across the bridges. But above bell and voice and footstep, he heard the last words he had read, chiming in his ear as though she had been speaking directly to him.

Shall I kiss you, child, shall I kiss you, man? Feel the teeth behind my lips when I do. I could kill you, as easily as I embrace you. The taste of power is the taste of blood—iron in my mouth, iron in my hand.

Sacrifice is required.

33

Midsummer's Eve

June 20, 1971

On Midsummer's Eve in Scotland, the sun hangs in the sky with the moon. Summer solstice, the feast of Litha, Alban Eilir. Nearly midnight, and the light was dim and milky white, but light nonetheless.

He could feel the stones long before he saw them. Claire and Geillis had both been right, he thought; the date mattered. They had been eerie on his earlier visits, but silent. Now he could hear them; not with his ears but with his skin—a low buzzing hum like the drone of bagpipes.

They came over the crest of the hill and paused, thirty feet from the circle. Below was dark glen, a mystery under the rising moon. He heard a small intake of breath at his elbow, and it occurred to him that Fiona was seriously afraid.

"Look, you don't need to be here," he told her. "If you're afraid, you should go on down; I'll be all right."

"It's not me I'm scairt for, fool," she muttered, thrusting her balled fists deeper into her pockets. She turned away, lowering her head like a little bull as she faced up the path. "Come on, then."

The alder bushes rustled near his shoulder and he shivered suddenly, feeling a cold qualm go over him, warmly as he was dressed. His dress seemed suddenly ridiculous; the long-skirted coat and the weskit in thick wool, the matching breeches and knitted stockings. A play at the college, he had told the tailor who made the costume.

"Fool is right," he muttered to himself.

Fiona went first into the circle; she would not let him come with her or watch. Obediently, he turned his back, letting her do whatever she intended. She had a plastic shopping bag, presumably containing items for her ceremonial. He had asked what was in it, and she had tersely told him to mind his own business. She was nearly as nervous as he was, he thought.

The humming noise disturbed him. It wasn't in his ears but in his body—under his skin, in his bones. It made the long bones of his arms and legs thrum like plucked strings, and itched in his blood, making him want constantly to scratch. Fiona couldn't hear it; he'd asked, to be sure she was safe before letting her help him.

He hoped to God he was right; that only those who heard the stones could pass through them. He'd never forgive himself if anything happened to Fiona—though as she'd pointed out, she'd been in this circle any number of times on the fire feasts, with no ill effect. He sneaked a look over one shoulder, saw a tiny flame burning at the base of the big cleft stone, and jerked his head back around.

She was singing, in a soft, high voice. He couldn't make out the words. All the other travelers he knew of were women; would it truly work for him?

It might, he thought. If the ability to pass through the stones was genetic—something like the ability to roll one's tongue into a cylinder or color-blindness—then why not? Claire had traveled, so had Brianna. Brianna was Claire's daughter. And he was a descendant of the only other time-traveler he knew of—Geillis the witch.

He stamped both feet and shook himself like a horse with flies, trying to rid himself of the humming. God, it was like being eaten by ants! Was Fiona's chanting making it worse, or was it only his imagination?

He rubbed violently at his chest, trying to ease the irritation, and felt the small round weight of his mother's locket, taken for luck and for its garnets. He had his doubts about Geillis's speculations—he wasn't about to try blood, though Fiona seemed to be supplying fire—but after all, the gems could do no harm, and if they helped . . . Christ, would Fiona not hurry? He twisted and strained inside his clothes, trying to get out of not only his clothing but his skin.

Seeking distraction, he patted his breast pocket again, feeling the locket. If it worked . . . if he could . . . it was a notion that had come to him only lately, as the possibility posed by the stones had matured into actual planning. But if it *were* possible . . . he fingered the small, round shape, seeing the face of Jerry MacKenzie on the dark surface of his mind.

Brianna had gone to find her father. Could he do the same? Jesus, Fiona! She *was* making it worse; the roots of his teeth ached, and his skin was burning. He shook his head violently, then stopped, feeling dizzy; the seams of his skull felt as though they were beginning to separate.

Then she was there, a small figure grasping his hand, saying something anxious as she led him into the circle. He couldn't hear her—the noise was much worse inside; now it was in his ears, in his head, blackening his sight, driving wedges of pain between the joints of his spine.

Gritting his teeth, he blinked back the buzzing darkness, long enough to fix his eyes on Fiona's round and fearful face.

Swiftly he bent and kissed her, full on the mouth.

"Don't tell Ernie," he said. He turned away from her and walked through the stone.

A faint scent came to him on the summer wind; the smell of burning. He turned his head, nostrils flared to catch it. There. A flame flared and bloomed on a nearby hilltop, a rose of Midsummer's fire.

There were faint stars overhead, half shadowed by a drifting cloud. He had no urge to move, nor to think. He felt bodiless, embraced by the sky, his mind turning free, reflecting starlit images like the glass bubble of a fisher's float, adrift in the surf. There was a soft and musical hum around him—the far-off song of siren stars, and the smell of coffee.

A vague feeling of wrongness intruded on his sense of peace. Sensation prodded at his mind, rousing tiny, painful sparks of confusion. He fought back feeling, wanting only to stay afloat in starlight, but the act of resistance woke him. All of a sudden, he had a body again, and it hurt.

"ROGER!" The star's voice blared in his ear, and he jerked. Searing pain shot through his chest, and he clapped a hand to the wound. Something seized his wrist and pulled it away, but not before he had felt wetness, and the silky roughness of ash on his breast. Was he bleeding?

"Oh, ye're wakin', thank God! Aye, there, that's a good lad. Easy, aye?" It was the cloud talking, not the star. He blinked, confused, and the cloud resolved itself into the curly silhouette of Fiona's head, dark against the sky. He jerked upright, more a convulsion than a conscious movement.

His body had come back with a vengeance. He felt desperately ill, and there was a horrible smell of coffee and burnt flesh in his nostrils. He rolled onto all fours, retching, then collapsed onto the grass. It was wet, and the coolness felt good on his scorched face.

Fiona's hands were on him, soothing, wiping his face and mouth.

"Are ye all right?" she said, for what he knew must be the hundredth time. This time, he summoned enough strength to answer.

"Aye," he whispered. "All right. Why—?"

Her head moved back and forth, wiping out half a sky of stars.

"I don't know. Ye went—ye were gone—and then there was a burst o' fire, and ye were lyin' in the circle, wi' your coat ablaze. I had to put ye out with the thermos bottle."

That accounted for the coffee, then, and the soggy feeling over his chest. He lifted a hand, groping, and this time she let him. There was a burnt patch on the wet cloth of his coat, maybe three inches across. The flesh of his chest was seared; he could feel the queer cushioned numbness of blisters through the hole in the cloth, and the nagging pain of a burn spread through his breast. His mother's locket was gone entirely.

"What happened, Rog?" Fiona was crouching by him, her face dim but visible; he could see the shiny tracks of tears on her face. What he had thought a Midsummer's Eve fire was the flame of her candle, burned down now to the last half inch. God, how long had he been out?

"I—" He had begun to say that he didn't know, but broke off. "Let me think a bit, aye?" He put his head on his knees, breathing in the smell of wet grass and scorched cloth.

He concentrated on breathing, let it come back. He had no real need to think—it was all there, distinct in his mind. But how did one describe such things? There was no sight—and yet he had the image of his father. No sound, no touch—and yet he had both heard and felt. The body seemed to make its own sense of things, translating the numinous phenomena of time into concretions.

He raised his head from his knees, and breathed deep, settling himself slowly back in his body.

"I was thinking of my father," he said. "When I stepped through the rock, I had just thought, if it works, could I go back and find him? And I . . . did."

"You did? Your dad? Was he a ghost, d'ye mean?" He felt, more than saw, the flicker of her hand as she made the horns against evil.

"No. Not exactly. I—I can't explain, Fiona. But I met him; I knew him." The feeling of peace had not left him altogether; it hovered there, fluttering gently in the back of his mind. "Then there was—sort of an explosion, is all I can describe it as. Something hit me, here." His fingers touched the burnt place on his chest. "The force of it pushed me . . . out, and that's all I knew till I woke." He touched her face gently. "Thanks, Fee; you saved me burning."

"Och, get on wi' ye." She made an impatient gesture, dismissing him. She sat back on her heels, rubbing her chin as she thought.

"I'm thinking, Rog—what it said in her book, about there maybe being some protection, if ye had a gemstone with ye. There were the wee jewels in your Mam's locket, no?" He could hear her swallow. "Maybe—if ye hadn't had that—ye might not have lived. She told about the folk who didn't. They were burned —and your burn's where the locket was."

"Yes. It could be." Roger was beginning to feel more like himself. He glanced curiously at Fiona.

"You always say 'her.' Why do you never say her name?"

Fiona's curls lifted in the dawn wind as she turned to look at him. It was light enough now to see her face clearly, with its expression of disconcerting directness.

"Ye dinna call something unless ye want it to come," she said. "Surely ye know that, and your father a minister?"

The hairs on his forearms prickled, despite the covering of shirt and coat.

"Now that you mention it," he said, trying for a joking tone, and failing utterly. "I wasn't quite calling my father's name, but perhaps . . . Dr. Randall said she thought of her husband, when she came back."

Fiona nodded, frowning. He could see her face clearly, and realized with a start that the light was growing. It was near dawn; the sky to the east was the shimmered color of a salmon's scales.

"Christ, it's almost morning! I've got to go!"

"Go?" Fiona's eyes went round with horror. "You're no going to try it *again?*"

"I am. I've got to." The lining of his mouth was cotton-dry, and he regretted that Fiona had used all the coffee extinguishing him. He fought down the hollow-bellied feeling and made it to his feet. His knees were wobbly, but he could walk.

"Are you mad, Rog? It'll kill ye, sure!"

He shook his head, eyes fixed on the tall cleft stone.

"No," he said, and hoped to hell he was right. "No, I know what went wrong. It won't happen again."

"You can't know, not for sure!"

"Aye, I do." He took her hand from his sleeve and held it between his own; it was small and cold. He smiled at her, though his face felt strangely numb. "I hope Ernie's not come home; he'll have the police looking for you. You'd best hurry back."

She shrugged, impatient.

"Och, he's at the fishin' with his cousin Neil; he'll no be back till Tuesday. What d'ye mean, it won't happen again—why won't it?"

This was the thing that was harder to explain than the rest of it. He owed it to her to try, though.

"When I said I was thinking of my father, I was thinking of him from what I knew of him—the pictures of him in his airman's kit, or with my mother. The thing is . . . I was born by that time. Do you see?" He searched her small, round face, and saw her blink slowly, comprehending. Her breath left her in a small sigh, of fear and wonder mingled.

"Ye didna only meet your Da, then, did ye?" she asked quietly.

He shook his head, wordless. No sight, no sound or smell or touch. There were no images at all to convey what it had been like to meet himself.

"I have to go," he repeated softly. He squeezed her hand. "Fiona, I cannot say enough to thank you."

She stared at him for a moment, her soft bottom lip thrust out, eyes glistening. Then she pulled loose, and twisting off her engagement ring, put it into his hand.

"It's a wee stone, but it's a real diamond," she said. "It'll maybe help."

"I can't take this!" He reached to give it back, but she took a step backward, and put her hands behind her back.

"Dinna worry, it's insured," she said. "Ernie's a great one for the insurance." She tried to smile at him, though the tears were running down her face now. "So am I."

There was nothing more to say. He put the ring in the side pocket of his coat, and glanced at the great cleft stone, its black sides starting to glimmer as bits of mica and threads of quartz picked up the dawning light. He could hear the hum, still, though now it felt more like the pulsing of his blood; something inside him.

No words, and no need. He touched her face once lightly in

farewell, and walked toward the stone, staggering slightly. He stepped into the cleft.

Fiona heard nothing, but the still, clear air of Midsummer's Day shimmered with an echoed name.

She waited for a long time, until the sun rested on top of the stone.

"Slan leat, a charaid chòir," she said, softly. "Luck to you, dear friend." She went slowly down the hill, and didn't look back.

34

Lallybroch

Scotland, June 1769

The sorrel horse's name was Brutus, but luckily it didn't seem indicative of character so far. More plodder than plotter, he was strong and faithful—or if not faithful, at least resigned. He had carried her through the summer-green glens and rock-lined gorges without a slip, taking her higher and higher along the good roads made by the English general Wade fifty years before, and the bad roads beyond the General's reach, splashing through brushy burns and climbing up to the places where the roads dwindled away to nothing more than a red deer's track across the moor.

Brianna let the reins lie on Brutus's neck, letting him rest after the last climb, and sat still, surveying the small valley below. The big white-harled farmhouse sat serenely in the middle of pale green fields of oats and barley, its windows and chimneys edged in gray stone, the walled kailyard and the numerous outbuildings clustering around it like chicks round a big white hen.

She had never seen it before, but she was sure. She had heard her mother's descriptions of Lallybroch often enough. And besides, it was the only substantial house for miles; she had seen nothing else in the last three days but the tiny stone-walled crofters' cottages, many deserted and tumbled down, some no more than fire-black ruins.

Smoke was rising from a chimney below; someone was home. It was nearly midday; perhaps everyone was inside, eating dinner.

She swallowed, dry-mouthed with excitement and apprehension. Who would it be? Whom would she see first? Ian? Jenny? And how would they take her appearance, and her declaration?

She had decided simply to tell the truth, as far as who she was, and what she was doing there. Her mother had said how much she looked like her father; she would have to count on that resemblance to convince them. The Highlanders she had met so far were wary of her looks and strange speech; perhaps the Murrays wouldn't believe her. Then she remembered and touched the pocket of her coat; no, they'd believe her; she had proof, after all.

A sudden thought hollowed her breastbone. Could they possibly be here now? Jamie Fraser and her mother? The thought hadn't occurred to her before. She had been so convinced that they were in America—but that wasn't necessarily so. She only knew they *would* be in America in 1776; there was no telling where they were right now.

Brutus flung up his head and whinnied loudly. An answering neigh came from behind them, and Brianna drew up the reins as Brutus swung around. He lifted his head and nickered, nostrils flaring with interest as a handsome bay horse came round the bend of the road, carrying a tall man in brown.

The man pulled up his horse for a moment when he saw them, then twitched a heel against the bay's side and came on, slowly. He was young, she saw, and deeply tanned despite his hat; he must spend a good deal of time outdoors. The skirt of his coat was rumpled and his stockings were covered with dust and foxtails.

He came up to her warily, nodding as he came within speaking distance. Then she saw him stiffen in surprise, and smiled to herself.

He had just noticed that she was a woman. The men's clothes she wore would fool no one up close; "boyish" was the last word one would use to describe her figure. They served their purpose well enough, though—they were comfortable for riding and, given her height, made her look like a man on horseback at a distance.

The man swept off his hat and bowed to her, surprise plain on his face. He wasn't strictly good-looking, but had a pleasant, strong sort of face, with feathery brows—presently raised high— and soft brown eyes under a thick cap of curly hair, black and glossy with good health.

"Madame," he said. "Might I assist ye?"

She took off her own hat and smiled at him.

"I hope so," she said. "Is this place Lallybroch?"

He nodded, wariness now added to his surprise as he heard her odd accent.

"It is, so. Will ye be having some business here?"

"Yes," she said firmly. "I will." She drew herself up straight in the saddle and took a deep breath. "I'm Brianna . . . Fraser."

It felt odd to say it aloud; she had never used the name before. It seemed strangely right, though.

The wariness on his face diminished, but the puzzlement didn't. He nodded cautiously.

"Your servant, ma'am. Jamie Fraser Murray," he added formally, bowing, "of Broch Tuarach."

"Young Jamie!" she exclaimed, startling him with her eagerness. "You're Young Jamie!"

"My family calls me so," he said stiffly, managing to give her the impression that he objected to having the name used wantonly by strange women in unsuitable clothes.

"Pleased to meet you," she said, undaunted. She extended a hand to him, leaning from her saddle. "I'm your cousin."

The brows, which had come down during the introductions, popped back up. He looked at her extended hand, then, incredulously, at her face.

"Jamie Fraser is my father," she said.

His jaw dropped, and he simply goggled at her for a moment. He looked her over minutely, head to toe, peered closely at her face, and then a wide, slow smile spread across his own.

"Damned if he isn't!" he said. He seized her hand and squeezed it tight enough to grind the bones together. "Christ, you've the look of him!"

He laughed, humor transforming his face.

"Jesus!" he said. "My mother will have kittens!"

The great rose brier that overhung the door was newly in leaf, hundreds of tiny green buds just forming. Brianna looked up at it as she followed Young Jamie, and caught sight of the lintel over the door.

Fraser, 1716 was carved into the weathered wood. She felt a small thrill at the sight, and stood staring up at the name for a moment, the sunwarm wood of the jamb solid under her hand.

"All right, Cousin?" Young Jamie had turned to look back at her inquiringly.

"Fine." She hurried into the house after him, automatically ducking her head, though there was no need.

"We're mostly tall, save my Mam and wee Kitty," Young Jamie said with a smile, seeing her duck. "My grandsire—your grandsire, too—built this house for his wife, who was a verra tall woman herself. It's the only house in the Highlands where ye can go through a doorway without ducking or bashing your head, I expect.''

. . . *Your grandsire, too.* The casual words made her feel suddenly warm, in spite of the cool dimness of the entry hall.

Frank Randall had been an only child, as had her mother; such relatives as she had were not close—only a couple of elderly great-aunts in England, and some long-distant second cousins in Australia. She had set out thinking only to find her father; she hadn't realized that she might discover a whole new family in the process.

A *lot* of family. As she entered the hallway, with its scarred paneling, a door opened and four small children ran out, closely pursued by a tall young woman with brown curly hair.

''Ah, run for it, run for it, wee fishies!'' she cried, rushing forward with outstretched hands snapping like pincers. ''The wicked crab will have ye eaten up, snap, snap!''

The children fled down the hall in a gale of giggles and shrieks, looking back over their shoulders in terrified delight. One of them, a little boy of four or so, saw Brianna and Young Jamie standing in the entry and instantly reversed his direction, charging down the hallway like a runaway locomotive, shouting, ''Daddy, Daddy, Daddy!''

The boy flung himself recklessly at Young Jamie's midriff. The latter caught him expertly, and hoisted the beaming little boy in his arms.

''Now, then, wee Matthew,'' he said sternly. ''What sort of manners is this your auntie Janet's teachin' you? What will your new cousin be thinkin', to see ye dashin' about wi' no more sense than a chicken after corn?''

The little boy giggled louder, not at all put off by the scolding. He peeked at Brianna, caught her eye, and promptly buried his face in his father's shoulder. Slowly he raised his head and peeked again, blue eyes wide.

''Da!'' he said. ''Is that a lady?''

''Of course she is, I've told ye, she's your cousin.''

''But she's got on breeks!'' Matthew stared at her in shock. ''Ladies dinna wear breeks!''

The young woman looked rather as though she subscribed to this opinion as well, but she interrupted firmly, moving to take the little boy from his father.

''Well, and I'm sure she's a fine reason for it, but it isna proper to be makin' remarks before people's faces. You go and get your-

self washed, aye?'' She set him down and turned him toward the
door at the end of the hallway, giving him a gentle push. He didn't
move, but turned back around to stare at Brianna.

"Where's Grannie, Matt?" his father asked.

"In the back parlor wi' Grandda and a lady and a man," Matthew replied promptly. "They've had two pots of coffee, a tray of
scones, and a whole Dundee cake, but Mama says they're hangin'
on in hopes of bein' fed dinner, too, and good luck to them
because it's only brose and a bit o' hough today, and damned—
oop!''—he pressed a hand over his mouth, glancing guiltily at his
father—"and drat if she'll gie them any of the gooseberry tart, no
matter how long they stay."

Young Jamie gave his son a narrow look, then glanced quizzically at his sister. "A lady and a man?"

Janet made a faint moue of distaste.

"The Grizzler and her brother," she said.

Young Jamie grunted, with a glance at Brianna.

"I imagine Mam will be pleased for an excuse to get away
from them, then." He nodded at Matthew. "Go and fetch your
Grannie, lad. Tell her I've brought a visitor she'll like to see. And
watch your language, aye?'' He turned Matthew toward the back
of the house and slapped him gently on the rump in dismissal.

The little boy went, but slowly, casting glances of intense fascination over his shoulder at Brianna as he went.

Young Jamie turned back to Brianna, smiling.

"That'll be my eldest," he said. "And this"—gesturing to the
young woman, "is my sister, Janet Murray. Janet—Mistress Brianna Fraser."

Brianna didn't know whether to offer to shake hands or not, and
instead contented herself with a nod and a smile. "I'm very
pleased to meet you," she said warmly.

Janet's eyes sprang wide with amazement, whether at what Brianna had said or at the accent with which she'd spoken, Brianna
couldn't tell.

Young Jamie grinned at his sister's surprise.

"You'll never guess who she is, Jen," he said. "Never in a
thousand years!"

Janet lifted one eyebrow, then narrowed her eyes at Brianna.

"Cousin," she murmured, looking their guest frankly up and
down. "She's the look o' the MacKenzies, surely. But she's a
Fraser, ye say . . ." Her eyes sprang suddenly wide.

"Oh, ye can't be," she said to Brianna. A wide smile began to

582 **Diana Gabaldon**

spread across her face, pointing up the family resemblance to her brother. "You *can't* be!"

Her brother's chortle was interrupted by the swish of a swinging door and the sound of light footsteps on the boards of the hallway.

"Aye, Jamie? Mattie says we've a guest—" The soft, brisk voice died suddenly, and Brianna looked up, her heart suddenly in her throat.

Jenny Murray was very small—no more than five feet tall—and delicately boned as a sparrow. She stood staring at Brianna, mouth slightly open. Her eyes were the deep blue of gentians, made the more striking by a face gone white as paper.

"Oh, my," she said softly. "Oh, my." Brianna smiled tentatively, nodding to her aunt—her mother's friend, her father's beloved only sister. *Oh, please!* she thought, suddenly suffused with a longing as intense as it was unexpected. *Please like me, please be happy I'm here!*

Young Jamie bowed elaborately to his mother, beaming.

"Mam, might I have the honor to present to ye—"

"Jamie Fraser! I kent he was back—I told ye, Jenny Murray!" The voice rang out from the back of the hallway in tones of high-pitched accusation. Glancing up in startlement, Brianna saw a woman emerging from the shadows, rustling with indignation.

"Amyas Kettrick *told* me he'd seen your brother riding near Balriggan! But no, ye wouldna have it, would ye, Jenny—telling me I'm a fool, telling me Amyas is blind, and Jamie in America! Liars the both of ye, you and Ian, trying to protect that wicked coward! Hobart!" she shouted, turning toward the back of the house, "Hobart! Come out here this minute!"

"Be quiet!" said Jenny impatiently. "Ye *are* a fool, Laoghaire!" She jerked at the woman's sleeve, urging her around. "And as for who's blind, look at her! Are ye too far past it to tell the difference between a grown man and a lass in breeks, for heaven's sake?" Her own eyes stayed fixed on Brianna, bright with speculation.

"A *lass*?"

The other woman turned, frowning nearsightedly at Brianna. Then she blinked once, anger erased as her round face went slack with surprise. She gasped, crossing herself.

"Mary, Margaret and Bride! Who in the name of God are *you*?"

Brianna took a deep breath, looking from one woman to the other as she answered, trying to keep her voice from shaking.

"My name is Brianna. I'm Jamie Fraser's daughter."

Both women's eyes popped wide. The woman called Laoghaire grew slowly red and seemed to swell, opening and closing her mouth in a futile search for words.

Jenny stepped forward, though, and seized Brianna's hands, looking up into her face. A soft pink bloomed in her cheeks, making her look suddenly young.

"Jamie's? You're truly Jamie's lassie?" She squeezed Brianna's hands hard between her own.

"My mother says so."

Brianna felt the answering smile on her own face. Jenny's hands were cool, but Brianna felt a rush of warmth nonetheless, which spread through her hands and up into her chest. She caught the faint, spicy scent of baking in the folds of Jenny's gown, and something else, more earthy and pungent, that she thought must be the smell of sheep's wool.

"Does she, so?" Laoghaire had recovered both her voice and her self-possession. She stepped forward, eyes narrowed. "Jamie Fraser's your father, aye? And just who might your mother be?"

Brianna stiffened.

"His wife," she said. "Who else?"

Laoghaire put back her head and laughed. It wasn't a nice laugh.

"Who else?" she said, mimicking. "Who else indeed, lassie! And just which wife would that be, now?"

Brianna felt the blood drain from her own face, and her hands grow stiff in Jenny's as the flood of realization washed over her. *You idiot*, she thought. *You stupid idiot. It was twenty years! Of course he would have married again. Of course. No matter how much he loved Mama.*

On the heels of this thought was another, more terrible. *Did she find him? Oh, God, did she find him with a new wife, and he sent her away? Oh, God, where is she?*

She turned blindly, wanting to run, not knowing where to go, what to do, only feeling that she must get out of here at once, and find her mother.

"You'll be wanting to sit down, I expect, Cousin. Come into the parlor, aye?" Young Jamie's voice was firm in her ear, and his arm was around her, turning her, urging her down the hall and through one of the doors that opened off it.

She scarcely heard the babble of voices around her, the confusion of explanations and accusations that popped around her ears like strings of firecrackers. She glimpsed a small, neat man with a face like the White Rabbit, looking vastly surprised, and another man, much taller, who rose as she came into the parlor and came toward her, his weathered, homely face creased in concern.

It was the tall man who calmed the racket and brought everyone to order, extracting from the confused muddle of voices an explanation of her presence.

"Jamie's daughter?" He glanced at her with interest, but looked much less surprised than anyone else so far. "What's your name, *a leannan*?"

"Brianna." She was too upset to smile at him, but he didn't seem to mind.

"Brianna." He eased himself down on a hassock, motioning her to a seat opposite, and she saw that he had a wooden leg that protruded stiffly to one side. He took her hand and smiled at her, the warm light in his soft brown eyes making her feel momentarily safer.

"I'm your uncle Ian, lass. Welcome to ye." Her own hand tightened on his involuntarily, clinging to the refuge he seemed to offer. He didn't flinch or draw back, just looked her over carefully, seeming amused by the way she was dressed.

"Been sleeping in the heather, have ye?" he said, seeing the dirt and plant stains on her clothes. "You'll have come some way to find us, niece."

"She *says* she's your niece," Laoghaire said. Recovered from her shock, she peered over Ian's shoulder, her round face pinched with dislike. "Belike she's only come to see what she can get."

"I shouldna be callin' the kettle black, Laoghaire," Ian said mildly. He twisted round to face her. "Or was it not you and Hobart a half-hour past, tryin' to squeeze five hundred pounds from me?"

Her lips pressed tight together, deepening the lines that bracketed her mouth.

"That money's mine," she snapped, "and well ye know it! It was agreed to; you witnessed the paper."

Ian sighed; evidently this wasn't the first he had heard of the matter today.

"I did," he said patiently. "And ye'll have your money—so soon as Jamie's able to send it. He's promised, and he's an honorable man. But—"

"Honorable, is it?" Laoghaire produced an unladylike snort. "Is it honorable to commit bigamy, then? Desert his wife and children? Steal away my daughter and ruin her? Honorable!" She looked at Brianna, eyes bright and hard as fresh-rolled steel.

"I'll ask again, lass—what's your mother's name?"

Brianna simply stared at her, overwhelmed. The stock around her throat was choking her, and her hands felt icy, despite Ian's grasp.

"Your mother," Laoghaire repeated, impatient. "Who was she?"

"It doesna matter who—" Jenny began, but Laoghaire rounded on her, face flushed with fury.

"Oh, it matters! If he got her on some army whore, or some slut of a maidservant when he was in England—that's one thing. But if she's—"

"Laoghaire!"

"Sister!"

"Ye foul-tongued besom!"

Brianna put a stop to the outcry simply by standing up. She was as tall as any of the men, and towered over the women. Laoghaire took one quick step back. Every face in the room was turned to her, marked with hostility, sympathy, or merely curiosity.

With a coolness that she didn't feel, Brianna reached for the inner pocket of her coat, the secret pocket she had sewed into the seam only a week before. It seemed like a century.

"My mother's name is Claire," she said, and dropped the necklace on the table.

There was utter silence in the room, save for the soft hissing of the peat fire, burning low on the hearth. The pearl necklace lay gleaming, the spring sun from the window picking out the gold pierced-work roundels like sparks.

It was Jenny who spoke first. Moving like a sleepwalker, she reached out a slender finger and touched one of the pearls. Freshwater pearls, the kind called baroque because of their singular, irregular, unmistakable shapes.

"Oh, my," Jenny said softly. She lifted her head and looked Brianna in the face, the slanted blue eyes shimmering with what looked like tears. "I am so very glad to see ye—Niece."

❧

"Where is my mother? Do you know?" Brianna glanced from face to face, her heart beating heavily in her ears. Laoghaire was not looking at her; her gaze was fastened to the pearls, face gone cold and frozen.

Jenny and Ian exchanged a quick glance, then Ian stood up, moving awkwardly to bring his leg under him.

"She's with your Da," he said quietly, touching Brianna's arm. "Dinna fash yourself, lassie; they're both safe."

Brianna resisted the impulse to collapse with relief. Instead, she let out her breath very carefully, feeling the knot of anxiety loosen slowly in her belly.

"Thank you," she said. She tried to smile at Ian, but her face felt slack and rubbery. *Safe. And together. Oh, thank you!* she thought, in wordless gratitude.

"Those are mine, by rights." Laoghaire nodded at the pearls. She wasn't angry now, but coldly self-possessed. Without the distortions of fury, Brianna could see that she had once been very pretty, and was still a handsome woman—tall for a Scot, and graceful in her movements. She had the kind of delicate fair coloring that fades quickly, and had thickened through the middle, but her figure was still erect and firm, and her face still showed the pride of a woman who has known herself beautiful.

"That they're not!" said Jenny, with a quick flash of temper. "They were my mother's jewels, that my father gave to Jamie for his wife, and—"

"And his wife I am," Laoghaire interrupted. She looked at Brianna then, a cold, gauging look.

"I am his wife," she repeated. "I married him in good faith, and he promised me payment for the wrong he did me." She turned her cold gaze on Jenny. "It's been more than a year since I've seen a penny. Am I to sell my shoes to feed my daughter— the one he's left to me?"

She lifted her chin and looked at Brianna.

"If you're his daughter, then his debts are yours as well. Tell her, Hobart!"

Hobart looked mildly embarrassed.

"Ah, now, Sister," he said, putting a hand on her arm in an attempt to be soothing. "I dinna think—"

"No, ye don't, and haven't since ye were born!" She shook him off in irritation, and stretched out a hand toward the pearls. "They're mine!"

It was pure reflex; the pearls were clutched tight in Brianna's hand before she had made the decision to snatch them. The gold roundels were cool against her skin, but the pearls were warm—the sign of a genuine pearl, her mother had told her.

"You wait just one minute here." The strength and coldness of her own voice surprised her. "I don't know who you are, and I don't know what happened between you and my father, but—"

"I am Laoghaire MacKenzie, and your bastard of a father married me four years ago—under false pretenses, I might add." Laoghaire's anger had not disappeared but seemed to have submerged; her face had a tight, stretched look, but she was not shouting, and the red had faded from her soft, plump cheeks.

Brianna took a deep breath, striving for calmness.

"Yes? But if my mother is with my father now—"

"He left me."

The words were spoken without heat, but they fell with the weight of stones in still water, spreading endless ripples of pain and betrayal. Young Jamie had been opening his mouth to speak; he shut it again, watching Laoghaire.

"He said that he could not bear it longer—to dwell in the same house with me, to share my bed." She spoke calmly, as though reciting a piece she had learned by heart, her eyes still fixed on the empty spot where the pearls had rested.

"So he left. And then he came back—with the witch. Flaunted her in my face; bedded her under my nose." Slowly, she raised her eyes to Brianna's, studying her with quiet intensity, searching out the mysteries of her face. Slowly, she nodded.

"It was she," she said, with a certainty that was faintly eerie in its calmness. "She cast her spells on him from the day she came to Leoch—and on me. She made me invisible. From the day she came, he could not see me."

Brianna felt a small shiver run up her spine, despite the hissing peat fire on the hearth.

"And then she was gone. Dead, they said. Killed in the Rising. And him come home again from England, free at long last." She shook her head very slightly; her eyes still rested on Brianna's face, but Brianna knew Laoghaire didn't see her any longer.

"But she wasna dead at all," Laoghaire said softly. "And he was not free. I knew that; I always knew that. Ye canna kill a witch with steel—they must burn." Laoghaire's pale blue eyes turned to Jenny.

"You saw her—at my wedding. Her fetch standing there, between me and him. Ye saw her, but ye didna say. I only heard it

later, when ye told Maisri the seer. You should ha' told me, then."
It was a not so much an accusation as a statement of fact.

Jenny's face had gone pale again, the slanted blue eyes dark
with something—perhaps fear. She licked her lips and started to
reply, but Laoghaire's attention had shifted to Ian.

"Ye'd best be wary, Ian Murray," she said, her tone now matter-of-fact. She nodded toward Brianna. "Look at her weel, man.
Is a right woman made so? Taller than most men, dressed as a
man, wi' hands as broad as a dinner plate, fit to choke the life
from one o' your weans, should she choose."

Ian didn't answer, though his long, homely face looked troubled. Young Jamie's fists clenched, though, and his jaw set tight.
Laoghaire saw it, and a small smile touched the corners of her
mouth.

"She is a witch's child," she said. "And ye know it, all of
you!" She glanced around the room, challenging each uncomfortable face. "They should have burned her mother in Cranesmuir,
save for the lovespell she'd put on Jamie Fraser. Aye, I say be
wary of what ye've brought into your house!"

Brianna brought the flat of her hand down on the table with a
thump, startling everyone.

"Hogwash," she said loudly. She could feel the blood rushing
to her face, and didn't care. All the faces were gawking, mouths
open, but she had no attention to spare for anyone but Laoghaire
MacKenzie.

"Hogwash," she said again, and pointed a finger at the woman.
"If they ought to be wary of anybody, it's you, you fucking
murderess!"

Laoghaire's mouth was open wider than anyone's, but no sound
came out.

"You didn't tell them *all* about Cranesmuir, did you? My
mother should have, but she didn't. She thought you were too
young to know what you were doing. You weren't, though, were
you?"

"What . . . ?" said Jenny, in a faint voice.

Young Jamie looked wildly at his father, who stood as though
poleaxed, staring at Brianna.

"She tried to kill my mother." Brianna was having trouble
controlling her voice; it cracked and trembled, but she got the
words out. "You did, didn't you? You told her Geillis Duncan was
ill and calling for her—you knew she'd go, she always went to
anybody sick, she's a doctor! You knew they were going to arrest

Geilie Duncan for witchcraft, and if my mother was there, they'd take her, too! You thought they'd burn her, and then you could have him—have Jamie Fraser.''

Laoghaire was white to the lips, her face set like stone. Even her eyes had no life; they were blank and dull as marbles.

''I could feel her hand on him,'' she whispered. ''In our bed. Lying there between us, wi' her hand on him, so he would stiffen and cry out to her in his sleep. She *was* a witch. I always knew.''

The room was silent, save for the hissing of the fire, and the tender singing of a small bird outside the window. Hobart MacKenzie stirred at last, coming forward to take his sister by the arm.

''Come away, *a leannan*,'' he said quietly. ''I'll see ye safe home now.'' He nodded to Ian, who returned the nod, with a small gesture that somehow conveyed both sympathy and regret.

Laoghaire allowed her brother to lead her away, unresisting, but at the door she stopped and turned back. Brianna stood still; she didn't think she could move if she tried.

''If you're Jamie Fraser's daughter,'' Laoghaire said, in a cold clear voice, ''and ye may be, given your looks—know this. Your father is a liar and a whoremaster, a cheat and a pander. I wish ye well of each other.'' She gave in then to Hobart's tugging at her sleeve, and the door swung to behind her.

The rage that had filled her drained suddenly away, and Brianna leaned forward, resting her weight on the palms of her hands, the necklace hard and lumpy under her hand. Her hair had come loose, and a thick strand fell over her face.

Her eyes were closed against the dizziness that threatened to engulf her; she felt, rather than saw, the hand that touched her and tenderly smoothed the locks back from her face.

''He went on loving her,'' she whispered, as much to herself as to anyone else. ''He didn't forget her.''

''Of course he didna forget her.'' She opened her eyes to see Ian's long face and kind brown eyes six inches away. A broad work-worn hand rested on hers, warm and hard, a hand even larger than her own.

''Neither did we,'' he said.

◄━━━

''Will ye no have a bit more, Cousin Brianna?'' Joan, Young Jamie's wife, smiled across the table, serving spoon poised invitingly above the crumbled remains of a gigantic gooseberry tart.

"Thank you, no. I couldn't eat another bite," Brianna said, smiling back. "I'm stuffed!"

This made Matthew and his little brother Henry giggle loudly, but a gimlet gleam from their grandmother's eye shut them up sharply. Looking round the table, though, Brianna could see suppressed laughter blooming on all the faces; from grown-ups to toddlers, they all seemed to find her slightest remark endlessly entertaining.

It was neither her unorthodox costume nor the sheer novelty of seeing a stranger, she thought—even one stranger than most. There was something else; some current of joy that ran among the members of the family, unseen but lively as electricity.

She realized only slowly what it was; a remark from Ian brought it into focus.

"We didna think that Jamie would ever have a bairn of his own." Ian's smile across the table was warm enough to melt ice. "You'll never have seen him, though?"

She shook her head, swallowing the remains of the last bite, smiling back in spite of her full mouth. That was it, she thought; they were delighted with her not so much for her sake, but for Jamie's. They loved him, and they were happy not for themselves but for him.

That realization brought tears to her eyes. Laoghaire's accusations had shaken her, wild as they were, and it was a great comfort to realize that to all of these people who knew him well, Jamie Fraser was neither a liar nor a wicked man; he was indeed the man her mother thought him.

Mistaking her emotion for choking, Young Jamie pounded her helpfully on the back, making her choke in good earnest.

"Will ye have written Uncle Jamie, then, to say as ye were coming to us?" he asked, ignoring her coughing and red-faced spluttering.

"No," she said hoarsely. "I don't know where he is."

Jenny's gull-winged brows went up.

"Aye, ye said that; I'd forgotten."

"Do you know where he is now? He and my mother?" Brianna bent forward anxiously, brushing pastry crumbs from her jabot.

Jenny smiled and rose from the table.

"Aye, I do—more or less. If ye've eaten your fill, d'ye come with me, lassie. I'll fetch his last letter for ye."

Brianna rose to follow Jenny, but stopped abruptly near the door. She had vaguely noticed some paintings on the walls of the parlor earlier, but hadn't really looked at them, in the rush of emotion and event. She looked at this one, though.

Two little boys with red-gold hair, stiffly solemn in kilts and jackets, white shirts with frills showing bright against the dark coat of a huge dog that sat beside them, tongue lolling in patient boredom.

The older boy was tall and fine-featured; he sat straight and proud, chin lifted, one hand resting on the dog's head, the other protectively on the shoulder of the small brother who stood between his knees.

It was the younger boy Brianna stared at, though. His face was round and snub-nosed, cheeks translucent and ruddy as apples. Wide blue eyes, slightly slanted, looked out under a bell of bright hair combed into an unnatural tidiness. The pose was formal, done in classic eighteenth-century style, but there was something in the robust, stocky little figure that made her smile and reach a finger to touch his face.

"Aren't you a sweetie," she said softly.

"Jamie was a sweet laddie, but a stubborn wee fiend, forbye." Jenny's voice by her ear startled her. "Beat him or coax him, it made no difference; if he'd made up his mind, it stayed made up. Come wi' me; there's another picture you'll like to see, I think."

The second portrait hung on the landing of the stairs, looking thoroughly out of place. From below she could see the ornate gilded frame, its heavy carving quite at odds with the solid, battered comfort of the house's other furnishings. It reminded her of pictures in museums; this homely setting seemed incongruous.

As she followed Jenny onto the landing the glare of light from the window disappeared, leaving the painting's surface flat and clear before her.

She gasped, and felt the hair rise on her forearms, under the linen of her shirt.

"It's remarkable, aye?" Jenny looked from the painting to Brianna and back again, her own features marked with something between pride and awe.

"Remarkable!" Brianna agreed, swallowing.

"Ye see why we kent ye at once," her aunt went on, laying a loving hand against the carved frame.

"Yes. Yes, I can see that."

"It will be my mother, aye? Your grandmother, Ellen MacKenzie."

"Yes," Brianna said. "I know." Dust motes stirred up by their footsteps whirled lazily through the afternoon light from the window. Brianna felt rather as though she was whirling with them, no longer anchored to reality.

Two hundred years from now, she had—I *will*? she thought wildly—stood in front of this portrait in the National Portrait Gallery, furiously denying the truth that it showed.

Ellen MacKenzie looked out at her now as she had then; long-necked and regal, slanted eyes showing a humor that did not quite touch the tender mouth. It wasn't a mirror image, by any means; Ellen's forehead was high, narrower than Brianna's, and the chin was round, not pointed, her whole face somewhat softer and less bold in its features.

But the resemblance was there, and pronounced enough to be startling; the wide cheekbones and lush red hair were the same. And around her neck was the string of pearls, gold roundels bright in the soft spring sun.

"Who painted it?" Brianna said at last, though she didn't need to hear the answer. The tag by the painting in the museum had given the artist as "Unknown." But having seen the portrait of the two little boys below, Brianna knew, all right. This picture was less skilled, an earlier effort—but the same hand had painted that hair and skin.

"My mother herself," Jenny was saying, her voice filled with a wistful pride. "She'd a great hand for drawing and painting. I often wished I had the gift."

Brianna felt her fingers curl unconsciously, the illusion of the brush between them momentarily so vivid she could have sworn she felt smooth wood.

That's where, she thought, with a small shiver, and heard an almost audible *click!* of recognition as a tiny piece of her past dropped into place. *That's where I got it.*

Frank Randall had joked that he couldn't draw a straight line; Claire that she drew nothing else. But Brianna had the gift of line and curve, of light and shadow—and now she had the source of the gift, as well.

What else? she thought suddenly. What else did she have that had once belonged to the woman in the picture, to the boy with the stubborn tilt to his head?

"Ned Gowan brought me this from Leoch," Jenny said, touching the frame with a certain reverence. "He saved it, when the English battered down the castle, after the Rising." She smiled faintly. "He's a great one for family, Ned is. He's a Lowlander from Edinburgh, wi' no kin of his own, but he's taken the Mac-Kenzies for his clan—even now the clan's no more.''

"No more?" Brianna blurted. "They're all dead?" The horror in her voice made Jenny glance at her, surprised.

"Och, no. I didna mean that, lass. But Leoch's gone," she added, in a softer tone. "And the last chiefs with it—Colum and his brother Dougal . . . they died for the Stuarts.''

She had known that, of course; Claire had told her. What was surprising was the sudden rush of an unexpected grief; regret for these strangers of her newfound blood. With an effort, she swallowed the thickening in her throat and turned to follow Jenny up the stairs.

"Was Leoch a great castle?" she asked. Her aunt paused, hand on the banister.

"I dinna ken," she said. Jenny glanced back at Ellen's picture, something like regret in her eyes.

"I never saw it—and now it's gone.''

Entering the bedroom on the second floor was like entering an undersea cavern. The room was small, as all the rooms were, with low beams smoked black from years of peat fires, but the walls were fresh and white, and the room itself was filled with a greenish, wavering light that spilled through two large windows, filtered by the leaves of the swaying rose brier.

Here and there some bright thing blinked or glowed like a reef fish in the soft gloom; a painted doll that lay on the hearthrug, abandoned by a grandchild, a Chinese basket with a pierced coin tied to its lid by way of ornament. A brass candlestick on the table, a small painting on the wall, rich colors deep against the whitewash.

Jenny went at once to the big armoire that stood at the side of the room, and stood on tiptoe to bring down a large morocco-covered box, its corners worn with age. As she put back the lid, Brianna caught the glint of metal and a small sharp flash, as of sunlight on jewels.

"Here it is." Jenny brought out a thick, folded wad of grimy paper, much traveled and much read by the looks of it, and put it into Brianna's hand. It had been sealed; a smudge of greasy wax still clung to the end of one sheet.

"They're in the Colony of North Carolina, but they dinna live near any town," Jenny explained. "Jamie writes a bit in the eve-

nings when he can, and keeps the bits all by him, till either he or
Fergus takes the journey down to Cross Creek, or a traveler passes
by who will carry the letter. That suits him; he doesna write easy
—especially since he broke his hand that time ago.''

Brianna started at the casual reference, but her aunt's calm face
showed no special awareness.

"Sit ye down, lassie." She waved a hand, giving Brianna the
choice of stool or bed.

"Thank you," Brianna murmured, taking the stool. So perhaps
Jenny didn't know everything about Jamie and Black Jack Randall? The notion that she might know things about this unseen
man that not even his beloved sister knew was in a way unsettling.
To dismiss the thought, she hurriedly opened the letter.

The scrawled words sprang out at her, black and vivid. She had
seen this writing before—its cramped, difficult letters, with the
big, looping tails, but that had been on a document two hundred
years old, its ink brown and faded, its writing constrained by
careful thought and formality. Here he had felt free—the writing
rolled across the page in a bold broken scrawl, the lines tilting
drunkenly up at the ends. It was untidy, but readable for all that.

Fraser's Ridge, Monday 19 September

My dearest Jenny,

.

*All here are in Good Health and Spirits, and trust that this
letter will find all in your Household likewise Content.*

*Your son sends his Most Affectionate Regards, and begs to be
Remembered to his Father, Brothers and Sisters. He bids you tell
Matthew and Henry that he sends them the Encloased Object,
which is the preserved Skull of an animal called Porpentine by
Reason of its Prodigious Spines (though it is not at all like the
small Hedge-creepie which you will know by that name, being
much Greater in Size and Dwelling in the Treetops, where it
Feasts upon the tender shoots). Tell Matthew and Henry that I do
not know why the Teeth are orange. No Doubt the animal finds it
Decorative.*

*Also enclosed you will find a small Present for yourself; the
Patterning is contrived by use of the Quills of this same Porpentine, which the Indians dye with the juices of several Plants, before weaving them in the Ingenious Manner you see before you.*

Claire has been recently much Interested by Conversation—if the term can be used for a Communication limited mostly to Gesticulations and the Making of Faces (she insists I note here that she does not Make Faces, to which I reply that I am in Better Case to judge of the matter, being able to see the Face in question, which she is not)—in Conversation with an old woman of the Indians, much Esteemed in this area as a Healer, who has Given her many such plants. In consequence, her fingers are Purple at present, which I find Most Decorative.

Tuesday, 20 Sept.

I have been much Occupied today in repair and strengthening of the penfold in which we keep our few cows, pigs, etc. at night, to protect them from the depredations of Bears, which are plentiful. In walking to the privy this morning, I espied a great Pawprint in the mud, which Measured quite the length of my own Foot. The stock appeared Nervous and disturbed, for which Condition I can scarce Blame them.

Do not, I pray you, suffer any Alarm on our account. The Black Bears of this country are wary of Humans, and Loath to approach even a Single Man. Also, our house is strongly built, and I have forbidden Ian to go Abroad after dark, save he is Well-armed.

In the matter of Armament, our situation is much Improved. Fergus has brought back from High Point both a fine Rifle of the new kind, and several excellent Knives.

Also a large boiling kettle, whose Acquisition we have Celebrated with a great quantity of tasty Stew, made with Venison, wild Onions from the wood, dried beans, and likewise some Tomatoe-fruits, dried from the Summer. None of us Died or suffered Ill-effects from Eating of this stew, so Claire is likely right, Tomatoes are not Poison.

Wednesday, 21 Sept.

The Bear has come again. I found large Prints and Scrapings on the new-turned ground of Claire's Garden today. The beast will be fattening for its Winter slumbers, and no doubt seeks to Digg for grubs in the fresh Earth.

I have Removed the Sow to our Pantry, since she is near Farrowing. Neither Claire nor the Sow was greatly pleased by this arrangement, but the Animal is valuable, having cost me three pound from Mr. Quillan.

Four Indians came today. They are of the kind called Tusca-

rora. I have met these men on several Occasions, and found them most Amiable.

The Savages having expressed a determination to hunt our particular Bear, I made them a Gift of some tobacco and a Knife, with which they seemed Pleasd.

They sat under the eaves of the House most of the morning, Smoking and talking among themselves, but then near midday made to Depart upon their Hunt. I inquired whether, the Bear seeming Fond of our Society, it would not be best for the Hunters to lie hidden nearby, in Hopes that the animal will return here.

I was Informed—with the Kindest Condescension possible through word and sign—that the appearance of the Animal's droppings indicated beyond any Doubt that it had Quitted the area, and was Bound upon some errand to the west.

Being of no Mind to take issue with such Expert practitioners, I wished them luck and bade them a cordial Farewell. I could not accompany them, having urgent Labors still to perform here, but Ian and Rollo have gone with them, as they have done before.

I have loaded my new Rifle and left it ready to Hand, lest our friends' apprehension as to the Bear's intent be Mistaken.

Thursday, 22 Sept.

I was roused from Sleep last night by a Hideous Noise. This was a great Scraping, which reverberated thru the wooden logs of the wall, accompanied by such Thumps and loud Wails that I bolted from my Bed, convinced that the house was like to Fall about our Ears.

The Sow, observing the nearness of an Enemy, burst through the door of the Pantry (which I will say was flimsily made) and took Refuge beneath our Bed, squealing in a Manner to deafen us. Perceiving that the Bear was at Hand, I seiz'd my new Rifle and ran outside.

It was a moonlit Night, though hazy, and I could plainly see my Adversary, a great black shape, which stretched upon its hind feet appeared near as Tall as Myself, and (to my anxious eyes) roughly three times as Wide, being at no Great Distance from me.

I fired at it, whereon it Dropped to all fours and Ran with amazing Speed toward the shelter of the nearby Wood, disappearing before I could make Shift to shoot any more.

Come Daylight, I searched the ground for sign of Blood and found none, so cannot say did my Shot find its Target. The side of the House is decorated with several long Scrapes, as might be made with a sharpened Adze or Chizl, showing white in the Wood.

We have since been at some Pains to persuade the Sow (she is a White Sow, of Prodigious Size, a most Stubborn Temper, and not lacking in Teeth) to quit our bed and repair to her Sanctuary in the pantry. She was Reluctant, but was at length persuaded by the Combination of a trail of shattered corn laid before her, and myself at her Rear, Armed with a Stout Broom.

Monday, 26th Sept.

Ian and his Red Companions have returned, their Prey having eluded them in the wood. I shewed them the Scratches upon the Side of the House, whereon they became Excited and talked among themselves at such a Rate I could not Follow their Words.

One man then detached a large tooth from his necklace of such items and presented it to me with great Ceremony, saying that it would serve to Identify me to the Bear-spirit, and thus protect me from Harm. I accepted this Token with all due Solemnity, and was then oblig'd to present him with a piece of Honeycomb in Exchange, thus the proprieties were observ'd.

Claire was called to provide the Honeycomb, and with her usual eye for such Matters, perceived that one of our guests was Unwell, being heavy-eyed, coughing, and distracted in Appearance. Claire says he is also Flushed with fever, though this is not obvious to look at him. He being too ill to continue with his Companions, we have laid him on a pallet in the corncrib.

The sow has Most Incontinently farrowed in the pantry. There are a dozen piglets, all healthy and of a Vigorous Appetite, for which God be thanked. Our own Appetites bid fair to be impoverished for the present, as the Sow viciously Attacks anyone who opens the door of the Pantry, roaring and gnashing her Teeth in Rage. I was given one egg to my supper, and informed that I shall get no more until I have Contriv'd a solution to this Difficulty.

Saturday, 1 October

A great Surprise today. Two Guests have come . . .

"It will be a wild place."

Brianna looked up, startled. Jenny nodded at the letter, her eyes fixed on Brianna.

"Savages and bears and porpentines and such. It's no much more than a wee cot, where they live, Jamie told me. And all alone, up in the high mountains. Verra wild, it will be.'' She looked at Brianna a little anxiously. "But ye'll still wish to go?"

Brianna realized suddenly that Jenny was afraid she would not; that she would be frightened by the thought of the long journey and the savage place at the end of it. A savage place rendered suddenly real by the scrawled black words on the sheet she held— but not nearly as real as the man who had written them.

"I'm going," she assured her aunt. "As soon as I can."

Jenny's face relaxed.

"Oh, good," she said. She held out her hand, showing Brianna a small leather pouch decorated with a panel made of porcupine's quills, stained in shades of red and black, with here and there a few quills left in their natural grayish color for contrast.

"This is the present he sent me."

Brianna took it, admiring the intricacy of the pattern, and the softness of the pale deer's hide.

"It's beautiful."

"Aye, it is." Jenny turned away, busying herself with unnecessary tidying of the small ornaments that stood on the bookshelf. Brianna had just turned her attention back to the letter when Jenny spoke abruptly.

"Will ye stay a bit?"

Brianna looked up, startled.

"Stay?"

"Only for a day or two." Jenny turned around, the light from the window halo-bright behind her, shadowing her face.

"I ken ye'll wish to be gone," she said. "I should wish so much to talk wi' ye for a bit, though."

Brianna looked at her, puzzled, but could read nothing in the pale, even features and the slanted eyes so like her own.

"Yes," she said slowly. "Of course I'll stay."

A smile touched the corner of Jenny's mouth. Her hair was deep black, streaked with white like a magpie.

"That's good," she said softly. The smile spread slowly as she looked at her niece.

"Dear Lord, you're like my brother!"

Left alone, Brianna returned to the letter, rereading the beginning slowly, letting the quiet room around her fade, disappearing as Jamie Fraser came to life in her hands, his voice so vivid in her inner ear that he might have stood before her, the sun from the window glinting on his red hair.

Saturday, 1 October

A great Surprise today. Two Guests have come from Cross Creek. You will recall, I think, my Telling you of Lord John Grey, whom I knew in Ardsmuir. I have not said that I had seen him since, in Jamaica, where he was Governor for the Crown.

He is perhaps the last Person one should expect to find in this Remote Place, so far Removed from all Traces of Civilization, let alone those Luxurious Offices and Trappings of Pomp to which he is Accustomed. Surely we were Most Astonish'd by his appearing at our door, though we at once made him Welcome.

It is a melancholy Event that has led him here, I am Sorry to say. His wife, embarked from England with her son, contracted a Fever on the voyage, and Died of it while on the Ocean. Fearing lest the Miasmas of the Tropics prove as Fatal to the Boy as to his Mother, Lord John determined that the lad must go to Virginia, where Lord John's family has Substantial Property, and Determined to escort him there himself, seeing that the Lad was greatly Desolated by loss of his Mother.

I Expressed Amazement, as well as Gratification, that they should chuse to make such Alteration in their Journey as required to visit this Distant Spot, but his Lordship dismisses this, saying that he would have the Boy see something of the different Colonies, so as to appreciate the Richness and Variety of this Land. The lad is most Desirous of encountering Red Indians—reminding me in this Respect of Ian, not so long ago.

He is a comely lad, tall and Well-form'd for his Years, which I believe are near Twelve. He is somewhat subject still to Melancholy from his Mother's death, but is most Pleasant in Conversation, and Mannerly, for all he is an Earl (Lord John is his stepfather, I believe; his father having been Earl of Ellesmere). His name is William.

Brianna turned the page over, expecting continuation, but the passage stopped on that abrupt note. There was a break of several days before the letter resumed, on the 4th of October.

Tuesday, 4 October

The Indian in the corncrib died early this morning, in spite of Claire's best efforts to save him. His face, body and limbs were entirely suffused with a dreadful Rash, giving him a most Grew-some and Mottled look.

Claire thinks he suffered from the Measle, and is much Con-cerned, this being a Vicious Disease, plaguish and quick to Spread. She would not suffer anyone to go near the Body save only herself—she says she is Safe from it, by means of some charm—but we did all Assemble near Midday, whereat I read some Scripture suitable to the Occasion, and we said a Prayer for the Repose of his soul—for I trust that even unbaptised Savages may find rest in God's Mercy.

We are in some doubt how this poor soul's Earthly Remains shall be Disposed. I would in common course send Ian to summon his Friends, that they might give him such Burial as is common among the Indians.

Claire says we must not do this, however, for the Corpse itself may Spread the Disease among the man's own People, a Disaster which he would not Chuse to bring upon his Friends. She advo-cates burying or Burning the Corpse ourselves, and yet I am reluctant to undertake such Action, which might be easily Misun-derstood by the man's Companions—they thinking that we Sought by this means to hide some Complicity in his Death.

I have said nothing of this Concern to our Guests. If Danger seems Imminent, I must send them away. Still, I am loathe to Part with their society, so isolated is our situation. For now, we have Laid the Body in a small Dry Cave in the hill above the House, wherein I had thought to build a Stable or Storehouse.

I ask your forgiveness for thus Unburdening my Mind at the cost of your own Peace. I think all will be Well in the end, but for the Moment, I confess to some Worry. Should Danger—either from Indians or Disease—seem to threaten, I will send this Letter at once in the care of our Guests, that it may be Certain of reaching you.

If all is Well, I will write quickly to tell you.

Your Most Loving Brother,
        Jamie Fraser

Brianna's mouth felt dry and she swallowed, forcing saliva. There were two sheets yet to the letter; they clung together for a moment, stubbornly resisting her efforts to separate them, and then gave way.

Postscriptum, 20 October

We are all Safe, though the Manner of our Deliverance is most Melancholy; I will tell you of it later, having no great Heart for the matter at present.

Ian has been Sick of the Measle, as has Lord John, but they are both Recovered, and Claire bids me say that Ian does Exceeding well, you shall have no Fear for him. He writes in his own Hand, that you may know it is the Truth.

—J.

On the last sheet was writing in a different hand, this one neat and carefully schooled to an even slant, though here and there a blot defaced the page, perhaps the result either of the writer's illness or a defective pen.

Dear Mam—

I have been Sick, but am all Right agayne. I had a Fever, with most Peculiar Dreams, full of odd things. There was a great Wolf that came and spoke to me in the Voice of a man, but Auntie Claire says this must have been Rollo, who Stayed by me all the time I was Ill, he is a very Good Dog and does not bite very often.

The Measles came out in small Bumps beneath my Skin, and itched like Fury. I should have thought I had sat down on an Anthill, or wandered into a Hornet's nest. My head felt twice its usual Size, and I sneezd quite Ferocious.

I had three Eggs to my Breakfast today, and porridge, and have Walked to the privy alone twice, so I am quite Well, though I thought at first the Sickness had left me Blind—I could see nothing but a great Dazzle of Light when I went outside, but Auntie said this would soon be remedied, and it was.

I will write more later—Fergus is waiting to take the Letter away.

Your most Obedient and Devoted Son,
    Ian Murray

P.S. The Porpentine skull is for Henry and Mattie, I hope they will like it.

Brianna sat on the stool for some time, the whitewashed wall cool at her back, smoothing the pages of the letter and staring absently at the bookcase, with its neat row of cloth and leather bindings. *Robinson Crusoe* popped out at her, the title picked out in gold on the spine.

A savage place, Jenny had said. A dangerous place, too, where life could shift within a heartbeat from the humorous difficulty of a hog in the pantry to the instant threat of death by violence.

"And I thought *this* was primitive," she murmured, with a glance at the peat fire on the hearth.

Not so primitive after all, she thought as she followed Ian through the barnyard and out past the outbuildings. Everything was well kept and tidy; the drystone walls and buildings all in good repair, if a little shabby. The chickens were carefully confined to their own yard, and a hovering cloud of flies behind the barn announced the presence of a discreet manure pit, well away from the house.

The only real difference between this farmyard and modern ones she had seen was the absence of rusting farm equipment; there was a shovel resting against the barn, and two or three battered plowshares in a shed that they passed, but no ramshackle tractor, no tangles of wire and scattered metal scraps.

The animals were healthy, too, if somewhat smaller than their modern counterparts. A loud "Baaah!" announced the presence of a small herd of fat sheep in a paddock on the hillside, who trotted eagerly up to the fence as they passed, woolly backs wobbling and yellow eyes agleam in anticipation.

"Spoilt bastards," Ian said, but with a smile. "Think anyone's come up here has come to feed ye, don't you? My wife's," he added, turning to Brianna. "She gives them all the cast-off truck from the kailyard, till ye'd think they'd burst."

The ram, a majestic creature with great coiled horns, extended his head over the fence and emitted an imperious *"Beheheh!"* that was immediately echoed by his faithful flock.

"Bugger off, Hughie," said Ian, with tolerant scorn. "You're no mutton yet, but the day'll come, aye?" He waved dismissively at the ram and turned up the hill, kilt swinging.

Brianna hung back a step, watching his stride in fascination. Ian wore his kilt with an air quite unlike anything she was used to; not a costume nor a uniform—with a conscious bearing, but more as though it were part of his body than an article of clothing. In spite of that, she knew it wasn't usual for him to wear it;

Jenny's eyes had opened wide when he had come down to breakfast; then she had bent her head, burying a smile in her cup. Young Jamie had flicked a dark brow at his father, got back a bland look, and settled to his sausage with a faint shrug, and one of those small subterranean noises common to Scottish males.

The plaid cloth was old—she could see the fading along the creases and the wornness at the hem—but carefully kept. It would have been hidden away after Culloden, along with the pistols and the swords, with the pipes and their pibrochs—all the symbols of pride conquered.

No, not quite conquered, she thought, with a queer small tug at her heart. She remembered Roger Wakefield, squatting beside her under a gray sky on the battlefield at Culloden, his face lean and dark, eyes shadowed with knowledge of the dead nearby.

"Scots have long memories," he'd said, "and they're not the most forgiving of people. There's a clan stone out there with the name of MacKenzie carved on it, and a good many of my relatives under it." He had smiled then, but not in jest. "I don't feel quite so personal about it as some, but I haven't forgotten either."

No, not conquered. Not through a thousand years of strife and treachery, and not now. Defeated, scattered, but still surviving. Like Ian, maimed but upright. Like her father, exiled but still a Highlander.

With an effort she put Roger from her mind, and hurried to keep up with Ian's long, limping stride.

His lean face had lighted with pleasure when she had asked him to show her Lallybroch. It had been arranged that Young Jamie would take her to Inverness in a week's time, to see her safely aboard a ship to the Colonies, and she meant to use her time here to good advantage.

They walked—at a good pace, despite Ian's leg—over the fields toward the small foothills that rimmed the valley to the north, rising toward the pass through the black crags. It was a beautiful place, she thought. The pale green fields of oats and barley rippled with shifting light, cloud-shadows scudding through the spring sunshine, driven by the breeze that bent the stems of budding grass.

One field lay in long, dark ridges, the dirt humped and bare. At the side of the field stood a large heap of rough stones, neatly stacked.

''Is that a cairn?'' she asked Ian, voice lowered in respect. Cairns were the memorials of the dead, her mother had told her— sometimes the very long dead—new rocks added to the heap by each passing visitor.

He glanced at her in surprise, caught the direction of her gaze, and grinned.

''Ah, no, lass. Those are the stones we turned up wi' the plow in the spring. Every year we take them out, and every year there come new ones. Damned if I ken where they come from,'' he added, shaking his head in resignation. ''Stone fairies come and sow them in the night, I expect.''

She didn't know whether this was a joke or not. Uncertain whether to laugh, she asked a question instead.

''What will you plant here?''

''Oh, it's planted already.'' Ian shaded his eyes, squinting across the long field with pride. ''This is the tattie field. The new vines will be up by the end of the month.''

''Tattie—oh, potatoes!'' She looked at the field with new interest. ''Mama told me about that.''

''Aye, it was Claire's notion—and a good one, too. There's more than once the tatties have kept us from starving.'' He smiled briefly but said nothing more, and moved off, heading for the wild hills beyond the fields.

It was a long walk. The day was breezy, but warm, and Brianna was sweating by the time they paused at last, halfway up a rough track through the heather. The narrow path seemed to perch precariously between a steep hillside and an even steeper fall down a sheer rock face into a small, splashing burn.

Ian stopped, wiping his brow with his sleeve, and motioned her to a seat amid the heaps of granite boulders. From this vantage point, the valley lay below them, the farmhouse seeming small and incongruous, its fields a feeble intrusion of civilization on the surrounding wilderness of crag and heather.

He brought out a stone bottle from the sack he carried, and drew the cork with his teeth.

''That'll be your mother's doing, too,'' he said with a grin, handing her the bottle. ''That I've kept my teeth, I mean.'' He passed the tip of his tongue meditatively over his front teeth, shaking his head.

''A great one for eatin' weeds, your mother, but who's to argue, eh? Half the men my age are eatin' naught but porridge now.''

"She was always telling me to eat up my vegetables, when I was little. And brush after every meal." Brianna took the bottle from him and tilted it into her mouth; the ale was strong and bitter, but welcomely cool after the long walk.

"When ye were little, eh?" Amused, Ian cast an eye over her length. "I've seldom seen a lass sae braw. I'd say your mother kent her business, aye?"

She smiled back and gave him back the bottle.

"She knew enough to marry a tall man, at least," she said wryly.

Ian laughed and wiped the back of his hand across his mouth. He gazed affectionately at her, brown eyes warm.

"Ah, it's fine to see ye, lassie. You're verra much like him, it's true. Christ, what I wouldna give to be there when Jamie sees you!"

She looked down at the ground, biting her lip. The ground was thick with bracken, and their path up the hill showed plain, where the green fronds that had overgrown the track had been crushed and knocked aside.

"I don't know whether he knows or not," she blurted. "About me." She glanced up at him. "He didn't tell you."

Ian rocked back a little, frowning.

"No, that's true," he said slowly. "But I am thinking he maybe hadna time to say, even if he knew. He'll not have been here long, that last time he came, with Claire. And then, it was such a moil, wi' all that happened—" He stopped, pursing his lips, and glanced at her.

"Your auntie's been troubled about that," he said. "Thinking that ye might blame her."

"Blame her for what?" She stared at him, puzzled.

"For Laoghaire." The brown eyes held hers, intent.

A faint chill came over Brianna at the memory of those pale eyes, cold as marbles, and the woman's hateful words. She had dismissed them as simple malice, but the echoes of "whoremaster" and "cheat" lingered unpleasantly in her ear.

"What did Aunt Jenny have to do with Laoghaire?"

Ian sighed, brushing back a thick lock of brown hair that fell down across his face.

"It was her doing that Jamie married the woman. She meant it well, mind," he said warningly. "We did think Claire was dead these many years."

His tone held a question, but Brianna merely nodded, looking

down and smoothing the fabric across her knee. This was dangerous ground; better to say nothing, if she could. After a moment,
Ian went on.

"It was after he'd come home from England—he was a prisoner there for some years after the Rising—"

"I know."

Ian's brows shot up in surprise, but he said nothing; simply
shook his head.

"Aye, well. When he came back, he was—different. Well, he
would be, aye?" He smiled briefly, then dropped his eyes, pleating the fabric of his kilt between his fingers.

"It was like talking to a ghost," he said quietly. "He would
look at me, and smile, and answer—but he wasna really there."
He took a deep breath, and she could see the lines between his
brows, carved deep in concentration.

"Before—after Culloden—it was different, then. He was sair
wounded—and he'd lost Claire—" He glanced briefly at her, but
she kept still, and he went on.

"But it was a desperate time then. A great many folk died; of
the fighting, of sickness or of starving. There were English
soldiers in the country, burning, killing. When it's like that, ye
canna even think of dying, only because the struggle to live and
keep your family takes all your time."

A small smile touched Ian's lips, the rue of memory oddly
lightened with a private amusement.

"Jamie hid," he said, with an abrupt gesture toward the hillside
above them. "There. There's a wee cave behind that big gorse
bush, halfway up. It's what I brought ye here to show ye."

She looked where he pointed, up the tangled slope of rock and
heather, the hillside a riot of tiny flowers. There was no sign of a
cave, but the gorse bush stood out in a blaze of yellow blossom,
brilliant as a torch.

"I came up to bring him food once, when he was sick of the
ague. I told him he must come down to the house wi' me; that
Jenny was scairt he'd die up here, all alone. He opened one eye,
all bright with the fever, and his voice was sae hoarse I could
scarcely hear him. He said Jenny needna be worrit; even though
everything in the world seemed set on killin' him, he didna mean
to make it easy for them. Then he closed his eye and went to
sleep."

Ian gave her a wry glance. "I wasna so sure he had that much
to say about whether he was going to die or no, so I stayed with

him through the night. But he was right, after all; he's verra stubborn, ye ken?'' His tone held a note of a mild apology.

Brianna nodded, but her throat felt too tight to speak. Instead she stood up abruptly, and headed up the hill. Ian made no protest, but stayed on his rock, watching her.

It was a steep climb, and small thorny plants caught at her stockings. Near the cave, she had to scramble upward on all fours, to keep her balance on the steep granite slope.

The cave mouth was little more than a crack in the rock, the opening widening into a small triangle at the bottom. She knelt down and thrust her head and shoulders inside.

The chill was immediate; she could feel dampness condense on her cheeks. It took a moment for her sight to adapt to the dark, but enough light trickled into the cave past her shoulders for her to see.

It was perhaps eight feet long and six feet wide, a dim, dirt-floored cavity, with a ceiling so low that one could stand upright only near the entrance. To stay inside for any length of time would be like being entombed.

She pulled her head out quickly, breathing in deep gulps of the fresh spring air. Her heart was beating heavily.

Seven years! Seven years to have lived here, in cold grime and gnawing hunger. *I wouldn't last seven days,* she thought.

Wouldn't you? said another part of her mind. And then it came again, that tiny click of recognition that she had felt when she had looked at Ellen's portrait, and felt her fingers close on an invisible brush.

She turned around slowly and sat down, the cave behind her. It was very quiet here on the mountainside, but quiet in the way of hills and forests, a quiet that was not silent at all, but composed of constant tiny sounds.

There were small buzzings in the gorse bush nearby, of bees working the yellow flowers, dusty with pollen. Far below was the rushing of the burn, a low note echoing the rush of the wind above, stirring leaves and rattling twigs, sighing past the jutting boulders.

She sat still, and listened, and thought she knew what Jamie Fraser had found here.

Not loneliness, but solitude. Not suffering, but endurance, the discovery of grim kinship with the rocks and sky. And the finding here of a harsh peace that would transcend bodily discomfort, a healing instead of the wounds of the soul.

He had perhaps found the cave not a tomb, but a refuge; drawn strength from its rocks, like Antaeus thrown to earth. For this place was part of him, who had been born here, as it was part of her, who had never seen it before.

Ian was still sitting patiently below; hands clasped about his knees, looking out over the valley. She reached up and carefully broke off a bit of the gorse-bush, mindful of its spines. She laid it at the entrance of the cave, weighted with a small stone, then stood and made her way precariously down the hill.

Ian must have heard her approach, but didn't turn around. She sat down beside him.

"It's safe for you to wear that, now?" she said abruptly, with a nod at his kilt.

"Oh, aye," he said. He glanced down, his fingers rubbing the soft, worn wool. "It's been some years now since the soldiers last came. After all, what's left?" He gestured over the valley below.

"They carried away all they could find of value. Ruined what they couldna carry. There's no much left, save the land, is there? And I think they hadna much interest in that." She could see he was disturbed in some way; his wasn't a face that hid its owner's feelings.

She watched him for a moment, then said quietly, "You're still here. You and Jenny."

His hand stilled, and lay against the plaid. His eyelids were closed, his homely, weathered face raised to the sun.

"Aye, that's true," he said at last. He opened his eyes again, and turned to look at her. "And so are you. We talked a bit last night, your auntie and I. When ye see Jamie, and all's well between ye—then ask him, if ye will, what would he have us do."

"Do? About what?"

"About Lallybroch." He waved, taking in the valley and the house below. He turned to her, eyes troubled.

"You'll maybe know—maybe not—that your father made a deed of sassine before Culloden, to give over the place to Young Jamie, should it all come to smash and he be killed or condemned as a traitor. But that would be before you were born; before he kent that he'd have a bairn of his own."

"Yes, I did know that." She had a sudden awareness of what he was leading up to, and put her hand on his arm, startling him with the touch.

"I didn't come for that, Uncle," she said softly. "Lallybroch isn't mine—and I don't want it. All I want is to see my father—and my mother.''

Ian's long face relaxed, and he put his hand over hers where it lay on her arm. He didn't say anything for a moment; then squeezed her hand gently and let it go.

"Aye, well. You'll tell him, nonetheless; if he wishes it—"

"He won't," she interrupted firmly.

Ian looked at her, a faint smile at the back of his eyes.

"Ye ken a lot about what he'll do, for a lass that's never met him.''

She smiled at him, the spring sun warm on her shoulders.

"Maybe I do."

The smile broke through to Ian's face.

"Aye, your mother will ha' told ye, I suppose. And she did know him, for all she was a Sassenach. But then, she was always . . . special, your mother.''

"Yes." She hesitated for a moment, wanting to hear more about the topic of Laoghaire, but unsure how to ask. Before she could think of something, he stood, brushed down his kilt, and started down the track, forcing her to rise and follow.

"What's a fetch, Uncle Ian?" she asked the back of his head. Preoccupied with the difficulties of descent, he didn't turn, but she saw him lurch slightly, wooden leg sinking into the loose earth. At the bottom of the hill he waited for her, leaning on his stick.

"You'll be thinking of what Laoghaire said?" he asked. Without waiting for her nod, he turned and began making his way along the bottom of the hill, toward the small stream that flowed down through the rocks.

"A fetch is the sight of a person, when the person himself is far awa'," he said. "Sometimes it will be a person that's died, far from home. It's ill luck to see one, but worse luck to meet your own—for if you do, ye die.''

It was the absolute matter-of-factness of his tone that made a shiver run down her spine.

"I hope I don't," she said. "But she said—Laoghaire—" She stumbled on the name.

"L'heery," Ian corrected. "Aye, well. It was at her wedding to Jamie that Jenny saw your mother's fetch, that's true. She kent then that it was a bad match, but it was too late to be undone.''

He knelt awkwardly on his good knee, and splashed water from the burn over his face. Brianna did likewise, and gulped several handfuls of the cold, peaty-tasting water. Having no towel, she pulled her long shirttail from her breeks and wiped her face. She caught Ian's scandalized look at the glimpse of her bare stomach thus afforded, and dropped the shirttail abruptly, her cheeks flushing.

"You were going to tell me why my father married her," she said, to hide her embarrassment.

Ian's cheeks had gone a dull red, and he turned hastily away, talking to cover his confusion.

"Aye. It was as I told ye—when Jamie came from England, it was like the spark had gone out o' him, and there was nothing here to kindle it again. I dinna ken what it was that happened in England, but something did, sure as I'm born."

He shrugged, the back of his neck fading to its normal sunburnt brown.

"After Culloden, he was bad hurt, but there was fighting still to do, of a kind, and that kept him alive. When he came home from England—there wasna anything here for him, really." He spoke quietly, eyes cast down, watching his footing on the rocky ground.

"So Jenny made the match for him, with Laoghaire." He glanced at her, eyes bright and shrewd.

"You'll maybe be old enough to know, for all you're unwed yet. What a woman can do for a man—or he for her, I suppose. To heal him, I mean. Fill his emptiness." He touched his maimed leg absently. "Jamie wed Laoghaire from pity, I think—and if she had truly needed him—aye, well." He shrugged again, and smiled at her.

"It's no use to say what might have been or should be, is it? But he had left Laoghaire's house some time before your mother came back, you should know that."

Brianna felt a small surge of relief.

"Oh. I'm glad to know that. And my mother—when she came back—"

"He was verra glad to see her," Ian said simply. This time the smile lighted his whole face, like sunshine. "So was I."

35

Bon Voyage

It reminded her uncomfortably of Boston's city dog pound. A large, half-dark space whose rafters rang with yelping, and an atmosphere dense with animal smells. The big building on the market square in Inverness sheltered a great many enterprises—food vendors, cattle and swine brokers, assurance agents, shipchandlers and Royal Navy recruiters, but it was the group of men, women and children bunched in one corner that lent most force to the illusion.

Here and there a man or a woman stood upright amid the group, chin out and shoulders set in a show of good health and spirit, putting themselves forward. But for the most part, the people who offered themselves for sale eyed the passersby warily, in darting glances whose expressions were fixed between hope and fear—much too reminiscent of the dogs in the animal shelter where her father had now and then taken her to adopt a pet.

There were several families, too, with children clinging to their mothers, or standing blank-faced beside their parents. She tried not to look at them; it was always the puppies that had broken her heart.

Young Jamie was sidling slowly around the group, hat held against his chest to save it being crushed by the crowd, eyes half closed as he considered the prospects on offer. Her uncle Ian had gone to the shipping office to arrange her passage to America, leaving her cousin Jamie to choose a servant to accompany her on the journey. In vain had she protested that she didn't need a servant; after all, she had—so far as they knew—traveled from France to Scotland by herself, in perfect safety.

The men had nodded and smiled and listened with every evidence of polite attention—and here she was, obediently following Young Jamie through the crowd like one of her aunt Jenny's sheep. She was beginning to understand exactly what her mother had meant by describing the Frasers as "stubborn as rocks."

Despite the hubbub around her and her annoyance at her male relatives, her heart gave a small, excited bounce at thought of her mother. It was only now, when she knew for sure that Claire was safe, that she could admit to herself how sorely she had missed her. And her father—that unknown Highlander who had come so suddenly and vividly to life for her as she read his letters. The minor fact of an intervening ocean seemed no more than a small inconvenience.

Her cousin Jamie interrupted these rosy thoughts by taking her arm and leaning close to shout in her ear.

"Yon fellow wi' the cast in one eye," he said in a subdued bellow, indicating the gentleman in question by pointing with his chin. "What d'ye say to him, Brianna?"

"I'd say he looks like the Boston Strangler," she muttered, then louder, shouting into her cousin's ear, "He looks like an ox! No!"

"He's strong, and he looks honest!"

Brianna thought the gentleman in question looked too stupid to be *dis*honest, but refrained from saying so, merely shaking her head emphatically.

Young Jamie shrugged philosophically and resumed his scrutiny of the would-be bondsmen, walking around those who took his particular interest and peering at them closely, in a way she might have thought exceedingly rude had a number of other potential employers not been doing likewise.

"Bridies! Hot bridies!" A high-pitched screech cut through the rumble and racket of the hall, and Brianna turned to see an old woman elbowing her way robustly through the crowd, a steaming tray hung round her neck and a wooden spatula in hand.

The heavenly scent of fresh hot dough and spiced meat cut through the other pungencies in the hall, noticeable as the old woman's calling. It had been a long time since breakfast, and Brianna dug in her pocket, feeling saliva fill her mouth.

Ian had taken her purse to pay for her passage, but she had two or three loose coins; she held one up and waved it to and fro. The bridie seller spotted the flash of silver and at once altered course, tacking through the chattering mob. She hove to in front of Brianna and reached up to snatch the coin.

"Mary save us, a giantess!" she said, showing strong yellow teeth in a grin as she tilted her head back to look up at Brianna.

"Ye'd best take twa, my dearie. One will never do a great lass like you!"

Heads turned, and faces grinned up at her. She stood half a head higher than most of the men nearby. Mildly embarrassed by the attention, Brianna gave the nearest offender a cold look. This seemed to entertain the young man quite a lot; he staggered back against his friend, clutching his breast and pretending to be overcome.

"My God!" he said. "She looked at me! I'm heartstruck!"

"Och, awa' wi' ye," his friend scoffed, shoving him upright. " 'Twas me she was looking at; who'd look at *you* if they'd a choice?"

"Nothing of the sort," his friend protested stoutly. "It was me —wasn't it, darlin'?" He languished, making calf's eyes at Brianna and looking so ridiculous that she laughed, along with the crowd around her.

"And what would ye be doing with her, if ye got her, eh? She'd make two of ye. Now, off wi' ye, spawn," the bridie seller said, casually smacking the young man across the buttocks with her wooden spatula. "I've business, if you haven't. And the young woman will starve if ye dinna leave off playin' the fool and let her buy her dinner, aye?"

"She looks in fine flesh to me, grannie." Brianna's admirer, ignoring both assault and admonition, ogled her shamelessly. "And as for the rest—fetch me a ladder, Bobby, I'm no afraid of heights!"

Amid gales of laughter, the young man was dragged away by his friends, making loud kissing noises over his shoulder as he moved reluctantly off. Brianna took her change in coppers and retired into a corner to eat two of the hot beef pasties, her face still warm with laughter and self-consciousness.

She hadn't been so aware of her height since she had been a gawky seventh-grader, towering over all her classmates. Among her tall cousins, she had felt at home, but it was true; here she stuck out like a sore thumb, despite her having abided by Jenny's insistence and changed from her men's clothes to a dress of her cousin Janet's, hastily altered and let out in the seams.

Her sense of self-consciousness was not helped by the fact that no underclothes went with the dress, beyond a shift. No one seemed to find any lack in this state of affairs, but she was intensely conscious of the unaccustomed feeling of airiness about her nether parts, and the odd feeling of her naked thighs sliding past each other as she walked, her silk stockings gartered just above the knee.

Both self-consciousness and drafts were forgotten as she bit into the first hot pastry. A bridie was a plump hot pie in a half-moon shape, filled with minced steak and suet and spiced with onion. A rush of hot, rich juice and flaky pastry filled her mouth, and she closed her eyes in bliss.

"The food was either terribly bad or terribly good," Claire had said, describing her adventures in the past. "That's because there's no way of keeping things; anything you eat has either been salted or preserved in lard, if it isn't half rancid—or else it's fresh off the hoof or out of the garden, in which case it can be bloody marvelous."

The bridie was bloody marvelous, Brianna decided, even if it did keep dropping crumbs down the top of her bodice. She brushed at her bosom, trying to be unobtrusive, but the crowd's attention had turned—no one was looking at her now.

Or almost no one. A slight, fair man in a shabby coat had materialized by her elbow, making small nervous movements as though he wanted to pluck her sleeve but hadn't quite got up the nerve. Not sure whether he was a beggar or another importunate suitor, she looked suspiciously down her nose at him.

"Yes?"

"You—you are requiring a servant, ma'am?"

She dropped her aloofness, realizing that he must be one of the crowd of indentures.

"Oh. Well, I wouldn't say I require one, exactly, but it looks as though I'm going to get one anyway." She glanced at Young Jamie, who was now interrogating a squat, beetle-browed individual with shoulders like the Village Blacksmith. Young Jamie's notion of the ideal servant seemed to be limited to muscle. She looked back at the small man in front of her; he wasn't much by Young Jamie's standards, but by hers . . .

"Are you interested?" she asked.

The expression of haggard nervousness didn't leave his face, but a fugitive gleam of hope showed in his eyes.

"It—I—that is—not me, no. But will you think—perhaps consider—will you take my daughter?" he said abruptly. "Please!"

"Your daughter?" Brianna looked down at him, startled, her half-eaten bridie forgotten.

"I beg you, ma'am!" To her surprise, tears stood in the man's eyes. "Ye cannot think how urgently I pray you, or what gratitude I must bear ye!"

"But—ah—" Brianna brushed crumbs from the corner of her mouth, feeling desperately awkward.

"She is a strong girl in spite of her appearance, and most willing! She will be content to do any service whatever for ye, ma'am, and ye'll buy her contract!"

"But why should—look, what's the trouble?" she said, moved past awkwardness by curiosity and pity for his obvious distress. She took him by the arm and drew him into the shelter of a corner, where the racket was slightly diminished.

"Now, why are you so anxious that I should hire your daughter?"

She could see the muscles move in his throat as he swallowed convulsively.

"There is a man. He—he desires her. Not as a servant. As a— as a—concubine." The words came out in a hoarse whisper, and a flood of ugly crimson stained his face.

"Mmphm," said Brianna, discovering all at once the utility of this ambiguous expression. "I see. But you needn't let your daughter go to him, surely?"

"I have no choice." His agony was patent. "Her contract has been bought by Mr. Ransom—the broker." He jerked his head backward, indicating a tough-looking gentleman in a tie-wig, who was talking to Young Jamie. "He can dispose of it to whom he will—and he will sell her without a moment's hesitation to this . . . this . . ." He choked, overcome by despair.

"Here, take this." She hastily untucked the wide kerchief from her bodice, took it off her neck, and handed it to him. It left her slightly less than modest, but this seemed like an emergency.

Clearly it was, to him. He swabbed blindly at his face, then dropped the cloth and seized her free hand in both of his.

"He is a drover; he has gone to the cattle market to sell his beasts. When he has done so, he will return with the money for her contract, and take her away to his house in Aberdeen. When I heard him say so to Ransom, I was thrown into the most violent despair. I prayed most urgently to the Lord for her deliverance. And then—" He gulped.

"I saw you—so proud and noble and kind-seeming—and it did come to me as my prayers were answered. Oh, ma'am, I pray ye, do not disdain a father's plea. Take her!"

"But I'm going to America! You'd never—" She bit her lip. "I mean, you wouldn't see her—for a very long time."

The desperate father went quite white at this. He closed his eyes, and seemed to sway slightly, giving at the knees.

"The Colonies?" he whispered. Then he opened his eyes once more and set his jaw.

"Better she should be gone from me forever to a wild place, than to meet dishonor before my eyes."

Brianna had no idea what to say to this. She glanced helplessly over the man's head at the sea of bobbing heads.

"Er . . . your daughter . . . which one . . . ?"

The flicker of hope in his eyes sprang into sudden flame, shocking in its intensity.

"Bless ye, lady! I will fetch her to ye directly!"

He pressed her hand fervently, then darted away into the crowd, leaving her staring after him. After a moment, she shrugged helplessly, and bent to pick up her fallen kerchief. How had *this* happened? And what in the name of goodness would her uncle and her cousin say, if she—

"This is Elizabeth," a voice announced breathlessly. "Do your duty to the lady, Lizzie."

Brianna looked down and found the decision made for her.

"Oh, dear," she murmured, seeing the neat white parting down the middle of the small head that bent in a deep curtsy before her. "A puppy."

The head bobbed upright, presenting her with a thin, starved-looking face, in which scared gray eyes occupied most of the available space.

"Your servant, mum," said the small, white-lipped mouth. Or at least that's what it looked like it said; the girl spoke so softly, she couldn't be heard above the surrounding racket.

"She will serve ye well, ma'am, aye, indeed she will!" The father's anxious voice was more audible. She glanced at him; there was a strong resemblance between father and daughter, both with the same flyaway fair hair, the same thin, anxious faces. They were nearly the same height, though the girl was so frail, she seemed like her father's shadow.

"Er . . . hello." She smiled at the girl, trying to seem reassuring. The girl's head tilted fearfully back, looking up. She swallowed visibly, and licked her lips.

"Ah . . . how old are you, Lizzie? May I call you Lizzie?"

The small head bobbed on a neck that looked like a wild mushroom's stalk; long, colorless, and infinitely fragile. The girl whispered something that Brianna didn't catch; she looked at the father, who answered eagerly.

"Fourteen, ma'am. But she's a rare hand with cooking and sewing, clean in her person and ye'll never find a soul more biddable and willing!"

He stood behind his daughter, hands on her shoulders, gripped tight enough to show his knuckles white. His eyes met Brianna's. They were pale blue, pleading. His lips moved—without sound, but she heard him clearly.

"Please," he said.

Beyond him, Brianna could see her uncle, who had come into the hall. He was talking to Young Jamie, smooth head and curly bent together in close conversation. In a moment they would be looking for her.

She took a deep breath and drew herself up to her full height. Well, and if you came right down to it, she thought, she was as much a Fraser as her cousin. Let them find out just how stubborn a rock could be.

She smiled at the girl and held out a hand, offering the second, uneaten bridie.

"It's a bargain, Lizzie. Will you have a bite to seal it?"

<hr/>

"She's eaten my food," Brianna said, with as much assurance as she could conjure up. "She's mine."

Rather to her surprise, this statement finally put a stop to the argument. Her cousin looked as though he meant to go on remonstrating, but her uncle put a hand on Young Jamie's arm to silence him. The look of surprise on Ian's face turned to a sort of amused respect.

"Has she, now?" He looked at Lizzie, cowering behind Brianna, and his lips twitched. "Mmphm. Well, then, not much more to be said, is there?"

Young Jamie evidently didn't share his father's assessment of this point; he could think of quite a lot more to be said.

"But a wee lassie like that—she's useless!" He waved a dismissive hand at Lizzie, frowning. "Why, she isna big enough even to carry baggage, let alone—"

"I'm big enough to carry my own bags, thanks," Brianna put in. She lowered her brows and gave her cousin back scowl for scowl, straightening up to emphasize her height.

He lifted an eyebrow in acknowledgment, but didn't give up.

"A woman shouldna be traveling alone—"

"I won't be alone, I'll have Lizzie."

"—and certainly not to a place like America! Why, it's—"

"You'd think it was the ends of the earth to hear you talk, and you haven't even seen it!" Brianna said in exasperation. "I was *born* in America, for heaven's sake!"

Uncle and cousin gaped at her, identical expressions of shock on their faces. She seized the opportunity to press her advantage.

"It's my money, and my servant, and my journey. I've given my word, and I'll keep it!"

Ian rubbed a knuckle across his upper lip, suppressing a grin. He shook his head.

"They say it's a wise bairn that kens its father, but I dinna think there's much doubt who yours is, lass. Ye might have had the lang nebbit and red locks from anyone, but ye didna get the stubbornness from any man but Jamie Fraser."

A self-conscious flush rose to her cheeks, but Brianna felt an odd flutter of something like pleasure.

His feathers ruffled from the argument, Young Jamie made one last attempt.

"It's verra unseemly for a woman to be givin' her opinions sae free, and her with menfolk to look after her," he said stiffly.

"You don't think women ought to have opinions?" Brianna asked sweetly.

"No, I don't!"

Ian gave his son a long look.

"And you'll have been marrit what, eight years?" He shook his head. "Aye, well, your Joan's a tactful woman." Ignoring Young Jamie's black look, he turned back to Lizzie.

"Verra well, then. Go and take farewell of your father, lassie. I'll see to the papers." He watched Lizzie scurry away, thin shoulders hunched against the crowd. He shook his head a little doubtfully, and turned back to Brianna.

"Well, she'll maybe be better company for ye than a man-servant, lass, but your cousin's right about the one thing—she'll be no protection. It'll be you lookin' out for her, likely."

Brianna straightened her shoulders and thrust out her chin, summoning up as much self-confidence as she could, in spite of the sudden hollow feeling that assailed her.

"I can manage," she said.

She kept her hand curled tight, holding on to the stone in her palm. It was something to cling to, as the Moray Firth widened into the sea, and the cradling shore of Scotland fell away to either side.

Why ought she to feel so strongly for a place she hardly knew? Lizzie, born and raised in Scotland, had spared no glance for the receding land but had gone below at once, to lay claim to their space and arrange the few belongings they had brought aboard.

Brianna had never thought of herself as Scottish—had not *known* she was Scottish until quite recently—yet she had scarcely felt more bereft by her mother's leaving or her father's death than by this parting from people and places she had known for so short a time.

Perhaps it was only the contagious emotion of the other passengers. Many of them were standing at the rail as she was, several weeping openly. Or fear of the long journey ahead. But she knew quite well it was none of those things.

"That's that, I expect." It was Lizzie, appearing at her elbow after all, to see the last sight of the land fade away. Her small pale face was expressionless, but Brianna didn't mistake lack of expression for lack of feeling.

"Yes, we're on our way." Moved by impulse, Brianna put out a hand and drew the girl to stand in front of her at the rail, sheltered alike from freshening wind and from jostling passengers and seamen. Lizzie was a good foot shorter than Brianna, and fine-boned as the delicate sooty terns that circled the masts, squawking overhead.

The sun did not really set at this time of year but hung low above the dark hills, and the air had grown quite cold in the Firth. The girl was thinly dressed; she shivered, and pressed quite un-selfconsciously against Brianna for warmth. Brianna had a blue woolen *arisaid* provided by Jenny; she wrapped her arms and the shawl ends around the younger girl, finding as much comfort in the embrace as she gave.

"It will be all right," she said, to herself as much as to Lizzie. The pale blond head bobbed briefly under her chin; she couldn't tell whether it was a nod, or only Lizzie's attempt to get the wind-whipped strands of hair out of her eyes. Elf-locks snatched from her own thick plait fluttered in the stiff salt breeze, echoing the pull of the huge sails above. Despite her misgivings, she felt her spirits start to rise with the wind. She had survived a good many partings so far; she would survive this. That was what made this leaving hard, she thought. She had already lost father, mother, lover, home, and friends. She was alone by necessity, and also by choice. But then to find both home and family again so unexpectedly at Lallybroch had caught her unaware. She would have given almost anything to stay—just a little longer.

But there were promises to keep, losses to be made good. Then she could come back. To Scotland. And to Roger.

She shifted her arm, feeling his thin silver band warm on her wrist under the shawl, the metal heated by her own flesh. *Un peu . . . beaucoup . . .* Her other hand gripped the cloth together, exposed to the wind and damp with sea spray. If it hadn't been so cold, she might not have noticed the sudden warmth of the drop that fell on the back of her hand.

Lizzie stood stiff as a stick, her arms hugged tight around herself. Her ears were large and transparent, her hair fine and thin, sleek to her skull. Her ears poked out like a mouse's, tender and fragile in the soft deep light of the low night sun.

Brianna reached up and wiped away the tears by touch. Her own eyes were dry, and her mouth set firm as she looked out at the land over Lizzie's head, but the cold face and quivering lips against her hand might as well have been her own.

They stood for some time silently, until the last of the land was gone.

36

You Can't Go Home Again

Inverness, July 1769

Roger walked slowly through the town, looking around him with a mixture of fascination and delight. Inverness had changed a bit in two hundred–odd years, no doubt of it, and yet it was recognizably the same town; a good deal smaller, to be sure, with half its muddy streets unpaved, and yet he *knew* this street he was walking down, had walked down it a hundred times before.

It was Huntly Street, and while most of the small shops and buildings were unfamiliar, across the river stood the Old High Church—not so Old, now—its stubby steeple blunt as ever. Surely if he went inside, Mrs. Dunvegan, the minister's wife, would be setting out flowers in the chancel, ready for the Sunday service. But she wouldn't—Mrs. Dunvegan hadn't happened yet, with her thick wool sweaters and the terrible pot pies with which she tormented the sick of her husband's parish. Yet the small stone kirk stood solid and familiar, in the charge of a stranger.

His father's own church wasn't here; it had been—would be?—built in 1837. Likewise the manse, which had always seemed so elderly and decrepit, had not been built until the early 1900s. He had passed the site on his way; there was nothing there now save a tangle of cinquefoil and sweet broom, and a single small rowan sapling that sprouted from the underbrush, leaves fluttering in the light wind.

There was the same damp coolness to the air, tingling with freshness—but the overlying stink of motor exhaust was gone, replaced by a distant reek of sewage. The most striking absence was the churches; where both banks of the river would one day sport a noble profusion of steeples and spires, now there was nothing save a scatter of small buildings.

There was only the one stone footbridge, but the River Ness itself was naturally much the same. The river was low and the same gulls sat in the riffles, squawking companionably to one another as they picked small fish from among the stones just under the water's surface.

"Luck to you, mate," he said to a fat gull who sat on the bridge, and crossed the river into the town.

Here and there, a gracious residence sat comfortably insulated by its wide grounds, a grand lady spreading her skirts, ignoring the presence of the hoi polloi nearby. There was Mountgerald in the distance, the big house looking precisely as he had always known it, save that the great copper beeches that would in future surround the house had not yet been planted; instead, a row of spindly Italian cypresses leaned dismally against the garden wall, looking homesick for their sunny birthplace.

For all its elegance, Mountgerald was reputed to have been built in the oldest of the old ways—with the foundation laid over the body of a human sacrifice. By report, a workman had been lured into the hole of the cellar, and a great stone dropped onto him from the top of the newly built wall, crushing him to death. He had—so local history said—been buried there in the cellar, his blood a propitiation to the hungry spirits of the earth, who thus satisfied, had allowed the edifice to stand prosperous and untroubled through the years.

The house could be no more than twenty or thirty years old now, Roger thought. There might easily be people in the town who had worked on its building; who knew exactly what had happened in that cellar, to whom, and why.

But he had other things to do; Mountgerald and its ghost would have to keep their secrets. With a mild pang of regret, he left the big house behind, and turned his scholar's nose into the road that led to the docks downriver.

With a feeling of what could only be called déjà vu, he pushed open the door of a pub. The half-timbered entry, with its stone flags, was as he had seen it a week before—and two hundred years hence—and the familiar smell of hops and yeast in the air was a comfort to his spirit. The name had changed, but not the smell of beer.

Roger took a deep gulp from his wooden cup and nearly choked. "All right, man?" The barman paused, a bucket of sand in his hand, to peer at Roger.

"Fine," Roger said hoarsely. "Just fine."

The barman nodded and went back to scattering sand, but kept

Drums of Autumn   623

a practiced eye on Roger in case he looked like vomiting on the
freshly swept and sanded floor.

Roger coughed and cleared his throat, then essayed a further
cautious sip. The flavor was fine; very good, in fact. It was the
alcohol content that was unexpected; this stuff packed a wallop
far greater than any modern beer Roger had ever encountered.
Claire had said that alcoholism was endemic to the time, and
Roger could easily see why. Still, if drunkenness were the greatest
hazard he faced, he could deal with that.

He sat quietly by the hearth and drank, savoring the dark, bitter
brew as he watched and listened.

It was a port pub, and a busy one. So near the docks on the
Moray Firth, it hosted sea captains and merchants, as well as
sailors from the ships in port and longshoremen and laborers from
the nearby warehouses. A great deal of business of one kind and
another was being transacted over the beer-stained surfaces of its
many small tables.

With half an ear Roger could hear a contract being arranged for
the shipping of three hundred bolts of cheap drugget cloth from
Aberdeen, bound for the Colonies, with an exchange to be made
for a cargo of rice and indigo from the Carolinas. A hundred head
of Galloway cattle, six hundredweight of rolled copper, casks of
sulfur, molasses, and wine. Quantities and prices, delivery dates
and conditions floated through the babble and beer fumes of the
pub like the thick blue clouds of tobacco smoke that floated near
the low ceiling-beams.

Not only goods were being bargained for. In one corner sat a
ship's captain, marked by the cut of his long, full-skirted coat and
the fine black tricorne that lay on the table by his elbow. He was
attended by a clerk, a ledger and a money box on the table before
him, interviewing a steady stream of people, emigrants seeking
passage to the Colonies for themselves and their families.

Roger watched the proceedings covertly. The ship was bound
for Virginia, and after listening for some time he deduced that the
cost of passage for a male passenger—for a gentleman, that is—
was ten pounds, eight shillings. Those willing to travel in the
steerage, packed like casks and cattle in the lower holds, might
ship aboard for four pounds, two shillings each, bringing their
own food for a six-weeks voyage. Fresh water, he gathered, was
provided.

For those desiring passage but lacking funds, there were other
means available.

"Indenturement for yourself, your wife, and your two elder sons?" The captain tilted his head appraisingly, looking over the family that stood before him. A small, wiry man, who might be in his early thirties but looked much older, shabby and bowed with labor. His wife, perhaps a little younger, standing behind her husband, eyes glued to the floor, tightly grasping the hands of two little girls. One of the girls held on to her baby brother, a lad of three or four. The elder boys stood by their father, trying to look manly. Roger thought they might be ten and twelve, allowing for the puny stature caused by malnutrition.

"Yourself and the boys, aye, that'll do," the captain said. He frowned at the woman, who didn't look up. "No one will buy a woman with so many young ones—she might keep one, perhaps. You'll have to sell the girls, though."

The man glanced back at his family. His wife kept her head down, unmoving, not looking at anything. One of the girls twitched and jerked, though, complaining in an undertone that her hand was being crushed. The man turned back.

"All right," he said, low-voiced. "Can they—might they—go together?"

The captain rubbed a hand across his mouth, and nodded indifferently.

"Likely enough."

Roger didn't wait to witness the details of the transaction. He got up abruptly and left the pub; the dark beer had lost its taste.

He paused in the street outside, fingering the coins in his pocket. It was all he had been able to collect of suitable money, in the time he'd had. He had thought that it would be enough, though; he was good-sized and had a fair amount of confidence in his own abilities. Still, the little scene he had witnessed in the pub had shaken him.

He had grown up with the history of the Highlands. He knew well enough the sorts of things that drove families to such a pitch of desperation that they would accept permanent separation and semislavery as the price of survival.

He knew all about the sale of lands that forced small crofters off the lands their families had tended for hundreds of years, all about the dreadful conditions of penury and starvation in the cities, the simple insupportableness of life in Scotland in these days. And not all his years of reading and study had prepared him for the look of that woman's face, her eyes fixed on the fresh-sanded floor, her daughters' hands clutched hard in her own.

Ten pounds, eight shillings. Or four pounds, two. Plus whatever it might cost for food. He had exactly fourteen shillings, three-pence in his pocket, together with a handful of copper doits and a couple of farthings.

He walked slowly down the lane that led along the seaside, glancing at the collection of ships that lay moored by the wooden docks. Fishing ketches, for the most part, small galleys and brigs that plied their trade up and down the Firth, or at most ran across the Channel, carrying cargo and passengers to France. Only three large ships lay at anchor in the Firth, those of a size to brave the winds of the Atlantic crossing.

He could cross to France, of course, and take ship from there. Or travel overland to Edinburgh, a much larger port than Inverness. But it would be late in the year then, for sailing. Brianna was six weeks before him already; he could waste no time in finding her—God knew what could happen to a woman alone here.

Four pounds, two shillings. Well, he could work, certainly. With neither children nor wife to support, he could save most of his earnings. But given that the average clerk earned something like twelve pounds per year, and that he was much more likely to find work shoveling stables than keeping accounts, the chances of his saving up passage money in any reasonable time were fairly slim.

"First things first," he muttered. "Be sure where she's gone, before you trouble about getting there yourself."

Taking his hand out of his pocket, he turned right between two warehouses, and into a narrow lane. His high spirits of the morning had largely evaporated, but they lifted slightly, nonetheless, when he saw that he had been right in his guess; the harbormaster's office was where he had known it must be—in the same squat stone building where it still would be, two hundred years hence. Roger smiled with wry humor; Scots were not inclined to make changes purely for the sake of change.

It was crowded and busy inside, with four harried clerks behind a battered wooden counter, scribbling and stamping, carrying bundles of paper to and fro, taking money and conveying it carefully into an inner office, from which they issued moments later, bearing receipts on japanned tin trays.

A crush of impatient men pressed against the counter, each endeavoring to signal by means of voice and posture that his business was much more urgent than that of the fellow standing next him. Once Roger had succeeded in capturing the attention of one of the clerks, though, there turned out to be no great difficulty in seeing the registers of the ships that had sailed from Inverness within the last few months.

"Here, wait," he said to the young man who pushed a large, leather-bound book across the counter to him.

"Aye?" The clerk was flushed with hurry, and had a smut of ink on his nose, but paused politely, arrested in flight.

"How much d'ye get paid for working here?" Roger asked.

The clerk's fair eyebrows lifted, but he was in too much hurry either to ask questions or to take offense at the inquiry.

"Six shillings the week," he said briefly, and promptly disappeared in response to an irritable shout of "Munro!" from the office beyond the counter.

"Mmphm." Roger pushed back through the crowd and took the book of registers away to a small table by the window, out of the main stream of traffic.

Having seen the conditions under which the clerks worked, Roger was impressed at the legibility of the handwritten registers. He was well accustomed to archaic spelling and eccentric punctuation, though those he was used to seeing were always yellowed and fragile, on the verge of disintegration. It gave him an odd little historian's thrill to see the page before him fresh and white, and just beyond, the clerk who sat at a high table, copying as fast as quill could write, shoulders hunched against the hubbub in the room.

You're shilly-shallying, said a cold little voice in the middle of his brain. *She's here or she's not; being afraid to look won't change it. Get on!*

Roger took a deep breath and flipped open the big ledger book. The ships' names were neatly lettered at the tops of pages, followed by the names of their masters and mates, their main cargoes and dates of sailing. *Arianna. Polyphemus. Merry Widow. Tiburon.* Despite his apprehensions, he couldn't help admiring the names of the ships as he thumbed through the pages.

Half an hour later, he had ceased to marvel over both poetry and picturesqueness, barely noting each ship's name as he ran his finger down the pages in increasing desperation. Not here, she wasn't here!

But she had to be, he argued with himself. She *had* to have taken a ship to the Colonies, where else could she bloody be? Unless she hadn't found the notice, after all . . . but the sick feeling under his ribs assured him that she had; nothing else would have made her risk the stones.

He took a deep breath and closed his eyes, which were starting to feel the strain of the handwritten pages. Then he opened his eyes, turned back to the first relevant register, and began to read again, doggedly muttering each name beneath his breath, to be sure of not missing one out.

Mr. Phineas Forbes, gentleman.
Mrs. Wilhelmina Forbes.
Master Joshua Forbes.
Mrs. Josephine Forbes.
Mrs. Eglantine Forbes.
Mrs. Charlotte Forbes . . .

He smiled to himself at the thought of Mr. Phineas Forbes, surrounded by his womenfolk. Even knowing that "Mrs." here was sometimes merely the abbreviated form of "Mistress," and thus used for both married and unmarried women—rather than the "Miss" for little girls—he found himself with an irresistible mental picture of Phineas marching stoutly aboard at the head of a train of four wives, Master Joshua no doubt bringing up the rear.

Mr. William Talbot, merchant.
Mr. Peter Talbot, merchant.
Mr. Jonathan Bicknell, physician.
Mr. Robert MacLeod, farmer.
Mr. Gordon MacLeod, farmer.
Mr. Martin MacLeod. . . .

No Randalls this time through, either. Not for the *Persephone,* the *Queen's Revenge,* or the *Phoebe.* He rubbed his aching eyes, and began on the register of the *Phillip Alonzo.* A Spanish name, but it was listed under Scottish registry. Sailing from Inverness, under the command of Captain Patrick O'Brian.

He hadn't given up, but had already begun to think what to do next, if she should not be listed in the registers. Lallybroch, of course. He had been there once, in his own time, to the abandoned remains of the estate; could he find it now, without the guidance of roads and signposts?

His thoughts stopped with a jolt as his gliding finger came to a halt, near the bottom of a page. Not Brianna Randall, not the name he'd been looking for, but a name that rang bells of recognition in his mind. *Fraser,* read the slanted, crisp black writing. *Mr.*

Brian Fraser. No, not Brian. And not Mr., either. He bent closer, squinting at the cramped black lettering.

He closed his eyes, feeling his heart thump hard in his chest, and relief flowed through him, intoxicating as the pub's special dark beer. *Mrs.*, not Mr. And what had first seemed merely an exuberant tail on the "n" of Brian was on closer inspection almost surely instead a careless "a."

Her, it was her, it had to be! It was an unusual first name—he had seen no other Briannas or Brianas anywhere in the massive register. And even Fraser made sense, of a sort; embarked on a quixotic quest to find her father, she had taken his name, the name she was entitled to by right of birth.

He slammed the register closed, as though to keep her from escaping from the pages, and sat for a moment, breathing. Got her! He saw the fair-haired clerk eyeing him curiously from the counter and, flushing, opened the book again.

The *Phillip Alonzo.* Sailed from Inverness on the fourth of July, Anno Domini 1769. For Charleston, South Carolina.

He frowned at the name, suddenly uncertain. South Carolina. Was that her real destination, or only as close as she could get? A quick glance at the rest of the registers showed no ships in July for North Carolina. Perhaps she had simply taken the first ship for the southern colonies, intending to journey overland.

Or maybe he was wrong. A chill gripped him that had nothing to do with the river wind seeping through the cracks of the window next to him. He looked at the page again, and was reassured. No, there was no profession given, as there was for all the men. It was certainly "Mrs." and therefore it must be "Briana" as well. And if "Briana" it was, then Brianna it was, too, he knew it.

He rose and handed the book·across the counter to his fair-haired acquaintance.

"Thanks, man," he said, relaxing into his own soft accent. "Can ye be tellin' me, is there a ship in port bound for the American Colonies soon, now?"

"Oh, aye," the clerk said, deftly stowing the register with one hand and accepting a bill of lading from a customer with the other. "Happen it will be *Gloriana;* she sails day after tomorrow for the Carolinas." He looked Roger up and down. "Emigrant or seaman?" he asked.

"Seaman," Roger said promptly. Ignoring the other's raised eyebrow, he waved toward the forest of masts visible through the paned windows. "Where do I go to sign on?"

Both eyebrows high, the clerk nodded in the direction of the door.

"Her master works from the Friars when he's in port. Likely he'll be there now—Captain Bonnet." He forbore adding what was obvious from his skeptical expression; if Roger was a sea-man, he, the clerk, was an African parrot.

"Right, *mo ghille*. Thanks." Sketching a salute, Roger turned away, but turned back at the door to find the clerk still watching him, ignoring the press of impatient customers.

"Wish me luck!" Roger called, with a grin.

The clerk's answering grin was tinged with something that might have been either admiration or wistfulness.

"Luck to ye, man!" he called, and waved in farewell. By the time the door swung shut, he was deep in conversation with the next customer, quill pen poised in readiness.

He found Captain Bonnet in the pub, as advertised, settled in a corner under a thick blue haze of smoke, to which the Captain's own cigar was adding.

"Your name?"

"MacKenzie," Roger said on sudden impulse. If Brianna could do it, so could he.

"MacKenzie. Any experience, Mr. MacKenzie?"

A bar of sunlight cut across the Captain's face, making him squint. Bonnet drew back into the shadow of the settle, and the lines around his eyes relaxed, leaving Roger exposed to a gaze of uncomfortable penetration.

"It is myself has fished the herring now and then, in the Minch."

It was no lie, at that; he'd had several teenage summers as hand on a herring boat captained by an acquaintance of the Reverend's. The experience had left him with a useful layer of muscle, an ear for the singsong cadence of the Isles, and a fixed dislike of her-ring. But he knew the feel of a rope in his hands, at least.

"Ah, ye're a good-sized lad. But a fisherman will not be the same as a sailor, sure." The man's soft Irish lilt left it open whether this was question, statement—or provocation.

"I shouldna have thought it an occupation requiring great skill." For no reason he could name, Captain Bonnet raised the hairs on the back of his neck.

The green eyes sharpened.

"Perhaps more than ye think—but sure it's nothing a willing man can't learn. But what would it be, now, that makes a fellow of your sort crave the sea of a sudden?"

The eyes flickered in the tavern's shadows, taking him in. *Of your sort.* What was it? Roger wondered. Not his speech—he had taken care to suppress any hint of the Oxford scholar, by taking on the "teuchter" cant of the Isles. Was he too well dressed for a would-be sailor? Or was it the singed collar and the burn mark on the breast of his coat?

"That will be none of your business, I am thinking," he answered evenly. With a minor effort, he kept his hands relaxed at his sides.

The pale green eyes studied him dispassionately, unblinking. Like a leopard watching a passing wildebeest, Roger thought, wondering whether it would be worth the chase.

The heavy lids dropped; not worth it—for the moment.

"You'll be aboard by sundown," Bonnet said. "Five shillings the month, meat three days in the week, plum duff on Sundays. You'll have a hammock, but find your own clothes. You will be free to leave the ship once the cargo is unloaded, not until that time. We are agreed, sir?"

"It is agreed," Roger said, suddenly dry-mouthed. He would have given a lot for a pint, but not now, not here, under that pale green gaze.

"Ask for Mr. Dixon when yez come aboard. He's paymaster." Bonnet leaned back, took a small leather-bound book from his pocket and flipped it open. Audience concluded.

Roger turned smartly and went out, without a backward glance. There was a small cold spot at the base of his skull. If he looked back, he knew, he would see that lucent green gaze fixed unwaveringly over the edge of the unread book, taking note of every weakness.

The cold spot, he thought, was where the teeth would meet.

37

Gloriana

Before shipping with the *Gloriana,* Roger had assumed himself to be in reasonably good condition. In fact, compared to most of the obviously malnourished and wizened specimens of humanity who constituted the rest of the crew, he considered himself well endowed, indeed. It took precisely fourteen hours—the length of one day's work—to disabuse him of this notion.

Blisters he had bargained for, and sore muscles; heaving crates, lifting spars, and hauling ropes was familiar labor, though he hadn't done it for some time.

What he had forgotten was the bone-deep fatigue that sprang as much from the constant chill of damp clothes as from the work. He welcomed the heavy labor in the cargo hold, because it warmed him temporarily, even though he knew the warmth would be succeeded by a fine, constant shiver as soon as he emerged on deck, where the wind could resume its icy probe of his sweat-soaked clothes.

Hands roughened and scraped by wet hemp were painful, but expected; by the end of his first day, his palms were black with tar, and the skin of his fingers cracked and bled at the joints, scraped raw. But the gnawing ache of hunger had been something of a surprise. He hadn't thought it possible to be as hungry as he was.

The knobbled lump of humanity working beside him—one Duff by name—was similarly damp, but seemed unfazed by the condition. The long, pointed nose that quested, ferret-like, from the upturned collar of a ragged jacket was blue at the tip and dripped regularly as a stalactite, but the pale eyes were sharp and the mouth beneath grinned wide, displaying teeth the color of the water in the Firth.

"Take hairt, man. Grub in twa bells." Duff gave him a companionable elbow in the ribs and disappeared nimbly down a hatchway, from whose cavernous recesses echoed blasphemous shouts and loud bangings.

Roger resumed his unloading of the cargo net, heartened indeed at the prospect of supper.

The after hold had already been half filled. The water casks were loaded; tier upon tier of wooden hogsheads, squatting in the shadowy gloom, each hundred-gallon cask weighing more than seven hundred pounds. But the forward hold still gaped empty, and a constant procession of loaders and quaymen streamed like ants across the dock, piling up such a heap of boxes and barrels, rolls and bundles, that it seemed inconceivable that the mass should ever be condensed sufficiently to fit within the ship.

It took two days to finish the loading: barrels of salt, bolts of cloth, huge crates of ironmongery that had to be lowered with rope slings because of their weight. It was here that Roger's size proved of benefit. At the end of a rope belayed round the capstan, he leaned back against the weight of a crate suspended at the other end and, muscles popping with the strain, lowered it slowly enough that the two men below could catch and guide it into place in the increasingly crowded hold.

The passengers came aboard in the late afternoon, a straggling line of emigrants, burdened with bags, bundles, caged chickens, and children. These were the cargo of the steerage—a space created by erection of a bulkhead across the forward hold—and as profitable in their way as the harder goods aft.

"Bondsmen and redemptioners," Duff had told him, looking over the incomers with a practiced eye. "Worth fifteen pund each on the hoof in the plantations, weans three or four. Bairns at the teat go free wi' their mithers."

The seaman coughed, a deep, rattling noise like an ancient motor starting up, and hawked a glob of phlegm, narrowly missing the side rail as he spat. He shook his head as he looked the shuffling line over.

"Happen some can pay their way, but no many in this lot. They'll have had a job to come up wi' twa pund a family for their feed on the voyage."

"The Captain doesn't feed them, then?"

"Oh, aye." Duff rumbled in his chest again, coughed and spat. "For a price." He grinned at Roger, wiped his mouth, and jerked his head toward the gangplank. "Go and lend a hand, laddie. We wouldna want the Captain's profit to be fallin' intae the water, now, would we?"

Surprised by the padded feel of a little girl as he swung her aboard, Roger looked closer and saw that the stout build of many of the women was illusion, occasioned by their wearing several layers of clothes; all they owned in the world, apparently, beyond small bundles of personal possessions, boxes of food put by for the journey—and the scrawny children for whose sake they took this desperate step.

Roger squatted, smiling at a reluctant toddler who clung to his mother's skirts. He was no more than two, still in smocks, with a riot of soft blond curls, his fat little mouth drawn down in fearful disapproval of everything around him.

"Come on, man," Roger said softly, putting out a hand in invitation. It was no longer an effort to control his accent; his usual clipped Oxbridge had elided to the gentler Highland speech with which he had grown up, and he used it now without conscious thought. "Your Mam can't be pickin' ye up now; you come with me."

Grossly mistrustful, the boy snuffled and glowered at him, but suffered him to peel the grubby little fingers away from his mother's skirts. Roger carried the little boy across the deck, the woman following him silently. She looked up at him as he handed her down the ladder, her eyes fixed on his; her face disappeared in the darkness like a white rock dropped down a well, and he turned away with a feeling of unease, as though he had abandoned someone to drowning.

As he turned back to his work, he saw a young woman, just coming down above the quay. She was the sort of girl called "bonny"—not beautiful, but lively and nicely made, with something about her that took the eye.

Perhaps it was only her posture; straight as a lily stem among the hunched and drooping backs around her. Or her face, which showed apprehension and uncertainty, but had still about it the brightness of curiosity. A darer, that one, he thought, and his heart—oppressed by so many downcast faces among the emigrants—lightened at the sight of her.

She hesitated at sight of the ship and the crowd around it. A tall fair-haired young man was with her, a baby in his arms. He touched her shoulder in reassurance, and she glanced up at him, an answering smile lighting her face like the striking of a match.

Watching them, Roger felt a mild pang of something that might have been envy.

"You, MacKenzie!" The bosun's shout pulled him from his contemplation. The bosun jerked his head aft. "There's cargo a-waitin'—it's no goin' to walk aboard by itself!"

Once embarked and under sail, the voyage went smoothly for some weeks. The stormy weather that accompanied their exodus from Scotland quickly diminished into good winds and rolling seas, and while the immediate effect of this on the passengers was to make the majority of them seasick, this ailment also faded in time. The smell of vomit from the steerage subsided, becoming only a minor note in the symphony of stinks aboard the *Gloriana*.

Roger had been born with an acute sense of smell, an attribute he was finding a marked liability in close quarters. Still, even the keenest nose grew accustomed in time, and within a day or so he had ceased to note any but the most novel stenches.

He was fortunately not subject to seasickness himself, though his experiences with the herring fishers had been enough to give him a keen appreciation of the weather, with the sailor's unsettling knowledge that his life might depend on whether the sun was shining that day.

His new shipmates were not friendly, but neither were they hostile. Whether it was his "teuchter" accent from the Isles—for most of the *Gloriana*'s hands were English-speakers from Dingwall or Peterhead—the occasional odd things that he said, or simply his size, they regarded him with a certain watchful distance. No overt antagonism—his size prevented that—but distance nonetheless.

Roger wasn't disturbed by the coolness. He was pleased enough to be left to his thoughts, his mind ranging free while his body dealt with the daily round of shipboard duties. There was plenty to think about.

He had taken no heed to the reputation of the *Gloriana* or her captain before signing on; he would have sailed with Captain Ahab, provided only that that gentleman was bound for North Carolina. Still, from the talk he heard among the crew, he gathered that Stephen Bonnet was known as a good captain; hard but fair, and a man whose voyages always turned a profit. To the seamen, many of whom sailed on shares rather than wages, this latter quality plainly more than compensated for any small defects of character or address.

Not that Roger had seen open evidence of such defects. But he did see that Bonnet stood always as though an invisible circle had been drawn around him, a circle that few were bold enough to enter. Only the first mate and the bosun spoke directly to the Captain; the crewmen kept their heads down as he passed. Roger remembered the cool green leopard-eyes that had looked him over; little wonder that no one wanted to attract their notice.

He was more interested in the passengers, though, than in either crew or captain. Little was seen of them normally, but they were allowed on deck briefly twice each day, to take a bit of air, to empty their slop jars over the side—for the ship's heads were woefully inadequate for so many—and to carry down again the small amounts of water carefully rationed to each family. Roger looked forward to these brief appearances, and tried to see to it that he was employed as often as possible near the end of the deck where they took their fleeting exercise.

His interest was both professional and personal; his historian's instincts were roused by their presence, and his loneliness soothed by the homeliness of their talk. Here were the seeds of the new country, the legacy of the old. What these poor emigrants knew and valued, was what would endure to be passed on.

If one were handpicking the repository of Scottish culture, he thought, it might not contain such things as the recipe for warts about which an elderly woman was berating her long-suffering daughter-in-law ("I did tell ye, Katie Mac, and why ye chose tae leave my nice dried toadie behind, when ye could find room to bring all yon rubbish that we be squattin' on and pickin' oot from under our hurdies day and night . . ."), but that would last too, right along with the folksongs and prayers, with the woven wool and the Celtic patterns of their art.

He glanced at his own hand; he vividly remembered Mrs. Graham rubbing a large wart on his third finger with what she *said* was a dried toad. He grinned, rubbing a thumb across the spot. Must have worked; he'd never had another.

"Sir," said a small voice by his side. "Sir, may we go and touch the iron?"

He glanced down and smiled at the tiny girl, holding two tinier brothers by their hands.

"Aye, *a leannan,*" he said. "Get on; yourself will be minding the men, though."

She nodded and the three of them pattered off, looking anxiously up and down to be sure they were not in the way, before
scrambling up to touch the horseshoe nailed to the mast for luck.
Iron was protection and healing; the mothers often sent the little
ones who were ailing to touch it.

They could have used iron to better effect internally, Roger
thought, seeing the rash on the pasty white faces, and hearing the
high-pitched complaints of itching boils, of loose teeth and fever.
He resumed his job, measuring out water by the dipperful into the
buckets and dishes the emigrants held out to him. They were
living on oatmeal, the lot of them—that, with dried peas now and
then and a bit of hard biscuit, was the sum total of the "provisions" supplied them for the voyage.

At that, he'd heard no complaint; the water was clean, the biscuit was not moldy, and if the allowance of "corn" was not
generous, neither was it niggardly. The crew was fed better, but
still on meat and starch, with only the occasional onion for relief.
He ran his tongue round his teeth, testing, as he did every few
days. The faint taste of iron was nearly always in his mouth now;
his gums were beginning to bleed from the lack of fresh vegetables.

Still, his teeth were strongly rooted, and he had no sign of the
swollen joints or bruised nails that several of the other crewmen
showed. He'd looked it up, during his weeks of waiting; a normal
adult male in good health should be able to endure from three to
six months of prolonged vitamin deficiency before suffering any
real symptoms. If the good weather held, they'd be across in only
two.

"It will be good weather tomorrow, aye?" His attention recalled by this apparent reading of his thoughts, he looked down to
find that it was the bonny brown-haired girl he'd admired on the
quay in Inverness. Morag, her friends called her.

"I am hoping it may be," he said, taking her bucket with an
answering smile. "Why do ye say so?"

She nodded, pointing over his shoulder with a small sharp chin.
"There's the new moon in the arms o' the old; if that means fine
weather on the land, I should think it is the same on the sea, no?"

He glanced back to see the pale clean curve of a silver moon,
holding a glowing orb in its cup. It rode high and perfect in an
endless evening sky of pale violet, its reflection swallowed by the
indigo sea.

"Dinna be wasting time chattering, lass—go on and ask him!"

He turned back in time to hear this hissed over Morag's shoulder by the middle-aged woman behind her. Morag glared back.

"Will ye hush?" she hissed back. "I'll not, I said I won't!"

"Ye're a stubborn lass, Morag," the older woman declared, stepping boldly forward, "and if ye willna be asking for yourself, I shall do it for ye!"

The good-lady laid a broad hand on Roger's arm and gave him a charming smile.

"And what might your name be, lad?"

"MacKenzie, ma'am," Roger said respectfully, holding back a smile.

"Ah, MacKenzie, is it! Well, there, ye see, Morag, and belike he'll be some kinsman of your man's, and happy to do ye a service, at that!" The woman turned triumphantly to the girl, then swung back to let Roger have the full force of her personality.

"She's suckling a wean, and dyin' o' thirst in the doin' of it. A woman needs to drink when she's giving suck, or her milk dries; everyone kens that weel enough. But the silly lass cannae bring herself to ask ye for a bittie more water. There's nane here grudge it to her—is there?" she demanded rhetorically, turning round to glare at the other women in line. Not surprisingly, all the heads shook back and forth like clockwork toys.

It was getting dark, but Morag's face was visibly pink. Lips pressed tight together, she accepted the brimming bucket of water with a brief bob of her head.

"I thank ye, Mr. MacKenzie," she murmured. She didn't look up until she had reached the hatchway—but then she stopped, and looked back over her shoulder at him, with a smile of such gratitude that he felt himself grow warm, in spite of the sharp evening wind that blew through his shirt and jacket.

He was sorry to see the water line finish and the emigrants go below, the hatch battened down over them for the night watches. He knew they told stories and sang songs to pass the time, and would have given much to hear them. Not only from curiosity, but from longing—what moved him was neither pity for their poverty nor thought of their uncertain future; it was envy of the sense of connection among them.

But the Captain, the crew, the passengers, even the all-important weather, occupied no more than a fragment of Roger's thoughts. What he thought about, day and night, wet or dry, hungry or fed, was Brianna.

He went down to the mess when the signal came for supper,

and ate without much noticing the contents of his trencher. His was the second watch; he went to his hammock after eating, choosing solitude and rest over the possibility of companionship on the forecastle.

Solitude was an illusion, of course. Swinging gently in his hammock, he could feel each twitch and turn of the man next to him, the sweating heat of sleeping flesh clammy against his own through the thick cotton mesh. Each man had eighteen inches of sleeping space to call his own, and Roger was uncomfortably aware that when he lay upon his back, his shoulders exceeded that allowance by a good two inches on either side.

After two nights of sleep interrupted by the bumps and muttered insults of his shipmates, he had swapped places and ended in the space next the bulkhead, where he would have only one companion to discommode. He learned to lie on one side, his face an inch or two from the wooden partition, back turned to his companions, and tune his ears to the sounds of the ship, blocking out the noises of the men around him.

A very musical thing was a ship—lines and hawsers singing in the wind, the timber knees creaking with each rise and fall, the faint thumps and murmurs on the far side of the bulkhead, in the dark recesses of the passengers' hold in the steerage. He stared at the dark wood, lit by the shadows of the swinging lantern overhead, and began to re-create her, the lines of face and hair and body all vivid in the dark. Too vivid.

He could conjure her face without difficulty. What lay behind it was a good deal harder.

Rest was also an illusion. When she had gone through the stones, she had taken with her all peace of mind. He lived in a mixture of fear and anger, spiced with the hurt of betrayal, rubbed like pepper into the wounds. The same questions ran round and round inside his mind without answers, a snake chasing its tail.

Why had she gone?
What was she doing?
Why didn't she tell him?

It was the effort to come up with an answer to the first of these that kept him going over and over it, as though the answer might afford him the key to the whole mystery of Brianna.

Yeah, he'd been lonely. Knew bloody well what it felt like to have no one in the world who belonged to you, or you to them. But surely that was one reason why they had reached out to each other—he and Brianna.

Claire knew, too, he thought suddenly. She'd been orphaned, lost her uncle—of course, she'd been married then. But she'd been separated from her husband during the war . . . yes, she knew a lot about being alone. And that was why she'd taken care not to leave Bree alone, to assure herself that her daughter was loved.

Well, he'd tried to love her properly—was still trying, he thought grimly, twisting uncomfortably in his hammock. During the day, the demands of work suppressed the growing needs of his body. At night, though . . . she was a deal too vivid, the Brianna of his memory.

He hadn't hesitated; he'd known from the first moment of realization that he must follow her. Sometimes, though, he was not sure whether he had come to save her or to savage her—anything, so long as it was settled once and for all between them. He'd said he'd wait—but he'd waited long enough.

The worst of it was not the loneliness, he thought, flinging restlessly over again, but the doubt. Doubt of her feelings, and of his. Panic that he did not truly know her.

For the first time since his passage through the stones, he realized what she had meant in refusing him, and knew her hesitance for wisdom. But *was* it wisdom, and not only fear?

If she had not gone through the stones—would she have turned to him at last, wholeheartedly? Or turned away, always looking for something else?

It was a leap of faith—to throw one's heart across a gulf, and trust another to catch it. His own was still in flight across the void, with no certainty of landing. But still in flight.

The sounds on the other side of the bulkhead had faded to silence, but now they started up again, in a stealthy, rhythmic fashion with which he was thoroughly familiar. They were at it again, whoever they were.

They did it almost every night, when the others had gone to sleep. At first the sounds had made him feel only his isolation, alone with the burning ghost of Brianna. There seemed no possibility of true human warmth, no joining of heart or mind, no more than the animal consolation of a body to cling to in the dark. Was there really any more for a man than this?

But then he began to hear something else in the sounds, half-caught words of tenderness, small furtive sounds of affirmation, that made him in some way not a voyeur, but a participant in their joining.

He couldn't tell, of course. It might have been any of the couples, or a random pairing of lust—and yet he put faces to them, this unknown pair; in his mind, he saw the tall, fair-haired young man, the brown-haired lass with the open face, saw them look at each other as they had on the quay, and would have sold his soul to know such certainty.

38

For Those in Peril on the Sea

A sudden hard squall kept the passengers belowdecks for three days, and the sailors at their posts with no more than scant minutes snatched for rest or food. At the end of it, when the *Gloriana* rode high on the dying storm-swell and the dawn sky was filled with racing mare's-tails, Roger staggered down to his hammock, too exhausted even to shuck his wet clothes.

Crumpled, damp, crusted with salt and feeling fit for nothing but a hot bath and another week's sleep, he answered the bosun's whistle for the afternoon watch after four hours rest, and staggered through his duties.

He was so tired by sunset that his muscles quivered as he helped to heave up a fresh water barrel from the hold. He caved in the top with a hatchet, thinking that he might just manage the exertion of ladling out water rations without falling headfirst into the barrel. Then again, he might not. He splashed a cool handful of the fresh water into his face, in hopes of soothing his burning eyes, and gulped down a whole dipperful, ignoring for once the strictures imposed by that constant contradiction of the sea—always both too much water, and too little.

The folk bringing up their jars and buckets to be filled looked as though they felt even worse than he did; green-gilled as mushrooms, bruised from being pitched to and fro in the hold like billiard balls, reeking of renewed seasickness and overflowing chamber pots.

In marked contrast to the general air of pallid malaise, one of his old acquaintances was skipping in rings around him, singing in a monotonous chant that grated on his ears.

> *"Seven herrings are a salmon's fill,*
> *Seven salmon are a seal's fill,*

Seven seals are a whale's fill,
And seven whales the fill of a Cirein Croin!"

Bubbling with the freedom of release from the hold, the little girl hopped around like a demented chickadee, making Roger smile in spite of his tiredness. She hopped to the rail, then stood on tiptoe, and peeked cautiously over.

"D'ye think 'twas a Cirein Croin caused the storming, Mr. MacKenzie? Grandda says it was, like enough. They lash their great huge tails about, ye ken," she informed him. "That's what makes the waves go sae big."

"I shouldna be thinking such a thing, myself. Where's your brothers, then, *a leannan*?"

"Fevered," the girl answered, indifferently. It was nothing out of the way; half the emigrants in line were coughing and sneezing, three days in darkness and damp clothes having done nothing for their precarious state of health.

"Have ye seen a Cirein Croin, then?" she asked, leaning far over the rail, a hand shading her eyes. "Are they really big enough to swallow the boat?"

"Myself has not seen one." Roger dropped his dipper and grabbed her by the apron sash, pulling her firmly off the rail. "Have a care, aye? It would take no more than a spratling to swallow *you*, lassie!"

"Look!" she shrieked, leaning farther over in spite of his grasp. "Look, it is, it *is*!"

Drawn as much by the terror in her voice as what she said, Roger leaned over the rail involuntarily. A dark shape hovered just below the surface, smooth and black, graceful as a bullet—and half the length of the ship. It kept pace for a few moments with the racing vessel, then was outdistanced and left behind.

"Shark," Roger said, shaken in spite of himself. He gave the girl a small shake, to stop her steam-whistle screeches. "It's no but a shark, hear? Ye ken what's a shark, do ye not? We ate one, only last week!"

She had quit shrieking, but was still white-faced and wide-eyed, tender mouth quivering.

"You're sure?" she said. "It—it wasna a Cirein Croin?"

"No," Roger said gently, and gave her a dipper of water to drink, by herself. "Only a shark." The biggest shark he had ever seen, with an air of blind ferocity that raised the hair on his forearms to see—but only a shark. They hung about the ship whenever her speed slowed, eager for the garbage and slops tossed overboard.

"Isobeàil!" An indignant cry summoned his erstwhile companion to come and lend a hand with the family chores. With dragging step and out-thrust lip, Isobeàil slouched off to help her mother with the water buckets, leaving Roger to finish his job without further distraction.

No further distraction than his thoughts, at least. For the most part, he succeeded in forgetting that the *Gloriana* had nothing below her save leagues of empty water; that the ship was not, in fact, the small and solid island that it seemed, but instead no more than a fragile shell, at the mercy of forces that could crush her in moments—and everyone aboard.

Had the *Phillip Alonzo* reached port in safety? he wondered. Ships did sink, and fairly often; he'd read enough accounts of it. Having lived through the last three days, he could only be amazed that more of them *didn't* sink. Well, and there was precisely nothing he could do about that prospect, except pray.

For those in peril on the deep, Lord, have mercy.

With sudden vividness, he understood exactly what the maker of that line had meant.

Finished, he dropped the dipper into the barrel and reached for a board to cover the open top; rats tended to fall in and drown otherwise. One of the women clutched him by the arm as he turned away. She gestured at the little boy she held, fussing against his mother's neck.

"Mr. MacKenzie, might the Captain gie us a wee rub wi' his ring? Our Gibbie has a touch o' sore eyes from bein' in the dark sae long."

Roger hesitated, but then ridiculed himself. He, like the rest of the crew, tended to steer clear of Bonnet, but there was no reason to refuse the woman's request; the Captain had obliged before with a rub of his gold ring, this being a popular remedy for sore eyes and inflammations.

"Yeah, sure," he said, forgetting himself for a moment. "Come on." The woman blinked in surprise, but followed him obediently. The Captain was on his quarterdeck, engaged in close conversation with the mate; Roger motioned to the woman to wait for a bit, and she nodded, shrinking modestly behind him.

The Captain looked as tired as any of them, the lines of dissipation carved deeper in his face. Lucifer after a week of running Hell, and finding it no picnic, Roger thought, sourly amused.

". . . damage to the tea chests?" Bonnet was saying to the mate.

"Only two, and not soaked through," Dixon replied. "We can salvage a bit; maybe get rid of it upriver in Cross Creek."

"Aye, they're more particular in Edenton and New Bern. We'll get the best prices there, though; we'll get rid of what we can before we go to Wilmington."

Bonnet turned slightly and caught sight of Roger. His expression hardened, but relaxed again when he heard the request. Without comment, he reached down and rubbed the gold ring he wore on his little finger gently over little Gilbert's closed eyes. A plain wide band, Roger saw; it almost looked like a wedding ring, though smaller—a woman's ring, maybe. The formidable Bonnet with a love token? Could be, Roger supposed; some women might find the Captain's air of subdued violence attractive.

"The wean's ailing," Dixon remarked. He pointed, there was a prickle of red bumps behind the boy's ears, and his pale cheeks bloomed with fever.

"No but milk fever," the woman said, pulling her child defensively against her bosom. "He's a new tooth coming, likely."

The Captain nodded indifferently and turned away. Roger escorted the woman to the galley to beg a bit of hard biscuit for the child to gnaw on, then sent her back to the forward hold with the others.

He had little thought for Gilbert's gums, though; as he climbed the ladderway to the deck, his mind was occupied by the conversation he had overheard.

Stops in New Bern and Edenton, before Wilmington. And plainly Bonnet was in no rush; he'd be looking for good prices for his cargo, and taking the time to broker the indentures of his passengers—Christ, it could be weeks before they made Wilmington!

It wouldn't do, Roger thought. God knew where Brianna could get to—or what sort of thing happen to her. The *Gloriana* had made swift passage, in spite of the squall—God willing, they'd make North Carolina in only eight weeks, if the winds held. He didn't want to sacrifice the valuable time so gained to lallygagging in the northern Carolina ports, mooching their way south.

He'd be off the *Gloriana* in the first port they touched, he resolved, and make his way south as best he could. True, he'd given his word to stay with the ship until the cargo was disposed of, but then, he wouldn't be taking his wages, either, so the exchange seemed fair enough.

The fresh cold air above decks did a little bit to rouse him. His head still felt stuffed with damp cotton wool, though, and the back of his throat was raspy with salt. Three hours more to go on his watch; he made his way forward for another dipper of water, hoping it would help him stay on his feet.

Dixon had left the Captain, and was strolling through the clusters of passengers, nodding to the men, stopping to say something to a woman with children. Odd, Roger thought. The mate wasn't a sociable man with the crew, let alone with the passengers, whom he regarded as nothing more than an unusually inconvenient form of cargo.

Something stirred in his mind at the mention of cargo, something uncomfortable, but he couldn't bring it to the forefront of recognition. It hung in the shadows of exhaustion, just out of sight, nearly close enough to smell. Yes, that was it, it had to do with a smell. But what—

"MacKenzie!" One of the seamen was calling from the afterdeck, waving for him to come and help with the mending of sails torn by the storm; huge stacks of folded canvas lay like dirty snowdrifts on the boards, their upper layers billowing in the wind.

Roger groaned, and stretched his aching muscles. No matter what happened in North Carolina, he would be very glad to get off this ship.

Two nights later, Roger was deep in dreams when the shouting roused him. His feet hit the deck and he was running for the companionway, heart pumping at full bore, before his mind had grasped the fact that he was awake. He sprang for the ladder, only to be knocked sprawling by a blow to his chest.

"Stay where ye are, fool!" Dixon's voice growled from the rungs above. He could see the mate's head, outlined against the starry square of the hatchway overhead.

"What is it? What's happening?" He shook off the confusion of his dreams, to find no less confusion in the waking.

There were others in the dark near him, he could feel bodies stumble over him as he struggled to his feet. All the noise was up above, though; a thunder of feet on the deck and a shouting and shrieking like nothing he had ever heard.

"Murderers!" A woman's voice cut through the racket, shrill

as a fife. "Wicked *mur*—" The voice cut off abruptly, with a heavy thump on the deck above.

"What is it?" On his feet again, Roger shoved his way through the men by the ladder, shouting up to Dixon, "What? Are we boarded?" His words were drowned by the shouting above; the steam-whistle shrieks of women and children, cutting through men's bellowing and curses.

Red light flickered somewhere above. Was the ship afire? He shoved through the press of men and grabbed the ladder, reached up and seized Dixon's foot.

"Gerrof!" The foot jerked free, aimed a kick at his head. "Stay down there! Christ, man, ye want to catch pox?"

"Pox? What the *hell* is going on up there?" Eyes accustomed to the dark by now, Roger grabbed the stabbing foot and gave it a vicious twist, jerked downward. Unprepared for assault, Dixon lost his grip on the ladder and fell heavily, sliding over Roger's head and into the men below.

Roger ignored the cries of rage and surprise behind him and clambered out onto the deck. There was a group of men clustered thick about the forward hatchway. Lanterns hung above in the rigging, shooting beams of red and white and yellow light that caught the gleam of blades.

He looked quickly for another ship, but the ocean was black and empty on all sides. No boarders, no pirates; all the struggle was taking place near the hatchway, where half the crew was gathered in a knot, armed with knives and clubs.

Mutiny? he thought, and dismissed it, even as he pushed forward; Bonnet's head showed above the crowd, hatless, fair hair gleaming in the flash of lantern light. Roger shoved his way into the mob, ruthlessly shouldering smaller seamen aside.

Shrieks and shouts echoed from the hold, and a flicker of light showed below. A bundle of rags was handed up, passed rapidly from hand to hand, disappeared behind the shifting mass of limbs and clubs. There was a heavy splash to port, and then another.

"What is it, what's happening?" He bellowed in the ear of the bosun, who stood near the hatchway, holding a lantern. The man jerked round and glared at him.

"You've not had pox, have you? Get below!" Hutchinson's attention had already gone back to the open hatchway.

"Yes, I have! What's that got to—"

The bosun swung back, surprised.

"You've had pox? You're not marked. Ach, let it go—get you down, then, we need all hands!"

"For what?" Roger leaned forward, to make himself heard above the noise from below.

"Smallpox!" the bosun bellowed back. He gestured at the open hatchway, as one of the seamen appeared at the top of the ladder, a child under one arm, feebly kicking. Hands clawed and beat at the man's hunched back, and a woman's voice rose high above the other noises, shrill with terror.

She got a grip on the seaman's blouse, and as Roger watched, she began to climb the man's body, dragging him backward as she struggled to reach the child, screaming as she clawed the man's back, digging handfuls of cloth and flesh.

The man roared and swatted at her, trying to dislodge her. The ladder was fixed, but the seaman, one-handed and pulled off balance, swayed wildly, his look of rage turning to alarm as his feet slipped on the rung.

Reflex alone made Roger lunge forward, grabbing the child like a rugger ball as the seaman threw his arms out in a last effort to save himself. Entangled like lovers, man and woman fell backward together into the open maw of the hatchway. There was a crash and more screams from below, then the sudden, momentary silence of shock. Then the outcries began again, below, and a muttering babble around him.

Roger righted the child, trying to stop its whimpering with awkward pats. It seemed curiously loose-jointed in his arms, and it felt hot, even through its layers of clothes. Light flashed over Roger as the bosun lifted his lantern high, looking at the child with distaste.

"Hope you *have* had the pox, MacKenzie," he said.

It was wee Gilbert, the lad with sore eyes—but two days had made such a change that Roger scarcely recognized him. The boy was thin as a wraith, the round face gone so thin that the skullbones showed. The fair, dirt-smudged skin had gone, too, submerged under a mass of suppurating pustules so thick that the eyes were mere slits in the lolling head.

He had barely time to register the sight before hands plucked the small, burning body from him. Before he could grasp the sudden emptiness in his arms, there was another splash to port.

He swung toward the rail in vain reflex, hands curled in fists of shock, but then turned back as a new roar came from the hatchway behind.

The passengers had recovered from the surprise of the attack. A rush of men boiled up the ladder, armed with anything they could seize, and fell upon the seamen at the top, bearing them down with sheer frenzy.

Someone cannoned into Roger and he fell, rolling to the side as a stool leg thudded into the deck near his head. He got to his hands and knees, was kicked in the ribs, shied and was pushed, heaved back against obstruction, and with a moment's opportunity, threw himself blindly at a pair of legs, having no idea whether he fought crew or passengers, fighting only for room to stand up and breathe.

The stink of sickness rolled out of the hold, a sweet, rotting smell that overlaid the usual harsh reek of ripe bodies and sewage. The lanterns swung with the wind, and light and shadow cut the scene to pieces, so that here showed a face, wild-eyed and shouting, there an arm upraised, here a naked foot, only to vanish in the darkness and be replaced at once by elbows and knives and thrusting knees, so the deck seemed awash in dismembered bodies.

So strong was the confusion that Roger felt dismembered himself; he glanced down, feeling numbness in his left arm, half expecting to find the limb struck off. It was there, though, and he raised it by reflex, fending off an unseen blow that jarred through bone.

Someone grasped his hair; he jerked free and swung round, elbowed someone hard in the ribs and swung again, hitting air. He found himself momentarily standing clear of the fight, gasping for breath. Two figures crouched before him, in the shadow of the rail; as he shook his head to clear it, the taller stood up and launched itself at him.

He reeled backward under the impact, clutching his attacker. They struck the foremast and fell together, then rolled over and over, hammering each other in blind earnest. Caught in the web of noise and blows, he paid no mind to the disjointed words that panted in his ear.

Then a boot struck him, and another, and as he loosed his hold on his opponent, two crewmen kicked them apart. Someone seized the other man and pulled him upright, and Roger saw the flash of the bosun's lantern held high, revealing the face of the tall fair-haired passenger—Morag MacKenzie's husband, green eyes dark and wild with fury.

MacKenzie was the worse for wear—so was Roger, as he discovered when he passed a hand across his face and felt his split lip—but his skin was clear of pustules.

"Good enough," said Hutchinson briefly, and the man was thrust unceremoniously toward the hatchway.

His comrades gave Roger a rough hand up, and then left him swaying, dazed and ignored, as they finished their work. The resistance had been short-lived; though armed with the fury of despair, the passengers were weakened by six weeks under hatches, by sickness and scanty food. The stronger had been clubbed into submission, the weaker forced back, and those sick of pox—

Roger looked out at the rail and the path of the moon's aisle, serene on the water. He grabbed the rail and vomited, retching till no more than bile came up, burning the back of nose and throat. The water below was black, and empty.

Drained and shaking from exertion, he made his way slowly across the deck. Those seamen he passed were silent, but from the battened forward hatchway, a single thin wail rose up, and up, an endless keen that drew no breath and knew no respite.

He nearly fell down the companionway into the crew's quarters, went to his hammock, ignoring all questions, and wrapped his blanket over his head, trying to shut out the sound of the wailing —to shut out everything.

But there was no oblivion to be found in the suffocating woolen folds, and he jerked the blanket off, heart pounding, with a sensation of drowning so strong in his chest that he gulped air, again and again until he felt dizzy, and still breathed deep, as though he must breathe for those who could not.

"It's for the best, lad," Hutchinson had said to him with gruff sympathy, passing by as he puked his guts out over the rail. "Pox spreads like wildfire; none in that hold would live to make landfall, did we not take out the sick."

And was this better than the slower death of scabs and fever? Not for those left behind; the wail went on and on, lancing the silence, piercing wood and heart alike.

Maimed pictures flashed in his mind, truncated scenes caught by the popping of invisible flashbulbs: the sailor's contorted face as he fell into the hold; the little boy's half-open mouth, the inside scabbed with pustules. Bonnet standing above the fray, with his face of a fallen angel, watching. And the dark hungry water, empty under the moon.

Something bumped softly, sliding past the hull, and he rolled into a shivering ball, oblivious alike to the sweltering heat in the hold, and the sleepy complaint of the man next to him. No, not empty. He had heard the seamen say that sharks never sleep.

"Oh, God," he said aloud. "Oh, God!" He should have been praying for the dead, but could not.

He rolled again, squirming, trying to escape, and in the echo of the futile prayer found memory—the misplaced hearing of those few frantic words, panted in his ear during those moments of unthinking frenzy.

For the love of God, man, the fair-haired man had said. *For the love of God, let her go!*

He straightened and lay stiff, bathed in cold sweat.

Two figures in the shadow. And the open hatchway to the stores hold some twenty feet away.

"Oh, God," he said again, but this time, it *was* a prayer.

It was the middle of the dogwatch next day before Roger found an opportunity to go down to the hold. He made no effort to avoid being seen; watching his shipmates had taught him quickly that in close quarters, nothing drew attention faster than furtiveness.

If anyone asked, he had heard a bumping noise, and thought perhaps the load had shifted. Close enough to the truth, at that.

He hung from the edge of the hatch by his hands; less chance of being followed if he didn't put down the ladder. He dropped into the dark and landed hard, jarring his bones. Anyone down here would have heard that—and by the same token, if anyone followed him, he would be warned.

He took a moment to recover from the shock of landing, then began to move cautiously through the looming dim bulks of the stacked cargo. Everything seemed blurred round the edges. It wasn't only the faint light, he thought; everything in the hold was vibrating very slightly, thrumming to the shiver of the hull beneath. He could hear it, if he listened closely; the lowest note in the ship's song.

Through the narrow aisles between the ranks of crates, past the huge bellies of the serried water casks. He breathed in; the air was full of the smell of wet wood, overlaid by the faint perfume of tea. There were rustlings and creakings, plenty of odd noises—but no sign of any human presence. Still, he was sure that someone was here.

And why are you *here, mate?* he thought. What if one of the steerage passengers *had* taken refuge here? If someone lay hidden here, chances were good that they had the pox; Roger could do nothing for them—why bother to look?

Because he couldn't not look, was the answer. He didn't reproach himself for failing to save the pox-stricken passengers; nothing could have helped them in any case, and perhaps a quick death by drowning was not in fact more terrible than the slow agony of the disease. He'd like to believe that.

But he hadn't slept; the events of the night filled him with such a sense of horror and sick futility that he could find no rest. Whether he could do anything now, or not, he must do *something*. He had to look.

Something small moved in the deep shadows of the hold. *Rat*, he thought, and turned reflexively to stamp on it. The movement saved him; a heavy object whizzed past his head and landed with a splash in the bilges below.

He put his head down and lunged in the direction of the movement, shoulders hunched against an expected blow. There was nowhere to run, and not much place to hide. He saw it again, lunged, and grabbed cloth. Jerked hard, and got flesh. A quick scuffle in the dark, and a cry of alarm, and he found himself pressing a body hard against a bulkhead, clutching the skinny wrist of Morag MacKenzie.

"What the *hell*?" She kicked at him, and tried to bite, but he ignored this. He got a good grip on the scruff of her neck and hauled her out of the shadows, into the dim brown light of the hold. "What are you doing here?"

"Nothing! Let go! Let me go, please! Please, I beg ye, sir—" Force not availing to free herself—she weighed perhaps half what he did—she turned to pleading, words pouring out in a half-whispered stream of desperation. "For the sake of your own mother, sir! Ye canna do it, please ye cannot let them kill him *please*!"

"I'm not going to kill anyone. For God's sake, hush yourself!" he said, and gave her a small shake.

From the blackest shadows behind the anchor chain came the high, thin wail of a fretful baby.

She gave a small gasp and looked up at him, frantic.

"They'll hear him! God, man, let me go to him!" Such was her desperation that she succeeded in wrenching herself free, and fled toward the sound, clambering over the great rusted links of the anchor chain, heedless of filth.

He followed, more slowly; she couldn't get away—there was nowhere for her to go. He found them in the darkest spot, crouched against one of the ship's knees, the huge angled timbers that framed the hull. There was barely a foot of clearance between the rough wood of the hull and the piled mass of the anchor chain; she was no more than a darker blot on the stygian blackness.

"I will not hurt you," he said softly. The shadow seemed to shrink away from him, but she didn't answer.

His eyes were slowly growing accustomed to the dark; even back here, a faint light seeped through from the distant hatch. A patch of white—her breast was bared, giving suck to the child. He could hear the small wet noises as it fed.

"What the hell are you doing here?" he asked, though he knew well enough. His stomach clenched tight, and not just because of the foul smell of the bilges. He squatted next to her, barely able to fit in the tiny space.

"I'm hiding!" she said fiercely. "Surely to goodness ye see that?"

"Is the child sick?"

"No!" She hunched herself over the baby, squirming as far away from him as she could get.

"Then—"

"It's no but a wee rash! All bairns get them, my mither said so!" He could hear the fear in her voice, underneath the furious denial.

"Are you sure?" he said, as gently as he could. He reached a tentative hand toward the dark blotch she held.

She struck at him, awkwardly one-handed, and he jerked back with a hiss of pain.

"Jesus! Ye stabbed me!"

"Stay back! I've my husband's dirk," she warned. "I won't let ye take him, I'll kill ye first, I swear I will!"

He believed her. Hand to his mouth, he could taste his own blood, sweet and salt on his tongue. It was no more than a scratch, but he believed her. She'd kill him—or die herself, which was a great deal more likely if one of the crew found her.

But no, he thought. She was worth money. Bonnet wouldn't kill her—only have her dragged on deck and forced to watch as her child was torn out of her arms and thrown into the sea. He remembered the dark shadows that dogged the ship, and shuddered with a cold that had nothing to do with the dank surroundings.

"I won't take him. But if it's the pox—"

"It's not! I swear to Bride, it's not!" A small hand shot out of the shadows and gripped him by the sleeve. "It's as I tell ye, it's no but a milk rash, I've seen it, man—a hundred times before! I'm the eldest o' nine, I ken weel enough when a bairn's sick and when he's but teething!''

He hesitated, then made up his mind abruptly. If she was wrong, and the child had smallpox, she was likely already infected; to return her to the hold would be only to spread the disease. And if she was right—he knew as well as she that it didn't matter; any rash would condemn the child on sight.

He could feel her quivering, on the brink of hysteria. He wanted to touch her in reassurance, but thought better of it. She wouldn't trust him, and no wonder.

"I won't give you away," he whispered.

He was met by suspicious silence.

"You need food, don't you? And fresh water. You'll have no milk soon, without it, and then what of the bairn?"

He could hear her breathing, ragged and phlegmy. She was ill, but it needn't be pox; all the hold passengers coughed and wheezed—the damp had got into their lungs early on.

"Show him to me."

"No!" Her eyes shone in the dark, fearful as a cornered rat's, and the edge of her lip lifted over small white teeth.

"I swear I will not take him from you. I need to see, though."

"What will ye swear on?"

He groped his memory for a suitable Celtic oath, then gave up and said what was in his mind.

"On my own woman's life," he said, "and on the heads of my unborn sons."

He could feel doubt, and then a small easing of the tension in her; the round knee pressed against his leg moved slightly as she relaxed. There was a stealthy rustling in the chains nearby. Real rats this time.

"I canna leave him here alone while I steal food." He saw the faint tilt of her head toward the noise. "They'll eat him alive; they've bitten me in my sleep already, the filthy vermin."

He reached out his hands, conscious all the time of the sounds from the deck above. It wasn't likely that anyone would come down here, but how long before he was missed above?

She still hesitated, but at last reached a finger toward her breast, and freed the child's mouth with a tiny *pop!* It made a small sound of protest, and wriggled slightly as he took it.

He hadn't held babies very often; the feel of the dirty little bundle was startling—inert but lively, soft yet firm.

"Mind his head!"

"I've got it." Cradling the warm round skull in one careful palm, he duck-walked backward a step or two, bringing the child's face into dim light.

The cheeks were splotched with reddish pustules, topped with white—they looked for all the world like pox to Roger, and he felt a tremor of revulsion in the palms of his hands. Immunity or not, it took courage to touch contagion and not flinch.

He squinted at the child, then carefully undid its wrappings, ignoring the mother's hissed protest. He slid a hand under its dress, feeling first the soggy clout that hung between its chubby legs, and then the smooth, silky skin of chest and stomach.

The child didn't really seem so sick; his eyes were clear, not gummy. And while the tiny boy seemed feverish, it wasn't the searing heat he had felt the night before. The baby whined and squirmed, true, but he kicked with a fretful strength in the tiny limbs, not the weak spasms of a dying child.

The very young go quickly, Claire had said. *You have no notion how fast disease moves, when there's nothing to fight it with.* He had some notion, after last night.

"All right," he whispered at last. "I think you're maybe right." He felt, rather than saw, the easing of her arm—she had held her dagger ready.

He gingerly handed back the child, with a mingled sense of relief and reluctance. And the terrifying realization of the responsibility he had accepted.

Morag was cooing to the boy, cuddling him against her breast as she hastily rewrapped him.

"Sweet Jemmy, aye, that's a good laddie. Hush, bittie, hush now, it'll be all right, Mammy's here for ye."

"How long?" Roger whispered, laying a hand on her arm. "How long will the rash last, if it's milk rash?"

"Maybe four days, maybe five," she whispered back. "But it's no but maybe twa more, and the rash will be different—less. Anyone can see then that it's not the pox. I can come out, then."

Two days. If it was pox, the child would be dead in two days. But if not—he might just manage. And so might she.

"Can you keep awake that long? The rats—"

"Aye, I can," she said fiercely. "I can do what I must. Will ye help me, then?"

He drew a deep breath, ignoring the stench.

"Aye, I will." He stood up, and gave her his hand. After a

moment's hesitation, she took it, and stood too. She was small, she barely reached his shoulder, and her hand in his was the size of a child's—in the shadows, she looked like a young girl cradling her doll.

"How old are you?" he asked suddenly.

He caught the gleam of her eyes, surprised, and then the flash of teeth.

"Yesterday I was two-and-twenty," she said dryly. "Today, I'm maybe a hundred."

The small damp hand pulled free of his, and she melted back into the darkness.

39

A Gambling Man

The fog gathered through the night. By dawn the ship rode in a cloud so thick that the sea below could not be seen from the rail, and only the susurrus of the hull's passage indicated that the *Gloriana* still floated on water, not air.

There was no sun, and little wind; the sails hung limp, shuddering now and then with a passing air. Oppressed by the dimness, men walked the decks like ghosts, appearing out of the murk with a suddenness that startled one another.

This obscurity served Roger well; he was able to pass almost unseen through the ship, and slip unobserved into the hold, the small store of food he had kept back from his own meals concealed in his shirt.

The fog had gotten into the hold as well; clammy white tendrils touched his face, drifting out between the looming water casks, and hovered near his feet. It was darker than ever here below, gone from dusty-gold dimness to the black-brown of cold, wet wood.

The child was asleep; Roger saw no more than the curve of its cheek, still spattered with red pustules. They looked angry and inflamed. Morag saw his look of doubt and said nothing, but took his hand in her own and pressed it to the baby's neck.

The tiny pulse went bump-bump-bump under his finger, and the soft creased skin was warm but damp. Reassured, he smiled at Morag, and she gave him back a tiny glimmer.

A month in steerage had left her thin and grimy; the last two days had stamped her face with permanent lines of fear. Her hair straggled lank around her face, caked with grease and thick with lice. Her eyes were bruised with tiredness, and she smelled of feces and urine, sour milk and stale sweat. Her lips were tight and pale as the rest of her face. Roger took her very gently by the shoulders, bent, and kissed her mouth.

At the top of the ladder, he looked back. She was still standing there looking up at him, the child in her arms.

The deck was quiet save for the murmur of helmsman and bosun, invisible at the wheel. Roger eased the hatch cover back in place, his heart beginning to slow again, the touch of her still warming his hands. Two days. Maybe three. Perhaps they would make it; Roger at least was convinced she was right, the child did not have pox.

There should be no occasion for anyone to go into the hold soon—a fresh water-cask had been brought up only the day before. He could contrive to feed her—if only she could stay awake long enough . . . the sharp *ting* of the ship's bell pierced the fog, a reminder of time that no longer seemed to exist, its passage unmarked by any change of light or dark.

It was as Roger crossed toward the stern that he heard it; a sudden loud *whoosh* in the mist off the rail, very near at hand. The next instant, the ship trembled slightly underfoot, her boards brushed by something huge.

"Whale!" came a cry from aloft. He could see two men near the mainmast, dimly outlined in the fog. At the cry, they froze, and he realized that he, too, was standing rigid, listening.

There was another *whoosh* nearby, another farther off. The crew of the *Gloriana* stood silent, each man charting in his head the great exhalations, marking an invisible map on which the ship drifted through moving shoals, mountains of silent, intelligent flesh.

How big were they? Roger wondered. Big enough to damage the ship? He strained his eyes, vainly trying to see anything at all through the fog.

It came again, a thump hard enough to jar the rail under his hands, followed by a long, grating rasp that shuddered through the boards. There were muffled cries of fear from below; to those in the steerage, it would be right next to them, no more than the planks of the hull between them and rupture—a sudden smash and the frightful inrush of the sea. Three-inch oak planks seemed no more substantial than tissue paper against the great beasts that floated nearby, breathing unseen in the fog.

"Barnacles," said a soft Irish voice from the mist behind him. Despite himself, Roger jumped, and a low chuckle materialized into Bonnet's shadowed bulk. The Captain held a cheroot between his teeth, a spill from the galley fire illumining the lines and planes of his face, dissolute in red light. The rasping shudder came again through the boards.

"They scratch themselves to rid their skins of parasites," Bonnet said casually. "We are no more to them than a floating stone." He drew heavily to start the flame, blew fragrant smoke, and tossed the burning paper overboard. It vanished in the mist like a falling star.

Roger let out a breath only slightly less noisy than the whales'. How close had Bonnet been? Had the Captain seen him coming out of the hold?

"They will not damage the ship, then?" he said, matching the Captain's casual tone.

Bonnet smoked for a moment in silence, concentrating on the draw of his cigar. Without the illumination of the open flame, he was once more a shadow, marked only by the glowing coal of the tip.

"Who knows?" he said at last, small spurts of smoke puffing out between his teeth as he spoke. "Any one of the beasts might sink us, should he have a mind in him for mischief. I saw a ship once—or what was left of it—battered to pieces by an angry whale. Three feet of board, and a bit of spar left floating—sunk with all hands, two hundred souls."

"You don't seem troubled by the possibility."

There was a long sound of exhalation, a faint echo of the whales' sighing, as Bonnet blew smoke between pursed lips.

" 'Twould be a waste of strength to worry myself. A wise man leaves those things beyond his power to the gods—and prays that Danu will be with him." The edge of the Captain's hat turned toward him. "Ye'll know of Danu, will ye, MacKenzie?"

"Danu?" Roger said stupidly, and then the penny dropped, an old chant coming back to him from the mists of childhood—something Mrs. Graham had taught him to say. "Come to me, Danu, change my luck. Make me bold. Give me wealth—and love to hold."

There was an amused grunt behind the coal.

"Ah, and you not even an Irishman. But sure I knew you from the first for a man of learning, MacKenzie."

"I know Danu the Luck-Giver," Roger said, hoping against hope that that particular Celtic goddess was both a good sailor and on his side. He took a step backward, meaning to go, but a hand descended on his wrist, holding tight.

"A man of learning," Bonnet repeated softly, all levity gone from his voice, "but no wisdom. And are you a praying man at all, MacKenzie?"

He tensed, but felt the force of Bonnet's grip and did not pull away. Strength gathered in his limbs, his body knowing before he did that the fight had come.

"I said a wise man does not trouble himself with things beyond his power—but on this ship, MacKenzie, everything is in my power." The grip on his wrist tightened. "And everyone."

Roger jerked his wrist sideways, breaking the grip. He stood alone, knowing there was neither help nor escape. There was no world beyond the ship, and within it, Bonnet was right—all were in the Captain's power. If he died, it would not help Morag—but that choice was made already.

"Why?" said Bonnet, sounding only mildly interested. "The woman's no looker, sure. And a man of such learning, too; would you risk my ship and my venture, then, only for the sake of a warm body?"

"No risk." The words came out hoarse, forced through a tight throat. *Come at me,* he thought, and his hands curled at his sides. *Come at me, and give me a chance to take you with me.* "The child doesn't have pox—a harmless rash."

"You will forgive my putting my ignorant opinion above your own, Mr. MacKenzie, but I am Captain here." The voice was still soft, but the venom was clear.

"It is a child, for God's sake!"

"It is—and of no value."

"No value to you, perhaps!"

There was a moment's silence, broken only by a distant *whoosh* in the empty white.

"And what value to you?" the voice asked, implacable. "Why?"

For the sake of a warm body. Yes, for that. For the touch of humanity, the memory of tenderness, for the feeling of life stubborn in the face of death.

"For pity," he said. "She is poor; there was no one to help her."

The rich perfume of tobacco reached him, narcotic, enchanting. He breathed it in, taking strength from it.

Bonnet moved, and he moved, too, settling himself in preparation. But there was no blow forthcoming; the shadow dug in a pocket, held out a ghostly hand in which he caught a magpie glitter from the diffuse lantern light—coins and bits of rubbish and what might have been a jewel's quick gleam. Then the Captain plucked out a silver shilling, and thrust the rest back into his pocket.

"Ah, pity," he said. "And did yez say you were a gambling man at all, MacKenzie?"

He held out the shilling, dropped it. Roger caught it, only by reflex.

"For the suckling's life, then," Bonnet said, and the tone of light amusement was back. "A gentleman's wager, shall we call it? Heads it lives, and tails it dies."

The coin was warm and solid in his palm, an alien thing in this world of drifting chill. His hands were slick with sweat, and yet his mind had gone cold and sharp, focused to an ice pick's point.

Heads he lives, and tails he dies, he thought quite calmly, and did not mean the child below. He marked throat and crotch on the other man; grip and lunge, a blow and heave—the rail was no more than a foot away, the empty realm of the whales beyond.

There was no room beyond his calculations for any sense of fear. He saw the coin spin up as though it were thrown by another hand, then fall to the deck. His muscles bunched themselves, slowly.

"It seems Danu is with ye the night, sir." Bonnet's soft Irish voice seemed to come to him from a great way off, as the Captain bent and picked up the coin.

Realization was only beginning to bloom in his chest, when the Captain gripped his shoulder, turning him down the deck.

"You'll walk with me awhile, MacKenzie."

Something had happened to his knees; he felt as though he would sink down with every step, and yet somehow stayed upright, keeping pace with the shadow. The ship was silent, the deck under his feet a mile away; but the sea beyond was a live thing, breathing. He felt the breath in his own lungs rise and fall with the shifting deck, and felt as though there were no boundaries to his body. It might have been wood under his feet, or water, for all he could feel.

It was some time before he made sense of Bonnet's words, and realized, with a vague sense of amazement, that the man seemed to be recounting the story of his life, in a quiet, matter-of-fact sort of way.

Orphaned in Sligo at an early age, he had learned quickly to fend for himself, he said, working as a cabin boy aboard trading ships. But one winter, with ships scarce, he had found work ashore in Inverness, digging the foundation for a grand house that was building near the town.

"I was just seventeen," he said. "The youngest of the crew of workmen. I could not say why it was they hated me. Mayhap it was my manner, for that was rough enough—or jealousy for my size and strength; they were an unchancy, whey-faced lot. Or maybe that the lasses smiled on me. Or maybe 'twas only that I was a stranger.

"Still, I knew well enough I was unpopular with them—little did I know quite *how* unpopular, though, until the day the cellar was finished and the foundation ready to be laid."

Bonnet paused to draw on his cigar, lest it go out. He let out puffs of smoke from the corners of his mouth, white wisps that curled past his head into the greater white of the fog.

"The trenches were dug," he went on, the cigar clenched between his teeth, "and the walls started; the great block of the cornerstone standin' ready. I had gone to my supper, and was just walkin' back to the place where I slept, when to my surprise I was caught up by a pair of the lads with whom I worked.

"They'd a bottle; they sat down on a wall and urged me to drink with them. I should've known better, for they were friendly, which they'd never been before. But I did drink, and drink again, and in no time at all I was reelin' drunk, for I'd no head for liquor, havin' never the money to buy strong drink. I was well fuddled by the time 'twas full dark, and scarcely thought to pull away when they took me by the arms and hastened me down the lane. Then they seized me, tossed me over a half-built wall, and to my surprise, I found myself lyin' in the damp dirt of the cellar I'd helped dig.

"All of them were there, the workmen. Another man was with them, too; one o' them had a lantern, and when he held it up, I could see the man was Daft Joey. Daft Joey was a beggarman that lived beneath the bridge—he had nay teeth, and he ate rotten fish and floating dung from the river, and he stank worse than a blackbirder's hold.

"I was so dazed with the whisky and the fall that I lay where I was, only half hearin' them as they talked—or argued, rather, for the chief o' the gang was angry that the two had brought me. The daftie would do, he said; a mercy to him, at that. But them that brought me said no, better me. Someone might miss the beggarman, they said. Then someone laughed and said aye, and they would not have to pay me my last week's wages, and 'twas then I began to know they meant to kill me.

"They'd talked before, while we worked. A sacrifice, they said, for the foundation, lest the earth tremble and the walls collapse. But I had not listened—and if I had, would not have guessed that they meant any more than to chop the head off a cockerel and bury it, as was usual."

He had not looked at Roger through this recital, his eyes instead fixed on the mist, as though the events he described were happening again, somewhere just beyond the white curtain of fog.

Roger's clothing hung on him, clinging, wringing wet with mist and cold sweat. His stomach clenched, and the cesspool smell of the steerage might have been the stink of Daft Joey in the cellar.

"So they palavered for a bit," Bonnet went on, "and the beggarman began to make noise, for he wanted more drink. And at last the chief said it was not worth so much talk, he would throw for the choice. Then he took a coin from his pocket and he said to me, laughin', 'Will ye take heads or tails, then, man?'

"I was too sick to say a word; the sky was black and whirling round and bits of light kept flickering at the edges of my eyes, like fallin' stars. So he said it for me; by Geordie's head should I live, and by his arse I should die, and he threw the shilling up in the air. It came down in the dirt by my head, but I had nay strength to turn and look.

"He bent to see and gave a grunt, then he stood up and took nay more notice of me."

They had reached the stern in their quiet pacing. Bonnet stopped there, hands on the rail, smoking silently. Then he took the cigar from his mouth.

"They pulled the daftie to the wall that was built, and made him sit down on the ground at its foot. I do remember his foolish face," he said softly. "He took a drink and he laughed wi' them, and his mouth was open—slack and wet as a old whore's cunt. The next moment, the stone came down from the top of the wall, and crushed his head."

Drops of moisture had gathered on the spikes of hair at the back of Roger's neck; he could feel them run down, one at a time, trickling cold down the crease of his back.

"They rolled me on my face and hit me," Bonnet continued matter-of-factly. "When I came to myself again, I was in the bottom of a fishing boat. The fisherman left me on the shore near

Peterhead and said he would advise me to find a new ship—he could see, he said, I was not meant for the land.''

He held up the cigar and tapped it gently with a finger to loosen the ash.

''At that,'' he said, ''they did give me my wages; when I came to look, the shilling was in my pocket. Ah, they were honest men, sure.''

Roger leaned against the rail, gripping its wood as the single solid thing in a world gone soft and nebulous.

''And did you go back to the land?'' he asked, and heard his own voice, preternaturally calm, as though it belonged to someone else.

''Did I find them, ye mean.'' Bonnet turned and leaned back against the rail, half facing Roger. ''Oh, yes. Years later. One at a time. But I found them all.'' He opened the hand that held the coin, and held it cupped thoughtfully before him, tilting it back and forth so the silver gleamed in the lantern light.

''Heads you live, and tails you die. A fair chance, would yez say, MacKenzie?''

''For them?''

''For you.''

The soft Irish voice was as unemphatic as it might be were it making observations of the weather.

As in a dream, Roger felt the weight of the shilling drop once more into his hands. He heard the suck and hiss of the water on the hull, the blowing of the whales—and the suck and hiss of Bonnet's breath as he drew on his cigar. *Seven whales the fill of a Cirein Croin.*

''A fair chance,'' Bonnet said. ''Luck was with you before, MacKenzie. See will Danu come for you again—or will it be the Soul-Eater this time?''

The fog had closed over the deck. There was nothing visible save the glowing coal of Bonnet's cigar, a burning cyclops in the mist. The man might be a devil indeed, one eye closed to human misery, one eye open to the dark. And here Roger stood quite literally between the devil and the deep blue sea, with his fate shining silver in the palm of his hand.

''It is my life; I'll make the call,'' he said, and was surprised to hear his voice calm and steady. ''Tails—tails is mine.'' He threw, and caught, clapped his one hand hard against the back of the other, trapped the coin and its unknown sentence.

He closed his eyes and thought just once of Brianna. *I'm sorry,* he said silently to her, and lifted his hand.

A warm breath passed over his skin, and then he felt a spot of coolness on the back of his hand as the coin was picked up, but he didn't move, didn't open his eyes.

It was some time before he realized that he stood alone.

PART NINE

Passionnément

40

Virgin Sacrifice

Wilmington, the Colony of North Carolina, September 1, 1769

This was the third attack, of whatever Lizzie's sickness was. She had seemed to recover after the first bad fever, and after a day spent regaining her strength, had insisted she was able to travel. They had got no more than a day's ride north of Charleston, though, before the fever struck again.

Brianna had hobbled the horses, and made a hasty camp near a small creek, then made trip after trip through the night, scrabbling up and down a muddy bank in the dark, carrying water in a small canteen to dribble down Lizzie's throat and over her steaming body. She wasn't afraid of dark woods or lurking animals, but the thought of Lizzie dying in the wilderness, miles from any sort of help, was terrifying enough to make her want to head straight back to Charleston as soon as Lizzie could sit a horse.

By morning, however, the fever had broken, and though Lizzie was weak and pale, she had been able to ride. Brianna had hesitated, but finally decided to press on toward Wilmington, rather than turn back. The urge that had driven her all this way now had a sharper spur; she *had* to find her mother, for Lizzie's sake as well as her own.

Brianna hadn't appreciated her size for most of a life spent looming in the back row of class pictures, but she had begun to feel the advantages of height and strength as she grew older. And the longer she spent in this miserable place, the more advantageous they seemed.

She braced one arm against the bed frame as she eased the chamber pot out from under Lizzie's frail white buttocks with the other hand. Lizzie was scrawny but surprisingly heavy, and no more than half conscious; she moaned and twitched restlessly, the twitch suddenly springing into the full-fledged convulsion of a chill.

The shivering was beginning to ease a little now, though Lizzie's teeth were still clenched hard enough to make the sharp bones of her jaws stand out like struts beneath her skin.

Malaria, Brianna thought, for the dozenth time. It must be, to keep coming back like this. A number of small pink welts showed on Lizzie's neck, reminders of the mosquitoes that had plagued them ever since the *Phillip Alonzo* drew within sight of land. They had made landfall too far south, and wasted three weeks in meandering through the shallow coastal waters to Charleston, gnawed incessantly by bloodsucking bugs.

"There now. Feeling a little better?"

Lizzie nodded feebly, and tried to smile, succeeding only in looking like a white mouse that had taken poisoned bait.

"Water, honey. Try a little, just a sip." Brianna held the cup to Lizzie's mouth, coaxing. She felt a strange sense of déjà vu and realized that her voice was the echo of her mother's, both in words and tone. The realization was oddly comforting, as though her mother somehow stood behind her, speaking through her.

If it were her mother speaking, though, next would have come the orange-flavored St. Joseph's aspirin, a tiny pill to be sucked and savored, as much treat as medicine, the aches and fever seeming to subside as quickly as the sweet tart pill dissolved on her tongue. Brianna cast a bleak glance at her saddlebags, bulging in the corner. No aspirin there; Jenny had sent a small bundle of what she called "simples," but the chamomile and peppermint tea had only made Lizzie vomit.

Quinine was what you gave people for malaria; that's what she needed. But she had no idea whether it was even *called* quinine here, or how it was administered. Malaria was an old disease, though, and quinine came from plants—surely a doctor would have some, whatever it was called?

Only the hope of finding medical help had kept her going through Lizzie's second bout. Afraid to stop on the road again, she had taken Lizzie up in front of her, cradling the girl's body against her as they rode, leading Lizzie's horse. Lizzie had alternately blazed with heat and shaken with chill, and both of them had arrived in Wilmington limp with exhaustion.

But here they were, in the midst of Wilmington, and as far from real help as they had ever been. Bree glanced at the bedside table, lips tight. A wadded cloth lay there, dabbled with blood.

The landlady had taken one look at Lizzie and sent for an apothecary. Despite what her mother had said about the primitive state of medicine and its practitioners here, Brianna had felt a sudden instinctive surge of relief at sight of the man.

The apothecary was a decently dressed young man with a kindly air and reasonably clean hands. No matter what his state of medical knowledge, he was likely to know as much about fevers as she herself did. More important, she could feel that she wasn't alone in caring for Lizzie.

Modesty prompted her to step outside when the apothecary drew down the linen sheet to make his examination, and it was not until she heard a small cry of distress that she flung open the door, to find the young apothecary, fleam in hand, and Lizzie, her face white as chalk, red blood streaming from a cut in the crook of her elbow.

"But it is to draw the humors, miss!" the apothecary had pleaded, trying to shield both himself and the body of his patient. "Do you not understand? You must draw the humors! If it is not done, hot bile will toxify within her organs and fill her body entirely, to her certain detriment!"

"It will be to *your* certain detriment if you don't leave," Brianna had informed him, through clenched teeth. "Get out of here this minute!"

Medical zeal disappearing in favor of self-preservation, the young man had picked up his case and left with what dignity he could, pausing at the foot of the stairs to shout dire warnings up at her.

The warnings kept echoing in her ears, between trips downstairs to fill the basin from the kitchen copper. Most of the apothecary's words were simple ignorance—ranting about humors and bad blood—but there were some that came back with uncomfortable force.

"If you will not take heedful advice, miss, you may well condemn your maid to death!" he had called, indignant face upturned in the darkness of the stairwell. "You do not know how to care for her yourself!"

She didn't. She didn't even know for sure what Lizzie's sickness was; the apothecary had called it an "ague," and the landlady had talked of "seasoning." It was quite common for new immigrants to fall ill repeatedly, exposed as they were to an unfamiliar array of new germs. From the landlady's unguarded remarks, it seemed apparent that it was also quite common for such immigrants not to survive this seasoning process.

The basin tilted, slopping hot water over her wrists. Water was the only thing she had. God knew whether the well behind the inn was sanitary or not; better to use the boiling water from the copper and let it cool, even if it took longer. There was cool water in the pitcher; she dribbled a little between Lizzie's dry, cracked lips, then eased the girl down on the bed. She washed Lizzie's face and neck, pulled back the quilt and soaked the linen nightdress again, the tiny nipples showing as dark pink points beneath.

Lizzie managed a small smile, eyelids drooping, then sank back with a tiny sigh and fell asleep, loose joints relaxing like a rag doll's.

Brianna felt as though her own stuffing had been removed as well. She dragged the single stool over to the window and collapsed on it, leaning on the sill in a vain effort to get a breath of fresh air. The atmosphere had lain on them like a thick blanket all the way from Charleston—little wonder that poor Lizzie had crumpled under its weight.

She scratched uneasily at a bite on her own thigh; the bugs were not nearly as fond of her as they were of Lizzie, but she had suffered a few bites. Malaria wasn't a danger; she had had the shots for that, as well as for typhoid, cholera, and anything else she could think of. But there was no vaccine for things like dengue fever, or any of a dozen other diseases that haunted the thick air like malevolent spirits. How many of those were spread by biting insects?

She closed her eyes and leaned her head against the wooden frame, blotting trickles of sweat from her breastbone with the folds of her shirt. She could smell herself; how long had she been wearing these clothes? It didn't matter; she had been awake for most of two days and two nights, and was too tired to undress, let alone make the effort to wash.

Lizzie's fever seemed to have broken—but for how long? If it kept coming back, it was sure to kill the little maidservant; she had already lost all the weight she had gained on the voyage, and her fair skin was beginning to show a yellow tinge in sunlight.

There was no help to be found in Wilmington. Brianna sat up straight, stretching and feeling the bones of her back pop into place. Tired or not, there was only one thing to do. She had to find her mother, and as quickly as possible.

She would sell the horses and find a boat to take them up the river. Even if the fever came back, she could take care of Lizzie as well on a boat as she could in this hot, smelly little room—and they would still be traveling toward their goal.

She got up and splashed a little water on her face, twisting her sweat-soaked hair up out of the way. She loosened the crumpled breeches and stepped out of them, making plans in a dreamy, disconnected sort of way.

A boat, on the river. Surely it would be cooler on the river. No more riding; her thigh muscles ached from four days in the saddle. They would sail to Cross Creek, find Jocasta MacKenzie.

"Aunt," she murmured, swaying slightly as she reached for the oil-dip lamp. "Great-aunt Jocasta." She imagined a kindly white-haired old lady who would greet her with the same joy she had found at Lallybroch. Family. It would be so good to have family again. Roger drifted into her thoughts, as he did so often. She resolutely pushed him out again; time enough to think of him when her mission was accomplished.

A tiny cloud of gnats hovered over the flame, and the wall nearby was spattered with the arrowed shapes of moths and lacewings, taking respite from their quest. She pinched out the flame, scarcely hotter than the air in the room, and pulled the shirt off over her head in darkness.

Jocasta would know exactly where Jamie Fraser and her mother were—would help her get to them. For the first time since stepping through the stones, she thought of Jamie Fraser with neither curiosity nor trepidation. Nothing mattered but finding her mother. Her mother would know what to do for Lizzie; her mother would know how to take care of everything.

She spread a folded quilt on the floor and lay down naked on it. She was asleep in moments, dreaming of the mountains, and clean white snow.

By the next evening, things looked better. The fever *had* broken, just as before, leaving Lizzie spent and weak, but clear-headed, and as cool as the climate allowed. Restored by a night's rest, Brianna had washed her hair and sponge-bathed in the basin, then had paid the landlady to keep an eye on Lizzie while she, dressed in breeches and coat, went about her business.

It had taken most of the day—and the suffering of a good many widened eyes and gaping mouths as men realized her sex—to sell the horses at what she hoped was an honest price. She had heard of a man named Viorst, who took passengers between Wilmington and Cross Creek in his canoe for a price. She hadn't found Viorst before dark, though—and wasn't about to hang around the docks at night, breeches or no breeches. Morning would be time enough.

Still more heartening, Lizzie had been downstairs when she returned to the inn toward sunset, being cosseted by the landlady and fed morsels of corn pudding and chicken fricassee.

"You're better!" Brianna exclaimed. Lizzie nodded, beaming, and gulped her mouthful.

"I am, so," she said. "I feel quite myself again, and Mrs. Smoots has been so kind as to let me wash all of our things. Oh, it's so nice to feel clean again!" she said fervently, laying a pale hand on her kerchief, which looked freshly ironed.

"You shouldn't be washing and ironing," Brianna scolded, sliding into the bench beside her maid. "You'll wear yourself out, and get sick again."

Lizzie looked down her thin nose, a prim smile perched at the corners of her mouth.

"Well, I didna think ye'd be wanting to meet your Da in clothes all spotted wi' filth. Not but what even a clarty gown would be better than what ye've got on." The little maid's eyes passed reprovingly over Brianna's breeches; she didn't approve at all of her mistress's penchant for male costume.

"Meet my Da? What do you—Lizzie, have you heard something?" A flare of hope shot up inside her, a sudden bright puff like the lighting of a gas stove.

Lizzie looked smug.

"I have that. And 'twas all because of the washin', too—my Da did always say as how virtue brings its reward."

"I'm sure it does," Brianna said dryly. "What did you find out, and how?"

"Well, I was just after hanging out your petticoat—the nice one, aye, wi' the lace about the hem—"

Brianna picked up a small jug of milk, and held it menacingly over her maid's head. Lizzie squeaked and ducked away, giggling.

"All right! I'm telling! I'm telling!"

In the middle of her washing, one of the tavern's patrons had come out into the yard to smoke a pipe, the day being fine. He had admired Lizzie's domestic skills and taken up a pleasant conversation, in the course of which it was revealed that this gentleman —one Andrew MacNeill by name—had not only heard of James Fraser but was well acquainted with him.

"He is? What did he say? Is this MacNeill still here?"

Lizzie put out a hand and made small quelling motions.

"I'm sayin' it as quick as I can. No, he's not here; I did try to make him stay, but he was bound for New Bern by the packet boat, and couldna bide." She was nearly as excited as Brianna; her cheeks were still pale and sallow, but the tip of her nose had gone pink.

"Mr. MacNeill knows your Da, and your great-auntie Cameron as well—she's a great lady, he says, verra rich, with a tremendous great house, and lots of slaves, and—"

"Never mind about that now, what did he say about my father? Did he mention my mother?"

"Claire," Lizzie said triumphantly. "Ye did say that was your Mam's name? I asked, and he said yes, Mrs. Fraser's name was Claire. And he said she was a most amazing healer—did ye not say as your mother was a fine physician? He said as he had seen her do a desperate operation on a man, laid him smack in the middle of the dinner table and cut off his ballocks and then stitched them back on, right there on the spot, wi' all the dinner party lookin' on!"

"That's my mother, all right." There were tears of what might have been laughter in the corners of her eyes. "Are they well? Had he seen them lately?"

"Och, that's the best of it!" Lizzie leaned forward, eyes big with the importance of her news. "He's in Cross Creek—your Da, Mr. Fraser! A man he knows is on trial there for assault, and your Da's come down to be witness for him." She patted her handkerchief against her temple, mopping up tiny beads of sweat.

"Mr. MacNeill says the court willna sit again till Monday week because the judge fell ill, and another is coming from Edenton, and the trial canna go on until he arrives."

Brianna brushed back a lock of hair and blew out her breath, hardly daring to believe their luck.

"A week from Monday . . . and it's Saturday now. God, I wonder how long it will take to get upriver?"

Lizzie crossed herself hastily in atonement for her mistress's casual blasphemy, but shared in her excitement.

"I dinna ken, but Mrs. Smoots did say as her son's made the trip once before—we could ask him."

Brianna swung round on her bench, looking over the room. Men and boys had begun coming in as darkness fell, stopping for a drink or a supper on their way from work to bed, and now there were fifteen or twenty people crammed into the small space.

"Which one is Junior Smoots?" Brianna asked, craning her neck to see through the press of bodies.

"Yonder—the laddie wi' the sweet brown eyes. I'll fetch him to ye, shall I?" Emboldened by excitement, Lizzie slipped out of her seat and pushed her way into the throng.

Brianna was still holding the jug of milk, but made no move to pour it into her cup. Her throat was too choked with excitement to swallow. Little more than a week!

Wilmington was a small town, Roger thought. How many places could she be? If she was here at all. He thought there was a good chance of it; inquiries in the dockside taverns in New Bern had given him the valuable information that the *Phillip Alonzo* had reached Charleston safely—and only ten days before the *Gloriana* had docked in Edenton.

It might have taken Brianna anything from two days to two weeks to make her way from Charleston to Wilmington—assuming that she was indeed headed there.

"She's here," he muttered. "Damn it, I *know* she's here!" Whether this conviction was the result of deduction, intuition, hope, or merely stubbornness, he clung to it like a drowning sailor to a spar.

He had managed the journey from Edenton to Wilmington with a fair amount of ease, himself. Put to work unloading cargo from the *Gloriana*'s hold, he had carried a chest of tea into a warehouse, set it down, walked back to the door, and busied himself in retying the sweat-soaked kerchief round his head. As soon as the next man had passed him, he stepped out onto the dock, turned right instead of left, and within seconds was headed up the narrow cobbled lane that led from docks to town. By the next morning he'd found a berth as loader on a small cargo boat, transporting naval stores from Edenton to the main depot at Wilmington, there to be transferred to a larger ship for transport to England.

He jumped ship again in Wilmington, without a moment's compunction. He hadn't time to waste; there was Brianna to be found.

He knew she was here. Fraser's Ridge was in the mountains; she'd need a guide, and Wilmington was the most likely port in which to find one. And if she was here, someone would have noticed her; he'd bet money on that. He could only hope the wrong sort of person hadn't noticed her already.

A quick reconnoiter of the main street and the harbor gave him a count of twenty-three taverns. Christ, these people drank like fish! There was the chance she'd taken a room in a private house, but the taverns were the place to start.

By evening he'd covered ten of the taverns, slowed by the necessity of avoiding any of his erstwhile shipmates. Being in the presence of so much drink, and he without an extra penny to spend, had given him a raging thirst. He hadn't eaten all day, either, which didn't help matters.

At the same time, he scarcely noticed the physical discomfort. A man in the fifth tavern had seen her, so had a woman in the seventh. "A tall *man* wi' red hair," the man had said, but "A great huge girl, dressed in men's breeches," the woman had said, clicking her tongue in shock. "Walkin' down the street, plain as you please, with her coat over her arm and her backside in view of everyone!"

Let Roger get that particular backside in *his* view, he thought with some grimness, and he'd know what to do with it. He begged a cup of water from a kindhearted landlady, and set off with renewed determination.

By the time it was full dark, he had covered another five taverns. The taprooms were full now, and he discovered that the tall redheaded girl in men's clothing had been causing public comment for nearly a week. The quality of some of this comment caused the blood to throb in his cheeks with outrage, and only the fear of being arrested kept him from outright assault.

As it was, he left the fifteenth tavern after an ugly exchange of words with two drunkards, boiling with fury. Christ, had the woman no sense at all? Did she have no notion what men were capable of?

He stopped in the street and wiped a sleeve across his sweating face. He breathed heavily, wondering what to do next. Keep on, he supposed, though if he didn't find something to eat soon, he was going to fall flat on his face in the road.

The Blue Bull, he decided. He'd glanced into the shed there as he passed earlier, and seen a good pile of clean straw. He'd spend a penny or two for dinner, and perhaps the owner would let him sleep in the stable for the sake of Christian kindness.

Turning, his eye caught sight of a sign on the house across the road.

WILMINGTON GAZETTEER, JNO. GILLETTE. PROP., it read. Wilmington's newspaper; one of few in the Colony of North Carolina. One too

many, if you asked Roger. He fought the urge to pick up a rock
and hurl it through Jno. Gillette's window. Instead, he yanked the
sodden band off his head and, making an effort to tidy himself
into some semblance of decency, turned toward the river and the
Blue Bull.

She was there.

She was sitting by the hearth, her tailed hair sparking in the
firelight, engaged in conversation with a young man whose smile
Roger wanted to wipe off forcibly. Instead, he slammed the door
behind him with a crash and started toward her. She turned, startled, and stared blankly at the bearded stranger. Recognition
flashed in her eyes, then joy, and a huge smile spread across her
face.

"Oh," she said. "It's you." Then her eyes changed, as realization flared up like a brushfire. She screamed. It was a good full-
bodied scream, and every head in the tavern snapped round at the
sound of it.

"Damn you!" He lunged across the table, and got her by the
arm. "What the devil do you think you're doing?"

Her face had gone dead white, her eyes round and dark with
shock. She jerked away, trying to free herself.

"Let go!"

"That I won't! You'll come with me, and ye'll do it this moment!"

Sidling round the table, he got hold of her other arm, jerked her
up, whirled her around and pushed her in front of him toward the
door.

"MacKenzie!" Damn, it was one of the seamen from the cargo
boat. Roger glowered at the man, willing him to keep out of it.
Luckily the man was both smaller and older than Roger; he hesitated, but then took courage from the company and lifted his chin
pugnaciously.

"What you doing to the lass, MacKenzie? Leave her be!"
There was a stir among the crowd, men turning from their drinks,
attracted by the uproar. He had to get out of here *now,* or he
wouldn't get out at all.

"Tell them it's all right, tell them you know me!" he whispered
into Brianna's ear.

"It's all right." Brianna spoke, voice husky with shock, but
loud enough to be heard over the growing hubbub. "It's all right.
I—I know him." The seaman dropped back a little, still dubious.
A scrawny young girl in the inglenook had gotten to her feet; she

looked frightened to death, but bravely clutched a stone ale bottle in one fist, evidently intending to hit Roger with it, if necessary. Her high-pitched voice rang out above the suspicious grumble of voices.

"Miss Bree! Ye'll not go wi' yon black villain, surely?"

Brianna made a sound that might have been laughter, choked by hysteria. Reaching up, she dug her nails hard into the back of his hand. Startled by the pain, he loosened his grip and she yanked her arm out of his grasp.

"It's all right," she repeated, more firmly to the room at large. "I know him." She made a small shooing gesture at the girl. "Lizzie, go on up to bed. I'll—I'll be back later." She whirled on her bootheel and headed for the door, walking fast. Roger gave the taproom a menacing glare, to discourage anyone who thought of interfering, and followed her.

She was waiting right outside the door; her fingers sank into his arm with a fierceness that might have been gratifying were it prompted solely by joy at seeing him. He doubted it.

"What are you *doing* here?" she asked.

He detached her fingers and gripped them firmly.

"Not here," he snapped. He took her arm and dragged her a little way down the road, to the shelter of a big horse-chestnut tree. The sky still glowed with the remnants of twilight, but the drooping branches reached nearly to the ground, and it was dark enough underneath to hide them from any curious souls who thought of venturing after them.

She whirled on him the instant they reached its shadows.

"What are you doing here, for God's sake?"

"Looking for you, ye wee fool! And what in the name of all holy are *you* doing here? And dressed like *that,* God damn you!" He'd had the briefest look at her in her breeches and shirt, but it was enough.

In her own time, the clothes would have been so baggy as to be sexless. After months of seeing women in long skirts and *arisaids,* though, the blatant division of her legs, the sheer bloody length of thigh and curve of calf, seemed so outrageous that he wanted to wrap a sheet around her.

"Bloody woman! You might as well walk down the street naked!"

"Don't be an idiot! What are you doing here?"

"I told you—looking for you."

He took her by the shoulders, then, and kissed her, hard. Fear, anger, and the sheer relief of finding her were fused at once into a solid bolt of desire, and he found he was shaking with it. So was she. She was clinging to him, shaking in his arms.

"It's all right," he whispered to her. He buried his mouth in her hair. "It's all right, I'm here. I'll take care of you."

She jerked upright, out of his arms.

"All *right*?" she cried. "How can you say that? For God's sake, you're *here*!"

There was no mistaking the horror in her voice. He grabbed her by the arm.

"And where the hell else should I be, with you tearing off into fucking nowhere and risking your bloody neck, and—why the hell did you do it?!"

"I'm looking for my parents. What *else* would I be doing here?"

"I know that, for God's sake! I mean why in *hell* did you not tell me what you meant to do?"

She jerked her arm out of his grasp and gave him a healthy shove in the chest that all but sent him staggering.

"Because you wouldn't have let me go, that's why! You'd have tried to stop me, and—"

"Damn right I would! God, I'd have locked you in a room, or tied you hand and foot! Of all the flea-brained notions—"

She hit him, a full-palmed slap that caught him hard across the cheekbone.

"Shut up!"

"Bloody woman! D'ye expect me to let you go off into—into *nothing*, and I sit at home twiddling my thumbs while you're having your womb paraded on a pike in the marketplace? What sort of man d'ye think I am?"

He felt her movement rather than saw it, and grabbed her wrist before she could slap him again.

"I'm in no mood for that, girl! Hit me once more, and by Christ, I will do you violence!"

She folded her other hand into a fist and punched him in the belly, quick as a striking snake.

He wanted to hit her back. Instead, he grabbed her, and with a handful of her hair wrapped round his fist, kissed her as hard as he could.

She squirmed and struggled against him, making strangled noises, but he didn't stop. Then she was kissing him back, and they sank to their knees together. Her arms came round his neck as he bore her down beneath him to the leaf-matted ground beneath the tree. Then she was crying in his arms, choking and gasping, tears running down her face as she clutched him.

"Why?" she sobbed. "Why did you have to follow me? Didn't you realize? Now what are we going to do!"

"Do? Do about what?" He couldn't tell whether she was crying from anger or fear—both, he thought.

She stared up at him through strands of tangled hair.

"Getting back! You have to have somebody to go to—somebody you care for. You're the only person I love at that end—or you were! How am I going to get back, if you're *here*? And how will you get back, if *I'm* here?"

He stopped dead, fear and anger both forgotten, and his hands clamped tight on her wrists to stop her hitting him again.

"That's why? That's why you wouldn't tell me? Because you *love* me? Jesus Christ!"

He let go of her wrists and lay on top of her instead. He grabbed her face with both hands and tried to kiss her again. She gave a sudden snap of her hips, swung her legs up on either side, and scissored him neatly across the back, crushing his ribs.

He rolled, breaking the hold, and brought her with him, ending on his back, with her on top. He got a hand in her hair and drew her face down to his, panting.

"Stop," he said. "Christ, what is this, a wrestling match?"

"Let go of my hair." She shook her head, trying to dislodge his grip. "I *hate* having my hair pulled."

He let go of her hair, and slid his hand up the length of her neck, fingers curled round the slender nape, a thumb resting on the pulse in her throat. It was going like a trip-hammer; so was his.

"Right, how are ye on being choked?"

"Don't like it."

"Neither do I. Get your arm off my neck, aye?"

Very slowly, her weight eased back. He still felt short of breath, but not from being choked. He didn't want to let go of her neck. Not from fear of her cutting loose again, but because he couldn't bear to lose the feel of her. It had been too long.

She reached up and took hold of his wrist, but didn't pull his hand away. He felt her swallow.

"Right," he whispered. "Say it. I want to hear it."

"I . . . love . . . you," she said, between her teeth. "Got it?"

"Aye, I've got it." He took her face between his hands, very gently, and drew her down. She came, arms trembling and giving way beneath her.

"You're sure?" he said.

"Yes. What are we going to *do*?" she said, and began to cry.

"We." She'd said *we*. She'd said she was sure.

Roger lay in the dust of the road, bruised, filthy, and starving, with a woman trembling and weeping against his chest, now and then giving him a small thump with her fist. He had never felt happier in his life.

"Hush," he whispered, half rocking her. "It's all right; there's another way. We'll get back; I know how. Don't worry, I'll take care of you."

Finally, she wore herself out, and lay still in the crook of his arm, sniffling and hiccuping. There was a large wet spot on the front of his shirt. The crickets in the tree, startled into silence by the uproar, cautiously resumed their songs overhead.

She freed herself and sat up, fumbling in the dark.

"I have to blow my dose," she said thickly. "Do you have a hadky?"

He gave her the damp rag he used to tie back his hair. She made whooshing noises, and he smiled in the dark.

"You sound like a can of shaving cream."

"And when was the last time you saw one of those?" She lay down on him again, head tucked into the curve of his shoulder, and reached up to touch his jaw. He'd shaved two days ago; there had been neither time nor opportunity since.

Her hair still smelled faintly of grass, though no longer of artificial flowers. It must be her natural scent.

She sighed deeply, tightened her arm around him.

"I'm sorry," she said. "I didn't want you to come after me. But . . . Roger, I'm awfully glad you're here!"

He kissed her temple; she was damp and salty with sweat and tears.

"So am I," he said, and for the moment all the trials and dangers of the past two months seemed insignificant. All but one.

"How long have you been planning this?" he asked. He thought he could have told her, to the day. Since her letters had begun to change.

"Oh . . . about six months," she said, confirming his guess. "It was when I went to Jamaica during last Easter vacation."

"Aye?" To Jamaica, instead of to Scotland. She'd asked him to join her, and he'd refused, foolishly hurt that she hadn't planned to come to him automatically.

She took a deep breath and let it out, blotting the neck of her shirt against her skin.

"I kept dreaming," she said. "About my father. Fathers. Both of them."

The dreams were little more than fragments; vivid glimpses of Frank Randall's face, longer stretches now and then, in which she saw her mother. And now and then a tall, red-haired man whom she knew to be the father she had never seen.

"There was one dream in particular . . ." It had been night in the dream, somewhere tropical, with fields of tall green plants that might have been sugarcane, and fires burning in the distance.

"There were drums beating, and I knew something was hiding, waiting in the canes; something horrible," she said. "My mother was there, drinking tea with a crocodile." Roger grunted, and her voice grew sharper. "It was a dream, all right?

"Then he stepped out of the canes. I couldn't see his face very well, because it was dark, but I could see that he had red hair; there were copper glints when he turned his head."

"Was he the dreadful thing in the canes?" Roger asked.

"No." He could hear the susurrus of her hair as she shook her head. It had gone quite dark by now, and she was little more than a comforting weight on his chest, a soft voice beside him, speaking from the shadows.

"He was standing between my mother and the awful thing. I couldn't see it, but I knew it was there, waiting." She gave a small, involuntary shudder and Roger tightened his hold on her.

"Then I knew my mother was going to stand up and walk right toward it. I tried to stop her, but I couldn't make her hear me or see me. So I turned to him, and I called to him to go with her—to save her from whatever it was. And he saw me!" The hand on his arm squeezed tight. "He did, he saw me, and he heard me. And then I woke up."

"Aye?" Roger said skeptically. "And this made you go to Jamaica, and—"

"It made me think," she said sharply. "You'd looked; you couldn't find them anywhere in Scotland after 1766, and you couldn't find them on any of the emigration rolls to the Colonies.

That was when you said you thought we should give up; that there wasn't any more we could find out.''

Roger was glad of the darkness that hid his guilt. He kissed the top of her head, quickly.

"But I wondered; the place I saw them in the dream was in the tropics. What if they were in the Indies?"

"I looked," Roger said. "I checked the passenger rolls of every ship that left Edinburgh or London in the late 1760s and '70s —headed for anyplace. I did tell you," he added, an edge in his voice.

"I know that," she said, with a matching edge. "But what if they weren't passengers? Why did people *go* to the Indies then— now, I mean?" She caught herself, voice cracking a little in realization.

"For trade, mostly."

"Right. So what if they went on a cargo ship? They wouldn't show up on the passenger rolls."

"Okay," he said slowly. "Right, they wouldn't. But then how would you look for them?"

"Warehouse registers, plantation account books, port manifests. I spent the whole vacation in libraries and museums. And—and I found them," she said, with a small catch in her voice.

Christ, she'd seen the notice.

"Aye?" he said, striving for calmness.

She laughed, a little tremulously.

"A Captain James Fraser, of a ship named *Artemis,* sold five tons of bat guano to a planter in Montego Bay on April 2, 1767."

Roger couldn't help a grunt of amusement, but at the same time, couldn't help objecting.

"Aye, but a ship's captain? After all your mother said about the man's seasickness? And not to be discouraging, but there must be literally hundreds of James Frasers; how could you possibly know—"

"There might; but on April the first, a woman named Claire Fraser bought a slave from the slave market in Kingston."

"She *what*?"

"I don't know why," Brianna said firmly, "but I'm sure she had a good reason."

"Well, sure, but—"

"The papers gave the slave's name as 'Temeraire,' and described him as having one arm. Makes him stand out, doesn't it?

Anyway, I started looking through collections of old newspapers; not just from the Indies, from all the southern colonies, looking for that name—my mother wouldn't keep a slave; if she bought him, she'd free him somehow, and the notices of manumission were sometimes printed in the local papers. I thought I could maybe find where the slave was freed.''

"And did you?"

"No." She was quiet for a minute. "I—I found something else. A notice of their . . . deaths. My parents."

Even knowing that she must have found it, to hear it from her lips was still a shock. He pulled her tight against him, wrapping his arms around her.

"Where?" he said softly. "How?"

He should have known better. He wasn't listening to her half-choked explanation; he was too busy cursing himself. He should have known she was too stubborn to be dissuaded. All he'd done with his fatheaded interference was to drive her into secrecy. And it had been he who'd paid for that—in months of worry.

"But we're in time," she said. "It said 1776; we've got time to find them." She sighed hugely. "I'm so glad you're here. I was so worried you'd find out before I could get back and I didn't know what you'd do."

"What I *did* do. . . . You know," he said conversationally, "I have a friend with a two-year-old child. He says that he'd never in life condone child abuse—but by God, he understands what makes people do it. I feel very much the same about wife beating just now."

There was a small quiver of laughter from the heavy weight on his chest.

"What do you mean by that?"

He slid a hand down her back and got a firm grip on one round buttock. She wore no underclothes beneath the loose breeches.

"I mean that were I a man of this time, instead of my own, nothing would give me greater pleasure than to lay my belt across your arse a dozen times or so."

She didn't seem to consider this a serious threat. In fact, he thought she was laughing.

"So since you're not from this time, you wouldn't do it? Or you would, but you wouldn't enjoy it?"

"Oh, I'd enjoy it," he assured her. "There's nothing I'd like better than to take a stick to you."

She *was* laughing.

Suddenly furious, he shoved her off and sat up.

"What's the matter with you?"

"I thought you'd found someone else! Your letters, the last few months . . . and then that last one. I was sure of it. It's that I want to beat you for—not for lying to me or going off without telling me—for making me think I'd lost you!"

She was silent for a moment. Her hand came out of darkness and touched his face, very softly.

"I'm sorry," she said quietly. "I never meant for you to think that. I only wanted to keep you from finding out, until it was too late." Her head turned toward him, silhouetted by the faint light from the road outside their refuge. "How *did* you find out?"

"Your boxes. They came to the college."

"What? But I told them not to send those until the end of May, when you'd be in Scotland!"

"I would have been; only for a last-minute conference that kept me in Oxford. They came the day before I left."

There was a sudden spill of light and noise as the door of the tavern opened, disgorging a knot of patrons into the road. Voices and footsteps passed by their refuge, startlingly close. Neither of them spoke until the sounds had disappeared. In the renewed silence, he heard the sound of a conker falling through the leaves, to bounce on the leaves nearby.

Brianna's voice was oddly husky.

"You thought I'd found somebody else . . . and you still came after me?"

He sighed, anger gone as suddenly as it had come, and wiped the damp hair off his face.

"I'd have come if you were married to the King of Siam. Bloody woman."

She was no more than a pale blur in the darkness; he saw the brief movement as she leaned to pick up the fallen conker, and sat toying with it. Finally, she drew a very deep breath and let it out slowly.

"You said *wife* beating."

He paused. The crickets had stopped again.

"You said you were sure. Did you mean it?"

There was a silence, long enough to fill a heartbeat, long enough to fill forever.

"Yes," she said softly.

"In Inverness, I said—"

"You said you'd have me all—or not at all. And I said I understood. I'm sure."

Her shirt had pulled free of her breeches in their struggle, and billowed loose around her in the faint hot breeze. He reached under the floating hem and touched bare skin, which rippled into gooseflesh at his touch. He pulled her close, ran his hands over bare back and bare shoulders under the cloth, buried his face in her hair, her neck, exploring, asking with his hands—did she mean it?

She gripped his shoulders and leaned back, urging him. Yes, she did. He answered, wordless, opening the front of her shirt, spreading it apart. Her breasts were white and soft.

"Please," she said. Her hand was at the back of his head, pulling him toward her. "Please!"

"If I take you now, it's for always," he whispered.

She scarcely breathed, but stood stock-still, letting his hands go where they would. .

"Yes," she said.

The tavern door opened again, startling them apart. He let her go and stood up, reaching down a hand to help her, then stood with her hand in his, waiting while the voices receded into distance.

"Come on," he said, and ducked under the drooping branches.

The shed was some distance from the tavern, dark and quiet. They stopped outside, waiting, but there was no sound from the back of the inn; all the windows on the upper floor were dark.

"I hope Lizzie's gone to bed."

He wondered dimly who Lizzie was, but didn't care. At this distance he could see her face clearly, though the night washed all color from her skin. She looked like a harlequin, he thought; white cheek planes slashed by leaf shadows, framed by the dark of her hair, her eyes black triangles set above a dash of vivid mouth.

He took her hand in his, palm to palm.

"D'ye know what handfasting is?"

"Not exactly. Sort of a temporary marriage?"

"A bit. In the Isles and the remoter parts of the Highlands, where folk were a long way from the nearest minister, a man and a woman now would be handfast; vowed to each other for a year and a day. At the end of it, they find a minister and wed more permanently—or they go their own ways.''

Her hand tightened in his.

''I don't want anything temporary.''

''Neither do I. But I don't think we'll find a minister easily. There are no churches here yet; the nearest minister is likely in New Bern.'' He lifted their linked hands. ''I did say I wanted it all, and if ye did not care enough to wed me . . .''

Her hand tightened, hard.

''I do.''

''All right.''

He took a deep breath and began.

''I, Roger Jeremiah, do take thee, Brianna Ellen, to be my lawful wedded wife. With my goods I thee endow, with my body I thee worship . . .'' Her hand twitched in his, and his balls tightened. Whoever had worded this vow had understood, all right.

''. . . in sickness and in health, in richness and in poverty, so long as we both shall live.''

If I make a vow like that, I'll keep it—no matter what it costs me. Was she thinking of that now?

She brought their linked hands down together, and spoke with great deliberation.

''I, Brianna Ellen, take thee, Roger Jeremiah . . .'' Her voice was scarcely louder than the beating of his own heart, but he heard every word. A breeze came through the tree, rattling the leaves, lifting her hair.

''. . . as long as we both shall live.''

The phrase meant a good bit more to each of them now, he thought, than it would have even a few months before. The passage through the stones was enough to impress anyone with the fragility of life.

There was a moment's silence, broken only by the rustle of leaves overhead and a distant murmur of voices from the tavern's taproom. He raised her hand to his mouth and kissed it, on the knuckle of her fourth finger, where one day—God willing—her ring would be.

It was more of a large shed than a barn, though some beast—a horse or mule—stirred in its stall at one end. There was a strong, clean tang of hops in the air, enough to overpower the milder scents of hay and manure; the Blue Bull brewed its own ale. Roger felt drunk, but not from alcohol.

The shed was very dark, and undressing her was both frustration and delight.

"And I thought it took blind people years to develop a keen sense of touch," he murmured.

The warm breath of her laugh brushed his neck, making the tiny hairs at his nape stir and prickle.

"You're sure it's not like the poem about the five blind men and the elephant?" she said. Her own hand groped, found the opening of his shirt, and slid inside.

" 'No, the beast is like a wall,' " she quoted. Her fingers curved and flattened, curiously exploring the sensitive flesh around his nipple. "A wall with hair. Goodness, a wall with goose bumps, too."

She laughed again, and he bent his head, finding her mouth on the first try, sightless and unerring as a bat snatching a moth from the air.

"Amphora," he murmured against the wide, sweet curve of her lips. His hands slid over the wide, sweet curve of her hips, cupping smoothness cool and solid, timeless and graceful as the swell of ancient pottery, promising abundance. "Like a Grecian vase. God, you've got the most beautiful arse!"

"Jug-butt, huh?"

She vibrated against him, the quiver of laughter passing from her lips to his and into his bloodstream like infection. Her hand slid down his own hip, and up, long fingers fumbling loose the flap of his breeches, groping hesitantly and then more surely, gradually rucking his shirt up to disentangle him from the layers of fabric.

" 'No, the beast is like a rope' . . . oops . . ."

"Stop laughing, damn you."

". . . like a snake . . . no . . . well, maybe a cobra . . . gosh, what would you call *that*?"

"I had a friend once who called it 'Mr. Happy,' " Roger said, feeling light-headed, "but that's a bit whimsical for my tastes." He grabbed her by the arms and kissed her again, long enough to put a stop to any further comparisons.

She was still quivering, but he didn't *think* it was laughter. He slid his arms around her and pulled her closely against him, amazed as always by the sheer size of her—a good deal more amazed now that she was naked, those complex planes of bone and muscle transformed to immediate sensation in his arms.

He paused for breath. He wasn't sure whether the sensation was more akin to drowning or to mountain climbing, but whatever it was, there wasn't much oxygen left between them.

"I've never been able to kiss a girl without stooping before," he said, making conversation in hopes of getting his breath back.

"Oh, good; we wouldn't want you to have a stiff *neck*." The quiver was back in her voice, and it definitely was laughter, though he thought it stemmed as much from nervousness as humor.

"Ha ha," he said, and grabbed her again, oxygen be damned. Her breasts were high and round, pressed against his chest with that unique mixture of softness and firmness that so intrigued him whenever he touched her. One of her hands slid hesitantly between them, groping, then withdrew.

He couldn't bring himself to stop kissing her long enough to finish undressing, but arched his back to let her push the breeches down over his hips. They were loose enough to fall in a puddle around his feet, and he stepped free of them, still holding her, only making a small noise in his throat when her hand came back between them.

She had eaten onions with her dinner. Blindness sharpened not only touch, but taste and smell as well. He tasted roast meat, and sour ale, and bread. And a faint sweet taste that he couldn't identify, that reminded him somehow of green meadows full of waving grass. Did he taste it, or smell it in her hair? He couldn't tell; he seemed to be losing track of his senses as he lost the boundaries between them, breathing her breath, feeling her heart beat as though it lay in his own chest.

She was grasping him a trifle too tightly for comfort, and he broke the kiss at last, breathing heavily.

"Would you consider letting go for a moment? I grant you, it's an effective handle, but it's got better uses."

Instead of letting go, she dropped to her knees.

Roger made a slight move back, startled.

"Christ, are you sure you want to do that?" He wasn't sure whether he hoped she did or not. Her hair tickled against his thighs, and his cock was quivering, desperate for engulfment. At the same time, he didn't want to frighten or repulse her.

"Don't you want me to?" Her hands moved up the backs of his thighs, tentative and ticklish. He could feel every hair on his body spring erect, from knees to waist. It made him feel like a satyr, goat-legged and reeking.

"Well . . . yes. But I haven't bathed in days," he said, rather awkwardly trying to detach himself.

Deliberately, she brushed her nose over his stomach and down, inhaling deeply. His skin pebbled with gooseflesh, the shiver having nothing to do with the temperature of the room.

"You smell good," she whispered. "Like some kind of big male animal."

He grasped her head hard, fingers twisted in the thick, silky hair.

"Too right about that," he whispered. Her hand rested on his wrist, light and warm—God, she was warm.

Without his actually intending it, his grip loosened; he felt the fall of her hair brush his thighs and then stopped thinking anything coherent, as all of the blood left his brain, heading south at a high rate of speed.

"Mi oing i' i'?"

"What?" He came out of his daze a few moments later as she drew back, brushing the hair away from her face.

"I said, am I doing it right?"

"Oh. Ah . . . I think so."

"You *think* so? You don't know for sure?" Brianna seemed to have been regaining her composure as fast as Roger had been losing his; he could hear the suppressed laughter in her voice.

"Well . . . no," he said. "I mean, I haven't . . . that is, no one's . . . yeah, I think so." He had hold of her head again, urging her gently forward.

He thought she was making a low humming noise, somewhere deep in her throat. It might be his own blood, though, thrumming through distended veins, purling in violent eddies like the trapped water of the ocean, seething through the rocks. Another minute, and he was going off like a waterspout.

He pulled away and before she could protest, lifted her to her feet, then urged her down, onto the heap of straw where he had thrown her clothes.

His eyes had adjusted to the dark, but the starlight from the window was still so faint that he could see no more of her than shapes and outlines, white as marble. Not cold, though; not cold at all.

He approached his own duty with mingled excitement and caution; he had tried this exactly once, only to be met with a faceful of a feminine hygiene product that smelled like the flowers in his father's church on Sunday—an off-putting idea if ever there was one.

Brianna was not hygienic. The scent of her was enough to make him want to dispense with any preliminaries and throw himself on her in a pure abandonment of lust.

Instead, he breathed deeply, and kissed her just above the dark smudge of curls.

"Damn," he said.

"What is it?" She sounded faintly alarmed. "Do I smell terrible?"

He closed his eyes and breathed. His head was spinning slightly, and he felt giddy with a combination of lust and laughter.

"No. It's only that I've been wondering for more than a year what color your hair is here." He tugged gently on the curls. "Now here I am face-to-face with it, and I still can't tell."

She giggled, the vibration making her belly shake gently under his hand.

"Do you want me to tell you?"

"No, let me be surprised in the morning." He bent his head to his work, surprised now by the amazing variety of textures, all in such a small space—a smoothness like glass, tickling roughness, a yielding rubberiness, and that sudden slippery slickness, musk and tang and salt together.

After a few moments, he felt her hands come to rest gently on his head, as though in benediction. He hoped the stubble of his beard wasn't hurting her, but she didn't seem to mind. A subterranean quiver ran through the warm flesh of her thighs and she made a small sound that made a similar quiver dart through his belly.

"Am I doing it right?" he inquired half jokingly, lifting his head.

"Oh, yeah," she said softly. "You sure are." Her hands tightened in his hair.

He had started to lower his head again, but jerked it up at this, staring up across the dim white reaches of her body toward the pale oval of her face.

"And just how the hell do you know *that*?" he asked. His only answer was a deep, gurgling laugh. Then he was beside her, with no real notion how he'd got there, his mouth on her mouth, the length of his body pressed to hers, aware only of the heat of her, burning like fever.

She tasted of him, and he of her, and God help him, he wasn't going to be able to go slowly.

He did, though. She was eager, but awkward, trying to lift her hips to him, touching him too quickly, too lightly. He took her hands, one at a time, and placed them flat against his chest. Her palms were hot, and his nipples tightened.

"Feel my heart," he said. His voice sounded thick to his own ears. "Tell me if it stops."

He hadn't actually meant to be funny, and was faintly surprised when she gave a nervous laugh. The laugh disappeared as he touched her. Her hands tightened on his chest; then he felt her relax, opening her legs to him.

"I love you," he murmured. "Oh, Bree, I do love you."

She didn't answer, but a hand floated up from the dark and lay along his cheek, gentle as a tendril of seaweed. She kept it there while he took her, laid open in trust, while her other hand held his beating heart.

He felt more drunk than before. Not groggy or sleepy, though; alive to everything. He could smell his own sweat; he could smell hers, smell the faint tang of fear that tinged her desire.

He closed his eyes and breathed. Tightened his grip on her shoulders. Pressed slowly. Slid in. Felt her tear and bit his own lip, hard enough to draw blood.

Her fingernails dug into his chest.

"Go on!" she whispered.

One sharp hard thrust, and he possessed her.

He stayed that way, eyes closed, breathing. Balanced on an edge of pleasure sharp enough to cause him pain. Dimly he wondered if the pain he felt was hers.

"Roger?"

"Ah?"

"Are you . . . really big, do you think?" Her voice was slightly tremulous.

"Ah . . ." He groped for remnants of coherence. "About the usual." A flash of concern penetrated the feelings of drunkenness. "Am I hurting you a lot?"

"N-no, not exactly. Just . . . can you not move for a minute?"

"A minute, an hour. All my life, if you want." He thought it would kill him not to move, and would have died gladly.

Her hands moved slowly down his back, touching his buttocks.

He shivered and ducked his head, eyes closed, painting her face before his mind's eye with a dozen small and mindless kisses.

"Okay." She whispered in his ear, and like an automaton he began to move, as slowly as he could, restrained as he went by the pressure of her hand on his back.

She stiffened very slightly and relaxed, stiffened and relaxed, he knew he was hurting her, did it again, he ought to stop, she lifted up against him, taking him, and there was a deep and bestial noise that he must have made, now, it had to be now, he had to . . .

Shaking and gasping like a landed fish, he jerked free of her body and lay on her, feeling her breasts crushed against him as he jerked and moaned.

Then he lay still, no longer drunk but wrapped in guilty peace, and felt her arms around him and the warm breath of the whisper in his ear.

"I love you," she said, her voice husky in the hop-scented air. "Stay with me."

"All my life," he said, and wrapped his arms around her.

They lay peacefully together, welded with the sweat of their efforts, listening to each other breathe. Roger stirred at last, lifting his face from her hair, his limbs at once weightless and heavy as lead.

"All right, love?" he whispered. "Have I hurt you?"

"Yes, but I didn't mind." Her hand passed lightly down the length of his back, making him shiver despite the heat. "Was it all right? Did I do it right?" She sounded faintly anxious.

"Oh, God!" He bent his head and kissed her, long and lingering. She tensed a little, but then her mouth relaxed under his.

"It was all right, then?"

"Oh, Jesus!"

"You certainly swear a lot, for a minister's son," she said, with a faint note of accusation. "Maybe those old ladies in Inverness were right; you *have* gone to the devil."

"Not blasphemy," he said. He put his forehead against her shoulder, breathing in the deep, ripe scent of her, of them. "Prayers of thanksgiving."

That made her laugh.

"Oh, it *was* all right, then," she said, with an unmistakable note of relief.

He lifted his head.

"Christ, yes," he said, making her laugh again. "How could you possibly think otherwise?"

"Well, you didn't say anything. You just lay there like somebody'd hit you over the head; I thought maybe you were disappointed."

Now it was his turn to laugh, his face half buried in the smooth damps of her neck.

"No," he said finally, coming up for air. "Behaving as though your spinal column's been removed is a fair indication of male satisfaction. No very gentleman-like, maybe, but honest."

"Oh, okay." She seemed satisfied with that. "The book didn't say anything about that, but then it wouldn't; it didn't bother with what happens afterward."

"What book is this?" He moved cautiously, their skins separating with a noise like two strips of flypaper being parted. "Sorry about the mess." He groped for his wadded shirt and handed it to her.

"The Sensuous Man." She took the shirt and dabbed fastidiously. "There was a lot of stuff about ice cubes and whipped cream that I thought was pretty extreme, but it was good about how to do things like fellatio, and—"

"You learned that from a *book*?" Roger felt as scandalized as one of the ladies of his father's congregation.

"Well, you don't think I go around doing that with people I go out with!" She sounded truly shocked in turn.

"They write books telling young women how to—that's terrible!"

"What's terrible about it?" she said, rather huffy. "How else would I know what to do?"

Roger rubbed a hand over his face, at a loss for words. If asked an hour before, he would have stoutly claimed to be in favor of sexual equality. Under the veneer of modernity, though, there was apparently enough of the Presbyterian minister's son left to feel that a nice young woman really ought to be an ignoramus on her wedding night.

Manfully suppressing this Victorian notion, Roger brought a hand up over the smooth white curves of hip and flank, and cupped a soft full breast.

"Not a thing," he said. "Only," he said, and dipped his head to touch his lips to hers, "there's a bit more to it," and lightly nipped her lower lip, "than ye read in books, aye?"

She moved suddenly, turning to bring all that long white heat against his bare skin, and he shuddered at the shock of it.

"Show me," she whispered, and bit the lobe of his ear.

A rooster crowed, somewhere nearby. Brianna woke from a light doze, berating herself for sleeping. She felt disoriented, tired enough from emotion and exertion to feel light-headed, as though she were floating a foot or two off the ground. At the same time, she didn't want to miss a moment.

Roger stirred by her side, feeling her move. He groped, put an arm around her, and rolled her over, curving himself to fit behind her, knees to knees, belly to buttocks. He brushed the tangles of her hair away from his face, making little *pfft!* noises that made her want to laugh.

He'd made love to her three times. She was very sore, and very happy. She'd imagined it a thousand times, and been wrong every time. There wasn't any way to imagine the sheer terrifying immediacy of being taken like that—stretched suddenly beyond the limits of flesh, penetrated, rent, *entered.* Nor was there any way she could have imagined the sense of power in it.

She had expected to be helpless, the object of desire. Instead, she had held him, felt him quiver with need, all his strength leashed for fear of hurting her—hers to unleash as she would. Hers, to touch and rouse, to call to her, to command.

Nor had she ever thought such tenderness existed as when he cried out and shuddered in her arms, pressing his forehead hard against her own, trusting her with that moment when his strength turned so suddenly to helplessness.

"I'm sorry," he said softly in her ear.

"For what?" She reached back, stroked his thigh. She could do that, now. She could touch him anywhere, delighting in the textures and tastes of his body. She couldn't wait for the daylight, to see him naked.

"For this." He made a small movement with his hand, encompassing the dark around them, the hard straw under them. "I should have waited. I wanted it to be . . . good for you."

"It was very good for me," she said softly. There was a shallow groove down the side of his thigh, where the muscle was indented.

He laughed, a little ruefully.

"I wanted you to have a proper wedding night. Soft bed, clean sheets . . . it should have been better, for your first time."

"I've had soft beds and clean sheets," she said. "But not this." She turned in his arms, reached down and cupped him, that fascinating mass of changeability between his legs. He stiffened for a second in surprise, then relaxed, letting her handle him as she liked. "It couldn't have been better," she said softly, and kissed him.

He kissed her back, slow and lazy, exploring all the depths and hollows of her mouth, letting her have his. He moaned a little, far back in his throat, and reached down to take her hand away.

"Oh, God, you're going to kill me, Bree."

"I'm sorry," she said, anxious. "Did I squeeze too hard? I didn't mean to hurt you."

He laughed at that.

"Not that. But give the poor thing a wee rest, hm?" With a firm hand, he turned her over again, nuzzling her shoulder.

"Roger?"

"Mm?"

"I don't think I've ever been so happy."

"Aye? Well, that's good, then." He sounded drowsy.

"Even if—if we don't get back, as long as we're together, I don't mind."

"We'll get back." His hand cupped her breast, gentle as seaweed coming to rest round a rock. "I told you, there's another way."

"There is?"

"I think so." He told her about the grimoire, the mixture of careful notes and crazed rambling—and about his own passage through the stones of Craigh na Dun.

"The second time, I thought of you," he said softly, and traced her features with a finger in the dark. "I lived. And I did come to the right time. But the diamond Fiona gave me was no more than a smear of lampblack in my pocket."

"So it might be possible to—to steer, somehow?" Brianna couldn't keep a hint of hope from her voice.

"There might be." He hesitated. "There was a—I suppose it must have been a poem, or maybe meant to be a spell—in the book." His hand fell away as he recited it.

"I raise my athame to the North
Where is the home of my power,

> *To the West*
>   *Where is the hearth of my soul,*
> *To the South*
>   *Where is the seat of friendship and refuge,*
> *To the East*
>   *From whence rises the Sun.*
>
> *"Then lay I my blade on the altar I have made.*
>   *I sit down amid three flames.*
>
> *"Three points define a plane, and I am fixed.*
> *Four points box the earth and mine is the fullness thereof.*
> *Five is the number of protection; let no demon hinder me.*
> *My left hand is wreathed in gold*
>   *And holds the power of the sun.*
> *My right hand is sheathed in silver*
>   *And the moon reigns serene.*
>
> *"I begin.*
> *Garnets rest in love about my neck.*
>   *I will be faithful."*

Brianna sat up, arms wrapped around her knees. She was silent for moment.

"That's *nuts*," she said, finally.

"Being certifiably insane is unfortunately no guarantee that someone is likewise wrong," Roger said dryly. He stretched, groaning, and sat up cross-legged on the straw.

"Part of it is traditional ritual, I think—given that the tradition is ancient Celt. The bits about the directions; those are the 'four airts,' which you'll find running through Celtic legend for some way back. As for the blade, the altar, and the flames, it's straight witchcraft."

"She stabbed her husband through the heart and set him on fire." She still remembered as well as he did the stink of petrol and burning flesh in the circle of Craigh na Dun, and shivered, though it was warm in the shed.

"I hope we won't be forced to find someone for a human sacrifice," Roger said, trying and failing to make a joke of it. "The metal, though, and the gems . . . were you wearing any jewelry when you came through, Bree?"

She nodded in reply.

"Your bracelet," she said softly. "And I had my grand-mother's pearl necklace in my pocket. The pearls weren't hurt, though; they came through fine."

"Pearls aren't gemstones," he reminded her. "They're organic —like people." He rubbed a hand across his face; it had been a long day, and his head was starting to throb. "Silver and gold, though; you had the silver bracelet, and the necklace has gold, as well as the pearls. Ah—and your mother; she wore both silver and gold, too, didn't she? Her wedding rings."

"Uh-huh. But 'three points define a plane, Four points box the earth, five is the number of protection . . .' " Brianna murmured under her breath. "Could she mean that you need gemstones to— to do whatever she was trying to do? Are those the 'points'?"

"Could be. She had drawings of triangles and pentagrams, and lists of different gemstones, with the supposed 'magickal' proper-ties listed alongside. She wasn't laying out her theories in any great detail—didn't need to, since she was talking to herself—but the general notion seemed to be that there are lines of force—'ley lines,' she called them—running through the earth. Every now and again, the lines run close to each other, and sort of curl up into knots; and wherever you get such a knot, you've got a place where time essentially doesn't exist."

"So if you step into one, you might step out again . . . any-time."

"Same place, different time. And if you believe that gemstones have a force of their own, which might warp the lines a bit . . ."

"Would any gemstone do?"

"God knows," Roger said. "But it's the best chance we have, aye?"

"Yes," Brianna agreed, after a pause. "But where are we going to find any?" She waved an arm toward the town and its harbor. "I haven't seen anything like that anywhere—in Inverness or here. I think you'd need to go to a large city—London, or maybe Boston or Philadelphia. And then—how much money do you have, Roger? I managed to get twenty pounds, and I still have most of it, but that wouldn't be nearly enough for—"

"That's the point," he interrupted. "I was thinking of that, while you were sleeping. I know—I think I know—where I might lay hands on one stone, at least. The thing is—" He hesitated. "I'll have to go at once, to find it. The man who has it is in New Bern right now, but he won't be there for long. If I take a bit of your money, I can get a boat in the morning and be in New Bern by the next day. I think it's best you stay here, though. Then—''

"I can't stay here!"

"Why not?" He reached for her, groping in the dark. "I don't want you with me. Or rather I do," he corrected himself, "but I think it's a lot safer for you here."

"I don't mean I want to come with you; I mean I can't stay here," she repeated, though she grasped his groping hand. She had nearly forgotten, but now all the excitement of discovery flooded back again. "Roger, I found him—I found Jamie Fraser!"

"Fraser? Where? Here?" He turned toward the door, startled.

"No, he's in Cross Creek, and I know where he'll be on Monday. I have to go, Roger. Don't you understand? He's so close—and I've come so far." She wanted suddenly and irrationally to weep, with the thought of seeing her mother again.

"Aye, I see." Roger sounded faintly anxious. "But could you not wait a few days? It's only a day or so by sea to New Bern, the same back—and I think I can manage what I have to do within a day or two."

"No," she said. "I can't. There's Lizzie."

"Who's Lizzie?"

"My maid—you saw her. She was going to hit you with a bottle." Brianna grinned at the memory. "Lizzie's very brave."

"Aye, I daresay," Roger said dryly. "Be that as it may—"

"But she's sick," Brianna interrupted him. "Didn't you see how pale she is? I think it's malaria; she has horrible fevers and chills that last for a day or so and then stop—and then a few days later, they're back again. I have to find my mother as soon as I can. I *have* to."

She could feel him struggling, choking back arguments. She reached out in the darkness and stroked his face.

"I have to," she repeated softly, and felt him surrender.

"All right," he said. "All right! I'll come to join you, as soon as may be. Do me the one favor, though, aye? Wear a bloody dress!"

"You don't like my breeches?" Laughter fizzed up like the bubbles in carbonated soda—then stopped abruptly, as something occurred to her.

"Roger," she said. "What you're going to do—are you going to steal this stone?"

"Yes," he said simply.

She was quiet for a minute, her long thumb rubbing slowly over the palm of his hand.

"Don't," she said at last, very quietly. "Don't do it, Roger."

"Don't trouble yourself over the man who's got it." Roger reached for her, trying to reassure her. "It's odds-on he stole it from someone else."

"It's not him I'm worried about—it's you!"

"Oh, I'll be all right," he assured her, with casual bravado.

"Roger, they *hang* people in this time for stealing!"

"I won't be caught." His hand sought hers in the darkness, found it, and squeezed. "I'll be with you before ye know it."

"But it isn't—"

"It will be all right," he said firmly. "I said I would take care of you, aye? I will."

"But—"

He rose up on one elbow and silenced her with his mouth. Very slowly, he brought her hand toward him, pressed it between his legs.

She swallowed, the hairs on her arms rising suddenly with anticipation.

"Mm?" he murmured, against her mouth, and without waiting for an answer, pulled her down on the straw, and rolled onto her, nudging her legs apart with his knee.

She gasped and bit his shoulder when he took her, but he made no sound.

"D'ye know," Roger said sleepily, some time later, "I think I've just married my great-aunt six times removed? I've only just thought."

"You *what*?"

"Don't worry, it's nowhere close enough to be incest," he assured her.

"Oh, good," she said, with a certain amount of sarcasm. "I was really worried about that. How can I be your great-aunt, for heaven's sake?"

"Well, as I said, I just thought; I hadn't realized it before. But your father's uncle was Dougal MacKenzie—and it was him that caused all the trouble by getting a child on Geilie Duncan, aye?"

It was the unsatisfactory method of contraception he had been forced to adopt that had caused him to think of it, in fact, but he thought it more tactful not to mention that. Neither shirt was fit to

be worn by now. All things considered, he supposed it was just as
well that Dougal MacKenzie hadn't had his sense of conscien-
tiousness, since that would effectively have prevented Roger's
own existence.

"Well, I don't think it was all *his* fault." Brianna sounded
pleasantly drowsy as well. It couldn't be much off dawn; birds
were already making noises outside, and the air had changed,
growing fresher as the wind came in off the harbor.

"So if Dougal is my great-uncle, and your six-times great-
grandfather . . . no, you're wrong. I'm about your sixth or seventh cousin, not your aunt."

"No, that would be right if we were in the same generation of
descent, but we're not; you're up about five—on your father's
side, at least."

Brianna was silent, trying to work this out in her head. Then
giving up, she rolled over with a faint groan, nestling her bottom
snugly into the hollow of his thighs.

"The hell with it," she said. "As long as you're sure it's not
incest."

He clasped her to his bosom, but his sleepy brain had grasped
the point and wouldn't let it go.

"I really hadn't thought of it," he marveled. "You know what
it means, though? I'm related to your father, too—in fact, I suppose he's my *only* living relation, besides you!" Roger felt thoroughly nonplussed by this discovery, and rather moved. He had
long since reconciled himself to having no close family at all—
not that a seven-times great-uncle was all that close, but—

"No, he isn't," Brianna mumbled.

"What?"

"Not the only one. Jenny, too. And her kids. And grandkids.
My aunt Jenny's your—hm, maybe you're right, after all. 'Cause
if she's my aunt, she's your umpty-great aunt, so maybe *I'm* your
. . . gahh." She let her head loll back against Roger's shoulder,
the spill of her hair soft against his chest. "Who'd you tell them
you were?"

"Who?"

"Jenny and Ian." She shifted, stretching. "When you went to
Lallybroch."

"Never been there." He shifted, too, fitting his body to hers.
His hand settled in the dip of her waist, and he sank back into
drowsiness, giving up the abstract complexities of genealogical
calculation for more immediate sensations.

"No? But then . . ." her voice died away. Fogged with sleep and the exhaustions of pleasure, Roger paid no attention, only snuggling closer with a luxurious moan. A moment later, her voice sliced through his personal fog like a knife through butter.

"How did you know where I was?" she said.

"Hm?"

She twisted suddenly, leaving him with empty arms, and a pair of dark eyes a few inches from his own, slanted with suspicion.

"How did you know where I was?" she repeated slowly, each word a splinter of ice. "How did you know I'd gone to the Colonies?"

"Ah . . . I . . . why . . ." Much too late, he woke to the realization of his danger.

"You didn't have any way of knowing I'd left Scotland," she said, "unless you went to Lallybroch, and they told you where I was going. But you've never been to Lallybroch."

"I . . ." He groped frantically for an explanation—any explanation—but there was none, other than the truth. And from the stiffening of her body, she had deduced that too.

"You knew," she said. Her voice wasn't much above a whisper, but the effect was as great as if she'd shouted in his ear. "You *knew,* didn't you?"

She was sitting up now, looming over him like one of the Erinyes.

"You *saw* that death notice! You already knew, you knew all the time, didn't you?"

"No," he said, trying to gather his scattered wits. "I mean yes, but—"

"How long have you known? Why didn't you *tell* me?" she cried. She stood up and snatched at the pile of clothes under them.

"Wait," he pleaded. "Bree—let me explain—"

"Yeah, explain! I want to hear you explain!" Her voice was ragged with fury, but she did stop her rummaging for a moment, waiting to hear.

"Look." He was up himself by now. "I did find it. Last spring. But I—" He took a deep breath, searching desperately for words that might make her understand.

"I knew it would hurt you. I didn't want to show it to you because I knew there was nothing you could do—there was no point in you breaking your heart for the sake of—"

"What do you mean there's nothing I could do?" She jerked a shirt over her head, and glared toward him, fists clenched.

"You can't change things, Bree! Don't you know that? Your parents tried—they knew about Culloden, and they did everything they possibly could have, to stop Charles Stuart—but they couldn't, could they? They failed! Geillis Duncan tried to make Stuart a king. She failed! They all failed!" He risked a hand on her arm; she was stiff as a statue.

"You can't help them, Bree," he said, more quietly. "It's part of history, it's part of the past—you're not from this time; you can't change what's going to happen."

"You don't know that." She was still rigid, but he thought he heard a hint of doubt in her voice.

"I do!" He wiped a bead of sweat from his jaw. "Listen—if I'd thought there was the slightest chance—but I didn't. I—God, Bree, I couldn't stand the thought of you being hurt!"

She stood still, breathing heavily through her nose. If she'd had the choice, he was sure it would have been fire and brimstone rather than air.

"It wasn't your business to make up my mind for me," she said, speaking through clenched teeth. "No matter what you thought. And about something so important— Roger, how could you *do* something like that!?"

The tone of betrayal in her voice was too much.

"Damn it, I was afraid if I told you, ye'd do just what you did!" he burst out. "You'd leave me! You'd try to go through the stones by yourself. And now look what you've done—here's the both of us in this godforsaken—"

"You're trying to blame *me* for you being here? When I did everything I possibly could to keep you from being such an idiot as to follow me?"

Months of toil and terror, days of worry and fruitless searching caught up with Roger in a scorching blast.

"An idiot? That's the thanks I get for killing myself to find you? For risking my fucking *life* to try to protect you?" He rose from the straw, meaning to get hold of her, not sure if he meant to shake her or bed her again. He had the chance to do neither; a hard shove caught him off balance, square in the chest, and he went sprawling into the hay.

She was hopping on one foot, cursing incoherently as she struggled into her breeches.

"You—bloody—arrogant—damn you, Roger!—*damn* you!" She jerked up the breeches and, leaning down, snatched up her shoes and stockings.

"Go!" she said. "Damn you, go! Go and get hanged if you want to! I'm going to find my parents! And I'm going to save them, too!"

She whirled away, reached the door and jerked it open before he could reach her. She stood for a moment, silhouetted in the paler square of the doorway, dark strands of hair afloat in the wind, live as the strands of Medusa's mane.

"I'm going. Come, or don't come, I don't care. Go back to Scotland—go back through the stones by yourself, for all I care! But by God, you can't stop me!"

And then she was gone.

Lizzie's eyes shot wide as the door banged open against the wall. She hadn't been asleep—how could she sleep?—but had been lying with her eyes closed. She struggled up out of the bedclothes and fumbled for the tinderbox.

"Are ye all right, Miss Bree?"

It didn't sound like it; Brianna was stamping to and fro, hissing through her teeth like a snake, stopping to kick the wardrobe with a resounding thud. There were two more thuds in succession; by the wavering light of the newly lit candle, Lizzie could see that these were caused by Brianna's shoes, which had hit the wall and fallen to the floor.

"Are ye all right?" she repeated, uncertainly.

"Fine!" said Brianna.

From the black air beyond the window a voice roared, "Brianna! I shall come for you! Do ye hear me! I *will come*!"

Her mistress made no answer, but strode to the window, seized the shutters and crashed them shut with a bang that made the room echo. Then she turned like a panther striking, and dashed the candlestick to the floor, plunging the room in suffocating dark.

Lizzie eased herself back into bed and lay frozen, afraid to move or speak. She could hear Brianna tearing off her clothes in silent frenzy, the hiss of indrawn breath punctuating the rustle of cloth and the stamp of bare feet on the wooden floor. Through the shutter, she heard outside the muffled sound of cursing, then nothing.

She had seen Brianna's face for a moment in the light; white as paper and hard as bone, with the eyes black holes. Her gentle, kindly mistress had vanished like smoke, taken over by a *deamhan*, a she-devil. Lizzie was a town lass, born long after

Culloden. She had never seen the wild clansmen of the glens, or a Highlander in the grip of blood fury—but she'd heard the auld stories, and now she knew them true. A person who looked like that might do anything at all.

She tried to breathe as though she were sleeping, but the air came through her mouth in strangled gasps. Brianna seemed not to notice, though; she walked about the room in quick, hard steps, poured water in the bowl and splashed it on her face, then slid between the quilts and lay flat, rigid as a board.

Summoning all her courage, she turned her head toward her mistress.

"Are ye . . . all right, *a bann-sielbheadair*?" she asked, in a voice so low that her mistress could pretend not to have heard it if she wanted.

For a moment she thought that Brianna meant to ignore her. Then, "Yes" came the answer, in a voice so flat and expressionless, it didn't sound like Brianna's at all. "Go to sleep."

She didn't, of course. A body didn't sleep, lying next to someone who might turn into a *ursiq* next thing. Her eyes had adjusted to the dark again, but she was afraid to look, in case the red hair lying on the pillow next to her should suddenly be a mane, and the delicate straight nose changed to a curved, soft muzzle, over teeth that would rend and devour.

It was a few moments before Lizzie realized that her mistress was trembling. Not weeping; there was no sound—but shaking hard enough to make the bedclothes rustle.

Fool, she scolded herself. *It's no but your friend and your lady, with something terrible that's happened to her—and you lyin' here sniveling over fancies!*

On impulse she rolled toward Brianna, reaching for the other girl's hand.

"Bree," she said softly. "Can I be helpin' ye at all, then?"

Brianna's hand curled round hers and squeezed, quick and hard, then let go.

"No," Brianna said, very softly. "Go to sleep, Lizzie; everything will be all right."

Lizzie took leave to doubt that, but said no more, lying back down and breathing quietly. It was a very long time, but at last Brianna's long body shuddered gently and relaxed into sleep. Lizzie couldn't sleep—with the fever gone again, she was alert and restless. The single quilt lay heavy and damp on her, and with the shutters closed, the air in the tiny room was like breathing hot molasses.

Finally, unable to stand it any longer, Lizzie slid quietly out of bed. Keeping an ear out for any sound from the bed, she crept to the window and eased open the shutters.

The air was still hot and muggy outside, but it had begun to move a little; the dawn breeze was coming, with the turn of the air from sea to land. It was still dark, but the sky had begun to lighten as well; she could make out the line of the road below, blessedly empty.

Not knowing what else to do, she did what she always did when troubled or confused; set about to make things tidy. Moving quietly about the room, she picked up the clothes Brianna had so violently discarded, and shook them out.

They were filthy; covered with streaks of leaf stain and dirt, riddled with bits of straw; she could see it even in the dim light from the window. What had Brianna been doing, rolling about on the ground? The instant the thought came into her head, she saw it in her mind, so plain that the notion froze her with shock—Brianna pinned to the ground, struggling with the black devil who had taken her away.

Her mistress was a fine big woman, but yon MacKenzie was a great tall brute of a man; he could have—she stopped herself abruptly, not wanting to imagine. She couldn't help it, though; her mind had gone too far already.

With great reluctance, she brought the shirt to her nose and sniffed. Yes, there it was, the reek of a man, strong and sour as the smell of a rutting goat. The thought of the wicked creature with his body pressed to Brianna's, rubbing against her, leaving his scent on her like a dog who marks his ground—she shuddered in revulsion.

Trembling, she snatched up the breeches and stockings, and bore all the clothes to the basin. She would wash them out, rinse away the reminder of MacKenzie with the dirt and the grass stains. And if the clothes were too wet for her mistress to wear in the morning . . . well, so much the better for that.

She still had the pot of soft yellow lye soap the landlady had given her for laundering; that would take care of it. She plunged the breeks into the water, added a finger's dollop of the soap, and began to work it into a scummy lather, pressing it through and through the fabric.

The window's square was lightening. She cast a stealthy glance over her shoulder at her mistress, but Brianna's breath came slow and steady; good, she wouldn't wake for a time yet.

She looked back to her work, and froze, feeling a chill colder than those that came with her fevers. The thin suds that covered her hands were dark, and small black eddies spread through the water like the ink stains of a cuttlefish.

She didn't want to look, but it was too late to pretend she hadn't seen. She turned back the wet fabric carefully, and there it was; a large, dark blotch, discoloring the cloth just where the seams crossed in the crotch of the breeks.

The rising sun oozed a sullen red through the hazy sky, turning the water in the basin, the air in the room, the whole spinning world, the color of fresh blood.

41

Journey's End

Brianna thought she might scream. Instead, she patted Lizzie's back and spoke softly.

"Don't worry, it'll be all right. Mr. Viorst says he'll wait for us. As soon as you feel better, we'll leave. But for now, don't worry about anything, just rest."

Lizzie nodded, but couldn't answer; her teeth were chattering too hard, in spite of the three blankets over her and the hot brick at her feet.

"I'll go and get your drink, honey. Just rest," Brianna repeated, and with a final pat, rose and left the room.

It wasn't Lizzie's fault, of course, Brianna thought, but she could scarcely have picked a worse moment to have another attack of fever. Brianna had slept late and restlessly after the dreadful scene with Roger, waking to find her clothes washed and hung to dry, her shoes polished, her stockings folded, the room ruthlessly swept and tidied—and Lizzie collapsed in a shivering heap on the empty hearth.

For the thousandth time, she counted the days. Eight days until Monday. If Lizzie's attack followed its usual pattern, she might be able to travel the day after tomorrow. Six days. And according to Junior Smoots and Hans Viorst, five to six days to make the trip upriver at this time of year.

She couldn't miss Jamie Fraser, she couldn't! She had to be in Cross Creek by Monday, come hell or high water. Who knew how long the trial might take, or whether he would leave as soon as it was over? She would have given anything to be able to go at once.

The burning ache to move, to go, was so intense it obliterated all the other aches and burnings of her body—even the deep heart-burning of Roger's betrayal—but there was nothing to be done. She could go nowhere until Lizzie was better.

The taproom was full; two new ships had come into the harbor during the day, and now at evening the benches were full of seamen, with a game of cards loud and lively at the table in the corner. Brianna edged through the blue clouds of tobacco smoke, ignoring the whistles and ribald remarks. Roger had wanted her to wear a dress, had he? Damn him. Her breeches normally kept men at a safe distance, but Lizzie had washed them, and they were still too damp to wear.

She gave one man who reached for her buttocks a glare fit to sear his eyebrows. He stopped in mid-grab, startled, and she slid by him, through the door to the kitchen breezeway.

On the way back, with the jug of steaming catmint tea wrapped in a cloth to keep from burning her, she made a detour around the edge of the room to avoid her would-be assailant. If he touched her, she would pour boiling water in his lap. And while that would be no more than he deserved, and some palliative to her own volcanic feelings, it would waste the tea, which Lizzie badly needed.

She stepped carefully sideways, squeezing between the raucous cardplayers and the wall. The table was scattered with coins and other small valuables: silver and gilt and pewter buttons, a snuff-box, a silver penknife, and scribbled scraps of paper—IOUs, she supposed, or the eighteenth-century equivalent. Then one of the men moved, and beyond his shoulder she caught the gleam of gold.

She glanced down, looked away, then looked back, startled. It was a ring, a plain gold band, but wider than most. It wasn't the gold alone that had caught her eye, though. The ring was no more than a foot away, and while the light in the taproom was more than dim, a candlestick sat on the cardplayers' table, shedding its light in the inner curve of the golden band.

She couldn't quite read the letters engraved there, but she knew the pattern so well that the legend sprang into her mind, unbidden.

She laid a hand on the shoulder of the man who had the ring, interrupting him in mid-jest. He turned, half frowning, the frown clearing as he saw who had touched him.

"Aye, sweetheart, and have ye come to change my luck, then?" He was a big man, with a heavy-boned, handsome face, a broad mouth and a broken nose, and a pair of light green eyes that moved over her with quick appraisal.

She forced her lips to smile at him.

"I hope so," she said. "Shall I give your ring a rub for luck?" Without waiting for permission, she snatched the ring from the table and gave it a brisk rub on her sleeve. Then holding it up to admire the shine, she could see plainly the words written inside.

From F. to C. with love. Always.

Her hand was trembling as she gave it back.

"It's very pretty," she said. "Where did you get it?"

He looked startled, then wary, and she hastened to add, "It's too small for you—won't your wife be angry if you lose her ring?" *How?* she thought wildly. *How did he get it? And what's happened to my mother?*

The full lips curved in a charming smile.

"And if I had a wife, sweetheart, sure I'd leave her for you." He looked her over more closely, long lashes dropping to hide his gaze. He touched her waist in a casual gesture of invitation.

"I'm busy just now, sweetheart, but later . . . eh?"

The jug was burning through the cloth, but her fingers felt cold. Her heart had congealed into a small lump of terror.

"Tomorrow," she said. "In the daylight."

He looked at her, startled, then threw his head back and laughed.

"Well, I've heard men say I'm not a one to be met in the dark, poppet, but the women seem to prefer it." He ran a thick finger down her forearm in play; the red-gold hairs rose at his touch.

"In the daylight, then, if ye like. Come to my ship—*Gloriana*, near the naval yard."

"Gracious, you vill not how long haf eaten?" Miss Viorst peered at Brianna's empty bowl with good-willed incredulity. About the same age as Brianna herself, she was a broad-built, placid-tempered Dutchwoman whose motherly manner made her seem a good deal older.

"Day before yesterday, I think." Brianna gratefully accepted a second helping of dumplings and broth, and yet another thick slab of salt-rising bread slathered with curls of fresh white butter. "Oh, thank you!" The food did something to fill the hollow space that yawned inside her, a small warm comfort around which to center herself.

Lizzie's fever had come on again, two days upriver. This time the attack was longer and more severe, and Brianna had been seriously afraid that Lizzie would die, right there in the middle of the Cape Fear River.

She had sat in mid-canoe for all of a day and a night, while

Viorst and his partner paddled like maniacs, she alternately pouring handfuls of water over Lizzie's head and wrapping her in all
the coats and blankets available, all the time praying to see the
girl's small bosom rise with the next breath.

"If I die, will ye tell my father?" Lizzie had whispered to her
in the rushing dark.

"I will, but you won't, so dinna fash yourself," Brianna said
firmly. It was successful; Lizzie's frail back quivered with laughter at Brianna's attempted Scots, and a small bony hand reached
up to hers, holding on until sleep loosened its grip and the
fleshless fingers slipped free.

Viorst, alarmed at Lizzie's state, had taken them to the house
he shared with his sister a little way below Cross Creek, carrying
Lizzie's blanket-wrapped body up the dusty trail from the river to
a small framed cottage. The girl's stubborn spirit had brought her
through once more, but Brianna thought that the fragile flesh
might not be equal to many more such demands.

She cut a dumpling in half and ate it slowly, savoring the rich
warm juices of chicken and onion. She was grubby, travel-worn,
starved, and exhausted, every bone in her body aching. They had
made it, though. They were in Cross Creek, and tomorrow was
Monday. Somewhere nearby was Jamie Fraser—and God willing,
Claire as well.

She touched the leg of her breeches, and the secret pocket sewn
into the seam. It was still there, the small round hardness of the
talisman. Her mother was still alive. That was all that mattered.

After eating, she went once more to check on Lizzie. Hanneke
Viorst was sitting by the bed darning socks. She nodded to Brianna, smiling.

"She is *gut.*"

Looking down at the wasted, sleeping face, Brianna wouldn't
have said that much. Still, the fever was gone; a hand on Lizzie's
brow came away cool and damp, and a half-empty bowl on the
table nearby showed that she had managed a little nourishment.

"You vill rest, too?" Hanneke half rose, gesturing toward the
trundle bed pulled out in readiness.

Brianna cast a glance of longing at the clean quilts and puffy
bolster, but shook her head.

"Not yet, thank you. What I'd really like is to borrow your
mule, if I might."

There was no telling where Jamie Fraser was now. Viorst had
told her that River Run was a good distance from the town; he

might be there, or he might be staying somewhere in Cross Creek, for convenience. She couldn't leave Lizzie long enough to ride all the way to River Run, but she did want to go into town and find the courthouse where the trial would be held tomorrow. She was taking no chance of missing him by not knowing where to go.

The mule was large and elderly, but not averse to ambling along the riverbank road. He walked somewhat slower than she could have done herself, but that didn't matter; she was in no hurry, now.

Despite her tiredness, she began to feel better as she rode, her bruised, stiff body relaxing into the easy rhythm of the mule's slow gait. It was a hot, humid day, but the sky was clear and blue, and great elms and hickory trees overhung the road, cool leaves filtering the sun.

Torn between Lizzie's illness and her own painful memories, she had noticed nothing of the second half of their voyage, taken no notice of change in the countryside they passed. Now it was like being magically transported during sleep, waking up in a different place. She put everything else aside, determined to forget the last few days and everything in them. She was going to find Jamie Fraser.

The sandy roads, scrub-pine forests, and marshy swamps of the coast were gone, replaced by thickets of cool green, by tall, thick-trunked, canopied trees, and a soft orange dirt that darkened to black mold where the dead leaves lay matted at the edge of the road. The shrieks of gulls and terns were gone, replaced by the muted chatter of a jay, and the soft liquid song of a whippoorwill, far back in the forest.

How would it be? she wondered. She had wondered the same thing a hundred times, and a hundred times imagined different scenes: what she would say, what he would say—would he be glad to see her? She hoped so; and yet he would be a stranger. Likely he would bear no resemblance at all to the man of her imagination. With some difficulty, she fought back the memory of Laoghaire's voice: *A liar and a cheat . . .* Her mother hadn't thought so.

" 'Sufficient unto the day is the evil thereof,' " she murmured to herself. She had come into the town of Cross Creek itself; the scattered houses thickened, and the dirt track widened into a cobbled street, lined with shops and larger houses. There were people about, but it was the hottest part of the afternoon, when the air lay still and heavy on the town. Those who could be, were inside in the shade.

The road curved out, following the riverbank. A small sawmill stood by itself on a point of land, and near it, a tavern. She'd ask there, she decided. Hot as it was, she could use something to drink.

She patted the pocket of her coat, to be sure she had money. She felt instead the prickly outline of a horse chestnut's hull, and pulled her hand away as though she'd been burned.

She felt hollow again, in spite of the food she'd eaten. Lips pressed tight together, she tethered the mule and ducked into the dark refuge of the tavern.

The room was empty save for the landlord, perched in somnolence on his stool. He roused himself at her step, and after the usual goggle of surprise at her appearance, served her beer and gave her courteous directions to the courthouse.

"Thank you." She wiped the sweat from her forehead with a coat sleeve—even inside, the heat was stifling.

"You'll have come for the trial, then?" the landlord ventured, still looking at her curiously.

"Yes—well, not really. Whose trial is it?" she asked, belatedly realizing that she had no idea.

"Oh, it'll be Fergus Fraser," the man said, as though assuming that naturally everyone knew who Fergus Fraser was. "Assault on an officer of the Crown is the charge. He'll be acquitted, though," the landlord went on matter-of-factly. "Jamie Fraser's come down from the mountain for him."

Brianna choked on her beer.

"You *know* Jamie Fraser?" she asked breathlessly, swabbing at the spilled foam on her sleeve.

The landlord's brows went up.

"Wait but a moment and you'll know him, too." He nodded at a pewter tankard full of beer, sitting on the nearby table. She hadn't noticed it when she came in. "He went out the back, just as you came in. He—hey!" He fell back with a cry of surprise as she dropped her own tankard on the floor, and shot out the back door like a bat out of hell.

The light outside was dazzling after the taproom's gloom. Brianna blinked, eyes tearing at the shafts of sun that stabbed through the shifting greens of a screen of maples. Then a movement caught her eye, below the flickering leaves.

He stood in the shade of the maples, half turned away from her,

head bent in absorption. A tall man, long-legged, lean and graceful, with his shoulders broad under a white shirt. He wore a faded
kilt in pale greens and browns, casually rucked up in front as he
urinated against a tree.

He finished and, letting the kilt fall, turned toward the post
house. He saw her then, standing there staring at him, and tensed
slightly, hands half curling. Then he saw past her men's clothes,
and the look of wary suspicion changed at once to surprise as he
realized that she was a woman.

There was no doubt in her mind, from the first glimpse. She
was at once surprised and not surprised at all; he was not quite
what she had imagined—he seemed smaller, only man-sized—but
his face had the lines of her own; the long, straight nose and
stubborn jaw, and the slanted cat-eyes, set in a frame of solid
bone.

He moved toward her out of the maples' shadow, and the sun
struck his hair with a spray of copper sparks. Half consciously she
raised a hand and pushed a strand of hair back from her face,
seeing from the corner of her eye the matching gleam of thick
red-gold.

"What d'ye want here, lassie?" he asked. Sharp, but not unkind. His voice was deeper than she had imagined; the Highland
burr slight but distinct.

"You," she blurted. Her heart seemed to have wedged itself in
her throat; she had trouble forcing any words past it.

He was close enough that she caught the faint whiff of his
sweat and the fresh smell of sawn wood; there was a golden
scatter of sawdust caught in the rolled sleeves of his linen shirt.
His eyes narrowed with amusement as he looked her up and
down, taking in her costume. One reddish eyebrow rose, and he
shook his head.

"Sorry, lass," he said, with a half-smile. "I'm a marrit man."

He made to pass by, and she made a small incoherent sound,
putting out a hand to stop him, but not quite daring to touch his
sleeve. He stopped and looked at her more closely.

"No, I meant it; I've a wife at home, and home's not far," he
said, evidently wishing to be courteous. "But—" He stopped,
close enough now to take in the grubbiness of her clothes, the
hole in the sleeve of her coat and the tattered ends of her stock.

"Och," he said in a different tone, and reached for the small
leather purse he wore tied at his waist. "Will ye be starved, then,
lass? I've money, if you must eat."

She could scarcely breathe. His eyes were dark blue, soft with kindness. Her eyes fixed on the open collar of his shirt, where the curly hairs showed, bleached gold against his sunburnt skin.

"Are you—you're Jamie Fraser, aren't you?"

He glanced sharply at her face.

"I am," he said. The wariness had returned to his face; his eyes narrowed against the sun. He glanced quickly behind him, toward the tavern, but nothing stirred in the open doorway. He took a step closer to her.

"Who asks?" he said softly. "Have you a message for me, lass?"

She felt an absurd desire to laugh welling up in her throat. Did she have a message?

"My name is Brianna," she said. He frowned, uncertain, and something flickered in his eyes. He knew it! He'd heard the name and it meant something to him. She swallowed hard, feeling her cheeks blaze as though they'd been seared by a candle flame.

"I'm your daughter," she said, her voice sounding choked to her own ears. "Brianna."

He stood stock-still, not changing expression in the slightest. He had heard her, though; he went pale, and then a deep, painful red washed up his throat and into his face, sudden as a brushfire, matching her own vivid color.

She felt a deep flash of joy at the sight, a rush through her midsection that echoed that blaze of blood, recognition of their fair-skinned kinship. Did it trouble him to blush so strongly? she wondered suddenly. Had he schooled his face to immobility, as she had learned to do, to mask that telltale surge?

Her own face felt stiff, but she gave him a tentative smile.

He blinked, and his eyes moved at last from her face, slowly taking in her appearance, and—with what seemed to her a new and horrified awareness—her height.

"My God," he croaked. "You're *huge*."

Her own blush had subsided, but now came back with a vengeance.

"And whose fault is *that*, do you think?" she snapped. She drew herself up straight and squared her shoulders, glaring. So close, at her full height, she could look him right in the eye, and did.

He jerked back, and his face did change then, mask shattering in surprise. Without it, he looked younger; underneath were shock, surprise, and a dawning expression of half-painful eagerness.

"Och, no, lassie!" he exclaimed. "I didna mean it that way, at all! It's only—" He broke off, staring at her in fascination. His hand lifted, as though despite himself, and traced the air, outlining her cheek, her jaw and neck and shoulder, afraid to touch her directly.

"It's true?" he whispered. "It is you, Brianna?" He spoke her name with a queer accent—*Bree*anah—and she shivered at the sound.

"It's me," she said, a little huskily. She made another attempt at a smile. "Can't you tell?"

His mouth was wide and full-lipped, but not like hers; wider, a bolder shape, that seemed to hide a smile in the corners of it, even in repose. It was twitching now, not certain what to do.

"Aye," he said. "Aye, I can."

He did touch her then, his fingers drawing lightly down her face, brushing back the waves of ruddy hair from temple and ear, tracing the delicate line of her jaw. She shivered again, though his touch was noticeably warm; she could feel the heat of his palm against her cheek.

"I hadna thought of you as grown," he said, letting his hand fall reluctantly away. "I saw the pictures, but still—I had ye in my mind somehow as a wee bairn always—as my babe. I never expected . . ." His voice trailed off as he stared at her, the eyes like her own, deep blue and thick-lashed, wide in fascination.

"Pictures," she said, feeling breathless with happiness. "You've seen pictures of me? Mama found you, didn't she? When you said you had a wife at home—"

"Claire," he interrupted. The wide mouth had made its decision; it split into a smile that lit his eyes like the sun in the dancing tree leaves. He grabbed her arms, tight enough to startle her.

"You'll not have seen her, then? Christ, she'll be mad wi' joy!"

The thought of her mother was overwhelming. Her face cracked, and the tears she had been holding back for days spilled down her cheeks in a flood of relief, half choking her as she laughed and cried together.

"Here, lassie, dinna weep!" he exclaimed in alarm. He let go of her arm and snatched a large, crumpled handkerchief from his sleeve. He patted tentatively at her cheeks, looking worried.

."Dinna weep, *a leannan,* dinna be troubled," he murmured. "It's all right, *m' annsachd;* it's all right."

"I'm all right; everything's all right. I'm just—happy," she said. She took the handkerchief, wiped her eyes and blew her nose. "What does that mean—*a leannan?* And the other thing you said?"

.'You'll not have the Gaelic, then?" he asked, and shook his head. "No, of course she wouldna have been taught," he murmured, as though to himself.

"I'll learn," she said firmly, giving her nose a last wipe. *"A leannan?"*

A slight smile reappeared on his face as he looked at her.

"It means 'darling,' " he said softly. *"M' annsachd*—my blessing."

The words hung in the air between them, shimmering like the leaves. They stood still, both stricken suddenly with shyness by the endearment, unable to look away from each other, unable to find more words.

"Fa—" Brianna started to speak, then stopped, suddenly seized with doubt. What should she call him? Not Daddy. Frank Randall had been Daddy to her all her life; it would be a betrayal to use that name to another man—any other man. Jamie? No, she couldn't possibly; rattled as he was by her appearance, he had still a formidable dignity that forbade such casual use. "Father" seemed remote and stern—and whatever Jamie Fraser might be, he wasn't that; not to her.

He saw her hesitate and flush, and recognized her trouble.

"You can . . . call me Da," he said. His voice was husky; he stopped and cleared his throat. "If—if ye want to, I mean," he added diffidently.

"Da," she said, and felt the smile bloom easily this time, unmarred by tears. "Da. Is that Gaelic?"

He smiled back, the corners of his mouth trembling slightly.

"No. It's only . . . simple."

And suddenly it was all simple. He held out his arms to her. She stepped into them and found that she had been wrong; he *was* as big as she'd imagined—and his arms were as strong about her as she had ever dared to hope.

◄————

Everything after that seemed to happen in a daze. Overcome by emotion and fatigue, Brianna was conscious of events more as a series of images, sharp as stop-frame photos, than as a moving flow of life.

Lizzie, gray eyes blinking in the sudden light, tiny and pale in the arms of a sturdy black groom with an improbable Scottish accent. A wagon piled with glass and fragrant wood. The polished rumps of horses, and the jolt and creak of wooden wheels. Her father's voice, deep and warm in her ear, describing a house to be built, high on a mountain ridge, explaining that the windows were a surprise for her mother.

"But no such a surprise as you, lassie!" And a laugh of deep joy that seemed to echo in her bones.

A long ride down dusty roads, and sleeping with her head on her father's shoulder, his free arm around her as he drove, breathing the unfamiliar scent of his skin, his strange long hair brushing her face when he turned his head.

Then the cool luxury of the big, breezy house, filled with the scent of beeswax and flowers. A tall woman with white hair and Brianna's face, and a blue-eyed gaze that looked disconcertingly beyond her. Long cool hands that touched her face and stroked her hair with abstract curiosity.

"Lizzie," she said, and a pretty woman bent over Lizzie, murmuring, "Jesuit bark," her black hands beautiful against the yellow porcelain of Lizzie's face.

Hands—so many hands. Everything was done as if by magic, with soft murmurs as they passed her from hand to hand. She was stripped and bathed before she could protest, scented water poured over her, firm, gentle fingers that massaged her scalp as lavender soap was sluiced from her hair. Linen towels and a small black girl who dried her feet and sprinkled them with rice powder.

A fresh cotton gown and floating barefoot over polished floors, to see her father's eyes light at sight of her. Food—cakes and trifles and jellies and scones—and hot, sweet tea that seemed to replace the blood in her veins.

A pretty blond girl with a frown on her face, who seemed peculiarly familiar; her father called her Marsali. Lizzie, washed and wrapped in a blanket, both frail hands round a mug of pungent liquid, looking like a stepped-on flower newly watered.

Talk, and people coming, and more talk, with only the occasional phrase penetrating through her growing fog.

". . . Farquard Campbell has more sense . . ."

"Fergus, Da, did ye see him? Is he all right?"

Da? she thought, half puzzled, faintly indignant that someone else should call him that, because . . . because . . .

Her aunt's voice, coming from a great distance, saying, "The poor child is asleep where she sits; I can hear her snoring. Ulysses, take her up to bed."

And then strong arms that lifted her with no sense of strain, but not the candlewax smell of the black butler; the sawdust and linen scent of her father. She gave up the struggle and fell asleep, her head on his chest.

Fergus Fraser might sound like a Scottish clansman; he looked like a French noble. A French noble on his way to the guillotine, Brianna silently amended her first impression.

Handsomely dark, slightly built, and not very tall, he sauntered into the dock, and turned to face the room, long nose lifted an inch above the usual. The shabby clothes, the unshaven jaw, and the large purple bruise over one eye subtracted nothing from his air of aristocratic disdain. Even the curved metal hook that he wore in replacement of a missing hand only added to his impression of disreputable glamour.

Marsali gave a small sigh at sight of him, and her lips grew tight. She leaned across to Brianna to whisper to Jamie.

"What have they done to him, the bastards?"

"Nothing that matters." He made a small motion, gesturing her back, and she subsided into her seat, glowering at bailiff and sheriff in turn.

They had been lucky to procure seats; every space in the small building was filled, and people were jostling and muttering at the back of the room, kept in order only by the presence of the red-coated soldiers who guarded the doors. Two more soldiers stood to attention at the front of the room, beside the Justice's bench, an officer of some sort lurking in the corner behind them.

Brianna saw the officer catch Jamie Fraser's eye, and a look of malign satisfaction crept over the man's broad features, a look almost of gloating. It made the small hairs rise on the back of her neck, but her father met the man's gaze squarely, then turned away, indifferent.

The Justice arrived and took his place, and the ceremonies of justice being duly performed, the trial began. Evidently, it was not intended to be a trial by jury, since no such body was present; only the Justice and his minions.

Brianna had made out little from the conversation the evening before, though over breakfast she had managed to disentangle the confusion of persons. The young black woman's name was Phaedre, one of Jocasta's slaves, and the tall homely boy with the charming smile was Jamie's nephew, Ian—her cousin, she thought, with the same small thrill of discovered kinship she had felt at Lallybroch. The lovely blond Marsali was Fergus's wife, and Fergus, of course, was the French orphan whom Jamie had informally adopted in Paris, before the Stuart Rising.

Mr. Justice Conant, a tidy gentleman of middle age, settled his wig, arranged his coat, and called for the charges to be read. These were, to wit, that one Fergus Claudel Fraser, resident of Rowan County, had on August 4 of this year of our Lord 1769, feloniously assaulted the person of one Hugh Berowne, a deputy sheriff of said county, and stolen from him Crown property, then lawfully in the deputy's custody.

The said Hugh, being called to the stand, proved to be a gangling fellow of some thirty years and a nervous disposition. He twitched and stammered through his testimony, averring that he had encountered the defendant on the Buffalo Trail Road, while he, Berowne, was in pursuit of his lawful duties. He had been roughly abused by the defendant in the French tongue, and upon his endeavoring to leave, had been pursued by the defendant, who had apprehended him, struck him in the face, and taken away the property of the Crown in Berowne's custody, to wit, one horse, with bridle and saddle.

Upon the invitation of the court, the witness here pulled back the right side of his mouth in a grimace, disclosing a broken tooth, suffered in the assault.

Mr. Justice Conant peered interestedly at the shattered remains of the tooth, and turned to the prisoner.

"Indeed. And now, Mr. Fraser, might we hear your account of this unfortunate event?"

Fergus lowered his nose half an inch, awarding the justice the same regard he might have bestowed on a cockroach.

"This loathsome wad of dung," he began in measured tones, "had—"

"The prisoner will refrain from insult," Justice Conant said coldly.

"The deputy," Fergus resumed, without turning a hair, "had come upon my wife as she returned from the flour mill, with my infant son upon her saddle. This—the deputy—hailed her, and without ceremony dragged her from the saddle, informed her that he was taking the horse and its equipment in payment of tax, and left her and the child on foot, five miles from my home, in the blazing sun!'' He glared ferociously at Berowne, who narrowed his own gaze in reply. Next to Brianna, Marsali exhaled strongly through her nose.

''What tax did the deputy claim was owed?''

A dark flush had mantled Fergus's cheeks.

''I owe nothing! It was his claim that my land is subject to an annual rent of three shillings, but it is not! My land is exempt from this tax, by virtue of the terms of a land grant made to James Fraser by Governor Tryon. I told the stinking *salaud* as much, when he visited my home to try to collect the money.''

''I heard nothing of such a grant,'' Berowne said sulkily. ''These folks will tell you any tale at all, to put off paying. Lallygags and cheats, the lot of them.''

''Oreilles en feuille de chou!''

A small ripple of laughter ran through the room, nearly drowning out the Justice's rebuke. Brianna's high-school French was just about adequate to translate this as ''Cauliflower ears!'' and she joined in the general smile.

The Justice lifted his head and peered into the courtroom.

''Is James Fraser present?''

Jamie rose and bowed respectfully.

''Here, milord.''

''Swear the witness, Bailiff.''

Jamie, having been duly sworn, attested to the facts that he was in fact the proprietor of a grant of land, that said grant had been made and its terms agreed to by Governor Tryon, that said terms did include a quitment of land rent to the Crown for a period of ten years, such period to expire some nine years hence, and finally, that Fergus Fraser did maintain a house upon and farm crops within the boundaries of the granted territory, under license from himself, James Alexander Malcolm MacKenzie Fraser.

Brianna's attention had at first been fixed upon her father; she could scarcely get enough of looking at him. He was the tallest man in the courtroom, and by far the most striking, attired in snowy linen and a coat of deep blue that set off his slanted eyes and fiery hair.

A movement in the corner attracted her eye, though, and she looked to see the officer she had noticed before. He was no longer looking at her father, but had fixed Hugh Berowne with a penetrating stare. Berowne gave the shadow of a nod, and sat back to await the end of Fraser's testimony.

"It would appear that Mr. Fraser's claim of exemption holds true, Mr. Berowne," the Justice said mildly. "I must therefore hold him acquitted of the charge of—"

"He cannot prove it!" Berowne blurted out. He glanced at the officer, as though for moral support, and stiffened his long chin. "There is no documentary proof; only James Fraser's word."

Another stir went through the courtroom; this one uglier in tone. Brianna had no trouble hearing the shock and outrage that her father's word had been called in question, and felt an unexpected pride.

Her father showed no anger, though; he rose again, and bowed to the Justice.

"And your Lordship will permit me." He reached into his coat and removed a folded sheet of parchment, with a blob of red sealing wax affixed.

"Your Lordship will be familiar with the Governor's seal, I am sure," he said, laying it on the table before Mr. Conant. The Justice raised one eyebrow, but looked carefully at the seal, then broke it open, examined the document within, and laid it down.

"This is a duly witnessed copy of the original grant of land," he announced, "signed by His Excellency, William Tryon."

"How did you get that?" Berowne blurted. "There wasn't time to get to New Bern and back!" Then all the blood drained from his face. Brianna looked at the officer; his pudgy face seemed to have acquired all the blood Berowne had lost.

The Justice cast him a sharp glance, but merely said, "Given that documentary proof *is* now entered in evidence, we find that the defendant is plainly not guilty of the charge of theft, since the property in question was his own. On the matter of assault, however—" At this point he noticed that Jamie had not sat down, but was still standing in front of the bench.

"Yes, Mr. Fraser? Had you something else to tell the court?" Justice Conant dabbed at a trickle of sweat that ran down from under his wig; with so many bodies packed into the small room, it was like a sweatbath.

"I beg the court might gratify my curiosity, your Lordship. Does Mr. Berowne's original charge describe more fully the attack upon him?"

The Justice raised both eyebrows, but shuffled quickly through the papers on the table before him, then handed one to the bailiff, pointing to a spot on the page.

"Complainant stated that one Fergus Fraser struck him in the face with his fist, causing complainant to fall stunned upon the ground, whereat the defendant seized the bridle of the horse, leapt upon it, and rode away, calling out remarks of an abusive nature in the French tongue. Complainant—"

A loud cough from the dock pulled all eyes to the defendant, who smiled charmingly at Mr. Justice Conant, plucked a handkerchief from his pocket and elaborately wiped his face—using the hook at the end of his left arm.

"Oh!" said the Justice, and swiveled cold eyes toward the witness chair, where Berowne squirmed in hot-faced agony.

"And would you care to explain, sir, how you have sustained injury upon the right side of your face, when struck by the left fist of a man who does not have one?"

"Yes, *crottin*," Fergus said cheerfully. "Explain that one."

Perhaps feeling that Berowne's attempts at explanation were best conducted in privacy, Justice Conant mopped his neck and put a summary end to the trial, dismissing Fergus Fraser with no stain upon his character.

"It was me," Marsali said proudly, clinging to the arm of her husband at the celebratory feast that followed the trial.

"You?" Jamie gave her an amused glance. "That fisted yon deputy in the face, ye mean?"

"Not my fist, my foot," she corrected. "When the wicked *salaud* tried to drag me off the horse, I kicked him in the jaw. He'd never ha' got me down," she added, glowering at the memory, "save he snatched Germaine from me, so of course I had to go and get him."

She petted the sleek blond head of the toddler who clung to her skirts, a piece of biscuit clutched in one grubby fist.

"I don't quite understand," Brianna said. "Did Mr. Berowne not want to admit that a woman hit him?"

"Ah, no," Jamie said, pouring another cup of ale and handing it to her. "It was only Sergeant Murchison making a nuisance of himself."

"Sergeant Murchison? That would be the army officer who was at the trial?" she asked. She took a small sip of the ale, for politeness' sake. "The one who looks like a half-roasted pig?"

Her father grinned at this characterization.

"Aye, that'll be the man. He's a mislike of me," he explained. "This wilna be the first time—or the last—that he's tried such a trick to cripple me."

"He could not hope to succeed with such a ridiculous charge," Jocasta chimed in, leaning forward and reaching out a hand. Ulysses, standing by, moved the plate of bannocks the necessary inch. She took one, unerringly, and turned her disconcerting blind eyes toward Jamie.

"Was it really necessary for you to subvert Farquard Campbell?" she asked, disapproving.

"Aye, it was," Jamie answered. Seeing Brianna's confusion, he explained.

"Farquard Campbell is the usual justice of this district. If he hadna fallen ill so conveniently"—and here he grinned again, mischief dancing in his eyes—"the trial would have been held last week. That was their plan, aye? Murchison and Berowne. They meant to bring the charge, arrest Fergus, and force me down from the mountain in the midst of the harvest—and they succeeded in that much, damn them," he added ruefully.

"But they counted on my not being able to obtain a copy of the grant from New Bern before the trial—as indeed I could not, had it been last week." He gave Ian a smile, and the boy, who had ridden hellbent to New Bern to procure the document, blushed pink and buried his face in a bowl of punch.

"Farquard Campbell is a friend, Auntie," Jamie said to Jocasta, "but ye ken as well as I that he's a man of the law; it wouldna make a bit of difference that he knows the terms of my grant as well as I do; if I couldna produce the proof in court, he would feel himself forced to rule against me.

"And if he had," he went on, returning to Brianna, "I should have been forced to appeal the verdict, which would mean Fergus being taken to prison in New Bern, and a new trial scheduled there. The end of it would have been the same—but it would have taken both Fergus and myself off the land for most of the harvest season, and cost me more in fees than the harvest will bring."

He looked at Brianna over the rim of his cup, blue eyes suddenly serious.

"You'll no be thinking me rich, I hope?" he asked.

"I hadn't thought of it at all," she replied, startled, and he smiled.

"That's as well," he said, "for while I've a good bit of land,

there's little of it under cultivation as yet; we've enough—barely
—to seed the fields and feed ourselves, wi' a bit left over for the
cattle. And capable as your mother is"—the smile widened—
"she canna bring in thirty acres of corn and barley by herself."
He set down his empty cup and stood up.

"Ian, will ye see to the supplies and drive up the wagon with
Fergus and Marsali? The lass and I will go ahead, I think." He
glanced down at Brianna questioningly.

"Jocasta will care for your wee maid here. Ye dinna mind
going so soon?"

"No," she said, putting down her cup and standing up too.
"Can we go today?"

I took down the bottles from the cupboard, one by one, uncork-
ing one now and then to sniff at the contents. If not thoroughly
dry before storage, fleshy-leaved herbs would rot in the bottle;
seeds would grow exotic molds.

The thought of molds made me think once more of my penicillin plantation. Or what I hoped might one day be one, were I
lucky enough, and observant enough to know my luck. Of the
hundreds of molds that grew easily on stale, damp bread, *Penicil-
lium* was only one. What were the odds of a stray spore of that
one precious mold taking root on the slices of bread I laid out
weekly? What were the odds of an exposed slice of bread surviving long enough for *any* spores to find it? And lastly, what were
the odds that I would recognize it if I saw it?

I had been trying for more than a year, with no success so far.

Even with the marigolds and yarrow I scattered for repellency,
it was impossible to keep the vermin away. Mice and rats, ants
and cockroaches; one day I had even found a party of burglarious
squirrels in the pantry, holding riot over scattered corn and the
gnawed ruins of half my seed potatoes.

The only recourse was to lock all edibles in the big hutch Jamie
had built—that, or keep them in thick wooden casks or lidded
jars, resistent to the efforts of tooth and claw. But to seal food
away from four-footed thieves was also to seal it away from the air
—and the air was the only messenger that might one day bring me
a real weapon against disease.

*Each of the plants carries an antidote to some illness—if we
only knew what it was.* I felt a renewed pang of loss when I
thought of Nayawenne; not only for herself but for her knowledge.

She had taught me only a fraction of the things she knew, and I regretted that most bitterly—though not as bitterly as the loss of my friend.

Still, I knew one thing she had not—the manifold virtues of that smallest of plants, the lowly bread mold. To find it would be difficult, to recognize it, and to use it, even more so. But I never doubted it was worth the search.

To leave bread exposed in the house was to draw the mice and rats inside. I had tried setting it on the sideboard—Ian had absent-mindedly consumed half of my budding antibiotic incubator, and mice and ants made short work of the rest while I was away from the house.

It was simply impossible, in summer, spring, or autumn, either to leave bread exposed and unguarded or to stay inside to look after it. There were too many urgent chores to be done outside, too many calls to attend births or illness, too much opportunity for foraging.

In the winter, of course, the vermin went away, to lay their eggs against the spring, and hibernate under a blanket of dead leaves, secure from the cold. But the air was cold, too; too cold to bring me living spores. The bread I laid out either curled and dried, or went soggy, depending on its distance from the fire; in either case, sporting nothing but the occasional orange or pink crust: the molds that lived in the crevices of the human body.

I would try again in the spring, I thought, sniffing at a bottle of dried marjoram. It was good; musky as incense, smelling of dreams. The new house on the ridge was already rising, foundation laid and rooms marked out. I could see the skeletal framework from the cabin door, black against the clear September sky on the ridge.

By the spring, it would be finished. I would have plastered walls and laid oak floors, glass windows with stout frames that kept out mice and ants—and a nice snug, sunny surgery in which to conduct my medical practice.

My glowing visions were interrupted by a raucous bellow from the penfold; Clarence announcing an arrival. I could hear voices in the distance, in between Clarence's shrieks of ecstasy, and I hastily began to tidy away the scatter of corks and bottles. It must be Jamie returning with Fergus and Marsali—or at least I hoped so.

Jamie had been confident of the trial's outcome, but I worried nonetheless. Raised to believe that British law in the abstract was one of the great achievements of civilization, I had seen a good deal too many of its concrete applications to have much faith in its avatars. On the other hand, I had quite a bit of faith in Jamie.

Clarence's vocalizations had dropped to the wheezing gargle he used for intimate converse, but the voices had stopped. That was odd. Perhaps things had gone wrong after all?

I thrust the last of the bottles back into the cupboard and went to the door. The dooryard was empty. Clarence hee-hawed enthusiastically at my appearance, but nothing else moved. Someone had come, though—the chickens had scattered, fleeing into the bushes.

A brisk chill ran up my spine and I whirled, trying to look in front of me and over my shoulder at the same time. Nothing. The chestnut trees behind the house sighed in the breeze, a shimmer of sun filtered through their yellowing leaves.

I knew beyond the shadow of a doubt that I wasn't alone. Damn, and I'd left my knife on the table inside!

"Sassenach." My heart nearly stopped at the sound of Jamie's voice. I spun toward it, relief being rapidly overcome by annoyance. What did he think he—

For a split second, I thought I was seeing double. They were sitting on the bench outside the door, side by side, the afternoon sun igniting their hair like matchheads.

My eyes focused on Jamie's face, alight with joy—then shifted right.

"Mama." It was the same expression; eagerness and joy and longing all together. I had no time even to think before she was in my arms, and I was in the air, knocked off my feet both literally and figuratively.

"Mama!"

I hadn't any breath; what hadn't been taken away by shock was being squeezed out by a rib-crushing hug.

"Bree!" I managed to gasp, and she put me down, though she didn't let go. I looked disbelievingly up, but she was real. I looked for Jamie, and found him standing beside her. He said nothing, but gave me an face-splitting grin, his ears bright pink with delight.

"I, ah, I wasn't expecting—" I said idiotically.

Brianna gave me a grin to match her father's, eyes bright as stars and damp with happiness.

"Nobody expects the Spanish Inquisition!"

"What?" said Jamie blankly.

PART TEN

Impaired Relations

42

Moonlight

September 1769

S he woke from a dreamless sleep, a hand on her shoulder. She jerked and started up on one elbow, blinking. Jamie's face was barely distinguishable above her in the gloom; the fire had burned down to nothing more than a glow, and it was nearly pitch-black in the cabin.

"I shall be hunting up the mountain, lass; will ye come wi' me?" he whispered.

She rubbed her eyes, trying to reassemble her sleep-scattered thoughts, and nodded.

"Good. Wear your breeks." He rose silently and went out, letting in a breath of piercing-sweet cold air as the door opened.

By the time she had pulled on breeks and stockings, he was back, moving just as silently, despite the armload of firewood he carried. He nodded to her and knelt to rekindle the fire; she thrust her arms into her coat and went out herself, in search of the privy.

The world outside was black and dreamlike; if not for the chill, she might have thought herself still asleep. Stars burned coldly bright, but seemed to hang low, as though they might fall from the sky any minute and be extinguished, sizzling, in the mist-damp trees on the ridges beyond.

What time was it? she wondered, shivering at the touch of damp wood on her sleep-warmed thighs. Somewhere in the small hours; surely it was a long time until dawn. Everything was hushed; no insects hummed yet in her mother's garden, and there were no rustlings, even from the dry corn-stooks propped in the field.

When she pushed open the door of the cabin, the air inside seemed almost solid; a block of stale smoke, fried food, and the smell of sleeping bodies. By contrast, the air outside was sweet but thin—she kept taking large gulps, to get enough.

He was ready; a leather bag was tied at his belt with ax and powder horn, a bigger canvas sack slung over his shoulder. She didn't come in, but stood in the doorway watching as he bent quickly and kissed her mother in the bed.

He knew she was there, of course—and it was no more than a light kiss on the forehead—but she felt like an intruder, a voyeur. The more so when Claire's long, pale hand floated up from the quilts and touched his face with a tenderness that squeezed her heart. Claire murmured something, but Brianna didn't hear it.

She turned away quickly, face hot in spite of the chilly air, and was standing by the edge of the clearing when he came out. He shut the door behind him, waiting for the *clunk* within as it was barred. He had a gun, a long-barreled thing that seemed nearly as tall as she was.

He didn't speak, but smiled at her and cocked his head toward the wood. She followed, keeping up easily as he took a faint trail that led through groves of spruce and chestnut. His feet knocked the dew from clumps of grass, and left a dark trail through tussocks of shimmering silver.

The trail wound to and fro, nearly level for a long time, but then began to head uphill. She felt the shift, rather than saw it. It was still very dark, but suddenly the silence was gone. In the next breath, a bird began to call from the wood nearby.

Then the whole mountainside was alive with birdsong, screeches and trills and whirrs. Under the calling was a sense of movement, of fluttering and scratching just below the threshold of hearing. He stopped, listening.

She stopped, too, looking at him. The light had changed so slowly that she was scarcely aware of it; her eyes adapted to the dark, she could see easily by the starlight, and knew the change to daylight only when she glanced from the ground and saw the vivid color of her father's hair.

He had food in his bag; they sat on a log and shared apples and bread. Then she drank from a trickle that dropped from a ledge, filling her hands with cold crystal. Looking back, she could no longer see any trace of the small settlement; houses and fields were gone, as though the mountain had silently drawn her forests together, swallowing them up.

She wiped her hands on the skirts of her coat, feeling the prickly shape of the conker in her pocket. No horse chestnuts on these wooded slopes; that was an English tree, planted by some expatriate in the hope of creating a memory of home; a living link to another life. She curled her hand around it briefly, wondering whether her own links had been severed for good, then let it go, and turned to follow her father uphill.

At first her heart had pounded and her thigh muscles strained at the unaccustomed labor of climbing, but then her body had found the rhythm of the ground. With the coming of light, she no longer stumbled. By the time they emerged at the top of a steep slope, her feet trod so lightly on the spongy leaves that she felt she might float off into the sky that seemed so near, cut free of the earth.

For a single moment, she wished that she could. But the links still held in the chain that bound her to the earth—her mother, her father, Lizzie . . . and Roger. The morning sun was rising, a great ball of flame above the mountains. She had to shut her eyes for a moment, not to be blinded.

Here it was; the place he had meant to bring her. At the foot of a towering escarpment, part of the rock had fallen into a loose tumble, overgrown by moss and lichen, small saplings jutting drunkenly from cracks in the rock. He tilted his head, gesturing her to follow him. There was a way through the huge boulders, hard to see, but there. He felt her hesitate behind him, and looked back.

She smiled and waved a hand at the rock. A huge piece of limestone had fallen and split in two; he stood between the pieces.

"It's all right," she said softly. "It just reminded me."

That reminded *him,* and raised the hairs on his forearms. He had to stop and watch as she stepped through, only to be sure. But it was fine; she stepped through carefully, and joined him. He felt the need to touch her, though, only to be sure; he held out a hand, and felt reassured by the solid clasp of his fingers around hers.

He had judged it right; the sun was just coming over the far-. . thest ridge as they came out into the open space at the top of the slope. Below them spread ridges and valleys, so full of mist that it looked like smoke boiling through the hollows. From the mountain opposite, the waterfall arched out and down in a thin white plume, falling into the mist.

"Here," he said, stopping at a place where the rocks lay scattered, surrounded by thick grass. "Let's rest for a bit." Chilly as the early mornings were, the climb had heated him; he sat on a flat rock, legs stretched out to let the air come under his kilt, and pushed the plaid off his shoulders.

"It feels so different here," she said, brushing back a lock of the soft red hair whose flames warmed him more than the sun. She glanced back at him, smiling. "Do you know what I mean? I rode from Inverness to Lallybroch, through the Great Glen, and that was wild enough"—she shivered slightly at the recollection —"but it wasn't like this at all."

"No," he said. He knew exactly what she meant; the wildness of the glens and the moors was inhabited, in a way that this place of forests and rushing waters was not.

"I think—" he began, then stopped. Would she think him daft? But she was looking up at him, wanting him to say. "The spirits that live there," he said, a little awkwardly. "They are auld, and they've seen men for thousands on thousands of years; they ken us weel, and they're none so wary of showing themselves. What lives here"—he laid a hand on the trunk of a chestnut tree that rose a hundred feet above them, whose girth measured more than thirty feet around—"they havena seen our like before."

She nodded, seeming not at all taken back.

"They're curious, though, aren't they," she said, "some of them?" and tipped back her head to look up into the dizzy spiral of the branches overhead. "Don't you feel them watching, now and then?"

"Now and then."

He sat on the rock beside her and watched the light spread, spilling over the edge of the mountain, lighting the distant falls the way kindling catches from a spark, filling the mist with a glow like pearls, then burning it away altogether. Together they saw the slope of the mountain come to the light of day, and he said a quiet word to the spirit of this place, in thanks. If it had no Gaelic, still it might catch his meaning.

She stretched her long legs, breathing in the scent of the morning.

"You didn't really mind, did you?" Her voice was soft, and she kept her eyes on the valley below, careful not to look at him. "Living in the cave near Broch Mhorda."

"No," he said. The sun was warm on his breast and face, and filled him with a sense of peace. "No, I didna mind it."

"Only hearing about it—I thought it must have been terrible. Cold and dirty and lonely, I mean." She did look at him then, and the morning sky lived in her eyes.

"It was," he said, and smiled a little.

"Ian—Uncle Ian—took me there to show me."

"Did he, then? It's none so bleak, in the summertime, when the yellow's on the broom."

"No. But even when it was—" She hesitated.

"No, I didna mind it." He closed his eyes and let the sun heat his eyelids.

At first he had thought the loneliness would kill him, but once he had learned it would not, he came to value the solitude of the mountainside. He could see the sun clear, though his eyes were closed; a great red ball, flaming round the edges. Was that how Jocasta saw it behind her blind eyes?

She was silent for a long time, and so was he, content to listen. There were wee birds working in the spruce nearby, hanging upside down from the branches, hunting the bugs that they ate and talking to themselves about what they found.

"Roger—" she said suddenly, and his heart was struck by a dart of jealousy, the more painful for being unexpected. Was he not to have her to himself, even for so short a time? He opened his eyes and did his best to look interested.

"I tried to tell him, once, about being alone. That I thought it maybe wasn't a bad thing." She sighed, the heavy brows drawn down. "I don't think he understood."

He made a noncommittal sound in his throat.

"I thought—" She hesitated, glanced at him, then away. "I thought maybe that was why it's—why you and Mama . . ." Her skin was so clear, he could see the blood bloom under it. She took a deep breath, hands braced on the rock.

"She's like that too. She doesn't mind being alone."

He glanced at her, wanting badly to know what made her say so. What had Claire's life been in their years apart to give her that knowledge? It was so; Claire knew the flavor of solitude. It was cold as spring water, and not all could drink it; for some it was not refreshment, but mortal chill. But she had lived daily with a husband; how had she drunk deep enough of loneliness to know?

Brianna could maybe tell him, but he wouldn't ask; the last name he wished to hear spoken in this place was Frank Randall's.

He coughed instead.

"Well, it's maybe true," he agreed cautiously. "I've seen women—and men too, sometimes—as canna bear the sound of their own thoughts, and they maybe dinna make such good matches with those who can."

"No," she said, brooding. "Maybe they don't."

The small pang of jealousy eased. So she had doubts about this

Wakefield, did she? She'd told him and Claire everything, about her search, the death notice, the journey from Scotland, the visit to Lallybroch—damn Laoghaire!—and about the man Wakefield, who'd come after her. She wasn't telling everything there, he thought, but that was as well; he didn't want to hear it. He was less bothered at the prospect of a distant death by fire than by the more imminent interruption of his idyll with his long-lost daughter.

He drew up his knees and sat quiet. Much as he wanted to recapture his sense of tranquility, he could not free his mind from the thought of Randall.

He had won. Claire was his; so was this glorious child—this young woman, he corrected himself, looking at her. But Randall had had the keeping of them for twenty years; there was no doubt he had set his mark on them. But what mark had it been?

"Look." Brianna's hand squeezed his arm as she breathed the word.

He followed her gaze and saw them; two does, standing just under the shadow of the trees, not twenty feet away. He didn't move, but breathed quietly. He could feel Brianna beside him, enchanted into stillness too.

The deer saw them; delicate heads upraised, dark, moist nostrils flaring for scent. After a moment, though, one doe stepped out, dainty, nervous footsteps leaving streaks in the dew-wet grass. The other followed, cautious, and they grazed along the grassy strips between the rocks, turning now and then to lift their head and cast tranquil eyes on the strange but harmless creatures on the ledge.

He couldn't have come within a mile of a Scottish red deer that had his scent. The red stags kent weel what a man was.

He watched the deer graze, with the innocence of perfect wildness, and felt the sun's benediction on his head. This was a new place, and he was content to be alone here with his daughter.

━━━◆

"What are we hunting, Da?" He was standing still, eyes squinted as he scanned the horizon, but she was reasonably sure he wasn't looking at an animal; she could speak without scaring the game.

They'd seen a good many animals in the course of the day; the two deer at dawn, a red fox that sat watching on a rock, licking dainty black paws until they came too close, then vanishing like a

blown-out flame. Squirrels—dozens of them—chattering through the treetops, playing hide-and-seek past the tree boles. Even a flock of wild turkey, with two males strutting, chests puffed and tail fans spread for the edification of a gobbling harem.

None of these were the chosen prey, for which she was glad. She had no objection to killing for food, but would have been sorry to have the beauty of the day soiled by blood.

"Bees," he said.

"*Bees?* How do you hunt bees?"

He picked up his gun and smiled at her, nodding downhill toward a brilliant patch of yellow.

"Look for flowers."

There were certainly bees in the flowers; close enough, and she could hear the hum. There were several different kinds: huge black bumblebees, a smaller kind, striped with black and yellow fuzz, and the smooth lethal shapes of wasps, bellies pointed as daggers.

"What ye want to do," her father told her, slowly circling the patch, "is to watch and see which direction the honeybees go. And not get stung."

A dozen times, they lost sight of the tiny messengers they followed, lost in the broken light over a stream, disappearing into brush too thick to follow. Each time, Jamie cast to and fro, finding another patch of flowers.

"There's some!" she cried, pointing to a flash of brilliant red in the distance.

He squinted at them and smiled, shaking his head.

"Nay, not red," he said. "The wee hummingbirds like the red ones, but bees like yellow and white—yellow's best." He plucked a small white daisy from the grass near her feet and handed it to her—the petals were streaked with pollen, fallen from the delicate stamens in the round yellow center of the bloom. Looking closer, she saw a tiny beetle the size of a pinhead crawl out of the center, its shiny black armor dusted with gold.

"The hummingbirds drink from the long-throated flowers," he explained. "But the bees canna get all the way inside. They like the broad, flat flowers like this, and the ones that grow in heavy bunches. They light on them and wallow, till they're covered over wi' the yellow."

They hunted up and down the mountainside, laughing as they dodged the bomber assaults of enraged bumblebees, hunting telltale patches of yellow and white. The bees liked the mountain laurel, but too many of those patches were too high to see over, too dense to pass through.

It was late afternoon before they found what they were looking for. A snag, the remnants of a good-sized tree, its branches reduced to stumps, bark worn away to show weathered silver wood beneath—and a wide split in the wood, through which the bees were crowding, hanging in a veil around it.

"Oh, good," Jamie said, with satisfaction at the sight. "Sometimes they hive in the rocks, and then there's little ye can do." He unslung the ax at his belt, and his bags, and gestured to Brianna to sit down on a nearby rock.

"It's best to wait till dark," he explained. "For then all the swarm will be inside the hive. Meanwhile, will ye have a bite to eat?"

They shared the rest of the food, and talked sporadically, watching the light fade from the nearby mountains. He let her fire the long musket when she asked, showing her how to load a new round: swab the barrel, patch the ball, ram home ball, patch, and wadding with a charge of powder from the cartridge; pour the rest of the powder into the priming pan of the flintlock.

"You're no a bad shot at all, lass," he said, surprised. He bent and picked up a small chunk of wood, setting it on top of a large boulder as a target. "Try again."

She did, and again, and again, growing used to the awkward weight of the weapon, finding the lovely balancing point of its length and its natural seat in the curve of her shoulder. It kicked less than she'd expected; black powder hadn't the force of modern cartridges. Twice chips flew from the boulder; the third time the chunk of wood disappeared in a shower of fragments.

"Verra nice," he said, one eyebrow raised. "And where in God's name did ye learn to shoot?"

"My father was a target shooter." She lowered the gun, cheeks flushed with pleasure. "He taught me to shoot with a pistol or a rifle. A shotgun, too." Then her cheeks flushed a deeper hue, remembering. "Um. You wouldn't have seen a shotgun."

"No, I dinna suppose I have," was all he said, his face a careful blank.

"How will you move the hive?" she asked, wanting to cover the awkward moment. He shrugged.

"Oh, once the bees have gone to their rest, I shall blow a bit o' smoke into the hive, to keep them stunned. Then chop free the part of the trunk that's got the combs in it, slide a bit of flat wood

beneath it, and wrap it in my plaid. Once at the house, I'll nail a bit of wood top and bottom, to make a bee gum." He smiled at her. "Come morning, the bees will come out, look around, and venture out for the nearest flowers."

"Won't they realize they aren't in their proper place?"

He shrugged again.

"And what will they do about it, if they do? They've no means to find their way back, and they'll have no home left here to come to. Nay, they'll be content in the new place." He reached for the gun. "Here, let me clean it; the light's too bad for shooting."

Conversation died, and they sat in silence for half an hour or so, watching darkness fill the hollows below, an invisible tide that crept higher by the minute, engulfing the trunks of the trees so that the green canopies seemed to float on a lake of darkness.

At last she cleared her throat, feeling that she must say *something*.

"Won't Mama be worried about us, coming back so late?"

He shook his head, but didn't answer; only sat, a grass blade drooping idle in his hand. The moon was edging its way above the trees, big and golden, lopsided as a smudged teardrop.

"Your mother did tell me once that men meant to fly to the moon," he said abruptly. "They hadna done it yet, that she knew, but they meant to. Will ye know about that?"

She nodded, eyes fixed on the rising moon.

"They did. They will, I mean. She smiled faintly. "*Apollo,* they called it—the rocket ship that took them."

She could see his smile in answer; the moon was high enough to shed its radiance on the clearing. He tilted his face up, considering.

"Aye? And what did they say of it, the men who went?"

"They didn't need to say anything—they sent back pictures. I told you about the television?"

He looked a little startled, and she knew that like most things she had told him from her time, he had no real grasp of the reality of moving, talking pictures, let alone the notion that such things could be sent through thin air.

"Aye?" he said, a little unsurely. "You've seen these pictures, then?"

"Yes." She rocked back a little, hands clasped around her knees, looking up at the misshapen globe above them. There was a faint nimbus of light around it, and farther out in the starlit sky, a perfect, hazy ring, as though it were a big yellow stone dropped into a black pond, frozen in place as the first ripple formed.

"Fair weather tomorrow," he said, looking up at it.

"Will it be?" She could see everything around them, almost as clearly as in the daylight, but the color had fled now; everything was black and gray—like the pictures she described.

"It took hours, waiting. No one could say exactly how long it would take them to land and get out in their space suits—you know there isn't any air on the moon?" She raised a questioning brow, and he nodded, attentive as a schoolboy.

"Claire told me so," he murmured.

"The camera—the thing that made the pictures—was looking out of the side of the ship, so we could see the foot of the ship itself, settled in the dust, and the dust rising up over it like a horse's hoof when it puts its foot down.

"It was flat where the ship came down; covered with a soft, powdery kind of dust, with little rocks scattered on it here and there. Then the camera moved—or maybe another one started sending pictures—and you could see that there were rocky cliffs off in the distance. It's barren—no plants, no water, no air—but sort of beautiful, in an eerie kind of way."

"It sounds like Scotland," he said. She laughed at the joke, but thought she heard under the humor his longing for those barren mountains.

Wanting to distract him, she waved upward at the stars, beginning to burn brighter in the velvet sky.

"The stars are really suns, like ours. It's only that they're so far away from us, they look tiny. They're so far away that it may take years and years for their light to reach us; in fact, sometimes a star has died and we still see its light."

"Claire told me that, long ago," he said softly. He sat a moment, then got up with an air of decision.

"Come then," he said. "Let's take the hive, and be off home."

The night was warm enough that we had left the hide window-covering unpinned and rolled aside. Occasional moths and June bugs blundered in to drown themselves in the cauldron or commit fiery suicide on the hearth, but the cool leaf-scented air that washed over us was worth it.

On the first night, Ian had gallantly given Brianna the trundle bed and gone off to sleep with Rollo on a pallet in the herb shed, assuring her that he liked the privacy. Leaving, his quilt over one arm, he had clapped Jamie solidly on the back and squeezed his shoulder in a surprisingly adult gesture of congratulation that made me smile.

Jamie had smiled, too; in fact, he had scarcely stopped smiling in several days. He wasn't smiling now, though his face bore a tender, inward look. There was a half-full moon riding the sky, and enough light came through the window for me to see him clearly as he lay on his back beside me.

I was surprised that he wasn't asleep yet. He had risen well before dawn and spent the day with Brianna on the mountain, returning long after dark with a plaid full of smoke-stunned bees, who were likely to be more than irritated when they woke in the morning and discovered the trick perpetrated on them. I made a mental note to keep away from the end of the garden where the row of bee gums sat; newly moved bees were inclined to sting first and ask questions afterward.

Jamie gave a massive sigh, and I rolled toward him, curving myself to fit against him. The night wasn't cold, but he wore a shirt to bed, in deference to Brianna's modesty.

"Can't sleep?" I asked softly. "Does the moonlight bother you?"

"No." He was looking out at the moon, though; it rode high above the ridge, not yet full, but a luminous white that flooded the sky.

"If it's not the moon, it's something." I rubbed his stomach lightly, and let my fingers curve around the wide arch of his ribs.

He sighed again, and squeezed my hand.

"Och, it's no more than a foolish regret, Sassenach." He turned his head toward the trundle bed, where the dark spill of Brianna's hair fell in a moon-polished mass across the pillow. "I am only sorry that we must lose her."

"Mm." I let my hand rest flat on his chest. I had known it would come—both the realization and the parting itself—but I hadn't wanted to speak of it, and break the temporary spell that had bound the three of us so closely.

"You can't really lose a child," I said softly, one finger tracing the small, smooth hollow in the center of his chest.

"She must go back, Sassenach—ye know it as well as I do." He stirred impatiently but didn't move away. "Look at her. She's like Louis's camel, no?"

Despite my own regrets, I smiled at the thought. Louis of

France kept a fine menagerie at Versailles, and on good days the keepers would exercise certain of the animals, leading them through the spreading gardens, to the edification of startled passersby.

We had been walking in the gardens one day, and turned a corner to find the Bactrian camel advancing toward us down the path, splendid and stately in its gold and silver harness, towering in calm disdain above a crowd of gawking spectators—strikingly exotic, and utterly out of place among the formalized white statues.

"Yes," I said, though with a reluctance that squeezed my heart. "Yes, of course she'll have to go back. She belongs there."

"I ken that well enough." He put his own hand over mine, but kept his face turned away, looking at Brianna. "I shouldna grieve for it—but I do."

"So do I." I put my forehead against his shoulder, breathing in the clean male scent of him. "It's true, though—what I said. You can't truly lose a child. Do you—do you remember Faith?"

My voice trembled slightly as I asked it; we had not spoken in years of our first daughter, stillborn in France.

His arm curled around me, pulling me against him.

"Of course I do," he said softly. "D'ye think I would ever forget?"

"No." The tears were flowing down my face, but I was not truly weeping; it was no more than the overflow of feeling. "That's what I mean. I never told you—when we were in Paris, to see Jared—I went to the Hôpital des Anges; I saw her grave there. I—I brought her a pink tulip."

He was quiet for a moment.

"I took her violets," he said, so softly I almost didn't hear him.

I was quite still for a moment, tears forgotten.

"You didn't tell me."

"Neither did you." His fingers traced the bumps of my spine, brushing softly up and down the line of my back.

"I was afraid you'd feel . . ." My voice trailed off. I had been afraid he would feel guilty, worry that I blamed him—I once had —for the loss. We were newly reunited, then; I had no wish to jeopardize the tender link between us.

"So was I."

"I'm sorry that you never saw her," I said at last, and felt him sigh. He turned toward me and put his arms around me, his lips brushing my forehead.

"It doesna matter, does it? Aye, it's true, what ye say, Sassenach. She was—and we will have her, always. And Brianna. If—when she goes—she will still be with us."

"Yes. It doesn't matter what happens; no matter where a child goes—how far or how long. Even if it's forever. You never lose them. You can't."

He didn't answer, but his arms tightened round me, and he sighed once more. The breeze stirred the air above us with the sound of angels' wings, and we fell slowly asleep together, as the moonlight bathed us in its ageless peace.

43

Whisky in the Jar

I didn't like Ronnie Sinclair. I never *had* liked him. I didn't like his half-handsome face, his foxy smile, or the way his eyes met mine: so direct, so openly honest, that you *knew* he was hiding something even when he wasn't. I particularly didn't like the way he was looking at my daughter.

I cleared my throat loudly, making him jump. He turned a sharp-toothed smile on me, idly turning a truss ring in his hands.

"Jamie says he'll need a dozen more of the small whisky casks by the end of the month, and I'll need a large barrel of hickory wood for the smoked meat, as soon as you can manage."

He nodded and made a number of cryptic marks on a slab of pine that hung on the wall. Oddly for a Scot, Sinclair couldn't write but had some sort of private shorthand that enabled him to keep track of orders and accounts.

"Right, Missus Fraser. Anything else?"

I paused, trying to reckon up all the possible necessities for cooperage that might spring up before snowfall. There would be fish and meat to salt down, but those did better in stoneware jars; wooden casks left them tasting of turpentine. I had a good seasoned barrel for apples and another for squash already; the potatoes would be stored on shelves to keep from rotting.

"No," I decided. "That will be all."

"Aye, missus." He hesitated, twirling the cask band faster. "Will Himself be coming down before the casks are ready?"

"No; he has the barley to get in, and the slaughtering to do, as well as the distilling. Everything's late, because of the trial." I raised an eyebrow at him. "Why, though? Do you have a message for him?"

Sited at the foot of the cove nearest the wagon road, the cooper's shop was the first building most visitors encountered, and thus a reception point for most gossip that came from outside Fraser's Ridge.

Sinclair tilted his gingery head, considering.

"Och, likely it's nothing. Only that I've heard of a stranger in the district, asking questions about Jamie Fraser."

From the corner of my eye, I saw Brianna's head snap round, distracted at once from her inspection of the spokeshavers, mallets, saws, and axes on the wall. She turned, skirt rustling in the wood shavings that littered the shop, ankle-deep.

"Do you know the stranger's name?" she asked anxiously. "Or what he looks like?"

Sinclair shot her a look of surprise. He was oddly proportioned, with slender shoulders but muscular arms, and hands so huge that they might have belonged to a man twice his height. He looked at her, and his broad thumb unconsciously stroked the metal of the ring, slowly, over and over again.

"Why, I couldna speak to his appearance, mistress," he said, politely enough, but with a hungry look in his eyes that made me want to take the truss ring away from him and wrap it around his neck. "He gave his name as Hodgepile, though."

Brianna's face lost its look of hope, though the muscle at the edge of her mouth curved slightly at the name.

"I don't suppose *that* could be Roger," she murmured to me.

"Likely not," I agreed. "He wouldn't have any reason to use a false name, anyway." I turned back to Sinclair.

"You won't have heard of a man called Wakefield, will you? Roger Wakefield?"

Sinclair shook his head decisively.

"No, missus. Himself has put word about that if such a one should come, he's to be taken to the Ridge at once. If yon Wakefield sets foot within the county, you'll hear of it as soon as I do."

Brianna sighed, and I heard her swallow her disappointment. It was mid-October, and while she said nothing, she was clearly growing more anxious by the day. She wasn't the only one, either; she had told us what Roger was trying to do, and the thought of the variety of disasters that might have befallen him in the attempt was enough to keep me wakeful at night.

"—about the whisky," Sinclair was saying, jerking my attention back to him.

"The whisky? Hodgepile was asking about Jamie and whisky?"

Sinclair nodded, and set down the truss ring.

"In Cross Creek. No one would say a word to him, o' course. But the one who told me did say as the one who spoke to the man thought him a soldier." He grimaced briefly. "Hard for a lobsterback to wash the flour from his hair."

"He wasn't dressed as a soldier, surely?" Foot soldiers wore their hair in a tight folded queue, wrapped round a core of lamb's wool and powdered with rice flour—which, in this climate, rapidly turned to paste as the flour mixed with sweat. Still, I imagined Sinclair meant the man's attitude rather than his appearance.

"Och, no; he did claim to be a fur trader—but he walked wi' a ramrod up his arse, and ye could hear the leather creak when he talked. So Geordie McClintock said."

"Likely one of Murchison's men. I'll tell Jamie—thank you."

I left the cooper's shop with Brianna, wondering just how much trouble this Hodgepile might prove to be. Likely not much; the sheer distance from civilization and the inaccessibility of the Ridge was protection against most intrusions; one of Jamie's purposes in choosing it. The multiple inconveniences of remoteness would be outweighed by its benefits, when it came to war. No battle would be fought on Fraser's Ridge, I was sure of that.

And no matter how virulent Murchison's grudge might be, or how good his spies, I couldn't see his superiors allowing him to mount an armed expedition more than a hundred miles into the mountains, for the sole purpose of extirpating an illegal distillery whose total output was less than a hundred gallons a year.

Lizzie and Ian were waiting for us outside, occupied in gathering kindling from Sinclair's rubbish heap. A cooper's work generated immense quantities of shavings, splinters, and discarded chunks of wood and bark, and it was worth the labor of picking them up, to save splitting kindling by hand at home.

"Can you and Ian load the barrels, honey?" I asked Brianna. "I want a look at Lizzie in the sunlight."

Brianna nodded, still looking abstracted, and went to help Ian heave the half-dozen small kegs outside the shop into the wagon. They were small, but heavy.

It was the skill that went into these particular barrels that had earned Ronnie Sinclair his land and shop, in spite of his less than prepossessing personality; not every cooper knew the trick of charring the inside of an oak barrel so as to lend a beautiful amber color and deep smoky flavor to the whisky aging gently inside.

"Come here, sweetie. Let me see your eyes." Lizzie obediently widened her eyes, and let me pull down the lower lid to see the white sclera of the eyeball.

The girl was still shockingly thin, but the nasty yellow tinge of jaundice was fading from her skin, and her eyes were nearly white again. I cupped my fingers gently under her jaw; lymph glands only slightly swollen—that was better, too.

"Feeling all right?" I asked. She smiled shyly, and nodded. It was the first time she had been outside the cabin since her arrival with Ian three weeks before; she was still wobbly as a new calf. Frequent infusions of Jesuit bark had helped, though; she had had no fresh attacks of fever in the last week, and I had hopes of clearing up the liver involvement in short order.

"Mrs. Fraser?" she said, and I jumped, startled to hear her talk. She was so shy that she could seldom bring herself to say anything to me or to Jamie directly; she murmured her needs to Brianna, who conveyed them to me.

"Yes, dear?"

"I—I couldna help hearing what yon cooper said—about how Mr. Fraser's asked word of Miss Brianna's man. I did wonder—" Her words trailed off in a spasm of shyness, and a faint rose-pink blush showed in her transparent cheeks.

"Yes?"

"Could he ask for my father, do ye think?" The words came out in a rush, and she blushed still harder.

"Oh, Lizzie! I'm sorry." Brianna, finished with the barrels, came and hugged her little maid. "I hadn't forgotten, but I hadn't thought, either. Just a minute, I'll go and tell Mr. Sinclair." With a whiff of skirts, she vanished into the cool dimness of the cooper's shop.

"Your father?" I asked. "Have you lost him?"

The girl nodded, pressing her lips together to prevent their quivering.

"He'll ha' gone as a bondsman, but I dinna ken where; only it would be to the southern colonies."

Well, that limited the search to several hundred thousand square miles, I thought. Still, it could do no harm to ask Ronnie Sinclair to put out word. Newspapers and other printed matter were scarce in the South; most real news still passed by word of mouth, handed on in shops and taverns, or carried by slaves and servants between far-flung plantations.

The thought of newspapers gave me a small nasty jolt of remembrance. Still, seven years seemed comfortingly far away—

and Brianna must be right; whether the house was doomed to burn on January 21 or not, surely it would be possible for us not to be in it on that date?

Brianna appeared, rather red in the face, swung aboard the wagon, and picked up the reins, waiting impatiently for the rest of us.

Ian, seeing her flushed face, frowned and glanced toward the cooper's shop.

"What is it, Coz? Did yon wee mannie say aught amiss to ye?" He flexed his hands, nearly as large as Sinclair's.

"No," she said tersely. "Not a word. Are we ready to go?"

Ian picked Lizzie up and swung her into the wagon bed, then put out a hand and helped me up on the seat by Brianna. He glanced at the reins in Brianna's hands; he had taught her to drive the mules, and took professional pride in her skill.

"Watch the bugger on the gee side," he advised her. "He'll no be pullin' his share o' the load, unless ye touch him up now and again wi' a slap across the rump."

He subsided into the wagon bed with Lizzie as we set off up the road. I could hear him telling her outlandish stories, and her faint giggle in reply. The baby of his own family, Ian was charmed by Lizzie and treated her like a younger sister, by turns nuisance and pet.

I glanced over my shoulder at the receding cooper's shop, then at Brianna.

"What did he do?" I asked, quietly.

"Nothing. I interrupted him." The flush across her wide cheekbones grew deeper.

"What on earth was he doing?"

"Drawing pictures on a piece of wood," she said, and bit the inside of her cheek. "Of naked women."

I laughed, as much from shock as from amusement.

"Well, he hasn't got a wife, and not likely to get one soon; women are very scarce in the colony generally, and even more so up here. I suppose one can't blame him."

I felt an unexpected pang of sympathy for Ronnie Sinclair. He'd been alone for a very long time, after all. His wife had died in the terrible days after Culloden, and he himself had spent more than ten years in prison before being transported to the Colonies. If he had made connections here, they had not endured; he was a solitary man, and suddenly I saw his avid questing for gossip, his

stealthy watching—even his use of Brianna for artistic inspiration
—in a different light. I knew what it was like to be lonely.

Brianna's embarrassment had faded, and she was whistling
softly under her breath, hunched casually over the reins—a
Beatles' tune, I thought, though I never could keep pop groups
straight.

The idle thought floated insidiously through my mind; if Roger
didn't come, she wouldn't be left alone for long, either here or
when she returned to the future. But that was ridiculous. He
would come. And if not . . .

A thought I had been trying to keep at bay sneaked past my
defenses and appeared in my mind, full-blown. *What if he had
chosen not to come?* I knew they had had some sort of argument,
though Brianna had been tight-lipped about it. Had he been so
infuriated that he would go back without her?

I rather thought the possibility had occurred to her, too; she had
stopped speaking much of Roger, but I saw the anxious light
spring up in her eyes whenever Clarence announced a visitor, and
saw it die each time the visitor proved to be one of Jamie's tenants, or some of Ian's Tuscaroran friends.

"Hurry up, you blighter," I muttered under my breath. Brianna
caught it, and smartly snapped the reins over the left mule's rump.

"Gee up!" she shouted, and the wagon rattled faster, jolting
over the narrow track toward home.

"It's a far cry from the still-cellar at Leoch," Jamie said, ruefully poking at the makeshift pot still at the edge of the small
clearing. "It does make whisky, though—of a sort."

In spite of his diffidence, Brianna could see that he was proud
of his infant distillery. It was nearly two miles from the cabin,
located—as he explained—close to Fergus's place, so that Marsali could come up several times a day to keep an eye on the
operation. In return for this service, she and Fergus had a slightly
larger share in the resulting whisky than did the other farmers on
the Ridge, who supplied the raw barley and helped in the distribution of the liquor.

"No, darlin', ye dinna want to be eating that nasty wee thing,"
Marsali said firmly. She grasped her son's wrist and began prying
open his fingers, one by one, in an effort to free the large and
madly wriggling insect that—in open contradiction of his
mother's adjuration—he very obviously *did* want to be eating.

"Feh!" Marsali dropped the cockroach on the ground and stamped on it.

Germaine, a stoic, stubby child, didn't cry at the loss of his treat, but glowered balefully under his blond fringe. The cockroach, nothing daunted by rough treatment, rose out of the leaf mold and walked off, staggering only slightly.

"Oh, I shouldna think it would do him harm," Ian said, amused. "I've eaten them, now and again, wi' the Indians. The locusts are better, though—especially the smoked ones."

Marsali and Brianna both made gagging noises, causing Ian to grin even wider. He picked up another bag of barley and poured a thick layer into a flat rush basket. Two more roaches, suddenly exposed to the light of day, skittered madly over the side of the basket, fell to the ground and dashed away, disappearing under the edge of the crudely built malting floor.

"No, I said!" Marsali kept a tight hold on Germaine's collar, preventing his determined attempts to follow them. "Stay, ye wee fiend, d'ye want to be smoked, too?" Small wisps of transparent smoke rose up through the cracks of the wooden platform, permeating the small clearing with the breakfast-like scent of roasting grain. Brianna felt her stomach gurgle; it was nearly suppertime.

"Maybe you should leave them in," she suggested, joking. "Smoked roaches might add a nice flavor to the whisky."

"I doubt they'd harm it any," her father agreed, coming up beside her. He wiped his face with a handkerchief, looked at it, and made a slight face at the sooty smudges on it before tucking it back up his sleeve. "All right, Ian?"

"Aye, it'll do. It's only the one bag that's spoilt all through, Uncle Jamie." Ian rose with his tray of raw barley, and kicked negligently at a split bag, where the soft green of mold and black tinge of rot showed the ill effects of seeping damp. Two more opened bags, with the spoiled top layer scooped off, sat by the edge of the malting floor.

"Let's finish, then," Jamie said. "I'm starved." He and Ian each seized a burlap bag and scattered the fresh barley in a thick layer over the clear space on the platform, using a flat wooden spade to flatten and turn the grain.

"How long does it all take?" Brianna poked her nose over the edge of the mash tub, where Marsali was stirring the fermenting grain of the last smoking. The mash had only begun to work; there was no more than a faint whiff of alcohol in the air.

"Oh, it will depend on the weather, a bit." Marsali cast an experienced eye skyward. It was late afternoon, and the sky had begun to darken into a clear deep blue, with no more than streaks of white cloud floating over the horizon. "Clear as it is, I should say—Germaine!" Germaine's bottom was the only part of him visible, the top half having disappeared under a log.

"I'll get him." Brianna took three quick strides across the clearing, and scooped him up. Germaine made a deep sound of protest at this unwarranted interference, and began to kick, hammering his sturdy heels against her legs.

"Ow!" Brianna set him on the ground, rubbing her thigh with one hand.

Marsali made a sound of exasperation and dropped her ladle. *"Now* what have ye got, ye wicked thing?" Germaine, having learned from experience, popped his latest acquisition into his mouth and swallowed convulsively. He immediately turned purple and began to choke.

With a cry of alarm, Marsali dropped to her knees and tried to pry his mouth open. Germaine gagged, wheezed, and staggered backward, shaking his head. His eyes bulged, and a thin line of drool snaked down his chin.

"Here!" Brianna grabbed the little boy by the arm, pulled his back against her, and with both hands fisted into his stomach, jerked them sharply back.

Germaine made a loud whooping noise, and something small and round shot out of his mouth. He gurgled, gasped for air, got a good lungful and started to howl, his face going from dusky purple to a healthy red within seconds.

"Is he all right?" Jamie peered anxiously at the little boy, who was crying in his mother's arms, then, satisfied, glanced at Brianna. "That was verra quick, lass. A good job."

"Thanks. I—thanks. I'm glad it worked."

Brianna felt a little shaky. Seconds. It hadn't taken more than a few seconds. Life to death and back again, in nothing flat. Jamie touched her arm, giving her a brief squeeze, and she felt a little better.

"Best take the laddie down to the house," he told Marsali. "Give him his supper and put him to bed. We'll finish here."

Marsali nodded, looking shaken herself. She brushed a strand of pale hair out of her eyes, and gave Brianna a poor attempt at a smile.

"I thank ye, good-sister."

Brianna felt a surprising small glow of pleasure at the title. She gave Marsali back the smile.

"I'm glad he's all right."

Marsali picked up her bag from the ground, and with a nod to Jamie, turned and made her way carefully down the steep path, toddler in her arms, Germaine's chubby fists twined tightly in her hair.

"That was pretty work, Coz." Ian had finished the spreading, and jumped down from the platform to congratulate her. "Where did ye learn a thing like that?"

"From my mother."

Ian nodded, looking impressed. Jamie bent over, searching the ground nearby.

"What is it the laddie swallowed, I wonder?"

"This." Brianna spotted the object, half buried under fallen leaves, and plucked it out. "It looks like a button." The object was a lopsided circle, crudely carved from wood, but indisputably a button, with a long shank and holes bored for thread.

"Let me see." Jamie held out a hand, and she dropped the button into it.

"You'll no be missing any buttons, will ye, Ian?" he asked, frowning at the small object in his palm.

Ian peered over Jamie's shoulder, and shook his head. "Maybe Fergus?" he suggested.

"Maybe, but I dinna think so. Our Fergus is too much the dandy to be wearin' something like this. All the buttons on his coat are made of polished horn." He shook his head slowly, still frowning, then shrugged. Picking up his sporran, he put the button into it before fastening it about his waist.

"Ah, well. I'll ask about. Will ye finish here, Ian? There's no much left to do." He smiled at Brianna and cocked his head toward the path. "Come then, lass; we'll ask at Lindseys', on our way home."

In the event, Kenny Lindsey was not at home.

"Duncan Innes came to fetch him, not an hour since," Mrs. Lindsey said, shading her eyes against the late sun as she stood in the doorway of her house. "I make nay doubt they'll be to your house the noo. Will ye and your lassie no step in, *Mac Dubh*, and have a taste of something?"

"Ah, no, I thank ye, Mrs. Kenny. My wife will be having the supper ready for us. But perhaps ye could be tellin' me whether this wee bawbee is from Kenny's coat?"

Mrs. Lindsey peered at the button in his hand, then shook her head.

"No, indeed. Have I not just finished sewing on a whole fresh set of buttons for him, that's he's carved from the bone of a deer? The bonniest things ye ever saw, too," she declared, with pride in her husband's craftsmanship. "Each one has got a wee face on it, grinnin' like an imp, and each one different!"

Her eye ran speculatively over Brianna.

"There's Kenny's brother, now," she said. "With a fine wee place near Cross Creek—twenty acres in tobacco, and a good creek through it. He'll be at the Gathering at Mount Helicon; perhaps you'll be going, *Mac Dubh*?"

Jamie shook his head, smiling at the bald hint. There were few available women in the colony, and even though Jamie had given it out that Brianna was promised elsewhere, this had not by any means put a stop to the matchmaking attempts.

"I fear not this year, Mrs. Kenny. Perhaps the next, but I canna spare the time just now."

They took their leave politely, and turned toward home, the sinking sun at their backs casting long shadows on the path ahead of them.

"Do you think the button's important?" Brianna asked curiously.

Jamie shrugged slightly. A light breeze lifted the hair on the crown of his head, and tugged at the leather thong that held it back.

"I canna say. It could be nothing—but it could be something, too. Your mother told me what Ronnie Sinclair said, about the man in Cross Creek, asking about the whisky."

"Hodgepile?" Brianna couldn't help smiling at the name. Jamie returned the smile briefly, then became serious again.

"Aye. If the button belongs to someone on the Ridge—they ken well enough where the still is, and they might stop to look and no harm done. But if it was to be a stranger . . ." He glanced at her and shrugged again.

"It's none so easy for a man to pass unnoticed here—unless he should be hiding a-purpose. A man come for any innocent reason would stop at a house for a bit of food and drink, and I'd hear of it the same day. But there's been nothing of the sort. Nor would it be an Indian; they dinna use such things in their clothing."

A gust of wind whirred across the path in a swirl of brown and yellow leaves, and they turned uphill, toward the cabin. They walked in near silence, affected by the growing quiet of the woods; the birds were still singing twilight songs, but the shadows were lengthening under the trees. The northern slope of the mountain across the valley had already gone dark and silent, as the sun edged behind it.

The cabin's clearing was still filled with sunlight, though, filtered through a yellow blaze of chestnut trees. Claire was in the palisaded garden, a basin on one hip, snapping beans from poled vines. Her slender figure was silhouetted dark against the sun, her hair a great aureole of curly gold.

"Innisfree," Brianna said involuntarily, stopping dead at the sight.

"Innisfree?" Jamie glanced at her, bewildered.

She hesitated, but there was no way out of explaining.

"It's a poem, or part of one. Daddy always used to say it, when he'd come home and find Mama puttering in her garden—he said she'd live out there if she could. He used to joke that she—that she'd leave us someday, and go find a place where she could live by herself, with nothing but her plants."

"Ah." Jamie's face was calm, its broad planes ruddy in the dying light. "How does the poem go, then?"

She was conscious of a small tightness round her heart as she said it.

> *"I will arise and go now, and go to Innisfree,*
> *And a small cabin build there, of clay and wattles*
> *   made:*
> *Nine bean-rows will I have there, a hive for the honey-bee.*
> *And live alone in the bee-loud glade."*

The thick red brows drew together slightly, sparking in the sun. "A poem, is it? And where is Innisfree?"

"Ireland, maybe. He was Irish," Brianna said in explanation. "The poet." The row of bee gums stood squat on their stones at the edge of the wood.

"Oh."

Tiny motes of gold and black drifted past them through honeyed air—bees homing from the fields. Her father made no move to go forward, but stood silent by her side, watching her mother pick beans, black and gold among the leaves.

Not alone, after all, she thought. But the small tightness stayed in her chest, not quite an ache.

Kenny Lindsey took a sip of whisky, closed his eyes, and rolled the liquor round his tongue like a professional wine taster. He paused, frowning in concentration, then swallowed with a convulsive gulp.

"Hoo!" He drew breath, shuddering all over.

"Christ," he said hoarsely. "That'll strip your tripes!"

Jamie grinned at the compliment, and poured another small measure, shoving it toward Duncan.

"Aye, it's better than the last," he agreed, with a cautious sniff before essaying his own drink. "This one doesna take the hide off your tongue—quite."

Lindsay wiped his mouth with the back of his hand, nodding in agreement.

"Weel, it'll find a good home. Woolam wants a cask—that'll last him a year, the way yon Quakers dole it out."

"Ye've agreed a price?"

Lindsay nodded, sniffing appreciatively at the platter of bannocks and savories that Lizzie set in front of him.

"A hundredweight of barley for the cask; another, if ye'll go halves wi' him in the whisky from it."

"That's fair." Jamie took a bannock and chewed absently for a moment. Then he raised one brow at Duncan, seated across the table.

"Will ye ask MacLeod on Naylor's Creek will he make us the same bargain? You'll pass that way going home, aye?"

Duncan nodded, chewing, and Jamie lifted his cup to me in a silent toast of celebration—Woolam's offer made a total of eight hundred pounds of barley, scraped together by barter and promise. More than the surplus output of every field on the Ridge; the raw material for next year's whisky.

"A cask each to the houses on the Ridge, two to Fergus—" Jamie pulled absently at his earlobe, calculating. "Two, maybe, to Nacognaweto, one kept back to age—aye, we can spare maybe a dozen casks for the Gathering, Duncan."

Duncan's coming was opportune. While Jamie had managed to barter the first year's crop of raw whisky to the Moravians in Salem for the tools, cloth, and other things we so urgently needed, there was no doubt that the wealthy Scottish planters of the Cape Fear would make a better market.

We couldn't possibly spare time away from the homestead for

long enough to make the week-long journey to Mount Helicon, but if Duncan could take the whisky down and sell it . . . I was already making lists in my head. Everyone brought things to sell, at a Gathering. Wool, cloth, tools, food, animals . . . I urgently needed a small copper kettle, and six lengths of fresh muslin for shifts, and . . .

"Do you think you should give alcohol to the Indians?" Brianna's question pulled me from my greedy reverie.

"Why not?" Lindsey asked, a little disapproving of her intrusion. "After all, we're no going to *give* it to them, lass. They've little silver, but they pay in hides—and they pay well."

Brianna glanced at me for support, then at Jamie.

"But Indians don't—I mean I've heard that they can't handle alcohol."

All three men looked at her uncomprehendingly, and Duncan looked at his cup, turning it round in his hand.

"Handle it?"

The corner of her mouth quirked inward.

"They get drunk easily, I mean."

Lindsey peered into his cup, then looked at her, rubbing a hand over the balding crown of his head.

"Ye've a point, lass?" he said, more or less politely.

Brianna's full mouth compressed itself, then relaxed.

"I *mean*," she said, "it seems wrong to encourage people to drink, who can't stop drinking if they start." She looked at me, a little helplessly. I shook my head.

" 'Alcoholic' isn't a noun yet," I said. "It's not a disease now —just weak character."

Jamie glanced up at her quizzically.

"Well, I'll tell ye, lass," he said, "I've seen many a drunkard in my day, but I've yet to see a bottle leap off a table and pour itself down anyone's throat."

There were general grunts of agreement with this, and another small round to accompany the change of subject.

"Hodgepile? No, I've not seen the man, though I do believe I've heard the name." Duncan swilled the rest of his drink and set down his cup, wheezing gently. "You'll want me to ask at the Gathering?"

Jamie nodded, and took another bannock. "Aye, if ye will, Duncan."

Lizzie was bent over the fire, stirring the stew for supper. I saw her shoulders tighten, but she was too shy to speak before so many men. Brianna suffered no such inhibitions.

"I have someone to ask after, too, Mr. Innes." She leaned over the table toward him, eyes fixed on him in earnest entreaty. "Will you ask for a man named Roger Wakefield? Please?"

"Och, indeed. Indeed I will." Duncan went pink at the proximity of Brianna's bosom, and in confusion drank down the rest of Kenny's whisky. "Is there aught else I can do?"

"Yes," I said, putting down a fresh cup in front of the disgruntled Lindsey. "While you're asking after Hodgepile and Bree's young man, would you also ask for a man named Joseph Wemyss? He'll be a bondsman." From the corner of my eye, I saw Lizzie's thin shoulders slump in relief.

Duncan nodded, his composure restored as Brianna disappeared into the pantry to fetch butter. Kenny Lindsey looked after her, interested.

"Bree? Is that the name ye call your daughter?" he asked.

"Yes," I said. "Why?"

A smile showed briefly on Lindsey's face. Then he glanced at Jamie, coughed, and buried the smile in his cup.

"It's a Scots word, Sassenach," Jamie said, a rather wry smile appearing on his own face. "A *bree* is a great disturbance."

44

Three-cornered Conversation

October 1769

The shock of impact juddered through his arms. With a rhythm born of long practice, Jamie jerked the axhead free, swung it back and brought it down in a *tchunk!* of splintered bark and yellow wood chips. He shifted his foot on the log and struck again, the ax blow judged to a nicety, sharp metal embedded in the wood a scant two inches from his toes.

He could have told Ian off to do the chopping, and gone himself to fetch the flour from the tiny mill at Woolam's Point, but the lad deserved the treat of a visit with the three unmarried Woolam daughters who worked with their father in the mill. They were Quaker girls, dressed drab as sparrows, but lively of wit and fair of face, and they made a pet of Ian, vying with each other to offer him small beer and meat pies when he came.

A good deal better the lad should spend his time flirting with virtuous Quakers than with the bold-eyed Indian lassies over the ridge, he thought, with a little grimness. He hadn't forgotten what Myers had said about Indian women taking men to their beds as they liked.

He had sent the wee bondmaid with Ian as well, thinking the brisk fall air might bring a bit of color to the lassie's face. The wean was white-skinned as Claire, but with the sickly blue-white cast of skimmed milk, not Claire's pale glow, rich and grainless as the silk-white heartwood of a poplar tree.

The log was nearly split; one more blow, and a twist of the ax, and two good chunks lay ready for the hearth, smelling clean and sharp with resin. He stacked them neatly on the growing woodpile next to the pantry, and rolled another half log into place beneath his foot.

The truth of it was that he liked chopping wood. Quite different from the damp, backbreaking, foot-freezing job of cutting peats, but with that same feeling of soul-deep satisfaction at seeing a good stock of fuel laid by, which only those who have spent winters shivering in thin clothes can know. The woodpile reached nearly to the eaves of the house by now, dry split chunks of pine and oak, hickory and maple, the sight of them warming his heart as much as the wood itself would warm his flesh.

Speak of warmth; it was a warm day for late October, and his shirt was clinging to his shoulders already. He wiped a sleeve across his face and examined the damp patch critically.

If he got wringing, Brianna would insist on washing it again, protest as he might that sweat was clean enough. "Phew," she would say, with a disapproving nostril-flare, wrinkling her long nose up like a possum. He had laughed out loud when he first saw her do it; as much from surprise as from amusement.

His mother had died long ago, in his childhood, and while the odd memory of her came now and then in dreams, he had mostly replaced her presence with static pictures, frozen images in his mind. But she had said "Phew!" to him when he came in mucky, and wrinkled up her long nose in just that way—it had come back with a flash when he saw Brianna do it.

What a mystery blood was—how did a tiny gesture, a tone of voice, endure through generations like the harder verities of flesh? He had seen it again and again, watching his nieces and nephews grow, and accepted without thought the echoes of parent and grandparent that appeared for brief moments, the shadow of a face looking back through the years—that vanished again into the face that was now.

Yet now that he saw it in Brianna . . . he could watch her for hours, he thought, and was reminded of his sister, bending close over each of her newborn bairns in fascination. Perhaps that was why parents watched their weans in such enchantment, he thought; finding out all the tiny links between them, that bound the chains of life, one generation to the next.

He shrugged, and pulled the shirt off. It was his own place, after all; there was no one to see the marks on his back, and no one whose business it would be to care if they did. The air was chill and sudden on his damp skin, but a few swings of the ax brought the warm blood pulsing back again.

He loved all Jenny's children deeply—especially Ian, the wee gowk whose mixture of foolishness and pigheaded courage reminded him so much of himself at that age. They were his blood, after all. But Brianna . . .

Brianna was his blood, and his flesh as well. An unspoken

promise kept to his own parents; his gift to Claire, and hers to him.

Not for the first time, he found himself wondering about Frank Randall. And what had Randall thought, holding the child of another man—and a man he had no cause to love?

Perhaps Randall had been the better man, come to that—to harbor a child for her mother's sake, and not his own; to search her face with joy only in its beauty, and not because he saw himself reflected there. He felt vaguely ashamed, and struck down with greater force to exorcise the feeling.

His mind was concerned entirely with its thoughts, and not at all with its actions. While he used it, though, the ax was as much a part of his body as the arms that swung it. Just as a twinge in wrist or elbow would have warned him instantly of damage, some faint vibration, some subtle shift in weight arrested him in midswing, so that the loosened axhead flew harmlessly across the clearing, rather than slamming into his vulnerable foot.

"Deo gratias," he muttered, with rather less thankfulness than the words indicated. He crossed himself perfunctorily and went to pick up the slab of metal. Damn the dry weather; it hadn't rained in nearly a month, and the shrunken haft of his ax was less worrying than the drooping heads of the plants in Claire's garden near the house.

He cast a glance at the half-dug well, shrugging in irritation. Another thing that must be done, which there wasn't time to do. It would have to wait a bit; they could haul water from the creek or melt snow, but without wood to burn they would starve or freeze, or both.

The door opened and Claire came out, cloak on against the chill of autumn shadows, her basket over her arm. Brianna was behind her, and at sight of them he forgot his annoyance.

"What have you done?" Claire said at once, seeing him with the axhead in one hand. Her eyes flicked over him quickly, looking for blood.

"Nay, I'm whole," he assured her. "It's only I've got to mend the handle. You'll be foraging?" He nodded at Claire's basket.

"I thought we'd try up the stream, for wood ears."

"Ah? Dinna go too far, aye? There are Indians hunting the far mountain. I smelt them on the ridge this morning."

"You smelled them?" Brianna asked.

One red brow went up in inquiry. He saw Claire glance from Brianna to him and smile slightly, to herself; it was one of his own gestures, then. He lifted one brow, looking at Claire, and saw her smile grow wider.

"It's autumn, and they're dryin' venison," he explained to Brianna. "Ye can smell the smoking fires a great ways away, if the wind sets right."

"We won't go far," Claire assured him. "Just above the trout pool."

"Aye, well. I daresay it's safe enough." He felt some reluctance at letting the women go, but he could scarcely keep them mewed up in the house only because there were savages nearby— the Indians were no doubt peacefully employed as he was himself, in making winter preparations.

If he knew for sure it was Nacognaweto's folk, he wouldn't worry, but as it was, the hunting parties often roamed far afield and it could as easily be Cherokee, or the odd small tribe that called themselves the Dog People. There was only one village of them left, and they were deeply suspicious of white strangers— not without reason.

Brianna's eyes rested on his bare chest for a moment, at the tiny knot of puckered scar tissue, but she showed no sign of disgust or curiosity—nor did she when she laid her hand briefly on his shoulder, kissing his cheek in goodbye, though he knew she must feel the healed welts beneath her fingers.

Claire would have told her, he supposed—all about Jack Randall, and the days before the Rising. Or perhaps not quite all. A small shiver that had nothing to do with cold ran up the crease of his spine, and he stepped back, away from her touch, though he still smiled at her.

"There's bread in the hutch, and a little stew left in the kettle for you and Ian and Lizzie." Claire reached up and flicked a stray wood chip from his hair. "Don't eat the pudding in the pantry; that's for supper."

He caught her fingers in his and kissed her knuckles lightly. She looked surprised, and then a faint warm glow came up under her skin. She came up a-tiptoe and kissed his mouth, then hurried after Brianna, already at the edge of the clearing.

"Be careful!" he called after them. They waved, and disappeared into the woods, leaving him with their kisses soft on his face.

"Deo gratias," he murmured again, watching them, and this time spoke with heartfelt gratitude. He waited until the last flicker of Brianna's cloak had vanished, before returning to his work.

He sat on the chopping block, a handful of square-headed nails on the ground beside him, carefully driving them one at a time into the end of the ax handle with a small mallet. The dry wood split and spread, but held by the iron enclosure of the axhead, could not splinter.

He twisted the head, then finding it firm, stood up and brought the ax down in a mighty blow on the chopping block, by way of test. It held.

He was chilled now, from sitting, and pulled his shirt back on. He was hungry, too, but he would wait a bit for the young ones. Not but what they had likely stuffed themselves already, he thought cynically. He could almost smell the meat pies Sarah Woolam made, the rich scent twining in his memory through the actual autumn smells of dead leaves and damp earth.

The thought of meat pies lingered in his mind as he went on with his work, along with the thought of winter. The Indians said it would be hard, this winter, not like the last. How would it be, hunting in deep snow? It snowed in Scotland, of course, but often enough it lay light on the ground, and the trodden paths of the red deer showed black on the steep, bare mountainsides.

Last winter had been like that. But this wilderness was given to extremes. He had heard stories of snowfalls that lay six feet deep, valleys where a man might sink to his oxters, and ice that froze so thick on the creeks that a bear could walk across. He smiled a little grimly, thinking of bears. Well, and that would be eating for the whole winter if he could kill another, and the skin would not come amiss, either.

His thoughts drifted slowly into the rhythm of his work, one part of his mind dimly occupied with the words to "Daddy's Gone A-Hunting," while the other was taken up with a intriguingly vivid picture of Claire's white skin, pale and intoxicant as Rhenish wine against the glossy black of a bearskin.

"Daddy's gone to fetch a skin / To wrap his baby bunting in," he murmured tunelessly under his breath.

He wondered just how much Claire *had* told Brianna. It was odd, though pleasant, their three-cornered way of talking; he and the lassie were a bit shy yet with each other—inclined to say personal things to Claire instead, confident that she would pass on their essence; their interpreter in this new and awkward language of the heart.

Thankful though he was for the miracle of his daughter, he wanted to make love to his wife in his bed again. It was getting overchilly to be having at it in the herb shed or the forest—though he would admit that floundering naked in the huge drifts of yellow chestnut leaves had a certain charm, even if it lacked dignity.

"Aye, well," he muttered, smiling slightly to himself. "And when did a man ever worry for his dignity, doin' *that*?"

He glanced thoughtfully at the pile of long, straight pine logs that lay at the side of the clearing, then at the sun. If Ian was quick enough returning, they might shape and notch a dozen or so before sunset.

Setting down the ax for a moment, he crossed to the house and began to pace out the dimensions of the new room he planned, to make do while the big house was a-building. She was a grown woman, Brianna—she should have a wee place of her own, to be private in, she and the maid. And if that restored his own privacy with Claire, well, so much the better, aye?

He heard the small crackling noises among the dried leaves in the yard, but didn't turn round. There was a tiny cough behind him, like a squirrel sneezing.

"Mrs. Lizzie," he said, eyes still on the ground. "And did ye enjoy your ride? I trust ye found all the Woolams well." Where was Ian and the wagon? he wondered. He hadn't heard it on the road below.

She didn't speak, but made an inarticulate noise that made him swing round in surprise to look at her.

She was pale and pinch-faced and looked like a scared white mouse. This was not unusual; he knew he frightened her with his size and deep voice, and so he spoke gently to her, slowly, as he would have done to a mistreated dog.

"Have ye had an accident, lass? Has something come amiss wi' the wagon or the horses?"

She shook her head, still wordless. Her eyes were nearly round, gray as the hem of her washed-out gown, and the tip of her nose had gone bright pink.

"Is Ian all right?" He didn't want to upset her further, but she was beginning to alarm him. *Something* had happened, that was sure.

"I'm fine, Uncle. So are the horses." Quiet as an Indian, Ian appeared round the corner of the cabin. He moved to Lizzie's side, offering her the support of his presence, and she took his arm as though by reflex.

He glanced from one to the other; Ian was outwardly calm, but his inner agitation was plain to see.

"What's happened?" he asked, more sharply than he'd intended. The lassie flinched.

"Ye'd better tell him," Ian said. "There might not be much time." He touched her shoulder in encouragement, and she seemed to take strength from his hand; she stood up straighter and bobbed her head.

"I—there was—I saw a man. At the mill, sir."

She tried to speak further, but her nerve had dried up; the tip of her tongue protruded between her teeth with effort, but no words came out.

"She kent him, Uncle," Ian said. He looked disturbed, but not afraid; excited, rather, in an unfamiliar way. "She'd seen him before—with Brianna."

"Aye?" He tried to speak encouragingly, but the hair on the back of his neck was rising with premonition.

"At Wilmington," Lizzie got out. "MacKenzie was his name; I heard a sailor call him so."

Jamie glanced quickly at Ian, who shook his head.

"He didna give his place, but I dinna ken any from Leoch like him. I saw him and heard him speak; he's maybe a Highlander, but schooled in the south, I'd say—an educated man."

"And did this Mr. MacKenzie seem to know my daughter?" he asked. Lizzie nodded, frowning in concentration.

"Oh, aye, sir! And she kent him, too—she was afraid of him."

"Afraid? Why?" He spoke sharply, and she blanched, but she was well started now, and the words came out, tripping and stumbling, but still coming.

"I dinna ken, sir. But she turned white when she saw him, sir, and let out a wee skelloch. Then she went red and white and red again—oh, she was fair upset, anyone could see it!"

"What did he do?"

"Why—why—nothing, then. He came close to her, and held her by the arms, and said to her that she must come awa' with him. Everyone in the taproom was looking. She pulled herself away, white as my shift, but she said to me as it was all right, I was to wait, and she would come back. And—and then she went out with him."

Lizzie drew in a quick breath and wiped the end of her nose, which had begun to drip.

"And ye let her go?"

The little bondmaid shrank back, cowering.

"Ooh, I should have gone after her, I ken weel I should, sir!" she cried, face twisted with misery. "But I was afraid, sir, and may God forgive me!"

With an effort, Jamie smoothed the frown from his face and spoke as patiently as he might.

"Aye, well. And what happened, then?"

"Oh, I went upstairs as she told me, and I lay in the bed, sir, prayin' for all I was worth!"

"Well, that was verra helpful, I'm sure!"

"Uncle—" Ian's voice was soft but not at all tentative, and his brown eyes were steady on Jamie's. "She's no but a wee lassie, Uncle; she did her best."

Jamie rubbed his hand hard over his scalp.

"Aye," he said. "Aye, I'm sorry, lass; I didna mean to bite your head off. But will ye no get on wi' it?"

A hot pink spot had begun to burn on each of Lizzie's cheeks.

"She—she didna come back till nearly dawn. And—and—"

Jamie had very little patience left, and no doubt it showed on his face.

"I could smell him on her," she whispered, voice dropping almost to inaudibility. "His . . . seed."

The surge of rage took him unaware, like a white-hot bolt of lightning through chest and belly. He felt half choked with it, but clamped it down tight, hoarding it like coals in a hearth.

"He bedded her, then; you're sure of that?"

Thoroughly mortified at this bluntness, the little bondmaid could do no more than nod.

Lizzie was twisting her hands in the stuff of her gown, leaving her skirt all bunched and crumpled. Her paleness was replaced with a hot flush; she looked like one of Claire's tomatoes. She couldn't look at him, but hung her head, staring at the ground.

"Oh, sir. She's wi' child, can ye not see? It must be him—she was virgin when he took her. He's come after her—and she's afraid of him."

Quite suddenly, he *could* see it, and felt the hairs rise all up his arms and shoulders. The autumn breeze struck cold through shirt and skin, and the rage turned to sickness. All the small things he had half seen and half thought, not allowing them to rise to the surface of his mind, came together at once in a logical pattern.

The look of her, and the way she acted; one moment lively and another lost in troubled thought. And the glow in her face that was not all from the sun. He knew the look of a woman breeding well enough; if he had known her before, he would have seen the change; but as it was . . .

Claire. Claire knew. The thought came to him, cold in its certainty. She knew her daughter, and she was a physician. She must know—and hadn't told him.

"Are ye sure of this?" The coldness froze his rage. He could feel it stuck in his chest—a dangerous, jagged object that seemed to point in every direction.

Lizzie nodded, wordless, and blushed deeper, if such a thing were possible.

"I am her maid, sir," she whispered, eyes on the ground.

"She means Brianna hasna had her courses in two months," Ian provided matter-of-factly. The youngest of a family containing several older sisters, he was not constrained by Lizzie's delicacy. "She's sure."

"I—I wouldna have said anything at all, sir," the girl went on wretchedly. "Only, when I saw the man . . ."

"D'ye think he's come to claim her, Uncle?" Ian interrupted. "We must stop him, aye?" The look of angry excitement was clear now, flushing the lad's lean cheeks with feeling.

Jamie took a deep breath, only then realizing that he had been holding it.

"I dinna ken," he said, surprised at the calmness of his own tone. He had barely had time to take in the news, let alone to draw conclusions, but the lad was right, there was a danger to be dealt with.

If this MacKenzie wished it, he might claim Brianna as his wife by right of common law, with the coming bairn as evidence of his claim. A court of law would not necessarily force a woman to wed a rapist, but any magistrate would uphold the right of a man to his wife and child—regardless of the wife's feelings in the matter.

His own parents had wed by such device: fleeing and hiding among the Highland crags until his mother was well with child, so that her brothers were forced to accept the unwelcome marriage. A child was a permanent, undeniable bond between man and woman, and he had cause to know it.

He glanced toward the path that came up through the lower wood.

"Will he not be here on your heels? The Woolams will have told him the way."

"Nooo," said Ian thoughtfully. "I shouldna think so. We took his horse, aye?" He grinned suddenly at Lizzie, who giggled faintly in reply.

"Aye? And what's to stop him taking the wagon, or one of the wagon mules?"

The grin widened substantially on Ian's face.

"I left Rollo in the wagon bed," he said. "I think he'll walk it, Uncle Jamie."

Jamie was forced to a grudging smile in return.

"That was quick of ye, Ian."

Ian shrugged modestly.

"Well, I didna want the bastard to take us unawares. And though I've not heard Cousin Brianna talk about her laddie lately —yon Wakefield, aye?" He paused delicately. "I didna think she'd want to see this MacKenzie. Especially if—"

"I should say Mr. Wakefield has left his coming ower-long," Jamie said. "Especially if." It was no wonder she had stopped looking forward to Wakefield's coming—once she'd realized. After all, how would a woman explain a swelling belly to a man who'd left her virgin?

He slowly and consciously unclenched his fists. There would be time enough for all that later. For the moment, there·was the one thing to be dealt with.

"Fetch my pistols from the house," he said, turning to Ian. "And you, lassie—" He gave Lizzie something intended for a smile, and reached for the coat he'd hung on the edge of the woodpile.

"Bide ye here, and wait for your mistress. Tell my wife—tell her I've gone to give Fergus a hand with his chimney. And dinna speak a word about this to my wife or daughter—or I'll have your guts for garters." This last threat was spoken half in jest, but the girl went white as though he'd meant it literally.

Lizzie sank down on the chopping block, her knees wabbling beneath her. She fumbled for the tiny medallion at her neck, seeking reassurance from the cold metal. She watched Mr. Fraser stride down the path, menacing as a great red wolf. His shadow stretched out black before him, and the late autumn sun touched him with fire.

The medal in her hand was cold as ice.

"O dear Mother," she murmured, over and over. "O Blessed Mother, what have I done?"

45

Fifty-fifty

The oak leaves were dry and crackling underfoot. There was a constant fall of leaves from the chestnut trees that towered overhead, a slow yellow rain that mocked the dryness of the ground.

"Is it true that Indians can move through the woods without making a sound, or is that just something they tell you in Girl Scouts?" Brianna kicked at a small drift of oak leaves, sending them flying. Dressed in wide skirts and petticoats that caught at leaves and twigs, we sounded like a herd of elephants ourselves.

"Well, they can't do it in dry weather like this, unless they swing through the trees like chimpanzees. In a wet spring, it's another story—even *I* could walk through here quietly then; the ground is like a sponge."

I drew in my skirts to keep them away from a big elderberry bush, and stooped to look at the fruit. It was dark red, but not yet showing the blackish tinge of true ripeness.

"Two more days," I said. "If we were going to use them for medicine, we'd pick them now. I want them for wine, though, and to dry like raisins—and for that, you want them to have a lot of sugar, so you wait until they're nearly ready to drop from their stems."

"Right. What landmark is it?" Brianna glanced around, and smiled. "No, don't tell me—it's that big rock that looks like an Easter Island head."

"Very good," I said approvingly. "Right, because it won't change with the seasons."

Reaching the edge of a small stream, we separated, working our way slowly down the banks. I had set Brianna to collect cress, while I poked about the trees in search of wood ears and other edible fungi.

I watched her covertly as I hunted, one eye on the ground, one on her. She was knee-deep in the stream with her skirts kilted up, showing an amazing stretch of long, muscular thigh as she waded slowly, eyes on the rippling water.

There was something wrong; had been for days. At first I had assumed her air of tension was due to the obvious stresses of the new situation in which she found herself. But over the past weeks she and Jamie had settled into a relationship that, while still marked by shyness on both sides, was increasingly warm. They delighted each other—and I was delighted to see them together.

Still, there was something troubling her. It had been three years since I had left her—four since she had left me, to live on her own, and she had changed; had grown entirely into a woman now. I could no longer read her as easily as I once had. She had Jamie's trick of hiding strong feeling behind a mask of calmness—I knew it well in both of them.

In part, I had arranged this foraging expedition as an excuse to talk to her alone; with Jamie, Ian, and Lizzie in the house, and the constant traffic of tenants and visitors come to see Jamie, private conversation there was impossible. And if what I suspected was true, this wasn't a conversation I wished to have where anyone could hear.

By the time I had my basket half filled with thick, fleshy orange wood ears, Brianna had emerged dripping from the stream, her own basket overflowing with clumps of wet green cress and bunches of jointed horsetail reeds to make into tapers.

She wiped her feet on the hem of her petticoat, and came to join me under one of the huge chestnut trees. I handed her the canteen of cider, and waited till she had had a drink.

"Is it Roger?" I said then, without preliminary.

She glanced at me, a flash of startlement visible in her eyes, and then I saw the tense line of her shoulder ease.

"I wondered whether you could still do that," she said.

"Do what?"

"Read my mind. I sort of hoped you could." Her wide mouth quirked awkwardly, trying to smile.

"I expect I'm a bit out of practice," I said. "But give me a moment." I reached up and smoothed the hair off her face. She looked at me, but beyond me, too shy to meet my eyes. A whippoorwill called in the far green shadows.

"It's all right, baby," I said quietly. "How far gone are you?"

The breath left her in a huge sigh. Her face went slack with relief.

"Two months."

Now she met my eyes, and I felt a small shock of difference, the kind I had been getting since her arrival. Once, her relief would have been a child's; a fear confided, and half eased already by the knowledge that I would somehow deal with it. But now it was only the relief of sharing an unbearable secret; she was not expecting me to remedy things. The knowledge that I *couldn't* do anything in any case didn't stop my irrational feeling of loss.

She squeezed my hand, as though reassuring *me,* and then sat down with her back against a tree trunk, stretching out her legs in front of her, long feet bare.

"Did you know already?"

I sat down next to her, less gracefully.

"I expect so; but I didn't know I knew, if that makes sense." Looking at her now, it was plain to see; the faint pallor of her skin and tiny alterations in her color, the fleeting look of inwardness. I had noticed, but had put the changes down to unfamiliarity and strain—to the flurry of emotions over finding me, meeting Jamie, to worry over Lizzie's sickness, worry over Roger.

That particular worry now took on a sudden new dimension.

"Oh, Jesus. Roger!"

She nodded, pale in the filtered yellow shade of the chestnut leaves overhead. She looked jaundiced, and no wonder.

"It's been nearly two months. He should have been here— unless something happened."

My mind was busy calculating.

"Two months, and now it's nearly November." The leaves under us lay thick and soft, yellow and brown, fresh-fallen from the hickory and chestnut trees. My heart dropped suddenly in my chest. "Bree—you've got to go back."

"What?" Her head jerked up. "Go back where?"

"To the stones." I waved a hand in agitation. "To Scotland, and right away!"

She stared at me, thick brows drawn down.

"*Now?* What for?"

I took a deep breath, feeling a dozen different emotions collide. Concern for Bree, fear for Roger, a terrible sorrow for Jamie, who would have to give her up again, so soon. And for myself.

"You can go through, pregnant. We know that much, because I did it, with you. But honey—you can't take a baby through that . . . that . . . you can't," I ended, helpless. "You know what it's like." It had been three years since I came through the stones, but I recalled the experience vividly.

Her eyes went black as the little blood remaining in her face drained away.

"You can't take a child through," I repeated, trying to get myself under control, think logically. "It would be like jumping off Niagara Falls with the baby in your arms. You'll have to go back before it's born, or—" I broke off, making calculations.

"It's almost November. Ships won't make the passage between late November and March. And you can't wait till March—that would mean making a two-month trip across the Atlantic, six or seven months pregnant. If you didn't deliver on the ship—which would likely kill you or the baby or both—you'd still have to ride thirty miles to the circle, and then make the passage, find your way to help on the other side . . . Brianna, you can't do it! You have to go now, as soon as we can manage."

"And if I do go now—how will I make sure I end up in the right time?"

She spoke quietly, but her fingers were pleating the fabric of her skirt.

"You—I think—well, *I* did," I said, my initial panic beginning to subside into rational thought.

"You had Daddy at the other end." She glanced up at me sharply. "Whether you wanted to go to him or not, you had strong feelings for him—he would have pulled you. Or me. But he isn't there anymore." Her face tightened, then relaxed.

"Roger knew—knows—how," she corrected herself. "Geillis Duncan's book said you could use gems to travel—for protection and navigation."

"But you and Roger are both only guessing!" I argued. "And so was bloody Geilie Duncan! You might not need either gemstones *or* a strong attachment. In the old fairy tales, when people go inside a fairy's dun and then return, it's always two hundred years. If that's the usual pattern, then—"

"Would you risk finding out it's not? And it's not—Geilie Duncan went *farther* than two hundred years."

It occurred to me, a little belatedly, that she had thought all this out herself. Nothing I was saying came as any surprise. And that meant she had also reached her own conclusion—which did not involve taking ship back to Scotland.

I rubbed a hand between my brows, making an effort to match

her calmness. The mention of Geillis had called to mind another memory—though one I had tried to forget.

"There's another way," I said, fighting for calm. "Another passage, I mean. It's on Haiti—they call it Hispaniola now. In the jungle, there are standing stones on a hill, but the crack, the passage, is underneath, in a cave."

The forest air was cool, but it wasn't the shadows that made my skin ripple into gooseflesh. I rubbed my forearms, trying to erase the chill. I would willingly have erased all memory of the cave of Abandawe as well—I'd tried—but it wasn't a place easily forgotten.

"You've been there?" She leaned forward, intent.

"Yes. It's a horrible place. But the Indies are a good deal closer than Scotland is, and ships sail between Charleston and Jamaica nearly all year." I took a deep breath, feeling a little better. "It wouldn't be easy to go through the jungle—but it would give you a little longer—long enough for us to find Roger." If he could still be found, I thought, but didn't say so. That particular fear could be dealt with later.

One of the chestnut leaves spiraled down onto Brianna's lap, vivid yellow against the soft brown homespun, and she picked it off, smoothing the waxy surface absently with her thumb. She looked at me, blue eyes intent.

"Does this place work like the other one?"

"I don't know how any of them work! It sounded different, a bell sound instead of a buzzing noise. But it was a passage, all right."

"You've been there," she said slowly, looking at me under her brows.

"Why? Did you want to go back? After you'd found—him?" There was still a slight hesitation in her voice; she couldn't quite bring herself to refer to Jamie as "my father."

"No. It was to do with Geillis Duncan. She found it."

Brianna's eyes sprang wide.

"She's *here*?"

"No. She's dead."

I took a deep breath, feeling the remembered shock and tingle of an ax blow run up my arm. Sometimes I thought of her, of Geillis, when I was alone in the forest. Sometimes I thought I heard her voice behind me, and turned around swiftly, but saw no more than the hemlock branches, soughing in the wind. But now and then I felt her eyes on me, green and bright as the springtime wood.

"Quite dead," I said firmly, and changed the subject. "How did this happen, anyway?"

There wasn't any pretence of not knowing what I was talking about. She gave me a straight look, one eyebrow raised.

"You're the doctor. How many ways *are* there?"

I gave her back the look, with interest.

"Didn't you even think of taking any precautions?"

She glowered, thick brows drawn down.

"I wasn't *planning* to have sex here!"

I clutched my head, digging my fingers into my scalp in exasperation.

"You think people *plan* it? Good God, how many times did I come to that school of yours and give talks about—"

"All the time! Every year! My mother the sex encyclopedia! Do you have any idea how mortifying it is to have your own mother standing up in front of everybody, drawing pictures of *penises*?"

Her face went the color of the scarlet maples, flushed with the memory.

"I must not have done it all that well," I said tartly, "since you seem not to have recognized one when you saw it."

Her face jerked toward me, blood in her eye, but then relaxed when she saw that I was joking—or trying to.

"Right," she said. "Well, they look different in 3-D."

Taken unawares, I laughed. After a moment's hesitation, she joined me, a hesitant giggle.

"You know what I mean. I gave you that prescription before I left."

She looked down her long, straight nose at me.

"Yes, and I was never so shocked in my life! You thought I'd run right out and have sex with everybody in sight the minute you left?"

"You're implying that it was only my presence stopping you?" The corner of her wide mouth twitched.

"Well, not *only* that," she conceded. "But you had something to do with it, you and Daddy. I mean, I—I wouldn't have wanted to disappoint you." The twitch had turned to a quiver in an instant, and I hugged her hard, her smooth bright hair against my cheek.

"You couldn't, baby," I murmured, rocking her slightly. "We'd never be disappointed in you, never."

I felt both tension and worry ebb as I held her. Finally, she took a deep breath and let go of me.

"Maybe not you or Daddy," she said. "But what about—?" She tilted her head toward the now invisible house.

"He won't—" I began, but then stopped. The truth was that I didn't know *what* Jamie would do. On the one hand, he was strongly inclined to think that Brianna hung the moon. On the other hand, he had opinions regarding sexual honor that could only be described—for obvious reasons—as old-fashioned, and no inhibitions at all about expressing them.

He was worldly, well educated, tolerant, and compassionate. This did not in any way, shape, or form mean that he shared or understood modern sensibilities; I knew quite well he didn't. And I couldn't think that his attitude toward Roger would be tolerant in the slightest.

"Well," I said dubiously, "I shouldn't wonder if he didn't want to punch Roger in the nose or something. But don't worry," I added, seeing her look of alarm. "He loves you," I said, and smoothed the tumbled hair off her flushed face. "He won't stop."

I got up, brushing yellow leaves from my skirt.

"We'll have a bit of time, then, but none to waste. Jamie can send word downriver, to keep an eye out for Roger. Speaking of Roger . . ." I hesitated, picking a bit of dried fern from my sleeve. "I don't suppose he knows about this, does he?"

Brianna took a deep breath, and her fist closed tight on the leaf in her hand, crushing it.

"Well, see, there's a problem about that," she said. She looked up at me, and suddenly she was my little girl again. "It isn't Roger's."

"What?" I said stupidly.

"It. Isn't. Roger's. Baby," she said, between clenched teeth.

I sank down beside her once more. Her worry over Roger suddenly took on new dimensions.

"Who?" I said. "Here, or there?" Even as I spoke, I was calculating—it had to be someone here, in the past. If it had been a man in her own time, she'd be farther along than two months. Not only in the past, then, but here, in the Colonies.

I wasn't planning to have sex, she'd said. No, of course not.

She hadn't told Roger, for fear he would follow her—he was her anchor, her key to the future. But in that case—

"Here," she said, confirming my calculations. She dug in the pocket of her skirt, and came out with something. She reached toward me, and I held out my hand automatically.

"Jesus H. Roosevelt Christ." The worn gold wedding band sparked in the sun, and my hand closed reflexively over it. It was warm from being carried next to her skin, but I felt a deep coldness seep into my fingers.

"Bonnet?" I said. "Stephen *Bonnet*?"

Her throat moved convulsively, and she swallowed, head jerking in a brief nod.

"I wasn't going to tell you—I couldn't; not after Ian told me about what happened on the river. At first I didn't know what Da would do; I was afraid he'd blame me. And then when I knew him a little better—I knew he'd try to find Bonnet—that's what Daddy would have done. I couldn't let him do that. You met that man, you know what he's like." She was sitting in the sun, but a shudder passed over her, and she rubbed her arms as though she was cold.

"I do," I said. My lips were stiff. Her words were ringing in my ears.

I wasn't planning to have sex. I couldn't tell . . . I was afraid he'd blame me.

"What did he do to you?" I asked, and was surprised that my voice sounded calm. "Did he hurt you, baby?"

She grimaced, and pulled her knees up to her chest, hugging them against herself.

"Don't call me that, okay? Not right now."

I reached to touch her, but she huddled closer into herself, and I dropped my hand.

"Do you want to tell me?" I didn't want to know; I wanted to pretend it hadn't happened, too.

She looked up at me, lips tightened to a straight white line.

"No," she said. "No, I don't want to. But I think I'd better."

◆───

She had stepped aboard the *Gloriana* in broad daylight, cautious, but feeling safe by reason of the number of people around; loaders, seamen, merchants, servants—the docks bustled with life. She had told a seaman on the deck what she wanted; he had vanished into the recesses of the ship, and a moment later, Stephen Bonnet had appeared.

He had on the same clothes as the night before; in the daylight, she could see that they were of fine quality, but stained and badly crumpled. Greasy candle wax had dripped on the silk cuff of his coat, and his jabot had crumbs in it.

Bonnet himself showed fewer marks of wear than did his clothes; he was fresh-shaven, and his green eyes were pale and alert. They passed over her quickly, lighting with interest.

"I did think ye comely last night by candlelight," he said, taking her hand and raising it to his lips. "But a-many seem so when the drink is flowin'. It's a good deal more rare to find a woman fairer in the sun than she is by the moon."

Brianna tried to extract her hand from his grasp, giving him a polite smile.

"Thank you. Do you still have the ring?" Her heart beat fast in her throat. He could still tell her about the ring—about her mother—even if he had lost it gambling. But she wanted very badly to have it in her hands. She suppressed the fear that had haunted her all night; that the ring might be all that was left of her mother. It couldn't be, not if the newspaper clipping was right, but—

"Oh, indeed. The luck of Danu herself was with me the night —and still is, by the looks of it." He gave her a charming smile, still keeping hold of her hand.

"I—ah, I wondered if you would sell it to me." She had brought nearly all the money she had with her, but had no idea what the cost of a gold ring might be.

"Why?" The blunt question took her unawares, and she fumbled for an answer.

"It—it looks like one my mother had," she answered, unable to invent an answer better than the truth. "Where did you get it?"

Something moved behind his eyes, though he still smiled at her. He gestured toward the dark companionway, and tucked her hand in the crook of his elbow. He was taller than she, a big man. She pulled, cautiously, but he held her hand fast.

"So ye want the ring? Come down to my cabin, my dear, and we shall see if an accommodation might be reached."

Below, he poured her brandy; she took the barest sip, but he drank deeply, draining one glass and pouring another.

"Where?" he said carelessly, in answer to her persistent questions. "Ah—well, a gentlemen should not be tellin' tales of his ladies, should he?'' He winked at her. "A love token," he whispered.

The smile on her own face felt stiff, and the sip of brandy she had taken burned in her stomach.

"The lady who—gave it to you," she said. "Is she in good health?"

He gaped at her, lower jaw fallen slightly open.

"Luck," she said hastily. "It's bad luck to wear jewelry that belongs to someone who's—who's dead."

"Is it?" The smile returned. "I cannot say I have noticed that effect myself." He set down the glass and gave a slight, pleasurable belch.

"Still, I can assure ye, the lady from whom I had that ring was both alive and well when I left her."

The burning sensation in her stomach eased slightly.

"Oh. I'm glad to hear that. Will you sell it to me, then?"

He rocked back in his chair, eyeing her, a small smile on his lips.

"Sell it. And what will ye offer me, sweetheart?"

"Fifteen pounds sterling." Her heart began to beat faster again, as he stood up. He was going to agree! Where did he keep it?

He stood up, took her hand, and pulled her up out of her chair.

"I've enough money, sweetheart," he said. "What color's the hair between your legs?"

She jerked her hand out of his grasp, and backed up as quickly as she could, slamming into the wall of the cabin within a few steps.

"You've mistaken me," she said. "I didn't mean—"

"Maybe not," he said, and the edges of his teeth showed in his smile. "But I do. And I do think perhaps you've mistaken *me,* sweetheart."

He took a step toward her. She snatched the brandy bottle from the table, and swung it at his head. He ducked adroitly, plucked the bottle from her hand, and slapped her hard across the face.

She staggered, half blinded by the sudden pain. He grasped her by the shoulders, and forced her to her knees. His fingers twisted tight in her hair, close to the scalp, and jerked her head, hard. He held her, head canted at an awkward angle, while he fumbled with the other hand at the front of his breeches. He grunted slightly with satisfaction and took a half step closer, thrusting his hips forward.

"Meet Leroi," he said.

Leroi was both uncircumcised and unwashed, and gave off a powerful smell of stale urine. She felt a bolus of vomit rise in her throat, and tried to turn her head away. The answer to that was a vicious yank on her hair that brought her back, stifling a cry of pain.

"Put out that little pink tongue and give us a kiss, sweetheart." Bonnet sounded cheerful and unconcerned, his grip on her hair tight as ever. She lifted her hands toward him in unspoken protest; he saw it and tightened his grip, making tears start in her eyes. She put out her tongue.

"Not bad, not bad," he said, judiciously. "All right, open your mouth." He let go of her hair quite suddenly and her head snapped back. Before she could jerk away, he had seized her by one ear, twisting slightly.

"Bite me, sweetheart, and I'll mash your nose flat. Eh?" He brushed his closed fist lightly under her nose, nudging the tip with a massive knuckle. Then he took a firm grip on her other ear, holding her head immobile between his big hands.

She concentrated on the taste of the blood from her cut lip, the taste and the pain of it. With her eyes closed, she could see the taste, salt and metal, a burnished copper, shining pure in the dark inside her eyes.

If she vomited, she would choke. She would choke, and he would not notice. She would strangle and die, and he wouldn't stop. She put her hands on his thighs to brace herself, and dug her fingers into the heavy muscle, pushing back as hard as she could, to resist the battering. He was humming, deep in his throat. *From Ushant to Scilly is thirty-five leagues.* Wiry hairs brushed her lips.

Then Leroi was gone. He let go of her ears and stepped back; unbalanced, she fell forward on hands and knees, gagging and coughing, the strings of saliva from her mouth tinged pink with blood. She coughed and spat, and spat again, trying to clear her mouth of foulness. Her lips were swollen, and throbbing with her heartbeat.

He lifted her effortlessly, hands under her arms, and kissed her, tongue thrusting, one palm cupping the back of her head to keep her from pulling away. He tasted overpoweringly of brandy, with a faint nastiness of decaying teeth. The other hand, at her waist, roamed slowly downward, kneading her buttocks.

"Mmm," he said, sighing pleasurably. "Bedtime, eh, sweetheart?"

She lowered her head and butted him in the face. Her forehead struck hard against bone, and he uttered a sharp cry of surprise and loosened his grip. She wrenched free and ran. Her flying skirt caught on the doorlatch and tore, disregarded as she hurled herself out into the dark companionway.

The sailors were at supper; twenty men sat at a long table in the mess at the end of the companionway, twenty faces turned toward her in expressions ranging from startlement to lascivious interest. It was the cook who tripped her, sticking out a foot as she dashed past the galley. Her knees hit the deck with numbing force.

"Like games, do you, sweetheart?" It was Bonnet's voice in her ear, jovial as ever, as a pair of hands scooped her up with disconcerting ease. He whirled her to face him, and smiled. She had hit him in the nose; a thick trickle of blood flowed down from one nostril. It ran over his upper lip, and followed the grooves of his smile, thin lines of red showing between his teeth, and dark drops dripping slowly from his chin.

His grip on her arms tightened, but the merry glint shone as ever in his light green eyes.

"That's all right, sweetheart," he said. "Leroi likes games. Don't you, Leroi?" He glanced down, and she followed his gaze. He had shed his breeches in the cabin, and stood half naked, Leroi brushing against her skirts, quivering with eagerness.

He took her by one elbow, and bowing gallantly, gestured toward the cabin. Numbly, she stepped forward, and he took his place beside her, arm in arm, nonchalantly exposing the white cheeks of his buttocks to the stares of his gaping crew.

"After that . . . it wasn't so bad." She could hear her own voice, unnaturally calm, as though it belonged to someone else. "I didn't—didn't fight him anymore."

He hadn't bothered to make her undress, merely untucked her kerchief. Her dress was made in the usual fashion, with a low, square neckline, and her breasts were high and round; it took no more than a casual downward yank to bare them, popping them up over the edge of the bodice like a pair of apples.

He mauled them idly for a moment, pinching her nipples between a large thumb and forefinger to make them stand up, then pushed her toward his tumbled bed.

The sheets were stained with spilled liquor and stank of perfume and wine, and overwhelmingly of the rank, heavy odor of Bonnet himself. He shoved up her skirt and arranged her legs to suit him, humming all the while beneath his breath. *Farewell to you all, ye fine Spanish ladies . . .*

In her mind's eye, she could see herself thrusting him away, flinging herself off the bed and running for the door, skimming light as a gull down the dark companionway and bursting up through the grated deck to freedom. She could feel the wooden boards under her bare feet, and the glare of the hot summer sun in her dark-blind eyes. Almost. She lay in the dim cabin, wooden as a figurehead, tasting blood in her mouth.

There was a blind, insistent prodding between her thighs and she convulsed in panic, scissoring her legs. Still humming, he thrust a muscular leg between her own, brutally nudging her thighs apart. Naked from the waist downward, he still wore his shirt and stock. The long tails drooped around Leroi's pale stalk as he rose up on his knees above her.

He stopped humming long enough to spit copiously into his palm. Rubbing roughly and thoroughly, he eased the path and then set to business. With one hand clutched firmly on her breast, he guided himself with the other to an inescapable berth, making a jovial remark about the snugness of the accommodation, and then loosed Leroi on his mindless—and mercifully brief—gallop to pleasure.

Two minutes, maybe three. And then it was over, and Bonnet lay heavily collapsed upon her, sweat crumpling his linen stock, one hand still crushing her breast. His lank fair hair fell soft against her cheek and his exhalations purled hot and damp on her neck. At least he'd stopped humming.

She lay frozen for endless long minutes, staring up at the ceiling, where the reflections from the water danced across the polished beams. He sighed at last, and rolled slowly off her onto his side. He smiled at her, dreamily scratching one bared and hairy hip.

"Not bad, sweetheart, though I've had livelier rides. Move your arse more next time, hm?" He sat up, yawned, and began to straighten his attire. She edged toward the side of the bed, then, sure that he didn't mean to restrain her, rolled abruptly off and onto her feet. She felt light-headed and desperately short of air, as though his bulk still pressed upon her.

Moving in a daze, she went to the door. It was bolted. As she struggled to lift the bolt, her hands shaking, she heard him say something behind her, and swung around in amazement.

"*What* did you say?"

"I said the ring's on the desk," he said, straightening up from retrieving his stockings. He sat down on the bed and began to pull them on, waving casually at the desk that stood against the wall. "There's money, too. Take what you want."

The top of the desk was a magpie's nest, littered with inkpots, trinkets, bits of jewelry, bills of lading, tattered quills, silver buttons, ragged bits of paper and crumpled clothing, and a scatter of coins in silver and bronze, copper and gold, currency of several colonies, several countries.

"You're offering me *money*?"

He looked up quizzically, fair brows arched.

"I pay for my pleasures," he said. "Did you think I wouldn't?"

Everything in the cabin seemed unnaturally vivid, detailed and individual as the objects in a dream, which would vanish with waking.

"I didn't think anything," she said, her voice sounding very clear, but distant, someone speaking from far away. Her kerchief lay on the floor where he had thrown it, by the desk. She walked there, carefully, trying not to think of the warm slipperiness that streaked down her thighs.

"I'm an honest man—for a pirate," he said behind her, and laughed. He stamped once on the deck to settle his foot in its shoe, then brushed past her and lifted the bolt easily with one hand.

"Help yourself, sweetheart," he said, with another casual wave toward the desk as he went out. "You were worth it."

She heard his footsteps going away down the companionway, a burst of laughter and a muffled remark as he met someone, then a shift of his voice, suddenly clear and harsh, shouting orders to someone above, and the tramp and scurry of feet overhead, rushing to obey. Back to business.

It was sitting in a bowl made of cowhorn, jumbled with a collection of bone buttons, string, and other bits of rubbish. Like him, she thought, with a cold clarity. Acquisition for its own sake; a reckless and savage delight in the taking, with no knowledge at all of the value of what he stole.

Her hand was shaking; she saw it with a vague sense of surprise. She tried to grasp the ring, failed, gave up. She scooped up

the bowl and emptied its contents into her pocket. She walked
down the dark companionway, her fist wrapped tight around the
pocket, holding it like a talisman. There were seamen all around,
too busy about their tasks to spare her more than a glance of lewd
speculation. Her shoes were perched on the end of the mess table,
bows perky in a shaft of light from the grating overhead.

She put them on, and with an even tread walked up the ladder,
across the deck and gangplank, onto the dock. Tasting blood.

"I thought at first I could just pretend it didn't happen." She
took a deep breath, and looked at me. Her hands folded over her
stomach, as though to hide it. "But I guess that won't work, will
it?"

I was silent for a moment, thinking. It was no time for delicacy.

"When?" I said. "How long after . . . um, after Roger?"

"Two days."

My eyebrows lifted at that.

"Why are you so sure it isn't Roger's, then? You weren't using
pills, obviously, and I'll bet my life Roger didn't use what passes
for condoms in these times."

She half smiled at that, and a small flush rose in her cheeks.

"No. He . . . um . . . he . . . ah . . ."

"Oh, coitus interruptus?"

She nodded.

I took a deep breath and blew it out through pursed lips.

"There is a word," I said, "for people who depend on that
particular method of birth control."

"What's that?" she asked, looking wary.

"Parents," I said.

46

Comes a Stranger

Roger bent his head and drank from cupped hands. A piece of luck, that flash of green, pointed out by a finger of sunlight stabbing down through the trees. Without it, he would never have seen the spring, so far off the trail as it was.

A clear trickle bubbled through a crack in the rock, cooling his hands and face. The rock itself was a smooth blackish green, and the ground all round was boggy, rumpled by tree roots and furred with a moss that grew brilliant as emeralds in the fleeting patch of sun.

The knowledge that he would see Brianna shortly—perhaps within the hour—soothed his annoyance as effectively as the cool water eased his dry throat. If he'd had to have his horse stolen, it was some consolation that he'd been close enough to reach his destination on foot.

The horse itself had been an ancient nag, barely worth stealing. At least he'd had the sense to keep his valuables on his person, not in the saddlebags. He clapped a hand against the side seam of his breeches, reassured to feel the small hardness snuggled against his thigh.

Beyond the horse itself, he hadn't lost much more than a pistol —nearly as ancient as the horse and not half so reliable—a bit of food, and a leather water flask. The loss of the flask had troubled him for the last few miles of hot, dusty walking, but now that minor inconvenience was remedied.

His feet sank into the damp ground as he stood up, leaving dark streaks in the emerald moss. He stepped back and wiped the mud from his shoe soles on the carpet of dry leaves and crusted needles. Then he dusted down the skirts of his coat as well as he could, and straightened the grimy stock at his throat. His knuckles rasped the stubble on his jaw; his razor had been in the saddlebag.

He looked a right villain, he thought ruefully. No way to meet your in-laws. In truth, though, he wasn't much concerned with what Claire and Jamie Fraser might think of him. His thoughts were all on Brianna.

She'd found her parents now; he could only hope that the re-union had been so satisfactory that she'd be in a mood to forgive his betrayal. Christ, he'd been stupid!

He made his way back toward the path, feet sinking in the soft leaf-layer. Stupid in underestimating her stubbornness, stupid not to have been honest with her, he amended. Stupid to have bullied her into secrecy. Trying to keep her safely in the future—no, that hadn't been stupid at all, he thought, with a grimace at the things he'd seen and heard in the last few months.

He pushed aside an overhanging limb of loblolly pine, then ducked with an exclamation of alarm, as something black shot past his head.

A hoarse *craawk!* announced that his assailant was a raven. Similar cries gave notice of the arrival of reinforcements in the trees nearby, and within seconds, another black missile whizzed past, within inches of his ear.

"Hey, bugger off!" he exclaimed, ducking away from yet an-other croaking buzz bomb. He was plainly near a nest, and the ravens didn't like it.

The first raven sailed back for another try. This pass knocked his hat into the dirt. The mobbing was unnerving, the sense of hostility out of all proportion to the size of his adversaries. An-other came in, zooming low, and struck him a glancing blow as its claws ripped at the shoulder of his coat. Roger snatched up his hat and ran.

A hundred yards up the trail, he slowed to a walk and looked round. The birds were nowhere in sight; he'd passed their nesting place, then.

"And where's Alfred Hitchcock when you need him?" he mut-tered to himself, trying to shake off the sense of danger.

His voice was damped at once by the thick vegetation; it was like talking into a pillow. He was breathing heavily, and his face felt flushed. All at once, it seemed very quiet in the forest. With the ceasing of the ravens' racket, all the other birds seemed to have stopped as well. It was no wonder the old Scots thought ravens birds of bad omen; spend much longer here, and all the old ways that had been no more than curiosities would be flourishing away in his mind.

Dangerous, dirty, and uncomfortable as it was, he had to admit the fascination of being here—of experiencing at firsthand things he'd read about, seeing objects he knew as museum artifacts being casually used in daily life. If it wasn't for Brianna, he might not regret the adventure, in spite of Stephen Bonnet and the things he had seen aboard the *Gloriana*.

Once more his hand went to his thigh. He had been luckier than he'd dared hope; Bonnet had had not one gemstone, but two. Would they really work? He ducked again, having to walk half crouched for several steps before the branches opened up again. Hard to believe that people lived up here, save that someone had cut this trail, and it must lead somewhere.

"You can't miss it," the girl at the mill had assured him, and he could see why. There wasn't anyplace else to go.

He shaded his eyes, looking up the trail, but the drooping branches of pine and maple hid everything, presenting only a shadowy, mysterious tunnel through the trees. No telling how far it might be to the top of the ridge.

"You'll make it by sundown, easy," the girl had told him, and it was late midafternoon now. But that had been when he had a horse. Not wanting to be caught on the mountainside in the dark, he picked up his pace, straining his eyes for sunlight ahead that would show him the openness of the ridge at the end of the trail.

As he walked, his thoughts ran inevitably ahead of him, quick with speculation.

And how had it gone, Brianna's reunion with her parents? What had she thought of Jamie Fraser? Was he the man she'd been imagining for the last year, or only a pale reflection of the image she had built up from her mother's stories?

At least she had a father to know, he thought, with a queer little pang at the memory of Midsummer's Eve, and that burst of light in the passage through the stones.

There it was! A lightening of the dense green shadow ahead; a brightening as tongues of sun struck autumn leaves in a flare of orange and yellow.

The sun dazzled him for a moment as he came out of the tunnel of greenery. He blinked once, and found himself not on the ridge, as he had expected, but in a small natural clearing, edged with scarlet maples and yellow scrub oak. It held the sunlight like a cup, dark forest spreading beyond on all sides.

As he turned about, searching for the continuation of the trail, he heard a horse's whicker and whirled to find his own elderly mount, jerking its head against the pull of a rein tied to a tree at the edge of the clearing.

"Well, I'll be buggered!" he exclaimed in astonishment. "How the hell did you get up here?"

"The same way you did," a voice answered him. A tall young man emerged from the wood beside the horse, and stood pointing a pistol at Roger; his own, he saw, with a sense of outrage as well as apprehension. He took a deep breath and choked down his fear.

"You've got my horse and my gun," Roger said coolly. "What else d'you want? My hat?" He held out the battered tricorne in invitation. The robber couldn't possibly know what else he carried; he hadn't shown them to anyone.

The young man—couldn't be more than in his teens, in spite of his size, Roger thought—didn't smile.

"A bit more than that, I expect." For the first time, the young man took his eyes off Roger, shifting his glance to one side. Following the direction of his gaze, Roger felt a jolt like an electric shock.

He hadn't seen the man at the edge of the clearing, though he must have been there all the time, standing motionless. He wore a faded hunting kilt whose browns and greens blended into the grass and brush, as his flaming hair blended with the brilliant leaves. He looked as if he'd grown out of the forest.

Beyond the sheer unexpectedness of his appearance, it was his looks that stunned Roger into speechlessness. It was one thing to have been told that Jamie Fraser resembled his daughter. It was another to see Brianna's bold features transmuted into power by the stamp of years, and fronting a personality not only thoroughly masculine, but fierce in aspect.

It was like lifting his hand from the fur of a handsome ginger cat, only to find himself staring into the unblinking gaze of a tiger. Roger barely kept himself from taking an involuntary step backward, thinking as he did so that Claire had not exaggerated a single thing in her descriptions of Jamie Fraser.

"You'll be Mr. MacKenzie," the man said. It wasn't a question. The voice was deep but not loud, barely lifted above the sound of the rustling leaves, but Roger had no difficulty hearing him.

"I am," he said, taking a step forward. "And you'll be . . . ah . . . Jamie Fraser?" He stretched out a hand, but quickly let it drop. Two pairs of eyes rested coldly on him.

"I am," said the red-haired man. "You'll know me?" The tone of the question was distinctly unfriendly.

Roger took a deep breath, cursing his own dishevelment. He didn't know how Brianna might have described him to her father, but Fraser had evidently expected something a good deal more prepossessing.

"Well, you—look quite a bit like your daughter."

The young man gave a loud snort, but Fraser didn't look around.

"And what business have ye wi' my daughter?" Fraser moved for the first time, stepping out from the shadow of the trees. No, Claire hadn't exaggerated. He *was* big, even an inch or two taller than Roger himself.

Roger felt a stab of alarm, mingled with his confusion. What the hell had Brianna told him? Surely she couldn't have been so angry that—well, he'd sort that out when he saw her.

"I've come to claim my wife," he said boldly.

Something changed in Fraser's eyes. Roger didn't know what it was, but it made him drop his hat, and half raise his hands in reflex.

"Oh, no, ye're not." It was the boy who had spoken, in an odd tone of satisfaction.

Roger glanced at him, and was still more alarmed to see the lad's big, bony knuckles white on the pistol's grip.

"Here be careful! You don't want that to go off by accident," he said.

The young man's lip lifted in a sneer.

"If it goes off, it'll be no accident."

"Ian." Fraser's voice stayed level, but the pistol lowered, reluctantly. The big man took another step forward. His eyes were fixed on Roger's, deep blue and slanted; unnervingly like Brianna's.

"I'll ask only the once, and I mean to hear the truth," he said, quite mildly. "Have ye taken my daughter's maidenheid?"

Roger felt his face grow hot as a flood of warmth washed up from chest to hairline. Christ, what had she told her father? And for God's sake, *why?* The last thing he had expected to meet was an infuriated father, bent on avenging his daughter's virtue.

"It's . . . ah . . . well, it's not what you think," he blurted. "I mean, we . . . that is . . . we meant to . . ."

"Did ye or no?" Fraser's face was no more than a foot away,

completely expressionless, save for whatever it was that burned, far back in his eyes.

"Look—I—damn it, yes! She wanted to—"

Fraser hit him, just under the ribs.

Roger doubled and staggered back, gasping from the blow. It didn't hurt—yet—but he'd felt the force of it all the way to his spine. His principal feeling was one of amazement, tinged with anger.

"Stop," he said, trying to get enough breath to talk. "Stop! For God's sake, I said I—"

Fraser hit him again, this time on the side of the jaw. That one hurt, a glancing blow that scraped the skin and left his jawbone throbbing. Roger jerked back, fear turning rapidly to fury. The bloody sod was trying to kill him!

Fraser swung at him again, but missed as Roger ducked and whirled. Well, to fuck with good family relations, then!

He took a giant step backward, shrugging out of his coat. To his surprise, Fraser didn't come after him, but stood there, fists at his sides, waiting.

The blood was drumming in Roger's ears, and he had no eyes for anyone but Fraser. If it was a fight the bugger wanted, that's what he'd get, then.

Roger crouched, hands up and ready. He'd been taken by surprise, but he wouldn't be caught that way again. No brawler, still he'd been in his share of pub fights. They were well matched for height and reach, and he had more than fifteen years' advantage on the man.

He saw Fraser's right, ducked and countered, felt his fist brush linen as it passed Fraser's side and then the left he hadn't seen took him in the eye. Bloody stars and streaks of light exploded through the side of his head, and tears ran down his cheek as he launched himself at Fraser, roaring.

He hit the man; he could feel his fists strike flesh, but it seemed to make no difference. Through his one sound eye, he could see that broad-boned face, set in eerie calm, like a Viking berserker. He swung, and it disappeared, bobbed up again; he swung, grazing an ear. A blow struck him in the shoulder; he swung half around with it, recovered, and launched himself headfirst.

"She's . . . mine," Roger gritted between clenched teeth. He had his arms wrapped around Fraser's body, felt the deep-sprung ribs give as he squeezed. He'd crack the bastard like a nut. "Mine . . . hear?"

Fraser rabbit-punched him in the back of the neck, a glancing blow, but hard enough to numb his left arm and shoulder. He let go his grip, hunched and drove his right shoulder hard into Fraser's chest, trying to drive the older man off his feet.

Fraser took a short step back and hooked him hard, but the blow struck his ribs, not the soft flesh below. Still, it was hard enough to make him grunt and jerk back, crouching to protect himself.

Fraser lowered his head and butted him, straight on; he flew backward and landed hard. Blood from his nose ran down his mouth and chin; with a sense of remoteness, he watched the spatter of dark red drops grow and run together into a splotch on his shirt.

He rolled to one side to avoid the kick he saw coming, but not far enough. As he rolled frantically the other way, it occurred to him, in a detached sort of way, that while he might be fifteen years younger than his opponent, Jamie Fraser had likely spent every one of those fifteen years engaged in physical combat.

He had got momentarily out of range. Gulping air, he rolled up onto his hands and knees. Blood gurgled through smashed cartilage with each breath; he could taste it in the back of his throat, a taste like sheared metal.

" 'Nuff,'' he panted. ''No. 'Nuff!''

A hand grabbed his hair and jerked back his head. Blue eyes glittered six inches away, and he felt the man's breath hot on his face.

''Not nearly enough,'' Fraser said, and kneed him in the mouth. He fell over and rolled once, then struggled to his feet. The clearing blurred in a throb of orange and yellow; only instinct got him up and moving.

He was fighting for his life, and knew it. He hurled himself blindly at the weaving figure, got a grip of Fraser's shirt and drove a punch at the man's belly, as hard as he could. Fabric tore and his fist struck bone. Fraser shifted like a snake and shot a hand down between them. He grabbed Roger's testicles and squeezed with all his strength.

Roger stood stock-still, then dropped as though his spinal cord had been severed. There was a split second, before the pain hit, when Roger was conscious of one last thought, cold and clear as a shard of ice. *My God,* he thought, *I'm going to die before I've been born.*

47

A Father's Song

It was well after dark before Jamie came in, and my nerves were thoroughly on edge from the waiting; I could only imagine Brianna's. We had eaten supper—or I should say, supper had been served. None of us had any appetite, either for food or conversation; even Lizzie's normal voracity was noticeably impaired. I hoped the girl wasn't ill; pale and silent, she had pled a headache and gone to bed in the herb shed. Still, it was fortunate in the circumstances; it saved me having to invent an excuse to get rid of her once Jamie did arrive.

The candles had been lit for over an hour when I finally heard the goats bleat in greeting at his step on the path. Brianna looked up at once at the sound, her face pale in the yellow light.

"It'll be all right," I said. She heard the confidence in my voice and nodded, slightly reassured. The confidence was authentic, but not unalloyed. I thought everything *would* be all right eventually —but God knew, it wasn't going to be a jolly family evening. Well as I knew Jamie, there were still a good many circumstances in which I had no idea how he would react—and hearing that his daughter was pregnant by a rapist was certainly one of them.

In the hours since Brianna had made my suspicions a certainty, I had envisioned virtually every possible response he *might* make, several of them involving shouting or the putting of his fists through solid objects, behavior which I always found upsetting. So might Bree, and I knew rather better what *she* might do when upset.

She was under a tight control for the moment, but I knew how precarious her calm demeanor was. Let him say a bruising word to her, and she would flare like a striking match. Beyond red hair and arresting height, she had from Jamie both a passionate nature and a perfect readiness to speak her mind.

So unfamiliar and so anxious to please each other, they had

both so far stepped delicately—but there seemed no delicate way of handling this. Unsure whether I should prepare myself to be advocate, interpreter, or referee, it was with rather a hollow feeling that I lifted the latch to let him in.

He had washed at the creek; his hair was damp at the temples, and he had wiped his face on his shirttail, judging by the moist patches on it.

"You're very late; where were you?" I asked, standing on tiptoe to give him a kiss: "And where's Ian?"

"Fergus came and asked could we give him a hand wi' his chimney stones, as he couldna manage verra well by himself. Ian's stayed ower, to help finish the job." He dropped an absent kiss on top of my head, and patted my bottom. He'd been working hard, I thought; he was warm to my touch and smelled pungently of sweat, though the skin of his face was cool and fresh from washing.

"Did Marsali feed you supper?" I peered at him in the gloom. Something seemed different about him, though I couldn't think what.

"No. I dropped a stone and I've maybe broken my blasted finger again; I thought I'd best come home and have ye tend to it." That was it, I thought; he'd patted me with his left hand instead of his right.

"Come into the light and let me see." I drew him to the fire, and made him sit down on one of the oak settles. Brianna was on the other, her sewing spread around her. She got up and came to look over my shoulder.

"Your poor hands, Da!" she said, seeing the swollen knuckles and scraped skin.

"Och, it's no great matter," he said, glancing dismissively at them. "Save for the bloody finger. Ow!"

I felt my way gently over the fourth finger of his right hand, from base to nail, disregarding his small grunt of pain. It was reddened and slightly swollen, but not visibly dislocated.

It always troubled me slightly to examine this hand. I had set a number of broken bones in it long ago, before I knew anything of formal surgery, and working under far from ideal conditions. I had managed; I had saved the hand from amputation, and he had good use of it, but there were small awkwardnesses; slight twistings and thickenings that I was aware of whenever I felt it closely. Still, at the moment, I blessed the opportunity for delay.

I closed my eyes, feeling the fire's warm flicker on my lids as I

concentrated. The fourth finger was always stiff; the middle joint
had been crushed, and healed frozen. I could see the bone in my
mind; not the polished dry surface of a laboratory specimen, but
the faintly luminous matte glow of living bone, all the tiny osteo-
blasts busily laying down their crystal matrix, and the hidden
pulse of the blood that fed them.

Once more, I drew my own finger down the length of his, then
took it gently between my thumb and index finger, just below the
distal joint. I could feel the crack in my mind, a thin dark line of
pain.

"There?" I asked, opening my eyes.

He nodded, a faint smile on his lips as he looked at me.

"Just there. I like the way ye look when ye do that, Sassenach."

"What way is that?" I asked, a bit startled to hear that I looked
any way in particular.

"I canna describe it, exactly," he said, head tilted to one side
as he examined me. "It's maybe like—"

"Madame Lazonga with her crystal ball," Brianna said, sounding amused.

I glanced up, taken aback to find Brianna gazing down at me,
head cocked at the same angle, with the same appraising look.
She switched her gaze to Jamie. "A fortune-teller, I mean. A
seer."

He laughed.

"Aye, I think you're maybe right, *a nighean.* Though it was a
priest I was thinking of; the way they look saying Mass, when
they look past the bread and see the flesh of Christ instead. Not
that I should think to compare my measly finger wi' the Body of
Our Lord, mind," he added, with a modest nod toward the offending digit.

Brianna laughed, and a smile curved his mouth on one side, as
he looked up at her, his eyes soft despite the lines of tiredness
round them. He'd had a long day, I thought. And likely to be a lot
longer. I would have given anything to hold that fleeting moment
of connection between them, but it had passed already.

"*I* think you are both ridiculous," I said. I touched his finger
lightly at the spot I'd held. "The bone is cracked, just there below
the joint. It's not bad, though; no more than a hairline fracture. I'll
splint it, just in case."

I got up and went to rummage through my medical chest for a
linen bandage and one of the long, flat wood chips I used as

tongue depressors. I glanced covertly over the raised lid, watching him. Something was definitely odd about him this evening, though I still couldn't put my finger on it.

I had sensed it from the first, even through my own agitation, and sensed it even more strongly when I held his hand to examine it; a sort of energy pulsed through him, as though he were excited or upset, though he gave no outward sign of it. He was bloody good at hiding things when he wanted to; what the hell had happened at Fergus's house?

Brianna said something to Jamie, too low for me to catch, and then turned away without waiting for an answer, and came to join me by the open chest.

"Do you have some ointment, for his hands?" she asked. Then, leaning close on pretext of looking into the chest, said in a low voice, "Should I tell him tonight? He's tired and he's hurt. Hadn't I better let him rest?"

I glanced at Jamie. He was leaning back against the settle, eyes wide open as he watched the flames, hands resting flat on his thighs. He wasn't relaxed, though; whatever strange current was flowing through him, it had him strung like a telegraph wire.

"He might rest better not knowing, but you won't," I said, equally low-voiced. "Go ahead and tell him. You might let him eat first, though," I added practically. I was a strong believer in meeting bad news on a full stomach.

I splinted Jamie's finger while Brianna sat down beside him and dabbed gentian ointment onto the abraded knuckles of his other hand. Her face was quite calm; no one would ever guess what was going on behind it.

"You've torn your shirt," I said, finishing off the last bandage with a small square knot. "Give it to me after supper and I'll mend it. How's that, then?"

"Verra nice, Madame Lazonga," he said, gingerly wiggling his freshly splinted finger. "I shall be getting quite spoilt, wi' so much attention paid me."

"When I start to chew your food for you, you can worry," I said tartly.

He laughed, and gave the splinted hand to Bree for anointing.

I went to the cupboard to fetch a plate for him. As I turned back toward the hearth, I saw him watching her intently. She kept her head bent, eyes on the large, callused hand she held between her own. I could imagine her search for words with which to begin, and my heart ached for her. Perhaps I should have told him privately myself, I thought; not let him near her until the first rush of feeling was safely past and he had himself in hand again.

"Ciamar a tha tu, mo chridhe?" he said suddenly. It was his customary greeting to her, the beginning of their evening Gaelic lesson, but his voice was different tonight; soft, and very gentle. *How are you, darling?* His hand turned and covered hers, cradling her long fingers.

"Tha mi gle mhath, athair," she replied, looking a bit surprised. *I am well, Father.* Normally he began the lesson after dinner.

Slowly he reached out with his other hand and rested it gently on her stomach.

"An e 'n fhirinn a th'agad?" he asked. *Do you tell me true?* I closed my eyes and let out a breath I didn't realize I'd been holding. No need to break *all* the news, after all. And now I knew the reason for his taut-strung strangeness; he knew, and whatever the knowledge cost him to hold, hold it he would, and treat her gently.

She didn't know enough Gaelic yet to tell what he'd asked, but she knew well enough what he meant. She stared at him for a moment, frozen, then lifted his sound hand to her cheek and bent her head over it, the loose hair hiding her face.

"Oh, Da," she said, very quietly. "I'm sorry."

She sat quite still, holding to his hand as though it were a lifeline.

"Ah, now, *m' annsachd,*" he said softly, "it will be all right."

"No, it won't," she said, her voice small but clear. "It can't ever be right. You know that."

He glanced at me out of habit, but only briefly. I couldn't tell him what to do, now. He drew a deep breath, took her by the shoulder and gave her a gentle shake.

"All I know," he said softly, "is that I'm here by ye, and your mother, too. We willna see ye shamed or hurt. Not ever. D'ye hear me?"

She didn't answer or look up, but kept her eyes on her lap, her face hidden by the rich fall of her hair. A maiden's hair, thick and unbound. His hand traced the shining curve of her head, then his fingers trailed along her jaw and lifted her chin so her eyes looked into his.

"Lizzie's right?" he asked gently. "It was rape?"

She pulled her chin away and looked down at her knotted hands, the gesture as much an admission as her nod.

"I didn't think she knew. I didn't tell her."

"She guessed. But it's no your fault, and dinna ever think so," he said firmly. "Come here to me, *a leannan*." He reached for her, and gathered her awkwardly onto his knee.

The oakwood creaked alarmingly under their combined weight, but Jamie had built it after his usual sturdy fashion; it could have held six of him. Tall as Brianna was, she looked almost small cradled in his arms, her head tucked into the curve of his shoulder. He stroked her hair gently, and murmured small things to her, half in Gaelic.

"I'll see ye safe marrit, and your bairn wi' a good father," he murmured to her. "I swear it to ye, *a nighean*."

"I can't marry anybody," she said, sounding choked. "It wouldn't be right. I can't take somebody else when I love Roger. And Roger won't want me now. When he finds out—"

"It'll make no difference to him," Jamie said, grasping her harder, almost fiercely, as though he could make things right by pure force of will. "If he's a decent man, it'll make no difference. And if it does—well, then he doesna deserve ye, and I shall beat him into pulp and stamp on the pieces, and then go and find ye a better man."

She gave a small laugh that turned into a sob, and buried her head in the cloth of his shoulder. He patted her, rocking and murmuring as though she were a tiny girl with a skinned knee, and his eyes met mine over her head.

I hadn't wept when she had told me; mothers are strong. But now she couldn't see me, and Jamie had taken the burden of strength from my shoulders for the moment.

She hadn't cried when she told me, either. But now she clung to him and wept, as much from relief, I thought, as from grief. He simply held her and let her cry, stroking her hair again and again, his eyes on my face.

I blotted my eyes on my sleeve, and he smiled at me, faintly. Brianna had subsided into long, sighing breaths, and he patted her gently on the back.

"I'm hungry, Sassenach," he said. "And I should imagine a wee drop wouldna come amiss for any of us, aye?"

"Right," I said, and cleared my throat. "I'll go and fetch some milk from the shed."

"That's no what I meant by drink!" he called after me in mock outrage.

Ignoring both this and Brianna's choked laugh, I pushed open the door.

The night outside was cold and bright, the autumn stars bright sparks overhead. I wasn't dressed to be outdoors—my face and hands were already beginning to tingle—but I stood quite still nonetheless, letting the cold wind sweep past me, taking with it the tension of the last quarter hour.

Everything was quiet; the crickets and cicadas had long since died or gone underground with the rustling mice, the skunks and possums who left off their endless search for food and went to dream their winter dreams, the rich fat of their efforts wrapped warm about their bones. Only wolves hunted in the cold, starry nights of late autumn, and they went silent, fur-footed on the frozen ground.

"What are we going to do?" I said softly, addressing the question to the overwhelming depths of the vast dark sky overhead.

I heard no sound but the rush of wind in the pine trees; no answer, save the form of my own question—the faint echo of "we" that rang in my ears. That much was true at least; whatever happened, none of us need face things alone. And I supposed that was after all as much answer as I needed, for now.

They were still on the settle when I came back in, red heads close together, haloed by the fire. The smell of gentian ointment mingled with the pungent scent of burning pine and the mouth-watering aroma of the venison stew—quite suddenly, I was hungry.

I let the door close quietly behind me, and slid to the heavy bolt. I went to poke the fire and lay a new supper, fetching down a fresh loaf of bread from the shelf, then went to get sweet butter from the crock in the pantry. I stayed a moment there, glancing over the loaded shelves.

"Put your trust in God, and pray for guidance. And when in doubt, eat." A Franciscan monk had once given me that advice, and on the whole, I had found it useful. I picked out a jar of black currant jam, a small round goat cheese, and a bottle of elderflower wine, to go with the meal.

Jamie was talking quietly when I came back. I finished my preparations, letting the deep lilt of his voice soothe me, as well as Brianna.

"I used to think of you, when ye were small," Jamie was saying to Bree, his voice very soft. "When I lived in the cave; I would imagine that I held ye in my arms, a wee babe. I would hold ye so, against my heart, and sing to ye there, watching the stars go by overhead.''

"What would you sing?" Brianna's voice was low, too, barely audible above the crackle of the fire. I could see her hand, resting on his shoulder. Her index finger touched a long, bright strand of his hair, tentatively stroking its softness.

"Old songs. Lullabies I could remember, that my mother sang to me, the same that my sister Jenny would sing to her bairns.''

She sighed, a long, slow sound.

"Sing to me now, please, Da.''

He hesitated, but then tilted his head toward hers and began to chant softly, an odd tuneless song in Gaelic. Jamie was tone-deaf; the song wavered oddly up and down, bearing no resemblance to music, but the rhythm of the words was a comfort to the ear.

I caught most of the words; a fisher's song, naming the fish of loch and sea, telling the child what he would bring home to her for food. A hunter's song, naming birds and beasts of prey, feathers for beauty and furs for warmth, meat to last the winter. It was a father's song—a soft litany of providence and protection.

I moved quietly around the room, taking down the pewter plates and wooden bowls for supper, coming back to cut bread and spread it with butter.

"Do you know something, Da?" Bree asked softly.

"What's that?" he said, momentarily suspending his song.

"You can't sing.''

There was a soft exhalation of laughter and the rustle of cloth as he shifted to make them both more comfortable.

"Aye, that's true. Shall I stop, then?''

"No." She snuggled closer, tucking her head into the curve of his shoulder.

He resumed his tuneless crooning, only to interrupt himself a few moments later.

"D'ye ken something yourself, *a leannan*?"

Her eyes were closed, her lashes casting deep shadows on her cheeks, but I saw her lips curve in a smile.

"What's that, Da?"

"Ye weigh as much as a full-grown deer."

"Shall I get off, then?" she asked, not moving.

"Of course not."

She reached up and touched his cheek.

"Mi gradhaich a thu, athair," she whispered. *My love to you, Father.*

He gathered her tightly against him, bent his head and kissed her forehead. The fire struck a knot of pitch and blazed up suddenly behind the settle, limning their faces in gold and black. His features were harsh-cut and bold; hers, a more delicate echo of his heavy, clean-edged bones. Both stubborn, both strong. And both, thank God, mine.

Brianna fell asleep after supper, worn out from emotion. I was feeling rather limp, myself, but not yet in any mood to sleep. I was at once exhausted and jittery, with that horrible battlefield feeling, of being in the midst of events beyond my ability to control, but which must be dealt with anyway.

I didn't want to deal with anything. What I wanted was to push away all thought of both present and future, and go back to the peace of the night before.

I wanted to crawl into bed with Jamie, and lie warm against him, the two of us sealed safe beneath the quilts against the growing chill of the room. Watch the embers fade as we talked softly, colloquy changing from the gossip and small jokes of the day to the language of the night. Let our talk go from words to touch, from breath to the small movements of the body that were in themselves question and answer; the completion of our conversation come at last to silence in the unity of sleep.

But trouble lay on the house tonight, and there was no peace between us.

He roamed the house like a caged wolf, picking things up and putting them down. I tidied away the things from dinner, watching him from the corners of my eyes. I wanted nothing more than to talk to him—and at the same time, dreaded it. I had promised Bree not to tell him about Bonnet. But I was a bad enough liar at any time—and he knew my face so well.

I filled a bucket of hot water from the big cauldron, and took the pewter plates outside to rinse clean.

I came back to find Jamie standing by the small shelf where he kept his inkhorn, quills and paper. He had not undressed for bed, but he made no move to take them down and begin the usual evening's work. But of course—he couldn't write, with his damaged hand.

"Do you want me to write something for you?" I asked, seeing him pick up a quill and put it down again.

He turned away with a restless gesture.

"No. I must write to Jenny, of course—and there are other things that must be done—but I canna bear to sit down and think just now."

"I know how you feel," I said sympathetically. He looked at me, a trifle startled.

"I canna tell quite how I feel myself, Sassenach," he said, with a queer laugh. "If ye think ye know, tell me."

"Tired," I said, and laid a hand on his arm. "Angry. Worried." I glanced at Brianna asleep in the trundle. "Heartbroken, maybe," I added softly.

"All of that," he said. "And a good bit more." He wore no stock, but plucked at the collar of his shirt, as though it choked him.

"I canna stay in here," he said. He glanced at me; I was still dressed in my day clothes; skirt, shift, and bodice. "Will ye come out and walk wi' me a bit?"

I went at once to fetch my cloak. It was dark outside; he wouldn't be able to watch my face.

We paced slowly together, across the dooryard and past the sheds, down to the penfold and the field beyond. I held his arm, feeling it tense and stiff under my fingers.

I had no notion how to begin, what to say. Perhaps I should simply keep quiet, I thought. Both of us were still upset, though we had done our best to be calm for Brianna.

I could feel the rage boiling just under his skin. Very understandable, but anger is as volatile as kerosene—bottled under pressure, with no target on which to unleash it. An unwary word of mine might be enough to trigger an explosion. And if he exploded at me, I might either cry or go for his throat—my own mood was far from certain.

We walked for quite a long time, through the trees to the dead cornfield, all round the edge and back, moving all the time soft-footed through a minefield of silence.

"Jamie," I said at last, as we reached the edge of the field, "what have you been doing with your hands?"

"What?" He swung toward me, startled.

"Your hands." I caught one of them, held it between my own. "You didn't do that kind of damage stacking chimney stones."

"Ah." He stood still, letting me touch the swollen knuckles of his hand.

"Brianna," he said. "She—she didna tell ye anything about the man? Did she tell ye his name?"

I hesitated—and was lost. He knew me very well.

"She did tell ye, no?" His voice was thick with danger.

"She made me promise not to tell you," I blurted. "I told her you'd know I was keeping something from you; but Jamie, I did promise—don't make me tell you, please!"

He snorted again, in half-amused disgust.

"Aye, I ken ye well, Sassenach; ye couldna keep a secret from anyone who knows ye in the slightest. Even wee Ian can read ye like a book."

He flapped a hand in dismissal.

"Dinna trouble your conscience. Let her tell me herself, when she will. I can wait." His bruised hand curled slowly against his kilt, and a small shiver ran up my back.

"Your hands," I said again.

He took a deep breath and held them out before him, backs up. He flexed them, slowly.

"D'ye recall, Sassenach, once when we were first acquent? Dougal deviled me to where I thought I must pound him, and yet I couldna do it, then. You told me, 'Hit something, you'll feel better.'" He gave me a wry, lopsided smile. "And I hit a tree. It hurt, but you were right, no? I did feel better, at least for a bit."

"Oh." I let out my breath, relieved that he didn't mean to press the matter. Let him wait, then; I doubted that he quite realized yet that his daughter could be as stubborn as he was himself.

"Did she—did she tell ye what happened?" I couldn't see his face, but the hesitation in his speech was noticeable. "I mean—" He drew in his breath with a deep hiss. "Did the man hurt her?"

"No, not physically."

I hesitated myself, imagining that I could feel the weight of the ring in my pocket, though of course I couldn't. Brianna had not asked me to keep anything to myself, other than Bonnet's name, but I would not tell Jamie any of the details she had told me, unless he asked. And I did not think he would ask; it was the last thing he would want to know.

He didn't ask; only muttered something under his breath in Gaelic and walked on, head bent.

The silence once broken, I found that I could not bear it any longer. Better to explode than suffocate. I took my hand from his arm.

"What are you thinking?"

"I am wondering—if it is as terrible to be—to be violated . . . if it is—is not . . . if there is not . . . damage." He shifted his shoulders restlessly, half shrugging as though his coat were too tight.

I knew very well what was in his mind. Wentworth prison, and the faint scars that webbed his back, a net of dreadful memory.

"Bad enough, I suppose," I said. "Though I expect you're right, it would be easier to stand if there were no physical reminder of it. But then, there *is* a physical reminder of it," I felt obliged to add. "And a bloody noticeable one, come to that!" His left hand curled at his side, clenching involuntarily.

"Aye, that's so," he muttered. He glanced uncertainly at me, the half-moon's light gilding the planes of his face. "But still— he didna hurt her, that's something. If he had . . . killing would be too good for him," he finished abruptly.

"There is the very minor detail that you don't precisely 'recover' from pregnancy," I said with a marked edge to my voice. "If he'd broken her bones or shed her blood, she'd heal. As it is —she isn't ever going to forget it, you know."

"I know!"

I flinched slightly, and he saw it. He made a sketchy gesture of apology.

"I didna mean to shout."

I gave him back a brief nod of acknowledgment, and we walked on, side by side, but not touching.

"It—" he began, and then broke off, glancing at me. He grimaced, impatient with himself.

"I do know," he said, more quietly. "Ye'll forgive me, Sassenach, but I ken the hell of a lot more about the matter than you do."

"I wasn't arguing with you. But you haven't borne a child; you can't know what that's like. It's—"

"You *are* arguing wi' me, Sassenach. Don't." He squeezed my arm, hard, and let it go. There was a touch of humor in his voice, but he was dead serious overall.

"I am trying to tell ye what *I* know." He stood still for a minute, gathering himself.

"I havena put myself in mind of Jack Randall for some good time," he said at last. "I dinna want to do it now. But there it is." He shrugged again, and rubbed a hand hard down one cheek.

"There is body, and there is soul, Sassenach," he said, speaking slowly, ordering his ideas with his words. "You're a physician; ye'll ken the one well. But the other is more important."

I opened my mouth to say that I knew that as well as he did, if not better—but then shut it without saying anything. He didn't notice; he wasn't seeing the dark cornfield, or the maple wood with its leaves gone silver with moonlight. His eyes were fixed on a small room with thick stone walls, furnished with a table and stools and a lamp. And a bed.

"Randall," he said, and his voice was meditative. "The most of what he did to me—I could have stood it." He spread out the fingers of his right hand; the dressing on the cracked finger shone white.

"I would have been afraid, been hurt; I would have meant to kill him for doing it. But I could have lived, after, and not felt his touch always on my skin, felt filthy in myself—were it not that he wasna satisfied with my body. He wanted my soul—and he had it." The white bandage vanished as his fist folded.

"Aye, well—ye ken all that." He turned away abruptly and began to walk. I had to scurry to catch him up.

"What I am saying, I suppose, is—was this man a stranger to her, who only took her for a moment's pleasure? If it was only her body that he wanted . . . then I think she will heal."

He took a deep breath and let it out again; I saw the faint white mist surround his head for a moment, the steam of his anger made visible.

"But if he knew her—was close enough to want *her,* and not just any woman—then perhaps it might be that he could touch her soul, and do real damage—"

"You don't think he did real damage?" My voice rose, despite myself. "Whether he knew her or not—"

"It is different, I tell ye!"

"No, it's not. I know what you mean—"

"You don't!"

"I do! But why—"

"Because it is not your body that matters when I take you," he said. "And ye ken that well enough, Sassenach!"

He turned and kissed me fiercely, taking me completely by surprise. He crushed my lips against my teeth, then took my whole mouth with his, half biting, demanding.

I knew what he wanted of me; the same thing I wanted so desperately of him—reassurance. But neither of us had it to give, tonight.

His fingers dug into my shoulders, slid upward and grasped my neck. The hairs rose up on my arms as he pressed me to him— and then he stopped.

"I can't," he said. He squeezed my neck hard, and then let go. His breath came raggedly. "I can't."

He stepped back and turned away from me, groping for the fence rail before him as though blind. He grasped the wood hard with both hands, and stood there, eyes closed.

I was shaking, my legs gone watery. I wrapped my arms around myself under my cloak and sat down at his feet. And waited, my heart beating painfully loud in my ears. The night wind moved through the trees on the ridge, murmuring through the pines. Somewhere, far away in the dark hills, a panther screamed, sounding like a woman.

"It's not that I dinna want ye," he said at last, and I caught the faint rustle of his coat as he turned toward me. He stood for a moment, head bowed, his bound hair gleaming in the moonlight, face hidden by the darkness, with the moon behind him. At last he leaned down and took my hand in his bruised one, lifting me to my feet.

"I want ye maybe more than I ever have," he said quietly. "And Christ! I do need ye, Claire. But I canna bear even to think of myself as a man just now. I cannot touch you, and think of what he—I can't."

I touched his arm.

"I do understand," I said, and did. I was glad that he hadn't asked for the details; I wished I didn't know them. How would it be, to make love with him, envisioning all the time an act identical in its motions, but utterly different in its essence?

"I understand, Jamie," I said again.

He opened his eyes and looked at me.

"Aye, ye do, don't you? And that's what I mean." He took my arm and drew me close to him.

"You could tear me limb from limb, Claire, without touching me," he whispered, "for ye know me." His fingers touched the side of my face. They were cold, and stiff. "And I could do the same to you."

"You could," I said, feeling a little faint. "But I really wish you wouldn't."

He smiled a little at that, bent and kissed me, very gently. We stood together, barely touching save our lips, breathing each other's breath.

Yes, we said silently to each other. *Yes, I am still here.* It was not rescue, but at least a tiny lifeline, stretched across the gulf that lay between us. I did know what he meant, about the difference between damage to body or soul; what I couldn't explain to him was the link between the two that centered in the womb. At last I stepped back, looking up at him.

"Bree's a very strong person," I said quietly. "Like you."

"Like me?" He gave a small snort. "God help her, then."

He sighed, then turned and began to walk slowly along the line of the fence. I followed, hurrying a little to catch up.

"This man, this Roger she speaks of. Will he stand by her?" he asked abruptly.

I took a deep breath and let it out slowly, not knowing how to answer. I'd known Roger only a few months. I liked him; was very fond of him, in fact. From everything I knew of him, he was a thoroughly decent, honorable young man—but how could I even pretend to know what he might think, do, or feel, upon finding that Brianna had been raped? Even worse, that she might well carry the rapist's child?

The best of men might not be able to deal with such a situation; in my years as a doctor, I had seen even well-established marriages shatter under the strain of smaller things. And those that did not shatter, but were crippled by mistrust . . . involuntarily, I pressed a hand against my leg, feeling the tiny hardness of the gold circle in my pocket. *From F. to C. with love. Always.*

"Would you do it?" I said at last. "If it were me?"

He glanced at me sharply, and opened his mouth as though to speak. Then he closed it and looked at me, searching my face, his brows knotted with troubled thought.

"I meant to say 'Aye, of course!' " he said slowly, at last. "But I did promise ye honesty once, did I not?"

"You did," I said, and felt my heart sink beneath its guilty burden. How could I force him to honesty when I couldn't give it him back? And yet he had asked.

He struck the fencepost a light blow with his fist.

"*Ifrinn!* Yes, damn it—I would. You would be mine, even if the child was not. And if you—yes. I would," he repeated firmly. "I should take you, and the child with ye, and damn the whole world!"

"And never think about it afterward?" I asked. "Never let it come into your mind when you came to my bed? Never see the father when you looked at the child? Never throw it back at me or let it make a difference between us?"

He opened his mouth to reply, but closed it without speaking.

Then I saw a change come over his features, a sudden shock of sick realization.

"Oh, Christ," he said. "Frank. Not me. It's Frank ye mean."

I nodded, and he gripped my shoulders.

"What did he do to ye?" he demanded. "What? Tell me, Claire!"

"He stood by me," I said, sounding choked even to my own ears. "I tried to make him go, but he wouldn't. And when the baby—when Brianna came—he loved her, Jamie. He wasn't sure, he didn't think he could—neither did I—but he truly did. I'm sorry," I added.

He took a deep breath and let go of my shoulders.

"Dinna be sorry for that, Sassenach," he said gruffly. "Never." He rubbed a hand across his face, and I could hear the faint rasp of his evening stubble.

"And what about you, Sassenach?" he said. "What ye said—when he came to your bed. Did he think—" He broke off abruptly, leaving all the questions hanging in the air between us, unstated, but asked nonetheless.

"It might have been me—my fault, I mean," I said at last, into the silence. "I couldn't forget, you see. If I could . . . it might have been different." I should have stopped there, but I couldn't; the words that had been dammed up all evening rushed out in a flood.

"It might have been easier—better—for him if it *had* been rape. That's what they told him, you know—the doctors; that I had been raped and abused, and was having delusions. That's what everyone believed, but I kept saying to him, no it wasn't that way, I insisted on telling him the truth. And after a time—he believed me, at least halfway. And that was the trouble; not that I'd had another man's child—but that I'd loved you. And I wouldn't stop. I couldn't," I added, in a softer tone. "He was better than me, Frank was. He could put the past away, at least for Bree's sake. But for me—" The words caught in my throat and I stopped.

He turned then, and looked at me for a long time, his face quite expressionless, eyes hidden by the shadows of his brows.

"And so ye lived twenty years with a man who couldna forgive ye for what was never your fault? I did that to ye, no?" he said. "I am sorry, too, Sassenach."

A small breath escaped me, not quite a sob.

"You said you could tear me limb from limb without touching me," I said. "You were right, damn you."

"I am sorry," he whispered again, but this time he reached for me, and held me tight against him.

"That I loved you? Don't be sorry for that," I said, my voice half muffled in his shirt. "Not ever."

He didn't answer, but bent his head and pressed his cheek against my hair. It was quiet; I could hear his heart beating, over and under the wind in the trees. My skin was cold; the tears on my cheeks chilled instantly.

At last I let my arms drop from around him and stepped back.

"We'd better go back to the house," I said, trying for a normal tone. "It's getting awfully late."

"Aye, I suppose so." He offered me his arm, and I took it. We passed in an easier silence down the path to the edge of the gorge above the stream. It was cold enough that tiny ice crystals glinted among the rocks where the starlight struck them, but the creek was far from frozen. Its gurgle and rush filled the air, and kept us from being too quiet.

"Aye, well," he said, as we turned up the path past the pigsty. "I hope Roger Wakefield is a better man than the two of us—Frank and I." He glanced at me. "Mind ye, if he's not, I shall beat him to a pudding."

Despite myself I laughed.

"That will be a *great* help to the situation, I'm sure."

He snorted briefly and walked on. At the bottom of the hill, we turned without speaking, and came back in the direction of the house. Just short of the path that led to the door, I stopped him.

"Jamie," I said hesitantly. "Do you believe I love you?"

He turned his head and looked down at me for a long moment before replying. The moon shone on his face, picking out his features as though they had been chiseled in marble.

"Well, if ye don't, Sassenach," he said at last, "ye've picked a verra poor time to tell me so."

I let out my breath in the ghost of a laugh.

"No, it's not that," I assured him. "But—" My throat tightened, and I swallowed hastily, needing to get the words out.

"I—I don't say it often. Perhaps it's only that I wasn't raised to say such things; I lived with my uncle, and he was affectionate, but not—well, I didn't know how married people—"

He put his hand lightly over my mouth, a faint smile touching his lips. After a moment, he took it away.

I took a deep breath, steadying my voice.

"Look, what I mean to say is—if I don't say it, how do you *know* I love you?"

He stood still, looking at me, then nodded in acknowledgment.

"I know because ye're here, Sassenach," he said quietly. "And that's what ye mean, aye? That he came after her—this Roger. And so perhaps he will love her enough?"

"It's not a thing you'd do, just for friendship's sake."

He nodded again, but I hesitated, wanting to tell him more, to impress him with the significance of it.

"I haven't told you a great deal about it, because—there aren't words for it. But one thing about it I could tell you. Jamie—" I shivered involuntarily, and not from the cold. "Not everyone who goes through the stones comes out again."

His look sharpened.

"How d'ye ken that, Sassenach?"

"I can—I could—hear them. Screaming."

I was shaking outright by this time, from a mixture of cold and memory, and he caught my hands between his own and drew me close. The autumn wind rattled the branches of the willows by the stream, a sound like dry, bare bones. He held me until the shivering stopped, then let me go.

"It's cold, Sassenach. Come inside." He turned toward the house, but I laid my hand on his shoulder to stop him again.

"Jamie?"

"Aye?"

"Should I—would you—do you need me to say it?"

He turned around and looked down at me. With the light behind him, he was haloed in moonlight, but his features were once more dark.

"I dinna need it, no." His voice was soft. "But I wouldna mind if ye wanted to say it. Now and again. Not too often, mind; I wouldna want to lose the novelty of it." I could hear the smile in his voice, and couldn't help smiling in return, whether he could see it or not.

"Once in a while wouldn't hurt, though?"

"No."

I stepped close to him and put my hands on his shoulders.

"I love you."

He looked down at me for a long moment.

"I'm glad of it, Claire," he said quietly, and touched my face. "Verra glad. Come to bed now; I'll warm ye."

48

Away in a Manger

The tiny stable was in a shallow cave under a rocky overhang, walled in along the front with a stockade of unpeeled cedar logs, sunk two feet deep in packed earth, stout enough to deter the most resolute bear. Light spilled out through the open upper half of the stable door, and ruddy, light-filled smoke shimmered up the face of the cliff above, rippling like bright water over the stone.

"Why a double door?" she had asked. It seemed excessive labor; an unnecessary refinement for such a crude structure.

"Ye must give the beasts a place to look out," her father had explained, showing her where to smooth the leather strap hinges tight around the curve of the wood. He picked up the hammer to tack down the leather and smiled at her, kneeling over the half-made gate. "Keeps them happy, aye?"

She didn't know if the animals were happy in the stable, but *she* was; cool and shadowy, smelling pungently of cut straw and the droppings of grass-fed animals, it was a peaceful refuge during the day, when its inhabitants were out grazing in the meadow. In bad weather or at night, the little stockade was a pocket of coziness; once she had passed near enough after dark to see the soft, misty exhalations of the animals drifting through the gap between wood and rock, as though the earth itself were breathing through pursed lips, warmly asleep in the autumn cold.

It was cold tonight, the stars sharp as needle points in the hard, clear air. It was only five minutes' walk from the house, but Brianna was shivering under her cloak by the time she reached the stable. The light spilling out came not only from a hanging lantern, she saw, but also from a small makeshift brazier in the corner, providing heat and light for the vigil within.

Her father lay curled up on a bed of straw, his plaid drawn over him, within arm's reach of the small brindled cow. The heifer lay on her chest, feet tucked to the side, grunting now and then, a look of mild concentration on her broad white face.

His head lifted abruptly at the sound of her step on the gravel, and his hand went by reflex to his belt, under his plaid.

"It's me," she said, and saw him relax as she came into the light. He swung his feet to the side and sat up, rubbing a hand over his face as she came in, carefully latching the lower gate behind her.

"Your mother's not back yet?" She was clearly alone, but he glanced briefly over her shoulder as though hoping to see Claire materialize out of the darkness.

Brianna shook her head. Claire had gone with Lizzie as escort to attend a birth at one of the farms at the far side of the cove; if the child hadn't arrived before sunset, they would stay the night at the Lachlans'.

"No. She said if she wasn't back, I was to bring you up some supper, though." She knelt and began to unpack the small basket she had brought, laying out small loaves of bread stuffed with cheese and tomato-pickle, a dried-apple tart, and two stone bottles —one of hot vegetable broth, the other of cider.

"That's kind, lassie." He smiled at her and picked up one of the bottles. "Will ye have eaten yet, yourself?"

"Oh, yes," she assured him. "Plenty." She *had* eaten, but couldn't resist a quick look of longing at the fresh rolls; the early faint sense of malaise had left her, replaced by an appetite mildly alarming in its intensity.

He saw her glance, and with a smile, drew his dirk and sliced one of the rolls in half, handing her the bigger piece.

They munched companionably for a few moments, sitting side by side on the straw, the silence broken only by soft snuffles and grunts from the stable's other inhabitants. The far end of the stable was fenced off to provide a pen for the gigantic sow and her new brood of piglets; Brianna could just make them out in the gloom—a row of plump bodies packed in the straw, prophetically sausage-shaped.

The rest of the small space was divided into three rough stalls. One belonged to the red cow, Magdalen, who lay in the straw peacefully chewing her cud, her month-old calf curled in sleep against her massive chest. The second stall was empty, filled with fresh straw, ready for the brindled cow and her tardy calf. The third stall held Ian's mare, sides glossy and bulging with the weight of an impending foal.

"It looks like a maternity ward in here," Brianna said, nodding toward Magdalen as she brushed crumbs off her skirt. Jamie smiled and raised a brow, as he always did when she said something he didn't understand.

"Oh, aye?"

"That's a special part of a hospital, where they put the new mothers and their babies," she explained. "Mama would take me to work with her sometimes, and let me go look at the nursery while she did her rounds."

She had a sudden memory of the smell of the hospital corridor, faintly acrid with the scent of disinfectant and floor polish, the babies lying bundled, plump as piglets in their bassinets, their blankets coded pink and blue. She always spent a long time going up and down the row, trying to pick which one she would take home with her, if she could keep one.

Pink or blue? For the first time, she wondered what the one she *would* now keep might wear. The thought of "it" as male or female was strangely upsetting, and she pushed the thought away with words.

"They put the babies all behind a glass wall, so you could look at them, but not breathe germs on them," she said, with a glance at Magdalen, contentedly oblivious to the strings of green saliva that dripped from her placidly moving jaws onto the head of her calf.

"Germs," he said thoughtfully. "Aye, I've heard about the germs. Dangerous wee beasties, are they not?"

"They can be." She had a vivid memory of her mother checking her box of medical supplies for the visit to Lachlans', carefully refilling the large glass bottle of distilled alcohol from the barrel in the pantry. And a more distant but equally vivid memory, of her mother explaining the past to Roger Wakefield.

"Childbirth was the most dangerous thing a woman could do," Claire had said, frowning in memory of the sights she had seen. "Infection, ruptured placenta, abnormal presentation, miscarriage, hemorrhage, puerperal fever—in most places, surviving birth was roughly a fifty-fifty proposition."

Brianna's fingers felt cold, in spite of the hissing pine chunks in the brazier, and her ravenous appetite seemed suddenly to have deserted her. She set the rest of her roll down on the straw, swallowing hard, feeling as though a bite of the thick bread had wedged itself in her throat.

Her father's broad hand touched her knee, warm even through the wool of her skirt.

"Your mother willna let ye come to harm," he said gruffly. "She's fought the germs before; I've seen her. She didna let them have the better of me, and she willna let them trouble you, either. She's a verra stubborn person, aye?"

She laughed, and the choking feeling eased.

"She'd say it takes one to know one."

"I expect she's right about that." He rose and walked around the brindled heifer, squatting down and squinting at her tail. He stood up, shaking his head, and came to sit down again. He settled comfortably back and picked up the discarded part of Brianna's roll.

"Is she doing all right?" Brianna bent and scooped up a twist of straw, holding it invitingly under the heifer's nose. The cow breathed heavily on her knuckles, but otherwise ignored the attention, the long-lashed brown eyes rolling restlessly to and fro. Now and then the bulging brindled sides rippled, the cow's thick winter coat rough but shining in the light of the hanging lantern.

Jamie frowned slightly.

"Aye, I think she'll maybe do all right. It's her first calf, though, and she's small for it. She's no much more than a yearling herself; she shouldna have been bred so early, but . . ." He shrugged, and took another bite of roll.

Brianna wiped the sticky moisture from her hand with a fold of her skirt. Feeling suddenly restless, she stood up and walked over to the pigpen.

The vast curve of the sow's belly rose up out of the hay like a swollen balloon, pink flesh visible beneath the soft, sparse white hair. The sow lay in stuporous dignity, breathing slow and deep, ignoring the squirms and squeaks of the hungry brood that scrabbled at her underside. One piglet was nudged too roughly by a fellow and momentarily lost his hold; there was a high-pitched shriek of protest, and a jet of milk spurted from the suddenly released nipple, hissing softly into the hay.

Brianna felt a slight tingle in her own breasts; they seemed suddenly heavier than usual, resting on her folded forearms as she leaned on the fence.

It wasn't a particularly aesthetic picture of motherhood—not exactly Madonna and Child—but there was something vaguely reassuring about the sow's nonchalant maternal torpor, nonetheless—a sort of careless confidence, a blind trust in natural processes.

Jamie had another look at the brindled cow, and came to stand beside Brianna by the pigpen.

"That's a good wee lass," he said approvingly, with a nod at the sow. As though in reply, the sow released a long, rumbling fart, and shifted a bit, stretching out in the straw with a voluptuous sigh.

"Well, she does look as though she knows what she's doing," Brianna agreed, biting her lip.

"That she does. She's a wicked temper, but she's an able mother, forbye. This will be her fourth litter, and not one lost or a runt weaned yet." He nodded approvingly at the sow, then glanced at the brindled heifer. "I could hope that one does half so well."

She took a deep breath.

"What if she doesn't?"

He didn't answer at once, but stood leaning on the fence, looking down at the gently squirming litter. Then his shoulders rose slightly.

"If she canna bring forth the calf alone, and I canna pull it for her, then I shall have to slaughter her," he said, matter-of-factly. "If I can save the calf, I can maybe foster it on Magdalen."

Her insides clenched tight, making lumps and knots of the food she'd eaten. She'd seen the dirk at his belt, of course, but it was so much a part of his normal costume, she hadn't thought to question its presence in this pastoral setting. The small round presence in her belly lay still and heavy, like a time bomb waiting.

He crouched beside the brindled heifer, and ran a light hand over the bulging flank. Evidently satisfied for the moment, he scratched the cow between the ears, muttering in Gaelic.

How could he murmur endearments to it, she thought, knowing that within hours he might be slicing into its living flesh? It seemed cold-blooded; did a butcher whisper "Sweet lass" to his victims? A small icy doubt dropped into her stomach, to join the other cold weights that lay there, like a collection of ball bearings.

He stood up and stretched himself, groaning as his spine crackled. He shifted his shoulders, settled, blinked, and smiled at her.

"Will I walk ye to the house, lassie? It will be some time before aught happens here."

She looked up at him, hesitating, but then made up her mind.

"No, I'll wait with you a little while. If you don't mind?"

Now, she decided on impulse. She would ask now. She had been waiting for days for the right time, but when could a time possibly *be* right for something like this? At least they would be alone now, with no chance of disturbance.

"As ye like. I shall be glad of the company."

Not for long, she thought, as he turned away to rummage in the basket she had brought. She would much have preferred darkness. It would have been a lot easier to ask what she needed to know, on the dark trail to the house. But words wouldn't be enough; she had to see his face.

Her mouth was dry; she accepted gratefully when he offered her a cup of cider. It was strong and rich, and the slight buzz of alcohol seemed to lighten the weight in her belly a little.

She gave him the cup but didn't wait for him to drink, afraid the momentary heartening effect of the cider would desert her before she could get the words out.

"Da—"

"Aye, lass?" He was pouring more cider, his eyes fixed on the cloudy golden stream.

"I need to ask you something."

"Mm?"

She took a deep breath and got it out in a rush.

"Did you kill Jack Randall?"

He froze for a moment, the jug still tilted over the cup. Then he turned the jug carefully upright, and set it down on the floor.

"And where will ye have heard that name?" he asked. He looked at her straight on, his voice as level as his eyes. "From your father, maybe? From Frank Randall?"

"Mother told me about him."

A muscle twitched near the corner of his mouth, the only outward indication of shock.

"Did she."

It wasn't a question, but she answered it anyway.

"She told me what—what happened. What he d-did to you. At Wentworth."

Her small spurt of courage was exhausted, but it didn't matter; she was in too deep to go back now. He simply sat and looked at her, the gourd cup forgotten in his hand. She longed to take it and drain it herself, but didn't dare.

It occurred to her, much too late, that he might think it a betrayal that Claire had told anyone, let alone her. She rushed ahead, babbling in her nervousness.

"It wasn't now; it was before—I didn't know you—she thought
I'd never meet you. I mean—I don't think—I know she didn't
mean to—" He raised one eyebrow at her.

"Be still, aye?"

She was only too glad to stop talking. She couldn't look at him,
but sat staring down at her lap, her fingers pleating the russet
cloth of her skirt. The silence lengthened, broken only by the
shiftings and muffled squeals of the piglets, and an occasional
digestive rumbling from Magdalen.

Why hadn't she found some other way? she wondered, in an
agony of embarrassment. *Thou shalt not uncover they father's
nakedness.* To invoke Jack Randall's name was to invoke the images of what he had done—and that was not something she could
bear even to think about. She should have asked her mother, let
Claire ask him . . . but no. There hadn't been any choice, not
really. She had to find out from him . . .

Her racing thoughts were interrupted by his words, calmly spoken.

"Why are ye asking, lass?"

She jerked her head up, to find him watching her over his
undrunk cider. He didn't look upset, and the jelly in her backbone
stiffened a little. She clenched her fists on her knees to steady
herself, and met his eyes, straight on.

"I need to know whether it will help. I want to kill . . . him.
The man who—" She made a vague gesture at her belly, and
swallowed hard. "But if I do, and it doesn't help—" She couldn't
go on.

He didn't seem shocked; abstracted, rather. He raised the cup to
his mouth and took a sip, slowly.

"Mmphm. And will ye have killed a man before?" He phrased
it as a question, but she knew it wasn't. The muscle quivered near
his mouth again—with amusement, she thought, not shock—and
she felt a quick spurt of anger.

"You think I can't, don't you? I can. You'd better believe me, I
can!" Her hands spread out, gripping her knees, broad and capable. She thought she could do it; though her image of how it
might happen wavered. In cold blood, shooting seemed the best,
perhaps the only certain way. But trying to imagine this, she had
realized vividly the truth of the old saying "Shooting's too good
for him."

It might be too good for Bonnet; it wouldn't be nearly good
enough for *her*. In the night when she flung off her blankets,

unable to bear even this slight weight and its reminder of restraint, she didn't just want him dead—she wanted to *kill* him, purely and passionately—kill him with her hands, taking back by the flesh what had been taken from her by that means.

And yet . . . what good would it be to murder him, if he would still haunt her? There was no way to know—unless her father could tell her.

"Will you tell me?" she blurted. "Did you kill him, finally—and did it help?"

He seemed to be thinking it over, his eyes traveling slowly over her, narrowed in assessment.

"And what would be helped by your doing murder?" he asked. "It willna take the child from your belly—or give ye back your maidenheid."

"I know that!" She felt her face flush hot, and turned away, irritated both with him and herself. They spoke of rape and murder, and she was embarrassed to have him mention her lost virginity? She forced herself to look back at him.

"Mama said you tried to kill Jack Randall in Paris, in a duel. What did *you* think you'd get back?"

He rubbed his chin hard, then drew in his breath through his nose and let it out slowly, eyes fixed on the stained rock of the ceiling.

"I meant to take back my manhood," he said softly. "My honor."

"You think my honor isn't worth taking back? Or do you figure it's the same thing as my *maidenheid*?" She mocked his accent nastily.

Sharp blue eyes swung back to hers.

"Is it the same thing to *you*?"

"No, it is not," she said, through clenched teeth.

"Good," he said, shortly.

"Then answer me, damn it!" She struck a fist on the straw, finding no satisfaction in the soundless blow. "Did killing him give you back your honor? Did it help? Tell me the truth!"

She stopped, breathing heavily. She glared at him, and he met her eyes with a cold stare. Then he raised the cup abruptly to his mouth, swallowed the cider in one gulp, and set the cup down on the hay beside him.

"The truth? The truth is that I dinna ken whether I killed him or no."

Her mouth dropped open in surprise.

"You don't *know* whether you killed him?"

"I said so." A slight jerk of the shoulders betrayed his impatience. He stood up abruptly, as if unable to sit any longer.

"He died at Culloden, and I was there. I woke on the moor after the battle, with Randall's corpse on top of me. I ken that much—and not much more." He paused as though thinking, then, mind made up, he thrust one knee forward, pulled up his kilt and nodded downward. "Look."

It was an old scar, but no less impressive for its age. It ran up the inner side of his thigh, nearly a foot in length, its lower end starred and knotted like the head of a mace, the rest of it a cleaner line, though thick and twisted.

"A bayonet, I expect," he said, looking at it dispassionately. He dropped the kilt, hiding the scar once more.

"I remember the feel of the blade strikin' bone, and no more. Not what came after—or before."

He took a deep, audible breath, and for the first time she realized that his apparent calmness was taking a good deal of effort to maintain.

"I thought it a blessing—that I couldna remember," he said at last. He wasn't looking at her, but into the shadows at the end of the stable. "There were gallant men who died there; men I loved well. If I didna know their deaths; if I couldna recall them or see them in my mind—then I didna have to think of them as dead. Maybe that was cowardice, maybe not. Perhaps I chose not to remember that day; perhaps I cannot if I would." He looked down at her, his eyes gone softer, but then turned away, plaid swinging, not waiting for an answer.

"Afterward—aye, well. Vengeance didna seem important, then. There were a thousand dead men on that field, and I thought I should be one of them in hours. Jack Randall . . ." He made an odd, impatient gesture, brushing aside the thought of Jack Randall as he might a biting deerfly. "He *was* one of them. I thought I could leave him to God. Then."

She took a deep breath, trying to keep her feelings under control. Curiosity and sympathy struggled with an overwhelming feeling of frustration.

"You're . . . all right, though. I mean—in spite of what he—did to you?"

He gave her a look of exasperation, understanding mingled with half-angry amusement.

"Not many die of it, lass. Not me. And not you."

"Not *yet*." Involuntarily, she put a hand over her belly. She stared up at him. "I guess we'll see in six months if I die of it."

That rattled him; she could see it. He blew out his breath and scowled at her.

"Ye'll do fine," he said curtly. "Ye're wider through the hip than yon wee heifer."

"Like your mother? Everybody says how much I'm like her. I guess she was wide through the hip, too, but it didn't save *her,* did it?"

He flinched. Quick and sharp as though she'd slapped him across the face with a stinging nettle. Perversely, seeing it filled her with panic, rather than the satisfaction she'd expected.

She understood then that his promise of protection was in good part illusion. He would kill for her, yes. Or willingly die himself, she had no doubt. He would—if she let him—avenge her honor, destroy her enemies. But he could not defend her from her own child; he was as powerless to save her from that threat as if she had never found him.

"I'll die," she said, cold certainty filling her belly like frozen mercury. "I know I will."

"Ye won't!" He rounded on her fiercely, and she felt his hands bite into her upper arms. "I will not let you!"

She would have given anything to believe him. Her lips were numb and stiff, rage giving way to a cold despair.

"You can't help," she said. "You can't do anything!"

"Your mother can," he said, but sounded only half convinced. His grip slackened, and she wrenched herself free.

"No, she can't—not without a hospital, without drugs and things. If it—if it goes wrong, all she can do is try to save the b-baby." Despite herself, her gaze flickered to his dirk, blade gleaming cold against the straw where he had left it.

Her knees felt watery, and she sat down suddenly. He snatched up the jug and slopped cider into a cup, pushing it under her nose.

"Drink it," he said. "Drink up, lass, you're pale as my sark." His hand was on the back of her head, urging her. She took a sip, but choked and drew back, waving him off. She drew a sleeve across her wet chin, wiping off the spilled cider.

"You know what's the worst? You said it wasn't my fault, but it is."

"It is not!"

She flapped a hand at him, bidding him be quiet.

"You talked about cowardice; you know what it is. Well, I was a coward. I should have fought, I shouldn't have let him . . . but I was scared of him. If I'd been brave enough, this wouldn't have happened, but I wasn't, I was scared! And now I'm even more scared,'' she said, voice breaking. She took a deep breath to steady herself, bracing her hands on the straw.

"You can't help, and neither can Mama, and I can't do anything either. And Roger—'' Her voice did crack then, and she bit her lip hard, forcing back tears.

"Brianna—*a leannan* . . .'' He made a move to comfort her, but she drew back, arms folded tight across her stomach.

"I keep thinking—if I kill him, that's something I can do. It's the *only* thing I can do. If I—if I have to die, at least I'll take him with me, and if I don't—then maybe I can forget, if he's dead.''

"Ye willna forget.'' The words were blunt and uncompromising as a blow to the stomach. He was still holding the cup of cider. Now he tilted back his head and drank, quite deliberately.

"It doesna matter, though,'' he said, setting down the cup with an air of businesslike finality. "We shall find you a husband, and once the babe's born, ye willna have much time to fret.''

"What?'' She gaped at him. "What do you mean, find me a husband?''

"You'll need one, aye?'' he said, in tones of mild surprise. "The bairn must have a father. And if ye willna tell me the name of the man who's given ye a swollen belly, so that I might make him do his duty by ye—''

"You think I'd *marry* the man who did this?'' Her voice cracked again, this time with astonishment.

His voice sharpened slightly.

"Well, I'm thinkin'—are ye maybe playin' wi' the truth a bit, lass? Perhaps it wasna rape at all; perhaps it was that ye took a mislike to the man, and ran—and made up the story later. Ye were not marked, after all. Hard to think a man could force a lass of your size, if ye were unwilling altogether.''

"You think I'm *lying*?''

He raised one brow in cynicism. Furious, she swung a hand at him, but he caught her by the wrist.

"Ah, now,'' he said, reprovingly. "Ye're no the first lass to make a slip and try to hide it, but—'' He caught the other wrist as she struck at him, and pulled them both up sharply.

"Ye dinna need to make such a fuss,'' he said. "Or is it that ye wanted the man and he threw ye over? Is that it?''

She swiveled in his grip, used her weight to swing aside,

brought her knee up hard. He turned only slightly, and her knee collided with his thigh, not the vulnerable flesh between his legs she had been aiming for.

The blow must have bruised him, but didn't lessen his grip on her wrists in the least. She twisted, kicking, cursing her skirts. She hit his shin dead-on at least twice, but he only chuckled, as though finding her struggles funny.

"Is that all ye can do, lassie?" He broke his grip then, but only to shift both her wrists to one hand. The other prodded her playfully in the ribs.

> *"There was a man*
> *In Muir of Skene,*
> *He had dirks*
> *And I had none;*
> *But I fell on him*
> *With my thumbs,*
> *And wot you how,*
> *I dirkit him,*
> *Dirkit him,*
> *Dirkit him?"*

With each repetition, he dug a thumb hard between her ribs.

"You fucking *bastard*!" she screamed. She braced her feet and yanked down on his arm as hard as she could, bringing it into biting range. She lunged at his wrist, but before she could sink her teeth in his flesh, she found herself jerked off her feet and whirled through the air.

She ended hard on her knees, one arm twisted up behind her back so tightly that her shoulder joint cracked. The strain on her elbow hurt; she writhed, trying to turn into the hold, but couldn't budge. An arm like an iron bar clamped across her shoulders, forcing her head down. And farther down.

Her chin drove into her chest; she couldn't breathe. And still he forced her head down. Her knees slid apart, her thighs forced wide by the downward pressure.

"Stop!" she grunted. It hurt to force sound through her constricted windpipe. "Gd's sk, stp!"

The relentless pressure paused, but did not ease. She could feel him there behind her, an inexorable, inexplicable force. She reached back with her free hand, groping for something to claw, something to hit or bend, but there was nothing.

"I could break your neck," he said, very quietly. The weight of his arm left her shoulders, though the twisted arm still held her bent forward, hair loose and tumbled, nearly touching the floor. A hand settled on her neck. She could feel thumb and index fingers on either side, pressing lightly on her arteries. He squeezed, and black spots danced before her eyes.

"I could kill you, so."

The hand left her neck, and touched her, deliberately, knee and shoulder, cheek and chin, emphasizing her helplessness. She jerked her head away, not letting him touch the wetness, not wanting to feel her tears of rage. Then the hand pressed sudden and brutal on the small of her back. She made a small, choked sound and arched her back to keep her arm from breaking, thrusting out her hips backward, legs spread to keep her balance.

"I could use ye as I would," he said, and there was a coldness in his voice. "Could you stop me, Brianna?"

She felt as though she would suffocate with rage and shame.

"Answer me." The hand took her by the neck again, and squeezed.

"No!"

She was free. So suddenly released, she pitched forward onto her face, barely getting one hand down in time to save herself.

She lay on the straw, panting and sobbing. There was a loud whuffle near her head—Magdalen, roused by the noise, leaning out of her stall to investigate. Slowly, painfully, she raised herself to a sitting position.

He was standing over her, arms folded.

"Damn you!" she gasped. She slammed a hand down in the hay. "God, I want to kill you!"

He stood quite still, looking down at her.

"Aye," he said quietly. "But ye can't, can you?"

She stared up at him, not understanding. His eyes were intent on hers, not angry, not mocking. Waiting.

"You *can't,*" he repeated, with emphasis.

And then realization came, flooding down her aching arms to her bruised fists.

"Oh, God," she said. "No. I can't. I couldn't. Even if I'd fought him . . . I *couldn't.*"

Quite suddenly she began to cry, the knots inside her slipping loose, the weights shifting, lifting, as a blessed relief spread through her body. It hadn't been her fault. If she had fought with all her strength—as she had fought just now—

"Couldn't," she said, and swallowed hard, gasping for air. "I couldn't have stopped him. I kept thinking, if only I'd fought harder . . . but it wouldn't have mattered. I couldn't have stopped him."

A hand touched her face, big and very gentle.

"You're a fine, braw lassie," he whispered. "But a lassie, nonetheless. Would ye fret your heart out and think yourself a coward because ye couldna fight off a lion wi' your bare hands? It's the same. Dinna be daft, now."

She wiped the back of her hand under her nose, and sniffed deeply.

He put a hand under her elbow and helped her up, his strength no longer either threat or mockery, but unutterable comfort. Her knees stung, where she had scraped them on the ground. Her legs wobbled, but she made it to the haypile, where he let her sit down.

"You could just have *told* me, you know," she said. "That it wasn't my fault."

He smiled faintly.

"I did. Ye couldna believe me, though, unless ye knew for yourself."

"No. I guess not." A profound but peaceful weariness had settled on her like a blanket. This time she had no urge to tear it off.

She watched, feeling too limp to move, as he wetted a cloth from the trough and wiped her face, straightened her twisted skirts, and poured out a drink for her.

When he handed her the freshly filled cup of cider, though, she laid a hand on his arm. Bone and muscle were solid, warm under her hand.

"You could have fought back. But you didn't."

He laid a big hand over hers, squeezed and let it go.

"No, I didna fight," he said quietly. "I gave my word—for your mother's life." His eyes met hers squarely, neither ice nor sapphire now, but clear as water. "I dinna regret it."

He took her by the shoulders, and eased her down onto the piled hay.

"Do ye rest a bit, *a leannan.*"

She lay down, but reached up to touch him as he knelt by her.

"Is it true—that I won't forget?"

He paused for a moment, hand on her hair.

"Aye, that's true," he said softly. "But it's true, too, that it willna matter after a time."

"Won't it?" She was too tired even to wonder what he might mean by this. She felt almost weightless; strangely remote, as though she no longer inhabited her troublesome body. "Even if I'm not strong enough to kill him?"

A clear cold draft from the open door cut through the warm fog of smoke, making all the animals stir. The brindled cow shifted her weight in sudden irritation and let out a low-throated *mwaaah,* not of distress so much as of querulous complaint.

She felt her father glance at the cow before turning back to her.

"You're a verra strong woman, *a bheanachd,*" he said at last, very softly.

"I'm not strong. You just proved I'm not—"

His hand on her shoulder stopped her.

"That's not what I mean." He stopped, thinking, his hand smoothing her hair, over and over.

"She was ten when our mother died, Jenny was," he said at last. "It was the day after the funeral when I came into the kitchen and found her kneeling on a stool, to be tall enough to stir the bowl on the table.

"She was wearing my mother's apron," he said softly, "folded up under the arms, and the strings wrapped twice about her waist. I could see she'd been weepin', like I had, for her face was all stained and her eyes red. But she just went on stirring, staring down into the bowl, and she said to me, 'Go and wash, Jamie; I'll have supper for you and Da directly.' "

His eyes closed altogether, and he swallowed once. Then he opened them, and looked down at her again.

"Aye, I ken fine how strong women are," he said quietly. "And you're strong enough for what must be done, *m' annsachd* —believe me."

He stood up then, and went to the cow. It had risen to its feet and was moving restlessly in a small circle, swaying and shuffling on its tether. He caught it by the tether rope, gentled it with hands and words, made his way behind the heifer, frowning in concentration. She saw him turn his head and look, to check his dirk, then turn back, murmuring.

Not a loving butcher, no. A surgeon in his way, like her mother. From this odd plateau of remoteness, she could see how much her parents—so wildly different in temperament and manner—were alike in this one respect; that odd ability to mingle compassion with sheer ruthlessness.

But they were different even in that, she thought; Claire could hold life and death together in her hands, and yet preserve herself, hold aloof; a doctor must go on living, for the sake of her patients, if not for her own sake. Jamie would be ruthless toward himself, as much as—or more than—he would be to anyone else.

He had thrown off his plaid; now he unfastened his shirt, with no haste but neither with any wasted motion. He pulled the pale linen over his head and laid it neatly aside, returning to his watching post at the heifer's tail, ready to assist.

A long ripple ran down the cow's rounded side, and the torchlight glimmered white on the tiny knot of a scar over his heart. Uncover his nakedness? He would strip himself to the bone, if he thought it necessary. And—a much less comforting thought—if he thought it necessary, he would do the same to her, without a moment's hesitation.

He had a hand at the base of the cow's tail, speaking to it in Gaelic, soothing, encouraging. She felt as though she could almost grasp the sense of his words—but not quite.

All might be well, or it might not. But whatever happened, Jamie Fraser would be there, fighting. It was a comfort.

Jamie paused by the upper fence of the cowpen, on the rise above the house. It was late, and he was more than tired, but his mind kept him wakeful. The calving completed, he had carried Brianna down to the cabin—she sleeping sound as a babe in his arms—and then gone out again, to seek relief in the solitude of the night.

His shins ached where she had kicked him, and there were deep bruises on his thighs; she was amazingly powerful for a woman. None of that troubled him in the least; in fact, he felt an odd and unexpected pride in this evidence of her strength. *She will be all right,* he thought. Surely she will.

There was more hope than confidence behind this thought. Yet it was on his own account that he was wakeful, and he felt at once troubled and foolish at the knowledge. He had thought himself thoroughly healed, old hurts so far behind him that they could safely be dismissed from mind. He had been wrong about that, and it unsettled him to find just how close to the surface the buried memories lay.

If he were to find rest tonight, they would have to be exhumed; the ghosts raised in order to lay them. Well, he had told the lass it took strength. He stopped, gripping the fence.

The rustle of night sounds faded slowly from his mind as he waited, listening for the voice. He had not heard it for years, had thought never to hear it again—but he had already heard its echo once tonight; seen the blaze of anger's phantom in his daughter's eyes, and felt its flames singe his own heart.

Better to call it forth and face it boldly than let it lie in ambush. If he could not face his own demons, he could not conquer hers. He touched a bruise on his thigh, finding an odd comfort in the soreness.

No one dies of it, he'd said. *Not you; not me.*

The voice did not come at first; for a moment he hoped it would not—perhaps it *had* been long enough . . . but then it was there again, whispering in his ear as though it had never left, its insinuations a caress that burned his memory as once they had burned his skin.

"Gently at first," it breathed. "Softly. Tender as though you were my infant son. Gently, but for so long you will forget there was a time I did not own your body."

The night stood still around him, paused as time had paused so long before, poised on the edge of a gulf of dread, waiting. Waiting for the next words, known beforehand and expected, but nonetheless . . .

"And then," the voice said, loving, "then I'll hurt you very badly. And you will thank me, and ask for more."

He stood quite still, face turned upward to the stars. Fought back the surge of fury as it murmured in his ear, the pulse of memory in his blood. Then made himself surrender, let it come. He trembled with remembered helplessness, and clenched his teeth in rage—but stared unblinking at the brightness of heaven overhead, invoking the names of the stars as the words of a prayer, abandoning himself to the vastness overhead as he sought to lose himself below.

Betelgeuse. Sirius. Orion. Antares. The sky is very large, and you are very small. Let the words wash through him, the voice and its memories pass over him, shivering his skin like the touch of a ghost, vanishing into darkness.

The Pleiades. Cassiopeia. Taurus. Heaven is wide, and you are very small. Dead, but none the less powerful for being dead. He spread his hands wide, gripping the fence—those were powerful, too. Enough to beat a man to death, enough to choke out a life. But even death was not enough to loose the bands of rage.

With great effort, he let go. Turned his hands palm upward, in gesture of surrender. He reached beyond the stars, searching. The words formed themselves quietly in his mind, by habit, so quietly he was not aware of them until he found them echoed in a whisper on his lips.

" '. . . *Forgive us our trespasses as we forgive those who trespass against us.*' "

He breathed slowly, deeply. Seeking, struggling; struggling to let go. " '*Lead us not into temptation, but deliver us from evil.*' "

Waited, in emptiness, in faith. And then grace came; the necessary vision; the memory of Jack Randall's face in Edinburgh, stricken to bare bone by the knowledge of his brother's death. And he felt once more the gift of pity, calm in its descent as the landing of a dove.

He closed his eyes, feeling the wounds bleed clean again as the succubus drew its claws from his heart.

He sighed, and turned his hands over, the rough wood of the fence comforting and solid under his palms. The demon was gone. He had been a man, Jack Randall; nothing more. And in the recognition of that common frail humanity, all power of past fear and pain vanished like smoke.

His shoulders slumped, relieved of their burden.

"Go in peace," he whispered, to the dead man and himself. "You are forgiven."

The night sounds had returned; the cry of a hunting cat rose sharp on the air, and rotting leaves crunched soft underfoot as he made his way back toward the house. The oiled hide that covered the window glowed golden in the dark, with the flame of the candle he had left burning in the hope of Claire's return. His sanctuary.

He thought that he should perhaps have told Brianna all this, too—but no. She couldn't understand what he *had* told her; he had had to show her, instead. How to tell her in words, then, what he had learned himself by pain and grace? That only by forgiveness could she forget—and that forgiveness was not a single act, but a matter of constant practice.

Perhaps she would find such grace herself; perhaps this unknown Roger Wakefield could be her sanctuary, as Claire had been his. He found his natural jealousy of the man dissolved in a passionate wish that Wakefield could indeed give her what he himself could not. Pray God he would come soon; pray God he would prove a decent man.

In the meantime, there were other matters to be dealt with. He

walked slowly down the hill, oblivious to the wind that blew the
kilt about his knees and billowed through his shirt and plaid.
Things must be done here; winter was coming, and he could not
leave his women here alone with only Ian to hunt for them and
defend them. He couldn't leave to search for Wakefield.

But if Wakefield did not come? Well, there were other ways; he
would see Brianna and the child protected, one way or another.
And at least his daughter was safe from the man who had harmed
her. Permanently safe. He rubbed a hand across his face, smelling
blood still on his skin from the calving.

*Forgive us our trespasses as we forgive those who trespass
against us.* Yes, but what of those who trespass against the ones
we love? He could not forgive on another's behalf—and would
not, if he could. But if not . . . how should he expect forgiveness in return?

Educated in the universities of Paris, confidant of kings and
friend to philosophers, still he was a Highlander, born to blood
and honor. The body of a warrior and the mind of a gentleman—
and the soul of a barbarian, he thought wryly, to whom neither
God's nor mortal law stood more sacred than the ties of blood.

Yes, there was forgiveness; she must find a way to forgive the
man, for her own sake. But he was a different matter.

'' *'Vengeance is mine, sayeth the Lord.'* '' He whispered it to
himself. Then he looked up, away from the safe small glow of
hearth and home, to the flaming glory of the stars above.

"The hell it is," he said, aloud, shamed but defiant. It was
ungrateful, he knew. And wrong, forbye. But there it was, and no
use to lie either to God or to himself about it.

"The hell it is," he repeated, louder. "And if I am damned for
what I've done—then let it be! She is my daughter."

He stood still for a moment, looking up, but there was no
answer from the stars. He nodded once, as though in reply, and
went on down the hill, the wind cold behind him.

49

Choices

November 1769

I opened Daniel Rawlings's box, and stared at the rows of bottles filled with the soft greens and browns of powdered root and leaf, the clear gold of distillations. There was nothing among the bottles to help. Very slowly, I lifted the covering that lay over the top compartment, over the blades.

I lifted out the scalpel with the curved edge, tasting cold metal in the back of my throat. It was a beautiful tool, sharp and sturdy, well balanced, part of my hand when I chose it to be. I balanced it on the end of my finger, letting it tilt gently back and forth.

I set it down, and picked up the long, thick root that lay on the table. Part of the stem was still attached, the remnants of leaves hanging limp and yellow. Only one. I had searched the woods for nearly two weeks, but it was so late in the year that the leaves of the smaller herbs had yellowed and fallen; it was impossible to recognize plants that were no more than brown sticks. I had found this one in a sheltered spot, a few of the distinctive fruits still clinging to its stalk. Blue cohosh, I was sure. But only one. It wasn't enough.

I had none of the European herbs, no hellebore, no wormwood. I could perhaps get wormwood, though with some difficulty; it was used to flavor absinthe.

"And who makes absinthe in the backwoods of North Carolina?" I said aloud, picking up the scalpel again.

"No one that I know of."

I jumped, and the blade jabbed deep into the side of my thumb. Blood spattered across the tabletop, and I snatched the corner of my apron, wadding the cloth hard against the wound in reflex.

"Christ, Sassenach! Are ye all right? I didna mean to startle ye."

It didn't hurt a great deal yet, but the shock of sudden injury made me bite my lower lip. Looking worried, Jamie took my wrist and lifted the edge of the wadded cloth. Blood promptly welled from the cut and ran down my hand, and he clamped the cloth back in place, squeezing tight.

"It's all right; just a cut. Where did you come from? I thought you were up at the still." I felt surprisingly shaky, perhaps from the shock.

"I was. The mash isna ready for distilling yet. You're bleeding like a pig, Sassenach. Are ye sure you're all right?" I *was* bleeding badly; besides the splashes of blood across the table, the corner of my apron was soaked with dark red.

"Yes. I probably severed a tiny vein. It's not an artery, though; it will stop. Hold my hand up, will you?" I fumbled one-handed with the strings of my apron, seeking to free it. Jamie undid it with a quick yank, wrapped the apron round my hand, and held the whole clumsy bundle up over my head.

"What were ye doing with your wee knife?" he asked, eyeing the dropped scalpel, where it lay alongside the twisted cohosh root.

"Ah . . . I was going to slice up that root," I said, waving weakly at it.

He gave me a sharp look, glanced across to the sideboard, where my paring knife lay in plain sight, then looked back at me with raised brows.

"Aye? I've never seen ye use one of these"—he nodded at the open array of scalpels and surgical blades—"save on people."

My hand twitched slightly in his, and he tightened his grip on my thumb, squeezing hard enough to make me catch my breath in pain. He loosened his grip, then looked intently into my face, frowning.

"What in heaven's name are ye about, Sassenach? Ye look as though I'd surprised ye about to commit murder."

My lips felt stiff and bloodless. I pulled my thumb out of his grasp and sat down, holding the wounded digit against my bosom with my other hand.

"I was . . . deciding," I said, with great reluctance. It was no good to lie; he would have to know, sooner or later, if Bree—

"Deciding what?"

"About Bree. What was the best way to do it."

"To do it?" His eyebrows shot up. He glanced at the open medicine case, then at the scalpel, and a look of sudden shocked comprehension washed over his face.

"You mean to—"

"If she wants me to." I touched the knife, its small blade stained with my own blood. "There are herbs—or this. There are awful risks to using herbs—convulsions, brain damage, hemorrhage—but it doesn't matter; I don't have enough of the right kind."

"Claire—have you done it before?"

I looked up, to see him looking down at me with something I had never seen in his eyes before—horror. I pressed my hands flat on the table, to stop them trembling. I didn't do as well with my voice.

"Would it make a difference to you if I had?"

He stared at me for a moment, then eased himself down on the bench opposite, slowly, as though afraid he might break something.

"Ye havena done it," he said softly. "I know it."

"No," I said. I stared down at his hand, covering mine. "No, I haven't."

I could feel the tension go out of his hand; it relaxed, curling over mine, enfolding it. But my own lay limp in his grasp.

"I knew ye couldna do murder," he said.

"I could. I have." I didn't look up at him, but spoke to the tabletop. "I killed a man, a patient in my care. I told you about Graham Menzies."

He was silent for a moment, but held on to my hand, squeezing slightly.

"I think it isna the same," he said at last. "To ease a doomed man to a death he wishes . . . it seems to me that that is mercy, not murder. And duty, too, perhaps."

"Duty?" That did make me look at him, startled. The look of shock had faded from his eyes, though he was still solemn.

"Do ye not recall Falkirk Hill, and the night Rupert died in the chapel there?"

I nodded. It wasn't something easily forgotten—the cold dark of the tiny church, the eerie sounds of pipes and battle far outside. Inside the black air thick with the sweat of frightened men, and Rupert dying slowly on the floor at my feet, choking on his blood. He had asked Dougal MacKenzie, as his friend and his chief, to hasten him . . . and Dougal had.

"It will be a doctor's duty, too, I think," Jamie said gently. "If you are sworn to heal—but cannot—and to save men pain—and can?"

"Yes." I took a deep breath and curled my hand around the

scalpel. "I *am* sworn—and by more than a doctor's oath. Jamie, she's my daughter. I would rather do anything in the world but this—anything." I looked up at him and blinked, holding back tears.

"Don't you think I haven't thought about it? That I don't know what the risks are? Jamie, I could kill her!" I pulled the cloth off my wounded thumb; the cut was still oozing.

"Look—it shouldn't bleed like that, it's a deep cut but not a bad one. But it does! I hit a vein. I could do the same to Bree and never know it, until she began to bleed—and if so . . . Jamie, I couldn't stop it! She'd bleed to death under my hand, and there isn't a thing I could do about it, not a thing!"

He looked at me, eyes dark with shock.

"How could ye think of doing such a thing, knowing that?" His voice was soft with disbelief.

I drew a deep, trembling breath, and felt despair wash over me. There was no way to make him understand, no way.

"Because I know other things," I said at last, very softly, not looking at him. "I know what it is to bear a child. I know what it is to have your body and your mind and your soul taken from you and changed without your will. I know what it is to be ripped out of the place you thought was yours, to have choice taken from you. *I know what it is,* do you hear me? and it isn't something anyone should do without being willing." I looked up at him, and my fist clenched hard on my wounded thumb.

"And you—for God's sake—*you* know what I don't; what it's like to live with the knowledge of violation. Do you mean to tell me that if I could have cut that from you after Wentworth, that you wouldn't have had me do it, no matter what the risks? Jamie, that may be a rapist's child!"

"Aye, I know," he began, and had to stop, too choked to finish. "I *know,*" he began again, and his jaw muscles bulged as he forced the words. "But I know the one thing else—if I dinna ken his father, I ken his grandsire well enough. Claire, that is a child of my blood!"

"*Your* blood?" I echoed. I stared at him, the truth dawning on me. "You want a grandchild badly enough to sacrifice your daughter?"

"Sacrifice? It isna me that's meaning to commit slaughter in cold blood!"

"You didn't mind the angel-makers at the Hôpital des Anges; you had pity for the women they helped, you said so."

"Those women had nay choice!" Too agitated to sit, he got up and paced restlessly back and forth in front of me. "They had no one to protect them, no way to feed a child—what else could they do, poor creatures? But it isna so, for Brianna! I will never let her be hungry or cold, never let aught harm her or the bairn, never!"

"That isn't all there is to it!"

He stared at me, brows drawn down in stubborn incomprehension.

"If she bears a child here, she won't leave," I said unsteadily. "She can't—not without tearing herself apart."

"So *you* mean to tear her apart?" I flinched, as though he'd struck me.

"You want her to stay," I said, striking back. "You don't care that she has a life somewhere else, that she *wants* to go back. If she'll stay—and better yet, if she'll give you a grandchild—then you bloody don't care what it does to her, do you?"

It was his turn to flinch, but he turned on me squarely.

"Aye, I care! That doesna mean I think it right for you to force her into—"

"What do you mean, force her?" The blood was burning hot in my cheeks. "For God's sake, you think I want to do this? No! But, by God, she'll have the choice if she wants it!"

I had to press my hands together to stop them shaking. The apron had fallen to the floor, stained with blood, reminding me much too vividly of operating theaters and battlefields—and of the terrible limits of my own skill.

I could feel his eyes on me, narrowed and burning. I knew that he was as torn in the matter as I was. He did indeed care desperately for Bree—but now I had spoken the truth, we both recognized it; deprived of his own children, living for so long as an exile, there was nothing he wanted more in life than a child of his blood.

But he couldn't stop me, and he knew it. He wasn't used to feeling helpless, and he didn't like it. He turned abruptly and went to the sideboard, where he stood, fists resting on top of it.

I had never felt so desolate, so in need of his understanding. Did he not realize how horrible the prospect was for me, as well as him? Worse, because it was my hand that must do the damage.

I came up behind him, and laid a hand on his back. He stood unmoving, and I stroked him lightly, taking some comfort from the simple fact of his presence, of the solid strength of him.

"Jamie." My thumb left a slight smear of red on the linen of his shirt. "It will be all right. I'm sure it will." I was talking to convince myself, as much as him. He didn't move, and I ventured to put my arm around his waist, laying my cheek against the curve of his back. I wanted him to turn and take me in his arms, to assure me that it would indeed somehow be all right—or at the least, that he would not blame me for whatever happened.

He moved abruptly, dislodging my hand.

"Ye've a high opinion of your power, have ye no?" He spoke coldly, turning to face me.

"What do you mean by that?"

He grasped my wrist in one hand, pinning it to the wall above my head. I could feel the tickle of blood down my wrist, flowing from my wounded thumb. His fingers wrapped around my hand, squeezing tight.

"Ye think it's yours alone to say? That life and death is yours?" I could feel the small bones of my hand grind together, and I stiffened, trying to pull free.

"It's not mine to say! But if *she* says—then yes, it's my power. And yes, I'll use it. Just like you would—like you *have,* when you've had to." I shut my eyes, fighting down fear. He wouldn't hurt me . . . surely? It occurred to me with a small shock that he could indeed stop me. If he broke my hand . . .

Very slowly, he bent his head and rested his forehead against mine.

"Look at me, Claire," he said, very quietly.

Slowly, I opened my eyes and looked. His eyes were no more than an inch away; I could see the tiny gold flecks near the center of his iris, the black ring surrounding it. My fingers in his were slippery with blood.

He let go of my hand, and touched my breast lightly, cupping it for a moment.

"Please," he whispered, and then was gone.

I stood quite still against the wall, and then slowly slid to the floor in a bloom of skirts, the cut on my thumb throbbing with my heartbeat.

I was so shaken by the quarrel with Jamie that I couldn't settle to anything. At last, I put on my cloak and went out, walking up the ridge. I avoided the path that led across the Ridge toward Fergus's cabin, and down toward the road. I didn't want to risk meeting anyone at all.

It was cold and cloudy, with a light rain sputtering intermittently among the leaf-bare branches. The air was heavy with cold moisture; let the temperature drop a few degrees more, and it would snow. If not tonight, tomorrow—or next week. Within a month at the most, the Ridge would be cut off from the lowlands.

Ought I to take Brianna to Cross Creek? Whether she decided to bear the child or not, might she be safer there?

I shuffled through layers of wet, yellow leaves. No. My impulse was to think that civilization must offer some advantage, but not in this case. There was nothing Cross Creek could offer that would truly be of help in case of any obstetrical emergency; in fact, she might well be in active danger from the medical practitioners of the time.

No, whatever she decided, she was better off here, with me. I wrapped my arms about myself under my cloak, and flexed my fingers, trying to work some warmth and suppleness into them, to feel some sense of surety in touch.

Please, he'd said. Please what? Please don't ask her, please don't do it if she asks? But I had to. *I swear by Apollo the physician . . . not to cut for the stone, nor to procure abortion . . .* Well, and Hippocrates was neither a surgeon, a woman . . . nor a mother. As I'd told Jamie, I'd sworn by something a lot older than Apollo the physician—and that oath was in blood.

I never had done an abortion though I had had some experience as a resident, in the post-care of miscarriage. On the rare occasions a patient had asked it of me, I had referred them to a colleague. I had no absolute objection; I had seen too many women killed in body or spirit by untimely children. If it was killing—and it was—then I thought it not murder, but a justifiable homicide, undertaken in desperate self-defense.

At the same time, I could not bring myself to do it. The surgeon's sense that gave me knowledge of the flesh under my hands gave me also an acute awareness for the living contents of the womb. I could touch a pregnant woman's belly, and feel in my fingertips the second beating heart; could trace unseeing the curve of limb and head, and the snakelike curl of the umbilicus with its rush of blood, all red and blue.

I could not bring myself to destroy it. Not until now; when it was a matter of killing my own flesh and blood.

How? It would have to be surgical. Dr. Rawlings had evidently not done such procedures; he had no uterine "spoon" for scraping the womb, nor any of the slender rods for dilation of the cervix. I could manage, though. One of the ivory knitting needles, its point blunted; the scalpel, bent to a shallow curve, its deadly edge sanded down for the delicate—but no less deadly—job of scraping.

When? Now. She was already three months gone; if it was to be done, it must be as soon as possible. Neither could I bear to be in the same room with Jamie while the matter was unresolved, feeling his anguish added to my own.

Brianna had taken Lizzie to Fergus's house. Lizzie was to stay and help Marsali, who had her hands full with the distillery, little Germaine, and the farm work that Fergus couldn't manage single-handed. It was a terrible load for an eighteen-year-old girl to be carrying, but she managed, with tenacity and style. Lizzie could at least help with the household chores, and mind the little fiend long enough to let his mother rest now and then.

Brianna would come back before suppertime. Ian was away, hunting with Rollo. Jamie . . . without being told, I knew that Jamie would not be back for some time. We would have a little while alone.

Would it be a suitable moment to ask her such a question, though—fresh from seeing Germaine's cherubic face? Though on reflection, exposure to a two-year-old boy was probably the best possible object lesson in the dangers of motherhood, I thought wryly.

Vaguely lightened by the faint whiff of humor, I turned back, drawing my cloak around me against the increasing wind. As I came down the hill I saw Brianna's horse in the penfold; she was home. My stomach clenched in dread, I went to lay the choice before her.

"I thought of it," she said, with a deep breath. "As soon as I realized. I wondered if you could do—something like that, here."

"It wouldn't be easy. It would be dangerous—and it would hurt. I don't even have any laudanum; only whisky. But yes, I can do it—if you want me to." I forced myself to sit still, watching her pace slowly back and forth before the hearth, hands folded behind her in thought.

"It would have to be surgical," I said, unable to keep quiet. "I don't have the right herbs—and they aren't always reliable, in any case. At least surgery is . . . certain." I laid the scalpel on the table; she should not be under any illusions as to what I was suggesting. She nodded at my words, but didn't stop her pacing. Like Jamie, she always thought better while moving.

A trickle of sweat ran down my back, and I shivered. The fire was warm enough, but my fingers were still cold as ice. Christ, if she wanted it, would I even be able to do it? My hands had begun to tremble, with the strain of waiting.

She turned at last to look at me, eyes clear and appraising under thick, ruddy brows.

"Would you have done it? If you could?"

"If I could—?"

"You said once that you hated me, when you were pregnant. If you could have not been—"

"God, not you!" I blurted, horror-stricken. "Not you, ever. It—" I knotted my hands together, to still their trembling. "No," I said, as positively as I could. "Never."

"You did say so," she said, looking at me intently. "When you told me about Da."

I rubbed a hand across my face, trying to focus my thoughts. Yes, I *had* told her that. Idiot.

"It was a horrible time. Terrible. We were starving, it was war —the world was coming apart at the seams." Wasn't hers? "At the time, it seemed as though there was no hope; I had to leave Jamie, and the thought drove almost everything else out of my mind. But there was one other thing," I said.

"What was that?"

"It wasn't rape," I said softly, meeting her eyes. "I loved your father."

She nodded, her face a little pale.

"Yes. But it *might* be Roger's. You did say that, didn't you?"

"Yes. It might. Is the possibility enough for you?"

She laid a hand over her stomach, long fingers gently curved.

"Yeah. Well. It isn't an it, to me. I don't know who it is, but—" She stopped suddenly and glanced at me, looking suddenly shy.

"I don't know if this sounds—well . . ." She shrugged abruptly, dismissing doubt. "I had this sharp pain that woke me up in the middle of the night, a few days . . . after. Quick, like somebody had stabbed me with a hatpin, but deep." Her fingers curled inward, her fist pressing just above her pubic bone, on the right side.

"Implantation," I said softly. "When the zygote takes root in the womb." When that first, eternal link is formed between mother and child. When the small blind entity, unique in its union of egg and sperm, comes to anchor from the perilous voyage of beginning, home from its brief, free-floating existence in the body, and settles to its busy work of division, drawing sustenance from the flesh in which it embeds itself, in a connection that belongs to neither side, but to both. That link, which cannot be severed, either by birth or by death.

She nodded. "It was the strangest feeling. I was still half asleep, but I . . . well, I just knew all of a sudden that I wasn't alone." Her lips curved in a faint smile, reminiscent of wonder. "And I said to . . . it . . ." Her eyes rested on mine, still lit by the smile, "I said, 'Oh, it's you.' And then I went back to sleep."

Her other hand crossed the first, a barricade across her belly.

"I thought it was a dream. That was a long time before I knew. But I remember. It *wasn't* a dream. I remember."

I remembered, too.

I looked down and saw beneath my hands not the wooden table-top nor gleaming blade, but the opal skin and perfect sleeping face of my first child, Faith, with slanted eyes that never opened on the light of earth.

Looked up into the same eyes, open now and filled with knowledge. I saw that baby, too, my second daughter, filled with bloody life, pink and crumpled, flushed with fury at the indignities of birth, so different from the calm stillness of the first—and just as magnificent in her perfection.

Two miracles I had been given, carried beneath my heart, born of my body, held in my arms, separated from me and part of me forever. I knew much too well that neither death nor time nor distance ever altered such a bond—because I had been altered by it, once and forever changed by that mysterious connection.

"Yes, I understand," I said. And then said, "Oh, but Bree!" as the knowledge of what her decision would mean to her flooded in on me anew.

She was watching me, brows drawn down, lines of trouble in her face, and it occurred to me belatedly that she might take my exhortations as the expression of my own regrets.

Appalled at the thought that she might think I had not wanted her, or had ever wished she had not been, I dropped the blade and reached out across the table to her.

"Bree," I said, seized with panic at the thought. "Brianna. I love you. Do you believe I love you?"

She nodded without speaking, and stretched out a hand toward me. I grasped it like a lifeline, like the cord that had once joined us.

She closed her eyes, and for the first time I saw the glitter of tears that clung to the delicate, thick curve of her lashes.

"I've always known that, Mama," she whispered. Her fingers tightened around mine; I saw her other hand press flat against her stomach. "From the beginning."

50

In Which All Is Revealed

By late November, the days as well as the nights were cold, and the rain clouds began to hang lower on the slopes above us. The weather unfortunately had no dampening effect on people's tempers; everyone was increasingly edgy, and for obvious reason: There was still no word of Roger Wakefield.

Brianna was still silent about the cause of their argument; in fact, she almost never referred to Roger anymore. She had made her decision; there was nothing to do but to wait, and let Roger make his—if he hadn't already. Still, I could see fear warring with anger when she left her face unguarded—and doubt hung over everyone like the clouds over the mountains.

Where was he? And what would happen when—or if—he finally appeared?

I took some respite from the prevailing mood of edginess by taking stock of the pantry. Winter was nearly here; the foraging was over, the garden harvested, the preserving done. The pantry shelves bulged with sacks of nuts, heaps of squash, rows of potatoes, jars of dried tomatoes, peaches, and apricots, bowls of dried mushrooms, wheels of cheese, and baskets of apples. Braids of onions and garlic and strings of dried fish hung from the ceiling; bags of flour and beans, barrels of salt beef and salt fish, and stone jars of sauerkraut stood on the floor.

I counted over my hoard like a squirrel reckoning nuts, and felt soothed by our abundance. No matter what else happened, we would neither starve nor go hungry.

Emerging from the pantry with a wedge of cheese in one hand and a bowl of dry beans in the other, I heard a tap on the door. Before I could call out, it opened and Ian's head poked in, cautiously surveying the room.

"Brianna's no here?" he asked. As she clearly wasn't, he

didn't wait for an answer but stepped in, trying to smooth back his hair.

"Have ye a bit o' looking glass, Auntie?" he asked. "And maybe a comb?"

"Yes, of course," I said. I set down the food, got my small mirror and the tortoiseshell comb from the drawer of the sideboy and handed them to him, peering upward at his gangling form.

His face seemed abnormally shiny, his lean cheeks blotched with red, as though he had not only shaved but had scrubbed the skin to the point of rawness. His hair, normally a thick, stubborn sheaf of soft brown, was now slicked straight back on the sides of his head with some kind of grease. Liberally pomaded with the same substance, it erupted in an untidy quiff over his forehead, making him look like a deranged porcupine.

"What have you got on your hair, Ian?" I asked. I sniffed at him and recoiled slightly at the result.

"Bear fat," he said. "But it stank a bit, so I mixed in a wee scoop of incense soap to make it smell better." He peered critically at himself in the mirror and made small jabs at his coiffure with the comb, which seemed pitifully inadequate to the task.

He was wearing his good coat, with a clean shirt and—unheard of touch for a workday—a clean, starched stock wrapped about his throat, looking tight enough to strangle him.

"You look very nice, Ian," I said, biting the inside of my cheek. "Um . . . are you going somewhere special?"

"Aye, well," he said awkwardly. "It's just if I'm meant to be courting, like, I thought I must try to look decent."

Courting? I wondered at his haste. While he was certainly interested in girls—and there were a few girls in the district who made no secret of returning his interest—he was barely seventeen. Men did marry that young, of course, and Ian had both his own land and a share in the whisky making, but I hadn't thought his affections so strongly engaged yet.

"I see," I said. "Ah . . . is the young lady anyone I know?" He rubbed at his jaw, raising a red flush along the bone.

"Aye, well. It's—it's Brianna." He wouldn't meet my eyes, but the flush rose slowly over his face.

"What?" I said incredulously. I set down the slice of bread I was holding and stared at him. "Did you say *Brianna*?"

His eyes were fixed on the floor, but his jaw was set stubbornly.

"Brianna," he repeated. "I've come to make her a proposal of marriage."

"Ian, you can't possibly mean that."

"I do," he said, sticking out his long, square chin in a determined manner. He glanced toward the window, and shuffled his feet. "Will she—is she comin' in soon, d'ye think?"

The sharp scent of nervous perspiration reached me, mingled with soap and bear fat, and I saw that his hands were clenched in fists, tight enough to make the knobby knuckles stand out white against his tanned skin.

"Ian," I said, torn between exasperation and tenderness, "are you doing this because of Brianna's baby?"

The whites of his eyes flashed as he glanced at me, startled. He nodded, shifting his shoulders uncomfortably inside the stiff coat.

"Aye, of course," he said, as though surprised that I should ask.

"Then you're not in love with her?" I knew the answer quite well, but thought we had better have it all out.

"Well . . . no," he said, the painful blush renewing itself. "But I'm no promised to anyone else," he hastened to add. "So that's all right."

"It is not all right," I said firmly. "Ian, that's a very, very kind notion of yours, but—"

"Oh, it's not mine," he interrupted, looking surprised. "Uncle Jamie thought of it."

"He *what*?" A loud, incredulous voice spoke behind me, and I whirled to find Brianna standing in the doorway, staring at Ian. She advanced slowly into the room, hands fisted at her sides. Just as slowly, Ian retreated, fetching up with a bump against the table.

"Cousin," he said, with a bob of his head that dislodged a spike of greased hair. He brushed at it, but it stuck out, hanging disreputably over one eye. "I . . . ah . . . I . . ." He saw the look on Brianna's face and promptly shut his eyes.

"I-have-come-to-express-my-desire-to-ask-for-your-hand-in-the-blessed-sacrament-of-matrimony," he said in one breath. He took in another, with an audible gasp. "I—"

"Shut up!"

Ian, his mouth opened to continue, immediately shut it. He opened one eye in a cautious slit, like one viewing a bomb momentarily expected to go off.

Bree glared from Ian to me. Even in the dim room, I could see the tight look of her mouth and the crimson rising in her cheeks. The tip of her nose was red, whether from the nippy air outside or from annoyance, I couldn't tell.

"Did you know about this?" she demanded of me.

"Of course not!" I said. "For heaven's sake, Bree—" Before I could finish, she had whirled on her heel and run out of the door. I could see the quick flash of her rusty skirts as she hurried up the slope leading to the stable.

I pulled off my apron and flung it hastily over the chair. "I'd better go after her."

"I'll go, too," Ian offered, and I didn't stop him. Reinforcements might be needed.

"What do you think she'll do?" he asked, panting in my wake as I hastened up the steep slope.

"God knows," I said. "But I'm afraid we're going to find out." I was entirely too familiar with the look of a Fraser roused to fury. Neither Bree nor Jamie lost their temper easily, but when they did, they lost it thoroughly.

"I'm glad she didna strike me," Ian said thankfully. "I thought for a moment she was going to." He pulled even with me, his long legs outstripping mine, hurrying though I was. I could hear uplifted voices from the open half-door of the stable.

"Why on earth would you put poor little Ian up to such a thing?" Brianna was saying, her voice high with indignation. "I've never heard of such a high-handed, arrogant—"

"Poor little Ian?" Ian said, vastly affronted. "What does she—"

"Oh, high-handed, am I?" Jamie's voice interrupted. He sounded both impatient and irritable, though not yet angry. Perhaps I was in time to avert full-scale hostilities. I peeked through the stable door, to see them face-to-face, glaring at each other over a large pile of half-dried manure.

"And what better choice could I make, will ye tell me that?" he demanded. "Let me tell ye, lassie, I thought of every bachelor in fifty miles before I settled on Ian. I wouldna have ye wed to a cruel man or a drunkard, nor yet a poor man—nor one auld enough to be your grandsire, either."

He shoved a hand through his hair, sure sign of mental agitation, but made a masterful effort to calm himself. He lowered his voice a bit, trying to be conciliatory.

"Why, I even put aside Tammas McDonald, for while he's a fine stretch of land and a good temper, and he's an age for you, he's a bittie wee fellow forbye, and I thought ye wouldna care to stand up side by side with him before a priest. Believe me, Brianna, I've done my best to see ye well wed."

Bree wasn't having any; her own hair had come loose during her dash up the hill, and was floating round her face like the flames of a vengeful archangel.

"And what makes you think I want to be married to anybody at all?"

His mouth dropped open.

"Want?" he said incredulously. "And what has *want* to do with it?"

"Everything!" She stamped her foot.

"Now there you're wrong, lassie," he advised her, turning to pick up his fork. He eyed her stomach with a nod. "You've a bairn coming, who needs a name. Your time to be choosy is long since past, aye?"

He dug his fork into the pile of manure and heaved the load into the waiting barrow, then dug again, with a smooth economy of motion born of years of labor.

"Now, Ian's a sweet-tempered lad, and a hard worker," he said, eyes on his task. "He's got his own land; he'll have mine, too, in time, and that will—"

"I am not going to marry anybody!" Brianna drew herself up to her full height, fists balled at her sides, and spoke in a voice loud enough to disturb the bats in the corners of the ceiling. One small dark form detached itself from the shadows and flittered out into the gathering dusk, ignored by the combatants underneath.

"Well, then, make your own choice," Jamie said shortly. "And I wish ye well of it!"

"You . . . are . . . not . . . listening!" Brianna said, grinding each word between her teeth. "I've made my choice. I said I won't . . . marry . . . *anyone*!" She punctuated this with another stamp of her foot.

Jamie thrust the fork into the pile with a thump. He straightened up and eyed Brianna, rubbing his fist across his jaw.

"Aye, well. I seem to recall hearin' a verra similar opinion expressed by your mother—the night before our wedding. I havena asked her lately does she regret bein' forced to wed me or not, but I flatter myself she's maybe not been miserable altogether. Perhaps ye should go and have a word wi' her?"

"It's not the same thing at all!" Brianna snapped.

"No, it's not," Jamie agreed, keeping a firm grip on his temper. The sun was low behind the hills, flooding the stable with a golden light in which the creeping tide of red in his skin was nonetheless quite visible. Still, he was making every attempt to be reasonable.

"Your mother wed me to save her life—and mine. It was a brave thing she did, and generous, too. I'll grant it's no a matter of life or death, but—have ye no idea what it is to live branded as a wanton—or as a fatherless bastard, come to that?"

Seeing her expression falter slightly at this, he pressed his advantage, stretching out a hand to her and speaking kindly.

"Come, lassie. Can ye not bring yourself to do it for the bairn's sake?"

Her face tightened again and she stepped back.

"No," she said, sounding strangled. "No. I can't."

He dropped his hand. I could see them both, despite the fading light, and saw the danger signs all too clearly, in the narrowing of his eyes and the set of his shoulders, squared for battle. "Is that how Frank Randall raised ye, lass, to have no regard for what's right or wrong?"

Brianna was trembling all over, like a horse that's run too far.

"My father always did what was right for me! And he would never have tried to pull something like this!" she said. "Never! *He* cared about me!"

At this, Jamie finally lost his temper, which went off with a bang.

"And I don't?" he said. "I am not trying my best to do what's right for ye? In spite of your being—"

"Jamie—" I turned toward him, saw his eyes gone black with anger, and turned toward her. "Bree—I know he didn't—you have to understand—"

"Of all the reckless, thoughtless, selfish ways in which to behave!"

"You self-righteous, insensitive bastard!"

"Bastard! Ye'll call *me* a bastard, and your belly swellin' like a pumpkin with a child that ye mean to doom to finger-pointing and calumny for all its days, and—"

"Anybody points a finger at my child, and I'll break it off and stuff it down their throat!"

"Ye senseless wee besom! Have ye no the faintest notion o' how things are? Ye'll be a scandal and a hissing! Folk will call ye whore to your face!"

"Let them try it!"

"Oh, let them try it? And ye mean me to stand by and listen, I suppose?"

"It's not your job to defend me!"

He was so furious that his face went white as fresh-bleached muslin.

"Not my job to defend you? For Christ's sake, woman, who *else* is meant to do it?"

Ian tugged gently on my arm, drawing me back.

"Ye've only the twa choices now, Auntie," he murmured in my ear. "Douse them both wi' a pan o' cold water, or come away with me and leave them to it. I've seen Uncle Jamie and my Mam go at it before. Believe me, ye dinna want to step between two Frasers wi' their dander up. My Da said he's tried once or twice, and got the scars to prove it."

I took a final glance at the situation and gave up. He was right; they were nose to nose, red hair bristling and eyes slitted like a couple of bobcats, circling, spitting and snarling. I could have set the hay on fire, and neither one would have spared an instant's notice.

It seemed remarkably quiet and peaceful outside. A whippoorwill sang in the aspen grove, and the wind was in the east, carrying the faint sounds of the waterfall to us. By the time we reached the dooryard, we couldn't hear the shouting anymore.

"Dinna be worrit, Auntie," Ian said comfortingly. "They'll get hungry, sooner or later."

In the event, it was unnecessary to starve them out; Jamie stamped down the hill a few minutes later and without a word, fetched his horse from the paddock, bridled him, mounted, and rode bareback at a gallop down the track toward Fergus's cabin. As I watched his departing form, Brianna stalked out of the stable, puffing like a steam engine, and made for the house.

"What does *nighean na galladh* mean?" she demanded, seeing me at the door.

"I don't know," I said. I did, but thought it much more prudent not to say. "I'm sure he didn't mean it," I added. "Er . . . whatever it means."

"Ha," she said, and with an angry snort, stomped into the house, reappearing moments later with the egg basket over her arm. Without a word, she disappeared into the bushes, making a rustling noise like a hurricane.

I took several deep breaths and went in to start supper, cursing Roger Wakefield.

Physical exertion seemed to have dissipated at least some of the negative energy in the household. Brianna spent an hour in the bushes, and returned with sixteen eggs and a calmer face. There were leaves and stickers in her hair, and from the look of her shoes, she had been kicking trees.

I didn't know what Jamie had been doing, but he returned at suppertime, sweaty and windblown but outwardly calm. They pointedly ignored each other, a reasonably difficult feat for two large persons confined in a twenty-foot-square log cabin. I glanced at Ian, who rolled his eyes skyward and came to help carry the big serving bowl to the table.

Conversation over supper was limited to requests to pass the salt, and afterward, Brianna cleared the dishes, then went to sit at the spinning wheel, working the foot treadle with unnecessary emphasis.

Jamie gave her back a glare, then jerked his head at me and went out. He was waiting on the path to the privy when I followed him a moment later.

"What am I to do?" he demanded, without preamble.

"Apologize," I said.

"Apologize?" His hair seemed to be standing on end, though it was likely only the effects of the wind. "But I havena done anything wrong!"

"Well, what difference does that make?" I said, exasperated. "You asked me what you should do, and I told you."

He exhaled strongly through his nose, hesitated a moment, then turned and stalked back into the house, shoulders set for martyrdom or battle.

"I apologize," he said, looming up in front of her.

Surprised, she nearly dropped the yarn, but caught it adeptly.

"Oh," she said, and flushed. She took her foot off the treadle, and the great wheel creaked and slowed.

"I was wrong," he said, with a quick look at me. I nodded encouragingly, and he cleared his throat. "I shouldna have—"

"It's all right." She spoke quickly, eager to meet him. "You didn't—I mean, you were only trying to help." She looked down at the thread, slowing as it ran through her fingers. "I'm sorry too —I shouldn't have been mad at you."

He closed his eyes briefly and sighed, then opened them and lifted one eyebrow at me. I smiled faintly and turned back to my work, pounding fennel seeds in the mortar.

He pulled up a stool and sat down beside her, and she turned toward him, putting one hand on the wheel to stop it.

"I know you meant well," she said. "You and Ian both. But don't you see, Da? I have to wait for Roger."

"But if something has happened to the man—if he's met with an accident of some kind . . ."

"He isn't dead. I *know* he isn't." She spoke with the fervency of someone who means to bend reality to her will. "He'll come back. And how would it be if he did, and found me married to Ian?"

Ian looked up, hearing his name. He sat on the floor by the fire, Rollo's great head resting on his knee, his yellow wolf-eyes mere slits of pleasure as Ian methodically combed through the thick pelt, pulling out ticks and burs as he found them.

Jamie ran his fingers through his hair in a gesture of frustration.

"I have had word out since ye told me of him, *a nighean.* I sent Ian to Cross Creek to leave word at River Run, and with Captain Freeman to pass to the other rivermen. I've sent Duncan wi' word, all through the Cape Fear valley and as far north as Edenton and New Bern, and wi' the packet boats that run from Virginia to Charleston."

He looked at me, pleading for understanding. "What more can I do? The man is nowhere to be found. If I thought there were the slightest chance—" He stopped, teeth set in his lip.

Brianna dropped her gaze to the yarn in her hand, and with a quick, sharp gesture, snapped it. Leaving the loose end to flap from the spindle, she got up and crossed the room, sitting down at the table with her back to us.

"I'm sorry, lass," Jamie said, more quietly. He reached out and laid a hand on her shoulder, gingerly, as though she might bite him.

She stiffened slightly, but didn't pull away. After a moment, she reached up and took his hand, squeezing it lightly, then putting it aside.

"I see," she said. "Thank you, Da." She sat, eyes fixed on the flames, her face and figure utterly still, but managing to radiate complete desolation. I put my hands on her shoulders, rubbing gently, but she felt like a wax manikin under my fingers—not resisting but not acknowledging the touch.

Jamie studied her for a moment, frowning, and glanced at me. Then, with an air of decision, he got up, reached to the shelf, brought down his inkhorn and quill jar, and set them on the table with a clank.

"Here's a thought," he said firmly. "Let us draw up a broadsheet, here, and I will take it to Gillette in Wilmington. He can print it up, and Ian and the Lindsey lads will take the copies up and down the coast, from Charleston to Jamestown. It may be that someone's not kent Wakefield, not hearing his name, but they'll maybe know him by his looks."

He shook ink powder made of iron and oak gall into the stained half-gourd he used as a well, and poured a little water from the pitcher, using the shaft of a quill to stir the ink. He smiled at Brianna, and took a sheet of paper from the drawer.

"Now, then, lass, how is this man of yours to look at?"

The suggestion of action had brought a spark of life back to Brianna's face. She sat up straighter, and a current of energy flowed up her spine, into my fingers.

"Tall," she said. "Nearly as tall as you, Da. People *would* notice; they always look at you. He has black hair, and green eyes —bright green; it's one of the first things you notice about him, isn't it, Mama?"

Ian gave a small start, and looked up from his grooming.

"Yes," I said, sitting down on the bench next to Brianna. "But you can maybe do better than just the written description. Bree's a good hand with a likeness," I explained to Jamie. "Can you draw Roger from memory, do you think, Bree?"

"Yes!" She reached for the quill, eager to try. "Yes, I'm sure I can—I've drawn him before."

Jamie surrendered the quill and paper, the vertical lines between his brows showing in a slight frown.

"Can the printer work from an ink sketch?" I asked, seeing it.

"Oh—aye, I expect so. It's no great matter to make a woodblock, if the lines are clear." He spoke abstractedly, eyes fixed on the paper in front of Brianna.

Ian pushed Rollo's head off his knee and came to stand by the table, looking over Bree's shoulder in what seemed a rather exaggerated curiosity.

Lower lip fixed between her teeth, she drew clean and swiftly. High forehead, with a thick lock of black hair that rose from an invisible cowlick, then dipped almost to the strongly marked black brows. She drew him in profile; a bold nose, not quite beaky, a clean-lined, sensitive mouth and a wide, slanted jaw. Thick-lashed eyes, deepset, with lines of good humor marking a strong, appealing face. She added a neat, flat ear, then turned her attention to the elegant curve of the skull, drawing thick, wavy dark hair pulled back in a short tail.

Ian made a small, strangled noise in his throat.

"Are you all right, Ian?" I looked up at him, but he wasn't looking at the drawing—he was looking across the table, at Jamie. He was wearing a glazed sort of expression, like a pig on a spit.

I turned, to find precisely the same expression on Jamie's face.

"What on earth is the matter?" I asked.

"Oh . . . nothing." The muscles of his throat moved in a convulsive swallow. The corner of his mouth twitched, and twitched again, as though he couldn't control it.

"Like hell it is!" Alarmed, I leaned across the table, seizing his wrist and groping for his pulse. "Jamie, what is it? Are you having chest pains? Do you feel ill?"

"*I* do." Ian was leaning over the table, looking as though he might be going to throw up any minute. "Coz—d'ye mean honestly to tell me that . . . *this*"—he gestured feebly at the sketch —"is Roger Wakefield?"

"Yes," she said, looking up at him in puzzlement. "Ian, are you all right? Did you eat something funny?"

He didn't answer, but dropped heavily onto the bench beside her, put his head in his hands, and groaned.

Jamie gently detached his hand from my grip. Even in the red of the firelight, I could see that he was white and strained. The hand on the table curled around the quill jar, as though seeking support.

"Mr. Wakefield," he said carefully to Brianna. "Has he by any chance . . . another name?"

"Yes," Brianna and I said in unison. I stopped and let her explain as I rose and went hurriedly to fetch a bottle of brandy from the pantry. I didn't know what was going on, but had the horrible feeling that it was about to be called for.

"—adopted. MacKenzie was his own family name," she was saying as I emerged with the bottle in hand. She glanced from father to cousin, frowning. "Why? You haven't heard of a Roger MacKenzie, have you?"

Jamie and Ian exchanged an appalled glance. Ian cleared his throat. So did Jamie.

"What?" Brianna demanded, leaning forward, glancing anxiously from one to the other. "What is it? Have you seen him? Where?"

I saw Jamie's jaw tighten as he summoned up words.

"Aye," he said carefully. "We have. On the mountain."

"What—here? On *this* mountain?" She stood up, pushing back the bench. Alarm and excitement played over her face like flames. "Where is he? What happened?"

"Well," Ian said defensively, "he *did* say as he'd taken your maidenheid, after all."

"He WHAT?" Brianna's eyes sprang open so far that a rim of white showed all around the iris.

"Well, your Da asked him, just to be sure, and he admitted that he'd—"

"You *what*?" Brianna rounded on Jamie, clenched fists on the table.

"Aye, well. It—was a mistake," Jamie said. He looked utterly wretched.

"You bet it was! What in the name of—what have you done?" Her own cheeks had blanched, and blue sparks glinted in her eyes, hot as the heart of a flame.

Jamie took a deep breath. He looked up, straight into her face, and set his jaw.

"The wee lassie," he said. "Lizzie. She told me that ye were with child, and that the man who'd got it on ye was a wicked brute called MacKenzie."

Brianna's mouth opened and shut, but no words came out. Jamie looked at her steadily.

"Ye did say to me that ye'd been violated, did ye no?"

She nodded, jerky as a badly sprung puppet.

"So, then. Ian and the lassie were at the mill, when MacKenzie came askin' for ye. They rode to fetch me, and Ian and I met him in the clearing just above the green spring."

Brianna had got her voice working, though only barely.

"What did you do to him?" she asked hoarsely. "What?"

"It was a fair fight," Ian said, still defensive. "I wanted to shoot him on sight, but Uncle Jamie said no, he meant to have his hands on the—the man."

"You *hit* him?"

"Aye, I did!" Jamie said, stung at last. "For God's sake, woman, what would ye have me do to the man who'd used ye that way? It was you wanting to do murder, aye?"

"Besides, he hit Uncle Jamie, too," Ian put in helpfully. "It was a fair fight I said."

"Be quiet, Ian, there's a good lad," I said. I poured two fingers, neat, and pushed the cup in front of Jamie.

"But it was—he *wasn't*—" Brianna was sputtering, like a firecracker with a short fuse lit. Then she caught fire, and slammed one fist on the table, going off like a rocket.

"WHAT HAVE YOU DONE WITH HIM?" she screamed.

Jamie blinked and Ian flinched. They exchanged haunted glances.

I put a hand on Jamie's arm, squeezing tight. I couldn't keep the quaver out of my own voice as I asked the necessary question.

"Jamie—did you kill him?"

He glanced at me, and the tension in his face relaxed, if only marginally.

"Ah . . . no," he said. "I gave him to the Iroquois."

"Och, now, Coz, it could have been worse." Ian patted Brianna tentatively on the back. "We didna kill him, after all."

Brianna made a small choking sound, and pulled her head up off her knees. Her face was white and damp as the inside of an oyster shell, her hair in a tangle round it. She hadn't vomited or fainted, but looked as though she still might do either.

"We did mean to," Ian went on, looking at her a little nervously. "I'd my pistol pressed behind his ear, but then I thought it was really Uncle Jamie's right to blow his brains out, but then he—"

Brianna choked again, and I hastily placed an ashet on the table in front of her, just in case.

"Ian, I really think she doesn't need to hear this just now," I said, narrowing my eyes at him.

"Yes, I do." Brianna pushed herself upright, hands gripping the edge of the table. "I have to hear it all, I have to." She turned her head slowly, as though her neck was stiff, toward Jamie.

"Why?" she said. "WHY?"

He was as white and ill-looking as she was. He had pushed away from the table and gone to the chimney corner, as though trying to get as far away as possible from the drawing, with its damning likeness of Roger MacKenzie Wakefield.

He looked as though he would have done anything rather than answer, but answer he did, his eyes steady on hers.

"I meant to kill him. I stopped Ian because shooting the prick seemed too easy a death—too quick for what he'd done." He took a deep breath, and I could see that the hand gripping his writing shelf was clenched so tight that the knuckles stood out white against his skin.

"I stopped to think, how it should be; what I must do. I left Ian with him, and I walked away." He swallowed; I could see the muscles move in his throat, but he didn't look away.

"I walked into the forest a wee way, and leaned my back against a tree to let my heart slow. It seemed best he should be awake, to know—but I didna think I could bear to hear him speak again. He'd said too much already. But then I began to hear it, over again, what he'd said."

"What? What did he say?" Even her lips were white.

So were Jamie's.

"He said . . . that ye'd asked him to your bed. That you—" He stopped and bit his lip, savagely.

"He said ye wanted him; that ye'd asked him to take your maidenheid," Ian said. He spoke coolly, his eyes on Brianna.

She drew in breath with a ragged sound, like paper being torn. "I did."

I glanced involuntarily at Jamie. His eyes were closed, his teeth fixed in his lip.

Ian made a shocked sound, and Brianna drew back a hand like lightning and slapped him across the face.

He jerked back, lost his balance, and half fell off the bench. He grabbed the edge of the table and staggered to his feet.

"How?" he shouted, his face contorted in sudden anger. "How could ye do such a thing? I told Uncle Jamie that ye'd never play the whore, never! But it's true, isn't it?"

She was on her feet like a leopard, her cheeks gone from white to blazing fury in a second.

"Well, damn you for a self-righteous prig, Ian! Who gave you the right to call me a whore?"

"Right?" He sputtered for a moment, at a loss for words. "I— you—he—"

Before I could intervene, she drew back a fist and punched him hard in the pit of the stomach. With a look of intense surprise, he sat down hard on the floor, mouth open like a suckling pig.

I moved, but Jamie was faster. In less than a second he was beside her, gripping her arm. She whirled, meaning to hit him, too, I think, but then froze. Her mouth was working soundlessly, tears of shock and fury running down her cheeks.

"Be still," he said, and his voice was very cold. I saw his

fingers dig into her flesh, and I made a small sound of protest. He paid no attention, too intent on Brianna.

"I didna want to believe it," he said, in a voice like ice. "I told myself he was only saying so to save himself, it wasna true. But if it was—" He seemed to become aware at last that he was hurting her. He let go of her arm.

"I couldna take the man's life, without being sure," he said, and paused, his eyes searching her face. For regret? I wondered. Or remorse? Whatever he might be looking for, all he found was a smoldering rage. Her face was the echo of his own, her blue eyes hot as his.

His own face changed, and he looked away.

"I did regret it," he said, very quietly. "When I came that night, and saw ye, I was sorry then that I hadna killed him. I held ye in my arms—and I felt my heart go sma' wi' shame, that I should doubt my daughter's virtue." He looked down, and I could see the mark where he had bitten his lip.

"Now my heart is shrunk altogether. Not only that ye should be impure but that ye should lie to me."

"Lie to you?" Her voice was no more than whisper. "*Lie* to you?"

"Aye, lie to me!" With sudden violence, he turned back to her. "That ye should bed a man from lust, and cry rape when ye find ye're with child! Do ye not realize that it's only chance I have not the sin of murder on my soul, and you the cause of it?"

She was too furious to speak; I saw her throat swell with words, and knew I had to do something, at once, before either of them had the opportunity to say more.

I couldn't speak, either. Blindly, I fumbled in the pocket of my gown, feeling for the ring. I found it, pulled it out, and dropped it on the table. It chimed against the wood; spun, and rattled to a stop, the gold of the tiny circlet gleaming red in the firelight.

From F. to C. with love. Always.

Jamie looked at it, his face gone completely blank. Brianna drew in her breath with a sob.

"That's your ring, Auntie," Ian said. He sounded dazed, and bent close to look, as though he couldn't believe his eyes. "Your gold ring. The one that Bonnet took from ye, on the river."

"Yes," I said. My knees felt weak. I sat down at the table, and laid my hand over the telltale ring as though to take it back, deny its presence.

Jamie took my wrist and lifted it. Like a man handling a dangerous insect, he picked the ring up gingerly between thumb and forefinger.

"Where did ye get this?" he asked, his voice almost casual. He looked at me, and a bolt of terror shot through me at the look in his eyes.

"I brought it to her." Brianna's tears had dried, evaporated by the heat of her fury. She stood behind me and gripped me by the shoulders. "Don't you look at her that way, don't you dare!"

He shifted the look to her, but she didn't flinch; only held on to me harder, her fingers digging into my shoulders.

"Where did ye get it?" he asked again, his voice no more than a whisper. "Where?"

"From him. From Stephen Bonnet." Her voice was shaking, but from rage, not fear. "When . . . he . . . raped . . . me."

Jamie's face cracked suddenly, as though some explosion had burst him from within. I made an incoherent sound of distress, and reached out for him, but he whirled away and stood rigid, back turned to us, in the middle of the room.

I felt Brianna draw herself upright, heard Ian say, rather stupidly, *"Bonnet?"* I heard the ticking of the clock on the sideboard, felt the draft from the door. I was dimly aware of all these things, but had no eyes for anything but Jamie.

I pushed back the bench, stumbled to my feet. He stood as though rooted into the floor, fists clenched into his belly like a man gut-shot, trying to hold back the inevitable fatal spill of his insides.

I should be able to do something, to say something. I should be able to help them, to take care of them. But I could do nothing. I could not help one without betraying the other—had already betrayed them both. I had sold Jamie's honor to keep him safe, and the doing of it had taken Roger and destroyed Bree's happiness.

I could go to neither of them now. All I could do was to stand there, feeling my heart crumble into small, jagged chunks.

Bree left me, and walked quietly around the table, across the room, around Jamie. She stood in front of him, looking up into his face, her own set like marble, cold as a saint's.

"Damn you," she said, scarcely audible. "Damn you very much, you bastard. I'm sorry I ever saw you."

PART ELEVEN

Pas Du Tout

51

Betrayal

October 1769

Roger opened his eyes and threw up. Or rather, down. It didn't matter; the burning rush of bile through his nose and the trickle of vomitus that ran into his hair were unimportant by comparison with the agony in head and groin.

A thumping swerve of movement jarred him, shooting kaleidoscopic colors from crotch to brain. A damp smell of canvas filled his nose. Then a voice spoke somewhere near, and formless panic took sudden, jagged shape among the colors.

Gloriana! They'd got him! He lurched in reflex, brought up short by a searing jolt through his temples—but brought up a split-second earlier by something round his wrists. Tied, he was tied up in the hold.

The shape of panic blew up bold and black against his mind. Bonnet. They'd caught him, taken back the stones. And now they'd kill him.

He jerked convulsively, yanking at his wrists, teeth clenched against the pain. The deck dropped beneath him with a startled snort, and he slammed down hard.

He vomited again, but his stomach was empty. He retched, ribs grating with each spasm against the canvas-wrapped bundles he lay across. Not sails; not a hold. Not the *Gloriana,* not a ship at all. A horse. He was tied hand and foot, belly down across a fucking horse!

The horse jolted on a few more steps, then stopped. Voices muttered, hands fumbled at him, then he was pulled off roughly and dropped on his feet. He fell down at once, unable either to stand or to break his fall.

He lay half doubled on the ground, concentrating on breathing. Without the jouncing, it was easier. Nobody troubled him, and gradually he began to be aware of his surroundings.

Awareness didn't help much. There were damp leaves under his cheek, cool and smelling of sweet rot. He cracked a cautious eye. Sky above, an impossible deep color, between blue and purple. The sound of trees, the rush of nearby water.

Everything seemed to be revolving slowly around him, painfully vivid. He closed his eyes and pressed his hands flat against the ground.

Jesus, where am I? The voices were talking casually, words half lost in the stamping and whickering of nearby horses. He listened intently but couldn't make out the words. He felt a moment's panic at the inability; he couldn't even put a name to the language.

There was a large, tender lump behind one ear, another on the back of his head, and a pain that made his temples throb; he'd been hit hard—but when? Had the blows ruptured vessels in his brain, deprived him of language? He opened his eyes all the way, and—with infinite caution—rolled onto his back.

A square brown face glanced down at him, with no particular expression of interest, then looked back to the horse the man was tending.

Indians. The shock was so great that he forgot momentarily about his pain, and sat up abruptly. He gasped and put his face on his knees, eyes closed as he fought to keep from passing out again, blood pounding through a splitting head.

Where was he? He bit his knee, grinding the cloth savagely between his teeth, fighting for memory. Fragments of images came back to him, in mocking bits that stubbornly refused to fit together into sense.

The creak of boards and the smell of bilges. Blinding sun through panes of glass. Bonnet's face, and the breathing of whales in the mist, and a little boy named . . . named . . .

Hands clasped in dark and the tang of hops. *I thee wed, with my body I thee worship* . . .

Bree. Brianna. Cold sweat rolled down his cheek and his jaw muscles ached with clenching. The images hopped around in his mind like fleas. Her face, her face, he must not let it go!

Not gentle, not a gentle face. A nose dead straight and cold blue eyes . . . no, not cold . . .

A hand on his shoulder yanked him from the tortured pursuit of memory into the all too immediate present. It was an Indian, knife in hand. Numb with confusion, Roger simply looked at the man.

The Indian, a middle-aged man with a bone in his roached hair, and an air of no-nonsense about him, took Roger by his own hair and tilted his head back and forth with a critical air. Confusion evaporated, as it occurred to Roger that he was about to be scalped as he sat there.

He flung himself backward and lashed out with his feet, catching the Indian in the knees. The man went down with a cry of surprise, and Roger rolled, lurching and stumbling to his feet, running for his life.

He ran like a drunken spider, spraddle-legged, staggering toward the trees. Shadows, refuge. There were shouts behind him, and the sound of quick feet scattering leaves. Then something jerked his feet from under him and he fell headlong with a bone-shaking thud.

They had him on his feet before he had his breath back. No good to struggle; there were four of them, including the one Roger had knocked down. That one came toward them, limping, still holding the knife.

"Not hurt you!" he said crossly. He slapped Roger briskly across the face, then leaned over and sawed through the leather thong that bound Roger's wrists. With a loud snort, he turned on his heel and went back to the horses.

The two men holding Roger promptly let go of him and walked off, too, leaving him swaying like a sapling in a high wind.

Great, he thought blankly, *I'm not dead. What the bloody hell?*

No answer to this presenting itself, he rubbed a hand gingerly over his face, discovering several bruises he'd missed earlier, and looked around.

He stood in a small clearing, surrounded by huge oaks and half-shed hickory trees; the ground was thick with brown and yellow leaves, and the squirrels had left heaps of acorn caps and nut hulls scattered over the ground. He stood on a mountain; the slope of the ground told him that, as the chill air and jewel-deep sky told him the time was near sunset.

The Indians—there were four, all men—ignored him completely, going about the business of camp-building without a glance in Roger's direction. He licked dry lips and took a cautious step toward the small stream that burbled over algae-furred rocks a few yards away.

He drank his fill, though the cold water made his teeth ache; nearly all the teeth were loose on one side of his mouth, and the lining of his cheek was badly cut. He rinsed his face gingerly, with a feeling of déjà vu. Sometime earlier, he had washed and drunk like this, cold water running over emerald rocks . . .

Fraser's Ridge. He sat back on his heels, memory dropping back in place, in large, ugly chunks.

Brianna, and Claire . . . and Jamie Fraser. Suddenly the confusing image he had sought so desperately came back unbidden; Brianna's face, with its broad, clean bones, blue eyes set slantwise above a long, straight nose. But Brianna's face grown older, weathered to bronze, rough-cut and toughened by masculinity and experience, blue eyes gone black with a murderous rage. Jamie Fraser.

"You bloody sod," Roger said softly. "You bloody, fucking *sod.* You tried to kill me."

His initial feeling was one of astonishment—but anger wasn't far behind.

He remembered everything now; the meeting in the clearing, the autumn leaves like fire and honey and the blazing man among them; the brown-haired youth—and who the hell was *he?* The fight—he touched a sore spot under his ribs with a grimace—and the end of it, lying flat in the leaves, sure that he was about to be killed.

Well, he hadn't been. He had a dim memory of hearing the man and the boy arguing somewhere over him—one of them had been for killing him on the spot, the other said no—but damned if he knew which one. Then one of them had hit him again, and he remembered nothing more until now.

And now—he glanced around. The Indians had a fire going, and a clay pot sitting by it. None of them paid him the least attention, though he was sure they were all aware of him.

Perhaps they had taken him from Fraser and the boy—why, though? More likely, Fraser had given him to the Indians. The man with the knife had said they didn't mean to hurt him. What *did* they mean to do with him?

He looked around. It would be night, soon; already, the distant shadows under the oaks had thickened.

So what, sport? If you slope off after dark, where're you going to? The only direction you know is down. The Indians were apparently ignoring him because they were confident that he wasn't going anywhere.

Dismissing the uncomfortable truth of this observation, he stood up. First things first. It was the last thing he wanted to do at the moment, but his bladder was bursting. His fingers were slow and clumsy, congested with blood, but he managed to fumble loose the lacing of his breeches.

His first feeling was one of relief; it wasn't as bad as it felt. Very sore, but ginger prodding seemed to indicate that he was basically intact and unruptured.

It was only as he turned back toward the fire that simple relief was succeeded by a burst of rage so pure and blinding as to burn away both pain and fear. On his right wrist was a smudged black oval—a thumbprint, clear and mocking as a signature.

"Christ," he said, very softly. Fury burned hot and thick in the pit of his belly. He could taste it, sour in his mouth. He looked down the mountainside behind him, not knowing whether he faced Fraser's Ridge or not.

"Wait for me, bugger," he said, under his breath. "*Both* of you —wait for me. I'm coming back."

Not right away, though. The Indians allowed him to share the food—a sort of stew, which they scooped up with their hands in spite of its near-boiling temperature—but were otherwise indifferent to him. He tried them in English, French—even the small bits of German that he knew, but got no response.

They did tie him when they lay down to sleep; his ankles were bound and a noose put round his neck, tied to the wrist of one of his captors. Whether from indifference or because there wasn't one, they didn't give him a blanket, and he spent the night shivering, huddled as close to the dwindling fire as he could get without choking himself.

He hadn't thought he could sleep, but did, exhausted with pain. It was a restless sleep, though, filled with violent, fragmentary dreams and broken by the constant illusion of being strangled.

In the morning, they set off again. No question of riding this time; he walked, and as fast as he could; the noose was left around his neck, hanging loose, but a short length of rope bound his wrists to the harness leathers of one of the horses. He stumbled and fell several times, but managed to scramble to his feet, in spite of bruises and aching muscles. He had the distinct impression that they would allow him to be dragged without compunction if he didn't.

They were heading roughly north; he could tell as much by the sun. Not that that helped a lot, since he had no notion where they had started from. Still, they could be no great distance from Fraser's Ridge; he couldn't have been unconscious for more than a few hours. He looked at the churning hooves of the horse beside him, trying to estimate its speed. No more than two or three miles per hour; he was managing to keep up without great strain.

Landmarks. There was no telling where they meant to take him —or why—but if he was ever to get back, he had to memorize the shape of the terrain through which they passed.

A cliff, forty feet high and overgrown with shaggy plants, a twisted persimmon tree protruding from a crack in the rock like a jack-in-the-box popping out, covered in bright orange bobbles.

They emerged onto the crest of a ridge, to a breathtaking view of distant mountains; three sharp peaks, clustered together against a blazing sky, the left one higher than the other two. He could remember that. A stream—a river?—that fell through a small gorge; they drove the horses through a shallow ford, soaking Roger to the waist in icy water.

The routine of travel lasted for days, moving ever northward. His captors did not talk to him, and by the fourth day he realized that he was beginning to lose track of time, falling into a dreamlike trance, overcome by fatigue and the silence of the mountains. He pulled a long thread from the hem of his coat and began to knot it, one knot for each day, both as some small hold on reality, and as a crude method of estimating the distance traveled.

He was going back. Whatever it took, he was going back to Fraser's Ridge.

It was on the eighth day that he found his chance. They were high in the mountains by now. They had crossed through one pass the day before, and come down a steep slope, the ponies grunting, slowing to brace each careful step as the loads on their saddles creaked and shifted.

Now they were headed up again, and the ponies slowed their pace still further as the ground sloped sharply upward. Roger was able to gain a little ground, to pull even with the pony's side and cling to the harness leather, letting the tough little beast pull him along.

The Indians had dismounted, walking and leading the ponies. He kept a narrow eye on the long black scalp lock hanging down the back of the brave leading the pony he clung to. He held on with one hand; the other was busy under cover of a hanging flap of canvas, picking at the knot that bound him to the harness.

Strand by strand, the hemp came free, until no more than a single thread of rope held him to the pony. He waited, sweat streaming down his ribs from fear and the effort of the climb, rejecting one opportunity after another, worrying from moment to moment that he had left it too late, that they would stop to make camp, that the brave who led his pony would turn and see him, would think to check.

But they didn't stop, and the brave didn't turn. *There,* he thought, and his heart beat fast, seeing the first pony in the string step out along a narrow deer trail cut into the hillside. The ground fell away sharply below the trail, then leveled out about six feet down. Below was a thickly wooded slope, ideal for concealment.

One pony, then another, negotiated the narrow stretch of trail, putting down their feet with finicking care. A third, and then it was Roger's turn. He squeezed in close to the pony's side, smelling the sweet, pungent foam of its sweat. One step, then another, and they were on the narrow trail.

He jerked the rope loose and jumped. He hit with a jolt and sank halfway to his knees, sprang up and ran downhill. His shoes came off and he left them behind. He splashed across a tiny creek, scrabbled up its bank on hands and knees, and clambered to his feet, running before he'd got upright.

He heard calls behind him, then silence, but knew he was pursued. He had no breath to waste; neither would they.

The landscape slid past in a blur of leaves and rocks as he swung his head from side to side, looking for which way to go, someplace to hide. He chose a grove of birch, burst through and into a sloping meadow, careened down across the slippery grass, bare feet stubbing on roots and rocks. At the far side, he took a second to glance back. Two of them; he saw the round dark heads among the leaves.

On into another copse, out again, zigzagging madly through a field of broken rocks, breath coming hard in his throat. One thing the bloody past had done for him, he thought grimly; improved his wind. Then there was no room for any thought—nothing but the blind instincts of flight.

And down again, a scrambling drop down the wet, cracked face of a twenty-foot cliff, grabbing at the plants as he half fell past them, roots ripping, hands sinking into pockets of mud, blunting his fingers on unseen rocks. He landed hard at the bottom, bent over, gasping.

One of them was right behind him, coming backward down the cliff. He snatched off the noose still around his neck, and whipped it hard at the Indian's hands. The man's hold slipped; he let go and slithered down, landing askew. Roger flung the noose over the man's head, gave it a vicious yank, and fled, leaving the man on his knees, choking and clawing at the rope round his neck.

Trees. He needed cover. He vaulted a fallen log, stumbled and rolled, was up again running. Up, a spruce thicket up a little way. Heart laboring, he jabbed his feet down hard, bounding up the slope.

He flung himself into the spruces, fighting through the pricks of a million needles, blind, eyes shut against the lashing twigs. Then the ground gave way underneath him and he fell in a blur of sky and branches.

He hit, half curled, his breath knocked out; had barely sense to curl up further and keep on rolling, bashing off rocks and saplings, setting off showers of dirt and fallen needles, bouncing and smashing his way to the bottom.

He fetched up with a crash amid a tangle of woody stems, hung a moment, then slid down, to end with a thud. Dazed and bleeding, he lay still for a moment, then rolled painfully onto his side, wiping dirt and blood from his face.

He looked up, searching. There they were. The two of them, at the top of the slope, coming carefully down beside the ledge he had fallen from.

On hands and knees, he dived between the woody stems, and crawled for his life. Twigs bent, sharp ends jabbed him, and cascades of dust, dead leaves and insects fell from the higher branches above as he heaved his way forward, forcing a passage through the close-grown stems, twisting and turning, following such openings as he found.

Hell was his first coherent thought. Then he realized that it was as much description as curse. He was in a rhododendron hell. With that belated realization, he slowed his flight—if crawling at roughly ten feet per hour could be called "flight."

The tunnel-like opening in which he found himself was too narrow to allow him to turn around, but he managed to see behind him by thrusting his head to one side and craning his neck. There was nothing there; nothing but damp and musty darkness, illumined by a faint scatter of light, swirling with dust motes. Nothing was visible but the stems and limber branches of the rhododendron thicket.

His shaking limbs gave way, and he collapsed. He lay for a moment, curled up between the stems, breathing the musk of rotting leaves and damp earth.

"You wanted cover, mate," he murmured to himself. Things were beginning to hurt. He was ripped and bleeding in a dozen places. Even in the dim light, the ends of his fingers looked like raw meat.

He took a slow inventory of the damage, listening all the while for sounds of pursuit. Not surprisingly, there were none. He had heard talk about rhododendron hells in the taverns in Cross Creek; half-boasting stories of hunting dogs who had chased a squirrel into one of the huge tangles and become hopelessly lost, never to be seen again.

Roger hoped there was a fair amount of exaggeration to these stories, though a good look around wasn't reassuring. What light there was had no direction. Any way he looked, looked the same. Drooping clusters of cool, leathery leaves, thick stems and slender branches laced together in a nearly impenetrable snarl.

With a slight feeling of panic, he realized that he had no idea from which direction he had come.

He put his head on his knees and breathed deeply, trying to think. All right, first things first. His right foot was bleeding freely from a deep gash on the edge of the sole. He took off his tattered stockings and used one to bind his foot. Nothing else seemed bad enough to need a bandage, save the shallow gouge in his scalp; that was still seeping blood, wet and sticky to his touch.

His hands were shaking; it was hard to tie the stocking round his head. Still, the small action made him feel better. Now, then. He'd climbed countless Munros in Scotland, those endless craggy peaks, and more than once had helped to find day-trippers lost among the rocks and heather.

If you were lost in the wilderness, the usual caution was to stay put; wait for someone to find you. That would seem not to apply, he thought, if the only people looking for you were ones you didn't want to be found by.

He looked upward, through the snarl of branches. He could see small patches of sky, but the rhododendrons rose nearly twelve feet over his head. There was no way to stand up; he could barely sit upright under the interlacing branches.

There was no way of telling how big this particular hell was; on their journey through the mountains, he had seen entire slopes covered with heath balds, valleys filled with the deep green of rhododendron, only a few ambitious trees protruding above the waving sea of leaves. Then again, they had detoured round small tangles of the stuff, no more than a hundred feet square. He knew he was fairly close to one edge of the thing, but that knowledge was useless, with no idea in which direction the edge lay.

He became aware that he was very cold, his hands still shaking. *Shock,* he thought dimly. What did you do for shock? Hot liquids, blankets. Brandy. Yeah, right. Elevate the feet. That much, he could do.

He scooped a shallow, awkward little depression and eased himself into it, scraping the clammy, half-rotted leaves over his chest and shoulders. He propped his heels in the fork of a stem and closed his eyes, shivering.

They wouldn't come in after him. Why should they? A lot better to wait, if they were in no hurry. He'd have to come out eventually—if he still could.

Any movement here below would shake the leaves above, and pinpoint his movements to the watchers. That was a cold thought; they undoubtedly knew where he was now, and were simply waiting for his next move. The patches of sky were the deep blue of sapphires; it was still afternoon. He would wait till dark before he moved, then.

Hands clasped together on his chest, he willed himself to rest, to think of something beyond his present situation. Brianna. Let him think of her. Without the rage or bewilderment, now; there was no time for that.

Let him pretend that all was still between them as it had been on that night, their night. Warm against him in the dark. Her hands, so frank and curious, eager on his body. The generosity of her nakedness, freely given. And his momentary, mistaken conviction that all was forever right with the world. Gradually, the shivering eased, and he slept.

He woke sometime after moonrise; he could see brightness suffusing the sky, though not the moon itself. He was stiff and cold, and very sore. Hungry, too, and with a desperate thirst. Well, if he got himself out of this bloody tangle, at least he could find water; streams were everywhere in these mountains. Feeling awkward as a turtle on its back, he turned slowly over.

One direction was as good as another. On hands and knees, he started off, pushing through crevices, breaking branches, trying his best to go in a straight line. One fear haunted him more than thought of the Indians; he could so easily lose his bearings, moving blindly through this maze. He could end by going in endless circles, trapped forever. The stories of the hunting dogs had lost any element of exaggeration.

Some small animal ran over his hand and he jerked, hitting his head on the branches overhead. He gritted his teeth and kept on, a few inches at a time. Crickets chirped all around him, and countless small rustlings let him know that the inhabitants of this particular hell didn't appreciate his intrusion. He couldn't see anything at all; it was almost pitch-black here below. There was the one good thing, though: The constant effort heated him; sweat stung the gouge in his scalp and dripped from his chin.

Whenever he had to stop for breath, he listened for some clue—to either his location or his pursuers'—but he heard nothing beyond the occasional night bird's call and the rustle of the leaves all around. He wiped his sweating face on his sleeve and pushed on.

He didn't know how long he had been going when he found the rock. Or not so much found it as ran headfirst into it. He reeled back, clutching his head and gritting his teeth to keep from crying out.

Blinking from the pain, he put out a hand and found what he had struck. Not a boulder; a flat-faced rock. A tall one, too; the hard surface extended up as high as he could reach.

He groped to the side, and made his way around the rock. There was a thick stem growing near it; his shoulders stuck in the narrow space between. He wrenched and heaved, squirming, and finally shot forward, losing his balance and landing on his face.

Doggedly, he rose up onto his hands again—and realized that he could *see* his hands. He looked up, and around, in complete amazement.

His head and shoulders protruded into a clear space. Not merely clear, but *empty*. Eagerly, he wriggled forward, out of the claustrophobic grip of the rhododendrons.

He was standing in an open space, facing a cliff wall that rose on the far side of a small clearing. It really was a clearing, too; nothing at all grew in the soft dirt beneath his feet. Astonished, he turned slowly round, gulping great lungfuls of cold, sharp air.

"My God in heaven," he said softly, aloud. The clearing was roughly oval in shape, ringed by standing stones, with one end of the oval closed by the cliff face. The stones were evenly spaced around the ring, a few of them fallen, a couple more dislodged from their places by the press of roots and stems behind them. He could see the dense black mass of the rhododendrons, showing between and above the stones—but not one plant grew within the perimeter of the ring.

Feeling gooseflesh ripple over his body, he walked softly toward the center of the ring. It couldn't be—but it was. And why not, after all? If Geillis Duncan had been right . . . he turned and saw in the moonlight the scratchings on the cliff face.

He walked closer to look at them. There were several petroglyphs, some the size of his hand, others nearly as tall as he was; spiral shapes, and what might be a bent man, dancing—or dying. A nearly closed circle, that looked like a snake chasing its tail. Warning signs.

He shuddered again, and his hand went to the seam of his breeches. They were still there: the two gems he had risked his life to get, tiny passports to safety—he hoped—for him and for Brianna.

He could hear nothing; no humming, no buzzing. The autumn air was cold, a light wind stirring the rhododendron leaves. Damn, what was the date? He didn't know, had lost track long since. He thought it had been near the beginning of September, though, when he left Brianna in Wilmington. It had taken much longer than he'd thought, to track Bonnet and find an opportunity to steal the gems. It must be nearly the end of October now—the feast of Samhain, the Eve of All Hallows, was nearly come, or only recently past.

Would this ring follow the same dates, though? He supposed that it would; if the Earth's lines of force shifted with its revolution around the sun, then all the passages should stand open or closed with the shift.

He stepped closer to the cliff and saw it; an opening near the base of the cliff, a split in the rock, perhaps a cave. A chill ran over him that had nothing to do with the cold night wind. His fingers closed tightly over the small round hardness of the gems. He heard nothing; was it open? If so . . .

Escape. It would be that. Escape to when, though? And how? The words of Geilie's spell chanted in his mind. *Garnets rest in love about my neck; I will be faithful.*

Faithful. To try that avenue of escape was to abandon Brianna. *And hasn't she abandoned you?*

"No, I'm damned if she has!" he whispered to himself. There was some reason for what she'd done, he knew it.

She's found her parents; she'll be safe enough. "And for this reason, a woman shall leave her parents, and cleave to her husband." Safety wasn't what mattered; love was. If he'd cared for safety, he wouldn't have crossed that desperate void to begin with.

His hands were sweating; he could feel the damp grain of the rough cloth under his fingers, and his torn fingertips burned and throbbed. He took one more step toward the split in the cliff face, his eyes fixed on the pitch-black inside. If he didn't step inside . . . there were only two things to do. Go back to the suffocating grip of the rhododendrons, or try to scale the cliff before him.

He tilted his head back to gauge its height. A face was looking down at him, featureless in the dark, silhouetted against the moon-bright sky. He hadn't time to move or think before the rope noose settled gently over his head and tightened, pressing his arms against his body.

52

Desertion

River Run, December 1769

It had been raining, and soon would be again. Drops of water hung trembling under the petals of the marble Jacobite roses on Hector Cameron's tomb, and the brick walk was dark with wet.

Semper Fidelis, it said, beneath his name and dates. Semper Fi. She had dated a Marine cadet once; he'd had it carved on the ring he had tried to give her. Always faithful. And who had Hector Cameron been faithful to? His wife? His prince?

She hadn't spoken to Jamie Fraser since that night. Nor he to her. Not since the final moment, when in a fury of fear and outrage, she had screamed at him, "My father would never have said such a thing!"

She could still see what his face had looked like when she spoke her final words to him; she wished she could forget. He had turned without a word and left the cabin. Ian had risen, and quietly gone after him; neither of them had come back that night.

Her mother had stayed with her, comforting, petting, stroking her head and murmuring small soothing things as she alternately raged and sobbed. But even as her mother held Brianna's head in her lap and wiped her face with cool cloths, Bree could feel a part of her yearning toward that man, wanting to follow him, wanting to comfort *him.* And she blamed him for that as well.

Her head throbbed with the effort of staying stone-faced. She didn't dare relax the muscles of eyes and jaw until she was sure they had left; it would be too easy to break down.

She hadn't; not since that night. Once she had pulled herself together, she had assured her mother that she was all right, insisted that Claire go to bed. She had herself sat up till dawn, eyes burning from rage and woodsmoke, with the drawing of Roger on the table before her.

He had come back at dawn, called her mother to him, not

looking at Brianna. Murmured a bit in the dooryard, and sent her mother back, face hollow-eyed with worry, to pack her things.

He had brought her here, down the mountain to River Run. She had wanted to go with them, had wanted to go at once to find Roger, without a moment's delay. But he had been obdurate, and so had her mother.

It was late December, and the winter snows lay thick on the mountainside. She was nearly four months gone; the taut curve of her belly was tightly rounded now. There was no telling how long the journey might take, and she was reluctantly compelled to admit that she didn't want to give birth on a raw mountainside. She might have overridden her mother's opinion, but not when it was buttressed by *his* stubbornness.

She leaned her forehead against the cool marble of the mausoleum; it was a cold day, spitting rain, but her face felt hot and swollen, as though she were coming down with a fever.

She couldn't stop hearing him, seeing him. His face, congested with rage, sharp-edged as a devil's mask. His voice, rough with fury and contempt, reproaching her—reproaching *her*!—for the loss of his bloody honor!

"*Your* honor?" she had said incredulously. "Your *honor*? Your fucking notion of honor is what's caused all the trouble in the first place!"

"Ye willna use that sort of language to me! Though if it's fucking we're speaking of—"

"I'll fucking well say anything I want!" she bellowed, and slammed a fist on the table, rattling the dishes.

She had, too. So had he. Her mother had tried once or twice to stop them—Brianna flinched at the belated memory of the distress in Claire's deep golden eyes—but neither of them had paid a moment's notice, too intent on the savagery of their mutual betrayal.

Her mother had told her once that she had a Scottish temper—slow-fused, but long-burning. Now she knew where it came from, but the knowing didn't help.

She put her folded arms against the tomb and rested her face on them, breathing in the faint sheep-smell of the wool. It reminded her of the hand-knit sweaters her father—her *real* father, she thought, with a fresh burst of desolation—had liked to wear.

"Why did you have to die?" she whispered to the hollow of damp wool. "Oh, why?" If Frank Randall hadn't died, none of this would have happened. He and Claire would still be there, in the house in Boston, her family and her life would be intact.

But her father was gone, replaced by a violent stranger; a man who had her face, but could not understand her heart, a man who had taken both family and home from her, and not satisfied with that, had taken love and safety, too, leaving her bereft in this strange, harsh land.

She pulled the shawl closer around her shoulders, shivering at the wind that cut through the loose weave. She should have brought a cloak. She had kissed her white-lipped mother goodbye and then left, running through the dead garden, not looking at him. She'd wait here until she was sure they were gone, no matter if she froze.

She heard a step on the brick path above her and stiffened, though she didn't turn around. Perhaps it was a servant, or Jocasta come to persuade her inside.

But it was a stride too long and a footfall too strong for any but one man. She blinked hard, and gritted her teeth. She wouldn't turn around, she wouldn't.

"Brianna," he said quietly behind her. She didn't answer, didn't move.

He made a small snorting noise—anger, impatience?

"I have a thing to say to ye."

"Say it," she said, and the words hurt her throat, as though she'd swallowed some jagged object.

It was beginning to rain again; fresh spatters slicked the marble in front of her, and she could feel the icy *pat*! of drops that struck through her hair.

"I will bring him home to you," Jamie Fraser said, still quiet, "or I will not come back myself."

She couldn't bring herself to turn around. There was a small sound, a click on the pavement behind her, and then the sound of his footsteps, going away. Before her tear-blurred eyes, the drops on the marble roses gathered weight and began to fall.

When at last she turned around, the brick-lined walk was empty. At her feet was a folded paper, damp with rain, weighted with a stone. She picked it up, and held it crumpled in her hand, afraid to open it.

February 1770

In spite of worry and anger, she found herself easily absorbed into the flow of daily life at River Run. Her great-aunt, delighted at her company, encouraged her to find distraction; finding that she had some skill in drawing, Jocasta had brought out her own painting equipment, urging Brianna to make use of it.

By comparison with the cabin on the ridge, life at River Run was so luxurious as to be almost decadent. Still, Brianna woke at dawn, out of habit. She stretched languorously, wallowing in the physical delight of a feather bed that embraced and yielded to her every move—a definite contrast to lumpy quilts spread over a chilly straw tick.

There was a fire burning on the hearth, and a large copper can on the washstand, its burnished sides glowing. Hot water for washing; she could see the tiny shimmers of heat wavering over the metal. There was still a chill in the room, and the light outside was winter-blue with cold; the servant who had come and gone in silence must have risen in the black predawn and broken ice to get the water.

She ought to feel guilty at being waited on by slaves, she thought drowsily. She must remember to, later. There were a lot of things she didn't mean to think about until later; one more wouldn't hurt.

For now, she was warm. Far away, she could hear small noises in the house; a comforting scuffle of domesticity. The room itself was wrapped in silence, the occasional pop of kindling from the fire the only sound.

She rolled onto her back and, mind still half afloat in sleep, began to reacquaint herself with her body. This was a morning ritual; something she had begun to do half consciously as a teenager, and found necessary to do on purpose now—to find and make peace with the small changes of the night, lest she look suddenly during the day and find herself a stranger in her own body.

One stranger in her body was enough, she thought. She pushed the bedclothes down, running her hands slowly over the dormant swell of her stomach. A tiny ripple ran across her flesh as the inhabitant stretched, turning slowly as she had turned in the bed a few minutes before, enclosed and embraced.

"Hi, there," she said softly. The bulge flexed briefly against her hand and then fell still, the occupant returned to its mysterious dreams.

Slowly, she ruffled up the nightgown—it was Jocasta's, warm soft flannel—registering the smooth long muscle at the top of each thigh, the soft hollow curving in at the top. Then up and down and over, bare skin to bare skin, palms to legs and belly and breasts. Smooth and soft, round and hard; muscle and bone . . . but now not all *her* muscle and bone.

Her skin felt different in the morning, like a snake's skin, newly shed, all tender and light-lucent. Later, when she rose, when the air got at it, it would be harder, a duller but more serviceable envelope.

She lay back against the pillow, watching the light fill the room. The house was awake beyond her. She could hear the myriad faint noises of people at work, and felt soothed. When she was small, she would wake on summer mornings to hear the chatter of her father's lawnmower underneath her window; his voice calling out in greeting to a neighbor. She had felt safe, protected, knowing he was there.

More recently, she had waked at dawn and heard Jamie Fraser's voice, speaking in soft Gaelic to his horses outside, and had felt that same feeling return with a rush. No more, though.

It had been true, what her mother said. She was removed, changed, altered without consent or knowledge, learning only after the fact. She threw aside the quilts and got up. She couldn't lie in bed mourning what was lost; it was no longer anyone's job to protect her. The job of protector was hers, now.

The baby was a constant presence—and, oddly enough, a constant reassurance. For the first time she felt blessing in it, and an odd reconciliation; her body had known this long before her mind. So that was true, too—her mother had said it often—"Listen to your body."

She leaned against the window frame, looking out on the patchy snow that lay on the kitchen garden. A slave, muffled in cloak and scarf, was kneeling on the path, digging overwintered carrots from one of the beds. Tall elms bordered the walled garden; somewhere beyond those stark bare branches lay the mountains.

She stayed still, listening to the rhythms of her body. The intruder in her flesh stirred a little, the tides of its movement merging with the pulsing of her blood—their blood. In the beating of her heart, she thought she heard the echo of that other, smaller heart, and in the sound found at last the courage to think clearly, with the assurance that if the worst happened—she pressed hard against the window frame, and felt it creak under the force of her urgency—if the worst happened, still she would not be totally alone.

53

Blame

Jamie spoke barely a word to anyone, between our departure
from Fraser's Ridge, and our arrival at the Tuscaroran village
of Tennago. I rode in a state of misery, torn between guilt at
leaving Brianna, fear for Roger, and pain at Jamie's silence. He
was short with Ian, and had said no more than absolutely necessary to Jocasta at Cross Creek. To me, he said nothing.

Plainly, he blamed me for not telling him at once about Stephen
Bonnet. In retrospect, I blamed myself bitterly, seeing what had
come of it. He had kept the gold ring I had thrown at him; I had
no idea what he had done with it.

The weather was intermittently bad, the clouds hanging so low
to the mountains that on the higher ridges, we traveled for days on
end through a thick, cold fog, water droplets condensing on the
horses' coats, so that a constant rain dripped from their manes and
moisture shone on their flanks. We slept at night in whatever
shelter we could find, each rolled in a damp cocoon of blankets,
lying separately around a smoldering fire.

Some of the Indians who had known us at Anna Ooka made us
welcome when we reached Tennago. I saw several men eye the
casks of whisky as we unloaded our pack mules, but no one made
any move to molest them. There were two mule-loads of whisky;
a dozen small casks, all of the Fraser share of the year's distilling
—most of our income for the year. A king's ransom, in terms of
trade. Enough to ransom one young Scotsman, I hoped.

It was the best—and the only—thing we had to trade with, but
it was also a dangerous one. Jamie presented one cask to the
sachem of the village, and he and Ian disappeared into one of the
longhouses to confer. Ian had given Roger to some of his friends
among the Tuscarora, but did not know where they had taken him.
I hoped against hope that it was Tennago. If so, we could be back
at River Run within a month.

This was a faint hope, though. In the midst of the bitter quarrel with Brianna, Jamie had admitted telling Ian to make sure that Roger didn't come back again. Tennago was about ten days journey from the Ridge; much too close for the purposes of an enraged father.

I wanted to ask the women who entertained me about Roger, but no one in the house had any French or English, and I had only enough words of Tuscaroran to allow for basic politeness. Better to let Ian and Jamie handle the diplomatic negotiations. Jamie, with his gift for languages, was competent in Tuscaroran; Ian, who spent half his time hunting with the Indians, was thoroughly fluent.

One of the women offered me a platter containing steaming mounds of grain cooked with fish. I leaned to scoop up a bit with the flat piece of wood provided for the purpose, and felt the amulet swing forward under my shirt, its small weight both a reminder of grief and a comfort to it.

I had brought both Nayawenne's amulet, and the carved opal I had found under the red cedar tree. I had brought the former, intending to give it back—to whom, I had no idea. The latter might augment the whisky, if additional bargaining power was needed. For the same reason, Jamie had brought every small valuable he possessed—not many—with the exception of his father's ruby ring, which Brianna had brought to him from Scotland.

We had left the ruby with Brianna, just in case we did not return—the possibility had to be faced. There was no telling whether Geillis Duncan had been right or wrong in her theories regarding the use of gemstones, but at least Brianna would have one.

She had hugged me fiercely and kissed me when we left River Run. I hadn't wanted to go. Nor had I wanted to stay. I was torn between them once more; between the necessity to stay and look after Brianna, and the equally urgent necessity to go with Jamie.

"You have to go," Brianna had said firmly. "I'll be fine; you said yourself I'm healthy as a horse. You'll be back a long time before I need you."

She had glanced at her father's back; he stood in the stableyard, supervising the loading of the horses and mules. She turned back to me, expressionless.

"You have to go, Mama. I trust you to find Roger." There was an uncomfortable emphasis on the *you*, and I hoped very much that Jamie couldn't hear her.

"Surely you don't think Jamie would—"

"I don't know," she interrupted. "I don't know what he'd do." Her jaw was set in a way I recognized all too well. Argument was futile, but I tried anyway.

"Well, *I* know," I said firmly. "He'd do anything for you, Brianna. Anything. And even if it weren't you, he'd do everything he possibly could to get Roger back. His sense of honor—" Her face shut up like a trap, and I realized my mistake.

"His honor," she said flatly. "That's what matters. I guess it's all right, though; as long as it makes him get Roger back." She turned away, bending her head against the wind.

"Brianna!" I said, but she only hunched her shoulders, pulling the shawl tight around them.

"Auntie Claire? We're ready now." Ian had appeared nearby, glancing from me to Brianna, his face troubled. I looked from him to Brianna, hesitating, not wanting to leave her like this.

"Bree?" I said again.

Then she had turned back in a flurry of wool and embraced me, her cheek cold against mine.

"Come back!" she whispered. "Oh, Mama—come back safe!"

"I can't leave you, Bree, I can't!" I held her tight, all strong bone and tender flesh, the child I had left, the child I had regained —and the woman who now put my arms away from her and stood straight, alone.

"You have to go," she whispered. The mask of indifference had fallen and her cheeks were wet. She glanced over my shoulder at the archway to the stableyard. "Bring him back. You're the only one who can bring him back."

She kissed me quickly, turned and ran, the sound of her steps ringing on the brick path.

Jamie came through the stable arch and saw her, flying through the stormy light like a banshee. He stood still, looking after her, his face expressionless.

"You can't leave her like this," I said. I wiped my own wet cheeks with the corner of my shawl. "Jamie, go after her. Please, go and say goodbye, at least."

He stood still for a moment, and I thought he was going to pretend he hadn't heard me. But then he turned and walked slowly down the path. The first drops of rain were beginning to fall, splatting on the dusty brick, and the wind belled his cloak as he went.

"Auntie?" Ian's hand was under my arm, gently urging. I went with him, and let him give me a hand under my foot to mount. Within a few minutes Jamie was back. He had mounted, not looking at me, and, with a signal to Ian, ridden out of the stableyard without looking back. *I* had looked back, but there was no sign of Brianna.

Night had long since fallen, and Jamie was still in the longhouse with Nacognaweto and the *sachem* of the village. I looked up whenever anyone came into the house, but it was never him. At length, though, the hide flap over the doorway lifted, and Ian came in, a small, round figure behind him.

"I've a surprise for ye, Auntie," he said, beaming, and stepped aside to show me the smiling round face of the slavewoman Pollyanne.

Or rather, the ex-slave. For here, of course, she was free. She sat down beside me, grinning like a jack-o'-lantern, and turned back the deerskin mantle she wore to show me the little boy in the crook of her arm, his face as round and beaming as her own.

With Ian as interpreter, her own bits of English and Gaelic, and the odd bit of female sign language, we were soon deep in conversation. She had, as Myers surmised, been welcomed by the Tuscarorans and adopted into the tribe, where her skills at healing were valued. She had taken as husband a man who had been widowed in the measles epidemic, and had presented him with this new addition to the family a few months before.

I was delighted that she had found both freedom and happiness, and congratulated her warmly. I was reassured, too; if the Tuscarorans had treated her so kindly, perhaps Roger had not fared as badly as I feared.

A thought struck me, and I pulled Nayawenne's amulet from the neck of my buckskin shirt.

"Ian—will you ask if she knows who I should give this to?"

He spoke to her in Tuscaroran, and she leaned forward, fingering the amulet curiously as he spoke. At last she shook her head and sat back, replying in her curious deep voice.

"She says they will not want it, Auntie," Ian translated. "It is the medicine bundle of a *shaman,* and it is dangerous. It should have been buried with the person to whom it belonged; no one here will touch it, for fear of attracting the *shaman*'s ghost."

I hesitated, holding the leather pouch in my hand. The strange sense of holding something alive had not recurred since Nayawenne's death. Surely it was no more than imagination that seemed to stir against my palm.

"Ask her—what if the *shaman* wasn't buried? If the body couldn't be found?"

Pollyanne's round face was solemn, listening. She shook her head when Ian had finished and replied.

"She says that in that case the ghost walks with you, Auntie. She says you should not show it to anyone here—they will be frightened."

"She isn't frightened, is she?" Pollyanne caught that on her own; she shook her head, and touched her massive bosom.

"Indian now," she said simply. "Not always." She turned to Ian, and explained through him that her own people revered the spirits of the dead; in fact, it was not unusual for a man to keep by him the head or some other part of his grandfather or other ancestor, for protection or advice. No, the thought of a ghost walking with me did not trouble her.

Nor did the notion trouble me. In fact, I found the thought of Nayawenne walking with me to be rather a comfort, under the circumstances. I put the amulet back in my shirt. It brushed soft and warm against my skin, like the touch of a friend.

We talked for some time, until long after the others in the longhouse had gone to their separate cubicles, and the sound of snoring filled the smoky air. We were surprised, in fact, by Jamie's arrival, which let in a draft of cold air.

It was as Pollyanne made her farewells that she hesitated, trying to decide whether to tell me something. She glanced at Jamie, then shrugged her massive shoulders and made up her mind. She leaned close to Ian, murmured something that sounded like honey trickling over rocks, putting both hands to her face, fingertips against the skin. She then embraced me quickly and left.

Ian stared after her in astonishment.

"What did she say, Ian?"

He turned back to me, his sketchy brows drawn together in concern.

"She says I should tell Uncle Jamie, that the night the woman died in the sawmill, she saw a man."

"What man?"

He shook his head, still frowning.

"She didna ken him. Only that he was a white man, heavy and square, not so tall as Uncle or I. She saw him come out of the mill, and walk fast into the forest. She was sitting in the door to her hut, in the dark, so she thinks he didna see her—but he passed close enough to the fire that she saw his face. She says he was pockmarked''—here he put his fingertips against his face, as she had—"with a face like a pig."

"Murchison?" My heart skipped a beat.

"Did the man wear a uniform?" Jamie asked, frowning.

"No. But she was curious to know what he had been doing there; he wasna one of the plantation owners, nor yet a hand or an overseer. So she crept to the mill to see, but when she put her head inside, she knew something evil had happened. She said she smelt blood, and then she heard voices, so she didna go in."

So it had been murder, and Jamie and I had missed preventing it by a matter of moments. It was warm in the longhouse, but I felt cold at the memory of the thick, bloody air in the sawmill, and the hardness of a kitchen skewer in my hand.

Jamie's hand settled on my shoulder. Without thinking, I reached up and took it. It felt very good in mine, and I realized that we had not purposely touched each other in nearly a month.

"The dead lass was an army laundress," he said quietly. "Murchison has a wife in England; I suppose he might have found a pregnant mistress to be an encumbrance."

"No wonder he was making such a fuss of hunting for whoever was responsible—and then seizin' on yon poor woman who couldna even speak for herself." Ian's face was flushed with indignation. "If he could have got her hanged for it, he'd ha' thought himself safe, I daresay, the wicked wee scut."

"Perhaps I will pay a call on the Sergeant, when we return," Jamie said. "Privately."

The thought made my blood run cold. His voice was soft and even, and his face calm when I turned to look, but I seemed to see the surface of a dark Scottish pool reflected in his eyes, the water ruffled as though something heavy had just sunk below.

"Don't you think you've enough vengeance to keep you occupied for the moment?"

I spoke more sharply than I intended, and his hand slipped abruptly out of mine.

"I expect so," he said, both face and voice without expression. He turned to Ian.

"Wakefield—or MacKenzie, or whatever the man's name is—is a good way to the north. They sold him to the Mohawk; a small village below the river. Your friend Onakara has agreed to guide us; we'll leave at first light."

He rose and walked away, toward the far end of the house. Everyone else had already retired for the night. Five hearths burned, down the length of the house, each with its own smokehole, and the far wall was divided into cubicles, one for each couple or family, with a low, wide shelf for sleeping and space beneath for storage.

Jamie stopped at the cubicle assigned for our use, where I had left our cloaks and bundles. He slipped off his boots, unbelted the plaid he wore over breeches and shirt, and disappeared into the darkness of the sleeping space without a backward glance.

I scrambled to my feet, meaning to follow him, but Ian stopped me with a hand on my arm.

"Auntie," he said hesitantly. "Will ye not forgive him?"

"Forgive *him*?" I stared at him. "For what? For Roger?"

He grimaced.

"No. It was a grievous mistake, but we would do the same again, thinking matters as we did. No—for Bonnet."

"For Stephen Bonnet? How can he possibly think I blame him for that? I've never said such a thing to him!" And I had been too busy thinking that he blamed *me,* to even consider it.

Ian scratched a hand through his hair.

"Well . . . do ye not see, Auntie? He blames himself for it. He has, ever since the man robbed us on the river; and now wi' what he's done to my cousin . . ." He shrugged, looking mildly embarrassed. "He's fair eaten up with it, and knowing that you're angry wi' him—"

"But I'm not angry with him! I thought he was angry with me, because I didn't tell him Bonnet's name right away."

"Och." Ian looked as though he didn't know whether to laugh or look distressed. "Well, I daresay it would ha' saved us a bit of trouble if ye had, but no, I'm sure it's not that, Auntie. After all, by the time Cousin Brianna told ye, we'd already met yon Mac-Kenzie on the mountainside and done him a bit of no good."

I took in a deep breath and blew it out again.

"But you think he thinks I'm angry at him?"

"Oh, anyone could see ye are, Auntie," he assured me earnestly. "Ye dinna look at him or speak to him save for what ye must—and," he said, clearing his throat delicately, "I havena seen ye go to his bed, anytime this month past."

"Well, he hasn't come to mine, either!" I said hotly, before reflecting that this was scarcely a suitable conversation to be having with a seventeen-year-old boy.

Ian hunched his shoulders and gave me an owlish look.

"Well, he's his pride, hasn't he?"

"God knows he has," I said, rubbing a hand over my face. "I —look, Ian, thank you for saying something to me."

He gave me one of the rare sweet smiles that transformed his long, homely face.

"Well, I do hate to see him suffer. I'm fond of Uncle Jamie, aye?"

"So am I," I said, and swallowed the small lump in my throat. "Good night, Ian."

I walked softly down the length of the house, past cubicles in which whole families slept together, the sound of their mingled breathing a peaceful descant to the anxious beating of my heart. It was raining outside; water dripped from the smokeholes, sizzling in the embers.

Why had I not seen what Ian had? That was easy to answer; it wasn't anger, but my own sense of guilt that had blinded me. I had kept back my knowledge of Bonnet's involvement as much because of the gold wedding ring as because Brianna had asked me to; I could have persuaded her to tell Jamie, had I tried.

She was right; he would undoubtedly go after Stephen Bonnet sooner or later. I had somewhat more confidence in Jamie's success than she did, though. No, it had been the ring that had made me keep silence.

And why should I feel guilty over that? There was no sensible answer; it had been instinct, not conscious thought, to hide the ring. I had not wanted to show it to Jamie, to put it back on my finger in front of him. And yet I had wanted—needed—to keep it.

My heart squeezed small, thinking of the past few weeks, of Jamie, going grimly about the necessities of reparation in loneliness and guilt. That was why I had come with him, after all—because I was afraid that if he went alone, he might not come back. Spurred by guilt and courage, he might go to reckless lengths; with me to consider, I knew he would be careful. And all the time he had thought himself not only alone but bitterly reproached by the one person who could—and should—have offered him comfort.

"Eaten up with it" indeed.

I paused by the cubicle. The shelf was some eight feet wide, and he lay well back; I could see little more of him than a humped shape under a blanket made of rabbit skins. He lay very still, but I knew he wasn't asleep.

I climbed onto the platform, and once safe within the shadows of the cubicle, slipped out of my clothes. It was fairly warm in the longhouse, but my bare skin prickled and my nipples tightened. My eyes had grown accustomed to the dimness; I could see that he lay on his side facing me. I caught the shine of his eyes in the dark, open and watching me.

I knelt down and slid under the blanket, the fur soft against my skin. Without stopping to think too much, I rolled to face him, pressing my nakedness against him, face buried in his shoulder.

"Jamie," I whispered to him. "I'm cold. Come and warm me. Please?"

He turned to me, wordless, with a quiet ferocity that I might have thought the hunger of desire long stifled—but knew now for simple desperation. I sought no pleasure for myself; I wanted only to give him comfort. But opening to him, urging him, some deep wellspring opened too, and I cleaved to him in a sudden need as blind and desperate as his own.

We clung tight together, shuddering, heads buried in each other's hair, unable to look at each other, unable to let go. Slowly, as the spasms died away, I became aware of things outside our own small mortal coil, and realized that we lay in the midst of strangers, naked and helpless, shielded only by darkness.

And yet we were alone, completely. We had the privacy of Babel; there was a conversation going on at the far end of the longhouse, but its words held no meaning. It might as well have been the hum of bees.

Smoke from the banked fire wavered up outside the sanctuary of our bed, fragrant and insubstantial as incense. It was dark as a confessional inside the cubicle; I could see no more of Jamie than the faint curve of light that rimmed his shoulder, a transient gleam in the locks of his hair.

"Jamie, I'm sorry," I said softly. "It wasn't your fault."

"Who else?" he said, with some bleakness.

"Everyone. No one. Stephen Bonnet, himself. But not you."

"Bonnet?" His voice was blank with surprise. "What has he to do with it?"

"Well . . . everything," I said, taken aback. "Er . . . doesn't he?"

He rolled halfway off me, brushing hair out of his face.

"Stephen Bonnet is a wicked creature," he said precisely, "and I shall kill him at the first opportunity I have. But I dinna see how I can blame him for my own failings as a man."

"What on earth are you talking about? What failings?"

He didn't answer right away, but bent his head, a humped shadow in the dark. His legs were still entangled with mine; I could feel the tension of his body, knotted in his joints, rigid in the hollows of his thighs.

"I hadna thought ever to be so jealous of a dead man," he whispered at last. "I shouldna have thought it possible."

"Of a dead man?" My own voice rose slightly, with astonishment, as it finally dawned on me. "Of *Frank*?"

He lay still, half on top of me. His hand touched the bones of my face, hesitant.

"Who else? I have been worm-eaten wi' it, all these days of riding. I see his face in my mind, waking and sleeping. Ye did say he looked like Jack Randall, no?"

I gathered him tight against myself, pressing his head down so that his ear was near my mouth. Thank God I hadn't mentioned the ring to him—but had my face, my traitorous, transparent face, somehow given away that I thought of it?

"How?" I whispered to him, squeezing hard. "How could you think of such a thing?"

He broke loose, rising on one elbow, his hair falling down over my face in a mass of flaming shadows, the firelight sparking gold and crimson through it.

"How could I not?" he demanded. "Ye heard her, Claire; ye ken well what she said to me!"

"Brianna?"

"She said she would gladly see me in hell, and sell her own soul to have her father back—her real father." He swallowed; I heard the sound of it, above the murmur of distant voices.

"I keep thinking he would not have made such a mistake. He would have trusted her; he would have known that she . . . I keep thinking that Frank Randall was a better man than I am. She thinks so." His hand faltered, then settled on my shoulder, squeezing tight. "I thought . . . perhaps ye felt the same, Sassenach."

"Fool," I whispered, and didn't mean him. I ran my hands down the long slope of his back, digging my fingers into the firmness of his buttocks. "Wee idiot. Come here."

He dropped his head, and made a small sound against my shoulder that might have been a laugh.

"Aye, I am. Ye dinna mind it so much, though?"

"No." His hair smelt of smoke and pinesap. There were still bits of needles caught in it; one pricked smooth and sharp against my lips.

"She didn't mean it," I said.

"Aye, she did," he said, and I felt him swallow the thickness in his throat. "I heard her."

"I heard you both." I rubbed slowly between his shoulder blades, feeling the faint traces of the old scars, the thicker, more recent welts left by the bear's claws. "She's just like you; she'll say things in a temper she'd never say in cold blood. You didn't mean all the things you said to her, did you?"

"No." I could feel the tightness in him lessening, the joints of his body loosening, yielding reluctantly to the persuasion of my fingers. "No, I didna mean it. Not all of it."

"Neither did she."

I waited a moment, stroking him as I had stroked Brianna, when she was small, and afraid.

"You can believe me," I whispered. "I love you both."

He sighed, deeply, and was quiet for a moment.

"If I can find the man and bring him back to her. If I do—d'ye think she'll forgive me one day?"

"Yes," I said. "I know it."

On the other side of the partition, I heard the small sounds of love-making begin; the shift and sigh, the murmured words that have no language.

"You have to go." Brianna had said to me. *"You're the only one who can bring him back."*

It occurred to me for the first time that perhaps she hadn't been speaking of Roger.

It was a long trek through the mountains, made longer by the winter weather. There were days when it was impossible to travel;

when we crouched all day under rocky overhangs or in the shelter of a grove of trees, huddled against the wind.

Once we were through the mountains, the traveling was somewhat easier, though the temperatures grew colder as we headed north. Some nights we ate cold food, unable to keep a fire alight in snow and wind. But each night I lay with Jamie, closely huddled together within a single cocoon of furs and blankets, sharing our warmth.

I kept close count of the days, marking them by means of a length of knotted twine. We had left River Run in early January; it was mid-February before Onakara pointed out to us the smoke rising in the distance that marked the Mohawk village where he and his companions had taken Roger Wakefield. "Snake-town," he said it was called.

Six weeks, and Brianna would be nearly six months gone. If we could get Roger back quickly—and if he was capable of travel, I added grimly to myself—we should be back well before the child was due. If Roger wasn't here, though—if the Mohawk had sold him elsewhere . . . or if he was dead—said a small cold voice inside my head, we would return without delay.

Onakara declined to accompany us into the village, which did absolutely nothing to increase my confidence in our prospects. Jamie thanked him and saw him off, with one of the horses, a good knife, and a flask of whisky in payment for his services.

We buried the rest of the whisky, hiding it carefully some distance outside the village.

"Will they understand what we want?" I asked, as we remounted. "Is Tuscaroran close enough to Mohawk for us to talk to them?"

"It's no quite the same, Auntie, but close," Ian said. It was snowing lightly, and the flakes clung melting to his eyelashes. "Like the differences between Italian and Spanish, maybe. But Onakara says that the *sachem* and a few others have a bit of English, though they mostly dinna choose to use it. But the Mohawk fought with the English against the French; there will be some who ken it."

"Well, then." Jamie smiled at us and laid his musket across the saddle in front of him. "Let's go and try our luck."

54

Captivity I

H e had been in the Mohawk village nearly three months, by the reckoning of his knotted string. At first he had not known who they were; only that they were a different kind of Indian than his captors—and that his captors were afraid of them.

He had stood numb with exhaustion while the men who had brought him talked and pointed. The new Indians were different; they were dressed for the cold, in fur and leather, and many of the men's faces were tattooed.

One of them prodded him with the point of a knife, and made him undress. He was forced to stand naked in the middle of a long wooden house while several men—and women—poked and jeered at him. His right foot was badly swollen; the deep cut had become infected. He could still walk, but each step sent jabs of pain through his leg, and he burned intermittently with fever.

They shoved him, pushing him to the door of the house. There was a lot of noise outside. He recognized the gauntlet; a double row of shouting savages, all armed with sticks and clubs. Someone behind poked him in the buttock with the point of a knife, and he felt a warm trickle of blood run down his leg. *"Cours!"* they said. Run.

The ground was trampled, snow packed into grimy ice. It burned his feet as a shove in his back sent him staggering into pandemonium.

He stayed upright most of the way, lurching one way, then another, as the clubs struck him to and fro and sticks lashed at his legs and back. There was no way to avoid the blows. All he could do was keep going, as fast as possible.

Close to the end, a club swung straight and took him hard across the belly; he doubled over and another swatted him behind the ear. He rolled bonelessly into the snow, barely feeling the cold on his broken skin.

A switch stung his legs, then lashed him hard just under the balls. He jerked his legs up in reflex, rolled again, and found himself on hands and knees, still somehow going, the blood from his nose and mouth mixing with the frozen mud.

He reached the end, and with the last blows still stinging on his back, grasped the poles of a longhouse and pulled himself slowly to his feet. He turned to face them, holding on to the poles to keep from falling. They liked that; they were laughing, with high-pitched yips that made them sound like a pack of dogs. He bowed low, and straightened up, head whirling. They laughed harder. He'd always known how to please a crowd.

They took him inside then, gave him water to wash with, some food. They gave him back his ragged shirt and filthy breeches, but not his coat or shoes. It was warm in the house; there were several fires burning at intervals down the length of the long structure, each with its own open smokehole above. He crawled into a corner and fell asleep, his hand on the lumpy seam of his breeches.

After this reception, the Mohawk treated him with general indifference but no great cruelty. He was the slave of the longhouse, at the use of anyone who lived there. If he did not understand an order, they would show him—once. If he refused or pretended not to understand, they beat him, and he refused no more. Still, he shared equally in their food and was given a decent place to sleep, at the end of the house.

As it was winter, the main work was in gathering wood and fetching water, though now and then a hunting party would take him along to help in butchering and carrying meat. The Indians made no great effort to communicate with him, but by careful listening he acquired a little of the language.

He began, with great caution, to try a few words. He chose a young girl to begin with, feeling her less dangerous. She stared at him, then laughed, delighted as if she had heard a crow talk. She called a friend to come and hear, and another, and the three of them crouched in front of him, laughing softly behind their hands and looking sideways at him from the corners of their eyes. He said all the words he knew, pointing at the objects—fire, pot, blanket, corn—then pointed at a string of dried fish overhead and raised his eyebrows.

"Yona'kensyonk," said his new friend promptly, and giggled when he repeated it. Over the next days and weeks, the girls

taught him a great deal; it was from them that he finally learned where he was. Or not where, precisely, but in whose hands.

They were *Kahnyen'kehaka,* they told him proudly, with looks of surprise that he did not know that. Mohawk. Keepers of the Eastern Gate of the Iroquois League. He, on the other hand, was *Kakonhoaerhas*. It took a certain amount of discussion to determine the exact meaning of this term; he finally discovered, when one of the girls dragged in a mongrel in illustration, that it meant "dogface."

"Thanks," he said, fingering the thick growth of his beard. He bared his teeth at them and growled, and they shrieked with laughter.

One of the girls' mothers became interested; seeing that his foot was still swollen, she brought ointment and bathed it, bandaging it for him with lichen and corn husks. The women began to speak to him when he brought them wood or water.

He made no attempt at escape; not yet. Winter kept its grip on the village, with frequent snows and bitter wind. He wouldn't get far, unarmed, lame, and with no protection from the weather. He bided his time. And he dreamed at night of lost worlds, waking often in the dawn to the smell of fresh grass, with the ache of his need spilled warm on his belly.

The edges of the river were still frozen when the Jesuit came.

Roger had the run of the village; he was outside when the dogs began to bark and yelps from the sentries signaled the arrival of visitors. People began to gather, and he went with them, curious.

The new arrivals were a large group of Mohawk, men and women both, all on foot, burdened with the usual bundles of traveling gear. That seemed odd; such visitors as had come to the village before were small hunting parties. What was odder was that the visitors had with them a white man—the pale winter sun gleamed on the man's fair hair.

Roger moved closer, eager to see, but was shoved back by some of the villagers. Not before seeing that the man was a priest, though; the tattered remnants of a long black robe showed beneath a bearskin cape, over leather leggings and moccasins.

The priest didn't act like a prisoner, nor was he bound. And yet Roger had the feeling that he traveled under compulsion; there were lines of strain in an otherwise young face. The priest and several of his companions disappeared into the longhouse where the *sachem* held council; Roger had never been inside, but had heard the women talk.

One of the older women from his own longhouse saw him loitering in the crowd, and ordered him sharply to fetch more wood. He went, and didn't see the priest again, though the faces of the new arrivals showed in the village, scattered among the longhouses to share the hospitality of their hearths.

Something was happening in the village; he could feel the currents of it eddying around him but did not understand them. The men sat later by the fires in the evenings, talking, and the women murmured to each other as they worked, but the discussion was far beyond the grasp of Roger's rudimentary comprehension. He asked one of the little girls about the new visitors; she could tell him only that they came from a village to the north—why they had come, she did not know, save it had to do with the Black Robe, the *Kahontsi'yatawi.*

It was more than a week later that Roger went out with a hunting party. The weather was cold but clear, and they traveled far, eventually finding and killing a moose. Roger was stunned, not only by the size of the thing but by its stupidity. He could understand the attitude of the hunters: There was no honor in killing such a thing; it was only meat.

It was a *lot* of meat. He was burdened like a pack mule, and the extra weight bore hard on his lame foot; by the time they returned to the village, he was limping so badly that he couldn't keep up with the hunting party, but lagged far behind, desperately trying to keep them in view lest he be lost in the forest.

To his surprise, several men were waiting for him when he finally limped into view of the village palisades. They grabbed him, relieved him of the burden of meat, and hustled him into the village. They didn't take him to his own longhouse, but to a small hut that stood at the far end of the central clearing.

He hadn't enough Mohawk to ask questions, and didn't think they would be answered in any case. They shoved him inside the hut, and left him.

There was a small fire burning, but the interior was so dark after the brightness of the day outside that he was momentarily blinded.

"Who are you?" said a startled voice in French.

Roger blinked several times, and made out a slight figure rising from its seat beside the fire. The priest.

"Roger MacKenzie," he said. *"Et vous?"* He experienced a

sudden and unexpected flood of happiness at the simple speaking of his name. The Indians didn't care what his name was; they called him dogface when they wanted him.

"Alexandre." The priest came forward, looking both pleased and incredulous. "Père Alexandre Ferigault. *Vous êtes anglais?*"

"Scots," said Roger, and sat down suddenly, his lame leg giving way.

"A Scotsman? How do you come here? You are a soldier?"

"A prisoner."

The priest squatted by him, looking him over curiously. He *was* fairly young—in his late twenties or early thirties, though his fair skin was chapped and weathered by the cold.

"You will eat with me?" He gestured to a small collection of clay pots and baskets that held food and water.

Speaking in his own language seemed to be as much a relief for the priest as speaking freely was for Roger. By the time the meal was concluded, they had gleaned a cautious knowledge of each other's basic past—if no explanation as yet for their present situation.

"Why have they put me here with you?" Roger asked, wiping grease from his mouth. He didn't think it was to provide the priest with company. Thoughtfulness was not an outstanding Mohawk characteristic, so far as he'd noticed.

"I cannot say. I was in fact astonished to see another white man."

Roger glanced at the door of the hut. It moved slightly; there was someone outside.

"Are you a prisoner?" he asked, in some surprise. The priest hesitated, then shrugged, with a small smile.

"I cannot say that, either. With the Mohawk, one is *Kahnyen'kehaka* or one is—other. And if one is other, the line between guest and prisoner can alter in a moment. Leave it that I have lived among them for several years—but I have not been adopted into the tribe. I am still 'other.' " He coughed and changed the subject. "How did you come to be taken captive?"

Roger hesitated, not really knowing how to answer.

"I was betrayed," he said at last. "Sold."

The priest nodded sympathetically.

"Is there anyone who might ransom you? They will take care to keep you alive if they have some hope of ransom."

Roger shook his head, feeling hollow as a drum.

"There's no one."

Conversation ceased as the light from the smokehole dimmed into dusk, leaving them in darkness below. There was a firepit, but no wood; the fire died out. The hut seemed to have been abandoned; there was a bed frame built of poles, but nothing else in the hut save a couple of tattered deerskins and a small heap of domestic debris in one corner.

"Have you been here—in this hut—long?" Roger asked at last, breaking the silence. He could barely see the other man, though the last remnants of twilight were visible through the smokehole.

"No. They brought me here today—shortly before you came." The priest coughed, shifting uneasily on the packed dirt floor.

That seemed sinister, but Roger thought it more tactful—and less frightening—not to mention it. It was no doubt as obvious to the priest as to himself that the line between "guest" and "prisoner" had been crossed. What had the man done?

"You are a Christian?" Alexandre broke the silence abruptly.

"Yes. My father was a minister."

"Ah. May I ask—if they take me away, will you pray for me?"

Roger felt a sudden chill that had nothing to do with the cheerless surroundings.

"Yes," he said awkwardly. "Of course. If you like."

The priest rose and began to walk restlessly about the confines of the hut, unable to keep still.

"It may be all right," he said, but it was the voice of a man trying to convince himself. "They are still deciding."

"Deciding what?"

He felt rather than saw the priest's shrug.

"Whether I live."

There seemed no good response to that, and they fell once more into silence. Roger sat huddled by the cold firepit, resting his lame foot, while the priest paced to and fro, finally settling beside him. Without comment, the two moved close together, pooling their warmth; it was going to be a cold night.

Roger had dozed off, one of the deerskins pulled over him, when there was a sudden noise at the door. He sat up, blinking, to a blaze of fire.

There were four Mohawk warriors in the hut; one dumped a load of wood into the firepit and thrust the brand he held into the pile. Ignoring Roger, the others pulled Père Ferigault to his feet and roughly stripped him of his clothes.

Roger moved instinctively, half rising, and was knocked flat. The priest gave him a quick, open-eyed look that begged him not to interfere.

One of the warriors held his own brand close to Père Ferigault's face. He said something that sounded like a question, then, receiving no answer, passed his brand downward, so close to the priest's body that the white skin glowed red.

Sweat stood out on Alexandre's face as the fire hovered near his genitals, but his face remained carefully blank. The warrior with the brand poked it suddenly at the priest, who could not keep from flinching. The Indians laughed, and did it again. This time he was prepared; Roger smelled singed hair, but the priest didn't move.

Tiring of this sport, two of the warriors seized the priest by the arms, and dragged him out of the hut.

If they take me away—pray for me. Roger sat up slowly, the hairs on his body prickling with dread. He could hear the voices of the Indians, talking among themselves, receding in the distance; no sound from the priest.

Alexandre's discarded clothes were flung around the hut; Roger picked them up, carefully beating the dust from them and folding them. His hands were shaking.

He tried to pray, but found it hard to focus his mind upon devotion. Over and around the words of his prayer, he could hear a small, cold voice, saying, *And when they come to take me away —who will pray for me?*

They had left him a fire; he tried to believe that meant that they did not mean to kill him right away. The granting of comforts to a condemned prisoner was not the Mohawk way, either. After a time he lay down under the deerskins, curled on his side, and watched the flames until he fell asleep, worn out by terror.

He was roused from uneasy sleep by the shuffle of feet and many voices. He sprang awake, rolled away from the fire and crouched, looking frantically for some means of defense.

The door flap lifted, and the naked body of the priest fell into the hut. The noises outside moved away.

Alexandre stirred and moaned. Roger came quickly and knelt by him. He could smell fresh blood, a hot-copper smell he recognized from the slaughtering of the moose.

"Are you hurt? What have they done?"

The answer to that was quick in coming. He turned the half-conscious priest over, to see blood streaming over face and neck in a shiny red glaze. He snatched the priest's discarded robe to stanch the wound, pushed back the matted blond hair, and found that the priest's right ear was missing. Something sharp had taken a patch of skin some three inches square from just behind the jaw, removing both ear and a section of scalp.

Roger clenched his stomach muscles and pressed the cloth tight against the raw wound. Holding it in place, he dragged the limp body to the fire, and piled the remnants of clothes and both deer-skins on top of Père Ferigault.

The man was moaning now. Roger washed his face, made him drink a little water.

"It's all right," he muttered, over and over, though he was uncertain whether the other could hear him. "It's all right, they didn't kill you." He couldn't help wondering whether it might have been better if they had; did they mean this only as a warning to the priest, or was it only the preliminary to greater tortures?

The fire had burned itself to coals; in the reddish light, the seeping blood was black.

Father Alexandre moved constantly in small jerks, the restless-ness of his body at once caused and constrained by the pain of his wound. He could not by any means settle to sleep, and conse-quently neither could Roger, nearly as aware as the priest of each interminably passing minute.

Roger cursed himself for helplessness; he would have given anything to assuage the other man's pain, even for a moment. It wasn't merely sympathy, and he knew it; Father Alexandre's small, breathless sounds kept the knowledge of the mutilation fresh in Roger's mind, and terror alive in his blood. If the priest could only sleep, the sounds would stop—and perhaps in the darkness, the horror would recede a bit.

For the first time, he thought he understood what it was that made Claire Randall tick; made her walk onto battlefields, to lay her hands on wounded men. To ease pain and death in another was to soothe the fear of it in oneself—and to soothe his own fear, he would do almost anything.

At last, unable to bear the whispered prayers and stifled whim-pering any longer, he lay down beside the priest, and took Alexan-dre in his arms.

"Hush," he said, his lips close to Père Alexandre's head. He hoped he had the side with the ear. "Be still now. *Reposez-vous.*"

The priest's lean body quivered against his own, the muscles knotted with cold and agony. Roger rubbed the man's back briskly, chafed his palms over the chilled limbs, and pulled both tattered deerskins over them.

"You'll be all right." Roger spoke in English, aware that it didn't matter what he said, only that he said something. "Here now, it's all right. Yes, go on, then." He talked as much to distract himself as the other man; the feel of Alexandre's naked body was vaguely shocking—as much because it didn't feel unnatural as because it did.

The priest clung to him, head pressed into his shoulder. He said nothing, but Roger could feel the wetness of tears against his skin. He made himself hug the priest tightly, rubbing up and down the spine with its small lumps of knobby bone, forcing himself to think only of stopping the terrible shaking.

"You could be a dog," Roger said. "A mistreated stray of some kind. I'd do it if you were a dog, of course I would. No, I wouldn't," he muttered to himself. "Call the ruddy RSPCA, I expect."

He patted Alexandre's head, careful where his fingers went, cold with gooseflesh at the thought of touching that raw, bloody patch by inadvertence. The hair at the priest's nape was lank with sweat, though the flesh of his neck and shoulders was like ice. His lower body was warmer, but not by much.

"Nobody'd treat a dog like this," he muttered. "Fucking savages. Set the police onto them. Put their bloody pictures in the *Times*. Complain to my MP."

A small ripple of something too frightened to be called laughter went through him. He gripped the priest fiercely, and rocked him to and fro in darkness.

"Reposez-vous, mon ami. C'est bien, là, c'est bien."

55

Captivity II

River Run, March 1770

Brianna rolled the wet brush along the edge of the palette, squeezing out the excess turps to form a good point. She touched the point briefly to the viridian–cobalt mix and added a fine line of shadow to the river's edge.

There were footsteps on the path behind her, coming from the house. She recognized the arrhythmic double step; it was the Deadly Duo. She tensed slightly, fighting the urge to snatch the wet canvas and put it out of sight behind Hector Cameron's mausoleum. She didn't mind Jocasta, who often came to sit with her while she painted in the mornings, to discuss techniques of painting, grinding pigments, and the like. In fact, she welcomed her great-aunt's company and treasured the older woman's stories of her girlhood in Scotland, of Brianna's grandmother, and of the other MacKenzies of Leoch. But when Jocasta brought her faithful Seeing-eye Dog along, it was a different matter.

"Good morning, Niece! Is it not too cold for you the morn?"

Jocasta halted, her own cloak drawn around her, and smiled at Brianna. If she hadn't known better, she wouldn't have realized her aunt's blindness.

"No, it's fine here; the . . . er . . . tomb blocks the wind. I'm finished for now, though." She wasn't, but stabbed her brush into the turpentine jar and began to scrape the palette. Damned if she'd paint with Ulysses describing her every brushstroke out loud.

"Ah? Well, leave your things, then; Ulysses will take them up for you."

Reluctantly abandoning her easel, Brianna picked up her private sketchbook and tucked it under one arm, giving her other to Jocasta. She wasn't leaving *that* for Mr. Sees-all, Tells-all to flip through.

"We have company today," Jocasta said, turning back toward

the house. "Judge Alderdyce, from Cross Creek, and his mother. I thought perhaps ye'd wish time to change, before luncheon." Brianna bit the inside of her cheek, to prevent any rejoinder to this less than subtle hint. More visitors.

Under the circumstances, she could scarcely refuse to meet her aunt's guests—or even to change clothes for them—but she could have wished that Jocasta were a good deal less sociable. There was a constant stream of visitors; for luncheon, for tea, for supper, overnight, for breakfast, come to buy horses, sell cows, trade lumber, borrow books, bring gifts, play music. They came from neighboring plantations, from Cross Creek, and from as far away as Edenton and New Bern.

The array of Jocasta's acquaintance was staggering. Still, Brianna had noticed an increasing tendency of late for the callers to be men. Single men.

Phaedre verified Brianna's suspicions, voiced as the maid dug in the wardrobe for a fresh morning gown.

"There ain't a lot of single women in the colony," Phaedre observed, when Brianna mentioned the peculiar coincidence that most of the recent visitors appeared to be bachelors. Phaedre cast an eye at Brianna's midsection, which was bulging noticeably under the loose muslin shift. " 'Specially not young ones. To say nothing of women who's got River Run a-coming to them."

"Who's got *what*?" Brianna said. She stopped, hair half pinned, and stared at the maid.

Phaedre laid one graceful hand across her mouth, eyes wide above it.

"Your auntie ain't told you yet? Thought sure you knew, or I'd not've said."

"Well, now you've said that much, go on saying. What do you mean?" Phaedre, a born gossip, took little coaxing.

"Your daddy and them hadn't been gone but a week, before Miss Jo sent for Lawyer Forbes and had her will changed. When Miss Jo dies, they's some little bits of money goes to your daddy, and some personal things to Mr. Farquard and some of her other friends—but everything else, that's yours. The plantation, the timber, the sawmill . . ."

"But I don't want it!"

Phaedre's elegantly lifted eyebrow expressed profound doubt, then dropped, dismissing it.

"Well, it ain't what you want, I reckon. Miss Jo is kind of inclined to get what *she* wants."

Brianna laid the hairbrush down, slowly.

"And just what *does* she want?" she asked. "Do you happen to know that, too?"

"Ain't any big secret. She wants River Run to last longer than she does—and to belong to somebody from her blood. Seems sense to me; she got no children, no grandchildren. Who else is there to carry on after her?"

"Well . . . there's my father."

Phaedre laid the fresh dress across the bed and frowned at it appraisingly, glancing back at Brianna's middle.

"This one going to last no more than another couple weeks, the way that belly's growing. Oh, yes, there's your daddy. She done tried to make him her heir, but the way I hears it, he wasn't havin' none of it." She pursed her lips in amusement.

"Now there's a stubborn man for you. Go off into the mountains and live like a red man, just to keep from doing what Miss Jo want him to do. But Mr. Ulysses reckons your daddy had the right of it, at that. Be him and Miss Jo buttin' heads day and night, if he'd a-stayed."

Brianna slowly twisted up the other side of her hair, but the hairpin slipped out again, letting it fall.

"Here, you be lettin' me do that, Miss Bree." Phaedre slid behind her, pulled out the slipshod pinning, and began deftly to braid the sides of her hair.

"And all these visitors—these men—"

"Miss Jo out to pick you a good one," Phaedre assured her. "You can't run the place alone, no more than Miss Jo can. That Mr. Duncan, he's a godsend; don't know what she'd do without him."

Sheer astonishment was giving way to outrage.

"She's trying to pick a husband for me? She's showing me off like—like some prize heifer?"

"Uh-huh." Phaedre appeared to see nothing wrong with this. She frowned, drawing a straying lock skillfully into the main braid.

"But she knows about Roger—about Mr. Wakefield! How can she be trying to marry me off to—"

Phaedre sighed, not without sympathy.

"I don't reckon she thinks they're going to find the man, tell you true. Miss Jo, she knows a bit about the Indians; we've all heard Mr. Myers tell about the Iroquois."

It was chilly in the room, but prickles of sweat broke out along Brianna's hairline and jaw.

"Besides," Phaedre went on, weaving a blue silk ribbon into the braid, "Miss Jo don't know this Wakefield. Might be he'd not be a good manager. Better—she thinks—to get you married to a man she knows will take good care of her place; add it to his own, maybe, make a truly grand place for you."

"I don't *want* a grand place! I don't want *this* place!" Outrage in turn was giving way to panic.

Phaedre tied the end of the ribbon with a small flourish.

"Well, like I say—it ain't so much what you want. It's what Miss Jo wants. Now, let's try this dress."

There was a sound in the hallway, and Brianna hastily flipped the page of her sketchbook over, to a half-finished charcoal drawing of the river and its trees. The steps went by, though, and she relaxed, turning back the page.

She wasn't working; the drawing was complete. She only wanted to look at it.

She'd drawn him in three-quarter profile, head turned to listen as he tuned his guitar strings. It was no more than a sketch, but it caught the line of head and body with a rightness that memory confirmed. She could look at this and conjure him, bring him close enough almost to touch.

There were others; some botched messes, some that came close. A few that were good drawings in themselves, but that failed to capture the man behind the lines. One or two, like this one, that she could use to comfort herself in the late gray afternoons, when the light began to fail and the fires burned low.

The light was fading over the river now, the water dimming from bright silver to the gentler glow of pewter.

There were others; sketches of Jamie Fraser, of her mother, of Ian. She had begun to draw them out of loneliness, and looked at them now with fear, hoping against hope that these fragments of paper were not the only remnants of the family she had known so briefly.

Tell you true, I don't reckon Miss Jo thinks they going to find the man . . . Miss Jo knows about Indians.

Her hands were damp; the charcoal smeared at the corner of a page. A soft step sounded just outside the parlor door, and she closed her book at once.

Ulysses came in, a lighted taper in his hand, and began to light the branches of the great candelabrum.

"You don't need to light all those for me." Brianna spoke as much from a desire not to disturb the quiet melancholy of the room as from modesty. "I don't mind the dark."

The butler smiled gently and went on with his work. He touched each wick precisely, and the tiny flames sprang up at once, jinni called up by a magician's wand.

"Miss Jo will be down soon," he said. "She can see the lights —and the fire—so she knows where she is in the room."

He finished and blew out the taper, then moved about the room in his usual soft-footed way, tidying the small disorder left by the afternoon guests, adding wood to the fire, puffing it into crackling life with the bellows.

.She watched him; the small, precise movements of the well-kept hands, his complete absorption in the correct placement of the whisky decanter and its glasses. How many times had he straightened this room? Put back each piece of furniture, each tiny ornament precisely in its place, so that its mistress's hand would fall upon it without groping?

A whole life devoted to the needs of someone else. Ulysses could read and write both French and English; could reckon numbers, could sing and play the harpsichord. All that skill and learning—used only for the entertainment of an autocratic old lady.

To say to one, "Come," and he cometh, to say to another "Go," and he goeth. Yes, that was Jocasta's way.

And if Jocasta had her way . . . she would own this man.

The thought was unconscionable. Worse, it was ridiculous! She shifted impatiently in her seat, trying to push it away. He caught the slight movement, and turned inquiringly, to see if anything was wanted.

"Ulysses," she blurted. "Do you want to be free?"

The moment the words were out, she bit her tongue, and felt her cheeks go red with mortification.

"I'm sorry," she said at once, and looked down at her hands, twisted in her lap. "That was a terribly rude question. Please forgive me."

The tall butler didn't say anything, but regarded her quizzically for a moment. Then he touched his wig lightly, as though to settle it in place, and turned back to his work, picking up the scattered sketches on the table and tapping them neatly into a stack.

"I was born free," he said at last, so quietly that she wasn't sure she'd heard him. His head was bent, eyes on the long black fingers that plucked the ivory counters from the game table and placed each one neatly in its box.

"My father had a tiny farm, not too far from here. But he died of a snake's bite, when I was six or so. My mother could not manage to keep us—she was not strong enough for farming—and so she sold herself, putting the money with a carpenter for my apprenticeship once I should come of age, that I might learn a useful trade."

He set the ivory box in its slot in the game table, and wiped away a crumb of tea cake that had fallen on the cribbage board.

"But then she died," he went on matter-of-factly. "And the carpenter, instead of taking me as an apprentice, claimed that as I was the child of a slave, I was by law a slave myself. And so he sold me."

"But that's not right!"

He looked at her in patient amusement, but didn't speak. And what had right ever had to do with it? his dark eyes said.

"I was fortunate," he said. "I was sold—cheaply, for I was very small and puny—to a schoolmaster, whom several plantation owners on the Cape Fear had hired to teach their children. He would ride from one house to another, staying in each for a week or a month, and I would go with him, perched behind him on the horse's rump, tending the horse when we stopped, and doing such small services as he required.

"And because the journeys were long and tedious, he would talk to me as we rode. He sang—he loved to sing, that man, and he had a most delightful voice—" To Brianna's surprise, Ulysses looked faintly nostalgic, but then he shook his head, recalling himself, and took out a cloth from his pocket, with which he wiped the sideboard.

"It was the schoolmaster who gave me the name Ulysses," he said, back turned to her. "He knew some Greek, and some Latin as well, and for his own amusement, he taught me to read, on the nights when darkness befell us and we were forced to encamp on the road."

The straight, lean shoulders rose in the faintest of shrugs.

"When the schoolmaster died as well, I was a young man of twenty or so. Hector Cameron bought me, and discovered my talents. Not all masters would value such endowments in a slave, but Mr. Cameron was not a common man." Ulysses smiled faintly.

"He taught me to play chess, and would wager upon my success, playing against his friends. He had me taught to sing, and to play the harpsichord, that I might provide entertainment for his guests. And when Miss Jocasta began to lose her sight, he gave me to her, to be her eyes."

"What was your name? Your real name?"

He paused, thinking, then gave her a smile that did not reach his eyes.

"I am not sure that I remember," he said politely, and went out.

56

Confessions of the Flesh

He woke a little before dawn. It was still black dark, but the air had changed; the embers had burned to staleness and the forest's breath moved past his face.

Alexandre was gone. He lay alone under the tattered deerskin, very cold.

"Alexandre?" he whispered hoarsely. "Père Ferigault?"

"I am here." The young priest's voice was soft, somehow remote, though he sat no more than a yard away.

Roger rose up on one elbow, squinting. Once the sleep had left his eyes, he could see dimly. Alexandre was sitting cross-legged, his back very straight, his face turned up to the square of the smokehole overhead.

"Are you all right?" One side of the priest's neck was stained dark with blood, though his face—what Roger could see of it—seemed serene.

"They will kill me soon. Perhaps today."

Roger sat up, clutching the deerskin to his chest. He was already cold; the calm tone of this froze him.

"No," he said, and had to cough to clear his throat of soot. "No, they won't."

Alexandre didn't bother contradicting him. Didn't move. He sat naked, oblivious of the cold morning air, looking up. At last he lowered his gaze, and turned his head toward Roger.

"Will you hear my confession?"

"I'm not a priest." Roger scrambled to his knees and scuffled across the floor, the skin held awkwardly before him. "Here, you'll freeze. Get under this."

"It does not matter."

Roger wasn't sure whether he meant being cold didn't matter, or whether Roger's not being a priest didn't matter. He laid a hand on Alexandre's bare shoulder. Whether it mattered or not, the man was cold as ice.

Roger sat down next to Alexandre, as close as could be managed, and spread the skin over them both. Roger could feel his own skin ripple into gooseflesh where the other man's icy skin touched him, but it didn't trouble him; he leaned closer, wanting urgently to give Alexandre some of his own warmth.

"Your father," Alexandre said. He had turned his head; his breath touched Roger's face, and his eyes were dark holes in his face. "You told me he was a priest."

"A minister. Yes, but I'm not."

He sensed, rather than saw, the other's small gesture of dismissal.

"In time of need, any man may do the office of a priest," Alexandre said. Cold fingers touched Roger's thigh, briefly. "Will you hear my confession?"

"If that's—yes, if you like." He felt awkward, but it couldn't hurt, and if it helped the other at all . . . The hut, and the village outside, were quiet around them. There was no sound but the wind in the pine trees.

He cleared his throat. Did Alexandre mean to begin, or was he to say something first?

As though the sound had been a signal, the Frenchman turned to face him, bowing his head so the soft light smoothed the gold hair of his crown.

"Bless me, brother, for I have sinned," Alexandre said in a low voice. And with his head bowed, hands folded in his lap, he made confession.

Sent out from Detroit with an escort of Hurons, he had ventured down the river as far as the settlement of Ste. Berthe de Ronvalle, to relieve the elderly priest in charge of the mission, whose health had broken down.

"I was happy there," Alexandre said, in the half-dreaming voice that men use for events that have taken place decades ago. "It was a wild place, but I was very young, and ardent in my faith. I welcomed hardship."

Young? The priest couldn't be much older than himself.

Alexandre shrugged, dismissing the past.

"I spent two years with the Huron, and converted many. Then I went with a group of them to Ft. Stanwix, where there was a great gathering of the tribes of the region. There I met Kennyanisi-t'ago, a war chief of the Mohawk. He heard me preach, and being moved of the Holy Spirit, invited me to return with him to his village.''

The Mohawk were notoriously wary of conversion; it had seemed a heaven-sent chance. So Père Ferigault had traveled down the river by canoe, in company with Kennyanisi-t'ago and his warriors.

"That was my first sin,'' he said quietly. "Pride.'' He lifted one finger to Roger, as though suggesting that he keep count. "Still, God was with me.'' The Mohawk had sided with the English during the recent French and Indian War, and were more than suspicious of the young French priest. He had persevered, learning the Mohawk language, that he might preach to them in their own tongue.

He had succeeded in converting a number of the village, though by no means all. However, among his converts was the war chief, so he was protected from interference. Unfortunately, the *sachem* of the village opposed his influence, and there was continued uneasiness between Christian and non-Christian in the village.

The priest licked dry lips, then picked up the water jar and drank.

"And then,'' he said, taking a deep breath, "then I committed my second sin.''

He had fallen in love with one of his own converts.

"Had you had women, before—?'' Roger choked off the question, but Alexandre answered quite simply, without hesitation.

"No, never.'' There was a breath there, not quite a laugh, of bitter self-mockery. "I had thought I was immune to *that* temptation. But man is frail in the face of Satan's fleshly lures.''

He had lived in the girl's longhouse for some months. Then, one morning, he had risen early, and going to the stream to wash, had seen his own reflection in the water.

"There was a sudden disturbance in the water, and the surface broke. A huge and gaping mouth rose through the surface, shattering the reflection of my face.''

It had been no more than a rising trout, leaping for a dragonfly, but the priest, shaken by the experience, had seen it as a sign from God that his soul was in danger of being swallowed by the mouth of Hell. He had gone at once to the longhouse and removed his things, going to live alone in a small shelter outside the village. However, he had left his lover pregnant.

"Was that what caused the trouble that brought you here?'' Roger asked.

"No, not in itself. They do not see matters of marriage and morality as we do," Alexandre explained. "Women take men as they will, and marriage is an agreement that endures so long as the partners are in amity; if they should fall out, then the woman may expel the man from her house—or he may leave. The children, if there are children, stay with the mother."

"But then—"

"The difficulty was that I had always, as a priest, refused to baptize infants unless both parents were Christian and in a state of grace. This is necessary, you understand, if the child is to be raised in faith—for the Indians are inclined otherwise to view the sacrament of baptism as no more than one of their pagan rituals."

Alexandre drew a deep breath.

"And of course I could not baptize this child. This offended and horrified Kennyanisi-t'ago, who insisted that I must do so. Upon my refusing, he ordered me to be tortured. My—the girl—interceded for me, and was abetted in this by her mother and several other influential persons."

Consequently the village had been torn by controversy and schism, and at last the *sachem* had decreed that they must take Père Alexandre to Onyarekenata, where an impartial council might judge what must be done to restore the harmony amongst them.

Roger scratched at his beard; perhaps the Indian dislike of hairy Europeans was the association with lice.

"I am afraid I don't quite understand," he said carefully. "You refused to baptize your own child because the mother was not a good Christian?"

Alexandre looked surprised.

"Ah, *non*! She retains her faith—though she would have every excuse if she did not," he added ruefully. He sighed. "No. I cannot baptize the child, not because of its mother—but because its father is not in a state of grace."

Roger rubbed his forehead, hoping his face didn't betray his astonishment.

"Ah. Is this why you wished to make confession to me? That you might be restored to a state of grace, and thus able to—"

The priest stopped him with a small gesture. He sat quietly for a moment, slender shoulders slumped. He must have brushed his wound accidentally; the clotted mass had cracked, and blood was once more seeping slowly down his neck.

"Forgive me," Alexandre said. "I should not have asked you;

it was only that I was so grateful to be able to speak in my own language; I could not resist the temptation to ease my soul by telling you. But it is no good; there can be no absolution for me.''

The man's despair was so plain, Roger laid a hand on the priest's forearm, wanting urgently to assuage it.

"Are you sure? You said that in time of need—"

"It is not that." He laid his hand on top of Roger's, squeezing tight, as though he might draw strength from the other's grip.

Roger said nothing. After a moment, Alexandre's head rose and the priest looked him in the face. The light outside had changed; there was a faint glow, a brightness in the air just short of light. His own breath rose white from his mouth, like smoke rising toward the hole above.

"Even though I confess, I will not be forgiven. There must be true repentance in order to obtain absolution; I must reject my sin. And that I cannot do."

He fell silent. Roger didn't know whether to speak, or what to say. A priest, he supposed, would have said something like "Yes, my son?" but he couldn't. Instead, he took Alexandre's other hand in his, and held it tightly.

"My sin was to love her," Alexandre said, very softly, "and that I cannot stop."

57

A Shattered Smile

"Two Spears is agreeable. The matter must be spoken of before the Council, and accepted, but I think it will be done." Jamie slouched against a pine tree, slumping a little in exhaustion. We had been in the village for a week; he had been with the *sachem* of the village for the greater part of the last three days. I had barely seen him or Ian, but had been entertained by the women, who were polite but distant. I kept my amulet carefully out of sight.

"Then they do have him?" I asked, and felt the knot of anxiety that had traveled with me for so long begin to loosen. "Roger's really here?" So far, the Mohawks had been unwilling to admit either to Roger's continued existence—or the alternative.

"Aye, well, as to that, the auld bugger's no admitting it—for fear I should try to steal him away, I suppose—but either he's here or he's not far off. If the Council approves the bargain, we'll exchange the whisky for the man in three days time—and be off." He glanced at the heavy-laden clouds that hid the distant mountains. "God, I hope that's rain coming, and not snow."

"Do you think there's any chance the Council won't agree?"

He sighed deeply and ran a hand through his hair. It was unbound and fell rumpled over his shoulders; evidently the negotiations had been difficult.

"Aye, there's a chance. They want the whisky, but they're wary of it. Some of the older men will be against the bargain, for fear of the damage liquor might do to the folk; the younger men are all for it. Some in the middle say aye, take it; they can use the liquor in trade if they're fearful of using it."

"Wakatihsnore told you all that?" I was surprised. The *sachem,* Acts Fast, seemed much too cool and wily a customer for such openness.

"Not him: wee Ian." Jamie smiled briefly. "The lad shows

great promise as a spy, I will say. He's eaten at every hearth in the village, and he's found a lassie who's taken a great liking to him. She tells Ian what the Council of Mothers is thinking.''

I hunched my shoulders and pulled my cloak tight around them; our perch on the rocks outside the village made us safe from interruption, but the price of visibility was exposure to the bitter wind.

''And what does the Council of Mothers say?'' A week spent in a longhouse had given me some idea of the importance of the women's opinions in the scheme of things; though they didn't make direct decisions about general affairs, very little would be done without their approval.

''They could wish I offered some ransom other than whisky, and they're none so sure about giving up the man; more than one lady has a small fancy for him. They wouldna mind adopting him into the tribe.'' Jamie's mouth twisted at that, and I laughed despite my worry.

''Roger's a nice-looking lad,'' I said.

''I've seen him,'' Jamie said shortly. ''Most of the men think he's an ugly, hairy bastard. Of course, they think that of me, too.'' One side of his mouth lifted reluctantly, as he brushed a hand over his jaw; knowing the Indians' dislike of facial hair, he was careful to shave every morning.

''As it is, that may be what makes the difference.''

''What, Roger's looks? Or yours?''

''The fact that more than one lady wants the bugger. Ian says his lassie says her aunt thinks it will make trouble to keep him; she's thinking better to give him back to us than to have ill-feeling amongst the women over him.''

I rubbed my cold-reddened knuckles over my lips, trying to keep from laughing.

''Has the men's Council any idea that some of the women are interested in Roger?''

''I dinna ken. Why?''

''Because if they knew, they'd give him to you for free.''

Jamie snorted at that, but gave me a reluctant lift of one eyebrow.

''Aye, maybe. I'll have Ian mention the matter among the young men. It canna hurt.''

''You said the women wished you would offer something instead of whisky. Did you mention the opal to Acts Fast?''

He sat up straight at that, interested.

"Aye, I did. They couldna have been taken more aback had I pulled a snake from my sporran. They got verra excited—angry and fearful both, and I think they might well have done me harm, save I'd already mentioned the whisky."

He reached into the breast of his coat and drew out the opal, dropping it into my hand.

"Best you take it, Sassenach. But I think you'll maybe not want to show it to anyone."

"How odd." I looked down at the stone, its spiral petroglyph shimmering with color. "So it did mean something to them."

"Oh, that it did," he assured me. "I couldna say what, but whatever it was, they didna like it a bit. The war chief demanded to know where I'd got it, and I told them ye'd found it. That made them back off a bit, but they were like a kettle on the boil over it."

"Why are you wanting me to take it?" The stone was warm from his body, and felt smooth and comfortable in my hand. Instinctively, my thumb ran round and round the spiraled carving.

"They were shocked when they saw it, as I said—and then angry. One or two of them made as though to strike me, but they held back. I watched for a bit, wi' the stone in my hand, and I realized that they were afraid of it; they wouldna touch me while I held it."

He reached out and closed my fist around the stone.

"Keep it by ye. If there should be danger, bring it out."

"You're more likely to be in danger than I am," I protested, trying to hand it back.

He shook his head, though, the ends of his hair lifting in the wind.

"No, not now they ken about the whisky. They'd not harm me until they've heard where it is."

"But why should I be in any danger?" The thought was disquieting; the women had been cautious but not hostile, and the men of the village had largely ignored me.

He frowned, and looked down toward the village. From here, little was visible save the outer palisades, with trails of smoke drifting above them from the unseen longhouses beyond.

"I canna say, Sassenach. Only that I have been a hunter—and I have been hunted. Ye ken how when something strange is near, the birds stop singing, and there is a stillness in the wood?"

He nodded toward the village, eyes fixed on the swirl of smoke as though some shape might emerge from it.

"There is a stillness there. Something is happening that I canna

see. I dinna think it is to do with us—and yet . . . I am uneasy,"
he said abruptly. "And I have lived too long to dismiss such a
feeling."

Ian, who joined us shortly at the rendezvous, seconded this
opinion.

"Aye, it's like holding the edge of a fishing net that's underwater," he said, frowning. "Ye can feel the wriggling through your
hands, and ye ken there's fish there—but ye canna see where."
The wind ruffled his thick brown hair; as usual, it was half plaited,
with strands coming loose. He thumbed one absently behind an
ear.

"There's something happening among the people; some disagreement, I think. And *something* happened last night, in the
Council house. Emily willna answer me when I ask about it; she
only looks away and tells me it's naught to do with us. But I think
it is, somehow."

"Emily?" Jamie lifted one eyebrow, and Ian grinned.

"It's what I call her for short," he said. "Her own name's
Wakyo'teyehsnonhsa; it means Works with Her Hands. She's a
rare carver, is wee Emily. See what she's made for me?" He
reached into his pouch and proudly displayed a tiny otter carved
in white soapstone. The animal stood alert, head up and ready for
mischief; just to look at it made me smile.

"Verra nice." Jamie examined the carving with approval,
stroking the sinuous curve of the body. "The lassie must like ye
fine, Ian."

"Aye, well, I like her too, Uncle." Ian was very casual, but his
lean cheeks were slightly redder than the cold wind could account
for. He coughed and changed the subject slightly.

"She said to me that she thinks the Council might be swayed a
bit in our favor, if ye were to give some of them a taste of the
whisky, Uncle Jamie. If it's all right wi' you, I'll fetch up a cask
and we'll have a wee *ceilidh* tonight. Emily will manage it."

Jamie lifted both eyebrows at that, but nodded after a moment.

"I'll trust your judgment, Ian," he said. "In the Council
House?"

Ian shook his head.

"Nay. Emily says it will be better if it's done at the longhouse
of her aunt—auld Tewaktenyonh is the Pretty Woman."

"Is what?" I asked, startled.

"The Pretty Woman," he explained, wiping his running nose on his sleeve. "One woman of influence in the village has it in her power to decide what's done wi' captives; they call her the Pretty Woman, no matter what she looks like. So ye ken, it's to our advantage if Tewaktenyonh can be convinced the bargain we offer is a good one."

"I suppose to a captive that's been freed, the woman would seem beautiful, regardless," Jamie said wryly. "Aye, I see. Go ahead then; can ye fetch the whisky by yourself?"

Ian nodded and turned to go.

"Wait a minute, Ian," I said, and held out the opal as he turned back to me. "Could you ask Emily if she knows anything about this?"

"Aye, Auntie Claire, I'll mention it. Rollo!" He whistled sharply through his teeth, and Rollo, who had been nosing suspiciously under a rock shelf, left off and bounded after his master. Jamie watched them go, a slight frown between his eyebrows.

"D'ye ken where Ian's spending his nights, Sassenach?"

"If you mean in which longhouse, yes. If you mean in whose bed, no. I could guess, though."

"Mmphm." He stretched and shook his hair back. "Come on, Sassenach, I'll see ye back to the village."

Ian's *ceilidh* got underway soon after dark; the invited guests included the most prominent members of the Council, who came one at a time to Tewaktenyonh's longhouse, paying their respects to the *sachem,* Two Spears, who sat at the main hearth with Jamie and Ian flanking him. A slight, pretty girl, who I assumed must be Ian's Emily, sat quietly behind him, on the keg of whisky.

With the exception of Emily, women were not involved in the whisky-tasting. I had come along, though, to watch, and sat at one of the smaller hearths, keeping an eye on the proceedings while helping two of the women to braid onions, exchanging occasional politenesses in a halting mixture of Tuscaroran, English, and French.

The woman at whose hearth I sat offered me a gourd of spruce beer and some kind of cornmeal mush as refreshment. I did my best to accept with cordiality, but my stomach was knotted too tightly to make more than a token attempt at eating.

Too much depended on this impromptu party. Roger was here; somewhere in the village, I knew it. He was alive; I could only hope he was well—well enough to travel, at least. I glanced at the far end of the longhouse, at the largest hearth. I could see no more of Tewaktenyonh than the curve of a white-streaked head; a queer jolt went through me at the sight, and I touched the small lump of Nayawenne's amulet, where it hung beneath my shirt.

Once the guests were assembled, a rough circle was formed around the hearth, and the opened keg of whisky brought into the center of it. To my surprise, the girl also came into the circle, and took a place beside the keg, a dipping gourd in her hand.

After some words from Two Spears, the festivities commenced, with the girl measuring out portions of the whisky. She did this not by pouring the whisky into the cups, but by taking mouthfuls from the gourd, carefully spitting three mouthfuls into each cup before passing it to one of the men in the circle. I glanced at Jamie, who looked momentarily taken aback, but who politely accepted his cup and drank without hesitation.

I rather wondered just how much whisky the girl was absorbing through the lining of her mouth. Not nearly as much as the men, though I thought it might take quite a bit to lubricate Two Spears, who was a taciturn old bastard with a face like a dyspeptic prune. Before the party had got well underway, though, I was distracted by the arrival of a young boy, the offspring of one of my companions. He came in silently and sat down by his mother, leaning heavily against her. She looked sharply at him, then set down her onions and rose with an exclamation of concern.

The firelight fell on the boy, and I could see at once the peculiar hunched way he sat. I rose hastily to my knees, pushing aside the basket of onions. I knelt forward and took him by the other arm, turning him toward me. His left shoulder had been slightly dislocated; he was sweating, his lips pressed tightly together in pain.

I gestured to his mother, who hesitated, frowning at me. The boy made a small, whimpering noise, and she pulled him away, holding him tight. With sudden inspiration, I pulled Nayawenne's amulet from my shirt; she wouldn't know whose it was but might recognize *what* it was. She did; her eyes widened at the sight of the tiny leather bag.

The boy made no more noise, but I could see the sweat run down his hairless chest, clear in the firelight. I fumbled at the thong that held the pouch shut, digging inside for the rough blue stone. *Pierre sans peur,* Gabrielle had called it. The fearless stone. I took the boy's good hand and pressed the stone firmly into his palm, folding his fingers around it.

"Je suis une sorciere," I said softly. *"C'est medecine, la."*
Trust me, I thought. Don't be afraid. I smiled at him.

The boy stared round-eyed at me; the two women at the hearth
exchanged a look, then as one, looked toward the distant hearth
where the old woman sat.

There was talk from the *ceilidh;* someone was telling an old
story—I recognized the rise and fall of the formal rhythms. I had
heard Highlanders tell their stories and legends in Gaelic, in just
that way; it sounded much the same.

The mother nodded; her sister went quickly down the length of
the house. I didn't turn, but felt the stir of interest behind me as
she passed the other hearths; heads were turning, looking toward
us. I kept my eyes on the boy's face, smiling, holding his hand
tightly in my own.

The sister's footsteps came softly behind me. The boy's mother
reluctantly released her hold on him, leaving him to me. Permission had been received.

It was a simple matter to put back the joint; he was a small boy
and the injury was minor. His bones were light under my hand. I
smiled at him as I felt the joint, assessing damage. Then a quick
bending of the arm, rotation of the elbow, whipping the arm upward—and it was done.

The boy looked intensely surprised. It was a most satisfactory
operation, in that pain was relieved almost instantly. He felt his
shoulder, then smiled shyly back at me. Very slowly, he opened
his hand and held out the stone to me.

The minor sensation created by this occupied my attention for
some time, with the women crowding close, touching the boy and
peering at him, summoning their friends to stare at the murky
sapphire. By the time I had attention to spare for the whisky party
at the far hearth, the festivities were well advanced. Ian was singing in Gaelic, very off-key, accompanied in a haphazard way by
one or two of the other men, who chimed in with the weird, high-
pitched *Haihai!* that I had heard now and then among
Nayawenne's people.

As though my thought had conjured her, I felt eyes on my back,
and turned, to see Tewaktenyonh watching me steadily from her
own hearth at the end of the longhouse. I met her eyes and nodded
to her. She leaned across to say something to one of the young
women at her hearth, who rose and came toward me, stepping
carefully around a couple of toddlers playing under their family
bed-cubicle.

"My grandmother asks if you will come to her." The young woman squatted beside me, speaking quietly in English. I was surprised, though not astonished, to hear it. Onakara had been right, some of the Mohawk had some English. They would not use it, though, except from necessity, preferring their own language.

I rose and accompanied her to Tewaktenyonh's hearth, wondering what necessity impelled the Pretty Woman. I had my own necessities; the thought of Roger, and of Brianna.

The old woman nodded to me, inviting me to sit down, and spoke to the girl, not taking her eyes off me.

"My grandmother asks if she may see your medicine."

"Of course." I could see the old lady's eyes on my amulet, watching curiously as I took out the sapphire. I had added to Nayawenne's woodpecker feather two of my own; a raven's stiff black wing quills.

"You are the wife of Bear Killer?"

"Yes. The Tuscarora call me White Raven," I said, and the girl jerked, startled. She translated quickly for her grandmother. The old lady's eyes flew wide and she glanced at me in consternation. Evidently this was not the most auspicious name she'd ever heard. I smiled at her, keeping my mouth closed; the Indians usually bared their teeth only when laughing.

The old lady handed me back the stone, very gingerly. She studied me narrowly, then spoke to her granddaughter, not taking her eyes off me.

"My grandmother has heard that your man bears a bright stone also," the girl said, interpreting. "She would hear more of this; what it is like, and how you came to have it."

"She's welcome to see it." The girl's eyes widened in surprise as I reached into the pouch at my waist and drew out the stone. I held out the opal to the old woman; she bent and peered closely at it, but made no move to take it from me.

Tewaktenyonh's arms were brown and hairless, wrinkled and smooth as weathered satinwood to the eye. But as I watched I saw the prick of gooseflesh rising, raising vanished hairs in vain defense. *She's seen it,* I thought. *Or at least she knows what it is.*

I didn't need the interpreter's words; her eyes met mine directly and I heard the question clearly, for all that the words were strange.

"How did this come to you?" she said, and the girl echoed it faithfully.

I let my hand lie open; the opal fit snugly in my palm, its weight belied by its colors, glimmering like a soap bubble in my hand.

"It came to me in a dream," I said at last, not knowing how else to explain.

The old woman's breath went out in a sigh. The fear didn't quite leave her eyes, but was overlaid with something else—curiosity, perhaps? She said something, and one of the women at the hearth rose, digging in a basket under the bed frame at her back. She came back and bent by the old lady, handing her something.

The old lady began to sing, quietly, in a voice cracked with age, but still strong. She rubbed her hands together over the fire, and a shower of small brown particles rained down, only to rise up again at once as smoke, thick with the scent of tobacco.

It was a quiet night; I could hear the rise and fall of voices and loud laughter from the far hearth, where the men were drinking. I could pick out the odd word in Jamie's voice—he was speaking French. Was Roger perhaps close enough to hear it too?

I took a deep breath. The smoke rose straight up from the fire in a thin white pillar, and the strong sweet scent of tobacco mingled with the smell of cold air, triggering incongruous memories of Brianna's high school football games; cozy scents of wool blankets and thermoses of cocoa, wisps of cigarette smoke drifting from the crowd. Farther back were other, harsher memories, of young men in uniform, in the shattered light of airfields, crushing out glowing fag ends and running to their battles, leaving no more of themselves behind than the smell of smoke on winter air.

Tewaktenyonh spoke, her eyes still on me, and the girl's soft voice chimed in.

"Tell me this dream."

Was it truly a dream I would tell her, or a memory like these, brought to life on the wings of smoke from a burning tree? It didn't matter; here, all my memories were dreams.

I told her what I could. The memory—of the storm and my refuge among the red cedar's roots, the skull buried with the stone —and the dream; the light on the mountain and the man with his face painted black—making no distinction between them.

The old lady leaned forward, the astonishment on her features mirroring that of her granddaughter.

"You have seen the Fire-Carrier?" the girl blurted. "You have seen his *face*?" She shrank away from me, as though I might be dangerous.

The old lady said something peremptory; her startlement had

faded into a piercing gaze of interest. She poked the girl, and repeated her question impatiently.

"My grandmother says, can you say what he looked like; what did he wear?"

"Nothing. A breech-clout, I mean. And he was painted."

"Painted. How?" the girl asked, in response to her grandmother's sharp question.

I described the body paint of the man I had seen, as carefully as I could. This wasn't difficult; if I closed my eyes, I could see him, as clearly as he had appeared to me on the mountainside.

"And his face was black, from forehead to chin," I ended, opening my eyes.

When I described the man, the interpreter became visibly upset; her lips trembled, and she glanced fearfully from me to her grandmother. The old woman listened intently, though, her eyes searching, straining to discern meaning from my face before the slower words could reach her ears.

When I finished, she sat silent, dark eyes still fastened on my own. At last she nodded, reached up a wrinkled hand and took hold of the purple wampum strings that lay across her shoulder. Myers had told me enough so that I recognized the gesture. The wampum was her family record, badge of her office; speech made while holding it was tantamount to testimony made upon the Bible.

"At the feast of Green Corn, this many years ago"—the interpreter's fingers flashed four times—"a man came among us from the north. His speech was strange, but we could understand him; he spoke like Canienga, or maybe Onondaga, but he would not tell us his tribe or village—only his clan, which was the Turtle.

"He was a wild man, but a brave one. He was a good hunter, and a warrior. Oh, a fine man; all the women liked to look at him, but we were afraid to come too close." Tewaktenyonh paused a moment, a far-off look in her eye that made me count back; she would have been a full-grown woman then, but perhaps young enough still to have been impressed by the frightening, intriguing stranger.

"The men were not so careful; men aren't." She gave a brief, sardonic glance at the *ceilidh,* growing louder by the minute. "So they would sit and smoke with him, and drink spruce beer and listen. He would talk from midday till the dark, and then again in the night by the fires. His face was always fierce, because he talked of war."

She sighed, fingers curling over the purple shell strands.

"Always war. Not against the frog-eaters of the next village, or the ones who eat moose dung. No, we must lift our tomahawks against the *O'seronni*. Kill them all, he said, from the oldest to the youngest, from the Treaty Line to the big water. Go to the Cayuga, send messengers to the Seneca, let the League of the Iroquois go forth as one. Go before it is too late, he said."

One frail shoulder lifted, fell.

" 'Too late for what?' the men asked. 'And why shall we make war for no cause? We need nothing this season; there is no war treaty'—this was before the Time of the French, you understand.

" 'It is our last chance,' he said to them. 'Already it may be too late. They seduce us with their metal, bring us close to them in the hope of knives and guns, and destroy us for the sake of cooking pots. Turn back, brothers! You have left the ways of years too great to count. Go back, I say—or you will be no more. Your stories will be forgotten. Kill them now or they will eat you.'

"And my brother—he was *sachem* then, and my other brother war chief—said that this was foolishness. Destroy us with tools? Eat us? The whites do not consume the hearts of their enemies, even in battle.

"The young men listened; they listen to anyone with a loud voice. But the older ones looked at the stranger with a narrow eye, and said nothing.

"He knew," she said, and the old lady nodded emphatically, speaking almost faster than her granddaughter could translate. "He knew what would happen—that the British and the French would fight with each other, and would seek our help, each against the other. He said that that would be the time; when they fought each other, then we must rise up against them both and cast them out.

"Tawineonawira—Otter-Tooth—that was his name—said to me, 'You live in the moment. You know the past, but you don't look to the future. Your men say, "We need nothing this season," and so they will not move. Your women think it is easier to cook in a iron kettle than to make clay pots. You don't see what will happen because of your laziness, your greed.'

" 'It's not true,' I said to him. 'We are not lazy. We scrape hides, we dry the meat and the corn, we press the oil from sunflowers and put it in jars; we take heed for the next season— always. If we didn't, we would die. And what have pots and kettles to do with it?'

"He laughed at that, but his eyes were sad. He was not always fierce with me, you see." The young woman's eyes slid toward her grandmother at this, but then she looked away, eyes once more on her lap.

" 'A woman's heed,' he said, and shook his head. 'You think of things to eat, what to wear. None of this matters. Men can't think of such things.'

" 'You can be *Hodeenosaunee* and think this?' I said. 'Where do you come from that you don't take heed of what the women think?'

"He shook his head again and said, 'You cannot see far enough.' I asked him how far then did *he* see, but he would not answer me."

I knew the answer to that, and my skin prickled with gooseflesh, too, in spite of the fire. I knew too bloody well how far he'd seen—and how dangerous the view was from that particular precipice.

"But nothing I said was any use," the old lady continued, "nor what my brothers said. Otter-Tooth grew more angry. One day he came out and danced the war dance. He was painted—his arms and legs were striped with red—and he sang and shouted through the village. Everyone came out to watch, to see who would follow him, and when he drove his tomahawk into the war tree and shouted that he went to gain horses and plunder from the Shawnee, a number of the young men followed him.

"They were gone for the rising and setting of a moon, and came back with horses, and with scalps. White scalps, and my brothers were angry. It would bring soldiers from the fort, they said—or revenge parties from the Treaty Line settlements, where they had taken the scalps.

"Otter-Tooth answered boldly that he hoped this was so; then we would be forced to fight. And he said plainly that he would lead such raids again—again and again, until the whole land was roused and we saw that it was as he said; that we must kill the *O'seronni* or die ourselves.

"No one could stop him doing what he said, and there were a few of the young men whose blood was hot; they would follow him, no matter what anyone said. My brother the *sachem* made his medicine tent, and called the Great Turtle to counsel with him. He stayed in the tent for a day and a night. The tent shook and heaved, and voices came out of it, and the people were afraid.

"When my brother came out of the tent, he said that Otter-

Tooth must leave the village. He would do what he would do, but we would not let him bring destruction to us. He caused disharmony among the people; he must go.

"Otter-Tooth became more angry then than we had ever seen him. He stood up in the center of the village and he shouted until the veins stood out in his neck and his eyes were red with rage." The girl's voice dropped. "He shouted terrible things.

"Then he became very quiet, and we were afraid. He said things that took the hearts from our bodies. Even those who had followed him were afraid of him, then.

"He didn't sleep or eat. For all of a day, and all of a night, and all of the next day, he went on talking, walking round and round the village, stopping at the doors of the houses and talking, until the people in the house drove him away. And then he left.

"But he came back again. And again. He would go away, and hide in the forest, but then he would be back again, by the fires at night, thin and hungry, with his eyes glowing like a fox's, always talking. His voice filled the village at night, and no one could sleep.

"We began to know that he had an evil spirit in him; perhaps it was Atatarho, from whose head Hiawatha combed the snakes; perhaps the snakes had come to this man, looking for a home. Finally, my brother the war chief said that it must stop; he must leave or we would kill him."

Tewaktenyonh paused. Her fingers, which had stroked the wampum continuously, as though she drew strength from it for her story, were now still.

"He was a stranger," she said softly. "But he didn't know he was a stranger. I think he never understood."

At the other end of the longhouse the drinking party was growing riotous; all the men were laughing, rocking to and fro with mirth. I could hear the girl Emily's voice, higher, laughing with them. Tewaktenyonh glanced that way, frowning slightly.

Mice were creeping briskly up and down my spine. A stranger. An Indian, by his face, by his speech; his slightly strange speech. An Indian—with silver fillings in his teeth. No, he hadn't understood. He had thought they were his people, after all. Knowing what their future held, he had come to try to save them. How could he believe that they meant to do him harm?

But they *had* meant it. They stripped him, said Tewaktenyonh, her face remote. They tied him to a pole in the center of the

village, and painted his face with an ink made from soot and oak
galls.

"Black is for death; prisoners who are to be killed are always
painted so," the girl said. One eyebrow lifted slightly. "You knew
this when you met the man on the mountain?"

I shook my head, mute. The opal had grown warm in my palm,
slick with sweat.

They had tortured him for a time; prodding his naked body with
sharpened sticks, and then with hot embers, so that blisters rose
up and burst, and his skin hung in tatters. He stood this well, not
crying out, and this pleased them. He seemed still strong, so they
left him overnight, still tied to the pole.

"In the morning, he was gone." The old woman's face was
smooth with secrets. If she had been pleased, or relieved, or distressed by the escape, no one would ever have known.

"I said that they should not follow him, but my brother said it
was no good; he would only come back again, if we did not finish
the matter."

So a party of warriors left the village, on Otter-Tooth's track.
Bloody as he was, it was not difficult to follow.

"They chased him to the south. They thought to catch him,
time after time, but he was strong. He ran on. For four days, they
followed him, and finally they caught him, in a grove of aspens,
leafless in the snow and their branches white as finger bones."

She saw the question in my eyes at this, and nodded.

"My brother the war chief was there. He told me, afterward.

"He was alone, and unarmed. He had no chance, and knew it.
But he faced them nonetheless—and he talked. Even after one of
the men had struck him in the mouth with a war club, he talked
through the blood, spitting out words with his broken teeth.

"He was a brave man," she said, reflectively. "He didn't beg.
He told them the same things he had said before, but my brother
said this time it was different. Before, he had been hot as fire;
dying, he was cold as snow—and because they were so cold, his
words terrified the warriors.

"Even when the stranger lay dead in the snow, his words
seemed to go on ringing in the warriors' ears. They lay down to
sleep, but his voice talked to them in their dreams, and kept them
from sleeping. *You will be forgotten,* he said. *The Nations of the
Iroquois will be no more. No one will tell your stories. Everything
you are and have been will be lost.*

"They turned toward home, but his voice followed them. At

night, they could not sleep for the evil words in their ears. In the day, they heard cries and whispers from the trees along their trail. Some of them said it was only ravens calling, but others said no, they heard him plainly.

"At last, my brother said it was clear this man was a sorcerer."

The old lady glanced sharply at me. *Je suis une sorciere,* I'd said. I swallowed, and my hand went to the amulet at my neck.

"The thing to do, my brother said, was to cut off his head, and then he would talk no more. So they went back, and they cut off his head, and tied it in the branches of a spruce. But when they slept that night, they still heard his voice, and they woke with shriveled hearts. The ravens had picked out his eyes, but the head still spoke.

"One man, very brave, said he would take the head, and bury it far away." She smiled briefly. "This brave man was my husband. He wrapped the head in a piece of deerskin, and he ran with it, far to the south, and the head still talking under his arm all the time, so he had to put plugs of beeswax in his ears. At last he saw a very big red cedar tree, and he knew this was the place, because the red cedar has a strong spirit for healing.

"So he buried the head under the tree's roots, and when he took the beeswax from his ears, he could hear nothing but the wind and water. So he came home, and no one has spoken the name of Otter-Tooth in this village, from that day until this one."

The girl finished this, eyes on her grandmother. Evidently this was true; she had never heard this story.

I swallowed, and tried to get a clear breath. The smoke had ceased to rise as she talked; it had gathered instead in a low cloud overhead, and the air was thick with narcotic perfume.

The hilarity from the drinking circle had lessened. One of the men got up and, stumbling, went outside. Two more lay on their sides by the fire, half asleep.

"And this?" I said, holding out the opal. "You've seen it? It was his?"

Tewaktenyonh reached out as though to touch the stone, but then drew back.

"There is a legend," the girl said softly, not taking her eyes from the opal. "Magic snakes carry stones in their heads. If you kill such a snake and take the stone, it will give you great power." She shifted uneasily, and I had no trouble imagining with her the size of the snake that might have carried a stone like this.

The old lady spoke suddenly, nodding at the stone. The girl jumped, but repeated the words obediently.

"It was his," she said. "He called it his *tika-ba*."

I looked at the interpreter, but she shook her head. "*Tika-ba*," she said, enunciating clearly. "This is not an English word?"

I shook my head.

Her story finished, the old woman sat back in her furs, watching me with deep speculation. Her eyes rested on the amulet around my neck.

"Why did he speak to you? Why has he given you that?" She nodded at my hand, and my fingers closed over the opal's curve in reflex.

"I don't know," I said—but she had taken me unaware; I had had no time to prepare my face.

She fixed me with a piercing look. She knew I was lying, all right—and yet how could I tell her the truth? Tell her what Otter-Tooth—whatever his real name—had been? Much less that his prophecies were true.

"I think perhaps he was a part of my . . . family," I said at last, thinking of what Pollyanne had told me about the ghosts of one's ancestors. There was no telling from where—or when—he had come; he must, I supposed, be an ancestor or a descendant. If not of me, then of someone like me.

Tewaktenyonh sat up very straight at that, and looked at me in astonishment. Slowly the look faded, and she nodded.

"He has sent you to me to hear this. He was wrong," she declared, with confidence. "My brother said that we must not speak of him; we must let him be forgotten. But a man is not forgotten, as long as there are two people left under the sky. One, to tell the story; the other, to hear it. So."

She reached out and touched my hand, careful not to touch the stone. The glitter of moisture in her black eyes might have been from the tobacco smoke.

"I am one. You are the other. He is not forgotten."

She motioned to the girl, who rose silently and brought us food and drink.

When I rose finally to go back to the longhouse where we were lodged, I glanced toward the drinking party. The ground was littered with snoring bodies, and the keg lay empty on its side. Two Spears lay peacefully on his back, a beatific smile creasing the wrinkles of his face. The girl, Ian, and Jamie were gone.

Jamie was outside, waiting for me. His breath rose white in the night air, and the scents of whisky and tobacco wafted from his plaid.

"You seemed to be having fun," I said, taking his arm. "Any progress, do you think?"

"I think so." We walked side by side across the big central clearing to the longhouse where we were lodged. "It went well. Ian was right, bless him; now they've seen this wee *ceilidh* did no harm, I think they'll maybe be disposed to make the bargain."

I glanced at the row of longhouses with their floating clouds of smoke, and the glow of firelight from smokeholes and doorways. Was Roger in one of them now? I counted automatically, as I did every day—seven months. The ground was thawing; if we traveled partway by river, we could perhaps make the trip in a month —six weeks at the most. Yes, if we left soon, we would be in time.

"And you, Sassenach? Ye seemed to be having a most earnest discussion wi' the auld lady. Did she ken aught of that stone?"

"Yes. Come inside and I'll tell you about it."

He lifted the skin over the doorway, and I walked inside, the opal a solid weight in my hand. They hadn't known what he had called it, but I did. The man called Otter-Tooth, who had come to raise a war, to save a nation—with silver fillings in his teeth. Yes, I knew what it was, the *tika-ba*.

His unused ticket back. My legacy.

58

Lord John Returns

River Run, March 1770

Phaedre had brought a dress, one of Jocasta's, yellow silk, very full in the skirt.

"We got better company tonight than ol' Mr. Cooper or Lawyer Forbes," Phaedre said with satisfaction. "We got us a real live *lord,* how 'bout *that*?"

She let down a huge armload of fabric on the bed and began to pull bits and pieces from the frothing billows, issuing instructions like a drill sergeant.

"Here, you strip off and put on these yere stays. You need somethin' strong, keep that belly pushed down. Ain't nobody but backcountry trash goes 'thout stays. Your auntie wasn't blind as a bat, she'd 'a had you fitted out proper long since—*long* since. Then put on the stockins and garters—ain't those pretty? I always did like that pair with the little bitty leaves on 'em—then we'll tie on the petticoats, and then—"

"What lord?" Brianna took the proferred stays and frowned at them. "My God, what's this made of, whalebones?"

"Uh-huh. Ain't no cheap tin or iron for Miss Jo, surely not." Phaedre burrowed like a terrier, frowning and muttering to herself. "Where that garter gone to?"

"I don't need these. And what lord is it that's coming?"

Phaedre straightened up, staring at Brianna over the folds of yellow silk.

"Don't need 'em?" she said censoriously. "And you with a six-month belly? What you thinking of, girl, come into dinner all pooched out, and a lordship sittin' by the soup a-gogglin' at you through his eyeglass?"

Brianna couldn't help smiling at this description, but replied with considerable dryness nonetheless.

"What difference would it make? The whole county knows by now that I'm having a baby. I wouldn't be surprised if that circuit rider—Mr. Urmstone, is it? didn't preach a sermon about me up on the Buttes."

Phaedre uttered a short laugh.

"He did," she said. "Two Sundays back. Mickey and Drusus was there—they thought it was right funny, but your auntie didn't. She set Lawyer Forbes on to law him for the slander, but ol' Reverend Urmstone, he said 'twasn't slander if it was the truth."

Brianna stared back at the maid.

"And just what did he say about me?"

Phaedre shook her head and resumed her rummaging.

"You don' want to know," she said darkly. "But be that as it might, whether the county knows ain't the same thing as you flauntin' your belly through the dining room and leavin' his lord-ship in no doubt, so you put on them stays."

Her authoritative tone left no room for argument. Brianna struggled resentfully into the stiff garment, and suffered Phaedre to lace it tight. Her waist was still slender, and the remaining bulge in front would be easily disguised by the full skirt and petticoats.

She stared at herself in the mirror, Phaedre's dark head bobbing near her thighs as the maid adjusted the green silk stockings to her own satisfaction. She couldn't breathe, and being squeezed like that *couldn't* be good for the baby. The stays laced in front; as soon as Phaedre left, she'd undo them. The hell with his Lord-ship, whoever he was.

"And who *is* this lord we're having for dinner?" she asked for the third time, stepping obediently into the billow of starched white linen the maid held for her.

"This be Lord John William Grey, of Mount Josiah plantation in Virginia." Phaedre rolled out the syllables with great cere-mony, though seeming rather disappointed by the unfortunately brief and simple names of the lord. She would, Brianna knew, have preferred a Lord FitzGerald Vanlandingham Walthamstead if she could have got one.

"He a friend of your daddy's, or so Miss Jo says," the maid added, more prosaically. "There, that's good. Lucky you got nice bosoms, this dress is made for 'em."

Brianna hoped this didn't mean the dress wasn't going to cover her breasts; the stays ended just beneath, pushing them up so that they swelled startlingly high, like something bubbling over the rim of a pot. Her nipples stared at her in the mirror, gone a rich dark color, like raspberry wine.

It wasn't worry over which bulges she was exposing that made her oblivious to the rest of Phaedre's brisk ministrations, though; it was the maid's casual *He a friend of your daddy's.*

It was not a crowd; Jocasta seldom had crowds. Dependent on her ears for the nuances of social byplay, she would not risk commotion. Still, there were more people here in the drawing room than was usual; Lawyer Forbes, of course, with his spinster sister; Mr. MacNeill and his son, Judge Alderdyce and his mother, a couple of Farquard Campbell's unmarried sons. No one, though, resembling Phaedre's lordship.

Brianna smiled sourly to herself. "Let 'em look, then," she murmured, straightening her back so that her bulge swelled proudly before her, glistening under the silk. She gave it an encouraging pat. "Come on, Osbert, let's be social."

Her entrance was greeted by a general outcry of cordiality that made her mildly ashamed of her cynicism. They were kind men and women, including Jocasta; and the situation, after all, was none of *their* doing.

Still, she did enjoy the expression of mild shock that the Judge tried to hide, and the too-sweet smile on his mother's face, as her beady little parrot eyes registered the blatant fact of Osbert's unbound presence. Jocasta might propose, but the Judge's mother would dispose, no doubt of that. Brianna met Mrs. Alderdyce's eye with a sweet smile of her own.

Mr. MacNeill's weatherbeaten face twitched slightly with amusement, but he bowed gravely and asked after her health with no sign of embarrassment. As for Lawyer Forbes, if he noticed anything amiss in her appearance, he drew the veil of his professional discretion over it and greeted her with his customary suavity.

"Ah, Miss Fraser!" he said. "Precisely whom we were wanting. Mrs. Alderdyce and myself have just been engaged in amiable dispute concerning a question of aesthetics. You, with your instinct for loveliness, would have a most valuable opinion, should you be willing to oblige me by giving it." Taking her arm, he drew her smoothly to his side—away from MacNeill, who twitched a bushy brow at her but made no move to interfere.

He led her to the hearthside, where four small wooden boxes sat on the table. Ceremoniously removing the lids of these, the lawyer displayed in turn four jewels, each the size of a marrow-fat pea, each nestled in a pad of dark blue velvet, the better to set off its brilliance.

"I think of purchasing one of these stones," Forbes explained. "To have made into a ring. I had them sent from Boston." He smirked at Brianna, plainly feeling that he had stolen a march on the competition—and judging from the faint glower on Mac-Neill's face, he had.

"Tell me, my dear—which do you prefer? The sapphire, the emerald, the topaz, or the diamond?" He rocked back on his heels, waistcoat swelling with his own cleverness.

For the first time in her pregnancy, Brianna felt a sudden qualm of nausea. Her head felt light and giddy, and her fingertips tingled with numbness.

Sapphire, emerald, topaz, diamond. And her father's ring held a ruby. Five stones of power, the points of a traveler's pentagram, the guarantors of safe passage. For how many? Without thinking, she spread a hand protectively over her belly.

She realized the trap Forbes thought he was luring her toward. Let her make a choice and he would present her with the unmounted stone on the spot, a public proposal that would—he thought—force her either to accept him at once, or cause an unpleasant scene by rejecting him outright. Gerald Forbes really knew nothing about women, she thought.

"I—ah—I should not like to venture my own opinion without first hearing Mrs. Alderdyce's choice," she said, forcing a cordial smile and a nod toward the Judge's mother, who looked both surprised and gratified by being so deferred to.

Brianna's stomach clenched, and she surreptitiously wiped sweaty hands on her skirt. There they were, all together and in one place—the four stones she had thought it would take a lifetime to find.

Mrs. Alderdyce was jabbing an arthritic finger at the emerald, explaining the virtues of her choice, but Brianna paid no attention to what the woman said. She glanced at Lawyer Forbes, his round face still reflecting smugness. A sudden wild impulse filled her.

If she said yes, now, tonight, while he still had all four stones . . . could she bring herself to that? Inveigle him, kiss him, lull him into complacency—and then steal the stones?

Yes, she could—and then what? Run off into the mountains with them? Leave Jocasta disgraced and the county in an uproar, run and hide like a common thief? And how would she get to the

Indies before the baby came? She counted in her head, knowing it was insanity, but still—it could be done.

The stones glittered and winked, temptation and salvation. Everyone had come to look, heads bent over the table, murmuring their admiration, herself temporarily overlooked.

She could hide, she thought, the steps of the plan unfolding inevitably before her mind's eye, quite without her willing it. Steal a horse, head up the Yadkin valley into the backcountry. Despite the nearness of the fire, she shivered, feeling cold at the thought of flight through the winter snows. But her mind ran on.

She could hide in the mountains, at her parents' cabin, and wait for them to come back with Roger. If they came back. If Roger was with them. Yes, and what if the baby came first, and she was there on the mountain, all alone with no one at hand, and nothing to help but a handful of stolen brightness?

Or should she ride at once for Wilmington and find a ship to the Indies? If Jocasta was right, Roger was never coming back. Was she sacrificing her only chance at return to wait for a man who was dead—or who, if not dead, might reject her and her child?

"Miss Fraser?"

Lawyer Forbes was waiting, swollen with expectation.

She took a deep breath, feeling sweat trickle down between her breasts, beneath the loosened stays.

"They're all very lovely," she said, surprised at how coolly she was able to speak. "I could not possibly choose among them— but then, I have no particular liking for gems. I have very simple tastes, I'm afraid."

She caught the flicker of a smile on Mr. MacNeill's face, and the deep flush of Forbes's round cheeks, but turned her back on the stones with a polite word.

"I think we will not wait dinner," Jocasta murmured in her ear. "If his Lordship should be delayed . . ."

On cue, Ulysses appeared in the doorway, elegant in full livery, to announce dinner. Instead, in a mellifluous voice that carried easily over the chatter, he said, "Lord John Grey, ma'am," and stepped aside.

Jocasta breathed a sigh of satisfaction, and urged Brianna forward, toward the slight figure that stood in the doorway.

"Good. You shall be his partner at dinner, my dear."

Brianna glanced back at the table by the hearth, but the stones were gone.

Lord John Grey was a surprise. She had heard her mother speak of John Grey—soldier, diplomat, nobleman—and expected someone tall and imposing. Instead, he was six inches shorter than she was, fine-boned and slight, with large, beautiful eyes, and a fair-skinned handsomeness that was saved from girlishness only by the firm set of mouth and jaw.

He had looked startled upon seeing her; many people did, taken aback by her size—but then had set himself to exercise his considerable charm, telling her amusing anecdotes of his travel, admiring the two paintings that Jocasta had hung upon the wall, and regaling the table at large with news of the political situation in Virginia.

What he did not mention was her father, and for that she was grateful.

Brianna listened to Miss Forbes's descriptions of her brother's importance with an absent smile. She felt more and more as though she were drowning in a sea of kind intentions. Could they not leave her alone? Could Jocasta not even have the decency to wait a few months?

". . . and then there's the wee sawmill he's just bought, up to Averasboro. Heavens, how the man manages, I couldna tell you!"

No, they couldn't, she thought, with a kind of despair. They couldn't leave her alone. They were Scots, kindly but practical, and with an iron conviction of their own rightness—the same conviction that had got half of them killed or exiled after Culloden.

Jocasta was fond of her, but clearly had made up her mind that it would be foolish to wait. Why sacrifice the chance of a good, solid, respectable marriage, to a will-o'-the-wisp hope of love?

The horrible thing was that she knew herself it was foolish to wait. Of all the things she had been trying not to think of for weeks, this was the worst—and here it was, rising up in her mind like the shadow of a dead tree, stark against snow.

If. If they came back—if, if, *IF*. If her parents came back at all, Roger would not be with them. She knew it. They wouldn't find the Indians who had taken him—how could they, in a trackless wilderness of snow and mud? Or they would find the Indians, only to learn that Roger was dead—of injuries, disease, torture.

Or he would be found, alive, and refuse to come back, not wanting to see her ever again. Or he would come back, with that maddening sense of Scottish honor, determined to take her, but hating her for it. Or he would come back, see the baby, and . . .

Or none of them would come back at all. *I will bring him home to you—or I will not come home myself.* And she would live here alone forever, drowned in the waves of her own guilt, her body bobbing in the swirl of good intentions, anchored by a rotting umbilical cord to the child whose dead weight had pulled her under.

"Miss Fraser! Miss Fraser, are ye quite weel, then?"

"Not very, no," she said. "I think I'm going to faint." And did, shaking the table with a crash as she fell forward into a whirling sea of china and white linen.

The tide had turned again, she thought. She was buoyed up on a flood of kindness as people bustled to and fro, fetching warm drinks and a brick to her feet, seeing her tucked up warmly on the sofa in the little parlor, with a pillow to her head and salts to her nose, a thick shawl round her knees.

At last they were gone. She could be alone. And now that the truth was out in her own mind, she could cry for all her losses—for father and lover, family and mother, for the loss of time and place and all that she should have been and would never be.

Except that she couldn't.

She tried. She tried to summon up the sense of terror she had felt in the drawing room, alone among the crowd. But now that she truly *was* alone, paradoxically she wasn't afraid anymore. One of the house slaves popped a head in, but she waved a hand, sending the girl away again.

Well, she was Scottish, too—"Well, half," she muttered, cupping a hand over her belly—and entitled to her own stubbornness. They *were* coming back. All of them; mother, father, Roger. If it felt as though that conviction were made of feathers rather than iron . . . still it was hers. And she was hanging on to it like a raft, until they pried her fingers off and let her sink.

The door to the small parlor opened, silhouetting the tall, spare figure of Jocasta against the lighted hall.

"Brianna?" The pale oval face turned unerringly toward the sofa; did she only guess where they had put her, or could she hear Brianna breathing?

"I'm here, Aunt."

Jocasta came into the room, followed by Lord John, with Ulysses bringing up the rear with a tea tray.

"How are you, child? Had I best send for Dr. Fentiman?" She frowned, laying a long hand across Brianna's forehead.

"No!" Brianna had met Dr. Fentiman, a small, damp-handed golliwog of a man with a strong faith in lye and leeches; the sight of him made her shudder. "Er . . . no. Thank you, but I'm quite all right; I was just taken queer for a moment."

"Ah, good." Jocasta turned blind eyes toward Lord John. "His Lordship will be going on to Wilmington in the morning; he wished to pay you his regards, if you are well enough."

"Yes, of course." She sat up, swinging her feet to the floor. So the lord wasn't going to linger; that would be a disappointment to Jocasta, if not to her. Still, she could be polite for a little while.

Ulysses set down the tray, and soft-footed out the door behind her aunt, leaving them alone.

He drew up an embroidered footstool and sat down, not waiting for invitation.

"Are you truly well, Miss Fraser? I have no desire to see you prostrate among the teacups." A smile pulled at the corner of his mouth, and she flushed.

"I'm fine," she said shortly. "Did you have something to say to me?"

He wasn't taken aback by her abruptness.

"Yes, but I thought perhaps you would prefer that I not mention it in the midst of the company. I understand that you are interested in the whereabouts of a man named Roger Wakefield?"

She had been feeling fine; at this, the wave of faintness threatened to return.

"Yes. How do you—do you know where he is?"

"No." He saw her face change, and took her hand between his. "No, I am sorry. Your father had written to me, some three months ago, asking me to assist him in finding this man. It had occurred to him that if Mr. Wakefield was anywhere in the ports, he might have been taken up by a press-gang, and thus be now at sea in one of His Majesty's ships. He asked if I would make use of my acquaintance in naval circles to determine whether such a fate had in fact befallen Mr. Wakefield."

Another wave of faintness passed over her, this one tinged with remorse, as she realized the lengths her father had gone to, in attempting to find Roger for her.

"He isn't on a ship."

He looked surprised at her tone of certainty.

"I have found no evidence that he was impressed anywhere between Jamestown and Charleston. Still, there is the possibility that he was taken up on the eve of sailing, in which case his presence on the crew would not be registered until the ship reached port. That is why I travel tomorrow to Wilmington, to make inquiries—"

"You don't need to. I know where he is." In as few words as possible, she acquainted him with the basic facts.

"Jamie—your father—that is, your parents—have gone to rescue this man from the Iroquois?" Looking shaken, he turned and poured two cups of tea, handing her one without asking if she wanted it.

She held it between her hands, finding a small comfort in the warmth; a greater comfort in being able to speak frankly to Lord John.

"Yes. I wanted to go with them, but—"

"Yes, I see." He glanced at her bulge and coughed. "I collect there is some urgency in finding Mr. Wakefield?"

She laughed, unhappily.

"I can wait. Can you tell me something, Lord John? Have you ever heard of handfasting?"

His fair brows drew together momentarily.

"Yes," he said slowly. "A Scottish custom of temporary marriage, is it not?"

"Yes. What I want to know is, is it legal here?"

He rubbed his jaw, thinking. Either he'd shaved recently or he had a light beard; late as it was, he showed no sign of stubble.

"I don't know," he said finally. "I have never seen the question addressed in law. Still, any couple who dwells together as man and wife are considered married, by common law. I should think handfasting would fall into that class, would it not?"

"It might, except that we're rather obviously not dwelling together," Brianna said. She sighed. "*I* think I'm married—but my aunt doesn't. She keeps insisting that Roger won't come back, or that if he does, I'm still not legally bound to him. Even by the Scots custom, I'm not bound beyond a year and a day. She wants to pick a husband for me—and God, she's trying! I thought you were the newest candidate, when you showed up."

Lord John looked amused at the idea.

"Oh. That would explain the oddly assorted company at dinner. I did notice that the rather florid gentleman—Alderdyce? A judge?—seemed inclined to pay you attention beyond the normal limits of gallantry.''

"Much good it will do him." Brianna snorted briefly. "You should have seen the looks Mrs. Alderdyce kept giving me, all through dinner. She's not going to have her ewe lamb—God, he must be forty, if he's a day—marry the local whore of Babylon. I'd be surprised if she ever lets him set foot over the doorstep again." She patted her small bulge. "I think I've seen to that."

One brow rose, and Grey smiled wryly at her. He set down his teacup and reached for the sherry decanter and a glass.

"Ah? Well, while I admire the boldness of your strategy, Miss Fraser—may I call you 'my dear'?—I regret to inform you that your tactics do not suit the terrain upon which you've chosen to employ them."

"What do you mean by that?"

He leaned back in his chair, glass in hand, surveying her kindly.

"Mrs. Alderdyce. Not being blind—though by no means as astute as your aunt—I did indeed observe her observing you. But you mistake the nature of her observations, I'm afraid." He shook his head, looking at her over the rim of his glass as he sipped.

"Not the look of outraged respectability, by any means. It's granny lust."

Brianna sat up straight.

"It's *what*?"

"Granny lust," he repeated. He sat up himself and topped his glass, pouring the golden liquid carefully. "You know; an elderly woman's urgent desire for grandchildren to dandle upon her knee, spoil with sweetmeats, and generally corrupt." He raised his glass to his nose and reverently breathed in the vapors. "Oh, ambrosia. I haven't had a decent sherry in two years, at least."

"What—you mean Mrs. Alderdyce thinks that I—I mean, because I've shown I'm—that I can have children, then she's sure to get grandchildren out of me later on? That's ridiculous! The Judge could pick any healthy girl—of good character," she added bitterly, "and be fairly sure of having children by her."

He took a drink, let it drift across his tongue, and swallowed, relishing the final ghost of the taste before answering. "Well. No. I rather think that she realizes he could not. Or would not; it makes no difference." He looked at her directly, pale blue eyes unblinking.

"You said it yourself—he is forty and unmarried."

"You mean he—but he's a judge!" The moment her horrified

exclamation came out, she realized the idiocy of it, and clapped a hand over her mouth, blushing furiously. Lord John laughed, though with a wry edge to it.

"The more certainty therefore," he said. "You are quite right; he could have his choice of any girl in the county. If he has not so chosen . . ." He paused delicately, then lifted his glass to her in ironic toast. "I rather think that Mrs. Alderdyce has realized that her son's marriage to you is her best—possibly her only—expectation of having the grandchild she so ardently desires."

"Damn!" She couldn't make a move right, she thought with despair. "It doesn't matter what I do. I'm doomed. They'll have me married off to *somebody,* no matter what I do!"

"You must give me leave to doubt that," he said. His smile quirked sideways, a little painfully. "From what I have seen of you, you have your mother's bluntness and your father's sense of honor. Either would be sufficient to preserve you from such entrapment."

"Don't talk to me about my father's honor," she said sharply. "He's who got me into this mess!"

His eyes dropped to her waistline, frankly ironical.

"You shock me," he said politely, seeming not shocked at all.

She felt the blood surge up in her face once more, hotter than before.

"You know perfectly well that's not what I mean!"

He hid a smile in his sherry cup, eyes crinkling at her.

"My apologies, Miss Fraser. What did you mean, then?"

She took a deep sip of tea to cover her confusion, and felt the comforting heat run down her throat and into her chest.

"I mean," she said through her teeth, "*this* particular mess; being put on show like a piece of bloodstock with doubtful lines. Being held up by the scruff of the neck like an orphaned kitten, in hopes somebody will take me in! Being—being left alone here in the first place," she ended, her voice trembling unexpectedly.

"Why are you alone here?" Lord John asked, quite gently. "I should have thought that your mother might have—"

"She wanted to. I wouldn't let her. Because she had to—that is, he—oh, it's all such a fucking *mess*!" She dropped her head into her hands and stared wretchedly at the tabletop; not crying, but not far from it, either.

"I can see that." Lord John leaned forward and put his empty glass back on the tray. "It's very late, my dear, and if you will pardon my observing it, you are in need of rest." He stood up and laid a hand lightly on her shoulder; oddly, it seemed only friendly, and not condescending, as another man's might.

"As it seems my journey to Wilmington is unnecessary, I think I will accept your aunt's kind invitation to remain here for a little. We will speak again, and see whether perhaps there is at least some palliative for your situation."

59

Blackmail

The commode was magnificent, a beautiful piece of smooth carved walnut that mingled appeal with convenience. Particularly convenient on a rainy, cold night like this. She fumbled sleepily with the lid in the dark, lit by lightning flashes from the window, then sat down, sighing with relief as the pressure on her bladder eased.

Evidently pleased with the additional internal space thus provided, Osbert performed a series of lazy somersaults, making her belly undulate in ghostly waves beneath her white flannel nightgown. She stood up slowly—she did almost everything slowly these days—feeling pleasantly drugged with sleep.

She paused by the rumpled bed, looking out at the stark beauty of the hills and the rain-lashed trees. The glass of the window was icy to the touch, and the clouds rolled down from the mountains, black-bellied and growling with thunder. It wasn't snowing, but it was a nasty night and no mistake.

And what was it like in the high mountains now? Had they reached a village that would shelter them? Had they found Roger? She shivered involuntarily, though the embers still glowed red in the hearth and the room was warm. She felt the irresistible pull of her bed, promising warmth and, even more, the lure of dreams in which she might escape the chronic nag of fear and guilt.

She turned to the door, though, and pulled her cloak from the peg behind it. The urgency of pregnancy might necessitate her using the commode in her room, but she was resolved that no slave would ever carry a chamber pot for her—not as long as she could walk. She wrapped the cloak tightly around her, took the lidded pewter receptacle from its cabinet, and stepped quietly into the corridor.

It was very late; all the candles had been put out, and the stale smell of dead fires lay in the stairwell, but she could see clearly enough by the flicker of the lightning as she made her way down-stairs. The kitchen door was unbolted, a piece of carelessness for which she blessed the cook; no need to make noise struggling one-handed with the heavy bolt.

Freezing rain struck her face and whooshed up beneath the hem of her nightgown, making her gasp. Once past the first shock of cold, though, she enjoyed it; the violence of it was exhilarating, the wind strong enough to lift her cloak in billowing surges that made her feel light on her feet for the first time in months.

She swept in a flurry to the necessary house, rinsed out the pot in the drench of rain that poured from its gutters, then stood in the paved yard, letting the fresh wind sweep into her face and slash her cheeks with rain. She wasn't sure if this was expiation or exultation—a need to share the discomfort her parents might be facing, or some more pagan rite—a need to lose herself by joining in the ferocity of the elements. Either or both, it didn't matter; she stepped deliberately under the spout of the gutter, letting the water pound against her scalp and soak her hair and shoulders.

Gasping and shaking water from her hair like a dog, she stepped back—and stopped, her eye caught by a sudden flash of light. Not lightning; a steady beam that shone for a moment, then vanished.

A door in the slave quarters opened for a moment, then closed. Was someone coming? Someone was; she could hear footsteps on the gravel, and took another step back into the shadows—the last thing she wanted was to explain what she was doing out here.

The lightning showed him clearly as he passed, and she felt a jar of recognition. Lord John Grey, hurrying shirt sleeved and bareheaded, his fair hair unbound and blowing in the wind, evidently oblivious to the cold and rain. He passed without seeing her, and vanished under the overhang of the kitchen porch.

Realizing that she was in danger of being locked out, she ran after him, awkward but still fast. He was just closing the door when she hit it with her shoulder. She burst into the kitchen and stood dripping, Lord John goggling at her in disbelief.

"Nice night for a walk," she said, half breathless. "Isn't it?" She wiped back her wet hair, and with a cordial nod slipped past him, out, and up the stairs, her bare feet leaving wet half-moon prints on the dark, polished wood. She listened, but heard no steps behind her as she reached her room.

She left cloak and gown spread out before the fire to dry, and having toweled her hair and face, climbed naked into bed. She was shivering, but the feel of the cotton sheets on her bare skin was wonderful. She stretched, wiggling her toes, then rolled on her side, curling tightly around her center of gravity, letting the constant heat from within tendril outward, gradually reaching her skin, forming a small cocoon of warmth around her.

She replayed the scene on the footpath once more in memory, and very gradually, the shadowy thoughts that had been rattling around in her mind for days fell together into a rational shape.

Lord John treated her always with attention and respect—often with amusement or admiration—but there was something missing. She had not been able to identify it—for some time had not even been aware of it—but now she knew what it was, without doubt.

She was accustomed, as are most striking women, to the open admiration of men, and this she had from Lord John as well. But below such admiration was usually a deeper awareness, more subtle than glance or gesture, a vibration like the distant chime of a bell, a visceral acknowledgment of herself as female. She had thought she felt it from Lord John when they met—but it had been gone on subsequent meetings, and she had concluded that she had mistaken it at first.

She should have guessed before, she thought; she'd encountered that inner indifference once before, in the roommate of a casual boyfriend. But then, Lord John hid it very well; she might never have guessed, were it not for that chance encounter in the yard. No, he didn't chime for her. But when he came out of the servants' quarters, he had been ringing like a firebell.

She wondered briefly if her father knew, but dismissed the possibility. After his experiences in Wentworth Prison, he couldn't possibly hold a man with that preference in such warm regard as she knew he felt for Lord John.

She rolled onto her back. The polished cotton of the sheet slid across the bare skin of breasts and thighs, caressing. She half noticed the feeling, and as her nipple hardened she raised a hand to cup her breast in reflex, felt Roger's large warm hand in memory, and a sudden surge of wanting. Then in memory she felt the sudden grasp of rougher hands, pinching and mauling, and wanting changed at once to sickened fury. She flipped onto her stomach, arms crossed beneath her breasts and face buried in her pillow, legs clenched and teeth gritted in futile defense.

The baby was a large, uncomfortable lump; impossible to lie

that way now. With a small half-spoken curse, she rolled over and jerked out of bed, out from under the betraying, seductive sheets.

She walked naked through the half-lit room, and stood again by the window, looking out at the pounding rain. Her hair hung damp down her back, and cold was coming through the glass, pebbling the white flesh of arms and thighs and belly. She made no move either to cover herself or to go back to bed, but only stood there, one hand on the gently squirming bulge, looking out.

It would be too late soon. She had known when they left that it was already too late—so had her mother. Neither of them had wanted to admit it to the other, though; they had both pretended that Roger would come back in time, that he and she would sail to Hispaniola, and find their way back through the stones—together.

She laid her other hand against the glass; at once, a mist of condensation sprang up, outlining her fingers. It was early March; maybe three months left, maybe less. It would take a week, maybe two, to travel to the coast. No ship would risk the treacherous Outer Banks in March, though. Early April, at the soonest, before a journey could be undertaken. How long to the West Indies? Two weeks, three?

The end of April, then. And a few days to make their way inland, find the cave; it would be slow, fighting through the jungle, more than eight months pregnant. And dangerous, though that didn't matter much, considering.

That would be if Roger were here now. But he wasn't. He might never come, though that was a possibility she fought hard against envisioning. If she didn't think about all the ways he could die, then he wouldn't die; it was one article of her stubborn faith; the others were that he wasn't dead yet, and that her mother would come back before the child was born. As to her father—rage boiled up again, as it did whenever she thought of him—him or Bonnet—so she tried to think of either of them as little as possible.

She prayed, of course, as hard as she could, but she wasn't constituted for praying and waiting; she was made for action. If only she could have gone with them, to find Roger!

She hadn't had a choice about that, though. Her jaw tightened, and her hand splayed flat against her belly. She hadn't had a choice about a lot of things. But she had made one choice—to keep her child—and now she'd have to live with the consequences of it.

She was beginning to shiver. Abruptly she turned away from

the storm, and went to the fire. A small tongue of flame played along the blackened back of a red-crackled log, the heart of the embers glowing gold and white.

She sank down on the hearth rug, closing her eyes as the heat of the fire sent waves of comfort over her cold skin, caressing as the stroke of a hand. This time she kept all thought of Bonnet at bay, refusing him entrance to her mind, concentrating fiercely instead on the few precious memories she had of Roger.

. . . put your hand on my heart. Tell me if it stops . . . She could hear him, half breathless, half choked between laughter and passion.

How the hell do you know that? The rough feel of curly hairs under her palms, the smooth hard curves of his shoulders, the throb of the pulse in the side of his throat when she'd pulled him down to her and put her mouth on him, wanting in her urgency to bite him, to taste him, to breathe the salt and dust of his skin.

The dark and secret places of him, that she knew only by feel, recalled as soft weight, rolling and vulnerable in her palm, a complexity of curve and depth that yielded reluctantly to her probing fingertips *(Oh, God, don't stop, but careful, aye? Oh!),* the strange wrinkled silk that grew taut and smooth, filled her hand rising, silent and incredible as the stalk of a night-blooming flower that opens as you watch.

His gentleness as he touched her *(Christ, I wish I could see your face, to know how it is for you, am I doing well by ye. Is it good, just here? Tell me, Bree, talk to me . . .),* as she explored him, and then the moment when she had pushed him too far, her mouth on his nipple. She felt again the sudden amazing surge of power in him, as he lost all sense of restraint and seized her, lifting her as though she weighed nothing, rolled her back against the straw and took her, half hesitating as he remembered her freshly riven flesh, then answering the demand of her nails in his back to come to her fiercely, forcing her past the fear of impalement, into acceptance, and welcome, and finally into a frenzy that matched his own, rupturing the last membrane of reticence between them, joining them forever in a flood of sweat and musk and blood and semen.

She moaned out loud, shuddered and lay still, too weak even to move her hand away. Her heart was thumping, very slowly. Her belly was tight as a drum, the last of the spasms slowly relaxing its grip on her swollen womb. One half of her body blazed with heat, the other was cool and dark.

After a moment she rolled onto her hands and knees, and crawled away from the fire. She hauled herself onto the bed like a wounded beast, and lay half stunned, ignoring the currents of heat and cold that played over her.

At last she stirred, pulled a single quilt over her, and lay staring at the wall, hands crossed in protection above her baby. Yes, it was too late. Sensation and yearning must be put aside, along with love and anger. She must resist the mindless pull of both body and emotion. There were decisions to be made.

It took three days to convince herself of the virtue of her plan, to overcome her own scruples, and, at last, to find a suitable time and place in which to catch him alone. But she was thorough and she was patient; she had all the time in the world—nearly three months of it.

On Tuesday, her opportunity came at last. Jocasta was closeted in her study with Duncan Innes and the account books, Ulysses—with a brief, inscrutable look at the closed door of the study—had gone to the kitchen to superintend the preparations for yet another lavish dinner in his Lordship's honor, and she had gotten rid of Phaedre by sending her on horseback to Barra Meadows to fetch a book Jenny Ban Campbell had promised her.

With a fresh blue camlet gown that matched her eyes, and a heart beating in her chest like a trip-hammer, she set out to stalk her victim. She found him in the library, reading the *Meditations* of Marcus Aurelius by the French windows, the morning sun streaming over his shoulder making his smooth fair hair gleam like buttered toffee.

He looked up from his book when she came in—a hippopotamus could have made a more graceful entrance, she thought crossly, catching her skirt on the corner of a bric-a-brac table in her nervousness—then graciously laid it aside, springing to his feet to bow over her hand.

"No, I don't want to sit down, thank you." She shook her head at the seat he was offering her. "I wondered—that is, I thought I'd go for a walk. Would you like to come with me?"

There was frost on the lower panes of the French door, a stiff breeze whining past the house, and soft chairs, brandy, and blazing fire within. But Lord John was a gentleman.

"There is nothing I should like better," he gallantly assured her, and abandoned Marcus Aurelius without a backward glance.

It was a bright day, but very cold. Muffled in thick cloaks, they turned into the kitchen garden, where the high walls gave them some shelter from the wind. They exchanged small, breathless comments on the brightness of the day, assured each other that they were not cold at all, and came through a small archway into the brick-walled herbary. Brianna glanced around them; they were quite alone, and she would be able to see anyone coming along the walk. Best not waste time, then.

"I have a proposal to make to you," she said.

"I am sure any notion of yours must necessarily be delightful, my dear," he said, smiling slightly.

"Well, I don't know about that," she said, and took a deep breath. "But here goes. I want you to marry me."

He kept smiling, evidently waiting for the punch line.

"I mean it," she said.

The smile didn't altogether go away, but it altered. She wasn't sure whether he was dismayed at her gaucherie or just trying not to laugh, but she suspected the latter.

"I don't want any of your money," she assured him. "I'll sign a paper saying so. And you don't need to live with me, either, though it's probably a good idea for me to go to Virginia with you, at least for a little while. As for what I could do for you . . ." She hesitated, knowing that hers was the weaker side of the bargain. "I'm strong, but that doesn't mean much to you, since you have servants. I'm a good manager, though—I can keep accounts, and I think I know how to run a farm. I *do* know how to build things. I could manage your property in Virginia while you were in England. And . . . you have a young son, don't you? I'll look after him; I'd be a good mother to him."

Lord John had stopped dead in the path during this speech. Now he leaned slowly back against the brick wall, casting his eyes up in a silent prayer for understanding.

"Dear God in heaven," he said. "That I should live to hear an offer like that!" Then he lowered his head and gave her a direct and piercing look.

"Are you out of your mind?"

"No," she said, with an attempt at keeping her own composure. "It's a perfectly reasonable suggestion."

"I have heard," he said, rather cautiously, with an eye to her belly, "that women in an expectant condition are somewhat . . . excitable, in consequence of their state. I confess, though, that my experience is distressingly limited with respect to . . . that is—perhaps I should send for Dr. Fentiman?''

She drew herself up to her full height, put a hand on the wall and leaned toward him, deliberately looking down on him, menacing him with her size.

''No, you should not,'' she said, in measured tones. ''Listen to me, Lord John. I'm not crazy, I'm not frivolous, and I don't mean it to be an inconvenience to you in any way—but I'm dead serious.''

The cold had reddened his fair skin, and there was a drop of moisture glistening on the tip of his nose. He wiped it on a fold of his cloak, eyeing her with something between interest and horror. At least he'd stopped laughing.

She felt mildly sick, but she'd have to do it. She'd hoped it could be avoided, but there seemed no other way.

''If you don't agree to marry me,'' she said, ''I'll expose you.''

''You'll do what?'' His usual mask of urbanity had disappeared, leaving puzzlement and the beginnings of wariness in its stead.

She was wearing woolen mittens, but her fingers felt frozen. So did everything else, except the warm lump of her slumbering child.

''I know what you were doing—the other night, at the slave quarters. I'll tell everyone; my aunt, Mr. Campbell, the sheriff. I'll write letters,'' she said, her lips feeling numb even as she uttered the ridiculous threat. ''To the Governor, and the Governor of Virginia. They put p-pederasts in the pillory here; Mr. Campbell told me so.''

A frown drew his brows together; they were so fair that they scarcely showed against his skin when he stood in strong light. They reminded her of Lizzie's.

''Stop looming over me, if you please.''

He took hold of her wrist and pulled it down with a force that surprised her. He was small but much stronger than she had supposed, and for the first time, she was slightly afraid of what she was doing.

He took her firmly by the elbow and propelled her into motion, away from the house. The thought struck her that perhaps he meant to take her down to the river, out of sight, and try to drown her. She thought it unlikely, but still resisted the direction of his urging, and turned back into the square-laid paths of the kitchen garden instead.

He made no demur, but went with her, though it meant walking head-on into the wind. He didn't speak until they had turned once more, and reached a sheltered corner by the onion bed.

"I am halfway tempted to submit to your outrageous proposal," he said at last, the corner of his mouth twitching—whether with fury or amusement, she couldn't tell.

"It would certainly please your aunt. It would outrage your mother. And it would teach *you* to play with fire, I do assure you." She caught a gleam in his eye that gave her a sudden surge of doubt about her conclusions as to his preferences. She drew back from him a bit.

"Oh. I hadn't thought of that—that you might . . . men and women both, I mean."

"I *was* married," he pointed out, with some sarcasm.

"Yes, but I thought that was probably the same kind of thing I'm suggesting now—just a formal arrangement, I mean. That's what made me think of it in the first place, once I realized that you—" She broke off with an impatient gesture. "Are you telling me that you *do* like to go to bed with women?"

He raised one eyebrow.

"Would that make a substantial difference to your plans?"

"Well . . ." she said uncertainly. "Yes. Yes, it would. If I'd known that, I wouldn't have suggested it."

" 'Suggested,' she says," he muttered. "Public denunciation? The pillory? *Suggested?*"

The blood burned so hotly in her cheeks, she was surprised not to see the cold air turn to steam around her face.

"I'm sorry," she said. "I wouldn't have done it. You have to believe me, I really wouldn't have said a word to anybody. It's only when you laughed, I thought—anyway, it doesn't matter. If you did want to sleep with me, I couldn't marry you—it wouldn't be right."

He closed his eyes very tight and held them squinched shut for a minute. Then he opened one light blue eye and looked at her.

"Why not?" he asked.

"Because of Roger," she said, and was infuriated to hear her voice break on the name. Still more infuriated to feel a hot tear escape to run down her cheek.

"Damn it!" she said. "Damn it to hell! I wasn't even going to *think* about him!"

She swiped the tear angrily away, and clenched her teeth.

"Maybe you're right," she said. "Maybe it is being pregnant. I cry all the time, over nothing."

"I rather doubt it is nothing," he said dryly.

She took a deep breath, the cold air hollowing her chest. There was one last card to play, then.

"If you do like women . . . I couldn't—I mean, I don't want to sleep with you regularly. And I wouldn't mind your sleeping with anybody else—male or female—"

"Thank you for that," he muttered, but she ignored him, bent only on the need to get it all out.

"But I can see that you might want a child of your own. It wouldn't be right for me to keep you from having one. I can give you that, I think." She glanced down at herself, arms clasped across the round of her belly. "Everyone says I'm made for childbearing," she went on steadily, eyes on her feet. "I'd—just until I got pregnant again, though. You'd have to put that in the contract, too—Mr. Campbell could draw it up."

Lord John massaged his forehead, evidently suffering the on-slaught of a massive headache. Then he dropped his hand and took her by the arm.

"Come and sit down, child," he said quietly. "You'd best tell me what the devil you're up to."

She took a deep, savage breath to steady her voice.

"I am not a child," she said. He glanced up at her and seemed to change his mind about something.

"No, you're not—God help us both. But before you startle Farquard Campbell into an apoplexy with your notion of a suit-able marriage contract, I beg you to sit with me for a moment and share the processes of your most remarkable brain." He motioned her through the archway into the ornamental garden, where they would be invisible from the house.

The garden was bleak, but orderly; all the dead stalks of the year before had been pulled out, the dry stems chopped and scat-tered as mulch over the beds. Only in the circular bed around the dry fountain were there signs of life; green crocus spikes poked up like tiny battering rams, vivid and intransigent.

They sat, but she couldn't sit. Not and face him. He got up with her, and walked beside her, not touching her but keeping pace, the wind whipping strands of blond hair across his face, not saying a word, but listening, listening as she told him almost everything.

"So I've been thinking, and thinking," she ended wretchedly. "And I never get anywhere. Do you see? Mother and—and Da, they're out there somewhere—'' She waved an arm toward the distant mountains. "Anything could happen to them—anything might have happened to Roger already. And here I sit, getting bigger and bigger, and there's nothing I can *do*!"

She glanced down at him and drew the back of a mittened hand under her dripping nose.

"I'm not crying," she assured him, though she was.

"Of course not," he said. He took her hand and drew it through his arm.

"Round and round," he murmured, eyes on the path of crazy paving as they circled the fountain.

"Yes, round and round the mulberry bush," she agreed. "And it'll be Pop! goes the weasel in three months or so. I have to do *something*," she ended, miserably.

"Believe it or not, in your case waiting *is* doing something, though I admit it may not seem so," he answered dryly. "Why is it that you will not wait to see whether your father's quest is successful? Is it that your sense of honor will not allow you to bear a fatherless child? Or—"

"It's not my honor," she said. "It's his. Roger's. He's—he followed me. He gave up—everything—and came after me, when I came here to find my father. I knew he would, and he did.

"When he finds out about this—" She grimaced, cupping a hand to the swell of her stomach. "He'll marry me; he'll feel as though he has to. And I can't let him do that."

"Why not?"

"Because I love him. I don't want him to marry me out of obligation. And I—" She clamped her lips tight on the rest of it. "I won't," she ended firmly. "I've made up my mind, and I won't."

Lord John pulled his cloak tighter as a fresh blast of wind came rocketing in off the river. It smelled of ice and dead leaves, but there was a hint of freshness in it; spring was coming.

"I see," he said. "Well, I quite agree with your aunt that you require a husband. Why me, though?" He raised one pale brow. "Is it my title or my wealth?"

"Neither one. It was because I was sure that you didn't like women," she said, giving him one of those candid blue looks.

"I do like women," he said, exasperated. "I admire and honor them, and for several of the sex I feel considerable affection—your mother among them, though I doubt the sentiment is reciprocated. I do not, however, seek pleasure in their beds. Do I speak plainly enough?''

''Yes,'' she said, the small lines between her eyes vanishing like magic. ''That's what I thought. See, it wouldn't be right for me to marry Mr. MacNeill or Barton McLachlan or any of those men, because I'd be promising something I couldn't give them. But you don't want that anyway, so there isn't any reason why I can't marry you.''

He repressed a strong urge to bang his head against the wall.

''There most assuredly is.''

''What?''

''To name only the most obvious, your father would undoubtedly break my neck!''

''What for?'' she demanded, frowning. ''He likes you; he says you're one of his best friends.''

''I am honored to be the recipient of his esteem,'' he said shortly. ''However, that esteem would very shortly cease to exist, upon Jamie Fraser's discovering that his daughter was serving as consort and brood mare to a degenerate sodomite.''

''And how would he discover that?'' she demanded. ''*I* wouldn't tell him.'' Then she flushed and, meeting his outraged eye, suddenly dissolved into laughter, in which he helplessly joined.

''Well, I'm sorry, but *you* said it,'' she gasped at last, sitting up and wiping her streaming eyes with the hem of her cloak.

''Oh, Christ. Yes, I did.'' Distracted, he thumbed a strand of hair out of his mouth, and wiped his running nose on his sleeve again. ''Damn, why haven't I a handkerchief? I said it because it's true. As for your father finding out, he's well aware of the fact.''

''He is?'' She seemed disproportionately surprised. ''But I thought he'd never—''

A flash of yellow apron interrupted her; one of the kitchen maids was in the adjoining garden. Without comment, Lord John stood up and gave her a hand; she got ponderously to her feet and they sailed out onto the dry brown scurf of the dead lawn, cloaks billowing like sails around them.

The stone bench under the willow tree was devoid of its usual charm at this time of year, but it was at least sheltered from the icy blasts off the river. Lord John saw her seated, sat down himself, and sneezed explosively. She opened her cloak and dug in the bosom of her dress, finally coming out with a crumpled handkerchief, which she handed to him with apologies.

It was warm and smelled of her—a disconcerting odor of girl-flesh, spiced with cloves and lavender.

"What you said about teaching me to play with fire," she said. "Just what did you mean by that?"

"Nothing," he said, but now it was his turn to flush.

"Nothing, hm?" she said, and gave him the ghost of an ironic smile. "That was a threat if I ever heard one."

He sighed, and wiped his face once more with her handkerchief.

"You have been frank with me," he said. "To the point of embarrassment and well beyond. So yes, I suppose I—no, it *was* a threat." He made a small gesture of surrender. "You look like your father, don't you see?"

She frowned at him, his words obviously meaning nothing. Then realization flickered, sprang to full life. She sat bolt upright, staring down at him.

"Not you—not Da! He wouldn't!!"

"No," Lord John said, very dryly. "He wouldn't. Though your shock is scarcely flattering. And for what the statement is worth, I would under no circumstances take advantage of your likeness to him—that was as much an idle threat as was your menacing me with exposure."

"Where did you . . . meet my father?" she asked carefully, her own troubles superseded for the moment by curiosity.

"In prison. You knew he was imprisoned, after the Rising?"

She nodded, frowning slightly.

"Yes. Well. Leave it as said that I harbor feelings of particular affection for Jamie Fraser, and have for some years." He shook his head, sighing.

"And here you come offering me your innocent body, with its echoes of his flesh—and add to that the promise of giving me a child who would mingle my blood with his—and all this, because your honor will not let you wed a man you love, or love a man you wed." He broke off and sank his head in his hands.

"Child, you would make an angel weep, and God knows I am no angel!"

"My mother thinks you are."

He glanced up at her, startled.

"She thinks *what*?"

"Maybe she wouldn't go quite *that* far," she amended, still frowning. "She says you're a good man, though. I think she likes you, but she doesn't want to. Of course, I understand that now;

I suppose she must know—how you . . . er . . . feel about . . .'' She coughed, hiding her blushes in a fold of her cloak.

"Hell," he muttered. "Oh, hell and thundering damnation. I ought never to have come out with you. Yes, she does. Though in all truth, I am not sure why she regards me with suspicion. It cannot be jealousy, surely."

Brianna shook her head, chewing thoughtfully on her lower lip.

"I think it's because she's afraid you'll hurt him, somehow: She's afraid for him, you know."

He glanced up at her, startled.

"Hurt him? How? Does she think I will overpower him and commit depraved indignities upon his person?"

He spoke lightly, but a flicker in her eyes froze the words in his throat. He tightened his grip on her arm. She bit her lip, then gently detached his hand, laying it on his knee.

"Have you ever seen my father with his shirt off?"

"Do you mean the scars on his back?"

She nodded.

He drummed his fingers restlessly on his knees, soundless on the fine broadcloth.

"Yes, I've seen them. I did that."

Her head jerked back, eyes wide. The end of her nose was cherry-red, but the rest of her skin so pale that her hair and eyebrows seemed to have leached all the life from it.

"Not all of it," he said, staring off into a bed of dead hollyhocks. "He'd been flogged before, which made it all the worse— that he knew what he was doing, when he did it."

"Did . . . what?" she asked. Slowly, she rearranged herself on the bench, not so much turning toward him as flowing in her garments, like a cloud changing shape in the wind.

"I was the commander at Ardsmuir prison; did he tell you? No, I thought not." He made an impatient gesture, brushing back the strands of fair hair that whipped across his face.

"He was an officer, a gentleman. The only officer there. He spoke for the Jacobite prisoners. We dined together, in my quarters. We played chess, we spoke of books. We had interests in common. We . . . became friends. And then . . . we were not."

He stopped speaking.

She drew away from him a bit, distaste in her eyes.

"You mean—you had him flogged because he wouldn't—"

"No, damn it, I did not!" He snatched the handkerchief and scrubbed angrily at his nose. He flung it down on the seat between them and glared at her. "How dare you suggest such a thing!"

"But you said yourself you did it!"

"*He* did it."

"You can't flog yourself!"

He started to reply, then snorted. He raised one brow at her, still angry, but with his feelings coming back under control.

"The hell you can't. You've been doing it for months, according to what you've told me."

"We aren't talking about me."

"Of course we are!"

"No, we're not!" She leaned toward him, heavy brows drawn down. "What the hell do you mean, he did it?"

The wind was blowing from behind her, into his face. It made his eyes sting and water, and he looked away.

"What am I doing here?" he muttered to himself. "I must be mad to be talking with you in this manner!"

"I don't care if you're mad or not," she said, and gripped him by the sleeve. "You tell me what happened!"

He pressed his lips tight together, and for a moment, she thought he wouldn't. But he had already said too much to stop, and he knew it. His shoulders rose under his cloak and dropped, slumping in surrender.

"We were friends. Then . . . he discovered my feeling for him. We were no longer friends, by his choice. But that was not enough for him; he wished a final severance. And so he deliberately brought about an occasion so drastic that it must alter our relation irrevocably and prevent any chance of friendship between us. So he lied. During a search of the prisoners' quarters, he claimed a piece of tartan publicly as his own. Possession was against the law, then—it still is, in Scotland."

He drew a deep breath and let it out. He wouldn't look at her, but kept his eyes focused on the ragged fringe of bare trees across the river, raw against the pale spring sky.

"I was the governor, charged with execution of the law. I was obliged to have him flogged. As he damn well knew I would be."

He tilted his head back, resting it against the carved stone back of the bench. His eyes were closed against the wind.

"I could forgive his not wanting me," he said, with quiet bitterness. "But I couldn't forgive him for making me use him in that fashion. Not forcing me merely to hurt him, but to degrade him. He could not merely refuse to acknowledge my feeling; he must destroy it. It was too much."

Bits of debris boiled past on the flood; storm-cracked twigs and branches, a broken board from the hull of a boat, wrecked somewhere upstream. Her hand covered his where it rested on his knee. It was slightly larger than his own, and warm from sheltering in her cloak.

"There was a reason. It wasn't you. But it's for him to tell you, if he wants to. You did forgive him, though," she said quietly. "Why?"

He sat up then, and shrugged, but didn't put away her hand.

"I had to." He glanced at her, eyes straight and level. "I hated him for as long as I could. But then I realized that loving him . . . that was part of me, and one of the best parts. It didn't matter that he couldn't love me, that had nothing to do with it. But if I could not forgive him, then I could not love him, and that part of me was gone. And I found eventually that I wanted it back." He smiled, faintly. "So you see, it was really entirely selfish."

He squeezed her hand then, stood up, and pulled her to her feet.

"Come, my dear. We shall both freeze solid if we sit here any longer."

They walked back toward the house, not talking, but walking close together, arm in arm. As they came back through the gardens he spoke abruptly.

"You're right, I think. To live with someone you love, knowing that they tolerate the relation only for the sake of obligation—no, I wouldn't do it, either. Were it only a matter of convenience and respect on both sides, then yes; such a marriage is one of honor. As long as both parties are honest—" His mouth twisted briefly as he glanced in the direction of the servants' quarters. "There is no need for shame on either side."

She looked down at him, brushing a strand of windblown copper hair out of her eyes with her free hand.

"Then you'll accept my proposal?" The hollow feeling in her chest didn't feel like the relief she had expected.

"No," he said bluntly. "I may have forgiven Jamie Fraser for what he did in the past—but he would never forgive *me* for marrying you." He smiled at her, and patted the hand he held tucked in the curve of his arm.

"I can give you some respite from both your suitors and your aunt, though." He glanced at the house, whose curtains hung unstirring against the glass.

"Do you suppose anyone's watching?"

"I'd say you can bet on it," she said, a little grimly.

"Good." Pulling off the sapphire ring he wore, he turned to face her and took her hand. He pulled off her mitten and ceremoniously slid the ring onto her little finger—the only one it would fit. Then he rose smoothly on his toes and kissed her on the lips. Leaving her no time to recover from surprise, he clasped her hand in his, and turned once more toward the house, his expression bland.

"Come along, my dear," he said. "Let us announce our engagement."

60

Trial By Fire

They were left alone all day. The fire was dead, and there was no food left. It didn't matter; neither man could eat, and no fire would have reached Roger's soul-deep chill.

The Indians came back in late afternoon. Several warriors, escorting an elderly man, dressed in a flowing lace shirt and a woven mantle, his face painted with red and ocher—the *sachem,* bearing a small clay pot in his hand, filled with black liquid.

Alexandre had put on his clothes; he stood when the *sachem* approached him, but neither spoke nor moved. The *sachem* began to sing in a cracked old voice, and as he sang, dipped a rabbit's foot into the pot and painted the priest's face in black, from forehead to chin.

The Indians left, and the priest sat down on the ground, his eyes closed. Roger tried to speak to him, to offer him water, or at least the knowledge of company, but Alexandre made no response, sitting as though he had been carved of stone.

In the last of the twilight, he spoke, finally.

"There is not much time," he said softly. "I asked you once before to pray for me. I did not know then what I would have you pray for—for the preservation of my life, or my soul. Now I know that neither is possible."

Roger moved to speak, but the priest twitched a hand, stopping him.

"There is only the only thing I can ask for. Pray for me, brother—that I might die well. Pray that I may die in silence." He looked at Roger for the first time, then, his eyes glinting with moisture. "I would not shame her by crying out."

It was some time after dark that the drums began. Roger had not heard them in his time in the village. Impossible to say how many there were; the sound seemed to come from everywhere. He felt it in the marrow of his bones and the soles of his feet.

The Mohawks returned. When they came in, the priest stood up at once. He undressed himself, and walked out, naked, without a backward glance.

Roger sat staring at the hide-covered doorway, praying—and listening. He knew what a drum could do; had done it himself—evoked awe and fury with the beating of a stretched hide, calling to the deep and hidden instincts of the listener. Knowing what was happening, though, didn't make it any less frightening.

He could not have said how long he sat there listening to the drums, hearing other sounds—voices, footsteps, the noises of a large assembly—trying not to listen for Alexandre's voice.

Suddenly the drumming stopped. It started again, no more than a few tentative thumps, and then quit altogether. There were shouts, and then a sudden cacophony of yells. Roger started up, and hobbled toward the door. The guard was still there, though; he thrust his head through the flap and gestured menacingly, one hand on his war club.

Roger stopped, but couldn't return to the fire. He stood in the half-dark, sweat rolling down his ribs, listening to the sounds outside.

It sounded like all the devils in hell had been let loose. What in God's name was going on out there? A terrific fight, obviously. But who, and why?

After the first salvo of shrieks, the vocal part of it had lessened, but there were still individual high-pitched yelps and ululations from every part of the central clearing. There were thuds, too; moans, and other noises indicative of violent combat. Something struck the wall of the longhouse; the wall shivered and a bark panel cracked down the middle.

Roger glanced at the door flap; no, the guard wasn't looking. He dashed across to the panel and tore at it with his fingers. No good; the wood fibers shredded away beneath his nails and wouldn't give him purchase. In desperation, he pressed his eye to the hole he had made, trying to see what was happening outside.

No more than a narrow slice of the central clearing was visible. He could see the longhouse opposite, a strip of churned earth between, and over everything, the flickering light of an enormous fire. Red and yellow shadows fought with black ones, peopling the air with fiery demons.

Some of the demons were real; two dark figures reeled past and out of sight, locked in violent embrace. More figures streaked across his line of sight, running toward the fire.

Then he stiffened, pressing his face against the wood. Among the incomprehensible Mohawk yells, he could have sworn he had heard someone bellowing in *Gaelic.*

He had.

"Caisteal Dhuni!" somebody shouted nearby, followed by a hair-raising screech. Scots—white men! He had to get to them! Roger smashed his fists on the shattered wood in a frenzy, trying to batter his way through the panel by main force. The Gaelic voice broke loose again.

"Caisteal Dhuni!" No, wait—God, it was *another* voice! And the first one, answering. *"Do mi! Do mi!"* To me! To me! And then a fresh wave of Mohawk shrieks rose up and drowned the voices—women, it was women screaming now, their voices even louder than the men's.

Roger flung himself at the panel, shoulder first; it cracked and splintered further, but would not give way. He tried again, and a third time, with no result. There was nothing in the longhouse that could be used as a weapon, nothing. In desperation he seized the lashings of one of the bed cubicles and tore at it with hands and teeth, ripping until he had loosened part of the frame.

He grabbed the wood, heaved; shook it and heaved again, until with a rending crack it came free in his hands, leaving him panting, holding a six-foot pole with a shattered, sharpened end. He tucked the butt end under his arm and charged the doorway, pointed end aimed like a spear at the hide flap.

He shot out into dark and flame, cold air and smoke, into noise that singed his blood. He saw a figure ahead of him, and charged it. The man danced aside, and raised a war club. Roger couldn't stop, couldn't turn, but threw himself flat, and the club smashed down inches from his head.

He rolled to the side and swung his pole wildly. It crashed against the Indian's head, and the man stumbled and went down, falling over Roger.

Whisky. The man reeked of whisky. Not stopping to wonder, Roger wriggled out from under the squirming body, staggering to his feet, pole still in his hand.

A scream came from behind him and he whirled, stabbing with all his strength as he pivoted on the ball of his foot. The shock of impact shuddered up his arms and through his chest. The man he had struck was clawing at the pole; it jerked and quivered, then was wrenched from his grasp as the man fell over.

He staggered, caught himself, then whirled toward the fire. It was an immense pyre; flames billowing in a wall of pure and ardent scarlet, vivid against the night. Through the bobbing heads of the watchers, he saw the black figure in the heart of the flame, arms spread in a gesture of benediction, lashed to the pole from which he hung. Long hair fluttered up, strands catching fire with a burst of flame, surrounding the head with a halo of gold, like Christ in a missal. Then something crashed down on Roger's head, and he dropped like a rock.

He didn't quite lose consciousness. He couldn't see or move, but he could still hear, dimly. There were voices near him. The yelling was still there, but fainter, almost a background noise, like the roar of the ocean.

He felt himself rise in the air, and the crackle of the flames got louder, it matched the roar in his ears . . . Christ, they were going to throw him into the fire! His head spun with effort and light blazed behind his shut lids, but his stubborn body wouldn't move.

The roar diminished, but paradoxically he felt warm air brush his face. He struck the ground, half bounced, and rolled, ending up on his face, his arms flung out. Cool earth was under his fingers.

He breathed. Mechanically, one breath at a time. Very slowly, the spinning sensation began to ebb.

There was noise, a long way away, but he couldn't hear anything near him but his own loud breathing. Very slowly, he opened one eye. Firelight flickered on poles and bark panels, a dim echo of the brilliance outside. Longhouse. He was inside again.

His breathing was loud and ragged in his ears. He tried to hold his breath, but couldn't. Then he realized that he *was* holding his breath; the gasping noise was coming from someone else.

It was behind him. With immense effort, he got his hands under him, and rose onto hands and knees, swaying, eyes squinted against the pain in his head.

"Jesus Christ," he muttered to himself. He rubbed a hand hard over his face and blinked, but the man was still there, six feet away.

Jamie Fraser. He was lying on his side in a huddle of limbs, a crimson plaid tangled round his body. Half his face was obscured with blood, but there wasn't any mistaking him.

For a moment, Roger just looked at him blankly. For months the greater part of his waking moments had been devoted to imagining a meeting with this man. Now it had happened, and it seemed simply impossible. There was room for no feeling beyond a sort of dull amazement.

He rubbed his face again, harder, forcing aside the fog of fear and adrenaline. What . . . *what* was Fraser doing here?

When thought and feeling connected again, his first recognizable feeling was neither fury nor alarm, but an absurd burst of joyful relief.

"She didn't," he muttered, and the words sounded queer and hoarse to his ears, after so long without spoken English. "Oh, God, she didn't do it!"

Jamie Fraser could be here for only one reason—to rescue him. And if that was so, it was because Brianna had made her father come. Whether it was misunderstanding or malevolence that had put him through the hell of the last few months, it had not been hers.

"Didn't," he said again. "She didn't." He shuddered, both with nausea from the blow and with relief.

He had thought he would be hollow forever, but suddenly there was something there; something small, but very solid. Something he could hold in the cup of his heart. *Brianna.* He had her back.

There was another set of high-pitched screams from just outside; ululations that went on and on, sticking into his flesh like a thousand pins. He jerked, and shuddered again, all other feelings subsumed in renewed realization.

Dying with the reassurance that Brianna loved him was better than dying without it—but he hadn't wanted to die in the first place. He remembered what he had seen outside, felt his gorge rise, and choked it down.

With a trembling hand he began the unfamiliar sign of the Cross. "In the name of the Father," he whispered, and then the words failed him. "Please," he whispered instead. "Please, don't let him have been right."

He crawled shakily to Fraser's body, hoping that the man was still alive. He was; blood was flowing from a gash on Fraser's temple, and when he thrust his fingers under the man's jaw, he could feel the steady bump of a pulse.

There was water in one of the pots under the shattered bed

frame; luckily it hadn't spilled. He dipped the end of the plaid in water and used it to mop Fraser's face. After a few minutes of this ministration, the man's eyelids began to flutter.

Fraser coughed, gagged heavily, turned his head to one side, and threw up. Then his eyes shot open, and before Roger could speak or move, Fraser had rolled up onto one knee, his hand on the *sgian dhu* in his stocking.

Blue eyes glared at him, and Roger raised an arm in instinctive defense. Then Fraser blinked, shook his head, groaned, and sat down heavily on the earthen floor.

"Oh, it's you," he said. He closed his eyes and groaned again. Then his head snapped up, eyes blue and piercing, but this time with alarm rather than fury.

"Claire!" he exclaimed. "My wife, where is she?"

Roger felt his jaw drop.

"Claire? You brought her *here*? You brought a woman into *this*?"

Fraser gave him a glance of extreme dislike, but wasted no words. Palming the knife from his stocking, he glanced at the doorway. The flap was down; no one was visible. The noise outside had died down, though the rumble of voices was still audible. Now and then one stood out, shouting or raised in exhortation.

"There's a guard," Roger said.

Fraser glanced at him and rose to his feet, smooth as a panther. Blood was still running down the side of his face, but it didn't seem to trouble him. Silently, he flattened himself along the wall, glided to the edge of the door flap, and eased the flap aside with the tip of the tiny dagger.

Fraser grimaced at whatever he saw. Letting the flap swing back in place, he returned and sat down, putting the knife away in his stocking.

"A good dozen of them just outside. Is that water?" He put out a hand, and Roger silently scooped a gourdful of water and handed it to him. He drank deeply, splashed water in his face, then poured the rest of it over his head.

Fraser wiped a hand over his battered face, then opened bloodshot eyes and looked at Roger.

"Wakefield, is it?"

"I go by my own name, these days. MacKenzie."

Fraser gave a brief, humorless snort.

"So I've heard." He had a wide, expressive mouth—like Bree's. His lips compressed briefly, then relaxed.

"I've done wrong to ye, MacKenzie, as ye'll know. I've come to put it right, so far as may be, but it may be as I'll not have the chance." He gestured briefly toward the door. "For now, you've my apology. For what satisfaction ye may want of me later—I'll bide your will. But I'd ask ye to let it wait until we're safe out of this."

Roger stared at him for a moment. Satisfaction for the last months of torment and uncertainty seemed as farfetched a notion as the thought of safety. He nodded.

"Done," he said.

They sat in silence for several moments. The fire in the hut was burning low, but the wood to feed it was outside; the guards kept charge of anything that might be used as a weapon.

"What happened?" Roger asked at last. He nodded toward the door. "Out there?"

Fraser took a deep breath and let it out in a sigh. For the first time, Roger noticed that he held the elbow of his right arm cradled in his left palm, the arm itself held close to the body.

"I will be damned if I know," he said.

"They did burn the priest? He's dead?" There could be no doubt of it after what he'd seen, but still Roger felt compelled to ask.

"He was a priest?" Thick reddish brows rose in surprise, then fell. "Aye, he's dead. And not only him." An involuntary shudder went over the Highlander's big frame.

Fraser hadn't known what they meant to do when the drums began to sound, and everyone went out to gather by the great fire. There was plenty of talk, but his knowledge of the Mohawk tongue was insufficient to make out what was happening, and his nephew, who spoke the tongue, was nowhere to be found.

The whites had not been invited, but no one made any move to keep them away. And so it was that he and Claire had come to be standing on the edge of the crowd, curious onlookers, when the *sachem* and the Council came out and the old man began to speak. Another man had spoken, too, very angrily.

"Then they brought the man out, naked as a tadpole, bound him to a stake, and started in upon him." He paused, eyes shadowed, and glanced at Roger.

"I'll tell ye, man, I've seen French executioners keep a man alive who wished he weren't. It wasna worse than that—but no a great deal better." Fraser drank again, thirstily, and lowered the cup.

"I tried to take Claire away—I didna ken but what they meant to attack us next." The crowd was pressed so tight around them, though, that movement was impossible; there was no choice but to go on watching.

Roger's mouth felt dry, and he reached for the cup. He didn't want to ask, but he felt a perverse need to know—whether for Alexandre's sake or for his own.

"Did he—cry out at all?"

Fraser gave him another glance of surprise, then something like understanding crossed his face.

"No," he said slowly. "He died verra well—by their lights. Ye will have been knowing the man?"

Roger nodded, wordless. It was difficult to believe Alexandre was gone, even hearing this. And *where* had he gone? Surely he could not have been right. *I will not be forgiven.* Surely not. No just God—

Roger shook his head hard, pushing the thought away. It was plain that Fraser had no more than half his mind on his story, horrific as it was. He kept glancing at the door, a look of anxious expectation on his face. Was he expecting rescue?

"How many men did you bring with you?"

The blue eyes flashed, surprised.

"My nephew Ian."

"That's all?" Roger tried to keep the stunned disbelief out of his voice, but patently failed.

"Ye were expecting the 78th Hieland regiment?" Fraser asked sarcastically. He got to his feet, swaying slightly, arm pressed to his side. "I brought whisky."

"Whisky? Did that have anything to do with the fighting?" Remembering the reek of the man who had fallen over him, Roger nodded toward the wall of the longhouse.

"It may have."

Fraser went to the wall with the cracked panel, and pressed an eye against the opening, staring out at the clearing for some time before returning to the dwindling fire. Things had gone quiet outside.

The big Highlander was looking more than unwell. His face was white and sheened with sweat under the streaks of dried blood. Roger silently poured more water; it was as silently accepted. He knew well enough what was wrong with Fraser, and it wasn't the effects of injury.

"When you last saw her—"

"When the fighting broke out." Unable to stay seated, Fraser set down the cup and got to his feet again, prowling the confines of the longhouse like a restless bear. He paused, glancing at Roger.

"Will ye maybe ken a bit what happened there?"

"I could guess." He acquainted Fraser with the priest's story, finding some small respite from worry in the telling.

"They wouldn't have harmed her," he said, trying to reassure himself as much as Fraser. "She'd nothing to do with it."

Fraser gave a derisory snort.

"Aye, she did." Without warning, he smashed a fist against the ground, in a muffled thump of fury. "Damn the woman!"

"She'll be all right," Roger repeated stubbornly. He couldn't bear to think otherwise, but he knew what Fraser plainly knew as well—if Claire Fraser was alive, unhurt, and free, nothing could have kept her from her husband's side. And as for the unknown nephew . . .

"I heard your nephew—in the fight. I heard him call out to you. He sounded all right." Even as he offered this bit of information, he knew how feeble it was as reassurance. Fraser nodded, though, head bent on his knees.

"He's a good lad, Ian," he murmured. "And he has friends among the Mohawk. God send they will protect him."

Roger's curiosity was coming back, as the shock of the evening began to fade.

"Your wife," he said. "What did she do? How could she possibly have been involved in this?"

Fraser sighed. He scrubbed his good hand over his face and through his hair, rubbing until the loose red locks stood up in knots and snarls.

"I shouldna have said so," he said. "It wasna her fault in the least. It's only—she'll not be killed, but God, if they've harmed her . . ."

"They won't," Roger said firmly. "What happened?"

Fraser shrugged and closed his eyes. Head tilted back, he described the scene as though he could still see it, engraved on the inside of his eyelids. Perhaps he could.

"I didna take heed of the girl, in such a crowd. I couldna even say what she looked like. It was only at the last that I saw her."

Claire had been by his side, white-faced and rigid in the press of shouting, swaying bodies. When the Indians had nearly finished with the priest, they untied him from the stake and fastened his hands instead to a long pole, held above his head, from which to suspend him in the flames.

Fraser glanced at him, wiping the back of a hand across his lips.

"I've seen a man's heart pulled beating from his chest before," he said. "But I hadna seen it eaten before his eyes." He spoke almost shyly, as though apologizing for his squeamishness. Shocked, he had looked to Claire. It was then that he had seen the Indian girl standing on Claire's other side, with a cradleboard in her arms.

With great calmness, the girl had handed the board to Claire, then turned and slipped through the crowd.

"She didna look to left or right, but walked straight into the fire."

"What?" Roger's throat closed with shock, the exclamation emerging in a strangled croak.

The flames had embraced the girl in moments. A head taller than the folk near him, Jamie had seen everything clearly.

"Her clothes caught, and then her hair. By the time she reached him, she was burning like a torch." Still, he had seen the dark silhouette of her arms, raised to embrace the empty body of the priest. Within moments, it was no longer possible to distinguish man or woman; there was only the one figure, black amid the towering flames.

"It was then everything went mad." Fraser's wide shoulders slumped a little, and he touched the gash in his temple. "All I ken is one woman set up a howl, and then there was the hell of a screech, and of a sudden, everyone was either fleeing or fighting."

He had himself tried to do both, shielding Claire and her burden while fighting his way out of the thrashing press of bodies. There were too many of them, though. Unable to escape, he had pushed Claire against the wall of a longhouse, seized a stick of wood with which to defend them, and shouted for Ian, while wielding his makeshift club on anyone reckless enough to come near.

"Then a wee fiend leapt out o' the smoke, and struck me with his club." He shrugged, one-shouldered. "I turned to fight him off, and then there were three of them on me." Something had caught him in the temple, and he had known no more till waking in the longhouse with Roger.

"I havena seen Claire since. Nor Ian."

The fire had burned itself to coals, and it was growing cold in the longhouse. Jamie unfastened his brooch and pulled the plaid around his shoulders as well as he could, one-handed, and leaned gingerly back against the wall.

His right arm might be broken; he'd taken a blow from one of the war clubs just below the shoulder, and the stricken spot went from numbness to blinding pain with no warning. That was of no moment, though, compared with his worry for Claire and wee Ian.

It was very late. If Claire hadn't been hurt in the fighting, she was likely safe enough, he told himself. The old woman wouldn't countenance harm done to her. As for Ian, though—he felt a moment's pride in the lad, in spite of his fear. Ian was a bonny fighter, and a credit to the uncle who'd taught him.

If he should have been overcome, though . . . there had been so many of the savages, and with the fighting so hot . . .

He shifted restlessly, trying not to think of facing his sister with ill news of her youngest boy. Christ, he'd rather have his own heart torn from his breast and eaten before his eyes; it would feel much the same.

Seeking distraction—any distraction—from his fears, he shifted again, taking random stock of the shadowy insides of the house. Bare as a Skyeman's cupboard, for the most part. A jug of water, a broken bed frame, and one or two tattered skins for bedding lying crumpled on the earthen floor.

MacKenzie was sitting hunched across the fire, heedless of the growing chill. His arms were wrapped about his knees, head bent in thought. He was half turned away, unaware of Jamie's eye on him.

He grudged to admit it, but the man was decently made. Long shanks and a good breadth through the shoulders; he'd have a fair reach with a sword. He was tall as the MacKenzies of Leoch— and why not? he thought suddenly. The man was Dougal's get, if a few generations onward.

He found that notion both disturbing and oddly comforting. He'd killed men when he must, and mostly their ghosts let him sleep at night with no great rattling of bones. Dougal's death, though, was one that he had lived through more than once, and woke from sweating, with the sound of those last silent words of Dougal's ringing in his ears; words mouthed in blood.

There'd been not the slightest choice; it was kill or be killed,

and a near thing either way. And yet . . . Dougal MacKenzie
had been his foster father, and if he was honest, a part of him had
loved the man.

Yes, it was some comfort to know that a small part of Dougal
was left. The other part of this MacKenzie's heritage was a wee
bit more troubling. He'd seen the man's eyes first thing when he
woke, bright green and intent, and for one second his wame had
shriveled up into a ball, thinking of Geillis Duncan.

Did he much want his daughter linked with a witch's spawn?
He eyed the man covertly. Perhaps it was as well if Brianna's
child was not of this man's blood.

"Brianna," MacKenzie said, lifting his head suddenly from his
knees. "Where is she?"

Jamie jerked, and a hot knife-blade seared his arm, leaving him
sweating.

"Where?" he said. "At River Run, with her aunt. She's safe."
His heart was thundering in his ears. Christ, was the man able to
read thoughts? Or had he the Sight?

The green eyes were steady, dark in the dim light.

"Why did you bring Claire, and not Brianna? Why did she not
come with you?"

Jamie returned the man's cool look. They'd see if it was a
matter of mind reading or not. If not, the last thing he meant to
tell MacKenzie now was the truth; time enough for that when—if
—they were safely away.

"I should have left Claire as well, if I thought I could. She's a
stubborn wee besom. Short of tying her hand and foot, I couldna
prevent her coming."

Something dark flickered in MacKenzie's eyes—doubt, or
pain?

"I should not have thought Brianna the kind of lass to mind her
father's word overmuch," he said. His voice had an edge to it—
yes, pain, and a sort of jealousy.

Jamie relaxed slightly. No mind reading.

"Did ye no? Well, and perhaps ye dinna ken her so well as all
that," he said. Pleasantly enough, but with a jeering undertone
that would make one sort of man go for his throat.

MacKenzie wasn't that sort. He sat up straight, and drew a deep
breath.

"I know her well," he said levelly. "She is my wife."

Jamie sat up straight in turn, and clenched his teeth on a hiss of
pain.

"The hell she is."

MacKenzie's black brows drew down at that.

"We are handfast, she and I. Did she not tell you that?"

She hadn't—but he hadn't given her much chance to tell him, either. Too furious at the thought of her willing to bed a man, stung at thinking she'd made a fool of him, proud as Lucifer and suffering the Devil's pains for it, in wishing her perfect and finding her only as human as himself.

"When?" Jamie asked.

"Early September, in Wilmington. When I—just before I left her." The admission came unwillingly, and through the black veil of his own guilt he saw a reflection of it on MacKenzie's face. As well deserved as his own, he thought viciously. If the coward had not left her . . .

"She didna tell me."

He saw the doubt and the pain in MacKenzie's eyes quite clearly now. The man worried that Brianna did not want him—for if she did, she would have come. He knew well enough that no power on earth or below it would keep Claire from *his* side if she thought him in danger—and felt a jolt of fear renewed at that thought; for where was she?

"I suppose she thought you wouldn't see handfasting as a legal form of marriage," MacKenzie said quietly.

"Or perhaps she didna see it so herself," Jamie suggested cruelly. He could relieve the man's mind by telling him a part of the truth—that Brianna had not come because she was with child—but he was in no charitable mood.

It was getting quite dark, but even so he could see MacKenzie's face flush at that, and his hands clench on the ragged deerskin.

"I saw it so," was all he said.

Jamie closed his eyes, and said no more. The last coals in the fire died slowly, leaving them in darkness.

61

The Office of a Priest

The smell of burnt things hung in the air. We passed close by the pit and I couldn't help seeing from the corner of my eye the heap of charred fragments, shattered ends frosted white with ash. I hoped it was wood. I was afraid to look directly.

I stumbled on the frozen ground, and my escort caught me by the arm. Pulled me up without comment and pushed me toward a longhouse where two men stood on guard, huddled against a cold wind that filled the air with drifting ashes.

I had not slept and had not eaten, though food was offered. My feet and my fingers were cold. There was keening from a longhouse at the far end of the village, and over it the louder formal chant of a death song. Was it for the girl that they sang, or someone else? I shivered.

The guards glanced at me and stood aside. I lifted the hide flap at the door and went in.

It was dark; the fire inside as dead as the one outside. Gray light from the smokehole gave me enough illumination to see an untidy heap of skins and cloth on the floor, though. A patch of red tartan showed amid the jumble, and I felt a surge of relief.

"Jamie!"

The pile heaved and came apart. Jamie's rumpled head popped up, alert but looking a good deal the worse for wear. Next to him was a dark, bearded man who seemed oddly familiar. Then he moved into the light, and I caught the flash of green eyes above the shrubbery.

"Roger!" I exclaimed.

Without a word he rose out of the blankets and clasped me in his arms. He held so tight, I could hardly breathe.

He was terribly thin; I could feel every one of his ribs. Not starved, though; he stank, but with the normal scents of dirt and stale sweat, not the yeasty effluvium of starvation.

"Roger, are you all right?" He let go, and I looked him up and down, searching for any signs of injury.

"Yes," he said. His voice was husky, from sleep and emotion. "Bree? She's all right?"

"She's fine," I assured him. "What's happened to your foot?" He wore nothing but a tattered shirt and a stained rag wrapped around one foot.

"A cut. Nothing. Where is she?" He clutched my arm, anxious.

"At a place called River Run, with her great-aunt. Didn't Jamie tell you? She's—"

I was interrupted by Jamie clutching my other arm.

"Are ye all right, Sassenach?"

"Yes, of course I—my God, what happened to you?" My attention was momentarily distracted from Roger by the sight of Jamie. It wasn't the nasty contusion on his temple or the dried blood on his shirt that struck my notice, so much as the unnatural way he held his right arm.

"My arm's maybe broken," he said. "Hurts like a bugger. Will ye come and tend to it?"

Without waiting for an answer he turned and walked away, sitting down heavily near the broken bed frame. I gave Roger a brief pat and went after him, wondering what the hell. Jamie wouldn't admit to being in pain in front of Roger Wakefield, if splintered raw bone were sticking out of his flesh.

"What are you up to?" I muttered, kneeling beside him. I felt the arm gingerly through his shirt—no compound fractures. I rolled it carefully up for a better look.

"I havena told him about Brianna," he said, very softly. "And I think it better you do not."

I stared at him.

"We can't do that! He has to know."

"Keep your voice down. Aye, he maybe should know about the bairn—but not the other, not Bonnet."

I bit my lip, feeling gingerly down the swell of his biceps. He had one of the worst bruises I had ever seen; a huge mottled splotch of purple-blue—but I was fairly sure the arm wasn't broken.

I wasn't so sure about his suggestion.

He could see the doubt on my face; he squeezed my hand hard.

"Not yet; not here. Let it wait, at least until we're safe away."

I thought for a moment, as I ripped the sleeve of his shirt and used it to make a rough sling. Learning that Brianna was pregnant was going to be a shock by itself. Perhaps Jamie was right; there was no telling how Roger would react to the news of the rape, and we were a long way from being home free yet. Better he should have his head clear. At last I nodded, reluctantly.

"All right," I said aloud, getting up. "I don't think it's broken, but the sling will help."

I left Jamie sitting on the ground and went to Roger, feeling like a Ping-Pong ball.

"How's the foot?" I knelt to unwrap the unsanitary-looking rag around it, but he stopped me with an urgent hand on my shoulder.

"Brianna. I know there's something wrong. Is she—"

"She's pregnant."

Whatever possibilities he had been turning over in his mind, that hadn't been among them. It isn't possible to mistake sheer amazement. He blinked, looking as though I'd hit him on the head with an ax.

"Are you sure?"

"She'll be seven months gone by now; it's noticeable." Jamie had come up so quietly that neither of us had heard him. He spoke coldly, and looked even colder, but Roger was well beyond noticing subtleties.

Excitement brightened his eyes, and his shocked face came alive beneath the black whiskers.

"Pregnant. My God, but how?"

Jamie made a derisive noise in the back of his throat. Roger glanced at him, then quickly away.

"That is, I never thought—"

"*How?* Aye, ye didna think, and it's my daughter left to pay the price of your pleasure!"

Roger's head snapped round at that, and he glared at Jamie.

"She is not left, in any way! I told you she is my wife!"

"She is?" I said, startled in the midst of my unwrapping.

"They're handfast," Jamie said, very grudgingly. "Why could the lass not have told us, though?"

I thought I could answer that one—in more than one way. The second answer wasn't one I could suggest in front of Roger, though.

She hadn't said, because she was with child, and thought it was Bonnet's. Believing that, she might have thought it better not to reveal their handfasting, so as to leave Roger an escape—if he wanted it.

"Most likely because she thought you wouldn't see that as a true marriage," I said. "I'd told her about our wedding; about the contract and how you insisted on marrying me in church, with a priest. She wouldn't want to tell you anything she thought you might not approve of—she wanted so badly to please you."

Jamie had the grace to look abashed at this, but Roger ignored the argument.

"Is she well?" he asked, leaning forward and grasping my arm.

"Yes, she's fine," I assured him, hoping it was still true. "She wanted to come with us, but of course we couldn't let her do that."

"She wanted to come?" His face lighted up, joy and relief plain to see, even through the hair and filth. "Then she didn't—" He stopped abruptly, and glanced from me to Jamie and back. "When I met . . . Mr. Fraser on the mountainside, he seemed to think that she—er—had said—"

"A terrible misunderstanding," I put in hastily. "She hadn't told us about the handfasting, so when she turned up pregnant, we, er . . . assumed . . ." Jamie was brooding, looking at Roger with no particular favor, but jerked into awareness when I nudged him sharply.

"Oh, aye," he said, a little grudgingly. "A mistake. I've given Mr. Wakefield my apologies and told him I shall do my best to see it right. But we've other things to think of now. Have ye seen Ian, Sassenach?"

"No." I became aware for the first time that Ian was not with them, and felt a small lurch of fear in the pit of my stomach. Jamie looked grim.

"Where have ye been all night, Sassenach?"

"I was with—oh, Jesus!"

I ignored his question for a moment, caught up in the sight of Roger's foot. The flesh was swollen and reddened over half his foot, with a severe ulceration on the outer margin of the sole. I pressed firmly, a little way in, and felt the nasty give of small pockets of pus under the skin.

"What happened here?"

"I cut it, trying to get away. They bound it and put things on it, but it's been infected on and off. It gets better, and then it gets worse." He shrugged; his attention wasn't on his foot, ugly as it was. He looked up at Jamie, evidently having come to a decision.

"Brianna didn't send you to meet me, then? She didn't ask you to—get rid of me?"

"No," Jamie said, taken by surprise. He smiled briefly, his features suffused with sudden charm. "That was my own notion."

Roger drew a deep breath and closed his eyes briefly.

"Thank God," he said, and opened them. "I thought perhaps she'd—we'd had a terrible argument, just before I left her, and I thought maybe that was why she hadn't told you about the hand-fasting; that she'd decided she didn't want to be married to me."

There was sweat on his forehead, either from the news or from my handling of his foot. He smiled, a little painfully. "Having me beaten to death or sold into slavery seemed a trifle extreme, though, even for a woman with her temper."

"Mmphm." Jamie was slightly flushed. "I did say I was sorry for it."

"I know." Roger looked at him for a minute, evidently making up his mind about something. He took a deep breath, then bent down and put my hand gently away from his foot. He straightened up and met Jamie's eyes, dead-on.

"I've something to tell you. What we fought over. Has she told you what brought her here—to find you?"

"The death notice? Aye, she's told us. Ye dinna think I'd allow Claire to come with me otherwise?"

"What?" Puzzled wariness showed in Roger's eyes.

"Ye canna have it both ways. If she and I are to die at Fraser's Ridge six years from now, we canna very well be killed by the Iroquois any time before that, now can we?"

I stared at him; that particular implication had escaped me. Rather staggering; practical immortality—for a time. But that was assuming—

"That's assuming that you can't change the past—that *we* can't, I mean. Do you believe that?" Roger leaned forward a little, intent.

"I will be damned if I know. Do *you* think so?"

"Yes," Roger said flatly. "I do think the past can't be changed. That's why I did it."

"Did what?"

He licked his lips, but went doggedly on.

"I found that death notice long before Brianna did. I thought, though, that it would be useless to try to change things. So I—I kept it from her." He looked from me to Jamie. "So now you know. I didn't want her to come; I did everything I could to keep her away from you. I thought it was too dangerous. And—I was afraid of losing her," he ended simply.

To my surprise, Jamie was looking at Roger with sudden approval.

"Ye tried to keep her safe, then? To protect her?"

Roger nodded, a certain relief lessening the tension in his shoulders.

"So you understand?"

"Aye, I do. That's the first thing I've heard that gives me a good opinion of ye, sir."

It wasn't an opinion I shared at the moment.

"You found that thing—and didn't tell her?" I could feel the blood climbing into my cheeks.

Roger saw the look on my face, and looked away.

"No. She . . . um . . . she saw it your way, I'm afraid. She thought—well, she said I'd betrayed her, and—"

"And you did! Her and us both! Of all the—Roger, how could you *do* such a thing?"

"He did right," Jamie said. "After all—" I turned on him fiercely, interrupting.

"He did *not*! He deliberately kept it from her, and tried to keep her from—don't you realize, if he'd succeeded, you'd never have seen her?"

"Aye, I do. And what's happened to her would not have happened." His eyes were deep blue, steady on mine. "I would it had been so."

I swallowed down my grief and anger, until I thought I could speak again without choking.

"I don't think *she* would have had it so," I said softly. "And it was hers to say."

Roger jumped in, before Jamie could reply.

"You said what's happened to her wouldn't have—you mean, being pregnant?" He didn't wait for a reply; he had plainly recovered from the shock of the news sufficiently to begin thinking, and was rapidly reaching the same unpleasant conclusions Brianna had come to, some months earlier. He swung his head toward me, eyes wide with shock.

"She's seven months along, you said. Jesus! She can't go back!"

"Not *now*," I said, with bitter emphasis. "She might have, when we first found out. I tried to make her go back to Scotland, or at least to the Indies—there's another . . . opening, there. But she wouldn't do it. She wouldn't go without finding out what happened to you.''

''What happened to me,'' he repeated, and glanced at Jamie. Jamie's shoulders tensed, and he set his jaw.

''Aye,'' he said. ''It's my fault, and no remedy for it. She's trapped here. And I can do nothing for her—save bring ye back to her.'' And that, I realized, was why he had not wanted to tell Roger anything; for fear that when he realized Brianna was trapped in the past, Roger would refuse to come back with us. Following her into the past was one thing; staying there forever with her was something else again. Neither was it guilt over Bonnet alone that had eaten Jamie up on our journey here; the Spartan boy with the fox gnawing at his vitals would have recognized a kindred soul on the spot, I thought, looking at him with exasperated tenderness.

Roger gazed at him, completely at a loss for words.

Before he could find any, a noise of shuffling footsteps approached the door of the hut. The flap lifted, and a large number of Mohawks came in, one after the other.

We looked at them in astonishment; there were about fifteen of them, men and women and children, all dressed for traveling, in leggings and furs. One of the older women held a cradleboard, and without hesitation she walked up to Roger and pressed it into his arms, saying something in Mohawk.

He frowned at her, not understanding. Jamie, suddenly alert, leaned toward her and said a few halting words. She repeated what she had said, impatiently, then looked behind her and motioned to a young man.

''You are . . . priest,'' he said haltingly to Roger. He pointed at the cradleboard. ''Water.''

''I'm not a priest.'' Roger tried to give the board back to the woman, but she refused to take it.

''Prees,'' she said definitely. ''Babtize.'' She motioned to one of the younger women, who stepped forward, holding a small bowl made of horn, filled with water.

''Father Alexandre—he say you priest, son of priest,'' said the young man. I saw Roger's face go pale beneath the beard.

Jamie had stepped aside, murmuring in French patois to a man he recognized among the crowd. Now he pushed his way back to us.

''These are what is left of the priest's flock,'' he said softly.

"The council has told them to leave. They mean to travel to the Huron mission at Ste. Berthe, but they would have the child baptized, lest it die on the journey." He glanced at Roger. "They think ye are a priest?"

"Evidently." Roger looked down at the child in his arms.

Jamie hesitated, glancing at the waiting Indians. They stood patiently, their faces calm. I could only guess what lay behind them. Fire and death, exile—what else? There were marks of sorrow on the face of the old woman who brought the baby; she would be its grandmother, I thought.

"In case of need," Jamie said quietly to Roger, "any man may do the office of a priest."

I wouldn't have thought it was possible for Roger to go any whiter, but he did. He swayed briefly, and the old lady, alarmed, reached out a hand to steady the cradleboard.

He caught himself, though, and nodded to the young woman with the water, to come closer.

"Parlez-vous français?" he asked, and heads nodded, some with certainty, some with less.

"C'est bien," he said, and taking a deep breath, lifted the cradleboard, showing the child to the congregation. The baby, a round-faced charmer with soft brown curls and a golden skin, blinked sleepily at the change of perspective.

"Hear the words of our Lord Jesus Christ," he said clearly in French. "Obeying the word of our Lord Jesus, and sure of his presence with us, we baptize those whom he has called to be his own."

Of course, I thought, watching him. He *was* the son of a priest, so to speak; he would often enough have seen the Reverend administer the sacrament of baptism. If he didn't recall the entire service, he seemed to know the general form of it.

He had the baby passed from hand to hand among the congregation—for so his agreement had made them—following and asking questions of each person there, in a low voice.

"Qui est votre Seigneur, votre Sauveur?" Who is your Lord and Savior?

"Voulez-vous placer votre foi en Lui?" Do you have faith in Him?

"Do you promise to tell this child the good news of the gospel, and all that Christ commands, and by your fellowship, to strengthen his family ties with the household of God?"

Head after head bobbed in reply.

"Oui, certainement. Je le promets. Nous le ferons." Yes, of course. I promise. We will.

At last Roger turned and gave the child to Jamie.

"Who is your Lord and Savior?"

"Jesus Christ," he answered without hesitation, and the baby was handed on to me.

"Do you trust in him?"

I looked down into the face of innocence, and answered for it. "I do."

He took the cradleboard, gave it to the grandmother, then dipping a sprig of juniper into the bowl of water, sprinkled water on the baby's head.

"I baptize you—" he began, and stopped, with a sudden panicked glance at me.

"It's a girl," I murmured, and he nodded, lifting the sprig of juniper again.

"I baptize you, Alexandra, in the name of the Father and of the Son and of the Holy Spirit, Amen."

After the small band of Christians had left, there were no more visitors. A warrior brought us wood for the fire, and some food, but he ignored Jamie's questions and left, saying nothing.

"Do you think they'll kill us?" Roger asked suddenly, after a period of silence. His mouth twitched in an attempted smile. "Kill me, I suppose I mean. Presumably the two of you are safe."

He didn't sound worried. Looking at the deep shadows and lines in his face, I thought that he was simply too exhausted to be afraid anymore.

"They won't kill us," I said, and pushed a hand through the tangle of my hair. I dimly realized that I, too, was exhausted; I had been without sleep for more than thirty-six hours.

"I started out to tell you. I spent last night in Tewaktenyonh's house. The Council of Mothers met there."

They hadn't told me everything; they never would. But at the end of the long hours of ceremony and discussion, the girl who spoke English had told me as much as they wanted me to know, before they sent me back to Jamie.

"Some of the young men found the whisky cache," I said. "They brought it back to the village yesterday, and started to drink. The women thought they didn't mean anything dishonest, that they thought the bargain was already made. But then some argument started among them, just before they lit the fire to—to execute the priest. A fight broke out, and some of the men ran into the crowd, and—one thing led to another.'' I rubbed a hand hard over my face, trying to keep my thoughts clear enough to speak.

"A man was killed in the fighting." I glanced at Roger. "They think you killed him; did you?"

He shook his head, shoulders slumping with tiredness.

"I don't know. I—probably. What will they do about it?"

"Well, it took them a long time to decide, and it isn't settled yet; they've sent word to the main Council, but the *sachem* hasn't made a decision yet." I took a deep breath.

"They won't kill you, because the whisky was taken, and that was offered as the price of your life. But since they've decided not to kill us in revenge for their dead, what they usually do instead is to adopt an enemy into the tribe, in replacement of the dead man."

That shook Roger out of his numbness.

"Adopt me? They want to keep me?"

"One of us. One of you. I don't suppose I'd be a suitable replacement, since I'm not a man." I tried to smile, but failed completely. All the muscles of my face had gone numb.

"Then it must be me," Jamie said quietly.

Roger's head jerked up, startled.

"You've said yourself, if the past canna be changed, then nothing will happen to me. Leave me, and as soon as it can be managed, I will escape and come home."

He laid a hand on my arm before I could protest.

"You and Ian will take MacKenzie back to Brianna." He looked at Roger, his face inscrutable. "After all," he said quietly, "it's the two of you she needs."

Roger started in at once to argue, but I butted in.

"May the Lord deliver me from stubborn Scotsmen!" I said. I glared at the two of them. "They haven't decided yet. That's only what the Council of Mothers says. So there's no sense in arguing about it until we know for sure. And speaking of knowing things for sure," I said, in hopes of distracting them, "where's Ian?"

Jamie stared at me.

"I don't know," he said, and I saw his throat ripple as he swallowed. "But I hope to God he's safe in that girl's bed."

No one came. The night passed quietly, though none of us slept well. I dozed fitfully, through sheer exhaustion, waking every time there was a sound outside, my dreams a vivid crazy-quilt of blood and fire and water.

It was midday before we heard the sound of voices approaching. My heart leapt as I recognized one of them, and Jamie was on his feet before the door flap lifted.

"Ian? Is that you?"

"Aye, Uncle. It's me."

His voice sounded odd; breathless and uncertain. He stepped into the light from the smokehole and I gasped, feeling as though I had been punched in the stomach.

The hair had been plucked from the sides of his skull; what was left stood up in a thick crest from his scalp, a long tail hanging down his back. One ear had been freshly pierced and sported a silver earring.

His face had been tattooed. Double crescent lines of small dark spots, most still scabbed with dried blood, ran across each cheekbone, to meet at the bridge of his nose.

"I—canna stay long, Uncle," Ian said. He looked pale, under the lines of tattooing, but stood erect. "I said they must let me come to say goodbye."

Jamie had gone white to the lips.

"Jesus, Ian," he whispered.

"The naming ceremony is tonight," Ian said, trying not to look at us. "They say that after that I will be Indian, and I must not speak any tongue but the *Kahnyen'kehaka;* I canna speak again in English, or the Gaelic." He smiled painfully. "And I ken ye didna have much Mohawk."

"Ian, ye canna be doing this!"

"I've done it, Uncle Jamie," Ian said softly. He looked at me then.

"Auntie. Will ye say to my mother that I willna forget her? My Da will know, I think."

"Oh, Ian!" I hugged him hard, and his arms went gently around me.

"Ye can leave in the morning," he said to Jamie. "They willna prevent ye."

I let him go, and he crossed the hut to where Roger stood, looking stunned. Ian offered him a hand.

"I am sorry for what we did to ye," he said quietly. "Ye'll take good care of my cousin and the bairn?"

Roger took his hand and shook it. He cleared his throat and found his voice.

"I will," he said. "I promise."

Then Ian turned to Jamie.

"No, Ian," he said. "God, no, lad. Let it be me!"

Ian smiled, though his eyes were full of tears. "Ye said to me once, that my life wasna meant to be wasted," he said. "It won't be." He held out his arms. "I willna forget you, either, Uncle Jamie."

They took Ian to the bank of the river, just before sunset. He stripped and waded into the freezing water, accompanied by three women, who ducked and pummeled him, laughing and scrubbing him with handfuls of sand. Rollo ran up and down the bank, barking madly, then plunged into the river and joined in what he plainly saw as fun and games, coming close to drowning Ian in the process.

All of the spectators who lined the bank found it hilarious— save the three whites.

Once the white blood had been thus ceremonially scrubbed from Ian's body, more women dried him, dressed him in fresh clothing, and took him to the Council longhouse for the naming ceremony.

Everyone crowded inside; all of the village was there. Jamie, Roger, and I stood silently in a corner, watching as the *sachem* sang and spoke over him, as the drums beat, as the pipe was lit and passed from hand to hand. The girl he called Emily stood near him, eyes shining as she looked at him. I saw him look back at her, and the light that sprang up in his own eyes did a little to ease the soreness of my heart.

They called him Wolf's Brother. His brother wolf sat panting at Jamie's feet, viewing the proceedings with interest.

At the end of the ceremony a small hush fell on the crowd, and at that moment Jamie stepped out of the corner. All heads turned as he crossed to Ian, and I saw more than one warrior tense in disapproval.

He unpinned the brooch from his plaid, unbelted it, and laid the length of bloodstained crimson tartan across his nephew's shoulder.

"*Cuimhnich,*" he said softly, and stepped back. *Remember.*

All of us were quiet as we made our way down the narrow trail
that led away from the village next morning. Ian had taken a
formal, white-faced farewell of us as he stood with his new family. I hadn't been so stalwart, though, and seeing my tears made
Ian bite his lip to hold back his own emotion. Jamie had embraced
him, kissed his mouth and left him, without speaking a word.

Jamie went about the business of setting camp that night with
his usual efficiency, but I could tell that his mind was somewhere
else. And no wonder if it was; my own was divided in worry
between Ian behind us and Brianna ahead of us, with very little
attention to spare for present circumstances.

Roger dumped an armload of wood beside the fire and sat down
next to me.

"I've been thinking," he said quietly. "About Brianna."

"Have you? So have I." I was so tired, I thought I might
tumble headfirst into the flames before I got the water boiling.

"You said there was another circle—opening, whatever it is—
in the Indies?"

"Yes." I thought briefly of telling him all about Geilie Duncan
and the cave at Abandawe, and dismissed it. I hadn't the energy.
Another time. Then I jerked out of my mental fog, catching what
he was saying.

"Another one? Here?" I looked wildly around, as though expecting to see a menhir standing menacingly at my back.

"Not *here,*" he said. "Somewhere between here and Fraser's
Ridge, though."

"Oh." I tried to gather my scattered thoughts. "Yes, I know
there is, but—" Then it penetrated, and I grabbed his arm. "You
mean you *know* where it is?"

"You knew about it?" He stared at me in astonishment.

"Yes, I—here, look . . ." I scrabbled in my pouch and came
up with the opal. He grabbed it from me before I could explain.

"Look! It's the same; this same symbol—it's carved on the
rock in the circle. Where the hell did you get this?"

"It's a long story," I said. "I'll tell you later. But for now—do
you know where this circle is? You've actually seen it?"

Jamie, attracted by our excitement, had come to see what was
going on.

"A circle?"

"A time-circle, an opening, a—a—"

"I've been there," Roger said, interrupting my stuttering explanations. "I found it by accident while I was trying to escape."

"Could you find it again? How far is it from River Run?" My mind was making frantic calculations. A little more than seven months. If it took six weeks to return, Brianna would be eight and a half months gone. Could we possibly take her into the mountains in time? And if we could—what would be the greater risk, to travel through a time-passage on the verge of delivery, or to stay in the past permanently?

Roger dug in the waistband of his ragged breeches and brought out a strand of thread, grimy and knotted. "Here," he said, grasping a double knot. "It was eight days past the day that they took me. Eight days from Fraser's Ridge."

"And a week, at least, from River Run to the Ridge." I let myself breathe again, not sure whether I felt disappointment or relief. "We'd never make it."

"But the weather is turning," Jamie said. He nodded toward a big blue spruce, its needles wet and dripping. "When we came, that tree was cased in ice." He looked at me. "The traveling may be easier; we may make better time—or not."

"Or not." I shook my head reluctantly. "You know as well as I do that spring means mud. And mud is worse to travel in than snow." I felt my heart begin to slow down, accepting it. "No, it's too late, too risky. She'll have to stay."

Jamie was gazing at Roger, over the fire.

"He doesn't," he said.

Roger looked at him, startled.

"I—" he began, then firmed his jaw and started over. "I do. You don't think I'd leave her? And my child?"

I opened my mouth, and felt Jamie stiffen beside me in warning.

"No," I said sharply. "No. We have to tell him. Brianna will. Better he should know now. If it makes a difference to him, then it's better he knows before he sees her."

Jamie's lips pressed tight together, but he nodded.

"Aye," he said. "Tell him, then."

"Tell me what?" Roger's dark hair was loose, rising around his head in the evening wind. He looked more alive than he had since we had found him, alarmed and excited at once. I bit the bullet.

"It may not be your child," I said.

His expression didn't change for a moment; then the words fell into place. He grabbed me by the arms, so suddenly that I yelped with alarm.

"What do you mean? What's happened?"

Jamie moved like a striking snake. He caught Roger a short, sharp blow under the chin that loosened his grip and sent him sprawling backward on the ground.

"She means that when ye left my daughter to her own devices, she was raped," he said roughly. "Two days past the time ye lay with her. So maybe the wean's yours, and maybe it's not."

He glared down at Roger.

"So. D'ye mean to stand by her, or no?"

Roger shook his head, trying to clear it, and got slowly back to his feet.

"Raped. Who? Where?"

"In Wilmington. A man named Stephen Bonnet. He—"

"Bonnet?" It was only too clear from Roger's expression that the name was familiar. He stared wildly from me to Jamie and back. "Brianna was raped by Stephen Bonnet?"

"So I said." Suddenly all the rage Jamie had been holding since our exit from the village broke loose. He seized Roger by the throat and slammed him into a tree trunk.

"And where were you when it was done, ye coward? She was angry with ye, and so ye ran away and left her! If ye thought ye must go, why did ye not see her safe into my keeping first?"

I grabbed Jamie's arm and yanked.

"Let go of him!"

He did, and whirled away, breathing hard. Roger, shaken and almost as furious as Jamie, shook down his ruffled clothing.

"I didn't leave because we argued! I left to find this!" He snatched a handful of his loose breeches, and ripped at the cloth. A spark of green brightness glowed in the palm of his hand.

"I risked my life to get that, to see her safe back through the stones! Do you know where I went to get it, who I got it from? Stephen Bonnet! That's why it took me so long to come to Fraser's Ridge; he wasn't where I expected him to be; I had to ride up and down the coast to find him."

Jamie was frozen, staring at the gemstone. So was I.

"I shipped with Stephen Bonnet, from Scotland." Roger was growing a little calmer. "He is a—a—"

"I ken what he is." Jamie stirred, breaking his trance. "But what he also may be, is the father of my daughter's child." He gave Roger a long, cold look. "So I'm askin' ye, MacKenzie; can ye go back to her, and live with her, knowing that it's likely Bonnet's child she bears? For if ye canna do it—then say so now, for I swear, if ye come to her and treat her badly . . . I will kill ye without a second thought.''

''For God's sake!'' I burst out. ''Give him a moment to think, Jamie! Can't you see that he hasn't had a chance even to take it in, yet?''

Roger's fist closed tight over the jewel, then opened. I could hear him breathing, harsh and ragged.

''I don't know,'' he said. ''I don't know!''

Jamie stooped and picked up the stone, where Roger had dropped it. He flung it hard between Roger's feet.

''Then go!'' he said. ''Take yon cursed stone and find your wicked circle. Get ye gone—for my daughter doesna need a coward!''

He had not yet unsaddled the horses; he seized his saddlebags and heaved them across the horse's back. He untied both his horse and mine, and mounted in one fluid motion.

''Come,'' he said to me. I looked helplessly at Roger. He was staring up at Jamie, green eyes glinting with firelight, bright as the emerald in his hand.

''Go,'' he said softly to me, not taking his eyes off Jamie. ''If I can—then I'll come.''

My hands and feet seemed not to belong to me; they moved smoothly, without my direction. I walked to my horse, put my foot in the stirrup, and was up.

When I looked back, even the light of the fire had disappeared. There was nothing behind us but the dark.

62

Three-thirds of a Ghost

River Run, April 1770

"They have captured Stephen Bonnet."

Brianna dropped the game box on the floor. Ivory counters exploded in every direction, and rolled off under the furniture. Speechless, she stood staring at Lord John, who set down his glass of brandy and came hastily to her side.

"Are you all right? Do you require to sit down? I apologize most profoundly. I should not have—"

"Yes, you should. No, not the sofa, I'll never get out of it." She waved away his offered hand, and made her way slowly toward a plain wooden chair near the windows. Once solidly on it, she gave him a long, level look.

"Where?" she said. "How?"

He didn't trouble asking whether he ought to send for wine or burnt feathers; she plainly wasn't going to swoon.

He drew up a stool beside her, but then thought better, and went to the parlor door. He glanced out into the dark hallway; sure enough, one of the maids was dozing on a stool in the curve of the staircase, available in case they should want anything. The woman's head snapped up at his step, eyes showing white in the dimness.

"Go to bed," he said. "We shall not require anything further this evening."

The slave nodded and shuffled off, relief in the droop of her shoulders; she would have been awake since dawn, and it was near midnight now. He was desperately tired himself, after the long ride from Edenton, but it wasn't news that could wait. He had arrived in the early evening, but this had been his first opportunity to make an excuse to see Brianna alone.

He closed the double doors and placed a footstool in front of them, to prevent any interruptions.

"He was taken here, in Cross Creek," he said without pream-

ble, sitting down beside her. "As to how, I could not say. The charge brought was smuggling. Once they discovered his identity, of course, there were others added."

"Smuggling what?"

"Tea and brandy. At least this time." He rubbed the back of his neck, trying to relieve the stiffness caused by hours in the saddle. "I heard of it in Edenton; evidently the man is notorious. His reputation extends from Charleston to Jamestown."

He looked closely at her; she was pale, but not ghastly.

"He is condemned," he said quietly. "He will hang next week, in Wilmington. I thought you would wish to know."

She took a deep breath, and let it out slowly, but said nothing. He stole a closer look at her, not wanting to stare, but amazed at the sheer size of her. By God, she was immense! In the two months since their engagement, she had doubled in size, at least.

One side of her enormous abdomen bulged suddenly out, startling him. He was having second thoughts about the wisdom of having told her; if the shock of his news brought on her confinement prematurely, he would never forgive himself. Jamie wouldn't forgive him, either.

She was staring off into space, her brow wrinkled in concentration. He'd seen broodmares in foal look that way; thoroughly absorbed in inward matters. It had been a mistake to send the slave away. He got his feet under him, meaning to go and fetch assistance, but the movement brought her out of her trance.

"Thank you," she said. The frown was still there, but her eyes had lost that distant look; they were fixed on him with a disconcerting blue directness—the more disconcerting for being so familiar.

"When will they hang him?" She leaned forward a little, hand pressed against her side. Another swell rippled across her belly in apparent response to the pressure.

He sat back, eyeing her stomach uneasily.

"Friday week."

"Is he in Wilmington now?"

Slightly reassured by her calm demeanor, he reached for his abandoned glass. He took a sip and shook his head, feeling the comfort of the warm liquor spread through his chest.

"No. He is still here; there was no need for trial, as he had been previously convicted."

"So they'll move him to Wilmington for the execution? When?"

"I have no idea." The distant look was back; with deep misgiving, he recognized it this time—not motherly abstraction; calculation.

"I want to see him."

Very deliberately, he swallowed the rest of the brandy.

"No," he said definitely, setting down the glass. "Even if your state allowed of travel to Wilmington—which it assuredly does not," he added, glancing sidelong at her dangerous-looking abdomen—"attendance at an execution could not but have the worst effects upon your child. Now, I am in complete sympathy with your feelings, my dear, but—"

"No you aren't. You don't know what my feelings are." She spoke without heat, but with complete conviction. He stared at her for a moment, then got up and went to fetch the decanter.

She watched the amber liquid purl up in the glass and waited for him to pick it up before she went on.

"I don't want to watch him die," she said.

"Thank God for that," he muttered, and took a mouthful of brandy.

"I want to talk to him."

The mouthful went down the wrong way and he choked, spluttering brandy over the frills of his shirt.

"Maybe you should sit down," she said, squinting at him. "You don't look so good."

"I can't think why." Nonetheless, he sat down, and groped for a kerchief to wipe his face.

"Now, I know what you're going to say," she said firmly, "so don't bother. Can you arrange for me to see him, before they take him to Wilmington? And before you say no, certainly not, ask yourself what I'll do if you *do* say that."

Having opened his mouth to say "No, certainly not," Lord John shut it and contemplated her in silence for a moment.

"I don't suppose you are intending to threaten me again, are you?" he asked conversationally. "Because if you are . . ."

"Of course not." She had the grace to blush slightly at that.

"Well, then, I confess I do not see quite what you—"

"I'll tell my aunt that Stephen Bonnet fathered my baby. And I'll tell Farquard Campbell. And Gerald Forbes. And Judge Alderdyce. And then I'll go down to the garrison headquarters—that must be where he is—and I'll tell Sergeant Murchison. If he won't let me in, I'll go to Mr. Campbell for a writ to make him admit me. I have a right to see him."

He looked at her narrowly, but he could see it was no idle threat. She sat there, solid and immobile as a piece of marble statuary, and just as susceptible of persuasion.

"You do not shrink from creating a monstrous scandal?" It was a rhetorical question; he sought only to buy himself a moment to think.

"No," she said calmly. "What have I got to lose?" She lifted one eyebrow in a half-humorous quirk.

"I suppose you'd have to break our engagement. But if the whole county knows who the baby's father is, I think that would have the same effect as the engagement, in terms of keeping men from wanting to marry me."

"Your reputation—" he began, knowing it was hopeless.

"Is not real hot to start with. Though come to that, why should it be worse for me to be pregnant because I was raped by a pirate than because I was wanton, as my father so charmingly put it?" There was a small note of bitterness in her voice that stopped him from saying any more.

"Anyway, Aunt Jocasta isn't likely to throw me out, just because I'm scandalous. I won't starve; neither will the baby. And I can't say I care whether the Misses MacNeill call on me or not."

He took up his glass and drank again, carefully this time, with an eye on her to prevent further shocks. He was curious to know what had passed between her and her father—but not reckless enough to ask. Instead he put down the glass and asked, "Why?"

"Why?"

"Why do you feel you must speak with Bonnet? You say I do not know your feelings, which is undeniably true." He allowed a tinge of wryness to creep into his voice. "Whatever they are, though, they must be exigent, to cause you to contemplate such drastic expedients."

A slow smile grew on her lips, spreading into her eyes.

"I really like the way you talk," she said.

"I am exceeding flattered. However, if you would contemplate answering my question . . ."

She sighed, deeply enough to make the flame of the candle flicker. She stood up, moving ponderously, and groped in the seam of her gown. She had evidently had a pocket sewn into it, for she extracted a small piece of paper, folded and worn with much handling.

"Read that," she said, handing it to him. She turned away, and went to the far end of the room, where her paints and easel stood in a corner by the hearth.

The black letters struck him with a small jolt of familiarity. He had seen Jamie Fraser's hand only once before, but once was enough; it was a distinctive scrawl.

Daughter—

I cannot say if I shall see you again. My fervent hope is that it shall be so, and that all may be mended between us, but that event must rest in the Hand of God. I write now in the event that He may will otherwise.

You asked me once whether it was right to kill in revenge of the great Wrong done you. I tell you that you must not. For the sake of your Soul, for the sake of your own Life, you must find the grace of forgiveness. Freedom is hard-won, but it is not the fruit of Murder.

Do not Fear that he will escape Vengeance. Such a man carries with him the seeds of his own Destruction. If he does not Die at my Hand, it will be by another. But it must not be your Hand that strikes him down.

Hear me, for the sake of the Love I bear you.

Below the text of the letter, he had written *Your most affection- ate and loving Father, James Fraser.* This was scratched out, and below it was written simply, *Da.*

"I never said goodbye to him."

Lord John looked up, startled. Her back was turned to him; she was staring at the half-finished landscape on the easel as though it were a window.

He crossed the carpet to stand beside her. The fire had burned down in the hearth, and it was growing cold in the room. She turned to face him, clutching her elbows against the chill.

"I want to be free," she said quietly. "Whether Roger comes back or not. Whatever happens."

The child was restless; he could see it kicking and squirming below her crossed arms, like a cat in a sack. He drew a deep breath, feeling chilled and apprehensive.

"You are sure you must see Bonnet?"

She gave him another of those long blue looks.

"I have to find a way to forgive him, Da says. I've been trying, ever since they left, but I can't do it. Maybe if I see him, I can. I have to try."

"All right." He let his breath out in a long sigh, shoulders slumping in capitulation.

A small light—relief?—showed in her eyes, and he tried to smile back.

"You'll do it?"

"Yes. God knows how, but I'll do it."

He put out all the candles save one, keeping that to light their way to bed. He gave her his arm and they walked in silence through the empty hall, the unpeopled quiet wrapping them in peace. At the foot of the stair, he paused, letting her go ahead of him.

"Brianna."

She turned, questioning, on the stair above him. He stood hesitant, not knowing how to ask for what he suddenly wanted so badly. He reached out a hand, lightly poised.

"May I—?"

Without speaking, she took his hand and pressed it against her belly. It was warm and very firm. They stood quite still for a moment, her hand locked over his. Then it came, a small hard push against his hand, which sent a thrill through his heart.

"My God," he said, in soft delight. "He's real."

Her eyes met his in rueful amusement.

"Yes," she said. "I know."

It was well past dark when they drove up beside the garrison headquarters. It was a small, unprepossessing little building, dwarfed by the loom of the warehouse behind it, and Brianna eyed it askance.

"They have him in there?" Her hands felt cold, in spite of being muffled under her cloak.

"No." Lord John glanced around, as he got down to tie the horses. A light burned in the window, but the small dirt yard was empty, the narrow street silent and deserted. There were no houses or shops nearby, and the warehousemen had long since gone home to their suppers and their beds.

He reached up both hands to help her down; alighting from a wagon was easier than getting out of a carriage, but still no small task.

"He's in the cellar below the warehouse," he told her, his voice pitched low. "I've bribed the soldier on duty to admit us."

"Not *us*," she said, her voice pitched as low as his, but no less firm for that. "Me. I'll see him alone."

She saw his lips compress tightly for a moment, then relax as he nodded.

"Private Hodgepile assures me he is in chains, or I would not countenance such a suggestion. As it is . . ." He shrugged, half irritably, and took her arm to guide her over the rutted ground.

"Hodgepile?"

"Private Arvin Hodgepile. Why? Are you acquainted?"

She shook her head, holding her skirts out of the way with her free hand.

"No. I've heard the name, but—"

The door of the building opened, spilling light into the yard.

"That'll be you, will it, my lord?" A soldier looked out warily. Hodgepile was slight and narrow-faced, tight-jointed as a marionette. He jerked, startled, as he saw her.

"Oh! I didn't realize—"

"You needn't." Lord John's voice was cool. "Show us the way, if you please."

With an apprehensive glance at Brianna's looming bulk, the private brought out a lantern, and led them to a small side door into the warehouse.

Hodgepile was short as well as slight, but held himself more erect than usual in compensation. *He walks with a ramrod up his arse.* Yes, she thought, watching him with interest as he marched ahead of them. It had to be the man Ronnie Sinclair had described to her mother. How many Hodgepiles could there be, after all? Perhaps she could talk to him when she'd finished with—her thoughts stopped abruptly as Hodgepile unlocked the warehouse door.

The April night was cool and fresh, but the air inside was thick with the reek of pitch and turpentine. Brianna felt suffocated. She could almost feel the tiny molecules of resin floating in the air, sticking to her skin. The sudden illusion of being trapped in a block of solidifying amber was so oppressive that she moved suddenly forward, almost dragging Lord John with her.

The warehouse was nearly full, its vast space crowded with bulky shapes. Kegs of pitch bled sticky black in the farthest shadows, while wooden racks near the huge double doors at the front held piles of barrels; brandy and rum, ready to roll down the ramps and out onto the dock, to barges waiting in the river below.

Private Hodgepile's shadow stretched and shrank by turns as he passed between the towering ranks of casks and boxes, his steps muffled by the thick layer of sawdust on the floor.

". . . must be careful of fire . . ." His high, thin voice floated back to her, and she saw his puppet shadow wave an etiolated hand. "You will be careful where you set the lantern, won't you? Though there should be no danger, no danger at all down below . . ."

The warehouse was built out over the river, to facilitate loading, and the front part of the floor was wood; the back half of the building was brick-floored. Brianna heard the echo of their foot-steps change as they crossed the boundary. Hodgepile paused by a trapdoor set into the bricks.

"You won't be long, my lord?"

"No longer than we can help," Lord John replied tersely. He took the lantern and waited in silence as Hodgepile heaved up the door and propped it. Brianna's heart was beating heavily; she could feel each separate thump, like a blow to the chest.

A flight of redbrick stairs ran down into darkness. Hodgepile took out his ring of keys and counted them over in the pool of lantern light, making sure of the right one before descending. He squinted dubiously at Brianna, then motioned them to follow him.

"It's a good thing they made the stairs wide enough for rum casks," she murmured to Lord John, holding on to his arm as she edged herself down, one step at a time.

She could see at once why Private Hodgepile wasn't worried about fire down here; the air was so damp, she wouldn't have been surprised to see mushrooms sprouting from the walls. There was a sound of dripping water somewhere, and the light of the lantern shone off wet brick. Cockroaches scattered in panic from the light, and the air smelled of mold and mildew.

She thought briefly of her mother's penicillin farm, less briefly of her mother, and her throat closed tight. Then they were there, and she could no longer distract herself from the realization of what she was doing.

Hodgepile struggled with the key, and the panic she had been suppressing all day swept over her. She had no idea what to say, what to do. What was she *doing* here?

Lord John squeezed her arm in encouragement. She took a

deep breath of the dank wet air, ducked her head, and stepped inside.

He sat on a bench at the far side of the cell, eyes fixed on the door. He'd clearly been expecting someone—he'd heard the footsteps outside—but it wasn't her. He jerked in startlement, and his eyes flashed briefly green as the light swept over him.

She heard a faint metallic clink; of course, they'd said he was in chains. The thought gave her a little courage. She took the lantern from Hodgepile, and shut the door behind her.

She leaned against the wooden door, studying him in silence. He seemed smaller than she remembered. Perhaps it was only that she was now so much bigger.

"Do you know who I am?" It was a tiny cell, low-ceilinged, with no echo. Her voice sounded small, but clear.

He cocked his head to one side, considering. His eyes traveled slowly over her.

"I don't think ye were after tellin' me your name, sweetheart."

"Don't call me that!" The spurt of rage took her by surprise, and she choked it back, clenching her fists behind her. If she had come here to administer forgiveness, it wasn't a good start.

He shrugged, good-natured but cool.

"As ye will. No, I don't know who you are. I'll know your face —and a few other things"—his teeth gleamed briefly in the blond stubble of his beard—"but not your name. I suppose you'll mean to tell me, though?"

"You do recognize me?"

He drew in air and blew it out through pursed lips, looking her over carefully. He was a good bit the worse for wear, but it hadn't impaired his assurance.

"Oh, indeed I do." He seemed amused, and she wanted to cross the room and slap him, hard. Instead, she took a deep breath. That was a mistake—she could smell him.

Without warning, her gorge rose suddenly and violently. She hadn't been sick before, but the stench of him brought up everything in her. She had barely time to turn away before the flood of bile and half-digested food came hurtling up, splattering the damp brick floor.

She leaned her forehead against the wall, waves of hot and cold running over her. Finally, she wiped her mouth and turned around.

He was still sitting there, watching her. She'd set the lantern on the floor. It threw a yellow flicker upward, carving his face from the shadows behind him. He might have been a beast, chained in its den; only wariness showed in the pale green eyes.

"My name is Brianna Fraser."

He nodded, repeating it.

"Brianna Fraser. A lovely name, sure." He smiled briefly, lips together. "And?"

"My parents are James and Claire Fraser. They saved your life, and you robbed them."

"Yes."

He said it with complete matter-of-factness, and she stared at him. He stared back.

She felt a wild urge to laugh, as unexpected as the surge of nausea had been. What had she expected? Remorse? Excuses? From a man who took things because he wanted them?

"If ye've come in the hopes of getting back the jewels, I'm afraid you've left it too late," he said pleasantly. "I sold the first to buy a ship, and the other two were stolen from me. Perhaps you'll find that justice; I should think it cold comfort, myself."

She swallowed, tasting bile.

"Stolen. When?"

Don't trouble yourself over the man who's got it, Roger had said. *It's odds-on he stole it from someone else.*

Bonnet shifted on the wooden bench and shrugged.

"Some four months gone. Why?"

"No reason." So Roger had made it; had got them—the gems that might have been safe transport for them both. Cold comfort.

"I recall there was a trinket, too—a ring, was it? But you got that back." He smiled, showing his teeth this time.

"I paid for it." One hand went unthinking to her belly, gone round and tight as a basketball under her cloak.

His gaze stayed on her face, mildly curious.

"Have we business still to do then, darlin'?"

She took a deep breath—through her mouth, this time.

"They told me you're going to hang."

"They told me the same thing." He shifted again on the hard wooden bench. He stretched his head to one side, to ease the muscles of his neck, and peered up sidelong at her. "You'll not have come from pity, though, I shouldn't think."

"No," she said, watching him thoughtfully. "To be honest, I'll rest a lot easier once you're dead."

He stared at her for a moment, then burst out laughing. He laughed hard enough that tears came to his eyes; he wiped them carelessly, bending his head to swipe his face against a shrugged shoulder, then straightened up, the marks of his laughter still on his face.

"What is it you want from me, then?"

She opened her mouth to reply, and quite suddenly, the link between them dissolved. She had not moved, but felt as though she had taken one step across an impassable abyss. She stood now safe on the other side, alone. Blessedly alone. He could no longer touch her.

"Nothing," she said, her voice clear in her own ears. "I don't want anything at all from you. I came to give you something."

She opened her cloak, and ran her hands over the swell of her abdomen. The small inhabitant stretched and rolled, its touch a blind caress of hand and womb, both intimate and abstract.

"Yours," she said.

He looked at the bulge, and then at her.

"I've had whores try to foist their spawn on me before," he said. But he spoke without viciousness, and she thought there was a new stillness behind the wary eyes.

"Do you think I'm a whore?" She didn't care if he did or not, though she doubted he did. "I've no reason to lie. I already told you, I don't want anything from you."

She drew the cloak back together, covering herself. She drew herself up then, feeling the ache in her back ease with the movement. It was done. She was ready to go.

"You're going to die," she said to him, and she who had not come for pity's sake was surprised to find she had some. "If it makes the dying easier for you, to know there's something of you left on earth—then you're welcome to the knowledge. But I've finished with you, now."

She turned to pick up the lantern, and was surprised to see the door half cracked ajar. She had no time to feel anger at Lord John for eavesdropping, when the door swung fully open.

"Well, 'twas a gracious speech, ma'am," Sergeant Murchison said judiciously. He smiled broadly then, and brought the butt of his musket up even with her belly. "But I can't say I've finished, quite, with you."

She took a quick step back, and swung the lantern at his head in a reflex of defense. He ducked with a yelp of alarm, and a grip of iron seized her wrist before she could dash the lamp at him again.

"Christ, that was close! You're fast, girl, if not quite so fast as

the good Sergeant." Bonnet took the lantern from her and released her wrist.

"You're not chained after all," she said stupidly, staring at
him. Then her wits caught up with the situation, and she whirled,
plunging for the door. Murchison shoved his musket in front of
her, blocking her way, but not before she had seen the darkened
corridor through the doorway—and the dim form sprawled
facedown on the bricks outside.

"You've killed him," she whispered. Her lips were numb with
shock, and a dread deeper than nausea sickened her to the bone.
"Oh, God, you've killed him."

"Killed who?" Bonnet held the lantern up, peering at the spill
of butter-yellow hair, blotched with blood. "Who the hell is
that?"

"A busybody," Murchison snapped. "Hurry, man! There's no
time to waste. I've taken care of Hodgepile and the fuses are lit."

"Wait!" Bonnet glanced from the Sergeant to Brianna, frowning.

"There's no time, I said." The Sergeant brought up his gun
and checked the priming. "Don't worry; no one will find them."

Brianna could smell the brimstone scent of the gunpowder in
the priming pan. The Sergeant swung the stock of the gun to his
shoulder, and turned toward her, but the quarters were too
cramped; with her belly in the way, there was no room to raise the
long muzzle.

The Sergeant grunted with irritation, reversed the gun, and
raised it high, to club her with the butt.

Her hand was clenched around the barrel before she knew she
had reached for it. Everything seemed to be moving very slowly,
Murchison and Bonnet both standing frozen. She herself felt quite
detached, as though she stood to one side, watching.

She plucked the musket from Murchison's grip as though it
were a broomstraw, swung it high, and smashed it down. The jolt
of it vibrated up her arms, into her body, her whole body charged
as though someone had thrown a switch and sent a white-hot
current pulsing through her.

She saw so clearly the man's face hanging drop-jawed in the air
before her, eyes passing from astonishment through horror to the
dullness of unconsciousness, so slowly that she saw the change.
Had time to see the vivid colors in his face. A plum lip caught on
a yellow tooth, half lifted in a sneer. Slow tiny blossoms of bril-

liant red unfolding in a graceful curve across his temple, Japanese water flowers blooming on a field of fresh-bruised blue.

She was entirely calm, no more than a conduit for the ancient savagery that men call motherhood, who mistake its tenderness for weakness. She saw her own hands, knuckles stark and tendons etched, felt the surge of power up her legs and back, through wrists and arms and shoulders, swung again, so slowly, it seemed so slowly, and yet the man was still falling, had not quite reached the floor when the gun butt struck again.

A voice was calling her name. Dimly, it penetrated through the crystal hum around her.

"Stop, for God's sake! Woman—Brianna—stop!"

There were hands on her shoulders, dragging, shaking. She pulled free of the grip and turned, the gun still in hand.

"Don't touch me," she said, and he took a quick step back, his eyes filled with surprise and wariness—perhaps a touch of fear. Afraid of her? Why would anyone be afraid of her? she thought dimly. He was talking; she saw his mouth moving, but she couldn't catch the words, it was just noise. The current in her was dying, making her dizzy.

Then time readjusted itself, began to move normally again. Her muscles quivered, all their fibers turned to jelly. She set the stained butt of the gun against the floor to balance herself.

"What did you say?"

Impatience flickered across his face.

"I said, it's no time we have to be wasting! Did ye not hear your man sayin' that the fuses are lit?"

"What fuses? Why?" She saw his eyes flick toward the door behind her. Before he could move, she stepped back into the doorway, bringing up the muzzle of the gun. He backed away from her instinctively, hitting the bench with the backs of his legs. He fell back, and struck the chains fastened to the wall; empty manacles chimed against the brick.

Shock was beginning to steal over her, but the memory of the white-hot current still burned through her spine, keeping her upright.

"You do not mean to kill me, surely?" He tried to smile, and failed; couldn't keep the panic from his eyes. She *had* said she would rest easier with him dead.

Freedom is hard-won, but is not the fruit of Murder. She had her hard-won freedom now, and would not give it back to him.

"No," she said, and took a firmer hold on the gun, the butt

snugged solid into her shoulder. "But I will by God shoot you through the knees and leave you here, if you don't tell me right this minute what the *hell* is going on!"

He shifted his weight, big body hovering, pale eyes on her, judging. She blocked the door entirely, her bulk filling it from side to side. She saw the doubt in his posture, the shift of his shoulders as he thought to rush her, and cocked the gun with a single loud *click*!

He stood six feet from the muzzle's end; too far to lunge and grab it from her. One move, one pull of her trigger finger. She couldn't miss, and he knew it.

His shoulders slumped.

"The warehouse above is laid with gunpowder and fuses," he said, speaking quick and sharp, anxious to get it done. "I can't say how long, but it's goin' up with an almighty bang. For God's sake, let me out of here!"

"Why?" Her hands were sweating, but solid on the gun. The baby stirred, a reminder that she had no time to waste, either. She would risk one minute to know, though. She had to know, with John Grey's body limp on the floor behind her. "You've killed a good man here, and I want to know *why*!"

He made a gesture of frustration.

"The smuggling!" he said. "We were partners, the Sergeant and I. I'd bring him in cheap contraband, he'd stamp it with the Crown's mark. He'd steal the licensed stuff, I'd sell it for a good price and split with him."

"Keep talking."

He was nearly dancing with impatience.

"A soldier—Hodgepile—he was on to it, asking questions. Murchison couldn't say if he'd told anyone, but it wasn't wise to wait and see, not once I was taken. The Sergeant moved the last of the liquor from the warehouse, substituted barrels of turpentine, and laid the fuses. It all goes up, no one can say it wasn't brandy burning—no evidence of theft. That's it, that's all. Now let me go!"

"All right." She lowered the musket a few inches, but didn't yet uncock it. "What about him?" She nodded toward the fallen Sergeant, who was beginning to snort and mumble.

He stared at her blankly.

"What about him?"

"Aren't you going to take him with you?"

"No." He sidled to one side, looking for a way past her. "For

Christ's sweet sake, woman, let me go, and leave yourself!
There's twelve hundredweight of pitch and turpentine overhead.
It'll go off like a bomb!''

"But he's still alive! We can't leave him here!''

Bonnet gave her a look of sheer exasperation, then crossed the
room in two strides. He bent, jerked the dagger from the Sergeant's belt, and drew it hard across the fat throat, just above the
leather stock. A thick spray of blood soaked Bonnet's shirt, and
whipped against the wall.

"There," he said, straightening up. "He's not alive. Leave
him.''

He dropped the dagger, pushed her aside, and lunged out into
the corridor. She could hear his footsteps going away, quick and
ringing on the brick.

Trembling all over with the shock of action and reaction, she
stood still for a second, staring down at John Grey's body. Grief
ripped through her, and her womb clenched hard. There was no
pain, but every fiber had contracted; her stomach bulged as
though she'd swallowed a basketball. She felt breathless, unable
to move.

No, she thought quite clearly, to the child inside. *I am* not *in
labor, I absolutely, positively am not. I won't have it. Stay put. I
haven't got time right now.*

She took two steps down the black corridor, then stopped. No,
she had to check, at least, make sure. She turned back, and knelt
by John Grey's body. He had looked dead when she first saw him
lying there, and still did; he hadn't moved or even twitched since
she had first seen his body.

She leaned forward but couldn't reach easily over the bulge of
her belly. She grasped his arm instead, and pulled at him, trying
to turn him over. A small, fine-boned man, he was still heavy. His
body tilted up, rolled boneless toward her, head lolling, and her
heart sank anew, seeing his half-closed eyes and slack mouth. But
she reached beneath the angle of his jaw, feeling frantically for a
pulse point.

Where the hell was it? She'd seen her mother do it in emergencies; faster to find than a wrist pulse, she'd said. She couldn't find
one. How long had it been, how long were the fuses set to burn?

She wiped a fold of her cloak across her clammy face, trying to
think. She looked back, judging the distance to the stairs. Jesus,
could she risk it, even alone? The thought of popping out into the
warehouse above, just as everything went off— She cast one look

upward, then bent to her work and tried again, pushing his head far back. There! She could see the damn vein under his skin—that's where the pulse should be, shouldn't it?

For a moment, she wasn't sure she felt it; it might be only the hammering of her own heart, beating in her fingertips. But no, it was—a different rhythm, faint and fluttering. He might be close to dead, but not quite.

"Close," she muttered, "but no cigar." She felt too frightened to be greatly relieved; now she'd have to get him out, too. She scrambled to her feet, and reached down to get hold of his arms, to drag him. But then she stopped, a memory of what she had seen a moment before penetrating her panic.

She turned and lumbered hastily back into the cell. Averting her eyes from the sodden red mound on the floor, she snatched up the lantern and brought it back to the corridor. She held it high, casting light on the low brick ceiling. Yes, she'd been right!

The bricks curved up from the floor in groynes, making arches all along both sides of the corridors. Storage alcoves and cells. Above the groynes, though, ran sturdy beams made of eight-inch pine. Over that, thick planking—and above the planks, the layer of bricks that formed the floor of the warehouse.

Going up like a bomb, Bonnet had said—but was he right? Turpentine burned, so did pitch; yes, they'd likely explode if they burned under pressure, but not like a bomb, no. Fuses. Fuses, in the plural. Long fuses, plainly, and likely running to small caches of gunpowder; that was the only true explosive Murchison would have; there were no high explosives now.

So the gunpowder would explode in several places, and ignite the barrels nearby. But the barrels would burn slowly; she'd seen Sinclair make barrels like those; the staves were half an inch thick, watertight. She remembered the reek as they walked through the warehouse; yes, Murchison would likely have opened the bungs of a few barrels, let the turpentine flow out, to help the fire along.

So the barrels would burn, but likely they wouldn't explode—or if they did, not all at once. Her breathing eased a little, making calculations. Not a bomb; a string of firecrackers, maybe.

So. She took a deep breath—as deep a breath as she could manage, with Osbert in the way. She put her hands across her stomach, feeling her racing heart begin to slow.

Even if some of the barrels did explode, the force of the explosion would be out, and up, through the thin plank walls and the roof. Very little force would be deflected down. And what was— she reached up a hand and pushed against a beam, reassuring herself of its strength.

She sat down quite suddenly on the floor, skirts puffed out around her.

"I think it'll be all right," she whispered, not sure if she was talking to John, to the baby, or to herself.

She sat huddled for a moment, shaking with relief, then rolled awkwardly onto her knees again, and began with fumbling fingers to administer first aid.

She was still struggling to tear a strip from the hem of her petticoat when she heard the footsteps. Coming fast, almost running. She turned sharply toward the stairs, but no—the footsteps came from the other way, behind her.

She whirled around, to see the form of Stephen Bonnet looming out of the darkness.

"Run!" he shouted at her. "For Christ's sweet sake, why have ye not gone?"

"Because it's safe here," she said. She had laid the musket down on the floor beside Grey's body; she stooped and picked it up, lifted it to her shoulder. "Go away."

He stared at her, mouth half open in the gloom.

"Safe? Woman, you're an eedjit! Did ye not hear—"

"I heard, but you're wrong. It's not going to explode. And if it did, it would still be safe down here."

"The hell it is! Sweet bleeding Jesus! Even if the cellar doesn't go, what happens when the fire burns through the floor?"

"It can't, it's brick." She jerked her chin upward, not taking her eyes off him.

"Back here it is—up front, by the river, it's wood, like the wharf. It'll burn through, then collapse. And what happens back here then, eh? Do ye no good for the ceiling to hold, when the smoke comes rolling back to smother ye!"

She felt a wave of sickness roil up from her depths.

"It's open? The cellar isn't sealed? The other end of the corridor's open?" Knowing even as she spoke that of course it was— he had run that way, heading for the river, not for the stairs.

"Yes! Now come!" He lunged forward, reaching for her arm, but she jerked away, back against the wall, the muzzle of the gun trained on him.

"I'm not going without him." She licked dry lips, nodding at the floor.

"The man's dead!"

"He's not! Pick him up!"

An extraordinary mixture of emotions crossed Bonnet's face; fury and astonishment preeminent among them.

"Pick him up!" she repeated fiercely. He stood still, staring at her. Then, very slowly, he squatted, and gathering John Grey's limp form into his arms, got the point of his shoulder into Grey's abdomen and heaved him up.

"Come on, then," he said, and without another glance at her started off into the dark. She hesitated for a second, then seized the lantern and followed him.

Within fifty feet, she smelled smoke. The brick corridor wasn't straight; it branched and turned, encompassing the many partitions of the cellar. But all the time it slanted down, heading toward the riverbank. As they descended through the multiple turnings, the scent of smoke thickened; a layer of acrid haze swirled lazily around them, visible in the lantern light.

Brianna held her breath, trying not to breathe. Bonnet was moving fast, despite Grey's weight. She could barely keep up, burdened with gun and lantern, but she didn't mean to give up either one, just yet. Her belly tightened again, another of those breathless moments.

"Not *yet*, I said!" she muttered through gritted teeth.

She had had to stop for a moment; Bonnet had disappeared into the haze ahead. Evidently he'd noticed the fading of the lantern light, though—she heard him bellow, from somewhere up ahead.

"Woman! Brianna!"

"I'm coming!" she called, and hurried as fast as she could, waddling, discarding any pretense of grace. The smoke was much thicker, and she could hear a faint crackle, somewhere in the distance—overhead? Before them?

She was breathing heavily, in spite of the smoke. She drew in a ragged gulp of air, and smelled water. Damp and mud, dead leaves and fresh air, slicing through the smoky murk like a knife.

A faint glow shone through the smoke and grew as they hurried toward it, dwarfing the light of her lantern. Then a dark square loomed ahead. Bonnet turned and seized her arm, dragging her out into the air.

They were under the wharf, she realized; dark water lapped ahead of them, brightness dancing on it. Reflection; the brightness came from up above, and so did the crackle of flame. Bonnet didn't stop or let go of her arm; he pulled her to one side, into the long, dank grass and mud of the bank. He let go within a few steps, but she followed, gasping for breath, slipping and sliding, tripping on the soggy edges of her skirts.

At last he stopped, in the shadow of the trees. He bent, and let Grey's body slide to the ground. He stayed bent for a moment, chest heaving, trying to get his breath back.

Brianna realized that she could see both men plainly; could see every bud on the twigs of the tree. She turned and looked back, to see the warehouse lighted like a jack-o'-lantern, flames licking through cracks in the wooden walls. The huge double doors had been left ajar; as she watched, the blast of hot air forced one open, and small tongues of fire began to creep across the dock, deceptively small and playful-looking.

She felt a hand on her shoulder, and whirled, looking up into Bonnet's face.

"I've a ship waiting," he said. "A little way upriver. Will you come with me, then?"

She shook her head. She still held the gun, but didn't need it now. He was no threat to her.

Still he didn't go, but lingered, staring down at her, a small frown between his brows. His face was gaunt, hollowed and shadowed by the distant fire. The surface of the river was aflame now, small tongues of fire flickering from the dark water as a slick of turpentine spread across it.

"Is it true?" he asked abruptly. He asked no permission, but set his hands on her belly. It tightened at his touch, rounding in another of those breathless, painless squeezes, and a look of astonishment crossed his face.

She jerked away from his touch, pulling her cloak together, and nodded, unable to speak.

He seized her chin in his hand and peered into her face— assessing her truthfulness, perhaps? Then he let go, and stuck a finger into his mouth, groping in the recesses of his cheek.

He took her hand, and put something wet and hard in her palm.

"For his maintenance, then," he said, and grinned at her. "Take care of him, sweetheart!"

And then he was gone, bounding long-legged up the riverbank, silhouetted like a demon in the flickering light. The turpentine flowing into the water had caught fire, and roiling billows of scarlet light shot upward, floating pillars of fire that lit the riverbank bright as day.

She half raised the musket, finger on the trigger. He was no

more than twenty yards away, a perfect shot. *Not by your hand.*
She lowered the gun, and let him go.

The warehouse was fully ablaze by now; the heat from it beat
against her cheeks and blew the hair back from her face.

"I have a ship upriver," he'd said. She squinted into the glare.
The fire had nearly filled the river, a great floating slick that
bloomed from bank to bank in a fiery garden of unfolding flames.
Nothing could come through that blinding wall of light.

Her other fist was still closed around the object he had given
her. She opened her hand and looked down at the wet black diamond that gleamed in her palm, the fire glowing red and bloody in
its facets.

PART TWELVE

Je T'aime

63

Forgiveness

River Run, May 1770

"That is the most stubborn woman I have ever met!" Brianna huffed into the room like a ship in full sail, and subsided onto the love seat by the bed, billowing.

Lord John Grey opened one eye, bloodshot under his turban of bandages.

"Your aunt?"

"Who else?"

"You have a looking glass in your room, do you not?" His mouth curved, and after a reluctant moment, so did hers.

"It's her bloody will. I *told* her I don't want River Run, I can't own slaves—but she won't change it! She just smiles as though I were a six-year-old having a tantrum and says by the time it happens, I'll be glad of it. Glad of it!" She snorted and flounced into a more comfortable position. "What am I going to do?"

"Nothing."

"Nothing?" She turned the force of her displeasure on him. "How can I do nothing?"

"To begin with, I should be extremely surprised if your aunt were not immortal; several of that particular race of Scots seem to be. However"—he waved a hand in dismissal—"should this prove untrue, and should she persist in her delusions that you would prove a good mistress to River Run—"

"What makes you think I wouldn't?" she said, pride stung.

"You cannot run a plantation of this size without slaves, and you decline to own them for reasons of conscience, or so I was given to understand. Though a less likely Quaker I have never seen." He narrowed his open eye, indicating the immense tent of purple-striped muslin in which she was swathed. "Returning to the point at issue—or one of them—should you find yourself the unwilling recipient of a number of slaves, arrangements can undoubtedly be made to free them."

"Not in North Carolina. The Assembly—"

"No, not in North Carolina," he agreed patiently. "If the occasion should arise, and you find yourself in possession of slaves, you will simply sell them to me."

"But that's—"

"And I will take them to Virginia, where manumission is much less stringently controlled. Once they are freed, you will return my money. At this point, you will be totally destitute and lacking in property, which appears to be your chief desire, second only to preventing any possibility of personal happiness by ensuring that you cannot marry the man you love."

She pleated a handful of muslin between her fingers, frowning at the big sapphire that shone on her hand.

"I promised I'd listen to him first." She cast a narrow eye at Lord John. "Though I still say it's emotional blackmail."

"So much more effective than any other kind," he agreed. "Almost worth a cracked pate, to finally hold the whip hand on a Fraser."

She ignored this.

"And I only said I'd listen. I still think when he knows everything, he'll—he can't." She put a hand on her enormous belly. "You couldn't, could you? Care—really care, I mean—for a child that wasn't yours?"

He moved higher on the pillow, grimacing slightly.

"For the sake of its parent? I expect I could." He opened both eyes and looked at her, smiling. "Indeed, I was under the impression that I had been doing so for some time."

She looked momentarily blank, before a tide of pink flowed up from the scooped neck of her bodice. She was charming when she blushed.

"You mean me? Well, yes, but—I mean—I'm not a baby, and you're not having to claim me as your own." She gave him a direct blue look, at odds with the lingering pinkness of her cheeks. "And I did hope it wasn't *all* for my father's sake."

He was quiet for a moment, then reached out and squeezed her hand.

"No, it wasn't," he said gruffly. He let go, and lay back with a small groan.

"Are you feeling worse?" she asked anxiously. "Shall I get you something? Some tea? A poultice?"

"No, it's only the blasted headache," he said. "The light makes it throb." He shut his eyes again.

"Tell me," he said without opening them, "why is it that you seem so convinced that a man could not care for a child unless it were the fruit of his loins? As it is, my dear, I did *not* mean to refer to you when I said I had been doing such a thing myself. My son—my stepson—is in fact the son of my late wife's sister. By tragic accident, both of his parents died within a day of each other, and my wife Isobel and her parents raised him from babyhood. I married Isobel when Willie was six or so. So you see, there is no blood between us at all—and yet were any man to impugn my affection for him, or to say he is not my son, I would call him out on the instant for it."

"I see," she said, after a moment. "I didn't know that." He cracked an eyelid; she was still twisting her ring, looking pensive.

"I think . . ." she began, and glanced at him. "I think I'm not so worried about Roger and the baby. If I'm honest—"

"Heaven forfend you should be otherwise," he murmured.

"If I'm honest," she went on, glowering at him, "I think I'm worried more about how it would be between us—between Roger and me." She hesitated, then took the plunge.

"I didn't know Jamie Fraser was my father," she said. "Not all the time I was growing up. After the Rising, my parents were separated; they each thought the other was dead. And so my mother married again. I thought Frank Randall was my father. I didn't find out otherwise until after he died."

"Ah." He viewed her with increased interest. "And was this Randall cruel to you?"

"No! He was . . . wonderful." Her voice broke slightly, and she cleared her throat, embarrassed. "No. He was the best father I could have had. It's just that I thought my parents had a good marriage. They cared for each other, they respected each other, they—well, I thought everything was fine."

Lord John scratched at his bandages. The doctor had shaved his head, a condition which, in addition to affronting his vanity, itched abominably.

"I fail to see the difficulty, as applied to your present situation."

She heaved a huge sigh.

"Then my father died, and . . . we found out that Jamie Fraser was still alive. My mother went to join him, and then I came. And—it was different. I saw how they looked at each other. I never saw her look at Frank Randall that way—or him at her."

"Ah, yes." A small gust of bleakness swept through him. He'd seen that look once or twice; the first time, he had wanted desperately to put a knife through Claire Randall's heart.

"Do you know how rare such a thing is?" he asked quietly. "That peculiar sort of mutual passion?" The one-sided kind was common enough.

"Yes." She had half turned, her arm along the back of the love seat, and was looking out through the French doors, over the burgeoning spread of the spring flower beds below.

"The thing is—I think I had it," she said, even more quietly. "For a little while. A very little while." She turned her head and looked at him, with eyes that let him see clear through her.

"If I've lost it—then I have. I can live with that—or without it. But I won't live with an imitation of it. I couldn't stand that."

"It looks like you may get me by default." Brianna put the breakfast tray over his lap and collapsed heavily into the love seat, making the joints groan.

"Don't riddle with a sick man," he said, picking up a piece of toast. "What do you mean?"

"Drusus just came racing into the cookhouse, saying he saw two riders coming down through Campbell's fields. He said he was sure one of them was my father—he said it was a big man with red hair; God knows there aren't that many like him."

"Not many, no." He smiled briefly, his eyes traveling over her. "So, two riders?"

"It must be Da and my mother. So they haven't found Roger. Or they did, and he—didn't want to come back." She twisted the big sapphire on her finger. "Good thing I have a fallback, isn't it?"

Lord John blinked, and made haste to swallow his mouthful of toast.

"If by that extraordinary metaphor, you mean that you intend to marry me after all, I assure you—"

"No." She gave him a halfhearted smile. "Just teasing."

"Oh, good." He took a gulp of tea, closing his eyes to enjoy the fragrant steam. "Two riders. Did your cousin not go with them?"

"Yes, he did," she said slowly. "God, I hope nothing's happened to Ian."

"It might be that they experienced any variety of disasters on the journey, which obliged your cousin and your mother to travel behind your father and Mr. MacKenzie. Or your cousin and Mac-Kenzie behind your parents.'' He waved a hand, indicating innumerable possibilities.

''I guess you're right.'' She still looked peaked, and Lord John suspected she had cause. Comforting possibilities were all very well for the short term, but the colder probabilities were inclined to triumph over the longer course—and whoever accompanied Jamie Fraser, they would be arriving shortly, with the answers to all questions.

He pushed back the unfinished breakfast and leaned back against his pillows.

''Tell me—how far does your remorse extend for having nearly gotten me killed?''

She colored and looked uncomfortable.

''What do you mean?''

''If I ask you to do something you do not wish to, will your sense of guilt and obligation compel you to do it nonetheless?''

''Oh, more blackmail. What is it?'' she asked warily.

''Forgive your father. Whatever has happened.''

Pregnancy had made her complexion more delicate; all her emotions ebbed and flowed just under the surface of that apricot skin. A touch would bruise her.

He reached out and laid a hand very gently along her cheek.

''For your sake, as well as his,'' he said.

''I already have.'' Her lashes covered her eyes as she looked down; her hands lay still in her lap, the blue fire of his sapphire glowing on her finger.

The sound of hooves came clearly through the open French doors, rattling on the gravel drive.

''Then I think you had better go down and tell him so, my dear.''

She pursed her lips, and nodded. Without a word, she stood up and floated out the door, disappearing like a storm cloud over the horizon.

''When we heard that there were two riders coming, and one of them Jamie, we feared lest something had happened to your nephew, or MacKenzie. Somehow, it occurred to neither of us to think that anything had happened to *you*.''

''I'm immortal,'' she murmured, peering alternately into his eyes. "Didn't you know?" The pressure of her thumbs lifted from his eyelids and he blinked, still feeling her touch.

"You have a slight enlargement of one pupil, but very small. Grip my fingers and squeeze as hard as you can." She held out her index fingers and he obliged, annoyed to feel the weakness of his grip.

"Did you find MacKenzie?" He was further annoyed not to be able to control his curiosity.

She gave him a quick, wary glance from those sherry-colored eyes, and returned her gaze to his hands.

"Yes. He'll be coming along. A little later."

"Will he?" She caught the tone of his question and hesitated, then looked at him directly.

"How much do you know?"

"Everything," he said, and had the momentary satisfaction of seeing her startled. Then one side of her mouth curved up.

"Everything?"

"Enough," he amended sardonically. "Enough to ask whether your statement of Mr. MacKenzie's return is knowledge on your part or wishful thinking."

"Call it faith." Without so much as a by-your-leave, she tugged loose the strings of his nightshirt and spread it open, exposing his chest. Rolling a sheet of parchment deftly into a tube, she applied one end of it to his breast, putting her ear to the other end.

"I beg your pardon, madame!"

"Hush, I can't hear," she said, making small shushing motions with one hand. She proceeded to move her tube to different parts of his chest, pausing now and then to thump experimentally or prod him in the liver.

"Have you moved your bowels yet today?" she inquired, poking him familiarly in the abdomen.

"I decline to say," he said, pulling his nightshirt back together with dignity.

She looked more outrageous even than usual. The woman must be forty at least, yet she showed no more sign of age than a fine webbing of lines at the corners of her eyes, and threadings of silver in that ridiculous mass of hair.

She was thinner than he remembered, though it was hard to judge of her figure, dressed as she was in a barbaric leather shirt and trouserings. She'd plainly been in the sun and weather for some time; her face and hands had baked a delicate soft brown, that made the big golden eyes that much more startling when they turned full on one—which they now did.

"Brianna says that Dr. Fentiman trephined your skull."

He shifted uncomfortably under the sheets.

"I am told that he did. I am afraid I was not aware of it at the time."

Her mouth quirked slightly.

"Just as well. Would you mind if I look at it? It's only curiosity," she went on, with unaccustomed delicacy. "Not medical necessity. It's only that I've never seen a trepanation."

He closed his eyes, giving up.

"Beyond the state of my bowels, I have no secrets from you, madame." He tilted his head, indicating the location of the hole in his head, and felt her cool fingers slide under the bandage, lifting the gauze and allowing a breath of air to soothe his hot head.

"Brianna is with her father?" he asked, eyes still closed.

"Yes." Her voice was softer. "She told me—us—a little of what you'd done for her. Thank you."

The fingers left his skin and he opened his eyes.

"It was my pleasure to be of service to her. Perforated skull and all."

She smiled faintly.

"Jamie will be up to see you in a bit. He's . . . talking to Brianna in the garden."

He felt a small stab of anxiety.

"Are they—in accord?"

"See for yourself." She put an arm behind him, and with amazing strength for a woman with such fine bones, levered him upright. Just beyond the balustrade he could see the two figures at the bottom of the garden, heads close together. As he watched, they embraced, then broke apart, laughing at the awkwardness caused by Brianna's shape.

"I think we got here just in time," Claire murmured, looking at her daughter with a practiced eye. "It isn't going to be much longer."

"I confess to some gratitude at your prompt arrival," he said, letting her ease him back onto the pillows and smooth his bedding. "I have barely survived the experience of being your daughter's nursemaid; I fear serving as her midwife would finish me completely."

"Oh, I nearly forgot." Claire reached into a nasty-looking

leather pouch around her neck. "Brianna said to give this back to you—she won't need it anymore."

He held out his hand, and a tiny spark of brilliant blue fell into his palm.

"Jilted, by God!" he said, and grinned.

64

Bottom of the Ninth

"It's like baseball," I assured her. "Long stretches of boredom, punctuated by short periods of intense activity."

She laughed, then stopped abruptly, grimacing.

"Ugh. Intense, yeah. Whew." She smiled, a little lopsidedly. "At least at baseball games you get to drink beer and eat hot dogs in the boring parts."

Jamie, grasping at the only part of this conversation that made sense, leaned forward.

"There's a crock of small beer, cool in the pantry," he said, peering anxiously at Brianna. "Will I fetch it in?"

"No," I said. "Not unless you want some; alcohol wouldn't be good for the baby."

"Ah. What about the hot dog?" He stood up and flexed his hands, obviously preparing to dash out and shoot one.

"It's a sort of sausage in a roll," I said, rubbing my upper lip in an effort not to laugh. I glanced at Brianna. "I don't think she wants one." Small beads of sweat had popped out quite suddenly on her wide brow, and she was looking white around the eye sockets.

"Oh, barf," she said faintly.

Correctly interpreting this remark from the look on her face, Jamie hastily applied the damp cloth to her face and neck.

"Put your head between your knees, lass."

She glared at him ferociously.

"I can't get . . . my head . . . *near* my knees!" she said, teeth clenched. Then the spasm relaxed and she took a deep breath, the color coming back into her face.

Jamie glanced from her to me, frowning worriedly. He took a hesitant step toward the door.

"I expect I'd best go, then, if you—"

"Don't leave me!"

"But it's—I mean, you've your mother, and—"

"Don't leave me!" she repeated. Agitated, she leaned over and grabbed his arm, shaking it for emphasis. "You can't!"

"You said I wouldn't die." She was staring intently into his face. "If you stay, it will be all right. I won't die." She spoke with such intensity that I felt a sudden spasm of fear clutch my own innards, hard as the pain of labor.

She was a big girl, strong and healthy. She should have no great trouble delivering. But I was large enough, healthy as well—and twenty-five years before, I had lost a stillborn child at six months, and nearly died myself. I might be able to protect her from child-bed fever, but there was no defense against a sudden hemorrhage; the best I could do under such circumstances would be to try to save her child via Caesarian section. I resolutely kept my eyes off the chest in which the sterile blade lay ready, just in case.

"You're not going to die, Bree," I said. I spoke as soothingly as I could, and put a hand on her shoulder, but she must have felt the fear under my professional facade. Her face twisted, and she grabbed my hand, clinging so tightly the bones rubbed together. She closed her eyes and breathed through her nose, but didn't cry out.

She opened her eyes and looked straight at me, her pupils dilated so that she seemed to be looking past me, into a future that only she could see.

"If I do . . ." she said, putting a hand to her swollen belly. Her mouth worked, but whatever she'd been meaning to say couldn't force its way out.

She struggled to her feet, then, and leaned heavily on Jamie, her face muffled in his shoulder, repeating, "Da, don't leave me, don't."

"I willna leave ye, *a leannan*. Dinna be afraid, I'll stay wi' ye." He put an arm around her, looking helplessly over her head at me.

"Walk her," I said to Jamie, seeing her restlessness. "Like a horse with colic," I added, as he looked blank.

That made her laugh. With the ginger air of a man approaching an armed bomb, he put an arm around her waist and towed her slowly around the room. Given their respective sizes, it sounded a lot like someone leading a horse, too.

"All right?" I heard him ask anxiously, on one circuit.

"I'll tell you when I'm not," she assured him.

It was warm for mid-May; I opened the windows wide, and the

scents of phlox and columbine flowed in, mixed with cool, damp air from the river.

The house was filled with an air of expectation: eagerness, with a hint of fear beneath. Jocasta walked up and down the terrace below, too nervous to stay put. Betty put her head in every few minutes to ask if anything was needed; Phaedre came up from the pantry with a jug of fresh buttermilk, just in case. Brianna, her eyes focused inwardly, merely shook her head at it; I sipped a glass myself, mentally checking off the preparations.

The fact was that there wasn't a hell of a lot you needed to do for a normal birth, and not the hell of a lot you *could* do if it wasn't. The bed was stripped and old quilts laid to protect the mattress; there was a stack of clean cloths to hand, and a can of hot water, renewed every half hour or so from the kitchen copper. Cool water for sipping and brow-mopping, a small vial of oil for rubbing, my suture kit to hand, just in case—and beyond that, everything was up to Brianna.

After nearly an hour's walking, she stopped dead in the middle of the floor, gripping Jamie's arm and breathing through her nose like a horse at the end of a twenty-furlong race.

"I want to lie down," she said.

Phaedre and I got her gown off, and got her safely onto the bed in her shift. I laid my hands on the huge mound of her belly, marveling at the sheer impossibility of what had happened already, and what was about to happen next.

The rigidity of the contraction passed off, and I could clearly feel the curves of the child below the thin rubbery covering of skin and muscle. It was large, I could tell that, but it seemed to be lying well, head down and fully engaged.

Normally, babies about to be born were fairly quiet, intimidated by the upheaval of their surroundings. This one was stirring; I felt a small, distinct surge against my hand as an elbow poked out.

"Daddy!" Brianna reached out blindly, flailing as a contraction took her unaware. Jamie lunged forward and caught her hand, squeezing tight.

"I'm here, *a bheanachd,* I'm here."

She breathed heavily, face bright red, then relaxed, and swallowed.

"How long?" she asked. She was facing me but not looking at me; she wasn't looking at anything outside.

"I don't know. Not an awfully long time, I don't think." The contractions were roughly five minutes apart, but I knew they could continue like that for a long time, or speed up abruptly; there was simply no telling.

There was a light breeze from the window, but she was sweating. I wiped her face and neck again, and rubbed her shoulders.

"You're doing fine, lovey," I murmured to her. "Just fine." I glanced up at Jamie, and smiled. "So are you."

He made a game try at returning the smile; he was sweating, too, but his face was white, not red.

"Talk to me, Da," she said suddenly.

"Och?" He looked at me, frantic. "What shall I say?"

"It doesn't matter," I said. "Tell her stories; anything to take her mind off things."

"Oh. Ah . . . will ye have heard the one about . . . Habetrot the spinstress?"

Brianna grunted in reply. Jamie looked apprehensive, but started in nonetheless.

"Aye, well. It happened that in an old farmhouse that stood by the river, there lived a fair maid called Maisie. She'd red hair and blue een, and was the bonniest maid in all the valley. But she had no husband, because . . ." He stopped, appalled. I glared at him.

He coughed and went on, plainly not knowing what else to do. "Ah . . . because in those days men were sensible, and instead of looking for lovely lasses to be their brides, they looked out for girls who could cook and spin, who might make notable housewives. But Maisie . . ."

Brianna made a deep inhuman noise. Jamie clenched his teeth for a moment, but went on, holding tight to both her hands.

"But Maisie loved the light in the fields and the birds of the glen . . ."

The light faded gradually from the room, and the smell of sun-warmed flowers was replaced by the damp green smell of the willows by the river, and the faint scent of woodsmoke from the cookhouse.

Brianna's shift was wet through, and stuck to her skin. I dug my thumbs into her back, just above the hips, and she squirmed hard against me, trying to ease the ache. Jamie sat with his head down, clinging doggedly to her hands, still talking soothingly, telling stories of silkies and seal catchers, of pipers and elves, of the great giants of Fingal's Cave, and the Devil's black horse that passes through the air faster than the thought between a man and a maid.

The pains were very close together. I motioned to Phaedre, who ran away and came back with a lighted taper, to light the candles in the sconces.

It was cool and dim in the room, the walls lit with flickering shadows. Jamie's voice was hoarse; Brianna's was nearly gone.

Suddenly she let go of him and sat up, grabbing at her knees, face dark red with effort, pushing.

"Now, then," I said. I stacked pillows quickly behind her, made her lean back against the bedstead, called Phaedre to hold the candlestick for me.

I oiled my fingers, reached under her shift, and touched flesh I had not touched since she was a baby herself. I rubbed slowly, gently, talking to her, knowing it made no great difference what I said.

I felt the strain, the sudden change under my fingers. A relaxation, then once more. There was a sudden gush of amniotic fluid, that splashed across the bed and dripped on the floor, filling the room with the scent of fecund rivers. I rubbed and eased, praying that it would not come too fast, not tear her.

The ring of flesh opened suddenly, and my fingers touched something wet and hard. Relaxation, and it moved back, away, leaving the ends of my fingers tingling with the knowledge that I had touched someone entirely new. Once more the great pressure, the stretching came, and once more eased slowly back. I pushed back the edge of the shift, and with the next push the ring stretched to impossible size, and a head like a Chinese gargoyle popped out, with a flood of amniotic fluid and blood.

I found myself nose to nose with a waxy-white head with a face like a fist, that grimaced at me in utter fury.

"What is it? Is it a boy?" Jamie's hoarse question cut through my startlement.

"I hope so," I said, hastily thumbing mucus from nose and mouth. "It's the ugliest thing I've ever seen; God help it if it's a girl."

Brianna made a noise that might have started as a laugh, and turned into an enormous grunt of effort. I barely had time to get my fingers in and turn the wide shoulders slightly to help. There was an audible *pop*, and a long, wet form slithered out onto the soggy quilt, wriggling like a landed trout.

I seized a clean linen towel and wrapped him—it was him, the scrotal sac swelled up round and purple between fat thighs— checking quickly for his Apgar signs: breathing, color, activity . . . all good. He was making thin, angry noises, short explosions of breath, not really crying, and punching the air with clenched tiny fists.

I laid him on the bed, one hand on the bundle as I checked Brianna. Her thighs were smeared with blood, but there was no sign of hemorrhage. The cord was still pulsing, a thick wet snake of connection between them.

She was panting, lying back on the crushed pillows, hair plastered wetly to her temples, an enormous smile of relief and triumph on her face. I laid a hand on her belly, suddenly flaccid. Deep inside, I felt the placenta give way, as her body surrendered its last physical link with her son.

"Once more, honey," I said softly to her. The last contraction shivered over her belly, and the afterbirth slid out. I tied off the cord and cut it, and placed the solid little bundle of her child in her arms.

"He's beautiful," I whispered.

I left him to her, and turned my attention to immediate matters, kneading her belly firmly with my fists, to encourage the uterus to contract and stop the bleeding. I could hear the babble of excitement spreading through the house as Phaedre rushed downstairs to spread the news. I glanced upward once, to see Brianna glowing, still smiling from ear to ear. Jamie was behind her, also smiling, his cheeks wet with tears. He said something to her in husky Gaelic, and brushing the hair away from her neck, leaned forward and kissed her gently, just behind the ear.

"Is he hungry?" Brianna's voice was deep and cracked, and she tried to clear her throat. "Shall I feed him?"

"Try him and see. Sometimes they're sleepy right afterward, but sometimes they want to nurse."

She fumbled at the neck of her shift and pulled loose the ribbon, baring one high, full breast. The bundle made small *growf* noises as she turned it awkwardly toward her, and her eyes sprang open in surprise as the mouth fastened on her nipple with sudden ferocity.

"Strong, isn't he?" I said, and realized that I was crying only when I tasted the salt of my tears running into the corners of my smile.

Sometime later, with mother and child cleaned up and made comfortable, food and drink brought for Brianna, and a last check assuring that all was well, I walked out into the deep shadows of the upper gallery. I felt pleasantly detached from reality, as though I were walking a foot or so off the ground.

Jamie had gone down to tell John; he was waiting for me at the foot of the stairs. He drew me into his arms without a word and kissed me; as he let me go I saw the deep red crescents of Brianna's nailmarks on his hands, not yet faded.

"Ye did brawly too," he whispered to me. Then the joy in his eyes bloomed bright and flowered in a face-splitting grin. "Grannie!"

"Is he dark or fair?" Jamie asked suddenly, rising on one elbow beside me in bed. "I counted his fingers, and I didna even think to look."

"You can't really tell yet," I said drowsily. I'd counted his toes, and I'd thought of it. "He's sort of reddish-purple, and he's still got the vernix—the white stuff—all over him. It will probably be a day or two before his skin fades into a natural color. He's got just a bit of dark hair, but it's the sort that rubs off soon after birth." I stretched, enjoying the pleasant ache in legs and back; labor was hard work, even for the midwife. "It wouldn't prove anything, even if he were fair, since Brianna is; he could be, either way."

"Aye . . . but if he were dark, we'd know for sure."

"Maybe not. Your father was dark; so was mine. He could have recessive genes and come out dark even if—"

"He could have *what*?"

I tried without success to think whether Gregor Mendel had yet started messing about with his pea plants, but gave up the effort, too sleepy to concentrate. Whether he had or not, Jamie evidently hadn't heard of him.

"He could be any color, and we wouldn't know for sure," I said. I yawned widely. "We won't know until he gets old enough to start resembling . . . somebody. And even then . . ." I trailed off. Did it matter a great deal who his father had been, if he wasn't going to have one?

Jamie rolled toward me and scooped me into a spooned embrace. We slept naked, and the hair on his body brushed against my skin. He kissed me softly on the back of the neck and sighed, his breath warm and tickling on my ear.

I hovered on the edge of sleep, too happy to fall completely over into dreams. Somewhere nearby, I heard a small stifled squawk, and the murmur of voices.

"Aye, well," Jamie's voice roused me, some moments later.

He sounded defiant. "If I dinna ken his father, at least I'm sure who his grandsire is."

I reached back and patted his leg.

"So am I—Grandpa. Hush up and go to sleep. 'Sufficient unto the day is the evil thereof.' "

He snorted, but his arms relaxed around me, hand curved on my breast, and in moments, he was asleep.

I lay wide-eyed, watching stars through the open window. Why had I said that? It was Frank's favorite quotation, one he always used to soothe Brianna or me when we worried over things: *Sufficient unto the day is the evil thereof.*

The air in the room was live; a light breeze stirred the curtains, and coolness touched my cheek.

"Do you know?" I whispered, soundless. "Do you know she has a son?"

There was no answer, but peace came gradually over me in the quiet of the night, and I fell at last over the edge of dreams.

65

Return to Fraser's Ridge

Jocasta was loath to part with her newest relative, but the spring planting was already very late, and the homestead sadly neglected; we needed to return to the Ridge without delay, and Brianna would not hear of staying behind. Which was a good thing, as it would have taken dynamite to separate Jamie from his grandson.

Lord John was well enough to travel; he came with us as far as the Great Buffalo Trail Road, where he kissed Brianna and the baby, embraced Jamie and—to my shock—me, before turning north toward Virginia and Willie.

"I'll trust you to take care of them," he said quietly to me, with a nod toward the wagon, where two bright heads bent together in mutual absorption over the bundle in Brianna's lap.

"You may," I said, and pressed his hand. "I'll trust you, too." He lifted my hand to his lips, briefly, smiled at me, and rode away without looking back.

A week later, we bumped over the grass-choked ruts to the ridge where the wild strawberries grew, green and white and red together, constancy and courage, sweetness and bitterness mingled in the shadows of the trees.

The cabin was dirty and uncared for, its sheds empty and full of dead leaves. The garden was a tangle of old dried stalks and random shoots, the paddock an empty shell. The framework of the new house stood black and skeletal, reproachful on the Ridge. The place looked barely habitable, a ruin.

I had never felt such joy in any homecoming, ever.

Name, I wrote, and paused. God knew, I thought. His last name was open to question; his Christian name not yet even considered.

I called him "sweetie" or "darling," Lizzie called him "dear lad," Jamie addressed him with Gaelic formality either as "grandson" or *"a Ruaidh,"* the Red One—his dark infant fuzz and dusky skin having given way to a blazing fair ruddiness that made it clear to the most casual observer just who his grandsire was—whoever his father might have been.

Brianna found no need to call him anything; she kept him always with her, guarding him with a fierce absorption that went beyond words. She would not give him a formal name, she said. Not yet.

"When?" Lizzie had asked, but Brianna didn't answer. I knew when; when Roger came.

"And if he doesna come," said Jamie privately to me, "I expect the poor wee lad will go to his grave wi' no name at all. Christ, that lass is stubborn!"

"She trusts Roger," I said evenly. "You might try to do the same."

He gave me a sharp look.

"There is a difference between trust and hope, Sassenach, and ye ken that as well as I do."

"Well, have a stab at hope, then, why don't you?" I snapped, and turned my back on him, dipping my quill and shaking it elaborately. Little Query Mark had a rash on his bottom, that had kept him—and everyone else in the house—awake all night. I was grainy-eyed and cross, and not inclined to tolerate any show of bad faith.

Jamie walked deliberately around the table and sat down opposite me, resting his chin on his folded arms, so that I was forced to look at him.

"I would," he said, a shadow of humor in his eyes. "If I could decide whether to hope he comes or hope he does not."

I smiled, then reached across and ran the feathered tip of my quill down the bridge of his nose in token of forgiveness, before returning to my work. He wrinkled his nose and sneezed, then sat up straight, peering at the paper.

"What's that you're doing, Sassenach?"

"Making out little Gizmo's birth certificate—so far as I can," I added.

"Gizmo?" he said doubtfully. "That will be a saint's name?"

"I shouldn't think so, though you never know, what with people named Pantaleon and Onuphrius. Or Ferreolus."

"Ferreolus? I dinna think I ken that one." He leaned back, hands linked over his knee.

"One of my favorites," I told him, carefully filling in the birthdate and time of birth—even that was an estimate, poor thing. There were precisely two bits of unequivocal information on this birth certificate—the date and the name of the doctor who'd delivered him.

"Ferreolus," I went on with some enjoyment, "is the patron saint of sick poultry. Christian martyr. He was a Roman tribune and a secret Christian. Having been found out, he was chained up in the prison cesspool to await trial—I suppose the cells must have been full. Sounds rather a daredevil; he slipped his chains and escaped through the sewer. They caught up with him, though, dragged him back and beheaded him."

Jamie looked blank.

"What has that got to do wi' chickens?"

"I haven't the faintest idea. Take it up with the Vatican," I advised him.

"Mmphm. Aye, well, I've always been fond of Saint Guignole, myself." I could see the glint in his eye, but couldn't resist.

"And what's he the patron of?"

"He's invoked against impotence." The glint got stronger. "I saw a statue of him in Brest once; they did say it had been there for a thousand years. 'Twas a miraculous statue—it had a cock like a gun muzzle, and—"

"A *what*?"

"Well, the size wasna the miraculous bit," he said, waving me to silence. "Or not quite. The townsfolk say that for a thousand years, folk have whittled away bits of it as holy relics, and yet the cock is still as big as ever." He grinned at me. "They do say that a man wi' a bit of St. Guignole in his pocket can last a night and a day without tiring."

"Not with the same woman, I don't imagine," I said dryly. "It does rather make you wonder what he did to merit sainthood, though, doesn't it?"

He laughed.

"Any man who's had his prayer answered could tell ye that, Sassenach." He swiveled on his stool, looking out the open door. Brianna and Lizzie sat on the grass, skirts blooming around them, watching the baby, who lay naked on an old shawl on his stomach, red-arsed as a baboon.

Brianna Ellen, I wrote neatly, then paused.

"Brianna Ellen Randall, do you think?" I asked. "Or Fraser? Or both?"

He didn't turn around, but his shoulder moved in the faintest of shrugs.

"Does it matter?"

"It might." I blew across the page, watching the shiny black letters go dull as the ink dried. "If Roger comes back—whether he stays or not—if he chooses to acknowledge little Anonymous, I suppose his name will be MacKenzie. If he doesn't or won't, then I imagine the baby takes his mother's name."

He was silent for a moment, watching the two girls. They had washed their hair in the creek that morning; Lizzie was combing out Brianna's mane, the long strands shimmering like red silk in the summer sun.

"She calls herself Fraser," he said softly. "Or she did."

I put down my quill and reached across the table to lay a hand on his arm.

"She's forgiven you," I said. "You know she has."

His shoulders moved; not quite a shrug, but the unconscious attempt to ease some inner tightness.

"For now," he said. "But if the man doesna come?"

I hesitated. He was quite right; Brianna had forgiven him for his original mistake. Still, if Roger did not appear soon, she would be bound to blame Jamie for it—not without reason, I was forced to admit.

"Use both," he said abruptly. "Let her choose." I didn't think he meant last names.

"He'll come," I said firmly, "and it will be all right."

I picked up the quill, and added, not quite under my breath. "I hope."

He stooped to drink, the water splashing over dark green rock. It was a warm day; spring now, not autumn, but the moss was still emerald-green underfoot.

The memory of a razor was far behind him; his beard was thick and his hair hung past his shoulders. He'd bathed in a creek the night before, and done his best to wash himself and his clothes, but he had no illusions about his appearance. Neither did he care, he told himself. What he looked like didn't matter.

He turned toward the path where he had left his horse, limping. His foot ached, but that didn't matter either.

He rode slowly through the clearing where he had first met Jamie Fraser. The leaves were new and green, and in the distance he could hear the raucous calling of the ravens. Nothing stirred among the trees but the wild grasses. He breathed deep and felt a stab of memory, a broken remnant from a past life, a shard sharp as glass.

He turned his horse's head toward the top of the Ridge and urged it on, kicking gently with his good foot. Soon now. He had no idea what his reception might be, but that didn't matter.

Nothing mattered now save the fact that he was here.

66

Child of My Blood

Some enterprising rabbit had dug its way under the stakes of my garden again. One voracious rabbit could eat a cabbage down to the roots, and from the looks of things, he'd brought friends. I sighed and squatted to repair the damage, packing rocks and earth back into the hole. The loss of Ian was a constant ache; at such moments as this, I missed his horrible dog as well.

I had brought a large collection of cuttings and seeds from River Run, most of which had survived the journey. It was mid-June, still time—barely—to put in a fresh crop of carrots. The small patch of potato vines was all right, so were the peanut bushes; rabbits wouldn't touch those, and didn't care for the aromatic herbs either, except the fennel, which they gobbled like licorice.

I wanted cabbages, though, to preserve as sauerkraut; come midwinter, we would want food with some taste to it, as well as some vitamin C. I had enough seed left, and could raise a couple of decent crops before the weather turned cold, if I could keep the bloody rabbits off. I drummed my fingers on the handle of my basket, thinking. The Indians scattered clippings of their hair around the edges of the fields, but that was more protection against deer than rabbits.

Jamie was the best repellent, I decided. Nayawenne had told me that the scent of carnivore urine would keep rabbits away—and a man who ate meat was nearly as good as a mountain lion, to say nothing of being more biddable. Yes, that would do; he'd shot a deer only two days ago; it was still hanging. I should brew a fresh bucket of spruce beer to go with the roast venison, though . . .

As I wandered toward the herb shed to see if I had any maypop fruits for flavoring, my eye caught a movement at the far edge of the clearing. Thinking it was Jamie, I turned to go and inform him of his new duty, only to be stopped dead in my tracks when I saw who it was.

He looked worse than he had the last time I'd seen him, which was saying quite a bit. He was hatless, hair and beard a glossy black tangle, and his clothes hung on him in tatters. He was barefoot, one foot wrapped in a bundle of filthy rags, and he limped badly.

He saw me at once, and stopped while I came up to him.

"I'm glad it's you," he said. "I wondered who I'd meet first." His voice sounded soft and rusty, and I wondered whether he had spoken to a living soul since we had left him in the mountains.

"Your foot, Roger—"

"It doesn't matter." He gripped my arm. "Are they all right? The baby? And Brianna?"

"They're fine. Everybody's in the house." His head turned toward the cabin, and I added, "You have a son."

He jerked sharply back toward me, green eyes wide with startlement.

"He's mine? *I* have a son?"

"I suppose you do," I said. "You're here, aren't you?" The look of startlement—and hope, I realized—faded slowly. He looked into my eyes and seemed to see how I felt, for he smiled—not easily, no more than a painful lifting of the corner of his mouth—but he smiled.

"I'm here," he said, and turned toward the cabin and its open doorway.

Jamie sat in his rolled-up shirt sleeves at the table, shoulder to shoulder with Brianna, frowning at a set of house drawings as she pointed with her quill. Both of them were liberally covered with ink, being inclined to enthusiasm when discussing architecture. The baby snored peacefully in his cradle nearby; Brianna was rocking it absently with one foot. Lizzie was spinning by the window, humming softly under her breath as the great wheel went round.

"Very domestic," Roger said under his breath, stopping in the dooryard. "Seems a shame to disturb them."

"Do you have a choice?" I said.

"Aye, I do," he replied. "But I've made it already." He walked purposefully up to the open door and stepped inside.

Jamie reacted instantly to this unfamiliar darkening of his door; he pushed Brianna off the bench and lunged for his pistols on the wall. He had one leveled at Roger's chest before he realized what

—or whom—he was looking at, and lowered it with a small exclamation of disgust.

"Oh, it's you," he said.

The baby, rudely wakened by the crash of the overturned bench,
was shrieking like a fire engine. Brianna scooped him out of his
cradle and clasped him to her breast, looking wild-eyed at the
apparition in the door.

I had forgotten that she hadn't had the benefit of seeing him
even as recently as I had; he must be substantially changed from
the young history professor who'd left her in Wilmington nearly a
year before.

Roger took a step toward her; instinctively, she took a step
back. He stood quite still, looking at the child. She sat down on
the nursing stool, fumbling at her bodice, bending protectively
over the baby. She pulled a shawl across her shoulder and gave
him a breast in its shelter, and he stopped squawking at once.

I saw Roger's eyes shift from the baby to Jamie. Jamie stood
beside Brianna with that utter stillness that so frightened me—
straight and still as a stick of dynamite, with a lit match laid a
hairsbreadth from the fuse.

The flame of Brianna's head moved slightly, looking from one
to the other, and I saw what she saw; the echo of Jamie's dangerous stillness in Roger. It was both unexpected and shocking; I had
never seen any resemblance between them at all—and yet at the
moment they might have been day and dark, images of fire and
night, each mirroring the other.

MacKenzie, I thought suddenly. Viking beasts, bloody-minded
and big. And saw the third echo of that flaming heritage blaze up
in Brianna's eyes, the only thing alive in her face.

I should say something, do something, to break the awful stillness. But my mouth was dry, and there was nothing I could say in
any case.

Roger's reached his hand toward Jamie, palm up, and the gesture held no hint of supplication.

"I don't imagine it pleases you any more than it does me," he
said, in his rusty voice, "but you are my nearest kinsman. Cut me.
I've come to swear an oath in our shared blood."

I couldn't tell whether Jamie hesitated or not; time seemed to
have stopped, the air in the room crystallized around us. Then I
watched Jamie's dirk cut the air, honed edge draw swift across the
thin, tanned wrist, and blood well red and sudden in its path.

To my surprise, Roger didn't look at Brianna, or reach for her hand. Instead, he swiped his thumb across his bleeding wrist, and stepped close to her, eyes on the baby. She pulled back instinctively, but Jamie's hand came down on her shoulder.

She stilled at once under its weight, at once a promise of restraint and protection, but she held the child tight, cradled against her breast. Roger knelt in front of her, and reaching out, pushed the shawl aside and smeared a broad red cross upon the downy curve of the baby's forehead.

"You are blood of my blood," he said softly, "and bone of my bone. I claim thee as my son before all men, from this day forever." He looked up at Jamie, challenging. After a long moment, Jamie gave the slightest nod of acknowledgment, and stepped back, letting his hand fall from Brianna's shoulder.

Roger's gaze shifted to Brianna.

"What do you call him?"

"Nothing—yet." Her eyes rested on him, questioning. It was only too clear that the man who had come back was not the man who'd left her.

Roger's eyes were fixed on hers as he stood. Blood was still dripping from his wrist. With a small shock, I realized that she was as changed to him as he to her.

"He's my son," Roger said quietly, nodding at the baby. "Are you my wife?"

Brianna had gone pale to the lips.

"I don't know."

"This man says that you are handfast." Jamie took a step closer to her, watching Roger. "Is that true?"

"We—we were."

"We still are." Roger took a deep breath, and I realized suddenly that he was about to fall over, whether from hunger, exhaustion, or the shock of being cut. I took his arm, made him sit down, sent Lizzie to the dairy shed for milk, and fetched down my small medical box to bind his wrist.

This small bustle of normality seemed to break the tension a little. Meaning to help things along in that direction, I broke out a bottle of brandy from River Run, pouring a cup for Jamie, and putting a good-sized dollop in Roger's milk. Jamie gave me a wry look, but sat back on the replaced bench and sipped his drink.

"Verra well, then," he said, calling the meeting to order. "If you're handfast, Brianna, then you're married and this man is your husband."

Brianna's flush deepened, but she looked at Roger, not Jamie.

"You said handfasting was good for a year and a day."

"And you said ye did not want anything temporary."

She flinched at that, but then set her lips firmly.

"I didn't. But I didn't know what was going to happen." She glanced at me and Jamie, then back at Roger. "They told you—that the baby isn't yours?"

Roger raised his eyebrows.

"Oh, but he is mine. Mm?" He lifted his bandaged wrist in illustration.

Brianna's face had lost its frostbitten look; she was pink around the edges.

"You know what I mean."

He met her eyes straight on.

"I know what you mean," he said softly. "I am sorry for it."

"It wasn't your fault."

Roger glanced at Jamie.

"Aye, it was," he said quietly. "I should have stayed with you; seen you safe."

Brianna's brows drew together.

"I told you to go, and I meant it." She twitched her shoulders impatiently. "But it doesn't matter now." She took a firmer hold on the baby and sat up straight.

"I just want to know one thing," she said, her voice trembling only a little. "I want to know why you came back."

He set his empty cup down deliberately.

"Did ye not want me to come back?"

"Never mind what I wanted. What I want now is to know. Did you come back because you wanted to—or because you thought you should?"

He looked at her for a long moment, then down at his hands, still clasped around the cup.

"Perhaps both. Perhaps neither. I don't know," he said very softly. "That's God's truth; I don't know."

"Did you go to the stone circle?" she asked. He nodded, not looking at her. He fumbled in his pocket, and laid the big opal stone on the table.

"I went there. That's why I was long in coming; it took me a long time to find it."

She was silent for a moment, then nodded.

"You didn't go back. But you can. Maybe you should." She looked at him straight on, her gaze the twin of her father's.

"I don't want to live with you, if you came back for duty," she said. She looked at me then, her eyes soft with pain. "I've seen a marriage made from obligation—and I've seen one made for love. If I hadn't—" She stopped and swallowed, then went on, looking at Roger. "If I hadn't seen both, I could have lived with obligation. But I *have* seen both—and I won't."

I felt as though someone had struck me in the breastbone. *My* marriages, she meant. I looked for Jamie, and found him looking at me with the same expression of shock I knew was on my own face. He coughed to break the silence, and cleared his throat, turning to Roger.

"When were ye handfast?"

"September the second," Roger answered promptly.

"And now it is mid-June." Jamie glanced from one to the other, frowning.

"Well, *mo nighean,* if you are handfast with this man, then you are bound to him; there's no question." He turned and gave Roger a dark blue stare. "So you'll live here, as her husband. And on September the third, she will choose whether she'll wed ye by priest and book—or whether ye'll leave and trouble her no more. Ye've that long to decide why you're here—and convince her of it."

Roger and Brianna both started to speak, to protest, but he stopped them, picking up the dirk he had left on the table. He lowered the blade gently, until it touched the cloth over Roger's chest.

"Ye'll live here as her husband, I said. But if ye touch her unwilling, I'll cut your heart out and feed it to the pig. Ye understand me?"

Roger stared down at the gleaming blade for a long moment, no expression visible beneath the thick beard, then lifted his head to meet Jamie's eyes.

"You think I'd trouble a woman who didn't want me?"

A rather awkward question, given that Jamie had beaten him to pulp under precisely that mistaken assumption. Roger put a hand on Jamie's and shoved the dirk point-first into the table. He pushed back his stool abruptly and stood up, turned on his heel, and left.

Just as quickly, Jamie stood and went after him, sheathing his dirk as he went.

Brianna looked at me helplessly.

"What do you think he'll—"

She was interrupted by a loud thud and an equally loud grunt, as a heavy body struck the wall outside.

"Treat her badly and I'll rip your balls off and cram them down your throat," Jamie's voice said softly, in Gaelic.

I glanced at Brianna, and saw that her mastery of Gaelic was sufficient to have appreciated the gist of this. Her mouth opened, but she didn't get a word out.

There was the sound of a quick scuffle outside, ending in an even louder thump, as of a head striking logs.

Roger didn't have Jamie's air of quiet menace, but his voice rang with sincerity. "Lay hands on me once more, you fucking sod, and I'll stuff your head back up your arse where it came from!"

There was a moment's silence, and then the sound of feet moving off. A moment later, Jamie made a Scottish noise deep in his throat, and moved off too.

Brianna's eyes were round as she looked at me.

"Testosterone poisoning," I said, with a shrug.

"Can you do anything about it?" she asked. The corner of her mouth twitched, though I couldn't tell whether with laughter or incipient hysteria.

I pushed a hand through my hair, considering.

"Well," I said finally, "there are only two things they do with it, and one of them is try to kill each other."

Brianna rubbed her nose.

"Uh-huh," she said. "And the other . . ." Our eyes met with a perfect understanding.

"I'll take care of your father," I said. "But Roger's up to you."

Life on the mountain was a trifle tense, with Brianna and Roger behaving respectively like a trapped hare and a cornered badger, Jamie fixing Roger with brooding looks of Gaelic disapproval over the supper table, Lizzie falling over her feet to apologize to everyone in sight, and the baby deciding that the time was ripe to have nightly attacks of screaming colic.

It was probably the colic that spurred Jamie into a frenzy of activity on the new house. Fergus and some of the tenants had kindly put in a small planting for us, so that while we would have no extra corn this year to sell, at least we would eat. Freed of the need to tend a large acreage, Jamie instead spent every free moment on the ridge, hammering and sawing.

Roger was doing his best to assist with the other farm chores, though hampered by his lame foot. He had several times brushed off my attempts to treat it, but now I refused to be put off any longer. A few days after his arrival, I made my preparations and informed him firmly that I meant to deal with it first thing in the morning.

The time come, I made him lie down, and unwrapped the layers of rags wound around his foot. The sweet-rotten smell of deep infection tickled my nose, but I thanked God to see neither the red streaks of blood poisoning nor the black tinges of incipient gangrene. It was bad enough, for all that.

"You've got chronic abscesses, deep in the tissue," I said, probing firmly with my thumbs. I could feel the squishy yielding of pockets of pus, and as I squeezed harder, the half-healed wounds broke open and a nasty yellow-gray slime oozed from an inflamed crack at the edge of the sole.

Roger went white under his tan, and his hands clenched on the wooden frame of the bed, but he didn't make a sound.

"You're lucky," I said, still working his foot back and forth, flexing the tiny joints of the metacarpals. "You've been breaking open the abscesses and partially draining them by walking on it. They re-form, of course, but the movement's kept the infection from moving much deeper, and it's kept your foot flexible."

"Oh, good," he said faintly.

"Bree, I need you to help," I said, turning casually toward the far end of the room, where the two girls sat, taking turns between baby and spinning wheel.

"I could; let me do it." Lizzie sprang up, eager to help. Remorseful over her part in Roger's ordeal, she had been trying to make amends in any way possible, constantly bringing him bits of food, offering to mend his clothes, and driving him mad generally with her expressions of contrition.

I smiled at her.

"Yes, you can help. Take the baby so Brianna can come here. Why don't you take him outside for a little air?"

With a dubious glance, Lizzie did as I said, scooping little Gizmo into her arms and murmuring endearments to him as they went out. Brianna came to stand beside me, carefully keeping her eyes off Roger's face.

"I'm going to open this up and drain it the best I can," I said, indicating the long black-crusted slit. "Then we'll have to debride the dead tissue, disinfect it, and hope for the best."

"And what exactly does 'debride' mean?" Roger asked. I let go of his foot and his body relaxed, very slightly.

"Cleansing of a wound by the surgical or nonsurgical removal of dead tissue or bone," I said. I touched his foot. "Luckily, I don't think the bone's been affected, though there may be a bit of damage in the cartilage between the metacarpals. Don't worry," I said, patting his leg. "The debridement isn't going to hurt."

"It isn't?"

"No. It's the draining and disinfecting that will hurt." I glanced up at Bree. "Go take hold of his hands, please."

She hesitated no more than a second, then moved to the head of the couch and held out her hands to him. He took them, his eyes on her. It was the first time they had touched each other in nearly a year.

"Hold on tight," I instructed them. "This is the nasty part."

I didn't look up, but worked quickly, opening the half-healed wounds cleanly with a scalpel, pressing out as much pus and dead matter as I could. I could feel the tension quivering in his leg muscles, and the slight arcing of his body as the pain lifted and bent him, but he didn't say a word.

"Do you want something to bite down on, Roger?" I asked, taking out my bottle of dilute alcohol–water mixture for irrigating. "It's going to sting a bit, now."

He didn't answer; Brianna did.

"He's all right," she said steadily. "Go ahead."

He made a muffled noise when I began to wash out the wounds, and rolled halfway onto his side, his leg convulsing. I kept tight hold of his foot and finished the job as quickly as possible. When I let go and recorked the bottle, I looked up toward the head of the bed. She was sitting on the bed, her arms locked tight around his shoulders. His face was buried in her lap, his arms around her waist. Her face was white, but she gave me a strained smile.

"Is it over?"

"The bad part is. Just a little more to do," I assured them. I had made my preparations two days before; at this time of year, there was no difficulty. I went outside to the smoking shed. The venison carcass hung in the shadows, bathing in clouds of protectively fragrant hickory smoke. My goal was less thoroughly preserved meat, though.

Good, it had been out long enough. I picked up the small saucer from its place near the door and carried it back to the house.

"Phew!" Brianna wrinkled her nose as I came in. "What's that? It smells like rotten meat."

"That's what it is." The partial remains of a snare-killed rabbit, to be exact, retrieved from the edge of the garden and set out to wait for visitors.

She was still holding his hands. I smiled to myself and resumed my place, picking up the wounded foot and reaching for my long-nosed forceps.

"Mama! What are you *doing*?"

"It won't hurt," I said. I squeezed the foot slightly, spreading one of my surgical incisions. I picked one of the small white grubs out of the stinking scraps of rabbit meat and inserted it deftly into the gaping slit.

Roger's eyes had been closed, his forehead sheened with sweat.

"What?" he said, lifting his head and squinting over his shoulder in an effort to see what I was doing. "What are you doing?"

"Putting maggots in the wounds," I said, intent on my work. "I learned it from an old Indian lady I used to know."

Twin sounds indicative of shock and nausea came from the bedhead, but I kept a tight hold on his foot and went on with it.

"It works," I said, frowning slightly as I opened another incision and deposited three of the wriggling white larvae. "Much better than the usual means of debridement; for that, I'd have to open up your foot much more extensively, and physically scrape out as much dead tissue as I could reach—which would not only hurt like the dickens, it would likely cripple you permanently. Our little friends here eat dead tissue, though; they can get into tiny places where I couldn't reach, and do a nice, thorough job."

"Our friends the maggots," Brianna muttered. "God, Mama!"

"What, exactly, is going to stop them eating my entire leg?" Roger asked with a thoroughly spurious attempt at detachment. "They . . . um . . . they *spread,* don't they?"

"Oh, no," I assured him cheerfully. "Maggots are larval forms; they don't breed. They also don't eat live tissue—only the nasty dead stuff. If there's enough to get them through their pupal cycle, they'll develop into tiny flies and fly off—if not, when the food's exhausted, they'll simply crawl out, searching for more."

Both faces were a pale green by now. Finished with the work, I wrapped the foot loosely in gauze bandages, and patted Roger's leg.

"There now," I said. "Don't worry, I've seen it before. One brave told me that they tickle a bit, gnawing, but it doesn't hurt at all."

I picked up the saucer and took it outside to wash. At the edge of the dooryard I met Jamie, coming down from the new house, Ruaidh in his arms.

"There's Grannie," he informed the baby, removing his thumb from Ruaidh's mouth and wiping saliva from it against the side of his kilt. "Is she no a bonny woman?"

"Gleh," said Ruaidh, focusing a slightly cross-eyed look on his grandfather's shirt button, which he began to mouth in a meditative fashion.

"Don't let him swallow that," I said, standing on tiptoe and kissing first Jamie, then the baby. "Where's Lizzie?"

"I found the lassie sitting on a stump, greetin'," he said. "So I took the lad and sent her off to be by herself for a bit."

"She was crying? What's the matter?"

A small shadow crossed Jamie's face.

"She'll be grieving for Ian, won't she?" Putting that and his own grief aside, he took my arm and turned back toward the trail up the ridge.

"Come up wi' me, Sassenach, and see what I've done the day. I've laid the floor for your surgery; all that's needed now is a bit of a temporary roof, and it'll do for sleeping." He glanced back toward the cabin. "I was thinking that MacKenzie might be put there—for the time being."

"Good idea." Even with the additional small room to the cabin that he had built for Brianna and Lizzie, conditions were more than crowded. And if Roger was to be bedridden for several days, I would as soon not have him lying in the middle of the cabin.

"How are they faring?" he asked, with assumed casualness.

"Who? Brianna and Roger, you mean?"

"Who else?" he asked, dropping the casualness. "Is it well between them?"

"Oh, I think so. They're getting used to each other again."

"They are?"

"Yes," I said, with a glance back at the cabin. "He's just thrown up in her lap.".

67

The Toss of a Coin

Roger rolled onto his side and sat up. There was no glass in the windows as yet—none needed, so long as the summer weather kept fine—and the surgery was at the front of the new house, facing the slope. If he craned his neck to one side, he could watch Brianna most of the way down to the cabin, before the chestnut trees hid her from view.

A last flick of rusty homespun, and she was gone. She'd come without the baby this evening; he didn't know whether that was progress or the reverse. They'd been able to talk without the incessant interruptions of wet diapers, squawking, fussing, feeding, and spitting up; that was a rare luxury.

She hadn't stayed as long as usual, though—he could feel the presence of the child pulling her away, as though she were tethered to it by a rubber band. He did not resent the little bugger, he told himself grimly. It was only that . . . well, only that he resented the little bugger. Didn't mean he didn't *like* him.

He hadn't eaten yet; hadn't wanted to waste any of their rare solitude. He uncovered the basket she'd brought and inhaled the warm, rich scent of squirrel stew and salt-rising bread with fresh butter. Apple tart, too.

His foot still throbbed, and it took considerable effort not to think of the helpful maggots, but in spite of that, his appetite had returned with a vengeance. He ate slowly, savoring both the food and the quiet dusk creeping over the mountainside below:

Fraser had known what he was about when he'd chosen the site of this house. It commanded the entire slope of the mountain, with a view that ran to the distant river and beyond, with mist-filled valleys in the distance and dark peaks that touched a star-strewn sky. It was one of the most solitary, magnificent, heart-wrenchingly romantic spots he had ever seen.

And Brianna was down below, nursing a small bald parasite, while he was here—alone with a few dozen of his own.

He put the empty basket on the floor, hopped to the slop jar in the corner, then back to his lonely bed on the new surgery table. Why in hell had he told her he didn't know, when she'd asked why he'd come back?

Well, because just then, he *hadn't* known. He'd been wandering in the bloody wilderness for months, half starved and off his head with solitude and pain. He hadn't seen her in nearly a year—a year in which he'd gone through hell and back. He'd sat on the cliff above that bloody stone circle for three solid days without food or fire, thinking things over, trying to decide. And in the end he'd simply gotten up and begun walking, knowing that it was the only possible choice.

Obligation? Love? How in hell could you have love *without* obligation?

He turned restlessly onto his other side, turning his back on the glorious night of scent and sun-warmed winds. The trouble with being restored to health was that some parts of him were getting a damn sight too healthy for comfort, given that the chance of their having any proper exercise was something below nil.

He couldn't even suggest such a thing to Brianna. One, she might think he'd come back solely for *that,* and two, the bloody Great Scot had not been joking about the pig.

He knew now. He'd come back because he couldn't live on the other side. If it were guilt over abandoning them—or the simple knowledge that he would die without her . . . either or both, take your choice. He knew what he was giving up, and none of it bloody mattered; he had to be here, that was all.

He flopped onto his back, staring up at the dim paleness of the pine boards that roofed his shelter. Thumps and skitterings announced the nightly visitation of squirrels from the nearby hickory tree, who found it a convenient shortcut.

How to tell her that, so she would believe it? Christ, she was so jumpy that she'd barely let him touch her. A brush of lips, a touch of hands, and she was sidling away. Except for the day when she'd held him while Claire had tortured his foot. Then, she'd been truly there for him, hanging on with all her strength. He could still feel her arms around him, and the memory gave him a small thump of satisfaction in the pit of his stomach.

Thinking on that, he wondered a bit. True, the doctoring had hurt like buggery, but it was nothing he couldn't have stood with a little tooth-gritting, and Claire, with her battlefield experience, would certainly have known that.

Done it on purpose, had she? Given Bree a chance to touch him without feeling pressured or pursued? Given him a chance to remember just how strong the pull between them was? He rolled again, onto his stomach this time, and lay with his chin on his folded arms, looking out into the soft dark outside.

She could have the other foot, if she'd do it again.

Claire looked in on him once or twice each day, but he waited until the end of the week, when she came to remove the bandages, the maggots having presumably done their dirty work and—he hoped to God—cleared out.

"Oh, lovely," she said, poking his foot with a surgeon's ghoulish delight. "Granulating beautifully; almost no inflammation left."

"Great," he said. "Are they gone?"

"The maggots? Oh, yes," she assured him. "They pupate within a few days. Did a nice job, didn't they?" She ran a delicate thumbnail along the side of his foot, which tickled.

"I'll take your word for it. I'm clear to walk on it, then?" He flexed the foot experimentally. It hurt a bit, but nothing compared to what it had before.

"Yes. Don't wear shoes for a few more days, though. And for God's sake, don't step on anything sharp."

She began to put away her things, humming to herself. She looked happy but tired; there were shadows under her eyes.

"Kid still howling at night?" he asked.

"Yes, poor thing. Can you hear him up here?"

"No. You just look tired."

"I'm not surprised. Nobody's had a good night's sleep all week, especially poor Bree, since she's the only one who can feed him." She yawned briefly and shook her head, blinking. "Jamie's got the back bedroom here nearly floored; he wants to move up here as soon as it's ready—give Bree and the baby more room, and, not incidentally, have a little peace and quiet ourselves."

"Good idea. Ah—speaking of Bree . . ."

"Mm?"

No use dragging it out; better say it straight.

"Look—I'm trying all I can. I love her, and I want to show her that, but—she sheers off. She comes and we talk, and it's great, but then I go to put an arm around her or kiss her, and suddenly she's across the room, picking leaves off the floor. Is there something wrong, something I should do?''

She gave him one of those disconcerting yellow looks of hers; straightforward and ruthless as a hawk.

''You were her first, weren't you? The first man she slept with, I mean.''

He felt the blood rising his cheeks.

''I—ah—yes.''

''Well, then. So far her entire experience of what one might call the delights of sex consists of being deflowered—and I don't care how gentle you were about it, it tends to hurt—being raped two days later, then giving birth. You think this is calculated to make her fall swooning into your arms in anticipation of your reclaiming your marital rights?''

You asked for it, he thought, *and you got it. Right between the eyes.* His cheeks burned hotter than they ever had with fever.

''I never thought of that,'' he muttered to the wall.

''Well, naturally not,'' she said, sounding torn between exasperation and amusement. ''You're a bloody *man.* That's why I'm telling you.''

He took a deep breath, and reluctantly turned back to face her.

''And just what *are* you telling me?''

''That she's afraid,'' she said. She cocked her head to one side, evaluating him. ''Though it's not you she's afraid of, by the way.''

''It's not?''

''No,'' she said bluntly. ''She may have convinced herself that she has to know why you came back, but that's not it—a regiment of blind men could see that. It's that she's afraid she won't be able to—mmphm.'' She raised one brow at him, encompassing a wealth of indelicate suggestion.

''I see,'' he said, taking a deep breath. ''And just what do you suggest I do about it?''

She picked up her basket and put it over her arm.

''I don't know,'' she said, giving him another yellow look. ''But I think you should be careful.''

He had just about recovered his equanimity after this unsettling consultation, when another visitor darkened his door. Jamie Fraser, bearing gifts.

"I've brought ye a razor," Fraser said, looking critically at him. "And some hot water."

Claire had clipped his beard short with her surgical scissors a few days earlier, but he had felt too shaky then to attempt shaving with what was called a "cutthroat" razor for good reason.

"Thanks."

Fraser had brought a small looking glass and a pot of shaving soap as well. Very thoughtful. He could have wished that Fraser might have left him alone, rather than leaning against the door-frame, lending a critical eye to the proceedings, but under the circumstances Roger could scarcely ask him to leave.

Even with the unwelcome spectator, it was a sublime relief to get rid of the beard. It itched like a fiend, and he hadn't seen his own face in months.

"Work going well?" He tried for a bit of polite conversation, rinsing the blade between strokes. "I heard you hammering in the back this morning."

"Oh, aye." Fraser's eyes followed his every move with interest —sizing him up, he thought. "I've got the floor laid, and a bit of roof on. Claire and I will sleep up here tonight, I think."

"Ah." Roger stretched his neck, negotiating the turn of his jaw. "Claire's told me I can walk again; let me know which chores I can take over."

Jamie nodded, arms crossed.

"Are ye handy wi' tools?"

"Haven't done a lot of building," Roger admitted. A birdhouse done in school didn't count, he suspected.

"I dinna suppose you'll be much hand wi' a plow, or a farrowing hog?" There was a definite glimmer of amusement in Fraser's eyes.

Roger lifted his chin, clearing the last of the stubble from his neck. He'd thought about it, the last few days. Not much call for the skills of either a historian or a folk singer, on an eighteenth-century hill farm.

"No," he said evenly, putting down the razor. "Nor do I know how to milk a cow, build a chimney, split shingles, drive horses, shoot bears, gut deer, or spit someone with a sword."

"No?" Overt amusement.

Roger splashed water on his face and toweled it dry, then turned to face Fraser.

"No. What I've got is a strong back. That do you?"

"Oh, aye. Couldna ask better, could I?" One side of Fraser's mouth curled up. "Know one end of a shovel from the other, do ye?"

"That much I know."

"Then ye'll do fine." Fraser shoved himself away from the doorframe. "Claire's garden needs spading, there's barley to be turned at the still, and there's an almighty heap of manure waitin' in the stable. After that, I'll show ye how to milk a cow."

"Thanks." He wiped the razor, put it back in the bag, and handed the lot over.

"Claire and I are going to Fergus's place the eve," Fraser said casually, accepting it. "Takin' the wee maid to help Marsali for a bit."

"Ah? Well . . . enjoy yourselves."

"Oh, I expect we will." Fraser paused in the doorway. "Brianna thought she'd stay; the bairn's settled a bit, and she doesna want to upset him wi' the walk."

Roger stared hard at the other man. You could read anything—or nothing—in those slanted blue eyes.

"Oh, aye?" he said. "So you're telling me they'll be alone? I'll keep an eye on them, then."

One ruddy brow lifted an inch.

"I'm sure ye will." Fraser's hand reached out and opened over the empty basin. There was a small metallic clink and a red spark glowed against the pewter. "Ye'll mind I told ye, MacKenzie—my daughter doesna need a coward."

Before he could reply, the brow dropped, and Fraser gave him a level blue look.

"Ye've cost me a lad I loved, and I'm no inclined to like ye for it." He glanced down at Roger's foot, then up. "But I've maybe cost ye more than that. I'll call the score settled—or not—at your word."

Astonished, Roger nodded, then found his voice.

"Done."

Fraser nodded, and disappeared as quickly as he'd come, leaving Roger staring at the empty doorway.

He lifted the latch and pushed gently on the cabin's door. It was bolted. So much for the notion of waking Sleeping Beauty with a kiss. He lifted a fist to knock, then stopped. Wrong heroine. Sleeping Beauty hadn't had an irascible dwarf in bed with her, ready to yell the house down at any disturbance.

He circled the small cabin, checking the windows, names like Sneezy and Grumpy drifting through the back of his mind. What would they call this one? Noisy? Smelly?

The house was snug as a drum, oiled skins nailed over the windows. He could punch one loose, but the last thing he wanted was to scare her by breaking in on her.

Slowly, he circled the house once more. The sensible thing was to go back to the surgery and wait till morning. He could talk to her then. Better than waking her out of a sound sleep, waking the kid.

Yes, that was plainly the thing to do. Claire would take the little bas—the baby, if he asked her. They could talk calmly, without fear of interruption, walk in the wood, get things settled between them. Right. That was it, then.

Ten minutes later he had circled the house twice more, and was standing in the grass at the back, looking at the faint glow of the window.

"What the hell do you think you are?" he muttered to himself. "A bloody moth?"

The creak of boards prevented his answering himself. He shot around the end of the house in time to see a white-gowned figure float ghostlike down the path toward the privy.

"Brianna?"

The figure whirled, with a small yelp of fright.

"It's me," he said, and saw the dark blotch of her hand press against the white of her nightdress, over her heart.

"What's the matter with you, sneaking up on me like that?" she demanded furiously.

"I want to talk to you."

She didn't answer, but whipped round and made off down the path.

"I said, I want to talk to you," he repeated more loudly, following.

"*I* want to go to the bathroom," she said. "Go away." She shut the door of the privy with a decisive slam.

He retreated a short distance up the path and waited for her to emerge. Her step slowed when she saw him, but there was no way around him without stepping into the long, wet grass.

"You shouldn't be up walking on that foot," she said.

"The foot's fine."

"I think you should go back to bed."

"All right," he said, and moved solidly into the center of the path in front of her. "Where?"

"Where?" She froze, but made no pretense of not understanding.

"Up there?" He jerked a thumb at the ridge. "Or here?"

"I—ah—"

Be careful, her mother said, and *my daughter doesna need a coward,* said her father. He could flip a bloody coin, but for the moment he was taking Jamie Fraser's advice, and damn the torpedoes.

"You said you'd seen a marriage of obligation and one of love. And do you think the one cuts out the other? Look—I spent three days in that godforsaken circle, thinking. And by God, I thought. I thought of staying, and I thought of going. And I stayed."

"So far. You don't know what you'd be giving up, if you stay for good."

"I do! And even if I did not, I know bloody well what I'd be giving up by going." He gripped her shoulder, the light gauze of her shift coarse under his hand. She was very warm.

"I could not go, and live with myself, thinking I'd left behind a child who might be mine—who *is* mine." His voice dropped a little. "And I could not go, and live without you."

She hesitated, drawing back, trying to escape his hand.

"My father—my fathers—"

"Look, I'm neither one of your bloody fathers! Give me credit for my own sins, at least!"

"You haven't committed any sins," she said, her voice sounding choked.

"No, and neither have you."

She looked up at him, and he caught the gleam of a dark, slanted eye.

"If I hadn't—" she began.

"And if I hadn't," he interrupted roughly. "Drop it, aye? It doesn't matter what you've done—or I. I said I was neither of your fathers, and I meant it. But there they are, the two of them, and you know them well—far better than I.

"Did Frank Randall not love you as his own? Take you as the child of his heart, *knowing* you were the blood of another man, and one he'd good reason to hate?"

He took her other shoulder and gave her a little shake.

"Did that redheaded bastard not love your mother more than

life? And love you enough to sacrifice even that love to save you?''

She made a small, choked noise, and a pang went through him at the sound, but he would not release her.

"If you believe it of them,'' he said, his voice little more than a whisper, ''then by God you must believe it of me. For I am a man like them, and by all I hold holy, I do love you.''

Slowly her head rose, and her breath was warm on his face.

"We have time,'' he said softly, and knew suddenly why it had been so important to talk to her now, here in the dark. He reached for her hand, clasped it flat against his breast.

"Do you feel it? Do you feel my heart beat?''

"Yes,'' she whispered, and slowly brought their linked hands to her own breast, pressing his palm against the thin white gauze.

"This is our time,'' he said. "Until that shall stop—for one of us, for both—it is our time. *Now.* Will ye waste it, Brianna, because you are afraid?''

"No,'' she said, and her voice was thick, but clear. "I won't.''

There was a sudden thin wail from the house, and a surprising gush of moist heat against his palm.

"I have to go,'' she said, pulling away. She took two steps, then turned. "Come in,'' she said, and ran up the path in front of him, fleet and white as the ghost of a deer.

By the time he reached the door, she had already fetched the baby from his cradle. She had been in bed; the quilt was thrown back and the hollow of her body was printed on the feather bed. Looking self-conscious, she sidled past him and lay down.

"I usually feed him in bed at night. He stays asleep longer if he's next to me.''

Roger made some murmur of assent, and drew up the low nursing chair before the fire. It was very warm in the room, and the air was thick with smells of cooking, used diapers—and Brianna. Her scent was slightly different these days; the tang of wild grass tempered with a light, sweet smell that he thought must be milk.

Her head was bent, loose red hair falling over her shoulders in a cascade of sparks and shadows. The front of her gown was open to her waist, and the full round curve of one breast showed plainly, only the nipple obscured by the roundness of the baby's head. There was a faint sound of sucking.

As though feeling his eyes on her, she raised her head.

"I'm sorry," he said softly, not to disturb the baby. "I cannot pretend not to be looking."

He couldn't tell if she flushed; the fire cast a red glow over face and breasts alike. She glanced down, though, as if she was embarrassed.

"Go ahead," she said. "Nothing much worth looking at."

Without a word, he stood up and began to undress.

"What are you doing?" Her voice was low, but shocked.

"Not fair for me to sit here gawking at you, is it? It's much less worth looking at, I expect, but . . ." He paused, frowning at a knot in the lacing of his breeches. "But at least you'll not feel you're on display."

"Oh." He didn't look up to see, but he thought that had made her smile. He'd got his shirt off; the fire felt good on his bare back. Feeling unspeakably self-conscious, he stood up and eased his breeches halfway down before stopping.

"Is this a striptease?" Brianna's mouth quivered as she tried to keep from laughing out loud, joggling the baby.

"I couldn't decide whether to turn my back or not." He paused. "Have you got a preference?"

"Turn your back," she said softly. "For now."

He did, and got the breeches off without falling into the fire.

"Stay that way for a minute," she said. "Please. I like to look at you."

He straightened up and stood still, looking into the fire. The heat played over him, uncomfortably warm, and he took a step back, a sudden memory of Father Alexandre vivid in his mind. Christ, and why would he think of that now?

"You have marks on your back, Roger," Brianna said, her voice softer than ever. "Who hurt you?"

"The Indians. It doesn't matter. Not now." He hadn't bound or cut his hair; it fell over his shoulders, tickling the bare skin of his back. He could imagine the tickle of her eyes, going lower, over back and arse and thighs and calves.

"I'm going to turn around now. All right?"

"I won't be shocked," she assured him. "I've seen pictures."

She had her father's trick of hiding her expressions when she wanted to. He couldn't tell a thing from the soft, wide mouth or the slanted cat-eyes. Was she shocked, frightened, amused? Why ought she to be any of those things? She had touched everything she was now looking at; had caressed and handled him with such intimacy that he had lost himself in her hands, yielded himself to her without reservation—and she to him.

But that had been a lifetime ago, in the freedom and frenzy of hot darkness. Now he stood before her for the first time naked in the light, and she sat there watching him with a baby in her arms. Which of them had changed more, since their wedding night?

She looked at him carefully, head on one side, then smiled, her eyes rising to meet his. She sat up, shifting the child easily to the other breast, leaving her gown open, the one breast bared.

He couldn't stand there any longer; the fire was singeing the hair on his arse. He moved to the side of the hearth and sat down again, watching her.

"What does that feel like?" he asked, partly from a need to break the silence before it got too heavy, partly from a deep curiosity.

"It feels good," she answered softly, head bent over the child. "Sort of a pulling. It tingles. When he starts to feed, something happens, and there's a rushing feeling, like everything in me is surging toward him."

"It's not—you don't feel drained? I should have thought it would feel like your substance being taken, somehow."

"Oh, no, not like that at all. Here, look." She put a finger in the infant's mouth and detached it with a soft *pop!* She lowered the small body for an instant, and Roger saw the nipple drawn up taut, milk jetting out in a thin stream of incredible force. Before the child could start to wail, she put him back, but not before Roger had felt the spray of tiny droplets, warm and then suddenly cool against the skin of his chest.

"My God," he said, half shocked. "I didn't know it did that! It's like a squirt gun."

"Neither did I." She smiled again, her hand cupping the tiny head. Then the smile faded. "There are lots of things I couldn't have imagined before they happened to me."

"Bree." He sat forward, forgetting his nakedness in the need to touch her. "Bree, I know you're scared. So am I. I don't want you to be afraid of me—but Bree, I do want ye so."

His hand rested on the round of her knee. After a moment, her free hand came down on his, light as a landing bird.

"I want you, too," she whispered. They sat frozen together for what seemed a long time; he had no notion what to do next, only that he must not go too fast, not frighten her. *Be careful.*

The tiny sucking sounds had ceased and the bundle had gone limp and heavy in the curve of her arm.

"He's asleep," she whispered. Moving as cautiously as one holding a vial of nitroglycerine, she scooted to the edge of the bed and stood up.

She might have meant to lay the child in its cradle, but Roger lifted his hands instinctively. She hesitated for no more than a second, then bent to lay the child in his arms. Her breasts hung full and heavy in the shadow of her open gown, and he smelled the deep musk of her body as she brushed him.

The baby was surprisingly heavy; dense, for the size of the bundle. He was amazingly warm, too; warmer even than his mother's body.

Roger boosted the tiny body cautiously, cuddling it against him; the small, curved buttocks fit in the palm of his hand. It—*he*— wasn't quite bald, after all. There was a soft red-blond fuzz all over the head. Tiny ears. Almost transparent; the one he could see was red and crumpled from being pressed against his mother's arm.

"You can't tell by looking." Brianna's voice jerked him out of his contemplation. "I've tried." She was standing across the room, one drawer of the sideboard open. He thought it might be regret on her face, but the shadows were too deep to tell.

"That wasn't what I was looking for." He lowered the baby carefully to his lap. "It's only—this is the first time I've had a proper look at my son." The words sounded peculiar, stiff to his tongue. She relaxed a little, though.

"Oh. Well, he's all there." There was a small note of pride in her voice that caught at his heart, and made him look closer. The little fists were curled up tight as snail shells; he picked one up and gently stroked it with his thumb. Slowly as an octopus moving, the hand opened, enough for him to insert the tip of his index finger. The fist closed again in reflex, astonishing in the strength of its grip.

He could hear a rhythmic *whish* across the room, and realized that she was brushing her hair. He would have liked to watch her, but was too fascinated to look up.

The body had feet like a frog's; wide at the toes, narrow at the heel. Roger stroked one with a fingertip, and smiled as the tiny toes sprang wide apart. Not webbed, at least.

My son, he thought, and wasn't sure what he felt at the thought. It would take time to get used to.

But he could be, came the next thought. Not just Brianna's child, to be loved for her sake—but his own flesh and blood. That thought was even more foreign. He tried to push it from his mind, but it kept coming back. That coupling in the dark, that bitter-sweet mix of pain and joy—had he started this, in the midst of that?

He hadn't meant to—but he hoped like hell he had.

The child was wearing some long thing made of white gauzy stuff; he lifted it, looking at the sagging diaper and the perfect oval of the tiny navel just above. Moved by a curiosity he didn't think to question, he hooked a finger in the edge of the clout and pulled it down.

"I told you he was all there." Brianna was standing at his elbow.

"Well, it's there," Roger said dubiously. "But isn't it a bit . . . small?"

She laughed.

"It'll grow," she assured him. "It's not like he needs it for much yet."

His own penis, gone flaccid between his thighs, gave a small twitch at that reminder.

"Shall I take him?" She reached for the baby, but he shook his head and picked up the child again.

"Not just yet." It—he—smelled of milk and something sweetly putrid. Something else, his own indefinable smell, like nothing else Roger had ever encountered.

"Eau de baby, Mama calls it." She sat on the bed, a faint smile on her face. "She says it's a natural protective device; one of the things babies use to keep their parents from killing them."

"Killing him? But he's a sweet wee lad," Roger protested.

One eyebrow quirked up in derision.

"You haven't been living with the little fiend for the last month. This is the first night he hasn't had colic in three weeks. I would have exposed him on a hillside if he wasn't mine."

If he wasn't mine. That certainty was a mother's reward, he supposed. She'd always know—had always known. For a brief, surprising moment, he envied her.

The baby stirred and made a small, faint *yawp!* noise against his neck. Before he could move, she was up and had the child back in her arms, patting the rounded little back. There was a soft belch, and he subsided into limpness once more.

Brianna set him on his stomach in the cradle, carefully, as if he were wired to a stick of dynamite. He could see the faint outline of her body through the gauze, highlighted by the fire behind her. When she turned around, he was ready.

"You could have gone back, once you knew. There would have been time." He held her eyes, not letting her look away. "So it's my turn to ask, then, isn't it? What made you wait for me? Love —or obligation?"

"Both," she said, her eyes nearly black. "Neither. I—just couldn't go without you."

He breathed deeply, feeling the last small doubt in the pit of his stomach melt away.

"Then you do know."

"Yes." She lifted her shoulders and let them fall, and the loose gown fell too, leaving her as naked as he was. It *was* red, by God. More than red; she was gold and amber, ivory and cinnabar, and he wanted her with a longing that went beyond flesh.

"You said that you loved me, by all you hold holy," she whispered. "What is it that's holy to you, Roger?"

He stood and reached for her, gently, carefully. Held her against his heart, and remembered the stinking hold of the *Gloriana* and a thin, ragged woman who smelled of milk and ordure. Of fire and drums and blood, and an orphan baptized with the name of the father who had sacrificed himself for fear of the power of love.

"You," he said, against her hair. "Him. Us. There isn't anything else, is there?"

68

Domestic Bliss

August 1770

It was a peaceful morning. The baby had slept all night, for which feat he was the recipient of general praise. Two hens had obligingly laid eggs in their coop rather than scattering them round the landscape, so I was not required to crawl through the blackberry bushes in search of breakfast before cooking it.

The bread had risen to a perfect snowy mound in its bowl, been molded into loaves by Lizzie, and—the new Dutch oven sharing the general mood of cooperation—had been baked into a delicate brown fragrance that suffused the house with contentment. Spiced ham and turkey hash sizzled pleasantly on the griddle, adding their aromas to the softer morning scents of damp grass and summer flowers that came through the open window.

These things all helped, but the general atmosphere of drowsy well-being owed more to the night before than to the events of the morning.

It had been a perfect moon-drenched night. Jamie had put out the candle and gone to bolt the door, but instead he stood, arms braced on the doorframe, looking down the valley.

"What is it?" I asked.

"Nothing," he said softly. "Come and see."

Everything seemed to be floating, deprived of depth by the eerie light. Far off, the spurt of the falls seemed frozen, suspended in air. The wind was toward us, though, and I could hear the faint rumble of tons of falling water.

The night air was scented with grass and water, and the breath of pine and spruce blew down cool from the mountaintops. I shivered in my shift, and drew closer to him for warmth. His shirttails were split at the side, open nearly to his waist. I slid my hand inside the opening nearest me, and cupped one round, warm buttock. The muscles tensed under my grip, then flexed as he turned.

He hadn't pulled away; only stepped back in order to yank the shirt off over his head. He stood on the porch naked, and held out a hand to me.

He was furred with silver and the moonlight carved his body from the night. I could see every small detail of him, long toes to flowing hair, clear as the clean black canes of the blackberry bushes at the bottom of the yard. Yet like them he was dimensionless; he might have been within hand's touch or a mile away.

I shrugged the shift from my shoulders and let it fall from my body, left it puddled by the door and took his hand. Without a word we had floated through the grass, walked wet-legged and cool-skinned into the forest, turned wordless toward each other's warmth and stepped together into the empty air beyond the ridge.

We had wakened in the dark after moonset, leaf-spattered, twig-strewn, bug-bitten, and stiff with cold. We had said not a word to each other, but laughing and staggering drunkenly, stumbling over roots and stones, had helped each other through the moonless wood and made our way back to bed for an hour's brief sleep before dawn.

I leaned over his shoulder now and deposited a bowl of oatmeal in front of him, pausing to pluck an oak leaf from his hair. I laid it on the table beside his bowl.

He turned his head, a smile hiding in his eyes, caught my hand and kissed it lightly. He let me go, and went back to his parritch. I touched the back of his neck, and saw the smile spread to his mouth.

I looked up, smiling myself, and found Brianna watching. One corner of her mouth turned up, and her eyes were warm with understanding. Then I saw her gaze shift to Roger, who was spooning in his parritch in a absentminded sort of way, his gaze intent on her.

This picture of domestic bliss was broken by the stentorian tones of Clarence, announcing a visitor. I missed Rollo, I reflected, going to the door to see, but at least Clarence didn't leap on visitors and knock them flat or chase them round the dooryard.

The visitor was Duncan Innes, who had come bearing an invitation.

"Your aunt asks if perhaps ye will be coming to the Gathering at Mount Helicon this autumn. She says ye did give her your word, twa year past."

Jamie shoved the platter of eggs in front of Duncan.

"I hadna thought of it," he said, frowning a little. "There's the devil of a lot to do, and I'm to have a roof on this place before snowfall.'' He gestured upward with his chin, indicating the slats and branches that were temporarily shielding us from the vagaries of weather.

"There's a priest coming, down from Baltimore," Duncan said, carefully avoiding looking at Roger or Brianna. "Miss Jo did think as how ye might be wishing to have the wean baptized."

"Oh." Jamie sat back, lips pursed in thought. "Aye, that's a thought. Perhaps we will go, then, Duncan."

"That's fine; your auntie will be pleased." Something appeared to be caught in Duncan's throat; he was turning slowly red as I watched. Jamie squinted at him and pushed a jug of cider in his direction.

"Ye've something in your throat, man?"

"Ah . . . no." Everyone had stopped eating by now, viewing the changes to Duncan's complexion in fascination. He had gone a sort of puce by the time he managed to squeeze out the next words.

"I—errr—wish to ask your consent, *an fhearr Mac Dubh,* to the marriage of Mistress Jocasta Cameron and . . . and—''

"And who?" Jamie asked, the corner of his mouth twitching. "The governor of the colony?"

"And myself!" Duncan seized the cup of cider and buried his face in it with the relief of a drowning man seeing a life raft float past.

Jamie burst out laughing, which seemed to be no great solace to Duncan's embarrassment.

"My consent? D'ye not think my aunt's of an age, Duncan? Or you, come to that?"

Duncan was breathing a little easier now, though the purple tinge hadn't yet begun to fade from his cheeks.

"I thought it only proper," he said, a little stiffly. "Seeing as how ye're her nearest kinsman." He swallowed, and unbent a bit. "And . . . it didna seem entirely right, *Mac Dubh,* that I should be takin' what might be yours."

Jamie smiled and shook his head.

"I've no claim on any of my aunt's property, Duncan—and wouldna take it when she offered. You'll be married at the Gathering? Tell her we'll come, then, and dance at the wedding."

69

Jeremiah

October 1770

Roger rode with Claire and Fergus, close to the wagon. Jamie, not trusting Brianna to drive a vehicle containing his grandson, insisted on driving, with Lizzie and Marsali in the wagon bed and Brianna on the seat beside him.

From his saddle Roger caught snatches of the discussion that had been going on ever since his arrival.

"John, for sure," Brianna was saying, frowning down at her son, who was burrowing energetically under her shawl. "But I don't know if it should be his first name. And if it was—should it maybe be Ian? That's 'John' in Gaelic—and I'd like to name him that, but would it be too confusing, with Uncle Ian and our Ian, too?"

"Since neither one of them is here, I think it wouldna be too troublesome," Marsali put in. She glanced up at her stepfather's back. "Did ye not say ye wanted to use one of Da's names, as well?"

"Yes, but which one?" Brianna twisted around to talk to Marsali. "Not James, that *would* be confusing. And I don't think I like Malcolm much. He'll already have MacKenzie, of course, so maybe—" She caught Roger's eye and smiled up at him.

"What about Jeremiah?"

"John Jeremiah Alexander Fraser MacKenzie?" Marsali frowned, saying the names over to taste them.

"I rather like Jeremiah," Claire chipped in. "Very Old Testament. It's one of your names, isn't it, Roger?" She smiled at him and drew closer to the wagon, leaning over to talk to Brianna.

"Besides, if Jeremiah seems too formal, you can call him Jemmy," she said. "Or is that too much like Jamie?"

Roger felt a small chill prickle down his spine, at the sudden recollection of another child whose mother had called him Jemmy

—a child whose father was fair-haired, with eyes as green as Roger's own.

He waited until Brianna had turned to rummage through her bag for a fresh diaper, handing the fussing baby to Lizzie to mind. He kneed his horse, urging it up close to Claire's mare.

"Do you recall something?" he asked in a low voice. "When you first came to call on me in Inverness, with Brianna—you'd had my genealogy researched beforehand."

"Yes?" She quirked a brow at him.

"It's been some time, and you likely wouldn't have noticed in any case . . ." He hesitated, but he had to know, if it could be known. "You pointed out the place on my family tree where the substitution was made; where Geilie Duncan's child by Dougal was adopted in place of another child who'd died, and given his name."

"William Buccleigh MacKenzie," she said promptly, and smiled at his look of surprise. "I went over that genealogy at some length," she said dryly. "I could probably tell you every name on it."

He took a deep breath, uneasiness curling at the back of his neck.

"Can you? What I'm wondering—do you know the name of the changeling's wife—my six-times great-grandmother? Her name wasn't listed on my own family tree; only William Buccleigh."

Soft lashes dropped over the golden eyes as she thought, lips pursed.

"Yes," she said at last, and looked at him. "Morag. Her name was Morag Gunn. Why?"

He only shook his head, too shaken to reply. He glanced at Brianna; the baby lay half naked in her lap, the soggy diaper in a heap on the seat beside her—and remembered the smooth damp skin and soggy clout of the little boy named Jemmy.

"And their son's name was Jeremiah," he said at last, so softly that Claire had to lean close to hear it.

"Yes." She watched him curiously, then turned her head to look down the twisting road ahead, disappearing between the dark pines.

"I asked Geilie," Claire said suddenly. "I asked her why. Why we can do it."

''And did she have an answer?'' Roger stared at a deerfly on his wrist without seeing it.

''She said—'To change things.' '' Claire smiled at him, her mouth curled wryly. ''I don't know whether that's an answer or not.''

70

The Gathering

It had been nearly thirty years since the last Gathering I had seen; the Gathering at Leoch, and the oath-taking of clan MacKenzie. Colum MacKenzie was dead now, and his brother Dougal—and all the clans with them. Leoch lay in ruins, and there would be no more Gatherings of the clans in Scotland.

Yet here were the plaids and the pipes, and the remnants of the Highlanders themselves, undiminished in fierce pride, among the new mountains they claimed for their own. MacNeills and Campbells, Buchanans and Lindseys, MacLeods and MacDonalds; families, slaves and servants, indentured men and lairds.

I looked out over the stir and bustle of the dozens of encampments to see if I could find Jamie, and spotted instead a familiar tall form, striding loose-jointed through the scattered throng. I stood up and waved, calling out to him.

"Myers! Mr. Myers!"

John Quincy Myers spotted me and, beaming, made his way up the slope to our encampment.

"Mrs. Claire!" he exclaimed, sweeping off his disreputable hat and bowing over my hand with his usual courtliness. "I'm right uplifted to see ye."

"The feeling is mutual," I assured him, smiling. "I didn't expect to see you here."

"Oh, I usually reckon to come to a Gathering," he said, straightening up and beaming down at me. "If I'm down from the mountains in time. Fine place to sell my hides; any little bits of things I have to get rid of. Speakin' of which . . ." He began a slow, methodical rummage through the contents of his big buckskin pouch.

"Will you have been far to the north, Mr. Myers?"

"Oh, 'deed I have, 'deed I have, Mrs. Claire. Halfway up the Mohawk River, to the place they call the Upper Castle."

"The Mohawk?" My heart began to beat faster.

"Mm." He withdrew something from his bag, squinted at it, put it back, and rummaged further. "Imagine my surprise, Mrs. Claire, when I stopped at a Mohawk village to the south, to see a familiar face."

"Ian! You've seen Ian? Is he all right?" I was so excited, I grasped him by the arm.

"Oh, aye," he assured me. "Fine-lookin' boy—though I will say it did give me a right turn to see him rigged out like a brave, and his face burnt dark enough that I might ha' taken him for one, did he not hail me by name."

At last he found what he was looking for, and handed me a small package wrapped in thin leather and tied with a strip of buckskin—a woodpecker's feather thrust through the knot.

"He trusted me with that, ma'am, to bring to you and your goodman." He smiled kindly. "Reckon as you'll want to read that right promptly; I'll meet up with ye a mite later, Mrs. Claire." He bowed with solemn formality, and walked away, hailing acquaintances as he passed.

I wouldn't read it without waiting for Jamie; luckily, he appeared no more than a few minutes later. The letter was written on what seemed to be the torn-out flyleaf of a book, its ink the pale brown of oak-galls, but legible enough. *Ian salutat avunculus Jacobus,* the note began, and a grin broke out on Jamie's face.

Ave! That exhausting my Remembrance of the Latin tongue, I must now lapse into Plain English, of which I recall much more. I am well, Uncle, and Happy—I ask you to believe it. I have been married, after the custom of the Mohawk, and live in the house of my Wife. You will remember Emily, who carves so cleverly. Rollo has sired a Great many puppies; the village is littered with small wolfish Replicas. I cannot hope to claim the same profligacy of Procreation—yet I hope you will write to my Mother with the wish that she has not yet so many Grandchildren that she will overlook the addition of one more. The birth will be in spring; I will send Word of its outcome so soon as I may. In the meantime, you will oblige me by Remembering me to all at Lallybroch, at River Run, and Fraser's Ridge. I remember them all most Fondly, and will, so long as I shall live. My love to Auntie Claire, to Cousin Brianna, and most of all to yourself. Your most affectionate nephew, Ian Murray. Vale, avunculus.

Jamie blinked once or twice, and folding the torn page carefully, tucked it in his sporran.

"It's *avuncule,* ye wee idiot," he said softly. "A greeting takes the vocative case."

Looking over the dotted campfires that evening, I would have said that every Scottish family between Philadelphia and Charleston had come—and yet more arrived with the dawn next day, and kept coming.

It was on the second day, while Lizzie, Brianna, and I were comparing babies with two of Farquard Campbell's daughters, that Jamie made his way through a mass of women and children, a wide smile on his face.

"Mrs. Lizzie," he said. "I've a wee surprise for ye. Fergus!"

Fergus, likewise beaming, came from behind a wagon, ushering a slight man with windblown, thin fair hair.

"Da!" Lizzie shrieked, and flung herself into his arms. Jamie put a finger in his ear and wiggled it, looking amazed.

"I dinna think I've ever heard her make a noise that loud before," he said. He grinned at me and handed me two pieces of paper; originally part of one document, they had been carefully torn apart so that the notched edge of one fitted the jagged edge of the other.

"That'll be Mr. Wemyss's indenture," he said. "Put it away for now, Sassenach; we'll burn it at the bonfire tonight."

Then he vanished back into the crowd, summoned by a wave and a shout of *Mac Dubh!* from across the clearing.

By the third day of the Gathering, I had heard so much news, gossip, and general chatter that my ears rang with the sound of Gaelic. Those who were not talking were singing; Roger was in his element, wandering through the grounds and listening. He was hoarse from singing himself; he had been up most of the night before, strumming a borrowed guitar and singing to a crowd of enchanted listeners while Brianna sat curled by his feet, looking smug.

"Is he any good?" Jamie had murmured to me, squinting dubiously at his putative son-in-law.

"Better than good," I assured him.

He lifted one eyebrow and shrugged, then leaned down to take the baby from me.

"Aye, well, I'll take your word for it. I think wee Ruaidh and I will go and find a game of dice."

"You're going gambling with a baby?"

"Of course," he said, and grinned at me. "He's never too young to learn an honest trade, in case he canna sing for his supper like his Da."

"When you make bashed neeps," I said, "be sure to boil the tops along with the turnips. Then save the pot liquor and give it to the children; you take some too—it's good for your milk."

Maisri Buchanan pressed her smallest child to her breast and nodded solemnly, committing my advice to memory. I could not persuade most of the new immigrants either to eat fresh greens or to feed them to their families, but now and then I found opportunity to introduce a bit of vitamin C surreptitiously into their usual diet—which consisted for the most part of oatmeal and venison.

I had tried the expedient of making Jamie eat a plate of sliced tomatoes in public view, in hopes that the sight of him would ease some of the new immigrants' fears. This had not been successful; most of them regarded him with a half-superstitious awe, and I was given to understand that Himself could naturally survive the eating of things that would kill a normal person dead on the spot.

I dismissed Maisri, and welcomed the next visitor to my impromptu clinic, a woman with two little girls, covered with an eczematous rash that I at first thought evidence of more nutritional deficiency, but which fortunately proved to be only poison ivy.

I became aware of a stir in the crowd, and paused in my ministrations, turning to see who had arrived. Sunlight glinted from metal near the edge of the clearing, and Jamie's was not the only hand to go to gun or knife hilt.

They came into the sun in marchstep, though their drums were muffled, with no more than a soft *tap-tap!* of stick on rim to guide them. Muskets pointing skyward, broadswords waggling like scorpion tails, they emerged from the grove in small bursts of scarlet, two by two, green kilts aswish around their knees.

Four, and six, and eight, and ten . . . I was counting silently, with everyone else. Forty men came on, eyes straight ahead beneath their bearskin caps, looking neither to left nor to right, with no sound but the shuffle of feet and the tap of their drum.

Across the clearing, I saw MacNeill of Barra rise from his seat and straighten up; there was a subtle stir around him, a few steps bringing his men to stand near him. I didn't need to look around to sense the same thing happening behind me; felt, rather than saw, the eddies of similar small rallyings around the mountain's foot, each group with one eye on the intruders, one eye on its chief for direction.

I looked for Brianna and was startled, if not surprised, to find her just behind me, the baby in her arms, watching intently over my shoulder.

"Who are they?" she asked, low-voiced, and I could hear the echo of the question running through the Gathering like ripples in water.

"A Highland regiment," I said.

"I see that," she said tartly. "Friend or foe?"

That was plainly the question—were they here as Scots, or as soldiers? But I didn't have an answer, nor did anyone else, judging from the shiftings and mutterings among the crowd. There were incidents of troops coming to disperse unruly groups, of course. But surely not a peaceable gathering like this, which had no political purpose?

At one time, though, the mere presence of a number of Scots in one place was a political declaration, and most of those present remembered those times. The murmuring got louder, Gaelic spoken with the muffled sibilance of vehemence, sighing round the mountain like the wind before a storm.

There were forty soldiers coming up the road with guns and swords. There were two hundred Scotsmen here, most of them armed, many with slaves and servants. But also with their wives and children.

I thought of the days after Culloden, and without looking round, said to Brianna, "If anything happens—anything at all— take the baby up into the rocks."

Roger appeared suddenly in front of me, his attention focused on the soldiers. He didn't look at Jamie but moved silently so they stood, shoulder to shoulder, a bulwark before us. All over the clearing, the same thing was happening; the women gave not an inch, but their men stepped out before them. Anyone coming into the clearing would think that the women had melted into invisibility, leaving an implacable phalanx of Scotsmen staring down the glen.

Then two men rode out from the shelter of the trees; an officer on horseback, his aide by his side, regimental banner flying. Spurring up, they rode past the column of soldiers into the edge of the crowd. I saw the aide lean down from his horse to ask a question, saw the officer's head turn toward us in acknowledgment of the answer.

The officer barked an order and the soldiers stood to rest, muskets planted in the dust, their checkered legs apart. The officer turned his horse into the crowd, slowly nosing his way among the throng, who gave way reluctantly before him.

He was coming toward us; I saw his eyes fix on Jamie from a distance, so conspicuous by his height and his hair, bright as scarlet maple leaves.

The man drew up before us, and took off his feathered cap. He slid off his horse, took two steps toward Jamie, and bowed, rigidly correct. He was a short man, but solid, maybe thirty, with dark eyes that glittered bright as the gorget at his throat. Closer now, I saw what I had missed before, the smaller bit of metal pinned to the shoulder of his red coat; a battered brooch of tarnished gilt.

"Ma name is Airchie Hayes," he said in broad Scots. His eyes were fixed on Jamie's face, dark with hope. "They say ye kent my faither."

71

Circle's Close

"I have a thing to say to you," Roger said. He'd waited for some time to catch Jamie Fraser alone. Fraser was much in demand; everyone wanted his ear for a moment. For this moment, though, he was by himself, sitting on the fallen log from which he held court. He looked up at Roger, brows raised, but nodded toward a seat on the log.

Roger sat down. He had the baby with him; Brianna and Lizzie were making the dinner, and Claire had gone to visit with the Camerons of Isle Fleur, whose fire was nearby. The night air was thick with the scent of woodsmoke rather than peat fires, but in many ways it might be Scotland, he thought.

Jamie's eye lighted on the curve of little Jemmy's skull, dusted with copper fuzz that shone in the firelight. He held out his arms, and with only the slightest hesitation, Roger carefully passed the sleeping baby to him.

"Balach Boidheach," Jamie murmured as the baby stirred against him. "There now, it's fine." He looked across at Roger. "You've a thing to say to me, you said."

Roger nodded.

"I have, though not on my own account. You might say it is a message to be passed on for someone else."

Jamie lifted one quizzical brow, in a gesture so reminiscent of Brianna that Roger felt a small internal start. To cover it, he coughed.

"I—ah—when Brianna went to the stones on Craigh na Dun, I was forced to wait a few weeks until I could follow after her."

"Aye?" Jamie looked wary, as he always did at any mention of stone circles.

"I went to Inverness," Roger continued, keeping his eyes on his father-in-law. "I stayed at the house that my father had lived in, and I spent part of the time in sorting through his papers; he was a great saver of letters and bits of old rubbish."

Jamie nodded, evidently wondering what Roger was on about, but too polite to interrupt him.

"I found a letter." Roger took a deep breath, feeling his heart thump in his chest. "I committed it to memory, thinking that if I found Claire, I would tell her of it. But then when I found her"— he shrugged—"I was not sure whether I should tell her or not— or tell Brianna."

"And you are asking me if you should tell them?" Fraser's brows rose, thick and ruddy, showing his puzzlement.

"Perhaps I am. But thinking on it, it occurred to me that the letter was perhaps of more concern to you than to them." Now that the moment was at hand, Roger found himself feeling some sympathy for Fraser.

"You'll know my father was a minister? The letter was to him. I suppose it was written under the seal of confession, in a way— but I imagine death has dissolved this particular seal."

Roger took a deep breath and closed his eyes, seeing the black letters slanting across the page, in the neat, angular handwriting. He'd read it over more than a hundred times; he was sure of every word.

Dear Reg (the letter said);

I've something the matter with my heart. Besides Claire, I mean (says he, with irony). The doctor says it might be years yet, with care, and I hope it is—but there's the odd chance. The nuns at Bree's school used to scare the kids into fits about the horrible fate in store for sinners who died unconfessed and unforgiven; damned (if you'll pardon the expression) if I'm afraid of whatever comes after—if anything. But again—there's the odd chance, isn't there?

Not a thing I could say to my parish priest, for obvious reasons. I doubt he'd see the sin in it, even if he didn't slip out to telephone discreetly for psychiatric help!

But you're a priest, Reg, if not a Catholic—and more importantly, you're my friend. You needn't reply to this; I don't suppose a reply is possible. But you can listen. One of your great gifts, listening. Had I told you that before?

I'm delaying, though I don't know why I should. Best have it out.

You'll recall the favor I asked you a few years ago—about the gravestones at St. Kilda's? Kind friend that you are, you never asked, but it's time I should tell you why.

God knows why old Black Jack Randall should have been left out there on a Scottish hill instead of taken home to Sussex for burial. Perhaps no one cared enough to bring him home. Sad to think of; I rather hope it wasn't that.

There he is, though. If Bree's ever interested in her history—in my history—she'll look, and she'll find him there; the location of his grave is mentioned in the family papers. That's why I asked you to have the other stone put up nearby. It will stand out—all the other stones in that kirkyard are crumbling away with age.

Claire will take her to Scotland one day; I'm sure of that much. If she goes to St. Kilda's, she'll see it—no one goes into an old churchyard and doesn't have a browse round the stones. If she wonders, if she cares to look further—if she asks Claire—well, that's as far as I'm prepared to go. I've made the gesture; I shall leave it to chance what happens when I've gone.

You know all the rubbish Claire talked when she came back. I did all I could to get it out of her head, but she wouldn't be budged; God, she is a stubborn woman!

You'll not credit this, perhaps, but when I came last to visit you, I hired a car and went to that damned hill—to Craigh na Dun. I told you about the witches dancing in the circle, just before Claire disappeared. With that eerie sight in mind, standing there in the early light among those stones—I could almost believe her. I touched one. Nothing happened, of course.

And yet. I looked. Looked for the man—for Fraser. And perhaps I found him. At least I found a man of that name, and what I could dredge up of his connections matched what Claire told me of him. Whether she was telling the truth, or whether she had grafted some delusion onto real experience . . . well, there was a man, I'm sure of that!

You'll scarcely credit this, but I stood there with my hand on that bloody stone, and wanted nothing more than that it should open, and put me face-to-face with James Fraser. Whoever he was, whenever he was, I wanted nothing more in life than to see him—and to kill him.

I have never seen him—I don't know that he existed!—and yet I hate this man as I have never hated anyone else. If what Claire said and what I found was true—then I've taken her from him, and kept her by me through these years by a lie. Maybe only a lie of omission, but nonetheless a lie for that. I could call that revenge, I suppose.

Priests and poets call revenge a two-edged sword; and the other edge of it is that I'll never know—if I gave her the choice, would she have stayed with me? Or if I told her that her Jamie survived Culloden, would she have been off to Scotland like a shot?

I cannot think Claire would leave her daughter. I hope she'd not leave me, either . . . but . . . if I had any certainty of it, I swear I'd have told her, but I haven't, and that's the truth of it.

Fraser—shall I curse him for stealing my wife, or bless him for giving me my daughter? I think these things, and then I stop, appalled that I should be giving a moment's credence to such a preposterous theory. And yet . . . I have the oddest sense of James Fraser, almost a memory, as though I must have seen him somewhere. Though likely this is just the product of jealousy and imagination—I know what the bastard looks like, well enough; I see his face on my daughter, day by day!

That's the queer side of it, though—a sense of obligation. Not just to Bree, though I do think she's a right to know—later. I told you I had a sense of the bastard? Funny thing is, it's stayed with me. I can almost feel him, sometimes, looking over my shoulder, standing across the room.

Hadn't thought of this before—do you suppose I'll meet him in the sweet by-and-by, if there is one? Funny to think of it. Should we meet as friends, I wonder, with the sins of the flesh behind us? Or end forever locked in some Celtic hell, with our hands wrapped round each other's throat?

I treated Claire badly—or well, depending how one looks at it. I won't go into the sordid details; leave it that I'm sorry.

So there it is, Reg. Hate, jealousy, lying, stealing, unfaithfulness, the lot. Not much to balance it save love. I do love her—love them. My women. Maybe it's not the right kind of love, or not enough. But it's all I've got.

Still, I won't die unshriven—and I'll trust you for a conditional absolution. I raised Bree as a Catholic; do you suppose there's some forlorn hope that she'll pray for me?

"It was signed, 'Frank,' of course," Roger said.

"Of course," Jamie echoed softly. He sat quite still, his face unreadable.

Roger didn't need to read it; he knew well enough the thoughts that were going through the other's mind. The same thoughts he'd wrestled with, during those weeks between Beltane and Midsummer's Eve, during the search for Brianna across the ocean, during his captivity—and at the last, in the circle in the rhododendron hell, hearing the song of the standing stones.

If Frank Randall had chosen to keep secret what he'd found, had never placed that stone at St. Kilda's—would Claire have learned the truth anyway? Perhaps; perhaps not. But it had been the sight of that spurious grave that had led her to tell her daughter the story of Jamie Fraser, and to set Roger on the path of discovery that had led them all to this place, this time.

It had been the stone that had at once sent Claire back to the arms of her Scottish lover—and possibly to her death in those arms. That had given Frank Randall's daughter back to her other father, and simultaneously condemned her to live in a time not her own; that had resulted in the birth of a red-haired boy who might otherwise not have been—the continuance of Jamie Fraser's blood. Interest on the debt owed? Roger wondered.

And then there were Roger's private thoughts, of another boy who might not have been, save for that cryptic stone hint, left by Frank Randall for the sake of forgiveness. Morag and William MacKenzie were not at the Gathering; Roger was unsure whether to be disappointed or relieved.

Jamie Fraser stirred at last, though his eyes stayed fixed on the fire.

"Englishman," he said softly, and it was a conjuration. The hair rose very slightly on the back of Roger's neck; he could believe he saw something move in the flames.

Jamie's big hands spread, cradling his grandson. His face was remote, the flames catching sparks from hair and brows.

"Englishman," he said, speaking to whatever he saw beyond the flames. "I could wish that we shall meet one day. And I could hope that we shall not."

Roger waited, hands loose on his knees. Fraser's eyes were shadowed, his face masked by the flicker of the dancing fire. At last, something like a shudder seemed to go over the big frame; he shook his head as though to clear it, and seemed to realize for the first time that Roger was still there.

"Do I tell her?" Roger said. "Claire?"

The big Highlander's eyes sharpened.

"Will ye have told Brianna?"

"Not yet; but I will." He gave back Fraser's stare, eye for eye. "She is my wife."

"For now."

"Forever—if she will."

Fraser looked toward the Camerons' fire. Claire's lithe shape was visible, dark against the brightness.

"I did promise her honesty," he said at last, very quietly. "Aye, tell her."

By the fourth day, the slopes of the mountain were filled with new arrivals. Just before dusk, the men began to bring wood, piling it in the burnt space at the foot of the mountain. Each family had its campfire, but here was the great fire, around which everyone gathered each night to see who had come during the day.

As the dark came on, the fires bloomed on the mountainside, dotted here and there among the shallow ledges and sandy pockets. For a moment, I had a vision of the MacKenzie clan badge—a "burning mountain"—and realized suddenly what it was. Not a volcano, as I had thought. No, it was the image of a Gathering like this one, the fires of families burning in the dark, a signal to all that the clan was present—and together. And for the first time, I understood the motto that went with the image:'*Luceo non uro; I shine, not burn.*

Soon the mountainside was alive with fires. Here and there were smaller, moving flames, as the head of each family or plantation thrust a brand into his fire and brought it down the hill, to add to the blazing pyre at the foot. From our perch high on the mountainside, the figures of the men showed small and dark in silhouette against the huge fire.

A dozen families had declared themselves before Jamie finished his conversation with Gerald Forbes, and rose himself. He handed me the baby, who was sleeping soundly in spite of all the racket around him, and bent to light a brand from our fire. The shouts came from far below, thin but audible on the clear autumn air.

"The MacNeills of Barra are here!"

"The Lachlans of Glen Linnhe are here!"

And after a little, Jamie's voice, loud and strong on the dark air.

''The Frasers of the Ridge are here!'' There was a brief spatter of applause from those around me—whoops and yelps from the tenants who had come with us, just as there had been from the followers of the other heads of families.

I sat quietly, enjoying the feel of the limp, heavy little body in my arms. He slept with the abandonment of total trust, tiny pink mouth half open, his breath warm and humid on the slope of my breast.

Jamie came back smelling of woodsmoke and whisky, and sat down on the log behind me. He took me by the shoulders and I leaned back against him, enjoying the feeling of him behind me. Across the fire, Brianna and Roger were talking earnestly, their heads close together. Their faces shone in the firelight, each reflecting the other.

''Ye dinna suppose they're going to change his name again, do you?'' Jamie said, frowning slightly at them.

''I don't think so,'' I said. ''There are other things ministers do besides christenings, you know.''

''Oh, aye?''

''It's well past the third of September,'' I said, tilting back my head to look at him. ''You did tell her to choose by then.''

''So I did.'' A lopsided moon floated low in the sky, shedding a soft light over his face. He leaned forward and kissed my forehead.

Then he reached down and took my free hand in his own.

''And will ye choose, too?'' he asked softly. He opened his hand, and I saw the glint of gold. ''Do ye want it back?''

I paused, looking up into his face, searching it for doubt. I saw none there, but something else; a waiting, a deep curiosity as to what I might say.

''It was a long time ago,'' I said softly.

''And a long time,'' he said. ''I am a jealous man, but not a vengeful one. I would take you from him, my Sassenach—but I wouldna take him from you.''

He paused for a moment, the fire glinting softly from the ring in his hand. ''It was your life, no?''

And he asked again, ''Do you want it back?''

I held up my hand in answer and he slid the gold ring on my finger, the metal warm from his body.

From F. to C. with love. Always.

''What did you say?'' I asked. He had murmured something in Gaelic above me, too low for me to catch.

"I said, 'Go in peace,' " he answered. "I wasna talking to you, though, Sassenach."

Across the fire, something winked red. I glanced across in time to see Roger lift Brianna's hand to his lips; Jamie's ruby shone dark on her finger, catching the light of moon and fire.

"I see she's chosen, then," Jamie said softly.

Brianna smiled, her eyes on Roger's face, and leaned to kiss him. Then she stood up, brushing sand from her skirts and bent to pick up a brand from the campfire. She turned and held it out to him, speaking in a voice loud enough to carry to us where we sat across the fire.

"Go down," she said, "and tell them the MacKenzies are here."

And don't miss the next
installment of the acclaimed
OUTLANDER series . . .

DIANA GABALDON'S

THE FIERY
CROSS

Available now
from Dell Books!

Read on for a preview. . . .

THE FIERY CROSS

On Sale Now

Mount Helicon
The Royal Colony of North Carolina
Late October, 1770

I WOKE TO THE PATTER OF RAIN on canvas, with the feel of my first husband's kiss on my lips. I blinked, disoriented, and by reflex put my fingers to my mouth. To keep the feeling, or to hide it? I wondered, even as I did so.

Jamie stirred and murmured in his sleep next to me, his movement rousing a fresh wave of scent from the cedar branches under our bottom quilt. Perhaps the ghost's passing had disturbed him. I frowned at the empty air outside our lean-to.

Go away, Frank, I thought sternly.

It was still dark outside, but the mist that rose from the damp earth was a pearly gray; dawn wasn't far off. Nothing stirred, inside or out, but I had the distinct sense of an ironic amusement that lay on my skin like the lightest of touches.

Shouldn't I come to see her married?

I couldn't tell whether the words had formed themselves in my thoughts, or whether they—and that kiss—were merely the product of my own subconscious. I had fallen asleep with my mind still busy with wedding preparations; little wonder that I should wake from dreams of weddings. And wedding nights.

I smoothed the rumpled muslin of my shift, uneasily aware that it was rucked up around my waist and that my skin was flushed with more than sleep. I didn't remember anything concrete about the dream that had wakened me; only a confused jumble of image and sensation. I thought perhaps that was a good thing.

I turned over on the rustling branches, nudging close to Jamie. He was warm and smelled pleasantly of woodsmoke and whisky, with a faint tang of sleepy maleness under it, like the deep note of a lingering chord. I stretched myself, very slowly, arching my back so that my pelvis nudged his hip. If he were sound asleep or disinclined, the gesture was slight enough to pass unnoticed; if he were not . . .

He wasn't. He smiled faintly, eyes still closed, and a big hand ran slowly down my back, settling with a firm grip on my bottom.

"Mmm?" he said. "Hmmmm." He sighed, and relaxed back into sleep, holding on.

I nestled close, reassured. The immediate physicality of Jamie was more than enough to banish the touch of lingering dreams. And Frank—if that *was* Frank—was right, so far as that went. I was sure that if such a thing were possible, Bree would want both her fathers at her wedding.

I was wide awake now, but much too comfortable to move. It was raining outside; a light rain, but the air was cold and damp enough to make the cozy nest of quilts more inviting than the distant prospect of hot coffee. Particularly since the getting of coffee would involve a trip to the stream for water, making up the campfire—oh, God, the wood would be damp, even if the fire hadn't gone completely out—grinding the coffee in a stone quern and brewing it, while wet leaves blew round my ankles and drips from overhanging tree branches slithered down my neck.

Shivering at the thought, I pulled the top quilt up over my bare shoulder and instead resumed the mental catalogue of preparations with which I had fallen asleep.

Food, drink . . . luckily I needn't trouble about that. Jamie's aunt Jocasta would deal with the arrangements; or rather, her black butler, Ulysses, would. Wedding guests—no difficulties there. We were in the middle of the largest Gathering of Scottish Highlanders in the Colonies, and food and drink were being provided. Engraved invitations would not be necessary.

Bree would have a new dress, at least; Jocasta's gift as well. Dark blue wool—silk was both too expensive and too impractical for life in the backwoods. It was a far cry from the white satin and orange blossom I had once envisioned her wearing to be married in—but then, this was scarcely the marriage anyone might have imagined in the 1960s.

I wondered what Frank might have thought of Brianna's husband. He likely would have approved; Roger was a historian—or once had been—like Frank himself. He was intelligent and humorous, a talented musician and a gentle man, thoroughly devoted to Brianna and little Jemmy.

Which is very admirable indeed, I thought in the direction of the mist, *under the circumstances.*

You admit that, do you? The words formed in my inner ear as though he had spoken them, ironic, mocking both himself and me.

Jamie frowned and tightened his grasp on my buttock, making small whuffling noises in his sleep.

You know I do, I said silently. *I always did, and you know it, so just bugger off, will you?!*

I turned my back firmly on the outer air and laid my head on Jamie's shoulder, seeking refuge in the feel of the soft, crumpled linen of his shirt.

I rather thought Jamie was less inclined than I—or perhaps Frank—to give Roger credit for accepting Jemmy as his own. To Jamie, it was a simple matter of obligation; an honorable man could not do otherwise. And I knew he had his doubts as to Roger's ability to support and protect a family in the Carolina wilderness. Roger was tall, well-built, and capable—but "bonnet, belt, and swordie" were the stuff of songs to Roger; to Jamie, they were the tools of his trade.

The hand on my bottom squeezed suddenly, and I started.

"Sassenach," Jamie said drowsily, "you're squirming like a toadling in a wee lad's fist. D'ye need to get up and go to the privy?"

"Oh, you're awake," I said, feeling mildly foolish.

"I am *now*," he said. The hand fell away, and he stretched, groaning. His bare feet popped out at the far end of the quilt, long toes spread wide.

"Sorry. I didn't mean to wake you."

"Och, dinna fash yourself," he assured me. He cleared his throat and rubbed a hand through the ruddy waves of his loosened hair, blinking. "I was dreaming like a fiend; I always do when I sleep cold." He lifted his head and peered down across the quilt, wiggling his exposed toes with disfavor. "Why did I not sleep wi' my stockings on?"

"Really? What were you dreaming about?" I asked, with a small stab of uneasiness. I rather hoped he hadn't been dreaming the same sort of thing I had.

"Horses," he said, to my immediate relief. I laughed.

"What sort of fiendish dreams could you be having about horses?"

"Oh, God, it was terrible." He rubbed his eyes with both fists and shook his head, trying to clear the dream from his mind. "All to do wi' the Irish kings. Ye ken what MacKenzie was sayin' about it, at the fire last night?"

"Irish ki—oh!" I remembered, and laughed again at the recollection. "Yes, I do."

Roger, flushed with the triumph of his new engagement, had regaled the company around the fireside the night before with songs, poems, and entertaining historical anecdotes—one of which concerned the rites with which the ancient Irish kings were said to have been crowned. One of these involved the successful candidate copulating with a white mare before the assembled multitudes, presumably to prove his virility—though I thought it would be a better proof of the gentleman's *sangfroid*, myself.

"I was in charge o' the horse," Jamie informed me. "And *everything* went wrong. The man was too short, and I had to find something for him to stand on. I found a rock, but I couldna lift it. Then a stool, but the leg came off in my hand. Then I tried to pile up bricks to make a platform, but they crumbled to sand. Finally they said it was all right, they would just cut the legs off the mare, and I was trying to stop them doing that, and the man who would be king was jerkin' at his breeks and complaining that his fly buttons wouldna come loose, and then someone noticed that it was a *black* mare, and that wouldna do at all."

I snorted, muffling my laughter in a fold of his shirt for fear of wakening someone camped near us.

"Is that when you woke up?"

"No. For some reason, I was verra much affronted at that. I said it *would* do, in fact the black was a much better horse, for everyone knows that white horses have weak een, and I said the offspring would be blind. And they said no, no, the black was ill luck, and I was insisting it was not, and . . ." He stopped, clearing his throat.

"And?"

He shrugged and glanced sideways at me, a faint flush creeping up his neck.

"Aye, well. I said it would do fine, I'd show them. And I had just grasped the mare's rump to stop her moving, and was getting ready to . . . ah . . . make myself king of Ireland. *That's* when I woke."

I snorted and wheezed, and felt his side vibrate with his own suppressed laughter.

"Oh, now I'm *really* sorry to have wakened you!" I wiped my eyes on the corner of the quilt. "I'm sure it was a great loss to the Irish. Though I do wonder how the queens of Ireland felt about that particular ceremony," I added as an afterthought.

"I canna think the ladies would suffer even slightly by comparison," Jamie assured me. "Though I have heard of men who prefer—"

"I wasn't thinking of *that*," I said. "It was more the hygienic implications, if you see what I mean. Putting the cart before the horse is one thing, but putting the horse before the queen . . ."

"The—oh, aye." He was flushed with amusement, but his skin darkened further at that. "Say what ye may about the Irish, Sassenach, but I do believe they wash now and then. And under the circumstances, the king might possibly even have found a bit of soap useful, in . . . in . . ."

"*In medias res*?" I suggested. "Surely not. I mean, after all, a horse is quite large, relatively speaking . . ."

"It's a matter of readiness, Sassenach, as much as room," he said, with a repressive glance in my direction. "And I can see that a man might require a bit of encouragement, under the circumstances. Though it's *in medias res*, in any case," he added. "Have ye never read Horace? Or Aristotle?"

"No. We can't all be educated. And I've never had much time for Aristotle, after hearing that he ranked women somewhere below worms in his classification of the natural world."

"The man can't have been married." Jamie's hand moved slowly up my back, fingering the knobs of my spine through my shift. "Surely he would ha' noticed the bones, else."

I smiled and lifted a hand to his own cheekbone, rising stark and clean above a tide of auburn stubble.

As I did so, I saw that the sky outside had lightened into dawn; his head was silhouetted by the pale canvas of our shelter, but I could see his face clearly. The expression on it reminded me exactly why he had taken off his stockings the night before. Unfortunately, we had both been so tired after the prolonged festivities that we had fallen asleep in mid-embrace.

I found that belated memory rather reassuring, offering as it did some explanation both for the state of my shift and for the dreams from which I had awakened. At the same time, I felt a chilly draft slide its fingers under the quilt, and shivered. Frank and Jamie were very different men, and there was no doubt in my mind as to who had kissed me, just before waking.

"Kiss me," I said suddenly to Jamie. Neither of us had yet brushed our teeth, but he obligingly skimmed my lips with his, then, when I caught the back of his head and pressed him closer, shifted his weight to one hand, the better to adjust the tangle of bedclothes round our lower limbs.

"Oh?" he said, when I released him. He smiled, blue eyes creasing into dark triangles in the dimness. "Well, to be sure, Sassenach. I must just step outside for a moment first, though."

He flung back the quilt and rose. From my position on the ground, I had a rather unorthodox view which provided me with engaging glimpses under the hem of his long linen shirt.

I did hope that what I was looking at was not the lingering result of his nightmare, but thought it better not to ask.

"You'd better hurry," I said. "It's getting light; people will be up and about soon."

He nodded and ducked outside. I lay still, listening. A few birds cheeped faintly in the distance, but this was autumn; not even full light would provoke the raucous choruses of spring and summer. The mountain and its many camps still lay slumbering, but I could feel small stirrings all around, just below the edge of hearing.

I ran my fingers through my hair, fluffing it out round my shoulders, and rolled over, looking for the water bottle. Feeling cool air on my back, I glanced over my shoulder, but dawn had come and the mist had fled; the air outside was gray but still.

I touched the gold ring on my left hand, restored to me the night before, and still unfamiliar after its long absence. Perhaps it was his ring that had summoned Frank to my dreams. Perhaps tonight at the wedding ceremony, I would touch it again, deliberately, and hope that he could see his daughter's happiness somehow through my eyes. For now, though, he was gone, and I was glad.

A small sound, no louder than the distant birdcalls, drifted through the air. The brief cry of a baby waking.

I had once thought that no matter the circumstances, there ought really to be no more than two people in a marriage bed. I still thought so. However, a baby was more difficult to banish than the ghost of a former love; Brianna and Roger's bed must perforce accommodate three.

The edge of the canvas lifted, and Jamie's face appeared, looking excited and alarmed.

"Ye'd best get up and dress, Claire," he said. "The soldiers are drawn up by the creek. Where are my stockings?"

I sat bolt upright, and far down the mountainside the drums began to roll.

COLD FOG LAY like smoke in the hollows all round; a cloud had settled on Mount Helicon like a broody hen on a single egg, and the air was thick with damp. I blinked blearily across a stretch of rough grass, to where a detachment of the 67th Highland regiment was drawn up in full splendor by the creek, drums rumbling and the company piper tootling away, grandly impervious to the rain.

I was very cold, and more than slightly cross. I'd gone to bed in the expectation of waking to hot coffee and a nourishing breakfast, this to be followed by two weddings, three christenings, two tooth extractions, the removal of an infected toenail, and other entertaining forms of wholesome social intercourse requiring whisky.

Instead, I'd been wakened by unsettling dreams, led into amorous dalliance, and then dragged out into a cold drizzle *in medias* bloody *res*, apparently to hear a proclamation of some sort. No coffee yet, either.

It had taken some time for the Highlanders in their camps to rouse themselves and stagger down the hillside, and the piper had gone quite purple in the face before he at last blew the final blast and left off with a discordant wheeze. The echoes were still ringing off the mountainside, as Lieutenant Archibald Hayes stepped out before his men.

Lieutenant Hayes's nasal Fife accent carried well, and the wind was with him. Still, I was sure the people farther up the mountain could hear very little. Standing as we did at the foot of the slope, though, we were no more than twenty yards from the Lieutenant and I could hear every word, in spite of the chattering of my teeth.

"By his EXCELLENCY, WILLIAM TRYON, Esquire, His Majesty's Captain-General, Governor, and Commander-in-Chief, in and over the said Province," Hayes read, lifting his voice in a bellow to carry above the noises of wind and water, and the premonitory murmurs of the crowd.

The moisture shrouded trees and rocks with dripping mist, the clouds spat intermittent sleet and freezing rain, and erratic winds had lowered the temperature by some thirty degrees. My left shin, sensitive to cold, throbbed at the spot where I had broken the bone two years before. A person given to portents and metaphors might have been tempted to draw comparisons between the nasty weather and the reading of the Governor's Proclamation, I thought—the prospects were similarly chill and foreboding.

"Whereas," Hayes boomed, glowering at the crowd over his paper, *"I have received information that a great Number of outrageous and disorderly Persons did tumultuously assemble themselves together in the Town of Hillsborough, on the 24th and 25th of last Month, during the sitting of the Superior Court of Justice of that District to oppose the Just Measures of Government and in open Violation of the Laws of their Country, audaciously attacking his Majesty's Associate Justice in the Execution of his Office, and barbarously beating and wounding several Persons in and during the sitting of said Court, and offering other enormous Indignities and Insults to his Majesty's Government, committing the most violent Outrages on the Persons and properties of the Inhabitants of the said Town, drinking Damnation to their lawful Sovereign King George and Success to the Pretender—"*

Hayes paused, gulping air with which to accomplish the next clause. Inflating his chest with an audible whoosh, he read on:

"To the End therefore, that the Persons concerned in the said outrageous Acts may be brought to Justice, I do, by the Advice and Consent of his Majesty's Council, issue this my Proclamation, hereby requiring and strictly enjoining all his Majesty's Justices of the Peace in this Government to make diligent Inquiry into the above recited Crimes, and to receive the Deposition of such Person or Persons as shall appear before them to make Information of and concerning the same; which Depositions are to be transmitted to me, in Order to be laid before the General Assembly, at New Bern, on the 30th day of November next, to which time it stands Prorogued for the immediate Dispatch of Public Business."

A final inhalation; Hayes's face was nearly as purple as the piper's by now.

"Given under my Hand, and the Great Seal of the Province, at New Bern, the 18th Day of October, in the 10th Year of his Majesty's Reign, Anno Domini 1770.

"Signed, William Tryon," Hayes concluded, with a final puff of steamy breath.

"Do you know," I remarked to Jamie, "I believe that was all one single sentence, bar the closing. Amazing, even for a politician."

"Hush, Sassenach," he said, his eyes still fixed on Archie Hayes. There was a subdued rumble from the crowd behind me, of interest and consternation—touched with a certain amount of amusement at the phrases regarding treasonous toasts.

This was a Gathering of Highlanders, many of them exiled to the Colonies in the wake of the Stuart Rising, and had Archie Hayes chosen to take official notice of what was said over the cups of ale and whisky passed round the fires the night before . . . but then, he had but forty soldiers with him, and whatever his own opinions of King George and that monarch's possible damnation, he kept them wisely to himself.

Some four hundred Highlanders surrounded Hayes's small beachhead on the creekbank, summoned by the tattoo of drums. Men and women sheltered among the trees above the clearing, plaids and arisaids pulled tight against the rising wind. They too were keeping their own counsel, judging from the array of stony faces visible under the flutter of scarves and bonnets. Of course, their expressions might derive from cold as much as from natural caution; my own cheeks were stiff, the end of my nose had gone numb, and I hadn't felt my feet anytime since daybreak.

"Any person wishing to make declaration concerning these most serious matters may entrust such statements safely to my care," Hayes announced, his round face an official blank. "I will remain in my tent with my clerk for the rest of the day. God save the King!"

He handed the Proclamation to his corporal, bowed to the crowd in dismissal, and turned smartly toward a large canvas tent that had been erected near the trees, regimental banners flapping wildly from a standard next to it.

Shivering, I slid a hand into the slit of Jamie's cloak and over the crook of his arm, my cold fingers comforted by the warmth of his body. Jamie pressed his elbow briefly to his side in acknowledgment of my frozen grasp, but didn't look down at me; he was studying Archie Hayes's retreating back, eyes narrowed against the sting of the wind.

A compact and solid man, of inconsequent height but considerable presence, the Lieutenant moved with great deliberation, as though oblivious of the crowd on the hillside above. He vanished into his tent, leaving the flap invitingly tied up.

Not for the first time, I reluctantly admired Governor Tryon's political instincts. This Proclamation was clearly being read in towns and villages throughout the colony; he could have relied on a local magistrate or sheriff to carry his message of official fury to this Gathering. Instead, he had taken the trouble to send Hayes.

Archibald Hayes had taken the field at Culloden by his father's side, at the age of twelve. Wounded in the fight, he had been captured and sent south. Presented with a choice of transportation or joining the army, he had taken the King's shilling and made the best of it. The fact that he had risen to be an officer in his mid-thirties, in a time when most commissions were bought rather than earned, was sufficient testimony to his abilities.

He was as personable as he was professional; invited to share our food and fire the day before, he had spent half the night talking with Jamie—and the other half moving from fire to fire under the aegis of Jamie's presence, being introduced to the heads of all the important families present.

And whose notion had that been? I wondered, looking up at Jamie. His long, straight nose was reddened by the cold, his eyes hooded from the wind, but his face gave no inkling of what he was thinking. And that, I thought, was a bloody good indication that he was thinking something rather dangerous. Had he known about this Proclamation?

No English officer, with an English troop, could have brought such news into a Gathering like this, with any hope of cooperation. But Hayes and his Highlanders, stalwart in their tartan . . . I didn't miss the fact that Hayes had had his tent erected with its back to a thick grove of pines; anyone who wished to speak to the Lieutenant in secret could approach through the woods, unseen.

"Does Hayes expect someone to pop out of the crowd, rush into his tent, and surrender on the spot?" I murmured to Jamie. I personally knew of at least a dozen men among those present who had taken part in the Hillsborough riots; three of them were standing within arm's length of us.

Jamie saw the direction of my glance and put his hand over mine, squeezing it in a silent adjuration of discretion. I lowered my brows at him; surely he didn't think I would give anyone away by inadvertence? He gave me a faint smile and one of those annoying marital looks that said, more plainly than words, *You know how ye are, Sassenach. Anyone who sees your face kens just what ye think.*

I sidled in a little closer, and kicked him discreetly in the ankle. I might have a glass face, but it certainly wouldn't arouse comment in a crowd like this! He didn't wince, but the smile spread a little wider. He slid one arm inside my cloak, and drew me closer, his hand on my back.

Hobson, MacLennan, and Fowles stood together just in front of us, talking quietly among themselves. All three came from a tiny settlement called Drunkard's Creek, some fifteen miles from our own place on Fraser's Ridge. Hugh Fowles was Joe Hobson's son-in-law, and very young, no more than twenty. He was doing his best to keep his composure, but his face had gone white and clammy as the Proclamation was read.

I didn't know what Tryon intended to do to anyone who could be proved to have had a part in the riot, but I could feel the currents of unrest created by the Governor's Proclamation passing through the crowd like the eddies of water rushing over rocks in the nearby creek.

Several buildings had been destroyed in Hillsborough, and a number of public officials dragged out and assaulted in the street. Gossip had it that one ironically titled justice of the peace had lost an eye to a vicious blow aimed with a horsewhip. No doubt taking this demonstration of civil disobedience to heart, Chief Justice Henderson had escaped out of a window and fled the town, thus effectively preventing the Court from sitting. It was clear that the Governor was *very* annoyed about what had happened in Hillsborough.

Joe Hobson glanced back at Jamie, then away. Lieutenant Hayes's presence at our fire the previous evening had not gone unremarked.

If Jamie saw the glance, he didn't return it. He lifted one shoulder in a shrug, tilting his head down to speak to me.

"I shouldna think Hayes expects anyone to give themselves up, no. It may be his duty to ask for information; I thank God it isna mine to answer." He hadn't spoken loudly, but loudly enough to reach the ears of Joe Hobson.

Hobson turned his head and gave Jamie a small nod of wry acknowledgment. He touched his son-in-law's arm, and they turned away, scrambling up the slope toward the scattered campsites above, where their womenfolk were tending the fires and the younger children.

This was the last day of the Gathering; tonight there would be marryings and christenings, the formal blessing of love and its riotous fruits, sprung from the loins of the unchurched multitude during the year before. Then the last songs would be sung, the last stories told, and dancing done amid the leaping flames of many fires—rain or no rain. Come morning, the Scots and their households would all disperse back to their homes, scattered from the settled banks of the Cape Fear River to the wild mountains of the west—carrying news of the Governor's Proclamation and the doings at Hillsborough.

I wiggled my toes inside my damp shoes and wondered uneasily who among the crowd might think it their duty to answer Hayes's invitation to confession or incrimination. Not Jamie, no. But others might. There had been a good deal of boasting about the riots in Hillsborough during the week of the Gathering, but not all the listeners were disposed to view the rioters as heroes, by any means.

I could feel as well as hear the mutter of conversation breaking out in the wake of the Proclamation; heads turning, families drawing close together, men moving from group to group, as the content of Hayes's speech was relayed up the hill, repeated to those who stood too far away to have heard it.

"Shall we go? There's a lot to do yet before the weddings."

"Aye?" Jamie glanced down at me. "I thought Jocasta's slaves were managing the food and drink. I gave Ulysses the barrels of whisky—he'll be *soghan*."

"Ulysses? Did he bring his wig?" I smiled at the thought. The *soghan* was the man who managed the dispensing of drink and refreshment at a Highland wedding; the term actually meant something like "hearty, jovial fellow." Ulysses was possibly the most dignified person I had ever seen— even without his livery and powdered horsehair wig.

"If he did, it's like to be stuck to his head by the evening." Jamie glanced up at the lowering sky and shook his head. "Happy the bride the sun shines on," he quoted. "Happy the corpse the rain falls on."

"That's what I like about Scots," I said dryly. "An appropriate proverb for all occasions. Don't you dare say that in front of Bree."

"What d'ye take me for, Sassenach?" he demanded, with a half-smile down at me. "I'm her father, no?"

"Definitely yes." I suppressed the sudden thought of Brianna's other father, and glanced over my shoulder, to be sure she wasn't in hearing.

There was no sign of her blazing head among those nearby. Certainly her father's daughter, she stood six feet tall in her stocking feet; nearly as easy as Jamie himself to pick out of a crowd.

"It's not the wedding feast I need to deal with, anyway," I said, turning back to Jamie. "I've got to manage breakfast, then do the morning clinic with Murray MacLeod."

"Oh, aye? I thought ye said wee Murray was a charlatan."

"I said he was ignorant, stubborn, and a menace to the public health," I corrected. "That's not the same thing— quite."

"Quite," said Jamie, grinning. "Ye mean to educate him, then—or poison him?"

"Whichever seems most effective. If nothing else, I might accidentally step on his fleam and break it; that's probably the only way I'll stop him bleeding people. Let's go, though, I'm freezing!"

"Aye, we'll away, then," Jamie agreed, with a glance at the soldiers, still drawn up along the creekbank at parade rest.

"No doubt wee Archie means to keep his lads there 'til the crowd's gone; they're going a wee bit blue round the edges."

Though fully armed and uniformed, the row of Highlanders was relaxed; imposing, to be sure, but no longer threatening. Small boys—and not a few wee girls—scampered to and fro among them, impudently flicking the hems of the soldiers' kilts or dashing in, greatly daring, to touch the gleaming muskets, dangling canteens, and the hilts of dirks and swords.

"Abel, *a charaid*!" Jamie had paused to greet the last of the men from Drunkard's Creek. "Will ye ha' eaten yet the day?"

MacLennan had not brought his wife to the Gathering, and thus ate where luck took him. The crowd was dispersing around us, but he stood stolidly in place, holding the ends of a red flannel handkerchief pulled over his balding head against the spatter of rain. Probably hoping to cadge an invitation to breakfast, I thought cynically.

I eyed his stocky form, mentally estimating his possible consumption of eggs, parritch, and toasted bread against the dwindling supplies in our hampers. Not that simple shortage of food would stop any Highlander from offering hospitality—certainly not Jamie, who was inviting MacLennan to join us, even as I mentally divided eighteen eggs by nine people instead of eight. Not fried, then; made into fritters with grated potatoes, and I'd best borrow more coffee from Jocasta's campsite on the way up the mountain.

We turned to go, and Jamie's hand slid suddenly downward over my backside. I made an undignified sound, and Abel MacLennan turned round to gawk at me. I smiled brightly at him, resisting the urge to kick Jamie again, less discreetly.

MacLennan turned away, and scrambled up the slope in front of us with alacrity, coattails bouncing in anticipation over worn breeks. Jamie put a hand under my elbow to help me over the rocks, bending down as he did so to mutter in my ear.

"Why the devil are ye not wearing a petticoat, Sassenach?" he hissed. "Ye've nothing at all on under your skirt—you'll catch your death of cold!"

"You're not wrong there," I said, shivering in spite of my cloak. I did in fact have on a linen shift under my gown, but it was a thin, ragged thing, suitable for rough camping-out in summertime, but quite insufficient to stem the wintry blasts that blew through my skirt as though it were cheesecloth.

"Ye had a fine woolen petticoat yesterday. What's become of it?"

"You don't want to know," I assured him.

His eyebrows went up at this, but before he could ask further questions, a scream rang out behind us.

"Germain!"

I turned to see a small blond head, hair flying as the owner streaked down the slope below the rocks. Two-year-old Germain had taken advantage of his mother's preoccupation with his newborn sister to escape custody and make a dash for the row of soldiers. Eluding capture, he charged headlong down the slope, picking up speed like a rolling stone.

"Fergus!" Marsali screamed. Germain's father, hearing his name, turned round from his conversation, just in time to see his son trip over a rock and fly headlong. A born acrobat, the little boy made no move to save himself, but collapsed gracefully, rolling into a ball like a hedgehog as he struck the grassy slope on one shoulder. He rolled like a cannonball through the ranks of soldiers, shot off the edge of a rocky shelf, and plopped with a splash into the creek.

There was a general gasp of consternation, and a number of people ran down the hill to help, but one of the soldiers had already hurried to the bank. Kneeling, he thrust the tip of his bayonet through the child's floating clothes and towed the soggy bundle to the shore.

Fergus charged into the icy shallows, reaching out to clasp his waterlogged son.

"Merci, mon ami, merci beaucoup," he said to the young soldier. *"Et toi, garnement,"* he said, addressing his spluttering offspring with a small shake. *"Comment vas-tu,* ye wee chowderheid?"

The soldier looked startled, but I couldn't tell whether the cause was Fergus's unique patois, or the sight of the gleaming hook he wore in place of his missing left hand.

"That's all right then, sir," he said, with a shy smile. "He'll no be damaged, I think."

Brianna appeared suddenly from behind a chinkapin tree, six-month-old Jemmy on one shoulder, and scooped baby Joan neatly out of Marsali's arms.

"Here, give Joanie to me," she said. "You go take care of Germain."

Jamie swung the heavy cloak from his shoulders and laid it in Marsali's arms in place of the baby.

"Aye, and tell the soldier laddie who saved him to come and share our fire," he told her. "We can feed another, Sassenach?"

"Of course," I said, swiftly readjusting my mental calculations. Eighteen eggs, four loaves of stale bread for toast—no, I should keep back one for the trip home tomorrow—three dozen oatcakes if Jamie and Roger hadn't eaten them already, half a jar of honey . . .

Marsali's thin face lighted with a rueful smile, shared among the three of us, then she was gone, hastening to the aid of her drenched and shivering menfolk.

Jamie looked after her with a sigh of resignation, as the wind caught the full sleeves of his shirt and belled them out with a muffled *whoomp*. He crossed his arms across his chest, hunching his shoulders against the wind, and smiled down at me, sidelong.

"Ah, well. I suppose we shall both freeze together, Sassenach. That's all right, though. I wouldna want to live without ye, anyway."

"Ha," I said amiably. "You could live naked on an ice floe, Jamie Fraser, and melt it. What have you done with your coat and plaid?" He wore nothing besides his kilt and sark save shoes and stockings, and his high cheekbones were reddened with cold, like the tips of his ears. When I slipped a hand back inside the crook of his arm, though, he was warm as ever.

"Ye dinna want to know," he said, grinning. He covered my hand with one large, callused palm. "Let's go; I'm starved for my breakfast."

"Wait," I said, detaching myself. Jemmy was indisposed

to share his mother's embrace with the newcomer, and howled and squirmed in protest, his small round face going red with annoyance under a blue knitted cap. I reached out and took him from Brianna, as he wriggled and fussed in his wrappings.

"Thanks, Mama." Brianna smiled briefly, boosting tiny Joan into a more secure position against her shoulder. "Are you sure you want that one, though? This one's quieter—and weighs half as much."

"No, he's all right. Hush, sweetie, come see Grannie." I smiled as I said it, with the still-new feeling of mingled surprise and delight that I could actually be someone's grandmother. Recognizing me, Jemmy abandoned his fuss and went promptly into his mussel-clinging-to-a-rock routine, chubby fists gripped tight in my hair. Disentangling his fingers, I peered over his head, but things below seemed under control.

Fergus, breeches and stockings soaking wet, Jamie's cloak draped round his shoulders, was wringing out his shirtfront one-handed, saying something to the soldier who had rescued Germain. Marsali had whipped off her arisaid and wrapped the little boy in it, her loosened blond hair flying out from under her kerch like cobwebs in the wind.

Lieutenant Hayes, attracted by the noise, was peering out from the flap of his tent like a whelk from its shell. He looked up, and caught my eye; I waved briefly, then turned to follow my own family back to our campsite.

Jamie was saying something to Brianna in Gaelic, as he helped her over a rocky patch in the trail ahead of me.

"Yes, I'm ready," she said, replying in English. "Where's your coat, Da?"

"I lent it to your husband," he said. "We dinna want him to look a beggar at your wedding, aye?"

Bree laughed, wiping a flying strand of red hair out of her mouth with her free hand.

"Better a beggar than an attempted suicide."

"A what?" I caught up with them as we emerged from the shelter of the rocks. The wind barreled across the open space, pelting us with sleet and bits of stinging gravel, and I pulled the knitted cap further down over Jemmy's ears, then pulled the blanket up over his head.

"Whoof!" Brianna hunched over the swaddled baby girl she carried, sheltering her from the blast. "Roger was shaving when the drums started up; he nearly cut his throat. The front of his coat is covered with bloodstains." She glanced at Jamie, eyes watering with the wind. "So you've seen him this morning. Where is he now, do you know?"

"The lad's in one piece," he assured her. "I told him to go and talk wi' Father Donahue, while Hayes was about his business." He gave her a sharp look. "Ye might have told me the lad was no a Catholic."

"I might," she said, unperturbed. "But I didn't. It's no big deal to me."

"If ye mean by that peculiar expression, that it's of no consequence—" Jamie began with a distinct edge in his voice, but was interrupted by the appearance of Roger himself, resplendent in a kilt of green-and-white MacKenzie tartan, with the matching plaid draped over Jamie's good coat and waistcoat. The coat fit decently—both men were of a size, long-limbed and broad-shouldered, though Jamie was an inch or two the taller—and the gray wool was quite as becoming to Roger's dark hair and olive skin as it was to Jamie's burnished auburn coloring.

"You look very nice, Roger," I said. "Where did you cut yourself?" His face was pink, with the raw look common to just-shaved skin, but otherwise unmarked.

Roger was carrying Jamie's plaid under his arm, a bundle of red and black tartan. He handed it over and tilted his head to one side, showing me the deep gash just under his jawbone.

"Just there. Not so bad, but it bled like the dickens. They don't call them cutthroat razors for nothing, aye?"

The gash had already crusted into a neat dark line, a cut some three inches long, angled down from the corner of his jaw across the side of his throat. I touched the skin near it briefly. Not bad; the blade of the razor had cut straight in, no flap of skin needing suture. No wonder it had bled a lot, though; it did look as though he had tried to cut his throat.

"A bit nervous this morning?" I teased. "Not having second thoughts, are you?"

"A little late for that," Brianna said dryly, coming up beside me. "Got a kid who needs a name, after all."

"He'll have more names than he knows what to do with," Roger assured her. "So will you—Mrs. MacKenzie."

A small flush lit Brianna's face at the name, and she smiled at him. He leaned over and kissed her on the forehead, taking the cocooned baby from her as he did so. A look of sudden shock crossed his face as he felt the weight of the bundle in his arms, and he gawked down at it.

"That's not ours," Bree said, grinning at his look of consternation. "It's Marsali's Joan. Mama has Jemmy."

"Thank God," he said, holding the bundle with a good deal more caution. "I thought he'd evaporated or something." He lifted the blanket slightly, exposing tiny Joan's sleeping face, and smiled—as people always did—at sight of her comical quiff of brown hair, which came to a point like a Kewpie doll's.

"Not a chance," I said, grunting as I hoisted a well-nourished Jemmy, now peacefully comatose in his own wrappings, into a more comfortable position. "I think he's gained a pound or two on the way uphill." I was flushed from exertion, and held the baby a little away from myself, as a sudden wave of heat flushed my cheeks and perspiration broke out under the waves of my disheveled hair.

Jamie took Jemmy from me, and tucked him expertly under one arm like a football, one hand cupping the baby's head.

"Ye've spoken wi' the priest, then?" he said, eyeing Roger skeptically.

"I have," Roger said dryly, answering the look as much as the question. "He's satisfied I'm no the Anti-Christ. So long as I'm willing the lad should be baptized Catholic, there's no bar to the wedding. I've said I'm willing."

Jamie grunted in reply, and I repressed a smile. While Jamie had no great religious prejudices—he had dealt with, fought with, and commanded far too many men, of every possible background—the revelation that his son-in-law was a Presbyterian—and had no intention of converting—had occasioned some small comment.

Bree caught my eye and gave me a sidelong smile, her own eyes creasing into blue triangles of catlike amusement.

"Very wise of you not to mention religion ahead of time," I murmured, careful not to speak loudly enough for Jamie to hear me. Both men were walking ahead of us, still rather stiff in their attitudes, though the formality of their demeanor was rather impaired by the trailing draperies of the babies they carried.

Jemmy let out a sudden squawk, but his grandfather swung him up without breaking stride, and he subsided, round eyes fixed on us over Jamie's shoulder, sheltered under the hooding of his blanket. I made a face at him, and he broke into a huge, gummy smile.

"Roger wanted to say something, but I told him to keep quiet." Bree stuck out her tongue and wiggled it at Jemmy, then fixed a wifely look on Roger's back. "I knew Da wouldn't make a stramash about it, if we waited 'til just before the wedding."

I noted both her astute evaluation of her father's behavior, and her easy use of Scots. She resembled Jamie in a good deal more than the obvious matter of looks and coloring; she had his talent for human judgment and his glibness with language. Still, there was something niggling at my mind, something to do with Roger and religion . . .

We had come up close enough behind the men to hear their conversation.

". . . about Hillsborough," Jamie was saying, leaning toward Roger so as to be heard over the wind. "Calling for information about the rioters."

"Oh, aye?" Roger sounded both interested and wary. "Duncan Innes will be interested to hear that. He was in Hillsborough during the troubles, did you know?"

"No." Jamie sounded more than interested. "I've barely seen Duncan to speak to this week. I'll ask him, maybe, after the wedding—if he lives through it." Duncan was to marry Jamie's aunt, Jocasta Cameron, in the evening, and was nervous to the point of prostration over the prospect.

Roger turned, shielding Joan from the wind with his body as he spoke to Brianna.

"Your aunt's told Father Donahue he can hold the weddings in her tent. That'll be a help."

"Brrrr!" Bree hunched her shoulders, shivering. "Thank goodness. It's no day to be getting married under the greenwood tree."

A huge chestnut overhead sent down a damp shower of yellow leaves, as though in agreement. Roger looked a little uneasy.

"I don't imagine it's quite the wedding you maybe thought of," he said. "When ye were a wee girl."

Brianna looked up at Roger and a slow, wide smile spread across her face. "Neither was the first one," she said. "But I liked it fine."

Roger's complexion wasn't given to blushing, and his ears were red with cold in any case. He opened his mouth as though to reply, caught Jamie's gimlet eye, and shut it again, looking embarrassed but undeniably pleased.

"Mr. Fraser!"

I turned to see one of the soldiers making his way up the hill toward us, his eyes fixed on Jamie.

"Corporal MacNair, your servant, sir," he said, breathing hard as he reached us. He gave a sharp inclination of the head. "The Lieutenant's compliments, and would ye be so good as to attend him in his tent?" He caught sight of me, and bowed again, less abruptly. "Mrs. Fraser. My compliments, ma'am."

"Your servant, sir." Jamie returned the Corporal's bow. "My apologies to the Lieutenant, but I have duties that require my attendance elsewhere." He spoke politely, but the Corporal glanced sharply up at him. MacNair was young, but not callow; a quick look of understanding crossed his lean, dark face. The last thing any man would want was to be seen going into Hayes's tent by himself, immediately following that Proclamation.

"The Lieutenant bids me request the attendance upon him of Mr. Farquard Campbell, Mr. Andrew MacNeill, Mr. Gerald Forbes, Mr. Duncan Innes, and Mr. Randall Lillywhite, as well as yourself, sir."

A certain amount of tension left Jamie's shoulders.

"Does he," he said dryly. So Hayes meant to consult the powerful men of the area: Farquard Campbell and Andrew MacNeill were large landowners and local magistrates; Gerald Forbes a prominent solicitor from Cross Creek, and a justice of the peace; Lillywhite a magistrate of the circuit court. And Duncan Innes was about to become the largest plantation owner in the western half of the colony, by virtue of his impending marriage to Jamie's widowed aunt. Jamie himself was neither rich nor an official of the Crown—but he *was* the proprietor of a large, if still largely vacant, land grant in the backcountry.

He gave a slight shrug and shifted the baby to his other shoulder, settling himself.

"Aye. Well, then. Tell the Lieutenant I shall attend him as soon as may be convenient."

Nothing daunted, MacNair bowed and went off, presumably in search of the other gentlemen on his list.

"And what's all that about?" I asked Jamie. "Oops." I reached up and skimmed a glistening strand of saliva from Jemmy's chin before it could reach Jamie's shirt. "Starting a new tooth, are we?"

"I've plenty of teeth," Jamie assured me, "and so have you, so far as I can see. As to what Hayes may want with me, I canna say for sure. And I dinna mean to find out before I must, either." He cocked one ruddy eyebrow at me, and I laughed.

"Oh, a certain flexibility in that word 'convenient,' is there?"

"I didna say it would be convenient for *him*," Jamie pointed out. "Now, about your petticoat, Sassenach, and why you're scampering about the forest bare-arsed—Duncan, *a charaid*!" The wry look on his face melted into genuine pleasure at sight of Duncan Innes, making his way toward us through a small growth of bare-limbed dogwood.

Duncan clambered over a fallen log, the process made rather awkward by his missing left arm, and arrived on the path beside us, shaking water droplets from his hair. He was already dressed for his wedding, in a clean ruffled shirt and starched linen stock above his kilt, and a coat of scarlet broadcloth trimmed in gold lace, the empty sleeve pinned up with a brooch. I had never seen Duncan look so elegant, and said so.

"Och, well," he said diffidently. "Miss Jo did wish it." He shrugged off the compliment along with the rain, carefully brushing away dead needles and bits of bark that had adhered to his coat in the passage through the pines.

"Brrr! A gruesome day, *Mac Dubh*, and no mistake." He looked up at the sky and shook his head. "Happy the bride the sun shines on; happy the corpse the rain falls on."

"I do wonder just how delighted you can expect the average corpse to be," I said, "whatever the meteorological conditions. But I'm sure Jocasta will be quite happy regardless," I added hastily, seeing a look of bewilderment spread itself across Duncan's features. "And you too, of course!"

"Oh . . . aye," he said, a little uncertainly. "Aye, of course. I thank ye, ma'am."

"When I saw ye coming through the wood, I thought perhaps Corporal MacNair was nippin' at your heels," Jamie said. "You're no on your way to see Archie Hayes, are you?"

Duncan looked quite startled.

"Hayes? No, what would the Lieutenant want wi' me?"

"You were in Hillsborough in September, aye? Here, Sassenach, take this wee squirrel away." Jamie interrupted himself to hand me Jemmy, who had decided to take a more active interest in the proceedings and was attempting to climb his grandfather's torso, digging in his toes and making loud grunting noises. The sudden activity, however, was not Jamie's chief motive for relieving himself of the burden, as I discovered when I accepted Jemmy.

"Thanks a lot," I said, wrinkling my nose. Jamie grinned at me, and turned Duncan up the path, resuming their conversation.

"Hmm," I said, sniffing cautiously. "Finished, are you? No, I thought not." Jemmy closed his eyes, went bright red, and emitted a popping noise like muffled machine-gun fire. I undid his wrappings sufficiently to peek down his back.

"Whoops," I said, and hastily unwound the blanket, just in time. "*What* has your mother been feeding you?"

Thrilled to have escaped his swaddling bands, Jemmy

churned his legs like a windmill, causing a noxious yellowish substance to ooze from the baggy legs of his diaper.

"Pew," I said succinctly, and holding him at arm's length, headed off the path toward one of the tiny rivulets that meandered down the mountainside, thinking that while I could perhaps do without such amenities as indoor plumbing and motorcars, there were times when I sincerely missed things like rubber pants with elasticated legs. To say nothing of toilet rolls.

I found a good spot on the edge of the little stream, with a thick coating of dead leaves. I knelt, laid out a fold of my cloak, and parked Jemmy on it on his hands and knees, pulling the soggy clout off without bothering to unpin it.

"Weee!" he said, sounding surprised as the cold air struck him. He clenched his fat little buttocks and hunched like a small pink toad.

"Ha," I told him. "If you think a cold wind up the bum is bad, just wait." I scooped up a handful of damp yellow-brown leaves, and cleaned him off briskly. A fairly stoic child, he wiggled and squirmed, but didn't screech, instead making high-pitched "Eeeeee" noises as I excavated his crevices.

I flipped him over, and with a hand held prophylactically over the danger zone, administered a similar treatment to his private parts, this eliciting a wide, gummy grin.

"Oh, you *are* a Hieland man, aren't you?" I said, smiling back.

"And just what d'ye mean by that remark, Sassenach?" I looked up to find Jamie leaning against a tree on the other side of the streamlet. The bold colors of his dress tartan and white linen sark stood out bright against the faded autumn foliage; face and hair, though, made him look like some denizen of the wood, all bronze and auburn, with the wind stirring his hair so the free ends danced like the scarlet maple leaves above.

"Well, he's apparently impervious to cold and damp," I said, concluding my labors and discarding the final handful of soiled leaves. "Beyond that . . . well, I've not had much to do with male infants before, but isn't this rather precocious?"

One corner of Jamie's mouth curled up, as he peered at

the prospect revealed under my hand. The tiny appendage stood up stiff as my thumb, and roughly the same size.

"Ah, no," he said. "I've seen a many wee lads in the raw. They all do that now and again." He shrugged, and the smile grew wider. "Now, whether it's only *Scottish* lads, I couldna be saying . . ."

"A talent that improves with age, I daresay," I said dryly. I tossed the dirty clout across the streamlet, where it landed at his feet with a splat. "Get the pins and rinse that out, will you?"

His long, straight nose wrinkled slightly, but he knelt without demur and picked the filthy thing up gingerly between two fingers.

"Oh, so *that's* what ye've done wi' your petticoat," he said. I had opened the large pocket I wore slung at my waist and extracted a clean, folded rectangle of cloth. Not the unbleached linen of the clout he held, but a thick, soft, oftenwashed wool flannel, dyed a pale red with the juice of currants.

I shrugged, checked Jemmy for the prospect of fresh explosions, and popped him onto the new diaper.

"With three babies all in clouts, and the weather too damp to dry anything properly, we were rather short of clean bits." The bushes around the clearing where we had made our family camp were all festooned with flapping laundry, most of it still wet, owing to the inopportune weather.

"Here." Jamie stretched across the foot-wide span of rock-strewn water to hand me the pins extracted from the old diaper. I took them, careful not to drop them in the stream. My fingers were stiff and chilly, but the pins were valuable; Bree had made them of heated wire, and Roger had carved the capped heads from wood, in accordance with her drawings. Honest-to-goodness safety pins, if a bit larger and cruder than the modern version. The only real defect was the glue used to hold the wooden heads to the wire; made from boiled milk and hoof parings, it was not entirely waterproof, and the heads had to be reglued periodically.

I folded the diaper snugly about Jemmy's loins and thrust a pin through the cloth, smiling at sight of the wooden cap.

Bree had taken one set and carved a small, comical frog—each with a wide, toothless grin—onto each one.

"All right, Froggie, here you go, then." Diaper securely fastened, I sat down and boosted him into my lap, smoothing down his smock and attempting to rewrap his blanket.

"Where did Duncan go?" I asked. "Down to see the Lieutenant?"

Jamie shook his head, bent over his task.

"I told him not to go yet. He *was* in Hillsborough during the troubles there. Best he should wait a bit; then if Hayes should ask, he can swear honestly there's no man here who took part in the riots." He looked up and smiled, without humor. "There won't be, come nightfall."

I watched his hands, large and capable, wringing out the rinsed clout. The scars on his right hand were usually almost invisible, but they stood out now, ragged white lines against his cold-reddened skin. The whole business made me mildly uneasy, though there seemed no direct connection with us.

For the most part, I could think of Governor Tryon with no more than a faint sense of edginess; he was, after all, safely tucked away in his nice new palace in New Bern, separated from our tiny settlement on Fraser's Ridge by three hundred miles of coastal towns, inland plantations, pine forest, piedmont, trackless mountains, and sheer howling wilderness. With all the other things he had to worry about, such as the self-styled "Regulators" who had terrorized Hillsborough, and the corrupt sheriffs and judges who had provoked the terror, I hardly thought he would have time to spare a thought for us. I hoped not.

The uncomfortable fact remained that Jamie held title to a large grant of land in the North Carolina mountains as the gift of Governor Tryon—and Tryon in turn held one small but important fact tucked away in his vest pocket: Jamie was a Catholic. And Royal grants of land could be made only to Protestants, by law.

Given the tiny number of Catholics in the colony, and the lack of organization among them, the question of religion was rarely an issue. There were no Catholic churches, no resident Catholic priests; Father Donahue had made the arduous journey down from Baltimore, at Jocasta's request. Jamie's aunt Jocasta and her late husband, Hector Cameron, had been influential among the Scottish community here for so long that no one would have thought of questioning their religious background, and I thought it likely that few of the Scots with whom we had been celebrating all week knew that we were Papists.

They were, however, likely to notice quite soon. Bree and Roger, who had been handfasted for a year, were to be married by the priest this evening, along with two other Catholic couples from Bremerton—and with Jocasta and Duncan Innes.

"Archie Hayes," I said suddenly. "Is he a Catholic?"

Jamie hung the wet clout from a nearby branch and shook water from his hands.

"I havena asked him," he said, "but I shouldna think so. That is, his father was not; I should be surprised if he was— and him an officer."

"True." The disadvantages of Scottish birth, poverty, and being an ex-Jacobite were sufficiently staggering; amazing enough that Hayes had overcome these to rise to his present position, without the additional burden of the taint of Papistry.

What was troubling me, though, was not the thought of Lieutenant Hayes and his men; it was Jamie. Outwardly, he was calm and assured as ever, with that faint smile always hiding in the corner of his mouth. But I knew him very well; I had seen the two stiff fingers of his right hand—maimed in an English prison—twitch against the side of his leg as he traded jokes and stories with Hayes the night before. Even now, I could see the thin line that formed between his brows when he was troubled, and it wasn't concern over what he was doing.

Was it simply worry over the Proclamation? I couldn't see why that should be, given that none of our folk had been involved in the Hillsborough riots.

". . . a Presbyterian," he was saying. He glanced over at me with a wry smile. "Like wee Roger."

The memory that had niggled at me earlier dropped suddenly into place.

"You knew that," I said. "You *knew* Roger wasn't a Catholic. You saw him baptize that child in Snaketown, when we . . . took him from the Indians." Too late, I saw the shadow cross his face, and bit my tongue. When we took Roger—and left in his place Jamie's dearly loved nephew Ian.

A shadow crossed his face momentarily, but he smiled, pushing away the thought of Ian.

"Aye, I did," he said.

"But Bree—"

"She'd marry the lad if he were a Hottentot," Jamie interrupted. "Anyone can see that. And I canna say I'd object overmuch to wee Roger if he *were* a Hottentot," he added, rather to my surprise.

"You wouldn't?"

Jamie shrugged, and stepped over the tiny creek to my side, wiping wet hands on the end of his plaid.

"He's a braw lad, and he's kind. He's taken the wean as his own and said no word to the lass about it. It's no more than a man should do—but not every man would."

I glanced down involuntarily at Jemmy, curled up cozily in my arms. I tried not to think of it myself, but could not help now and then searching his bluntly amiable features for any trace that might reveal his true paternity.

Brianna had been handfast with Roger, lain with him for one night—and then been raped two days later, by Stephen Bonnet. There was no way to tell for sure who the father had been, and so far Jemmy gave no indication of resembling either man in the slightest. He was gnawing his fist at the moment, with a ferocious scowl of concentration, and with his soft fuzz of red-gold plush, he looked like no one so much as Jamie himself.

"Mm. So why all the insistence on having Roger vetted by a priest?"

"Well, they'll be married in any case," he said logically. "I want the wee lad baptized a Catholic, though." He laid a large hand gently on Jemmy's head, thumb smoothing the tiny red brows. "So if I made a bit of a fuss about MacKenzie, I thought they'd be pleased to agree about *an gille ruaidh* here, aye?"

I laughed, and pulled a fold of blanket up around Jemmy's ears.

"And I thought Brianna had *you* figured out!"

"So does she," he said, with a grin. He bent suddenly and kissed me.

His mouth was soft and very warm. He tasted of bread and butter, and he smelled strongly of fresh leaves and unwashed male, with just the faintest trace of effluvium of diaper.

"Oh, that's nice," I said with approval. "Do it again."

The wood around us was still, in the way of woods. No bird, no beast, just the sough of leaves above and the rush of water underfoot. Constant movement, constant sound—and at the center of it all, a perfect peace. There were a good many people on the mountain, and most of them not that far away—yet just here, just now, we might have been alone on Jupiter.

I opened my eyes and sighed, tasting honey. Jamie smiled at me, and brushed a fallen yellow leaf from my hair. The baby lay in my arms, a heavy, warm weight, the center of the universe.

Neither of us spoke, not wishing to disturb the stillness. It was like being at the tip of a spinning top, I thought—a whirl of events and people going on all round, and a step in one direction or another would plunge us back into that spinning frenzy, but here at the very center—there was peace.

I reached up and brushed a scatter of maple seeds from his shoulder. He seized my hand, and brought it to his mouth with a sudden fierceness that startled me. And yet his lips were tender, the tip of his tongue warm on the fleshy mound at the base of my thumb—the mount of Venus, it's called, love's seat.

He raised his head, and I felt the sudden chill on my hand, where the ancient scar showed white as bone. A letter "J," cut in the skin, his mark on me.

He laid his hand against my face, and I pressed it there with my own, as though I could feel the faded "C" he bore on his own palm, against the cold skin of my cheek. Neither of us spoke, but the pledge was made, as we had made it once before, in a place of sanctuary, our feet on a scrap of bedrock in the shifting sands of threatened war.

It was not near; not yet. But I heard it coming, in the sound of drums and proclamation, saw it in the glint of steel, knew the fear of it in heart and bone when I looked in Jamie's eyes.

The chill had gone, and hot blood throbbed in my hand as though to split the ancient scar and spill my heart's blood for him once again. It would come, and I could not stop it.

But this time, I wouldn't leave him.

   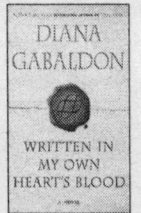
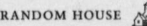

Also by **DIANA GABALDON**

THE COMPANION
VOLUME

THE OUTLANDER
GRAPHIC NOVEL

THE
LORD JOHN
SERIES

Lord John and the Private Matter
Lord John and the Brotherhood of the Blade
Lord John and the Hand of Devils
The Scottish Prisoner

Continue the saga with original eNovellas,
engrossing tales to complement the Outlander series.

A Plague of Zombies

*The Custom of
the Army*

*A Leaf on the Wind
of All Hallows*

The Space Between

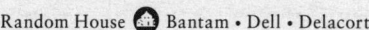

DianaGabaldon.com
f AuthorDianaGabaldon   🐦 @Writer_DG

Random House 🅡🅗 Bantam • Dell • Delacorte

OUTLANDER

SEASON ONE
THE ULTIMATE COLLECTION

THE ULTIMATE COLLECTION comes with:

- A Keepsake Box

- A Collectible Behind-the-Scenes Book

- An Engraved Flask with one of three unique quotes from the series

- A Curated Collection of Photographs and a Frame

- The Complete First Season Blu-ray™ & Soundtrack
  with Three Exclusive Tracks

VOLUMES 1 & 2 ALSO AVAILABLE ON BLU-RAY™

By Diana Gabaldon

(in chronological order)
Outlander
Dragonfly in Amber
Voyager
Drums of Autumn
The Fiery Cross
A Breath of Snow and Ashes
An Echo in the Bone
Written in My Own Heart's Blood

The Outlandish Companion
(nonfiction)

The Exile
(graphic novel)

The Outlandish Companion, Volume Two
(nonfiction)

(in chronological order)
Lord John and the Hellfire Club (novella)
Lord John and the Private Matter
Lord John and the Succubus (novella)
Lord John and the Brotherhood of the Blade
Lord John and the Haunted Soldier (novella)
The Custom of the Army (novella)
Lord John and the Hand of Devils (collected novellas)
The Scottish Prisoner
A Plague of Zombies (novella)

Other Outlander-related novellas
A Leaf on the Wind of All Hallows
The Space Between

DIANA GABALDON

VOYAGER

A DELL BOOK

Published by
Bantam Dell
a division of
Random House, Inc.

LIBRARY OF CONGRESS CATALOG CARD NUMBER:
93-021907

ISBN: 978-0-440-21756-5

Reprinted by arrangement with Delacorte Press

MANUFACTURED IN THE UNITED STATES OF AMERICA

Published simultaneously in Canada

Dell mass market edition/November 1994
Dell reissue/September 2002

60 59 58 57 56 55 54
OPM

*To my children,
Laura Juliet,
Samuel Gordon,
and Jennifer Rose,*

*Who gave me the heart, the blood, and the bones
of this book.*

Acknowledgments

The author's deepest thanks to:

Jackie Cantor, as always, for being the rare and marvelous sort of editor who thinks it's all right if a book is long as long as it's good; my husband, Doug Watkins, for his literary eye, his marginal notes (e.g., "nipples *again*?"), and the jokes he insists I steal from him to give to Jamie Fraser; my elder daughter, Laura, who says, "If you come talk to my class about writing again, just talk about books and don't tell them about whale penises, okay?"; my son, Samuel, who walks up to total strangers in the park and says, "Have you read my mother's book?"; my younger daughter, Jenny, who says, "Why don't you wear makeup like on your book covers *all* the time, Mommy?"; Margaret J. Campbell, scholar; Barry Fodgen, English poet; and Pindens Cinola Oleroso Loventon Greenpeace Ludovic, dog, for generously allowing me to use their personae as the basis for the excesses of imagination (Mr. Fodgen wishes to note for the record that his dog Ludo has never actually tried to copulate with anyone's leg, wooden or not, but does understand the concept of artistic license); Perry Knowlton, who as well as being an excellent literary agent is also a fount of knowledge about bowlines, mainsails, and matters nautical, as well as the niceties of French grammar and the proper way to gut a deer; Robert Riffle, noted authority on what plants grow where, and what they look like while doing so; Kathryn (whose last name was either Boyle or Frye; all I remember is that it had to do with cooking), for the useful information on tropical diseases, particu-

viii   *Acknowledgments*

larly the picturesque habits of loa loa worms; Michael Lee West, for detailed descriptions of Jamaica, including regional dialect and folklore anecdotes; Dr. Mahlon West, for advice on typhoid fever; William Cross, Paul Block (and Paul's father), and Chrystine Wu (and Chrystine's parents), for invaluable assistance with Chinese vocabulary, history, and cultural attitudes; my father-in-law, Max Watkins, who, as always, provided useful comments on the appearance and habits of horses, including which way they face when the wind is blowing; Peggy Lynch, for wanting to know what Jamie would say if he saw a picture of his daughter in a bikini; Lizy Buchan, for telling me the story about her husband's ancestor who escaped Culloden; Dr. Gary Hoff, for medical detail; Fay Zachary, for lunch and critical comment; Sue Smiley, for critical reading and suggesting the blood vow; David Pijawka, for the materials on Jamaica and his most poetic description of what the air feels like after a Caribbean rainstorm; Iain MacKinnon Taylor, and his brother Hamish Taylor, for their most helpful suggestions and corrections of Gaelic spelling and usages; and as always, the various members of the CompuServe Literary Forum, including Janet McConnaughey, Marte Brengle, Akua Lezli Hope, John L. Myers, John E. Simpson, Jr., Sheryl Smith, Alit, Norman Shimmel, Walter Hawn, Karen Pershing, Margaret Ball, Paul Solyn, Diane Engel, David Chaifetz, and many others, for being interested, providing useful discussion, and laughing in the right places.

Prologue

When I was small, I never wanted to step in puddles. Not because of any fear of drowned worms or wet stockings; I was by and large a grubby child, with a blissful disregard for filth of any kind.

It was because I couldn't bring myself to believe that that perfect smooth expanse was no more than a thin film of water over solid earth. I believed it was an opening into some fathomless space. Sometimes, seeing the tiny ripples caused by my approach, I thought the puddle impossibly deep, a bottomless sea in which the lazy coil of tentacle and gleam of scale lay hidden, with the threat of huge bodies and sharp teeth adrift and silent in the far-down depths.

And then, looking down into reflection, I would see my own round face and frizzled hair against a featureless blue sweep, and think instead that the puddle was the entrance to another sky. If I stepped in there, I would drop at once, and keep on falling, on and on, into blue space.

The only time I would dare to walk through a puddle was at twilight, when the evening stars came out. If I looked in the water and saw one lighted pinprick there, I could splash through unafraid—for if I should fall into the puddle and on into space, I could grab hold of the star as I passed, and be safe.

Even now, when I see a puddle in my path, my mind half-halts—though my feet do not—then hurries on, with only the echo of the thought left behind.

What if, this time, you fall?

PART ONE

Battle, and the Loves of Men

1

The Corbies' Feast

Many a Highland chieftain fought,
Many a gallant man did fall.
Death itself were dearly bought,
All for Scotland's King and law.

—*"Will Ye No Come Back Again?"*

April 16, 1746

He was dead. However, his nose throbbed painfully, which he thought odd in the circumstances. While he placed considerable trust in the understanding and mercy of his Creator, he harbored that residue of elemental guilt that made all men fear the chance of hell. Still, all he had ever heard of hell made him think it unlikely that the torments reserved for its luckless inhabitants could be restricted to a sore nose.

On the other hand, this couldn't be heaven, on several counts. For one, he didn't deserve it. For another, it didn't look it. And for a third, he doubted that the rewards of the blessed included a broken nose, any more than those of the damned.

While he had always thought of Purgatory as a gray sort of place, the faint reddish light that hid everything around him seemed suitable. His mind was clearing a bit, and his power to reason was coming back, if slowly. Someone, he thought rather crossly, ought to see him and tell him just what the sentence was, until he should have suffered enough to be purified, and at last to enter the Kingdom of God. Whether he was expecting a demon or an angel was uncertain. He had no idea of the staffing requirements of Purgatory; it wasn't a matter the dominie had addressed in his schooldays.

While waiting, he began to take stock of whatever other torments he might be required to endure. There were numerous cuts, gashes, and bruises here and there, and he was fairly sure he'd broken the fourth finger of his right hand again—difficult to protect it, the way it stuck out so stiff, with the joint frozen. None of that was too bad, though. What else?

Claire. The name knifed across his heart with a pain that was more racking than anything his body had ever been called on to withstand.

If he had had an actual body anymore, he was sure it would have doubled up in agony. He had known it would be like this, when he sent her back to the stone circle. Spiritual anguish could be taken as a standard condition in Purgatory, and he had expected all along that the pain of separation would be his chief punishment—sufficient, he thought, to atone for anything he'd ever done: murder and betrayal included.

He did not know whether persons in Purgatory were allowed to pray or not, but tried anyway. *Lord,* he prayed, *that she may be safe. She and the child.* He was sure she would have made it to the circle itself; only two months gone with child, she was still light and fleet of foot—and the most stubbornly determined woman he had ever met. But whether she had managed the dangerous transition back to the place from which she had come—sliding precariously through whatever mysterious layers lay between then and now, powerless in the grip of the rock—that he could never know, and the thought of it was enough to make him forget even the throbbing in his nose.

He resumed his interrupted inventory of bodily ills, and became inordinately distressed at the discovery that his left leg appeared to be missing. Sensation stopped at the hip, with a sort of pins-and-needles tingling at the joint. Presumably he would get it back in due time, either when he finally arrived in Heaven, or at the least, at Judgment Day. And after all, his brother-in-law Ian managed very well on the wooden peg he wore to replace *his* missing leg.

Still, his vanity was troubled. Ah, that must be it; a punishment meant to cure him of the sin of vanity. He mentally set his teeth, determined to accept whatever came to him with fortitude, and such humility as he could manage. Still, he couldn't help reaching an exploratory hand (or whatever he was using for a hand) tentatively downward, to see just where the limb now ended.

The hand struck something hard, and the fingers tangled in wet, snarled hair. He sat up abruptly, and with some effort, cracked the layer of dried blood that had sealed his eyelids shut. Memory flooded back, and he groaned aloud. He had been mistaken. This *was* hell. But James Fraser was unfortunately not dead, after all.

The body of a man lay across his own. Its dead weight crushed his left leg, explaining the absence of feeling. The head, heavy as a spent cannonball, pressed facedown into his abdomen, the damp, matted hair a dark spill on the wet linen of his shirt. He jerked upward in sudden panic; the head rolled sideways into his lap and a half-open eye stared sightlessly up behind the sheltering strands of hair.

It was Jack Randall, his fine red captain's coat so dark with the wet it looked almost black. Jamie made a fumbling effort to push the body away, but found himself amazingly weak; his hand splayed feebly against Randall's shoulder, and the elbow of his other arm buckled suddenly as he tried to support himself. He found himself lying once more flat on his back, the sleeting sky pale gray and whirling dizzily overhead. Jack Randall's head moved obscenely up and down on his stomach with each gasping breath.

He pressed his hands flat against the boggy ground—the water rose up cold through his fingers and soaked the back of his shirt—and wriggled sideways. Some warmth was trapped between them; as the limp dead weight slid slowly free, the freezing rain struck his newly exposed flesh with a shock like a blow, and he shivered violently with sudden chill.

As he squirmed on the ground, struggling with the crumpled, mud-stained folds of his plaid, he could hear sounds above the keening of the April wind; far-off shouts and a moaning and wailing, like the calling of ghosts in the wind. And overall, the raucous calling of crows. Dozens of crows, from the sound.

That was strange, he thought dimly. Birds shouldn't fly in a storm like this. A final heave freed the plaid from under him, and he fumbled it over his body. As he reached to cover his legs, he saw that his kilt and left leg were soaked with blood. The sight didn't distress him; it seemed only vaguely interesting, the dark red smears a contrast to the grayish green of the moor plants around him. The echoes of battle faded from his ears, and he left Culloden Field to the calling of the crows.

He was wakened much later by the calling of his name.

"Fraser! Jamie Fraser! Are ye here?"

No, he thought groggily. I'm not. Wherever he had been while unconscious, it was a better place than this. He lay in a small declivity, half-filled with water. The sleeting rain had stopped, but the wind hadn't; it whined over the moor, piercing and chilling. The sky had darkened nearly to black; it must be near evening, then.

"I saw him go down here, I tell ye. Right near a big clump of gorse." The voice was at a distance, fading as it argued with someone.

There was a rustle near his ear, and he turned his head to see the crow. It stood on the grass a foot away, a blotch of wind-ruffled black feathers, regarding him with a bead-bright eye. Deciding that he posed no threat, it swiveled its neck with casual ease and jabbed its thick sharp bill into Jack Randall's eye.

Jamie jerked up with a cry of revulsion and a flurry of movement that sent the crow flapping off, squawking with alarm.

"Ay! Over there!"

There was a squelching through boggy ground, and a face before him, and the welcome feel of a hand on his shoulder.

"He's alive! Come on, MacDonald! D'ye lend a hand here; he'll no be walkin' on his own." There were four of them, and with a good deal of effort, they got him up, arms draped helpless about the shoulders of Ewan Cameron and Iain MacKinnon.

He wanted to tell them to leave him; his purpose had returned to him with the waking, and he remembered that he had meant to die. But the sweetness of their company was too much to resist. The rest had restored the feeling in his dead leg, and he knew the seriousness of the wound. He would die soon in any case; thank God that it need not be alone, in the dark.

"Water?" The edge of the cup pressed against his lip, and he roused himself long enough to drink, careful not to spill it. A hand pressed briefly against his forehead and dropped away without comment.

He was burning; he could feel the flames behind his eyes when he closed them. His lips were cracked and sore from the heat, but it was better than the chills that came at intervals. At least when he was fevered, he could lie still; the shaking of the chills woke the sleeping demons in his leg.

Murtagh. He had a terrible feeling about his godfather, but no memory to give it shape. Murtagh was dead; he knew that must be it, but didn't know why or how he knew. A good half of the Highland army was dead, slaughtered on the moor—so much he had gathered from the talk of the men in the farmhouse, but he had no memory of the battle himself.

He had fought with armies before, and knew such loss of memory was not uncommon in soldiers; he had seen it, though never before suffered it himself. He knew the memories would come back, and hoped he would be dead before they did. He shifted at the thought, and the movement sent a jolt of white-hot pain through his leg that made him groan.

"All right, Jamie?" Ewan rose on one elbow next to him, worried face wan in the dawning light. A bloodstained bandage circled his head, and there were rusty stains on his collar, from the scalp wound left by a bullet's graze.

"Aye, I'll do." He reached up a hand and touched Ewan's shoulder in gratitude. Ewan patted it, and lay back down.

The crows were back. Black as night themselves, they had gone to roost with the darkness, but with the dawn they were back—birds of war, the corbies had come to feast on the flesh of the fallen. It could as well be his own eyes the cruel beaks picked out, he thought. He could feel the shape of his eyeballs beneath his lids, round and hot, tasty bits of jelly rolling restless to and fro, looking vainly for oblivion, while the rising sun turned his lids a dark and bloody red.

Four of the men were gathered near the single window of the farmhouse, talking quietly together.

"Make a run for it?" one said, with a nod outside. "Christ, man, the best of us can barely stagger—and there's six at least canna walk at all."

"If ye can go, be going," said a man from the floor. He grimaced toward his own leg, wrapped in the remains of a tattered quilt. "Dinna linger on our account."

Duncan MacDonald turned from the window with a grim smile,

shaking his head. The window's light shone off the rough planes of his face, deepening the lines of fatigue.

"Nay, we'll bide," he said. "For one thing, the English are thick as lice on the ground; ye can see them swarm from the window. There's no man would get away whole from Drumossie now."

"Even those that fled the field yesterday will no get far," MacKinnon put in softly. "Did ye no hear the English troops passing in the night at the quick-march? D'ye think it will be hard for them to hunt down our ragtag lot?"

There was no response to this; all of them knew the answer too well. Many of the Highlanders had been barely able to stand on the field before the battle, weakened as they were by cold, fatigue, and hunger.

Jamie turned his face to the wall, praying that his men had started early enough. Lallybroch was remote; if they could get far enough from Culloden, it was unlikely they would be caught. And yet Claire had told him that Cumberland's troops would ravage the Highlands, ranging far afield in their thirst for revenge.

The thought of her this time caused only a wave of terrible longing. God, to have her here, to lay her hands on him, to tend his wounds and cradle his head in her lap. But she was gone—gone away two hundred years from him—and thank the Lord that she was! Tears trickled slowly from under his closed lids, and he rolled painfully onto his side, to hide them from the others.

Lord, that she might be safe, he prayed. *She and the child.*

Toward midafternoon, the smell of burning came suddenly on the air, wafting through the glassless window. It was thicker than the smell of black-powder smoke, pungent, with an underlying odor that was faintly horrible in its reminiscent smell of roasting meat.

"They are burning the dead," said MacDonald. He had scarcely moved from his seat by the window in all the time they had been in the cottage. He looked like a death's-head himself, hair coal-black and matted with dirt, scraped back from a face in which every bone showed.

Here and there, a small, flat crack sounded on the moor. Gun-shots. The coups de grace, administered by those English officers with a sense of compassion, before a tartan-clad wretch should be stacked on the pyre with his luckier fellows. When Jamie looked up, Duncan MacDonald still sat by the window, but his eyes were closed.

Next to him, Ewan Cameron crossed himself. "May we find as much mercy," he whispered.

They did. It was just past noon on the second day when booted feet at last approached the farmhouse, and the door swung open on silent leather hinges.

"Christ." It was a muttered exclamation at the sight within the farmhouse. The draft from the door stirred the fetid air over grimed, bedraggled, bloodstained bodies that lay or sat huddled on the packed-dirt floor.

There had been no discussion of the possibility of armed resistance; they had no heart and there was no point. The Jacobites simply sat, waiting the pleasure of their visitor.

He was a major, all fresh and new in an uncreased uniform, with polished boots. After a moment's hesitation to survey the inhabitants, he stepped inside, his lieutenant close behind.

"I am Lord Melton," he said, glancing around as though seeking the leader of these men, to whom his remarks might most properly be addressed.

Duncan MacDonald, after a glance of his own, stood slowly, and inclined his head. "Duncan MacDonald, of Glen Richie," he said. "And others"—he waved a hand—"late of the forces of His Majesty, King James."

"So I surmised," the Englishman said dryly. He was young, in his early thirties, but he carried himself with a seasoned soldier's confidence. He looked deliberately from man to man, then reached into his coat and produced a folded sheet of paper.

"I have here an order from His Grace, the Duke of Cumberland," he said. "Authorizing the immediate execution of any man found to have engaged in the treasonous rebellion just past." He glanced around the confines of the cottage once more. "Is there any man here who claims innocence of treason?"

There was the faintest breath of laughter from the Scots. Innocence, with the smoke of battle still black on their faces, here on the edge of the slaughter-field?

"No, my lord," said MacDonald, the faintest of smiles on his lips. "Traitors all. Shall we be hanged, then?"

Melton's face twitched in a small grimace of distaste, then settled back into impassivity. He was a slight man, with small, fine bones, but carried his authority well, nonetheless.

"You will be shot," he said. "You have an hour, in which to prepare yourselves." He hesitated, shooting a glance at his lieutenant, as though afraid to sound overgenerous before his subordinate, but continued. "If any of you wish writing materials—to compose a letter, perhaps—the clerk of my company will attend you." He nodded briefly to MacDonald, turned on his heel, and left.

It was a grim hour. A few men availed themselves of the offer of pen and ink, and scribbled doggedly, paper held against the slanted wooden chimney for lack of another firm writing surface. Others prayed quietly, or simply sat, waiting.

MacDonald had begged mercy for Giles McMartin and Frederick Murray, arguing that they were barely seventeen, and should not be held to the same account as their elders. This request was denied, and the boys sat together, white-faced against the wall, holding each other's hands.

For them, Jamie felt a piercing sorrow—and for the others here, loyal friends and gallant soldiers. For himself, he felt only relief. No more to worry, nothing more to do. He had done all he could for his men, his wife, his unborn child. Now let this bodily misery be ended, and he would go grateful for the peace of it.

More for form's sake than because he felt the need of it, he closed his eyes and began the Act of Contrition, in French, as he always said it. *Mon Dieu, je regrette* . . . And yet he didn't; it was much too late for any sort of regret.

Would he find Claire at once when he died? he wondered. Or perhaps, as he expected, be condemned to separation for a time? In any case, he would see her again; he clung to the conviction much more firmly than he embraced the tenets of the Church. God had given her to him; He would restore her.

Forgetting to pray, he instead began to conjure her face behind his eyelids, the curve of cheek and temple, a broad fair brow that always moved him to kiss it, just there, in that small smooth spot between her eyebrows, just at the top of her nose, between clear amber eyes. He fixed his attention on the shape of her mouth, carefully imagining the full, sweet curve of it, and the taste and the feel and the joy of it. The sounds of praying, the pen-scratching and the small, choked sobs of Giles McMartin faded from his ears.

It was midafternoon when Melton returned, this time with six soldiers in attendance, as well as the Lieutenant and the clerk. Again, he paused in the doorway, but MacDonald rose before he could speak.

"I'll go first," he said, and walked steadily across the cottage. As he bent his head to go through the door, though, Lord Melton laid a hand on his sleeve.

"Will you give your full name, sir? My clerk will make note of it."

MacDonald glanced at the clerk, a small bitter smile tugging at the corner of his mouth.

"A trophy list, is it? Aye, well." He shrugged and drew himself upright. "Duncan William MacLeod MacDonald, of Glen Richie." He bowed politely to Lord Melton. "At your service— sir." He passed through the door, and shortly there came the sound of a single pistol-shot from near at hand.

The boys were allowed to go together, hands still clutched tightly as they passed through the door. The rest were taken one by one, each asked for his name, that the clerk might make a record of it. The clerk sat on a stool by the door, head bent to the papers in his lap, not looking up as the men passed by.

When it came Ewan's turn, Jamie struggled to prop himself on his elbows, and grasped his friend's hand, as hard as he could.

"I shall see ye soon again," he whispered.

Ewan's hand shook in his, but the Cameron only smiled. Then he leaned across simply and kissed Jamie's mouth, and rose to go.

They left the six who could not walk to the last.

"James Alexander Malcolm MacKenzie Fraser," he said, speaking slowly to allow the clerk time to get it down right. "Laird of Broch Tuarach." Patiently, he spelled it, then glanced up at Melton.

"I must ask your courtesy, my lord, to give me help to stand."

Melton didn't answer him, but stared down at him, his expression of remote distaste altering to one of mingled astonishment and something like dawning horror.

"Fraser?" he said. "Of Broch Tuarach?"

"I am," Jamie said patiently. Would the man not hurry a bit?

Being resigned to being shot was one thing, but listening to your friends being killed in your hearing was another, and not just calculated to settle the nerves. His arms were trembling with the strain of propping him, and his bowels, not sharing the resignation of his higher faculties, were twitching with a gurgling dread.

"Bloody hell," the Englishman muttered. He bent and peered at Jamie where he lay in the shadow of the wall, then turned and beckoned to his lieutenant.

"Help me get him into the light," he ordered. They weren't gentle about it, and Jamie grunted as the movement sent a bolt of pain from his leg right up through the top of his head. It made him dizzy for a moment, and he missed what Melton was saying to him.

"Are you the Jacobite they call 'Red Jamie'?" he asked again, impatiently.

A streak of fear went through Jamie at that; let them know he was the notorious Red Jamie, and they wouldn't shoot him. They'd take him in chains to London to be tried—a prize of war. And after that, it would be the hangman's rope, and lying half strangled on the gallows platform while they slit his belly and ripped out his bowels. His bowels gave another long, rumbling gurgle; they didn't think much of the notion either.

"No," he said, with as much firmness as he could manage. "Just get on wi' it, eh?"

Ignoring this, Melton dropped to his knees, and ripped open the throat of Jamie's shirt. He gripped Jamie's hair and jerked back his head.

"Damn!" Melton said. Melton's finger prodded him in the throat, just above the collarbone. There was a small triangular scar there, and this appeared to be what was causing his interrogator's concern.

"James Fraser of Broch Tuarach; red hair and a three-cornered scar on his throat." Melton let go of the hair and sat back on his heels, rubbing his chin in a distracted sort of way. Then he pulled himself together and turned to the Lieutenant, gesturing at the five men remaining in the farm cottage.

"Take the rest," he ordered. His fair brows were knitted together in a deep frown. He stood over Jamie, scowling, while the other Scottish prisoners were removed.

"I have to think," he muttered. "Damme, I must think!"

"Do that," said Jamie, "if you're able. I must lie down, myself." They had propped him sitting against the far wall, his leg stretched out in front of him, but sitting upright after two days of lying flat was more than he could manage; the room was tilting drunkenly, and small flashing lights kept coming before his eyes. He leaned to one side, and eased himself down, hugging the dirt floor, eyes closed as he waited for the dizziness to pass.

Melton was muttering under his breath, but Jamie couldn't make out the words; didn't care greatly in any case. Sitting up in the sunlight, he had seen his leg clearly for the first time, and he was fairly sure that he wouldn't live long enough to be hanged.

The deep angry red of inflammation spread from midthigh upward, much brighter than the remaining smears of dried blood. The wound itself was purulent; with the stench of the other men lessening, he could smell the faint sweet-foul odor of the discharge. Still, a quick bullet through the head seemed much preferable to the pain and delirium of death by infection. Did you hear the bang? he wondered, and drifted off, the cool pounded dirt smooth and comforting as a mother's breast under his hot cheek.

He wasn't really asleep, only drifting in a feverish doze, but Melton's voice in his ear jerked him to alertness.

"Grey," the voice was saying, "John William Grey! Do you know that name?"

"No," he said, mazy with sleep and fever. "Look, man, either shoot me or go away, aye? I'm ill."

"Near Carryarrick." Melton's voice was prodding, impatient. "A boy, a fair-haired boy, about sixteen. You met him in the wood."

Jamie squinted up at his tormentor. The fever distorted his vision, but there seemed something vaguely familiar about the fine-boned face above him, with those large, almost girlish eyes.

"Oh," he said, catching a single face from the flood of images that swirled erratically through his brain. "The wee laddie that tried to kill me. Aye, I mind him." He closed his eyes again. In the odd way of fever, one sensation seemed to blend into another. He had broken John William Grey's arm; the memory of the boy's fine bone beneath his hand became the bone of Claire's forearm as he tore her from the grip of the stones. The cool misty breeze stroked his face with Claire's fingers.

"Wake up, damn you!" His head snapped on his neck as Melton shook him impatiently. "Listen to me!"

Jamie opened his eyes wearily. "Aye?"

"John William Grey is my brother," Melton said. "He told me of his meeting with you. You spared his life, and he made you a promise—is that true?"

With great effort, he cast his mind back. He had met the boy two days before the first battle of the rebellion; the Scottish victory at Prestonpans. The six months between then and now seemed a vast chasm; so much had happened in between.

"Aye, I recall. He promised to kill me. I dinna mind if you do it for him, though." His eyelids were drooping again. Did he have to be awake in order to be shot?

"He said he owed you a debt of honor, and he does." Melton stood up, dusting the knees of his breeches, and turned to his lieutenant, who had been watching the questioning with considerable bewilderment.

"It's the deuce of a situation, Wallace. This . . . this Jacobite scut is famous. You've heard of Red Jamie? The one on the broadsheets?" The Lieutenant nodded, looking curiously down at the bedraggled form in the dirt at his feet. Melton smiled bitterly.

"No, he doesn't look so dangerous now, does he? But he's still Red Jamie Fraser, and His Grace would be more than pleased to hear of such an illustrious prisoner. They haven't yet found Charles Stuart, but a few well-known Jacobites would please the crowds at Tower Hill nearly as much."

"Shall I send a message to His Grace?" The Lieutenant reached for his message box.

"No!" Melton wheeled to glare down at his prisoner. "That's the difficulty! Besides being prime gallows bait, this filthy wretch is also the man who captured my youngest brother near Preston, and rather than shooting the brat, which is what he deserved, spared his life and returned him to his companions. Thus," he said through his teeth, "incurring a bloody great debt of honor upon my family!"

"Dear me," said the Lieutenant. "So you can't give him to His Grace, after all."

"No, blast it! I can't even shoot the bastard, without dishonoring my brother's sworn word!"

The prisoner opened one eye. "I willna tell anyone if you don't," he suggested, and promptly closed it again.

"Shut up!" Losing his temper entirely, Melton kicked the prisoner, who grunted at the impact, but said nothing more.

"Perhaps we could shoot him under an assumed name," the Lieutenant suggested helpfully.

Lord Melton gave his aide a look of withering scorn, then looked out the window to judge the time.

"It will be dark in three hours. I'll oversee the burial of the other executed prisoners. Find a small wagon, and have it filled with hay. Find a driver—pick someone discreet, Wallace, that means bribable, Wallace—and have them here as soon as it's dark."

"Yes, sir. Er, sir? What about the prisoner?" The Lieutenant gestured diffidently toward the body on the floor.

"What about him?" Melton said brusquely. "He's too weak to crawl, let alone walk. He isn't going anywhere—at least not until the wagon gets here."

"Wagon?" The prisoner was showing signs of life. In fact, under the stimulus of agitation, he had managed to raise himself onto one arm. Bloodshot blue eyes gleamed wide with alarm, under the spikes of matted red hair. "Where are ye sending me?" Turning from the door, Melton cast him a glance of intense dislike.

"You're the laird of Broch Tuarach, aren't you? Well, that's where I'm sending you."

"I dinna want to go home! I want to be shot!"

The Englishmen exchanged a look.

"Raving," the Lieutenant said significantly, and Melton nodded.

"I doubt he'll live through the journey—but his death won't be on my head, at least."

The door shut firmly behind the Englishmen, leaving Jamie Fraser quite alone—and still alive.

2

The Hunt Begins

Inverness
May 2, 1968

"Of course he's dead!" Claire's voice was sharp with agitation; it rang loudly in the half-empty study, echoing among the rifled bookshelves. She stood against the cork-lined wall like a prisoner awaiting a firing squad, staring from her daughter to Roger Wakefield and back again.

"I don't think so." Roger felt terribly tired. He rubbed a hand over his face, then picked up the folder from the desk; the one containing all the research he'd done since Claire and her daughter had first come to him, three weeks before, and asked his help.

He opened the folder and thumbed slowly through the contents. The Jacobites of Culloden. The Rising of the '45. The gallant Scots who had rallied to the banner of Bonnie Prince Charlie, and cut through Scotland like a blazing sword—only to come to ruin and defeat against the Duke of Cumberland on the gray moor at Culloden.

"Here," he said, plucking out several sheets clipped together. The archaic writing looked odd, rendered in the black crispness of a photocopy. "This is the muster roll of the Master of Lovat's regiment."

He thrust the thin sheaf of papers at Claire, but it was her daughter, Brianna, who took the sheets from him and began to turn the pages, a slight frown between her reddish brows.

"Read the top sheet," Roger said. "Where it says 'Officers.' "

"All right. 'Officers,' " she read aloud, " 'Simon, Master of Lovat' . . ."

"The Young Fox," Roger interrupted. "Lovat's son. And five more names, right?"

Brianna cocked one brow at him, but went on reading.

" 'William Chisholm Fraser, Lieutenant; George D'Amerd Fraser Shaw, Captain; Duncan Joseph Fraser, Lieutenant; Bayard Murray Fraser, Major,' " she paused, swallowing, before reading the last name, " '. . . James Alexander Malcolm MacKenzie Fraser, Captain.' " She lowered the papers, looking a little pale. "My father."

Claire moved quickly to her daughter's side, squeezing the girl's arm. She was pale, too.

"Yes," she said to Roger. "I know he went to Culloden. When he left me . . . there at the stone circle . . . he meant to go back to Culloden Field, to rescue his men who were with Charles Stuart. And we know he did"—she nodded at the folder on the desk, its manila surface blank and innocent in the lamplight—"you found their names. But . . . but . . . Jamie . . ." Speaking the name aloud seemed to rattle her, and she clamped her lips tight.

Now it was Brianna's turn to support her mother.

"He meant to go back, you said." Her eyes, dark blue and encouraging, were intent on her mother's face. "He meant to take his men away from the field, and then go back to the battle."

Claire nodded, recovering herself slightly.

"He knew he hadn't much chance of getting away; if the English caught him . . . he said he'd rather die in battle. That's what he meant to do." She turned to Roger, her gaze an unsettling amber. Her eyes always reminded him of hawk's eyes, as though she could see a good deal farther than most people. "I can't believe he didn't die there—so many men did, and *he* meant to!"

Almost half the Highland army had died at Culloden, cut down in a blast of cannonfire and searing musketry. But not Jamie Fraser.

"No," Roger said doggedly. "That bit I read you from Linklater's book—" He reached to pick it up, a white volume, entitled *The Prince in the Heather.*

" *'Following the battle,' "* he read, " *'eighteen wounded Jacobite officers took refuge in the farmhouse near the moor. Here they lay in pain, their wounds untended, for two days. At the end of that time, they were taken out and shot. One man, a Fraser of the*

*Master of Lovat's regiment, escaped the slaughter. The rest are
buried at the edge of the domestic park.'*

"See?" he said, laying the book down and looking earnestly at
the two women over its pages. "An officer, of the Master of
Lovat's regiment." He grabbed up the sheets of the muster roll.

"And here they are! Just six of them. Now, we know the man in
the farmhouse can't have been Young Simon; he's a well-known
historical figure, and we know very well what happened to him.
He retreated from the field—unwounded, mind you—with a group
of his men, and fought his way north, eventually making it back to
Beaufort Castle, near here." He waved vaguely at the full-length
window, through which the nighttime lights of Inverness twinkled
faintly.

"Nor was the man who escaped Leanach farmhouse any of the
other four officers—William, George, Duncan, or Bayard," Roger
said. "Why?" He snatched another paper out of the folder and
brandished it, almost triumphantly. "Because they all *did* die at
Culloden! All four of them were killed on the field—I found their
names listed on a plaque in the church at Beauly."

Claire let out a long breath, then eased herself down into the old
leather swivel chair behind the desk.

"Jesus H. Christ," she said. She closed her eyes and leaned
forward, elbows on the desk, and her head against her hands, the
thick, curly brown hair spilling forward to hide her face. Brianna
laid a hand on Claire's back, face troubled as she bent over her
mother. She was a tall girl, with large, fine bones, and her long red
hair glowed in the warm light of the desk lamp.

"If he didn't die . . ." she began tentatively.

Claire's head snapped up. "But he *is* dead!" she said. Her face
was strained, and small lines were visible around her eyes. "For
God's sake, it's two hundred years; whether he died at Culloden or
not, he's dead now!"

Brianna stepped back from her mother's vehemence, and lowered her head, so the red hair—her father's red hair—swung down
beside her cheek.

"I guess so," she whispered. Roger could see she was fighting
back tears. And no wonder, he thought. To find out in short order
that first, the man you had loved and called "Father" all your life
really *wasn't* your father, secondly, that your real father was a
Highland Scot who had lived two hundred years ago, and thirdly,

to realize that he had likely perished in some horrid fashion, unthinkably far from the wife and child he had sacrificed himself to save . . . enough to rattle one, Roger thought.

He crossed to Brianna and touched her arm. She gave him a brief, distracted glance, and tried to smile. He put his arms around her, even in his pity for her distress thinking how marvelous she felt, all warm and soft and springy at once.

Claire still sat at the desk, motionless. The yellow hawk's eyes had gone a softer color now, remote with memory. They rested sightlessly on the east wall of the study, still covered from floor to ceiling with the notes and memorabilia left by the Reverend Wakefield, Roger's late adoptive father.

Looking at the wall himself, Roger saw the annual meeting notice sent by the Society of the White Rose—those enthusiastic, eccentric souls who still championed the cause of Scottish independence, meeting in nostalgic tribute to Charles Stuart, and the Highland heroes who had followed him.

Roger cleared his throat slightly.

"Er . . . if Jamie Fraser didn't die at Culloden . . ." he said.

"Then he likely died soon afterward." Claire's eyes met Roger's, straight on, the cool look back in the yellow-brown depths. "You have no idea how it was," she said. "There was a famine in the Highlands—none of the men had eaten for days before the battle. He was wounded—we know that. Even if he escaped, there would have been . . . no one to care for him." Her voice caught slightly at that; she was a doctor now, had been a healer even then, twenty years before, when she had stepped through a circle of standing stones, and met destiny with James Alexander Malcolm MacKenzie Fraser.

Roger was conscious of them both; the tall, shaking girl he held in his arms, and the woman at the desk, so still, so poised. She had traveled through the stones, through time; been suspected as a spy, arrested as a witch, snatched by an unimaginable quirk of circumstance from the arms of her first husband, Frank Randall. And three years later, her second husband, James Fraser, had sent her back through the stones, pregnant, in a desperate effort to save her and the unborn child from the onrushing disaster that would soon engulf him.

Surely, he thought to himself, she's been through enough? But Roger was a historian. He had a scholar's insatiable, amoral curiosity, too powerful to be constrained by simple compassion. More than that, he was oddly conscious of the third figure in the family tragedy in which he found himself involved—Jamie Fraser.

"If he didn't die at Culloden," he began again, more firmly, "then perhaps I can find out what did happen to him. Do you want me to try?" He waited, breathless, feeling Brianna's warm breath through his shirt.

Jamie Fraser had had a life, and a death. Roger felt obscurely that it was his duty to find out all the truth; that Jamie Fraser's women deserved to know all they could of him. For Brianna, such knowledge was all she would ever have of the father she had never known. And for Claire—behind the question he had asked was the thought that had plainly not yet struck her, stunned with shock as she was: she had crossed the barrier of time twice before. She could, just possibly, do it again. And if Jamie Fraser had not died at Culloden . . .

He saw awareness flicker in the clouded amber of her eyes, as the thought came to her. She was normally pale; now her face blanched white as the ivory handle of the letter opener before her on the desk. Her fingers closed around it, clenching so the knuckles stood out in knobs of bone.

She didn't speak for a long time. Her gaze fixed on Brianna and lingered there for a moment, then returned to Roger's face.

"Yes," she said, in a whisper so soft he could barely hear her. "Yes. Find out for me. Please. Find out."

3

Frank and Full Disclosure

Inverness
May 9, 1968

The foot traffic was heavy on the bridge over the River
Ness, with folk streaming home to their teas. Roger moved
in front of me, his wide shoulders protecting me from the
buffets of the crowd around us.

I could feel my heart beating heavily against the stiff cover of
the book I was clutching to my chest. It did that whenever I paused
to think what we were truly doing. I wasn't sure which of the two
possible alternatives was worse; to find that Jamie had died at
Culloden, or to find that he hadn't.

The boards of the bridge echoed hollowly underfoot, as we
trudged back toward the manse. My arms ached from the weight
of the books I carried, and I shifted the load from one side to the
other.

"Watch your bloody wheel, man!" Roger shouted, nudging me
adroitly to the side, as a workingman on a bicycle plowed head-
downward through the bridge traffic, nearly running me against
the railing.

"Sorry!" came back the apologetic shout, and the rider gave a
wave of the hand over his shoulder, as the bike wove its way
between two groups of schoolchildren, coming home for their
teas. I glanced back across the bridge, in case Brianna should be
visible behind us, but there was no sign of her.

Roger and I had spent the afternoon at the Society for the
Preservation of Antiquities. Brianna had gone down to the Highland Clans office, there to collect photocopies of a list of documents Roger had compiled.

"It's very kind of you to take all this trouble, Roger," I said, raising my voice to be heard above the echoing bridge and the river's rush.

"It's all right," he said, a little awkwardly, pausing for me to catch him up. "I'm curious," he added, smiling a little. "You know historians—can't leave a puzzle alone." He shook his head, trying to brush the windblown dark hair out of his eyes without using his hands.

I did know historians. I'd lived with one for twenty years. Frank hadn't wanted to leave this particular puzzle alone, either. But neither had he been willing to solve it. Frank had been dead for two years, though, and now it was my turn—mine and Brianna's.

"Have you heard yet from Dr. Linklater?" I asked, as we came down the arch of the bridge. Late in the afternoon as it was, the sun was still high, so far north as we were. Caught among the leaves of the lime trees on the riverbank, it glowed pink on the granite cenotaph that stood below the bridge.

Roger shook his head, squinting against the wind. "No, but it's been only a week since I wrote. If I don't hear by the Monday, I'll try telephoning. Don't worry"—he smiled sideways at me—"I was very circumspect. I just told him that for purposes of a study I was making, I needed a list—if one existed—of the Jacobite officers who were in Leanach farmhouse after Culloden, and if any information exists as to the survivor of that execution, could he refer me to the original sources?"

"Do you know Linklater?" I asked, easing my left arm by tilting the books sideways against my hip.

"No, but I wrote my request on the Balliol College letterhead, and made tactful reference to Mr. Cheesewright, my old tutor, who *does* know Linklater." Roger winked reassuringly, and I laughed.

His eyes were a brilliant, lucent green, bright against his olive skin. Curiosity might be his stated reason for helping us to find out Jamie's history, but I was well aware that his interest went a good bit deeper—in the direction of Brianna. I also knew that the interest was returned. What I didn't know was whether Roger realized that as well.

Back in the late Reverend Wakefield's study, I dropped my armload of books on the table in relief, and collapsed into the wing chair by the hearth, while Roger went to fetch a glass of lemonade from the manse's kitchen.

My breathing slowed as I sipped the tart sweetness, but my pulse stayed erratic, as I looked over the imposing stack of books we had brought back. Was Jamie in there somewhere? And if he was . . . my hands grew wet on the cold glass, and I choked the thought off. Don't look too far ahead, I cautioned myself. Much better to wait, and see what we might find.

Roger was scanning the shelves in the study, in search of other possibilities. The Reverend Wakefield, Roger's late adoptive father, had been both a good amateur historian, and a terrible pack rat; letters, journals, pamphlets and broadsheets, antique and contemporary volumes—all were crammed cheek by jowl together on the shelves.

Roger hesitated, then his hand fell on a stack of books sitting on the nearby table. They were Frank's books—an impressive achievement, so far as I could tell by reading the encomiums printed on the dust jackets.

"Have you ever read this?" he asked, picking up the volume entitled *The Jacobites*.

"No," I said. I took a restorative gulp of lemonade, and coughed. "No," I said again. "I couldn't." After my return, I had resolutely refused to look at any material dealing with Scotland's past, even though the eighteenth century had been one of Frank's areas of specialty. Knowing Jamie dead, and faced with the necessity of living without him, I avoided anything that might bring him to mind. A useless avoidance—there was no way of keeping him out of my mind, with Brianna's existence a daily reminder of him —but still, I could not read books about the Bonnie Prince—that terrible, futile young man—or his followers.

"I see. I just thought you might know whether there might be something useful in here." Roger paused, the flush deepening over his cheekbones. "Did—er, did your husband—Frank, I mean," he added hastily. "Did you tell him . . . um . . . about . . . ?" His voice trailed off, choked with embarrassment.

"Well, of course I did!" I said, a little sharply. "What did you think—I'd just stroll back into his office after being gone for three years and say, 'Oh, hullo there, darling, and what would you like for supper tonight?' "

"No, of course not," Roger muttered. He turned away, eyes fixed on the bookshelves. The back of his neck was deep red with embarrassment.

"I'm sorry," I said, taking a deep breath. "It's a fair question to ask. It's only that it's—a bit raw, yet." A good deal more than a bit. I was both surprised and appalled to find just how raw the wound still was. I set the glass down on the table at my elbow. If we were going on with this, I was going to need something stronger than lemonade.

"Yes," I said. "I told him. All about the stones—about Jamie. Everything."

Roger didn't reply for a moment. Then he turned, halfway, so that only the strong, sharp lines of his profile were visible. He didn't look at me, but down at the stack of Frank's books, at the back-cover photo of Frank, leanly dark and handsome, smiling for posterity.

"Did he believe you?" Roger asked quietly.

My lips felt sticky from the lemonade, and I licked them before answering.

"No," I said. "Not at first. He thought I was mad; even had me vetted by a psychiatrist." I laughed, shortly, but the memory made me clench my fists with remembered fury.

"Later, then?" Roger turned to face me. The flush had faded from his skin, leaving only an echo of curiosity in his eyes. "What did he think?"

I took a deep breath and closed my eyes. "I don't know."

The tiny hospital in Inverness smelled unfamiliar, like carbolic disinfectant and starch.

I couldn't think, and tried not to feel. The return was much more terrifying than my venture into the past had been, for there, I had been shrouded by a protective layer of doubt and disbelief about where I was and what was happening, and had lived in constant hope of escape. Now I knew only too well where I was, and I knew that there was no escape. Jamie was dead.

The doctors and nurses tried to speak kindly to me, to feed me and bring me things to drink, but there was no room in me for anything but grief and terror. I had told them my name when they asked, but wouldn't speak further.

I lay in the clean white bed, fingers clamped tight together over my vulnerable belly, and kept my eyes shut. I visualized

*over and over the last things I had seen before I stepped
through the stones—the rainy moor and Jamie's face—knowing that if I looked too long at my new surroundings, these
sights would fade, replaced by mundane things like the
nurses and the vase of flowers by my bed. I pressed one
thumb secretly against the base of the other, taking an obscure comfort in the tiny wound there, a small cut in the
shape of a* J. *Jamie had made it, at my demand—the last of
his touch on my flesh.*

*I must have stayed that way for some time; I slept some-
times, dreaming of the last few days of the Jacobite Rising—I
saw again the dead man in the wood, asleep beneath a coverlet of bright blue fungus, and Dougal MacKenzie dying on the
floor of an attic in Culloden House; the ragged men of the
Highland army, asleep in the muddy ditches; their last sleep
before the slaughter.*

*I would wake screaming or moaning, to the scent of disin-
fectant and the sound of soothing words, incomprehensible
against the echoes of Gaelic shouting in my dreams, and fall
asleep again, my hurt clutched tight in the palm of my hand.*

*And then I opened my eyes and Frank was there. He stood
in the door, smoothing back his dark hair with one hand,
looking uncertain—and no wonder, poor man.*

*I lay back on the pillows, just watching him, not speaking.
He had the look of his ancestors, Jack and Alex Randall; fine,
clear, aristocratic features and a well-shaped head, under a
spill of straight dark hair. His face had some indefinable
difference from theirs, though, beyond the small differences of
feature. There was no mark of fear or ruthlessness on him;
neither the spirituality of Alex nor the icy arrogance of Jack.
His lean face looked intelligent, kind, and slightly tired, unshaven and with smudges beneath his eyes. I knew without
being told that he had driven all night to get here.*

*"Claire?" He came over to the bed, and spoke tentatively,
as though not sure that I really was Claire.*

*I wasn't sure either, but I nodded and said, "Hullo,
Frank." My voice was scratchy and rough, unaccustomed to
speech.*

He took one of my hands, and I let him have it.

"Are you . . . all right?" he said, after a minute. He was frowning slightly as he looked at me.

"I'm pregnant." That seemed the important point, to my disordered mind. I had not thought of what I would say to Frank, if I ever saw him again, but the moment I saw him standing in the door, it seemed to come clear in my mind. I would tell him I was pregnant, he would leave, and I would be alone with my last sight of Jamie's face, and the burning touch of him on my hand.

His face tightened a bit, but he didn't let go of my other hand. *"I know. They told me."* He took a deep breath and let it out. *"Claire—can you tell me what happened to you?"*

I felt quite blank for a moment, but then shrugged.

"I suppose so," I said. I mustered my thoughts wearily; I didn't want to be talking about it, but I had some feeling of obligation to this man. Not guilt, not yet; but obligation nonetheless. I had been married to him.

"Well," I said, *"I fell in love with someone else, and I married him. I'm sorry,"* I added, in response to the look of shock that crossed his face, *"I couldn't help it."*

He hadn't been expecting that. His mouth opened and closed for a bit and he gripped my hand, hard enough to make me wince and jerk it out of his grasp.

"What do you mean?" he said, his voice sharp. *"Where have you been, Claire?"* He stood up suddenly, looming over the bed.

"Do you remember that when I last saw you, I was going up to the stone circle on Craigh na Dun?"

"Yes?" He was staring down at me with an expression somewhere between anger and suspicion.

"Well"—I licked my lips, which had gone quite dry—*"the fact is, I walked through a cleft stone in that circle, and ended up in 1743."*

"Don't be facetious, Claire!"

"You think I'm being funny?" The thought was so absurd that I actually began to laugh, though I felt a good long way from real humor.

"Stop that!"

I quit laughing. Two nurses appeared at the door as though

*by magic; they must have been lurking in the hall nearby.
Frank leaned over and grabbed my arm.*

*"Listen to me," he said through his teeth. "You are going
to tell me where you've been and what you've been doing!"*

*"I am telling you! Let go!" I sat up in bed and yanked at
my arm, pulling it out of his grasp. "I told you; I walked
through a stone and ended up two hundred years ago. And I
met your bloody ancestor, Jack Randall, there!"*

Frank blinked, entirely taken aback. "Who?"

*"Black Jack Randall, and a bloody, filthy, nasty pervert he
was, too!"*

*Frank's mouth hung open, and so did the nurses'. I could
hear feet coming down the corridor behind them, and hurried
voices.*

*"I had to marry Jamie Fraser to get away from Jack Ran-
dall, but then—Jamie—I couldn't help it, Frank, I loved him
and I would have stayed with him if I could, but he sent me
back because of Culloden, and the baby, and—" I broke off,
as a man in a doctor's uniform pushed past the nurses by the
door.*

*"Frank," I said tiredly, "I'm sorry. I didn't mean it to
happen, and I tried all I could to come back—really, I did—
but I couldn't. And now it's too late."*

*Despite myself, tears began to well up in my eyes and roll
down my cheeks. Mostly for Jamie, and myself, and the child I
carried, but a few for Frank as well. I sniffed hard and swallowed, trying to stop, and pushed myself upright in the bed.*

*"Look," I said, "I know you won't want to have anything
more to do with me, and I don't blame you at all. Just—just
go away, will you?"*

*His face had changed. He didn't look angry anymore, but
distressed, and slightly puzzled. He sat down by the bed,
ignoring the doctor who had come in and was groping for my
pulse.*

*"I'm not going anywhere," he said, quite gently. He took
my hand again, though I tried to pull it away. "This—Jamie.
Who was he?"*

*I took a deep, ragged breath. The doctor had hold of my
other hand, still trying to take my pulse, and I felt absurdly*

panicked, as though I were being held captive between them. I fought down the feeling, though, and tried to speak steadily.

"James Alexander Malcolm MacKenzie Fraser," I said, spacing the words, formally, the way Jamie had spoken them to me when he first told me his full name—on the day of our wedding. The thought made another tear overflow, and I blotted it against my shoulder, my hands being restrained.

"He was a Highlander. He was k-killed at Culloden." It was no use, I was weeping again, the tears no anodyne to the grief that ripped through me, but the only response I had to unendurable pain. I bent forward slightly, trying to encapsulate it, wrapping myself around the tiny, imperceptible life in my belly, the only remnant left to me of Jamie Fraser.

Frank and the doctor exchanged a glance of which I was only half-conscious. Of course, to them, Culloden was part of the distant past. To me, it had happened only two days before.

"Perhaps we should let Mrs. Randall rest for a bit," the doctor suggested. "She seems a wee bit upset just now."

Frank looked uncertainly from the doctor to me. "Well, she certainly does seem upset. But I really want to find out . . . what's this, Claire?" Stroking my hand, he had encountered the silver ring on my fourth finger, and now bent to examine it. It was the ring Jamie had given me for our marriage; a wide silver band in the Highland interlace pattern, the links engraved with tiny, stylized thistle blooms.

"No!" I exclaimed, panicked, as Frank tried to twist it off my finger. I jerked my hand away and cradled it, fisted, beneath my bosom, cupped in my left hand, which still wore Frank's gold wedding band. "No, you can't take it, I won't let you! That's my wedding ring!"

"Now, see here, Claire—" Frank's words were interrupted by the doctor, who had crossed to Frank's side of the bed, and was now bending down to murmur in his ear. I caught a few words—"not trouble your wife just now. The shock"— and then Frank was on his feet once more, being firmly urged away by the doctor, who gave a nod to one of the nurses in passing.

I barely felt the sting of the hypodermic needle, too engulfed in the fresh wave of grief to take notice of anything. I dimly heard Frank's parting words, "All right—but Claire, I

will know!" And then the blessed darkness came down, and I
slept without dreaming, for a long, long time.

———————

Roger tilted the decanter, bringing the level of the spirit in the glass up to the halfway point. He handed it to Claire with a half-smile.

"Fiona's grannie always said whisky is good for what ails ye."

"I've seen worse remedies." Claire took the glass and gave him back the half-smile in exchange.

Roger poured out a drink for himself, then sat down beside her, sipping quietly.

"I tried to send him away, you know," she said suddenly, lowering her glass. "Frank. I told him I knew he couldn't feel the same for me, no matter what he believed had happened. I said I would give him a divorce; he must go away and forget about me—take up the life he'd begun building without me."

"He wouldn't do it, though," Roger said. It was growing chilly in the study as the sun went down, and he bent and switched on the ancient electric fire. "Because you were pregnant?" he guessed.

She shot him a sudden sharp look, then smiled, a little wryly.

"Yes, that was it. He said no one but a cad would dream of abandoning a pregnant woman with virtually no resources. Particularly one whose grip on reality seemed a trifle tenuous," she added ironically. "I wasn't quite without resources—I had a bit of money from my uncle Lamb—but Frank wasn't a cad, either." Her glance shifted to the bookshelves. Her husband's historical works stood there, side by side, spines gleaming in the light of the desklamp.

"He was a very decent man," she said softly. She took another sip of her drink, closing her eyes as the alcoholic fumes rose up.

"And then—he knew, or suspected, that he couldn't have children himself. Rather a blow, for a man so involved in history and genealogies. All those dynastic considerations, you see."

"Yes, I can see that," Roger said slowly. "But wouldn't he feel —I mean, another man's child?"

"He might have." The amber eyes were looking at him again, their clearness slightly softened by whisky and reminiscence. "But as it was, since he didn't—*couldn't*—believe anything I said about Jamie, the baby's father was essentially unknown. If he didn't know who the man was—and convinced himself that I didn't really know either, but had just made up these delusions out of traumatic shock—well, then, there was no one ever to say that the child *wasn't* his. Certainly not me," she added, with just a tinge of bitterness.

She took a large swallow of whisky that made her eyes water slightly, and took a moment to wipe them.

"But to make sure, he took me clean away. To Boston," she went on. "He'd been offered a good position at Harvard, and no one knew us there. That's where Brianna was born."

———————————

The fretful crying jarred me awake yet again. I had gone back to bed at 6:30, after getting up five times during the night with the baby. A bleary-eyed look at the clock showed the time now as 7:00. A cheerful singing came from the bathroom, Frank's voice raised in "Rule, Britannia," over the noise of rushing water.

I lay in bed, heavy-limbed with exhaustion, wondering whether I had the strength to endure the crying until Frank got out of the shower and could bring Brianna to me. As though the baby knew what I was thinking, the crying rose two or three tones and escalated to a sort of periodic shriek, punctuated by frightening gulps for air. I flung back the covers and was on my feet, propelled by the same sort of panic with which I had greeted air raids during the War.

I lumbered down the chilly hall and into the nursery, to find Brianna, aged three months, lying on her back, yelling her small red head off. I was so groggy from lack of sleep that it took a moment for me to realize that I had left her on her stomach.

"Darling! You turned over! All by yourself!" Terrorized by her audacious act, Brianna waved her little pink fists and squalled louder, eyes squeezed shut.

I snatched her up, patting her back and murmuring to the top of her red-fuzzed head.

"Oh, you precious darling! What a clever girl you are!"

"What's that? What's happened?" Frank emerged from the bathroom, toweling his head, a second towel wrapped about his loins. "Is something the matter with Brianna?"

He came toward us, looking worried. As the birth grew closer, we had both been edgy; Frank irritable and myself terrified, having no idea what might happen between us, with the appearance of Jamie Fraser's child. But when the nurse had taken Brianna from her bassinet and handed her to Frank, with the words "Here's Daddy's little girl," his face had grown blank, and then—looking down at the tiny face, perfect as a rosebud—gone soft with wonder. Within a week, he had been hers, body and soul.

I turned to him, smiling. "She turned over! All by herself!"

"Really?" His scrubbed face beamed with delight. "Isn't it early for her to do that?"

"Yes, it is. Dr. Spock says she oughtn't to be able to do it for another month, at least!"

"Well, what does Dr. Spock know? Come here, little beauty; give Daddy a kiss for being so precocious." He lifted the soft little body, encased in its snug pink sleep-suit, and kissed her button of a nose. Brianna sneezed, and we both laughed.

I stopped then, suddenly aware that it was the first time I had laughed in nearly a year. Still more, that it was the first time I had laughed with Frank.

He realized it too; his eyes met mine over the top of Brianna's head. They were a soft hazel, and at the moment, filled with tenderness. I smiled at him, a little tremulous, and suddenly very much aware that he was all but naked, with water droplets sliding down his lean shoulders and shining on the smooth brown skin of his chest.

The smell of burning reached us simultaneously, jarring us from this scene of domestic bliss.

"The coffee!" Thrusting Bree unceremoniously into my arms, Frank bolted for the kitchen, leaving both towels in a heap at my feet. Smiling at the sight of his bare buttocks, gleaming an incongruous white as he sprinted into the kitchen, I followed him more slowly, holding Bree against my shoulder.

He was standing at the sink, naked, amid a cloud of malodorous steam rising from the scorched coffeepot.

"Tea, maybe?" I asked, adroitly anchoring Brianna on my

hip with one arm while I rummaged in the cupboard. "None of the orange pekoe leaf left, I'm afraid; just Lipton's teabags."

Frank made a face; an Englishman to the bone, he would rather lap water out of the toilet than drink tea made from teabags. The Lipton's had been left by Mrs. Grossman, the weekly cleaning woman, who thought tea made from loose leaves messy and disgusting.

"No, I'll get a cup of coffee on my way to the university. Oh, speaking of which, you recall that we're having the Dean and his wife to dinner tonight? Mrs. Hinchcliffe is bringing a present for Brianna."

"Oh, right," I said, without enthusiasm. I had met the Hinchcliffes before, and wasn't all that keen to repeat the experience. Still, the effort had to be made. With a mental sigh, I shifted the baby to the other side and groped in the drawer for a pencil to make a grocery list.

Brianna burrowed into the front of my red chenille dressing gown, making small voracious grunting noises.

"You can't be hungry again," I said to the top of her head. "I fed you not two hours ago." My breasts were beginning to leak in response to her rooting, though, and I was already sitting down and loosening the front of my gown.

"Mrs. Hinchcliffe said that a baby shouldn't be fed every time it cries," Frank observed. "They get spoilt if they aren't kept to a schedule."

It wasn't the first time I had heard Mrs. Hinchcliffe's opinions on child-rearing.

"Then she'll be spoilt, won't she?" I said coldly, not looking at him. The small pink mouth clamped down fiercely, and Brianna began to suck with mindless appetite. I was aware that Mrs. Hinchcliffe also thought breast-feeding both vulgar and insanitary. I, who had seen any number of eighteenth-century babies nursing contentedly at their mothers' breasts, didn't.

Frank sighed, but didn't say anything further. After a moment, he put down the pot holder and sidled toward the door.

"Well," he said awkwardly. "I'll see you around six then, shall I? Ought I to bring home anything—save you going out?"

I gave him a brief smile, and said, "No, I'll manage."

"Oh, good." He hesitated a moment, as I settled Bree more comfortably on my lap, head resting on the crook of my arm, the round of her head echoing the curve of my breast. I looked up from the baby, and found him watching me intently, eyes fixed on the swell of my half-exposed bosom.

My own eyes flicked downward over his body. I saw the beginnings of his arousal, and bent my head over the baby, to hide my flushing face.

"Goodbye," I muttered, to the top of her head.

He stood still a moment, then leaned forward and kissed me briefly on the cheek, the warmth of his bare body unsettlingly near.

"Goodbye, Claire," he said softly. *"I'll see you tonight."*

He didn't come into the kitchen again before leaving, so I had a chance to finish feeding Brianna and bring my own feelings into some semblance of normality.

I hadn't seen Frank naked since my return; he had always dressed in bathroom or closet. Neither had he tried to kiss me before this morning's cautious peck. The pregnancy had been what the obstetrician called "high-risk," and there had been no question of Frank's sharing my bed, even had I been so disposed—which I wasn't.

I should have seen this coming, but I hadn't. Absorbed first in sheer misery, and then in the physical torpor of oncoming motherhood, I had pushed away all considerations beyond my bulging belly. After Brianna's birth, I had lived from feeding to feeding, seeking small moments of mindless peace, when I could hold her oblivious body close and find relief from thought and memory in the pure sensual pleasure of touching and holding her.

Frank, too, cuddled the baby and played with her, falling asleep in his big chair with her stretched out atop his lanky form, rosy cheek pressed flat against his chest, as they snored together in peaceful companionship. He and I did not touch each other, though, nor did we truly talk about anything beyond our basic domestic arrangements—except Brianna.

The baby was our shared focus; a point through which we could at once reach each other, and keep each other at arm's

length. It looked as though arm's length was no longer close
enough for Frank.

I could do it—physically, at least. I had seen the doctor for
a checkup the week before, and he had—with an avuncular
wink and a pat on the bottom—assured me that I could resume "relations" with my husband at any time.

I knew Frank hadn't been celibate since my disappearance.
In his late forties, he was still lean and muscular, dark and
sleek, a very handsome man. Women clustered about him at
cocktail parties like bees round a honeypot, emitting small
hums of sexual excitement.

There had been one girl with brown hair whom I had
noticed particularly at the departmental party; she stood in
the corner and stared at Frank mournfully over her drink.
Later she became tearfully and incoherently drunk, and was
escorted home by two female friends, who took turns casting
evil looks at Frank and at me, standing by his side, silently
bulging in my flowered maternity dress.

He'd been discreet, though. He was always home at night,
and took pains not to have lipstick on his collar. So, now he
meant to come home all the way. I supposed he had some
right to expect it; was that not a wifely duty, and I once more
his wife?

There was only one small problem. It wasn't Frank I
reached for, deep in the night, waking out of sleep. It wasn't
his smooth, lithe body that walked my dreams and roused me,
so that I came awake moist and gasping, my heart pounding
from the half-remembered touch. But I would never touch that
man again.

"Jamie," I whispered, "Oh, Jamie." My tears sparkled in
the morning light, adorning Brianna's soft red fuzz like scattered pearls and diamonds.

It wasn't a good day. Brianna had a bad diaper rash,
which made her cross and irritable, needing to be picked up
every few minutes. She nursed and fussed alternately, pausing to spit up at intervals, making clammy wet patches on
whatever I wore. I changed my blouse three times before
eleven o'clock.

The heavy nursing bra I wore chafed under the arms, and

my nipples felt cold and chapped. Midway through my laborious tidying-up of the house, there was a whooshing clank from under the floorboards, and the hot-air registers died with a feeble sigh.

"No, next week won't do," I said over the telephone to the furnace-repair shop. I looked at the window, where the cold February fog was threatening to seep under the sill and engulf us. "It's forty-two degrees in here, and I have a three-month-old baby!" The baby in question was sitting in her baby seat, swaddled in all her blankets, squalling like a scalded cat. Ignoring the quacking of the person on the other end, I held the receiver next to Brianna's wide open mouth for several seconds.

"See?" I demanded, lifting the phone to my ear again.

"Awright, lady," said a resigned voice on the other end of the line. "I'll come out this afternoon, sometime between noon and six."

"Noon and six? Can't you narrow it down a little more than that? I have to get out to the market," I protested.

"You ain't the only dead furnace in town, lady," the voice said with finality, and hung up. I glanced at the clock; eleven-thirty. I'd never be able to get the marketing done and get back in half an hour. Marketing with a small baby was more like a ninety-minute expedition into Darkest Borneo, requiring massive amounts of equipment and tremendous expenditures of energy.

Gritting my teeth, I called the expensive market that delivered, ordered the necessities for dinner, and picked up the baby, who was by now the shade of an eggplant, and markedly smelly.

"That looks ouchy, darling. You'll feel much better if we get it off, won't you?" I said, trying to talk soothingly as I wiped the brownish slime off Brianna's bright-red bottom. She arched her back, trying to escape the clammy washcloth, and shrieked some more. A layer of Vaseline and the tenth clean diaper of the day; the diaper service truck wasn't due 'til tomorrow, and the house reeked of ammonia.

"All right, sweetheart, there, there." I hoisted her up on my shoulder, patting her, but the screeching went on and on. Not that I could blame her; her poor bottom was nearly raw.

Ideally, she should be let to lie about on a towel with nothing on, but with no heat in the house, that wasn't feasible. She and I were both wearing sweaters and heavy winter coats, which made the frequent feedings even more of a nuisance than usual; excavating a breast could take several minutes, while the baby screamed.

Brianna couldn't sleep for more than ten minutes at a time. Consequently, neither could I. When we did drift off together at four o'clock, we were roused within a quarter of an hour by the crashing arrival of the furnace man, who pounded on the door, not bothering to set down the large wrench he was holding.

Jiggling the baby against my shoulder with one hand, I began cooking the dinner with the other, to the accompaniment of screeches in my ear and the sounds of violence from the cellar below.

"I ain't promising nothin', lady, but you got heat for now." The furnace man appeared abruptly, wiping a smear of grease from his creased forehead. He leaned forward to inspect Brianna, who was lying more or less peacefully across my shoulder, loudly sucking her thumb.

"How's that thumb taste, sweetie?" he inquired. "They say you shouldn't oughta let 'em suck their thumbs, you know," he informed me, straightening up. "Gives 'em crooked teeth and they'll need braces."

"Is that so?" I said through my own teeth. "How much do I owe you?"

Half an hour later, the chicken lay in its pan, stuffed and basted, surrounded by crushed garlic, sprigs of rosemary, and curls of lemon peel. A quick squeeze of lemon juice over the buttery skin, and I could stick it in the oven and get myself and Brianna dressed. The kitchen looked like the result of an incompetent burglary, with cupboards hanging open and cooking paraphernalia strewn on every horizontal surface. I banged shut a couple of cupboard doors, and then the kitchen door itself, trusting that that would keep Mrs. Hinchcliffe out, even if good manners wouldn't.

Frank had brought a new pink dress for Brianna to wear. It was a beautiful thing, but I eyed the layers of lace around the neck dubiously. They looked not only scratchy, but delicate.

"Well, we'll give it a try," I told her. *"Daddy will like you to look pretty. Let's try not to spit up in it, hm?"*

Brianna responded by shutting her eyes, stiffening, and grunting as she extruded more slime.

"Oh, well done!" I said, sincerely. It meant changing the crib sheet, but at least it wouldn't make the diaper rash worse. The mess attended to and a fresh diaper in place, I shook out the pink dress, and paused to carefully wipe the snot and drool from her face before popping the garment over her head. She blinked at me and gurgled enticingly, windmilling her fists.

I obligingly lowered my head and went *"Pfffft!"* into her navel, which made her squirm and gurgle with joy. We did it a few more times, then began the painstaking job of getting into the pink dress.

Brianna didn't like it; she started to complain as I put it over her head, and as I crammed her chubby little arms into the puffed sleeves, put back her head and let out a piercing cry.

"What is it?" I demanded, startled. I knew all her cries by now and mostly, what she meant by them, but this was a new one, full of fright and pain. *"What's the matter, darling?"*

She was screaming furiously now, tears rolling down her face. I turned her frantically over and patted her back, thinking she might have had a sudden attack of colic, but she wasn't doubled up. She was struggling violently, though, and as I turned her back over to pick her up, I saw the long red line running up the tender inside of her waving arm. A pin had been left in the dress, and had scored her flesh as I forced the sleeve up her arm.

"Oh, baby! Oh, I'm so sorry! Mummy's so sorry!" Tears were running down my own face as I eased the stabbing pin free and removed it. I clutched her to my shoulder, patting and soothing, trying to calm my own feelings of panicked guilt. Of course I hadn't meant to hurt her, but she wouldn't know that.

"Oh, darling," I murmured. *"It's all right now. Yes, Mummy loves you, it's all right."* Why hadn't I thought to check for pins? For that matter, what sort of maniac would package a baby's clothes using straight pins? Torn between

fury and distress, I eased Brianna into the dress, wiped her chin, and carried her into the bedroom, where I laid her on my twin bed while I hastily changed to a decent skirt and a fresh blouse.

The doorbell rang as I was pulling on my stockings. There was a hole in one heel, but no time to do anything about it now. I stuck my feet into the pinching alligator pumps, snatched up Brianna, and went to answer the door.

It was Frank, too laden with packages to use his key. One-handed, I took most of them from him and parked them on the hall table.

"Dinner all ready, dear? I've brought a new tablecloth and napkins—thought ours were a bit shabby. And the wine, of course." He lifted the bottle in his hand, smiling, then leaned forward to peer at me, and stopped smiling. He looked disapprovingly from my disheveled hair to my blouse, freshly stained with spit-up milk.

"Christ, Claire," he said. "Couldn't you fix yourself up a bit? I mean, it's not as though you have anything else to do, at home all day—couldn't you take a few minutes for a—"

"No," I said, quite loudly. I pushed Brianna, who was wailing again with fretful exhaustion, into his arms.

"No," I said again, and took the wine bottle from his unresisting hand.

"NO!" I shrieked, stamping my foot. I swung the bottle widely, and he dodged, but it was the doorjamb I struck, and purplish splatters of Beaujolais flew across the stoop, leaving glass shards glittering in the light from the entryway.

I flung the shattered bottle into the azaleas and ran coat-less down the walk and into the freezing fog. At the foot of the walk, I passed the startled Hinchcliffes, who were arriving half an hour early, presumably in hopes of catching me in some domestic deficiency. I hoped they'd enjoy their dinner.

I drove aimlessly through the fog, the car's heater blasting on my feet, until I began to get low on gas. I wasn't going home; not yet. An all-night cafe? Then I realized that it was Friday night, and getting on for twelve o'clock. I had a place to go, after all. I turned back toward the suburb where we lived, and the Church of St. Finbar.

At this hour, the chapel was locked to prevent vandalism and burglary. For the late adorers, there was a push-button lock set just below the door handle. Five buttons, numbered one to five. By pushing three of them, in the proper combination, the latch could be sprung to allow lawful entry.

I moved quietly along the back of the chapel, to the log-book that sat at the feet of St. Finbar, to record my arrival.

"St. Finbar?" Frank had said incredulously. "There isn't such a saint. There can't possibly be."

"There is," I said, with a trace of smugness. "An Irish bishop, from the twelfth century."

"Oh, Irish," said Frank dismissively. "That explains it. But what I can't understand," he said, careful to be tactful, "is, er, well . . . why?"

"Why what?"

"Why go in for this Perpetual Adoration business? You've never been the least devout, no more than I have. And you don't go to Mass or anything; Father Beggs asks me every week where you are."

I shook my head. "I can't really say, Frank. It's just something . . . I need to do." I looked at him, helpless to explain adequately. "It's . : . peaceful there," I said, finally.

He opened his mouth as though to speak further, then turned away, shaking his head.

It was *peaceful. The car park at the church was deserted, save for the single car of the adorer on duty at this hour, gleaming an anonymous black under the arc lights. Inside, I signed my name to the log and walked forward, coughing tactfully to alert the eleven o'clock adorer to my presence without the rudeness of direct speech. I knelt behind him, a heavyset man in a yellow windcheater. After a moment, he rose, genuflected before the altar, turned and walked to the door, nodding briefly as he passed me.*

The door hissed shut and I was alone, save for the Sacrament displayed on the altar, in the great golden sunburst of the monstrance. There were two candles on the altar, big ones. Smooth and white, they burned steadily in the still air, without a flicker. I closed my eyes for a moment, just listening to the silence.

Everything that had happened during the day whirled

through my mind in a disjointed welter of thoughts and feelings. Coatless, I was shaking with cold from the short walk through the parking lot, but slowly I grew warm again, and my clenched hands relaxed in my lap.

At last, as usually happened here, I ceased to think. Whether it was the stoppage of time in the presence of eternity, or only the overtaking of a bone-deep fatigue, I didn't know. But the guilt over Frank eased, the wrenching grief for Jamie lessened, and even the constant tug of motherhood upon my emotions receded to the level of background noise, no louder than the slow beating of my own heart, regular and comforting in the dark peace of the chapel.

"O Lord," I whispered, "I commend to Your mercy the soul of Your servant James." And mine, I added silently. And mine.

I sat there without moving, watching the flickering glow of the candle flames in the gold surface of the monstrance, until the soft footsteps of the next adorer came down the aisle behind me, ending in the heavy creak of genuflection. They came once each hour, day and night. The Blessed Sacrament was never left alone.

I stayed for a few minutes more, then slid out of the pew, with my own nod toward the altar. As I walked toward the back of the chapel, I saw a figure in the back row, under the shadow of the statue of St. Anthony. It stirred as I approached, then the man rose to his feet and made his way to the aisle to meet me.

"What are you doing here?" I whispered.

Frank nodded toward the form of the new adorer, already kneeling in contemplation, and took my elbow to guide me out.

I waited until the chapel door had closed behind us before pulling away and whirling to confront him.

"What is this?" I said angrily. "Why did you come after me?"

"I was worried about you." He gestured toward the empty car park, where his large Buick nestled protectively next to my small Ford. "It's dangerous, a lone woman walking about in the very late night in this part of town. I came to see you home. That's all."

He didn't mention the Hinchcliffes, or the dinner party. My annoyance ebbed a bit.

"Oh," I said. "What did you do with Brianna?"

"Asked old Mrs. Munsing from next door to keep an ear out in case she cried. But she seemed dead asleep; I didn't think there was much chance. Come along now, it's cold out."

It was; the freezing air off the bay was coiling in white tendrils around the posts of the arc lights, and I shivered in my thin blouse.

"I'll meet you at home, then," I said.

The warmth of the nursery reached out to embrace me as I went in to check Brianna. She was still asleep, but restless, turning her russet head from side to side, the groping little mouth opening and closing like the breathing of a fish.

"She's getting hungry," I whispered to Frank, who had come in behind me and was hovering over my shoulder, peering fondly at the baby. "I'd better feed her before I come to bed; then she'll sleep later in the morning."

"I'll get you a hot drink," and he vanished through the door to the kitchen as I picked up the sleepy, warm bundle.

She had only drained one side, but she was full. The slack mouth pulled slowly away from the nipple, rimmed with milk, and the fuzzy head fell heavily back on my arm. No amount of gentle shaking or calling would rouse her to nurse on the other side, so at last I gave up and tucked her back in her crib, patting her back softly until a faint, contented belch wafted up from the pillow, succeeded by the heavy breathing of absolute satiation.

"Down for the night, is she?" Frank drew the baby blanket, decorated with yellow bunnies, up over her.

"Yes." I sat back in my rocking chair, mentally and physically too exhausted to get up again. Frank came to stand behind me; his hand rested lightly on my shoulder.

"He's dead, then?" he asked gently.

I told you so, I started to say. Then I stopped, closed my mouth and only nodded, rocking slowly, staring at the dark crib and its tiny occupant.

My right breast was still painfully swollen with milk. No

matter how tired I was, I couldn't sleep until I took care of it. With a sigh of resignation, I reached for the breast pump, an ungainly and ridiculous-looking rubber contraption. Using it was undignified and uncomfortable, but better than waking up in an hour in bursting pain, sopping wet from overflowing milk.

I waved a hand at Frank, dismissing him.

"Go ahead. It will only take a few minutes, but I have to . . ."

Instead of leaving or answering, he took the pump from my hand and laid it down on the table. As though it moved of its own will, without direction from him, his hand rose slowly through the warm, dark air of the nursery and cupped itself gently around the swollen curve of my breast.

His head bowed and his lips fastened softly on my nipple. I groaned, feeling the half-painful prickle of the milk rushing through the tiny ducts. I put a hand behind his head, and pressed him slightly closer.

"Harder," I whispered. His mouth was soft, gentle in its pressure, nothing like the relentless grasp of a baby's hard, toothless gums, that fasten on like grim death, demanding and draining, releasing the bounteous fountain at once in response to their greed.

Frank knelt before me, his mouth a supplicant. Was this how God felt, I wondered, seeing the adorers before Him— was He, too, filled with tenderness and pity? The haze of fatigue made me feel as though everything happened in slow motion, as though we were under water. Frank's hands moved slowly as sea fronds, swaying in the current, moving over my flesh with a touch as gentle as the brush of kelp leaves, lifting me with the strength of a wave, and laying me down on the shore of the nursery rug. I closed my eyes, and let the tide carry me away.

The front door of the old manse opened with a screech of rusty hinges, announcing the return of Brianna Randall. Roger was on his feet and into the hall at once, drawn by the sound of girls' voices.

"A pound of best butter—that's what you told me to ask for,

and I did, but I kept wondering whether there was such a thing as second-best butter, or worst butter—'' Brianna was handing over wrapped packages to Fiona, laughing and talking at once.

"Well, and if ye got it from that auld rascal Wicklow, worst is what it's likely to be, no matter what he says," Fiona interrupted. "Oh, and ye've got the cinnamon, that's grand! I'll make cinnamon scones, then; d'ye want to come and watch me do it?"

"Yes, but first I want supper. I'm starved!" Brianna stood on tiptoe, sniffing hopefully in the direction of the kitchen. "What are we having—haggis?"

"Haggis! Gracious, ye silly Sassenach—ye dinna have haggis in the spring! Ye have it in the autumn when the sheep are killed."

"Am I a Sassenach?" Brianna seemed delighted at the name.

"Of course ye are, gowk. But I like ye fine, anyway."

Fiona laughed up at Brianna, who towered over the small Scottish girl by nearly a foot. Fiona was nineteen, prettily charming and slightly plump; next to her, Brianna looked like a medieval carving, strong-boned and severe. With her long, straight nose and the long hair glowing red-gold beneath the glass bowl of the ceiling fixture, she might have walked out of an illuminated manuscript, vivid enough to endure a thousand years unchanged.

Roger was suddenly conscious of Claire Randall, standing near his elbow. She was looking at her daughter, with an expression in which love, pride, and something else were mingled—memory, perhaps? He realized, with a slight shock, that Jamie Fraser too must have had not only the striking height and Viking red hair he had bequeathed to his daughter, but likely the same sheer physical presence.

It was quite remarkable, he thought. She didn't do or say anything so out of the ordinary, and yet Brianna undeniably drew people. There was some attraction about her, almost magnetic, that drew everyone near into the glow of her orbit.

It drew him; Brianna turned and smiled at him, and without consciousness of having moved, he found himself near enough to see the faint freckles high on her cheekbones, and smell the whiff of pipe tobacco that lingered in her hair from her expeditions to the shops.

"Hullo," he said, smiling. "Any luck with the Clans office, or have you been too busy playing dogsbody for Fiona?"

"Dogsbody?" Brianna's eyes slanted into blue triangles of

amusement. *"Dogsbody?* First I'm a Sassenach, and now I'm a dogsbody. What do you Scots call people when you're trying to be *nice*?"

"Darrrrlin'," he said, rolling his *r*'s exaggeratedly, and making both girls laugh.

"You sound like an Aberdeen terrier in a bad mood," Claire observed. "Did you find anything at the Highland Clans library, Bree?"

"Lots of stuff," Brianna replied, rummaging through the stack of photocopies she had set down on the hall table. "I managed to read most of it while they were making the copies—this one was the most interesting." She pulled a sheet from the stack and handed it to Roger.

It was an extract from a book of Highland legends; an entry headed "Leap O' the Cask."

"Legends?" said Claire, peering over his shoulder. "Is that what we want?"

"Could be." Roger was perusing the sheet, and spoke absently, his attention divided. "So far as the Scottish Highlands go, most of the history is oral, up to the mid-nineteenth century or so. That means there wasn't a great distinction made between stories about real people, stories of historical figures, and the stories about mythical things like water horses and ghosts and the doings of the Auld Folk. Scholars who wrote the stories down often didn't know for sure which they were dealing with, either—sometimes it was a combination of fact and myth, and sometimes you could tell that it was a real historical occurrence being described.

"This one, for instance"—he passed the paper to Claire—"sounds like a real one. It's describing the story behind the name of a particular rock formation in the Highlands."

Claire brushed the hair behind her ear and bent her head to read, squinting in the dim light of the ceiling fixture. Fiona, too accustomed to musty papers and boring bits of history to be interested, disappeared back into her kitchen to see to the dinner.

" 'Leap O' the Cask,' " Claire read. " '*This unusual formation, located some distance above a burn, is named after the story of a Jacobite laird and his servant. The laird, one of the few fortunates to escape the disaster of Culloden, made his way with difficulty to his home, but was compelled to lie hidden in a cave on his lands for nearly seven years, while the English hunted the*

Highlands for the fugitive supporters of Charles Stuart. The laird's tenants loyally kept his presence a secret, and brought food and supplies to the laird in his hiding place. They were careful always to refer to the hidden man only as the "Dunbonnet," in order to avoid any chance of giving him away to the English patrols who frequently crossed the district.

"'One day, a boy bringing a cask of ale up the trail to the laird's cave met a group of English dragoons. Bravely refusing either to answer the soldiers' questions, or to give up his burden, the boy was attacked by one of the dragoons, and dropped the cask, which bounded down the steep hill, and into the burn below.'"

She looked up from the paper, raising her eyebrows at her daughter.

"Why this one? We know—or we think we know," she corrected, with a wry nod toward Roger, "that Jamie escaped from Culloden, but so did a lot of other people. What makes you think this laird might have been Jamie?"

"Because of the Dunbonnet bit, of course," Brianna answered, as though surprised that she should ask.

"What?" Roger looked at her, puzzled. "What about the Dunbonnet?"

In answer, Brianna picked up a hank of her thick red hair and waggled it under his nose.

"Dunbonnet!" she said impatiently. "A dull brown bonnet, right? He wore a hat all the time, because he had hair that could be recognized! Didn't you say the English called him 'Red Jamie'? They knew he had red hair—he had to hide it!"

Roger stared at her, speechless. The hair floated loose on her shoulders, alive with fiery light.

"You could be right," Claire said. Excitement made her eyes bright as she looked at her daughter. "It was like yours—Jamie's hair was just like yours, Bree." She reached up and softly stroked Brianna's hair. The girl's face softened as she looked down at her mother.

"I know," she said. "I was thinking about that while I was reading—trying to see him, you know?" She stopped and cleared her throat, as though something might be caught in it. "I could see him, out in the heather, hiding, and the sun shining off his hair. You said he'd been an outlaw; I just—I just thought he must have known pretty well . . . how to hide. If people were trying to kill him," she finished softly.

"Right." Roger spoke briskly, to dispel the shadow in Brianna's eyes. "That's a marvelous job of guesswork, but maybe we can tell for sure, with a little more work. If we can find Leap O' the Cask on a map—"

"What kind of dummy do you think I am?" Brianna said scornfully. "I thought of that." The shadow disappeared, replaced by an expression of smugness. "That's why I was so late; I made the clerk drag out every map of the Highlands they had." She withdrew another photocopied sheet from the stack and poked a finger triumphantly near the upper edge.

"See? It's so tiny, it doesn't show up on most maps, but this one had it. Right there; there's the village of Broch Mordha, which Mama says is near the Lallybroch estate, and there"—her finger moved a quarter-inch, pointing to a line of microscopic print. "See?" she repeated. "He went back to his estate—Lallybroch— and that's where he hid."

"Not having a magnifying glass to hand, I'll take your word for it that that says 'Leap O' the Cask,' " Roger said, straightening up. He grinned at Brianna. "Congratulations, then," he said. "I think you've found him—that far, at least."

Brianna smiled, her eyes suspiciously bright. "Yeah," she said softly. She touched the two sheets of paper with a gentle finger. "My father."

Claire squeezed her daughter's hand. "If you have your father's hair, it's nice to see you have your mother's brains," she said, smiling. "Let's go and celebrate your discovery with Fiona's dinner."

"Good job," Roger said to Brianna, as they followed Claire toward the dining room. His hand rested lightly on her waist. "You should be proud of yourself."

"Thanks," she said, with a brief smile, but the pensive expression returned almost at once to the curve of her mouth.

"What is it?" Roger asked softly, stopping in the hall. "Is something the matter?"

"No, not really." She turned to face him, a small line visible between the ruddy brows. "It's only—I was just thinking, trying to imagine—what do you think it was like for him? Living in a cave for seven years? And what happened to him then?"

Moved by an impulse, Roger leaned forward and kissed her lightly between the brows.

"I don't know, darlin'," he said. "But maybe we'll find out."

PART TWO

Lallybroch

4

The Dunbonnet

He came down to the house once a month to shave, when one of the boys brought him word it was safe. Always at night, moving soft-footed as a fox through the dark. It seemed necessary, somehow, a small gesture toward the concept of civilization.

He would slip like a shadow through the kitchen door, to be met with Ian's smile or his sister's kiss, and would feel the transformation begin. The basin of hot water, the freshly stropped razor would be laid ready for him on the table, with whatever there was for shaving soap. Now and then it was real soap, if Cousin Jared had sent some from France; more often just half-rendered tallow, eye-stinging with lye.

He could feel the change begin with the first scent of the kitchen —so strong and rich, after the wind-thin smells of loch and moor and wood—but it wasn't until he had finished the ritual of shaving that he felt himself altogether human once more.

They had learned not to expect him to talk until he had shaved; words came hard after a month's solitude. Not that he could think of nothing to say; it was more that the words inside formed a logjam in his throat, battling each other to get out in the short time he had. He needed those few minutes of careful grooming to pick and choose, what he would say first and to whom.

There was news to hear and to ask about—of English patrols in the district, of politics, of arrests and trials in London and Edinburgh. That he could wait for. Better to talk to Ian about the estate, to Jenny about the children. If it seemed safe, the children would be brought down to say hello to their uncle, to give him sleepy hugs and damp kisses before stumbling back to their beds.

"He'll be getting a man soon" had been his first choice of conversation when he came in September, with a nod toward Jenny's eldest child, his namesake. The ten-year-old sat at the table with a certain constraint, immensely conscious of the dignity of his temporary position as man of the house.

"Aye, all I need's another of the creatures to worry over," his sister replied tartly, but she touched her son's shoulder in passing, with a pride that belied her words.

"Have ye word from Ian, then?" His brother-in-law had been arrested—for the fourth time—three weeks before, and taken to Inverness under suspicion of being a Jacobite sympathizer.

Jenny shook her head, bringing a covered dish to set before him. The thick warm smell of partridge pie drifted up from the pricked crust, and made his mouth water so heavily, he had to swallow before he could speak.

"It's naught to fret for," Jenny said, spooning out the pie onto his plate. Her voice was calm, but the small vertical line between her brows deepened. "I've sent Fergus to show them the deed of sasine, and Ian's discharge from his regiment. They'll send him home again, so soon as they realize he isna the laird of Lallybroch, and there's naught to be gained by deviling him." With a glance at her son, she reached for the ale jug. "Precious chance they have of provin' a wee bairn to be a traitor."

Her voice was grim, but held a note of satisfaction at the thought of the English court's confusion. The rain-spattered deed of sasine that proved transfer of the title of Lallybroch from the elder James to the younger had made its appearance in court before, each time foiling the Crown's attempt to seize the estate as the property of a Jacobite traitor.

He would feel it begin to slip away when he left—that thin veneer of humanity—more of it gone with each step away from the farmhouse. Sometimes he would keep the illusion of warmth and family all the way to the cave where he hid; other times it would disappear almost at once, torn away by a chill wind, rank and acrid with the scent of burning.

The English had burned three crofts, beyond the high field. Pulled Hugh Kirby and Geoff Murray from their firesides and shot them by their own doorsteps, with no question or word of formal accusation. Young Joe Fraser had escaped, warned by his wife, who had seen the English coming, and had lived three weeks with Jamie in the cave, until the soldiers were well away from the district—and Ian with them.

In October, it had been the older lads he spoke to; Fergus, the French boy he had taken from a Paris brothel, and Rabbie MacNab, the kitchenmaid's son, Fergus's best friend.

He had drawn the razor slowly down one cheek and round the angle of his jaw, then wiped the lathered blade against the edge of the basin. From the corner of one eye, he caught a faint glimpse of fascinated envy on the face of Rabbie MacNab. Turning slightly, he saw that the three boys—Rabbie, Fergus, and Young Jamie—were all watching him intently, mouths slightly open.

"Have ye no seen a man shave before?" he asked, cocking one brow.

Rabbie and Fergus glanced at each other, but left it to Young Jamie, as titular owner of the estate, to answer.

"Oh, well . . . aye, Uncle," he said, blushing. "But . . . I m-mean"—he stammered slightly and blushed even harder—"with my da gone, and even when he's home, we dinna see him shave himself always, and well, you've just such a lot of *hair* on your face, Uncle, after a whole month, and it's only we're so glad to see you again, and . . ."

It dawned on Jamie quite suddenly that to the boys he must seem a most romantic figure. Living alone in a cave, emerging at dark to hunt, coming down out of the mist in the night, filthy and wild-haired, beard all in a fierce red sprout—yes, at their age, it likely seemed a glamorous adventure to be an outlaw and live hidden in the heather, in a dank, cramped cave. At fifteen and sixteen and ten, they had no notion of guilt or bitter loneliness, of the weight of a responsibility that could not be relieved by action.

They might understand fear, of a sort. Fear of capture, fear of death. Not the fear of solitude, of his own nature, fear of madness. Not the constant, chronic fear of what his presence might do to them—if they thought about that risk at all, they dismissed it, with the casual assumption of immortality that was the right of boys.

"Aye, well," he had said, turning casually back to the looking glass as Young Jamie stuttered to a halt. "Man is born to sorrow and whiskers. One of the plagues of Adam."

"Of Adam?" Fergus looked openly puzzled, while the others tried to pretend they had the slightest idea what Jamie was talking about. Fergus, as a Frenchie, was not expected to know everything.

"Oh, aye." Jamie pulled his upper lip down over his teeth and scraped delicately beneath his nose. "In the beginning, when God made man, Adam's chin was as hairless as Eve's. And their bodies both smooth as a newborn child's," he added, seeing Young Jamie's eyes dart toward Rabbie's crotch. Beardless Rabbie still was, but the faint dark down on his upper lip bespoke new sproutings elsewhere.

"But when the angel wi' the flaming sword drove them out of Eden, no sooner had they passed the gate of the garden, when the hair began to sprout and itch on Adam's chin, and ever since, man has been cursed with shaving." He finished his own chin with a final flourish, and bowed theatrically to his audience.

"But what about the other hair?" Rabbie demanded. "Ye dinna shave *there*!" Young Jamie giggled at the thought, going red again.

"And a damn good thing, too," his elder namesake observed. "Ye'd need the devil of a steady hand. No need of a looking glass, though," he added, to a chorus of giggles.

"What about the ladies?" Fergus said. His voice broke on the word "ladies," in a bullfrog croak that made the other two laugh harder. "Certainly *les filles* have hair there, too, but they do not shave it—usually not, anyway," he added, clearly thinking of some of the sights of his early life in the brothel.

Jamie heard his sister's footsteps coming down the hall.

"Oh, well, that's no a curse," he told his rapt audience, picking up the basin and tossing the contents neatly through the open window. "God gave that as a consolation to man. If ye've ever the privilege of seeing a woman in her skin, gentlemen," he said, looking over his shoulder toward the door and lowering his voice confidentially, "ye'll observe that the hair there grows in the shape of an arrow—pointing the way, ye ken, so as a poor ignorant man can find his way safe home."

He turned grandly away from the guffawing and sniggers behind him, to be struck suddenly with shame as he saw his sister, coming down the hall with the slow, waddling stride of advanced pregnancy. She was holding the tray with his supper on top of her swelling stomach. How could he have demeaned her so, for a crude jest and the sake of a moment's camaraderie with the boys?

"Be still!" he had snapped at the boys, who stopped giggling abruptly and stared at him in puzzlement. He hastened forward to take the tray from Jenny and set it on the table.

It was a savoury made of goat's meat and bacon, and he saw Fergus's prominent Adam's apple bob in the slender throat at the smell of it. He knew they saved the best of the food for him; it didn't take much looking at the pinched faces across the table. When he came, he brought what meat he could, snared rabbits or grouse, sometimes a nest of plover's eggs—but it was never enough, for a house where hospitality must stretch to cover the needs of not only family and servants, but the families of the murdered Kirby and Murray. At least until spring, the widows and children of his tenants must bide here, and he must do his best to feed them.

"Sit down by me," he said to Jenny, taking her arm and gently guiding her to a seat on the bench beside him. She looked surprised—it was her habit to wait on him when he came—but sat down gladly enough. It was late, and she was tired; he could see the dark smudges beneath her eyes.

With great firmness, he cut a large slab of the savoury and set the plate before her.

"But that's all for you!" Jenny protested. "I've eaten."

"Not enough," he said. "Ye need more—for the babe," he added, with inspiration. If she would not eat for herself, she would for the child. She hesitated a moment longer, but then smiled at him, picked up her spoon, and began to eat.

Now it was November, and the chill struck through the thin shirt and breeches he wore. He hardly noticed, intent on his tracking. It was cloudy, but with a thin-layered mackerel sky, through which the full moon shed plenty of light.

Thank God it wasn't raining; impossible to hear through the pattering of raindrops, and the pungent scent of wet plants masked the smell of animals. His nose had grown almost painfully acute through the long months of living outdoors; the smells of the house sometimes nearly knocked him down when he stepped inside.

He wasn't quite close enough to smell the musky scent of the

stag, but he heard the telltale rustle of its brief start when it
scented *him*. Now it would be frozen, one of the shadows that
rippled across the hillside around him, under the racing clouds.

He turned as slowly as he possibly could toward the spot where
his ears had told him the stag stood. His bow was in his hand, an
arrow ready to the string. He would have one shot—maybe—when
the stag bolted.

Yes, there! His heart sprang into his throat as he saw the antlers,
pricking sharp and black above the surrounding gorse. He steadied
himself, took a deep breath, and then the one step forward.

The crash of a deer's flight was always startlingly loud, to
frighten back a stalker. This stalker was prepared, though. He
neither startled nor pursued, but stood his ground, sighting along
the shaft of the arrow, following with his eye the track of the
springing deer, judging the moment, holding fire, and then the
bowstring slapped his wrist with stinging force.

It was a clean shot, just behind the shoulder, and a good thing,
too; he doubted he had the strength to run down a full-grown stag.
It had fallen in a clear spot behind a clump of gorse, legs stuck
out, stiff as sticks, in the oddly helpless way of dying ungulates.
The hunter's moon lit its glazing eye, so the soft dark stare was
hidden, the mystery of its dying shielded by blank silver.

He pulled the dirk from his belt and knelt by the deer, hastily
saying the words of the gralloch prayer. Old John Murray, Ian's
father, had taught him. His own father's mouth had twisted
slightly, hearing it, from which he gathered that this prayer was
perhaps not addressed to the same God they spoke to in church on
Sunday. But his father had said nothing, and he had mumbled the
words himself, scarcely noticing what he said, in the nervous
excitement of feeling old John's hand, steady on his own, for the
first time pressing down the knife blade into hairy hide and steaming flesh.

Now, with the sureness of practice, he thrust up the sticky
muzzle in one hand, and with the other, slit the deer's throat.

The blood spurted hot over knife and hand, pumping two or
three times, the jet dying away to a steady stream as the carcass
drained, the great vessels of the throat cut through. Had he paused
to think, he might not have done it, but hunger and dizziness and
the cold fresh intoxication of the night had taken him far past the

point of thinking. He cupped his hands beneath the running stream and brought them steaming to his mouth.

The moon shone black on his cupped, spilling hands, and it was as though he absorbed the deer's substance, rather than drank it. The taste of the blood was salt and silver, and the heat of it was his own. There was no startlement of hot or cold as he swallowed, only the taste of it, rich in his mouth, and the head-swimming, hot-metal smell, and the sudden clench and rumble of his belly at the nearness of food.

He closed his eyes and breathed, and the cold damp air came back, between the hot reek of the carcass and his senses. He swallowed once, then wiped the back of his hand across his face, cleaned his hands on the grass, and set about the business at hand.

There was the sudden effort of moving the limp, heavy carcass, and then the gralloch, the long stroke of mingled strength and delicacy that slit the hide between the legs, but did not penetrate the sac that held the entrails. He forced his hands into the carcass, a hot wet intimacy, and again there was an effortful tug that brought out the sac, slick and moon-shining in his hands. A slash above and another below, and the mass slid free, the transformation of black magic that changed a deer to meat.

It was a small stag, although it had points to its antlers. With luck, he could carry it alone, rather than leave it to the mercy of foxes and badgers until he could bring help to move it. He ducked a shoulder under one leg, and slowly rose, grunting with effort as he shifted the burden to a solid resting place across his back.

The moon cast his shadow on a rock, humped and fantastic, as he made his slow, ungainly way down the hill. The deer's antlers bobbed above his shoulder, giving him in shadowed profile the semblance of a horned man. He shivered slightly at the thought, remembering tales of witches' sabbats, where the Horned One came, to drink the sacrifice of goat's or rooster's blood.

He felt a little queasy, and more than a little light-headed. More and more, he felt the disorientation, the fragmenting of himself between day and night. By day, he was a creature of the mind alone, as he escaped his damp immobility by a stubborn, disciplined retreat into the avenues of thought and meditation, seeking refuge in the pages of books. But with the rising of the moon, all sense fled, succumbing at once to sensation, as he emerged into the fresh air like a beast from its lair, to run the dark hills beneath

the stars, and hunt, driven by hunger, drunk with blood and moonlight.

He stared at the ground as he walked, night-sight keen enough
to keep his footing, despite the heavy burden. The deer was limp
and cooling, its stiff, soft hair scratching against the back of his
neck, and his own sweat cooling in the breeze, as though he shared
his prey's fate.

It was only as the lights of Lallybroch manor came into view
that he felt at last the mantle of humanity fall upon him, and mind
and body joined as one again as he prepared himself to greet his
family.

5

To Us a Child Is Given

Three weeks later, there was still no word of Ian's return. No word of any kind, in fact. Fergus had not come to the cave in several days, leaving Jamie in a fret of worry over how things might be at the house. If nothing else, the deer he had shot would have gone long since, with all the extra mouths to feed, and there would be precious little from the kailyard at this time of year.

He was sufficiently worried to risk an early visit, checking his snares and coming down from the hills just before sunset. Just in case, he was careful to pull on the woolen bonnet, knitted of rough dun yarn, that would hide his hair from any telltale fingering of late sunbeams. His size alone might provoke suspicion, but not certainty, and he had full confidence in the strength of his legs to carry him out of harm's way should he have the ill luck to meet with an English patrol. Hares in the heather were little match for Jamie Fraser, given warning.

The house was strangely quiet as he approached. There was none of the usual racket made by children: Jenny's five, and the six bairns belonging to the tenants, to say nothing of Fergus and Rabbie MacNab, who were a long way from being too old to chase each other round the stables, screeching like fiends.

The house felt strangely empty round him, as he paused just inside the kitchen door. He was standing in the back hall, the pantry to one side, the scullery to the other, and the main kitchen just beyond. He stood stock-still, reaching out with all his senses, listening as he inhaled the overpowering smells of the house. No, there was someone here; the faint sound of a scrape, followed by a soft, regular clinking came from behind the cloth-padded door that kept the heat of the kitchen from seeping out into the chilly back pantry.

It was a reassuringly domestic sound, so he pushed open the door cautiously, but without undue fear. His sister, Jenny, alone and vastly pregnant, was standing at the table, stirring something in a yellow bowl.

"What are you doing in here? Where's Mrs. Coker?"

His sister dropped the spoon with a startled shriek.

"Jamie!" Pale-faced, she pressed a hand to her breast and closed her eyes. "Christ! Ye scairt the bowels out of me." She opened her eyes, dark blue like his own, and fixed him with a penetrating stare. "And what in the name of the Holy Mother are ye doing here now? I wasna expecting ye for a week at least."

"Fergus hasna come up the hill lately; I got worried," he said simply.

"Ye're a sweet man, Jamie." The color was coming back into her face. She smiled at her brother and came close to hug him. It was an awkward business, with the impending baby in the way, but pleasant, nonetheless. He rested his cheek for a moment on the sleek darkness of her head, breathing in her complex aroma of candle wax and cinnamon, tallow-soap and wool. There was an unusual element to her scent this evening; he thought she was beginning to smell of milk.

"Where is everyone?" he asked, releasing her reluctantly.

"Well, Mrs. Coker's dead," she answered, the faint crease between her brows deepening.

"Aye?" he said softly, and crossed himself. "I'm sorry for it." Mrs. Coker had been first housemaid and then housekeeper for the family, since the marriage of his own parents, forty-odd years before. "When?"

"Yesterday forenoon. 'Twasn't unexpected, poor soul, and it was peaceful. She died in her own bed, like she wanted, and Father McMurtry prayin' over her."

Jamie glanced reflexively toward the door that led to the servants' rooms, off the kitchen. "Is she still here?"

His sister shook her head. "No. I told her son they should have the wake here at the house, but the Cokers thought, everything being like it is"—her small moue encompassed Ian's absence, lurking Redcoats, refugee tenants, the dearth of food, and his own inconvenient presence in the cave—"they thought better to have it at Broch Mordha, at her sister's place. So that's where everyone's gone. I told them I didna feel well enough to go," she added, then smiled, raising an impish brow. "But it was really that I wanted a few hours' peace and quiet, wi' the lot of them gone."

"And here I've come, breakin' in on your peace," Jamie said ruefully. "Shall I go?"

"No, clot-heid," his sister said affably. "Sit ye down, and I'll get on wi' the supper."

"What's to eat, then?" he asked, sniffing hopefully.

"Depends on what ye've brought," his sister replied. She moved heavily about the kitchen, taking things from cupboard and hutch, pausing to stir the large kettle hung over the fire, from which a thin steam was rising.

"If ye've brought meat, we'll have it. If not, it's brose and hough."

He made a face at this; the thought of boiled barley and shin-beef, the last remnants of the salted beef carcass they'd bought two months before, was unappealing.

"Just as well I had luck, then," he said. He upended his game bag and let the three rabbits fall onto the table in a limp tumble of gray fur and crumpled ears. "And blackthorn berries," he added, tipping out the contents of the dun bonnet, now stained inside with the rich red juice.

Jenny's eyes brightened at the sight. "Hare pie," she declared. "There's no currants, but the berries will do even better, and there's enough butter, thank God." Catching a tiny blink of movement among the gray fur, she slapped her hand down on the table, neatly obliterating the minuscule intruder.

"Take them out and skin 'em, Jamie, or the kitchen will be hopping wi' fleas."

Returning with the skinned carcasses, he found the piecrust well advanced, and Jenny with smears of flour on her dress.

"Cut them into collops and break the bones for me, will ye, Jamie?" she said, frowning at *Mrs. McClintock's Receipts for Cookery and Pastry-Work,* laid open on the table beside the pie pan.

"Surely ye can make hare pie without looking in the wee book?" he said, obligingly taking the big bone-crushing wooden mallet from the top of the hutch where it was kept. He grimaced as he took it into his hand, feeling the weight of it. It was very like the one that had broken his right hand several years before, in an English prison, and he had a sudden vivid memory of the shattered bones in a hare pie, splintered and cracked, leaking salty blood and marrow-sweetness into the meat.

"Aye, I can," his sister answered abstractedly, thumbing through the pages. "It's only that when ye havena got half the things ye need to make a dish, sometimes there's something else you'll come across in here, that ye can use instead." She frowned at the page before her. "Ordinarily, I'd use claret in the sauce, but we've none in the house, save one of Jared's casks in the priest hole, and I dinna want to broach that yet—we might need it."

He didn't need telling what she might use it for. A cask of claret might grease the skids for Ian's release—or at least pay for news of his welfare. He stole a sidewise glance at the great round of Jenny's belly. It wasn't for a man to say, but to his not inexperienced eyes, she looked damn near her time. Absently, he reached over the kettle and swished the blade of his dirk to and fro in the scalding liquid, then pulled it out and wiped it clean.

"Whyever did ye do that, Jamie?" He turned to find Jenny staring at him. The black curls were coming undone from their ribbon, and it gave him a pang to see the glimmer of a single white hair among the ebony.

"Oh," he said, too obviously offhand as he picked up one carcass, "Claire—she told me ye ought to wash off a blade in boiling water before ye touched food with it."

He felt rather than saw Jenny's eyebrows rise. She had asked him about Claire only once, when he had come home from Culloden, half-conscious and mostly dead with fever.

"She is gone," he had said, and turned his face away. "Dinna speak her name to me again." Loyal as always, Jenny had not, and neither had he. He could not have said what made him say it today; unless perhaps it was the dreams.

He had them often, in varying forms, and it always unsettled him the day after, as though for a moment Claire had really been near enough to touch, and then had drawn away again. He could swear that sometimes he woke with the smell of her on him, musky and rich, pricked with the sharp, fresh scents of leaves and green herbs. He had spilled his seed in his sleep more than once while dreaming, an occurrence that left him faintly shamed and uneasy in mind. To distract both of them, he nodded at Jenny's stomach.

"How close is it?" he asked, frowning at her swollen midsection. "Ye look like a puffball mushroom—one touch, and poof!" He flicked his fingers wide in illustration.

"Oh, aye? Well, and I could wish it was as easy as poof." She arched her back, rubbing at the small of it, and making her belly protrude in an alarming fashion. He pressed back against the wall, to give it room. "As for when, anytime, I expect. No telling for sure." She picked up the cup and measured out the flour; precious little left in the bag, he noted with some grimness.

"Send up to the cave when it starts," he said suddenly. "I'll come down, Redcoats or no."

Jenny stopped stirring and stared at him.

"You? Why?"

"Well, Ian's not here," he pointed out, picking up one skinned carcass. With the expertise of long practice, he neatly disjointed a thigh and cut it free from the backbone. Three quick smacks with the boning mallet and the pale flesh lay flattened and ready for the pie.

"And a great lot of help he'd be if he was," Jenny said. "He took care of his part o' the business nine months ago." She wrinkled her nose at her brother and reached for the plate of butter.

"Mmphm." He sat down to continue his work, which brought her belly close to his eye-level. The contents, awake and active, was shifting to and fro in a restless manner, making her apron twitch and bulge as she stirred. He couldn't resist reaching out to put a light hand against the monstrous curve, to feel the surprising strong thrusts and kicks of the inhabitant, impatient of its cramped confinement.

"Send Fergus for me when it's time," he said again.

She looked down at him in exasperation and batted his hand away with the spoon. "Have I no just been telling ye, I dinna need ye? For God's sake, man, have I not enough to worry me, wi' the house full of people, and scarce enough to feed them, Ian in gaol in Inverness, and Redcoats crawling in at the windows every time I look round? Should I have to worry that ye'll be taken up, as well?"

"Ye needna be worrit for me; I'll take care." He didn't look at her, but focused his attention on the forejoint he was slicing through.

"Well, then, have a care and stay put on the hill." She looked down her long, straight nose, peering at him over the rim of the bowl. "I've had six bairns already, aye? Ye dinna think I can manage by now?"

"No arguing wi' you, is there?" he demanded.

"No," she said promptly. "So you'll stay."

"I'll come."

Jenny narrowed her eyes and gave him a long, level look.

"Ye're maybe the most stubborn gomerel between here and Aberdeen, no?"

A smile spread across her brother's face as he looked up at her.

"Maybe so," he said. He reached across and patted her heaving belly. "And maybe no. But I'm coming. Send Fergus when it's time."

It was near dawn three days later that Fergus came panting up the slope to the cave, missing the trail in the dark, and making such a crashing through the gorse bushes that Jamie heard him coming long before he reached the opening.

"Milord . . ." he began breathlessly as he emerged by the head of the trail, but Jamie was already past the boy, pulling his cloak around his shoulders as he hurried down toward the house.

"But, milord . . ." Fergus's voice came behind him, panting and frightened. "Milord, the soldiers . . ."

"Soldiers?" He stopped suddenly and turned, waiting impatiently for the French lad to make his way down the slope. "What soldiers?" he demanded, as Fergus slithered the last few feet.

"English dragoons, milord. Milady sent me to tell you—on no account are you to leave the cave. One of the men saw the soldiers yesterday, camped near Dunmaglas."

"Damn."

"Yes, milord." Fergus sat down on a rock and fanned himself, narrow chest heaving as he caught his breath.

Jamie hesitated, irresolute. Every instinct fought against going back into the cave. His blood was heated by the surge of excitement caused by Fergus's appearance, and he rebelled at the thought of meekly crawling back into hiding, like a grub seeking refuge beneath its rock.

"Mmphm," he said. He glanced down at Fergus. The changing light was beginning to outline the boy's slender form against the blackness of the gorse, but his face was still a pale smudge, marked with a pair of darker smudges that were his eyes. A certain suspicion was stirring in Jamie. Why had his sister sent Fergus at this odd hour?

If it had been necessary urgently to warn him about the dragoons, it would have been safer to send the boy up during the night. If the need was not urgent, why not wait until the next night? The answer to that was obvious—because Jenny thought she might not be able to send him word the next night.

"How is it with my sister?" he asked Fergus.

"Oh, well, milord, quite well!" The hearty tone of this assurance confirmed all Jamie's suspicions.

"She's having the child, no?" he demanded.

"No, milord! Certainly not!"

Jamie reached down and clamped a hand on Fergus's shoulder. The bones felt small and fragile beneath his fingers, reminding him uncomfortably of the rabbits he had broken for Jenny. Nonetheless, he forced his grip to tighten. Fergus squirmed, trying to ease away.

"Tell me the truth, man," Jamie said.

"No, milord! Truly!"

The grip tightened inexorably. "Did she tell you not to tell me?"

Jenny's prohibition must have been a literal one, for Fergus answered this question with evident relief.

"Yes, milord!"

"Ah." He relaxed his grip and Fergus sprang to his feet, now talking volubly as he rubbed his scrawny shoulder.

"She said I must not tell you anything except about the soldiers, milord, for if I did, she would cut off my cods and boil them like turnips and sausage!"

Jamie could not repress a smile at this threat.

"Short of food we may be," he assured his protégé, "but not that short." He glanced at the horizon, where a thin line of pink showed pure and vivid behind the black pines' silhouette. "Come along, then; it'll be full light in half an hour."

There was no hint of silent emptiness about the house this dawn. Anyone with half an eye could see that things were not as usual at Lallybroch; the wash kettle sat on its plinth in the yard, with the fire gone out under it, full of cold water and sodden clothes. Moaning cries from the barn—like someone being strangled—indicated that the sole remaining cow urgently required milking. An irritable blatting from the goat shed let him know that the female inhabitants would like some similar attention as well.

As he came into the yard, three chickens ran past in a feathery squawk, with Jehu the rat terrier in close pursuit. With a quick dart, he leapt forward and booted the dog, catching it just under the ribs. It flew into the air with a look of intense surprise on its face, then, landing with a yip, picked itself up and made off.

He found the children, the older boys, Mary MacNab, and the other housemaid, Sukie, all crammed into the parlor, under the watchful eye of Mrs. Kirby, a stern and rock-ribbed widow, who was reading to them from the Bible.

" *'And Adam was not deceived, but the woman being deceived was in the transgression,'* " read Mrs. Kirby. There was a loud, rolling scream from upstairs, which seemed to go on and on. Mrs. Kirby paused for a moment, to allow everyone to appreciate it, before resuming the reading. Her eyes, pale gray and wet as raw oysters, flickered toward the ceiling, then rested with satisfaction on the row of strained faces before her.

" *'Notwithstanding, she shall be saved in childbearing, if she continue in faith and charity and holiness with sobriety,'* " she read. Kitty burst into hysterical sobbing and buried her head in her sister's shoulder. Maggie Ellen was growing bright red beneath her freckles, while her elder brother had gone dead-white at the scream.

"Mrs. Kirby," said Jamie. "Be still, if ye please."

The words were civil enough, but the look in his eyes must have been the one that Jehu saw just before his boot-assisted flight, for Mrs. Kirby gasped and dropped the Bible, which landed on the floor with a papery thump.

Jamie bent and picked it up, then showed Mrs. Kirby his teeth. The expression evidently was not successful as a smile, but had some effect nonetheless. Mrs. Kirby went quite pale, and put a hand to her ample bosom.

"Perhaps ye'd go to the kitchen and make yourself useful," he said, with a jerk of his head that sent Sukie the kitchenmaid scuttling out like a windblown leaf. With considerably more dignity, but no hesitation, Mrs. Kirby rose and followed her.

Heartened by this small victory, Jamie disposed of the parlor's other occupants in short order, sending the widow Murray and her daughters out to deal with the wash kettle, the smaller children out to catch chickens under the supervision of Mary MacNab. The older lads departed, with obvious relief, to tend the stock.

The room empty at last, he stood for a moment, hesitating as to what to do next. He felt obscurely that he should stay in the house, on guard, though he was acutely aware that he could—as Jenny had said—do nothing to help, whatever happened. There was an unfamiliar mule hobbled in the dooryard; presumably the midwife was upstairs with Jenny.

Unable to sit, he prowled restlessly around the parlor, the Bible in his hand, touching things. Jenny's bookshelf, battered and scarred from the last incursion of Redcoats, three months ago. The big silver epergne. That was slightly dented, but had been too heavy to fit into a soldier's knapsack, and so had escaped the pilfering of smaller objects. Not that the English had got so much; the few truly valuable items, along with the tiny store of gold they had left, were safely tucked away in the priest hole with Jared's wine.

Hearing a prolonged moan from above, he glanced down involuntarily at the Bible in his hand. Not really wanting to, still he let the book fall open, showing the page at the front where the marriages, births, and deaths of the family were recorded.

The entries began with his parents' marriage. Brian Fraser and Ellen MacKenzie. The names and the date were written in his mother's fine round hand, with underneath, a brief notation in his father's firmer, blacker scrawl. *Marrit for love,* it said—a pointed observation, in view of the next entry, which showed Willie's birth, which had occurred scarcely two months past the date of the marriage.

Jamie smiled, as always, at sight of the words, and glanced up at the painting of himself, aged two, standing with Willie and Bran, the huge deerhound. All that was left of Willie, who had died of the smallpox at eleven. The painting had a slash through the canvas—the work of a bayonet, he supposed, taking out its owner's frustration.

"And if ye hadna died," he said softly to the picture, "then what?"

Then what, indeed. As he closed the book, his eye caught the last entry—*Caitlin Maisri Murray, born December 3, 1749, died December 3, 1749.* Aye, if. If the Redcoats had not come on December 2, would Jenny have borne the child too early? If they had had enough food, so that she, like the rest of them, was no more than skin and bones and the bulge of her belly, would that have helped?

"No telling, is there?" he said to the painting. Willie's painted hand rested on his shoulder; he had always felt safe, with Willie standing behind him.

Another scream came from upstairs, and a spasm of fear clenched his hands on the book.

"Pray for us, Brother," he whispered, and crossing himself, laid down the Bible and went out to the barn to help with the stock.

There was little to do here; Rabbie and Fergus between them were more than able to take care of the few animals that remained, and Young Jamie, at ten, was big enough to be a substantial help. Looking about for something to do, Jamie gathered up an armful of scattered hay and took it down the slope to the midwife's mule. When the hay was gone, the cow would have to be slaughtered; unlike the goats, it couldn't get enough forage on the winter hills to sustain it, even with the picked grass and weeds the small children brought in. With luck, the salted carcass would last them through 'til spring.

As he came back into the barn, Fergus looked up from his manure fork.

"This is a proper midwife, of good repute?" Fergus demanded. He thrust out a long chin aggressively. "Madame should not be entrusted to the care of a peasant, surely!"

"How should I know?" Jamie said testily. "D'ye think I had anything to do wi' engaging midwives?" Mrs. Martin, the old midwife who had delivered all previous Murray children, had died —like so many others—during the famine in the year following Culloden. Mrs. Innes, the new midwife, was much younger; he hoped she had sufficient experience to know what she was doing.

Rabbie seemed inclined to join the argument as well. He scowled blackly at Fergus. "Aye, and what d'ye mean 'peasant'? Ye're a peasant, too, or have ye not noticed?"

Fergus stared down his nose at Rabbie with some dignity, despite the fact that he was forced to tilt his head backward in order to do so, he being several inches shorter than his friend.

"Whether I am a peasant or not is of no consequence," he said loftily. "I am not a midwife, am I?"

"No, ye're a fiddle-ma-fyke!" Rabbie gave his friend a rough push, and with a sudden whoop of surprise, Fergus fell backward, to land heavily on the stable floor. In a flash, he was up. He lunged at Rabbie, who sat laughing on the edge of the manger, but Jamie's hand snatched him by the collar and pulled him back.

"None of that," said his employer. "I willna have ye spoilin' what little hay's left." He set Fergus back on his feet, and to distract him, asked, "And what d'ye ken of midwives anyway?"

"A great deal, milord." Fergus dusted himself off with elegant gestures. "Many of the ladies at Madame Elise's were brought to bed while I was there—"

"I daresay they were," Jamie interjected dryly. "Or is it childbed ye mean?"

"Childbed, certainly. Why, I was born there myself!" The French boy puffed his narrow chest importantly.

"Indeed." Jamie's mouth quirked slightly. "Well, and I trust ye made careful observations at the time, so as to say how such matters should be arranged?"

Fergus ignored this piece of sarcasm.

"Well, of course," he said, matter-of-factly, "the midwife will naturally have put a knife beneath the bed, to cut the pain."

"I'm none so sure she did that," Rabbie muttered. "At least it doesna sound much like it." Most of the screaming was inaudible from the barn, but not all of it.

"And an egg should be blessed with holy water and put at the foot of the bed, so that the woman shall bring forth the child easily," Fergus continued, oblivious. He frowned.

"I gave the woman an egg myself, but she did not appear to know what to do with it. And I had been keeping it especially for the last month, too," he added plaintively, "since the hens scarcely lay anymore. I wanted to be sure of having one when it was needed.

"Now, following the birth," he went on, losing his doubts in the enthusiasm of his lecture, "the midwife must brew a tea of the placenta, and give it to the woman to drink, so that her milk will flow strongly."

Rabbie made a faint retching sound. "Of the *afterbirth,* ye mean?" he said disbelievingly. "God!"

Jamie felt a bit queasy at this exhibition of modern medical knowledge himself.

"Aye, well," he said to Rabbie, striving for casualness, "they eat frogs, ye know. And snails. I suppose maybe afterbirth isna so strange, considering." Privately, he wondered whether it might not be long before they were all eating frogs and snails, but thought that a speculation better kept to himself.

Rabbie made mock puking noises. "Christ, who'd be a Frenchie!"

Fergus, standing close to Rabbie, whirled and shot out a lightning fist. Fergus was small and slender for his age, but strong for all that, and with a deadly aim for a man's weak points, knowledge acquired as a juvenile pickpocket on the streets of Paris. The blow caught Rabbie squarely in the wind, and he doubled over with a sound like a stepped-on pig's bladder.

"Speak with respect of your betters, if you please," Fergus said haughtily. Rabbie's face turned several shades of red and his mouth opened and closed like a fish's, as he struggled to get his breath back. His eyes bulged with a look of intense surprise, and he looked so ridiculous that it was a struggle for Jamie not to laugh, despite his worry over Jenny and his irritation at the boys' squabbling.

"Will ye wee doiters no keep your paws off—" he began, when he was interrupted by a cry from Young Jamie, who had until now been silent, fascinated by the conversation.

"What?" Jamie whirled, hand going automatically to the pistol he carried whenever he left the cave, but there was not, as he had half-expected, an English patrol in the stableyard.

"What the hell is it?" he demanded. Then, following Young Jamie's pointing finger, he saw them. Three small black specks, drifting across the brown crumple of dead vines in the potato field.

"Ravens," he said softly, and felt the hair rise on the back of his neck. For those birds of war and slaughter to come to a house during a birth was the worst sort of ill luck. One of the filthy beasts was actually settling on the rooftree, as he watched.

With no conscious thought, he took the pistol from his belt and braced the muzzle across his forearm, sighting carefully. It was a long shot, from the door of the stable to the rooftree, and sighted upward, too. Still . . .

The pistol jerked in his hand and the raven exploded in a cloud of black feathers. Its two companions shot into the air as though blown there by the explosion, and flapped madly away, their hoarse cries fading quickly on the winter air.

"Mon Dieu!" Fergus exclaimed. *"C'est bien, ça!"*

"Aye, bonny shooting, sir." Rabbie, still red-faced and a little breathless, had recovered himself in time to see the shot. Now he nodded toward the house, pointing with his chin. "Look, sir, is that the midwife?"

It was. Mrs. Innes poked her head out of the second-story window, fair hair flying loose as she leaned out to peer into the yard below. Perhaps she had been drawn by the sound of the shot, fearing some trouble. Jamie stepped into the stableyard and waved at the window to reassure her.

"It's all right," he shouted. "Only an accident." He didn't mean to mention the ravens, lest the midwife tell Jenny.

"Come up!" she shouted, ignoring this. "The bairn's born, and your sister wants ye!"

Jenny opened one eye, blue and slightly slanted like his own. "So ye came, aye?"

"I thought someone should be here—if only to pray for ye," he said gruffly.

She closed the eye and a small smile curved her lips. She looked, he thought, very like a painting he had seen in France—an old one by some Italian fellow, but a good picture, nonetheless.

"Ye're a silly fool—and I'm glad of it," she said softly. She opened her eyes and glanced down at the swaddled bundle she held in the crook of her arm.

"D'ye want to see him?"

"Oh, a him, is it?" With hands experienced by years of unclehood, he lifted the tiny package and cuddled it against himself, pushing back the flap of blanket that shaded its face.

Its eyes were closed tight shut, the lashes not visible in the deep crease of the eyelids. The eyelids themselves lay at a sharp angle above the flushed smooth rounds of the cheeks, giving promise that it might—in this one recognizable feature, at least—resemble its mother.

The head was oddly lumpy, with a lopsided appearance that made Jamie think uncomfortably of a kicked-in melon, but the small fat mouth was relaxed and peaceful, the moist pink underlip quivering faintly with the snore attendant on the exhaustion of being born.

"Hard work, was it?" he said, speaking to the child, but it was the mother who answered him.

"Aye, it was," Jenny said. "There's whisky in the armoire— will ye fetch me a glass?" Her voice was hoarse and she had to clear her throat before finishing the request.

"Whisky? Should ye not be having ale wi' eggs beaten up in it?" he asked, repressing with some difficulty a mental vision of Fergus's suggestion of appropriate sustenance for newly delivered mothers.

"Whisky," his sister said definitely. "When ye were lyin' downstairs crippled and your leg killin' ye, did I give ye ale wi' eggs beaten up in it?"

"Ye fed me stuff a damn sight worse than that," her brother said, with a grin, "but ye're right, ye gave me whisky, too." He laid the sleeping child carefully on the coverlet, and turned to get the whisky.

"Has he a name, yet?" he asked, nodding toward the baby as he poured out a generous cup of the amber liquid.

"I'll call him Ian, for his da." Jenny's hand rested gently for a moment on the rounded skull, lightly furred with a gold-brown fuzz. A pulse beat visibly in the soft spot on top; it seemed hideously fragile to Jamie, but the midwife had assured him the babe was a fine, lusty lad, and he supposed he must take her word for it. Moved by an obscure impulse to protect that nakedly exposed soft spot, he picked up the baby once more, pulling the blanket up over its head.

"Mary MacNab told me about you and Mrs. Kirby," Jenny remarked, sipping. "Pity I didna see it—she said the wretched auld besom nearly swallowed her tongue when ye spoke to her."

Jamie smiled in return, gently patting the baby's back as it lay against his shoulder. Dead asleep, the little body lay inert as a boneless ham, a soft comforting weight.

"Too bad she didn't. How can ye stand the woman, living in the same house wi' ye? I'd strangle her, were I here every day."

His sister snorted and closed her eyes, tilting her head back to let the whisky slide down her throat.

"Ah, folk fash ye as much as ye let them; I dinna let her, much. Still," she added, opening her eyes, "I canna say as I'll be sorry to be rid of her. I have it in my mind to palm her off on auld Kettrick, down at Broch Mordha. His wife and his daughter both died last year, and he'll be wanting someone to do for him."

"Aye, but if I were Samuel Kettrick, I'd take the widow Murray," Jamie observed, "not the widow Kirby."

"Peggy Murray's already provided for," his sister assured him. "She'll wed Duncan Gibbons in the spring."

"That's fast work for Duncan," he said, a little surprised. Then a thought occurred to him, and he grinned at her. "Does either o' them know it yet?"

"No," she said, grinning back. Then the smile faded into a speculative look.

"Unless you were thinking of Peggy yourself, that is?"

"Me?" Jamie was as startled as if she had suddenly suggested he might wish to jump out of the second-story window.

"She's only five and twenty," Jenny pursued. "Young enough for more bairns, and a good mother."

"How much of that whisky have ye had?" Her brother bent forward and pretended to examine the level of the decanter, cupping the baby's head in one palm to prevent it wobbling. He straightened up and gave his sister a look of mild exasperation.

"I'm living like an animal in a cave, and ye wish me to take a wife?" He felt suddenly hollow inside. To prevent her seeing that the suggestion had upset him, he rose and walked up and down the room, making unnecessary small humming noises to the bundle in his arms.

"How long is it since ye've lain wi' a woman, Jamie?" his sister asked conversationally behind him. Shocked, he turned on his heel to stare at her.

"What the hell sort of question is that to ask a man?"

"You've not gone wi' any of the unwed lasses between Lallybroch and Broch Mordha," she went on, paying no attention.

"Or I'd have heard of it. None of the widows, either, I dinna think?" She paused delicately.

"Ye know damn well I haven't," he said shortly. He could feel his cheeks flushing with annoyance.

"Why not?" his sister asked bluntly.

"Why *not*?" He stared at her, his mouth slightly open. "Have ye lost your senses? What d'ye think, I'm the sort of man would slink about from house to house, bedding any woman who didna drive me out wi' a girdle in her hand?"

"As if they would. No, you're a good man, Jamie." Jenny smiled, half sadly. "Ye wouldna take advantage of any woman. Ye'd marry first, no?"

"No!" he said violently. The baby twitched and made a sleepy sound, and he transferred it automatically to his other shoulder, patting, as he glared at his sister. "I dinna mean to marry again, so ye just abandon all thought of matchmaking, Jenny Murray! I willna have it, d'ye hear?"

"Oh, I hear," she said, unperturbed. She pushed herself higher on the pillow, so as to look him in the eye.

"Ye mean to live a monk to the end of your days?" she asked. "Go to your grave wi' no son to bury you or bless your name?"

"Mind your own business, damn ye!" Heart pounding, he turned his back on her and strode to the window, where he stood staring sightlessly out over the stableyard.

"I ken ye mourn Claire." His sister's voice came softly from behind him. "D'ye think I could forget Ian, if he doesna come back? But it's time ye went on, Jamie. Ye dinna think Claire would mean ye to live alone all your life, with no one to comfort ye or bear your children?"

He didn't answer for a long time, just stood, feeling the soft heat of the small fuzzy head pressed against the side of his neck. He could see himself dimly in the misted glass, a tall dirty gangle of a man, the round white bundle incongruous beneath his own grim face.

"She was with child," he said softly at last, speaking to the reflection. "When she—when I lost her." How else could he put it? There was no way to tell his sister where Claire was—where he hoped she was. That he could not think of another woman, hoping that Claire still lived, even knowing her truly lost to him for good.

There was a long silence from the bed. Then Jenny said quietly, "Is that why ye came today?"

He sighed and turned sideways toward her, leaning his head against the cool glass. His sister was lying back, her dark hair loose on the pillow, eyes gone soft as she looked at him.

"Aye, maybe," he said. "I couldna help my wife; I suppose I thought I might help you. Not that I could," he added, with some bitterness. "I am as useless to you as I was to her."

Jenny stretched out a hand to him, face filled with distress. "Jamie, *mo chridhe*," she said, but then stopped, eyes widening in sudden alarm as a splintering crash and the sound of screams came from the house below.

"Holy Mary!" she said, growing even whiter. "It's the English!"

"Christ." It was as much a prayer as an exclamation of surprise. He glanced quickly from the bed to the window, judging the possibilities of hiding versus those of escape. The sounds of booted feet were already on the stair.

"The cupboard, Jamie!" Jenny whispered urgently, pointing. Without hesitation, he stepped into the armoire, and pulled the door to behind him.

The door of the chamber sprang open with a crash a moment later, to be filled with a red-coated figure in a cocked hat, holding a drawn sword before him. The Captain of dragoons paused, and darted his eyes all round the chamber, finally settling on the small figure in the bed.

"Mrs. Murray?" he said.

Jenny struggled to pull herself upright.

"I am. And what in flaming hell are ye doing in my house?" she demanded. Her face was pale and shiny with sweat, and her arms trembled, but she held her chin up and glared at the man. "Get out!"

Disregarding her, the man moved into the room and over to the window; Jamie could see his indistinct form disappear past the edge of the wardrobe, then reappear, back turned as he spoke to Jenny.

"One of my scouts reported hearing a shot from the vicinity of this house, not long since. Where are your men?"

"I have none." Her trembling arms would not support her longer, and Jamie saw his sister ease herself back, collapsing on the pillows. "You've taken my husband already—my eldest son is no more than ten." She did not mention Rabbie or Fergus; boys of their age were old enough to be treated—or mistreated—as men, should the Captain take the notion. With luck, they would have taken to their heels at the first sight of the English.

The Captain was a hard-bitten man of middle age, and not overly given to credulity.

"The keeping of weapons in the Highlands is a serious offense," he said, and turned to the soldier who had come into the room behind him. "Search the house, Jenkins."

He had to raise his voice in the giving of the order, for there was a rising commotion in the stairwell. As Jenkins turned to leave the room, Mrs. Innes, the midwife, burst past the soldier who tried to bar her way.

"Leave the poor lady alone!" she cried, facing the Captain with fists clenched at her sides. The midwife's voice shook and her hair was coming down from its snood, but she stood her ground. "Get out, ye wretches! Leave her be!"

"I am not mistreating your mistress," the Captain said, with some irritation, evidently mistaking Mrs. Innes for one of the maids. "I am merely—"

"And her not delivered but an hour since! It isna decent even for ye to lay eyes on her, so much as—"

"Delivered?" The Captain's voice sharpened, and he glanced from the midwife to the bed in sudden interest. "You have borne a child, Mrs. Murray? Where is the infant?"

The infant in question stirred inside its wrappings, disturbed by the tightened grip of its horror-stricken uncle.

From the depths of the wardrobe, he could see his sister's face, white to the lips and set like stone.

"The child is dead," she said.

The midwife's mouth dropped open in shock, but luckily the Captain's attention was riveted on Jenny.

"Oh?" he said slowly. "Was it—"

"Mama!" The cry of anguish came from the doorway as Young Jamie broke free of a soldier's grip and hurled himself at his mother. "Mama, the baby's dead? No, no!" Sobbing, he flung himself on his knees and buried his head in the bedclothes.

As though to refute his brother's statement, baby Ian gave evidence of his living state by kicking his legs with considerable

vigor against his uncle's ribs and emitting a series of small snuffling grunts, which fortunately went unheard in the commotion
outside.

Jenny was trying to comfort Young Jamie, Mrs. Innes was futilely attempting to raise the boy, who kept a death grip on his
mother's sleeve, the Captain was vainly trying to make himself
heard above Young Jamie's grief-stricken wails, and over all, the
muted sound of boots and shouting vibrated through the house.

Jamie rather thought the Captain was inquiring as to the location of the infant's body. He clutched the body in question closer,
joggling it in an attempt to prevent any disposition on its part to
cry. His other hand went to the hilt of his dirk, but it was a vain
gesture; it was doubtful that even cutting his own throat would be
of help, if the wardrobe was opened.

Baby Ian made an irascible noise, suggesting that he disliked
being joggled. With visions of the house in flames and the inhabitants slaughtered, the noise sounded as loud to Jamie as his elder
nephew's anguished howls.

"You did it!" Young Jamie had gotten to his feet, face wet and
swollen with tears and rage, and was advancing on the Captain,
curly black head lowered like a small ram's. "You killed my
brother, ye English prick!"

The Captain was somewhat taken aback by this sudden attack,
and actually took a step back, blinking at the boy. "No, boy,
you're quite mistaken. Why, I only—"

"Prick! Cod! *A mhic an diabhoil!*" Entirely beside himself,
Young Jamie was stalking the Captain, yelling every obscenity he
had ever heard used, in Gaelic or English.

"Enh," said baby Ian in the elder Jamie's ear. "Enh, enh!"
This sounded very much like the preliminary to a full-fledged
screech, and in a panic, Jamie let go of his dirk and thrust his
thumb into the soft, moist opening from which the sounds were
issuing. The baby's toothless gums clamped on to his thumb with
a ferocity that nearly made him exclaim aloud.

"Get out! Get out! Get out or I'll kill ye!" Young Jamie was
screaming at the Captain, face contorted with rage. The Redcoat
looked helplessly at the bed, as though to ask Jenny to call off this
implacable small foe, but she lay as though dead with her eyes
closed.

"I shall wait for my men downstairs," the Captain said, with what dignity he could, and withdrew, shutting the door hastily behind him. Deprived of his enemy, Young Jamie fell to the floor and collapsed into helpless weeping.

Through the crack in the door, Jamie saw Mrs. Innes look at Jenny, mouth opening to ask a question. Jenny shot up from the bedclothes like Lazarus, scowling ferociously, finger pressed to her lips to enjoin silence. Baby Ian champed viciously at the thumb, growling at its failure to yield any sustenance.

Jenny swung herself to the side of the bed and sat there, waiting. The sounds of the soldiers below throbbed and eddied through the house. Jenny was shaking with weakness, but she reached out a hand toward the armoire where her men lay hidden.

Jamie drew a deep breath and braced himself. It would have to be risked; his hand and wrist were wet with saliva, and the baby's growls of frustration were growing louder.

He stumbled from the wardrobe, drenched with sweat, and thrust the infant at Jenny. Baring her breast with a single wrench, she pressed the small head to her nipple, and bent over the tiny bundle, as though to protect it. The beginnings of a squawk disappeared into the muffled sounds of vigorous sucking, and Jamie sat down on the floor quite suddenly, feeling as though someone had run a sword behind his knees.

Young Jamie had sat up at the sudden opening of the wardrobe, and now sat spraddled against the door, his face blank with bewildered shock as he looked from his mother to his uncle and back again. Mrs. Innes knelt beside him, whispering urgently in his ear, but no sign of comprehension showed on the small, tear-streaked face.

By the time shouts and the creaking of harness outside betokened the soldiers' departure, Young Ian lay replete and snoring in his mother's arms. Jamie stood by the window, just out of sight, watching them go.

The room was silent, save for the liquid noise of Mrs. Innes, drinking whisky. Young Jamie sat close against his mother, cheek pressed to her shoulder. She had not looked up once since taking the baby, and still sat, head lowered over the child in her lap, her black hair hiding her face.

Jamie stepped forward and touched her shoulder. The warmth of her seemed shocking, as though cold dread were his natural state and the touch of another person somehow foreign and unnatural.

"I'll go to the priest hole," he said softly, "and to the cave when it's dark."

Jenny nodded, but without looking up at him. There were several white hairs among the black, he saw, glinting silver by the parting down the center of her head.

"I think . . . I should not come down again," he said at last. "For a time."

Jenny said nothing, but nodded once more.

6

Being Now Justified by His Blood

A s it was, he did come down to the house once more. For two months, he stayed close hidden in the cave, scarcely daring to come out at night to hunt, for the English soldiers were still in the district, quartered at Comar. The troops went out by day in small patrols of eight or ten, combing the countryside, looting what little there was to steal, destroying what they could not use. And all with the blessing of the English Crown.

A path led close by the base of the hill where his cavern was concealed. No more than a rude track, it had begun as a deer path, and still largely served that use, though it was a foolish stag that would venture within smelling distance of the cave. Still, sometimes when the wind was right, he would see a small group of the red deer on the path, or find fresh spoor in the exposed mud of the track next day.

It was helpful as well for such people as had business on the mountainside—few enough as those were. The wind had been blowing downwind from the cave, and he had no expectation of seeing deer. He had been lying on the ground just within the cave entrance, where enough light filtered through the overhanging screen of gorse and rowan for him to read on fine days. There were not a great many books, but Jared managed still to smuggle a few with his gifts from France.

This violent rain forced me to a new work, viz., to cut a hole through my new fortification, like a sink, to let the water go out, which would else have drowned my cave. After I had

*been in my cave some time, and found still no more shocks of
the earthquake follow, I began to be more composed; and
now, to support my spirits, which indeed wanted it very much,
I went to my little store and took a small sup of rum, which
however, I did then and always very sparingly, knowing I
could have no more when that was gone.*

*It continued raining all that night, and great part of the
next day, so that I could not stir abroad; but my mind being
more composed, I began to think . . .*

The shadows across the page moved as the bushes above him
stirred. Instincts attuned, he caught the shift of the wind at once—
and on it, the sound of voices.

He sprang to his feet, hand on the dirk that never left his side.
Barely pausing to put the book carefully on its ledge, he grasped
the knob of granite that he used as a handhold and pulled himself
up into the steep narrow crevice that formed the cave's entrance.

The bright flash of red and metal on the path below hit him with
a blow of shock and annoyance. Damn. He had little fear that any
of the soldiers would leave the path—they were poorly equipped
for making their way even through the normal stretches of open,
spongy peat and heather, let alone an overgrown, brambly slope
like this—but having them so close meant he could not risk leaving the cave before dark, even to get water or relieve himself. He
cast a quick glance at his water jug, knowing as he did so that it
was nearly empty.

A shout pulled his attention back to the track below, and he
nearly lost his grip on the rock. The soldiers had bunched themselves around a small figure, humped under the weight of a small
cask it bore on its shoulder. Fergus, on his way up with a cask of
fresh-brewed ale. Damn, and damn again. He could have done
with that ale; it had been months since he'd had any.

The wind had changed again, so he caught only small snatches
of words, but the small figure seemed to be arguing with the
soldier in front of him, gesticulating violently with its free hand.

"Idiot!" said Jamie, under his breath. "Give it to them and
begone, ye wee clot!"

One soldier made a two-handed grab at the cask, and missed as
the small dark-haired figure jumped nimbly back. Jamie smacked
himself on the forehead with exasperation. Fergus could never

resist insolence when confronted with authority—especially English authority.

The small figure now was skipping backward, shouting something at his pursuers.

"Fool!" Jamie said violently. "Drop it and run!"

Instead of either dropping the cask or running, Fergus, apparently sure of his own speed, turned his back on the soldiers and waggled his rump insultingly at them. Sufficiently incensed to risk their footing in the soggy vegetation, several of the Redcoats jumped the path to follow.

Jamie saw their leader raise an arm and shout in warning. It had evidently dawned on him that Fergus might be a decoy, trying to lead them into ambush. But Fergus too was shouting, and evidently the soldiers knew enough gutter French to interpret what he was saying, for while several of the men halted at their leader's shout, four of the soldiers hurled themselves at the dancing boy.

There was a scuffle and more shouting as Fergus dodged, twisting like an eel between the soldiers. In all the commotion and above the whining wind, Jamie could not have heard the rush of the saber being drawn from its scabbard, but ever after felt as though he had, as though the faint swish and ring of drawn metal had been the first inkling of disaster. It seemed to ring in his ears whenever he remembered the scene—and he remembered it for a very long time.

Perhaps it was something in the attitudes of the soldiers, an irritableness of mood that communicated itself to him in the cave. Perhaps only the sense of doom that had clung to him since Culloden, as though everything in his vicinity were tainted; at risk by virtue only of being near him. Whether he had heard the sound of the saber or not, his body had tensed itself to spring before he saw the silver arc of the blade swing through the air.

It moved almost lazily, slowly enough for his brain to have tracked its arc, deduced its target, and shouted, wordless, *no*! Surely it moved slowly enough that he could have darted down into the midst of the swarming men, seized the wrist that wielded the sword and twisted the deadly length of metal free, to tumble harmless to the ground.

The conscious part of his brain told him this was nonsense, even as it froze his hands around the granite knob, anchoring him against the overwhelming impulse to heave himself out of the earth and run forward.

You can't, it said to him, a thready whisper under the fury and the horror that filled him. *He has done this for you; you cannot make it senseless. You can't,* it said, cold as death beneath the searing rush of futility that drowned him. *You can do nothing.*

And he did nothing, nothing but watch, as the blade completed its lazy swing, crashed home with a small, almost inconsequential thunk! and the disputed cask tumbled end over end over end down the slope of the burn, its final splash lost in the merry gurgle of brown water far below.

The shouting ceased abruptly in shocked silence. He scarcely heard when it resumed; it sounded so much like the roaring in his ears. His knees gave way, and he realized dimly that he was about to faint. His vision darkened into reddish black, shot with stars and streaks of light—but not even the encroaching dark would blot out the final sight of Fergus's hand, that small and deft and clever pickpocket's hand, lying still in the mud of the track, palm turned upward in supplication.

He waited for forty-eight long, dragging hours before Rabbie MacNab came to whistle on the path below the cave.

"How is he?" he said without preliminary.

"Mrs. Jenny says he'll be all right," Rabbie answered. His young face was pale and drawn; plainly he had not yet recovered from the shock of his friend's accident. "She says he's not fevered, and there's no trace of rot yet in the"—he swallowed audibly—"in the . . . stump."

"The soldiers took him down to the house, then?" Not waiting for an answer, he was already making his way down the hillside.

"Aye, they were all amoil wi' it. I think"—Rabbie paused to distentangle his shirt from a clinging brier, and had to hurry to catch up with his employer—"I think they were sorry about it. The Captain said so, at least. And he gave Mrs. Jenny a gold sovereign—for Fergus."

"Oh, aye?" Jamie said. "Verra generous." And did not speak again, until they reached the house.

* * *

Fergus was lying in state in the nursery, ensconced in a bed by the window. His eyes were closed when Jamie entered the room, long lashes lying softly against thin cheeks. Seen without its customary animation, his usual array of grimaces and poses, his face looked quite different. The slightly beaked nose above the long, mobile mouth gave him a faintly aristocratic air, and the bones hardening beneath the skin gave some promise that his face might one day pass from boyish charm to outright handsomeness.

Jamie moved toward the bed, and the dark lashes lifted at once.

"Milord," Fergus said, and a weak smile restored his face at once to its familiar contours. "You are safe here?"

"God, laddie, I'm sorry." Jamie sank to his knees by the bed. He could scarcely bear to look at the slender forearm that lay across the quilt, its frail bandaged wrist ending in nothing, but forced himself to grip Fergus's shoulder in greeting, and rub a palm gently over the shock of dark hair.

"Does it hurt much?" he asked.

"No, milord," Fergus said. Then a sudden belying twinge of pain crossed his features, and he grinned shamefacedly. "Well, not so much. And Madame has been most generous with the whisky."

There was a tumbler full of it on the sidetable, but no more than a thimbleful had been drunk. Fergus, weaned on French wine, did not really like the taste of whisky.

"I'm sorry," Jamie said again. There was nothing else to say. Nothing he *could* say, for the tightening in his throat. He looked hastily down, knowing that it would upset Fergus to see him weep.

"Ah, milord, do not trouble yourself." There was a note of the old mischief in Fergus's voice. "Me, I have been fortunate."

Jamie swallowed hard before replying.

"Aye, you're alive—and thank God for it!"

"Oh, beyond that, milord!" He glanced up to see Fergus smiling, though still very pale. "Do you not recall our agreement, milord?"

"Agreement?"

"Yes, when you took me into your service in Paris. You told me then that should I be arrested and executed, you would have Masses said for my soul for the space of a year." The remaining hand fluttered toward the battered greenish medal that hung about his neck—St. Dismas, patron saint of thieves. "But if I should lose an ear or a hand while doing your service—"

"I would support you for the rest of your life." Jamie was unsure whether to laugh or cry, and contented himself with patting the hand that now lay quiet on the quilt. "Aye, I remember. You may trust me to keep the bargain."

"Oh, I have always trusted you, milord," Fergus assured him. Clearly he was growing tired; the pale cheeks were even whiter than they had been, and the shock of black hair fell back against the pillow. "So I am fortunate," he murmured, still smiling. "For in one stroke, I am become a gentleman of leisure, *non*?"

Jenny was waiting for him when he left Fergus's room.

"Come down to the priest hole wi' me," he said, taking her by the elbow. "I need to talk wi' ye a bit, and I shouldna stay in the open longer."

She followed him without comment, down to the stone-floored back hall that separated kitchen and pantry. Set into the flags of the floor was a large wooden panel, perforated with drilled holes, apparently mortared into the floorstones. Theoretically, this gave air to the root cellar below, and in fact—should any suspicious person choose to investigate, the root cellar, reached by a sunken door outside the house, did have just such a panel set into its ceiling.

What was not apparent was that the panel also gave light and air to a small priest hole that had been built just behind the root cellar, which could be reached by pulling up the panel, mortared frame and all, to reveal a short ladder leading down into the tiny room.

It was no more than five feet square, equipped with nothing in the way of furniture beyond a rude bench, a blanket, and a chamber pot. A large jug of water and a small box of hard biscuit completed the chamber's accoutrements. It had in fact been added to the house only within the last few years, and therefore was not really a priest hole, as no priest had occupied it or was likely to. A hole it definitely was, though.

Two people could occupy the hole only by sitting side by side on the bench, and Jamie sat down beside his sister as soon as he had replaced the panel overhead and descended the ladder. He sat still for a moment, then took a breath and started.

"I canna bear it anymore," he said. He spoke so softly that Jenny was forced to bend her head close to hear him, like a priest receiving some penitent's confession. "I can't. I must go."

They sat so close together that he could feel the rise and fall of her breast as she breathed. Then she reached out and took hold of his hand, her small firm fingers tight on his.

"Will ye try France again, then?" He had tried to escape to France twice before, thwarted each time by the tight watch the English placed on all ports. No disguise was sufficient for a man of his remarkable height and coloring.

He shook his head. "No. I shall let myself be captured."

"Jamie!" In her agitation, Jenny allowed her voice to rise momentarily, then lowered it again in response to the warning squeeze of his hand.

"Jamie, ye canna do that!" she said, lower. "Christ, man, ye'll be hangit!"

He kept his head bent as though in thought, but shook it, not hesitating.

"I think not." He glanced at his sister, then quickly away. "Claire—she had the Sight." As good an explanation as any, he thought, if not quite the truth. "She saw what would happen at Culloden—she knew. And she told me what would come after."

"Ah," said Jenny softly. "I wondered. So that was why she bade me plant potatoes—and build this place."

"Aye." He gave his sister's hand a small squeeze, then let go and turned slightly on the narrow seat to face her. "She told me that the Crown would go on hunting Jacobite traitors for some time—and they have," he added wryly. "But that after the first few years, they would no longer execute the men that were captured—only imprison them."

"Only!" his sister echoed. "If ye mun go, Jamie, take to the heather then, but to give yourself up to an English prison, whether they'll hang ye or no—"

"Wait." His hand on her arm stopped her. "I havena told it all to ye yet. I dinna mean just to walk up to the English and surrender. There's a goodly price on my head, no? Be a shame to let that go to waste, d'ye not think?" He tried to force a smile in his voice; she heard it and glanced sharply up at him.

"Holy Mother," she whispered. "So ye mean to have someone betray ye?"

"Seemingly, aye." He had decided upon the plan, alone in the cave, but it had not seemed quite real until now. "I thought perhaps Joe Fraser would be best for it."

Jenny rubbed her fist hard against her lips. She was quick; he knew she had grasped the plan at once—and all its implications.

"But Jamie," she whispered. "Even if they dinna hang ye outright—and that's the hell of a risk to take—Jamie, ye could be killed when they take ye!"

His shoulders slumped suddenly, under the weight of misery and exhaustion.

"God, Jenny," he said, "d'ye think I care?"

There was a long silence before she answered.

"No, I don't," she said. "And I canna say as I blame ye, either." She paused a moment, to steady her voice. "But *I* still care." Her fingers gently touched the back of his head, stroking his hair. "So ye'll mind yourself, won't ye, clot-heid?"

The ventilation panel overhead darkened momentarily, and there was the tapping sound of light footsteps. One of the kitchenmaids, on her way to the pantry, perhaps. Then the dim light came back, and he could see Jenny's face once more.

"Aye," he whispered at last. "I'll mind."

It took more than two months to complete the arrangements. When at last word came, it was full spring.

He sat on his favorite rock, near the cave's entrance, watching the evening stars come out. Even in the worst of the year after Culloden, he had always been able to find a moment of peace at this time of the day. As the daylight faded, it was as though objects became faintly lit from within, so they stood outlined against sky or ground, perfect and sharp in every detail. He could see the shape of a moth, invisible in the light, now limned in the dusk with a triangle of deeper shadow that made it stand out from the trunk it hid upon. In a moment, it would take wing.

He looked out across the valley, trying to stretch his eyes as far as the black pines that edged the distant cliffside. Then up, among the stars. Orion there, striding stately over the horizon. And the Pleiades, barely visible in the darkening sky. It might be his last sight of the sky for some time, and he meant to enjoy it. He thought of prison, of bars and locks and solid walls, and remem-

bered Fort William. Wentworth Prison. The Bastille. Walls of
stone, four feet thick, that blocked all air and light. Filth, stench,
hunger, entombment . . .

He shrugged such thoughts away. He had chosen his way, and
was satisfied with it. Still, he searched the sky, looking for Taurus.
Not the prettiest of constellations, but his own. Born under the
sign of the bull, stubborn and strong. Strong enough, he hoped, to
do what he intended.

Among the growing night sounds, there was a sharp, high whistle. It might have been the homing song of a curlew on the loch,
but he recognized the signal. Someone was coming up the path—a
friend.

It was Mary MacNab, who had become kitchenmaid at Lallybroch, after the death of her husband. Usually it was her son
Rabbie, or Fergus, who brought him food and news, but she had
come a few times before.

She had brought a basket, unusually well supplied, with a cold
roast partridge, fresh bread, several young green onions, a bunch
of early cherries, and a flask of ale. Jamie examined the bounty,
then looked up with a wry smile.

"My farewell feast, eh?"

She nodded, silent. She was a small woman, dark hair heavily
streaked with gray, and her face lined by the difficulties of life.
Still, her eyes were soft and brown, and her lips still full and gently
curved.

He realized that he was staring at her mouth, and hastily turned
again to the basket.

"Lord, I'll be so full I'll not be able to move. Even a cake, now!
However did ye ladies manage that?"

She shrugged—she wasn't a great chatterer, Mary MacNab—
and taking the basket from him, proceeded to lay the meal on the
wooden tabletop, balanced on stones. She laid places for both of
them. This was nothing out of the ordinary; she had supped with
him before, to give him the gossip of the district while they ate.
Still, if this was his last meal before leaving Lallybroch, he was
surprised that neither his sister nor the boys had come to share it.
Perhaps the farmhouse had visitors that would make it difficult for
them to leave undetected.

He gestured politely for her to sit first, before taking his own
place, cross-legged on the hard dirt floor.

"Ye've spoken wi' Joe Fraser? Where is it to be, then?" he asked, taking a bite of cold partridge.

She told him the details of the plan; a horse would be brought before dawn, and he would ride out of the narrow valley by way of the pass. Then turn, cross the rocky foothills and come down, back into the valley by Feesyhant's Burn, as though he were coming home. The English would meet him somewhere between Struy and Eskadale, most likely at Midmains; it was a good place for an ambush, for the glen rose steeply there on both sides, but with a wooded patch by the stream where several men could conceal themselves.

After the meal, she packed the basket tidily, leaving out enough food for a small breakfast before his dawn leaving. He expected her to go then, but she did not. She rummaged in the crevice where he kept his bedding, spread it neatly upon the floor, turned back the blankets and knelt beside the pallet, hands folded on her lap.

He leaned back against the wall of the cave, arms folded. He looked down at the crown of her bowed head in exasperation.

"Oh, like that, is it?" he demanded. "And whose idea was this? Yours, or my sister's?"

"Does it matter?" She was composed, her hands perfectly still on her lap, her dark hair smooth in its snood.

He shook his head and bent down to pull her to her feet.

"No, it doesna matter, because it's no going to happen. I appreciate your meaning, but—"

His speech was interrupted by her kiss. Her lips *were* as soft as they looked. He grasped her firmly by both wrists and pushed her away from him.

"No!" he said. "It isna necessary, and I dinna want to do it." He was uncomfortably aware that his body did not agree at all with his assessments of necessity, and still more uncomfortable at the knowledge that his breeches, too small and worn thin, made the magnitude of the disagreement obvious to anyone who cared to look. The slight smile curving those full, sweet lips suggested that she was looking.

He turned her toward the entrance and gave her a light push, to which she responded by stepping aside and reaching behind her for the fastenings to her skirt.

"Don't do that!" he exclaimed.

"How d'ye mean to stop me?" she asked, stepping out of the

garment and folding it tidily over the single stool. Her slender fingers went to the laces of her bodice.

"If ye won't leave, then I'll have to," he replied with decision. He whirled on his heel and headed for the cave entrance, when he heard her voice behind him.

"My lord!" she said.

He stopped, but did not turn around. "It isna suitable to call me that," he said.

"Lallybroch is yours," she said. "And will be so long as ye live. If ye're its laird, I'll call ye so."

"It isna mine. The estate belongs to Young Jamie."

"It isna Young Jamie that's doing what you are," she answered with decision. "And it isna your sister that's asked me to do what I'm doin'. Turn round."

He turned, reluctantly. She stood barefoot in her shift, her hair loose over her shoulders. She was thin, as they all were these days, but her breasts were larger than he had thought, and the nipples showed prominently through the thin fabric. The shift was as worn as her other garments, frayed at the hem and shoulders, almost transparent in spots. He closed his eyes.

He felt a light touch on his arm, and willed himself to stand still.

"I ken weel enough what ye're thinkin'," she said. "For I saw your lady, and I know how it was between the two of ye. I never had that," she added, in a softer voice, "not wi' either of the two men I wed. But I know the look of a true love, and it's not in my mind to make ye feel ye've betrayed it."

The touch, feather-light, moved to his cheek, and a work-worn thumb traced the groove that ran from nose to mouth.

"What I want," she said quietly, "is to give ye something different. Something less, mayhap, but something ye can use; something to keep ye whole. Your sister and the bairns canna give ye that—but I can." He heard her draw breath, and the touch on his face lifted away.

"Ye've given me my home, my life, and my son. Will ye no let me gi'e ye this small thing in return?"

He felt tears sting his eyelids. The weightless touch moved across his face, wiping the moisture from his eyes, smoothing the roughness of his hair. He lifted his arms, slowly, and reached out.

She stepped inside his embrace, as neatly and simply as she had laid the table and the bed.

"I . . . havena done this in a long time," he said, suddenly shy.

"Neither have I," she said, with a tiny smile. "But we'll remember how 'tis."

PART THREE

When I Am Thy Captive

7

A Faith in Documents

Inverness
May 25, 1968

The envelope from Linklater arrived in the morning post.
"Look how fat it is!" Brianna exclaimed. "He's sent something!" The tip of her nose was pink with excitement.

"Looks like it," said Roger. He was outwardly calm, but I could see the pulse beating in the hollow of his throat. He picked up the thick manila envelope and held it for a moment, weighing it. Then he ripped the flap recklessly with his thumb, and yanked out a sheaf of photocopied pages.

The cover letter, on heavy university stationery, fluttered out. I snatched it from the floor and read it aloud, my voice shaking a little.

" 'Dear Dr. Wakefield,' " I read. " 'This is in reply to your inquiry regarding the execution of Jacobite officers by the Duke of Cumberland's troops following the Battle of Culloden. The main source of the quote in my book to which you refer, was the private journal of one Lord Melton, in command of an infantry regiment under Cumberland at the time of Culloden. I have enclosed photocopies of the relevant pages of the journal; as you will see, the story of the survivor, one James Fraser, is an odd and touching one. Fraser is not an important historical character, and not in line with the thrust of my own work, but I have often thought of investigating further, in hopes of determining his eventual fate. Should you find that he did survive the journey to his own estate, I should be happy if you would inform me. I have always rather hoped that he did, though his situation as described by Melton

makes the possibility seem unlikely. Sincerely yours, Eric Link-
later.' ''

The paper rattled in my hand, and I set it down, very carefully,
on the desk.

"Unlikely, huh?" Brianna said, standing on tiptoe to see over
Roger's shoulder. "Ha! He *did* make it back, we know he did!"

"We think he did," Roger corrected, but it was only scholarly
caution; his grin was as broad as Brianna's.

"Will ye be havin' tea or cocoa to your elevenses?" Fiona's
curly dark head poked through the study doorway, interrupting the
excitement. "There's fresh ginger-nut biscuits, just baked." The
scent of warm ginger came into the study with her, wafting enticingly from her apron.

"Tea, please," said Roger, just as Brianna said, "Oh, cocoa
sounds great!" Fiona, wearing a smug expression, pushed in the
tea cart, sporting both tea cozy and pot of cocoa, as well as a plate
of fresh ginger-nut biscuits.

I accepted a cup of tea myself, and sat down in the wing chair
with the pages of Melton's journal. The flowing eighteenth-century handwriting was surprisingly clear, in spite of the archaic
spelling, and within minutes, I was in the confines of Leanach
farmhouse, imagining the sound of buzzing flies, the stir of close-
packed bodies, and the harsh smell of blood soaking into the
packed-dirt floor.

*". . . in satisfaction of my brother's debt of honor, I could not
do otherwise than to spare Fraser's life. I therefore omitted his
name from the list of traitors executed at the farmhouse, and have
made arrangement for his transport to his own estate. I cannot feel
myself either altogether merciful toward Fraser in the taking of
this action, nor yet altogether culpable with respect to my service
toward the Duke, as Fraser's situation, with a great wound in his
leg festering and pustulent, makes it unlikely that he will survive
the journey to his home. Still, honor prevents my acting otherwise,
and I will confess that my spirit was lightened to see the man
removed, still living, from the field, as I turned my own attentions
to the melancholy task of disposing of the bodies of his comrades.
So much killing as I have seen these last two days oppresses me,''*
the entry ended simply.

I laid the pages down on my knee, swallowing heavily. *"A great
wound . . . festering and pustulent . . ."* I knew, as Roger and

Brianna could not, just how serious such a wound would have been, with no antibiotics, nothing in the way of proper medical treatment; not even the crude herbal poultices available to a High- land charmer at the time. How long would it have taken, jolting from Culloden to Broch Tuarach in a wagon? Two days? Three? How could he have lived, in such a state, and neglected for so long?

"He did, though." Brianna's voice broke in upon my thoughts, answering what seemed to be a similar thought expressed by Roger. She spoke with simple assurance, as though she had seen all the events described in Melton's journal, and were sure of their outcome. "He did get back. He was the Dunbonnet, I know it."

"The Dunbonnet?" Fiona, tut-tutting over my cold cup of un- drunk tea, looked over her shoulder in surprise. "Heard of the Dunbonnet, have ye?"

"Have *you*?" Roger looked at the young housekeeper in aston- ishment.

She nodded, casually dumping my tea into the aspidistra that stood by the hearth and refilling my cup with fresh steaming brew.

"Oh, aye. My grannie tellt me that tale, often and often."

"Tell us!" Brianna leaned forward, intent, her cocoa cupped between her palms. "Please, Fiona! What's the story?"

Fiona seemed mildly surprised to find herself suddenly the cen- ter of so much attention, but shrugged good-naturedly.

"Och, it's just the story of one o' the followers o' the Bonnie Prince. When there was the great defeat at Culloden, and sae many were killed, a few escaped. Why, one man fled the field and swam the river to get away, but the Redcoats were after him, nonetheless. He came to a kirk along his way, and a service going on inside, and he dashing in, prayed mercy from the minister. The minister and the people took pity on him, and he put on the minister's robe, so when the Redcoats burst in moments later, there he was, stand- ing at the pulpit, preachin' the sermon, and the water from his beard and clothes puddled up about his feet. The Redcoats thought they were mistaken, and went on down the road, and so he escaped —and everyone in the kirk said 'twas the best sermon they ever heard!" Fiona laughed heartily, while Brianna frowned, and Roger looked puzzled.

"That was the Dunbonnet?" he said. "But I thought—"

"Och, no!" she assured him. "That was no the Dunbonnet—

only the Dunbonnet was another o' the men who got away from
Culloden. He came back to his own estate, but because the Sassenachs were hunting men all across the Highlands, he lay hidden
there in a cave for seven years.''

Hearing this, Brianna slumped back in her chair with a sigh of
relief. ''And his tenants called him the Dunbonnet so as not to
speak his name and betray him,'' she murmured.

''Ye ken the story?'' Fiona asked, astonished. ''Aye, that's
right.''

''And did your grannie say what happened to him after that?''
Roger prompted.

''Oh, aye!'' Fiona's eyes were round as butterscotch drops.
''That's the best part o' the story. See, there was a great famine
after Culloden; folk were starvin' in the glens, turned out of their
houses in winter, the men shot and the cots set afire. The Dunbonnet's tenants managed better than most, but even so, there came a
day when the food ran out, and their bellies garbeled from dawn
'til dark—no game in the forest, nay grain in the field, and the
weans dyin' in their mothers' arms for lack o' milk to feed them.''

A cold chill swept over me at her words. I saw the faces of the
Lallybroch inhabitants—the people I had known and loved—
pinched with cold and starvation. Not only horror filled me; there
was guilt, too. I had been safe, warm, and well fed, instead of
sharing their fate—because I had done as Jamie wanted, and left
them. I looked at Brianna, smooth red head bent in absorption, and
the tight feeling in my chest eased a bit. She too had been safe for
these past years, warm, well fed, and loved—because I had done
as Jamie wanted.

''So he made a bold plan, the Dunbonnet did,'' Fiona was
continuing. Her round face was alight with the drama of her tale.
''He arranged that one of his tenants should go to the English, and
offer to betray him. There was a good price on his head, for he'd
been a great warrior for the Prince. The tenant would take the gold
o' the reward—to use for the folk on the estate, o' course—and
tell the English where the Dunbonnet might be taken.''

My hand clenched so convulsively at this that the delicate handle of my teacup snapped clean off.

''Taken?'' I croaked, my voice hoarse with shock. ''Did they
hang him?''

Fiona blinked at me in surprise. ''Why, no,'' she said. ''They wanted to, my grannie said, and took him to trial for treason, but in the end, they shut him up in a prison instead—but the gold went to his tenants, and so they lived through the famine," she ended cheerfully, obviously regarding this as the happy ending.

"Jesus Christ," Roger breathed. He set his cup down carefully, and sat staring into space, transfixed. "Prison."

"You sound like that's *good*," Brianna protested. The corners of her mouth were tight with distress, and her eyes slightly shiny.

"It is," Roger said, not noticing her distress. "There weren't that many prisons where the English imprisoned Jacobite traitors, and they all kept official records. Don't you see?" he demanded, looking from Fiona's bewilderment to Brianna's scowl, then settling on me in hope of finding understanding. "If he went to prison, I can find him." He turned then, to look up at the towering shelves of books that lined three walls of the study, holding the late Reverend Wakefield's collection of Jacobite arcana.

"He's in there," Roger said softly. "On a prison roll. In a document—real evidence! Don't you see?" he demanded again, turning back to me. "Going to prison made him a part of written history again! And somewhere in there, we'll find him!"

"And what happened to him then," Brianna breathed. "When he was released."

Roger's lips pressed tight together, to cut off the alternative that sprang to his mind, as it had to mine—"or died."

"Yes, that's right," he said, taking Brianna's hand. His eyes met mine, deep green and unfathomable. "When he was released."

A week later, Roger's faith in documents remained unshaken. The same could not be said for the eighteenth-century table in the late Reverend Wakefield's study, whose spindly legs wobbled and creaked alarmingly beneath their unaccustomed burden.

This table normally was asked to accommodate no more than a small lamp, and a collection of the Reverend's smaller artifacts; it was pressed into service now only because every other horizontal surface in the study already overflowed with papers, journals, books, and bulging manila envelopes from antiquarian societies, universities, and research libraries across England, Scotland, and Ireland.

"If you set one more page on that thing, it's going to collapse," Claire observed, as Roger carelessly reached out, meaning to drop the folder he was carrying on the little inlaid table.

"Ah? Oh, right." He switched direction in midair, looked vainly for another place to put the folder, and finally settled for placing it on the floor at his feet.

"I've just about finished with Wentworth," Claire said. She indicated a precarious stack on the floor with her toe. "Have we got in the records for Berwick yet?"

"Yes, just this morning. Where did I put them, though?" Roger stared vaguely about the room, which strongly resembled the sacking of the library at Alexandria, just before the first torch was lit. He rubbed his forehead, trying to concentrate. After a week of spending ten-hour days thumbing the handwritten registers of British prisons, and the letters, journals, and diaries of their governors, searching for any official trace of Jamie Fraser, Roger was beginning to feel as though his eyes had been sandpapered.

"It was blue," he said at last. "I distinctly remember it was blue. I got those from McAllister, the History Lecturer at Trinity at Cambridge, and Trinity College uses those big envelopes in pale blue, with the college's coat of arms on the front. Maybe Fiona's seen it. Fiona!"

He stepped to the study door and called down the hall toward the kitchen. Despite the lateness of the hour, the light was still on, and the heartening scent of cocoa and freshly baked almond cake lingered in the air. Fiona would never abandon her post while there was the faintest possibility that someone in her vicinity might require nourishment.

"Och, aye?" Fiona's curly brown head poked out of the kitchen. "There'll be cocoa ready directly," she assured him. "I'm only waiting for the cake to be out of the oven."

Roger smiled at her with deep affection. Fiona had not the slightest use herself for history—never read anything beyond *My Weekly* magazine—but she never questioned his activities, tranquilly dusting the heaps of books and papers daily, without bothering about their contents.

"Thanks, Fiona," he said. "I was only wondering, though; have you seen a big blue envelope—a fat one, about so?" He measured with his hands. "It came in the morning post, but I've misplaced it."

"Ye left it in the upstairs bath," she said promptly. "There's that great thick book wi' the gold writing and the picture of the Bonnie Prince on the front up there, and three letters ye'd just opened, and there's the gas bill, too, which ye dinna want to be forgetting, it's due on the fourteenth o' the month. I've put it all on the top of the geyser, so as to be out of the way." A tiny, sharp ding! from the oven timer made her withdraw her head abruptly with a smothered exclamation.

Roger turned and went up the stairs two at a time, smiling. Given other inclinations, Fiona's memory might have made her a scholar. As it was, she was no mean research assistant. So long as a particular document or book could be described on the basis of its appearance, rather than its title or contents, Fiona was bound to know exactly where it was.

"Och, it's nothing," she had assured Roger airily, when he had tried to apologize earlier for the mess he was making of the house. "Ye'd think the Reverend was still alive, wi' such a moil of papers strewn everywhere. It's just like old times, no?"

Coming down more slowly, with the blue envelope in his hands, he wondered what his late adoptive father might have thought of this present quest.

"In it up to the eyebrows, I shouldn't wonder," he murmured to himself. He had a vivid memory of the Reverend, bald head gleaming under the old-fashioned bowl lamps that hung from the hall ceiling, as he pottered from his study to the kitchen, where old Mrs. Graham, Fiona's grandmother, would have been manning the stove, supplying the old man's bodily needs during bouts of late-night scholarship, just as Fiona was now doing for him.

It made one wonder, he thought, as he went into the study. In the old days, when a man's son usually followed his father's profession, was that only a matter of convenience—wanting to keep the business in the family—or was there some sort of family predisposition for some kinds of work? Were some people actually born to be smiths, or merchants, or cooks—born to an inclination and an aptitude, as well as to the opportunity?

Clearly it didn't apply to everyone; there were always the people who left their homes, went a-wandering, tried things hitherto unknown in their family circles. If that weren't so, probably there would be no inventors, no explorers; still, there seemed to be a certain affinity for some careers in some families, even in these restless modern times of widespread education and easy travel.

What he was really wondering about, he thought to himself, was Brianna. He watched Claire, her curly gold-shot head bent over the desk, and found himself wondering how much Brianna would be like her, and how much like the shadowy Scot—warrior, farmer, courtier, laird—who had been her father?

His thoughts were still running on such lines a quarter-hour later, when Claire closed the last folder on her stack and sat back, sighing.

"Penny for your thoughts?" she asked, reaching for her drink.

"Not worth that much," Roger replied with a smile, coming out of his reverie. "I was only wondering how people come to be what they are. How did you come to be a doctor, for instance?"

"How did I come to be a doctor?" Claire inhaled the steam from her cup of cocoa, decided it was too hot to drink, and set it back on the desk, among the litter of books and journals and pencil-scribbled sheets of paper. She gave Roger a half-smile and rubbed her hands together, dispersing the warmth of the cup.

"How did you come to be a historian?"

"More or less honestly," he answered, leaning back in the Reverend's chair and waving at the accumulation of papers and trivia all around them. He patted a small gilt traveling clock that sat on the desk, an elegant bit of eighteenth-century workmanship, with miniature chimes that struck the hour, the quarter, and the half.

"I grew up in the midst of it all; I was ferreting round the Highlands in search of artifacts with my father from the time I could read. I suppose it just seemed natural to keep doing it. But you?"

She nodded and stretched, easing her shoulders from the long hours of stooping over the desk. Brianna, unable to stay awake, had given up and gone to bed an hour before, but Claire and Roger had gone on with their search through the administrative records of British prisons.

"Well, it was something like that for me," she said. "It wasn't so much that I suddenly decided I must become a doctor—it was just that I suddenly realized one day that I'd *been* one for a long time—and then I wasn't, and I missed it."

She spread her hands out on the desk and flexed her fingers, long and supple, the nails buffed into neat, shiny ovals.

"There used to be an old song from the First World War," she said reflectively. "I used to hear it sometimes when some of Uncle Lamb's old army friends would come round and stay up late and get drunk. It went, 'How You Gonna Keep 'em Down on the Farm, After They've Seen Paree?' " She sang the first line, then broke off with a wry smile.

"I'd seen Paree," she said softly. She looked up from her hands, alert and present, but with the traces of memory in her eyes, fixed on Roger with the clarity of a second sight. "And a lot of other things besides. Caen and Amiens, Preston, and Falkirk, the Hôpital des Anges and the so-called surgery at Leoch. I'd *been* a doctor, in every way there is—I'd delivered babies, set bones, stitched wounds, treated fevers . . ." She trailed off, and shrugged. "There was a terrible lot I didn't know, of course. I knew how much I could learn—and that's why I went to medical school. But it didn't really make a difference, you know." She dipped a finger into the whipped cream floating on her cocoa, and licked it off. "I have a diploma with an M.D. on it—but I was a doctor long before I set foot in medical school."

"It can't possibly have been as easy as you make it sound." Roger blew on his own cocoa, studying Claire with open interest. "There weren't many women in medicine then—there aren't that many women doctors *now,* come to that—and you had a family, besides."

"No, I can't say it was easy at all." Claire looked at him quizzically. "I waited until Brianna was in school, of course, and we had enough money to afford someone to come in to cook and clean—but . . ." She shrugged and smiled ironically. "I stopped sleeping for several years, there. That helped a bit. And oddly enough, Frank helped, too."

Roger tested his own cup and found it almost cool enough to drink. He held it between his hands, enjoying the heat of the thick white porcelain seeping into his palms. Early June it might be, but the nights were cool enough to make the electric fire still a necessity.

"Really?" he said curiously. "Only from the things you've said about him, I shouldn't have thought he'd have liked your wanting to go to medical school or be a doctor."

"He didn't." Her lips pressed tight together; the motion told Roger more than words might, recalling arguments, conversations half-finished and abandoned, an opposition of stubbornness and devious obstruction rather than of open disapproval.

What a remarkably expressive face she had, he thought, watching her. He wondered quite suddenly whether his own was as easily readable. The thought was so unsettling that he dipped his face into his mug, gulping the cocoa, although it was still a bit too hot.

He emerged from the cup to find Claire watching him, slightly sardonic.

"Why?" he asked quickly, to distract her. "What made him change his mind?"

"Bree," she said, and her face softened as it always did at the mention of her daughter. "Bree was the only thing really important to Frank."

I had, as I'd said, waited until Brianna began school before beginning medical school myself. But even so, there was a large gap between her hours and my own, which we filled haphazardly with a series of more or less competent housekeepers and baby-sitters; some more, most of them less.

My mind went back to the frightful day when I had gotten a call at the hospital, telling me that Brianna was hurt. I had dashed out of the place, not pausing to change out of the green linen scrub-suit I was wearing, and raced for home, ignoring all speed limits, to find a police car and an ambulance lighting the night with bloodred pulses, and a knot of interested neighbors clustered on the street outside.

As we pieced the story together later, what had happened was that the latest temporary sitter, annoyed at my being late yet again, had simply put on her coat at quitting time and left, abandoning seven-year-old Brianna with instructions to "wait for Mommy." This she had obediently done, for an hour or so. But as it began to get dark, she had become frightened in the house alone, and determined to go out and find me. Making her way across one of the busy streets near our house, she had been struck by a car turning into the street.

She wasn't—thank God!—hurt badly; the car had been moving slowly, and she had only been shaken and bruised by the experience. Not nearly as shaken as I was, for that matter. Nor as bruised, when I came into the living room to find her lying on the sofa, and she looked at me, tears welling afresh on her stained cheeks and said, "Mommy! Where were you? I couldn't find you!"

It had taken just about all my reserves of professional composure to comfort her, to check her over, re-tend her cuts and scrapes, thank her rescuers—who, to my fevered mind, all glared accusingly at me—and put her to bed with her teddy bear clutched securely in her arms. Then I sat down at the kitchen table and cried myself.

Frank patted me awkwardly, murmuring, but then gave it up, and with more practicality, went to make tea.

"I've decided," I said, when he set the steaming cup in front of me. I spoke dully, my head feeling thick and clogged. "I'll resign. I'll do it tomorrow."

"Resign?" Frank's voice was sharp with astonishment. "From the school? What for?"

"I can't stand it anymore." I never took cream or sugar in my tea. Now I added both, stirring and watching the milky tendrils swirl through the cup. "I can't stand leaving Bree, and not knowing if she's well cared for—and knowing she isn't happy. You know she doesn't really like any of the sitters we've tried."

"I know that, yes." He sat opposite me, stirring his own tea. After a long moment, he said, "But I don't think you should resign."

It was the last thing I had expected; I had thought he would greet my decision with relieved applause. I stared at him in astonishment, then blew my nose yet again on the wadded tissue from my pocket.

"You don't?"

"Ah, Claire." He spoke impatiently, but with a tinge of affection nonetheless. "You've known forever who you are. Do you realize at all how unusual it is to know that?"

"No." I wiped my nose with the shredding tissue, dabbing carefully to keep it in one piece.

Frank leaned back in his chair, shaking his head as he looked at me.

"No, I suppose not," he said. He was quiet for a minute, looking down at his folded hands. They were long-fingered, narrow; smooth and hairless as a girl's. Elegant hands, made for casual gestures and the emphasis of speech.

He stretched them out on the table and looked at them as though he'd never seen them before.

"I haven't got that," he said quietly at last. "I'm good, all right. At what I do—the teaching, the writing. Bloody splendid sometimes, in fact. And I like it a good bit, enjoy what I do. But the thing is—" He hesitated, then looked at me straight on, hazel-eyed and earnest. "I could do something else, and be as good. Care as much, or as little. I haven't got that absolute conviction that there's something in life I'm meant to do—and you have."

"Is that good?" The edges of my nostrils were sore, and my eyes puffed from crying.

He laughed shortly. "It's damned inconvenient, Claire. To you and me and Bree, all three. But my God, I do envy you sometimes."

He reached out for my hand, and after a moment's hesitation, I let him have it.

"To have that passion for anything"—a small twitch tugged the corner of his mouth—"or anyone. That's quite splendid, Claire, and quite terribly rare." He squeezed my hand gently and let it go, turning to reach behind him for one of the books on the shelf beside the table.

It was one of his references, Woodhill's Patriots, *a series of profiles of the American Founding Fathers.*

He laid his hand on the cover of the book, gently, as though reluctant to disturb the rest of the sleeping lives interred there.

"These were people like that. The ones who cared so terribly much—enough to risk everything, enough to change and do things. Most people aren't like that, you know. It isn't that they don't care, but that they don't care so greatly." He took my hand again, this time turning it over. One finger traced the lines that webbed my palm, tickling as it went.

"Is it there, I wonder?" he said, smiling a little. "Are

*some people destined for a great fate, or to do great things?
Or is it only that they're born somehow with that great passion—and if they find themselves in the right circumstances,
then things happen? It's the sort of thing you wonder, studying history . . . but there's no way of telling, really. All we
know is what they accomplished.*

"But Claire—" His eyes held a definite note of warning,
as he tapped the cover of his book. "They paid for it," he
said.

"I know." I felt very remote now, as though I were watching us from a distance; I could see it quite clearly in my
mind's eye; Frank, handsome, lean, and a little tired, going
beautifully gray at the temples. Me, grubby in my surgical
scrubs, my hair coming down, the front of my shirt crumpled
and stained with Brianna's tears.

We sat in silence for some time, my hand still resting in
Frank's. I could see the mysterious lines and valleys, clear as
a road map—but a road to what unknown destination?

I had had my palm read once years before, by an old
Scottish lady named Graham—Fiona's grandmother, in fact.
"The lines in your hand change as you change," she had
said. "It's no so much what you're born with, as what ye
make of yourself."

And what had I made of myself, what was I making? A
mess, that was what. Neither a good mother, nor a good wife,
nor a good doctor. A mess. Once I had thought I was whole—
had seemed to be able to love a man, to bear a child, to heal
the sick—and know that all these things were natural parts of
me, not the difficult, troubled fragments into which my life
had now disintegrated. But that had been in the past, the man
I had loved was Jamie, and for a time, I had been part of
something greater than myself.

"I'll take Bree."

I was so deep in miserable thought that for a moment
Frank's words didn't register, and I stared at him stupidly.

"What did you say?"

"I said," he repeated patiently, "that I'll take Bree. She
can come from her school to the university, and play at my
office until I'm ready to come home."

I rubbed my nose. "I thought you didn't think it appropri-

*ate for staff to bring their children to work." He had been
quite critical of Mrs. Clancy, one of the secretaries, who had
brought her grandson to work for a month when his mother
was sick.*

He shrugged, looking uncomfortable.

*"Well, circumstances alter cases. And Brianna's not likely
to be running up and down the halls shrieking and spilling
ink like Bart Clancy."*

*"I wouldn't bet my life on it," I said wryly. "But you'd do
that?" A small feeling was growing in the pit of my clenched
stomach; a cautious, unbelieving feeling of relief. I might not
trust Frank to be faithful to me—I knew quite well he wasn't
—but I did trust him unequivocally to care for Bree.*

*Suddenly the worry was removed. I needn't hurry home
from the hospital, filled with dread because I was late, hating
the thought of finding Brianna crouched in her room sulking
because she didn't like the current sitter. She loved Frank; I
knew she would be ecstatic at the thought of going to his
office every day.*

*"Why?" I asked bluntly. "It isn't that you're dead keen on
my being a doctor; I know that."*

*"No," he said thoughtfully. "It isn't that. But I do think
there isn't any way to stop you—perhaps the best I can do is
to help, so that there will be less damage to Brianna." His
features hardened slightly then, and he turned away.*

"So far as he ever felt he had a destiny—something he was
really meant to do—he felt that Brianna was it," Claire said. She
stirred her cocoa meditatively.

"Why do you care, Roger?" she asked him suddenly. "Why
are you asking me?"

He took a moment to answer, slowly sipping his cocoa. It was
rich and dark, made with new cream and a sprinkle of brown
sugar. Fiona, always a realist, had taken one look at Brianna and
given up her attempts to lure Roger into matrimony via his stomach, but Fiona was a cook the same way Claire was a doctor; born
to skill, and unable not to use it.

"Because I'm a historian, I suppose," he answered finally. He watched her over the rim of his cup. "I need to know. What people really did, and why they did it."

"And you think I can tell you that?" She glanced sharply at him. "Or that I know?"

He nodded, sipping. "You know, better than most people. Most of a historian's sources haven't your"—he paused and gave her a grin—"your unique perspective, shall we say?"

There was a sudden lessening of tension. She laughed and picked up her own cup. "We shall say that," she agreed.

"The other thing," he went on, watching her closely, "is that you're honest. I don't think you *could* lie, even if you wanted to."

She glanced at him sharply, and gave a short, dry laugh.

"Everyone can lie, young Roger, given cause enough. Even me. It's only that it's harder for those of us who live in glass faces; we have to think up our lies ahead of time."

She bent her head and shuffled through the papers before her, turning the pages over slowly, one by one. They were lists of names, these sheets, lists of prisoners, copied from the ledger books of British prisons. The task was complicated by the fact that not all prisons had been well run.

Some governors kept no official lists of their inmates, or listed them haphazardly in their journals, in among the notations of daily expenditure and maintenance, making no great distinction between the death of a prisoner and the slaughter of two bullocks, salted for meat.

Roger thought Claire had abandoned the conversation, but a moment later she looked up again.

"You're quite right, though," she said. "I'm honest—from default, more than anything. It isn't easy for me *not* to say what I'm thinking. I imagine you see it because you're the same way."

"Am I?" Roger felt absurdly pleased, as though someone had given him an unexpected present.

Claire nodded, a small smile on her lips as she watched him.

"Oh, yes. It's unmistakable, you know. There aren't many people like that—who will tell you the truth about themselves and anything else right out. I've only met three people like that, I think —four now," she said, her smile widening to warm him.

"There was Jamie, of course." Her long fingers rested lightly on the stack of papers, almost caressing in their touch. "Master

Raymond, the apothecary I knew in Paris. And a friend I met in medical school—Joe Abernathy. Now you. I think.''

She tilted her cup and swallowed the last of the rich brown liquid. She set it down and looked directly at Roger.

''Frank was right, in a way, though. It isn't necessarily easier if you know what it is you're meant to do—but at least you don't waste time in questioning or doubting. If you're honest—well, that isn't necessarily easier, either. Though I suppose if you're honest with yourself and know what you are, at least you're less likely to feel that you've wasted your life, doing the wrong thing.''

She set aside the stack of papers and drew up another—a set of folders with the characteristic logo of the British Museum on the covers.

''Jamie had that,'' she said softly, as though to herself. ''He wasn't a man to turn away from anything he thought his job. Dangerous or not. And I think he won't have felt himself wasted—no matter what happened to him.''

She lapsed into silence, then, absorbed in the spidery tracings of some long-dead writer, looking for the entry that might tell her what Jamie Fraser had done and been, and whether his life had been wasted in a prison cell, or ended in a lonely dungeon.

The clock on the desk struck midnight, its chimes surprisingly deep and melodious for such a small instrument. The quarter-hour struck, and then the half, punctuating the monotonous rustle of pages. Roger put down the sheaf of flimsy papers he had been thumbing through, and yawned deeply, not troubling to cover his mouth.

''I'm so tired I'm seeing double,'' he said. ''Shall we go on with it in the morning?''

Claire didn't answer for a moment; she was looking into the glowing bars of the electric fire, a look of unutterable distance on her face. Roger repeated his question, and slowly she came back from wherever she was.

''No,'' she said. She reached for another folder, and smiled at Roger, the look of distance lingering in her eyes. ''You go on, Roger,'' she said. ''I'll—just look a little longer.''

When I finally found it, I nearly flipped right past it. I had not been reading the names carefully, but only skimming the pages for the letter "J." "John, Joseph, Jacques, James." There were James Edward, James Alan, James Walter, ad infinitum. Then it was there, the writing small and precise across the page: "Jms. Mac-Kenzie Fraser, of Brock Turac."

I put the page down carefully on the table, shut my eyes for a moment to clear them, then looked again. It was still there.

"Jamie," I said aloud. My heart was beating heavily in my chest. "Jamie," I said again, more quietly.

It was nearly three o'clock in the morning. Everyone was asleep, but the house, in the manner of old houses, was still awake around me, creaking and sighing, keeping me company. Strangely enough, I had no desire to leap up and wake Brianna or Roger, to tell them the news. I wanted to keep it to myself for a bit, as though I were alone here in the lamp-lit room with Jamie himself.

My finger traced the line of ink. The person who had written that line had seen Jamie—perhaps had written this with Jamie standing in front of him. The date at the top of the page was May 16, 1753. It had been close to this time of year, then. I could imagine how the air had been, chilly and fresh, with the rare spring sun across his shoulders, lighting sparks in his hair.

How had he worn his hair then—short, or long? He had preferred to wear it long, plaited or tailed behind. I remembered the casual gesture with which he would lift the weight of it off his neck to cool himself in the heat of exercise.

He would not have worn his kilt—the wearing of all tartans had been outlawed after Culloden. Breeks, then, likely, and a linen shirt. I had made such sarks for him; I could feel the softness of the fabric in memory, the billowing length of the three full yards it took to make one, the long tails and full sleeves that let the Highland men drop their plaids and sleep or fight with a sark their only garment. I could imagine his shoulders broad beneath the rough-woven cloth, his skin warm through it, hands touched with the chill of the Scottish spring.

He had been imprisoned before. How would he have looked, facing an English prison clerk, knowing all too well what waited for him? Grim as hell, I thought, staring down that long, straight nose with his eyes a cold, dark blue—dark and forbidding as the waters of Loch Ness.

I opened my own eyes, realizing only then that I was sitting on the edge of my chair, the folder of photocopied pages clasped tight to my chest, so caught up in my conjuration that I had not even paid attention to which prison these registers had come from.

There were several large prisons that the English had used regularly in the eighteenth century, and a number of minor ones. I turned the folder over, slowly. Would it be Berwick, near the border? The notorious Tolbooth of Edinburgh? Or one of the southern prisons, Leeds Castle or even the Tower of London?

"Ardsmuir," said the notecard neatly stapled to the front of the folder.

"Ardsmuir?" I said blankly. "Where the hell is *that*?"

8

Honor's Prisoner

**Ardsmuir, Scotland
February 15, 1755**

"Ardsmuir is the carbuncle on God's bum," Colonel Harry Quarry said. He raised his glass sardonically to the young man by the window. "I've been here a twelvemonth, and that's eleven months and twenty-nine days too long. Give you joy of your new posting, my lord."

Major John William Grey turned from the window over the courtyard, where he had been surveying his new domain.

"It does appear a trifle incommodious," he agreed dryly, picking up his own glass. "Does it rain *all* the time?"

"Of course. It's Scotland—and the backside of bloody Scotland, at that." Quarry took a deep pull at his whisky, coughed, and exhaled noisily as he set down the empty glass.

"The drink is the only compensation," he said, a trifle hoarsely. "Call on the local booze-merchants in your best uniform, and they'll make you a decent price. It's astounding cheap, without the tariff. I've left you a note of the best stills." He nodded toward the massive oaken desk at the side of the room, planted four-square on its island of carpet like a small fortress confronting the barren room. The illusion of fortifications was enhanced by the banners of regiment and nation that hung from the stone wall behind it.

"The guards' roster is here," Quarry said, rising and groping in the top desk drawer. He slapped a battered leather folder on the desktop, and added another on top of that. "And the prisoners' roll. You have one hundred and ninety-six at the moment; two hundred is the usual count, give or take a few deaths from sickness or the odd poacher taken up in the countryside."

"Two hundred," Grey said. "And how many in the guards' barracks?"

"Eighty-two, by number. In use, about half that." Quarry reached into the drawer again and withdrew a brown glass bottle with a cork. He shook it, heard it slosh, and smiled sardonically. "The commander isn't the only one to find consolation in drink. Half the sots are usually incapable at roll call. I'll leave this for you, shall I? You'll need it." He put the bottle back and pulled out the lower drawer.

"Requisitions and copies here; the paperwork's the worst of the post. Not a great deal to do, really, if you've a decent clerk. You haven't, at the moment; I had a corporal who wrote a fairish hand, but he died two weeks ago. Train up another, and you'll have nothing to do save to hunt for grouse and the Frenchman's Gold." He laughed at his own joke; rumors of the gold that Louis of France had supposedly sent to his cousin Charles Stuart were rife in this end of Scotland.

"The prisoners are not difficult?" Grey asked. "I had understood them to be mostly Jacobite Highlanders."

"They are. But they're docile enough." Quarry paused, looking out of the window. A small line of ragged men was issuing from a door in the forbidding stone wall opposite. "No heart in them after Culloden," he said matter-of-factly. "Butcher Billy saw to that. And we work them hard enough that they've no vigor left for troublemaking."

Grey nodded. Ardsmuir fortress was undergoing renovation, rather ironically using the labor of the Scots incarcerated therein. He rose and came to join Quarry at the window.

"There's a work crew going out now, for peat-cutting." Quarry nodded at the group below. A dozen bearded men, ragged as scarecrows, formed an awkward line before a red-coated soldier, who walked up and down, inspecting them. Evidently satisfied, he shouted an order and jerked a hand toward the outer gate.

The prisoners' crew was accompanied by six armed soldiers, who fell in before and behind, muskets held in marching order, their smart appearance a marked contrast to the ragged Highlanders. The prisoners walked slowly, oblivious to the rain that soaked their rags. A mule-drawn wagon creaked behind, a bundle of peat knives gleaming dully in its bed.

Quarry frowned, counting them. "Some must be ill; a work

crew is eighteen men—three prisoners to a guard, because of the knives. Though surprisingly few of them try to run,'' he added, turning away from the window. "Nowhere to go, I suppose." He left the desk, kicking aside a large woven basket that sat on the hearth, filled with crude chunks of a rough dark-brown substance.

"Leave the window open, even when it's raining," he advised. "The peat smoke will choke you, otherwise." He took a deep breath in illustration and let it out explosively. "God, I'll be glad to get back to London!"

"Not much in the way of local society, I collect?" Grey asked dryly. Quarry laughed, his broad red face creasing in amusement at the notion.

"Society? My dear fellow! Bar one or two passable blowzabellas down in the village, 'society' will consist solely of conversation with your officers—there are four of them, one of whom is capable of speaking without the use of profanity—your orderly, and one prisoner."

"A prisoner?" Grey looked up from the ledgers he had been perusing, one fair brow lifted in inquiry.

"Oh, yes." Quarry was prowling the office restlessly, eager to be off. His carriage was waiting; he had stayed only to brief his replacement and make the formal handover of command. Now he paused, glancing at Grey. One corner of his mouth curled up, enjoying a secret joke.

"You've heard of Red Jamie Fraser, I expect?"

Grey stiffened slightly, but kept his face as unmoved as possible.

"I should imagine most people have," he said coldly. "The man was notorious during the Rising." Quarry had heard the story, damn him! All of it, or only the first part?

Quarry's mouth twitched slightly, but he merely nodded.

"Quite. Well, we have him. He's the only senior Jacobite officer here; the Highlander prisoners treat him as their chief. Consequently, if any matters arise involving the prisoners—and they will, I assure you—he acts as their spokesman." Quarry was in his stocking feet; now he sat and tugged on long cavalry boots, in preparation for the mud outside.

"*Seumas, mac an fhear dhuibh,* they call him, *or just Mac Dubh*. Speak Gaelic, do you? Neither do I—Grissom does, though; he says it means 'James, son of the Black One.' Half the guards are afraid of him—those that fought with Cope at Preston-pans. Say he's the Devil himself. Poor devil, now!'' Quarry gave a brief snort, forcing his foot into the boot. He stamped once, to settle it, and stood up.

''The prisoners obey him without question; but give orders without his putting his seal to them, and you might as well be talking to the stones in the courtyard. Ever had much to do with Scots? Oh, of course; you fought at Culloden with your brother's regiment, didn't you?'' Quarry struck his brow at his pretended forgetfulness. Damn the man! He *had* heard it all.

''You'll have an idea, then. Stubborn does not begin to describe it.'' He flapped a hand in the air as though to dismiss an entire contingent of recalcitrant Scots.

''Which means,'' Quarry paused, enjoying it, ''you'll need Fraser's goodwill—or at least his cooperation. I had him take supper with me once a week, to talk things over, and found it answered very well. You might try the same arrangement.''

''I suppose I might.'' Grey's tone was cool, but his hands were clenched tight at his sides. When icicles grew in hell, he might take supper with James Fraser!

''He's an educated man,'' Quarry continued, eyes bright with malice, fixed on Grey's face. ''A great deal more interesting to talk to than the officers. Plays chess. You have a game now and then, do you not?''

''Now and then.'' The muscles of his abdomen were clenched so tightly that he had trouble drawing breath. Would this bullet-headed fool not stop talking and leave?

''Ah, well, I'll leave you to it.'' As though divining Grey's wish, Quarry settled his wig more firmly, then took his cloak from the hook by the door and swirled it rakishly about his shoulders. He turned toward the door, hat in hand, then turned back.

''Oh, one thing. If you do dine with Fraser alone—don't turn your back on him.'' The offensive jocularity had left Quarry's face; Grey scowled at him, but could see no evidence that the warning was meant as a joke.

''I mean it,'' Quarry said, suddenly serious. ''He's in irons, but it's easy to choke a man with the chain. And he's a very large fellow, Fraser.''

''I know.'' To his fury, Grey could feel the blood rising in his cheeks. To hide it, he swung about, letting the cold air from the half-open window play on his countenance. "Surely," he said, to the rain-slick gray stones below, "if he is the intelligent man you say, he would not be so foolish as to attack me in my own quarters, in the midst of the prison? What would be the purpose in it?"

Quarry didn't answer. After a moment, Grey turned around, to find the other staring at him thoughtfully, all trace of humor gone from the broad, ruddy face.

"There's intelligence," Quarry said slowly. "And then there are other things. But perhaps you're too young to have seen hate and despair at close range. There's been a deal of it in Scotland, these last ten years." He tilted his head, surveying the new commander of Ardsmuir from his vantage point of fifteen years' seniority.

Major Grey *was* young, no more than twenty-six, and with a fair-complexioned face and girlish lashes that made him look still younger than his years. To compound the problem, he was an inch or two shorter than the average, and fine-boned, as well. He drew himself up straight.

"I am aware of such things, Colonel," he said evenly. Quarry was a younger son of good family, like himself, but still his superior in rank; he must keep his temper.

Quarry's bright hazel gaze rested on him in speculation.

"I daresay."

With a sudden motion, he clapped his hat on his head. He touched his cheek, where the darker line of a scar sliced across the ruddy skin; a memento of the scandalous duel that had sent him into exile at Ardsmuir.

"God knows what you did to be sent here, Grey," he said, shaking his head. "But for your own sake, I hope you deserved it! Luck to you!" And with a swirl of blue cloak, he was gone.

<hr/>

"Better the Devil ye ken than the Devil ye don't," Murdo Lindsay said, shaking his head lugubriously. "Handsome Harry was nain sae bad."

"No, he wasna, then," agreed Kenny Lesley. "But ye'll ha' been here when he came, no? He was a deal better than that shite-face Bogle, aye?"

"Aye," said Murdo, looking blank. "What's your meaning, man?"

"So if Handsome was better than Bogle," Lesley explained patiently, "then Handsome was the Devil we didna ken, and Bogle the one that we did—but Handsome was better, in spite of that, so you're wrong, man."

"I am?" Murdo, hopelessly confused by this bit of reasoning, glowered at Lesley. "No, I'm not!"

"Ye are, then," Lesley said, losing patience. "Ye're always wrong, Murdo! Why d'ye argue, when ye're never in the right of it?"

"I'm no arguin'!" Murdo protested indignantly. "Ye're takin' exception to *me,* not t'other way aboot."

"Only because ye're wrong, man!" Lesley said. "If ye were right, I'd have said not a word."

"I'm not wrong! At least I dinna think so," Murdo muttered, unable to recall precisely what he had said. He turned, appealing to the large figure seated in the corner. "Mac Dubh, was I wrong?"

The tall man stretched himself, the chain of his irons chiming faintly as he moved, and laughed.

"No, Murdo, ye're no wrong. But we canna say if ye're right yet awhile. Not 'til we see what the new Devil's like, aye?" Seeing Lesley's brows draw down in preparation for further dispute, he raised his voice, speaking to the room at large. "Has anyone seen the new Governor yet? Johnson? MacTavish?"

"I have," Hayes said, pushing gladly forward to warm his hands at the fire. There was only one hearth in the large cell, and room for no more than six men before it at a time. The other forty were left in bitter chill, huddling together in small groups for warmth.

Consequently, the agreement was that whoever had a tale to tell or a song to sing might have a place by the hearth, for as long as he spoke. Mac Dubh had said this was a bard-right, that when the bards came to the old castles, they would be given a warm place and plenty to eat and drink, to the honor of the laird's hospitality. There was never food or drink to spare here, but the warm place was certain.

Hayes relaxed, eyes closed and a beatific smile on his face as he spread his hands to the warmth. Warned by restive movement to either side, though, he hastily opened his eyes and began to speak.

"I saw him when he came in from his carriage, and then again, when I brought up a platter o' sweeties from the kitchens, whilst he and Handsome Harry were nattering to ain another.'' Hayes frowned in concentration.

''He's fair-haired, wi' long yellow locks tied up wi' blue ribbon. And big eyes and long lashes, too, like a lassie's.'' Hayes leered at his listeners, batting his own stubby lashes in mock flirtation.

Encouraged by the laughter, he went on to describe the new Governor's clothes—''fine as a laird's''—his equipage and servant—''one of they Sassenachs as talks like he's burnt his tongue''—and as much as had been overheard of the new man's speech.

''He talks sharp and quick, like he'll know what's what,'' Hayes said, shaking his head dubiously. ''But he's verra young, forbye—he looks scarce more than a wean, though I'd reckon he's older than his looks.''

''Aye, he's a bittie fellow, smaller than wee Angus,'' Baird chimed in, with a jerk of the head at Angus MacKenzie, who looked down at himself in startlement. Angus had been twelve when he fought beside his father at Culloden. He had spent nearly half his life in Ardsmuir, and in consequence of the poor fare of prison, had never grown much bigger.

''Aye,'' Hayes agreed, ''but he carries himself well; shoulders square and a ramrod up his arse.''

This gave rise to a burst of laughter and ribald comment, and Hayes gave way to Ogilvie, who knew a long and scurrilous story about the laird of Donibristle and the hogman's daughter. Hayes left the hearth without resentment, and went—as was the custom —to sit beside Mac Dubh.

Mac Dubh never took his place on the hearth, even when he told them the long stories from the books that he'd read—*The Adventures of Roderick Random, The History of Tom Jones, a Foundling,* or everyone's favorite, *Robinson Crusoe.* Claiming that he needed the room to accommodate his long legs, Mac Dubh sat always in his same spot in the corner, where everyone might hear him. But the men who left the fire would come, one by one, and sit down on the bench beside him, to give him the warmth that lingered in their clothes.

''Shall ye speak to the new Governor tomorrow, d'ye think, Mac Dubh?'' Hayes asked as he sat. ''I met Billy Malcolm, coming in from the peat-cutting, and he shouted to me as the rats were grown uncommon bold in their cell just now. Six men bitten this sennight as they slept, and two of them festering.''

Mac Dubh shook his head, and scratched at his chin. He had been allowed a razor before his weekly audiences with Harry Quarry, but it had been five days since the last of these, and his chin was thick with red stubble.

"I canna say, Gavin," he said. "Quarry did say as he'd tell the new fellow of our arrangement, but the new man might have his own ways, aye? If I'm called to see him, though, I shall be sure to say about the rats. Did Malcolm ask for Morrison to come and see to the festering, though?'' The prison had no doctor; Morrison, who had a touch for healing, was permitted by the guards to go from cell to cell to tend the sick or injured, at Mac Dubh's request.

Hayes shook his head. "He hadna time to say more—they were marching past, aye?"

"Best I send Morrison," Mac Dubh decided. "He can ask Billy is there aught else amiss there." There were four main cells where the prisoners were kept in large groups; word passed among them by means of Morrison's visits and the mingling of men on the work crews that went out daily to haul stone or cut peats on the nearby moor.

Morrison came at once when summoned, pocketing four of the carved rats' skulls with which the prisoners improvised games of chess. Mac Dubh groped under the bench where he sat, drawing out the cloth bag he carried when he went to the moor.

"Och, not more o' the damn thistles," Morrison protested, seeing Mac Dubh's grimace as he groped in the bag. "I canna make them eat those things; they all say, do I think them kine, or maybe pigs?"

Mac Dubh gingerly set down a fistful of wilted stalks, and sucked his pricked fingers.

"They're stubborn as pigs, to be sure," he remarked. "It's only milk thistle. How often must I tell ye, Morrison? Take the thistle heads off, and mash the leaves and stems fine, and if they're too prickly to eat spread on a bannock, then make a tea of them and have them drink it. I've yet to see pigs drink tea, tell them."

Morrison's lined face cracked in a grin. An elderly man, he knew well enough how to handle recalcitrant patients; he only liked to complain for the fun of it.

"Aye, well, I'll say have they ever seen a toothless cow?" he said, resigned, as he tucked the limp greens carefully into his own sack. "But you'll be sure to bare your teeth at Joel McCulloch, next time ye see him. He's the worst o' them, for not believin' as the greens do help wi' the scurvy."

"Say as I'll bite him in the arse," Mac Dubh promised, with a flash of his excellent teeth, "if I hear he hasna eaten his thistles."

Morrison made the small amused noise that passed for a belly laugh with him, and went to gather up the bits of ointment and the few herbs he had for medicines.

Mac Dubh relaxed for the moment, glancing about the room to be sure no trouble brewed. There were feuds at the moment; he'd settled Bobby Sinclair and Edwin Murray's trouble a week back, and while they were not friends, they were keeping their distance from one another.

He closed his eyes. He was tired; he had been hauling stone all day. Supper would be along in a few minutes—a tub of parritch and some bread to be shared out, a bit of brose too if they were lucky—and likely most of the men would go to sleep soon after, leaving him a few minutes of peace and semiprivacy, when he need not listen to anyone or feel he must do anything.

He had had no time as yet even to wonder about the new Governor, important as the man would be to all their lives. Young, Hayes had said. That might be good, or might be bad.

Older men who had fought in the Rising were often prejudiced against Highlanders—Bogle, who had put him in irons, had fought with Cope. A scared young soldier, though, trying to keep abreast of an unfamiliar job, could be more rigid and tyrannical than the crustiest of old colonels. Aye, well, and nothing to be done but wait to see.

He sighed and shifted his posture, incommoded—for the ten-thousandth time—by the manacles he wore. He shifted irritably, banging one wrist against the edge of the bench. He was large enough that the weight of the irons didn't trouble him overmuch, but they chafed badly with the work. Worse was the inability to spread his arms more than eighteen inches apart; this gave him cramp and a clawing feeling, deep in the muscle of chest and back, that left him only when he slept.

"Mac Dubh," said a soft voice beside him. "A word in your ear, if I might?" He opened his eyes to see Ronnie Sutherland perched alongside, pointed face intent and foxlike in the faint glow from the fire.

"Aye, Ronnie, of course." He pushed himself upright, and put both his irons and the thought of the new Governor firmly from his mind.

Dearest Mother, John Grey wrote, later that night.

I am arrived safely at my new post, and find it comfortable. Colonel Quarry, my predecessor—he is the Duke of Clarence's nephew, you recall?—made me welcome and acquainted with my charge. I am provided with a most excellent servant, and while I am bound to find many things about Scotland strange at first, I am sure I will find the experience interesting. I was served an object for my supper that the steward told me was called a "haggis." Upon inquiry, this proved to be the interior organ of a sheep, filled with a mixture of ground oats and a quantity of unidentifiable cooked flesh. Though I am assured the inhabitants of Scotland esteem this dish a particular delicacy, I sent it to the kitchens and requested a plain boiled saddle of mutton in its place. Having thus made my first— humble!—meal here, and being somewhat fatigued by the long journey—of whose details I shall inform you in a subsequent missive—I believe I shall now retire, leaving further descriptions of my surroundings—with which I am imperfectly acquainted at present, as it is dark—for a future communication.

He paused, tapping the quill on the blotter. The point left small dots of ink, and he abstractedly drew lines connecting these, making the outlines of a jagged object.

Dared he ask about George? Not a direct inquiry, that wouldn't do, but a reference to the family, asking whether his mother had happened to encounter Lady Everett lately, and might he ask to be remembered to her son?

He sighed and drew another point on his object. No. His widowed mother was ignorant of the situation, but Lady Everett's husband moved in military circles. His brother's influence would keep the gossip to a minimum, but Lord Everett might catch a whiff of it, nonetheless, and be quick enough to put two and two together. Let him drop an injudicious word to his wife about George, and the word pass on from Lady Everett to his mother . . . the Dowager Countess Melton was not a fool.

She knew quite well that he was in disgrace; promising young officers in the good graces of their superiors were not sent to the arse-end of Scotland to oversee the renovation of small and unimportant prison-fortresses. But his brother Harold had told her that the trouble was an unfortunate affair of the heart, implying sufficient indelicacy to stop her questioning him about it. She likely thought he had been caught with his colonel's wife, or keeping a whore in his quarters.

An unfortunate affair of the heart! He smiled grimly, dipping his pen. Perhaps Hal had a greater sensitivity than he'd thought, in so describing it. But then, all his affairs had been unfortunate, since Hector's death at Culloden.

With the thought of Culloden, the thought of Fraser came back to him; something he had been avoiding all day. He looked from the blotter to the folder which held the prisoners' roll, biting his lip. He was tempted to open it, and look to see the name, but what point was there in that? There might be scores of men in the Highlands named James Fraser, but only one known also as Red Jamie.

He felt himself flush as waves of heat rolled over him, but it was not nearness to the fire. In spite of that, he rose and went to the window, drawing in great lungfuls of air as though the cold draft could cleanse him of memory.

"Pardon, sir, but will ye be wantin' yer bed warmed now?" The Scottish speech behind him startled him, and he whirled round to find the tousled head of the prisoner assigned to tend his quarters poking through the door that led to his private rooms.

"Oh! Er, yes. Thank you . . . MacDonell?" he said doubtfully.

"MacKay, my lord," the man corrected, without apparent resentment, and the head vanished.

Grey sighed. There was nothing that could be done tonight. He came back to the desk and gathered up the folders, to put them away. The jagged object he had drawn on the blotter looked like one of those spiked maces, with which ancient knights had crushed the heads of their foes. He felt as though he had swallowed one, though perhaps this was no more than indigestion occasioned by half-cooked mutton.

He shook his head, pulled the letter to him and signed it hastily. *With all affection, your obt. son, John Wm. Grey.* He shook sand over the signature, sealed the missive with his ring and set it aside to be posted in the morning.

He rose and stood hesitating, surveying the shadowy reaches of the office. It was a great, cold, barren room, with little in it bar the huge desk and a couple of chairs. He shivered; the sullen glow of the peat bricks on the hearth did little to warm its vast spaces, particularly with the freezing wet air coming in at the window.

He glanced once more at the prisoners' roll. Then he bent, opened the lower drawer of the desk, and drew out the brown glass bottle. He pinched out the candle, and made his way toward his bed by the dull glow of the hearth.

The mingled effects of exhaustion and whisky should have sent him to sleep at once, but sleep kept its distance, hovering over his bed like a bat, but never lighting. Every time he felt himself sinking into dreams, a vision of the wood at Carryarrick came before his eyes, and he found himself lying once more wide-awake and sweating, his heart thundering in his ears.

He had been sixteen then, excited beyond bearing by his first campaign. He had not got his commission then, but his brother Hal had taken him along with the regiment, so that he might get a taste of soldiering.

Camped at night near a dark Scottish wood, on their way to join General Cope at Prestonpans, John had found himself too nervous to sleep. What would the battle be like? Cope was a great general, all Hal's friends said so, but the men around the fires told frightful stories of the fierce Highlanders and their bloody broadswords. Would he have the courage to face the dreadful Highland charge?

He couldn't bring himself to mention his fears even to Hector. Hector loved him, but Hector was twenty, tall and muscular and fearless, with a lieutenant's commission and dashing stories of battles fought in France.

He didn't know, even now, whether it had been an urge to emulate Hector, or merely to impress him, that had led him to do it. In either case, when he saw the Highlander in the wood, and recognized him from the broadsheets as the notorious Red Jamie Fraser, he had determined to kill or capture him.

The notion of returning to camp for help *had* occurred to him, but the man was alone—at least John had thought he was alone—and evidently unawares, seated quietly upon a log, eating a bit of bread.

And so he had drawn his knife from his belt and crept quietly through the wood toward that shining red head, the haft slippery in his grasp, his mind filled with visions of glory and Hector's praise.

Instead, there had been a glancing blow as his knife flashed down, his arm locked tight round the Scot's neck to choke him, and then—

Lord John Grey flung himself over in his bed, hot with remembrance. They had fallen back, rolling together in the crackling oak-leaf dark, grappling for the knife, thrashing and fighting—for his life, he had thought.

First the Scot had been under him, then twisting, somehow over. He had touched a great snake once, a python that a friend of his uncle's had brought from the Indies, and that was what it had been like, Fraser's touch, lithe and smooth and horribly powerful, moving like the muscular coils, never where you expected it to be.

He had been flung ignominiously on his face in the leaves, his wrist twisted painfully behind his back. In a frenzy of terror, convinced he was about to be slain, he had wrenched with all his strength at his trapped arm, and the bone had snapped, with a red-black burst of pain that rendered him momentarily senseless.

He had come to himself moments later, slumped against a tree, facing a circle of ferocious-looking Highlanders, all in their plaids. In the midst of them stood Red Jamie Fraser—and the woman.

Grey clenched his teeth. Curse that woman! If it hadn't been for her—well, God knew what might have happened. What *had* happened was that she had spoken. She was English, a lady by her speech, and he—idiot that he was!—had leapt at once to the conclusion that she was a hostage of the vicious Highlanders, no doubt kidnapped for the purpose of ravishment. Everyone said that Highlanders indulged in rapine at every opportunity, and took delight in dishonoring Englishwomen; how should he have known otherwise!

And Lord John William Grey, aged sixteen and filled to the brim with regimental notions of gallantry and noble purpose, bruised, shaken, and fighting the pain of his broken arm, had tried to bargain, to save her from her fate. Fraser, tall and mocking, had played him like a salmon, stripping the woman half-naked before him to force from him information about the position and strength of his brother's regiment. And then, when he had told all he could, Fraser had laughingly revealed that the woman was his wife. They'd all laughed; he could hear the ribald Scottish voices now, hilarious in memory.

Grey rolled over, shifting his weight irritably on the unaccustomed mattress. And to make it all worse, Fraser had not even had the decency to kill him, but instead had tied him to a tree, where he would be found by his friends in the morning. By which time Fraser's men had visited the camp and—with the information *he* had given them!—had immobilized the cannon they were bringing to Cope.

Everyone had found out, of course, and while excuses were made because of his age and his noncommissioned status, he had been a pariah and an object of scorn. No one would speak to him, save his brother—and Hector. Loyal Hector.

He sighed, rubbing his cheek against the pillow. He could see Hector still, in his mind's eye. Dark-haired and blue-eyed, tender-mouthed, always smiling. It had been ten years since Hector had died at Culloden, hacked to pieces by a Highland broadsword, and still John woke in the dawn sometimes, body arched in clutching spasm, feeling Hector's touch.

And now this. He had dreaded this posting, being surrounded by Scots, by their grating voices, overwhelmed with the memory of what they had done to Hector. But never, in the most dismal moments of anticipation, had he thought he would ever meet James Fraser again.

The peat fire on the hearth died gradually to hot ash, then cold, and the window paled from deep black to the sullen gray of a rainy Scottish dawn. And still John Grey lay sleepless, burning eyes fixed on the smoke-blackened beams above him.

Grey rose in the morning unrested, but with his mind made up. He was here. Fraser was here. And neither could leave, for the foreseeable future. So. He must see the man now and again—he would be speaking to the assembled prisoners in an hour, and must inspect them regularly thereafter—but he would not see him privately. If he kept the man himself at a distance, perhaps he could also keep at bay the memories he stirred. And the feelings.

For while it was the memory of his past rage and humiliation that had kept him awake to begin with, it was the other side of the present situation that had left him still wakeful at dawn. The slowly dawning realization that Fraser was now *his* prisoner; no longer his tormentor, but a prisoner, like the others, entirely at his mercy.

He rang the bell for his servant and padded to the window to see how the weather kept, wincing at the chill of the stone under his bare feet.

It was, not surprisingly, raining. In the courtyard below, the prisoners were already being formed up in work crews, wet to the skin. Shivering in his shirt, Grey pulled in his head and shut the window halfway; a nice compromise between death from suffocation and death from the ague.

It had been visions of revenge that kept him tossing in his bed as the window lightened and the rain pattered on the sill; thoughts of Fraser confined to a tiny cell of freezing stone, kept naked through the winter nights, fed on slops, stripped and flogged in the courtyard of the prison. All that arrogant power humbled, reduced to groveling misery, dependent solely on his word for a moment's relief.

Yes, he thought all those things, imagined them in vivid detail, reveled in them. He heard Fraser beg for mercy, imagined himself disdaining, haughty. He thought these things, and the spiked object turned over in his guts, piercing him with self-disgust.

Whatever he might once have been to Grey, Fraser now was a beaten foe; a prisoner of war, and the charge of the Crown. He was *Grey's* charge, in fact; a responsibility, and his welfare the duty of honor.

His servant had brought hot water for shaving. He splashed his cheeks, feeling the warmth soothe him, laying to rest the tormented fancies of the night. That was all they were, he realized—fancies, and the realization brought him a certain relief.

He might have met Fraser in battle and taken a real and savage pleasure in killing or maiming him. But the inescapable fact was that so long as Fraser was his prisoner, he could not in honor harm the man. By the time he had shaved and his servant had dressed him, he was recovered enough to find a certain grim humor in the situation.

His foolish behavior at Carryarrick had saved Fraser's life at Culloden. Now, that debt discharged, and Fraser in his power, Fraser's sheer helplessness as a prisoner made him completely safe. For whether foolish or wise, naive or experienced, all the Greys were men of honor.

Feeling somewhat better, he met his gaze in the looking glass, set his wig to rights, and went to eat breakfast before giving his first address to the prisoners.

"Will you have your supper served in the sitting room, sir, or in here?" MacKay's head, uncombed as ever, poked into the office.

"Um?" Grey murmured, absorbed in the papers spread out on the desk. "Oh," he said, looking up. "In here, if you please." He waved vaguely at the corner of the huge desk and returned to his work, scarcely looking up when the tray with his food arrived sometime later.

Quarry had not been joking about the paperwork. The sheer quantity of food alone required endless orders and requisitions— all orders to be submitted in duplicate to London, *if* he pleased!— let alone the hundreds of other necessities required by the prisoners, the guards, and the men and women from the village who came in by the day to clean the barracks and work in the kitchens. He had done nothing all day but write and sign requisitions. He *must* find a clerk soon, or die of sheer ennui.

Two hundred lb. wheat flowr, he wrote, *for prisoners' use. Six hogsheads ale, for use of barracks.* His normally elegant handwriting had quickly degenerated into a utilitarian scrawl, his stylish signature become a curt *J. Grey.*

He laid down his pen with a sigh and closed his eyes, massaging the ache between his brows. The sun had not bothered to show its face once since his arrival, and working all day in a smoky room by candlelight left his eyes burning like lumps of coal. His books had arrived the day before, but he had not even unpacked them, too exhausted by nightfall to do more than bathe his aching eyes in cold water and go to sleep.

He heard a small, stealthy sound, and sat up abruptly, his eyes popping open. A large brown rat sat on the corner of his desk, a morsel of plum cake held in its front paws. It didn't move, but merely looked at him speculatively, whiskers twitching.

"Well, God damn my eyes!" Grey exclaimed in amazement. "Here, you bugger! That's *my* supper!"

The rat nibbled pensively at the plum cake, bright beady eyes fixed on the Major.

"Get out of it!" Enraged, Grey snatched up the nearest object and let fly at the rat. The ink bottle exploded on the stone floor in a spray of black, and the startled rat leapt off the desk and fled precipitously, galloping between the legs of the even more startled MacKay, who appeared at the door to see what the noise was.

"Has the prison got a cat?" Grey demanded, dumping the contents of his supper tray into the waste can by his desk.

"Aye, sir, there's cats in the storerooms," MacKay offered, crawling backward on hands and knees to wipe up the small black footprints the rat had left in its precipitous flight through the ink puddle.

"Well, fetch one up here, if you please, MacKay," Grey ordered. "At once." He grunted at the memory of that obscenely naked tail draped nonchalantly over his plate. He had encountered rats often enough in the field, of course, but there was something about having his own personal supper molested before his eyes that seemed particularly infuriating.

He strode to the window and stood there, trying to clear his head with fresh air, as MacKay finished his mopping-up. Dusk was drawing down, filling the courtyard with purple shadows. The stones of the cell wing opposite looked even colder and more dreary than usual.

The turnkeys were coming through the rain from the kitchen wing; a procession of small carts laden with the prisoners' food; huge pots of steaming oatmeal and baskets of bread, covered with cloths against the rain. At least the poor devils had hot food after their wet day's work in the stone quarry.

A thought struck him as he turned from the window.

"Are there many rats in the cells?" he asked MacKay.

"Aye, sir, a great many," the prisoner replied, with a final swipe to the threshold. "I'll tell the cook to make ye up a fresh tray, shall I, sir?"

"If you please," Grey said. "And then if you will, Mr. Mac-Kay, please see that each cell is provided with its own cat."

MacKay looked slightly dubious at this. Grey paused in the act of retrieving his scattered papers.

"Is there something wrong, MacKay?"

"No, sir," MacKay replied slowly. "Only the wee brown beasties do keep down the cockchafers. And with respect, sir, I dinna think the men would care to have a cat takin' all their rats."

Grey stared at the man, feeling mildly queasy.

"The prisoners eat the rats?" he asked, with a vivid memory of sharp yellow teeth nibbling at his plum cake.

"Only when they're lucky enough to catch one, sir," MacKay said. "Perhaps the cats would be a help wi' that, after all. Will that be all for tonight, sir?"

9

The Wanderer

Grey's resolve concerning James Fraser lasted for two weeks. Then the messenger arrived from the village of Ardsmuir, with news that changed everything.

"Does he still live?" he asked the man sharply. The messenger, one of the inhabitants of Ardsmuir village who worked for the prison, nodded.

"I saw him mysel', sir, when they brought him in. He's at the Lime Tree now, being cared for—but I didna think he looked as though care would be enough, sir, if ye take my meaning." He raised one brow significantly.

"I take it," Grey answered shortly. "Thank you, Mr.—"

"Allison, sir, Rufus Allison. Your servant, sir." The man accepted the shilling offered him, bowed with his hat under his arm, and took his leave.

Grey sat at his desk, staring out at the leaden sky. The sun had scarcely shone for a day since his arrival. He tapped the end of the quill with which he had been writing on the desk, oblivious to the damage he was inflicting on the sharpened tip.

The mention of gold was enough to prick up any man's ears, but especially his.

A man had been found this morning, wandering in the mist on the moor near the village. His clothes were soaked not only with the damp, but with seawater, and he was out of his mind with fever.

He had talked unceasingly since he was found, babbling for the most part, but his rescuers were unable to make much sense of his ravings. The man appeared to be Scottish, and yet he spoke in an incoherent mixture of French and Gaelic, with here and there the odd word of English thrown in. And one of those words had been "gold."

The combination of Scots, gold, and the French tongue, mentioned in this area of the country, could bring only one thought to the mind of anyone who had fought through the last days of the Jacobite rising. The Frenchman's Gold. The fortune in gold bullion that Louis of France had—according to rumor—sent secretly to the aid of his cousin, Charles Stuart. But sent far too late.

Some stories said that the French gold had been hidden by the Highland army during the last headlong retreat to the North, before the final disaster at Culloden. Others held that the gold had never reached Charles Stuart, but had been left for safekeeping in a cave near the place where it had come ashore on the northwestern coast.

Some said that the secret of the hiding place had been lost, its guardian killed at Culloden. Others said that the hiding place was still known, but a close-kept secret, held among the members of a single Highland family. Whatever the truth, the gold had never been found. Not yet.

French and Gaelic. Grey spoke passable French, the result of several years fighting abroad, but neither he nor any of his officers spoke the barbarous Gaelic, save a few words Sergeant Grissom had learned as a child from a Scottish nursemaid.

He could not trust a man from the village; not if there was anything to this tale. The Frenchman's Gold! Beyond its value as treasure—which would belong to the Crown in any case—the gold had a considerable and personal value to John William Grey. The finding of that half-mythical hoard would be his passport out of Ardsmuir—back to London and civilization. The blackest disgrace would be instantly obscured by the dazzle of gold.

He bit the end of the blunted quill, feeling the cylinder crack between his teeth.

Damn. No, it couldn't be a villager, nor one of his officers. A prisoner, then. Yes, he could use a prisoner without risk, for a prisoner would be unable to make use of the information for his own ends.

Damn again. All of the prisoners spoke Gaelic, many had some

English as well—but only one spoke French besides. *He is an educated man,* Quarry's voice echoed in his memory.

"Damn, damn, *damn!*" Grey muttered. It couldn't be helped. Allison had said the wanderer was very ill; there was no time to look for alternatives. He spat out a shred of quill.

"Brame!" he shouted. The startled corporal poked his head in. "Yes, sir?"

"Bring me a prisoner named James Fraser. At once."

The Governor stood behind his desk, leaning on it as though the huge slab of oak were in fact the bulwark it looked. His hands were damp on the smooth wood, and the white stock of his uniform felt tight around his neck.

His heart leapt violently as the door opened. The Scot came in, his irons chinking slightly, and stood before the desk. The candles were all lit, and the office nearly as bright as day, though it was nearly full dark outside.

He had seen Fraser several times, of course, standing in the courtyard with the other prisoners, red head and shoulders above most of the other men, but never close enough to see his face clearly.

He looked different. That was both shock and relief; for so long, he had seen a clean-shaven face in memory, dark with threat or alight with mocking laughter. This man was short-bearded, his face calm and wary, and while the deep blue eyes were the same, they gave no sign of recognition. The man stood quietly before the desk, waiting.

Grey cleared his throat. His heart was still beating too fast, but at least he could speak calmly.

"Mr. Fraser," he said. "I thank you for coming."

The Scot bent his head courteously, but did not answer that he had had no choice in the matter; his eyes said that.

"Doubtless you wonder why I have sent for you," Grey said. He sounded insufferably pompous to his own ears, but was unable to remedy it. "I find that a situation has arisen in which I require your assistance."

"What is that, Major?" The voice was the same—deep and precise, marked with a soft Highland burr.

He took a deep breath, bracing himself on the desk. He would rather have done anything but ask help of this particular man, but there was no bloody choice. Fraser was the only possibility.

"A man has been found wandering the moor near the coast," he said carefully. "He appears to be seriously ill, and his speech is deranged. However, certain . . . matters to which he refers appear to be of . . . substantial interest to the Crown. I require to talk with him, and discover as much as I can of his identity, and the matters of which he speaks."

He paused, but Fraser merely stood there, waiting.

"Unfortunately," Grey said, taking another breath, "the man in question has been heard to speak in a mixture of Gaelic and French, with no more than a word or two of English."

One of the Scot's ruddy eyebrows stirred. His face didn't change in any appreciable way, but it was evident that he had grasped the implications of the situation.

"I see, Major." The Scot's soft voice was full of irony. "And you would like my assistance to interpret for ye what this man might have to say."

Grey couldn't trust himself to speak, but merely jerked his head in a short nod.

"I fear I must decline, Major." Fraser spoke respectfully, but with a glint in his eye that was anything but respectful. Grey's hand curled tight around the brass letter-opener on his blotter.

"You decline?" he said. He tightened his grasp on the letter-opener in order to keep his voice steady. "Might I inquire why, Mr. Fraser?"

"I am a prisoner, Major," the Scot said politely. "Not an interpreter."

"Your assistance would be—appreciated," Grey said, trying to infuse the word with significance without offering outright bribery. "Conversely"—his tone hardened—"a failure to render legitimate assistance—"

"It is not legitimate for ye either to extort my services or to threaten me, Major." Fraser's voice was a good deal harder than Grey's.

"I did not threaten you!" The edge of the letter-opener was cutting into his hand; he was forced to loosen his grip.

"Did ye no? Well, and I'm pleased to hear it." Fraser turned toward the door. "In that case, Major, I shall bid ye good night."

Grey would have given a great deal simply to have let him go. Unfortunately, duty called.

"Mr. Fraser!" The Scot stopped, a few feet from the door, but didn't turn.

Grey took a deep breath, steeling himself to it.

"If you do what I ask, I will have your irons struck off," he said.

Fraser stood quite still. Young and inexperienced Grey might be, but he was not unobservant. Neither was he a poor judge of men. Grey watched the rise of his prisoner's head, the increased tension of his shoulders, and felt a small relaxation of the anxiety that had gripped him since the news of the wanderer had come.

"Mr. Fraser?" he said.

Very slowly, the Scot turned around. His face was quite expressionless.

"You have a bargain, Major," he said softly.

It was well past midnight when they arrived in the village of Ardsmuir. No lights showed in the cottages they passed, and Grey found himself wondering what the inhabitants thought, as the sound of hooves and the jingle of arms passed by their windows late at night, a faint echo of the English troops who had swept through the Highlands ten years before.

The wanderer had been taken to the Lime Tree, an inn so called because for many years, it had boasted a huge lime tree in the yard; the only tree of any size for thirty miles. There was nothing left now but a broad stump—the tree, like so many other things, had perished in the aftermath of Culloden, burned for firewood by Cumberland's troops—but the name remained.

At the door, Grey paused and turned to Fraser.

"You will recall the terms of our agreement?"

"I will," Fraser answered shortly, and brushed past him.

In return for having the irons removed, Grey had required three things: firstly, that Fraser would not attempt to escape during the journey to or from the village. Secondly, Fraser would undertake to give a full and true account of all that the vagrant should say. And thirdly, Fraser would give his word as a gentleman to speak to no one but Grey of what he learned.

There was a murmur of Gaelic voices inside; a sound of sur-

prise as the innkeeper saw Fraser, and deference at the sight of the
Redcoat behind him. The goodwife stood on the stair, an oil-dip in
her hand making the shadows dance around her.

Grey laid a hand on the innkeeper's arm, startled.

"Who is that?" There was another figure on the stairs, an
apparition, clothed all in black.

"That is the priest," Fraser said quietly, beside him. "The man
will be dying, then."

Grey took a deep breath, trying to steady himself for what
might come.

"Then there is little time to waste," he said firmly, setting a
booted foot on the stair. "Let us proceed."

The man died just before dawn, Fraser holding one of his hands,
the priest the other. As the priest leaned over the bed, mumbling in
Gaelic and Latin, making Popish signs over the body, Fraser sat
back on his stool, eyes closed, still holding the small, frail hand in
his own.

The big Scot had sat by the man's side all night, listening,
encouraging, comforting. Grey had stood by the door, not wishing
to frighten the man by the sight of his uniform, both surprised and
oddly touched at Fraser's gentleness.

Now Fraser laid the thin weathered hand gently across the still
chest, and made the same sign as the priest had, touching forehead, heart, and both shoulders in turn, in the sign of a cross. He
opened his eyes, and rose to his feet, his head nearly brushing the
low rafters. He nodded briefly to Grey, and preceded him down
the narrow stair.

"In here." Grey motioned to the door of the taproom, empty at
this hour. A sleepy-eyed barmaid laid the fire for them and
brought bread and ale, then went out, leaving them alone.

He waited for Fraser to refresh himself before asking.

"Well, Mr. Fraser?"

The Scot set down his pewter mug and wiped a hand across his
mouth. Already bearded, with his long hair neatly plaited, he
didn't look disheveled by the long night watch, but there were dark
smudges of tiredness under his eyes.

"All right," he said. "It doesna make a great deal of sense,
Major," he added warningly, "but this is all he said." And he

spoke carefully, pausing now and then to recall a word, stopping again to explain some Gaelic reference. Grey sat listening in deepening disappointment; Fraser had been correct—it didn't make much sense.

"The white witch?" Grey interrupted. "He spoke of a white witch? And seals?" It scarcely seemed more farfetched than the rest of it, but still he spoke disbelievingly.

"Aye, he did."

"Say it to me again," Grey commanded. "As best you remember. If you please," he added.

He felt oddly comfortable with the man, he realized, with a feeling of surprise. Part of it was sheer fatigue, of course; all his usual reactions and feelings were numbed by the long night and the strain of watching a man die by inches.

The entire night had seemed unreal to Grey; not least was this odd conclusion, wherein he found himself sitting in the dim dawn light of a country tavern, sharing a pitcher of ale with Red Jamie Fraser.

Fraser obeyed, speaking slowly, stopping now and then to recall. With the difference of a word here or there, it was identical to the first account—and those parts of it that Grey himself had been able to understand were faithfully translated.

He shook his head, discouraged. Gibberish. The man's ravings had been precisely that—ravings. If the man had ever seen any gold—and it did sound as though he had, at one time—there was no telling where or when from this hodgepodge of delusion and feverish delirium.

"You are quite positive that is all he said?" Grey grasped at the slim hope that Fraser might have omitted some small phrase, some statement that would yield a clue to the lost gold.

Fraser's sleeve fell back as he lifted his cup; Grey could see the deep band of raw flesh about his wrist, dark in the gray early light of the taproom. Fraser saw him looking at it, and set down the cup, the frail illusion of companionship shattered.

"I keep my bargains, Major," Fraser said, with cold formality. He rose to his feet. "Shall we be going back now?"

They rode in silence for some time. Fraser was lost in his own thoughts, Grey sunk in fatigue and disappointment. They stopped at a spring to refresh themselves, just as the sun topped the small hills to the north.

Grey drank cold water, then splashed it on his face, feeling the shock of it revive him momentarily. He had been awake for more than twenty-four hours, and was feeling slow and stupid.

Fraser had been awake for the same twenty-four hours, but gave no sign of being troubled by the fact. He was crawling busily around the spring on his hands and knees, evidently plucking some sort of weed from the water.

"What are you doing, Mr. Fraser?" Grey asked, in some bewilderment.

Fraser looked up, mildly surprised, but not embarrassed in the slightest.

"I am picking watercress, Major."

"I see that," Grey said testily. "What for?"

"To eat, Major," Fraser replied evenly. He took the stained cloth bag from his belt and dropped the dripping green mass into it.

"Indeed? Are you not fed sufficiently?" Grey asked blankly. "I have never heard of people eating watercress."

"It's green, Major."

In his fatigued state, the Major had suspicions that he was being practiced upon.

"What in damnation other color ought a weed to be?" he demanded.

Fraser's mouth twitched slightly, and he seemed to be debating something with himself. At last he shrugged slightly, wiping his wet hands on the sides of his breeks.

"I only meant, Major, that eating green plants will stop ye getting scurvy and loose teeth. My men eat such greens as I take them, and cress is better-tasting than most things I can pick on the moor."

Grey felt his brows shoot up.

"Green plants stop scurvy?" he blurted. "Wherever did you get that notion?"

"From my wife!" Fraser snapped. He turned away abruptly, and stood, tying the neck of his sack with hard, quick movements.

Grey could not prevent himself asking.

"Your wife, sir—where is she?"

The answer was a sudden blaze of dark blue that seared him to the backbone, so shocking was its intensity.

Perhaps you are too young to know the power of hate and

despair. Quarry's voice spoke in Grey's memory. He was not; he recognized them at once in the depths of Fraser's eyes.

Only for a moment, though; then the man's normal veil of cool politeness was back in place.

"My wife is gone," Fraser said, and turned away again, so abruptly that the movement verged on rudeness.

Grey felt himself shaken by an unexpected feeling. In part it was relief. The woman who had been both cause of and party to his humiliation was dead. In part, it was regret.

Neither of them spoke again on the journey back to Ardsmuir.

Three days later, Jamie Fraser escaped. It had never been a difficult matter for prisoners to escape from Ardsmuir; no one ever did, simply because there was no place for a man to go. Three miles from the prison, the coast of Scotland dropped into the ocean in a spill of crumbled granite. On the other three sides, nothing but empty moorland stretched for miles.

Once, a man might take to the heather, depending on clan and kinsmen for support and protection. But the clans were crushed, the kin dead, the Scottish prisoners removed far away from their own clan lands. Starving on the bleak moor was little improvement on a prison cell. Escape was not worth it—to anyone but Jamie Fraser, who evidently had a reason.

The dragoons' horses kept to the road; while the surrounding moor looked smooth as a velvet counterpane, the purpling heather was a thin layer, deceptively spread over a foot or more of wet, spongy peat moss. Even the red deer didn't walk at random in that boggy mass—Grey could see four of the animals now, stick figures a mile away, the line of their track through the heather seeming no wider than a thread.

Fraser, of course, was not mounted. That meant that the escaped prisoner might be anywhere on the moor, free to follow the red deer's paths.

It was John Grey's duty to pursue his prisoner and attempt his recapture. It was something more than duty that had made him strip the garrison for his search party, and urge them on with only the briefest of stops for rest and food. Duty, yes, and an urgent desire to find the French gold and win approval from his masters —and reprieve from this desolate Scottish exile. But there was anger, too, and an odd sense of personal betrayal.

Grey wasn't sure whether he was more angry at Fraser for breaking his word, or at himself, for having been fool enough to believe that a Highlander—gentleman or not—held a sense of honor equal to his own. But angry he was, and determined to search every deer path on this moor if necessary, in order to lay James Fraser by the heels.

They reached the coast the next night, well after dark, after a laborious day of combing the moor. The fog had thinned away over the rocks, swept out by the offshore wind, and the sea spread out before them, cradled by cliffs and strewn with tiny barren islets.

John Grey stood beside his horse on the clifftops, looking down at the wild black sea. It was a clear night on the coast, thank God, and the moon was at the half; its gleam painted the spray-wet rocks, making them stand out hard and shining as silver ingots against black velvet shadows.

It was the most desolate place he had ever seen, though it had a sort of terrible beauty about it that made the blood run cold in his veins. There was no sign of James Fraser. No sign of life at all.

One of the men with him gave a sudden exclamation of surprise, and drew his pistol.

"There!" he said. "On the rocks!"

"Hold your fire, fool," said another of the soldiers, grabbing his companion's arm. He made no effort to disguise his contempt. "Have you ne'er seen seals?"

"Ah . . . no," said the first man, rather sheepishly. He lowered his pistol, staring out at the small dark forms on the rocks below.

Grey had never seen seals, either, and he watched them with fascination. They looked like black slugs from this distance, the moonlight gleaming wetly on their coats as they raised restless heads, seeming to roll and weave unsteadily as they made their awkward way on land.

His mother had had a cloak made of sealskin, when he was a boy. He had been allowed to touch it once, marveling at the feel of it, dark and warm as a moonless summer night. Amazing that such thick, soft fur came from these slick, wet creatures.

"The Scots call them silkies," said the soldier who had recognized them. He nodded at the seals with the proprietary air of special knowledge.

"Silkies?" Grey's attention was caught; he stared at the man with interest. "What else do you know about them, Sykes?"

The soldier shrugged, enjoying his momentary importance. "Not a great deal, sir. The folk hereabout have stories about them, though; they say sometimes one of them will come ashore and leave off its skin, and inside is a beautiful woman. If a man should find the skin, and hide it, so she can't go back, why then—she'll be forced to stay and be his wife. They make good wives, sir, or so I'm told."

"At least they'd always be wet," murmured the first soldier, and the men erupted in guffaws that echoed among the cliffs, raucous as seabirds.

"That's enough!" Grey had to raise his voice, to be heard above the rash of laughter and crude suggestions.

"Spread out!" Grey ordered. "I want the cliffs searched in both directions—and keep an eye out for boats below; God knows there's room enough to hide a sloop behind some of those islands."

Abashed, the men went without comment. They returned an hour later, wet from spray and disheveled with climbing, but with no sign of Jamie Fraser—or the Frenchman's Gold.

At dawn, as the light stained the slippery rocks red and gold, small parties of dragoons were sent off to search the cliffs in both directions, making their way carefully down the rocky clefts and tumbled piles of stone.

Nothing was found. Grey stood by a fire on the clifftop, keeping an eye on the search. He was swathed in his greatcoat against the biting wind, and fortified periodically by hot coffee, supplied by his servant.

The man at the Lime Tree had come from the sea, his clothes soaked in saltwater. Whether Fraser had learned something from the man's words that he had not told, or had decided only to take the chance of looking for himself, surely he also would have gone to the sea. And yet there was no sign of James Fraser, anywhere along this stretch of coast. Worse yet, there was no sign of the gold.

"If he went in anywhere along this stretch, Major, you'll have

seen the last of him, I'm thinking.'' It was Sergeant Grissom,
standing beside him, gazing down at the crash and whirl of water
through the jagged rocks below. He nodded at the furious water.

''They call this spot the Devil's Cauldron, because of the way it
boils all the time. Fishermen drowned off this coast are seldom
found; there are wicked currents to blame for it, of course, but folk
say the Devil seizes them and pulls them below.''

''Do they?'' Grey said bleakly. He stared down into the smash
and spume forty feet below. ''I wouldn't doubt it, Sergeant.''

He turned back toward the campfire.

''Give orders to search until nightfall, Sergeant. If nothing is
found, we'll start back in the morning.''

Grey lifted his gaze from his horse's neck, squinting through
the dim early light. His eyes felt swollen from peat smoke and lack
of sleep, and his bones ached from several nights spent lying on
damp ground.

The ride back to Ardsmuir would take no more than a day. The
thought of a soft bed and a hot supper was delightful—but then he
would have to write the official dispatch to London, confessing
Fraser's escape—the reason for it—and his own shameful failure
to recapture the man.

The feeling of bleakness at this prospect was reinforced by a
deep griping in the major's lower abdomen. He raised a hand,
signaling a halt, and slid wearily to the ground.

''Wait here,'' he said to his men. There was a small hillock a
few hundred feet away; it would afford him sufficient privacy for
the relief he sorely needed; his bowels, unaccustomed to Scottish
parritch and oatcake, had rebelled altogether at the exigencies of a
field diet.

The birds were singing in the heather. Away from the noise of
hooves and harness, he could hear all the tiny sounds of the waking moor. The wind had changed with the dawn, and the scent of
the sea came inland now, whispering through the grass. Some
small animal made a rustling noise on the other side of a gorse
bush. It was all very peaceful.

Straightening up from what too late struck him as a most undignified posture, Grey raised his head and looked straight into the
face of James Fraser.

He was no more than six feet away. He stood still as one of the red deer, the moor wind brushing over him, with the rising sun tangled in his hair.

They stood frozen, staring at each other. The smell of the sea came faintly on the wind. There was no sound but the sea wind and the singing of meadowlarks for a moment. Then Grey drew himself up, swallowing to bring his heart down from his throat.

"I fear you take me at a disadvantage, Mr. Fraser," he said coolly, fastening his breeches with as much self-possession as he could muster.

The Scot's eyes were the only part of him to move, down over Grey and slowly back up. Looked over his shoulder, to where six armed soldiers stood, pointing their muskets. Dark blue eyes met his, straight on. At last, the edge of Fraser's mouth twitched, and he said, "I think ye take me at the same, Major."

10

White Witch's Curse

Jamie Fraser sat shivering on the stone floor of the empty store-room, clutching his knees and trying to get warm. He thought he likely would never be warm again. The chill of the sea had seeped into his bones, and he could still feel the churn of the crashing breakers, deep in his belly.

He wished for the presence of the other prisoners—Morrison, Hayes, Sinclair, Sutherland. Not only for company, but for the heat of their bodies. On bitter nights, the men would huddle close together for warmth, breathing each other's stale breath, tolerating the bump and knock of close quarters for the sake of warmth.

He was alone, though. Likely they would not return him to the large cell with the other men until after they had done whatever they meant to do to him as punishment for escaping. He leaned back against the wall with a sigh, morbidly aware of the bones of his spine pressing against the stone, and the fragility of the flesh covering them.

He was very much afraid of being flogged, and yet he hoped that would be his punishment. It would be horrible, but it would be soon over—and infinitely more bearable than being put back in irons. He could feel in his flesh the crash of the smith's hammer, echoing through the bones of his arm as the smith pounded the fetters firmly into place, holding his wrist steady on the anvil.

His fingers sought the rosary around his neck. His sister had given it to him when he left Lallybroch; the English had let him keep it, as the string of beechwood beads had no value.

"Hail Mary, full of grace," he muttered, "blessed art thou amongst women."

He hadn't much hope. That wee yellow-haired fiend of a major had seen, damn his soul—he knew just how terrible the fetters had been.

"Blessed is the fruit of thy womb, Jesus. Holy Mary, Mother of God, pray for us sinners . . ."

The wee Major had made him a bargain, and he had kept it. The major would not be thinking so, though.

He had kept his oath, had done as he promised. Had relayed the words spoken to him, one by one, just as he had heard them from the wandering man. It was no part of his bargain to tell the Englishman that he knew the man—or what conclusions he had drawn from the muttered words.

He had recognized Duncan Kerr at once, changed though he was by time and mortal illness. Before Culloden, he had been a tacksman of Colum MacKenzie, Jamie's uncle. After, he had escaped to France, to eke out what living might be made there.

"Be still, *a charaid; bi sàmhach,*" he had said softly in Gaelic, dropping to his knees by the bed where the sick man lay. Duncan was an elderly man, his worn face wasted by illness and fatigue, and his eyes were bright with fever. At first he had thought Duncan too far gone to know him, but the wasted hand had gripped his with surprising strength, and the man had repeated through his rasping breath *"mo charaid."* My kinsman.

The innkeeper was watching, from his place near the door, peering over Major Grey's shoulder. Jamie had bent his head and whispered in Duncan's ear, "All you say will be told to the English. Speak wary." The landlord's eyes narrowed, but the distance between them was too far; Jamie was sure he hadn't heard. Then the Major had turned and ordered the innkeeper out, and he was safe.

He couldn't tell whether it was the effect of his warning, or only the derangement of fever, but Duncan's speech wandered with his mind, often incoherent, images of the past overlapping with those of the present. Sometimes he had called Jamie "Dougal," the name of Colum's brother, Jamie's other uncle. Sometimes he dropped into poetry, sometimes he simply raved. And within the ravings and the scattered words, sometimes there was a grain of sense—or more than sense.

"It is cursed," Duncan whispered. "The gold is cursed. Do ye be warned, lad. It was given by the white witch, given for the King's son. But the Cause is lost, and the King's son fled, and she will not let the gold be given to a coward."

"Who is she?" Jamie asked. His heart had sprung up and choked him at Duncan's words, and it beat madly as he asked. "The white witch—who is she?"

"She seeks a brave man. A MacKenzie, it is for Himself. MacKenzie. It is theirs, she says it, for the sake of him who is dead."

"Who is the witch?" Jamie asked again. The word Duncan used was *ban-druidh*—a witch, a wisewoman, a white lady. They had called his wife that, once. Claire—his own white lady. He squeezed Duncan's hand tight in his own, willing him to keep his senses.

"Who?" he said again. "Who is the witch?"

"The witch," Duncan muttered, his eyes closing. "The witch. She is a soul-eater. She is death. He is dead, the MacKenzie, he is dead."

"Who is dead? Colum MacKenzie?"

"All of them, all of them. All dead. All dead!" cried the sick man, clutching tight to his hand. "Colum, and Dougal, and Ellen, too."

Suddenly his eyes opened, and fixed on Jamie's. The fever had dilated his pupils, so his gaze seemed a pool of drowning black.

"Folk do say," he said, with surprising clarity, "as how Ellen MacKenzie did leave her brothers and her home, and go to wed with a silkie from the sea. She heard them, aye?" Duncan smiled dreamily, the black stare swimming with distant vision. "She heard the silkies singing, there upon the rocks, one, and two, and three of them, and she saw from her tower, one and two, and three of them, and so she came down, and went to the sea, and so under it, to live wi' the silkies. Aye? Did she no?"

"So folk say," Jamie had answered, mouth gone dry. Ellen had been his mother's name. And that was what folk had said, when she had left her home, to elope with Brian Dubh Fraser, a man with the shining black hair of a silkie. The man for whose sake he was himself now called Mac Dubh—Black Brian's son.

Major Grey stood close, on the other side of the bed, brow furrowed as he watched Duncan's face. The Englishman had no Gaelic, but Jamie would have been willing to wager that he knew the word for gold. He caught the Major's eye, and nodded, bending again to speak to the sick man.

"The gold, man," he said, in French, loud enough for Grey to hear. "Where is the gold?" He squeezed Duncan's hand as hard as he could, hoping to convey some warning.

Duncan's eyes closed, and he rolled his head restlessly, to and fro upon the pillow. He muttered something, but the words were too faint to catch.

"What did he say?" the Major demanded sharply. "What?"

"I don't know." Jamie patted Duncan's hand to rouse him. "Speak to me, man, tell me again."

There was no response save more muttering. Duncan's eyes had rolled back in his head, so that only a thin line of gleaming white showed beneath the wrinkled lids. Impatient, the Major leaned forward and shook him by one shoulder.

"Wake up!" he said. "Speak to us!"

At once Duncan Kerr's eyes flew open. He stared up, up, past the two faces bending over him, seeing something far beyond them.

"She will tell you," he said, in Gaelic. "She will come for you." For a split second, his attention seemed to return to the inn room where he lay, and his eyes focused on the men with him. "For both of you," he said distinctly.

Then he closed his eyes, and spoke no more, but clung ever tighter to Jamie's hand. Then after a time, his grip relaxed, his hand slid free, and it was over. The guardianship of the gold had passed.

And so, Jamie Fraser had kept his word to the Englishman—and his obligation to his countrymen. He had told the Major all that Duncan had said, and the devil of a help to him that had been! And when the opportunity of escape offered, he had taken it—gone to the heather and sought the sea, and done what he could with Duncan Kerr's legacy. And now he must pay the price of his actions, whatever that turned out to be.

There were footsteps coming down the corridor outside. He clutched his knees harder, trying to quell the shivering. At least it would be decided now, either way.

". . . pray for us sinners now, and at the hour of our death, amen."

The door swung open, letting in a shaft of light that made him blink. It was dark in the corridor, but the guard standing over him held a torch.

"On your feet." The man reached down and pulled him up against the stiffness of his joints. He was pushed toward the door, stumbling. "You're wanted upstairs."

"Upstairs? Where?" He was startled at that—the smith's forge was downstairs from where he was, off the courtyard. And they wouldn't flog him so late in the evening.

The man's face twisted, fierce and ruddy in the torchlight. "To the Major's quarters," the guard said, grinning. "And may God have mercy on your soul, Mac Dubh."

"No, sir, I will not say where I have been." He repeated it firmly, trying not to let his teeth chatter. He had been brought not to the office, but to Grey's private sitting room. There was a fire on the hearth, but Grey was standing in front of it, blocking most of the warmth.

"Nor why you chose to escape?" Grey's voice was cool and formal.

Jamie's face tightened. He had been placed near the bookshelf, where the light of a triple-branched candlestick fell on his face; Grey himself was no more than a silhouette, black against the fire's glow.

"That is my private affair," he said.

"Private affair?" Grey echoed incredulously. "Did you say your private affair?"

"I did."

The Governor inhaled strongly through his nose.

"That is possibly the most outrageous thing I have heard in my life!"

"Your life has been rather brief, then, Major," Fraser said. "If you will pardon my saying so." There was no point in dragging it out or trying to placate the man. Better to provoke a decision at once and get it over with.

He had certainly provoked something; Grey's fists clenched tight at his sides, and he took a step toward him, away from the fire.

"Have you any notion what I could do to you for this?" Grey inquired, his voice low and very much controlled.

"Aye, I have. Major." More than a notion. He knew from experience what they might do to him, and he wasn't looking forward to it. It wasn't as though he'd a choice about it, though.

Grey breathed heavily for a moment, then jerked his head.

"Come here, Mr. Fraser," he ordered. Jamie stared at him, puzzled.

"Here!" he said peremptorily, pointing to a spot directly before him on the hearthrug. "Stand here, sir!"

"I am not a dog, Major!" Jamie snapped. "Ye'll do as ye like wi' me, but I'll no come when ye call me to heel!"

Taken by surprise, Grey uttered a short, involuntary laugh.

"My apologies, Mr. Fraser," he said dryly. "I meant no offense by the address. I merely wish you to approach nearer. If you will?" He stepped aside and bowed elaborately, gesturing to the hearth.

Jamie hesitated, but then stepped warily onto the patterned rug. Grey stepped close to him, nostrils flared. So close, the fine bones and fair skin of his face made him look almost girlish. The Major put a hand on his sleeve, and the long-lashed eyes sprang wide in shock.

"You're wet!"

"Yes, I am wet," Jamie said, with elaborate patience. He was also freezing. A fine, continuous shiver ran through him, even this close to the fire.

"Why?"

"Why?" Jamie echoed, astonished. "Did you not order the guards to douse me wi' water before leaving me in a freezing cell?"

"I did not, no." It was clear enough that the Major was telling the truth; his face was pale under the ruddy flush of the firelight, and he looked angry. His lips thinned to a fine line.

"I apologize for this, Mr. Fraser."

"Accepted, Major." Small wisps of steam were beginning to rise from his clothes, but the warmth was seeping through the damp cloth. His muscles ached from the shivering, and he wished he could lie down on the hearthrug, dog or not.

"Did your escape have anything to do with the matter of which you learned at the Lime Tree Inn?"

Jamie stood silent. The ends of his hair were drying, and small wisps floated across his face.

"Will you swear to me that your escape had *nothing* to do with that matter?"

Jamie stood silent. There seemed no point in saying anything, now.

The little Major was pacing up and down the hearth before him, hands locked behind his back. Now and then, the Major glanced up at him, and then resumed his pacing.

Finally he stopped in front of Jamie.

"Mr. Fraser," he said formally. "I will ask you once more— why did you escape from the prison?"

Jamie sighed. He wouldn't get to stand by the fire much longer.

"I cannot tell you, Major."

"Cannot or will not?" Grey asked sharply.

"It doesna seem a useful distinction, Major, as ye willna hear anything, either way." He closed his eyes and waited, trying to soak up as much heat as possible before they took him away.

Grey found himself at a loss, both for words and action. *Stubborn does not begin to describe it,* Quarry had said. It didn't.

He took a deep breath, wondering what to do. He found himself embarrassed by the petty cruelty of the guards' revenge; the more so because it was just such an action he had first contemplated upon hearing that Fraser was his prisoner.

He would be perfectly within his rights now to order the man flogged, or put back in irons. Condemned to solitary confinement, put on short rations—he could in justice inflict any of a dozen different punishments. And if he did, the odds of his ever finding the Frenchman's Gold became vanishingly small.

The gold *did* exist. Or at least there was a good probability that it did. Only a belief in that gold would have stirred Fraser to act as he had.

He eyed the man. Fraser's eyes were closed, his lips set firmly. He had a wide, strong mouth, whose grim expression was somewhat belied by the sensitive lips, set soft and exposed in their curly nest of red beard.

Grey paused, trying to think of some way to break past the man's wall of bland defiance. To use force would be worse than useless—and after the guards' actions, he would be ashamed to order it, even had he the stomach for brutality.

The clock on the mantelpiece struck ten. It was late; there was no sound in the fortress, save the occasional footsteps of the soldier on sentry in the courtyard outside the window.

Clearly neither force nor threat would work in gaining the truth. Reluctantly, he realized that there was only one course open to him, if he still wished to pursue the gold. He must put aside his feelings about the man and take Quarry's suggestion. He must pursue an acquaintance, in the course of which he might worm out of the man some clue that would lead him to the hidden treasure.

If it existed, he reminded himself, turning to his prisoner. He took a deep breath.

"Mr. Fraser," he said formally, "will you do me the honor to take supper tomorrow in my quarters?"

He had the momentary satisfaction of having startled the Scottish bastard, at least. The blue eyes opened wide, and then Fraser regained the mastery of his face. He paused for a moment, and then bowed with a flourish, as though he wore a kilt and swinging plaid, and not damp prison rags.

"It will be my pleasure to attend ye, Major," he said.

March 7, 1755

Fraser was delivered by the guard and left to wait in the sitting room, where a table was laid. When Grey came through the door from his bedroom a few moments later, he found his guest standing by the bookshelf, apparently absorbed in a copy of *La Nouvelle Héloïse*.

"You are interested in French novels?" he blurted, not realizing until too late how incredulous the question sounded.

Fraser glanced up, startled, and snapped the book shut. Very deliberately, he returned it to its shelf.

"I *can* read, Major," he said. He had shaved; a slight flush burned high on his cheekbones.

"I—yes, of course I did not mean—I merely—" Grey's own cheeks were more flushed than Fraser's. The fact was that he *had* subconsciously assumed that the other did not read, his evident education notwithstanding, merely because of his Highland accent and shabby dress.

While his coat might be shabby, Fraser's manners were not. He ignored Grey's flustered apology, and turned to the bookshelf.

"I have been telling the men the story, but it has been some time since I read it; I thought I would refresh my memory as to the sequence of the ending."

"I see." Just in time, Grey stopped himself from saying "They understand it?"

Fraser evidently read the unspoken question in his face, for he said dryly, "All Scottish children are taught their letters, Major. Still, we have a great tradition of storytelling in the Highlands."

"Ah. Yes. I see."

The entry of his servant with dinner saved him from further awkwardness, and the supper passed uneventfully, though there was little conversation, and that little, limited to the affairs of the prison.

The next time, he had had the chess table set up before the fire, and invited Fraser to join him in a game before the supper was served. There had been a brief flash of surprise from the slanted blue eyes, and then a nod of acquiescence.

That had been a small stroke of genius, Grey thought in retrospect. Relieved of the need for conversation or social courtesies, they had slowly become accustomed to each other as they sat over the inlaid board of ivory and ebony-wood, gauging each other silently by the movements of the chessmen.

When they had at length sat down to dine, they were no longer quite strangers, and the conversation, while still wary and formal, was at least true conversation, and not the awkward affair of starts and stops it had been before. They discussed matters of the prison, had a little conversation of books, and parted formally, but on good terms. Grey did not mention gold.

And so the weekly custom was established. Grey sought to put his guest at ease, in the hopes that Fraser might let drop some clue to the fate of the Frenchman's Gold. It had not come so far, despite careful probing. Any hint of inquiry as to what had transpired during the three days of Fraser's absence from Ardsmuir met with silence.

Over the mutton and boiled potatoes, he did his best to draw his odd guest into a discussion of France and its politics, by way of discovering whether there might exist any links between Fraser and a possible source of gold from the French Court.

Much to his surprise, he was informed that Fraser had in fact spent two years living in France, employed in the wine business, prior to the Stuart rebellion.

A certain cool humor in Fraser's eyes indicated that the man was well aware of the motives behind this questioning. At the same time, he acquiesced gracefully enough in the conversation, though taking some care always to lead questions away from his personal life, and instead toward more general matters of art and society.

Grey had spent some time in Paris, and despite his attempts at probing Fraser's French connections, found himself becoming interested in the conversation for its own sake.

"Tell me, Mr. Fraser, during your time in Paris, did you chance to encounter the dramatic works of Monsieur Voltaire?"

Fraser smiled. "Oh, aye, Major. In fact, I was privileged to entertain Monsieur Arouet—Voltaire being his nom de plume, aye?—at my table, on more than one occasion."

"Really?" Grey cocked a brow in interest. "And is he as great a wit in person as with the pen?"

"I couldna really say," Fraser replied, tidily forking up a slice of mutton. "He seldom said anything at all, let alone much sparkling with wit. He only sat hunched over in his chair, watching everyone, wi' his eyes rolling about from one to another. I shouldna be at all surprised to hear that things said at my dinner table later appeared on the stage, though fortunately I never encountered a parody of myself in his work." He closed his eyes in momentary concentration, chewing his mutton.

"Is the meat to your taste, Mr. Fraser?" Grey inquired politely. It was gristled, tough, and seemed barely edible to him. But then, he might well think differently, had he been eating oatmeal, weeds, and the occasional rat.

"Aye, it is, Major, I thank ye." Fraser dabbed up a bit of wine sauce and brought the last bite to his lips, making no demur when Grey signaled MacKay to bring back the platter.

"Monsieur Arouet wouldna appreciate such an excellent meal, I'm afraid," Fraser said, shaking his head as he helped himself to more mutton.

"I should expect a man so feted in French society to have

somewhat more exacting tastes," Grey answered dryly. Half his own meal remained on his plate, destined for the supper of the cat Augustus.

Fraser laughed. "Scarcely that, Major," he assured Grey. "I have never seen Monsieur Arouet consume anything beyond a glass of water and a dry biscuit, no matter how lavish the occasion. He's a wizened wee scrap of a man, ye ken, and a martyr to the indigestion."

"Indeed?" Grey was fascinated. "Perhaps that explains the cynicism of some of the sentiments I have seen expressed in his plays. Or do you not think that the character of an author shows in the construction of his work?"

"Given some of the characters that I have seen appear in plays and novels, Major, I should think the author a bit depraved who drew them entirely from himself, no?"

"I suppose that is so," Grey answered, smiling at the thought of some of the more extreme fictional characters with whom he was acquainted. "Though if an author constructs these colorful personages from life, rather than from the depths of imagination, surely he must boast a most varied acquaintance!"

Fraser nodded, brushing crumbs from his lap with the linen napkin.

"It was not Monsieur Arouet, but a colleague of his—a lady novelist—who remarked to me once that writing novels was a cannibal's art, in which one often mixed small portions of one's friends and one's enemies together, seasoned them with imagination, and allowed the whole to stew together into a savory concoction."

Grey laughed at the description, and beckoned to MacKay to take away the plates and bring in the decanters of port and sherry.

"A delightful description, indeed! Speaking of cannibals, though, have you chanced to be acquainted with Mr. Defoe's *Robinson Crusoe*? It has been a favorite of mine since boyhood."

The conversation turned then to romances, and the excitement of the tropics. It was very late indeed when Fraser returned to his cell, leaving Major Grey entertained, but no wiser concerning either the source or the disposition of the Frenchman's Gold.

April 2, 1755

John Grey opened the packet of quills his mother had sent from London. Swan's quills, both finer and stronger than common goose-quills. He smiled faintly at the sight of them; an unsubtle reminder that his correspondence was in arrears.

His mother would have to wait until tomorrow, though. He took out the small monogrammed penknife he always carried, and slowly trimmed a quill to his liking, composing in his mind what he meant to say. By the time he dipped his quill into the ink, the words were clear in his mind, and he wrote quickly, seldom pausing.

2 April, 1755
To Harold, Lord Melton, Earl of Moray

My dear Hal, he wrote, *I write to inform you of a recent occurrence that has much engaged my attention. It may amount in the end to nothing, but if there be any substance in the matter, it is of great import.* The details of the wandering man's appearance, and the report of his ravings followed swiftly, but Grey found himself slowing as he told of Fraser's escape and recapture.

The fact that Fraser vanished from the precincts of the prison so soon following these events suggests strongly to me that there was in truth some substance in the vagrant's words.

If this was the case, however, I find myself at a loss to account for Fraser's subsequent actions. He was recaptured within three days of his escape, at a point no more than a mile from the coast. The countryside beyond the prison is deserted for a great many miles beyond the village of Ardsmuir, and there is little likelihood of his meeting with a confederate to whom he might pass word of the treasure. Every house in the village has been searched, as was Fraser himself, with no trace discovered of any gold. It is a remote district, and I am reasonably sure that he communicated with no one outside the prison prior to his escape—I am positive that he has not done so since, for he is closely watched.

Grey stopped, seeing once more the windswept figure of James Fraser, wild as the red stags and as much at home on the moor as one of them.

He had not the slightest doubt that Fraser could have eluded the dragoons easily, had he so chosen, but he had not. He had deliberately allowed himself to be recaptured. Why? He resumed writing, more slowly.

It may be, of course, that Fraser failed to find the treasure, or that such a treasure does not exist. I find myself somewhat inclined to this belief, for if he were in possession of a great sum, surely he would have departed from the district at once. He is a strong man, well accustomed to rough living, and entirely capable, I believe, of making his way overland to some point on the coast from which he might make an escape by sea.

Grey bit the end of the quill gently, tasting ink. He made a face at the bitterness, rose, and spat out the window. He stood there for a minute, looking out into the cold spring night, absently wiping his mouth.

It had finally occurred to him to ask; not the question he had been asking all along, but the more important one. He had done it at the conclusion of a game of chess, which Fraser had won. The guard was standing at the door, ready to escort Fraser back to his cell; as the prisoner had risen from his seat, Grey had stood up, too.

"I shall not ask you again why you left the prison," he had said, calmly conversational. "But I will ask you—why did you come back?"

Fraser had frozen briefly, startled. He turned back and met Grey's eyes directly. For a moment he said nothing. Then his mouth curled up in a smile.

"I suppose I must value the company, Major; I can tell ye, it's not the food."

Grey snorted slightly, remembering. Unable to think of a suitable response, he had allowed Fraser to leave. It was only later that night that he had laboriously arrived at an answer, at last having had the wit to ask questions of himself rather than of Fraser. What would he, Grey, have done, had Fraser *not* returned?

The answer was that his next step would have been an inquiry into Fraser's family connections, in case the man had sought refuge or help from them.

And that, he was fairly sure, was the answer. Grey had not taken part in the subjugation of the Highlands—he had been posted to Italy and France—but he had heard more than enough of that particular campaign. He had seen the blackened stones of too many charred cottages, rising like cairns amid the ruined fields, as he traveled north to Ardsmuir.

The fierce loyalties of the Scottish Highlanders were legendary. A Highlander who had seen those cots in flames might well choose to suffer prison, irons, or even flogging, to save his family a visitation from English soldiers.

Grey sat and took up his quill, dipping it afresh.

You will know, I think, the mettle of the Scots, he wrote. That one in particular, he thought wryly.

> *It is unlikely that any force or threat I can exert will induce Fraser to reveal the whereabouts of the gold—should it exist, and if it does not, I can still less expect any threat to be effective! I have instead chosen to begin a formal acquaintance with Fraser, in his capacity as chief of the Scottish prisoners, in hopes of surprising some clue from his conversation. So far, I have gained nothing from this process. One further avenue of approach suggests itself, however.*

For obvious reasons, he went on, writing slowly as he formed the thought, *I do not wish to make this matter known officially.* To call attention to a hoard that might well prove to be chimerical was dangerous; the chance of disappointment was too great. Time enough, if the gold was found, to inform his superiors and collect his deserved reward—escape from Ardsmuir; a posting back to civilization.

> *Therefore I approach you, dear brother, and ask your help in discovering what particulars may obtain regarding the family of James Fraser. I pray you, do not let anyone*

*be alarmed by your inquiries; if such family connections
exist, I would have them ignorant of my interest for the
present. My deepest thanks for any efforts you may be
able to exert on my behalf, and believe me always,*

He dipped the pen once more and signed with a small flourish,

Your humble servant and most affectionate brother,
John William Grey

May 15, 1755

"The men sick of *la grippe*," Grey inquired, "how do they
fare?" Dinner was over, and with it their conversation of books.
Now it was time for business.

Fraser frowned over the single glass of sherry that was all he
would accept in the way of drink. He still had not tasted it, though
dinner had been over for some time.

"None so well. I have more than sixty men ill, fifteen of them
verra badly off." He hesitated. "Might I ask . . ."

"I can promise nothing, Mr. Fraser, but you may ask," Grey
answered formally. He had barely sipped his own sherry, nor more
than tasted his dinner; his stomach had been knotted with anticipation all day.

Jamie paused a moment longer, calculating his chances. He
wouldn't get everything; he must try for what was most important,
but leave Grey room to reject some requests.

"We have need of more blankets, Major, more fires, and more
food. And medicines."

Grey swirled the sherry in his cup, watching the light from the
fire play in the vortex. Ordinary business first, he reminded himself. Time enough for the other, later.

"We have no more than twenty spare blankets in store," he
answered, "but you may have those for the use of the very sick. I
fear I cannot augment the ration of food; the rat-spoilage has been
considerable, and we lost a great quantity of meal in the collapse
of the storeroom two months ago. We have limited resources,
and—"

"It is not so much a question of more," Fraser put in quickly.

"But rather of the type of food. Those who are most ill cannot readily digest the bread and parritch. Perhaps a substitution of some sort might be arranged?" Each man was given, by law, a quart of oatmeal parritch and a small wheaten loaf each day. Thin barley brose supplemented this twice each week, with a quart of meat stew added on Sunday, to sustain the needs of men working at manual labor for twelve to sixteen hours per day.

Grey raised one eyebrow. "What are you suggesting, Mr. Fraser?"

"I assume that the prison does have some allowance for the purchase of salt beef, turnips and onions, for the Sunday stew?"

"Yes, but that allowance must provide for the next quarter's supplies."

"Then what I suggest, Major, is that you might use that money now to provide broth and stew for those who are sick. Those of us who are hale will willingly forgo our share of meat for the quarter."

Grey frowned. "But will the prisoners not be weakened, with no meat at all? Will they not be unable to work?"

"Those who die of the grippe will assuredly not work," Fraser pointed out acerbically.

Grey snorted briefly. "True. But those of you who remain healthy will not be healthy long, if you give up your rations for so long a time." He shook his head. "No, Mr. Fraser, I think not. It is better to let the sick take their chances than to risk many more falling ill."

Fraser was a stubborn man. He lowered his head for a moment, then looked up to try again.

"Then I would ask your leave to hunt for ourselves, Major, if the Crown cannot supply us with adequate food."

"Hunt?" Grey's fair brows rose in astonishment. "Give you weapons and allow you to wander the moors? God's teeth, Mr. Fraser!"

"I think God doesna suffer much from the scurvy, Major," Jamie said dryly. "*His* teeth are in no danger." He saw the twitch of Grey's mouth and relaxed slightly. Grey always tried to suppress his sense of humor, no doubt feeling that put him at a disadvantage. In his dealings with Jamie Fraser, it did.

Emboldened by that telltale twitch, Jamie pressed on.

"Not weapons, Major. And not wandering. Will ye give us

leave to set snares upon the moor when we cut peats, though? And to keep such meat as we take?'' A prisoner would now and then contrive a snare as it was, but as often as not, the catch would be taken from him by the guards.

Grey drew a deep breath and blew it out slowly, considering.

"Snares? Would you not require materials for the construction of these snares, Mr. Fraser?"

"Only a bit of string, Major," Jamie assured him. "A dozen balls, no more, of any sort of twine or string, and ye may leave the rest to us."

Grey rubbed slowly at his cheek in contemplation, then nodded.

"Very well." The Major turned to the small secretary, plucked the quill out of its inkwell and made a note. "I shall give orders to that effect tomorrow. Now, as to the rest of your requests . . ."

A quarter-hour later, it was settled. Jamie sat back at last, sighing, and finally took a sip of his sherry. He considered that he had earned it.

He had permission not only for the snares, but for the peat-cutters to work an extra half-hour per day, the extra peats to provide for an additional small fire in each cell. No medicines were to be had, but he had leave for Sutherland to send a message to a cousin in Ullapool, whose husband was an apothecary. If the cousin's husband was willing to send medicines, the prisoners could have them.

A decent evening's work, Jamie thought. He took another sip of sherry and closed his eyes, enjoying the warmth of the fire against his cheek.

Grey watched his guest beneath lowered lids, seeing the broad shoulders slump a little, tension eased now that their business was finished. Or so Fraser thought. Very good, Grey thought to himself. Yes, drink your sherry and relax. I want you thoroughly off guard.

He leaned forward to pick up the decanter, and felt the crackle of Hal's letter in his breast pocket. His heart began to beat faster.

"Will you not take a drop more, Mr. Fraser? And tell me—how does your sister fare these days?"

He saw Fraser's eyes spring open, and his face whiten with shock.

"How are matters there at—Lallybroch, they call it, do they

not?'' Grey pushed aside the decanter, keeping his eyes fixed on his guest.

"I could not say, Major." Fraser's voice was even, but his eyes were narrowed to slits.

"No? But I daresay they do very well these days, what with the gold you have provided them."

The broad shoulders tightened suddenly, bunched under the shabby coat. Grey carelessly picked up one of the chessmen from the nearby board, tossing it casually from one hand to the other.

"I suppose Ian—your brother-in-law is named Ian, I think?—will know how to make good use of it."

Fraser had himself under control again. The dark blue eyes met Grey's directly.

"Since you are so well informed as to my connections, Major," he said evenly, "I must suppose that you also are aware that my home lies well over a hundred miles from Ardsmuir. Perhaps you will explain how I might have traveled that distance twice within the space of three days?"

Grey's eyes stayed on the chess piece, rolling idly from hand to hand. It was a pawn, a cone-headed little warrior with a fierce face, carved from a cylinder of walrus ivory.

"You might have met someone upon the moor who would have borne word of the gold—or borne the gold itself—to your family."

Fraser snorted briefly.

"On Ardsmuir? How likely is it, Major, that I should by happenstance encounter a person known to me on that moor? Much less that it should be a person whom I would trust to convey a message such as you suggest?" He set down his glass with finality. "I met no one on the moor, Major."

"And should I trust *your* word to that effect, Mr. Fraser?" Grey allowed considerable skepticism to show in his voice. He glanced up, brows raised.

Fraser's high cheekbones flushed slightly.

"No one has ever had cause to doubt my word, Major," he said stiffly.

"Have they not, indeed?" Grey was not altogether feigning his anger. "I believe you gave *me* your word, upon the occasion of my ordering your irons stricken off!"

"And I kept it!"

"Did you?" The two men sat upright, glaring at each other over the table.

"You asked three things of me, Major, and I have kept that bargain in every particular!"

Grey gave a contemptuous snort.

"Indeed, Mr. Fraser? And if that is so, pray what was it caused you suddenly to despise the company of your fellows and seek congress with the coneys on the moor? Since you assure me that you met no one else—you give me *your word* that it is so." This last was spoken with an audible sneer that brought the color surging into Fraser's face.

One of the big hands curled slowly into a fist.

"Aye, Major," he said softly. "I give ye *my word* that that is so." He seemed to realize at this point that his fist was clenched; very slowly, he unfolded it, laying his hand flat on the table.

"And as to your escape?"

"And as to my escape, Major, I have told you that I will say nothing." Fraser exhaled slowly and sat back in his chair, eyes fixed on Grey under thick, ruddy brows.

Grey paused for a moment, then sat back himself, setting the chess piece on the table.

"Let me speak plainly, Mr. Fraser. I do you the honor of assuming you to be a sensible man."

"I am deeply sensible of the honor, Major, I do assure you."

Grey heard the irony, but did not respond; he held the upper hand now.

"The fact is, Mr. Fraser, that it is of no consequence whether you did in fact communicate with your family regarding the matter of the gold. You might have done so. That possibility alone is sufficient to warrant my sending a party of dragoons to search the premises of Lallybroch—thoroughly—and to arrest and interrogate the members of your family."

He reached into his breast pocket and withdrew a piece of paper. Unfolding it, he read the list of names.

"Ian Murray—your brother-in-law, I collect? His wife, Janet. That would be your sister, of course. Their children, James—named for his uncle, perhaps?"—he glanced up briefly, long enough to catch a glimpse of Fraser's face, then returned to his list—"Margaret, Katherine, Janet, Michael, and Ian. Quite a brood," he said, in a tone of dismissal that equated the six younger Murrays with a litter of piglets. He laid the list on the table beside the chess piece.

"The three eldest children are old enough to be arrested and interrogated with their parents, you know. Such interrogations are frequently ungentle, Mr. Fraser."

In this, he spoke no less than the truth, and Fraser knew it. All color had faded from the prisoner's face, leaving the strong bones stark under the skin. He closed his eyes briefly, then opened them.

Grey had a brief memory of Quarry's voice, saying *"If you dine alone with the man, don't turn your back on him."* The hair rose briefly on the back of his neck, but he controlled himself, returning Fraser's blue stare.

"What do you want of me?" The voice was low, and hoarse with fury, but the Scot sat motionless, a figure carved in cinnabar, gilded by the flame.

Grey took a deep breath.

"I want the truth," he said softly.

There was no sound in the chamber save the pop and hiss of the peats in the grate. There was a flicker of movement from Fraser, no more than the twitch of his fingers against his leg, and then nothing. The Scot sat, head turned, staring into the fire as though he sought an answer there.

Grey sat quietly, waiting. He could afford to wait. At last, Fraser turned back to face him.

"The truth, then." He took a deep breath; Grey could see the breast of his linen shirt swell with it—he had no waistcoat.

"I kept my word, Major. I told ye faithfully all that the man said to me that night. What I didna tell ye was that some of what he said had meaning to me."

"Indeed." Grey held himself still, scarcely daring to move. "And what meaning was that?"

Fraser's wide mouth compressed to a thin line.

"I—spoke to you of my wife," he said, forcing the words out as though they hurt him.

"Yes, you said that she was dead."

"I said that she was *gone,* Major," Fraser corrected softly. His eyes were fixed on the pawn. "It is likely she is dead, but—" He stopped and swallowed, then went on more firmly.

"My wife was a healer. What they call in the Highlands a charmer, but more than that. She was a white lady—a wisewoman." He glanced up briefly. "The word in Gaelic is *ban-druidh;* it also means witch."

"The white witch." Grey also spoke softly, but excitement was thrumming through his blood. "So the man's words referred to your wife?"

"I thought they might. And if so—" The wide shoulders stirred in a slight shrug. "I had to go," he said simply. "To see."

"How did you know where to go? Was that also something you gleaned from the vagrant's words?" Grey leaned forward slightly, curious. Fraser nodded, eyes still fixed on the ivory chess piece.

"There is a spot I knew of, not too far distant from this place, where there is a shrine to St. Bride. St. Bride was also called 'the white lady,' " he explained, looking up. "Though the shrine has been there a verra long time—since long before St. Bride came to Scotland."

"I see. And so you assumed that the man's words referred to this spot, as well as to your wife?"

Again the shrug.

"I did not know," Fraser repeated. "I couldna say whether he meant anything to do with my wife, or whether 'the white witch' only meant St. Bride—was only meant to direct me to the place— or perhaps neither. But I felt I must go."

He described the place in question, and at Grey's prodding, gave directions for reaching it.

"The shrine itself is a small stone in the shape of an ancient cross, so weathered that the markings scarce show on it. It stands above a small pool, half-buried in the heather. Ye can find small white stones in the pool, tangled among the roots of the heather that grows on the bank. The stones are thought to have great powers, Major," he explained, seeing the other's blank look. "But only when used by a white lady."

"I see. And your wife . . . ?" Grey paused delicately.

Fraser shook his head briefly.

"There was nothing there to do with her," he said softly. "She is truly gone." His voice was low and controlled, but Grey could hear the undertone of desolation.

Fraser's face was normally calm and unreadable; he did not change expression now, but the marks of grief were clear, etched in the lines beside mouth and eyes, thrown into darkness by the flickering fire. It seemed an intrusion to break in upon such a depth of feeling, unstated though it was, but Grey had his duty.

"And the gold, Mr. Fraser?" he asked quietly. "What of that?"

Fraser heaved a deep sigh.

"It was there," he said flatly.

"What!" Grey sat bolt upright in his chair, staring at the Scot. "You found it?"

Fraser glanced up at him then, and his mouth twisted wryly.

"I found it."

"Was it indeed the French gold that Louis sent for Charles Stuart?" Excitement was racing through Grey's bloodstream, with visions of himself delivering great chests of gold louis d'or to his superiors in London.

"Louis never sent gold to the Stuarts," Fraser said, with certainty. "No, Major, what I found at the saint's pool was gold, but not French coin."

What he had found was a small box, containing a few gold and silver coins, and a small leather pouch, filled with jewels.

"Jewels?" Grey blurted. "Where the devil did they come from?"

Fraser cast him a glance of mild exasperation.

"I havena the slightest notion, Major," he said. "How should I know?"

"No, of course not," Grey said, coughing to cover his confusion. "Certainly. But this treasure—where is it now?"

"I threw it into the sea."

Grey stared blankly at him.

"You—what?"

"I threw it into the sea," Fraser repeated patiently. The slanted blue eyes met Grey's steadily. "Ye'll maybe have heard of a place called the Devil's Cauldron, Major? It's no more than half a mile from the saint's pool."

"Why? Why would you have done such a thing?" Grey demanded. "It isn't sense, man!"

"I wasna much concerned with sense at the time, Major," Fraser said softly. "I had gone there hoping—and with that hope gone, the treasure seemed no more to me than a wee box of stones and bits of tarnished metal. I had no use for it." He looked up, one brow slightly raised in irony. "But I didna see the 'sense' in giving it to King Geordie, either. So I flung it into the sea."

Grey sat back in his chair and mechanically poured out another cup of sherry, hardly noticing what he was doing. His thoughts were in turmoil.

Fraser sat, head turned away and chin propped on his fist, gazing into the fire, his face gone back to its usual impassivity. The light glowed behind him, lighting the long, straight line of his nose and the soft curve of his lip, shadowing jaw and brow with sternness.

Grey took a good-sized swallow of his drink and steadied himself.

"It is a moving story, Mr. Fraser," he said levelly. "Most dramatic. And yet there is no evidence that it is the truth."

Fraser stirred, turning his head to look at Grey. Jamie's slanted eyes narrowed, in what might have been amusement.

"Aye, there is, Major," he said. He reached under the waistband of his ragged breeches, fumbled for a moment, and held out his hand above the tabletop, waiting.

Grey extended his own hand in reflex, and a small object dropped into his open palm.

It was a sapphire, dark blue as Fraser's own eyes, and a good size, too.

Grey opened his mouth, but said nothing, choked with astonishment.

"There is your evidence that the treasure existed, Major." Fraser nodded toward the stone in Grey's hand. His eyes met Grey's across the tabletop. "And as for the rest—I am sorry to say, Major, that ye must take my word for it."

"But—but—you said—"

"I did." Fraser was as calm as though they had been discussing the rain outside. "I kept that one wee stone, thinking that it might be some use, if I were ever to be freed, or that I might find some chance of sending it to my family. For ye'll appreciate, Major"—a light glinted derisively in Jamie's blue eyes—"that my family couldna make use of a treasure of that sort, without attracting a deal of unwelcome attention. One stone, perhaps, but not a great many of them."

Grey could scarcely think. What Fraser said was true; a Highland farmer like his brother-in-law would have no way of turning such a treasure into money without causing talk that would bring down the King's men on Lallybroch in short order. And Fraser himself might well be imprisoned for the rest of his life. But still, to toss away a fortune so lightly! And yet, looking at the Scot, he could well believe it. If ever there was a man whose judgment would not be distorted by greed, James Fraser was it. Still—

"How did you keep this by you?" Grey demanded abruptly. "You were searched to the skin when you were brought back."

The wide mouth curved slightly in the first genuine smile Grey had seen.

"I swallowed it," Fraser said.

Grey's hand closed convulsively on the sapphire. He opened his hand and rather gingerly set the gleaming blue thing on the table by the chess piece.

"I see," he said.

"I'm sure ye do, Major," said Fraser, with a gravity that merely made the glint of amusement in his eyes more pronounced. "A diet of rough parritch has its advantages, now and again."

Grey quelled the sudden urge to laugh, rubbing a finger hard over his lip.

"I'm sure it does, Mr. Fraser." He sat for a moment, contemplating the blue stone. Then he looked up abruptly.

"You are a Papist, Mr. Fraser?" He knew the answer already; there were few adherents of the Catholic Stuarts who were not. Without waiting for a reply, he rose and went to the bookshelf in the corner. It took a moment to find; a gift from his mother, it was not part of his usual reading.

He laid the calf-bound Bible on the table, next to the stone.

"I am myself inclined to accept your word as a gentleman, Mr. Fraser," he said. "But you will understand that I have my duty to consider."

Fraser gazed at the book for a long moment, then looked up at Grey, his expression unreadable.

"Aye, I ken that fine, Major," he said quietly. Without hesitation, he laid a broad hand on the Bible.

"I swear in the name of Almighty God and by His Holy Word," he said firmly. "The treasure is as I told you." His eyes glowed in the firelight, dark and unfathomable. "And I swear on my hope of heaven," he added softly, "that it rests now in the sea."

11

The Torremolinos Gambit

With the question of the French gold thus settled, they returned to what had become their routine; a brief period of formal negotiation over the affairs of the prisoners, followed by informal conversation and sometimes a game of chess. This evening, they had come from the dinner table, still discussing Samuel Richardson's immense novel *Pamela*.

"Do you think that the size of the book is justified by the complexity of the story?" Grey asked, leaning forward to light a cheroot from the candle on the sideboard. "It must after all be a great expense to the publisher, as well as requiring a substantial effort from the reader, a book of that length."

Fraser smiled. He did not smoke himself, but had chosen to drink port this evening, claiming that to be the only drink whose taste would be unaffected by the stink of tobacco.

"What is it—twelve hundred pages? Aye, I think so. After all, it is difficult to sum up the complications of a life in a short space with any hope of constructing an accurate account."

"True. I have heard the point made, though, that the novelist's skill lies in the artful selection of detail. Do you not suppose that a volume of such length may indicate a lack of discipline in such selection, and hence a lack of skill?"

Fraser considered, sipping the ruby liquid slowly.

"I have seen books where that is the case, to be sure," he said. "An author seeks by sheer inundation of detail to overwhelm the reader into belief. In this case, however, I think it isna so. Each character is most carefully considered, and all the incidents chosen seem necessary to the story. No, I think it is true that some stories simply require a greater space in which to be told.'' He took another sip and laughed.

"Of course, I admit to some prejudice in that regard, Major. Given the circumstances under which I read *Pamela,* I should have been delighted had the book been twice as long as it was.''

"And what circumstances were those?'' Grey pursed his lips and blew a careful smoke ring that floated toward the ceiling.

"I lived in a cave in the Highlands for several years, Major,'' Fraser said wryly. "I seldom had more than three books with me, and those must last me for months at a time. Aye, I'm partial to lengthy tomes, but I must admit that it is not a universal preference.''

"That's certainly true,'' Grey agreed. He squinted, following the track of the first smoke ring, and blew another. Just off target, it drifted to the side.

"I remember,'' he continued, sucking fiercely on his cheroot, encouraging it to draw, "a friend of my mother's—saw the book —in Mother's drawing room—'' He drew deeply, and blew once more, giving a small grunt of satisfaction as the new ring struck the old, dispersing it into a tiny cloud.

"Lady Hensley, it was. She picked up the book, looked at it in that helpless way so many females affect and said, 'Oh, Countess! You are so *courageous* to attack a novel of such stupendous size. I fear I should never dare to start so lengthy a book myself.' '' Grey cleared his throat and lowered his voice from the falsetto he had affected for Lady Hensley.

"To which Mother replied,'' he went on in his normal voice, " 'Don't worry about it for a moment, my dear; you wouldn't understand it anyway.' ''

Fraser laughed, then coughed, waving away the remnants of another smoke ring.

Grey quickly snuffed out the cheroot, and rose from his seat. "Come along, then; we've just time for a quick game.''

They were not evenly matched; Fraser was much the better player, but Grey could now and then contrive to rescue a match through sheer bravado of play.

Tonight, he tried the Torremolinos Gambit. It was a risky opening, a queen's knight opening. Successfully launched, it paved the way for an unusual combination of rook and bishop, depending for its success upon a piece of misdirection by the king's knight and king bishop's pawn. Grey used it seldom, for it was a trick that would not work on a mediocre player, one not sharp enough to detect the knight's threat, or its possibilities. It was a gambit for use against a shrewd and subtle mind, and after nearly three months of weekly games, Grey knew quite well what sort of mind he was facing across the tinted ivory squares.

He forced himself not to hold his breath as he made the next-to-final move of the combination. He felt Fraser's eyes rest on him briefly, but didn't meet them, for fear of betraying his excitement. Instead, he reached to the sideboard for the decanter, and refilled both glasses with the sweet dark port, keeping his eyes carefully on the rising liquid.

Would it be the pawn, or the knight? Fraser's head was bent over the board in contemplation, small reddish lights winking in his hair as he moved slightly. The knight, and all was well; it would be too late. The pawn, and all was likely lost.

Grey could feel his heart beating heavily behind his breastbone as he waited. Fraser's hand hovered over the board, then suddenly decided, swooped down and touched the piece. The knight.

He must have let his breath out too noisily, for Fraser glanced sharply up at him, but it was too late. Careful to keep any overt expression of triumph off his face, Grey castled.

Fraser frowned at the board for a long moment, eyes flicking among the pieces, assessing. Then he jerked slightly, seeing it, and looked up, eyes wide.

"Why ye cunning wee bastard!" he said, in a tone of surprised respect. "Where in the bloody hell did ye learn *that* trick?"

"My elder brother taught it to me," Grey answered, losing his customary wariness in a rush of delight at his success. He normally beat Fraser no more than three times in ten, and victory was sweet.

Fraser uttered a short laugh, and reaching out a long index finger, delicately tipped his king over.

"I should have expected something like that from a man like my Lord Melton," he observed casually.

Grey stiffened in his seat. Fraser saw the movement, and arched one brow quizzically.

"It is Lord Melton ye mean, is it not?" he said. "Or perhaps you have another brother?"

"No," Grey said. His lips felt slightly numb, though that might only be the cheroot. "No, I have only one brother." His heart had begun to pound again, but this time with a heavy, dull beat. Had the Scottish bastard remembered all the time who he was?

"Our meeting was necessarily rather brief," the Scot said dryly. "But memorable." He picked up his glass and took a drink, watching Grey across the crystal rim. "Perhaps ye didna know that I had met Lord Melton, on Culloden Field?"

"I knew. I fought at Culloden." All Grey's pleasure in his victory had evaporated. He felt slightly nauseated from the smoke. "I didn't know that you would recall Hal, though—or know of the relationship between us."

"As I have that meeting to thank for my life, I am not likely to forget it," Fraser said dryly.

Grey looked up. "I understand that you were not so thankful when Hal met you at Culloden."

The line of Fraser's mouth tightened, then relaxed.

"No," he said softly. He smiled without humor. "Your brother verra stubbornly refused to shoot me. I wasna inclined to be grateful for the favor at the time."

"You wished to be shot?" Grey's eyebrows rose.

The Scot's eyes were remote, fixed on the chessboard, but clearly seeing something else.

"I thought I had reason," he said softly. "At the time."

"What reason?" Grey asked. He caught a gimlet glance and added hastily, "I mean no impertinence in asking. It is only—at that time, I—I felt similarly. From what you have said of the Stuarts, I cannot think that the loss of their cause would have led you to such despair."

There was a faint flicker near Fraser's mouth, much too faint to be called a smile. He inclined his head briefly, in acknowledgment.

"There were those who fought for love of Charles Stuart—or from loyalty to his father's right of kingship. But you are right; I wasna one of those."

He didn't explain further. Grey took a deep breath, keeping his eyes fixed on the board.

"I said that I felt much as you did, at the time. I—lost a particular friend at Culloden," he said. With half his mind he wondered why he should speak of Hector to this man, of all men; a

Scottish warrior who had slashed his way across that deadly field, whose sword might well have been the one . . . At the same time, he could not help but speak; there was no one to whom he *could* speak of Hector, save this man, this prisoner who could speak to no one else, whose words could do him no damage.

"He made me go and look at the body—Hal did, my brother," Grey blurted. He looked down at his hand, where the deep blue of Hector's sapphire burned against his skin, a smaller version of the one Fraser had reluctantly given him.

"He said that I must; that unless I saw him dead, I should never really believe it. That unless I knew Hector—my friend—was really gone, I would grieve forever. If I saw, and knew, I would grieve, but then I should heal—and forget." He looked up, with a painful attempt at a smile. "Hal is generally right, but not always."

Perhaps he had healed, but he would never forget. Certainly he would not forget his last sight of Hector, lying wax-faced and still in the early morning light, long dark lashes resting delicately on his cheeks as they did when he slept. And the gaping wound that had half-severed his head from his body, leaving the windpipe and large vessels of the neck exposed in butchery.

They sat silent for a moment. Fraser said nothing, but picked up his glass and drained it. Without asking, Grey refilled both glasses for the third time.

He leaned back in his chair, looking curiously at his guest.

"Do you find your life greatly burdensome, Mr. Fraser?"

The Scot looked up then, and met his eyes with a long, level gaze. Evidently, Fraser found nothing in his own face save curiosity, for the broad shoulders across the board relaxed their tension somewhat, and the wide mouth softened its grim line. The Scot leaned back, and flexed his right hand slowly, opening and closing it to stretch the muscles. Grey saw that the hand had been damaged at one time; small scars were visible in the firelight, and two of the fingers were set stiffly.

"Perhaps not greatly so," the Scot replied slowly. He met Grey's eyes with dispassion. "I think perhaps the greatest burden lies in caring for those we cannot help."

"Not in having no one for whom to care?"

Fraser paused before answering; he might have been weighing the position of the pieces on the table.

"That is emptiness," he said at last, softly. "But no great burden."

It was late; there was no sound from the fortress around them save the occasional step of the soldier on sentry in the courtyard below.

"Your wife—she was a healer, you said?"

"She was. She . . . her name was Claire." Fraser swallowed, then lifted his cup and drank, as though trying to dislodge something stuck in his throat.

"You cared very much for her, I think?" Grey said softly.

He recognized in the Scot the same compulsion he had had a few moments earlier—the need to speak a name kept hidden, to bring back for a moment the ghost of a love.

"I had meant to thank you sometime, Major," the Scot said softly.

Grey was startled.

"Thank me? For what?"

The Scot looked up, eyes dark over the finished game.

"For that night at Carryarrick where we first met." His eyes were steady on Grey's. "For what ye did for my wife."

"You remembered," Grey said hoarsely.

"I hadna forgotten," Fraser said simply. Grey steeled himself to look across the table, but when he did so, he found no hint of laughter in the slanted blue eyes.

Fraser nodded at him, gravely formal. "Ye were a worthy foe, Major; I wouldna forget you."

John Grey laughed bitterly. Oddly enough, he felt less upset than he had thought he would, at having the shameful memory so explicitly recalled.

"If you found a sixteen-year-old shitting himself with fear a worthy foe, Mr. Fraser, then it is little wonder that the Highland army was defeated!"

Fraser smiled faintly.

"A man that doesna shit himself with a pistol held to his head, Major, has either no bowels, or no brains."

Despite himself, Grey laughed. One edge of Fraser's mouth turned slightly up.

"Ye wouldna speak to save your own life, but ye would do it to save a lady's honor. The honor of my own lady," Fraser said softly. "That doesna seem like cowardice to me."

The ring of truth was too evident in the Scot's voice to mistake or ignore.

"I did nothing for your wife," Grey said, rather bitterly. "She was in no danger, after all!"

"Ye didna ken that, aye?" Fraser pointed out. "Ye thought to save her life and virtue, at the risk of your own. Ye did her honor by the notion—and I have thought of it now and again, since I— since I lost her." The hesitation in Fraser's voice was slight; only the tightening of the muscles in his throat betrayed his emotion.

"I see." Grey breathed deep, and let it out slowly. "I am sorry for your loss," he added formally.

They were both quiet for a moment, alone with their ghosts. Then Fraser looked up and drew in his breath.

"Your brother was right, Major," he said. "I thank ye, and I'll bid ye good e'en." He rose, set down his cup and left the room.

It reminded him in some ways of his years in the cave, with his visits to the house, those oases of life and warmth in the desert of solitude. Here, it was the reverse, going from the crowded, cold squalor of the cells up to the Major's glowing suite, able for a few hours to stretch both mind and body, to relax in warmth and conversation and the abundance of food.

It gave him the same odd sense of dislocation, though; that sense of losing some valuable part of himself that could not survive the passage back to daily life. Each time, the passage became more difficult.

He stood in the drafty passageway, waiting for the turnkey to unlock the cell door. The sounds of sleeping men buzzed in his ears and the smell of them wafted out as the door opened, pungent as a fart.

He filled his lungs with a quick deep breath, and ducked his head to enter.

There was a stir among the bodies on the floor as he stepped into the room, his shadow falling black across the prone and bundled shapes. The door swung closed behind him, leaving the cell in darkness, but there was a ripple of awareness through the room, as men stirred awake to his coming.

"You're back late, Mac Dubh," said Murdo Lindsay, voice rusty with sleep. "Ye'll be sair tuckered tomorrow."

"I'll manage, Murdo," he whispered, stepping over bodies. He pulled off his coat and laid it carefully over the bench, then took up the rough blanket and sought his space on the floor, his long shadow flickering across the moon-barred window.

Ronnie Sinclair turned over as Mac Dubh lay down beside him. He blinked sleepily, sandy lashes nearly invisible in the moonlight.

"Did Wee Goldie feed ye decent, Mac Dubh?"

"He did, Ronnie, thank ye." He shifted on the stones, seeking a comfortable position.

"Ye'll tell us about it tomorrow?" The prisoners took an odd pleasure in hearing what he had been served for dinner, taking it as an honor that their chief should be well fed.

"Aye, I will, Ronnie," Mac Dubh promised. "But I must sleep now, aye?"

"Sleep well, Mac Dubh," came a whisper from the corner where Hayes was rolled up, curled like a set of teaspoons with MacLeod, Innes, and Keith, who all liked to sleep warm.

"Sweet dreams, Gavin," Mac Dubh whispered back, and little by little, the cell settled back into silence.

He dreamed of Claire that night. She lay in his arms, heavy-limbed and fragrant. She was with child; her belly round and smooth as a muskmelon, her breasts rich and full, the nipples dark as wine, urging him to taste them.

Her hand cupped itself between his legs, and he reached to return the favor, the small, fat softness of her filling his hand, pressing against him as she moved. She rose over him, smiling, her hair falling down around her face, and threw her leg across him.

"Give me your mouth," he whispered, not knowing whether he meant to kiss her or to have her take him between her lips, only knowing he must have her somehow.

"Give me yours," she said. She laughed and leaned down to him, hands on his shoulders, her hair brushing his face with the scent of moss and sunlight, and he felt the prickle of dry leaves against his back and knew they lay in the glen near Lallybroch, and her the color of the copper beeches all around; beech leaves and beechwood, gold eyes and a smooth white skin, skimmed with shadows.

Then her breast pressed against his mouth, and he took it eagerly, drawing her body tight against him as he suckled her. Her milk was hot and sweet, with a faint taste of silver, like a deer's blood.

"Harder," she whispered to him, and put her hand behind his head, gripping the back of his neck, pressing him to her. "Harder."

She lay at her length upon him, his hands holding for dear life to the sweet flesh of her buttocks, feeling the small solid weight of the child upon his own belly, as though they shared it now, protecting the small round thing between their bodies.

He flung his arms about her, tight, and she held him tight as he jerked and shuddered, her hair in his face, her hands in his hair and the child between them, not knowing where any of the three of them began or ended.

He came awake suddenly, panting and sweating, half-curled on his side beneath one of the benches in the cell. It was not yet quite light, but he could see the shapes of the men who lay near him, and hoped he had not cried out. He closed his eyes at once, but the dream was gone. He lay quite still, his heart slowing, and waited for the dawn.

June 18, 1755

John Grey had dressed carefully this evening, with fresh linen and silk stockings. He wore his own hair, simply plaited, rinsed with a tonic of lemon-verbena. He had hesitated for a moment over Hector's ring, but at last had put it on, too. The dinner had been good; a pheasant he had shot himself, and a salad of greens, in deference to Fraser's odd tastes for such things. Now they sat over the chessboard, lighter topics of conversation set aside in the concentration of the midgame.

"Will you have sherry?" He set down his bishop, and leaned back, stretching.

Fraser nodded, absorbed in the new position.

"I thank ye."

Grey rose and crossed the room, leaving Fraser by the fire. He reached into the cupboard for the bottle, and felt a thin trickle of sweat run down his ribs as he did so. Not from the fire, crackling across the room; from sheer nervousness.

He brought the bottle back to the table, holding the goblets in his other hand; the Waterford crystal his mother had sent. The liquid purled into the glasses, shimmering amber and rose in the firelight. Fraser's eyes were fixed on the cup, watching the rising sherry, but with an abstraction that showed he was deep in his thoughts. The dark blue eyes were hooded. Grey wondered what he was thinking; not about the game—the outcome of that was certain.

Grey reached out and moved his queen's bishop. It was no more than a delaying move, he knew; still, it put Fraser's queen in danger, and might force the exchange of a rook.

Grey got up to put a brick of peat on the fire. Rising, he stretched himself, and strolled behind his opponent to view the situation from this angle.

The firelight shimmered as the big Scot leaned forward to study the board, picking up the deep red tones of James Fraser's hair, echoing the glow of the light in the crystalline sherry.

Fraser had bound his hair back with a thin black cord, tied in a bow. It would take no more than a slight tug to loosen it. John Grey could imagine running his hand up under that thick, glossy mass, to touch the smooth, warm nape beneath. To touch . . .

His palm closed abruptly, imagining sensation.

"It is your move, Major." The soft Scots voice brought him to himself again, and he took his seat, viewing the chessboard through sightless eyes.

Without really looking, he was intensely aware of the other's movements, his presence. There was a disturbance of the air around Fraser; it was impossible not to look at him. To cover his glance, he picked up his sherry glass and sipped, barely noticing the liquid gold taste of it.

Fraser sat still as a statue of cinnabar, only the deep blue eyes alive in his face as he studied the board. The fire had burned down, and the lines of his body were limned with shadow. His hand, all gold and black with the light of the fire on it, rested on the table, still and exquisite as the captured pawn beside it.

The blue stone in John Grey's ring glinted as he reached for his queen's bishop. *Is it wrong, Hector?* he thought. *That I should love a man who might have killed you?* Or was it a way at last to put things right; to heal the wounds of Culloden for them both?

The bishop made a soft thump as he set the felted base down with precision. Without stopping, his hand rose, as though it moved without his volition. The hand traveled the short distance through the air, looking as though it knew precisely what it wanted, and set itself on Fraser's, palm tingling, curved fingers gently imploring.

The hand under his was warm—so warm—but hard, and motionless as marble. Nothing moved on the table but the shimmer of the flame in the heart of the sherry. He lifted his eyes then, to meet Fraser's.

"Take your hand off me," Fraser said, very, very softly. "Or I will kill you."

The hand under Grey's did not move, nor did the face above, but he could feel the shiver of revulsion, a spasm of hatred and disgust that rose from the man's core, radiating through his flesh.

Quite suddenly, he heard once more the memory of Quarry's warning, as clearly as though the man spoke in his ear this moment.

If you dine with him alone—don't turn your back on him.

There was no chance of that; he could not turn away. Could not even look away or blink, to break the dark blue gaze that held him frozen. Moving as slowly as though he stood atop an unexploded mine, he drew back his hand.

There was a moment's silence, broken only by the rain's patter and the hissing of the peat fire, when neither of them seemed to breathe. Then Fraser rose without a sound, and left the room.

12

Sacrifice

The rain of late November pattered down on the stones of the courtyard, and on the sullen rows of men, standing huddled under the downpour. The Redcoats who stood on guard over them didn't look much happier than the sodden prisoners.

Major Grey stood under the overhang of the roof, waiting. It wasn't the best weather for conducting a search and cleaning of the prisoners' cells, but at this time of year, it was futile to wait for good weather. And with more than two hundred prisoners in Ardsmuir, it was necessary to swab the cells at least monthly in order to prevent major outbreaks of illness.

The doors to the main cell block swung back, and a small file of prisoners emerged; the trusties who did the actual cleaning, closely watched by the guards. At the end of the line, Corporal Dunstable came out, his hands full of the small bits of contraband a search of this sort usually turned up.

"The usual rubbish, sir," he reported, dumping the collection of pitiful relics and anonymous junk onto the top of a cask that stood near the Major's elbow. "Just this, you might take notice of."

"This" was a small strip of cloth, perhaps six inches by four, in a green tartan check. Dunstable glanced quickly at the lines of standing prisoners, as if intending to catch someone in a telltale action.

Grey sighed, then straightened his shoulders. "Yes, I suppose so." The possession of any Scottish tartan was strictly forbidden by the Diskilting Act that had likewise disarmed the Highlanders and prevented the wearing of their native dress. He stepped in front of the rows of men, as Corporal Dunstable gave a sharp shout to attract their attention.

"Whose is this?" The corporal raised the scrap high, and raised his voice as well. Grey glanced from the scrap of bright cloth to the row of prisoners, mentally ticking off the names, trying to match them to his imperfect knowledge of tartans. Even within a single clan, the patterns varied so wildly that a given pattern couldn't be assigned with any certainty, but there were general patterns of color and design.

MacAlester, Hayes, Innes, Graham, MacMurtry, MacKenzie, MacDonald . . . stop. MacKenzie. That one. It was more an officer's knowledge of men than any identification of the plaid with a particular clan that made him sure. MacKenzie was a young prisoner, and his face was a shade too controlled, too expressionless.

"It's yours, MacKenzie. Isn't it?" Grey demanded. He snatched the scrap of cloth from the corporal and thrust it under the young man's nose. The prisoner was white-faced under the blotches of dirt. His jaw was clamped hard, and he was breathing hard through his nose with a faint whistling sound.

Grey fixed the young man with a hard, triumphant stare. The young Scot had that core of implacable hate that they all had, but he hadn't managed to build the wall of stoic indifference that held it in. Grey could feel the fear building in the lad; another second and he would break.

"It's mine." The voice was calm, almost bored, and spoke with such flat indifference that neither MacKenzie nor Grey registered it at once. They stood locked in each other's eyes, until a large hand reached over Angus MacKenzie's shoulder and gently plucked the scrap of cloth from the officer's hand.

John Grey stepped back, feeling the words like a blow in the pit of his stomach. MacKenzie forgotten, he lifted his eyes the several inches necessary to look Jamie Fraser in the face.

"It isn't a Fraser tartan," he said, feeling the words force their way past wooden lips. His whole face felt numb, a fact for which he was dimly grateful; at least his expression couldn't betray him before the ranks of the watching prisoners.

Fraser's mouth widened slightly. Grey kept his gaze fastened on it, afraid to meet the dark blue eyes above.

"No, it isn't," Fraser agreed. "It's MacKenzie. My mother's clan."

In some far-off corner of his mind, Grey stored away another tiny scrap of information with the small hoard of facts kept in the jeweled coffer labeled "Jamie"—his mother was a MacKenzie. He knew that was true, just as he knew that the tartan didn't belong to Fraser.

He heard his voice, cool and steady, saying "Possession of clan tartans is illegal. You know the penalty, of course?"

The wide mouth curled in a one-sided smile.

"I do."

There was a shifting and a muttering among the ranks of the prisoners; there was little actual movement, but Grey could feel the alignment changing, as though they were in fact drawing toward Fraser, circling him, embracing him. The circle had broken and re-formed, and he was alone outside it. Jamie Fraser had gone back to his own.

With an effort of will, Grey forced his gaze away from the soft, smooth lips, slightly chapped from exposure to sun and wind. The look in the eyes above them was what he had been afraid of; neither fear nor anger—but indifference.

He motioned to a guard.

"Take him."

Major John William Grey bent his head over the work on his desk, signing requisitions without reading them. He seldom worked so late at night, but there had not been time during the day, and the paperwork was piling up. The requisitions must be sent to London this week.

"Two hundred pound wheat flowr," he wrote, trying to concentrate on the neatness of the black squiggles under his quill. The trouble with such routine paperwork was that it occupied his attention but not his mind, allowing memories of the day to creep in unawares.

"Six hogsheds ale, for use of barracks." He set down the quill and rubbed his hands briskly together. He could still feel the chill that had settled in his bones in the courtyard that morning. There

was a hot fire, but it didn't seem to be helping. He didn't go nearer; he had tried that once, and stood mesmerized, seeing the images of the afternoon in the flames, roused only when the cloth of his breeches began to scorch.

He picked up the quill and tried again to banish the sights of the courtyard from his mind.

It was better not to delay execution of sentences of this kind; the prisoners became restless and nervy in anticipation and there was considerable difficulty in controlling them. Executed at once, though, such discipline often had a salutary effect, showing the prisoners that retribution would be swift and dire, enhancing their respect for those who held their guardianship. Somehow John Grey suspected that this particular occasion had not much enhanced his prisoners' respect—for him, at least.

Feeling little more than the trickle of ice water through his veins, he had given his orders, swift and composed, and they had been obeyed with equal competence.

The prisoners had been drawn up in ranks around the four sides of the courtyard square, with shorter lines of guards arranged facing them, bayonets fixed to the ready, to prevent any unseemly outbreak.

But there had been no outbreak, seemly or otherwise. The prisoners had waited in a chill silence in the light rain that misted the stones of the courtyard, with little sound other than the normal coughs and throat-clearings of any assemblage of men. It was the beginning of winter, and catarrh was almost as common a scourge in the barracks as it was in the damp cells.

He had stood watching impassively, hands folded behind his back, as the prisoner was led to the platform. Watched, feeling the rain seep into the shoulders of his coat and run in tiny rivulets down the neck of his shirt, as Jamie Fraser stood on the platform a yard away and stripped to the waist, moving without haste or hesitation, as though this were something he had done before, an accustomed task, of no importance in itself.

He had nodded to the two privates, who seized the prisoner's unresisting hands and raised them, binding them to the arms of the whipping post. They gagged him, and Fraser stood upright, the rain running down his raised arms, and down the deep seam of his backbone, to soak the thin cloth of his breeches.

Another nod, to the sergeant who held the charge sheet, and a small surge of annoyance as the gesture caused a cascade of collected rain from one side of his hat. He straightened his hat and sodden wig, and resumed his stance of authority in time to hear the charge and sentence read.

". . . in contravention of the Diskilting Act, passed by His Majesty's Parliament, for which crime the sentence of sixty lashes shall be inflicted."

Grey glanced with professional detachment at the sergeant-farrier designated to give the punishment; this was not the first time for any of them. He didn't nod this time; the rain was still falling. A half-closing of the eyes instead, as he spoke the usual words:

"Mr. Fraser, you will take your punishment."

And he stood, eyes front and steady, watching, and hearing the thud of the landing flails and the grunt of the prisoner's breath, forced past the gag by the blow.

The man's muscles tightened in resistance to the pain. Again and again, until each separate muscle stood hard under the skin. His own muscles ached with tension, and he shifted inconspicuously from one leg to another, as the brutal tedium continued. Thin streams of red ran down the prisoner's spine, blood mixed with water, staining the cloth of his breeches.

Grey could feel the men behind him, soldiers and prisoners both, all eyes fixed on the platform and its central figure. Even the coughing was silenced.

And over it all like a sticky coat of varnish sealing off Grey's feelings was a thin layer of self-disgust, as he realized that his eyes were fixed on the scene not out of duty, but from sheer inability to look away from the sheen of mingled rain and blood that gleamed on muscle, tightened in anguish to a curve of wrenching beauty.

The sergeant-farrier paused only briefly between blows. He was hurrying it slightly; everyone wanted to get it over and get out of the rain. Grissom counted each stroke in a loud voice, noting it on his sheet as he did so. The farrier checked the lash, running the strands with their hard-waxed knots between his fingers to free them of blood and bits of flesh, then raised the cat once more, swung it slowly twice round his head, and struck again. "Thirty!" said the sergeant.

Major Grey pulled out the lowest drawer of his desk, and was neatly sick, all over a stack of requisitions.

His fingers were dug hard into his palms, but the shaking wouldn't stop. It was deep in his bones, like the winter cold.

"Put a blanket over him; I'll tend him in a moment."

The English surgeon's voice seemed to come from a long way off; he felt no connection between the voice and the hands that gripped him firmly by both arms. He cried out as they shifted him, the torsion splitting the barely clotted wounds on his back. The trickle of warm blood across his ribs made the shaking worse, despite the rough blanket they laid over his shoulders.

He gripped the edges of the bench on which he lay, cheek pressed against the wood, eyes closed, struggling against the shaking. There was a stir and a shuffle somewhere in the room, but he couldn't take notice, couldn't take his attention from the clenching of his teeth and the tightness of his joints.

The door closed, and the room grew quiet. Had they left him alone?

No, there were footsteps near his head, and the blanket over him lifted, folded back to his waist.

"Mm. Made a mess of you, didn't he, boy?"

He didn't answer; no answer seemed expected, in any case. The surgeon turned away for a moment; then he felt a hand beneath his cheek, lifting his head. A towel slid beneath his face, cushioning it from the rough wood.

"I'm going to cleanse the wounds now," the voice said. It was impersonal, but not unfriendly.

He drew in his breath through his teeth as a hand touched his back. There was an odd whimpering noise. He realized he had made it, and was ashamed.

"How old are you, boy?"

"Nineteen." He barely got the word out, before biting down hard on a moan.

The doctor touched his back gently here and there, then stood up. He heard the sound of the bolt being shot to, then the doctor's steps returning.

"No one will come in now," the voice said kindly. "Go ahead and cry."

"Hey!" the voice was saying. "Wake up, man!"

He came slowly to consciousness; the roughness of wood beneath his cheek brought dream and waking together for a moment, and he couldn't remember where he was. A hand came out of the darkness, touching him tentatively on the cheek.

"Ye were greetin' in your sleep, man," the voice whispered. "Does it pain ye much?"

"A bit." He realized the other link between dreaming and waking as he tried to raise himself and the pain crackled over his back like sheet lightning. He let out his breath in an involuntary grunt and dropped back on the bench.

He had been lucky; he had drawn Dawes, a stout middle-aged soldier who didn't really like flogging prisoners, and did it only because it was part of his job. Still, sixty lashes did damage, even if applied without enthusiasm.

"Nah, then, that's too hot by half. Want to scald him, do ye?" It was Morrison's voice, scolding. It would be Morrison, of course.

Odd, he thought dimly. How whenever you had a group of men, they seemed to find their proper jobs, no matter whether it was a thing they'd done before. Morrison had been a cottar, like most of them. Likely a good hand with his beasts, but not thinking much about it. Now he was the natural healer for the men, the one they turned to with a griping belly or a broken thumb. Morrison knew little more than the rest, but the men turned to him when they were hurt, as they turned to Seumus Mac Dubh for reassurance and direction. And for justice.

The steaming cloth was laid across his back and he grunted with the sting of it, pressing his lips tight to keep from crying out. He could feel the shape of Morrison's small hand, lightly laid in the center of his back.

"Bide ye, man, 'til the heat passes."

As the nightmare faded, he blinked for a moment, adjusting himself to the nearby voices and the perception of company. He was in the large cell, in the shadowy nook by the chimney breast. Steam rose from the fire; there must be a cauldron boiling. He saw Walter MacLeod lower a fresh armful of rags into its depths, the fire touching MacLeod's dark beard and brows with red. Then, as the heated rags on his back cooled to a soothing warmth, he closed his eyes and sank back into a half-doze, lulled by the soft conversation of the men nearby.

It was familiar, this state of dreamy detachment. He had felt much the same ever since the moment when he had reached over young Angus's shoulder and closed his fist on the scrap of tartan cloth. As though with that choice, some curtain had come down between him and the men around him; as though he were alone, in some quiet place of infinite remoteness.

He had followed the guard who took him, stripped himself when told, but all without feeling as though he had truly waked. Taken his place on the platform and heard the words of crime and sentence pronounced, without really listening. Not even the rough bite of the rope on his wrists or the cold rain on his naked back had roused him. These seemed all things that had happened before; nothing he said or did could change a thing; it was all fated.

As for the flogging, he had borne it. There was no room then for thought or regret, or for anything beyond the stubborn, desperate struggle such bodily insult required.

"Still, now, still." Morrison's hand rested on his neck, to prevent his moving as the sodden rags were taken off and a fresh, hot poultice applied, momentarily rousing all the dormant nerves to fresh startlement.

One consequence of his odd state of mind was that all sensations seemed of equal intensity. He could, if he tried, feel each separate stripe across his back, see each one in his mind's eye as a vivid streak of color across the dark of imagination. But the pain of the gash that ran from ribs to shoulder was of no more weight or consequence than the almost pleasant feeling of heaviness in his legs, the soreness in his arms, or the soft tickling brush of his hair across his cheek.

His pulse beat slow and regular in his ears; the sigh of his breath was a thing apart from the heave of his chest as he breathed. He existed only as a collection of fragments, each small piece with its own sensations, and none of them of any particular concern to the central intelligence.

"Here, Mac Dubh," said Morrison's voice, next to his ear. "Lift your head, and drink this."

The sharp scent of whisky struck him, and he tried to turn his head away.

"I don't need it," he said.

"That ye do," Morrison said, with that firm matter-of-factness that all healers seemed to have, as though they always knew better than you did what you felt like or what you required. Lacking strength or will to argue, he opened his mouth and sipped the whisky, feeling his neck muscles quiver under the strain of holding his head up.

The whisky added its own bit to the chorus of sensations that filled him. A burn in throat and belly, sharp tingle up the back of the nose, and a sort of whirling in his head that told him he had drunk too much, too fast.

"A bit more, now, aye, that's it," Morrison said, coaxing. "Good lad. Aye, that'll be better, won't it?" Morrison's thick body moved, so his vision of the darkened room was obscured. A draft blew from the high window, but there seemed more stir about him than was accounted for by the wind.

"Now, how's the back? Ye'll be stiff as a cornstook by the morrow, but I think it's maybe no so bad as it might be. Here, man, ye'll have a sup more." The rim of the horn cup pressed insistently against his mouth.

Morrison was still talking, rather loudly, of nothing in particular. There was something wrong about that. Morrison was not a talkative man. Something was happening, but he couldn't see. He lifted his head, searching for what was wrong, but Morrison pressed it down again.

"Dinna trouble yourself, Mac Dubh," he said softly. "Ye canna stop it, anyway."

Surreptitious sounds were coming from the far corner of the cell, the sounds Morrison had tried to keep him from hearing. Scraping noises, brief mutters, a thud. Then the muffled sound of blows, slow and regular, and a heavy gasping of fright and pain, punctuated with a small whimpering sound of indrawn breath.

They were beating young Angus MacKenzie. He braced his hands beneath his chest, but the effort made his back blaze and his head swim. Morrison's hand was back, forcing him down.

"Be still, Mac Dubh," he said. His tone was a mixture of authority and resignation.

A wave of dizziness washed through him, and his hands slipped off the bench. Morrison was right in any case, he realized. He couldn't stop them.

He lay still then under Morrison's hand, eyes closed, and waited for the sounds to stop. Despite himself, he wondered who it was, that administrator of blind justice in the dark. Sinclair. His mind supplied the answer without hesitation. And Hayes and Lindsay helping, no doubt.

They could no more help themselves than he could, or Morrison. Men did as they were born to. One man a healer, another a bully.

The sounds had stopped, except for a muffled, sobbing gasp. His shoulders relaxed, and he didn't move as Morrison took away the last wet poultice and gently blotted him dry, the draft from the window making him shiver in sudden chill. He pressed his lips tight, to make no noise. They had gagged him this afternoon, and he was glad of it; the first time he had been flogged, years ago, he had bitten his lower lip nearly in two.

The cup of whisky pressed against his mouth, but he turned his head aside, and it disappeared without comment to some place where it would find a more cordial reception. Milligan, likely, the Irishman.

One man with the weakness for drink, another with a hatred of it. One man a lover of women, and another . . .

He sighed and shifted slightly on the hard plank bed. Morrison had covered him with a blanket and gone away. He felt drained and empty, still in fragments, but with his mind quite clear, perched at some far remove from the rest of him.

Morrison had taken away the candle as well; it burned at the far end of the cell, where the men sat hunched companionably together, the light making black shapes of them, one indistinguishable from another, rimmed in gold light like the pictures of faceless saints in old missals.

He wondered where they came from, these gifts that shaped a man's nature. From God?

Was it like the descent of the Paraclete, and the tongues of fire that came to rest on the apostles? He remembered the picture in the Bible in his mother's parlor, the apostles all crowned with fire, and looking fair daft with the shock of it, standing about like a crowd of beeswax candles, lit for a party.

He smiled to himself at the memory, and closed his eyes. The candle shadows wavered red on his lids.

Claire, his own Claire—who knew what had sent her to him, had thrust her into a life she had surely not been born to? And yet she had known what to do, what she was meant to be, despite that. Not everyone was so fortunate as to know their gift.

There was a cautious shuffling in the darkness beside him. He
opened his eyes and saw no more than a shape, but knew nonetheless who it was.

"How are ye, Angus?" he said softly in Gaelic.

The youngster knelt awkwardly by him, and took his hand.

"I am . . . all right. But you—sir, I mean . . . I—I'm
sorry . . ."

Was it experience or instinct that made him tighten his own
hand in reassurance?

"I am all right, too," he said. "Lay ye down, wee Angus, and
take your rest."

The shape bent its head in an oddly formal gesture, and pressed
a kiss on the back of his hand.

"I—may I stay by ye, sir?"

His hand weighed a ton, but he lifted it nonetheless and laid it
on the young man's head. Then it slipped away, but he felt
Angus's tension relax, as the comfort flowed from his touch.

He had been born a leader, then bent and shaped further to fit
such a destiny. But what of a man who had not been born to the
role he was required to fill? John Grey, for one. Charles Stuart for
another.

For the first time in ten years, from this strange distance, he
could find it in himself to forgive that feeble man who had once
been his friend. Having so often paid the price exacted by his own
gift, he could at last see the more terrible doom of having been
born a king, without the gift of kingship.

Angus MacKenzie sat slumped against the wall next to him,
head bowed upon his knees, his blanket over his shoulders. A
small, gurgling snore came from the huddled form. He could feel
sleep coming for him, fitting back the shattered, scattered parts of
himself as it came, and knew he would wake whole—if very sore
—in the morning.

He felt relieved at once of many things. Of the weight of immediate responsibility, of the necessity for decision. Temptation was
gone, along with the possibility of it. More important, the burden
of anger had lifted; perhaps it was gone for good.

So, he thought, through the gathering fog, John Grey had given
him back his destiny.

Almost, he could be grateful.

13

Midgame

I t was Roger who found her in the morning, curled up on the study sofa under the hearthrug, papers scattered carelessly over the floor where they had spilled from one of the folders.

The light from the floor-length windows streamed in, flooding the study, but the high back of the sofa had shaded Claire's face and prevented the dawn from waking her. The light was just now pouring over the curve of dusty velvet to flicker among the strands of her hair.

A glass face in more ways than one, Roger thought, looking at her. Her skin was so fair that the blue veins showed through at temple and throat, and the sharp, clear bones were so close beneath that she might have been carved of ivory.

The rug had slipped half off, exposing her shoulders. One arm lay relaxed across her chest, trapping a single, crumpled sheet of paper against her body. Roger lifted her arm carefully, to pull the paper loose without waking her. She was limp with sleep, her flesh surprisingly warm and smooth in his grasp.

His eyes found the name at once; he had known she must have found it.

"James MacKenzie Fraser," he murmured. He looked up from the paper to the sleeping woman on the sofa. The light had just touched the curve of her ear; she stirred briefly and turned her head, then her face lapsed back into somnolence.

"I don't know who you were, mate," he whispered to the unseen Scot, "but you must have been something, to deserve her."

Very gently, he replaced the rug over Claire's shoulders, and lowered the blind of the window behind her. Then he squatted and gathered up the scattered papers from the Ardsmuir folder. Ardsmuir. That was all he needed for now; even if Jamie Fraser's eventual fate was not recorded in the pages in his hands, it would be somewhere in the history of Ardsmuir prison. It might take another foray into the Highland archives, or even a trip to London, but the next step in the link had been forged; the path was clear.

Brianna was coming down the stairs as he pulled the door of the study closed, moving with exaggerated caution. She arched a brow in question and he lifted the folder, smiling.

"Got him," he whispered.

She didn't speak, but an answering smile spread across her face, bright as the rising sun outside.

PART FOUR

The Lake District

14

Geneva

"I think," Grey said carefully, "that you might consider changing your name."

He didn't expect an answer; in four days of travel, Fraser had not spoken a single word to him, managing even the awkward business of sharing an inn room without direct communication. Grey had shrugged and taken the bed, while Fraser, without gesture or glance, had wrapped himself in his threadbare cloak and lain down before the hearth. Scratching an assortment of bites from fleas and bedbugs, Grey thought that Fraser might well have had the better end of the sleeping arrangements.

"Your new host is not well disposed toward Charles Stuart and his adherents, having lost his only son at Prestonpans," he went on, addressing the iron-set profile visible next to him. Gordon Dunsany had been only a few years older than himself, a young captain in Bolton's regiment. They might easily have died together on that field—if not for that meeting in the wood near Carryarrick.

"You can scarcely hope to conceal the fact that you are a Scot, and a Highlander at that. If you will condescend to consider a piece of well-meant advice, it might be judicious not to use a name which would be as easily recognized as your own."

Fraser's stony expression didn't alter in the slightest particular. He nudged his horse with a heel and guided it ahead of Grey's bay, seeking the remains of the track, washed out by a recent flood.

It was late afternoon when they crossed the arch of Ashness Bridge and started down the slope toward Watendlath Tarn. The

Lake District of England was nothing like Scotland, Grey reflected, but at least there were mountains here. Round-flanked, fat
and dreamy mountains, not sternly forbidding like the Highland
crags, but mountains nonetheless.

Watendlath Tarn was dark and ruffled in the early autumn wind,
its edges thick with sedge and marsh grass. The summer rains had
been more generous even than usual in this damp place, and the
tips of drowned shrubs poked limp and tattered above water that
had run over its banks.

At the crest of the next hill, the track split, going off in two
directions. Fraser, some distance ahead, pulled his horse to a stop
and waited for direction, the wind ruffling his hair. He had not
plaited it that morning, and it blew free, the flaming strands lifting
wild about his head.

Squelching his way up the slope, John William Grey looked up
at the man above him, still as a bronze statue on his mount, save
for that rippling mane. The breath dried in his throat, and he licked
his lips.

"O Lucifer, thou son of the morning," he murmured to himself, but forbore to add the rest of the quotation.

For Jamie, the four-day ride to Helwater had been torture. The
sudden illusion of freedom, combined with the certainty of its
immediate loss, gave him a dreadful anticipation of his unknown
destination.

This, with the anger and sorrow of his parting from his men
fresh in memory—the wrenching loss of leaving the Highlands,
with the knowledge that the parting might well be permanent—
and his waking moments suffused with the physical pain of long-
unused saddle muscles, were together enough to have kept him in
torment for the whole of the journey. Only the fact that he had
given his parole kept him from pulling Major John William Grey
off his horse and throttling him in some peaceful lane.

Grey's words echoed in his ears, half-obliterated by the thrumming beat of his angry blood.

"As the renovation of the fortress has largely been completed—
with the able assistance of yourself and your men"—Grey had
allowed a tinge of irony to show in his voice—"the prisoners are

to be removed to other accommodation, and the fortress of Ardsmuir garrisoned by troops of His Majesty's Twelfth Dragoons.

"The Scottish prisoners of war are to be transported to the American Colonies," he continued. "They will be sold under bond of indenture, for a term of seven years."

Jamie had kept himself carefully expressionless, but at that news, had felt his face and hands go numb with shock.

"Indenture? That is no better than slavery," he said, but did not pay much attention to his own words. America! A land of wilderness and savages—and one to be reached across three thousand miles of empty, roiling sea! Indenture in America was a sentence tantamount to permanent exile from Scotland.

"A term of indenture is not slavery," Grey had assured him, but the Major knew as well as he that the difference was merely a legality, and true only insofar as indentured servants would—if they survived—regain their freedom upon some predetermined date. An indentured servant *was* to most other intents and purposes the slave of his or her master—to be misused, whipped or branded at will, forbidden by law to leave the master's premises without permission.

As James Fraser was now to be forbidden.

"You are not to be sent with the others." Grey had not looked at him while speaking. "You are not merely a prisoner of war, you are a convicted traitor. As such, you are imprisoned at the pleasure of His Majesty; your sentence cannot be commuted to transportation without royal approval. And His Majesty has not seen fit to give that approval."

Jamie was conscious of a remarkable array of emotions; beneath his immediate rage was fear and sorrow for the fate of his men, mingled with a small flicker of ignominious relief that, whatever his own fate was to be, it would not involve entrusting himself to the sea. Shamed by the realization, he turned a cold eye on Grey.

"The gold," he said flatly. "That's it, aye?" So long as there remained the slightest chance of his revealing what he knew about that half-mythical hoard, the English Crown would take no chance of having him lost to the sea demons or the savages of the Colonies.

The Major still would not look at him, but gave a small shrug, as good as assent.

"Where am I to go, then?" His own voice had sounded rusty to his ears, slightly hoarse as he began to recover from the shock of the news.

Grey had busied himself putting away his records. It was early September, and a warm breeze blew through the half-open window, fluttering the papers.

"It's called Helwater. In the Lake District of England. You will be quartered with Lord Dunsany, to serve in whatever menial capacity he may require." Grey did look up then, the expression in his light blue eyes unreadable. "I shall visit you there once each quarter—to ensure your welfare."

He eyed the Major's red-coated back now, as they rode single-file through the narrow lanes, seeking refuge from his miseries in a satisfying vision of those wide blue eyes, bloodshot and popping in amazement as Jamie's hands tightened on that slender throat, thumbs digging into the sun-reddened flesh until the Major's small, muscular body should go limp as a killed rabbit in his grasp.

His Majesty's pleasure, was it? He was not deceived. This had been Grey's doing; the gold only an excuse. He was to be sold as a servant, and kept in a place where Grey could see it, and gloat. This was the Major's revenge.

He had lain before the inn hearth each night, aching in every limb, acutely aware of every twitch and rustle and breath of the man in the bed behind him, and deeply resentful of that awareness. By the pale gray of dawn, he was keyed to fury once more, longing for the man to rise from his bed and make some disgraceful gesture toward him, so that he might release his fury in the passion of murder. But Grey had only snored.

Over Helvellyn Bridge and past another of the strange grassy tarns, the red and yellow leaves of maple and larch whirling down in showers past the lightly sweated quarters of his horse, striking his face and sliding past him with a papery, whispering caress.

Grey had stopped just ahead, and turned in the saddle, waiting. They had arrived, then. The land sloped steeply down into a valley, where the manor house lay half-concealed in a welter of autumn-bright trees.

Helwater lay before him, and with it, the prospect of a life of shameful servitude. He stiffened his back and kicked his horse, harder than he intended.

Grey was received in the main drawing room, Lord Dunsany being cordially dismissive of his disheveled clothes and filthy boots, and Lady Dunsany, a small round woman with faded fair hair, fulsomely hospitable.

"A drink, Johnny, you must have a drink! And Louisa, my dear, perhaps you should fetch the girls down to greet our guest."

As Lady Dunsany turned to give orders to a footman, his Lordship leaned close over the glass to murmur to him. "The Scottish prisoner—you've brought him with you?"

"Yes," Grey said. Lady Dunsany, now in animated conversation with the butler about the altered dispositions for dinner, was unlikely to overhear, but he thought it best to keep his own voice low. "I left him in the front hall—I wasn't sure quite what you meant to do with him."

"You said the fellow's good with horses, eh? Best make him a groom then, as you suggested." Lord Dunsany glanced at his wife, and carefully turned so that his lean back was to her, further guarding their conversation. "I haven't told Louisa who he is," the baronet muttered. "All that scare about the Highlanders during the Rising—country was quite paralyzed with fear, you know? And she's never got over Gordon's death."

"I quite see." Grey patted the old man's arm reassuringly. He didn't think Dunsany himself had got over the death of his son, though he had rallied himself gamely for the sake of his wife and daughters.

"I'll just tell her the man's a servant you've recommended to me. Er . . . he's safe, of course? I mean . . . well, the girls . . ." Lord Dunsany cast an uneasy eye toward his wife.

"Quite safe," Grey assured his host. "He's an honorable man, and he's given his parole. He'll neither enter the house nor leave the boundaries of your property, save with your express permission." Helwater covered more than six hundred acres, he knew. It was a long way from freedom, and from Scotland as well, but perhaps something better than either the narrow stones of Ardsmuir or the distant hardships of the Colonies.

A sound from the doorway swung Dunsany around, restored to beaming joviality by the appearance of his two daughters.

"You'll remember Geneva, Johnny?" he asked, urging his guest forward. "Isobel was still in the nursery last time you came —how time does fly, does it not?" And he shook his head in mild dismay.

Isobel was fourteen, small and round and bubbly and blond, like her mother. Grey didn't, in fact, remember Geneva—or rather he did, but the scrawny schoolgirl of years past bore little resemblance to the graceful seventeen-year-old who now offered him her hand. If Isobel resembled their mother, Geneva rather took after her father, at least in the matter of height and leanness. Lord Dunsany's grizzled hair might once have been that shining chestnut, and the girl had Dunsany's clear gray eyes.

The girls greeted the visitor with politeness, but were clearly more interested in something else.

"Daddy," said Isobel, tugging on her father's sleeve. "There's a *huge* man in the hall! He watched us all the time we were coming down the stairs! He's scary-looking!"

"Who is he, Daddy?" Geneva asked. She was more reserved than her sister, but clearly also interested.

"Er . . . why, that must be the new groom John's brought us," Lord Dunsany said, obviously flustered. "I'll have one of the footmen take him—" The baronet was interrupted by the sudden appearance of a footman in the doorway.

"Sir," he said, looking shocked at the news he bore, "there is a Scotchman in the hall!" Lest this outrageous statement not be believed, he turned and gestured widely at the tall, silent figure standing cloaked behind him.

At this cue, the stranger took a step forward, and spotting Lord Dunsany, politely inclined his head.

"My name is Alex MacKenzie," he said, in a soft Highland accent. He bowed toward Lord Dunsany, with no hint of mockery in his manner. "Your servant, my lord."

For one accustomed to the strenuous life of a Highland farm or a labor prison, the work of a groom on a Lake District stud farm was no great strain. For a man who had been mewed up in a cell for two months—since the others had left for the Colonies—it was the hell of a sweat. For the first week, while his muscles reaccustomed themselves to the sudden demands of constant movement, Jamie Fraser fell into his hayloft pallet each evening too tired even to dream.

He had arrived at Helwater in such a state of exhaustion and mental turmoil that he had at first seen it only as another prison—and one among strangers, far away from the Highlands. Now that he was ensconced here, imprisoned as securely by his word as by bars, he found both body and mind growing easier, as the days passed by. His body toughened, his feelings calmed in the quiet company of horses, and gradually he found it possible to think rationally again.

If he had no true freedom, he did at least have air, and light, space to stretch his limbs, and the sight of mountains and the lovely horses that Dunsany bred. The other grooms and servants were understandably suspicious of him, but inclined to leave him alone, out of respect for his size and forbidding countenance. It was a lonely life—but he had long since accepted the fact that, for him, life was unlikely ever to be otherwise.

The soft snows came down upon Helwater, and even Major Grey's official visit at Christmas—a tense, awkward occasion—passed without disturbing his growing feelings of content.

Very quietly, he made such arrangements as could be managed, to communicate with Jenny and Ian in the Highlands. Aside from the infrequent letters that reached him by indirect means, which he read and then destroyed for safety's sake, his only reminder of home was the beechwood rosary he wore about his neck, concealed beneath his shirt.

A dozen times a day he touched the small cross that lay over his heart, conjuring each time the face of a loved one, with a brief word of prayer—for his sister, Jenny; for Ian and the children—his namesake, Young Jamie, Maggie, and Katherine Mary, for the twins Michael and Janet, and for Baby Ian. For the tenants of Lallybroch; the men of Ardsmuir. And always, the first prayer at morning, the last at night—and many between—for Claire. *Lord, that she may be safe. She and the child.*

As the snow passed and the year brightened into spring, Jamie Fraser was aware of only one fly in the ointment of his daily existence—the presence of the Lady Geneva Dunsany.

Pretty, spoilt, and autocratic, the Lady Geneva was accustomed to get what she wanted when she wanted it, and damn the convenience of anyone standing in her way. She was a good horse-woman—Jamie would give her that—but so sharp-tongued and whim-ridden that the grooms were given to drawing straws to determine who would have the misfortune of accompanying her on her daily ride.

Of late, though, the Lady Geneva had been making her own choice of companion—Alex MacKenzie.

"Nonsense," she said, when he pleaded first discretion, and then temporary indisposition, to avoid accompanying her into the secluded mist of the foothills above Helwater; a place she was forbidden to ride, because of the treacherous footing and danger-ous fogs. "Don't be silly. Nobody's going to see us. Come on!" And kicking her mare brutally in the ribs, was off before he could stop her, laughing back over her shoulder at him.

Her infatuation with him was sufficiently obvious as to make the other grooms grin sidelong and make low-voiced remarks to each other when she entered the stable. He had a strong urge, when in her company, to boot her swiftly where it would do most good, but so far had settled for maintaining a strict silence when in her company, replying to all overtures with a mumpish grunt.

He trusted that she would get tired of this taciturn treatment sooner or later, and transfer her annoying attentions to another of the grooms. Or—pray God—she would soon be married, and well away from both Helwater and him.

It was a rare sunny day for the Lake Country, where the differ-ence between the clouds and the ground is often imperceptible, in terms of damp. Still, on this May afternoon it was warm, warm enough for Jamie to have found it comfortable to remove his shirt. It was safe enough up here in the high field, with no likelihood of company beyond Bess and Blossom, the two stolid drayhorses pulling the roller.

It was a big field, and the horses old and well-trained to the task, which they liked; all he need do was twitch the reins occasionally, to keep their noses heading straight. The roller was made of wood, rather than the older kind of stone or metal, and constructed with a narrow slit between each board, so that the interior could be filled with well-rotted manure, which dribbled out in a steady stream as the roller turned, lightening the heavy contrivance as it drained.

Jamie thoroughly approved this innovation. He must tell Ian about it; draw a diagram. The Gypsies would be coming soon; the kitchenmaids and grooms were all talking of it. He would maybe have time to add another installment to the ongoing letter he kept, sending the current crop of pages whenever a band of roving tinkers or Gypsies came onto the farm. Delivery might be delayed for a month, or three, or six, but eventually the packet would make its way into the Highlands, passed from hand to hand, and on to his sister at Lallybroch, who would pay a generous fee for its reception.

Replies from Lallybroch came by the same anonymous route—for as a prisoner of the Crown, anything he sent or received by the mails must be inspected by Lord Dunsany. He felt a moment's excitement at the thought of a letter, but tried to damp it down; there might be nothing.

"Gee!" he shouted, more as a matter of form than anything. Bess and Blossom could see the approaching stone fence as well as he could, and were perfectly well aware that this was the spot to begin the ponderous turnabout. Bess waggled one ear and snorted, and he grinned.

"Aye, I know," he said to her, with a light twitch of the rein. "But they pay me to say it."

Then they were settled in the new track, and there was nothing more to do until they reached the wagon standing at the foot of the field, piled high with manure for refilling the roller. The sun was on his face now, and he closed his eyes, reveling in the feel of warmth on his bare chest and shoulders.

The sound of a horse's high whinny stirred him from somnolence a quarter-hour later. Opening his eyes, he could see the rider coming up the lane from the lower paddock, neatly framed between Blossom's ears. Hastily, he sat up and pulled the shirt back over his head.

"You needn't be modest on my account, MacKenzie." Geneva Dunsany's voice was high and slightly breathless as she pulled her mare to a walk beside the moving roller.

"Mmphm." She was dressed in her best habit, he saw, with a cairngorm brooch at her throat, and her color was higher than the temperature of the day warranted.

"What are you doing?" she asked, after they had rolled and paced in silence for some moments.

"I am spreading shit, my lady," he answered precisely, not looking at her.

"Oh." She rode on for the space of half a track, before venturing further into conversation.

"Did you know I am to be married?"

He did; all the servants had known it for a month, Richards the butler having been in the library, serving, when the solicitor came from Derwentwater to draw up the wedding contract. The Lady Geneva had been informed two days ago. According to her maid, Betty, the news had not been well received.

He contented himself with a noncommittal grunt.

"To Ellesmere," she said. The color rose higher in her cheeks, and her lips pressed together.

"I wish ye every happiness, my lady." Jamie pulled briefly on the reins as they came to the end of the field. He was out of the seat before Bess had set her hooves; he had no wish at all to linger in conversation with the Lady Geneva, whose mood seemed thoroughly dangerous.

"Happiness!" she cried. Her big gray eyes flashed and she slapped the thigh of her habit. "Happiness! Married to a man old enough to be my own grandsire?"

Jamie refrained from saying that he suspected the Earl of Ellesmere's prospects for happiness were somewhat more limited than her own. Instead, he murmured, "Your pardon, my lady," and went behind to unfasten the roller.

She dismounted and followed him. "It's a filthy bargain between my father and Ellesmere! He's selling me, that's what it is. My father cares not the slightest trifle for me, or he'd never have made such a match! Do you not think I am badly used?"

On the contrary, Jamie thought that Lord Dunsany, a most devoted father, had probably made the best match possible for his spoilt elder daughter. The Earl of Ellesmere *was* an old man. There was every prospect that within a few years, Geneva would be left as an extremely wealthy young widow, and a countess, to boot. On the other hand, such considerations might well not weigh heavily with a headstrong miss—a stubborn, spoilt bitch, he corrected, seeing the petulant set of her mouth and eyes—of seventeen.

"I am sure your father acts always in your best interests, my lady," he answered woodenly. Would the little fiend not go away?

She wouldn't. Assuming a more winsome expression, she came and stood close to his side, interfering with his opening the loading hatch of the roller.

"But a match with such a dried-up old man?" she said. "Surely it is heartless of Father to give me to such a creature." She stood on tiptoe, peering at Jamie. "How old are *you*, MacKenzie?"

His heart stopped beating for an instant.

"A verra great deal older than you, my lady," he said firmly. "Your pardon, my lady." He slid past her as well as he might without touching her, and leapt up onto the manure wagon, whence he was reasonably sure she wouldn't follow him.

"But not ready for the boneyard yet, are you, MacKenzie?" Now she was in front of him, shading her eyes with her hand as she peered upward. A breeze had come up, and wisps of her chestnut hair floated about her face. "Have you ever been married, MacKenzie?"

He gritted his teeth, overcome with the urge to drop a shovelful of manure over her chestnut head, but mastered it and dug the shovel into the pile, merely saying "I have," in a tone that brooked no further inquiries.

The Lady Geneva was not interested in other people's sensitivities. "Good," she said, satisfied. "You'll know what to do, then."

"To do?" He stopped short in the act of digging, one foot braced on the shovel.

"In bed," she said calmly. "I want you to come to bed with me."

In the shock of the moment, all he could think of was the ludicrous vision of the elegant Lady Geneva, skirts thrown up over her face, asprawl in the rich crumble of the manure wagon.

He dropped the shovel. "*Here?*" he croaked.

"No, silly," she said impatiently. "In bed, in a proper bed. In my bedroom."

"You have lost your mind," Jamie said coldly, the shock receding slightly. "Or I should think you had, if ye had one to lose."

Her face flamed and her eyes narrowed. "How dare you speak that way to me!"

"How dare ye speak so to *me*?" Jamie replied hotly. "A wee lassie of breeding to be makin' indecent proposals to a man twice

her age? And a groom in her father's house?'' he added, recollecting who he was. He choked back further remarks, recollecting
also that this dreadful girl *was* the Lady Geneva, and he *was* her
father's groom.

"I beg your pardon, my lady,'' he said, mastering his choler
with some effort. ''The sun is verra hot today, and no doubt it has
addled your wits a bit. I expect ye should go back to the house at
once and ask your maid to put cold cloths on your head.''

The Lady Geneva stamped her morocco-booted foot. ''My wits
are not addled in the slightest!''

She glared up at him, chin set. Her chin was little and pointed,
so were her teeth, and with that particular expression of determination on her face, he thought she looked a great deal like the
bloody-minded vixen she was.

"Listen to me,'' she said. ''I cannot prevent this abominable
marriage. But I am''—she hesitated, then continued firmly—''I
am *damned* if I will suffer my maidenhood to be given to a disgusting, depraved old monster like Ellesmere!''

Jamie rubbed a hand across his mouth. Despite himself, he felt
some sympathy for her. But *he* would be damned if he allowed this
skirted maniac to involve him in her troubles.

"I am fully sensible of the honor, my lady,'' he said at last, with
a heavy irony, ''but I really cannot—''

"Yes, you can.'' Her eyes rested frankly on the front of his
filthy breeches. ''Betty says so.''

He struggled for speech, emerging at first with little more than
incoherent splutterings. Finally he drew a deep breath and said,
with all the firmness he could muster, ''Betty has not the slightest
basis for drawing conclusions as to my capacity. I havena laid a
hand on the lass!''

Geneva laughed delightedly. ''So you didn't take her to bed?
She said you wouldn't, but I thought perhaps she was only trying
to avoid a beating. That's good; I couldn't possibly share a man
with my maid.''

He breathed heavily. Smashing her on the head with the shovel
or throttling her were unfortunately out of the question. His inflamed temper slowly calmed. Outrageous she might be, but essentially powerless. She could scarcely force him to go to her bed.

"Good day to ye, my lady,'' he said, as politely as possible. He turned his back on her and began to shovel manure into the hollow roller.

"If you don't," she said sweetly, "I'll tell my father you made improper advances to me. He'll have the skin flayed off your back."

His shoulders hunched involuntarily. She couldn't possibly know. He had been careful never to take his shirt off in front of anyone since he came here.

He turned carefully and stared down at her. The light of triumph was in her eye.

"Your father may not be so well acquent' with me," he said, "but he's kent *you* since ye were born. Tell him, and be damned to ye!"

She puffed up like a game cock, her face growing bright red with temper. "Is that so?" she cried. "Well, look at this, then, and be damned to *you*!" She reached into the bosom of her habit and pulled out a thick letter, which she waved under his nose. His sister's firm black hand was so familiar that a glimpse was enough.

"Give me that!" He was down off the wagon and after her in a flash, but she was too fast. She was up in the saddle before he could grab her, backing with the reins in one hand, waving the letter mockingly in the other.

"Want it, do you?"

"Yes, I want it! Give it to me!" He was so furious, he could easily have done her violence, could he get his hands on her. Unfortunately, her bay mare sensed his mood, and backed away, snorting and pawing uneasily.

"I don't think so." She eyed him coquettishly, the red of ill temper fading from her face. "After all, it's really my duty to give this to my father, isn't it? He ought really to know that his servants are carrying on clandestine correspondences, shouldn't he? Is Jenny your sweetheart?"

"You've read my letter? Ye filthy wee bitch!"

"Such language," she said, wagging the letter reprovingly. "It's my duty to help my parents, by letting them know what sorts of dreadful things the servants are up to, isn't it? And I am a dutiful daughter, am I not, submitting to this marriage without a squeak?" She leaned forward on her pommel, smiling mockingly, and with a fresh spurt of rage, he realized that she was enjoying this very much indeed.

"I expect Papa will find it very interesting reading," she said. "Especially the bit about the gold to be sent to Lochiel in France. Isn't it still considered treason to be giving comfort to the King's enemies? *Tsk,*" she said, clicking her tongue roguishly. "How wicked."

He thought he might be sick on the spot, from sheer terror. Did she have the faintest idea how many lives lay in that manicured white hand? His sister, Ian, their six children, all the tenants and families of Lallybroch—perhaps even the lives of the agents who carried messages and money between Scotland and France, maintaining the precarious existence of the Jacobite exiles there.

He swallowed, once, and then again, before he spoke.

"All right," he said. A more natural smile broke out on her face, and he realized how very young she was. Aye, well, and a wee adder's bite was as venomous as an auld one's.

"I won't tell," she assured him, looking earnest. "I'll give you your letter back afterward, and I won't ever say what was in it. I promise."

"Thank you." He tried to gather his wits enough to make a sensible plan. Sensible? Going into his master's house to ravish his daughter's maidenhood—at her request? He had never heard of a less sensible prospect.

"All right," he said again. "We must be careful." With a feeling of dull horror, he felt himself being drawn into the role of conspirator with her.

"Yes. Don't worry, I can arrange for my maid to be sent away, and the footman drinks; he's always asleep before ten o'clock."

"Arrange it, then," he said, his stomach curdling. "Mind ye choose a safe day, though."

"A safe day?" She looked blank.

"Sometime in the week after ye've finished your courses," he said bluntly. "You're less likely to get wi' child then."

"Oh." She blushed rosily at that, but looked at him with a new interest.

They looked at each other in silence for a long moment, suddenly linked by the prospect of the future.

"I'll send you word," she said at last, and wheeling her horse about, galloped away across the field, the mare's hooves kicking up spurts of the freshly spread manure.

Cursing fluently and silently, he crept beneath the row of larches. There wasn't much moon, which was a blessing. Six yards of open lawn to cross in a dash, and he was knee-deep in the columbine and germander of the flowerbed.

He looked up the side of the house, its bulk looming dark and forbidding above him. Yes, there was the candle in the window, as she'd said. Still, he counted the windows carefully, to verify it. Heaven help him if he chose the wrong room. Heaven help him if it was the right one, too, he thought grimly, and took a firm hold on the trunk of the huge gray creeper that covered this side of the house.

The leaves rustled like a hurricane and the stems, stout as they were, creaked and bent alarmingly under his weight. There was nothing for it but to climb as swiftly as possible, and be ready to hurl himself off into the night if any of the windows should suddenly be raised.

He arrived at the small balcony panting, heart racing, and drenched in sweat, despite the chilliness of the night. He paused a moment, alone beneath the faint spring stars, to draw breath. He used it to damn Geneva Dunsany once more, and then pushed open her door.

She had been waiting, and had plainly heard his approach up the ivy. She rose from the chaise where she had been sitting and came toward him, chin up, chestnut hair loose over her shoulders.

She was wearing a white nightgown of some sheer material, tied at the throat with a silk bow. The garment didn't look like the nightwear of a modest young lady, and he realized with a shock that she was wearing her bridal-night apparel.

"So you came." He heard the note of triumph in her voice, but also the faint quaver. So she hadn't been sure of him?

"I hadn't much choice," he said shortly, and turned to close the French doors behind him.

"Will you have some wine?" Striving for graciousness, she moved to the table, where a decanter stood with two glasses. How had she managed that? he wondered. Still, a glass of something wouldn't come amiss in the present circumstances. He nodded, and took the full glass from her hand.

He looked at her covertly as he sipped it. The nightdress did little to conceal her body, and as his heart gradually slowed from the panic of his ascent, he found his first fear—that he wouldn't be able to keep his half of the bargain—allayed without conscious effort. She was built narrowly, slim-hipped and small-breasted, but most definitely a woman.

Finished, he set down the glass. No point in delay, he thought.

"The letter?" he said abruptly.

"Afterward," she said, tightening her mouth.

"Now, or I leave." And he turned toward the window, as though about to execute the threat.

"Wait!" He turned back, but eyed her with ill-disguised impatience.

"Don't you trust me?" she said, trying to sound winsome and charming.

"No," he said bluntly.

She looked angry at that, and thrust out a petulant lower lip, but he merely looked stonily over his shoulder at her, still facing the window.

"Oh, all right, then," she said at last, with a shrug. Digging under the layers of embroidery in a sewing box, she unearthed the letter and tossed it onto the washing stand beside him.

He snatched it up and unfolded the sheets, to be sure of it. He felt a surge of mingled fury and relief at the sight of the violated seal, and Jenny's familiar hand within, neat and strong.

"Well?" Geneva's voice broke in upon his reading, impatient. "Put that down and come here, Jamie. I'm ready." She sat on the bed, arms curled around her knees.

He stiffened, and turned a very cold blue look on her, over the pages in his hands.

"You'll not use that name to me," he said. She lifted the pointed chin a trifle more and raised her plucked brows.

"Why not? It's yours. Your sister calls you so."

He hesitated for a moment, then deliberately laid the letter aside, and bent his head to the laces of his breeches.

"I'll serve ye properly," he said, looking down at his working fingers, "for the sake of my own honor as a man, and yours as a woman. But"—he raised his head and the narrowed blue eyes bored into hers—"having brought me to your bed by means of threats against my family, I'll not have ye call me by the name they give me." He stood motionless, eyes fixed on hers. At last she gave a very small nod, and her eyes dropped to the quilt.

She traced the pattern with a finger.

"What must I call you, then?" she asked at last, in a small voice. "I *can't* call you MacKenzie!"

The corners of his mouth lifted slightly as he looked at her. She looked quite small, huddled into herself with her arms locked around her knees and her head bowed. He sighed.

"Call me Alex, then. It's my own name, as well."

She nodded without speaking. Her hair fell forward in wings about her face, but he could see the brief shine of her eyes as she peeped out from behind its cover.

"It's all right," he said gruffly. "You can watch me." He pushed the loose breeches down, rolling the stockings off with them. He shook them out and folded them neatly over a chair before beginning to unfasten his shirt, conscious of her gaze, still shy, but now direct. Out of some idea of thoughtfulness, he turned to face her before removing the shirt, to spare her for a moment the sight of his back.

"Oh!" The exclamation was soft, but enough to stop him.

"Is something wrong?" he asked.

"Oh, no . . . I mean, it's only that I didn't expect . . ." The hair swung forward again, but not before he had seen the telltale reddening of her cheeks.

"You've not seen a man naked before?" he guessed. The shiny brown head swayed back and forth.

"Noo," she said doubtfully, "I have, only . . . it wasn't . . ."

"Well, it usually isn't," he said matter-of-factly, sitting down on the bed beside her. "But if one is going to make love, it has to be, ye see."

"I see," she said, but still sounded doubtful. He tried to smile, to reassure her.

"Don't worry. It doesna get any bigger. And it wilna do anything strange, if ye want to touch it." At least he hoped it wouldn't. Being naked, in such close proximity to a half-clad girl, was doing terrible things to his powers of self-control. His traitorous, deprived anatomy didn't care a whit that she was a selfish,

blackmailing little bitch. Perhaps fortunately, she declined his offer, shrinking back a little toward the wall, though her eyes stayed
on him. He rubbed his chin dubiously.

"How much do you . . . I mean, have ye any idea how it's
done?"

Her gaze was clear and guileless, though her cheeks flamed.

"Well, like the horses, I suppose?" He nodded, but felt a pang,
recalling his wedding night, when he too had expected it to be like
horses.

"Something like that," he said, clearing his throat. "Slower,
though. More gentle," he added, seeing her apprehensive look.

"Oh. That's good. Nurse and the maids used to tell stories,
about . . . men, and, er, getting married, and all . . . it sounded
rather frightening." She swallowed hard. "W-will it hurt much?"
She raised her head suddenly and looked him in the eye.

"I don't mind if it does," she said bravely, "it's only that I'd
like to know what to expect." He felt an unexpected small liking
for her. She might be spoilt, selfish, and reckless, but there was
some character to her, at least. Courage, to him, was no small
virtue.

"I think not," he said. "If I take my time to ready you" (if he
could take his time, amended his brain), "I think it will be not
much worse than a pinch." He reached out and nipped a fold of
skin on her upper arm. She jumped and rubbed the spot, but
smiled.

"I can stand that."

"It's only the first time it's like that," he assured her. "The
next time it will be better."

She nodded, then after a moment's hesitation, edged toward
him, reaching out a tentative finger.

"May I touch you?" This time he really did laugh, though he
choked the sound off quickly.

"I think you'll have to, my lady, if I'm to do what you asked of
me."

She ran her hand slowly down his arm, so softly that the touch
tickled, and his skin shivered in response. Gaining confidence, she
let her hand circle his forearm, feeling the girth of it.

"You're quite . . . big." He smiled, but stayed motionless,
letting her explore his body, at as much length as she might wish.
He felt the muscles of his belly tighten as she stroked the length of

one thigh, and ventured tentatively around the curve of one buttock. Her fingers approached the twisting, knotted line of the scar
that ran the length of his left thigh, but stopped short.

"It's all right," he assured her. "It doesna hurt me anymore."
She didn't reply, but drew two fingers slowly along the length of
the scar, exerting no pressure.

The questing hands, growing bolder, slid up over the rounded
curves of his broad shoulders, slid down his back—and stopped
dead. He closed his eyes and waited, following her movements by
the shifting of weight on the mattress. She moved behind him, and
was silent. Then there was a quivering sigh, and the hands touched
him again, soft on his ruined back.

"And you weren't afraid, when I said I'd have you flogged?"
Her voice was queerly hoarse, but he kept still, eyes closed.

"No," he said. "I am not much afraid of things, anymore." In
fact, he was beginning to be afraid that he wouldn't be able to keep
his hands off her, or to handle her with the necessary gentleness,
when the time came. His balls ached with need, and he could feel
his heartbeat, pounding in his temples.

She got off the bed, and stood in front of him. He rose suddenly,
startling her so that she stepped back a pace, but he reached out
and rested his hands on her shoulders.

"May I touch *you*, my lady?" The words were teasing, but the
touch was not. She nodded, too breathless to speak, and his arms
came around her.

He held her against his chest, not moving until her breathing
slowed. He was conscious of an extraordinary mixture of feelings.
He had never in his life taken a woman in his arms without some
feeling of love, but there was nothing of love in this encounter, nor
could there be, for her own sake. There was some tenderness for
her youth, and pity at her situation. Rage at her manipulation of
him, and fear at the magnitude of the crime he was about to
commit. But overall there was a terrible lust, a need that clawed at
his vitals and made him ashamed of his own manhood, even as he
acknowledged its power. Hating himself, he lowered his head and
cupped her face between his hands.

He kissed her softly, briefly, then a bit longer. She was trembling against him as his hands undid the tie of her gown and slid it
back off her shoulders. He lifted her and laid her on the bed.

He lay beside her, cradling her in one arm as the other hand caressed her breasts, one and then the other, cupping each so she felt the weight and the warmth of them, even as he did.

"A man should pay tribute to your body," he said softly, raising each nipple with small, circling touches. "For you are beautiful, and that is your right."

She let out her breath in a small gasp, then relaxed under his touch. He took his time, moving as slowly as he could make himself do it, stroking and kissing, touching her lightly all over. He didn't like the girl, didn't want to be here, didn't want to be doing this, but—it had been more than three years since he'd touched a woman's body.

He tried to gauge when she might be readiest, but how in hell could he tell? She was flushed and panting, but she simply lay there, like a piece of porcelain on display. Curse the girl, could she not even give him a clue?

He rubbed a trembling hand through his hair, trying to quell the surge of confused emotion that pulsed through him with each heartbeat. He was angry, scared, and most mightily roused, most of which feelings were of no great use to him now. He closed his eyes and breathed deeply, striving for calm, seeking for gentleness.

No, of course she couldn't show him. She'd never touched a man before. Having forced him here, she was, with a damnable, unwanted, unwarrantable trust, leaving the conduct of the whole affair up to him!

He touched the girl, gently, stroking her between the thighs. She didn't part them for him, but didn't resist. She was faintly moist there. Perhaps it would be all right now?

"All right," he murmured to her. "Be still, *mo chridhe.*" Murmuring what he hoped sounded like reassurances, he eased himself on top of her, and used his knee to spread her legs. He felt her slight start at the heat of his body covering her, at the touch of his cock, and he wrapped his hands in her hair to steady her, still muttering things in soft Gaelic.

He thought dimly that it was a good thing he was speaking Gaelic, as he was no longer paying any attention at all to what he was saying. Her small, hard breasts poked against his chest.

"Mo nighean," he murmured.

"Wait a minute," said Geneva. "I think perhaps . . ."

The effort of control made him dizzy, but he did it slowly, only easing himself the barest inch within.

"Ooh!" said Geneva. Her eyes flew wide.

"Uh," he said, and pushed a bit farther.

"Stop it! It's too big! Take it out!" Panicked, Geneva thrashed beneath him. Pressed beneath his chest, her breasts wobbled and rubbed, so that his own nipples leapt erect in pinpoints of abrupt sensation.

Her struggles were accomplishing by force what he had tried to do with gentleness. Half-dazed, he fought to keep her under him, while groping madly for something to say to calm her.

"But—" he said.

"Stop it!"

"I—"

"Take it *out*!" she screamed.

He clapped one hand over her mouth and said the only coherent thing he could think of.

"No," he said definitely, and shoved.

What might have been a scream emerged through his fingers as a strangled "Eep!" Geneva's eyes were huge and round, but dry.

In for a penny, in for a pound. The saying drifted absurdly through his head, leaving nothing in its wake but a jumble of incoherent alarms and a marked feeling of terrible urgency down between them. There was precisely one thing he was capable of doing at this point, and he did it, his body ruthlessly usurping control as it moved into the rhythm of its inexorable pagan joy.

It took no more than a few thrusts before the wave came down upon him, churning down the length of his spine and erupting like a breaker striking rocks, sweeping away the last shreds of conscious thought that clung, barnacle-like, to the remnants of his mind.

He came to himself a moment later, lying on his side with the sound of his own heartbeat loud and slow in his ears. He cracked one eyelid, and saw the shimmer of pink skin in lamplight. He must see if he'd hurt her much, but God, not just this minute. He shut his eye again and merely breathed.

"What . . . what are you thinking?" The voice sounded hesitant, and a little shaken, but not hysterical.

Too shaken himself to notice the absurdity of the question, he answered it with the truth.

"I was wondering why in God's name men want to bed virgins."

There was a long moment of silence, and then a tremulous intake of breath.

"I'm sorry," she said in a small voice. "I didn't know it would hurt you too."

His eyes popped open in astonishment, and he raised himself on one elbow to find her looking at him like a startled fawn. Her face was pale, and she licked dry lips.

"Hurt me?" he said, in blank astonishment. "It didna hurt *me.*"

"But"—she frowned as her eyes traveled slowly down the length of his body—"I thought it must. You made the most terrible face, as though it hurt awfully, and you . . . you *groaned* like a—"

"Aye, well," he interrupted hastily, before she could reveal any more unflattering observations of his behavior. "I didna mean . . . I mean . . . that's just how men act, when they . . . do that," he ended lamely.

Her shock was fading into curiosity. "Do all men act like that when they're . . . doing that?"

"How should I—?" he began irritably, then stopped himself with a shudder, realizing that he did in fact know the answer to that.

"Aye, they do," he said shortly. He pushed himself up to a sitting position, and brushed the hair back from his forehead. "Men are disgusting horrible beasts, just as your nurse told you. Have I hurt ye badly?"

"I don't think so," she said doubtfully. She moved her legs experimentally. "It did hurt, just for a moment, like you said it would, but it isn't so bad now."

He breathed a sigh of relief as he saw that while she had bled, the stain on the towel was slight, and she seemed not to be in pain. She reached tentatively between her thighs and made a face of disgust.

"Ooh!" she said. "It's all nasty and sticky!"

The blood rose to his face in mingled outrage and embarrassment.

"Here," he muttered, and reached for a washcloth from the stand. She didn't take it, but opened her legs and arched her back slightly, obviously expecting him to attend to the mess. He had a strong urge to stuff the rag down her throat instead, but a glance at the stand where his letter lay stopped him. It was a bargain, after all, and she'd kept her part.

Grimly, he wet the cloth and began to sponge her, but he found the trust with which she presented herself to him oddly moving. He carried out his ministrations quite gently, and found himself, at the end, planting a light kiss on the smooth slope of her belly.

"There."

"Thank you," she said. She moved her hips tentatively, and reached out a hand to touch him. He didn't move, letting her fingers trail down his chest and toy with the deep indentation of his navel. The light touch hesitantly descended.

"You said . . . it would be better next time," she whispered.

He closed his eyes and took a deep breath. It was a long time until the dawn.

"I expect it will," he said, and stretched himself once more beside her.

"Ja—er, Alex?"

He felt as though he had been drugged, and it was an effort to answer her. "My lady?"

Her arms came around his neck and she nestled her head in the curve of his shoulder, breath warm against his chest.

"I love you, Alex."

With difficulty, he roused himself enough to put her away from him, holding her by the shoulders and looking down into the gray eyes, soft as a doe's.

"No," he said, but gently, shaking his head. "That's the third rule. You may have no more than the one night. You may not call me by my first name. And you may not love me."

The gray eyes moistened a bit. "But if I can't help it?"

"It isna love you feel now." He hoped he was right, for his sake as well as her own. "It's only the feeling I've roused in your body. It's strong, and it's good, but it isna the same thing as love."

"What's the difference?"

He rubbed his hands hard over his face. She *would* be a philosopher, he thought wryly. He took a deep breath and blew it out before answering her.

''Well, love's for only one person. This, what you feel from me
—ye can have that with any man, it's not particular.''

Only one person. He pushed the thought of Claire firmly away,
and wearily bent again to his work.

He landed heavily in the earth of the flowerbed, not caring that
he crushed several small and tender plants. He shivered. This hour
before dawn was not only the darkest, but the coldest, as well, and
his body strongly protested being required to rise from a warm,
soft nest and venture into the chilly blackness, shielded from the
icy air by no more than a thin shirt and breeks.

He remembered the heated, rosy curve of the cheek he had bent
to kiss before leaving. The shapes of her lingered, warm in his
hands, curving his fingers in memory, even as he groped in the
dark for the darker line of the stableyard's stone wall. Drained as
he was, it was a dreadful effort to haul himself up and climb over,
but he couldn't risk the creak of the gate awakening Hughes, the
head groom.

He felt his way across the inner yard, crowded with wagons and
packed bales, ready for the journey of the Lady Geneva to the
home of her new lord, following the wedding on Thursday next. At
last he pushed open the stable door and found his way up the
ladder to his loft. He lay down in the icy straw and pulled the
single blanket over him, feeling empty of everything.

15

By Misadventure

Appropriately enough, the weather was dark and stormy when the news reached Helwater. The afternoon exercise had been canceled, owing to the heavy downpour, and the horses were snug in their stalls below. The homely, peaceful sounds of munching and blowing rose up to the loft above, where Jamie Fraser reclined in a comfortable, hay-lined nest, an open book propped on his chest.

It was one of several he had borrowed from the estate's factor, Mr. Grieves, and he was finding it absorbing, despite the difficulty of reading by the poor light from the owl-slits beneath the eaves.

> *My lips, which I threw in his way, so as that he could not escape kissing them, fix'd, fir'd and embolden'd him: and now, glancing my eyes towards that part of his dress which cover'd the essential object of enjoyment, I plainly discover'd the swell and commotion there; and as I was now too far advanc'd to stop in so fair a way, and was indeed no longer able to contain myself, or wait the slower progress of his maiden bashfulness, I stole my hand upon his thighs, down one of which I could both see and feel a stiff hard body, confin'd by his breeches, that my fingers could discover no end to.*

"Oh, aye?" Jamie muttered skeptically. He raised his eyebrows and shifted himself on the hay. He had been aware that books like this existed, of course, but—with Jenny ordering the reading matter at Lallybroch—had not encountered one personally before. The type of mental engagement demanded was somewhat different from that required for the works of Messieurs Defoe and Fielding, but he was not averse to variety.

> *Its prodigious size made me shrink again; yet I could not, without pleasure, behold, and even ventur'd to feel, such a length, such a breadth of animated ivory! perfectly well turn'd and fashion'd, the proud stiffness of which distended its skin, whose smooth polish and velvet softness might vie with that of the most delicate of our sex, and whose exquisite whiteness was not a little set off by a sprout of black curling hair round the root; then the broad and blueish casted incarnate of the head, and blue serpentines of its veins, altogether compos'd the most striking assemblage of figures and colors in nature. In short, it stood an object of terror and delight!*

Jamie glanced at his own crotch and snorted briefly at this, but flipped the page, the crash of thunder outside meriting no more than a twinge of his attention. He was so absorbed that at first he failed to hear the noises down below, the sound of voices drowned in the heavy rush and beat of the rain on the planks a few feet above his head.

"MacKenzie!" The repeated stentorian bellow finally penetrated his awareness, and he rolled hastily to his feet, quickly straightening his clothes as he went toward the ladder.

"Aye?" He thrust his head over the edge of the loft to see Hughes, just opening his mouth for another bellow.

"Oh, there 'ee are." Hughes shut his mouth, and beckoned with one gnarled hand, wincing as he did so. Hughes suffered mightily from rheumatics in damp weather; he had been riding out the storm snug in the small chamber beside the tack room, where he kept a bed and a jug of crudely distilled spirits. The aroma was perceptible from the loft, and grew substantially stronger as Jamie descended the ladder.

"You're to help ready the coach to drive Lord Dunsany and Lady Isobel to Ellesmere," Hughes told him, the moment his foot touched the flags of the stable floor. The old man swayed alarmingly, hiccuping softly to himself.

"Now? Are ye daft, man? Or just drunk?" He glanced at the

open half-door behind Hughes, which seemed a solid sheet of streaming water. Even as he looked, the sky beyond lit up with a sudden flare of lightning that threw the mountain beyond into sudden sharp relief. Just as suddenly, it disappeared, leaving its afterimage printed on his retina. He shook his head to clear the image, and saw Jeffries, the coachman, making his way across the yard, head bowed against the force of wind and water, cloak clutched tight about him. So it wasn't only a drunken fancy of Hughes's.

"Jeffries needs help wi' the horses!" Hughes was forced to lean close and shout to be heard over the noise of the storm. The smell of rough alcohol was staggering at close distance.

"Aye, but why? Why must Lord Dunsany—ah, feckit!" The head groom's eyes were red-rimmed and bleary; clearly there was no sense to be got out of him. Disgusted, Jamie pushed past the man and mounted the ladder two rungs at a time.

A moment to wrap his own worn cloak about him, a moment more to thrust the book he had been reading under the hay—stable lads were no respecters of property—and he was slithering down the ladder again, and out into the roar of the storm.

It was a hellish journey. The wind screamed through the pass, striking the bulky coach and threatening to overturn it at any moment. Perched aloft beside Jeffries, a cloak was little protection against the driving rain; still less was it a help when he was forced to dismount—as he did every few minutes, it seemed—and put his shoulder to the wheel to free the miserable contrivance from the clinging grip of a mudhole.

Still, he scarcely noticed the physical inconvenience of the journey, preoccupied as he was with the possible reasons for it. There couldn't be many matters of such urgency as to force an old man like Lord Dunsany outside on a day like this, let alone over the rutted road to Ellesmere. Some word had come from Ellesmere, and it could only concern the Lady Geneva or her child.

Hearing through the servants' gossip that Lady Geneva was due to be deliverd in January, he had counted quickly backward, cursed Geneva Dunsany once more, and then said a hasty prayer for her safe delivery. Since then, he had done his best not to think about it. He had been with her only three days before her wedding; he couldn't be sure.

A week before, Lady Dunsany had gone to Ellesmere to be with her daughter. Since then, she had sent daily messengers home, to fetch the dozen things she had forgotten to take and must have at once, and each of them, upon arrival at Helwater, had reported "No news yet." Now there was news, and it was plainly bad.

Passing back toward the front of the coach, after the latest battle with the mud, he saw the Lady Isobel's face peering out from beneath the isinglass sheet that covered the window.

"Oh, MacKenzie!" she said, her face contorted in fear and distress. "Please, is it much farther?"

He leaned close to shout in her ear, over the gurgle and rush of the gullies running down both sides of the road.

"Jeffries says it's four mile yet, milady! Two hours, maybe." If the damned and hell-bent coach didn't tip itself and its hapless passengers off the Ashness Bridge into Watendlath Tarn, he added silently to himself.

Isobel nodded her thanks, and lowered the window, but not before he had seen that the wetness upon her cheeks was due as much to tears as to the rain. The snake of anxiety wrapped round his heart slithered lower, to twist in his guts.

It was closer to three hours by the time the coach rolled at last into the courtyard at Ellesmere. Without hesitation, Lord Dunsany scrambled down and, scarcely pausing to give his younger daughter an arm, hurried into the house.

It took nearly another hour to unharness the team, rub down the horses, wash the caked-on mud from the coach's wheels, and put everything away in Ellesmere's stables. Numb with cold, fatigue, and hunger, he and Jeffries sought refuge and sustenance in Ellesmere's kitchens.

"Poor fellows, you're gone right blue wi' the cold," the cook observed. "Sit ye down 'ere, and I'll soon 'ave yer a hot bite." A sharp-faced, spare-framed woman, her figure belied her skill, for within minutes, a huge, savoury omelet was laid before them, garnished with liberal amounts of bread and butter, and a small pot of jam.

"Fair, quite fair," Jeffries pronounced, casting an appreciative eye on the spread. He winked at the cook. "Not as it wouldn' go down easier wi' a drop o' something to pave the way, eh? You look the sort would have mercy on a pair o' poor half-frozen chaps, wouldn't ye, darlin'?''

Whether it was this piece of Irish persuasion or the sight of their dripping, steaming clothes, the argument had its effect, and a bottle of cooking brandy made its appearance next to the peppermill. Jeffries poured a large tot and drank it off without hesitation, smacking his lips.

"Ah, that's more like! Here, boyo." He passed the bottle to Jamie, then settled himself comfortably to a hot meal and gossip with the female servants. "Well, then, what's to do here? Is the babe born yet?''

"Oh, yes, last night!" the kitchen maid said eagerly. "We were up all night, with the doctor comin', and fresh sheets and towels called for, and the house all topsle-turvy. But the babe's the least of it!''

"Now, then," the cook broke in, frowning censoriously. "There's too much work to be standin' about gossiping. Get yer on, Mary Ann—up to the study, and see if his Lordship'll be wantin' anything else served now."

Jamie, wiping his plate with a slice of bread, observed that the maid, far from being abashed at this rebuke, departed with alacrity, causing him to deduce that something of considerable interest was likely transpiring in the study.

The undivided attention of her audience thus obtained, the cook allowed herself to be persuaded into imparting the gossip with no more than a token demur.

"Well, it started some months ago, when the Lady Geneva started to show, poor thing. His Lordship'd been nicer than pie to 'er, ever since they was married couldn't do enough for 'er, anything she wanted ordered from Lunnon, always askin' was she warm enough, 'ad she what she wanted to eat—fair dotin', 'is Lordship was. But then, when 'e found she was with child!'' The cook paused, to screw up her face portentously.

Jamie wanted desperately to know about the child; what was it, and how did it fare? There seemed no way to hurry the woman, though, so he composed his face to look as interested as possible, leaning forward encouragingly.

"Why, the shouting, and the carrryings-on!" the cook said, throwing up her hands in dismayed illustration, " 'im shoutin', and 'er cryin', and the both of 'em stampin' up and down and slammin' doors, and 'im callin' 'er names as isn't fit to be used in a stableyard—and so I told Mary Ann, when she told me . . ."

"Was his Lordship not pleased about the child, then?" Jamie interrupted. The omelet was settling into a hard lump somewhere under his breastbone. He took another gulp of brandy, in hopes of dislodging it.

The cook turned a bright, birdlike eye on him, eyebrow cocked in appreciation at his intelligence. "Well, you'd think as 'e would be, wouldn't yer? But no indeed! Far from it," she added with emphasis.

"Why not?" said Jeffries, only mildly interested.

"'E said," the cook said, dropping her voice in awe at the scandalousness of the information, "as the child wasn't 'is!"

Jeffries, well along with his second glass, snorted in contemptuous amusement. "Old goat with a young gel? I should think it like enough, but how on earth would his Lordship know for sure whose the spawn was? Could be his as much as anyone's, couldn't it, with only her Ladyship's word to go by, eh?"

The cook's thin mouth stretched in a bright, malicious smile. "Oh, I don't say as 'e'd know whose it *was*, now—but there's one sure way 'e'd know it wasn't *'is*, now isn't there?"

Jeffries stared at the cook, tilting back on his chair. "What?" he said. "You mean to tell me his Lordship's incapable?" A broad grin at this juicy thought split his weatherbeaten face. Jamie felt the omelet rising, and hastily gulped more brandy.

"Well, *I* couldn't say, I'm sure." The cook's mouth assumed a prim line, then split asunder to add, "though the chambermaid did say as the sheets she took off the weddin' bed was as white as when they'd gone on, to be sure."

It was too much. Interrupting Jeffries's delighted cackle, Jamie set down his glass with a thump, and bluntly said, "Did the child live?"

The cook and Jeffries both stared in astonishment, but the cook, after a moment's startlement, nodded in answer.

"Oh, yes, to be sure. Fine 'ealthy little lad, 'e is, too, or so I 'ear. I thought you knew a'ready. It's 'is mother that's dead."

That blunt statement struck the kitchen with silence. Even Jeffries was still for a moment, sobered by death. Then he crossed himself quickly, muttered "God rest her soul," and swallowed the rest of his brandy.

Jamie could feel his own throat burning, whether with brandy or tears, he could not say. Shock and grief choked him like a ball of yarn wedged in his gullet; he could barely manage to croak "When?"

"This morning," the cook said, wagging her head mournfully. "Just afore noon, poor girl. They thought for a time as she'd be all right, after the babe was born; Mary Ann said she was sittin' up, holdin' the wee thing and laughin'." She sighed heavily at the thought. "But then near dawn, she started to bleed again bad. They called back the doctor, and he came fast as could be, but—"

The door slamming open interrupted her. It was Mary Ann, eyes wide under her cap, gasping with excitement and exertion.

"Your master wants you!" she blurted out, eyes flicking between Jamie and the coachman. "The both of ye, at once, and oh, sir"—she gulped, nodding at Jeffries—"he says for God's sake, to bring your pistols!"

The coachman exchanged a glance of consternation with Jamie, then leapt to his feet and dashed out, in the direction of the stables. Like most coachmen, he carried a pair of loaded pistols beneath his seat, against the possibility of highwaymen.

It would take Jeffries a few minutes to find the arms, and longer if he waited to check that the priming had not been harmed by the wet weather. Jamie rose to his feet and gripped the dithering maidservant by the arm.

"Show me to the study," he said. "Now!"

The sound of raised voices would have led him there, once he had reached the head of the stair. Pushing past Mary Ann without ceremony, he paused for a moment outside the door, uncertain whether he should enter at once, or wait for Jeffries.

"That you can have the sheer heartless effrontery to make such accusations!" Dunsany was saying, his old man's voice shaking with rage and distress. "And my poor lamb not cold in her bed! You blackguard, you poltroon! I will not suffer the child to stay a single night under your roof!"

"The little bastard stays here!" Ellesmere's voice rasped hoarsely. It would have been apparent to a far less experienced observer that his Lordship was well the worse for drink. "Bastard that he is, he's my heir, and he stays with me! He's bought and paid for, and if his dam was a whore, at least she gave me a boy."

"Damn you!" Dunsany's voice had reached such a pitch of

shrillness that it was scarcely more than a squeak, but the outrage in it was clear nonetheless. "Bought? You—you—you dare to suggest . . ."

"I don't suggest." Ellesmere's voice was still hoarse, but under better control. "You sold me your daughter—and under false pretenses, I might add," the hoarse voice said sarcastically. "I paid thirty thousand pound for a virgin of good name. The first condition wasn't met, and I take leave to doubt the second." The sound of liquid being poured came through the door, followed by the scrape of a glass across a wooden tabletop.

"I would suggest that your burden of spirits is already excessive, sir," Dunsany said. His voice shook with an obvious attempt at mastery of his emotions. "I can only attribute the disgusting slurs you have cast upon my daughter's purity to your apparent intoxication. That being so, I shall take my grandson, and go."

"Oh, your *grand*son, is it?" Ellesmere's voice was slurred and sneering. "You seem damned sure of your daughter's 'purity.' Sure the brat isn't yours? She said—"

He broke off with a cry of astonishment, accompanied by a crash. Not daring to wait longer, Jamie plunged through the door, to find Ellesmere and Lord Dunsany entangled on the hearthrug, rolling to and fro in a welter of coats and limbs, both heedless of the fire behind them.

He took a moment to appraise the situation, then, seizing a fortuitous opening, reached into the fray and snatched his employer upright.

"Be still, my lord," he muttered in Dunsany's ear, dragging him back from Ellesmere's gasping form. Then, "Give over, ye auld fool!" he demanded, as Dunsany went on mindlessly struggling to reach his opponent. Ellesmere was almost as old as Dunsany, but more strongly built and clearly in better health, despite his drunkenness.

The Earl staggered to his feet, sparse hair disheveled and bloodshot eyes glaring fixedly at Dunsany. He wiped his spittle-flecked mouth with the back of his hand, fat shoulders heaving.

"Filth," he said, almost conversationally. "Lay hands . . . on me, would you?" Still gasping for breath, he lurched toward the bell rope.

It was by no means certain that Lord Dunsany would stay on his feet, but there was no time to worry about that. Jamie let go of his employer, and lunged for Ellesmere's groping hand.

"No, my lord," he said, as respectfully as possible. Holding Ellesmere in a crude bear-leading embrace, he forced the heavyset Earl back across the room. "I think it would be . . . unwise . . . to involve your . . . servants." Grunting, he pushed Ellesmere into a chair.

"Best stay there, my lord." Jeffries, a drawn pistol in each hand, advanced warily into the room, his darting glance divided between Ellesmere, struggling to rise from the depths of the armchair, and Lord Dunsany, who clung precariously to a table edge, his aged face white as paper.

Jeffries glanced at Dunsany for instructions, and seeing none forthcoming, instinctively looked to Jamie. Jamie was conscious of a monstrous irritation; why should he be expected to deal with this imbroglio? Still, it was important that the Helwater party remove themselves from the premises with all haste. He stepped forward and took Dunsany by the arm.

"Let us go now, my lord," he said. Detaching the wilting Dunsany from the table, he tried to edge the tall old nobleman toward the door. Just at this moment of escape, though, the door was blocked.

"William?" Lady Dunsany's round face, splotched with the marks of recent grief, showed a sort of dull bewilderment at the scene in the study. In her arms was what looked like a large, untidy bundle of washing. She lifted this in a movement of vague inquiry. "The maid said you wanted me to bring the baby. What—" A roar from Ellesmere interrupted her. Heedless of the pointing pistols, the Earl sprang from his chair and shoved the gawking Jeffries out of the way.

"He's mine!" Knocking Lady Dunsany roughly against the paneling, Ellesmere snatched the bundle from her arms. Clutching it to his bosom, the Earl retreated toward the window. He glared at Dunsany, panting like a cornered beast.

"Mine, d'ye hear?"

The bundle emitted a loud shriek, as if in protest at this asseveration, and Dunsany, roused from his shock by the sight of his grandson in Ellesmere's arms, started forward, his features contorted in fury.

"Give him to me!"

"Go to hell, you codless scut!" With an unforeseen agility, Ellesmere dodged away from Dunsany. He flung back the draperies and cranked the window open with one hand, clutching the wailing child with the other.

"Get—out—of—my—house!" he panted, gasping with each revolution that edged the casement wider. "Go! Now, or I'll drop the little bastard, I swear I will!" To mark his threat, he thrust the yelling bundle toward the sill, and the empty dark where the wet stones of the courtyard waited, thirty feet below.

Past all conscious thought or any fear of consequence, Jamie Fraser acted on the instinct that had seen him through a dozen battles. He snatched one pistol from the transfixed Jeffries, turned on his heel, and fired in the same motion.

The roar of the shot struck everyone silent. Even the child ceased to scream. Ellesmere's face went quite blank, thick eyebrows raised in question. Then he staggered, and Jamie leapt forward, noting with a sort of detached clarity the small round hole in the baby's trailing drapery, where the pistol ball had passed through it.

He stood then rooted on the hearthrug, heedless of the fire scorching the backs of his legs; of the still-heaving body of Ellesmere at his feet; of the regular, hysterical shrieks of Lady Dunsany, piercing as a peacock's. He stood, eyes tight closed, shaking like a leaf, unable either to move or to think, arms wrapped tight about the shapeless, squirming, squawking bundle that contained his son.

"I wish to speak to MacKenzie. Alone."

Lady Dunsany looked distinctly out of place in the stable. Small, plump, and impeccable in black linen, she looked like a china ornament, removed from its spot of cherished safety on the mantelpiece, and in imminent and constant peril of breakage, here in this world of rough animals and unshaven men.

Hughes, with a glance of complete astonishment at his mistress, bowed and tugged at his forelock before retreating to his den behind the tack room, leaving MacKenzie face-to-face with her.

Close to, the impression of fragility was heightened by the paleness of her face, touched faintly with pink at the corners of nose and eyes. She looked like a very small and dignified rabbit, dressed in mourning. Jamie felt that he should ask her to sit down, but there was no place for her to sit, save on a pile of hay or an upturned barrow.

"The coroner's court met this morning, MacKenzie," she said.

"Aye, milady." He had known that—they all had, and the other grooms had kept their distance from him all morning. Not out of respect; out of the dread for one who suffers from a deadly disease. Jeffries knew what had happened in the drawing room at Ellesmere, and that meant all the servants knew. But no one spoke of it.

"The verdict of the court was that the Earl of Ellesmere met his death by misadventure. The coroner's theory is that his Lordship was—distraught''—she made a faint moue of distaste—"over my daughter's death." Her voice quivered faintly, but did not break. The fragile Lady Dunsany had borne up much better beneath the tragedy than had her husband; the servants' rumor had it that his Lordship had not risen from his bed since his return from Ellesmere.

"Aye, milady?" Jeffries had been called to give evidence. MacKenzie had not. So far as the coroner's court was concerned, the groom MacKenzie had never set foot on Ellesmere.

Lady Dunsany's eyes met his, straight on. They were a pale bluish-green, like her daughter Isobel's, but the blond hair that glowed on Isobel was faded on her mother, touched with white strands that shone silver in the sun from the open door of the stable.

"We are grateful to you, MacKenzie," she said quietly.

"Thank ye, milady."

"Very grateful," she repeated, still gazing at him intently. "MacKenzie isn't your real name, is it?" she said suddenly.

"No, milady." A sliver of ice ran down his spine, despite the warmth of the afternoon sun on his shoulders. How much had the Lady Geneva told her mother before her death?

She seemed to feel his stiffening, for the edge of her mouth lifted in what he thought was meant as a smile of reassurance.

"I think I need not ask what it is, just yet," she said. "But I do have a question for you. MacKenzie—do you want to go home?"

"Home?" He repeated the word blankly.

"To Scotland." She was watching him intently. "I know who

you are," she said. "Not your name, but that you're one of John's Jacobite prisoners. My husband told me."

Jamie watched her warily, but she didn't seem upset; no more so than would be natural in a woman who has just lost a daughter and gained a grandson, at least.

"I hope you will forgive the deception, milady," he said. "His Lordship—"

"Wished to save me distress," Lady Dunsany finished for him. "Yes, I know. William worries too much." Still, the deep line between her brows relaxed a bit at the thought of her husband's concern. The sight, with its underlying echo of marital devotion, gave him a faint and unexpected pang.

"We are not rich—you will have gathered that from Ellesmere's remarks," Lady Dunsany went on. "Helwater is rather heavily in debt. My grandson, however, is now the possessor of one of the largest fortunes in the county."

There seemed nothing to say to this but "Aye, milady?" though it made him feel rather like the parrot who lived in the main salon. He had seen it as he crept stealthily through the flowerbeds at sunset the day before, taking the chance of approaching the house while the family were dressing for dinner, in an attempt to catch a glimpse through a window of the new Earl of Ellesmere.

"We are very retired here," she went on. "We seldom visit London, and my husband has little influence in high circles. But—"

"Aye, milady?" He had some inkling by now of where her Ladyship was heading with this roundabout conversation, and a feeling of sudden excitement hollowed the space beneath his ribs.

"John—Lord John Grey, that is—comes from a family with considerable influence. His stepfather is—well, that's of no consequence." She shrugged, the small black-linen shoulders dismissing the details.

"The point is that it might be possible to exert sufficient influence on your behalf to have you released from the conditions of your parole, so that you might return to Scotland. So I have come to ask you—do you want to go home, MacKenzie?"

He felt quite breathless, as though someone had punched him very hard in the stomach.

Scotland. To go away from this damp, spongy atmosphere, set foot on that forbidden road and walk it with a free, long stride, up into the crags and along the deer trails, to feel the air clearing and sharpening with the scent of gorse and heather. To go home!

To be a stranger no longer. To go away from hostility and loneliness, come down into Lallybroch, and see his sister's face light with joy at the sight of him, feel her arms around his waist, Ian's hug about his shoulders and the pummeling, grasping clutch of the children's hands, tugging at his clothes.

To go away, and never to see or hear of his own child again. He stared at Lady Dunsany, his face quite blank, so that she should not guess at the turmoil her offer had caused within him.

He had, at last, found the baby yesterday, lying asleep in a basket near the nursery window on the second floor. Perched precariously on the branch of a huge Norway spruce, he had strained his eyes to see through the screen of needles that hid him.

The child's face had been visible only in profile, one fat cheek resting on its ruffled shoulder. Its cap had slipped awry, so he could see the smooth, arching curve of the tiny skull, lightly dusted with a pale gold fuzz.

"Thank God it isn't red," had been his first thought, and he had crossed himself in reflexive thanksgiving.

"God, he's so small!" had been his second, coupled with an overwhelming urge to step through the window and pick the boy up. The smooth, beautifully shaped head would just fit, resting in the palm of his hand, and he could feel in memory the small squirming body that he had held so briefly to his heart.

"You're a strong laddie," he had whispered. "Strong and braw and bonny. But my God, you are so small!"

Lady Dunsany was waiting patiently. He bowed his head respectfully to her, not knowing whether he was making a terrible mistake, but unable to do otherwise.

"I thank ye, milady, but—I think I shall not go . . . just yet."

One pale eyebrow quivered slightly, but she inclined her head to him with equal grace.

"As you wish, MacKenzie. You have only to ask."

She turned like a tiny clockwork figure and left, going back to the world of Helwater, a thousand times more his prison now than it had ever been.

To his extreme surprise, the next few years were in many ways among the happiest of Jamie Fraser's life, aside from the years of his marriage.

Relieved of responsibility for tenants, followers, or anyone at all beyond himself and the horses in his charge, life was relatively simple. While the coroner's court had taken no notice of him, Jeffries had let slip enough about the death of Ellesmere that the other servants treated him with distant respect, but did not presume on his company.

He had enough to eat, sufficient clothes to keep warm and decent, and the occasional discreet letter from the Highlands reassured him that similar conditions obtained there.

One unexpected benefit of the quiet life at Helwater was that he had somehow resumed his odd half-friendship with Lord John Grey. The Major had, as promised, appeared once each quarter, staying each time for a few days to visit with the Dunsanys. He had made no attempt to gloat, though, or even to speak with Jamie, beyond the barest formal inquiry.

Very slowly, Jamie had realized all that Lady Dunsany had implied, in her offer to have him released. "John—Lord John Grey, that is—comes from a family with considerable influence. His stepfather is—well, that's of no consequence," she had said. It was of consequence, though. It had not been His Majesty's pleasure that had brought him here, rather than condemning him to the perilous ocean crossing and near-slavery in America; it had been John Grey's influence.

And he had not done it for revenge or from indecent motives, for he never gloated, made no advances; never said anything beyond the most commonplace civilities. No, he had brought Jamie here because it was the best he could do; unable simply to release him at the time, Grey had done his best to ease the conditions of captivity—by giving him air, and light, and horses.

It took some effort, but he did it. When Grey next appeared in the stableyard on his quarterly visit, Jamie had waited until the Major was alone, admiring the conformation of a big sorrel gelding. He had come to stand beside Grey, leaning on the fence. They watched the horse in silence for several minutes.

"King's pawn to king four," Jamie said quietly at last, not looking at the man beside him.

He felt the other's start of surprise, and felt Grey's eyes on him, but didn't turn his head. Then he felt the creak of the wood beneath his forearm as Grey turned back, leaning on the fence again.

"Queen's knight to queen bishop three," Grey replied, his voice a little huskier than usual.

Since then, Grey had come to the stables during each visit, to spend an evening perched on Jamie's crude stool, talking. They had no chessboard and seldom played verbally, but the late-night conversations continued—Jamie's only connection with the world beyond Helwater, and a small pleasure to which both of them looked forward once each quarter.

Above everything else, he had Willie. Helwater was dedicated to horses; even before the boy could stand solidly on his feet, his grandfather had him propped on a pony to be led round the paddock. By the time Willie was three, he was riding by himself—under the watchful eye of MacKenzie, the groom.

Willie was a strong, courageous, bonny little lad. He had a blinding smile, and could charm birds from the trees if he liked. He was also remarkably spoilt. As the ninth Earl of Ellesmere and the only heir to both Ellesmere and Helwater, with neither mother nor father to keep him under control, he ran roughshod over his doting grandparents, his young aunt, and every servant in the place—except MacKenzie.

And that was a near thing. So far, threats of not allowing the boy to help him with the horses had sufficed to quash Willie's worst excesses in the stables, but sooner or later, threats alone were not going to be sufficient, and MacKenzie the groom found himself wondering just what was going to happen when he finally lost his own control and clouted the wee fiend.

As a lad, he would himself have been beaten senseless by the nearest male relative within earshot, had he ever dared to address a woman the way he had heard Willie speak to his aunt and the maidservants, and the impulse to haul Willie into a deserted box stall and attempt to correct his manners was increasingly frequent.

Still, for the most part, he had nothing but joy in Willie. The boy adored MacKenzie, and as he grew older would spend hours in his company, riding on the huge draft horses as they pulled the heavy roller through the high fields, and perched precariously on the hay wagons as they came down from the upper pastures in summer.

There was a threat to this peaceful existence, though, which grew greater with each passing month. Ironically, the threat came from Willie himself, and was one he could not help.

"What a handsome little lad he is, to be sure! And such a lovely little rider!" It was Lady Grozier who spoke, standing on the veranda with Lady Dunsany to admire Willie's peregrinations on his pony around the edge of the lawn.

Willie's grandmother laughed, eyeing the boy fondly. "Oh, yes. He loves his pony. We have a terrible time getting him even to come indoors for meals. And he's even more fond of his groom. We joke sometimes that he spends so much time with MacKenzie that he's even starting to *look* like MacKenzie!"

Lady Grozier, who had of course paid no attention to a groom, now glanced in MacKenzie's direction.

"Why, you're right!" she exclaimed, much amused. "Just look; Willie's got just that same cock to his head, and the same set to his shoulders! How funny!"

Jamie bowed respectfully to the ladies, but felt cold sweat pop out on his face.

He had seen this coming, but hadn't wanted to believe the resemblance was sufficiently pronounced as to be visible to anyone but himself. Willie as a baby had been fat and pudding-faced, and resembled no one at all. As he had grown, though, the pudginess had vanished from cheeks and chin, and while his nose was still the soft snub of childhood, the hint of high, broad cheekbones was apparent, and the slaty-blue eyes of babyhood had grown dark blue and clear, thickly fringed with sooty lashes, and slightly slanted in appearance.

Once the ladies had gone into the house, and he could be sure no one was watching, Jamie passed a hand furtively over his own features. Was the resemblance truly that great? Willie's hair was a soft middle brown, with just a tinge of his mother's chestnut gleam. And those large, translucent ears—surely his own didn't stick out like that?

The trouble was that Jamie Fraser had not actually seen himself clearly for several years. Grooms did not have looking glasses, and he had sedulously avoided the company of the maids, who might have provided him with one.

Moving to the watering trough, he bent over it, casually, as though inspecting one of the water striders that skated over its surface. Beneath the wavering surface, flecked with floating bits of hay and crisscrossed by the dimpling striders, his own face stared up at him.

He swallowed, and saw the reflection's throat move. It was by no means a complete resemblance, but it was definitely there. More in the set and shape of the head and shoulders, as Lady Grozier had observed—but most definitely the eyes as well. Fraser eyes; his father, Brian, had had them, and his sister, Jenny, as well. Let the boy's bones go on pressing through his skin; let the child-snub nose grow long and straight, and the cheekbones still broader —and anyone would be able to see it.

The reflection in the trough vanished as he straightened up, and stood, staring blindly at the stable that had been home for the last several years. It was July and the sun was hot, but it made no impression on the chill that numbed his fingers and sent a shiver up his back.

It was time to speak to Lady Dunsany.

By the middle of September, everything had been arranged. The pardon had been procured; John Grey had brought it the day before. Jamie had a small amount of money saved, enough for traveling expenses, and Lady Dunsany had given him a decent horse. The only thing that remained was to bid farewell to his acquaintances at Helwater—and Willie.

"I shall be leaving tomorrow." Jamie spoke matter-of-factly, not taking his eyes off the bay mare's fetlock. The horny growth he was filing flaked away, leaving a dust of coarse black shavings on the stable floor.

"Where are you going? To Derwentwater? Can I come with you?" William, Viscount Dunsany, ninth Earl of Ellesmere, hopped down from the edge of the box stall, landing with a thump that made the bay mare start and snort.

"Don't do that," Jamie said automatically. "Have I not told ye to move quiet near Milly? She's skittish."

"Why?"

"You'd be skittish, too, if I squeezed your knee." One big hand darted out and pinched the muscle just above the boy's knee. Willie squeaked and jerked back, giggling.

"Can I ride Millyflower when you're done, Mac?"

"No," Jamie answered patiently, for the dozenth time that day. "I've told ye a thousand times, she's too big for ye yet."

"But I *want* to ride her!"

Jamie sighed but didn't answer, instead moving around to the other side of Mille Fleurs and picking up the left hoof.

"I *said* I want to ride Milly!"

"I heard ye."

"Then saddle her for me! Right now!"

The ninth Earl of Ellesmere had his chin thrust out as far as it would go, but the defiant look in his eye was tempered with a certain doubt as he intercepted Jamie's cold blue gaze. Jamie set the horse's hoof down slowly, just as slowly stood up, and drawing himself to his full height of six feet four, put his hands on his hips, looked down at the Earl, three feet six, and said, very softly, "No."

"Yes!" Willie stamped his foot on the hay-strewn floor. "You *have* to do what I tell you!"

"No, I don't."

"Yes, you do!"

"No, I . . ." Shaking his head hard enough to make the red hair fly about his ears, Jamie pressed his lips tight together, then squatted down in front of the boy.

"See here," he said, "I havena got to do what ye say, for I'm no longer going to be groom here. I told ye, I shall be leaving tomorrow."

Willie's face went quite blank with shock, and the freckles on his nose stood out dark against the fair skin.

"You can't!" he said. "You can't leave."

"I have to."

"No!" The small Earl clenched his jaw, which gave him a truly startling resemblance to his paternal great-grandfather. Jamie thanked his stars that no one at Helwater had likely ever seen Simon Fraser, Lord Lovat. "I won't *let* you go!"

"For once, my lord, ye have nothing to say about it," Jamie replied firmly, his distress at leaving tempered somewhat by finally being allowed to speak his mind to the boy.

"If you leave . . ." Willie looked around helplessly for a threat, and spotted one easily to hand. "If you leave," he repeated more confidently, "I'll scream and shout and scare all the horses, so there!"

"Make a peep, ye little fiend, and I'll smack ye a good one!" Freed from his usual reserve, and alarmed at the thought of this spoiled brat upsetting the high-strung and valuable horses, Jamie glared at the boy.

The Earl's eyes bulged with rage, and his face went red. He took a deep breath, then whirled and ran down the length of the stable, shrieking and waving his arms.

Mille Fleurs, already on edge from having her hoofs fiddled with, reared and plunged, neighing loudly. Her distress was echoed by kicks and high-pitched whinnying from the box stalls nearby, where Willie was roaring out all the bad words he knew— no small store—and kicking frenziedly at the doors of the stalls.

Jamie succeeded in catching Mille Fleurs's lead-rope and with considerable effort, managed to get the mare outside without damage to himself or the horse. He tied her to the paddock fence, and then strode back into the stable to deal with Willie.

"Damn, damn, *damn!*" the Earl was shrieking. "Sluire! Quim! Shit! Swive!"

Without a word, Jamie grabbed the boy by the collar, lifted him off his feet and carried him, kicking and squirming, to the farrier's stool he had been using. Here he sat down, flipped the Earl over his knee, and smacked his buttocks five or six times, hard. Then he jerked the boy up and set him on his feet.

"I *hate* you!" The Earl's tear-smudged face was bright red and his fists trembled with rage.

"Well, I'm no verra fond of you either, ye little bastard!" Jamie snapped.

Willie drew himself up, fists clenched, purple in the face.

"I'm not a bastard!" he shrieked. "I'm not, I'm not! Take it back! Nobody can say that to me! Take it *back,* I said!"

Jamie stared at the boy in shock. There *had* been talk, then, and Willie had heard it. He had delayed his going too long.

He drew a deep breath, and then another, and hoped that his voice would not tremble.

"I take it back," he said softly. "I shouldna have used the word, my lord."

He wanted to kneel and embrace the boy, or pick him up and comfort him against his shoulder—but that was not a gesture a groom might make to an earl, even a young one. The palm of his left hand stung, and he curled his fingers tight over the only fatherly caress he was ever likely to give his son.

Willie knew how an earl should behave; he was making a masterful effort to subdue his tears, sniffing ferociously and swiping at his face with a sleeve.

"Allow me, my lord." Jamie did kneel then, and wiped the little boy's face gently with his own coarse handkerchief. Willie's eyes looked at him over the cotton folds, red-rimmed and woeful.

"Have you really got to go, Mac?" he asked, in a very small voice.

"Aye, I have." He looked into the dark blue eyes, so heartbreakingly like his own, and suddenly didn't give a damn what was right or who saw. He pulled the boy roughly to him, hugging him tight against his heart, holding the boy's face close to his shoulder, that Willie might not see the quick tears that fell into his thick, soft hair.

Willie's arms went around his neck and clung tight. He could feel the small, sturdy body shake against him with the force of suppressed sobbing. He patted the flat little back, and smoothed Willie's hair, and murmured things in Gaelic that he hoped the boy would not understand.

At length, he took the boy's arms from his neck and put him gently away.

"Come wi' me to my room, Willie; I shall give ye something to keep."

He had long since moved from the hayloft, taking over

Hughes's snuggery beside the tack room when the elderly head groom retired. It was a small room, and very plainly furnished, but it had the twin virtues of warmth and privacy.

Besides the bed, the stool, and a chamber pot, there was a small table, on which stood the few books that he owned, a large candle in a pottery candlestick, and a smaller candle, thick and squat, that stood to one side before a small statue of the Virgin. It was a cheap wooden carving that Jenny had sent him, but it had been made in France, and was not without artistry.

"What's that little candle for?" Willie asked. "Grannie says only stinking Papists burn candles in front of heathen images."

"Well, I am a stinking Papist," Jamie said, with a wry twist of his mouth. "It's no a heathen image, though; it's a statue of the Blessed Mother."

"You are?" Clearly this revelation only added to the boy's fascination. "Why do Papists burn candles before statues, then?"

Jamie rubbed a hand through his hair. "Aye, well. It's . . . maybe a way of praying—and remembering. Ye light the candle, and say a prayer and think of people ye care for. And while it burns, the flame remembers them for ye."

"Who do you remember?" Willie glanced up at him. His hair was standing on end, rumpled by his earlier distress, but his blue eyes were clear with interest.

"Oh, a good many people. My family in the Highlands—my sister and her family. Friends. My wife." And sometimes the candle burned in memory of a young and reckless girl named Geneva, but he did not say that.

Willie frowned. "You haven't got a wife."

"No. Not anymore. But I remember her always."

Willie put out a stubby forefinger and cautiously touched the little statue. The woman's hands were spread in welcome, a tender maternity engraved on the lovely face.

"I want to be a stinking Papist, too," Willie said firmly.

"Ye canna do that!" Jamie exclaimed, half-amused, half-touched at the notion. "Your grandmama and your auntie would go mad."

"Would they froth at the mouth, like that mad fox you killed?" Willie brightened.

"I shouldna wonder," Jamie said dryly.

"I want to do it!" The small, clear features were set in determi-

nation. "I won't tell Grannie or Auntie Isobel; I won't tell anybody. Please, Mac! Please let me! I want to be like you!"

Jamie hesitated, both touched by the boy's earnestness, and
suddenly wanting to leave his son with something more than the
carved wooden horse he had made to leave as a farewell present.
He tried to remember what Father McMurtry had taught them in
the schoolroom about baptism. It was all right for a lay person to
do it, he thought, provided that the situation was an emergency,
and no priest was to hand.

It might be stretching a point to call the present situation an
emergency, but . . . a sudden impulse made him reach down the
jug of water that he kept on the sill.

The eyes that were like his watched, wide and solemn, as he
carefully brushed the soft brown hair back from the high brow. He
dipped three fingers into the water and carefully traced a cross on
the lad's forehead.

"I baptize thee William James," he said softly, "in the name o'
the Father, the Son, and the Holy Ghost. Amen."

Willie blinked, crossing his eyes as a drop of water rolled down
his nose. He stuck out his tongue to catch it, and Jamie laughed,
despite himself.

"Why did you call me William James?" Willie asked curiously. "My other names are Clarence Henry George." He made a
face; Clarence wasn't his idea of a good name.

Jamie hid a smile. "Ye get a new name when you're baptized;
James is your special Papist name. It's mine, too."

"It is?" Willie was delighted. "I'm a stinking Papist now, like
you?"

"Aye, as much as I can manage, at least." He smiled down at
Willie, then, struck by another impulse, reached into the neck of
his shirt.

"Here. Keep this, too, to remember me by." He laid the beechwood rosary gently over Willie's head. "Ye canna let anyone see
that, though," he warned. "And for God's sake, dinna tell anyone
you're a Papist."

"I won't," Willie promised. "Not a soul." He tucked the rosary into his shirt, patting carefully to be sure that it was hidden.

"Good." Jamie reached out and ruffled Willie's hair in dismissal. "It's almost time for your tea; ye'd best go on up to the
house now."

Willie started for the door, but stopped halfway, suddenly distressed again, with a hand pressed flat to his chest.

"You said to keep this to remember you. But I haven't got anything for you to remember me by!"

Jamie smiled slightly. His heart was squeezed so tight, he thought he could not draw breath to speak, but he forced the words out.

"Dinna fret yourself," he said. "I'll remember ye."

17

Monsters Rising

B rianna blinked, brushing back a bright web of hair caught by the wind. "I'd almost forgotten what the sun looks like," she said, squinting at the object in question, shining with unaccustomed ferocity on the dark waters of Loch Ness.

Her mother stretched luxuriously, enjoying the light wind. "To say nothing of what fresh air is like. I feel like a toadstool that's been growing in the dark for weeks—all pale and squashy."

"Fine scholars the two of you would make," Roger said, but grinned. All three of them were in high spirits. After the arduous slog through the prison records to narrow the search to Ardsmuir, they had had a run of luck. The records for Ardsmuir were complete, in one spot, and—in comparison to most others—remarkably clear. Ardsmuir had been a prison for only fifteen years; following its renovation by Jacobite prison-labor, it had been converted into a small permanent garrison, and the prison population dispersed—mostly transported to the American Colonies.

"I still can't imagine why Fraser wasn't sent along to America with the rest," Roger said. He had had a moment's panic there, going over and over the list of transported convicts from Ardsmuir, searching the names one by one, nearly letter by letter, and still finding no Frasers. He had been certain that Jamie Fraser had died in prison, and had been in a cold sweat of fear over the thought of telling the Randall women—until the flip of a page had showed him Fraser's parole to a place named Helwater.

"I don't know," Claire said, "but it's a bloody good thing he wasn't. He's—he *was*—" she caught herself quickly, but not quickly enough to stop Roger noticing the slip—"terribly, terribly seasick." She gestured at the surface of the loch before them, dancing with tiny waves. "Even going out on something like that would turn him green in minutes."

Roger glanced at Brianna with interest. "Are you seasick?"

She shook her head, bright hair lifting in the wind. "Nah." She patted her bare midriff smugly. "Cast-iron."

Roger laughed. "Want to go out, then? It's your holiday, after all."

"Really? Could we? Can you fish in there?" Brianna shaded her eyes, looking eagerly out over the dark water.

"Certainly. I've caught salmon and eels many a time in Loch Ness," Roger assured her. "Come along; we'll rent a wee boat at the dock in Drumnadrochit."

The drive to Drumnadrochit was a delight. The day was one of those clear, bright summer days that cause tourists from the South to stampede into Scotland in droves during August and September. With one of Fiona's larger breakfasts inside him, one of her lunches stowed in a basket in the trunk, and Brianna Randall, long hair blowing in the wind, seated beside him, Roger was strongly disposed to consider that all was right with the world.

He allowed himself to dwell with satisfaction on the results of their researches. It had meant taking additional leave from his college for the summer term, but it had been worth it.

After finding the record of James Fraser's parole, it had taken another two weeks of slog and inquiry—even a quick weekend trip by Roger and Bree to the Lake District, another by all three of them to London—and then the sight that had made Brianna whoop out loud in the middle of the British Museum's sacrosanct Reading Room, causing their hasty departure amid waves of icy disapproval. The sight of the Royal Warrant of Pardon, stamped with the seal of George III, *Rex Angleterre,* dated 1764, bearing the name of "James Alex*dr* M'Kensie Frazier."

"We're getting close," Roger had said, gloating over the photocopy of the Warrant of Pardon. "Bloody close!"

"Close?" Brianna had said, but then had been distracted by the sight of their bus approaching, and had not pursued the matter.

Roger had caught Claire's eye on him, though; she knew very well what he meant.

She would, of course, have been thinking of it; he wondered whether Brianna had. Claire had disappeared into the past in 1945, vanishing through the circle of standing stones on Craigh na Dun and reappearing in 1743. She had lived with Jamie Fraser for nearly three years, then returned through the stones. And she had come back nearly three years past the time of her original disappearance, in April of 1948.

All of which meant—just possibly—that if she were disposed to try the trip back through the stones once more, she would likely arrive twenty years past the time she had left—in 1766. And 1766 was only two years past the latest known date at which Jamie Fraser had been located, alive and well. If he had survived another two years, and if Roger could find him . . .

"There it is!" Brianna said suddenly. " 'Boats for Rent.' " She pointed at the sign in the window of the dockside pub, and Roger nosed the car into a parking slot outside, with no further thought of Jamie Fraser.

"I wonder why short men are so often enamored of very tall women." Claire's voice behind him echoed Roger's thoughts with an uncanny accuracy—and not for the first time.

"Moth and flame syndrome, perhaps?" Roger suggested, frowning at the diminutive barman's evident fascination with Brianna. He and Claire were standing before the counter for rentals, waiting for the clerk to write up the receipt while Brianna bought bottles of Coca-Cola and brown ale to augment their lunch.

The young barman, who came up approximately to Brianna's armpit, was hopping to and fro, offering pickled eggs and slices of smoked tongue, eyes worshipfully upturned to the yellow-haltered goddess before him. From her laughter, Brianna appeared to think the man "cute."

"I always told Bree not to get involved with short men," Claire observed, watching this.

"Did you?" Roger said dryly. "Somehow I didn't envision you being all that much in the motherly advice line."

She laughed, disregarding his momentary sourness. "Well, I'm not, all that much. When you notice an important principle like that, though, it seems one's motherly duty to pass it along.''

"Something wrong with short men, is there?'' Roger inquired.

"They tend to turn mean if they don't get their way," Claire answered. "Like small yapping dogs. Cute and fluffy, but cross them and you're likely to get a nasty nip in the ankle.''

Roger laughed. "This observation is the result of years of experience, I take it?''

"Oh, yes.'' She nodded, glancing up at him. "I've never met an orchestra conductor over five feet tall. Vicious specimens, practically all of them. But tall men''—her lips curved slightly as she surveyed his six-feet-three-inch frame—"tall men are almost always very sweet and gentle.''

"Sweet, eh?'' said Roger, with a cynical glance at the barman, who was cutting up a jellied eel for Brianna. Her face expressed a wary distaste, but she leaned forward, wrinkling her nose as she took the bite offered on a fork.

"With women,'' Claire amplified. "I've always thought it's because they realize that they don't have anything to prove; when it's perfectly obvious that they can do anything they like whether you want them to or not, they don't need to try to prove it.''

"While a short man—'' Roger prompted.

"While a short one knows he can't do anything unless you let him, and the knowledge drives him mad, so he's always trying something on, just to prove he can.''

"Mmphm.'' Roger made a Scottish noise in the back of his throat, meant to convey both appreciation of Claire's acuity, and general suspicion of what the barman might be wanting to prove to Brianna.

"Thanks,'' he said to the clerk, who shoved the receipt across the counter to him. "Ready, Bree?'' he asked.

The loch was calm and the fishing slow, but it was pleasant on the water, with the August sun warm on their backs and the scent of raspberry canes and sun-warmed pine trees wafting from the nearby shore. Full of lunch, they all grew drowsy, and before long, Brianna was curled up in the bow, asleep with her head pillowed on Roger's jacket. Claire sat in the stern, blinking, but still awake.

"What about short and tall women?'' Roger asked, resuming

their earlier conversation as he sculled slowly across the loch. He glanced over his shoulder at the amazing length of Brianna's legs, awkwardly curled under her. "Same thing? The little ones nasty?"

Claire shook her head meditatively, the curls beginning to work their way loose from her hairclip. "No, I don't think so. It doesn't seem to have anything to do with size. I think it's more a matter of whether they see men as The Enemy, or just see them as men, and on the whole, rather like them for it."

"Oh, to do with women's liberation, is it?"

"No, not at all," Claire said. "I saw just the same kinds of behavior between men and women in 1743 that you see now. Some differences, of course, in how they each behave, but not so much in how they behave to each other."

She looked out over the dark waters of the loch, shading her eyes with her hand. She might have been keeping an eye out for otters and floating logs, but Roger thought that far-seeing gaze was looking a bit farther than the cliffs of the opposite shore.

"You like men, don't you?" he said quietly. "Tall men."

She smiled briefly, not looking at him.

"One," she said softly.

"Will you go, then—if I can find him?" He rested his oars momentarily, watching her.

She drew a deep breath before answering. The wind flushed her cheeks with pink and molded the fabric of the white shirt to her figure, showing off a high bosom and a slender waist. Too young to be a widow, he thought, too lovely to be wasted.

"I don't know," she said, a little shakily. "The thought of it— or rather, the *thoughts* of it! On the one hand, to find Jamie—and then, on the other, to . . . go through again." A shudder went through her, closing her eyes.

"It's indescribable, you know," she said, eyes still closed as though she saw inside them the ring of stones on Craigh na Dun. "Horrible, but horrible in a way that isn't like other horrible things, so you can't say." She opened her eyes and smiled wryly at him.

"A bit like trying to tell a man what having a baby is like; he can more or less grasp the idea that it's painful, but he isn't equipped actually to understand what it feels like."

Roger grunted with amusement. "Oh, aye? Well, there's some

difference, you know. I've actually heard those bloody stones."
He shivered himself, involuntarily. The memory of the night, three
months ago, when Gillian Edgars had gone through the stones,
was not one he willingly called to mind; it had come back to him
in nightmares several times, though. He heaved strongly on the
oars, trying to erase it.

"Like being torn apart, isn't it?" he said, his eyes intent on
hers. "There's something pulling at you, ripping, dragging, and
not just outside—inside you as well, so you feel your skull will fly
to pieces any moment. And the filthy noise." He shuddered again.
Claire's face had gone slightly pale.

"I didn't know you could hear them," she said. "You didn't tell
me."

"It didn't seem important." He studied her a moment, as he
pulled, then added quietly, "Bree heard them as well."

"I see." She turned to look back over the loch, where the wake
of the tiny boat spread its V-shaped wings. Far behind, the waves
from the passage of a larger boat reflected back from the cliffs and
joined again in the center of the loch, making a long, humped
form of glistening water—a standing wave, a phenomenon of the
loch that had often been mistaken for a sighting of the monster.

"It's there, you know," she said suddenly, nodding down into
the black, peat-laden water.

He opened his mouth to ask what she meant, but then realized
that he *did* know. He had lived near Loch Ness for most of his life,
fished for eels and salmon in its waters, and heard—and laughed at
—every story of the "fearsome beastie" that had ever been told in
the pubs of Drumnadrochit and Fort Augustus.

Perhaps it was the unlikeliness of the situation—sitting here,
calmly discussing whether the woman with him should or should
not take the unimaginable risk of catapulting herself into an unknown past. Whatever the cause of his certainty, it seemed suddenly not only possible, but sure, that the dark water of the loch
hid unknown but fleshly mystery.

"What do you think it is?" he asked, as much to give his
disturbed feelings time to settle, as out of curiosity.

Claire leaned over the side, watching intently as a log drifted
into view.

"The one I saw was probably a plesiosaur," she said at last. She
didn't look at Roger, but kept her gaze astern. "Though I didn't

take notes at the time.'' Her mouth twisted in something not quite a smile.

"How many stone circles are there?" she asked abruptly. "In Britain, in Europe. Do you know?"

"Not exactly. Several hundred, though," he answered cautiously. "Do you think they're all—"

"How should I know?" she interrupted impatiently. "The point is, they may be. They were set up to mark something, which means there may be the hell of a lot of places where that something has happened." She tilted her head to one side, wiping the windblown hair out of her face, and gave him a lopsided smile.

"That would explain it, you know."

"Explain what?" Roger felt fogged by the rapid shifts of her conversation.

"The monster." She gestured out over the water. "What if there's another of those—places—under the loch?"

"A time corridor—passage—whatever?" Roger looked out over the purling wake, staggered by the idea.

"It would explain a lot." There was a smile hiding at the corner of her mouth, behind the veil of blowing hair. He couldn't tell whether she was serious or not. "The best candidates for monster are all things that have been extinct for hundreds of thousands of years. If there's a time passage under the loch, that would take care of that little problem."

"It would also explain why the reports are sometimes different," Roger said, becoming intrigued by the idea. "If it's different creatures who come through."

"And it would explain why the creature—or creatures—haven't been caught, and aren't seen all that often. Maybe they go back the other way, too, so they aren't in the loch all the time."

"What a marvelous idea!" Roger said. He and Claire grinned at each other.

"You know what?" she said. "I'll bet that isn't going to make it on the list of popular theories."

Roger laughed, catching a crab, and droplets of water sprayed over Brianna. She snorted, sat up abruptly, blinking, then sank back down, face flushed with sleep, and was breathing heavily within seconds.

"She was up late last night, helping me box up the last set of records to go back to the University of Leeds," Roger said, defensive on her behalf.

Claire nodded abstractedly, watching her daughter.

"Jamie could do that," she said softly. "Lie down and sleep anywhere."

She fell silent. Roger rowed steadily on, toward the point of the loch where the grim bulk of the ruins of Castle Urquhart stood amid its pines.

"The thing is," Claire said at last, "it gets harder. Going through the first time was the most terrible thing I'd ever had happen to me. Coming back was a thousand times worse." Her eyes were fixed on the looming castle.

"I don't know whether it was because I didn't come back on the right day—it was Beltane when I went, and two weeks before, when I came back."

"Geilie—Gillian, I mean—she went on Beltane, too." In spite of the heat of the day, Roger felt slightly cold, seeing again the figure of the woman who had been both his ancestor and his contemporary, standing in the light of a blazing bonfire, fixed for a moment in the light, before disappearing forever into the cleft of the standing stones.

"That's what her notebook said—that the door is open on the Sun Feasts and the Fire Feasts. Perhaps it's only partly open as you near those times. Or perhaps she was wrong altogether; after all, she thought you had to have a human sacrifice to make it work."

Claire swallowed heavily. The petrol-soaked remains of Greg Edgars, Gillian's husband, had been recovered from the stone circle by the police, on May Day. The record concluded of his wife only, "Fled, whereabouts unknown."

Claire leaned over the side, trailing a hand in the water. A small cloud drifted over the sun, turning the loch a sudden gray, with dozens of small waves rising on the surface as the light wind increased. Directly below, in the wake of the boat, the water was darkly impenetrable. Seven hundred feet deep is Loch Ness, and bitter cold. What can live in a place like that?

"Would you go down there, Roger?" she asked softly. "Jump overboard, dive in, go on down through that dark until your lungs were bursting, not knowing whether there are things with teeth and great heavy bodies waiting?"

Roger felt the hair on his arms rise, and not only because the sudden wind was chilly.

"But that's not all the question," she continued, still staring into the blank, mysterious water. "Would you go, if Brianna were down there?" She straightened up and turned to face him.

"Would you go?" The amber eyes were intent on his, unblinking as a hawk's.

He licked his lips, chapped and dried by the wind, and cast a quick look over his shoulder at Brianna, sleeping. He turned back to face Claire.

"Yes. I think I would."

She looked at him for a long moment, and then nodded, unsmiling.

"So would I."

PART FIVE

You Can't Go Home Again

18

Roots

The woman next to me probably weighed three hundred pounds. She wheezed in her sleep, lungs laboring to lift the burden of her massive bosom for the two-hundred-thousandth time. Her hip and thigh and pudgy arm pressed against mine, unpleasantly warm and damp.

There was no escape; I was pinned on the other side by the steel curve of the plane's fuselage. I eased one arm upward and flicked on the overhead light in order to see my watch. Ten-thirty, by London time; at least another six hours before the landing in New York promised escape.

The plane was filled with the collective sighs and snorts of passengers dozing as best they might. Sleep for me was out of the question. With a sigh of resignation, I dug into the pocket in front of me for the half-finished romance novel I had stashed there. The tale was by one of my favorite authors, but I found my attention slipping from the book—either back to Roger and Brianna, whom I had left in Edinburgh, there to continue the hunt, or forward, to what awaited me in Boston.

I wasn't sure just what *did* await me, which was part of the problem. I had been obliged to come back, if only temporarily; I had long since exhausted my vacation, plus several extensions. There were matters to be dealt with at the hospital, bills to be collected and paid at home, the maintenance of the house and yard to be attended to—I shuddered to think what heights the lawn in the backyard must have attained by now—friends to be called on . . .

One friend in particular. Joseph Abernathy had been my closest friend, from medical school on. Before I made any final—and likely irrevocable—decisions, I wanted to talk to him. I closed the book in my lap and sat tracing the extravagant loops of the title with one finger, smiling a little. Among other things, I owed a taste for romance novels to Joe.

I had known Joe since the beginning of my medical training. He stood out among the other interns at Boston General, just as I did. I was the only woman among the budding doctors; Joe was the only black intern.

Our shared singularity gave us each a special awareness for the other; both of us sensed it clearly, though neither mentioned it. We worked together very well, but both of us were wary—for good reason—of exposing ourselves, and the tenuous bond between us, much too nebulous to be called friendship, remained unacknowledged until near the end of our internship.

I had done my first unassisted surgery that day—an uncomplicated appendectomy, done on a teenage boy in good health. It had gone well, and there was no reason to think there would be postoperative complications. Still, I felt an odd kind of possessiveness about the boy, and didn't want to go home until he was awake and out of Recovery, even though my shift had ended. I changed clothes and went to the doctors' lounge on the third floor to wait.

The lounge wasn't empty. Joseph Abernathy sat in one of the rump-sprung stuffed chairs, apparently absorbed in a copy of *U.S. News & World Report.* He looked up as I entered, and nodded briefly to me before returning to his reading.

The lounge was equipped with stacks of magazines—salvaged from the waiting rooms—and a number of tattered paperbacks, abandoned by departing patients. Seeking distraction, I thumbed past a six-month-old copy of *Studies in Gastroenterology,* a ragged copy of *Time* magazine, and a neat stack of *Watchtower* tracts. Finally picking up one of the books, I sat down with it.

It had no cover, but the title page read *The Impetuous Pirate.* "A sensuous, compelling love story, boundless as the Spanish Main!" said the line beneath the title. The Spanish Main, eh? If escape was what I wanted, I couldn't do much better, I thought, and opened the book at random. It fell open automatically to page 42.

Tipping up her nose scornfully, Tessa tossed her lush blond tresses back, oblivious to the fact that this caused her voluptuous breasts to become even more prominent in the low-necked dress. Valdez's eyes widened at the sight, but he gave no outward sign of the effect such wanton beauty had on him.

"I thought that we might become better acquainted, Señorita," he suggested, in a low, sultry voice that made little shivers of anticipation run up and down Tessa's back.

"I have no interest in becoming acquainted with a . . . a . . . filthy, despicable, underhanded pirate!" she said.

Valdez's teeth gleamed as he smiled at her, his hand stroking the handle of the dagger at his belt. He was impressed by her fearlessness; so bold, so impetuous . . . and so beautiful.

I raised an eyebrow, but went on reading, fascinated.

With an air of imperious possession, Valdez swooped an arm about Tessa's waist.

"You forget, Señorita," he murmured, the words tickling her sensitive earlobe, "you are a prize of war; and the Captain of a pirate ship has first choice of the booty!"

Tessa struggled in his powerful arms as he bore her to the berth and tossed her lightly onto the jeweled coverlet. She struggled to catch her breath, watching in terror as he undressed, laying aside his azure-blue velvet coat and then the fine ruffled white linen shirt. His chest was magnificent, a smooth expanse of gleaming bronze. Her fingertips ached to touch it, even though her heart pounded deafeningly in her ears as he reached for the waistband of his breeches.

"But no," he said, pausing. "It is unfair of me to neglect you, Señorita. Allow me." With an irresistible smile, he bent and gently cupped Tessa's breasts in the heated palms of his calloused hands, enjoying the voluptuous weight of them through the thin silken fabric. With a small scream, Tessa shrank away from his probing touch, pressing back against the lace-embroidered feather pillow.

"You resist? What a pity to spoil such fine clothing, Señorita . . ." He took a firm grasp on her jade-silk bodice and

*yanked, causing Tessa's fine white breasts to leap out of their
concealment like a pair of plump partridges taking wing.*

I made a sound, causing Dr. Abernathy to look sharply over the
top of his *U.S. News & World Report.* Hastily rearranging my face
into a semblance of dignified absorption, I turned the page.

*Valdez's thick black curls swept her chest as he fastened
his hot lips on Tessa's rose-pink nipples, making waves of
anguished desire wash through her being. Weakened by the
unaccustomed feelings that his ardor aroused in her, she was
unable to move as his hand stealthily sought the hem of her
gown and his blazing touch traced tendrils of sensation up
the length of her slender thigh.*

"Ah, mi amor," *he groaned. "So lovely, so pure. You
drive me mad with desire,* mi amor. *I have wanted you since I
first saw you, so proud and cold on the deck of your father's
ship. But not so cold now, my dear, eh?"*

*In fact, Valdez's kisses were wreaking havoc on Tessa's
feelings. How, how could she be feeling such things for this
man, who had cold-bloodedly sunk her father's ship, and
murdered a hundred men with his own hands? She should be
recoiling in horror, but instead she found herself gasping for
breath, opening her mouth to receive his burning kisses,
arching her body in involuntary abandon beneath the demanding pressure of his burgeoning manhood.*

"Ah, mi amor," *he gasped. "I cannot wait. But . . . I do
not wish to hurt you. Gently,* mi amor, *gently."*

*Tessa gasped as she felt the increasing pressure of his
desire making its presence known between her legs.*

*"Oh!" she said. "Oh, please! You can't! I don't want you
to!"* [Fine time to start making protests, I thought.]

"Don't worry, mi amor. *Trust me."*

*Gradually, little by little, she relaxed under the touch of his
hypnotic caresses, feeling the warmth in her stomach grow
and spread. His lips brushed her breast, and his hot breath,
murmuring reassurances, took away all her resistance. As
she relaxed, her thighs opened without her willing it. Moving
with infinite slowness, his engorged shaft teased aside the
membrane of her innocence . . .*

I let out a whoop and lost my grasp on the book, which slid off my lap and fell on the floor with a plop near Dr. Abernathy's feet.

"Excuse me," I murmured, and bent to retrieve it, my face flaming. As I came up with *The Impetuous Pirate* in my sweaty grasp, though, I saw that far from preserving his usual austere mien, Dr. Abernathy was grinning widely.

"Let me guess," he said. "Valdez just teased aside the membrane of her innocence?"

"Yes," I said, breaking out into helpless giggling again. "How did you know?"

"Well, you weren't too far into it," he said, taking the book from my hand. His short, blunt fingers flicked the pages expertly. "It had to be that one, or maybe the one on page 73, where he laves her pink mounds with his hungry tongue."

"He *what*?"

"See for yourself." He thrust the book back into my hands, pointing to a spot halfway down the page.

Sure enough, *". . . lifting aside the coverlet, he bent his coal-black head and laved her pink mounds with his hungry tongue. Tessa moaned and . . ."* I gave an unhinged shriek.

"You've actually *read* this?" I demanded, tearing my eyes away from Tessa and Valdez.

"Oh, yeah," he said, the grin widening. He had a gold tooth, far back on the right side. "Two or three times. It's not the best one, but it isn't bad."

"The best one? There are *more* like this?"

"Sure. Let's see . . ." He rose and began digging through the pile of tattered paperbacks on the table. "You want to look for the ones with no covers," he explained. "Those are the best."

"And here I thought you never read anything but *Lancet* and the *Journal of the AMA*," I said.

"What, I spend thirty-six hours up to my elbows in people's guts, and I want to come up here and read 'Advances in Gallbladder Resection'? Hell, no—I'd rather sail the Spanish Main with Valdez." He eyed me with some interest, the grin still not quite gone. "I didn't think you read anything but *The New England Journal of Medicine,* either, Lady Jane," he said. "Appearances are deceiving, huh?"

"Must be," I said dryly. "What's this 'Lady Jane'?"

"Oh, Hoechstein started that one," he said, leaning back with his fingers linked around one knee. "It's the voice, that accent that sounds like you just drank tea with the Queen. That's what you've got, keeps the guys from bein' worse than they are. See, you sound like Winston Churchill—if Winston Churchill was a lady, that is—and that scares them a little. You've got somethin' else, though"—he viewed me thoughtfully, rocking back in his chair. "You have a way of talking like you expect to get your way, and if you don't, you'll know the reason why. Where'd you learn that?"

"In the war," I said, smiling at his description.

His eyebrows went up. "Korea?"

"No, I was a combat nurse during the Second World War; in France. I saw a lot of Head Matrons who could turn interns and orderlies to jelly with a glance." And later, I had had a good deal of practice, where that air of inviolate authority—assumed though it might be—had stood me in good stead against people with a great deal more power than the nursing staff and interns of Boston General Hospital.

He nodded, absorbed in my explanation. "Yeah, that makes sense. I used Walter Cronkite, myself."

"Walter *Cron*kite?" I goggled at him.

He grinned again, showing his gold tooth. "You can think of somebody better? Besides, I got to hear him for free on the radio or the TV every night. I used to entertain my mama—she wanted me to be a preacher." He smiled, half ruefully. "If I talked like Walter Cronkite where we lived in those days, I wouldn't have *lived* to go to med school."

I was liking Joe Abernathy more by the second. "I hope your mother wasn't disappointed that you became a doctor instead of a preacher."

"Tell you the truth, I'm not sure," he said, still grinning. "When I told her, she stared at me for a minute, then heaved a big sigh and said, 'Well, at least you can get my rheumatism medicine for me cheap.' "

I laughed wryly. "I didn't get *that* much enthusiasm when I told my husband I was going to be a doctor. He stared at me, and finally said if I was bored, why didn't I volunteer to write letters for the inmates of the nursing home."

Joe's eyes were a soft golden brown, like toffee drops. There was a glint of humor in them as they fixed on me.

"Yeah, folks still think it's fine to say to your face that you can't be doing what you're doing. 'Why are you here, little lady, and not home minding your man and child?' '' he mimicked.

He grinned wryly, and patted my hand. "Don't worry, they'll give it up sooner or later. They mostly don't ask me to my face anymore why I ain't cleanin' the toilets, like God made me to."

Then the nurse had come with word that my appendix was awake, and I had left, but the friendship begun on page 42 had flourished, and Joe Abernathy had become one of my best friends; possibly the only person close to me who truly understood what I did, and why.

I smiled a little, feeling the slickness of the embossing on the cover. Then I leaned forward and put the book back into the seat pocket. Perhaps I didn't want to escape just now.

Outside, a floor of moonlit cloud cut us off from the earth below. Up here, everything was silent, beautiful and serene, in marked contrast to the turmoil of life below.

I had the odd feeling of being suspended, motionless, cocooned in solitude, even the heavy breathing of the woman next to me only a part of the white noise that makes up silence, one with the tepid rush of the air-conditioning and the shuffle of the steward-esses' shoes along the carpet. At the same time, I knew we were rushing on inexorably through the air, propelled at hundreds of miles per hour to some end—as for it being a safe one, we could only hope.

I closed my eyes, in suspended animation. Back in Scotland, Roger and Bree were hunting Jamie. Ahead, in Boston, my job—and Joe—were waiting. And Jamie himself? I tried to push the thought away, determined not to think of him until the decision was made.

I felt a slight ruffling of my hair, and one lock brushed against my cheek, light as a lover's touch. But surely it was no more than the rush of air from the vent overhead, and my imagination that the stale smells of perfume and cigarettes were suddenly underlaid by the scents of wool and heather.

19

To Lay a Ghost

Home at last, to the house on Furey Street, where I had lived with Frank and Brianna for nearly twenty years. The azaleas by the door were not quite dead, but their leaves hung in limp, shabby clusters, a thick layer of fallen leaves curling on the dry-baked bed underneath. It was a hot summer—there wasn't any other kind in Boston—and the August rains hadn't come, even though it was mid-September by now.

I set my bags by the front door and went to turn on the hose. It had been lying in the sun; the green rubber snake was hot enough to burn my hand, and I shifted it uneasily from palm to palm until the rumble of water brought it suddenly alive and cooled it with a burst of spray.

I didn't like azaleas all that much to start with. I would have pulled them out long since, but I had been reluctant to alter any detail of the house after Frank's death, for Brianna's sake. Enough of a shock, I thought, to begin university and have your father die in one year, without more changes. I had been ignoring the house for a long time; I could go on doing so.

"All right!" I said crossly to the azaleas, as I turned off the hose. "I hope you're happy, because that's all you get. I want to go have a drink myself. And a bath," I added, seeing their mud-spattered leaves.

I sat on the edge of the big sunken tub in my dressing gown, watching the water thunder in, churning the bubble bath into

clouds of perfumed sea-foam. Steam rose from the boiling surface; the water would be almost too hot.

I turned it off—one quick, neat twist of the tap—and sat for a
moment, the house around me still save for the crackle of popping
bath bubbles, faint as the sounds of a far-off battle. I realized
perfectly well what I was doing. I had been doing it ever since I
stepped aboard the Flying Scotsman in Inverness, and felt the
thrum of the track come alive beneath my feet. I was testing
myself.

I had been taking careful note of the machines—all the contrivances of modern daily life—and more important, of my own response to them. The train to Edinburgh, the plane to Boston, the
taxicab from the airport, and all the dozens of tiny mechanical
flourishes attending—vending machines, streetlights, the plane's
mile-high lavatory, with its swirl of nasty blue-green disinfectant,
whisking waste and germs away with the push of a button. Restaurants, with their tidy certificates from the Department of Health,
guaranteeing at least a better than even chance of escaping food
poisoning when eating therein. Inside my own house, the omnipresent buttons that supplied light and heat and water and cooked
food.

The question was—did I care? I dipped a hand into the steaming bathwater and swirled it to and fro, watching the shadows of
the vortex dancing in the marble depths. Could I live without all
the "conveniences," large and small, to which I was accustomed?

I had been asking myself that with each touch of a button, each
rumble of a motor, and was quite sure that the answer was "yes."
Time didn't make all the difference, after all; I could walk across
the city and find people who lived without many of these conveniences—farther abroad and there were entire countries where
people lived in reasonable content and complete ignorance of electricity.

For myself, I had never cared a lot. I had lived with my uncle
Lamb, an eminent archaeologist, since my own parents' death
when I was five. Consequently, I had grown up in conditions that
could conservatively be called "primitive," as I accompanied him
on all his field expeditions. Yes, hot baths and light bulbs were
nice, but I had lived without them during several periods of my life
—during the war, for instance—and never found the lack of them
acute.

The water had cooled enough to be tolerable. I dropped the dressing gown on the floor and stepped in, feeling a pleasant shiver as the heat at my feet made my shoulders prickle in cool contrast.

I subsided into the tub and relaxed, stretching my legs. Eighteenth-century hip baths were barely more than large barrels; one normally bathed in segments, immersing the center of the body first, with the legs hanging outside, then stood up and rinsed the upper torso while soaking the feet. More frequently, one bathed from a pitcher and basin, with the aid of a cloth.

No, conveniences and comforts were merely that. Nothing essential, nothing I couldn't do without.

Not that conveniences were the only issue, by a long chalk. The past was a dangerous country. But even the advances of so-called civilization were no guarantee of safety. I had lived through two major "modern" wars—actually served on the battlefields of one of them—and could see another taking shape on the telly every evening.

"Civilized" warfare was, if anything, more horrifying than its older versions. Daily life might be safer, but only if one chose one's walk in it with care. Parts of Roxbury now were as dangerous as any alley I had walked in the Paris of two hundred years past.

I sighed and pulled up the plug with my toes. No use speculating about impersonal things like bathtubs, bombs, and rapists. Indoor plumbing was no more than a minor distraction. The real issue was the people involved, and always had been. Me, and Brianna, and Jamie.

The last of the water gurgled away. I stood up, feeling slightly light-headed, and wiped away the last of the bubbles. The big mirror was misted with steam, but clear enough to show me myself from the knees upward, pink as a boiled shrimp.

Dropping the towel, I looked myself over. Flexed my arms, raised them overhead, checking for bagginess. None; biceps and triceps all nicely defined, deltoids neatly rounded and sloping into the high curve of the pectoralis major. I turned slightly to one side, tensing and relaxing my abdominals—obliques in decent tone, the rectus abdominis flattening almost to concavity.

"Good thing the family doesn't run to fat," I murmured. Uncle Lamb had remained trim and taut to the day of his death at seventy-five. I supposed my father—Uncle Lamb's brother—had been constructed similarly, and wondered suddenly what my mother's backside had looked like. Women, after all, had a certain amount of excess adipose tissue to contend with.

I turned all the way round and peered back over my shoulder at the mirror. The long columnar muscles of my back gleamed wetly as I twisted; I still had a waist, and a good narrow one, too.

As for my own backside—"Well, no dimples, anyway," I said aloud. I turned around and stared at my reflection.

"It could be a lot worse," I said to it.

Feeling somewhat heartened, I put on my nightgown and went about the business of putting the house to bed. No cats to put out, no dogs to feed—Bozo, the last of our dogs, had died of old age the year before, and I had not wanted to get another, with Brianna off at school and my own hours at the hospital long and irregular.

Adjust the thermostat, check the locks of windows and doors, see that the burners of the stove were off. That was all there was to it. For eighteen years, the nightly route had included a stop in Brianna's room, but not since she had left for university.

Moved by a mixture of habit and compulsion, I pushed open the door to her room and clicked on the light. Some people have the knack of objects, and others haven't. Bree had it; scarcely an inch of wall space showed between the posters, photographs, dried flowers, scraps of tie-dyed fabric, framed certificates and other impedimenta on the walls.

Some people have a way of arranging everything about them, so the objects take on not only their own meaning, and a relation to the other things displayed with them, but something more besides —an indefinable aura that belongs as much to their invisible owner as to the objects themselves. *I am here because Brianna placed me here,* the things in the room seemed to say. *I am here because she is who she is.*

It was odd that she should have that, really, I thought. Frank had had it; when I had gone to empty his university office after his death, I had thought it like the fossilized cast of some extinct animal; books and papers and bits of rubbish holding exactly the shape and texture and vanished weight of the mind that had inhabited the space.

For some of Brianna's objects, the relation to her was obvious —pictures of me, of Frank, of Bozo, of friends. The scraps of fabric were ones she had made, her chosen patterns, the colors she liked—a brilliant turquoise, deep indigo, magenta, and clear yellow. But other things—why should the scatter of dried freshwater snail shells on the bureau say to me "Brianna"? Why that one lump of rounded pumice, taken from the beach at Truro, indistinguishable from a hundred thousand others—except for the fact that she had taken it?

I didn't have a way with objects. I had no impulse either to acquire or to decorate—Frank had often complained of the Spartan furnishings at home, until Brianna grew old enough to take a hand. Whether it was the fault of my nomadic upbringing, or only the way I was, I lived mostly inside my skin, with no impulse to alter my surroundings to reflect me.

Jamie was the same. He had had the few small objects, always carried in his sporran for utility or as talismans, and beyond that, had neither owned nor cared for things. Even during the short period when we had lived luxuriously in Paris, and the longer time of tranquillity at Lallybroch, he had never shown any disposition to acquire objects.

For him as well, it might have been the circumstances of his early manhood, when he had lived like a hunted animal, never owning anything beyond the weapons he depended on for survival. But perhaps it was natural to him also, this isolation from the world of things, this sense of self-sufficiency—one of the things that had made us seek completion in each other.

Odd all the same, that Brianna should have so much resembled both her fathers, in their very different ways. I said a silent good night to the ghost of my absent daughter, and put out the light.

The thought of Frank went with me into the bedroom. The sight of the big double bed, smooth and untroubled under its dark blue satin spread, brought him suddenly and vividly to mind, in a way I had not thought of him in many months.

I supposed it was the possibility of impending departure that made me think of him now. This room—this bed, in fact—was where I had said goodbye to him for the last time.

"Can't you come to bed, Claire? It's past midnight." Frank looked up at me over the edge of his book. He was already in bed himself, reading with the book propped upon his knees. The soft pool of light from the lamp made him look as though he were floating in a warm bubble, serenely isolated from the dark chilliness of the rest of the room. It was early January, and despite the furnace's best efforts, the only truly warm place at night was bed, under heavy blankets.

I smiled at him, and rose from my chair, dropping the heavy wool dressing gown from my shoulders.

"Am I keeping you up? Sorry. Just reliving this morning's surgery."

"Yes, I know," he said dryly. *"I can tell by looking at you. Your eyes glaze over and your mouth hangs open."*

"Sorry," I said again, matching his tone. *"I can't be responsible for what my face is doing when I'm thinking."*

"But what good does thinking do?" he asked, sticking a bookmark in his book. *"You've done whatever you could—worrying about it now won't change . . . ah, well."* He shrugged irritably and closed the book. *"I've said it all before."*

"You have," I said shortly.

I got into bed, shivering slightly, and tucked my gown down round my legs. Frank scooted automatically in my direction, and I slid down under the sheets beside him, huddling together to pool our warmth against the cold.

"Oh, wait; I've got to move the phone." I flung back the covers and scrambled out again, to move the phone from Frank's side of the bed to mine. He liked to sit in bed in the early evening, chatting with students and colleagues while I read or made surgical notes beside him, but he resented being wakened by the late calls that came from the hospital for me. Resented it enough that I had arranged for the hospital to call only for absolute emergencies, or when I left instructions to keep me informed of a specific patient's progress. Tonight I had left instructions; it was a tricky bowel resection. If things went wrong, I might have to go back in in a hurry.

Frank grunted as I turned out the light and slipped into bed again, but after a moment, he rolled toward me, throwing an arm across my middle. I rolled onto my side and curled against him, gradually relaxing as my chilled toes thawed.

I mentally replayed the details of the operation, feeling again the chill at my feet from the refrigeration in the operating room and the initial, unsettling feeling of the warmth in the patient's belly as my gloved fingers slid inside. The diseased bowel itself, coiled like a viper, patterned with the purple splotches of ecchymosis and the slow leakage of bright blood from tiny ruptures.

"I'd been thinking." *Frank's voice came out of the darkness behind me, excessively casual.*

"Mm?" *I was still absorbed in the vision of the surgery, but struggled to pull myself back to the present.* "About what?"

"My sabbatical." *His leave from the university was due to start in a month. He had planned to make a series of short trips through the northeastern United States, gathering material, then go to England for six months, returning to Boston to spend the last three months of the sabbatical writing.*

"I'd thought of going to England straight off," *he said carefully.*

"Well, why not? The weather will be dreadful, but if you're going to spend most of the time in libraries . . ."

"I want to take Brianna with me."

I stopped dead, the cold in the room suddenly coalescing into a small lump of suspicion in the pit of my stomach.

"She can't go now; she's only a semester from graduation. Surely you can wait until we can join you in the summer? I've put in for a long vacation then, and perhaps . . ."

"I'm going now. For good. Without you."

I pulled away and sat up, turning on the light. Frank lay blinking up at me, dark hair disheveled. It had gone gray at the temples, giving him a distinguished air that seemed to have alarming effects on the more susceptible of his female students. I felt quite astonishingly composed.

"Why now, all of a sudden? The latest one putting pressure on you, is she?"

The look of alarm that flashed into his eyes was so pronounced as to be comical. I laughed, with a noticeable lack of humor.

"You actually thought I didn't know? God, Frank! You are the most . . . oblivious man!"

He sat up in bed, jaw tight.

"I thought I had been most discreet."

"You may have been at that," *I said sardonically.* "I counted *six over the last ten years—if there were really a dozen or so, then you were quite the model of discretion.''*

His face seldom showed great emotion, but a whitening beside his mouth told me that he was very angry indeed.

"This one must be something special," I said, folding my arms and leaning back against the headboard in assumed casualness. "But still—why the rush to go to England now, and why take Bree?"

"She can go to boarding school for her last term," he said shortly. "Be a new experience for her."

"Not one I expect she wants," I said. "She won't want to leave her friends, especially not just before graduation. And certainly not to go to an English boarding school!" I shuddered at the thought. I had come within inches of being immured in just such a school as a child; the scent of the hospital cafeteria sometimes evoked memories of it, complete with the waves of terrified helplessness I had felt when Uncle Lamb had taken me to visit the place.

"A little discipline never hurt anyone," Frank said. He had recovered his temper, but the lines of his face were still tight. "Might have done you some good." He waved a hand, dismissing the topic. "Let that be. Still, I've decided to go back to England permanently. I've a good position offered at Cambridge, and I mean to take it up. You won't leave the hospital, of course. But I don't mean to leave my daughter behind."

"Your daughter?" I felt momentarily incapable of speech. So he had a new job all set, and a new mistress to go along. He'd been planning this for some time, then. A whole new life—but not with Brianna.

"My daughter," he said calmly. "You can come to visit whenever you like, of course . . ."

"You . . . bloody . . . bastard!" I said.

"Do be reasonable, Claire." He looked down his nose, giving me Treatment A, long-suffering patience, reserved for students appealing failing grades. "You're scarcely ever home. If I'm gone, there will be no one to look after Bree properly."

"You talk as though she's eight, not almost eighteen! For heaven's sake, she's nearly grown."

"All the more reason she needs care and supervision," he

snapped. *"If you'd seen what I'd seen at the university—the drinking, the drugging, the . . ."*

"I do see it," I said through my teeth. *"At fairly close range in the emergency room. Bree is not likely to—"*

"She damn well is! Girls have no sense at that age—she'll be off with the first fellow who—"

"Don't be idiotic! Bree's very sensible. Besides, all young people experiment, that's how they learn. You can't keep her swaddled in cotton wool all her life."

"Better swaddled than fucking a black man!" he shot back. A mottled red showed faintly over his cheekbones. *"Like mother, like daughter, eh? But that's not how it's going to be; damn it, not if I've anything to say about it!"*

I heaved out of bed and stood up, glaring down at him.

"You," I said, *"have not got one bloody, filthy, stinking thing to say, about Bree or anything else!"* I was trembling with rage, and had to press my fists into the sides of my legs to keep from striking him. *"You have the absolute, unmitigated gall to tell me that you are leaving me to live with the latest of a succession of mistresses, and then imply that I have been having an affair with Joe Abernathy? That is what you mean, isn't it?"*

He had the grace to lower his eyes slightly.

"Everyone thinks you have," he muttered. *"You spend all your time with the man. It's the same thing, so far as Bree is concerned. Dragging her into . . . situations, where she's exposed to danger, and . . . and to those sorts of people . . ."*

"Black people, I suppose you mean?"

"I damn well do," he said, looking up at me with eyes flashing. *"It's bad enough to have the Abernathys to parties all the time, though at least he's educated. But that obese person I met at their house with the tribal tattoos and the mud in his hair? That repulsive lounge lizard with the oily voice? And young Abernathy's taken to hanging round Bree day and night, taking her to marches and rallies and orgies in low dives . . ."*

"I shouldn't think there are any high dives," I said, repressing an inappropriate urge to laugh at Frank's unkind but accurate assessment of two of Leonard Abernathy's more outré friends. *"Did you know Lenny's taken to calling himself Muhammad Ishmael Shabazz now?"*

"Yes, he told me," he said shortly, *"and I am taking no risk of having my daughter become Mrs. Shabazz."*

"I don't think Bree feels that way about Lenny," I assured him, struggling to suppress my irritation.

"She isn't going to, either. She's going to England with me."

"Not if she doesn't want to," I said, with great finality.

No doubt feeling that his position put him at a disadvantage, Frank climbed out of bed and began groping for his slippers.

"I don't need your permission to take my daughter to England," he said. *"And Bree's still a minor; she'll go where I say. I'd appreciate it if you'd find her medical records; the new school will need them."*

"Your daughter?" I said again. I vaguely noticed the chill in the room, but was so angry that I felt hot all over. *"Bree's my daughter, and you'll take her bloody nowhere!"*

"You can't stop me," he pointed out, with aggravating calmness, picking up his dressing gown from the foot of the bed.

"The hell I can't," I said. *"You want to divorce me? Fine. Use any grounds you like—with the exception of adultery, which you can't prove, because it doesn't exist. But if you try to take Bree away with you, I'll have a thing or two to say about adultery. Do you want to know how many of your discarded mistresses have come to see me, to ask me to give you up?"*

His mouth hung open in shock.

"I told them all that I'd give you up in a minute," I said, *"if you asked."* I folded my arms, tucking my hands into my armpits. I was beginning to feel the chilliness again. *"I did wonder why you never asked—but I supposed it was because of Brianna."*

His face had gone quite bloodless now, and showed white as a skull in the dimness on the other side of the bed.

"Well," he said, with a poor attempt at his usual self-possession, *"I shouldn't have thought you minded. It's not as though you ever made a move to stop me."*

I stared at him, completely taken aback.

"Stop you?" I said. *"What should I have done? Steamed open your mail and waved the letters under your nose? Made a scene at the faculty Christmas party? Complained to the Dean?"*

His lips pressed tight together for a moment, then relaxed.

"You might have behaved as though it mattered to you," he said quietly.

"It mattered." My voice sounded strangled.

He shook his head, still staring at me, his eyes dark in the lamplight.

"Not enough." He paused, face floating pale in the air above his dark dressing gown, then came round the bed to stand by me.

"Sometimes I wondered if I could rightfully blame you," he said, almost thoughtfully. *"He looked like Bree, didn't he? He was like her?"*

"Yes."

He breathed heavily, almost a snort.

"I could see it in your face—when you'd look at her, I could see you thinking of him. Damn you, Claire Beauchamp," he said, very softly. *"Damn you and your face that can't hide a thing you think or feel."*

There was a silence after this, of the sort that makes you hear all the tiny unhearable noises of creaking wood and breathing houses—only in an effort to pretend you haven't heard what was just said.

"I did love you," I said softly, at last. *"Once."*

"Once," he echoed. *"Should I be grateful for that?"*

The feeling was beginning to come back to my numb lips.

"I did tell you," I said. *"And then, when you wouldn't go . . . Frank, I did try."*

Whatever he heard in my voice stopped him for a moment.

"I did," I said, very softly.

He turned away and moved toward my dressing table, where he touched things restlessly, picking them up and putting them down at random.

"I couldn't leave you at the first—pregnant, alone. Only a cad would have done that. And then . . . Bree." He stared sightlessly at the lipstick he held in one hand, then set it gently back on the glassy tabletop. *"I couldn't give her up,"* he said softly. He turned to look at me, eyes dark holes in a shadowed face.

"Did you know I couldn't sire a child? I . . . had myself tested, a few years ago. I'm sterile. Did you know?"

I shook my head, not trusting myself to speak.

"Bree is mine, my daughter," he said, as though to himself. *"The only child I'll ever have. I couldn't give her up."* He gave a short laugh. *"I couldn't give her up, but you couldn't see her*

without thinking of him, could you? Without that constant memory, I wonder—would you have forgotten him, in time?"

"No." The whispered word seemed to go through him like an electric shock. He stood frozen for a moment, then whirled to the closet and began to jerk on his clothes over his pajamas. I stood, arms wrapped around my body, watching as he pulled on his overcoat and stamped out of the room, not looking at me. The collar of his blue silk pajamas stuck up over the astrakhan trim of his coat.

A moment later, I heard the closing of the front door—he had sufficient presence of mind not to slam it—and then the sound of a cold motor turning reluctantly over. The headlights swept across the bedroom ceiling as the car backed down the drive, and then were gone, leaving me shaking by the rumpled bed.

Frank didn't come back. I tried to sleep, but found myself lying rigid in the cold bed, mentally reliving the argument, listening for the crunch of his tires in the drive. At last, I got up and dressed, left a note for Bree, and went out myself.

The hospital hadn't called, but I might as well go and have a look at my patient; it was better than tossing and turning all night. And, to be honest, I would not have minded had Frank come home to find me gone.

The streets were slick as butter, black ice gleaming in the streetlights. The yellow phosphor glow lit whorls of falling snow; within an hour, the ice that lined the streets would be concealed beneath fresh powder, and twice as perilous to travel. The only consolation was that there was no one on the streets at 4:00 A.M. to be imperiled. No one but me, that is.

Inside the hospital, the usual warm, stuffy institutional smell wrapped itself round me like a blanket of familiarity, shutting out the snow-filled black night outside.

"He's okay," the nurse said to me softly, as though a raised voice might disturb the sleeping man. "All the vitals are stable, and the count's okay. No bleeding." I could see that it was true; the patient's face was pale, but with a faint undertone of pink, like the veining in a white rose petal, and the pulse in the hollow of his throat was strong and regular.

I let out the deep breath I hadn't realized I was holding.

"That's good," I said. *"Very good."* The nurse smiled warmly at me, and I had to resist the impulse to lean against him and dissolve. The hospital surroundings suddenly seemed like my only refuge.

There was no point in going home. I checked briefly on my remaining patients, and went down to the cafeteria. It still smelled like a boarding school, but I sat down with a cup of coffee and sipped it slowly, wondering what I would tell Bree.

It might have been a half-hour later when one of the ER nurses hurried through the swinging doors and stopped dead at the sight of me. Then she came on, quite slowly.

I knew at once; I had seen doctors and nurses deliver the news of death too often to mistake the signs. Very calmly, feeling nothing whatever, I set down the almost full cup, realizing as I did so that for the rest of my life, I would remember that there was a chip in the rim, and that the *"B"* of the gold lettering on the side was almost worn away.

". . . said you were here. Identification in his wallet . . . police said . . . snow on black ice, a skid . . . DOA . . ." The nurse was talking, babbling, as I strode through the bright white halls, not looking at her, seeing the faces of the nurses at the station turn toward me in slow motion, not knowing, but seeing from a glance at me that something final had happened.

He was on a gurney in one of the emergency room cubicles; a spare, anonymous space. There was an ambulance parked outside —perhaps the one that had brought him here. The double doors at the end of the corridor were open to the icy dawn. The ambulance's red light was pulsing like an artery, bathing the corridor in blood.

I touched him briefly. His flesh had the inert, plastic feel of the recently dead, so at odds with the lifelike appearance. There was no wound visible; any damage was hidden beneath the blanket that covered him. His throat was smooth and brown; no pulse moved in its hollow.

I stood there, my hand on the motionless curve of his chest, looking at him, as I had not looked for some time. A strong and delicate profile, sensitive lips, and a chiseled nose and jaw. A handsome man, despite the lines that cut deep beside his mouth, lines of disappointment and unspoken anger, lines that even the relaxation of death could not wipe away.

I stood quite still, listening. I could hear the wail of a new ambulance approaching, voices in the corridor. The squeak of gurney wheels, the crackle of a police radio, and the soft hum of a fluorescent light somewhere. I realized with a start that I was listening for Frank, expecting . . . what? That his ghost would be hovering still nearby, anxious to complete our unfinished business?

I closed my eyes, to shut out the disturbing sight of that motionless profile, going red and white and red in turn as the light throbbed through the open doors.

"Frank," I said softly, to the unsettled, icy air, "if you're still close enough to hear me—I did love you. Once. I did."

Then Joe was there, pushing through the crowded corridor, face anxious over his green scrub suit. He had come straight from surgery; there was a small spray of blood across the lenses of his glasses, a smear of it on his chest.

"Claire," he said, "God, Claire!" and then I started to shake. In ten years, he had never called me anything but "Jane" or "L.J." If he was using my name, it must be real. My hand showed startlingly white in Joe's dark grasp, then red in the pulsing light, and then I had turned to him, solid as a tree trunk, rested my head on his shoulder, and—for the first time—wept for Frank.

I leaned my face against the bedroom window of the house on Furey Street. It was hot and humid on this blue September evening, filled with the sound of crickets and lawn sprinklers. What I saw, though, was the uncompromising black and white of that winter's night two years before—black ice and the white of hospital linen, and then the blurring of all judgments in the pale gray dawn.

My eyes blurred now, remembering the anonymous bustle in the corridor and the pulsing red light of the ambulance that had washed the silent cubicle in bloody light, as I wept for Frank.

Now I wept for him for the last time, knowing even as the tears slid down my cheeks that we had parted, once and for all, twenty-odd years before, on the crest of a green Scottish hill.

My weeping done, I rose and laid a hand on the smooth blue coverlet, gently rounded over the pillow on the left—Frank's side.

"Goodbye, my dear," I whispered, and went out to sleep downstairs, away from the ghosts.

It was the doorbell that woke me in the morning, from my makeshift bed on the sofa.

"Telegram, ma'am," the messenger said, trying not to stare at my nightgown.

Those small yellow envelopes have probably been responsible for more heart attacks than anything besides fatty bacon for breakfast. My own heart squeezed like a fist, then went on beating in a heavy, uncomfortable manner.

I tipped the messenger and carried the telegram down the hall. It seemed important not to open it until I had reached the relative safety of the bathroom, as though it were an explosive device that must be defused under water.

My fingers shook and fumbled as I opened it, sitting on the edge of the tub, my back pressed against the tiled wall for reinforcement.

It was a brief message—of course, a Scot would be thrifty with words, I thought absurdly.

HAVE FOUND HIM STOP, it read. WILL YOU COME BACK QUERY ROGER.

I folded the telegram neatly and put it back into its envelope. I sat there and stared at it for quite a long time. Then I stood up and went to dress.

20

Diagnosis

Joe Abernathy was seated at his desk, frowning at a small rectangle of pale cardboard he held in both hands.

"What's that?" I said, sitting on the edge of his desk without ceremony.

"A business card." He handed the card to me, looking at once amused and irritated.

It was a pale gray laid-finish card; expensive stock, fastidiously printed in an elegant serif type. *Muhammad Ishmael Shabazz III,* the center line read, with address and phone number below.

"Lenny?" I asked, laughing. "Muhammad Ishmael Shabazz the *Third*?"

"Uh-huh." Amusement seemed to be getting the upper hand. The gold tooth flashed briefly as he took the card back. "He says he's not going to take a white man's name, no slave name. He's going to reclaim his African heritage," he said sardonically. "All right, I say; I ask him, you gonna go round with a bone through your nose next thing? It's not enough he's got his hair out to *here*"—he gestured, fluffing his hands on either side of his own close-cropped head—"and he's going round in a thing down to his knees, looks like his sister made it in Home Ec class. No, Lenny—excuse me, Muhammad—he's got to be *African* all the way."

Joe waved a hand out the window, at his privileged vista over the park. "I tell him, look around, man, you see any lions? This look like Africa to you?" He leaned back in his padded chair, stretching out his legs. He shook his head in resignation. "There's no talkin' to a boy that age."

"True," I said. "But what's this 'Third' about?"

A reluctant gleam of gold answered me. "Well, he was talking all about his 'lost tradition' and his 'missing history' and all. He says, 'How am I going to hold my head up, face-to-face with all these guys I meet at Yale named Cadwallader IV and Sewell Lodge, Jr., and I don't even know my own grandaddy's name, I don't know where I come from?' "

Joe snorted. "I told him, you want to know where you come from, kid, look in the mirror. Wasn't the *Mayflower,* huh?"

He picked up the card again, a reluctant grin on his face.

"So he says, if he's taking back his heritage, why not take it back all the way? If his grandaddy wouldn't give him a name, he'll give his grandaddy one. And the only trouble with *that,*" he said, looking up at me under a cocked brow, "is that it kind of leaves me man in the middle. Now I have to be Muhammad Ishmael Shabazz, *Junior,* so Lenny can be a 'proud African American.' "

He thrust himself back from the desk, chin on his chest, staring balefully at the pale gray card.

"You're lucky, L.J.," he said. "At least Bree isn't giving you grief about who her granddaddy was. All you have to worry about is will she be doing dope. and getting pregnant by some draft dodger who takes off for Canada."

I laughed, with more than a touch of irony. "That's what *you* think," I told him.

"Yeah?" He cocked an interested eyebrow at me, then took off his gold-rimmed glasses and wiped them on the end of his tie. "So how was Scotland?" he asked, eyeing me. "Bree like it?"

"She's still there," I said. "Looking for *her* history."

Joe was opening his mouth to say something when a tentative knock on the door interrupted him.

"Dr. Abernathy?" A plump young man in a polo shirt peered doubtfully into the office, leaning over the top of a large cardboard box he held clutched to his substantial abdomen.

"Call me Ishmael," Joe said genially.

"What?" The young man's mouth hung slightly open, and he glanced at me in bewilderment, mingled with hope. "Are *you* Dr. Abernathy?"

"No," I said, "he is, when he puts his mind to it." I rose from the desk, brushing down my skirts. "I'll leave you to your appointment, Joe, but if you have time later—"

"No, stay a minute, L.J.," he interrupted, rising. He took the box from the young man, then shook his hand formally. "You'd be Mr. Thompson? John Wicklow called to tell me you'd be coming. Pleased to meet you."

"Horace Thompson, yes," the young man said, blinking slightly. "I brought, er, a specimen . . ." He waved vaguely at the cardboard box.

"Yes, that's right. I'd be happy to look at it for you, but I think Dr. Randall here might be of assistance, too." He glanced at me, the glint of mischief in his eyes. "I just want to see can you do it to a dead person, L.J."

"Do *what* to a dead—" I began, when he reached into the opened box and carefully lifted out a skull.

"Oh, pretty," he said in delight, turning the object gently to and fro.

"Pretty" was not the first adjective that struck me; the skull was stained and greatly discolored, the bone gone a deep streaky brown. Joe carried it to the window and held it in the light, his thumbs gently stroking the small bony ridges over the eye sockets.

"Pretty lady," he said softly, talking as much to the skull as to me or Horace Thompson. "Full-grown, mature. Maybe late forties, middle fifties. Do you have the legs?" he asked, turning abruptly to the plump young man.

"Yeah, right here," Horace Thompson assured him, reaching into the box. "We have the whole body, in fact."

Horace Thompson was probably someone from the coroner's office, I thought. Sometimes they brought bodies to Joe that had been found in the countryside, badly deteriorated, for an expert opinion as to the cause of death. This one looked considerably deteriorated.

"Here, Dr. Randall." Joe leaned over and carefully placed the skull in my hands. "Tell me whether this lady was in good health, while I check her legs."

"Me? I'm not a forensic scientist." Still, I glanced automatically down. It was either an old specimen, or had been weathered extensively; the bone was smooth, with a gloss that fresh specimens never had, stained and discolored by the leaching of pigments from the earth.

"Oh, all right." I turned the skull slowly in my hands, watching the bones, naming them each in my mind as I saw them. The smooth arch of the parietals, fused to the declivity of the temporal, with the small ridge where the jaw muscle originated, the jutting projection that meshed itself with the maxillary into the graceful curve of the squamosal arch. She had had lovely cheekbones, high and broad. The upper jaw had most of its teeth—straight and white.

Deep eyes. The scooped bone at the back of the orbits was dark with shadow; even by tilting the skull to the side, I couldn't get light to illuminate the whole cavity. The skull felt light in my hands, the bone fragile. I stroked her brow and my hand ran upward, and down behind the occiput, my fingers seeking the dark hole at the base, the foramen magnum, where all the messages of the nervous system pass to and from the busy brain.

Then I held it close against my stomach, eyes closed, and felt the shifting sadness, filling the cavity of the skull like running water. And an odd faint sense—of surprise?

"Someone killed her," I said. "She didn't want to die." I opened my eyes to find Horace Thompson staring at me, his own eyes wide in his round, pale face. I handed him the skull, very gingerly. "Where did you find her?" I asked.

Mr. Thompson exchanged glances with Joe, then looked back at me, both eyebrows still high.

"She's from a cave in the Caribbean," he said. "There were a lot of artifacts with her. We think she's maybe between a hundred fifty and two hundred years old."

"She's *what*?"

Joe was grinning broadly, enjoying his joke.

"Our friend Mr. Thompson here is from the anthropology department at Harvard," he said. "His friend Wicklow knows me; asked me would I have a look at this skeleton, to tell them what I could about it."

"The nerve of you!" I said indignantly. "I thought she was some unidentified body the coroner's office dragged in."

"Well, she's unidentified," Joe pointed out. "And certainly liable to stay that way." He rooted about in the cardboard box like a terrier. The end flap said PICT-SWEET CORN.

"Now what have we got here?" he said, and very carefully drew out a plastic sack containing a jumble of vertebrae.

"She was in pieces when we got her," Horace explained.

"Oh, de headbone connected to de . . . neckbone," Joe sang softly, laying out the vertebrae along the edge of the desk. His stubby fingers darted skillfully among the bones, nudging them into alignment. "De neckbone connected to de . . . backbone . . ."

"Don't pay any attention to him," I told Horace. "You'll just encourage him."

"Now hear . . . de word . . . of de Lawd!" he finished triumphantly. "Jesus Christ, L.J., you're somethin' else! Look here." Horace Thompson and I bent obediently over the line of spiky vertebral bones. The wide body of the axis had a deep gouge; the posterior zygapophysis had broken clean off, and the fracture plane went completely through the centrum of the bone.

"A broken neck?" Thompson asked, peering interestedly.

"Yeah, but more than that, I think." Joe's finger moved over the line of the fracture plane. "See here? The bone's not just cracked, it's *gone* right there. Somebody tried to cut this lady's head clean off. With a dull blade," he concluded with relish.

Horace Thompson was looking at me queerly. "How did you know she'd been killed, Dr. Randall?" he asked.

I could feel the blood rising in my face. "I don't know," I said. "I—she—*felt* like it, that's all."

"Really?" He blinked a few times, but didn't press me further. "How odd."

"She does it all the time," Joe informed him, squinting at the femur he was measuring with a pair of calipers. "Mostly on live people, though. Best diagnostician I ever saw." He set down the calipers and picked up a small plastic ruler. "A *cave,* you said?"

"We think it was a . . . er, secret slave burial," Mr. Thompson explained, blushing, and I suddenly realized why he had seemed so abashed when he realized which of us was the Dr. Abernathy he had been sent to see. Joe shot him a sudden sharp glance, but then bent back to his work. He kept humming "Dem Dry Bones" faintly to himself as he measured the pelvic inlet, then went back to the legs, this time concentrating on the tibia. Finally he straightened up, shaking his head.

"Not a slave," he said.

Horace blinked. "But she must have been," he said. "The things we found with her . . . a clear African influence . . ."

"No," Joe said flatly. He tapped the long femur, where it rested on his desk. His fingernail clicked on the dry bone. "She wasn't black."

"You can tell that? From bones?" Horace Thompson was visibly agitated. "But I thought—that paper by Jensen, I mean—theories about racial physical differences—largely exploded—" He blushed scarlet, unable to finish.

"Oh, they're there," said Joe, very dryly indeed. "If you want to think blacks and whites are equal under the skin, be my guest, but it ain't scientifically so." He turned and pulled a book from the shelf behind him. *Tables of Skeletal Variance,* the title read.

"Take a look at this," Joe invited. "You can see the differences in a lot of bones, but especially in the leg bones. Blacks have a completely different femur-to-tibia ratio than whites do. And that lady"—he pointed to the skeleton on his desk—"was white. Caucasian. No question about it."

"Oh," Horace Thompson murmured. "Well. I'll have to think —I mean—it was very kind of you to look at her for me. Er, thank you," he added, with an awkward little bow. We silently watched him bundle his bones back into the PICT-SWEET box, and then he was gone, pausing at the door to give us both another brief bob of the head.

Joe gave a short laugh as the door closed behind him. "Want to bet he takes her down to Rutgers for a second opinion?"

"Academics don't give up theories easily," I said, shrugging. "I lived with one long enough to know that."

Joe snorted again. "So you did. Well, now that we've got Mr. Thompson and his dead white lady sorted out, what can I do for *you,* L.J.?"

I took a deep breath and turned to face him.

"I need an honest opinion, from somebody I can depend on to be objective. No," I amended, "I take that back. I need an opinion and then—depending on the opinion—maybe a favor."

"No problem," Joe assured me. "Especially the opinion. My specialty, opinions." He rocked back in his chair, unfolded his gold-rimmed glasses and set them firmly atop his broad nose. Then he folded his hands across his chest, fingers steepled, and nodded at me. "Shoot."

"Am I sexually attractive?" I demanded. His eyes always reminded me of toffee drops, with their warm golden-brown color. Now they went completely round, enhancing the resemblance.

Then they narrowed, but he didn't answer immediately. He looked me over carefully, head to toe.

"It's a trick question, right?" he said. "I give you an answer and one of those women's libbers jumps out from behind the door, yells 'Sexist pig!' and hits me over the head with a sign that says 'Castrate Male Chauvinists.' Huh?"

"No," I assured him. "A sexist male chauvinist answer is basically what I want."

"Oh, okay. As long as we're straight, then." He resumed his perusal, squinting closely as I stood up straight.

"Skinny white broad with too much hair, but a great ass," he said at last. "Nice tits, too," he added, with a cordial nod. "That what you want to know?"

"Yes," I said, relaxing my rigid posture. "That's exactly what I wanted to know. It isn't the sort of question you can ask just anybody."

He pursed his lips in a silent whistle, then threw back his head and roared with delight.

"Lady Jane! You've got you a *man*!"

I felt the blood rising in my cheeks, but tried to keep my dignity. "I don't know. Maybe. Just maybe."

"Maybe, hell! Jesus Christ on a piece of toast, L.J., it's about *time*!"

"Kindly quit cackling," I said, lowering myself into his visitor's chair. "It doesn't become a man of your years and station."

"My years? O*ho*," he said, peering shrewdly at me through the glasses. "He's younger than you? That's what you're worried about?"

"Not a lot," I said, the blush beginning to recede. "But I haven't seen him in twenty years. You're the only person I know who's known me for a long time; have I changed terribly since we met?" I looked at him straight on, demanding honesty.

He looked at me, took off his glasses and squinted, then replaced them.

"No," he said. "You wouldn't, though, unless you got fat."

"I wouldn't?"

"Nah. Ever been to your high school reunion?"

"I didn't go to a high school."

His sketchy brows flicked upward. "No? Well, I have. And I tell you what, L.J.; you see all these people you haven't seen for twenty years, and there's this split second when you meet somebody you used to know, when you think, 'My *God,* he's changed!,' and then all of a sudden, he hasn't—it's just like the twenty years weren't there. I mean"—he rubbed his head vigorously, struggling for meaning—"you see they've got some gray, and some lines, and maybe they aren't just the same as they were, but two minutes past that shock, and you don't see it anymore. They're just the same people they always were, and you have to make yourself stand back a ways to see that they aren't eighteen anymore.

"Now, if people get fat," he said meditatively, "*they* change some. It's harder to see who they were, because the faces change. But you"—he squinted at me again—"you're never going to be fat; you don't have the genes for it."

"I suppose not," I said. I looked down at my hands, clasped together in my lap. Slender wristbones; at least I wasn't fat yet. My rings gleamed in the autumn sun from the window.

"Is it Bree's daddy?" he asked softly.

I jerked my head up and stared at him. "How the hell did you know that?" I said.

He smiled slightly. "I've known Bree how long? Ten years, at least." He shook his head. "She's got a lot of you in her, L.J., but I've never seen anything of Frank. Daddy's got red hair, huh?" he asked. "And he's one big son of a bitch, or everything I learned in Genetics 101 was a damn lie."

"Yes," I said, and felt a kind of delirious excitement at that simple admission. Until I had told Bree herself and Roger about Jamie, I had said nothing about him for twenty years. The joy of suddenly being able to talk freely about him was intoxicating.

"Yes, he's big and red-haired, and he's Scottish," I said, making Joe's eyes go round once more.

"And Bree's in Scotland now?"

I nodded. "Bree is where the favor comes in."

Two hours later, I left the hospital for the last time, leaving behind me a letter of resignation, addressed to the Hospital Board, all the necessary documents for the handling of my property until

Brianna should be of age, and another one, to be executed at that
time, turning everything over to her. As I drove out of the parking
lot, I experienced a feeling of mingled panic, regret, and elation. I
was on my way.

21

Q.E.D.

"I found the deed of sasine." Roger's face was flushed with excitement. He had hardly been able to contain himself, waiting with open impatience at the train station in Inverness while Brianna hugged me and my bags were retrieved. He had barely got us stuffed into his tiny Morris and the car's ignition started before blurting out his news.

"What, for Lallybroch?" I leaned over the seat back between him and Brianna, in order to hear him over the noise of the motor.

"Yes, the one Jamie—your Jamie—wrote, deeding the property to his nephew, the younger Jamie."

"It's at the manse," Brianna put in, twisting to look at me. "We were afraid to bring it with us; Roger had to sign his name in blood to get it out of the SPA collection." Her fair skin was pinkened by excitement and the chilly day, raindrops in her ruddy hair. It was always a shock to me to see her again after an absence —mothers always think their children beautiful, but Bree really was.

I smiled at her, glowing with affection tinged with panic. Could I really be thinking of leaving her? Mistaking the smile for one of pleasure in the news, she went on, gripping the back of the seat in excitement.

"And you'll never guess what else we found!"

"What *you* found," Roger corrected, squeezing her knee with one hand as he negotiated the tiny orange car through a round-about. She gave him a quick glance and a reciprocal touch with an air of intimacy about it that set off my maternal alarm bells on the spot. Like that already, was it?

I seemed to feel Frank's shade glaring accusingly over my shoulder. Well, at least Roger wasn't black. I coughed and said, "Really? What is it?"

They exchanged a glance and grinned widely at each other.

"Wait and see, Mama," said Bree, with irritating smugness.

➤

"See?" she said, twenty minutes later, as I bent over the desk in the manse's study. On the battered surface of the late Reverend Wakefield's desk lay a sheaf of yellowed papers, foxed and browned at the edges. They were carefully enclosed in protective plastic covers now, but obviously had been carelessly used at one time; the edges were tattered, one sheet was torn roughly in half, and all the sheets had notes and annotations scribbled in the margins and inserted in the text. This was obviously someone's rough draft—of something.

"It's the text of an article," Roger told me, shuffling through a pile of huge folio volumes that lay on the sofa. "It was published in a sort of journal called *Forrester's,* put out by a printer called Alexander Malcolm, in Edinburgh, in 1765."

I swallowed, my shirtwaist dress feeling suddenly too tight under the arms; 1765 was almost twenty years past the time when I had left Jamie.

I stared at the scrawling letters, browned with age. They were written by someone of difficult penmanship, here cramped and there sprawling, with exaggerated loops on "g" and "y." Perhaps the writing of a left-handed man, who wrote most painfully with his right hand.

"See, here's the published version." Roger brought the opened folio to the desk and laid it before me, pointing. "See the date? It's 1765, and it matches this handwritten manuscript almost exactly; only a few of the marginal notes aren't included."

"Yes," I said. "And the deed of sasine . . ."

"Here it is." Brianna fumbled hastily in the top drawer and pulled out a much crumpled paper, likewise encased in protective plastic. Protection here was even more after the fact than with the manuscript; the paper was rain-spattered, filthy and torn, many of

the words blurred beyond recognition. But the three signatures at
the bottom still showed plainly.

By my hand, read the difficult writing, here executed with such
care that only the exaggerated loop of the "y" showed its kinship
with the careless manuscript, *James Alexander Malcolm MacKenzie Fraser.* And below, the two lines where the witnesses had
signed. In a thin, fine script, *Murtagh FitzGibbons Fraser,* and,
below that, in my own large, round hand, *Claire Beauchamp Fraser.*

I sat down quite suddenly, putting my hand over the document
instinctively, as though to deny its reality.

"That's it, isn't it?" said Roger quietly. His outward composure was belied by his hands, trembling slightly as he lifted the
stack of manuscript pages to set them next to the deed. "You
signed it. Proof positive—if we needed it," he added, with a quick
glance at Bree.

She shook her head, letting her hair fall down to hide her face.
They didn't need it, either of them. The vanishing of Geilie
Duncan through the stones five months before had been all the
evidence anyone could need as to the truth of my story.

Still, having it all laid out in black and white was rather staggering. I took my hand away and looked again at the deed, and then at
the handwritten manuscript.

"Is it the same, Mama?" Bree bent anxiously over the pages,
her hair brushing softly against my hand. "The article wasn't
signed—or it was, but with a pseudonym." She smiled briefly.
"The author signed himself 'Q.E.D.' It looked the same to us, but
we aren't either of us handwriting experts and we didn't want to
give these to an expert until you'd seen them."

"I think so." I felt breathless, but quite certain at the same
time, with an upwelling of incredulous joy. "Yes, I'm almost sure.
Jamie wrote this." Q.E.D., indeed! I had an absurd urge to tear the
manuscript pages out of their plastic shrouds and clutch them in
my hands, to feel the ink and paper he had touched; the certain
evidence that he had survived.

"There's more. Internal evidence." Roger's voice betrayed his
pride. "See there? It's an article against the Excise Act of 1764,
advocating the repeal of the restrictions on export of liquor from
the Scottish Highlands to England. Here it is"—his racing finger
stopped suddenly on a phrase—" 'for as has been known for ages

past, "Freedom and Whisky gang tegither." ' See how he's put that Scottish dialect phrase in quotes? He got it from somewhere else."

"He got it from me," I said softly. "I told him that—when he was setting out to steal Prince Charles's port."

"I remembered." Roger nodded, eyes shining with excitement. "But it's a quote from Burns," I said, frowning suddenly. "Perhaps the writer got it there—wasn't Burns alive then?"

"He was," said Bree smugly, forestalling Roger. "But Robert Burns was six years old in 1765."

"And Jamie would be forty-four." Suddenly, it all seemed real. He was alive—had been alive, I corrected myself, trying to keep my emotions in check. I laid my fingers flat against the manuscript pages, trembling.

"And if—" I said, and had to stop to swallow again.

"And if time goes on in parallel, as we think it does—" Roger stopped, too, looking at me. Then his eyes shifted to Brianna.

She had gone quite pale, but both lips and eyes were steady, and her fingers were warm when she touched my hand.

"Then you can go back, Mama," she said softly. "You can find him."

The plastic hangers rattled against the steel tubing of the dress rack as I thumbed my way slowly through the available selection.

"Can I be helpin' ye at all, miss?" The salesgirl peered up at me like a helpful Pekingese, blue-ringed eyes barely visible through bangs that brushed the top of her nose.

"Have you got any more of these old-fashioned sorts of dresses?" I gestured at the rack before me, thick with examples of the current craze—laced-bodiced, long-skirted dresses in gingham cotton and velveteen.

The salesgirl's mouth was caked so thickly that I expected the white lipstick to crack when she smiled, but it didn't.

"Oh, aye," she said. "Got a new lot o' the Jessica Gutenburgs in just today. Aren't they the grooviest, these old-style gowns?" She ran an admiring finger over a brown velvet sleeve, then whirled on her ballet flats and pointed toward the center of the store. "Just there, aye? Where it says, on the sign."

The sign, stuck on the top of a circular rack, said CAPTURE THE

CHARM OF THE EIGHTEENTH CENTURY in large white letters across the top. Just below, in curlicue script, was the signature, *Jessica Gutenburg*.

Reflecting on the basic improbability of anyone actually being named Jessica Gutenburg, I waded through the contents of the rack, pausing at a truly stunning number in cream velvet, with satin inserts and a good deal of lace.

"Look lovely on, that would." The Pekingese was back, pug nose sniffing hopefully for a sale.

"Maybe so," I said, "but not very practical. You'd get filthy just walking out of the store." I pushed the white dress away with some regret, proceeding to the next size ten.

"Oh, I just love the red ones!" The girl clasped her hands in ecstasy at the brilliant garnet fabric.

"So do I," I murmured, "but we don't want to look too garish. Wouldn't do to be taken for a prostitute, would it?" The Peke gave me a startled look through the thickets, then decided I was joking, and giggled appreciatively.

"Now, that one," she said decisively, reaching past me, "that's perfect, that is. That's your color, here."

Actually, it *was* almost perfect. Floor-length, with three-quarter sleeves edged with lace. A deep, tawny gold, with shimmers of brown and amber and sherry in the heavy silk.

I lifted it carefully off the rack and held it up to examine it. A trifle fancy, but it might do. The construction seemed halfway decent; no loose threads or unraveling seams. The machine-made lace on the bodice was just tacked on, but that would be easy enough to reinforce.

"Want to try it on? The dressing rooms are just over there." The Peke was frisking about near my elbow, encouraged by my interest. Taking a quick look at the price tag, I could see why; she must work on commission. I took a deep breath at the figure, which would cover a month's rent on a London flat, but then shrugged. After all, what did I need money for?

Still, I hesitated.

"I don't know . . ." I said doubtfully, "it is lovely. But . . ."

"Oh, don't worry a bit about it's being too young for you," the Pekingese reassured me earnestly. "You don't look a day over twenty-five! Well . . . maybe thirty," she concluded lamely, after a quick glance at my face.

"Thanks," I said dryly. "I wasn't worried about that, though. I don't suppose you have any without zippers, do you?"

"Zippers?" Her small round face went quite blank beneath the makeup. "Erm . . . no. Don't think we do."

"Well, not to worry," I said, taking the dress over my arm and turning toward the dressing room. "If I go through with this, zippers will be the least of it."

22

All Hallows' Eve

"Two golden guineas, six sovereigns, twenty-three shillings, eighteen florins ninepence, ten halfpence, and . . . twelve farthings." Roger dropped the last coin on the tinkling pile, then dug into his shirt pocket, lean face absorbed as he searched. "Oh, here." He brought out a small plastic bag and carefully poured a handful of tiny copper coins into a pile alongside the other money.

"Doits," he explained. "The smallest denomination of Scottish coinage of the time. I got as many as I could, because that's likely what you'd use most of the time. You wouldn't use the large coins unless you had to buy a horse or something."

"I know." I picked up a couple of sovereigns and tilted them in my hand, letting them clink together. They were heavy—gold coins, nearly an inch in diameter. It had taken Roger and Bree four days in London, going from one rare-coin dealer to the next, to assemble the small fortune gleaming in the lamplight before me.

"You know, it's funny; these coins are worth a lot more now than their face value," I said, picking up a golden guinea, "but in terms of what they'll buy, they were worth then just about as much as now. This is six months' income for a small farmer."

"I was forgetting," Roger said, "that you know all this already; what things were worth and how they were sold."

"It's easy to forget," I said, eyes still on the money. From the corner of my vision, I saw Bree draw suddenly close to Roger, and his hand go out to her automatically.

I took a deep breath and looked up from the tiny heaps of gold and silver. "Well, that's that. Shall we go and have some dinner?"

Dinner—at one of the pubs on River Street—was a largely silent affair. Claire and Brianna sat side by side on the banquette, with Roger opposite. They barely looked at each other while they ate, but Roger could see the frequent small touches, the tiny nudges of shoulder and hip, the brushing of fingers that went on.

How would he manage, he wondered to himself. If it were his choice, or his parent? Separation came to all families, but most often it was death that intervened, to sever the ties between parent and child. It was the element of choice here that made it so difficult—not that it could ever be easy, he thought, forking in a mouthful of hot shepherd's pie.

As they rose to leave after supper, he laid a hand on Claire's arm.

"Just for the sake of nothing," he said, "will you try something for me?"

"I expect so," she said, smiling. "What is it?"

He nodded at the door. "Close your eyes and step out of the door. When you're outside, open them. Then come in and tell me what's the first thing you saw."

Her mouth twitched with amusement. "All right. We'll hope the first thing I see isn't a policeman, or you'll have to come bail me out of jail for being drunk and disorderly."

"So long as it isn't a duck."

Claire gave him a queer look, but obediently turned toward the door of the pub and closed her eyes. Brianna watched her mother disappear through the door, hand extended to the paneling of the entry to keep her bearings. She turned to Roger, copper eyebrows raised.

"What are you up to, Roger? *Ducks*?"

"Nothing," he said, eyes still fixed on the empty entrance. "It's just an old custom. Samhain—Hallowe'en, you know?— that's one of the feasts when it was customary to try to divine the future. And one of the ways of divination was to walk to the end of the house, and then step outside with your eyes closed. The first thing you see when you open them is an omen for the near future."

"Ducks are bad omens?"

"Depends what they're doing," he said absently, still watching the entry. "If they have their heads under their wings, that's death. What's keeping her?"

"Maybe we'd better go see," Brianna said nervously. "I don't expect there are a lot of sleeping ducks in downtown Inverness, but with the river so close . . ."

Just as they reached the door, though, its stained-glass window darkened and it swung open to reveal Claire, looking mildly flustered.

"You'll never believe what's the first thing I saw," she said, laughing as she saw them.

"Not a duck with its head under its wing?" asked Brianna anxiously.

"No," her mother said, giving her a puzzled look. "A policeman. I turned to the right and ran smack into him."

"He was coming toward you, then?" Roger felt inexplicably relieved.

"Well, he was until I ran into him," she said. "Then we waltzed round the pavement a bit, clutching each other." She laughed, looking flushed and pretty, with her brown-sherry eyes sparkling in the amber pub lights. "Why?"

"That's good luck," Roger said, smiling. "To see a man coming toward you on Samhain means you'll find what you seek."

"Does it?" Her eyes rested on his, quizzical, then her face lit with a sudden smile. "Wonderful! Let's go home and celebrate, shall we?"

The anxious constraint that had lain on them over dinner seemed suddenly to have vanished, to be replaced with a sort of manic excitement, and they laughed and joked on the trip back to the manse, where they drank toasts to past and future—Loch Minneaig Scotch for Claire and Roger, Coca-Cola for Brianna—and talked excitedly about the plans for the next day. Brianna had insisted on carving a pumpkin into a jack-o'-lantern, which sat on the sideboard, grinning benevolently on the proceedings.

"You've got the money, now," Roger said, for the tenth time.

"And your cloak," Brianna chimed in.

"Yes, yes, yes," Claire said impatiently. "Everything I need— or everything I can manage, at least," she amended. She paused, then impulsively reached out and took both Bree and Roger by the hand.

"Thank you both," she said, squeezing their hands. Her eyes shone moist, and her voice was suddenly husky. "Thank you. I can't say what I feel. I can't. But—oh, my dears, I will miss you!"

Then she and Bree were in each other's arms, Claire's head tucked into her daughter's neck, both of them hugged tight, as though simple force could somehow express the depth of feeling between them.

Then they broke apart, eyes wet, and Claire laid a hand on her daughter's cheek. "I'd better go up now," she whispered. "There are things to do, still. I'll see you in the morning, baby." She rose on tiptoe to plant a kiss on her daughter's nose, then turned and hurried from the room.

After her mother's exit, Brianna sat down again with her glass of Coke, and heaved a deep sigh. She didn't speak, but sat looking into the fire, turning the glass slowly between her hands.

Roger busied himself, setting the room to rights for the night, closing the windows, tidying the desk, putting away the reference books he had used to help Claire prepare for her journey. He paused by the jack-o'-lantern, but it looked so jolly, with the candlelight streaming from its slanted eyes and jagged mouth, that he couldn't bring himself to blow it out.

"I shouldn't think it's likely to set anything on fire," he remarked. "Shall we leave it?"

There was no answer. When he glanced at Brianna, he found her sitting still as stone, eyes fixed on the hearth. She hadn't heard him. He sat down beside her and took her hand.

"She might be able to come back," he said gently. "We don't know."

Brianna shook her head slowly, not taking her eyes from the leaping flames.

"I don't think so," she said softly. "She told you what it was like. She may not even make it through." Long fingers drummed restlessly on a denimed thigh.

Roger glanced at the door, to be sure that Claire was safely upstairs, then sat down on the sofa next to Brianna.

"She belongs with him, Bree," he said. "Can ye not see it? When she speaks of him?"

"I see it. I know she needs him." The full lower lip trembled slightly. "But . . . I need *her*!" Brianna's hands clenched suddenly tight on her knees, and she bent forward, as though trying to contain some sudden pain.

Roger stroked her hair, marveling at the softness of the glowing strands that slid through his fingers. He wanted to take her into his arms, as much for the feel of her as to offer comfort, but she was rigid and unresponsive.

"You're grown, Bree," he said softly. "You live on your own now, don't you? You may love her, but you don't need her anymore—not the way you did when you were small. Has she no right to her own joy?"

"Yes. But . . . Roger, you don't understand!" she burst out. She pressed her lips tight together and swallowed hard, then turned to him, eyes dark with distress.

"She's all that's left, Roger! The only one who really *knows* me. She and Daddy—Frank"—she corrected herself—"they were the ones who knew me from the beginning, the ones who saw me learn to walk and were proud of me when I did something good in school, and who—" She broke off, and the tears overflowed, leaving gleaming tracks in the firelight.

"This sounds really *dumb*," she said with sudden violence. "Really, really *dumb*! But it's—" she groped, helpless, then sprang to her feet, unable to stay still.

"It's like—there are all these things I don't even know!" she said, pacing with quick, angry steps. "Do you think I remember what I looked like, learning to walk, or what the first word I said was? No, but Mama does! And that's so *stupid,* because what difference does it make, it doesn't make any difference at all, but it's important, it matters because *she* thought it was, and . . . oh, Roger, if she's gone, there won't be a soul left in the world who cares what I'm like, or thinks I'm special not because of anything, but just because I'm me! She's the only person in the world who really, really cares I was born, and if she's gone . . ." She stood still on the hearthrug, hands clenched at her sides, and mouth twisted with the effort to control herself, tears wet on her cheeks. Then her shoulders slumped and the tension went out of her tall figure.

"And that's just really dumb and selfish," she said, in a quietly reasonable tone. "And you don't understand, and you think I'm awful."

"No," Roger said quietly. "I think maybe not." He stood and came behind her, putting his arms around her waist, urging her to lean back against him. She resisted at first, stiff in his arms, but then yielded to the need for physical comfort and relaxed, his chin propped on her shoulder, head tilted to touch her own.

"I never realized," he said. "Not 'til now. D'ye remember all those boxes in the garage?"

"Which ones?" she said, with a sniffling attempt at a laugh. "There are hundreds."

"The ones that say 'Roger' on them." He gave her a slight squeeze and brought his arms up, crisscrossed on her chest, holding her snug against himself.

"They're full of my parents' old clobber," he said. "Pictures and letters and baby clothes and books and old bits of rubbish. The Reverend packed them up when he took me to live with him. Treated them just like his most precious historical documents—double-boxing, and mothproofing and all that."

He rocked slowly back and forth, swaying from side to side, carrying her with him as he watched the fire over her shoulder.

"I asked him once why he bothered to keep them—I didn't want any of it, didn't care. But he said we'd keep it just the same; it was my history, he said—and everyone needs a history."

Brianna sighed, and her body seemed to relax still further, joining him in his rhythmic, half-unconscious sway.

"Did you ever look inside them?"

He shook his head. "It isn't important what's in them," he said. "Only that they're there."

He let go of her then, and stepped back so that she turned to face him. Her face was blotched and her long, elegant nose a little swollen.

"You're wrong, you know," he said softly, and held out his hand to her. "It isn't only your mother who cares."

Brianna had gone to bed long since, but Roger sat on in the study, watching the flames die down in the hearth. Hallowe'en had always seemed to him a restless night, alive with waking spirits. Tonight was even more so, with the knowledge of what would happen in the morning. The jack-o'-lantern on the desk grinned in anticipation, filling the room with the homely scent of baking pies.

The sound of a footfall on the stair roused him from his thoughts. He had thought it might be Brianna, unable to sleep, but the visitor was Claire.

"I thought you might still be awake," she said. She was in her nightdress, a pale glimmer of white satin against the dark hallway.

He smiled and stretched out a hand, inviting her in. "No. I never could sleep on All Hallows'. Not after all the stories my father told me; I always thought I could hear ghosts talking outside my window."

She smiled, coming into the firelight. "And what did they say?"

" 'See'st thou this great gray head, with jaws which have no meat?' " Roger quoted. "You know the story? The little tailor who spent the night in a haunted church, and met the hungry ghost?"

"I do. I think if I'd heard *that* outside my window, I'd have spent the rest of the night hiding under the bedclothes."

"Oh, I usually did," Roger assured her. "Though once, when I was seven or so, I got up my nerve, stood up on the bed and peed on the windowsill—the Reverend had just told me that pissing on the doorposts is supposed to keep a ghost from coming in the house."

Claire laughed delightedly, the firelight dancing in her eyes. "Did it work?"

"Well, it would have worked better had the window been open," Roger said, "but the ghosts didn't come in, no."

They laughed together, and then one of the small awkward silences that had punctuated the evening fell between them, the sudden realization of enormity gaping beneath the tightrope of conversation. Claire sat beside him, watching the fire, her hands moving restlessly among the folds of her gown. The light winked from her wedding rings, silver and gold, in sparks of fire.

"I'll take care of her, you know," Roger said quietly, at last. "You do know that, don't you?"

Claire nodded, not looking at him.

"I know," she said softly. He could see the tears, caught trembling at the edge of her lashes, glowing with firelight. She fumbled in the pocket of her gown, and drew out a long white envelope.

"You'll think me a dreadful coward," she said, "and I am. But I . . . I honestly don't think I can do it—say goodbye to Bree, I mean.'' She stopped, to bring her voice under control, and then held out the envelope to him.

''I wrote it all down for her—everything I could. Will you . . . ?''

Roger took the envelope. It was warm from resting next to her body. From some obscure feeling that it must not be allowed to grow cold before it reached her daughter, he thrust it into his own breast pocket, feeling the crackle of paper as the envelope bent.

''Yes,'' he said, hearing his own voice thicken. ''Then you'll go . . .''

''Early,'' she said, taking a deep breath. ''Before dawn. I've arranged for a car to pick me up.'' Her hands twisted together in her lap. ''If I—'' She bit her lip, then looked at Roger pleadingly. ''I don't know, you see,'' she said. ''I don't know whether I can do it. I'm very much afraid. Afraid to go. Afraid not to go. Just—afraid.''

''I would be, too.'' He held out his hand and she took it. He held it for a long time, feeling the pulse in her wrist, light and fast against his fingers.

After a long time, she squeezed his hand gently and let go.

''Thank you, Roger,'' she said. ''For everything.'' She leaned over and kissed him lightly on the lips. Then she rose and went out, a white ghost in the darkness of the hall, borne on the Hallowe'en wind.

Roger sat on for some time alone, feeling her touch still warm on his skin. The jack-o'-lantern was nearly burned out. The smell of candle wax rose strongly in the restless air, and the pagan gods looked out for the last time, through eyes of guttering flame.

23

Craigh na Dun

The early morning air was cold and misty, and I was glad of the cloak. It had been twenty years since I'd worn one, but with the sorts of things people wore nowadays, the Inverness tailor who'd made it for me had not found an order for a woolen cloak with a hood at all odd.

I kept my eyes on the path. The crest of the hill had been invisible, wreathed in mist, when the car had left me on the road below.

"Here?" the driver had said, peering dubiously out of his window at the deserted countryside. "Sure, mum?"

"Yes," I'd said, half-choked with terror. "This is the place."

"Aye?" He looked dubious, in spite of the large note I put in his hand. "D'ye want me to wait, mum? Or to come later, to fetch ye back?"

I was sorely tempted to say yes. After all, what if I lost my nerve? At the moment, my grip on that slippery substance seemed remarkably feeble.

"No," I said, swallowing. "No, that won't be necessary." If I couldn't do it, I would just have to walk back to Inverness, that was all. Or perhaps Roger and Brianna would come; I thought that would be worse, to be ignominiously retrieved. Or would it be a relief?

The granite pebbles rolled beneath my feet and a clod of dirt fell in a small rushing shower, dislodged by my passage. I couldn't possibly really be doing this, I thought. The weight of the money in my reinforced pocket swung against my thigh, the heavy certainty of gold and silver a reminder of reality. I *was* doing it.

I couldn't. Thoughts of Bree as I had seen her late last night, peacefully asleep in her bed, assaulted me. The tendrils of remembered horror reached out from the hilltop above, as I began to sense the nearness of the stones. Screaming, chaos, the feeling of being torn in pieces. I couldn't.

I couldn't, but I kept on climbing, palms sweating, my feet moving as though no longer under my control.

It was full dawn by the time I reached the top of the hill. The mist lay below, and the stones stood clear and dark against a crystal sky. The sight of them left me wet-palmed with apprehension, but I walked forward, and passed into the circle.

They were standing on the grass in front of the cleft stone, facing each other. Brianna heard my footsteps and whirled around to face me.

I stared at her, speechless with astonishment. She was wearing a Jessica Gutenburg dress, very much like the one I had on, except that hers was a vivid lime green, with plastic jewels stitched across the bosom.

"That's a perfectly horrible color for you," I said.

"It's the only one they had in my size," she answered calmly.

"What in the name of goodness are you doing here?" I demanded, recovering some remnant of coherence.

"We came to see you off," she said, and a hint of a smile flickered on her lips. I looked at Roger, who shrugged slightly and gave me a lopsided smile of his own.

"Oh. Yes. Well," I said. The stone stood behind Brianna, twice the height of a man. I could look through the foot-wide crack, and see the faint morning sun shining on the grass outside the circle.

"You're going," she said firmly, "or I am."

"You! Are you out of your mind?"

"No." She glanced at the cleft stone and swallowed. It might have been the lime-green dress that made her face look chalk-white. "I can do it—go through, I mean. I know I can. When Geilie Duncan went through the stones, I heard them. Roger did too." She glanced at him as though for reassurance, then fixed her gaze firmly on me.

"I don't know whether I could find Jamie Fraser or not; maybe only you can. But if you won't try, then I will."

My mouth opened, but I couldn't find anything to say.

"Don't you see, Mama? He has to know—has to know he did it, he did what he meant to for us." Her lips quivered, and she pressed them together for a minute.

"We owe it to him, Mama," she said softly. "Somebody has to find him, and tell him." Her hand touched my face, briefly. "Tell him I was born."

"Oh, Bree," I said, my voice so choked I could barely speak. "Oh, Bree!"

She was holding my hands tight between her own, squeezing hard.

"He gave you to me," she said, so low I could hardly hear her. "Now I have to give you back to him, Mama."

The eyes that were so like Jamie's looked down at me, blurred by tears.

"If you find him," she whispered, "when you find my father— give him this." She bent and kissed me, fiercely, gently, then straightened and turned me toward the stone.

"Go, Mama," she said, breathless. "I love you. Go!"

From the corner of my eye, I saw Roger move toward her. I took one step, and then another. I heard a sound, a faint roaring. I took the last step, and the world disappeared.

PART SIX

Edinburgh

24

A. Malcolm, Printer

y first coherent thought was "It's raining. This must be Scotland." My second thought was that this observation was no great improvement over the random images jumbling around inside my head, banging into each other and setting off small synaptic explosions of irrelevance.

I opened one eye, with some difficulty. The lid was stuck shut, and my entire face felt cold and puffy, like a submerged corpse's. I shuddered faintly at the thought, the slight movement making me aware of the sodden fabric all around me.

It was certainly raining—a soft, steady drum of rain that raised a faint mist of droplets above the green moor. I sat up, feeling like a hippopotamus emerging from a bog, and promptly fell over backward.

I blinked and closed my eyes against the downpour. Some small sense of who I was—and where I was—was beginning to come back to me. *Bree.* Her face emerged suddenly into memory, with a jolt that made me gasp as though I'd been punched in the stomach. Jagged images of loss and the rip of separation pulled at me, a faint echo of the chaos in the stone passage.

Jamie. There it was; the anchor point to which I had clung, my single hold on sanity. I breathed slow and deep, hands folded over my pounding heart, summoning Jamie's face. For a moment, I thought I had lost him, and then it came, clear and bold in my mind's eye.

Once again, I struggled upright, and this time stayed, propped by my outstretched hands. Yes, certainly it was Scotland. It could hardly be anything else, of course, but it was also the Scotland of the past. At least, I *hoped* it was the past. It wasn't the Scotland I'd left, at any rate. The trees and bushes grew in different patterns; there was a patch of maple saplings just below me that hadn't been there when I'd climbed the hill—when? That morning? Two days ago?

I had no idea how much time had passed since I had entered the standing stones, or how long I had lain unconscious on the hillside below the circle. Quite a while, judging from the sogginess of my clothing; I was soaked through to the skin, and small chilly rivulets ran down my sides under my gown.

One numbed cheek was beginning to tingle; putting my hand to it, I could feel a pattern of incised bumps. I looked down and saw a layer of fallen rowan berries, gleaming red and black among the grass. Very appropriate, I thought, vaguely amused. I had fallen down under a rowan—the Highland protection against witchcraft and enchantment.

I grasped the smooth trunk of the rowan tree, and laboriously hauled myself to my feet. Still holding onto the tree for support, I looked to the northeast. The rain had faded the horizon to a gray invisibility, but I knew that Inverness lay in that direction. No more than an hour's trip by car, along modern roads.

The road existed; I could see the outline of a rough track that led along the base of the hill, a dark, silvery line in the gleaming green wetness of the moor plants. However, forty-odd miles on foot was a far cry from the journey by car that had brought me here.

I was beginning to feel somewhat better, standing up. The weakness in my limbs was fading, along with the feeling of chaos and disruption in my mind. It had been as bad as I'd feared, this passage; perhaps worse. I could feel the terrible presence of the stones above me, and shuddered, my skin prickling with cold.

I was alive, though. Alive, and with a small feeling of certainty, like a tiny glowing sun beneath my ribs. *He was here.* I knew it now, though I hadn't known it when I threw myself between the stones; that had been a leap of faith. But I had cast out my thought of Jamie like a lifeline tossed into a raging torrent—and the line had tightened in my grasp, and pulled me free.

I was wet, cold, and felt battered, as though I had been washing about in the surf against a rocky shore. But I was here. And somewhere in this strange country of the past was the man I had come to find. The memories of grief and terror were receding, as I realized that my die was cast. I could not go back; a return trip would almost surely be fatal. As I realized that I was likely here to stay, all hesitations and terrors were superseded by a strange calm, almost exultant. I could not go back. There was nothing to do but go forward—to find him.

Cursing my carelessness in not having thought to tell the tailor to make my cloak with a waterproof layer between fabric and lining, I pulled the water-soaked garment closer. Even wet, the wool held some warmth. If I began to move, I would grow warmer. A quick pat reassured me that my bundle of sandwiches had made the trip with me. That was good; the thought of walking forty miles on an empty stomach was a daunting one.

With luck, I wouldn't have to. I might find a village or a house that had a horse I could buy. But if not, I was prepared. My plan was to go to Inverness—by whatever means offered itself—and there take a public coach to Edinburgh.

There was no telling where Jamie was at the moment. He might be in Edinburgh, where his article had been published, but he might easily be somewhere else. If I could not find him there, I could go to Lallybroch, his home. Surely his family would know where he was—if any of them were left. The sudden thought chilled me, and I shivered.

I thought of a small bookstore that I passed every morning on my way from the parking lot to the hospital. They had been having a sale on posters; I had seen the display of psychedelic examples when I left Joe's office for the last time.

"Today is the first day of the rest of your life," said one poster, above an illustration of a foolish-looking chick, absurdly poking its head out of an eggshell. In the other window, another poster showed a caterpillar, inching its way up a flower stalk. Above the stalk soared a brilliantly colored butterfly, and below was the motto "A journey of a thousand miles begins with a single step."

The most irritating thing about clichés, I decided, was how frequently they were true. I let go of the rowan tree, and started down the hill toward my future.

It was a long, jolting ride from Inverness to Edinburgh, crammed cheek by jowl into a large coach with two other ladies, the small and whiny son of one of the ladies, and four gentlemen of varying sizes and dispositions.

Mr. Graham, a small and vivacious gentleman of advanced years who was seated next to me, was wearing a bag of camphor and asafoetida about his neck, to the eyewatering discomfort of the rest of the coach.

"Capital for dispelling the evil humors of influenza," he explained to me, waving the bag gently under my nose like a censer. "I have worn this daily through the autumn and winter months, and haven't been sick a day in nearly thirty years!"

"Amazing!" I said politely, trying to hold my breath. I didn't doubt it; the fumes probably kept everyone at such a distance that germs couldn't reach him.

The effects on the little boy didn't seem nearly so beneficial. After a number of loud and injudicious remarks about the smell in the coach, Master Georgie had been muffled in his mother's bosom, from which he now peeped, looking rather green. I kept a close eye on him, as well as on the chamber pot beneath the seat opposite, in case quick action involving a conjunction of the two should be called for.

I gathered that the chamber pot was for use in inclement weather or other emergency, as normally the ladies' modesty required stops every hour or so, at which point the passengers would scatter into the roadside vegetation like a covey of quail, even those who did not require relief of bladder or bowels seeking some relief from the stench of Mr. Graham's asafoetida bag.

After one or two changes, Mr. Graham found his place beside me superseded by Mr. Wallace, a plump young lawyer, returning to Edinburgh after seeing to the disposition of the estate of an elderly relative in Inverness, as he explained to me.

I didn't find the details of his legal practice nearly as fascinating as he did, but under the circumstances, his evident attraction to me was mildly reassuring, and I passed several hours in playing with him upon a small chess set that he produced from a pocket and laid upon his knee.

My attention was distracted both from the discomforts of the journey and the intricacies of chess by anticipation of what I might find in Edinburgh. A. Malcolm. The name kept running through my mind like an anthem of hope. A. Malcolm. It had to be Jamie, it simply had to! James Alexander Malcolm MacKenzie Fraser.

"Considering the way the Highland rebels were treated after Culloden, it would be very reasonable for him to use an assumed name in a place like Edinburgh," Roger Wakefield had explained to me. "Particularly him—he was a convicted traitor, after all. Made rather a habit of it, too, it looks like," he had added critically, looking over the scrawled manuscript of the antitax diatribe. "For the times, this is bloody near sedition."

"Yes, that sounds like Jamie," I had said dryly, but my heart had leapt at the sight of that distinctively untidy scrawl, with its boldly worded sentiments. My Jamie. I touched the small hard rectangle in my skirt pocket, wondering how long it would be, before we reached Edinburgh.

The weather kept unseasonably fine, with no more than the occasional drizzle to hinder our passage, and we completed the journey in less than two days, stopping four times to change horses and refresh ourselves at posthouse taverns.

The coach debouched into a yard at the back of Boyd's Whitehorse tavern, near the foot of the Royal Mile in Edinburgh. The passengers emerged into the watery sunshine like newly hatched chrysalids, rumpled of wing and jerky in movement, unaccustomed to mobility. After the dimness of the coach, even the cloudy gray light of Edinburgh seemed blinding.

I had pins and needles in my feet from so long sitting, but hurried nonetheless, hoping to escape from the courtyard while my erstwhile companions were busy with the retrieval of their belongings. No such luck; Mr. Wallace caught up with me near the street.

"Mrs. Fraser!" he said. "Might I beg the pleasure of accompanying you to your destination? You will surely require some assistance in the removal of your luggage." He looked over his shoulder toward the coach, where the ostlers were heaving the bags and portmanteaux apparently at random into the crowd, to the accompaniment of incoherent grunts and shouts.

"Er . . ." I said. "Thank you, but I . . . er, I'm leaving my luggage in charge of the landlord. My . . . my . . ." I groped frantically. "My husband's servant will come fetch it later."

His plump face fell slightly at the word "husband," but he rallied gallantly, taking my hand and bowing low over it.

"I quite see. May I express my profound appreciation for the pleasure of your company on our journey, then, Mrs. Fraser? And perhaps we shall meet again." He straightened up, surveying the crowd that eddied past us. "Is your husband meeting you? I should be delighted to make his acquaintance."

While Mr. Wallace's interest in me had been rather flattering, it was rapidly becoming a nuisance.

"No, I shall be joining him later," I said. "So nice to have met you, Mr. Wallace; I'll hope to see you again sometime." I shook Mr. Wallace's hand enthusiastically, which disconcerted him enough for me to slither off through the throng of passengers, ostlers, and food sellers.

I didn't dare pause near the coachyard for fear he would come out after me. I turned and darted up the slope of the Royal Mile, moving as quickly as my voluminous skirts would allow, jostling and bumping my way through the crowd. I had had the luck to pick a market day for my arrival, and I was soon lost to sight from the coachyard among the luckenbooths and oyster sellers who lined the street.

Panting like an escaped pickpocket, I stopped for breath halfway up the hill. There was a public fountain here, and I sat down on the rim to catch my breath.

I was here. Really here. Edinburgh sloped up behind me, to the glowering heights of Edinburgh Castle, and down before me, to the gracious majesty of Holyrood Palace at the foot of the city.

The last time I had stood by this fountain, Bonnie Prince Charlie had been addressing the gathered citizenry of Edinburgh, inspiring them with the sight of his royal presence. He had bounded exuberantly from the rim to the carved center finial of the fountain, one foot in the basin, clinging to one of the spouting heads for support, shouting "On to England!" The crowd had roared, pleased at this show of youthful high spirits and athletic prowess. I would myself have been more impressed had I not noticed that the water in the fountain had been turned off in anticipation of the gesture.

I wondered where Charlie was now. He had gone back to Italy after Culloden, I supposed, there to live whatever life was possible for royalty in permanent exile. What he was doing, I neither knew nor cared. He had passed from the pages of history, and from my life as well, leaving wreck and ruin in his wake. It remained to be seen what might be salvaged now.

I was very hungry; I had had nothing to eat since a hasty breakfast of rough parritch and boiled mutton, made soon after dawn at a posthouse in Dundaff. I had one last sandwich remaining in my pocket, but had been reluctant to eat it in the coach, under the curious gaze of my fellow travelers.

I pulled it out and carefully unwrapped it. Peanut butter and jelly on white bread, it was considerably the worse for wear, with the purple stains of the jelly seeping through the limp bread, and the whole thing mashed into a flattened wodge. It was delicious.

I ate it carefully, savoring the rich, oily taste of the peanut butter. How many mornings had I slathered peanut butter on bread, making sandwiches for Brianna's school lunches? Firmly suppressing the thought, I examined the passersby for distraction. They did look somewhat different from their modern equivalents; both men and women tended to be shorter, and the signs of poor nutrition were evident. Still, there was an overwhelming familiarity to them—these were people I knew, Scots and English for the most part, and hearing the rich burring babble of voices in the street, after so many years of the flat nasal tones of Boston, I had quite an extraordinary feeling of coming home.

I swallowed the last rich, sweet bite of my old life, and crumpled the wrapper in my hand. I glanced around, but no one was looking in my direction. I opened my hand, and let the bit of plastic film fall surreptitiously to the ground. Wadded up, it rolled a few inches on the cobbles, crinkling and unfolding itself as though alive. The light wind caught it, and the small transparent sheet took sudden wing, scudding over the gray stones like a leaf.

The draft of a set of passing wheels sucked it under a drayman's cart; it winked once with reflected light, and was gone, disappearing without notice from the passersby. I wondered whether my own anachronistic presence would cause as little harm.

"You are dithering, Beauchamp," I said to myself. "Time to get on." I took a deep breath and stood up.

"Excuse me," I said, catching the sleeve of a passing baker's boy. "I'm looking for a printer—a Mr. Malcolm. Alexander Malcolm." A feeling of mingled dread and excitement gurgled through my middle. What if there was no printshop run by Alexander Malcolm in Edinburgh?

There was, though; the boy's face screwed up in thought and then relaxed.

"Oh, aye, mum—just down the way and to your left. Carfax Close." And hitching his loaves up under his arm with a nod, he plunged back into the crowded street.

Carfax Close. I edged my way back into the crowd, pressing close to the buildings, to avoid the occasional shower of slops that splattered into the street from the windows high above. There were several thousand people in Edinburgh, and the sewage from all of them was running down the gutters of the cobbled street, depending on gravity and the frequent rain to keep the city habitable.

The low, dark opening to Carfax Close yawned just ahead, across the expanse of the Royal Mile. I stopped dead, looking at it, my heart beating hard enough to be heard a yard away, had anyone been listening.

It wasn't raining, but was just about to, and the dampness in the air made my hair curl. I pushed it off my forehead, tidying it as best I could without a mirror. Then I caught sight of a large plate-glass window up ahead, and hurried forward.

The glass was misty with condensation, but provided a dim reflection, in which my face looked flushed and wide-eyed, but otherwise presentable. My hair, however, had seized the opportunity to curl madly in all directions, and was writhing out of its hairpins in excellent imitation of Medusa's locks. I yanked the pins out impatiently, and began to twist up my curls.

There was a woman inside the shop, leaning across the counter. There were three small children with her, and I watched with half an eye as she turned from her business to address them impatiently, swatting with her reticule at the middle one, a boy who was fiddling with several stalks of fresh anise that stood in a pail of water on the floor.

It was an apothecary's shop; glancing up, I saw the name "Haugh" above the door, and felt a thrill of recognition. I had bought herbs here, during the brief time I had lived in Edinburgh. The decor of the window had been augmented sometime since by the addition of a large jar of colored water, in which floated something vaguely humanoid. A fetal pig, or perhaps an infant baboon; it had leering, flattened features that pressed against the rounded side of the jar in a disconcerting fashion.

"Well, at least I look better than *you*!" I muttered, shoving in a recalcitrant pin.

I looked better than the woman inside, too, I thought. Her business concluded, she was stuffing her purchase into the bag she carried, her thin face frowning as she did so. She had the rather pasty look of a city dweller, and her skin was deeply lined, with sharp creases running from nose to mouth, and a furrowed forehead.

"De'il tak' ye, ye wee ratten," she was saying crossly to the little boy as they all clattered out of the shop together. "Have I no told ye time and again to keep yer paws in yer pockets?"

"Excuse me." I stepped forward, interrupting, impelled by a sudden irresistible curiosity.

"Aye?" Distracted from maternal remonstration, she looked blankly at me. Up close, she looked even more harried. The corners of her mouth were pinched, and her lips folded in—no doubt because of missing teeth.

"I couldn't help admiring your children," I said, with as much pretense of admiration as I could manage on short notice. I beamed kindly at them. "Such pretty babies! Tell me, how old are they?"

Her jaw dropped, confirming the absence of several teeth. She blinked at me, then said, "Oh! Well, that's maist kind o' ye, mum. Ah . . . Maisri here is ten," she said, nodding at the eldest girl, who was in the act of wiping her nose on her sleeve, "Joey's eight —tak' yer finger out o' yer nose, ye clattie imp!" she scolded, then turned and proudly patted her youngest on the head. "And wee Polly's just turned six this May."

"Really!" I gazed at the woman, affecting astonishment. "You scarcely look old enough to have children of that age. You must have married very young."

She preened slightly, smirking.

"Och, no! Not so young as all that; why, I was all o' nineteen when Maisri was born."

"Amazing," I said, meaning it. I dug in my pocket and offered the children each a penny, which they took with shy bobs of thanks. "Good day to you—and congratulations on your lovely family," I said to the woman, and walked away with a smile and a wave.

Nineteen when the eldest was born, and Maisri was ten now.

She was twenty-nine. And I, blessed by good nutrition, hygiene, and dentistry, not worn down by multiple pregnancies and hard physical labor, looked a good deal younger than she. I took a deep breath, pushed back my hair, and marched into the shadows of Carfax Close.

It was a longish, winding close, and the printshop was at the foot. There were thriving businesses and tenements on either side, but I had no attention to spare for anything beyond the neat white sign that hung by the door.

A. MALCOLM

PRINTER AND BOOKSELLER

it said, and beneath this, *Books, calling cards, pamphlets, broadsheets, letters, etc.*

I stretched out my hand and touched the black letters of the name. A. Malcolm. Alexander Malcolm. James Alexander Malcolm MacKenzie Fraser. Perhaps.

Another minute, and I would lose my nerve. I shoved open the door and walked in.

There was a broad counter across the front of the room, with an open flap in it, and a rack to one side that held several trays of type. Posters and notices of all sorts were tacked up on the opposite wall; samples, no doubt.

The door into the back room was open, showing the bulky angular frame of a printing press. Bent over it, his back turned to me, was Jamie.

"Is that you, Geordie?" he asked, not turning around. He was dressed in shirt and breeches, and had a small tool of some kind in his hand, with which he was doing something to the innards of the press. "Took ye long enough. Did ye get the—"

"It isn't Geordie," I said. My voice was higher than usual. "It's me," I said. "Claire."

He straightened up very slowly. He wore his hair long; a thick tail of a deep, rich auburn sparked with copper. I had time to see that the neat ribbon that tied it back was green, and then he turned around.

He stared at me without speaking. A tremor ran down the muscular throat as he swallowed, but still he didn't say anything.

It was the same broad, good-humored face, dark blue eyes aslant the high, flat cheekbones of a Viking, long mouth curling at the ends as though always on the verge of smiling. The lines surrounding eyes and mouth were deeper, of course. The nose had changed just a bit. The knife-edge bridge was slightly thickened near the base by the ridge of an old, healed fracture. It made him look fiercer, I thought, but lessened that air of aloof reserve, and lent his appearance a new rough charm.

I walked through the flap in the counter, seeing nothing but that unblinking stare. I cleared my throat.

"When did you break your nose?"

The corners of the wide mouth lifted slightly.

"About three minutes after I last saw ye—Sassenach."

There was a hesitation, almost a question in the name. There was no more than a foot between us. I reached out tentatively and touched the tiny line of the break, where the bone pressed white against the bronze of his skin.

He flinched backward as though an electric spark had arced between us, and the calm expression shattered.

"You're real," he whispered. I had thought him pale already. Now all vestiges of color drained from his face. His eyes rolled up and he slumped to the floor in a shower of papers and oddments that had been sitting on the press—he fell rather gracefully for such a large man, I thought abstractedly.

It was only a faint; his eyelids were beginning to flutter by the time I knelt beside him and loosened the stock at his throat. I had no doubts at all by now, but still I looked automatically as I pulled the heavy linen away. It was there, of course, the small triangular scar just above the collarbone, left by the knife of Captain Jonathan Randall, Esquire, of His Majesty's Eighth Dragoons.

His normal healthy color was returning. I sat cross-legged on the floor and hoisted his head onto my thigh. His hair felt thick and soft in my hand. His eyes opened.

"That bad, is it?" I said, smiling down at him with the same words he had used to me on the day of our wedding, holding my head in his lap, twenty-odd years before.

"That bad, and worse, Sassenach," he answered, mouth twitching with something almost a smile. He sat up abruptly, staring at me.

"God in heaven, you *are* real!"

"So are you." I lifted my chin to look up at him. "I th-thought you were dead." I had meant to speak lightly, but my voice betrayed me. The tears spilled down my cheeks, only to soak into the rough cloth of his shirt as he pulled me hard against him.

I shook so that it was some time before I realized that he was shaking, too, and for the same reason. I don't know how long we sat there on the dusty floor, crying in each other's arms with the longing of twenty years spilling down our faces.

His fingers twined hard in my hair, pulling it loose so that it tumbled down my neck. The dislodged pins cascaded over my shoulders and pinged on the floor like pellets of hail. My own fingers were clasped around his forearm, digging into the linen as though I were afraid he would disappear unless physically restrained.

As though gripped by the same fear, he suddenly grasped me by the shoulders and held me away from him, staring desperately into my face. He put his hand to my cheek, and traced the bones over and over again, oblivious to my tears and to my abundantly running nose.

I sniffed loudly, which seemed to bring him to his senses, for he let go and groped hastily in his sleeve for a handkerchief, which he used clumsily to swab first my face, then his own.

"Give me that." I grabbed the erratically waving swatch of cloth and blew my nose firmly. "Now you." I handed him the cloth and watched as he blew his nose with a noise like a strangled goose. I giggled, undone with emotion.

He smiled too, knuckling the tears away from his eyes, unable to stop staring at me.

Suddenly I couldn't bear not to be touching him. I lunged at him, and he got his arms up just in time to catch me. I squeezed until I could hear his ribs crack, and felt his hands roughly caressing my back as he said my name over and over.

At last I could let go, and sat back a little. He glanced down at the floor between his legs, frowning.

"Did you lose something?" I asked, surprised.

He looked up and smiled, a little shyly.

"I was afraid I'd lost hold altogether and pissed myself, but it's all right. I've just sat on the alepot."

Sure enough, a pool of aromatic brown liquid was spreading slowly beneath him. With a squeak of alarm, I scrambled to my feet and helped him up. After trying vainly to assess the damage behind, he shrugged and unfastened his breeches. He pushed the tight fabric down over his haunches, then stopped and looked at me, blushing slightly.

"It's all right," I said, feeling a rich blush stain my own cheeks. "We're married." I cast my eyes down, nonetheless, feeling a little breathless. "At least, I suppose we are."

He stared at me for a long moment, then a smile curved his wide, soft mouth.

"Aye, we are," he said. Kicking free of the stained breeches, he stepped toward me.

I stretched out a hand toward him, as much to stop as to welcome him. I wanted more than anything to touch him again, but was unaccountably shy. After so long, how were we to start again?

He felt the constraint of mingled shyness and intimacy as well. Stopping a few inches from me, he took my hand. He hesitated for a moment, then bent his head over it, his lips barely brushing my knuckles. His fingers touched the silver ring and stopped there, holding the metal lightly between thumb and forefinger.

"I never took it off," I blurted. It seemed important he should know that. He squeezed my hand lightly, but didn't let go.

"I want—" He stopped and swallowed, still holding my hand. His fingers found and touched the silver ring once more. "I want verra much to kiss you," he said softly. "May I do that?"

The tears were barely dammed. Two more welled up and overflowed; I felt them, full and round, roll down my cheeks.

"Yes," I whispered.

He drew me slowly close to him, holding our linked hands just under his breast.

"I havena done this for a verra long time," he said. I saw the hope and the fear dark in the blue of his eyes. I took the gift and gave it back to him.

"Neither have I," I said softly.

His hands cupped my face with exquisite gentleness, and he set his mouth on mine.

I didn't know quite what I had been expecting. A reprise of the

pounding fury that had accompanied our final parting? I had remembered that so often, lived it over in memory, helpless to
change the outcome. The half-rough, timeless hours of mutual
possession in the darkness of our marriage bed? I had longed for
that, wakened often sweating and trembling from the memory of
it.

But we were strangers now, barely touching, each seeking the
way toward joining, slowly, tentatively, seeking and giving unspoken permission with our silent lips. My eyes were closed, and I
knew without looking that Jamie's were, as well. We were, quite
simply, afraid to look at each other.

Without raising his head, he began to stroke me lightly, feeling
my bones through my clothes, familiarizing himself again with the
terrain of my body. At last his hand traveled down my arm and
caught my right hand. His fingers traced my hand until they found
the ring again, and circled it, feeling the interlaced silver of the
Highland pattern, polished with long wear, but still distinct.

His lips moved from mine, across my cheeks and eyes. I gently
stroked his back, feeling through his shirt the marks I couldn't see,
the remnants of old scars, like my ring, worn but still distinct.

"I've seen ye so many times," he said, his voice whispering
warm in my ear. "You've come to me so often. When I dreamed
sometimes. When I lay in fever. When I was so afraid and so
lonely I knew I must die. When I needed you, I would always see
ye, smiling, with your hair curling up about your face. But ye
never spoke. And ye never touched me."

"I can touch you now." I reached up and drew my hand gently
down his temple, his ear, the cheek and jaw that I could see. My
hand went to the nape of his neck, under the clubbed bronze hair,
and he raised his head at last, and cupped my face between his
hands, love glowing strong in the dark blue eyes.

"Dinna be afraid," he said softly. "There's the two of us
now."

We might have gone on standing there gazing at each other
indefinitely, had the shop bell over the door not rung. I let go of
Jamie and looked around sharply, to see a small, wiry man with
coarse dark hair standing in the door, mouth agape, holding a
small parcel in one hand.

"Oh, there ye are, Geordie! What's kept ye?" Jamie said.

Geordie said nothing, but his eyes traveled dubiously over his employer, standing bare-legged in his shirt in the middle of the shop, his breeches, shoes, and stockings discarded on the floor, and me in his arms, with my gown all crumpled and my hair coming down. Geordie's narrow face creased into a censorious frown.

"I quit," he said, in the rich tones of the West Highlands. "The printing's one thing—I'm wi' ye there, and ye'll no think otherwise—but I'm Free Church and my daddy before me and my grandsire before him. Workin' for a Papist is one thing—the Pope's coin's as good as any, aye?—but workin' for an immoral Papist is another. Do as ye like wi' your own soul, man, but if it's come to orgies in the shop, it's come too far, that's what I say. I quit!"

He placed the package precisely in the center of the counter, spun on his heel and stalked toward the door. Outside, the Town Clock on the Tolbooth began to strike. Geordie turned in the doorway to glare accusingly at us.

"And it not even noon yet!" he said. The shop door slammed behind him.

Jamie stared after him for a moment, then sank slowly down onto the floor again, laughing so hard, the tears came to his eyes.

"And it's not even noon yet!" he repeated, wiping the tears off his cheeks. "Oh, God, Geordie!" He rocked back and forth, grasping his knees with both hands.

I couldn't help laughing myself, though I was rather worried.

"I didn't mean to cause you trouble," I said. "Will he come back, do you think?"

He sniffed and wiped his face carelessly on the tail of his shirt.

"Oh, aye. He lives just across the way, in Wickham Wynd. I'll go and see him in a bit, and . . . and explain," he said. He looked at me, realization dawning, and added, "God knows how!" It looked for a minute as though he might start laughing again, but he mastered the impulse and stood up.

"Have you got another pair of breeches?" I asked, picking up the discarded ones and draping them across the counter to dry.

"Aye, I have—upstairs. Wait a bit, though." He snaked a long arm into the cupboard beneath the counter, and came out with a neatly lettered notice that said GONE OUT. Attaching this to the outside of the door, and firmly bolting the inside, he turned to me.

"Will ye step upstairs wi' me?" he said. He crooked an arm invitingly, eyes sparkling. "If ye dinna think it immoral?"

"Why not?" I said. The impulse to explode in laughter was just below the surface, sparkling in my blood like champagne. "We're married, aren't we?"

The upstairs was divided into two rooms, one on either side of the landing, and a small privy closet just off the landing itself. The back room was plainly devoted to storage for the printing business; the door was propped open, and I could see wooden crates filled with books, towering bundles of pamphlets neatly tied with twine, barrels of alcohol and powdered ink, and a jumble of odd-looking hardware that I assumed must be spare parts for a printing press.

The front room was spare as a monk's cell. There was a chest of drawers with a pottery candlestick on it, a washstand, a stool, and a narrow cot, little more than a camp bed. I let out my breath when I saw it, only then realizing that I had been holding it. He slept alone.

A quick glance around confirmed that there was no sign of a feminine presence in the room, and my heart began to beat with a normal rhythm again. Plainly no one lived here but Jamie; he had pushed aside the curtain that blocked off a corner of the room, and the row of pegs revealed there supported no more than a couple of shirts, a coat and long waistcoat in sober gray, a gray wool cloak, and the spare pair of breeches he had come to fetch.

He had his back turned to me as he tucked in his shirt and fastened the new breeches, but I could see the self-consciousness in the tense line of his shoulders. I could feel a similar tension in the back of my own neck. Given a moment to recover from the shock of seeing each other, we were both stricken now with shyness. I saw his shoulders straighten and then he turned around to face me. The hysterical laughter had left us, and the tears, though his face still showed the marks of so much sudden feeling, and I knew mine did, too.

"It's verra fine to see ye, Claire," he said softly. "I thought I never . . . well." He shrugged slightly, as though to ease the tightness of the linen shirt across his shoulders. He swallowed, then met my eyes directly.

"The child?" he said. Everything he felt was evident on his face; urgent hope, desperate fear, and the struggle to contain both.

I smiled at him, and put out my hand. "Come here."

I had thought long and hard about what I might bring with me, should my journey through the stones succeed. Given my previous brush with accusations of witchcraft, I had been very careful. But there was one thing I had had to bring, no matter what the consequences might be if anyone saw them.

I pulled him down to sit beside me on the cot, and pulled out of my pocket the small rectangular package I had done up with such care in Boston. I undid its waterproof wrapping, and thrust its contents into his hands. "There," I said.

He took them from me, gingerly, like one handling an unknown and possibly dangerous substance. His big hands framed the photographs for a moment, holding them confined. Brianna's round newborn face was oblivious between his fingers, tiny fists curled on her blanket, slanted eyes closed in the new exhaustion of existence, her small mouth slightly open in sleep.

I looked up at his face; it was absolutely blank with shock. He held the pictures close to his chest, unmoving, wide-eyed and staring as though he had just been transfixed by a crossbow bolt through the heart—as I supposed he had.

"Your daughter sent you this," I said. I turned his blank face toward me and gently kissed him on the mouth. That broke the trance; he blinked and his face came to life again.

"My . . . she . . ." His voice was hoarse with shock. "Daughter. My daughter. She . . . knows?"

"She does. Look at the rest." I slid the first picture from his grasp, revealing the snapshot of Brianna, uproariously festooned with the icing of her first birthday cake, a four-toothed smile of fiendish triumph on her face as she waved a new plush rabbit overhead.

Jamie made a small inarticulate sound, and his fingers loosened. I took the small stack of photographs from him and gave them back, one at a time.

Brianna at two, stubby in her snowsuit, cheeks round and flushed as apples, feathery hair wisping from under her hood.

Bree at four, hair a smooth bell-shaped gleam as she sat, one ankle propped on the opposite knee as she smiled for the photographer, proper and poised in a white pinafore.

At five, in proud possession of her first lunchbox, waiting to board the school bus to kindergarten.

"She wouldn't let me go with her; she wanted to go alone. She's very b-brave, not afraid of anything . . ." I felt half-choked as I explained, displayed, pointed to the changing images that fell from his hands and slid down to the floor as he began to snatch each new picture.

"Oh, God!" he said, at the picture of Bree at ten, sitting on the kitchen floor with her arms around Smoky, the big Newfoundland. That one was in color; her hair a brilliant shimmer against the dog's shiny black coat.

His hands were shaking so badly that he couldn't hold the pictures anymore; I had to show him the last few—Bree full-grown, laughing at a string of fish she'd caught; standing at a window in secretive contemplation; red-faced and tousled, leaning on the handle of the ax she had been using to split kindling. These showed her face in all the moods I could capture, always that face, long-nosed and wide-mouthed, with those high, broad, flat Viking cheekbones and slanted eyes—a finer-boned, more delicate version of her father's, of the man who sat on the cot beside me, mouth working wordlessly, and the tears running soundless down his own cheeks.

He splayed a hand out over the photographs, trembling fingers not quite touching the shiny surfaces, and then he turned and leaned toward me, slowly, with the improbable grace of a tall tree falling. He buried his face in my shoulder and went very quietly and thoroughly to pieces.

I held him to my breast, arms tight around the broad, shaking shoulders, and my own tears fell on his hair, making small dark patches in the ruddy waves. I pressed my cheek against the top of his head, and murmured small incoherent things to him as though he were Brianna. I thought to myself that perhaps it was like surgery—even when an operation is done to repair existing damage, the healing still is painful.

"Her name?" He raised his face at last, wiping his nose on the back of his hand. He picked up the pictures again, gently, as though they might disintegrate at his touch. "What did ye name her?"

"Brianna," I said proudly.

"Brianna?" he said, frowning at the pictures. "What an awful name for a wee lassie!"

I started back as though struck. "It is not awful!" I snapped. "It's a beautiful name, and besides you *told* me to name her that! What do you mean, it's an awful name?"

"*I* told ye to name her that?" He blinked.

"You most certainly did! When we—when we—the last time I saw you." I pressed my lips tightly together so I wouldn't cry again. After a moment, I had mastered my feelings enough to add, "You told me to name the baby for your father. His name was Brian, wasn't it?"

"Aye, it was." A smile seemed to be struggling for dominance of the other emotions on his face. "Aye," he said. "Aye, you're right, I did. It's only—well, I thought it would be a boy, is all."

"And you're sorry she wasn't?" I glared at him, and began snatching up the scattered photographs. His hands on my arms stopped me.

"No," he said. "No, I'm not sorry. Of course not!" His mouth twitched slightly. "But I willna deny she's the hell of a shock, Sassenach. So are you."

I sat still for a moment, looking at him. I had had months to prepare myself for this, and still my knees felt weak and my stomach was clenched in knots. He had been taken completely unawares by my appearance; little wonder if he was reeling a bit under the impact.

"I expect I am. Are you sorry I came?" I asked. I swallowed. "Do—do you want me to go?"

His hands clamped my arms so tightly that I let out a small yelp. Realizing that he was hurting me, he loosened his grip, but kept a firm hold nonetheless. His face had gone quite pale at the suggestion. He took a deep breath and let it out.

"No," he said, with an approximation of calmness. "I don't. I—" He broke off abruptly, jaw clamped. "No," he said again, very definitely.

His hand slid down to take hold of mine, and with the other he reached down to pick up the photographs. He laid them on his knee, looking at them with head bent, so I couldn't see his face.

"Brianna," he said softly. "Ye say it wrong, Sassenach. Her name is Brianna." He said it with an odd Highland lilt, so that the first syllable was accented, the second barely pronounced. *Bree*-anah.

"*Bree*anah?" I said, amused. He nodded, eyes still fixed on the pictures.

"Brianna," he said. "It's a beautiful name."

"Glad you like it," I said.

He glanced up then, and met my eyes, with a smile hidden in the corner of his long mouth.

"Tell me about her." One forefinger traced the pudgy features of the baby in the snowsuit. "What was she like as a wee lassie? What did she first say, when she learned to speak?"

His hand drew me closer, and I nestled close to him. He was big, and solid, and smelled of clean linen and ink, with a warm male scent that was as exciting to me as it was familiar.

" 'Dog,' " I said. "That was her first word. The second one was 'No!' "

The smile widened across his face. "Aye, they all learn that one fast. She'll like dogs, then?" He fanned the pictures out like cards, searching out the one with Smoky. "That's a lovely dog with her there. What sort is that?"

"A Newfoundland." I bent forward to thumb through the pictures. "There's another one here with a puppy a friend of mine gave her . . ."

The dim gray daylight had begun to fade, and the rain had been pattering on the roof for some time, before our talk was interrupted by a fierce subterranean growl emanating from below the lace-trimmed bodice of my Jessica Gutenburg. It had been a long time since the peanut butter sandwich.

"Hungry, Sassenach?" Jamie asked, rather unnecessarily, I thought.

"Well, yes, now that you mention it. Do you still keep food in the top drawer?" When we were first married, I had developed the habit of keeping small bits of food on hand, to supply his constant appetite, and the top drawer of any chest of drawers where we lived generally provided a selection of rolls, small cakes, or bits of cheese.

He laughed and stretched. "Aye, I do. There's no much there just now, though, but a couple of stale bannocks. Better I take ye down to the tavern, and—" The look of happiness engendered by perusing the photographs of Brianna faded, to be replaced by a look of alarm. He glanced quickly at the window, where a soft purplish color was beginning to replace the pale gray, and the look of alarm deepened.

"The tavern! Christ! I've forgotten Mr. Willoughby!" He was on his feet and groping in the chest for fresh stockings before I could say anything. Coming out with the stockings in one hand and two bannocks in the other, he tossed the latter into my lap and sat down on the stool, hastily yanking on the former.

"Who's Mr. Willoughby?" I bit into a bannock, scattering crumbs.

"Damn," he said, more to himself than me, "I said I'd come for him at noon, but it went out o' my head entirely! It must be four o'clock by now!"

"It is; I heard the clock strike a little while ago."

"Damn!" he repeated. Thrusting his feet into a pair of pewter-buckled shoes, he rose, snatched his coat from the peg, and then paused at the door.

"You'll come wi' me?" he asked anxiously.

I licked my fingers and rose, pulling my cloak around me.

"Wild horses couldn't stop me," I assured him.

"Who is Mr. Willoughby?" I inquired, as we paused under the arch of Carfax Close to peer out at the cobbled street.

"Er . . . he's an associate of mine," Jamie replied, with a wary glance at me. "Best put up your hood, it's pouring."

It was in fact raining quite hard; sheets of water fell from the arch overhead and gurgled down the gutters, cleansing the streets of sewage and rubbish. I took a deep breath of the damp, clean air, feeling exhilarated by the wildness of the evening and the closeness of Jamie, tall and powerful by my side. I had found him. I had found him, and whatever unknowns life now held, they didn't seem to matter. I felt reckless and indestructible.

I took his hand and squeezed it; he looked down and smiled at me, squeezing back.

"Where are we going?"

"To The World's End." The roar of the water made conversation difficult. Without further speech, Jamie took me by the elbow to help me across the cobbles, and we plunged down the steep incline of the Royal Mile.

Luckily, the tavern called The World's End was no more than a hundred yards away; hard as the rain was, the shoulders of my cloak were scarcely more than dampened when we ducked beneath the low lintel and into the narrow entry-hall.

The main room was crowded, warm and smoky, a snug refuge from the storm outside. There were a few women seated on the benches that ran along the walls, but most of the patrons were

men. Here and there was a man in the well-kept dress of a merchant, but most men with homes to go to were in them at this hour;
the tavern hosted a mix of soldiers, wharf rats, laborers and apprentices, with here and there the odd drunkard for variety.

Heads looked up at our appearance, and there were shouts of
greeting, and a general shuffling and pushing, to make room at one
of the long tables. Clearly Jamie was well-known in The World's
End. A few curious glances came my way, but no one said anything. I kept my cloak pulled close around me, and followed Jamie
through the crush of the tavern.

"Nay, mistress, we'll no be stayin'," he said to the young
barmaid who bustled forward with an eager smile. "I've only
come for himself."

The girl rolled her eyes. "Oh, aye, and no before time, either!
Mither's put him doon the stair."

"Aye, I'm late," Jamie said apologetically. "I had . . . business that kept me."

The girl looked curiously at me, but then shrugged and dimpled
at Jamie.

"Och, it's no trouble, sir. Harry took him doon a stoup of
brandy, and we've heard little more of him since."

"Brandy, eh?" Jamie sounded resigned. "Still awake, is he?"
He reached into the pocket of his coat and brought out a small
leather pouch, from which he extracted several coins, which he
dropped into the girl's outstretched hand.

"I expect so," she said cheerfully, pocketing the money. "I
heard him singin' a whiles since. Thankee, sir!"

With a nod, Jamie ducked under the lintel at the back of the
room, motioning me to follow. A tiny, barrel-ceilinged kitchen lay
behind the main taproom, with a huge kettle of what looked like
oyster stew simmering in the hearth. It smelled delicious, and I
could feel my mouth starting to water at the rich aroma. I hoped
we could do our business with Mr. Willoughby over supper.

A fat woman in a grimy bodice and skirt knelt by the hearth,
stuffing billets of wood into the fire. She glanced up at Jamie and
nodded, but made no move to get up.

He lifted a hand in response, and headed for a small wooden
door in the corner. He lifted the bolt and swung the door open to
reveal a dark stairway leading down, apparently into the bowels of

the earth. A light flickered somewhere far below, as though elves were mining diamonds beneath the tavern.

Jamie's shoulders filled the narrow stairwell, obstructing my view of whatever lay below us. When he stepped out into the open space below, I could see heavy oak rafters, and a row of huge casks standing on a long plank set on hurdles against the stone wall.

Only a single torch burned at the foot of the stair. The cellar was shadowy, and its cavelike depths seemed quite deserted. I listened, but didn't hear anything but the muffled racket of the tavern upstairs. Certainly no singing.

"Are you sure he's down here?" I bent to peer beneath the row of casks, wondering whether perhaps the bibulous Mr. Willoughby had been overcome with an excess of brandy and sought some secluded spot to sleep it off.

"Oh, aye." Jamie sounded grim, but resigned. "The wee bugger's hiding, I expect. He knows I dinna like it when he drinks in public houses."

I raised an eyebrow at this, but he merely strode into the shadows, muttering under his breath. The cellar stretched some way, and I could hear him, shuffling cautiously in the dark, long after I lost sight of him. Left in the circle of torchlight near the stairs, I looked around with interest.

Besides the row of casks, there were a number of wooden crates stacked near the center of the room, against an odd little chunk of wall that stood by itself, rising some five feet out of the cellar floor, running back into the darkness.

I had heard of this feature of the tavern when we had stayed in Edinburgh twenty years before with His Highness Prince Charles, but what with one thing and another, I had never actually seen it before. It was the remnant of a wall constructed by the city fathers of Edinburgh, following the disastrous Battle of Flodden Field in 1513. Concluding—with some justice—that no good was likely to come of association with the English to the south, they had built a wall defining both the city limits and the limit of the civilized world of Scotland. Hence "The World's End," and the name had stuck through several versions of the tavern that had eventually been built upon the remnants of the old Scots' wishful thinking.

"Damned little bugger." Jamie emerged from the shadows, a

cobweb stuck in his hair, and a frown on his face. "He must be back of the wall."

Turning, he put his hands to his mouth and shouted something. It sounded like incomprehensible gibberish—not even like Gaelic. I dug a finger dubiously into one ear, wondering whether the trip through the stones had deranged my hearing.

A sudden movement caught the corner of my eye, causing me to look up, just in time to see a ball of brilliant blue fly off the top of the ancient wall and smack Jamie squarely between the shoulder-blades.

He hit the cellar floor with a frightful thump, and I dashed toward his fallen body.

"Jamie! Are you all right?"

The prone figure made a number of coarse remarks in Gaelic and sat up slowly, rubbing his forehead, which had struck the stone floor a glancing blow. The blue ball, meanwhile, had resolved itself into the figure of a very small Chinese, who was giggling in unhinged delight, sallow round face shining with glee and brandy.

"Mr. Willoughby, I presume?" I said to this apparition, keeping a wary eye out for further tricks.

He appeared to recognize his name, for he grinned and nodded madly at me, his eyes creased to gleaming slits. He pointed to himself, said something in Chinese, and then sprang into the air and executed several backflips in rapid succession, bobbing up on his feet in beaming triumph at the end.

"Bloody flea." Jamie got up, wiping the skinned palms of his hands gingerly on his coat. With a quick snatch, he caught hold of the Chinaman's collar and jerked him off his feet.

"Come on," he said, parking the little man on the stairway and prodding him firmly in the back. "We need to be going, and quick now." In response, the little blue-clad figure promptly sagged into limpness, looking like a bag of laundry resting on the step.

"He's all right when he's sober," Jamie explained apologetically to me, as he hoisted the Chinese over one shoulder. "But he really shouldna drink brandy. He's a terrible sot."

"So I see. Where on earth did you get him?" Fascinated, I followed Jamie up the stairs, watching Mr. Willoughby's pigtail swing back and forth like a metronome across the felted gray wool of Jamie's cloak.

"On the docks." But before he could explain further, the door above opened, and we were back in the tavern's kitchen. The stout proprietor saw us emerge, and came toward us, her fat cheeks puffed with disapproval.

"Now, Mr. Malcolm," she began, frowning, "ye ken verra weel as you're welcome here, and ye'll ken as weel that I'm no a fussy woman, such not bein' a convenient attitude when maintainin' a public hoose. But I've telt ye before, yon wee yellow mannie is no—"

"Aye, ye've mentioned it, Mrs. Patterson," Jamie interrupted. He dug in his pocket and came up with a coin, which he handed to the stout publican with a bow. "And your forbearance is much appreciated. It willna happen again. I hope," he added under his breath. He placed his hat on his head, bowed again to Mrs. Patterson, and ducked under the low lintel into the main tavern.

Our reentry caused another stir, but a negative one this time. People fell silent, or muttered half-heard curses under their breath. I gathered that Mr. Willoughby was perhaps not this local's most popular patron.

Jamie edged his way through the crowd, which gave way reluctantly. I followed as best I could, trying not to meet anyone's eyes, and trying not to breathe. Unused as I was to the unhygienic miasma of the eighteenth century, the stench of so many unwashed bodies in a small space was nearly overwhelming.

Near the door, though, we met trouble, in the person of a buxom young woman whose dress was a notch above the sober drab of the landlady and her daughter. Her neckline was a notch lower, and I hadn't much trouble in guessing her principal occupation. Absorbed in flirtatious conversation with a couple of apprentice lads when we emerged from the kitchen, she looked up as we passed, and sprang to her feet with a piercing scream, knocking over a cup of ale in the process.

"It's him!" she screeched, pointing a wavering finger at Jamie. "The foul fiend!" Her eyes seemed to have trouble focusing; I gathered that the spilled ale wasn't her first of the evening, early as it was.

Her companions stared at Jamie with interest, the more so when the young lady advanced, stabbing her finger in the air like one leading a chorus. "Him! The wee poolie I telt ye of—him that did the disgustin' thing to me!"

I joined the rest of the crowd in looking at Jamie with interest, but quickly realized, as did they, that the young woman was not talking to him, but rather to his burden.

"Ye neffit qurd!" she yelled, addressing her remarks to the seat of Mr. Willoughby's blue-silk trousers. "Hiddie-pyke! Slug!"

This spectacle of maidenly distress was rousing her companions; one, a tall, burly lad, stood up, fists clenched, and leaned on the table, eyes gleaming with ale and aggro.

"S'him, aye? Shall I knivvle him for ye, Maggie?"

"Dinna try, laddie," Jamie advised him shortly, shifting his burden for better balance. "Drink your drink, and we'll be gone."

"Oh, aye? And you're the little ked's pimpmaster, are ye?" The lad sneered unbecomingly, his flushed face turning in my direction. "At least your other whore's no yellow—le's ha' a look at her." He flung out a paw and grabbed the edge of my cloak, revealing the low bodice of the Jessica Gutenburg.

"Looks pink enough to me," said his friend, with obvious approval. "Is she like it all over?" Before I could move, he snatched at the bodice, catching the edge of the lace. Not designed for the rigors of eighteenth-century life, the flimsy fabric ripped halfway down the side, exposing quite a lot of pink.

"Leave off, ye whoreson!" Jamie swung about, eyes blazing, free fist doubled in threat.

"Who ye miscallin', ye skrae-shankit skoot?" The first youth, unable to get out from behind the table, leapt on top of it, and launched himself at Jamie, who neatly sidestepped the lad, allowing him to crash face-first into the wall.

Jamie took one giant step toward the table, brought his fist down hard on top of the other apprentice's head, making the lad's jaw go slack, then grabbed me by the hand and dragged me out the door.

"Come on!" he said, grunting as he shifted the Chinaman's slippery form for a better grip. "They'll be after us any moment!"

They were; I could hear the shouting as the more boisterous elements poured out of the tavern into the street behind us. Jamie took the first opening off the Royal Mile, into a narrow, dark wynd, and we splashed through mud and unidentifiable slops, ducked through an archway, and down another twisting alleyway that seemed to lead through the bowels of Edinburgh. Dark walls flashed past, and splintered wooden doors, and then we were round a corner, in a small courtyard, where we paused for breath.

"What . . . on earth . . . did he do?" I gasped. I couldn't imagine what the little Chinese could have done to a strapping young wench like the recent Maggie. From all appearances, she could have squashed him like a fly.

"Well, it's the feet, ye ken," Jamie explained, with a glance of resigned irritation at Mr. Willoughby.

"Feet?" I glanced involuntarily at the tiny Chinese man's feet, neat miniatures shod in felt-soled black satin.

"Not his," Jamie said, catching my glance. "The women's."

"What women?" I asked.

"Well, so far it's only been whores," he said, glancing through the archway in search of pursuit, "but ye canna tell what he may try. No judgment," he explained briefly. "He's a heathen."

"I see," I said, though so far, I didn't. "What—"

"There they are!" A shout at the far end of the alley interrupted my question.

"Damn, I thought they'd give it up. Come on, this way!"

We were off once more, down an alley, back onto the Royal Mile, a few steps down the hill, and back into a close. I could hear shouts and cries behind us on the main street, but Jamie grasped my arm and jerked me after him through an open doorway, into a yard full of casks, bundles, and crates. He looked frantically about, then heaved Mr. Willoughby's limp body into a large barrel filled with rubbish. Pausing only long enough to drop a piece of canvas on the Chinese's head for concealment, he dragged me behind a wagon loaded with crates, and pulled me down beside him.

I was gasping from the unaccustomed exertion, and my heart was racing from the adrenaline of fear. Jamie's face was flushed with cold and exercise, and his hair was sticking up in several directions, but he was scarcely breathing hard.

"Do you do this sort of thing all the time?" I asked, pressing a hand to my bosom in a vain effort to make my heart slow down.

"Not exactly," he said, peering warily over the top of the wagon in search of pursuit.

The echo of pounding feet came faintly, then disappeared, and everything was quiet, save for the patter of rain on the boxes above us.

"They've gone past. We'd best stay here a bit, to make sure, though." He lifted down a crate for me to sit on, procured another for himself, and sat down sighing, pushing the loose hair out of his face with one hand.

He gave me a lopsided smile. "I'm sorry, Sassenach. I didna think it would be quite so . . ."

"Eventful?" I finished for him. I smiled back and pulled out a handkerchief to wipe a drop of moisture from the end of my nose. "It's all right." I glanced at the large barrel, where stirrings and rustlings indicated that Mr. Willoughby was returning to a more or less conscious state. "Er . . . how do you know about the feet?"

"He told me; he's a taste for the drink, ye ken," he explained, with a glance at the barrel where his colleague lay concealed. "And when he's taken a drop too much, he starts talkin' about women's feet, and all the horrible things he wants to do wi' them."

"What sort of horrible things can you do with a foot?" I was fascinated. "Surely the possibilities are limited."

"No, they aren't," Jamie said grimly. "But it isna something I want to be talking about in the public street."

A faint singsong came from the depths of the barrel behind us. It was hard to tell, amid the natural inflections of the language, but I thought Mr. Willoughby was asking a question of some sort.

"Shut up, ye wee poutworm," Jamie said rudely. "Another word, and I'll walk on your damn face myself; see how ye like that." There was a high-pitched giggle, and the barrel fell silent.

"He wants someone to walk on his face?" I asked.

"Aye. You," Jamie said briefly. He shrugged apologetically, and his cheeks flushed a deeper red. "I hadna time to tell him who ye were."

"Does he speak English?"

"Oh, aye, in a way, but not many people understand him when he does. I mostly talk to him in Chinee."

I stared at him. "You speak Chinese?"

He shrugged, tilting his head with a faint smile. "Well, I speak Chinee about as well as Mr. Willoughby speaks English, but then, he hasna got all that much choice in who he talks to, so he puts up wi' me."

My heart showed signs of returning to normal, and I leaned back against the wagon bed, my hood farther forward against the drizzle.

"Where on earth did he get a name like Willoughby?" I asked.

While I was curious about the Chinese, I was even more curious about what a respectable Edinburgh printer was doing with one, but I felt a certain hesitance in prying into Jamie's life. Freshly returned from the supposed dead—or its equivalent—I could hardly demand to know all the details of his life on the spot.

Jamie rubbed a hand across his nose. "Aye, well. It's only that his real name's Yi Tien Cho. He says it means 'Leans against heaven.' "

"Too hard for the local Scots to pronounce?" Knowing the insular nature of most Scots, I wasn't surprised that they were disinclined to venture into strange linguistic waters. Jamie, with his gift for tongues, was a genetic anomaly.

He smiled, teeth a white gleam in the gathering darkness. "Well, it's no that, so much. It's only, if ye say his name just a wee bit off, like, it sounds verra much like a coarse word in Gaelic. I thought Willoughby would maybe do better."

"I see." I thought perhaps under the circumstances, I shouldn't ask just what the indelicate Gaelic word was. I glanced over my shoulder, but the coast seemed clear.

Jamie caught the gesture and rose, nodding. "Aye, we can go now; the lads will ha' gone back to the tavern by now."

"Won't we have to pass by The World's End on the way back to the printshop?" I asked dubiously. "Or is there a back way?" It was full dark by now, and the thought of stumbling through the middens and muddy back passages of Edinburgh was unappealing.

"Ah . . . no. We willna be going to the printshop." I couldn't see his face, but there seemed a certain reserve in his manner. Perhaps he had a residence somewhere else in the city? I felt a certain hollowness at the prospect; the room above the printshop was very clearly a monk's cell; but perhaps he had an entire house somewhere else—with a family in it? There had been no time for any but the most essential exchange of information at the printshop. I had no way of knowing what he had done over the last twenty years, or what he might now be doing.

Still, he had plainly been glad—to say the least—to see me, and the air of frowning consideration he now bore might well have to do with his inebriated associate, rather than with me.

He bent over the barrel, saying something in Scots-accented Chinese. This was one of the odder sounds I had ever heard; rather

like the squeaks of a bagpipe tuning up, I thought, vastly entertained by the performance.

Whatever he'd said, Mr. Willoughby replied to it volubly, interrupting himself with giggles and snorts. At last, the little Chinese
climbed out of the barrel, his diminutive figure silhouetted by the
light of a distant lantern in the alleyway. He sprang down with fair
agility and promptly prostrated himself on the ground before me.

Bearing in mind what Jamie had told me about the feet, I took a
quick step back, but Jamie laid a reassuring hand on my arm.

"Nay, it's all right, Sassenach," he said. "He's only makin'
amends for his disrespect to ye earlier."

"Oh. Well." I looked dubiously at Mr. Willoughby, who was
gabbling something to the ground under his face. At a loss for the
proper etiquette, I stooped down and patted him on the head.
Evidently that was all right, for he leapt to his feet and bowed to
me several times, until Jamie told him impatiently to stop, and we
made our way back to the Royal Mile.

The building Jamie led us to was discreetly hidden down a
small close just above the Kirk of the Canongate, perhaps a quarter-mile above Holyrood Palace. I saw the lanterns mounted by the
gates of the palace below, and shivered slightly at the sight. We
had lived with Charles Stuart in the palace for nearly five weeks,
in the early, victorious phase of his short career. Jamie's uncle,
Colum MacKenzie, had died there.

The door opened to Jamie's knock, and all thoughts of the past
vanished. The woman who stood peering out at us, candle in hand,
was petite, dark-haired, and elegant. Seeing Jamie, she drew him
in with a glad cry, and kissed his cheek in greeting. My insides
squeezed tight as a fist, but then relaxed again, as I heard him
greet her as "Madame Jeanne." Not what one would call a wife—
nor yet, I hoped, a mistress.

Still, there was something about the woman that made me uneasy. She was clearly French, though she spoke English well—not
so odd; Edinburgh was a seaport, and a fairly cosmopolitan city.
She was dressed soberly, but richly, in heavy silk cut with a flair,
but she wore a good deal more rouge and powder than the average
Scotswoman. What disturbed me was the way she was looking at
me—frowning, with a palpable air of distaste.

"Monsieur Fraser," she said, touching Jamie on the shoulder

with a possessive air that I didn't like at all, "if I might have a word in private with you?"

Jamie, handing his cloak to the maid who came to fetch it, took a quick look at me, and read the situation at once.

"Of course, Madame Jeanne," he said courteously, reaching out a hand to draw me forward. "But first—allow me to introduce my wife, Madame Fraser."

My heart stopped beating for a moment, then resumed, with a force that I was sure was audible to everyone in the small entry hall. Jamie's eyes met mine, and he smiled, the grip of his fingers tightening on my arm.

"Your . . . wife?" I couldn't tell whether astonishment or horror was more pronounced on Madame Jeanne's face. "But Monsieur Fraser . . . you bring her *here*? I thought . . . a woman . . . well enough, but to insult our own *jeunes filles* is not good . . . but then . . . a *wife* . . ." Her mouth hung open unbecomingly, displaying several decayed molars. Then she shook herself suddenly back into an attitude of flustered poise, and inclined her head to me with an attempt at graciousness. *"Bonsoir . . . Madame."*

"Likewise, I'm sure," I said politely.

"Is my room ready, Madame?" Jamie said. Without waiting for an answer, he turned toward the stair, taking me with him. "We shall be spending the night."

He glanced back at Mr. Willoughby, who had come in with us. He had sat down at once on the floor, where he sat dripping rain, a dreamy expression on his small, flat face.

"Er . . . ?" Jamie made a small questioning motion toward Mr. Willoughby, his eyebrows raised at Madame Jeanne. She stared at the little Chinese for a moment as though wondering where he had come from, then, returned to herself, clapped her hands briskly for the maid.

"See if Mademoiselle Josie is at liberty, if you please, Pauline," she said. "And then fetch up hot water and fresh towels for Monsieur Fraser and his . . . wife." She spoke the word with a sort of stunned amazement, as though she still didn't quite believe it.

"Oh, and one more thing, if you would be so kind, Madame?" Jamie leaned over the banister, smiling down at her. "My wife will require a fresh gown; she has had an unfortunate accident to her wardrobe. If you could provide something suitable by morning? Thank you, Madame Jeanne. *Bonsoir*!''

I didn't speak, as I followed him up four flights of winding stairs to the top of the house. I was much too busy thinking, my mind in a whirl. ''Pimpmaster,'' the lad in the pub had called him. But surely that was only an epithet—such a thing was absolutely impossible. For the Jamie Fraser I had known, it was impossible, I corrected myself, looking up at the broad shoulders under the dark gray serge coat. But for this man?

I didn't know quite what I had been expecting, but the room was quite ordinary, small and clean—though that was extraordinary, come to think of it—furnished with a stool, a simple bed and chest of drawers, upon which stood a basin and ewer and a clay candlestick with a beeswax candle, which Jamie lighted from the taper he had carried up.

He shucked off his wet coat and draped it carelessly on the stool, then sat down on the bed to remove his wet shoes.

''God,'' he said, ''I'm starving. I hope the cook's not gone to bed yet.''

''Jamie . . .'' I said.

''Take off your cloak, Sassenach,'' he said, noticing me still standing against the door. ''You're soaked.''

''Yes. Well . . . yes.'' I swallowed, then went on. ''There's just . . . er . . . Jamie, why have you got a regular room in a brothel?'' I burst out.

He rubbed his chin, looking mildly embarrassed. ''I'm sorry, Sassenach,'' he said. ''I know it wasna right to bring ye here, but it was the only place I could think of where we might get your dress mended at short notice, besides finding a hot supper. And then I had to put Mr. Willoughby where he wouldna get in more trouble, and as we had to come here anyway . . . well''—he glanced at the bed—''it's a good deal more comfortable than my cot at the printshop. But perhaps it was a poor idea. We can leave, if ye feel it's not—''

''I don't mind about that,'' I interrupted. ''The question is— why have you got a room in a brothel? Are you such a good customer that—''

''A customer?'' He stared up at me, eyebrows raised. ''Here? God, Sassenach, what d'ye think I am?''

"Damned if I know," I said. "That's why I'm asking. Are you going to answer my question?"

He stared at his stocking feet for a moment, wiggling his toes on the floorboard. At last he looked up at me, and answered calmly, "I suppose so. I'm not a customer of Jeanne's, but she's a customer of mine—and a good one. She keeps a room for me because I'm often abroad late on business, and I'd as soon have a place I can come to where I can have food and a bed at any hour, and privacy. The room is part of my arrangement with her."

I had been holding my breath. Now I let out about half of it. "All right," I said. "Then I suppose the next question is, what business has the owner of a brothel got with a printer?" The absurd thought that perhaps he printed advertising circulars for Madame Jeanne flitted through my brain, to be instantly dismissed.

"Well," he said slowly. "No. I dinna think that's the question."

"It's not?"

"No." With one fluid move, he was off the bed and standing in front of me, close enough for me to have to look up into his face. I had a sudden urge to take a step backward, but didn't, largely because there wasn't room.

"The question is, Sassenach, why have ye come back?" he said softly.

"That's a hell of a question to ask me!" My palms pressed flat against the rough wood of the door. "Why do you *think* I came back, damn you?"

"I dinna ken." The soft Scottish voice was cool, but even in the dim light, I could see the pulse throbbing in the open throat of his shirt.

"Did ye come to be my wife again? Or only to bring me word of my daughter?" As though he sensed that his nearness unnerved me, he turned away suddenly, moving toward the window, where the shutters creaked in the wind.

"You are the mother of my child—for that alone, I owe ye my soul—for the knowledge that my life hasna been in vain—that my child is safe." He turned again to face me, blue eyes intent.

"But it has been a time, Sassenach, since you and I were one. You'll have had your life—then—and I have had mine here. You'll know nothing of what I've done, or been. Did ye come now because ye wanted to—or because ye felt ye must?''

My throat felt tight, but I met his eyes.

"I came now because before . . . I thought you were dead. I thought you'd died at Culloden."

His eyes dropped to the windowsill, where he picked at a splinter.

"Aye, I see," he said softly. "Well . . . I meant to be dead." He smiled, without humor, eyes intent on the splinter. "I tried hard enough." He looked up at me again.

"How did ye find out I hadna died? Or where I was, come to that?''

"I had help. A young historian named Roger Wakefield found the records; he tracked you to Edinburgh. And when I saw 'A. Malcolm,' I knew . . . I thought . . . it might be you," I ended lamely. Time enough for the details later.

"Aye, I see. And then ye came. But still . . . why?"

I stared at him without speaking for a moment. As though he felt the need of air, or perhaps only for something to do, he fumbled with the latch of the shutters and thrust them halfway open, flooding the room with the sound of rushing water, and the cold, fresh smell of rain.

"Are you trying to tell me you don't want me to stay?" I said, finally. "Because if so . . . I mean, I know you'll have a life now . . . maybe you have . . . other ties . . ." With unnaturally acute senses, I could hear the small sounds of activity throughout the house below, even above the rush of the storm, and the pounding of my own heart. My palms were damp, and I wiped them surreptitiously against my skirt.

He turned from the window to stare at me.

"Christ!" he said. "Not want ye?" His face was pale now, and his eyes unnaturally bright.

"I have burned for you for twenty years, Sassenach," he said softly. "Do ye not know that? Jesus!" The breeze stirred the loose wisps of hair around his face, and he brushed them back impatiently.

"But I'm no the man ye knew, twenty years past, am I?" He turned away, with a gesture of frustration. "We know each other now less than we did when we wed.''

"Do you want me to go?" The blood was pounding thickly in my ears.

"No!" He swung quickly toward me, and gripped my shoulder tightly, making me pull back involuntarily. "No," he said, more quietly. "I dinna want ye to go. I told ye so, and I meant it. But . . . I must know." He bent his head toward me, his face alive with troubled question.

"Do ye want me?" he whispered. "Sassenach, will ye take me —and risk the man that I am, for the sake of the man ye knew?"

I felt a great wave of relief, mingled with fear. It ran from his hand on my shoulder to the tips of my toes, weakening my joints.

"It's a lot too late to ask that," I said, and reached to touch his cheek, where the rough beard was starting to show. It was soft under my fingers, like stiff plush. "Because I've already risked everything I had. But whoever you are now, Jamie Fraser—yes. Yes, I do want you."

The light of the candle flame glowed blue in his eyes, as he held out his hands to me, and I stepped wordless into his embrace. I rested my face against his chest, marveling at the feel of him in my arms; so big, so solid and warm. Real, after the years of longing for a ghost I could not touch.

Disentangling himself after a moment, he looked down at me, and touched my cheek, very gently. He smiled slightly.

"You've the devil's own courage, aye? But then, ye always did."

I tried to smile at him, but my lips trembled.

"What about you? How do you know what *I'm* like? You don't know what I've been doing for the last twenty years, either. I might be a horrible person, for all you know!"

The smile on his lips moved into his eyes, lighting them with humor. "I suppose ye might, at that. But, d'ye know, Sassenach— I dinna think I care?"

I stood looking at him for another minute, then heaved a deep sigh that popped a few more stitches in my gown.

"Neither do I."

It seemed absurd to be shy with him, but shy I was. The adventures of the evening, and his words to me, had opened up the chasm of reality—those twenty unshared years that gaped between us, and the unknown future that lay beyond. Now we had come to the place where we would begin to know each other again, and discover whether we were in fact the same two who had once existed as one flesh—and whether we might be one again.

A knock at the door broke the tension. It was a small servingmaid, with a tray of supper. She bobbed shyly to me, smiled at Jamie, and laid both supper—cold meat, hot broth, and warm oatbread with butter—and the fire with a quick and practiced hand, then left us with a murmured "Good e'en to ye."

We ate slowly, talking carefully only of neutral things; I told him how I had made my way from Craigh na Dun to Inverness, and made him laugh with stories of Mr. Graham and Master Georgie. He in turn told me about Mr. Willoughby; how he had found the little Chinese, half-starved and dead drunk, lying behind a row of casks on the docks at Burntisland, one of the shipping ports near Edinburgh.

We said nothing much of ourselves, but as we ate, I became increasingly conscious of his body, watching his fine, long hands as he poured wine and cut meat, seeing the twist of his powerful torso under his shirt, and the graceful line of neck and shoulder as he stooped to retrieve a fallen napkin. Once or twice, I thought I saw his gaze linger on me in the same way—a sort of hesitant avidity—but he quickly glanced away each time, hooding his eyes so that I could not tell what he saw or felt.

As the supper concluded, the same thought was uppermost in both our minds. It could scarcely be otherwise, considering the place in which we found ourselves. A tremor of mingled fear and anticipation shot through me.

At last, he drained his wineglass, set it down, and met my eyes directly.

"Will ye . . ." He stopped, the flush deepening on his features, but met my eyes, swallowed once, and went on. "Will ye come to bed wi' me, then? I mean," he hurried on, "it's cold, and we're both damp, and—"

"And there aren't any chairs," I finished for him. "All right." I pulled my hand loose from his, and turned toward the bed, feeling a queer mix of excitement and hesitance that made my breath come short.

He pulled off his breeches and stockings quickly, then glanced at me.

"I'm sorry, Sassenach; I should have thought ye'd need help wi' your laces."

So he didn't undress women often, I thought, before I could stop myself, and my lips curved in a smile at the thought.

"Well, it's not laces," I murmured, "but if you'd give a hand in the back there . . ." I laid aside my cloak, and turned my back to him, lifting my hair to expose the neck of the dress.

There was a puzzled silence. Then I felt a finger sliding slowly down the groove of my backbone.

"What's that?" he said, sounding startled.

"It's called a zipper," I said, smiling, though he couldn't see me. "See the little tab at the top? Just take hold of that, and pull it straight down."

The zipper teeth parted with a muted ripping noise, and the remnants of Jessica Gutenburg sagged free. I pulled my arms out of the sleeves and let the dress drop heavily around my feet, turning to face Jamie before I lost my nerve.

He jerked back, startled by this sudden chrysalis-shedding. Then he blinked, and stared at me.

I stood in front of him in nothing but my shoes and gartered rose-silk stockings. I had an overwhelming urge to snatch the dress back up, but I resisted it. I stiffened my spine, raised my chin, and waited.

He didn't say a word. His eyes gleamed in the candlelight as he moved his head slightly, but he still had that trick of hiding all his thoughts behind an inscrutable mask.

"Will you bloody say something?" I demanded at last, in a voice that shook only a little.

His mouth opened, but no words came out. He shook his head slowly from side to side.

"Jesus," he whispered at last. "Claire . . . you are the most beautiful woman I have ever seen."

"You," I said with conviction, "are losing your eyesight. It's probably glaucoma; you're too young for cataracts."

He laughed at that, a little unsteadily, and then I saw that he was in fact blinded—his eyes shone with moisture, even as he smiled. He blinked hard, and held out his hand.

"I," he said, with equal conviction, "ha' got eyes like a hawk, and always did. Come here to me."

A little reluctantly, I took his hand, and stepped out of the inadequate shelter of the remains of my dress. He drew me gently in, to stand between his knees as he sat on the bed. Then he kissed me softly, once on each breast, and laid his head between them, his breath coming warm on my bare skin.

"Your breast is like ivory," he said softly, the word almost "breest" in the Highland Scots that always grew broad when he was truly moved. His hand rose to cup one breast, his fingers tanned into darkness against my own pale glow.

"Only to see them, sae full and sae round—Christ, I could lay my head here forever. But to touch ye, my Sassenach . . . you wi' your skin like white velvet, and the sweet long lines of your body . . ." He paused, and I could feel the working of his throat muscles as he swallowed, his hand moving slowly down the curving slope of waist and hip, the swell and taper of buttock and thigh.

"Dear God," he said, still softly. "I couldna look at ye, Sassenach, and keep my hands from you, nor have ye near me, and not want ye." He lifted his head then, and planted a kiss over my heart, then let his hand float down the gentle curve of my belly, lightly tracing the small marks left there by Brianna's birth.

"You . . . really don't mind?" I said hesitantly, brushing my own fingers over my stomach.

He smiled up at me with something half-rueful in his expression. He hesitated for a moment, then drew up the hem of his shirt.

"Do you?" he asked.

The scar ran from midthigh nearly to his groin, an eight-inch length of twisted, whitish tissue. I couldn't repress a gasp at its appearance, and dropped to my knees beside him.

I laid my cheek on his thigh, holding tight to his leg, as though I would keep him now—as I had not been able to keep him then. I could feel the slow, deep pulse of the blood through his femoral artery under my fingers—a bare inch away from the ugly gully of that twisting scar.

"It doesna fright ye, nor sicken ye, Sassenach?" he asked, laying a hand on my hair. I lifted my head and stared up at him.

"Of course not!"

"Aye, well." He reached to touch my stomach, his eyes holding mine. "And if ye bear the scars of your own battles, Sassenach," he said softly, "they dinna trouble me, either."

He lifted me to the bed beside him then, and leaned to kiss me. I kicked off my shoes, and curled my legs up, feeling the warmth of him through his shirt. My hands found the button at the throat, fumbling to open it.

"I want to see you."

"Well, it's no much to see, Sassenach," he said, with an uncertain laugh. "But whatever it is, it's yours—if ye want it."

He pulled the shirt over his head and tossed it on the floor, then leaned back on the palms of his hands, displaying his body.

I didn't know quite what I had been expecting. In fact, the sight of his naked body took my breath away. He was still tall, of course, and beautifully made, the long bones of his body sleek with muscle, elegant with strength. He glowed in the candlelight, as though the light came from within him.

He had changed, of course, but the change was subtle; as though he had been put into an oven and baked to a hard finish. He looked as though both muscle and skin had drawn in just a bit, grown closer to the bone, so he was more tightly knit; he had never seemed gawky, but the last hint of boyish looseness had vanished.

His skin had darkened slightly, to a pale gold, burned to bronze on face and throat, paling down the length of his body to a pure white, tinged with blue veins, in the hollow of his thighs. His pubic hair stood out in a ferocious auburn bush, and it was quite obvious that he had not been lying; he did want me, and very badly.

My eyes met his, and his mouth quirked suddenly.

"I did say once I would be honest with ye, Sassenach."

I laughed, feeling tears sting my eyes at the same time, a rush of confused emotion surging up in me.

"So did I." I reached toward him, hesitant, and he took my hand. The strength and warmth of it were startling, and I jerked slightly. Then I tightened my grasp, and he rose to his feet, facing me.

We stood still then, awkwardly hesitating. We were intensely aware of each other—how could we not be? It was quite a small room, and the available atmosphere was completely filled with a charge like static electricity, almost strong enough to be visible. I had a feeling of empty-bellied terror, like the sort you get at the top of a roller coaster.

"Are you as scared as I am?" I finally said, sounding hoarse to my own ears.

He looked me over carefully, and raised one eyebrow.

"I dinna think I can be," he said. "You're covered wi' goose-flesh. Are ye scairt, Sassenach, or only cold?"

"Both," I said, and he laughed.

"Get in, then," he said. He released my hand and bent to turn back the quilt.

I didn't stop shaking when he slid under the quilt beside me, though the heat of his body was a physical shock.

"God, you're not cold!" I blurted. I turned toward him, and the warmth of him shimmered against my skin from head to toes. Instinctively drawn, I pressed close against him, shivering. I could feel my nipples tight and hard against his chest, and the sudden shock of his naked skin against my own.

He laughed a little uncertainly. "No, I'm not. I suppose I must be afraid, aye?" His arms came around me, gently, and I touched his chest, feeling hundreds of tiny goose bumps spring up under my fingertips, among the ruddy curling hairs.

"When we were afraid of each other before," I whispered, "on our wedding night—you held my hands. You said it would be easier if we touched."

He made a small sound as my fingertip found his nipple.

"Aye, I did," he said, sounding breathless. "Lord, touch me like that again." His hands tightened suddenly, holding me against him.

"Touch me," he said again softly, "and let me touch you, my Sassenach." His hand cupped me, stroking, touching, and my breast lay taut and heavy in his palm. I went on trembling, but now he was doing it, too.

"When we wed," he whispered, his breath warm against my cheek, "and I saw ye there, so bonny in your white dress—I couldna think of anything but when we'd be alone, and I could undo your laces and have ye naked, next to me in the bed."

"Do you want me now?" I whispered, and kissed the sun-burned flesh in the hollow above his collarbone. His skin was faintly salty to the taste, and his hair smelled of woodsmoke and pungent maleness.

He didn't answer, but moved abruptly, so I felt the hardness of him, stiff against my belly.

It was terror as much as desire that pressed me close against him. I wanted him, all right; my breasts ached and my belly was tight with it, the unaccustomed rush of arousal slippery between my legs, opening me for him. But as strong as lust, was the desire simply to be taken, to have him master me, quell my doubts in a moment of rough usage, take me hard and swiftly enough to make me forget myself.

I could feel the urge to do it tremble in the hands that cupped my buttocks, in the involuntary jerk of his hips, brought up short as he stopped himself.

Do it, I thought, in an agony of apprehension. For God's sake, do it now and don't be gentle!

I couldn't say it. I saw the need of it on his face, but he couldn't say it, either; it was both too soon and too late for such words between us.

But we had shared another language, and my body still recalled it. I pressed my hips against him sharply, grasping his, the curves of his buttocks clenched hard under my hands. I turned my face upward, urgent to be kissed, at the same moment that he bent abruptly to kiss me.

My nose hit his forehead with a sickening crunch. My eyes watered profusely as I rolled away from him, clutching my face.
"Ow!"

"Christ, have I hurt ye, Claire?" Blinking away the tears, I could see his face, hovering anxiously over me.

"No," I said stupidly. "My nose is broken, though, I think."

"No, it isn't," he said, gently feeling the bridge of my nose. "When ye break your nose, it makes a nasty crunching sound, and ye bleed like a pig. It's all right."

I felt gingerly beneath my nostrils, but he was right; I wasn't bleeding. The pain had receded quickly, too. As I realized that, I also realized that he was lying on me, my legs sprawled wide beneath him, his cock just touching me, no more than a hairs-breadth from the moment of decision.

I saw the realization dawn in his eyes as well. Neither of us moved, barely breathing. Then his chest swelled as he took a deep breath, reached and took both my wrists in one hand. He pulled them up, over my head, and held me there, my body arched taut and helpless under him.

"Give me your mouth, Sassenach," he said softly, and bent to me. His head blotted out the candlelight, and I saw nothing but a dim glow and the darkness of his flesh as his mouth touched mine.

Gently, brushing, then pressing, warm, and I opened to him with a little gasp, his tongue seeking mine.

I bit his lip, and he drew back a little, startled.

"Jamie," I said against his lips, my own breath warm between us. "Jamie!" That was all I could say, but my hips jerked against him, and jerked again, urging violence. I turned my head and fastened my teeth in the flesh of his shoulder.

He made a small sound deep in his throat and came into me hard. I was tight as any virgin and cried out, arching under him.

"Don't stop!" I said. "For God's sake, don't stop!"

His body heard me and answered in the same language, his grasp of my wrists tightening as he plunged hard into me, the force of it reaching my womb with each stroke.

Then he let go of my wrists and half-fell on me, the weight of him pinning me to the bed as he reached under, holding my hips hard, keeping me immobile.

I whimpered and writhed against him, and he bit my neck.

"Be still," he said in my ear. I was still, only because I couldn't move. We lay pressed tight together, shuddering. I could feel the pounding against my ribs, but didn't know whether it was my heart, or his.

Then he moved in me, very slightly, a question of the flesh. It was enough; I convulsed in answer, held helpless under him, and felt the spasms of my release stroke him, stroke him, seize and release him, urging him to join me.

He reared up on both hands, back arched and head thrown back, eyes closed and breathing hard. Then very slowly, he bent his head forward and opened his eyes. He looked down at me with unutterable tenderness, and the candlelight gleamed briefly on the wetness on his cheek, maybe sweat or maybe tears.

"Oh, Claire," he whispered. "Oh, God, Claire."

And his release began, deep inside me, without his moving, shivering through his body so that his arms trembled, the ruddy hairs quivering in the dim light, and he dropped his head with a sound like a sob, his hair hiding his face as he spilled himself, each jerk and pulse of his flesh between my legs rousing an echo in my own.

When it was over, he held himself over me, still as stone for a long moment. Then, very gently, he lowered himself, pressed his head against mine, and lay as if dead.

I stirred at last from a deep, contented stupor, lifting my hand to lay it over the spot where his pulse beat slow and strong, just at the base of his breastbone.

"It's like bicycle riding, I expect," I said. My head rested peacefully in the curve of his shoulder, my hand idly playing with the red-gold curls that sprang up in thickets across his chest. "Did you know you've got lots more hairs on your chest than you used to?"

"No," he said drowsily, "I dinna usually count them. Have bye-sickles got lots of hair, then?"

It caught me by surprise, and I laughed.

"No," I said. "I just meant that we seemed to recall what to do all right."

Jamie opened one eye and looked down at me consideringly. "It would take a real daftie to forget *that,* Sassenach," he said. "I may be lacking practice, but I havena lost all my faculties yet."

We were still for a long time, aware of each other's breathing, sensitive to each small twitch and shifting of position. We fitted well together, my head curled into the hollow of his shoulder, the territory of his body warm under my hand, both strange and familiar, awaiting rediscovery.

The building was a solid one, and the sound of the storm outside drowned most noises from within, but now and then the sounds of feet or voices were dimly audible below us; a low, masculine laugh, or the higher voice of a woman, raised in professional flirtation.

Hearing it, Jamie stirred a little uncomfortably.

"I should maybe have taken ye to a tavern," he said. "It's only—"

"It's all right," I assured him. "Though I must say, of all the places I'd imagined being with you again, I somehow never thought of a brothel." I hesitated, not wanting to pry, but curiosity got the best of me. "You . . . er . . . don't *own* this place, do you, Jamie?"

He pulled back a little, staring down at me.

"Me? God in heaven, Sassenach, what d'ye think I am?"

"Well, I don't know, do I?" I pointed out, with some asperity. "The first thing you do when I find you is faint, and as soon as

I've got you back on your feet, you get me assaulted in a pub and chased through Edinburgh in company with a deviant Chinese, ending up in a brothel—whose madam seems to be on awfully familiar terms with you, I might add.'' The tips of his ears had gone pink, and he seemed to be struggling between laughter and indignation.

"You then take off your clothes, announce that you're a terrible person with a depraved past, and take me to bed. What did you *expect* me to think?"

Laughter won out.

"Well, I'm no a saint, Sassenach," he said. "But I'm no a pimp, either."

"Glad to hear it," I said. There was a momentary pause, and then I said, "Do you mean to tell me what you *are,* or shall I go on running down the disreputable possibilities until I come close?"

"Oh, aye?" he said, entertained by this suggestion. "What's your best guess?"

I looked him over carefully. He lay at ease amid the tumbled sheets, one arm behind his head, grinning at me.

"Well, I'd bet my shift you're not a printer," I said.

The grin widened.

"Why not?"

I poked him rudely in the ribs. "You're much too fit. Most men in their forties have begun to go soft round the middle, and you haven't a spare ounce on you."

"That's mostly because I havena got anyone to cook for me," he said ruefully. "If you ate in taverns all the time, ye wouldna be fat, either. Luckily, it looks as though ye eat regularly." He patted my bottom familiarly, and then ducked, laughing, as I slapped at his hand.

"Don't try to distract me," I said, resuming my dignity. "At any rate, you didn't get muscles like that slaving over a printing press."

"Ever tried to work one, Sassenach?" He raised a derisive eyebrow.

"No." I furrowed my brow in thought. "I don't suppose you've taken up highway robbery?"

"No," he said, the grin widening. "Guess again."

"Embezzlement."

"No."

"Well, likely not kidnapping for ransom," I said, and began to tick other possibilities off on my fingers. "Petty thievery? No. Piracy? No, you couldn't possibly, unless you've got over being seasick. Usury? Hardly." I dropped my hand and stared at him. "You were a traitor when I last knew you, but that scarcely seems a good way of making a living."

"Oh, I'm still a traitor," he assured me. "I just havena been convicted lately."

"Lately?"

"I spent several years in prison for treason, Sassenach," he said, rather grimly. "For the Rising. But that was some time back."

"Yes, I knew that."

His eyes widened. "Ye knew that?"

"That and a bit more," I said. "I'll tell you later. But putting that all aside for the present and returning to the point at issue— what *do* you do for a living these days?"

"I'm a printer," he said, grinning widely.

"And a traitor?"

"And a traitor," he confirmed, nodding. "I've been arrested for sedition six times in the last two years, and had my premises seized twice, but the court wasna able to prove anything."

"And what happens to you if they *do* prove it, one of these times?"

"Oh," he said airily, waving his free hand in the air, "the pillory. Ear-nailing. Flogging. Imprisonment. Transportation. That sort of thing. Likely not hanging."

"What a relief," I said dryly. I felt a trifle hollow. I hadn't even tried to imagine what his life might be like, if I found him. Now that I had, I was a little taken aback.

"I did warn ye," he said. The teasing was gone now, and the dark blue eyes were serious and watchful.

"You did," I said, and took a deep breath.

"Do ye want to leave now?" He spoke casually enough, but I saw his fingers clench and tighten on a fold of the quilt, so that the knuckles stood out white against the sun-bronzed skin.

"No," I said. I smiled at him, as best I could manage. "I didn't come back just to make love with you once. I came to be with you —if you'll have me," I ended, a little hesitantly.

"If I'll have you!" He let out the breath he had been holding, and sat up to face me, cross-legged on the bed. He reached out and took my hands, engulfing them between his own.

"I—canna even say what I felt when I touched you today, Sassenach, and knew ye to be real," he said. His eyes traveled over me, and I felt the heat of him, yearning, and my own heat, melting toward him. "To find you again—and then to lose ye . . ." He stopped, throat working as he swallowed.

I touched his face, tracing the fine, clean line of cheekbone and jaw.

"You won't lose me," I said. "Not ever again." I smiled, smoothing back the thick ruff of ruddy hair behind his ear. "Not even if I find out you've been committing bigamy and public drunkenness."

He jerked sharply at that, and I dropped my hand, startled.

"What is it?"

"Well—" he said, and stopped. He pursed his lips and glanced at me quickly. "It's just—"

"Just what? Is there something else you haven't told me?"

"Well, printing seditious pamphlets isna all that profitable," he said, in explanation.

"I don't suppose so," I said, my heart starting to speed up again at the prospect of further revelations. "What else have you been doing?"

"Well, it's just that I do a wee bit of smuggling," he said apologetically. "On the side, like."

"A *smuggler*?" I stared. "Smuggling what?"

"Well, whisky mostly, but rum now and then, and a fair bit of French wine and cambric."

"So that's it!" I said. The pieces of the puzzle all settled into place—Mr. Willoughby, the Edinburgh docks, and the riddle of our present surroundings. "That's what your connection is with this place—what you meant by saying Madame Jeanne is a customer?"

"That's it." He nodded. "It works verra well; we store the liquor in one of the cellars below when it comes in from France. Some of it we sell directly to Jeanne; some she keeps for us until we can ship it on."

"Um. And as part of the arrangements . . ." I said delicately, "you, er . . ."

The blue eyes narrowed at me.

"The answer to what you're thinking, Sassenach, is no," he said very firmly.

"Oh, is it?" I said, feeling extremely pleased. "Mind reader, are you? And what am I thinking?"

"You were wondering do I take out my price in trade sometimes, aye?" He lifted one brow at me.

"Well, I was," I admitted. "Not that it's any of my business."

"Oh, isn't it, then?" He raised both ruddy brows and took me by both shoulders, leaning toward me.

"Is it?" he said, a moment later. He sounded a little breathless.

"Yes," I said, sounding equally breathless. "And you don't—"

"I don't. Come here."

He wrapped his arms around me, and pulled me close. The body's memory is different from the mind's. When I thought, and wondered, and worried, I was clumsy and awkward, fumbling my way. Without the interference of conscious thought, my body knew him, and answered him at once in tune, as though his touch had left me moments before, and not years.

"I was more afraid this time than on our wedding night," I murmured, my eyes fixed on the slow, strong pulsebeat in the hollow of his throat.

"Were ye, then?" His arm shifted and tightened round me. "Do I frighten ye, Sassenach?"

"No." I put my fingers on the tiny pulse, breathing the deep musk of his effort. "It's only . . . the first time . . . I didn't think it would be forever. I meant to go, then."

He snorted faintly, the sweat gleaming lightly in the small hollow in the center of his chest.

"And ye did go, and came again," he said. "You're here; there's no more that matters, than that."

I raised myself slightly to look at him. His eyes were closed, slanted and catlike, his lashes that striking color I remembered so well because I had seen it so often; deep auburn at the tips, fading to a red so pale as nearly to be blond at the roots.

"What did you think, the first time we lay together?" I asked. The dark blue eyes opened slowly, and rested on me.

"It has always been forever, for me, Sassenach," he said simply.

Sometime later, we fell asleep entwined, with the sound of the rain falling soft against the shutters, mingling with the muffled sounds of commerce below.

It was a restless night. Too tired to stay awake a moment longer, I was too happy to fall soundly asleep. Perhaps I was afraid he would vanish if I slept. Perhaps he felt the same. We lay close together, not awake, but too aware of each other to sleep deeply. I felt every small twitch of his muscles, every movement of his breathing, and knew he was likewise aware of me.

Half-dozing, we turned and moved together, always touching, in a sleepy, slow-motion ballet, learning again in silence the language of our bodies. Somewhere in the deep, quiet hours of the night, he turned to me without a word, and I to him, and we made love to each other in a slow, unspeaking tenderness that left us lying still at last, in possession of each other's secrets.

Soft as a moth flying in the dark, my hand skimmed his leg, and found the thin deep runnel of the scar. My fingers traced its invisible length and paused, with the barest of touches at its end, wordlessly asking, "How?"

His breathing changed with a sigh, and his hand lay over mine.

"Culloden," he said, the whispered word an evocation of tragedy. Death. Futility. And the terrible parting that had taken me from him.

"I'll never leave you," I whispered. "Not again."

His head turned on the pillow, his features lost in darkness, and his lips brushed mine, light as the touch of an insect's wing. He turned onto his back, shifting me next to him, his hand resting heavy on the curve of my thigh, keeping me close.

Sometime later, I felt him shift again, and turn the bedclothes back a little way. A cool draft played across my forearm; the tiny hairs prickled upright, and then flattened beneath the warmth of his touch. I opened my eyes, to find him turned on his side, absorbed in the sight of my hand. It lay still on the quilt, a carved white thing, all the bones and tendons chalked in gray as the room began its imperceptible shift from night to day.

"Draw her for me," he whispered, head bent as he gently traced the shapes of my fingers, long and ghostly beneath the darkness of his own touch.

"What has she of you, of me? Can ye tell me? Are her hands

like yours, Claire, or mine? Draw her for me, let me see her.'' He laid his own hand down beside my own. It was his good hand, the fingers straight and flat-jointed, the nails clipped short, square and clean. ·

''Like mine,'' I said. My voice was low and hoarse with waking, barely loud enough to register above the drumming of the rain outside. The house beneath was silent. I raised the fingers of my immobile hand an inch in illustration.

''She has long, slim hands like mine—but bigger than mine, broad across the backs, and a deep curve at the outside, near the wrist—like that. Like yours; she has a pulse just there, where you do.'' I touched the spot where a vein crossed the curve of his radius, just where the wrist joins the hand. He was so still I could feel his heartbeat under my fingertip.

''Her nails are like yours; square, not oval like mine. But she has the crooked little finger on her right hand that I have,'' I said, lifting it. ''My mother had it, too; Uncle Lambert told me.'' My own mother had died when I was five. I had no clear memory of her, but thought of her whenever I saw my own hand unexpectedly, caught in a moment of grace like this one. I laid the hand with the crooked finger on his, then lifted it to his face.

''She has this line,'' I said softly, tracing the bold sweep from temple to cheek. ''Your eyes, exactly, and those lashes and brows. A Fraser nose. Her mouth is more like mine, with a full bottom lip, but it's wide, like yours. A pointed chin, like mine, but stronger. She's a big girl—nearly six feet tall.'' I felt his start of astonishment, and nudged him gently, knee to knee. ''She has long legs, like yours, but very feminine.''

''And has she that small blue vein just there?'' His hand touched my own face, thumb tender in the hollow of my temple. ''And ears like tiny wings, Sassenach?''

''She always complained about her ears—said they stuck out,'' I said, feeling the tears sting my eyes as Brianna came suddenly to life between us.

''They're pierced. You don't mind, do you?'' I said, talking fast to keep the tears at bay. ''Frank did; he said it looked cheap, and she shouldn't, but she wanted to do it, and I let her, when she was sixteen. Mine were; it didn't seem right to say she couldn't when I did, and her friends all did, and I didn't—didn't want—''

''Ye were right,'' he said, interrupting the flow of half-hysterical words. ''Ye did fine,'' he repeated, softly but firmly, holding me close. ''Ye were a wonderful mother, I know it.''

I was crying again, quite soundlessly, shaking against him. He held me gently, stroking my back and murmuring. ''Ye did well,'' he kept saying. ''Ye did right.'' And after a little while, I stopped crying.

''Ye gave me a child, *mo nighean donn*,'' he said softly, into the cloud of my hair. ''We are together for always. She is safe; and we will live forever now, you and I.'' He kissed me, very lightly, and laid his head upon the pillow next to me. ''Brianna,'' he whispered, in that odd Highland way that made her name his own. He sighed deeply, and in an instant, was asleep. In another, I fell asleep myself, my last sight his wide, sweet mouth, relaxed in sleep, half-smiling.

26

Whore's Brunch

From years of answering the twin calls of motherhood and medicine, I had developed the ability to wake from even the soundest sleep at once and completely. I woke so now, immediately aware of the worn linen sheets around me, the dripping of the eaves outside, and the warm scent of Jamie's body mingling with the cold, sweet air that breathed through the crack of the shutters above me.

Jamie himself was not in bed; without reaching out or opening my eyes, I knew that the space beside me was empty. He was close by, though. There was a sound of stealthy movement, and a faint scraping noise nearby. I turned my head on the pillow and opened my eyes.

The room was filled with a gray light that washed the color from everything, but left the pale lines of his body clear in the dimness. He stood out against the darkness of the room, solid as ivory, vivid as though he were etched upon the air. He was naked, his back turned to me as he stood in front of the chamber pot he had just pulled from its resting place beneath the washstand.

I admired the squared roundness of his buttocks, the small muscular hollow that dented each one, and their pale vulnerability. The groove of his backbone, springing in a deep, smooth curve from hips to shoulders. As he moved slightly, the light caught the faint silver shine of the scars on his back, and the breath caught in my throat.

He turned around then, face calm and faintly abstracted. He saw me watching him, and looked slightly startled.

I smiled but stayed silent, unable to think of anything to say. I kept looking at him, though, and he at me, the same smile upon his lips. Without speaking, he moved toward me and sat on the bed, the mattress shifting under his weight. He laid his hand open on the quilt, and I put my own into it without hesitation.

"Sleep well?" I asked idiotically.

A grin broadened across his face. "No," he said. "Did you?"

"No." I could feel the heat of him, even at this distance, in spite of the chilly room. "Aren't you cold?"

"No."

We fell quiet again, but could not take our eyes away from each other. I looked him over carefully in the strengthening light, comparing memory to reality. A narrow blade of early sun knifed through the shutters' crack, lighting a lock of hair like polished bronze, gilding the curve of his shoulder, the smooth flat slope of his belly. He seemed slightly larger than I had remembered, and one hell of a lot more immediate.

"You're bigger than I remembered," I ventured. He tilted his head, looking down at me in amusement.

"You're a wee bit smaller, I think."

His hand engulfed mine, fingers delicately circling the bones of my wrist. My mouth was dry; I swallowed and licked my lips.

"A long time ago, you asked me if I knew what it was between us," I said.

His eyes rested on mine, so dark a blue as to be nearly black in a light like this.

"I remember," he said softly. His fingers tightened briefly on mine. "What it is—when I touch you; when ye lie wi' me."

"I said I didn't know."

"I didna ken either." The smile had faded a bit, but was still there, lurking in the corners of his mouth.

"I still don't," I said. "But—" and stopped to clear my throat.

"But it's still there," he finished for me, and the smile moved from his lips, lighting his eyes. "Aye?"

It was. I was still as aware of him as I might have been of a lighted stick of dynamite in my immediate vicinity, but the feeling between us had changed. We had fallen asleep as one flesh, linked by the love of the child we had made, and had waked as two people —bound by something different.

"Yes. Is it—I mean, it's not just because of Brianna, do you think?"

The pressure on my fingers increased.

"Do I want ye because you're the mother of my child?" He raised one ruddy eyebrow in incredulity. "Well, no. Not that I'm no grateful," he added hastily. "But—no." He bent his head to look down at me intently, and the sun lit the narrow bridge of his nose and sparked in his lashes.

"No," he said. "I think I could watch ye for hours, Sassenach, to see how you have changed, or how ye're the same. Just to see a wee thing, like the curve of your chin"—he touched my jaw gently, letting his hand slide up to cup my head, thumb stroking my earlobe—"or your ears, and the bittie holes for your earbobs. Those are all the same, just as they were. Your hair—I called ye *mo nighean donn,* d'ye recall? My brown one." His voice was little more than a whisper, his fingers threading my curls between them.

"I expect that's changed a bit," I said. I hadn't gone gray, but there were paler streaks where my normal light brown had faded to a softer gold, and here and there, the glint of a single silver strand.

"Like beechwood in the rain," he said, smiling and smoothing a lock with one forefinger, "and the drops coming down from the leaves across the bark."

I reached out and stroked his thigh, touching the long scar that ran down it.

"I wish I could have been there to take care of you," I said softly. "It was the most horrible thing I ever did—leaving you, knowing . . . that you meant to be killed." I could hardly bear to speak the word.

"Well, I tried hard enough," he said, with a wry grimace that made me laugh, in spite of my emotion. "It wasna my fault I didna succeed." He glanced dispassionately at the long, thick scar that ran down his thigh. "Not the fault of the Sassenach wi' the bayonet, either."

I heaved myself up on one elbow, squinting at the scar. "A *bayonet* did that?"

"Aye, well. It festered, ye see," he explained.

"I know; we found the journal of the Lord Melton who sent you home from the battlefield. He didn't think you'd make it." My hand tightened on his knee, as though to reassure myself that he was in fact here before me, alive.

He snorted. "Well, I damn nearly didn't. I was all but dead when they pulled me out of the wagon at Lallybroch." His face darkened with memory.

"God, sometimes I wake up in the night, dreaming of that wagon. It was two days' journey, and I was fevered or chilled, or both together. I was covered wi' hay, and the ends of it sticking in my eyes and my ears and through my shirt, and fleas hopping all through it and eating me alive, and my leg killing me at every jolt in the road. It was a verra bumpy road, too," he added broodingly.

"It sounds horrible," I said, feeling the word quite inadequate. He snorted briefly.

"Aye. I only stood it by imagining what I'd do to Melton if I ever met him again, to get back at him for not shooting me."

I laughed again, and he glanced down at me, a wry smile on his lips.

"I'm not laughing because it's funny," I said, gulping a little. "I'm laughing because otherwise I'll cry, and I don't want to— not now, when it's over."

"Aye, I know." He squeezed my hand.

I took a deep breath. "I—I didn't look back. I didn't think I could stand to find out—what happened." I bit my lip; the admission seemed a betrayal. "It wasn't that I tried—that I wanted—to forget," I said, groping clumsily for words. "I couldn't forget you; you shouldn't think that. Not ever. But I—"

"Dinna fash yourself, Sassenach," he interrupted. He patted my hand gently. "I ken what ye mean. I try not to look back myself, come to that."

"But if I had," I said, staring down at the smooth grain of the linen, "if I had—I might have found you sooner."

The words hung in the air between us like an accusation, a reminder of the bitter years of loss and separation. Finally he sighed, deeply, and put a finger under my chin, lifting my face to his.

"And if ye had?" he said. "Would ye have left the lassie there without her mother? Or come to me in the time after Culloden, when I couldna care for ye, but only watch ye suffer wi' the rest, and feel the guilt of bringing ye to such a fate? Maybe see ye die of the hunger and sickness, and know I'd killed ye?'' He raised one eyebrow in question, then shook his head.

''No. I told ye to go, and I told ye to forget. Shall I blame ye for doing as I said, Sassenach? No.''

''But we might have had more time!'' I said. ''We might have—'' He stopped me by the simple expedient of bending and putting his mouth on mine. It was warm and very soft, and the stubble of his face was faintly scratchy on my skin.

After a moment he released me. The light was growing, putting color in his face. His skin glowed bronze, sparked with the copper of his beard. He took a deep breath.

''Aye, we might. But to think of that—we cannot.'' His eyes met mine steadily, searching. ''I canna look back, Sassenach, and live,'' he said simply. ''If we have no more than last night, and this moment, it is enough.''

''Not for me, it isn't!'' I said, and he laughed.

''Greedy wee thing, are ye no?''

''Yes,'' I said. The tension broken, I returned my attention to the scar on his leg, to keep away for the moment from the painful contemplation of lost time and opportunity.

''You were telling me how you got that.''

''So I was.'' He rocked back a little, squinting down at the thin white line down the top of his thigh.

''Well, it was Jenny—my sister, ye ken?'' I did indeed remember Jenny; half her brother's size, and dark as he was blazing fair, but a match and more for him in stubbornness.

''She said she wasna going to let me die,'' he said, with a rueful smile. ''And she didn't. My opinion didna seem to have anything to do wi' the matter, so she didna bother to ask me.''

''That sounds like Jenny.'' I felt a small glow of comfort at the thought of my sister-in-law. Jamie hadn't been alone as I feared, then; Jenny Murray would have fought the Devil himself to save her brother—and evidently had.

''She dosed me for the fever, and put poultices on my leg to draw the poison, but nothing worked, and it only got worse. It swelled and stank, and then began to go black and rotten, so they thought they must take the leg off, if I was to live.''

He recounted this quite matter-of-factly, but I felt a little faint at the thought.

''Obviously they didn't,'' I said. ''Why not?''

Jamie scratched his nose and rubbed a hand back through his hair, wiping the wild spill of it out of his eyes. "Well, that was Ian," he said. "He wouldna let her do it. He said he kent well enough what it was like to live wi' one leg, and while he didna mind it so much himself, he thought I wouldna like to—all things considered," he added, with a wave of the hand and a glance at me that encompassed everything—the loss of the battle, of the war, of me, of home and livelihood—of all the things of his normal life. I thought Ian might well have been right.

"So instead Jenny made three of the tenants come to sit on me and hold me still, and then she slit my leg to the bone wi' a kitchen knife and washed the wound wi' boiling water," he said casually.

"Jesus H. Christ!" I blurted, shocked into horror.

He smiled faintly at my expression. "Aye, well, it worked."

I swallowed heavily, tasting bile. "Jesus. I'd think you'd have been a cripple for life!"

"Well, she cleansed it as best she could, and stitched it up. She said she wasna going to let me die, and she wasna going to have me be a cripple, and she wasna going to have me lie about all the day feelin' sorry for myself, and—" He shrugged, resigned. "By the time she finished tellin' me all the things she wouldna let me do, it seemed the only thing left to me was to get well."

I echoed his laugh, and his smile broadened at the memory. "Once I could get up, she made Ian take me outside after dark and make me walk. Lord, we must ha' been a sight, Ian wi' his wooden leg, and me wi' my stick, limping up and down the road like a pair of lame cranes!"

I laughed again, but had to blink back tears; I could see all too well the two tall, limping figures, struggling stubbornly against darkness and pain, leaning on each other for support.

"You lived in a cave for a time, didn't you? We found the story of it."

His eyebrows went up in surprise. "A story about it? About me, ye mean?"

"You're a famous Highland legend," I told him dryly, "or you will be, at least."

"For living in a cave?" He looked half-pleased, half-embarrassed. "Well, that's a foolish thing to make a story about, aye?"

"Arranging to have yourself betrayed to the English for the

price on your head was maybe a little more dramatic," I said, still
more dryly. "Taking rather a risk there, weren't you?"

The end of his nose was pink, and he looked somewhat abashed.

"Well," he said awkwardly, "I didna think prison would be
verra dreadful, and everything considered. . . ."

I spoke as calmly as I could, but I wanted to shake him, suddenly and ridiculously furious with him in retrospect.

"Prison, my arse! You knew perfectly well you might have been
hanged, didn't you? And you bloody did it anyway!"

"I had to do something," he said, shrugging. "And if the
English were fool enough to pay good money for my lousy carcass
—well, there's nay law against takin' advantage of fools, is
there?" One corner of his mouth quirked up, and I was torn
between the urge to kiss him and the urge to slap him.

I did neither, but sat up in bed and began combing the tangles
out of my hair with my fingers.

"I'd say it's open to question who the fool was," I said, not
looking at him, "but even so, you should know that your daughter's very proud of you."

"She is?" He sounded thunderstruck, and I looked up at him,
laughing despite my irritation.

"Well, of course she is. You're a bloody hero, aren't you?"

He went quite red in the face at this, and stood up, looking
thoroughly disconcerted.

"Me? No!" He rubbed a hand through his hair, his habit when
thinking or disturbed in his mind.

"No. I mean," he said slowly, "I wasna heroic at all about it. It
was only . . . I couldna bear it any longer. To see them all starving, I mean, and not be able to care for them—Jenny, and Ian and
the children; all the tenants and their families." He looked helplessly down at me. "I really didna care if the English hanged me
or not," he said. "I didna think they would, because of what ye'd
told me, but even if I'd known for sure it meant that—I would ha'
done it, Sassenach, and not minded. But it wasna bravery—not at
all." He threw up his hands in frustration, turning away. "There
was nothing else I could do!"

"I see," I said softly, after a moment. "I understand." He was
standing by the chiffonier, still naked, and at this, he turned half-
round to face me.

"Do ye, then?" His face was serious.

"I know you, Jamie Fraser." I spoke with more certainty than I had felt at any time since the moment I stepped through the rock.

"Do ye, then?" he asked again, but a faint smile shadowed his mouth.

"I think so."

The smile on his lips widened, and he opened his mouth to reply. Before he could speak, though, there was a knock upon the chamber door.

I started as though I had touched a hot stove. Jamie laughed, and bent to pat my hip as he went to the door.

"I expect it's the chambermaid with our breakfast, Sassenach, not the constable. And we *are* marrit, aye?" One eyebrow rose quizzically.

"Even so, shouldn't you put something on?" I asked, as he reached for the doorknob.

He glanced down at himself.

"I shouldna think it's likely to come as a shock to anyone in this house, Sassenach. But to honor your sensibilities—" He grinned at me, and taking a linen towel from the washstand, wrapped it casually about his loins before pulling open the door.

I caught sight of a tall male figure standing in the hall, and promptly pulled the bedclothes over my head. This was a reaction of pure panic, for if it had been the Edinburgh constable or one of his minions, I could scarcely expect much protection from a couple of quilts. But then the visitor spoke, and I was glad that I was safely out of sight for the moment.

"Jamie?" The voice sounded rather startled. Despite the fact that I had not heard it in twenty years, I recognized it at once. Rolling over, I surreptitiously lifted a corner of the quilt and peeked out beneath it.

"Well, of course it's me," Jamie was saying, rather testily. "Have ye no got eyes, man?" He pulled his brother-in-law, Ian, into the room and shut the door.

"I see well enough it's you," Ian said, with a note of sharpness. "I just didna ken whether to believe my eyes!" His smooth brown hair showed threads of gray, and his face bore the lines of a good many years' hard work. But Joe Abernathy had been right; with his first words, the new vision merged with the old, and this was the Ian Murray I had known before.

"I came here because the lad at the printshop said ye'd no been there last night, and this was the address Jenny sends your letters to,'' he was saying. He looked round the room with wide, suspicious eyes, as though expecting something to leap out from behind the armoire. Then his gaze flicked back to his brother-in-law, who was making a perfunctory effort to secure his makeshift loincloth.

''I never thought to find ye in a kittle-hoosie, Jamie!'' he said. ''I wasna sure, when the . . . the lady answered the door downstairs, but then—''

''It's no what ye think, Ian,'' Jamie said shortly.

''Oh, it's not, aye? And Jenny worrying that ye'd make yourself ill, living without a woman so long!'' Ian snorted. ''I'll tell her she needna concern herself wi' your welfare. And where's my son, then, down the hall with another o' the harlots?''

''Your son?'' Jamie's surprise was evident. ''Which one?''

Ian stared at Jamie, the anger on his long, half-homely face fading into alarm.

''Ye havena got him? Wee Ian's not here?''

''Young Ian? Christ, man, d'ye think I'd bring a fourteen-year-old lad into a brothel?''

Ian opened his mouth, then shut it, and sat down on the stool.

''Tell ye the truth, Jamie, I canna say what ye'd do anymore,'' he said levelly. He looked up at his brother-in-law, jaw set. ''Once I could. But not now.''

''And what the hell d'ye mean by that?'' I could see the angry flush rising in Jamie's face.

Ian glanced at the bed, and away again. The red flush didn't recede from Jamie's face, but I saw a small quiver at the corner of his mouth. He bowed elaborately to his brother-in-law.

''Your pardon, Ian, I was forgettin' my manners. Allow me to introduce ye to my companion.'' He stepped to the side of the bed and pulled back the quilts.

''No!'' Ian cried, jumping to his feet and looking frantically at the floor, the wardrobe, anywhere but at the bed.

''What, will ye no give your regards to my wife, Ian?'' Jamie said.

''Wife?'' Forgetting to look away, Ian goggled at Jamie in horror. ''Ye've marrit a whore?'' he croaked.

''I wouldn't call it that, exactly,'' I said. Hearing my voice, Ian jerked his head in my direction.

"Hullo," I said, waving cheerily at him from my nest of bed-clothes. "Been a long time, hasn't it?"

I'd always thought the descriptions of what people did when seeing ghosts rather exaggerated, but had been forced to revise my opinions in light of the responses I had been getting since my return to the past. Jamie had fainted dead away, and if Ian's hair was not literally standing on end, he assuredly looked as though he had been scared out of his wits.

Eyes bugging out, he opened and closed his mouth, making a small gobbling noise that seemed to entertain Jamie quite a lot.

"That'll teach ye to go about thinkin' the worst of my charac-ter," he said, with apparent satisfaction. Taking pity on his quiver-ing brother-in-law, Jamie poured out a tot of brandy and handed him the glass. "Judge not, and ye'll no be judged, eh?"

I thought Ian was going to spill the drink on his breeches, but he managed to get the glass to his mouth and swallow.

"What—?" He wheezed, eyes watering as he stared at me. "How—?"

"It's a long story," I said, with a glance at Jamie. He nodded briefly. We had had other things to think about in the last twenty-four hours besides how to explain me to people, and under the circumstances, I rather thought explanations could wait.

"I don't believe I know Young Ian. Is he missing?" I asked politely.

Ian nodded mechanically, not taking his eyes off me.

"He stole away from home last Friday week," he said, sound-ing rather dazed. "Left a note that he'd gone to his uncle." He took another swig of brandy, coughed and blinked several times, then wiped his eyes and sat up straighter, looking at me.

"It'll no be the first time, ye see," he said to me. He seemed to be regaining his self-confidence, seeing that I appeared to be flesh and blood, and showed no signs either of getting out of bed or of putting my head under my arm and strolling round without it, in the accepted fashion of Highland ghosts.

Jamie sat down on the bed next to me, taking my hand in his.

"I've not seen Young Ian since I sent him home wi' Fergus six months ago," he said. He was beginning to look as worried as Ian. "You're sure he said he was coming to me?"

"Well, he hasna got any other uncles that I know of," Ian said, rather acerbically. He tossed back the rest of the brandy and set the cup down.

"Fergus?" I interrupted. "Is Fergus all right, then?" I felt a surge of joy at the mention of the French orphan whom Jamie had once hired in Paris as a pickpocket, and brought back to Scotland as a servant lad.

Distracted from his thoughts, Jamie looked down at me.

"Oh, aye, Fergus is a bonny man now. A bit changed, of course." A shadow seemed to cross his face, but it cleared as he smiled, pressing my hand. "He'll be fair daft at seein' you once more, Sassenach."

Uninterested in Fergus, Ian had risen and was pacing back and forth across the polished plank floor.

"He didna take a horse," he muttered. "So he'd have nothing anyone would rob him for." He swung round to Jamie. "How did ye come, last time ye brought the lad here? By the land round the Firth, or did ye cross by boat?"

Jamie rubbed his chin, frowning as he thought. "I didna come to Lallybroch for him. He and Fergus crossed through the Carryarrick Pass and met me just above Loch Laggan. Then we came down through Struan and Weem and . . . aye, now I remember. We didna want to cross the Campbell lands, so we came to the east, and crossed the Forth at Donibristle."

"D'ye think he'd do that again?" Ian asked. "If it's the only way he knows?"

Jamie shook his head doubtfully. "He might. But he kens the coast is dangerous."

Ian resumed his pacing, hands clasped behind his back. "I beat him 'til he could barely stand, let alone sit, the last time he ran off," Ian said, shaking his head. His lips were tight, and I gathered that Young Ian was perhaps rather a trial to his father. "Ye'd think the wee fool would think better o' such tricks, aye?"

Jamie snorted, but not without sympathy.

"Did a thrashing ever stop you from doing anything you'd set your mind on?"

Ian stopped his pacing and sat down on the stool again, sighing.

"No," he said frankly, "but I expect it was some relief to my father." His face cracked into a reluctant smile, as Jamie laughed.

"He'll be all right," Jamie declared confidently. He stood up and let the towel drop to the floor as he reached for his breeches.

"I'll go and put about the word for him. If he's in Edinburgh, we'll hear of it by nightfall."

Ian cast a glance at me in the bed, and stood up hastily.

"I'll go wi' ye."

I thought I saw a shadow of doubt flicker across Jamie's face, but then he nodded and pulled the shirt over his head.

"All right," he said, as his head popped through the slit. He frowned at me.

"I'm afraid ye'll have to stay here, Sassenach," he said.

"I suppose I will," I said dryly. "Seeing that I haven't any clothes." The maid who brought our supper had removed my dress, and no replacement had as yet appeared.

Ian's feathery brows shot up to his hairline, but Jamie merely nodded.

"I'll tell Jeanne on the way out," he said. He frowned slightly, thinking. "It may be some time, Sassenach. There are things—well, I've business to take care of." He squeezed my hand, his expression softening as he looked at me.

"I dinna want to leave ye," he said softly. "But I must. You'll stay here until I come again?"

"Don't worry," I assured him, waving a hand at the linen towel he had just discarded. "I'm not likely to go anywhere in that."

The thud of their feet retreated down the hall and faded into the sounds of the stirring house. The brothel was rising, late and languid by the stern Scottish standards of Edinburgh. Below me I could hear the occasional slow muffled thump, the clatter of shutters thrust open nearby, a cry of "Gardyloo!" and a second later, the splash of slops flung out to land on the street far below.

Voices somewhere far down the hall, a brief inaudible exchange, and the closing of a door. The building itself seemed to stretch and sigh, with a creaking of timbers and a squeaking of stairs, and a sudden puff of coal-smelling warm air came out from the back of the cold hearth, the exhalation of a fire lit on some lower floor, sharing my chimney.

I relaxed into the pillows, feeling drowsy and heavily content. I was slightly and pleasantly sore in several unaccustomed places, and while I had been reluctant to see Jamie go, there was no denying that it was nice to be alone for a bit to mull things over.

* * *

I felt much like one who has been handed a sealed casket containing a long-lost treasure. I could feel the satisfying weight and the shape of it, and know the great joy of its possession, but still did not know exactly what was contained therein.

I was dying to know everything he had done and said and thought and been, through all the days between us. I had of course known that if he had survived Culloden, he would have a life—and knowing what I did of Jamie Fraser, it was unlikely to be a simple one. But knowing that, and being confronted with the reality of it, were two different things.

He had been fixed in my memory for so long, glowing but static, like an insect frozen in amber. And then had come Roger's brief historical sightings, like peeks through a keyhole; separate pictures like punctuations, alterations; adjustments of memory, each showing the dragonfly's wings raised or lowered at a different angle, like the single frames of a motion picture. Now time had begun to run again for us, and the dragonfly was in flight before me, flickering from place to place, so I saw little more yet than the glitter of its wings.

There were so many questions neither of us had had a chance to ask yet—what of his family at Lallybroch, his sister Jenny and her children? Obviously Ian was alive, and well, wooden leg notwithstanding—but had the rest of the family and the tenants of the estate survived the destruction of the Highlands? If they had, why was Jamie here in Edinburgh?

And if they were alive—what would we tell them about my sudden reappearance? I bit my lip, wondering whether there was *any* explanation—short of the truth—which might make sense. It might depend on what Jamie had told them when I disappeared after Culloden; there had seemed no need to concoct a reason for my vanishing at the time; it would simply be assumed that I had perished in the aftermath of the Rising, one more of the nameless corpses lying starved on the rocks or slaughtered in a leafless glen.

Well, we'd manage that when we came to it, I supposed. I was more curious just now about the extent and the danger of Jamie's less legitimate activities. Smuggling and sedition, was it? I was aware that smuggling was nearly as honorable a profession in the Scottish Highlands as cattle-stealing had been twenty years before, and might be conducted with relatively little risk. Sedition was something else, and seemed like an occupation of dubious safety for a convicted ex-Jacobite traitor.

That, I supposed, was the reason for his assumed name—or one reason, at any rate. Disturbed and excited as I had been when we arrived at the brothel the night before, I had noticed that Madame Jeanne referred to him by his own name. So presumably he smuggled under his own identity, but carried out his publishing activities—legal and illegal—as Alex Malcolm.

I had seen, heard and felt enough, during the all too brief hours of the night, to be fairly sure that the Jamie Fraser I had known still existed. How many other men he might be now remained to be seen.

There was a tentative rap at the door, interrupting my thoughts. Breakfast, I thought, and not before time. I was ravenous.

"Come in," I called, and sat up in bed, pulling up the pillows to lean against.

The door opened very slowly, and after quite a long pause, a head poked its way through the opening, much in the manner of a snail emerging from its shell after a hailstorm.

It was topped with an ill-cut shag of dark brown hair so thick that the cropped edges stuck out like a shelf above a pair of large ears. The face beneath was long and bony; rather pleasantly homely, save for a pair of beautiful brown eyes, soft and huge as a deer's, that rested on me with a mingled expression of interest and hesitancy.

The head and I regarded each other for a moment.

"Are you Mr. Malcolm's . . . woman?" it asked.

"I suppose you could say so," I replied cautiously. This was obviously not the chambermaid with my breakfast. Neither was it likely to be one of the other employees of the establishment, being evidently male, though very young. He seemed vaguely familiar, though I was sure I hadn't seen him before. I pulled the sheet a bit higher over my breasts. "And who are you?" I inquired.

The head thought this over for some time, and finally answered, with equal caution, "Ian Murray."

"Ian Murray?" I shot up straight, rescuing the sheet at the last moment. "Come in here," I said peremptorily. "If you're who I think you are, why aren't you where you're supposed to be, and what are you doing here?" The face looked rather alarmed, and showed signs of withdrawal.

"Stop!" I called, and put a leg out of bed to pursue him. The big brown eyes widened at the sight of my bare limb, and he froze. "Come in, I said."

Slowly, I withdrew the leg beneath the quilts, and equally slowly, he followed it into the room.

He was tall and gangly as a fledgling stork, with perhaps nine stone spread sparsely over a six-foot frame. Now that I knew who he was, the resemblance to his father was clear. He had his mother's pale skin, though, which blushed furiously red as it occurred to him suddenly that he was standing next to a bed containing a naked woman.

"I . . . er . . . was looking for my . . . for Mr. Malcolm, I mean," he murmured, staring fixedly at the floorboards by his feet.

"If you mean your uncle Jamie, he's not here," I said.

"No. No, I suppose not." He seemed unable to think of anything to add to this, but remained staring at the floor, one foot twisted awkwardly to the side, as though he were about to draw it up under him, like the wading bird he so much resembled.

"Do ye ken where . . ." he began, lifting his eyes, then, as he caught a glimpse of me, lowered them, blushed again and fell silent.

"He's looking for you," I said. "With your father," I added. "They left here not half an hour ago."

His head snapped up on its skinny neck, goggling.

"My father?" he gasped. "My father was here? Ye know him?"

"Why, yes," I said, without thinking. "I've known Ian for quite a long time."

He might be Jamie's nephew, but he hadn't Jamie's trick of inscrutability. Everything he thought showed on his face, and I could easily trace the progression of his expressions. Raw shock at learning of his father's presence in Edinburgh, then a sort of awestruck horror at the revelation of his father's long-standing acquaintance with what appeared to be a woman of a certain occupation, and finally the beginnings of angry absorption, as the young man began an immediate revision of his opinions of his father's character.

"Er—" I said, mildly alarmed. "It isn't what you think. I mean, your father and I—it's really your uncle and I, I mean—" I was trying to figure out how to explain the situation to him without getting into even deeper waters, when he whirled on his heel and started for the door.

"Wait a minute," I said. He stopped, but didn't turn around. His well-scrubbed ears stood out like tiny wings, the morning light illuminating their delicate pinkness. "How old are you?" I asked.

He turned around to face me, with a certain painful dignity. "I'll be fifteen in three weeks," he said. The red was creeping up his cheeks again. "Dinna worry, I'm old enough to know—what sort of place this is, I mean." He jerked his head toward me in an attempt at a courtly bow.

"Meaning no offense to ye, mistress. If Uncle Jamie—I mean, I—" He groped for suitable words, failed to find any, and finally blurted, "Verra pleased to meet ye, mum!" turned and bolted through the door, which shut hard enough to rattle in its frame.

I fell back against the pillows, torn between amusement and alarm. I did wonder what the elder Ian was going to say to his son when they met—and vice versa. As long as I was wondering, I wondered what had brought the younger Ian here in search of Jamie. Evidently, he knew where his uncle was likely to be found; yet judging from his diffident attitude, he had never before ventured into the brothel.

Had he extracted the information from Geordie at the print-shop? That seemed unlikely. And yet, if he hadn't—then that meant he had learned of his uncle's connection with this place from some other source. And the most likely source was Jamie himself.

But in that case, I reasoned, Jamie likely already knew that his nephew was in Edinburgh, so why pretend he hadn't seen the boy? Ian was Jamie's oldest friend; they had grown up together. If whatever Jamie was up to was worth the cost of deceiving his brother-in-law, it was something serious.

I had got no further with my musings, when there came another knock on the door.

"Come in," I said, smoothing out the quilts in anticipation of the breakfast tray to be placed thereon.

When the door opened, I had directed my attention at a spot about five feet above the floor, where I expected the chambermaid's head to materialize. Upon the last opening of the door, I had had to adjust my vision upward a foot, to accommodate the appearance of Young Ian. This time, I was obliged to drop it.

"What in the bloody hell are you doing here?" I demanded as the diminutive figure of Mr. Willoughby entered on hands and knees. I sat up and hastily tucked my feet underneath me, pulling not only sheet but quilts well up around my shoulders.

In answer, the Chinese advanced to within a foot of the bed, then let his head fall to the floor with a loud clunk. He raised it and repeated the process with great deliberation, making a horrid sound like a melon being cleaved with an ax.

"Stop that!" I exclaimed, as he prepared to do it a third time.

"Thousand apology," he explained, sitting up on his heels and blinking at me. He was quite a bit the worse for wear, and the dark red mark where his forehead had smacked the floor didn't add anything to his appearance. I trusted he didn't mean he'd been going to hit his head on the floor a thousand times, but I wasn't sure. He obviously had the hell of a hangover; for him to have attempted it even once was impressive.

"That's quite all right," I said, edging cautiously back against the wall. "There's nothing to apologize for."

"Yes, apology," he insisted. "Tsei-mi saying wife. Lady being most honorable First Wife, not stinking whore."

"Thanks a lot," I said. "Tsei-mi? You mean Jamie? Jamie Fraser?"

The little man nodded, to the obvious detriment of his head. He clutched it with both hands and closed his eyes, which promptly disappeared into the creases of his cheeks.

"Tsei-mi," he affirmed, eyes still closed. "Tsei-mi saying apology to most honored First Wife. Yi Tien Cho most humble servant." He bowed deeply, still holding on to his head. "Yi Tien Cho," he added, opening his eyes and tapping his chest to indicate that that was his name, in case I should be confusing him with any other humble servants in the vicinity.

"That's quite all right," I said. "Er, pleased to meet you."

Evidently heartened by this, he slid bonelessly onto his face, prostrating himself before me.

"Yi Tien Cho lady's servant," he said. "First Wife please to walk on humble servant, if like."

"Ha," I said coldly. "I've heard about you. Walk on you, eh? Not bloody likely!"

A slit of gleaming black eye showed, and he giggled, so irre-pressibly that I couldn't help laughing myself. He sat up again, smoothing down the spikes of dirt-stiffened black hair that sprang, porcupine-like, from his skull.

"I wash First Wife's feet?" he offered, grinning widely.

"Certainly not," I said. "If you really want to do something helpful, go and tell someone to bring me breakfast. No, wait a minute," I said, changing my mind. "First, tell me where you met Jamie. If you don't mind," I added, to be polite.

He sat back on his heels, head bobbing slightly. "Docks," he said. "Two year ago. I come China, long way, no food. Hiding barrel," he explained, reaching his arms in a circle, to demon-strate his means of transportation.

"A stowaway?"

"Trade ship," he nodded. "On docks here, stealing food. Steal-ing brandy one night, getting stinking drunk. Very cold to sleep; die soon, but Tsei-mi find." He jabbed a thumb at his chest once more. "Tsei-mi's humble servant. Humble servant First Wife." He bowed to me, swaying alarmingly in the process, but came upright again without mishap.

"Brandy seems to be your downfall," I observed. "I'm sorry I haven't anything to give you for your head; I don't have any medicines with me at the moment."

"Oh, not worry," he assured me. "I having healthy balls."

"How nice for you," I said, trying to decide whether he was gearing up for another attempt on my feet, or merely still too drunk to distinguish basic anatomy. Or perhaps there was some connection, in Chinese philosophy, between the well-being of head and testicles? Just in case, I looked round for something that might be used as a weapon, in case he showed a disposition to begin burrowing under the bedclothes.

Instead, he reached into the depths of one baggy blue-silk sleeve and with the air of a conjuror, drew out a small white silk bag. He upended this, and two balls dropped out into his palm. They were larger than marbles and smaller than baseballs; about the size, in fact, of the average testicle. A good deal harder, though, being apparently made of some kind of polished stone, greenish in color.

"Healthy balls," Mr. Willoughby explained, rolling them to-gether in his palm. They made a pleasant clicking noise.

"Streaked jade, from Canton," he said. "Best kind of healthy balls."

"Really?" I said, fascinated. "And they're medicinal—good for you, that's what you're saying?"

He nodded vigorously, then stopped abruptly with a faint moan. After a pause, he spread out his hand, and rolled the balls to and fro, keeping them in movement with a dextrous circling of his fingers.

"All body one part; hand all parts," he said. He poked a finger toward his open palm, touching delicately here and there between the smooth green spheres. "Head there, stomach there, liver there," he said. "Balls make all good."

"Well, I suppose they're as portable as Alka-Seltzer," I said. Possibly it was the reference to stomach that caused my own to emit a loud growl at this point.

"First Wife wanting food," Mr. Willoughby observed shrewdly.

"Very astute of you," I said. "Yes, I do want food. Do you suppose you could go and tell someone?"

He dumped the healthy balls back into their bag at once, and springing to his feet, bowed deeply.

"Humble servant go now," he said, and went, crashing rather heavily into the door post on his way out.

This was becoming ridiculous, I thought. I harbored substantial doubt as to whether Mr. Willoughby's visit would result in food; he'd be lucky to make it to the bottom of the stair without falling on his head, if I was any judge of his condition.

Rather than go on sitting here in the nude, receiving random deputations from the outside world, I thought it time to take steps. Rising and carefully wrapping a quilt around my body, I took a few, out into the corridor.

The upper floor seemed deserted. Aside from the room I had left, there were only two other doors up here. Glancing up, I could see unadorned rafters overhead. We were in the attic, then; chances were that the other rooms here were occupied by servants, who were presumably now employed downstairs.

I could hear faint noises drifting up the stairwell. Something else drifted up, as well—the scent of frying sausage. A loud gustatory rumble informed me that my stomach hadn't missed this, and furthermore, that my innards considered the consumption of one peanut butter sandwich and one bowl of soup in one twenty-four-hour period a wholly inadequate level of nutrition.

I tucked the ends of the quilt in, sarong-fashion, just above my breasts, and picking up my trailing skirts, followed the scent of food downstairs.

The smell—and the clinking, clattering, sloshing noises of a number of people eating—were coming from a closed door on the first floor above ground level. I pushed it open, and found myself at the end of a long room equipped as a refectory.

The table was surrounded by twenty-odd women, a few gowned for day, but most of them in a state of dishabille that made my quilt modest by comparison. A woman near the end of the table caught sight of me hovering in the doorway, and beckoned, companionably sliding over to make room for me on the end of the long bench.

"You'll be the new lass, aye?" she said, looking me over with interest. "You're a wee bit older than Madame usually takes on— she likes 'em no more than five and twenty. You're no bad at all, though," she assured me hastily. "I'm sure you'll do fine."

"Good skin and a pretty face," observed the dark-haired lady across from us, sizing me up with the detached air of one appraising horseflesh. "And nice bubbies, what I can see." She lifted her chin slightly, peering across the table at what could be seen of my cleavage.

"Madame doesna like us to take the kivvers off the beds," my original acquaintance said reprovingly. "Ye should wear your shift, if ye havena something pretty to show yourself in yet."

"Aye, be careful with the quilt," advised the dark-haired girl, still scrutinizing me. "Madame'll dock your wages, an' ye get spots on the bedclothes."

"What's your name, my dearie?" A short, rather plump girl with a round, friendly face leaned past the dark girl's elbow to smile at me. "Here we're all chatterin' at ye, and not welcomed ye proper at all. I'm Dorcas, this is Peggy"—she jerked a thumb at the dark-haired girl, then pointed across the table to the fair-haired woman beside me—"and that's Mollie."

"My name is Claire," I said, smiling and hitching the quilt a bit higher in self-consciousness. I wasn't sure how to correct their impression that I was Madame Jeanne's newest recruit; for the moment, that seemed less important than getting some breakfast.

Apparently divining my need, the friendly Dorcas reached to the sideboard behind her, passed me a wooden plate, and shoved a large dish of sausages in my direction.

The food was well cooked and would have been good in any case; starved as I was, it was ambrosial. A hell of a lot better than the hospital cafeteria's breakfasts, I observed to myself, taking another ladle of fried potatoes.

"Had a rough one for your first, aye?" Millie, next to me, nodded at my bosom. Glancing down, I was mortified to see a large red patch peeking above the edge of my quilt. I couldn't see my neck, but the direction of Millie's interested gaze made it clear that the small tingling sensations there were evidence of further bite-marks.

"Your nose is a wee bit puffed, too," Peggy said, frowning at me critically. She reached across the table to touch it, disregarding the fact that the gesture caused her flimsy wrap to fall open to the waist. "Slap ye, did he? If they get too rough, ye should call out, ye know; Madame doesna allow the customers to mistreat us— give a good screech and Bruno will be in there in a moment."

"Bruno?" I said, a little faintly.

"The porter," Dorcas explained, busily spooning eggs into her mouth. "Big as a bear—that's why we call him Bruno. What's his name really?" she asked the table at large, "Horace?"

"Theobald," corrected Millie. She turned to call to a serv-ingmaid at the end of the room, "Janie, will ye fetch in more ale? The new lassie's had none yet!"

"Aye, Peggy's right," she said, turning back to me. She wasn't at all pretty, but had a nicely shaped mouth and a pleasant expres-sion. "If ye get a man likes to play a bit rough, that's one thing— and don't sic Bruno on a good customer, or there'll be hell to pay, and you'll do the paying. But if ye think ye might really be dam-aged, then just give a good skelloch. Bruno's never far away during the night. Oh, here's the ale," she added, taking a big pewter mug from the servingmaid and plonking it in front of me.

"She's no damaged," Dorcas said, having completed her sur-vey of the visible aspects of my person. "A bit sore between the legs, though, aye?" she said shrewdly, grinning at me.

"Ooh, look, she's *blushing*," said Mollie, giggling with delight. "Ooh, you *are* a fresh one, aren't ye?"

I took a deep gulp of the ale. It was dark, rich, and extremely welcome, as much for the width of the cup rim that hid my face as for its taste.

"Never mind." Mollie patted my arm kindly. "After breakfast, I'll show ye where the tubs are. Ye can soak your parts in warm water, and they'll be good as new by tonight."

"Be sure to show her where the jars are, too," put in Dorcas. "Sweet herbs," she explained to me. "Put them in the water before ye sit in it. Madame likes us to smell sweet."

"Eef ze men want to lie wiz a feesh, zey would go to ze docks; eet ees more cheap," Peggy intoned, in what was patently meant to be an imitation of Madame Jeanne. The table erupted in giggles, which were rapidly quelled by the sudden appearance of Madame herself, who entered through a door at the end of the room.

Madame Jeanne was frowning in a worried fashion, and seemed too preoccupied to notice the smothered hilarity.

"*Tsk!*" murmured Mollie, seeing the proprietor. "An early customer. I hate it when they come in the middle o' breakfast," she grumbled. "Stop ye digesting your food proper, it does."

"Ye needn't worry, Mollie; it's Claire'll have to take him," Peggy said, tossing her dark plait out of the way. "Newest lass takes the ones no one wants," she informed me.

"Stick your finger up his bum," Dorcas advised me. "That brings 'em off faster than anything. I'll save ye a bannock for after, if ye like."

"Er . . . thanks," I said. Just then, Madame Jeanne's eye lit upon me, and her mouth dropped open in a horrified "O."

"What are *you* doing here?" she asked, rushing up to grab me by the arm.

"Eating," I said, in no mood to be snatched at. I detached my arm from her grasp and picked up my ale cup.

"*Merde!*" she said. "Did no one bring you food this morning?"

"No," I said. "Nor yet clothes." I gestured at the quilt, which was in imminent danger of falling off.

"*Nez de Cléopatre!*" she said violently. She stood up and glanced around the room, eyes flashing daggers. "I will have the worthless scum of a maid flayed for this! A thousand apologies, Madame!''

"That's quite all right," I said graciously, aware of the looks of astonishment on the faces of my breakfast companions. "I've had a wonderful meal. Nice to have met you all, ladies," I said, rising and doing my best to bow graciously while clutching my quilt. "Now, Madame . . . about my gown?"

Amid Madame Jeanne's agitated protestations of apology, and reiterated hopes that I would not find it necessary to tell Monsieur Fraser that I had been exposed to an undesirable intimacy with the working members of the establishment, I made my clumsy way up two more flights of stairs, and into a small room draped with hanging garments in various stages of completion, with bolts of cloth stacked here and there in the corners of the chamber.

"A moment, please," Madame Jeanne said, and with a deep bow, left me to the company of a dressmaker's dummy, with a large number of pins protruding from its stuffed bosom.

Apparently this was where the costuming of the inmates took place. I walked around the room, quilt trailing, and observed several flimsy silk wrappers under construction, together with a couple of elaborate gowns with very low necks, and a number of rather imaginative variations on the basic shift and camisole. I removed one shift from its hook, and put it on.

It was made of fine cotton, with a low, gathered neck, and embroidery in the form of multiple hands that curled enticingly under the bosom and down the sides of the waist, spreading out into a rakish caress atop the hips. It hadn't been hemmed, but was otherwise complete, and gave me a great deal more freedom of movement than had the quilt.

I could hear voices in the next room, where Madame was apparently haranguing Bruno—or so I deduced the identity of the male rumble.

"I do not care *what* the miserable girl's sister has done," she was saying, "do you not realize that the wife of Monsieur Jamie was left naked and starving—"

"Are you sure she's his wife?" the deep male voice asked. "I had heard—"

"So had I. But if he says this woman is his wife, I am not

disposed to argue, *n'est-ce pas*?" Madame sounded impatient. "Now, as to this wretched Madeleine—"

"It's not her fault, Madame," Bruno broke in. "Have you not heard the news this morning—about the Fiend?"

Madame gave a small gasp. "No! Not another?"

"Yes, Madame." Bruno's voice was grim. "No more than a few doors away—above the Green Owl tavern. The girl was Madeleine's sister; the priest brought the news just before breakfast. So you can see—"

"Yes, I see." Madame sounded a little breathless. "Yes, of course. Of course. Was it—the same?" Her voice quivered with distaste.

"Yes, Madame. A hatchet or a big knife of some sort." He lowered his voice, as people do when recounting horrid things. "The priest told me that her head had been completely severed. Her body was near the door of her room, and her head"—his voice dropped even lower, almost to a whisper—"her head was sitting on the mantelpiece, looking into the room. The landlord swooned when he found her."

A heavy thud from the next room suggested that Madame Jeanne had done likewise. Gooseflesh rippled up my arms, and my own knees felt a trifle watery. I was beginning to agree with Jamie's fear that his installing me in a house of prostitution had been injudicious.

At any rate, I was now clad, if not entirely dressed, and I went into the room next door, to find Madame Jeanne in semi-recline on the sofa of a small parlor, with a burly, unhappy-looking man sitting on the hassock near her feet.

Madame started up at the sight of me. "Madame Fraser! Oh, I am so sorry! I did not mean to leave you waiting, but I have had . . ." she hesitated, looking for some delicate expression ". . . some distressing news."

"I'd say so," I said. "What's this about a Fiend?"

"You heard?" She was already pale; now her complexion went a few shades whiter, and she wrung her hands. "What will he say? He will be furious!" she moaned.

"Who?" I asked. "Jamie, or the Fiend?"

"Your husband," she said. She looked about the parlor, distracted. "When he hears that his wife has been so shamefully neglected, mistaken for a *fille de joie* and exposed to—to—"

"I really don't think he'll mind," I said. "But I would like to hear about the Fiend."

"You would?" Bruno's heavy eyebrows rose. He was a big man, with sloping shoulders and long arms that made him look rather like a gorilla; a resemblance enhanced by a low brow and a receding chin. He looked eminently suited to the role of bouncer in a brothel.

"Well." He hesitated, glancing at Madame Jeanne for guidance, but the proprietor caught sight of the small enameled clock on the mantelpiece and jumped to her feet with an exclamation of shock.

"Crottin!" she exclaimed. "I must go!" And with no more than a perfunctory wave in my direction, she sped from the room, leaving Bruno and me looking after her in surprise.

"Oh," he said, recovering himself. "That's right, it was coming at ten o'clock." It was a quarter-past ten, by the enamel clock. Whatever "it" was, I hoped it would wait.

"Fiend," I prompted.

Like most people, Bruno was only too willing to reveal all the gory details, once past a pro forma demur for the sake of social delicacy.

The Edinburgh Fiend was—as I had deduced from the conversation thus far—a murderer. Like an early-day Jack the Ripper, he specialized in women of easy virtue, whom he killed with blows from a heavy-bladed instrument. In some cases, the bodies had been dismembered or otherwise "interfered with," as Bruno said, in lowered voice.

The killings—eight in all—had occurred at intervals over the last two years. With one exception, the women had been killed in their own rooms; most lived alone—two had been killed in brothels. Hence Madame's agitation, I supposed.

"What was the exception?" I asked.

Bruno crossed himself. "A nun," he whispered, the words evidently still a shock to him. "A French Sister of Mercy."

The Sister, coming ashore at Edinburgh with a group of nuns bound for London, had been abducted from the docks, without any of her companions noticing her absence in the confusion. By the time she was discovered in one of Edinburgh's wynds, after nightfall, it was far too late.

"Raped?" I asked, with clinical interest.

Bruno eyed me with considerable suspicion.

"I do not know," he said formally. He rose heavily to his feet, his simian shoulders drooping with fatigue. I supposed he had been on duty all night; it must be his bedtime now. "If you will excuse me, Madame," he said, with remote formality, and went out.

I sat back on the small velvet sofa, feeling mildly dazed. Somehow I hadn't realized that quite so much went on in brothels in the daytime.

There was a sudden loud hammering at the door. It didn't sound like knocking, but as though someone really were using a metal-headed hammer to demand admittance. I got to my feet to answer the summons, but without further warning, the door burst open, and a slender imperious figure strode into the room, speaking French in an accent so pronounced and an attitude so furious that I could not follow it all.

"Are you looking for Madame Jeanne?" I managed to put in, seizing a small pause when he stopped to draw breath for more invective. The visitor was a young man of about thirty, slightly built and strikingly handsome, with thick black hair and brows. He glared at me under these, and as he got a good look at me, an extraordinary change went across his face. The brows rose, his black eyes grew huge, and his face went white.

"Milady!" he exclaimed, and flung himself on his knees, embracing me about the thighs as he pressed his face into the cotton shift at crotch level.

"Let go!" I exclaimed, shoving at his shoulders to detach him. "I don't work here. Let go, I say!"

"Milady!" he was repeating in tones of rapture. "Milady! You have come back! A miracle! God has restored you!"

He looked up at me, smiling as tears streamed down his face. He had large white perfect teeth. Suddenly memory stirred and shifted, showing me the outlines of an urchin's face beneath the man's bold visage.

"Fergus!" I said. "Fergus, is that really you? Get up, for God's sake—let me see you!"

He rose to his feet, but didn't pause to let me inspect him. He gathered me into a rib-cracking hug, and I clutched him in return, pounding his back in the excitement of seeing him again. He had

been ten or so when I last saw him, just before Culloden. Now he
was a man, and the stubble of his beard rasped against my cheek.

"I thought I was seeing a ghost!" he exclaimed. "It is really
you, then?"

"Yes, it's me," I assured him.

"You have seen milord?" he asked excitedly. "He knows you
are here?"

"Yes."

"Oh!" He blinked and stepped back half a pace, as something
occurred to him. "But—but what about—" He paused, clearly
confused.

"What about what?"

"There ye are! What in the name of God are ye doing up here,
Fergus?" Jamie's tall figure loomed suddenly in the doorway. His
eyes widened at the sight of me in my embroidered shift. "Where
are your clothes?" he asked. "Never mind," he said then, waving
his hand impatiently as I opened my mouth to answer. "I havena
time just now. Come along, Fergus, there's eighteen ankers of
brandy in the alleyway, and the excisemen on my heels!"

And with a thunder of boots on the wooden staircase, they were
gone, leaving me alone once more.

I wasn't sure whether I should join the party downstairs or not,
but curiosity got the better of discretion. After a quick visit to the
sewing room in search of more extensive covering, I made my way
down, a large shawl half-embroidered with hollyhocks flung round
my shoulders.

I had gathered only a vague impression of the layout of the
house the night before, but the street noises that filtered through
the windows made it clear which side of the building faced the
High Street. I assumed the alleyway to which Jamie had referred
must be on the other side, but wasn't sure. The houses of Edinburgh were frequently constructed with odd little wings and twisting walls, to take advantage of every inch of space.

I paused on the large landing at the foot of the stairs, listening
for the sound of rolling casks as a guide. As I stood there, I felt a
sudden draft on my bare feet, and turned to see a man standing in
the open doorway from the kitchen.

He seemed as surprised as I, but after blinking at me, he smiled and stepped forward to grip me by the elbow.

"And a good morning to you, my dear. I didn't expect to find any of you ladies up and about so early in the morning."

"Well, you know what they say about early to bed and early to rise," I said, trying to extricate my elbow.

He laughed, showing rather badly stained teeth in a narrow jaw. "No, what do they say about it?"

"Well, it's something they say in America, come to think of it," I replied, suddenly realizing that Benjamin Franklin, even if currently publishing, probably didn't have a wide readership in Edinburgh.

"Got a wit about you, chuckie," he said, with a slight smile. "Send you down as a decoy, did she?"

"No. Who?" I said.

"The madam," he said, glancing around. "Where is she?"

"I have no idea," I said. "Let go!"

Instead, he tightened his grip, so that his fingers dug uncomfortably into the muscles of my upper arm. He leaned closer, whispering in my ear with a gust of stale tobacco fumes.

"There's a reward, you know," he murmured confidentially. "A percentage of the value of the seized contraband. No one would need to know but you and me." He flicked one finger gently under my breast, making the nipple stand up under the thin cotton. "What d'ye say, chuck?"

I stared at him. "The excisemen are on my heels," Jamie had said. This must be one, then; an officer of the Crown, charged with the prevention of smuggling and the apprehension of smugglers. What had Jamie said? "The pillory, transportation, flogging, imprisonment, ear-nailing," waving an airy hand as though such penalties were the equivalent of a traffic ticket.

"Whatever are you talking about?" I said, trying to sound puzzled. "And for the last time, let go of me!" He couldn't be alone, I thought. How many others were there around the building?

"Yes, please let go," said a voice behind me. I saw the exciseman's eyes widen as he glanced over my shoulder.

Mr. Willoughby stood on the second stair in rumpled blue silk, a large pistol gripped in both hands. He bobbed his head politely at the excise officer.

"Not stinking whore," he explained, blinking owlishly. "Honorable wife."

The exciseman, clearly startled by the unexpected appearance of a Chinese, gawked from me to Mr. Willoughby and back again.

"Wife?" he said disbelievingly. "You say she's your *wife*?"

Mr. Willoughby, clearly catching only the salient word, nodded pleasantly.

"Wife," he said again. "Please letting go." His eyes were mere bloodshot slits, and it was apparent to me, if not to the exciseman, that his blood was still approximately 80 proof.

The exciseman pulled me toward himself and scowled at Mr. Willoughby. "Now, listen here—" he began. He got no further, for Mr. Willoughby, evidently assuming that he had given fair warning, raised the pistol and pulled the trigger.

There was a loud crack, an even louder shriek, which must have been mine, and the landing was filled with a cloud of gray powder-smoke. The exciseman staggered back against the paneling, a look of intense surprise on his face, and a spreading rosette of blood on the breast of his coat.

Moving by reflex, I leapt forward and grasped the man under the arms, easing him gently down to the floorboards of the landing. There was a flurry of noise from above, as the inhabitants of the house crowded, chattering and exclaiming, onto the upper landing, attracted by the shot. Bounding footsteps came up the lower stairs two at a time.

Fergus burst through what must be the cellar door, a pistol in his hand.

"Milady," he gasped, catching sight of me sitting in the corner with the exciseman's body sprawled across my lap. "What have you done?"

"Me?" I said indignantly. "*I* haven't done anything; it's Jamie's pet Chinaman." I nodded briefly toward the stair, where Mr. Willoughby, the pistol dropped unregarded by his feet, had sat down on the step and was now regarding the scene below with a benign and bloodshot eye.

Fergus said something in French that was too colloquial to translate, but sounded highly uncomplimentary to Mr. Willoughby. He strode across the landing, and reached out a hand to grasp the little Chinaman's shoulder—or so I assumed, until I saw that the arm he extended did not end in a hand, but in a hook of gleaming dark metal.

"Fergus!" I was so shocked at the sight that I stopped my attempts to stanch the exciseman's wound with my shawl. "What —what—" I said incoherently.

"What?" he said, glancing at me. Then, following the direction of my gaze, said, "Oh, that," and shrugged. "The English. Don't worry about it, milady, we haven't time. You, *canaille,* get downstairs!" He jerked Mr. Willoughby off the stairs, dragged him to the cellar door and shoved him through it, with a callous disregard for safety. I could hear a series of bumps, suggesting that the Chinese was rolling downstairs, his acrobatic skills having temporarily deserted him, but had no time to worry about it.

Fergus squatted next to me, and lifted the exciseman's head by the hair. "How many companions are with you?" he demanded. "Tell me quickly, *cochon,* or I slit your throat!"

From the evident signs, this was a superfluous threat. The man's eyes were already glazing over. With considerable effort, the corners of his mouth drew back in a smile.

"I'll see . . . you . . . burn . . . in . . . hell," he whispered, and with a last convulsion that fixed the smile in a hideous rictus upon his face, he coughed up a startling quantity of bright red foamy blood, and died in my lap.

More feet were coming up the stairs at a high rate of speed. Jamie charged through the cellar door and barely stopped himself before stepping on the excise officer's trailing legs. His eyes traveled up the body's length and rested on my face with horrified amazement.

"What have ye done, Sassenach?" he demanded.

"Not her—the yellow pox," Fergus put in, saving me the trouble. He thrust the pistol into his belt and offered me his real hand. "Come, milady, you must get downstairs!"

Jamie forestalled him, bending over me as he jerked his head in the direction of the front hall.

"I'll manage here," he said. "Guard the front, Fergus. The usual signal, and keep your pistol hidden unless there's need."

Fergus nodded and vanished at once through the door to the hall.

Jamie had succeeded in bundling the corpse awkwardly in the shawl; he lifted it off me, and I scrambled to my feet, greatly relieved to be rid of it, in spite of the blood and other objectionable substances soaking the front of my shift.

"Ooh! I think he's *dead*!" An awestruck voice floated down from above, and I looked up to see a dozen prostitutes peering down like cherubim from on high.

"Get back to your rooms!" Jamie barked. There was a chorus of frightened squeals, and they scattered like pigeons.

Jamie glanced around the landing for traces of the incident, but luckily there were none—the shawl and I had caught everything.

"Come on," he said.

The stairs were dim and the cellar at the foot pitch-black. I stopped at the bottom, waiting for Jamie. The exciseman had not been lightly built, and Jamie was breathing hard when he reached me.

"Across to the far side," he said, gasping. "A false wall. Hold my arm."

With the door above shut, I couldn't see a thing; luckily Jamie seemed able to steer by radar. He led me unerringly past large objects that I bumped in passing, and finally came to a halt. I could smell damp stone, and putting out a hand, felt a rough wall before me.

Jamie said something loudly in Gaelic. Apparently it was the Celtic equivalent of "open sesame," for there was a short silence, then a grating noise, and a faint glowing line appeared in the darkness before me. The line widened into a slit, and a section of the wall swung out, revealing a small doorway, made of a wooden framework, upon which cut stones were mounted so as to look like part of the wall.

The concealed cellar was a large room, at least thirty feet long. Several figures were moving about, and the air was ripely suffocating with the smell of brandy. Jamie dumped the body unceremoniously in a corner, then turned to me.

"God, Sassenach, are ye all right?" The cellar seemed to be lighted with candles, dotted here and there in the dimness. I could just see his face, skin drawn tight across his cheekbones.

"I'm a little cold," I said, trying not to let my teeth chatter. "My shift is soaked with blood. Otherwise I'm all right. I think."

"Jeanne!" He turned and called toward the far end of the cellar, and one of the figures came toward us, resolving itself into a very worried-looking madam. He explained the situation in a few words, causing the worried expression to grow considerably worse.

"Horreur!" she said. "Killed? On my premises? With *witnesses*?"

"Aye, I'm afraid so." Jamie sounded calm. "I'll manage about it. But in the meantime, ye must go up. He might not have been alone. You'll know what to do."

His voice held a tone of calm assurance, and he squeezed her arm. The touch seemed to calm her—I hoped that was why he had done it—and she turned to leave.

"Oh, and Jeanne," Jamie called after her. "When ye come back, can ye bring down some clothes for my wife? If her gown's not ready, I think Daphne is maybe the right size."

"Clothes?" Madame Jeanne squinted into the shadows where I stood. I helpfully stepped out into the light, displaying the results of my encounter with the exciseman.

Madame Jeanne blinked once or twice, crossed herself, and turned without a word, to disappear through the concealed doorway, which swung to behind her with a muffled thud.

I was beginning to shake, as much with reaction as with the cold. Accustomed as I was to emergency, blood, and even sudden death, the events of the morning had been more than a little harrowing. It was like a bad Saturday night in the emergency room.

"Come along, Sassenach," Jamie said, putting a hand gently on the small of my back. "We'll get ye washed." His touch worked on me as well as it had on Madame Jeanne; I felt instantly better, if still apprehensive.

"Washed? In what? Brandy?"

He gave a slight laugh at that. "No, water. I can offer ye a bathtub, but I'm afraid it will be cold."

It was extremely cold.

"Wh-wh-where did this water come from?" I asked, shivering. "Off a glacier?" The water gushed out of a pipe set in the wall, normally kept plugged with an insanitary-looking wad of rags, wrapped to form a rough seal around the chunk of wood that served as a plug.

I pulled my hand out of the chilly stream and wiped it on the shift, which was too far gone for anything to make much difference. Jamie shook his head as he maneuvered the big wooden tub closer to the spout.

"Off the roof," he answered. "There's a rainwater cistern up there. The guttering pipe runs down the side of the building, and the cistern pipe is hidden inside it." He looked absurdly proud of himself, and I laughed.

"Quite an arrangement," I said. "What do you use the water for?"

"To cut the liquor," he explained. He gestured at the far side of the room, where the shadowy figures were working with notable industry among a large array of casks and tubs. "It comes in a hundred and eighty degrees above proof. We mix it here wi' pure water, and recask it for sale to the taverns."

He shoved the rough plug back into the pipe, and bent to pull the big tub across the stone floor. "Here, we'll take it out of the way; they'll be needing the water." One of the men was in fact standing by with a small cask clasped in his arms; with no more than a curious glance at me, he nodded to Jamie and thrust the cask beneath the stream of water.

Behind a hastily arranged screen of empty barrels, I peered dubiously down into the depths of my makeshift tub. A single candle burned in a puddle of wax nearby, glimmering off the surface of the water and making it look black and bottomless. I stripped off, shivering violently, thinking that the comforts of hot water and modern plumbing had seemed a hell of a lot easier to renounce when they were close at hand.

Jamie groped in his sleeve and pulled out a large handkerchief, at which he squinted dubiously.

"Aye, well, it's maybe cleaner than your shift," he said, shrugging. He handed it to me, then excused himself to oversee operations at the other end of the room.

The water was freezing and so was the cellar, and as I gingerly sponged myself, the icy trickles running down my stomach and thighs brought on small fits of shivering.

Thoughts of what might be happening overhead did little to ease my feelings of chilly apprehension. Presumably, we were safe enough for the moment, so long as the false cellar wall deceived any searching excisemen.

But if the wall failed to hide us, our position was all but hopeless. There appeared to be no way out of this room but by the door in the false wall—and if that wall was breached, we would not only be caught red-handed in possession of quite a lot of contraband brandy, but also in custody of the body of a murdered King's Officer.

And surely the disappearance of that officer would provoke an intensive search? I had visions of excisemen combing the brothel, questioning and threatening the women, emerging with complete descriptions of myself, Jamie, and Mr. Willoughby, as well as several eyewitness accounts of the murder. Involuntarily, I glanced at the far corner, where the dead man lay beneath his bloodstained shroud, covered with pink and yellow hollyhocks. The Chinaman was nowhere to be seen, having apparently passed out behind the ankers of brandy.

"Here, Sassenach. Drink this; your teeth are chattering so, you're like to bite through your tongue." Jamie had reappeared by my seal hole like a St. Bernard dog, bearing a firkin of brandy.

"Th-thanks." I had to drop the washcloth and use both hands to steady the wooden cup so it wouldn't clack against my teeth, but the brandy helped; it dropped like a flaming coal into the pit of my stomach and sent small curling tendrils of warmth through my frigid extremities as I sipped.

"Oh, God, that's better," I said, stopping long enough to gasp for breath. "Is this the uncut version?"

"No, that would likely kill ye. This is maybe a little stronger than what we sell, though. Finish up and put something on; then ye can have a bit more." Jamie took the cup from my hand and gave me back the handkerchief washcloth. As I hurriedly finished my chilly ablutions, I watched him from the corner of my eye. He was frowning as he gazed at me, clearly deep in thought. I had imagined that his life was complicated; it hadn't escaped me that my presence was undoubtedly complicating it a good bit more. I would have given a lot to know what he was thinking.

"What are you thinking about, Jamie?" I said, watching him sidelong as I swabbed the last of the smudges from my thighs. The water swirled around my calves, disturbed by my movements, and the candlelight lit the waves with sparks, as though the dark blood I had washed from my body now glowed once more live and red in the water.

The frown vanished momentarily as his eyes cleared and fixed on my face.

"I am thinking that you're verra beautiful, Sassenach," he said softly.

"Maybe if one has a taste for gooseflesh on a large scale," I said tartly, stepping out of the tub and reaching for the cup.

He grinned suddenly at me, teeth flashing white in the dimness of the cellar.

"Oh, aye," he said. "Well, you're speaking to the only man in Scotland who has a terrible cockstand at sight of a plucked chicken."

I spluttered in my brandy and choked, half-hysterical from tension and terror.

Jamie quickly shrugged out of his coat and wrapped the garment around me, hugging me close against him as I shivered and coughed and gasped.

"Makes it hard to pass a poulterer's stall and stay decent," he murmured in my ear, briskly rubbing my back through the fabric. "Hush, Sassenach, hush now. It'll be fine."

I clung to him, shaking. "I'm sorry," I said. "I'm all right. It's my fault, though. Mr. Willoughby shot the exciseman because he thought he was making indecent advances to me."

Jamie snorted. "That doesna make it your fault, Sassenach," he said dryly. "And for what it's worth, it's no the first time the Chinaman's done something foolish, either. When he's drink taken, he'll do anything, and never mind how mad it is."

Suddenly Jamie's expression changed as he realized what I had said. He stared down at me, eyes wide. "Did ye say 'exciseman,' Sassenach?"

"Yes, why?"

He didn't answer, but let go my shoulders and whirled on his heel, snatching the candle off the cask in passing. Rather than be left in the dark, I followed him to the corner where the corpse lay under its shawl.

"Hold this." Jamie thrust the candle unceremoniously into my hand and knelt by the shrouded figure, pulling back the stained fabric that covered the face.

I had seen quite a few dead bodies; the sight was no shock, but it still wasn't pleasant. The eyes had rolled up beneath half-closed lids, which did nothing to help the generally ghastly effect. Jamie frowned at the dead face, drop-jawed and waxy in the candlelight, and muttered something under his breath.

"What's wrong?" I asked. I had thought I would never be warm again, but Jamie's coat was not only thick and well-made, it held the remnants of his own considerable body heat. I was still cold, but the shivering had eased.

"This isna an exciseman," Jamie said, still frowning. "I know all the Riding Officers in the district, and the Superintending Officers, too. But I've no seen this fellow before." With some distaste, he turned back the sodden flap of the coat and groped inside.

He felt about gingerly but thoroughly inside the man's clothing, emerging at last with a small penknife, and a small booklet bound in red paper.

" 'New Testament,' " I read, with some astonishment.

Jamie nodded, looking up at me with one brow raised. "Exciseman or no, it seems a peculiar thing to bring with ye to a kittlehoosie." He wiped the little booklet on the shawl, then drew the folds of fabric quite gently back over the face, and rose to his feet, shaking his head.

"That's the only thing in his pockets. Any Customs inspector or exciseman must carry his warrant upon his person at all times, for otherwise he's no authority to carry out a search of premises or seize goods." He glanced up, eyebrows raised. "Why did ye think he was an exciseman?"

I hugged the folds of Jamie's coat around myself, trying to remember what the man had said to me on the landing. "He asked me whether I was a decoy, and where the madam was. Then he said that there was a reward—a percentage of seized contraband, that's what he said—and that no one would know but him and me. And you'd said there were excisemen after you," I added. "So naturally I thought he was one. Then Mr. Willoughby turned up and things rather went to pot."

Jamie nodded, still looking puzzled. "Aye, well. I havena got any idea who he is, but it's a good thing that he isna an exciseman. I thought at first something had come verra badly unstuck, but it's likely all right."

"Unstuck?"

He smiled briefly. "I've an arrangement with the Superintending Customs Officer for the district, Sassenach."

I gaped at him. "Arrangement?"

He shrugged. "Well, bribery then, if ye like to be straight out about it." He sounded faintly irritated.

"No doubt that's standard business procedure?" I said, trying to sound tactful. One corner of his mouth twitched slightly.

"Aye, it is. Well, in any case, there's an understanding, as ye might say, between Sir Percival Turner and myself, and to find him sending excise officers into this place would worry me considerably."

"All right," I said slowly, mentally juggling all the half-understood events of the morning, and trying to make a pattern of them. "But in that case, what did you mean by telling Fergus the excisemen were on your heels? And why has everyone been racing round like chickens with their heads off?"

"Oh, that." He smiled briefly, and took my arm, turning me away from the corpse at our feet. "Well, it's an arrangement, as I said. And part of it is that Sir Percival must satisfy his own masters in London, by seizing sufficient amounts of contraband now and again. So we see to it that he's given the opportunity. Wally and the lads brought down two wagonloads from the coast; one of the best brandy, and the other filled with spiled casks and the punked wine, topped off with a few ankers of cheap swill, just to give it all flavor.

"I met them just outside the city this morning, as we planned, and then we drove the wagons in, takin' care to attract the attention of the Riding Officer, who just happened to be passing with a small number of dragoons. They came along and we led them a canty chase through the alleyways, until the time for me and the good tubs to part company wi' Wally and his load of swill. Wally jumped off his wagon then, and made awa', and I drove like hell down here, wi' two or three dragoons following, just for show, like. Looks good in a report, ye ken." He grinned at me, quoting, *" 'The smugglers escaped in spite of industrious pursuit, but His Majesty's valiant soldiers succeeded in capturing an entire wagonload of spirits, valued at sixty pounds, ten shillings.'* You'll know the sort of thing?"

"I expect so," I said. "Then it was you and the good liquor that was arriving at ten? Madame Jeanne said—"

"Aye," he said, frowning. "She was meant to have the cellar door open and the ramp in place at ten sharp—we havena got long to get everything unloaded. She was bloody late this morning; I had to circle round twice to keep from bringing the dragoons straight to the door."

"She was a bit distracted," I said, remembering suddenly about the Fiend. I told Jamie about the murder at the Green Owl, and he grimaced, crossing himself.

"Poor lass," he said.

I shuddered briefly at the memory of Bruno's description, and moved closer to Jamie, who put an arm about my shoulders. He kissed me absently on the forehead, glancing again at the shawl-covered shape on the ground.

"Well, whoever he was, if he wasna an exciseman, there are likely no more of them upstairs. We should be able to get out of here soon."

"That's good." Jamie's coat covered me to the knees, but I felt the covert glances cast from the far end of the room at my bare calves, and was all too uncomfortably aware that I was naked under it. "Will we be going back to the printshop?" What with one thing and another, I didn't think I wanted to take advantage of Madame Jeanne's hospitality any longer than necessary.

"Maybe for a bit. I'll have to think." Jamie's tone was abstracted, and I could see that his brow was furrowed in thought. With a brief hug, he released me, and began to walk about the cellar, staring meditatively at the stones underfoot.

"Er . . . what did you do with Ian?"

He glanced up, looking blank; then his face cleared.

"Oh, Ian. I left him making inquiries at the taverns above the Market Cross. I'll need to remember to meet him, later," he muttered, as though making a note to himself.

"I met Young Ian, by the way," I said conversationally.

Jamie looked startled. "He came here?"

"He did. Looking for you—about a quarter of an hour after you left, in fact."

"Thank God for small mercies!" He rubbed a hand through his hair, looking simultaneously amused and worried. "I'd have had the devil of a time explaining to Ian what his son was doing here."

"You *know* what he was doing here?" I asked curiously.

"No, I don't! He was supposed to be—ah, well, let it be. I canna be worrit about it just now." He relapsed into thought, emerging momentarily to ask, "Did Young Ian say where he was going, when he left ye?"

I shook my head, gathering the coat around myself, and he nodded, sighed, and took up his slow pacing once more.

I sat down on an upturned tub and watched him. In spite of the general atmosphere of discomfort and danger, I felt absurdly happy simply to be near him. Feeling that there was little I could do to help the situation at present, I settled myself with the coat wrapped round me, and abandoned myself to the momentary pleasure of looking at him—something I had had no chance to do, in the tumult of events.

In spite of his preoccupation, he moved with the surefooted grace of a swordsman, a man so aware of his body as to be able to forget it entirely. The men by the casks worked by torchlight; it gleamed on his hair as he turned, lighting it like a tiger's fur, with stripes of gold and dark.

I caught the faint twitch as two fingers of his right hand flickered together against the fabric of his breeches, and felt a strange little lurch of recognition in the gesture. I had seen him do that a thousand times as he was thinking, and seeing it now again, felt as though all the time that had passed in our separation was no more than the rising and setting of a single sun.

As though catching my thought, he paused in his strolling and smiled at me.

"You'll be warm enough, Sassenach?" he asked.

"No, but it doesn't matter." I got off my tub and went to join him in his peregrinations, slipping a hand through his arm. "Making any progress with the thinking?"

He laughed ruefully. "No. I'm thinking of maybe half a dozen things together, and half of them things I canna do anything about. Like whether Young Ian's where he should be."

I stared up at him. "Where he should be? Where do you think he should be?"

"He *should* be at the printshop," Jamie said, with some emphasis. "But he *should* ha' been with Wally this morning, and he wasn't."

"With Wally? You mean you knew he wasn't at home, when his father came looking for him this morning?"

He rubbed his nose with a finger, looking at once irritated and amused. "Oh, aye. I'd promised Young Ian I wouldna say anything to his da, though, until he'd a chance to explain himself. Not that an explanation is likely to save his arse," he added.

Young Ian had, as his father said, come to join his uncle in Edinburgh without the preliminary bother of asking his parents' leave. Jamie had discovered this dereliction fairly quickly, but had not wanted to send his nephew alone back to Lallybroch, and had not yet had time to escort him personally.

"It's not that he canna look out for himself," Jamie explained, amusement winning in the struggle of expressions on his face. "He's a nice capable lad. It's just—well, ye ken how things just happen around some folk, without them seeming to have anything much to do wi' it?"

"Now that you mention it, yes," I said wryly. "I'm one of them."

He laughed out loud at that. "God, you're right, Sassenach! Maybe that's why I like Young Ian so well; he 'minds me of you."

"He reminded me a bit of *you*," I said.

Jamie snorted briefly. "God, Jenny will maim me, and she hears her baby son's been loitering about a house of ill repute. I hope the wee bugger has the sense to keep his mouth shut, once he's home."

"I hope he *gets* home," I said, thinking of the gawky almost-fifteen-year-old I had seen that morning, adrift in an Edinburgh filled with prostitutes, excisemen, smugglers, and hatchet-wielding Fiends. "At least he isn't a girl," I added, thinking of this last item. "The Fiend doesn't seem to have a taste for young boys."

"Aye, well, there are plenty of others who have," Jamie said sourly. "Between Young Ian and you, Sassenach, I shall be lucky if my hair's not gone white by the time we get out of this stinking cellar."

"Me?" I said in surprise. "You don't need to worry about me."

"I don't?" He dropped my arm and rounded on me, glaring. "I dinna need to worry about ye? Is that what ye said? Christ! I leave ye safely in bed waiting for your breakfast, and not an hour later, I find ye downstairs in your shift, clutching a corpse to your bosom! And now you're standing in front of me bare as an egg, with fifteen men over there wondering who in hell ye are—and how d'ye think I'm going to explain ye to them, Sassenach? Tell me that, eh?" He shoved a hand through his hair in exasperation.

"Sweet bleeding Jesus! And I've to go up the coast in two days without fail, but I canna leave ye in Edinburgh, not wi' Fiends creepin' about with hatchets, and half the people who've seen ye thinking you're a prostitute, and . . . and . . ." The lacing around his pigtail broke abruptly under the pressure, and his hair fluffed out round his head like a lion's mane. I laughed. He glared for a moment longer, but then a reluctant grin made its way slowly through the frown.

"Aye, well," he said, resigned. "I suppose I'll manage."

"I suppose you will," I said, and stood on tiptoe to brush his hair back behind his ears. Working on the same principle that causes magnets of opposing polarities to snap together when placed in close proximity, he bent his head and kissed me.

"I had forgotten," he said, a moment later.

"Forgotten what?" His back was warm through the thin shirt.

"Everything." He spoke very softly, mouth against my hair. "Joy. Fear. Fear, most of all." His hand came up and smoothed my curls away from his nose.

"I havena been afraid for a verra long time, Sassenach," he whispered. "But now I think I am. For there is something to be lost, now."

I drew back a little, to look up at him. His arms were locked tight around my waist, his eyes dark as bottomless water in the dimness. Then his face changed and he kissed me quickly on the forehead.

"Come along, Sassenach," he said, taking me by the arm. "I'll tell the men you're my wife. The rest of it will just have to bide."

27

Up in Flames

The dress was a trifle lower cut than necessary, and a bit tight in the bosom, but on the whole, not a bad fit.

"And how did you know Daphne would be the right size?" I asked, spooning up my soup.

"I said I didna bed wi' the lasses," Jamie replied circumspectly. "I never said I didna look at them." He blinked at me like a large red owl—some congenital tic made him incapable of closing one eye in a wink—and I laughed.

"That gown becomes ye a good deal more than it did Daphne, though." He cast a glance of general approval at my bosom and waved at a servingmaid carrying a platter of fresh bannocks.

Moubray's tavern was doing a thriving dinner business. Several cuts above the snug, smoky atmosphere to be found in The World's End and similar serious drinking establishments, Moubray's was a large and elegant place, with an outside stair that ran up to the second floor, where a commodious dining room accommodated the appetites of Edinburgh's prosperous tradesmen and public officials.

"Who are you at the moment?" I asked. "I heard Madame Jeanne call you 'Monsieur Fraser'—are you Fraser in public, though?"

He shook his head and broke a bannock into his soup bowl. "No, at the moment, I'm Sawney Malcolm, Printer and Publisher."

"Sawney? That's a nickname for Alexander, is it? I should have thought 'Sandy' was more like it, especially considering your hair.'' Not that his hair was sandy-colored in the least, I reflected, looking at it. It was like Bree's hair—very thick, with a slight wave to it, and all the colors of red and gold mixed; copper and cinnamon, auburn and amber, red and roan and rufous, all mingled together.

I felt a sudden wave of longing for Bree; at the same time, I longed to untie Jamie's hair from its formal plait and run my hands up under it, to feel the solid curve of his skull, and the soft strands tangled in my fingers. I could still recall the tickle of it, spilling loose and rich across my breasts in the morning light.

My breath coming a little short, I bent my head to my oyster stew.

Jamie appeared not to have noticed; he added a large pat of butter to his bowl, shaking his head as he did so.

"Sawney's what they say in the Highlands," he informed me. "And in the Isles, too. Sandy's more what ye'd hear in the Lowlands—or from an ignorant Sassenach." He lifted one eyebrow at me, smiling, and raised a spoonful of the rich, fragrant stew to his mouth.

"All right," I said. "I suppose more to the point, though—who am *I*?"

He had noticed, after all. I felt one large foot nudge mine, and he smiled at me over the rim of his cup.

"You're my wife, Sassenach," he said gruffly. "Always. No matter who I may be—you're my wife."

I could feel the flush of pleasure rise in my face, and see the memories of the night before reflected in his own. The tips of his ears were faintly pink.

"You don't suppose there's too much pepper in this stew?" I asked, swallowing another spoonful. "Are you sure, Jamie?"

"Aye," he said. "Aye, I'm sure," he amended, "and no, the pepper's fine. I like a wee bit of pepper." The foot moved slightly against mine, the toe of his shoe barely brushing my ankle.

"So I'm Mrs. Malcolm," I said, trying out the name on my tongue. The mere fact of saying "Mrs." gave me an absurd little thrill, like a new bride. Involuntarily, I glanced down at the silver ring on my right fourth finger.

Jamie caught the glance, and raised his cup to me.

"To Mrs. Malcolm," he said softly, and the breathless feeling came back.

He set down the cup and took my hand; his own was big and so warm that a general feeling of glowing heat spread rapidly through my fingers. I could feel the silver ring, separate from my flesh, its metal heated by his touch.

"To have and to hold," he said, smiling.

"From this day forward," I said, not caring in the least that we were attracting interested glances from the other diners.

Jamie bent his head and pressed his lips against the back of my hand, an action that turned the interested glances into frank stares. A clergyman was seated across the room; he glared at us and said something to his companions, who turned round to stare. One was a small, elderly man; the other, I was surprised to see, was Mr. Wallace, my companion from the Inverness coach.

"There are private rooms upstairs," Jamie murmured, blue eyes dancing over my knuckles, and I lost interest in Mr. Wallace.

"How interesting," I said. "You haven't finished your stew."

"Damn the stew."

"Here comes the servingmaid with the ale."

"Devil take her." Sharp white teeth closed gently on my knuckle, making me jerk slightly in my seat.

"People are watching you."

"Let them, and I trust they've a fine day for it."

His tongue flicked gently between my fingers.

"There's a man in a green coat coming this way."

"To hell—" Jamie began, when the shadow of the visitor fell upon the table.

"A good day to you, Mr. Malcolm," said the visitor, bowing politely. "I trust I do not intrude?"

"You do," said Jamie, straightening up but keeping his grip on my hand. He turned a cool gaze on the newcomer. "I think I do not know ye, sir?"

The gentleman, an Englishman of maybe thirty-five, quietly dressed, bowed again, not intimidated by this marked lack of hospitality.

"I have not had the pleasure of your acquaintance as yet, sir," he said deferentially. "My master, however, bade me greet you, and inquire whether you—and your companion—might be so agreeable as to take a little wine with him."

The tiny pause before the word "companion" was barely discernible, but Jamie caught it. His eyes narrowed.

"My wife and I," he said, with precisely the same sort of pause before "wife," "are otherwise engaged at the moment. Should your master wish to speak wi' me—"

"It is Sir Percival Turner who sends to ask, sir," the secretary—for so he must be—put in quickly. Well-bred as he was, he couldn't resist a tiny flick of one eyebrow, as one who uses a name he expects to conjure with.

"Indeed," said Jamie dryly. "Well, with all respect to Sir Percival, I am preoccupied at present. If you will convey him my regrets?" He bowed, with a politeness so pointed as to come within a hair of rudeness, and turned his back on the secretary. That gentleman stood for a moment, his mouth slightly open, then pivoted smartly on his heel and made his way through the scatter of tables to a door on the far side of the dining room.

"Where was I?" Jamie demanded. "Oh, aye—to hell wi' gentlemen in green coats. Now, about these private rooms—"

"How are you going to explain me to people?" I asked.

He raised one eyebrow.

"Explain what?" He looked me up and down. "Why must I make excuses for ye? You're no missing any limbs; you're not poxed, hunchbacked, toothless or lame—"

"You know what I mean," I said, kicking him lightly under the table. The lady sitting near the wall nudged her companion and widened her eyes disapprovingly at us. I smiled nonchalantly at them.

"Aye, I do," he said, grinning. "However, what wi' Mr. Willoughby's activities this morning, and one thing and another, I havena had much chance to think about the matter. Perhaps I'll just say—"

"My dear fellow, so you are married! Capital news! Simply capital! My deepest congratulations, and may I be—dare I hope to be?—the first to extend my felicitations and best wishes to your lady?"

A small, elderly gentleman in a tidy wig leaned heavily on a gold-knobbed stick, beaming genially at us both. It was the little gentleman who had been sitting with Mr. Wallace and the clergyman.

"You will pardon the minor discourtesy of my sending Johnson to fetch you earlier, I am sure," he said deprecatingly. "It is only that my wretched infirmity prevents rapid movement, as you see."

Jamie had risen to his feet at the appearance of the visitor, and with a polite gesture, now drew out a chair.

"You'll join us, Sir Percival?" he said.

"Oh, no, no indeed! Shouldn't dream of intruding on your new happiness, my dear sir. Truly, I had no idea—" Still protesting gracefully, he sank down into the proffered chair, wincing as he extended his foot beneath the table.

"I am a martyr to gout, my dear," he confided, leaning close enough for me to smell his foul old-man's breath beneath the wintergreen that spiced his linen.

He didn't look corrupt, I thought—breath notwithstanding—but then appearances could be deceiving; it was only about four hours since I had been mistaken for a prostitute.

Making the best of it, Jamie called for wine, and accepted Sir Percival's continued effusions with some grace.

"It is rather fortunate that I should have encountered you here, my dear fellow," the elderly gentleman said, breaking off his flowery compliments at last. He laid a small, manicured hand on Jamie's sleeve. "I had something particular to say to you. In fact, I had sent a note to the printshop, but my messenger failed to find you there."

"Ah?" Jamie cocked an eyebrow in question.

"Yes," Sir Percival went on. "I believe you had spoken to me —some weeks ago, I scarce recall the occasion—of your intention to travel north on business. A matter of a new press, or something of the sort?" Sir Percival had quite a sweet face, I thought, hand-somely patrician despite his years, with large, guileless blue eyes.

"Aye, that's so," Jamie agreed courteously. "I am invited by Mr. McLeod of Perth, to see a new style of letterpress he's re-cently put in use."

"Quite." Sir Percival paused to remove a snuffbox from his pocket, a pretty thing enameled in green and gold, with cherubs on the lid.

"I really should not advise a trip to the north just now," he said, opening the box and concentrating on its contents. "Really I should not. The weather is like to be inclement at this season; I am sure it would not suit Mrs. Malcolm." Smiling at me like an elderly angel, he inhaled a large pinch of snuff and paused, linen handkerchief at the ready.

Jamie sipped at his wine, his face blandly composed.

"I am grateful for your advice, Sir Percival," he said. "You'll perhaps have received word from your agents of recent storms to the north?"

Sir Percival sneezed, a small, neat sound, like a mouse with a cold. He was rather like a white mouse altogether, I thought, seeing him dab daintily at his pointed pink nose.

"Quite," he said again, putting away the kerchief and blinking benevolently at Jamie. "No, I would—as a particular friend with your welfare at heart—most strongly advise that you remain in Edinburgh. After all," he added, turning the beam of his benevolence on me, "you surely have an inducement to remain comfortably at home now, do you not? And now, my dear young people, I am afraid I must take my leave; I must not detain you any longer from what must be your wedding breakfast."

With a little assistance from the hovering Johnson, Sir Percival got up and tottered off, his gold-knobbed stick tap-tapping on the floor.

"He seems a nice old gent," I remarked, when I was sure he was far enough away not to hear me.

Jamie snorted. "Rotten as a worm-riddled board," he said. He picked up his glass and drained it. "Ye'd think otherwise," he said meditatively, putting it down and staring after the wizened figure, now cautiously negotiating the head of the stairs. "A man as close as Sir Percival is to Judgment Day, I mean. Ye'd think fear o' the Devil would prevent him, but not a bit."

"I suppose he's like everyone else," I said cynically. "Most people think they're going to live forever."

Jamie laughed, his exuberant spirits returning with a rush.

"Aye, that's true," he said. He pushed my wineglass toward me. "And now you're here, Sassenach, I'm convinced of it. Drink up, *mo nighean donn,* and we'll go upstairs."

"Post coitum omne animalium triste est," I remarked, with my eyes closed.

There was no response from the warm, heavy weight on my chest, save the gentle sigh of his breathing. After a moment, though, I felt a sort of subterranean vibration, which I interpreted as amusement.

"That's a verra peculiar sentiment, Sassenach," Jamie said, his voice blurred with drowsiness. "Not your own, I hope?"

"No." I stroked the damp bright hair back from his forehead, and he turned his face into the curve of my shoulder, with a small contented snuffle.

The private rooms at Moubray's left a bit to be desired in the way of amorous accommodation. Still, the sofa at least offered a padded horizontal surface, which, if you came right down to it, was all that was necessary. While I had decided that I was not past wanting to commit passionate acts after all, I was still too old to want to commit them on the bare floorboards.

"I don't know who said it—some ancient philosopher or other. It was quoted in one of my medical textbooks; in the chapter on the human reproductive system."

The vibration made itself audible as a small chuckle.

"Ye'd seem to have applied yourself to your lessons to good purpose, Sassenach," he said. His hand passed down my side and wormed its way slowly underneath to cup my bottom. He sighed with contentment, squeezing slightly.

"I canna think when I have felt less *triste*," he said.

"Me either," I said, tracing the whorl of the small cowlick that lifted the hair from the center of his forehead. "That's what made me think of it—I rather wondered what led the ancient philosopher to that conclusion."

"I suppose it depends on the sorts of *animaliae* he'd been fornicating with," Jamie observed. "Maybe it was just that none o' them took to him, but he must ha' tried a fair number, to make such a sweeping statement."

He held tighter to his anchor as the tide of my laughter bounced him gently up and down.

"Mind ye, dogs sometimes do look a trifle sheepish when they've done wi' mating," he said.

"Mm. And how do sheep look, then?"

"Aye, well, female sheep just go on lookin' like sheep—not havin' a great deal of choice in the matter, ye ken."

"Oh? And what do the male sheep look like?"

"Oh, they look fair depraved. Let their tongues hang out, drooling, and their eyes roll back, while they make disgusting noises. Like most male animals, aye?" I could feel the curve of his grin against my shoulder. He squeezed again, and I pulled gently on the ear closest to hand.

"I didn't notice your tongue hanging out."

"Ye werena noticing; your eyes were closed."

"I didn't hear any disgusting noises, either."

"Well, I couldna just think of any on the spur of the moment," he admitted. "Perhaps I'll do better next time."

We laughed softly together, and then were quiet, listening to each other breathe.

"Jamie," I said softly at last, smoothing the back of his head, "I don't think I've ever been so happy."

He rolled to one side, shifting his weight carefully so as not to squash me, and lifted himself to lie face-to-face with me.

"Nor me, my Sassenach," he said, and kissed me, very lightly, but lingering, so that I had time just to close my lips in a tiny bite on the fullness of his lower lip.

"It's no just the bedding, ye ken," he said, drawing back a little at last. His eyes looked down at me, a soft deep blue like the warm tropic sea.

"No," I said, touching his cheek. "It isn't."

"To have ye with me again—to talk wi' you—to know I can say anything, not guard my words or hide my thoughts—God, Sassenach," he said, "the Lord knows I am lust-crazed as a lad, and I canna keep my hands from you—or anything else—" he added, wryly, "but I would count that all well lost, had I no more than the pleasure of havin' ye by me, and to tell ye all my heart."

"It was lonely without you," I whispered. "So lonely."

"And me," he said. He looked down, long lashes hiding his eyes, and hesitated for a moment.

"I willna say that I have lived a monk," he said quietly. "When I had to—when I felt that I must or go mad—"

I laid my fingers against his lips, to stop him.

"Neither did I," I said. "Frank—"

His own hand pressed gently against my mouth. Both dumb, we looked at each other, and I could feel the smile growing behind my hand, and my own under his, to match it. I took my hand away.

"It doesna signify," he said. He took his hand off my mouth.

"No," I said. "It doesn't matter." I traced the line of his lips with my finger.

"So tell me all your heart," I said. "If there's time."

He glanced at the window to gauge the light—we were to meet Ian at the printshop at five o'clock, to check the progress of the search for Young Ian—and then rolled carefully off me.

"There's two hours, at least, before we must go. Sit up and put your clothes on, and I'll have them bring some wine and biscuits."

This sounded wonderful. I seemed to have been starving ever since I found him. I sat up and began to rummage through the pile of discarded clothes on the floor, looking for the set of stays the low-necked gown required.

"I'm no ways sad, but I do maybe feel a bit ashamed," Jamie observed, wriggling long, slender toes into a silk stocking. "Or I should, at least."

"Why is that?"

"Well, here I am, in paradise, so to speak, wi' you and wine and biscuits, while Ian's out tramping the pavements and worrying for his son."

"Are you worried about Young Ian?" I asked, concentrating on my laces.

He frowned slightly, pulling on the other stocking.

"Not so much worried for him as afraid he may not turn up before tomorrow."

"What happens tomorrow?" I asked, and then belatedly re-called the encounter with Sir Percival Turner. "Oh, your trip to the north—that was supposed to be tomorrow?"

He nodded. "Aye, there's a rendezvous set at Mullin's Cove, tomorrow being the dark of the moon. A lugger from France, wi' a load of wine and cambric."

"And Sir Percival was warning you not to make that rendez-vous?"

"So it seems. What's happened, I canna say, though I expect I'll find out. Could be as there's a visiting Customs Officer in the district, or he's had word of some activity on the coast there that has nothing to do wi' us, but could interfere." He shrugged and finished his last garter.

He spread out his hands upon his knees then, palm up, and slowly curled the fingers inward. The left curled at once into a fist, compact and neat, a blunt instrument ready for battle. The fingers of his right hand curled more slowly; the middle finger was crooked, and would not lie along the second. The fourth finger would not curl at all, but stuck out straight, holding the little finger at an awkward angle beside it.

He looked from his hands to me, smiling.

"D'ye remember the night when ye set my hand?"

"Sometimes, in my more horrible moments." That night was one to remember—only because it couldn't be forgotten. Against all odds, I had rescued him from Wentworth Prison and a death sentence—but not in time to prevent his being cruelly tortured and abused by Black Jack Randall.

I picked up his right hand and transferred it to my own knee. He let it lie there, warm, heavy and inert, and didn't object as I felt each finger, pulling gently to stretch the tendons and twisting to see the range of motion in the joints.

"My first orthopedic surgery, that was," I said wryly.

"Have ye done a great many things like that since?" he asked curiously, looking down at me.

"Yes, a few. I'm a surgeon—but it doesn't mean then what it means now," I added hastily. "Surgeons in my time don't pull teeth and let blood. They're more like what's meant now by the word 'physician'—a doctor with training in all the fields of medicine, but with a specialty."

"Special, are ye? Well, ye've always been that," he said, grinning. The crippled fingers slid into my palm and his thumb stroked my knuckles. "What is it a surgeon does that's special, then?"

I frowned, trying to think of the right phrasing. "Well, as best I can put it—a surgeon tries to effect healing . . . by means of a knife."

His long mouth curled upward at the notion.

"A nice contradiction, that; but it suits ye, Sassenach."

"It does?" I said, startled.

He nodded, never taking his eyes off my face. I could see him studying me closely, and wondered self-consciously what I must look like, flushed from lovemaking, with my hair in wild disorder.

"Ye havena been lovelier, Sassenach," he said, smile growing wider as I reached up to smooth my hair. He caught my hand, and kissed it gently. "Leave your curls be.

"No," he said, holding my hands trapped while he looked me over, "no, a knife is verra much what you are, now I think of it. A clever-worked scabbard, and most gorgeous to see, Sassenach"—he traced the line of my lips with a finger, provoking a smile—

"but tempered steel for a core . . . and a wicked sharp edge, I do think."

"Wicked?" I said, surprised.

"Not heartless, I don't mean," he assured me. His eyes rested on my face, intent and curious. A smile touched his lips. "No, never that. But you can be ruthless strong, Sassenach, when the need is on ye."

I smiled, a little wryly. "I can," I said.

"I have seen that in ye before, aye?" His voice grew softer and his grasp on my hand tightened. "But now I think ye have it much more than when ye were younger. You'll have needed it often since, no?"

I realized quite suddenly why he saw so clearly what Frank had never seen at all.

"You have it too," I said. "And you've needed it. Often." Unconsciously, my fingers touched the jagged scar that crossed his middle finger, twisting the distal joints.

He nodded.

"I have wondered," he said, so low I could scarcely hear him. "Wondered often, if I could call that edge to my service, and sheathe it safe again. For I have seen a great many men grow hard in that calling, and their steel decay to dull iron. And I have wondered often, was I master in my soul, or did I become the slave of my own blade?

"I have thought again and again," he went on, looking down at our linked hands . . . "that I had drawn my blade too often, and spent so long in the service of strife that I wasna fit any longer for human intercourse."

My lips twitched with the urge to make a remark, but I bit them instead. He saw it, and smiled, a little wryly.

"I didna think I should ever laugh again in a woman's bed, Sassenach," he said. "Or even come to a woman, save as a brute, blind with need." A note of bitterness came into his voice.

I lifted his hand, and kissed the small scar on the back of it.

"I can't see you as a brute," I said. I meant it lightly, but his face softened as he looked at me, and he answered seriously.

"I know that, Sassenach. And it is that ye canna see me so that gives me hope. For I am—and know it—and yet perhaps . . ." He trailed off, watching me intently.

"You have that—the strength. Ye have it, and your soul as well. So perhaps my own may be saved."

I had no notion what to say to this, and said nothing for a while, but only held his hand, caressing the twisted fingers and the large, hard knuckles. It was a warrior's hand—but he was not a warrior, now.

I turned the hand over and smoothed it on my knee, palm up. Slowly, I traced the deep lines and rising hillocks, and the tiny letter "C" at the base of his thumb; the brand that marked him mine.

"I knew an old lady in the Highlands once, who said the lines in your hand don't predict your life; they reflect it."

"Is that so, then?" His fingers twitched slightly, but his palm lay still and open.

"I don't know. She said you're born with the lines of your hand —with a life—but then the lines change, with the things you do, and the person you are." I knew nothing about palmistry, but I could see one deep line that ran from wrist to midpalm, forking several times.

"I think that might be the one they call a life-line," I said. "See all the forks? I suppose that would mean you'd changed your life a lot, made a lot of choices."

He snorted briefly, but with amusement rather than derision.

"Oh, aye? Well, that's safe enough to say." He peered into his palm, leaning over my knee. "I suppose the first fork would be when I met Jack Randall, and the second when I wed you—see, they're close together, there."

"So they are." I ran my finger slowly along the line, making his fingers twitch slightly as it tickled. "And Culloden maybe would be another?"

"Perhaps." But he did not wish to talk of Culloden. His own finger moved on. "And when I went to prison, and came back again, and came to Edinburgh."

"And became a printer." I stopped and looked up at him, brows raised. "How on earth *did* you come to be a printer? It's the last thing I would have thought of."

"Oh, that." His mouth widened in a smile. "Well—it was an accident, aye?"

To start with he had only been looking for a business that would help to conceal and facilitate the smuggling. Possessed of a sizable sum from a recent profitable venture, he had determined to purchase a business whose normal operations involved a large wagon and team of horses, and some discreet premises that could be used for the temporary storage of goods in transit.

Carting suggested itself, but was rejected precisely because the operations of that business made its practitioners subject to more or less constant scrutiny from the Customs. Likewise, the ownership of a tavern or inn, while superficially desirable because of the large quantities of supplies brought in, was too vulnerable in its legitimate operation to hide an illegitimate one; tax collectors and Customs agents hung about taverns like fleas on a fat dog.

"I thought of printing, when I went to a place to have some notices made up," he explained. "As I was waiting to put in my order, I saw the wagon come rumbling up, all loaded wi' boxes of paper and casks of alcohol for the ink powder, and I thought, by God, that's it! For excisemen would never be troubling a place like that."

It was only after purchasing the shop in Carfax Close, hiring Geordie to run the press, and actually beginning to fill orders for posters, pamphlets, folios, and books, that the other possibilities of his new business had occurred to him.

"It was a man named Tom Gage," he explained. He loosed his hand from my grasp, growing eager in the telling, gesturing and rubbing his hands through his hair as he talked, disheveling himself with enthusiasm.

"He brought in small orders for this or that—innocent stuff, all of it—but often, and stayed to talk over it, taking trouble to talk to me as well as to Geordie, though he must have seen I knew less about the business than he did himself."

He smiled at me wryly.

"I didna ken much about printing, Sassenach, but I do ken men."

It was obvious that Gage was exploring the sympathies of Alexander Malcolm; hearing the faint sibilance of Jamie's Highland speech, he had prodded delicately, mentioning this acquaintance and that whose Jacobite sympathies had led them into trouble after the Rising, picking up the threads of mutual acquaintance, skillfully directing the conversation, stalking his prey. Until at last, the amused prey had bluntly told him to bring what he wanted made; no King's man would hear of it.

"And he trusted you." It wasn't a question; the only man who had ever trusted Jamie Fraser in error was Charles Stuart—and in that case, the error was Jamie's.

"He did." And so an association was begun, strictly business in the beginning, but deepening into friendship as time went on. Jamie had printed all the materials generated by Gage's small group of radical political writers—from publicly acknowledged articles to anonymous broadsheets and pamphlets filled with material incriminating enough to get the authors summarily jailed or hanged.

"We'd go to the tavern down the street and talk, after the printing was done. I met a few of Tom's friends, and finally Tom said I should write a small piece myself. I laughed and told him that, with my hand, by the time I'd penned anything that could be read, we'd all be dead—of old age, not hanging.

"I was standing by the press as we were talking, setting the type wi' my left hand, not even thinking. He just stared at me, and then he started to laugh. He pointed at the tray, and at my hand, and went on laughing, 'til he had to sit down on the floor to stop."

He stretched out his arms in front of him, flexing his hands and studying them dispassionately. He curled one hand into a fist and bent it slowly up toward his face, making the muscles of his arm ripple and swell under the linen.

"I'm hale enough," he said. "And with luck, may be so for a good many years yet—but not forever, Sassenach. I ha' fought wi' sword and dirk many times, but to every warrior comes the day when his strength will fail him." He shook his head and stretched out a hand toward his coat, which lay on the floor.

"I took these, that day wi' Tom Gage, to remind me of it," he said.

He took my hand and put into it the things he had taken from his pocket. They were cool, and hard to the touch, small heavy oblongs of lead. I didn't need to feel the incised ends to know what the letters on the type slugs were.

"Q.E.D.," I said.

"The English took my sword and dirk away," he said softly. His finger touched the slugs that lay in my palm. "But Tom Gage put a weapon into my hands again, and I think I shall not lay it down."

We walked arm in arm down the cobbled slope of the Royal Mile at a quarter to five, suffused with a glow engendered by several bowls of well-peppered oyster stew and a bottle of wine, shared at intervals during our "private communications."

The city glowed all around us, as though sharing our happiness. Edinburgh lay under a haze that would soon thicken to rain again, but for now, the light of the setting sun hung gold and pink and red in the clouds, and shone in the wet patina of the cobbled street, so that the gray stones of the buildings softened and streamed with reflected light, echoing the glow that warmed my cheeks and shone in Jamie's eyes when he looked at me.

I drifted down the street in this state of soft-headed self-absorption, it was several minutes before I noticed anything amiss. A man, impatient of our meandering progress, stepped briskly around us, and then came to a dead stop just in front of me, making me trip on the wet stones and throw a shoe.

He flung up his head and stared skyward for a moment, then hurried off down the street, not running, but walking as fast as he could go.

"What's the matter with him?" I said, stooping to retrieve my shoe. Suddenly I noticed that all around us, folk were stopping, staring up, and then starting to rush down the street.

"What do you think—?" I began, but when I turned to Jamie, he too was staring intently upward. I looked up, too, and it took only a moment to see that the red glow in the clouds above was a good deal deeper than the general color of the sunset sky, and seemed to flicker in an uneasy fashion most uncharacteristic of sunsets.

"Fire," he said. "God, I think it's in Leith Wynd!"

At the same moment, someone farther down the street raised the cry of "Fire!" and as though this official diagnosis had given them leave to run at last, the hurrying figures below broke loose and cascaded down the street like a herd of lemmings, anxious to fling themselves into the pyre.

A few saner souls ran upward, past us, also shouting "Fire!"

but presumably with the intent of alerting whatever passed for a fire department.

Jamie was already in motion, tugging me along as I hopped awkwardly on one foot. Rather than stop, I kicked the other shoe off, and followed him, slipping and stubbing my toes on the cold wet cobbles as I ran.

The fire was not in Leith Wynd, but next door, in Carfax Close. The mouth of the close was choked with excited onlookers, shoving and craning in an effort to see, shouting incoherent questions at one another. The smell of smoke struck hot and pungent through the damp evening air, and waves of crackling heat beat against my face as I ducked into the close.

Jamie didn't hesitate, but plunged into the crowd, making a path by main force. I pressed close behind him before the human waves could close again, and elbowed my way through, unable to see anything but Jamie's broad back ahead of me.

Then we popped out in the front of the crowd, and I could see all too well. Dense clouds of gray smoke rolled out of both the printshop's lower windows, and I could hear a whispering, crackling noise that rose above the noise of the spectators as though the fire were talking to itself.

"My press!" With a cry of anguish, Jamie darted up the front step and kicked in the door. A cloud of smoke rolled out of the open doorway and engulfed him like a hungry beast. I caught a brief glimpse of him, staggering from the impact of the smoke; then he dropped to his knees and crawled into the building.

Inspired by this example, several men from the crowd ran up the steps of the printshop, and likewise disappeared into the smoke-filled interior. The heat was so intense that I felt my skirts blow against my legs with the wind of it, and wondered how the men could stand it, there inside.

A fresh outbreak of shouting in the crowd behind me announced the arrival of the Town Guard, armed with buckets. Obviously accustomed to this task, the men flung off their wine-red uniform coats and began at once to attack the fire, smashing the windows and flinging pails of water through them with a fierce abandon. Meanwhile, the crowd swelled, its noise augmented by a constant cascade of pattering feet down the many staircases of the close, as families on the upper floors of the surrounding buildings hastily ushered hordes of excited children down to safety.

I couldn't think that the efforts of the bucket brigade, valiant as they were, would have much effect on what was obviously a fire well under way. I was edging back and forth on the pavement, trying vainly to see anything moving within, when the lead man in the bucket line uttered a startled cry and leapt back, just in time to avoid being crowned by a tray of lead type that whizzed through the broken window and landed on the cobbles with a crash, scattering slugs in all directions.

Two or three urchins wriggled through the crowd and snatched at the slugs, only to be cuffed and driven off by indignant neighbors. One plump lady in a kertch and apron darted forward, risking life and limb, and took custody of the heavy type-tray, dragging it back to the curb, where she crouched protectively over it like a hen on a nest.

Before her companions could scoop up the fallen type, though, they were driven back by a hail of objects that rained from both windows: more type trays, roller bars, inking pads, and bottles of ink, which broke on the pavement, leaving big spidery blotches that ran into the puddles spilled by the fire fighters.

Encouraged by the draft from the open door and windows, the voice of the fire had grown from a whisper into a self-satisfied, chuckling roar. Prevented from flinging water through the windows by the rain of objects being thrown out of them, the leader of the Town Guard shouted to his men, and holding a soaked handkerchief over his nose, ducked and ran into the building, followed by a half-dozen of his fellows.

The line quickly re-formed, full buckets coming hand to hand round the corner from the nearest pump and up the stoop, excited lads snatching the empty buckets that bounced down the step, to race back with them to the pump for refilling. Edinburgh is a stone city, but with so many buildings crammed cheek by jowl, all equipped with multiple hearths and chimneys, fire must be still a frequent occurrence.

Evidently so, for a fresh commotion behind me betokened the belated arrival of the fire engine. The waves of people parted like the Red Sea, to allow passage of the engine, drawn by a team of men rather than horses, which could not have negotiated the tight quarters of the wynds.

The engine was a marvel of brass, glowing like a coal itself in the reflected flames. The heat was becoming more intense; I could feel my lungs dry and labor with each gulp of hot air, and was terrified for Jamie. How long could he breathe, in that hellish fog of smoke and heat, let alone the danger of the flames themselves?

"Jesus, Mary, and Joseph!" Ian, forcing his way through the crowd despite his wooden leg, had appeared suddenly by my elbow. He grabbed my arm to keep his balance as another rain of objects forced the people around us back again.

"Where's Jamie?" he shouted in my ear.

"In there!" I bellowed back, pointing.

There was a sudden bustle and commotion at the door of the printshop, with a confused shouting that rose even over the sound of the fire. Several sets of legs appeared, shuffling to and fro beneath the emergent plume of smoke that billowed from the door. Six men emerged, Jamie among them, staggering under the weight of a huge piece of bulky machinery—Jamie's precious printing press. They eased it down the step and pushed it well into the crowd, then turned back to the printshop.

Too late for any more rescue maneuvers; there was a crash from inside, a fresh blast of heat that sent the crowd scuttling backward, and suddenly the windows of the upper story were lit with dancing flames inside. A small stream of men issued from the building, coughing and choking, some of them crawling, blackened with soot and dampened with the sweat of their efforts. The engine crew pumped madly, but the thick stream of water from their hose made not the slightest impression on the fire.

Ian's hand clamped down on my arm like the jaws of a trap.

"Ian!" he shrieked, loud enough to be heard above the noises of crowd and fire alike.

I looked up in the direction of his gaze, and saw a wraithlike shape at the second-story window. It seemed to struggle briefly with the sash, and then to fall back or be enveloped in the smoke.

My heart leapt into my mouth. There was no telling whether the shape was indeed Young Ian, but it was certainly a human form. Ian had lost no time in gaping, but was stumping toward the door of the printshop with all the speed his leg would allow.

"Wait!" I shouted, running after him.

Jamie was leaning on the printing press, chest heaving as he tried to catch his breath and thank his assistants at the same time.

"Jamie!" I snatched at his sleeve, ruthlessly jerking him away from a red-faced barber, who kept excitedly wiping sooty hands on his apron, leaving long black streaks among the smears of dried soap and the spots of blood.

"Up there!" I shouted, pointing. "Young Ian's upstairs!"

Jamie stepped back, swiping a sleeve across his blackened face, and stared wildly at the upper windows. Nothing was to be seen but the roiling shimmer of the fire against the panes.

Ian was struggling in the hands of several neighbors who sought to prevent his entering the shop.

"No, man, ye canna go in!" the Guard captain cried, trying to grasp Ian's flailing hands. "The staircase has fallen, and the roof will go next!"

Despite his stringy build and the handicap of his leg, Ian was tall and vigorous, and the feeble grasp of his well-meaning Town Guard captors—mostly retired pensioners from the Highland regiments—was no match for his mountain-hardened strength, reinforced as it was by parental desperation. Slowly but surely, the whole confused mass jerked by inches up the steps of the printshop as Ian dragged his would-be rescuers with him toward the flames.

I felt Jamie draw breath, gulping air as deep as he could with his seared lungs, and then he was up the steps as well, and had Ian round the waist, dragging him back.

"Come down, man!" he shouted hoarsely. "Ye'll no manage—the stair is gone!" He glanced round, saw me, and thrust Ian bodily backward, off-balance and staggering, into my arms. "Hold him," he shouted, over the roar of the flames. "I'll fetch down the lad!"

With that, he turned and dashed up the steps of the adjoining building, pushing his way through the patrons of the ground-floor chocolate shop, who had emerged onto the pavement to gawk at the excitement, pewter cups still clutched in their hands.

Following Jamie's example, I locked my arms tight around Ian's waist and didn't let go. He made an abortive attempt to follow Jamie, but then stopped and stood rigid in my arms, his heart beating wildly just under my cheek.

"Don't worry," I said, pointlessly. "He'll do it; he'll get him out. He will. I know he will."

Ian didn't answer—might not have heard—but stood still and stiff as a statue in my grasp, breath coming harshly with a sound like a sob. When I released my hold on his waist, he didn't move or turn, but when I stood beside him, he snatched my hand and held it hard. My bones would have ground together, had I not been squeezing back just as hard.

It was no more than a minute before the window above the chocolate shop opened and Jamie's head and shoulders appeared, red hair glowing like a stray tongue of flame escaped from the main fire. He climbed out onto the sill, and cautiously turned, squatting, until he faced the building.

Rising to his stocking feet, he grasped the gutter of the roof overhead and pulled, slowly raising himself by the strength of his arms, long toes scrabbling for a grip in the crevices between the mortared stones of the housefront. With a grunt audible even over the sound of fire and crowd, he eeled over the edge of the roof and disappeared behind the gable.

A shorter man could not have managed. Neither could Ian, with his wooden leg. I heard Ian say something under his breath; a prayer I thought, but when I glanced at him, his jaw was clenched, face set in lines of fear.

"What in hell is he going to do up there?" I thought, and was unaware that I had spoken aloud until the barber, shading his eyes next to me, replied.

"There's a trapdoor built in the roof o' the printshop, ma'am. Nay doubt Mr. Malcolm means to gain access to the upper story so. Is it his 'prentice up there, d'ye know?"

"No!" Ian snapped, hearing this. "It's my son!"

The barber shrank back before Ian's glare, murmuring "Oh, aye, just so, sir, just so!" and crossing himself. A shout from the crowd grew into a roar as two figures appeared on the roof of the chocolate shop, and Ian dropped my hand, springing forward.

Jamie had his arm round Young Ian, who was bent and reeling from the smoke he had swallowed. It was reasonably obvious that neither of them was going to be able to negotiate a return through the adjoining building in his present condition.

Just then, Jamie spotted Ian below. Cupping his hand around his mouth, he bellowed "Rope!"

Rope there was; the Town Guard had come equipped. Ian snatched the coil from an approaching Guardsman, leaving that worthy blinking in indignation, and turned to face the house.

I caught the gleam of Jamie's teeth as he grinned down at his brother-in-law, and the look of answering wryness on Ian's face.

How many times had they thrown a rope between them, to raise hay to the barn loft, or bind a load to the wagon for carrying?

The crowd fell back from the whirl of Ian's arm, and the heavy coil flew up in a smooth parabola, unwinding as it went, landing on Jamie's outstretched arm with the precision of a bumblebee lighting on a flower. Jamie hauled in the dangling tail, and disappeared momentarily, to anchor the rope about the base of the building's chimney.

A few precarious moments' work, and the two smoke-blackened figures had come to a safe landing on the pavement below. Young Ian, rope slung under his arms and round his chest, stood upright for a moment, then, as the tension of the rope slackened, his knees buckled and he slid into a gangling heap on the cobbles.

"Are ye all right? *A bhalaich,* speak to me!" Ian fell to his knees beside his son, anxiously trying to unknot the rope round Young Ian's chest, while simultaneously trying to lift up the lad's lolling head.

Jamie was leaning against the railing of the chocolate shop, black in the face and coughing his lungs out, but otherwise apparently unharmed. I sat down on the boy's other side, and took his head on my lap.

I wasn't sure whether to laugh or cry at the sight of him. When I had seen him in the morning, he had been an appealing-looking lad, if no great beauty, with something of his father's homely, good-natured looks. Now, at evening, the thick hair over one side of his forehead had been singed to a bleached red stubble, and his eyebrows and lashes had been burned off entirely. The skin beneath was the soot-smeared bright pink of a suckling pig just off the spit.

I felt for a pulse in the spindly neck and found it, reassuringly strong. His breathing was hoarse and irregular, and no wonder; I hoped the lining of his lungs had not been burned. He coughed, long and rackingly, and the thin body convulsed on my lap.

"Is he all right?" Ian's hands instinctively grabbed his son beneath the armpits and sat him up. His head wobbled to and fro, and he pitched forward into my arms.

"I think so; I can't tell for sure." The boy was still coughing, but not fully conscious; I held him against my shoulder like an enormous baby, patting his back futilely as he retched and gagged.

"Is he all right?" This time it was Jamie, squatting breathless alongside me. His voice was so hoarse I wouldn't have recognized it, roughened as it was by smoke.

"I think so. What about you? You look like Malcolm X," I said, peering at him over Young Ian's heaving shoulder.

"I do?" He put a hand to his face, looking startled, then grinned reassuringly. "Nay, I canna say how I look, but I'm no an ex-Malcolm yet; only a wee bit singed round the edges."

"Get back, get back!" The Guard captain was at my side, gray beard bristling with anxiety, plucking at my sleeve. "Move yourself, ma'am, the roof's going!"

Sure enough, as we scrambled to safety, the roof of the printshop fell in, and an awed sound rose from the watching crowd as an enormous fountain of sparks whirled skyward, brilliant against the darkening sky.

As though heaven resented this intrusion, the spume of fiery ash was answered by the first pattering of raindrops, plopping heavily on the cobbles all around us. The Edinburghians, who surely ought to have been accustomed to rain by now, made noises of consternation and began to scuttle back into the surrounding buildings like a herd of cockroaches, leaving nature to complete the fire engine's work.

A moment later, Ian and I were alone with Young Ian. Jamie, having dispensed money liberally to the Guard and other assistants, and having arranged for his press and its fittings to be housed in the barber's storeroom, trudged wearily toward us.

"How's the lad?" he asked, wiping a hand down his face. The rain had begun to come down more heavily, and the effect on his soot-blackened countenance was picturesque in the extreme. Ian looked at him, and for the first time, the anger, worry, and fear faded somewhat from his countenance. He gave Jamie a lopsided smile.

"He doesna look a great deal better than ye do yourself, man— but I think he'll do now. Give us a hand, aye?"

Murmuring small Gaelic endearments suitable for babies, Ian bent over his son, who was by this time sitting up groggily on the curbstone, swaying to and fro like a heron in a high wind.

By the time we reached Madame Jeanne's establishment, Young Ian could walk, though still supported on either side by his father and uncle. Bruno, who opened the door, blinked incredulously at the sight, and then swung the door open, laughing so hard he could barely close it after us.

I had to admit that we were nothing much to look at, wet through and streaming with rain. Jamie and I were both barefoot, and Jamie's clothes were in rags, singed and torn and covered with streaks of soot. Ian's dark hair straggled in his eyes, making him look like a drowned rat with a wooden leg.

Young Ian, though, was the focus of attention, as multiple heads came popping out of the drawing room in response to the noise Bruno was making. With his singed hair, swollen red face, beaky nose, and lashless, blinking eyes, he strongly resembled the fledgling young of some exotic bird species—a newly hatched flamingo, perhaps. His face could scarcely grow redder, but the back of his neck flamed crimson, as the sound of feminine giggles followed us up the stairs.

Safely ensconced in the small upstairs sitting room, with the door closed, Ian turned to face his hapless offspring.

"Going to live, are ye, ye wee bugger?" he demanded.

"Aye, sir," Young Ian replied in a dismal croak, looking rather as though he wished the answer were "No."

"Good," his father said grimly. "D'ye want to explain yourself, or shall I just belt hell out of ye now and save us both time?"

"Ye canna thrash someone who's just had his eyebrows burnt off, Ian," Jamie protested hoarsely, pouring out a glass of porter from the decanter on the table. "It wouldna be humane." He grinned at his nephew and handed him the glass, which the boy clutched with alacrity.

"Aye, well. Perhaps not," Ian agreed, surveying his son. One corner of his mouth twitched. Young Ian was a pitiable sight; he was also an extremely funny one. "That doesna mean ye aren't going to get your arse blistered later, mind," he warned the boy, "and that's besides whatever your mother means to do to ye when she sees ye again. But for now, lad, take your ease."

Not noticeably reassured by the magnanimous tone of this last statement, Young Ian didn't answer, but sought refuge in the depths of his glass of porter.

I took my own glass with a good deal of pleasure. I had realized belatedly just why the citizens of Edinburgh reacted to rain with such repugnance; once one was wet through, it was the devil to get dry again in the damp confines of a stone house, with no change of clothes and no heat available but a small hearthfire.

I plucked the damp bodice away from my breasts, caught Young Ian's interested glance, and decided regretfully that I really couldn't take it off with the boy in the room. Jamie seemed to have been corrupting the lad to quite a sufficient extent already. I gulped the porter instead, feeling the rich flavor purl warmingly through my innards.

"D'ye feel well enough to talk a bit, lad?" Jamie sat down opposite his nephew, next to Ian on the hassock.

"Aye . . . I think so," Young Ian croaked cautiously. He cleared his throat like a bullfrog and repeated more firmly, "Aye, I can."

"Good. Well, then. First, how did ye come to be in the printshop, and then, how did it come to be on fire?"

Young Ian pondered that one for a minute, then took another gulp of his porter for courage and said, "I set it."

Jamie and Ian both sat up straight at that. I could see Jamie revising his opinion as to the advisability of thrashing people without eyebrows, but he mastered his temper with an obvious effort, and said merely, "Why?"

The boy took another gulp of porter, coughed, and drank again, apparently trying to decide what to say.

"Well," he began uncertainly, "there was a man," and came to a dead stop.

"A man," Jamie prompted patiently when his nephew showed signs of having become suddenly deaf and dumb. "What man?"

Young Ian clutched his glass in both hands, looking deeply unhappy.

"Answer your uncle this minute, clot," Ian said sharply. "Or I'll take ye across my knee and tan ye right here."

With a mixture of similar threats and promptings, the two men managed to extract a more or less coherent story from the boy.

Young Ian had been at the tavern at Kerse that morning, where he had been told to meet Wally, who would come down from the rendezvous with the wagons of brandy, there to load the punked casks and spoiled wine to be used as subterfuge.

"Told?" Ian asked sharply. "Who told ye?"

"I did," Jamie said, before Young Ian could speak. He waved a hand at his brother-in-law, urging silence. "Aye, I kent he was here. We'll talk about it later, Ian, if ye please. It's important we know what happened today."

Ian glared at Jamie and opened his mouth to disagree, then shut it with a snap. He nodded to his son to go on.

"I was hungry, ye see," Young Ian said.

"When are ye not?" his father and uncle said together, in perfect unison. They looked at each other, snorted with sudden laughter, and the strained atmosphere in the room eased slightly.

"So ye went into the tavern to have a bite," Jamie said. "That's all right, lad, no harm done. And what happened while ye were there?"

That, it transpired, was where he had seen the man. A small, ratty-looking fellow, with a seaman's pigtail, and a blind eye, talking to the landlord.

"He was askin' for you, Uncle Jamie," Young Ian said, growing easier in his speech with repeated applications of porter. "By your own name."

Jamie started, looking surprised. "Jamie Fraser, ye mean?" Young Ian nodded, sipping. "Aye. But he knew your other name as well—Jamie Roy, I mean."

"Jamie Roy?" Ian turned a puzzled glance on his brother-in-law, who shrugged impatiently.

"It's how I'm known on the docks. Christ, Ian, ye know what I do!"

"Aye, I do, but I didna ken the wee laddie was helpin' ye to do it." Ian's thin lips pressed tight together, and he turned his attention back to his son. "Go on, lad. I willna interrupt ye again."

The seaman had asked the tavernkeeper how best an old seadog, down on his luck and looking for employment, might find one Jamie Fraser, who was known to have a use for able men. The landlord pleading ignorance of that name, the seaman had leaned closer, pushed a coin across the table, and in a lowered voice asked whether the name "Jamie Roy" was more familiar.

The landlord remaining deaf as an adder, the seaman had soon left the tavern, with Young Ian right behind him.

"I thought as how maybe it would be good to know who he was, and what he meant," the lad explained, blinking.

"Ye might have thought to leave word wi' the publican for Wally," Jamie said. "Still, that's neither here nor there. Where did he go?"

Down the road at a brisk walk, but not so brisk that a healthy boy could not follow at a careful distance. An accomplished walker, the seaman had made his way into Edinburgh, a distance of some five miles, in less than an hour, and arrived at last at the Green Owl tavern, followed by Young Ian, near wilted with thirst from the walk.

I started at the name, but didn't say anything, not wanting to interrupt the story.

"It was terrible crowded," the lad reported. "Something happened in the morning, and everyone was talking of it—but they shut up whenever they saw me. Anyway, it was the same there." He paused to cough and clear his throat. "The seaman ordered drink—brandy—then asked the landlord was he acquainted wi' a supplier of brandy named Jamie Roy or Jamie Fraser."

"Did he, then?" Jamie murmured. His gaze was intent on his nephew, but I could see the thoughts working behind his high forehead, making a small crease between his thick brows.

The man had gone methodically from tavern to tavern, dogged by his faithful shadow, and in each establishment had ordered brandy and repeated his question.

"He must have a rare head, to be drinkin' that much brandy," Ian remarked.

Young Ian shook his head. "He didna drink it. He only smelt it."

His father clicked his tongue at such a scandalous waste of good spirit, but Jamie's red brows climbed still higher.

"Did he taste any of it?" he asked sharply.

"Aye. At the Dog and Gun, and again at the Blue Boar. He had nay more than a wee taste, though, and then left the glass untouched. He didna drink at all at the other places, and we went to five o' them, before . . ." He trailed off, and took another drink.

Jamie's face underwent an astonishing transformation. From an expression of frowning puzzlement, his face went completely blank, and then resolved itself into an expression of revelation.

"Is that so, now," he said softly to himself. "Indeed." His attention came back to his nephew. "And then what happened, lad?"

Young Ian was beginning to look unhappy again. He gulped, the tremor visible all the way down his skinny neck.

"Well, it was a terrible long way from Kerse to Edinburgh," he began, "and a terrible dry walk, too . . ."

His father and uncle exchanged jaundiced glances.

"Ye drank too much," Jamie said, resigned.

"Well, I didna ken he was going to so many taverns, now, did I?" Young Ian cried in self-defense, going pink in the ears.

"No, of course not, lad," Jamie said kindly, smothering the beginning of Ian's more censorious remarks. "How long did ye last?"

Until midway down the Royal Mile, it turned out, where Young Ian, overcome by the cumulation of early rising, a five-mile walk, and the effects of something like two quarts of ale, had dozed off in a corner, waking an hour later to find his quarry long gone.

"So I came here," he explained. "I thought as how Uncle Jamie should know about it. But he wasna here." The boy glanced at me, and his ears grew still pinker.

"And just why did ye think he *should* be here?" Ian favored his offspring with a gimlet eye, which then swiveled to his brother-in-law. The simmering anger Ian had been holding in check since the morning suddenly erupted. "The filthy gall of ye, Jamie Fraser, takin' my son to a bawdy house!"

"A fine one you are to talk, Da!" Young Ian was on his feet, swaying a bit, but with his big, bony hands clenched at his sides.

"Me? And what d'ye mean by that, ye wee gomerel?" Ian cried, his eyes going wide with outrage.

"I mean you're a damned hypocrite!" his son shouted hoarsely. "Preachin' to me and Michael about purity and keepin' to one woman, and all the time ye're slinkin' about the city, sniffin' after whores!"

"What?" Ian's face had gone entirely purple. I looked in some alarm to Jamie, who appeared to be finding something funny in the present situation.

"You're a . . . a . . . goddamned whited sepulchre!" Young Ian came up with the simile triumphantly, then paused as though trying to think of another to equal it. His mouth opened, though nothing emerged but a soft belch.

"That boy is rather drunk," I said to Jamie.

He picked up the decanter of porter, eyed the level within, and set it down.

"You're right," he said. "I should ha' noticed sooner, but it's hard to tell, scorched as he is."

The elder Ian wasn't drunk, but his expression strongly resembled his offspring's, what with the suffused countenance, popping eyes, and straining neck cords.

"What the bloody, stinking hell d'ye mean by that, ye whelp?" he shouted. He moved menacingly toward Young Ian, who took an involuntary step backward and sat down quite suddenly as his calves met the edge of the sofa.

"Her," he said, startled into monosyllables. He pointed at me, to make it clear. "Her! You deceivin' my mam wi' this filthy whore, that's what I mean!"

Ian fetched his son a clout over the ear that knocked him sprawling on the sofa.

"Ye great clot!" he said, scandalized. "A fine way to speak o' your auntie Claire, to say nothing o' me and your mam!"

"Aunt?" Young Ian gawped at me from the cushions, looking so like a nestling begging for food that I burst out laughing despite myself.

"You left before I could introduce myself this morning," I said.

"But you're dead," he said stupidly.

"Not yet," I assured him. "Unless I've caught pneumonia from sitting here in a damp dress."

His eyes had grown perfectly round as he stared at me. Now a fugitive gleam of excitement came into them.

"Some o' the auld women at Lallybroch say ye were a wise-woman—a white lady, or maybe even a fairy. When Uncle Jamie came home from Culloden without ye, they said as how ye'd maybe gone back to the fairies, where ye maybe came from. Is that true? D'ye live in a dun?"

I exchanged a glance with Jamie, who rolled his eyes toward the ceiling.

"No," I said. "I . . . er, I . . ."

"She escaped to France after Culloden," Ian broke in suddenly, with great firmness. "She thought your uncle Jamie was killed in the battle, so she went to her kin in France. She'd been one of Prince *Tearlach*'s particular friends—she couldna come back to Scotland after the war without puttin' herself in sore danger. But then she heard of your uncle, and as soon as she kent that her husband wasna deid after all, she took ship at once and came to find him.''

Young Ian's mouth hung open slightly. So did mine.

"Er, yes," I said, closing it. "That's what happened."

The lad turned large, shining eyes from me to his uncle.

"So ye've come back to him," he said happily. "God, that's romantic!"

The tension of the moment was broken. Ian hesitated, but his eyes softened as he looked from Jamie to me.

"Aye," he said, and smiled reluctantly. "Aye, I suppose it is."

"I didna expect to be doing this for him for a good two or three years yet," Jamie remarked, holding his nephew's head with an expert hand as Young Ian retched painfully into the spittoon I was holding.

"Aye, well, he's always been forward," Ian answered resignedly. "Learnt to walk before he could stand, and was forever tumblin' into the fire or the washpot or the pigpen or the cowbyre." He patted the skinny, heaving back. "There, lad, let it come."

A little more, and the lad was deposited in a wilted heap on the sofa, there to recover from the effects of smoke, emotion, and too much porter under the censoriously mingled gaze of uncle and father.

"Where's that damn tea I sent for?" Jamie reached impatiently for the bell, but I stopped him. The brothel's domestic arrangements were evidently still disarranged from the excitements of the morning.

"Don't bother," I said. "I'll go down and fetch it." I scooped up the spittoon and carried it out with me at arm's length, hearing Ian say behind me, in a reasonable tone of voice, "Look, fool—"

I found my way to the kitchen with no difficulty, and obtained the necessary supplies. I hoped Jamie and Ian would give the boy a few minutes' respite; not only for his own sake, but so that I would miss nothing of his story.

I had clearly missed *something;* when I returned to the small sitting room, an air of constraint hung over the room like a cloud, and Young Ian glanced up and then quickly away to avoid my eye. Jamie was his usual imperturbable self, but the elder Ian looked almost as flushed and uneasy as his son. He hurried forward to take the tray from me, murmuring thanks, but would not meet my eye.

I raised one eyebrow at Jamie, who gave me a slight smile and a shrug. I shrugged back and picked up one of the bowls on the tray.

"Bread and milk," I said, handing it to Young Ian, who at once looked happier.

"Hot tea," I said, handing the pot to his father.

"Whisky," I said, handing the bottle to Jamie, "and cold tea for the burns." I whisked the lid off the last bowl, in which a number of napkins were soaking in cold tea.

"Cold tea?" Jamie's ruddy brows lifted. "Did the cook have no butter?"

"You don't put butter on burns," I told him. "Aloe juice, or the juice of a plantain or plantago, but the cook didn't have any of that. Cold tea is the best we could manage."

I poulticed Young Ian's blistered hands and forearms and blotted his scarlet face gently with the tea-soaked napkins while Jamie and Ian did the honors with teapot and whisky bottle, after which we all sat down, somewhat restored, to hear the rest of Ian's story.

"Well," he began, "I walked about the city for a bit, tryin' to think what best to do. And finally my head cleared a bit, and I reasoned that if the man I'd been followin' was goin' from tavern to tavern down the High Street, if I went to the other end and started *up* the street, I could maybe find him that way."

"That was a bright thought," Jamie said, and Ian nodded approvingly, the frown lifting a bit from his face. "Did ye find him?"

Young Ian nodded, slurping a bit. "I did, then."

Running down the Royal Mile nearly to the Palace of Holyrood at the foot, he had toiled his way painstakingly up the street, stopping at each tavern to inquire for the man with the pigtail and one eye. There was no word of his quarry anywhere below the Canongate, and he was beginning to despair of his idea, when suddenly he had seen the man himself, sitting in the taproom of the Holyrood Brewery.

Presumably this stop was for respite, rather than information, for the seaman was sitting at his ease, drinking beer. Young Ian had darted behind a hogshead in the yard, and remained there, watching, until at length the man rose, paid his score, and made his leisurely way outside.

"He didna go to any more taverns," the boy reported, wiping a stray drop of milk off his chin. "He went straight to Carfax Close, to the printshop."

Jamie said something in Gaelic under his breath. "Did he? And what then?"

"Well, he found the shop shut up, of course. When he saw the door was locked, he looked careful like, up at the windows, as though he was maybe thinking of breaking in. But then I saw him look about, at all the folk coming and going—it was a busy time of day, wi' all the folk coming to the chocolate shop. So he stood on the stoop a moment, thinking, and then he set off back up the close—I had to duck into the tailor's shop on the corner so as not to be seen."

The man had paused at the entrance of the close, then, making up his mind, had turned to the right, gone down a few paces, and disappeared into a small alley.

"I kent as how the alley led up to the court at the back of the close," Young Ian explained. "So I saw at once what he meant to be doing."

"There's a wee court at the back of the close," Jamie explained, seeing my puzzled look. "It's for rubbish and deliveries and such—but there's a back door out of the printshop opens onto it."

Young Ian nodded, putting down his empty bowl. "Aye. I thought it must be that he meant to get into the place. And I thought of the new pamphlets."

"Jesus," Jamie said. He looked a little pale.

"Pamphlets?" Ian raised his brows at Jamie. "What kind of pamphlets?"

"The new printing for Mr. Gage," Young Ian explained.

Ian still looked as blank as I felt.

"Politics," Jamie said bluntly. "An argument for repeal of the last Stamp Act—with an exhortation to civil opposition—by violence, if necessary. Five thousand of them, fresh-printed, stacked in the back room. Gage was to come round and get them in the morning, tomorrow."

"Jesus," Ian said. He had gone even paler than Jamie, at whom he stared in a sort of mingled horror and awe. "Have ye gone straight out o' your mind?" he inquired. "You, wi' not an inch on your back unscarred? Wi' the ink scarce dry on your pardon for treason? You're mixed up wi' Tom Gage and his seditious society, and got my son involved as well?"

His voice had been rising throughout, and now he sprang to his feet, fists clenched.

"How could ye do such a thing, Jamie—how? Have we not suffered enough for your actions, Jenny and me? All through the war and after—Christ, I'd think you'd have your fill of prisons and blood and violence!"

"I have," Jamie said shortly. "I'm no part of Gage's group. But my business is printing, aye? He paid for those pamphlets."

Ian threw up his hands in a gesture of vast irritation. "Oh, aye! And that will mean a great deal when the Crown's agents arrest ye and take ye to London to be hangit! If those things were to be found on your premises—" Struck by a sudden thought, he stopped and turned to his son.

"Oh, that was it?" he asked. "Ye kent what those pamphlets were—that's why ye set them on fire?"

Young Ian nodded, solemn as a young owl.

"I couldna move them in time," he said. "Not five thousand. The man—the seaman—he'd broke out the back window, and he was reachin' in for the doorlatch."

Ian whirled back to face Jamie.

"Damn you!" he said violently. "Damn ye for a reckless, harebrained fool, Jamie Fraser! First the Jacobites, and now this!"

Jamie had flushed up at once at Ian's words, and his face grew darker at this.

"Am I to blame for Charles Stuart?" he said. His eyes flashed angrily and he set his teacup down with a thump that sloshed tea and whisky over the polished tabletop. "Did I not try all I could to stop the wee fool? Did I not give up everything in that fight—*everything,* Ian! My land, my freedom, my wife—to try to save us all?" He glanced at me briefly as he spoke, and I caught one very small quick glimpse of just what the last twenty years had cost him.

He turned back to Ian, his brows lowering as he went on, voice growing hard.

"And as for what I've cost your family—what have ye profited,

Ian? Lallybroch belongs to wee James now, no? To *your* son, not mine!''

Ian flinched at that. ''I never asked—'' he began.

''No, ye didn't. I'm no accusing ye, for God's sake! But the fact's there—Lallybroch's no mine anymore, is it? My father left it to me, and I cared for it as best I could—took care o' the land and the tenants—and ye helped me, Ian.'' His voice softened a bit. ''I couldna have managed without you and Jenny. I dinna begrudge deeding it to Young Jamie—it had to be done. But still . . .'' He turned away for a moment, head bowed, broad shoulders knotted tight beneath the linen of his shirt.

I was afraid to move or speak, but I caught Young Ian's eye, filled with infinite distress. I put a hand on his skinny shoulder for mutual reassurance, and felt the steady pounding of the pulse in the tender flesh above his collarbone. He set his big, bony paw on my hand and held on tight.

Jamie turned back to his brother-in-law, struggling to keep his voice and temper under control. ''I swear to ye, Ian, I didna let the lad be put in danger. I kept him out of the way so much as I possibly could—didna let the shoremen see him, or let him go out on the boats wi' Fergus, hard as he begged me.'' He glanced at Young Ian and his expression changed, to an odd mixture of affection and irritation.

''I didna ask him to come to me, Ian, and I told him he must go home again.''

''Ye didna *make* him go, though, did you?'' The angry color was fading from Ian's face, but his soft brown eyes were still narrow and bright with fury. ''And ye didna send word, either. For God's sake, Jamie, Jenny hasna slept at night anytime this month!''

Jamie's lips pressed tight. ''No,'' he said, letting the words escape one at a time. ''No. I didn't. I—'' He glanced at the boy again, and shrugged uncomfortably, as though his shirt had grown suddenly too tight.

''No,'' he said again. ''I meant to take him home myself.''

''He's old enough to travel by himself,'' Ian said shortly. ''He got here alone, no?''

''Aye. It wasna that.'' Jamie turned aside restlessly, picking up a teacup and rolling it to and fro between his palms. ''No, I meant to take him, so that I could ask your permission—yours and Jenny's—for the lad to come live wi' me for a time.''

Ian uttered a short, sarcastic laugh. ''Oh, aye! Give our permission for him to be hangit or transported alongside you, eh?''

The anger flashed across Jamie's features again as he looked up from the cup in his hands.

''Ye know I wouldna let any harm come to him,'' he said. ''For Christ's sake, Ian, I care for the lad as though he were my own son, and well ye ken it, too!''

Ian's breath was coming fast; I could hear it from my place behind the sofa. ''Oh, I ken it well enough,'' he said, staring hard into Jamie's face. ''But he's not your son, aye? He's mine.''

Jamie stared back for a long moment, then reached out and gently set the teacup back on the table. ''Aye,'' he said quietly. ''He is.''

Ian stood for a moment, breathing hard, then wiped a hand carelessly across his forehead, pushing back the thick dark hair.

''Well, then,'' he said. He took one or two deep breaths, and turned to his son.

''Come along, then,'' he said. ''I've a room at Halliday's.''

Young Ian's bony fingers tightened on mine. His throat worked, but he didn't move to rise from his seat.

''No, Da,'' he said. His voice quivered, and he blinked hard, not to cry. ''I'm no going wi' ye.''

Ian's face went quite pale, with a deep red patch over the angular cheekbones, as though someone had slapped him hard on both cheeks.

''Is that so?'' he said.

Young Ian nodded, swallowing. ''I—I'll go wi' ye in the morning, Da; I'll go home wi' ye. But not now.''

Ian looked at his son for a long moment without speaking. Then his shoulders slumped, and all the tension went out of his body.

''I see,'' he said quietly. ''Well, then. Well.''

Without another word, he turned and left, closing the door very carefully behind him. I could hear the awkward thump of his wooden leg on each step, as he made his way down the stair. There was a brief sound of shuffling as he reached the bottom, then Bruno's voice in farewell, and the thud of the main door shutting. And then there was no sound in the room but the hiss of the hearthfire behind me.

The boy's shoulder was shaking under my hand, and he was holding tighter than ever to my fingers, crying without making a sound.

Jamie came slowly to sit beside him, his face full of troubled helplessness.

"Ian, oh, wee Ian," he said. "Christ, laddie, ye shouldna have done that."

"I had to." Ian gasped and gave a sudden snuffle, and I realized that he had been holding his breath. He turned a scorched countenance on his uncle, raw features contorted in anguish.

"I didna want to hurt Da," he said. "I didn't!"

Jamie patted his knee absently. "I know, laddie," he said, "but to say such a thing to him—"

"I couldna tell him, though, and I had to tell you, Uncle Jamie!"

Jamie glanced up, suddenly alert at his nephew's tone.

"Tell me? Tell me what?"

"The man. The man wi' the pigtail."

"What about him?"

Young Ian licked his lips, steeling himself.

"I think I kilt him," he whispered.

Startled, Jamie glanced at me, then back at Young Ian.

"How?" he asked.

"Well . . . I lied a bit," Ian began, voice trembling. The tears were still welling in his eyes, but he brushed them aside. "When I went into the printshop—I had the key ye gave me—the man was already inside."

The seaman had been in the backmost room of the shop, where the stacks of newly printed orders were kept, along with the stocks of fresh ink, the blotting papers used to clean the press, and the small forge where worn slugs were melted down and recast into fresh type.

"He was taking some o' the pamphlets from the stack, and putting them inside his jacket," Ian said, gulping. "When I saw him, I screeched at him to put them back, and he whirled round at me wi' a pistol in his hand."

The pistol had discharged, scaring Young Ian badly, but the ball had gone wild. Little daunted, the seaman had rushed at the boy, raising the pistol to club him instead.

"There was no time to run, or to think," he said. He had let go my hand by now, and his fingers twisted together upon his knee. "I reached out for the first thing to hand and threw it."

The first thing to hand had been the lead-dipper, the long-handled copper ladle used to pour molten lead from the melting pot into the casting molds. The forge had been still alight, though well banked, and while the melting pot held no more than a small puddle, the scalding drops of lead had flown from the dipper into the seaman's face.

"God, how he screamed!" A strong shudder ran through Young Ian's slender frame, and I came round the end of the sofa to sit next to him and take both his hands.

The seaman had reeled backward, clawing at his face, and upset the small forge, knocking live coals everywhere.

"That was what started the fire," the boy said. "I tried to beat it out, but it caught the edge of the fresh paper, and all of a sudden, something went *whoosh!* in my face, and it was as though the whole room was alight."

"The barrels of ink, I suppose," Jamie said, as though to himself. "The powder's dissolved in alcohol."

The sliding piles of flaming paper fell between Young Ian and the back door, a wall of flame that billowed black smoke and threatened to collapse upon him. The seaman, blinded and screaming like a banshee, had been on his hands and knees between the boy and the door into the front room of the printshop and safety.

"I—I couldna bear to touch him, to push him out o' the way," he said, shuddering again.

Losing his head completely, he had run up the stairs instead, but then found himself trapped as the flames, racing through the back room and drawing up the stair like a chimney, rapidly filled the upper room with blinding smoke.

"Did ye not think to climb out the trapdoor onto the roof?" Jamie asked.

Young Ian shook his head miserably. "I didna ken it was there."

"Why *was* it there?" I asked curiously.

Jamie gave me the flicker of a smile. "In case of need. It's a foolish fox has but one exit to his bolthole. Though I must say, it wasna fire I was thinking of when I had it made." He shook his head, ridding himself of the distraction.

"But ye think the man didna escape the fire?" he asked.

"I dinna see how he could," Young Ian answered, beginning to sniffle again. "And if he's dead, then I killed him. I couldna tell Da I was a m-mur—mur—" He was crying again, too hard to get the word out.

"You're no a murderer, Ian," Jamie said firmly. He patted his nephew's shaking shoulder. "Stop now, it's all right—ye havena done wrong, laddie. Ye haven't, d'ye hear?"

The boy gulped and nodded, but couldn't stop crying or shaking. At last I put my arms around him, turned him and pulled his head down onto my shoulder, patting his back and making the sort of small soothing noises one makes to little children.

He felt very odd in my arms; nearly as big as a full-grown man, but with fine, light bones, and so little flesh on them that it was like holding a skeleton. He was talking into the depths of my bosom, his voice so disjointed by emotion and muffled by fabric that it was difficult to make out the words.

". . . mortal sin . . ." he seemed to be saying, ". . . damned to hell . . . couldna tell Da . . . afraid . . . canna go home ever . . ."

Jamie raised his brows at me, but I only shrugged helplessly, smoothing the thick, bushy hair on the back of the boy's head. At last Jamie leaned forward, took him firmly by the shoulders and sat him up.

"Look ye, Ian," he said. "No, look—look at me!"

By dint of supreme effort, the boy straightened his drooping neck and fixed brimming, red-rimmed eyes on his uncle's face.

"Now, then." Jamie took hold of his nephew's hands and squeezed them lightly. "First—it's no a sin to kill a man that's trying to kill you. The Church allows ye to kill if ye must, in defense of yourself, your family, or your country. So ye havena committed mortal sin, and you're no damned."

"I'm not?" Young Ian sniffed mightily, and mopped at his face with a sleeve.

"No, you're not." Jamie let the hint of a smile show in his eyes. "We'll go together and call on Father Hayes in the morning, and ye'll make your confession and be absolved then, but he'll tell ye the same as I have."

"Oh." The syllable held profound relief, and Young Ian's scrawny shoulders rose perceptibly, as though a burden had rolled off them.

Jamie patted his nephew's knee again. "For the second thing, ye needna fear telling your father."

"No?" Young Ian had accepted Jamie's word on the state of his soul without hesitation, but sounded profoundly dubious about this secular opinion.

"Well, I'll not say he'll no be upset," Jamie added fairly. "In fact, I expect it will turn the rest of his hair white on the spot. But he'll understand. He isna going to cast ye out or disown ye, if that's what you're scairt of."

"You think he'll understand?" Young Ian looked at Jamie with eyes in which hope battled with doubt. "I—I didna think he . . . has my da ever killed a man?" he asked suddenly.

Jamie blinked, taken aback by the question. "Well," he said slowly, "I suppose—I mean, he's fought in battle, but I—to tell ye the truth, Ian, I dinna ken." He looked a little helplessly at his nephew.

"It's no the sort of thing men talk much about, aye? Except sometimes soldiers, when they're deep in drink."

Young Ian nodded, absorbing this, and sniffed again, with a horrid gurgling noise. Jamie, groping hastily in his sleeve for a handkerchief, looked up suddenly, struck by a thought.

"That's why ye said ye must tell me, but not your da? Because ye knew I've killed men before?"

His nephew nodded, searching Jamie's face with troubled, trusting eyes. "Aye. I thought . . . I thought ye'd know what to do."

"Ah." Jamie drew a deep breath, and exchanged a glance with me. "Well . . ." His shoulders braced and broadened, and I could see him accept the burden Young Ian had laid down. He sighed.

"What ye do," he said, "is first to ask yourself if ye had a choice. You didn't, so put your mind at ease. Then ye go to confession, if ye can; if not, say a good Act of Contrition—that's good enough, when it's no a mortal sin. Ye harbor no fault, mind," he said earnestly, "but the contrition is because ye greatly regret the necessity that fell on ye. It does sometimes, and there's no preventing it.

"And then say a prayer for the soul of the one you've killed," he went on, "that he may find rest, and not haunt ye. Ye ken the prayer called Soul Peace? Use that one, if ye have leisure to think of it. In a battle, when there is no time, use Soul Leading—'Be this soul on Thine arm, O Christ, Thou King of the City of Heaven, Amen.' "

"Be this soul on Thine arm, O Christ, Thou King of the City of Heaven, Amen," Young Ian repeated under his breath. He nodded slowly. "Aye, all right. And then?"

Jamie reached out and touched his nephew's cheek with great gentleness. "Then ye live with it, laddie," he said softly. "That's all."

28

Virtue's Guardian

"You think the man Young Ian followed has something to do with Sir Percival's warning?" I lifted a cover on the supper tray that had just been delivered and sniffed appreciatively; it seemed a very long time since Moubray's stew.

Jamie nodded, picking up a sort of hot stuffed roll.

"I should be surprised if he had not," he said dryly. "While there's likely more than one man willing to do me harm, I canna think it likely that gangs o' them are roaming about Edinburgh." He took a bite and chewed industriously, shaking his head.

"Nay, that's clear enough, and nothing to be greatly worrit over."

"It's not?" I took a small bite of my own roll, then a bigger one. "This is delicious. What is it?"

Jamie lowered the roll he had been about to take a bite of, and squinted at it. "Pigeon minced wi' truffles," he said, and stuffed it into his mouth whole.

"No," he said, and paused to swallow. "No," he said again, more clearly. "That's likely just a matter of a rival smuggler. There are two gangs that I've had a wee bit of difficulty with now and then." He waved a hand, scattering crumbs, and reached for another roll.

"The way the man behaved—smellin' the brandy, but seldom tasting it—he may be a *dégustateur de vin*; someone that can tell from a sniff where a wine was made, and from a taste, which year it was bottled. A verra valuable fellow," he added thoughtfully, "and a choice hound to set on my trail."

Wine had come along with the supper. I poured out a glass and passed it under my own nose.

"He could track you—you, personally—through the brandy?" I asked curiously.

"More or less. You'll remember my cousin Jared?"

"Of course I do. You mean he's still alive?" After the slaughter of Culloden and the erosions of its aftermath, it was wonderfully heartening to hear that Jared, a wealthy Scottish émigré with a prosperous wine business in Paris, was still among the quick, and not the dead.

"I expect they'll have to head him up in a cask and toss him into the Seine to get rid of him," Jamie said, teeth gleaming white in his soot-stained countenance. "Aye, he's not only alive, but enjoying it. Where d'ye think I get the French brandy I bring into Scotland?"

The obvious answer was "France," but I refrained from saying so. "Jared, I suppose?" I said instead.

Jamie nodded, mouth full of another roll. "Hey!" He leaned forward and snatched the plate out from under the tentative reach of Young Ian's skinny fingers. "You're no supposed to be eating rich stuff like that when your wame's curdled," he said, frowning and chewing. He swallowed and licked his lips. "I'll call for more bread and milk for ye."

"But Uncle," said Young Ian, looking longingly at the savory rolls. "I'm awfully hungry." Purged by confession, the boy had recovered his spirits considerably, and evidently, his appetite as well.

Jamie looked at his nephew and sighed. "Aye, well. Ye swear you're no going to vomit on me?"

"No, Uncle," Young Ian said meekly.

"All right, then." Jamie shoved the plate in the boy's direction, and returned to his explanation.

"Jared sends me mostly the second-quality bottling from his own vineyards in the Moselle, keepin' the first quality for sale in France, where they can tell the difference."

"So the stuff you bring into Scotland is identifiable?"

He shrugged, reaching for the wine. "Only to a *nez,* a *dégustateur,* that is. But the fact is, that wee Ian here saw the man taste the wine at the Dog and Gun and at the Blue Boar, and those are the two taverns on the High Street that buy brandy from me exclusively. Several others buy from me, but from others as well.

"In any case, as I say, I'm none so concerned at havin' someone look for Jamie Roy at a tavern." He lifted his wineglass and passed it under his own nose by reflex, made a slight, unconscious face, and drank. "No," he said, lowering the glass, "what worries me is that the man should have found his way to the printshop. For I've taken considerable pains to make sure that the folk who see Jamie Roy on the docks at Burntisland are not the same ones who pass the time o' day in the High Street with Mr. Alec Malcolm, the printer."

I knitted my brows, trying to work it out.

"But Sir Percival called you Malcolm, and he knows you're a smuggler," I protested.

Jamie nodded patiently. "Half the men in the ports near Edinburgh are smugglers, Sassenach," he said. "Aye, Sir Percival kens fine I'm a smuggler, but he doesna ken I'm Jamie Roy—let alone James Fraser. He thinks I bring in bolts of undeclared silk and velvet from Holland—because that's what I pay him in." He smiled wryly. "I trade brandy for them, to the tailor on the corner. Sir Percival's an eye for fine cloth, and his lady even more. But he doesna ken I've to do wi' the liquor—let alone how much—or he'd be wanting a great deal more than the odd bit of lace and yardage, I'll tell ye."

"Could one of the tavern owners have told the seaman about you? Surely they've seen you."

He ruffled a hand through his hair, as he did when thinking, making a few short hairs on the crown stand up in a whorl of tiny spikes.

"Aye, they've seen me," he said slowly, "but only as a customer. Fergus handles the business dealings wi' the taverns—and Fergus is careful never to go near the printshop. He always meets me here, in private." He gave me a crooked grin. "No one questions a man's reasons for visiting a brothel, aye?"

"Could that be it?" I asked, struck by a sudden thought. "Any man can come here without question. Could the seaman Young Ian followed have seen you here—you and Fergus? Or heard your description from one of the girls? After all, you're not the most inconspicuous man I've ever seen." He wasn't, either. While there might be any number of redheaded men in Edinburgh, few of them towered to Jamie's height, and fewer still strode the streets with the unconscious arrogance of a disarmed warrior.

"That's a verra useful thought, Sassenach," he said, giving me a nod. "It will be easy enough to find out whether a pigtailed seaman with one eye has been here recently; I'll have Jeanne ask among her lassies."

He stood up, and stretched rackingly, his hands nearly touching the wooden rafters.

"And then, Sassenach, perhaps we'll go to bed, aye?" He lowered his arms and blinked at me with a smile. "What wi' one thing and another, it's been the bloody hell of a day, no?"

"It has, rather," I said, smiling back.

Jeanne, summoned for instructions, arrived together with Fergus, who opened the door for the madam with the easy familiarity of a brother or cousin. Little wonder if he felt at home, I supposed; he had been born in a Paris brothel, and spent the first ten years of his life there, sleeping in a cupboard beneath the stairs, when not making a living by picking pockets on the street.

"The brandy is gone," he reported to Jamie. "I have sold it to MacAlpine—at a small sacrifice in price, I regret, milord. I thought a quick sale the best."

"Better to have it off the premises," Jamie said, nodding. "What have ye done wi' the body?"

Fergus smiled briefly, his lean face and dark forelock lending him a distinctly piratical air.

"Our intruder also has gone to MacAlpine's tavern, milord—suitably disguised."

"As what?" I demanded.

The pirate's grin turned on me; Fergus had turned out a very handsome man, the disfigurement of his hook notwithstanding.

"As a cask of crème de menthe, milady," he said.

"I do not suppose anyone has drunk crème de menthe in Edinburgh anytime in the last hundred years," observed Madame Jeanne. "The heathen Scots are not accustomed to the use of civilized liqueurs; I have never seen a customer here take anything beyond whisky, beer, or brandywine."

"Exactly, Madame," Fergus said, nodding. "We do not want Mr. MacAlpine's tapmen broaching the cask, do we?"

"Surely somebody's going to look in that cask sooner or later," I said. "Not to be indelicate, but—"

"Exactly, milady," Fergus said, with a respectful bow to me. "Though crème de menthe has a very high content of alcohol. The tavern's cellar is but a temporary resting place on our unknown friend's journey to his eternal rest. He goes to the docks tomorrow, and thence to somewhere quite far away. It is only that I did not want him cluttering up Madame Jeanne's premises in the meantime."

Jeanne addressed a remark in French to St. Agnes that I didn't quite catch, but then shrugged and turned to go.

"I will make inquiries of *les filles* concerning this seaman tomorrow, Monsieur, when they are at leisure. For now—"

"For now, speaking of leisure," Fergus interrupted, "might Mademoiselle Sophie find herself unemployed this evening?"

The madam favored him with a look of ironic amusement. "Since she saw you come in, *mon petit saucisson,* I expect that she has kept herself available." She glanced at Young Ian, slouched against the cushions like a scarecrow from which all the straw stuffing has been removed. "And will I find a place for the young gentleman to sleep?"

"Oh, aye." Jamie looked consideringly at his nephew. "I suppose ye can lay a pallet in my room."

"Oh, no!" Young Ian blurted. "You'll want to be alone wi' your wife, will ye not, Uncle?"

"What?" Jamie stared at him uncomprehendingly.

"Well, I mean . . ." Young Ian hesitated, glancing at me, and then hastily away. "I mean, nay doubt you'll be wanting to . . . er . . . mmphm?" A Highlander born, he managed to infuse this last noise with an amazing wealth of implied indelicacy.

Jamie rubbed his knuckles hard across his upper lip.

"Well, that's verra thoughtful of ye, Ian," he said. His voice quivered slightly with the effort of not laughing. "And I'm flattered that ye have such a high opinion of my virility as to think I'm capable of anything but sleeping in bed after a day like this. But I think perhaps I can forgo the satisfaction of my carnal desires for one night—fond as I am of your auntie," he added, giving me a faint grin.

"But Bruno tells me the establishment is not busy tonight," Fergus put in, glancing round in some bewilderment. "Why does the boy not—"

"Because he's no but fourteen, for God's sake!" Jamie said, scandalized.

"Almost fifteen!" Young Ian corrected, sitting up and looking interested.

"Well, that is certainly sufficient," Fergus said, with a glance at Madame Jeanne for confirmation. "Your brothers were no older when I first brought them here, and they acquitted themselves honorably."

"You *what*?" Jamie goggled at his protégé.

"Well, someone had to," Fergus said, with slight impatience. "Normally, a boy's father—but of course, le Monsieur is not—meaning no disrespect to your esteemed father, of course," he added, with a nod to Young Ian, who nodded back like a mechanical toy, "but it is a matter for experienced judgment, you understand?

"Now"—he turned to Madame Jeanne, with the air of a gourmand consulting the wine steward—"Dorcas, do you think, or Penelope?"

"No, no," she said, shaking her head decidedly, "it should be the second Mary, absolutely. The small one."

"Oh, with the yellow hair? Yes, I think you are right," Fergus said approvingly. "Fetch her, then."

Jeanne was off before Jamie could manage more than a strangled croak in protest.

"But—but—the lad canna—" he began.

"Yes, I can," Young Ian said. "At least, I think I can." It wasn't possible for his face to grow any redder, but his ears were crimson with excitement, the traumatic events of the day completely forgotten.

"But it's—that is to say—I canna be letting ye—" Jamie broke off and stood glaring at his nephew for a long moment. Finally, he threw his hands up in the air in exasperated defeat.

"And what am I to say to your mother?" he demanded, as the door opened behind him.

Framed in the door stood a very short young girl, plump and soft as a partridge in her blue silk chemise, her round sweet face beaming beneath a loose cloud of yellow hair. At the sight of her, Young Ian froze, scarcely breathing.

When at last he must draw breath or die, he drew it, and turned to Jamie. With a smile of surpassing sweetness, he said, "Well,

Uncle Jamie, if I were you"—his voice soared up in a sudden
alarming soprano, and he stopped, clearing his throat before resuming in a respectable baritone—"I wouldna tell her. Good night
to ye, Auntie," he said, and walked purposefully forward.

"I canna decide whether I must kill Fergus or thank him."
Jamie was sitting on the bed in our attic room, slowly unbuttoning
his shirt.

I laid the damp dress over the stool and knelt down in front of
him to unbuckle the knee buckles of his breeches.

"I suppose he was trying to do his best for Young Ian."

"Aye—in his bloody immoral French way." Jamie reached
back to untie the lace that held his hair back. He had not plaited it
again when we left Moubray's, and it fell soft and loose on his
shoulders, framing the broad cheekbones and long straight nose,
so that he looked like one of the fiercer Italian angels of the
Renaissance.

"Was it the Archangel Michael who drove Adam and Eve out
of the Garden of Eden?" I asked, stripping off his stockings.

He gave a slight chuckle. "Do I strike ye so—as the guardian o'
virtue? And Fergus as the wicked serpent?" His hands came under my elbows as he bent to lift me up. "Get up, Sassenach; ye
shouldna be on your knees, serving me."

"You've had rather a time of it today yourself," I answered,
making him stand up with me. "Even if you didn't have to kill
anyone." There were large blisters on his hands, and while he had
wiped away most of the soot, there was still a streak down the side
of his jaw.

"Mm." My hands went around his waist to help with the waistband of his breeches, but he held them there, resting his cheek for
a moment against the top of my head.

"I wasna quite honest wi' the lad, ye ken," he said.

"No? I thought you did wonderfully with him. He felt better
after he talked to you, at least."

"Aye, I hope so. And maybe the prayers and such will help—
they canna hurt him, at least. But I didna tell him everything."

"What else is there?" I tilted up my face to his, touching his
lips softly with my own. He smelled of smoke and sweat.

"What a man most often does, when he's soul-sick wi' killing, is to find a woman, Sassenach,'' he answered softly. ''His own, if he can; another, if he must. For she can do what he cannot—and heal him.''

My fingers found the lacing of his fly; it came loose with a tug.

''That's why you let him go with the second Mary?''

He shrugged, and stepping back a pace, pushed the breeches down and off. ''I couldna stop him. And I think perhaps I was right to let him, young as he is.'' He smiled crookedly at me. ''At least he'll not be fashing and fretting himself over that seaman tonight.''

''I don't imagine so. And what about you?'' I pulled the chemise off over my head.

''Me?'' He stared down at me, eyebrows raised, the grimy linen shirt hanging loose upon his shoulders.

I glanced behind him at the bed.

''Yes. You haven't killed anyone, but do you want to . . . mmphm?'' I met his gaze, raising my own brows in question.

The smile broadened across his face, and any resemblance to Michael, stern guardian of virtue, vanished. He lifted one shoulder, then the other, and let them fall, and the shirt slid down his arms to the floor.

''I expect I do,'' he said. ''But you'll be gentle wi' me, aye?''

29

Culloden's Last Victim

I n the morning, I saw Jamie and Ian off on their pious errand, and then set off myself, stopping to purchase a large wicker basket from a vendor in the street. It was time I began to equip myself again, with whatever I could find in the way of medical supplies. After the events of the preceding day, I was beginning to fear I would have need of them before long.

Haugh's apothecary shop hadn't changed at all, through English occupation, Scottish Rising, and the Stuarts' fall, and my heart rose in delight as I stepped through the door into the rich, familiar smells of hartshorn, peppermint, almond oil, and anise.

The man behind the counter was Haugh, but a much younger Haugh than the middle-aged man I had dealt with twenty years before, when I had patronized this shop for tidbits of military intelligence, as well as for nostrums and herbs.

The younger Haugh did not know me, of course, but went courteously about the business of finding the herbs I wanted, among the neatly ranged jars on his shelves. A good many were common—rosemary, tansy, marigold—but a few on my list made the young Haugh's ginger eyebrows rise, and his lips purse in thoughtfulness as he looked over the jars.

There was another customer in the shop, hovering near the counter, where tonics were dispensed and compounds ground to order. He strode back and forth, hands clasped behind his back, obviously impatient. After a moment, he came up to the counter.

"How long?" he snapped at Mr. Haugh's back.

"I canna just say, Reverend." The apothecary's voice was apologetic. "Louisa did say as 'twould need to be boiled."

The only reply to this was a snort, and the man, tall and narrow-shouldered in black, resumed his pacing, glancing from time to time at the doorway to the back room, where the invisible Louisa was presumably at work. The man looked slightly familiar, but I had no time to think where I had seen him before.

Mr. Haugh was squinting dubiously at the list I had given him. "Aconite, now," he muttered. "Aconite. And what might that be, I wonder?"

"Well, it's a poison, for one thing," I said. Mr. Haugh's mouth dropped open momentarily.

"It's a medicine, too," I assured him. "But you have to be careful in the use of it. Externally, it's good for rheumatism, but a very tiny amount taken by mouth will lower the rate of the pulse. Good for some kinds of heart trouble."

"Really," Mr. Haugh said, blinking. He turned to his shelves, looking rather helpless. "Er, do ye ken what it smells like, maybe?"

Taking this for invitation, I came round the counter and began to sort through the jars. They were all carefully labeled, but the labels of some were clearly old, the ink faded, and the paper peeling at the edges.

"I'm afraid I'm none so canny wi' the medicines as my da yet," young Mr. Haugh was saying at my elbow. "He'd taught me a good bit, but then he passed on a year ago, and there's things here as I dinna ken the use of, I'm afraid."

"Well, that one's good for cough," I said, taking down a jar of elecampane with a glance at the impatient Reverend, who had taken out a handkerchief and was wheezing asthmatically into it. "Particularly sticky-sounding coughs."

I frowned at the crowded shelves. Everything was dusted and immaculate, but evidently not filed according either to alphabetical or botanical order. Had old Mr. Haugh merely remembered where things were, or had he a system of some kind? I closed my eyes and tried to remember the last time I had been in the shop.

To my surprise, the image came back easily. I had come for foxglove then, to make the infusions for Alex Randall, younger brother of Black Jack Randall—and Frank's six-times great-grandfather. Poor boy, he had been dead now twenty years, though he had lived long enough to sire a son. I felt a twinge of curiosity at the thought of that son, and of his mother, who had been my friend, but I forced my mind away from them, back to the image of Mr. Haugh, standing on tiptoe to reach up to his shelves, over near the right-hand side . . .

"There." Sure enough, my hand rested near the jar labeled FOXGLOVE. To one side of it was a jar labeled HORSETAIL, to the other, LILY OF THE VALLEY ROOT. I hesitated, looking at them, running over in my mind the possible uses of those herbs. Cardiac herbs, all of them. If aconite was to be found, it would be close by, then.

It was. I found it quickly, in a jar labeled AULD WIVES HUID.

"Be careful with it." I handed the jar gingerly to Mr. Haugh. "Even a bit of it will make your skin go numb. Perhaps I'd better have a glass bottle for it." Most of the herbs I'd bought had been wrapped up in squares of gauze or twisted in screws of paper, but the young Mr. Haugh nodded and carried the jar of aconite into the back room, held at arm's length, as though he expected it to explode in his face.

"Ye'd seem to know a good deal more about the medicines than the lad," said a deep, hoarse voice behind me.

"Well, I've somewhat more experience than he has, likely." I turned to find the minister leaning on the counter, watching me under thick brows with pale blue eyes. I realized with a start where I had seen him; in Moubray's, the day before. He gave no sign of recognizing me; perhaps because my cloak covered Daphne's dress. I had noticed that many men took relatively little notice of the face of a woman *en décolletage,* though it seemed a regrettable habit in a clergyman. He cleared his throat.

"Mmphm. And d'ye ken what to do for a nervous complaint, then?"

"What sort of nervous complaint?"

He pursed his lips and frowned, as though unsure whether to trust me. The upper lip came to a slight point, like an owl's beak, but the lower was thick and pendulous.

"Well . . . 'tis a complicated case. But to speak generally, now"—he eyed me carefully—"what would ye give for a sort of . . . fit?"

"Epileptic seizure? Where the person falls down and twitches?"

He shook his head, showing a reddened band about his neck, where the high white stock had chafed it.

"No, a different kind of fit. Screaming and staring."

"Screaming *and* staring?"

"Not at once, ye ken," he added hastily. "First the one, and then the other—or rather, roundabout. First she'll do naught but stare for days on end, not speaking, and then of a sudden, she'll scream fit to wake the deid."

"That sounds very trying." It did; if he had a wife so afflicted, it could easily explain the deep lines of strain that bracketed his mouth and eyes, and the blue circles of exhaustion beneath his eyes.

I tapped a finger on the counter, considering. "I don't know; I'd have to see the patient."

The minister's tongue touched his lower lip. "Perhaps . . . would ye be willing maybe, to come and see her? It isn't far," he added, rather stiffly. Pleading didn't come naturally to him, but the urgency of his request communicated itself despite the stiffness of his figure.

"I can't, just now," I told him. "I have to meet my husband. But perhaps this afternoon—"

"Two o'clock," he said promptly. "Henderson's, in Carrubber's Close. Campbell is the name, the Reverend Archibald Campbell."

Before I could say yes or no, the curtain between the front room and the back twitched aside, and Mr. Haugh appeared with two bottles, one of which he handed to each of us.

The Reverend eyed his with suspicion, as he groped in his pocket for a coin.

"Weel, and there's your price," he said ungraciously, slapping it on the counter. "And we'll hope as you've given me the right one, and no the lady's poison."

The curtain rustled again and a woman looked out after the departing form of the minister.

"Good riddance," she remarked. "Happence for an hour's work, and insult on the top of it! The Lord might ha' chosen better, is all I can say!"

"Do you know him?" I asked, curious whether Louisa might have any helpful information about the afflicted wife.

"Not to say I ken him weel, no," Louisa said, staring at me in frank curiosity. "He's one o' they Free Church meenisters, as is always rantin' on the corner by the Market Cross, tellin' folk as their behavior's of nay consequence at all, and all that's needful for salvation is that they shall 'come to grips wi' Jesus'—like as if Our Lord was to be a fair-day wrestler!" She sniffed disdainfully at this heretical viewpoint, crossing herself against contamination.

"I'm surprised the likes of the Reverend Campbell should come in our shop, hearin' what he thinks o' Papists by and large." Her eyes sharpened at me.

"But you'll maybe be Free Church yoursel', ma'am; meanin' no offense to ye, if so."

"No, I'm a Catholic—er, a Papist, too," I assured her. "I was only wondering whether you knew anything about the Reverend's wife, and her condition."

Louisa shook her head, turning to deal with a new customer.

"Nay, I've ne'er seen the lady. But whatever's the matter with her," she added, frowning after the departed Reverend, "I'm sure that livin' wi' *him* doesna improve it any!"

The weather was chill but clear, and only a faint hint of smoke lingered in the Rectory garden as a reminder of the fire. Jamie and I sat on a bench against the wall, absorbing the pale winter sunshine as we waited for Young Ian to finish his confession.

"Did you tell Ian that load of rubbish he gave Young Ian yesterday? About where I'd been all this time?"

"Oh, aye," he said. "Ian's a good deal too canny to believe it, but it's a likely enough story, and he's too good a friend to insist on the truth."

"I suppose it will do, for general consumption," I agreed. "But shouldn't you have told it to Sir Percival, instead of letting him think we were newlyweds?"

He shook his head decidedly. "Och, no. For the one thing, Sir Percival has no notion of my real name, though I'll lay a year's takings he knows it isna Malcolm. I dinna want him to be thinking of me and Culloden together, by any means. And for another, a story like the one I gave Ian would cause the devil of a lot more talk than the news that the printer's taken a wife."

" 'Oh, what a tangled web we weave,' " I intoned, " 'when first we practice to deceive.' "

He gave me a quick blue glance, and the corner of his mouth lifted slightly.

"It gets a bit easier with practice, Sassenach," he said. "Try living wi' me for a time, and ye'll find yourself spinning silk out of your arse easy as sh—, er, easy as kiss-my-hand."

I burst out laughing.

"I want to see you do that," I said.

"You already have." He stood up and craned his neck, trying to see over the wall into the Rectory garden.

"Young Ian's being the devil of a time," he remarked, sitting down again. "How can a lad not yet fifteen have that much to confess?"

"After the day and night he had yesterday? I suppose it depends how much detail Father Hayes wants to hear," I said, with a vivid recollection of my breakfast with the prostitutes. "Has he been in there all this time?"

"Er, no." The tips of Jamie's ears grew slightly pinker in the morning light. "I, er, I had to go first. As an example, ye ken."

"No wonder it took some time," I said, teasing. "How long has it been since you've been to confession?"

"I told Father Hayes it was six months."

"And was it?"

"No, but I supposed if he was going to shrive me for thieving, assault, and profane language, he might as well shrive me for lying, too."

"What, no fornication or impure thoughts?"

"Certainly not," he said austerely. "Ye can think any manner of horrible things without sin, and it's to do wi' your wife. It's only if you're thinking it about other ladies, it's impure."

"I had no idea I was coming back to save your soul," I said primly, "but it's nice to be useful."

He laughed, bent and kissed me thoroughly.

"I wonder if that counts as an indulgence," he said, pausing for breath. "It ought to, no? It does a great deal more to keep a man from the fires of hell than saying the rosary does. Speaking of which," he added, digging into his pocket and coming out with a rather chewed-looking wooden rosary, "remind me that I must say my penance sometime today. I was about to start on it, when ye came up."

"How many Hail Marys are you supposed to say?" I asked,

fingering the beads. The chewed appearance wasn't illusion; there were definite small toothmarks on most of the beads.

"I met a Jew last year," he said, ignoring the question. "A natural philosopher, who'd sailed round the world six times. He told me that in both the Musselman faith and the Jewish teachings, it was considered an act of virtue for a man and his wife to lie wi' each other.

"I wonder if that has anything to do wi' both Jews and Musselmen being circumcised?" he added thoughtfully. "I never thought to ask him that—though perhaps he would ha' found it indelicate to say."

"I shouldn't think a foreskin more or less would impair the virtue," I assured him.

"Oh, good," he said, and kissed me once more.

"What happened to your rosary?" I asked, picking up the string where it had fallen on the grass. "It looks like the rats have been at it."

"Not rats," he said. "Bairns."

"What bairns?"

"Oh, any that might be about." He shrugged, tucking the beads back in his pocket. "Young Jamie has three now, and Maggie and Kitty two each. Wee Michael's just married, but his wife's breeding." The sun was behind him, darkening his face, so that his teeth flashed suddenly white when he smiled. "Ye didna ken ye were a great-aunt seven times over, aye?"

"A great-aunt?" I said, staggered.

"Well, I'm a great-uncle," he said cheerfully, "and I havena found it a terrible trial, except for having my beads gnawed when the weans are cutting teeth—that, and bein' expected to answer to 'Nunkie' a lot."

Sometimes twenty years seemed like an instant, and sometimes it seemed like a very long time indeed.

"Er . . . there isn't a feminine equivalent of 'Nunkie,' I hope?"

"Oh, no," he assured me. "They'll all call ye Great-Auntie Claire, and treat ye wi' the utmost respect."

"Thanks a lot," I muttered, with visions of the hospital's geriatric wing fresh in my mind.

Jamie laughed, and with a lightness of heart no doubt engendered by being newly freed from sin, grasped me around the waist and lifted me onto his lap.

"I've never before seen a great-auntie wi' a lovely plump arse like that," he said with approval, bouncing me slightly on his knees. His breath tickled the back of my neck as he leaned forward. I let out a small shriek as his teeth closed lightly on my ear.

"Are ye all right, Auntie?" said Young Ian's voice just behind us, full of concern.

Jamie started convulsively, nearly unshipping me from his lap, then tightened his hold on my waist.

"Oh, aye," he said. "It's just your auntie saw a spider."

"Where?" said Young Ian, peering interestedly over the bench.

"Up there." Jamie rose, standing me on my feet, and pointed to the lime tree, where—sure enough—the web of an orb weaver stretched across the crook of two branches, sparkling with damp. The weaver herself sat in the center, round as a cherry, wearing a gaudy pattern of green and yellow on her back.

"I was telling your auntie," Jamie said, as Young Ian examined the web in lashless fascination, "about a Jew I met, a natural philosopher. He'd made a study of spiders, it seems; in fact, he was in Edinburgh to deliver a learned paper to the Royal Society, in spite of being a Jew."

"Really? Did he tell ye a lot about spiders?" Young Ian asked eagerly.

"A lot more than I cared to know," Jamie informed his nephew. "There are times and places for talkin' of spiders that lay eggs in caterpillars so the young hatch out and devour the poor beast while it's still alive, but during supper isna one of them. He did say one thing I thought verra interesting, though," he added, squinting at the web. He blew gently on it, and the spider scuttled briskly into hiding.

"He said that spiders spin two kinds of silk, and if ye have a lens—and can make the spider sit still for it, I suppose—ye can see the two places where the silk comes out; spinnerets, he called them. In any case, the one kind of silk is sticky, and if a wee bug touches it, he's done for. But the other kind is dry silk, like the sort ye'd embroider with, but finer."

The orb weaver was advancing cautiously toward the center of her web again.

"See where she walks?" Jamie pointed to the web, anchored by a number of spokes, supporting the intricate netlike whorl. "The spokes there, those are spun of the dry silk, so the spider can walk over it herself wi' no trouble. But the rest o' the web is the sticky kind of silk—or mostly so—and if ye watch a spider careful for quite a long time, you'll see that she goes only on the dry strands, for if she walked on the sticky stuff, she'd be stuck herself."

"Is that so?" Ian breathed reverently on the web, watching intently as the spider moved away along her nonskid road to safety.

"I suppose there's a moral there for web weavers," Jamie observed to me, sotto voce. "Be sure ye know which of your strands are sticky."

"I suppose it helps even more if you have the kind of luck that will conjure up a handy spider when you need one," I said dryly.

He laughed and took my arm.

"That's not luck, Sassenach," he told me. "It's watchfulness. Ian, are ye coming?"

"Oh, aye." Young Ian abandoned the web with obvious reluctance and followed us to the kirkyard gate.

"Oh, Uncle Jamie, I meant to ask, can I borrow your rosary?" he said, as we emerged onto the cobbles of the Royal Mile. "The priest told me I must say five decades for my penance, and that's too many to keep count of on my fingers."

"Surely." Jamie stopped and fished in his pocket for the rosary. "Be sure to give it back, though."

Young Ian grinned. "Aye, I reckon you'll be needing it yourself, Uncle Jamie. The priest told me he was verra wicked," Young Ian confided to me, with a lashless wink, "and told me not to be like him."

"Mmphm." Jamie glanced up and down the road, gauging the speed of an approaching handcart, edging its way down the steep incline. Freshly shaved that morning, his cheeks had a rosy glow about them.

"How many decades of the rosary are you supposed to say as penance?" I asked curiously.

"Eighty-five," he muttered. The rosiness of his freshly shaved cheeks deepened.

Young Ian's mouth dropped open in awe.

"How long has it been since ye went to confession, Uncle?" he asked.

"A long time," Jamie said tersely. "Come on!"

Jamie had an appointment after dinner to meet with a Mr. Harding, representative of the Hand in Hand Assurance Society, which had insured the premises of the printshop, to inspect the ashy remains with him and verify the loss.

"I willna need ye, laddie," he said reassuringly to Young Ian, who looked less than enthusiastic about the notion of revisiting the scene of his adventures. "You go wi' your auntie to see this madwoman."

"I canna tell how ye do it," he added to me, raising one brow. "You're in the city less than two days, and all the afflicted folk for miles about are clutching at your hems."

"Hardly all of them," I said dryly. "It's only one woman, after all, and I haven't even seen her yet."

"Aye, well. At least madness isna catching—I hope." He kissed me briefly, then turned to go, clapping Young Ian companionably on the shoulder. "Look after your auntie, Ian."

Young Ian paused for a moment, looking after the tall form of his departing uncle.

"Do you want to go with him, Ian?" I asked. "I can manage alone, if you—"

"Oh, no, Auntie!" He turned back to me, looking rather abashed. "I dinna want to go, at all. It's only—I was wondering—well, what if they . . . find anything? In the ashes?"

"A body, you mean," I said bluntly. I had realized, of course, that the distinct possibility that Jamie and Mr. Harding *would* find the body of the one-eyed seaman was the reason Jamie had told Ian to accompany me.

The boy nodded, looking ill at ease. His skin had faded to a sort of rosy tan, but was still too dark to show any paleness due to emotion.

"I don't know," I said. "If the fire was a very hot one, there may be nothing much left to find. But don't worry about it." I touched his arm in reassurance. "Your uncle will know what to do."

"Aye, that's so." His face brightened, full of faith in his uncle's ability to handle any situation whatever. I smiled when I saw his expression, then realized with a small start of surprise that I had that faith, too. Be it drunken Chinese, corrupt Customs agents, or Mr. Harding of the Hand in Hand Assurance Society, I hadn't any doubt that Jamie would manage.

"Come on, then," I said, as the bell in the Canongate Kirk began to ring. "It's just on two now."

Despite his visit to Father Hayes, Ian had retained a certain air of dreamy bliss, which returned to him now, and there was little conversation as we made our way up the slope of the Royal Mile to Henderson's lodging house, in Carrubber's Close.

It was a quiet hotel, but luxurious by Edinburgh standards, with a patterned carpet on the stairs and colored glass in the street window. It seemed rather rich surroundings for a Free Church minister, but then I knew little about Free Churchmen; perhaps they took no vow of poverty as the Catholic clergy did.

Showed up to the third floor by a young boy, we found the door opened to us at once by a heavyset woman wearing an apron and a worried expression. I thought she might be in her mid-twenties, though she had already lost several of her front teeth.

"You'll be the lady as the Reverend said would call?" she asked. Her expression lightened a bit at my nod, and she swung the door wider.

"Mr. Campbell's had to go oot the noo," she said in a broad Lowland accent, "but he said as how he'd be most obliged to hae yer advice regardin' his sister, mum."

Sister, not wife. "Well, I'll do my best," I said. "May I see Miss Campbell?"

Leaving Ian to his memories in the sitting room, I accompanied the woman, who introduced herself as Nellie Cowden, to the back bedroom.

Miss Campbell was, as advertised, staring. Her pale blue eyes were wide open, but didn't seem to be looking at anything—certainly not at me.

She sat in the sort of wide, low chair called a nursing chair, with her back to the fire. The room was dim, and the backlighting made her features indistinct, except for the unblinking eyes. Seen closer to, her features were still indistinct; she had a soft, round face, undistinguished by any apparent bone structure, and baby-fine brown hair, neatly brushed. Her nose was small and snub, her chin double, and her mouth hung pinkly open, so slack as to obscure its natural lines.

"Miss Campbell?" I said cautiously. There was no response from the plump figure in the chair. Her eyes did blink, I saw, though much less frequently than normal.

"She'll nae answer ye, whilst she's in this state," Nellie Cowden said behind me. She shook her head, wiping her hands upon her apron. "Nay, not a word."

"How long has she been like this?" I picked up a limp, pudgy hand and felt for the pulse. It was there, slow and quite strong.

"Oh, for twa days so far, this time." Becoming interested, Miss Cowden leaned forward, peering into her charge's face. "Usually she stays like that for a week or more—thirteen days is the longest she's done it."

Moving slowly—though Miss Campbell seemed unlikely to be alarmed—I began to examine the unresisting figure, meanwhile asking questions of her attendant. Miss Margaret Campbell was thirty-seven, Miss Cowden told me, the only relative of the Reverend Archibald Campbell, with whom she had lived for the past twenty years, since the death of their parents.

"What starts her doing this? Do you know?"

Miss Cowden shook her head. "No tellin', mum. Nothin' seems to start it. One minute she'll be lookin' aboot, talkin' and laughin', eatin' her dinner like the sweet child she is, and the next—wheesht!" She snapped her fingers, then, for effect, leaned forward and snapped them again, deliberately, just under Miss Campbell's nose.

"See?" she said. "I could hae six men wi' trumpets pass through the room, and she'd pay it nay more mind."

I was reasonably sure that Miss Campbell's trouble was mental, not physical, but I made a complete examination, anyway—or as complete as could be managed without undressing that clumsy, inert form.

"It's when she comes oot of it that's the worst, though," Miss Cowden assured me, squatting next to me as I knelt on the floor to check Miss Campbell's plantar reflexes. Her feet, loosed from shoes and stockings, were damp and smelled musty.

I drew a fingernail firmly down the sole of each foot in turn, checking for a Babinski reflex that might indicate the presence of a brain lesion. Nothing, though; her toes curled under, in normal startlement.

"What happens then? Is that the screaming the Reverend mentioned?" I rose to my feet. "Will you bring me a lighted candle, please?"

"Oh, aye, the screamin'." Miss Cowden hastened to oblige, lighting a wax taper from the fire. "She do shriek somethin' awful then, on and on 'til she's worn herself oot. Then she'll fall asleep —sleep the clock around, she will—and wake as though nothin' had happened."

"And she's quite all right when she wakes?" I asked. I moved the candle flame slowly back and forth, a few inches before the patient's eyes. The pupils shrank in automatic response to the light, but the irises stayed fixed, not following the flame. My hand itched for the solid handle of an ophthalmoscope, to examine the retinas, but no such luck.

"Well, not to say all right," Miss Cowden said slowly. I turned from the patient to look at her and she shrugged, massive shoulders powerful under the linen of her blouse.

"She's 'saft in the heid, puir dear," she said, matter-of-factly. "Has been for nigh on twenty year."

"You haven't been taking care of her all that time, surely?"

"Oh, no! Mr. Campbell had a woman as cared for her where they lived, in Burntisland, but the woman was none so young, and didna wish to leave her home. So when the Reverend made up his mind to take up the Missionary Society's offer, and to take his sister wi' him to the West Indies—why, he advertised for a strong woman o' good character who wouldna mind travel to be an abigail for her . . . and here I am." Miss Cowden gave me a gaptoothed smile in testimony to her own virtues.

"The West Indies? He's planning to take Miss Campbell on a ship to the West Indies?" I was staggered; I knew just enough of sailing conditions to think that any such trip would be a major ordeal to a woman in good health. This woman—but then I reconsidered. All things concerned, Margaret Campbell might endure such a trip better than a normal woman—at least if she remained in her trance.

"He thought as the change of climate might be good for her," Miss Cowden was explaining. "Get her away from Scotland, and all the dreadful memories. Ought to ha' done it long since, is what I say.''

"What sort of dreadful memories?'' I asked. I could see by the gleam in Miss Cowden's eye that she was only too ready to tell me. I had finished the examination by this time, and concluded that there was little physically wrong with Miss Campbell save inactivity and poor diet, but there was the chance that something in her history might suggest some treatment.

"Weel,'' she began, sidling toward the table, where a decanter and several glasses stood on a tray, "it's only what Tilly Lawson told me, her as looked after Miss Campbell for sae long, but she did swear it was the truth, and her a godly woman. If ye'd care to take a drop of cordial, mum, for the sake o' the Reverend's hospitality?''

The chair Miss Campbell sat on was the only one in the room, so Miss Cowden and I perched inelegantly on the bed, side by side, and watched the silent figure before us, as we sipped our blackberry cordial, and she told me Margaret Campbell's story.

Margaret Campbell had been born in Burntisland, no more than five miles from Edinburgh, across the Firth of Forth. At the time of the '45, when Charles Stuart had marched into Edinburgh to reclaim his father's throne, she had been seventeen.

"Her father was a Royalist, o' course, and her brother in a government regiment, marching north to put down the wicked rebels,'' said Miss Cowden, taking a tiny sip of the cordial to make it last. "But not Miss Margaret. Nay, she was for the Bonnie Prince, and the Hielan' men that followed him.''

One, in particular, though Miss Cowden did not know his name. But a fine man he must have been, for Miss Margaret stole away from her home to meet him, and told him all the bits of information that she gleaned from listening to her father and his friends, and from her brother's letters home.

But then had come Falkirk; a victory, but a costly one, followed by retreat. Rumor had attended the flight of the Prince's army to the north, and not a soul doubted but that their flight led to destruction. Miss Margaret, desperate at the rumors, left her home at dead of night in the cold March spring, and went to find the man she loved.

Now here the account had been uncertain—whether it was that she had found the man and he had spurned her, or that she had not found him in time, and been forced to turn back from Culloden Moor—but in any case, turn back she did, and the day after the battle, she had fallen into the hands of a band of English soldiers.

"Dreadful, what they did to her," Miss Cowden said, lowering her voice as though the figure in the chair could hear. "Dreadful!" The English soldiers, blind with the lust of the hunt and the kill, pursuing the fugitives of Culloden, had not stopped to ask her name or the sympathies of her family. They had known by her speech that she was a Scot, and that knowledge had been enough.

They had left her for dead in a ditch half full of freezing water, and only the fortuitous presence of a family of tinkers, hiding in the nearby brambles for fear of the soldiers, had saved her.

"I canna help but think it a pity they did save her, un-Christian thing it is to say," Miss Cowden whispered. "If not, the puir lamb might ha' slippit her earthly bonds and gone happy to God. But as it is—" She gestured clumsily at the silent figure, and drank down the last drops of her cordial.

Margaret had lived, but did not speak. Somewhat recovered, but silent, she traveled with the tinkers, moving south with them to avoid the pillaging of the Highlands that took place in the wake of Culloden. And then one day, sitting in the yard of a pothouse, holding the tin to collect coppers as the tinkers busked and sang, she had been found by her brother, who had stopped with his Campbell regiment to refresh themselves on the way back to their quarters at Edinburgh.

"She kent him, and him her, and the shock o' their meeting gave her back her voice, but not her mind, puir thing. He took her home, o' course, but she was always as though she was in the past —sometime before she met the Hielan' man. Her father was dead then, from the influenza, and Tilly Lawson said as the shock o' seeing her like that kilt her mother, but could be as that were the influenza, too, for there was a great deal of it about that year."

The whole affair had left Archibald Campbell deeply embittered against both Highland Scots and the English army, and he had resigned his commission. With his parents dead, he found himself middling well-to-do, but the sole support of his damaged sister.

"He couldna marry," Miss Cowden explained, "for what woman would have him, and she"—with a nod toward the fire—"was thrown into the bargain?"

In his difficulties, he had turned to God, and become a minister. Unable to leave his sister, or to bear the confinement of the family house at Burntisland with her, he had purchased a coach, hired a woman to look after Margaret, and begun to make brief journeys into the surrounding countryside to preach, often taking her with him.

In his preaching he had found success, and this year had been asked by the Society of Presbyterian Missionaries if he would undertake his longest journey yet, to the West Indies, there to organize churches and appoint elders on the colonies of Barbados and Jamaica. Prayer had given him his answer, and he had sold the family property in Burntisland and moved his sister to Edinburgh while he made preparations for the journey.

I glanced once more at the figure by the fire. The heated air from the hearth stirred the skirts about her feet, but beyond that small movement, she might have been a statue.

"Well," I said with a sigh, "there's not a great deal I can do for her, I'm afraid. But I'll give you some prescriptions—receipts, I mean—to have made up at the apothecary's before you go."

If they didn't help, they couldn't hurt, I reflected, as I copied down the short lists of ingredients. Chamomile, hops, rue, tansy, and verbena, with a strong pinch of peppermint, for a soothing tonic. Tea of rose hips, to help correct the slight nutritional deficiency I had noted—spongy, bleeding gums, and a pale, bloated look about the face.

"Once you reach the Indies," I said, handing Miss Cowden the paper, "you must see that she eats a great deal of fruit—oranges, grapefruit, and lemons, particularly. You should do the same," I added, causing a look of profound suspicion to flit across the maid's wide face. I doubted she ate any vegetable matter beyond the occasional onion or potato, save her daily parritch.

The Reverend Campbell had not returned, and I saw no real reason to wait for him. Bidding Miss Campbell adieu, I pulled open the door of the bedroom, to find Young Ian standing on the other side of it.

"Oh!" he said, startled. "I was just comin' to find ye, Auntie. It's nearly half-past three, and Uncle Jamie said—"

"Jamie?" The voice came from behind me, from the chair beside the fire.

Miss Cowden and I whirled to find Miss Campbell sitting bolt upright, eyes still wide but focused now. They were focused on the doorway, and as Young Ian stepped inside, Miss Campbell began to scream.

Rather unsettled by the encounter with Miss Campbell, Young Ian and I made our way thankfully back to the refuge of the brothel, where we were greeted matter-of-factly by Bruno and taken to the rear parlor. There we found Jamie and Fergus deep in conversation.

"True, we do not trust Sir Percival," Fergus was saying, "but in this case, what point is there to his telling you of an ambush, save that such an ambush is in fact to occur?"

"Damned if I ken why," Jamie said frankly, leaning back and stretching in his chair. "And that being so, we do, as ye say, conclude that there's meant to be an ambush by the excisemen. Two days, he said. That would be Mullen's Cove." Then, catching sight of me and Ian, he half-rose, motioning us to take seats.

"Will it be the rocks below Balcarres, then?" Fergus asked.

Jamie frowned in thought, the two stiff fingers of his right hand drumming slowly on the tabletop.

"No," he said at last. "Let it be Arbroath; the wee cove under the abbey there. Just to be sure, aye?"

"All right." Fergus pushed back the half-empty plate of oat-cakes from which he had been refreshing himself, and rose. "I shall spread the word, milord. Arbroath, in four days." With a nod to me, he swirled his cloak about his shoulders and went out.

"Is it the smuggling, Uncle?" Young Ian asked eagerly. "Is there a French lugger coming?" He picked up an oatcake and bit into it, scattering crumbs over the table.

Jamie's eyes were still abstracted, thinking, but they cleared as he glanced sharply at his nephew. "Aye, it is. And *you,* Young Ian, are having nothing to do with it."

"But I could help!" the boy protested. "You'll need someone to hold the mules, at least!"

"After all your da said to you and me yesterday, wee Ian?" Jamie raised his brows. "Christ, ye've a short memory, lad!"

Ian looked mildly abashed at this, and took another oatcake to cover his confusion. Seeing him momentarily silent, I took the opportunity to ask my own questions.

"You're going to Arbroath to meet a French ship that's bringing in smuggled liquor?" I asked. "You don't think that's dangerous, after Sir Percival's warning?"

Jamie glanced at me with one brow still raised, but answered patiently enough.

"No. Sir Percival was warning me that the rendezvous in two days' time is known. That was to take place at Mullen's Cove. I've an arrangement wi' Jared and his captains, though. If a rendezvous canna be kept for some reason, the lugger will stand offshore and come in again the next night—but to a different place. And there's a third fallback as well, should the second meeting not come off."

"But if Sir Percival knows the first rendezvous, won't he know the others, too?" I persisted.

Jamie shook his head and poured out a cup of wine. He quirked a brow at me to ask whether I wanted any, and upon my shaking my head, sipped it himself.

"No," he said. "The rendezvous points are arranged in sets of three, between me and Jared, sent by sealed letter inside a packet addressed to Jeanne, here. Once I've read the letter, I burn it. The men who'll help meet the lugger will all know the first point, of course—I suppose one o' them will have let something slip," he added, frowning into his cup. "But no one—not even Fergus— kens the other two points unless we need to make use of one. And when we do, all the men ken well enough to guard their tongues."

"But then it's bound to be safe, Uncle!" Young Ian burst out. "Please let me come! I'll keep well back out o' the way," he promised.

Jamie gave his nephew a slightly jaundiced look.

"Aye, ye will," he said. "You'll come wi' me to Arbroath, but you and your auntie will stay at the inn on the road above the abbey until we've finished. I've got to take the laddie home to Lallybroch, Claire," he explained, turning to me. "And mend things as best I can with his parents." The elder Ian had left Halliday's that morning before Jamie and Young Ian arrived, leaving no message, but presumably bound for home. "Ye willna mind the journey? I wouldna ask it, and you just over your travel from Inverness"—his eyes met mine with a small, conspiratorial smile —"but I must take him back as soon as may be."

"I don't mind at all," I assured him. "It will be good to see Jenny and the rest of your family again."

"But Uncle—" Young Ian blurted. "What about—"

"Be still!" Jamie snapped. "That will be all from you, laddie. Not another word, aye?"

Young Ian looked wounded, but took another oatcake and inserted it into his mouth in a marked manner, signifying his intention to remain completely silent.

Jamie relaxed then, and smiled at me.

"Well, and how was your visit to the madwoman?"

"Very interesting," I said. "Jamie, do you know any people named Campbell?"

"Not above three or four hundred of them," he said, a smile twitching his long mouth. "Had ye a particular Campbell in mind?"

"A couple of them." I told him the story of Archibald Campbell and his sister, Margaret, as related to me by Nellie Cowden.

He shook his head at the tale, and sighed. For the first time, he looked truly older, his face tightened and lined by memory.

"It's no the worst tale I've heard, of the things that happened after Culloden," he said. "But I dinna think—wait." He stopped, and looked at me, eyes narrowed in thought. "Margaret Campbell. Margaret. Would she be a bonny wee lass—perhaps the size o' the second Mary? And wi' soft brown hair like a wren's feather, and a verra sweet face?"

"She probably was, twenty years ago," I said, thinking of that still, plump figure sitting by the fire. "Why, do you know her after all?"

"Aye, I think I do." His brow was furrowed in thought, and he looked down at the table, drawing a random line through the spilled crumbs. "Aye, if I'm right, she was Ewan Cameron's sweetheart. You'll mind Ewan?"

"Of course." Ewan had been a tall, handsome joker of a man, who had worked with Jamie at Holyrood, gathering bits of intelligence that filtered through from England. "What's become of Ewan? Or should I not ask?" I said, seeing the shadow come over Jamie's face.

"The English shot him," he said quietly. "Two days after Culloden." He closed his eyes for a moment, then opened them and smiled tiredly at me.

"Well, then, may God bless the Reverend Archie Campbell. I'd heard of him, a time or two, during the Rising. He was a bold soldier, folk said, and a brave one—and I suppose he'll need to be now, poor man." He sat a moment longer, then stood up with decision.

"Aye, well, there's a great deal to be done before we leave Edinburgh. Ian, you'll find the list of the printshop customers upstairs on the table; fetch it down to me and I'll mark off for ye the ones with orders outstanding. Ye must go to see each one and offer back their money. Unless they choose to wait until I've found new premises and laid in new stock—that might take as much as two months, though, tell them."

He patted his coat, where something made a small jingling sound.

"Luckily the assurance money will pay back the customers, and have a bit left over. Speaking of which"—he turned and smiled at me—"your job, Sassenach, is to find a dressmaker who will manage ye a decent gown in two days' time. For I expect Daphne would like her dress back, and I canna take ye home to Lallybroch naked."

The chief entertainment of the ride north to Arbroath was watching the conflict of wills between Jamie and Young Ian. I knew from long experience that stubbornness was one of the major components of a Fraser's character. Ian seemed not unduly handicapped in that respect, though only half a Fraser; either the Murrays were no slouches with regard to stubbornness, or the Fraser genes were strong ones.

Having had the opportunity to observe Brianna at close range for many years, I had my own opinion about that, but kept quiet, merely enjoying the spectacle of Jamie having for once met his match. By the time we passed Balfour, he was wearing a distinctly hunted look.

This contest between immovable object and irresistible force continued until early evening of the fourth day, when we reached Arbroath to find that the inn where Jamie had intended to leave Ian and myself no longer existed. No more than a tumbled-down stone wall and one or two charred roof-beams remained to mark the spot; otherwise, the road was deserted for miles in either direction.

Jamie looked at the heap of stones in silence for some time. It was reasonably obvious that he could not just leave us in the middle of a desolate, muddy road. Ian, wise enough not to press the advantage, kept also silent, though his skinny frame fairly vibrated with eagerness.

"All right, then," Jamie said at last, resigned. "Ye'll come. But only so far as the cliff's edge, Ian—d'ye hear? You'll take care of your auntie."

"I hear, Uncle Jamie," Young Ian replied, with deceptive meekness. I caught Jamie's wry glance, though, and understood that if Ian was to take care of auntie, auntie was also to take care of Ian. I hid a smile, nodding obediently.

The rest of the men were timely, arriving at the rendezvous point on the cliffside just after dark. A couple of the men seemed vaguely familiar, but most were just muffled shapes; it was two days past the dark of the moon, but the tiny sliver rising over the horizon made conditions here little more illuminating than those obtaining in the brothel's cellars. No introductions were made, the men greeting Jamie with unintelligible mutters and grunts.

There was one unmistakable figure, though. A large mule-drawn wagon appeared, rattling its way down the road, driven by Fergus and a diminutive object that could only be Mr. Willoughby, whom I had not seen since he had shot the mysterious man on the stairs of the brothel.

"He hasn't a pistol with him tonight, I hope," I murmured to Jamie.

"Who?" he said, squinting into the gathering gloom. "Oh, the Chinee? No, none of them have." Before I could ask why not, he had gone forward, to help back the wagon around, ready to make a getaway toward Edinburgh, so soon as the contraband should be loaded. Young Ian pressed his way forward, and I, mindful of my job as custodian, followed him.

Mr. Willoughby stood on tiptoe to reach into the back of the wagon, emerging with an odd-looking lantern, fitted with a pierced metal top and sliding metal sides.

"Is that a dark lantern?" I asked, fascinated.

"Aye, it is," said Young Ian, importantly. "Ye keep the slides shut until we see the signal out at sea." He reached for the lantern. "Here, give it me; I'll take it—I ken the signal."

Mr. Willoughby merely shook his head, pulling the lantern out of Young Ian's grasp. "Too tall, too young," he said. "Tsei-mi say so," he added, as though that settled the matter once and for all.

"What?" Young Ian was indignant. "What d'ye mean too tall and too young, ye wee—"

"He means," said a level voice behind us, "that whoever's holding the lantern is a bonny target, should we have visitors. Mr. Willoughby kindly takes the risk of it, because he's the smallest man among us. You're tall enough to see against the sky, wee Ian, and young enough to have nay sense yet. Stay out o' the way, aye?''

Jamie gave his nephew a light cuff over the ear, and passed by to kneel on the rocks by Mr. Willoughby. He said something low-voiced in Chinese, and there was the ghost of a laugh from the Chinaman. Mr. Willoughby opened the side of the lantern, holding it conveniently to Jamie's cupped hands. A sharp click, repeated twice, and I caught the flicker of sparks struck from a flint.

It was a wild piece of coast—not surprising, most of Scotland's coast was wild and rocky—and I wondered how and where the French ship would anchor. There was no natural bay, only a curving of the coastline behind a jutting cliff that sheltered this spot from observation from the road.

Dark as it was, I could see the white lines of the surf purling in across the small half-moon beach. No smooth tourist beach this— small pockets of sand lay ruffled and churned between heaps of seaweed and pebbles and juts of rock. Not an easy footing for men carrying casks, but convenient to the crevices in the surrounding rocks, where the casks could be hidden.

Another black figure loomed up suddenly beside me.

"Everyone's settled, sir," it said softly. "Up in the rocks."

"Good, Joey." A sudden flare lit Jamie's profile, intent on the newly caught wick. He held his breath as the flame steadied and grew, taking up oil from the lantern's reservoir, then let it out with a sigh as he gently closed the metal slide.

"Fine, then," he said, standing up. He glanced up at the cliff to the south, observing the stars over it, and said, "Nearly nine o'clock. They'll be in soon. Mind ye, Joey—no one's to move 'til I call out, aye?"

"Aye, sir." The casual tone of the answer made it apparent that this was a customary exchange, and Joey was plainly surprised when Jamie gripped his arm.

"Be sure of it," Jamie said. "Tell them all again—no one moves 'til I give the word."

"Aye, sir," Joey said again, but this time with more respect. He faded back into the night, making no sound on the rocks.

"Is something wrong?" I asked, pitching my voice barely loud enough to be heard over the breakers. Though the beach and cliffs were evidently deserted, the dark setting and the secretive conduct of my companions compelled caution.

Jamie shook his head briefly; he'd been right about Young Ian, I thought—his own dark silhouette was clear against the paler black of the sky behind him.

"I dinna ken." He hesitated for a moment, then said, "Tell me, Sassenach—d'ye smell anything?"

Surprised, I obligingly took a deep sniff, held it for a moment, and let it out. I smelled any number of things, including rotted seaweed, the thick smell of burning oil from the dark lantern, and the pungent body odor of Young Ian, standing close beside me, sweating with a mix of excitement and fear.

"Nothing odd, I don't think," I said. "Do you?"

The silhouette's shoulders rose and dropped in a shrug. "Not now. A moment ago, I could ha' sworn I smelt gunpowder."

"I dinna smell anything," Young Ian said. His voice broke from excitement, and he hastily cleared his throat, embarrassed. "Willie MacLeod and Alec Hays searched the rocks. They didna find any sign of excisemen."

"Aye, well." Jamie's voice sounded uneasy. He turned to Young Ian, grasping him by the shoulder.

"Ian, you're to take charge of your auntie, now. The two of ye get back of the gorse bushes there. Keep well away from the wagon. If anything should happen—"

The beginnings of Young Ian's protest were cut off, apparently by a tightening of Jamie's hand, for the boy jerked back with a small grunt, rubbing his shoulder.

"*If* anything should happen," Jamie continued, with emphasis, "you're to take your auntie and go straight home to Lallybroch. Dinna linger."

"But—" I said.

"Uncle!" Young Ian said.

"Do it," said Jamie, in tones of steel, and turned aside, the discussion concluded.

Young Ian was grim on the trip up the cliff trail, but did as he was told, dutifully escorting me some distance past the gorse bushes and finding a small promontory where we might see out some way over the water.

"We can see from here," he whispered unnecessarily.

We could indeed. The rocks fell away in a shallow bowl beneath us, a broken cup filled with darkness, the light of the water spilling from the broken edge where the sea hissed in. Once I caught a tiny movement, as a metal buckle caught the faint light, but for the most part, the ten men below were completely invisible.

I squinted, trying to pick out the location of Mr. Willoughby with his lantern, but saw no sign of light, and concluded that he must be standing behind the lantern, shielding it from sight from the cliff.

Young Ian stiffened suddenly next to me.

"Someone's coming!" he whispered. "Quick, get behind me!" Stepping courageously out in front of me, he plunged a hand under his shirt, into the band of his breeches, and withdrew a pistol; dark as it was, I could see the faint gleam of starlight along the barrel.

He braced himself, peering into the dark, slightly hunched over the gun with both hands clamped on the weapon.

"Don't shoot, for God's sake!" I hissed in his ear. I didn't dare grab his arm for fear of setting off the pistol, but was terrified lest he make any noise that might attract attention to the men below.

"I'd be obliged if ye'd heed your auntie, Ian," came Jamie's soft, ironic tones from the blackness below the cliff edge. "I'd as soon not have ye blow my head off, aye?"

Ian lowered the pistol, shoulders slumping with what might have been a sigh either of relief or disappointment. The gorse bushes quivered, and then Jamie was before us, brushing gorse prickles from the sleeve of his coat.

"Did no one tell ye not to come armed?" Jamie's voice was mild, with no more than a note of academic interest. "It's a hanging offense to draw a weapon against an officer of the King's Customs," he explained, turning to me. "None o' the men are armed, even wi' so much as a fish knife, in case they're taken."

"Aye, well, Fergus said they wouldna hang me, because my beard's not grown yet," Ian said awkwardly. "I'd only be transported, he said."

There was a soft hiss as Jamie drew in his breath through his teeth in exasperation.

"Oh, aye, and I'm sure your mother will be verra pleased to hear ye've been shipped off to the Colonies, even if Fergus was right!" He put out his hand. "Give me that, fool.

"Where did ye get it, anyway?" he asked, turning the pistol over in his hand. "Already primed, too. I knew I smelt gunpowder. Lucky ye didna blow your cock off, carrying it in your breeches.''

Before Young Ian could answer, I interrupted, pointing out to sea.

''Look!''

The French ship was little more than a blot on the face of the sea, but its sails shone pale in the glimmer of starlight. A two-masted ketch, it glided slowly past the cliff and stood off, silent as one of the scattered clouds behind it.

Jamie was not watching the ship, but looking downward, toward a point where the rock face broke in a tumble of boulders, just above the sand. Looking where he was looking, I could just make out a tiny prickle of light. Mr. Willoughby, with the lantern.

There was a brief flash of light that glistened across the wet rocks and was gone. Young Ian's hand was tense on my arm. We waited, breaths held, to the count of thirty. Ian's hand squeezed my arm, just as another flash lit the foam on the sand.

''What was that?'' I said.

''What?'' Jamie wasn't looking at me, but out at the ship.

''On the shore; when the light flashed, I thought I saw something half-buried in the sand. It looked like—''

The third flash came, and a moment later, an answering light shone from the ship—a blue lantern, an eerie dot that hung from the mast, doubling itself in reflection in the dark water below.

I forgot the glimpse of what appeared to be a rumpled heap of clothing, carelessly buried in the sand, in the excitement of watching the ship. Some movement was evident now, and a faint splash reached our ears as something was thrown over the side.

''The tide's coming in,'' Jamie muttered in my ear. ''The ankers float; the current will carry them ashore in a few minutes.''

That solved the problem of the ship's anchorage—it didn't need one. But how then was the payment made? I was about to ask when there was a sudden shout, and all hell broke loose below.

Jamie thrust his way at once through the gorse bushes, followed in short order by me and Young Ian. Little could be seen distinctly, but there was a considerable turmoil taking place on the sandy beach. Dark shapes were stumbling and rolling over the sand, to the accompaniment of shouting. I caught the words ''Halt, in the King's name!'' and my blood froze.

''Excisemen!'' Young Ian had caught it, too.

Jamie said something crude in Gaelic, then threw back his head and shouted himself, his voice carrying easily across the beach below.

"*Eirich 'illean!*" he bellowed. "*Suas am bearrach is teich!*"

Then he turned to Young Ian and me. "Go!" he said.

The noise suddenly increased as the clatter of falling rocks joined the shouting. Suddenly a dark figure shot out of the gorse by my feet and made off through the dark at high speed. Another followed, a few feet away.

A high-pitched scream came from the dark below, high enough to be heard over the other noises.

"That's Willoughby!" Young Ian exclaimed. "They've got him!"

Ignoring Jamie's order to go, we both crowded forward to peer through the screen of gorse. The dark-lantern had fallen atilt and the slide had come open, shooting a beam of light like a spotlight over the beach, where the shallow graves in which the Customs men had buried themselves gaped in the sand. Black figures swayed and struggled and shouted through the wet heaps of seaweed. A dim glow of light around the lantern was sufficient to show two figures clasped together, the smaller kicking wildly as it was lifted off its feet.

"I'll get him!" Young Ian sprang forward, only to be pulled up with a jerk as Jamie caught him by the collar.

"Do as you're told and see my wife safe!"

Gasping for breath, Young Ian turned to me, but I wasn't going anywhere, and set my feet firmly in the dirt, resisting his tug on my arm.

Ignoring us both, Jamie turned and ran along the clifftop, stopping several yards away. I could see him clearly in silhouette against the sky, as he dropped to one knee and readied the pistol, bracing it on his forearm to sight downward.

The sound of the shot was no more than a small cracking noise, lost amid the tumult. The result of it, though, was spectacular. The lantern exploded in a shower of burning oil, abruptly darkening the beach and silencing the shouting.

The silence was broken within seconds by a howl of mingled pain and indignation. My eyes, momentarily blinded by the flash of the lantern, adapted quickly, and I saw another glow—the light of several small flames, which seemed to be moving erratically up and down. As my night vision cleared, I saw that the flames rose from the coat sleeve of a man, who was dancing up and down as he howled, beating ineffectually at the fire started by the burning oil that had splashed him.

The gorse bushes quivered violently as Jamie plunged over the cliffside and was lost to view below.

"Jamie!"

Roused by my cry, Young Ian yanked harder, pulling me half off my feet and forcibly dragging me away from the cliff.

"Come on, Auntie! They'll be up here, next thing!"

This was undeniably true; I could hear the shouts on the beach coming closer, as the men swarmed up the rocks. I picked up my skirts and went, following the boy as fast as we could go through the rough marrow-grass of the clifftop.

I didn't know where we were going, but Young Ian seemed to. He had taken off his coat and the white of his shirt was easily visible before me, floating like a ghost through the thickets of alder and birch that grew farther inland.

"Where are we?" I panted, coming up alongside him when he slowed at the bank of a tiny stream.

"The road to Arbroath's just ahead," he said. He was breathing heavily, and a dark smudge of mud showed down the side of his shirt. "It'll be easier going in a moment. Are ye all right, Auntie? Shall I carry ye across?"

I politely declined this gallant offer, privately noting that I undoubtedly weighed as much as he did. I took off my shoes and stockings, and splashed my way knee-deep across the streamlet, feeling icy mud well up between my toes.

I was shivering violently when I emerged, and did accept Ian's offer of his coat—excited as he was, and heated by the exercise, he was clearly in no need of it. I was chilled not only by the water and the cold November wind, but by fear of what might be happening behind us.

We emerged panting onto the road, the wind blowing cold in our faces. My nose and lips were numb in no time, and my hair blew loose behind me, heavy on my neck. It's an ill wind that blows nobody good, though; it carried the sound of voices to us, moments before we would have walked into them.

"Any signal from the cliff?" a deep male voice asked. Ian stopped so abruptly in his tracks that I bumped into him.

"Not yet," came the reply. "I thought I heard a bit of shouting that way, but then the wind turned."

"Well, get up that tree again then, heavy-arse," the first voice said impatiently. "If any o' the whoresons get past the beach, we'll nibble 'em here. Better us get the headmoney than the buggers on the beach."

"It's cold," grumbled the second voice. "Out in the open where the wind gnaws your bones. Wish we'd drawn the watch at the abbey—at least it would be warm there."

Young Ian's hand was clutching my upper arm tight enough to leave bruises. I pulled, trying to loosen his grip, but he paid no attention.

"Aye, but less chance o' catching the big fish," the first voice said. "Ah, and what I might do with fifty pound!"

"Awright," said the second voice, resigned. "Though how we're to see red hair in the dark, I've no notion."

"Just lay 'em by the heels, Oakie; we'll look at their heads later."

Young Ian was finally roused from his trance by my tugging, and stumbled after me off the road and into the bushes.

"What do they mean, by the watch at the abbey?" I demanded, as soon as I thought we were out of earshot of the watchers on the road. "Do you know?"

Young Ian's dark thatch bobbed up and down. "I think so, Auntie. It must be Arbroath abbey. That's the meeting point, aye?"

"Meeting point?"

"If something should go wrong," he explained. "Then it's every man for himself, all to meet at the abbey as soon as they can."

"Well, it couldn't go more wrong," I observed. "What was it your uncle shouted when the Customs men popped up?"

Young Ian had half-turned to listen for pursuit from the road; now the pale oval of his face turned back to me. "Oh—he said, 'Up, lads! Over the cliff and run!' "

"Sound advice," I said dryly. "So if they followed it, most of the men may have gotten away."

"Except Uncle Jamie and Mr. Willoughby." Young Ian was running one hand nervously through his hair; it reminded me forcibly of Jamie, and I wished he would stop.

"Yes." I took a deep breath. "Well, there's nothing we can do about them just now. The other men, though—if they're headed for the abbey—"

"Aye," he broke in, "that's what I was tryin' to decide; ought I do as Uncle Jamie said, and take ye to Lallybroch, or had I best try to get to the abbey quick and warn the others as they come?"

"Get to the abbey," I said, "as fast as you can."

"Well, but—I shouldna like to leave ye out here by yourself, Auntie, and Uncle Jamie said—"

"There's a time to follow orders, Young Ian, and a time to think for yourself," I said firmly, tactfully ignoring the fact that I was in fact doing the thinking for him. "Does this road lead to the abbey?"

"Aye, it does. No more than a mile and a quarter." Already he was shifting to and fro on the balls of his feet, eager to be gone.

"Good. You cut round the road and head for the abbey. I'll walk straight along the road, and see if I can distract the excisemen until you're safely past. I'll meet you at the abbey. Oh, wait—you'd best take your coat."

I surrendered the coat reluctantly; besides being loath to part with its warmth, it felt like giving up my last link with a friendly human presence. Once Young Ian was away, I would be completely alone in the cold dark of the Scottish night.

"Ian?" I held his arm, to keep him a moment longer.

"Aye?"

"Be careful, won't you?" On impulse, I stood on tiptoe and kissed his cold cheek. I was near enough to see his brows arch in surprise. He smiled, and then he was gone, an alder branch snapping back into place behind him.

It was very cold. The only sounds were the *whish* of the wind through the bushes and the distant murmur of the surf. I pulled the woolen shawl tightly round my shoulders, shivering, and headed back toward the road.

Ought I to make a noise? I wondered. If not, I might be attacked without warning, since the waiting men might hear my footsteps but couldn't see that I wasn't an escaping smuggler. On the other hand, if I strolled through singing a jaunty tune to indicate that I was a harmless woman, they might just lie hidden in silence, not wanting to give away their presence—and giving away their presence was exactly what I had in mind. I bent and picked up a rock from the side of the road. Then, feeling even colder than before, I stepped out onto the road and walked straight on, without a word.

31

Smugglers' Moon

The wind was high enough to keep the trees and bushes in a constant stir, masking the sound of my footsteps on the road—and those of anyone who might be stalking me, too. Less than a fortnight past the feast of Samhain, it was the sort of wild night that made one easily believe that spirits and evil might well be abroad.

It wasn't a spirit that grabbed me suddenly from behind, hand clamped tight across my mouth. Had I not been prepared for just such an eventuality, I would have been startled senseless. As it was, my heart gave a great leap and I jerked convulsively in my captor's grasp.

He had grabbed me from the left, pinning my left arm tight against my side, his right hand over my mouth. *My* right arm was free, though. I drove the heel of my shoe into his kneecap, buckling his leg, and then, taking advantage of his momentary stagger, leaned forward and smashed backward at his head with the rock in my hand.

It was of necessity a glancing blow, but it struck hard enough that he grunted with surprise, and his grip loosened. I kicked and squirmed, and as his hand slipped across my mouth, I got my teeth onto a finger and bit down as hard as I could.

"The maxillary muscles run from the sagittal crest at the top of the skull to an insertion on the mandible," I thought, dimly recalling the description from *Grey's Anatomy*. "This gives the jaw and teeth considerable crushing power; in fact, the average human jaw is capable of exerting over three hundred pounds of force."

I didn't know whether I was bettering the average, but I was undeniably having an effect. My assailant was thrashing frantically to and fro in a futile effort to dislodge the death grip I had on his finger.

His hold on my arm had loosened in the struggle, and he was forced to lower me. As soon as my feet touched the dirt once more, I let go of his hand, whirled about, and gave him as hearty a root in the stones with my knee as I could manage, given my skirts.

Kicking men in the testicles is vastly overrated as a means of defense. That is to say, it does work—and spectacularly well—but it's a more difficult maneuver to carry out than one might think, particularly when one is wearing heavy skirts. Men are extremely careful of those particular appendages, and thoroughly wary of any attempt on them.

In this case, though, my attacker was off guard, his legs wide apart to keep his balance, and I caught him fairly. He made a hideous wheezing noise like a strangled rabbit and doubled up in the roadway.

"Is that you, Sassenach?" The words were hissed out of the darkness to my left. I leapt like a startled gazelle, and uttered an involuntary scream.

For the second time within as many minutes, a hand clapped itself over my mouth.

"For God's sake, Sassenach!" Jamie muttered in my ear. "It's me."

I didn't bite him, though I was strongly tempted to.

"I know," I said, through my teeth, when he released me. "Who's the other fellow that grabbed me, though?"

"Fergus, I expect." The amorphous dark shape moved away a few feet and seemed to be prodding another shape that lay on the road, moaning faintly. "Is it you, Fergus?" he whispered. Receiving a sort of choked noise in response, he bent and hauled the second shape to its feet.

"Don't talk!" I urged them in a whisper. "There are excisemen just ahead!"

"Is that so?" said Jamie, in a normal voice. "They're no verra curious about the noise we're making, are they?"

He paused, as though waiting for an answer, but no sound came but the low keening of the wind through the alders. He laid a hand on my arm and shouted into the night.

"MacLeod! Raeburn!"

"Aye, Roy," said a mildly testy voice in the shrubbery. "We're here. Innes, too, and Meldrum, is it?"

"Aye, it's me."

Shuffling and talking in low voices, more shapes emerged from the bushes and trees.

". . . four, five, six," Jamie counted. "Where are Hays and the Gordons?"

"I saw Hays go intae the water," one of the shapes volunteered. "He'll ha' gone awa' round the point. Likely the Gordons and Kennedy did, too. I didna hear anything as though they'd been taken."

"Well enough," Jamie said. "Now, then, Sassenach. What's this about excisemen?"

Given the nonappearance of Oakie and his companion, I was beginning to feel rather foolish, but I recounted what Ian and I had heard.

"Aye?" Jamie sounded interested. "Can ye stand yet, Fergus? Ye can? Good lad. Well, then, perhaps we'll have a look. Meldrum, have ye a flint about ye?"

A few moments later, a small torch struggling to stay alight in his hand, he strode down the road, and around the bend. The smugglers and I waited in tense silence, ready either to run or to rush to his assistance, but there were no noises of ambush. After what seemed like an eternity, Jamie's voice floated back along the road.

"Come along, then," he said, sounding calm and collected.

He was standing in the middle of the road, near a large alder. The torchlight fell round him in a flickering circle, and at first I saw nothing but Jamie. Then there was a gasp from the man beside me, and a choked sound of horror from another.

Another face appeared, dimly lit, hanging in the air just behind Jamie's left shoulder. A horrible, congested face, black in the torchlight that robbed everything of color, with bulging eyes and tongue protruding. The hair, fair as dry straw, rose stirring in the wind. I felt a fresh scream rise in my throat, and choked it off.

"Ye were right, Sassenach," Jamie said. "There *was* an exciseman." He tossed something to the ground, where it landed with a small plop! "A warrant," he said, nodding toward the object. "His name was Thomas Oakie. Will any of ye ken him?"

"Not like he is now," a voice muttered behind me. "Christ, his mither wouldna ken him!" There was a general mutter of negation, with a nervous shuffling of feet. Clearly, everyone was as anxious to get away from the place as I was.

"All right, then." Jamie stopped the retreat with a jerk of his head. "The cargo's lost, so there'll be no shares, aye? Will anyone need money for the present?" He reached for his pocket. "I can provide enough to live on for a bit—for I doubt we'll be workin' the coast for a time."

One or two of the men reluctantly advanced within clear sight of the thing hanging from the tree to receive their money, but the rest of the smugglers melted quietly away into the night. Within a few minutes, only Fergus—still white, but standing on his own— Jamie, and I were left.

"Jesu!" Fergus whispered, looking up at the hanged man. "Who will have done it?"

"I did—or so I expect the tale will be told, aye?" Jamie gazed upward, his face harsh in the sputtering torchlight. "We'll no tarry longer, shall we?"

"What about Ian?" I said, suddenly remembering the boy. "He went to the abbey, to warn you!"

"He did?" Jamie's voice sharpened. "I came from that direction, and didna meet him. Which way did he go, Sassenach?"

"That way," I said, pointing.

Fergus made a small sound that might have been laughter.

"The abbey's the other way," Jamie said, sounding amused. "Come on, then; we'll catch him up when he realizes his mistake and comes back."

"Wait," said Fergus, holding up a hand. There was a cautious rustling in the shrubbery, and Young Ian's voice said, "Uncle Jamie?"

"Aye, Ian," his uncle said dryly. "It's me."

The boy emerged from the bushes, leaves stuck in his hair, eyes wide with excitement.

"I saw the light, and thought I must come back to see that Auntie Claire was all right," he explained. "Uncle Jamie, ye mustna linger about wi' a torch—there are excisemen about!"

Jamie put an arm about his nephew's shoulders and turned him, before he should notice the thing hanging from the alder tree.

"Dinna trouble yourself, Ian," he said evenly. "They've gone."

Swinging the torch through the wet shrubbery, he extinguished it with a hiss.

"Let's go," he said, his voice calm in the dark. "Mr. Willoughby's down the road wi' the horses; we'll be in the Highlands by dawn."

PART SEVEN

Home Again

32

The Prodigal's Return

It was a four-day journey on horseback to Lallybroch from Arbroath, and there was little conversation for most of it. Both Young Ian and Jamie were preoccupied, presumably for different reasons. For myself, I was kept busy wondering, not only about the recent past, but about the immediate future.

Ian must have told Jamie's sister, Jenny, about me. How would she take my reappearance?

Jenny Murray had been the nearest thing I had ever had to a sister, and by far the closest woman friend of my life. Owing to circumstance, most of my close friends in the last fifteen years had been men; there were no other female doctors, and the natural gulf between nursing staff and medical staff prevented more than casual acquaintance with other women working at the hospital. As for the women in Frank's circle, the departmental secretaries and university wives . . .

More than any of that, though, was the knowledge that of all the people in the world, Jenny was the one who might love Jamie Fraser as much—if not more—than I did. I was eager to see Jenny again, but could not help wondering how she would take the story of my supposed escape to France, and my apparent desertion of her brother.

The horses had to follow each other in single file down the narrow track. My own bay slowed obligingly as Jamie's chestnut paused, then turned aside at his urging into a clearing, half-hidden by an overhang of alder branches.

A gray stone cliff rose up at the edge of the clearing, its cracks and bumps and ridges so furred with moss and lichen that it looked like the face of an ancient man, all spotted with whiskers and freckled with warts. Young Ian slid down from his pony with a sigh of relief; we had been in the saddle since dawn.

"Oof!" he said, frankly rubbing his backside. "I've gone all numb."

"So have I," I said, doing the same. "I suppose it's better than being saddlesore, though." Unaccustomed to riding for long stretches, both Young Ian and I had suffered considerably during the first two days of the journey; in fact, too stiff to dismount by myself the first night, I had had to be ignominiously hoisted off my horse and carried into the inn by Jamie, much to his amusement.

"How does Uncle Jamie do it?" Ian asked me. "His arse must be made of leather."

"Not to look at," I replied absently. "Where's he gone, though?" The chestnut, already hobbled, was nibbling at the grass under an oak to one side of the clearing, but of Jamie himself, there was no sign.

Young Ian and I looked blankly at each other; I shrugged, and went over to the cliff face, where a trickle of water ran down the rock. I cupped my hands beneath it and drank, grateful for the cold liquid sliding down my dry throat, in spite of the autumn air that reddened my cheeks and numbed my nose.

This tiny glen clearing, invisible from the road, was characteristic of most of the Highland scenery, I thought. Deceptively barren and severe, the crags and moors were full of secrets. If you didn't know where you were going, you could walk within inches of a deer, a grouse, or a hiding man, and never know it. Small wonder that many of those who had taken to the heather after Culloden had managed to escape, their knowledge of the hidden places making them invisible to the blind eyes and clumsy feet of the pursuing English.

Thirst slaked, I turned from the cliff face and nearly ran into Jamie, who had appeared as though sprung out of the earth by magic. He was putting his tinderbox back into the pocket of his coat, and the faint smell of smoke clung to his coat. He dropped a small burnt stick to the grass and ground it to dust with his foot.

"Where did you come from?" I said, blinking at this apparition. "And where have you been?"

"There's a wee cave just there," he explained, jerking a thumb behind him. "I only wanted to see whether anyone's been in it."

"Have they?" Looking closely, I could see the edge of the outcrop that concealed the cave's entrance. Blending as it did with the other deep cracks in the rock face, it wouldn't be visible unless you were deliberately looking for it.

"Aye, they have," he said. His brows were slightly furrowed, not in worry, but as though he were thinking about something. "There's charcoal mixed wi' the earth; someone's had a fire there."

"Who do you think it was?" I asked. I stuck my head around the outcrop, but saw nothing but a narrow bar of darkness, a small rift in the face of the mountain. It looked thoroughly uninviting.

I wondered whether any of his smuggling connections might have traced him all the way from the coast to Lallybroch. Was he worried about pursuit, or an ambush? Despite myself, I looked over my shoulder, but saw nothing but the alders, dry leaves rustling in the autumn breeze.

"I dinna ken," he said absently. "A hunter, I suppose; there are grouse bones scattered about, too."

Jamie didn't seem perturbed by the unknown person's possible identity, and I relaxed, the feeling of security engendered by the Highlands wrapping itself about me once more. Both Edinburgh and the smugglers' cove seemed a long way away.

Young Ian, fascinated by the revelation of the invisible cave, had disappeared through the crevice. Now he reappeared, brushing a cobweb out of his hair.

"Is this like Cluny's Cage, Uncle?" he asked, eyes bright.

"None so big, Ian," Jamie answered with a smile. "Poor Cluny would scarce fit through the entrance o' this one; he was a stout big fellow, forbye, near twice my girth." He touched his chest ruefully, where a button had been torn loose by squeezing through the narrow entrance.

"What's Cluny's Cage?" I asked, shaking the last drops of icy water from my hands and thrusting them under my armpits to thaw out.

"Oh—that's Cluny MacPherson," Jamie replied. He bent his head, and splashed the chilly water up into his face. Lifting his head, he blinked the sparkling drops from his lashes and smiled at me. "A verra ingenious man, Cluny. The English burnt his house, and pulled down the foundation, but Cluny himself escaped. He built himself a wee snuggery in a nearby cavern, and sealed over the entrance wi' willow branches all woven together and chinked wi' mud. Folk said ye could stand three feet away, and no notion that the cave was there, save the smell of the smoke from Cluny's pipe.''

''Prince Charles stayed there too, for a bit, when he was hunted by the English,'' Young Ian informed me. ''Cluny hid him for days. The English bastards hunted high and low, but never found His Highness—or Cluny, either!'' he concluded, with considerable satisfaction.

''Come here and wash yourself, Ian,'' Jamie said, with a hint of sharpness that made Young Ian blink. ''Ye canna face your parents covered wi' filth.''

Ian sighed, but obediently bent his head over the trickle of water, sputtering and gasping as he splashed his face, which while not strictly speaking filthy, undeniably bore one or two small stains of travel.

I turned to Jamie, who stood watching his nephew's ablutions with an air of abstraction. Did he look ahead, I wondered, to what promised to be an awkward meeting at Lallybroch, or back to Edinburgh, with the smoldering remains of his printshop and the dead man in the basement of the brothel? Or back further still, to Charles Edward Stuart, and the days of the Rising?

''What do you tell your nieces and nephews about him?'' I asked quietly, under the noise of Ian's snorting. ''About Charles?''

Jamie's gaze sharpened and focused on me; I had been right, then. His eyes warmed slightly, and the hint of a smile acknowledged the success of my mind-reading, but then both warmth and smile disappeared.

''I never speak of him,'' he said, just as quietly, and turned away to catch the horses.

Three hours later, we came through the last of the windswept passes, and out onto the final slope that led down to Lallybroch. Jamie, in the lead, drew up his horse and waited for me and Young Ian to come up beside him.

"There it is," he said. He glanced at me, smiling, one eyebrow raised. "Much changed, is it?"

I shook my head, rapt. From this distance, the house seemed completely unchanged. Built of white harled stone, its three stories gleamed immaculately amid its cluster of shabby outbuildings and the spread of stone-dyked brown fields. On the small rise behind the house stood the remains of the ancient broch, the circular stone tower that gave the place its name.

On closer inspection, I could see that the outbuildings had changed a bit; Jamie had told me that the English soldiery had burned the dovecote and the chapel the year after Culloden, and I could see the gaps where they had been. A space where the wall of the kailyard had been broken through had been repaired with stone of a different color, and a new shed built of stone and scrap lumber was evidently serving as a dovecote, judging from the row of plump feathered bodies lined up on the rooftree, enjoying the late autumn sun.

The rose brier planted by Jamie's mother, Ellen, had grown up into a great, sprawling tangle latticed to the wall of the house, only now losing the last of its leaves.

A plume of smoke rose from the western chimney, carrying away toward the south on a wind from the sea. I had a sudden vision of the fire in the hearth of the sitting room, its light rosy on Jenny's clear-cut face in the evening as she sat in her chair, reading aloud from a novel or book of poems while Jamie and Ian sat absorbed in a game of chess, listening with half an ear. How many evenings had we spent that way, the children upstairs in their beds, and me sitting at the rosewood secretary, writing down receipts for medicines or doing some of the interminable domestic mending?

"Will we live here again, do you think?" I asked Jamie, careful to keep any trace of longing from my voice. More than any other place, the house at Lallybroch had been home to me, but that had been a long time ago—and any number of things had changed since then.

He paused for a long minute, considering. Finally he shook his head, gathering up the reins in his hand. "I canna say, Sassenach," he said. "It would be pleasant, but—I dinna ken how things may be, aye?" There was a small frown on his face, as he looked down at the house.

"It's all right. If we live in Edinburgh—or even in France—it's all right, Jamie." I looked up into his face and touched his hand in reassurance. "As long as we're together."

The faint look of worry lifted momentarily, lightening his features. He took my hand, raised it to his lips, and kissed it gently.

"I dinna mind much else myself, Sassenach, so long as ye'll stay by me."

We sat gazing into each other's eyes, until a loud, self-conscious cough from behind alerted us to Young Ian's presence. Scrupulously careful of our privacy, he had been embarrassingly circumspect on the trip from Edinburgh, crashing off through the heather to a great distance when we camped, and taking remarkable pains so as not inadvertently to surprise us in an indiscreet embrace.

Jamie grinned and squeezed my hand before letting it go and turning to his nephew.

"Almost there, Ian," he said, as the boy negotiated his pony up beside us. "We'll be there well before supper if it doesna rain," he added, squinting under his hand to gauge the possibilities of the clouds drifting slowly over the Monadhliath Mountains.

"Mmphm." Young Ian didn't sound thrilled at the prospect, and I glanced at him sympathetically.

" 'Home is the place where, when you have to go there, they have to take you in,' " I quoted.

Young Ian gave me a wry look. "Aye, that's what I'm afraid of, Auntie."

Jamie, hearing this exchange, glanced back at Young Ian, and blinked solemnly—his own version of an encouraging wink.

"Dinna be downhearted, Ian. Remember the story o' the Prodigal Son, aye? Your mam will be glad to see ye safe back."

Young Ian cast him a glance of profound disillusion.

"If ye expect it's the fatted calf that's like to be kilt, Uncle Jamie, ye dinna ken my mother so well as ye think."

The lad sat gnawing his lower lip for a moment, then drew himself up in the saddle with a deep breath.

"Best get it over, aye?" he said.

"Will his parents really be hard on him?" I asked, watching Young Ian pick his way carefully down the rocky slope.

Jamie shrugged.

"Well, they'll forgive him, of course, but he's like to get a rare ballocking and his backside tanned before that. I'll be lucky to get off wi' the same," he added wryly. "Jenny and Ian are no going to be verra pleased wi' me, either, I'm afraid." He kicked up his mount, and started down the slope.

"Come along, Sassenach. Best get it over, aye?"

I wasn't sure what to expect in terms of a reception at Lallybroch, but in the event, it was reassuring. As on all previous arrivals, our presence was heralded by the barking of a miscellaneous swarm of dogs, who galloped out of hedge and field and kailyard, yapping first with alarm, and then with joy.

Young Ian dropped his reins and slid down into the furry sea of welcome, dropping into a crouch to greet the dogs who leapt on him and licked his face. He stood up smiling with a half-grown puppy in his arms, which he brought over to show me.

"This is Jocky," he said, holding up the squirming brown and white body. "He's mine; Da gave him to me."

"Nice doggie," I told Jocky, scratching his floppy ears. The dog barked and squirmed ecstatically, trying to lick me and Ian simultaneously.

"You're getting covered wi' dog hairs, Ian," said a clear, high voice, in tones of marked disapproval. Looking up from the dog, I saw a tall, slim girl of seventeen or so, rising from her seat by the side of the road.

"Well, you're covered wi' foxtails, so there!" Young Ian retorted, swinging about to address the speaker.

The girl tossed a headful of dark brown curls and bent to brush at her skirt, which did indeed sport a number of the bushy grass-heads, stuck to the homespun fabric.

"Da says ye dinna deserve to have a dog," she remarked. "Running off and leaving him like ye did."

Young Ian's face tightened defensively. "I did think o' taking him," he said, voice cracking slightly. "But I didna think he'd be safe in the city." He hugged the dog tighter, chin resting between the furry ears. "He's grown a bit; I suppose he's been eating all right?"

"Come to greet us, have ye, wee Janet? That's kind." Jamie's voice spoke pleasantly from behind me, but with a cynical note that made the girl glance up sharply and blush at the sight of him.

"Uncle Jamie! Oh, and . . ." Her gaze shifted to me, and she ducked her head, blushing more furiously.

"Aye, this is your auntie Claire." Jamie's hand was firm under my elbow as he nodded toward the girl. "Wee Janet wasna born yet, last ye were here, Sassenach. Your mother will be to home, I expect?" he said, addressing Janet.

The girl nodded, wide-eyed, not taking her fascinated gaze from my face. I leaned down from my horse and extended a hand, smiling.

"I'm pleased to meet you," I said.

She stared for a long moment, then suddenly remembered her manners, and dropped into a curtsy. She rose and took my hand gingerly, as though afraid it might come off in her grasp. I squeezed hers, and she looked faintly reassured at finding me merely flesh and blood.

"I'm . . . pleased, mum," she murmured.

"Are Mam and Da verra angry, Jen?" Young Ian gently put the puppy on the ground near her feet, breaking her trance. She glanced at her younger brother, her expression of impatience tinged with some sympathy.

"Well, and why wouldn't they be, clot-heid?" she said. "Mam thought ye'd maybe met a boar in the wood, or been taken by Gypsies. She scarcely slept until they found out where ye'd gone," she added, frowning at her brother.

Ian pressed his lips tight together, looking down at the ground, but didn't answer.

She moved closer, and picked disapprovingly at the damp yellow leaves adhering to the sleeves of his coat. Tall as she was, he topped her by a good six inches, gangly and rawboned next to her trim competence, the resemblance between them limited to the rich darkness of their hair and a fugitive similarity of expression.

"You're a sight, Ian. Have ye been sleepin' in your clothes?"

"Well, of course I have," he said impatiently. "What d'ye think, I ran away wi' a nightshirt and changed into it every night on the moor?"

She gave a brief snort of laughter at this picture, and his expression of annoyance faded a bit.

"Oh, come on, then, gowk," she said, taking pity on him. "Come into the scullery wi' me, and we'll get ye brushed and combed before Mam and Da see ye."

He glared at her, then turned to look up at me, with an expression of mingled bewilderment and annoyance. "Why in the name o' heaven," he demanded, his voice cracking with strain, "does everyone think bein' *clean* will help?"

Jamie grinned at him, and dismounting, clapped him on the shoulder, raising a small cloud of dust.

"It canna hurt anything, Ian. Go along wi' ye; I think perhaps it's as well if your parents havena got so many things to deal with all at once—and they'll be wanting to see your auntie first of all."

"Mmphm." With a morose nod of assent, Young Ian moved reluctantly off toward the back of the house, towed by his determined sister.

"What have ye been eating?" I heard her say, squinting up at him as they went. "You've a great smudge of filth all round your mouth."

"It isna filth, it's whiskers!" he hissed furiously under his breath, with a quick backward glance to see whether Jamie and I had heard this exchange. His sister stopped dead, peering up at him.

"Whiskers?" she said loudly and incredulously. *"You?"*

"Come on!" Grabbing her by the elbow, he hustled her off through the kailyard gate, his shoulders hunched in self-consciousness.

Jamie lowered his head against my thigh, face buried in my skirts. To the casual observer, he might have been occupied in loosening the saddlebags, but the casual observer couldn't have seen his shoulders shaking or felt the vibration of his soundless laughter.

"It's all right, they're gone," I said, a moment later, gasping for breath myself from the strain of silent mirth.

Jamie raised his face, red and breathless, from my skirts, and used a fold of the cloth to dab his eyes.

"Whiskers? *You?*" he croaked in imitation of his niece, setting us both off again. He shook his head, gulping for air. "Christ, she's like her mother! That's just what Jenny said to me, in just that voice, when she caught me shavin' for the first time. I nearly cut my throat." He wiped his eyes again on the back of his hand, and rubbed a palm tenderly across the thick, soft stubble that coated his own jaws and throat with an auburn haze.

"Do you want to go and shave yourself before we meet Jenny and Ian?" I asked, but he shook his head.

"No," he said, smoothing back the hair that had escaped from its lacing. "Young Ian's right; bein' clean won't help."

◄━━━━━━━━►

They must have heard the dogs outside; both Ian and Jenny were in the sitting room when we came in, she on the sofa knitting woolen stockings, while he stood before the fire in plain brown coat and breeks, warming the backs of his legs. A tray of small cakes with a bottle of home-brewed ale was set out, plainly in readiness for our arrival.

It was a very cozy, welcoming scene, and I felt the tiredness of the journey drop away as we entered the room. Ian turned at once as we came in, self-conscious but smiling, but it was Jenny that I looked for.

She was looking for me, too. She sat still on the couch, her eyes wide, turned to the door. My first impression was that she was quite different, the second, that she had not changed at all. The black curls were still there, thick and lively, but blanched and streaked with a deep, rich silver. The bones, too, were the same—the broad, high cheekbones, strong jaw, and long nose that she shared with Jamie. It was the flickering firelight and the shadows of the gathering afternoon that gave the strange impression of change, one moment deepening the lines beside her eyes and mouth 'til she looked like a crone; the next erasing them with the ruddy glow of girlhood, like a 3-D picture in a box of Cracker Jack.

On our first meeting in the brothel, Ian had acted as if I were a ghost. Jenny did much the same now, blinking slightly, her mouth slightly open, but not otherwise changing expression as I crossed the room toward her.

Jamie was just behind me, his hand at my elbow. He squeezed it lightly as we reached the sofa, then let go. I felt rather as though I were being presented at Court, and resisted the impulse to curtsy.

"We're home, Jenny," he said. His hand rested reassuringly on my back.

She glanced quickly at her brother, then stared at me again.

"It's you, then, Claire?" Her voice was soft and tentative, familiar, but not the strong voice of the woman I remembered.

"Yes, it's me," I said. I smiled and reached out my hands to her. "It's good to see you, Jenny."

She took my hands, lightly. Then her grip strengthened and she rose to her feet. "Christ, it *is* you!" she said, a little breathless, and suddenly the woman I had known was back, dark blue eyes alive and dancing, searching my face with curiosity.

"Well, of course it is," Jamie said gruffly. "Surely Ian told ye; did ye think he was lying?"

"You'll scarce have changed," she said, ignoring her brother as she touched my face wonderingly. "Your hair's a bit lighter, but my God, ye look the same!" Her fingers were cool; her hands smelled of herbs and red-currant jam, and the faint hint of ammonia and lanolin from the dyed wool she was knitting.

The long-forgotten smell of the wool brought everything back at once—so many memories of the place, and the happiness of the time I had lived here—and my eyes blurred with tears.

She saw it, and hugged me hard, her hair smooth and soft against my face. She was much shorter than I, fine-boned and delicate to look at, but still I had the feeling of being enveloped, warmly supported and strongly held, as though by someone larger than myself.

She released me after a moment, and stood back, half-laughing. "God, ye even smell the same!" she exclaimed, and I burst out laughing, too.

Ian had come up; he leaned down and embraced me gently, brushing his lips against my cheek. He smelled faintly of dried hay and cabbage leaves, with the ghost of peat smoke laid over his own deep, musky scent.

"It's good to see ye back again, Claire," he said. His soft brown eyes smiled at me, and the sense of homecoming deepened. He stood back a little awkwardly, smiling. "Will ye eat something, maybe?" He gestured toward the tray on the table.

I hesitated a moment, but Jamie moved toward it with alacrity.

"A drop wouldna come amiss, Ian, thank ye kindly," he said. "You'll have some, Claire?"

Glasses were filled, the biscuits passed, and small spoken pleasantries murmured through mouthfuls as we sat down around the fire. Despite the outward cordiality, I was strongly aware of an underlying tension, not all of it to do with my sudden reappearance.

Jamie, seated beside me on the oak settle, took no more than a sip of his ale, and the oatcake sat untasted on his knee. I knew he hadn't accepted the refreshments out of hunger, but in order to mask the fact that neither his sister nor his brother-in-law had offered him a welcoming embrace.

I caught a quick glance passing between Ian and Jenny; and a longer stare, unreadable, exchanged between Jenny and Jamie. A stranger here in more ways than one, I kept my own eyes cast down, observing under the shelter of my lashes. Jamie sat to my left; I could feel the tiny movement between us as the two stiff fingers of his right hand drummed their small tattoo against his thigh.

The conversation, what there was of it, petered out, and the room fell into an uncomfortable silence. Through the faint hissing of the peat fire, I could hear a few distant thumps in the direction of the kitchen, but nothing like the sounds I remembered in this house, of constant activity and bustling movement, feet always pounding on the stair, and the shouts of children and squalling of babies splitting the air in the nursery overhead.

"How are all of your children?" I asked Jenny, to break the silence. She started, and I realized that I had inadvertently asked the wrong question.

"Oh, they're well enough," she replied hesitantly. "All verra bonny. And the grandchildren, too," she added, breaking into a sudden smile at the thought of them.

"They've mostly gone to Young Jamie's house," Ian put in, answering my real question. "His wife's had a new babe just the week past, so the three girls have gone to help a bit. And Michael's up in Inverness just now, to fetch down some things come in from France."

Another glance flicked across the room, this one between Ian and Jamie. I felt the small tilt of Jamie's head, and saw Ian's not-quite-nod in response. And what in hell was *that* about? I wondered. There were so many invisible cross-currents of emotion in the room that I had a sudden impulse to stand up and call the meeting to order, just to break the tension.

Apparently Jamie felt the same. He cleared his throat, looking directly at Ian, and addressed the main point on the agenda, saying, "We've brought the lad home with us."

Ian took a deep breath, his long, homely face hardening slightly.

"Have ye, then?" The thin layer of pleasantry spread over the occasion vanished suddenly, like morning dew.

I could feel Jamie beside me, tensing slightly as he prepared to defend his nephew as best he might.

"He's a good lad, Ian," he said.

"Is he, so?" It was Jenny who answered, her fine black brows drawn down in a frown. "Ye couldna tell, the way he acts at home. But perhaps he's different wi' you, Jamie." There was a strong note of accusation in her words, and I felt Jamie tense at my side.

"It's kind of ye to speak up for the lad, Jamie," Ian put in, with a cool nod in his brother-in-law's direction. "But I think we'd best hear from Young Ian himself, if ye please. Will he be upstairs?"

A muscle near Jamie's mouth twitched, but he answered noncommittally. "In the scullery, I expect; he wanted to tidy himself a bit before seein' ye." His right hand slid down and pressed against my leg in warning. He hadn't mentioned meeting Janet, and I understood; she had been sent away with her siblings, so that Jenny and Ian could deal with the matters of my appearance and their prodigal son in some privacy, but had crept back unbeknownst to her parents, wanting either to catch a glimpse of her notorious aunt Claire, or to offer succor to her brother.

I lowered my eyelids, indicating that I understood. No point in mentioning the girl's presence, in a situation already so fraught with tension.

The sound of feet and the regular thump of Ian's wooden leg sounded in the uncarpeted passage. Ian had left the room in the direction of the scullery; now he returned, grimly ushering Young Ian before him.

The prodigal was as presentable as soap, water, and razor could make him. His bony jaws were reddened with scraping and the hair on his neck was clotted in wet spikes, most of the dust beaten from his coat, and the round neck of his shirt neatly buttoned to the collarbone. There was little to be done about the singed half of his head, but the other side was neatly combed. He had no stock, and there was a large rip in the leg of his breeks, but all things considered, he looked as well as someone could who expects momentarily to be shot.

"Mam," he said, ducking his head awkwardly in his mother's direction.

"Ian," she said softly, and he looked up at her, clearly startled at the gentleness of her tone. A slight smile curved her lips as she saw his face. "I'm glad you're safe home, *mo chridhe*," she said.

The boy's face cleared abruptly, as though he had just heard the reprieve read to the firing squad. Then he caught a glimpse of his father's face, and stiffened. He swallowed hard, and bent his head again, staring hard at the floorboards.

"Mmphm," Ian said. He sounded sternly Scotch; much more like the Reverend Campbell than the easygoing man I had known before. "Now then, I want to hear what ye've got to say for yourself, laddie."

"Oh. Well . . . I . . ." Young Ian trailed off miserably, then cleared his throat and had another try. "Well . . . nothing, really, Father," he murmured.

"Look at me!" Ian said sharply. His son reluctantly raised his head and looked at his father, but his gaze kept flicking away, as though afraid to rest very long on the stern countenance before him.

"D'ye ken what ye did to your mother?" Ian demanded. "Disappeared and left her thinkin' ye dead or hurt? Gone off without a word, and not a smell of ye for three days, until Joe Fraser brought down the letter ye left? Can ye even think what those three days were like for her?"

Either Ian's expression or his words seemed to have a strong effect on his errant offspring; Young Ian bowed his head again, eyes fixed on the floor.

"Aye, well, I thought Joe would bring the letter sooner," he muttered.

"Aye, that letter!" Ian's face was growing more flushed as he talked. " 'Gone to Edinburgh,' it said, cool as dammit." He slapped a hand flat on the table, with a smack that made everyone jump. "Gone to Edinburgh! Not a 'by your leave,' not an 'I'll send word,' not a thing but 'Dear Mother, I have gone to Edinburgh. Ian'!"

Young Ian's head snapped up, eyes bright with anger.

"That's not true! I said 'Don't worry for me,' and I said *'Love, Ian*'! I did! Did I no, Mother?" For the first time, he looked at Jenny, appealing.

She had been still as a stone since her husband began to talk, her face smooth and blank. Now her eyes softened, and the hint of a curve touched her wide, full mouth again.

"Ye did, Ian," she said softly. "It was kind to say—but I did worry, aye?"

His eyes fell, and I could see the oversized Adam's apple bobble in his lean throat as he swallowed.

"I'm sorry, Mam," he said, so low I could scarcely hear him. "I—I didna mean . . ." His words trailed off, ending in a small shrug.

Jenny made an impulsive movement, as though to extend a hand to him, but Ian caught her eye, and she let the hand fall to her lap.

"The thing is," Ian said, speaking slowly and precisely, "it's no the first time, is it, Ian?"

The boy didn't answer, but made a small twitching movement that might have been assent. Ian took a step closer to his son. Close as they were in height, the differences between them were obvious. Ian was tall and lanky, but firmly muscled for all that, and a powerful man, wooden leg or no. By comparison, his son seemed almost frail, fledgling-boned and gawky.

"No, it's not as though ye had no idea what ye were doing; not like we'd never told ye the dangers, not like we'd no forbidden ye to go past Broch Mordha—not like ye didna ken we'd worry, aye? Ye kent all that—and ye did it anyway."

This merciless analysis of his behavior caused a sort of indefinite quiver, like an internal squirm, to go through Young Ian, but he kept up a stubborn silence.

"Look at me, laddie, when I'm speakin' to ye!" The boy's head rose slowly. He looked sullen now, but resigned; evidently he had been through scenes like this before, and knew where they were heading.

"I'm not even going to ask your uncle what ye've been doing," Ian said. "I can only hope ye weren't such a fool in Edinburgh as ye've been here. But ye've disobeyed me outright, and broken your mother's heart, whatever else ye've done."

Jenny moved again, as though to speak, but a brusque movement of Ian's hand stopped her.

"And what did I tell ye the last time, wee Ian? What did I say when I gave ye your whipping? You tell me that, Ian!"

The bones in Young Ian's face stood out, but he kept his mouth shut, sealed in a stubborn line.

"Tell me!" Ian roared, slamming his hand on the table again. Young Ian blinked in reflex, and his shoulder blades drew together, then apart, as though he were trying to alter his size, and unsure whether to grow larger or try to be smaller. He swallowed hard, and blinked once more.

"Ye said—ye said ye'd skin me. Next time." His voice broke in a ridiculous squeak on the last word, and he clamped his mouth hard shut on it.

Ian shook his head in heavy disapproval. "Aye. And I thought ye'd have enough sense to see there was no next time, but I was wrong about that, hm?" He breathed in heavily and let it out with a snort.

"I'm fair disgusted wi' ye, Ian, and that's the truth." He jerked his head toward the doorway. "Go outside. I'll see ye by the gate, presently."

There was a tense silence in the sitting room, as the sound of the miscreant's dragging footsteps disappeared down the passage. I kept my own eyes carefully on my hands, folded in my lap. Beside me, Jamie drew a slow, deep breath and sat up straighter, steeling himself.

"Ian." Jamie spoke mildly to his brother-in-law. "I wish ye wouldna do that."

"What?" Ian's brow was still furrowed with anger as he turned toward Jamie. "Thrash the lad? And what have you to say about it, aye?"

Jamie's jaw tensed, but his voice stayed calm.

"I've nothing to say about it, Ian—he's your son; you'll do as ye like. But maybe you'll let me speak for the way he's acted?"

"How he's acted?" Jenny cried, starting suddenly to life. She might leave dealing with her son to Ian, but when it came to her brother, no one was likely to speak for her. "Sneakin' away in the night like a thief, ye mean? Or perhaps ye'll mean consorting wi' criminals, and risking his neck for a cask of brandy!"

Ian silenced her with a quick gesture. He hesitated, still frowning, but then nodded abruptly at Jamie, giving permission.

"Consorting wi' criminals like me?" Jamie asked his sister, a definite edge to his voice. His eyes met hers straight on, matching slits of blue.

"D'ye ken where the money comes from, Jenny, that keeps you and your bairns and everyone here in food, and the roof from fallin' in over your head? It's not from me printing up copies o' the Psalms in Edinburgh!''

''And did I think it was?'' she flared at him. ''Did I ask ye what ye did?''

''No, ye didn't,'' he flashed back. ''I think ye'd rather not know —but ye do know, don't you?''

''And will ye blame me for what ye do? It's *my* fault that I've children, and that they must eat?'' She didn't flush red like Jamie did; when Jenny lost her temper, she went dead white with fury.

I could see him struggling to keep his own temper. ''Blame ye? No, of course I dinna blame ye—but is it right for you to blame me, that Ian and I canna keep ye all just working the land?''

Jenny too was making an effort to subdue her rising temper. ''No,'' she said. ''Ye do what ye must, Jamie. Ye ken verra well I didna mean you when I said 'criminals,' but—''

''So ye mean the men who work for me? I do the same things, Jenny. If they're criminals, what am I, then?'' He glared at her, eyes hot with resentment.

''You're my brother,'' she said shortly, ''little pleased as I am to say so, sometimes. Damn your eyes, Jamie Fraser! Ye ken quite well I dinna mean to quarrel wi' whatever ye see fit to do! If ye robbed folk on the highway, or kept a whorehouse in Edinburgh, 'twould be because there was no help for it. That doesna mean I want ye takin' my son to be part of it!''

Jamie's eyes tightened slightly at the corners at the mention of whorehouses in Edinburgh, and he darted a quick glance of accusation at Ian, who shook his head. He looked mildly stunned at his wife's ferocity.

''I've said not a word,'' he said briefly. ''Ye ken how she is.''

Jamie took a deep breath and turned back to Jenny, obviously determined to be reasonable.

''Aye, I see that. But ye canna think I would take Young Ian into danger—God, Jenny, I care for him as though he were my own son!''

''Aye?'' Her skepticism was pronounced. ''So that's why ye encouraged him to run off from his home, and kept him with ye, wi' no word to ease our minds about where he was?''

Jamie had the grace to look abashed at this.

''Aye, well, I'm sorry for that,'' he muttered. ''I meant to—'' He broke off with an impatient gesture. ''Well, it doesna matter what I meant; I should have sent word, and I didna. But as for encouraging him to run off—''

"No, I dinna suppose ye did," Ian interrupted. "Not directly, anyway." The anger had faded from his long face. He looked tired now, and a little sad. The bones in his face were more pronounced, leaving him hollow-cheeked in the waning afternoon light.

"It's only that the lad loves ye, Jamie," he said quietly. "I see him listen when ye visit, and talk of what ye do; I can see his face. He thinks it's all excitement and adventure, how ye live, and a good long way from shoveling goat-shit for his mother's garden." He smiled briefly, despite himself.

Jamie gave his brother-in-law a quick smile in return, and a lifted shoulder. "Well, but it's usual for a lad of that age to want a bit of adventure, no? You and I were the same."

"Whether he wants it or no, he shouldna be having the sort of adventures he'll get with you," Jenny interrupted sharply. She shook her head, the line between her brows growing deeper as she looked disapprovingly at her brother. "The good Lord kens as there's a charm on your life, Jamie, or ye'd ha' been dead a dozen times."

"Aye, well. I suppose He had something in mind to preserve me for." Jamie glanced at me with a brief smile, and his hand sought mine. Jenny darted a glance at me, too, her face unreadable, then returned to the subject at hand.

"Well, that's as may be," she said. "But I canna say as the same's true for Young Ian." Her expression softened slightly as she looked at Jamie.

"I dinna ken everything about the way ye live, Jamie—but I ken *you* well enough to say it's likely not the way a wee laddie should live."

"Mmphm." Jamie rubbed a hand over his stubbled jaw, and tried again. "Aye, well, that's what I mean about Young Ian. He's carried himself like a man this last week. I dinna think it right for ye to thrash him like a wee laddie, Ian."

Jenny's eyebrows rose, graceful wings of scorn.

"A man, now, is he? Why, he's but a baby, Jamie—he's not but fourteen!''

Despite his annoyance, one side of Jamie's mouth curled slightly.

"I was a man at fourteen, Jenny," he said softly.

She snorted, but a film of moisture shone suddenly over her eyes.

"Ye thought ye were." She stood and turned away abruptly, blinking. "Aye, I mind ye then," she said, face turned to the bookshelf. She reached out a hand as though to support herself, grasping the edge.

"Ye were a bonny lad, Jamie, riding off wi' Dougal to your first raid, and your dirk all bright on your thigh. I was sixteen, and I thought I'd never seen a sight so fair as you on your pony, so straight and tall. And I mind ye coming back, too, all covered in mud, and a scratch down the side of your face from falling in brambles, and Dougal boasting to Da how brawly ye'd done— driven off six kine by yourself, and had a dunt on the head from the flat of a broadsword, and not made a squeak about it." Her face once more under control, she turned back from her contemplation of the books to face her brother. "That's what a man is, aye?"

A hint of humor stole back into Jamie's face as he met her gaze.

"Aye, well, there's maybe a bit more to it than that," he said.

"Is there," she said, more dryly still. "And what will that be? To be able to bed a girl? Or to kill a man?"

I had always thought Janet Fraser had something of the Sight, particularly where her brother was concerned. Evidently the talent extended to her son, as well. The flush over Jamie's cheekbones deepened, but his expression didn't change.

She shook her head slowly, looking steadily at her brother. "Nay, Young Ian's not a man yet—but you are, Jamie; and ye ken the difference verra well."

Ian, who had been watching the fireworks between the two Frasers with the same fascination as I had, now coughed briefly.

"Be that as it may," he said dryly. "Young Ian's been waiting for his whipping for the last quarter-hour. Whether or not it's suitable to beat him, to make him wait any longer for it is a bit cruel, aye?"

"Have ye really got to do it, Ian?" Jamie made one last effort, turning to appeal to his brother-in-law.

"Well," said Ian slowly, "as I've told the lad he's going to be thrashed, and he kens verra well he's earned it, I canna just go back on my word. But as for me doing it—no, I dinna think I will." A faint gleam of humor showed in the soft brown eyes. He reached into a drawer of the sideboard, drew out a thick leather strap, and thrust it into Jamie's hand. "You do it."

"Me?" Jamie was horror-struck. He made a futile attempt to shove the strap back into Ian's hand, but his brother-in-law ignored it. "I canna thrash the lad!"

"Oh, I think ye can," Ian said calmly, folding his arms. "Ye've said often enough ye care for him as though he were your son." He tilted his head to one side, and while his expression stayed mild, the brown eyes were implacable. "Well, I'll tell ye, Jamie— it's no that easy to be his da; best ye go and find that out now, aye?"

Jamie stared at Ian for a long moment, then looked to his sister. She raised one eyebrow, staring him down.

"You deserve it as much as he does, Jamie. Get ye gone."

Jamie's lips pressed tight together and his nostrils flared white. Then he whirled on his heel and was gone without speaking. Rapid steps sounded on the boards, and a muffled slam came from the far end of the passage.

Jenny cast a quick glance at Ian, a quicker one at me, and then turned to the window. Ian and I, both a good deal taller, came to stand behind her. The light outside was failing rapidly, but there was still enough to see the wilting figure of Young Ian, leaning dispiritedly against a wooden gate, some twenty yards from the house.

Looking around in trepidation at the sound of footsteps, he saw his uncle approaching and straightened up in surprise.

"Uncle Jamie!" His eye fell on the strap then, and he straightened a bit more. "Are . . . are *you* goin' to whip me?"

It was a still evening, and I could hear the sharp hiss of air through Jamie's teeth.

"I suppose I'll have to," he said frankly. "But first I must apologize to ye, Ian."

"To me?" Young Ian sounded mildly dazed. Clearly he wasn't used to having his elders think they owed him an apology, especially before beating him. "Ye dinna need to do that, Uncle Jamie."

The taller figure leaned against the gate, facing the smaller one, head bent.

"Aye, I do. It was wrong of me, Ian, to let ye stay in Edinburgh, and it was maybe wrong, too, to tell ye stories and make ye think of running away to start with. I took ye to places I shouldna, and might have put ye in danger, and I've caused more of a moil wi' your parents than maybe ye should be in by yourself. I'm sorry for it, Ian, and I'll ask ye to forgive me."

"Oh." The smaller figure rubbed a hand through his hair, plainly at a loss for words. "Well . . . aye. Of course I do, Uncle."

"Thank ye, Ian."

They stood in silence for a moment, then Young Ian heaved a sigh and straightened his drooping shoulders.

"I suppose we'd best do it, then?"

"I expect so." Jamie sounded at least as reluctant as his nephew, and I heard Ian, next to me, snort slightly, whether with indignation or amusement, I couldn't tell.

Resigned, Young Ian turned and faced the gate without hesitation. Jamie followed more slowly. The light was nearly gone and we could see no more than the outlines of figures at this distance, but we could hear clearly from our position at the window. Jamie was standing behind his nephew, shifting uncertainly, as though unsure what to do next.

"Mmphm. Ah, what does your father . . ."

"It's usually ten, Uncle." Young Ian had shed his coat, and tugged at his waist now, speaking over his shoulder. "Twelve if it's pretty bad, and fifteen if it's really awful."

"Was this only bad, would ye say, or pretty bad?"

There was a brief, unwilling laugh from the boy.

"If Father's makin' *you* do it, Uncle Jamie, it's really awful, but I'll settle for pretty bad. Ye'd better give me twelve."

There was another snort from Ian at my elbow. This time, it was definitely amusement. "Honest lad," he murmured.

"All right, then." Jamie drew in his breath and pulled his arm back, but was interrupted by Young Ian.

"Wait, Uncle, I'm no quite ready."

"Och, ye've got to do that?" Jamie's voice sounded a bit strangled.

"Aye. Father says only girls are whipped wi' their skirts down," Young Ian explained. "Men must take it bare-arsed."

"He's damn well right about *that* one," Jamie muttered, his quarrel with Jenny obviously still rankling. "Ready now?"

The necessary adjustments made, the larger figure stepped back and swung. There was a loud crack, and Jenny winced in sympathy with her son. Beyond a sudden intake of breath, though, the lad was silent, and stayed so through the rest of the ordeal, though I blanched a bit myself.

Finally Jamie dropped his arm, and wiped his brow. He held out a hand to Ian, slumped over the fence. "All right, lad?" Young Ian straightened up, with a little difficulty this time, and pulled up his breeks. "Aye, Uncle. Thank ye." The boy's voice was a little thick, but calm and steady. He took Jamie's outstretched hand. To my surprise, though, instead of leading the boy back to the house, Jamie thrust the strap into Ian's other hand.

"Your turn," he announced, striding over to the gate and bending over.

Young Ian was as shocked as those of us in the house.

"What!" he said, stunned.

"I said it's your turn," his uncle said in a firm voice. "I punished you; now you've got to punish me."

"I canna do that, Uncle!" Young Ian was as scandalized as though his uncle had suggested he commit some public indecency.

"Aye, ye can," said Jamie, straightening up to look his nephew in the eye. "Ye heard what I said when I apologized to ye, did ye no?" Ian nodded in a dazed fashion. "Weel, then. I've done wrong just as much as you, and I've to pay for it, too. I didna like whipping you, and ye're no goin' to like whipping me, but we're both goin' through wi' it. Understand?"

"A-aye, Uncle," the boy stammered.

"All right, then." Jamie tugged down his breeches, tucked up his shirttail, and bent over once more, clutching the top rail. He waited a second, then spoke again, as Ian stood paralyzed, strap dangling from his nerveless hand.

"Go on." His voice was steel; the one he used with the whisky smugglers; not to obey was unthinkable. Ian moved timidly to do as he was ordered. Standing back, he took a halfhearted swing. There was a dull thwacking sound.

"That one didna count," Jamie said firmly. "Look, man, it was just as hard for me to do it to you. Make a proper job of it, now."

The thin figure squared its shoulders with sudden determination and the leather whistled through the air. It landed with a crack like lightning. There was a startled yelp from the figure on the fence, and a suppressed giggle, at least half shock, from Jenny.

Jamie cleared his throat. "Aye, that'll do. Finish it, then."

We could hear Young Ian counting carefully to himself under his breath between strokes of the leather, but aside from a smothered "Christ!" at number nine, there was no further sound from his uncle.

With a general sigh of relief from inside the house, Jamie rose off the fence after the last stroke, and tucked his shirt into his breeks. He inclined his head formally to his nephew. "Thank ye, Ian." Dropping the formality, he then rubbed his backside, saying in a tone of rueful admiration, "Christ, man, ye've an arm on ye!"

"So've you, Uncle," said Ian, matching his uncle's wry tones. The two figures, barely visible now, stood laughing and rubbing themselves for a moment. Jamie flung an arm about his nephew's shoulders and turned him toward the house. "If it's all the same to you, Ian, I dinna want to have to do that again, aye?" he said, confidentially.

"It's a bargain, Uncle Jamie."

A moment later, the door opened at the end of the passage, and with a look at each other, Jenny and Ian turned as one to greet the returning prodigals.

33

Buried Treasure

"You look rather like a baboon," I observed.

"Oh, aye? And what's one of those?" In spite of the freezing November air pouring in through the half-open window, Jamie showed no signs of discomfort as he dropped his shirt onto the small pile of clothing.

He stretched luxuriously, completely naked. His joints made little popping noises as he arched his back and stretched upward, fists resting easily on the smoke-dark beams overhead.

"Oh, God, it feels good not to be on a horse!"

"Mm. To say nothing of having a real bed to sleep in, instead of wet heather." I rolled over, luxuriating in the warmth of the heavy quilts, and the relaxation of sore muscles into the ineffable softness of the goose-down mattress.

"D'ye mean to tell me what's a baboon, then?" Jamie inquired, "Or are ye just makin' observations for the pleasure of it?" He turned to pick up a frayed willow twig from the washstand, and began to clean his teeth. I smiled at the sight; if I had had no other impact during my earlier sojourn in the past, I had at least been instrumental in seeing that virtually all of the Frasers and Murrays of Lallybroch retained their teeth, unlike most Highlanders—unlike most Englishmen, for that matter.

"A baboon," I said, enjoying the sight of his muscular back flexing as he scrubbed, "is a sort of very large monkey with a red behind."

He snorted with laughter and choked on the willow twig. "Well," he said, removing it from his mouth, "I canna fault your observations, Sassenach.'' He grinned at me, showing brilliant white teeth, and tossed the twig aside. ''It's been thirty years since anyone took a tawse to me,'' he added, passing his hands tenderly over the still-glowing surfaces of his rear. ''I'd forgot how much it stings.''

''And here Young Ian was speculating that your arse was tough as saddle leather,'' I said, amused. ''Was it worth it, do you think?''

''Oh, aye,'' he said, matter-of-factly, sliding into bed beside me. His body was hard and cold as marble, and I squeaked but didn't protest as he gathered me firmly against his chest. ''Christ, you're warm,'' he murmured. ''Come closer, hm?'' His legs insinuated themselves between mine, and he cupped my bottom, drawing me in.

He gave a sigh of pure content, and I relaxed against him, feeling our temperatures start to equalize through the thin cotton of the nightdress Jenny had lent me. The peat fire in the hearth had been lit, but hadn't been able to do much yet toward dispelling the chill. Body heat was much more effective.

''Oh, aye, it was worth it,'' he said. ''I could have beaten Young Ian half-senseless—his father has, once or twice—and it would ha' done nothing but make him more determined to run off, once he got the chance. But he'll walk through hot coals before he risks havin' to do something like that again.''

He spoke with certainty, and I thought he was undoubtedly right. Young Ian, looking bemused, had received absolution from his parents, in the form of a kiss from his mother and a swift hug from his father, and then retired to his bed with a handful of cakes, there no doubt to ponder the curious consequences of disobedience.

Jamie too had been absolved with kisses, and I suspected that this was more important to him than the effects of his performance on Young Ian.

''At least Jenny and Ian aren't angry with you any longer,'' I said.

''No. It's no really that they were angry so much, I think; it's only that they dinna ken what to do wi' the lad,'' he explained. ''They've raised two sons already, and Young Jamie and Michael are fine lads both; but both of them are more like Ian—soft-spoke, and easy in their manner. Young Ian's quiet enough, but he's a great deal more like his mother—and me.''

"Frasers are stubborn, eh?" I said, smiling. This bit of clan doctrine was one of the first things I had learned when I met Jamie, and nothing in my subsequent experience had suggested that it might be in error.

He chuckled, soft and deep in his chest.

"Aye, that's so. Young Ian may look like a Murray, but he's a Fraser born, all right. And it's no use to shout at a stubborn man, or beat him, either; it only makes him more set on having his way.''

"I'll bear that in mind," I said dryly. One hand was stroking my thigh, gradually inching the cotton nightdress upward. Jamie's internal furnace had resumed its operations, and his bare legs were warm and hard against mine. One knee nudged gently, seeking an entrance between my thighs. I cupped his buttocks and squeezed gently.

"Dorcas told me that a number of gentlemen pay very well for the privilege of being smacked at the brothel. She says they find it . . . arousing.''

Jamie snorted briefly, tensing his buttocks, then relaxing as I stroked them lightly.

"Do they, then? I suppose it's true, if Dorcas says so, but I canna see it, myself. There are a great many more pleasant ways to get a cockstand, if ye ask me. On the other hand," he added fairly, "perhaps it makes a difference if it's a bonny wee lassie in her shift on the other end o' the strap, and not your father—or your nephew, come to that.''

"Perhaps it does. Shall I try sometime?" The hollow of his throat lay just by my face, sunburned and delicate, showing the faint white triangle of a scar just above the wide arch of his collarbone. I set my lips on the pulsebeat there, and he shivered, though neither of us was cold any longer.

"No," he said, a little breathless. His hand fumbled at the neck of my shift, pulling loose the ribbons. He rolled onto his back then, lifting me suddenly above him as though I weighed nothing at all. A flick of his finger brought the loosened chemise down over my shoulders, and my nipples rose at once as the cold air struck them.

His eyes were more slanted than usual as he smiled up at me, half-lidded as a drowsing cat, and the warmth of his palms encircled both breasts.

"I said I could think of more pleasant ways, aye?"

The candle had guttered and gone out, the fire on the hearth burned low, and a pale November starlight shone through the misted window. Dim as it was, my eyes were so adapted to the dark that I could pick out all the details of the room; the thick white porcelain jug and basin, its blue band black in the starlight, the small embroidered sampler on the wall, and the rumpled heap of Jamie's clothes on the stool by the bed.

Jamie was clearly visible, too; covers thrown back, chest gleaming faintly from exertion. I admired the long slope of his belly, where small whorls of dark auburn hair spiraled up across the pale, fresh skin. I couldn't keep my fingers from touching him, tracing the lines of the powerfully sprung ribs that shaped his torso.

"It's so good," I said dreamily. "So good to have a man's body to touch."

"D'ye like it still, then?" He sounded half-shy, half-pleased, as I fondled him. His own arm came around my shoulder, stroking my hair.

"Mm-hm." It wasn't a thing I had consciously missed, but having it now reminded me of the joy of it; that drowsy intimacy in which a man's body is as accessible to you as your own, the strange shapes and textures of it like a sudden extension of your own limbs.

I ran my hand down the flat slope of his belly, over the smooth jut of hipbone and the swell of muscled thigh. The remnants of firelight caught the red-gold fuzz on arms and legs, and glowed in the auburn thicket nested between his thighs.

"God, you are a wonderful hairy creature," I said. "Even there." I slid my hand down the smooth crease of his thigh and he spread his legs obligingly, letting me touch the thick, springy curls in the crease of his buttocks.

"Aye, well, no one's hunted me yet for my pelt," he said comfortably. His hand cupped my own rear firmly, and a large thumb passed gently over the rounded surface. He propped one arm behind his head, and looked lazily down the length of my body.

"You're even less worth the skinning than I am, Sassenach."

"I should hope so." I moved slightly to accommodate his touch as he extended his explorations, enjoying the warmth of his hand on my naked back.

"Ever seen a smooth branch that's been in still water a long time?" he asked. A finger passed lightly up my spine, raising a ripple of gooseflesh in its wake. "There are tiny wee bubbles on it, hundreds and thousands and millions of them, so it looks as though it's furred all about wi' a silver frost." His fingers brushed my ribs, my arms, my back, and the tiny down-hairs rose everywhere in the wake of his touch, tingling.

"That's what ye look like, my Sassenach," he said, almost whispering. "All smooth and naked, dipped in silver."

Then we lay quiet for a time, listening to the drip of rain outside. A cold autumn air drifted through the room, mingling with the fire's smoky warmth. He rolled onto his side, facing away from me, and drew the quilts up to cover us.

I curled up behind him, knees fitting neatly behind his own. The firelight shone dully from behind me now, gleaming over the smooth round of his shoulder and dimly illuminating his back. I could see the faint lines of the scars that webbed his shoulders, thin streaks of silver on his flesh. At one time, I had known those scars so intimately, I could have traced them with my fingers, blindfolded. Now there was a thin half-moon curve I didn't know; a diagonal slash that hadn't been there before, the remnants of a violent past I hadn't shared.

I touched the half-moon, tracing its length.

"No one's hunted you for your pelt," I said softly, "but they've hunted you, haven't they?"

His shoulder moved slightly, not quite a shrug. "Now and then," he said.

"Now?" I asked.

He breathed slowly for a moment or two before answering.

"Aye," he said. "I think so."

My fingers moved down to the diagonal slash. It had been a deep cut; old and well healed as the damage was, the line was sharp and clear beneath my fingertips.

"Do you know who?"

"No." He was quiet for a moment; then his hand closed over my own, where it lay across his stomach. "But I maybe ken why."

The house was very quiet. With most of the children and grand-children gone, there were only the far-off servants in their quarters behind the kitchen, Ian and Jenny in their room at the far end of the hall, and Young Ian somewhere upstairs—all asleep. We could have been alone at the end of the world; both Edinburgh and the smugglers' cove seemed very far away.

"Do ye recall, after the fall of Stirling, not so long before Culloden, when all of a sudden there was gossip from everywhere, about gold being sent from France?"

"From Louis? Yes—but he never sent it." Jamie's words sum-moned up those brief frantic days of Charles Stuart's reckless rise and precipitous fall, when rumor had been the common currency of conversation. "There was always gossip—about gold from France, ships from Spain, weapons from Holland—but nothing came of most of it."

"Oh, something came—though not from Louis—but no one kent it, then."

He told me then of his meeting with the dying Duncan Kerr, and the wanderer's whispered words, heard in the inn's attic under the watchful eye of an English officer.

"He was fevered, Duncan, but not crazed wi' it. He kent he was dying, and he kent me, too. It was his only chance to tell someone he thought he could trust—so he told me."

"White witches and seals?" I repeated. "I must say, it sounds like gibberish. But you understood it?"

"Well, not all of it," Jamie admitted. He rolled over to face me, frowning slightly. "I've no notion who the white witch might be. At the first, I thought he meant you, Sassenach, and my heart nearly stopped when he said it." He smiled ruefully, and his hand tightened on mine, clasped between us.

"I thought all at once that perhaps something had gone wrong —maybe ye'd not been able to go back to Frank and the place ye came from—maybe ye'd somehow ended in France, maybe ye were there right then—all kinds o' fancies went through my head."

"I wish it had been true," I whispered.

He gave me a lopsided smile, but shook his head.

"And me in prison? And Brianna would be what—just ten or so? No, dinna waste your time in regretting, Sassenach. You're here now, and ye'll never leave me again." He kissed me gently on the forehead, then resumed his tale.

"I didna have any idea where the gold had come from, but I kent his telling me where it was, and why it was there. It was Prince *Tearlach*'s, sent for him. And the bit about the silkies—" He raised his head a little and nodded toward the window, where the rose brier cast its shadows on the glass.

"Folk said when my mother ran away from Leoch that she'd gone to live wi' the silkies; only because the maid that saw my father when he took her said as he looked like a great silkie who'd shed his skin and come to walk on the land like a man. And he did." Jamie smiled and passed a hand through his own thick hair, remembering. "He had hair thick as mine, but a black like jet. It would shine in some lights, as though it was wet, and he moved quick and sleekit, like a seal through the water." He shrugged suddenly, shaking off the recollection of his father.

"Well, so. When Duncan Kerr said the name Ellen, I kent it was my mother he meant—as a sign that he knew my name and my family, kent who I was; that he wasna raving, no matter how it sounded. And knowin' that—" He shrugged again. "The Englishman had told me where they found Duncan, near the coast. There are hundreds of bittie isles and rocks all down that coast, but only one place where the silkies live, at the ends of the MacKenzie lands, off Coigach."

"So you went there?"

"Aye, I did." He sighed deeply, his free hand drifting to the hollow of my waist. "I wouldna have done it—left the prison, I mean—had I not still thought it maybe had something to do wi' you, Sassenach."

Escape had been an enterprise of no great difficulty; prisoners were often taken outside in small gangs, to cut the peats that burned on the prison's hearths, or to cut and haul stone for the ongoing work of repairing the walls.

For a man to whom the heather was home, disappearing had been easy. He had risen from his work and turned aside by a hummock of grass, unfastening his breeches as though to relieve himself. The guard had looked politely away, and looking back a moment later, beheld nothing but an empty moor, holding no trace of Jamie Fraser.

"See, it was little trouble to slip off, but men seldom did," he explained. "None of us were from near Ardsmuir—and had we been, there was little left for most o' the men to gang to."

The Duke of Cumberland's men had done their work well. As one contemporary had put it, evaluating the Duke's achievement later, "He created a desert and called it peace." This modern approach to diplomacy had left some parts of the Highlands all but deserted; the men killed, imprisoned, or transported, crops and houses burned, the women and children turned out to starve or seek refuge elsewhere as best they might. No, a prisoner escaping from Ardsmuir would have been truly alone, without kin or clan to turn to for succor.

Jamie had known there would be little time before the English commander realized where he must be heading and organized a party of pursuit. On the other hand, there were no real roads in this remote part of the kingdom, and a man who knew the country was at a greater advantage on foot than were the pursuing outlanders on horseback.

He had made his escape in midafternoon. Taking his bearings by the stars, he had walked through the night, arriving at the coast near dawn the next day.

"See, I kent the silkies' place; it's well known amongst the MacKenzies, and I'd been there once before, wi' Dougal."

The tide had been high, and the seals mostly out in the water, hunting crabs and fish among the fronds of floating kelp, but the dark streaks of their droppings and the indolent forms of a few idlers marked the seals' three islands, ranged in a line just inside the lip of a small bay, guarded by a clifflike headland.

By Jamie's interpretation of Duncan's instructions, the treasure lay on the third island, the farthest away from the shore. It was nearly a mile out, a long swim even for a strong man, and his own strength was sapped from the hard prison labor and the long walk without food. He had stood on the clifftop, wondering whether this was a wild-goose chase, and whether the treasure—if there was one—was worth the risk of his life.

"The rock was all split and broken there; when I came too close to the edge, chunks would fall awa' from my feet and plummet down the cliff. I didna see how I'd ever reach the water, let alone the seals' isle. But then I was minded what Duncan said about Ellen's tower," Jamie said. His eyes were open, fixed not on me, but on that distant shore where the crash of falling rock was lost in the smashing of the waves.

The "tower" was there; a small spike of granite that stuck up no more than five feet from the tip of the headland. But below that spike, hidden by the rocks, was a narrow crack, a small chimney that ran from top to bottom of the eighty-foot cliff, providing a possible passage, if not an easy one, for a determined man.

From the base of Ellen's tower to the third island was still over a quarter-mile of heaving green water. Undressing, he had crossed himself, and commending his soul to the keeping of his mother, he had dived naked into the waves.

He made his way slowly out from the cliff, floundering and choking as the waves broke over his head. No place in Scotland is that far from the sea, but Jamie had been raised inland, his experience of swimming limited to the placid depths of lochs and the pools of trout streams.

Blinded by salt and deafened by the roaring surf, he had fought the waves for what seemed hours, then thrust his head and shoulders free, gasping for breath, only to see the headland looming—not behind, as he had thought, but to his right.

"The tide was goin' out, and I was goin' with it," he said wryly. "I thought, well, that's it, then, I'm gone, for I knew I could never make my way back. I hadna eaten anything in two days, and hadn't much strength left."

He ceased swimming then, and simply spread himself on his back, giving himself to the embrace of the sea. Light-headed from hunger and effort, he had closed his eyes against the light and searched his mind for the words of the old Celtic prayer against drowning.

He paused for a moment then, and was quiet for so long that I wondered whether something was wrong. But at last he drew breath and said shyly, "I expect ye'll think I'm daft, Sassenach. I havena told anyone about it—not even Jenny. But—I heard my mother call me, then, right in the middle of praying." He shrugged, uncomfortable.

"It was maybe only that I'd been thinking of her when I left the shore," he said. "And yet—" He fell silent, until I touched his face.

"What did she say?" I asked quietly.

"She said, 'Come here to me, Jamie—come to me, laddie!' "

He drew a deep breath and let it out slowly. "I could hear her plain as day, but I couldna see anything; there was no one there, not even a silkie. I thought perhaps she was callin' me from Heaven—and I was so tired I really would not ha' minded dying then, but I rolled myself over and struck out toward where I'd heard her voice. I thought I would swim ten strokes and then stop again to rest—or to sink."

But on the eighth stroke, the current had taken him.

"It was just as though someone had picked me up," he said, sounding still surprised at the memory of it. "I could feel it under me and all around; the water was a bit warmer than it had been, and it carried me with it. I didna have to do anything but paddle a bit, to keep my head above water."

A strong, curling current, eddying between headland and islands, it had taken him to the edge of the third islet, where no more than a few strokes brought him within reach of its rocks.

It was a small lump of granite, fissured and creviced like all the ancient rocks of Scotland, and slimed with seaweed and seal droppings to boot, but he crawled on shore with all the thankfulness of a shipwrecked sailor for a land of palm trees and white-sand beaches. He fell down upon his face on the rocky shelf and lay there, grateful for breath, half-dozing with exhaustion.

"Then I felt something looming over me, and there was a terrible stink o' dead fish," he said. "I got up onto my knees at once, and there he was—a great bull seal, all sleek and wet, and his black eyes starin' at me, no more than a yard away."

Neither fisher nor seaman himself, Jamie had heard enough stories to know that bull seals were dangerous, particularly when threatened by intrusions upon their territory. Looking at the open mouth, with its fine display of sharp, peglike teeth, and the burly rolls of hard fat that girdled the enormous body, he was not disposed to doubt it.

"He weighed more than twenty stone, Sassenach," he said. "If he wasna inclined to rip the flesh off my bones, still he could ha' knocked me into the sea wi' one swipe, or dragged me under to drown."

"Obviously he didn't, though," I said dryly. "What happened?"

He laughed. "I think I was too mazed from tiredness to do

anything sensible," he said. "I just looked at him for a moment, and then I said, 'It's all right; it's only me.' "

"And what did the seal do?"

Jamie shrugged slightly. "He looked me over for a bit longer—silkies dinna blink much, did ye know that? It's verra unnerving to have one look at ye for long—then he gave a sort of a grunt and slid off the rock into the water."

Left in sole possession of the tiny islet, Jamie had sat blankly for a time, recovering his strength, and then at last began a methodical search of the crevices. Small as the area was, it took little time to find a deep split in the rock that led down to a wide hollow space, a foot below the rocky surface. Floored with dry sand and located in the center of the island, the hollow would be safe from flooding in all but the worst storms.

"Well, don't keep me in suspense," I said, poking him in the stomach. "Was the French gold there?"

"Well, it was and it wasn't, Sassenach," he answered, neatly sucking in his stomach. "I'd been expecting gold bullion; that's what the rumor said that Louis would send. And thirty thousand pounds' worth of gold bullion would make a good-sized hoard. But all there was in the hollow was a box, less than a foot long, and a small leather pouch. The box did have gold in it, though—and silver, too."

Gold and silver indeed. The wooden box had contained two hundred and five coins, gold ones and silver ones, some as sharply cut as though new-minted, some with their markings worn nearly to blankness.

"Ancient coins, Sassenach."

"Ancient? What, you mean very old—"

"Greek, Sassenach, and Roman. Verra old indeed."

We lay staring at each other in the dim light for a moment, not speaking.

"That's incredible," I said at last. "It's treasure, all right, but not—"

"Not what Louis would send, to help feed an army, no," he finished for me. "No, whoever put this treasure there, it wasna Louis or any of his ministers."

"What about the bag?" I said, suddenly remembering. "What was in the pouch you found?"

"Stones, Sassenach. Gemstones. Diamonds and pearls and

emeralds and sapphires. Not many, but nicely cut and big enough." He smiled, a little grimly. "Aye, big enough."

He had sat on a rock under the dim gray sky, turning the coins and the jewels over and over between his fingers, stunned into bewilderment. At last, roused by a sensation of being watched, he had looked up to find himself surrounded by a circle of curious seals. The tide was out, the females had come back from their fishing, and twenty pairs of round black eyes surveyed him cautiously.

The huge black male, emboldened by the presence of his harem, had come back too. He barked loudly, darting his head threateningly from side to side, and advanced on Jamie, sliding his three-hundred-pound bulk a few feet closer with each booming exclamation, propelling himself with his flippers across the slick rock.

"I thought I'd best leave, then," he said. "I'd found what I came to find, after all. So I put the box and the pouch back where I'd found them—I couldna carry them ashore, after all, and if I did —what then? So I put them back, and crawled down into the water, half-frozen wi' cold."

A few strokes from the island had taken him again into the current heading landward; it was a circular current, like most eddies, and the gyre had carried him to the foot of the headland within half an hour, where he crawled ashore, dressed, and fell asleep in a nest of marrow-grass.

He paused then, and I could see that while his eyes were open and fixed on me, it wasn't me they saw.

"I woke at dawn," he said softly. "I have seen a great many dawns, Sassenach, but never one like that one.

"I could feel the earth turn beneath me, and my own breath coming wi' the breathing of the wind. It was as though I had no skin nor bone, but only the light of the rising sun inside me."

His eyes softened, as he left the moor and came back to me.

"So then the sun came up higher," he said, matter-of-factly. "And when it warmed me enough to stand, I got up and went inland toward the road, to meet the English."

"But why did you go back?" I demanded. "You were free! You had money! And—"

"And where would I spend such money as that, Sassenach?" he asked. "Walk into a cottar's hearth and offer him a gold denarius, or a wee emerald?'' He smiled at my indignation and shook his head.

"Nay," he said gently, "I had to go back. Aye, I could ha' lived on the moor for a time—half-starved and naked, but I might have managed. But they were hunting me, Sassenach, and hunting hard, for thinking that I might know where the gold was hid. No cot near Ardsmuir would be safe from the English, so long as I was free, and might be thought to seek refuge there.

"I've seen the English hunting, ye ken," he added, a harder note creeping into his voice. "Ye'll have seen the panel in the entry hall?"

I had; one panel of the glowing oak that lined the hall below had been smashed in, perhaps by a heavy boot, and the crisscross scars of saber slashes marred the paneling from door to stairs.

"We keep it so to remember," he said. "To show to the weans, and tell them when they ask—this is what the English are."

The suppressed hate in his voice struck me low in the pit of the stomach. Knowing what I knew of what the English army had done in the Highlands, there was bloody little I could say in argument. I said nothing, and he continued after a moment.

"I wouldna expose the folk near Ardsmuir to that kind of attention, Sassenach." At the word "Sassenach," his hand squeezed mine and a small smile curved the corner of his mouth. Sassenach I might be to him, but not English.

"For that matter," he went on, "were I not taken, the hunt would likely come here again—to Lallybroch. If I would risk the folk near Ardsmuir, I would not risk my own. And even without that—" He stopped, seeming to struggle to find words.

"I had to go back," he said slowly. "For the sake of the men there, if for nothing else."

"The men in the prison?" I said, surprised. "Were some of the Lallybroch men arrested with you?"

He shook his head. The small vertical line that appeared between his brows when he thought hard was visible, even by starlight.

"No. There were men there from all over the Highlands—from every clan, almost. Only a few men from each clan—remnants and ragtag. But the more in need of a chief, for all that."

"And that's what you were to them?" I spoke gently, restraining the urge to smooth the line away with my fingers.

"For lack of any better," he said, with the flicker of a smile.

He had come from the bosom of family and tenants, from a strength that had sustained him for seven years, to find a lack of hope and a loneliness that would kill a man faster than the damp and the filth and the quaking ague of the prison.

And so, quite simply, he had taken the ragtag and remnants, the castoff survivors of the field of Culloden, and made them his own, that they and he might survive the stones of Ardsmuir as well. Reasoning, charming, and cajoling where he could, fighting where he must, he had forced them to band together, to face their captors as one, to put aside ancient clan rivalries and allegiances, and take him as their chieftain.

"They were mine," he said softly. "And the having of them kept me alive." But then they had been taken from him and from each other—wrenched apart and sent into indenture in a foreign land. And he had not been able to save them.

"You did your best for them. But it's over now," I said softly.

We lay in each other's arms in silence for a long time, letting the small noises of the house wash over us. Different from the comfortable commercial bustle of the brothel, the tiny creaks and sighing spoke of quiet, and home, and safety. For the first time, we were truly alone together, removed from danger and distraction.

There was time, now. Time to hear the rest of the story of the gold, to hear what he had done with it, to find out what had happened to the men of Ardsmuir, to speculate about the burning of the printshop, Young Ian's one-eyed seaman, the encounter with His Majesty's Customs on the shore by Arbroath, to decide what to do next. And since there was time, there was no need to speak of any of that, now.

The last peat broke and fell apart on the hearth, its glowing interior hissing red in the cold. I snuggled closer to Jamie, burying my face in the side of his neck. He tasted faintly of grass and sweat, with a whiff of brandy.

He shifted his body in response, bringing us together all down our naked lengths.

"What, again?" I murmured, amused. "Men your age aren't supposed to do it again so soon."

His teeth nibbled gently on my earlobe. "Well, you're doing it too, Sassenach," he pointed out. "And you're older than I am."

"That's different," I said, gasping a little as he moved suddenly over me, his shoulders blotting out the starlit window. "I'm a woman."

"And if ye weren't a woman, Sassenach," he assured me, settling to his work, "I wouldna be doing it either. Hush, now."

I woke just past dawn to the scratching of the rose brier against the window, and the muffled thump and clang of breakfast fixing in the kitchen below. Peering over Jamie's sleeping form, I saw that the fire was dead out. I slid out of bed, quietly so as not to wake him. The floorboards were icy under my feet and I reached, shivering, for the first available garment.

Swathed in the folds of Jamie's shirt, I knelt on the hearth and went about the laborious business of rekindling the fire, thinking rather wistfully that I might have included a box of safety matches in the short list of items I had thought worthwhile to bring. Striking sparks from a flint to catch kindling does work, but not usually on the first try. Or the second. Or . . .

Somewhere around the dozenth attempt, I was rewarded by a tiny black spot on the twist of tow I was using for kindling. It grew at once and blossomed into a tiny flame. I thrust it hastily but carefully beneath the little tent of twigs I had prepared, to shelter the blooming flame from the cold breeze.

I had left the window ajar the night before, to ensure not being suffocated by the smoke—peat fires burned hot, but dully, with a lot of smoke, as the blackened beams overhead attested. Just now, though, I thought we could dispense with fresh air—at least until I got the fire thoroughly under way.

The pane was rimed at the bottom with a light frost; winter was not far off. The air was so crisp and fresh that I paused before shutting the window, breathing in great gulps of dead leaf, dried apples, cold earth, and damp, sweet grass. The scene outside was perfect in its still clarity, stone walls and dark pines drawn sharp as black quillstrokes against the gray overcast of the morning.

A movement drew my eye to the top of the hill, where the rough track led to the village of Broch Mordha, ten miles distant. One by one, three small Highland ponies came up over the rise, and started down the hill toward the farmhouse.

They were too far away for me to make out the faces, but I could see by the billowing skirts that all three riders were women.

Perhaps it was the girls—Maggie, Kitty, and Janet—coming back from Young Jamie's house. My own Jamie would be glad to see them.

I pulled the shirt, redolent of Jamie, around me against the chill, deciding to take advantage of what privacy might remain to us this morning by thawing out in bed. I shut the window, and paused to lift several of the light peat bricks from the basket by the hearth and feed them carefully to my fledgling fire, before shedding the shirt and crawling under the covers, numb toes tingling with delight at the luxurious warmth.

Jamie felt the chill of my return, and rolled instinctively toward me, gathering me neatly in and curling round me spoon-fashion. He sleepily rubbed his face against my shoulder.

"Sleep well, Sassenach?" he muttered.

"Never better," I assured him, snuggling my cold bottom into the warm hollow of his thighs. "You?"

"Mmmmm." He responded with a blissful groan, wrapping his arms about me. "Dreamed like a fiend."

"What about?"

"Naked women, mostly," he said, and set his teeth gently in the flesh of my shoulder. "That, and food." His stomach rumbled softly. The scent of biscuits and fried bacon in the air was faint but unmistakable.

"So long as you don't confuse the two," I said, twitching my shoulder out of his reach.

"I can tell a hawk from a handsaw, when the wind sets north by nor'west," he assured me, "and a sweet, plump lassie from a salt-cured ham, too, appearances notwithstanding." He grabbed my buttocks with both hands and squeezed, making me yelp and kick him in the shins.

"Beast!"

"Oh, a beast, is it?" he said, laughing. "Well, then . . ." Growling deep in his throat, he dived under the quilt and proceeded to nip and nibble his way up the insides of my thighs, blithely ignoring my squeaks and the hail of kicks on his back and shoulders. Dislodged by our struggles, the quilt slid off onto the floor, revealing the tousled mass of his hair, flying wild over my thighs.

"Perhaps there's less difference than I thought," he said, his head popping up between my legs as he paused for breath. He pressed my thighs flat against the mattress and grinned up at me, spikes of red hair standing on end like a porcupine's quills. "Ye do taste a bit salty, come to try it. What do ye—"

He was interrupted by a sudden bang as the door flew open and rebounded from the wall. Startled, we turned to look. In the doorway stood a young girl I had never seen before. She was perhaps fifteen or sixteen, with long flaxen hair and big blue eyes. The eyes were somewhat bigger than normal, and filled with an expression of horrified shock as she stared at me. Her gaze moved slowly from my tangled hair to my bare breasts, and down the slopes of my naked body, until it encountered Jamie, lying prone between my thighs, white-faced with a shock equal to hers.

"Daddy!" she said, in tones of total outrage. "*Who* is that woman?"

34

Daddy

"**D**addy?" I said blankly. *"Daddy?"*

Jamie had turned to stone when the door opened. Now he shot bolt upright, snatching at the fallen quilt. He shoved the disheveled hair out of his face, and glared at the girl.

"What in the name of bloody hell are you doing here?" he demanded. Red-bearded, naked, and hoarse with fury, he was a formidable sight, and the girl took a step backward, looking uncertain. Then her chin firmed and she glared back at him.

"I came with Mother!"

The effect on Jamie could not have been greater had she shot him through the heart. He jerked violently, and all the color went out of his face.

It came flooding back, as the sound of rapid footsteps sounded on the wooden staircase. He leapt out of bed, tossing the quilt hastily in my direction, and grabbed his breeks.

He had barely pulled them on when another female figure burst into the room, skidded to a halt, and stood staring, bug-eyed, at the bed.

"It's true!" She whirled toward Jamie, fists clenched against the cloak she still wore. "It's true! It's the Sassenach witch! How could ye do such a thing to me, Jamie Fraser?"

"Be still, Laoghaire!" he snapped. "I've done nothing to ye!"

I sat up against the wall, clutching the quilt to my bosom and staring. It was only when he spoke her name that I recognized her. Twenty-odd years ago, Laoghaire MacKenzie had been a slender sixteen-year-old, with rose-petal skin, moonbeam hair, and a vio-

lent—and unrequited—passion for Jamie Fraser. Evidently, a few
things had changed.

She was nearing forty and no longer slender, having thickened
considerably. The skin was still fair, but weathered, and stretched
plumply over cheeks flushed with anger. Strands of ashy hair
straggled out from under her respectable white kertch. The pale
blue eyes were the same, though—they turned on me again, with
the same expression of hatred I had seen in them long ago.

"He's mine!" she hissed. She stamped her foot. "Get ye back
to the hell that ye came from, and leave him to me! Go, I say!"

As I made no move to obey, she glanced wildly about in search
of a weapon. Catching sight of the blue-banded ewer, she seized it
and drew back her arm to fling it at me. Jamie plucked it neatly
from her hand, set it back on the bureau, and grasped her by the
upper arm, hard enough to make her squeal.

He turned her and shoved her roughly toward the door. "Get
ye downstairs," he ordered. "I'll speak wi' ye presently,
Laoghaire."

"You'll speak wi' me? Speak wi' me, is it!" she cried. Face
contorted, she swung her free hand at him, raking his face from
eye to chin with her nails.

He grunted, grabbed her other wrist, and dragging her to the
door, pushed her out into the passage and slammed the door to and
turned the key.

By the time he turned around again, I was sitting on the edge of
the bed, fumbling with shaking hands as I tried to pull my stockings on.

"I can explain it to ye, Claire," he said.

"I d-don't think so," I said. My lips were numb, along with the
rest of me, and it was hard to form words. I kept my eyes fixed on
my feet as I tried—and failed—to tie my garters.

"Listen to me!" he said violently, bringing his fist down on the
table with a crash that made me jump. I jerked my head up, and
caught a glimpse of him towering over me. With his red hair
tumbled loose about his shoulders, his face unshaven, bare-
chested, and the raw marks of Laoghaire's nails down his cheek,
he looked like a Viking raider, bent on mayhem. I turned away to
look for my shift.

It was lost in the bedclothes; I scrabbled about among the
sheets. A considerable pounding had started up on the other side

of the door, accompanied by shouts and shrieks, as the commotion attracted the other inhabitants of the house.

"You'd best go and explain things to your daughter," I said, pulling the crumpled cotton over my head.

"She's not my daughter!"

"No?" My head popped out of the neck of the shift, and I lifted my chin to stare up at him. "And I suppose you aren't married to Laoghaire, either?"

"I'm married to you, damn it!" he bellowed, striking his fist on the table again.

"I don't think so." I felt very cold. My stiff fingers couldn't manage the lacing of the stays; I threw them aside, and stood up to look for my gown, which was somewhere on the other side of the room—behind Jamie.

"I need my dress."

"You're no going anywhere, Sassenach. Not until—"

"Don't call me that!" I shrieked it, surprising both of us. He stared at me for a moment, then nodded.

"All right," he said quietly. He glanced at the door, now reverberating under the force of the pounding. He drew a deep breath and straightened, squaring his shoulders.

"I'll go and settle things. Then we'll talk, the two of us. Stay here, Sass—Claire." He picked up his shirt and yanked it over his head. Unlocking the door, he stepped out into the suddenly silent corridor and closed it behind him.

I managed to pick up the dress, then collapsed on the bed and sat shaking all over, the green wool crumpled across my knees.

I couldn't think in a straight line. My mind spun in small circles around the central fact; he was married. Married to Laoghaire! And he had a family. And yet he had wept for Brianna.

"Oh, Bree!" I said aloud. "Oh, God, Bree!" and began to cry —partly from shock, partly at the thought of Brianna. It wasn't logical, but this discovery seemed a betrayal of her, as much as of me—or of Laoghaire.

The thought of Laoghaire turned shock and sorrow to rage in a moment. I rubbed a fold of green wool savagely across my face, leaving the skin red and prickly.

Damn him! How dare he? If he had married again, thinking me

dead, that was one thing. I had half-expected, half-feared it. But to marry that woman—that spiteful, sneaking little bitch who had tried to murder me at Castle Leoch . . . but he likely didn't know that, a small voice of reason in my head pointed out.

"Well, he *should* have known!" I said. "Damn him to hell, how could he take her, anyway?" The tears were rolling heedlessly down my face, hot spurts of loss and fury, and my nose was running. I groped for a handkerchief, found none, and in desperation, blew my nose at last on a corner of the sheet.

It smelled of Jamie. Worse, it smelled of the two of us, and the faint, musky lingerings of our pleasure. There was a small tingling spot on the inside of my thigh, where Jamie had nipped me, a few minutes before. I brought the flat of my hand down hard on the spot in a vicious slap, to kill the feeling.

"Liar!" I screamed. I grabbed the pitcher Laoghaire had tried to throw at me, and hurled it myself. It crashed against the door in an explosion of splinters.

I stood in the middle of the room, listening. It was quiet. There was no sound from below; no one was coming to see what had made the crash. I imagined they were all much too concerned with soothing Laoghaire to worry about me.

Did they live here, at Lallybroch? I recalled Jamie, taking Fergus aside, sending him ahead, ostensibly to tell Ian and Jenny we were coming. And, presumably, to warn them about me, and get Laoghaire out of the way before I arrived.

What in the name of God did Jenny and Ian think about this? Clearly they must know about Laoghaire—and yet they had received me last night, with no sign of it on their faces. But if Laoghaire had been sent away—why did she come back? Even trying to think about it made my temples throb.

The act of violence had drained enough rage for me to be able once more to control my shaking fingers. I kicked the stays into a corner and pulled the green gown over my head.

I had to get out of there. That was the only half-coherent thought in my head, and I clung to it. I had to leave. I couldn't stay, not with Laoghaire and her daughters in the house. They belonged there—I didn't.

I managed to tie up the garters this time, do up the laces of the dress, fasten the multiple hooks of the overskirt, and find my shoes. One was under the washstand, the other by the massive oak armoire, where I had kicked them the night before, dropping my clothes carelessly anywhere in my eagerness to crawl into the welcoming bed and nestle warmly in Jamie's arms.

I shivered. The fire had gone out again, and there was an icy draft from the window. I felt chilled to the bone, despite my clothes.

I wasted some time in searching for my cloak before realizing that it was downstairs; I had left it in the parlor the day before. I pushed my fingers through my hair, but was too upset to look for a comb. The strands crackled with electricity from having the woolen dress pulled over my head, and I slapped irritably at the floating hairs that stuck to my face.

Ready. Ready as I'd be, at least. I paused for one last look around, then heard footsteps coming up the stair.

Not fast and light, like the last ones. These were heavier, and slow, deliberate. I knew without seeing him that it was Jamie coming—and that he wasn't anxious to see me.

Fine. I didn't want to see him, either. Better just to leave at once, without speaking. What was there to say?

I backed away as the door opened, unaware that I was moving, until my legs hit the edge of the bed. I lost my balance and sat down. Jamie paused in the doorway, looking down at me.

He had shaved. That was the first thing I noticed. In echo of Young Ian the day before, he had hastily shaved, brushed his hair back and tidied himself before facing trouble. He seemed to know what I was thinking; the ghost of a smile passed over his face, as he rubbed his freshly scraped chin.

"D'ye think it will help?" he asked.

I swallowed, and licked dry lips, but didn't answer. He sighed, and answered himself.

"No, I suppose not." He stepped into the room and closed the door. He stood awkwardly for a moment, then moved toward the bed, one hand extended toward me. "Claire—"

"Don't touch me!" I leapt to my feet and backed away, circling toward the door. His hand fell to his side, but he stepped in front of me, blocking the way.

"Will ye no let me explain, Claire?"

"It seems to be a little late for that," I said, in what I meant to be a cold, disdainful tone. Unfortunately, my voice shook.

He pushed the door shut behind him.

"Ye never used to be unreasonable," he said quietly.

"And don't tell me what I used to be!" The tears were much too near the surface, and I bit my lip to hold them back.

"All right." His face was very pale; the scratches Laoghaire had given him showed as three red lines, livid down his cheek.

"I dinna live with her," he said. "She and the girls live at Balriggan, over near Broch Mordha." He watched me closely, but I said nothing. He shrugged a little, settling the shirt on his shoulders, and went on.

"It was a great mistake—the marriage between us."

"With two children? Took you a while to realize, didn't it?" I burst out.

His lips pressed tight together.

"The lassies aren't mine; Laoghaire was a widow wi' the two bairns when I wed her."

"Oh." It didn't make any real difference, but still, I felt a small wave of something like relief, on Brianna's behalf. She was the sole child of Jamie's heart, at least, even if I—

"I've not lived wi' them for some time; I live in Edinburgh, and send money to them, but—"

"You don't need to tell me," I interrupted. "It doesn't make any difference. Let me by, please—I'm going."

The thick, ruddy brows drew sharply together.

"Going where?"

"Back. Away. I don't know—let me by!"

"You aren't going anywhere," he said definitely.

"You can't stop me!"

He reached out and grabbed me by both arms.

"Aye, I can," he said. He could; I jerked furiously, but couldn't budge the iron grip on my biceps.

"Let go of me this minute!"

"No, I won't!" He glared at me, eyes narrowed, and I suddenly realized that calm as he might seem outwardly, he was very nearly as upset as I was. I saw the muscles of his throat move as he swallowed, controlling himself enough to speak again.

"I willna let ye go until I've explained to ye, why . . ."

"What is there to explain?" I demanded furiously. "You married again! What else is there?"

The color was rising in his face; the tips of his ears were already red, a sure sign of impending fury.

"And have you lived a nun for twenty years?" he demanded, shaking me slightly. "Have ye?"

"No!" I flung the word at his face, and he flinched slightly. "No, I bloody haven't! And I don't think you've been a monk, either—I never did!"

"Then—" he began, but I was much too furious to listen anymore.

"You lied to me, damn you!"

"I never did!" The skin was stretched tight over his cheekbones, as it was when he was very angry indeed.

"You did, you bastard! You know you did! Let go!" I kicked him sharply in the shin, hard enough to numb my toes. He exclaimed in pain, but didn't let go. Instead, he squeezed harder, making me yelp.

"I never said a thing to ye—"

"No, you didn't! But you lied, anyway! You let me think you weren't married, that there wasn't anyone, that you—that you—" I was half-sobbing with rage, gasping between words. "You should have told me, the minute I came! Why in hell didn't you tell me?" His grip on my arms slackened, and I managed to wrench myself free. He took a step toward me, eyes glittering with fury. I wasn't afraid of him; I drew back my fist and hit him in the chest.

"Why?" I shrieked, hitting him again and again and again, the sound of the blows thudding against his chest. "Why, why, *why*!"

"Because I was afraid!" He got hold of my wrists and threw me backward, so I fell across the bed. He stood over me, fists clenched, breathing hard.

"I am a coward, damn you! I couldna tell ye, for fear ye would leave me, and unmanly thing that I am, I thought I couldna bear that!"

"Unmanly? With two wives? Ha!"

I really thought he would slap me; he raised his arm, but then his open palm clenched into a fist.

"Am I a man? To want you so badly that nothing else matters? To see you, and know I would sacrifice honor or family or life itself to lie wi' you, even though ye'd left me?"

"You have the filthy, unmitigated, bleeding gall to say such a thing to me?" My voice was so high, it came out as a thin and vicious whisper. "You'll blame *me*?"

He stopped then, chest heaving as he caught his breath.

"No. No, I canna blame you." He turned aside, blindly. "How could it have been your fault? Ye wanted to stay wi' me, to die with me."

"I did, the more fool I," I said. "*You* sent me back, you made me go! And now you want to blame me for going?"

He turned back to me, eyes dark with desperation.

"I had to send ye away! I had to, for the bairn's sake!" His eyes went involuntarily to the hook where his coat hung, the pictures of Brianna in its pocket. He took one deep, quivering breath, and calmed himself with a visible effort.

"No," he said, much more quietly. "I canna regret that, whatever the cost. I would have given my life, for her and for you. If it took my heart and soul, too . . ."

He drew a long, quivering breath, mastering the passion that shook him.

"I canna blame ye for going."

"You blame me for coming back, though."

He shook his head as though to clear it.

"No, God no!"

He grabbed my hands tight between his own, the strength of his grip grinding the bones together.

"Do ye know what it is to live twenty years without a heart? To live half a man, and accustom yourself to living in the bit that's left, filling in the cracks wi' what mortar comes handy?"

"Do I know?" I echoed. I struggled to loose myself, to little effect. "Yes, you bloody bastard, I know that! What did you think, I'd gone straight back to Frank and lived happy ever after?" I kicked at him as hard as I could. He flinched, but didn't let go.

"Sometimes I hoped ye did," he said, speaking through clenched teeth. "And then sometimes I could see it—him with you, day and night, lyin' with ye, taking your body, holding my child! And God, I could kill ye for it!"

Suddenly, he dropped my hands, whirled, and smashed his fist through the side of the oak armoire. It was an impressive blow; the armoire was a sturdy piece of furniture. It must have bruised his knuckles considerably, but without hesitation, he drove the other fist into the oak boards as well, as though the shining wood were Frank's face—or mine.

"Feel like that about it, do you?" I said coldly, as he stepped back, panting. "I don't even have to imagine you with Laoghaire —I've bloody *seen* her!"

"I dinna care a fig for Laoghaire, and never have!"

"Bastard!" I said again. "You'd marry a woman without wanting her, and then throw her aside the minute—"

"Shut up!" he roared. "Hold your tongue, ye wicked wee bitch!" He slammed a fist down on the washstand, glaring at me. "I'm damned the one way or the other, no? If I felt anything for her, I'm a faithless womanizer, and if I didn't, I'm a heartless beast."

"You should have told me!"

"And if I had?" He grabbed my hand and jerked me to my feet, holding me eye to eye with him. "You'd have turned on your heel and gone without a word. And having seen ye again—I tell ye, I would ha' done far worse than lie to keep you!"

He pressed me tight against his body and kissed me, long and hard. My knees turned to water, and I fought to keep my feet, buttressed by the vision of Laoghaire's angry eyes, and her voice, echoing shrill in my ears. *He's mine!*

"This is senseless," I said, pulling away. Fury had its own intoxication, but the hangover was setting in fast, a black dizzy vortex. My head swam so that I could hardly keep my balance. "I can't think straight. I'm leaving."

I lurched toward the door, but he caught me by the waist, yanking me back.

He whirled me toward himself and kissed me again, hard enough to leave a quicksilver taste of blood in my mouth. It was neither affection nor desire, but a blind passion, a determination to possess me. He was through talking.

So was I. I pulled my mouth away and slapped him hard across the face, fingers curved to rake his flesh.

He jerked back, cheek scraped raw, then twisted his fingers tight in my hair, bent and took my mouth again, deliberate and savage, ignoring the kicks and blows I rained on him.

He bit my lower lip, hard, and when I opened my lips, gasping, thrust his tongue into my mouth, stealing breath and words together.

He threw me bodily onto the bed where we had lain laughing an hour before, and pinned me there at once with the weight of his body.

He was most mightily roused.

So was I.

Mine, he said, without uttering a word. *Mine!*

I fought him with boundless fury and no little skill, and *Yours,* my body echoed back. *Yours, and may you be damned for it!*

I didn't feel him rip my gown, but I felt the heat of his body on my bare breasts, through the thin linen of his shirt, the long, hard muscle of his thigh straining against my own. He took his hand off my arm to tear at his breeches, and I clawed him from ear to breast, striping his skin with pale red.

We were doing our level best to kill each other, fueled by the rage of years apart—mine for his sending me away, his for my going, mine for Laoghaire, his for Frank.

"Bitch!" he panted. "Whore!"

"Damn you!" I got a hand in his own long hair, and yanked, pulling his face down to me again. We rolled off the bed and landed on the floor in a tangled heap, rolling to and fro in a welter of half-uttered curses and broken words.

I didn't hear the door open. I didn't hear anything, though she must have called out, more than once. Blind and deaf, I knew nothing but Jamie until the shower of cold water struck us, sudden as an electric shock. Jamie froze. All the color left his face, leaving the bones jutting stark beneath the skin.

I lay dazed, drops of water dripping from the ends of his hair onto my breasts. Just behind him, I could see Jenny, her face as white as his, holding an empty pan in her hands.

"Stop it!" she said. Her eyes were slanted with a horrified anger. "How could ye, Jamie? Rutting like a wild beast, and not carin' if all the house hears ye!"

He moved off me, slowly, clumsy as a bear. Jenny snatched a quilt from the bed and flung it over my body.

On all fours, he shook his head like a dog, sending droplets of water flying. Then, very slowly, he got to his feet, and pulled his ripped breeches back into place.

"Are ye no ashamed?" she cried, scandalized.

Jamie stood looking down at her as though he had never seen

any creature quite like her, and was making up his mind what she might be. The wet ends of his hair dripped over his bare chest.

"Yes," he said at last, quite mildly. "I am."

He seemed dazed. He closed his eyes and a brief, deep shudder went over him. Without a word, he turned and went out.

35

Flight from Eden

Jenny helped me to the bed, making small clucking noises; whether of shock or concern, I couldn't tell. I was vaguely conscious of hovering figures in the doorway—servants, I supposed—but wasn't disposed to pay much attention.

"I'll find ye something to put on," she murmured, fluffing a pillow and pushing me back onto it. "And perhaps a bit of a drink. You're all right?"

"Where's Jamie?"

She glanced at me quickly, sympathy mixed with a gleam of curiosity.

"Dinna be afraid; I'll no let him at ye again." She spoke firmly, then pressed her lips tight together, frowning as she tucked the quilt around me. "How he could do such a thing!"

"It wasn't his fault—not this." I ran a hand through my tangled hair, indicating my general dishevelment. "I mean—I did it, as much as he did. It was both of us. He—I—" I let my hand fall, helpless to explain. I was bruised and shaken, and my lips were swollen.

"I see," was all Jenny said, but she gave me a long, assessing look, and I thought it quite possible that she did see.

I didn't want to talk about the recent happenings, and she seemed to sense this, for she kept quiet for a bit, giving a soft-voiced order to someone in the hall, then moving about the room, straightening furniture and tidying things. I saw her pause for a moment as she saw the holes in the armoire, then she stooped to pick up the larger pieces of the shattered ewer.

As she dumped them into the basin, there was a faint thud from the house below; the slam of the big main door. She stepped to the window and pushed the curtain aside.

"It's Jamie," she said. She glanced at me, and let the curtain fall. "He'll be going up to the hill; he goes there, if he's troubled. That, or he gets drunk wi' Ian. The hill's better."

I gave a small snort.

"Yes, I expect he's troubled, all right."

There was a light step in the hallway, and the younger Janet appeared, carefully balancing a tray of biscuits, whisky, and water. She looked pale and scared.

"Are ye . . . well, Aunt?" she asked tentatively, setting down the tray.

"I'm fine," I assured her, pushing myself upright and reaching for the whisky decanter.

A sharp glance having assured Jenny of the same, she patted her daughter's arm and turned toward the door.

"Stay wi' your auntie," she ordered. "I'll go and find a dress." Janet nodded obediently, and sat down by the bed on a stool, watching me as I ate and drank.

I began to feel physically much stronger with a little food inside me. Internally, I felt quite numb; the recent events seemed at once dreamlike and yet completely clear in my mind. I could recall the smallest details; the blue calico bows on the dress of Laoghaire's daughter, the tiny broken veins in Laoghaire's cheeks, a rough-torn fingernail on Jamie's fourth finger.

"Do you know where Laoghaire is?" I asked Janet. The girl had her head down, apparently studying her own hands. At my question, she jerked upright, blinking.

"Oh!" she said. "Oh. Aye, she and Marsali and Joan went back to Balriggan, where they live. Uncle Jamie made them go."

"Did he," I said flatly.

Janet bit her lip, twisting her hands in her apron. Suddenly she looked up at me.

"Aunt—I'm so awfully sorry!" Her eyes were a warm brown, like her father's, but swimming now with tears.

"It's all right," I said, having no idea what she meant, but trying to be soothing.

"But it was me!" she burst out. She looked thoroughly miserable, but determined to confess. "I—I told Laoghaire ye were here. That's why she came."

"Oh." Well, that explained that, I supposed. I finished the whisky and set the glass carefully back on the tray.

"I didna think—I mean, I didna have it in mind to cause a kebbie-lebbie, truly not. I didna ken that you—that she—"

"It's all right," I said again. "One of us would have found out sooner or later." It made no difference, but I glanced at her with some curiosity. "Why did you tell her, though?"

The girl glanced cautiously over her shoulder, hearing steps start up from below. She leaned close to me.

"Mother told me to," she whispered. And with that, she rose and hastily left the room, brushing past her mother in the doorway.

I didn't ask. Jenny had found a dress for me—one of the elder girls'—and there was no conversation beyond the necessary as she helped me into it.

When I was dressed and shod, my hair combed and put up, I turned to her.

"I want to go," I said. "Now."

She didn't argue, but only looked me over, to see that I was strong enough. She nodded then, dark lashes covering the slanted blue eyes so like her brother's.

"I think that's best," she said quietly.

It was late morning when I left Lallybroch for what I knew would be the last time. I had a dagger at my waist, for protection, though it was unlikely I would need it. My horse's saddlebags held food and several bottles of ale; enough to see me back to the stone circle. I had thought of taking back the pictures of Brianna from Jamie's coat, but after a moment's hesitation, had left them. She belonged to him forever, even if I didn't.

It was a cold autumn day, the morning's gray promise fulfilled with a mourning drizzle. No one was in sight near the house, as Jenny led the horse out of the stable, and held the bridle for me to mount.

I pulled the hood of my cloak farther forward, and nodded to her. Last time, we had parted with tears and embraces, as sisters. She let go the reins, and stood back, as I turned the horse's head toward the road.

"Godspeed!" I heard her call behind me. I didn't answer, nor did I look back.

I rode most of the day, without really noticing where I was going; taking heed only for the general direction, and letting the gelding pick his own way through the mountain passes.

I stopped when the light began to go; hobbled the horse to graze, lay down wrapped in my cloak, and dropped straight asleep, unwilling to stay awake for fear I might think, and remember. Numbness was my only refuge. I knew it would go, but I clung to its gray comfort so long as I might.

It was hunger that brought me unwillingly back to life the next day. I had not paused to eat through all the day before, nor when rising in the morning, but by noon my stomach had begun to register loud protests, and I stopped in a small glen beside a sparkling burn, and unwrapped the food that Jenny had slipped into my saddlebag.

There were oatcakes and ale, and several small loaves of fresh-baked bread, slit down the middle, stuffed with sheepmilk cheese and homemade pickle. Highland sandwiches, the hearty fare of shepherds and warriors, as characteristic of Lallybroch as peanut butter had been of Boston. Very suitable, that my quest should end with one of these.

I ate a sandwich, drank one of the stone bottles of ale, and swung back into the saddle, turning the horse's head to the northeast once more. Unfortunately, while the food had brought fresh strength to my body, it had given fresh life to my feelings as well. As we climbed higher and higher into the clouds, my spirits fell lower—and they hadn't been high to begin with.

The horse was willing enough, but I wasn't. Near midafternoon, I felt that I simply couldn't go on. Leading the horse far enough into a small thicket that it wouldn't be noticeable from the road, I hobbled it loosely, and walked farther under the trees myself, 'til I came to the trunk of a fallen aspen, smooth-skinned, stained green with moss.

I sat slumped over, elbows on my knees and head on my hands. I ached in every joint. Not really from the encounter of the day before, or from the rigors of riding; from grief.

Constraint and judgment had been a great deal of my life. I had learned at some pains the art of healing; to give and to care, but always stopping short of that danger point where too much was given to make me effective. I had learned detachment and disengagement, to my cost.

With Frank, too, I had learned the balancing act of civility; kindness and respect that did not pass those unseen boundaries into passion. And Brianna? Love for a child cannot be free; from the first signs of movement in the womb, a devotion springs up as powerful as it is mindless, irresistible as the process of birth itself. But powerful as it is, it is a love always of control; one is in charge, the protector, the watcher, the guardian—there is great passion in it, to be sure, but never abandon.

Always, always, I had had to balance compassion with wisdom, love with judgment, humanity with ruthlessness.

Only with Jamie had I given everything I had, risked it all. I had thrown away caution and judgment and wisdom, along with the comforts and constraints of a hard-won career. I had brought him nothing but myself, been nothing but myself with him, given him soul as well as body, let him see me naked, trusted him to see me whole and cherish my frailties—because he once had.

I had feared he couldn't, again. Or wouldn't. And then had known those few days of perfect joy, thinking that what had once been true was true once more; I was free to love him, with everything I had and was, and be loved with an honesty that matched my own.

The tears slid hot and wet between my fingers. I mourned for Jamie, and for what I had been, with him.

Do you know, his voice said, whispering, *what it means, to say again "I love you," and to mean it?*

I knew. And with my head in my hands beneath the pine trees, I knew I would never mean it again.

Sunk as I was in miserable contemplation, I didn't hear the footsteps until he was nearly upon me. Startled by the crack of a branch nearby, I rocketed off the fallen tree like a rising pheasant and whirled to face the attacker, heart in my mouth and dagger in hand.

"Christ!" My stalker shied back from the open blade, clearly as startled as I was.

"What the hell are you doing here?" I demanded. I pressed my free hand to my chest. My heart was pounding like a kettledrum and I was sure I was as white as he was.

"Jesus, Auntie Claire! Where'd ye learn to pull a knife like that? Ye scairt hell out of me." Young Ian passed a hand over his brow, Adam's apple bobbing as he swallowed.

"The feeling is mutual," I assured him. I tried to sheathe the dagger, but my hand was shaking too much with reaction to manage it. Knees wobbling, I sank back on the aspen trunk and laid the knife on my thigh.

"I repeat," I said, trying to gain mastery of myself, "what are you doing here?" I had a bloody good idea what he was doing there, and I wasn't having any. On the other hand, I needed a moment's recovery from the fright before I could reliably stand up.

Young Ian bit his lip, glanced around, and at my nod of permission, sat down awkwardly on the trunk beside me.

"Uncle Jamie sent me—" he began. I didn't pause to hear more, but got up at once, knees or no knees, thrusting the dagger into my belt as I turned away.

"Wait, Aunt! Please!" He grabbed at my arm, but I jerked loose, pulling away from him.

"I'm not interested," I said, kicking the fronds of bracken aside. "Go home, wee Ian. I've places to go." I hoped I had, at least.

"But it isn't what you think!" Unable to stop me leaving the clearing, he was following me, arguing as he ducked low branches. "He needs you, Aunt, really he does! Ye must come back wi' me!"

I didn't answer him; I had reached my horse, and bent to undo the hobbles.

"Auntie Claire! Will ye no listen to me?" He loomed up on the far side of the horse, gawky height peering at me over the saddle. He looked very much like his father, his good-natured, half-homely face creased with anxiety.

"No," I said briefly. I stuffed the hobbles into the saddlebag, and put my foot into the stirrup, swinging up with a satisfyingly majestic swish of skirts and petticoats. My dignified departure was hampered at this point by the fact that Young Ian had the horse's reins in a death grip.

"Let go," I said peremptorily.

"Not until ye hear me out," he said. He glared up at me, jaw clenched with stubbornness, soft brown eyes ablaze. I glared back at him. Gangling as he was, he had Ian's skinny muscularity; unless I was prepared to ride him down, there seemed little choice but to listen to him.

All right, I decided. Fat lot of good it would do, to him or his double-dealing uncle, but I'd listen.

"Talk," I said, mustering what patience I could.

He drew a deep breath, eyeing me warily to see whether I meant it. Deciding that I did, he blew his breath out, making the soft brown hair over his brow flutter, and squared his shoulders to begin.

"Well," he started, seeming suddenly unsure. "It . . . I . . . he . . ."

I made a low sound of exasperation in my throat. "Start at the beginning," I said. "But don't make a song and dance of it, hm?"

He nodded, teeth set in his upper lip as he concentrated.

"Well, there was the hell of a stramash broke out at the house, after ye left, when Uncle Jamie came back," he began.

"I'll just bet there was," I said. Despite myself, I was conscious of a small stirring of curiosity, but fought it down, assuming an expression of complete indifference.

"I've never seen Uncle Jamie sae furious," he said, watching my face carefully. "Nor Mother, either. They went at it hammer and tongs, the two o' them. Father tried to quiet them, but it was like they didna even hear him. Uncle Jamie called Mother a meddling besom, and a *lang-nebbit* . . . and . . . and a lot of worse names," he added, flushing.

"He shouldn't have been angry with Jenny," I said. "She was only trying to help—I think." I felt sick with the knowledge that I had caused this rift, too. Jenny had been Jamie's mainstay since the death of their mother when both were children. Was there no end to the damage I had caused by coming back?

To my surprise, Jenny's son smiled briefly. "Well, it wasna all one-sided," he said dryly. "My mother's no the person to be taking abuse lying down, ye ken. Uncle Jamie had a few tooth-marks on him before the end of it." He swallowed, remembering.

"In fact, I thought they'd damage each other, surely; Mother went for Uncle Jamie wi' an iron girdle, and he snatched it from her and threw it through the kitchen window. Scairt the chickens out o' the yard," he added, with a feeble grin.

"Less about chickens, Young Ian," I said, looking down at him coldly. "Get on with it; I want to leave."

"Well, then Uncle Jamie knocked over the bookshelf in the parlor—I dinna think he did it on purpose," the lad added hastily, "he was just too fashed to see straight—and went out the door. Father stuck his head out the window and shouted at him where was he going, and he said he was going to find you."

"Then why are you here, and not him?" I was leaning forward slightly, watching his hand on the reins; if his fingers showed signs of relaxation, perhaps I could twitch the rein out of his grasp.

Young Ian sighed. "Well, just as Uncle Jamie was setting out on his horse, Aunt . . . er . . . I mean his wi—" He blushed miserably. "Laoghaire. She . . . she came down the hill and into the dooryard."

At this point, I gave up pretending indifference.

"And what happened then?"

He frowned. "There was an awful collieshangie, but I couldna hear much. Auntie . . . I mean Laoghaire—she doesna seem to know how to fight properly, like my mam and Uncle Jamie. She just weeps and wails a lot. Mam says she snivels," he added.

"Mmphm," I said. "And so?"

Laoghaire had slid off her own mount, clutched Jamie by the leg, and more or less dragged him off as well, according to Young Ian. She had then subsided into a puddle in the dooryard, clutching Jamie about the knees, weeping and wailing as was her usual habit.

Unable to escape, Jamie had at last hauled Laoghaire to her feet, flung her bodily over his shoulder, and carried her into the house and up the stairs, ignoring the fascinated gazes of his family and servants.

"Right," I said. I realized that I had been clenching my jaw, and consciously unclenched it. "So he sent you after me because he was too occupied with his *wife*. Bastard! The gall of him! He thinks he can just send someone to fetch me back, like a hired girl, because it doesn't suit his convenience to come himself? He thinks he can have his cake and eat it, does he? Bloody arrogant, selfish, overbearing . . . Scot!" Distracted as I was by the pic-

ture of Jamie carrying Laoghaire upstairs, "Scot" was the worst
epithet I could come up with on short notice.

My knuckles were white where my hand clutched the edge of
the saddle. Not caring about subtlety anymore, I leaned down,
snatching for the reins.

"Let go!"

"But Auntie Claire, it's not that!"

"What's not that?" Caught by his tone of desperation, I
glanced up. His long, narrow face was tight with the anguished
need to make me understand.

"Uncle Jamie didna stay to tend Laoghaire!"

"Then why did he send you?"

He took a deep breath, renewing his grip on my reins.

"She shot him. He sent me to find ye, because he's dying."

"If you're lying to me, Ian Murray," I said, for the dozenth
time, "you'll regret it to the end of your life—which will be
short!"

I had to raise my voice to be heard. The rising wind came
whooshing past me, lifting my hair in streamers off my shoulders,
whipping my skirts tight around my legs. The weather was suitably
dramatic; great black clouds choked the mountain passes, boiling
over the crags like seafoam, with a faint distant rumble of thunder,
like far-off surf on packed sand.

Lacking breath, Young Ian merely shook his bowed head as he
leaned into the wind. He was afoot, leading both ponies across a
treacherously boggy stretch of ground near the edge of a tiny loch.
I glanced instinctively at my wrist, missing my Rolex.

It was difficult to tell where the sun was, with the in-rolling
storm filling half the western sky, but the upper edge of the dark-
tinged clouds glowed a brilliant white that was almost gold. I had
lost the knack of telling time by sun and sky, but thought it was no
more than midafternoon.

Lallybroch lay several hours ahead; I doubted we would reach it
by dark. Meaching my way reluctantly toward Craigh na Dun, I
had taken nearly two days to reach the small wood where Young
Ian had caught up with me. He had, he said, spent only one day in
the pursuit; he had known roughly where I was headed, and he
himself had shod the pony I rode; my tracks had been plain to him,

where they showed in the mud-patches among the heather on the open moor.

Two days since I had left, and one—or more—on the journey back. Three days, then, since Jamie had been shot.

I could get few useful details from Young Ian; having succeeded in his mission, he wanted only to return to Lallybroch as fast as possible, and saw no point in further conversation. Jamie's gunshot wound was in the left arm, he said. That was good, so far as it went. The ball had penetrated into Jamie's side, as well. That wasn't good. Jamie was conscious when last seen—that was good —but was starting a fever. Not good at all. As to the possible effects of shock, the type or severity of the fever, or what treatment had so far been administered, Young Ian merely shrugged.

So perhaps Jamie was dying; perhaps he wasn't. It wasn't a chance I could take, as Jamie himself would know perfectly well. I wondered momentarily whether he might conceivably have shot himself, as a means of forcing me to return. Our last interview could have left him in little doubt as to my response had he come after me, or used force to make me return.

It was beginning to rain, in soft spatters that caught in my hair and lashes, blurring my sight like tears. Past the boggy spot, Young Ian had mounted again, leading the way upward to the final pass that led to Lallybroch.

Jamie was devious enough to have thought of such a plan, all right, and certainly courageous enough to have carried it out. On the other hand, I had never known him to be reckless. He had taken plenty of bold risks—marrying me being one of them, I thought ruefully—but never without an estimation of the cost, and a willingness to pay it. Would he have thought drawing me back to Lallybroch worth the chance of actually dying? That hardly seemed logical, and Jamie Fraser was a very logical man.

I pulled the hood of my cloak further over my head, to keep the increasing downpour out of my face. Young Ian's shoulders and thighs were dark with wet, and the rain dripped from the brim of his slouch hat, but he sat straight in the saddle, ignoring the weather with the stoic nonchalance of a trueborn Scot.

Very well. Given that Jamie likely hadn't shot himself, was he shot at all? He might have made up the story, and sent his nephew to tell it. On consideration, though, I thought it highly unlikely that

Young Ian could have delivered the news so convincingly, were it false.

I shrugged, the movement sending a cold rivulet down inside the front of my cloak, and set myself to wait with what patience I could for the journey to be ended. Years in the practice of medicine had taught me not to anticipate; the reality of each case was bound to be unique, and so must be my response to it. My emotions, however, were much harder to control than my professional reactions.

Each time I had left Lallybroch, I had thought I would never return. Now here I was, going back once more. Twice now, I had left Jamie, knowing with certainty that I would never see him again. And yet here I was, going back to him like a bloody homing pigeon to its loft.

"I'll tell you one thing, Jamie Fraser," I muttered under my breath. "If you aren't at death's door when I get there, you'll live to regret it!"

36

Practical and Applied Witchcraft

It was several hours past dark when we arrived at last, soaked to the skin. The house was silent, and dark, save for two dimly lighted windows downstairs in the parlor. There was a single warning bark from one of the dogs, but Young Ian shushed the animal, and after a quick, curious nosing at my stirrup, the black-and-white shape faded back into the darkness of the dooryard.

The warning had been enough to alert someone; as Young Ian led me into the hall, the door to the parlor opened. Jenny poked her head out, her face drawn with worry.

At the sight of Young Ian, she popped out into the hallway, her expression transformed to one of joyous relief, at once superseded by the righteous anger of a mother confronted by an errant offspring.

"Ian, ye wee wretch!" she said. "Where have ye been all this time? Your da and I ha' been worrit sick for ye!" She paused long enough to look him over anxiously. "You're all right?"

At his nod, her lips grew tight again. "Aye, well. You're for it now, laddie, I'll tell ye! And just where the devil *have* ye been, anyway?"

Gangling, knob-jointed, and dripping wet, Young Ian looked like nothing so much as a drowned scarecrow, but he was still large enough to block me from his mother's view. He didn't answer Jenny's scolding, but shrugged awkwardly and stepped aside, exposing me to his mother's startled gaze.

If my resurrection from the dead had disconcerted her, this second reappearance stunned her. Her deep blue eyes, normally as slanted as her brother's, opened so wide, they looked round. She stared at me for a long moment, without saying anything, then her gaze swiveled once more to her son.

"A cuckoo," she said, almost conversationally. "That's what ye are, laddie—a great cuckoo in the nest. God knows whose son ye were meant to be; it wasna mine."

Young Ian flushed hotly, dropping his eyes as the red burned in his cheeks. He pushed the feathery damp hair out of his eyes with the back of one hand.

"I—well, I just . . ." he began, eyes on his boots, "I couldna just . . ."

"Oh, never mind about it now!" his mother snapped. "Get ye upstairs to your bed; your da will deal wi' ye in the morning."

Ian glanced helplessly at the parlor door, then at me. He shrugged once more, looked at the sodden hat in his hands as though wondering how it had got there, and shuffled slowly down the hall.

Jenny stood quite still, eyes fixed on me, until the padded door at the end of the hallway closed with a soft thump behind Young Ian. Her face showed lines of strain, and the shadows of sleeplessness smudged her eyes. Still fine-boned and erect, for once she looked her age, and more.

"So you're back," she said flatly.

Seeing no point in answering the obvious, I nodded briefly. The house was quiet around us, and full of shadows, the hallway lighted only by a three-pronged candlestick set on the table.

"Never mind about it now," I said, softly, so as not to disturb the house's slumber. There was, after all, only one thing of importance at the moment. "Where's Jamie?"

After a small hesitation, she nodded as well, accepting my presence for the moment. "In there," she said, waving toward the parlor door.

I started toward the door, then paused. There was the one thing more. "Where's Laoghaire?" I asked.

"Gone," she said. Her eyes were flat and dark in the candlelight, unreadable.

I nodded in response, and stepped through the door, closing it gently but firmly behind me.

Too long to be laid on the sofa, Jamie lay on a camp bed set up before the fire. Asleep or unconscious, his profile rose dark and sharp-edged against the light of the glowing coals, unmoving.

Whatever he was, he wasn't dead—at least not yet. My eyes growing accustomed to the dim light of the fire, I could see the slow rise and fall of his chest beneath nightshirt and quilt. A flask of water and a brandy bottle sat on the small table by the bed. The padded chair by the fire had a shawl thrown over its back; Jenny had been sitting there, watching over her brother.

There seemed no need now for haste. I untied the strings at the neck of my cloak, and spread the soggy garment over the chairback, taking the shawl in substitute. My hands were cold; I put them under my arms, hugging myself, to bring them to something like a normal temperature before I touched him.

When I did venture to place a thawed hand on his forehead, I nearly jerked it back. He was hot as a just-fired pistol, and he twitched and moaned at my touch. Fever, indeed. I stood looking down at him for a moment, then carefully moved to the side of the bed and sat down in Jenny's chair. I didn't think he would sleep long, with a temperature like that, and it seemed a shame to wake him needlessly soon, merely to examine him.

The cloak behind me dripped water on the floor, a slow, arrhythmic patting. It reminded me unpleasantly of an old Highland superstition—the "death-drop." Just before a death occurs, the story goes, the sound of water dripping is heard in the house, by those sensitive to such things.

I wasn't, thank heaven, subject to noticing supernatural phenomena of that sort. No, I thought wryly, it takes something like a crack through time to get *your* attention. The thought made me smile, if only briefly, and dispelled the frisson I had felt at the thought of the death-drop.

As the rain chill left me, though, I still felt uneasy, and for obvious reasons. It wasn't that long ago that I had stood by another makeshift bed, deep in the night-watches, and contemplated death, and the waste of a marriage. The thoughts I had begun in the wood hadn't stopped on the hasty journey back to Lallybroch, and they continued now, without my conscious volition.

Honor had led Frank to his decision—to keep me as his wife, and raise Brianna as his own. Honor, and an unwillingness to decline a responsibility he felt was his. Well, here before me lay another honorable man.

Laoghaire and her daughters, Jenny and her family, the Scots prisoners, the smugglers, Mr. Willoughby and Geordie, Fergus and the tenants—how many other responsibilities had Jamie shouldered, through our years apart?

Frank's death had absolved me of one of my own obligations; Brianna herself of another. The Hospital Board, in their eternal wisdom, had severed the single great remaining tie that bound me to that life. I had had time, with Joe Abernathy's help, to relieve myself of the smaller responsibilities, to depute and delegate, divest and resolve.

Jamie had had neither warning nor choice about my reappearance in his life; no time to make decisions or resolve conflicts. And he was not one to abandon his responsibilities, even for the sake of love.

Yes, he'd lied to me. Hadn't trusted me to recognize his responsibilities, to stand by him—or to leave him—as his circumstances demanded. He'd been afraid. So had I; afraid that he wouldn't choose me, confronted with the struggle between a twenty-year-old love and a present-day family. So I'd run away.

"Who you jiving, L.J.?" I heard Joe Abernathy's voice say, derisive and affectionate. I had fled toward Craigh na Dun with all the speed and decision of a condemned felon approaching the steps of the gallows. Nothing had slowed my journey but the hope that Jamie would come after me.

True, the pangs of conscience and wounded pride had spurred me on, but the one moment when Young Ian had said, "He's dying," had shown those up for the flimsy things they were.

My marriage to Jamie had been for me like the turning of a great key, each small turn setting in play the intricate fall of tumblers within me. Bree had been able to turn that key as well, edging closer to the unlocking of the door of myself. But the final turn of the lock was frozen—until I had walked into the printshop in Edinburgh, and the mechanism had sprung free with a final, decisive click. The door now was ajar, the light of an unknown future shining through its crack. But it would take more strength than I had alone to push it open.

I watched the rise and fall of his breath, and the play of light and shadow on the strong, clean lines of his face, and knew that nothing truly mattered between us but the fact that we both still lived.

So here I was. Again. And whatever the cost of it might be to him or me, here I stayed.

I didn't realize that his eyes had opened until he spoke.

"Ye came back, then," he said softly. "I knew ye would."

I opened my mouth to reply, but he was still talking, eyes fixed on my face, pupils dilated to pools of darkness.

"My love," he said, almost whispering. "God, ye do look so lovely, wi' your great eyes all gold, and your hair so soft round your face." He brushed his tongue across dry lips. "I knew ye must forgive me, Sassenach, once ye knew."

Once I knew? My brows shot up, but I didn't speak; he had more to say.

"I was so afraid to lose ye again, *mo chridhe*," he murmured. "So afraid. I havena loved anyone but you, my Sassenach, never since the day I saw ye—but I couldna . . . I couldna bear . . ." His voice drifted off in an unintelligible mumble, and his eyes closed again, lashes lying dark against the high curve of his cheek.

I sat still, wondering what I should do. As I watched, his eyes opened suddenly once again. Heavy and drowsy with fever, they sought my face.

"It willna be long, Sassenach," he said, as though reassuring me. One corner of his mouth twitched in an attempt at a smile. "Not long. Then I shall touch ye once more. I do long to touch you."

"Oh, Jamie," I said. Moved by tenderness, I reached out and laid my hand along his burning cheek.

His eyes snapped wide with shock, and he jerked bolt upright in bed, letting out a bloodcurdling yell of anguish as the movement jarred his wounded arm.

"Oh God, oh Christ, oh Jesus Lord God Almighty!" he said, bent half-breathless and clutching at his left arm. "You're real! Bloody stinking filthy pig-swiving hell! Oh, Christ!"

"Are you all right?" I said, rather inanely. I could hear startled exclamations from the floor above, muffled by the thick planks, and the thump of feet as one after another of Lallybroch's inhabitants leapt from their beds to investigate the uproar.

Jenny's head, eyes even wider than before, poked through the parlor door. Jamie saw her, and somehow found sufficient breath to roar "Get *out*!" before doubling up again with an agonized groan.

"Je-sus," he said between clenched teeth. "What in God's holy name are ye doing here, Sassenach?"

"What do you mean, what am I doing here?" I said. "You sent for me. And what do you mean, I'm real?"

He unclenched his jaw and tentatively loosened his grip on his left arm. The resultant sensation proving unsatisfactory, he promptly grabbed it again and said several things in French involving the reproductive organs of assorted saints and animals.

"For God's sake, lie down!" I said. I took him by the shoulders and eased him back onto the pillows, noting with some alarm how close his bones were to the surface of his heated skin.

"I thought ye were a fever dream, 'til you touched me," he said, gasping. "What the hell d'ye mean, popping up by my bed and scarin' me to death?" He grimaced in pain. "Christ, it feels like my damn arm's come off at the shoulder. Och, bugger it!" he exclaimed, as I firmly detached the fingers of his right hand from his left arm.

"Didn't you send Young Ian to tell me you were dying?" I said, deftly rolling back the sleeve of his nightshirt. The arm was wound in a huge bandage above the elbow, and I groped for the end of the linen strip.

"Me? No! Ow, that hurts!"

"It'll hurt worse before I'm through with you," I said, carefully unwrapping. "You mean the little bastard came after me on his own? You didn't *want* me to come back?"

"Want ye back? No! Want ye to come back to me for nothing but pity, the same as ye might show for a dog in a ditch? Bloody hell! No! I forbade the little bugger to go after ye!" He scowled furiously at me, ruddy brows knitting together.

"I'm a doctor," I said coldly, "not a veterinarian. And if you didn't want me back, what was all that you were saying before you realized I was real, hm? Bite the blanket or something; the end's stuck, and I'm going to pull it loose."

He bit his lip instead, and made no noise but a swift intake of air through his nose. It was impossible to judge his color in the firelight, but his eyes closed briefly, and small beads of sweat popped out on his forehead.

I turned away for a moment, groping in the drawer of Jenny's desk where the extra candles were kept. I needed more light before I did anything.

"I suppose Young Ian told me you were dying just to get me back here. He must have thought I wouldn't come otherwise." The candles were there; fine beeswax, from the Lallybroch hives.

"For what it's worth, I am dying." His voice came from behind me, dry and blunt, despite his breathlessness.

I turned back to him in some surprise. His eyes rested on my face quite calmly, now that the pain in his arm had lessened a bit, but his breath was still coming unevenly, and his eyes were heavy and bright with fever. I didn't respond at once, but lit the candles I had found, placing them in the big candelabra that usually decorated the sideboard, unused save for great occasions. The flames of five additional candles brightened the room as though in preparation for a party. I bent over the bed, noncommital.

"Let's have a look at it."

The wound itself was a ragged dark hole, scabbed at the edges and faintly blue-tinged. I pressed the flesh on either side of the wound; it was red and angry-looking, and there was a considerable seepage of pus. Jamie stirred uneasily as I drew my fingertips gently but firmly down the length of the muscle.

"You have the makings of a very fine little infection there, my lad," I said. "Young Ian said it went into your side; a second shot, or did it go through your arm?"

"It went through. Jenny dug the ball out of my side. That wasna so bad, though. Just an inch or so in." He spoke in brief spurts, lips tightening involuntarily between sentences.

"Let me see where it went through."

Moving very slowly, he turned his hand to the outside, letting the arm fall away from his side. I could see that even that small movement was intensely painful. The exit wound was just above the elbow joint, on the inside of the upper arm. Not directly opposite the entrance wound, though; the ball had been deflected in its passage.

"Hit the bone," I said, trying not to imagine what that must have felt like. "Do you know if the bone's broken? I don't want to poke you more than I need to."

"Thanks for small mercies," he said, with an attempt at a smile. The muscles of his face trembled, though, and went slack with exhaustion.

"No, I think it's not broken," he said. "I've broken my collarbone and my hand before, and it's no like that, though it hurts a bit.''

"I expect it does." I felt my way carefully up the swell of his biceps, testing for tenderness. "How far up does the pain go?"

He glanced at his wounded arm, almost casually. "Feels like I've a hot poker in my arm, not a bone. But it's no just the arm pains me now; my whole side's gone stiff and sore." He swallowed, licking his lips again. "Will ye give me a taste of the brandy?" he asked. "It hurts to feel my heart beating," he added apologetically.

Without comment, I poured a cup of water from the flask on the table, and held it to his lips. He raised one brow, but drank thirstily, then let his head fall back against the pillow. He breathed deeply for a moment, eyes closed, then opened them and looked directly at me.

"I've had two fevers in my life that near killed me," he said. "I think this one likely will. I wouldna send for ye, but . . . I'm glad you're here." He swallowed once, then went on. "I . . . wanted to say to ye that I'm sorry. And to bid ye a proper farewell. I wouldna ask ye to stay 'til the end, but . . . would ye . . . would ye stay wi' me—just for a bit?"

His right hand was pressed flat against the mattress, steadying him. I could see that he was fighting hard to keep any note of pleading from his voice or eyes, to make it a simple request, one that could be refused.

I sat down on the bed beside him, careful not to jar him. The firelight glowed on one side of his face, sparking the red-gold stubble of his beard, picking up the small flickers of silver here and there, leaving the other side masked in shadow. He met my eyes, not blinking. I hoped the yearning that showed in his face was not quite so apparent on my own.

I reached out and ran a hand gently down the side of his face, feeling the soft scratchiness of beard stubble.

"I'll stay for a bit," I said. "But you're not going to die."

He raised one eyebrow. "You brought me through one bad fever, using what I still think was witchcraft. And Jenny got me through the next, wi' naught but plain stubbornness. I suppose wi' the both of ye here, ye might just manage it, but I'm no at all sure I want to go through such an ordeal again. I think I'd rather just die and ha' done with it, if it's all the same to you."

"Ingrate," I said. "Coward." Torn between exasperation and tenderness, I patted his cheek and stood up, groping in the deep pocket of my skirt. There was one item I had carried on my person at all times, not trusting it to the vagaries of travel.

I laid the small, flat case on the table and flipped the latch. "I'm not going to let you die this time either," I informed him, "greatly as I may be tempted." I carefully extracted the roll of gray flannel and laid it on the table with a soft clinking noise. I unrolled the flannel, displaying the gleaming row of syringes, and rummaged in the box for the small bottle of penicillin tablets.

"What in God's name are those?" Jamie asked, eyeing the syringes with interest. "They look wicked sharp."

I didn't answer, occupied in dissolving the penicillin tablets in the vial of sterile water. I selected a glass barrel, fitted a needle, and pressed the tip through the rubber covering the mouth of the bottle. Holding it up to the light, I pulled back slowly on the plunger, watching the thick white liquid fill the barrel, checking for bubbles. Then pulling the needle free, I depressed the plunger slightly until a drop of liquid pearled from the point and rolled slowly down the length of the spike.

"Roll onto your good side," I said, turning to Jamie, "and pull up your shirt."

He eyed the needle in my hand with keen suspicion, but reluctantly obeyed. I surveyed the terrain with approval.

"Your bottom hasn't changed a bit in twenty years," I remarked, admiring the muscular curves.

"Neither has yours," he replied courteously, "but I'm no insisting you expose it. Are ye suffering a sudden attack of lustfulness?"

"Not just at present," I said evenly, swabbing a patch of skin with a cloth soaked in brandy.

"That's a verra nice make of brandy," he said, peering back over his shoulder, "but I'm more accustomed to apply it at the other end."

"It's also the best source of alcohol available. Hold still now, and relax." I jabbed deftly and pressed the plunger slowly in.

"Ouch!" Jamie rubbed his posterior resentfully.

"It'll stop stinging in a minute." I poured an inch of brandy into the cup. "Now you can have a bit to drink—a very little bit."

He drained the cup without comment, watching me roll up the

collection of syringes. Finally he said, "I thought ye stuck pins in ill-wish dolls when ye meant to witch someone; not in the people themselves."

"It's not a pin, it's a hypodermic syringe."

"I dinna care what ye call it; it felt like a bloody horseshoe nail. Would ye care to tell me why jabbing pins in my arse is going to help my arm?"

I took a deep breath. "Well, do you remember my once telling you about germs?"

He looked quite blank.

"Little beasts too small to see," I elaborated. "They can get into your body through bad food or water, or through open wounds, and if they do, they can make you ill."

He stared at his arm with interest. "I've germs in my arm, have I?"

"You very definitely have." I tapped a finger on the small flat box. "The medicine I just shot into your backside kills germs, though. You get another shot every four hours 'til this time tomorrow, and then we'll see how you're doing."

I paused. Jamie was staring at me, shaking his head.

"Do you understand?" I asked. He nodded slowly.

"Aye, I do. I should ha' let them burn ye, twenty years ago."

After giving him a shot and settling him comfortably, I sat
watching until he fell asleep again, allowing him to hold
my hand until his own grip relaxed in sleep and the big
hand dropped slack by his side.

I sat by his bed for the rest of the night, dozing sometimes, and
rousing myself by means of the internal clock all doctors have,
geared to the rhythms of a hospital's shift changes. Two more
shots, the last at daybreak, and by then the fever had loosed its
hold perceptibly. He was still very warm to the touch, but his flesh
no longer burned, and he rested easier, falling asleep after the last
shot with no more than a few grumbles and a faint moan as his
arm twinged.

"Bloody eighteenth-century germs are no match for penicillin," I told his sleeping form. "No resistance. Even if you had
syphilis, I'd have it cleaned up in no time."

And what then? I wondered, as I staggered off to the kitchen in
search of hot tea and food. A strange woman, presumably the cook
or the housemaid, was firing up the brick oven, ready to receive
the daily loaves that lay rising in their pans on the table. She didn't
seem surprised to see me, but cleared away a small space for me to
sit down, and brought me tea and fresh girdle-cakes with no more
than a quick "Good mornin' to ye, mum" before returning to her
work.

Evidently, Jenny had informed the household of my presence.
Did that mean she accepted it herself? I doubted it. Clearly, she
had wanted me to go, and wasn't best pleased to have me back. If I

was going to stay, there was plainly going to be a certain amount of explanation about Laoghaire, from both Jenny and Jamie. And I *was* going to stay.

"Thank you," I said politely to the cook, and taking a fresh cup of tea with me, went back to the parlor to wait until Jamie saw fit to wake up again.

People passed by the door during the morning, pausing now and then to peep through, but always went on hurriedly when I looked up. At last, Jamie showed signs of waking, just before noon; he stirred, sighed, groaned as the movement jarred his arm, and subsided once more.

I gave him a few moments to realize that I was there, but his eyes stayed shut. He wasn't asleep, though; the lines of his body were slightly tensed, not relaxed in slumber. I had watched him sleep all night; I knew the difference.

"All right," I said. I leaned back in the chair, settling myself comfortably, well out of his reach. "Let's hear it, then."

A small slit of blue showed under the long auburn lashes, then disappeared again.

"Mmmm?" he said, pretending to wake slowly. The lashes fluttered against his cheeks.

"Don't stall," I said crisply. "I know perfectly well you're awake. Open your eyes and tell me about Laoghaire."

The blue eyes opened and rested on me with an expression of some disfavor.

"You're no afraid of giving me a relapse?" he inquired. "I've always heard sick folk shouldna be troubled owermuch. It sets them back."

"You have a doctor right here," I assured him. "If you pass out from the strain, I'll know what to do about it."

"That's what I'm afraid of." His narrowed gaze flicked to the little case of drugs and hypodermics on the table, then back to me. "My arse feels like I've sat in a gorse bush wi' no breeks on."

"Good," I said pleasantly. "You'll get another one in an hour. Right now, you're going to talk."

His lips pressed tight together, but then relaxed as he sighed. He pushed himself laboriously upright against the pillows, one-handed. I didn't help him.

"All right," he said at last. He didn't look at me, but down at the quilt, where his finger traced the edge of the starred design.

"Well, it was when I'd come back from England."

He had come up from the Lake District and over the Carter's Bar, that great ridge of high ground that divides England from Scotland, on whose broad back the ancient courts and markets of the Borders had been held.

"There's a stone there to mark the border, maybe you'll know; it looks the sort of stone to last awhile." He glanced at me, questioning, and I nodded. I did know it; a huge menhir, some ten feet tall. In my time, someone had carved on its one face ENGLAND, and on the other, SCOTLAND.

There he stopped to rest, as thousands of travelers had stopped over the years, his exiled past behind him, the future—and home —below and beyond, past the hazy green hollows of the Lowlands, up into the gray crags of the Highlands, hidden by fog.

His good hand ran back and forth through his hair, as it always did when he thought, leaving the cowlicks on top standing up in small, bright whorls.

"You'll not know how it is, to live among strangers for so long."

"Won't I?" I said, with some sharpness. He glanced up at me, startled, then smiled faintly, looking down at the coverlet.

"Aye, maybe ye will," he said. "Ye change, no? Much as ye want to keep the memories of home, and who ye are—you're changed. Not one of the strangers; ye could never be that, even if ye wanted to. But different from who ye were, too."

I thought of myself, standing silent beside Frank, a bit of flotsam in the eddies of university parties, pushing a pram through the chilly parks of Boston, playing bridge and talking with other wives and mothers, speaking the foreign language of middle-class domesticity. Strangers indeed.

"Yes," I said. "I know. Get on."

He sighed, rubbing his nose with a forefinger. "So I came back," he said. He looked up, a smile hidden in the corner of his mouth. "What is it ye told wee Ian? 'Home is the place where, when ye have to go there, they have to take ye in'?"

"That's it," I said. "It's a quotation from a poet called Frost. But what do you mean? Surely your family was glad to see you!"

He frowned, fingering the quilt. "Aye, they were," he said slowly. "It's not that—I dinna mean they made me feel unwelcome, not at all. But I had been away so long—Michael and wee

Janet and Ian didna even remember me.'' He smiled ruefully. ''They'd heard about me, though. When I came into the kitchen, they'd squash back against the walls and stare at me, wi' their eyes gone round.''

He leaned forward a little, intent on making me understand.

''See, it was different, when I hid in the cave. I wasna in the house, and they seldom saw me, but I was always *here,* I was always part of them. I hunted for them; I kent when they were hungry, or cold, or when the goats were ill or the kail crop poor, or a new draft under the kitchen door.

''Then I went to prison,'' he said abruptly. ''And to England. I wrote to them—and they to me—but it canna be the same, to see a few black words on the paper, telling things that happened months before.

''And when I came back—'' He shrugged, wincing as the movement jarred his arm. ''It was different. Ian would ask me what I thought of fencing in auld Kirby's pasture, but I'd know he'd already set Young Jamie to do it. I'd walk through the fields, and folk would squint at me, suspicious, thinking me a stranger. Then their eyes would go big as they'd seen a ghost, when they knew me.''

He stopped, looking out at the window, where the brambles of his mother's rose beat against the glass as the wind changed. ''I *was* a ghost, I think.'' He glanced at me shyly. ''If ye ken what I mean.''

''Maybe,'' I said. Rain was streaking the glass, with drops the same gray as the sky outside.

''You feel like your ties to the earth are broken,'' I said softly. ''Floating through rooms without feeling your footsteps. Hearing people speak to you, and not making sense of it. I remember that —before Bree was born.'' But I had had one tie then; I had her, to anchor me to life.

He nodded, not looking at me, and then was quiet for a minute. The peat fire hissed on the hearth behind me, smelling of the Highlands, and the rich scent of cock-a-leekie and baking bread spread through the house, warm and comforting as a blanket.

''I was here,'' he said softly, ''but not home.''

I could feel the pull of it around me—the house, the family, the place itself. I, who couldn't remember a childhood home, felt the urge to sit down here and stay forever, enmeshed in the thousand strands of daily life, bound securely to this bit of earth. What would it have meant to him, who had lived all his life in the strength of that bond, endured his exile in the hope of coming back to it, and then arrived to find himself still rootless?

"And I suppose I was lonely," he said quietly. He lay still on the pillow, eyes closed.

"I suppose you were," I said, careful to let no tone either of sympathy or condemnation show. I knew something of loneliness, too.

He opened his eyes then, and met my gaze with a naked honesty. "Aye, there was that too," he said. "Not the main thing, no —but aye, that too."

Jenny had tried, with varying degrees of gentleness and insistence, to persuade him to marry again. She had tried intermittently since the days after Culloden, presenting first one and then another personable young widow, this and that sweet-tempered virgin, all to no avail. Now, bereft of the feelings that had sustained him so far, desperately seeking some sense of connection—he had listened.

"Laoghaire was married to Hugh MacKenzie, one of Colum's tacksmen," he said, eyes closed once more. "Hugh was k..ed at Culloden, though, and two years later, Laoghaire married Simon MacKimmie of clan Fraser. The two lassies—Marsali and Joan— they're his. The English arrested him a few years later, and took him to prison in Edinburgh." He opened his eyes, looking up at the dark ceiling beams overhead. "He had a good house, and property worth seizing. That was enough to make a Highland man a traitor, then, whether he'd fought for the Stuarts openly or not." His voice was growing hoarse, and he stopped to clear his throat.

"Simon wasn't as lucky as I was. He died in prison, before they could bring him to trial. The Crown tried for some time to take the estate, but Ned Gowan went to Edinburgh, and spoke for Laoghaire, and he managed to save the main house and a little money, claiming it was her dower right."

"Ned Gowan?" I spoke with mingled surprise and pleasure. "He can't still be alive, surely?" It was Ned Gowan, a small and elderly solicitor who advised the MacKenzie clan on legal matters, who had saved me from being burned as a witch, twenty years before. I had thought him quite ancient then.

Jamie smiled, seeing my pleasure. "Oh, aye. I expect they'll have to knock him on the head wi' an ax to kill him. He looks just the same as he always did, though he must be past seventy now."

"Does he still live at Castle Leoch?"

He nodded, reaching to the table for the tumbler of water. He drank awkwardly, right-handed, and set it back.

"What's left of it. Aye, though he's traveled a great deal these last years, appealing treason cases and filing lawsuits to recover property." Jamie's smile had a bitter edge. "There's a saying, aye? 'After a war, first come the corbies to eat the flesh; and then the lawyers, to pick the bones.' "

His right hand went to his left shoulder, massaging it unconsciously.

"No, he's a good man, is Ned, in spite of his profession. He goes back and forth to Inverness, to Edinburgh—sometimes even to London or Paris. And he stops here from time to time, to break his journey."

It was Ned Gowan who had mentioned Laoghaire to Jenny, returning from Balriggan to Edinburgh. Pricking up her ears, Jenny had inquired for further details, and finding these satisfactory, had at once sent an invitation to Balriggan, for Laoghaire and her two daughters to come to Lallybroch for Hogmanay, which was near.

The house was bright that night, with candles lit in the windows, and bunches of holly and ivy fixed to the staircase and the doorposts. There were not so many pipers in the Highlands as there had been before Culloden, but one had been found, and a fiddler as well, and music floated up the stairwell, mixed with the heady scent of rum punch, plum cake, almond squirts, and Savoy biscuits.

Jamie had come down late and hesitant. Many people here he had not seen in nearly ten years, and he was not eager to see them now, feeling changed and distant as he did. But Jenny had made him a new shirt, brushed and mended his coat, and combed his hair smooth and plaited it for him before going downstairs to see to the cooking. He had no excuse to linger, and at last had come down, into the noise and swirl of the gathering.

"Mister Fraser!" Peggy Gibbons was the first to see him; she hurried across the room, face glowing, and threw her arms about him, quite unabashed. Taken by surprise, he hugged her back, and within moments was surrounded by a small crowd of women, exclaiming over him, holding up small children born since his departure, kissing his cheeks and patting his hands.

The men were shyer, greeting him with a gruff word of welcome or a slap on the back as he made his way slowly through the rooms, until, quite overwhelmed, he had escaped temporarily into the laird's study.

Once his father's room, and then his own, it now belonged to his brother-in-law, who had run Lallybroch through the years of his absence. The ledgers and stockbooks and accounts were all lined up neatly on the edge of the battered desk; he ran a finger along the leather spines, feeling a sense of comfort at the touch. It was all in here; the planting and the harvests, the careful purchases and acquisitions, the slow accumulations and dispersals that were the rhythm of life to the tenants of Lallybroch.

On the small bookshelf, he found his wooden snake. Along with everything else of value, he had left it behind when he went to prison. A small icon carved of cherrywood, it had been the gift of his elder brother, dead in childhood. He was sitting in the chair behind the desk, stroking the snake's well-worn curves, when the door of the study opened.

"Jamie?" she had said, hanging shyly back. He had not bothered to light a lamp in the study; she was silhouetted by the candles burning in the hall. She wore her pale hair loose, like a maid, and the light shone through it, haloing her unseen face.

"You'll remember me, maybe?" she had said, tentative, reluctant to come into the room without invitation.

"Aye," he said, after a pause. *"Aye, of course I do."*

"The music's starting," she said. It was; he could hear the whine of the fiddle and the stamp of feet from the front parlor, along with an occasional shout of merriment. It showed signs of being a good party already; most of the guests would be asleep on the floor come morning.

"Your sister says you're a bonny dancer," she said, still shy, but determined.

"It will ha' been some time since I tried," he said, feeling shy himself, and painfully awkward, though the fiddle music ached in his bones and his feet twitched at the sound of it.

"It's 'Tha mo Leabaidh 'san Fhraoch'—'In the Heather's my Bed'—you'll ken that one. Will ye come and try wi' me?" *She had held out a hand to him, small and graceful in the half-dark. And he had risen, clasped her outstretched hand in his own, and taken his first steps in pursuit of himself.*

"It was in here," he said, waving his good hand at the room where we sat. "Jenny had had the furniture cleared away, all but one table wi' the food and the whisky, and the fiddler stood by the window there, wi' a new moon over his shoulder." He nodded at the window, where the rose vine trembled. Something of the light of that Hogmanay feast lingered on his face, and I felt a small pang, seeing it.

"We danced all that night, sometimes wi' others, but mostly with each other. And at the dawn, when those still awake went to the end o' the house to see what omens the New Year might bring, the two of us went, too. The single women took it in turns to spin about, and walk through the door wi' their eyes closed, then spin again and open their eyes to see what the first thing they might see would be—for that tells them about the man they'll marry, ye ken."

There had been a lot of laughter, as the guests, heated by whisky and dancing, pushed and shoved at the door. Laoghaire had held back, flushed and laughing, saying it was a game for young girls, and not for a matron of thirty-four, but the others had insisted, and try she had. Spun three times clockwise and opened the door, stepped out into the cold dawnlight and spun again. And when she opened her eyes, they had rested on Jamie's face, wide with expectation.

"So . . . there she was, a widow wi' two bairns. She needed a man, that was plain enough. I needed . . . something." He gazed into the fire, where the low flame glimmered through the red mass of the peat; heat without much light. "I supposed that we might help each other."

They had married quietly at Balriggan, and he had moved his

few possessions there. Less than a year later, he had moved out again, and gone to Edinburgh.

"What on earth happened?" I asked, more than curious.

He looked up at me, helpless.

"I canna say. It wasna that anything was wrong, exactly—only that nothing was right." He rubbed a hand tiredly between his brows. "It was me, I think; my fault. I always disappointed her somehow. We'd sit down to supper and all of a sudden the tears would well up in her eyes, and she'd leave the table sobbing, and me sitting there wi' not a notion what I'd done or said wrong."

His fist clenched on the coverlet, then relaxed. "God, I *never* knew what to do for her, or what to say! Anything I said just made it worse, and there would be days—nay, weeks!—when she'd not speak to me, but only turn away when I came near her, and stand staring out the window until I went away again."

His fingers went to the parallel scratches down the side of his neck. They were nearly healed now, but the marks of my nails still showed on his fair skin. He looked at me wryly.

"You never did that to me, Sassenach."

"Not my style," I agreed, smiling faintly. "If I'm mad at you, you'll bloody know why, at least."

He snorted briefly and lay back on his pillows. Neither of us spoke for a bit. Then he said, staring up at the ceiling, "I thought I didna want to hear anything about what it was like—wi' Frank, I mean. I was maybe wrong about that."

"I'll tell you anything you want to know," I said. "But not just now. It's still your turn."

He sighed and closed his eyes.

"She was afraid of me," he said softly, a minute later. "I tried to be gentle wi' her—God, I tried again and again, everything I knew to please a woman. But it was no use."

His head turned restlessly, making a hollow in the feather pillow.

"Maybe it was Hugh, or maybe Simon. I kent them both, and they were good men, but there's no telling what goes on in a marriage bed. Maybe it was bearing the children; not all women can stand it. But something hurt her, sometime, and I couldna heal it for all my trying. She shrank away when I touched her, and I could see the sickness and the fear in her eyes." There were lines

of sorrow around his own closed eyes, and I reached impulsively
for his hand.

He squeezed it gently and opened his eyes. "That's why I left,
finally," he said softly. "I couldna bear it anymore."

I didn't say anything, but went on holding his hand, putting a
finger on his pulse to check it. His heartbeat was reassuringly slow
and steady.

He shifted slightly in the bed, moving his shoulders and making
a grimace of discomfort as he did so.

"Arm hurt a lot?" I asked.

"A bit."

I bent over him, feeling his brow. He was very warm, but not
feverish. There was a line between the thick ruddy brows, and I
smoothed it with a knuckle.

"Head ache?"

"Yes."

"I'll go and make you some willow-bark tea." I made to rise,
but his hand on my arm stopped me.

"I dinna need tea," he said. "It would ease me, though, if
maybe I could lay my head in your lap, and have ye rub my
temples a bit?" Blue eyes looked up at me, limpid as a spring sky.

"You don't fool me a bit, Jamie Fraser," I said. "I'm not going
to forget about your next shot." Nonetheless, I was already moving the chair out of the way, and sitting down beside him on the
bed.

He made a small grunting sound of content as I moved his head
into my lap and began to stroke it, rubbing his temples, smoothing
back the thick wavy mass of his hair. The back of his neck was
damp; I lifted the hair away and blew softly on it, seeing the
smooth fair skin prickle into gooseflesh at the nape of his neck.

"Oh, that feels good," he murmured. Despite my resolve not to
touch him beyond the demands of caretaking until everything
between us was resolved, I found my hands molding themselves to
the clean, bold lines of his neck and shoulders, seeking the hard
knobs of his vertebrae and the broad, flat planes of his shoulder
blades.

He was firm and solid under my hands, his breath a warm caress
on my thigh, and it was with some reluctance that I at last eased
him back onto the pillow and reached for the ampule of penicillin.

"All right," I said, turning back the sheet and reaching for the hem of his shirt. "A quick stick, and you'll—" My hand brushed over the front of his nightshirt, and I broke off, startled.

"Jamie!" I said, amused. "You can't possibly!"

"I dinna suppose I can," he agreed comfortably. He curled up on his side like a shrimp, his lashes dark against his cheek. "But a man can dream, no?"

I didn't go upstairs to bed that night, either. We didn't talk much, just lay close together in the narrow bed, scarcely moving, so as not to jar his injured arm. The rest of the house was quiet, everyone safely in bed, and there was no sound but the hissing of the fire, the sigh of the wind, and the scratch of Ellen's rosebush at the window, insistent as the demands of love.

"Do ye know?" he said softly, somewhere in the black, small hours of the night. "Do ye know what it's like to be with someone that way? To try all ye can, and seem never to have the secret of them?"

"Yes," I said, thinking of Frank. "Yes, I do know."

"I thought perhaps ye did." He was quiet for a moment, and then his hand touched my hair lightly, a shadowy blur in the firelight.

"And then . . ." he whispered, "then to have it back again, that knowing. To be free in all ye say or do, and know that it is right."

"To say 'I love you,' and mean it with all your heart," I said softly to the dark.

"Aye," he answered, barely audible. "To say that."

His hand rested on my hair, and without knowing quite how it happened, I found myself curled against him, my head just fitting in the hollow of his shoulder.

"For so many years," he said, "for so long, I have been so many things, so many different men." I felt him swallow, and he shifted slightly, the linen of his nightshirt rustling with starch.

"I was 'Uncle' to Jenny's children, and 'Brother' to her and Ian. 'Milord' to Fergus, and 'Sir' to my tenants. 'Mac Dubh' to the men of Ardsmuir and 'MacKenzie' to the other servants at Helwater. 'Malcolm the printer,' then, and 'Jamie Roy' at the docks." The hand stroked my hair, slowly, with a whispering sound like the wind outside. "But here," he said, so softly I could barely hear him, "here in the dark, with you . . . I have no name."

I lifted my face toward his, and took the warm breath of him between my own lips.

"I love you," I said, and did not need to tell him how I meant it.

38

I Meet a Lawyer

As I had predicted, eighteenth-century germs were no match for a modern antibiotic. Jamie's fever had virtually disappeared within twenty-four hours, and within the next two days the inflammation in his arm began to subside as well, leaving no more than a reddening about the wound itself and a very slight oozing of pus when pressed.

On the fourth day, after satisfying myself that he was mending nicely, I dressed the wound lightly with coneflower salve, bandaged it again, and left to dress and make my own toilet upstairs.

Ian, Janet, Young Ian, and the servants had all put their heads in at intervals over the last few days, to see how Jamie progressed. Jenny had been conspicuously absent from these inquiries, but I knew that she was still entirely aware of everything that happened in her house. I hadn't announced my intention of coming upstairs, yet when I opened the door to my bedroom, there was a large pitcher of hot water standing by the ewer, gently steaming, and a fresh cake of soap laid alongside it.

I picked it up and sniffed. Fine-milled French soap, perfumed with lily of the valley, it was a delicate comment on my status in the household—honored guest, to be sure; but not one of the family, who would all make do as a matter of course with the usual coarse soap made of tallow and lye.

"Right," I muttered. "Well, we'll see, won't we?" and lathered the cloth for washing.

As I was arranging my hair in the glass a half-hour later, I heard the sounds below of someone arriving. Several someones, in fact, from the sounds of it. I came down the stairs to find a small mob of children in residence, streaming in and out of the kitchen and front parlor, with here and there a strange adult visible in the midst of them, who stared curiously at me as I came down the stairs.

Entering the parlor, I found the camp bed put away and Jamie, shaved and in a fresh nightshirt, neatly propped up on the sofa under a quilt with his left arm in a sling, surrounded by four or five children. These were shepherded by Janet, Young Ian, and a smiling young man who was a Fraser of sorts by the shape of his nose, but otherwise bore only the faintest resemblances to the tiny boy I had seen last at Lallybroch twenty years before.

"There she is!" Jamie exclaimed with pleasure at my appearance, and the entire roomful of people turned to look at me, with expressions ranging from pleasant greeting to gape-mouthed awe.

"You'll remember Young Jamie?" the elder Jamie said, nodding to the tall, broad-shouldered young man with curly black hair and a squirming bundle in his arms.

"I remember the curls," I said, smiling. "The rest has changed a bit."

Young Jamie grinned down at me. "I remember ye well, Auntie," he said, in a deep-brown voice like well-aged ale. "Ye held me on your knee and played Ten Wee Piggies wi' my toes."

"I can't possibly have," I said, looking up at him in some dismay. While it seemed to be true that people really didn't change markedly in appearance between their twenties and their forties, they most assuredly did so between four and twenty-four.

"Perhaps ye can have a go wi' wee Benjamin here," Young Jamie suggested with a smile. "Maybe the knack of it will come back to ye." He bent and carefully laid his bundle in my arms.

A very round face looked up at me with that air of befuddlement so common to new babies. Benjamin appeared mildly confused at having me suddenly exchanged for his father, but didn't object. Instead, he opened his small pink mouth very wide, inserted his fist and began to gnaw on it in a thoughtful manner.

A small blond boy in homespun breeks leaned on Jamie's knee, staring up at me in wonder. "Who's that, Nunkie?" he asked in a loud whisper.

"That's your great-auntie Claire," Jamie said gravely. "Ye'll have heard about her, I expect?"

"Oh, aye," the little boy said, nodding madly. "Is she as old as Grannie?"

"Even older," Jamie said, nodding back solemnly. The lad gawked up at me for a moment, then turned back to Jamie, face screwed up in scorn.

"Get on wi' ye, Nunkie! She doesna look anything like as old as Grannie! Why, there's scarce a bit o' silver in her hair!"

"Thank you, child," I said, beaming at him.

"Are ye sure that's our great-auntie Claire?" the boy went on, looking doubtfully at me. "Mam says Great-Auntie Claire was maybe a witch, but this lady doesna look much like it. She hasna got a single wart on her nose that *I* can see!"

"Thanks," I said again, a little more dryly. "And what's your name?"

He turned suddenly shy at being thus directly addressed, and buried his head in Jamie's sleeve, refusing to speak.

"This is Angus Walter Edwin Murray Carmichael," Jamie answered for him, ruffling the silky blond hair. "Maggie's eldest son, and most commonly known as Wally."

"We call him Snot-rag," a small red-haired girl standing by my knee informed me. " 'Cause his neb is always clotted wi' gook."

Angus Walter jerked his face out of his uncle's shirt and glared at his female relation, his features beet-red with fury.

"Is *not!"* he shouted. "Take it back!" Not waiting to see whether she would or not, he flung himself at her, fists clenched, but was jerked off his feet by his great-uncle's hand, attached to his collar.

"Ye dinna hit girls," Jamie informed him firmly. "It's not manly."

"But she said I was snotty!" Angus Walter wailed. "I *must* hit her!"

"And it's no verra civil to pass remarks about someone's personal appearance, Mistress Abigail," Jamie said severely to the little girl. "Ye should apologize to your cousin."

"Well, but he *is* . . ." Abigail persisted, but then caught Jamie's stern eyes and dropped her own, flushing scarlet. "Sorry, Wally," she murmured.

Wally seemed at first indisposed to consider this adequate compensation for the insult he had suffered, but was at last prevailed upon to cease trying to hit his cousin by his uncle promising him a story.

"Tell the one about the kelpie and the horseman!" my red-haired acquaintance exclaimed, pushing forward to be in on it.

"No, the one about the Devil's chess game!" chimed in one of the other children. Jamie seemed to be a sort of magnet for them; two boys were plucking at his coverlet, while a tiny brown-haired girl had climbed up onto the sofa back by his head, and begun intently plaiting strands of his hair.

"Pretty, Nunkie," she murmured, taking no part in the hail of suggestions.

"It's Wally's story," Jamie said firmly, quelling the incipient riot with a gesture. "He can choose as he likes." He drew a clean handkerchief out from under the pillow and held it to Wally's nose, which was in fact rather unsightly.

"Blow," he said in an undertone, and then, louder, "and then tell me which you'll have, Wally."

Wally snuffled obligingly, then said, "St. Bride and the geese, please, Nunkie."

Jamie's eyes sought me, resting on my face with a thoughtful expression.

"All right," he said, after a pause. "Well, then. Ye'll ken that the greylag mate for life? If ye kill a grown goose, hunting, ye must always wait, for the mate will come to mourn. Then ye must try to kill the second, too, for otherwise it will grieve itself to death, calling through the skies for the lost one."

Little Benjamin shifted in his wrappings, squirming in my arms. Jamie smiled and shifted his attention back to Wally, hanging open-mouthed on his great-uncle's knee.

"So," he said, "it was a time, more hundreds of years past than you could ken or dream of, that Bride first set foot on the stone of the Highlands, along with Michael the Blessed . . ."

Benjamin let out a small squawk at this point, and began to rootle at the front of my dress. Young Jamie and his siblings seemed to have disappeared, and after a moment's patting and joggling had proved vain, I left the room in search of Benjamin's mother, leaving the story in progress behind me.

I found the lady in question in the kitchen, embedded in a large company of girls and women, and after turning Benjamin over to her, spent some time in introductions, greeting, and the sort of ritual by which women appraise each other, openly and otherwise.

The women were all very friendly; evidently everyone knew or had been told who I was, for while they introduced me from one to another, there was no apparent surprise at the return of Jamie's first wife—either from the dead or from France, depending on what they'd been told.

Still, there were very odd undercurrents passing through the gathering. They scrupulously avoided asking me questions; in another place, this might be mere politeness, but not in the Highlands, where any stranger's life history was customarily extracted in the course of a casual visit.

And while they treated me with great courtesy and kindness, there were small looks from the corner of the eye, the passing of glances exchanged behind my back, and casual remarks made quietly in Gaelic.

But strangest of all was Jenny's absence. She was the hearthfire of Lallybroch; I had never been in the house when it was not suffused with her presence, all the inhabitants in orbit about her like planets about the sun. I could think of nothing less like her than that she should leave her kitchen with such a mob of company in the house.

Her presence was as strong now as the perfume of the fresh pine boughs that lay in a large pile in the back pantry, their presence beginning to scent the house; but of Jenny herself, not a hair was to be seen.

She had avoided me since the night of my return with Young Ian —natural enough, I supposed, under the circumstances. Neither had I sought an interview with her. Both of us knew there was a reckoning to be made, but neither of us would seek it then.

It was warm and cozy in the kitchen—too warm. The intermingled scents of drying cloth, hot starch, wet diapers, sweating bodies, oatcake frying in lard, and bread baking were becoming a bit too heady, and when Katherine mentioned the need of a pitcher of cream for the scones, I seized the opportunity to escape, volunteering to fetch it down from the dairy shed.

After the press of heated bodies in the kitchen, the cold, damp air outside was so refreshing that I stood still for a minute, shaking the kitchen smells out of my petticoats and hair before making my way to the dairy shed. This shed was some distance away from the main house, convenient to the milking shed, which in turn was built to adjoin the two small paddocks in which sheep and goats were kept. Cattle were kept in the Highlands, but normally for beef, rather than milk, cow's milk being thought suitable only for invalids.

To my surprise, as I came out of the dairy shed, I saw Fergus leaning on the paddock fence, staring moodily at the mass of milling wooly backs below. I had not expected to see him here, and wondered whether Jamie knew he had returned.

Jenny's prized Merino sheep—imported, hand-fed and a great deal more spoilt than any of her grandchildren—spotted me as I passed, and rushed en masse for the side of their pen, blatting frenziedly in hope of tidbits. Fergus looked up, startled at the racket, then waved halfheartedly. He called something, but it was impossible to hear him over the uproar.

There was a large bin of frost-blasted cabbage heads near the pen; I pulled out a large, limp green head, and doled out leaves to a dozen or so pairs of eagerly grasping lips, in hopes of shutting them up.

The ram, a huge wooly creature named Hughie, with testicles that hung nearly to the ground like wool-covered footballs, shouldered his massive way into the front rank with a loud and autocratic *Bahh!* Fergus, who had reached my side by this time, picked up a whole cabbage and hurled it at Hughie with considerable force and fair accuracy.

"Tais-toi!" he said irritably.

Hughie shied and let out an astonished, high-pitched *Beh!* as the cabbage bounced off his padded back. Then, shaking himself back into some semblance of dignity, he trotted off, testes swinging with offended majesty. His flock, sheeplike, trailed after him, uttering a low chorus of discontented *bahs* in his wake.

Fergus glowered malevolently after them.

"Useless, noisy, smelly beasts," he said. Rather ungratefully, I thought, given that the scarf and stockings he was wearing had almost certainly been woven from their wool.

"Nice to see you again, Fergus," I said, ignoring his mood. "Does Jamie know you're back yet?" I wondered just how much Fergus knew of recent events, if he had just arrived at Lallybroch.

"No," he said, rather listlessly. "I suppose I should tell him I am here." In spite of this, he made no move toward the house, but continued staring into the churned mud of the paddock. Something was obviously eating at him; I hoped nothing had gone wrong with his errand.

"Did you find Mr. Gage all right?" I asked.

He looked blank for a moment, then a spark of animation came back into his lean face.

"Oh, yes. Milord was right; I went with Gage to warn the other members of the Society, and then we went together to the tavern where they were to meet. Sure enough, there was a nest of Customs men there waiting, disguised. And may they be waiting as long as their fellow in the cask, ha ha!"

The gleam of savage amusement died out of his eyes then, and he sighed.

"We cannot expect to be paid for the pamphlets, of course. And even though the press was saved, God knows how long it may be until milord's business is reestablished."

He spoke with such mournfulness that I was surprised.

"You don't help with the printing business, do you?" I asked.

He raised one shoulder and let it fall. "Not to say help, milady. But milord was kind enough to allow me to invest a part of my share of the profits from the brandy in the printing business. In time, I should have become a full partner."

"I see," I said sympathetically. "Do you need money? Perhaps I can—"

He shot me a glance of surprise, and then a smile that displayed his perfect, square white teeth.

"Thank you, milady, but no. I myself need very little, and I have enough." He patted the side pocket of his coat, which jingled reassuringly.

He paused, frowning, and thrust both wrists deep into the pockets of his coat.

"Noo . . ." he said slowly. "It is only—well, the printing business is most respectable, milady."

"I suppose so," I said, slightly puzzled. He caught my tone and smiled, rather grimly.

"The difficulty, milady, is that while a smuggler may be in possession of an income more than sufficient for the support of a wife, smuggling as a sole profession is not likely to appeal to the parents of a respectable young lady.''

"Oho," I said, everything becoming clear. "You want to get married? To a respectable young lady?''

He nodded, a little shyly.

"Yes, madame. But her mother does not favor me.''

I couldn't say I blamed the young lady's mother, all things considered. While Fergus was possessed of dark good looks and a dashing manner that might well win a young girl's heart, he lacked a few of the things that might appeal somewhat more to conservative Scottish parents, such as property, income, a left hand, and a last name.

Likewise, while smuggling, cattle-lifting, and other forms of practical communism had a long and illustrious history in the Highlands, the French did not. And no matter how long Fergus himself had lived at Lallybroch, he remained as French as Notre Dame. He would, like me, always be an outlander.

"If I were a partner in a profitable printing firm, you see, perhaps the good lady might be induced to consider my suit," he explained. "But as it is . . .'' He shook his head disconsolately.

I patted his arm sympathetically. "Don't worry about it," I said. "We'll think of something. Does Jamie know about this girl? I'm sure he'd be willing to speak to her mother for you.''

To my surprise, he looked quite alarmed.

"Oh, no, milady! Please, say nothing to him—he has a great many things of more importance to think of just now.''

On the whole, I thought this was probably true, but I was surprised at his vehemence. Still, I agreed to say nothing to Jamie. My feet were growing chilly from standing in the frozen mud, and I suggested that we go inside.

"Perhaps a little later, milady," he said. "For now, I believe I am not suitable company even for sheep." With a heavy sigh, he turned and trudged off toward the dovecote, shoulders slumped.

To my surprise, Jenny was in the parlor with Jamie. She had been outside; her cheeks and the end of her long, straight nose were pink with the cold, and the scent of winter mist lingered in her clothes.

"I've sent Young Ian to saddle Donas," she said. She frowned at her brother. "Can ye stand to walk to the barn, Jamie, or had he best bring the beast round for ye?"

Jamie stared up at her, one eyebrow raised.

"I can walk wherever it's needful to go, but I'm no going anywhere just now."

"Did I not tell ye he'd be coming?" Jenny said impatiently. "Amyas Kettrick stopped by here late last night, and said he'd just come from Kinwallis. Hobart's meaning to come today, he said." She glanced at the pretty enameled clock on the mantel. "If he left after breakfast, he'll be here within the hour."

Jamie frowned at his sister, tilting his head back against the sofa.

"I told ye, Jenny, I'm no afraid of Hobart MacKenzie," he said shortly. "Damned if I'll run from him!"

Jenny's brows rose as she looked coldly at her brother.

"Oh, aye?" she said. "Ye weren't afraid of Laoghaire, either, and look where that got ye!" She jerked her head at the sling on his arm.

Despite himself, Jamie's mouth curled up on one side.

"Aye, well, it's a point," he said. "On the other hand, Jenny, ye ken guns are scarcer than hen's teeth in the Highlands. I dinna think Hobart's going to come and ask to borrow my own pistol to shoot me with."

"I shouldna think he'd bother; he'll just walk in and spit ye through the gizzard like the silly gander ye are!" she snapped.

Jamie laughed, and she glared at him. I seized the moment to interrupt.

"Who," I inquired, "is Hobart MacKenzie, and why exactly does he want to spit you like a gander?"

Jamie turned his head to me, the light of amusement still in his eyes.

"Hobart is Laoghaire's brother, Sassenach," he explained. "As for spitting me or otherwise—"

"Laoghaire's sent for him from Kinwallis, where he lives," Jenny interrupted, "and told him about . . . all this." A slight, impatient gesture encompassed me, Jamie, and the awkward situation in general.

"The notion being that Hobart's meant to come round and expunge the slight upon his sister's honor by expunging me,"

Jamie explained. He seemed to find the idea entertaining. I wasn't so sure about it, and neither was Jenny.

"You're not worried about this Hobart?" I asked.

"Of course not," he said, a little irritably. He turned to his sister. "For God's sake, Jenny, ye ken Hobart MacKenzie! The man couldna stick a pig without cutting off his own foot!"

She looked him up and down, evidently gauging his ability to defend himself against an incompetent pigsticker, and reluctantly concluding that he might manage, even one-handed.

"Mmphm," she said. "Well, and what if he comes for ye and ye kill him, aye? What then?"

"Then he'll be dead, I expect," Jamie said dryly.

"And ye'll be hangit for murder," she shot back, "or on the run, wi' all the rest of Laoghaire's kin after ye. Want to start a blood feud, do ye?"

Jamie narrowed his eyes at his sister, emphasizing the already marked resemblance between them.

"What I want," he said, with exaggerated patience, "is my breakfast. D'ye mean to feed me, or d'ye mean to wait until I faint from hunger, and then hide me in the priest hole 'til Hobart leaves?"

Annoyance struggled with humor on Jenny's fine-boned face as she glared at her brother. As usual with both Frasers, humor won out.

"It's a thought," she said, teeth flashing in a brief, reluctant smile. "If I could drag your stubborn carcass that far, I'd club ye myself." She shook her head and sighed.

"All right, Jamie, ye'll have it your way. But ye'll try not to make a mess on my good Turkey carpet, aye?"

He looked up at her, long mouth curling up on one side.

"It's a promise, Jenny," he said. "Nay bloodshed in the parlor."

She snorted. "Clot," she said, but without rancor. "I'll send Janet wi' your parritch." And she was gone, in a swirl of skirts and petticoats.

"Did she say Donas?" I asked, looking after her in bemusement. "Surely it isn't the same horse you took from Leoch!"

"Och, no." Jamie tilted his head back, smiling up at me. "This is Donas's grandson—or one of them. We give the name to the sorrel colts in his honor."

I leaned over the back of the sofa, gently feeling down the length of the injured arm from the shoulder.

"Sore?" I asked, seeing him wince as I pressed a few inches above the wound. It was better; the day before, the area of soreness had started higher.

"Not bad," he said. He removed the sling and tried gingerly extending the arm, grimacing. "I dinna think I'll turn handsprings awhile yet, though."

I laughed.

"No, I don't suppose so." I hesitated. "Jamie—this Hobart. You really don't think—"

"I don't," he said firmly. "And if I did, I'd still want my breakfast first. I dinna mean to be killed on an empty stomach."

I laughed again, somewhat reassured.

"I'll go and get it for you," I promised.

As I stepped out into the hall, though, I caught sight of a flutter through one of the windows, and stopped to look. It was Jenny, cloaked and hooded against the cold, headed up the slope to the barn. Seized by a sudden impulse, I snatched a cloak from the hall tree and darted out after her. I had things to say to Jenny Murray, and this might be the best chance of catching her alone.

I caught up with her just outside the barn; she heard my step behind her and turned, startled. She glanced about quickly, but saw we were alone. Realizing that there was no way of putting off a confrontation, she squared her shoulders under the woolen cloak and lifted her head, meeting my eyes straight on.

"I thought I'd best tell Young Ian to unsaddle the horse," she said. "Then I'm going to the root cellar to fetch up some onions for a tart. Will ye come with me?"

"I will." Pulling my cloak tight around me against the winter wind, I followed her into the barn.

It was warm inside, at least by contrast with the chill outdoors, dark, and filled with the pleasant scent of horses, hay, and manure. I paused a moment to let my eyes adapt to the dimness, but Jenny walked directly down the central aisle, footsteps light on the stone floor.

Young Ian was sprawled at length on a pile of fresh straw; he sat up, blinking at the sound.

Jenny glanced from her son to the stall, where a soft-eyed sorrel was peacefully munching hay from its manger, unburdened by saddle or bridle.

"Did I not tell ye to ready Donas?" she asked the boy, her voice sharp.

Young Ian scratched his head, looking a little sheepish, and stood up.

"Aye, mam, ye did," he said. "But I didna think it worth the time to saddle him, only to have to unsaddle him again."

Jenny stared up at him.

"Oh, aye?" she said. "And what made ye so certain he wouldna be needed?"

Young Ian shrugged, and smiled down at her.

"Mam, ye ken as well as I do that Uncle Jamie wouldna run away from anything, let alone Uncle Hobart. Don't ye?" he added, gently.

Jenny looked up at her son and sighed. Then a reluctant smile lighted her face and she reached up, smoothing the thick, untidy hair away from his face.

"Aye, wee Ian. I do." Her hand lingered along his ruddy cheek, then dropped away.

"Go along to the house, then, and have second breakfast wi' your uncle," she said. "Your auntie and I are goin' to the root cellar. But ye come and fetch me smartly, if Mr. Hobart MacKenzie should come, aye?"

"Right away, Mam," he promised, and shot for the house, impelled by the thought of food.

Jenny watched him go, moving with the clumsy grace of a young whooping crane, and shook her head, the smile still on her lips.

"Sweet laddie," she murmured. Then, recalled to the present circumstances, she turned to me with decision.

"Come along, then," she said. "I expect ye want to talk to me, aye?"

Neither of us said anything until we reached the quiet sanctuary of the root cellar. It was a small room dug under the house, pungent with the scent of the long braided strings of onions and garlic that hung from the rafters, the sweet, spicy scent of dried apples, and the moist, earthy smell of potatoes, spread in lumpy brown blankets over the shelves that lined the cellar.

"D'ye remember telling me to plant potatoes?" Jenny asked, passing a hand lightly over the clustered tubers. "That was a lucky thing; 'twas the potato crop kept us alive, more than one winter after Culloden."

I remembered, all right. I had told her as we stood together on a cold autumn night, about to part—she to return to a newborn baby, I to hunt for Jamie, an outlaw in the Highlands, under sentence of death. I had found him, and saved him—and Lallybroch, evidently. And she had tried to give them both to Laoghaire.

"Why?" I said softly, at last. I spoke to the top of her head, bent over her task. Her hand went out with the regularity of clockwork, pulling an onion from the long hanging braid, breaking the tough, withered stems from the plait and tossing it into the basket she carried.

"Why did you do it?" I said. I broke off an onion from another braid, but instead of putting it in the basket, held it in my hands, rolling it back and forth like a baseball, hearing the papery skin rustle between my palms.

"Why did I do what?" Her voice was perfectly controlled again; only someone who knew her well could have heard the note of strain in it. I knew her well—or had, at one time.

"Why did I make the match between my brother and Laoghaire, d'ye mean?" She glanced up quickly, smooth black brows raised in question, but then bent back to the braid of onions. "You're right; he wouldna have done it, without I made him."

"So you did make him do it," I said. The wind rattled the door of the root cellar, sending a small sifting of dirt down upon the cut-stone steps.

"He was lonely," she said, softly. "So lonely. I couldna bear to see him so. He was wretched for so long, ye ken, mourning for you."

"I thought he was dead," I said quietly, answering the unspoken accusation.

"He might as well have been," she said, sharply, then raised her head and sighed, pushing back a lock of dark hair.

"Aye, maybe ye truly didna ken he'd lived; there were a great many who didn't, after Culloden—and it's sure he thought *you* were dead and gone then. But he was sair wounded, and not only his leg. And when he came home from England—'' She shook her head, and reached for another onion. "He was whole enough to look at, but not—" She gave me a look, straight on, with those slanted blue eyes, so disturbingly like her brother's. "He's no the sort of man should sleep alone, aye?"

"Granted," I said shortly. "But we did live, the both of us. Why did you send for Laoghaire when we came back with Young Ian?"

Jenny didn't answer at first, but only went on reaching for onions, breaking, reaching, breaking, reaching.

"I liked you," she said at last, so low I could barely hear her. "Loved ye, maybe, when ye lived here with Jamie, before."

"I liked you, too," I said, just as softly. "Then why?"

Her hands stilled at last and she looked up at me, fists balled at her sides.

"When Ian told me ye'd come back," she said slowly, eyes fastened on the onions, "ye could have knocked me flat wi' a down-feather. At first, I was excited, wanting to see ye—wanting to know where ye'd been—" she added, arching her brows slightly in inquiry. I didn't answer, and she went on.

"But then I was afraid," she said softly. Her eyes slid away, shadowed by their thick fringe of black lashes.

"I saw ye, ye ken," she said, still looking off into some unseeable distance. "When he wed Laoghaire, and them standing by the altar—ye were there wi' them, standing at his left hand, betwixt him and Laoghaire. And I kent that meant ye would take him back."

The hair prickled slightly on the nape of my neck. She shook her head slowly, and I saw she had gone pale with the memory. She sat down on a barrel, the cloak spreading out around her like a flower.

"I'm not one of those born wi' the Sight, nor one who has it regular. I've never had it before, and hope never to have it again. But I saw ye there, as clear as I see ye now, and it scairt me so that I had to leave the room, right in the midst o' the vows." She swallowed, looking at me directly.

"I dinna ken who ye are," she said softly. "Or . . . or . . . what. We didna ken your people, or your place. I never asked ye, did I? Jamie chose ye, that was enough. But then ye were gone, and after so long—I thought he might have forgot ye enough to wed again, and be happy.''

"He wasn't, though,'' I said, hoping for confirmation from Jenny.

She gave it, shaking her head.

"No,'' she said quietly. "But Jamie's a faithful man, aye? No matter how it was between the two of them, him and Laoghaire, if he'd sworn to be her man, he wouldna leave her altogether. It didna matter that he spent most of his time in Edinburgh; I kent he'd always come back here—he'd be bound here, to the Highlands. But then you came back.''

Her hands lay still in her lap, a rare sight. They were still finely shaped, long-fingered and deft, but the knuckles were red and rough with years of work, and the veins stood out blue beneath the thin white skin.

"D'ye ken,'' she said, looking into her lap, "I have never been further than ten miles from Lallybroch, in all my life?''

"No,'' I said, slightly startled. She shook her head slowly, then looked up at me.

"You have, though,'' she said. "You've traveled a great deal, I expect.'' Her gaze searched my face, looking for clues.

"I have.''

She nodded, as though thinking to herself.

"You'll go again,'' she said, nearly whispering. "I kent ye would go again. You're not bound here, not like Laoghaire—not like me. And he would go with ye. And I should never see him again.'' She closed her eyes briefly, then opened them, looking at me under her fine dark brows.

"That's why,'' she said. "I thought if ye kent about Laoghaire, ye'd go again at once—you did—'' she added, with a faint grimace, "and Jamie would stay. But ye came back.'' Her shoulders rose in a faint, helpless shrug. "And I see it's no good; he's bound to ye, for good or ill. It's you that's his wife. And if ye leave again, he will go with ye.''

I searched helplessly for words to reassure her. "But I won't. I won't go again. I only want to stay here with him—always.''

I laid a hand on her arm and she stiffened slightly. After a moment, she laid her own hand over mine. It was chilled, and the tip of her long, straight nose was red with cold.

"Folk say different things of the Sight, aye?'' she said after a moment. "Some say it's doomed; whatever ye see that way must come to pass. But others say nay, it's no but a warning; take heed and ye can change things. What d'ye think, yourself?" She looked sideways at me, curiously.

I took a deep breath, the smell of onions stinging the back of my nose. This was hitting home in no uncertain terms.

"I don't know," I said, and my voice shook slightly. "I'd always thought that of course you could change things if you knew about them. But now . . . I don't know," I ended softly, thinking of Culloden.

Jenny watched me, her eyes so deep a blue as almost to be black in the dim light. I wondered again just how much Jamie had told her—and how much she knew without the telling.

"But ye must try, even so," she said, with certainty. "Ye couldna just leave it, could ye?"

I didn't know whether she meant this personally, but I shook my head.

"No," I said. "You couldn't. You're right; you have to try."

We smiled at each other, a little shyly.

"You'll take good care of him?" Jenny said suddenly. "Even if ye go? Ye will, aye?"

I squeezed her cold fingers, feeling the bones of her hand light and fragile-seeming in my grasp.

"I will," I said.

"Then that's all right," she said softly, and squeezed back.

We sat for a moment, holding each other's hands, until the door of the root cellar swung open, admitting a blast of rain and wind down the stairs.

"Mam?" Young Ian's head poked in, eyes bright with excitement. "Hobart MacKenzie's come! Da says to come quick!"

Jenny sprang to her feet, barely remembering to snatch up the basket of onions.

"Has he come armed, then?" she asked anxiously. "Has he brought a pistol or a sword?"

Ian shook his head, his dark hair lifting wildly in the wind.

"Oh, no, Mam!" he said. "It's worse. He's brought a lawyer!"

Anything less resembling vengeance incarnate than Hobart MacKenzie could scarcely be imagined. A small, light-boned man of about thirty, he had pale blue, pale-lashed eyes with a tendency to water, and indeterminate features that began with a receding hairline and dwindled down into a similarly receding chin that seemed to be trying to escape into the folds of his stock.

He was smoothing his hair at the mirror in the hall when we came in the front door, a neatly curled bob wig sitting on the table beside him. He blinked at us in alarm, then snatched up the wig and crammed it on his head, bowing in the same motion.

"Mrs. Jenny," he said. His small, rabbity eyes flicked in my direction, away, then back again, as though he hoped I really wasn't there, but was very much afraid I was.

Jenny glanced from him to me, sighed deeply, and took the bull by the horns.

"Mr. MacKenzie," she said, dropping him a formal curtsy. "Might I present my good-sister, Claire? Claire, Mr. Hobart Mac-Kenzie of Kinwallis."

His mouth dropped open and he simply gawked at me. I started to extend a hand to him, but thought better of it. I would have liked to know what Emily Post had to recommend in a situation like this, but as Miss Post wasn't present, I was forced to improvise.

"How nice to meet you," I said, smiling as cordially as possible.

"Ah . . ." he said. He bobbed his head tentatively at me. "Um . . . your . . . servant, ma'am."

Fortunately, at this point in the proceedings, the door to the parlor opened. I looked at the small, neat figure framed in the doorway, and let out a cry of delighted recognition.

"Ned! Ned Gowan!"

It was indeed Ned Gowan, the elderly Edinburgh lawyer who had once saved me from burning as a witch. He was noticeably more elderly now, shrunken with age and so heavily wrinkled as to look like one of the dried apples I had seen in the root cellar.

The bright black eyes were the same, though, and they fastened on me at once with an expression of joy.

"My dear!" he exclaimed, hastening forward at a rapid hobble. He seized my hand, beaming, and pressed it to his withered lips in fervent gallantry.

"I had heard that you—"

"How did you come to be—"

"—so delightful to see you!"

"—so happy to see you again, but—"

A cough from Hobart MacKenzie interrupted this rapturous exchange, and Mr. Gowan looked up, startled, then nodded.

"Oh, aye, of course. Business first, my dear," he said, with a gallant bow to me, "and then if ye will, I should be most charmed to hear the tale of your adventures."

"Ah . . . I'll do my best," I said, wondering just how much he would insist on hearing.

"Splendid, splendid." He glanced about the hall, bright little eyes taking in Hobart and Jenny, who had hung up her cloak and was smoothing her hair. "Mr. Fraser and Mr. Murray are already in the parlor. Mr. MacKenzie, if you and the ladies would consent to join us, perhaps we can settle your affairs expeditiously, and proceed to more congenial matters. If you will allow me, my dear?" He crooked a bony arm to me invitingly.

Jamie was still on the sofa where I had left him, and in approximately the same condition—that is, alive. The children were gone, with the exception of one chubby youngster who was curled up on Jamie's lap, fast asleep. Jamie's hair now sported several small plaits on either side, with silk ribbons woven gaily through them, which gave him an incongruously festive air.

"You look like the Cowardly Lion of Oz," I told him in an undertone, sitting down on a hassock behind his sofa. I didn't think it likely that Hobart MacKenzie intended any outright mischief, but if anything happened, I meant to be in close reach of Jamie.

He looked startled, and put a hand to his head.

"I do?"

"Shh," I said, "I'll tell you later."

The other participants had now arranged themselves around the parlor, Jenny sitting down by Ian on the other love seat, and Hobart and Mr. Gowan taking two velvet chairs.

"We are assembled?" Mr. Gowan inquired, glancing around the room. "All interested parties are present? Excellent. Well, to begin with, I must declare my own interest. I am here in the capacity of solicitor to Mr. Hobart MacKenzie, representing the interests of Mrs. James Fraser"—he saw me start, and added, with precision—"that is, the *second* Mrs. James Fraser, née Laoghaire MacKenzie. That is understood?"

He glanced inquiringly at Jamie, who nodded.

"It is."

"Good." Mr. Gowan picked up a glass from the table next to him and took a tiny sip. "My clients, the MacKenzies, have accepted my proposal to seek a legal solution to the imbroglio, which I understand has resulted from the sudden and unexpected —though of course altogether happy and fortuitous—" he added, with a bow to me, "return of the first Mrs. Fraser."

He shook his head reprovingly at Jamie.

"You, my dear young man, have contrived to entangle yourself in considerable legal difficulties, I am sorry to say."

Jamie raised one eyebrow and looked at his sister.

"Aye, well, I had help," he said dryly. "Just what difficulties are we speakin' of?"

"Well, to begin with," Ned Gowan said cheerily, his sparkling black eyes sinking into nets of wrinkles as he smiled at me, "the first Mrs. Fraser would be well within her rights to bring a civil suit against ye for adultery, and criminal fornication, forbye. Penalties for which include—"

Jamie glanced back at me, with a quick blue gleam.

"I think I'm no so worrit by that possibility," he told the lawyer. "What else?"

Ned Gowan nodded obligingly and held up one withered hand, folding down the fingers as he ticked off his points.

"With respect to the second Mrs. Fraser—née Laoghaire Mac-Kenzie—ye could, of course, be charged wi' bigamous misconduct, intent to defraud, actual fraud committed—whether wi' intent or no, which is a separate question—felonious misrepresentation"—he happily folded down his fourth finger and drew breath for more—"and . . ."

Jamie had been listening patiently to this catalogue. Now he interrupted, leaning forward.

"Ned," he said gently, "what the hell does the bloody woman want?"

The small lawyer blinked behind his spectacles, lowered his hand, and cast up his eyes to the beams overhead.

"Weel, the lady's chief desire as stated," he said circumspectly, "is to see ye castrated and disemboweled in the market square at Broch Mordha, and your head mounted on a stake over her gate."

Jamie's shoulders vibrated briefly, and he winced as the movement jarred his arm.

"I see," he said, his mouth twitching.

A smile gathered up the wrinkles by Ned's ancient mouth.

"I was obliged to inform Mrs.—that is, the lady—" he amended, with a glance at me and a slight cough, "that her remedies under the law were somewhat more limited than would accommodate her desires."

"Quite," Jamie said dryly. "But I assume the general idea is that she doesna particularly want me back as a husband?"

"No," Hobart put in unexpectedly. "Crow's bait, maybe, but not a husband."

Ned cast a cold glance at his client.

"Ye willna compromise your case by admitting things in advance of settlement, aye?" he said reprovingly. "Or what are ye payin' me for?" He turned back to Jamie, professional dignity unimpaired.

"While Miss MacKenzie does not wish to resume a marital position wi' regard to you—an action which would be impossible in any case," he added fairly, "unless ye should wish to divorce the present Mrs. Fraser, and remarry—"

"No, I dinna want to do that," Jamie assured him hurriedly, with another glance at me.

"Well, in such case," Ned went on, unruffled, "I should advise my clients that it is more desirable where possible to avoid the cost —and the publicity—" he added, cocking an invisible eyebrow in admonition to Hobart, who nodded hastily, "of a suit at law, with a public trial and its consequent exposure of facts. That being the case—"

"How much?" Jamie interrupted.

"Mr. Fraser!" Ned Gowan looked shocked. "I havena mentioned anything in the nature of a pecuniary settlement as yet—"

"Only because ye're too busy enjoying yourself, ye wicked auld rascal," Jamie said. He was irritated—a red patch burned over each cheekbone—but amused, too. "Get to it, aye?"

Ned Gowan inclined his head ceremoniously.

"Weel, ye must understand," he began, "that a successful suit brought under the charges as described might result in Miss Mac-

Kenzie and her brother mulcting ye in substantial damages—verra
substantial indeed," he added, with a faint lawyerly gloating at the
prospect.

"After all, Miss MacKenzie has not only been subject to public
humiliation and ridicule leading to acute distress of mind, but is
also threatened with loss of her chief means of support—"

"She isna threatened wi' any such thing," Jamie interrupted
heatedly. "I told her I should go on supporting her and the two
lassies! What does she think I am?"

Ned exchanged a glance with Hobart, who shook his head.

"Ye dinna want to know what she thinks ye are," Hobart assured Jamie. "I wouldna have thought she kent such words, myself. But ye do mean to pay?"

Jamie nodded impatiently, rubbing his good hand through his
hair.

"Aye, I will."

"Only until she's marrit again, though." Everyone's head
turned in surprise toward Jenny, who nodded firmly to Ned
Gowan.

"If Jamie's married to Claire, the marriage between him and
Laoghaire wasna valid, aye?"

The lawyer bowed.

"That is true, Mrs. Murray."

"Well, then," Jenny said, in a decided manner. "She's free to
marry again at once, is she no? And once she does, my brother
shouldna be providing for her household."

"An excellent point, Mrs. Murray." Ned Gowan took up his
quill and scratched industriously. "Well, we make progress," he
declared, laying it down again and beaming at the company.
"Now, the next point to be covered . . ."

An hour later, the decanter of whisky was empty, the sheets of
foolscap on the table were filled with Ned Gowan's chicken-
scratchings, and everyone lay limp and exhausted—except Ned
himself, spry and bright-eyed as ever.

"Excellent, excellent," he declared again, gathering up the
sheets and tapping them neatly into order. "So—the main provisions of the settlement are as follows: Mr. Fraser agrees to pay to
Miss MacKenzie the sum of five hundred pounds in compensation
for distress, inconvenience, and the loss of his conjugal services"
—Jamie snorted slightly at this, but Ned affected not to hear him,

continuing his synopsis—"and in addition, agrees to maintain her household at the rate of one hundred pounds per annum, until such time as the aforesaid Miss MacKenzie may marry again, at which time such payment shall cease. Mr. Fraser agrees also to provide a bride-portion for each of Miss MacKenzie's daughters, of an additional three hundred pounds, and as a final provision, agrees not to pursue a prosecution against Miss MacKenzie for assault with intent to commit murder. In return, Miss MacKenzie acquits Mr. Fraser of any and all other claims. This is in accordance with your understanding and consent, Mr. Fraser?" He quirked a brow at Jamie.

"Aye, it is," Jamie said. He was pale from sitting up too long, and there was a fine dew of sweat at his hairline, but he sat straight and tall, the child still asleep in his lap, thumb firmly embedded in her mouth.

"Excellent," Ned said again. He rose, beaming, and bowed to the company. "As our friend Dr. John Arbuthnot says, 'Law is a bottomless pit.' But not more so at the moment than my stomach. Is that delectable aroma indicative of a saddle of mutton in our vicinity, Mrs. Jenny?"

At table, I sat to one side of Jamie, Hobart MacKenzie to the other, now looking pink and relaxed. Mary MacNab brought in the joint, and by ancient custom, set it down in front of Jamie. Her gaze lingered on him a moment too long. He picked up the long, wicked carving knife with his good hand and offered it politely to Hobart.

"Will ye have a go at it, Hobart?" he said.

"Och, no," Hobart said, waving it away. "Better let your wife carve it. I'm no hand wi' a knife—likely cut my finger off instead. You know me, Jamie," he said comfortably.

Jamie gave his erstwhile brother-in-law a long look over the saltcellar.

"Once I would ha' thought, so, Hobart," he said. "Pass me the whisky, aye?"

"The thing to do is to get her married at once," Jenny declared. The children and grandchildren had all retired, and Ned and Hobart had departed for Kinwallis, leaving the four of us to take stock over brandy and cream cakes in the laird's study.

Jamie turned to his sister. "The matchmaking's more in your line, aye?" he said, with a noticeable edge to his voice. "I expect you can think of a suitable man or two for the job, if ye put your mind to it?"

"I expect I can," she said, matching his edge with one of her own. She was embroidering; the needle stabbed through the linen fabric, flashing in the lamplight. It had begun to sleet heavily outside, but the study was cozy, with a small fire on the hearth and the pool of lamplight spilling warmth over the battered desk and its burden of books and ledgers.

"There's the one thing about it," she said, eyes on her work. "Where d'ye mean to get twelve hundred pounds, Jamie?"

I had been wondering that myself. The insurance settlement on the printshop had fallen far short of that amount, and I doubted that Jamie's share of the smuggling proceeds amounted to anything near that magnitude. Certainly Lallybroch itself could not supply the money; survival in the Highlands was a chancy business, and even several good years in a row would provide only the barest surplus.

"Well, there's only the one place, isn't there?" Ian looked from his sister to his brother-in-law and back. After a short silence, Jamie nodded.

"I suppose so," he said reluctantly. He glanced at the window, where the rain was slashing across the glass in slanting streaks. "A vicious time of year for it, though."

Ian shrugged, and sat forward a bit in his chair. "The spring tide will be in a week."

Jamie frowned, looking troubled.

"Aye, that's so, but . . ."

"There's no one has a better right to it, Jamie," Ian said. He reached out and squeezed his friend's good arm, smiling. "It was meant for Prince Charles's followers, aye? And ye were one of those, whether ye wanted to be or no."

Jamie gave him back a rueful half-smile.

"Aye, I suppose that's true." He sighed. "In any case, it's the only thing I can see to do." He glanced back and forth between Ian and Jenny, evidently debating whether to add something else. His sister knew him even better than I did. She lifted her head from her work and looked at him sharply.

"What is it, Jamie?" she said.

He took a deep breath.

"I want to take Young Ian," he said.

"No," she said instantly. The needle had stopped, stuck halfway through a brilliant red bud in the pattern, the color of blood against the white smock.

"He's old enough, Jenny," Jamie said quietly.

"He's not!" she objected. "He's but barely fifteen; Michael and Jamie were both sixteen at least, and better grown."

"Aye, but wee Ian's a better swimmer than either of his brothers," Ian said judiciously. His forehead was furrowed with thought. "It will have to be one of the lads, after all," he pointed out to Jenny. He jerked his head toward Jamie, cradling his arm in its sling. "Jamie canna very well be swimming himself, in his present condition. Or Claire, for that matter," he added, with a smile at me.

"Swim?" I said, utterly bewildered. "Swim *where*?"

Ian looked taken aback for a moment; then he glanced at Jamie, brows lifted.

"Oh. Ye hadna told her?"

Jamie shook his head. "I had, but not all of it." He turned to me. "It's the treasure, Sassenach—the seals' gold."

Unable to take the treasure with him, he had concealed it in its place and returned to Ardsmuir.

"I didna ken what best to do about it," he explained. "Duncan Kerr gave the care of it to me, but I had no notion who it belonged to, or who put it there, or what I was to do with it. 'The white witch' was all Duncan said, and that meant nothing to me but you, Sassenach."

Reluctant to make use of the treasure himself, and yet feeling that someone should know about it, lest he die in prison, he had sent a carefully coded letter to Jenny and Ian at Lallybroch, giving the location of the cache, and the use for which it had—presumably—been meant.

Times had been hard for Jacobites then, sometimes even more so for those who had escaped to France—leaving lands and fortunes behind—than for those who remained to face English persecution in the Highlands. At about the same time, Lallybroch had experienced two bad crops in a row, and letters had reached them from France, asking for any help possible to succor erstwhile companions there, in danger of starvation.

"We had nothing to send; in fact, we were damn close to starving here," Ian explained. "I sent word to Jamie, and he said as he thought perhaps it wouldna be wrong to use a small bit of the treasure to help feed Prince *Tearlach*'s followers."

"It seemed likely it was put there by one of the Stuarts' supporters," Jamie chimed in. He cocked a ruddy brow at me, and his mouth quirked up at one corner. "I thought I wouldna send it to Prince Charles, though."

"Good thinking," I said dryly. Any money given to Charles Stuart would have been wasted, squandered within weeks, and anyone who had known Charles intimately, as Jamie had, would know that very well.

Ian had taken his eldest son, Jamie, and made his way across Scotland to the seals' cove near Coigach. Fearful of any word of the treasure getting out, they had not sought a fisherman's boat, but instead Young Jamie had swum to the seals' rock as his uncle had several years before. He had found the treasure in its place, abstracted two gold coins and three of the smaller gemstones, and secreting these in a bag tied securely round his neck, had replaced the rest of the treasure and made his way back through the surf, arriving exhausted.

They had made their way to Inverness then, and taken ship to France, where their cousin Jared Fraser, a successful expatriate wine merchant, had helped them to change the coins and jewels discreetly into cash, and taken the responsibility of distributing it among the Jacobites in need.

Three times since, Ian had made the laborious trip to the coast with one of his sons, each time to abstract a small part of the hidden fortune to supply a need. Twice the money had gone to friends in need in France; once it had been needed to purchase fresh planting-stock for Lallybroch and provide the food to see its tenants through a long winter when the potato crop failed.

Only Jenny, Ian, and the two elder boys, Jamie and Michael, knew of the treasure. Ian's wooden leg prevented his swimming to the seals' island, so one of his sons must always make the trip with him. I gathered that it had been something of a rite of passage for both Young Jamie and Michael, entrusted with such a great secret. Now it might be Young Ian's turn.

"No," Jenny said again, but I thought her heart wasn't in it. Ian was already nodding thoughtfully.

"Would ye take him with ye to France, too, Jamie?"

Jamie nodded.

"Aye, that's the thing. I shall have to leave Lallybroch, and stay away for a good bit, for Laoghaire's sake—I canna be living here with you, under her nose," he said apologetically to me, "at least not until she's suitably wed to someone else." He switched his attention back to Ian.

"I havena told ye everything that's happened in Edinburgh, Ian, but all things considered, I think it likely best I stay away from there for a time, too."

I sat quiet, trying to digest this news. I hadn't realized that Jamie meant to leave Lallybroch—leave Scotland altogether, it sounded like.

"So what d'ye mean to do, Jamie?" Jenny had given up any pretense of sewing, and sat with her hands in her lap.

He rubbed his nose, looking tired. This was the first day he had been up; I privately thought he should have been back in bed hours ago, but he had insisted upon staying up to preside over dinner and visit with everyone.

"Well," he said slowly, "Jared's offered more than once to take me into his firm. Perhaps I shall stay in France, at least for a year. I was thinking Young Ian could go with us, and be schooled in Paris."

Jenny and Ian exchanged a long look, one of those in which long-married couples are capable of carrying out complete conversations in the space of a few heartbeats. At last, Jenny tilted her head a bit to one side. Ian smiled and took her hand.

"It'll be all right, *mo nighean dubh,*" he said to her in a low, tender voice. Then he turned to Jamie.

"Aye, take him. It'll be a great chance for the lad."

"You're sure?" Jamie hesitated, speaking to his sister, rather than Ian. Jenny nodded. Her blue eyes glistened in the lamplight, and the end of her nose was slightly red.

"I suppose it's best we give him his freedom while he still thinks it's ours to give," she said. She looked at Jamie, then at me, straight and steady. "But you'll take good care of him, aye?"

39

Lost, and by the Wind Grieved

This part of Scotland was as unlike the leafy glens and lochs near Lallybroch as the North Yorkshire moors. Here there were virtually no trees; only long sweeps of rock-strewn heather, rising into crags that touched the lowering sky and disappeared abruptly into curtains of mist.

As we got nearer to the seacoast, the mist became heavier, setting in earlier in the afternoon, lingering longer in the morning, so that only for a couple of hours in the middle of the day did we have anything like clear riding. The going was consequently slow, but none of us minded greatly, except Young Ian, who was beside himself with excitement, impatient to arrive.

"How far is it from the shore to the seals' island?" he asked Jamie for the tenth time.

"A quarter mile, I make it," his uncle replied.

"I can swim that far," Young Ian repeated, for the tenth time. His hands were clenched tightly on the reins, and his bony jaw set with determination.

"Aye, I know ye can," Jamie assured him patiently. He glanced at me, the hint of a smile hidden in the corner of his mouth. "Ye willna need to, though; just swim straight for the island, and the current will carry ye."

The boy nodded, and lapsed into silence, but his eyes were bright with anticipation.

The headland above the cove was mist-shrouded and deserted. Our voices echoed oddly in the fog, and we soon stopped talking, out of an abiding sense of eeriness. I could hear the seals barking far below, the sound wavering and mixing with the crash of the surf, so that now and then it sounded like sailors hallooing to one another over the sound of the sea.

Jamie pointed out the rock chimney of Ellen's tower to Young Ian, and taking a coil of rope from his saddle, picked his way over the broken rock of the headland to the entrance.

"Keep your shirt on 'til you're down," he told the lad, shouting to be heard above the wave. "Else the rock will tear your back to shreds."

Ian nodded understanding, then, the rope tied securely round his middle, gave me a nervous grin, took two jerky steps, and disappeared into the earth.

Jamie had the other end of the rope wrapped round his own waist, paying out the length of it carefully with his sound hand as the boy descended. Crawling on hands and knees, I made my way over the short turf and pebbles to the crumbling edge of the cliff, where I could look over to the half-moon beach below.

It seemed a very long time, but finally I saw Ian emerge from the bottom of the chimney, a small, antlike figure. He untied his rope, peered around, spotted us at the top of the cliff, and waved enthusiastically. I waved back, but Jamie merely muttered, "All right, get on, then," under his breath.

I could feel him tense beside me as the boy stripped off to his breeks and scrambled down the rocks to the water, and I felt his flinch as the small figure dived headlong into the gray-blue waves.

"Brrr!" I said, watching. "The water must be freezing!"

"It is," Jamie said with feeling. "Ian's right; it's a vicious time of year to be swimming."

His face was pale and set. I didn't think it was the result of discomfort from his wounded arm, though the long ride and the exercise with the rope couldn't have done it any good. While he had shown nothing but encouraging confidence while Ian was making his descent, he wasn't making any effort to hide his worry now. The fact was that there was no way for us to reach Ian, should anything go wrong.

"Maybe we should have waited for the mist to lift," I said, more to distract him than because I thought so.

"If we had 'til next Easter, we might," he agreed ironically. "Though I'll grant ye, I've seen it clearer than this," he added, squinting into the swirling murk below.

The three islands were only intermittently visible from the cliff as the fog swept across them. I had been able to see the bobbing dot of Ian's head for the first twenty yards as he left the shore, but now he had disappeared into the mist.

"Do you think he's all right?" Jamie bent to help me scramble upright. The cloth of his coat was damp and rough under my fingers, soaked with mist and the fine droplets of ocean spray.

"Aye, he'll do. He's a bonny swimmer; and it's none so difficult a swim, either, once he's into the current." Still, he stared into the mist as though sheer effort could pierce its veils.

On Jamie's advice, Young Ian had timed his descent to begin when the tide began to go out, so as to have as much assistance as possible from the tide-race. Looking over the edge, I could see a floating mass of bladder wrack, half-stranded on the widening strip of beach.

"Perhaps two hours before he comes back." Jamie answered my unspoken question. He turned reluctantly from his vain perusal of the mist-hidden cove. "Damn, I wish I'd gone myself, arm or no arm."

"Both Young Jamie and Michael have done it," I reminded him. He gave me a rueful smile.

"Oh, aye. Ian will do fine. It's only that it's a good deal easier to do something that's a bit dangerous than it is to wait and worry while someone else does it."

"Ha," I told him. "So now you know what it's like being married to *you*."

He laughed.

"Oh, aye, I suppose so. Besides, it would be a shame to cheat Young Ian of his adventure. Come on, then, let's get out of the wind."

We moved inland a bit, away from the crumbling edge of the cliff, and sat down to wait, using the horses' bodies as shelter. Rough, shaggy Highland ponies, they appeared unmoved by the unpleasant weather, merely standing together, heads down, tails turned against the wind.

The wind was too high for easy conversation. We sat quietly, leaning together like the horses, with our backs to the windy shore.

"What's that?" Jamie raised his head, listening.

"What?"

"I thought I heard shouting."

"I expect it's the seals," I said, but before the words were out of my mouth, he was up and striding toward the cliff's edge.

The cove was still full of curling mist, but the wind had uncovered the seals' island, and it was clearly visible, at least for the moment. There were no seals on it now, though.

A small boat was drawn up on a sloping rock shelf at one side of the island. Not a fisherman's boat; this one was longer and more pointed at the prow, with one set of oars.

As I stared, a man appeared from the center of the island. He carried something under one arm, the size and shape of the box Jamie had described. I didn't have long to speculate as to the nature of this object, though, for just then a second man came up the far slope of the island and into sight.

This one was carrying Young Ian. He had the boy's half-naked body slung carelessly over one shoulder. It swung head down, arms dangling with a limpness that made it clear the boy was unconscious or dead.

"Ian!" Jamie's hand clamped over my mouth before I could shout again.

"Hush!" He dragged me to my knees to keep me out of sight. We watched, helpless, as the second man heaved Ian carelessly into the boat, then took hold of the gunwales to run it back into the water. There wasn't a chance of making the descent down the chimney and the swim to the island before they succeeded in making their escape. But escape to where?

"Where did they come from?" I gasped. Nothing else stirred in the cove below, save the mist and the shifting kelp-beds, turning in the tide.

"A ship. It's a ship's boat." Jamie added something low and heartfelt in Gaelic, and then was gone. I turned to see him fling himself on one of the horses and wrench its head around. Then he was off, riding hell-for-leather across the headland, away from the cove.

Rough as the footing across the headland was, the horses were shod for it better than I was. I hastily mounted and followed Jamie, a high-pitched whinny of protest from Ian's hobbled mount ringing in my ears.

It was less than a quarter of a mile to the ocean side of the headland, but it seemed to take forever to reach it. I saw Jamie ahead of me, his hair flying loose in the wind, and beyond him, the ship, lying to offshore.

The ground broke away in a tumble of rock that fell down to the ocean, not so steep as the cliffs of the cove, but much too rough to take a horse down. By the time I had reined up, Jamie was off his horse, and picking his way down the rubble toward the water.

To the left, I could see the longboat from the island, pulling round the curve of the headland. Someone on the ship must have been looking out for them, for I heard a faint hail from the direction of the ship, and saw small figures suddenly appear in the rigging.

One of these must also have seen us, for there was a sudden agitation aboard, with heads popping up above the rail and more yelling. The ship was blue, with a broad black band painted all around it. There was a line of gunports set in this band, and as I watched, the forward one opened, and the round black eye of the gun peeked out.

"Jamie!" I shrieked, as loudly as I could. He looked up from the rocks at his feet, saw where I was pointing, and hurled himself flat in the rubble as the gun went off.

The report wasn't terribly loud, but there was a sort of whistling noise past my head that made me duck instinctively. Several of the rocks around me exploded in puffs of flying rock chips, and it occurred to me, rather belatedly, that the horses and I were a great deal more visible there at the top of the headland than Jamie was on the cliff below.

The horses, having grasped this essential fact long before I did, were on their way back to where we had left their hobbled fellow well before the dust had settled. I flung myself bodily over the edge of the headland, slid several feet in a shower of gravel, and wedged myself into a deep crevice in the cliff.

There was another explosion somewhere above my head, and I pressed myself even closer into the rock. Evidently the people on board the ship were satisfied with the effect of their last shot, for relative silence now descended.

My heart was hammering against my ribs, and the air around my face was full of a fine gray dust that gave me an irresistible urge to cough. I risked a look over my shoulder, and was in time to see the longboat being hoisted aboard ship. Of Ian and his two captors, there was no sign.

The gunport closed silently as I watched, and the rope that held the anchor slithered up, streaming water. The ship turned slowly, seeking wind. The air was light and the sails barely puffed, but even that was enough. Slowly, then faster, she was moving toward the open sea. By the time Jamie had reached my roosting place, the ship had all but vanished in the thick cloudbank that obscured the horizon.

"Jesus" was all he said when he reached me, but he clutched me hard for a moment. "Jesus."

He let go then, and turned to look out over the sea. Nothing moved save a few tendrils of slow-floating mist. The whole world seemed stricken with silence; even the occasional cries of the murres and shearwaters had been cut off by the cannon's boom.

The gray rock near my foot showed a fresh patch of lighter gray, where shot had struck off a wide flake of stone. It was no more than three feet above the crevice where I had taken refuge.

"What shall we do?" I felt numbed, both by the shock of the afternoon, and by the sheer enormity of what had happened. Impossible to believe that in less than an hour, Ian had disappeared from us as completely as though he had been wiped off the face of the earth. The fogbank loomed thick and impenetrable, a little way off the coast before us, a barrier as impassible as the curtain between earth and the underworld.

My mind kept replaying images: the mist, drifting over the outlines of the silkies' island, the sudden appearance of the boat, the men coming over the rocks, Ian's lanky, teenage body, white-skinned as the mist, skinny limbs dangling like a disjointed doll's. I had seen everything with that clarity that attends tragedy; every detail fixed in my mind's eye, to be shown again and again, always with that half-conscious feeling that, this time, I should be able to alter it.

Jamie's face was set in rigid lines, the furrows cut deep from nose to mouth.

"I don't know," he said. "Damn me to hell, I don't *know* what to do!" His hands flexed suddenly into fists at his sides. He shut his eyes, breathing heavily.

I felt even more frightened at this admission. In the brief time I had been back with him, I had grown once more accustomed to having Jamie always know what to do, even in the direst circumstances. This confession seemed more upsetting than anything that had yet happened.

A sense of helplessness swirled round me like the mist. Every nerve cried out to do *something*. But what?

I saw the streak of blood on his cuff then; he had gashed his hand, climbing down the rocks. That, I could help, and I felt a sense of thankfulness that there was, after all, one thing I could do, however small.

"You've cut yourself," I said. I touched his injured hand. "Let me see; I'll wrap it for you."

"No," he said. He turned away, face strained, still looking desperately out into the fog. When I reached for him again, he jerked away.

"No, I said! Leave it be!"

I swallowed hard and wrapped my arms about myself under my cloak. There was little wind now, even on the headland, but it was cold and clammy nonetheless.

He rubbed his hand carelessly against the front of his coat, leaving a rusty smear. He was still staring out to sea, toward the spot where the ship had vanished. He closed his eyes, and pressed his lips tight together. Then he opened them, made a small gesture of apology toward me, and turned toward the headland.

"I suppose we must catch the horses," he said quietly. "Come on."

We walked back across the thick, short turf and strewn rocks without speaking, silent with shock and grief. I could see the horses, small stick-legged figures in the distance, clustered together with their hobbled companion. It seemed to have taken hours to run from the headland to the outer shore; going back seemed much longer.

"I don't think he was dead," I said, after what seemed like a year. I laid a hand tentatively on Jamie's arm, meaning to be comforting, but he wouldn't have noticed if I had struck him with a blackjack. He walked on slowly, head down.

"No," he said, and I saw him swallow hard. "No, he wasn't dead, or they'd not have taken him."

"*Did* they take him aboard the ship?" I pressed. "Did you see them?" I thought it might be better for him if he would talk.

He nodded. "Aye, they passed him aboard; I saw it clear. I suppose that's some hope," he muttered, as though to himself. "If

they didna knock him on the head at once, maybe they won't.''
Suddenly remembering that I was there, he turned and looked at
me, eyes searching my face.

"You're all right, Sassenach?"

I was scraped raw in several places, covered with filth, and
shaky-kneed with fright, but basically sound.

"I'm fine." I put my hand on his arm again. This time he let it
stay.

"That's good," he said softly, after a moment. He tucked my
hand into the crook of his elbow, and we went on.

"Have you any idea who they were?" I had to raise my voice
slightly to be heard above the wash of the surf behind us, but I
wanted to keep him talking if I could.

He shook his head, frowning. The effort of talking seemed to be
bringing him slowly out of his own shock.

"I heard one of the sailors shout to the men in the boat, and he
spoke in French. But that proves nothing—sailors come from everywhere. Still, I have seen enough of ships at the docks to think
that this one didna have quite the look of a merchant—nor the
look of an English ship at all," he added, "though I couldna say
why, exactly. The way the sails were rigged, maybe."

"It was blue, with a black line painted round it," I said. "That
was all I had time to see, before the guns started firing."

Was it possible to trace a ship? The germ of the idea gave me
hope; perhaps the situation was not so hopeless as I had first
thought. If Ian was not dead, and we could find out where the ship
was going . . .

"Did you see a name on it?" I asked.

"A name?" He looked faintly surprised at the notion. "What,
on the ship?"

"Do ships not usually have their names painted on the sides?" I
asked.

"No, what for?" He sounded honestly puzzled.

"So you could bloody tell who they are!" I said, exasperated.
Taken by surprise by my tone, he actually smiled a little.

"Aye, well, I should expect that perhaps they dinna much want
anyone telling who they are, given their business," he said dryly.

We paced on together for a few moments, thinking. Then I said
curiously, "Well, but how do legitimate ships tell who each other
is, if they haven't got names painted on?"

He glanced at me, one eyebrow raised.

"I should know you from another woman," he pointed out, "and ye havena got your name stitched upon your bosom."

"Not so much as a letter 'A,' " I said, flippantly, but seeing his blank look, added, "You mean ships look different enough—and there are few enough of them—that you can tell one from another just by looking?"

"Not me," he said honestly. "I know a few; ships where I ken the captain, and have been aboard to do business, or a few like the packet boats, that go back and forth so often that I've seen them in port dozens of times. But a sailing man would ken a great deal more."

"Then it *might* be possible to find out what the ship that took Ian is called?"

He nodded, looking at me curiously. "Aye, I think so. I have been trying to call to mind everything about it as we walked, so as to tell Jared. He'll know a great many ships, and a great many more captains—and perhaps one of them will know a blue ship, wide in the beam, with three masts, twelve guns, and a scowling figurehead."

My heart bounded upward. "So you *do* have a plan!"

"I wouldna call it so much a plan," he said. "It's only I canna think of anything else to do." He shrugged, and wiped a hand over his face. Tiny droplets of moisture were condensing on us as we walked, glistening in the ruddy hairs of his eyebrows and coating his cheeks with a wetness like tears. He sighed.

"The passage is arranged from Inverness. The best I can see to do is to go; Jared will be expecting us in Le Havre. When we see him, perhaps he can help us to find out what the blue ship is called, and maybe where it's bound. Aye," he said dryly, anticipating my question, "ships have home ports, and if they dinna belong to the navy, they have runs they commonly make, and papers for the harbormaster, too, showing where they're bound."

I began to feel better than I had since Ian had descended Ellen's tower.

"If they're not pirates or privateers, that is," he added, with a warning look which put an immediate damper on my rising spirits.

"And if they are?"

"Then God knows, but I don't," he said briefly, and would not say any more until we reached the horses.

They were grazing on the headland near the tower where we had left Ian's mount, behaving as though nothing had happened, pretending to find the tough sea grass delicious.

"Tcha!" Jamie viewed them disapprovingly. "Silly beasts." He grabbed the coil of rope and wrapped it twice round a projecting stone. Handing me the end, with a terse instruction to hold it, he dropped the free end down the chimney, shed his coat and shoes, and disappeared down the rope himself without further remark.

Sometime later, he came back up, sweating profusely, with a small bundle tucked under his arm. Young Ian's shirt, coat, shoes and stockings, with his knife and the small leather pouch in which the lad kept such valuables as he had.

"Do you mean to take them home to Jenny?" I asked. I tried to imagine what Jenny might think, say, or do at the news, and succeeded all too well. I felt a little sick, knowing that the hollow, aching sense of loss I felt was as nothing to what hers would be.

Jamie's face was flushed from the climb, but at my words, the blood drained from his cheeks. His hands tightened on the bundle.

"Oh, aye," he said, very softly, with great bitterness. "Aye, I shall go home and tell my sister that I have lost her youngest son? She didna want him to come wi' me, but I insisted. I'll take care of him, I said. And now he is hurt and maybe dead—but here are his clothes, to remember him by?" His jaw clenched, and he swallowed convulsively.

"I'd rather be dead myself," he said.

He knelt on the ground then, shaking out the articles of clothing, folding them carefully, and laying them together in a pile. He folded the coat carefully around the other things, stood up, and stuffed the bundle into his saddlebag.

"Ian will be needing them, I expect, when we find him," I said, trying to sound convinced.

Jamie looked at me, but after a moment, he nodded.

"Aye," he said softly. "I expect he will."

It was too late in the day to begin the ride to Inverness. The sun was setting, announcing the fact with a dull reddish glow that barely penetrated the gathering mist. Without speaking, we began to make camp. There was cold food in the saddlebags, but neither of us had the heart to eat. Instead, we rolled ourselves up in cloaks and blankets and lay down to sleep, cradled in small hollows that Jamie had scooped in the earth.

I couldn't sleep. The ground was hard and stony beneath my hips and shoulders, and the thunder of the surf below would have been sufficient to keep me awake, even had my mind not been filled with thoughts of Ian.

Was he badly hurt? The limpness of his body had bespoken some damage, but I had seen no blood. Presumably, he had merely been hit on the head. If so, what would he feel when he woke, to find himself abducted, and being carried farther from home and family with each passing minute?

And how were we ever to find him? When Jamie had first mentioned Jared, I had felt hopeful, but the more I thought of it, the slimmer seemed the prospects of actually finding a single ship, which might now be sailing in any direction at all, to anyplace in the world. And would his captors bother to keep Ian, or would they, on second thoughts, conclude that he was a dangerous nuisance, and pitch him overboard?

I didn't think I slept, but I must have dozed, my dreams full of trouble. I woke shivering with cold, and edged out a hand, reaching for Jamie. He wasn't there. When I sat up, I found that he had spread his blanket over me while I dozed, but it was a poor substitute for the heat of his body.

He was sitting some distance away, with his back to me. The offshore wind had risen with the setting of the sun, and blown some of the mist away; a half-moon shed enough light through the clouds to show me his hunched figure clearly.

I got up and walked over to him, folding my cloak tight about me against the chill. My steps made a light crunching sound on the crumbled granite, but the sound was drowned in the sighing rumble of the sea below. Still, he must have heard me; he didn't turn around, but gave no sign of surprise when I sank down beside him.

He sat with his chin in his hands, his elbows on his knees, eyes wide and sightless as he gazed out into the dark water of the cove. If the seals were awake, they were quiet tonight.

"Are you all right?" I said quietly. "It's beastly cold." He was wearing nothing but his coat, and in the small, chilled hours of the night, in the wet, cold air above the sea, that was far from enough. I could feel the tiny, constant shiver that ran through him when I set my hand on his arm.

"Aye, I'm fine," he said, with a marked lack of conviction.

I merely snorted at this piece of prevarication, and sat down next to him on another chunk of granite.

"It wasn't your fault," I said, after we had sat in silence for some time, listening to the sea.

"Ye should go and sleep, Sassenach." His voice was even, but with an undertone of hopelessness that made me move closer to him, trying to embrace him. He was clearly reluctant to touch me, but I was shivering very obviously myself by this time.

"I'm not going anywhere."

He sighed deeply and pulled me closer, settling me upon his knee, so that his arms came inside my cloak, holding tight. Little by little, the shivering eased.

"What are you doing out here?" I asked at last.

"Praying," he said softly. "Or trying to."

"I shouldn't have interrupted you." I made as though to move away, but his hold on me tightened.

"No, stay," he said. We stayed clasped close; I could feel the warmth of his breathing in my ear. He drew in his breath as though about to speak, but then let it out without saying anything. I turned and touched his face.

"What is it, Jamie?"

"Is it wrong for me to have ye?" he whispered. His face was bone-white, his eyes no more than dark pits in the dim light. "I keep thinking—is it my fault? Have I sinned so greatly, wanting you so much, needing ye more than life itself?"

"Do you?" I took his face between my hands, feeling the wide bones cold under my palms. "And if you do—how can that be wrong? I'm your wife." In spite of everything, the simple word "wife" made my heart lighten.

He turned his face slightly, so his lips lay against my palm, and his hand came up, groping for mine. His fingers were cold, too, and hard as driftwood soaked in seawater.

"I tell myself so. God has given ye to me; how can I not love you? And yet—I keep thinking, and canna stop."

He looked down at me then, brow furrowed with trouble.

"The treasure—it was all right to use it when there was need, to feed the hungry, or to rescue folk from prison. But to try to buy my freedom from guilt—to use it only so that I might live free at

Lallybroch with you, and not trouble myself over Laoghaire—I think maybe that was wrong to do.''

I drew his hand down around my waist, and pulled him close. He came, eager for comfort, and laid his head on my shoulder.

"Hush," I said to him, though he hadn't spoken again. "Be still. Jamie, have you ever done something for yourself alone—not with any thought of anyone else?"

His hand rested gently on my back, tracing the seam of my bodice, and his breathing held the hint of a smile.

"Oh, many and many a time," he whispered. "When I saw you. When I took ye, not caring did ye want me or no, did ye have somewhere else to be, someone else to love."

"Bloody man," I whispered in his ear, rocking him as best I could. "You're an awful fool, Jamie Fraser. And what about Brianna? That wasn't wrong, was it?"

"No." He swallowed; I could hear the sound of it clearly, and feel the pulse beat in his neck where I held him. "But now I have taken ye back from her, as well. I love you—and I love Ian, like he was my own. And I am thinking maybe I cannot have ye both."

"Jamie Fraser," I said again, with as much conviction as I could put into my voice, "you're a terrible fool." I smoothed the hair back from his forehead and twisted my fist in the thick tail at his nape, pulling his head back to make him look at me.

I thought my face must look to him as his did to me; the bleached bones of a skull, with the lips and eyes dark as blood.

"You didn't force me to come to you, or snatch me away from Brianna. I came, because I wanted to—because I wanted *you,* as much as you did me—and my being here has nothing to do with what's happened. We're *married,* blast you, by any standard you care to name—before God, man, Neptune, or what-have-you."

"Neptune?" he said, sounding a little stunned.

"Be quiet," I said. "We're married, I say, and it isn't wicked for you to want me, or to have me, and no God worth his salt would take your nephew away from you because you wanted to be happy. So there!

"Besides," I added, pulling back and looking up at him a moment later, "I'm not bloody going back, so what could you do about it, anyway?"

The small vibration in his chest this time was laughter, not cold.

"Take ye and be damned for it, I expect," he said. He kissed my forehead gently. "Loving you has put me through hell more than once, Sassenach; I'll risk it again, if need be."

"Bah," I said. "And you think loving *you*'s been a bed of roses, do you?"

This time he laughed out loud.

"No," he said, "but you'll maybe keep doing it?"

"Maybe I will, at that."

"You're a verra stubborn woman," he said, the smile clear in his voice.

"It bloody takes one to know one," I said, and then we were both quiet for quite some time.

It was very late—perhaps four o'clock in the morning. The half-moon was low in the sky, seen only now and then through the moving clouds. The clouds themselves were moving faster; the wind was shifting and the mist breaking up, in the turning hour between dark and dawn. Somewhere below, one of the seals barked loudly, once.

"Do ye think perhaps ye could stand to go now?" Jamie said suddenly. "Not wait for the daylight? Once off the headland, the going's none so bad that the horses canna manage in the dark."

My whole body ached from weariness, and I was starving, but I stood up at once, and brushed the hair out of my face.

"Let's go," I said.

PART EIGHT

On the Water

40

I Shall Go Down to the Sea

"It will have to be the *Artemis*." Jared flipped shut the cover of his portable writing desk and rubbed his brow, frowning. Jamie's cousin had been in his fifties when I knew him before, and was now well past seventy, but the snub-nosed hatchet face, the spare, narrow frame, and the tireless capacity for work were just the same. Only his hair marked his age, gone from lank darkness to a scanty, pure and gleaming white, jauntily tied with a red silk ribbon.

"She's no more than a midsized sloop, with a crew of forty or so," he remarked. "But it's late in the season, and we'll not likely do better—all of the Indiamen will have gone a month since. *Artemis* would have gone with the convoy to Jamaica, was she not laid up for repair."

"I'd sooner have a ship of yours—and one of your captains," Jamie assured him. "The size doesna matter."

Jared cocked a skeptical eyebrow at his cousin. "Oh? Well, and ye may find it matters more than ye think, out at sea. It's like to be squally, this late in the season, and a sloop will be bobbin' like a cork. Might I ask how ye weathered the Channel crossing in the packet boat, cousin?"

Jamie's face, already drawn and grim, grew somewhat grimmer at this question. The completest of landlubbers, he was not just prone to seasickness, but prostrated by it. He had been violently ill all the way from Inverness to Le Havre, though sea and weather had been quite calm. Now, some six hours later, safe ashore in

Jared's warehouse by the quay, there was still a pale tinge to his lips and dark circles beneath his eyes.

"I'll manage," he said shortly.

Jared eyed him dubiously, well aware of his response to seagoing craft of any kind. Jamie could scarcely set foot on a ship at anchor without going green; the prospect of his crossing the Atlantic, sealed inescapably in a small and constantly tossing ship for two or three months, was enough to boggle the stoutest mind. It had been troubling mine for some time.

"Well, I suppose there's no help for it," Jared said with a sigh, echoing my thought. "And at least you'll have a physician to hand," he added, with a smile at me. "That is, I suppose you intend accompanying him, my dear?"

"Yes indeed," I assured him. "How long will it be before the ship is ready? I'd like to find a good apothecary's, to stock my medicine chest before the voyage."

Jared pursed his lips in concentration. "A week, God willing," he said. "*Artemis* is in Bilbao at the moment; she's to carry a cargo of tanned Spanish hides, with a load of copper from Italy—she'll ship that here, once she arrives, which should be day after tomorrow, with a fair wind. I've no captain signed on for the voyage yet, but a good man in mind; I may have to go to Paris to fetch him, though, and that will be two days there and two back. Add a day to complete stores, fill the water casks, add all the bits and pieces, and she should be ready to leave at dawn tomorrow week."

"How long to the West Indies?" Jamie asked. The tension in him showed in the lines of his body, little affected either by our journey or by the brief rest. He was strung taut as a bow, and likely to remain so until we had found Young Ian.

"Two months, in the season," Jared replied, the small frown still lining his forehead. "But you're a month past the season now; hit the winter gales and it could be three. Or more."

Or never, but Jared, ex-seaman that he was, was too superstitious—or too tactful—to voice this possibility. Still, I saw him touch the wood of his desk surreptitiously for luck.

Neither would he voice the other thought that occupied my mind; we had no positive proof that the blue ship was headed for the West Indies. We had only the records Jared had obtained for us from the Le Havre harbormaster, showing two visits by the ship—

aptly named *Bruja*—within the last five years, each time giving her home port as Bridgetown, on the island of Barbados.

"Tell me about her again—the ship that took Young Ian," Jared said. "How did she ride? High in the water, or sunk low, as if she were loaded heavy for a voyage?"

Jamie closed his eyes for a moment, concentrating, then opened them with a nod. "Heavy-laden, I could swear it. Her gunports were no more than six feet from the water."

Jared nodded, satisfied. "Then she was leaving port, not coming in. I've messengers out to all the major ports in France, Portugal, and Spain. With luck, they'll find the port she shipped from, and then we'll know her destination for sure from her papers." His thin lips quirked suddenly downward. "Unless she's turned pirate, and sailing under false papers, that is."

The old wine merchant carefully set aside the lap desk, its carved mahogany richly darkened by years of use, and rose to his feet, moving stiffly.

"Well, that's the most that can be done for the moment. Let's go to the house, now; Mathilde will have supper waiting. Tomorrow I'll take ye over the manifests and orders, and your wife can find her bits of herbs."

It was nearly five o'clock, and full dark at this time of year, but Jared had two linksmen waiting to escort us the short distance to his house, equipped with torches to light the way and armed with stout clubs. Le Havre was a thriving port city, and the quay district was no place to walk alone after dark, particularly if one was known as a prosperous wine merchant.

Despite the exhaustion of the Channel crossing, the oppressive clamminess and pervasive fish-smell of Le Havre, and a gnawing hunger, I felt my spirits rise as we followed the torches through the dark, narrow streets. Thanks to Jared, we had at least a chance of finding Young Ian.

Jared had concurred with Jamie's opinion that if the pirates of the *Bruja*—for so I thought of them—had not killed Young Ian on the spot, they were likely to keep him unharmed. A healthy young male of any race could be sold as a slave or indentured servant in the West Indies for upward of two hundred pounds; a respectable sum by current standards.

If they did intend so to dispose of Young Ian profitably, *and* if we knew the port to which they were sailing, it should be a reasonably easy matter to find and recover the boy. A gust of wind and a few chilly drops from the hovering clouds dampened my optimism slightly, reminding me that while it might be no great matter to find Ian once we had reached the West Indies, both the *Bruja* and the *Artemis* had to reach the islands first. And the winter storms were beginning.

The rain increased through the night, drumming insistently on the slate roof above our heads. I would normally have found the sound soothing and soporific; under the circumstances, the low thrum seemed threatening, not peaceful.

Despite Jared's substantial dinner and the excellent wines that accompanied it, I found myself unable to sleep, my mind summoning images of rain-soaked canvas and the swell of heavy seas. At least my morbid imaginings were keeping only myself awake; Jamie had not come up with me but had stayed to talk with Jared about the arrangements for the upcoming voyage.

Jared was willing to risk a ship and a captain to help in the search. In return, Jamie would sail as supercargo.

"As *what*?" I had said, hearing this proposal.

"The supercargo," Jared had explained patiently. "That's the man whose duty it is to oversee the loading, the unloading, and the sale and disposition of the cargo. The captain and the crew merely sail the ship; someone's got to look after the contents. In a case where the welfare of the cargo will be affected, the supercargo's orders may override even the captain's authority."

And so it was arranged. While Jared was more than willing to go to some risk in order to help a kinsman, he saw no reason not to profit from the arrangement. He had therefore made quick provision for a miscellaneous cargo to be loaded from Bilbao and Le Havre; we would sail to Jamaica to unload the bulk of it, and would arrange for the reloading of the *Artemis* with rum produced by the sugarcane plantation of Fraser et Cie on Jamaica, for the return trip.

The return trip, however, would not occur until good sailing weather returned, in late April or early May. For the time between arrival on Jamaica in February and return to Scotland in May, Jamie would have disposal of the *Artemis* and her crew, to travel to

Barbados—or other places—in search of Young Ian. Three months. I hoped it would be enough.

It was a generous arrangement. Still, Jared, who had been an expatriate wine-seller for many years in France, was wealthy enough that the loss of a ship, while distressing, would not cripple him. The fact did not escape me that while Jared was risking a small portion of his fortune, we were risking our lives.

The wind seemed to be dying; it no longer howled down the chimney with quite such force. Sleep proving still elusive, I got out of bed, and with a quilt wrapped round my shoulders for warmth, went to the window.

The sky was a deep, mottled gray, the scudding rain clouds edged with brilliant light from the moon that hid behind them, and the glass was streaked with rain. Still, enough light seeped through the clouds for me to make out the masts of the ships moored at the quay, less than a quarter of a mile away. They swayed to and fro, their sails furled tight against the storm, rising and falling in uneasy rhythm as the waves rocked the boats at anchor. In a week's time, I would be on one.

I had not dared to think what life might be like once I had found Jamie, lest I not find him after all. Then I *had* found him, and in quick succession, had contemplated life as a printer's wife among the political and literary worlds of Edinburgh, a dangerous and fugitive existence as a smuggler's lady, and finally, the busy, settled life of a Highland farm, which I had known before and loved.

Now, in equally quick succession, all these possibilities had been jerked away, and I faced an unknown future once more.

Oddly enough, I was not so much distressed by this as excited by it. I had been settled for twenty years, rooted as a barnacle by my attachments to Brianna, to Frank, to my patients. Now fate— and my own actions—had ripped me loose from all those things, and I felt as though I were tumbling free in the surf, at the mercy of forces a great deal stronger than myself.

My breath had misted the glass. I traced a small heart in the cloudiness, as I had used to do for Brianna on cold mornings. Then, I would put her initials inside the heart—B.E.R., for Brianna Ellen Randall. Would she still call herself Randall? I wondered, or Fraser, now? I hesitated, then drew two letters inside the outline of the heart—a "J" and a "C."

I was still standing before the window when the door opened and Jamie came in.

"Are ye awake still?" he asked, rather unnecessarily.

"The rain kept me from sleeping." I went and embraced him, glad of his warm solidity to dispel the cold gloom of the night.

He hugged me, resting his cheek against my hair. He smelt faintly of seasickness, much more strongly of candlewax and ink.

"Have you been writing?" I asked.

He looked down at me in astonishment. "I have, but how did ye know that?"

"You smell of ink."

He smiled slightly, stepping back and running his hand through his hair. "You've a nose as keen as a truffle pig's, Sassenach."

"Why, thank you, what a graceful compliment," I said. "What were you writing?"

The smile disappeared from his face, leaving him looking strained and tired.

"A letter to Jenny," he said. He went to the table, where he shed his coat and began to unfasten his stock and jabot. "I didna want to write her until we'd seen Jared, and I could tell her what plans we had, and what the prospects were for bringing Ian home safe." He grimaced, and pulled the shirt over his head. "God knows what she'll do when she gets it—and thank God, I'll be at sea when she does," he added wryly, emerging from the folds of linen.

It couldn't have been an easy piece of composition, but I thought he seemed easier for the writing of it. He sat down to take off his shoes and stockings, and I came behind him to undo the clubbed queue of his hair.

"I'm glad the writing's over, at least," he said, echoing my thought. "I'd been dreading telling her, more than anything else."

"You told her the truth?"

He shrugged. "I always have."

Except about me. I didn't voice the thought, though, but began to rub his shoulders, kneading the knotted muscles.

"What did Jared do with Mr. Willoughby?" I asked, massage bringing the Chinese to mind. He had accompanied us on the Channel crossing, sticking to Jamie like a small blue-silk shadow. Jared, used to seeing everything on the docks, had taken Mr. Willoughby in stride, bowing gravely to him and addressing him with a few words of Mandarin, but his housekeeper had viewed this unusual guest with considerably more suspicion.

"I believe he's gone to sleep in the stable." Jamie yawned, and stretched himself luxuriously. "Mathilde said she wasna accustomed to have heathens in the house and didna mean to start now. She was sprinkling the kitchen wi' holy water after he ate supper there." Glancing up, he caught sight of the heart I had traced on the windowpane, black against the misted glass, and smiled.

"What's that?"

"Just silliness," I said.

He reached up and took my right hand, the ball of his thumb caressing the small scar at the base of my own thumb, the letter "J" he had made with the point of his knife, just before I left him, before Culloden.

"I didna ask," he said, "whether ye wished to come with me. I could leave ye here; Jared would have ye stay wi' him and welcome, here or in Paris. Or ye could go back to Lallybroch, if ye wished."

"No, you didn't ask," I said. "Because you knew bloody well what the answer would be."

We looked at each other and smiled. The lines of heartsickness and weariness had lifted from his face. The candlelight glowed softly on the burnished crown of his head as he bent and gently kissed the palm of my hand.

The wind still whistled in the chimney, and the rain ran down the glass like tears outside, but it no longer mattered. Now I could sleep.

The sky had cleared by morning. A brisk, cold breeze rattled the windowpanes of Jared's study, but couldn't penetrate to the cozy room inside. The house at Le Havre was much smaller than his lavish Paris residence, but still boasted three stories of solid half-timbered comfort.

I pushed my feet farther toward the crackling fire, and dipped my quill into the inkwell. I was making up a list of all the things I thought might be needed in the medical way for a two-month voyage. Distilled alcohol was both the most important and the easiest to obtain; Jared had promised to get me a cask in Paris.

"We'd best label it something else, though," he'd told me. "Or the sailors will have drunk it before you've left port."

Purified lard, I wrote slowly, *St.-John's-wort; garlic, ten pounds; yarrow.* I wrote *borage,* then shook my head and crossed it out, replacing it with the older name by which it was more likely known now, *bugloss.*

It was slow work. At one time, I had known the medicinal uses of all the common herbs, and not a few uncommon ones. I had had to; they were all that was available.

At that, many of them were surprisingly effective. Despite the skepticism—and outspoken horror—of my supervisors and colleagues at the hospital in Boston, I had used them occasionally on my modern patients to good effect. ("Did you *see* what Dr. Randall did?" a shocked intern's cry echoed in memory, making me smile as I wrote. "She fed the stomach in 134B *boiled flowers*!")

The fact remained that one wouldn't use yarrow and comfrey on a wound if iodine were available, nor treat a systemic infection with bladderwort in preference to penicillin.

I had forgotten a lot, but as I wrote the names of the herbs, the look and the smell of each one began to come back to me—the dark, bituminous look and pleasant light smell of birch oil, the sharp tang of the mint family, the dusty sweet smell of chamomile and the astringency of bistort.

Across the table, Jamie was struggling with his own lists. A poor penman, he wrote laboriously with his crippled right hand, pausing now and then to rub the healing wound above his left elbow and mutter curses under his breath.

"Have ye lime juice on your list, Sassenach?" he inquired, looking up.

"No. Ought I to have?"

He brushed a strand of hair out of his face and frowned at the sheet of paper in front of him.

"It depends. Customarily, it would be the ship's surgeon who provides the lime juice, but in a ship the size of the *Artemis,* there generally isn't a surgeon, and the provision of foodstuffs falls to the purser. But there isn't a purser, either; there's no time to find a dependable man, so I shall fill that office, too."

"Well, if you'll be purser and supercargo, I expect I'll be the closest thing to a ship's surgeon," I said, smiling slightly. "I'll get the lime juice."

"All right." We returned to a companionable scratching, unbroken until the entrance of Josephine, the parlormaid, to announce the arrival of a person. Her long nose wrinkled in unconscious disapproval at the information.

"He waits upon the doorstep. The butler tried to send him away, but he insists that he has an appointment with you, Monsieur James?" The questioning tone of this last implied that nothing could seem more unlikely, but duty compelled her to relay the improbable suggestion.

Jamie's eyebrows rose. "A person? What sort of person?" Josephine's lips primmed together as though she really could not bring herself to say. I was becoming curious to see this person, and ventured over to the window. Sticking my head far out, I could see the top of a very dusty black slouch hat on the doorstep, and not much more.

"He looks like a peddler; he's got a bundle of some kind on his back," I reported, craning out still farther, hands on the sill. Jamie clutched me by the waist and drew me back, thrusting his own head out in turn.

"Och, it's the coin dealer Jared mentioned!" he exclaimed. "Bring him up, then."

With an eloquent expression on her narrow face, Josephine departed, returning in short order with a tall, gangling youth of perhaps twenty, dressed in a badly outmoded style of coat, wide unbuckled breeches that flapped limply about his skinny shanks, drooping stockings and the cheapest of wooden sabots.

The filthy black hat, courteously removed indoors, revealed a thin face with an intelligent expression, adorned with a vigorous, if scanty, brown beard. Since virtually no one in Le Havre other than a few seamen wore a beard, it hardly needed the small shiny black skullcap on the newcomer's head to tell me he was a Jew.

The boy bowed awkwardly to me, then to Jamie, struggling with the straps of his peddler's pack.

"Madame," he said, with a bob that made his curly sidelocks dance, "Monsieur. It is most good of you to receive me." He spoke French oddly, with a singsong intonation that made him hard to follow.

While I entirely understood Josephine's reservations about this . . . person, still, he had wide, guileless blue eyes that made me smile at him despite his generally unprepossessing appearance.

"It's we who should be grateful to you," Jamie was saying. "I had not expected you to come so promptly. My cousin tells me your name is Mayer?"

The coin dealer nodded, a shy smile breaking out amid the sprigs of his youthful beard.

"Yes, Mayer. It is no trouble; I was in the city already."

"Yet you come from Frankfort, no? A long way," Jamie said politely. He smiled as he looked over Mayer's costume, which looked as though he had retrieved it from a rubbish tip. "And a dusty one, too, I expect," he added. "Will you take wine?"

Mayer looked flustered at this offer, but after opening and closing his mouth a few times, finally settled on a silent nod of acceptance.

His shyness vanished, though, once the pack was opened. Though from the outside the shapeless bundle looked as though it might contain, at best, a change of ragged linen and Mayer's midday meal, once opened it revealed several small wooden racks, cleverly fitted into a framework inside the pack, each rack packed carefully with tiny leather bags, cuddling together like eggs in a nest.

Mayer removed a folded square of fabric from beneath the racks, whipped it open, and spread it with something of a flourish on Jamie's desk. Then one by one, Mayer opened the bags and drew out the contents, placing each gleaming round reverently on the deep blue velvet of the cloth.

"An Aquilia Severa aureus," he said, touching one small coin that glowed with the deep mellowness of ancient gold from the velvet. "And here, a Sestercius of the Calpurnia family." His voice was soft and his hands sure, stroking the edge of a silver coin only slightly worn, or cradling one in his palm to demonstrate the weight of it.

He looked up from the coins, eyes bright with the reflections of the precious metal.

"Monsieur Fraser tells me that you desire to inspect as many of the Greek and Roman rarities as possible. I have not my whole stock with me, of course, but I have quite a few—and I could send to Frankfort for others, if you desire."

Jamie smiled, shaking his head. "I'm afraid we haven't time, Mr. Mayer. We—"

"Just Mayer, Monsieur Fraser," the young man interrupted, perfectly polite, but with a slight edge in his voice.

"Indeed." Jamie bowed slightly. "I hope my cousin shall not have misled you. I shall be most happy to pay the cost of your journey, and something for your time, but I am not wishful to purchase any of your stock myself . . . Mayer."

The young man's eyebrows rose in inquiry, along with one shoulder.

"What I wish," Jamie said slowly, leaning forward to look closely at the coins on display, "is to compare your stock with my recollection of several ancient coins I have seen, and then—should I see any that are similar—to inquire whether you—or your family, I should say, for I expect you are too young yourself—should be familiar with anyone who might have purchased such coins twenty years ago."

He glanced up at the young Jew, who was looking justifiably astonished, and smiled.

"That may be asking a bit much of you, I know. But my cousin tells me that your family is one of the few who deals in such matters, and is by far the most knowledgeable. If you can acquaint me likewise with any persons in the West Indies with interests in this area, I should be deeply obliged to you."

Mayer sat looking at him for a moment, then inclined his head, the sunlight winking from the border of small jet beads that adorned his skullcap. It was plain that he was intensely curious, but he merely touched his pack and said, "My father or my uncle would have sold such coins, not me; but I have here the catalogue and record of every coin that has passed through our hands in thirty years. I will tell you what I can."

He drew the velvet cloth toward Jamie and sat back.

"Do you see anything here like the coins you remember?"

Jamie studied the rows of coins with close attention, then gently nudged a silver piece, about the size of an American quarter. Three leaping porpoises circled its edge, surrounding a charioteer in the center.

"This one," he said. "There were several like it—small differences, but several with these porpoises." He looked again, picked out a worn gold disc with an indistinct profile, then a silver one, somewhat larger and in better condition, with a man's head shown both full-face and in profile.

"These," he said. "Fourteen of the gold ones, and ten of the ones with two heads."

"Ten!" Mayer's bright eyes popped wide with astonishment. "I should not have thought there were so many in Europe."

Jamie nodded. "I'm quite certain—I saw them closely; handled them, even."

"These are the twin heads of Alexander," Mayer said, touching the coin with reverence. "Very rare indeed. It is a tetradrachm, struck to commemorate the battle fought at Amphipolos, and the founding of a city on the site of the battlefield."

Jamie listened with attention, a slight smile on his lips. While he had no great interest in ancient money himself, he did have a great appreciation for a man with a passion.

A quarter of an hour more, another consultation of the catalogue, and the business was complete. Four Greek drachmas of a type Jamie recognized had been added to the collection, several small gold and silver coins, and a thing called a quintinarius, a Roman coin in heavy gold.

Mayer bent and reached into his pack once more, this time pulling out a sheaf of foolscap pages furled into a roll and tied with ribbon. Untied, they showed row upon row of what looked from a distance like bird tracks; on closer inspection, they proved to be Hebraic writing, inked small and precise.

He thumbed slowly through the pages, stopping here and there with a murmured "Um," then passing on. At last he laid the pages on his shabby knee and looked up at Jamie, head cocked to one side.

"Our transactions are naturally carried out in confidence, Monsieur," he said, "and so while I could tell you, for example, that certainly we had sold such and such a coin, in such and such a year, I should not be able to tell you the name of the purchaser." He paused, evidently thinking, then went on.

"We did in fact sell coins of your description—three drachmas, two each of the heads of Egalabalus and the double head of Alexander, and no fewer than six of the gold Calpurnian aurei in the year 1745." He hesitated.

"Normally, that is all I could tell you. However . . . in this case, Monsieur, I happen to know that the original buyer of these coins is dead—has been dead for some years, in fact. Really, I cannot see that under the circumstances . . . ." He shrugged, making up his mind.

"The purchaser was an Englishman, Monsieur. His name was Clarence Marylebone, Duke of Sandringham."

"Sandringham!" I exclaimed, startled into speech.

Mayer looked curiously at me, then at Jamie, whose face betrayed nothing beyond polite interest.

"Yes, Madame," he said. "I know that the Duke is dead, for he possessed an extensive collection of ancient coins, which my uncle bought from his heirs in 1746—the transaction is listed here." He raised the catalogue slightly, and let it fall.

I knew the Duke of Sandringham was dead, too, and by more immediate experience. Jamie's godfather, Murtagh, had killed him, on a dark night in March 1746, soon before the battle of Culloden brought an end to the Jacobite rebellion. I swallowed briefly, recalling my last sight of the Duke's face, its blueberry eyes fixed in an expression of intense surprise.

Mayer's eyes went back and forth between us, then he added hesitantly, "I can tell you also this; when my uncle purchased the Duke's collection after his death, there were no tetradrachms in it."

"No," Jamie murmured, to himself. "There wouldn't have been." Then, recollecting himself, he stood and reached for the decanter that stood on the sideboard.

"I thank you, Mayer," he said formally. "And now, let us drink to you and your wee book, there."

A few minutes later, Mayer was kneeling on the floor, doing up the fastenings of his ragged pack. The small pouch filled with silver livres that Jamie had given him in payment was in his pocket. He rose and bowed in turn to Jamie and to me before straightening and putting on his disreputable hat.

"I bid you goodbye, Madame," he said.

"Goodbye to you, too, Mayer," I replied. Then I asked, somewhat hesitantly, "Is 'Mayer' really your only name?"

Something flickered in the wide blue eyes, but he answered politely, heaving the heavy sack onto his back, "Yes, Madame. The Jews of Frankfort are not allowed to use family names." He looked up and smiled lopsidedly. "For the sake of convenience, the neighbors call us after an old red shield that was painted on the

front of our house, many years ago. But beyond that . . . no,
Madame. We have no name."

Josephine came then to conduct our visitor to the kitchen, taking care to walk several paces in front of him, her nostrils pinched
white as though smelling something foul. Mayer stumbled after
her, his clumsy sabots clattering on the polished floor.

Jamie relaxed in his chair, eyes abstracted in deep thought.

I heard the door close downstairs a few minutes later, with what
was almost a slam, and the click of sabots on the stone steps
below. Jamie heard it too, and turned toward the window.

"Well, Godspeed to ye, Mayer Red-Shield," he said, smiling.

"Jamie," I said, suddenly thinking of something, "do you
speak German?"

"Eh? Oh, aye," he said vaguely, his attention still fixed on the
window and the noises outside.

"What is 'red shield' in German?" I asked.

He looked blank for a moment, then his eyes cleared as his
brain made the proper connection.

"*Rothschild,* Sassenach," he said. "Why?"

"Just a thought," I said. I looked toward the window, where the
clatter of wooden shoes was long since lost in the noises of the
street. "I suppose everyone has to start somewhere."

"Fifteen men on a dead man's chest," I observed. "Yo-ho-ho,
and a bottle of rum."

Jamie gave me a look.

"Oh, aye?" he said.

"The Duke being the dead man," I explained. "Do you think
the seals' treasure was really his?"

"I couldna say for sure, but it seems at least likely." Jamie's
two stiff fingers tapped briefly on the table in a meditative rhythm.
"When Jared mentioned Mayer the coin dealer to me, I thought it
worth inquiring—for surely the most likely person to have sent the
Bruja to retrieve the treasure was the person who put it there."

"Good reasoning," I said, "but evidently it wasn't the same
person, if it was the Duke who put it there. Do you think the whole
treasure amounted to fifty thousand pounds?"

Jamie squinted at his reflection in the rounded side of the decanter, considering. Then he picked it up and refilled his glass, to assist thought.

"Not as metal, no. But did ye notice the prices that some of those coins in Mayer's catalogue have sold for?"

"I did."

"As much as a thousand pound—sterling!—for a moldy bit of metal!" he said, marveling.

"I don't think metal molds," I said, "but I take your point. Anyway," I said, dismissing the question with a wave of my hand, "the point here is this: Do you suppose the seals' treasure could have been the fifty thousand pounds that the Duke had promised to the Stuarts?"

In the early days of 1744, when Charles Stuart had been in France, trying to persuade his royal cousin Louis to grant him some sort of support, he had received a ciphered offer from the Duke of Sandringham, of fifty thousand pounds—enough to hire a small army—on condition that he enter England to retake the throne of his ancestors.

Whether it had been this offer that finally convinced the vacillating Prince Charles to undertake his doomed excursion, we would never know. It might as easily have been a challenge from someone he was drinking with, or a slight—real or imagined—by his mistress, that had sent him to Scotland with nothing more than six companions, two thousand Dutch broadswords, and several casks of brandywine with which to charm the Highland chieftains.

In any case, the fifty thousand pounds had never been received, because the Duke had died before Charles reached England. Another of the speculations that troubled me on sleepless nights was the question of whether that money would have made a difference. If Charles Stuart had received it, would he have taken his ragged Highland army all the way to London, retaken the throne and regained his father's crown?

If he had—well, if he had, the Jacobite rebellion might have succeeded, Culloden might not have happened, I should never have gone back through the circle of stone . . . and I and Brianna would likely both have died in childbed and been dust these many years past. Surely twenty years should have been enough to teach me the futility of "if."

Jamie had been considering, meditatively rubbing the bridge of his nose.

"It might have been," he said at last. "Given a proper market for the coins and gems—ye ken such things take time to sell; if ye must dispose of them quickly, you'll get but a fraction of the price. But given long enough to search out good buyers—aye, it might reach fifty thousand."

"Duncan Kerr was a Jacobite, wasn't he?"

Jamie frowned, nodding. "He was. Aye, it could be—though God knows it's an awkward kind of fortune to be handing to the commander of an army to pay his troops!"

"Yes, but it's also small, portable, and easy to hide," I pointed out. "And if you were the Duke, and busy committing treason by dealing with the Stuarts, that might be important to you. Sending fifty thousand pounds in sterling, with strongboxes and carriages and guards, would attract the hell of a lot more attention than sending one man secretly across the Channel with a small wooden box."

Jamie nodded again. "Likewise, if ye had a collection of such rarities already, it would attract no attention to be acquiring more, and no one would likely notice what coins ye had. It would be a simple matter to take out the most valuable, replace them with cheap ones, and no one the wiser. No banker who might talk, were ye to shift money or land." He shook his head admiringly.

"It's a clever scheme, aye, whoever made it." He looked up inquiringly at me.

"But then, why did Duncan Kerr come, nearly ten years after Culloden? And what happened to him? Did he come to leave the fortune on the silkies' isle then, or to take it away?"

"And who sent the *Bruja* now?" I finished for him. I shook my head, too.

"Damned if I know. Perhaps the Duke had a confederate of some sort? But if he did, we don't know who it was."

Jamie sighed, and impatient with sitting for so long, stood up and stretched. He glanced out the window, estimating the height of the sun, his usual method of telling time, whether a clock was handy or not.

"Aye, well, we'll have time for speculation once we're at sea. It's near on noon, now, and the Paris coach leaves at three o'clock."

The apothecary's shop in the Rue de Varennes was gone. In its place were a thriving tavern, a pawnbroker's, and a small gold-smith's shop, crammed companionably cheek by jowl.

"Master Raymond?" The pawnbroker knitted grizzled brows. "I have heard of him, Madame"—he darted a wary glance at me, suggesting that whatever he had heard had not been very admira-ble—"but he has been gone for several years. If you are requiring a good apothecary, though, Krasner in the Place d'Aloes, or per-haps Madame Verrue, near the Tuileries . . ." He stared with interest at Mr. Willoughby, who accompanied me, then leaned over the counter to address me confidentially.

"Might you be interested in selling your Chinaman, Madame? I have a client with a marked taste for the Orient. I could get you a very good price—with no more than the usual commission, I assure you."

Mr. Willoughby, who did not speak French, was peering with marked contempt at a porcelain jar painted with pheasants, done in an Oriental style.

"Thank you," I said, "but I think not. I'll try Krasner."

Mr. Willoughby had attracted relatively little attention in Le Havre, a port city teeming with foreigners of every description. On the streets of Paris, wearing a padded jacket over his blue-silk pajamas, and with his queue wrapped several times around his head for convenience, he caused considerable comment. He did, however, prove surprisingly knowledgeable about herbs and me-dicinal substances.

"Bai jei ai," he told me, picking up a pinch of mustard seed from an open box in Krasner's emporium. "Good for *shen-yen*—kidneys."

"Yes, it is," I said, surprised. "How did you know?"

He allowed his head to roll slightly from side to side, as I had learned was his habit when pleased at being able to astonish some-one.

"I know healers one time," was all he said, though, before turning to point at a basket containing what looked like balls of dried mud.

"Shan-yü," he said authoritatively. "Good—*very* good—cleanse blood, liver he work good, no dry skin, help see. You buy."

I stepped closer to examine the objects in question and found them to be a particularly homely sort of dried eel, rolled into balls and liberally coated with mud. The price was quite reasonable, though, so to please him, I added two of the nasty things to the basket over my arm.

The weather was mild for early December, and we walked back toward Jared's house in the Rue Tremoulins. The streets were bright with winter sunshine, and lively with vendors, beggars, prostitutes, shopgirls, and the other denizens of the poorer part of Paris, all taking advantage of the temporary thaw.

At the corner of the Rue du Nord and the Allée des Canards, though, I saw something quite out of the ordinary; a tall, slope-shouldered figure in black frock coat and a round black hat.

"Reverend Campbell!" I exclaimed.

He whirled about at being so addressed; then, recognizing me, bowed and removed his hat.

"Mistress Malcolm!" he said. "How most agreeable to see you again." His eye fell on Mr. Willoughby, and he blinked, features hardening in a stare of disapproval.

"Er . . . this is Mr. Willoughby," I introduced him. "He's an . . . associate of my husband's. Mr. Willoughby, the Reverend Archibald Campbell."

"Indeed." The Reverend Campbell normally looked quite austere, but contrived now to look as though he had breakfasted on barbed wire, and found it untasty.

"I thought that you were sailing from Edinburgh to the West Indies," I said, in hopes of taking his gelid eye off the Chinaman. It worked; his gaze shifted to me, and thawed slightly.

"I thank you for your kind inquiries, Madame," he said. "I still harbor such intentions. However, I had urgent business to transact first in France. I shall be departing from Edinburgh on Thursday week."

"And how is your sister?" I asked. He glanced at Mr. Willoughby with dislike, then taking a step to one side so as to be out of the Chinaman's direct sight, lowered his voice.

"She is somewhat improved, I thank you. The draughts you prescribed have been most helpful. She is much calmer, and sleeps quite regularly now. I must thank you again for your kind attentions."

"That's quite all right," I said. "I hope the voyage will agree with her." We parted with the usual expressions of good will, and

Mr. Willoughby and I walked down the Rue du Nord, back toward Jared's house.

"Reverend meaning most holy fella, not true?" Mr. Willoughby said, after a short silence. He had the usual Oriental difficulty in pronouncing the letter "r," which made the word "Reverend" more than slightly picturesque, but I gathered his meaning well enough.

"True," I said, glancing down at him curiously. He pursed his lips and pushed them in and out, then grunted in a distinctly amused manner.

"Not so holy, *that* Reverend fella," he said.

"What makes you say so?"

He gave me a bright-eyed glance, full of shrewdness.

"I see him one time, Madame Jeanne's. Not loud talking then. Very quiet then, Reverend fella."

"Oh, really?" I turned to look back, but the Reverend's tall figure had disappeared into the crowd.

"Stinking whores," Mr. Willoughby amplified, making an extremely rude gesture in the vicinity of his crotch in illustration.

"Yes, I gathered," I said. "Well, I suppose the flesh is weak now and then, even for Scottish Free Church ministers."

At dinner that night, I mentioned seeing the Reverend, though without adding Mr. Willoughby's remarks about the Reverend's extracurricular activities.

"I ought to have asked him where in the West Indies he was going," I said. "Not that he's a particularly scintillating companion, but it might be useful to know someone there."

Jared, who was consuming veal patties in a businesslike way, paused to swallow, then said, "Dinna trouble yourself about that, my dear. I've made up a list for you of useful acquaintances. I've written letters for ye to carry to several friends there, who will certainly lend ye assistance."

He cut another sizable chunk of veal, wiped it through a puddle of wine sauce, and chewed it, while looking thoughtfully at Jamie.

Having evidently come to a decision of some kind, he swallowed, took a sip of wine, and said in a conversational voice, "We met on the level, Cousin."

I stared at him in bewilderment, but Jamie, after a moment's pause, replied, "And we parted on the square."

Jared's narrow face broke into a wide smile.

"Ah, that's a help!" he said. "I wasna just sure, aye? but I thought it worth the trial. Where were ye made?"

"In prison," Jamie replied briefly. "It will be the Inverness lodge, though."

Jared nodded in satisfaction. "Aye, well enough. There are lodges on Jamaica and Barbados—I'll have letters for ye to the Masters there. But the largest lodge is on Trinidad—better than two thousand members there. If ye should need great help in finding the lad, that's where ye must ask. Word of everything that happens in the islands comes through that lodge, sooner or later."

"Would you care to tell me what you're talking about?" I interrupted.

Jamie glanced at me and smiled.

"Freemasons, Sassenach."

"You're a Mason?" I blurted. "You didn't tell me that!"

"He's not meant to," Jared said, a bit sharply. "The rites of Freemasonry are secret, known only to the members. I wouldna have been able to give Jamie an introduction to the Trinidad lodge, had he not been one of us already."

The conversation became general again, as Jamie and Jared fell to discussing the provisioning of the *Artemis,* but I was quiet, concentrating on my own veal. The incident, small as it was, had reminded me of all the things I didn't know about Jamie. At one time, I should have said I knew him as well as one person can know another.

Now, there would be moments, talking intimately together, falling asleep in the curve of his shoulder, holding him close in the act of love, when I felt I knew him still, his mind and heart as clear to me as the lead crystal of the wineglasses on Jared's table.

And others, like now, when I would stumble suddenly over some unsuspected bit of his past, or see him standing still, eyes shrouded with recollections I didn't share. I felt suddenly unsure and alone, hesitating on the brink of the gap between us.

Jamie's foot pressed against mine under the table, and he looked across at me with a smile hidden in his eyes. He raised his glass a little, in a silent toast, and I smiled back, feeling obscurely comforted. The gesture brought back a sudden memory of our wedding night, when we had sat beside each other sipping wine, strangers frightened of each other, with nothing between us but a marriage contract—and the promise of honesty.

There are things ye maybe canna tell me, he had said. *I willna ask ye, or force ye. But when ye do tell me something, let it be the truth. There is nothing between us now but respect, and respect has room for secrets, I think—but not for lies.*

I drank deeply from my own glass, feeling the strong bouquet of the wine billow up inside my head, and a warm flush heat my cheeks. Jamie's eyes were still fixed on me, ignoring Jared's solil-oquy about ship's biscuit and candles. His foot nudged mine in silent inquiry, and I pressed back in answer.

"Aye, I'll see to it in the morning," he said, in reply to a question from Jared. "But for now, Cousin, I think I shall retire. It's been a long day." He pushed back his chair, stood up, and held out his arm to me.

"Will ye join me, Claire?"

I stood up, the wine rushing through my limbs, making me feel warm all over and slightly giddy. Our eyes met with a perfect understanding. There was more than respect between us now, and room for all our secrets to be known, in good time.

In the morning, Jamie and Mr. Willoughby went with Jared, to complete their errands. I had another errand of my own—one that I preferred to do alone. Twenty years ago, there had been two people in Paris whom I cared for deeply. Master Raymond was gone; dead or disappeared. The chances that the other might still be living were slim, but still, I had to see, before I left Europe for what might be the last time. With my heart beating erratically, I stepped into Jared's coach, and told the coachman to drive to the Hôpital des Anges.

The grave was set in the small cemetery reserved for the con-vent, under the buttresses of the nearby cathedral. Even though the air from the Seine was damp and cold, and the day cloudy, the walled cemetery held a soft light, reflected from the blocks of pale limestone that sheltered the small plot from wind. In the winter, there were no shrubs or flowers growing, but leafless aspens and larches spread a delicate tracery against the sky, and a deep green moss cradled the stones, thriving despite the cold.

It was a small stone, made of a soft white marble. A pair of cherub's wings spread out across the top, sheltering the single word that was the stone's only other decoration. "Faith," it read.

I stood looking down at it until my vision blurred. I had brought a flower; a pink tulip—not the easiest thing to find in Paris in December, but Jared kept a conservatory. I knelt down and laid it on the stone, stroking the soft curve of the petal with a finger, as though it were a baby's cheek.

"I thought I wouldn't cry," I said a little later.

I felt the weight of Mother Hildegarde's hand on my head.

"Le Bon Dieu orders things as He thinks best," she said softly. "But He seldom tells us why."

I took a deep breath and wiped my cheeks with a corner of my cloak. "It was a long time ago, though." I rose slowly to my feet and turned to find Mother Hildegarde watching me with an expression of deep sympathy and interest.

"I have noticed," she said slowly, "that time does not really exist for mothers, with regard to their children. It does not matter greatly how old the child is—in the blink of an eye, the mother can see the child again as it was when it was born, when it learned to walk, as it was at any age—at any time, even when the child is fully grown and a parent itself."

"Especially when they're asleep," I said, looking down again at the little white stone. "You can always see the baby then."

"Ah." Mother nodded, satisfied. "I thought you had had more children; you have the look, somehow."

"One more." I glanced at her. "And how do you know so much about mothers and children?"

The small black eyes shone shrewdly under heavy brow ridges whose sparse hairs had gone quite white.

"The old require very little sleep," she said, with a deprecatory shrug. "I walk the wards at night, sometimes. The patients talk to me."

She had shrunk somewhat with advancing age, and the wide shoulders were slightly bowed, thin as a wire hanger beneath the black serge of her habit. Even so, she was still taller than I, and towered over most of the nuns, more scarecrow-like, but imposing as ever. She carried a walking stick but strode erect, firm of tread and with the same piercing eye, using the stick more frequently to prod idlers or direct underlings than to lean on.

I blew my nose and we turned back along the path to the convent. As we walked slowly back, I noticed other small stones set here and there among the larger ones.

"Are those all children?" I asked, a little surprised.

"The children of the nuns," she said matter-of-factly. I gaped at her in astonishment, and she shrugged, elegant and wry as always.

"It happens," she said. She walked a few steps farther, then added, "Not often, of course." She gestured with her stick around the confines of the cemetery.

"This place is reserved for the sisters, a few benefactors of the Hôpital—and those they love."

"The sisters or the benefactors?"

"The sisters. Here, you lump!"

Mother Hildegarde paused in her progress, spotting an orderly leaning idly against the church wall, smoking a pipe. As she berated him in the elegantly vicious Court French of her girlhood, I stood back, looking around the tiny cemetery.

Against the far wall, but still in consecrated ground, was a row of small stone tablets, each with a single name, "Bouton." Below each name was a Roman numeral, I through XV. Mother Hildegarde's beloved dogs. I glanced at her current companion, the sixteenth holder of that name. This one was coal-black, and curly as a Persian lamb. He sat bolt upright at her feet, round eyes fixed on the delinquent orderly, a silent echo of Mother Hildegarde's outspoken disapproval.

The sisters, and those they love.

Mother Hildegarde came back, her fierce expression altering at once to the smile that transformed her strong gargoyle features into beauty.

"I am so pleased that you have come again, *ma chère*," she said. "Come inside; I shall find things that may be useful to you on your journey." Tucking the stick in the crook of her arm, she instead took my forearm for support, grasping it with a warm bony hand whose skin had grown paper-thin. I had the odd feeling that it was not I who supported her, but the other way around.

As we turned into the small yew alley that led to the entrance to the Hôpital, I glanced up at her.

"I hope you won't think me rude, Mother," I said hesitantly, "but there is one question I wanted to ask you . . ."

"Eighty-three," she replied promptly. She grinned broadly,

showing her long yellow horse's teeth. "Everyone wants to know," she said complacently. She looked back over her shoulder toward the tiny graveyard, and lifted one shoulder in a dismissive Gallic shrug.

"Not yet," she said confidently. "*Le Bon Dieu* knows how much work there is still to do."

41

We Set Sail

It was a cold, gray day—there is no other kind in Scotland in December—when the *Artemis* touched at Cape Wrath, on the northwest coast.

I peered out of the tavern window into a solid gray murk that hid the cliffs along the shore. The place was depressingly reminiscent of the landscape near the silkies' isle, with the smell of dead seaweed strong in the air, and the crashing of waves so loud as to inhibit conversation, even inside the small pothouse by the wharf. Young Ian had been taken nearly a month before. Now it was past Christmas, and here we were, still in Scotland, no more than a few miles from the seals' island.

Jamie was striding up and down the dock outside, in spite of the cold rain, too restless to stay indoors by the fire. The sea journey from France back to Scotland had been no better for him than the first Channel crossing, and I knew the prospect of two or three months aboard the *Artemis* filled him with dread. At the same time, his impatience to be in pursuit of the kidnappers was so acute that any delay filled him with frustration. More than once I had awakened in the middle of the night to find him gone, walking the streets of Le Havre alone.

Ironically, this final delay was of his own making. We had touched at Cape Wrath to retrieve Fergus, and with him, the small group of smugglers whom Jamie had sent him to fetch, before leaving ourselves for Le Havre.

"There's no telling what we shall find in the Indies, Sassenach," Jamie had explained to me. "I dinna mean to go up against a shipload of pirates single-handed, nor yet to fight wi' men I dinna ken alongside me.'' The smugglers were all men of the shore, accustomed to boats and the ocean, if not to ships; they would be hired on as part of the *Artemis*'s crew, shorthanded in consequence of the late season in which we sailed.

Cape Wrath was a small port, with little traffic at this time of year. Besides the *Artemis,* only a few fishing boats and a ketch were tied up at the wooden wharf. There was a small pothouse, though, in which the crew of the *Artemis* cheerfully passed their time while waiting, the men who would not fit inside the house crouching under the eaves, swilling pots of ale passed through the windows by their comrades indoors. Jamie walked on the shore, coming in only for meals, when he would sit before the fire, the wisps of steam rising from his soggy garments symptomatic of his increasing aggravation of soul.

Fergus was late. No one seemed to mind the wait but Jamie and Jared's captain. Captain Raines, a small, plump, elderly man, spent most of his time on the deck of his ship, keeping one weather eye on the overcast sky, and the other on his barometer.

''That's verra strong-smelling stuff, Sassenach,'' Jamie observed, during one of his brief visits to the taproom. ''What is it?''

''Fresh ginger,'' I answered, holding up the remains of the root I was grating. ''It's the thing most of my herbals say is best for nausea.''

''Oh, aye?'' He picked up the bowl, sniffed at the contents, and sneezed explosively, to the vast amusement of the onlookers. I snatched back the bowl before he could spill it.

''You don't take it like snuff,'' I said. ''You drink it in tea. And I hope to heaven it works, because if it doesn't, we'll be scooping you out of the bilges, if bilges are what I think they are.''

''Oh, not to worry, missus,'' one of the older hands assured me, overhearing. ''Lots o' green hands feel a bit queerlike the first day or two. But usually they comes round soon enough; by the third day, they've got used to the pitch and roll, and they're up in the rigging, happy as larks.''

I glanced at Jamie, who was markedly unlarklike at the moment. Still, this comment seemed to give him some hope, for he brightened a bit, and waved to the harassed servingmaid for a glass of ale.

''It may be so,'' he said. ''Jared said the same; that seasickness doesna generally last more than a few days, provided the seas aren't too heavy.'' He took a small sip of his ale, and then, with growing confidence, a deeper swallow. ''I can stand three days of it, I suppose.''

Late in the afternoon of the second day, six men appeared, winding their way along the stony shore on shaggy Highland ponies.

''There's Raeburn in the lead,'' Jamie said, shading his eyes and squinting to distinguish the identities of the six small dots. ''Kennedy after him, then Innes—he's missing the left arm, see? —and Meldrum, and that'll be MacLeod with him, they always ride together like that. Is the last man Gordon, then, or Fergus?''

''It must be Gordon,'' I said, peering over his shoulder at the approaching men, ''because it's much too fat to be Fergus.''

''Where the devil is Fergus, then?'' Jamie asked Raeburn, once the smugglers had been greeted, introduced to their new shipmates, and sat down to a hot supper and a cheerful glass.

Raeburn bobbed his head in response, hastily swallowing the remains of his pasty.

''Weel, he said to me as how he'd some business to see to, and would I see to the hiring of the horses, and speak to Meldrum and MacLeod about coming, for they were out wi' their own boat at the time, and not expected back for a day or twa more, and . . .''

''What business?'' Jamie said sharply, but got no more than a shrug in reply. Jamie muttered something under his breath in Gaelic, but returned to his own supper without further comment.

The crew being now complete—save Fergus—preparations began in the morning for getting under way. The deck was a scene of organized confusion, with bodies darting to and fro, popping up through hatchways, and dropping suddenly out of the rigging like dead flies. Jamie stood near the wheel, keeping out of the way, but lending a hand whenever a matter requiring muscle rather than skill arose. For the most part, though, he simply stood, eyes fixed on the road along the shore.

''We shall have to sail by midafternoon, or miss the tide.'' Captain Raines spoke kindly, but firmly. ''We'll have surly weather in twenty-four hours; the glass is falling, and I feel it in my neck.'' The Captain tenderly massaged the part in question, and nodded at the sky, which had gone from pewter to lead-gray since early morning. "I'll not set sail in a storm if I can help it, and if we mean to make the Indies as soon as possible—"

"Aye, I understand, Captain," Jamie interrupted him. "Of course; ye must do as seems best." He stood back to let a bustling seaman go past, and the Captain disappeared, issuing orders as he went.

As the day wore on, Jamie seemed composed as usual, but I noticed that the stiff fingers fluttered against his thigh more and more often, the only outward sign of worry. And worried he was. Fergus had been with him since the day twenty years before, when Jamie had found him in a Paris brothel, and hired him to steal Charles Stuart's letters.

More than that; Fergus had lived at Lallybroch since before Young Ian was born. The boy had been a younger brother to Fergus, and Jamie the closest thing to a father that Fergus had ever known. I could not imagine any business so urgent that it would have kept him from Jamie's side. Neither could Jamie, and his fingers beat a silent tattoo on the wood of the rail.

Then it was time, and Jamie turned reluctantly away, tearing his eyes from the empty shore. The hatches were battened, the lines coiled, and several seamen leapt ashore to cast free the mooring hawsers; there were six of them, each a rope as thick around as my wrist.

I put a hand on Jamie's arm in silent sympathy.

"You'd better come down below," I said. "I've got a spirit lamp. I'll brew you some hot ginger tea, and then you—"

The sound of a galloping horse echoed along the shore, the scrunch of hoofbeats on gravel echoing from the cliffside well in advance of its appearance.

"There he is, the wee fool," Jamie said, his relief evident in voice and body. He turned to Captain Raines, one brow raised in question. "There's enough of the tide left? Aye, then, let's go."

"Cast off!" the Captain bellowed, and the waiting hands sprang into action. The last of the lines tethering us to the piling was slipped free and neatly coiled, and all around us, lines tightened and sails snapped overhead, as the bosun ran up and down the deck, bawling orders in a voice like rusty iron.

"She moves! She stirs! 'She seems to feel / the thrill of life along her keel!' " I declaimed, delighted to feel the deck quiver beneath my feet as the ship came alive, the energy of all the crew poured into its inanimate hulk, transmuted by the power of the wind-catching sails.

"Oh, God," said Jamie hollowly, feeling the same thing. He grasped the rail, closed his eyes, and swallowed.

"Mr. Willoughby says he has a cure for seasickness," I said, watching him sympathetically.

"Ha," he said, opening his eyes. "I ken what he means, and if he thinks I'll let him—what the bloody hell!"

I whirled to look, and saw what had caused him to break off. Fergus was on deck, reaching up to help down a girl perched awkwardly above him on the railing, her long blond hair whipping in the wind. Laoghaire's daughter—Marsali MacKimmie.

Before I could speak, Jamie was past me and striding toward the pair.

"What in the name of holy God d'ye mean by this, ye wee coofs?" he was demanding, by the time I made my way into earshot through the obstacle course of lines and seamen. He loomed menacingly over the pair, a foot taller than either of them.

"We are married," Fergus said, bravely moving in front of Marsali. He looked both scared and excited, his face pale beneath the shock of black hair.

"Married!" Jamie's hands clenched at his sides, and Fergus took an involuntary step backward, nearly treading on Marsali's toes. "What d'ye mean, 'married'?"

I assumed this was a rhetorical question, but it wasn't; Jamie's appreciation of the situation had, as usual, outstripped mine by yards and seized at once upon the salient point.

"Have ye bedded her?" he demanded bluntly. Standing behind him, I couldn't see his face, but I knew what it must look like, if only because I could see the effect of his expression on Fergus. The Frenchman turned a couple of shades paler and licked his lips.

"Er . . . no, milord," he said, just as Marsali, eyes blazing, thrust her chin up and said defiantly, "Yes, he has!"

Jamie glanced briefly back and forth between the two of them, snorted loudly, and turned away.

"Mr. Warren!" he called down the deck to the ship's sailing master. "Put back to the shore, if ye please!"

Mr. Warren stopped, openmouthed, in the middle of an order addressed to the rigging, and stared, first at Jamie, then—quite elaborately—at the receding shoreline. In the few moments since the appearance of the putative newlyweds, the *Artemis* had moved more than a thousand yards from the shore, and the rocks of the cliffs were slipping by with increasing speed.

"I don't believe he can," I said. "I think we're already in the tide-race."

No sailor himself, Jamie had spent sufficient time in the company of seamen at least to understand the notion that time and tide wait for no one. He breathed through his teeth for a moment, then jerked his head toward the ladder that led belowdecks.

"Come down, then, the both of ye."

Fergus and Marsali sat together in the tiny cabin, huddled on one berth, hands clutched tight. Jamie waved me to a seat on the other berth, then turned to the pair, hands on his hips.

"Now, then," he said. "What's this nonsense of bein' married?"

"It is true, milord," Fergus said. He was quite pale, but his dark eyes were bright with excitement. His one hand tightened on Marsali's, his hook resting across his thigh.

"Aye?" Jamie said, with the maximum of skepticism. "And who married ye?"

The two glanced at each other, and Fergus licked his lips briefly before replying.

"We—we are handfast."

"Before witnesses," Marsali put in. In contrast to Fergus's paleness, a high color burned in her cheeks. She had her mother's roseleaf skin, but the stubborn set of her jaw had likely come from somewhere else. She put a hand to her bosom, where something crackled under the fabric. "I ha' the contract, and the signatures, here."

Jamie made a low growling noise in his throat. By the laws of Scotland, two people could in fact be legally married by clasping hands before witnesses—handfasting—and declaring themselves to be man and wife.

"Aye, well," he said. "But ye're no bedded, yet, and a contract's not enough, in the eyes o' the Church." He glanced out of the stern casement, where the cliffs were just visible through the ragged mist, then nodded with decision.

"We'll stop at Lewes for the last provisions. Marsali will go ashore there; I'll send two seamen to see her home to her mother."

"Ye'll do no such thing!" Marsali cried. She sat up straight, glaring at her stepfather. "I'm going wi' Fergus!"

"Oh, no, you're not, my lassie!" Jamie snapped. "D'ye have no feeling for your mother? To run off, wi' no word, and leave her to be worrit—"

"I left word." Marsali's square chin was high. "I sent a letter from Inverness, saying I'd married Fergus and was off to sail wi' you."

"Sweet bleeding Jesus! She'll think I kent all about it!" Jamie looked horror-stricken.

"We—I—did ask the lady Laoghaire for the honor of her daughter's hand, milord," Fergus put in. "Last month, when I came to Lallybroch."

"Aye. Well, ye needna tell me what she said," Jamie said dryly, seeing the sudden flush on Fergus's cheeks. "Since I gather the general answer was no."

"She said he was a bastard!" Marsali burst out indignantly. "And a criminal, and—and—"

"He is a bastard and a criminal," Jamie pointed out. "And a cripple wi' no property, either, as I'm sure your mother noticed."

"I dinna care!" Marsali gripped Fergus's hand and looked at him with fierce affection. "I want him."

Taken aback, Jamie rubbed a finger across his lips. Then he took a deep breath and returned to the attack.

"Be that as it may," he said, "ye're too young to be married."

"I'm fifteen; that's plenty old enough!"

"Aye, and he's thirty!" Jamie snapped. He shook his head, "Nay, lassie, I'm sorry about it, but I canna let ye do it. If it were nothing else, the voyage is too dangerous—"

"You're taking *her*!" Marsali's chin jerked contemptuously in my direction.

"You'll leave Claire out of this," Jamie said evenly. "She's none of your concern, and—"

"Oh, she's not? You leave my mother for this English whore, and make her a laughingstock for the whole countryside, and it's no my concern, is it?" Marsali leapt up and stamped her foot on the deck. "And you ha' the hellish nerve to tell me what *I* shall do?"

"I have," Jamie said, keeping hold of his temper with some difficulty. "My private affairs are not your concern—"

"And mine aren't any of yours!"

Fergus, looking alarmed, was on his feet, trying to calm the girl.

"Marsali, *ma chère,* you must not speak to milord in such a way. He is only—"

"I'll speak to him any way I want!"

"No, you will not!" Surprised at the sudden harshness in Fergus's tone, Marsali blinked. Only an inch or two taller than his new wife, the Frenchman had a certain wiry authority that made him seem much bigger than he was.

"No," he said more softly. "Sit down, *ma p'tite.*" He pressed her back down on the berth, and stood before her.

"Milord has been to me more than a father," he said gently to the girl. "I owe him my life a thousand times. He is also your stepfather. However your mother may regard him, he has without doubt supported and sheltered her and you and your sister. You owe him respect, at the least."

Marsali bit her lip, her eyes bright. Finally she ducked her head awkwardly at Jamie.

"I'm sorry," she murmured, and the air of tension in the cabin lessened slightly.

"It's all right, lassie," Jamie said gruffly. He looked at her and sighed. "But still, Marsali, we must send ye back to your mother."

"I won't go." The girl was calmer now, but the set of her pointed chin was the same. She glanced at Fergus, then at Jamie. "He says we havena bedded together, but we have. Or at any rate, I shall say we have. If ye send me home, I'll tell everyone that he's had me; so ye see—I shall either be married or ruined." Her tone was reasonable and determined. Jamie closed his eyes.

"May the Lord deliver me from women," he said between his teeth. He opened his eyes and glared at her.

"All right!" he said. "You're married. But you'll do it right, before a priest. We'll find one in the Indies, when we land. And until ye've been blessed, Fergus doesna touch you. Aye?" He turned a ferocious gaze on both of them.

"Yes, milord," said Fergus, his features suffused with joy. *"Merci beaucoup!"* Marsali narrowed her eyes at Jamie, but seeing that he wasn't to be moved, she bowed her head demurely, with a sidelong glance at me.

"Yes, Daddy," she said.

The question of Fergus's elopement had at least distracted Jamie's mind temporarily from the motion of the ship, but the palliative effect didn't last. He held on grimly nevertheless, turning greener by the moment, but refusing to leave the deck and go below, so long as the shore of Scotland was in sight.

"I may never see it again," he said gloomily, when I tried to persuade him to go below and lie down. He leaned heavily on the rail he had just been vomiting over, eyes resting longingly on the unprepossessingly bleak coast behind us.

"No, you'll see it," I said, with an unthinking surety. "You're coming back. I don't know when, but I know you'll come back."

He turned his head to look up at me, puzzled. Then the ghost of a smile crossed his face.

"You've seen my grave," he said softly. "Haven't ye?"

I hesitated, but he didn't seem upset, and I nodded.

"It's all right," he said. He closed his eyes, breathing heavily. "Don't . . . don't tell me when, though, if ye dinna mind."

"I can't," I said. "There weren't any dates on it. Just your name—and mine."

"Yours?" His eyes popped open.

I nodded again, feeling my throat tighten at the memory of that granite slab. It had been what they call a "marriage stone," a quarter-circle carved to fit with another in a complete arch. I had, of course, seen only the one half.

"It had all your names on it. That's how I knew it was you. And underneath, it said 'Beloved husband of Claire.' At the time, I didn't see how—but now, of course, I do."

He nodded slowly, absorbing it. "Aye, I see. Aye, well, I suppose if I shall be in Scotland, and still married to you—then maybe 'when' doesna matter so much." He gave me a shadow of his usual grin, and added wryly, "It also means we'll find Young Ian safe, for I'll tell ye, Sassenach, I willna set foot in Scotland again without him."

"We'll find him," I said, with an assurance I didn't altogether feel. I put a hand on his shoulder and stood beside him, watching Scotland slowly recede in the distance.

By the time evening set in, the rocks of Scotland had disappeared in the sea mists, and Jamie, chilled to the bone and pale as a sheet, suffered himself to be led below and put to bed. At this point, the unforeseen consequences of his ultimatum to Fergus became apparent.

There were only two small private cabins, besides the Captain's; if Fergus and Marsali were forbidden to share one until their union was formally blessed, then clearly Jamie and Fergus would have to take one, and Marsali and I the other. It seemed destined to be a rough voyage, in more ways than one.

I had hoped that the sickness might ease, if Jamie couldn't see the slow heave and fall of the horizon, but no such luck.

"Again?" said Fergus, sleepily rousing on one elbow in his berth, in the middle of the night. "How can he? He has eaten nothing all day!"

"Tell *him* that," I said, trying to breathe through my mouth as I sidled toward the door, a basin in my hands, making my way with difficulty through the tiny, cramped quarters. The deck rose and fell beneath my unaccustomed feet, making it hard to keep my balance.

"Here, milady, allow me." Fergus swung bare feet out of bed and stood up beside me, staggering and nearly bumping into me as he reached for the basin.

"You should go and sleep now, milady," he said, taking it from my hands. "I will see to him, be assured."

"Well . . ." The thought of my berth was undeniably tempting. It had been a long day.

"Go, Sassenach," Jamie said. His face was a ghastly white, sheened with sweat in the dim light of the small oil light that burned on the wall. "I'll be all right."

This was patently untrue; at the same time, it was unlikely that my presence would help particularly. Fergus could do the little that could be done; there was no known cure for seasickness, after all. One could only hope that Jared was right, and that it would ease of itself as the *Artemis* made its way out into the longer swells of the Atlantic.

"All right," I said, giving in. "Perhaps you'll feel better in the morning."

Jamie opened one eye for a moment, then groaned, and shivering, closed it again.

"Or perhaps I'll be dead," he suggested.

On that cheery note, I made my way out into the dark companionway, only to stumble over the prostrate form of Mr. Willoughby, curled up against the door of the cabin. He grunted in surprise, then, seeing that it was only me, rolled slowly onto all fours and crawled into the cabin, swaying with the rolling of the ship. Ignoring Fergus's exclamation of distaste, he curled himself about the pedestal of the table, and fell promptly back asleep, an expression of beatific content on his small round face.

My own cabin was just across the companionway, but I paused for a moment, to breathe in the fresh air coming down from the deck above. There was an extraordinary variety of noises, from the creak and crack of timbers all around, to the snap of sails and the whine of rigging above, and the faint echo of a shout somewhere on deck.

Despite the racket and the cold air pouring in down the companionway, Marsali was sound asleep, a humped black shape in one of the two berths. Just as well; at least I needn't try to make awkward conversation with her.

Despite myself, I felt a pang of sympathy for her; this was likely not what she had expected of her wedding night. It was too cold to undress; fully clothed, I crawled into my small box-berth and lay listening to the sounds of the ship around me. I could hear the hissing of the water passing the hull, only a foot or two beyond my head. It was an oddly comforting sound. To the accompaniment of the song of the wind and the faint sound of retching across the corridor, I fell peacefully asleep.

The *Artemis* was a tidy ship, as ships go, but when you cram thirty-two men—and two women—into a space eighty feet long and twenty-five wide, together with six tons of rough-cured hides, forty-two barrels of sulfur, and enough sheets of copper and tin to sheathe the *Queen Mary,* basic hygiene is bound to suffer.

By the second day, I had already flushed a rat—a small rat, as Fergus pointed out, but still a rat—in the hold where I went to retrieve my large medicine box, packed away there by mistake during the loading. There was a soft shuffling noise in my cabin at night, which when the lantern was lit proved to be the footsteps of several dozen middling-size cockroaches, all fleeing frantically for the shelter of the shadows.

The heads, two small quarter-galleries on either side of the ship toward the bow, were nothing more than a pair of boards—with a strategic slot between them—suspended over the bounding waves eight feet below, so that the user was likely to get an unexpected dash of cold seawater at some highly inopportune moment. I suspected that this, coupled with a diet of salt pork and hardtack, likely caused constipation to be epidemic among seamen.

Mr. Warren, the ship's master, proudly informed me that the decks were swabbed regularly every morning, the brass polished, and everything generally made shipshape, which seemed a desirable state of affairs, given that we were in fact aboard a ship. Still, all the holystoning in the world could not disguise the fact that thirty-four human beings occupied this limited space, and only one of us bathed.

Given such circumstances, I was more than startled when I opened the door of the galley on the second morning, in search of boiling water.

I had expected the same dim and grubby conditions that obtained in the cabins and holds, and was dazzled by the glitter of sunlight through the overhead lattice on a rank of copper pans, so scrubbed that the metal of their bottoms shone pink. I blinked against the dazzle, my eyes adjusting, and saw that the walls of the galley were solid with built-in racks and cupboards, so constructed as to be proof against the roughest seas.

Blue and green glass bottles of spice, each tenderly jacketed in felt against injury, vibrated softly in their rack above the pots. Knives, cleavers, and skewers gleamed in deadly array, in a quantity sufficient to deal with a whale carcass, should one present itself. A rimmed double shelf hung from the bulkhead, thick with bulb glasses and shallow plates, on which a quantity of fresh-cut turnip tops were set to sprout for greens. An enormous pot bubbled softly over the stove, emitting a fragrant steam. And in the midst of all this spotless splendor stood the cook, surveying me with baleful eye.

"Out," he said.

"Good morning," I said, as cordially as possible. "My name is Claire Fraser."

"Out," he repeated, in the same graveled tones.

"I am Mrs. Fraser, the wife of the supercargo, and ship's surgeon for this voyage," I said, giving him eyeball for eyeball. "I require six gallons of boiling water, when convenient, for cleaning of the head."

His small, bright blue eyes grew somewhat smaller and brighter, the black pupils of them training on me like gun barrels.

"I am Aloysius O'Shaughnessy Murphy," he said. "Ship's cook. And I require ye to take yer feet off my fresh-washed deck. I do not allow women in my galley." He glowered at me under the edge of the black cotton kerchief that swathed his head. He was several inches shorter than I, but made up for it by measuring about three feet more in circumference, with a wrestler's shoulders and a head like a cannonball, set upon them without apparent benefit of an intervening neck. A wooden leg completed the ensemble.

I took one step back, with dignity, and spoke to him from the relative safety of the passageway.

"In that case," I said, "you may send up the hot water by the messboy."

"I may," he agreed. "And then again, I may not." He turned his broad back on me in dismissal, busying himself with a chopping block, a cleaver, and a joint of mutton.

I stood in the passageway for a moment, thinking. The thud of the cleaver sounded regularly against the wood. Mr. Murphy reached up to his spice rack, grasped a bottle without looking, and sprinkled a good quantity of the contents over the diced meat. The dusty scent of sage filled the air, superseded at once by the pungency of an onion, whacked in two with a casual swipe of the cleaver and tossed into the mixture.

Evidently the crew of the *Artemis* did not subsist entirely upon salt pork and hardtack, then. I began to understand the reasons for Captain Raines's rather pear-shaped physique. I poked my head back through the door, taking care to stand outside.

"Cardamom," I said firmly. "Nutmeg, whole. Dried this year. Fresh extract of anise. Ginger root, two large ones, with no blemishes." I paused. Mr. Murphy had stopped chopping, cleaver poised motionless above the block.

"And," I added, "half a dozen whole vanilla beans. From Ceylon."

He turned slowly, wiping his hands upon his leather apron.

Unlike his surroundings, neither the apron nor his other apparel was spotless.

He had a broad, florid face, edged with stiff sandy whiskers like a scrubbing brush, which quivered slightly as he looked at me, like the antennae of some large insect. His tongue darted out to lick pursed lips.

"Saffron?" he asked hoarsely.

"Half an ounce," I said promptly, taking care to conceal any trace of triumph in my manner.

He breathed in deeply, lust gleaming bright in his small blue eyes.

"Ye'll find a mat just outside, ma'am, should ye care to wipe yer boots and come in."

One head sterilized within the limits of boiling water and Fergus's tolerance, I made my way back to my cabin to clean up for luncheon. Marsali was not there; she was undoubtedly attending to Fergus, whose labors at my insistence had been little short of heroic.

I rinsed my own hands with alcohol, brushed my hair, and then went across the passage to see whether—by some wild chance—Jamie wanted anything to eat or drink. One glance disabused me of this notion.

Marsali and I had been given the larger cabin, which meant that each of us had approximately six square feet of space, not including the beds. These were box-berths, a sort of enclosed bed built into the wall, about five and a half feet long. Marsali fitted neatly into hers, but I was forced to adopt a slightly curled position, like a caper on toast, which caused me to wake up with pins and needles in my feet.

Jamie and Fergus had similar berths. Jamie was lying on his side, wedged into one of these like a snail into its shell; one of which beasts he strongly resembled at the moment, being a pale and viscid gray in color, with streaks of green and yellow that contrasted nastily with his red hair. He opened one eye when he heard me come in, regarded me dimly for a moment, and closed it again.

"Not so good, hm?" I said sympathetically.

The eye opened again, and he seemed to be preparing to say

something. He opened his mouth, changed his mind, and closed it again.

"No," he said, and shut the eye once more.

I tentatively smoothed his hair, but he seemed too sunk in misery to notice.

"Captain Raines says it will likely be calmer by tomorrow," I offered. The sea wasn't terribly rough as it was, but there was a noticeable rise and fall.

"It doesna matter," he said, not opening his eyes. "I shall be dead by then—or at least I hope so."

"Afraid not," I said, shaking my head. "Nobody dies of seasickness; though I must say it seems a wonder that they don't, looking at you."

"Not that." He opened his eyes, and struggled up on one elbow, an effort that left him clammy with sweat and white to the lips.

"Claire. Be careful. I should have told ye before—but I didna want to worry ye, and I thought—" His face changed. Familiar as I was with expressions of bodily infirmity, I had the basin there just in time.

"Oh, God." He lay limp and exhausted, pale as the sheet.

"What should you have told me?" I asked, wrinkling my nose as I put the basin on the floor near the door. "Whatever it was, you should have told me before we sailed, but it's too late to think of that."

"I didna think it would be so bad," he murmured.

"You never do," I said, rather tartly. "What did you want to tell me, though?"

"Ask Fergus," he said. "Say I said he must tell ye. And tell him Innes is all right."

"What are you talking about?" I was mildly alarmed; delirium wasn't a common effect of seasickness.

His eyes opened, and fixed on mine with great effort. Beads of sweat stood out on his brow and upper lip.

"Innes," he said. "He canna be the one. He doesna mean to kill me."

A small shiver ran up my spine.

"Are you quite all right, Jamie?" I asked. I bent and wiped his face, and he gave me the ghost of an exhausted smile. He had no fever, and his eyes were clear.

"Who?" I said carefully, with a sudden feeling that there were eyes fixed on my back. "Who *does* mean to kill you?"

"I don't know." A passing spasm contorted his features, but he clamped his lips tight, and managed to subdue it.

"Ask Fergus," he whispered, when he could talk again. "In private. He'll tell ye."

I felt exceedingly helpless. I had no notion what he was talking about, but if there was any danger, I wasn't about to leave him alone.

"I'll wait until he comes down," I said.

One hand was curled near his nose. It straightened slowly and slid under the pillow, coming out with his dirk, which he clasped to his chest.

"I shall be all right," he said. "Go on, then, Sassenach. I shouldna think they'd try anything in daylight. If at all."

I didn't find this reassuring in the slightest, but there seemed nothing else to do. He lay quite still, the dirk held to his chest like a stone tomb-figure.

"Go," he murmured again, his lips barely moving.

Just outside the cabin door, something stirred in the shadows at the end of the passage. Peering sharply, I made out the crouched silk shape of Mr. Willoughby, chin resting on his knees. He spread his knees apart, and bowed his head politely between them.

"Not worry, honorable First Wife," he assured me in a sibilant whisper. "I watch."

"Good," I said, "keep doing it." And went, in considerable distress of mind, to find Fergus.

Fergus, found with Marsali on the after deck, peering into the ship's wake at several large white birds, was somewhat more reassuring.

"We are not sure that anyone intends actually to kill milord," he explained. "The casks in the warehouse might have been an accident—I have seen such things happen more than once—and likewise the fire in the shed, but—"

"Wait one minute, young Fergus," I said, gripping him by the sleeve. "*What* casks, and *what* fire?"

"Oh," he said, looking surprised. "Milord did not tell you?"

"Milord is sick as a dog, and incapable of telling me anything more than that I should ask you."

Fergus shook his head, clicking his tongue in a censorious French way.

"He never thinks he will be so ill," he said. "He always is, and yet every time he must set foot on a ship, he insists that it is only a matter of will; his mind will be master, and he will not allow his stomach to be dictating his actions. Then within ten feet of the dock, he has turned green."

"He never told me that," I said, amused at this description. "Stubborn little fool."

Marsali had been hanging back behind Fergus with an air of haughty reserve, pretending that I wasn't there. At this unexpected description of Jamie, though, she was surprised into a brief snort of laughter. She caught my eye and turned hastily away, cheeks flaming, to stare out to sea.

Fergus smiled and shrugged. "You know what he is like, milady," he said, with tolerant affection. "He could be dying, and one would never know."

"You'd know if you went down and looked at him now," I said tartly. At the same time, I was conscious of surprise, accompanied by a faint feeling of warmth in the pit of my stomach. Fergus had been with Jamie almost daily for twenty years, and still Jamie would not admit to him the weakness that he would readily let me see. Were he dying, *I* would know about it, all right.

"Men," I said, shaking my head.

"Milady?"

"Never mind," I said. "You were telling me about casks and fires."

"Oh, indeed, yes." Fergus brushed back his thick shock of black hair with his hook. "It was the day before I met you again, milady, at Madame Jeanne's."

The day I had returned to Edinburgh, no more than a few hours before I had found Jamie at the printshop. He had been at the Burntisland docks with Fergus and a gang of six men during the night, taking advantage of the late dawn of winter to retrieve several casks of unbonded Madeira, smuggled in among a shipment of innocent flour.

"Madeira does not soak through the wood so quickly as some other wines do," Fergus explained. "You cannot bring in brandy under the noses of the Customs like that, for the dogs will smell it at once, even if their masters do not. But not Madeira, provided it has been freshly casked.''

"Dogs?"

"Some of the Customs inspectors have dogs, milady, trained to smell out such contraband as tobacco and brandy.'' He waved away the interruption, squinting his eyes against the brisk sea wind.

"We had removed the Madeira safely, and brought it to the warehouse—one of those belonging apparently to Lord Dundas, but in fact it belongs jointly to milord and Madame Jeanne.''

"Indeed," I said, again with that minor dip of the stomach I had felt when Jamie opened the door of the brothel on Queen Street. "Partners, are they?''

"Well, of a sort.'' Fergus sounded regretful. "Milord has only a five percent share, in return for his finding the place, and making the arrangements. Printing as an occupation is much less profitable than keeping a *hôtel de joie*.'' Marsali didn't look round, but I thought her shoulders stiffened further.

"I daresay," I said. Edinburgh and Madame Jeanne were a long way behind us, after all. "Get on with the story. Someone may cut Jamie's throat before I find out why.''

"Of course, milady.'' Fergus bobbed his head apologetically.

The contraband had been safely hidden, awaiting disguise and sale, and the smugglers had paused to refresh themselves with a drink in lieu of breakfast, before making their way home in the brightening dawn. Two of the men had asked for their shares at once, needing the money to pay gaming debts and buy food for their families. Jamie agreeing to this, he had gone across to the warehouse office, where some gold was kept.

As the men relaxed over their whisky in a corner of the warehouse, their joking and laughter was interrupted by a sudden vibration that shook the floor beneath their feet.

"Come-down!'' shouted MacLeod, an experienced warehouseman, and the men had dived for cover, even before they had seen the great rack of hogsheads near the office quiver and rumble, one two-ton cask rolling down the stack with ponderous grace, to smash in an aromatic lake of ale, followed within seconds by a cascade of its monstrous fellows.

"Milord was crossing in front of the rank,'' Fergus said, shaking his head. "It was only by the grace of the Blessed Virgin herself that he was not crushed." A bounding cask had missed him by inches, in fact, and he had escaped another only by diving headfirst out of its way and under an empty wine rack that had deflected its course.

"As I say, such things happen often," Fergus said, shrugging. "A dozen men are killed each year in such accidents, in the warehouses near Edinburgh alone. But with the other things . . ."

The week before the incident of the casks, a small shed full of packing straw had burst into flames while Jamie was working in it. A lantern placed between him and the door had apparently fallen over, setting the straw alight and trapping Jamie in the windowless shed, behind a sudden wall of flame.

"The shed was fortunately of a most flimsy construction, and the boards half-rotted. It went up like matchwood, but milord was able to kick a hole in the back wall and crawl out, with no injury. We thought at first that the lantern had merely fallen of its own accord, and were most grateful for his escape. It was only later that milord told me he thought that he had heard a noise—perhaps a shot, perhaps only the cracking noises an old warehouse makes as its boards settle—and when he turned to see, found the flames shooting up before him."

Fergus sighed. He looked rather tired, and I wondered whether perhaps he had stayed awake to stand watch over Jamie during the night.

"So," he said, shrugging once more. "We do not know. Such incidents may have been no more than accident—they may not. But taking such occurrences together with what happened at Arbroath—"

"You may have a traitor among the smugglers," I said.

"Just so, milady." Fergus scratched his head. "But what is more disturbing to milord is the man whom the Chinaman shot at Madame Jeanne's."

"Because you think he was a Customs agent, who'd tracked Jamie from the docks to the brothel? Jamie said he couldn't be, because he had no warrant."

"Not proof," Fergus noted. "But worse, the booklet he had in his pocket."

"The New Testament?" I saw no particular relevance to that, and said so.

"Oh, but there is, milady—or might be, I should say," Fergus corrected himself. "You see, the booklet was one that milord himself had printed."

"I see," I said slowly, "or at least I'm beginning to."

Fergus nodded gravely. "To have the Customs trace brandy from the points of delivery to the brothel would be bad, of course, but not fatal—another hiding place could be found; in fact, milord has arrangements with the owners of two taverns that . . . but that is of no matter." He waved it away. "But to have the agents of the Crown connect the notorious smuggler Jamie Roy with the respectable Mr. Malcolm of Carfax Close . . ." He spread his hands wide. "You see?"

I did. Were the Customs to get too close to his smuggling operations, Jamie could merely disperse his assistants, cease frequenting his smugglers' haunts, and disappear for a time, retreating into his guise as a printer until it seemed safe to resume his illegal activities. But to have his two identities both detected and merged was not only to deprive him of both his sources of income, but to arouse such suspicion as might lead to discovery of his real name, his seditious activities, and thence to Lallybroch and his history as rebel and convicted traitor. They would have evidence to hang him a dozen times—and once was enough.

"I certainly do see. So Jamie wasn't only worried about Laoghaire and Hobart MacKenzie, when he told Ian he thought it would be as well for us to skip to France for a bit."

Paradoxically, I felt somewhat relieved by Fergus's revelations. At least I hadn't been single-handedly responsible for Jamie's exile. My reappearance might have precipitated the crisis with Laoghaire, but I had had nothing to do with any of this.

"Exactly, milady. And still, we do not know for certain that one of the men has betrayed us—or whether, even if there should be a traitor among them, he should wish to kill milord."

"That's a point." It was, but not a large one. If one of the smugglers had undertaken to betray Jamie for money, that was one thing. If it was for some motive of personal vengeance, though, the man might well feel compelled to take matters into his own hands, now that we were—temporarily, at least—out of reach of the King's Customs.

"If so," Fergus was continuing, "it will be one of six men—the six milord sent me to collect, to sail with us. These six were present both when the casks fell, and when the shed caught fire; all have been to the brothel." He paused. "And all of them were present on the road at Arbroath, when we were ambushed, and found the exciseman hanged."

"Do they all know about the printshop?"

"Oh, no, milady! Milord has always been most careful to let none of the smuggling men know of that—but it is always possible that one of them shall have seen him on the streets in Edinburgh, followed him to Carfax Close, and so learned of A. Malcolm." He smiled wryly. "Milord is not the most inconspicuous of men, milady."

"Very true," I said, matching his tone. "But now all of them know Jamie's real name—Captain Raines calls him Fraser."

"Yes," he said, with a faint, grim smile. "That is why we must discover whether we do indeed sail with a traitor—and who it is."

I looked at him, and it occurred to me for the first time that Fergus was indeed a grown man now—and a dangerous one. I had known him as an eager, squirrel-toothed boy of ten, and to me, something of that boy would always remain in his face. But some time had passed since he had been a Paris street urchin.

Marsali had remained staring out to sea during most of this discussion, preferring to take no risk of having to converse with me. She had obviously been listening, though, and now I saw a shiver pass through her thin shoulders—whether of cold or apprehension, I couldn't tell. She likely hadn't planned on shipping with a potential murderer when she had agreed to elope with Fergus.

"You'd better take Marsali below," I said to Fergus. "She's going blue round the edges. Don't worry," I said to Marsali, in a cool voice, "I shan't be in the cabin for some time."

"Where are you going, milady?" Fergus was squinting at me, slightly suspicious. "Milord will not wish you to be—"

"I don't mean to," I assured him. "I'm going to the galley."

"The galley?" His fine black brows shot up.

"To see whether Aloysius O'Shaughnessy Murphy has anything to suggest for seasickness," I said. "If we don't get Jamie back on his feet, he isn't going to care whether anyone cuts his throat or not."

Murphy, sweetened by an ounce of dried orange peel and a bottle of Jared's best claret, was quite willing to oblige. In fact, he seemed to consider the problem of keeping food in Jamie's stomach something of a professional challenge, and spent hours in mystic contemplation of his spice rack and pantries—all to no avail.

We encountered no storms, but the winter winds drove a heavy swell before them, and the *Artemis* rose and fell ten feet at a time, laboring up and down the great glassy peaks of the waves. There were times, watching the hypnotic rise and lurch of the taffrail against the horizon, when I felt a few interior qualms of my own, and turned hastily away.

Jamie showed no signs of being about to fulfill Jared's heartening prophecy and spring to his feet, suddenly accustomed to the motion. He remained in his berth, the color of rancid custard, moving only to stagger to the head, and guarded in turns day and night by Mr. Willoughby and Fergus.

On the positive side of things, none of the six smugglers made any move that might be considered threatening. All expressed a sympathetic concern for Jamie's welfare, and—carefully watched —all had visited him briefly in his cabin, with no suspicious circumstances attending.

For my part, I spent the days in exploring the ship, attending to such small medical emergencies as arose from the daily business of sailing—a smashed finger, a cracked rib, bleeding gums and an abscessed tooth—and pounding herbs and making medicines in a corner of the galley, allowed to work there by Murphy's grace.

Marsali was absent from our shared cabin when I rose, already asleep when I returned to it, and silently hostile when the cramped confines of shipboard forced us to meet on deck or over meals. I assumed that the hostility was in part the result of her natural feelings for her mother, and in part the result of frustration over passing her night hours in my company, rather than Fergus's.

For that matter, if she remained untouched—and judging from her sullen demeanor, I was reasonably sure she did—it was owing entirely to Fergus's respect for Jamie's dictates. In terms of his role as guardian of his stepdaughter's virtue, Jamie himself was a negligible force at the moment.

"Wot, not the broth, too?" Murphy said. The cook's broad red face lowered menacingly. "Which I've had folk rise from their deathbeds after a sup of that broth!"

He took the pannikin of broth from Fergus, sniffed at it critically, and thrust it under my nose.

"Here, smell that, missus. Marrow bones, garlic, caraway seed, and a lump o' pork fat to flavor, all strained careful through muslin, same as some folks bein' poorly to their stomachs can't abide chunks, but chunks you'll not find there, not a one!"

The broth was in fact a clear golden brown, with an appetizing smell that made my own mouth water, despite the excellent breakfast I had made less than an hour before. Captain Raines had a delicate stomach, and in consequence had taken some pains both in the procurement of a cook and the provisioning of the galley, to the benefit of the officers' table.

Murphy, with a wooden leg and the general dimensions of a rum cask, looked the picture of a thoroughgoing pirate, but in fact had a reputation as the best sea-cook in Le Havre—as he had told me himself, without the least boastfulness. He considered cases of seasickness a challenge to his skill, and Jamie, still prostrate after four days, was a particular affront to him.

"I'm sure it's wonderful broth," I assured him. "It's just that he can't keep *anything* down."

Murphy grunted dubiously, but turned and carefully poured the remains of the broth into one of the numerous kettles that steamed day and night over the galley fire.

Scowling horribly and running one hand through the wisps of his scanty blond hair, he opened a cupboard and closed it, then bent to rummage through a chest of provisions, muttering under his breath.

"A bit o' hardtack, maybe?" he muttered. "Dry, that's what's wanted. Maybe a whiff o' vinegar, though; tart pickle, say . . ."

I watched in fascination as the cook's huge, sausage-fingered hands flicked deftly through the stock of provisions, plucking dainties and assembling them swiftly on a tray.

" 'Ere, let's try this, then," he said, handing me the finished tray. "Let 'im suck on the pickled gherkins, but don't let 'im bite 'em yet. Then follow on with a bite of the plain hardtack—there ain't no weevils in it yet, I don't think—but see as he don't drink water with it. Then a bite of gherkin, well-chewed, to make the spittle flow, a bite of hardtack, and so to go on with. That much stayin' down, then, we can proceed to the custard, which it's fresh-made last evening for the Captain's supper. Then if that sticks . . ." His voice followed me out of the galley, continuing the catalogue of available nourishment. ". . . milk toast, which it's made with goat's milk, and fresh-milked, too . . .

". . . syllabub beat up well with whisky and a nice *egg* . . ." boomed down the passageway as I negotiated the narrow turn with the loaded tray, carefully stepping over Mr. Willoughby, who was as usual crouched in a corner of the passage by Jamie's door like a small blue lapdog.

One step inside the cabin, though, I could see that the exercise of Murphy's culinary skill was going to be once again in vain. In the usual fashion of a man feeling unwell, Jamie had managed to arrange his surroundings to be as depressing and uncomfortable as possible. The tiny cabin was dank and squalid, the cramped berth covered with a cloth so as to exclude both light and air, and half-piled with a tangle of clammy blankets and unwashed clothes.

"Rise and shine," I said cheerfully. I set down the tray and pulled off the makeshift curtain, which appeared to be one of Fergus's shirts. What light there was came from a large prism embedded in the deck overhead. It struck the berth, illuminating a countenance of ghastly pallor and baleful mien.

He opened one eye an eighth of an inch.

"Go away," he said, and shut it again.

"I've brought you some breakfast," I said firmly.

The eye opened again, coldly blue and gelid.

"Dinna mention the word 'breakfast' to me," he said.

"Call it luncheon then," I said. "It's late enough." I pulled up a stool next to him, picked a gherkin from the tray, and held it invitingly under his nose. "You're supposed to suck on it," I told him.

Slowly, the other eye opened. He said nothing, but the pair of blue orbs swiveled around, resting on me with an expression of such ferocious eloquence that I hastily withdrew the pickle.

The eyelids drooped slowly shut once more.

I surveyed the wreckage, frowning. He lay on his back, his knees drawn up. While the built-in berth provided more stability for the sleeper than the crew's swinging hammocks, it was de-signed to accommodate the usual run of passengers, who—judging from the size of the berth—were assumed to be no more than a modest five feet three or so.

"You can't be at all comfortable in there," I said.

"I am not."

"Would you like to try a hammock instead? At least you could stretch—"

"I would not."

"The captain says he requires a list of the cargo from you—at your convenience."

He made a brief and unrepeatable suggestion as to what Captain Raines might do with his list, not bothering to open his eyes.

I sighed, and picked up his unresisting hand. It was cold and damp, and his pulse was fast.

"Well," I said after a pause. "Perhaps we could try something I used to do with surgical patients. It seemed to help sometimes."

He gave a low groan, but didn't object. I pulled up a stool and sat down, still holding his hand.

I had developed the habit of talking with the patients for a few minutes before they were taken to surgery. My presence seemed to reassure them, and I had found that if I could fix their attention on something beyond the impending ordeal, they seemed to do better —there was less bleeding, the postanesthetic nausea was less, and they seemed to heal better. I had seen it happen often enough to believe that it was not imagination; Jamie hadn't been altogether wrong when assuring Fergus that the power of mind over flesh was possible.

"Let's think of something pleasant," I said, pitching my voice to be as low and soothing as possible. "Think of Lallybroch, of the hillside above the house. Think of the pine trees there—can you smell the needles? Think of the smoke coming up from the kitchen chimney on a clear day, and an apple in your hand. Think about how it feels in your hand, all hard and smooth, and then—"

"Sassenach?" Both Jamie's eyes were open, and fixed on me in intense concentration. Sweat gleamed in the hollow of his temples.

"Yes?"

"Go away."

"What?"

"Go away," he repeated, very gently, "or I shall break your neck. Go away *now*."

I rose with dignity and went out.

Mr. Willoughby was leaning against an upright in the passage, peering thoughtfully into the cabin.

"Don't have those stone balls with you, do you?" I asked.

"Yes," he answered, looking surprised. "Wanting healthy balls for Tsei-mi?" He began to fumble in his sleeve, but I stopped him with a gesture.

"What I want to do is bash him on the head with them, but I suppose Hippocrates would frown on that."

Mr. Willoughby smiled uncertainly and bobbed his head several times in an effort to express appreciation of whatever I thought I meant.

"Never mind," I said. I glared back over my shoulder at the heap of reeking bedclothes. It stirred slightly, and a groping hand emerged, patting gingerly around the floor until it found the basin that stood there. Grasping this, the hand disappeared into the murky depths of the berth, from which presently emerged the sound of dry retching.

"Bloody man!" I said, exasperation mingled with pity—and a slight feeling of alarm. The ten hours of a Channel crossing were one thing; what would his state be like after two months of this?

"Head of pig," Mr. Willoughby agreed, with a lugubrious nod. "He is rat, you think, or maybe dragon?"

"He smells like a whole zoo," I said. "Why dragon, though?"

"One is born in Year of Dragon, Year of Rat, Year of Sheep, Year of Horse," Mr. Willoughby explained. "Being different, each year, different people. You are knowing is Tsei-mi rat, or dragon?"

"You mean which year was he born in?" I had vague memories of the menus in Chinese restaurants, decorated with the animals of the Chinese zodiac, with explanations of the supposed character traits of those born in each year. "It was 1721, but I don't know offhand which animal that was the year of."

"I am thinking rat," said Mr. Willoughby, looking thoughtfully at the tangle of bedclothes, which were heaving in a mildly agitated manner. "Rat very clever, very lucky. But dragon, too, could be. He is most lusty in bed, Tsei-mi? Dragons most passionate people."

"Not so as you would notice lately," I said, watching the heap of bedclothes out of the corner of my eye. It heaved upward and fell back, as though the contents had turned over suddenly.

"I have Chinese medicine," Mr. Willoughby said, observing this phenomenon thoughtfully. "Good for vomit, stomach, head, all making most peaceful and serene."

I looked at him with interest. "Really? I'd like to see that. Have you tried it on Jamie yet?"

The little Chinese shook his head regretfully.

"Not want," he replied. "Say damn-all, throwing overboard if I am come near."

Mr. Willoughby and I looked at each other with a perfect understanding.

"You know," I said, raising my voice a decibel or two, "prolonged dry retching is very bad for a person."

"Oh, most bad, yes." Mr. Willoughby had shaved the forward part of his skull that morning; the bald curve shone as he nodded vigorously.

"It erodes the stomach tissues, and irritates the esophagus."

"This is so?"

"Quite so. It raises the blood pressure and strains the abdominal muscles, too. Can even tear them, and cause a hernia."

"Ah."

"And," I continued, raising my voice just a trifle, "it can cause the testicles to become tangled round each other inside the scrotum, and cuts off the circulation there."

"Ooh!" Mr. Willoughby's eyes went round.

"If *that* happens," I said ominously, "the only thing to do, usually, is to amputate before gangrene sets in."

Mr. Willoughby made a hissing sound indicative of understanding and deep shock. The heap of bedclothes, which had been tossing to and fro in a restless manner during this conversation, was quite still.

I looked at Mr. Willoughby. He shrugged. I folded my arms and waited. After a minute, a long foot, elegantly bare, was extruded from the bedclothes. A moment later, its fellow joined it, resting on the floor.

"Damn the pair of ye," said a deep Scottish voice, in tones of extreme malevolence. "Come in, then."

Fergus and Marsali were leaning over the aft rail, cozily shoulder to shoulder, Fergus's arm about the girl's waist, her long fair hair fluttering in the wind.

Hearing approaching footsteps, Fergus glanced back over his shoulder. Then he gasped, whirled round, and crossed himself, eyes bulging.

"Not . . . one . . . word, if ye please," Jamie said between clenched teeth.

Fergus opened his mouth, but nothing came out. Marsali, turning to look too, emitted a shrill scream.

"Da! What's happened to ye?"

The obvious fright and concern in her face stopped Jamie from whatever acerbic remark he had been about to make. His face relaxed slightly, making the slender gold needles that protruded from behind his ears twitch like ant's feelers.

"It's all right," he said gruffly. "It's only some rubbish of the Chinee's, to cure the puking."

Wide-eyed, Marsali came up to him, gingerly extending a finger to touch the needles embedded in the flesh of his wrist below the palm. Three more flashed from the inside of his leg, a few inches above the ankle.

"Does—does it work?" she asked. "How does it feel?"

Jamie's mouth twitched, his normal sense of humor beginning to reassert itself.

"I feel like a bloody ill-wish doll that someone's been poking full o' pins," he said. "But then I havena vomited in the last quarter-hour, so I suppose it must work." He shot a quick glare at me and Mr. Willoughby, standing side by side near the rail.

"Mind ye," he said, "I dinna feel like sucking on gherkins just yet, but I could maybe go so far as to relish a glass of ale, if ye mind where some might be found, Fergus."

"Oh. Oh, yes, milord. If you will come with me?" Unable to refrain from staring, Fergus reached out a tentative hand to take Jamie's arm, but thinking better of it, turned in the direction of the after gangway.

"Shall I tell Murphy to start cooking your luncheon?" I called after Jamie as he turned to follow Fergus. He gave me a long, level look over one shoulder. The golden needles sprouted through his hair in twin bunches, gleaming in the morning light like a pair of devil's horns.

"Dinna try me too high, Sassenach," he said. "I'm no going to forget, ye ken. Tangled testicles—pah!"

Mr. Willoughby had been ignoring this exchange, squatting on his heels in the shadow of the aft-deck scuttlebutt, a large barrel filled with water for refreshment of the deck watch. He was counting on his fingers, evidently absorbed in some kind of calculation. As Jamie stalked away, he looked up.

"Not rat," he said, shaking his head. "Not dragon, too. Tsei-mi born in Year of Ox."

"Really?" I said, looking after the broad shoulders and red head, lowered stubbornly against the wind. "How appropriate."

42

The Man in the Moon

Voyager

As his title suggested, Jamie's job as supercargo was not onerous. Beyond checking the contents of the hold against the bills of lading to ensure that the *Artemis* was in fact carrying the requisite quantities of hides, tin, and sulfur, there was nothing for him to do while at sea. His duties would begin once we reached Jamaica, when the cargo must be unloaded, rechecked, and sold, with the requisite taxes paid, commissions deducted, and paperwork filed.

In the meantime, there was little for him—or me—to do. While Mr. Picard, the bosun, eyed Jamie's powerful frame covetously, it was obvious that he would never make a seaman. Quick and agile as any of the crew, his ignorance of ropes and sails made him useless for anything beyond the occasional situation where sheer strength was required. It was plain he was a soldier, not a sailor.

He did assist with enthusiasm at the gunnery practice that was held every other day, helping to run the four huge guns on their carriages in and out with a tremendous racket, and spending hours in rapt discussion of esoteric cannon lore with Tom Sturgis, the gunner. During these thunderous exercises, Marsali, Mr. Willoughby, and I sat safely out of the way under the care of Fergus, who was excluded from the fireworks because of his missing hand.

Somewhat to my surprise, I had been accepted as the ship's surgeon with little question from the crew. It was Fergus who explained that in small merchant ships, even barber-surgeons were uncommon. It was commonly the gunner's wife—if he had one—who dealt with the small injuries and illnesses of the crew.

I saw the normal run of crushed fingers, burnt hands, skin infections, abscessed teeth, and digestive ills, but in a crew of only thirty-two men, there was seldom enough work to keep me busy beyond the hour of sick call each morning.

In consequence, both Jamie and I had a great deal of free time. And, as the *Artemis* drew gradually south into the great gyre of the Atlantic, we began to spend most of this time with each other.

For the first time since my return to Edinburgh, there was time to talk; to relearn all the half-forgotten things we knew of each other, to find out the new facets that experience had polished, and simply to take pleasure in each other's presence, without the distractions of danger and daily life.

We strolled the deck constantly, up and down, marking off miles as we conversed of everything and nothing, pointing out to each other the phenomena of a sea voyage; the spectacular sunrises and sunsets, schools of strange green and silver fish, enormous islands of floating seaweed, harboring thousands of tiny crabs and jellyfish, the sleek dolphins that appeared for several days in a row, swimming parallel with the ship, leaping out of the water now and then, as though to get a look at the curious creatures above the water.

The moon rose huge and fast and golden, a great glowing disc that slid upward, out of the water and into the sky like a phoenix rising. The water was dark now, and the dolphins invisible, but I thought somehow that they were still there, keeping pace with the ship on her flight through the dark.

It was a scene breathtaking enough even for the sailors, who had seen it a thousand times, to stop and sigh with pleasure at the sight, as the huge orb rose to hang just over the edge of the world, seeming almost near enough to touch.

Jamie and I stood close together by the rail, admiring it. It seemed so close that we could make out with ease the dark spots and shadows on its surface.

"It seems so close ye could speak to the Man in the Moon," he said, smiling, and waved a hand in greeting to the dreaming golden face above.

" 'The weeping Pleiads wester / and the moon is under seas,' " I quoted. "And look, it is, down there, too." I pointed over the rail, to where the trail of moonlight deepened, glowing in the water as though a twin of the moon itself were sunken there.

"When I left," I said, "men were getting ready to fly to the moon. I wonder whether they'll make it."

"Do the flying machines go so high, then?" Jamie asked. He squinted at the moon. "I should say it's a great way, for all it looks so close just now. I read a book by an astronomer—he said it was perhaps three hundred leagues from the earth to the moon. Is he wrong, then, or is it only that the—airplanes, was it?—will fly so far?"

"It takes a special kind, called a rocket," I said. "Actually, it's a lot farther than that to the moon, and once you get far away from the earth, there's no air to breathe in space. They'll have to carry air with them on the voyage, like food and water. They put it in sort of canisters."

"Really?" He gazed up, face full of light and wonder. "What will it look like there, I wonder?"

"I know that," I said. "I've seen pictures. It's rocky, and barren, with no life at all—but very beautiful, with cliffs and mountains and craters—you can see the craters from here; the dark spots." I nodded toward the smiling moon, then smiled at Jamie myself. "It's not unlike Scotland—except that it isn't green."

He laughed, then evidently reminded by the word "pictures," reached into his coat and drew out the little packet of photographs. He was cautious about them, never taking them out where they might be seen by anyone, even Fergus, but we were alone back here, with little chance of interruption.

The moon was bright enough to see Brianna's face, glowing and mutable, as he thumbed slowly through the pictures. The edges were becoming frayed, I saw.

"Will she walk about on the moon, d'ye think?" he asked softly, pausing at a shot of Bree looking out a window, secretly dreaming, unaware of being photographed. He glanced up again at the orb above us, and I realized that for him, a voyage to the moon seemed very little more difficult or farfetched than the one in which we were engaged. The moon, after all, was only another distant, unknown place.

"I don't know," I said, smiling a bit.

He thumbed through the pictures slowly, absorbed as he always was by the sight of his daughter's face, so like his own. I watched him quietly, sharing his silent joy at this promise of our immortality.

I thought briefly of that stone in Scotland, engraved with his name, and took comfort from its distance. Whenever our parting might come, chances were it would not be soon. And even when and where it did—Brianna would still be left of us.

More of Housman's lines drifted through my head—*Halt by the headstone naming / The heart no longer stirred, / And say the lad that loved you / Was one that kept his word.*

I drew close to him, feeling the heat of his body through coat and shirt, and rested my head against his arm as he turned slowly through the small stack of photographs.

"She is beautiful," he murmured, as he did every time he saw the pictures. "And clever, too, did ye not say?"

"Just like her father," I told him, and felt him chuckle softly.

I felt him stiffen slightly as he turned one picture over, and lifted my head to see which one he was looking at. It was one taken at the beach, when Brianna was about sixteen. It showed her standing thigh-deep in the surf, hair in a sandy tangle, kicking water at her friend, a boy named Rodney, who was backing away, laughing too, hands held up against the spray of water.

Jamie frowned slightly, lips pursed.

"That—" he began. "Do they—" He paused and cleared his throat. "I wouldna venture to criticize, Claire," he said, very carefully, "but do ye not think this is a wee bit . . . indecent?"

I suppressed an urge to laugh.

"No," I said, composedly. "That's really quite a modest bathing suit—for the time." While the suit in question *was* a bikini, it was by no means skimpy, rising to at least an inch below Bree's navel. "I chose this picture because I thought you'd want to, er . . . see as much of her as possible."

He looked mildly scandalized at this thought, but his eyes returned to the picture, drawn irresistibly. His face softened as he looked at her.

"Aye, well," he said. "Aye, she's verra lovely, and I'm glad to know it." He lifted the picture, studying it carefully. "No, it's no the thing she's wearing I meant; most women who bathe outside do it naked, and their skins are no shame to them. It's only—this lad. Surely she shouldna be standing almost naked before a man?"

He scowled at the hapless Rodney, and I bit my lip at the thought of the scrawny little boy, whom I knew very well, as a masculine threat to maidenly purity.

"Well," I said, drawing a deep breath. We were on slightly delicate ground here. "No. I mean, boys and girls do play together —like that. You know people dress differently then; I've told you. No one's really covered up a great deal except when the weather's cold."

"Mmphm," he said. "Aye, ye've told me." He managed to convey the distinct impression that on the basis of what I'd told him, he was not impressed with the moral conditions under which his daughter was living.

He scowled at the picture again, and I thought it was fortunate that neither Bree nor Rodney was present. I had seen Jamie as lover, husband, brother, uncle, laird, and warrior, but never before in his guise as a ferocious Scottish father. He was quite formidable.

For the first time, I thought that perhaps it was not altogether a bad thing that he wasn't able to oversee Bree's life personally; he would have frightened the living daylights out of any lad bold enough to try to court her.

Jamie blinked at the picture once or twice, then took a deep breath, and I could feel him brace himself to ask.

"D'ye think she is—a virgin?" The halt in his voice was barely perceptible, but I caught it.

"Of course she is," I said firmly. I thought it very likely, in fact, but this wasn't a situation in which to admit the possibility of doubt. There were things I could explain to Jamie about my own time, but the idea of sexual freedom wasn't one of them.

"Oh." The relief in his voice was inexpressible, and I bit my lip to keep from laughing. "Aye, well, I was sure of it, only I—that is—" He stopped and swallowed.

"Bree's a very good girl," I said. I squeezed his arm lightly. "Frank and I may not have got on so well together, but we were both good parents to her, if I do say so."

"Aye, I know ye were. I didna mean to say otherwise." He had the grace to look abashed, and tucked the beach picture carefully back into the packet. He put the pictures back into his pocket, patting them to be sure they were safe.

He stood looking up at the moon, then his brows drew together in a slight frown. The sea wind lifted strands of his hair, tugging them loose from the ribbon that bound it, and he brushed them back absentmindedly. Clearly there was still something on his mind.

"Do ye think," he began slowly, not looking at me. "Do ye think that it was quite wise to come to me now, Claire? Not that I dinna want ye," he added hastily, feeling me stiffen beside him. He caught my hand, preventing my turning away.

"No, I didna mean that at all! Christ, I do want ye!" He drew me closer, pressing my hand in his against his heart. "I want ye so badly that sometimes I think my heart will burst wi' the joy of having ye," he added more softly. "It's only—Brianna's alone now. Frank is gone, and you. She has no husband to protect her, no men of her family to see her safely wed. Will she not have need of ye awhile yet? Should ye no have waited a bit, I mean?"

I paused before answering, trying to get my own feelings under control.

"I don't know," I said at last; my voice quivered, in spite of my struggle to control it. "Look—things aren't the same then."

"I know that!"

"You don't!" I pulled my hand loose, and glared at him. "You don't know, Jamie, and there isn't any way for me to tell you, because you won't believe me. But Bree's a grown woman; she'll marry when and as she likes, not when someone arranges it for her. She doesn't *need* to marry, for that matter. She's having a good education; she can earn her own living—women do that. She won't have to have a man to protect her—"

"And if there's no need for a man to protect a woman, and care for her, then I think it will be a verra poor time!" He glared back at me.

I drew a deep breath, trying to be calm.

"I didn't say there's no need for it." I placed a hand on his shoulder, and spoke in a softer tone. "I said, she can choose. She needn't take a man out of necessity; she can take one for love."

His face began to relax, just slightly.

"You took me from need," he said. "When we wed."

"And I came back for love," I said. "Do you think I needed you any less, only because I could feed myself?"

The lines of his face eased, and the shoulder under my hand relaxed a bit as he searched my face.

"No," he said softly. "I dinna think that."

He put his arm around me and drew me close. I put my arms around his waist and held him, feeling the small flat patch of Brianna's pictures in his pocket under my cheek.

"I did worry about leaving her," I whispered, a little later. "She made me go; we were afraid that if I waited longer, I might not be able to find you. But I did worry."

"I know. I shouldna ha' said anything." He brushed my curls away from his chin, smoothing them down.

"I left her a letter," I said. "It was all I could think to do—knowing I might . . . might not see her again." I pressed my lips tight together and swallowed hard.

His fingertips stroked my back, very softly.

"Aye? That was good, Sassenach. What did ye say to her?"

I laughed, a little shakily.

"Everything I could think of. Motherly advice and wisdom—what I had of it. All the practical things—where the deed to the house and the family papers were. And everything I knew or could think of, about how to live. I expect she'll ignore it all, and have a wonderful life—but at least she'll know I thought about her."

It had taken me nearly a week, going through the cupboards and desk drawers of the house in Boston, finding all of the business papers, the bankbooks and mortgage papers and the family things. There were a good many bits and pieces of Frank's family lying about; huge scrapbooks and dozens of genealogy charts, albums of photographs, cartons of saved letters. My side of the family was a good deal simpler to sum up.

I lifted down the box I kept on the shelf of my closet. It was a small box. Uncle Lambert was a saver, as all scholars are, but there had been little to save. The essential documents of a small family—birth certificates, mine and my parents', their marriage lines, the registration for the car that had killed them—what ironic whim had prompted Uncle Lamb to save that? More likely he had never opened the box, but only kept it, in a scholar's blind faith that information must never be destroyed, for who knew what use it might be, and to whom?

I had seen its contents before, of course. There had been a period in my teens when I opened it nightly to look at the few photos it contained. I remembered the bone-deep longing for the mother I didn't remember, and the vain effort to imagine her, to bring her back to life from the small dim images in the box.

The best of them was a close-up photograph of her, face turned toward the camera, warm eyes and a delicate mouth, smiling under the brim of a felt cloche hat. The photograph had been hand-tinted; the cheeks and lips were an unnatural rose-pink, the eyes soft brown. Uncle Lamb said that that was wrong; her eyes had been gold, he said, like mine.

I thought perhaps that time of deep need had passed for Brianna, but was not sure. I had had a studio portrait made of myself the week before; I placed it carefully in the box and closed it, and put the box in the center of my desk, where she would find it. Then I sat down to write.

My dear Bree— I wrote, and stopped. I couldn't. Couldn't possibly be contemplating abandoning my child. To see those three black words stark on the page brought the whole mad idea into a cold clarity that struck me to the bone.

My hand shook, and the tip of the pen made small wavering circles in the air above the paper. I put it down, and clasped my hands between my thighs, eyes closed.

"Get a grip on yourself, Beauchamp," I muttered. "Write the bloody thing and have done. If she doesn't need it, it will do no harm, and if she does, it will be there." I picked up the pen and began again.

I don't know if you will ever read this, but perhaps it's as well to set it down. This is what I know of your grandparents (your real ones), your great-grandparents, and your medical history . . .

I wrote for some time, covering page after page. My mind grew calmer with the effort of recall, and the necessity of setting down the information clearly, and then I stopped, thinking.

What could I tell her, beyond those few bare bloodless facts? How to impart what sparse wisdom I had gained in forty-eight years of a fairly eventful life? My mouth twisted wryly in consideration of that. Did any daughter listen? Would I, had my mother been there to tell me?

It made no difference, though; I would just have to set it down, to be of use if it could.

But what was true, that would last forever, in spite of changing times and ways, what would stand her in good stead? Most of all, how could I tell her just how much I loved her?

The enormity of what I was about to do gaped before me, and my fingers clenched tight on the pen. I couldn't think—not and do this. I could only set the pen to the paper and hope.

Baby— I wrote, and stopped. Then swallowed hard, and started again.

> *You are my baby, and always will be. You won't know what that means until you have a child of your own, but I tell you now, anyway—you'll always be as much a part of me as when you shared my body and I felt you move inside. Always.*
>
> *I can look at you, asleep, and think of all the nights I tucked you in, coming in the dark to listen to your breathing, lay my hand on you and feel your chest rise and fall, knowing that no matter what happens, everything is right with the world because you are alive.*
>
> *All the names I've called you through the years—my chick, my pumpkin, precious dove, darling, sweetheart, dinky, smudge . . . I know why the Jews and Muslims have nine hundred names for God; one small word is not enough for love.*

I blinked hard to clear my vision, and went on writing, fast; I didn't dare take time to choose my words, or I would never write them.

> *I remember everything about you, from the tiny line of golden down that zigged across your forehead when you were hours old to the bumpy toenail on the big toe you broke last year, when you had that fight with Jeremy and kicked the door of his pickup truck.*
>
> *God, it breaks my heart to think it will stop now—that watching you, seeing all the tiny changes—I won't know when you stop biting your nails, if you ever do—seeing you grow suddenly taller than I, and your face take its shape. I always will remember, Bree, I always will.*
>
> *There's probably no one else on earth, Bree, who knows*

*what the back of your ears looked like when you were
three years old. I used to sit beside you, reading "One
Fish, Two Fish, Red Fish, Blue Fish," or "The Three Billy
Goats Gruff," and see those ears turn pink with happiness.
Your skin was so clear and fragile, I thought a touch would
leave fingerprints on you.*

*You look like Jamie, I told you. You have something from
me, too, though—look at the picture of my mother, in the
box, and the little black-and-white one of her mother and
grandmother. You have that broad clear brow they have;
so do I. I've seen a good many of the Frasers, too—I think
you'll age well, if you take care of your skin.*

*Take care of everything, Bree—oh, I wish—well, I have
wished I could take care of you and protect you from everything all your life, but I can't, whether I stay or go. Take
care of yourself, though—for me.*

The tears were puckering the paper now; I had to stop to blot
them, lest they smear the ink beyond reading. I wiped my face, and
resumed, slower now.

*You should know, Bree—I don't regret it. In spite of ev-
erything, I don't regret it. You'll know something now, of
how lonely I was for so long, without Jamie. It doesn't
matter. If the price of that separation was your life, neither
Jamie nor I can regret it—I know he wouldn't mind my
speaking for him.*

*Bree . . . you are my joy. You're perfect, and wonder-
ful—and I hear you saying now, in that tone of exasperation, "But of course you think that—you're my mother!"
Yes, that's how I know.*

*Bree, you are worth everything—and more. I've done a
great many things in my life so far, but the most important
of them all was to love your father and you.*

I blew my nose and reached for another fresh sheet of paper.
That was the most important thing; I could never say all I felt, but
this was the best I could do. What might I add, to be of aid in
living well, in growing up and growing old? What had I learned,
that I might pass on to her?

Choose a man like your father, I wrote. *Either of them.* I shook my head over that—could there be two men more different? —but left it, thinking of Roger Wakefield. *Once you've chosen a man, don't try to change him,* I wrote, with more confidence. *It can't be done. More important—don't let him try to change you. He can't do it either, but men always try.*

I bit the end of the pen, tasting the bitter tang of India ink. And finally I put down the last and the best advice I knew, on growing older.

> *Stand up straight and try not to get fat.*
> *With All My Love Always,*
> *Mama*

Jamie's shoulders shook as he leaned against the rail, whether with laughter or some other emotion, I couldn't tell. His linen glowed white with moonlight, and his head was dark against the moon. At last he turned and pulled me to him.

"I think she will do verra well," he whispered. "For no matter what poor gowk has fathered her, no lass has ever had a better mother. Kiss me, Sassenach, for believe me—I wouldna change ye for the world."

43

Phantom Limbs

Fergus, Mr. Willoughby, Jamie, and I had all kept careful watch upon the six Scottish smugglers since our departure from Scotland, but there was not the slightest hint of suspicious behavior from any of them, and after a time, I found myself relaxing my wariness around them. Still, I felt some reserve toward most of them, save Innes. I had finally realized why neither Fergus nor Jamie thought him a possible traitor; with but one arm, Innes was the only smuggler who could not have strung up the exciseman on the Arbroath road.

Innes was a quiet man. None of the Scots was what one might call garrulous, but even by their high standards of taciturnity, he was reserved. I was therefore not surprised to see him grimacing silently one morning, bent over behind a hatch cover, evidently engaged in some silent internal battle.

"Have you a pain, Innes?" I asked, stopping.

"Och!" He straightened, startled, but then fell back into his half-crouched position, his one arm locked across his belly. "Mmphm," he muttered, his thin face flushing at being so discovered.

"Come along with me," I said, taking him by the elbow. He looked frantically about for salvation, but I towed him, resisting but not audibly protesting, back to my cabin, where I forced him to sit upon the table and removed his shirt so that I could examine him.

I palpated his lean and hairy abdomen, feeling the firm, smooth mass of the liver on one side, and the mildly distended curve of the

stomach on the other. The intermittent way in which the pains
came on, causing him to writhe like a worm on a hook, then
passing off, gave me a good idea that what troubled him was
simple flatulence, but best to be thorough.

I probed for the gallbladder, just in case, wondering as I did so
just what I would do, should it prove to be an acute attack of
cholecystitis or an inflamed appendix. I could envision the cavity
of the belly in my mind, as though it lay open in fact before me,
my fingers translating the soft, lumpy shapes beneath the skin into
vision—the intricate folds of the intestines, softly shielded by their
yellow quilting of fat-padded membrane, the slick, smooth lobes
of the liver, deep purple-red, so much darker than the vivid scarlet
of the heart's pericardium above. Opening that cavity was a risky
thing to do, even equipped with modern anesthetics and antibiotics. Sooner or later, I knew, I would be faced with the necessity of
doing it, but I sincerely hoped it would be later.

"Breathe in," I said, hands on his chest, and saw in my mind
the pink-flushed grainy surface of a healthy lung. "Breathe out,
now," and felt the color fade to soft blue. No rales, no halting, a
nice clear flow. I reached for one of the thick sheets of vellum
paper I used for stethoscopes.

"When did you last move your bowels?" I inquired, rolling the
paper into a tube. The Scot's thin face turned the color of fresh
liver. Fixed with my gimlet eye, he mumbled something incoherent, in which the word "four" was just distinguishable.

"Four *days*?" I said, forestalling his attempts to escape by
putting a hand on his chest and pinning him flat to the table.
"Hold still, I'll just have a listen here, to be sure."

The heart sounds were reassuringly normal; I could hear the
valves open and close with their soft, meaty clicks, all in the right
places. I was quite sure of the diagnosis—had been virtually from
the moment I had looked at him—but by now there was an audience of heads peering curiously round the doorway; Innes's mates,
watching. For effect, I moved the end of my tubular stethoscope
down farther, listening for belly sounds.

Just as I thought, the rumble of trapped gas was clearly audible
in the upper curve of the large intestine. The lower sigmoid colon
was blocked, though; no sound at all down there.

"You have belly gas," I said, "and constipation."

"Aye, I ken that fine," Innes muttered, looking frantically for his shirt.

I put my hand on the garment in question, preventing him from leaving while I catechized him about his diet of late. Not surprisingly, this consisted almost entirely of salt pork and hardtack.

"What about the dried peas and the oatmeal?" I asked, surprised. Having inquired as to the normal fare aboard ship, I had taken the precaution of stowing—along with my surgeon's cask of lime juice and the collection of medicinal herbs—three hundred pounds of dried peas and a similar quantity of oatmeal, intending that this should be used to supplement the seamen's normal diet.

Innes remained tongue-tied, but this inquiry unleashed a flood of revelation and grievance from the onlookers in the doorway.

Jamie, Fergus, Marsali, and I all dined daily with Captain Raines, feasting on Murphy's ambrosia, so I was unaware of the deficiencies of the crew's mess. Evidently the difficulty was Murphy himself, who, while holding the highest culinary standards for the captain's table, considered the crew's dinner to be a chore rather than a challenge. He had mastered the routine of producing the crew's meals quickly and competently, and was highly resistant to any suggestions for an improved menu that might require further time or trouble. He declined absolutely to trouble with such nuisances as soaking peas or boiling oatmeal.

Compounding the difficulty was Murphy's ingrained prejudice against oatmeal, a crude Scottish mess that offended his aesthetic sense. I knew what he thought about that, having heard him muttering things about "dog's vomit" over the trays of breakfast that included the bowls of parritch to which Jamie, Marsali, and Fergus were addicted.

"Mr. Murphy says as how salt pork and hardtack is good enough for every crew he's had to feed for thirty year—given figgy-dowdy or plum duff for pudding, and beef on Sundays, too —though if that's beef, I'm a Chinaman—and it's good enough for us," Gordon burst in.

Accustomed to polyglot crews of French, Italian, Spanish, and Norwegian sailors, Murphy was also accustomed to having his meals accepted and consumed with a voracious indifference that transcended nationalities. The Scots' stubborn insistence on oatmeal roused all his own Irish intransigence, and the matter, at first a small, simmering disagreement, was now beginning to rise to a boil.

"We knew as there was meant to be parritch," MacLeod explained, "for Fergus did say so, when he asked us to come. But it's been nothing but the meat and biscuit since we left Scotland, which is a wee bit griping to the belly if ye're not used to it."

"We didna like to trouble Jamie Roy ower such a thing," Raeburn put in. "Geordie's got his girdle, and we've been makin' our own oatcake ower the lamps in the crew quarters. But we've run through what corn we brought in our bags, and Mr. Murphy's got the keys to the pantry store." He glanced shyly at me under his sandy blond lashes. "We didna like to ask, knowin' what he thought of us."

"Ye wouldna ken what's meant by the term 'spalpeens,' would ye, Mistress Fraser?" MacRae asked, raising one bushy brow.

While listening to this outpouring of woe, I had been selecting assorted herbs from my box—anise and angelica, two large pinches of horehound, and a few sprigs of peppermint. Tying these into a square of gauze, I closed the box and handed Innes his shirt, into which he burrowed at once, in search of refuge.

"I'll speak to Mr. Murphy," I promised the Scots. "Meanwhile," I said to Innes, handing him the gauze bundle, "brew you a good pot of tea from that, and drink a cupful at every watch change. If we've had no results by tomorrow, we'll try stronger measures."

As if in answer to this, a high, squeaking fart emerged from under Innes, to an ironic cheer from his colleagues.

"Aye, that's right, Mistress Fraser; maybe ye can scare the shit out o' him," MacLeod said, a broad grin splitting his face.

Innes, scarlet as a ruptured artery, took the bundle, bobbed his head in inarticulate thanks, and fled precipitously, followed in more leisurely fashion by the other smugglers.

A rather acrimonious debate with Murphy followed, terminating without bloodshed, but with the compromise that *I* would be responsible for the preparation of the Scots' morning parritch, permitted to do so under provision that I confined myself to a single pot and spoon, did not sing while cooking, and was careful not to make a mess in the precincts of the sacred galley.

It was only that night, tossing restlessly in the cramped and chilly confines of my berth, that it occurred to me how odd the morning's incident had been. Were this Lallybroch, and the Scots Jamie's tenants, not only would they have had no hesitation in approaching him about the matter, they would have had no need to. He would have known already what was wrong, and taken steps to remedy the situation. Accustomed as I had always been to the intimacy and unquestioning loyalty of Jamie's own men, I found this distance troubling.

Jamie was not at the captain's table next morning, having gone out in the small boat with two of the sailors to catch whitebait, but I met him on his return at noon, sunburned, cheerful, and covered with scales and fish blood.

"What have ye done to Innes, Sassenach?" he said, grinning. "He's hiding in the starboard head, and says ye told him he mustna come out at all until he'd shit."

"I didn't tell him *that,* exactly," I explained. "I just said if he hadn't moved his bowels by tonight, I'd give him an enema of slippery elm."

Jamie glanced over his shoulder in the direction of the head.

"Well, I suppose we will hope that Innes's bowels cooperate, or I doubt but he'll spend the rest of the voyage in the head, wi' a threat like that hangin' ower him."

"Well, I shouldn't worry; now that he and the others have their parritch back, their bowels ought to take care of themselves without undue interference from me."

Jamie glanced down at me, surprised.

"Got their parritch back? Whatever d'ye mean, Sassenach?"

I explained the genesis of the Oatmeal War, and its outcome, as he fetched a basin of water to clean his hands. A small frown drew his brows close together as he pushed his sleeves up his arms.

"They ought to have come to me about it," he said.

"I expect they would have, sooner or later," I said. "I only happened to find out by accident, when I found Innes grunting behind a hatch cover."

"Mmphm." He set about scouring the bloodstains off his fingers, rubbing the clinging scales free with a small pumice stone.

"These men aren't like your tenants at Lallybroch, are they?" I said, voicing the thought I had had.

"No," he said quietly. He dipped his fingers in the basin, leaving tiny shimmering circles where the fish scales floated. "I'm no their laird; only the man who pays them."

"They like you, though," I protested, then remembered Fergus's story and amended this rather weakly to, "or at least five of them do."

I handed him the towel. He took it with a brief nod, and dried his hands. Looking down at the strip of cloth, he shook his head.

"Aye, MacLeod and the rest like me well enough—or five of them do," he repeated ironically. "And they'll stand by me if it's needful—five of them. But they dinna ken me much, nor me them, save Innes."

He tossed the dirty water over the side, and tucking the empty basin under his arm, turned to go below, offering me his arm.

"There was more died at Culloden than the Stuart cause, Sassenach," he said. "You'll be coming for your dinner now?"

I did not find out why Innes was different, until the next week. Perhaps emboldened by the success of the purgative I had given him, Innes came voluntarily to call upon me in my cabin a week later.

"I am wondering, mistress," he said politely, "whether there might be a medicine for something as isna there."

"What?" I must have looked puzzled at this description, for he lifted the empty sleeve of his shirt in illustration.

"My arm," he explained. "It's no there, as ye can plainly see. And yet it pains me something terrible sometimes." He blushed slightly.

"I did wonder for some years was I only a bit mad," he confided, in lowered tones. "But I spoke a bit wi' Mr. Murphy, and he tells me it's the same with his leg that got lost, and Fergus says he wakes sometimes, feeling his missing hand slide into someone's pocket." He smiled briefly, teeth a flash under his drooping mustache. "So I thought maybe if it was a common thing, to feel a limb that wasn't there, perhaps there was something that might be done about it."

"I see." I rubbed my chin, pondering. "Yes, it is common; it's called a phantom limb, when you still have feelings in a part that's been lost. As for what to do about it. . . ." I frowned, trying to think whether I had ever heard of anything therapeutic for such a situation. To gain time, I asked, "How did you happen to lose the arm?"

"Oh, 'twas the blood poison," he said, casually. "I tore a small hole in my hand wi' a nail one day, and it festered."

I stared at the sleeve, empty from the shoulder.

"I suppose it did," I said faintly.

"Oh, aye. It was a lucky thing, though; it was that stopped me bein' transported wi' the rest."

"The rest of whom?"

He looked at me, surprised. "Why, the other prisoners from Ardsmuir. Did Mac Dubh not tell ye about that? When they stopped the fortress from being a prison, they sent off all of the Scottish prisoners to be indenture men in the Colonies—all but Mac Dubh, for he was a great man, and they didna want him out o' their sight, and me, for I'd lost the arm, and was no good for hard labor. So Mac Dubh was taken somewhere else, and I was let go— pardoned and set free. So ye see, it was a most fortunate accident, save only for the pain that comes on sometimes at night." He grimaced, and made as though to rub the nonexistent arm, stopping and shrugging at me in illustration of the problem.

"I see. So you were with Jamie in prison. I didn't know that." I was turning through the contents of my medicine chest, wondering whether a general pain reliever like willow-bark tea or horehound with fennel would work on a phantom pain.

"Oh, aye." Innes was losing his shyness, and beginning to speak more freely. "I should have been dead of starvation by now, had Mac Dubh not come to find me, when he was released himself."

"He went looking for you?" Out of the corner of my eye, I spotted a flash of blue, and beckoned to Mr. Willoughby, who was passing by.

"Aye. When he was released from his parole, he came to inquire, to see whether he could trace any of the men who'd been taken to America—to see whether any might have returned." He shrugged, the missing arm exaggerating the gesture. "But there were none in Scotland, save me."

"I see. Mr. Willoughby, have you a notion what might be done about this?" Motioning to the Chinese to come and look, I explained the problem, and was pleased to hear that he did indeed have a notion. We stripped Innes of his shirt once again, and I watched, taking careful notes, as Mr. Willoughby pressed hard with his fingers at certain spots on the neck and torso, explaining as best he might what he was doing.

"Arm is in the ghost world," he explained. "Body not; here in upper world. Arm tries to come back, for it does not like to be away from body. This—*An-mo*—press-press—this stops pain. But also we tell arm not come back."

"And how d'ye do that?" Innes was becoming interested in the procedure. Most of the crew would not let Mr. Willoughby touch them, regarding him as heathen, unclean, and a pervert to boot, but Innes had known and worked with the Chinese for the last two years.

Mr. Willoughby shook his head, lacking words, and burrowed in my medicine box. He came up with the bottle of dried hot peppers, and shaking out a careful handful, put it into a small dish.

"Have fire?" he inquired. I had a flint and steel, and with these he succeeded in kindling a spark to ignite the dried herb. The pungent smell filled the cabin, and we all watched as a small plume of white rose up from the dish and formed a small, hovering cloud over the dish.

"Send smoke of *fan jiao* messenger to ghost world, speak arm," Mr. Willoughby explained. Inflating his lungs and puffing out his cheeks like a blowfish, he blew lustily at the cloud, dispersing it. Then, without pausing, he turned and spat copiously on Innes's stump.

"Why, ye heathen bugger!" Innes cried, eyes bulging with fury. "D'ye dare spit on me?"

"Spit on ghost," Mr. Willoughby explained, taking three quick steps backward, toward the door. "Ghost afraid spittle. Not come back now right away."

I laid a restraining hand on Innes's remaining arm.

"Does your missing arm hurt now?" I asked.

The rage began to fade from his face as he thought about it.

"Well . . . no," he admitted. Then he scowled at Mr. Willoughby. "But that doesna mean I'll have ye spit on me whenever the fancy takes ye, ye wee poutworm!"

"Oh, no," Mr. Willoughby said, quite cool. "I not spit. You spit now. Scare you own ghost."

Innes scratched his head, not sure whether to be angry or amused.

"Well, I will be damned," he said finally. He shook his head, and picking up his shirt, pulled it on. "Still," he said, "I think perhaps next time, I'll try your tea, Mistress Fraser."

"I," said Jamie, "am a fool." He spoke broodingly, watching Fergus and Marsali, who were absorbed in close conversation by the rail on the opposite side of the ship.

"What makes you think so?" I asked, though I had a reasonably good idea. The fact that all four of the married persons aboard were living in unwilling celibacy had given rise to a certain air of suppressed amusement among the members of the crew, whose celibacy was involuntary.

"I have spent twenty years longing to have ye in my bed," he said, verifying my assumption, "and within a month of having ye back again, I've arranged matters so that I canna even kiss ye without sneakin' behind a hatch cover, and even then, half the time I look round to find Fergus looking cross-eyed down his nose at me, the little bastard! And no one to blame for it but my own foolishness. What did I think I was doing?" he demanded rhetorically, glaring at the pair across the way, who were nuzzling each other with open affection.

"Well, Marsali *is* only fifteen," I said mildly. "I expect you thought you were being fatherly—or stepfatherly."

"Aye, I did." He looked down at me with a grudging smile. "The reward for my tender concern being that I canna even touch my own wife!"

"Oh, you can touch me," I said. I took one of his hands, caressing the palm gently with my thumb. "You just can't engage in acts of unbridled carnality."

We had had a few abortive attempts along those lines, all frustrated by either the inopportune arrival of a crew member or the sheer uncongeniality of any nook aboard the *Artemis* sufficiently secluded as to be private. One late-night foray into the after hold had ended abruptly when a large rat had leapt from a stack of hides onto Jamie's bare shoulder, sending me into hysterics and depriving Jamie abruptly of any desire to continue what he was doing.

He glanced down at our linked hands, where my thumb continued to make secret love to his palm, and narrowed his eyes at me, but let me continue. He closed his fingers gently round my hand, his own thumb feather-light on my pulse. The simple fact was that we couldn't keep our hands off each other—no more than Fergus and Marsali could—despite the fact that we knew very well such behavior would lead only to greater frustration.

"Aye, well, in my own defense, I meant well," he said ruefully, smiling down into my eyes.

"Well, you know what they say about good intentions."

"What do they say?" His thumb was stroking gently up and down my wrist, sending small fluttering sensations through the pit of my stomach. I thought it must be true what Mr. Willoughby said, about sensations on one part of the body affecting another.

"They pave the road to Hell." I gave his hand a squeeze, and tried to take mine away, but he wouldn't let go.

"Mmphm." His eyes were on Fergus, who was teasing Marsali with an albatross's feather, holding her by one arm and tickling her beneath the chin as she struggled ineffectually to get away.

"Verra true," he said. "I meant to make sure the lass had a chance to think what she was about before the matter was too late for mending. The end result of my interference being that I lie awake half the night trying not to think about you, and listening to Fergus lust across the cabin, and come up in the morning to find the crew all grinning in their beards whenever they see me." He aimed a vicious glare at Maitland, who was passing by. The beardless cabin boy looked startled, and edged carefully away, glancing nervously back over his shoulder.

"How do you hear someone lust?" I asked, fascinated.

He glanced down at me, looking mildly flustered.

"Oh! Well . . . it's only . . ."

He paused for a moment, then rubbed the bridge of his nose, which was beginning to redden in the sharp breeze.

"Have ye any idea what men in a prison do, Sassenach, having no women for a verra long time?"

"I could guess," I said, thinking that perhaps I didn't really want to hear, firsthand. He hadn't spoken to me before about his time in Ardsmuir.

"I imagine ye could," he said dryly. "And ye'd be right, too. There's the three choices; use each other, go a bit mad, or deal with the matter by yourself, aye?"

He turned to look out to sea, and bent his head slightly to look down at me, a slight smile visible on his lips. "D'ye think me mad, Sassenach?"

"Not most of the time," I replied honestly, turning round beside him. He laughed and shook his head ruefully.

"No, I dinna seem able to manage it. I now and then wished I *could* go mad"—he said thoughtfully "—it seemed a great deal easier than having always to think what to do next—but it doesna seem to come natural to me. Nor does buggery," he added, with a wry twist of his mouth.

"No, I shouldn't think so." Men who might in the ordinary way recoil in horror from the thought of using another man could still bring themselves to the act, out of desperate need. Not Jamie. Knowing what I did of his experiences at the hands of Jack Randall, I suspected that he very likely *would* have gone mad before seeking such resort himself.

He shrugged slightly, and stood silent, looking out to sea. Then he glanced down at his hands, spread before him, clutching the rail.

"I fought them—the soldiers who took me. I'd promised Jenny I wouldn't—she thought they'd hurt me—but when the time came, I couldna seem to help it." He shrugged again, and slowly opened and closed his right hand. It was his crippled hand, the third finger marked by a thick scar that ran the length of the first two joints, the fourth finger's second joint fused into stiffness, so that the finger stuck out awkwardly, even when he made a fist.

"I broke this again then, against a dragoon's jaw," he said ruefully, waggling the finger slightly. "That was the third time; the second was at Culloden. I didna mind it much. But they put me in chains, and I minded that a great deal."

"I'd think you would." It was hard—not difficult, but surprisingly painful—to think of that lithe, powerful body subdued by metal, bound and humbled.

"There's nay privacy in prison," he said. "I minded that more than the fetters, I think. Day and night, always in sight of someone, wi' no guard for your thoughts but to feign sleep. As for the other . . ." He snorted briefly, and shoved the loose hair back behind his ear. "Well, ye wait for the light to go, for the only modesty there is, is darkness."

The cells were not large, and the men lay close together for warmth in the night. With no modesty save darkness, and no privacy save silence, it was impossible to remain unaware of the accommodation each man made to his own needs.

"I was in irons for more than a year, Sassenach," he said. He lifted his arms, spread them eighteen inches apart, and stopped abruptly, as though reaching some invisible limit. "I could move that far—and nay more," he said, staring at his immobile hands. "And I couldna move my hands at all without the chain makin' a sound."

Torn between shame and need, he would wait in the dark, breathing in the stale and brutish scent of the surrounding men, listening to the murmurous breath of his companions, until the stealthy sounds nearby told him that the telltale clinking of his irons would be ignored.

"If there's one thing I ken verra well, Sassenach," he said quietly, with a brief glance at Fergus, "it's the sound of a man makin' love to a woman who's not there."

He shrugged and jerked his hands suddenly, spreading them wide on the rail, bursting his invisible chains. He looked down at me then with a half-smile, and I saw the dark memories at the back of his eyes, under the mocking humor.

I saw too the terrible need there, the desire strong enough to have endured loneliness and degradation, squalor and separation.

We stood quite still, looking at each other, oblivious of the deck traffic passing by. He knew better than any man how to hide his thoughts, but he wasn't hiding them from me.

The hunger in him went bone-deep, and my own bones seemed to dissolve in recognition of it. His hand was an inch from mine, resting on the wooden rail, long-fingered and powerful. . . . If I touched him, I thought suddenly, he would turn and take me, here, on the deck boards.

As though hearing my thought, he took my hand suddenly, pressing it tight against the hard muscle of his thigh.

"How many times have we lain together, since ye came back to me?" he whispered. "Once, twice, in the brothel. Three times in the heather. And then at Lallybroch, again in Paris." His fingers tapped lightly against my wrist, one after the other, in time with my pulse.

"Each time, I left your bed as hungry as ever I came to it. It takes no more to ready me now than the scent of your hair brushing past my face, or the feel of your thigh against mine when we sit to eat. And to see ye stand on deck, wi' the wind pressing your gown tight to your body . . ."

The corner of his mouth twitched slightly as he looked at me. I could see the pulse beat strong in the hollow of his throat, his skin flushed with wind and desire.

"There are moments, Sassenach, when for one copper penny, I'd have ye on the spot, back against the mast and your skirts about your waist, and devil take the bloody crew!"

My fingers convulsed against his palm, and he tightened his grasp, nodding pleasantly in response to the greeting of the gunner, coming past on his way toward the quarter-gallery.

The bell for the Captain's dinner sounded beneath my feet, a sweet metallic vibration that traveled up through the soles of my feet and melted the marrow of my bones. Fergus and Marsali left their play and went below, and the crew began preparations for the changing of the watch, but we stayed standing by the rail, fixed in each other's eyes, burning.

"The Captain's compliments, Mr. Fraser, and will you be joining him for dinner?" It was Maitland, the cabin boy, keeping a cautious distance as he relayed this message.

Jamie took a deep breath, and pulled his eyes away from mine.

"Aye, Mr. Maitland, we'll be there directly." He took another breath, settled his coat on his shoulders, and offered me his arm.

"Shall we go below, Sassenach?"

"Just a minute." I drew my hand out of my pocket, having found what I was looking for. I took his hand and pressed the object into his palm.

He stared down at the image of King George III in his hand, then up at me.

"On account," I said. "Let's go and eat."

The next day found us on deck again; though the air was still chilly, the cold was far preferable to the stuffiness of the cabins. We took our usual path, down one side of the ship and up the other, but then Jamie stopped, pausing to lean against the rail as he told me some anecdote about the printing business.

A few feet away, Mr. Willoughby sat cross-legged in the protection of the mainmast, a small cake of wet black ink by the toe of his slipper and a large sheet of white paper on the deck before him. The tip of his brush touched the paper lightly as a butterfly, leaving surprising strong shapes behind.

As I watched, fascinated, he began again at the top of the page. He worked rapidly, with a sureness of stroke that was like watching a dancer or a fencer, sure of his ground.

One of the deckhands passed dangerously close to the edge of the paper, almost—but not quite—placing a large dirty foot on the snowy white. A few moments later, another man did the same thing, though there was plenty of room to pass by. Then the first man came back, this time careless enough to kick over the small cake of black ink as he passed.

"Tck!" the seaman exclaimed in annoyance. He scuffed at the black splotch on the otherwise immaculate deck. "Filthy heathen! Look 'ere, wot he's done!"

The second man, returning from his brief errand, paused in interest. "On the clean deck? Captain Raines won't be pleased, will he?" He nodded at Mr. Willoughby, mock-jovial. "Best hurry and lick it up, little fella, before the Captain comes."

"Aye, that'll do; lick it up. Quick, now!" The first man moved a step nearer the seated figure, his shadow falling on the page like a blot. Mr. Willoughby's lips tightened just a shade, but he didn't look up. He completed the second column, righted the ink cake and dipped his brush without taking his eyes from the page, and began a third column, hand moving steadily.

"I *said,*" began the first seaman, loudly, but stopped in surprise as a large white handkerchief fluttered down on the deck in front of him, covering the inkblot.

"Your pardon, gentlemen," said Jamie. "I seem to have dropped something." With a cordial nod to the seamen, he bent down and swept up the handkerchief, leaving nothing but a faint smear on the decking. The seamen glanced at each other, uncertain, then at Jamie. One man caught sight of the blue eyes over the blandly smiling mouth, and blanched visibly. He turned hastily away, tugging at his mate's arm.

"Norratall, sir," he mumbled. "C'mon, Joe, we're wanted aft."

Jamie didn't look either at the departing seamen or at Mr. Willoughby, but came toward me, tucking his handkerchief back in his sleeve.

"A verra pleasant day, is it not, Sassenach?" he said. He threw back his head, inhaling deeply. "Refreshing air, aye?"

"More so for some than for others, I expect," I said, amused. The air at this particular spot on deck smelled rather strongly of the alum-tanned hides in the hold below.

"That was kind of you," I said as he leaned back against the rail next to me. "Do you think I should offer Mr. Willoughby the use of my cabin to write?"

Jamie snorted briefly. "No. I've told him he can use my cabin, or the table in the mess between meals, but he'd rather be here— stubborn wee fool that he is."

"Well, I suppose the light's better," I said dubiously, eyeing the small hunched figure, crouched doggedly against the mast. As I watched, a gust of wind lifted the edge of the paper; Mr. Willoughby pinned it at once, holding it still with one hand while continuing his short, sure brushstrokes with the other. "It doesn't look comfortable, though."

"It's not." Jamie ran his fingers through his hair in mild exasperation. "He does it on purpose, to provoke the crew."

"Well, if that's what he's after, he's doing a good job," I observed. "What on earth for, though?"

Jamie leaned back against the rail beside me, and snorted once more.

"Aye, well, that's complicated. Ever met a Chinaman before, have ye?"

"A few, but I suspect they're a bit different in my time," I said dryly. "They tend not to wear pigtails and silk pajamas, for one thing, nor do they have obsessions about ladies' feet—or if they did, they didn't tell me about it," I added, to be fair.

Jamie laughed and moved a few inches closer, so that his hand on the rail brushed mine.

"Well, it's to do wi' the feet," he said. "Or that's the start of it, anyway. See, Josie, who's one of the whores at Madame Jeanne's, told Gordon about it, and of course he's told everyone now."

"What on earth is it about the feet?" I demanded, curiosity becoming overwhelming. "What does he *do* to them?"

Jamie coughed, and a faint flush rose in his cheeks. "Well, it's a bit . . ."

"You couldn't possibly tell me anything that would shock me," I assured him. "I *have* seen quite a lot of things in my life, you know—and a good many of them with you, come to that."

"I suppose ye have, at that," he said, grinning. "Aye, well, it's no so much what he does, but—well, in China, the highborn ladies have their feet bound."

"I've heard of that," I said, wondering what all the fuss was about. "It's supposed to make their feet small and graceful."

Jamie snorted again. "Graceful, aye? D'ye know how it's done?" And proceeded to tell me.

"They take a tiny lassie—nay more than a year old, aye?—and turn under the toes of her feet until they touch her heel, then tie bandages about the foot to hold it so."

"Ouch!" I said involuntarily.

"Yes, indeed," he said dryly. "Her nanny will take the bandages off now and then to clean the foot, but puts them back directly. After some time, her wee toes rot and fall off. And by the time she's grown, the poor lassie's little more at the end of her legs than a crumple of bones and skin, smaller than the size o' my fist." His closed fist knocked softly against the wood of the rail in illustration. "But she's considered verra beautiful then," he ended. "Graceful, as ye say."

"That's perfectly disgusting!" I said. "But what has that got to do with—" I glanced at Mr. Willoughby, but he gave no sign of hearing us; the wind was blowing from him toward us, carrying our words out to sea.

"Say this was a lassie's foot, Sassenach," he said, stretching his right hand out flat before him. "Curl the toes under to touch the heel, and what have ye in the middle?" He curled his fingers loosely into a fist in illustration.

"What?" I said, bewildered. Jamie extended the middle finger of his left hand, and thrust it abruptly through the center of his fist in an unmistakably graphic gesture.

"A hole," he said succinctly.

"You're kidding! *That's* why they do it?"

His forehead furrowed slightly, then relaxed. "Oh, am I jesting? By no means, Sassenach. He says"—he nodded delicately at Mr. Willoughby—"that it's a most remarkable sensation. To a man."

"Why, that perverted little beast!"

Jamie laughed at my indignation.

"Aye, well, that's about what the crew thinks, too. Of course, he canna get quite the same effect wi' a European woman, but I gather he . . . tries, now and then."

I began to understand the general feeling of hostility toward the little Chinese. Even a short acquaintance with the crew of the *Artemis* had taught me that seamen on the whole tended to be gallant creatures, with a strong romantic streak where women were concerned—no doubt because they did without female company for a good part of the year.

"Hm," I said, with a glance of suspicion at Mr. Willoughby. "Well, that explains them, all right, but what about him?"

"That's what's a wee bit complicated." Jamie's mouth curled upward in a wry smile. "See, to Mr. Yi Tien Cho, late of the Heavenly Kingdom of China, *we're* the barbarians."

"Is that so?" I glanced up at Brodie Cooper, coming down the ratlines above, the filthy, callused soles of his feet all that was visible from below. I rather thought both sides had a point. "Even you?"

"Oh, aye. I'm a filthy, bad-smelling *gwao-fe*—that means a foreign devil, ye ken—wi' the stink of a weasel—I think that's what *huang-shu-lang* means—and a face like a gargoyle," he finished cheerfully.

"He *told* you all that?" It seemed an odd recompense for saving someone's life. Jamie glanced down at me, cocking one eyebrow.

"Have ye noticed, maybe, that verra small men will say *any-thing* to ye, when they've drink taken?" he asked. "I think brandy makes them forget their size; they think they're great hairy brutes, and swagger something fierce."

He nodded at Mr. Willoughby, industriously painting. "He's a bit more circumspect when he's sober, but it doesna change what he thinks. It fair galls him, aye? Especially knowing that if it wasna for me, someone would likely knock him on the head or put him through the window into the sea some quiet night.''

He spoke with simple matter-of-factness, but I hadn't missed the sideways looks directed at us by the passing seamen, and had already realized just why Jamie was passing time in idle conversation by the rail with me. If anyone had been in doubt about Mr. Willoughby's being under Jamie's protection, they would be rapidly disabused of the notion.

"So you saved his life, gave him work, and keep him out of trouble, and he insults you and thinks you're an ignorant barbarian," I said dryly. "Sweet little fellow."

"Aye, well." The wind had shifted slightly, blowing a lock of Jamie's hair free across his face. He thumbed it back behind his ear and leaned farther toward me, our shoulders nearly touching. "Let him say what he likes; I'm the only one who understands him."

"Really?" I laid a hand over Jamie's where it rested on the rail.

"Well, maybe not to say understand him," he admitted. He looked down at the deck between his feet. "But I do remember," he said softly, "what it's like to have nothing but your pride—and a friend."

I remembered what Innes had said, and wondered whether it was the one-armed man who had been his friend in time of need. I knew what he meant; I had had Joe Abernathy, and knew what a difference it made.

"Yes, I had a friend at the hospital . . ." I began, but was interrupted by loud exclamations of disgust emanating from under my feet.

"Damn! Blazing Hades! That filth-eating son of a pig-fart!"

I looked down, startled, then realized, from the muffled Irish oaths proceeding from below, that we were standing directly over the galley. The shouting was loud enough to attract attention from the hands forward, and a small group of sailors gathered with us, watching in fascination as the cook's black-kerchiefed head poked out of the hatchway, glaring ferociously at the crowd.

"Burry-arsed swabs!" he shouted. "What're ye lookin' at? Two of yer idle barsteds tumble arse down here and toss this muck over the side! D'ye mean me to be climbin' ladders all day, and me with half a leg?" The head disappeared abruptly, and with a good-natured shrug, Picard motioned to one of the younger sailors to come along below.

Shortly there was a confusion of voices and a bumping of some large object down below, and a terrible smell assaulted my nostrils.

"Jesus Christ on a piece of toast!" I snatched a handkerchief from my pocket and clapped it to my nose; this wasn't the first smell I had encountered afloat, and I usually kept a linen square soaked in wintergreen in my pocket, as a precaution. "What's that?"

"By the smell of it, dead horse. A verra old horse, at that, and a long time dead." Jamie's long, thin nose looked a trifle pinched around the nostrils, and all around, sailors were gagging, holding their noses, and generally commenting unfavorably on the smell.

Maitland and Grosman, faces averted from their burden, but slightly green nonetheless, manhandled a large cask through the hatchway and onto the deck. The top had been split, and I caught a brief glimpse of a yellowish-white mass in the opening, glistening faintly in the sun. It seemed to be moving. Maggots, in profusion.

"Eew!" The exclamation was jerked from me involuntarily. The two sailors said nothing, their lips being pressed tightly together, but both of them looked as though they agreed with me. Together, they manhandled the cask to the rail and heaved it up and over.

Such of the crew as were not otherwise employed gathered at the rail to watch the cask bobbing in the wake, and be entertained by Murphy's outspokenly blasphemous opinion of the ship's chandler who had sold it to him. Manzetti, a small Italian seaman with a thick russet pigtail, was standing by the rail, loading a musket.

"Shark," he explained with a gleam of teeth beneath his mustache, seeing me watching him. "Very good to eat."

"Ar," said Sturgis approvingly.

Such of the crew as were not presently occupied gathered at the stern, watching. There were sharks, I knew; Maitland had pointed out to me two dark, flexible shapes hovering in the shadow of the hull the evening before, keeping pace with the ship with no apparent effort save a small and steady oscillation of sickled tails.

"There!" A shout went up from several throats as the cask jerked suddenly in the water. A pause, and Manzetti fixed his aim carefully in the vicinity of the floating cask. Another jerk, as though something had bumped it violently, and another.

The water was a muddy gray, but clear enough for me to catch a glimpse of something moving under the surface, fast. Another jerk, the cask heeled to one side, and suddenly the sharp edge of a fin creased the surface of the water, and a gray back showed briefly, tiny waves purling off it.

The musket discharged next to me with a small roar and a cloud of black-powder smoke that left my eyes stinging. There was a universal shout from the observers, and when the watering of my eyes subsided, I could see a small brownish stain spreading round the cask.

"Did he hit the shark, or the horsemeat?" I asked Jamie, in a low-voiced aside.

"The cask," he said with a smile. "Still, it's fine shooting."

Several more shots went wild, while the cask began to dance an agitated jig, the frenzied sharks striking it repeatedly. Bits of white and brown flew from the broken cask, and a large circle of grease, rotten blood, and debris spread round the shark's feast. As though by magic, seabirds began to appear, one and two at a time, diving for tidbits.

"No good," said Manzetti at last, lowering the musket and wiping his face with his sleeve. "Too far." He was sweating and stained from neck to hairline with black powder; the wiping left a streak of white across his eyes, like a raccoon's mask.

"I could relish a slab of shark," said the Captain's voice near my ear. I turned to see him peering thoughtfully over the rail at the scene of carnage. "Perhaps we might lower a boat, Mr. Picard."

The bosun turned with an obliging roar, and the *Artemis* hauled her wind, coming round in a small circle to draw near the remains of the floating cask. A small boat was launched, containing Manzetti, with musket, and three seamen armed with gaffs and rope.

By the time they reached the spot, there was nothing left of the cask but a few shattered bits of wood. There was still plenty of activity, though; the water roiled with the sharks' thrashing beneath the surface, and the scene was nearly obscured by a raucous cloud of seabirds. As I watched, I saw a pointed snout rise suddenly from the water, mouth open, seize one of the birds and disappear beneath the waves, all in the flick of an eyelash.

"Did you see that?" I said, awed. I was aware, in a general way, that sharks were well-equipped with teeth, but this practical demonstration was more striking than any number of *National Geographic* photographs.

"Why, Grandmother dear, what big teeth ye have!" said Jamie, sounding suitably impressed.

"Oh, they do indeed," said a genial voice nearby. I glanced aside to find Murphy grinning at my elbow, broad face shining with a savage glee. "Little good it will do the buggers, with a ball blown clean through their fucking brains!" He pounded a hamlike fist on the rail, and shouted, "Get me one of them jagged buggers, Manzetti! There's a bottle o' cookin' brandy waitin' if ye do!"

"Is it a personal matter to ye, Mr. Murphy?" Jamie asked politely. "Or professional concern?"

"Both, Mr. Fraser, both," the cook replied, watching the hunt with a fierce attention. He kicked his wooden leg against the side, with a hollow clunk. "They've had a taste o' me," he said with grim relish, "but I've tasted a good many more o' them!"

The boat was barely visible through the flapping screen of birds, and their screams made it hard to hear anything other than Murphy's war cries.

"Shark steak with mustard!" Murphy was bellowing, eyes mere slits in an ecstasy of revenge. "Stewed liver wi' piccalilli! I'll make soup o' yer fins, and jelly yer eyeballs in sherry wine, ye wicked barsted!"

I saw Manzetti, kneeling in the bows, take aim with his musket, and the puff of black smoke as he fired. And then I saw Mr. Willoughby.

I hadn't seen him jump from the rail; no one had, with all eyes fixed on the hunt. But there he was, some distance away from the melee surrounding the boat, his shaven head glistening like a fishing float as he wrestled in the water with an enormous bird, its wings churning the water like an eggbeater.

Alerted by my cry, Jamie tore his eyes from the hunt, goggled for an instant, and before I could move or speak, was perched on the rail himself.

My shout of horror coincided with a surprised roar from Murphy, but Jamie was gone, too, lancing into the water near the Chinaman with barely a splash.

There were shouts and cries from the deck—and a shrill screech from Marsali—as everyone realized what had happened. Jamie's wet red head emerged next to Mr. Willoughby, and in seconds, he had an arm tight about the Chinaman's throat. Mr. Willoughby clung tightly to the bird, and I wasn't sure, just for the moment, whether Jamie intended rescue or throttling, but then he kicked strongly, and began to tow the struggling mass of bird and man back toward the ship.

Triumphant shouts from the boat, and a spreading circle of deep red in the water. There was a tremendous thrashing as one shark was gaffed and hauled behind the small boat by a rope about its tail. Then everything was confusion, as the men in the boat noticed what else was going on in the water nearby.

Lines were thrown over one side and then the other, and crewmen rushed back and forth in high excitement, undecided whether to help with rescue or shark, but at last Jamie and his burdens were hauled in to starboard, and dumped dripping on the deck, while the captured shark—several large bites taken out of its body by its hungry companions—was drawn in, still feebly snapping, to port.

"Je . . . sus . . . Christ," Jamie said, chest heaving. He lay flat on the deck, gasping like a landed fish.

"Are you all right?" I knelt beside him, and wiped the water off his face with the hem of my skirt. He gave me a lopsided smile and nodded, still gasping.

"Jesus," he said at last, sitting up. He shook his head and sneezed. "I thought I was eaten, sure. Those fools in the boat started toward us, and there were sharks all round them, under the water, bitin' at the gaffed one." He tenderly massaged his calves. "It's nay doubt oversensitive of me, Sassenach, but I've always dreaded the thought of losing a leg. It seems almost worse than bein' killed outright."

"I'd as soon you didn't do either," I said dryly. He was beginning to shiver; I pulled off my shawl and wrapped it around his shoulders, then looked about for Mr. Willoughby.

The little Chinese, still clinging stubbornly to his prize, a young pelican nearly as big as he was, ignored both Jamie and the considerable abuse flung in his direction. He squelched below, dripping, protected from physical castigation by the clacking bill of his captive, which discouraged anyone from getting too close to him.

A nasty chunking sound and a crow of triumph from the other

side of the deck announced Murphy's use of an ax to dispatch his erstwhile nemesis. The seamen clustered round the corpse, knives drawn, to get pieces of the skin. Further enthusiastic chopping, and Murphy came strolling past, beaming, a choice section of tail under his arm, the huge yellow liver hanging from one hand in a bag of netting, and the bloody ax slung over his shoulder.

"Not drowned, are ye?" he said, ruffling Jamie's damp hair with his spare hand. "I can't see why ye'd bother wi' the little bugger, myself, but I'll say 'twas bravely done. I'll brew ye up a fine broth from the tail, to keep off the chill," he promised, and stumped off, planning menus aloud.

"Why did he do it?" I asked. "Mr. Willoughby, I mean."

Jamie shook his head and blew his nose on his shirttail.

"Damned if I know. He wanted the bird, I expect, but I couldna say why. To eat, maybe?"

Murphy overheard this and swung round at the head of the galley ladder, frowning.

"Ye can't eat pelicans," he said, shaking his head in disapproval. "Fishy-tasting, no matter how ye cook 'em. And God knows what one's doing out here anyway; they're shorebirds, pelicans. Blown out by a storm I suppose. Awkward buggers." His bald head disappeared into his realm, murmuring happily of dried parsley and cayenne.

Jamie laughed and stood up.

"Aye, well, perhaps it's only he wants the feathers to make quills of. Come along below, Sassenach. Ye can help me dry my back."

He had spoken jokingly, but as soon as the words were out of his mouth, his face went blank. He glanced quickly to port, where the crew was arguing and jostling over the remains of the shark, while Fergus and Marsali cautiously examined the severed head, lying gape-jawed on the deck. Then his eyes met mine, with a perfect understanding.

Thirty seconds later, we were below in his cabin. Cold drops from his wet hair rained over my shoulders and slid down my bosom, but his mouth was hot and urgent. The hard curves of his back glowed warm through the soaked fabric of the shirt that stuck to them.

"Ifrinn!" he said breathlessly, breaking loose long enough to

yank at his breeches. "Christ, they're stuck to me! I canna get them off!"

Snorting with laughter, he jerked at the laces, but the water had soaked them into a hopeless knot.

"A knife!" I said. "Where's a knife?" Snorting myself at the sight of him, struggling frantically to get his drenched shirttail out of his breeches, I began to rummage through the drawers of the desk, tossing out bits of paper, bottle of ink, a snuffbox—everything but a knife. The closest thing was an ivory letter opener, made in the shape of a hand with a pointing finger.

I seized upon this and grasped him by the waistband, trying to saw at the tangled laces.

He yelped in alarm and backed away.

"Christ, be careful wi' that, Sassenach! It's no going to do ye any good to get my breeks off, and ye geld me in the process!"

Half-crazed with lust as we were, that seemed funny enough to double us both up laughing.

"Here!" Rummaging in the chaos of his berth, he snatched up his dirk and brandished it triumphantly. An instant later, the laces were severed and the sopping breeks lay puddled on the floor.

He seized me, picked me up bodily, and laid me on the desk, heedless of crumpled papers and scattered quills. Tossing my skirts up past my waist, he grabbed my hips and half-lay on me, his hard thighs forcing my legs apart.

It was like grasping a salamander; a blaze of heat in a chilly shroud. I gasped as the tail of his sopping shirt touched my bare belly, then gasped again as I heard footsteps in the passage.

"Stop!" I hissed in his ear. "Someone's coming!"

"Too late," he said, with breathless certainty. "I must have ye, or die."

He took me, with one quick, ruthless thrust, and I bit his shoulder hard, tasting salt and wet linen, but he made no sound. Two strokes, three, and I had my legs locked tight around his buttocks, my cry muffled in his shirt, not caring either who else might be coming.

He had me, quickly and thoroughly, and thrust himself home, and home, and home again, with a deep sound of triumph in his throat, shuddering and shaking in my arms.

Two minutes later, the cabin door swung open. Innes looked slowly round the wreckage of the room. His soft brown gaze traveled from the ravaged desk to me, sitting damp and disheveled, but respectably clothed, upon the berth, and rested at last on Jamie, who sat collapsed on a stool, still clad in his wet shirt, chest heaving and the deep red color fading slowly from his face.

Innes's nostrils flared delicately, but he said nothing. He walked into the cabin, nodding at me, and bent to reach under Fergus's berth, whence he pulled out a bottle of brandywine.

"For the Chinee," he said to me. "So as he mightn't take a chill." He turned toward the door and paused, squinting thoughtfully at Jamie.

"Ye might should have Mr. Murphy make ye some broth on that same account, Mac Dubh. They do say as 'tis dangerous to get chilled after hard work, aye? Ye dinna want to take the ague." There was a faint twinkle in the mournful brown depths.

Jamie brushed back the salty tangle of his hair, a slow smile spreading across his face.

"Aye, well, and if it should come to that, Innes, at least I shall die a happy man."

We found out the next day what Mr. Willoughby wanted the pelican for. I found him on the afterdeck, the bird perched on a sail-chest beside him, its wings bound tight to its body by means of strips of cloth. It glared at me with round yellow eyes, and clacked its bill in warning.

Mr. Willoughby was pulling in a line, on the end of which was a small, wriggling purple squid. Detaching this, he held it up in front of the pelican and said something in Chinese. The bird regarded him with deep suspicion, but didn't move. Quickly, he seized the upper bill in his hand, pulled it up, and tossed the squid into the bird's pouch. The pelican, looking surprised, gulped convulsively and swallowed it.

"Hao-liao," Mr. Willoughby said approvingly, stroking the bird's head. He saw me watching, and beckoned me to come closer. Keeping a cautious eye on the wicked bill, I did so.

"Ping An," he said, indicating the pelican. "Peaceful one." The bird erected a small crest of white feathers, for all the world as though it were pricking up its ears at its name, and I laughed.

"Really? What are you going to do with him?"

"I teach him hunt for me," the little Chinese said matter-of-factly. "You watch."

I did. After several more squid and a couple of small fish had been caught and fed to the pelican, Mr. Willoughby removed another strip of soft cloth from the recesses of his costume, and wrapped this snugly round the bird's neck.

"Not want choke," he explained. "Not swallow fish." He then tied a length of light line tightly to this collar, motioned to me to stand back, and with a swift jerk, released the bindings that held the bird's wings.

Surprised at the sudden freedom, the pelican waddled back and forth on the locker, flapped its huge bony wings once or twice, and then shot into the sky in an explosion of feathers.

A pelican on the ground is a comical thing, all awkward angles, splayed feet, and gawky bill. A soaring pelican, circling over water, is a thing of wonder, graceful and primitive, startling as a pterodactyl among the sleeker forms of gulls and petrels.

Ping An, the peaceful one, soared to the limit of his line, struggled to go higher, then, as though resigned, began to circle. Mr. Willoughby, eyes squinted nearly shut against the sun, spun slowly round and round on the deck below, playing the pelican like a kite. All the hands in the rigging and on deck nearby stopped what they were doing to watch in fascination.

Sudden as a bolt from a crossbow, the pelican folded its wings and dived, cleaving the water with scarcely a splash. As it popped to the surface, looking mildly surprised, Mr. Willoughby began to tow it in. Aboard once more, the pelican was persuaded with some difficulty to give up its catch, but at last suffered its captor to reach cautiously into the leathery subgular pouch and extract a fine, fat sea bream.

Mr. Willoughby smiled pleasantly at a gawking Picard, took out a small knife, and slit the still-living fish down the back. Pinioning the bird in one wiry arm, he loosened the collar with his other hand, and offered it a flapping piece of bream, which Ping An eagerly snatched from his fingers and gulped.

"His," Mr. Willoughby explained, wiping blood and scales carelessly on the leg of his trousers. "Mine," nodding toward the half-fish still sitting on the locker, now motionless.

Within a week, the pelican was entirely tame, able to fly free, collared, but without the tethering line, returning to his master to regurgitate a pouchful of shining fish at his feet. When not fishing, Ping An either took up a position on the crosstrees, much to the displeasure of the crewmen responsible for swabbing the deck beneath, or followed Mr. Willoughby around the deck, waddling absurdly from side to side, eight-foot wings half-spread for balance.

The crew, both impressed by the fishing and wary of Ping An's great snapping bill, steered clear of Mr. Willoughby, who made his words each day beside the mast, weather permitting, secure under the benign yellow eye of his new friend.

I paused one day to watch Mr. Willoughby at his work, staying out of sight behind the shelter of the mast. He sat for a moment, a look of quiet satisfaction on his face, contemplating the finished page. I couldn't read the characters, of course, but the shape of the whole thing was somehow very pleasing to look at.

Then he glanced quickly around, as though checking to see that no one was coming, picked up the brush, and with great care, added a final character, in the upper left corner of the page. Without asking, I knew it was his signature.

He sighed then, and lifted his face to look out over the rail. Not inscrutable, by any means, his expression was filled with a dreaming delight, and I knew that whatever he saw, it was neither the ship nor the heaving ocean beyond.

At last, he sighed again and shook his head, as though to himself. He laid hands on the paper, and quickly, gently, folded it, once, and twice, and again. Then rising to his feet, he went to the rail, extended his hands over the water, and let the folded white shape fall.

It tumbled toward the water. Then the wind caught it and whirled it upward, a bit of white receding in the distance, looking much like the gulls and terns who squawked behind the ship in search of scraps.

Mr. Willoughby didn't stay to watch it, but turned away from the rail and went below, the dream still stamped on his small round face.

45

Mr. Willoughby's Tale

As we passed the center of the Atlantic gyre and headed south, the days and evenings became warm, and the off-duty crew began to congregate on the forecastle for a time after supper, to sing songs, dance to Brodie Cooper's fiddle, or listen to stories. With the same instinct that makes children camping in the wood tell ghost stories, the men seemed particularly fond of horrible tales of shipwreck and the perils of the sea.

As we passed farther south, and out of the realm of Kraken and sea serpent, the mood for monsters passed, and the men began instead to tell stories of their homes.

It was after most of these had been exhausted that Maitland, the cabin boy, turned to Mr. Willoughby, crouched as usual against the foot of the mast, with his cup cradled to his chest.

"How was it that you came from China, Willoughby?" Maitland asked curiously. "I've not seen more than a handful of Chinese sailors, though folk do say as there's a great many people in China. Is it such a fine place that the inhabitants don't care to take leave of it, perhaps?"

At first demurring, the little Chinese seemed mildly flattered at the interest provoked by this question. With a bit more urging, he consented to tell of his departure from his homeland—requiring only that Jamie should translate for him, his own English being inadequate to the task. Jamie readily agreeing, he sat down beside Mr. Willoughby, and cocked his head to listen.

"I was a Mandarin," Mr. Willoughby began, in Jamie's voice, "a Mandarin of letters, one gifted in composition. I wore a silk gown, embroidered in very many colors, and over this, the scholar's blue silk gown, with the badge of my office embroidered upon breast and back—the figure of a *feng-huang*—a bird of fire.''

"I think he means a phoenix," Jamie added, turning to me for a moment before directing his attention back to the patiently waiting Mr. Willoughby, who began speaking again at once.

"I was born in Pekin, the Imperial City of the Son of Heaven—"

"That is how they call their emperor," Fergus whispered to me. "Such presumption, to equate their king with the Lord Jesus!"

"Shh," hissed several people, turning indignant faces toward Fergus. He made a rude gesture at Maxwell Gordon, but fell silent, turning back to the small figure sitting crouched against the mast.

"I was found early to have some skill in composition, and while I was not at first adept in the use of brush and ink, I learned at last with great effort to make the representations of my brush resemble the ideas that danced like cranes within my mind. And so I came to the notice of Wu-Xien, a Mandarin of the Imperial Household, who took me to live with him, and oversaw my training.

"I rose rapidly in merit and eminence, so that before my twenty-sixth birthday, I had attained a globe of red coral upon my hat. And then came an evil wind, that blew the seeds of misfortune into my garden. It may be that I was cursed by an enemy, or perhaps that in my arrogance I had omitted to make proper sacrifice—for surely I was not lacking in reverence to my ancestors, being careful always to visit my family's tomb each year, and to have joss sticks always burning in the Hall of Ancestors—"

"If his compositions were always so long-winded, no doubt the Son of Heaven lost patience and tossed him in the river," Fergus muttered cynically.

"—but whatever the cause," Jamie's voice continued, "my poetry came before the eyes of Wan-Mei, the Emperor's Second Wife. Second Wife was a woman of great power, having borne no less than four sons, and when she asked that I might become part of her own household, the request was granted at once."

"And what was wrong wi' that?" demanded Gordon, leaning forward in interest. "A chance to get on in the world, surely?"

Mr. Willoughby evidently understood the question, for he nodded in Gordon's direction as he continued, and Jamie's voice took up the story.

"Oh, the honor was inestimable; I should have had a large house of my own within the walls of the palace, and a guard of soldiers to escort my palanquin, with a triple umbrella borne before me in symbol of my office, and perhaps even a peacock feather for my hat. My name would have been inscribed in letters of gold in the Book of Merit."

The little Chinaman paused, scratching at his scalp. The hair had begun to sprout from the shaved part, making him look rather like a tennis ball.

"However, there is a condition of service within the Imperial Household; all the servants of the royal wives must be eunuchs."

A gasp of horror greeted this, followed by a babble of agitated comment, in which the remarks "Bloody heathen!" and "Yellow bastards!" were heard to predominate.

"What is a eunuch?" Marsali asked, looking bewildered.

"Nothing you need ever concern yourself with, *chérie,*" Fergus assured her, slipping an arm about her shoulders. "So you ran, *mon ami*?" he addressed Mr. Willoughby in tones of deepest sympathy. "I should do the same, without doubt!"

A deep murmur of heartfelt approbation reinforced this sentiment. Mr. Willoughby seemed somewhat heartened by such evident approval; he bobbed his head once or twice at his listeners before resuming his story.

"It was most dishonorable of me to refuse the Emperor's gift. And yet—it is a grievous weakness—I had fallen in love with a woman."

There was a sympathetic sigh at this, most sailors being wildly romantic souls, but Mr. Willoughby stopped, jerking at Jamie's sleeve and saying something to him.

"Oh, I'm wrong," Jamie corrected himself. "He says it was not '*a* woman'—just 'Woman'—all women, or the idea of women in general, he means. That's it?" he asked, looking down at Mr. Willoughby.

The Chinaman nodded, satisfied, and sat back. The moon was full up by now, three-quarters full, and bright enough to show the little Mandarin's face as he talked.

"Yes," he said, through Jamie, "I thought much of women; their grace and beauty, blooming like lotus flowers, floating like milkweed on the wind. And the myriad sounds of them, sometimes like the chatter of ricebirds, or the song of nightingales;

sometimes the cawing of crows," he added with a smile that creased his eyes to slits and brought his hearers to laughter, "but even then I loved them.

"I wrote all my poems to Woman—sometimes they were addressed to one lady or another, but most often to Woman alone. To the taste of breasts like apricots, the warm scent of a woman's navel when she wakens in the winter, the warmth of a mound that fills your hand like a peach, split with ripeness."

Fergus, scandalized, put his hands over Marsali's ears, but the rest of his hearers were most receptive.

"No wonder the wee fellow was an esteemed poet," Raeburn said with approval. "It's verra heathen, but I like it!"

"Worth a red knob on your hat, any day," Maitland agreed.

"Almost worth learning a bit of Chinee for," the master's mate chimed in, eyeing Mr. Willoughby with fresh interest. "Does he have a lot of those poems?"

Jamie waved the audience—by now augmented by most of the off-duty hands—to silence and said, "Go on, then," to Mr. Willoughby.

"I fled on the Night of Lanterns," the Chinaman said. "A great festival, and one when people would be thronging the streets; there would be no danger of being noticed by the watchmen. Just after dark, as the processions were assembling throughout the city, I put on the garments of a traveler—"

"That's like a pilgrim," Jamie interjected, "they go to visit their ancestors' tombs far away, and wear white clothes—that's for mourning, ye ken?"

"—and I left my house. I made my way through the crowds without difficulty, carrying a small anonymous lantern I had bought—one without my name and place of residence painted on it. The watchmen were hammering upon their bamboo drums, the servants of the great households beating gongs, and from the roof of the palace, fireworks were being set off in great profusion."

The small round face was marked by nostalgia, as he remembered.

"It was in a way a most appropriate farewell for a poet," he said. "Fleeing nameless, to the sound of great applause. As I passed the soldiers' garrison at the city gate, I looked back, to see the many roofs of the Palace outlined by bursting flowers of red and gold. It looked like a magic garden—and a forbidden one, for me."

Yi Tien Cho had made his way without incident through the night, but had nearly been caught the next day.

"I had forgotten my fingernails," he said. He spread out a hand, small and short-fingered, the nails bitten to the quicks. "For a Mandarin has long nails, as symbol that he is not obliged to work with his hands, and my own were the length of one of my finger joints."

A servant at the house where he had stopped for refreshment next day saw them, and ran to tell the guard. Yi Tien Cho ran, too, and succeeded at last in eluding his pursuers by sliding into a wet ditch and lying hidden in the bushes.

"While lying there, I destroyed my nails, of course," he said. He waggled the little finger of his right hand. "I was obliged to tear that nail out, for it had a golden *da zi* inlaid in it, which I could not dislodge."

He had stolen a peasant's clothes from a bush where they had been hung to dry, leaving the torn-out nail with its golden character in exchange, and made his way slowly across country toward the coast. At first he paid for his food with the small store of money he had brought away, but outside Lulong he met with a band of robbers, who took his money but left him his life.

"And after that," he said simply, "I stole food when I could, and starved when I could not. And at last the wind of fortune changed a little, and I met with a group of traveling apothecaries, on their way to the physicians' fair near the coast. In return for my skill at drawing banners for their booth and composing labels extolling the virtues of their medicines, they carried me along with them."

Once reaching the coast, he had made his way to the waterfront, and tried there to pass himself off as a seaman, but failed utterly, as his fingers, so skillful with brush and ink, knew nothing of the art of knots and lines. There were several foreign ships in port; he had chosen the one whose sailors looked the most barbarous as being likely to carry him farthest away, and seizing his chance, had slipped past the deck guard and into the hold of the *Serafina,* bound for Edinburgh.

"You had always meant to leave the country altogether?" Fergus asked, interested. "It seems a desperate choice."

"Emperor's reach very long," Mr. Willoughby said softly in English, not waiting for translation. "I am exile, or I am dead."

His listeners gave a collective sigh at the awesome contemplation of such bloodthirsty power, and there was a moment of silence, with only the whine of the rigging overhead, while Mr. Willoughby picked up his neglected cup and drained the last drops of his grog.

He set it down, licking his lips, and laid his hand once more on Jamie's arm.

"It is strange," Mr. Willoughby said, and the air of reflection in his voice was echoed exactly by Jamie's, "but it was my joy of women that Second Wife saw and loved in my words. Yet by desiring to possess me—and my poems—she would have forever destroyed what she admired."

Mr. Willoughby uttered a small chuckle, whose irony was unmistakable.

"Nor is that the end of the contradiction my life has become. Because I could not bring myself to surrender my manhood, I have lost all else—honor, livelihood, country. By that, I mean not only the land itself, with the slopes of noble fir trees where I spent my summers in Tartary, and the great plains of the south, the flowing of rivers filled with fish, but also the loss of myself. My parents are dishonored, the tombs of my ancestors fall into ruin, and no joss burns before their images.

"All order, all beauty is lost. I am come to a place where the golden words of my poems are taken for the clucking of hens, and my brushstrokes for their scratchings. I am taken as less than the meanest beggar who swallows serpents for the entertainment of the crowds, allowing passersby to draw the serpent from my mouth by its tail for the tiny payment that will let me live another day."

Mr. Willoughby glared round at his hearers, making his parallel evident.

"I am come to a country of women coarse and rank as bears." The Chinaman's voice rose passionately, though Jamie kept to an even tone, reciting the words, but stripping them of feeling. "They are creatures of no grace, no learning, ignorant, bad-smelling, their bodies gross with sprouting hair, like dogs! And these— these! disdain me as a yellow worm, so that even the lowest whores will not lie with me.

"For the love of Woman, I am come to a place where no woman is worthy of love!" At this point, seeing the dark looks on the seamen's faces, Jamie ceased translating, and instead tried to calm the Chinaman, laying a big hand on the blue-silk shoulder.

"Aye, man, I quite see. And I'm sure there's no a man present would have done otherwise, given the choice. Is that not so, lads?" he asked, glancing over his shoulder with eyebrows raised significantly.

His moral force was sufficient to extort a grudging murmur of agreement, but the crowd's sympathy with the tale of Mr. Willoughby's travails had been quite dissipated by his insulting conclusion. Pointed remarks were made about licentious, ungrateful heathen, and a great many extravagantly admiring compliments paid to Marsali and me, as the men dispersed aft.

Fergus and Marsali left then, too, Fergus pausing en route to inform Mr. Willoughby that any further remarks about European women would cause him, Fergus, to be obliged to wrap his, Willoughby's, queue about his neck and strangle him with it.

Mr. Willoughby ignored remarks and threats alike, merely staring straight ahead, his black eyes shining with memory and grog. Jamie at last stood up, too, and held out a hand to help me down from my cask.

It was as we were turning to leave that the Chinaman reached down between his legs. Completely without lewdness, he cupped his testicles, so that the rounded mass pressed against the silk. He rolled them slowly in the palm of his hand, staring at the bulge in deep meditation.

"Sometime," he said, as though to himself, "I think not worth it."

46

We Meet a Porpoise

I had been conscious for some time that Marsali was trying to get up the nerve to speak to me. I had thought she would, sooner or later; whatever her feelings toward me, I was the only other woman aboard. I did my best to help, smiling kindly and saying "Good morning," but the first move would have to be hers.

She made it, finally, in the middle of the Atlantic Ocean, a month after we had left Scotland.

I was writing in our shared cabin, making surgical notes on a minor amputation—two smashed toes on one of the foredeck hands. I had just completed a drawing of the surgical site, when a shadow darkened the doorway of the cabin, and I looked up to see Marsali standing there, chin thrust out pugnaciously.

"I need to know something," she said firmly. "I dinna like ye, and I reckon ye ken that, but Da says you're a wisewoman, and I think you're maybe an honest woman, even if ye are a whore, so you'll maybe tell me."

There were any number of possible responses to this remarkable statement, but I refrained from making any of them.

"Maybe I will," I said, putting down the pen. "What is it you need to know?"

Seeing that I wasn't angry, she slid into the cabin and sat down on the stool, the only available spot.

"Weel, it's to do wi' bairns," she explained. "And how ye get them."

I raised one eyebrow. "Your mother didn't tell you where babies come from?"

She snorted impatiently, her small blond brows knotted in fierce scorn. "O' course I ken where they come from! Any fool knows that much. Ye let a man put his prick between your legs, and there's the devil to pay, nine months later. What I want to know is how ye *don't* get them."

"I see." I regarded her with considerable interest. "You don't want a child? Er . . . once you're properly married, I mean? Most young women seem to."

"Well," she said slowly, twisting a handful of her dress. "I think I maybe would like a babe sometime. For itself, I mean. If it maybe had dark hair, like Fergus." A hint of dreaminess flitted across her face, but then her expression hardened once more.

"But I can't," she said.

"Why not?"

She pushed out her lips, thinking, then pulled them in again. "Well, because of Fergus. We havena lain together yet. We havena been able to do more than kiss each other now and again behind the hatch covers—thanks to Da and his bloody-minded notions," she added bitterly.

"Amen," I said, with some wryness.

"Eh?"

"Never mind." I waved a hand, dismissing it. "What has that got to do with not wanting babies?"

"I want to like it," she said matter-of-factly. "When we get to the prick part."

I bit the inside of my lower lip.

"I . . . er . . . imagine that has something to do with Fergus, but I'm afraid I don't quite see what it has to do with babies."

Marsali eyed me warily. Without hostility for once, more as though she was estimating me in some fashion.

"Fergus likes ye," she said.

"I'm fond of him, too," I answered cautiously, not sure where the conversation was heading. "I've known him for quite a long time, ever since he was a boy."

She relaxed suddenly, some of the tension going out of the slender shoulders.

"Oh. You'll know about it, then—where he was born?"

Suddenly I understood her wariness.

"The brothel in Paris? Yes, I know about that. He told you, then?"

She nodded. "Aye, he did. A long time ago, last Hogmanay."
Well, I supposed a year was a long time to a fifteen-year-old.

"That's when I told him I loved him," she went on. Her eyes
were fixed on her skirt, and a faint tinge of pink showed in her
cheeks. "And he said he loved me, too, but my mother wasna
going to ever agree to the match. And I said why not, there was
nothing so awful about bein' French, not everybody could be
Scots, and I didna think his hand mattered a bit either—after all,
there was Mr. Murray wi' his wooden leg, and Mother liked *him*
well enough—but then he said, no, it was none of those things,
and then he told me—about Paris, I mean, and being born in a
brothel and being a pickpocket until he met Da."

She raised her eyes, a look of incredulity in the light blue
depths. "I think he thought I'd *mind*," she said, wonderingly.
"He tried to go away, and said he wouldna see me anymore.
Well—" she shrugged, tossing her fair hair out of the way, "I
soon took care of that." She looked at me straight on then, hands
clasped in her lap.

"It's just I didna want to mention it, in case ye didn't know
already. But since ye do . . . well, it's no Fergus I'm worried
about. He says he knows what to do, and I'll like it fine, once
we're past the first time or two. But that's not what my mam told
me."

"What *did* she tell you?" I asked, fascinated.

A small line showed between the light brows. "Well . . ."
Marsali said slowly, "it wasna so much she said it—though she
did say, when I told her about Fergus and me, that he'd do terrible
things to me because of living wi' whores and having one for a
mother—it was more she . . . she acted like it."

Her face was a rosy pink now, and she kept her eyes in her lap,
where her fingers twisted themselves in the folds of her skirt. The
wind seemed to be picking up; small strands of blond hair rose
gently from her head, wafted by the breeze from the window.

"When I started to bleed the first time, she told me what to do,
and about how it was part o' the curse of Eve, and I must just put
up wi' it. And I said, what was the curse of Eve? And she read me
from the Bible all about how St. Paul said women were terrible,
filthy sinners because of what Eve did, but they could still be
saved by suffering and bearing children."

"I never did think a lot of St. Paul," I observed, and she looked up, startled.

"But he's in the Bible!" she said, shocked.

"So are a lot of other things," I said dryly. "Heard that story about Gideon and his daughter, have you? Or the fellow who sent his lady out to be raped to death by a crowd of ruffians, so they wouldn't get *him*? God's chosen men, just like Paul. But go on, do."

She gaped at me for a minute, but then closed her mouth and nodded, a little stunned.

"Aye, well. Mother said as how it meant I was nearly old enough to be wed, and when I did marry, I must be sure to remember it was a woman's duty to do as her husband wanted, whether she liked it or no. And she looked so sad when she told me that . . . I thought whatever a woman's duty was, it must be awful, and from what St. Paul said about suffering and bearing children . . ."

She stopped and sighed. I sat quietly, waiting. When she resumed, it was haltingly, as though she had trouble choosing her words.

"I canna remember my father. I was only three when the English took him away. But I was old enough when my mother wed —wed Jamie—to see how it was between them." She bit her lip; she wasn't used to calling Jamie by his name.

"Da—Jamie, I mean—he's kind, I think; he always was to Joan and me. But I'd see, when he'd lay his hand on my mother's waist and try to draw her close—she'd shrink away from him." She gnawed her lip some more, then continued.

"I could see she was afraid; she didna like him to touch her. But I couldna see that he ever did anything to be afraid *of,* not where we could see—so I thought it must be something he did when they were in their bed, alone. Joan and I used to wonder what it could be; Mam never had marks on her face or her arms, and she didna limp when she walked—not like Magdalen Wallace, whose husband always beats her when he's drunk on market day— so we didna think Da hit her."

Marsali licked her lips, dried by the warm salt air, and I pushed the jug of water toward her. She nodded in thanks and poured a cupful.

"So I thought," she said, eyes fixed on the stream of water, "that it must be because Mam had had children—had us—and she knew it would be terrible again and so she didna want to go to bed with—with Jamie for fear of it."

She took a drink, then set down the cup and looked at me directly, firming her chin in challenge.

"I saw ye with my da," she said. "Just that minute, before he saw me. I—I think ye liked what he was doing to you in the bed."

I opened my mouth, and closed it again.

"Well . . . yes," I said, a little weakly. "I did."

She grunted in satisfaction. "Mmphm. And ye like it when he touches ye; I've seen. Well, then. Ye havena got any children. And I'd heard there are ways not to have them, only nobody seems to know just how, but you must, bein' a wisewoman and all."

She tilted her head to one side, studying me.

"I'd like a babe," she admitted, "but if it's got to be a babe or liking Fergus, then it's Fergus. So it won't be a babe—if you'll tell me how."

I brushed the curls back behind my ear, wondering where on earth to start.

"Well," I said, drawing a deep breath, "to begin with, I have had children."

Her eyes sprang wide and round at this.

"Ye do? Does Da—does Jamie know?"

"Well, of course he does," I replied testily. "They were his."

"I never heard Da had any bairns at all." The pale eyes narrowed with suspicion.

"I don't imagine he thought it was any of your business," I said, perhaps a trifle more sharply than necessary. "And it's not, either," I added, but she just raised her brows and went on looking suspicious.

"The first baby died," I said, capitulating. "In France. She's buried there. My—our second daughter is grown now; she was born after Culloden."

"So he's never seen her? The grown one?" Marsali spoke slowly, frowning.

I shook my head, unable to speak for a moment. There seemed to be something stuck in my throat, and I reached for the water. Marsali pushed the jug absently in my direction, leaning against the swing of the ship.

"That's verra sad," she said softly, to herself. Then she glanced up at me, frowning once more in concentration as she tried to work it all out.

"So ye've had children, and it didna make a difference to you? Mmphm. But it's been a long while, then—did ye have other men whilst ye were away in France?" Her lower lip came up over the upper one, making her look very much like a small and stubborn bulldog.

"That," I said firmly, putting the cup down, "is definitely none of your business. As to whether childbirth makes a difference, possibly it does to some women, but not all of them. But whether it does or not, there are good reasons why you might not want to have a child right away."

She withdrew the pouting underlip and sat up straight, interested.

"So there is a way?"

"There are a lot of ways, and unfortunately most of them don't work," I told her, with a pang of regret for my prescription pad and the reliability of contraceptive pills. Still, I remembered well enough the advice of the *maîtresses sages-femmes,* the experienced midwives of the Hôpital des Anges, where I had worked in Paris twenty years before.

"Hand me the small box in the cupboard over there," I said, pointing to the doors above her head. "Yes, that one.

"Some of the French midwives make a tea of bayberry and valerian," I said, rummaging in my medicine box. "But it's rather dangerous, and not all that dependable, I don't think."

"D'ye miss her?" Marsali asked abruptly. I glanced up, startled. "Your daughter?" Her face was abnormally expressionless, and I suspected the question had more to do with Laoghaire than with me.

"Yes," I said simply. "But she's grown; she has her own life." The lump in my throat was back, and I bent my head over the medicine box, hiding my face. The chances of Laoghaire ever seeing Marsali again were just about as good as the chances that I would ever see Brianna; it wasn't a thought I wanted to dwell on.

"Here," I said, pulling out a large chunk of cleaned sponge. I took one of the thin surgical knives from the fitted slots in the lid of the box and carefully sliced off several thin pieces, about three inches square. I searched through the box again and found the small bottle of tansy oil, with which I carefully saturated one square under Marsali's fascinated gaze.

"All right," I said. "That's about how much oil to use. If you haven't any oil, you can dip the sponge in vinegar—even wine will work, in a pinch. You put the bit of sponge well up inside you before you go to bed with a man—mind you do it even the first time; you can get with child from even once."

Marsali nodded, her eyes wide, and touched the sponge gently with a forefinger. "Aye? And—and after? Do I take it out again, or—"

An urgent shout from above, coupled with a sudden heeling of the *Artemis* as she backed her mainsails, put an abrupt end to the conversation. Something was happening up above.

"I'll tell you later," I said, pushing the sponge and bottle toward her, and headed for the passage.

Jamie was standing with the Captain on the afterdeck, watching the approach of a large ship behind us. She was perhaps three times the size of the *Artemis,* three-masted, with a perfect forest of rigging and sail, through which small black figures hopped like fleas on a bedsheet. A puff of white smoke floated in her wake, token of a cannon recently fired.

"Is she firing on us?" I asked in amazement.

"No," Jamie said grimly. "A warning shot only. She means to board us."

"Can they?" I addressed the question to Captain Raines, who was looking even more glum than usual, the downturned corners of his mouth sunk in his beard.

"They can," he said. "We'll not outrun her in a stiff breeze like this, on the open sea."

"What is she?" Her ensign flew at the masthead, but seen against the sun at this distance, it looked completely black.

Jamie glanced down at me, expressionless. "A British man-o-war, Sassenach. Seventy-four guns. Perhaps ye'd best go below."

This was bad news. While Britain was no longer at war with France, relations between the two countries were by no means cordial. And while the *Artemis* was armed, she had only four twelve-pound guns; sufficient to deter small pirates, but no match for a man-of-war.

"What can they want of us?" Jamie asked the Captain. Raines shook his head, his soft, plump face set grimly.

"Likely pressing," he answered. "She's shorthanded; you can see by her rigging—and her foredeck all ahoo," he noted disapprovingly, eyes fixed on the man-of-war, now looming as she drew alongside. He glanced at Jamie. "They can press any of our hands who look to be British—which is something like half the crew. And yourself, Mr. Fraser—unless you wish to pass for French?"

"Damn," Jamie said softly. He glanced at me and frowned. "Did I not tell ye to get below?"

"You did," I said, not going. I drew closer to him, my eyes fixed on the man-of-war, where a small boat was now being lowered. One officer, in a gilded coat and laced hat, was climbing down the side.

"If they press the British hands," I asked Captain Raines, "what will happen to them?"

"They'll serve aboard the *Porpoise*—that's her," he nodded at the man-of-war, which sported a puff-lipped fish as the figurehead, "as members of the Royal Navy. She may release the pressed hands when she reaches port—or she may not."

"What? You mean they can just kidnap men and make them serve as sailors for as long as they please?" A thrill of fear shot through me, at the thought of Jamie's being abruptly taken away.

"They can," the Captain said shortly. "And if they do, we'll have a job of it to reach Jamaica ourselves, with half a crew." He turned abruptly and went forward, to greet the arriving boat.

Jamie gripped my elbow and squeezed.

"They'll not take Innes or Fergus," he said. "They'll help ye to hunt for Young Ian. If they take us"— I noted the "us" with a sharp pang —"you'll go on to Jared's place at Sugar Bay, and search from there." He looked down and gave me a brief smile. "I'll meet ye there," he said, and gave my elbow a reassuring squeeze. "I canna say how long it might be, but I'll come to ye there."

"But you could pass as a Frenchman!" I protested. "You know you could!"

He looked at me for a moment, and shook his head, smiling faintly.

"No," he said softly. "I canna let them take my men, and stay behind, hiding under a Frenchman's name."

"But—" I started to protest that the Scottish smugglers were *not* his men, had no claim on his loyalty, and then stopped, realizing that it was useless. The Scots might not be his tenants or his kin, and one of them might well be a traitor. But he had brought them here, and if they went, he would go with them.

"Dinna mind it, Sassenach," he said softly. "I shall be all right, one way or the other. But I think it is best if our name is Malcolm, for the moment."

He patted my hand, then released it and went forward, shoulders braced to meet whatever was coming. I followed, more slowly. As the gig pulled alongside, I saw Captain Raines's eyebrows rise in astonishment.

"God save us, what is this?" he murmured under his breath, as a head appeared above the *Artemis*'s rail.

It was a young man, evidently in his late twenties, but with his face drawn and shoulders slumping with fatigue. A uniform coat that was too big for him had been tugged on over a filthy shirt, and he staggered slightly as the deck of the *Artemis* rose beneath him.

"You are the captain of this ship?" The Englishman's eyes were red-rimmed from tiredness, but he picked Raines from the crowd of grim-faced hands at a glance. "I am acting captain Thomas Leonard, of His Majesty's ship *Porpoise*. For the love of God," he said, speaking hoarsely, "have you a surgeon aboard?"

Over a warily offered glass of port below, Captain Leonard explained that the *Porpoise* had suffered an outbreak of some infectious plague, beginning some four weeks before.

"Half the crew are down with it," he said, wiping a crimson drop from his stubbled chin. "We've lost thirty men so far, and look fair to lose a lot more."

"You lost your captain?" Raines asked.

Leonard's thin face flushed slightly. "The—the captain and the two senior lieutenants died last week, and the surgeon and the surgeon's mate, as well. I was third lieutenant." That explained both his surprising youth and his nervous state; to be landed suddenly in sole command of a large ship, a crew of six hundred men, and a rampant infection aboard, was enough to rattle anyone.

"If you have anyone aboard with some medical experience . . ." He looked hopefully from Captain Raines to Jamie, who stood by the desk, frowning slightly.

"I'm the *Artemis*'s surgeon, Captain Leonard," I said, from my place in the doorway. "What symptoms do your men have?"

"You?" The young captain's head swiveled to stare at me. His jaw hung slackly open, showing the furred tongue and stained teeth of a tobacco-chewer.

"My wife's a rare healer, Captain," Jamie said mildly. "If it's help ye came for, I'd advise ye to answer her questions, and do as she tells ye."

Leonard blinked once, but then took a deep breath and nodded. "Yes. Well, it seems to start with griping pains in the belly, and a terrible flux and vomiting. The afflicted men complain of headache, and they have considerable fever. They—"

"Do some of them have a rash on their bellies?" I interrupted.

He nodded eagerly. "They do. And some of them bleed from the arse as well. Oh, I beg pardon, ma'am," he said, suddenly flustered. "I meant no offense, only that—"

"I think I know what that might be," I interrupted his apologies. A feeling of excitement began to grow in me; the feeling of a diagnosis just under my hands, and the sure knowledge of how to proceed with it. The call of trumpets to a warhorse, I thought with wry amusement. "I'd need to look at them, to be sure, but—"

"My wife would be pleased to advise ye, Captain," Jamie said firmly. "But I'm afraid she canna go aboard your ship."

"Are you sure?" Captain Leonard looked from one to the other of us, eyes desperate with disappointment. "If she could only look at my crew . . ."

"No," Jamie said, at the same moment I replied, "Yes, of course!"

There was an awkward silence for a moment. Then Jamie rose to his feet, said politely, "You'll excuse us, Captain Leonard?" and dragged me bodily out of the cabin, down the passage to the afterhold.

"Are ye daft?" he scowled, still clutching me by one arm. "Ye canna be thinking of setting foot on a ship wi' the plague! Risk your life and the crew and Young Ian, all for the sake of a pack of Englishmen?"

"It isn't plague," I said, struggling to get free. "And I wouldn't be risking my life. Let go of my arm, you bloody Scot!"

He let go, but stood blocking the ladder, glowering at me.

"Listen," I said, striving for patience. "It isn't plague; I'm almost sure it's typhoid fever—the rash sounds like it. I can't catch that, I've been vaccinated for it."

Momentary doubt flitted across his face. Despite my explanations, he was still inclined to consider germs and vaccines in the same league with black magic.

"Aye?" he said skeptically. "Well, perhaps that's so, but still . . ."

"Look," I said, groping for words. "I'm a doctor. They're sick, and I can do something about it. I . . . it's . . . well, I have to, that's all!"

Judging from its effect, this statement appeared to lack something in eloquence. Jamie raised one eyebrow, inviting me to go on.

I took a deep breath. How should I explain it—the need to touch, the compulsion to heal? In his own way, Frank had understood. Surely there was a way to make it clear to Jamie.

"I took an oath," I said. "When I became a physician."

Both eyebrows went up. "An oath?" he echoed. "What sort of oath?"

I had said it aloud only the one time. Still, I had had a framed copy in my office; Frank had given it to me, a gift when I graduated from medical school. I swallowed a small thickening in my throat, closed my eyes, and read what I could remember from the scroll before my mind's eye.

"I swear by Apollo the physician, by Aesculapius, Hygeia, and Panacea, and I take to witness all the gods, all the goddesses, to keep according to my ability and my judgment the following Oath:

I will prescribe regimen for the good of my patients according to my ability and my judgment and never do harm to anyone. To please no one will I prescribe a deadly drug, nor give advice which may cause his death. But I will preserve the purity of my life and my art. In every house where I come I will enter only for the good of my patients, keeping myself far from all intentional ill-doing and all seduction, and especially from the pleasures of love with women or with men, be they free or slaves. All that may come to my knowledge in the exercise of my profession or outside of my profession or in daily commerce with men, which ought not to be spread abroad, I will keep secret and will never reveal. If I keep

*this oath faithfully, may I enjoy my life and practice my art, re-
spected by all men and in all times; but if I swerve from it or
violate it, may the reverse be my lot."*

I opened my eyes, to find him looking down at me thoughtfully.
"Er . . . parts of it are just for tradition," I explained.

The corner of his mouth twitched slightly. "I see," he said.
"Well, the first part sounds a wee bit pagan, but I like the part
about how ye willna seduce anyone."

"I thought you'd like that one," I said dryly. "Captain Leonard's virtue is safe with me."

He gave a small snort and leaned back against the ladder, running one hand slowly through his hair.

"Is that how it's done, then, in the company of physicians?" he
asked. "Ye hold yourself bound to help whoever calls for it, even
an enemy?"

"It doesn't make a great difference, you know, if they're ill or
hurt." I looked up, searching his face for understanding.

"Aye, well," he said slowly. "I've taken an oath now and then,
myself—and none of them lightly." He reached out and took my
right hand, his fingers resting on my silver ring. "Some weigh
heavier than others, though," he said, watching my face in turn.

He was very close to me, the sun from the hatchway overhead
striping the linen of his sleeve, the skin of his hand a deep ruddy
bronze where it cradled my own white fingers, and the glinting
silver of my wedding ring.

"It does," I said softly, speaking to his thought. "You know it
does." I laid my other hand against his chest, its gold ring glowing
in a bar of sunlight. "But where one vow can be kept, without
damage to another . . . ?"

He sighed, deeply enough to move the hand on his chest, then
bent and kissed me, very gently.

"Aye, well, I wouldna have ye be forsworn," he said, straightening up with a wry twist to his mouth. "You're sure of this
vaccination of yours? It does work?"

"It works," I assured him.

"Perhaps I should go with ye," he said, frowning slightly.

"You can't—you haven't been vaccinated, and typhoid's awfully contagious."

"You're only thinking it's typhoid, from what Leonard says," he pointed out. "Ye dinna ken for sure that it's that."

"No," I admitted. "But there's only one way to find out."

I was assisted up onto the deck of the *Porpoise* by means of a bosun's chair, a terrorizing swing over empty air and frothing sea. I landed ignominiously in a sprawl on the deck. Once I regained my feet, I was astonished to find how solid the deck of the man-of-war felt, compared to the tiny, pitching quarterdeck of the *Artemis,* far below. It was like standing on the Rock of Gibraltar.

My hair had blown loose during the trip between the ships; I twisted it up and repinned it as best I could, then reached to take the medicine box I had brought from the midshipman who held it.

"You'd best show me where they are," I said. The wind was brisk, and I was aware that it was taking a certain amount of work on the part of both crews to keep the two ships close together, even as both drifted leeward.

It was dark in the tween-decks, the confined space lit by small oil lamps that hung from the ceiling, swaying gently with the rise and fall of the ship, so that the ranks of hammocked men lay in deep shadow, blotched with dim patches of light from above. They looked like pods of whales, or sleeping sea beasts, lying humped and black, side by side, swaying with the movement of the sea beneath.

The stench was overpowering. What air there was came down through crude ventilator shafts that reached the upper deck, but that wasn't a lot. Worse than unwashed seamen was the reek of vomitus and the ripe, throat-clogging smell of blood-streaked diarrhea, which liberally spattered the decking beneath the hammocks, where sufferers had been too ill to reach the few available chamber pots. My shoes stuck to the deck, coming away with a nasty sucking noise as I made my way cautiously into the area.

"Give me a better light," I said peremptorily to the apprehensive-looking young midshipman who had been told to accompany me. He was holding a kerchief to his face and looked both scared and miserable, but he obeyed, holding up the lantern he carried so that I could peer into the nearest hammock.

The occupant groaned and turned away his face as the light struck him. He was flushed with fever, and his skin hot to the touch. I pulled his shirt up and felt his stomach; it too was hot, the skin distended and hard. As I prodded gently here and there, the man writhed like a worm on a hook, uttering piteous groans.

"It's all right," I said soothingly, urging him to flatten out again. "Yes, I'll help you; it will feel better soon. Let me look into your eyes, now. Yes, that's right."

I pulled back the eyelid; his pupil shrank in the light, leaving his eyes brown and red-rimmed with suffering.

"Christ, take away the light!" he gasped, jerking his head away. "It splits my head!" Fever, vomiting, abdominal cramps, headache.

"Do you have chills?" I asked, waving back the midshipman's lantern.

The answer was more a moan than a word, but in the affirmative. Even in the shadows, I could see that many of the men in the hammocks were wrapped in their blankets, though it was stifling hot here below.

If not for the headache, it could be simple gastroenteritis—but not with this many men stricken. Something very contagious indeed, and I was fairly sure what. Not malaria, coming *from* Europe to the Caribbean. Typhus was a possibility; carried by the common body louse, it was prone to rapid spread in close quarters like these, and the symptoms were similar to those I saw around me— with one distinctive difference.

That seaman didn't have the characteristic belly rash, nor the next, but the third one did. The light red rosettes were plain on the clammy white skin. I pressed firmly on one, and it disappeared, blinking back into existence a moment later, as the blood returned to the skin. I squeezed my way between the hammocks, the heavy, sweating bodies pressing in on me from either side, and made my way back to the companionway where Captain Leonard and two more of his midshipmen waited for me.

"It's typhoid," I told the Captain. I was as sure as I could be, lacking a microscope and blood culture.

"Oh?" His drawn face remained apprehensive. "Do you know what to do for it, Mrs. Malcolm?"

"Yes, but it won't be easy. The sick men need to be taken above, washed thoroughly, and laid where they can have fresh air to breathe. Beyond that, it's a matter of nursing; they'll need to have a liquid diet—and lots of water—*boiled* water, that's very important!—and sponging to bring down the fever. The most important thing is to avoid infecting any more of your crew, though. There are several things that need to be done—"

"Do them," he interrupted. "I shall give orders to have as many of the healthy men as can be spared to attend you; order them as you will."

"Well," I said, with a dubious glance at the surroundings. "I can make a start, and tell you how to be going on, but it's going to be a big job. Captain Raines and my husband will be anxious to be on our way."

"Mrs. Malcolm," the Captain said earnestly, "I shall be eternally grateful for any assistance you can render us. We are most urgently bound for Jamaica, and unless the remainder of my crew can be saved from this wicked illness, we will never reach that island." He spoke with profound seriousness, and I felt a twinge of pity for him.

"All right," I said with a sigh. "Send me a dozen healthy crewmen, for a start."

Climbing to the quarterdeck, I went to the rail and waved at Jamie, who was standing by the *Artemis*'s wheel, looking upward. I could see his face clearly, despite the distance; it was worried, but relaxed into a broad smile when he saw me.

"Are ye comin' down now?" he shouted, cupping his hands.

"Not yet!" I shouted back. "I need two hours!" Holding up two fingers to make my meaning clear in case he hadn't heard, I stepped back from the rail, but not before I saw the smile fade from his face. He'd heard.

I saw the sick men removed to the afterdeck, and a crew of hands set to strip them of their filthy clothes, and hose and sponge them with seawater from the pumps. I was in the galley, instructing the cook and galley crew in food-handling precautions, when I felt the movement of the deck under my feet.

The cook to whom I was talking snaked out a hand and snapped shut the latch of the cupboard behind him. With the utmost dispatch, he grabbed a loose pot that leapt off its shelf, thrust a large ham on a spit into the lower cupboard, and whirled to clap a lid on the boiling pot hung over the galley fire.

I stared at him in astonishment. I had seen Murphy perform this same odd ballet, whenever the *Artemis* cast off or changed course abruptly.

"What—" I said, but then abandoned the question, and headed for the quarterdeck, as fast as I could go. We were under way; big and solid as the *Porpoise* was, I could feel the vibration that ran through the keel as she took the wind.

I burst onto the deck to find a cloud of sails overhead, set and drawing, and the *Artemis* falling rapidly behind us. Captain Leonard was standing by the helmsman, looking back to the *Artemis,* as the master bawled commands to the men overhead.

"What are you doing?" I shouted. "You bloody little bastard, what's going on here?"

The Captain glanced at me, plainly embarrassed, but with his jaw set stubbornly.

"We must get to Jamaica with the utmost dispatch," he said. His cheeks were chapped red with the rushing sea wind, or he might have blushed. "I am sorry, Mrs. Malcolm—indeed I regret the necessity, but—"

"But nothing!" I said, furious. "Put about! Heave to! Drop the bloody anchor! You can't take me away like this!"

"I regret the necessity," he said again, doggedly. "But I believe that we require your continuing services most urgently, Mrs. Malcolm. Don't worry," he said, striving for a reassurance that he didn't achieve. He reached out as though to pat my shoulder, but then thought better of it. His hand dropped to his side.

"I have promised your husband that the navy will provide you accommodation in Jamaica until the *Artemis* arrives there."

He flinched backward at the look on my face, evidently afraid that I might attack him—and not without reason.

"What do you *mean,* you promised my husband?" I said, through gritted teeth. "Do you mean that J—that Mr. Malcolm *permitted* you to abduct me?"

"Er . . . no. No, he didn't." The Captain appeared to be finding the interview a strain. He dragged a filthy handkerchief from his pocket and wiped his brow and the back of his neck. "He was most intransigent, I'm afraid."

"Intransigent, eh? Well, so am I!" I stamped my foot on the deck, aiming for his toes, and missing only because he leapt agilely backward. "If you expect me to help you, you bloody kidnapper, just bloody think again!"

The Captain tucked his handkerchief away and set his jaw. "Mrs. Malcolm. You compel me to tell you what I told your husband. The *Artemis* sails under a French flag, and with French papers, but more than half her crew are Englishmen or Scots. I could have pressed these men to service here—and I badly need them. Instead, I have agreed to leave them unmolested, in return for the gift of your medical knowledge.''

''So you've decided to press me instead. And my husband *agreed* to this . . . this *bargain*?''

''No, he didn't,'' the young man said, rather dryly. ''The captain of the *Artemis,* however, perceived the force of my argument.'' He blinked down at me, his eyes swollen from days without sleep, the too-big jacket flapping around his slender torso. Despite his youth and his slovenly appearance, he had considerable dignity.

''I must beg your pardon for what must seem the height of ungentlemanly behavior, Mrs. Malcolm—but the truth is that I am desperate,'' he said simply. ''You may be our only chance. I must take it.''

I opened my mouth to reply, but then closed it. Despite my fury —and my profound unease about what Jamie was going to say when I saw him again—I felt some sympathy for his position. It was quite true that he stood in danger of losing most of his crew, without help. Even with my help, we would lose some—but that wasn't a prospect I cared to dwell on.

''All right,'' I said, through my teeth. ''All . . . *right*!'' I looked out over the rail, at the dwindling sails of the *Artemis*. I wasn't prone to seasickness, but I felt a distinct hollowing in the pit of my stomach as the ship—and Jamie—fell far behind. ''I wouldn't appear to have a lot of choice in the matter. If you can spare as many men as possible to scrub down the tween-decks— oh, and have you any alcohol on board?''

He looked mildly surprised. ''Alcohol? Well, there is the rum for the hands' grog, and possibly some wine from the gun room locker. Will that do?''

''If that's what you have, it will have to do.'' I tried to push aside my own emotions, long enough to deal with the situation. ''I suppose I must speak to the purser, then.''

''Yes, of course. Come with me.'' Leonard started toward the companionway that led belowdecks, then, flushing, stood back and gestured awkwardly to let me go first—lest my descent expose my

lower limbs indelicately, I supposed. Biting my lip with a mixture
of anger and amusement, I went.

I had just reached the bottom of the ladder when I heard a
confusion of voices above.

"No, I tell 'ee, the Captain's not to be disturbed! Whatever you
have to say will—"

"Leave go! I tell *you,* if you don't let me speak to him now, it
will be too late!"

And then Leonard's voice, suddenly sharp as he turned to the
interlopers. "Stevens? What is this? What's the matter?"

"No matter, sir," said the first voice, suddenly obsequious.
"Only that Tompkins here is sure as he knows the cove what was
on that ship—the big 'un, with the red hair. He says—"

"I haven't time," the Captain said shortly. "Tell the mate,
Tompkins, and I shall attend to it later."

I was, naturally, halfway back up the ladder by the time these
words were spoken, and listening for all I was worth.

The hatchway darkened as Leonard began the backward descent
down the ladder. The young man glanced at me sharply, but I kept
my face carefully blank, saying only, "Have you many food stores
left, Captain? The sick men will need to be fed very carefully. I
don't suppose there would be any milk aboard, but—"

"Oh, there's milk," he said, suddenly more cheerful. "We have
six milch goats, in fact. The gunner's wife, Mrs. Johansen, does
quite wonderfully with them. I'll send her to talk with you, after
we've seen the purser."

Captain Leonard introduced me briefly to Mr. Overholt, the
purser, and then left, with the injunction that I should be afforded
every possible service. Mr. Overholt, a small, plump man with a
bald and shining head, peered at me out of the deep collar of his
coat like an undersized Humpty-Dumpty, murmuring unhappily
about the scarcity of everything near the end of a cruise, and how
unfortunate everything was, but I scarcely attended to him. I was
much too agitated, thinking of what I had overheard.

Who was this Tompkins? The voice was entirely unfamiliar, and
I was sure I had never heard the name before. More important,
what did he know about Jamie? And what was Captain Leonard
likely to do with the information? As it was, there was nothing I
could do now, save contain my impatience, and with the half of my

mind not busy with fruitless speculation, work out with Mr. Overholt what supplies were available for use in sickroom feeding.

Not a great deal, as it turned out.

"No, they certainly can't eat salt beef," I said firmly. "Nor yet hardtack, though if we soak the biscuit in boiled milk, perhaps we can manage that as they begin to recover. If you knock the weevils out first," I added, as an afterthought.

"Fish," Mr. Overholt suggested, in a hopeless sort of way. "We often encounter substantial schools of mackerel or even bonita, as we approach the Caribbean. Sometimes the crew will have luck with baited lines."

"Maybe that would do," I said, absently. "Boiled milk and water will be enough in the early stages, but as the men begin to recover, they should have something light and nourishing—soup, for instance. I suppose we could make a fish soup? Unless you have something else that might be suitable?"

"Well . . ." Mr. Overholt looked profoundly uneasy. "There *is* a small quantity of dried figs, ten pound of sugar, some coffee, a quantity of Naples biscuit, and a large cask of Madeira wine, but of course we cannot use that."

"Why not?" I stared at him, and he shuffled his feet uneasily.

"Why, those supplies are intended for the use of our passenger," he said.

"What sort of passenger?" I asked blankly.

Mr. Overholt looked surprised. "The Captain did not tell you? We are carrying the new governor for the island of Jamaica. That is the cause—well, *one* cause"—he corrected himself, dabbing nervously at his bald head with a handkerchief—"of our haste."

"If he's not sick, the Governor can eat salt beef," I said firmly. "Be good for him, I shouldn't wonder. Now, if you'll have the wine taken to the galley, I've work to do."

Aided by one of the remaining midshipmen, a short, stocky youth named Pound, I made a rapid tour of the ship, ruthlessly dragooning supplies and hands. Pound, trotting beside me like a small, ferocious bulldog, firmly informed surprised and resentful cooks, carpenters, sweepers, swabbers, sailmakers, and holdsmen that all my wishes—no matter how unreasonable—must be gratified instantly, by the Captain's orders.

Quarantine was the most important thing. As soon as the tween-decks had been scrubbed and aired, the patients would have to be carried down again, but the hammocks restrung with plenty of space between—the unaffected crew would have to sleep on deck —and provided with adequate toilet facilities. I had seen a pair of large kettles in the galley that I thought might do. I made a quick note on the mental list I was keeping, and hoped the chief cook was not as possessive of his receptacles as Murphy was.

I followed Pound's round head, covered with close-clipped brown curls, down toward the hold in search of worn sails that might be used for cloths. Only half my mind was on my list; with the other half, I was contemplating the possible source of the typhoid outbreak. Caused by a bacillus of the *Salmonella* genus, it was normally spread by ingestion of the bacillus, carried on hands contaminated by urine or feces.

Given the sanitary habits of seamen, any one of the crew could be the carrier of the disease. The most likely culprit was one of the food handlers, though, given the widespread and sudden nature of the outbreak—the cook or one of his two mates, or possibly one of the stewards. I would have to find out how many of these there were, which messes they served, and whether anyone had changed duties four weeks ago—no, five, I corrected myself. The outbreak had begun four weeks ago, but there was an incubation period for the disease to be considered, too.

"Mr. Pound," I called, and a round face peered up at me from the foot of the ladder.

"Yes, ma'am?"

"Mr. Pound—what's your first name, by the way?" I asked.

"Elias, ma'am," he said, looking mildly bewildered.

"Do you mind if I call you so?" I dropped off the foot of the ladder and smiled at him. He smiled hesitantly back.

"Er . . . no, ma'am. The Captain might mind, though," he added cautiously. " 'Tisn't really naval, you know."

Elias Pound couldn't be more than seventeen or eighteen; I doubted that Captain Leonard was more than five or six years older. Still, protocol was protocol.

"I'll be very naval in public," I assured him, suppressing a smile. "But if you're going to work with me, it will be easier to call you by name." I knew, as he didn't, what lay ahead—hours and days and possibly weeks of labor and exhaustion, when the

senses would blur, and only bodily habit and blind instinct—and
the leadership of a tireless chief—would keep those caring for the
sick on their feet.

I was far from tireless, but the illusion would have to be kept up.
This could be done with the help of two or three others, whom I
could train; substitutes for my own hands and eyes, who could
carry on when I must rest. Fate—and Captain Leonard—had designated Elias Pound as my new right hand; best to be on comfortable terms with him at once.

"How long have you been at sea, Elias?" I asked, stopping to
peer after him as he ducked under a low platform that held enormous loops of a huge, evil-smelling chain, each link more than
twice the size of my fist. The anchor chain? I wondered, touching
it curiously. It looked strong enough to moor the *Queen Elizabeth,*
which seemed a comforting thought.

"Since I was seven, ma'am," he said, working his way out
backward, dragging a large chest. He stood up puffing slightly
from the exertion, and wiped his round, ingenuous face. "My
uncle's commander in *Triton,* so he was able to get me a berth in
her. I come to join the *Porpoise* just this voyage, though, out of
Edinburgh." He flipped open the chest, revealing an assortment of
rust-smeared surgical implements—at least I hoped it was rust—
and a jumbled collection of stoppered bottles and jugs. One of the
jars had cracked, and a fine white dust like plaster of Paris lay over
everything in the chest.

"This is what Mr. Hunter, the surgeon, had with him, ma'am,"
he said. "Will you have use for it?"

"God knows," I said, peering into the chest. "But I'll have a
look. Have someone else fetch it up to the sickbay, though, Elias. I
need you to come and speak firmly to the cook."

As I oversaw the scrubbing of the tween-decks with boiling
seawater, my mind was occupied with several distinct trains of
thought.

First, I was mentally charting the necessary steps to take in
combating the disease. Two men, far gone from dehydration and
malaise, had died during the removal from the tween-decks, and
now lay at the far end of the afterdeck, where the sailmaker was
industriously stitching them into their hammocks for burial, a pair

of round shot sewn in at their feet. Four more weren't going to make it through the night. The remaining forty-five had chances ranging from excellent to slim; with luck and skill, I might save most of them. But how many new cases were brewing, undetected, among the remaining crew?

Huge quantities of water were boiling in the galley at my order; hot seawater for cleansing, boiled fresh water for drinking. I made another tick on my mental list; I must see Mrs. Johansen, she of the milch goats, and arrange for the milk to be sterilized as well.

I must interview the galley hands about their duties; if a single source of infection could be found and isolated, it would do a lot to halt the spread of the disease. Tick.

All of the available alcohol on the ship was being gathered in the sickbay, to the profound horror of Mr. Overholt. It could be used in its present form, but it would be better to have purified alcohol. Could a means be found of distilling it? Check with the purser. Tick.

All the hammocks must be boiled and dried before the healthy hands slept in them. That would have to be done quickly, before the next watch went to its rest. Send Elias for a crew of swabbers and sweepers; laundry duty seemed most in their line. Tick.

Under the growing mental list of necessities were vague but continuing thoughts of the mysterious Tompkins and his unknown information. Whatever it was, it had not resulted in our changing course to return to the *Artemis*. Either Captain Leonard had not taken it seriously, or he was simply too eager to get to Jamaica to allow anything to hinder his progress.

I had paused for a moment by the rail, to organize my thoughts. I pushed back the hair from my forehead, and lifted my face to the cleansing wind, letting it blow away the stench of sickness. Puffs of ill-smelling steam rose from the nearby hatchway, from the hot-water cleansing going on below. It would be better down there when they had finished, but a long way from fresh air.

I looked out over the rail, hoping vainly for the glimpse of a sail, but the *Porpoise* was alone, the *Artemis*—and Jamie—left far behind.

I pushed away the sudden rush of loneliness and panic. I must speak soon with Captain Leonard. Answers to two, at least, of the problems that concerned me lay with him; the possible source of the typhoid outbreak—and the role of the unknown Mr. Tompkins in Jamie's affairs. But for the moment, there were more pressing matters.

"Elias!" I called, knowing he would be somewhere within reach of my voice. "Take me to Mrs. Johansen and the goats, please."

47

Plague Ship

Two days later, I had still not found time to speak to Captain Leonard. Twice, I had gone to his cabin, but found the young Captain gone or unavailable—taking position, I was told, or consulting charts, or otherwise engaged in some bit of sailing arcana.

Mr. Overholt had taken to avoiding me and my insatiable demands, locking himself in his cabin with a pomander of dried sage and hyssop tied round his neck to ward off plague. The able-bodied crewmen assigned to the work of cleaning and shifting had been lethargic and dubious at first, but I had chivvied and scolded, glared and shouted, stamped my foot and shrieked, and got them gradually moving. I felt more like a sheepdog than a doctor—snapping and growling at their heels, and hoarse now with the effort.

It was working, though; there was a new feeling of hope and purpose among the crew—I could feel it. Four new deaths today, and ten new cases reporting, but the sounds of groaning distress from the tween-decks were much less, and the faces of the still-healthy showed the relief that comes of doing something—anything. I had so far failed to find the source of the contagion. If I could do that, and prevent any fresh outbreaks, I might—just possibly—halt the devastation within a week, while the *Porpoise* still had hands enough to sail her.

A quick canvass of the surviving crew had turned up two men pressed from a county jail where they had been imprisoned for brewing illicit liquor. I had seized on these gratefully and put them to work building a still in which—to the horror of the crew—half the ship's store of rum was being distilled into pure alcohol for disinfection.

I had posted one of the surviving midshipmen by the entrance to the sick bay and another by the galley, each armed with a basin of pure alcohol and instructions to see that no one went in or came out without dipping their hands. Beside each midshipman stood a marine with his rifle, charged with the duty of seeing that no one should drink the grimy contents of the barrel into which the used alcohol was emptied when it became too filthy to be used any longer.

In Mrs. Johansen, the gunner's wife, I had found an unexpected ally. An intelligent woman in her thirties, she had understood—despite her having only a few words of broken English, and my having no Swedish at all—what I wanted done, and had done it.

If Elias was my right hand, Annekje Johansen was the left. She had single-handedly taken over the responsibility of scalding the goats' milk, patiently pounding hard biscuit—removing the weevils as she did so—to be mixed with it, and feeding the resulting mixture to those hands strong enough to digest it.

Her own husband, the chief gunner, was one of the victims of the typhoid, but he fortunately seemed one of the lighter cases, and I had every hope that he might recover—as much because of his wife's devoted nursing as because of his own hardy constitution.

"Ma'am, Ruthven says as somebody's been a-drinking of the pure alcohol again." Elias Pound popped up at my elbow, his round pink face looking drawn and wan, substantially thinned by the pressures of the last few days.

I said something extremely bad, and his brown eyes widened.

"Sorry," I said. I wiped the back of a hand across my brow, trying to get my hair out of my eyes. "Don't mean to offend your tender ears, Elias."

"Oh, I've heard it before, ma'am," Elias assured me. "Just not from a lady, like."

"I'm not a lady, Elias," I said tiredly. "I'm a doctor. Have someone go and search the ship for whoever it was; they'll likely be unconscious by now." He nodded and whirled on one foot.

"I'll look in the cable tier," he said. "That's where they usually hide when they're drunk."

This was the fourth in the last three days. Despite all guards set over the still and the purified alcohol, the hands, living on half their usual daily ration of grog, were so desperate for drink that they contrived somehow to get at the pure grain alcohol meant for sterilization.

"Goodness, Mrs. Malcolm," the purser had said, shaking his bald head when I complained about the problem. "Seamen will drink *anything*, ma'am! Spoilt plum brandy, peaches mashed inside a rubber boot and left to ferment—why, I've even known a hand caught stealing the old bandages from the surgeon's quarters and soaking them, in hopes of getting a whiff of alcohol. No, ma'am, telling them that drinking it will kill them certainly won't stop them."

Kill them it did. One of the four men who had drunk it had died; two more were in their own boarded-off section of the sick bay, deeply comatose. If they survived, they were likely to be permanently brain-damaged.

"Not that being on a bloody floating hellhole like this isn't likely to brain-damage anyone," I remarked bitterly to a tern who alighted on the rail nearby. "As if it isn't enough, trying to save half the miserable lot from typhoid, now the other half is trying to kill themselves with my alcohol! Damn the bloody lot of them!"

The tern cocked its head, decided I was not edible, and flew away. The ocean stretched empty all around—before us, where the unknown West Indies concealed Young Ian's fate, and behind, where Jamie and the *Artemis* had long since vanished. And me in the middle, with six hundred drink-mad English sailors and a hold full of inflamed bowels.

I stood fuming for a moment, then turned with decision toward the forward gangway. I didn't care if Captain Leonard was personally pumping the bilges, he was going to talk to me.

I stopped just inside the door of the cabin. It was not yet noon, but the Captain was asleep, head pillowed on his forearms, on top of an outspread book. The quill had fallen from his fingers, and the glass inkstand, cleverly held in its anchored bracket, swayed gently with the motion of the ship. His face was turned to the side, cheek pressed flat on his arm. Despite the heavy beard stubble, he looked absurdly young.

I turned, meaning to come back later, but in moving, brushed against the locker, where a stack of books was precariously balanced amid a rubble of papers, navigational instruments, and half-rolled charts. The top volume fell with a thump to the deck.

The sound was scarcely audible above the general sounds of creaking, flapping, whining rigging, and shouting that made up the background of life on shipboard, but it brought him awake, blinking and looking startled.

"Mrs. Fra—Mrs. Malcolm!" he said. He rubbed a hand over his face, and shook his head quickly, trying to wake himself. "What—that is—you required something?"

"I didn't mean to wake you," I said. "But I do need more alcohol—if necessary, I can use straight rum—and you really must speak to the hands, to see if there is some way of stopping them trying to drink the distilled alcohol. We've had another that's poisoned himself today. And if there's any way of bringing more fresh air down to the sick bay . . ." I stopped, seeing that I was overwhelming him.

He blinked and scratched, slowly pulling his thoughts into order. The buttons on his sleeve had left two round red imprints on his cheek, and his hair was flattened on that side.

"I see," he said, rather stupidly. Then, as he began to wake, his expression cleared. "Yes. Of course. I will give orders to have a windsail rigged, to bring more air below. As for the alcohol—I must beg leave to consult the purser, as I do not myself know our present capacities in that regard." He turned and took a breath, as though to shout, but then remembered that his steward was no longer within earshot, being now below in the sick bay. Just then, the *ting* of the ship's bell came faintly from above.

"I beg your pardon, Mrs. Malcolm," he said, politeness recovered. "It is nearly noon; I must go and take our position. I will send the purser to you, should you care to remain here for a moment."

"Thank you." I sat down in the chair he had just vacated. He turned to go, making an attempt to straighten the too-large braided coat over his shoulders.

"Captain Leonard?" I said, moved by a sudden impulse. He turned back, questioning.

"If you don't mind my asking—how old are you?"

He blinked and his face tightened, but he answered me.

"I am nineteen, ma'am. Your servant, ma'am." And with that, he vanished through the door. I could hear him in the companionway, calling out in a voice half-cracked with fatigue.

Nineteen! I sat quite still, paralyzed with shock. I had thought him very young, but not nearly that young. His face weathered from exposure and lined with strain and sleeplessness, he had looked to be at least in his mid-twenties. *My God!* I thought, appalled. *He's no more than a baby!*

Nineteen. Just Brianna's age. And to be suddenly thrust into command not only of a ship—and not just a ship, but an English man-of-war—and not merely a man-of-war, but one with a plague aboard that had deprived her suddenly of a quarter of her crew and virtually all her command—I felt the fright and fury that had bubbled inside me for the last few days begin to ebb, as I realized that the high-handedness that had led him to kidnap me was in fact not arrogance or ill-judgment, but the result of sheer desperation.

He had to have help, he had said. Well, he was right, and I was it. I took a deep breath, visualizing the mess I had left behind in the sick bay. That was mine, and mine alone, to do the best I could with.

Captain Leonard had left the logbook open on the desk, his entry half-complete. There was a small damp spot on the page; he had drooled slightly in his sleep. In a spasm of irritated pity, I flipped over the page, wishing to hide this further evidence of his vulnerability.

My eye caught a word on the new page, and I stopped, a chill snaking down from the nape of my neck as I remembered something. When I had wakened him unexpectedly, the captain had started up, seen me, and said, "Mrs. Fra—" before catching himself. And the name on the page before me, the word that had caught my attention, was "Fraser." He knew who I was—and who Jamie was.

I rose quickly and shut the door, dropping the bolt. At least I would have warning if anyone came. Then I sat down at the Captain's desk, pressed flat the pages, and began to read.

I flipped back to find the record of the meeting with the *Artemis,* three days before. Captain Leonard's entries were distinct from those of his predecessor, and mostly quite brief—not surprising, considering how much he had had to deal with of late. Most entries contained only the usual navigational information, with a brief note of the names of those men who had died since the previous day. The meeting with the *Artemis* was noted, though, and my own presence.

> 3 February 1767. Met near eight bells with *Artemis,* a small two-masted brig under French colors. Hailed her and requested the assistance of her surgeon, C. Malcolm, who was taken on board and remains with us to assist with the sick.

C. Malcolm, eh? No mention of my being a woman; perhaps he thought it irrelevant, or wished to avoid any inquiries over the propriety of his actions. I went on to the next entry.

> 4 February 1767. I have rec'd information this day from Harry Tompkins, able seaman, that the supercargo of the brig *Artemis* is known to him as a criminal by the name of James Fraser, known also by the names of Jamie Roy and of Alexandr Malcolm. This Fraser is a seditionist, and a notorious smuggler, for whose capture a substantial reward is offered by the King's Customs. Information was received from Tompkins after we had parted company with *Artemis;* I thought it not expeditious to pursue *Artemis,* as we are ordered with all possible dispatch for Jamaica, because of our passenger. However, as I have promised to return the *Artemis*'s surgeon to them there, Fraser may be arrested at that time.
>
> Two men dead of the plague—which the *Artemis*'s surgeon informs me is the Typhoide. Jno. Jaspers, able seaman, DD, Harty Kepple, cook's mate, DD.

That was all; the next day's entry was confined entirely to navigation and the recording of the death of six men, all with "DD" written beside their names. I wondered what it meant, but was too distracted to worry about it.

I heard steps coming down the passageway, and barely got the bolt lifted before the purser's knock sounded on the door. I scarcely heard Mr. Overholt's apologies; my mind was too busy trying to make sense of this new revelation.

Who in blinking, bloody hell was this man Tompkins? No one I had ever seen or heard about, I was sure, and yet he obviously knew a dangerous amount about Jamie's activities. Which led to two questions: How had an English seaman come by such information—and who else knew it?

". . . cut the grog rations further, to give you an additional cask of rum," Mr. Overholt was saying dubiously. "The hands won't like it, but we might manage; we're only two weeks out of Jamaica now."

"Whether they like it or not, I need the alcohol more than they need grog," I answered brusquely. "If they complain too much, tell them if I don't have the rum, none of them may *make* it to Jamaica."

Mr. Overholt sighed, and wiped small beads of sweat from his shiny brow.

"I'll tell them, ma'am," he said, too beaten down to object.

"Fine. Oh, Mr. Overholt?" He turned back, questioning. "What does the legend 'DD' mean? I saw the Captain write it in his log."

A small flicker of humor lighted in the purser's deep-sunk eyes.

"It means 'Discharged, Dead,' ma'am," he replied. "The only sure way for most of us, of leaving His Majesty's Navy."

As I oversaw the bathing of bodies and the constant infusions of sweetened water and boiled milk, my mind continued to work on the problem of the unknown Tompkins.

I knew nothing of the man, save his voice. He might be one of the faceless horde overhead, the silhouettes that I saw in the rigging when I came up on deck for air, or one of the hurrying anonymous bodies, hurtling up and down the decks in a vain effort to do the work of three men.

I would meet him, of course, if he became infected; I knew the names of each patient in the sick bay. But I could hardly allow the matter to wait, in the rather ghoulish hope that Tompkins would contract typhoid. At last I made up my mind to ask; the man presumably knew who I was, anyway. Even if he found out that I had been asking about him, it was unlikely to do any harm.

Elias was the natural place to begin. I waited until the end of the day to ask, trusting to fatigue to dull his natural curiosity.

"Tompkins?" The boy's round face drew together in a brief

frown, then cleared. "Oh, yes, ma'am. One o' the forecastle hands."

"Where did he come aboard, do you know?" There was no good way of accounting for this sudden interest in a man I had never met, but luckily, Elias was much too tired to wonder about it.

"Oh," he said vaguely, "at Spithead, I think. Or—no! I remember now, 'twas Edinburgh." He rubbed his knuckles under his nose to stifle a yawn. "That's it, Edinburgh. I wouldn' remember, only he was a pressed man, and a unholy fuss he made about it, claimin' as how they couldn' press him, he was protected, account of he worked for Sir Percival Turner, in the Customs." The yawn got the better of him and he gaped widely, then subsided. "But he didn' have no written protection from Sir Percival," he concluded, blinking, "so there wasn' nothing to be done."

"A Customs agent, was he?" *That* went quite some way toward explaining things, all right.

"Mm-hm. Yes, mum, I mean." Elias was trying manfully to stay awake, but his glazing eyes were fixed on the swaying lantern at the end of the sick bay, and he was swaying with it.

"You go on to bed, Elias," I said, taking pity on him. "I'll finish here."

He shook his head quickly, trying to shake off sleep.

"Oh, no, ma'am! I ain't sleepy, not a bit!" He reached clumsily for the cup and bottle I held. "You give me that, mum, and go to rest yourself." He would not be moved, but stubbornly insisted on helping to administer the last round of water before staggering off to his cot.

I was nearly as tired as Elias by the time we finished, but sleep would not come. I lay in the dead surgeon's cabin, staring up at the shadowy beam above my head, listening to the creak and rumble of the ship about me, wondering.

So Tompkins worked for Sir Percival. And Sir Percival assuredly knew that Jamie was a smuggler. But was there more to it than that? Tompkins knew Jamie by sight. How? And if Sir Percival had been willing to tolerate Jamie's clandestine activities in return for bribes, then—well, perhaps none of those bribes had made it to Tompkins's pockets. But in that case . . . and what about the ambush at Arbroath cove? Was there a traitor among the smugglers? And if so . . .

My thoughts were losing coherence, spinning in circles like the revolutions of a dying top. The powdered white face of Sir Percival faded into the purple mask of the hanged Customs agent on the Arbroath road, and the gold and red flames of an exploding lantern lit the crevices of my mind. I rolled onto my stomach, clutching the pillow to my chest, the last thought in my mind that I must find Tompkins.

As it was, Tompkins found me. For more than two days, the situation in the sick bay was too pressing for me to leave for more than the barest space of time. On the third day, though, matters seemed easier, and I retired to the surgeon's cabin, intending to wash myself and rest briefly before the midday drum beat for the noon meal.

I was lying on the cot, a cool cloth over my tired eyes, when I heard the sound of bumping and voices in the passage outside my door. A tentative knock sounded on my door, and an unfamiliar voice said, "Mrs. Malcolm? There's been a h'accident, if you please, ma'am."

I swung open the door to find two seamen supporting a third, who stood storklike on one leg, his face white with shock and pain.

It took no more than a single glance for me to know whom I was looking at. The man's face was ridged down one side with the livid scars of a bad burn, and the twisted eyelid on that side exposed the milky lens of a blind eye, had I needed any further confirmation that here stood the one-eyed seaman Young Ian had thought he'd killed, lank brown hair grew back from a balding brow to a scrawny pigtail that drooped over one shoulder, exposing a pair of large, transparent ears.

"Mr. Tompkins," I said with certainty, and his remaining eye widened in surprise. "Put him down over there, please."

The men deposited Tompkins on a stool by the wall, and went back to their work; the ship was too shorthanded to allow for distraction. Heart beating heavily, I knelt down to examine the wounded leg.

He knew who I was, all right; I had seen it in his face when I

opened the door. There was a great deal of tension in the leg under
my hand. The injury was gory, but not serious, given suitable care;
a deep gash scored down the calf of the leg. It had bled substantially, but there were no deep arteries cut; it had been well-
wrapped with a piece of someone's shirt, and the bleeding had
nearly stopped when I unwound the homemade bandage.

"How did you do this, Mr. Tompkins?" I asked, standing up
and reaching for the bottle of alcohol. He glanced up, his single
eye alert and wary.

"Splinter wound, ma'am," he answered, in the nasal tones I
had heard once before. "A spar broke as I was a-standing on it."
The tip of his tongue stole out, furtively wetting his lower lip.

"I see." I turned and flipped open the lid of my empty medicine box, pretending to survey the available remedies. I studied
him out of the corner of one eye, while I tried to think how best to
approach him. He was on his guard; tricking him into revelations
or winning his trust was clearly out of the question.

My eyes flicked over the tabletop, seeking inspiration. And
found it. With a mental apology to the shade of Aesculapius the
physician, I picked up the late surgeon's bone-saw, a wicked thing
some eighteen inches long, of rust-flecked steel. I looked at this
thoughtfully, turned, and laid the toothed edge of the instrument
gently against the injured leg, just above the knee. I smiled charmingly into the seaman's terrified single eye.

"Mr. Tompkins," I said, "let us talk frankly."

An hour later, able-bodied seaman Tompkins had been restored
to his hammock, stitched and bandaged, shaking in every limb, but
able-bodied still. For my part, I felt a little shaky as well.

Tompkins was, as he had insisted to the press-gang in Edinburgh, an agent of Sir Percival Turner. In that capacity, he went
about the docks and warehouses of all the shipping ports in the
Firth of Forth, from Culross and Donibristle to Restalrig and Mus-
selburgh, picking up gossip and keeping his beady eye sharp-
peeled to catch any evidence of unlawful activity.

The attitude of Scots toward English tax laws being what it was,
there was no lack of such activity to report. What was done with
such reports, though, varied. Small smugglers, caught red-handed
with a bottle or two of unbonded rum or whisky, might be sum-

marily arrested, tried and convicted, and sentenced to anything from penal servitude to transportation, with forfeiture of all their property to the Crown.

The bigger fish, though, were reserved to Sir Percival's private judgment. In other words, allowed to pay substantial bribes for the privilege of continuing their operations under the blind eye (here Tompkins laughed sardonically, touching the ruined side of his face) of the King's agents.

"Sir Percival's got ambitions, see?" While not noticeably relaxed, Tompkins had at least unbent enough to lean forward, one eye narrowing as he gestured in explanation. "He's in with Dundas and all them. Everything goes right, and he might have a peerage, not just a knighthood, eh? But that'll take more than money."

One thing that could help was some spectacular demonstration of competence and service to the Crown.

"As in the sort of arrest that might make 'em sit up and take notice, eh? Ooh! That smarts, missus. You sure of what you're a-doing of, there?" Tompkins squinted dubiously downward, to where I was sponging the site of the injury with dilute alcohol.

"I'm sure," I said. "Go on, then. I suppose a simple smuggler wouldn't have been good enough, no matter how big?"

Evidently not. However, when word had reached Sir Percival that there might just possibly be a major political criminal within his grasp, the old gentleman had nearly blown a gasket with excitement.

"But sedition's a harder thing to prove than smuggling, eh? You catch one of the little fish with the goods, and they're saying not a thing will lead you further on. Idealists, them seditionists," Tompkins said, shaking his head with disgust. "Never rat on each other, they don't."

"So you didn't know who you were looking for?" I stood and took one of my cat-gut sutures from its jar, threading it through a needle. I caught Tompkins's apprehensive look, but did nothing to allay his anxiety. I wanted him anxious—and voluble.

"No, we didn't know who the big fish was—not until another of Sir Percival's agents had the luck to tumble to one of Fraser's associates, what gave 'em the tip he was Malcolm the printer, and told his real name. Then it all come clear, o' course."

My heart skipped a beat.

"Who was the associate?" I asked. The names and faces of the six smugglers darted through my mind—little fish. Not idealists, any of them. But to which of them was loyalty no bar?

"I don't know. No, it's true, missus, I swear! Ow!" he said frantically as I jabbed the needle under the skin.

"I'm not trying to hurt you," I assured him, in as false a voice as I could muster. "I have to stitch the wound, though."

"Oh! Ow! I don't know, to be sure I don't! I'd tell, if I did, as God's my witness!"

"I'm sure you would," I said, intent on my stitching.

"Oh! Please, missus! Stop! Just for a moment! All I know is it was an Englishman! That's all!"

I stopped, and stared up at him. "An Englishman?" I said blankly.

"Yes, missus. That's what Sir Percival said." He looked down at me, tears trembling on the lashes of both his eyes. I took the final stitch, as gently as I could, and tied the suture knot. Without speaking, I got up, poured a small tot of brandy from my private bottle, and handed it to him.

He gulped it gratefully, and seemed much restored in consequence. Whether out of gratitude, or sheer relief for the end of the ordeal, he told me the rest of the story. In search of evidence to support a charge of sedition, he had gone to the printshop in Carfax Close.

"I know what happened there," I assured him. I turned his face toward the light, examining the burn scars. "Is it still painful?"

"No, Missus, but it hurt precious bad for some time," he said. Being incapacitated by his injuries, Tompkins had taken no part in the ambush at Arbroath cove, but he had heard—"not direct-like, but I heard, you know," he said, with a shrewd nod of the head—what had happened.

Sir Percival had given Jamie warning of an ambush, to lessen the chances of Jamie's thinking him involved in the affair, and possibly revealing the details of their financial arrangements in quarters where such revelations would be detrimental to Sir Percival's interests.

At the same time, Sir Percival had learned—from the associate, the mysterious Englishman—of the fallback arrangement with the French delivery vessel, and had arranged the grave-ambush on the beach at Arbroath.

"But what about the Customs officer who was killed on the road?" I asked sharply. I couldn't repress a small shudder, at memory of that dreadful face. "Who did that? There were only five men among the smugglers who could possibly have done it, and none of them are Englishmen!"

Tompkins rubbed a hand over his mouth; he seemed to be debating the wisdom of telling me or not. I picked up the brandy bottle and set it by his elbow.

"Why, I'm much obliged, Missus Fraser! You're a true Christian, missus, and so I shall tell anyone who asks!"

"Skip the testimonials," I said dryly. "Just tell me what you know about the Customs officer."

He filled the cup and drained it, sipping slowly. Then, with a sigh of satisfaction, he set it down and licked his lips.

"It wasn't none of the smugglers done him in, missus. It was his own mate."

"What!" I jerked back, startled, but he nodded, blinking his good eye in token of sincerity.

"That's right, missus. There was two of 'em, wasn't there? Well, the one of them had his instructions, didn't he?"

The instructions had been to wait until whatever smugglers escaped the ambush on the beach had reached the road, whereupon the Customs officer was to drop a noose over his partner's head in the dark and strangle him swiftly, then string him up and leave him as evidence of the smugglers' murderous wrath.

"But why?" I said, bewildered and horrified. "What was the point of doing that?"

"Do you not see?" Tompkins looked surprised, as though the logic of the situation should be obvious. "We'd failed to get the evidence from the printshop that would have proved the case of sedition against Fraser, and with the shop burnt to the ground, no possibility of another chance. Nor had we ever caught Fraser red-handed with the goods himself, only some of the small fish who worked for him. One of the other agents thought he'd a clue where the stuff was kept, but something happened to him—perhaps Fraser caught him or bought him off, for he disappeared one day in November, and wasn't heard of again, nor the hiding place for the contraband, neither."

"I see." I swallowed, thinking of the man who had accosted me on the stairs of the brothel. What had become of that cask of crème de menthe? "But—"

"Well, I'm telling you, missus, just you wait." Tompkins raised a monitory hand. "So—here's Sir Percival, knowing as he's got a rare case, with a man's not only one of the biggest smugglers on the Firth, *and* the author of some of the most first-rate seditious material it's been my privilege to see, *but* is also a pardoned Jacobite traitor, whose name will make the trial a sensation from one end of the kingdom to the other. The only trouble being"—he shrugged—"as there's no evidence."

It began to make a hideous sort of sense, as Tompkins explained the plan. The murder of a Customs officer killed in pursuit of duty would not only make any smuggler arrested for the crime subject to a capital charge, but was the sort of heinous crime that would cause a major public outcry. The matter-of-fact acceptance that smugglers enjoyed from the populace would not protect them in a matter of such callous villainy.

"Your Sir Percival has got the makings of a really first-class son of a bitch," I observed. Tompkins nodded meditatively, blinking into his cup.

"Well, you've the right of it there, missus, I'll not say you're wrong."

"And the Customs officer who was killed—I suppose he was just a convenience?"

Tompkins sniggered, with a fine spray of brandy. His one eye seemed to be having some trouble focusing.

"Oh, very convenient, missus, more ways than one. Don't you grieve none on his account. There was a good many folk glad enough to see Tom Oakie swing—and not the least of 'em, Sir Percival."

"I see." I finished fastening the bandage about his calf. It was getting late; I would have to get back to the sick bay soon.

"I'd better call someone to take you to your hammock," I said, taking the nearly empty bottle from his unresisting hand. "You should rest your leg for at least three days; tell your officer I said you can't go aloft until I've taken out the stitches."

"I'll do that, missus, and I thank you for your kindness to a poor unfortunate sailor." Tompkins made an abortive attempt to stand, looking surprised when he failed. I got a hand under his armpit and heaved, getting him on his feet, and—he declining my offer to summon him assistance—helped him to the door.

"You needn't worry about Harry Tompkins, missus," he said, weaving unsteadily into the corridor. He turned and gave me an exaggerated wink. "Old Harry always ends up all right, no matter what." I looked at him, with his long nose, pink-tipped from liquor, his large, transparent ears, and his single sly brown eye. It came to me suddenly what he reminded me of.

"When were you born, Mr. Tompkins?" I asked.

He blinked for a moment, uncomprehending, but then said, "The Year of Our Lord 1713, missus. Why?"

"No reason," I said, and waved him off, watching as he caromed slowly down the corridor, dropping out of sight at the ladder like a bag of oats. I would have to check with Mr. Willoughby to be sure, but at the moment, I would have wagered my chemise that 1713 had been a Year of the Rat.

48

Moment of Grace

Over the next few days, a routine set in, as it does in even the most desperate circumstances, provided that they continue long enough. The hours after a battle are urgent and chaotic, with men's lives hanging on a second's action. Here a doctor can be heroic, knowing for certain that the wound just stanched has saved a life, that the quick intervention will save a limb. But in an epidemic, there is none of that.

Then come the long days of constant watching and battles fought on the field of germs—and with no weapons suited to that field, it can be no more than a battle of delay, doing the small things that may not help but must be done, over and over and over again, fighting the invisible enemy of disease, in the tenuous hope that the body can be supported long enough to outlast its attacker.

To fight disease without medicine is to push against a shadow; a darkness that spreads as inexorably as night. I had been fighting for nine days, and forty-six more men were dead.

Still, I rose each day at dawn, splashed water into my grainy eyes, and went once more to the field of war, unarmed with anything save persistence—and a barrel of alcohol.

There were some victories, but even these left a bitter taste in my mouth. I found the likely source of infection—one of the messmates, a man named Howard. First serving on board as a member of one of the gun crews, Howard had been transferred to galley duty six weeks before, the result of an accident with a recoiling gun-carriage that had crushed several fingers.

Howard had served the gun room, and the first known case of

the disease—taken from the incomplete records of the dead surgeon, Mr. Hunter—was one of the marines who messed there. Four more cases, all from the gun room, and then it had begun to spread, as infected but still ambulatory men left the deadly contamination smeared in the ship's heads, to be picked up there and passed to the crew at large.

Howard's admission that he had seen sickness like this before, on other ships where he had served, was enough to clinch the matter. However, the cook, shorthanded as everyone else aboard, had declined absolutely to part with a valuable hand, only because of "a goddamned female's silly notion!"

Elias could not persuade him, and I had been obliged to summon the Captain himself, who—misunderstanding the nature of the disturbance, had arrived with several armed marines. There was a most unpleasant scene in the galley, and Howard was removed to the brig—the only place of certain quarantine—protesting in bewilderment, and demanding to know his crime.

As I came up from the galley, the sun was going down into the ocean in a blaze that paved the western sea with gold like the streets of Heaven. I stopped for a moment, just a moment, transfixed by the sight.

It had happened many times before, but it always took me by surprise. Always in the midst of great stress, wading waist-deep in trouble and sorrow, as doctors do, I would glance out a window, open a door, look into a face, and there it would be, unexpected and unmistakable. A moment of peace.

The light spread from the sky to the ship, and the great horizon was no longer a blank threat of emptiness, but the habitation of joy. For a moment, I lived in the center of the sun, warmed and cleansed, and the smell and sight of sickness fell away; the bitterness lifted from my heart.

I never looked for it, gave it no name; yet I knew it always, when the gift of peace came. I stood quite still for the moment that it lasted, thinking it strange and not strange that grace should find me here, too.

Then the light shifted slightly and the moment passed, leaving me as it always did, with the lasting echo of its presence. In a reflex of acknowledgment, I crossed myself and went below, my tarnished armor faintly gleaming.

Elias Pound died of the typhoid four days later. It was a virulent
infection; he came to the sick bay heavy-eyed with fever and
wincing at the light; six hours later he was delirious and unable to
rise. The next dawn he pressed his cropped round head against my
bosom, called me "Mother," and died in my arms.

I did what had to be done throughout the day, and stood by
Captain Leonard at sunset, when he read the burial service. The
body of Midshipman Pound was consigned to the sea, wrapped in
his hammock.

I declined the Captain's invitation to dinner, and went instead to
sit in a remote corner of the afterdeck, next to one of the great
guns, where I could look out over the water, showing my face to
no one. The sun went down in gold and glory, succeeded by a
night of starred velvet, but there was no moment of grace, no
peace in either sight for me.

As the darkness settled over the ship, all her movements began
to slow. I leaned my head against the gun, the polished metal cool
under my cheek. A seaman passed me at a fast walk, intent on his
duties, and then I was alone.

I ached desperately; my head throbbed, my back was stiff and
my feet swollen, but none of these was of any significance, compared to the deeper ache that knotted my heart.

Any doctor hates to lose a patient. Death is the enemy, and to
lose someone in your care to the clutch of the dark angel is to be
vanquished yourself, to feel the rage of betrayal and impotence,
beyond the common, human grief of loss and the horror of death's
finality. I had lost twenty-three men between dawn and sunset of
this day. Elias was only the first.

Several had died as I sponged their bodies or held their hands;
others, alone in their hammocks, had died uncomforted even by a
touch, because I could not reach them in time. I thought I had
resigned myself to the realities of this time, but knowing—even as
I held the twitching body of an eighteen-year-old seaman as his
bowels dissolved in blood and water—that penicillin would have
saved most of them, and I had none, was galling as an ulcer, eating
at my soul.

The box of syringes and ampules had been left behind on the
Artemis, in the pocket of my spare skirt. If I had had it, I could not

have used it. If I had used it, I could have saved no more than one or two. But even knowing that, I raged at the futility of it all, clenching my teeth until my jaw ached as I went from man to man, armed with nothing but boiled milk and biscuit, and my two empty hands.

My mind followed the same dizzying lines my feet had traveled earlier, seeing faces—faces contorted in anguish or smoothing slowly in the slackness of death, but all of them looking at me. At me. I lifted my futile hand and slammed it hard against the rail. I did it again, and again, scarcely feeling the sting of the blows, in a frenzy of furious rage and grief.

"Stop that!" a voice spoke behind me, and a hand seized my wrist, preventing me from slapping the rail yet again.

"Let go!" I struggled, but his grip was too strong.

"Stop," he said again, firmly. His other arm came around my waist, and he pulled me back, away from the rail. "You mustn't do that," he said. "You'll hurt yourself."

"I don't bloody care!" I wrenched against his grasp, but then slumped, defeated. What did it matter?

He let go of me then, and I turned to find myself facing a man I had never seen before. He wasn't a sailor; while his clothes were crumpled and stale with long wear, they had originally been very fine; the dove-gray coat and waistcoat had been tailored to flatter his slender frame, and the wilted lace at his throat had come from Brussels.

"Who the hell are you?" I said in astonishment. I brushed at my wet cheeks, sniffed, and made an instinctive effort to smooth down my hair. I hoped the shadows hid my face.

He smiled slightly, and handed me a handkerchief, crumpled, but clean.

"My name is Grey," he said, with a small, courtly bow. "I expect that you must be the famous Mrs. Malcolm, whose heroism Captain Leonard has been so strongly praising." I grimaced at that, and he paused.

"I am sorry," he said. "Have I said something amiss? My apologies, Madame, I had no notion of offering you offense." He looked anxious at the thought, and I shook my head.

"It is not heroic to watch men die," I said. My words were thick, and I stopped to blow my nose. "I'm just here, that's all. Thank you for the handkerchief." I hesitated, not wanting to hand the used handkerchief back to him, but not wanting simply to pocket it, either. He solved the dilemma with a dismissive wave of his hand.

"Might I do anything else for you?" He hesitated, irresolute. "A cup of water? Some brandy, perhaps?" He fumbled in his coat, drawing out a small silver pocket flask engraved with a coat of arms, which he offered to me.

I took it, with a nod of thanks, and took a swallow deep enough to make me cough. It burned down the back of my throat, but I sipped again, more cautiously this time, and felt it warm me, easing and strengthening. I breathed deeply and drank again. It helped.

"Thank you," I said, a little hoarsely, handing back the flask. That seemed somewhat abrupt, and I added, "I'd forgotten that brandy is good to drink; I've been using it to wash people in the sick bay." The statement brought back the events of the day to me with crushing vividness, and I sagged back onto the powder box where I had been sitting.

"I take it the plague continues unabated?" he asked quietly. He stood in front of me, the glow of a nearby lantern shining on his dark blond hair.

"Not unabated, no." I closed my eyes, feeling unutterably bleak. "There was only one new case today. There were four the day before, and six the day before that."

"That sounds hopeful," he observed. "As though you are defeating the disease."

I shook my head slowly. It felt dense and heavy as one of the cannonballs piled in the shallow bins by the guns.

"No. All we're doing is to stop more men being infected. There isn't a bloody thing I can do for the ones who already have it."

"Indeed." He stooped and picked up one of my hands. Surprised, I let him have it. He ran a thumb lightly over the blister where I had burned myself scalding milk, and touched my knuckles, reddened and cracked from the constant immersion in alcohol.

"You would appear to have been very active, Madame, for someone who is doing nothing," he said dryly.

"Of course I'm doing something!" I snapped, yanking my hand back. "It doesn't do any good!"

"I'm sure—" he began.

"It doesn't!" I slammed my fist on the gun, the noiseless blow seeming to symbolize the pain-filled futility of the day. "Do you know how many men I lost today? Twenty-three! I've been on my feet since dawn, elbow-deep in filth and vomit and my clothes stuck to me, and none of it's been any good! I couldn't help! Do you hear me? I couldn't help!"

His face was turned away, in shadow, but his shoulders were stiff.

"I hear you," he said quietly. "You shame me, Madame. I had kept to my cabin at the Captain's orders, but I had no idea that the circumstances were such as you describe, or I assure you that I should have come to help, in spite of them."

"Why?" I said blankly. "It isn't your job."

"Is it yours?" He swung around to face me, and I saw that he was handsome, in his late thirties, perhaps, with sensitive, fine-cut features, and large blue eyes, open in astonishment.

"Yes," I said.

He studied my face for a moment, and his own expression changed, fading from surprise to thoughtfulness.

"I see."

"No, you don't, but it doesn't matter." I pressed my fingertips hard against my brow, in the spot Mr. Willoughby had shown me, to relieve headache. "If the Captain means you to keep to your cabin, then you likely should. There are enough hands to help in the sick bay; it's just that . . . nothing helps," I ended, dropping my hands.

He walked over to the rail, a few feet away from me, and stood looking out over the expanse of dark water, sparked here and there as a random wave caught the starlight.

"I do see," he repeated, as though talking to the waves. "I had thought your distress due only to a woman's natural compassion, but I see it is something quite different." He paused, hands gripping the rail, an indistinct figure in the starlight.

"I have been a soldier, an officer," he said. "I know what it is, to hold men's lives in your hand—and to lose them."

I was quiet, and so was he. The usual shipboard sounds went on in the distance, muted by night and the lack of men to make them. At last he sighed and turned toward me again.

"What it comes to, I think, is the knowledge that you are not God." He paused, then added, softly, "And the very real regret that you cannot be."

I sighed, feeling some of the tension drain out of me. The cool wind lifted the weight of my hair from my neck, and the curling ends drifted across my face, gentle as a touch.

"Yes," I said.

He hesitated a moment, as though not knowing what to say next, then bent, picked up my hand, and kissed it, very simply, without affectation.

"Good night, Mrs. Malcolm," he said, and turned away, the sound of his footsteps loud on the deck.

He was no more than a few yards past me when a seaman, hurrying by, spotted him and stopped with a cry. It was Jones, one of the stewards.

"My Lord! You shouldn't ought to be out of your cabin, sir! The night air's mortal, and the plague loose on board—and the Captain's orders—whatever is your servant a-thinking of, sir, to let you walk about like this?"

My acquaintance nodded apologetically.

"Yes, yes, I know. I shouldn't have come up; but I thought that if I stayed in the cabin a moment longer I should be stifled altogether."

"Better stifled than dead o' the bloody flux, sir, and you'll pardon of my saying so," Jones replied sternly. My acquaintance made no remonstrance to this, but merely murmured something and disappeared in the shadows of the afterdeck.

I reached out a hand and grasped Jones by the sleeve as he passed, causing him to start, with a wordless yelp of alarm.

"Oh! Mrs. Malcolm," he said, coming to earth, a bony hand splayed across his chest. "Christ, I did think you was a ghost, mum, begging your pardon."

"I beg yours," I said, politely. "I only wanted to ask—who was the man you were just talking to?"

"Oh, him?" Jones twisted about to look over his shoulder, but the aptly named Mr. Grey had long since vanished. "Why, that's Lord John Grey, mum, him as is the new governor of Jamaica." He frowned censoriously in the direction taken by my acquaintance. "He ain't supposed to be up here; the Captain's give strict orders he's to stay safe below, out o' harm's way. All we need's to come into port with a dead political aboard, and there'll be the devil to pay, mum, savin' your presence."

He shook his head disapprovingly, then turned to me with a bob of the head.

"You'll be retiring, mum? Shall I bring you down a nice cup of tea and maybe a bit o' biscuit?"

"No, thank you, Jones," I said. "I'll go and check the sick bay again before I go to bed. I don't need anything."

"Well, you do, mum, and you just say. Anytime. Good night to you, mum." He touched his forelock briefly and hurried off.

I stood at the rail alone for a moment before going below, drawing in deep breaths of the clean, fresh air. It would be a good many hours yet until dawn; the stars burned bright and clear over my head, and I realized, quite suddenly, that the moment of grace I had wordlessly prayed for had come, after all.

"You're right," I said at last, aloud, to the sea and sky. "A sunset wouldn't have been enough. Thank you," I added, and went below.

49

Land Ho!

I t's true, what the sailors say. You can smell land, a long time
before you see it.

Despite the long voyage, the goat pen in the hold was a
surprisingly pleasant place. By now, the fresh straw had been
exhausted, and the goats' hooves clicked restlessly to and fro on
bare boards. Still, the heaps of manure were swept up daily, and
neatly piled in baskets to be heaved overboard, and Annekje Johansen brought dry armloads of hay to the manger each morning.
There was a strong smell of goat, but it was a clean, animal scent,
and quite pleasant by contrast with the stench of unwashed sailors.

"Komma, komma, komma, dyr get," she crooned, luring a yearling within reach with a twiddled handful of hay. The animal
stretched out cautious lips, and was promptly seized by the neck
and pulled forward, its head secured under Annekje's brawny arm.

"Ticks, is it?" I asked, coming forward to help. Annekje
looked up and gave me her broad, gap-toothed smile.

"God Morgon, Mrs. Claire," she said. *"Ja,* tick. Here." She took
the young goat's drooping ear in one hand and turned up the silky
edge to show me the blueberry bulge of a blood-gorged tick, burrowed deep in the tender skin.

She clutched the goat to hold it still, and dug into the ear,
pinching the tick viciously between her nails. She pulled it free
with a twist, and the goat blatted and kicked, a tiny spot of blood
welling from its ear where the tick had been detached.

"Wait," I said, when she would have released the animal. She
glanced at me, curious, but kept her hold and nodded. I took the

bottle of alcohol I wore slung at my belt like a sidearm, and poured a few drops on the ear. It was soft and tender, the tiny veins clearly visible beneath the satin skin. The goat's square-pupiled eyes bulged farther and its tongue stuck out in agitation as it bleated.

"No sore ear," I said, in explanation, and Annekje nodded in approval.

Then the goatling was free, and went plunging back into the herd, to butt its head against its mother's side in a frantic search for milky reassurance. Annekje looked about for the discarded tick and found it lying on the deck, tiny legs helpless to move its swollen body. She smashed it casually under the heel of her shoe, leaving a tiny dark blotch on the board.

"We come to land?" I asked, and she nodded, with a wide, happy smile. She waved expansively upward, where sunlight fell through the grating overhead.

"*Ja.* Smell?" she said, sniffing vigorously in illustration. She beamed. "Land, *ja*! Water, grass. Is goot, goot!"

"I need to go to land," I said, watching her carefully. "Go quiet. Secret. Not tell."

"Ah?" Annekje's eyes widened, and she looked at me speculatively. "Not tell Captain, *ja*?"

"Not tell anyone," I said, nodding hard. "You can help?"

She was quiet for a moment, thinking. A big, placid woman, she reminded me of her own goats, adapting cheerfully to the queer life of shipboard, enjoying the pleasures of hay and warm company, thriving despite the lurching deck and stuffy shadows of the hold.

With that same air of capable adaptation, she looked up at me and nodded calmly.

"*Ja,* I help."

It was past midday when we anchored off what one of the midshipmen told me was Watlings Island.

I looked over the rail with considerable curiosity. This flat island, with its wide white beaches and lines of low palms, had once been called San Salvador. Renamed for the present in honor of a notorious buccaneer of the last century, this dot of land was presumably Christopher Columbus's first sight of the New World.

I had the substantial advantage over Columbus of having known for a fact that the land was here, but still I felt a faint echo of the joy and relief that the sailors of those tiny wooden caravels had felt at that first landfall.

Long enough on a rolling ship, and you forget what it is to walk on land. Getting sea legs, they call it. It's a metamorphosis, this leg-getting, like the change from tadpole to frog, a painless shift from one element to another. But the smell and sight of land makes you remember that you were born to the earth, and your feet ache suddenly for the touch of solid ground.

The problem at the moment was actually getting my feet *on* solid ground. Watlings Island was no more than a pause, to replenish our severely depleted water supply before the run through the Windward Isles down to Jamaica. It would be at least another week's sail, and the presence of so many invalids aboard requiring vast infusions of liquid had run the great water casks in the hold nearly dry.

San Salvador was a small island, but I had learned from careful questioning of my patients that there was a fair amount of shipping traffic through its main port in Cockburn Town. It might not be the ideal place to escape, but it looked as though there would be little other choice; I had no intention of enjoying the navy's "hospitality" on Jamaica, serving as the bait that would lure Jamie to arrest.

Starved as the crew was for the sight and feel of land, no one was allowed to go ashore save the watering party, now busy with their casks and sledges up Pigeon Creek, at whose foot we were anchored. One of the marines stood at the head of the gangway, blocking any attempt at leaving.

Such members of the crew as were not involved in watering or on watch stood by the rail, talking and joking or merely gazing at the island, the dream of hope fulfilled. Some way down the deck, I caught sight of a long, blond tail of hair, flying in the shore breeze. The Governor too had emerged from seclusion, pale face upturned to the tropic sun.

I would have gone to speak to him, but there was no time. Annekje had already gone below for the goat. I wiped my hands on my skirt, making my final estimations. It was no more than two hundred yards to the thick growth of palms and underbrush. If I could get down the gangway and into the jungle, I thought I had a good chance of getting away.

Anxious as he was to be on his way to Jamaica, Captain Leonard was unlikely to waste much time in trying to catch me. And if they did catch me—well, the Captain could hardly punish me for trying to leave the ship; I was neither a seaman nor a formal captive, after all.

The sun shone on Annekje's blond head as she made her way carefully up the ladder, a young goat cozily nestled against her wide bosom. A quick glance, to see that I was in place, and she headed for the gangway.

Annekje spoke to the sentry in her queer mixture of English and Swedish, pointing to the goat and then ashore, insisting that it must have fresh grass. The marine appeared to understand her, but stood firm.

"No, ma'am," he said, respectfully enough, "no one is to go ashore save the watering party; Captain's orders."

Standing just out of sight, I watched as she went on arguing, thrusting her goatling urgently in his face, forcing him a step back, a step to the side, maneuvering him artfully just far enough that I could slip past behind him. No more than a moment, now; he was almost in place. When she had drawn him away from the head of the gangplank, she would drop the goat and cause sufficient confusion in the catching of it that I would have a minute or two to make my escape.

I shifted nervously from foot to foot. My feet were bare; it would be easier to run on the sandy beach. The sentry moved, his red-coated back fully turned to me. A foot more, I thought, just a foot more.

"Such a fine day, is it not, Mrs. Malcolm?"

I bit my tongue.

"Very fine, Captain Leonard," I said, with some difficulty. My heart seemed to have stopped dead when he spoke. It now resumed beating much faster than usual, to make up for lost time.

The Captain stepped up beside me and looked over the rail, his young face shining with Columbus's joy. Despite my strong desire to push him overboard, I felt myself smile grudgingly at the sight of him.

"This landfall is as much your victory as mine, Mrs. Malcolm," he said. "Without you, I doubt we should ever have brought the *Porpoise* to land." He very shyly touched my hand, and I smiled again, a little less grudgingly.

"I'm sure you would have managed, Captain," I said. "You seem to be a most competent sailor."

He laughed, and blushed. He had shaved in honor of the land, and his smooth cheeks glowed pink and raw.

"Well, it is mostly the hands, ma'am; I may say they have done nobly. And their efforts, of course, are due in turn to your skill as a physician." He looked at me, brown eyes shining earnestly.

"Indeed, Mrs. Malcolm—I cannot say what your skill and kindness have meant to us. I—I mean to say so, too, to the Governor and to Sir Greville—you know, the King's Commissioner on Antigua. I shall write a letter, a most sincere testimonial to you and to your efforts on our behalf. Perhaps—perhaps it will help." He dropped his eyes.

"Help with what, Captain?" My heart was still beating fast.

Captain Leonard bit his lip, then looked up.

"I had not meant to say anything to you, ma'am. But I—really I cannot in honor keep silence. Mrs. Fraser, I know your name, and I know what your husband is."

"Really?" I said, trying to keep control of my own emotions. "What is he?"

The boy looked surprised at that. "Why, ma'am, he is a criminal." He paled a little. "You mean—you did not know?"

"Yes, I knew that," I said dryly. "Why are you telling me, though?"

He licked his lips, but met my eyes bravely enough. "When I discovered your husband's identity, I wrote it in the ship's log. I regret that action now, but it is too late; the information is official. Once I reach Jamaica, I must report his name and destination to the authorities there, and likewise to the commander at the naval barracks on Antigua. He will be taken when the *Artemis* docks." He swallowed. "And if he is taken—"

"He'll be hanged," I said, finishing what he could not. The boy nodded, wordless. His mouth opened and closed, seeking words.

"I have seen men hanged," he said at last. "Mrs. Fraser, I just —I—" He stopped then, fighting for control, and found it. He drew himself up straight and looked at me straight on, the joy of his landing drowned in sudden misery.

"I am sorry," he said softly. "I cannot ask you to forgive me; I can only say that I am most terribly sorry."

He turned on his heel and walked away. Directly before him

stood Annekje Johansen and her goat, still in heated conversation with the sentry.

"What is this?" Captain Leonard demanded angrily. "Remove this animal from the deck at once! Mr. Holford, what are you thinking of?"

Annekje's eyes flicked from the Captain to my face, instantly divining what had gone wrong. She stood still, head bowed to the Captain's scolding, then marched away toward the hatchway to the goats' hold, clutching her yearling. As she passed, one big blue eye winked solemnly. We would try again. But how?

Racked by guilt and bedeviled by contrary winds, Captain Leonard avoided me, seeking refuge on his quarterdeck as we made our cautious way past Acklin Island and Samana Cay. The weather aided him in this evasion; it stayed bright, but with odd, light breezes alternating with sudden gusts, so that constant adjustment of the sails was required—no easy task, in a ship so shorthanded.

It was four days later, as we shifted course to enter the Caicos Passage, that a sudden booming gust of wind struck the ship out of nowhere, catching her ill-rigged and unprepared.

I was on deck when the gust struck. There was a sudden *whoosh* that sent my skirts billowing and propelled me flying down the deck, followed by a sharp, loud *crack!* somewhere overhead. I crashed head-on into Ramsdell Hodges, one of the forecastle crew, and we whirled together in a mad pirouette before falling entangled to the deck.

There was confusion all around, with hands running and orders shouted. I sat up, trying to collect my scattered wits.

"What is it?" I demanded of Hodges, who staggered to his feet and reached down to lift me up. "What's happened?"

"The fucking mainmast's split," he said succinctly. "Saving your presence, ma'am, but it has. And now there'll be hell to pay."

The *Porpoise* limped slowly south, not daring to risk the banks and shoals of the passage without a mainmast. Instead, Captain

Leonard put in for repairs at the nearest convenient anchorage, Bottle Creek, on the shore of North Caicos Island.

This time, we were allowed ashore, but no great good did it do me. Tiny and dry, with few sources of fresh water, the Turks and Caicos provided little more than numerous tiny bays that might shelter passing ships caught in storms. And the idea of hiding on a foodless, waterless island, waiting for a convenient hurricane to blow me a ship, did not appeal.

To Annekje, though, our change of course suggested a new plan.

"I know these island," she said, nodding wisely. "We go round now, Grand Turk, Mouchoir. Not Caicos."

I looked askance, and she squatted, drawing with a blunt forefinger in the yellow sand of the beach.

"See—Caicos Passage," she said, sketching a pair of lines. At the top, between the lines, she sketched the small triangle of a sail. "Go through," she said, indicating the Caicos Passage, "but mast is gone. Now—" She quickly drew several irregular circles, to the right of the passage. "North Caicos, South Caicos, Caicos, Grand Turk," she said, stabbing a finger at each circle in turn. "Go round now—reefs. Mouchoir." And she drew another pair of lines, indicating a passage to the southeast of Grand Turk Island.

"Mouchoir Passage?" I had heard the sailors mention it, but had no idea how it applied to my potential escape from the *Porpoise.*

Annekje nodded, beaming, then drew a long, wavy line, some way below her previous illustrations. She pointed at it proudly. "Hispaniola. St. Domingue. Big island, is there towns, lots ships."

I raised my eyebrows, still baffled. She sighed, seeing that I didn't understand. She thought a moment, then stood up, dusting her heavy thighs. We had been gathering whelks from the rocks in a shallow pan. She seized this, dumped out the whelks, and filled it with seawater. Then, laying it on the sand, she motioned to me to watch.

She stirred the water carefully, in a circular motion, then lifted her finger out, stained dark with the purple blood of the whelks. The water continued to move, swirling past the tin sides.

Annekje pulled a thread from the raveling hem of her skirt, bit off a short piece, and spat it into the water. It floated, following the swirl of the water in lazy circles round the pan.

"You," she said, pointing at it. "Vater move you." She pointed back to her drawing in the sand. A new triangle, in the Mouchoir Passage. A line, curving from the tiny sail down to the left, indicating the ship's course. And now, the blue thread representing me, rescued from its immersion. She placed it by the tiny sail representing the *Porpoise,* then dragged it off, down the Passage toward the coast of Hispaniola.

"Jump," she said simply.

"You're crazy!" I said in horror.

She chuckled in deep satisfaction at my understanding. "*Ja,*" she said. "But it vork. Vater move you." She pointed to the end of the Mouchoir Passage, to the coast of Hispaniola, and stirred the water in the pan once more. We stood side by side, watching the ripples of her manufactured current die away.

Annekje glanced thoughtfully sideways at me. "You try not drown, *ja*?"

I took a deep breath and brushed the hair out of my eyes.

"*Ja,*" I said. "I'll try."

50

I Meet a Priest

The sea was remarkably warm, as seas go, and like a warm bath as compared to the icy surf off Scotland. On the other hand, it was extremely wet. After two or three hours of immersion, my feet were numb and my fingers chilled where they gripped the ropes of my makeshift life preserver, made of two empty casks.

The gunner's wife was as good as her word, though. The long, dim shape I had glimpsed from the *Porpoise* grew steadily nearer, its low hills dark as black velvet against a silver sky. Hispaniola—Haiti.

I had no way of telling time, and yet two months on shipboard, with its constant bells and watch-changes, had given me a rough feeling for the passage of the night hours. I thought it must have been near midnight when I left the *Porpoise;* now it was likely near 4:00 A.M., and still over a mile to the shore. Ocean currents are strong, but they take their time.

Worn out from work and worry, I twisted the rope awkwardly about one wrist to prevent my slipping out of the harness, laid my forehead on one cask, and drifted off to sleep with the scent of rum strong in my nostrils.

The brush of something solid beneath my feet woke me to an opal dawn, the sea and sky both glowing with the colors found inside a shell. With my feet planted in cold sand, I could feel the strength of the current flowing past me, tugging on the casks. I disentangled myself from the rope harness and with considerable relief, let the unwieldy things go bobbing toward the shore.

There were deep red indentations on my shoulders. The wrist I had twisted through the wet rope was rubbed raw; I was chilled, exhausted, and very thirsty, and my legs were rubbery as boiled squid.

On the other hand, the sea behind me was empty, the *Porpoise* nowhere in sight. I had escaped.

Now, all that remained to be done was to get ashore, find water, find some means of quick transport to Jamaica, and find Jamie and the *Artemis,* preferably before the Royal Navy did. I thought I could just about manage the first item on the agenda.

Such little as I knew of the Caribbean from postcards and tourist brochures had led me to think in terms of white-sand beaches and crystal lagoons. In fact, prevailing conditions ran more toward a lot of dense and ugly vegetation, embedded in extremely sticky dark-brown mud.

The thick bushlike plants must be mangroves. They stretched as far as I could see in either direction; there was no alternative but to clamber through them. Their roots rose out of the mud in big loops like croquet wickets, which I tripped over regularly, and the pale, smooth gray twigs grew in bunches like finger bones, snatching at my hair as I passed.

Squads of tiny purple crabs ran off in profound agitation at my approach. My feet sank into the mud to the ankles, and I thought better of putting on my shoes, wet as they were. I rolled them up in my wet skirt, kirtling it up above my knees and took out the fish knife Annekje had given me, just in case. I saw nothing threatening, but felt better with a weapon in my hand.

The rising sun on my shoulders at first was welcome, as it thawed my chilled flesh and dried my clothes. Within an hour, though, I wished that it would go behind a cloud. I was sweating heavily as the sun rose higher, caked to the knees with drying mud, and growing thirstier by the moment.

I tried to see how far the mangroves extended, but they rose above my head, and tossing waves of narrow, gray-green leaves were all I could see.

"The whole bloody island can't be mangroves," I muttered, slogging on. "There has to be solid land *someplace.*" And water, I hoped.

A noise like a small cannon going off nearby startled me so that I dropped the fish knife. I groped frantically in the mud for it, then dived forward onto my face as something large whizzed past my head, missing me by inches.

There was a loud rattling of leaves, and then a sort of conversational-sounding *"Kwark?"*

"What?" I croaked. I sat up cautiously, knife in one hand, and wiped the wet, muddy curls out of my face with the other. Six feet away, a large black bird was sitting on a mangrove, regarding me with a critical eye.

He bent his head, delicately preening his sleek black feathers, as though to contrast his immaculate appearance with my own dishevelment.

"Well, la-di-dah," I said sarcastically. "You've got wings, mate."

The bird stopped preening and eyed me censoriously. Then he lifted his beak into the air, puffed his chest, and as though to further establish his sartorial superiority, suddenly inflated a large pouch of brilliant red skin that ran from the base of his neck halfway down his body.

"Bwoom!" he said, repeating the cannon-like noise that had startled me before. It startled me again, but not so much.

"Don't *do* that," I said irritably. Paying no attention, the bird slowly flapped its wings, settled back on its branch, and boomed again.

There was a sudden harsh cry from above, and with a loud flapping of wings, two more large black birds plopped down, landing in a mangrove a few feet away. Encouraged by the audience, the first bird went on booming at regular intervals, the skin of his pouch flaming with excitement. Within moments, three more black shapes had appeared overhead.

I was reasonably sure they weren't vultures, but I still wasn't inclined to stay. I had miles to go before I slept—or found Jamie. The chances of finding him in time were something I preferred not to dwell on.

A half-hour later, I had made so little progress that I could still hear the intermittent booming of my fastidious acquaintance, now joined by a number of similarly vocal friends. Panting with exertion, I picked a thickish root and sat down to rest.

My lips were cracked and dry, and the thought of water was occupying my mind to the exclusion of virtually everything else, even Jamie. I had been struggling through the mangroves for what seemed like forever, yet I could still hear the sound of the ocean. In fact, the tide must have been following me, for as I sat, a thin sheet of foaming, dirty seawater came purling through the mangrove roots to touch my toes briefly before receding.

"Water, water everywhere," I said ruefully, watching it, "nor any drop to drink."

A small movement on the damp mud caught my eye. Bending down, I saw several small fishes, of a sort I had never seen before. So far from flopping about, gasping for breath, these fish were sitting upright, propped on their pectoral fins, looking as though the fact that they were out of water was of no concern at all.

Fascinated, I bent closer to inspect them. One or two shifted on their fins, but they seemed not to mind being looked at. They goggled solemnly back at me, eyes bulging. It was only as I looked closer that I realized that the goggling appearance was caused by the fact that each fish appeared to have four eyes, not two.

I stared at one for a long minute, feeling the sweat trickle down between my breasts.

"Either I'm hallucinating," I told it conversationally, "or *you* are."

The fish didn't answer, but hopped suddenly, landing on a branch several inches above the ground. Perhaps it sensed something, for a moment later, another wave washed through, this one splashing up to my ankles.

A sudden welcome coolness fell on me. The sun had obligingly gone behind a cloud, and with its vanishing, the whole feel of the mangrove forest changed.

The gray leaves rattled as a sudden wind came up, and all the tiny crabs and fish and sand fleas disappeared as though by magic. They obviously knew something I didn't, and I found their going rather sinister.

I glanced up at the cloud where the sun had vanished, and gasped. A huge purple mass of boiling cloud was coming up behind the hills, so fast that I could actually see the leading edge of the mass, blazing white with shielded sunlight, moving forward toward me.

The next wave came through, two inches higher than the last, and taking longer to recede. I was neither a fish nor a crab, but by this time I had tumbled to the fact that a storm was on its way, and moving with amazing speed.

I glanced around, but saw nothing more than the seemingly infinite stretch of mangroves before me. Nothing that could be used for shelter. Still, being caught out in a rainstorm was hardly the worst that could happen, under the circumstances. My tongue felt dry and sticky, and I licked my lips at the thought of cool, sweet rain falling on my face.

The swish of another wave halfway up my shins brought me to a sudden awareness that I was in danger of more than getting wet. A quick glance into the upper branches of the mangroves showed me dried tufts of seaweed tangled in the twigs and crotches—high-tide level—and well above my head.

I felt a moment's panic, and tried to calm myself. If I lost my bearings in this place, I was done for. "Hold on, Beauchamp," I muttered to myself. I remembered a bit of advice I'd learned as an intern—"The first thing to do in a cardiac arrest is take your own pulse." I smiled at the memory, feeling panic ebb at once. As a gesture, I did take my pulse; a little fast, but strong and steady.

All right, then, which way? Toward the mountain; it was the only thing I could see above the sea of mangroves. I pushed my way through the branches as fast as I could, ignoring the ripping of my skirts and the increasing pull of each wave on my legs. The wind was coming from the sea behind me, pushing the waves higher. It blew my hair constantly into my eyes and mouth, and I wiped it back again and again, cursing out loud for the comfort of hearing a voice, but my throat was soon so dry that it hurt to talk.

I squelched on. My skirt kept pulling loose from my belt, and somewhere I dropped my shoes, which disappeared at once in the boiling foam that now washed well above my knees. It didn't seem to matter.

The tide was midthigh when the rain hit. With a roar that drowned the rattle of the leaves, it fell in drenching sheets that soaked me to the skin in moments. At first I wasted time vainly tilting my head back, trying to direct the rivulets that ran down my face into my open mouth. Then sense reasserted itself; I took off the kerchief tucked around my shoulders, let the rain soak it and wrung it out several times, to remove the vestiges of salt. Then I let it soak in the rain once more, lifted the wadded fabric to my mouth, and sucked the water from it. It tasted of sweat and sea-weed and coarse cotton. It was delicious.

I had kept going, but was still in the clutches of the mangroves.

The incoming tide was nearly waist-deep, and the walking getting much harder. Thirst slaked momentarily, I put my head down and pushed forward as fast as I could.

Lightning flashed over the mountains, and a moment later came the growl of thunder. The wash of the tide was so strong now that I could move forward only as each wave came in, half-running as the water shoved me along, then clinging to the nearest mangrove stem as the wash sucked back, dragging my trailing legs.

I was beginning to think that I had been over-hasty in abandoning Captain Leonard and the *Porpoise*. The wind was rising still further, dashing rain into my face so that I could barely see. Sailors say every seventh wave is higher. I found myself counting, as I slogged forward. It was the ninth wave, in fact, that struck me between the shoulder blades and knocked me flat before I could grasp a branch.

I floundered, helpless and choking in a blur of sand and water, then found my feet and stood upright again. The wave had half-drowned me, but had also altered my direction. I was no longer facing the mountain. I was, however, facing a large tree, no more than twenty feet away.

Four more waves, four more surging rushes forward, four more grim clutchings as the tide-race sought to pull me back, and I was on the muddy bank of a small inlet, where a tiny stream ran through the mangroves and out to sea. I crawled up it, slipping and staggering as I clambered into the welcoming embrace of the tree.

From a perch twelve feet up, I could see the stretch of the mangrove swamp behind me, and beyond that, the open sea. I changed my mind once more about the wisdom of my leaving the *Porpoise;* no matter how awful things were on land, they were a good deal worse out there.

Lightning shattered over a surface of boiling water, as wind and tide-race fought for control of the waves. Farther out, in the Mouchoir Passage, the swell was so high, it looked like rolling hills. The wind was high enough now to make a thin, whistling scream as it passed by, chilling me to the skin in my wet clothes. Thunder cracked together with the lightning flashes now, as the storm moved over me.

The *Artemis* was slower than the man-of-war; slow enough, I hoped, to be still safe, far out in the Atlantic.

I saw one clump of mangroves struck, a hundred feet away; the water hissed back, boiled away, and the dry land showed for a moment, before the waves rolled back, drowning the black wire of the blasted stems. I wrapped my arms about the trunk of the tree, pressed my face against the bark, and prayed. For Jamie, and the *Artemis.* For the *Porpoise,* Annekje Johansen and Tom Leonard and the Governor. And for me.

It was full daylight when I woke, my leg wedged between two branches, and numb from the knee down. I half-climbed, half-fell from my perch, landing in the shallow water of the inlet. I scooped up a handful of the water, tasted it, and spat it out. Not salt, but too brackish to drink.

My clothes were damp, but I was parched. The storm was long gone; everything around me was peaceful and normal, with the exception of the blackened mangroves. In the distance, I could hear the booming of the big black birds.

Brackish water here promised fresher water farther up the inlet. I rubbed my leg, trying to work out the pins-and-needles, then limped up the bank.

The vegetation began to change from the gray-green mangroves to a lusher green, with a thick undergrowth of grass and mossy plants that obliged me to walk in the water. Tired and thirsty as I was, I could go only a short distance before having to sit down and rest. As I did so, several of the odd little fish hopped up onto the bank beside me, goggling as though in curiosity.

"Well, I think you look rather peculiar, too," I told one.

"Are you English?" said the fish incredulously. The impression of Alice in Wonderland was so pronounced that I merely blinked stupidly at it for a moment. Then my head snapped up, and I stared into the face of the man who had spoken.

His face was weathered and sunburned to the color of mahogany, but the black hair that curled back from his brow was thick and ungrizzled. He stepped out from behind the mangrove, moving cautiously, as though afraid to startle me.

He was a bit above middle height and burly, thick through the shoulder, with a broad, boldly carved face, whose naturally friendly expression was tinged with wariness. He was dressed shabbily, with a heavy canvas bag slung across his shoulder—and a canteen made of goatskin hung from his belt.

"Vous êtes anglaise?" he asked, repeating his original question in French. *"Comment ça va?"*

"Yes, I'm English," I said, croaking. "May I have some water, please?"

His eyes popped wide open—they were a light hazel—but he didn't say anything, just took the skin bag from his belt and handed it to me.

I laid the fish knife on my knee, close within reach, and drank deeply, scarcely able to gulp fast enough.

"Careful," he said. "It's dangerous to drink too fast."

"I know," I said, slightly breathless as I lowered the bag. "I'm a doctor." I lifted the canteen and drank again, but forced myself to swallow more slowly this time.

My rescuer was regarding me quizzically—and little wonder, I supposed. Sea-soaked and sun-dried, mud-caked and sweat-stained, with my hair straggling down over my face, I looked like a beggar, and probably a demented one at that.

"A doctor?" he said in English, showing that his thoughts had been traveling in the direction I suspected. He eyed me closely, in a way strongly reminiscent of the big black bird I had met earlier. "A doctor of *what,* if I might ask?"

"Medicine," I said, pausing briefly between gulps.

He had strongly drawn black brows. These rose nearly to his hairline.

"Indeed," he said, after a noticeable pause.

"Indeed," I said in the same tone of voice, and he laughed.

He inclined his head toward me in a formal bow. "In that case, Madame Physician, allow me to introduce myself. Lawrence Stern, Doctor of Natural Philosophy, of the Gesellschaft von Naturwissenschaft Philosophieren, Munich."

I blinked at him.

"A naturalist," he elaborated, gesturing at the canvas bag over his shoulder. "I was making my way toward those frigate birds in hopes of observing their breeding display, when I happened to overhear you, er . . ."

"Talking to a fish," I finished. "Yes, well . . . have they really got four eyes?" I asked, in hopes of changing the subject.

"Yes—or so it seems." He glanced down at the fish, who appeared to be following the conversation with rapt attention. "They seem to employ their oddly shaped optics when submerged, so that the upper pair of eyes observes events above the surface of the water, and the lower pair similarly takes note of happenings below it."

He looked then at me, with a hint of a smile. "Might I perhaps have the honor of knowing your name, Madame Physician?"

I hesitated, unsure what to tell him. I pondered the assortment of available aliases and decided on the truth.

"Fraser," I said. "Claire Fraser. Mrs. James Fraser," I added for good measure, feeling vaguely that marital status might make me seem slightly more respectable, appearances notwithstanding. I fingered back the curl hanging in my left eye.

"Your servant, Madame," he said with a gracious bow. He rubbed the bridge of his nose thoughtfully, looking at me.

"You have been shipwrecked, perhaps?" he ventured. It seemed the most logical—if not the only—explanation of my presence, and I nodded.

"I need to find a way to get to Jamaica," I said. "Do you think you can help me?"

He stared at me, frowning slightly, as though I were a specimen he couldn't quite decide how to classify, but then he nodded. He had a broad mouth that looked made for smiling; one corner turned up, and he extended a hand to help me up.

"Yes," he said. "I can help. But I think maybe first we find you some food, and maybe clothes, eh? I have a friend, who lives not so far away. I will take you there, shall I?"

What with parching thirst and the general press of events, I had paid little attention to the demands of my stomach. At the mention of food, however, it came immediately and vociferously to life.

"That," I said loudly, in hopes of drowning it out, "would be very nice indeed." I brushed back the tangle of my hair as well as I could, and ducking under a branch, followed my rescuer into the trees.

As we emerged from a palmetto grove, the ground opened out into a meadow-like space, then rose up in a broad hill before us. At the top of the hill, I could see a house—or at least a ruin. Its yellow plaster walls were cracked and overrun by pink bougainvillaeas and straggling guavas, the tin roof sported several visible holes, and the whole place gave off an air of mournful dilapidation.

"Hacienda de la Fuente," my new acquaintance said, with a nod toward it. "Can you stand the walk up the hill, or—" He hesitated, eyeing me as though estimating my weight. "I could carry you, I suppose," he said, with a not altogether flattering tone of doubt in his voice.

"I can manage," I assured him. My feet were bruised and sore, and punctured by fallen palmetto fronds, but the path before us looked relatively smooth.

The hillside leading up to the house was crisscrossed with the faint lines of sheep trails. There were a number of these animals present, peacefully grazing under the hot Hispaniola sun. As we stepped out of the trees, one sheep spotted us and uttered a short bleat of surprise. Like clockwork, every sheep on the hillside lifted its head in unison and stared at us.

Feeling rather self-conscious under this unblinking phalanx of suspicious eyes, I picked up my muddy skirts and followed Dr. Stern toward the main path—trodden by more than sheep, to judge from its width—that led up and over the hill.

It was a fine, bright day, and flocks of orange and white butterflies flickered through the grass. They lighted on the scattered blooms with here and there a brilliant yellow butterfly shining like a tiny sun.

I breathed in deeply, a lovely smell of grass and flowers, with minor notes of sheep and sun-warmed dust. A brown speck lighted for a moment on my sleeve and clung, long enough for me to see the velvet scales on its wing, and the tiny curled hose of its proboscis. The slender abdomen pulsed, breathing to its wing-beats, and then it was gone.

It might have been the promise of help, the water, the butterflies, or all three, but the burden of fear and fatigue under which I had labored for so long began to lift. True, I still had to face the problem of finding transport to Jamaica, but with thirst assuaged, a friend at hand, and the possibility of lunch just ahead, that no longer appeared the impossible task it had seemed in the mangroves.

"There he is!" Lawrence stopped, waiting for me to come up alongside him on the path. He gestured upward, toward a slight, wiry figure, picking its way carefully down the hillside toward us.

I squinted at the figure as it wandered through the sheep, who took no apparent notice of his passage.

"Jesus!" I said. "It's St. Francis of Assisi."

Lawrence glanced at me in surprise.

"No, neither one. I told you he's English." He raised an arm and shouted, *"¡Hola!* Señor Fogden!"

The gray-robed figure paused suspiciously, one hand twined protectively in the wool of a passing ewe.

"¿Quien es?"

"Stern!" called Lawrence. "Lawrence Stern! Come along," he said, and extended a hand to pull me up the steep hillside onto the sheep path above.

The ewe was making determined efforts to escape her protector, which distracted him from our approach. A slender man a bit taller than I, he had a lean face that might have been handsome if not disfigured by a reddish beard that straggled dust-mop-like round the edges of his chin. His long and straying hair had gone to gray in streaks and runnels, and fell forward into his eyes with some frequency. An orange butterfly took wing from his head as we reached him.

"Stern?" he said, brushing back the hair with his free hand and blinking owlishly in the sunlight. "I don't know any . . . oh, it's you!" His thin face brightened. "Why didn't you say it was the shitworm man; I should have known you at once!"

Stern looked mildly embarrassed at this, and glanced at me apologetically. "I . . . ah . . . collected several interesting parasites from the excrement of Mr. Fogden's sheep, upon the occasion of my last visit," he explained.

"Horrible great worms!" Father Fogden said, shuddering violently in recollection. "A foot long, some of them, at least!"

"No more than eight inches," Stern corrected, smiling. He glanced at the nearest sheep, his hand resting on his collecting bag as though in anticipation of further imminent contributions to science. "Was the remedy I suggested effective?"

Father Fogden looked vaguely doubtful, as though trying to remember quite what the remedy had been.

"The turpentine drench," the naturalist prompted.

"Oh, yes!" The sun broke out on the priest's lean countenance, and he beamed fondly upon us. "Of course, of course! Yes, it worked splendidly. A few of them died, but the rest were quite cured. Capital, entirely capital!"

Suddenly it seemed to dawn on Father Fogden that he was being less than hospitable.

"But you must come in!" he said. "I was just about to partake of the midday meal; I insist you must join me." The priest turned to me. "This will be Mrs. Stern, will it?"

Mention of eight-inch intestinal worms had momentarily suppressed my hunger pangs, but at the mention of food, they came gurgling back in full force.

"No, but we should be delighted to partake of your hospitality," Stern answered politely. "Pray allow me to introduce my companion—a Mrs. Fraser, a countrywoman of yours."

Fogden's eyes grew quite round at this. A pale blue, with a tendency to water in bright sun, they fixed wonderingly upon me.

"An Englishwoman?" he said, disbelieving. "Here?" The round eyes took in the mud and salt stains on my crumpled dress, and my general air of disarray. He blinked for a moment, then stepped forward, and with the utmost dignity, bowed low over my hand.

"Your most obedient servant, Madame," he said. He rose and gestured grandly at the ruin on the hill. *"Mi casa es su casa."* He whistled sharply, and a small King Charles cavalier spaniel poked its face inquiringly out of the weeds.

"We have a guest, Ludo," the priest said, beaming. "Isn't that nice?" Tucking my hand firmly under one elbow, he took the sheep by its topknot of wool and towed us both toward the Hacienda de la Fuente, leaving Stern to follow.

The reason for the name became clear as we entered the dilapidated courtyard; a tiny cloud of dragonflies hovered like blinking lights over an algae-filled pool in one corner; it looked like a natural spring that someone had curbed in when the house was built. At least a dozen jungle fowl sprang up from the shattered pavement and flapped madly past our feet, leaving a small cloud of dust and feathers behind them. From other evidences left behind, I deduced that the trees overhanging the patio were their customary roost, and had been for some time.

"And so I was fortunate enough to encounter Mrs. Fraser among the mangroves this morning," Stern concluded. "I thought that perhaps you might . . . oh, look at that beauty! A magnificent Odonata!''

A tone of amazed delight accompanied this last statement, and he pushed unceremoniously past us to peer up into the shadows of the palm-thatched patio roof, where an enormous dragonfly, at least four inches across, was darting to and fro, blue body catching fire when it crossed one of the errant rays of sunshine poking through the tattered roof.

"Oh, do you want it? Be my guest." Our host waved a gracious hand at the dragonfly. "Here, Becky, trot in there and I'll see to your hoof in a bit." He shooed the ewe into the patio with a slap on the rump. It snorted and galloped off a few feet, then fell at once to browsing on the scattered fruit of a huge guava that overhung the ancient wall.

In fact, the trees around the patio had grown up to such an extent that the branches at many points interlaced. The whole of the courtyard seemed roofed with them, a sort of leafy tunnel, leading down the length of the patio into the gaping cavern of the house's entrance.

Drifts of dust and the pink paper leaves of bougainvillaea lay heaped against the sill, but just beyond, the dark wood floor gleamed with polish, bare and immaculate. It was dark inside, after the brilliance of the sunlight, but my eyes quickly adapted to the surroundings, and I looked around curiously.

It was a very plain room, dark and cool, furnished with no more than a long table, a few stools and chairs, and a small sideboard, over which hung a hideous painting in the Spanish style—an emaciated Christ, goateed and pallid in the gloom, indicating with one skeletal hand the bleeding heart that throbbed in his chest.

This ghastly object so struck my eye that it was a moment before I realized there was someone else in the room. The shadows in one corner of the room coalesced, and a small round face emerged, wearing an expression of remarkable malignity. I blinked and took a step back. The woman—for so she was—took a step forward, black eyes fixed on me, unblinking as the sheep.

She was no more than four feet tall, and so thick through the body as to seem like a solid block, without joint or indentation. Her head was a small round knob atop her body, with the smaller knob of a sparse gray bun scraped tightly back behind it. She was a light mahogany color—whether from the sun or naturally, I couldn't tell—and looked like nothing so much as a carved wooden doll. An ill-wish doll.

"Mamacita," said the priest, speaking Spanish to the graven image, "what good fortune! We have guests who will eat with us. You remember Señor Stern?" he added, gesturing at Lawrence.

"Sí, claro," said the image, through invisible wooden lips. "The Christ-killer. And who is the *puta alba*?"

"And this is Señora Fraser," Father Fogden went on, beaming as though she had not spoken. "The poor lady has had the misfortune to be shipwrecked; we must assist her as much as we can."

Mamacita looked me over slowly from top to toe. She said nothing, but the wide nostrils flared with infinite contempt.

"Your food's ready," she said, and turned away.

"Splendid!" the priest said happily. "Mamacita welcomes you; she'll bring us some food. Won't you sit down?"

The table was already laid with a large cracked plate and a wooden spoon. The priest took two more plates and spoons from the sideboard, and distributed them haphazardly about the table, gesturing hospitably at us to be seated.

A large brown coconut sat on the chair at the head of the table. Fogden tenderly picked this up and set it alongside his plate. The fibrous husk was darkened with age, and the hair was worn off it in patches, showing an almost polished appearance; I thought he must have had it for some time.

"Hallo there," he said, patting it affectionately. "And how are you keeping this fine day, Coco?"

I glanced at Stern, but he was studying the portrait of Christ, a small frown between his thick black brows. I supposed it was up to me to open a conversation.

"You live alone here, Mr.—ah, Father Fogden?" I inquired of our host. "You, and—er, Mamacita?"

"Yes, I'm afraid so. That's why I'm so pleased to see you. I haven't any real company but Ludo and Coco, you know," he explained, patting the hairy nut once more.

"Coco?" I said politely, thinking that on the evidence to hand so far, Coco wasn't the only nut among those present. I darted another glance at Stern, who looked mildly amused, but not alarmed.

"Spanish for bugbear—*coco,*" the priest explained. "A hobgoblin. See him there, wee button nose and his dark little eyes?'' Fogden jabbed two long, slender fingers suddenly into the depressions in the end of the coconut and jerked them back, chortling.

''Ah-ah!'' he cried. ''Mustn't stare, Coco, it's rude, you know!''

The pale blue eyes darted a piercing glance at me, and with some difficulty, I removed my teeth from my lower lip.

''Such a pretty lady,'' he said, as though to himself. ''Not like my Ermenegilda, but very pretty nonetheless—isn't she, Ludo?''

The dog, thus addressed, ignored me, but bounded joyfully at its master, shoving its head under his hand and barking. He scratched its ears affectionately, then turned his attention back to me.

''Would one of Ermenegilda's dresses fit you, I wonder?''

I didn't know whether to answer this or not. Instead, I merely smiled politely, and hoped what I was thinking didn't show on my face. Fortunately, at this point Mamacita came back, carrying a steaming clay pot wrapped in towels. She slapped a ladleful of the contents on each plate, then went out, her feet—if she had any— moving invisibly beneath the shapeless skirt.

I stirred the mess on my plate, which appeared to be vegetable in nature. I took a cautious bite, and found it surprisingly good.

''Fried plantain, mixed with manioc and red beans,'' Lawrence explained, seeing my hesitation. He took a large spoonful of the steaming pulp himself and ate it without pausing for it to cool.

I had expected something of an inquisition about my presence, identity, and prospects. Instead, Father Fogden was singing softly under his breath, keeping time on the table with his spoon between bites.

I darted a glance at Lawrence, eyebrows up. He merely smiled, raised one shoulder in a slight shrug, and bent to his own food.

No real conversation occurred until the conclusion of the meal, when Mamacita—''unsmiling'' seemed an understatement of her expression—removed the plates, replacing them with a platter of fruit, three cups, and a gigantic clay pitcher.

''Have you ever drunk sangria, Mrs. Fraser?''

I opened my mouth to say ''Yes,'' thought better of it, and said, ''No, what is it?'' Sangria had been a popular drink in the 1960s, and I had had it many times at faculty parties and hospital social events. But for now, I was sure that it was unknown in England

and Scotland; Mrs. Fraser of Edinburgh would never have heard of sangria.

"A mixture of red wine and the juices of orange and lemon," Lawrence Stern was explaining. "Mulled with spices, and served hot or cold, depending upon the weather. A most comforting and healthful beverage, is it not, Fogden?"

"Oh, yes. Oh, yes. Most comforting." Not waiting for me to find out for myself, the priest drained his cup, and reached for the pitcher before I had taken the first sip.

It was the same; the same sweet, throat-rasping taste, and I suffered the momentary illusion that I was back at the party where I had first tasted it, in company with a marijuana-smoking graduate student and a professor of botany.

This illusion was fostered by Stern's conversation, which dealt with his collections, and by Father Fogden's behavior. After several cups of sangria, he had risen, rummaged through the sideboard, and emerged with a large clay pipe. This he packed full of a strong-smelling herb shaken out of a paper twist, and proceeded to smoke.

"Hemp?" Stern asked, seeing this. "Tell me, do you find it settling to the digestive processes? I have heard it is so, but the herb is unobtainable in most European cities, and I have no first-hand observations of its effect."

"Oh, it is most genial and comforting to the stomach," Father Fogden assured him. He drew in a huge breath, held it, then exhaled long and dreamily, blowing a stream of soft white smoke that floated in streamers of haze near the room's low ceiling. "I shall send a packet home with you, dear fellow. Do say, now, what do you mean doing, you and this shipwrecked lady you have rescued?"

Stern explained his plan; after a night's rest, we intended to walk as far as the village of St. Luis du Nord, and from there see whether a fishing boat might carry us to Cap-Haïtien, thirty miles distant. If not, we would have to make our way overland to Le Cap, the nearest port of any size.

The priest's sketchy brows drew close together, frowning against the smoke.

"Mm? Well, I suppose there isn't much choice, is there? Still, you must go careful, particularly if you go overland to Le Cap. Maroons, you know."

"Maroons?" I glanced quizzically at Stern, who nodded, frowning.

"That's true. I did meet with two or three small bands as I came north through the valley of the Artibonite. They didn't molest me, though—I daresay I looked little better off than they, poor wretches. The Maroons are escaped slaves," he explained to me. "Having fled the cruelty of their masters, they take refuge in the remote hills, where the jungle hides them."

"They might not trouble you," Father Fogden said. He sucked deeply on his pipe, with a low, slurping noise, held his breath for a long count and then let it out reluctantly. His eyes were becoming markedly bloodshot. He closed one of them and examined me rather blearily with the other. "She doesn't look worth robbing, really."

Stern smiled broadly, looking at me, then quickly erased the smile, as though feeling he had been less than tactful. He coughed and took another cup of sangria. The priest's eyes gleamed over the pipe, red as a ferret's.

"I believe I need a little fresh air," I said, pushing back my chair. "And perhaps a little water, to wash with?"

"Oh, of course, of course!" Father Fogden cried. He rose, swaying unsteadily, and thumped the coals from his pipe carelessly out onto the sideboard. "Come with me."

The air in the patio seemed fresh and invigorating by comparison, despite its mugginess. I inhaled deeply, looking on with interest as Father Fogden fumbled with a bucket by the fountain in the corner.

"Where does the water come from?" I asked. "Is it a spring?" The stone trough was lined with soft tendrils of green algae, and I could see these moving lazily; evidently there was a current of some kind.

It was Stern who answered.

"Yes, there are hundreds of such springs. Some of them are said to have spirits living in them—but I do not suppose you subscribe to such superstition, sir?"

Father Fogden seemed to have to think about this. He set the half-filled bucket down on the coping and squinted into the water, trying to fix his gaze on one of the small silver fish that swam there.

"Ah?" he said vaguely. "Well, no. Spirits, no. Still—oh, yes, I had forgotten. I had something to show you.'' Going to a cupboard set into the wall, he pulled open the cracked wooden door and removed a small bundle of coarse unbleached muslin, which he put gingerly into Stern's hands.

"It came up in the spring one day last month,'' he said. "It died when the noon sun struck it, and I took it out. I'm afraid the other fish nibbled it a bit,'' he said apologetically, "but you can still see.''

Lying in the center of the cloth was a small dried fish, much like those darting about in the spring, save that this one was pure white. It was also blind. On either side of the blunt head, there was a small swelling where an eye should have been, but that was all.

"Do you think it is a ghost fish?'' the priest inquired. "I thought of it when you mentioned spirits. Still, I can't think what sort of sin a fish might have committed, so as to be doomed to roam about like that—eyeless, I mean. I mean''—he closed one eye again in his favorite expression—"one doesn't think of fish as having souls, and yet, if they don't, how can they become ghosts?''

"I shouldn't think they do, myself,'' I assured him. I peered more closely at the fish, which Stern was examining with the rapt joy of the born naturalist. The skin was very thin, and so transparent that the shadows of the internal organs and the knobbly line of the vertebrae were clearly visible, yet it did have scales, tiny and translucent, though dulled by dryness.

"It is a blind cave fish,'' Stern said, reverently stroking the tiny blunt head. "I have seen one only once before, in a pool deep inside a cave, at a place called Abandawe. And that one escaped before I could examine it closely. My dear fellow—'' He turned to the priest, eyes shining with excitement. "Might I have it?''

"Of course, of course.'' The priest fluttered his fingers in off-hand generosity. "No use to me. Too small to eat, you know, even if Mamacita would think of cooking it, which she wouldn't.'' He glanced around the patio, kicking absently at a passing hen. "Where *is* Mamacita?''

"Here, *cabrón,* where else?'' I hadn't seen her come out of the house, but there she was, a dusty, sun-browned little figure stooping to fill another bucket from the spring.

A faintly musty, unpleasant smell reached my nostrils, and they twitched uneasily. The priest must have noticed, for he said, "Oh, you mustn't mind, it's only poor Arabella."

"Arabella?"

"Yes, in here." The priest held aside a ragged curtain of burlap that screened off a corner of the patio, and I glanced behind it.

A ledge jutted out of the stone wall at waist-height. On it were ranged a long row of sheep's skulls, pure white and polished.

"I can't bear to part with them, you see." Father Fogden gently stroked the heavy curve of a skull. "This was Beatriz—so sweet and gentle. She died in lambing, poor thing." He indicated two much smaller skulls nearby, shaped and polished like the rest.

"Arabella is a—a sheep, too?" I asked. The smell was much stronger here, and I thought I really didn't want to know where it was coming from at all.

"A member of my flock, yes, certainly." The priest turned his oddly bright blue eyes on me, looking quite fierce. "She was murdered! Poor Arabella, such a gentle, trusting soul. How they can have had the wickedness to betray such innocence for the sake of carnal lusts!"

"Oh, dear," I said, rather inadequately. "I'm terribly sorry to hear that. Ah—who murdered her?"

"The sailors, the wicked heathen! Killed her on the beach and roasted her poor body over a gridiron, just like St. Lawrence the Martyr."

"Heavens," I said.

The priest sighed, and his spindly beard appeared to droop with mourning.

"Yes, I must not forget the hope of Heaven. For if Our Lord observes the fall of every sparrow, He can scarcely have failed to observe Arabella. She must have weighed near on ninety pounds, at least, such a good grazer as she was, poor child."

"Ah," I said, trying to infuse the remark with a suitable sympathy and horror. It then occurred to me what the priest had said.

"Sailors?" I asked. "When did you say this—this sad occurrence took place?" It couldn't be the *Porpoise,* I thought. Surely, Captain Leonard would not have thought me so important that he had risked bringing his ship in so close to the island, in order to pursue me? But my hands grew damp at the thought, and I wiped them unobtrusively on my robe.

"This morning," Father Fogden replied, setting back the

lamb's skull he had picked up to fondle. "But," he added, his manner brightening a bit, "I must say they're making wonderful progress with her. It usually takes more than a week, and already you can quite see . . ."

He opened the cupboard again, revealing a large lump, covered with several layers of damp burlap. The smell was markedly stronger now, and a number of small brown beetles scuttled away from the light.

"Are those members of the Dermestidae you have there, Fogden?" Lawrence Stern, having tenderly committed the corpse of his cave fish to a jar of alcoholic spirits, had come to join us. He peered over my shoulder, sunburned features creased in interest.

Inside the cupboard, the white maggot larvae of dermestid beetles were hard at work, polishing the skull of Arabella the sheep. They had made a good start on the eyes. The manioc shifted heavily in my stomach.

"Is that what they are? I suppose so; dear voracious little fellows." The priest swayed alarmingly, catching himself on the edge of the cupboard. As he did so, he finally noticed the old woman, standing glaring at him, a bucket in either hand.

"Oh, I had quite forgotten! You will be needing a change of clothing, will you not, Mrs. Fraser?"

I looked down at myself. The dress and shift I was wearing were ripped in so many places that they were barely decent, and so soaked and sodden with water and swamp-mud that I was scarcely tolerable, even in such undemanding company as that of Father Fogden and Lawrence Stern.

Father Fogden turned to the graven image. "Have we not something this unfortunate lady might wear, Mamacita?" he asked in Spanish. He seemed to hesitate, swaying gently. "Perhaps, one of the dresses in—"

The woman bared her teeth at me. "They are much too small for such a cow," she said, also in Spanish. "Give her your old robe, if you must." She cast an eye of scorn on my tangled hair and mud-streaked face. "Come," she said in English, turning her back on me. "You wash."

She led me to a smaller patio at the back of the house, where she provided me with two buckets of cold, fresh water, a worn linen towel, and a small pot of soft soap, smelling strongly of lye. Adding a shabby gray robe with a rope belt, she bared her teeth at me again and left, remarking genially in Spanish, "Wash away the blood on your hands, Christ-killing whore."

I shut the patio gate after her with a considerable feeling of relief, stripped off my sticky, filthy clothes with even more relief, and made my toilet as well as might be managed with cold water and no comb.

Clad decently, if oddly, in Father Fogden's extra robe, I combed out my wet hair with my fingers, contemplating my peculiar host. I wasn't sure whether the priest's excursions into oddness were some form of dementia, or only the side effects of long-term alcoholism and cannabis intoxication, but he seemed a gentle, kindly soul, in spite of it. His servant—if that's what she was—was another question altogether.

Mamacita made me more than slightly nervous. Mr. Stern had announced his intention of going down to the seaside to bathe, and I was reluctant to go back into the house until he returned. There had been quite a lot of sangria left, and I suspected that Father Fogden—if he was still conscious—would be little protection by this time against that basilisk glare.

Still, I couldn't stay outside all afternoon; I was very tired, and wanted to sit down at least, though I would have preferred to find a bed and sleep for a week. There was a door opening into the house from my small patio; I pushed it open and stepped into the dark interior.

I was in a small bedroom. I looked around, amazed; it didn't seem part of the same house as the Spartan main room and the shabby patios. The bed was made up with feather pillows and a coverlet of soft red wool. Four huge patterned fans were spread like bright wings across the whitewashed walls, and wax candles in a branched brass candelabrum sat on the table.

The furniture was simply but carefully made, and polished with oil to a soft, deep gloss. A curtain of striped cotton hung across the end of the room. It was pushed partway back, and I could see a row of dresses hung on hooks behind it, in a rainbow of silken color.

These must be Ermenegilda's dresses, the ones that Father Fogden had mentioned. I walked forward to look at them, my bare feet quiet on the floor. The room was dustless and clean, but very quiet, without the scent or vibration of human occupancy. No one lived in this room anymore.

The dresses were beautiful; all of silk and velvet, moiré and satin, mousseline and panne. Even hanging lifeless here from their hooks, they had the sheen and beauty of an animal's pelt, where some essence of life lingers in the fur.

I touched one bodice, purple velvet, heavy with embroidered silver pansies, centered with pearls. She had been small, this Ermenegilda, and slightly built—several of the dresses had ruffles and pads cleverly sewn inside the bodices, to add to the illusion of a bust. The room was comfortable, though not luxurious; the dresses were splendid—things that might have been worn at Court in Madrid.

Ermenegilda was gone, but the room still seemed inhabited. I touched a sleeve of peacock blue in farewell and tiptoed away, leaving the dresses to their dreams.

I found Lawrence Stern on the veranda at the back of the house, overlooking a precipitous slope of aloe and guava. In the distance, a small humped island sat cradled in a sea of glimmering turquoise. He rose in courtesy, giving me a small bow and a look of surprise.

"Mrs. Fraser! You are in greatly improved looks, I must say. The Father's robe suits you somewhat more than it does him." He smiled at me, hazel eyes creasing in a flattering expression of admiration.

"I expect the absence of dirt has more to do with it," I said, sitting down in the chair he offered me. "Is that something to drink?" There was a pitcher on the rickety wooden table between the chairs; moisture had condensed in a heavy dew on the sides and droplets ran enticingly down the sides. I had been thirsty so long that the sight of anything liquid automatically made my cheeks draw in with longing.

"More sangria," Stern said. He poured out a small cupful for each of us, and sipped his own, sighing with enjoyment. "I hope you will not think me intemperate, Mrs. Fraser, but after months of tramping country, drinking nothing but water and the slaves' crude rum—" He closed his eyes in bliss. "Ambrosia."

I was rather disposed to agree.

"Er . . . is Father Fogden . . . ?" I hesitated, looking for some tactful way of inquiring after our host's state. I needn't have bothered.

"Drunk," Stern said frankly. "Limp as a worm, laid out on the table in the *sala*. He nearly always is, by the time the sun's gone down,'' he added.

"I see." I settled back in the chair, sipping my own sangria. "Have you known Father Fogden long?"

Stern rubbed a hand over his forehead, thinking. "Oh, for a few years." He glanced at me. "I was wondering—do you by chance know a James Fraser, from Edinburgh? I realize it is a common name, but—oh, you do?"

I hadn't spoken, but my face had given me away, as it always did, unless I was carefully prepared to lie.

"My husband's name is James Fraser," I said.

Stern's face lighted with interest. "Indeed!" he exclaimed. "And is he a very large fellow, with—"

"Red hair," I agreed. "Yes, that's Jamie." Something occurred to me. "He told me he'd met a natural philosopher in Edinburgh, and had a most interesting conversation about . . . various things." What I was wondering was where Stern had learned Jamie's real name. Most people in Edinburgh would have known him only as "Jamie Roy," the smuggler, or as Alexander Malcolm, the respectable printer of Carfax Close. Surely Dr. Stern, with his distinct German accent, couldn't be the "Englishman" Tompkins had spoken of?

"Spiders," Stern said promptly. "Yes, I recall perfectly. Spiders and caves. We met in a—a—" His face went blank for a moment. Then he coughed, masterfully covering the lapse. "In a, um, drinking establishment. One of the—ah—female employees happened to encounter a large specimen of *Arachnida* hanging from the ceiling in her—that is, from the ceiling as she was engaged in . . . ah, conversation with me. Being somewhat frightened in consequence, she burst into the passageway, shrieking incoherently." Stern took a large gulp of sangria as a restorative, evidently finding the memory stressful.

"I had just succeeded in capturing the animal and securing it in a specimen jar when Mr. Fraser burst into the room, pointed a species of firearm at me, and said—" Here Stern developed a prolonged coughing fit, pounding himself vigorously on the chest.

"Eheu! Do you not find this particular pitcher perhaps a trifle strong, Mrs. Fraser? I suspect that the old woman has added too many sliced lemons."

I suspected that Mamacita would have added cyanide, had she any to hand, but in fact the sangria was excellent.

"I hadn't noticed," I said, sipping. "But do go on. Jamie came in with a pistol and said—?"

"Oh. Well, in fact, I cannot say I recall precisely what was said. There appeared to have been a slight misapprehension, owing to his impression that the lady's outcry was occasioned by some inopportune motion or speech of my own, rather than by the arachnid. Fortunately, I was able to display the beast to him, whereupon the lady was induced to come so far as the door—we could not persuade her to enter the room again—and identify it as the cause of her distress."

"I see," I said. I could envision the scene very well indeed, save for one point of paramount interest. "Do you happen to recall what he was wearing? Jamie?"

Lawrence Stern looked blank. "Wearing? Why . . . no. My impression is that he was clad for the street, rather than in dishabille, but—"

"That's quite all right," I assured him. "I only wondered." "Clad," after all, was the operative word. "So he introduced himself to you?"

Stern frowned, running a hand through his thick black curls. "I don't believe he did. As I recall, the lady referred to him as Mr. Fraser; sometime later in the conversation—we availed ourselves of suitable refreshment and remained conversing nearly until the dawn, finding considerable interest in each other's company, you see. At some point, he invited me to address him by his given name." He raised one eyebrow sardonically. "I trust you do not think it overfamiliar of me to have done so, upon such brief acquaintance?"

"No, no. Of course not." Wanting to change the subject, I continued, "You said you talked about spiders and caves? Why caves?"

"By way of Robert the Bruce and the story—which your husband was inclined to think apocryphal—regarding his inspiration to persevere in his quest for the throne of Scotland. Presumably, the Bruce was in hiding in a cave, pursued by his enemies, and—"

"Yes, I know the story," I interrupted.

"It was James's opinion that spiders do not frequent caves in which humans dwell; an opinion with which I basically concurred, though pointing out that in the larger type of cave, such as occurs on this island—''

''There are caves here?'' I was surprised, and then felt foolish. ''But of course, there must be, if there are cave fish, like the one in the spring. I always thought Caribbean islands were made of coral, though. I shouldn't have thought you'd find caves in coral.''

''Well, it is possible, though not highly likely,'' Stern said judiciously. ''However, the island of Hispaniola is not a coral atoll but is basically volcanic in origin—with the addition of crystalline schists, fossiliferous sedimentary deposits of a considerable antiquity, and widespread deposits of limestone. The limestone is particularly karstic in spots.''

''You don't say.'' I poured a fresh cup of spiced wine.

''Oh, yes.'' Lawrence leaned over to pick up his bag from the floor of the veranda. Pulling out a notebook, he tore a sheet of paper from it and crumpled it in his fist.

''There,'' he said, holding out his hand. The paper slowly unfolded itself, leaving a mazed topography of creases and crumpled peaks. ''That is what this island is like—you remember what Father Fogden was saying about the Maroons? The runaway slaves who have taken refuge in these hills? It is not lack of pursuit on the part of their masters that allows them to vanish with such ease. There are many parts of this island where no man—white or black, I daresay—has yet set foot. And in the lost hills, there are caves still more lost, whose existence no one knows save perhaps the aboriginal inhabitants of this place—and they are long gone, Mrs. Fraser.

''I have seen one such cave,'' he added reflectively. ''Abandawe, the Maroons call it. They consider it a most sinister and sacred spot, though I do not know why.''

Encouraged by my close attention, he took another gulp of sangria and continued his natural history lecture.

''Now that small island''—he nodded at the floating island visible in the sea beyond—''that is the Ile de la Tortue—Tortuga. That one is in fact a coral atoll, its lagoon long since filled in by the actions of the coral animalculae. Did you know it was once the haunt of pirates?'' he asked, apparently feeling that he ought to infuse his lecture with something of more general interest than karstic formations and crystalline schists.

"Real pirates? Buccaneers, you mean?" I viewed the little island with more interest. "That's rather romantic."

Stern laughed, and I glanced at him in surprise.

"I am not laughing at you, Mrs. Fraser," he assured me. A smile lingered on his lips as he gestured at the Ile de la Tortue. "It is merely that I had occasion once to talk with an elderly resident of Kingston, regarding the habits of the buccaneers who had at one point made their headquarters in the nearby village of Port Royal."

He pursed his lips, decided to speak, decided otherwise, then, with a sideways glance at me, decided to risk it. "You will pardon the indelicacy, Mrs. Fraser, but as you are a married woman, and as I understand, have some familiarity with the practice of medicine—" He paused, and might have stopped there, but he had drunk nearly two-thirds of the pitcher; the broad, pleasant face was deeply flushed.

"You have perhaps heard of the abominable practices of sodomy?" he asked, looking at me sideways.

"I have," I said. "Do you mean—"

"I assure you," he said, with a magisterial nod. "My informant was most discursive upon the habits of the buccaneers. Sodomites to a man," he said, shaking his head.

"What?"

"It was a matter of public knowledge," he said. "My informant told me that when Port Royal fell into the sea some sixty years ago, it was widely assumed to be an act of divine vengeance upon these wicked persons in retribution for their vile and unnatural usages."

"Gracious," I said. I wondered what the voluptuous Tessa of *The Impetuous Pirate* would have thought about this.

He nodded, solemn as an owl.

"They say you can hear the bells of the drowned churches of Port Royal when a storm is coming, ringing for the souls of the damned pirates."

I thought of inquiring further into the precise nature of the vile and unnatural usages, but at this point in the proceedings, Mamacita stumped out onto the veranda, said curtly, "Food," and disappeared again.

"I wonder which cave Father Fogden found *her* in," I said, shoving back my chair.

Stern glanced at me in surprise. "Found her? But I forgot," he said, face clearing, "you don't know." He peered at the open door where the old woman had vanished, but the interior of the house was quiet and dark as a cave.

"He found her in Habana," he said, and told me the rest of the story.

Father Fogden had been a priest for ten years, a missionary of the order of St. Anselm, when he had come to Cuba fifteen years before. Devoted to the needs of the poor, he had worked among the slums and stews of Habana for several years, thinking of nothing more than the relief of suffering and the love of God—until the day he met Ermenegilda Ruiz Alcantara y Meroz in the marketplace.

"I don't suppose he knows, even now, how it happened," Stern said. He wiped away a drop of wine that ran down the side of his cup, and drank again. "Perhaps she didn't know, either, or perhaps she planned it from the moment she saw him."

In any case, six months later the city of Habana was agog at the news that the young wife of Don Armando Alcantara had run away—with a priest.

"And her mother," I said, under my breath, but he heard me, and smiled slightly.

"Ermenegilda would never leave Mamacita behind," he said. "Nor her dog Ludo."

They would never have succeeded in escaping—for the reach of Don Armando was long and powerful—save for the fact that the English conveniently chose the day of their elopement to invade the island of Cuba, and Don Armando had many things more important to worry him than the whereabouts of his runaway young wife.

The fugitives rode to Bayamo—much hampered by Ermenegilda's dresses, with which she would not part—and there hired a fishing boat, which carried them to safety on Hispaniola.

"She died two years later," Stern said abruptly. He set down his cup, and refilled it from the sweating pitcher. "He buried her himself, under the bougainvillaea."

"And here they've stayed since," I said. "The priest, and Ludo and Mamacita."

"Oh, yes." Stern closed his eyes, his profile dark against the setting sun. "Ermenegilda would not leave Mamacita, and Mamacita will never leave Ermenegilda."

He tossed back the rest of his cup of sangria.

"No one comes here," he said. "The villagers won't set foot on the hill. They're afraid of Ermenegilda's ghost. A damned sinner, buried by a reprobate priest in unhallowed ground—of course she will not lie quiet."

The sea breeze was cool on the back of my neck. Behind us, even the chickens in the patio had grown quiet with falling twilight. The Hacienda de la Fuente lay still.

"You come," I said, and he smiled. The scent of oranges rose up from the empty cup in my hands, sweet as bridal flowers.

"Ah, well," he said. "I am a scientist. I don't believe in ghosts." He extended a hand to me, somewhat unsteadily. "Shall we dine, Mrs. Fraser?"

After breakfast the next morning, Stern was ready to set off for St. Luis. Before leaving, though, I had a question or two about the ship the priest had mentioned; if it was the *Porpoise,* I wanted to steer clear of it.

"What sort of ship was it?" I asked, pouring a cup of goat's milk to go with the breakfast of fried plantain.

Father Fogden, apparently little the worse for his excesses of the day before, was stroking his coconut, humming dreamily to himself.

"Ah?" he said, startled out of his reverie by Stern's poking him in the ribs. I patiently repeated my query.

"Oh." He squinted in deep thought, then his face relaxed. "A wooden one."

Lawrence bent his broad face over his plate, hiding a smile. I took a breath and tried again.

"The sailors who killed Arabella—did you see them?"

His narrow brows rose.

"Well, of course I saw them. How else would I know they had done it?"

I seized on this evidence of logical thought.

"Naturally. And did you see what they were wearing? I mean" —I saw him opening his mouth to say "clothes," and hastily forestalled him —"did they seem to be wearing any sort of uniform?'' The crew of the *Porpoise* commonly wore "slops" when not performing any ceremonial duty, but even these rough clothes bore the semblance of a uniform, being mostly all of a dirty white and similar in cut.

Father Fogden laid down his cup, leaving a milky mustache across his upper lip. He brushed at this with the back of his hand, frowning and shaking his head.

"No, I think not. All I recall of them, though, is that the leader wore a hook—missing a hand, I mean." He waggled his own long fingers at me in illustration.

I dropped my cup, which exploded on the tabletop. Stern sprang up with an exclamation, but the priest sat still, watching in surprise as a thin white stream ran across the table and into his lap.

"Whatever did you do that for?" he said reproachfully.

"I'm sorry," I said. My hands were trembling so that I couldn't even manage to pick up the shards of the shattered cup. I was afraid to ask the next question. "Father—has the ship sailed away?"

"Why no," he said, looking up in surprise from his damp robe. "How could it? It's on the beach."

Father Fogden led the way, his skinny shanks a gleaming white as he kirtled his cassock about his thighs. I was obliged to do the same, for the hillside above the house was thick with grass and thorny shrubs that caught at the coarse wool skirts of my borrowed robe.

The hill was crisscrossed with sheep paths, but these were narrow and faint, losing themselves under the trees and disappearing abruptly in thick grass. The priest seemed confident about his destination, though, and scampered briskly through the vegetation, never looking back.

I was breathing hard by the time we reached the crest of the hill, even though Lawrence Stern had gallantly assisted me, pushing branches out of my way, and taking my arm to haul me up the steeper slopes.

"Do you think there really is a ship?" I said to him, low-voiced, as we approached the top of the hill. Given our host's behavior so far, I wasn't so sure he might not have imagined it, just to be sociable.

Stern shrugged, wiping a trickle of sweat that ran down his bronzed cheek.

"I suppose there will be *something* there," he replied. "After all, there is a dead sheep."

A qualm ran over me in memory of the late departed Arabella. Someone *had* killed the sheep, and I walked as quietly as I could, as we approached the top of the hill. It couldn't be the *Porpoise;* none of her officers or men wore a hook. I tried to tell myself that it likely wasn't the *Artemis,* either, but my heart beat still faster as we came to a stand of giant agave on the crest of the hill.

I could see the Caribbean glowing blue through the succulents' branches, and a narrow strip of white beach. Father Fogden had come to a halt, beckoning us to his side.

"There they are, the wicked creatures," he muttered. His blue eyes glittered bright with fury, and his scanty hair fairly bristled, like a moth-eaten porcupine. "Butchers!" he said, hushed but vehement, as though talking to himself. "Cannibals!"

I gave him a startled look, but then Lawrence Stern grasped my arm, drawing me to a wider opening between two trees.

"Oy! There *is* a ship," he said.

There was. It was lying tilted on its side, drawn up on the beach, its masts unstepped, untidy piles of cargo, sails, rigging, and water casks scattered all about it. Men crawled over the beached carcass like ants. Shouts and hammer blows rang out like gunshots, and the smell of hot pitch was thick on the air. The unloaded cargo gleamed dully in the sun; copper and tin, slightly tarnished by the sea air. Tanned hides had been laid flat on the sand, brown stiff blotches drying in the sun.

"It *is* them! It's the *Artemis*!" The matter was settled by the appearance near the hull of a squat, one-legged figure, head shaded from the sun by a gaudy kerchief of yellow silk.

"Murphy!" I shouted. "Fergus! *Jamie*!" I broke from Stern's grasp and ran down the far side of the hill, his cry of caution disregarded in the excitement of seeing the *Artemis.*

Murphy whirled at my shout, but was unable to get out of my way. Carried by momentum and moving like a runaway freight, I crashed straight into him, knocking him flat.

"Murphy!" I said, and kissed him, caught up in the joy of the moment.

"Hoy!" he said, shocked. He wriggled madly, trying to get out from under me.

"Milady!" Fergus appeared at my side, crumpled and vivid, his beautiful smile dazzling in a sun-dark face. "Milady!" He helped me off the grunting Murphy, then grabbed me to him in a rib-cracking hug. Marsali appeared behind him, a broad smile on her face.

"Merci aux saints!" he said in my ear. "I was afraid we would never see you again!" He kissed me heartily himself, on both cheeks and the mouth, then released me at last.

I glanced at the *Artemis,* lying on her side on the beach like a stranded whale. "What on earth happened?"

Fergus and Marsali exchanged a glance. It was the sort of look in which questions are asked and answered, and it rather startled me to see the depths of intimacy between them. Fergus drew a deep breath and turned to me.

"Captain Raines is dead," he said.

The storm that had come upon me during my night in the mangrove swamp had also struck the *Artemis.* Carried far off her path by the howling wind, she had been forced over a reef, tearing a sizable hole in her bottom.

Still, she had remained afloat. The aft hold filling rapidly, she had limped toward the small inlet that opened so near, offering shelter.

"We were no more than three hundred yards from the shore when the accident happened," Fergus said, his face drawn by the memory. The ship had heeled suddenly over, as the contents of the aft hold had shifted, beginning to float. And just then, an enormous wave, coming from the sea, had struck the leaning ship, washing across the tilting quarterdeck, and carrying away Captain Raines, and four seamen with him.

"The shore was so near!" Marsali said, her face twisted with distress. "We were aground ten minutes later! If only—"

Fergus stopped her with a hand on her arm.

"We cannot guess God's ways," he said. "It would have been the same, if we had been a thousand miles at sea, save that we would not have been able to give them decent burial." He nodded toward the far edge of the beach, near the jungle, where five small mounds, topped with crude wooden crosses, marked the final resting places of the drowned men.

"I had some holy water that Da brought me from Notre Dame in Paris," Marsali said. Her lips were cracked, and she licked them. "In a little bottle. I said a prayer, and sprinkled it on the graves. D'ye—d'ye think they would have l-liked that?"

I caught the quaver in her voice, and realized that for all her self-possession, the last two days had been a terrifying ordeal for the girl. Her face was grimy, her hair coming down, and the sharpness was gone from her eyes, softened by tears.

"I'm sure they would," I said gently, patting her arm. I glanced at the faces crowding around, searching for Jamie's great height and fiery head, even as the realization dawned that he was not there.

"Where *is* Jamie?" I said. My face was flushed from the run down the hill. I felt the blood begin to drain from my cheeks, as a trickle of fear rose in my veins.

Fergus was staring at me, lean face mirroring mine.

"He is not with you?" he said.

"No. How could he be?" The sun was blinding, but my skin felt cold. I could feel the heat shimmer over me, but to no effect. My lips were so chilled, I could scarcely form the question.

"Where is he?"

Fergus shook his head slowly back and forth, like an ox stunned by the slaughterer's blow.

"I don't know."

51

In Which Jamie Smells a Rat

Jamie Fraser lay in the shadows under the *Porpoise*'s jolly boat, chest heaving with effort. Getting aboard the man-of-war without being seen had been no small task; his right side was bruised from being slammed against the side of the ship as he hung from the boarding nets, struggling to pull himself up to the rail. His arms felt as though they had been jerked from their sockets and there was a large splinter in one hand. But he was here, and so far unseen.

He chewed delicately at his palm, groping for the end of the splinter with his teeth, as he got his bearings. Russo and Stone, *Artemis* hands who had served aboard men-of-war, had spent hours describing to him the structure of a large ship, the compartments and decks, and the probable location of the surgeon's quarters. Hearing something described and being able to find your way about in it were two different things, though. At least the miserable thing rocked less than the *Artemis,* though he could still feel the subtle, nauseating heave of the deck beneath him.

The end of the splinter worked free; nipping it between his teeth, he drew it slowly out and spat it on the deck. He sucked the tiny wound, tasting blood, and slid cautiously out from under the jolly boat, ears pricked to catch the sound of an approaching footstep.

The deck below this one, down the forward companionway. The officers' quarters would be there, and with luck, the surgeon's cabin as well. Not that she was likely to be in her quarters; not her.

She'd cared enough to come tend the sick—she would be with them.

He had waited until dark to have Robbie MacRae row him out. Raines had told him that the *Porpoise* would likely weigh anchor with the evening tide, two hours from now. If he could find Claire and escape over the side before that—he could swim ashore with her, easily—the *Artemis* would be waiting for them, concealed in a small cove on the other side of Caicos Island. If he couldn't—well, he would deal with that when he came to it.

Fresh from the cramped small world of the *Artemis,* the below-decks of the *Porpoise* seemed huge and sprawling; a shadowed warren. He stood still, nostrils flaring as he deliberately drew the fetid air deep into his lungs. There were all the nasty stenches associated with a ship at sea for a long time, overlaid with the faint floating stink of feces and vomit.

He turned to the left and began to walk softly, long nose twitching. Where the smell of sickness was the strongest; that was where he would find her.

Four hours later, in mounting desperation, he made his way aft for the third time. He had covered the entire ship—keeping out of sight with some difficulty—and Claire was nowhere to be found.

"Bloody woman!" he said under his breath. "Where have ye gone, ye fashious wee hidee?"

A small worm of fear gnawed at the base of his heart. She had said her vaccine would protect her from the sickness, but what if she had been wrong? He could see for himself that the man-of-war's crew had been badly diminished by the deadly sickness—knee-deep in it, the germs might have attacked her too, vaccine or not.

He thought of germs as small blind things, about the size of maggots, but equipped with vicious razor teeth, like tiny sharks. He could all too easily imagine a swarm of the things fastening on to her, killing her, draining her flesh of life. It was just such a vision that had made him pursue the *Porpoise*—that, and a murderous rage toward the English bugger who had had the filth-eating insolence to steal away his wife beneath his very nose, with a vague promise to return her, once they'd made use of her.

Leave her to the Sassenachs, unprotected?

"Not bloody likely," he muttered under his breath, dropping down into a dark cargo space. She wouldn't be in such a place, of course, but he must think a moment, what to do. Was this the cable tier, the aft cargo hatch, the forward stinking God knew what? Christ, he hated boats!

He drew in a deep breath and stopped, surprised. There were animals here; goats. He could smell them plainly. There was also a light, dimly visible around the edge of a bulkhead, and the murmur of voices. Was one of them a woman's voice?

He edged forward, listening. There were feet on the deck above, a patter and thump that he recognized; bodies dropping from the rigging. Had someone above seen him? Well, and if they had? It was no crime, so far as he knew, for a man to come seeking his wife.

The *Porpoise* was asail; he had felt the thrum of the sails, passing through the wood all the way to the keel as she took the wind. They had long since missed the rendezvous with the *Artemis*.

That being so, there was likely nothing to lose by appearing boldly before the Captain and demanding to see Claire. But perhaps she was here—it *was* a woman's voice.

It was a woman's figure, too, silhouetted against the lantern's light, but the woman wasn't Claire. His heart leapt convulsively at the gleam of light on her hair, but then fell at once as he saw the thick, square shape of the woman by the goat pen. There was a man with her; as Jamie watched, the man bent and picked up a basket. He turned and came toward Jamie.

He stepped into the narrow aisle between the bulkheads, blocking the seaman's way.

"Here, what do you mean—" the man began, and then, raising his eyes to Jamie's face, stopped, gasping. One eye was fixed on him in horrified recognition; the other showed only as a bluish-white crescent beneath the withered lid.

"God preserve us!" the seaman said. "What are *you* doing here?" The seaman's face gleamed pale and jaundiced in the dim light.

"Ye ken me, do ye?" Jamie's heart was hammering against his ribs, but he kept his voice level and low. "I have not the honor to know your own name, I think?"

"I should prefer to leave that particular circumstance un-

changed, your honor, if you've no objection." The one-eyed seaman began to edge backward, but was forestalled as Jamie gripped
his arm, hard enough to elicit a small yelp.

"Not quite so fast, if ye please. Where is Mrs. Malcolm, the
surgeon?"

It would have been difficult for the seaman to look more
alarmed, but at this question, he managed it.

"I don't know!" he said.

"You do," Jamie said sharply. "And ye'll tell me this minute,
or I shall break your neck."

"Well, now, I can't be tellin' you anything if you break my
neck, can I?" the seaman pointed out, beginning to recover his
nerve. He lifted his chin pugnaciously over his basket of manure.
"Now, you leave go of me, or I'll call—" The rest was lost in a
squawk as a large hand fastened about his neck and began inexorably to squeeze. The basket fell to the deck, and balls of goat
manure exploded out of it like shrapnel.

"Ak!" Harry Tompkins's legs thrashed wildly, scattering goat
dung in every direction. His face turned the color of a beetroot as
he clawed ineffectually at Jamie's arm. Judging the results clini-
cally, Jamie let go as the man's eye began to bulge. He wiped his
hand on his breeches, disliking the greasy feel of the man's sweat
on his palm.

Tompkins lay on the deck in a sprawl of limbs, wheezing
faintly.

"Ye're quite right," Jamie said. "On the other hand, if I break
your arm, I expect you'll still be able to speak to me, aye?" He
bent, grasped the man by one skinny arm and jerked him to his
feet, twisting the arm roughly behind his back.

"I'll tell you, I'll tell you!" The seaman wriggled madly, panicked. "Damn you, you're as wicked cruel as she was!"

"Was? What do you mean, 'was'?" Jamie's heart squeezed
tight in his chest, and he jerked the arm, more roughly than he had
meant to do. Tompkins let out a screech of pain, and Jamie slackened the pressure slightly.

"Let go! I'll tell you, but for pity's sake, let go!" Jamie lessened his grasp, but didn't let go.

"Tell me where my wife is!" he said, in a tone that had made
stronger men than Harry Tompkins fall over their feet to obey.

"She's lost!" the man blurted. "Gone overboard!"

"What!" He was so stunned that he let go his hold. Overboard. Gone overboard. Lost.

"When?" he demanded. "How? Damn you, tell me what happened!" He advanced on the seaman, fists clenched.

The seaman was backing away, rubbing his arm and panting, a look of furtive satisfaction in his one eye.

"Don't worry, your honor," he said, a queer, jeering tone in his voice. "You won't be lonesome long. You'll join her in hell in a few days—dancing from the yardarm over Kingston Harbor!"

Too late, Jamie heard the footfall on the boards behind him. He had no time even to turn his head before the blow fell.

He had been struck in the head frequently enough to know that the sensible thing was to lie still until the giddiness and the lights that pulsed behind your eyelids with each heartbeat stopped. Sit up too soon and the pain made you vomit.

The deck was rising and falling, rising and falling under him, in the horrible way of ships. He kept his eyes tight closed, concentrating on the knotted ache at the base of his skull in order not to think of his stomach.

Ship. He should be on a ship. Yes, but the surface under his cheek was wrong—hard wood, not the linen of his berth's bedding. And the smell, the smell was wrong, it was—

He shot bolt upright, memory shooting through him with a vividness that made the pain in his head pale by comparison. The darkness moved queasily around him, blinking with colored lights, and his stomach heaved. He closed his eyes and swallowed hard, trying to gather his scattered wits about the single appalling thought that had lanced through his brain like a spit through mutton.

Claire. Lost. Drowned. Dead.

He leaned to the side and threw up. He retched and coughed, as though his body were trying forcibly to expel the thought. It didn't work; when he finally stopped, leaning against the bulkhead in exhaustion, it was still with him. It hurt to breathe, and he clenched his fists on his thighs, trembling.

There was the sound of a door opening, and bright light struck him in the eyes with the force of a blow. He winced, closing his eyes against the glare of the lantern.

"Mr. Fraser," a soft, well-bred voice said. "I am—truly sorry. I wish you to know that, at least."

Through a cracked eyelid, he saw the drawn, harried face of young Leonard—the man who had taken Claire. The man wore a look of regret. Regret! Regret, for killing her.

Fury pulled him up against the weakness, and sent him lunging across the slanted deck in an instant. There was an outcry as he hit Leonard and bore him backward into the passage, and a good, juicy *thunk!* as the bugger's head hit the boards. People were shouting, and shadows leapt crazily all round him as the lanterns swayed, but he paid no attention.

He smashed Leonard's jaw with one great blow, his nose with the next. The weakness mattered nothing. He would spend all his strength and die here glad, but let him batter and maim now, feel the bones crack and the blood hot and slick on his fists. Blessed Michael, let him avenge her first!

There were hands on him, snatching and jerking, but they didn't matter. They would kill him now, he thought dimly, and that didn't matter, either. The body under him jerked and twitched between his legs, and lay still.

When the next blow came, he went willingly into the dark.

The light touch of fingers on his face awakened him. He reached drowsily up to take her hand, and his palm touched . . .

"Aaaah!"

With an instinctive revulsion, he was on his feet, clawing at his face. The big spider, nearly as frightened as he was, made off toward the shrubbery at high speed, long hairy legs no more than a blur.

There was an outburst of giggling behind him. He turned around, his heart pounding like a drum, and found six children, roosting in the branches of a big green tree, all grinning down at him with tobacco-stained teeth.

He bowed to them, feeling dizzy and rubber-legged, the start of fright that had got him up now dying in his blood.

"Mesdemoiselles, messieurs," he said, croaking, and in the half-awake recesses of his brain wondered what had made him speak to them in French? Had he half-heard them speaking, as he lay asleep?

French they were, for they answered him in that language, strongly laced with a gutteral sort of creole accent that he had never heard before.

"Vous êtes matelot?" the biggest boy asked, eyeing him with interest.

His knees gave way and he sat down on the ground, suddenly enough to make the children laugh again.

"Non," he replied, struggling to make his tongue work. *"Je suis guerrier."* His mouth was dry and his head ached like a fiend. Faint memories swam about in the parritch that filled his head, too vague to grasp.

"A soldier!" exclaimed one of the smaller children. His eyes were round and dark as sloes. "Where is your sword and *pistola,* eh?"

"Don't be silly," an older girl told him loftily. "How could he swim with a *pistola*? It would be ruined. Don't you know any better, guava-head?"

"Don't call me that!" the smaller boy shouted, face contorting in rage. "Shitface!"

"Frog-guts!"

"Caca-brains!"

The children were scrabbling through the branches like monkeys, screaming and chasing each other. Jamie rubbed a hand hard over his face, trying to think.

"Mademoiselle!" He caught the eye of the older girl and beckoned to her. She hesitated for a moment, then dropped from her branch like a ripe fruit, landing on the ground before him in a puff of yellow dust. She was barefoot, wearing nothing but a muslin shift and a colored kerchief round her dark, curly hair.

"Monsieur?"

"You seem a woman of some knowledge, Mademoiselle," he said. "Tell me, please, what is the name of this place?"

"Cap-Haïtien," she replied promptly. She eyed him with considerable curiosity. "You talk funny," she said.

"I am thirsty. Is there water nearby?" Cap-Haïtien. So he was on the island of Hispaniola. His mind was slowly beginning to function again; he had a vague memory of terrible effort, of swimming for his life in a frothing cauldron of heaving waves, and rain pelting his face so hard that it made little difference whether his head was above or below the surface. And what else?

"This way, this way!" The other children had dropped out of the tree, and a little girl was tugging his hand, urging him to follow.

He knelt by the little stream, splashing water over his head, gulping delicious cool handfuls, while the children scampered over the rocks, pelting each other with mud.

Now he remembered—the rat-faced seaman, and Leonard's surprised young face, the deep-red rage and the satisfying feel of flesh crushed against bone under his fist.

And Claire. The memory came back suddenly, with a sense of confused emotion—loss and terror, succeeded by relief. What had happened? He stopped what he was doing, not hearing the questions the children were flinging at him.

"Are you a deserter?" one of the boys asked again. "Have you been in a fight?" The boy's eyes rested curiously on his hands. His knuckles were cut and swollen, and his hands ached badly; the fourth finger felt as though he had cracked it again.

"Yes," he said absently, his mind occupied. Everything was coming back; the dark, stuffy confines of the brig where they had left him to wake, and the dreadful waking, to the thought that Claire was dead. He had huddled there on the bare boards, too shaken with grief to notice at first the increasing heave and roll of the ship, or the high-pitched whine of the rigging, loud enough to filter down even to his oubliette.

But after a time, the motion and noise were great enough to penetrate even the cloud of grief. He had heard the sounds of the growing storm, and the shouts and running overhead, and then was much too occupied to think of anything.

There was nothing in the small room with him, nothing to hold to. He had bounced from wall to wall like a dried pea in a wean's rattle, unable to tell up from down, right from left in the heaving dark, and not much caring, either, as waves of seasickness rolled through his body. He had thought then of nothing but death, and that with a fervor of longing.

He had been nearly unconscious, in fact, when the door to his prison had opened, and a strong smell of goat assailed his nostrils. He had no idea how the woman had got him up the ladder to the afterdeck, or why. He had only a confused memory of her babbling urgently to him in broken English as she pulled him along, half-supporting his weight as he stumbled and slid on the rain-wet decking.

He remembered the last thing she had said, though, as she pushed him toward the tilting taffrail.

"She is not dead," the woman had said. "She go there"— pointing at the rolling sea—"you go, too. Find her!" and then she had bent, got a hand in his crutch and a sturdy shoulder under his rump, and heaved him neatly over the rail and into the churning water.

"You are not an Englishman," the boy was saying. "It's an English ship, though, isn't it?"

He turned automatically, to look where the boy pointed, and saw the *Porpoise,* riding at anchor far out in the shallow bay. Other ships were scattered throughout the harbor, all clearly visible from this vantage point on a hill just outside the town.

"Yes," he said to the boy. "An English ship."

"One for me!" the boy exclaimed happily. He turned to shout to another lad. "Jacques! I was right! English! That's four for me, and only two for you this month!"

"Three!" Jacques corrected indignantly. "I get Spanish *and* Portuguese. *Bruja* was Portuguese, so I can count that, too!"

Jamie reached out and caught the older boy's arm.

"*Pardon,* Monsieur," he said. "Your friend said *Bruja*?"

"Yes, she was in last week," the boy answered. "Is *Bruja* a Portuguese name, though? We weren't sure whether to count it Spanish or Portuguese."

"Some of the sailors were in my *maman*'s taverna," one of the little girls chimed in. "They sounded like they were talking Spanish, but it wasn't like Uncle Geraldo talks."

"I think I should like to talk to your *maman, chérie,*" he said to the little girl. "Do any of you know, perhaps, where this *Bruja* was going when she left?"

"Bridgetown," the oldest girl put in promptly, trying to regain his attention. "I heard the clerk at the garrison say so."

"The garrison?"

"The barracks are next door to my *maman*'s taverna," the smaller girl chimed in, tugging at his sleeve. "The ship captains all go there with their papers, while the sailors get drunk. Come, come! *Maman* will feed you if I tell her to."

"I think your *maman* will throw me out the door," he told her, rubbing a hand across the heavy stubble on his chin. "I look like a vagabond." He did. There were stains of blood and vomit on his clothes despite the swim, and he knew by the feel of his face that it was bruised and bloodshot.

"*Maman* has seen much worse than you," the little girl assured him. "Come on!"

He smiled and thanked her, and allowed them to lead him down the hill, staggering slightly, as his land legs had not yet returned. He found it odd but somehow comforting that the children should not be frightened of him, horrible as he no doubt looked.

Was this what the goat-woman had meant? That Claire had swum ashore on this island? He felt a welling of hope that was as refreshing to his heart as the water had been to his parched throat. Claire was stubborn, reckless, and had a great deal more courage than was safe for a woman, but she was by no means such a fool as to fall off a man-of-war by accident.

And the *Bruja*—and Ian—were nearby! He would find them both, then. The fact that he was barefoot, penniless, and a fugitive from the Royal Navy seemed of no consequence. He had his wits and his hands, and with dry land once more beneath his feet, all things seemed possible.

52

A Wedding Takes Place

There was nothing to be done, but to repair the *Artemis* as quickly as possible, and make sail for Jamaica. I did my best to put aside my fear for Jamie, but I scarcely ate for the next two days, my appetite impeded by the large ball of ice that had taken up residence in my stomach.

For distraction, I took Marsali up to the house on the hill, where she succeeded in charming Father Fogden by recalling—and mixing for him—a Scottish recipe for a sheep-dip guaranteed to destroy ticks.

Stern helpfully pitched in with the labor of repair, delegating to me the guardianship of his specimen bag, and charging me with the task of searching the nearby jungle for any curious specimens of *Arachnida* that might come to hand as I looked for medicinal plants. While thinking privately that I would prefer to meet any of the larger specimens of *Arachnida* with a good stout boot, rather than my bare hands, I accepted the charge, peering into the internal water-filled cups of bromeliads in search of the bright-colored frogs and spiders who inhabited these tiny worlds.

I returned from one of these expeditions on the afternoon of the third day, with several large lily-roots, some shelf fungus of a vivid orange, and an unusual moss, together with a live tarantula—carefully trapped in one of the sailor's stocking caps and held at arm's length—large and hairy enough to send Lawrence into paroxysms of delight.

When I emerged from the jungle's edge, I saw that we had reached a new stage of progress; the *Artemis* was no longer canted on her side, but was slowly regaining an upright position on the sand, assisted by ropes, wedges, and a great deal of shouting.

"It's nearly finished, then?" I asked Fergus, who was standing near the stern, doing a good bit of the shouting as he instructed his crew in the placement of wedges. He turned to me, grinning and wiping the sweat from his forehead.

"Yes, milady! The caulking is complete. Mr. Warren gives it as his opinion that we may launch the ship near evening, when the day is grown cool, so the tar is hardened."

"That's marvelous!" I craned my neck back, looking up at the naked mast that towered high above. "Have we got sails?"

"Oh, yes," he assured me. "In fact, we have everything except—"

A shout of alarm from MacLeod interrupted whatever he had been about to say. I whirled to look toward the distant road out of the palmettos, where the sun winked off the glint of metal.

"Soldiers!" Fergus reacted faster than anyone, leaping from the scaffolding to land in a thudding spray of sand beside me. "Quick, milady! To the wood! Marsali!" he shouted, looking wildly about for the girl.

He licked sweat from his upper lip, eyes darting from the jungle to the approaching soldiers. "Marsali!" he shouted, once more.

Marsali appeared round the edge of the hull, pale and startled. Fergus grasped her by the arm and shoved her toward me. "Go with milady! Run!"

I snatched Marsali's hand and ran for the forest, sand spurting beneath our feet. There were shouts from the road behind us, and a shot cracked overhead, followed by another.

Ten steps, five, and then we were in the shadow of the trees. I collapsed behind the shelter of a thorny bush, gasping for breath against the stabbing pain of a stitch in my side. Marsali knelt on the earth beside me, her cheeks streaked with tears.

"What?" she gasped, struggling for breath. "Who are they? What—will they—do? To Fergus. What?"

"I don't know." Still breathing heavily, I grasped a cedar sapling and pulled myself to my knees. Peering through the underbrush on all fours, I could see that the soldiers had reached the ship.

It was cool and damp under the trees, but the lining of my

mouth was dry as cotton. I bit the inside of my cheek, trying to encourage a little saliva to flow.

"I think it will be all right." I patted Marsali's shoulder, trying to be reassuring. "Look, there are only ten of them," I whispered, counting as the last soldier trotted out of the palmetto grove. "They're French; the *Artemis* has French papers. It may be all right."

And then again, it might not. I was well aware that a ship aground and abandoned was legal salvage. It was a deserted beach. And all that stood between these soldiers and a rich prize were the lives of the *Artemis*'s crew.

A few of the seamen had pistols to hand; most had knives. But the soldiers were armed to the teeth, each man with musket, sword, and pistols. If it came to a fight, it would be a bloody one, but the odds were heavily on the mounted soldiers.

The men near the ship were silent, grouped close together behind Fergus, who stood out, straight-backed and grim, as the spokesman. I saw him push back his shock of hair with his hook, and plant his feet solidly in the sand, ready for whatever might come. The creak and jingle of harness seemed muted in the damp, hot air, and the horses moved slowly, hooves muffled in the sand.

The soldiers came to a halt ten feet away from the little knot of seamen. A big man who seemed to be in command raised one hand in an order to stay, and swung down from his horse.

I was watching Fergus, rather than the soldiers. I saw his face change, then freeze, white under his tan. I glanced quickly at the soldier coming toward him across the sand, and my own blood froze.

"*Silence, mes amis,*" said the big man, in a voice of pleasant command. "*Silence, et restez, s'il vous plaît.*" Silence, my friends, and do not move, if you please.

I would have fallen, were I not already on my knees. I closed my eyes in a wordless prayer of thanksgiving.

Next to me, Marsali gasped. I opened my eyes and clapped a hand over her open mouth.

The commander took off his hat, and shook out a thick mass of sweat-soaked auburn hair. He grinned at Fergus, teeth white and wolfish in a short, curly red beard.

"You are in charge here?" Jamie said in French. "You, come with me. The rest"—he nodded at the crew, several of whom were goggling at him in open amazement—"you stay where you are. Don't talk," he added, offhandedly.

Marsali jerked at my arm, and I realized how tightly I had been holding her.

"Sorry," I whispered, letting go, but not taking my eyes from the beach.

"What is he doing?" Marsali hissed in my ear. Her face was pale with excitement, and the little freckles left by the sun stood out on her nose in contrast. "How did he get here?"

"I don't know! Be quiet, for God's sake!"

The crew of the *Artemis* exchanged glances, waggled their eyebrows, and nudged each other in the ribs, but fortunately also obeyed orders and didn't speak. I hoped to heaven that their obvious excitement would be construed merely as consternation over their impending fate.

Jamie and Fergus had walked over toward the shore, conferring in low voices. Now they separated, Fergus coming back toward the hull with an expression of grim determination, Jamie calling the soldiers to dismount and gather round him.

I couldn't tell what Jamie was saying to the soldiers, but Fergus was close enough for us to hear.

"These are soldiers from the garrison at Cap-Haïtien," he announced to the crew members. "Their commander—Captain Alessandro—" he said, lifting his eyebrows and grimacing hideously to emphasize the name, "says that they will assist us in launching the *Artemis.*" This announcement was greeted with faint cheers from some of the men, and looks of bewilderment from others.

"But how did Mr. Fraser—" began Royce, a rather slow-witted seaman, his heavy brows drawn together in a puzzled frown. Fergus allowed no time for questions, but plunged into the midst of the crew, putting an arm about Royce's shoulders and dragging him toward the scaffolding, talking loudly to drown out any untoward remarks.

"Yes, is it not a most fortunate accident?" he said loudly. I could see that he was twisting Royce's ear with his sound hand. "Most fortunate indeed! Captain Alessandro says that a *habitant* on his way from his plantation saw the ship aground, and reported it to the garrison. With so much help, we will have the *Artemis* aswim in no time at all.'' He let go of Royce and clapped his hand sharply against his thigh.

"Come, come, let us set to work at once! Manzetti—up you go! MacLeod, MacGregor, seize your hammers! Maitland—'' He spotted Maitland, standing on the sand gawking at Jamie. Fergus whirled and clapped the cabin boy on the back hard enough to make him stagger.

"Maitland, *mon enfant!* Give us a song to speed our efforts!'' Looking rather dazed, Maitland began a tentative rendition of "The Nut-Brown Maid.'' A few of the seamen began to climb back onto the scaffolding, glancing suspiciously over their shoulders.

"Sing!'' Fergus bellowed, glaring up at them. Murphy, who appeared to be finding something extremely funny, mopped his sweating red face and obligingly joined in the song, his wheezing bass reinforcing Maitland's pure tenor.

Fergus stalked up and down beside the hull, exhorting, directing, urging—and making such a spectacle of himself that few telltale glances went in Jamie's direction. The uncertain tap of hammers started up again.

Meanwhile, Jamie was giving careful directions to his soldiers. I saw more than one Frenchman glance at the *Artemis* as he talked, with a look of dimly concealed greed that suggested that a selfless desire to help their fellow beings was perhaps not the motive uppermost in the soldiers' minds, no matter what Fergus had announced.

Still, the soldiers went to work willingly enough, stripping off their leather jerkins and laying aside most of their arms. Three of the soldiers, I noticed, did not join the work party, but remained on guard, fully armed, eyes sharp on the sailors' every move. Jamie alone remained aloof, watching everything.

"Should we come out?'' Marsali murmured in my ear. "It seems safe, now.''

"No,'' I said. My eyes were fixed on Jamie. He stood in the shade of a tall palmetto, at ease, but erect. Behind the unfamiliar beard, his expression was unreadable, but I caught the faint movement at his side, as the two stiff fingers flickered once against his thigh.

"No,'' I said again. "It isn't over yet.''

The work went on through the afternoon. The stack of wooden rollers mounted, cut ends scenting the air with the tang of fresh sap. Fergus's voice was hoarse, and his shirt clung wetly to his lean torso. The horses, hobbled, wandered slowly under the edge of the forest, browsing. The sailors had given up singing now, and had settled to work, with no more than an occasional glance toward the palmetto where Captain Alessandro stood in the shade, arms folded.

The sentry near the trees paced slowly up and down, musket carried at the ready, a wistful eye on the cool green shadows. He passed close enough on one circuit for me to see the dark, greasy curls dangling down his neck, and the pockmarks on his plump cheeks. He creaked and jingled as he walked. The rowel was missing from one of his spurs. He looked hot, and fairly cross.

It was a long wait, and the inquisitiveness of the forest midges made it longer still. After what seemed forever, though, I saw Jamie give a nod to one of the guards, and come from the beach toward the trees. I signed to Marsali to wait, and ducking under branches, ignoring the thick brush, I dodged madly toward the place where he had disappeared.

I popped breathlessly out from behind a bush, just as he was doing up the laces of his flies. His head jerked up at the sound, his eyes widened, and he let out a yell that would have summoned Arabella the sheep back from the dead, let alone the waiting sentry.

I dodged back into hiding, as crashing boots and shouts of inquiry headed in our direction.

"C'est bien!" Jamie shouted. He sounded a trifle shaken. *"Ce n'est qu'un serpent!"*

The sentry spoke an odd dialect of French, but appeared to be asking rather nervously whether the serpent was dangerous.

"Non, c'est innocent," Jamie answered. He waved at the sentry, whose inquiring head I could just see, peering reluctantly over the bush. The sentry, who seemed unenthusiastic about snakes, however innocent, disappeared promptly back to his duty.

Without hesitation, Jamie plunged into the bush.

"Claire!" He crushed me tight against his chest. Then he grabbed me by the shoulders and shook me, hard.

"Damn you!" he said, in a piercing whisper. "I thought ye were dead for sure! How dare ye do something harebrained like jump off a ship in the middle of the night! Have ye no sense at all?"

"Let go!" I demanded. The shaking had made me bite my lip. "Let go, I say! What do you mean, how dare *I* do something harebrained? You idiot, what possessed you to follow me?"

His face was darkened by the sun; now a deep red began to darken it further, washing up from the edges of his new beard.

"What possessed me?" he repeated. "You're my wife, for the Lord's sake! Of course I would follow ye; why did ye not wait for me? Christ, if I had time, I'd—" The mention of time evidently reminded him that we hadn't much, and with a noticeable effort, he choked back any further remarks, which was just as well, because I had a number of things to say in that vein myself. I swallowed them, with some difficulty.

"What in bloody hell are you doing here?" I asked instead.

The deep flush subsided slightly, succeeded by the merest hint of a smile amid the unfamiliar foliage.

"I'm the Captain," he said. "Did ye not notice?"

"Yes, I noticed! Captain Alessandro, my foot! What do you mean to do?"

Instead of answering, he gave me a final, gentle shake and divided a glare between me and Marsali, who had poked an inquiring head out.

"Stay here, the both of ye, and dinna stir a foot or I swear I'll beat ye senseless."

Without pausing for a response, he whirled and strode back through the trees, toward the beach.

Marsali and I exchanged stares, which were interrupted a second later, when Jamie, breathless, hurtled back into the small clearing. He grabbed me by both arms, and kissed me briefly but thoroughly.

"I forgot. I love you," he said, giving me another shake for emphasis. "And I'm glad you're no dead. Dinna do that again!" Letting go, he crashed back into the brush and disappeared.

I felt breathless, myself, and more than a little rattled, but undeniably happy.

Marsali's eyes were round as saucers.

"What shall we do?" she asked. "What's Da going to do?"

"I don't know," I said. My cheeks were flushed, and I could still feel the touch of his mouth on mine, and the unfamiliar tingling left by the brush of beard and mustache. My tongue touched the small stinging place where I had bitten my lip. "I don't know what he's going to do," I repeated. "I suppose we'll have to wait and see."

It was a long wait. I was dozing against the trunk of a huge tree, near dusk, when Marsali's hand on my shoulder brought me awake.

"They're launching the ship!" she said in an excited whisper.

They were; under the eyes of the sentries, the remaining soldiers and the crew of the *Artemis* were all manning the ropes and rollers that would move her down the beach into the waters of the inlet. Even Fergus, Innes, and Murphy joined in the labor, missing limbs notwithstanding.

The sun was going down; its disc shone huge and orange-gold, blinding above a sea gone the purple of whelks. The men were no more than black silhouettes against the light, anonymous as the slaves of an Egyptian wall-painting, tethered by ropes to their massive burden.

The monotonous "Heave!" of the bosun's shout was succeeded by a weak cheer as the hull slid the last few feet, drawn away from the shore by towropes from the *Artemis*'s jolly boat and cutter.

I saw the flash of red hair as Jamie moved up the side and swung aboard, then the gleam of metal as one of the soldiers followed him. They stood guard together, red hair and black no more than dots at the head of the rope ladder, as the crew of the *Artemis* entered the jolly boat, rowed out and came up the ladder, interspersed with the rest of the French soldiers.

The last man disappeared up the ladder. The men in the boats sat on their oars, looking up, tense and alert. Nothing happened.

Next to me, I heard Marsali exhale noisily, and realized I had been holding my own breath much too long.

"What are they *doing*?" she said, in exasperation.

As though in answer to this, there was one loud, angry shout from the *Artemis*. The men in the boats jerked up, ready to lunge aboard. No other signal came, though. The *Artemis* floated serenely on the rising waters of the inlet, perfect as an oil painting.

"I've had enough," I said suddenly to Marsali. "Whatever those bloody men are doing, they've done it. Come on."

I drew in a fresh gulp of the cool evening air, and walked out of the trees, Marsali behind me. As we came down the beach, a slim black figure dropped over the ship's side and galloped through the shallows, gleaming gouts of green and purple seawater spouting from his footsteps.

"Mo chridhe chérie!" Fergus ran dripping toward us, face beaming, and seizing Marsali, swung her off her feet with exuberance and whirled her round.

"Done!" he crowed. "Done without a shot fired! Trussed like geese and packed like salted herrings in the hold!" He kissed Marsali heartily, then set her down on the sand, and turning to me, bowed ceremoniously, with the elaborate flourish of an imaginary hat.

"Milady, the captain of the *Artemis* desires you will honor him with your company over supper."

The new captain of the *Artemis* was standing in the middle of his cabin, eyes closed and completely naked, blissfully scratching his testicles.

"Er," I said, confronted with this sight. His eyes popped open and his face lit with joy. The next moment, I was enfolded in his embrace, face pressed against the red-gold curls of his chest.

We didn't say anything for quite some time. I could hear the thrum of footsteps on the deck overhead, the shouts of the crew, ringing with joy at the imminence of escape, and the creak and flap of sails being rigged. The *Artemis* was coming back to life around us.

My face was warm, tingling from the rasp of his beard. I felt suddenly strange and shy holding him, he naked as a jay and myself as bare under the remnants of Father Fogden's tattered robe.

The body that pressed against my own with mounting urgency was the same from the neck down, but the face was a stranger's, a Viking marauder's. Besides the beard that transformed his face, he smelled unfamiliar, his own sweat overlaid with rancid cooking oil, spilled beer, and the reek of harsh perfume and unfamiliar spices.

I let go, and took a step back.

"Shouldn't you dress?" I asked. "Not that I don't enjoy the

scenery," I added, blushing despite myself. "I—er . . . I think I like the beard. Maybe," I added doubtfully, scrutinizing him.

"I don't," he said frankly, scratching his jaw. "I'm crawling wi' lice, and it itches like a fiend."

"Eew!" While I was entirely familiar with *Pediculus humanus,* the common body louse, acquaintance had not endeared me. I rubbed a hand nervously through my own hair, already imagining the prickle of feet on my scalp, as tiny sestets gamboled through the thickets of my curls.

He grinned at me, white teeth startling in the auburn beard.

"Dinna fash yourself, Sassenach," he assured me. "I've already sent for a razor and hot water."

"Really? It seems rather a pity to shave it off right away." Despite the lice, I leaned forward to peer at his hirsute adornment. "It's like your hair, all different colors. Rather pretty, really."

I touched it, warily. The hairs were odd; thick and wiry, very curly, in contrast to the soft thick smoothness of the hair on his head. They sprang exuberantly from his skin in a profusion of colors; copper, gold, amber, cinnamon, a roan so deep as almost to be black. Most startling of all was a thick streak of silver that ran from his lower lip to the line of his jaw.

"That's funny," I said, tracing it. "You haven't any white hairs on your head, but you have right here."

"I have?" He put a hand to his jaw, looking startled, and I suddenly realized that he likely had no idea what he looked like. Then he smiled wryly, and bent to pick up the pile of discarded clothes from the floor.

"Aye, well, little wonder if I have; I wonder I've not gone white-haired altogether from the things I've been through this month." He paused, eyeing me over the wadded white breeches. "And speaking of that, Sassenach, as I was saying to ye in the trees—"

"Yes, speaking of that," I interrupted. "What in the name of God did you *do*?"

"Oh, the soldiers, ye mean?" He scratched his chin meditatively. "Well, it was simple enough. I told the soldiers that as soon as the ship was launched, we'd gather everyone on deck, and at my signal, they were to fall on the crew and push them into the hold." A broad grin blossomed through the foliage. "Only Fergus had mentioned it to the crew, ye see; so when each soldier came aboard, two of the crewmen snatched him by the arms while a third gagged him, bound his arms, and took away his weapons. Then we pushed all of *them* into the hold. That's all.'' He shrugged, modestly nonchalant.

"Right," I said, exhaling. "And as for just how you happened to be here in the first place . . .''

At this juncture we were interrupted by a discreet knock on the cabin's door.

"Mr. Fraser? Er . . . Captain, I mean?" Maitland's angular young face peered round the jamb, cautious over a steaming bowl. "Mr. Murphy's got the galley fire going, and here's your hot water, with his compliments.''

"Mr. Fraser will do," Jamie assured him, taking the tray with bowl and razor in one hand. "A less seaworthy captain doesna bear thinking of." He paused, listening to the thump of feet above our heads.

"Though since I *am* the captain," he said slowly, "I suppose that means I shall say when we sail and when we stop?''

"Yes, sir, that's one thing a captain does,'' Maitland said. He added helpfully, "The captain also says when the hands are to have extra rations of food and grog.''

"I see." The upward curl of Jamie's mouth was still visible, beard notwithstanding. "Tell me, Maitland—how much d'ye think the hands can drink and still sail the ship?''

"Oh, quite a lot, sir,'' Maitland said earnestly. His brow wrinkled in thought. "Maybe—an extra double ration all round?''

Jamie lifted one eyebrow. "Of brandy?''

"Oh, no, sir!'' Maitland looked shocked. "Grog. If it was to be brandy, only an extra half-ration, or they'd be rolling in the bilges.''

"Double grog, then." Jamie bowed ceremoniously to Maitland, unhampered by the fact that he was still completely unclad. "Make it so, Mr. Maitland. And the ship will not lift anchor until I have finished my supper.''

"Yes, sir!'' Maitland bowed back; Jamie's manners were catching. "And shall I desire the Chinee to attend you directly after the anchor is weighed?''

"Somewhat before that, Mr. Maitland, thank ye kindly.''

Maitland was turning to leave, with a last admiring glance at Jamie's scars, but I stopped him.

"One more thing, Maitland," I said.

"Oh, yes, mum?"

"Will you go down to the galley and ask Mr. Murphy to send up a bottle of his strongest vinegar? And then find where the men have put some of my medicines, and fetch them as well?"

His narrow forehead creased in puzzlement, but he nodded obligingly. "Oh, yes, mum. This direct minute."

"Just what d'ye mean to do wi' the vinegar Sassenach?" Jamie observed me narrowly, as Maitland vanished into the corridor.

"Souse you in it to kill the lice," I said. "I don't intend to sleep with a seething nest of vermin."

"Oh," he said. He scratched the side of his neck meditatively. "Ye mean to sleep with me, do you?" He glanced at the berth, an uninviting hole in the wall.

"I don't know where, precisely, but yes, I do," I said firmly. "And I wish you wouldn't shave your beard just yet," I added, as he bent to set down the tray he was holding.

"Why not?" He glanced curiously over his shoulder at me, and I felt the heat rising in my cheeks.

"Er . . . well. It's a bit . . . different."

"Oh, aye?" He stood up and took a step toward me. In the cramped confines of the cabin, he seemed even bigger—and a lot more naked—than he ever had on deck.

The dark blue eyes had slanted into triangles of amusement.

"How, different?" he asked.

"Well, it . . . um . . ." I brushed my fingers vaguely past my burning cheeks. "It feels different. When you kiss me. On my .. . . skin."

His eyes locked on mine. He hadn't moved, but he seemed much closer.

"Ye have verra fine skin, Sassenach," he said softly. "Like pearls and opals." He reached out a finger and very gently traced the line of my jaw. And then my neck, and the wide flare of collarbone and back, and down, in a slow-moving serpentine that brushed the tops of my breasts, hidden in the deep cowl neck of the priest's robe. "Ye have a *lot* of verra fine skin, Sassenach," he added. One eyebrow quirked up. "If that's what ye were thinking?"

I swallowed and licked my lips, but didn't look away.

"That's more or less what I was thinking, yes."

He took his finger away and glanced at the bowl of steaming water.

"Aye, well. It seems a shame to waste the water. Shall I send it back to Murphy to make soup, or shall I drink it?"

I laughed, both tension and strangeness dissolving at once.

"You shall sit down," I said, "and wash with it. You smell like a brothel."

"I expect I do," he said, scratching. "There's one upstairs in the tavern where the soldiers go to drink and gamble." He took up the soap and dropped it in the hot water.

"Upstairs, eh?" I said.

"Well, the girls come down, betweentimes," he explained. "It wouldna be mannerly to stop them sitting on your lap, after all."

"And your mother brought you up to have nice manners, I expect," I said, very dryly.

"Upon second thoughts, I think perhaps we shall anchor here for the night," he said thoughtfully, looking at me.

"Shall we?"

"And sleep ashore, where there's room."

"Room for *what*?" I asked, regarding him with suspicion.

"Well, I have it planned, aye?" he said, sloshing water over his face with both hands.

"You have *what* planned?" I asked. He snorted and shook the excess water from his beard before replying.

"I have been thinking of this for months, now," he said, with keen anticipation. "Every night, folded up in that godforsaken nutshell of a berth, listening to Fergus grunt and fart across the cabin. I thought it all out, just what I would do, did I have ye naked and willing, no one in hearing, and room enough to serve ye suitably." He lathered the cake of soap vigorously between his palms, and applied it to his face.

"Well, I'm willing enough," I said, intrigued. "And there's room, certainly. As for naked . . ."

"I'll see to that," he assured me. "That's part o' the plan, aye? I shall take ye to a private spot, spread out a quilt to lie on, and commence by sitting down beside you."

"Well, that's a start, all right," I said. "What then?" I sat down next to him on the berth. He leaned close and bit my earlobe very delicately.

"As for what next, then I shall take ye on my knee and kiss ye."

He paused to illustrate, holding my arms so I couldn't move. He let go a minute later, leaving my lips slightly swollen, tasting of ale, soap, and Jamie.

"So much for step one," I said, wiping soapsuds from my mouth. "What then?"

"Then I shall lay ye down upon the quilt, twist your hair up in my hand and taste your face and throat and ears and bosom wi' my lips," he said. "I thought I would do that until ye start to make squeaking noises."

"I don't make squeaking noises!"

"Aye, ye do," he said. "Here, hand me the towel, aye?"

"Then," he went on cheerfully, "I thought I would begin at the other end. I shall lift up your skirt and—" His face disappeared into the folds of the linen towel.

"And what?" I asked, thoroughly intrigued.

"And kiss the insides of your thighs, where the skin's so soft. The beard might help there, aye?" He stroked his jaw, considering.

"It might," I said, a little faintly. "What am I supposed to be doing while you do this?"

"Well, ye might moan a bit, if ye like, to encourage me, but otherwise, ye just lie still."

He didn't sound as though he needed any encouragement whatever. One of his hands was resting on my thigh as he used the other to swab his chest with the damp towel. As he finished, the hand slid behind me, and squeezed.

"My beloved's arm is under me," I quoted. "And his hand behind my head. Comfort me with apples, and stay me with flagons, For I am sick of love."

There was a flash of white teeth in his beard.

"More like grapefruit," he said, one hand cupping my behind. "Or possibly gourds. Grapefruit are too small."

"Gourds?" I said indignantly.

"Well, wild gourds get that big sometimes," he said. "But aye, that's next." He squeezed once more, then removed the hand in order to wash the armpit on that side. "I lie upon my back and have ye stretched at length upon me, so that I can get hold of your buttocks and fondle them properly." He stopped washing to give me a quick example of what he thought proper, and I let out an involuntary gasp.

"Now," he went on, resuming his ablutions, "should ye wish to kick your legs a bit, or make lewd motions wi' your hips and pant in my ear at that point in the proceedings, I should have no great objection."

"I do not pant!"

"Aye, ye do. Now, about your breasts—"

"Oh, I thought you'd forgotten those."

"Never in life," he assured me. "No," he went blithely on, "that's when I take off your gown, leaving ye in naught but your shift."

"I'm not wearing a shift."

"Oh? Well, no matter," he said, dismissing this. "I meant to suckle ye through the thin cotton, 'til your nipples stood up hard in my mouth, and then take it off, but it's no great concern; I'll manage without. So, allowing for the absence of your shift, I shall attend to your breasts until ye make that wee bleating noise—"

"I don't—"

"And then," he said, interrupting, "since ye will, according to the plan, be naked, and—provided I've done it right so far—possibly willing as well—"

"Oh, just possibly," I said. My lips were still tingling from step one.

"—then I shall spread open your thighs, take down my breeks, and—" He paused, waiting.

"And?" I said, obligingly.

The grin widened substantially.

"And we'll see what sort of noise it is ye don't make then, Sassenach."

There was a slight cough in the doorway behind me.

"Oh, your pardon, Mr. Willoughby," Jamie said apologetically. "I wasna expecting ye so soon. Perhaps ye'd care to go and have a bit of supper? And if ye would, take those things along and ask Murphy will he burn them in the galley fire." He tossed the remains of his uniform to Mr. Willoughby, and bent to rummage in a sealocker for fresh clothing.

"I never thought to meet Lawrence Stern again," he remarked, burrowing through the tangled linen. "How does he come to be here?"

"Oh, he *is* the Jewish natural philosopher you told me about?"

"He is. Though I shouldna think there are so many Jewish philosophers about as to cause great confusion."

I explained how I had come to meet Stern in the mangroves. ". . . and then he brought me up to the priest's house," I said, and stopped, suddenly reminded. "Oh, I almost forgot! You owe the priest two pounds sterling, on account of Arabella."

"I do?" Jamie glanced at me, startled, a shirt in his hand.

"You do. Maybe you'd best ask Lawrence if he'll act as ambassador; the priest seems to get on with him."

"All right. What's happened to this Arabella, though? Has one of the crew debauched her?"

"I suppose you might say that." I drew breath to explain further, but before I could speak, another knock sounded on the door.

"Can a man not dress in peace?" Jamie demanded irritably. "Come, then!"

The door swung open, revealing Marsali, who blinked at the sight of her nude stepfather. Jamie hastily swathed his midsection in the shirt he was holding, and nodded to her, sangfroid only slightly impaired.

"Marsali, lass. I'm glad to see ye unhurt. Did ye require something?"

The girl edged into the room, taking up a position between the table and a sea chest.

"Aye, I do," she said. She was sunburned, and her nose was peeling, but I thought she seemed pale nonetheless. Her fists were clenched at her sides, and her chin lifted as for battle.

"I require ye to keep your promise," she said.

"Aye?" Jamie looked wary.

"Your promise to let me and Fergus be married, so soon as we came to the Indies." A small wrinkle appeared between her fair eyebrows. "Hispaniola *is* in the Indies, no? The Jew said so."

Jamie scratched at his beard, looking reluctant.

"It is," he said. "And aye, I suppose if I . . . well, aye. I did promise. But—you're still sure of yourselves, the two of ye?" She lifted her chin higher, jaw set firmly.

"We are."

Jamie lifted one eyebrow.

"Where's Fergus?"

"Helping stow the cargo. I kent we'd be under way soon, so I thought I'd best come and ask now."

"Aye. Well." Jamie frowned, then sighed with resignation. "Aye, I said. But I did say as ye must be blessed by a priest, did I no? There's no priest closer than Bayamo, and that's three days' ride. But perhaps in Jamaica . . ."

"Nay, you're forgetting!" Marsali said triumphantly. "We've a priest right here. Father Fogden can marry us."

I felt my jaw drop, and hastily closed it. Jamie was scowling at her.

"We sail first thing in the morning!"

"It won't take long," she said. "It's only a few words, after all. We're already married, by law; it's only to be blessed by the Church, aye?" Her hand flattened on her abdomen where her marriage contract presumably resided beneath her stays.

"But your mother . . ." Jamie glanced helplessly at me for reinforcement. I shrugged, equally helpless. The task of trying either to explain Father Fogden to Jamie or to dissuade Marsali was well beyond me.

"He likely won't do it, though." Jamie came up with this objection with a palpable air of relief. "The crew have been trifling with one of his parishioners named Arabella. He willna want anything to do wi' us, I'm afraid."

"Yes, he will! He'll do it for me—he likes me!" Marsali was almost dancing on her toes with eagerness.

Jamie looked at her for a long moment, eyes fixed on hers, reading her face. She was very young.

"You're sure, then, lassie?" he said at last, very gently. "Ye want this?"

She took a deep breath, a glow spreading over her face.

"I am, Da. I truly am. I want Fergus! I love him!"

Jamie hesitated a moment, then rubbed a hand through his hair and nodded.

"Aye, then. Go and send Mr. Stern to me, then fetch Fergus and tell him to make ready."

"Oh, Da! Thank you, thank you!" Marsali flung herself at him and kissed him. He held her with one arm, clutching the shirt about his middle with the other. Then he kissed her on the forehead and pushed her gently away.

"Take care," he said, smiling. "Ye dinna want to go to your bridal covered wi' lice."

"Oh!" This seemed to remind her of something. She glanced at me and blushed, putting up a hand to her own pale locks, which were matted with sweat and straggling down her neck from a careless knot.

"Mother Claire," she said shyly, "I wonder—would ye—could ye lend me a bit of the special soap ye make wi' the chamomile? I —if there's time—" she added, with a hasty glance at Jamie, "I should like to wash my hair."

"Of course," I said, and smiled at her. "Come along and we'll make you pretty for your wedding." I looked her over appraisingly, from glowing round face to dirty bare feet. The crumpled muslin of her sea-shrunk gown stretched tight over her bosom, slight as it was, and the grubby hem hovered several inches above her sandy ankles.

A thought struck me, and I turned to Jamie. "She should have a nice dress to be married in," I said.

"Sassenach," he said, with obviously waning patience, "we havena—"

"No, but the priest does," I interrupted. "Tell Lawrence to ask Father Fogden whether we might borrow one of his gowns; Ermenegilda's, I mean. I think they're almost the right size."

Jamie's face went blank with surprise above his beard.

"Ermenegilda?" he said. "Arabella? Gowns?" He narrowed his eyes at me. "What sort of priest *is* this man, Sassenach?"

I paused in the doorway, Marsali hovering impatiently in the passage beyond.

"Well," I said, "he drinks a bit. And he's rather fond of sheep. But he might remember the words to the wedding ceremony."

It was one of the more unusual weddings I had attended. The sun had long since sunk into the sea by the time all arrangements were made. To the disgruntlement of Mr. Warren, the ship's master, Jamie had declared that we would not leave until the next day, so as to allow the newlyweds one night of privacy ashore.

"Damned if I'd care to consummate a marriage in one of those godforsaken pesthole berths," he told me privately. "If they got coupled in there to start wi', we'd never pry them out. And the thought of takin' a maidenhead in a hammock—"

"Quite," I said. I poured more vinegar on his head, smiling to myself. "Very thoughtful of you."

Now Jamie stood by me on the beach, smelling rather strongly of vinegar, but handsome and dignified in blue coat, clean stock and linen, and gray serge breeks, with his hair clubbed back and ribboned. The wild red beard was a bit incongruous above his otherwise sober garb, but it had been neatly trimmed and fine-combed with vinegar, and stocking feet notwithstanding, he made a fine picture as father of the bride.

Murphy, as one chief witness, and Maitland, as the other, were somewhat less prepossessing, though Murphy had washed his hands and Maitland his face. Fergus would have preferred Lawrence Stern as a witness, and Marsali had asked for me, but both were dissuaded; first on grounds that Stern was not a Christian, let alone a Catholic, and then, by consideration that while I was religiously qualified, that fact was unlikely to weigh heavily with Laoghaire, once she found out about it.

"I've told Marsali she must write to her mother to say she's wed," Jamie murmured to me as we watched the preparations on the beach go forward. "But perhaps I shall suggest she doesna say much more about it than that."

I saw his point; Laoghaire was not going to be pleased at hearing that her eldest daughter had eloped with a one-handed ex-pickpocket twice her age. Her maternal feelings were unlikely to be assuaged by hearing that the marriage had been performed in the middle of the night on a West Indian beach by a disgraced—if not actually defrocked—priest, witnessed by twenty-five seamen, ten French horses, a small flock of sheep—all gaily beribboned in honor of the occasion—and a King Charles spaniel, who added to the generally festive feeling by attempting to copulate with Murphy's wooden leg at every opportunity. The only thing that could make things worse, in Laoghaire's view, would be to hear that I had participated in the ceremony.

Several torches were lit, bound to stakes pounded into the sand, and the flames streamed seaward in tails of red and orange, bright against the black velvet night. The brilliant stars of the Caribbean shone overhead like the lights of heaven. While it was not a church, few brides had had a more beautiful setting for their nuptials.

I didn't know what prodigies of persuasion had been required on Lawrence's part, but Father Fogden was there, frail and insubstantial as a ghost, the blue sparks of his eyes the only real signs of life. His skin was gray as his robe, and his hands trembled on the worn leather of his prayer book.

Jamie glanced sharply at him, and appeared to be about to say something, but then merely muttered under his breath in Gaelic and pressed his lips tightly together. The spicy scent of sangria wafted from Father Fogden's vicinity, but at least he had reached the beach under his own power. He stood swaying between two torches, laboriously trying to turn the pages of his book as the light offshore wind jerked them fluttering from his fingers.

At last he gave up, and dropped the book on the sand with a little *plop!*

"Um," he said, and belched. He looked about and gave us a small, saintlike smile. "Dearly beloved of God."

It was several moments before the throng of shuffling, murmuring spectators realized that the ceremony had started, and began to poke each other and straighten to attention.

"Wilt thou take this woman?" Father Fogden demanded, suddenly rounding ferociously on Murphy.

"No!" said the cook, startled. "I don't hold wi' women. Messy things."

"You don't?" Father Fogden closed one eye, the remaining orb bright and accusing. He looked at Maitland.

"Do *you* take this woman?"

"Not me, sir, no. Not that anyone wouldn't be pleased," he added hastily. "Him, please." Maitland pointed at Fergus, who stood next to the cabin boy, glowering at the priest.

"Him? You're sure? He hasn't a hand," Father Fogden said doubtfully. "Won't she mind?"

"I will not!" Marsali, imperious in one of Ermenegilda's gowns, blue silk encrusted with gold embroidery along the low, square neckline and puffed sleeves, stood beside Fergus. She looked lovely, with her hair clean and bright as fresh straw, brushed to a gloss and floating loose round her shoulders, as became a maiden. She also looked angry.

"Go on!" She stamped her foot, which made no noise on the sand, but seemed to startle the priest.

"Oh, yes," he said nervously, taking one step back. "Well, I don't suppose it's an impt—impeddy—impediment, after all. Not as though he'd lost his cock, I mean. He hasn't, has he?" the priest inquired anxiously, as the possibility occurred to him. "I can't marry you if he has. It's not allowed."

Marsali's face was already bathed in red by torchlight. The expression on it at this point reminded me strongly of how her mother had looked upon finding me at Lallybroch. A visible tremor ran through Fergus's shoulders, whether of rage or laughter, I couldn't tell.

Jamie quelled the incipient riot by striding firmly into the middle of the wedding and placing a hand on the shoulders of Fergus and Marsali.

"This man," he said, with a nod toward Fergus, "and this woman," with another toward Marsali. "Marry them, Father. Now. Please," he added, as an obvious afterthought, and stood back a pace, restoring order among the audience by dint of dark glances from side to side.

"Oh, quite. Quite," Father Fogden repeated, swaying gently. "Quite, quite." A long pause followed, during which the priest squinted at Marsali.

"Name," he said abruptly. "I have to have a name. Can't get married without a name. Just like a cock. Can't get married without a name; can't get married without a c—"

"Marsali Jane MacKimmie Joyce!" Marsali spoke up loudly, drowning him out.

"Yes, yes," he said hurriedly. "Of course it is. Marsali. Marsa-lee. Just so. Well, then, do you Mar-sa-lee take this man—even though he's missing a hand and possibly other parts not visible—to be your lawful husband? To have and to hold, from this day forward, forsaking . . ." At this point he trailed off, his attention fixed on one of the sheep that had wandered into the light and was chewing industriously on a discarded stocking of striped wool.

"I do!"

Father Fogden blinked, brought back to attention. He made an unsuccessful attempt to stifle another belch, and transferred his bright blue gaze to Fergus.

"You have a name, too? *And* a cock?"

"Yes," said Fergus, wisely choosing not to be more specific. "Fergus."

The priest frowned slightly at this. "Fergus?" he said. "Fergus. Fergus. Yes, Fergus, got that. That's all? No more name? Need more names, surely."

"Fergus," Fergus repeated, with a note of strain in his voice. Fergus was the only name he had ever had—bar his original French name of Claudel. Jamie had given him the name Fergus in Paris, when they had met, twenty years before. But naturally a brothel-born bastard would have no last name to give a wife.

"Fraser," said a deep, sure voice beside me. Fergus and Marsali both glanced back in surprise, and Jamie nodded. His eyes met Fergus's, and he smiled faintly.

"Fergus Claudel Fraser," he said, slowly and clearly. One eyebrow lifted as he looked at Fergus.

Fergus himself looked transfixed. His mouth hung open, eyes wide black pools in the dim light. Then he nodded slightly, and a glow rose in his face, as though he contained a candle that had just been lit.

"Fraser," he said to the priest. His voice was husky, and he cleared his throat. "Fergus Claudel Fraser."

Father Fogden had his head tilted back, watching the sky, where a crescent of light floated over the trees, holding the black orb of the moon in its cup. He lowered his head to face Fergus, looking dreamy.

"Well, that's good," he said. "Isn't it?"

A small poke in the ribs from Maitland brought him back to an awareness of his responsibilities.

"Oh! Um. Well. Man and wife. Yes, I pronounce you man—no, that's not right, you haven't said whether you'd take her. She has both hands," he added helpfully.

"I will," Fergus said. He had been holding Marsali's hand; now he let go and dug hastily in his pocket, coming out with a small gold ring. He must have bought it in Scotland, I realized, and kept it ever since, not wanting to make the marriage official until it had been blessed. Not by a priest—by Jamie.

The beach was silent as he slid the ring on her finger, all eyes fixed on the small gold circle and the two heads bent close together over it, one bright, one dark.

So she had done it. One fifteen-year-old girl, with nothing but stubbornness as a weapon. "I want him," she had said. And kept saying it, through her mother's objections and Jamie's arguments, through Fergus's scruples and her own fears, through three thousand miles of homesickness, hardship, ocean storm, and shipwreck.

She raised her face, shining, and found her mirror in Fergus's eyes. I saw them look at each other, and felt the tears prickle behind my lids.

"I want him." I had not said that to Jamie at our marriage; I had not wanted him, then. But I had said it since, three times; in two moments of choice at Craigh na Dun, and once again at Lallybroch.

"I want him." I wanted him still, and nothing whatever could stand between us.

He was looking down at me; I could feel the weight of his gaze, dark blue and tender as the sea at dawn.

"What are ye thinking, *mo chridhe*?" he asked softly.

I blinked back the tears and smiled at him. His hands were large and warm on mine.

"What I tell you three times is true," I said. And standing on tiptoe, I kissed him as the sailors' cheer went up.

PART NINE

Worlds Unknown

PART NINE

WRITING WORKSHOP

53

Bat Guano

Bat guano is a slimy blackish green when fresh, a powdery light brown when dried. In both states, it emits an eye-watering reek of musk, ammonia, and decay.

"*How* much of this stuff did you say we're taking?" I asked, through the cloth I had wrapped about my lower face.

"Ten tons," Jamie replied, his words similarly muffled. We were standing on the upper deck, watching as the slaves trundled barrowloads of the reeking stuff down the gangplank and over to the open hatchway of the after hold.

Tiny particles of the dried guano blew from the barrows and filled the air around us with a deceptively beautiful cloud of gold, that sparked and glimmered in the late afternoon sun. The men's bodies were coated with the stuff as well; the runnels of sweat carved dark channels in the dust on their bare torsos, and the constant tears ran down their faces and chests, so that they were striped in black and gold like exotic zebras.

Jamie dabbed at his own streaming eyes as the wind veered slightly toward us. "D'ye ken how to keelhaul someone, Sassenach?"

"No, but if it's Fergus you have in mind as a candidate, I'm with you. How far is it to Jamaica?" It was Fergus, making inquiries in the marketplace on King's Street in Bridgetown, who had gained the *Artemis* her first commission as a trading and hauling vessel; the shipment of ten cubic tons of bat guano from Barbados to Jamaica, for use as fertilizer on the sugar plantation of one Mr. Grey, planter.

Fergus himself was rather self-consciously overseeing the loading of the huge quarried blocks of dried guano, which were tipped from their barrows and handed down one by one into the hold. Marsali, never far from his side, had in this case moved as far as the forecastle, where she sat on a barrel filled with oranges, the lovely new shawl Fergus had bought her in the market wrapped over her face.

"We are meant to be traders, no?" Fergus had argued. "We have an empty hold to fill. Besides," he had added logically, clinching the argument, "Monsieur Grey will pay us more than adequately."

"How far, Sassenach?" Jamie squinted at the horizon, as though hoping to see land rising from the sparkling waves. Mr. Willoughby's magic needles rendered him seaworthy, but he submitted to the process with no real enthusiasm. "Three or four days' sail, Warren says," he admitted with a sigh, "and the weather holds fair."

"Maybe the smell will be better at sea," I said.

"Oh, yes, milady," Fergus assured me, overhearing as he passed. "The owner tells me that the stench dissipates itself significantly, once the dried material is removed from the caves where it accumulates." He leapt into the rigging and went up, climbing like a monkey despite his hook. Reaching the top rigging, Fergus tied the red kerchief that was the signal to hands on shore to come aboard, and slid down again, pausing to say something rude to Ping An, who was perched on the lowest crosstrees, keeping a bright yellow eye on the proceedings below.

"Fergus seems to be taking quite a proprietary interest in this cargo," I observed.

"Aye, well, he's a partner," Jamie said. "I told him if he'd a wife to support, he must think of how to do it. And as it may be some time before we're in the printing business again, he must turn his hand to what offers. He and Marsali have half the profit on this cargo—against the dowry I promised her," he added wryly, and I laughed.

"You know," I said, "I really would like to read the letter Marsali's sending to her mother. First Fergus, I mean, then Father Fogden and Mamacita, and now a dowry of ten tons of bat shit."

"I shall never be able to set foot in Scotland again, once

Laoghaire reads it," said Jamie, but he smiled nonetheless. "Have ye thought yet what to do wi' your new acquisition?"

"Don't remind me," I said, a little grimly. "Where is he?"

"Somewhere below," Jamie said, his attention distracted by a man coming down the wharf toward us. "Murphy's fed him, and Innes will find a place for him. Your pardon, Sassenach; I think this will be someone looking for me." He swung down from the rail and went down the gangplank, neatly skipping around a slave coming up with a barrowload of guano.

I watched with interest as he greeted the man, a tall colonial in the dress of a prosperous planter, with a weathered red face that spoke of long years in the islands. He extended a hand toward Jamie, who took it in a firm clasp. Jamie said something, and the man replied, his expression of wariness changing to an instant cordiality.

This must be the result of Jamie's visit to the Masonic lodge in Bridgetown, where he had gone immediately upon landing the day before, mindful of Jared's suggestion. He had identified himself as a member of the brotherhood, and spoken to the Master of the lodge, describing Young Ian and asking for any news of either the boy or the ship *Bruja*. The Master had promised to spread the word among such Freemasons as might have occasion to frequent the slave market and the shipping docks. With luck, this was the fruit of that promise.

I watched eagerly as the planter reached into his coat and withdrew a paper, which he unfolded and showed to Jamie, apparently explaining something. Jamie's face was intent, his ruddy brows drawn together with concentration, but showed neither exultation nor disappointment. Maybe it was not news of Ian at all. After our visit to the slave market the day before, I was half-inclined to hope not.

Lawrence, Fergus, Marsali, and I had gone to the slave market under the cranky chaperonage of Murphy, while Jamie called on the Masonic Master. The slave market was near the docks, down a dusty road lined with sellers of fruit and coffee, dried fish and coconuts, yams and red cochineal bugs, sold for dye in small, corked glass bottles.

Murphy, with his passion for order and propriety, had insisted that Marsali and I must each have a parasol, and had forced Fergus to buy two from a roadside vendor.

"All the white women in Bridgetown carry parasols," he said firmly, trying to hand me one.

"I don't need a parasol," I said, impatient at talk of something so inconsequential as my complexion, when we might be near to finding Ian at last. "The sun isn't that hot. Let's go!"

Murphy glowered at me, scandalized.

"Ye don't want folk to think ye ain't respectable, that ye don't care enough to keep yer skin fine!"

"I wasn't planning to take up residence here," I said tartly. "I don't care *what* they think." Not pausing to argue further, I began walking down the road, toward a distant murmur of noise that I took to be the slave market.

"Yer face will . . . get . . . red!" Murphy said, huffing indignantly alongside me, attempting to open the parasol as he stumped along.

"Oh, a fate worse than death, I'm sure!" I snapped. My nerves were strung tight, in anticipation of what we might find. "All right, then, give me the bloody thing!" I snatched it from him, snapped it open, and set it over my shoulder with an irritable twirl.

As it was, within minutes I was grateful for Murphy's intransigence. While the road was shaded by tall palms and cecropia trees, the slave market itself was held in a large, stone-paved space without the grace of any shade, save that provided by ramshackle open booths roofed with sheets of tin or palm fronds, in which the slave-dealers and auctioneers sought occasional refuge from the sun. The slaves themselves were mostly held in large pens at the side of the square, open to the elements.

The sun *was* fierce in the open, and the light bouncing off the pale stones was blinding after the green shade of the road. I blinked, eyes watering, and hastily adjusted my parasol over my head.

So shaded, I could see a bewildering array of bodies, naked or nearly so, gleaming in every shade from pale café au lait to a deep blue-black. Bouquets of color blossomed in front of the auction blocks, where the plantation owners and their servants gathered to inspect the wares, vivid amid the stark blacks and whites.

The stink of the place was staggering, even to one accustomed to the stenches of Edinburgh and the reeking tween-decks of the

Porpoise. Heaps of wet human excrement lay in the corners of the slave pens, buzzing with flies, and a thick oily reek floated on the air, but the major component of the smell was the unpleasantly intimate scent of acres of hot bare flesh, baking in the sun.

"Jesu," Fergus muttered next to me. His dark eyes flicked right and left in shocked disapproval. "It's worse than the slums in Montmartre." Marsali didn't say a word, but drew closer to his side, her nostrils pinched.

Lawrence was more matter-of-fact; I supposed he must have seen slave markets before during his explorations of the islands.

"The whites are at that end," he said, gesturing toward the far side of the square. "Come; we'll ask for news of any young men sold recently." He placed a large square hand in the center of my back and urged me gently forward through the crowd.

Near the edge of the market, an old black woman squatted on the ground, feeding charcoal to a small brazier. As we drew near, a little group of people approached her: a planter, accompanied by two black men dressed in rough cotton shirts and trousers, evidently his servants. One of them was holding the arm of a newly purchased female slave; two other girls, naked but for small strips of cloth wrapped about their middles, were led by ropes around their necks.

The planter bent and handed the old woman a coin. She turned and drew several short brass rods from the ground behind her, holding them up for the man's inspection. He studied them for a moment, picked out two, and straightened up. He handed the branding irons to one of his servants, who thrust the ends into the old woman's brazier.

The other servant stepped behind the girl and pinioned her arms. The first man then pulled the irons from the fire and planted both together on the upper slope of her right breast. She shrieked, a high steam-whistle sound loud enough to turn a few heads nearby. The irons pulled away, leaving the letters HB in raw pink flesh.

I had stopped dead at the sight of this. Not realizing that I was no longer with them, the others had gone on. I turned round and round, looking vainly for any trace of Lawrence or Fergus. I never had any difficulty finding Jamie in crowds; his bright head was always visible above everyone else's. But Fergus was a small man, Murphy, no taller, and Lawrence, no more than middle height;

even Marsali's yellow parasol was lost among the many others in the square.

I turned away from the brazier with a shudder, hearing screams and whimpers behind me, but not wanting to look back. I hurried past several auction blocks, eyes averted, but then was slowed and finally stopped by a thickening of the crowd around me.

The men and women blocking my way were listening to an auctioneer who was touting the virtues of a one-armed slave who stood naked on the block for inspection. He was a short man, but broadly built, with massive thighs and a strong chest. The missing arm had been crudely amputated above the elbow; sweat dripped from the end of the stump.

"No good for field work, that's true," the auctioneer was admitting. "But a sound investment for breeding. Look at those legs!" He carried a long rattan cane, which he flicked against the slave's calves, then grinned fatly at the crowd.

"Will you give a guarantee of virility?" the man standing behind me said, with a distinct tone of skepticism. "I had a buck three year past, big as a mule, and not a foal dropped on his account; couldn't do a thing, the juba-girls said."

The crowd tittered at that, and the auctioneer pretended to be offended.

"Guarantee?" he said. He wiped a hand theatrically over his jowls, gathering oily sweat on the palm. "See for yourselves, O ye of little faith!" Bending slightly, he grasped the slave's penis and began to massage it vigorously.

The man grunted in surprise and tried to draw back, but was prevented by the auctioneer's assistant, who clutched him firmly by his single arm. There was an outburst of laughter from the crowd, and a few scattered cheers as the soft black flesh hardened and began to swell.

Some small thing inside me suddenly snapped; I heard it, distinctly. Outraged by the market, the branding, the nakedness, the crude talk and casual indignity, outraged most of all by my own presence here, I could not even think what I was doing, but began to do it, all the same. I felt very oddly detached, as though I stood outside myself, watching.

"Stop it!" I said, very loudly, hardly recognizing my own voice. The auctioneer looked up, startled, and smiled ingratiatingly at me. He looked directly into my eyes, with a knowing leer.

"Sound breeding stock, ma'am," he said. "Guaranteed, as you see."

I folded my parasol, lowered it, and stabbed the pointed end of it as hard as I could into his fat stomach. He jerked back, eyes bulging in surprise. I yanked the parasol back and smashed it on his head, then dropped it and kicked him, hard.

Somewhere deep inside, I knew it would make no difference, would not help in any way, would do nothing but harm. And yet I could not stand here, consenting by silence. It was not for the branded girls, the man on the block, not for any of them that I did it; it was for myself.

There was a good deal of noise around me, and hands snatched at me, pulling me off the auctioneer. This worthy, recovered sufficiently from his initial shock, grinned nastily at me, took aim, and slapped the slave hard across the face.

I looked around for reinforcements, and caught a quick glimpse of Fergus, face contorted in rage, lunging through the crowd toward the auctioneer. There was a shout, and several men turned in his direction. People began to push and shove. Someone tripped me and I sat down hard on the stones.

Through a haze of dust, I saw Murphy, six feet away. With a resigned expression on his broad red face, he bent, detached his wooden leg, straightened up, and hopping gracefully forward, brought it down with great force on the auctioneer's head. The man tottered and fell, as the crowd surged back, trying to get out of the way.

Fergus, baffled of his prey, skidded to a halt by the fallen man and glared ferociously round. Lawrence, dark, grim, and bulky, came striding through the crowd from the other direction, hand on the cane-knife at his belt.

I sat on the ground, shaken. I no longer felt detached. I felt sick, and terrified, realizing that I had just committed an act of folly that was likely to result in Fergus, Lawrence, and Murphy being badly beaten, if nothing worse.

And then Jamie was there.

"Stand up, Sassenach," he said quietly, stooping over me and giving me his hands. I managed it, knees shaking. I saw Raeburn's long mustache twitching at one side, MacLeod behind him, and realized that his Scots were with him. Then my knees gave way, but Jamie's arms held me up.

"Do something," I said in a choked voice into his chest. "Please. Do something."

He had. With his usual presence of mind, he had done the only thing that would quell the riot and prevent harm. He had bought the one-armed man. And as the ironic result of my little outburst of sensibilities, I was now the appalled owner of a genuine male Guinea slave, one-armed, but in glowing health and of guaranteed virility.

I sighed, trying not to think of the man, presumably now somewhere under my feet, fed, and—I hoped—clad. The papers of ownership, which I had refused even to touch, said that he was a full-blooded Gold Coast Negro, a Yoruba, sold by a French planter from Barbuda, one-armed, bearing a brand on the left shoulder of a fleur-de-lys and the initial "A," and known by the name Temeraire. The Bold One. The papers did not suggest what in the name of God I was to do with him.

Jamie had finished looking at the papers his Masonic acquaintance had brought—they were very like the ones I had received for Temeraire, so far as I could see from the rail of the ship. He handed them back with a bow of thanks, a slight frown on his face. The men exchanged a few more words, and parted with another handshake.

"Is everyone aboard?" Jamie asked, stepping off the gangplank. There was a light breeze; it fluttered the dark blue ribbon that tied back the thick tail of his hair.

"Aye, sir," said Mr. Warren, with the casual jerk of the head that passed for a salute in a merchant ship. "Shall we make sail?"

"We shall, if ye please. Thank ye, Mr. Warren." With a small bow, Jamie passed him and came to stand beside me.

"No," he said quietly. His face was calm, but I could feel the depths of his disappointment. Interviews the day before with the two men who dealt in white indentured labor at the slave market had provided no useful information—the Masonic planter had been a beacon of last-minute hope.

There wasn't anything helpful to be said. I put my hand over his where it lay on the rail, and squeezed lightly. Jamie looked down and gave me a faint smile. He took a deep breath and straightened his shoulders, shrugging to settle his coat over them.

"Aye, well. I've learned something, at least. That was a Mr. Villiers, who owns a large sugar plantation here. He bought six slaves from the captain of the ship *Bruja,* three days ago—but none of them Ian."

"Three days?" I was startled. "But—the *Bruja* left Hispaniola more than two weeks ago!"

He nodded, rubbing his cheek. He had shaved, a necessity before making public inquiries, and his skin glowed fresh and ruddy above the snowy linen of his stock.

"She did. And she arrived here on Wednesday—five days ago."

"So she'd been somewhere else, before coming to Barbados! Do we know where?"

He shook his head.

"Villiers didna ken. He said he had spoken some time wi' the captain of the *Bruja,* and the man seemed verra secretive about where he'd been and what he'd been doing. Villiers thought no great thing of it, knowin' as the *Bruja* has a reputation as a crook ship—and seein' as how the captain was willing to sell the slaves for a good price."

"Still"—he brightened slightly—"Villiers did show me the papers for the slaves he'd bought. Ye'll have seen those for your slave?"

"I wish you wouldn't call him that," I said. "But yes. Were the ones you saw the same?"

"Not quite. Three o' the papers gave no previous owner—though Villiers says they were none of them fresh from Africa; all of them have a few words of English, at least. One listed a previous owner, but the name had been scratched out; I couldna read it. The other two gave a Mrs. Abernathy of Rose Hall, Jamaica, as the previous owner."

"Jamaica? How far—"

"I dinna ken," he interrupted. "But Mr. Warren will know. It may be right. In any case, I think we must go to Jamaica next—if only to dispose of our cargo before we all die o' disgust." He wrinkled his long nose fastidiously and I laughed.

"You look like an anteater when you do that," I told him.

The attempt to distract him was successful; the wide mouth curved upward slightly.

"Oh, aye? There's a beastie eats ants, is there?" He did his best to respond to the teasing, turning his back on the Barbados docks.

He leaned against the rail and smiled down at me. "I shouldna think they'd be verra filling."

"I suppose it must eat a lot of them. They can't be any worse than haggis, after all." I took a breath before going on, and let it out quickly, coughing. "God, what's that?"

The *Artemis* had by now slid free of the loading wharf and out into the harbor. As we came about into the wind, a deep, pungent smell struck the ship, a lower and more sinister note in the olfactory dockside symphony of dead barnacles, wet wood, fish, rotted seaweed, and the constant warm breath of the tropical vegetation on shore.

I pressed my handkerchief hard over my nose and mouth. "What is it?"

"We're passing the burning ground, mum, at the foot o' the slave market," Maitland explained, overhearing my question. He pointed toward the shore, where a plume of white smoke rose from behind a screen of bayberry bushes. "They burn the bodies of the slaves who don't survive their passage from Africa," he explained. "First they unload the living cargo, and then, as the ship is swabbed out, the bodies are removed and thrown onto the pyre here, to prevent sickness spreading into the town."

I looked at Jamie, and found the same fear in his face that showed in my own.

"How often do they burn bodies?" I asked. "Every day?"

"Don't know, mum, but I don't think so. Maybe once a week?" Maitland shrugged and went on about his duties.

"We have to look," I said. My voice sounded strange to my own ears, calm and clear. I didn't feel that way.

Jamie had gone very pale. He had turned round again, and his eyes were fixed on the plume of smoke, rising thick and white from behind the palm trees.

His lips pressed tight, then, and his jaw set hard.

"Aye," was all he said, and turned to tell Mr. Warren to put about.

The keeper of the flames, a wizened little creature of indistinguishable color and accent, was vociferously shocked at the notion that a lady should enter the burning ground, but Jamie elbowed him brusquely aside. He didn't try to prevent me following him, or turn to see that I did; he knew I would not leave him alone here.

It was a small hollow, set behind a screen of trees, convenient to a small wharf that extended into the river. Black-smeared pitch barrels and piles of dry wood stood in grim sticky clumps amid the brilliant greens of tree-ferns and dwarf poinciana. To the right, a huge pyre had been built, with a platform of wood, onto which the bodies had been thrown, dribbled with pitch.

This had been lit only a short time before; a good blaze had started at one side of the heap, but only small tongues of flame licked up from the rest. It was smoke that obscured the bodies, rolling up over the heap in a wavering thick veil that gave the outflung limbs a horrid illusion of movement.

Jamie had stopped, staring at the heap. Then he sprang onto the platform, heedless of smoke and scorching, and began jerking bodies loose, grimly pawing through the grisly remains.

A smaller heap of gray ashes and shards of pure white friable bone lay nearby. The curve of an occiput lay on top of the heap, fragile and perfect as an eggshell.

"Makee fine crop." The soot-smeared little creature who tended the fire was at my elbow, offering information in evident hopes of reward. He—or she—pointed at the ashes. "Put on crop; makee grow-grow."

"No, thank you," I said faintly. The smoke obscured Jamie's figure for a moment, and I had the terrible feeling that he had fallen, was burning in the pyre. The horrible, jolly smell of roasting meat rose on the air, and I thought I would be sick.

"Jamie!" I called. *"Jamie!"*

He didn't answer, but I heard a deep, racking cough from the heart of the fire. Several long minutes later, the veil of smoke parted, and he staggered out, choking.

He made his way down the platform and stood bent over, coughing his lungs out. He was covered with an oily soot, his hands and clothes smeared with pitch. He was blind with the smoke; tears poured down his cheeks, making runnels in the soot.

I threw several coins to the keeper of the pyre, and taking Jamie by the arm, led him, blind and choking, out of the valley of death. Under the palms, he sank to his knees and threw up.

"Don't touch me," he gasped, when I tried to help him. He

retched over and over again, but finally stopped, swaying on his knees. Then he slowly staggered to his feet.

"Don't touch me," he said again. His voice, roughened by smoke and sickness, was that of a stranger.

He walked to the edge of the dock, removed his coat and shoes, and dived into the water, fully clothed. I waited for a moment, then stooped and picked up the coat and shoes, holding them gingerly at arm's length. I could see in the inner pocket the faint rectangular bulge of Brianna's pictures.

I waited until he came back and hoisted himself out of the water, dripping. The pitch smears were still there, but most of the soot and the smell of the fire were gone. He sat on the wharf, head on his knees, breathing hard. A row of curious faces edged the *Artemis*'s rail above us.

Not knowing what else to do, I leaned down and laid a hand on his shoulder. Without raising his head, he reached up a hand and grasped mine.

"He wasn't there," he said, in his muffled, rasping stranger's voice.

The breeze was freshening; it stirred the tendrils of wet hair that lay across his shoulders. I looked back, to see that the plume of smoke rising from the little valley had changed to black. It flattened and began to drift out over the sea, the ashes of the dead slaves fleeing on the wind, back toward Africa.

bit. He was a cane-cutter until he lost his arm, and doesna ken how to do anything else much.''

I laid the roll down, barely tasted, and frowned unhappily at the papers. The mere idea of owning a slave frightened and disgusted me, but it was beginning to dawn on me that it might not be so simple to divest myself of the responsibility.

The man had been taken from a barracoon on the Guinea coast, five years before. My original impulse, to return him to his home, was clearly impossible; even had it been possible to find a ship headed for Africa that would agree to take him as a passenger, the overwhelming likelihood was that he would be immediately enslaved again, either by the ship that accepted him, or by another slaver in the West African ports.

Traveling alone, one-armed and ignorant, he would have no protection at all. And even if he should by some miracle reach Africa safely and keep himself out of the hands of both European and African slavers, there was virtually no chance of his ever finding his way back to his village. Should he do so, Lawrence had kindly explained, he would likely be killed or driven away, as his own people would regard him now as a ghost, and a danger to them.

''I dinna suppose ye would consider selling him?'' Jamie put the question delicately, raising one eyebrow. ''To someone we could be sure would treat him kindly?''

I rubbed two fingers between my brows, trying to soothe the growing headache.

''I can't see that that's any better than owning him ourselves,'' I protested. ''Worse, probably, because we couldn't be sure what the new owners would do with him.''

Jamie sighed. He had spent most of the day climbing through the dark, reeking cargo holds with Fergus, making up inventories against our arrival in Jamaica, and he was tired.

''Aye, I see that,'' he said. ''But it's no kindness to free him to starve, that I can see.''

''No.'' I fought back the uncharitable wish that I had never seen the one-armed slave. It would have been a great deal easier for me if I had not—but possibly not for him.

Jamie rose from the berth and stretched himself, leaning on the desk and flexing his shoulders to ease them. He bent and kissed me on the forehead, between the brows.

54

"The Impetuous Pirate"

"I can't own anyone, Jamie," I said, looking in dismay at the papers spread out in the lamplight before me. "I just *can't*. It isn't right."

"Well, I'm inclined to agree wi' ye, Sassenach. But what are we to do with the fellow?" Jamie sat on the berth next to me, close enough to see the ownership documents over my shoulder. He rubbed a hand through his hair, frowning.

"We could set him free—that would seem the right thing—and yet, if we do—what will happen to him then?" He hunched forward, squinting down his nose to read the papers. "He's no more than a bit of French and English; no skills to speak of. If we were to set him free, or even give him a bit of money—can he manage to live, on his own?"

I nibbled thoughtfully on one of Murphy's cheese rolls. It was good, but the smell of the burning oil in the lamp blended oddly with the aromatic cheese, underlaid—as everything was—with the insidious scent of bat guano that permeated the ship.

"I don't know," I said. "Lawrence told me there are a lot of free blacks on Hispaniola. Lots of Creoles and mixed-race people, and a good many who own their own businesses. Is it like that on Jamaica, too?"

He shook his head, and reached for a roll from the tray.

"I dinna think so. It's true, there are some free blacks who earn a living for themselves, but those are the ones who have some skill —sempstresses and fishers and such. I spoke to this Temeraire a

"Dinna fash, Sassenach. I'll speak to the manager at Jared's plantation. Perhaps he can find the man some employment, or else—"

A warning shout from above interrupted him.

"Ship ahoy! Look alive, below! Off the port bow, ahoy!" The lookout's cry was urgent, and there was a sudden rush and stir, as hands began to turn out. Then there was a lot more shouting, and a jerk and shudder as the *Artemis* backed her sails.

"What in the name of God—" Jamie began. A rending crash drowned his words, and he pitched sideways, eyes wide with alarm, as the cabin tilted. The stool I was on fell over, throwing me onto the floor. The oil lamp had shot from its bracket, luckily extinguishing itself before hitting the floor, and the place was in darkness.

"Sassenach! Are ye all right?" Jamie's voice came out of the murk close at hand, sharp with anxiety.

"Yes," I said, scrambling out from under the table. "Are you? What happened? Did someone hit us?"

Not pausing to answer any of these questions, Jamie had reached the door and opened it. A babel of shouts and thumps came down from the deck above, punctuated by the sudden popcorn-sound of small-arms fire.

"Pirates," he said briefly. "We've been boarded." My eyes were becoming accustomed to the dim light; I saw his shadow lunge for the desk, reaching for the pistol in the drawer. He paused to snatch the dirk from under the pillow of his berth, and made for the door, issuing instructions as he went.

"Take Marsali, Sassenach, and get below. Go aft as far as ye can get—the big hold where the guano blocks are. Get behind them, and stay there." Then he was gone.

I spent a moment feeling my way through the cupboard over my berth, in search of the morocco box Mother Hildegarde had given me when I saw her in Paris. A scalpel might be little use against pirates, but I would feel better with a weapon of some kind in my hand, no matter how small.

"Mother Claire?" Marsali's voice came from the door, high and scared.

"I'm here," I said. I caught the gleam of pale cotton as she moved, and pressed the ivory letter-opener into her hand. "Here, take this, just in case. Come on; we're to go below."

With a long-handled amputation blade in one hand, and a cluster of scalpels in the other, I led the way through the ship to the after hold. Feet thundered on the deck overhead, and curses and shouts rang through the night, overlaid with a dreadful groaning, scraping noise that I thought must be caused by the rubbing of the *Artemis*'s timbers against those of the unknown ship that had rammed us.

The hold was black as pitch and thick with dusty fumes. We made our way slowly, coughing, toward the back of the hold.

"Who are they?" Marsali asked. Her voice had a strangely muffled sound, the echoes of the hold deadened by the blocks of guano stacked around us. "Pirates, d'ye think?"

"I expect they must be." Lawrence had told us that the Caribbean was a rich hunting ground for pirate luggers and unscrupulous craft of all kinds, but we had expected no trouble, as our cargo was not particularly valuable. "I suppose they must not have much sense of smell."

"Eh?"

"Never mind," I said. "Come sit down; there's nothing we can do but wait."

I knew from experience that waiting while men fought was one of the most difficult things in life to do, but in this case, there wasn't any sensible alternative.

Down here, the sounds of the battle were muted to a distant thumping, though the constant rending groan of the scraping timbers echoed through the whole ship.

"Oh, God, Fergus," Marsali whispered, listening, her voice filled with agony. "Blessed Mary, save him!"

I silently echoed the prayer, thinking of Jamie somewhere in the chaos overhead. I crossed myself in the dark, touching the small spot between my brows that he had kissed a few minutes before, not wanting to think that it could so easily be the last touch of him I would ever know.

Suddenly, there was an explosion overhead, a roar that sent vibrations through the jutting timbers we were sitting on.

"They're blowing up the ship!" Marsali jumped to her feet, panicked. "They'll sink us! We must get out! We'll drown down here!"

"Wait!" I called. "It's only the guns!" but she had not waited to hear. I could hear her, blundering about in a blind panic, whimpering among the blocks of guano.

"Marsali! Come back!" There was no light at all in the hold; I took a few steps through the smothering atmosphere, trying to locate her by sound, but the deadening effect of the crumbling blocks hid her movements from me. There was another booming explosion overhead, and a third close on its heels. The air was filled with dust loosed from the vibrations, and I choked, eyes watering.

I wiped at my eyes with a sleeve, and blinked. I was not imagining it; there was a light in the hold, a dim glow that limned the edge of the nearest block.

"Marsali?" I called. "Where are you?"

The answer was a terrified shriek, from the direction of the light. I dashed around the edge of the block, dodged between two others, and emerged into the space by the ladder, to find Marsali in the clutches of a large, half-naked man.

He was hugely obese, the rolling layers of his fat decorated with a stipple of tattoos, a jangling necklace of coins and buttons hung round his neck. Marsali slapped at him, shrieking, and he jerked his face away, impatient.

Then he caught sight of me, and his eyes widened. He had a wide, flat face, and a tarred topknot of black hair. He grinned nastily at me, showing a marked lack of teeth, and said something that sounded like slurred Spanish.

"Let her go!" I said loudly. *"Basta, cabrón!"* That was as much Spanish as I could summon; he seemed to think it funny, for he grinned more widely, let go of Marsali, and turned toward me. I threw one of my scalpels at him.

It bounced off his head, startling him, and he ducked wildly. Marsali dodged past him, and sprang for the ladder.

The pirate waffled for a moment, torn between us, but then turned to the ladder, leaping up several rungs with an agility that belied his weight. He caught Marsali by the foot as she dived through the hatch, and she screamed.

Cursing incoherently under my breath, I ran to the bottom of the ladder, and reaching up, swung the long-handled amputation knife at his foot, as hard as I could. There was a high-pitched screech from the pirate. Something flew past my head, and a spray of blood spattered across my cheek, wet-hot on my skin.

Startled, I dropped back, looking down by reflex to see what had fallen. It was a small brown toe, callused and black-nailed, smudged with dirt.

The pirate hit the deck beside me with a thud that shivered the floorboards, and lunged. I ducked, but he caught a handful of my sleeve. I yanked away, ripping fabric, and jabbed at his face with the blade in my hand.

Jerking back in surprise, he slipped on his own blood and fell. I jumped for the ladder and climbed for my life, dropping the blade.

He was so close behind me that he succeeded in catching hold of the hem of my skirt, but I pulled it from his grasp and lunged upward, lungs burning from the dust of the choking hold. The man was shouting, a language I didn't know. Some dim recess of my brain, not occupied with immediate survival, speculated that it might be Portuguese.

I burst out of the hold onto the deck, into the midst of a surging chaos. The air was thick with black-powder smoke, and small knots of men were pushing and shoving, cursing and stumbling all over the deck.

I couldn't take time to look around; there was a hoarse bellow from the hatchway behind me, and I dived for the rail. I hesitated for a moment, balanced on the narrow wooden strip. The sea spun past in a dizzy churn of black below. I grasped the rigging and began to climb.

It was a mistake; I knew that almost at once. He was a sailor, I was not. Neither was he hampered by wearing a dress. The ropes danced and jerked in my hands, vibrating under the impact of his weight as he hit the lines below me.

He was coming up the underside of the lines, climbing like a gibbon, even as I made my slower way across the upper slope of the rigging. He drew even with me, and spat in my face. I kept climbing, propelled by desperation; there was nothing else to do. He kept pace with me, easily, hissing words through an evil half-toothed grin. It didn't matter what language he was speaking; his meaning was perfectly clear. Hanging by one hand, he drew the cutlass from his sash, and swung it in a vicious cut that barely missed me.

I was too frightened even to scream. There was nowhere to go, nothing to do. I squeezed my eyes tight shut, and hoped it would be quick.

It was. There was a sort of thump, a sharp grunt, and a strong smell of fish.

I opened my eyes. The pirate was gone. Ping An was sitting on the crosstrees, three feet away, crest erect with irritation, wings half-spread to keep his balance.

"Gwa!" he said crossly. He turned a beady little yellow eye on me, and clacked his bill in warning. Ping An hated noise and commotion. Evidently, he didn't like Portuguese pirates, either.

There were spots before my eyes, and I felt light-headed. I clung tight to the rope, shaking, until I thought I could move again. The noise below had slackened now, and the tenor of the shouting had changed. Something had happened; I thought it was over.

There was a new noise, a sudden flap of sails, and a long, grinding sound, with a vibration that made the line I was holding sing in my hand. It *was* over; the pirate ship was moving away. On the far side of the *Artemis,* I saw the web of the pirate's mast and rigging begin to move, black against the silver Caribbean sky. Very, very slowly, I began the long trip back down.

The lanterns were still lit below. A haze of black-powder smoke lay over everything, and bodies lay here and there about the deck. My glance flickered over them as I lowered myself, searching for red hair. I found it, and my heart leapt.

Jamie was sitting on a cask near the wheel, with his head tilted back, eyes closed, a cloth pressed to his brow, and a cup of whisky in his hand. Mr. Willoughby was on his knees alongside, administering first aid—in the form of more whisky—to Willie MacLeod, who sat against the foremast, looking sick.

I was shaking all over from exertion and reaction. I felt giddy and slightly cold. Shock, I supposed, and no wonder. I could do with a bit of that whisky as well.

I grasped the smaller lines above the rail, and slid the rest of the way to the deck, not caring that my palms were skinned raw. I was sweating and cold at the same time, and the down-hairs on my face were prickling unpleasantly.

I landed clumsily, with a thump that made Jamie straighten up and open his eyes. The look of relief in them pulled me the few feet to him. I felt better, with the warm solid flesh of his shoulder under my hand.

"Are you all right?" I said, leaning over him to look.

"Aye, it's no more than a wee dunt," he said, smiling up at me.

There was a small gash at his hairline, where something like a pistol butt had caught him, but the blood had clotted already. There were stains of dark, drying blood on the front of his shirt, but the sleeve of his shirt was also bloody. In fact, it was nearly soaked, with fresh bright red.

"Jamie!" I clutched at his shoulder, my vision going white at the edges. "You aren't all right—look, you're bleeding!"

My hands and feet were numb, and I only half-felt his hands grasp my arms as he rose from the cask in sudden alarm. The last thing I saw, amid flashes of light, was his face, gone white beneath the tan.

"My God!" said his frightened voice, out of the whirling blackness. "It's no my blood, Sassenach, it's yours!"

"I am not going to die," I said crossly, "unless it's from heat exhaustion. Take some of this bloody stuff off me!"

Marsali, who had been tearfully pleading with me not to expire, looked rather relieved at this outburst. She stopped crying and sniffed hopefully, but made no move to remove any of the cloaks, coats, blankets, and other impedimenta in which I was swaddled.

"Oh, I canna do that, Mother Claire!" she said. "Da says ye must be kept warm!"

"Warm? I'm being boiled alive!" I was in the captain's cabin, and even with the stern windows wide open, the atmosphere belowdecks was stifling, hot with sun and acrid with the fumes of the cargo.

I tried to struggle out from under my wrappings, but got no more than a few inches before a bolt of lightning struck me in the right arm. The world went dark, with small bright flashes zigging through my vision.

"Lie still," said a stern Scots voice, through a wave of giddy sickness. An arm was under my shoulders, a large hand cradling my head. "Aye, that's right, lie back on my arm. All right now, Sassenach?"

"No," I said, looking at the colored pinwheels inside my eyelids. "I'm going to be sick."

I was, and a most unpleasant process it was, too, with fiery knives being jabbed into my right arm with each spasm.

"Jesus H. Roosevelt Christ," I said at last, gasping.

"Finished, are ye?" Jamie lowered me carefully and eased my head back onto the pillow.

"If you mean am I dead, the answer is unfortunately no." I cracked one eyelid open. He was kneeling by my berth, looking no end piratical himself, with a bloodstained strip of cloth bound round his head, and still wearing his blood-soaked shirt.

He stayed still, and so did the cabin, so I cautiously opened the other eye. He smiled faintly at me.

"No, you're no dead; Fergus will be glad to hear it."

As though this had been a signal, the Frenchman's head poked anxiously into the cabin. Seeing me awake, his face broke into a dazzling smile and disappeared. I could hear his voice overhead, loudly informing the crew of my survival. To my profound embarrassment, the news was greeted with a rousing cheer from the upper deck.

"What happened?" I asked.

"What *happened*?" Jamie, pouring water into a cup, stopped and stared over the rim at me. He knelt down again beside me, snorting, and raised my head for a sip of water.

"What happened, she says! Aye, what indeed? I tell ye to stay all snug below wi' Marsali, and next thing I ken, ye've dropped out of the sky and landed at my feet, sopping wi' blood!"

He shoved his face into the berth and glared at me. Sufficiently impressive when clean-shaven and unhurt, he was considerably more ferocious when viewed, stubbled, bloodstained, and angry, at a distance of six inches. I promptly shut my eyes again.

"Look at me!" he said peremptorily, and I did, against my better judgment.

Blue eyes bored into mine, narrowed with fury.

"D'ye ken ye came damn close to dying?" he demanded. "Ye've a bone-deep slash down your arm from oxter to elbow, and had I not got a cloth round it in time, ye'd be feeding the sharks this minute!"

One big fist crashed down on the side of the berth next to me, making me start. The movement hurt my arm, but I didn't make a sound.

"Damn ye, woman! Will ye never do as you're told?"

"Probably not," I said meekly.

He turned a black scowl on me, but I could see the corner of his mouth twitching under the copper stubble.

"God," he said longingly. "What I wouldna give to have ye tied facedown over a gun, and me wi' a rope's end in my hand." He snorted again, and pulled his face out of the berth.

"Willoughby!" he bellowed. In short order, Mr. Willoughby trotted in, beaming, with a steaming pot of tea and a bottle of brandy on a tray.

"Tea!" I breathed, struggling to sit up. "Ambrosia." In spite of the stifling atmosphere of the cabin, the hot tea was just what I needed. The delightful, brandy-laced stuff slid down my throat and glowed peacefully in the pit of my quivering stomach.

"Nobody makes tea better than the English," I said, inhaling the aroma, "except the Chinese."

Mr. Willoughby beamed in gratification and bowed ceremoniously. Jamie snorted again, bringing his total up to three for the afternoon.

"Aye? Well, enjoy it while ye can."

This sounded more or less sinister, and I stared at him over the rim of the cup. "And just what do you mean by that?" I demanded.

"I'm going to doctor your arm when you're finished," he informed me. He picked up the pot and peered into it.

"How much blood did ye tell me a person has in his body?" he asked.

"About eight quarts," I said, bewildered. "Why?"

He lowered the pot and glared at me.

"Because," he said precisely, "judging from the amount ye left on the deck, you've maybe four of them left. Here, have some more." He refilled the cup, set down the pot, and stalked out.

"I'm afraid Jamie's rather annoyed with me," I observed ruefully to Mr. Willoughby.

"Not angry," he said comfortingly. "Tsei-mi scared very bad." The little Chinaman laid a hand on my right shoulder, delicate as a resting butterfly. "This hurts?"

I sighed. "To be perfectly honest," I said, "yes, it does."

Mr. Willoughby smiled and patted me gently. "I help," he said consolingly. "Later."

In spite of the throbbing in my arm, I was feeling sufficiently restored to inquire about the rest of the crew, whose injuries, as reported by Mr. Willoughby, were limited to cuts and bruises, plus one concussion and a minor arm fracture.

A clatter in the passage heralded Jamie's return, accompanied by Fergus, who carried my medicine box under one arm, and yet another bottle of brandy in his hand.

"All right," I said, resigned. "Let's have a look at it."

I was no stranger to horrible wounds, and this one—technically speaking—was not all that bad. On the other hand, it was my own personal flesh involved here, and I was not disposed to be technical.

"Ooh," I said rather faintly. While being a bit picturesque about the nature of the wound, Jamie had also been quite accurate. It was a long, clean-edged slash, running at a slight angle across the front of my biceps, from the shoulder to an inch or so above the elbow joint. And while I couldn't actually see the bone of my humerus, it was without doubt a very deep wound, gaping widely at the edges.

It was still bleeding, in spite of the cloth that had been wrapped tightly round it, but the seepage was slow; no major vessels seemed to have been severed.

Jamie had flipped open my medical box and was rootling meditatively through it with one large forefinger.

"You'll need sutures and a needle," I said, feeling a sudden jolt of alarm as it occurred to me that I was about to have thirty or forty stitches taken in my arm, with no anesthesia bar brandy.

"No laudanum?" Jamie asked, frowning into the box. Evidently, he had been thinking along the same lines.

"No. I used it all on the *Porpoise.*" Controlling the shaking of my left hand, I poured a sizable tot of straight brandy into my empty teacup, and took a healthy mouthful.

"That was thoughtful of you, Fergus," I said, nodding at the fresh brandy bottle as I sipped, "but I don't think it's going to take *two* bottles." Given the potency of Jared's French brandy, it was unlikely to take more than a teacupful.

I was wondering whether it was more advisable to get dead drunk at once, or to stay at least half-sober in order to supervise operations; there wasn't a chance in hell that I could do the suturing myself, left-handed and shaking like a leaf. Neither could Fergus do it one-handed. True, Jamie's big hands could move with amazing lightness over some tasks, but . . .

Jamie interrupted my apprehensions, shaking his head and picking up the second bottle.

"This one's no for drinking, Sassenach, that's for washing out the wound."

"What!" In my state of shock, I had forgotten the necessity for disinfection. Lacking anything better, I normally washed out wounds with distilled grain alcohol, cut half and half with water, but I had used my supply of that as well, in our encounter with the man-of-war.

I felt my lips go slightly numb, and not just because the internal brandy was taking effect. Highlanders were among the most stoic and courageous of warriors, and seamen as a class weren't far behind. I had seen such men lie uncomplaining while I set broken bones, did minor surgery, sewed up terrible wounds, and put them through hell generally, but when it came to disinfection with alcohol, it was a different story—the screams could be heard for miles.

"Er . . . wait a minute," I said. "Maybe just a little boiled water. . . ."

Jamie was watching me, not without sympathy.

"It willna get easier wi' waiting, Sassenach," he said. "Fergus, take the bottle." And before I could protest, he had lifted me out of the berth and sat down with me on his lap, holding me tight about the body, pinning my left arm so I couldn't struggle, while he took my right wrist in a firm grip and held my wounded arm out to the side.

I believe it was bloody old Ernest Hemingway who said you're supposed to pass out from pain, but unfortunately you never do. All I can say in response to that is that either Ernest had a fine distinction for states of consciousness, or else no one ever poured brandy on several cubic inches of *his* raw flesh.

To be fair, I suppose I must not absolutely have lost consciousness myself, since when I began noticing things again, Fergus was saying, "Please, milady! You must not scream like that; it upsets the men."

Clearly it upset Fergus; his lean face was pale, and droplets of sweat ran down his jaw. He was right about the men, too—several faces were peering into the cabin from door and window, wearing expressions of horror and concern.

I summoned the presence of mind to nod weakly at them. Jamie's arm was still locked about my middle; I couldn't tell which of us was shaking; both, I thought.

I made it into the wide captain's chair, with considerable assistance, and lay back palpitating, the fire in my arm still sizzling. Jamie was holding one of my curved suture needles and a length of sterilized cat-gut, looking as dubious over the prospects as I felt.

It was Mr. Willoughby who intervened, quietly taking the needle from Jamie's hands.

"I can do this," he said, in tones of authority. "A moment." And he disappeared aft, presumably to fetch something.

Jamie didn't protest, and neither did I. We heaved twin sighs of relief, in fact, which made me laugh.

"And to think," I said, "I once told Bree that big men were kind and gentle, and the short ones tended to be nasty."

"Well, I suppose there's always the exception that proves the rule, no?" He mopped my streaming face with a wet cloth, quite gently.

"I dinna want to know how ye did this," he said, with a sigh, "but for God's sake, Sassenach, don't do it again!"

"Well, I didn't *intend* to do anything . . ." I began crossly, when I was interrupted by the return of Mr. Willoughby. He was carrying the little roll of green silk I had seen when he cured Jamie's seasickness.

"Oh, ye've got the wee stabbers?" Jamie peered interestedly at the small gold needles, then smiled at me. "Dinna fash yourself, Sassenach, they don't hurt . . . or not much, anyway," he added.

Mr. Willoughby's fingers probed the palm of my right hand, prodding here and there. Then he grasped each of my fingers, wiggled it, and pulled it gently, so that I felt the joints pop slightly. Then he laid two fingers at the base of my wrist, pressing down in the space between the radius and the ulna.

"This is the Inner Gate," he said softly. "Here is quiet. Here is peace." I sincerely hoped he was right. Picking up one of the tiny gold needles, he placed the point over the spot he had marked, and with a dexterous twirl of thumb and forefinger, pierced the skin.

The prick made me jump, but he kept a tight, warm hold on my hand, and I relaxed again.

He placed three needles in each wrist, and a rakish, porcupine-like spray on the crest of my right shoulder. I was getting interested, despite my guinea pig status. Beyond an initial prick at placement, the needles caused no discomfort. Mr. Willoughby was humming, in a low, soothing sort of way, tapping and pressing places on my neck and shoulder.

I couldn't honestly tell whether my right arm was numbed, or whether I was simply distracted by the goings-on, but it did feel somewhat less agonized—at least until he picked up the suture needle and began.

Jamie was sitting on a stool by my left side, holding my left hand as he watched my face. After a moment, he said, rather gruffly, "Let your breath out, Sassenach; it's no going to get any worse than that."

I let go of the breath I hadn't realized I was holding, and realized as well what he was telling me. It was dread of being hurt that had me rigid as a board in the chair. The actual pain of the stitches was unpleasant, all right, but nothing I couldn't stand.

I let my breath out cautiously, and gave him a rough approximation of a smile. Mr. Willoughby was singing under his breath in Chinese. Jamie had translated the words for me a week earlier; it was a pillow-song, in which a young man catalogued the physical charms of his partner, one by one. I hoped he would finish the stitching before he got to her feet.

"That's a verra wicked slash," Jamie said, eyes on Mr. Willoughby's work. I preferred not to look myself. "A parang, was it, or a cutlass, I wonder."

"I think it was a cutlass," I said. "In fact, I know it was. He came after . . ."

"I wonder what led them to attack us," Jamie said, not paying any attention to me. His brows were drawn in speculation. "It canna ha' been the cargo, after all."

"I shouldn't think so," I said. "But maybe they didn't know what we were carrying?" This seemed grossly unlikely; any ship that came within a hundred yards of us would have known—the ammoniac reek of bat guano hovered round us like a miasma.

"Perhaps it's only they thought the ship small enough to take. The *Artemis* itself would bring a fair price, cargo or no."

I blinked as Mr. Willoughby paused in his song to tie a knot. I thought he was down to the navel by now, but wasn't paying close attention.

"Do we know the name of the pirate ship?" I asked. "Granted, there's likely a lot of pirates in these waters, but we do know that the *Bruja* was in this area three days ago, and—"

"That's what I'm wondering," he said. "I couldna see a great deal in the darkness, but she was the right size, wi' that wide Spanish beam."

"Well, the pirate that was after me spoke——" I started, but the sound of voices in the corridor made me stop.

Fergus edged in, shy of interrupting, but obviously bursting with excitement. He held something shiny and jingling in one hand.

"Milord," he said, "Maitland has found a dead pirate on the forward deck."

Jamie's red brows went up, and he looked from Fergus to me. "Dead?"

"Very dead, milord," said Fergus, with a small shudder. Maitland was peeking over his shoulder, anxious to claim his share of the glory. "Oh, yes, sir," he assured Jamie earnestly. "Dead as a doornail; his poor head's bashed in something shocking!"

All three men turned and stared at me. I gave them a modest little smile.

Jamie rubbed a hand over his face. His eyes were bloodshot, and a trickle of blood had dried in front of his ear.

"Sassenach," he began, in measured tones.

"I tried to tell you," I said virtuously. With the shock, brandy, acupuncture, and the dawning realization of survival, I was beginning to feel quite pleasantly light-headed. I scarcely noticed Mr. Willoughby's final efforts.

"He was wearing this, milord." Fergus stepped forward and laid the pirate's necklace on the table in front of us. It had the silver buttons from a military uniform, polished *kona* nuts, several large shark's teeth, pieces of polished abalone shell and chunks of mother of pearl, and a large number of jingling coins, all pierced for stringing on a leather thong.

"I thought you should see this at once, milord," Fergus continued. He reached out a hand and lifted one of the shimmering coins. It was silver, untarnished, and through the gathering brandy haze, I could see on its face the twin heads of Alexander. A tetradrachm, of the fourth century B.C. Mint condition.

Thoroughly worn out by the events of the afternoon, I had fallen asleep at once, the pain in my arm dulled by brandy. Now it was full dark, and the brandy had worn off. My arm seemed to swell and throb with each beat of my heart, and any small movement sent tiny jabs of a sharper pain whipping through my arm, like warning flicks of a scorpion's tail.

The moon was three-quarters full, a huge lopsided shape like a golden teardrop, hanging just above the horizon. The ship heeled slightly, and the moon slid slowly out of sight, the Man in the Moon leering rather unpleasantly as he went. I was hot, and possibly a trifle feverish.

There was a jug of water in the cupboard on the far side of the cabin. I felt weak and giddy as I swung my feet over the edge of the berth, and my arm registered a strong protest against being disturbed. I must have made some sound, for the darkness on the floor of the cabin stirred suddenly, and Jamie's voice came drowsily from the region of my feet.

"Are ye hurting, Sassenach?"

"A little," I said, not wanting to be dramatic about it. I set my lips and rose unsteadily to my feet, cradling my right elbow in my left hand.

"That's good," he said.

"That's *good*?" I said, my voice rising indignantly.

There was a soft chuckle from the darkness, and he sat up, his head popping suddenly into sight as it rose above the shadows into the moonlight.

"Aye, it is," he said. "When a wound begins to hurt ye, it means it's healing. Ye didna feel it when it happened, did you?"

"No," I admitted. I certainly felt it now. The air was a good deal cooler out on the open sea, and the salt wind coming through the window felt good on my face. I was damp and sticky with sweat, and the thin chemise clung to my breasts.

"I could see ye didn't. That's what frightened me. Ye never feel a fatal wound, Sassenach," he said softly.

I laughed shortly, but cut it off as the movement jarred my arm.

"And how do you know that?" I asked, fumbling left-handed to pour water into a cup. "Not the sort of thing you'd learn firsthand, I mean."

"Murtagh told me."

The water seemed to purl soundlessly into the cup, the sound of its pouring lost in the hiss of the bow-wave outside. I set down the jug and lifted the cup, the surface of the water black in the moonlight. Jamie had never mentioned Murtagh to me, in the months of our reunion. I had asked Fergus, who told me that the wiry little Scot had died at Culloden, but he knew no more than the bare fact.

"At Culloden." Jamie's voice was barely loud enough to be heard above the creak of timber and the whirring of the wind that bore us along. "Did ye ken they burnt the bodies there? I wondered, listening to them do it—what it would be like inside the fire when it came my turn." I could hear him swallow, above the creaking of the ship. "I found that out, this morning."

The moonlight robbed his face of depth and color; he looked like a skull, with the broad, clean planes of cheek and jawbone white and his eyes black empty pits.

"I went to Culloden meaning to die," he said, his voice scarcely more than a whisper. "Not the rest of them. I should have been happy to stop a musket ball at once, and yet I cut my way across the field and halfway back, while men on either side o' me were blown to bloody bits." He stood up, then, looking down at me.

"Why?" he said. "Why, Claire? Why am I alive, and they are not?"

"I don't know," I said softly. "For your sister, and your family, maybe? For me?"

"They had families," he said. "Wives, and sweethearts; children to mourn them. And yet they are gone. And I am still here."

"I don't know, Jamie," I said at last. I touched his cheek, already roughened by newly sprouting beard, irrepressible evidence of life. "You aren't ever going to know."

He sighed, his cheekbone pressed against my palm for a moment.

"Aye, I ken that well enough. But I canna help the asking, when I think of them—especially Murtagh." He turned restlessly away, his eyes empty shadows, and I knew he walked Drumossie Moor again, with the ghosts.

"We should have gone sooner; the men had been standing for hours, starved and half-frozen. But they waited for His Highness to give the order to charge."

And Charles Stuart, perched safely on a rock, well behind the line of battle, having seized personal command of his troops for the first time, had dithered and delayed. And the English cannon had had time to bear squarely on the lines of ragged Highlanders, and opened fire.

"It was a relief, I think," Jamie said softly. "Every man on the field knew the cause was lost, and we were dead. And still we stood there, watching the English guns come up, and the cannon mouths open black before us. No one spoke. I couldna hear anything but the wind, and the English soldiers shouting, on the other side of the field."

And then the guns had roared, and men had fallen, and those still standing, rallied by a late and ragged order, had seized their swords and charged the enemy, the sound of their Gaelic shrieking drowned by the guns, lost in the wind.

"The smoke was so thick, I couldna see more than a few feet before me. I kicked off my shoon and ran into it, shouting." The bloodless line of his lips turned up slightly.

"I was happy," he said, sounding a bit surprised. "Not scairt at all. I meant to die, after all; there was nothing to fear except that I might be wounded and not die at once. But I would die, and then it would be all over, and I would find ye again, and it would be all right."

I moved closer to him, and his hand rose up from the shadows to take mine.

"Men fell to either side of me, and I could hear the grapeshot and the musket balls hum past my head like bumblebees. But I wasna touched."

He had reached the British lines unscathed, one of very few Highlanders to have completed the charge across Culloden Moor. An English gun crew looked up, startled, at the tall Highlander who burst from the smoke like a demon, the blade of his broadsword gleaming with rain and then dull with blood.

"There was a small part of my mind that asked why I should be killin' them," he said reflectively. "For surely I knew that we were lost; there was no gain to it. But there is a lust to killing—you'll know that?" His fingers tightened on mine, questioning, and I squeezed back in affirmation.

"I couldna stop—or I would not." His voice was quiet, without bitterness or recrimination. "It's a verra old feeling, I think; the wish to take an enemy with ye to the grave. I could feel it there, a

hot red thing in my chest and belly, and . . . I gave myself to it,"
he ended simply.

There were four men tending the cannon, none armed with
more than a pistol and knife, none expecting attack at such close
quarters. They stood helpless against the berserk strength of his
despair, and he killed them all.

"The ground shook under my feet," he said, "and I was near
deafened by the noise. I couldna think. And then it came to me
that I was behind the English guns." A soft chuckle came from
below. "A verra poor place to try to be killed, no?"

So he had started back across the moor, to join the Highland
dead.

"He was sitting against a tussock near the middle of the field—
Murtagh. He'd been struck a dozen times at least, and there was a
dreadful wound in his head—I knew he was dead."

He hadn't been, though; when Jamie had fallen to his knees
beside his godfather and taken the small body in his arms, Murtagh's eyes had opened.

"He saw me. And he smiled." And then the older man's hand
had touched his cheek briefly. "Dinna be afraid, *a bhalaich,*"
Murtagh had said, using the endearment for a small, beloved boy.
"It doesna hurt a bit to die."

I stood quietly for a long time, holding Jamie's hand. Then he
sighed, and his other hand closed very, very gently about my
wounded arm.

"Too many folk have died, Sassenach, because they knew me—
or suffered for the knowing. I would give my own body to save ye
a moment's pain—and yet I could wish to close my hand just now,
that I might hear ye cry out and know for sure that I havena killed
you, too."

I leaned forward, pressing a kiss on the skin of his chest. He
slept naked in the heat.

"You haven't killed me. You didn't kill Murtagh. And we'll find
Ian. Take me back to bed, Jamie."

Sometime later, as I drowsed on the edge of sleep, he spoke
from the floor beside my bed.

"Ye know, I seldom wanted to go home to Laoghaire," he said
contemplatively. "And yet, at least when I did, I'd find her where
I'd left her."

I turned my head to the side, where his soft breathing came

from the darkened floor. "Oh? And is that the kind of wife you want? The sort who stays put?"

He made a small sound between a chuckle and a cough, but didn't answer, and after a few moments, the sound of his breathing changed to a soft, rhythmic snore.

55

Ishmael

I slept restlessly, and woke up late and feverish, with a throbbing headache just behind my eyes. I felt ill enough not to protest when Marsali insisted on bathing my forehead, but relaxed gratefully, eyes closed, enjoying the cool touch of the vinegar-soaked cloth on my pounding temples.

It was so soothing, in fact, that I drifted off to sleep again after she left. I was dreaming uneasily of dark mine shafts and the chalk of charred bones, when I was suddenly roused by a crash that brought me bolt upright and sent a shaft of pure white pain ripping through my head.

"What?" I exclaimed, clutching my head in both hands, as though this might prevent it falling off. "What is it?" The window had been covered to keep the light from disturbing me, and it took a moment for my stunned vision to adapt to the dimness.

On the opposite side of the cabin, a large figure was mimicking me, clutching its own head in apparent agony. Then it spoke, releasing a volley of very bad language, in a mixture of Chinese, French, and Gaelic.

"Damn!" it said, the exclamations tapering off into milder English. "Goddamn it to hell!" Jamie staggered to the window, still rubbing the head he had smashed on the edge of my cupboard. He shoved aside the covering and pushed the window open, bringing in a welcome draft of fresh air in along with a dazzle of light.

"What in the name of bloody hell do you think you're doing?" I demanded, with considerable asperity. The light jabbed my tender eyeballs like needles, and the movement involved in clutch-ing my head had done the stitches in my arm no good at all.

"I was looking for your medicine box," he replied, wincing as he felt the crown of his head. "Damn, I've caved in my skull. Look at that!" He thrust two fingers, slightly smeared with blood, under my nose. I dropped the vinegar-soaked cloth over the fingers and collapsed back on my pillow.

"Why do you need the medicine box, and why didn't you ask me in the first place, instead of bumping around like a bee in a bottle?" I said irritably.

"I didna want to wake ye from your sleep," he said, sheepishly enough that I laughed, despite the various throbbings going on in my anatomy.

"That's all right; I wasn't enjoying it," I assured him. "Why do you need the box? Is someone hurt?"

"Aye. I am," he said, dabbing gingerly at the top of his head with the cloth and scowling at the result. "Ye dinna want to look at my head?"

The answer to this was "Not especially," but I obligingly mo-tioned to him to bend over, presenting the top of his head for inspection. There was a reasonably impressive lump under the thick hair, with a small cut from the edge of the shelf, but the damage seemed a bit short of concussion.

"It's not fractured," I assured him. "You have the thickest skull I've ever seen." Moved by an instinct as old as motherhood, I leaned forward and kissed the bump gently. He lifted his head, eyes wide with surprise.

"That's supposed to make it feel better," I explained. A smile tugged at the corner of his mouth.

"Oh. Well, then." He bent down and gently kissed the bandage on my wounded arm.

"Better?" he inquired, straightening up.

"Lots."

He laughed, and reaching for the decanter, poured out a tot of whisky, which he handed to me.

"I wanted that stuff ye use to wash out scrapes and such," he explained, pouring another for himself.

"Hawthorn lotion. I haven't got any ready-made, because it doesn't keep," I said, pushing myself upright. "If it's urgent, though, I can brew some; it doesn't take long." The thought of getting up and walking to the galley was daunting, but perhaps I'd feel better once I was moving.

"Not urgent," he assured me. "It's only there's a prisoner in the hold who's a bit bashed about."

I lowered my cup, blinking at him.

"A prisoner? Where did we get a prisoner?"

"From the pirate ship." He frowned at his whisky. "Though I dinna think he's a pirate."

"What is he?"

He tossed off the whisky neatly, in one gulp, and shook his head.

"Damned if I know. From the scars on his back, likely a runaway slave, but in that case, I canna think why he did what he did."

"What did he do?"

"Dived off the *Bruja* into the sea. MacGregor saw him go, and then after the *Bruja* made sail, he saw the man bobbing about in the waves and threw him a rope."

"Well, that is funny; why should he do that?" I asked. I was becoming interested, and the throbbing in my head seemed to be lessening as I sipped my whisky.

Jamie ran his fingers through his hair, and stopped, wincing.

"I dinna ken, Sassenach," he said, gingerly smoothing the hair on his crown flat. "It wouldna be likely for a crew like ours to try to board the pirate—any merchant would just fight them off; there's no reason to try to take them. But if he didna mean to escape from us—perhaps he meant to escape from them, aye?"

The last golden drops of the whisky ran down my throat. It was Jared's special blend, the next-to-last bottle, and thoroughly justified the name he had given it—*Ceò Gheasacach.* "Magic Mist." Feeling somewhat restored, I pushed myself upright.

"If he's hurt, perhaps I should take a look at him," I suggested, swinging my feet out of the berth.

Given Jamie's behavior of the day before, I fully expected him to press me flat and call for Marsali to come and sit on my chest. Instead, he looked at me thoughtfully, and nodded.

"Aye, well. If ye're sure ye can stand, Sassenach?"

I wasn't all that sure, but gave it a try. The room tilted when I stood up, and black and yellow spots danced before my eyes, but I stayed upright, clinging to Jamie's arm. After a moment, a small amount of blood reluctantly consented to reenter my head, and the spots went away, showing Jamie's face looking anxiously down at me.

"All right," I said, taking a deep breath. "Carry on."

The prisoner was below in what the crew called the orlop, a lower-deck space full of miscellaneous cargo. There was a small timbered area, walled off at the bow of the ship, that sometimes housed drunk or unruly seamen, and here he had been secured.

It was dark and airless down in the bowels of the ship, and I felt myself becoming dizzy again as I made my way slowly along the companionway behind Jamie and the glow of his lantern.

When he unlocked the door, at first I saw nothing at all in the makeshift brig. Then, as Jamie stooped to enter with his lantern, the shine of the man's eyes betrayed his presence. "Black as the ace of spades" was the first thought that popped into my slightly addled mind, as the edges of face and form took shape against the darkness of the timbers.

No wonder Jamie had thought him a runaway slave. The man looked African, not island-born. Besides the deep red-black of his skin, his demeanor wasn't that of a man raised as a slave. He was sitting on a cask, hands bound behind his back and feet tied together, but I saw his head rise and his shoulders straighten as Jamie ducked under the lintel of the tiny space. He was very thin, but very muscular, clad in nothing but a ragged pair of trousers. The lines of his body were clear; he was tensed for attack or defense, but not submission.

Jamie saw it, too, and motioned me to stay well back against the wall. He placed the lantern on a cask, and squatted down before the captive, at eye-level.

"*Amiki,*" he said, spreading out his empty hands, palm up. "*Amiki. Bene-bene.*" Friend. Is good. It was taki-taki, the all-purpose pidgin polyglot that the traders from Barbados to Trinidad spoke in the ports.

The man stared impassively at Jamie for a moment, eyes still as tide pools. Then one eyebrow flicked up and he extended his bound feet before him.

"*Bene-bene, amiki?*" he said, with an ironic intonation that couldn't be missed, whatever the language. Is good, friend?

Jamie snorted briefly, amused, and rubbed a finger under his nose.

"It's a point," he said in English.

"Does he speak English, or French?" I moved a little closer. The captive's eyes rested on me for a moment, then passed away, indifferent.

"If he does, he'll no admit it. Picard and Fergus tried talking to him last night. He willna say a word, just stares at them. What he just said is the first he's spoken since he came aboard. *¿Habla Español?*" he said suddenly to the prisoner. There was no response. The man didn't even look at Jamie; just went on staring impassively at the square of open doorway behind me.

"Er, *sprechen Sie Deutsch?*" I said tentatively. He didn't answer, which was just as well, as the question had exhausted my own supply of German. "*Nicht* Hollander, either, I don't suppose."

Jamie shot me a sardonic look. "I canna tell much about him, Sassenach, but I'm fairly sure he's no a Dutchman."

"They have slaves on Eleuthera, don't they? That's a Dutch island," I said irritably. "Or St. Croix—that's Danish, isn't it?" Slowly as my mind was working this morning, it hadn't escaped me that the captive was our only clue to the pirates' whereabouts —and the only frail link to Ian. "Do you know enough taki-taki to ask him about Ian?"

Jamie shook his head, eyes intent on the prisoner. "No. Besides what I said to him already, I ken how to say '*not* good,' 'how much?' 'give it to me,' and 'drop that, ye bastard,' none of which seems a great deal to the point at present."

Stymied for the moment, we stared at the prisoner, who stared impassively back.

"To hell with it," Jamie said suddenly. He drew the dirk from his belt, went behind the cask, and sawed through the thongs around the prisoner's wrists.

He cut the ankle bindings as well, then sat back on his heels, the knife laid across his thigh.

"Friend," he said firmly in taki-taki. "Is good?"

The prisoner didn't say anything, but after a moment, he nodded slightly, his expression warily quizzical.

"There's a chamber pot in the corner," Jamie said in English, rising and sheathing his dirk. "Use it, and then my wife will tend your wounds."

A very faint flicker of amusement crossed the man's face. He nodded once more, this time in acceptance of defeat. He rose slowly from the cask and turned, stiff hands fumbling at his trousers. I looked askance at Jamie.

"It's one of the worst things about being bound that way," he explained matter-of-factly. "Ye canna take a piss by yourself."

"I see," I said, not wanting to think about how he knew that.

"That, and the pain in your shoulders," he said. "Be careful touching him, Sassenach." The note of warning in his voice was clear, and I nodded. It wasn't the man's shoulders he was concerned about.

I still felt light-headed, and the stuffiness of the surroundings had made my headache throb again, but I was less battered than the prisoner, who had indeed been "bashed about" at some stage of the proceedings.

Bashed though he was, his injuries seemed largely superficial. A swollen knot rose on the man's forehead, and a deep scrape had left a crusted reddish patch on one shoulder. He was undoubtedly bruised in a number of places, but given the remarkably deep shade of his skin and the darkness of the surroundings, I couldn't tell where.

There were deep bands of rawness on ankles and wrists, where he had pulled against the thongs. I hadn't made any of the hawthorn lotion, but I had brought the jar of gentian salve. I eased myself down on the deck next to him, but he took no more notice of me than of the deck beneath his feet, even when I began to spread the cool blue cream on his wounds.

What was more interesting than the fresh injuries, though, were the healed ones. At close range, I could see the faint white lines of three parallel slashes, running across the slope of each cheekbone, and a series of three short vertical lines on the high, narrow forehead, just between his brows. Tribal scars. African-born for sure, then; such scars were made during manhood rituals, or so Murphy had told me.

His flesh was warm and smooth under my fingers, slicked with sweat. I felt warm, too; sweaty and unwell. The deck rose gently beneath me, and I put my hand on his back to keep my balance. The thin, tough lines of healed whipstrokes webbed his shoulders, like the furrows of tiny worms beneath his skin. The feel of them was unexpected; so much like the feel of the marks on Jamie's own back. I swallowed, feeling queasy, but went on with my doctoring.

The man ignored me completely, even when I touched spots I knew must be painful. His eyes were fixed on Jamie, who was watching the prisoner with equal intentness.

The problem was plain. The man was almost certainly a runaway slave. He hadn't wanted to speak to us, for fear that his speech would give away his owner's island, and that we would then find out his original owner and return him to captivity.

Now we knew that he spoke—or at least understood—English, it was bound to increase his wariness. Even if we assured him that it was not our intention either to return him to an owner or to enslave him ourselves, he was unlikely to trust us. I couldn't say that I blamed him, under the circumstances.

On the other hand, this man was our best—and possibly the only—chance of finding out what had happened to Ian Murray aboard the *Bruja*.

When at length I had bandaged the man's wrists and ankles, Jamie gave me a hand to rise, then spoke to the prisoner.

"You'll be hungry, I expect," he said. "Come along to the cabin, and we'll eat." Not waiting for a response, he took my good arm and turned to the door. There was silence behind us as we moved into the corridor, but when I looked back, the slave was there, following a few feet behind.

Jamie led us to my cabin, disregarding the curious glances of the sailors we passed, only stopping by Fergus long enough to order food to be sent from the galley.

"Back to bed with ye, Sassenach," he said firmly, when we reached the cabin. I didn't argue. My arm hurt, my head hurt, and I could feel little waves of heat flickering behind my eyes. It looked as though I would have to break down and use a little of the precious penicillin on myself, after all. There was still a chance that my body could throw off the infection, but I couldn't afford to wait too long.

Jamie had poured out a glass of whisky for me, and another for our guest. Still wary, the man accepted it, and took a sip, eyes widening in surprise. I supposed Scotch whisky must be a novelty to him.

Jamie took a glass for himself and sat down, motioning the slave to the other seat, across the small table.

"My name is Fraser," he said. "I am captain here. My wife," he added, with a nod toward my berth.

The prisoner hesitated, but then set down his glass with an air of decision.

"They be callin' me Ishmael," he said, in a voice like honey poured over coal. "I ain't no pirate. I be a cook."

"Murphy's going to like that," I remarked, but Jamie ignored me. There was a faint line between the ruddy brows, as he felt his way into the conversation.

"A ship's cook?" he asked, taking care to make his voice sound casual. Only the tap of his two stiff fingers against his thigh betrayed him—and that, only to me.

"No, mon, I don't got nothin' to do with that ship!" Ishmael was vehement. "They taken me off the shore, say they kill me, I don' go long by them, be easy. I ain't no pirate!" he repeated, and it dawned on me belatedly that of course he wouldn't wish to be taken for a pirate—whether he was one or not. Piracy was punishable by hanging, and he could have no way of knowing that we were as eager as he to stay clear of the Royal Navy.

"Aye, I see." Jamie hit the right balance, between soothing and skeptical. He leaned back slightly in the big wheel-backed chair. "And how did the *Bruja* come to take ye prisoner, then? Not where," he added quickly, as a look of alarm flitted across the prisoner's face.

"Ye needna tell me where ye came from; that's of no concern to me. Only I should care to know how ye came to fall into their hands, and how long ye've been with them. Since, as ye say, ye werena one of them." The hint was broad enough to spread butter on. We didn't mean to return him to his owner; however, if he didn't oblige with information, we might just turn him over to the Crown as a pirate.

The prisoner's eyes darkened; no fool, he had grasped the point at once. His head twitched briefly sideways, and his eyes narrowed.

"I be catchin' fish by the river," he said. "Big ship, he come sailin' up the river slow, little boats be pullin' him. Men in the little boat, they see me, holler out. I drop the fish, be runnin', but they close by. They men jump out, kotch me by the cane field, figure they take me to sell. Tha's all, mon." He shrugged, signaling the conclusion of his story.

"Aye, I see." Jamie's eyes were intent on the prisoner. He hesitated, wanting to ask where the river was, but not quite daring to, for fear the man would clam up again. "While ye were on the ship—did ye see any boys among the crew, or as prisoners, too? Boys, young men?"

The man's eyes widened slightly; he hadn't been expecting that. He paused warily, but then nodded, with a faintly derisive glint in his eye.

"Yes, mon, they have boys. Why? You be wantin' one?" His glance flicked to me and then back to Jamie, one eyebrow raised.

Jamie's head jerked, and a slight flush rose on his cheekbones at the implication.

"I do," he said levelly. "I am looking for a young kinsman who was taken by pirates. I should feel myself greatly obliged to anyone who might assist me in finding him." He lifted one eyebrow significantly.

The prisoner grunted slightly, his nostrils flaring.

"That so? What you be doin' for me, I be helpin' you fin' this boy?"

"I should set you ashore at any port of your choosing, with a fair sum in gold," Jamie replied. "But of course I should require proof that ye did have knowledge of my nephew's whereabouts, aye?"

"Huh." The prisoner was still wary, but beginning to relax. "You tell me, mon—what this boy be like?"

Jamie hesitated for a moment, studying the prisoner, but then shook his head.

"No," he said thoughtfully. "I dinna think that will work. *You* describe to *me* such lads as ye saw on the pirate vessel."

The prisoner eyed Jamie for a moment, then broke out in a low, rich laugh.

"You no particular fool, mon," he said. "You know that?"

"I know that," Jamie said dryly. "So long as ye know it as well. Tell me, then."

Ishmael snorted briefly, but complied, pausing only to refresh himself from the tray of food Fergus had brought. Fergus himself lounged against the door, watching the prisoner through half-lidded eyes.

"They be twelve boys talkin' strange, like you."

Jamie's eyebrows shot up, and he exchanged a glance of astonishment with me. Twelve?

"Like me?" He said. "White boys, English? Or Scots, d'ye mean?"

Ishmael shook his head in incomprehension; "Scot" was not in his vocabulary.

"Talkin' like dogs fightin'," he explained. "Grrrr! Wuff!" He growled, shaking his head in illustration like a dog worrying a rat, and I saw Fergus's shoulders shake in suppressed hilarity.

"Scots for sure," I said, trying not to laugh. Jamie shot me a brief dirty look, then returned his attention to Ishmael.

"Verra well, then," he said, exaggerating his natural soft burr. "Twelve Scottish lads. What did they look like?"

Ishmael squinted dubiously, chewing a piece of mango from the tray. He wiped the juice from the corner of his mouth and shook his head.

"I only see them once, mon. Tell you all I see, though." He closed his eyes and frowned, the vertical lines on his forehead drawing close together.

"Four boys be yellow-haired, six brown, two with black hair. Two shorter than me, one maybe the size that *griffon* there"—he nodded toward Fergus, who stiffened in outrage at the insult—"one big, not so big as you . . ."

"Aye, and how will they have been dressed?" Slowly, carefully, Jamie drew him through the descriptions, asking for details, demanding comparisons—how tall? how fat? what color eyes?—carefully concealing the direction of his interest as he drew the man further into conversation.

My head had stopped spinning, but the fatigue was still there, weighting my senses. I let my eyes close, obscurely soothed by the deep, murmuring voices. Jamie *did* sound rather like a big, fierce dog, I thought, with his soft growling burr and the abrupt, clipped sound of his consonants.

"Wuff," I murmured under my breath, and my belly muscles quivered slightly under my folded hands.

Ishmael's voice was just as deep, but smooth and low, rich as hot chocolate made with cream. I began to drift, lulled by the sound of it.

He sounded like Joe Abernathy, I thought drowsily, dictating an autopsy report—unvarnished and unappetizing physical details, related in a voice like a deep golden lullaby.

I could see Joe's hands in memory, dark on the pale skin of an accident victim, moving swiftly as he made his verbal notes to the tape recorder.

"Deceased is a tall man, approximately six feet in height, and slender in build. . . ."

A tall man, slender.

"—that one, he bein' tall, bein' thin . . ."

I came awake suddenly, heart pounding, hearing the echo of Joe's voice coming from the table a few feet away.

"No!" I said, quite suddenly, and all three men stopped and looked at me in surprise. I pushed back the weight of my damp hair and waved weakly at them.

"Don't mind me; I was dreaming, I think."

They returned to their conversation, and I lay still, eyes half-closed, but no longer sleepy.

There was no physical resemblance. Joe was stocky and bear-like; this Ishmael slender and lean, though the swell of muscle over the curve of his shoulder suggested considerable strength.

Joe's face was broad and amiable; this man's narrow and wary-eyed, with a high forehead that made his tribal scars the more striking. Joe's skin was the color of fresh coffee, Ishmael's the deep red-black of a burning ember, which Stern had told me was characteristic of slaves from the Guinea coast—not so highly prized as the blue-black Senegalese, but more valuable than the yellow-brown Yaga and Congolese.

But if I closed my eyes entirely, I could hear Joe's voice speaking, even allowing for the faint Caribbean lilt of slave-English. I cracked my eyelids and looked carefully, searching for any signs of resemblance. There were none, but I did see what I had seen before, and not noticed, among the other scars and marks on the man's battered torso. What I had thought merely a scrape was in fact a deep abrasion that overlay a wide, flat scar, cut in the form of a rough square just below the point of the shoulder. The mark was raw and pink, newly healed. I should have seen it at once, if not for the darkness of the orlop, and the scrape that obscured it.

I lay quite still, trying to remember. "No *slave* name," Joe had said derisively, referring to his son's self-christening. Clearly, Ishmael had cut away an owner's brand, to prevent identification, should he be recaptured. But whose? And surely the name Ishmael was no more than coincidence.

Maybe not so farfetched a one, though; "Ishmael" almost certainly wasn't the man's real name. "They be *callin'* me Ishmael," he had said. That, too, was a slave name, given him by one owner or another. And if young Lenny had been climbing his family tree, as it seemed, what more likely than that he should have chosen one of his ancestors' given names in symbol? If. But if he was . . .

I lay looking up at the claustrophobic ceiling of the berth, suppositions spinning through my head. Whether this man had any link with Joe or not, the possibility had reminded me of something.

Jamie was catechizing the man about the personnel and structure of the *Bruja*—for so the ship that had attacked us had been—but I was paying no attention. I sat up, cautiously, so as not to make the dizziness worse, and signaled to Fergus.

"I need air," I said. "Help me up on deck, will you?" Jamie glanced at me with a hint of worry, but I smiled reassuringly at him, and took Fergus's arm.

"Where are the papers for that slave we bought on Barbados?" I demanded, as soon as we were out of earshot of the cabin. "And where's the slave, for that matter?"

Fergus looked at me curiously, but obligingly rummaged in his coat.

"I have the papers here, milady," he said, handing them to me. "As for the slave, I believe he is in the crew's quarters. Why?" he added, unable to restrain his curiosity.

I ignored the question, fumbling through the grubby, repellent bits of paper.

"There it is," I said, finding the bit I remembered Jamie reading to me. "Abernathy! It *was* Abernathy! Branded on the left shoulder with a fleur-de-lys. Did you notice that mark, Fergus?"

He shook his head, looking mildly bewildered.

"No, milady."

"Then come with me," I said, turning toward the crew's quarters. "I want to see how big it is."

The mark was about three inches long and three wide; a flower, surmounting the initial "A," burned into the skin a few inches below the point of the shoulder. It was the right size, and in the right place, to match the scar on the man Ishmael. It wasn't, however, a fleur-de-lys; that had been the mistake of a careless transcriber. It was a sixteen-petaled rose—the Jacobite emblem of Charles Stuart. I blinked at it in amazement; what patriotic exile had chosen this bizarre method of maintaining allegiance to the vanquished Stuarts?

"Milady, I think you should return to your bed," Fergus said. He was frowning at me as I stooped over Temeraire, who bore this inspection as stolidly as everything else. "You are the color of goose turds, and milord will not like it at all if I allow you to fall down on the deck."

"I won't fall down," I assured him. "And I don't care what color I am. I think we've just had a stroke of luck. Listen, Fergus, I want you to do something for me."

"Anything, milady," he said, grabbing me by the elbow as a shift in the wind sent me staggering across the suddenly tilting deck. "But not," he added firmly, "until you are safely back in your bed."

I allowed him to lead me back to the cabin, for I really didn't feel at all well, but not before giving him my instructions. As we entered the cabin, Jamie stood up from the table to greet us.

"There ye are, Sassenach! Are ye all right?" he asked, frowning down at me. "Ye've gone a nasty color, like a spoilt custard."

"I am perfectly fine," I said, through my teeth, easing myself down on the bunk to avoid jarring my arm. "Have you and Mr. Ishmael finished your conversation?"

Jamie glanced at the prisoner, and I saw the flat black gaze that locked with his. The atmosphere between them was not hostile, but it was charged in some way. Jamie nodded in dismissal.

"We've finished—for the moment," he said. He turned to Fergus. "See our guest below, will ye, Fergus, and see to it that he's fed and clothed?" He remained standing until Ishmael had left under Fergus's wing. Then he sat down beside my berth and squinted into the darkness at me.

"Ye look awful," he said. "Had I best fetch your kit and be feeding ye a wee tonic or somesuch?"

"No," I said. "Jamie, listen—I think I know where our friend Ishmael came from."

He lifted one brow.

"You do?"

I explained about the scar on Ishmael, and the almost matching brand on the slave Temeraire, without mentioning what had given me the idea in the first place.

"Five will get you ten that they came from the same place—from this Mrs. Abernathy's, on Jamaica." I said.

"Five will . . . ? Och," he said, waving away my confusing reference in the interests of continuing the discussion. "Well, ye could be right, Sassenach, and I hope so. The wily black bastard wouldna say where he was from. Not that I can blame him," he added fairly. "God, if I'd got away from such a life, there's no power on earth would take me back!" He spoke with a surprising vehemence.

"No, I wouldn't blame him either," I said. "But what did he tell you, about the boys? Has he seen Young Ian?"

The frowning lines of his face relaxed.

"Aye, I'm almost sure he has." One fist curled on his knee in anticipation. "Two of the lads he described could be Ian. And knowin' it was the *Bruja,* I canna think otherwise. And if you're right about where he's come from, Sassenach, we might have him —we may find him at last!" Ishmael, while refusing to give any clue as to where the *Bruja* had picked him up, had gone so far as to say that the twelve boys—all prisoners—had been taken off the ship together, soon after his own capture.

"Twelve lads," Jamie repeated, his momentary look of excitement fading back into a frown. "What in the name of God would someone be wanting, to kidnap twelve lads from Scotland?"

"Perhaps he's a collector," I said, feeling more light-headed by the moment. "Coins, and gems, and Scottish boys."

"Ye think whoever's got Ian has the treasure as well?" He glanced curiously at me.

"I don't know," I said, feeling suddenly very tired. I yawned rackingly. "We may know for sure about Ishmael, though. I told Fergus to see that Temeraire gets a look at him. If they are from the same place . . ." I yawned again, my body seeking the oxygen that loss of blood had deprived me of.

"That's verra sensible of ye, Sassenach," Jamie said, sounding faintly surprised that I was capable of sense. For that matter, I was a little surprised myself; my thoughts were becoming more fragmented by the moment, and it was an effort to keep talking logically.

Jamie saw it; he patted my hand and stood up.

"Ye dinna trouble yourself about it now, Sassenach. Rest, and I'll send Marsali down wi' some tea."

"Whisky," I said, and he laughed.

"All right, then, whisky," he agreed. He smoothed my hair back, and leaning into the berth, kissed my hot forehead.

"Better?" he asked, smiling.

"Lots." I smiled back and closed my eyes.

56

Turtle Soup

When I woke again, in the late afternoon, I ached all over. I had thrown off the covers in my sleep, and lay sprawled in my shift, my skin hot and dry in the soft air. My arm ached abominably, and I could feel each of Mr. Willoughby's forty-three elegant stitches like red-hot safety pins stuck through my flesh.

No help for it; I was going to have to use the penicillin. I might be proof against smallpox, typhoid, and the common cold in its eighteenth-century incarnation, but I wasn't immortal, and God only knew what insanitary substances the Portuguese had been employing his cutlass on before applying it to me.

The short trip across the room to the cupboard where my clothes hung left me sweating and shivering, and I had to sit down quite suddenly, the skirt clutched to my bosom, in order to avoid falling.

"Sassenach! Are ye all right?" Jamie poked his head through the low doorway, looking worried.

"No," I said. "Come here a minute, will you? I need you to do something."

"Wine? A biscuit? Murphy's made a wee broth for ye, special." He was beside me in a moment, the back of his hand cool against my flushed cheek. "God, you're burning!"

"Yes, I know," I said. "Don't worry, though; I have medicine for it."

I fumbled one-handed in the pocket of the skirt, and pulled out the case containing the syringes and ampules. My right arm was sore enough that any movement made me clench my teeth.

"Your turn," I said wryly, shoving the case across the table toward Jamie. "Here's your chance for revenge, if you want it."

He looked blankly at the case, then at me.

"What?" he said. "Ye want me to stab ye with one of these spikes?"

"I wish you wouldn't put it quite that way, but yes," I said.

"In the bum?" His lips twitched.

"Yes, damn you!"

He looked at me for a moment, one corner of his mouth curling slightly upward. Then he bowed his head over the case, red hair glowing in the shaft of sun from the window.

"Tell me what to do, then," he said.

I directed him carefully, guiding him through the preparation and filling of the syringe, and then took it myself, checking for air bubbles, clumsily left-handed. By the time I had given it back to him and arranged myself on the berth, he had ceased to find anything faintly funny about the situation.

"Are ye sure ye want me to do it?" he said doubtfully. "I'm no verra good with my hands."

That made me laugh, in spite of my throbbing arm. I had seen him do everything with those hands, from delivering foals and building walls, to skinning deer and setting type, all with the same light and dextrous touch.

"Well, aye," he said, when I said as much. "But it's no quite the same, is it? The closest thing I've done to this is to dirk a man in the wame, and it feels a bit strange to think of doin' such a thing to you, Sassenach."

I glanced back over my shoulder, to find him gnawing dubiously on his lower lip, the brandy-soaked pad in one hand, the syringe held gingerly in the other.

"Look," I said. "I did it to you; you *know* what it feels like. It wasn't that bad, was it?" He was beginning to make me rather nervous.

"Mmphm." Pressing his lips together, he knelt down by the bed and gently wiped a spot on my backside with the cool, wet pad. "Is this all right?"

"That's fine. Press the point in at a bit of an angle, not straight in—you see how the point of the needle's cut at an angle? Push it in about a quarter-inch—don't be afraid to jab a bit, skin's tougher than you think to get through—and then push down the plunger very slowly, you don't want to do it too fast.''

I closed my eyes and waited. After a moment, I opened them and looked back. He was pale, and a faint sheen of sweat glimmered over his cheekbones.

''Never mind.'' I heaved myself upright, bracing against the wave of dizziness. ''Here, give me that.'' I snatched the pad from his hand and swiped a patch across the top of my thigh. My hand trembled slightly from the fever.

''But—''

''Shut up!'' I took the syringe and aimed it as well as I could, left-handed, then plunged it into the muscle. It hurt. It hurt more when I pressed down on the plunger, and my thumb slipped off.

Then Jamie's hands were there, one steadying my leg, the other on the needle, slowly pressing down until the last of the white liquid had vanished from the tube. I took one quick, deep breath when he pulled it out.

''Thanks,'' I said, after a moment.

''I'm sorry,'' he said softly, a minute later. His hand came behind my back, easing me down.

''It's all right.'' My eyes were closed, and there were little colored patterns on the inside of my eyelids. They reminded me of the lining of a doll's suitcase I had had as a child; tiny pink and silver stars on a dark background. ''I'd forgotten; it's hard to do it the first few times. I suppose sticking a dirk in someone *is* easier,'' I added. ''You aren't worried about hurting them, after all.''

He didn't say anything, but exhaled rather strongly through his nose. I could hear him moving about the room, putting the case of syringes away and hanging up my skirt. The site of the injection felt like a knot under my skin.

''I'm sorry,'' I said. ''I didn't mean it that way.''

''Well, ye should,'' he said evenly. ''It *is* easier to kill someone to save your own life than it is to hurt someone to save theirs. Ye're a deal braver than I am, and I dinna mind your saying so.''

I opened my eyes and looked at him.

''The hell you don't.''

He stared down at me, blue eyes narrowed. The corner of his mouth turned up.

''The hell I don't,'' he agreed.

I laughed, but it hurt my arm.

"I'm not, and you aren't, and I didn't mean it that way, anyway," I said, and closed my eyes again.

"Mmphm."

I could hear the thump of feet on the deck above, and Mr. Warren's voice, raised in organized impatience. We had passed Great Abaco and Eleuthera in the night, and were now headed south toward Jamaica, with the wind behind us.

"*I* wouldn't risk being shot and hacked at, and arrested and hanged, if there were any choice about it," I said.

"Neither would I," he said dryly.

"But you—" I began, and then stopped. I looked at him curiously. "You really think that," I said slowly. "That you don't have a choice about it. Don't you?"

He was turned slightly away from me, eyes fixed on the port. The sun shone on the bridge of his long, straight nose and he rubbed a finger slowly up and down it. The broad shoulders rose slightly, and fell.

"I'm a man, Sassenach," he said, very softly. "If I thought there was a choice . . . then I maybe couldna do it. Ye dinna need to be so brave about things if ye ken ye canna help it, aye?" He looked at me then, with a faint smile. "Like a woman in childbirth, aye? Ye must do it, and it makes no difference if you're afraid—ye'll do it. It's only when ye ken ye can say no that it takes courage."

I lay quiet for a bit, watching him. He had closed his eyes and leaned back in the chair, auburn lashes long and absurdly childish against his cheeks. They contrasted strangely with the smudges beneath his eyes and the deeper lines at the corners. He was tired; he'd barely slept since the sighting of the pirate vessel.

"I haven't told you about Graham Menzies, have I?" I said at last. The blue eyes opened at once.

"No. Who was he?"

"A patient. At the hospital in Boston."

Graham had been in his late sixties when I knew him; a Scottish immigrant who hadn't lost his burr, despite nearly forty years in Boston. He was a fisherman, or had been; when I knew him he owned several lobster boats, and let others do the fishing for him.

He was a lot like the Scottish soldiers I had known at Prestonpans and Falkirk; stoic and humorous at once, willing to joke about anything that was too painful to suffer in silence.

"You'll be careful, now, lassie," was the last thing he said to me as I watched the anesthetist set up the intravenous drip that would maintain him while I amputated his cancerous left leg. "Be sure ye're takin' off the right one, now."

"Don't worry," I assured him, patting the weathered hand that lay on the sheet. "I'll get the right one."

"Ye will?" His eyes widened in simulated horror. "I thought 'twas the *left* one was bad!" He was still chuckling asthmatically as the gas mask came down over his face.

The amputation had gone well, and Graham had recovered and gone home, but I was not really surprised to see him back again, six months later. The lab report on the original tumor had been dubious, and the doubts were now substantiated; metastasis to the lymph nodes in the groin.

I removed the cancerous nodes. Radiation treatment was applied. Cobalt. I removed the spleen, to which the disease had spread, knowing that the surgery was entirely in vain, but not willing to give up.

"It's a lot easier not to give up, when it isn't you that's sick," I said, staring up at the timbers overhead.

"Did he give up, then?" Jamie asked.

"I don't think I'd call it that, exactly."

"I have been thinking," Graham announced. The sound of his voice echoed tinnily through the earpieces of my stethoscope.

"Have you?" I said. "Well, don't do it out loud 'til I've finished here, that's a good lad."

He gave a brief snort of laughter, but lay quietly as I auscultated his chest, moving the disc of the stethoscope swiftly from ribs to sternum.

"All right," I said at last, slipping the tubes out of my ears and letting them fall over my shoulders. "What have you been thinking about?"

"Killing myself."

His eyes met mine straight on, with just a hint of challenge. I glanced behind me, to be sure that the nurse had left, then pulled up the blue plastic visitor's chair and sat down next to him.

"Pain getting bad?" I asked. "There are things we can do, you know. You only need to ask." I hesitated before adding the last; he never had asked. Even when it was obvious that he needed medication, he never mentioned his discomfort. To mention it myself seemed an invasion of his privacy; I saw the small tightening at the corners of his mouth.

"I've a daughter," he said. "And two grandsons; bonny lads. But I'm forgetting; you'll have seen them last week, aye?"

I had. They came at least twice a week to see him, bringing scribbled school papers and autographed baseballs to show their grandpa.

"And there's my mother, living up to the rest home on Canterbury," he said thoughtfully. "It costs dearly, that place, but it's clean, and the food's good enough she enjoys complainin' about it while she eats."

He glanced dispassionately at the flat bedsheet, and lifted his stump.

"A month, d'ye think? Four? Three?"

"Maybe three," I said. "With luck," I added idiotically.

He snorted at me, and jerked his head at the IV drip above him.

"Tcha! And worse luck I wouldna wish on a beggar." He looked around at all the paraphernalia; the automatic respirator, the blinking cardiac monitor, the litter of medical technology. "Nearly a hundred dollars a day it's costing, to keep me here," he said. "Three months, that would be—great heavens, ten thousand dollars!" He shook his head, frowning.

"A bad bargain, I call that. Not worth it." His pale gray eyes twinkled suddenly up at me. "I'm Scots, ye know. Born thrifty, and not likely to get over it now."

"So I did it for him," I said, still staring upward. "Or rather, we did it together. He was prescribed morphia for the pain—that's like laudanum, only much stronger. I drew off half of each ampule and replaced the missing bit with water. It meant he didn't get the relief of a full dose for nearly twenty-four hours, but that was the safest way to get a big dose with no risk of being found out.

"We talked about using one of the botanical medicines I was studying; I knew enough to make up something fatal, but I wasn't sure of it being painless, and he didn't want to risk me being accused, if anyone got suspicious and did a forensic examination." I saw Jamie's eyebrow lift, and flapped a hand. "It doesn't matter; it's a way of finding out how someone died."

"Ah. Like a coroner's court?"

"A bit. Anyway, he'd be supposed to have morphia in his blood; that wouldn't prove ànything. So that's what we did."

I drew a deep breath.

"There would have been no trouble, if I'd given him the injection, and left. That's what he'd asked me to do."

Jamie was quiet, eyes fixed intently on me.

"I couldn't do it, though." I looked at my left hand, seeing not my own smooth flesh, but the big, swollen knuckles of a commercial fisherman, and the fat green veins that crossed his wrist.

"I got the needle in," I said. I rubbed a finger over the spot on the wrist, where a large vein crosses the distal head of the radius. "But I couldn't press down the plunger."

In memory, I saw Graham Menzies's other hand rise from his side, trailing tubes, and close over my own. He hadn't much strength, then, but enough.

"I sat there until he was gone, holding his hand." I felt it still, the steady beat of the wrist-pulse under my thumb, growing slower, and slower still, as I held his hand, and then waiting for a beat that did not come.

I looked up at Jamie, shaking off the memory.

"And then a nurse came in." It had been one of the younger nurses—an excitable girl, with no discretion. She wasn't very experienced, but knew enough to tell a dead man when she saw one. And me just sitting there, doing nothing—most undoctorlike conduct. And the empty morphia syringe, lying on the table beside me.

"She talked, of course," I said.

"I expect she would."

"I had the presence of mind to drop the syringe into the incinerator chute after she left, though. It was her word against mine, and the whole matter was just dismissed."

My mouth twisted wryly. "Except that the next week, they offered me a job as head of the whole department. Very important. A lovely office on the sixth floor of the hospital—safely away from the patients, where I couldn't murder anyone else."

My finger was still rubbing absently across my wrist. Jamie reached out and stopped it by laying his own hand over mine.

"When was this, Sassenach?" he asked, his voice very gentle.

"Just before I took Bree and went to Scotland. That's why I went, in fact; they gave me an extended leave—said I'd been working too hard, and deserved a nice vacation." I didn't try to keep the irony out of my voice.

"I see." His hand was warm on mine, despite the heat of my fever. "If it hadna been for that, for losing your work—would ye have come, Sassenach? Not just to Scotland. To me?"

I looked up at him and squeezed his hand, taking a deep breath.

"I don't know," I said. "I really don't. If I hadn't come to Scotland, met Roger Wakefield, found out that you—" I stopped and swallowed, overwhelmed. "It was Graham who sent me to Scotland," I said at last, feeling slightly choked. "He asked me to go someday—and say hello to Aberdeen for him." I glanced up at Jamie suddenly.

"I didn't! I never did go to Aberdeen."

"Dinna trouble yourself, Sassenach." Jamie squeezed my hand. "I'll take ye there myself—when we go back. Not," he added practically, "that there's anything to see there."

It was growing stuffy in the cabin. He rose and went to open one of the stern windows.

"Jamie," I said, watching his back, "what do you want?"

He glanced around, frowning slightly in thought.

"Oh—an orange would be good," he said. "There's some in the desk, aye?" Without waiting for a reply, he rolled back the lid of the desk, revealing a small bowl of oranges, bright among the litter of quills and papers. "D'ye want one, too?"

"All right," I said, smiling. "That wasn't really what I meant, though. I meant—what do you want to do, once we've found Ian?"

"Oh." He sat down by the berth, an orange in his hands, and stared at it for a moment.

"D'ye know," he said at last, "I dinna think anyone has ever asked me that—what it was I wanted to do." He sounded mildly surprised.

"Not as though you very often had a choice about it, is it?" I said dryly. "Now you do, though."

"Aye, that's true." He rolled the orange between his palms, head bent over the dimpled sphere. "I suppose it's come to ye that we likely canna go back to Scotland—at least for a time?" he said. I had told him of Tompkins's revelations about Sir Percival and his machinations, of course, but we had had little time to discuss the matter—or its implications.

"It has," I said. "That's why I asked."

I was quiet then, letting him come to terms with it. He had lived as an outlaw for a good many years, hiding first physically, and then by means of secrecy and aliases, eluding the law by slipping from one identity to another. But now all these were known; there was no way for him to resume any of his former activities—or even to appear in public in Scotland.

His final refuge had always been Lallybroch. But even that avenue of retreat was lost to him now. Lallybroch would always be his home, but it was no longer his; there was a new laird now. I knew he would not begrudge the fact that Jenny's family possessed the estate—but he must, if he was human, regret the loss of his heritage.

I could hear his faint snort, and thought he had probably reached the same point in his thinking that I had in mine.

"Not Jamaica or the English-owned islands, either," he observed ruefully. "Tom Leonard and the Royal Navy may think us both dead for the moment, but they'll be quick enough to notice otherwise if we stay for any length of time."

"Have you thought of America?" I asked this delicately. "The Colonies, I mean."

He rubbed his nose doubtfully.

"Well, no. I hadna really thought of it. It's true we'd likely be safe from the Crown there, but . . ." He trailed off, frowning. He picked up his dirk and scored the orange, quickly and neatly, then began to peel it.

"No one would be hunting you there," I pointed out. "Sir Percival hasn't got any interest in you, unless you're in Scotland, where arresting you would do him some good. The British Navy can't very well follow you ashore, and the West Indian governors haven't anything to say about what goes on in the Colonies, either."

"That's true," he said slowly. "But the Colonies . . ." He took the peeled orange in one hand, and began to toss it lightly, a few inches in the air. "It's verra primitive, Sassenach," he said. "A wilderness, aye? I shouldna like to take ye into danger."

That made me laugh, and he glanced sharply at me, then, catching my thought, relaxed into a half-rueful smile.

"Aye, well, I suppose draggin' ye off to sea and letting ye be kidnapped and locked up in a plague ship is dangerous enough. But at least I havena let ye be eaten by cannibals, yet."

I wanted to laugh again, but there was a bitter note to his voice that made me bite my lip instead.

"There aren't any cannibals in America," I said.

"There are!" he said heatedly. "I printed a book for a society of Catholic missionaries, that told all about the heathen Iroquois in the north. They tie up their captives and chop bits off of them, and then rip out their hearts and eat them before their eyes!"

"Eat the hearts first and then the eyes, do they?" I said, laughing in spite of myself. "All right," I said, seeing his scowl, "I'm sorry. But for one thing, you can't believe everything you read, and for another—"

I didn't get to finish. He leaned forward and grasped my good arm, tight enough to make me squeak with surprise.

"Damn you, listen to me!" he said. "It's no light matter!"

"Well . . . no, I suppose not," I said, tentatively. "I didn't mean to make fun of you—but, Jamie, I *did* live in Boston for nearly twenty years. You've never set foot in America!"

"That's true," he said evenly. "And d'ye think the place ye lived in is anything like what it's like now, Sassenach?"

"Well—" I began, then paused. While I had seen any number of historic buildings near Boston Common, sporting little brass plaques attesting to their antiquity, the majority of them had been built later than 1770; many a lot later. And beyond a few buildings . . .

"Well, no," I admitted. "It's not; I know it's not. But I don't think it's a complete wilderness. There *are* cities and towns now; I know that much."

He let go of my arm and sat back. He still held the orange in his other hand.

"I suppose that's so," he said slowly. "Ye dinna hear so much of the towns—only that it's such a wild savage place, though verra beautiful. But I'm no a fool, Sassenach." His voice sharpened slightly, and he dug his thumb savagely into the orange, splitting it in half.

"I dinna believe something only because someone's set words down in a book—for God's sake, I print the damn things! I ken verra well just what charlatans and fools some writers are—I see them! And surely I ken the difference between a romance and a fact set down in cold blood!"

"All right," I said. "Though I'm not sure it's all that easy to tell the difference between romance and fact in print. But even if it's dead true about the Iroquois, the whole continent isn't swarming with bloodthirsty savages. I *do* know that much. It's a very big place, you know," I added, gently.

"Mmphm," he said, plainly unconvinced. Still, he bent his attention to the orange, and began to divide it into segments.

"This is very funny," I said ruefully. "When I made up my mind to come back, I read everything I could find about England and Scotland and France about this time, so I'd know as much as I could about what to expect. And here we end up in a place I know nothing about, because it never dawned on me we'd cross the ocean, with you being so seasick."

That made him laugh, a little grudgingly.

"Aye, well, ye never ken what ye can do 'til ye have to. Believe me, Sassenach, once I've got Ian safely back, I shall never set foot on a filthy, godforsaken floating plank in my life again—except to go home to Scotland, when it's safe," he added, as an afterthought. He offered me an orange segment and I took it, token of a peace offering.

"Speaking of Scotland, you still have your printing press there, safe in Edinburgh," I said. "We could have it sent over, maybe—if we settled in one of the larger American cities."

He looked up at that, startled.

"D'ye think it would be possible to earn a living, printing? There are that many people? It takes a fair-sized city, ye ken, to need a printer or bookseller."

"I'm sure you could. Boston, Philadelphia . . . not New York yet, I don't think. Williamsburg, maybe? I don't know which ones, but there are several places big enough to need printing—the shipping ports, certainly.'' I remembered the flapping posters, advertising dates of embarkation and arrival, sales of goods and recruitment of seamen, that decorated the walls of every seaside tavern in Le Havre.

''Mmphm.'' This one was a thoughtful noise. ''Aye, well, if we might do that . . .''

He poked a piece of fruit into his mouth and ate it slowly.

''What about you?'' he said abruptly.

I glanced at him, startled.

''What about me?''

His eyes were fixed intently on me, reading my face.

''Would it suit ye to go to such a place?'' He looked down then, carefully separating the other half of the fruit. ''I mean—you've your work to do as well, aye?'' He looked up and smiled, wryly.

''I learned in Paris that I couldna stop ye doing it. And ye said yourself, ye might not have come, had Menzies's death not stopped you, where ye were. Can ye be a healer in the Colonies, d'ye think?''

''I expect I can,'' I said slowly. ''There are people sick and injured, almost anywhere you go, after all.'' I looked at him, curious.

''You're a very odd man, Jamie Fraser.''

He laughed at that, and swallowed the rest of his orange.

''Oh, I am, aye? And what d'ye mean by that?''

''Frank loved me,'' I said slowly. ''But there were . . . pieces of me, that he didn't know what to do with. Things about me that he didn't understand, or maybe that frightened him.'' I glanced at Jamie. ''Not you.''

His head was bent over a second orange, hands moving swiftly as he scored it with his dirk, but I could see the faint smile in the corner of his mouth.

''No, Sassenach, ye dinna frighten me. Or rather ye do, but only when I think ye may kill yourself from carelessness.''

I snorted briefly.

''You scare me, for the same reason, but I don't suppose there's anything I can do about it.''

His chuckle was deep and easy.

"And ye think I canna do anything about it, either, so I shouldna be worrit?"

"I didn't say you shouldn't worry—do you think I don't worry? But no, you probably can't do anything about me."

I saw him opening his mouth to disagree. Then he changed his mind, and laughed again. He reached out and popped an orange segment into my mouth.

"Well, maybe no, Sassenach, and maybe so. But I've lived a long enough time now to think it maybe doesna matter so much— so long as I can love you."

Speechless with orange juice, I stared at him in surprise.

"And I do," he said softly. He leaned into the berth and kissed me, his mouth warm and sweet. Then he drew back, and gently touched my cheek.

"Rest now," he said firmly. "I'll bring ye some broth, in a bit."

I slept for several hours, and woke up still feverish, but hungry. Jamie brought me some of Murphy's broth—a rich green concoction, swimming in butter and reeking with sherry—and insisted, despite my protests, on feeding it to me with a spoon.

"I have a perfectly good hand," I said crossly.

"Aye, and I've seen ye use it, too," he replied, deftly gagging me with the spoon. "If ye're clumsy with a spoon as wi' that needle, you'll have this all spilt down your bosom and wasted, and Murphy will brain me wi' the ladle. Here, open up."

I did, my resentment gradually melting into a sort of warm and glowing stupor as I ate. I hadn't taken anything for the pain in my arm, but as my empty stomach expanded in grateful relief, I more or less quit noticing it.

"Will ye have another bowl?" Jamie asked, as I swallowed the last spoonful. "Ye'll need your strength kept up." Not waiting for an answer, he uncovered the small tureen Murphy had sent, and refilled the bowl.

"Where's Ishmael?" I asked, during the brief hiatus.

"On the after deck. He didna seem comfortable belowdecks— and I canna say I blame him, having seen the slavers at Bridgetown. I had Maitland sling him a hammock."

"Do you think it's safe to leave him loose like that? What kind of soup is this?'' The last spoonful had left a delightful, lingering taste on my tongue; the next revived the full flavor.

"Turtle; Stern took a big hawksbill last night. He sent word he's saving ye the shell to make combs of, for your hair.'' Jamie frowned slightly, whether at the thought of Lawrence Stern's gallantry or Ishmael's presence, I couldn't tell. "As for the black, he's not loose—Fergus is watching him.''

"Fergus is on his honeymoon,'' I protested. "You shouldn't make him do it. Is this really turtle soup? I've never had it before. It's marvelous.''

Jamie was unmoved by contemplation of Fergus's tender state.

"Aye, well, he'll be wed a long time,'' he said callously. "Do him no harm to keep his breeches on for one night. And they do say that abstinence makes the heart grow firmer, no?''

"Absence,'' I said, dodging the spoon for a moment. "And fonder. If anything's growing firmer from abstinence, it wouldn't be his heart.''

"That's verra bawdy talk for a respectable marrit woman,'' Jamie said reprovingly, sticking the spoon in my mouth. "And inconsiderate, forbye.''

I swallowed. "Inconsiderate?''

"I'm a wee bit firm myself at the moment,'' he replied evenly, dipping and spooning. "What wi' you sitting there wi' your hair loose and your nipples starin' me in the eye, the size of cherries.''

I glanced down involuntarily, and the next spoonful bumped my nose. Jamie clicked his tongue, and picking up a cloth, briskly blotted my bosom with it. It was quite true that my shift was made of thin cotton, and even when dry, reasonably easy to see through.

"It's not as though you haven't seen them before,'' I said, amused.

He laid down the cloth and raised his brows.

"I have drunk water every day since I was weaned,'' he pointed out. "It doesna mean I canna be thirsty, still.'' He picked up the spoon. "You'll have a wee bit more?''

"No, thanks,'' I said, dodging the oncoming spoon. "I want to hear more about this firmness of yours.''

"No, ye don't; you're ill.''

"I feel much better,'' I assured him. "Shall I have a look at it?'' He was wearing the loose petticoat breeches the sailors wore, in which he could easily have concealed three or four dead mullet, let alone a fugitive firmness.

"You shall not," he said, looking slightly shocked. "Someone might come in. And I canna think your looking at it would help a bit."

"Well, you can't tell that until I *have* looked at it, can you?" I said. "Besides, you can bolt the door."

"Bolt the door? What d'ye think I'm going to do? Do I look the sort of man would take advantage of a woman who's not only wounded and boiling wi' fever, but drunk as well?" he demanded. He stood up, nonetheless.

"I am not drunk," I said indignantly. "You can't get drunk on turtle soup!" Nonetheless, I was conscious that the glowing warmth in my stomach seemed to have migrated somewhat lower, taking up residence between my thighs, and there was undeniably a slight lightness of head not strictly attributable to fever.

"You can if ye've been drinking turtle soup as made by Aloysius O'Shaughnessy Murphy," he said. "By the smell of it, he's put at least a full bottle o' the sherry in it. A verra intemperate race, the Irish."

"Well, I'm still not drunk." I straightened up against the pillows as best I could. "You told me once that if you could still stand up, you weren't drunk."

"You aren't standing up," he pointed out.

"You are. And I could if I wanted to. Stop trying to change the subject. We were talking about your firmness."

"Well, ye can just stop talking about it, because——" He broke off with a small yelp, as I made a fortunate grab with my left hand.

"Clumsy, am I?" I said, with considerable satisfaction. "Oh, my. Heavens, you *do* have a problem, don't you?"

"Will ye leave go of me?" he asked, looking frantically over his shoulder at the door. "Someone could come in any moment!"

"I told you you should have bolted the door," I said, not letting go. Far from being a dead mullet, the object in my hand was exhibiting considerable liveliness.

He eyed me narrowly, breathing through his nose.

"I wouldna use force on a sick woman," he said through his teeth, "but you've a damn healthy grip for someone with a fever, Sassenach. If you——"

"I told you I felt better," I interrupted, "but I'll make you a bargain; you bolt the door and I'll prove I'm not drunk." I rather regretfully let go, to indicate good faith. He stood staring at me for a moment, absentmindedly rubbing the site of my recent assault on his virtue. Then he lifted one ruddy eyebrow, turned, and went to bolt the door.

By the time he turned back, I had made it out of the berth and was standing—a trifle shakily, but still upright—against the frame. He eyed me critically.

"It's no going to work, Sassenach," he said, shaking his head. He looked rather regretful, himself. "We'll never stay upright, wi' a swell like there is underfoot tonight, and ye know I'll not fit in that berth by myself, let alone wi' you."

There was a considerable swell; the lantern on its swivel-bracket hung steady and level, but the shelf above it tilted visibly back and forth as the *Artemis* rode the waves. I could feel the faint shudder of the boards under my bare feet, and knew Jamie was right. At least he was too absorbed in the discussion to be seasick.

"There's always the floor," I suggested hopefully. He glanced down at the limited floor space and frowned. "Aye, well. There is, but we'd have to do it like snakes, Sassenach, all twined round each other amongst the table legs."

"I don't mind."

"No," he said, shaking his head, "it would hurt your arm." He rubbed a knuckle across his lower lip, thinking. His eyes passed absently across my body at about hip level, returned, fixed, and lost their focus. I thought the bloody shift must be more transparent than I realized.

Deciding to take matters into my own hands, I let go my hold on the frame of the berth and lurched the two paces necessary to reach him. The roll of the ship threw me into his arms, and he barely managed to keep his own balance, clutching me tightly round the waist.

"Jesus!" he said, staggered, and then, as much from reflex as from desire, bent his head and kissed me.

It was startling. I was accustomed to be surrounded by the warmth of his embrace; now it was I who was hot to the touch and he who was cool. From his reaction, he was enjoying the novelty as much as I was.

Light-headed, and reckless with it, I nipped the side of his neck with my teeth, feeling the waves of heat from my face pulsate against the column of his throat. He felt it, too.

"God, you're like holding a hot coal!" His hands dropped lower and pressed me hard against him.

"Firm is it? Ha," I said, getting my mouth free for a moment. "Take those baggy things off." I slid down his length and onto my knees in front of him, fumbling mazily at his flies. He freed the laces with a quick jerk, and the petticoat breeches ballooned to the floor with a whiff of wind.

I didn't wait for him to remove his shirt; just lifted it and took him. He made a strangled sound and his hands came down on my head as though he wanted to restrain me, but hadn't the strength.

"Oh, Lord!" he said. His hands tightened in my hair, but he wasn't trying to push me away. "This must be what it's like to make love in Hell," he whispered. "With a burning she-devil."

I laughed, which was extremely difficult under the circumstances. I choked, and pulled back a moment, breathless.

"Is this what a succubus does, do you think?"

"I wouldna doubt it for a moment," he assured me. His hands were still in my hair, urging me back.

A knock sounded on the door, and he froze. Confident that the door was indeed bolted, I didn't.

"Aye? What is it?" he said, with a calmness rather remarkable for a man in his position.

"Fraser?" Lawrence Stern's voice came through the door. "The Frenchman says the black is asleep, and may he have leave to go to bed now?"

"No," said Jamie shortly. "Tell him to stay where he is; I'll come along and relieve him in a bit."

"Oh." Stern's voice sounded a little hesitant. "Surely. His . . . um, his wife seems . . . eager for him to come now."

Jamie inhaled sharply.

"Tell her," he said, a small note of strain becoming evident in his voice, "that he'll be there . . . presently."

"I will say so." Stern sounded dubious about Marsali's reception of this news, but then his voice brightened. "Ah . . . is Mrs. Fraser feeling somewhat improved?"

"Verra much," said Jamie, with feeling.

"She enjoyed the turtle soup?"

"Greatly. I thank ye." His hands on my head were trembling.

"Did you tell her that I've put aside the shell for her? It was a fine hawksbill turtle; a most elegant beast."

"Aye. Aye, I did." With an audible gasp, Jamie pulled away and reaching down, lifted me to my feet.

"Good night, Mr. Stern!" he called. He pulled me toward the berth; we struggled four-legged to keep from crashing into tables and chairs as the floor rose and fell beneath us.

"Oh." Lawrence sounded faintly disappointed. "I suppose Mrs. Fraser is asleep, then?"

"Laugh, and I'll throttle ye," Jamie whispered fiercely in my ear. "She is, Mr. Stern," he called through the door. "I shall give her your respects in the morning, aye?"

"I trust she will rest well. There seems to be a certain roughness to the sea this evening."

"I . . . have noticed, Mr. Stern." Pushing me to my knees in front of the berth, he knelt behind me, groping for the hem of my shift. A cool breeze from the open stern window blew over my naked buttocks, and a shiver ran down the backs of my thighs.

"Should you or Mrs. Fraser find yourselves discommoded by the motion, I have a most capital remedy to hand—a compound of mugwort, bat dung, and the fruit of the mangrove. You have only to ask, you know."

Jamie didn't answer for a moment.

"Oh, Christ!" he whispered. I took a sizable bite of the bed-clothes.

"Mr. Fraser?"

"I said, 'Thank you'!" Jamie replied, raising his voice.

"Well, I shall bid you a good evening, then."

Jamie let out his breath in a long shudder that was not quite a moan.

"Mr. Fraser?"

"Good evening, Mr. Stern!" Jamie bellowed.

"Oh! Er . . . good evening."

Stern's footsteps receded down the companionway, lost in the sound of the waves that were now crashing loudly against the hull. I spit out the mouthful of quilt.

"Oh . . . my . . . God!"

His hands were large and hard and cool on my heated flesh.

"You've the roundest arse I've ever seen!"

A lurch by the *Artemis* here aiding his efforts to an untoward degree, I uttered a loud shriek.

"Shh!" He clasped a hand over my mouth, bending over me so that he lay over my back, the billowing linen of his shirt falling around me and the weight of him pressing me to the bed. My skin, crazed with fever, was sensitive to the slightest touch, and I shook in his arms, the heat inside me rushing outward as he moved within me.

His hands were under me then, clutching my breasts, the only anchor as I lost my boundaries and dissolved, conscious thought a displaced element in the chaos of sensations—the warm damp of tangled quilts beneath me, the cold sea wind and misty spray that wafted over us from the rough sea outside, the gasp and brush of Jamie's warm breath on the back of my neck, and the sudden prickle and flood of cold and heat, as my fever broke in a dew of satisfied desire.

Jamie's weight rested on my back, his thighs behind mine. It was warm, and comforting. After a long time, his breathing eased, and he rose off me. The thin cotton of my shift was damp, and the wind plucked it away from my skin, making me shiver.

Jamie closed the window with a snap, then bent and picked me up like a rag doll. He lowered me into the berth, and pulled the quilt up over me.

"How is your arm?" he said.

"What arm?" I murmured drowsily. I felt as though I had been melted and poured into a mold to set.

"Good," he said, a smile in his voice. "Can ye stand up?"

"Not for all the tea in China."

"I'll tell Murphy ye liked the soup." His hand rested for a moment on my cool forehead, passed down the curve of my cheek in a light caress, and then was gone. I didn't hear him leave.

"It's persecution!" Jamie said indignantly. He stood behind me, looking over the rail of the *Artemis*. Kingston Harbor stretched to our left, glowing like liquid sapphires in the morning light, the town above half-sunk in jungle green, cubes of yellowed ivory and pink rose-quartz in a lush setting of emerald and malachite. And on the cerulean bosom of the water below floated the majestic sight of a great three-masted ship, furled canvas white as gull wings, gun decks proud and brass gleaming in the sun. His Majesty's man-of-war *Porpoise*.

"The filthy boat's pursuing me," he said, glaring at it as we sailed past at a discreet distance, well outside the harbor mouth. "Everywhere I go, there it is again!"

I laughed, though in truth, the sight of the *Porpoise* made me slightly nervous, too.

"I don't suppose it's personal," I told him. "Captain Leonard did say they were bound for Jamaica."

"Aye, but why would they no head straight to Antigua, where the naval barracks and the navy shipyards are, and them in such straits as ye left them?" He shaded his eyes, peering at the *Porpoise*. Even at this distance, small figures were visible in the rigging, making repairs.

"They had to come here first," I explained. "They were carrying a new governor for the colony." I felt an absurd urge to duck below the rail, though I knew that even Jamie's red hair would be indistinguishable at this distance.

"Aye? I wonder who's that?" Jamie spoke absently; we were

no more than an hour away from arrival at Jared's plantation on Sugar Bay, and I knew his mind was busy with plans for finding Young Ian.

"A chap named Grey," I said, turning away from the rail. "Nice man; I met him on the ship, just briefly."

"Grey?" Startled, Jamie looked down at me. "Not Lord John Grey, by chance?"

"Yes, that was his name? Why?" I glanced up at him, curious. He was staring at the *Porpoise* with renewed interest.

"Why?" He heard me when I repeated the question a second time, and glanced down at me, smiling. "Oh. It's only that I ken Lord John; he's a friend of mine."

"Really?" I was no more than mildly surprised. Jamie's friends had once included the French minister of finance and Charles Stuart, as well as Scottish beggars and French pickpockets. I supposed it was not remarkable that he should now count English aristocrats among his acquaintance, as well as Highland smugglers and Irish seacooks.

"Well, that's luck," I said. "Or at least I suppose it is. Where do you know Lord John from?"

"He was the Governor of Ardsmuir prison," he replied, surprising me after all. His eyes were still fixed on the *Porpoise,* narrowed in speculation.

"And he's a *friend* of yours?" I shook my head. "I'll never understand men."

He turned and smiled at me, taking his attention at last from the English ship.

"Well, friends are where ye find them, Sassenach," he said. He squinted toward the shore, shading his eyes with his hand. "Let us hope this Mrs. Abernathy proves to be one."

◆━━━

As we rounded the tip of the headland, a lithe black figure materialized next to the rail. Now clothed in spare seaman's clothes, with his scars hidden, Ishmael looked less like a slave and a good deal more like a pirate. Not for the first time, I wondered just how much of what he had told us was the truth.

"I be leavin' now," he announced abruptly.

Jamie lifted one eyebrow and glanced over the rail, into the soft blue depths.

"Dinna let me prevent ye," he said politely. "But would ye not rather have a boat?"

Something that might have been humor flickered briefly in the black man's eyes, but didn't disturb the severe outlines of his face.

"You say you put me ashore where I want, I be tellin' you 'bout those boys," he said. He nodded toward the island, where a riotous growth of jungle spilled down the slope of a hill to meet its own green shadow in the shallow water. "That be where I want."

Jamie looked thoughtfully from the uninhabited shore to Ishmael, and then nodded.

"I'll have a boat lowered." He turned to go to the cabin. "I promised ye gold as well, no?"

"Don't be wantin' gold, mon." Ishmael's tone, as well as his words, stopped Jamie in his tracks. He looked at the black man with interest, mingled with a certain reserve.

"Ye'll have something else in mind?"

Ishmael jerked his head in a short nod. He didn't seem outwardly nervous, but I noticed the faint gleam of sweat on his temples, despite the mild noon breeze.

"I be wantin' that one-arm nigger." He stared boldly at Jamie as he spoke, but there was a diffidence under the confident facade.

"Temeraire?" I blurted out in astonishment. "Why?"

Ishmael flicked a glance at me, but addressed his words to Jamie, half-bold, half-cajoling.

"He ain't no good to you, mon; can't be doin' field work or ship work neither, ain't got but one arm."

Jamie didn't reply directly, but stared at Ishmael for a moment. Then he turned and called for Fergus to bring up the one-armed slave.

Temeraire, brought up on deck, stood expressionless as a block of wood, barely blinking in the sun. He too had been provided with seaman's clothes, but he lacked Ishmael's raffish elegance in them. He looked like a stump upon which someone had spread out washing to dry.

"This man wants you to go with him, to the island there," Jamie said to Temeraire, in slow, careful French. "Do you want to do this thing?"

Temeraire did blink at that, and a brief look of startlement widened his eyes. I supposed that no one had asked him what he wanted in many years—if ever. He glanced warily from Jamie to Ishmael and back again, but didn't say anything.

Jamie tried again.

"You do not have to go with this man," he assured the slave. "You may come with us, and we will take care of you. No one will hurt you. But you can go with him, if you like."

Still the slave hesitated, eyes flicking right and left, clearly startled and disturbed by the unexpected choice. It was Ishmael who decided the matter. He said something, in a strange tongue full of liquid vowels and syllables that repeated like a drumbeat.

Temeraire let out a gasp, fell to his knees, and pressed his forehead to the deck at Ishmael's feet. Everyone on deck stared at him, then looked at Ishmael, who stood with arms folded with a sort of wary defiance.

"He be goin' with me," he said.

And so it was. Picard rowed the two blacks ashore in the dinghy, and left them on the rocks at the edge of the jungle, supplied with a small bag of provisions, each equipped with a knife.

"Why there?" I wondered aloud, watching the two small figures make their way slowly up the wooded slope. "There aren't any towns nearby, are there? Or any plantations?" To the eye, the shore presented an unbroken expanse of jungle.

"Oh, there are plantations," Lawrence assured me. "Far up in the hills; that's where they grow the coffee and indigo—the sugar-cane grows better near the coast." He squinted toward the shore, where the two dark figures had disappeared. "It is more likely that they have gone to join a band of Maroons, though," he said.

"There are Maroons on Jamaica as well as on Hispaniola?" Fergus asked, interested.

Lawrence smiled, a little grimly.

"There are Maroons wherever there are slaves, my friend," he said. "There are always men who prefer to take the chance of dying like animals, rather than live as captives."

Jamie turned his head sharply to look at Lawrence, but said nothing.

Jared's plantation at Sugar Bay was called Blue Mountain House, presumably for the sake of the low, hazy peak that rose inland a mile behind it, blue with pines and distance. The house itself was set near the shore, in the shallow curve of the bay. In fact, the veranda that ran along one side of the house overhung a small lagoon, the building set on sturdy silvered-wood pilings that rose from the water, crusted with a spongy growth of tunicates and mussels and the fine green seaweed called mermaid's hair.

We were expected; Jared had sent a letter by a ship that left Le Havre a week before the *Artemis*. Owing to our delay on Hispaniola, the letter had arrived nearly a month in advance of ourselves, and the overseer and his wife—a portly, comfortable Scottish couple named MacIvers—were relieved to see us.

"I thought surely the winter storms had got ye," Kenneth MacIver said for the fourth time, shaking his head. He was bald, the top of his head scaly and freckled from long years' exposure to the tropic sun. His wife was a plump, genial, grandmotherly soul—who, I realized to my shock, was roughly five years younger than myself. She herded Marsali and me off for a quick wash, brush, and nap before supper, while Fergus and Jamie went with Mr. MacIver to direct the partial unloading of the *Artemis*'s cargo and the disposition of her crew.

I was more than willing to go; while my arm had healed sufficiently to need no more than a light bandage, it had prevented me from bathing in the sea as was my usual habit. After a week aboard the *Artemis,* unbathed, I looked forward to fresh water and clean sheets with a longing that was almost hunger.

I had no landlegs yet; the worn wooden floorboards of the plantation house gave the disconcerting illusion of seeming to rise and fall beneath my feet, and I staggered down the hallway after Mrs. MacIver, bumping into walls.

The house had an actual bathtub in a small porch; wooden, but filled—*mirabile dictu!*—with hot water, by the good offices of two black slave women who heated kettles over a fire in the yard and carried them in. I should have felt much too guilty at this exploitation to enjoy my bath, but I didn't. I wallowed luxuriously, scrubbing the salt and grime from my skin with a loofah sponge and lathering my hair with a shampoo made from chamomile, geranium oil, fat-soap shavings, and the yolk of an egg, graciously supplied by Mrs. MacIver.

Smelling sweet, shiny-haired, and languid with warmth, I collapsed gratefully into the bed I was given. I had time only to think how delightful it was to stretch out at full length, before I fell asleep.

When I woke, the shadows of dusk were gathering on the veranda outside the open French doors of my bedroom, and Jamie lay naked beside me, hands folded on his belly, breathing deep and slow.

He felt me stir, and opened his eyes. He smiled sleepily and reaching up a hand, pulled me down to his mouth. He had had a bath, too; he smelled of soap and cedar needles. I kissed him at length, slowly and thoroughly, running my tongue across the wide curve of his lip, finding his tongue with mine in a soft, dark joust of greeting and invitation.

I broke loose, finally, and came up for air. The room was filled with a wavering green light, reflections from the lagoon outside, as though the room itself were underwater. The air was at once warm and fresh, smelling of sea and rain, with tiny currents of breeze that caressed the skin.

"Ye smell sweet, Sassenach," he murmured, voice husky with sleep. He smiled, reaching up to twine his fingers into my hair. "Come here to me, curly-wig."

Freed from pins and freshly washed, my hair was clouding over my shoulders in a perfect explosion of Medusa-like curls. I reached up to smooth it back, but he tugged gently, bending me forward so the veil of brown and gold and silver fell loose over his face.

I kissed him, half-smothered in clouds of hair, and lowered myself to lie on top of him, letting the fullness of my breasts squash gently against his chest. He moved slightly, rubbing, and sighed with pleasure.

His hands cupped my buttocks, trying to move me upward enough to enter me.

"Not bloody yet," I whispered. I pressed my hips down, rolling them, enjoying the feel of the silky stiffness trapped beneath my belly. He made a small breathless sound.

"We haven't had room or time to make love properly in months," I told him. "So we're taking our time about it now, right?"

"Ye take me at something of a disadvantage, Sassenach," he murmured into my hair. He squirmed under me, pressing upward urgently. "Ye dinna think we could take our time next time?"

"No, we couldn't," I said firmly. "Now. Slow. Don't move."

He made a sort of rumbling noise in his throat, but sighed and relaxed, letting his hands fall away to the sides. I squirmed lower on his body, making him inhale sharply, and set my mouth on his nipple.

I ran my tongue delicately round the tiny nub, making it stand up stiff, enjoying the coarse feel of the curly auburn hairs that surrounded it. I felt him tense under me, and put my hands on his upper arms to hold him still while I went on with it, biting gently, sucking and flicking with my tongue.

A few minutes later, I raised my head, brushed my hair back with one hand, and asked, "What's that you're saying?"

He opened one eye.

"The rosary," he informed me. "It's the only way I'm going to stand it." He closed his eyes and resumed murmuring in Latin. *"Ave Maria, gratia plena . . ."*

I snorted and went to work on the other one.

"You're losing your place," I said, next time I came up for air. "You've said the Lord's Prayer three times in a row."

"I'm surprised to hear I'm still makin' any sense at all." His eyes were closed, and a dew of moisture gleamed on his cheekbones. He moved his hips with increasing restiveness. "Now?"

"Not yet." I dipped my head lower and seized by impulse, went *Pffft!* into his navel. He convulsed, and taken by surprise, emitted a noise that could only be described as a giggle.

"Don't do that!" he said.

"Will if I want to," I said, and did it again. "You sound just like Bree," I told him. "I used to do that to her when she was a baby; she loved it."

"Well, I'm no a wee bairn, if ye hadna noticed the difference," he said a little testily. "If ye must do that, at least try it a bit lower, aye?"

I did.

"You don't have any hair at all at the tops of your thighs," I said, admiring the smooth white skin there. "Why is that, do you think?"

"The cow licked it all off last time she milked me," he said between his teeth. "For God's sake, Sassenach!"

I laughed, and returned to my work. At last I stopped and raised myself on my elbows.

"I think you've had enough," I said, brushing hair out of my eyes. "You haven't said anything but 'Jesus Christ' over and over again for the last few minutes."

Given the cue, he surged upward, and flipped me onto my back, pinning me with the solid weight of his body.

"You're going to live to regret this, Sassenach," he said with a grim satisfaction.

I grinned at him, unrepentant.

"Am I?"

He looked down at me, eyes narrowed. "Take my time, was it? You'll beg for it, before I've done wi' ye."

I tugged experimentally at my wrists, held tight in his grasp, and wriggled slightly under him with anticipation.

"Ooh, mercy," I said. "You beast."

He snorted briefly, and bent his head to the curve of my breast, white as pearl in the dim green water-light.

I closed my eyes and lay back against the pillows.

"Pater noster, qui es in coelis . . ." I whispered.

We were very late to supper.

◄━━━━━►

Jamie lost no time over supper in asking about Mrs. Abernathy of Rose Hall.

"Abernathy?" MacIver frowned, tapping his knife on the table to assist thought. "Aye, seems I've heard the name, though I canna just charge my memory."

"Och, ye ken Abernathy's fine," his wife interrupted, pausing in her instructions to a servant for the preparation of the hot pudding. "It's that place up the Yallahs River, in the mountains. Cane, mostly, but a wee bit of coffee, too."

"Oh, aye, to be sure!" her husband exclaimed. "What a memory ye've got, Rosie!" He beamed fondly at his wife.

"Well, I might not ha' brought it to mind mysel'," she said modestly, "only as how that minister over to New Grace kirk last week was askin' after Mrs. Abernathy, too."

"What minister is this, ma'am?" Jamie asked, taking a split roast chicken from the huge platter presented to him by a black servant.

"Such a fine braw appetite as ye have, Mr. Fraser!" Mrs. Mac-

Iver exclaimed admiringly, seeing his loaded plate. "It's the is-land air does it, I expect."

The tips of Jamie's ears turned pink.

"I expect it is," he said, carefully not looking at me. "This minister . . . ?"

"Och, aye. Campbell, his name was, Archie Campbell." I started, and she glanced quizzically at me. "You'll know him?"

I shook my head, swallowing a pickled mushroom. "I've met him once, in Edinburgh."

"Oh. Well, he's come to be a missionary, and bring the heathen blacks to the salvation of Our Lord Jesus." She spoke with admi-ration, and glared at her husband when he snorted. "Now, ye'll no be makin' your Papist remarks, Kenny! The Reverend Campbell's a fine holy man, and a great scholar, forbye. I'm Free Church myself," she said, leaning toward me confidingly. "My parents disowned me when I wed Kenny, but I told them I was sure he'd come to see the light sooner or later."

"A lot later," her husband remarked, spooning jam onto his plate. He grinned at his wife, who sniffed and returned to her story.

"So, 'twas on account of the Reverend's bein' a great scholar that Mrs. Abernathy had written him, whilst he was still in Edin-burgh, to ask him questions. And now that he's come here, he had it in mind to go and see her. Though after all Myra Dalrymple and the Reverend Davis telt him, I should be surprised he'd set foot on her place," she added primly.

Kenny MacIver grunted, motioning to a servant in the doorway with another huge platter.

"I wouldna put a great deal of stock in anything the Reverend Davis says, myself," he said. "The man's too godly to shit. But Myra Dalrymple's a sensible woman. Ouch!" He snatched back the fingers his wife had just cracked with a spoon, and sucked them.

"What did Miss Dalrymple have to say of Mrs. Abernathy?" Jamie inquired, hastily intervening before full-scale marital war-fare could break out.

Mrs. MacIver's color was high, but she smoothed the frown from her brow as she turned to answer him.

"Well, a great deal of it was no more than ill-natured gossip," she admitted. "The sorts of things folk will always say about a woman as lives alone. That she's owerfond of the company of her men-slaves, aye?''

''But there was the talk when her husband died,'' Kenny interrupted. He slid several small, rainbow-striped fish off the platter the stooping servant held for him. ''I mind it well, now I come to think on the name.''

Barnabas Abernathy had come from Scotland, and had purchased Rose Hall five years before. He had run the place decently, turning a small profit in sugar and coffee, causing no comment among his neighbors. Then, two years ago, he had married a woman no one knew, bringing her home from a trip to Guadeloupe.

''And six months later, he was dead,'' Mrs. MacIver concluded with grim relish.

''And the talk is that Mrs. Abernathy had something to do with it?'' Having some idea of the plethora of tropical parasites and diseases that attacked Europeans in the West Indies, I was inclined to doubt it, myself. Barnabas Abernathy could easily have died of anything from malaria to elephantiasis, but Rosie MacIver was right—folk were partial to ill-natured gossip.

''Poison,'' Rosie said, low-voiced, with a quick glance at the door to the kitchen. ''The doctor who saw him said so. Mind, it could ha' been the slave-women. There was talk about Barnabas and his female slaves, and it's more common than folk like to say for a plantation cook-girl to be slipping something into the stew, but—'' She broke off as another servant came in, carrying a cut-glass relish pot. Everyone was silent as the woman placed it on the table and left, curtsying to her mistress.

''You needn't worry,'' Mrs. MacIver said reassuringly, seeing me look after the woman. ''We've a boy who tastes everything, before it's served. It's all quite safe.''

I swallowed the mouthful of fish I had taken, with some difficulty.

''Did the Reverend Campbell go to see Mrs. Abernathy, then?'' Jamie put in.

Rosie took the distraction gratefully. She shook her head, agitating the lace ruffles on her cap.

''No, I'm sure not, for 'twas the very next day there was the stramash about his sister.''

In the excitement of tracking Ian and the *Bruja,* I had nearly forgotten Margaret Jane Campbell.

"What happened to his sister?" I asked, curious.

"Why, she's disappeared!" Mrs. MacIver's blue eyes went wide with importance. Blue Mountain House was remote, some ten miles out of Kingston by land, and our presence provided an unparalleled opportunity for gossip.

"What?" Fergus had been addressing himself to his plate with single-minded devotion, but now looked up, blinking. "Disappeared? Where?"

"The whole island's talking of it," Kenny put in, snatching the conversational ball from his wife. "Seems the Reverend had a woman engaged as abigail to his sister, but the woman died of a fever on the voyage."

"Oh, that's too bad!" I felt a real pang for Nellie Cowden, with her broad, pleasant face.

"Aye." Kenny nodded offhandedly. "Well, and so the Reverend found a place for his sister to lodge. Feebleminded, I understand?" He lifted a brow at me.

"Something like that."

"Aye, well, the lass seemed quiet and biddable, and Mrs. Forrest, who had the house where she lodged, would take her to sit on the veranda in the cool part of the day. So Tuesday last, a boy comes to say as Mrs. Forrest is wanted quicklike to come to her sister, who's having a child. And Mrs. Forrest got flustered and went straight off, forgetting Miss Campbell on the veranda. And when she thought of it, and sent someone back to see—why Miss Campbell was gone. And not a smell of her since, in spite of the Reverend raising heaven and earth, ye might say." MacIver rocked back on his chair, puffing out his sun-mottled cheeks.

Mrs. MacIver wagged her head, *tsk*ing mournfully.

"Myra Dalrymple told the Reverend as how he should go to the Governor for help to find her," she said. "But the Governor's scarce settled, and not yet ready to receive anyone. He's having a great reception this coming Thursday, for to meet all the important folk o' the island. Myra said as the Reverend must go, and speak to the Governor there, but he's no of a mind to do that, it bein' such a worldly occasion, aye?"

"A reception?" Jamie set down his spoon, looking at Mrs. MacIver with interest. "Is it by invitation, d'ye know?"

"Oh, no," she said, shaking her head. "Anyone may come as likes to, or so I've heard."

"Is that so?" Jamie glanced at me, smiling. "What d'ye think, Sassenach—would ye care to step out wi' me at the Governor's Residence?"

I stared at him in astonishment. I should have thought that the last thing he would wish to do was show himself in public. I was also surprised that he would let anything at all stop his visiting Rose Hall at the earliest opportunity.

"It's a good opportunity to ask about Ian, no?" he explained. "After all, he might not be at Rose Hall, but someplace else on the island."

"Well, aside from the fact that I've nothing to wear . . ." I temporized, trying to figure out what he was really up to.

"Och, that's no trouble," Rosie MacIver assured me. "I've one of the cleverest sempstresses on the island; she'll have ye tricked out in no time."

Jamie was nodding thoughtfully. He smiled, eyes slanting as he looked at me over the candle flame.

"Violet silk, I think," he said. He plucked the bones delicately from his fish and set them aside. "And as for the other—dinna fash, Sassenach. I've something in mind. You'll see."

58

Masque of the Red Death

"Oh who is that young sinner with the handcuffs on his wrists?
And what has he been after that they groan and shake their
    fists?
And wherefore is he wearing such a conscience-stricken air?
Oh they're taking him to prison for the colour of his hair."

Jamie put down the wig in his hand and raised one eyebrow at
me in the mirror. I grinned at him and went on, declaiming with
gestures:

" 'Tis a shame to human nature, such a head of hair as his;
In the good old time 'twas hanging for the colour that it is;
Though hanging isn't bad enough and flaying would be fair
For the nameless and abominable colour of his hair!"

"Did ye not tell me ye'd studied for a doctor, Sassenach?" he
inquired. "Or was it a poet, after all?"

"Not me," I assured him, coming to straighten his stock.
"Those sentiments are by one A. E. Housman."

"Surely one of him is sufficient," Jamie said dryly. "Given the
quality of his opinions." He picked up the wig and fitted it carefully on his head, raising little puffs of scented powder as he poked
it here and there. "Is Mr. Housman an acquaintance of yours,
then?"

"You might say so." I sat down on the bed to watch. "It's only
that the doctors' lounge at the hospital I worked at had a copy of

Housman's collected works that someone had left there. There isn't time between calls to read most novels, but poems are ideal. I expect I know most of Housman by heart, now.''

He looked warily at me, as though expecting another outburst of poetry, but I merely smiled at him, and he returned to his work. I watched the transformation in fascination.

Red-heeled shoes and silk stockings clocked in black. Gray satin breeches with silver knee buckles. Snowy linen, with Brussels lace six inches deep at cuff and jabot. The coat, a masterpiece in heavy gray with blue satin cuffs and crested silver buttons, hung behind the door, awaiting its turn.

He finished the careful powdering of his face, and licking the end of one finger, picked up a false beauty mark, dabbed it in gum arabic, and affixed it neatly near the corner of his mouth.

"There," he said, swinging about on the dressing stool to face me. "Do I look like a red-heided Scottish smuggler?"

I inspected him carefully, from full-bottomed wig to morocco-heeled shoes.

"You look like a gargoyle," I said. His face flowered in a wide grin. Outlined in white powder, his lips seemed abnormally red, his mouth even wider and more expressive than it usually was.

"Non!" said Fergus indignantly, coming in in time to hear this. "He looks like a Frenchman."

"Much the same thing," Jamie said, and sneezed. Wiping his nose on a handkerchief, he assured the young man, "Begging your pardon, Fergus."

He stood up and reached for the coat, shrugging it over his shoulders and settling the edges. In three-inch heels, he towered to a height of six feet seven; his head nearly brushed the plastered ceiling.

"I don't know," I said, looking up at him dubiously. "I've never seen a Frenchman that size."

Jamie shrugged, his coat rustling like autumn leaves. "Aye, well, there's no hiding my height. But so long as my hair is hidden, I think it will be all right. Besides," he added, gazing with approval at me, "folk willna be looking at me. Stand up and let me see, aye?"

I obliged, rotating slowly to show off the deep flare of the violet silk skirt. Cut low in the front, the décolletage was filled with a froth of lace that rippled down the front of the bodice in a series of

V's. Matching lace cascaded from the elbow-length sleeves in graceful white falls that left my wrists bare.

"Rather a pity I don't have your mother's pearls," I remarked. I didn't regret their lack; I had left them for Brianna, in the box with the photographs and family documents. Still, with the deep décolletage and my hair twisted up in a knot, the mirror showed a long expanse of bare neck and bosom, rising whitely out of the violet silk.

"I thought of that." With the air of a conjuror, Jamie produced a small box from his inside pocket and presented it to me, making a leg in his best Versailles fashion.

Inside was a small, gleaming fish, carved in a dense black material, the edges of its scales touched with gold.

"It's a pin," he explained. "Ye could maybe wear it fastened to a white ribbon round your neck?"

"It's beautiful!" I said, delighted. "What's it made of? Ebony?"

"Black coral," he said. "I got it yesterday, when Fergus and I were in Montego Bay." He and Fergus had taken the *Artemis* round the island, disposing at last of the cargo of bat guano, delivered to its purchaser.

I found a length of white satin ribbon, and Jamie obligingly tied it about my neck, bending to peer over my shoulder at the reflection in the mirror.

"No, they won't be looking at me," he said. "Half o' them will be lookin' at you, Sassenach, and the other half at Mr. Willoughby."

"Mr. Willoughby? Is that safe? I mean—" I stole a look at the little Chinese, sitting patiently cross-legged on a stool, gleaming in clean blue silk, and lowered my voice. "I mean, they'll have wine, won't they?"

Jamie nodded. "And whisky, and cambric, and claret cup, and port, and champagne punch—and a wee cask of the finest French brandy—contributed by the courtesy of Monsieur Etienne Marcel de Provac Alexandre." He put a hand on his chest and bowed again, in an exaggerated pantomime that made me laugh. "Nay worry," he said, straightening up. "He'll behave, or I'll have his coral globe back—will I no, ye wee heathen?" he added with a grin to Mr. Willoughby.

The Chinese scholar nodded with considerable dignity. The

embroidered black silk of his round cap was decorated with a small carved knob of red coral—the badge of his calling, restored to him by the chance encounter with a coral trader on the docks at Montego, and Jamie's good nature.

"You're quite sure we have to go?" The palpitations I was experiencing were due in part to the tightness of the stays I was wearing, but in greater degree to recurring visions of Jamie's wig falling off and the reception coming to a complete stop as the entire assemblage paused to stare at his hair before calling en masse for the Royal Navy.

"Aye, we do." He smiled at me reassuringly. "Dinna worry, Sassenach; if anyone's there from the *Porpoise,* it's not likely they'll recognize me—not like this."

"I hope not. Do you think anyone from the ship *will* be there tonight?"

"I doubt it." He scratched viciously at the wig above his left ear. "Where did ye get this thing, Fergus? I believe it's got lice."

"Oh, no, milord," Fergus assured him. "The wigmaker from whom I rented it assured me that it had been well dusted with hyssop and horse nettle to prevent any such infestations." Fergus himself was wearing his own hair, thickly powdered, and was handsome—if less startling than Jamie—in a new suit of dark blue velvet.

There was a tentative knock at the door, and Marsali stepped in. She too had had her wardrobe refurbished, and glowed in a dress of soft pink, with a deep rose sash.

She glowed somewhat more than I thought the dress accounted for, in fact, and as we made our way down the narrow corridor to the carriage, pulling in our skirts to keep them from brushing the walls, I managed to lean forward and murmur in her ear.

"Are you using the tansy oil?"

"Mm?" she said absently, her eyes on Fergus as he bowed and held open the carriage door for her. "What did ye say?"

"Never mind," I said, resigned. That was the least of our worries at the moment.

The Governor's mansion was ablaze with lights. Lanterns were perched along the low wall of the veranda, and hung from the trees along the paths of the ornamental garden. Gaily dressed people were emerging from their carriages on the crushed-shell drive, passing into the house through a pair of huge French doors.

We dismissed our own—or, rather, Jared's—carriage, but stood for a moment on the drive, waiting for a brief lull in the arrivals. Jamie seemed mildly nervous—for him; his fingers twitched now and then against the gray satin, but his manner was outwardly as calm as ever.

There was a short reception line in the foyer; several of the minor dignitaries of the island had been invited to assist the new governor in welcoming his guests. I passed ahead of Jamie down the line, smiling and nodding to the Mayor of Kingston and his wife. I quailed a bit at the sight of a fully decorated admiral next in line, resplendent in gilded coat and epaulettes, but no sign of anything beyond a mild amazement crossed his features as he shook hands with the gigantic Frenchman and the tiny Chinese who accompanied me.

There was my acquaintance from the *Porpoise;* Lord John's blond hair was hidden under a formal wig tonight, but I recognized the fine, clear features and slight, muscular body at once. He stood a little apart from the other dignitaries, alone. Rumor had it that his wife had refused to leave England to accompany him to this posting.

He turned to greet me, his face fixed in an expression of formal politeness. He looked, blinked, and then broke into a smile of extraordinary warmth and pleasure.

"Mrs. Malcolm!" he exclaimed, seizing my hands. "I am vastly pleased to see you!"

"The feeling is entirely mutual," I said, smiling back at him. "I didn't know you were the Governor, last time we met. I'm afraid I was a bit informal."

He laughed, his face glowing with the light of the candles in the wall sconces. Seen clearly in the light for the first time, I realized what a remarkably handsome man he was.

"You might be thought to have had an excellent excuse," he said. He looked me over carefully. "May I say that you are in remarkable fine looks this evening? Clearly the island air must agree with you somewhat more than the miasmas of shipboard. I had hoped to meet you again before leaving the *Porpoise,* but when I inquired for you, I was told by Mr. Leonard that you were unwell. I trust you are entirely recovered?"

"Oh, entirely," I told him, amused. Unwell, eh? Evidently Tom Leonard was not about to admit to losing me overboard. I wondered whether he had put my disappearance in the log.

"May I introduce my husband?" I turned to wave at Jamie, who had been detained in animated conversation with the admiral, but who was now advancing toward us, accompanied by Mr. Willoughby.

I turned back to find the Governor gone green as a gooseberry. He stared from Jamie to me, and back again, pale as though confronted by twin specters.

Jamie came to a stop beside me, and inclined his head graciously toward the Governor.

"John," he said softly. "It's good to see ye, man."

The Governor's mouth opened and shut without making a sound.

"Let us make an opportunity to speak, a bit later," Jamie murmured. "But for now—my name is Etienne Alexandre." He took my arm, and bowed formally. "And may I have the pleasure to present to you my wife, Claire?" he said aloud, shifting effortlessly into French.

"Claire?" The Governor looked wildly at me. *"Claire?"*

"Er, yes," I said, hoping he wasn't going to faint. He looked very much as though he might, though I had no idea why the revelation of my Christian name ought to affect him so strongly.

The next arrivals were waiting impatiently for us to move out of the way. I bowed, fluttering my fan, and we walked into the main salon of the Residence. I glanced back over my shoulder to see the Governor shaking hands mechanically with the new arrival, staring after us with a face like white paper.

The salon was a huge room, low-ceilinged and filled with people, noisy and bright as a cageful of parrots. I felt some relief at the sight. Among this crowd, Jamie wouldn't be terribly conspicuous, despite his size.

A small orchestra played at one side of the room, near a pair of doors thrown open to the terrace outside. I saw a number of people strolling there, evidently seeking either a breath of air or sufficient quiet to hold a private conversation. At the other side of the room, yet another pair of doors opened into a short hallway, where the retiring rooms were.

We knew no one, and had no social sponsor to make introductions. However, due to Jamie's foresight, we had no need of one. Within moments of our arrival, women had begun to cluster around us, fascinated by Mr. Willoughby.

"My acquaintance, Mr. Yi Tien Cho," Jamie introduced him to a stout young woman in tight yellow satin. "Late of the Celestial Kingdom of China, Madame."

"Ooh!" The young lady fluttered her fan before her face, impressed. "Really from China? But what an unthinkable distance you must have come! Do let me welcome you to our small island, Mr.—Mr. Cho?" She extended a hand to him, clearly expecting it to be kissed.

Mr. Willoughby bowed deeply, hands in his sleeves, and obligingly said something in Chinese. The young woman looked thrilled. Jamie looked momentarily startled, and then the mask of urbanity dropped back over his face. I saw Mr. Willoughby's shining black eyes fix on the tips of the lady's shoes, protruding from under the hem of her dress, and wondered just what he had said to her.

Jamie seized the opportunity—and the lady's hand—bowing over it with extreme politeness.

"Your servant, Madame," he said in thickly accented English. "Etienne Alexandre. And might I present to you my wife, Claire?"

"Oh, yes, so pleased to meet you!" The young woman, flushed with excitement, took my hand and squeezed it. "I'm Marcelline Williams; perhaps you'll be acquainted with my brother, Judah? He owns Twelvetrees—you know, the large coffee plantation? I've come to stay with him for the season, and I'm having ever so marvelous a time!"

"No, I'm afraid we don't know anyone here," I said apologetically. "We've only just arrived ourselves—from Martinique, where my husband's sugar business is."

"Oh," Miss Williams cried, her eyes flying wide open. "But you must allow me to make you acquainted with my particular friends, the Stephenses! I believe they once visited Martinique, and Georgina Stephens is such a charming person—you will like her at once, I promise!"

And that was all there was to it. Within an hour, I had been introduced to dozens of people, and was being carried slowly round the room, eddying from one group to the next, passed hand to hand by the current of introductions launched by Miss Williams.

Across the room, I could see Jamie, standing head and shoulders above his companions, the picture of aristocratic dignity. He was conversing cordially with a group of men, all eager to make the acquaintance of a prosperous businessman who might offer useful contacts with the French sugar trade. I caught his eye once, in passing, and he gave me a brilliant smile and a gallant French bow. I still wondered what in the name of God he thought he was up to, but shrugged mentally. He would tell me when he was ready.

Fergus and Marsali, as usual needing no one's company but each other's, were dancing at one end of the floor, her glowing pink face smiling into his. For the sake of the occasion, Fergus had forgone his useful hook, replacing it with a black leather glove filled with bran, pinned to the sleeve of his coat. This rested against the back of Marsali's gown, a trifle stiff-looking, but not so unnatural as to provoke comment.

I danced past them, revolving sedately in the arms of a short, tubby English planter named Carstairs, who wheezed pleasantries into my bosom, red face streaming sweat.

As for Mr. Willoughby, he was enjoying an unparalleled social triumph, the center of attention of a cluster of ladies who vied with each other in pressing dainties and refreshments on him. His eyes were bright, and a faint flush shone on his sallow cheeks.

Mr. Carstairs deposited me among a group of ladies at the end of the dance, and gallantly went to fetch a cup of claret. I at once returned to the business of the evening, asking the ladies whether they might be familiar with people to whose acquaintance I had been recommended, named Abernathy.

"Abernathy?" Mrs. Hall, a youngish matron, fluttered her fan and looked blank. "No, I cannot say I am acquainted with them. Do they take a great part in society, do you know?"

"Oh, no, Joan!" Her friend, Mrs. Yoakum, looked shocked, with the particular kind of enjoyable shock that precedes some juicy revelation. "You've heard of the Abernathys! You remember, the man who bought Rose Hall, up on the Yallahs River?"

"Oh, yes!" Mrs. Hall's blue eyes widened. "The one who died so soon after buying it?"

"Yes, that's the one," another lady chimed in, overhearing.

"Malaria, they *said* it was, but *I* spoke to the doctor who attended him—he had come to dress Mama's bad leg, you know she is such a martyr to the dropsy—and *he* told me—in strictest confidence, of course . . ."

The tongues wagged merrily. Rosie MacIver had been a faithful reporter; all the stories she had conveyed were here, and more. I caught hold of the conversational thread and gave it a jerk in the desired direction.

"Does Mrs. Abernathy have indentured labor, as well as slaves?"

Here opinion was more confused. Some thought that she had several indentured servants, some thought only one or two—no one present had actually set foot in Rose Hall, but of course people *said* . . .

A few minutes later, the gossip had turned to fresh meat, and the *incredible* behavior of the new curate, Mr. Jones, with the widowed Mrs. Mina Alcott, but then, what could be expected of a woman with *her* reputation, and surely it was not entirely the young man's fault, and she so much older, though of course, one in Holy Orders might be expected to be held to a higher standard . . . I made an excuse and slipped away to the ladies' retiring room, my ears ringing.

I saw Jamie as I went, standing near the refreshment table. He was talking to a tall, red-haired girl in embroidered cotton, a trace of unguarded tenderness lingering in his eyes as he looked at her. She was smiling eagerly up at him, flattered by his attention. I smiled at the sight, wondering what the young lady would think, did she realize that he was not really looking at her at all, but imagining her as the daughter he had never seen.

I stood in front of the looking glass in the outer retiring room, tucking in stray curls loosened by the exertion of dancing, and took pleasure in the temporary silence. The retiring room was luxuriously appointed, being in fact three separate chambers, with the privy facilities and a room for the storage of hats, shawls, and extraneous clothing opening off the main room, where I stood. This had not only a long pier-glass and a fully appointed dressing table, but also a chaise longue, covered in red velvet. I eyed it with some wistfulness—the slippers I was wearing were pinching my feet badly—but duty called.

So far, I had learned nothing beyond what we already knew

about the Abernathy plantation, though I had compiled a useful list of several other plantations near Kingston that employed indentured labor. I wondered whether Jamie intended to call upon his friend the Governor to help in the search for Ian—that might possibly justify risking an appearance here tonight.

But Lord John's response to the revelation of my identity was both puzzling and disturbing; you would think the man had seen a ghost. I squinted at my violet reflection, admiring the glitter of the black-and-gold fish at my throat, but failed to see anything unsettling in my appearance. My hair was tucked up with pins decorated with seed pearls and brilliants, and discreet use of Mrs. MacIver's cosmetics had darkened my lids and blushed my cheeks quite becomingly, if I did say so myself.

I shrugged, fluttered my lashes seductively at my image, then patted my hair and returned to the salon.

I made my way toward the long tables of refreshments, where a huge array of cakes, pastries, savories, fruits, candies, stuffed rolls, and a number of objects I couldn't put a name to but presumed edible were displayed. As I turned absentmindedly from the refreshment table with a plate of fruit, I collided headlong with a dark-hued waistcoat. Apologizing to its owner in confusion, I found myself looking up into the dour face of the Reverend Archibald Campbell.

"Mrs. Malcolm!" he exclaimed in astonishment.

"Er . . . Reverend Campbell," I replied, rather weakly. "What a surprise." I dabbed tentatively at a smear of mango on his abdomen, but he took a marked step backward, and I desisted.

He looked rather coldly at my décolletage.

"I trust I find you well, Mrs. Malcolm?" he said.

"Yes, thank you," I said. I wished he would stop calling me Mrs. Malcolm before someone to whom I had been introduced as Madame Alexandre heard him.

"I was so sorry to hear about your sister," I said, hoping to distract him. "Have you any word of her yet?"

He bent his head stiffly, accepting my sympathy.

"No. My own attempts at instigating a search have of course been limited," he said. "It was at the suggestion of one of my parishioners that I accompanied him and his wife here tonight, with the intention of putting my case before the Governor, and begging his assistance in locating my sister. I assure you, Mrs.

Malcolm, no less weighty a consideration would have impelled my attendance at a function such as this.''

He cast a glance of profound dislike at a laughing group nearby, where three young men were competing with each other in the composition of witty toasts to a group of young ladies, who received these attentions with much giggling and energetic fan-fluttering.

''I'm truly sorry for your misfortune, Reverend,'' I said, edging aside. ''Miss Cowden told me a bit about your sister's tragedy. If I should be able to be of help . . .''

''No one can help,'' he interrupted. His eyes were bleak. ''It was the fault of the Papist Stuarts, with their wicked attempt upon the throne, and the licentious Highlanders who followed them. No, no one can help, save God. He has destroyed the house of Stuart; he will destroy the man Fraser as well, and on that day, my sister will be healed.''

''Fraser?'' The trend of the conversation was making me distinctly uneasy. I glanced quickly across the room, but luckily Jamie was nowhere in sight.

''That is the name of the man who seduced Margaret from her family and her proper loyalties. His may not have been the hand that struck her down, but it was on his account that she had left her home and safety, and placed herself in danger. Aye, God will requite James Fraser fairly,'' he said with a sort of grim satisfaction at the thought.

''Yes, I'm sure he will,'' I murmured. ''If you will excuse me, I believe I see a friend . . .'' I tried to escape, but a passing procession of footmen bearing dishes of meat blocked my way.

''God will not suffer lewdness to endure forever,'' the Reverend went on, evidently feeling that the Almighty's opinions coincided largely with his own. His small gray eyes rested with icy disapproval on a group nearby, where several ladies fluttered around Mr. Willoughby like bright moths about a Chinese lantern.

Mr. Willoughby was brightly lit, too, in more than one sense of the word. His high-pitched giggle rose above the laughter of the ladies, and I saw him lurch heavily against a passing servant, nearly upsetting a tray of sorbet cups.

''Let the women learn with all sobriety,'' the Reverend was intoning, ''avoiding all gaudiness of clothing and broided hair.'' He seemed to be hitting his stride; no doubt Sodom and Gomorrah would be up next. "A woman who has no husband should devote herself to the service of the Lord, not be disporting herself with abandon in public places. Do you see Mrs. Alcott? And she a widow, who should be engaged in pious works!"

I followed the direction of his frown and saw that he was looking at a chubby, jolly-looking woman in her thirties, with light brown hair done in gathered ringlets, who was giggling at Mr. Willoughby. I looked at her with interest. So this was the infamous merry widow of Kingston!

The little Chinese had now got down upon his hands and knees and was crawling around on the floor, pretending to look for a lost earring, while Mrs. Alcott squeaked in mock alarm at his forays toward her feet. I thought perhaps I had better find Fergus without delay, and have him detach Mr. Willoughby from his new acquaintance before matters went too far.

Evidently offended beyond bearing by the sight, the Reverend abruptly put down the cup of lemon squash he had been holding, turned and made his way through the crowd toward the terrace, vigorously elbowing people out of his way.

I breathed a sigh of relief; conversation with the Reverend Campbell was a lot like exchanging frivolities with the public hangman—though, in fact, the only hangman with whom I had been personally acquainted was much better company than the Reverend.

Suddenly I saw Jamie's tall figure, heading for a door on the far side of the room, where I assumed the Governor's private quarters to be. He must be going to talk to Lord John now. Moved by curiosity, I decided to join him.

The floor was by now so crowded that it was difficult to make my way across it. By the time I reached the door through which Jamie had gone, he had long since disappeared, but I pushed my way through.

I was in a long hallway, dimly lighted by candles in sconces, and pierced at intervals by long casement windows, through which red light from the torches on the terrace outside flickered, picking up the gleam of metal from the decorations on the walls. These were largely military, consisting of ornamental sprays of pistols, knives, shields and swords. Lord John's personal souvenirs? I wondered, or had they come with the house?

Away from the clamor of the salon, it was remarkably quiet. I walked down the hallway, my steps muffled by the long Turkey carpet that covered the parquet.

There was an indistinguishable murmur of male voices ahead. I turned a corner into a shorter corridor and saw a door ahead from which light spilled—that must be the Governor's private office. Inside, I heard Jamie's voice.

"Oh, God, John!" he said.

I stopped dead, halted much more by the tone of that voice than by the words—it was broken with an emotion I had seldom heard from him.

Walking very quietly, I drew closer. Framed in the half-open door was Jamie, head bowed as he pressed Lord John Grey tight in a fervent embrace.

I stood still, completely incapable of movement or speech. As I watched, they broke apart. Jamie's back was turned to me, but Lord John faced the hallway; he could have seen me easily, had he looked. He wasn't looking toward the hallway, though. He was staring at Jamie, and on his face was a look of such naked hunger that the blood rushed to my own cheeks when I saw it.

I dropped my fan. I saw the Governor's head turn, startled at the sound. Then I was running down the hall, back toward the salon, my heartbeat drumming in my ears.

I shot through the door into the salon and came to a halt behind a potted palm, heart pounding. The wrought-iron chandeliers were thick with beeswax candles, and pine torches burned brightly on the walls, but even so, the corners of the room were dark. I stood in the shadows, trembling.

My hands were cold, and I felt slightly sick. What in the name of God was going on?

The Governor's shock at learning that I was Jamie's wife was now at least partially explained; that one glimpse of unguarded, painful yearning had told me exactly how matters stood on his side. Jamie was another question altogether.

He was the Governor of Ardsmuir prison, he had said, casually. And less casually, on another occasion, *D'ye ken what men in prison do?*

I did know, but I would have sworn on Brianna's head that Jamie didn't; hadn't, couldn't, under any circumstances whatever. At least I would have sworn that before tonight. I closed my eyes, chest heaving, and tried not to think of what I had seen.

I couldn't, of course. And yet, the more I thought of it, the more impossible it seemed. The memories of Jack Randall might have faded with the physical scars he had left, but I could not believe that they would ever fade sufficiently for Jamie to tolerate the physical attentions of another man, let alone to welcome them.

But if he knew Grey so intimately as to make what I had witnessed plausible in the name of friendship alone, then why had he not told me of him before? Why go to such lengths to see the man, as soon as he learned that Grey was in Jamaica? My stomach dropped once more, and the feeling of sickness returned. I wanted badly to sit down.

As I leaned against the wall, trembling in the shadows, the door to the Governor's quarters opened, and the Governor came out, returning to his party. His face was flushed and his eyes shone. I could at that moment easily have murdered him, had I anything more lethal than a hairpin to hand.

The door opened again a few minutes later, and Jamie emerged, no more than six feet away. His mask of cool reserve was in place, but I knew him well enough to see the marks of a strong emotion under it. But while I could see it, I couldn't interpret it. Excitement? Apprehension? Fear and joy mingled? Something else? I had simply never seen him look that way before.

He didn't seek conversation or refreshments, but instead began to stroll about the room, obviously looking for someone. For me.

I swallowed heavily. I couldn't face him—not in front of a crowd. I stayed where I was, watching him, until he finally went out onto the terrace. Then I left my hiding place, and crossed the room as quickly as I could, heading for the refuge of the retiring room. At least there I would be able to sit down for a moment.

I pushed open the heavy door and stepped inside, relaxing at once as the warm, comforting scents of women's perfume and powder surrounded me. Then the other smell struck me. It too was a familiar scent—one of the smells of my profession. But not expected here.

The retiring room was still quiet; the loud rumble from the salon had dropped abruptly to a faint murmur, like a far-off thunderstorm. It was, however, no longer a place of refuge.

Mina Alcott lay sprawled across the red velvet chaise, her head hanging backward over the edge, her skirts in disarray about her neck. Her eyes were open, fixed in upside-down surprise. The blood from her severed throat had turned the velvet black beneath her, and dripped down into a large pool beneath her head. Her light brown hair had come loose from its dressing, the matted ends of her ringlets dangling in the puddle.

I stood frozen, too paralyzed even to call for help. Then I heard the sound of gay voices in the hallway outside, and the door pushed open. There was a moment's silence as the women behind me saw it too.

Light from the corridor spilled through the door and across the floor, and in the moment before the screaming began, I saw the footprints leading toward the window—the small neat prints of a felt-soled foot, outlined in blood.

59

In Which Much Is Revealed

They had taken Jamie somewhere. I, shaking and incoherent, had been put—with a certain amount of irony—in the Governor's private office with Marsali, who insisted on trying to bathe my face with a damp towel, in spite of my resistance.

"They canna think Da had anything to do with it!" she said, for the fifth time.

"They don't." I finally pulled myself together enough to talk to her. "But they think Mr. Willoughby did—and Jamie brought him here."

She stared at me, wide-eyed with horror.

"Mr. Willoughby? But he couldn't!"

"I wouldn't have thought so." I felt as though someone had been beating me with a club; everything ached. I sat slumped on a small velvet love seat, aimlessly twirling a glass of brandy between my hands, unable to drink it.

I couldn't even decide what I *ought* to feel, let alone sort out the conflicting events and emotions of the evening. My mind kept jumping between the grisly scene in the retiring room, and the tableau I had seen a half-hour earlier, in this very room.

I sat looking at the Governor's big desk. I could still see the two of them, Jamie and Lord John, as though they had been painted on the wall before me.

"I just don't believe it," I said out loud, and felt slightly better for the saying.

"Neither do I," said Marsali. She was pacing the floor, her

footsteps changing from the click of heels on parquet to a muffled thump as she hit the flowered carpet. "He can't have! I ken he's a heathen, but we've lived wi' the man! We *know* him!"

Did we? Did I know Jamie? I would have sworn I did, and yet . . . I kept remembering what he had said to me at the brothel, during our first night together. *Will ye take me, and risk the man that I am, for the sake of the man ye knew?* I had thought then— and since—that there was not so much difference between them. But if I were wrong?

"I'm not wrong!" I muttered, clutching my glass fiercely. "I'm not!" If Jamie could take Lord John Grey as a lover, and hide it from me, he wasn't remotely the man I thought he was. There had to be some other explanation.

He didn't tell you about Laoghaire, said an insidious little voice inside my head.

"That's different," I said to it stoutly.

"What's different?" Marsali was looking at me in surprise.

"I don't know; don't mind me." I brushed a hand across my face, trying to wipe away confusion and weariness. "It's taking them a long time."

The walnut case-clock had struck two o'clock in the morning before the door of the office opened and Fergus came in, accompanied by a grim-looking militiaman.

Fergus was somewhat the worse for wear; most of the powder had gone from his hair, shaken onto the shoulders of his dark blue coat like dandruff. What was left gave his hair a grayish cast, as though he had aged twenty years overnight. No surprise; I felt as though I had.

"We can go now, *chérie,*" he said quietly to Marsali. He turned to me. "Will you come with us, milady, or wait for milord?"

"I'll wait," I said. I wasn't going to bed until I had seen Jamie, no matter how long it took.

"I will have the carriage return for you, then," he said, and put a hand on Marsali's back to usher her out.

The militiaman said something under his breath as they passed him. I didn't catch it, but evidently Fergus did. He stiffened, eyes narrowing, and turned back toward the man. The militiaman rocked up onto the balls of his feet, smiling evilly and looking expectant. Clearly he would like nothing better than an excuse to hit Fergus.

To his surprise, Fergus smiled charmingly at him, square white teeth gleaming.

"My thanks, *mon ami*," he said, "for your assistance in this most trying situation." He thrust out a black-gloved hand, which the militiaman accepted in surprise.

Then Fergus jerked his arm suddenly backward. There was a brief rip, and a pattering sound, as a small stream of bran struck the parquet floor.

"Keep it," he told the militiaman graciously. "A small token of my appreciation." And then they were gone, leaving the man slack-jawed, staring down in horror at the apparently severed hand in his grasp.

It was another hour before the door opened again, this time to admit the Governor. He was still handsome and neat as a white camellia, but definitely beginning to turn brown round the edges. I set the untouched glass of brandy down and got to my feet to face him.

"Where is Jamie?"

"Still being questioned by Captain Jacobs, the militia commander." He sank into his chair, looking bemused. "I had no notion he spoke French so remarkably well."

"I don't suppose you know him all that well," I said, deliberately baiting. What I wanted badly to know was just how well he *did* know Jamie. He didn't rise to it, though; merely took off his formal wig and laid it aside, running a hand through his damp blond hair with relief.

"Can he keep up such an impersonation, do you think?" he asked, frowning, and I realized that he was so occupied with thoughts of the murder and of Jamie that he was paying little, if any, attention to me.

"Yes," I said shortly. "Where do they have him?" I got up, heading for the door.

"In the formal parlor," he said. "But I don't think you should—"

Not pausing to listen, I yanked open the door and poked my head into the hall, then hastily drew it back and slammed the door.

Coming down the hall was the Admiral I had met in the receiving line, face set in lines of gravity suitable to the situation. Admirals I could deal with. However, he was accompanied by a flotilla of junior officers, and among the entourage I had spotted a face I knew, though he was now wearing the uniform of a first lieutenant, instead of an oversized captain's coat.

He was shaved and rested, but his face was puffy and discolored; someone had beaten him up in the not too distant past. Despite the differences in his appearance, I had not the slightest difficulty in recognizing Thomas Leonard. I had the distinct feeling that he wouldn't have any trouble recognizing me, either, violet silk notwithstanding.

I looked frantically about the office for someplace to hide, but short of crawling into the kneehole of the desk, there was no place at all. The Governor was watching me, fair brows raised in astonishment.

"What—" he began, but I rounded on him, finger to my lips.

"Don't give me away, if you value Jamie's life!" I whispered melodramatically, and so saying, flung myself onto the velvet love seat, snatched up the damp towel and dropped it on my face, and —with a superhuman effort of will—forced all my limbs to go limp.

I heard the door open, and the Admiral's high, querulous voice.

"Lord John—" he began, and then evidently noticed my supine form, for he broke off and resumed in a slightly lower voice, "Oh! I collect you are engaged?"

"Not precisely engaged, Admiral, no." Grey had fast reflexes, I would say that for him; he sounded perfectly self-possessed, as though he were quite used to being found in custody of unconscious females. "The lady was overcome by the shock of discovering the body."

"Oh!" said the Admiral again, this time dripping with sympathy. "I quite see that. Beastly shock for a lady, to be sure." He hesitated, then dropping his voice to a sort of hoarse whisper, said, "D'you think she's asleep?"

"I should think so," the Governor assured him. "She's had enough brandy to fell a horse." My fingers twitched, but I managed to lie still.

"Oh, quite. Best thing for shock, brandy." The Admiral went on whispering, sounding like a rusted hinge. "Meant to tell you I have sent to Antigua for additional troops—quite at your disposal

—guards, search the town—if the militia don't find the fellow first," he added.

"I hope they may not," said a viciously determined voice among the officers. "I'd like to catch the yellow bugger myself. There wouldn't be enough of him left to hang, believe me!"

A deep murmur of approval at this sentiment went through the men, to be sternly quelled by the Admiral.

"Your sentiments do you credit, gentlemen," he said, "but the law will be observed in all respects. You will make that clear to the troops in your command; when the miscreant is taken, he is to be brought to the Governor, and justice will be properly executed, I assure you." I didn't like the way he emphasized the word "executed," but he got a grudging chorus of assent from his officers.

The Admiral, having delivered this order in his ordinary voice, dropped back into a whisper to take his leave.

"I shall be staying in the town, at MacAdams Hotel," he croaked. "Do not hesitate to send to me for any assistance, Your Excellency."

There was a general shuffle and murmur as the naval officers took their leave, observing discretion for the sake of my slumbers. Then came the sound of a single pair of footsteps, and then the *whoosh* and creak of someone settling heavily into a chair. There was silence for a moment.

Then Lord John said "You can get up now, if you wish. I am supposing that you are not in fact prostrate with shock," he added, ironically. "Somehow I suspect that a mere murder would not be sufficient to discompose a woman who could deal single-handedly with a typhoid epidemic."

I removed the towel from my face and swung my feet off the chaise, sitting up to face him. He was leaning on his desk, chin in his hands, staring at me.

"There are shocks," I said precisely, smoothing back my damp curls and giving him an eyeball, "and then there are shocks. If you know what I mean."

He looked surprised; then a flicker of understanding came into his expression. He reached into the drawer of his desk, and pulled out my fan, white silk embroidered with violets.

"This is yours, I suppose? I found it in the corridor." His mouth twisted wryly as he looked at me. "I see. I suppose, then, you will have some notion of how your appearance earlier this evening affected *me*.''

''I doubt it very much,'' I said. My fingers were still icy, and I felt as though I had swallowed some large, cold object that pressed uncomfortably under my breastbone. I breathed deeply, trying to force it down, to no avail. ''You didn't know that Jamie was married?''

He blinked, but not in time to keep me from seeing a small grimace of pain, as though someone had struck him suddenly across the face.

''I knew he *had* been married,'' he corrected. He dropped his hands, fiddling aimlessly with the small objects that littered his desk. ''He told me—or gave me to understand, at least—that you were dead.''

Grey picked up a small silver paperweight, and turned it over and over in his hands, eyes fixed on the gleaming surface. A large sapphire was set in it, winking blue in the candlelight.

''Has he never mentioned me?'' he asked softly. I wasn't sure whether the undertone in his voice was pain or anger. Despite myself, I felt some small sense of pity for him.

''Yes, he did,'' I said. ''He said you were his friend.'' He glanced up, the fine-cut face lightening a bit.

''Did he?''

''You have to understand,'' I said. ''He—I—we were separated by the war, the Rising. Each of us thought the other was dead. I found him again only—my God, was it only four months ago?'' I felt staggered, and not only by the events of the evening. I felt as though I had lived several lifetimes since the day I had opened the door of the printshop in Edinburgh, to find A. Malcolm bending over his press.

The lines of stress in Grey's face eased a little.

''I see,'' he said slowly. ''So—you have not seen him since— my God, that's twenty years!'' He stared at me, dumbfounded. ''And four months? Why—how—'' He shook his head, brushing away the questions.

''Well, that's of no consequence just now. But he did not tell you—that is—has he not told you about Willie?''

I stared at him blankly.

''Who's Willie?''

Instead of explaining, he bent and opened the drawer of his

desk. He pulled out a small object and laid it on the desk, motioning me to come closer.

It was a portrait, an oval miniature, set in a carved frame of some fine-grained dark wood. I looked at the face, and sat down abruptly, my knees gone to water. I was only dimly aware of Grey's face, floating above the desk like a cloud on the horizon, as I picked up the miniature to look at it more closely.

He might have been Bree's brother, was my first thought. The second, coming with the force of a blow to the solar plexus, was "My God in heaven, he *is* Bree's brother!"

There couldn't be much doubt about it. The boy in the portrait was perhaps nine or ten, with a childish tenderness still lingering about his face, and his hair was a soft chestnut brown, not red. But the slanted blue eyes looked out boldly over a straight nose a fraction of an inch too long, and the high Viking cheekbones pressed tight against smooth skin. The tilt of the head held the same confident carriage as that of the man who had given him that face.

My hands trembled so violently that I nearly dropped it. I set it back on the desk, but kept my hand over it, as though it might leap up and bite me. Grey was watching me, not without sympathy.

"You didn't know?" he said.

"Who—" My voice was hoarse with shock, and I had to stop and clear my throat. "Who is his mother?"

Grey hesitated, eyeing me closely, then shrugged slightly.

"Was. She's dead."

"Who was she?" The ripples of shock were still spreading from an epicenter in my stomach, making the crown of my head tingle and my toes go numb, but at least my vocal cords were coming back under my control. I could hear Jenny saying, *He's no the sort of man should sleep alone, aye?* Evidently he wasn't.

"Her name was Geneva Dunsany," Grey said. "My wife's sister."

My mind was reeling, in an effort to make sense of all this, and I suppose I was less than tactful.

"Your *wife*?" I said, goggling at him. He flushed deeply and looked away. If I had been in any doubt about the nature of the look I had seen him give Jamie, I wasn't any longer.

"I think you had better bloody well explain to me just what you have to do with Jamie, and this Geneva, and this boy," I said, picking up the portrait once more.

He raised one brow, cool and reserved; he had been shocked, too, but the shock was wearing off.

"I cannot see that I am under any particular obligation to do so," he said.

I fought back the urge to rake my nails down his face, but the impulse must have shown on my face, for he pushed back his chair and got his feet under him, ready to move quickly. He eyed me warily across the expanse of dark wood.

I took several deep breaths, unclenched my fists, and spoke as calmly as I could.

"Right. You're not. But I would appreciate it very much if you did. And why did you show me the picture if you didn't mean me to know?" I added. "Since I know that much, I'll certainly find out the rest from Jamie. You might as well tell me your side of it now." I glanced at the window; the slice of sky that showed between the half-open shutters was still a velvet black, with no sign of dawn. "There's time."

He breathed deeply, and laid down the paperweight. "I suppose there is." He jerked his head abruptly at the decanter. "Will you have brandy?"

"I will," I said promptly, "and I strongly suggest you have some, too. I expect you need it as much as I do."

A slight smile showed briefly at the corner of his mouth.

"Is that a medical opinion, Mrs. Malcolm?" he asked dryly.

"Absolutely," I said.

This small truce established, he sat back, rolling his beaker of brandy slowly between his hands.

"You said Jamie mentioned me to you," he said. I must have flinched slightly at his use of Jamie's name, for he frowned at me. "Would you prefer that I referred to him by his surname?" he said, coldly. "I should scarcely know which to use, under the circumstances."

"No." I waved it away, and took a sip of brandy. "Yes, he mentioned you. He said you had been the Governor of the prison at Ardsmuir, and that you were a friend—and that he could trust you," I added reluctantly. Possibly Jamie felt he could trust Lord John Grey, but I was not so sanguine.

The smile this time was not quite so brief.

"I am glad to hear that," Grey said softly. He looked down into the amber liquid in his cup, swirling it gently to release its heady bouquet. He took a sip, then set the cup down with decision.

"I met him at Ardsmuir, as he said," he began. "And when the prison was shut down and the other prisoners sold to indenture in America, I arranged that Jamie should be paroled instead to a place in England, called Helwater, owned by friends of my family." He looked at me, hesitating, then added simply, "I could not bear the thought of never seeing him again, you see."

In a few brief words, he acquainted me with the bare facts of Geneva's death and Willie's birth.

"Was he in love with her?" I asked. The brandy was doing its bit to warm my hands and feet, but it didn't touch the large cold object in my stomach.

"He has never spoken to me of Geneva," Grey said. He gulped the last of his brandy, coughed, and reached to pour another cup. It was only when he finished this operation that he looked at me again, and added, "But I doubt it, having known her." His mouth twisted wryly.

"He never told me about Willie, either, but there was a certain amount of gossip about Geneva and old Lord Ellesmere, and by the time the boy was four or five, the resemblance made it quite clear who his father was—to anyone who cared to look." He took another deep swallow of brandy. "I suspect that my mother-in-law knows, but of course she would never breathe a word."

"She wouldn't?"

He stared at me over the rim of his cup.

"No, would you? If it were a choice of your only grandchild being either the ninth Earl of Ellesmere, and heir to one of the wealthiest estates in England, or the penniless bastard of a Scottish criminal?"

"I see." I drank some more of my own brandy, trying to imagine Jamie with a young English girl named Geneva—and succeeding all too well.

"Quite," Grey said dryly. "Jamie saw, too. And very wisely arranged to leave Helwater before it became obvious to everyone."

"And that's where you come back into the story, is it?" I asked.

He nodded, eyes closed. The Residence was quiet, though there was a certain distant stir that made me aware that people were still about.

"That's right," he said. "Jamie gave the boy to me."

The stable at Ellesmere was well-built; cozy in the winter, it was a cool haven in summer. The big bay stallion flicked its ears lazily at a passing fly, but stood stolidly content, enjoying the attentions of his groom.

"Isobel is most displeased with you," Grey said.

"Is she?" Jamie's voice was indifferent. There was no need any longer to worry about displeasing any of the Dunsanys.

"She said you had told Willie you were leaving, which upset him dreadfully. He's been howling all day."

Jamie's face was turned away, but Grey saw the faint tightening at the side of his throat. He rocked backward, leaning against the stable wall as he watched the curry comb come down and down and down in hard, even strokes that left dark trails across the shimmering coat.

"Surely it would have been easier to say nothing to the boy?" Grey said quietly.

"I suppose it would—for Lady Isobel." Fraser turned to put up the curry comb, and slapped a hand on the stallion's rump in dismissal. Grey thought there was an air of finality in the gesture; tomorrow Jamie would be gone. He felt a slight thickening in his own throat, but swallowed it. He rose and followed Fraser toward the door of the stall.

"Jamie—" he said, putting his hand on Fraser's shoulder. The Scot swung round, his features hastily readjusting themselves, but not fast enough to hide the misery in his eyes. He stood still, looking down at the Englishman.

"You're right to go," Grey said. Alarm flared in Fraser's eyes, quickly supplanted by wariness.

"Am I?" he said.

"Anyone with half an eye could see it," Grey said dryly. "If anyone ever actually looked at a groom, someone would have noticed long before now." He glanced back at the bay stallion, and cocked one brow. "Some sires stamp their get. I have the distinct impression that any offspring of yours would be unmistakable."

Jamie said nothing, but Grey fancied that he had grown a shade paler than usual.

"Surely you can see—well, no, perhaps not," he corrected himself, "I don't suppose you have a looking glass, have you?"

Jamie shook his head mechanically. "No," he said absently. "I shave in the reflection from the trough." He drew in a deep breath, and let it out slowly.

"Aye, well," he said. He glanced toward the house, where the French doors were standing open onto the lawn. Willie was accustomed to play there after lunch on fine days.

Fraser turned to him with sudden decision. "Will ye walk with me?" he said.

Not pausing for an answer, he set off past the stable, turning down the lane that led from the paddock to the lower pasture. It was nearly a quarter-mile before he came to a halt, in a sunny clearing by a clump of willows, near the edge of the mere.

Grey found himself puffing slightly from the quick pace—too much soft living in London, he chided himself. Fraser, of course, was not even sweating, despite the warmth of the day.

Without preamble, turning to face Grey, he said, "I wish to ask a favor of ye." The slanted blue eyes were direct as the man himself.

"If you think I would tell anyone . . ." Grey began, then shook his head. "Surely you don't think I could do such a thing. After all, I have known—or at least suspected—for some time."

"No." A faint smile lifted Jamie's mouth. "No, I dinna think ye would. But I would ask ye . . ."

"Yes," Grey said promptly. The corner of Jamie's mouth twitched.

"Ye dinna wish to know what it is first?"

"I should imagine that I know; you wish me to look out for Willie; perhaps to send you word of his welfare."

Jamie nodded.

"Aye, that's it." He glanced up the slope, to where the house lay half-hidden in its nest of fiery maples. "It's an imposition, maybe, to ask ye to come all the way from London to see him now and then."

"Not at all," Grey interrupted. "I came this afternoon to give you some news of my own; I am to be married."

"Married?" The shock was plain on Fraser's face. "To a woman?"

"I think there are not many alternatives," Grey replied dryly. "But yes, since you ask, to a woman. To the Lady Isobel."

"Christ, man! Ye canna do that!"

"I can," Grey assured him. He grimaced. "I made trial of my capacity in London; be assured that I shall make her an adequate husband. You needn't necessarily enjoy the act in order to perform it—or perhaps you were aware of that?"

There was a small reflexive twitch at the corner of Jamie's eye; not quite a flinch, but enough for Grey to notice. Jamie opened his mouth, then closed it again and shook his head, obviously thinking better of what he had been about to say.

"Dunsany is growing too old to take a hand in the running of the estate," Grey pointed out. "Gordon is dead, and Isobel and her mother cannot manage the place alone. Our families have known each other for decades. It is an entirely suitable match."

"Is it, then?" The sardonic skepticism in Jamie's voice was clear. Grey turned to him, fair skin flushing as he answered sharply.

"It is. There is more to a marriage than carnal love. A great deal more."

Fraser swung sharply away. He strode to the edge of the mere, and stood, boots sunk in the reedy mud, looking over the ruffled waves for some time. Grey waited patiently, taking the time to unribbon his hair and reorder the thick blond mass.

At long last, Fraser came back, walking slowly, head down as though still thinking. Face-to-face with Grey he looked up again.

"You are right," he said quietly. "I have no right to think ill of you, if ye mean no dishonor to the lady."

"Certainly not," Grey said. "Besides," he added more cheerfully, "it means I will be here permanently, to see to Willie."

"You mean to resign your commission, then?" One copper eyebrow flicked upward.

"Yes," Grey said. He smiled, a little ruefully. "It will be a relief, in a way. I was not meant for army life, I think."

Fraser seemed to be thinking. "I should be . . . grateful, then," he said, "if you would stand as stepfather to—to my son." He had likely never spoken the word aloud before, and the sound of it seemed to shock him. "I . . . would be obliged to you." Jamie sounded as though his collar were too tight, though in fact his shirt was open at the throat. Grey looked curiously at him, and saw that his countenance was slowly turning a dark and painful red.

"In return . . . If you want . . . I mean, I would be willing to . . . that is . . ."

Grey suppressed the sudden desire to laugh. He laid a light hand on the big Scot's arm, and saw Jamie brace himself not to flinch at the touch.

"My dear Jamie," he said, torn between laughter and exasperation. "Are you actually offering me your body in payment for my promise to look after Willie?"

Fraser's face was red to the roots of his hair.

"Aye, I am," he snapped, tight-lipped. "D'ye want it, or no?"

At this, Grey did laugh, in long gasping whoops, finally having to sit down on the grassy bank in order to recover himself.

"Oh, dear God," he said at last, wiping his eyes. "That I should live to hear an offer like that!"

Fraser stood above him, looking down, the morning light silhouetting him, lighting his hair in flames against the pale blue sky. Grey thought he could see a slight twitch of the wide mouth in the darkened face—humor, tempered with a profound relief.

"Ye dinna want me, then?"

Grey got to his feet, dusting the seat of his breeches. "I shall probably want you to the day I die," he said matter-of-factly. "But tempted as I am—" He shook his head, brushing wet grass from his hands.

"Do you really think that I would demand—or accept—any payment for such a service?" he asked. "Really, I should

*feel my honor most grossly insulted by that offer, save that I
know the depth of feeling which prompted it.''*

"Aye, well," Jamie muttered. "I didna mean to insult ye."

Grey was not sure at this point whether to laugh or cry.
Instead, he reached a hand up and gently touched Jamie's
cheek, fading now to its normal pale bronze. More quietly, he
said, "Besides, you cannot give me what you do not have."

Grey felt, rather than saw, the slight relaxation of tension
in the tall body facing him.

"You shall have my friendship," Jamie said softly, "if that
has any value to ye."

"A very great value indeed." The two men stood silent
together for a moment, then Grey sighed and turned to look
up at the sun. "It's getting late. I suppose you will have a
great many things to do today?"

Jamie cleared his throat. "Aye, I have. I suppose I should
be about my business."

"Yes, I suppose so."

Grey tugged down the points of his waistcoat, ready to go.
But Jamie lingered awkwardly a moment, and then, as though
suddenly making up his mind to it, stepped forward and bending down, cupped Grey's face between his hands.

Grey felt the big hands warm on the skin of his face, light
and strong as the brush of an eagle's feather, and then Jamie
Fraser's soft wide mouth touched his own. There was a fleeting impression of tenderness and strength held in check, the
faint taste of ale and fresh-baked bread. Then it was gone,
and John Grey stood blinking in the brilliant sun.

"Oh," he said.

Jamie gave him a shy, crooked smile.

"Aye, well," he said. "I suppose I'm maybe not
poisoned." He turned then, and disappeared into the screen
of willows, leaving Lord John Grey alone by the mere.

The Governor was quiet for a moment. Then he looked up with
a bleak smile.

"That was the first time that he ever touched me willingly," he
said quietly. "And the last—until this evening, when I gave him
the other copy of that miniature."

I sat completely motionless, the brandy glass unregarded in my hands. I wasn't sure *what* I felt; shock, fury, horror, jealousy, and pity all washed through me in successive waves, mingling in eddies of confused emotion.

A woman had been violently done to death nearby, within the last few hours. And yet the scene in the retiring room seemed unreal by comparison with that miniature; a small and unimportant picture, painted in tones of red. For the moment, neither Lord John nor I was concerned with crime or justice—or with anything beyond what lay between us.

The Governor was examining my face, with considerable absorption.

"I suppose I should have recognized you on the ship," he said. "But of course, at the time, I had thought you long dead."

"Well, it was dark," I said, rather stupidly. I shoved a hand through my curls, feeling dizzy from brandy and sleeplessness. Then I realized what he had said.

"Recognized me? But you'd never met me!"

He hesitated, then nodded.

"Do you recall a dark wood, near Carryarrick in the Scottish Highlands, twenty years ago? And a young boy with a broken arm? You set it for me." He lifted one arm in demonstration.

"Jesus H. Roosevelt Christ." I picked up the brandy and took a swallow that made me cough and gasp. I blinked at him, eyes watering. Knowing now who he was, I could make out the fine, light bones and see the slighter, softer outline of the boy he had been.

"Yours were the first woman's breasts I had ever seen," he said wryly. "It was a considerable shock."

"From which you appear to have recovered," I said, rather coldly. "You seem to have forgiven Jamie for breaking your arm and threatening to shoot you, at least."

He flushed slightly, and set down his beaker.

"I—well—yes," he said, abruptly.

We sat there for quite some time, neither of us having any idea what to say. He took a breath once or twice, as though about to say something, but then abandoned it. At last, he closed his eyes as though commending his soul to God, opened them and looked at me.

"Do you know—" he began, then stopped. He looked down at

his clenched hands, then, not at me. A blue stone winked on one knuckle, bright as a teardrop.

"Do you know," he said again, softly, addressing his hands, "what it is to love someone, and never—never!—be able to give them peace, or joy, or happiness?"

He looked up then, eyes filled with pain. "To know that you cannot give them happiness, not through any fault of yours or theirs, but only because you were not born the right person for them?"

I sat quiet, seeing not his, but another handsome face; dark, not fair. Not feeling the warm breath of the tropical night, but the icy hand of a Boston winter. Seeing the pulse of light like heart's blood, spilling across the cold snow of hospital linens.

. . . *only because you were not born the right person for them.*

"I know," I whispered, hands clenched in my lap. I had told Frank—Leave me. But he could not, no more than I could love him rightly, having found my match elsewhere.

Oh, Frank, I said, silently. Forgive me.

"I suppose I am asking whether you believe in fate," Lord John went on. The ghost of a smile wavered on his face. "You, of all people, would seem best suited to say."

"You'd think so, wouldn't you?" I said bleakly. "But I don't know, any more than you."

He shook his head, then reached out and picked up the miniature.

"I have been more fortunate than most, I suppose," he said quietly. "There was the one thing he would take from me." His expression softened as he looked down into the face of the boy in the palm of his hand. "And he has given me something most precious in return."

Without thinking, I let my hand spread out across my belly. Jamie had given me that same precious gift—and at the same great cost to himself.

The sound of footsteps came down the hall, muffled by the carpet. There was a sharp rap at the door, and a militiaman stuck his head into the office.

"Is the lady recovered yet?" he asked. "Captain Jacobs has finished his questions, and Monsieur Alexandre's carriage has returned."

I got hastily to my feet.

"Yes, I'm fine." I turned to the Governor, not knowing what to say to him. "I—thank you for—that is—"

He bowed formally to me, coming around the desk to see me out.

"I regret extremely that you should have been subjected to such a shocking experience, ma'am," he said, with no trace of anything but diplomatic regret in his voice. He had resumed his official manner, smooth and polished as his parquet floors.

I followed the militiaman, but at the door I turned impulsively.

"When we met, that night aboard the *Porpoise*—I'm glad you didn't know who I was. I . . . liked you. Then."

He stood for a second, polite, remote. Then the mask dropped away.

"I liked you, too," he said quietly. "Then."

I felt as though I were riding next to a stranger. The light was beginning to gray toward dawn, and even in the dimness of the coach, I could see Jamie sitting opposite me, his face drawn with weariness. He had taken off the ridiculous wig as soon as we drove away from Government House, discarding the facade of the polished Frenchman to let the disheveled Scot beneath show through. His unbound hair lay in waves over his shoulders, dark in that predawn light that robs everything of color.

"Do you think he did it?" I asked at last, only for something to say.

His eyes were closed. At this, they opened and he shrugged slightly.

"I don't know," he said. He sounded exhausted. "I have asked myself that a thousand times tonight—and been asked it even more." He rubbed his knuckles hard over his forehead.

"I canna imagine a man I know to do such a thing. And yet . . . well, ye ken he'll do anything when he's drink taken. And he's killed before, drunk—you'll mind the Customs man at the brothel?" I nodded, and he leaned forward, elbows on his knees, sinking his head into his hands.

"This is different, though," he said. "I canna think—but maybe so. Ye ken what he said about women on the ship. And if this Mrs. Alcott was to have toyed wi' him—"

"She did," I said. "I saw her."

He nodded without looking up. "So did any number of other people. But if she led him to think she meant more than she maybe did, and then perhaps she put him off, maybe laughed at him . . . and him fu' as a puggie wi' drink, and knives to hand on every wall of the place . . ." He sighed and sat up.

"God knows," he said bleakly. "I don't." He ran a hand backward through his hair, smoothing it.

"There's something else about it. I had to tell them that I scarcely knew Willoughby—that we'd met him on the packet boat from Martinique, and thought it kindly to introduce him about, but didna ken a thing of where he came from, or the sort of fellow he truly was."

"Did they believe it?"

He glanced at me wryly.

"So far. But the packet boat comes in again in six days—at which point, they'll question the captain and discover that he's never laid eyes on Monsieur Etienne Alexandre and his wife, let alone a wee yellow murdering fiend."

"That might be a trifle awkward," I observed, thinking of Fergus and the militiaman. "We're already rather unpopular on Mr. Willoughby's account."

"Nothing to what we will be, if six days pass and they havena found him," he assured me. "Six days is also maybe as long as it will take for gossip to spread from Blue Mountain House to Kingston about the MacIvers' visitors—for ye ken the servants there all know who we are."

"Damn."

He smiled briefly at that, and my heart turned over to see it.

"You've a nice way wi' words, Sassenach. Aye, well, all it means is that we must find Ian within six days. I shall go to Rose Hall at once, but I think I must just have a wee rest before setting out." He yawned widely behind his hand and shook his head, blinking.

We didn't speak again until after we had arrived at Blue Mountain House and made our way on tiptoe through the slumbering house to our room.

I changed in the dressing room, dropping the heavy stays on the floor with relief, and taking out the pins to let my hair fall free. Wearing only a silk chemise, I came into the bedroom, to see

Jamie standing by the French door in his shirt, looking out over the lagoon.

He turned when he heard me, and beckoned, putting a finger to his lips.

"Come see," he whispered.

There was a small herd of manatees in the lagoon, big gray bodies gliding under the dark crystal water, rising gleaming like smooth, wet rocks. Birds were beginning to call in the trees near the house; besides this, the only sound was the frequent *whoosh* of the manatees' breath as they rose for air, and now and then an eerie sound like a hollow, distant wail, as they called to each other.

We watched them in silence, side by side. The lagoon began to turn green as the first rays of sun touched its surface. In that state of extreme fatigue where every sense is preternaturally heightened, I was as aware of Jamie as though I were touching him.

John Grey's revelations had relieved me of most of my fears and doubts—and yet there remained the fact that Jamie had not told me about his son. Of course he had reasons—and good ones —for his secrecy, but did he not think he could trust me to keep his secret? It occurred to me suddenly that perhaps he had kept quiet because of the boy's mother. Perhaps he had loved her, in spite of Grey's impressions.

She was dead; could it matter if he had? The answer was that it did. I had thought Jamie dead for twenty years, and it had made no difference at all in what I felt for him. What if he had loved this young English girl in such a way? I swallowed a small lump in my throat, trying to find the courage to ask him.

His face was abstracted, a small frown creasing his forehead, despite the dawning beauty of the lagoon.

"What are you thinking?" I asked at last, unable to ask for reassurance, fearing to ask for the truth.

"It's only that I had a thought," he answered, still staring out at the manatees. "About Willoughby, aye?"

The events of the night seemed far away and unimportant. Yet murder had been done.

"What was that?"

"Well, I couldna think at first that Willoughby could do such a thing—how could any man?" He paused, drawing a finger through the light mist of condensation that formed on the window-panes as the sun rose. "And yet . . ." He turned to face me.

"Perhaps I can see." His face was troubled. "He was alone—verra much alone."

"A stranger, in a strange land," I said quietly, remembering the poems, painted in the open secrecy of bold black ink, sent flying toward a long-lost home, committed to the sea on wings of white paper.

"Aye, that's it." He stopped to think, rubbing a hand slowly through his hair, gleaming copper in the new daylight. "And when a man is alone that way—well, it's maybe no decent to say it, but making love to a woman is maybe the only thing will make him forget it for a time."

He looked down, turning his hands over, stroking the length of his scarred middle finger with the index finger of his left hand.

"That's what made me wed Laoghaire," he said quietly. "Not Jenny's nagging. Not pity for her or the wee lassies. Not even a pair of aching balls." His mouth turned up briefly at one corner, then relaxed. "Only needing to forget I was alone," he finished softly.

He turned restlessly, back to the window.

"So I am thinking that if the Chinee came to her, wanting that—needing that—and she wouldna take him . . ." He shrugged, staring out across the cool green of the lagoon. "Aye, maybe he could have done it," he said.

I stood beside him. Out in the center of the lagoon, a single manatee drifted lazily to the surface, turning on her back to hold the infant on her chest toward the sunlight.

He was silent for several minutes, and I was as well, not knowing how to take the conversation back to what I had seen and heard at Government House.

I felt rather than saw him swallow, and he turned from the window to face me. There were lines of tiredness in his face, but his expression was filled with a sort of determination—the sort of look he wore facing battle.

"Claire," he said, and at once I stiffened. He called me by my name only when he was most serious. "Claire, I must tell ye something."

"What?" I had been trying to think how to ask, but suddenly I didn't want to hear. I took half a step back, away from him, but he grabbed my arm.

He had something hidden in his fist. He took my unresisting

hand and put the object into it. Without looking, I knew what it was; I could feel the carving of the delicate oval frame and the slight roughness of the painted surface.

"Claire." I could see the slight tremor at the side of his throat as he swallowed. "Claire—I must tell ye. I have a son."

I didn't say anything, but opened my hand. There it was; the same face I had seen in Grey's office, a childish, cocky version of the man before me.

"I should ha' told ye before." He was searching my face for some clue to my feelings, but for once, my giveaway countenance must have been perfectly blank. "I would have—only—" He took a deep breath for strength to go on.

"I havena ever told anyone about him," he said. "Not even Jenny."

That startled me enough to speak.

"Jenny doesn't know?"

He shook his head, and turned away to watch the manatees. Alarmed by our voices, they had retreated a short distance, but then had settled down again, feeding on the water weed at the edge of the lagoon.

"It was in England. It's—he's—I couldna say he was mine. He's a bastard, aye?" It might have been the rising sun that flushed his cheeks. He bit his lip and went on.

"I havena seen him since he was a wee lad. I never will see him again—except it might be in a wee painting like this." He took the small picture from me, cradling it in the palm of his hand like a baby's head. He blinked, head bent over it.

"I was afraid to tell ye," he said, low-voiced. "For fear ye would think that perhaps I'd gone about spawning a dozen bastards . . . for fear ye'd think that I wouldna care for Brianna so much, if ye kent I had another child. But I do care, Claire—a great deal more than I can tell ye." He lifted his head and looked directly at me.

"Will ye forgive me?"

"Did you—" The words almost choked me, but I had to say them. "Did you love her?"

An extraordinary expression of sadness crossed his face, but he didn't look away.

"No," he said softly. "She . . . wanted me. I should have found a way—should have stopped her, but I could not. She wished me to lie wi' her. And I did, and . . . she died of it.'' He did look down then, long lashes hiding his eyes. ''I am guilty of her death, before God; perhaps the more guilty—because I did not love her.''

I didn't say anything, but put up a hand to touch his cheek. He pressed his own hand over it, hard, and closed his eyes. There was a gecko on the wall beside us, nearly the same color as the yellow plaster behind it, beginning to glow in the gathering daylight.

''What is he like?'' I asked softly. ''Your son?''

He smiled slightly, without opening his eyes.

''He's spoilt and stubborn,'' he said softly. ''Ill-mannered. Loud. Wi' a wicked temper.'' He swallowed. ''And braw and bonny and canty and strong,'' he said, so softly I could barely hear him.

''And yours,'' I said. His hand tightened on mine, holding it against the soft stubble of his cheek.

''And mine,'' he said. He took a deep breath, and I could see the glitter of tears under his closed lids.

''You should have trusted me,'' I said at last. He nodded, slowly, then opened his eyes, still holding my hand.

''Perhaps I should,'' he said quietly. ''And yet I kept thinking —how should I tell ye everything, about Geneva, and Willie, and John—will ye know about John?'' He frowned slightly, then relaxed as I nodded.

''He told me. About everything.'' His brows rose, but he went on.

''Especially after ye found out about Laoghaire. How could I tell ye, and expect ye to know the difference?''

''What difference?''

''Geneva—Willie's mother—she wanted my body,'' he said softly, watching the gecko's pulsing sides. ''Laoghaire needed my name, and the work of my hands to keep her and her bairns.'' He turned his head then, dark blue eyes fixed on mine. ''John—well.'' He lifted his shoulders and let them drop. ''I couldna give him what he wanted—and he is friend enough not to ask it.

''But how shall I tell ye all these things,'' he said, the line of his mouth twisting. ''And then say to you—it is only you I have ever loved? How should you believe me?''

The question hung in the air between us, shimmering like the reflection from the water below.

"If you say it," I said, "I'll believe you."

"You will?" He sounded faintly astonished. "Why?"

"Because you're an honest man, Jamie Fraser," I said, smiling so that I wouldn't cry. "And may the Lord have mercy on you for it."

"Only you," he said, so softly I could barely hear him. "To worship ye with my body, give ye all the service of my hands. To give ye my name, and all my heart and soul with it. Only you. Because ye will not let me lie—and yet ye love me."

I did touch him then.

"Jamie," I said softly, and laid my hand on his arm. "You aren't alone anymore."

He turned then and took me by the arms, searching my face.

"I swore to you," I said. "When we married. I didn't mean it then, but I swore—and now I mean it." I turned his hand over in both mine, feeling the thin, smooth skin at the base of his wrist, where the pulse beat under my fingers, where the blade of his dirk had cut his flesh once, and spilled his blood to mingle with mine forever.

I pressed my own wrist against his, pulse to pulse, heartbeat to heartbeat.

"Blood of my blood . . ." I whispered.

"Bone of my bone." His whisper was deep and husky. He knelt quite suddenly before me, and put his folded hands in mine; the gesture a Highlander makes when swearing loyalty to his chieftain.

"I give ye my spirit," he said, head bent over our hands.

" 'Til our life shall be done," I said softly. "But it isn't done yet, Jamie, is it?"

Then he rose and took the shift from me, and I lay back on the narrow bed naked, pulled him down to me through the soft yellow light, and took him home, and home, and home again, and we were neither one of us alone.

60

The Scent of Gemstones

Rose Hall was ten miles out of Kingston, up a steep and winding road of reddish dust that led into blue mountains. The road was overgrown, so narrow that we must ride in single file most of the way. I followed Jamie through the dark, sweet-scented caverns of cedar boughs, under trees nearly a hundred feet high. Huge ferns grew in the shade below, the fiddle-heads nearly the size of real violin necks.

Everything was quiet, save for the calling of birds in the shrubbery—and even that fell silent as we passed. Jamie's horse stopped dead, once, and backed up, snorting; we waited as a tiny green snake wriggled across the path and into the undergrowth. I looked after it, but could see no farther than ten feet from the edge of the road; everything beyond was cool green shadow. I half-hoped that Mr. Willoughby had come this way—no one would ever find him, in a place like this.

The Chinaman had not been found in spite of an intensive search of the town by the island militia. The special detachment of marines from the barracks on Antigua was expected to arrive tomorrow. In the meantime, every house in Kingston was shut up like a bank vault, the owners armed to the teeth.

The mood of the town was thoroughly dangerous. Like the naval officers; it was the militia colonel's opinion that if the Chinaman were found, he would be lucky to survive long enough to be hanged.

"Be torn to pieces, I expect," Colonel Jacobs had said as he escorted us from the Residence on the night of the murder. "Have

his balls ripped off and thrust down his stinking throat, I daresay,"
he added, with obvious grim satisfaction at the thought.

"I daresay," Jamie had murmured in French, assisting me into
the carriage. I knew that the question of Mr. Willoughby was still
troubling him; he had been quiet and thoughtful on the ride
through the mountains. And yet there was nothing we could do. If
the little Chinese was innocent, we could not save him; if he was
guilty, we could not give him up. The best we might hope for was
that he would not be found.

And in the meantime, we had five days to find Young Ian. If he
was indeed at Rose Hall, all might be well. If he was not . . .

A fence and small gate marked the division of the plantation
from the surrounding forest. Inside, the ground had been cleared,
and planted in sugarcane and coffee. Some distance from the
house, on a separate rise, a large, plain, mud-daub building stood,
roofed with palm thatch. Dark-skinned people were going in and
out, and the faint, cloying scent of burnt sugar hung over the place.

Below the refinery—or so I assumed the building to be—stood
a large sugar press. A primitive-looking affair, this consisted of a
pair of huge timbers crossed in the shape of an X, set on an
enormous spindle, surmounting the boxlike body of the press. Two
or three men were clambering over the press, but it was not working at present; the oxen who drove it were hobbled some distance
away, grazing.

"How do they ever get the sugar down from here?" I asked,
curious, thinking of the narrow trail we had come up. "On
mules?" I brushed cedar needles off the shoulders of my coat,
making myself presentable.

"No," Jamie answered absently. "They send it down the river
on barges. The river's just over there, down the wee pass ye can
see beyond the house." He pointed with his chin, reining up with
one hand, and using the other to beat the dust of travel from the
skirts of his coat.

"Ready, Sassenach?"

"As I'll ever be."

Rose Hall was a two-storied house; long and graciously proportioned, with a roof laid in expensive slates, rather than in the
sheets of tin that covered most of the planters' residences. A long

veranda ran all along one side of the house, with long windows and French doors opening onto it.

A great yellow rosebush grew by the front door, climbing on a trellis and spilling over the edge of the roof. The scent of its perfume was so heady that it made breathing difficult; or perhaps it was only excitement that made my breath come short and stick in my throat. I glanced around as we waited for the door to be answered, trying to catch a glimpse of any white-skinned figure near the sugar refinery above.

"Yes, sah?" A middle-aged slave woman opened the door, looking out curiously at us. She was wide-bodied, dressed in a white cotton smock, with a red turban wrapped round her head, and her skin was the deep, rich gold in the heart of the flowers on the trellis.

"Mr. and Mrs. Malcolm, to call upon Mrs. Abernathy, if ye please," Jamie said politely. The woman looked rather taken aback, as though callers were not a common occurrence, but after a moment's indecision, she nodded and stepped back, swinging the door wide.

"You be waitin' in the salon, please, sah," she said, in a soft lilt that made it "*sall*ong." "I be askin' the mistress will she see you."

It was a large room, long and graciously proportioned, lit by huge casement windows all down one side. At the far end of the room was the fireplace, an enormous structure with a stone overmantel and a hearth of polished slates that occupied nearly the whole wall. You could have roasted an ox in it without the slightest difficulty, and the presence of a large spit suggested that the owner of the house did so on occasion.

The slave had shown us to a wicker sofa and invited us to be seated. I sat, looking about, but Jamie strolled restlessly about the room, peering through the windows that gave a view of the cane fields below the house.

It was an odd room; comfortably furnished with wicker and rattan furniture, well-equipped with fat, soft cushions, but ornamented with small, uncommon curios. On one window ledge sat a row of silver handbells, graduated from small to large. Several squat figures of stone and terra-cotta sat together on the table by my elbow; some sort of primitive fetishes or idols.

All of them were in the shape of women, hugely pregnant, or

with enormous, rounded breasts and exaggerated hips, and all with a vivid and mildly disturbing sexuality about them. It was not a prudish age, by any means, but I wouldn't have expected to find such objects in a drawing room in any age.

Somewhat more orthodox were the Jacobite relics. A silver snuffbox, a glass flagon, a decorated fan, a large serving platter—even the large woven rug on the floor; all decorated with the square white rose of the Stuarts. That wasn't so odd—a great many Jacobites who had fled Scotland after Culloden had come to the West Indies to seek the repair of their fortunes. I found the sight encouraging. A householder with Jacobite sympathies might be welcoming to a fellow Scot, and willing to oblige in the matter of Ian. *If he's here,* a small voice in my head warned.

Steps sounded in the inner part of the house, and there was a flutter at the door by the hearth. Jamie made a small grunting sound, as though someone had hit him, and I looked up, to see the mistress of the house step into the room.

I rose to my feet, and the small silver cup I had picked up fell to the floor with a clank.

"Kept your girlish figure, I see, Claire." Her head was tilted to one side, green eyes gleaming with amusement.

I was too paralyzed with surprise to respond aloud, but the thought drifted through my stunned mind that I couldn't say the same for her.

Geillis Duncan had always had a voluptuous abundance of creamy bosom and a generous swell of rounded hip. While still creamy-skinned, she was considerably more abundant and generous, in every dimension visible. She wore a loose muslin gown, under which the soft, thick flesh wobbled and swayed as she moved. The delicate bones of her face had long since been submerged in swelling plumpness, but the brilliant green eyes were the same, filled with malice and humor.

I took a deep breath, and got my voice back.

"I trust you won't take this the wrong way," I said, sinking slowly back onto the wicker sofa, "but why aren't you dead?"

She laughed, the silver in her voice as clear as a young girl's.

"Think I should have been, do you? Well, you're no the first—and I daresay you'll no be the last to think so, either."

Eyes creased to bright green triangles by amusement, she sank into her own chair, nodded casually to Jamie, and clapped her hands sharply to summon a servant. "Shall we have a dish of tea?" she asked me. "Do, and I'll read the leaves in your cup for ye, after. I've a reputation as a reader, after all; a fine teller o' the future, to be sure—and why not?" She laughed again, plump cheeks pinkening with mirth. If she had been as shocked by my appearance as I was at hers, she disguised it masterfully.

"Tea," she said, to the black maidservant who appeared in response to the summons. "The special kind in the blue tin, aye? And the bittie cakes wi' the nuts in, too."

"You'll take a bite?" she asked, turning back to me. " 'Tis something of an occasion, after all. I did wonder," she said, tilting her head to one side, like a gull judging the chances of snatching a fish, "whether our paths might cross again, after that day at Cranesmuir."

My heart was beginning to slow, the shock overcome in a great wave of curiosity. I could feel the questions bubbling up by the dozens, and picked one off the top at random.

"Did you know me?" I asked. "When you met me in Cranesmuir?"

She shook her head, the strands of cream-white hair coming loose from their pins and sliding down her neck. She poked haphazardly at her knot, still surveying me with interest.

"Not at the first, no. Though sure and I thought there was a great strangeness about ye—not that I was the only one to think that. Ye didna come through the stones prepared, did ye? Not on purpose, I mean?"

I bit back the words, "Not that time," and said instead, "No, it was an accident. You came on purpose, though—from 1967?"

She nodded, studying me intently. The thickened flesh between her brows was creased, and the crease deepened slightly as she looked at me.

"Aye—to help Prince *Tearlach*." Her mouth twisted to one side, as though she tasted something bad, and quite suddenly, she turned her head and spat. The globule of saliva hit the polished wooden floor with an audible *plop*.

"An gealtaire salach Atailteach!" she said. "Filthy Italian coward!" Her eyes darkened and shone with no pleasant light. "Had I known, I should have made my way to Rome and killed him, while there was time. His brother Henry might ha' been no better, though—a ballock-less, sniveling priest, that one. Not that

it made a difference. After Culloden, any Stuart would be as use-less as"another.''

She sighed, and shifted her bulk, the rattan of the chair creaking beneath her. She waved a hand impatiently, dismissing the Stuarts.

"Still, that's done with for now. Ye came by accident—walked through the stones near the date of a Fire Feast, did ye? That's how it usually happens."

"Yes," I said, startled. "I came through on Beltane. But what do you mean, 'usually happens'? Have you met a great many others—like . . . us?" I ended hesitantly.

She shook her head rather absently. "Not many." She seemed to be pondering something, though perhaps it was only the ab-sence of her refreshments; she picked up the silver bell and rang it violently.

"Damn that Clotilda! Like us?" she said, returning to the ques-tion at hand. "No, I haven't. Only one besides you, that I ken. Ye could ha' knocked me over wi' a feather, when I saw the wee scar on your arm, and kent ye for one like myself." She touched the great swell of her own upper arm, where the small vaccination scar lay hidden beneath the puff of white muslin. She tilted her head in that bird-like way again, surveying me with one bright green eye.

"No, when I said that's how it usually happens, I meant, judg-ing from the stories. Folk who disappear in fairy rings and the stone circles, I mean. They usually walk through near Beltane or Samhain; a few near the Sun Feasts—Midsummer's Day or the winter solstice."

"That's what the list was!" I said suddenly, reminded of the gray notebook I had left with Roger Wakefield. "You had a list of dates and initials—nearly two hundred of them. I didn't know what they were, but I saw that the dates were mostly in late April or early May, or near the end of October."

"Aye, that's right." She nodded, eyes still fixed on me in spec-ulation. "So ye found my wee book? Is that how ye knew to come and look for me on Craigh na Dun? It *was* you, no? That shouted my name, just before I stepped through the stones?"

"Gillian," I said, and saw her pupils widen at the name that had once been hers, though her face stayed smooth. "Gillian Edgars. Yes, it was me. I didn't know if you saw me in the dark." I could see in memory the night-black circle of stones—and in the center, the blazing bonfire, and the figure of a slim girl standing by it, pale hair flying in the heat of the fire.

"I didn't see ye," she said. " 'Twas only later, when I heard ye call out at the witch trial and thought I'd heard your voice before. And then, when I saw the mark on your arm . . ." She shrugged massively, the muslin tight across her shoulders as she settled back. "Who was with ye, that night?" she asked curiously. "There were two I saw—a bonnie dark lad, and a girl."

She closed her eyes, concentrating, then opened them again to stare at me. "Later on, I thought I kent her—but I couldna put a name to her, though I could swear I'd seen the face. Who was she?"

"Mistress Duncan? Or is it Mistress Abernathy, now?" Jamie interrupted, stepping forward and bowing to her formally. The first shock of her appearance was fading, but he was still pale, his cheekbones prominent under the stretched skin of his face.

She glanced at him, then looked again, as though noticing him for the first time.

"Well, and if it's no the wee fox cub!" she said, looking amused. She looked him carefully up and down, noting every detail of his appearance with interest.

"Grown to a bonny man, have ye no?" she said. She leaned back in the chair, which creaked loudly under her weight, and squinted appraisingly at him. "You've the look of the MacKenzies about ye, laddie. Ye always did, but now you're older, you've the look of both your uncles in your face."

"I am sure both Dougal and Colum would be pleased ye'd remember them so well." Jamie's eyes were fixed on her as intently as hers on him. He had never liked her—and was unlikely to change his opinion now—but he could not afford to antagonize her; not if she had Ian here somewhere.

The arrival of the tea interrupted whatever reply she might have made. Jamie moved to my side, and sat with me on the sofa, while Geilie carefully poured the tea and handed us each a cup, behaving exactly like a conventional hostess at a tea party. As though wishing to preserve this illusion, she offered the sugar bowl and milk jug, and sat back to make light conversation.

"If ye dinna mind my asking, Mrs. Abernathy," Jamie said, "how did ye come to this place?" Politely left unspoken was the larger question—*How did you escape being burned as a witch?*

She laughed, lowering her long lashes coquettishly over her eyes.

''Well, and ye'll maybe recall I was wi' child, back at Cranesmuir?''

''I seem to recall something of the sort.'' Jamie took a sip of his tea, the tips of his ears turning slightly pink. He had cause to remember that, all right; she had torn off her clothes in the midst of the witch trial, disclosing the secret bulge that would save her life—at least temporarily.

A small pink tongue poked out and delicately skimmed the tea droplets from her upper lip.

''Have ye had children yourself?'' she asked, cocking an eyebrow at me.

''I have.''

''Terrible chore, isn't it? Dragging about like a mud-caked sow, and then being ripped apart for the sake of something looks like a drowned rat.'' She shook her head, making a low noise of disgust in her throat. ''The beauty o' motherhood, is it? Still, I should not complain, I suppose—the wee ratling saved my life for me. And wretched as childbirth is, it's better than being burnt at the stake.''

''I'd suppose so,'' I said, ''though not having tried the latter, I couldn't say for sure.''

Geillis choked in her tea, spraying brown droplets over the front of her dress. She mopped at them carelessly, eyeing me with amusement.

''Well, I've not done it either, but I've seen them burn, poppet. And I think perhaps even lyin' in a muddy hole watching your belly grow is better than that.''

''They kept you in the thieves' hole all the time?'' The silver spoon was cool in my hand, but my palm grew sweaty at the memory of the thieves' hole in Cranesmuir. I had spent three days there with Geillis Duncan, accused as a witch. How long had she stayed there?

''Three months,'' she said, staring meditatively into her tea. ''Three mortal months of frozen feet and crawling vermin, stinking scraps of food and the grave-smell clinging to my skin day and night.''

She looked up then, mouth twisting in bitter amusement. ''But I bore the child in style, at the end. When my pains began, they took me from the hole—little chance I'd run then, aye?—and the babe was born in my own old bedroom; in the fiscal's house.''

Her eyes were slightly clouded, and I wondered whether the liquid in her glass was entirely tea.

"I had diamond-paned windows, do ye recall? All in shades of purple and green and white—the finest house in the village.'' She smiled reminiscently. ''They gave me the bairn to hold, and the green light fell over his face. He looked as though he was drowned indeed. I thought he should be cold to the touch, like a corpse, but he wasn't; he was warm. Warm as his father's balls.'' She laughed suddenly, an ugly sound.

"Why are men such fools? Ye can lead them anywhere by the cock—for a while. Then give them a son and ye have them by the balls again. But it's all ye are to them, whether they're coming in or going out—a cunt.''

She was leaning back in her chair. At this, she spread her thighs wide, and hoisted her glass in ironic toast above her pubic bone, squinting down across the swelling bulge of belly.

"Well, here's to it, I say! Most powerful thing in the world. The niggers know that, at least.'' She took a deep, careless swig of her drink. ''They carve wee idols, all belly and cunt and breasts. Same as men do where we came from—you and I.'' She squinted at me, teeth bared in amusement. ''Seen the dirty mags men buy under the counters then, aye?''

The bloodshot green eyes swiveled to Jamie. ''And you'll know the pictures and the books the men pass about among themselves in Paris now, won't ye, fox? It's all the same.'' She waved a hand and drank again, deeply. ''The only difference is the niggers have the decency to worship it.''

"Verra perceptive of them,'' Jamie said calmly. He was sitting back in his chair, long legs stretched out in apparent relaxation, but I could see the tension in the fingers of the hand that gripped his own cup. ''And how d'ye ken the pictures men look at in Paris, Mistress—Abernathy, is it now?''

She might be tipsy, but was by no means fuddled. She looked up sharply at the tone of his voice, and gave him a twisted smile.

"Oh, Mistress Abernathy will do well enough. When I lived in Paris, I had another name—Madame Melisande Robicheaux. Like that one? I thought it a bit grand, but your uncle Dougal gave it me, so I kept it—out of sentiment.''

My free hand curled into a fist, out of sight in the folds of my skirt. I had heard of Madame Melisande, when we lived in Paris. Not a part of society, she had had some fame as a seer of the future; ladies of the court consulted her in deepest secrecy, for advice on their love lives, their investments, and their pregnancies.

"I imagine you could have told the ladies some interesting things," I said dryly.

Her laugh this time was truly amused. "Oh, I could, indeed! Seldom did, though. Folk don't usually pay for the truth, ye know. Sometimes, though—did ye ken that Jean-Paul Marat's mother meant to name her bairn Rudolphe? I told her I thought Rudolphe was ill-omened. I wondered now and then about that—would he grow up a revolutionary with a name like Rudolphe, or would he take it all out in writing poems, instead? Ever think that, fox—that a name might make a difference?" Her eyes were fixed on Jamie, green glass.

"Often," he said, and set down his cup. "It was Dougal got ye away from Cranesmuir, then?"

She nodded, stifling a small belch. "Aye. He came to take the babe—alone, for fear someone would find out he was the father, aye? I wouldna let it go, though. And when he came near to wrest it from me—why, I snatched the dirk from his belt and pressed it to the child's throat." A small smile of satisfaction at the memory curved her lovely lips.

"Told him I'd kill it, sure, unless he swore on his brother's life and his own soul to get me safe away."

"And he believed you?" I felt mildly ill at the thought of any mother holding a knife to the throat of her newborn child, even in pretense.

Her gaze swiveled back to me. "Oh, yes," she said softly, and the smile widened. "He knew me, did Dougal."

Sweating, even in the chill of December, and unable to take his eyes off the tiny face of his sleeping son, Dougal had agreed.

"When he leaned over me to take the child, I thought of plunging the dirk into his own throat instead," she said, reminiscently. "But it would have been a good deal harder to get away by myself, so I didn't."

Jamie's expression didn't change, but he picked up his tea and took a deep swallow.

Dougal had summoned the locksman, John MacRae, and the

church sexton, and by means of discreet bribery, ensured that the hooded figure dragged on a hurdle to the pitch barrel next morning would not be that of Geillis Duncan.

"I thought they'd use straw, maybe," she said, "but he was a cleverer man than that. Auld Grannie Joan MacKenzie had died three days before, and was meant to be burying that same afternoon. A few rocks in the coffin and the lid nailed down tight, and Bob's your uncle, eh? A real body, fine for burning." She laughed, and gulped the last swallow of her drink.

"Not everyone's seen their own funeral; fewer still ha' seen their own execution, aye?"

It had been the dead of winter, and the small grove of rowan trees outside the village stood bare, drifted with their own dead leaves, the dried red berries showing here and there on the ground like spots of blood.

It was a cloudy day, with the promise of sleet or snow, but the whole village turned out nonetheless; a witch-burning was not an event to be missed. The village priest, Father Bain, had died himself three months before, of fever brought on by a festering sore, but a new priest had been imported for the occasion from a village nearby. Perfuming his way with a censer held before him, the priest had come down the path to the grove, chanting the service for the dead. Behind him came the locksman and his two assistants, dragging the hurdle and its black-robed burden.

"I expect Grannie Joan would have been pleased," Geilie said, white teeth gleaming at the vision. "She couldna have expected more nor four or five people to her burying—as it was, she had the whole village, and the incense and special prayers to boot!"

MacRae had untied the body and carried it, lolling, to the barrel of pitch ready waiting.

"The court granted me the mercy to be weirrit before the burning," Geillis explained ironically. "So they expected the body to be dead—no difficulty there, if I was strangled already. The only thing anyone might ha' seen was that Grannie Joan weighed half what I did, newly delivered as I was, but no one seemed to notice she was light in MacRae's arms."

"You were *there*?" I said.

She nodded smugly. "Oh, aye. Well muffled in a cloak—everyone was, because o' the weather—but I wouldna have missed it."

As the priest finished his last prayer against the evils of enchantment, MacRae had taken the pine torch from his assistant and stepped forward.

"God, omit not this woman from Thy covenant, and the many evils that she in the body committed," he had said, and flung the fire into the pitch.

"It was faster than I thought it would be," Geillis said, sounding mildly surprised. "A great *whoosh!* of fire—there was a blast of hot air and a cheer from the crowd, and naught to be seen but the flames, shooting up high enough to singe the rowan branches overhead."

The fire had subsided within a minute, though, and the dark figure within was clear enough to be seen through the pale daylight flames. The hood and the hair had burned away with the first scorching rush, and the face itself was burned beyond recognition. A few moments more, and the clean dark shapes of the bones emerged from the melted flesh, an airy superstructure rising above the charring barrel.

"Only great empty holes where her eyes had been," she said. The moss-green eyes turned toward me, clouded by memory. "I thought perhaps she was looking at me. But then the skull exploded, and it was all over, and folk began to come away—all except a few who stayed in hopes of picking up a bit of bone as a keepsake."

She rose and went unsteadily to the small table near the window. She picked up the silver bell and rang it, hard.

"Aye," she said, her back turned to us. "Childbirth is maybe easier."

"So Dougal got ye away to France," Jamie said. The fingers of his right hand twitched slightly. "How came ye here to the West Indies?"

"Oh, that was later," she said carelessly. "After Culloden." She turned then, and smiled from Jamie to me.

"And what might bring the two of ye here to this place? Surely not the pleasure of my company?"

I glanced at Jamie, seeing the slight tensing of his back as he sat up straighter. His face stayed calm, though, only his eyes bright with wariness.

"We've come to seek a young kinsman of mine," he said. "My nephew, Ian Murray. We've some reason to think he is indentured here."

Geilie's pale brows rose high, making soft ridges in her forehead.

"Ian Murray?" she said, and shook her head in puzzlement. "I've no indentured whites at all, here. No whites, come to that. The only free man on the place is the overseer, and he's what they call a *griffon;* one-quarter black."

Unlike me, Geillis Duncan was a very good liar. Impossible to tell, from her expression of mild interest, whether she had ever heard the name Ian Murray before. But lying she was, and I knew it.

Jamie knew it, too; the expression that flashed through his eyes was not disappointment, but fury, quickly suppressed.

"Indeed?" he said politely. "And are ye not fearful, then, alone wi' your slaves here, so far from town?"

"Oh, no. Not at all."

She smiled broadly at him, then lifted her double chin and waggled it gently in the direction of the terrace behind him. I turned my head, and saw that the French door was filled from jamb to doorpost with an immense black man, several inches taller than Jamie, from whose rolled-up shirt sleeves protruded arms like tree trunks, knotted with muscle.

"Meet Hercules," Geilie said, with a tiny laugh. "He has a twin brother, too."

"Named Atlas, by chance?" I asked, with an edge to my voice.

"You guessed! Is she no the clever one, eh, fox?" She winked conspiratorially at Jamie, the rounded flesh of her cheek wobbling with the movement. The light caught her from the side as she turned her head, and I saw the red spiderwebs of tiny broken capillaries that netted her jowls.

Hercule took no note of this, or of anything else. His broad face was slack and dull, and there was no life in the deep-sunk eyes beneath the bony brow ridge. It gave me a very uneasy feeling to look at him, and not only because of his threatening size; looking at him was like passing by a haunted house, where something lurks behind blind windows.

"That will do, Hercule; ye can go back to work now." Geilie picked up the silver bell and tinkled it gently, once. Without a word, the giant turned and lumbered off the veranda. "I have no fear o' the slaves," she explained. "They're afraid o' me, for they think I'm a witch. Verra funny, considering, is it not?'' Her eyes twinkled behind little pouches of fat.

"Geilie—that man.'' I hesitated, feeling ridiculous in asking such a question. "He's not a—a zombie?''

She laughed delightedly at that, clapping her hands together.

"Christ, a zombie? Jesus, Claire!'' She chortled with glee, a bright pink rising from throat to hair roots.

"Well, I'll tell ye, he's no verra bright,'' she said at last, still gasping and wheezing. "But he's no dead, either!'' and went off into further gales of laughter.

Jamie stared at me, puzzled.

"Zombie?''

"Never mind,'' I said, my face nearly as pink as Geilie's. "How many slaves have you got here?'' I asked, wanting to change the subject.

"Hee hee,'' she said, winding down into giggles. "Oh, a hundred or so. It's no such a big place. Only three hundred acres in cane, and a wee bit of coffee on the upper slopes.''

She pulled a lace-trimmed handkerchief from her pocket and patted her damp face, sniffing a bit as she regained her composure. I could feel, rather than see, Jamie's tension. I was sure he was as convinced as I that Geilie knew something about Ian Murray—if nothing else, she had betrayed no surprise whatever at our appearance. Someone had told her about us, and that someone could only be Ian.

The thought of threatening a woman to extract information wasn't one that would come naturally to Jamie, but it would to me. Unfortunately, the presence of the twin pillars of Hercules had put a stop to that line of thought. The next best idea seemed to be to search the house and grounds for any trace of the boy. Three hundred acres was a fair piece of ground, but if he was on the property, he would likely be in or near the buildings—the house, the sugar refinery, or the slave quarters.

I came out of my thoughts to realize that Geilie had asked me a question.

"What's that?''

"I said,'' she repeated patiently, "that ye had a great deal of talent for the healing when I knew ye in Scotland; you'll maybe know more now?''

"I expect I might.'' I looked her over cautiously. Did she want my skill for herself? She wasn't healthy; a glance at her mottled complexion and the dark circles beneath her eyes was enough to show that. But was she actively ill?

"Not for me," she said, seeing my look. "Not just now, anyway. I've two slaves gone sick. Maybe ye'd be so kind as to look at them?"

I glanced at Jamie, who gave me the shadow of a nod. It was a chance to get into the slave quarters and look for Ian.

"I saw when we came in as ye had a bit of trouble wi' your sugar press," he said, rising abruptly. He gave Geilie a cool nod. "Perhaps I shall have a look at it, whilst you and my wife tend the sick." Without waiting for an answer, he took off his coat and hung it on the peg by the door. He went out by the veranda, rolling up the sleeves of his shirt, sunlight glinting on his hair.

"A handy sort, is he?" Geilie looked after him, amused. "My husband Barnabas was that sort—couldna keep his hands off any kind of machine. Or off the slave girls, either," she added. "Come along, the sick ones are back o' the kitchen."

The kitchen was in a separate small building of its own, connected to the house by a breezeway covered with blooming jasmine. Walking through it was like floating through a cloud of perfume, surrounded by a hum of bees loud enough to be felt on the skin, like the low drone of a bagpipe.

"Ever been stung?" Geillis swiped casually at a low-flying furry body, batting it out of the air.

"Now and then."

"So have I," she said. "Any number of times, and nothing worse than a red welt on my skin to show for it. One of these wee buggers stung one o' the kitchen slaves last spring, though, and the wench swelled up like a toad and died, right before my eyes!" She glanced at me, eyes wide and mocking. "Did wonders for my reputation, I can tell ye. The rest o' the slaves put it about I'd witched the lass; put a spell on her to kill her for burning the sponge cake. I havena had so much as a scorched pot, since." Shaking her head, she waved away another bee.

While appalled at her callousness, I was somewhat relieved by the story. Perhaps the other gossip I had heard at the Governor's ball had as little foundation in fact.

I paused, looking out through the jasmine's lacy leaves at the cane fields below. Jamie was in the clearing by the sugar press, looking up at the gigantic crossbars of the machine while a man I assumed to be the overseer pointed and explained. As I watched, he said something, gesturing, and the overseer nodded emphatically, waving his hands in voluble reply. If I didn't find any trace of Ian in the kitchen quarters, perhaps Jamie would learn something from the overseer. Despite Geilie's denials, every instinct I had insisted that the boy was here—somewhere.

There was no sign of him in the kitchen itself; only three or four women, kneading bread and snapping peas, who looked up curiously as we came through. I caught the eye of one young woman, and nodded and smiled at her; perhaps I would have a chance to come back and talk, later. Her eyes widened in surprise, and she bent her head at once, eyes on the bowl of peapods in her lap. I saw her steal a quick glance at me as we crossed the long room, and noticed that she balanced the bowl in front of the small bulge of an early pregnancy.

The first sick slave was in a small pantry off the kitchen itself, lying on a pallet laid under shelves stacked high with gauze-wrapped cheeses. The patient, a young man in his twenties, sat up blinking at the sudden ray of light when I opened the door.

"What's the trouble with him?" I knelt down beside the man and touched his skin. Warm, damp, no apparent fever. He didn't seem in any particular distress, merely blinking sleepily as I examined him.

"He has a worm."

I glanced at Geilie in surprise. From what I had seen and heard so far in the islands, I thought it likely that at least three-quarters of the black population—and not a few of the whites—suffered from internal parasites. Nasty and debilitating as these could be, though, most were actively threatening only to the very young and the very old.

"Probably a lot more than one," I said. I pushed the slave gently onto his back and began to palpate his stomach. The spleen was tender and slightly enlarged—also a common finding here—but I felt no suspicious masses in the abdomen that might indicate a major intestinal infestation. "He seems moderately healthy; why have you got him in here in the dark?"

As though in answer to my question, the slave suddenly wrenched himself away from my hand, let out a piercing scream, and rolled up into a ball. Rolling and unrolling himself like a yo-yo, he reached the wall and began to bang his head against it, still screaming. Then, as suddenly as the fit had come on, it passed off, and the young man sank back onto the pallet, panting heavily and soaked with sweat.

"Jesus H. Roosevelt Christ," I said. "What was *that*?"

"A *loa-loa* worm," Geilie said, looking amused at my reaction. "They live in the eyeballs, just under the lining. They cross back and forth, from one eye to the other, and when they go across the bridge o' the nose, I'm told it's rather painful." She nodded at the slave, still quivering slightly on his pallet.

"The dark keeps them from moving so much," she explained. "The fellow from Andros who told me about them says ye must catch them when they've just come in one eye, for they're right near the surface, and ye can lift them out with a big darning needle. If ye wait, they go deeper, and ye canna get them." She turned back to the kitchen and shouted for a light.

"Here, I brought the needle, just in case." She groped in the bag at her waist and drew out a square of felt, with a three-inch steel needle thrust through it, which she extended helpfully to me.

"Are you out of your mind?" I stared at her, appalled.

"No. Did ye not say ye were a good healer?" she asked reasonably.

"I am, but—" I glanced at the slave, hesitated, then took the candle one of the kitchenmaids was holding out to me.

"Bring me some brandy, and a small sharp knife," I said. "Dip the knife—and the needle—in the brandy, then hold the tip in a flame for a moment. Let it cool, but don't touch it." As I spoke, I was gently pulling up one eyelid. The man's eye looked up at me, an oddly irregular, blotched brown iris in a bloodshot sclera the yellow of heavy cream. I searched carefully, bringing the candle flame close enough to shrink the pupil, then drawing it away, but saw nothing there.

I tried the other eye, and nearly dropped the candle. Sure enough, there was a small, transparent filament, *moving* under the conjunctiva. I gagged slightly at the sight, but controlled myself, and reached for the freshly sterilized knife, still holding back the eyelid.

"Take him by the shoulders," I said to Geilie. "Don't let him move, or I may blind him."

The surgery itself was horrifying to contemplate, but surprisingly simple to perform. I made one quick, small incision along the inside corner of the conjunctiva, lifted it slightly with the tip of the needle, and as the worm undulated lazily across the open field, I slipped the tip of the needle under the body and drew it out, neat as a loop of yarn.

Repressing a shudder of distaste, I flicked the worm away. It hit the wall with a tiny wet splat! and vanished in the shadows under the cheese.

There was no blood; after a brief debate with myself, I decided to leave it to the man's own tear ducts to irrigate the incision. That would have to be left to heal by itself; I had no fine sutures, and the wound was small enough not to need more than a stitch or two in any case.

I tied a clean pad of cloth over the closed eye with a bandage round the head, and sat back, reasonably pleased with my first foray into tropical medicine.

"Fine," I said, pushing back my hair. "Where's the other one?"

The next patient was in a shed outside the kitchen, dead. I squatted next to the body, that of a middle-aged man with grizzled hair, feeling both pity and outrage.

The cause of death was more than obvious: a strangulated hernia. The loop of twisted, gangrenous bowel protruded from one side of the belly, the stretched skin over it already tinged with green, though the body itself was still nearly as warm as life. An expression of agony was fixed on the broad features, and the limbs were still contorted, giving an unfortunately accurate witness to just what sort of death it had been.

"Why did you wait?" I stood up, glaring at Geilie. "For God's sake, you kept me drinking tea and chatting, while *this* was going on? He's been dead less than an hour, but he must have been in trouble a long time since—days! Why didn't you bring me out here at once?"

"He seemed pretty far gone this morning," she said, not at all disturbed by my agitation. She shrugged. "I've seen them so before; I didna think you could do anything much. It didna seem worth hurrying."

I choked back further recrimination. She was right; I could have operated, had I come sooner, but the chances of it doing any good were slim to nonexistent. The hernia repair was something I might have managed, even with such difficult conditions; after all, that was nothing more than pushing back the bowel protrusion and pulling the ruptured layers of abdominal muscle back together with sutures; infection was the only real danger. But once the loop of escaped intestine had twisted, so that the blood supply was cut off and the contents began to putrefy, the man was doomed.

But to allow the man to die here in this stuffy shed, alone . . . well, perhaps he would not have found the presence of one white woman more or less a comfort, in any case. Still, I felt an obscure sense of failure; the same I always felt in the presence of death. I wiped my hands slowly on a brandy-soaked cloth, mastering my feelings.

One to the good, one to the bad—and Ian still to be found.

"Since I'm here now, perhaps I'd best have a look at the rest of your slaves," I suggested. "An ounce of prevention, you know."

"Oh, they're well enough." Geilie waved a careless hand. "Still, if ye want to take the time, you're welcome. Later, though; I've a visitor coming this afternoon, and I want to talk more with ye, first. Come back to the house, now—someone will take care o' this." A brief nod disposed of "this," the slave's contorted body. She linked her arm in mine, urging me out of the shed and back toward the kitchen with soft thrustings of her weight.

In the kitchen, I detached myself, motioning toward the pregnant slave, now on her hands and knees, scrubbing the hearthstones.

"You go along; I want to have a quick look at this girl. She looks a bit toxic to me—you don't want her to miscarry."

Geilie gave me a curious glance, but then shrugged.

"She's foaled twice with no trouble, but you're the doctor. Aye, if that's your notion of fun, go ahead. Don't take too long, though; that parson said he'd come at four o'clock."

I made some pretense of examining the bewildered woman, until Geilie's draperies had disappeared into the breezeway.

"Look," I said. "I'm looking for a young white boy named Ian; I'm his aunt. Do you know where he might be?"

The girl—she couldn't be more than seventeen or eighteen—looked startled. She blinked, and darted a glance at one of the older women, who had quit her own work and come across the room to see what was going on.

"No, ma'am," the older woman said, shaking her head. "No white boys here. None at all."

"No, ma'am," the girl obediently echoed. "We don' know nothin' 'bout your boy." But she hadn't said that at first, and her eyes wouldn't meet mine.

The older woman had been joined now by the other two kitchen-maids, coming to buttress her. I was surrounded by an impenetrable wall of bland ignorance, and no way to break through it. At the same time, I was aware of a current running among the women —a feeling of common warning; of wariness and secrecy. It might be only the natural reaction to the sudden appearance of a white stranger in their domain—or it might be something more.

I couldn't take longer; Geilie would be coming back to look for me. I fumbled quickly in my pocket, and pulled out a silver florin, which I pressed into the girl's hand.

"If you should see Ian, tell him that his uncle is here to find him." Not waiting for an answer, I turned and hurried out of the kitchen.

I glanced down toward the sugar mill as I passed through the breezeway. The sugar press stood abandoned, the oxen grazing placidly in the long grass at the edge of the clearing. There was no sign of Jamie or the overseer; had he come back to the house?

I came through the French windows into the salon, and stopped short. Geilie sat in her wicker chair, Jamie's coat across the arm, and the photographs of Brianna spread over her lap. She heard my step and looked up, one pale brow arched over an acid smile.

"What a pretty lassie, to be sure. What's her name?"

"Brianna." My lips felt stiff. I walked slowly toward her, fighting the urge to snatch the pictures from her hands and run.

"Looks a great deal like her father, doesn't she? I thought she seemed familiar, that tall red-haired lass I saw that night on Craigh na Dun. He *is* her father, no?" She inclined her head toward the door where Jamie had vanished.

"Yes. Give them to me." It made no difference; she had seen the pictures already. Still, I couldn't stand to see her thick white fingers cupping Brianna's face.

Her mouth twitched as though she meant to refuse, but she tapped them neatly into a square and handed them to me without demur. I held them against my chest for a moment, not knowing what to do with them, then thrust them back into the pocket of my skirt.

"Sit ye down, Claire. The coffee's come." She nodded toward the small table, and the chair alongside. Her eyes followed me as I moved to it, alive with calculation.

She gestured for me to pour the coffee for both of us, and took her own cup without words. We sipped silently for a few moments. The cup trembled in my hands, spilling hot liquid across my wrist. I put it down, wiping my hand on my skirt, wondering in some dim recess of my mind why I should be afraid.

"Twice," she said suddenly. She looked at me with something akin to awe. "Sweet Christ Jesus, ye went through *twice*! Or no— *three* times, it must have been, for here ye are now." She shook her head, marveling, never taking her bright green eyes from my face.

"How?" she asked. "How could ye do it so many times, and live?"

"I don't know." I saw the look of hard skepticism flash across her face, and answered it, defensively. "I don't! I just—went."

"Was it not the same for you?" The green eyes had narrowed into slits of concentration. "What was it like, there between? Did ye not feel the terror? And the noise, fit to split your skull and spill your brains?"

"Yes, it was like that." I didn't want to talk about it; didn't even like to think of the time-passage. I had blocked it deliberately from my mind, the roar of death and dissolution and the voices of chaos that urged me to join them.

"Did ye have blood to protect you, or stones? I wouldna think ye'd the nerve for blood—but maybe I'm wrong. For surely ye're stronger than I thought, to have done it three times, and lived through it."

"Blood?" I shook my head, confused. "No. Nothing. I told you —I . . . went. That's all." Then I remembered the night she had gone through the stones in 1968; the blaze of fire on Craigh na Dun, and the twisted, blackened shape in the center of that fire. "Greg Edgars," I said. The name of her first husband. "You didn't just kill him because he found you and tried to stop you, did you? He was—"

"The blood, aye." She was watching me, intent. "I didna think it could be done at all, the crossing—not without the blood." She sounded faintly amazed. "The auld ones—they always used the blood. That and the fire. They built great wicker cages, filled wi' their captives, and set them alight in the circles. I thought that was how they opened the passage."

My hands and my lips felt cold, and I picked up the cup to warm them. Where in the name of God was Jamie?

"And ye didna use stones, either?"

I shook my head. "What stones?"

She looked at me for a moment, debating whether to tell me. Her little pink tongue flicked over her lip, and then she nodded, deciding. With a small grunt, she heaved herself up from the chair and went toward the great hearth at the far end of the room, beckoning me to follow.

She knelt, with surprising grace for one of her figure, and pressed a greenish stone set into the mantelpiece, a foot or so above the hearth. It moved slightly, and there was a soft *click!* as one of the hearth slates rose smoothly out of its mortared setting.

"Spring mechanism," Geilie explained, lifting the slate carefully and setting it aside. "A Danish fellow named Leiven from St. Croix made it for me."

She reached into the cavity beneath and drew out a wooden box, about a foot long. There were pale brown stains on the smooth wood, and it looked swollen and split, as though it had been immersed in seawater at some time. I bit my lip hard at its appearance, and hoped my face didn't give anything away. If I had had any doubts about Ian being here, they had vanished—for here, unless I was very much mistaken, was the silkies' treasure. Fortunately, Geilie wasn't looking at me, but at the box.

"I learned about the stones from an Indian—not a red Indian, a Hindoo from Calcutta," she explained. "He came to me, looking for thornapple, and he told me about how to make medicines from the gemstones."

I looked over my shoulder for Jamie, but there was no sign of him. Where the hell was he? Had he found Ian, somewhere on the plantation?

"Ye can get the powdered stones from a London apothecary," she was saying, frowning slightly as she pushed at the sliding lid. "But they're mostly poor quality, and the *bhasmas* doesn't work so well. Best to have a stone at least of the second quality—what they call a *nagina* stone. That's a goodish-sized stone that's been polished. A stone of the first quality is faceted, and unflawed for preference, but most folk canna afford to burn those to ash. The ashes of the stone are the *bhasmas*," she explained, turning to look up at me. "That's what ye use in the medicines. Here, can ye pry this damn thing loose? It's been spoilt in seawater, and the locking bit swells whenever the weather's damp—which it is all the time, this season of the year," she added, making a face over her shoulder at the clouds rolling in over the bay, far below.

She thrust the box into my hands and rose heavily to her feet, grunting with the effort.

It was a Chinese puzzle-box, I saw; a fairly simple one, with a small sliding panel that unlocked the main lid. The problem was that the smaller panel had swollen, sticking in its slot.

"It's bad luck to break one," Geilie observed, watching my attempts. "Else I'd just smash the thing and be done with it. Here, maybe this will help." She produced a small mother-of-pearl pen-knife from the recesses of her gown and handed it to me, then went to the window ledge and rang another of her silver bells.

I pried gently upward with the blade of the knife. I felt it catch in the wood, and wiggled it gingerly. Little by little, the small rectangle of wood edged out of its place, until I could get hold of it between thumb and forefinger and pull it all the way loose.

"There you go," I said, handing her back the box with some reluctance. It felt heavy, and there was an unmistakable metallic chinking as I tilted it.

"Thanks." As she took it, the black servingmaid came in through the far door. Geilie turned to order the girl to bring a tray of fresh tarts, and I saw that she had slipped the box between the folds of her skirts, hiding it.

"Nosy creatures," she said, frowning toward the departing maid's back as the girl passed through the door. "One of the difficulties wi' slaves; it's hard to have secrets." She put the box on the table, and pushed at the top; with a small, sharp *skreek!* of protest, the lid slid back.

She reached into the box and drew out her closed hand. She smiled mischievously at me, saying, "Little Jackie Horner sat in the corner, eating her Christmas pie. She put in her thumb, and pulled out a plum"—she opened her hand with a flourish—"and said 'What a good girl am I!' "

I had been expecting them, of course, but had no difficulty in looking impressed anyway. The reality of a gem is both more immediate and more startling than its description. Six or seven of them flashed and glimmered in her palm, flaming fire and frozen ice, the gleam of blue water in the sun, and a great gold stone like the eye of a lurking tiger.

Without meaning to, I drew near enough to look down into the well of her hand, staring with fascination. "Big enough," Jamie had described them as being, with a characteristic Scottish talent for understatement. Well, smaller than a breadbox, I supposed.

"I got them for the money, to start," Geilie was saying, prodding the stones with satisfaction. "Because they were easier to carry than a great weight of gold or silver, I mean; I didna think then what other use they might have."

"What, as *bhasmas*?" The idea of burning any of those glowing things to ash seemed a sacrilege.

"Oh, no, not these." Her hand closed on the stones, dipped into her pocket, and back into the box for more. A small shower of liquid fire dropped into her pocket, and she patted it affectionately. "No, I've a lot o' the smaller stones for that. These are for something else."

She eyed me speculatively, then jerked her head toward the door at the end of the room.

"Come along up to my workroom," she said. "I've a few things there you'll maybe be interested to see."

"Interested" was putting it mildly, I thought.

It was a long, light-filled room, with a counter down one side. Bunches of drying herbs hung from hooks overhead and lay on gauze-covered drying racks along the inner wall. Drawered cabinets and cupboards covered the rest of the wall space, and there was a small glass-fronted bookcase at the end of the room.

The room gave me a mild sense of déjà-vu; after a moment, I realized that it was because it strongly resembled Geilie's workroom in the village of Cranesmuir, in the house of her first husband—no, second, I corrected myself, remember the flaming body of Greg Edgars.

"How many times have you been married?" I asked curiously. She had begun building her fortune with her second husband, procurator fiscal of the district where they lived, forging his signature in order to divert money to her own use, and then murdering him. Successful with this modus operandi, I imagined she had tried it again; she was a creature of habit, was Geilie Duncan.

She paused a moment to count up. "Oh, five, I think. Since I came here," she added casually.

"Five?" I said, a little faintly. Not just a habit, it seemed; a positive addiction.

"A verra unhealthy atmosphere for Englishmen it is in the tropics," she said, and smiled slyly at me. "Fevers, ulcers, festering stomachs; any little thing will carry them off." She had evidently been mindful of her oral hygiene; her teeth were still very good.

She reached out and lightly caressed a small bottle that stood on the lowest shelf. It wasn't labeled, but I had seen crude white arsenic before. On the whole, I was glad I hadn't taken any food.

"Oh, you'll be interested in this," she said, spying a jar on an upper shelf. Grunting slightly as she stood on tiptoe, she reached it down and handed it to me.

It contained a very coarse powder, evidently a mixture of several substances, brown, yellow, and black, flecked with shreds of a semitranslucent material.

"What's this?"

"Zombie poison," she said, and laughed. "I thought ye'd like to see."

"Oh?" I said coldly. "I thought you told me there was no such thing."

"No," she corrected, still smiling. "I told ye Hercule wasn't dead; and he's not." She took the jar from me and replaced it on the shelf. "But there's no denying that he's a good bit more manageable if he's had a dose of this stuff once a week, mixed with his grain."

"What the hell is it?"

She shrugged, offhanded. "A bit of this and a bit of that. The main thing seems to be a kind of fish—a little square thing wi' spots; verra funny-looking. Ye take the skin and dry it, and the liver as well. But there are a few other things ye put in with it—I wish I kent what," she added.

"You don't know what's in it?" I stared at her. "Didn't you make it?"

"No. I had a cook," Geilie said, "or at least they sold him to me as a cook, but damned if I'd feel safe eating a thing he turned

out of the kitchen, the sly black devil. He was a *houngan,*
though.''

''A what?''

''Houngan is what the blacks call one of their medicine-priests;
though to be quite right about it, I believe Ishmael said his sort of
black called him an *oniseegun,* or somesuch.''

''Ishmael, hm?'' I licked my dry lips. ''Did he come with that
name?''

''Oh, no. He had some heathen name wi' six syllables, and the
man who sold him called him 'Jimmy'—the auctioneers call all
the bucks Jimmy. I named him Ishmael, because of the story the
seller told me about him.''

Ishmael had been taken from a barracoon on the Gold Coast of
Africa, one of a shipment of six hundred slaves from the villages
of Nigeria and Ghana, stowed between decks of the slave ship
Persephone, bound for Antigua. Coming through the Caicos Passage, the *Persephone* had run into a sudden squall, and been run
aground on Hogsty Reef, off the island of Great Inagua. The ship
had broken up, with barely time for the crew to escape in the
ship's boats.

The slaves, chained and helpless between decks, had all
drowned. All but one man who had earlier been taken from the
hold to assist as a galley mate, both messboys having died of the
pox en route from Africa. This man, left behind by the ship's
crew, had nonetheless survived the wreck by clinging to a cask of
spirits, which floated ashore on Great Inagua two days later.

The fishermen who discovered the castaway were more interested in his means of salvation than in the slave himself. Breaking
open the cask, however, they were shocked and appalled to find
inside the body of a man, somewhat imperfectly preserved by the
spirits in which he had been soaking.

''I wonder if they drank the crème de menthe anyway,'' I murmured, having observed for myself that Mr. Overholt's assessment
of the alcoholic affinities of sailors was largely correct.

''I daresay,'' said Geilie, mildly annoyed at having her story
interrupted. ''In any case, when I heard of it, I named him Ishmael
straight off. Because of the floating coffin, aye?''

''Very clever,'' I congratulated her. ''Er . . . did they find out
who the man in the cask was?''

''I don't think so.'' She shrugged carelessly. ''They gave him to the Governor of Jamaica, who had him put in a glass case, wi' fresh spirits, as a curiosity.''

"*What?*" I said incredulously.

"Well, not so much the man himself, but some odd fungi that were growing on him," Geilie explained. "The Governor's got a passion for such things. The old Governor, I mean; I hear there's a new one, now."

"Quite," I said, feeling a bit queasy. I thought the ex-governor was more likely to qualify as a curiosity than the dead man, on the whole.

Her back was turned, as she pulled out drawers and rummaged through them. I took a deep breath, hoping to keep my voice casual.

"This Ishmael sounds an interesting sort; do you still have him?"

"No," she said indifferently. "The black bastard ran off. He's the one who made the zombie poison for me, though. Wouldn't tell me how, no matter what I did to him," she added, with a short, humorless laugh, and I had a sudden vivid memory of the weals across Ishmael's back. "He said it wasn't proper for women to make medicine, only men could do it. Or the verra auld women, once they'd quit bleeding. Hmph!"

She snorted, and reached into her pocket, pulling out a handful of stones.

"Anyway, that's not what I brought ye up to show ye."

Carefully, she laid five of the stones in a rough circle on the countertop. Then she took down from a shelf a thick book, bound in worn leather.

"Can ye read German?" she asked, opening it carefully.

"Not much, no," I said. I moved closer, to look over her shoulder. *Hexenhammer,* it said, in a fine, handwritten script.

"Witches' Hammer?" I asked. I raised one eyebrow. "Spells? Magic?"

The skepticism in my voice must have been obvious, for she glared at me over one shoulder.

"Look, fool," she said. "Who are ye? Or what, rather?"

"What am I?" I said, startled.

"That's right." She turned and leaned against the counter, studying me through narrowed eyes. "What are ye? Or me, come to that? What are we?"

I opened my mouth to reply, then closed it again.

"That's right," she said softly, watching. "It's not everyone can go through the stones, is it? Why us?"

"I don't know," I said. "And neither do you, I'll be bound. It doesn't mean we're witches, surely!"

"Doesn't it?" She lifted one brow, and turned several pages of the book.

"Some people can leave their bodies and travel miles away," she said, staring meditatively at the page. "Other people see them out wandering, and recognize them, and ye can bloody *prove* they were really tucked up safe in bed at the time. I've seen the records, all the eyewitness testimony. Some people have stigmata ye can see and touch—I've seen one. But not everybody. Only certain people."

She turned another page. "If everyone can do it, it's science. If only a few can, then it's witchcraft, or superstition, or whatever you like to call it," she said. "But it's real." She looked up at me, green eyes bright as a snake's over the crumbling book. "*We're* real, Claire—you and me. And special. Have ye never asked yourself why?"

I had. Any number of times. I had never gotten a reasonable answer to the question, though. Evidently, Geilie thought she had one.

She turned back to the stones she had laid on the counter, and pointed at them each in turn. "Stones of protection; amethyst, emerald, turquoise, lapis lazuli, and a male ruby."

"A *male* ruby?"

"Pliny says rubies have a sex to them; who am I to argue?" she said impatiently. "The male stones are what ye use, though; the female ones don't work."

I suppressed the urge to ask precisely how one distinguished the sex of rubies, in favor of asking, "Work for *what*?"

"For the travel," she said, glancing curiously at me. "Through the stones. They protect ye from the . . . whatever it is, out there." Her eyes grew slightly shadowed at the thought of the time-passage, and I realized that she was deathly afraid of it. Little wonder; so was I.

"When did ye come? The first time?" Her eyes were intent on mine.

"From 1945," I said slowly. "I came to 1743, if that's what

you mean." I was reluctant to tell her too much; still, my own curiosity was overwhelming. She was right about one thing; she and I were different. I might never again have the chance to talk to another person who knew what she did. For that matter, the longer I could keep her talking, the longer Jamie would have to look for Ian.

"Hm." She grunted in a satisfied manner. "Near enough. It's two hundred year, in the Highland tales—when folk fall asleep on fairy duns and end up dancing all night wi' the Auld Folk; it's usually two hundred year later when they come back to their own place."

"You didn't, though. You came from 1968, but you'd been in Cranesmuir several years before I came there."

"Five years, aye." She nodded, abstracted. "Aye, well, that was the blood."

"Blood?"

"The sacrifice," she said, suddenly impatient. "It gives ye a greater range. And at least a bit of control, so ye have some notion how far ye're going. How did ye get to and fro three times, without blood?" she demanded.

"I . . . just came." The need to find out as much as I could made me add the little else I knew. "I think—I think it has something to do with being able to fix your mind on a certain person who's in the time you go to."

Her eyes were nearly round with interest.

"Really," she said softly. "Think o' that, now." She shook her head slowly, thinking. "Hm. That might be so. Still, the stones should work as well; there's patterns ye make, wi' the different gems, ye ken."

She pulled another fistful of shining stones from her pocket and spread them on the wooden surface, pawing through them.

"The protection stones are the points of the pentacle," she explained, intent on her rummaging, "but inside that, ye lay the pattern wi' different stones, depending which way ye mean to go, and how far. And ye lay a line of quicksilver between them, and fire it when ye speak the spells. And of course ye draw the pentacle wi' diamond dust."

"Of course," I murmured, fascinated.

"Smell it?" she asked, looking up for a moment and sniffing.

"Ye wouldna think stones had a scent, aye? But they do, when ye grind them to powder."

I inhaled deeply, and did seem to find a faint, unfamiliar scent among the smell of dried herbs. It was a dry scent, pleasant but indescribable—the scent of gemstones.

She held up one stone with a small cry of triumph.

"This one! This is the one I needed; couldna find one anywhere in the islands, and finally I thought o' the box I'd left in Scotland." The stone she held was a black crystal of some kind; the light from the window passed through it, and yet it glittered like a piece of jet between her white fingers.

"What is it?"

"An adamant; a black diamond. The auld alchemists used them. The books say that to wear an adamant brings ye the knowledge of the joy in all things." She laughed, a short, sharp sound, devoid of her usual girlish charm. "If anything can bring knowledge o' joy in that passage through the stones, I want one!"

Something was beginning to dawn on me, rather belatedly. In defense of my slowness, I can only argue that I was simultaneously listening to Geilie and keeping an ear out for any sign of Jamie returning below.

"You mean to go back, then?" I asked, as casually as I could.

"I might." A small smile played around the corners of her mouth. "Now that I've got the things I need. I tell ye, Claire, I wouldna risk it, without." She stared at me, shaking her head. "Three times, wi' no blood," she murmured. "So it can be done.

"Well, best we go down now," she said, suddenly brisk, sweeping the stones up and dumping them back into her pocket. "The fox will be back—Fraser is his name, is it no? I thought Clotilda said something else, but the stupid bitch likely got it wrong."

As we made our way down the long workroom, something small and brown darted across the floor in front of me. Geilie was quick, despite her size; her small foot stamped on the centipede before I could react.

She watched the half-crushed beast wriggling on the floor for a moment, then stooped and slid a sheet of paper under it. Scooping it up, she decanted the thing thriftily into a glass jar.

"Ye dinna want to believe in witches and zombies and things that go bump in the night?" she said, with a small, sly smile at me. She nodded at the centipede, struggling round and round in frenzied, lopsided circles. "Well, legends are many-legged beasties, aye? But they generally have at least one foot on the truth."

She took down a clear brown-glass jug and poured the liquid into the centipede's bottle. The pungent scent of alcohol rose in the air. The centipede, washed up by the wave, kicked frantically for a moment, then sank to the bottom of the bottle, legs moving spasmodically. She corked the bottle neatly, and turned to go.

"You asked me why I thought we can pass through the stones," I said to her back. "Do you know why, Geilie?" She glanced over her shoulder at me.

"Why, to change things," she said, sounding surprised. "Why else? Come along; I hear your man down there."

Whatever Jamie had been doing, it had been hard work; his shirt was dampened with sweat, and clung to his shoulders. He swung around as we entered the room, and I saw that he had been looking at the wooden puzzle-box that Geilie had left on the table. It was obvious from his expression that I had been correct in my surmise —it was the box he had found on the silkies' isle.

"I believe I have succeeded in mending your sugar press, mistress," he said, bowing politely to Geilie. "A matter of a cracked cylinder, which your overseer and I contrived to stuff with wedges. Still, I fear ye may be needing another soon."

Geilie quirked her eyebrows, amused.

"Well, and I'm obliged to ye, Mr. Fraser. Can I not offer ye some refreshment after your labor?" Her hand hovered over the row of bells, but Jamie shook his head, picking up his coat from the sofa.

"I thank ye, mistress, but I fear we must take our leave. It's quite some way back to Kingston, and we must be on our way, if we mean to reach it before dark." His face went suddenly blank, and I knew he must have felt the pocket of his coat and realized that the photographs were missing.

He glanced quickly at me, and I gave him a brief nod, touching the side of my skirt where they lay.

"Thank you for your hospitality," I said, snatching up my hat, and moving toward the door with alacrity. Now that Jamie was back, I wanted nothing so much as to get quickly away from Rose Hall and its owner. Jamie hung back a moment, though.

"I wondered, Mistress Abernathy—since ye mentioned having lived in Paris for a time—whether ye might have been acquainted there wi' a gentleman of my own acquaintance. Did ye by chance ken the Duke of Sandringham?"

She cocked her cream-blond head at him inquisitively, but as he said no more, she nodded.

"Aye, I kent him. Why?"

Jamie gave her his most charming smile. "No particular reason, mistress; only a curiosity, ye might say."

The sky was completely overcast by the time we passed the gate, and it was clear that we weren't going to make it back to Kingston without getting soaked. Under the circumstances, I didn't care.

"Ye've got Brianna's pictures?" was the first thing Jamie asked, reining up for a moment.

"Right here." I patted my pocket. "Did you find any sign of Ian?"

He glanced back over his shoulder, as though fearing we might be pursued.

"I couldna get anything out of the overseer or any o' the slaves —they're bone-scairt of that woman, and I canna say I blame them a bit. But I know where he is." He spoke with considerable satisfaction.

"Where? Can we sneak back and get him?" I rose slightly in my saddle, looking back; the slates of Rose Hall were all that was visible through the treetops. I would have been most reluctant to set foot on the place again for any reason—except for Ian.

"Not now." Jamie caught at my bridle, turning the horse's head back to the trail. "I'll need help."

Under the pretext of finding material to repair the damaged sugar press, Jamie had managed to see most of the plantation within a quarter-mile of the house, including a cluster of slave huts, the stables, a disused drying shed for tobacco, and the building that housed the sugar refinery. Everyplace he went, he suffered no interference beyond curious or hostile glances—except near the refinery.

"That big black bugger who came up onto the porch was sitting on the ground outside," he said. "When I got too close to him, it made the overseer verra nervous indeed; he kept calling me away, warning me not to get too close to the fellow."

"That sounds like a really excellent idea," I said, shuddering slightly. "Not getting close to him, I mean. But you think he has something to do with Ian?"

"He was sitting in front of a wee door fixed into the ground, Sassenach." Jamie guided his horse adroitly around a fallen log in the path. "It must lead to a cellar beneath the refinery." The man had not moved an inch, in all the time that Jamie contrived to spend around the refinery. "If Ian's there, that's where he is."

"I'm fairly sure he's there, all right." I told him quickly the details of my visit, including my brief conversation with the kitchen-maids. "But what are we going to do?" I concluded. "We can't just leave him there! After all, we don't know what Geillis wants with him, but it can't be innocent, if she wouldn't admit he was there, can it?"

"Not innocent at all," he agreed, grim-faced. "The overseer wouldna speak to me of Ian, but he told me other things that would curl your hair, if it wasna already curled up like sheep's wool." He glanced at me, and a half-smile lit his face, in spite of his obvious perturbation.

"Judging by the state of your hair, Sassenach, I should say that it's going to rain verra soon now."

"How observant of you," I said sarcastically, vainly trying to tuck in the curls and tendrils that were escaping from under my hat. "The fact that the sky's black as pitch and the air smells like lightning wouldn't have a thing to do with your conclusions, of course."

The leaves of the trees all round us were fluttering like tethered butterflies, as the edge of the storm rose toward us up the slope of the mountain. From the small rise where we stood, I could see the storm clouds sweep in across the bay below, with a dark curtain of rain hanging beneath it like a veil.

Jamie rose in his saddle, looking over the terrain. To my unpracticed eye, our surroundings looked like solid, impenetrable jungle, but other possibilities were visible to a man who had lived in the heather for seven years.

"We'd best find a bit of shelter while we can, Sassenach," he said. "Follow me."

On foot, leading the horses, we left the narrow path and pressed into the forest, following what Jamie said was a wild pigs' trail. Within a few moments, he had found what he was looking for; a small stream that cut deep through the forest floor, with a steep bank, overgrown with ferns and dark, glossy bushes, interspersed with stands of slender saplings.

He set me to gathering ferns, each frond the length of my arm, and by the time I had returned with as many as I could carry, he had the framework of a tidy snug, formed by the arch of the bent saplings, tied to a fallen log, and covered over with branches cut from the nearby bushes. Hastily roofed with the spread ferns, it was not quite waterproof, but a great deal better than being caught in the open. Ten minutes later, we were safe inside.

There was a moment of absolute quiet as the wind on the edge of the storm passed by us. No birds chattered, no insects sang; they were as well equipped as we were to predict the rain. A few large drops fell, splattering on the foliage with an explosive sound like snapping twigs. Then the storm broke.

Caribbean rainstorms are abrupt and vigorous. None of the misty mousing about of an Edinburgh drizzle. The heavens blacken and split, dropping gallons of water within a minute. For as long as the rain lasts, speech is impossible, and a light fog rises from the ground like steam, vapor raised by the force of the raindrops striking the ground.

The rain pelted the ferns above us, and a faint mist filled the green shadows of our shelter. Between the clatter of the rain and the constant thunder that boomed among the hills, it was impossible to talk.

It wasn't cold, but there was a leak overhead, which dripped steadily on my neck. There was no room to move away; Jamie took off his coat and wrapped it around me, then put his arm around me to wait out the storm. In spite of the terrible racket outside, I felt suddenly safe, and peaceful, relieved of the strain of the last few hours, the last few days. Ian was as good as found, and nothing could touch us, here.

I squeezed his free hand; he smiled at me, then bent and kissed me gently. He smelled fresh and earthy, scented with the sap of the branches he had cut and the smell of his own healthy sweat.

It was nearly over, I thought. We had found Ian, and God willing, would get him back safely, very soon. And then what? We would have to leave Jamaica, but there were other places, and the world was wide. There were the French colonies of Martinique and Grenada, the Dutch-held island of Eleuthera; perhaps we would even venture as far as the continent—cannibals notwith-standing. So long as I had Jamie, I was not afraid of anything.

The rain ceased as abruptly as it had started. Drops fell singly from the shrubs and trees, with a pit-a-pat drip that echoed the ringing left in my ears by the storm's roar. A soft, fresh breeze came up the stream bed, carrying away humidity, lifting the damp curls from my neck with delicious coolness. The birds and the insects began again, quietly, and then in full voice, and the air itself seemed to dance with green life.

I stirred and sighed, pushing myself upright and shrugging off Jamie's coat.

"You know, Geilie showed me a special stone, a black diamond called an adamant," I said. "She said it's a stone the alchemists used; it gives a knowledge of the joy in all things. I think there might be one under this spot."

Jamie smiled at me.

"I shouldna be surprised at all, Sassenach," he said. "Here, ye've water all down your face."

He reached into his coat for a handkerchief, then stopped.

"Brianna's pictures," he said suddenly.

"Oh, I forgot." I dug in my pocket, and handed him back the pictures. He took them and thumbed rapidly through them, stopped, then went through them again, more slowly.

"What's wrong?" I asked, suddenly alarmed.

"One of them's gone," he said quietly. I felt an inexpressible feeling of dread begin to grow in the pit of my stomach, and the joy of a moment before began to ebb away.

"Are you sure?"

"I know them as well as I know your face, Sassenach," he said. "Aye, I'm sure. It's the one of her by the fire."

I remembered the picture in question well; it showed Brianna as an adult, sitting on a rock, outdoors by a campfire. Her knees were drawn up, her elbows resting on them, and she was looking di-rectly into the camera, but with no knowledge of its presence, her face filled with firelit dreams, her hair blown back away from her face.

"Geilie must have taken it. She found the pictures in your coat while I was in the kitchen, and I took them away from her. She must have stolen it then."

"Damn the woman!" Jamie turned sharply to look toward the

road, eyes dark with anger. His hand was tight on the remaining photographs. "What does she want with it?"

"Perhaps it's only curiosity," I said, but the feeling of dread would not go away. "What *could* she do with it, after all? She isn't likely to show it to anyone—who would come here?"

As though in answer to this question, Jamie's head lifted suddenly, and he grasped my arm in adjuration to be still. Some distance below, a loop of the road was visible through the overgrowth, a thin ribbon of yellowish mud. Along this ribbon came a plodding figure on horseback, a man dressed in black, small and dark as an ant at this distance.

Then I remembered what Geilie had said. *I'm expecting a visitor.* And later, *That parson said he'd come at four o'clock.*

"It's a parson, a minister of some kind," I said. "She said she was expecting him."

"It's Archie Campbell, is who it is," Jamie said, with some grimness. "What the devil—or perhaps I shouldna use that particular expression, wi' respect to Mistress Duncan."

"Perhaps he's come to exorcise her," I suggested, with a nervous laugh.

"He's his work cut out for him, if so." The angular figure disappeared into the trees, but it was several minutes before Jamie deemed him safely past us.

"What do you plan to do about Ian?" I asked, once we had made our way back to the path.

"I'll need help," he answered briskly. "I mean to come up the river with Innes and MacLeod and the rest. There's a landing there, no great distance from the refinery. We'll leave the boat there, go ashore and deal wi' Hercules—and Atlas, too, if he's a mind to be troublesome—break open the cellar, snatch Ian, and make off again. The dark o' the moon's in two days—I wish it could be sooner, but it will likely take that long to get a suitable boat and what arms we'll need."

"Using what for money?" I inquired bluntly. The expenditure for new clothes and shoes had taken a substantial portion of Jamie's share of profit from the bat guano. What was left would feed us for several weeks, and possibly be sufficient to rent a boat for a day or two, but it wouldn't stretch to buying large quantities of weapons.

Neither pistols nor swords were manufactured on the island; all weapons were imported from Europe and were in consequence expensive. Jamie himself had Captain Raines's two pistols; the Scots had nothing but their fish knives and the odd cutlass—insufficient for an armed raid.

He grimaced slightly, then glanced at me sidelong.

"I must ask John for help," he said simply. "Must I not?"

I rode silently for a moment, then nodded in acquiescence.

"I suppose you'll have to." I didn't like it, but it wasn't a question of my liking; it was Ian's life. "One thing, though, Jamie—"

"Aye, I know," he said, resigned. "Ye mean to come with me, no?"

"Yes," I said, smiling. "After all, what if Ian's hurt, or sick, or—"

"Aye, ye can come!" he said, rather testily. "Only do me the one wee favor, Sassenach. Try verra hard not to be killed or cut to pieces, aye? It's hard on a man's sensibilities."

"I'll try," I said, circumspectly. And nudging my horse closer to his, rode side by side down toward Kingston, through the dripping trees.

61

The Crocodile's Fire

There was a surprising amount of traffic on the river at night. Lawrence Stern, who had insisted on accompanying the expedition, told me that most of the plantations up in the hills used the river as their main linkage with Kingston and the harbor; roads were either atrocious or nonexistent, swallowed by lush growth with each new rainy season.

I had expected the river to be deserted, but we passed two small craft and a barge headed downstream as we tacked laboriously up the broad waterway, under sail. The barge, an immense dark shape stacked high with casks and bales, passed us like a black iceberg, huge, humped, and threatening. The low voices of the slaves poling it carried across the water, talking softly in a foreign tongue.

"It was kind of ye to come, Lawrence," Jamie said. We had a small, single-masted open boat, which barely held Jamie, myself, the six Scottish smugglers, and Stern. Despite the crowded quarters, I too was grateful for Stern's company; he had a stolid, phlegmatic quality about him that was very comforting under the circumstances.

"Well, I confess to some curiosity," Stern said, flapping the front of his shirt to cool his sweating body. In the dark, all I could see of him was a moving blotch of white. "I have met the lady before, you see."

"Mrs. Abernathy?" I paused, then asked delicately, "Er . . . what did you think of her?"

"Oh . . . she was a very pleasant lady; most . . . gracious."
Dark as it was, I couldn't see his face, but his voice held an odd

note, half-pleased, half-embarrassed, that told me he had found
the widow Abernathy quite attractive indeed. From which I concluded that Geilie had wanted something from the naturalist; I had
never known her treat a man with any regard, save for her own
ends.

"Where did you meet her? At her own house?" According to
the attendees at the Governor's ball, Mrs. Abernathy seldom or
never left her plantation.

"Yes, at Rose Hall. I had stopped to ask permission to collect a
rare type of beetle—one of the Cucurlionidae—that I had found
near a spring on the plantation. She invited me in, and . . . made
me most welcome." This time there was a definite note of self-
satisfaction in his voice. Jamie, handling the tiller next to me,
heard it and snorted briefly.

"What did she want of ye?" he asked, no doubt having formed
conclusions similar to mine about Geilie's motives and behavior.

"Oh, she was most gratifyingly interested in the specimens of
flora and fauna I had collected on the island; she asked me about
the locations and virtues of several different herbs. Ah, and about
the other places I had been. She was particularly interested in my
stories of Hispaniola." He sighed, momentarily regretful. "It is
difficult to believe that such a lovely woman might engage in such
reprehensible behavior as you describe, James."

"Lovely, aye?" Jamie's voice was dryly amused. "A bit smit-
ten, were ye, Lawrence?"

Lawrence's voice echoed Jamie's smile. "There is a sort of
carnivorous fly I have observed, friend James. The male fly,
choosing a female to court, takes pains to bring her a bit of meat
or other prey, tidily wrapped in a small silk package. While the
female is engaged in unwrapping her tidbit, he leaps upon her,
performs his copulatory duties, and hastens away. For if she
should finish her meal before he has finished his own activities, or
should he be so careless as not to bring her a tasty present—she
eats him." There was a soft laugh in the darkness. "No, it was an
interesting experience, but I think I shall not call upon Mrs. Abernathy again."

"Not if we're lucky about it, no," Jamie agreed.

The men left me by the riverbank to mind the boat, and melted into the darkness, with instructions from Jamie to stay put. I had a primed pistol, given to me with the stern injunction not to shoot myself in the foot. The weight of it was comforting, but as the minutes dragged by in black silence, I found the dark and the solitude more and more oppressive.

From where I stood, I could see the house, a dark oblong with only the lower three windows lighted; that would be the salon, I thought, and wondered why there was no sign of any activity by the slaves. As I watched, though, I saw a shadow cross one of the lighted windows, and my heart jumped into my throat.

It wasn't Geilie's shadow, by any conceivable stretch of the imagination. It was tall, thin, and gawkily angular.

I looked wildly around, wanting to call out; but it was too late. The men were all out of earshot, headed for the refinery. I hesitated for a moment, but there was really nothing else to do. I kilted up my skirts and stepped into the dark.

By the time I stepped onto the veranda, I was damp with perspiration, and my heart was beating loudly enough to drown out all other sounds. I edged silently next to the nearest window, trying to peer in without being seen from within.

Everything was quiet and orderly within. There was a small fire on the hearth, and the glow of the flames gleamed on the polished floor. Geilie's rosewood secretary was unfolded, the desk shelf covered with piles of handwritten papers and what looked like very old books. I couldn't see anyone inside, but I couldn't see the whole room, either.

My skin prickled with imagination, thinking of the dead-eyed Hercules, silently stalking me in the dark. I edged farther down the veranda, looking over my shoulder with every other step.

There was an odd sense of desertion about the place this evening. There were none of the subdued voices of slaves that had attended my earlier visit, muttering to one another as they went about their tasks. But that might mean nothing, I told myself. Most of the slaves would stop work and go to their own quarters at sundown. Still, ought there not to be house servants, to tend the fire and fetch food from the kitchen?

The front door stood open. Spilled petals from the yellow rose lay across the doorstep, glowing like ancient gold coins in the faint light from the entryway.

I paused, listening. I thought I heard a faint rustle from inside the salon, as of someone turning the pages of a book, but I couldn't be sure. Taking my courage in both hands, I stepped across the threshold.

The feeling of desertion was more pronounced in here. There were unmistakable signs of neglect visible; a vase of wilted flowers on the polished surface of a chest, a teacup and saucer left to sit on an occasional table, the dregs dried to a brown stain in the bottom of the cup. Where the hell was everybody?

I stopped at the door into the salon and listened again. I heard the quiet crackle of the fire, and again, that soft rustle, as of turning pages. By poking my head around the jamb, I could just see that there was someone seated in front of the secretary now. Someone undeniably male, tall and thin-shouldered, dark head bent over something before him.

"Ian!" I shouted, as loudly as I dared. "Ian!"

The figure started, pushed back the chair, and stood up quickly, blinking toward the shadows.

"Jesus!" I said.

"Mrs. Malcolm?" said the Reverend Archibald Campbell, astonished.

I swallowed, trying to force my heart down out of my throat. The Reverend looked nearly as startled as I, but it lasted only a moment. Then his features hardened, and he took a step toward the door.

"What are you doing here?" he demanded.

"I'm looking for my husband's nephew," I said; there was no point in lying, and perhaps he knew where Ian was. I glanced quickly round the room, but it was empty, save for the Reverend, and the one small lighted lamp he had been using. "Where's Mrs. Abernathy?"

"I have no idea," he said, frowning. "She appears to have left. What do you mean, your husband's nephew?"

"Left?" I blinked at him. "Where has she gone?"

"I don't know." He scowled, his pointed upper lip clamped beaklike over the lower one. "She was gone when I rose this morning—and all of the servants with her, apparently. A fine way to treat an invited guest!"

I relaxed slightly, despite my alarm. At least I was in no danger

of running into Geilie. I thought I could deal with the Reverend
Campbell.

"Oh," I said. "Well, that does seem a bit inhospitable, I admit.
I suppose you haven't seen a boy of about fifteen, very tall and
thin, with thick dark brown hair? No, I didn't think you had. In
that case, I expect I should be go—"

"Stop!" He grabbed me by the upper arm, and I stopped,
surprised and unsettled by the strength of his grip.

"What is your husband's true name?" he demanded.

"Why—Alexander Malcolm," I said, tugging at my captive
arm. "You know that."

"Indeed. And how is it, then, that when I described you and
your husband to Mrs. Abernathy, she told me that your family
name is Fraser—that your husband in fact is James Fraser?"

"Oh." I took a deep breath, trying to think of something plausible, but failed. I never had been good at lying on short notice.

"Where is your husband, woman?" he demanded.

"Look," I said, trying to extract myself from his grasp,
"you're quite wrong about Jamie. He had nothing to do with your
sister, he told me. He—"

"You've spoken to him about Margaret?" His grip tightened. I
gave a small grunt of discomfort and yanked a bit harder.

"Yes. He says that it wasn't him—he wasn't the man she went
to see at Culloden. It was a friend of his, Ewan Cameron."

"Ye're lying," he said flatly. "Or he is. It makes little difference. Where is he?" He gave me a small shake, and I jerked hard,
managing to detach my arm from his grip.

"I tell you, he had nothing to do with what happened to your
sister!" I was backing away, wondering how to get away from him
without setting him loose to blunder about the grounds in search
of Jamie, making noise and drawing unwelcome attention to the
rescue effort. Eight men were enough to overcome the pillars of
Hercules, but not enough to withstand a hundred roused slaves.

"Where?" The Reverend was advancing on me, eyes boring
into mine.

"He's in Kingston!" I said. I glanced to one side; I was near a
pair of French doors opening onto the veranda. I thought I could
get out without his catching me, but then what? Having him chase
me through the grounds would be worse than keeping him talking
in here.

I looked back at the Reverend, who was scowling at me in disbelief, and then what I had seen on the terrace registered in my mind's eye, and I jerked my head back around, staring.

I *had* seen it. There was a large white pelican perched on the veranda railing, head turned back, beak buried comfortably in its feathers. Ping An's plumage glinted silver against the night in the dim light from the doorway.

"What is it?" Reverend Campbell demanded. "Who is it? Who's out there?"

"Just a bird," I said, turning back to him. My heart was beating in a jerky rhythm. Mr. Willoughby must surely be nearby. Pelicans were common, near the mouths of rivers, near the shore, but I had never seen one so far inland. But if Mr. Willoughby was in fact lurking nearby, what ought I to do about it?

"I doubt very much that your husband is in Kingston," the Reverend was saying, narrowed eyes fixed on me with suspicion. "However, if he is, he will presumably be coming here, to retrieve you."

"Oh, no!" I said.

"No," I repeated, with as much assurance as I could manage. "Jamie isn't coming here. I came by myself, to visit Geillis—Mrs. Abernathy. My husband isn't expecting me back until next month."

He didn't believe me, but there was nothing he could do about it, either. His mouth pursed up in a tiny rosette, then unpuckered enough to ask, "So you are staying here?"

"Yes," I said, pleased that I knew enough about the geography of the place to pretend to be a guest. If the servants were gone, there was no one to say I wasn't, after all.

He stood still, regarding me narrowly for a long moment. Then his jaw tightened and he nodded grudgingly.

"Indeed. Then I suppose ye'll have some notion as to where our hostess has taken herself, and when she proposes to return?"

I was beginning to have a rather unsettling notion of where—if not exactly *when*—Geillis Abernathy might have gone, but the Reverend Campbell didn't seem the proper person with whom to share it.

"No, I'm afraid not," I said. "I . . . ah, I've been out visiting since yesterday, at the neighboring plantation. Just came back this minute."

The Reverend eyed me closely, but I was in fact wearing a riding habit—because it was the only decent set of clothes I owned, besides the violet ball dress and two wash-muslin gowns—and my story passed unchallenged.

"I see," he said. "Mmphm. Well, then." He fidgeted restlessly, his big bony hands clenching and unclenching themselves, as though he were not certain what to do with them.

"Don't let me disturb you," I said, with a charming smile and a nod at the desk. "I'm sure you must have important work to do."

He pursed his lips again, in that objectionable way that made him look like an owl contemplating a juicy mouse. "The work has been completed. I was only preparing copies of some documents that Mrs. Abernathy had requested."

"How interesting," I said automatically, thinking that with luck, after a few moments' small talk, I could escape under the pretext of retiring to my theoretical room—all the first-floor rooms opened onto the veranda, and it would be a simple matter to slip off into the night to meet Jamie.

"Perhaps you share our hostess's—and my own—interest in Scottish history and scholarship?" His gaze had sharpened, and with a sinking heart I recognized the fanatical gleam of the passionate researcher in his eyes. I knew it well.

"Well, it's very interesting, I'm sure," I said, edging toward the door, "but I must say, I really don't know very much about—" I caught sight of the top sheet on his pile of documents, and stopped dead.

It was a genealogy chart. I had seen plenty of those, living with Frank, but I recognized this particular one. It was a chart of the Fraser family—the bloody thing was even *headed* "Fraser of Lovat"—beginning somewhere around the 1400s, so far as I could see, and running down to the present. I could see Simon, the late —and not so lamented, in some quarters—Jacobite lord, who had been executed for his part in Charles Stuart's Rising, and his descendants, whose names I recognized. And down in one corner, with the sort of notation indicating illegitimacy, was Brian Fraser —Jamie's father. And beneath him, written in a precise black hand, *James A. Fraser*.

I felt a chill ripple up my back. The Reverend had noticed my reaction, and was watching with a sort of dry amusement.

"Yes, it is interesting that it should be the Frasers, isn't it?"

"That . . . *what* should be the Frasers?" I said. Despite myself, I moved slowly toward the desk.

"The subject of the prophecy, of course," he said, looking faintly surprised. "Do ye not know of it? But perhaps, your husband being an illegitimate descendant . . ."

"I don't know of it, no."

"Ah." The Reverend was beginning to enjoy himself, seizing the opportunity to inform me. "I thought perhaps Mrs. Abernathy had spoken of it to you; she being so interested as to have written to me in Edinburgh regarding the matter." He thumbed through the stack, extracting one paper that appeared to be written in Gaelic.

"This is the original language of the prophecy," he said, shoving Exhibit A under my nose. "By the Brahan Seer; you'll have heard of the Brahan Seer, surely?" His tone held out little hope, but in fact, I had heard of the Brahan Seer, a sixteenth-century prophet along the lines of a Scottish Nostradamus.

"I have. It's a prophecy concerning the Frasers?"

"The Frasers of Lovat, aye. The language is poetic, as I pointed out to Mistress Abernathy, but the meaning is clear enough." He was gathering enthusiasm as he went along, notwithstanding his suspicions of me. "The prophecy states that a new ruler of Scotland will spring from Lovat's lineage. This is to come to pass following the eclipse of 'the kings of the white rose'—a clear reference to the Papist Stuarts, of course." He nodded at the white roses woven into the carpet. "There are somewhat more cryptic references included in the prophecy, of course; the time in which this ruler will appear, and whether it is to be a king or a queen— there is some difficulty in interpretation, owing to mishandling of the original . . ."

He went on, but I wasn't listening. If I had had any doubt about where Geilie had gone, it was fast disappearing. Obsessed with the rulers of Scotland, she had spent the better part of ten years in working for the restoration of a Stuart Throne. That attempt had failed most definitively at Culloden, and she had then expressed nothing but contempt for all extant Stuarts. And little wonder, if she thought she knew what was coming next.

But where would she go? Back to Scotland, perhaps, to involve herself with Lovat's heir? No, she was thinking of making the leap through time again; that much was clear from her conversation

with me. She was preparing herself, gathering her resources—
retrieving the treasure from the silkies' isle—and completing her
researches.

I stared at the paper in a kind of fascinated horror. The genealogy, of course, was only recorded to the present. Did Geilie know
who Lovat's descendants would be, in the future?

I looked up to ask the Reverend Campbell a question, but the
words froze on my lips. Standing in the door to the veranda was
Mr. Willoughby.

The little Chinese had evidently been having a rough time; his
silk pajamas were torn and stained, and his round face was beginning to show the hollows of hunger and fatigue. His eyes passed
over me with only a remote flicker of acknowledgment; all his
attention was for the Reverend Campbell.

"Most holy fella," he said, and his voice held a tone I had
never heard in him before; an ugly taunting note.

The Reverend whirled, so quickly that his elbow knocked
against a vase; water and yellow roses cascaded over the rosewood
desk, soaking the papers. The Reverend gave a cry of rage, and
snatched the papers from the flood, shaking them frantically to
remove the water before the ink should run.

"See what ye've done, ye wicked, murdering heathen!"

Mr. Willoughby laughed. Not his usual high giggle, but a low
chuckle. It didn't sound at all amused.

"I murdering?" He shook his head slowly back and forth, eyes
fixed on the Reverend. "Not me, holy fella. Is you, murderer."

"Begone, fellow," Campbell said coldly. "You should know
better than to enter a lady's house."

"I know you." The Chinaman's voice was low and even, his
gaze unwavering. "I see you. See you in red room, with the
woman who laughs. See you too with stinking whores, in Scotland." Very slowly, he lifted his hand to his throat and drew it
across, precise as a blade. "You kill pretty often, holy fella, I
think."

The Reverend Campbell had gone pale, whether from shock or
rage, I couldn't tell. I was pale, too—from fear. I wet my dry lips
and forced myself to speak.

"Mr. Willoughby—"

"Not Willoughby." He didn't look at me; the correction was
almost indifferent. "I am Yi Tien Cho."

Seeking escape from the present situation, my mind wondered absurdly whether the proper form of address would be Mr. Yi, or Mr. Cho?

"Get out at once!" The Reverend's paleness came from rage. He advanced on the little Chinese, massive fists clenched. Mr. Willoughby didn't move, seemingly indifferent to the looming minister.

"Better you leave, First Wife," he said, softly. "Holy fella liking women—not with cock. With knife."

I wasn't wearing a corset, but felt as though I were. I couldn't get enough breath to form words.

"Nonsense!" the Reverend said sharply. "I tell you again—get out! Or I shall—"

"Just stand still, please, Reverend Campbell," I said. Hands shaking, I drew the pistol Jamie had given me out of the pocket of my habit and pointed it at him. Rather to my surprise, he did stand still, staring at me as though I had just grown two heads.

I had never held anyone at gunpoint before; the sensation was quite oddly intoxicating, in spite of the way the pistol's barrel wavered. At the same time, I had no real idea what to do.

"Mr.—" I gave up, and used all his names. "Yi Tien Cho. Did you see the Reverend at the Governor's ball with Mrs. Alcott?"

"I see him kill her," Yi Tien Cho said flatly. "Better shoot, First Wife."

"Don't be ridiculous! My dear Mrs. Fraser, surely you cannot believe the word of a savage, who is himself—" The Reverend turned toward me, trying for a superior expression, which was rather impaired by the small beads of sweat that had formed at the edge of his receding hairline.

"But I think I do," I said. "You were there. I saw you. And you were in Edinburgh when the last prostitute was killed there. Nellie Cowden said you'd lived in Edinburgh for two years; that's how long the Fiend was killing girls there." The trigger was slippery under my forefinger.

"That's how long *he* had lived there, too!" The Reverend's face was losing its paleness, becoming more flushed by the moment. He jerked his head toward the Chinese.

"Will you take the word of the man who betrayed your husband?"

"Who?"

"Him!" The Reverend's exasperation roughened his voice. "It is this wicked creature who betrayed Fraser to Sir Percival Turner. Sir Percival told me!"

I nearly dropped the gun. Things were happening a lot too fast for me. I hoped desperately that Jamie and his men had found Ian and returned to the river—surely they would come to the house, if I was not at the rendezvous.

I lifted the pistol a little, meaning to tell the Reverend to go down the breezeway to the kitchen; locking him in one of the storage pantries was the best thing I could think of to do.

"I think you'd better—" I began, and then he lunged at me.

My finger squeezed the trigger in reflex. Simultaneously, there was a loud report, the weapon kicked in my hand, and a small cloud of black-powder smoke rolled past my face, making my eyes water.

I hadn't hit him. The explosion had startled him, but now his face settled into new lines of satisfaction. Without speaking, he reached into his coat and drew out a chased-metal case, six inches long. From one end of this protruded a handle of white staghorn.

With the horrible clarity that attends crisis of all kinds, I noted everything, from the nick in the edge of the blade as he drew it from the case, to the scent of the rose he crushed beneath one foot as he came toward me.

There was nowhere to run. I braced myself to fight, knowing fight was useless. The fresh scar of the cutlass slash burned on my arm, a portent of what was coming that made my flesh shrink. There was a flash of blue in the corner of my vision, and a juicy *thunk*! as though someone had dropped a melon from some height. The Reverend turned very slowly on one shoe, eyes wide open and quite, quite blank. For that one moment, he looked like Margaret. Then he fell.

He fell all of a piece, not putting out a hand to save himself. One of the satinwood tables went flying, scattering potpourri and polished stones. The Reverend's head hit the floor at my feet, bounced slightly and lay still. I took one convulsive step back and stood trapped, back against the wall.

There was a dreadful contused depression in his temple. As I watched, his face changed color, fading before my eyes from the red of choler to a pasty white. His chest rose, fell, paused, rose again. His eyes were open; so was his mouth.

"Tsei-mi is here, First Wife?" The Chinese was putting the bag that held the stone balls back into his sleeve.

"Yes, he's here—out there." I waved vaguely toward the veranda. "What—he—did you really—?" I felt the waves of shock creeping over me and fought them back, closing my eyes and drawing in a breath as deep as I could manage.

"Was it you?" I said, my eyes still closed. If he was going to cave in my head as well, I didn't want to watch. "Did he tell the truth? Was it you who gave away the meeting place at Arbroath to Sir Percival? Who told him about Malcolm, and the printshop?"

There was neither answer nor movement, and after a moment, I opened my eyes. He was standing there, watching the Reverend Campbell.

Archibald Campbell lay still as death, but was not yet dead. The dark angel was coming, though; his skin had taken on the faint green tinge I had seen before in dying men. Still, his lungs moved, taking air with a high wheezing sound.

"It wasn't an Englishman, then," I said. My hands were wet, and I wiped them on my skirt. "An English *name*. Willoughby."

"Not Willoughby," he said sharply. "I am Yi Tien Cho!"

"Why!" I said, almost shouting. "Look at me, damn you! *Why*?"

He did look at me then. His eyes were black and round as marbles, but they had lost their shine.

"In China," he said, "there are . . . stories. Prophecy. That one day the ghosts will come. Everyone fear ghost." He nodded once, twice, then glanced again at the figure on the floor.

"I leave China to save my life. Waking up long time—I see ghosts. All round me, ghosts," he said softly.

"A big ghost comes—horrible white face, most horrible, hair on fire. I think he will eat my soul." His eyes had been fixed on the Reverend; now they rose to my face, remote and still as standing water.

"I am right," he said simply, and nodded again. He had not shaved his head recently, but the scalp beneath the black fuzz gleamed in the light from the window.

"He eat my soul, Tsei-mi. I am no more Yi Tien Cho."

"He saved your life," I said. He nodded once more.

"I know. Better I die. Better die than be Willoughby. Willoughby! Ptah!" He turned his head and spat. His face contorted, suddenly angry.

"He talks my words, Tsei-mi! He eats my soul!" The fit of anger seemed to pass as quickly as it had come on. He was sweating, though the room was not terribly warm. He passed a trembling hand over his face, wiping away the moisture.

"There is a man I see in tavern. Ask for Mac-Doo. I am drunk," he said dispassionately. "Wanting woman, no woman come with me—laugh, saying yellow worm, point . . ." He waved a hand vaguely toward the front of his trousers. He shook his head, his queue rustling softly against the silk.

"No matter what *gwao-fei* do; all same to me. I am drunk," he said again. "Ghost-man wants Mac-Doo, ask I am knowing. Say yes, I know Mac-Doo." He shrugged. "It is not important what I say."

He was staring at the minister again. I saw the narrow black chest rise slowly, fall . . . rise once more, fall . . . and remain still. There was no sound in the room; the wheezing had stopped.

"It is a debt," Yi Tien Cho said. He nodded toward the still body. "I am dishonored. I am stranger. But I pay. Your life for mine, First Wife. You tell Tsei-mi."

He nodded once more, and turned toward the door. There was a faint rustling of feathers from the dark veranda. On the threshold he turned back.

"When I wake on dock, I am thinking ghosts have come, are all around me," Yi Tien Cho said softly. His eyes were dark and flat, with no depth to them. "But I am wrong. It is me; I am the ghost."

There was a stir of breeze at the French windows, and he was gone. The quick soft sound of felt-shod feet passed down the veranda, followed by the rustle of spread wings, and a soft, plaintive *Gwaaa!* that faded into the night-sounds of the plantation.

I made it to the sofa before my knees gave way. I bent down and laid my head on my knees, praying that I would not faint. The blood hammered in my ears. I thought I heard a wheezing breath, and jerked up my head in panic, but the Reverend Campbell lay quite still.

I could not stay in the same room with him. I got up, circling as far around the body as I could get, but before I reached the veranda door, I had changed my mind. All the events of the evening were colliding in my head like the bits of glass in a kaleidoscope.

I could not stop now to think, to make sense of it all. But I remembered the Reverend's words, before Yi Tien Cho had come. If there was any clue here to where Geillis Abernathy had gone, it would be upstairs. I took a candle from the table, lighted it, and made my way through the dark house to the staircase, resisting the urge to look behind me. I felt very cold.

The workroom was dark, but a faint, eerie violet glow hovered over the far end of the counter. There was an odd burnt smell in the room, that stung the back of my nose and made me sneeze. The faint metallic aftertaste in the back of my throat reminded me of a long-ago chemistry class.

Quicksilver. Burning mercury. The vapor it gave off was not only eerily beautiful, but highly toxic as well. I snatched out a handkerchief and plastered it over my nose and mouth as I went toward the site of the violet glow.

The lines of the pentacle had been charred into the wood of the counter. If she had used stones to mark a pattern, she had taken them with her, but she had left something else behind.

The photograph was heavily singed at the edges, but the center was untouched. My heart gave a thump of shock. I seized the picture, clutching Brianna's face to my chest with a mingled feeling of fury and panic.

What did she mean by this—this desecration? It couldn't have been meant as a gesture toward me or Jamie, for she could not have expected either of us ever to have seen it.

It must be magic—or Geilie's version of it. I tried frantically to recall our conversation in this room; what had she said? She had been curious about how I had traveled through the stones—that was the main thing. And what had I said? Only something vague, about fixing my attention on a person—yes, that was it—I said I had fixed my attention on a specific person inhabiting the time to which I was drawn.

I drew a deep breath, and discovered that I was trembling, both with delayed reaction from the scene in the salon, and from a dreadful, growing apprehension. It might be only that Geilie had decided to try my technique—if one could dignify it with such a word—as well as her own, and use the image of Brianna as a point of fixation for her travel. Or—I thought of the Reverend's piles of neat, handwritten papers, the carefully drawn genealogies, and thought I might just faint.

"One of the Brahan Seer's prophecies," he had said. "Concerning the Frasers of Lovat. Scotland's ruler will come from that lineage." But thanks to Roger Wakefield's researches, I knew—what Geilie almost certainly knew as well, obsessed as she was with Scottish history—that Lovat's direct line had failed in the 1800s. To all visible intents and purposes, that is. There was in fact one survivor of that line living in 1968—Brianna.

It took a moment for me to realize that the low, growling sound I heard was coming from my own throat, and a moment more of conscious effort to unclench my jaws.

I stuffed the mutilated photograph into the pocket of my skirt and whirled, running for the door as though the workroom were inhabited by demons. I had to find Jamie—now.

They were not there. The boat floated silently, empty in the shadows of the big cecropia where we had left it, but of Jamie and the rest, there was no sign at all.

One of the cane fields lay a short distance to my right, between me and the looming rectangle of the refinery beyond. The faint caramel smell of burnt sugar lingered over the field. Then the wind changed, and I smelled the clean, damp scent of moss and wet rocks from the stream, with all the tiny pungencies of the water plants intermingled.

The stream bank rose sharply here, going up in a mounded ridge that ended at the edge of the cane field. I scrambled up the slope, my palm slipping in soft sticky mud. I shook it off with a muffled exclamation of disgust and wiped my hand on my skirt. A thrill of anxiety ran through me. Bloody *hell,* where was Jamie? He should have been back long since.

Two torches burned by the front gate of Rose Hall, small dots of flickering light at this distance. There was a closer light as well; a glow from the left of the refinery. Had Jamie and his men met trouble there? I could hear a faint singing from that direction, and see a deeper glow that bespoke a large open fire. It seemed peaceful, but something about the night—or the place—made me very uneasy.

Suddenly I became aware of another scent, above the tang of watercress and burnt sugar—a strong putrid-sweet smell that I recognized at once as the smell of rotten meat. I took a cautious step, and all hell promptly broke loose underfoot.

It was as though a piece of the night had suddenly detached itself from the rest and sprung into action at about the level of my knees. A very large object exploded into movement close to me, and there was a stunning blow across my lower legs that knocked me off my feet.

My involuntary shriek coincided with a truly awful sound—a sort of loud, grunting hiss that confirmed my impression that I was in close juxtaposition to something large, alive, and reeking of carrion. I didn't know what it was, but I wanted no part of it.

I had landed very hard on my bottom. I didn't pause to see what was happening, but flipped over and made off through the mud and leaves on all fours, followed by a repetition of the grunting hiss, only louder, and a scrabbling, sliding sort of rush. Something hit my foot a glancing blow, and I stumbled to my feet, running.

I was so panicked that I didn't realize that I suddenly could see, until the man loomed up before me. I crashed into him, and the torch he was carrying dropped to the ground, hissing as it struck the wet leaves.

Hands grabbed my shoulders, and there were shouts behind me. My face was pressed against a hairless chest with a strong musky smell about it. I regained my balance, gasping, and leaned back to look into the face of a tall black slave, who was gaping down at me in perplexed dismay.

"Missus, what you be doin' here?" he said. Before I could answer, though, his attention was distracted from me to what was going on behind me. His grip on my shoulders relaxed, and I turned to see.

Six men surrounded the beast. Two carried torches, which they held aloft to light the other four, dressed only in loin cloths, who cautiously circled, holding sharpened wooden poles at the ready.

My legs were still stinging and wobbly from the blow they had taken; when I saw what had struck me, they nearly gave way again. The thing was nearly twelve feet long, with an armored body the size of a rum cask. The great tail whipped suddenly to one side;

the man nearest leapt aside, shouting in alarm, and the saurian's head turned, jaws opening slightly to emit another hiss.

The jaws clicked shut with an audible snap, and I saw the telltale carnassial tooth, jutting up from the lower jaw in an expression of grim and spurious pleasantry.

"Never smile at a crocodile," I said stupidly.

"No, ma'am, I surely won't," the slave said, leaving me and edging cautiously toward the scene of action.

The men with the poles were poking at the beast, evidently trying to irritate it. In this endeavor, they appeared to be succeeding. The fat, splayed limbs dug hard into the ground, and the crocodile charged, roaring. It lunged with astonishing speed; the man before it yelped and jumped back, lost his footing on the slippery mud and fell.

The man who had collided with me launched himself through the air and landed on the crocodile's back. The men with the torches danced back and forth, yelling encouragement, and one of the pole men, bolder than the others, dashed forward and whacked his pole across the broad, plated head to distract it, while the fallen slave scrabbled backward, bare heels scooping trenches in the black mud.

The man on the crocodile's back was groping—with what seemed to me suicidal mania—for the beast's mouth. Getting a hold with one arm about the thick neck, he managed to grab the end of the snout with one hand, and holding the mouth shut, screamed something to his companions.

Suddenly a figure I hadn't noticed before stepped out of the shadow of the cane. It went down on one knee before the struggling pair, and without hesitation, slipped a rope noose around the crocodile's jaws. The shouting rose in a yell of triumph, cut off by a sharp word from the kneeling figure.

He rose and motioned violently, shouting commands. He wasn't speaking English, but his concern was obvious; the great tail was still free, lashing from side to side with a force that would have felled any man who came within range of it. Seeing the power of that stroke, I could only marvel that my own legs were merely bruised, and not broken.

The pole men dashed in closer, in response to the commands of their leader. I could feel the half-pleasant numbness of shock stealing over me, and in that state of unreality, it somehow seemed no surprise to see that the leader was the man called Ishmael.

"Huwe!" he said, making violent upward gestures with his palms that made his meaning obvious. Two of the pole men had gotten their poles shoved under the belly; a third now managed a lucky strike past the tossing head, and lodged his pole under the chest.

"Huwe!" Ishmael said again, and all three threw themselves hard upon their poles. With a sucking *splat*! the reptile flipped over and landed thrashing on its back, its underside a sudden gleaming white in the torchlight.

The torchbearers were shouting again; the noise rang in my ears. Then Ishmael stopped them with a word, his hand thrown out in demand, palm up. I couldn't tell what the word was, but it could as easily have been "Scalpel!" The intonation—and the result—were the same.

One of the torchbearers hastily tugged the cane-knife from his loincloth, and slapped it into his leader's hand. Ishmael turned on his heel and in the same movement, drove the point of the knife deep into the crocodile's throat, just where the scales of the jaw joined those of the neck.

The blood welled black in the torchlight. All the men stepped back then, and stood at a safe distance, watching the dying frenzy of the great reptile with a respect mingled with deep satisfaction. Ishmael straightened, shirt a pale blur against the dark canes; unlike the other men, he was fully dressed, save for bare feet, and a number of small leather bags swung at his belt.

Owing to some freak of the nervous system, I had kept standing all this time. The increasingly urgent messages from my legs made it through to my brain at this point, and I sat down quite suddenly, my skirts billowing on the muddy ground.

The movement attracted Ishmael's notice; the narrow head turned in my direction, and his eyes widened. The other men, seeing him, turned also, and a certain amount of incredulous comment in several languages followed.

I wasn't paying much attention. The crocodile was still breathing, in stertorous, bubbling gasps. So was I. My eyes were fixed on the long scaled head, its eye with a slit pupil glowing the greenish gold of tourmaline, its oddly indifferent gaze seeming fixed in turn on me. The crocodile's grin was upside down, but still in place.

The mud was cool and smooth beneath my cheek, black as the thick stream that flowed between the reptile's scales. The tone of the questions and comments had changed to concern, but I was no longer listening.

I hadn't actually lost consciousness; I had a vague impression of jostling bodies and flickering light, and then I was lifted into the air, clutched tight in someone's arms. They were talking excitedly, but I caught only a word now and then. I dimly thought I should tell them to lay me down and cover me with something, but my tongue wasn't working.

Leaves brushed my face as my escort ruthlessly shouldered the canes aside; it was like pushing through a cornfield that had no ears, all stalks and rustling leaves. There was no conversation among the men now; the susurrus of our passage drowned even the sound of footsteps.

By the time we entered the clearing by the slave huts, both sight and wits had returned to me. Bar scrapes and bruises, I wasn't hurt, but I saw no point in advertising the fact. I kept my eyes closed and stayed limp as I was carried into one of the huts, fighting back panic, and hoping to come up with some sensible plan before I was obliged to wake up officially.

Where in bloody hell were Jamie and the others? If all went well —or worse, if it didn't—what were they going to do when they arrived at the landing place and found me gone, with traces— traces? the place was a bloody wallow!—of a struggle where I had been?

And what about friend Ishmael? What in the name of all merciful God was *he* doing here? I knew one thing—he wasn't bloody well cooking.

There was a good deal of festive noise outside the open door of the hut, and the scent of something alcoholic—not rum, something raw and pungent—floated in, a high note in the fuggy air of the hut, redolent of sweat and boiled yams. I cracked an eye and saw the reflected glimmer of firelight on the beaten earth. Shadows moved back and forth in front of the open door; I couldn't leave without being seen.

There was a general shout of triumph, and all the figures disappeared abruptly, in what I assumed was the direction of the fire.

Presumably they were doing something to the crocodile, who had arrived when I did, swinging upside-down from the hunters' poles.

I rolled cautiously up onto my knees. Could I steal away while they were occupied with whatever they were doing? If I could make it to the nearest cane field, I was fairly sure they couldn't find me, but I was by no means so sure that I could find the river again, alone in the pitch-dark.

Ought I to make for the main house, instead, in hopes of running into Jamie and his rescue party? I shuddered slightly at the thought of the house, and the long, silent black form on the floor of the salon. But if I didn't go to either house or boat, how was I to find them, on a moonless night black as the Devil's armpit?

My planning was interrupted by a shadow in the doorway that momentarily blocked the light. I risked a peek, then sat bolt upright and screamed.

The figure came swiftly in and knelt by my pallet.

"Don' you be makin' that noise, woman," Ishmael said. "It ain't but me."

"Right," I said. Cold sweat prickled on my jaws and I could feel my heart pounding like a triphammer. "Knew it all the time."

They had cut off the crocodile's head and sliced out the tongue and the floor of the mouth. He wore the huge, cold-eyed thing like a hat, his eyes no more than a gleam in the depths beneath the portcullised teeth. The empty lower jaw sagged, fat-jowled and grimly jovial, hiding the lower half of his face.

"The *egungun,* he didn't hurt you none?" he asked.

"No," I said. "Thanks to the men. Er . . . you wouldn't consider taking that off, would you?"

He ignored the request and sat back on his heels, evidently considering me. I couldn't see his face, but every line of his body expressed the most profound indecision.

"Why you bein' here?" he asked at last.

For lack of any better idea, I told him. He didn't mean to bash me on the head, or he would have done it already, when I collapsed below the cane field.

"Ah," he said, when I had finished. The reptile's snout dipped slightly toward me as he thought. A drop of moisture fell from the valved nostril onto my bare hand, and I wiped it quickly on my skirt, shuddering.

"The missus not here tonight," he said, at last, as though wondering whether it was safe to trust me with the information.

"Yes, I know," I said. I gathered my feet under me, preparing to rise. "Can you—or one of the men—take me back to the big tree by the river? My husband will be looking for me," I added pointedly.

"Likely she be takin' the boy with her," Ishmael went on, ignoring me.

My heart had lifted when he had verified that Geilie was gone; now it fell, with a distinct thud in my chest.

"She's taken Ian? Why?"

I couldn't see his face, but the eyes inside the crocodile mask shone with a gleam of something that was partly amusement—but only partly.

"Missus likes boys," he said, the malicious tone making his meaning quite clear.

"Does she," I said flatly. "Do you know when she'll be coming back?"

The long, toothy snout turned suddenly up, but before he could reply, I sensed someone standing behind me, and swung around on the pallet.

"I know you," she said, a small frown puckering the wide, smooth forehead as she looked down at me. "Do I not?"

"We've met," I said, trying to swallow the heart that had leapt into my mouth in startlement. "How—how do you do, Miss Campbell?"

Better than when last seen, evidently, in spite of the fact that her neat wool challis gown had been replaced with a loose smock of coarse white cotton, sashed with a broad, raggedly torn strip of the same, stained dark blue with indigo. Both face and figure had grown more slender, though, and she had lost the pasty, sagging look of too many months spent indoors.

"I am well, I thank ye, ma'am," she said politely. The pale blue eyes had still that distant, unfocused look to them, and despite the new sun-glow on her skin, it was clear that Miss Margaret Campbell was still not altogether in the here and now.

This impression was borne out by the fact that she appeared not to have noticed Ishmael's unconventional attire. Or to have noticed Ishmael himself, for that matter. She went on looking at me, a vague interest passing across her snub features.

"It is most civil in ye to call upon me, ma'am," she said. "Might I offer ye refreshment of some kind? A dish of tea, perhaps? We keep no claret, for my brother holds that strong spirits are a temptation to the lusts of the flesh."

"I daresay they are," I said, feeling that I could do with a brisk spot of temptation at the moment.

Ishmael had risen, and now bowed deeply to Miss Campbell, the great head slipping precariously.

"You ready, *bébé*?" he asked softly. "The fire is waiting."

"Fire," she said. "Yes, of course," and turned to me.

"Will ye not join me, Mrs. Malcolm?" she asked graciously. "Tea will be served shortly. I do so enjoy looking into a nice fire," she confided, taking my arm as I rose. "Do you not find yourself sometimes imagining that you see things in the flames?"

"Now and again," I said. I glanced at Ishmael, who was standing in the doorway. His indecision was apparent in his stance, but as Miss Campbell moved inexorably toward him, towing me after her, he shrugged very slightly, and stepped aside.

Outside, a small bonfire burned brightly in the center of the clearing before the row of huts. The crocodile had already been skinned; the raw hide was stretched on a frame near one of the huts, throwing a headless shadow on the wooden wall. Several sharpened sticks were thrust into the ground around the fire, each strung with chunks of meat, sizzling with an appetizing smell that nonetheless made my stomach clench.

Perhaps three dozen people, men, women and children, were gathered near the fire, laughing and talking. One man was still singing softly, curled over a battered guitar.

As we appeared, one man caught sight of us, and turned sharply, saying something that sounded like "Hau!" At once, the talk and laughter stopped, and a respectful silence fell upon the crowd.

Ishmael walked slowly toward them, the crocodile's head grinning in apparent delight. The firelight shone off faces and bodies like polished jet and melted caramel, all with deep black eyes that watched us come.

There was a small bench near the fire, set on a sort of dais made of stacked planks. This was evidently the seat of honor, for Miss Campbell made for it directly, and gestured politely for me to sit down next to her.

I could feel the weight of eyes upon me, with expressions ranging from hostility to guarded curiosity, but most of the attention
was for Miss Campbell. Glancing covertly around the circle of
faces, I was struck by their strangeness. These were the faces of
Africa, and alien to me; not faces like Joe's, that bore only the
faint stamp of his ancestors, diluted by centuries of European
blood. Black or not, Joe Abernathy was a great deal more like me
than like these people—different to the marrow of their bones.

The man with the guitar had put it aside, and drawn out a small
drum that he set between his knees. The sides were covered with
the hide of some spotted animal; goat, perhaps. He began to tap it
softly with the palms of his hands, in a half-halting rhythm like the
beating of a heart.

I glanced at Miss Campbell, sitting tranquil beside me, hands
carefully folded in her lap. She was gazing straight ahead, into the
leaping flames, with a small, dreaming smile on her lips.

The swaying crowd of slaves parted, and two little girls came
out, carrying a large basket between them. The handle of the
basket was twined with white roses, and the lid jerked up and
down, agitated by the movements of something inside.

The girls set the basket at Ishmael's feet, casting awed glances
up at his grotesque headdress. He rested a hand on each of their
heads, murmured a few words, and then dismissed them, his upraised palms a startling flash of yellow-pink, like butterflies rising
from the girls' knotted hair.

The attitude of the spectators had so far been quiet and respectful. It continued so, but now they crowded closer, necks craning to
see what would happen next, and the drum began to beat faster,
still softly. One of the women was holding a stone bottle, she took
one step forward, handed it to Ishmael, and melted back into the
crowd.

Ishmael took up the bottle of liquor and poured a small amount
on the ground, moving carefully in a circle around the basket. The
basket, momentarily quiescent, heaved to and fro, evidently disturbed by the movement or the pungent scent of alcohol.

A man holding a stick wrapped in rags stepped forward, and
held the stick in the bonfire until the rags blazed up, bright red. At
a word from Ishmael, he dipped his torch to the ground where the
liquor had been poured. There was a collective "Ah!" from the
watchers as a ring of flame sprang up, burned blue and died away

at once, as quickly as it came. From the basket came a loud "Cock-a-doodle-dooo!"

Miss Campbell stirred beside me, eyeing the basket with suspicion.

As though the crowing had been a signal—perhaps it was—a flute began to play, and the humming of the crowd rose to a higher pitch.

Ishmael came toward the makeshift dais where we sat, holding a red headrag between his hands. This he tied about Margaret's wrist, placing her hand gently back in her lap when he had finished.

"Oh, there is my handkerchief!" she exclaimed, and quite unselfconsciously raised her wrist and wiped her nose.

No one but me seemed to notice. The attention was on Ishmael, who was standing before the crowd, speaking in a language I didn't recognize. The cock in the basket crowed again, and the white roses on the handle quivered violently with its struggles.

"I do wish it wouldn't do that," said Margaret Campbell, rather petulantly. "If it does again, it will be three times, and that's bad luck, isn't it?"

"Is it?" Ishmael was now pouring the rest of the liquor in a circle round the dais. I hoped the flame wouldn't startle her.

"Oh, yes, Archie says so. 'Before the cock crows thrice, thou wilt betray me.' Archie says women are always betrayers. Is that so, do you think?"

"Depends on your point of view, I suppose," I murmured, watching the proceedings. Miss Campbell seemed oblivious to the swaying, humming slaves, the music, the twitching basket, and Ishmael, who was collecting small objects handed to him out of the crowd.

"I'm hungry," she said. "I do hope the tea will be ready soon."

Ishmael heard this. To my amazement, he reached into one of the bags at his waist and unwrapped a small bundle, which proved to hold a cup of chipped and battered porcelain, the remnants of gold leaf still visible on the rim. This he placed ceremoniously on her lap.

"Oh, goody," Margaret said happily, clapping her hands together. "Perhaps there'll be biscuits."

I rather thought not. Ishmael had placed the objects given him by the crowd along the edge of the dais. A few small bones, with lines carved across them, a spray of jasmine, and two or three crude little figures made of wood, each one wrapped in a scrap of cloth, with little shocks of hair glued to the head-nubbins with clay.

Ishmael spoke again, the torch dipped, and a sudden whiff of blue flame shot up around the dais. As it died away, leaving the scent of scorched earth and burnt brandy heavy in the cool night air, he opened the basket and brought out the cock.

It was a large, healthy bird, black feathers glistening in the torchlight. It struggled madly, uttering piercing squawks, but it was firmly trussed, its feet wrapped in cloth to prevent scratching. Ishmael bowed low, saying something, and handed the bird to Margaret.

"Oh, thank you," she said graciously.

The cock stretched out its neck, wattles bright red with agitation, and crowed piercingly. Margaret shook it.

"Naughty bird!" she said crossly, and raising it to her mouth, bit it just behind the head.

I heard the soft crack of the neck bones and the little grunt of effort as she flung her head up, wrenching off the head of the hapless cock.

She clutched the gurgling, struggling trussed carcass tight against her bosom, crooning, "Now, then, now, then, it's all right, darling," as the blood spurted and sprayed into the teacup and all over her dress.

The crowd had cried out at first, but now was quite still, watching. The flute, too, had fallen silent, but the drum beat on, sounding much louder than before.

Margaret dropped the drained carcass carelessly to one side, where a boy darted out of the crowd to retrieve it. She brushed absently at the blood on her skirt, picking up the teacup with her red-swathed hand.

"Guests first," she said politely. "Will you have one lump, Mrs. Malcolm, or two?"

I was fortunately saved from answering by Ishmael, who thrust a crude horn cup into my hands, indicating that I should drink from it. Considering the alternative, I raised it to my mouth without hesitation.

It was fresh-distilled rum, sharp and raw enough to strip the throat, and I choked, wheezing. The tang of some herb rose up the back of my throat and into my nose; something had been mixed with the liquor, or soaked in it. It was faintly tart, but not unpleasant.

Other cups like mine were making their way from hand to hand through the crowd. Ishmael made a sharp gesture, indicating that I should drink more. I obediently raised the cup to my lips, but let the fiery liquid lap against my mouth without swallowing. Whatever was happening here, I thought I might need such wits as I had.

Beside me, Miss Campbell was drinking from her teetotal cup with genteel sips. The feeling of expectancy among the crowd was rising; they were swaying now, and a woman had begun to sing, low and husky, her voice an offbeat counterpoint to the thump of the drum.

The shadow of Ishmael's headdress fell across my face, and I looked up. He too was swaying slowly, back and forth. The collarless white shirt he wore was speckled over the shoulders with black dots of blood, and stuck to his breast with sweat. I thought suddenly that the raw crocodile's head must weigh thirty pounds at least, a terrible weight to support; the muscles of his neck and shoulders were taut with effort.

He raised his hands and began to sing as well. I felt a shiver run down my back and coil at the base of my spine, where my tail would have been. With his face masked, the voice could have been Joe's; deep and honeyed, with a power that commanded attention. If I closed my eyes, it *was* Joe, with the light glinting off his spectacles, and catching the gold tooth far back as he smiled.

Then I opened my eyes again, half-shocked to see instead the crocodile's sinister yawn, and the fire gold-green in the cold, cruel eyes. My mouth was dry and there was a faint buzzing in my ears, weaving around the strong, sweet words.

He was getting attention, all right; the night by the fire was full of eyes, black-wide and shiny, and small moans and shouts marked the pauses in the song.

I closed my eyes and shook my head hard. I grabbed the edge of the wooden bench, clinging to its rough reality. I wasn't drunk, I knew; whatever herb had been mixed with the rum was potent. I could feel it creeping snakelike through my blood, and kept my eyes tight closed, fighting its progress.

I couldn't block my ears, though, or the sound of that voice, rising and falling.

I didn't know how much time had passed. I came back to myself with a start, suddenly aware that the drum and the singing had stopped.

There was an absolute silence around the fire. I could hear the small rush of flame, and the rustle of cane leaves in the night wind; the quick darting scuttle of a rat in the palm-frond roof of the hut behind me.

The drug was still in my bloodstream, but the effects were dying; I could feel clarity coming back to my thoughts. Not so for the crowd; the eyes were fixed in a single, unblinking stare, like a wall of mirrors, and I thought suddenly of the voodoo legends of my time—of zombies and the *houngans* who made them. What had Geilie said? *Every legend has one foot on the truth.*

Ishmael spoke. He had taken off the crocodile's head. It lay on the ground at our feet, eyes gone dark in the shadow.

"Ils sont arrivés," Ishmael said quietly. *They have come.* He lifted his wet face, lined with exhaustion, and turned to the crowd. "Who asks?"

As though in response, a young woman in a turban moved out of the crowd, still swaying, half-dazed, and sank down on the ground before the dais. She put her hand on one of the carved images, a crude wooden icon in the shape of a pregnant woman.

Her eyes looked up with hope, and while I didn't recognize the words she spoke, it was clear what she asked.

"Aya, gado." The voice spoke from beside me, but it wasn't Margaret Campbell's. It was the voice of an old woman, cracked and high, but confident, answering in the affirmative.

The young woman gasped with joy, and prostrated herself on the ground. Ishmael nudged her gently with a foot; she got up quickly and backed into the crowd, clutching the small image and bobbing her head, murmuring *"Mana, mana,"* over and over.

Next was a young man, by his face the brother of the first young woman, who squatted respectfully upon his haunches, touching his head before he spoke.

"Grandmère," he began, in high, nasal French. Grandmother? I thought.

He asked his question looking shyly down at the ground. "Does the woman I love return my love?'' His was the jasmine spray; he held it so that it brushed the top of a bare, dusty foot.

The woman beside me laughed, her ancient voice ironic but not unkind. *''Certainement,''* she answered. "She returns it; and that of three other men, besides. Find another; less generous, but more worthy.''

The young man retired, crestfallen, to be replaced by an older man. This one spoke in an African language I did not know, a tone of bitterness in his voice as he touched one of the clay figures.

''Setato hoye,'' said—who? The voice had changed. The voice of a man this time, full-grown but not elderly, answering in the same language with an angry tone.

I stole a look to the side, and despite the heat of the fire, felt the chill ripple up my forearms. It was Margaret's face no longer. The outlines were the same, but the eyes were bright, alert and focused on the petitioner, the mouth set in grim command, and the pale throat swelled like a frog's with the effort of strong speech as whoever-it-was argued with the man.

"They are here," Ishmael had said. "They," indeed. He stood to one side, silent but watchful, and I saw his eyes rest on me for a second before coming back to Margaret. Or whatever had been Margaret.

"They." One by one the people came forward, to kneel and ask. Some spoke in English, some French, or the slave patois, some in the African speech of their vanished homes. I couldn't understand all that was said, but when the questions were in French or English, they were often prefaced by a respectful "Grandfather," or "Grandmother," once by "Aunt."

Both the face and the voice of the oracle beside me changed, as "they" came to answer their call; male and female, mostly middle-aged or old, their shadows dancing on her face with the flicker of the fire.

Do you not sometimes imagine that you see things in the fire? The echo of her own small voice came back to me, thin and childish.

Listening, I felt the hair rise on the back of my neck, and understood for the first time what had brought Ishmael back to this place, risking recapture and renewed slavery. Not friendship, not love, nor any loyalty to his fellow slaves, but power.

What price is there for the power to tell the future? Any price, was the answer I saw, looking out at the rapt faces of the congregation. He had come back for Margaret.

It went on for some time. I didn't know how long the drug would last, but I saw people here and there sink down to the ground, and nod to sleep; others melted silently back to the darkness of the huts, and after a time, we were almost alone. Only a few remained around the fire, all men.

They were all husky and confident, and from their attitude, accustomed to command some respect, among slaves at least. They had hung back, together as a group, watching the proceedings, until at last one, clearly the leader, stepped forward.

"They be done, mon," he said to Ishmael, with a jerk of his head toward the sleeping forms around the fire. "Now you ask."

Ishmael's face showed nothing but a slight smile, yet he seemed suddenly nervous. Perhaps it was the closing in of the other men. There was nothing overtly menacing about them, but they seemed both serious and intent—not upon Margaret, for a change, but upon Ishmael.

At last he nodded, and turned to face Margaret. During the hiatus, her face had gone blank; no one at home.

"Bouassa," he said to her. "Come you, Bouassa."

I shrank involuntarily away, as far as I could get on the bench without falling into the fire. Whoever Bouassa was, he had come promptly.

"I be hearin'." It was a voice as deep as Ishmael's, and should have been as pleasant. It wasn't. One of the men took an involuntary step backward.

Ishmael stood alone; the other men seemed to shrink away from him, as though he suffered some contamination.

"Tell me what I want to know, you Bouassa," he said.

Margaret's head tilted slightly, a light of amusement in the pale blue eyes.

"What you want to know?" the deep voice said, with mild scorn. "For why, mon? You be goin', I tell you anything or not."

The small smile on Ishmael's face echoed that on Bouassa's.

"You say true," he said softly. "But these—" He jerked his head toward his companions, not taking his eyes from the face. "They be goin' with me?"

"Might as well," the deep voice said. It chuckled, rather unpleasantly. "The Maggot dies in three days. Won't be nothin' for them here. That all you be wantin' with me?'' Not waiting for an answer, Bouassa yawned widely, and a loud belch erupted from Margaret's dainty mouth.

Her mouth closed, and her eyes resumed their vacant stare, but the men weren't noticing. An excited chatter erupted from them, to be hushed by Ishmael, with a significant glance at me. Abruptly quiet, they moved away, still muttering, glancing at me as they went.

Ishmael closed his eyes as the last man left the clearing, and his shoulders sagged. I felt a trifle drained myself.

''What—'' I began, and then stopped. Across the fire, a man had stepped from the shelter of the sugarcane. Jamie, tall as the cane itself, with the dying fire staining shirt and face as red as his hair.

He raised a finger to his lips, and I nodded. I gathered my feet cautiously beneath me, picking up my stained skirt in one hand. I could be up, past the fire, and into the cane with him before Ishmael could reach me. But Margaret?

I hesitated, turned to look at her, and saw that her face had come alive once again. It was lifted, eager, lips parted and shining eyes narrowed so that they seemed slightly slanted, as she stared across the fire.

''Daddy?'' said Brianna's voice beside me.

The hairs rippled softly erect on my forearms. It was Brianna's voice, Brianna's face, blue eyes dark and slanting with eagerness.

''Bree?'' I whispered, and the face turned to me.

''Mama,'' said my daughter's voice, from the throat of the oracle.

''Brianna,'' said Jamie, and she turned her head sharply to look at him.

''Daddy,'' she said, with great certainty. ''I knew it was you. I've been dreaming about you.''

Jamie's face was white with shock. I saw his lips form the word ''Jesus,'' without sound, and his hand moved instinctively to cross himself.

''Don't let Mama go alone,'' said the voice with great certainty. ''You go with her. I'll keep you safe.''

There was no sound save the crackling of the fire. Ishmael stood transfixed, staring at the woman beside me. Then she spoke again, in Brianna's soft, husky tones.

"I love you, Daddy. You too, Mama." She leaned toward me, and I smelled the fresh blood. Then her lips touched mine, and I screamed.

I was not conscious of leaping to my feet, or of crossing the clearing. All I knew was that I was clinging to Jamie, my face buried in the cloth of his coat, shaking.

His heart was pounding under my cheek, and I thought that he was shaking, too. I felt his hand trace the sign of the cross upon my back, and his arm lock tight about my shoulders.

"It's all right," he said, and I could feel his ribs swell and brace with the effort of keeping his voice steady. "She's gone."

I didn't want to look, but forced myself to turn my head toward the fire.

It was a peaceful scene. Margaret Campbell sat quietly on her bench, humming to herself, twiddling a long black tailfeather upon her knee. Ishmael stood behind her, one hand smoothing her hair in what looked like tenderness. He murmured something to her in a low, liquid tongue—a question—and she smiled placidly.

"Oh, I'm not a scrap tired!" she assured him, turning to look fondly up into the scarred face that hovered in the darkness above her. "Such a nice party, wasn't it?"

"Yes, *bébé*," he said gently. "But you rest now, eh?" He turned and clicked his tongue loudly. Suddenly two of the turbaned women materialized out of the night; they must have been waiting, just within call. Ishmael said something to them, and they came at once to tend Margaret, lifting her to her feet and leading her away between them, murmuring soft endearments in African and French.

Ishmael remained, watching us across the fire. He was still as one of Geilie's idols, carved out of night.

"I did not come alone," Jamie said. He gestured casually over his shoulder toward the cane field behind him, implying armed regiments.

"Oh, you be alone, mon," Ishmael said, with a slight smile. "No matter. The *loa* speak to you; you be safe from me." He glanced back and forth between us, appraising.

"Huh," he said, in a tone of interest. "Never did hear a *loa* speak to *buckra*." He shook his head then, dismissing the matter.

"You be going now," he said, quietly but with considerable authority.

"Not yet." Jamie's arm dropped from my shoulder, and he straightened up beside me. "I have come for the boy Ian; I will not go without him."

Ishmael's brows went up, compressing the three vertical scars between them.

"Huh," he said again. "You forget that boy; he be gone."

"Gone where?" Jamie asked sharply.

The narrow head tilted to one side, as Ishmael looked him over carefully.

"Gone with the Maggot, mon," he said. "And where she go, you don' be going. That boy gone, mon," he said again, with finality. "You leave too, you a wise man." He paused, listening. A drum was talking, somewhere far away, the pulse of it little more than a disturbance of the night air.

"The rest be comin' soon," he remarked. "You safe from me, mon, not from them."

"Who are the rest?" I asked. The terror of the encounter with the *loa* was ebbing, and I was able to talk once more, though my spine still rippled with fear of the dark cane field at my back.

"Maroons, I expect," Jamie said. He raised a brow at Ishmael. "Or ye will be?"

The priest nodded, one formal bob of the head.

"That be true," he said. "You hear Bouassa speak? His *loa* bless us, we go." He gestured toward the huts and the dark hills behind them. "The drum callin' them down from the hills, those strong enough to go."

He turned away, the conversation obviously at an end.

"Wait!" Jamie said. "Tell us where she has gone—Mrs. Abernathy and the boy!"

Ishmael turned back, shoulders mantled in the crocodile's blood.

"To Abandawe," he said.

"And where's that?" Jamie demanded impatiently. I put a hand on his arm.

"I know where it is," I said, and Ishmael's eyes widened in astonishment. "At least—I know it's on Hispaniola. Lawrence told me. That was what Geilie wanted from him—to find out where it was."

"*What* is it? A town, a village? Where?" I could feel Jamie's arm tense under my hand, vibrating with the urgency to be gone.

"It's a cave," I said, feeling cold in spite of the balmy air and the nearness of the fire. "An old cave."

"Abandawe a magic place," Ishmael put in, deep voice soft, as though he feared to speak of it out loud. He looked at me hard, reassessing. "Clotilda say the Maggot take you to the room upstairs. You maybe be knowin' what she do there?"

"A little." My mouth felt dry. I remembered Geilie's hands, soft and plump and white, laying out the gems in their patterns, talking lightly of blood.

As though he caught the echo of this thought, Ishmael took a sudden step toward me.

"I ask you, woman—you still bleed?"

Jamie jerked under my hand, but I squeezed his arm to be still.

"Yes," I said. "Why? What has that to do with it?"

The *oniseegun* was plainly uneasy; he glanced from me back toward the huts. A stir was perceptible in the dark behind him; many bodies were moving to and fro, with a mutter of voices like the whisper of the cane fields. They were getting ready to go.

"A woman bleeds, she kill magic. You bleed, got your womanpower, the magic don't work for you. The old women do magic; witch someone, call the *loas*, make sick, make well." He gave me a long, appraising look, and shook his head.

"You ain' gone do the magic, what the Maggot do. That magic kill her, sure, but it kill you, too." He gestured behind him, toward the empty bench. "You hear Bouassa speak? He say the Maggot die, three days. She taken the boy, he die. You go follow them, mon, you die, too, sure."

He stared at Jamie, and raised his hands in front of him, wrists crossed as though bound together. "I tell you, *amiki*," he said. He let his hands fall, jerking them apart, breaking the invisible bond. He turned abruptly, and vanished into the darkness, where the shuffle of feet was growing louder, punctuated with bumps as heavy objects were shifted.

"Holy Michael defend us," muttered Jamie. He ran a hand hard through his hair, making fiery wisps stand out in the flickering light. The fire was dying fast, with no one left to tend it.

"D'ye ken this place, Sassenach? Where Geillis has gone wi' Ian?"

"No, all I know is that it's somewhere up in the far hills on Hispaniola, and that a stream runs through it."

"Then we must take Stern," he said with decision. "Come on; the lads are by the river wi' the boat."

I turned to follow him, but paused on the edge of the cane field to look back.

"Jamie! Look!" Behind us lay the embers of the *egungun*'s fire, and the shadowy ring of slave huts. Farther away, the bulk of Rose Hall made a light patch against the hillside. But farther still, beyond the shoulder of the hill, the sky glowed faintly red.

"That will be Howe's place, burning," he said. He sounded oddly calm, without emotion. He pointed to the left, toward the flank of the mountain, where a small orange dot glowed, no more at this distance than a pinprick of light. "And that will be Twelvetrees, I expect."

The drum-voice whispered through the night, up and down the river. What had Ishmael said? *The drum callin' them down from the hills—those strong enough to go.*

A small line of slaves was coming down from the huts, women carrying babies and bundles, cooking pots slung over their shoulders, heads turbaned in white. Next to one young woman, who held her arm with careful respect, walked Margaret Campbell, likewise turbaned.

Jamie saw her, and stepped forward.

"Miss Campbell!" he said sharply. "Margaret!"

Margaret and her attendant stopped; the young woman moved as though to step between her charge and Jamie, but he held up both hands as he came, to show he meant no harm, and she reluctantly stepped back.

"Margaret," he said. "Margaret, do ye not know me?"

She stared vacantly at him. Very slowly, he touched her, holding her face between his hands.

"Margaret," he said to her, low-voiced, urgent. "Margaret, hear me! D'ye ken me, Margaret?"

She blinked once, then twice, and the smooth round face melted and thawed into life. It was not like the sudden possession of the *loas;* this was a slow, tentative coming, of something shy and fearful.

"Aye, I ken ye, Jamie," she said at last. Her voice was rich and pure, a young girl's voice. Her lips curled up, and her eyes came alive once more, her face still held in the hollow of his hands.

"It's been lang since I saw ye, Jamie," she said, looking up into his eyes. "Will ye have word of Ewan, then? Is he well?"

He stood very still for a minute, his face that careful blank mask that hid strong feeling.

"He is well," he whispered at last. "Verra well, Margaret. He gave me this, to keep until I saw ye." He bent his head and kissed her gently.

Several of the women had stopped, standing silently by to watch. At this, they moved and began to murmur, glancing uneasily at each other. When he released Margaret Campbell and stepped back, they closed in around her, protective and wary, nodding him back.

Margaret seemed oblivious; her eyes were still on Jamie's face, the smile on her lips.

"I thank ye, Jamie!" she called, as her attendant took her arm and began to urge her away. "Tell Ewan I'll be with him soon!" The little band of white-clothed women moved away, disappearing like ghosts into the darkness by the cane field.

Jamie made an impulsive move in their direction, but I stopped him with a hand on his arm.

"Let her go," I whispered, mindful of what lay on the floor in the salon of the plantation house. "Jamie, let her go. You can't stop her; she's better with them."

He closed his eyes briefly, then nodded.

"Aye, you're right." He turned, then stopped suddenly, and I whirled about to see what he had seen. There were lights in Rose Hall now. Torchlight, flickering behind the windows, upstairs and down. As we watched, a surly glow began to swell in the windows of the secret workroom on the second floor.

"It's past time to go," Jamie said. He seized my hand and we went quickly, diving into the dark rustle of the canes, fleeing through air suddenly thick with the smell of burning sugar.

62

Abandawe

"You can take the Governor's pinnace; that's small, but it's seaworthy." Grey fumbled through the drawer of his desk. "I'll write an order for the dockers to hand it over to you."

"Aye, we'll need the boat—I canna risk the *Artemis;* as she's Jared's—but I think we'd best steal it, John." Jamie's brows were drawn together in a frown. "I wouldna have ye be involved wi' me in any visible way, aye? You'll be having trouble enough with things, without that."

Grey smiled unhappily. "Trouble? Yes, you might call it trouble, with four plantation houses burnt, and over two hundred slaves gone—God knows where! But I vastly doubt that anyone will take notice of my social acquaintance, under the circumstances. Between fear of the Maroons and fear of the Chinaman, the whole island is in such a panic that a mere smuggler is the most negligible of trivialities."

"It's a great relief to me to be thought trivial," Jamie said, very dryly. "Still, we'll steal the boat. And if we're taken, ye've never heard my name or seen my face, aye?"

Grey stared at him, a welter of emotions fighting for mastery of his features, amusement, fear, and anger among them.

"Is that right?" he said at last. "Let you be taken, watch them hang you, and keep quiet about it—for fear of smirching my reputation? For God's sake, Jamie, what do you take me for?"

Jamie's mouth twitched slightly.

"For a friend, John," he said. "And if I'll take your friendship

—and your damned boat!—then you'll take mine, and keep quiet. Aye?"

The Governor glared at him for a moment, lips pressed tight, but then his shoulders sagged in defeat.

"I will," he said shortly. "But I should regard it as a great personal favor if you would endeavor not to be captured."

Jamie rubbed a knuckle across his mouth, hiding a smile.

"I'll try verra hard, John."

The Governor sat down, wearily. There were deep circles under his eyes, and his impeccable linen was wilted; obviously he had not changed his clothes from the day before.

"All right. I don't know where you're going, and it's likely better I don't. But if you can, keep out of the sea-lanes north of Antigua. I sent a boat this morning, to ask for as many men as the barracks there can supply, marines and sailors both. They'll be heading this way by the day after tomorrow at the latest, to guard the town and harbor against the escaped Maroons in case of an outright rebellion."

I caught Jamie's eye, and raised one brow in question, but he shook his head, almost imperceptibly. We had told the Governor of the uprising on the Yallahs River, and the escape of the slaves— something he had heard about from other sources, anyway. We had not told him what we had seen later that night, lying to under cover of a tiny cove, sails taken down to hide their whiteness.

The river was dark as onyx, but with a fugitive gleam from the broad expanse of water. We had heard them coming, and had time to hide before the ship came down upon us; the beating of drums and a savage exultation of many voices echoing through the river valley as the *Bruja* sailed past us, carried by the downward current. The bodies of the pirates no doubt lay somewhere upriver, left to rot peacefully among the frangipani and cedar.

The escaped slaves of the Yallahs River had not gone into the mountains of Jamaica, but out to sea, presumably to join Bouassa's followers on Hispaniola. The townsfolk of Kingston had nothing to fear from the escaped slaves—but it was a good deal better that the Royal Navy should concentrate their attention here than on Hispaniola, where we were bound.

Jamie rose to take our leave, but Grey stopped him.

"Wait. Will you not require a safe place for your—for Mrs. Fraser?" He didn't look at me, but at Jamie, eyes steady. "I should be honored if you would entrust her to my protection. She could stay here, in the Residence, until you return. No one would trouble her—or even need to know she was here.''

Jamie hesitated, but there was no gentle way to phrase it.

''She must go with me, John,'' he said. ''There is no choice about it; she must.''

Grey's glance flickered to me, then away, but not before I had seen the look of jealousy in his eyes. I felt sorry for him, but there was nothing I could say; no way to tell him the truth.

''Yes,'' he said, and swallowed noticeably. ''I see. Quite.''

Jamie held out a hand to him. He hesitated for a moment, but then took it.

''Good luck, Jamie,'' he said, voice a little husky. ''God go with you.''

Fergus had been somewhat more difficult to deal with. He had insisted absolutely on accompanying us, offering argument after argument, and arguing the more vehemently when he found that the Scottish smugglers would sail with us.

''You take them, but you will go without *me*?'' Fergus's face was alive with indignation.

''I will,'' Jamie said firmly. ''The smugglers are widowers or bachelors, all, but you're a marrit man.'' He glanced pointedly at Marsali, who stood watching the discussion, her face drawn with anxiety. ''I thought she was oweryoung to be wed, and I was wrong; but I *know* she's oweryoung to be widowed. You'll stay.'' And he turned aside, the matter settled.

It was full dark when we set sail in Grey's pinnace, a thirty-foot, single-decked sloop, leaving two docksmen bound and gagged in the boathouse behind us. It was a small, single-masted ship, bigger than the fishing boat in which we had traveled up the Yallahs River, but barely large enough to qualify for the designation ''ship.''

Nonetheless, she seemed seaworthy enough, and we were soon out of Kingston Harbor, heeling over in a brisk evening breeze, on our way toward Hispaniola.

The smugglers handled the sailing among them, leaving Jamie,

Lawrence, and me to sit on one of the long benches along the rail. We chatted desultorily of this and that, but after a time, fell silent, absorbed in our own thoughts.

Jamie yawned repeatedly, and finally, at my urging, consented to lie down upon the bench, his head resting in my lap. I was myself strung too tightly to want to sleep.

Lawrence too was wakeful, staring upward into the sky, hands folded behind his head.

"There is moisture in the air tonight," he said, nodding upward toward the silver sliver of the crescent moon. "See the haze about the moon? It may rain before dawn; unusual for this time of year."

Talk about the weather seemed sufficiently boring to soothe my jangled nerves. I stroked Jamie's hair, thick and soft under my hand.

"Is that so?" I said. "You and Jamie both seem able to read the weather from the sky. All I know is the old bit about 'Red sky at night, sailor's delight; red sky at morning, sailor take warning.' I didn't notice what color the sky was tonight, did you?"

Lawrence laughed comfortably. "Rather a light purple," he said. "I cannot say whether it will be red in the morning, but it is surprising how frequently such signs are reliable. But of course there is a scientific principle involved—the refraction of light from the moisture in the air, just as I observed presently of the moon."

I lifted my chin, enjoying the breeze that lifted the heavy hair that fell on my neck.

"But what about odd phenomena? Supernatural things?" I asked him. "What about things where the rules of science seem not to apply?" *I am a scientist,* I heard him say in memory, his slight accent seeming only to reinforce his matter-of-factness. *I don't believe in ghosts.*

"Such as what, these phenomena?"

"Well—" I groped for a moment, then fell back on Geilie's own examples. "People who have bleeding stigmata, for example? Astral travel? Visions, supernatural manifestations . . . odd things, that can't be explained rationally."

Lawrence grunted, and settled his bulk more comfortably on the bench beside me.

"Well, I say it is the place of science only to observe," he said. "To seek cause where it may be found, but to realize that there are many things in the world for which no cause shall *be* found; not because it does not exist, but because we know too little to find it. It is not the place of science to insist on explanation—but only to observe, in hopes that the explanation will manifest itself."

"That may be science, but it isn't human nature," I objected. "People go on wanting explanations."

"They do." He was becoming interested in the discussion; he leaned back, folding his hands across his slight paunch, in a lecturer's attitude. "It is for this reason that a scientist constructs hypotheses—suggestions for the cause of an observation. But a hypothesis must never be confused with an explanation—with proof.

"I have seen a great many things which might be described as peculiar. Fish-falls, for instance, where a great many fish—all of the same species, mind you, all the same size—fall suddenly from a clear sky, over dry land. There would appear to be no rational cause for this—and yet, is it therefore suitable to attribute the phenomenon to supernatural interference? On the face of it, does it seem more likely that some celestial intelligence should amuse itself by flinging shoals of fish at us from the sky, or that there is some meteorological phenomenon—a waterspout, a tornado, something of the kind?— that while not visible to us, is still in operation? And yet"—his voice became more pensive—"why— and how!—might a natural phenomenon such as a waterspout remove the heads—and only the heads—of all the fish?"

"Have you seen such a thing yourself?" I asked, interested, and he laughed.

"There speaks a scientific mind!" he said, chuckling. "The first thing a scientist asks—how do you know? Who has seen it? Can I see it myself? Yes, I have seen such a thing—three times, in fact, though in one case the precipi- tation was of frogs, rather than fish."

"Were you near a seashore or a lake?"

"Once near a shore, once near a lake—that was the frogs—but the third time, it took place far inland; some twenty miles from the nearest body of water. And yet the fish were of a kind I have seen only in the deep ocean. In none of the cases did I see any sort of disturbance of the upper air—no clouds, no great wind, none of the fabled spouts of water that rise from the sea into the sky, assuredly. And yet the fish fell; so much is a fact, for I have seen them."

"And it isn't a fact if you haven't seen it?" I asked dryly.

He laughed in delight, and Jamie stirred, murmuring against my thigh. I smoothed his hair, and he relaxed into sleep again.

"It may be so; it may not. But a scientist could not say, could he? What is it the Christian Bible says—'Blest are they who have not seen, but have believed'?"

"That's what it says, yes."

"Some things must be accepted as fact without provable cause." He laughed again, this time without much humor. "As a scientist who is also a Jew, I have perhaps a different perspective on such phenomena as stigmata—and the idea of resurrection of the dead, which a very great proportion of the civilized world accepts as fact beyond question. And yet, this skeptical view is not one I could even breathe, to anyone save yourself, without grave danger of personal harm."

"Doubting Thomas was a Jew, after all," I said, smiling. "To begin with."

"Yes; and only when he ceased to doubt, did he become a Christian—and a martyr. One could argue that it was surety that killed him, no?" His voice was heavy with irony. "There is a great difference between those phenomena which are accepted on faith, and those which are proved by objective determination, though the cause of both may be equally 'rational' once known. And the chief difference is this: that people will treat with disdain such phenomena as are proved by the evidence of the senses, and commonly experienced—while they will defend to the death the reality of a phenomenon which they have neither seen nor experienced.

"Faith is as powerful a force as science," he concluded, voice soft in the darkness, "—but far more dangerous."

We sat quietly for a time, looking over the bow of the tiny ship, toward the thin slice of darkness that divided the night, darker than the purple glow of the sky, or the silver-gray sea. The black island of Hispaniola, drawing inexorably closer.

"Where did you see the headless fish?" I asked suddenly, and was not surprised to see the faint inclination of his head toward the bow.

"There," he said. "I have seen a good many odd things among these islands—but perhaps more there than anywhere else. Some places are like that."

I didn't speak for several minutes, pondering what might lie ahead—and hoping that Ishmael had been right in saying that it was Ian whom Geillis had taken with her to Abandawe. A thought occurred to me—one that had been lost or pushed aside during the events of the last twenty-four hours.

"Lawrence—the other Scottish boys. Ishmael told us he saw twelve of them, including Ian. When you were searching the plantation . . . did you find any trace of the others?"

He drew in his breath sharply, but did not answer at once. I could feel him, turning over words in his mind, trying to decide how to say what the chill in my bones had already told me.

The answer, when it came, was not from Lawrence, but from Jamie.

"We found them," he said softly, from the darkness. His hand rested on my knee, and squeezed gently. "Dinna ask more, Sassenach—for I willna tell ye."

I understood. Ishmael had to have been right; it must be Ian with Geilie, for Jamie could bear no other possibility. I laid a hand on his head, and he stirred slightly, turning so that his breath touched my hand.

"Blest are they who have not seen," I whispered under my breath, *"but have believed."*

We dropped anchor near dawn, in a small, nameless bay on the northern coast of Hispaniola. There was a narrow beach, faced with cliffs, and through a split in the rock, a narrow, sandy trail was visible, leading into the interior of the island.

Jamie carried me the few steps to shore, set me down, and then turned to Innes, who had splashed ashore with one of the parcels of food.

"I thank ye, *a charaid,*" he said formally. "We shall part here; with the Virgin's blessing, we will meet here again in four days' time."

Innes's narrow face contracted in surprised disappointment; then resignation settled on his features.

"Aye," he said. "I'll mind the boatie then, 'til ye all come back."

Jamie saw the expression, and shook his head, smiling.

"Not just you, man; did I need a strong arm, it would be yours I should call on first. No, all of ye shall stay, save my wife and the Jew."

Resignation was replaced by sheer surprise.

"Stay here? All of us? But will ye not have need of us, Mac Dubh?" He squinted anxiously at the cliffs, with their burden of flowering vines. "It looks a fearsome place to venture into, without friends."

"I shall count it the act of greatest friendship for ye to wait here, as I say, Duncan," Jamie said, and I realized with a slight shock that I had never known Innes's given name.

Innes glanced again at the cliffs, his lean face troubled, then bent his head in acquiescence.

"Well, it's you as shall say, Mac Dubh. But ye ken we are willing—all of us."

Jamie nodded, his face turned away.

"Aye, I ken that fine, Duncan," he said softly. Then he turned back, held out an arm, and Innes embraced him, his one arm awkwardly thumping Jamie's back.

"If a ship should come," Jamie said, letting go, "then I wish ye to take heed for yourselves. The Royal Navy will be looking for that pinnace, aye? I doubt they shall come here, looking, but if they should—or if anything else at all should threaten ye—then leave. Sail away at once."

"And leave ye here? Nay, ye can order me to do a great many things, Mac Dubh, and do them I shall—but not that."

Jamie frowned and shook his head; the rising sun struck sparks from his hair and the stubble of his beard, wreathing his head in fire.

"It will do me and my wife no good to have ye killed, Duncan. Mind what I say. If a ship comes—go." He turned aside then, and went to take leave of the other Scots.

Innes sighed deeply, his face etched with disapproval, but he made no further protest.

It was hot and damp in the jungle, and there was little talk among the three of us as we made our way inland. There was nothing to say, after all; Jamie and I could not speak of Brianna before Lawrence, and there were no plans to be made until we reached Abandawe, and saw what was there. I dozed fitfully at night, waking several times to see Jamie, back against a tree near me, eyes fixed sightless on the fire.

At noon of the second day, we reached the place. A steep and rocky hillside of gray limestone rose before us, sprouted over with spiky aloes and a ruffle of coarse grass. And on the crest of the hill, I could see them. Great standing stones, megaliths, in a rough circle about the crown of the hill.

"You didn't say there was a stone circle," I said. I felt faint, and not only from the heat and damp.

"Are you quite well, Mrs. Fraser?" Lawrence peered at me in some alarm, his genial face flushed beneath its tan.

"Yes," I said, but my face must as usual have given me away, for Jamie was there in a moment, taking my arm and steadying me with a hand about my waist.

"For God's sake, be careful, Sassenach!" he muttered. "Dinna go near those things!"

"We have to know if Geilie's there, with Ian," I said. "Come on." I forced my reluctant feet into motion, and he came with me, still muttering under his breath in Gaelic—I thought it was a prayer.

"They were put up a very long time ago," Lawrence said, as we came up onto the crest of the hill, within a few feet of the stones. "Not by slaves—by the aboriginal inhabitants of the islands."

The circle was empty, and innocent-looking. No more than a staggered circle of large stones, set on end, motionless under the sun. Jamie was watching my face anxiously.

"Can ye hear them, Claire?" he said. Lawrence looked startled, but said nothing as I advanced carefully toward the nearest stone.

"I don't know," I said. "It isn't one of the proper days—not a Sun Feast, or a Fire Feast, I mean. It may not be open now; I don't know."

Holding tightly to Jamie's hand, I edged forward, listening. There seemed a faint hum in the air, but it might be no more than the usual sound of the jungle insects. Very gently, I laid the palm of my hand against the nearest stone.

I was dimly conscious of Jamie calling my name. Somewhere, my mind was struggling on a physical level, making the conscious effort to lift and lower my diaphragm, to squeeze and release the chambers of my heart. My ears were filled with a pulsating hum, a vibration too deep for sound, that throbbed in the marrow of my bones. And in some small, still place in the center of the chaos was Geilie Duncan, green eyes smiling into mine.

"Claire!"

I was lying on the ground, Jamie and Lawrence bending over me, faces dark and anxious against the sky. There was dampness on my cheeks, and a trickle of water ran down my neck. I blinked, cautiously moving my extremities, to be sure I still possessed them.

Jamie put down the handkerchief with which he had been bathing my face, and lifted me to a sitting position.

"Are ye all right, Sassenach?"

"Yes," I said, still mildly confused. "Jamie—she's here!"

"Who? Mrs. Abernathy?" Lawrence's heavy eyebrows shot up, and he glanced hastily behind him, as though expecting her to materialize on the spot.

"I heard her—saw her—whatever." My wits were coming slowly back. "She's here. Not in the circle; close by."

"Can ye tell where?" Jamie's hand was resting on his dirk, as he darted quick glances all around us.

I shook my head, and closed my eyes, trying—reluctantly—to recapture that moment of seeing. There was an impression of darkness, of damp coolness, and the flicker of red torchlight.

"I think she's in a cave," I said, amazed. "Is it close by, Lawrence?"

"It is," he said, watching my face with intense curiosity. "The entrance is not far from here."

"Take us there." Jamie was on his feet, lifting me to mine.

"Jamie." I stopped him with a hand on his arm.

"Aye?"

"Jamie—she knows I'm here, too."

That stopped him, all right. He paused, and I saw him swallow. Then his jaw tightened, and he nodded.

"A Mhìcheal bheannaichte, dìon sinn bho dheamhainnean," he said softly, and turned toward the edge of the hill. Blessed Michael, defend us from demons.

The blackness was absolute. I brought my hand to my face; felt my palm brush my nose, but saw nothing. It wasn't an empty blackness, though. The floor of the passage was uneven, with small sharp particles that crunched underfoot, and the walls in some places grew so close together that I wondered how Geilie had ever managed to squeeze through.

Even in the places where the passage grew wider, and the stone walls were too far away for my outstretched hands to brush against, I could feel them. It was like being in a dark room with another person—someone who kept quite silent, but whose presence I could feel, never more than an arm's length away.

Jamie's hand was tight on my shoulder, and I could feel his presence behind me, a warm disturbance in the cool void of the cave.

"Are we headed right?" he asked, when I stopped for a moment to catch my breath. "There are passages to the sides; I feel them as we pass. How can ye tell where we're going?"

"I can hear. Hear them. It. Don't you hear?" It was a struggle to speak, to form coherent thoughts. The call here was different; not the beehive sound of Craigh na Dun, but a hum like the vibration of the air following the striking of a great bell. I could feel it ringing in the long bones of my arms, echoing through pectoral girdle and spine.

Jamie gripped my arm hard.

"Stay with me!" he said. "Sassenach—don't let it take ye; stay!"

I reached blindly out and he caught me tight against his chest. The thump of his heart against my temple was louder than the hum.

"Jamie. Jamie, hold on to me." I had never been more frightened. "Don't let me go. If it takes me—Jamie, I can't come back again. It's worse every time. It will kill me, Jamie!"

His arms tightened round me 'til I felt my ribs crack, and gasped for breath. After a moment, he let go, and putting me gently aside, moved past me into the passage, taking care to keep his hand always on me.

"I'll go first," he said. "Put your hand in my belt, and dinna let go for anything."

Linked together, we moved slowly down, farther into the dark. Lawrence had wanted to come, but Jamie would not let him. We had left him at the mouth of the cave, waiting. If we should not return, he was to go back to the beach, to keep the rendezvous with Innes and the other Scots.

If we should not return . . .

He must have felt my grip tighten, for he stopped, and drew me alongside him.

"Claire," he said softly. "I must say something."

I knew already, and groped for his mouth to stop him, but my hand brushed by his face in the dark. He gripped my wrist, and held tight.

"If it will be a choice between her and one of us—then it must be me. Ye know that, aye?"

I knew that. If Geilie should be there, still, and one of us might be killed in stopping her, it must be Jamie to take the risk. For with Jamie dead, I would be left—and I could follow her through the stone, which he could not.

"I know," I whispered at last. I knew also what he did not say, and what he knew as well; that should Geilie have gone through already, then I must go as well.

"Then kiss me, Claire," he whispered. "And know that you are more to me than life, and I have no regret."

I couldn't answer, but kissed him, first his hand, its crooked fingers warm and firm, and the brawny wrist of a sword-wielder, and then his mouth, haven and promise and anguish all mingled, and the salt of tears in the taste of him.

Then I let go, and turned toward the left-hand tunnel.

"This way," I said. Within ten paces, I saw the light.

It was no more than a faint glow on the rocks of the passage, but it was enough to restore the gift of sight. Suddenly, I could see my hands and feet, though dimly. My breath came out in something like a sob, of relief and fear. I felt like a ghost taking shape as I walked toward the light and the soft bell-hum before me.

The light was stronger, now, then dimmed again as Jamie slid in front of me, and his back blocked my view. Then he bent and stepped through a low archway. I followed, and stood up in light.

It was a good-sized chamber, the walls farthest from the torch still cold and black with the slumber of the cave. The wall before us had wakened, though. It flickered and gleamed, particles of embedded mineral reflecting the flames of a pine torch, fixed in a crevice.

"So ye came, did you?" Geillis was on her knees, eyes fixed on a glittering stream of white powder that fell from her folded fist, drawing a line on the dark floor.

I heard a small sound from Jamie, half relief, half horror, as he saw Ian. The boy lay in the middle of the pentacle on his side, hands bound behind him, gagged with a strip of white cloth. Next to him lay an ax. It was made of a shiny dark stone, like obsidian, with a sharp, chipped edge. The handle was covered with gaudy beadwork, in an African pattern of stripes and zigzags.

"Don't come any closer, fox." Geilie sat back on her heels, showing her teeth to Jamie in an expression that was not a smile. She held a pistol in one hand; its fellow, charged and cocked, was thrust through the leather belt she wore about her waist.

Eyes fixed on Jamie, she reached into the pouch suspended from the belt and withdrew another handful of diamond dust. I could see beads of sweat standing on her broad white brow; the bell-hum from the time-passage must be reaching her as it reached me. I felt sick, and the sweat ran down my body in trickles under my clothes.

The pattern was almost finished. With the pistol carefully trained, she dribbled out the thin, shining stream until she had completed the pentagram. The stones were already laid inside it—they glinted from the floor in sparks of color, connected by a gleaming line of poured quicksilver.

"There, then." She sat back on her heels with a sigh of relief, and wiped the thick, creamy hair back with one hand. "Safe. The diamond dust keeps out the noise," she explained to me. "Nasty, isn't it?"

She patted Ian, who lay bound and gagged on the ground in front of her, his eyes wide with fear above the white cloth of the gag. "There, there, *mo chridhe*. Dinna fret, it will be soon over."

"Take your hand off him, ye wicked bitch!" Jamie took an impulsive step forward, hand on his dirk, then stopped, as she lifted the barrel of the pistol an inch.

"Ye mind me o' your uncle Dougal, *a sionnach*," she said, tilting her head to one side coquettishly. "He was older when I met him than you are now, but you've the look of him about ye, aye? Like ye'd take what ye pleased and damn anyone who stands in your way."

Jamie looked at Ian, curled on the floor, then up at Geilie.

"I'll take what's mine," he said softly.

"But ye can't, now, can ye?" she said, pleasantly. "One more step, and I kill ye dead. I spare ye now, only because Claire seems fond of ye.'' Her eyes shifted to me, standing in the shadows behind Jamie. She nodded to me.

"A life for a life, sweet Claire. Ye tried to save me once, on Craigh na Dun; I saved you from the witch-trial at Cranesmuir. We're quits now, aye?"

Geilie picked up a small bottle, uncorked it, and poured the contents carefully over Ian's clothes. The smell of brandy rose up, strong and heady, and the torch flared brighter as the fumes of alcohol reached it. Ian bucked and kicked, making a strained noise of protest, and she kicked him sharply in the ribs.

"Be still!" she said.

"Don't do it, Geilie," I said, knowing that words would do no good.

"I have to," she said calmly. "I'm meant to. I'm sorry I shall have to take the girl, but I'll leave ye the man."

"What girl?" Jamie's fists were clenched tight at his side, knuckles white even in the dim torchlight.

"Brianna? That's the name, isn't it?" She shook back her heavy hair, smoothing it out of her face. "The last of Lovat's line." She smiled at me. "What luck ye should have come to see me, aye? I'd never ha' kent it, otherwise. I thought they'd all died out before 1900."

A thrill of horror shot through me. I could feel the same tremor run through Jamie as his muscles tightened.

It must have shown on his face. Geilie cried out sharply and leapt back. She fired as he lunged at her. His head snapped back, and his body twisted, hands still reaching for her throat. Then he fell, his body limp across the edge of the glittering pentagram. There was a strangled moan from Ian.

I felt rather than heard a sound rise in my throat. I didn't know what I had said, but Geilie turned her face in my direction, startled.

When Brianna was two, a car had carelessly sideswiped mine, hitting the back door next to where she was sitting. I slowed to a stop, checked briefly to see that she was unhurt, and then bounded out, headed for the other car, which had pulled over a little way ahead.

The other driver was a man in his thirties, quite large, and probably entirely self-assured in his dealings with the world. He looked over his shoulder, saw me coming, and hastily rolled up his window, shrinking back in his seat.

I had no consciousness of rage or any other emotion; I simply *knew,* with no shadow of doubt, that I could—and would—shatter the window with my hand, and drag the man out through it. He knew it, too.

I thought no further than that, and didn't have to; the arrival of a police car had recalled me to my normal state of mind, and then I started to shake. But the memory of the look on that man's face stayed with me.

Fire is a poor illuminator, but it would have taken total darkness to conceal that look on Geilie's face; the sudden realization of what was coming toward her.

She jerked the other pistol from her belt and swung it to bear on me; I saw the round hole of the muzzle clearly—and didn't care. The roar of the discharge caromed through the cave, the echoes sending down showers of rocks and dirt, but by then I had seized the ax from the floor.

I noted quite clearly the leather binding, ornamented with a beaded pattern. It was red, with yellow zigzags and black dots. The dots echoed the shiny obsidian of the blade, and the red and yellow picked up the hues of the flaming torch behind her.

I heard a noise behind me, but didn't turn. Reflections of the fire burned red in the pupils of her eyes. *The red thing,* Jamie had called it. *I gave myself to it,* he had said.

I didn't need to give myself; it had taken me.

There was no fear, no rage, no doubt. Only the stroke of the swinging ax.

The shock of it echoed up my arm, and I let go, my fingers numbed. I stood quite still, not even moving when she staggered toward me.

Blood in firelight is black, not red.

She took one blind step forward and fell, all her muscles gone limp, making no attempt to save herself. The last I saw of her face was her eyes; set wide, beautiful as gemstones, a green water-clear and faceted with the knowledge of death.

Someone was speaking, but the words made no sense. The cleft in the rock buzzed loudly, filling my ears. The torch flickered, flaring sudden yellow in a draft; the beating of the dark angel's wings, I thought.

The sound came again, behind me.

I turned and saw Jamie. He had risen to his knees, swaying. Blood was pouring from his scalp, dyeing one side of his face red-black. The other side was white as a harlequin's mask.

Stop the bleeding, said some remnant of instinct in my brain, and I fumbled for a handkerchief. But by then he had crawled to where Ian lay, and was groping at the boy's bonds, jerking loose the leather straps, drops of his blood pattering on the lad's shirt. Ian squirmed to his feet, his face ghastly pale, and put out a hand to help his uncle.

Then Jamie's hand was on my arm. I looked up, numbly offering the cloth. He took it and wiped it roughly over his face, then jerked at my arm, pulling me toward the tunnel mouth. I stumbled and nearly fell, caught myself, and came back to the present.

"Come!" he was saying. "Can ye not hear the wind? There is a storm coming, above."

Wind? I thought. In a cave? But he was right; the draft had not been my imagination; the faint exhalation from the crack near the entrance had changed to a steady, whining wind, almost a keening that rang in the narrow passage.

I turned to look over my shoulder, but Jamie grasped my arm hard and pushed me forward. My last sight of the cave was a blurred impression of jet and rubies, with a still white shape in the middle of the floor. Then the draft came in with a roar, and the torch went out.

"Jesus!" It was Young Ian's voice, filled with terror, somewhere close by. "Uncle Jamie!"

"Here." Jamie's voice came out of the darkness just in front of me, surprisingly calm, raised to be heard above the noise. "Here, lad. Come here to me, Ian. Dinna be afraid; it's only the cave breathing."

It was the wrong thing to say. When he said it, I could *feel* the cold breath of the rock touch my neck, and the hairs there rose up prickling. The image of the cave as a living thing, breathing all around us, blind and malevolent, struck me cold with horror.

Apparently the notion was as terrifying to Ian as it was to me, for I heard a faint gasp, and then his groping hand struck me and clung for dear life to my arm.

I clutched his hand with one of mine and probed the dark ahead with the other, finding Jamie's reassuringly large shape almost at once.

"I've got Ian," I said. "For God's sake, let's get out of here!"

He gripped my hand in answer, and linked together, we began to make our way back down the winding tunnel, stumbling through the pitch dark and stepping on each other's heels. And all the time, that ghostly wind whined at our backs.

I could see nothing; no hint of Jamie's shirt in front of my face, snowy white as I knew it to be, not even a flicker of the movement of my own light-colored skirts, though I heard them swish about my feet as I walked, the sound blending with that of the wind.

The thin rush of air rose and fell in pitch, whispering and wailing. I tried to force my mind away from the memory of what lay behind us, away from the morbid fancy that the wind held sighing voices, whispering secrets just past hearing.

"I can hear her," Ian said suddenly behind me. His voice rose, cracking with panic. "I can hear her! God, oh God, she's coming!"

I froze in my tracks, a scream wedged in my throat. The cool observer in my head knew quite well it was not so—only the wind and Ian's fright—but that made no difference to the spurt of sheer terror that rose from the pit of my stomach and turned my bowels to water. I knew she was coming, too, and screamed out loud.

Then Jamie had me, and Ian too, gripped tight against him, one in each arm, our ears muffled against his chest. He smelled of pine smoke and sweat and brandy, and I nearly sobbed in relief at the closeness of him.

"Hush!" he said fiercely. "Hush, the both of ye! I willna let her touch ye. Never!" He pressed us to him, hard; I felt his heart beating fast beneath my cheek and Ian's bony shoulder, squeezed against mine, and then the pressure relaxed.

"Come along now," Jamie said, more quietly. "It's but wind. Caves blow through their cracks when the weather changes aboveground. I've heard it before. There is a storm coming, outside. Come, now."

The storm was a brief one. By the time we had stumbled to the surface, blinking against the shock of sunlight, the rain had passed, leaving the world reborn in its wake.

Lawrence was sheltering under a dripping palm near the cave's entrance. When he saw us, he sprang to his feet, a look of relief relaxing the creases of his face.

"It is all right?" he said, looking from me to a blood-stained Jamie.

Jamie gave him half a smile, nodding.

"It is all right," he said. He turned and motioned to Ian. "May I present my nephew, Ian Murray? Ian, this is Dr. Stern, who's been of great assistance to us in looking for ye."

"I'm much obliged to ye, Doctor," Ian said, with a bob of his head. He wiped a sleeve across his streaked face, and glanced at Jamie.

"I knew ye'd come, Uncle Jamie," he said, with a tremulous smile, "but ye left it a bit late, aye?" The smile widened, then broke, and he began to tremble. He blinked hard, fighting back tears.

"I did then, and I'm sorry, Ian. Come here, *a bhalaich*." Jamie reached out and took him in a close embrace, patting his back and murmuring to him in Gaelic.

I watched for a moment, before I realized that Lawrence was speaking to me.

"Are you quite well, Mrs. Fraser?" he was asking. Without waiting for an answer, he took my arm.

"I don't quite know." I felt completely empty. Exhausted as though by childbirth, but without the exultation of spirit. Nothing seemed quite real; Jamie, Ian, Lawrence, all seemed like toy figures that moved and talked at a distance, making noises that I had to strain to understand.

"I think perhaps we should leave this place," Lawrence said, with a glance at the cave mouth from which we had just emerged. He looked slightly uneasy. He didn't ask about Mrs. Abernathy.

"I think you are right." The picture of the cave we had left was vivid in my mind—but just as unreal as the vivid green jungle and gray stones around us. Not waiting for the men to follow, I turned and walked away.

The feeling of remoteness increased as we walked. I felt like an automaton, built around an iron core, walking by clockwork. I followed Jamie's broad back through branches and clearings, shadow and sun, not noticing where we were going. Sweat ran down my sides and into my eyes, but I barely stirred to wipe it away. At length, toward sunset, we stopped in a small clearing near a stream, and made our primitive camp.

I had already discovered that Lawrence was a most useful person to have along on a camping trip. He was not only as good at finding or building shelter as was Jamie, but was sufficiently familiar with the flora and fauna of the area to be able to plunge into the jungle and return within half an hour bearing handfuls of edible roots, fungi, and fruit with which to augment the Spartan rations in our packs.

Ian was set to gather firewood while Lawrence foraged, and I sat Jamie down with a pan of water, to tend the damage to his head. I washed away the blood from face and hair, to find to my surprise that the ball had in fact not plowed a furrow through his scalp as I had thought. Instead, it had pierced the skin just above his hairline and—evidently—vanished into his head. There was no sign of an exit wound. Unnerved by this, I prodded his scalp with increasing agitation, until a sudden cry from the patient announced that I had discovered the bullet.

There was a large, tender lump on the back of his head. The pistol ball had traveled under the skin, skimming the curve of his skull, and come to rest just over his occiput.

"Jesus H. Christ!" I exclaimed. I felt it again, unbelieving, but there it was. "You always said your head was solid bone, and I'll be damned if you weren't right. She shot you point-blank, and the bloody ball bounced off your skull!"

Jamie, supporting his head in his hands as I examined him, made a sound somewhere between a snort and a groan.

"Aye, well," he said, his voice somewhat muffled in his hands, "I'll no say I'm not thick-heided, but if Mistress Abernathy had used a full charge of powder, it wouldna have been nearly thick enough."

"Does it hurt a lot?"

"Not the wound, no, though it's sore. I've a terrible headache, though."

"I shouldn't wonder. Hold on a bit; I'm going to take the ball out."

Not knowing in what condition we might find Ian, I had brought the smallest of my medical boxes, which fortunately contained a bottle of alcohol and a small scalpel. I shaved away a little of Jamie's abundant mane, just below the swelling, and soused the area with alcohol for disinfection. My fingers were chilled from the alcohol, but his head was warm and comfortingly live to the touch.

"Three deep breaths and hold on tight," I murmured. "I'm going to cut you, but it will be fast."

"All right." The back of his neck looked a little pale, but the pulse was steady. He obligingly drew in his breath deeply, and exhaled, sighing. I held the area of scalp taut between the index and third fingers of my left hand. On the third breath, I said, "Right now," and drew the blade hard and quick across the scalp. He grunted slightly, but didn't cry out. I pressed gently with my right thumb against the swelling, slightly harder—and the ball popped out of the incision I had made, falling into my left hand like a grape.

"Got it," I said, and only then realized that I had been holding my breath. I dropped the little pellet—somewhat flattened by its contact with his skull—into his hand, and smiled, a little shakily. "Souvenir," I said. I pressed a pad of cloth against the small wound, wound a strip of cloth round his head to hold it, and then quite suddenly, with no warning whatever, began to cry.

I could feel the tears rolling down my face, and my shoulders shaking, but I felt still detached; somehow outside my body. I was conscious mostly of a mild amazement.

"Sassenach? Are ye all right?" Jamie was peering up at me, eyes worried under the rakish bandage.

"Yes," I said, stuttering from the force of my crying. "I d-don't k-know why I'm c-crying. I d-don't know!"

"Come here." He took my hand and drew me down onto his knee. He wrapped his arms around me and held me tight, resting his cheek on the top of my head.

"It will be all right," he whispered. "It's fine now, *mo chridhe,* it's fine." He rocked me gently, one hand stroking my hair and neck, and murmured small unimportant things in my ear. Just as suddenly as I had been detached, I was back inside my body, warm and shaking, feeling the iron core dissolve in my tears.

Gradually I stopped weeping, and lay still against his chest, hiccuping now and then, feeling nothing but peace and the comfort of his presence.

I was dimly aware that Lawrence and Ian had returned, but paid no attention to them. At one point, I heard Ian say, with more curiosity than alarm, "You're bleeding all down the back of your neck, Uncle Jamie."

"Perhaps you'll fix me a new bandage, then, Ian," Jamie said. His voice was soft and unconcerned. "I must just hold your auntie now." And sometime later I went to sleep, still held tight in the circle of his arms.

I woke up later, curled on a blanket next to Jamie. He was leaning against a tree, one hand resting on my shoulder. He felt me wake, and squeezed gently. It was dark, and I could hear a rhythmic snoring somewhere close at hand. It must be Lawrence, I thought drowsily, for I could hear Young Ian's voice, on the other side of Jamie.

"No," he was saying slowly, "it wasna really so bad, on the ship. We were all kept together, so there was company from the other lads, and they fed us decently, and let us out two at a time to walk about the deck. Of course, we were all scairt, for we'd no notion why we'd been taken—and none of the sailors would tell us anything—but we were not mistreated."

The *Bruja* had sailed up the Yallahs River, and delivered her human cargo directly to Rose Hall. Here the bewildered boys had been warmly welcomed by Mrs. Abernathy, and promptly popped into a new prison.

The basement beneath the sugar mill had been fitted up comfortably enough, with beds and chamber pots, and aside from the noise of the sugar-making above during the days, it was comfortable enough. Still, none of the boys could think why they were there, though any number of suggestions were made, each more improbable than the last.

"And every now and then, a great black fellow would come down into the place with Mrs. Abernathy. We always begged to know what it was we were there for, and would she not be letting us go, for mercy's sake? but she only smiled and patted us and said we would see, in good time. Then she would choose a lad, and the black fellow would clamp on to the lad's arm and take him awa' wi' them." Ian's voice sounded distressed, and little wonder.

"Did the lads come back again?" Jamie asked. His hand patted me softly, and I reached up and pressed it.

"No—or not usually. And that scairt us all something dreadful."

Ian's turn had come eight weeks after his arrival. Three lads had gone and not returned by then, and when Mistress Abernathy's bright green eyes rested on him, he was not disposed to cooperate.

"I kicked the black fellow, and hit him—I even bit his hand," Ian said ruefully, "and verra nasty he tasted, too—all over some kind of grease, he was. But it made nay difference; he only clouted me over the head, hard enough to make my ears ring, then picked me up and carried me off in his arms, as though I was no more than a wee bairn."

Ian had been taken into the kitchen, where he was stripped, bathed, dressed in a clean shirt—but nothing else—and taken to the main house.

"It was just at night," he said wistfully, "and all the windows lighted. It looked verra much like Lallybroch, when ye come down from the hills just at dark, and Mam's just lit the lamps—it almost broke my heart to see it, and think of home."

He had had little opportunity to feel homesick, though. Hercules—or Atlas—had marched him up the stairs into what was obviously Mistress Abernathy's bedroom. Mrs. Abernathy was waiting for him, dressed in a soft, loose sort of gown with odd-looking figures embroidered round the hem of it in red and silver thread.

She had been cordial and welcoming, and had offered him a drink. It smelled strange, but not nasty, and as he had little choice in the matter, he had drunk it.

There were two comfortable chairs in the room, on either side of a long, low table, and a great bed at one side, swagged and canopied like a king's. He had sat in one chair, Mrs. Abernathy in the other, and she had asked him questions.

"What sorts of questions?" Jamie asked, prompting as Ian seemed hesitant.

"Well, all about my home, and my family—she asked the names of all my sisters and brothers, and my aunts and uncles"— I jerked a bit. So that *was* why Geilie had betrayed no surprise at our appearance! —"and all sorts of things, Uncle. Then she—she asked me had I—had I ever lain wi' a lassie. Just as though she were asking did I have parritch to my breakfast!" Ian sounded shocked at the memory.

"I didna want to answer her, but I couldna seem to help myself.

I felt verra warm, like I was fevered, and I couldna seem to move easy. But I answered all her questions, and her just sitting there, pleasant as might be, watching me close wi' those big green eyes.''

"So ye told her the truth?"

"Aye. Aye, I did." Ian spoke slowly, reliving the scene. "I said I had, and I told her about—about Edinburgh, and the printshop, and the seaman, and the brothel, and Mary, and—everything."

For the first time, Geilie had seemed displeased with one of his answers. Her face had grown hard and her eyes narrowed, and for a moment, Ian was seriously afraid. He would have run, then, but for the heaviness in his limbs, and the presence of the giant who stood against the door, unmoving.

"She got up and stamped about a bit, and said I was ruined, then, as I wasna a virgin, and what business did a bittie wee lad like me have, to be goin' wi' the lassies and spoiling myself?"

Then she had stopped her ranting, poured a glass of wine and drank it off, and her temper had seemed to cool.

"She laughed then, and looked at me careful, and said as how I might not be such a loss, after all. If I was no good for what she had in mind, perhaps I might have other uses." Ian's voice sounded faintly constricted, as though his collar were too tight. Jamie made a soothing interrogatory sound, though, and he took a deep breath, determined to go on.

"Well, she—she took my hand and made me stand up. Then she took off the shirt I was wearing, and she—I swear it's true, Uncle! —she knelt on the floor in front of me, and took my cock into her mouth!"

Jamie's hand tightened on my shoulder, but his voice betrayed no more than a mild interest.

"Aye, I believe ye, Ian. She made love to ye, then?"

"Love?" Ian sounded dazed. "No—I mean, I dinna ken. It—she—well, she got my cock to stand up, and then she made me come to the bed and lie down and she did things. But it wasna at all like it was with wee Mary!"

"No, I shouldna suppose it was," his uncle said dryly.

"God, it felt queer!" I could sense Ian's shudder from the tone of his voice. "I looked up in the middle, and there was the black man, standing right by the bed, holding a candlestick. She told him to lift it higher, so that she could see better." He paused, and I heard a small glugging noise as he drank from one of the bottles. He let out a long, quivering breath.

"Uncle. Have ye ever—lain wi' a woman, when ye didna want to do it?"

Jamie hesitated a moment, his hand tight on my shoulder, but then he said quietly, "Aye, Ian. I have."

"Oh." The boy was quiet, and I heard him scratch his head. "D'ye ken how it can be, Uncle? How ye can do it, and not want to a bit, and hate doing it, and—and still it—it feels good?"

Jamie gave a small, dry laugh.

"Well, what it comes to, Ian, is that your cock hasna got a conscience, and you have." His hand left my shoulder as he turned toward his nephew. "Dinna trouble yourself, Ian," he said. "Ye couldna help it, and it's likely that it saved your life for ye. The other lads—the ones who didna come back to the cellar—d'ye ken if they were virgins?"

"Well—a few I know were for sure—for we had a great deal of time to talk, aye? and after a time we kent a lot about one another. Some o' the lads boasted of havin' gone wi' a lassie, but I thought —from what they said about it, ye ken—that they hadna done it, really." He paused for a moment, as though reluctant to ask what he knew he must.

"Uncle—d'ye ken what happened to them? The rest of the lads with me?"

"No, Ian," Jamie said, evenly. "I've no notion." He leaned back against the tree, sighing deeply. "D'ye think ye can sleep, wee Ian? If ye can, ye should, for it will be a weary walk to the shore tomorrow."

"Oh, I can sleep, Uncle," Ian assured him. "But should I not keep watch? It's you should be resting, after bein' shot and all that." He paused and then added, rather shyly, "I didna say thank ye, Uncle Jamie."

Jamie laughed, freely this time.

"You're verra welcome, Ian," he said, the smile still in his voice. "Lay your head and sleep, laddie. I'll wake ye if there's need."

Ian obligingly curled up and within moments, was breathing heavily. Jamie sighed and leaned back against the tree.

"Do you want to sleep too, Jamie?" I pushed myself up to sit beside him. "I'm awake; I can keep an eye out."

His eyes were closed, the dying firelight dancing on the lids. He smiled without opening them and groped for my hand.

"No. If ye dinna mind sitting with me for a bit, though, you can watch. The headache's better if I close my eyes."

We sat in contented silence for some time, hand in hand. An occasional odd noise or far-off scream from some jungle animal came from the dark, but nothing seemed threatening now.

"Will we go back to Jamaica?" I asked at last. "For Fergus and Marsali?"

Jamie started to shake his head, then stopped, with a stifled groan.

"No," he said, "I think we shall sail for Eleuthera. That's Dutch-owned, and neutral. We can send Innes back wi' John's boatie, and he can take a message to Fergus to come and join us. I would as soon not set foot on Jamaica again, all things considered."

"No, I suppose not." I was quiet for a moment, then said, "I wonder how Mr. Willoughby—Yi Tien Cho, I mean—will manage. I don't suppose anyone will find him, if he stays in the mountains, but—"

"Oh, he may manage brawly," Jamie interrupted. "He's the pelican to fish for him, after all." One side of his mouth turned up in a smile. "For that matter, if he's canny, he'll find a way south, to Martinique. There's a small colony there of Chinese traders. I'd told him of it; said I'd take him there, once our business on Jamaica was finished."

"You aren't angry at him now?" I looked at him curiously, but his face was smooth and peaceful, almost unlined in the firelight.

This time he was careful not to move his head, but lifted one shoulder in a shrug, and grimaced.

"Och, no." He sighed and settled himself more comfortably. "I dinna suppose he had much thought for what he did, or understood at all what might be the end of it. And it would be foolish to hate a man for not giving ye something he hasna got in the first place." He opened his eyes then, with a faint smile, and I knew he was thinking of John Grey.

Ian twitched in his sleep, snorted loudly, and rolled over onto his back, arms flung wide. Jamie glanced at his nephew, and the smile grew wider.

"Thank God," he said. "*He* goes back to his mother by the first ship headed for Scotland."

"I don't know," I said, smiling. "He might not want to go back to Lallybroch, after all this adventure."

"I dinna care whether he wants to or not," Jamie said firmly. "He's going, if I must pack him up in a crate. Are ye looking for something, Sassenach?" he added, seeing me groping in the dark.

"I've got it," I said, pulling the flat hypodermic case out of my pocket. I flipped it open to check the contents, squinting to see by the waning light. "Oh, good; there's enough left for one whopping dose."

Jamie sat up a little straighter.

"I'm not fevered a bit," he said, eyeing me warily. "And if ye have it in mind to shove that filthy spike into my head, ye can just think again, Sassenach!"

"Not you," I said. "Ian. Unless you mean to send him home to Jenny riddled with syphilis and other interesting forms of the clap."

Jamie's eyebrows rose toward his hairline, and he winced at the resultant sensation.

"Ow. Syphilis? Ye think so?"

"I shouldn't be a bit surprised. Pronounced dementia is one of the symptoms of the advanced disease—though I must say it would be hard to tell in her case. Still, better safe than sorry, hm?"

Jamie snorted briefly with amusement.

"Well, that may teach Young Ian the price o' dalliance. I'd best distract Stern while ye take the lad behind a bush for his penance, though; Lawrence is a bonny man for a Jew, but he's curious. I dinna want ye burnt at the stake in Kingston, after all."

"I expect that would be awkward for the Governor," I said dryly. "Much as he might enjoy it, personally."

"I shouldna think he would, Sassenach." His dryness matched my own. "Is my coat within reach?"

"Yes." I found the garment folded on the ground near me, and handed it to him. "Are you cold?"

"No." He leaned back, the coat laid across his knees. "It's only that I wanted to feel the bairns all close to me while I sleep." He smiled at me, folded his hands gently atop the coat and its pictures, and closed his eyes again. "Good night, Sassenach."

63

Out of the Depths

In the morning, buoyed by rest and a breakfast of biscuit and plantain, we pressed on toward the shore in good heart—even Ian, who ceased to limp ostentatiously after the first quarter-mile. As we came down the defile that led onto the beach, though, a remarkable sight met our eyes.

"Jesus God, it's them!" Ian blurted. "The pirates!" He turned, ready to flee back into the hills, but Jamie grasped him by the arm.

"Not pirates," he said. "It's the slaves. Look!"

Unskilled in the seamanship of large vessels, the escaped slaves of the Yallahs River plantations had evidently made a slow and blundering passage toward Hispaniola, and having somehow arrived at that island, had promptly run the ship aground. The *Bruja* lay canted on her side in the shallows, her keel sunk deep in the sandy mud. A very agitated group of slaves surrounded her, some rushing up and down the beach shouting, others dashing off toward the refuge of the jungle, a few remaining to help the last of their number off the beached hulk.

A quick glance out to sea showed the cause of their agitation. A patch of white showed on the horizon, growing in size even as we watched.

"A man-of-war," Lawrence said, sounding interested.

Jamie said something under his breath in Gaelic, and Ian glanced at him, shocked.

"Out of here," Jamie said tersely. He pulled Ian about and gave him a shove up the defile, then grabbed my hand.

"Wait!" said Lawrence, shading his eyes. "There's another ship coming. A little one."

The Governor of Jamaica's private pinnace, to be exact, leaning at a perilous angle as she shot round the curve of the bay, her canvas bellied by the wind on her quarter.

Jamie stood for a split second, weighing the possibilities, then grabbed my hand again.

"Let's go!" he said.

By the time we reached the edge of the beach, the pinnace's small boat was plowing through the shallows, Raeburn and Mac-Leod pulling hard at the oars. I was wheezing and gulping air, my knees rubbery from the run. Jamie snatched me up bodily into his arms and ran into the surf, followed by Lawrence and Ian, gasping like whales.

I saw Gordon, a hundred yards out in the pinnace's bow, aim a gun at the shore, and knew we were followed. The musket discharged with a puff of smoke, and Meldrum, behind him, promptly raised his own weapon and fired. Taking it in turns, the two of them covered our splashing advance, until friendly hands could pull us over the side and raise the boat.

"Come about!" Innes, manning the wheel, barked the order, and the boom swung across, the sails filling at once. Jamie hauled me to my feet and deposited me on a bench, then flung himself down beside me, panting.

"Holy God," he wheezed. "Did I no—tell ye to—stay away— Duncan?"

"Save your breath, Mac Dubh," Innes said, a wide grin spreading under his mustache. "Ye havena enough to be wasting it." He shouted something to MacLeod, who nodded and did something to the lines. The pinnace heeled over, changed her course, and came about, headed straight out of the tiny cove—and straight toward the man-of-war, now close enough for me to see the fat-lipped porpoise grinning beneath its bowsprit.

MacLeod bellowed something in Gaelic, accompanied by a gesture that left the meaning of what he had said in no doubt. To a triumphant yodel from Innes, we shot past the *Porpoise*, directly under her bow and close enough to see surprised-looking heads poking out from the rail above.

I looked back as we left the cove, to see the *Porpoise* still heading in, massive under her three great masts. The pinnace could never outrace her on the open sea, but in close quarters, the little sloop was light and maneuverable as a feather by comparison to the leviathan man-of-war.

"It's the slave ship they'll be after," Meldrum said, turning to look alongside me. "We saw the man-o'-war pick her up, three miles off the island. We thought whilst they were otherwise occupied, we might as well nip in and pick ye all off the beach."

"Good enough," Jamie said with a smile. His chest was still heaving, but he had recovered his breath. "I hope the *Porpoise* will be sufficiently occupied for the time being."

A warning shout from Raeburn indicated that this was not to be, however. Looking back, I could see the gleam of brass on the *Porpoise*'s deck as the pair of long guns called stern chasers were uncovered and began their process of aiming.

Now it was us at gunpoint, and I found the sensation very objectionable. Still, we were moving, and fast, at that. Innes put the wheel hard over, then hard again, tacking a zigzag path past the headland.

The stern chasers boomed together. There was a splash off the port bow, twenty yards away, but a good deal too close for comfort, given the fact that a twenty-four-pound ball through the floor of the pinnace would sink us like a rock.

Innes cursed and hunched his shoulders over the wheel, his missing arm giving him an odd, lopsided appearance. Our course became still more erratic, and the next three tries came nowhere near. Then came a louder boom, and I looked back to see the side of the canted *Bruja* erupt in splinters, as the *Porpoise* came in range and trained her forward guns on the grounded ship.

A rain of grapeshot hit the beach, striking dead in the center of a group of fleeing slaves. Bodies—and parts of bodies—flew into the air like black stick-figures and fell to the sand, staining it with red blotches. Severed limbs were scattered over the beach like driftwood.

"Holy Mary, Mother of God." Ian, white to the lips, crossed himself, staring in horror at the beach as the shelling went on. Two more shots struck the *Bruja,* opening up a great hole in her side. Several landed harmlessly in the sand, and two more found their mark among the fleeing people. Then we were round the edge of the headland, and heading into the open sea, the beach and its carnage lost to view.

"Pray for us sinners, now and at the hour of our death." Ian finished his prayer in a whisper, and crossed himself again.

There was little conversation in the boat, beyond Jamie's giving Innes instructions for Eleuthera, and a conference between Innes and MacLeod as to the proper heading. The rest of us were too appalled by what we had just seen—and too relieved at our own escape—to want to talk.

The weather was fair, with a bright, brisk breeze, and we made good way. By sundown, the island of Hispaniola had dropped below the horizon, and Grand Turk Island was rising to the left.

I ate my small share of the available biscuit, drank a cup of water, and curled myself in the bottom of the boat, lying down between Ian and Jamie to sleep. Innes, yawning, took his own rest in the bow, while MacLeod and Meldrum took it in turns to man the helm through the night.

A shout woke me in the morning. I rose on one elbow, blinking with sleep and stiff from a night spent on bare, damp boards. Jamie was standing by me, his hair blowing back in the morning breeze.

"What?" I asked Jamie. "What is it?"

"I dinna believe it," he said, staring aft over the rail. "It's that bloody boat again!"

I scrambled to my feet, to find that it was true; far astern were tiny white sails.

"Are you sure?" I said, squinting. "Can you tell at this distance?"

"I can't, no," Jamie said frankly, "but Innes and MacLeod can, and they say it's the bloodsucking English, right enough. They'll have guessed our heading, maybe, and come after us, as soon as they'd dealt with those poor black buggers on Hispaniola." He turned away from the rail, shrugging.

"Damned little to be done about it, save to hope we stay ahead of them. Innes says there's a hope of giving them the slip off Cat Island, if we reach there by dark."

As the day wore on, we kept just out of firing distance, but Innes looked more and more worried.

The sea between Cat Island and Eleuthera was shallow, and filled with coral heads. A man-of-war could never follow us into the maze—but neither could we move swiftly enough through it to avoid being sunk by the *Porpoise*'s long guns. Once in those treacherous shoals and channels, we would be sitting ducks.

At last, reluctantly, the decision was made to head east, out to sea; we could not risk slowing, and there was a slight chance of giving the man-of-war the slip in the dark.

When dawn came, all sight of land had disappeared. The *Porpoise*, unfortunately, had not. She was no closer, but as the wind rose along with the sun, she shook out more sail, and began to gain. With every scrap of sail already hoisted, and nowhere to hide, there was nothing we could do but run—and wait.

All through the long hours of the morning, the *Porpoise* grew steadily larger astern. The sky had begun to cloud over, and the wind had risen considerably, but this helped the *Porpoise*, with her huge spread of canvas, a great deal more than it did us.

By ten o'clock, she was close enough to risk a shot. It fell far astern, but was frightening, nonetheless. Innes squinted back over his shoulder, judging the distance, then shook his head and settled grimly to his course. There was nothing to be gained by tacking now; we must head straight on, as long as we could, taking evasive action only when it was too late for anything else.

By eleven, the *Porpoise* had drawn within a quarter-mile, and the monotonous boom of her forward guns had begun to sound every ten minutes, as her gunner tried the range. If I closed my eyes, I could imagine Erik Johansen, bent sweating and powder-stained over his gun, the smoking slow-match in his hand. I hoped that Annekje had been left on Antigua with her goats.

By eleven-thirty, it had begun to rain, and a heavy sea was running. A sudden gust of wind struck us sideways, and the boat heeled over far enough to bring the port rail within a foot of the water. Dumped onto the deck by the motion, we disentangled ourselves as Innes and MacLeod skillfully righted the pinnace. I glanced back, as I did every few minutes, despite myself, and saw the seamen scampering aloft in the *Porpoise*, reefing the topsails.

"That's luck!" MacGregor shouted in my ear, nodding where I was looking. "That'll slow them."

By twelve-thirty, the sky had gone a peculiar purple-green, and the wind had risen to an eerie whine. The *Porpoise* had taken in yet more canvas, and in spite of the action, had had a staysail carried away, the scrap of canvas jerked from the mast and whipped away, flapping like an albatross. She had long since stopped firing on us, unable to aim at such a small target in the heavy swell.

With the sun gone from sight, I could no longer estimate time. The storm caught us squarely, perhaps an hour later. There was no possibility of hearing anything; by sign language and grimaces, Innes made the men lower the sails; to keep canvas flying, or even reefed, was to risk having the mast ripped from the floorboards.

I clung tight to the rail with one hand, to Ian's hand with the other. Jamie crouched behind us, arms spread to give us the shelter of his back. The rain lashed past, hard enough to sting the skin, driven almost horizontal by the wind, and so thick that I barely saw the faint shape on the horizon that I thought was Eleuthera.

The sea had risen to terrifying heights, with swells rolling forty feet high. The pinnace rode them lightly, carried up and up and up to dizzy heights, then dropped abruptly into a trough. Jamie's face was dead white in the storm-light, his sodden hair pasted against his scalp.

It was near dark that it happened. The sky was nearly black, but there was an eerie green glow all across the horizon that silhouetted the skeletal shape of the *Porpoise* behind us. Another of the rain squalls slammed us sideways, lurching and swaying atop a huge wave.

As we picked ourselves up from yet another bruising spill, Jamie grabbed my arm, and pointed behind us. The *Porpoise*'s foremast was oddly bent, the top of it leaning far to one side. Before I had time to realize what was happening, the top fifteen feet of the mast had split off and pitched into the sea, carrying with it rigging and spars.

The man-of-war swung heavily round this impromptu anchor, and came sliding sideways down the face of a wave. The wall of water towered over the ship, and came crashing down, catching her broadside. The *Porpoise* heeled, spun around once. The next wave rose, and took her stern first, pulling the high aft deck below the water, whipping the masts through the air like snapping twigs.

It took three more waves to sink her; no time for escape for her hapless crew, but plenty for those of us watching to share their terror. There was a great bubbling flurry in the trough of a wave, and the man-of-war was gone.

Jamie's arm was rigid as iron beneath my hand. All the men

stared back, faces gone empty with horror. All save Innes, who crouched doggedly over the wheel, meeting each wave as it came.

A new wave rose up beside the rail and seemed to hover there, looming above me. The great wall of water was glassy clear; I could see suspended in it the debris and the men of the wrecked *Porpoise,* limbs outflung in grotesque ballet. The body of Thomas Leonard hung no more than ten feet from me, drowned mouth open in surprise, his long soft hair aswirl above the gilded collar of his coat.

Then the wave struck. I was snatched off the deck, and at once engulfed in chaos. Blind and deaf, unable to breathe, I was tumbled through space, my arms and legs wrenched awry by the force of the water.

Everything was dark; there was nothing but sensation, and all of that intense but indistinguishable. Pressure and noise and overwhelming cold. I couldn't feel the pull of my clothing, or the jerk of the rope—if it was still there—around my waist. A sudden faint warmth swathed my legs, distinct in the surrounding cold as a cloud in a clear sky. Urine, I thought, but didn't know whether it was my own, or the last touch of another human body, swallowed as I was in the belly of the wave.

My head hit something with a sickening crack, and suddenly I was coughing my lungs out on the deck of the pinnace, still miraculously afloat. I sat up slowly, choking and wheezing. My rope was still in place, yanked so tight about my waist that I was sure my lower ribs were broken. I jerked feebly at it, trying to breathe, and then Jamie was there, one arm around me, the other groping at his belt for a knife.

"Are ye all right?" he bellowed, his voice barely audible above the shrieking wind.

"No!" I tried to shout back, but it came out as no more than a wheeze. I shook my head, fumbling at my waist.

The sky was a queer purple-green, a color I had never seen before. Jamie sawed at the rope, his bent head spray-soaked and the color of mahogany, hair whipped across his face by the fury of the wind.

The rope popped and I gulped in air, ignoring a stabbing pain in my side and the stinging of raw skin about my waist. The ship was pitching wildly, the deck swinging up and down like a lawn glider. Jamie fell down on the deck, pulling me with him, and began to work his way on hands and knees toward the mast, some six feet away, dragging me.

My garments had been drenched through, plastered to me from my immersion in the wave. Now the blast of the wind was so great that it plucked my skirts away from my legs and flung them up, half-dried, to beat about my face like goose wings.

Jamie's arm was tight as an iron bar across my chest. I clung to him, trying to aid our progress by shoving with my feet on the slippery deckboards. Smaller waves washed over the rail, sousing us intermittently, but no more huge monsters followed them.

Reaching hands grasped us and hauled us the last few feet, into the nominal shelter of the mast. Innes had tied the wheel over long since; as I looked forward, I saw lightning strike the sea ahead, making the spokes of the wheel spring out black, leaving an image like a spider's web printed on my retina.

Speech was impossible—and unnecessary. Raeburn, Ian, Meldrum, and Lawrence were huddled against the mast, all tied; frightful as it was on deck, no one wanted to go below, to be tossed to and fro in bruising darkness, with no notion of what was happening overhead.

I was sitting on the deck, legs splayed, with the mast at my back and the line passed across my chest. The sky had gone lead-gray on one side, a deep, lucent green on the other, and lightning was striking at random over the surface of the sea, bright jags of brilliance across the dark. The wind was so loud that even the thunderclaps reached us only now and then, as muffled booms, like ships' guns firing at a distance.

Then a bolt crashed down beside the ship, lightning and thunder together, close enough to hear the hiss of boiling water in the ringing aftermath of the thunderclap. The sharp reek of ozone flooded the air. Innes turned from the light, his tall, thin figure so sharply cut against the flash that he looked momentarily like a skeleton, black bones against the sky.

The momentary dazzle and his movement made it seem for an instant that he stood whole once more, two arms swinging, as though his missing limb had emerged from the ghost world to join him, here on the brink of eternity.

Oh, de headbone connected to de . . . neckbone. Joe Abernathy's voice sang softly in memory. *And de neckbone connected to de . . . backbone . . .* I had a sudden hideous vision of the scattered limbs I had seen on the beach by the corpse of the *Bruja*, animated by the lightning, squirming and wriggling to reunite.

> *Dem bones, dem bones, are gonna walk around.*
> *Now, hear de word of de Lawd!*

Another clap of thunder and I screamed, not at the sound, but at the lightning bolt of memory. A skull in my hands, with empty eyes that had once been the green of the hurricane sky.

Jamie shouted something in my ear, but I couldn't hear him. I could only shake my head in speechless shock, my skin rippling with horror.

My hair, like my skirts, was drying in the wind; the strands of it danced on my head, pulling at the roots. As it dried, I felt the crackle of static electricity where my hair brushed my cheek. There was a sudden movement among the sailors around me and I looked up, to see the spars and rigging above coated in the blue phosphorescence of St. Elmo's fire.

A fireball dropped to the deck and rolled toward us, streaming phosphorescence. Jamie struck at it and it hopped delicately into the air and rolled away along the rail, leaving a scent of burning in its wake.

I looked up at Jamie to see if he was all right, and saw the loose ends of his hair standing out from his head, coated with fire and streaming backward like a demon's. Streaks of vivid blue outlined the fingers of his hand when he brushed the hair from his face. Then he looked down, saw me, and grasped my hand. A jolt of electricity shot through us both with the touch, but he didn't let go.

I couldn't say how long it lasted; hours or days. Our mouths dried from the wind, and grew sticky with thirst. The sky went from gray to black, but there was no telling whether it was night, or only the coming of rain.

The rain, when it did come, was welcome. It came with the drenching roar of a tropical shower, a drumming audible even above the wind. Better yet, it was hail, not rain; the hailstones hit my skull like pebbles, but I didn't care. I gathered the icy globules in both hands, and swallowed them half-melted, a cool benison to my tortured throat.

Meldrum and MacLeod crawled about the deck on hands and

knees, scooping the hailstones into buckets and pots, anything that would hold water.

I slept intermittently, head lolling on Jamie's shoulder, and woke to find the wind still screaming. Numb to terror now, I only waited. Whether we lived or died seemed of little consequence, if only the dreadful noise would stop.

There was no telling day from night, no way to keep time, while the sun hid its face. The darkness seemed a little lighter now and then, but whether it was by virtue of daylight or moonlight, I couldn't tell. I slept, and woke, and slept again.

Then I woke, to find the wind a little quieter. The seas still heaved, and the tiny boat pitched like a cockleshell, throwing us up and dropping us with stomach-churning regularity. But the noise was less; I could hear, when MacGregor shouted to Ian to pass a cup of water. The men's faces were chapped and raw, their lips cracked to bleeding by the whistling wind, but they were smiling.

"It's gone by." Jamie's voice was low and husky in my ear, rusted by weather. "The storm's past."

It was; there were breaks in the lead-gray sky, and small flashes of a pale, fresh blue. I thought it must be early morning, sometime just past dawn, but couldn't tell for sure.

While the hurricane had ceased to blow, there was still a strong wind, and the storm surge carried us at an amazing speed. Meldrum took the wheel from Innes, and bending to check the compass, gave a cry of surprise. The fireball that had come aboard during the storm had harmed no one, but the compass was now a melted mass of silver metal, the wooden casing around it untouched.

"Amazing!" said Lawrence, touching it reverently with one finger.

"Aye, and inconvenient, forbye," said Innes dryly. He looked upward, toward the ragged remnants of the dashing clouds. "Much of a hand at celestial navigation, are ye, Mr. Stern?"

After much squinting at the rising sun and the remnants of the morning stars, Jamie, Innes, and Stern determined that our heading was roughly northeast.

"We must turn to the west," Stern said, leaning over the crude chart with Jamie and Innes. "We do not know where we are, but any land must surely be to the west."

Innes nodded, peering soberly at the chart, which showed a sprinkle of islands like coarse-ground pepper, floating on the waters of the Caribbean.

"Aye, that's so," he said. "We've been headed out to sea for God knows how long. The hull's in one piece, but that's all I'd say for it. As for the mast and sails—well, they'll maybe hold for a time." He sounded dubious in the extreme. "God knows where we may fetch up, though."

Jamie grinned at him, dabbing at a trickle of blood from his cracked lip.

"So long as it's land, Duncan, I'm no verra choosy about where."

Innes quirked an eyebrow at him, a slight smile on his lips.

"Aye? And here I thought ye'd settled for sure on a sailor's life, Mac Dubh; ye're sae canty on deck. Why, ye havena puked once in the last twa days!"

"That's because I havena eaten anything in the last twa days," Jamie said wryly. "I dinna much care if the island we find first is English, French, Spanish, or Dutch, but I should be obliged if ye'd find one with food, Duncan."

Innes wiped a hand across his mouth and swallowed painfully; the mention of food made everyone salivate, despite dry mouths.

"I'll do my best, Mac Dubh," he promised.

"Land! It's land!" The call came at last, five days later, in a voice rendered so hoarse by wind and thirst that it was no more than a faint croak, but full of joy, nonetheless. I dashed up on deck to see, my feet slipping on the ladder rungs. Everyone was hanging over the rail, looking at the humped black shape on the horizon. It was far off, but undeniably land, solid and distinct.

"Where do you think we are?" I tried to say, but my voice was so hoarse, the words came out in a tiny whisper, and no one heard. It didn't matter; if we were headed straight for the naval barracks at Antigua, I didn't care.

The waves were running in huge, smooth swells, like the backs of whales. The wind was gusting now, and Innes called for the helmsman to bring the bow another point nearer the wind.

I could see a line of large birds flying, a stately procession skimming down the distant shoreline. Pelicans, searching the shallows for fish, with the sun gleaming on their wings.

I tugged at Jamie's sleeve and pointed at them.

"Look—" I began, but got no further. There was a sharp *crack!* and the world exploded in black and fire. I came to in the water. Dazed and half-choked, I floundered and fought in a world of dark green. Something was wrapped about my legs, dragging me down.

I flailed wildly, kicking to free my leg of the deadly grip. Something floated past my head, and I grabbed for it. Wood, blessed wood, something to hold on to in the surging waves.

A dark shape sleeked by like a seal beneath the water, and a red head bobbed up six feet away, gasping.

"Hold on!" Jamie said. He reached me with two strokes, and ducking under the piece of wood I held, dived down. I felt a tugging at my leg, a sharp pain, and then the dragging tension eased. Jamie's head popped up again, across the spar. He grasped my wrists and hung there, gulping air, as the rolling swell carried us, up and down.

I couldn't see the ship anywhere; had it sunk? A wave broke over my head, and Jamie disappeared temporarily. I shook my head, blinking, and he was there again. He smiled at me, a savage grin of effort, and his grip on my wrists tightened harder.

"Hold on!" he rasped again, and I did. The wood was harsh and splintery under my hands, but I clung for all I was worth. We drifted, half-blinded by spray, spinning like a bit of flotsam, so that sometimes I saw the distant shore, sometimes nothing but the open sea from which we had come. And when the waves washed over us, I saw nothing but water.

There was something wrong with my leg; a strange numbness, punctuated with flashes of sharp pain. The vision of Murphy's peg and the razor-grin of an openmouthed shark drifted through my mind; had my leg been taken by some toothy beast? I thought of my tiny hoard of warm blood, streaming from the stump of a bitten limb, draining away into the cold vastness of the sea, and I panicked, trying to snatch my hand from Jamie's grasp in order to reach down and see for myself.

He snarled something unintelligible at me and held on to my wrists like grim death. After a moment of frenzied thrashing, reason returned, and I calmed myself, thinking that if my leg were indeed gone, I would have lost consciousness by now.

At that, I *was* beginning to lose consciousness. My vision was growing gray at the edges, and floating bright spots covered Jamie's face. Was I really bleeding to death, or was it only cold and shock? It hardly seemed to matter, I thought muzzily; the effect was the same.

A sense of lassitude and utter peace stole gradually over me. I couldn't feel my feet or legs, and only Jamie's crushing grip on my hands reminded me of their existence. My head went under water, and I had to remind myself to hold my breath.

The wave subsided and the wood rose slightly, bringing my nose above water. I breathed, and my vision cleared slightly. A foot away was the face of Jamie Fraser, hair plastered to his head, wet features contorted against the spray.

"Hold on!" he roared. "Hold on, God damn you!"

I smiled gently, barely hearing him. The sense of great peace was lifting me, carrying me beyond the noise and chaos. There was no more pain. Nothing mattered. Another wave washed over me, and this time I forgot to hold my breath.

The choking sensation roused me briefly, long enough to see the flash of terror in Jamie's eyes. Then my vision went dark again.

"Damn you, Sassenach!" his voice said, from a very great distance. His voice was choked with passion. "Damn you! I swear if ye die on me, I'll *kill* you!"

I was dead. Everything around me was a blinding white, and there was a soft, rushing noise like the wings of angels. I felt peaceful and bodiless, free of terror, free of rage, filled with quiet happiness. Then I coughed.

I wasn't bodiless, after all. My leg hurt. It hurt a lot. I became gradually aware that a good many other things hurt, too, but my left shin took precedence in no uncertain terms. I had the distinct impression that the bone had been removed and replaced with a red-hot poker.

At least the leg was demonstrably there. When I cracked my eyes open to look, the haze of pain that floated over my leg seemed almost visible, though perhaps that was only a product of the general fuzziness in my head. Whether mental or physical in origin, the general effect was of a sort of whirling whiteness, shot with flickers of a brighter light. Watching it hurt my eyes, so I shut them again.

"Thank God, you're awake!" said a relieved-sounding Scottish voice near my ear.

"No I'm not," I said. My own voice emerged as a salt-crusted croak, rusty with swallowed seawater. I could feel seawater in my sinuses, too, which gave my head an unpleasant gurgling feel. I coughed again, and my nose began to run profusely. Then I sneezed.

"Eugh!" I said, in complete revulsion at the resultant cascade of slime over my upper lip. My hand seemed far off and insubstantial, but I made the effort to raise it, swiping clumsily at my face.

"Be still, Sassenach; I'll take care of ye." There was a definite note of amusement in the voice, which irritated me enough to open my eyes again. I caught a brief glimpse of Jamie's face, intent on mine, before vision vanished once again in the folds of an immense white handkerchief.

He wiped my face thoroughly, ignoring my strangled noises of protest and impending suffocation, then held the cloth to my nose.

"Blow," he said.

I did as he said. Rather to my surprise, it helped quite a lot. I could think more or less coherently, now that my head was unclogged.

Jamie smiled down at me. His hair was rumpled and stiff with dried salt, and there was a wide abrasion on his temple, an angry dark red against the bronzed skin. He seemed not to be wearing a shirt, but had a blanket of some kind draped about his shoulders.

"Do ye feel verra bad?" he asked.

"Horrible," I croaked in reply. I was also beginning to be annoyed at being alive, after all, and being required to take notice of things again. Hearing the rasp in my voice, Jamie reached for a jug of water on the table by my bed.

I blinked in confusion, but it really was a bed, not a berth or a hammock. The linen sheets contributed to the overwhelming impression of whiteness that had first engulfed me. This was reinforced by the whitewashed walls and ceiling, and the long white muslin draperies that bellied in like sails, rustling in the breeze from the open windows.

The flickering light came from reflections that shimmered over the ceiling; apparently there was water close by outside, and sun shining on it. It seemed altogether cozier than Davy Jones's locker. Still, I felt a brief moment of intense regret for the sense of infinite peace I had experienced in the heart of the wave—a regret made more keen by the slight movement that sent a bolt of white agony up my leg.

"I think your leg is broken, Sassenach," Jamie told me unnecessarily. "Ye likely shouldna move it much."

"Thanks for the advice," I said, through gritted teeth. "Where in bloody hell are we?"

He shrugged briefly. "I dinna ken. It's a fair-sized house, is all I could say. I wasna taking much note when they brought us in. One man said the place is called Les Perles." He held the cup to my lips and I swallowed gratefully.

"What happened?" So long as I was careful not to move, the pain in my leg was bearable. Automatically, I placed my fingers under the angle of my jaw to check my pulse; reassuringly strong. I wasn't in shock; my leg couldn't be badly fractured, much as it hurt.

Jamie rubbed a hand over his face. He looked very tired, and I noticed that his hand trembled with fatigue. There was a large bruise on his cheek, and a line of dried blood where something had scratched the side of his neck.

"The topmast snapped, I think. One of the spars fell and knocked ye overboard. When ye hit the water, ye sank like a stone, and I dived in after you. I got hold of you—and the spar, too, thank God. Ye had a bit of rigging tangled round your leg, dragging ye down, but I managed to get that off." He heaved a deep sigh, and rubbed his head.

"I just held to ye; and after a time, I felt sand under my feet. I carried ye ashore, and a bit later, some men found us and brought us here. That's all." He shrugged.

I felt cold, despite the warm breeze coming in through the windows.

"What happened to the ship? And the men? Ian? Lawrence?"

"Safe, I think. They couldna reach us, with the mast broken— by the time they'd rigged a makeshift sail, we were long gone." He coughed roughly, and rubbed the back of his hand across his mouth. "But they're safe; the men who found us said they'd seen a small ketch go aground on a mud flat a quarter-mile south of here; they've gone down to salvage and bring back the men."

He took a swallow of water, swished it about his mouth, and going to the window, spat it out.

"I've sand in my teeth," he said, grimacing, as he returned. "And my ears. And my nose, and the crack of my arse, too, I shouldna wonder."

I reached out and took his hand again. His palm was heavily callused, but still showed the tender swelling of rising blisters, with shreds of ragged skin and raw flesh, where earlier blisters had burst and bled.

"How long were we in the water?" I asked, gently tracing the lines of his swollen palm. The tiny "C" at the base of his thumb was faded almost to invisibility, but I could still feel it under my finger. "Just how long did you hold on?"

"Long enough," he said simply.

He smiled a little, and held my hand more tightly, despite the soreness of his own. It dawned on me suddenly that I wasn't wearing anything; the linen sheets were smooth and cool on my bare skin, and I could see the swell of my nipples, rising under the thin fabric.

"What happened to my clothes?"

"I couldna hold ye up against the drag of your skirts, so I ripped them off," he explained. "What was left didna seem worth saving."

"I don't suppose so," I said slowly, "but Jamie—what about you? Where's your coat?"

He shrugged, then let his shoulders drop, and smiled ruefully.

"At the bottom of the sea with my shoon, I expect," he said. And the pictures of Willie and Brianna there, too.

"Oh, Jamie. I'm so sorry." I reached for his hand and held it tightly. He looked away, and blinked once or twice.

"Aye, well," he said softly. "I expect I will remember them." He shrugged again, with a lopsided smile. "And if not, I can look in the glass, no?" I gave a laugh that was half a sob; he swallowed painfully, but went on smiling.

He glanced down at his tattered breeches then, and seeming to think of something, leaned back and worked a hand into the pocket.

"I didna come away completely empty-handed," he said, pulling a wry face. "Though I would as soon it had been the pictures I kept, and lost these."

He opened his hand, and I saw the gleam and glitter in his ruined palm. Stones of the first quality, cut and faceted, suitable for magic. An emerald, a ruby—male, I supposed—a great fiery opal, a turquoise blue as the sky I could see out the window, a golden stone like sun trapped in honey, and the strange crystal purity of Geilie's black diamond.

"You have the adamant," I said, touching it gently. It was still cool to the touch, in spite of being worn so close to his body.

"I have," he said, but he was looking at me, not at the stone, a slight smile on his face. "What is it an adamant gives ye? The knowledge of joy in all things?"

"So I was told." I lifted my hand to his face and stroked it lightly, feeling hard bone and lively flesh, warm to the touch, and joyful to behold above all things.

"We have Ian," I said softly. "And each other."

"Aye, that's true." The smile reached his eyes then. He dropped the stones in a glittering heap on the table and leaned back in his chair, cradling my hand between his.

I relaxed, feeling a warm peace begin to steal over me, in spite of the aches and scrapes and the pain in my leg. We were alive, safe and together, and very little else mattered; surely not clothes, nor a fractured tibia. Everything would be managed in time—but not now. For now, it was enough only to breathe, and look at Jamie.

We sat in a peaceful silence for some time, watching the sunlit curtains and the open sky. It might have been ten minutes later, or as much as an hour, when I heard the sound of light footsteps outside, and a delicate rap at the door.

"Come in," Jamie said. He sat up straighter, but didn't let go of my hand.

The door opened, and a woman stepped in, her pleasant face lit by welcome, tinged with curiosity.

"Good morning," she said, a little shyly. "I must beg your pardon, not to have waited upon you before; I was in the town, and learned of your—arrival"—she smiled at the word —"only when I returned, just now."

"We must thank ye, Madame, most sincerely, for the kind treatment afforded to us," Jamie said. He rose and bowed formally to her, but kept hold of my hand. "Your servant, ma'am. Have ye word of our companions?"

She blushed slightly, and bobbed a curtsy in reply to his bow. She was young, only in her twenties, and seemed unsure quite how to conduct herself under the circumstances. She had light brown hair, pulled back in a knot, fair pink skin, and what I thought was a faint West Country accent.

"Oh, yes," she said. "My servants brought them back from the ship; they're in the kitchen now, being fed."

"Thank you," I said, meaning it. "That's terribly kind of you." She blushed rosily with embarrassment.

"Not at all," she murmured, then glanced shyly at me. "I must beg your pardon for my lack of manners, ma'am," she said. "I am remiss in not introducing myself. I am Patsy Olivier—Mrs. Joseph Olivier, that is." She looked expectantly from me to Jamie, clearly expecting reciprocation.

Jamie and I exchanged a glance. Where, exactly, were we? Mrs. Olivier was English, that was clear enough. Her husband's name was French. The bay outside gave no clue; this could be any of the Windward Isles—Barbados, the Bahamas, the Exumas, Andros— even the Virgin Islands. Or—the thought struck me—we might have been blown south by the hurricane, and not north; in which case, this might even be Antigua—in the lap of the British Navy! —or Martinique, or the Grenadines . . . I looked at Jamie and shrugged.

Our hostess was still waiting, glancing expectantly from one to the other of us. Jamie tightened his hold on my hand and drew a deep breath.

"I trust ye willna think this an odd question, Mistress Olivier— but could ye tell me where we are?"

Mrs. Olivier's brows rose to the edge of her widow's peak, and she blinked in astonishment.

"Well . . . yes," she said. "We call it Les Perles."

"Thank you," I put in, seeing Jamie taking breath to try again, "but what we mean is—what island is this?"

A broad smile of understanding broke out on her round pink face.

"Oh, I see!" she said. "Of course, you were cast away by the storm. My husband was saying last night that he'd never seen such a dreadful blow at this time of year. What a mercy it is that you were saved! But you came from the islands to the south, then?"

The south. This couldn't be Cuba. Might we have come as far as

St. Thomas, or even Florida? We exchanged a quick glance, and I squeezed Jamie's hand. I could feel the pulse beating in his wrist.

Mrs. Olivier smiled indulgently. "You are not on an island at all. You are on the mainland; in the Colony of Georgia."

"Georgia," Jamie said. "America?" He sounded slightly stunned, and no wonder. We had been blown at least six hundred miles by the storm.

"America," I said softly. "The New World." The pulse beneath my fingers had quickened, echoing my own. A new world. Refuge. Freedom.

"Yes," said Mrs. Olivier, plainly having no idea what the news meant to us, but still smiling kindly from one to the other. "It is America."

Jamie straightened his shoulders and smiled back at her. The clean bright air stirred his hair like kindling flames.

"In that case, ma'am," he said, "my name is Jamie Fraser." He looked then at me, eyes blue and brilliant as the sky behind him, and his heart beat strong in the palm of my hand.

"And this is Claire," he said. "My wife."

If you loved VOYAGER,
then be sure to read the next
book in the acclaimed
OUTLANDER series . . .

DIANA GABALDON'S

DRUMS OF AUTUMN

Available now
from Dell Books!

Read on for a preview. . . .

DRUMS OF AUTUMN
On Sale Now

Charleston, June 1767

I heard the drums long before they came in sight. The beating echoed in the pit of my stomach, as though I too were hollow. The sound traveled through the crowd, a harsh military rhythm meant to be heard over speech or gunfire. I saw heads turn as the people fell silent, looking up the stretch of East Bay Street, where it ran from the half-built skeleton of the new Customs House toward White Point Gardens.

It was a hot day, even for Charleston in June. The best places were on the seawall, where the air moved; here below, it was like being roasted alive. My shift was soaked through, and the cotton bodice clung between my breasts. I wiped my face for the tenth time in as many minutes and lifted the heavy coil of my hair, hoping vainly for a cooling breeze upon my neck.

I was morbidly aware of necks at the moment. Unobtrusively, I put my hand up to the base of my throat, letting my fingers circle it. I could feel the pulse beat in my carotid arteries, along with the drums, and when I breathed, the hot wet air clogged my throat as though I were choking.

I quickly took my hand down, and drew in a breath as deep as I could manage. That was a mistake. The man in front of me hadn't bathed in a month or more; the edge of the stock about his thick neck was dark with grime and his clothes smelled sour and musty, pungent even amid the sweaty reek of the crowd. The smell of hot bread and frying pig fat from the food vendors' stalls lay heavy over a musk of rotting seagrass from the marsh, only slightly relieved by a whiff of salt-breeze from the harbor.

There were several children in front of me, craning and gawking, running out from under the oaks and palmettos to look up the street, being called back by anxious parents. The girl nearest me had a neck like the white part of a grass stalk, slender and succulent.

There was a ripple of excitement through the crowd; the gallows procession was in sight at the far end of the street. The drums grew louder.

"Where is he?" Fergus muttered beside me, craning his own neck to see. "I knew I should have gone with him!"

"He'll be here." I wanted to stand on tiptoe, but didn't, feeling that this would be undignified. I did glance around, though, searching. I could always spot Jamie in a crowd; he stood head and shoulders above most men, and his hair caught the light in a blaze of reddish gold. There was no sign of him yet, only a bobbing sea of bonnets and tricornes, sheltering from the heat those citizens come too late to find a place in the shade.

The flags came first, fluttering above the heads of the excited crowd, the banners of Great Britain and of the Royal Colony of South Carolina. And another, bearing the family arms of the Lord Governor of the colony.

Then came the drummers, walking two by two in step, their sticks an alternate beat and blur. It was a slow march, grimly inexorable. A dead march, I thought they called that particular cadence; very suitable under the circumstances. All other noises were drowned by the rattle of the drums.

Then came the platoon of red-coated soldiers and in their midst, the prisoners.

There were three of them, hands bound before them, linked together by a chain that ran through rings on the iron collars about their necks. The first man was small and elderly, ragged and disreputable, a shambling wreck who lurched and staggered so that the dark-suited clergyman who walked beside the prisoners was obliged to grasp his arm to keep him from falling.

"Is that Gavin Hayes? He looks sick," I murmured to Fergus.

"He's drunk." The soft voice came from behind me, and I whirled, to find Jamie standing at my shoulder, eyes fixed on the pitiful procession.

The small man's disequilibrium was disrupting the progress of the parade, as his stumbling forced the two men chained to him to zig and zag abruptly in order to keep their feet. The general impression was of three inebriates rolling home from the local tavern; grossly at odds with the solemnity of the occasion. I could hear the rustle of laughter over the drums, and shouts and jeers from the crowds on the wrought-iron balconies of the houses on East Bay Street.

"Your doing?" I spoke quietly, so as not to attract notice, but I could have shouted and waved my arms; no one had eyes for anything but the scene before us.

I felt rather than saw Jamie's shrug, as he moved forward to stand beside me.

"It was what he asked of me," he said. "And the best I could manage for him."

"Brandy or whisky?" asked Fergus, evaluating Hayes' appearance with a practiced eye.

"The man's a Scot, wee Fergus." Jamie's voice was as calm as his face, but I heard the small note of strain in it. "Whisky's what he wanted."

"A wise choice. With luck, he won't even notice when they hang him," Fergus muttered. The small man had slipped from the preacher's grasp and fallen flat on his face in the sandy road, pulling one of his companions to his knees; the last prisoner, a tall young man, stayed on his feet but swayed wildly from side to side, trying desperately to keep his balance. The crowd on the point roared with glee.

The captain of the guard glowed crimson between the white of his wig and the metal of his gorget, flushed with fury as much as with sun. He barked an order as the drums continued their somber roll, and a soldier scrambled hastily to remove the chain that bound the prisoners together. Hayes was jerked unceremoniously to his feet, a soldier grasping each arm, and the procession resumed, in better order.

There was no laughter by the time they reached the gallows—a mule-drawn cart placed beneath the limbs of a huge live oak. I could feel the drums beating through the soles of my feet. I felt slightly sick from the sun and the smells. The drums stopped abruptly, and my ears rang in the silence.

"Ye dinna need to watch it, Sassenach," Jamie whispered to me. "Go back to the wagon." His own eyes were fixed unblinkingly on Hayes, who swayed and mumbled in the soldiers' grasp, looking blearily around.

The last thing I wanted was to watch. But neither could I leave Jamie to see it through alone. He had come for Gavin Hayes; I had come for him. I touched his hand.

"I'll stay."

Jamie drew himself straighter, squaring his shoulders. He moved a pace forward, making sure that he was visible in the crowd. If Hayes was still sober enough to see anything, the last thing he saw on earth would be the face of a friend.

He could see; Hayes glared to and fro as they lifted him into the cart, twisting his neck, desperately looking.

"Gabhainn! A charaid!" Jamie shouted suddenly. Hayes' eyes found him at once, and he ceased struggling.

The little man stood swaying slightly as the charge was read: theft in the amount of six pounds, ten shillings. He was covered in reddish dust, and pearls of sweat clung trembling to the gray stubble of his beard. The preacher was leaning close, murmuring urgently in his ear.

Then the drums began again, in a steady roll. The hangman guided the noose over the balding head and fixed it tight, knot positioned precisely, just under the ear. The captain of the guard stood poised, saber raised.

Suddenly, the condemned man drew himself up straight. Eyes on Jamie, he opened his mouth, as though to speak.

The saber flashed in the morning sun, and the drums stopped, with a final *thunk*!

I looked at Jamie; he was white to the lips, eyes fixed wide. From the corner of my eye, I could see the twitching rope, and the faint, reflexive jerk of the dangling sack of clothes. A sharp stink of urine and feces struck through the thick air.

On my other side, Fergus watched dispassionately.

"I suppose he noticed, after all," he murmured, with regret.

The body swung slightly, a dead weight oscillating like a plumb-bob on its string. There was a sigh from the crowd, of awe and release. Terns squawked from the burning sky, and the harbor sounds came faint and smothered through the heavy air, but the point was wrapped in silence. From where I stood, I could hear the small *plit . . . plat . . . plit* of the drops that fell from the toe of the corpse's dangling shoe.

I hadn't known Gavin Hayes, and felt no personal grief for his death, but I was glad it had been quick. I stole a glance at him, with an odd feeling of intrusion. It was a most public way of accomplishing a most private act, and I felt vaguely embarrassed to be looking.

The hangman had known his business; there had been no undignified struggle, no staring eyes, no protruding tongue; Gavin's small round head tilted sharply to the side, neck grotesquely stretched but cleanly broken.

It was a clean break in more ways than one. The captain of the guard, satisfied that Hayes was dead, motioned with his saber for the next man to be brought to the gibbet. I saw his eyes travel down the red-clad file, and then widen in outrage.

At the same moment, there was a cry from the crowd, and a ripple of excitement that quickly spread. Heads turned and people pushed each against his neighbor, striving to see where there was nothing to be seen.

"He's gone!"

"There he goes!"

"Stop him!"

It was the third prisoner, the tall young man, who had seized the moment of Gavin's death to run for his life, sliding past the guard who should have been watching him, but who had been unable to resist the gallows' fascination.

I saw a flicker of movement behind a vendor's stall, a flash of dirty blond hair. Some of the soldiers saw it, too, and ran in that direction, but many more were rushing in other directions, and among the collisions and confusion, nothing was accomplished.

The captain of the guard was shouting, face purple, his voice barely audible over the uproar. The remaining prisoner, looking stunned, was seized and hustled back in the direction of the Court of Guard as the redcoats began hastily to sort themselves back into order under the lash of their captain's voice.

Jamie snaked an arm around my waist and dragged me out of the way of an oncoming wave of humanity. The crowd fell back before the advance of squads of soldiers, who formed up and marched briskly off to quarter the area, under the grim and furious direction of their sergeant.

"We'd best find Ian," Jamie said, fending off a group of excited apprentices. He glanced at Fergus, and jerked his head toward the gibbet and its melancholy burden. "Claim the body, aye? We'll meet at the Willow Tree later."

"Do you think they'll catch him?" I asked, as we pushed through the ebbing crowd, threading our way down a cobbled lane toward the merchants' wharves.

"I expect so. Where can he go?" He spoke abstractedly, a narrow line visible between his brows. Plainly the dead man was still on his mind, and he had little attention to spare for the living.

"Did Hayes have any family?" I asked. He shook his head.

"I asked him that, when I brought him the whisky. He thought he might have a brother left alive, but no notion where. The brother was transported soon after the Rising—to Virginia, Hayes thought, but he'd heard nothing since."

Not surprising if he hadn't; an indentured laborer would have had no facilities for communicating with kin left behind in Scotland, unless the bondsman's employer was kind enough to send a letter on his behalf. And kind or not, it was unlikely that a letter would have found Gavin Hayes, who had spent ten years in Ardsmuir prison before being transported in his turn.

"Duncan!" Jamie called out, and a tall, thin man turned and raised a hand in acknowledgment. He made his way through the crowd in a corkscrew fashion, his single arm swinging in a wide arc that fended off the passersby.

"Mac Dubh," he said, bobbing his head in greeting to Jamie. "Mrs. Claire." His long, narrow face was furrowed with sadness. He too had once been a prisoner at Ardsmuir, with Hayes and with Jamie. Only the loss of his arm to a blood infection had prevented his being transported with the others. Unfit to be sold for labor, he had instead been pardoned and set free to starve— until Jamie had found him.

"God rest poor Gavin," Duncan said, shaking his head dolorously.

Jamie muttered something in response in Gaelic, and crossed himself. Then he straightened, casting off the oppression of the day with a visible effort.

"Aye, well. I must go to the docks and arrange about Ian's passage, and then we'll think of burying Gavin. But I must have the lad settled first."

We struggled through the crowd toward the docks, squeezing our way between knots of excited gossipers, eluding the drays and barrows that came and went through the press with the ponderous indifference of trade.

A file of red-coated soldiers came at the quick-march from the other end of the quay, splitting the crowd like vinegar dropped on mayonnaise. The sun glittered hot on the line of bayonet points and the rhythm of their tramping beat through the noise of the crowd like a muffled drum. Even the rumbling sledges and handcarts stopped abruptly to let them pass by.

"Mind your pocket, Sassenach," Jamie murmured in my ear, ushering me through a narrow space between a turban-clad slave clutching two small children and a street preacher perched on a box. He was shouting sin and repentance, but with only one word in three audible through the noise.

"I sewed it shut," I assured him, nonetheless reaching to touch the small weight that swung against my thigh. "What about yours?"

He grinned and tilted his hat forward, dark blue eyes narrowing against the bright sunlight.

"It's where my sporran would be, did I have one. So long as I dinna meet with a quick-fingered harlot, I'm safe."

I glanced at the slightly bulging front of his breeches, and then up at him. Broad-shouldered and tall, with bold, clean features and a Highlander's proud carriage, he drew the glance of every woman he passed, even with his bright hair covered by a sober blue tricorne. The breeches, which were borrowed, were substantially too tight, and did nothing whatever to detract from the general effect—an effect enhanced by the fact that he himself was totally ignorant of it.

"You're a walking inducement to harlots," I said. "Stick by me; I'll protect you."

He laughed and took my arm as we emerged into a small clear space.

"Ian!" he shouted, catching sight of his nephew over the heads of the crowd. A moment later, a tall, stringy gawk of a boy popped out of the crowd, pushing a thatch of brown hair out of his eyes and grinning widely.

"I thought I should never find ye, Uncle!" he exclaimed. "Christ, there are more folk here than at the Lawnmarket in Edinburgh!" He wiped a coat sleeve across his long, half-homely face, leaving a streak of grime down one cheek.

Jamie eyed his nephew askance.

"Ye're lookin' indecently cheerful, Ian, for having just seen a man go to his death."

Ian hastily altered his expression into an attempt at decent solemnity.

"Oh, no, Uncle Jamie," he said. "I didna see the hanging." Duncan raised one brow and Ian blushed slightly. "I—I wasna afraid to see; it was only I had . . . something else I wanted to do."

Jamie smiled slightly and patted his nephew on the back.

"Don't trouble yourself, Ian; I'd as soon not have seen it myself, only that Gavin was a friend."

"I know, Uncle. I'm sorry for it." A flash of sympathy showed in the boy's large brown eyes, the only feature of his face with any claim to beauty. He glanced at me. "Was it awful, Auntie?"

"Yes," I said. "It's over, though." I pulled the damp handkerchief out of my bosom and stood on tiptoe to rub away the smudge on his cheek.

Duncan Innes shook his head sorrowfully. "Aye, poor Gavin. Still, it's a quicker death than starving, and there was little left for him but that."

"Let's go," Jamie interrupted, unwilling to spend time in useless lamenting. "The *Bonnie Mary* should be near the far end of the quay." I saw Ian glance at Jamie and draw himself up as though about to speak, but Jamie had already turned toward the harbor and was shoving his way through the crowd. Ian glanced at me, shrugged, and offered me an arm.

We followed Jamie behind the warehouses that lined the docks, sidestepping sailors, loaders, slaves, passengers, customers and merchants of all sorts. Charleston was a major shipping port, and business was booming, with as many as a hundred ships a month coming and going from Europe in the season.

The *Bonnie Mary* belonged to a friend of Jamie's cousin Jared Fraser, who had gone to France to make his fortune in the wine business and succeeded brilliantly. With luck, the *Bonnie Mary*'s captain might be persuaded for Jared's sake to take Ian with him back to Edinburgh, allowing the boy to work his passage as a cabin lad.

Ian was not enthused at the prospect, but Jamie was determined to ship his errant nephew back to Scotland at the earliest opportunity. It was—among other concerns—news of the *Bonnie Mary*'s presence in Charleston that had brought us here from Georgia, where we had first set foot in America—by accident—two months before.

As we passed a tavern, a slatternly barmaid came out with a bowl of slops. She caught sight of Jamie and stood, bowl braced against her hip, giving him a slanted brow and a pouting smile. He passed without a glance, intent on his goal. She tossed her head, flung the slops to the pig who slept by the step, and flounced back inside.

He paused, shading his eyes to look down the row of towering ships' masts, and I came up beside him. He twitched unconsciously at the front of his breeches, easing the fit, and I took his arm.

"Family jewels still safe, are they?" I murmured.

"Uncomfortable, but safe," he assured me. He plucked at the

lacing of his flies, grimacing. "I would ha' done better to hide them up my bum, I think."

"Better you than me, mate," I said, smiling. "I'd rather risk robbery, myself."

The family jewels were just that. We had been driven ashore on the coast of Georgia by a hurricane, arriving soaked, ragged, and destitute—save for a handful of large and valuable gemstones.

I hoped the captain of the *Bonnie Mary* thought highly enough of Jared Fraser to accept Ian as a cabin boy, because if not, we were going to have a spot of difficulty about the passage.

In theory, Jamie's pouch and my pocket contained a sizable fortune. In practice, the stones might have been beach pebbles so far as the good they were to us. While gems were an easy, compact way of transporting wealth, the problem was changing them back into money.

Most trade in the southern colonies was conducted by means of barter—what wasn't, was handled by the exchange of scrip or bills written on a wealthy merchant or banker. And wealthy bankers were thin on the ground in Georgia; those willing to tie up their available capital in gemstones rarer still. The prosperous rice farmer with whom we had stayed in Savannah had assured us that he himself could scarcely lay his hand on two pounds sterling in cash—indeed, there was likely not ten pounds in gold and silver to be had in the whole colony.

Nor was there any chance of selling one of the stones in the endless stretches of salt marsh and pine forest through which we had passed on our journey north. Charleston was the first city we had reached of sufficient size to harbor merchants and bankers who might help to liquidate a portion of our frozen assets.

Not that anything was likely to stay frozen long in Charleston in summer, I reflected. Rivulets of sweat were running down my neck and the linen shift under my bodice was soaked and crumpled against my skin. Even so close to the harbor, there was no wind at this time of day, and the smells of hot tar, dead fish, and sweating laborers were nearly overwhelming.

Despite their protestations, Jamie had insisted on giving one of our gemstones to Mr. and Mrs. Olivier, the kindly people who had taken us in when we were shipwrecked virtually on their doorstep, as some token of thanks for their hospitality. In return, they had provided us with a wagon, two horses, fresh clothes for traveling, food for the journey north, and a small amount of money.

Of this, six shillings and threepence remained in my pocket, constituting the entirety of our disposable fortune.

"This way, Uncle Jamie," Ian said, turning and beckoning his uncle eagerly. "I've got something to show ye."

"What is it?" Jamie asked, threading his way through a throng of sweating slaves, who were loading dusty bricks of dried indigo into an anchored cargo ship. "And how did ye get whatever it is? Ye havena got any money, have you?"

"No, I won it, dicing." Ian's voice floated back, his body invisible as he skipped around a cartload of corn.

"Dicing! Ian, for God's sake, ye canna be gambling when ye've not a penny to bless yourself with!" Holding my arm, Jamie shoved a way through the crowd to catch up to his nephew.

"You do it all the time, Uncle Jamie," the boy pointed out, pausing to wait for us. "Ye've been doing it in every tavern and inn where we've stayed."

"My God, Ian, that's cards, not dice! And I know what I'm doing!"

"So do I," said Ian, looking smug. "I won, no?"

Jamie rolled his eyes toward heaven, imploring patience.

"Jesus, Ian, but I'm glad you're going home before ye get your head beaten in. Promise me ye willna be gambling wi' the sailors, aye? Ye canna get away from them on a ship."

Ian was paying no attention; he had come to a half-crumbled piling, around which was tied a stout rope. Here he stopped and turned to face us, gesturing at an object by his feet.

"See? It's a dog," Ian said proudly.

I took a quick half-step behind Jamie, grabbing his arm.

"Ian," I said, "that is not a dog. It's a wolf. It's a bloody *big* wolf, and I think you ought to get away from it before it takes a bite out of your arse."

The wolf twitched one ear negligently in my direction, dismissed me, and twitched it back. It continued to sit, panting with the heat, its big yellow eyes fixed on Ian with an intensity that might have been taken for devotion by someone who hadn't met a wolf before. I had.

"Those things are dangerous," I said. "They'd bite you as soon as look at you."

Disregarding this, Jamie stooped to inspect the beast.

"It's not quite a wolf, is it?" Sounding interested, he held out a loose fist to the so-called dog, inviting it to smell his knuckles. I closed my eyes, expecting the imminent amputation of his hand.

Hearing no shrieks, I opened them again to find him squatting on the ground, peering up the animal's nostrils.

"He's a handsome creature, Ian," he said, scratching the thing familiarly under the chin. The yellow eyes narrowed slightly, either in pleasure at the attention or—more likely, I thought—in anticipation of biting off Jamie's nose. "Bigger than a wolf, though; it's broader through the head and chest, and a deal longer in the leg."

"His mother was an Irish wolfhound." Ian was hunkered down by Jamie, eagerly explaining as he stroked the enormous gray-brown back. "She got out in heat, into the woods, and when she came back in whelp—"

"Oh, aye, I see." Now Jamie was crooning in Gaelic to the monster while he picked up its huge foot and fondled its hairy toes. The curved black claws were a good two inches long. The thing half closed its eyes, the faint breeze ruffling the thick fur at its neck.

I glanced at Duncan, who arched his eyebrows at me, shrugged slightly, and sighed. Duncan didn't care for dogs.

"Jamie—" I said.

"*Balach Boidheach,*" Jamie said to the wolf. "Are ye no the bonny laddie, then?"

"What would he eat?" I asked, somewhat more loudly than necessary.

Jamie stopped caressing the beast.

"Oh," he said. He looked at the yellow-eyed thing with some regret. "Well." He rose to his feet, shaking his head reluctantly.

"I'm afraid your auntie's right, Ian. How are we to feed him?"

"Oh, that's no trouble, Uncle Jamie," Ian assured him. "He hunts for himself."

"Here?" I glanced around at the warehouses, and the stuccoed row of shops beyond. "What does he hunt, small children?"

Ian looked mildly hurt.

"Of course not, Auntie. Fish."

Seeing three skeptical faces surrounding him, Ian dropped to his knees and grabbed the beast's muzzle in both hands, prying his mouth open.

"He does! I swear, Uncle Jamie! Here, just smell his breath!"

Jamie cast a dubious glance at the double row of impressively gleaming fangs on display, and rubbed his chin.

"I—ah, I shall take your word for it, Ian. But even so—for Christ's sake, be careful of your fingers, lad!" Ian's grip had loosened, and the massive jaws clashed shut, spraying droplets of saliva over the stone quay.

"I'm all right, Uncle," Ian said cheerfully, wiping his hand on his breeks. "He wouldn't bite me, I'm sure. His name is Rollo."

Jamie rubbed his knuckles across his upper lip.

"Mmphm. Well, whatever his name is, and whatever he eats, I dinna think the captain of the *Bonnie Mary* will take kindly to his presence in the crew's quarters."

Ian didn't say anything, but the look of happiness on his face didn't diminish. In fact, it grew. Jamie glanced at him, caught sight of his glowing face, and stiffened.

"No," he said, in horror. "Oh, no."

"Yes," said Ian. A wide smile of delight split his bony face. "She sailed three days ago, Uncle. We're too late."

Jamie said something in Gaelic that I didn't understand. Duncan looked scandalized.

"Damn!" Jamie said, reverting to English. "Bloody damn!" Jamie took off his hat and rubbed a hand over his face, hard. He looked hot, disheveled, and thoroughly disgruntled. He opened his mouth, thought better of whatever he had been going to say, closed it, and ran his fingers roughly through his hair, jerking loose the ribbon that tied it back.

Ian looked abashed.

"I'm sorry, Uncle. I'll try not to be a worry to ye, truly I will. And I can work; I'll earn enough for my food."

Jamie's face softened as he looked at his nephew. He sighed deeply, and patted Ian's shoulder.

"It's not that I dinna want ye, Ian. You know I should like nothing better than to keep ye with me. But what in hell will your mother say?"

The glow returned to Ian's face.

"I dinna ken, Uncle," he said, "but she'll be saying it in Scotland, won't she? And we're here." He put his arms around Rollo and hugged him. The wolf seemed mildly taken aback by the gesture, but after a moment, put out a long pink tongue and daintily licked Ian's ear. Testing him for flavor, I thought cynically.

"Besides," the boy added, "she kens well enough that I'm safe; you wrote from Georgia to say I was with you."

Jamie summoned a wry smile.

"I canna say that that particular bit of knowledge will be ower-comforting to her, Ian. She's known me a long time, aye?"

He sighed and clapped the hat back on his head, and turned to me.

"I badly need a drink, Sassenach," he said. "Let's find that tavern."

The Willow Tree was dark, and might have been cool, had there been fewer people in it. As it was, the benches and tables were crowded with sightseers from the hanging and sailors from the docks, and the atmosphere was like a sweatbath. I inhaled as I stepped into the taproom, then let my breath out, fast. It was like breathing through a wad of soiled laundry, soaked in beer.

Rollo at once proved his worth, parting the crowd like the Red Sea as he stalked through the taproom, lips drawn back from his teeth in a constant, inaudible growl. He was evidently no stranger to taverns. Having satisfactorily cleared out a corner bench, he curled up under the table and appeared to go to sleep.

Out of the sun, with a large pewter mug of dark ale foaming gently in front of him, Jamie quickly regained his normal self-possession.

"We've the two choices," he said, brushing back the sweat-soaked hair from his temples. "We can stay in Charleston long enough to maybe find a buyer for one of the stones, and perhaps book passage for Ian to Scotland on another ship. Or we can make our way north to Cape Fear, and maybe find a ship for him out of Wilmington or New Bern."

"I say north," Duncan said, without hesitation. "Ye've kin in Cape Fear, no? I mislike the thought of staying ower-long among strangers. And your kinsman would see we were not cheated nor robbed. Here—" He lifted one shoulder in eloquent indication of the un-Scottish—and thus patently dishonest—persons surrounding us.

"Oh, do let's go north, Uncle!" Ian said quickly, before Jamie could reply to this. He wiped away a small mustache of ale foam with his sleeve. "The journey might be dangerous; you'll need an extra man along for protection, aye?"

Jamie buried his expression in his own cup, but I was seated close enough to feel a subterranean quiver go through him. Jamie was indeed very fond of his nephew. The fact remained that Ian was the sort of person to whom things happened. Usually through no fault of his own, but still, they happened.

The boy had been kidnapped by pirates the year before, and it was the necessity of rescuing him that had brought us by circuitous and often dangerous means to America. Nothing had happened recently, but I knew Jamie was anxious to get his fifteen-year-old nephew back to Scotland and his mother before something did.

"Ah . . . to be sure, Ian," Jamie said, lowering his cup. He carefully avoided meeting my gaze, but I could see the corner of his mouth twitching. "Ye'd be a great help, I'm sure, but . . ."

"We might meet with Red Indians!" Ian said, eyes wide. His face, already a rosy brown from the sun, glowed with a flush of pleasurable anticipation. "Or wild beasts! Dr. Stern told me that the wilderness of Carolina is alive wi' fierce creatures—bears and wildcats and wicked panthers—and a great foul thing the Indians call a skunk!"

I choked on my ale.

"Are ye all right, Auntie?" Ian leaned anxiously across the table.

"Fine," I wheezed, wiping my streaming face with my kerchief. I blotted the drops of spilled ale off my bosom, pulling the fabric of my bodice discreetly away from my flesh in hopes of admitting a little air.

Then I caught a glimpse of Jamie's face, on which the expression of suppressed amusement had given way to a small frown of concern.

"Skunks aren't dangerous," I murmured, laying a hand on his knee. A skilled and fearless hunter in his native Highlands, Jamie was inclined to regard the unfamiliar fauna of the New World with caution.

"Mmphm." The frown eased, but a narrow line remained between his brows. "Maybe so, but what of the other things? I canna say I wish to be meeting a bear or a pack o' savages, wi' only this to hand." He touched the large sheathed knife that hung from his belt.

Our lack of weapons had worried Jamie considerably on the trip from Georgia, and Ian's remarks about Indians and wild animals had brought the concern to the forefront of his mind once more. Besides Jamie's knife, Fergus bore a smaller blade, suitable for cutting rope and trimming twigs for kindling. That was the full extent of our armory—the Oliviers had had neither guns nor swords to spare.

On the journey from Georgia to Charleston, we had had the company of a group of rice and indigo farmers—all bristling with knives, pistols, and muskets—bringing their produce to the port to be shipped north to Pennsylvania and New York. If we left for Cape Fear now, we would be alone, unarmed, and essentially defenseless against anything that might emerge from the thick forests.

At the same time, there were pressing reasons to travel north, our lack of available capital being one. Cape Fear was the largest settlement of Scottish Highlanders in the American Colonies, boasting several towns whose inhabitants had emigrated from Scotland during the last twenty years, following the upheaval after Culloden. And among these emigrants were Jamie's kin, who I knew would willingly offer us refuge: a roof, a bed, and time to establish ourselves in this new world.

Jamie took another drink and nodded at Duncan.

"I must say I'm of your mind, Duncan." He leaned back against the wall of the tavern, glancing casually around the crowded room. "D'ye no feel the eyes on your back?"

A chill ran down my own back, despite the trickle of sweat doing likewise. Duncan's eyes widened fractionally, then narrowed, but he didn't turn around.

"Ah," he said.

"*Whose* eyes?" I asked, looking rather nervously around. I didn't see anyone taking particular notice of us, though anyone might be watching surreptitiously; the tavern was seething with alcohol-soaked humanity, and the babble of voices was loud enough to drown out all but the closest conversation.

"Anyone's, Sassenach," Jamie answered. He glanced sideways at me, and smiled. "Dinna look so scairt about it, aye? We're in no danger. Not here."

"Not yet," Innes said. He leaned forward to pour another cup of ale. "*Mac Dubh* called out to Gavin on the gallows, d'ye see? There will be those who took notice—*Mac Dubh* bein' the bittie wee fellow he is," he added dryly.

"And the farmers who came with us from Georgia will have sold their stores by now, and be takin' their ease in places like this," Jamie said, evidently absorbed in studying the pattern of his cup. "All of them are honest men—but they'll talk, Sassenach. It makes a good story, no? The folk cast away by the hurricane? And what are the chances that at least one of them kens a bit about what we carry?"

"I see," I murmured, and did. We had attracted public interest by our association with a criminal, and could no longer pass as inconspicuous travelers. If finding a buyer took some time, as was likely, we risked inviting robbery from unscrupulous persons, or scrutiny from the English authorities. Neither prospect was appealing.

Jamie lifted his cup and drank deeply, then set it down with a sigh.

"No. I think it's perhaps not wise to linger in the city. We'll see Gavin buried decently, and then we'll find a safe spot in the woods outside the town to sleep. Tomorrow we can decide whether to stay or go."

The thought of spending several more nights in the woods— with or without skunks—was not appealing. I hadn't taken my dress off in eight days, merely rinsing the outlying portions of my anatomy whenever we paused in the vicinity of a stream.

I had been looking forward to a real bed, even if flea-infested, and a chance to scrub off the grime of the last week's travel. Still, he had a point. I sighed, ruefully eyeing the hem of my sleeve, gray and grubby with wear.

The tavern door flung suddenly open at this point, distracting me from my contemplation, and four red-coated soldiers shoved their way into the crowded room. They wore full uniform, held muskets with bayonets fixed, and were obviously not in pursuit of ale or dice.

Two of the soldiers made a rapid circuit of the room, glancing under tables, while another disappeared into the kitchen beyond. The fourth remained on watch by the door, pale eyes flicking over the crowd. His gaze lighted on our table, and rested on us for a moment, full of speculation, but then passed on, restlessly seeking.

Jamie was outwardly tranquil, sipping his ale in apparent obliviousness, but I saw the hand in his lap clench slowly into a fist. Duncan, less able to control his feelings, bent his head to hide his expression. Neither man would ever feel at ease in the presence of a red coat, and for good reason.

No one else appeared much perturbed by the soldiers' presence. The little knot of singers in the chimney corner went on with an interminable version of "Fill Every Glass," and a loud argument broke out between the barmaid and a pair of apprentices.

The soldier returned from the kitchen, having evidently found nothing. Stepping rudely through a dice game on the hearth, he rejoined his fellows by the door. As the soldiers shoved their way out of the tavern, Fergus's slight figure squeezed in, pressing against the doorjamb to avoid swinging elbows and musket butts.

I saw one soldier's eyes catch the glint of metal and fasten with interest on the hook Fergus wore in replacement of his missing left hand. He glanced sharply at Fergus, but then shouldered his musket and hurried after his companions.

Fergus shoved through the crowd and plopped down on the bench beside Ian. He looked hot and irritated.

"Blood-sucking *salaud,*" he said, without preamble.

Jamie's brows went up.

"The priest," Fergus elaborated. He took the mug Ian pushed in his direction and drained it, lean throat glugging until the cup was empty. He lowered it, exhaled heavily, and sat blinking, looking noticeably happier. He sighed and wiped his mouth.

"He wants ten shillings to bury the man in the churchyard," he said. "An Anglican church, of course; there are no Catholic churches here. Wretched usurer! He knows we have no choice about it. The body will scarcely keep till sunset, as it is." He ran a finger inside his stock, pulling the sweat-wilted cotton away from his neck, then banged his fist several times on the table to attract the attention of the servingmaid, who was being run off her feet by the press of patrons.

"I told the super-fatted son of a pig that you would decide whether to pay or not. We could just bury him in the wood, after all. Though we should have to purchase a shovel," he added, frowning. "These grasping townsfolk know we are strangers; they'll take our last coin if they can."

Last coin was perilously close to the truth. I had enough to pay for a decent meal here and to buy food for the journey north; perhaps enough to pay for a couple of nights' lodging. That was all. I saw Jamie's eyes flick round the room, assessing the possibilities of picking up a little money at hazard or loo.

Soldiers and sailors were the best prospects for gambling, but there were few of either in the taproom—likely most of the garrison was still searching the town for the fugitive. In one corner, a small group of men was being loudly convivial over several pitchers of brandywine; two of them were singing, or trying to, their attempts causing great hilarity among their comrades. Jamie gave an almost imperceptible nod at sight of them, and turned back to Fergus.

"What have ye done with Gavin for the time being?" Jamie asked. Fergus hunched one shoulder.

"Put him in the wagon. I traded the clothes he was wearing to a ragwoman for a shroud, and she agreed to wash the body as part of the bargain." He gave Jamie a faint smile. "Don't worry, milord; he's seemly. For now," he added, lifting the fresh mug of ale to his lips.

"Poor Gavin." Duncan Innes lifted his own mug in a half salute to his fallen comrade.

"Slàinte," Jamie replied, and lifted his own mug in reply. He set it down and sighed.

"He wouldna like being buried in the wood," he said.

"Why not?" I asked, curious. "I shouldn't think it would matter to him one way or the other."

"Oh, no, we couldna do that, Mrs. Claire." Duncan was shaking his head emphatically. Duncan was normally a most reserved man, and I was surprised at so much apparent feeling.

"He was afraid of the dark," Jamie said softly. I turned to stare at him, and he gave me a lopsided smile. "I lived wi' Gavin Hayes nearly as long as I've lived with you, Sassenach—and in much closer quarters. I kent him well."

"Aye, he was afraid of being alone in the dark," Duncan chimed in. "He was most mortally scairt of *tannagach*—of spirits, aye?"

His long, mournful face bore an inward look, and I knew he was seeing in memory the prison cell that he and Jamie had shared with Gavin Hayes—and with forty other men—for three long years. "D'ye recall, *Mac Dubh,* how he told us one night of the *tannasq* he met?"

"I do, Duncan, and could wish I did not." Jamie shuddered despite the heat. "I kept awake myself half the night after he told us that one."

"What was it, Uncle?" Ian was leaning over his cup of ale, round-eyed. His cheeks were flushed and streaming, and his stock crumpled with sweat.

Jamie rubbed a hand across his mouth, thinking.

"Ah. Well, it was a time in the late, cold autumn in the Highlands, just when the season turns, and the feel of the air tells ye the ground will be shivered wi' frost come dawn," he said. He settled himself in his seat and sat back, alecup in hand. He smiled wryly, plucking at his own throat. "Not like now, aye?

"Well, Gavin's son brought back the kine that night, but there was one beast missing—the lad had hunted up the hills and down the corries, but couldna find it anywhere. So Gavin set the lad to milk the two others, and set out himself to look for the lost cow."

He rolled the pewter cup slowly between his hands, staring down into the dark ale as though seeing in it the bulk of the night-black Scottish peaks and the mist that floats in the autumn glens.

"He went some distance, and the cot behind him disappeared. When he looked back, he couldna see the light from the window anymore, and there was no sound but the keening of the wind. It was cold, but he went on, tramping through the mud and the heather, hearing the crackle of ice under his boots.

"He saw a small grove through the mist, and thinking the cow might have taken shelter beneath the trees, he went toward it. He said the trees were birches, standing there all leafless, but with their branches grown together so he must bend his head to squeeze beneath the boughs.

"He came into the grove and saw it was not a grove at all, but a circle of trees. There were great tall trees, spaced verra evenly, all around him, and smaller ones, saplings, grown up between to make a wall of branches. And in the center of the circle stood a cairn."

Hot as it was in the tavern, I felt as though a sliver of ice had slid melting down my spine. I had seen ancient cairns in the Highlands myself, and found them eerie enough in the broad light of day.

Jamie took a sip of ale, and wiped away a trickle of sweat that ran down his temple.

"He felt quite queer, did Gavin. For he kent the place—everyone did, and kept well away from it. It was a strange place. And it seemed even worse in the dark and the cold, from what it did in the light of day. It was an auld cairn, the kind laid wi' slabs of rock, all heaped round with stones, and he could see before him the black opening of the tomb.

"He knew it was a place no man should come, and he without a powerful charm. Gavin had naught but a wooden cross about his neck. So he crossed himself with it and turned to go."

Jamie paused to sip his ale.

"But as Gavin went from the grove," he said softly, "he heard footsteps behind him."

I saw the Adam's apple bob in Ian's throat as he swallowed. He reached mechanically for his own cup, eyes fixed on his uncle.

"He didna turn to see," Jamie went on, "but kept walking. And the steps kept pace wi' him, step by step, always following.

And he came through the peat where the water seeps up, and it was crusted with ice, the weather bein' so cold. He could hear the peat crackle under his feet, and behind him the crack! crack! of breaking ice.

"He walked and he walked, through the cold, dark night, watching ahead for the light of his own window, where his wife had set the candle. But the light never showed, and he began to fear he had lost his way among the heather and the dark hills. And all the time, the steps kept pace with him, loud in his ears.

"At last he could bear it no more, and seizing hold of the crucifix he wore round his neck, he swung about wi' a great cry to face whatever followed."

"What did he see?" Ian's pupils were dilated, dark with drink and wonder. Jamie glanced at the boy, and then at Duncan, nodding at him to take up the story.

"He said it was a figure like a man, but with no body," Duncan said quietly. "All white, like as it might have been made of the mist. But wi' great holes where its eyes should be, and empty black, fit to draw the soul from his body with dread."

"But Gavin held up his cross before his face, and he prayed aloud to the Blessed Virgin." Jamie took up the story, leaning forward intently, the dim firelight outlining his profile in gold. "And the thing came no nearer, but stayed there, watching him.

"And so he began to walk backward, not daring to face round again. He walked backward, stumbling and slipping, fearing every moment as he might tumble into a burn or down a cliff and break his neck, but fearing worse to turn his back on the cold thing.

"He couldna tell how long he'd walked, only that his legs were trembling wi' weariness, when at last he caught a glimpse of light through the mist, and there was his own cottage, wi' the candle in the window. He cried out in joy, and turned to his door, but the cold thing was quick, and slippit past him, to stand betwixt him and the door.

"His wife had been watching out for him, and when she heard him cry out, she came at once to the door. Gavin shouted to her not to come out, but for God's sake to fetch a charm to drive away the *tannasq*. Quick as thought, she snatched the pot from beneath her bed, and a twig of myrtle bound wi' red thread and black, that she'd made to bless the cows. She dashed the water against the doorposts, and the cold thing leapt upward, astride the lintel. Gavin rushed in beneath and barred the door, and stayed inside in his wife's arms until the dawn. They let the candle burn all the night, and Gavin Hayes never again left his house past sunset—until he went to fight for Prince *Tearlach*."

Even Duncan, who knew the tale, sighed as Jamie finished speaking. Ian crossed himself, then looked about self-consciously, but no one seemed to have noticed.

"So, now Gavin has gone into the dark," Jamie said softly. "But we willna let him lie in unconsecrated ground."

"Did they find the cow?" Fergus asked, with his usual practicality. Jamie quirked one eyebrow at Duncan, who answered.

"Oh, aye, they did. The next morning they found the poor beast, wi' her hooves all clogged wi' mud and stones, staring mad and lathered about the muzzle, and her sides heavin' fit to burst." He glanced from me to Ian and back to Fergus. "Gavin did say," he said precisely, "that she looked as though she'd been ridden to Hell and back."

"Jesus." Ian took a deep gulp of his ale, and I did the same. In the corner, the drinking society was making attempts on a round of "Captain Thunder," breaking down each time in helpless laughter.

Ian put down his cup on the table.

"What happened to them?" he asked, his face troubled. "To Gavin's wife, and his son?"

Jamie's eyes met mine, and his hand touched my thigh. I knew, without being told, what had happened to the Hayes family. Without Jamie's own courage and intransigence, the same thing would likely have happened to me and to our daughter Brianna.

"Gavin never knew," Jamie said quietly. "He never heard aught of his wife—she will have been starved, maybe, or driven out to die of the cold. His son took the field beside him at Culloden. Whenever a man who had fought there came into our cell, Gavin would ask—"Have ye maybe seen a bold lad named Archie Hayes, about so tall?'" He measured automatically, five feet from the floor, capturing Hayes' gesture. "'A lad about fourteen,' he'd say, "wi' a green plaidie and a small gilt brooch.' But no one ever came who had seen him for sure—either seen him fall or seen him run away safe."

Jamie took a sip of the ale, his eyes fixed on a pair of British officers who had come in and settled in the corner. It had grown dark outside, and they were plainly off duty. Their leather stocks were unfastened on account of the heat, and they wore only sidearms, glinting under their coats; nearly black in the dim light save where the firelight touched them with red.

"Sometimes he hoped the lad might have been captured and transported," he said. "Like his brother."

"Surely that would be somewhere in the records?" I said. "Did they—do they—keep lists?"

"They did," Jamie said, still watching the soldiers. A small, bitter smile touched the corner of his mouth. "It was such a list that saved me, after Culloden, when they asked my name before shooting me, so as to add it to their roll. But a man like Gavin would have no way to see the English dead-lists. And if he could have found out, I think he would not." He glanced at me. "Would you choose to know for sure, and it was your child?"

I shook my head, and he gave me a faint smile and squeezed my hand. Our child was safe, after all. He picked up his cup and drained it, then beckoned to the serving maid.

The girl brought the food, skirting the table widely in order to avoid Rollo. The beast lay motionless under the table, his head protruding into the room and his great hairy tail lying heavily across my feet, but his yellow eyes were wide open, watching everything. They followed the girl intently, and she backed nervously away, keeping an eye on him until she was safely out of biting distance.

Seeing this, Jamie cast a dubious look at the so-called dog.

"Is he hungry? Must I ask for a fish for him?"

"Oh, no, Uncle," Ian reassured him. "Rollo catches his own fish."

Jamie's eyebrows shot up, but he only nodded, and with a wary glance at Rollo, took a platter of roasted oysters from the tray.

"Ah, the pity of it." Duncan Innes was quite drunk by now. He sat slumped against the wall, his armless shoulder riding higher than the other, giving him a strange, hunchbacked appearance. "That a dear man like Gavin should come to such an end!" He shook his head lugubriously, swinging it back and forth over his alecup like the clapper of a funeral bell.

"No family left to mourn him, cast alone into a savage land— hanged as a felon, and to be buried in an unconsecrated grave. Not even a proper lament to be sung for him!" He picked up the cup, and with some difficulty, found his mouth with it. He drank deep and set it down with a muffled clang.

"Well, he *shall* have a *caithris*!" He glared belligerently from Jamie to Fergus to Ian. "Why not?"

Jamie wasn't drunk, but he wasn't completely sober either. He grinned at Duncan and lifted his own cup in salute.

"Why not, indeed?" he said. "Only it will have to be you singin' it, Duncan. None of the rest knew Gavin, and I'm no singer. I'll shout along wi' ye, though."

Duncan nodded magisterially, bloodshot eyes surveying us. Without warning, he flung back his head and emitted a terrible howl. I jumped in my seat, spilling half a cup of ale into my lap. Ian and Fergus, who had evidently heard Gaelic laments before, didn't turn a hair.

All over the room, benches were shoved back, as men leapt to their feet in alarm, reaching for their pistols. The barmaid leaned out of the serving hatch, eyes big. Rollo came awake with an explosive *"Woof!"* and glared round wildly, teeth bared.

"Tha sinn cruinn a chaoidh ar caraid, Gabhainn Hayes," Duncan thundered, in a ragged baritone. I had just about enough Gaelic to translate this as "We are met to weep and cry out to heaven for the loss of our friend, Gavin Hayes!"

"Èisd ris!" Jamie chimed in.

"Rugadh e do Sheumas Immanuel Hayes agus Louisa N'ic a Liallainn an am baile Chill-Mhartainn, ann an sgire Dhun Domhnuill, anns a bhliadhnaseachd ceud deug agus a haon!" He was born of Seaumais Emmanuel Hayes and of Louisa Maclellan, in the village of Kilmartin in the parish of Dodanil, in the year of our Lord seventeen hundred and one!

"Èisd ris!" This time Fergus and Ian joined in on the chorus, which I translated roughly as "Hear him!"

Rollo appeared not to care for either verse or refrain; his ears lay flat against his skull, and his yellow eyes narrowed to slits. Ian scratched his head in reassurance, and he lay down again, muttering wolf curses under his breath.

The audience, having caught on to it that no actual violence threatened, and no doubt bored with the inferior vocal efforts of the drinking society in the corner, settled down to enjoy the show. By the time Duncan had worked his way into an accounting of the names of the sheep Gavin Hayes had owned before leaving his croft to follow his laird to Culloden, many of those at the surrounding tables were joining enthusiastically in the chorus, shouting *"Èisd ris!"* and banging their mugs on the tables, in perfect ignorance of what was being said, and a good thing too.

Duncan, drunker than ever, fixed the soldiers at the next table with a baleful glare, sweat pouring down his face.

"A Shasunnaich na galladh, 's olc a thig e dhuibh fanaid air bàs gasgaich. Gun toireadh an diabhul fhein leis anns a bhàs

sibh, direach do Fhirinn!!" Wicked Sassenach dogs, eaters of dead flesh! Ill does it become you to laugh and rejoice at the death of a gallant man! May the devil himself seize upon you in the hour of your death and take you straight to hell!

Ian blanched slightly at this, and Jamie cast Duncan a narrow look, but they stoutly shouted *"Èisd ris!"* along with the rest of the crowd.

Fergus, seized by inspiration, got up and passed his hat among the crowd, who, carried away by ale and excitement, happily flung coppers into it for the privilege of joining in their own denunciation.

I had as good a head for drink as most men, but a much smaller bladder. Head spinning from the noise and fumes as much as from alcohol, I got up and edged my way out from behind the table, through the mob, and into the fresh air of the early evening.

It was still hot and sultry, though the sun was long since down. Still, there was a lot more air out here, and a lot fewer people sharing it.

Having relieved the internal pressure, I sat down on the tavern's chopping block with my pewter mug, breathing deeply. The night was clear, with a bright half-moon peeping silver over the harbor's edge. Our wagon stood nearby, no more than its outline visible in the light from the tavern windows. Presumably, Gavin Hayes' decently shrouded body lay within. I trusted he had enjoyed his *caithris*.

Inside, Duncan's chanting had come to an end. A clear tenor voice, wobbly with drink, but sweet nonetheless, was singing a familiar tune, audible over the babble of talk.

> *"To Anacreon in heav'n, where he sat in full glee,*
> *A few sons of harmony sent a petition,*
> *That he their inspirer and patron would be!*
> *When this answer arrived from the jolly old Grecian:*
> *'Voice, fiddle, and flute,*
> > *No longer be mute!*
> *I'll lend you my name and inspire you to boot.'"*

The singer's voice cracked painfully on "voice, fiddle, and flute," but he sang stoutly on, despite the laughter from his audience. I smiled wryly to myself as he hit the final couplet,

> *"'And, besides, I'll instruct you like me to entwine,*
> *The Myrtle of Venus with Bacchus's vine!'"*

I lifted my cup in salute to the wheeled coffin, softly echoing the melody of the singer's last lines.

> *"Oh, say, does that star-spangled banner yet wave*
> *O'er the land of the free and the home of the brave?"*

I drained my cup and sat still, waiting for the men to come out.

OUTLANDER

SEASON ONE
THE ULTIMATE COLLECTION

THE ULTIMATE COLLECTION comes with:

- A Keepsake Box

- A Collectible Behind-the-Scenes Book

- An Engraved Flask with one of three unique quotes from the series

- A Curated Collection of Photographs and a Frame

- The Complete First Season Blu-ray™ & Soundtrack with Three Exclusive Tracks

VOLUMES 1 & 2 ALSO AVAILABLE ON BLU-RAY™

A STARZ ORIGINAL SERIES

OUTLANDER

STARZ